PEARS

CYCLOPAEDIA

1990–91

A BOOK OF BACKGROUND INFORMATION
AND REFERENCE FOR EVERYDAY USE

EDITED BY

CHRISTOPHER COOK

M.A. Cantab., D.Phil. Oxon., F.R. Hist. S.

Ninety-ninth Edition

The Editor desires to express his gratitude to readers for their criticisms and suggestions and to all those who in one way or another have contributed to the making of this edition. Correspondence on editorial matters should be addressed to Dr. Christopher Cook, "Pears Cyclopaedia", Pelham Books Ltd., 27 Wrights Lane, Kensington, London W8 5TZ.

PELHAM BOOKS/Stephen Greene Press

Published by the Penguin Group
27 Wrights Lane, London W8 5TZ, England
Stephen Greene Press, 15 Muzzey Street, Lexington, Massachusetts 02173, USA
Viking Penguin Inc., 40 West 23rd Street, New York, New York 10010, USA
Penguin Books Australia Ltd, Ringwood, Victoria, Australia
Penguin Books Canada Ltd, 2801 John Street, Markham, Ontario, Canada L3R 1B4
Penguin Books (NZ) Ltd, 182–190 Wairau Road, Auckland 10, New Zealand

Penguin Books Ltd, Registered Offices: Harmondsworth, Middlesex, England

First published 1897

Printed in England by Clays Ltd., St Ives plc

A CIP catalogue record for this book is available from the British Library.
0-7207-1968-2

CONTENTS

Sections are arranged alphabetically, or chronologically, or have a detailed Table of Contents.

HISTORICAL EVENTS

Historical events from the earliest times to the present. For events in pre-history the reader may also like to consult the relevant sections on geology and our early ancestors in the Science section. This edition includes a detailed chronicle of the dramatic events in the world as the 1980s came to a close and the new decade opened.

CHRONICLE OF EVENTS

Note.—For classical history and for the past millennium most dates are well established. For other periods there is sometimes considerable uncertainty. Many of the dates in ancient history are either dubious or approximate, sometimes both. For dates on evolution prior to 100 million years ago the reader is invited to consult the table on **F48.**

B.C.   **PREHISTORY**

70,000,000   Earliest known primate (*Plesiadapis*).

35,000,000   *Aegyptopithecus*, ancestral ape from the Fayum.

20,000,000   *Proconsul*, possible ancestor of hominids in East Africa.

3,700,000   First hominids in East Africa – *Australopithecus.*

2,100,000   First hominid stone toolmaker – *Homo habilis*; present in Africa until 1,800,000 years ago.

1,600,000   Earliest *Homo erectus* in East Africa, present there and in Europe and Far East until 200,000 years ago.

500,000   Archaic modern man, *Homo sapiens*, present in Africa until 30,000 years ago.

100,000   Neanderthal Man, present in Europe until 35,000 years ago: Anatomically modern man, *Homo sapiens sapiens* present in Africa, dispersed worldwide.

70,000   Neanderthalers (Europe, Asia, N. Africa). Rhodesian Man (S. Africa). Solo Man (Java). Flake tools.

40,000   First cold phase ends. Neanderthal race becoming extinct. Second cold phase. *Homo sapiens* (modern man). Implements show significant advances: small knife-blades, engraving tools. Paintings and sculpture; magic rites and ceremonies. Cro-Magnons with Aurignacian culture.

18,000   Final culmination of last ice age. Aurignacian culture dying out to be replaced by Solutrean and then by the Magdalenian cultures. Great flowering of Palaeolithic art.

15,000   First immigrants from Asia to cross Behring Straits?

15,000   Last glaciers in Britain disappeared. Proto-Neolithic in Middle East. Agricultural settlements (*e.g.*, Jericho). Settled way of life leading eventually to such skills as weaving, metallurgy; inventions as ox-drawn plough, wheeled cart.

5,000   Britain becomes an island (land connection with continent severed by melting ice-sheets).

B.C. CIVILISATION IN THE MIDDLE EAST

4000   Susa founded.

3500   Sumerian civilisation flourishes. Cuneiform writing.

3100   First Egyptian Dynasty. Hieratic writing already perfected.
Early Minoan Age (Crete). Pictorial writing, copper, silver, gold in use. Early Mycenaean civilisation begins.

2980   Memphis, capital of Egypt.

2870   First settlements at Troy.

2850   Golden Age of China begins (legendary).

B.C.
2700   Great Pyramid age in Egypt begins.

2400   Aryan migrations.

2371   Sargon founds Akkad: Akkadian empire.

2205   Hsia Dynasty begins in China (legendary).

2200   Middle Minoan Age: pottery, linear writing in pen and ink.

2100–1600   Building and rebuilding of Stonehenge.

1720–1550   Hyksos in Egypt. War chariots introduced. Hebrews entered Egypt (Joseph) c. 1600.

1751   Code of Hammurabi at Babylon.

1600   Late Minoan Age: Linear B script.

1600–1027   Shang Dynasty in China.

1546   18th Dynasty in Egypt commences. Civilisation at peak (under Tuthmosis III, 1490). Chronology more certain.

1500   Powerful Mitanni (Aryan) kingdom in Asia Minor. Phoenicia thriving—trade with Egypt and Babylonia. Vedic literature in India.

1450   Zenith of Minoan civilisation.

1400   Ugarit (N. Syria) culture at its zenith. Cretan civilisation ends: Knossos burnt. Temple at Luxor built.

1379   Amenhotep IV (Akhnaten), the "heretic" Pharaoh.

1350   Zenith of Hittite civilisation.

1300   Israelite oppression (Rameses II); Exodus from Egypt (Moses). Phoenician settlements—Hellas and Spain (Cadiz). Tyre flourishing.

1250   Israelites invade Palestine (Joshua).

1200   Attacks on Egypt by "Peoples of the Sea". Downfall of Hittite kingdom. Siege of Troy (Homeric). Beginning of sea-power of independent Phoenician cities. Probably all these are connected with Achaean and other migrations in Aegean area.

1115   Magnetic needle reputed in China.

1027–249   Chou Dynasty in China.

1005–925   Kingdom of David and Solomon: Jerusalem as Sanctuary.

1000   *Rig Veda* (India).

925–722   Israel and Judah divided.

893   Assyrian chronological records begin.

850   Foundation of Carthage (traditional).

781   Chinese record of an eclipse.

776   First Olympiad to be used for chronological purposes.

753   Foundation of Rome (traditional).

750   Greek colonists settling in Southern Italy.

745   Accession of Tiglath-Pileser III; Assyrian Power at its height.

722   Capture of Samaria by Sargon II: Israel deported to Nineveh.

700   Homer's poems probably written before this date. Spread of the iron-using Celtic Hallstatt culture about this time.

625   Neo-Babylonian (Chaldean) Empire (Nineveh destroyed 612).

621   Publication of Athenian laws by Draco.

610   Spartan constitution, made rigid after Messenian Wars: later attributed to Lycurgus.

B.C.

594 Athenian constitution reformed by Solon.

586 Capture of Jerusalem: Judah deported to Babylon (partial return 538).

561 Pisistratus tyrant of Athens.

560 Accession of Croesus—great prosperity of Lydia.

538 Babylon taken by Persians: Empire founded by Cyrus, soon covers almost all of civilised Middle East.

509 Foundation of Roman Republic (traditional).

508 Democratic constitution proclaimed in Athens.

500 Etruscans at height of their power in Northern Italy.

GREAT AGE OF GREECE

499 Revolt of Ionian Greek cities against Persian king Darius.

494 Secession of Plebeians from Rome. Tribunes established.

490 Battle of Marathon: Athenian repulse of Persian attack.

480 Death of Buddha. Battle of Thermopylae: Spartans under Leonidas wiped out by Persians. Battle of Salamis: Persian fleet defeated by Athenians under Themistocles; Persian invasion of Greece halted.

479 Battles of Plataea and Mycale: Greek victories by land and sea respectively destroy Persian invasion force. Death of Confucius.

477 League of Delos founded by Athens for defence against Persia; soon becomes Athenian Empire. (467 Naxos kept in by force.)

461 Pericles comes to power in Athens.

458 Cincinnatus saves Rome (traditional).

456 Death of Aeschylus.

447 Building of Parthenon begun.

431 Death of Phidias. Outbreak of Great Peloponnesian War between Athens and Sparta. Pericles "Funeral Oration" (according to Thucydides).

425 Death of Herodotus.

416 Massacre of Melos by Athenians.

415 Sicilian Expedition: flight of Alcibiades from Athens to Sparta.

413 Loss of entire Athenian expeditionary force at Syracuse.

406 Death of Euripides and Sophocles.

405 Battle of Aegospotami: Athenian navy destroyed by Sparta.

404 Athenian surrender to Sparta: beginning of Spartan hegemony in Greece.

403 Beginning of epoch of Warring States in China.

400 Death of Thucydides, Greek historian (?).

399 Execution of Socrates.

390 Occupation of Rome by Gauls under Brennus.

371 Battle of Leuctra: Spartans defeated by Thebans: beginning of Theban hegemony in Greece.

370 Death of Hippocrates of Cos (?).

347 Death of Plato.

338 Battle of Chaeronea: Greek city-states defeated by Philip II of Macedon, who becomes supreme in Greece.

336 Assassination of Philip of Macedon: accession of Alexander.

334 Alexander's invasion of Persion Empire. Battle of Granicus, first victory.

333 Battle of Issus: Alexander defeats Darius of Persia.

332 Alexander's siege and capture of Tyre, occupation of Egypt.

B.C

331 Battle of Arbela (Gaugamela)—final defeat of Darius.

330 Death of Darius and end of Persian Empire. Alexander heir to civilisations of Middle East.

326 Battle of Hydaspes: Alexander conquers the Punjab.

323 Death of Alexander at Babylon. Beginning of Hellenistic Age in Middle East and Eastern Mediterranean. Ptolemy I founds dynasty in Egypt. Alexandria becomes intellectual centre of Hellenic world.

322 Death of Demosthenes.

321 Death of Aristotle, Maurya dynasty unites N. India.

312 Seleucus I founds dynasty in Asia.

300 Zeno the Stoic, Epicurus and Euclid flourishing.

ROME: CONQUESTS AND DECAY OF REPUBLICAN INSTITUTIONS

290 End of Third Samnite War. Rome dominates Central Italy.

280 Translation of Pentateuch into Greek.

275 Battle of Beneventum: Rome finally defeats Pyrrhus and the Greek cities of Southern Italy. Rome dominates all Italy.

274 Asoka becomes ruler of two-thirds of Indian sub-continent.

264 Beginning of First Punic War (Rome v. Carthage).

260 Battle of Mylae: first great Roman naval victory.

255 Defeat and capture of Regulus by Carthaginians.

250 Incursion of "La Tène" Iron Age people into Britain.

241 End of First Punic War. Sicily becomes first Province of Rome.

221 Kingdom of Ch'in completes conquest of all Chinese states under Shih Huang-ti.

218 Outbreak of Second Punic War: Hannibal crosses Alps.

216 Battle of Cannae: Hannibal wipes out great Roman army.

214 Great Wall of China constructed (by linking existing walls).

213 Burning of Chinese classics.

212 Capture of Syracuse by Romans and death of Archimedes.

207 Battle of Metaurus: defeat and death of Hasdrubal. End of Hannibal's hopes of overcoming Rome.

205 Roman provinces organised in Spain.

202 Battle of Zama: Hannibal defeated by Scipio Africanus, 202-A.D. 220 Han Dynasty in China.

201 End of Second Punic War. Rome dominates Western Mediterranean.

196 After defeating Macedon, Rome proclaims independence of Greek city-states. Death of Eratosthenes the geographer (?).

160 Death in battle of Judas Maccabaeus: Jewish revolt against Seleucids continues successfully.

149 Outbreak of Third Punic War.

146 Carthage destroyed. Roman province of Africa formed. Roman provinces of Macedonia and Achaea formed, and most of remainder of Greece reduced to vassal status.

134 First Servile War; Revolt of slaves in Sicily under Eunus. Suppressed 132.

133 Siege and destruction of Numantia by Romans. Tiberius Gracchus Tribune. Attempted land reforms. Murdered 132.

129 Roman province of Asia formed from lands bequeathed by Attalus of Pergamum.

124 Chinese Grand College to train Civil Service officials.

123 Caius Gracchus Tribune. Attempted land reforms. Murdered 121.

110 Chinese expansion to include most of south-east of modern China, under Emperor Wu Ti. Commercial activity in Indian Ocean.

B.C.

106 Jugurtha captured by Marius and Sulla.

104 Second Servile War: revolt of slaves in Sicily under Tryphon and Athenion. Suppressed 101.

102 Chinese expedition to Ferghana and possible knowledge of West.

101 Battle of Vercellae: Marius ends threat of Cimbri to Rome.

91 Social War: revolt of Italian cities against Rome. Suppressed 88. Roman franchise granted to most Italians.

88 Civil Wars of Marius and Sulla begin.

87 Massacre in Rome by Marius.

82 Proscriptions in Rome by Sulla.

75 Belgic invasion of south-eastern Britain.

73 Third Servile War: revolt of slaves in southern Italy under Spartacus the gladiator. Suppressed 71.

63 Conspiracy of Catiline exposed by Cicero.

60 First Triumvirate: Pompey, Caesar, Crassus.

58 Beginning of Caesar's conquest of Gaul.

55 Caesar's first British expedition: second, 54.

53 Battle of Carrhae: destruction of Roman army under Crassus by Persians.

52 Revolt of Vercingetorix against Caesar.

50 Migration to Britain of Commius and his followers.

49 Caesar crosses the Rubicon. Beginning of war against Pompey and the Senate.

48 Battle of Pharsalus: defeat of Pompey by Caesar.

46 Caeser's calendar reforms.

44 Murder of Caesar.

43 Second Triumvirate: Antony, Octavian, Lepidus.

42 Battle of Philippi: defeat and death of Brutus and his associates.

31 Battle of Actium: naval victory of Octavian over Antony and Cleopatra. Octavian unchallenged master of the Roman world.

THE ROMAN EMPIRE

27 Octavian given the title of Augustus by the Senate.

19 Death of Virgil.

8 Death of Horace.

4 Birth of Jesus (date not certain).

A.D.

6 Civil Service Examination system in China.

9 Radical reforms by Wang Mang (short Hsin dynasty 9–23). Annihilation of Roman army under Varus by Teutonic tribesmen under Arminius.

10 Cunobelinus reigning over much of south-east Britain from Colchester.

14 Death of Augustus.

17 Death of Livy.

18 Death of Ovid.

30 Crucifixion of Jesus (date not certain).

43 Roman invasion of Britain under Aulus Plautius.

51 Caractacus taken to Rome as prisoner.

60 Revolt of Boudicca.

63 Great Fire of Rome.

64 Death of St. Paul (date not certain).

65 Death of Seneca.

66 Jews of Palestine rebelled against Roman rule.

68 Death of Nero—end of Julio-Claudian line of Roman Emperors.

70 Jerusalem taken and Jewish revolt suppressed by Titus.

79 Destruction of Pompeii and Herculaneum by eruption of Vesuvius.

A.D

80 Completion of Colosseum (Flavian Amphitheatre).

83 Battle of Mons Graupius: Agricola crushes Caledonians.

96 Accession of Nerva: first of the "Five Good Emperors."

97 Chinese expedition under Kang Yin (lieutenant of Pan Ch'ao) penetrates to Persian Gulf.

117 Death of Trajan, accession of Hadrian. Roman Empire at its greatest extent.

122 Beginning of Hadrian's Wall (Tyne–Solway) by Aulus Platorius Nepos.

135 Suppression of Bar-Cochba's revolt and Dispersion of Jews.

142 Construction of Antonine Wall (Forth–Clyde) by Quintus Lollius Urbicus.

180 Death of Marcus Aurelius, last of the "Five Good Emperors." Beginning of the "Decline" of the Roman Empire (Gibbon).

193 Praetorian guards murder Emperor Pertinax, sell Empire to highest bidder (Didius Julianus).

196 Clodius Albinus, governor, withdraws forces from Britain to support his attempt to become Emperor. Northern Britain overrun by barbarians.

208 Septimius Severus visits Britain to punish Caledonians (death at York 211).

212 Edict of Caracalla. Roman citizenship conferred on all free inhabitants of Empire.

220 End of Han Dynasty: China divided and frequently invaded for next three centuries.

227 Sassanid Empire in Persia.

230 Emperor Sulin—Japanese history emerging from legendary stage.

251 Goths defeat and kill Emperor Decius.

259 Break-away "Gallic Emp..." set up: suppressed 273.

273 Defeat of Zenobia and destruction of Palmyra by Emperor Aurelian.

284 Accession of Diocletian, who reorganises Roman Empire (293) with rigid social laws and heavy taxation.

287 Carausius attempts to found independent "Empire of Britain": suppressed 297.

306 Constantine proclaimed Emperor at York.

313 Edict of Milan. Christianity tolerated in Roman Empire.

320 Gupta dynasty reunites India.

325 Council of Nicaea: first general Council of the Church.

367 Successful attack on Britain by Picts, Scots, Saxons.

369 Restoration of Roman authority in Britain by Theodosius.

378 Battle of Adrianople: Goths defeat and kill Eastern Roman Emperor Valens.

383 Magnus Maximus withdraws forces from Britain to support his attempt to conquer north-western part of Empire.

388 Magnus Maximus defeated and killed in Italy.

395 Death of Emperor Theodosius the Great: the division of the Empire into East and West at his death proves eventually to be the final one.

406 Usurper Constantine III withdraws forces from Britain to support his claims: probable end of Roman military occupation of Britain.

410 Sack of Rome by Alaric the Goth. Emperor Honorius tells Britons to arrange for their own defence.

THE BARBARIAN INVASIONS

415 Visigoths begin conquest of Spain.

419 Visigothic kingdom of Toulouse recognised by Roman government.

429 Vandals begin conquest of North Africa.

432 St. Patrick begins mission in Ireland.

A.D.

446 "Groans of the Britons"—last appeal to Rome (traditional).

451 Châlons: Attila the Hun repelled from Gaul by mixed Roman–Barbarian forces.

452 Attila's raid into Italy: destruction of Aquilea and foundation of Venice by refugees.

455 Rome pillaged by Vandals.

476 Romulus Augustulus, last Western Roman Emperor, deposed by Odovacar: conventionally the end of the Western Roman Empire.

481 Clovis becomes King of the Franks, who eventually conquer Gaul (d. 511).

493 Theodoric founds Ostrogothic Kingdom in Italy (d. 526).

515 Battle of Mount Badon: West Saxon advance halted by Britons, perhaps led by Arthur (?).

BYZANTIUM AND ISLAM

527 Accession of Justinian I (d. 565).

529 Code of Civil Law published by Justinian. Rule of St. Benedict put into practice at Monte Cassino (traditional).

534 Byzantines under Belisarius reconquer North Africa from Vandals.

552 Byzantine reconquest of Italy complete.

563 St. Columba founds mission in Iona.

568 Lombard Kingdom founded in Italy.

570 Birth of Mohammed.

577 Battle of Deorham: West Saxon advance resumed.

581–618 Sui Dynasty in China.

590 Gregory the Great becomes Pope.

597 St. Augustine lands in Kent.

605 Grand Canal of China constructed.

618–907 T'ang Dynasty in China: their administrative system lasts in essentials for 1,300 years.

622 Hejira or flight from Mecca to Medina of Mohammed: beginning of Mohammedan era.

627 Battle of Nineveh: Persians crushed by Byzantines under Heraclius.

632 Death of Mohammed: all Arabia now Moslem. Accession of Abu Bakr, the first Caliph.

634 Battle of Heavenfield: Oswald becomes king of Northumbria, brings in Celtic Christianity.

638 Jerusalem captured by Moslems.

641 Battle of Mehawand: Persia conquered by Moslems.

643 Alexandria taken by Moslems.

645 Downfall of Soga clan in Japan, after establishing Buddhism: beginning of period of imitation of Chinese culture.

650 Slav occupation of Balkans now complete.

663 Synod of Whitby: Roman Christianity triumphs over Celtic Christianity in England.

685 Nectansmere: end of Northumbrian dominance in England.

698 Carthage taken by Moslems.

711 Tarik leads successful Moslem invasion of Spain.

718 Failure of second and greatest Moslem attack on Constantinople. Pelayo founds Christian kingdom of Asturias in Northern Spain.

726 Byzantine Emperor Leo III begins Iconoclast movement: opposed by Pope Gregory II, and an important cause of difference between Roman and Byzantine churches.

THE HOLY ROMAN EMPIRE AND THE TRIUMPH OF CHRISTIANITY IN EUROPE: NORSEMEN AND NORMANS

732 Poitiers: Moslem western advance halted by Charles Martel.

735 Death of Bede.

750 Beginning of Abbasid Caliphate (replacing Omayyads)

A.D

751 Pepin King of the Franks: founds Carolingian dynasty. Ravenna taken by Lombards: end of Byzantine power in the West.

754 Pepin promises central Italy to Pope: beginning of temporal power of the Papacy.

778 Roncesvalles: defeat and death of Roland.

786 Accession of Haroun-al-Rashid in Baghdad.

793 Sack of Lindisfarne: Viking attacks on Britain begin.

795 Death of Offa: end of Mercian dominance in England.

800 Coronation of Charlemagne as Emperor by Pope Leo III in Rome.

814 Death of Charlemagne: division of empire.

825 Ellandun: Egbert defeats Mercians and Wessex becomes leading kingdom in England.

827 Moslem invasion of Sicily.

840 Moslems capture Bari and occupy much of Southern Italy.

843 Treaty of Verdun: final division of Carolingian Empire, and beginning of France and Germany as separate states.

844 Kenneth MacAlpin becomes king of Picts as well as Scots: the kingdom of Alban.

862 Rurik founds Viking state in Russia: first at Novgorod, later at Kiev.

866 Fujiwara period begins in Japan. Viking "Great Army" in England: Northumbria, East Anglia and Mercia subsequently overwhelmed.

868 Earliest dated printed book in China.

872 Harold Fairhair King of Norway.

874 Iceland settled by Norsemen.

885–6 Viking attack on Paris.

893 Simeon founds first Bulgar Empire in Balkans.

896 Arpad and the Magyars in Hungary.

899 Death of Alfred the Great.

900 Ghana at the height of its power in North West Africa.

907–960 Five Dynasties in China: partition.

910 Abbey of Cluny founded: monastic reforms spread from here.

911 Rolf (or Rollo) becomes ruler of Normandy.

912 Accession of Abderrahman III: the most splendid period of the Omayyad Caliphate of Cordova (d. 961).

928 Brandenburg taken from the Slavs by Henry the Fowler, King of Germany.

929 Death of Wenceslas, Christian King of Bohemia.

937 Battle of Brunanburh: crowning victory of Athelstan. West Saxon kings now masters of England.

955 Battle of Lechfeld: Magyars finally defeated by Otto the Great and settle in Hungary.

960–1279 Sung Dynasty in China.

965 Harold Bluetooth king of Denmark, accepts Christianity.

966 Mieszko I king of Poland, accepts Christianity.

968 Fatimids begin their rule in Egypt.

982 Discovery of Greenland by Norsemen.

987 Hugh Capet king of France: founder of Capetian dynasty.

988 Vladimir of Kiev accepts Christianity.

991 Battle of Maldon: defeat of Byrhtnoth of Essex by Vikings—renewed Viking raids on England.

993 Olof Skutkonung, king of Sweden, accepts Christianity.

1000 Leif Ericsson discovers North America.

1001 Coronation of St. Stephen of Hungary with crown sent by the Pope.

1002 Massacre of St. Brice's Day: attempt by Ethelred to exterminate Danes in England.

A.D.

1014 Battle of Clontarf: victory of Irish under Brian Boru over Vikings.

1016 Canute becomes king of England; builds short-lived Danish "empire."

1018 Byzantines under Basil 11 complete subjection of Bulgars.

1040 Attempts to implement Truce of God from about this time.

1046 Normans under Robert Guiscard in southern Italy.

1054 Beginning of Almoravid (Moslem) conquests in West Africa.

1060 Normans invade Sicily.

1066 Norman conquest of England under William I.

1069 Reforms of Wang An-Shih in China.

THE CRUSADES

1071 Manzikert: Seljuk Turks destroy Byzantine army and overrun Anatolia.

1073 Hildebrand (Gregory VII) becomes Pope. Church discipline and Papal authority enforced.

1075 Seljuk Turks capture Jerusalem.

1076 Kumbi, capital of Ghana, sacked by Almoravids: subsequent break-up of Ghana Empire.

1084 Carthusians founded by St. Bruno at Chartreuse.

1086 Compilation of Domesday Book.

1094 El Cid takes Valencia.

1095 Council of Clermont: Urban II preaches First Crusade.

1098 Cistercians founded by St. Robert at Citeaux.

1099 First Crusade under Godfrey of Bouillon takes Jerusalem.

1100 Death of William Rufus in the New Forest. Baldwin I: Latin Kingdom of Jerusalem founded.

1106 Tinchebrai: Henry I of England acquires Normandy, captures his brother Robert.

1115 Abelard teaching at Paris. St. Bernard founds monastery at Clairvaux.

1119 Order of Knights Templars founded.

1120 Loss of the White Ship and heir to English throne.

1122 Concordat of Worms: Pope and Emperor compromise on the Investiture Controversy, but continue to quarrel over other matters (Guelfs and Ghibellines).

1135 Stephen takes English crown: civil wars with Matilda and anarchy ensue.

1143 Alfonso Henriques proclaimed first king of Portugal.

1144 Moslems take Christian stronghold of Edessa.

1148 Second Crusade fails to capture Damascus.

1150 Carmelites founded about this time by Berthold.

1152 Accession of Emperor Frederick Barbarossa.

1154 Henry of Anjou succeeds Stephen: first of Plantagenet kings of England.

1161 Explosives used in warfare in China.

1169 Strongbow invades Ireland: beginning of Anglo-Norman rule. Saladin ruling in Egypt.

1170 Murder of Thomas Becket in Canterbury cathedral.

1171 Spanish knightly Order of Santiago founded.

1176 Battle of Legnano: Frederick Barbarossa defeated by the Lombard League. Italian autonomy established.

1185 Kamakura Period in Japan: epoch of feudalism: until 1333.

1187 Hattin: destruction of Latin kingdom of Jerusalem by Saladin.

A.D

1189 Third Crusade launched: leaders—Frederick Barbarossa, Philip Augustus of France, Richard Lionheart of England.

1191 Capture of Acre by Crusaders.

1192 End of Third Crusade without regaining Jerusalem. Richard I seized and held to ransom in Austria on return journey.

1198 Innocent III becomes Pope.

1202 Fourth Crusade, diverted by Venetians takes Zara from Byzantines.

1204 Fourth Crusade captures Constantinople, founds Latin Empire. King John of England loses Normandy to France.

1206 Temujin proclaimed Genghiz Khan (Very Mighty King) of all the Mongols: soon controls all of Central Asia.

1208 Albigensian Crusade launched: the first against Christians.

1212 Battle of Las Navas de Tolosa: decisive victory of Spaniards over Moors. The Children's Crusade.

THE CULMINATION OF THE MIDDLE AGES

1215 Fourth Lateran Council: the authority of the mediaeval Church and Papacy at its zenith. Dominicans recognised by the Pope. Magna Carta extorted by barons from John.

1223 Franciscans recognised by the Pope.

1229 Emperor Frederick II, through diplomacy, recognised by Moslems as King of Jerusalem.

1230 Teutonic Knights established in Prussia.

1237 Golden Horde (Mongols) begin subjugation of Russia.

1241 Mongol incursions into Central Europe.

1250 St. Louis of France captured on his Crusade in Egypt. Mamelukes become rulers of Egypt. Mandingo king declares his independence of Ghana and embraces Islam.

1256 Conference of Baltic ports; the first form of the Hanseatic League.

1258 Provisions of Oxford: barons under Simon de Montfort force reforms on Henry III of England. Baghdad destroyed by Mongols.

1264 Battle of Lewes: Montfort's party become rulers of England.

1265 Simon de Montfort's Parliament, Battle of Evesham: defeat and death of de Montfort.

1274 Death of Thomas Aquinas.

1279–1368 Mongol Dynasty in China (Kublai Khan).

1281 Repulse of Mongol attack on Japan.

1282 Sicilian Vespers: rising of Sicilians against French ruler.

1284 Completion of Edward I of England's conquest of Wales.

1290 Expulsion of Jews from England. Death of Maid of Norway: Edward I begins attempts to rule Scotland.

1291 Fall of Acre: end of Crusading in Holy Land. Everlasting League of Uri: beginnings of Swiss Confederation.

1294 Death of Roger Bacon, the founder of experimental science.

1295 "Model Parliament" of Edward I (anticipated in 1275).

1308 Death of Duns Scotus.

THE DECLINE OF THE MIDDLE AGES

1309 Papacy moves to Avignon: beginning of the Babylonish Captivity.

1312 Suppression of Templars by king of France and Pope.

1314 Battle of Bannockburn: victory of Robert Bruce secures Scottish independence.

1321 Death of Dante.

1325 Zenith of Mandingo Empire of Mali (North West Africa) under Mansa Musa; superseded at end of 15th century by Songhai empire.

1327 Deposition of Edward II; subsequently murdered.

A.D.
1336 Ashikaga Period in Japan: great feudal lords semi-independent of authority of Shogun.

1337 Death of Giotto.

1338 Beginning of Hundred Years' War between England and France.

1340 Battle of Sluys: English capture French fleet.

1344 Swabian League: weakness of Imperial authority in Germany obliges towns to form leagues for mutual protection.

1346 Battles of Crecy and Neville's Cross: spectacular English victories over French and Scots.

1347 Calais taken by Edward III of England. Cola di Rienzi attempts to reform government of Rome: killed 1354.

1348 Black Death reaches Europe (England 1349, Scotland 1350).

1351 Statute of Labourers: attempt by English Parliament to freeze wages.

1353 Statute of Praemunire: restraints placed on Papal intervention in England.

1354 Ottoman Turks make first settlement in Europe, at Gallipoli.

1355 Death of Stephen Dushan: collapse of Serbian Empire which he had built.

1356 Battle of Poitiers: capture of King John of France by Black Prince. "Golden Bull" regulates Imperial elections in such a way as to place power in the hands of the German princes: valid until 1806.

1358 The Jacquerie: rising of French peasants.

1360 Peace of Bretigny: Edward III makes great territorial gains in France.

1362 English becomes the official language in Parliament and the Law Courts.

1363 Timur (Tamerlane) begins his career of conquest in Asia.

1368–1644 Ming Dynasty in China.

1370 Bertrand du Guesclin Constable of France: regains much territory from the English. Peace of Stralsund: Hansa in complete control of Baltic Sea.

1377 Pope returns to Rome: End of Babylonish Captivity.

1378 Disputed Papal Election: Beginning of Western Schism.

1380 Battle of Chioggia: decisive victory of Venice over Genoa. Battle of Kulikovo: Dmitri Donskoi of Moscow wins first major Russian victory over Golden Horde.

1381 Peasants' Revolt in England under Wat Tyler.

1384 Death of John Wyclif.

1385 Battle of Aljubarotta: Portugal safeguards independence from Castile.

1386 Battle of Sempach: Swiss safeguard independence from Habsburgs. Jagiello (Vladislav V) unites Lithuania and Poland.

1389 Battle of Kossovo: crushing defeat of Serbs and neighbouring nations by Turks.

1396 Battle of Nicopolis: "the last crusade" annihilated by Turks.

1397 Union of Kalmar: Denmark, Norway and Sweden united under one crown: dissolved 1448.

1398 Timur invades and pillages Northern India.

1399 Richard II deposed by Henry IV: first of the Lancastrian kings of England.

1400 Owen Glendower revolts in Wales. Death of Chaucer.

1401 De Haeretico Comburendo: the burning of heretics made legal in England.

1410 Battle of Tannenberg: Poles and Lithuanians break power of Teutonic Knights.

1415 Battle of Agincourt: great success of Henry V of England in France. Council of Constance ends Western Schism, burns John Hus.

1420 Treaty of Troyes: English claims to French throne recognised. Hussite Wars begin: Bohemian heretics defend themselves successfully.

A.D
1429 Relief of Orleans by Joan of Arc.

1431 Burning of Joan of Arc.

1433 Rounding of Cape Bojador: first great achievement in exploration ordered by Henry the Navigator.

1434 Cosimo die Medici begins his family's control of Florence.

1435 Congress of Arras: Burgundians withdraw support from England, in favour of France.

1438 Albert II became German king and began Hapsburg rule over Holy Roman Empire, 1438–1806.

1440 Death of Jan van Eyck.

1450 Rebellion of Jack Cade against government of Henry VI of England.

1453 Battle of Castillon: final English defeat and end of Hundred Years' War. Constantinople taken by Turks: end of Byzantine or Eastern Roman Empire.

RENAISSANCE, DISCOVERIES, "NEW MONARCHIES"

1454 First dated printing from movable types in Europe: Papal indulgence printed at Mainz.

1455 First battle of St. Albans: beginning of Wars of the Roses.

1458 Mathias Corvinus becomes king of Hungary. George of Podiebrad becomes king of Bohemia.

1461 Battle of Towton: Yorkist victory in a particularly bloody battle. Louis XI becomes king of France.

1467 Charles the Bold becomes Duke of Burgundy.

1469 Marriage of Ferdinand of Aragon with Isabella of Castile: union of the main kingdoms of Spain (1474). Lorenzo the Magnificent becomes ruler of Florence.

1470 Warwick ("The Kingmaker") turns Lancastrian, dethrones Edward IV.

1471 Return of Edward IV: Lancastrians crushed at Barnet and Tewkesbury. Ivan III of Moscow takes Novgorod: Muscovy rising to supremacy in Russia.

1476 Caxton sets up his press at Westminster.

1477 Battle of Nancy: defeat and death of Charles the Bold: end of the greatness of Burgundy.

1479 Pazzi conspiracy against the Medici in Florence.

1481 Inquisition becomes active in Castile (1484 in Aragon).

1485 Battle of Bosworth Field: beginning of Tudor period in England.

1487 Lambert Simnel's rising fails.

1488 Bartholomew Diaz rounds Cape of Good Hope.

1491 Brittany acquired by King of France (by marriage).

1492 Rodrigo Borgia becomes Pope Alexander VI. Granada, last Moorish foothold in Western Europe, conquered by Spain. Christopher Columbus discovers the West Indies.

1493 Sonni Ali brings Songhai Empire to height of its prestige: Timbuktu renowned centre of literary culture.

1494 Italy invaded by French led by Charles VIII: beginning of Italian Wars and "modern" European diplomacy and international relations. Treaty of Tordesillas: Spain and Portugal agree to divide unexplored part of world; subsequently approved by Pope.

1496 Hapsburg–Spanish marriages: foundation of later empires.

1497 Perkin Warbeck captured by Henry VII (hanged 1499). John Cabot discovers Newfoundland.

1498 Savonarola burned. Vasco da Gama at Calicut: the sea route to India found.

1499 Amerigo Vespucci charts part of the South American coast.

A.D.
1500 Brazil discovered by Pedro Cabral.

1503 Casa de Contratación established at Seville; beginnings of Spanish colonial government. Fall of Caesar Borgia.

1507 Alfonso de Albuquerque becomes Viceroy of Portuguese Empire in the East.

1513 Accession of Pope Leo X, zenith of Renaissance Papacy. Machiavelli writes *The Prince*. Balboa discovers the Pacific (South Sea). Battle of Flodden: James IV of Scotland defeated and killed by English.

1514 Battle of Chaldiran: Turkish victory begins long series of wars between Turkish and Persian Empires.

REFORMATION, HAPSBURG–VALOIS WARS

1515 Francis I becomes king of France: victory of Marignano ends legend of Swiss invincibility. Thomas Wolsey becomes Lord Chancellor of England and Cardinal.

1516 Algiers taken by Barbarossa; beginning of the Corsairs.

1517 Martin Luther nails up his Ninety-five Theses: beginning of the Reformation. Turks conquer Egypt.

1519 Charles V inherits Hapsburg lands and elected emperor. Magellan begins first circumnavigation of the world. Death of Leonardo da Vinci.

1520 Suleiman the Magnificent becomes Sultan; Turkish power at its height. Field of Cloth of Gold; celebrated diplomatic meeting, spectacular but with no results.

1521 Mexico conquered by Hernando Cortes. Belgrade taken by the Turks. Diet of Worms; Luther commits himself irrevocably. Charles V divides his dominions: Austrian and Spanish Hapsburgs.

1522 Rhodes taken by the Turks; Knights of St. John move to Malta. Election of Adrian VI, first non-Italian Pope since 1378.

1523 Swedes expel Danish overlords, elect Gustavus Vasa King.

1524 Peasants' War in Germany (suppressed 1525).

1525 Battle of Pavia: defeat and capture of Francis I by Imperialists.

1526 Battle of Mohács: Turkish victory ends Hungarian independence. Foundation of Danubian Hapsburg Monarchy (Hungarian and Bohemian crowns united with Austrian patrimony of Hapsburgs): Holy Roman Empire prolonged for 300 years. Battle of Panipat: Babar begins Moslem conquest of India, founds Mogul Empire.

1527 Sack of Rome by Imperialists. Italy under control of Charles V.

1529 Siege of Vienna by the Turks. Peace of Cambrai; pause in Hapsburg–Valois struggle, end of serious French intervention in Italy. Diet of Speyer: origin of the name Protestant.

1532 Peru conquered by Francisco Pizarro.

1533 Ivan IV (the Terrible) becomes Tsar. Marriage of Henry VIII and Catherine of Aragon declared null.

1534 Act of Supremacy: Henry VIII asserts control over English Church.

1535 Coverdale's English Bible printed. Execution of Thomas More and John Fisher.

1536 Execution of Anne Boleyn. Dissolution of smaller Monasteries by Henry VIII and Thomas Cromwell (remainder dissolved 1539). Pilgrimage of Grace: Northern rising because of religious grievances.

1538 Chibchas of Bogota conquered by Gonzalo de Quesada.

1540 Francisco de Coronado begins explorations in North America. Society of Jesus recognised by Pope.

1541 John Calvin regains authority in Geneva.

1542 First Portuguese reach Japan. New Laws of the Indies: first attempt to legislate for welfare of colonial natives, by Spanish government.

1543 Death of Copernicus.

1545 Opening of Council of Trent: the Counter-Reformation.

A.D
1547 Death of Henry VIII: Somerset Protector in the name of the boy king, Edward VI.

1549 First English Book of Common Prayer. Kett's Rebellion in Norfolk, because of economic grievances.

1550 Deposition of Protector Somerset: Northumberland rules England.

1553 Lady Jane Grey proclaimed Queen by Northumberland on death of Edward VI: Mary I succeeds. Servetus burned by Calvin.

1555 Latimer and Ridley burned by Mary. Religious Peace of Augsburg: policy of *cuius regio, eius religio* accepted in Germany.

1556 Charles V abdicated imperial powers in favour of brother Ferdinand. Cranmer burned. Akbar becomes Mogul Emperor (d. 1605).

1557 Macao becomes permanent Portuguese port in China.

1558 Calais lost by English to French. Elizabeth I becomes Queen of England.

1559 Peace of Cateau-Cambrésis: end of Hapsburg–Valois duel.

RELIGIOUS WARS

1561 Mary, Queen of Scots, returns to Scotland.

1562 First War of Religion in France: wars continue intermittently until 1598.

1563 Thirty-nine Articles define Elizabethan Church settlement.

1564 Birth of Shakespeare; death of Michelangelo.

1565 Malta beats off Turks.

1567 Deposition of Mary, Queen of Scots. Alva in the Netherlands: severe rule.

1568 Flight of Mary, Queen of Scots, to England: imprisonment. San Juan de Ulua: defeat of Hawkins, and end of his slave-trading voyages. Beginning of Anglo-Spanish maritime feud. Revolt of Moriscos of Granada (suppressed 1570).

1569 Rebellion of Northern Earls (Catholic) in England.

1570 Elizabeth I anathematised by Pope.

1571 Battle of Lepanto: spectacular defeat of Turkish sea-power by Don John of Austria. Bornu (or Kanem) in Central Sudan at its zenith under Idris III.

1572 Dutch "Sea Beggars" take Brill. Massacre of St. Bartholomew in France. Polish Crown elective again, on death of Sigismund II.

1576 Catholic League formed in France, led by Guise family.

1577 Drake begins voyage round world (returns 1580).

1578 Battle of Alcazar-Quivir: death of King Sebastian of Portugal. Parma re-establishes Spanish rule in Southern Netherlands.

1579 Union of Utrecht: seven northern provinces of Netherlands form what becomes Dutch Republic. Death of Grand Vizier Sokolli: decline of Turkish power begins.

1580 Philip II of Spain becomes king of Portugal.

1582 Gregorian Calendar (or New Style) introduced by Pope Gregory XIII.

1584 Assassination of William the Silent.

1585 Hidéyoshi Dictator of Japan: unification of the country. English intervention in Spanish–Dutch War.

1587 Execution of Mary, Queen of Scots. Drake "singes King of Spain's beard." Shah Abbas I (the Great) becomes ruler of Persia (d. 1629).

1588 Spanish Armada defeated.

1589 Death of Catherine de' Medici, Queen-Mother of France.

1592 Moorish conquest of African Songhai Empire.

1593 Henry IV of France becomes Catholic.

1598 Edict of Nantes: French Protestants guaranteed liberty of worship. End of French Wars of Religion.

1600 English East India Company founded. Tokugawa Period begins in Japan (Ieyasu takes title of Shogun, 1603): lasts until 1868.

A.D.

1601 Rebellion and execution of Earl of Essex. Elizabethan Poor Law.

1602 Dutch East India Company founded.

1603 Irish revolts finally suppressed by Mountjoy. Accession of James VI of Scotland as James I of England: Union of English and Scottish Crowns.

1604 Hampton Court Conference: James I disappoints Puritans.

1605 Gunpowder Plot.

1607 Virginia colonised by London company: Jamestown founded.

1608 Quebec founded by Champlain.

1609 Twelve Years' Truce between Spain and United Provinces: Dutch independence in fact secured. Expulsion of Moriscos from Spain.

1610 Assassination of Henry IV of France.

1611 Plantation of Ulster with English and Scottish colonists. Authorised Version of the Bible in England.

1613 Michael Romanov becomes Tsar: the first of the dynasty.

1614 Napier publishes his explanation of logarithms.

1616 Death of Shakespeare and Cervantes. Edict of Inquisition against Galileo's astronomy.

1618 "Defenestration of Prague": Bohemian assertion of independence begins Thirty Years' War.

1620 Pilgrim Fathers settle in New England.

1624 "Massacre of Amboina": English driven out of spice islands by Dutch. Richelieu becomes Chief Minister in France.

1628 Murder of Duke of Buckingham. Petition of Right by Commons to Charles I. Fall of La Rochelle: French Protestants lose political power. Harvey publishes his work on the circulation of blood.

1629 Charles I begins Personal Rule.

1630 Gustavus Adolphus of Sweden enters Thirty Years' War, turns tide against Imperialists.

1631 Sack of Magdeburg, one of the worst incidents of the Thirty Years' War.

1632 Battle of Lützen: death of Gustavus Adolphus.

1633 William Laud appointed Archbishop of Canterbury. Thomas Wentworth takes up his post as Lord Deputy of Ireland.

1634 Dismissal and murder of Imperialist general Wallenstein.

1635 John Hampden refuses to pay Ship Money.

1636 Japanese forbidden to go abroad.

1637 Russian pioneers reach shores of Pacific.

1638 Covenant widely signed in Scotland.

1639 First Bishops' War: Charles I comes to terms with Scots.

1640 Second Bishops' War: Charles I defeated by Scots. Long Parliament begins: abolition of Royal prerogatives. Great Elector (Frederick William) becomes ruler of Brandenburg. Revolt of Catalonia (finally suppressed 1659). Revolt of Portugal: Duke of Braganza proclaimed king.

1641 Japanese exclude all foreigners (except for small Dutch trading fleet). Massacre of Protestants in Ireland. Wentworth (Earl of Strafford) executed. Grand Remonstrance of Commons to Charles I.

1642 Charles I attempts to arrest the Five Members. Outbreak of English Civil War: first general engagement, Edgehill. Death of Richelieu.

1643 Mazarin becomes Chief Minister of France. Battle of Rocroi: French victory, end of Spanish reputation for invincibility. English Parliament agrees to Solemn League and Covenant, secures services of Scots army.

1644 Marston Moor: decisive battle of English Civil War. North lost to Charles I. Tippemuir: Montrose begins victorious Royalist

A.D

campaign in Scotland. 1644–1911 Manchu dynasty in China.

1645 Formation of New Model Army. Naseby: main Royalist army crushed. Battle of Philiphaugh: Montrose's army destroyed.

1646 Charles I surrenders to Scots.

1647 Charles I handed over to Parliament. Charles I seized by Army. Charles I flees to Carisbrooke Castle.

1648 Second Civil War: New Model Army defeats Scots and Royalists. "Pride's Purge": Parliament refashioned by Army. Peace of Westphalia ends Thirty Years' War.

ASCENDANCY OF FRANCE

1649 Charles I executed. England governed as Commonwealth. Cromwell in Ireland. New Code of Laws in Russia completes establishment of serfdom.

1651 Battle of Worcester: Cromwell's final victory, now master of all Britain. First English Navigation Act. Hobbes' *Leviathan* published.

1652 Foundation of Cape Colony by Dutch under Van Riebeek. First Anglo-Dutch War begins (ends 1654).

1653 Cromwell dissolves Rump, becomes Protector.

1655 Major-Generals appointed to supervise districts of England. Jamaica seized by English.

1656 Grand Vizier Kiuprili: revival of Turkish government.

1658 Death of Cromwell.

1659 Peace of the Pyrenees: France replaces Spain as greatest power in Western Europe.

1660 Restoration of monarch in Britain: Charles II. Royal Society founded.

1661 Death of Mazarin: Louis XIV now rules in person. "Clarendon Code"; beginning of persecution of Non-conformists in England.

1664 New York taken by English: Second Anglo-Dutch War ensues (ends 1667).

1665 Great Plague of London.

1666 Great Fire of London. Newton's discovery of law of gravitation.

1667 Dutch fleet in the Medway. War of Devolution begins: first of Louis XIV's aggressions.

1668 Portuguese Independence recognised by Spain.

1669 Death of Rembrandt.

1670 Secret Treaty of Dover between Charles II and Louis XIV. Revolt of peasants and Don Cossacks under Stenka Razin (suppressed 1671).

1672 Third Anglo-Dutch War begins (ends 1674). Murder of De Witt brothers: William of Orange becomes leader of Dutch against French invasion.

1673 Test Act deprives English Catholics and Non-conformists of public offices. Death of Molière.

1675 Battle of Fehrbellin: Swedes defeated by Great Elector; rise of Prussian military power. Greenwich Royal Observatory founded.

1678 "Popish Plot" of Titus Oates utilised by Shaftesbury and the Whigs to bring pressure on Charles II.

1679 Bothwell Brig: suppression of Scottish Covenanters. Habeas Corpus Act passed.

1680 Chambers of Reunion: Louis XIV uses legal arguments to complete annexation of Alsace.

1681 Oxford Parliament: Charles II overcomes his opponents, begins to rule without Parliament.

1683 Rye House Plot. Siege of Vienna by the Turks: last major Turkish attack on Europe.

1685 Sedgemoor: Monmouth's rebellion crushed by James II. Revocation of Edict of Nantes: persecution of French Protestants by Louis XIV.

A.D.

1688 Seven Bishops protest against James II's policy of toleration, and are acquitted. William of Orange lands in England: flight of James II. "The Glorious Revolution."

1689 Derry relieved: failure of James II to subdue Irish Protestants. Killiecrankie: death of Dundee and collapse of Highland rising. Bill of Rights defines liberties established by "Glorious Revolution."

1690 Locke's *Two Treatises on Government* published. Beachy Head: French victory over Anglo-Dutch fleet. Boyne: defeat of James II by William III.

1691 Capitulation of Limerick: surrender of Irish supporters of James II on conditions which are not fulfilled.

1692 Massacre of Glencoe: Government's "lesson" to Highlanders. La Hogue: Anglo-Dutch fleet regains command of the sea.

1693 National Debt of England begun.

1694 Bank of England founded.

1695 Press licensing abandoned: freedom of the press in England.

1696 Peter the Great sole Czar.

1697 Peace of Ryswyck between Louis XIV and William III. Peter journeys "incognito" to the West.

1699 Treaty of Karlowitz: great Turkish concessions to Austrians. Death of Racine.

1700 Great Northern War, involving all Baltic powers, begins (ends 1721). Battle of Narva: Russians defeated by Charles XII of Sweden. Death of Charles II of Spain: under French influence Louis XIV's grandson Philip of Anjou named successor.

1701 War of the Spanish Succession begins. Hungarian revolt led by Francis Rakoczi against Austrians. Elector of Brandenburg receives title of King of Prussia. Act of Settlement establishes Protestant Hanoverian Succession in England.

1703 Methuen Treaty between England and Portugal. St. Petersburg founded.

1704 Gibraltar taken by Rooke. Blenheim: Marlborough stops France from winning war.

1706 Ramillies: Marlborough's second great victory. Turin: Eugene defeats French in Italy.

1707 Almanza: Anglo-Austrian forces in Spain defeated by French under Berwick. Act of Union: English and Scottish Parliaments united. Death of Aurungzib, last powerful Mogul.

1708 Oudenarde: Marlborough's third great victory.

1709 Pultava: Charles XII's invasion of Russia smashed by Peter the Great. Malplaquet: Marlborough's fourth great victory—at great cost in lives.

1710 Tory government in England.

1711 Dismissal of Marlborough.

1713 Peace of Utrecht: England makes advantageous peace with Louis XIV. Bourbon king of Spain grants Asiento (monopoly of Spanish American slave trade) to England.

1714 Peace of Rastatt between France and Austria. Death of Queen Anne: accession of George I. Beginning of Hanoverian Dynasty in Britain. Whig oligarchy rules.

1715 Jacobite Rising defeated at Preston and Sheriffmuir. Death of Louis XIV. France under Regent Orleans.

ENLIGHTENED DESPOTS: FIRST BRITISH EMPIRE

1716 Septennial Act: English Parliament prolongs its life from three to seven years. Prince Eugène of Savoy defeated Turks at Petrovaradin (Yugoslavia).

1720 Collapse of Law's system of banking ("Mississippi Bubble") in France. "South Sea Bubble" in England.

A.D

1721 Robert Walpole becomes first Prime Minister. Peace of Nystad: Sweden no longer a major power at end of Great Northern War. Russian gains.

1723 Death of Christopher Wren.

1727 First Indemnity Act for Non-conformists.

1729 Methodists begin at Oxford.

1730 Resignation from government of Townshend, who becomes agricultural pioneer.

1733 First Family Compact between Bourbon kings of France and Spain. Withdrawal of Walpole's Excise Bill. John Kay invents flying shuttle, first of the great textile inventions. Jethro Tull publishes *The Horse-Hoeing Husbandry*, advocating new agricultural methods.

1738 Lorraine ceded to France.

1739 Nadir Shah with Persian army sacks Delhi, ruins Mogul power. War of Jenkins' Ear begins between Spain and Britain.

1740 Frederick II (the Great) becomes king of Prussia. Maria Theresa succeeds to Austrian dominions. Frederick seizes Silesia, begins War of the Austrian Succession.

1742 Fall of Walpole.

1743 Dettingen: George II, last British king to command his army in the field, defeats French.

1745 Fontenoy: Duke of Cumberland defeated by Marshal Saxe. Jacobite Rebellion under Prince Charles Edward: initial success, victory of Prestonpans, march to Derby.

1746 Culloden: Jacobites destroyed by Cumberland.

1748 Treaty of Aix-la-Chapelle: Frederick retains Silesia, elsewhere status quo.

1750 Death of J. S. Bach.

1751 First volume of the *Encyclopédie* published in France. Clive takes and holds Arcot: checks plans of Dupleix in Southern India. Chinese conquest of Tibet.

1752 Britain adopts New Style calendar.

1753 British Museum begun by government purchase of Sloane's collection.

1755 Lisbon earthquake. Braddock's defeat and death at the hands of French and Indians.

1756 Diplomatic Revolution (alliance of Austria with France) achieved by Kaunitz; Britain and Prussia perforce became allies. Seven Years' War begins. Minorca taken from British by French (Byng executed 1757). Black Hole of Calcutta: suffocation of many British prisoners.

1757 Pitt Secretary of State, main influence in British government. Rossbach: one of Frederick II's numerous victories against heavy odds. Plassey: Clive conquers Bengal.

1759 "Year of Victories" for Britain: Quebec, Minden, Lagos, Quiberon Bay. James Brindley designs Worsley–Manchester Canal: the beginning of this form of transport in Britain. Voltaire publishes *Candide*. Death of Handel.

1760 Wandewash: decisive defeat of French in India, by Coote.

1761 Panipat: Mahrattas heavily defeated by Afghans. Fall of Pitt.

1762 Catherine II (the Great) becomes Czarina. Rousseau's *Social Contract* and *Emile* published.

1763 Peace of Paris: British colonial gains, First British Empire at its height. Peace of Hubertusburg: Frederick II retains his gains. Pontiac's Conspiracy: failure of Red Indian attempt to destroy British power.

1764 John Wilkes expelled from Commons. James Hargreaves invents spinning jenny.

1766 Henry Cavendish proves hydrogen to be an element.

1768 Royal Academy of Arts founded.

1769 Richard Arkwright erects spinning mill (invention of water frame).

1770 Struensee comes to power in Denmark (executed 1772). "Boston Massacre." James Cook discovers New South Wales.

1772 First Partition of Poland between Russia, Prussia and Austria.

A.D.

1773 Society of Jesus suppressed by Pope (restored 1814). Revolt led by Pugachov in Russia (suppressed 1775). "Boston Tea Party."

1774 Warren Hastings appointed first Governor-General of India. Treaty of Kutchuk Kainarji; great Turkish concessions to Russia. Karl Scheele discovers chlorine. Joseph Priestley's discovery of oxygen.

1775 Watt and Boulton in partnership at Soho Engineering Works, Birmingham. Lexington: first action in American War of Independence.

1776 American Declaration of Independence. Adam Smith's *Wealth of Nations* published.

1777 Saratoga: surrender of British army under Burgoyne to Americans.

1779 Beginning of great Franco-Spanish siege of Gibraltar (raised finally, 1783). Samuel Crompton invents spinning mule.

1780 Joseph II assumes sole power in Austria. Armed neutrality of maritime nations to restrain British interference with shipping.

1781 Joseph II introduces religious toleration, abolishes serfdom in Austria. Yorktown: surrender of British under Cornwallis.

1782 Battle of the Saints: Rodney's victory save British West Indies.

1783 Treaty of Versailles: American independence recognised. Pitt the Younger becomes Prime Minister of Britain. First flights in hot-air (Montgolfier) and hydrogen (Charles) balloons.

1784 Death of Dr. Samuel Johnson.

1785 Edmund Cartwright invents the power loom.

1787 American Constitution drafted.

1788 Impeachment of Warren Hastings begins (ends 1795): English fleet commanded by Captain Arthur Phillip landed in Australia.

FRENCH REVOLUTION AND NAPOLEON

1789 Washington first President of U.S.A. French Revolution begins. Storming of the Bastille (July 14).

1790 Civil constitution of the Clergy in France.

1791 Flight of Louis XVI and Marie Antoinette to Varennes.

1792 Battle of Valmy: French Revolution saved from intervention of European kings. Denmark becomes first country to prohibit slave trade. France becomes a Republic.

1793 Louis XVI beheaded. Second partition of Poland.

1794 "Glorious First of June." Fall of Robespierre and end of Jacobin Republic. Negro revolt in Haiti led by Toussaint L'Ouverture.

1795 The Directory established. "Whiff of Grapeshot": Napoleon Bonaparte disperses Paris mob, Oct. 5. Batavian Republic set up by France.

1796 First Italian campaign of Bonaparte: victories of Lodi, Arcola.

1797 Treaty of Campo Formio: Bonaparte compels Austria to make peace. Britain left to fight France alone.

1798 Bonaparte goes to Egypt. Battle of the Nile. Vinegar Hill rebellion in Ireland suppressed.

1799 New coalition against France: Suvorov and Russians victorious in Italy. Bonaparte returns to France. *Coup d'état* of Brumaire, Nov. 9. Consulate set up.

1800 Parliamentary Union of Great Britain and Ireland.

1801 Treaty of Lunéville: Austria makes peace; great French gains in Germany.

1802 Peace of Amiens between Britain and France. *Charlotte Dundas*, first practical steamship, on Clyde.

1803 Insurrection in Ireland under Robert Emmet. Britain again at war with France.

A.D

1804 Bonaparte becomes Emperor. Spain declares war against Great Britain. Serbian revolt against Turks under Kara George.

1805 Battle of Trafalgar, Nelson's great victory and death, Oct. 21. Battle of Austerlitz, Dec. 2.

1806 Death of Pitt, Jan. 23. Confederation of the Rhine: Napoleon's reorganisation of Germany, July 12. End of Holy Roman Empire, Aug. 6. Prussia overthrown at Jena. Napoleon declares Great Britain in a state of blockade—"Continental System."

1807 Slave trade abolished in British Empire. Treaty of Tilsit: with Alexander of Russia his friend, Napoleon controls all of Europe. Occupation of Portugal by French, to enforce Continental Blockade.

1808 Occupation of Spain by French. Spanish rising: guerilla warfare. Peninsular War begins. Battle of Vimeiro (defeat of French by Wellington), Aug. 21.

1809 Battle of Corunna and death of Sir John Moore, Jan. 16. Attempted risings in Germany against Napoleon: Austria renews war. Treaty of Schönbrunn, Oct. 14.

1810 Self-government established in Argentina: first South American state to become independent of Spain.

1811 Massacre of Mamelukes at Cairo. Luddite riots.

1812 Retreat from Moscow: destruction of Napoleon's Grand Army.

1813 War of Liberation starts in Germany. Defeat of French by Wellington at Vitoria, June 21

1814 Soult defeated by Wellington at Toulouse, April 10. Abdication of Napoleon, April 11; Louis XVIII king of France. Congress of Vienna (concluded June 1815) under guidance of Metternich. Resettlement of Europe, usually by restoration of kings. Germanic Confederation under Austrian supervision. Poland ruled by Czar. Kingdom of Netherlands to include Belgium.

THE OLD ORDER RESTORED

1815 Escape of Napoleon from Elba. Battle of Waterloo, June 18. Corn Law in Britain to safeguard agricultural interests by keeping up prices. Quadruple Alliance (Austria, Russia, Prussia, Britain) to maintain Vienna settlement and hold regular meetings ("Congress System") —frequently confused with Holy Alliance, which was simply a declaration of Christian principles. Napoleon sent to St. Helena, Oct. 16.

1818 Bernadotte made king of Sweden (Charles XIV), Feb. 6.

1819 Singapore founded by Stamford Raffles. Beginning of Zollverein (Customs Union) in Germany under Prussian influence. Parliamentary reform meeting at Manchester dispersed by military ("Peterloo"), Aug. 16.

1820 Death of George III, Jan. 29.

1821 Death of Napoleon at St. Helena, May 5.

1822 Congress of Verona: congress system breaks down with refusal of Britain (Canning) to intervene against revolutions.

1823 "Monroe Doctrine" announced by U.S.A. President, Dec. 2.

1824 Repeal of Combination Acts in Britain which had forbidden Trades Unions. Charles X king of France.

1825 Independence of all Spanish American mainland now achieved. Nicholas I Czar of Russia. First railway, Stockton to Darlington, opened.

1826 First crossing of Atlantic under steam by Dutch ship *Curaçao*. Menai suspension bridge opened.

1827 Battle of Navarino, Turkish and Egyptian fleet destroyed. Death of Beethoven.

1828 Death of Chaka, great Zulu conqueror.

1829 Greece independent. Catholic Emancipation Act in Britain. Metropolitan Police established.

A.D.
1830 Death of George IV, June 26. Louis Philippe ousts Charles X. Belgium breaks away from Holland. Russian Poland revolts.

1831 First Reform Bill introduced by Lord John Russell. Leopold of Saxe-Coburg becomes king of independent Belgium. British Association founded. Faraday discovers electromagnetic induction.

1832 Reform Bill passed, June 7. Walter Scott, Jeremy Bentham, and Goethe die. Electric telegraph invented by Morse.

1833 Beginning of "Oxford Movement" in English Church. First government grant made to English schools. First British Factory Act.

1834 Poor Law Amendment Act: tightening up of relief in Britain. "Tolpuddle Martyrs" victimised to discourage British working-class movement. Carlist wars begin in Spain.

1835 Municipal Reform Act revises British local government. The word "socialism" first used. "Tamworth Manifesto" of Peel defines aims of Conservative Party.

1836 People's Charter states programme of Chartists. Great Trek of Boers from British South African territory. Texas achieves independence of Mexico.

1837 Queen Victoria succeeds to the throne.

1838 National Gallery opened.

1839 First Afghan war begins. Chartist riots at Birmingham and Newport. Anti-Corn Law League founded. Aden annexed by Britain.

1840 Penny postage instituted. Queen Victoria marries Prince Albert of Saxe-Coburg-Gotha. "Opium War" with China begins. Union Act gives Canada responsible government. Last convicts landed in New South Wales.

1841 Hong Kong acquired by Britain.

1842 Chartists present second national petition and put themselves at the head of strikes. Great potato famine in Ireland begins.

1846 Repeal of the Corn Laws. Peel resigns.

1847 British Museum opened.

REVOLUTIONS AND NEW NATIONS

1848 Monster meeting of Chartists on Kennington Common, procession abandoned, Apr. 10. General revolutionary movement throughout the Continent. Louis Philippe abdicates: French Republic proclaimed. Swiss Federal Constitution established after defeat of Sonderbund (Catholic succession movement). Rising in Vienna: flight of Metternich, accession of Francis Joseph. Nationalist risings in Bohemia and Hungary. Frankfurt Parliament: attempt to unite Germany on liberal principles. Communist Manifesto produced by Marx and Engels. U.S.A. makes great territorial gains from Mexico. Gold discovered in California.

1849 Collapse of revolutionary movements. Rome republic besieged by French (June 3), defended by Garibaldi, holds out until July 2. Austrians take Venice, Aug. 22. Repeal of old Navigation Laws. Punjab annexed by Britain.

1850 Cavour becomes Prime Minister of Sardinia. Don Pacifico affair: privileges of British citizenship at their highest defended by Palmerston.

1851 Great Exhibition in Hyde Park. First satisfactory submarine telegraph cable between Dover and Calais laid. Gold in Australia.

1852 Independence of Transvaal recognised by Britain. Napoleon III Emperor of the French.

1853 U.S. Commodore Perry lands in Japan: beginning of Western influence. Russia and Turkey at war.

1854 War declared against Russia by France and Britain. Allied armies land in Crimea, Sept. 14 (Alma, Siege of Sevastopol, Balaklava, Inkerman). Orange Free State set up.

1855 Sardinia joins Britain and France against Russia. Fall of Sevastopol and end of Crimean War. Alexander II Czar of Russia.

A.D
1856 Peace Treaty signed at Paris. Bessemer invents process for large-scale production of steel. Livingstone completes journey across Africa.

1857 Indian Mutiny. Relief of Lucknow. Canton captured by English and French.

1858 *Great Eastern* launched. Crown assumes government of India. Treaty of Aigun, by which China cedes Amur region to Russia.

1859 Darwin publishes *Origin of Species*. French support for Piedmont in war with Austria (Magenta, Solferino). Piedmont receives Lombardy. Harper's Ferry raid: John Brown hanged, Dec. 2.

1860 Garibaldi and the Thousand Redshirts in Sicily and Naples; most of Italy united to Piedmont. Vladivostok founded; Russia strongly established on N.W. Pacific.

1861 Abraham Lincoln takes office as Pres. of U.S. American Civil War commences with 11 states breaking away to form Southern Confederacy. Bull Run (July 21) Confederate success ends Federal hopes of easy victory. Victor Emmanuel proclaimed by first Italian Parliament as king of Italy. Emancipation of Serfs in Russia. Death of Prince Albert, Dec. 14.

1862 Bismarck becomes leading minister in Prussia. Garibaldi attempts to seize Rome but wounded at Aspromonte. Aug. 29. Cotton famine in Lancashire.

1863 Polish rising against Russia (suppressed 1864). French in Mexico. Battle of Gettysburg, July 1–3. Maximilian of Austria made emperor of Mexico.

1864 Cession of Schleswig-Holstein to Prussia and Austria. First Socialist International formed. Taiping rebellion in China ended. Federal army enters Atlanta, Sept. 2: General Sherman captures Savannah ("From Atlanta to the sea"). Dec. 22. Geneva Convention originated.

1865 Death of Cobden, Apr. 2. General Lee surrenders to Grant, Apr. 9. Lincoln assassinated, Apr. 14. Thirteenth Amendment to Constitution: slavery abolished in U.S. Death of Palmerston, Oct. 18. Lister introduces antiseptic surgery in Glasgow. Tashkent becomes centre of Russian expansion in Central Asia. Mendel experiments on heredity. William Booth founds Salvation Army.

1866 Austro-Prussian War over Schleswig-Holstein ("Seven Weeks War"). Prussian victory at Sadowa (July 3). Venice secured for Italy, who had, however, been defeated by Austrians at Custozza (June 24) and Lissa (July 20). Treaty of Prague, Aug. 23.

1867 North German Confederation founded. Emperor Maximilian of Mexico shot. Dominion of Canada established. Russia sells Alaska to America for $7 million. Garibaldi makes second attempt to seize Rome, but defeated by Pope with French support at Mentana, Nov. 3. Second Parliamentary Reform Bill passed (Disraeli "dished the Whigs").

1868 Shogunate abolished in Japan: Meiji period of rapid Westernisation under Imperial leadership begins. Ten Years' War (1868–78): struggle for Cuban independence from Spain. Disraeli succeeds Derby as Prime Minister but defeated in general election by Gladstone, Nov.

1869 General Grant, Pres. of U.S. Irish Church disestablished. Suez Canal formally opened.

1870 Napoleon III declares war against Prussia. French defeated at Woerth, Gravelotte, and Sedan. Paris besieged. Rome and Papal states annexed to kingdom of Italy. Irish Land Act passed. Forster's Education Act puts elementary education within reach of all British children. Papal Infallibility announced.

1871 William I of Prussia proclaimed German emperor at Versailles, Jan. 18. Paris capitulates, Jan. 28. Commune of Paris proclaimed, Mar. 28. Peace signed at Frankfurt-on-Main, May 10. Government troops enter Paris and

A.D.

crush Communards, May 28. Thiers President of the Republic, Aug. 31. Mont Cenis tunnel opened. Trade Unions in Britain legalised.

RIVAL IMPERIAL POWERS

1872 Secret ballot introduced in Britain. Death of Mazzini, Mar. 10.

1873 Death of Livingstone, May 4. Ashanti war.

1874 Disraeli succeeds Gladstone as Prime Minister.

1875 England purchases Khedive's shares in Suez Canal, Nov.

1876 Bulgarian massacres. Serbo-Turkish war. Bell invents the telephone. Custer defeated and killed in last large-scale Red Indian success. Porfirio Diaz in power in Mexico (until 1911). Victoria declared Empress of India.

1877 Transvaal annexed to British Empire. War between Russia and Turkey. Satsuma rebellion in Japan: final unsuccessful attempt to halt new ideas.

1878 Congress of Berlin: general Balkan settlement. Cyprus leased to Britain (annexed 1914). Second war with Afghanistan (ended 1880). Edison and Swan produce first successful incandescent electric light.

1879 Dual control (Britain and France) in Egypt. Zulu War. Gladstone's Midlothian Campaign. Tay Bridge destroyed, Dec. 28.

1880 Beaconsfield ministry succeeded by second Gladstone ministry. Transvaal declared a republic.

1881 British defeat at Majuba: independence of Transvaal recognised. France occupies Tunis. Gambetta becomes Prime Minister of France. Revolt of the Mahdi in the Sudan. Pasteur's famous immunisation experiment to show that inoculated animals can survive anthrax.

1882 Lord Frederick Cavendish, Irish Secretary, assassinated in Phoenix Park, Dublin, May 6. Triple Alliance (Germany, Austria, Italy) first formed. Alexandria bombarded, July 11. Cairo occupied by British troops, Sept. 14.

1883 National Insurance begun in Germany. Death of Wagner.

1884 Wolseley heads expedition to Khartoum to rescue Gordon. French establish complete protectorate in Indo-China. Evelyn Baring takes over administration of Egypt. Russians capture Merv. Berlin Conference defines rights of European Powers in Africa. Third Parliamentary Reform Bill. Parsons invents his turbine. Greenwich meridian internationally recognised as prime meridian. Fabian Society founded.

1885 Khartoum captured; Gordon slain, Jan. 26.

1886 Upper Burma annexed by Britain. Home Rule Bill defeated in Commons. All Indians in U.S.A. now in Reservations. Daimler produces his first motor car. Completion of Canadian Pacific Railway. Gold discovered in the Transvaal.

1887 Queen Victoria's Jubilee celebration, June 21.

1888 William II German Emperor. County Councils set up in Britain.

1889 Mayerling: tragic death of Prince Rudolf of Austria, Jan. 30. Flight of General Boulanger, after attempting to become master of France. Second Socialist International set up. Great London dock strike, Aug. 15–Sept. 16. Parnell Commission concludes sittings, Nov. 23 (129th day).

1890 Parnell ruined by divorce case: Irish politicians split. Sherman Anti-Trust Law: first attempt in U.S.A. to break cartels. Opening of Forth Bridge, Mar. 4. Bismarck resigns, Mar. 17. Caprivi succeeds. Heligoland ceded to Germany.

1891 The United States of Brazil formed.

1892 Panama Canal financial scandals in France.

1893 Home Rule Bill passes third reading in Commons, Sept. 1: Lords reject Bill, Sept. 8.

1894 Opening of Manchester Ship Canal, Jan. 1.

A.D

Gladstone resigns, Mar. 3, Lord Rosebery succeeds. Armenian massacres by Turks: repeated at intervals for next quarter of century. Japan declares war against China. Dreyfus convicted of treason.

1895 Opening of Kiel canal, June 21. Rosebery resigns, June 22; Salisbury Ministry succeeds. Treaty of Shimonoseki: Japan gets Formosa, free hand in Korea. New Cuban revolution breaks out against Spanish. Marconi sends message over a mile by wireless. Röntgen discovers X-rays. Freud publishes his first work on psycho-analysis. Jameson Raid, Dec. 29.

1896 Jameson raiders defeated by Boers, Jan. 1. Adowa: Italian disaster at hands of Abyssinians, the first major defeat of a white colonising power by "natives." Gold discovered in the Klondike.

1897 Cretan revolt leads to Greek–Turkish War. Hawaii annexed by U.S.A. Queen Victoria's Diamond Jubilee, June 22. Great Gold Rush began.

1898 Port Arthur ceded to Russia. Spanish–American War. *Maine*, U.S. warship blown up in Havana harbour. Treaty of Paris, Dec. 10: Cuba freed, Puerto Rico and Guam ceded to U.S.A., Phillippines surrendered for $20 million. Death of Gladstone, May 19. Battle of Omdurman, decisive defeat of Mahdists, Sept. 2. Empress of Austria assassinated, Sept. 10. The Curies discovered Radium.

1899 Boer War begins, Oct. 10.

1900 Boers attack Ladysmith, Jan. 6. Battle of Spion Kop, Buller repulsed with severe losses, Jan. 14. Relief of Kimberley, Feb. 15. Ladysmith relieved, Feb. 28. Mafeking relieved, May 17. Boxer outbreak in China, May. Annexation of Orange Free State, May 26. Roberts occupies Johannesburg, May 31. "Khaki Election." Annexation of the Transvaal, Oct. 25. Australian Commonwealth proclaimed, Dec. 30.

1901 Queen Victoria dies, Jan. 22. Trans-Siberian Railway opened for single-track traffic.

1902 Anglo-Japanese Alliance, Jan. 30. Death of Cecil Rhodes, Mar. 26. Treaty of Vereeniging ends Boer War, May 31.

1903 Congo scandal: celebrated case of misrule and exploitation. Royal family of Serbia assassinated, May 29. First controlled flight in heavier-than-air machine—Orville and Wilbur Wright at Kitty Hawk, U.S.A., Dec. 17.

1904 Russo-Japanese War begins, Feb. 8. Japanese victory at Yalu River, May 1. British forces under Younghusband reach Lhasa, Aug. 3. Treaty with Tibet signed at Lhasa, Sept. 7.

1905 Port Arthur falls to Japanese, Jan. 3. "Bloody Sunday" massacre at St. Petersburg, Jan. 22. Destruction of Russian fleet under Rozhdestvenski at Tsushima by Admiral Togo (May). Treaty of Portsmouth (U.S.A.) ends Russo-Japanese war. Separation of Church and State in France. Norway separates itself from Sweden.

1906 General strike in Russia. San Francisco destroyed by earthquake and fire, Apr. 18. Simplon tunnel opened for railway traffic, June 1. First Duma (Parliament with limited powers) in Russia. Liberal "landslide" majority in Britain: Labour M.P.s appear. Movement for Women's Suffrage becomes active in Britain. Algeciras Conference: Franco-German crises resolved in favour of France. Death of Ibsen. Vitamins discovered by F. G. Hopkins.

1907 New Zealand becomes a dominion.

1908 Annexation of Congo by Belgium. Young Turk revolution. Annexation of Bosnia and Herzegovina by Austria: severe rebuff for Russia. Asquith becomes Prime Minister of Britain.

1909 Old Age Pensions in Britain. Peary reaches North Pole. Blériot makes first cross-Channel flight. House of Lords rejects Lloyd George's budget. Union of South Africa formed. Henry Ford concentrates on producing Model T chassis: beginnings of cheap motors.

A.D.
1910 Accession of George V on death of Edward VII, May 6. Liberals win two General Elections. Labour Exchanges established in Britain. Death of Tolstoy and Florence Nightingale.

1911 Parliament Act: power of Lords decisively reduced. British M.P.s paid for first time. National Insurance in Britain. Great British rail strike. Tripoli taken from Turkey by Italy. Chinese Revolution. Amundsen reaches South Pole, Dec. 14.

1912 China becomes a Republic under Sun Yat Sen. *Titanic* disaster off Cape Race, Apr. 14–15. Great British coal strike. Scott's last expedition. Outbreak of Balkan Wars.

1913 Treaty of Bucharest: most of Turkey-in-Europe divided among Balkan states.

FIRST WORLD WAR

1914 Archduke Francis Ferdinand, heir to the Hapsburg thrones, assassinated at Sarajevo, June 28. Austria–Hungary declares war against Serbia, July 28. Germany declares war against Russia, Aug. 1. Germany declares war against France, Aug. 3. German invasion of Belgium: Great Britain declares war against Germany, Aug. 4. Great Britain declares war on Austria–Hungary, Aug. 12. British Expeditionary Force concentrated before Mauberge, Aug. 20. Battle of Mons; Japan declared war on Germany, Aug. 23. Battle of the Marne, Sept. 5–9. Trench warfare began on Aisne salient, Sept. 16. Three British cruisers (*Aboukir*, *Hogue*, and *Cressy*) sunk by one U-boat, Sept. 22. First Battle of Ypres, Oct. 12–Nov. 11. Raiding of German cruiser *Emden* until destroyed, Nov. 9. Battle of Coronel: German cruisers *Scharnhorst* and *Gneisenau* sink British cruisers *Good Hope* and *Monmouth*, Nov. 1. Great Britain declares war against Turkey, Nov. 5. Destruction of German squadron off Falkland Is., Dec. 8. British protectorate over Egypt proclaimed, Dec. 17. First Zeppelin appeared over British coast, Dec. 20.

1915 Turkish army defeated in Caucasus, Jan 5. Great Britain declared blockade of Germany, Mar. 1. Battle of Neuve Chapelle, Mar. 10–13. Naval attack on Dardanelles called off, Mar. 22. First landing of British, Australian, New Zealand troops on Gallipoli Peninsula, Apr. 25. Second Battle of Ypres, Apr. 22–May 25: Germans first used gas. Sinking of *Lusitania*, May 7. Battle of Aubers Ridge, May 9–25. Italy declares war on Austria, May 22. British Coalition Government formed, May 26. Italian army crosses Isonzo, June 2. Zeppelin destroyed by R. A. J. Warneford, June 7. Second landing of Allied troops on Suvla Bay. Italy declares war on Turkey, Aug. 20. Turks defeated at Kut-el-Amara, Sept 28. Serbia conquered by Austria and Bulgaria, Nov. 28. French and British troops occupy Salonika, Dec. 13. British troops withdraw from Anzac and Suvla, Dec. 20.

1916 Evacuation of Gallipoli completed, Jan 8. Opening of Battle of Verdun, Feb. 21. Republican rising in Ireland, Apr. 24. First Daylight Saving Bill passed. Fall of Kut, Apr. 29. Battle of Jutland, May 31. Brusilov's offensive in Galicia begins, June 4. Kitchener drowned when *Hampshire* struck mine, June 5. Battle of the Somme, July 1–Nov. 13: British losses: 420,000. Italians capture Gorizia, Aug. 10. Hindenburg and Ludendorff chiefs of German staff, Aug. 27. Rumania declares war against Austria and Germany. Aug. 27. Tanks first used by British, Sept. 15. Death of Francis Joseph of Austria, Nov. 21. Lloyd George forms War Cabinet, Dec. 6. Joffre replaced by Nivelle, early Dec.

1917 Unrestricted submarine warfare begins, Feb. 1. British troops occupy Baghdad, Mar. 11. Revolution in Russia, Mar. 12. U.S.A. declares war on Germany, April 6. Battle of Arras, Apr. 9–14: Vimy Ridge taken by Canadians, Apr. 10. Pétain replaced Nivelle, May 15. Messines Ridge taken by British, June 7. First American contingents arrive in France, June 26. Allenby assumes Palestine

A.D
command, June 29. Third Battle of Ypres opened, July 31. Russia proclaimed a Republic, Sept. 15. British victory on Passchendaele Ridge, Oct. 4. French victory on the Aisne, Oct. 23. Caporetto: Italians severely defeated by Austrians. Oct. 24. Bolshevik Revolution, Nov. 7 (Oct. 25 O.S.). Passchendaele captured by British, Nov. 6. Balfour declaration recognised Palestine as "a national home" for the Jews, Nov. 8. Hindenburg Lines smashed on 10-mile front, Nov. 20. Fall of Jerusalem, Dec. 9. Russo-German armistice signed, Dec. 15.

1918 Treaty of Brest-Litovsk, Mar. 3. German offensive against British opened on Somme, Mar. 21. Battle of Arras, Mar. 21–Apr. 4. Second German offensive against British, Apr. 9–25. British naval raid on Zeebrugge and Ostend, Apr. 23. Foch appointed C.-in-C. Allied armies, Apr. 14. Peace signed between Rumania and Central Powers, May 7. *Vindictive* sunk in Ostend harbour, May 9. Last German offensive against French, July 15. British, Canadians, and Australians attack in front of Amiens, Aug. 8. Allenby destroyed last Turkish army at Megiddo, Sept. 19. Bulgarians signed armistice, Sept. 29. General Allied offensive in West began, Sept. 26. Germans accepted Wilson's Fourteen Points, Oct. 23. Great Italian advance, Oct. 24. Turkey surrenders, Oct 30. Austria accepts imposed terms, Nov. 3. Popular government in Poland (Lublin), Nov. 7. Revolutionary movement begins in Germany, Nov. 8. Kaiser abdicates and escapes to Holland, Nov. 9. Armistice signed by Germans, Nov. 11. Proclamation of Kingdom of Serbs, Croats and Slovenes in Belgrade, Dec. 1.

THE TWENTIES AND THIRTIES

1919 Peace Conference in Paris, Jan. 18. Einstein's theory of Relativity confirmed experimentally during solar eclipse, March 29. First direct flight across Atlantic by Sir J. Alcock and Sir A. W. Brown, June 15. Interned German fleet scuttled at Scapa Flow, June 19. Treaty of Peace with Germany signed at Versailles, June 28. Treaty of St. Germain: break-up of Austrian Empire, Sept. 10.

1920 Peace Treaty ratified in Paris. First meeting of League of Nations, from which Germany, Austria, Russia, and Turkey are excluded, and at which the U.S.A. is not represented. Prohibition in U.S.A. Peace Treaty with Turkey signed at Sèvres: Ottoman Empire broken up Aug. 10. Degrees first open to women at Oxford Univ., Oct. 14.

1921 Riots in Egypt, May 23. In complete disregard of the League of Nations, Greece makes war on Turkey. Heligoland fortresses demolished, Oct. 14. Irish Free State set up by Peace Treaty with Britain, Dec. 6.

1922 Four-Power Pacific Treaty ratified by U.S. Senate, Mar. 24. Heavy fighting in Dublin, the Four Courts blown up, July 2. Defeat of Greek armies by the Turks, Aug.–Sept. Mussolini's Fascist "March on Rome," Oct. 28.

1923 French troops despatched to Ruhr, Jan. 11. Treaty of Lausanne, July 24. Earthquake in Japan, Tokyo and Yokohama in ruins, Sept. 1. Rhine Republic proclaimed, Bavaria defies the Reich, Oct. 20. Turkish Republic proclaimed; Kemal Pasha, first President, Oct. 29.

1924 Lenin dies, Jan. 21. First Labour Ministry in Britain under MacDonald, Jan. 22; lasts 9 months. George II of Greece deposed and a Republic declared, Mar. 25. Dawes Plan accepted by London conference; Ruhr evacuation agreed to, Aug. 16.

1925 Hindenburg elected German President, Mar. 26. Treaty of Locarno signed in London, Dec. 1. Summer Time Act made permanent.

1926 Ibn Saud proclaimed king of the Hedjaz in Jeddah, Jan. 11. Evacuation of Cologne by British forces, Jan. 31. General strike in Britain.

1927 Lindbergh flies Atlantic alone, May 21.

1928 Earthquake in Greece, Corinth destroyed. Apr. 23. Capt. Kingsford-Smith flies the

A.D.
Pacific, June 9. General Nobile rescued by aeroplane from Arctic one month after disaster, June 24. Kellogg Pact accepted by Gt. Britain, July 18. German airship with 60 persons crosses Atlantic, Oct. 15. Women in Britain enfranchised on same basis as men.

1929 Second Labour Ministry under MacDonald. Graf Zeppelin makes numerous successful intercontinental flights. Commander Byrd flies over South Pole, Nov. 30. American slump and Wall Street crash.

1930 *R.101* destroyed in France on first flight to India, 48 lives lost, Oct. 5—end of British interest in airships.

1931 Great floods in China. Resignation of Labour Government and formation of Coalition under MacDonald. Invergordon naval mutiny.

1932 Manchuria erected into Japanese puppet state of Manchukuo, Feb. 18. Sydney Harbour Bridge opened, Mar. 19. Ottawa Imperial Conference.

1933 Hitler appointed Chancellor by Hindenburg, Jan. 30, and step by step gains supreme control. German Reichstag set on fire, Feb. 27.

1934 Dollfuss, Austrian Chancellor, murdered by Austrian Nazis, July 25. Death of Hindenburg, Aug. 2. Hitler becomes Dictator. Alexander of Yugoslavia assassinated in Marseilles, Oct. 9.

1935 Saar plebiscite for return to Germany, Jan. 13. Baldwin succeeds MacDonald as Prime Minister, June 7. War begins between Italy and Abyssinia, Oct. 3. Ineffectual economic "sanctions" by League of Nations against Italy, Nov. 18.

1936 Accession of King Edward VIII, Jan. 20. Repudiation of Locarno Treaty by Germany, Mar. 7. Remilitarisation of Rhineland, Mar. 8. Italian troops occupy Addis Ababa, May 5. Civil War breaks out in Spain, July 18. King Edward VIII abdicates after a reign of 325 days, Dec. 10. The Duke of York succeeds his brother as King George VI, Dec. 12.

1937 Coalition Ministry under Chamberlain, May 28. Japanese begin attempted conquest of China—"China incident," July 7.

1938 Austria annexed by Germany, Mar. 13. British navy mobilised, Sept. 28. Munich Agreement between Chamberlain, Daladier, Hitler, and Mussolini, Sept. 29.

1939

February 27 Great Britain recognises General Franco's Government.

March 16 Bohemia and Moravia annexed by Hitler and proclaimed a German Protectorate. **22** Memel ceded to Germany by Lithuania. **28** Anti-Polish press campaign begun by Germany.

April 1 Spanish War ends. **7** Italy seizes Albania. **14** First British talks with Russia. **27** Conscription introduced in Great Britain. **28** Hitler denounces Anglo-German Naval agreement and the Polish Non-Aggression Treaty.

May 12 Great Britain signs defensive agreement with Turkey. **22** Italy and Germany sign pact. **23** France and Turkey sign defensive agreement. **25** Anglo-Polish treaty signed in London.

July 10 Chamberlain re-affirms British pledge to Poland.

August 23 German-Soviet Pact signed by von Ribbentrop. **25** Japan breaks away from the Anti-Comintern Pact. **28** Holland mobilises. **31** British fleet mobilised.

SECOND WORLD WAR

September 1 Poland invaded by German forces. Great Britain and France mobilise. **1–4** Evacuation schemes put in motion in England and Wales: 1,200,000 persons moved. **2** Compulsory military service for all men in Britain aged 18 to 41. **3** War declared (11 a.m.) between Britain and Germany as from 5 p.m. **4** British liner *Athenia* sunk by submarine. R.A.F. raid the Kiel Canal entrance and bomb German warships. **6** First enemy air raid on Britain. **8** Russia mobilises. Russian troops on Polish border. **11** British troops on French soil. **17**

A.D
Russian troops cross the Polish frontier along its entire length. Russian and German troops meet near Brest Litovsk: loss of *Courageous*. **27** Capitulation of Warsaw. **29** Nazi-Soviet pact signed in Moscow approving partition of Poland.

October 14 *Royal Oak* sunk in Scapa Flow with a loss of 810 lives.

November 8 Bomb explosion in the Bürgerbräukeller at Munich after Hitler's speech. Germans using magnetic mines. **29** Diplomatic relations between Russia and Finland severed. **30** Finland attacked by Russia.

December 11 Italy leaves the League of Nations. **13** Battle of the River Plate: engagement of German warship *Admiral Graf Spee* by H.M. cruisers *Exeter*, *Ajax*, and *Achilles*. **14** Rejection by Russia of the League of Nations' offer of mediation in the Russo-Finnish war. Russia expelled from the League of Nations. **17** *Admiral Graf Spee* scuttles herself in the entrance of Montevideo harbour.

1940

February 14 Finnish advanced posts captured by Russians. **16** 299 British prisoners taken off the German Naval Auxiliary *Altmark* in Norwegian waters. **26** Finns lose the island fortress of Kolvisto. Finns retreat from Petsamo.

March 12 British ships to be fitted with a protective device against magnetic mines. Finland concludes a peace treaty whereby she cedes to Russia the Karelian Isthmus, the town of Vipuri and a military base on Hango Peninsula.

April 9 Invasion of Denmark and Norway by Germany. **15** British troops arrive in Norway. **19** British soldiers land in the Faroes.

May 2 British troops withdrawn from Norway. **10** Holland, Belgium and Luxembourg invaded by German forces. Parachute troops landed near Rotterdam. British troops cross the Belgian border. British troops land in Iceland. Rotterdam bombed. **11** National Government formed under Churchill. **13** Queen Wilhelmina arrives in London. **14** Rotterdam captured. Holland ceases fighting. Allied troops land near Narvik. **17** Belgian Government moves to Ostend. **24** German forces enter Boulogne. **27** Belgian army capitulates on the order of King Leopold. British forces to be withdrawn from Flanders. Narvik captured by Allied forces. **29** Ostend, Ypres, Lille and other Belgian and French towns lost to the Germans.

June Evacuation of British army from Dunkirk (May 27–June 4): 299 British warships and 420 other vessels under constant attack evacuate 335,490 officers and men. **5** Hitler proclaims a war of total annihilation against his enemies. **8** German armoured forces penetrate French defences in the West near Rouen. **10** Italy declares war on Great Britain and France. **14** Paris captured by German forces. **15** Soviet troops occupy Lithuania, Latvia and Estonia. **22** French delegates accept terms for an Armistice. **25** Hostilities in France cease at 12.35 a.m.

July 1 Channel Islands occupied by Germany. **3** French naval squadron at Oran immobilised. **10** Battle of Britain began.

August 19 British withdrew from British Somaliland. **25** British began night bombing of Germany.

September 6 King Carol of Rumania abdicates in favour of his son Michael. **7** London sustains severe damage in the largest aerial attack since war commenced. **15** Battle of Britain ends with British victory: German aeroplanes destroyed, 1,733; R.A.F. losses, 915. **23** Japanese troops enter Indo-China.

October 7 German troops enter Rumania. **28** Greece rejects an Italian ultimatum.

November 1 Greeks repel Italian attacks, **5** H.M.S. *Jervis Bay* lost defending Atlantic convoy from German warship *Admiral Scheer*. **11** Italian fleet at Taranto crippled by Fleet Air Arm. **14** Coventry heavily attacked, the Cathedral destroyed. **22** Albanian town of Koritza captured by the Greeks.

December 2 Bristol heavily bombed. **11** Sidi Barrani captured by British forces: beginning

A.D.

of Wavell's destruction of Italian forces in Cyrenaica. **29** City of London severely burned by incendiary bombs: Guildhall and eight Wren Churches destroyed.

1941

January 5 Bardia captured. **22** Tobruk captured by Australian troops.

February 7 Benghazi captured. **26** Mogadishu, capital of Italian Somaliland, occupied by Imperial troops. German mechanised troops in Libya.

March 4 British raid Lofoten Islands. **11** U.S. Lease and Lend Bill signed by Roosevelt. **27** Keren—main battle in British conquest of Abyssinia and Somaliland. **28** Cape Matapan: Italian fleet routed by British. **30** Rommel opens attack in N. Africa.

April 4 Addis Ababa entered by Imperial troops. **6** Greece and Yugoslavia invaded by German troops. **8** Massawa capitulates. **11** Belgrade occupied by German forces. **13** Bardia given up by British. Tobruk holds out. **24** Empire forces withdrawing from Greece. **27** Athens captured by the Germans.

May 2 Evacuation from Greece completed. **10** Rudolf Hess descends by parachute in Scotland. **20** Crete invaded by German air-borne troops. **24** H.M.S. *Hood* sunk. **27** German battleship. *Bismark* sunk; British forces withdrawn from Crete.

June 2 Clothes rationing commences. **4** William II (ex-Kaiser of Germany) dies. **18** Treaty of friendship between Turkey and Germany signed. **22** Germany attacks Russia. **24** Russia loses Brest Litovsk.

July 3 Palmyra (Syria) surrenders to Allied forces. **7** U.S. forces arrive in Iceland. **9** General Dentz, the French High Commissioner in Syria, asks for Armistice terms. **25** Fighting round Smolensk.

August 25 British and Russian troops enter Persia. **27** The Dnepropetrovsk dam blown up by the Russians.

September 18 Crimea cut off from mainland. **19** Kiev entered by Germans.

October 6 German attack on Moscow. **16** Soviet Government leaves Moscow. Odessa occupied by German and Rumanian troops. **19** Taganrog on Sea of Azov captured by Germans. **26** Kharkov captured by the Germans.

November 14 *Ark Royal* sunk. **18** Libyan battle opens: Eighth Army's first offensive. **23** Bardia and Fort Capuzzo captured by British. **24** H.M.S. *Dunedin* torpedoed. **25** H.M.S. *Barham* sunk. **30** Russians re-take Rostov.

December 1 Points rationing scheme in force in Britain. **4** German attack on Moscow halted. **7** Japanese attack on Pearl Harbor. **8** Japanese forces land in Malaya. **9** British forces in Tobruk relieved. **10** H.M.S. *Repulse* and *Prince of Wales* sunk off Malaya by Japanese. Phillippines invaded by Japanese. **25** Hongkong surrenders to Japanese.

1942

January 2 Manila and Cavite taken by Japanese. **23** Japanese forces land in New Guinea and the Solomon Islands.

February 9 Soap rationed. **12** Escape through English Channel of German ships *Scharnhorst*, *Gneisenau*, and *Prinz Eugen*. **15** Singapore surrenders to Japanese. **27** Battle of Java Sea.

March 9 Surrender of Java to Japanese.

April 15 George Cross awarded to the island of Malta.

May 4–8 Battle of Coral Sea. **7** Madagascar invaded by British forces. **7** U.S. forces sink 11 Japanese warships off the Solomon islands. **30** Over 1,000 bombers raid Cologne. Canterbury bombed.

June 3–7 Midway Island: U.S. naval victory turns tide in Pacific. **20** Tobruk captured by the Germans.

July 16 R.A.F. make first daylight raid on the Ruhr.

August 6 Germans advancing towards the Caucasus. **10** American forces land in the Solomon

A.D

Islands. **11** Malta convoy action (loss of H.M.S. *Eagle, Manchester, Cairo,* and one destroyer). **19** Raid on Dieppe. **23–25** Battle of Solomons.

September 6 Germans halted at Stalingrad.

October 23 El Alamein: Allied offensive opens in Egypt.

November 4 Rommel's army in full retreat. **5** Red Army holding firm at Stalingrad. **7** Allied invasion of N. Africa. **27** German forces enter Toulon. French Fleet scuttled.

December 2 First self-sustained, controlled nuclear chain reaction in uranium achieved by group working under Enrico Fermi at Chicago. **24** Admiral Darlan assassinated.

1943

January 6 German armies in the Caucasus and the Don elbow in retreat. **18** Leningrad 16-month siege ended. **23** Tripoli occupied by the Eighth Army. **27** American bombers make their first attack on Germany. **31** Remnants of the German army outside Stalingrad surrender.

February 9 Guadalcanal Island cleared of Japanese troops. **16** Kharkov retaken by the Russians.

March 1–3 Battle of Bismarck Sea. **23** 8th Army penetrates the Mareth Line.

May 7 Tunis and Bizerta captured by Allies. **12** All organised German resistance in Tunisia ceases. **16** Dams in the Ruhr breached by the R.A.F. **22** Moscow dissolves the Comintern.

June 3 French Committee for National Liberation formed in Algiers.

July 10 Allied invasion of Sicily. **25** Mussolini overthrown. **28** Fascist Party in Italy dissolved.

August 17 Sicily in Allied hands.

September 3 Italian mainland invaded. **7** Italy surrenders. **9** British and American troops land near Naples. **10** Rome seized by the Germans. **14** Salamaua captured from the Japanese. **23** *Tirpitz* severely damaged (sunk Nov. 12, 1944). **25** Smolensk taken by the Russians.

October 1 Naples taken. **25** Russians capture Dnepropetrovsk and Dneprodzerzhinck.

November 6 Kiev taken by the Russians. **26** Second Battle of Solomons. **28** Churchill, Roosevelt, and Stalin meet in Teheran.

December 2 Men between 18 and 25 to be directed to the mining industry by ballot in Britain. **26** Sinking of German battleship *Scharnhorst*.

1944

January 22 Allied landings at Anzio. **28** Argentina breaks with the Axis Powers.

February 1 American forces land on the Marshall Islands. **2** Russians penetrate Estonia.

March 15 Cassino (Italy) destroyed by Allied bombers.

May 9 Sevastopol captured by Russians. **18** Capture of Cassino and Abbey by Allies. **19** 50 Allied officers shot after escaping from a German prison camp. **30** Battle for Rome commences.

June 4 Allied forces enter Rome. King of Italy signs decree transferring his powers to Prince Umberto, his son. **6** *D-Day*: invasion of Europe (over 4,000 ships in invasion fleet). **7** Defeat of Japanese thrust at India, outside Imphal. **9** Heavy fighting near Caen. **12** First V-1 falls on England. **18** Cherbourg peninsula cut by the Americans. Russians break through the Mannerheim Line.

July 3 Minsk captured by Russians. **9** Caen captured by Allies. **20** "Bomb plot" on Hitler's life. **21** Guam captured by Americans.

August 1 Uprising in Warsaw. **15** Myitkyina falls to Allied forces. **15** Allied forces land in southern France. Marseilles taken. Rumania surrenders. **25** Paris liberated. Rumania declares war on Germany.

September 3 Allies in Belgium. **4** Antwerp and Brussels taken by Allies. Holland entered. Finland "ceases fire." **6** Bulgaria asks for an armistice. **7** Boulogne entered by Allies. Bulgaria declares war on Germany. **8** First V-2 falls on England. **11** Allied forces fighting on

A.D.

Reich territory. **17** Allied air-borne troops land near Arnhem. **22** First Battle of Philippines.

October 3 Warsaw rising crushed by the Germans. **5** British troops land on the mainland of Greece. **14** Athens occupied by Allies. **15** Hungary asks for armistice terms. **20** Aachen captured by the Americans. **25** Battle of Leyte Gulf: end of Japanese sea-power. **28** Second Battle of Philippines.

December 6 Civil war breaks out in Athens. **16** German forces counter-attack in the Ardennes: last German offensive in the West. **26** Budapest encircled by Russians.

1945

January 5 Organized fighting in Athens ceases. **11** U.S. forces land on Island of Luzon. **17** Warsaw captured by the Russians. **23** Burma road to China re-opened.

February 4 Yalta conference. **14** Bombing of Dresden. **19** Americans land on Iwojima Island.

March 6 Cologne captured by Allies.

April 1 U.S. Invasion of Okinawa. **5** Russian Government denounces the Soviet-Japan neutrality pact. Japanese Cabinet resigns. **11** Russian Army enters Vienna after 7-day battle. **12** Death of President Roosevelt. **25** Berlin surrounded by Russian troops. **27** Russians and Americans link up in Germany. **28** Mussolini and his mistress shot by Italian partisans. **30**. Hitler killed himself and his mistress.

May 2 German armies in Italy surrender. Berlin captured by the Russians. **3** Rangoon captured by British. **4** German forces in N.W. Germany, Holland and Denmark surrender. **8** End of World War II against Germany officially declared to be one minute past midnight (Tuesday). **28** Naval air attacks on Japan.

June 26 United Nations Charter signed at San Francisco.

July 5 Polish Government in Warsaw recognised by Allies. **26** Striking Labour victory in general election; Attlee became Prime Minister.

August 6 Atomic bomb first used against Japan: Hiroshima laid waste. **8** Russia declares war against Japan. **9** Russia advances into Manchuria. Nagasaki target for atomic bomb No. 2. **14** Japan surrenders unconditionally to the Allies. **15** VJ Day celebrated. **17** Lend-Lease terminated.

September 5 Singapore re-occupied by the Allies.

"COLD WAR": AFRO-ASIAN INDEPENDENCE

October 9 U.S.A. to keep secret of manufacture of atomic bomb. **15** Laval executed.

November 20 Trial of major war criminals opens at Nuremberg.

1946

February 1 Mr. Trygve Lie elected Secretary-General of UNO.

April 19 League of Nations formally wound up.

June 30 United States atom bomb tests at Bikini.

July 13 United States House of Representatives approves loan to Britain. **22** Bread rationing in Britain. British H.Q. in Jerusalem blown up. **24** Underwater atom bomb test at Bikini.

August 1 Peace Conference opens in Paris.

September 6 United Nations F.A.O. considers establishment of World Food Board.

October 16 Nuremberg sentences on Nazis carried out, Goering commits suicide. **23** General Assembly of the United Nations opens in New York.

November 10 Communists head poll in French General Elections.

December 2 Agreement signed for economic fusion of British and American zones in Germany.

A.D

1947

January 1 British coal industry nationalised. **14** M. Vincent-Auriol elected first President of Fourth Republic.

March 24 Netherlands Government and Indonesian Cabinet sign agreement in Batavia for a United States of Indonesia.

April 1 School leaving age raised to 15 in Great Britain.

June 5 Inauguration of "Marshall Aid".

August 3 Dutch military action in Indonesia ends. **15** India and Pakistan assume Dominion Status. Viscount Mountbatten appointed Governor-General of India and Mr. Jinnah Governor-General of Pakistan. **29** Palestine Committee agrees British Mandate should end, majority report recommends partition.

September 22 First Atlantic automatic flight by U.S. pilotless aircraft.

October 6 Cominform, new international Communist organization, set up in Belgrade.

November 20 Marriage of Princess Elizabeth. **29** Palestine Committee of U.N. Assembly votes in favour of partition of Palestine into Jewish and Arab States.

December 15 Breakdown of 4-Power Conference on Germany. **30** King Michael of Romania abdicates; Rumania becomes a People's Republic.

1948

January 1 British Railways nationalised. **4** Burma becomes independent Republic. **30** Mahatma Gandhi assassinated in New Delhi.

February 1 New Malayan federal constitution comes into force. **4** Ceylon Independence Act. **25** New Czechoslovak Government formed under Communist leadership.

April 1 British electricity industry nationalised. **5** First European Aid shipments sail from America. **16** O.E.E.C. established.

May 3 Mr. Rajagopalachari appointed Gov.-Gen. of India in succession to Earl Mountbatten. **14** British Mandate for Palestine ended at midnight. Jews proclaim new State of Israel.

June 28 Yugoslavia expelled from Cominform.

July 1 "Berlin Airlift": American, British and French zones of Berlin supplied by air. **5** Establishment of National Health Service. **29** Bread rationing in Great Britain ends.

August 15 Republic of Korea proclaimed.

September 17 Count Bernadotte, U.N. Mediator for Palestine, assassinated.

October 30 Chinese Communist forces capture Mukden.

November 3 Mr. Truman elected U.S. President. **14** Birth of a son to Princess Elizabeth.

December 21 Republic of Ireland Bill signed in Dublin.

1949

March 15 Clothes rationing ends in Great Britain. **31** Russia protests against Atlantic Pact.

April 1 Newfoundland becomes part of Canada.

May 1 Gas Industry nationalised. **3** Ten-power conference in London establishes Council of Europe. **12** Berlin blockade lifted.

August 24 North Atlantic Treaty comes into force.

September 12 Professor Theodor Heuss elected first President of West German Republic. **21** General Mao Tse-Tung proclaims People's Republic of China.

October 2 Russia recognises newly-established Chinese People's Republic. **11** Herr Wilhelm Pieck elected first President of East German Republic.

December 8 Chinese Nationalist Government leaves mainland and sets up H.Q. in Formosa. **27** United States of Indonesia come into being.

1950

January 6 Britain recognises Communist Government of China: 24 Dr. Rajendra Prasad elected first President of Indian Republic; **26** New Constitution of Indian Republic comes into force.

February 14 30-year treaty of alliance between Russia and China signed in Moscow; **23** Labour

A.D.

Party wins General Election with narrow majority.

April 1 Italy takes over from Britain administration of Somaliland; **13** First shipment of military aid to France under N.A. Pact unloaded at Cherbourg.

May 19 Points rationing ends in Britain after 8 years; **25** Middle East Tripartite Declaration by Britain, France, and U.S.A.; **26** Petrol rationing ends in Britain.

June 25 N. Korean troops advance into S. Korea; Security Council calls for cease fire; **27** Pres. Truman orders U.S. air, and sea forces to support S. Korea and protect Formosa; U.N. Commission in Korea proposes neutral mediator; military assistance to S. Korea endorsed by Security Council; **30** Pres. Truman authorizes use of American ground troops in Korea.

July 2 American troops land in S. Korea; **8** Gen. MacArthur designated C.-in-C. of U.N. forces in Korea.

August 1 Security Council meets under chairmanship of M. Malik, the Soviet delegate; **7** American forces in Korea open offensive and halt drive on Pusan; **15** Princess Elizabeth gives birth to a daughter; **17** Independence Day in Indonesia.

September 6 British troops in action in Korea; **9** Soap rationing ends in Britain.

October 9 U.N. forces across the 38th parallel in strength; **19** Pyongyang, N. Korean capital, captured by U.N. forces; **26** New Chamber of House of Commons opened at Westminster; **29** King Gustav V of Sweden dies.

December 4 Pyongyang occupied by Chinese; **19** Gen. Eisenhower appointed Supreme Commander of West European Defence Forces set up by Atlantic Powers; **25** Stone of Scone stolen from Westminster Abbey.

1951

January 30 U.N. Assembly rejects resolution of 12 Asian and Arab nations calling for 7-nation conference for peaceful settlement of Korean question; **31** Decree confiscating property of Alfred Krupp cancelled.

February 15 Vesting date for Iron and Steel.

April 11 Gen. MacArthur relieved of all his commands by Pres. Truman and replaced by Lt.-Gen. Ridgway; **13** Coronation Stone returned to Westminster Abbey.

May 2 Persian oil industry nationalized; Germany admitted to Council of Europe; **3** H.M. the King opens Festival of Britain from steps of St. Paul's.

July 1 Colombo plan comes into force; **9** State of war between Britain and Germany officially ended; **10** Armistice negotiations open at Kaesong; **17** King Leopold abdicates in favour of his son Baudouin; **20** King Abdullah of Jordan assassinated.

September 1 Tripartite Security Treaty between U.S.A., Australia and New Zealand signed in San Francisco; **8** Japanese Peace Treaty signed at San Francisco; **23** H.M. the King undergoes successful operation.

October 8 Princess Elizabeth and Duke of Edinburgh leave for Canadian tour; **15** Egyptian Parliament passes unanimously Bills abrogating Anglo-Egyptian treaty of 1936 and 1899 Sudan Condominion Agreement; **16** Assassination of Liaquat Ali Khan; **25** General Election won by Conservatives with small majority.

December 17 London foreign-exchange market reopens after 12 years; **24** Libya becomes independent state.

1952

January 2 Mutual Security Agency replaces Economic Co-operation Administration; **31** Princess Elizabeth and Duke of Edinburgh leave London on the first stage of Commonwealth tour.

February 6 King George VI died at Sandringham aged 56; **7** Queen Elizabeth II and the Duke of

A.D

Edinburgh arrive home by air from Kenya; **21** Identity cards abolished.

April 11 H.M. the Queen declares that she wishes her children and descendants to bear the name of Windsor; **23** Japan regains status as sovereign and independent power.

May 5 H.M. the Queen takes up residence at Buckingham Palace; **27** Treaty setting up European Defence Community signed in Paris.

June 23 Power plants along Yalu River attacked by U.S. aircraft in biggest raid of Korean war.

July 7 American ship *United States* wins Atlantic Blue Riband; **23** Military *coup d'état* takes place in Cairo.

August 1 Ratification of Bonn Agreement, by which W. Germany again becomes independent nation, and Treaty of Paris, which sets up the European Defence Community, approved by Government against Labour opposition; **16** Severe thunderstorms in Somerset and N. Devon bring devastation to Lynmouth; **26** Passive resistance campaign against racial laws in S. Africa gains momentum.

September 8 New Egyptian Cabinet appoints Gen. Neguib military Gov.-Gen. of Egypt and approves land reforms.

October 3 Britain's first atomic weapon exploded in Monte Bello Islands, off N.W. Australia; **5** Tea derationed and decontrolled; **20** State of emergency declared in Kenya as a result of Mau Mau activities.

November 1 Reported explosion of U.S. hydrogen bomb at Eniwetok atoll in mid-Pacific; **4** Gen. Eisenhower, Republican candidate, wins sweeping victory in American Presidential election.

1953

January 31 Violent N.E. gales combined with surging high tides caused extensive flooding with loss of life along coasts of eastern England, the Netherlands, and Belgium.

February 4 Sweet rationing ended; **23** War-time deserters in Britain granted amnesty.

March 6 Marshal Stalin died, aged 74; **24** Death of Queen Mary at Marlborough House, aged 85; **31** Mr. Dag Hammarskjöld elected U.N. Sec.-Gen. in succession to Mr. Trygve Lie.

April 15 Dr. Malan's National Party again returned to power in S. Africa with increased majority; **24** Mr. Churchill created a Knight of the Garter by the Queen.

May 4 Duke of Edinburgh received his pilot's "wings"; **29** E. P. Hillary and Sherpa Tenzing of the Everest Expedition led by Colonel John Hunt reached summit of Everest (29,002 ft.).

June 2 Coronation of H.M. Elizabeth II in Westminster Abbey amid scenes of magnificent pageantry; ceremony televised; **26** Republic of Egypt accorded *de facto* recognition by Britain.

July 4 German–Austrian Expedition reached summit of Nanga Parbat in the Himalayas; **13** De-nationalisation of British steel industry; **14** Royal Assent given to Central African Federation Bill; **27** Korean Armistice signed at Panmunjom.

August 9–12 Disastrous earthquakes in Greek Ionian Islands; **12** Explosion of Russian hydrogen bomb reported.

September 26 Sugar rationing ended after nearly 14 years.

October 15 Sir Winston Churchill awarded 1953 Nobel Prize for Literature.

November 11 Great bell at Notre Dame rung by electricity for first time; **21** Piltdown skull, discovered in Sussex in 1911, found by anthropologists to be partial hoax; **23** The Queen and Duke of Edinburgh began 6 months' tour of Commonwealth.

December 1 Agreement signed for laying first transatlantic telephone cable; **23** M. René Coty elected President of France at the 13th ballot; L. P. Beria, former chief of Soviet Secret Police, and six associates sentenced to death and shot; **25** The Queen gave her Christmas broadcast from Auckland; **31** Mildest December for 20 years, and before that for over 200 years.

A.D.
1954

January 9 Self-government began in the Sudan; **12** M. Le Trouquer (Socialist) elected President of French National Assembly; **16** M. René Coty became President of France in succession to M. Vincent Auriol.

February 3 First Parliament of newly formed Federation of Rhodesia and Nyasaland opened in Salisbury; **5** Britain's first "breeder" pile in operation at Harwell.

March 1 American hydrogen bomb exploded at Bikini; **22** London gold market reopened after 15 years.

April 3 Oxford won 100th Boat Race; **21** Russia joined UNESCO.

May 6 Roger Bannister ran first under 4 minute mile; **7** Fortress of Dien Bien Phu fell to Viet-Minh; **18** Liverpool Cotton Exchange reopened.

June 1 Television licence fee raised from £2 to £3 a year; **2** Mr. John A. Costello (Fine Gael) elected Prime Minister of Ireland; **17** Indo-Chinese crisis brought M. Mendès-France to power in France; **22** First all-African Cabinet in British Africa appointed in the Gold Coast; **27** First electric power station using atomic energy began working in Soviet Union; **30** Eclipse of the sun.

July 3 Food rationing officially ended in Britain; **27** Agreement reached in Cairo for withdrawal of British troops from Suez Canal Zone; **31** K2 climbed by Italian team.

August 5 Persian oil dispute settled; **11** Cessation of hostilities in Indo-China after 8 years of fighting.

September 14 Sheffield–Manchester electrified railway opened.

October 14 Mr. Anthony Eden created a Knight of the Garter; **19** Anglo-Egyptian Suez Canal Agreement.

November 1 French settlements in India passed under Indian control; **30** Sir Winston Churchill celebrated his 80th birthday.

1955

January 31 Princess Margaret left for tour of W. Indies.

February 8 Marshal Bulganin succeeded Mr. Malenkov as chairman of the Soviet Council of Ministers; **17** Britain to proceed with manufacture of hydrogen bombs; **24** Restrictions on hire purchase announced; Dr. Albert Schweitzer appointed honorary member of the Order of Merit; Turco–Iraqi pact signed at Baghdad (Britain, Pakistan, and Persia acceded later).

April 5 Sir Winston Churchill resigned as Prime Minister; **6** Sir Anthony Eden succeeded as Prime Minister; **18** Afro-Asian conference (29 nations) opened at Bandung; **20** Signor Gronchi elected President of Italy.

May 5 Ratification of London and Paris agreements completed; Germany attained full sovereignty and Western European Union came into being; **26** British general election resulted in Conservative majority of 59.

June 15 U.S. and Britain agreed to co-operate on atomic energy; **16** Revolt against the Perón government in Argentina.

July 18 First meeting in Geneva between heads of Government since Potsdam, 1945; **27** Austrian State Treaty came into force.

August 8 International conference on peaceful uses of atomic energy opened in Geneva.

September 16 Universal Copyright convention came into force; **19** General Perón resigned after rebels threatened to bombard Buenos Aires; **22** Independent television service began.

October 2 City of London became a "smokeless zone"; **12** British and Soviet warships exchanged courtesy visits; **20** Syria and Egypt signed mutual defence treaty.

November 5 Vienna State Opera House re-opened; **23** *Hamlet* played on Russian stage by British company, the first since Tsarist times.

December 7 Mr. Attlee announced his retirement and was created an earl; **12** Completion of 830-mile pipeline through Urals; **14** Mr. Hugh Gaitskell elected leader of Labour Party.

A.D
1956

January 1 Sudan proclaimed an independent republic; **27** The Queen and the Duke of Edinburgh left for tour of Nigeria; 200th anniversary of birth of Mozart celebrated.

February 1 Britain had coldest day since 1895; **13** Referendum in Malta resulted in vote in favour of integration with Britain; **16** Bank rate increased from 4½ to 5½ per cent. (highest since 1932); **25** Khrushchev denounced Stalin.

March 2 King Hussein of Jordan discharged Lieut.-Gen. J. B. Glubb; **5** Telephone weather forecast began; **9** Archbishop Makarios with leaders of Enosis movement in Cyprus deported to the Seychelles; **23** The Queen laid foundation stone of new Coventry Cathedral; Pakistan proclaimed an Islamic republic within the Commonwealth.

April 6 Earl Attlee created Knight of the Garter; **11** Five-day week for Civil Servants announced; **18** Cease-fire between Israel and Egypt came into force; **29** French occupation of Indo-China ended after 80 years.

May 23 First atomic power station in Britain started working at Calder Hall; **24** 2,500th anniversary of the death of Buddha celebrated in India; **31** May was the sunniest month at Kew since 1922 and the driest since 1896.

June 3 Third-class travel abolished on British Railways to conform to continental practice; **13** Last British troops left Suez; **24** Col. Nasser elected Pres. of Egypt.

July 26 Pres. Nasser announced nationalisation of Suez Canal Company.

August 30 French troops arrived in Cyprus.

September 25 Submarine telephone cable linking Britain and America opened to public service.

October 3 Bolshoi Ballet danced at Covent Garden; **15** Duke of Edinburgh left on world tour; **23** Insurrection broke out in Budapest and spread throughout Hungary; **29** Israeli forces invaded Egypt and after 5 days' fighting had control of Sinai peninsula; **30** Britain and France issued 12-hour ultimatum to Israel and Egypt to cease fighting; **31** Anglo-French offensive launched against military targets in Egypt.

November 4 Soviet forces launched attack on Budapest to crush Hungarian uprising; **5** Anglo-French troops landed at Port Said; **6** Pres. Eisenhower reelected President with Congress controlled by Democrats; Anglo-French forces ceased fire at midnight; **7** Egypt accepted cease fire on UN conditions; **15** UN Emergengy Force left Naples for Suez; **16** Suez Canal blocked by 49 ships; **17** First refugees from Hungary arrived in Britain; **22** Duke of Edinburgh opened 16th Olympic Games in Melbourne; **28** Sir Anthony Eden flew to Jamaica for rest cure; **24** UN for third time called upon Britain, France, and Israel to withdraw troops from Egypt.

December 5 140 people arrested in S. Africa for alleged treason; Anglo-French forces began to leave Port Said; **19** Lord Radcliffe's proposals for a constitution for Cyprus published; **29** Suez Canal clearing operation by UN salvage fleet began.

1957

January 1 Anglo-Egyptian treaty of 1954 abrogated by Pres. Nasser as from October 31, 1956; Saar became tenth *Land* of German Federal Republic; **5** Eisenhower Doctrine for Middle East announced; **9** Resignation of Sir Anthony Eden as Prime Minister; **10** Mr. Harold Macmillan appointed Prime Minister; **20** India's first atomic reactor, *Apsara*, inaugurated; **31** Trans-Iranian oil pipeline from Abadan to Teheran (600 m.) completed.

February 15 Mr. Gromyko replaced Mr. Shepilov as Soviet Foreign Minister; **16** The Queen flew to Portugal on State visit; **22** Duke of Edinburgh granted title of Prince.

March 1 Mass protest in Tokyo against nuclear weapon tests in Pacific; **5** Fianna Fail majority in Irish general election; **6** Ghana celebrated independence; Israeli withdrawal from Sinai completed; **11** Warning by WHO of genetic effects of radiation; **21** Homicide Act in force (death

A.D.

penalty retained only for five categories of "capital murder"); **25** European Common Market and Euratom treaties signed by France, Germany, Italy, and Benelux.

April 8 The Queen and Prince Philip arrived in France on State visit; **9** Suez Canal cleared and opened to all shipping; **17** Archbishop Makarios arrived in Athens from exile.

May 14 Petrol rationing (imposed 17.12.56) ended; **15** First British H-bomb exploded in Central Pacific near Christmas I.; **16** M. Spaak succeeded Lord Ismay as NATO Sec. Gen.; **18** The Queen and Prince Philip left for State visit to Denmark.

June 1 New Copyright Act came into force; First drawing of Premium Bond prizes; **30** The IGY opened at midnight.

July 1 First Egyptian general election since revolution of 1952; **25** Tunisia declared a republic.

August 1 Sir Christopher Hinton appointed chairman of new C.E.G.B., responsible for new nuclear power stations.

September 15 German general election (Dr. Adenauer re-elected Chancellor Oct. 22); **30** Network Three introduced by B.B.C.

October 4 First earth satellite launched by Russia; **11** Radio telescope at Jodrell Bank inaugurated.

November 3 Satellite launched with dog on board.

December 4 90 killed in Lewisham rail crash; **25** Queen's Christmas broadcast televised for the first time.

CO-EXISTENCE AND REALIGNMENT: THE NEW EUROPE

1958

January 1 Treaties establishing EEC (Common Market) and EAEC (Euratom) came into force; **3** Inauguration of West Indian Federation; Sir Edmund Hillary and New Zealand party reached South Pole; **4** *Sputnik I* disintegrated after completing 1,367 circuits of the Earth and travelling 43 million miles; **7** Mr. Macmillan left for 6-week tour of Commonwealth; **31** First American earth satellite *Explorer I* launched.

February 1 Union of Egypt and Syria in the United Arab Republic; **14** Merger of Iraq and Jordan: lasted only 6 months; **25** Campaign for Nuclear Disarmament launched under presidency of Lord Russell.

March 2 IGY Commonwealth Trans-Antarctic Expedition, led by Dr. Vivian Fuchs, completed first crossing of Antarctic (2,200 miles in 99 days); **8** Federal union between UAR and Yemen; **21** Opening of London planetarium; **27** Mr. Khrushchev elected Soviet Prime Minister in succession to Mr. Bulganin.

April 4 First CND protest march from London to Aldermaston; **17** Nationalist Party of S. Africa returned with increased majority.

May 24 Nuclear reactor at Dounreay began working.

June 1 General de Gaulle became Prime Minister of France; Clean Air Act banning emission of dark smoke came into force; **9** Gatwick Airport opened by the Queen; **20** London bus strike ended after 7 weeks; **21** Greek Government rejected British plan for Cyprus.

July 1 Conference of scientists, including Russian delegation, met at Geneva to discuss ways of detecting nuclear tests; **14** Iraq monarchy overthrown. King Faisal assassinated; establishment of Republic; **15** US marines landed in Lebanon; **17** British troops flown to Jordan to restore order; **24** First life barons and baronesses under Life Peerages Act named; **26** H.M. the Queen created her son, Charles, Prince of Wales.

August 1 British Government recognised Republic of Iraq; **5** U.S. nuclear submarine *Nautilus* passed under North Pole; **17** Britain to resume nuclear tests on Christmas Island; **23** Bombardment by Chinese of Quemoy; American warships joined Seventh Fleet in Formosa Strait.

A.D

September 1 International conference on peaceful uses of atomic energy opened in Geneva; **7** Britain successfully fired ballistic rocket (Black Knight) from Woomera; **16** Relaxations in hire-purchase; **29** Lord Goddard retired as Lord Chief Justice; succeeded by Lord Justice Parker.

October 2 French Guinea proclaimed Republic of Guinea; **8** Martial law began in Pakistan; **9** Death of Pope Pius XII; **11** US *Pioneer* successfully launched; **21** First women peers introduced to House of Lords; **28** State opening of Parliament and Queen's Speech televised; Cardinal Roncalli, Patriarch of Venice, elected as Pope John XXIII at age of 76; **31** Conference opened in Geneva (Russia, Britain, and the US) on suspension of nuclear tests.

December 18 Empire Day to be known as Commonwealth Day; **21** General de Gaulle elected President of France; **27** Partial convertibility between £ and $ announced; UAR and Russia signed agreement on Russian co-operation in Aswan high dam project; **28** General de Gaulle announced devaluation of the franc.

1959

January 1 Batista Government in Cuba overthrown by revolutionary movement under Dr. Fidel Castro; **2** Russian launched planet round the sun (*Lunik I*); **3** Alaska became 49th state of American Union.

February 1 Votes for women rejected by Swiss national poll; **21** Mr. Macmillan arrived in Moscow on official visit; **23** Archbishop Makarios returned to Cyprus after 3-year exile. Cyprus to become a republic with Greek Pres. and Turkish Vice-Pres.; **26** State of emergency declared in Southern Rhodesia; **27** Riots in Malta dockyard due to dismissal of workers.

March 3 State of emergency declared in Nyasaland; British scientists isolated basic molecule of penicillin; **17** Uprising in Lhasa against Chinese rule; Flight of Dalai Lama to India; **24** Iraq withdrew from Baghdad Pact.

April 5 Panchen Lama took over local government of Tibet.

May 15 Jodrell Bank radioed message to United States via moon; **30** Auckland Harbour Bridge officially opened.

June 17 Mr. de Valera elected Pres. of Rep. of Ireland; **26** St. Lawrence Seaway formally opened.

July 3 Tancarville suspension bridge, opened; **5** Recovery in good condition of 3 animals from outer space; **21** First nuclear merchant ship *Savannah* launched.

September 13 Russian launched *Lunik II* which landed on moon; **25** Mr. Bandaranaike, Prime Min. of Ceylon, assassinated.

October 8 General Election returned Conservatives with 100 overall majority.

November 1 Basic travel allowance for British tourists ended; **2** First section of London–Yorkshire motorway (M1) opened to traffic; **14** Dounreay fast breeder reactor went into operation.

December 1 State of emergency in Cyprus ended; Bursting of dam at Fréjus killed 384 people; **5** Opening of 400-mile Sahara pipeline by French Prime Minister; **10** Raising of school-leaving age to 16 recommended by Crowther Report; **14** Archbishop Makarios elected first Pres. of Cyprus; **26** Soviet Antarctic expedition reached South Pole.

1960

January 1 Republic of Cameroun (formerly French Cameroons) became independent. **9** Work begun on Aswan High Dam. **12** State of emergency ended in Kenya after 8 years; Army rising in Algeria.

February 3 Mr. Macmillan addressed S. African Parliament ("wind of change" speech). **13** First French atomic test in Sahara. **17** British agreement to U.S. ballistic missile early-warning system at Fylingdales Moor,

A.D.
Yorkshire. **19** Prince Andrew born. **29** Agadir destroyed by earthquake.

March 17 New £1 notes issued in Britain. **18** Last steam locomotive of British Railways named. **21** 67 shot dead by police in Sharpeville in S. Africa: State of emergency.

April 1 U.N. Security Council adopted resolution deploring shootings in S. Africa. Dr. Hastings Banda, released from detention in S. Rhodesia. **5** Pres. de Gaulle on state visit to Britain. **9** Attempt on life of Dr. Verwoerd. **27** Togoland became independent as Togo.

May 1 U.S. aircraft engaged in military reconnaissance flight over Soviet territory shot down. **6** Wedding of Princess Margaret and Mr. A. Armstrong-Jones. **7** Mr. Leonid Brezhnev became President of Soviet Union. **16** Opening and breakdown of Summit conference in Paris. **17** The Queen Mother officially opened Kariba Dam. **21** Earthquake disaster in Chile. **25** Everest climbed by 3 Chinese; Army seized control in Turkey; End of U.S. foreign aid to Cuba.

June 25 Completion of second Saharan oil pipe-line (Edjelé to La Skirra on Tunisian coast). **26** Madagascar became independent state within French Community. **29** House of Commons rejected Wolfenden Committee's recommendations on homosexuality. **30** Belgian Congo became independent as the Congo Republic.

July 1 Ghana proclaimed a Republic; Somali Republic came into being. **6** Army mutiny in Congo. **11** Ivory Coast, Dahomey, Niger, and Upper Volta became independent; M. Tshombe, Congolese provincial leader, declared Katanga independent: M. Lumumba asked for U.N. help. **12** Congo (French), Chad and Central African Rep. became independent.

August 8 Military *coup d'état* in Laos. **16** Cyprus became independent. **25** Olympic Games opened in Rome. **29** Prime Minister of Jordan assassinated.

September 5 M. Lumumba dismissed as Prime Minister of Congo.

October 1 Nigeria became independent. **21** Royal Navy's first nuclear submarine *Dreadnought* launched by the Queen.

November 9 Senator John Kennedy elected Pres. of United States. **28** Islamic Republic of Mauritania proclaimed its independence.

December 2 Archbishop of Canterbury visited the Pope at the Vatican. **14** Fighting in Laos, between right-wing and left-wing forces. **15** Marriage of King Baudouin of Belgium. **27** Union of Ghana, Guinea, and Mali. **31** Farthing ceased to be legal tender.

1961

January 18 M. Lumumba, first Prime Min. of the independent Congo, sent to Katanga for imprisonment. **20** The Queen and the Duke of Edinburgh left for tour of India, Pakistan, Nepal and Iran.

February 13 Death of M. Lumumba announced (violent demonstrations in many countries). **15** Total eclipse of the sun visible from Europe.

March 8 First Polaris submarines arrived at Holy Loch. **14** The New English Bible (New Testament) published. **25** Russian satellite with dog aboard launched and brought safely back to earth.

April 12 Major Yuri Gagarin made first flight into space and back. **17** Unsuccessful invasion of Cuba by rebel forces. **23** Census held in Great Britain. **24** Gen. de Gaulle ordered blockade of Algeria. **25** Both sides in Laos agreed to ceasefire. **26** Collapse of mutiny in Algeria. **27** Independence of Sierra Leone.

May 1 Betting and Gaming Act came into force in Britain: betting shops opened. **5** Commander Alan Shepard made first American flight

A.D
into space; The Queen and the Duke of Edinburgh visited Pope John XXIII at the Vatican. **16** International conference on Laos opened in Geneva; Army in South Korea seized power. **17** Guildford Cathedral consecrated. **31** Gen. Trujillo, dictator of Dominican Republic, assassinated; South Africa became a Republic and withdrew from British Commonwealth.

June 3 Meeting of Pres. Kennedy and M. Khrushchev in Vienna. **27** Enthronement of Dr. Ramsey as Archbishop of Canterbury in Canterbury Cathedral.

July 21 New Runcorn–Widnes Bridge opened.

August 13 Soviet sector of Berlin sealed off from Western sectors. **14** Jomo Kenyatta freed. **15** U.N. recognised M. Adoula's government as the central government of the Congo. **16** Dr. Hastings Banda's Malawi Congress Party won control in the Nyasaland Legislative Assembly.

September 18 Mr. Hammarskjöld killed in plane crash when flying from Leopoldville, to Ndola, to arrange ceasefire between U.N. and Katanga forces. **28** Syria seceded from the United Arab Republic.

October 1 S. Cameroons gained independence as part of Cameroun. **3** Mr. A. Armstrong-Jones created Earl of Snowdon. **10** Volcanic eruption on Tristan da Cunha; whole population evacuated to Britain. **30** Russia tested a bomb of over 60 megatons amid world-wide protest. **31** Hurricane struck British Honduras, Belize devastated; Stalin's body removed from the Lenin Mausoleum in Red Square.

November 3 Birth of son to Princess Margaret and Lord Snowdon. **7** Dr. Adenauer re-elected Chancellor of Fed. German Rep. for fourth time. **8** Official negotiations for entry of Britain into Common Market opened in Brussels. **9** The Queen and the Duke of Edinburgh left for tour of Ghana, Liberia, and Sierra Leone. **20** Admission of Russian Orthodox Church to World Council of churches. **28** South Africa's apartheid policy condemned by U.N.

December 9 Tanganyika became independent sovereign state. **15** Adolf Eichmann sentenced to death by Israeli court for crimes against the Jewish people and against humanity: executed June 1962. **17** Indian troops took over Portuguese colony of Goa. **20** Mr. Adoula and Mr. Tshombe agreed on Katanga's subordinate status. **27** Belgium and the Congo resumed diplomatic relations.

1962

January 11 Smallpox outbreak in Britain.

March 7 Publication of Royal College of Physician's Report on dangers to health from cigarette smoking. **14** Opening of 17-nation disarmament conference at Geneva. **19** End of Algerian war.

April 1 Government's "pay pause" ended. **5** Completion of Gt. St. Bernard road tunnel. **13** International agreement (40 countries) to stop oil pollution of seas and beaches. **26** Britain's first satellite, *Ariel*, launched from Cape Canaveral.

May 6 Signor Segni elected Pres. of Italy. **8** Trolleybuses ran for last time in London. **13** Dr. Radhakrishnan elected Pres. of India. **25** Consecration of new Coventry Cathedral.

June 15 Nuclear power station at Berkeley, Glos., began electricity supply to national grid. **18** Conservatives (Mr. Diefenbaker) won Canadian general election by small majority. **23** Ceasefire in Laos.

July 1 Burundi and Rwanda became independent; French colonial rule in Algeria ended; Commonwealth Immigrants Act came into force. **10** First live television between U.S. and Europe via *Telstar*.

August 6 Jamaica became independent. **14** Completion of Mont Blanc tunnel (7½ m.). **21**

A.D.

Maiden voyage of *Savannah*, world's first nuclear-powered merchant ship. **31** Trinidad and Tobago became independent.

September 3 Opening of Trans-Canada highway. **27** Republic proclaimed in Yemen.

October 9 Uganda became independent. **11** 21st Oecumenical Council opened at Rome. **24** Commencement of U.S. naval quarantine of Cuba. **28** Dismantling of missile base in Cuba agreed by Russia.

November 1 Russia sent spacecraft on 7-month journey to Mars. **20** Cuba blockade ended. **21** Ceasefire declaration by China on Sino-Indian border dispute. **30** U Thant unanimously elected Sec.-Gen. of U.N.

December 5 British nuclear device exploded underground in Nevada. **9** Tanganyika became republic and Dr. Julius Nyerere its first president. **12** British troops in control of Brunei uprising. **14** N. Rhodesia's first African dominated government formed. **15** Sir Edgar Whitehead's party lost to right-wing party in S. Rhodesian general election. **25** Europe snowbound with freezing temperatures. **31** British Transport Commission replaced by British Railways Board with Dr. Beeching as chairman.

1963

January 29 Britain was refused entry to EEC.

February 1 Nyasaland became self-governing protectorate. **8** Overthrow of Iraq government and execution of Gen. Kassim. **12** Seventeen-nation disarmament conference resumed in Geneva. **14** Harold Wilson elected leader of Labour Party.

March 5–6 First frost-free night in Britain since Dec. 22. **8** Syrian government overthrown by military coup. **17** Typhoid broke out in Zermatt. **27** Publication of Beeching Report on British Railways.

April 6 Polaris missile agreement signed between U.S. and Britain. **8** Mr. Diefenbaker's Conservative Party defeated by Liberals in Canadian general election.

May 20 Life presidency for Pres. Sukarno of Indonesia.

June 3 Death of Pope John XXIII. **14–19** Bykovsky-Tereshkova space flights (first woman astronaut). **20** House of Commons censure on Mr. John Profumo, former Sec. of State for War. **30** Pope Paul VI inaugurated.

July 26 Skopje destroyed by earthquake.

August 1 Minimum prison age raised to 17. **3** First successful solo climb on north wall of Eiger by Michel Darbellay. **5** Partial nuclear-test ban treaty signed in Moscow by America, Russia, and Britain. **7** Security Council resolution to stop sale and shipment of arms to S. Africa. **8** Glasgow-London mail train robbery (£2·5 million). **21** Buddhists arrested and martial law imposed in South Vietnam. **28** Great Negro "freedom march" on Washington. **31** The "hot-line" linking Kremlin with White House went into service.

September 16 New state of Malaysia (Malaya, Singapore, North Borneo and Sarawak) came into being. **17** Malaysia broke off diplomatic relations with Indonesia; Fylingdales ballistic missile early warning station came into operation. **25** Denning report on Profumo affair published.

October 1 Nigeria became a republic within the Commonwealth. **15** Dr. Adenauer succeeded by Prof. Ludwig Erhard. **18** Mr. Macmillan resigned as Prime Minister; succeeded by the Earl of Home. **23** Robbins report on higher education published.

November 1 Diem oligarchy of S. Vietnam overthrown by military coup. **7** Sir Alec Douglas-Home elected at Kinross and W. Perthshire. **18** Opening of Dartford tunnel. **22** Assassination of

A.D

President Kennedy in Dallas, Texas; Vice-President Lyndon Johnson sworn in as new President.

December 9 Zanzibar became independent. **12** Kenya became independent. **31** Dissolution of Federation of Rhodesia and Nyasaland.

1964

January 4–6 Pope Paul made pilgrimage to Holy Land.

February 11 Fighting between Greeks and Turks at Limassol, Cyprus.

March 10 Birth of Prince Edward. **27** U.N. peacekeeping force in Cyprus operational.

April 9 First Greater London Council election; Labour 64, Conservatives 36. **10** Mr. Macmillan declined earldom and Order of the Garter. **13** Mr. Ian Smith became Prime Minister of S. Rhodesia. **21** Opening of BBC-2. **26** Tanganyika and Zanzibar united (United Republic of Tanzania).

May 1 Birth of a daughter to Princess Margaret and Lord Snowdon. **26** Typhoid outbreak in Aberdeen. **27** Death of Jawaharlal Nehru.

June 2 Mr. Lal Bahadur Shastri elected Prime Minister of India. **5** First flight into space of Britain's *Blue Streak* rocket. **12** Life imprisonment imposed on Nelson Mandela and others in Rivonia trial, Pretoria; 20-year treaty of friendship signed between Soviet Union and E. Germany.

July 2 Enactment of U.S. Civil Rights Bill. **6** Nyasaland became independent state of Malawi. **10** M. Tshombe succeeded M. Adoula as Prime Minister of the Congo. **15** Mr. Mikoyan succeeded Mr. Brezhnev as President of the Soviet Union. **27** Last appearance of Sir Winston Churchill in House of Commons.

August 2 U.S. destroyer attacked by N. Vietnam torpedo boats off N. Vietnam. **5** Congolese rebels captured Stanleyville; U.S. air raid on N. Vietnam.

September 2 Indonesian landings in Malaya. **4** Opening of new Forth bridge. **7** People's Republic of the Congo declared by Congolese rebels. **21** Malta became independent.

October 5 The Queen and the Duke of Edinburgh in Canada on week's visit. **10** Opening of Olympic Games in Tokyo. **15** Mr. Khrushchev replaced in posts of First Secretary of the CPSU and Prime Minister by Mr. Brezhnev and Mr. Kosygin; General election in Britain; Labour won with overall majority of five. **16** Mr. Harold Wilson became Prime Minister; China exploded an atomic device. **24** Northern Rhodesia achieved independence as Republic of Zambia; S. Rhodesia became officially known as Rhodesia. **26** Government proposed 15% import surcharge and export tax rebate to deal with balance of payments crisis.

November 2 Deposition of King Saud of Saudi Arabia and accession of his brother Faisal. **3** U.S. Presidential election: sweeping victory for President Johnson over Senator Goldwater. **17** Government to ban export of arms to S. Africa. **24** Belgian paratroops landed at Stanleyville to rescue rebel-held hostages.

December 2 The Pope welcomed in Bombay. **12** Kenya became Republic within Commonwealth. **16** Statement of Intent on productivity, prices and incomes signed by Government, T.U.C. and Employers' organisations.

1965

January 21 Prime Minister of Iran assassinated. **24** Death of Sir Winston Churchill.

February 1 The Queen and Duke of Edinburgh in Ethiopia on state visit. **7** First U.S. retaliatory raids against N. Vietnam. **18** Gambia became independent. **24** U.S. jets bombed Vietcong in S. Vietnam.

A.D.

March 7 First of 3,500 American marines landed in S. Vietnam. **18** Alexei Leonov became first man to leave a spaceship and float in space. **25** Defeat of Mrs. Bandaranaike in Ceylon elections; Mr. Senanayake became Prime Minister.

April 6 Launching of *Early Bird* commercial communication satellite; Cancellation of TSR 2. **29** Australian troops to be sent to S. Vietnam.

May 11 Cyclone and tidal wave disaster in E. Pakistan killing 16,000 people. **13** Conservatives made big gains in U.K. local government elections. **18** The Queen and the Duke of Edinburgh on 10-day state visit to Fed. German Republic. **28** 267 miners killed in Indian colliery disaster.

June 1 237 miners killed in Japanese colliery explosion. **7** 128 miners killed in Yugoslav mine disaster. **19** Pres. Ben Bella of Algeria deposed by Revolutionary Council under Col. Boumedienne.

July 15 King Constantine of Greece dismissed his Prime Minister, Mr. Papandreou. **22** Sir Alec Douglas-Home resigned as leader of the Conservative Party; succeeded by Mr. Edward Heath (July 28).

August 1 Television ban on cigarette advertising. **9** Singapore seceded from Malaysia. **11** Negro riots in Los Angeles. **12** Appointment of first woman High Court judge. **24** Pres. Nasser and King Faisal signed ceasefire agreement in Yemen.

September 1 Pakistan forces crossed Kashmir ceasefire line. **12** American division 20,000 strong landed in S. Vietnam: General election in Norway: Labour Government defeated. **21** British Petroleum struck oil in North Sea.

October 1 Attempt to overthrow Pres. Sukarno of Indonesia: reprisals against communists. **8** Rhodesian independence talks failed. **13** Pres. Kasavubu of the Congo dismissed Mr. Tshombe. **17** Demonstrations throughout U.S. and in London against war in Vietnam. **22** Pakistan and India accepted ceasefire call of Security Council. **26** Dr. Horace King elected Speaker of House of Commons. **28** Parliament passed Bill abolishing death penalty for murder.

November 11 UDI in Rhodesia: Britain declared régime illegal and introduced economic sanctions. **20** Security Council called on all states to sever economic relations with Rhodesia, and urged oil embargo. **25** General Mobuto deposed Pres. Kasavubu.

December 8 The Second Vatican Council closed. **9** Mr.Mikoyan retired as President of the Soviet Union; replaced by Mr. Nikolai Podgorny. **17** Britain imposed oil embargo on Rhodesia. **22** 70 m.p.h. speed limit on British roads came into force.

1966

January 15 Army coup in Nigeria; Fed Prime Min. killed. **16** General Ironsi, C.-in-C. of Nigerian army, took over command to restore law and order. **31** U.S. bombing of N. Vietnam resumed after 37 days; British Government banned all trade with Rhodesia.

February 3 Successful soft landing on moon by *Luna 9*. **24** Army coup in Ghana while Dr. Nkrumah absent in Far East.

March 4 Britain recognised new régime in Ghana. **23** Historic meeting in Rome of Archbishop of Canterbury and the Pope. **31** British General Election: Labour victory with overall majority of 97.

May 16 Seamen's strike began (ended 1 July). **26** British Guiana became independent state of Guyana.

June 11 Commonwealth Day (the Queen's official birthday) to be observed on this date in future.

July 3 Resignation of Mr. Frank Cousins as Minister of Technology over prices and incomes policy. **6** Malawi became a Republic. **20** Prime

A.D

Minister announced six-month freeze on wages, salaries, and prices. **21** Successful landing of *Gemini 10*: docking manœuvre and space walk. **29** Mutiny by section of Nigerian army; General Ironsi killed. **30** World Cup won by England.

August 1–2 Plenary session of Central Committee of Chinese Communist Party: Marshal Lin Piao officially recognised as Mao Tse-tung's successor. **3** Post Office to become public corporation. **4** Sir Edmund Compton named Britain's first Ombudsman. **10** Cabinet reshuffle: Mr. George Brown became Foreign Secretary. **11** Indonesian–Malaysian peace agreement signed in Djakarta. **18** Start of the "cultural revolution" in China; Earthquake in E. Turkey: over 2,000 killed.

September 5 Selective Employment Tax came into force. **6** Dr. Verwoerd assassinated in Parliament, Cape Town. **8** Opening of new Severn road bridge. **13** Mr. John Vorster chosen as S. Africa's new Prime Minister. **30** Bechuanaland became Republic of Botswana.

October 4 Basutoland became independent kingdom of Lesotho. **21** Aberfan disaster avalanche from coal tip slid down upon mining village killing 144, including 116 children.

November 23 Red Guards demanded dismissal of Liu Shao-ch'i, China's Head of State. **26** Australian General Election: Liberal–Country Party Coalition Government led by Mr. Harold Holt returned; New Zealand General Election: Mr. Keith Holyoake's National Party returned. **30** Barbados became independent.

December 1 Dr. Kiesinger took office as Chancellor of German Federal Republic. **2** Meeting of Prime Minister and Mr. Ian Smith of Rhodesia on board H.M.S. *Tiger* off Gibraltar. **5** Mr. Ian Smith rejected working document. **16** U.N. Security Council voted for British resolution for mandatory sanctions (including oil) against Rhodesia.

1967

January 18 Mr. Jeremy Thorpe, elected Leader of Liberal Party following resignation of Mr. Grimond. **27** 3 American astronauts killed in fire during ground test at Cape Kennedy.

February 9 Historic meeting between the Queen and Mr. Kosygin at Buckingham Palace. **22** Pres. Sukarno of Indonesia surrendered rule to Gen. Suharto.

March 12 Mrs. Indira Gandhi re-elected Prime Minister of India. **13** Gaullists gained bare majority in French National Assembly. **18** *Torrey Canyon* ran aground off Land's End with 120,000 tons of crude oil aboard. **22** Army in Sierra Leone seized power.

April 13 Conservatives gained landslide victory in GLC elections. **21** Army coup in Greece. **27** Opening in Montreal of Expo 67.

May 11 Britain presented application to join Common Market. **28** Francis Chichester arrived in Plymouth after solo circumnavigation of world. **30** Secession of Eastern Region (Biafra) from Nigerian Federation.

June 5 Outbreak of six-day war in Middle East: lightning attack by Israel caused severe Arab losses and capture of territory, mainly from Egypt and Jordan. **17** China exploded her first H-bomb. **28** Israel took over control of the Old City of Jerusalem.

July 1 Mr. Tshombe kidnapped in mid-flight and arrested in Algeria; Colour television began in Britain on BBC-2. **7** Francis Chichester knighted by the Queen at Greenwich. **10** Last use of steam engines on British Rail Southern Region. **12** Negro riots in Newark, N.J. **13** Public Record Act passed: public records now closed for only 30 years. **18** Defence cuts announced: withdrawal from East of Suez by mid-1970s.

August 3 Aberfan tribunal report blamed N.C.B. for the disaster; Lord Robens' resignation not

A.D.
accepted. **13** U.S. bombed N. Vietnam 10 miles from Chinese border.

September 3 Chinese Red Guards ordered to cease violence: Sweden's traffic changed from left to right. **20** Launching on Clydebank of Cunard Liner *Queen Elizabeth II*. **27** *Queen Mary* arrived at Southampton at end of her last transatlantic voyage.

October 9 Road Safety Act dealing with drink and driving came into force. **22** Big demonstrations against Vietnam war in Washington, London and other capitals. **25** Foot-and-mouth epidemic began at Oswestry. **30** Russians performed first automatic link-up and separation of unmanned spacecraft.

November 14 State visit to Malta by the Queen. **26** Lisbon area floods—464 dead. **27** End of eight-week unofficial London dock strike. **29** Aden independent as Republic of South Yemen.

December 3 First human heart transplant operation at Cape Town. **17** Mr. Harold Holt, Australian P.M., drowned in swimming accident.

1968

January 9 Senator John G. Gorton elected P.M. of Australia. **23** Seizure by N. Korea of *USS Pueblo* off N. Korean coast.

February 13 U.S. planes bombed outskirts of Saigon. **18** Introduction of British Standard Time. **19** Decision of Rann of Kutch Tribunal: nine-tenths to India and rest to Pakistan. **24** End of 25-day defence of Hué by Vietcong.

March 6 Africans in Rhodesia hanged in defiance of the Queen's reprieve. **12** Mauritius became independent. **14** Rush for gold in leading financial centres: U.S. Bank rate raised. Stock Exchange and Banks closed in Britain; Resignation of Mr. George Brown as Foreign Secretary. **17–18** Summit Meeting of Western Central Bankers: two-tier system for gold agreed.

April 4 Assassination of Martin Luther King at Memphis, Tennessee.

May 10 Violent clashes between students and security police in Paris.

June 5–6 Senator Robert Kennedy shot and died in Los Angeles. **10** National Health prescription charge introduced. **26** Pierre Trudeau's Liberal Party won Canadian election. **30** Gaullists increased their majority in French election.

July 4 Mr. Alec Rose landed at Portsmouth after sailing single-handed round the world. **29** Pope issued encyclical condemning all forms of artificial birth control.

August 20 Soviet and Warsaw Pact forces entered Czechoslovakia. **27** Death of Princess Marina, Duchess of Kent.

September 6 Swaziland independent. **11** Departure of Soviet troops from Prague. **15** Worst flooding in England since 1953. **16** Two-tier postal system began in Britain. **21–22** Clashes between students and police in Mexico City. **26** Theatres Act, abolishing censorship, in force. **27** French vetoed British entry into Common Market.

October 1 Federal Nigerian troops captured Okigwi in Biafra. **5** Clashes between police and crowds in Londonderry (beginning of disturbances in N. Ireland). **9** H.M.S. *Fearless* talks on Rhodesia failed. **12** Olympic Games in Mexico City. **16** Treaty signed providing for stationing of Soviet troops in Czechoslovakia. **27** Czechoslovakia became a two-state federation.

November 8 Mr Richard Nixon won U.S. Presidential elections.

December 28 Israeli commandos destroyed 13 Arab aircraft at Beirut after two Israeli airliners attacked by Arabs at Athens.

A.D
1969

January 16 First manned docking operation in orbit by Soviet *Soyuz 4* and *5*.

March 2 Maiden flight of French-built *Concorde*; Mrs. Golda Meir chosen as Israel's P.M. **7** Opening of London's Victoria Line. **13** B.P. found Alaskan oil deposits.

April 9 Maiden flight of British-built *Concorde*. **14** Lin Piao declared Mao's successor. **17** Mr. Dubcek replaced as first Secretary of Czechoslovak Communist Party by Dr. Husak. **21** British Army units to guard key points in N. Ireland. **23** Biafran capital of Umuahia captured by Federal forces. **28** Gen. de Gaulle resigned as President of France after defeat on referendum.

May 1 Maj. James Chichester-Clark became P.M. of N. Ireland after resignation of Mr. Terence O'Neill. **12** Voting age became 18.

June 15 M. Georges Pompidou elected President of France. **18** Government dropped plans to put legal restraints on unofficial strikers in return for T.U.C. pledge to deal with disputes. **24** Resignation of Sir Humphrey Gibbs as Governor of Rhodesia.

July 1 Investiture of Prince Charles as 21st Prince of Wales at Caernarvon Castle. **8** Church of England rejected scheme for unity with Methodists; Methodists accepted it. **21** Armstrong and Aldrin first men to land on the Moon at 3·56 a.m. (B.S.T.). **22** Prince Juan Carlos named future King of Spain by Gen. Franco. **31** Halfpennies ceased to be legal tender in Britain.

August 12 Three-day street battle in Londonderry after apprentice boys march. **19** Army took over security and police in N. Ireland.

September 10 Barricades dismantled in Belfast and Army's "peace line" erected. **28** Herr Brandt became Chancellor of W. Germany.

October 10 Hunt Committee report on N. Ireland recommended disarming police and disbanding B specials. **14** 50p (10s.) piece introduced.

November 11 Owners of *Torrey Canyon* agreed to pay £1·5 million each to Britain and France for oil damage. **14** Colour programmes began on BBC-1 and ITV. **24** Soviet Union and U.S. ratified Nuclear Non-Proliferation Treaty. **25** U.S. renounced use of biological warfare.

December 1–2 EEC Summit Meeting at The Hague agreed on negotiations for British entry by June 1970. **16–18** Houses of Commons and Lords voted for permanent abolition of the death penalty. **27** Ruling Liberal Democratic Party won sweeping victory in Japanese General Election.

1970

January 12 Gen. Effilong proclaimed end of Biafran secession.

February 1 Pope reaffirmed celibacy as a fundamental law of the Latin church; Serious clash on Golan Heights between Israel and Syria. **5** Special Public Order Act for N. Ireland passed.

March 2 Rhodesia proclaimed a republic. **16** Publication of the complete *New English Bible*.

April 18 Splashdown of *Apollo 13* after complex rescue operation (Lovell, Halse and Swigert). **21** Pres. Nixon announced withdrawal of another 150,000 U.S. troops from Vietnam in next year. **28** ELDO decided to abandon British *Blue Streak* in favour of French rocket. **30** U.S. combat troops entered Cambodia.

May 4 4 students shot dead during demonstration at Kent state University, U.S.A. **15** S. Africa expelled from International Olympic Committee. **22** Britain cancelled S. African cricket tour.

June 4 Tonga independent. **7** Fighting between Jordan troops and Palestinian guerrillas. **11** Warmest night in Britain for a century. **18** General Election in Britain; Conservative overall majority

A.D.

of 30. **23** Arrival of steamship *Great Britain* at Bristol from Falklands. **26** Mr. Dubcek expelled from Czechoslovak Communist Party. **29** British Government to end restrictions on sale of Council houses; Britain made third application to join EEC; Circular 10/70 issued, with Conservative policy on secondary education.

July 6 Government to resume arms sales to S. Africa. **30** Damages awarded to 28 deformed thalidomide children and their parents.

August 2 Army fired rubber bullets during Belfast disturbances. **7** Ceasefire in force along Suez Canal.

September 4 World Council of Churches proposed financial aid to African guerrillas. **17** Civil War in Jordan between King Hussein's army and Palestinian guerillas. **27** Agreement to end Jordan Civil War signed in Cairo by King Hussein, guerrilla leaders and leaders of eight Arab states. **29** Death of Pres. Nasser (later succeeded by Mr. Anwar Sadat).

October 15 Canonisation of 40 English and Welsh martyrs. **24** Dr. Salvador Allende, Marxist Socialist, elected President of Chile.

November 9 Death of Gen. de Gaulle. **20** U.N. voted to admit China but without necessary two-thirds majority. **21** U.S. bombed N. Vietnam after two-year halt.

December 18 Divorce became legal in Italy.

1971

January 1 Divorce Reform Act (1969) came into force; Kentucky mine disaster. **2** Ibrox Park disaster in Glasgow. **3** Open University on the air. **10** Highest ever January temperatures recorded in London. **25** Pres. Obote of Uganda deposed by Maj. Gen. Amin, Army Commander.

February 4 Financial collapse of Rolls Royce Ltd. **7** Male referendum in Switzerland gave women right to vote in national elections. **15** Decimal Day in Britain. **24** Immigration Bill published, placing Commonwealth and alien immigrants under one system of control.

March 11 Landslide victory for Mrs. Gandhi in Indian General Election. **20** Resignation of Maj. Chichester-Clark as N. Ireland's P.M. (succeeded by Mr Brian Faulkner). **26** Civil war erupted in E. Pakistan after arrest of Sheikh Mujibar Rahman. **29** Lieut. Calley convicted of murder of 22 people in My Lai massacre in S.Vietnam. **30** Soviet Union agreed to outlaw germ warfare.

April 17 Egypt, Syria and Libya formed new Federation of Arab republics.

May 10 Flotation of Deutsche Mark and Dutch guilder following Common Market currency crisis. **20–21** Heath–Pompidou talks on Common Market in Paris. **27** 15-year treaty of friendship and co-operation signed by Egypt and Russia.

June 10 Lifting of 21-year embargo on trade with China by U.S. **21** Labour Party victory in Malta General Election, Mr. Dom Mintoff Prime Minister. **30** Russian space tragedy; 3 astronauts killed just before touchdown.

August 9 Internment without trial introduced in Northern Ireland. **22** Right wing coup in Bolivia. **23** Foreign Exchange markets reopened: sterling allowed to float upwards to new parity against the U.S. dollar.

September. 9 Parliament recalled for special debate on Northern Ireland. **24** Britain expelled 105 Russian diplomats for espionage. **27** Meeting of Prime Ministers Heath, Lynch and Faulkner at Chequers.

October 26 U.N. General Assembly voted to admit China and expel Taiwan. **28** House of Commons (and Lords) voted in favour of joining Common Market on terms presented by Government: 69

A.D

Labour M.P.s voted with the Government. **31** Explosion at Post Office tower in London wrecked three floors.

November 16 Compton Report on Interrogation in Northern Ireland found "some ill-treatment but no brutality." **25** Terms of a Rhodesia settlement announced.

December 3 Outbreak of Indo-Pakistan war after prolonged friction and many border disputes. **17** End of Indo-Pakistan War. **18** Pres. Yahya Khan of Pakistan ousted and succeeded by Mr. Ali Bhutto; Group of Ten agreed on terms for re-alignment of currencies. **24** Signor Leone elected new President of Italy after 24 ballots. **29** British troops began withdrawal from Malta.

1972

January 9 *Queen Elizabeth* destroyed by fire in Hong Kong harbour; Miners' strike began with widespread power cuts and industrial disruption. **12** Sheikh Mujibar Rahman appointed Prime Minister of Bangladesh. **13** Dr. Busia's government in Ghana overthrown. **22** Britain, Ireland, Norway and Denmark signed European Economic Community treaty. **30** "Bloody Sunday" in Londonderry: 13 civilians killed.

February 9 State of emergency in power crisis declared and large-scale power cuts began. **15** Over 1·5 million workers laid off at height of power crisis. **17** Second reading of European Communities Bill carried by only eight votes. **18** Wilberforce Enquiry's terms for settling the miners' dispute published. **22** Seven killed in IRA bomb explosion at Aldershot. **25** Miners voted to return to work.

March 4 Belfast restaurant explosion killed two and injured 136. **29** Tutankhamun exhibition opened at the British Museum; Berlin Wall opened for the first time in six years. **30** Direct rule came into force in Northern Ireland.

April 10 46 countries signed a convention outlawing biological weapons. **18** Bangladesh admitted to the Commonwealth. **19** National Industrial Relations Court ordered 14-day cooling-off period in rail dispute.

May 3 Church of England Synod failed to reach required vote in favour of Anglican-Methodist union. **9** Black September hijackers killed at Lydda airport by Israeli soldiers. **15** The Queen began state visit to France. **22** President Nixon arrived in Moscow for talks; Ceylon became the republic of Sri Lanka. **23** Pearce Commission reported that the Rhodesians were not generally in favour of settlement proposals. **28** Duke of Windsor died in Paris.

June 6 430 killed in Wankie Colliery explosion in Rhodesia. **16** 120 killed in tunnel rail crash near Soissons, France; 5 burglars caught in Watergate building, Democratic Party's campaign H.Q. **23** Government decision to "float" the pound.

July 9 Ceasefire in Northern Ireland ended and six people were shot dead in Belfast. **28** Start of national dock strike following rejection of Jones-Aldington proposals for the modernisation of the docks.

August 4 President Amin ordered expulsion of 40,000 British Asians in Uganda. **28** Prince William of Gloucester killed in air race crash.

September 1 Iceland extended fishing limits from 12 to 50 miles. **5** Arab guerrillas held Israeli athletes hostage in Munich: the hostages, 5 guerrillas and a policeman were killed in gun battle at Fürstenfeldbruk airport. **25** Darlington conference on the future of Northern Ireland opened.

October 2 Denmark voted to join European Economic Community. **5** Congregational Church in England and Wales and Presbyterian Church of England combined to form the United Reformed Church. **10** Sir John Betjeman appointed Poet Laureate. **13** Bank rate abolished (now called minimum lending rate).

A.D.
November 6 Government imposed immediate 90-day freeze on prices, pay, rent and dividend increases. **7** President Nixon elected for a further term of office. **19** Herr Brandt re-elected in West German poll. **20** Silver Wedding anniversary of the Queen and Duke of Edinburgh.

December 2 Mr. G. Whitlam became first Labour Prime Minister in Australia since 1946. **18** United States resumed bombing of North Vietnam. **21** Treaty signed between West and East Germany. **23** Earthquake in Nicaragua devastated the capital Managua.

1973

January 1 Britain, Ireland and Denmark became members of the European Economic Community. **27** Vietnam ceasefire agreement signed.

February 1 The Common Agricultural Policy of the EEC came into operation. **5** First Protestant loyalists detained without trial in Northern Ireland. **12** First group of American prisoners released from North Vietnam. **21** Israeli fighters brought down a Libyan Boeing 727 with the loss of 104 lives.

March 1 Fine Gael and Labour Party coalition won Irish General Election: Mr. Liam Cosgrave became Prime Minister. **8** One killed and 238 injured in two bomb blasts in central London. **9** Result of Northern Ireland referendum showed 591,820 in favour of retaining links with Britain, and 6,463 for links with the Republic. **11** Gaullists and their allies won an absolute majority of seats in the French General Election. **18** Icelandic patrol vessel fired live shots across bow of a British trawler. **29** Last American soldier left Vietnam.

April 1 VAT introduced in Britain.

May 7 President Nixon denied all knowledge of Watergate. **10** Elections held for 36 new metropolitan district councils. **11** Charges dismissed in Pentagon papers case in Washington. **17** Senate Select Committee hearings on Watergate opened. **18** Royal Navy frigates sent to protect British trawlers in disputed 50-mile limit off Iceland. **25** 3 American astronauts docked with crippled Skylab. **31** Mr. Erskine Childers succeeded Mr. de Valera as President of Ireland.

June 1 Greece declared a republic. **7** Skylab astronauts freed solar panels and saved mission. **21** Mr. Brezhnev and President Nixon signed agreement on arms limitation.

July 31 First sitting of new Ulster Assembly ended in chaos.

August 2 50 killed in Summerland fire at Douglas, Isle of Man. **19** Mr. George Papadopoulos became first President of Greece.

September 3 Dr. Henry Kissinger became U.S. Secretary of State. **7** Mr. Len Murray succeeded Mr. Vic Feather as TUC General Secretary. **10** Bombs in London stations injured 13 people. **11** Allende government overthrown in Chile. **14** Death of King Gustav of Sweden. **20** Bomb exploded in Chelsea barracks. **25** Skylab astronauts returned after 59 days in space.

October 6 Start of Arab–Israeli war. **8** Britain's first commercial radio station opened. **10** Mr. Spiro Agnew resigned as Vice-President of U.S.A. **12** General Peron became President of Argentina and his wife Vice-President. **16** Government placed embargo on arms sales to Middle East. **17** Arab oil producers announced cut in oil supplies until Israel withdrew from occupied territories. **22** UN proposal for ceasefire agreed by Israel, Egypt and Jordan (marred by subsequent clashes). **31** 3 Provisional IRA leaders freed from Mountjoy prison by hijacked helicopter.

November 8 End of "cod war" between Britain and Iceland. **12** Miners started overtime ban and ambulance drivers began selective strikes. **14** Wedding of Princess Anne and Captain Mark Philips. **25** Army coup in Greece.

December 5 50 mile/h speed limit imposed to conserve fuel. **6** Mr. Gerald Ford became Vice-Presi-

A.D
dent of U.S.A. **12** Rail drivers' union ASLEF began ban on overtime. **13** Further series of measures to conserve fuel announced: three-day working week from 31 December. **17** Emergency budget included cuts in consumer credit and reduction in public expenditure. **20** Admiral Carrero Blanco, Prime Minister of Spain, assassinated in Madrid. **23** Iran announced doubling of price of Persian Gulf oil. **28** Power engineers called off ban on out-of-hours working.

1974

January 1 Direct rule by U.K. Govt. in N. Ireland ended: New Ulster Executive took office; Mrs. Golda Meir won narrow victory in Israeli General Election. **8** Lord Carrington became Secretary for Energy at head of new department. **9** Parliament recalled for two-day debate on energy crisis. **18** Israel and Egypt signed agreement on separation of forces. **22** Loyalists expelled from N. Ireland Assembly after angry scenes.

February 4 Miners' strike ballot showed 81% in favour of strike action. **7** Prime Minister called for General Election on 28 February; Island of Grenada achieved independence. **10** Miners' strike began. **28** Election in Britain resulted in no clear majority.

March 4 Mr. Edward Heath resigned and a minority Labour Government took office. **9** Britain returned to five-day week. **11** Miners returned to work.

April 10 Resignation of Mrs. Golda Meir and her Cabinet after 5 years as Prime Minister. **14** Heaviest fighting on Golan Heights and Mount Hermon since ceasefire in Oct. 1973. **24** General election in S. Africa: Nationalist Party returned for seventh successive time; Progressive Party won 6 seats. **25** Army uprising in Portugal: authoritarian régime in power since 1926 overthrown.

May 6 Resignation of Herr Brandt on discovery of chancellery aide spying for E. Germany. **15** General Spinola became President of Portugal; in Israeli village of Ma'alot schoolchildren killed when Israeli troops stormed school where children held hostage by Arab terrorists. **16** Herr Schmidt became Chancellor of West Germany. **19** Victory for M. Giscard d'Estaing in French general election. **28** Collapse of N.I. executive. **29** Ulster Workers' Council called off strike; Assembly suspended: direct rule from Westminster resumed.

June 1 Explosion at Flixborough Nypro chemical works: 29 dead. **3** Mr. Rabin became Prime Minister of Israel; Michael Gaughan, Irish hunger striker, died at Parkhurst. **17** Bomb exploded beside Westminster Hall, injuring 11 people. **27** Foreign husbands and fiancés of British women to be allowed to live in Britain.

July 9 Canadian general election gave Trudeau overall majority of 18. **13** Final Report of Ervin Senate Watergate Committee published. **15** Coup d'etat in Cyprus: President Makarios overthrown and replaced by Nicos Sampson. **17** Bomb exploded with no warning in Tower of London: one killed, 41 injured. **18** Abolition of Pay Board and end of statutory incomes policy. **20** Turkish invasion of Cyprus. **26** Junta in Greece collapsed: Mr. Karamanlis returned to power. **24** Supreme Court ordered surrender of 64 White House tape recordings subpoenaed by Mr. Leon Jaworski, the special Watergate prosecutor. **27–30** Three articles of impeachment adopted by Judiciary Committee of the House of Representatives against President Nixon.

August 8 President Nixon resigned. **9** Mr. Gerald Ford sworn in as 38th President of USA. **14** Failure of peace talks on Cyprus: Turks renewed offensive and took control of most of north-east third of island. **26** Guinea-Bissau became independent.

September 8 President Ford granted full pardon to Richard Nixon. **12** Emperor Haile Selassie deposed by military command. **30** General

A.D.

Spinola resigned as President of Portuguese Republic: succeeded by General Francisco da Costa Gomes.

October 5 Two bombs in Guildford public houses killed five people and injured 70. **10** General Election in Britain: Labour returned with overall majority of 3. **15** Rioting in the Maze prison. **31** Hostages held for 6 days at Scheveningen gaol freed by Dutch commandos.

November 2–3 Summit meeting between President Ford and Mr. Brezhnev at Vladivostok. **7** 2 killed in bomb attack on Woolwich pubs. **17** Greece held first general elections since 1967: victory for Mr. Constantine Karamanlis. **21** 21 killed and 120 injured in bomb blasts in two Birmingham bars. **29** Anti-Terrorism Bill proscribing the IRA and giving police wider powers received Royal Assent.

December 3 Defence cuts announced: £4,700 million over next 10 years. **7** Archbishop Makarios returned to Cyprus. **9** Mr. Tanaka resigned as Prime Minister of Japan. **11** House of Commons voted against restoration of capital punishment for terrorism. **18–22** New wave of bombs in London: outside Selfridges; at Harrods; and at the home of Mr. Edward Heath. **25** Devastation of Darwin, Australia, by cyclone Tracy.

1975

January 1 Watergate defendants Mitchell, Haldeman, Ehrlichman and Mardian found guilty of conspiracy and of obstruction of justice. **24** Dr. Coggan enthroned 101st Archbishop of Canterbury. **25** End of democracy in Bangladesh: Shaikh Mujibur Rahman became President of one-party state.

February 11 Mrs. Thatcher elected leader of the Conservative Party. **13** Declaration by Turkish Cypriots of separate state in Cyprus.

March 13 Portugal's new Supreme Revolutionary Council headed by President Gomes took power. **25** Assassination of King Faisal of Saudi Arabia. **26** Evacuation of Hué by S. Vietnamese forces. **30** Da Nang abandoned by S. Vietnamese forces after panic and confusion.

April 1 Departure of Marshal Lon Nol from beseiged capital Phnom Penh. **17** Phnom Penh government surrendered to Khmer Rouge. **21** President Thieu resigned as N. Vietnamese forces encircled Saigon. **23** Massive airlift of refugees from Vietnam to USA. **25** Elections in Portugal the first for 50 years: Socialist Party (PSP) 38% of votes, the largest single party. **30** End of Vietnam war.

May 30–31 Coldest May night in Britain since records began.

June 5 UK voted "Yes" by 2 to 1 majority in EEC referendum. **5** Reopening of Suez Canal to international shipping after 8 years of closure. **9** First live radio broadcast of House of Commons sitting. **12** Mrs. Gandhi convicted of illegally using Government officials in her campaign for Parliament in 1971.

July 1 Mr. S. S. Ramphal succeeded Mr. Arnold Smith as Commonwealth Secretary-General. **5** Cape Verde Islands achieved independence from Portugal. **11** £6 a week limit on pay increases till 1 Aug. 1976; Independence of Portuguese Sao Tomé and Principe. **29** Military coup in Nigeria: new head of state Brigadier Murtala Mohammed.

August 7 Hottest August day in London since records began in 1940 (32·3°C). **15** Assassination of Mujibur Rahman of Bangladesh. **27–28** Bombs at Caterham and London.

September 9 Return after 5½ years of exile of Prince Sihanouk to Cambodia as titular head of state. **16** Independence of Papua New Guinea. **24** Government announced £175m package of measures to check unemployment; Dougal Haston and Doug Scott climbed Everest by south-west face.

October 3 Dr. Herrema, a Dutch industrialist, kidnapped in Limerick: released 7 Nov. **15** Iceland unilaterally extended its fishing rights from 50 to 200 miles. **21** In Britain, unemployment rose to over one million for first time since the war. **23**

A.D

Bomb placed under car of Mr. Hugh Fraser MP in London killed Professor Fairley, leading cancer expert. **26** In Beirut, clashes between right-wing Christian Phalangists and left-wing Muslims developed into full-scale battles.

November 3 Queen formally inaugurated the flow of North Sea oil from the BP Forties field. **11** Independence of Angola after 500 years of Portuguese rule; Australia's Labour Government, led by Gough Whitlam, dismissed by the Governor-General, Sir John Kerr. **22** Prince Juan Carlos crowned King of Spain. **25** Surinam (Dutch Guiana) became independent.

December 2 BAC signed contract to supply Iran with Rapier anti-aircraft missile system. **4** End of detention without trial in N. Ireland after 4½ years. **10** First shots fired in "cod war". **11** House of Commons voted 361–232 not to restore death penalty; End of Balcombe Street siege in London: Mr. and Mrs. Matthews held in flat by IRA terrorists since 6 Dec. **14** End of Dutch train siege at Beilen; Landslide victory in Australia for Liberal Country Party. **18** Education Bill compelling comprehensive school education published. **29** Sex Discrimination and Equal Pay Acts came into force.

1976

January 19 Government majority of 158 at end of 4-day devolution debate. **21** Concorde entered supersonic passenger service.

February 11 Recognition of MPLA as legal government of Angola by OAU. **13** Assassination of General Murtala Mohammed, Nigerian head of state, in unsuccessful coup. **19** Iceland broke off diplomatic relations with Britain over fishing dispute.

March 5 Ulster Convention dissolved: direct rule from Westminster continued. **16** Resignation of Mr. Wilson as Prime Minister. **19** Official announcement of separation of Princess Margaret and Lord Snowdon. **24** Senora Perón of Argentina deposed. **25** Basil Hume installed as Archbishop of Westminster.

April 5 Mr. James Callaghan became Prime Minister. **27** Britain began exporting North Sea oil.

May 10 Resignation of Mr. Jeremy Thorpe as leader of the Liberal Party. **12** Mr. Jo Grimond agreed to resume leadership of the Liberal Party for a temporary period. **24** Concordes from England and France flew to Washington for first time. **28** Soviet-American treaty controlling underground nuclear explosions for non-military purposes signed.

June 1 Interim agreement signed in Oslo ending "cod war" between Britain and Iceland. **16** Riots began in African township of Soweto near Johannesburg. **24** Vietnam reunified: recognition by British. **27** Gen. Antonio Ramalho Eanes, Army Chief of Staff, elected President of Portugal. **29** Independence of Seychelles as republic within Commonwealth.

July 2 Government emergency powers to control water shortage in Britain. **4** Israeli attack on Entebbe airport to free 100 Israeli hostages. **7** The Queen arrived in Washington for bicentennial celebrations; Mr. David Steel elected leader of the Liberal Party. **10** Explosion at Hoffman-La Roche's Seveso plant near Milan: poisonous chemical contaminated area of 7 km radius. **14** Official handing over to Tanzania and Zambia of Chinese-built Tanzam railway (1,860 km). **21** Mr. Christopher Ewart-Biggs, British Ambassador to Irish Republic, and a member of his staff, assassinated by landmine. **28** Major earthquake destroyed Chinese mining town of Tangshan; Britain broke off diplomatic relations with Uganda.

August 1 Trinidad and Tobago became independent republic within Commonwealth. **4** Renewed violence in South African township of Soweto. **6** Drought Act 1976 came into force. **25** Resignation of M. Chirac, Prime Minister of France.

September 2 European Commission on Human

A.D.
Rights found Britain guilty of torturing detainees in Ulster. **10** Mid-air collision of 2 airliners near Zagreb: 176 killed. **20** Electoral defeat of Sweden's Social Democratic Party after 44 years in power. **24** Mr. Ian Smith announced acceptance of British and American proposals for majority rule in Rhodesia in two years.

October 3 Bishop Muzorewa returned to Rhodesia from exile. **4** British Rail's high-speed train came into service. **6** Military coup in Thailand and the end of civilian rule after 3 years. **25** Official opening of the National Theatre by the Queen. **28** Conference on future of Rhodesia, chaired by Mr. Ivor Richard, opened in Geneva. **29** Opening of world's largest mining complex at Selby, Yorks.

November 1 Mr. Jimmy Carter elected President of the USA with Democratic majorities in both Houses. **15** Formal end of civil war in Lebanon as Syrian troops (as part of Arab peacekeeping force) moved into heart of Beirut. **27** Rally in Trafalgar Square in support of N. Ireland Peace People.

December 16 Landslide victory for Mr. Michael Manley in Jamaica's general election. **17** Exchange of Vladimir Bukovsky, Soviet dissident, and Señor Corvalán, veteran leader of Chileán Communist Party.

1977

January 1 Britain together with EEC countries extended fishing limits to 200 miles offshore (with effect from 1 April). **24** Collapse of second round of Rhodesian talks: Mr. Ian Smith rejected British proposals for transition to black majority rule.

February 15 Deaths in England and Wales exceeded number of live births in 1976 (for first time since records began in 1837). **17** Uganda's Anglican archbishop and two cabinet ministers killed in mysterious circumstances while under arrest.

March 1 Mr. Callaghan's Government went into minority. **7** The Queen arrived in Australia on her Jubilee tour; Landslide victory for Mr. Bhutto in Pakistan's national assembly election. **22** Resignation of Mrs. Gandhi after loss of seat in general election and defeat of Congress Party after 30 years in power. **23** Lib-Lab pact: Conservative motion of no-confidence defeated by 322 to 298. **24** Janata Government sworn in with Mr Moraji Desai as Prime Minister of India. **27** Collision on runway of two jumbo-jets at Tenerife: 577 killed.

April 21 Imposition of martial law in Karachi, Hyderabad and Lahore following 6 weeks of political violence in Pakistan. **22** Norwegian Ekofisk Bravo oilfield disaster.

May 5 Conservative gains in local government elections in England and Wales. **13** Collapse of Ulster 11-day strike despite widespread intimidation. **17** Israeli Labour Party defeated in general election: right-wing Likud Party, led by Mr. Menachem Begin, emerged as largest party. **18** International Commission of Jurists reported to UN horrifying massacres and murders in Uganda under Amin's rule.

June 1 Change in road traffic speed limits in UK: 70 mile/h, dual roads, 60 mile/h, single. **5** Bloodless coup in the Seychelles. **7** Silver Jubilee Thanksgiving celebrations with state pageantry in London. **11** End of 11-day Dutch sieges by South Moluccan terrorists after storming of train and school by Dutch Marines and police: 2 hostages and 6 Moluccans died. **15** General election in Spain, first since 1936: victory for Union of Democratic Centre (UCD) led by Prime Minister Suarez. **16** Britain severed last diplomatic link with Uganda; Irish Republic's coalition Fine Gael–Labour government defeated in general election by Mr. Jack Lynch's Fianna Fail. **26** Independence for Djibouti (Afars and Issas).

July 5 Army took charge in Pakistan and deposed Mr. Bhutto. **11** Trade union demonstration outside Grunwick factory. **15** Pay rises in next 12 months to be limited to 10%. **21** Mrs. Bandar-

A.D
anaike and her Sri Lanka Freedom Party suffered defeat in general election.

August 10 Conclusion of new Panama Canal Agreement: gradual takeover by Panama of the zone and canal by the year 2000. **13** National Front march in Lewisham, London, brought violent clashes. **31** Mr. Spyros Kyprianou became President of Cyprus. **25** Scarman Report on Grunwick dispute recommended company to re-employ strikers, but company rejected report.

September 1 Dr. Owen presented Mr. Ian Smith with Anglo-American proposals for a Rhodesian settlement. **25** Skytrain service to New York began.

October 16 The Queen began her Canadian Jubilee tour. **31** Effective revaluation of the £: Government allowed it to float upwards.

November 4 Mandatory arms embargo imposed by UN Security Council against S. Africa. **14** First day of firemen's strike after their claim for a 30% pay increase had been rejected: armed forces dealt with fires. **15** A son (Peter Mark Andrew) born to Princess Anne. **19** Historic meeting in Israel between President Sadat of Egypt and Prime Minister Menachem Begin of Israel; Coastal belt off Bay of Bengal hit by cyclone: estimated death toll 20,000–25,000. **29** Home Secretary granted amnesty for immigrants who had entered the country illegally before 1 Jan. 1976. **30** South African general election: Mr. Vorster's governing National Party vanquished both liberal and ultra right-wing political parties.

December 8 Fall of Dr. Soares' minority Socialist Government in Portugal. **10** Resignation of Gough Whitlam as Australia's Labour leader after general election when Malcolm Fraser's Conservative coalition was returned. **14** House of Lords dismissed appeal by Advisory, Conciliation and Arbitration Service (ACAS) in Grunwick dispute. **16** Extension of Piccadilly tube line to Heathrow opened by the Queen. **21** OPEC countries froze oil prices for next 6 months.

1978

January 1 Air India jumbo jet crashed in sea off Bombay: all 213 people on board killed. **4** Said Hammani, PLO's London representative, shot dead in Mayfair. **20** Mario Soares re-appointed Prime Minister of Portugal. **21** Special Liberal Party Assembly voted 1727–520 to continue Lib-Lab pact until July. **25** Serious Government defeats on the Scottish Devolution Bill. **29** Talks in Malta on future of Rhodesia with leaders of the Patriotic Front, Joshua Nkomo and Robert Mugabe: in Rhodesia itself, Ian Smith began negotiations for an internal settlement.

February 4 Major Ethiopian offensive launched in the Ogaden: Somalia appealed to the West for aid. **7** Government majority of 14 in Commons for its policy of sanctions against companies breaking the pay guideline (the "black list"). **19** Egyptian commandos stormed hi-jacked airliner at Larnaca airport in Cyprus: 15 commandos killed and 14 others injured. **21** All-Party Speakers' Conference recommended increased Ulster representation at Westminster: number of seats to be increased from 12 to 17.

March 3 Internal settlement agreed in Rhodesia between Ian Smith and three black Nationalist leaders: majority rule to become effective by 31 December 1978. **8** Agreement reached in Italy on formation of new government to be headed by Giulio Andreotti. **15** Massive Israeli thrust into south Lebanon. **16** Aldo Moro, five times Prime Minister of Italy, kidnapped by "Red Brigade" terrorists: body found 9 May; *Amoco Cadiz* supertanker ran aground off the Brittany coast: major pollution of Brittany coastal waters.

April 3 First regular radio broadcasts of proceedings in Parliament commenced. **9** Attempted *coup* in Somalia crushed. **10** The Transkei, the first tribal homeland in South Africa to be granted independence, severed diplomatic links with South Africa. **17** World Health Organisation

A.D.

(WHO) announced no cases of smallpox reported anywhere in the world during the previous year. **26** Arab terrorist attack on bus in Nablus in Israeli-occupied West Bank. **27** President Daoud deposed in pro-Soviet *coup* in Afghanistan.

May 1 First May Day holiday celebrated in Britain. **24** Princess Margaret obtained a divorce from Lord Snowdon. **25** David Steel, the Liberal leader announced that the Lib-Lab pact would terminate at the end of July.

June 3 Presidential election in Bangladesh resulted in easy victory for General Zia ur-Rahman. **10** Riots in Londonderry. **12** Provisional IRA leader Seamus Twomey sentenced in Dublin. **19** OPEC agreed to peg oil prices until December.

July 5 Resignation of General Acheampong, head of state in Ghana. **7** Independence of Solomon Islands. **9** Former P.M. of Iraq, General Abdul Razzale al-Naif, shot in London. **18** Talks began at Leeds Castle between Egyptian and Israeli foreign ministers and the US Secretary of State. **25** World's first "test-tube" baby born in Oldham. **26** Queen began official visit to Canada. **31** Devolution Bills for Scotland and Wales received royal assent.

August 6 Death of Pope Paul VI. **13** Bomb in PLO headquarters in Beirut killed at least 100 people. **22** Gunmen held hundreds hostage in Nicaraguan Parliament and succeeded in gaining release of 83 political prisoners. **26** Cardinal Albino Luciani of Venice elected as Pope John Paul I. **30** Case of smallpox confirmed in Birmingham; Janet Parker died on 11 September.

September 7 Prime Minister announced that he was not calling a general election in the autumn. **8** Martial law declared in Tehran and 11 Iranian cities: riots resulted in which many were killed. **11** Martial law declared in part of Nicaragua. **16** Earthquake in Tabas in north-east Iran killed 11,000. **17** Camp David talks between Sadat and Begin concluded with signing of a framework for a Middle East peace treaty. **20** P.M. of South Africa, John Vorster, resigned because of ill health. **27** Disastrous floods in India caused deaths of at least 1,200 and 43m displaced. **28** Pope John Paul I died after only 33 days as pontiff; Pieter Botha became P.M. of South Africa. **30** Ellice Islands became independent nation of Tuvalu.

October 7 Declaration of ceasefire in Lebanon. **9** Britain agreed to accept 346 Vietnamese refugees. **10** Daniel Arap Moi became President of Kenya. **12** *Christos Bitas* grounded off St. David's Head: oil slick threatened South Wales coastline. **15** Cardinal Karol Wojtyla of Cracow became first non-Italian Pope for 450 years as Pope John Paul II. **20** 4-week siege of Beirut lifted.

November 3 Dominica achieved independence from Britain. **5** Serious riots in Tehran. **25** National Party returned to power in New Zealand with reduced majority. **26** Clashes in Iran during 24-hour general strike. **27** Japanese P.M., Takeo Fukuda, resigned. **30** Publication of *The Times* suspended until agreement reached on new technology and manning levels: returned 13 Nov 1979.

December 7 Masayoshi Ohira became P.M. of Japan. **15** Government won a vote of confidence. **17** OPEC announced rise in oil prices in four stages in 1979; IRA bomb explosions in Southampton, Bristol, Manchester and Coventry. **18** Further bombs exploded or were discovered in London, Southampton and Bristol. **20** Bomb explosion in Jerusalem and Israeli attack on terrorist bases in Lebanon.

1979

January 1 Dr. Bakhtiar became new P.M. of Iran. **4** Guadeloupe summit talks held between UK, US, W. Germany and France. **7** Phnom Penh, the Cambodian capital, captured by Vietnamese and rebel forces. **15** Secondary picketing in road haul-

A.D

age strike caused growing problems: about 150,000 laid off as result of strike. **16** Shah left Iran amidst great rejoicing. **17** IRA bomb attacks on gas-holder in Greenwich and oil depot on Canvey Island; Britain to admit a further 1,500 Vietnamese refugees. **18** Code on picketing distributed to road haulage strikers: shortages continued and lay-offs mounted. **30** Rhodesian referendum among whites voted by 6:1 majority in favour of Ian Smith's proposals for transfer to majority rule. **31** Resignation of Italian government.

February 1 Muslim leader, the Ayatollah Khomeini, returned to Iran from exile in Paris. **5** Dr. Mehdi Bazargan nominated by Ayatollah Khomeini as P.M. of Iran. **6** Dr. Bhutto's appeal against the death sentence rejected by 4–3 by Pakistan Supreme Court. **11** Dr. Bakhtiar finally resigned as P.M. of Iran. **12** Remaining royalist guards surrendered to Khomeini supporters. **14** "Concordat" between government and TUC announced together with agreement on target of 5% inflation within 3 years. **15** Power handed over to army in Chad. **16** Execution of pro-Shah generals in Iran. **21** Volcano erupted in Jakarta resulting in 175 deaths. **22** St. Lucia became independent. **27** Mineworkers reached pay agreement with NCB. **28** Final meeting of white Rhodesian House of Assembly.

March 1 32·5% of Scots voted in favour of devolution proposals, thus failing to reach 40% requirement; in Wales there was an overwhelming vote against devolution. **4** Trade agreement between China and Britain signed. **6** Commander of Rhodesian army dismissed. **12** Iran and Pakistan withdrew from Central Treaty Organisation. **13** Government of Sir Eric Gairy in Grenada overthrown. **26** Peace treaty between Israel and Egypt signed in Washington. **28** Government defeated by 1 vote on no confidence motion; Radiation leak at Three Mile Island nuclear power plant in Pennsylvania led to declaration of emergency. **29** Prime Minister announced general election for 3 May. **30** Assassination of Airey Neave, Conservative M.P. and Shadow Northern Ireland Secretary; Ilie Verdel became Prime Minister of Romania. **31** Final withdrawal of British navy from Malta.

April 1 Islamic Republic declared in Iran. **2** First visit of Israeli Prime Minister to Egypt; Adolfo Suarez became Spain's first elected Prime Minister for more than 40 years. **4** Former Prime Minister of Pakistan, Zulfikar Ali Bhutto, executed. **11** Kampala captured by Tanzanian troops and Ugandan exiles: Professor Yusufo Lule became new leader of Uganda. **23** Teacher killed and 300 people arrested after clashes in Southall between National Front and Anti-Nazi League. **27** Exchange of prisoners between Russia and USA.

May 3 General Election in Britain. **4** Margaret Thatcher became first woman Prime Minister in Britain: Conservatives won election with overall majority of 43. **16** Government removed legal compulsion on LEAs to reorganise education on comprehensive lines. **22** Progressive Conservatives led by Mr. Joe Clark formed minority government in Canada. **23** Prof. Karl Carstens elected Federal President of West Germany. **24** Conservative team led by Lord Boyd reported that the Rhodesian elections had been fair. **25** Sinai capital of El Arish returned to Egypt. **27** Border between Egypt and Israel re-opened. **29** Bishop Abel Muzorewa sworn in as Zimbabwe Rhodesia's first black P.M.

June 3 Christian Democrats maintained position in Italian elections as largest single party. **4** John Vorster resigned as President of South Africa after publication of Erasmus Report on the "Muldergate" scandal; Ghanaian forces led by Flight-Lieut. Rawlings seized power. **11** Tories took 60 seats, Labour 17 and SNP 1 in European election. **16** General Acheampong, former ruler of Ghana, executed by firing squad. **18** Presidents Carter and Brezhnev signed SALT II treaty in Vienna. **20** President Lule deposed as Ugandan leader after only 2 months: succeeded by Mr. Godfrey Binaisa. **22** Jeremy Thorpe and 3 others acquitted in Old Bailey conspiracy trial.

A.D.
July 12 Gilbert Islands became independent nation of Kiribati. **13** Majority of 144 on bill to tighten abortion law. **17** President Somoza of Nicaragua resigned and fled to Miami. **19** Death penalty rejected by 119 votes in Commons.

August 1 Leaders of Lambeth, Southwark and Lewisham AHA stripped of powers after refusal to make spending cuts; Queen Mother installed as Warden of the Cinque Ports. **14** Gale-force winds brought havoc and 17 deaths in Fastnet yacht race. **18** Heart transplant operation carried out at Papworth Hospital near Cambridge. **19** Former Cambodian leader, Pol Pot, convicted in his absence of causing the death of 3m people. **20** Indian P.M. Charan Singh resigned after 24 days in office. **27** Earl Mountbatten, 2 relatives and a young boy killed by bomb explosion on boat in Sligo.

September 10 Zimbabwe Rhodesia constitutional talks opened in Lancaster House in London. **17** Environment Secretary announced the abolition of 57 quangos. **18** ILEA voted to abolish corporal punishment in schools. **19** The 3-party non-Socialist coalition won Swedish general election. **20** Emperor Bokassa of the Central African Empire ousted in coup by the former President David Dacko. **26** Government announced abandonment of compulsory metrication orders. **29** Pope arrived in Ireland for first-ever papal visit.

October 1 Civilian rule restored in Nigeria. **16** General Zia of Pakistan cancelled elections due to be held on 17 November. **17** Army colonels who carried out coup in El Salvador imposed martial law. **19** End of ITV strike announced after 11-week black-out; programmes resumed on 24 October. **23** Government announced removal of all foreign exchange controls.

November 1 Military coup in Bolivia; BL workers overwhelmingly endorsed recovery plans for the company. **2** Irish security forces seized up to £500,000 weapons and ammunition in Dublin harbour. **4** Iranian students occupied US embassy in Tehran taking hostages. **6** PM Bazargan resigned in Iran. **9** Computer fault led to full-scale nuclear alert in US; UN Security Council called for release of American hostages. **12** President Carter ordered cessation of all American oil imports from Iran. **13** Commons completed all stages of bill restoring legality to Zimbabwe Rhodesia and lifting sanctions; *The Times* returned after nearly a year. **14** All Iranian assets in US frozen in retaliation for embassy occupation. **23** Thomas MacMahon sentenced to life imprisonment for murder of Lord Mountbatten. **26** Government to reintroduce political honours.

December 5 Jack Lynch, Irish PM, resigned. **6** Britain withdrew recognition of Pol Pot regime in Kampuchea; Dutch parliament rejected NATO plan for stationing of cruise missiles in Holland. **7** Charles Haughey elected leader of Ireland's governing party; Lord Soames appointed governor of Rhodesia. **11** BSC announced axing of 52,000 jobs; Charles Haughey confirmed as Irish PM after bitter debate. **12** NATO approved stationing of 572 American missiles in Europe. **15** Ex-Shah given asylum in Panama. **27** Rhodesian treaty signed at Lancaster House. **27** President Hafizullah Amin of Afghanistan ousted in Soviet-backed coup.

1980

January 7 Mrs. Gandhi's Congress Party won absolute majority in Indian general election; USSR blocked Security Council call for immediate Russian withdrawal from Afghanistan. **9** 63 beheaded in Saudi Arabia for attacking Grand Mosque in Mecca. **13** Joshua Nkomo returned to Rhodesia after 3½ years exile. **16** Diplomatic links with Chile restored after 4 years. **22** Dr. Andrei Sakharov, winner of 1975 Nobel Peace Prize sent into internal exile in the city of Gorky. **27** Border between Egypt and Israel in Sinai reopened; Robert Mugabe returned to Rhodesia from exile to fight election.

A.D
February 12 Publication of Brandt report "North South: a programme for survival". **13** Opening of winter Olympic Games at Lake Placid. **18** Pierre Trudeau returned to power in Canadian general election after nine months out of office. **28** 5 orchestras to be scrapped in economy package announced by BBC; Government defeated no confidence motion in Commons, majority of 59.

March 4 Robert Mugabe invited to form government in Zimbabwe Rhodesia after winning absolute majority: his ZANU(PF) party won 57 seats. **11** Zimbabwe cabinet included Joshua Nkomo and 2 white Rhodesians. **24** Archbishop Romero shot dead at altar in San Salvador. **25** Enthronement of Robert Runcie as Archbishop of Canterbury. **26** British Olympic Association voted in favour of attending Moscow Olympics. **27** The *Alexander Keilland*, an oil accommodation rig, overturned in North Sea: 124 dead. **30** 39 persons killed and 100 injured in gun battle in San Salvador during Archbishop Romero's funeral.

April 2 Rioting and street fighting in St. Pauls area of Bristol: 19 police hurt, many arrests. **3** Return to work after 13-week steel strike. **9** Israeli troops moved into Lebanon; Resignation of Belgian PM, Wilfried Martens. **13** US Olympic committee voted two-to-one to accept President Carter's boycott of games. **18** Rhodesia became independent nation of Zimbabwe, with Robert Mugabe as Prime Minister and the Rev. Canaan Banana as President. **20** 67 arrests and 4 hurt in Lewisham National Front and Anti-Nazi League marches. **25** President Carter announced unsuccessful attempt to free US hostages in Iran: 8 Americans killed in collision on ground in desert. **28** American Secretary of State, Cyrus Vance, resigned in protest against hostage mission: replaced by Edward Muskie. **30** Armed men seized Iranian Embassy in London; Queen Beatrix invested as Queen of the Netherlands: riots in Amsterdam by anti-monarchist groups.

May 5 Following shooting of 2 hostages, SAS commandos stormed Iranian Embassy and released hostages: all but one of the gunmen killed. **11** Much damage caused by forest fires after dry weather: Forestry Commission lost at least 3000 acres. **18** Eruption of Mount St. Helens volcano began. **24** Entries for Olympic Games officially closed with 85 out of 145 accepting: 27 countries failed to reply. **27** Ex-President Obote returned to Uganda after 9 years' exile.

June 1 Start of Musicians' Union strike in protest against BBC cuts. **8** US computer sent out second false war alert in a week; Wave of bombings in Ulster. **22** Liberals won Japanese general election. **23** Sanjay Gandhi, son of Indian PM, died in plane crash. **27** All 67 British athletes selected for Moscow agreed to go. **30** Ms. Vigdis Finnbogadottir elected head of state in Iceland.

July 3 Mr. George Howard appointed chairman of BBC. **16** Government dismissed Brandt Commission's proposals. **17** Military coup in Bolivia. **19** Opening of 22nd Olympic Games in Moscow. **22** Lifting of arms embargo on Chile. **23** Dispute between Musicians' Union and BBC settled: 3 orchestras reprieved. **27** Death of deposed Shah of Iran. **30** New Hebrides became independent nation of Vanuatu.

August 4 Queen Mother's 80th birthday. **10** Violence in Ulster to mark 9th anniversary of internment. **13** 18 pickets arrested in Brixton; Start of French fishermen's blockade of Channel ports: continued until 30 August. **24** Polish PM dismissed. **31** Polish government agreed to establish independent trade unions and recognise right to strike.

September 5 Edward Gierek, Polish leader, replaced by Stanislav Kania after heart attack; Opening of 10-mile road tunnel in St. Gotthard massif. **7** Hua Guofeng resigned as Chinese leader, replaced by Zhao Ziyang. **10** Libya and Syria announced merger into unitary Arab state. **17** Ex-dictator of

A.D.
Nicaragua, Anastasio Somoza assassinated in Paraguay; President Husain of Iraq abrogated 1975 border agreement with Iran. **18** Environment Secretary withdrew £200m government money from local councils. **22** Outbreak of war between Iran and Iraq.

October 5 Helmut Schmidt re-elected Chancellor of West Germany. **10** Earthquakes destroyed Algerian town of El-Asnam: death toll over 4000. **14** ICI, Britain's largest industrial company, announced 4500 redundancies; Launch of new Mini Metro at Motor Show; Ivor Richard appointed as Britain's second member of European Commission. **15** James Callaghan announced retirement from leadership of Labour Party. **17** Queen met Pope in Vatican. **18** Liberal and Country coalition in Australia led by Malcolm Fraser returned to power. **22** Chief executive of Thomson announced sale of *The Times* and *Sunday Times*. **23** Alexei Kosygin resigned as Soviet PM. **24** Solidarity, Polish independent trade union, recognised by Polish authorities. **27** 7 Republican prisoners at Maze prison began hunger strike.

November 4 American Presidential election: Ronald Reagan won landslide victory. **6** Government announced 6% ceiling on pay increases in public sector. **10** Michael Foot elected new leader of Labour Party by 10 votes. **13** Labour MPs involved in clashes in Commons to prevent Black Rod proroguing Parliament: Government forced to postpone council house rent rises. **23** Violent earthquake in Southern Italy caused enormous devastation and loss of life.

December 8 Summit meeting in Dublin between Thatcher and Haughey: agreed programme for wider future cooperation. **12** 6 UDA men began hunger strike at Maze prison. **15** Dr. Milton Obote sworn in as President of Uganda. **16** 3 prisoners escaped from Brixton gaol: included Gerard Tuite, alleged IRA bomber. **17** Heseltine announced reduced rate-support grant; Prof. Alan Walters appointed personal economic adviser to PM at salary of £50,000. **18** IRA hunger strike called off as one of the strikers was close to death. **19** Resignations from Polish parliament included that of Edward Gierek. **21** Iran demanded £10,000m for release of hostages.

1981

January 1 Greece became 10th member of EEC. **3** Death of Princess Alice, Countess of Athlone. **10** Dr. Francisco Pinto Balsemao became PM of Portugal. **20** US hostages finally left Iran. **21** Sir Norman Stronge and his son, both former Stormont MPs, killed by IRA. **24** Wembley Labour Party conference voted for election of party leader by electoral college. **25** "Gang of Four", Roy Jenkins, Shirley Williams, William Rodgers and David Owen announced launching of a Council for Social Democracy; In China Mao's widow Jiang Qing found guilty but death penalty suspended for 2 years. **27** Joshua Nkomo appointed Minister without Portfolio in attempt to prevent confrontation in Zimbabwe.

February 3 Dr. Gro Harlem Brundtland elected Norway's first woman PM. **12** Rupert Murdoch announced purchase of *The Times*; Ian Paisley suspended from Commons for 4 days after calling N. Ireland Secretary a liar. **14** 48 young people killed in disco fire in Dublin. **15** First Sunday games in Football League. **20** Peter Sutcliffe charged with murder of 13 women in north of England. **23** Abortive military coup in Spain: right-wing guards held MPs hostage in lower house. **24** Prince Charles and Lady Diana Spencer announced engagement.

March 16 Government majority cut to 14 after backbench rebellion on petrol tax increase. **17** EEC announced £1m in food aid for China. **26** Social Democratic Party launched at public meeting. **29** First London marathon run. **30** President Reagan shot outside Hilton Hotel in Washington: gun man John Hinckley detained.

April 5 President Brezhnev flew to Czechoslovakia for talks on Polish crisis; Census day in Britain. **11** Start of weekend of violence in Brixton. **13** Lord Scarman to head inquiry into Brixton riots.

A.D
25 Snowy weekend in Britain: worst April blizzards this century. **27** *Now!* magazine closed after £6m losses.

May 5 Death of Bobby Sands after 66-day fast. **9** Bomb explosion at Sullom Voe oil terminal while Queen and King Olav were inaugurating the complex. **10** François Mitterrand won French presidential election; Government announced cut in lead content in petrol. **12** 2nd IRA hunger striker Francis Hughes died on 59th day of fast. **13** Pope John Paul shot by Turkish gunman Mehmet Ali Agca. **15** Princess Anne gave birth to daughter, later named Zara Anne Elizabeth. **18** Weekend referendum in Italy showed majority in favour of retaining liberal abortion laws. **22** Peter Sutcliffe sentenced to life imprisonment for Yorkshire Ripper murders. **30** Assassination of General Zia ur Rahman, President of Bangladesh.

June 8 Israeli air force destroyed Iraqi nuclear reactor: widespread international condemnation. **10** Polish President Stanislav Kania survived attempt by hard-liners to remove him; 8 leading IRA prisoners made armed escape from Crumlin Road gaol. **13** Blanks fired at the Queen during Trooping of the Colour. **16** Working alliance between Liberals and SDP announced. **21** Socialists won general election in France. **22** President Bani-Sadr dismissed by Ayatollah Khomeni. **24** First traffic crossed new Humber Bridge. **30** General election in Israel: Begin secured continuation of coalition by agreement with National Religious Party; Dr Garret Fitz-Gerald elected PM of Irish Republic by 3-vote majority; End of 5½-year Nazi war crimes trial: sentences ranging from 3 years to life.

July 2 UGC announced massive cuts in university spending. **3** Riots in Southall after coaches of skinheads arrived for punk concert; Shot fired at Ian Paisley in Markets district of Belfast. **4** Weekend of serious riots in Toxteth: savage conflict between police and youths. **8** Riots in Moss Side, Manchester and Wood Green, London. **10** Further riots in British cities: continued until 26 July. **15** Northern Ireland office asked Red Cross to mediate at the Maze. **22** Mehmet Ali Agca sentenced to life imprisonment for shooting the Pope. **29** Wedding of Prince Charles and Lady Diana Spencer. **30** President of Gambia deposed whilst attending royal wedding: coup finally put down on 6 August; End of 21-week civil servants' strike.

August 8 Rioting in Northern Ireland after death of 9th hunger striker and 10 years of internment. **20** Bank of England suspended MLR. **24** Mark David Chapman gaoled for murder of John Lennon. **25** South African troops crossed border into Angola. **30** Iran's President and PM assassinated in bomb explosion in Tehran.

September 1 Army seized control in Central African Republic. **4** French ambassador to Lebanon assassinated in Beirut. **6** Solidarity's first national congress in Gdansk, Poland. **17** Soviet Union delivered ultimatum to Polish leadership to act against Solidarity. **18** France abolished capital punishment. **21** Belize became independent. **27** Denis Healey won Labour deputy leadership election.

October 4 End of hunger strike at Maze prison: 10 men had died during 7-month campaign. **6** President Sadat of Egypt assassinated at a military parade. **10** 2 killed in IRA bomb explosion in Chelsea: aimed at Irish Guards' coach. **14** Hosni Mubarak sworn in as President of Egypt. **17** Car bomb injured Lt.-Gen. Sir Steuart Pringle. **18** Left-wing victory in Greek general election; General Wojciech Jaruzelski became leader of Polish Communist Party. **26** Bomb disposal expert killed by IRA bomb in Oxford Street.

November 6 Anglo-Irish summit ended with agreement on new Anglo-Irish Intergovernmental Council. **14** Unionist MP Rev. Robert Bradford shot dead in Belfast. **17** Northern Ireland Secretary attacked by mob at funeral of Robert Bradford. **19** Tony Benn lost place in Shadow Cabinet election. **25** Scarman Report on summer riots published.

A.D.

December 8 Sudden heavy falls of snow caused chaos in Britain; Arthur Scargill elected leader of National Union of Mineworkers. **9** Labour National Executive agreed to investigate activities of Militant Tendency. **11** Javier Perez de Cuellar chosen as Secretary General of United Nations. **13** Martial law imposed in Poland: General Jaruzelski seized emergency powers. **14** Israel annexed Golan Heights, captured from Syria during Six Day War in 1967; Labour Party returned to power in Malta for third term. **15** Bomb in Iraqi embassy in Beirut killed at least 20 and injured 95. **17** Law Lords ruled that GLC cheap fares policy and supplementary rate were illegal; American general James Dozier kidnapped by Red Brigades in Verona. **19** Crew of Penlee lifeboat drowned during attempt to rescue crew of coaster *Union Star*. **31** Military coup in Ghana.

1982

January 4 EEC governments voted against following US economic sanctions against Poland and Soviet Union. **8** Blizzards swept Britain at start of weekend of chaos. **13** 81 dead after Air Florida Boeing 737 crashed into bridge in central Washington. **24** World Airways DC10 crashed into Boston harbour: all 208 on board rescued. **26** Unemployment reached 3m or 1:8 of working population. **27** Irish budget defeated by a single vote: PM asked for dissolution of parliament. **28** Brigadier-General James Dozier rescued from Red Brigades by Italian police: 5 guerrillas arrested.

February 1 Massive price increases in Poland. **5** Collapse of Laker Airways with debts of over £210m. **8** Japan Air Lines DC8 crashed into Tokyo Bay: 24 killed. **15** *Ocean Ranger* oil rig sank off Newfoundland: all 84 on board drowned. **17** Joshua Nkomo dropped from Zimbabwe cabinet; Settlement of rail strike. **19** De Lorean car company in Belfast went into liquidation. **25** Scenes in Stock Market when Amersham International shares went on sale.

March 3 Queen opened Barbican Centre in City of London. **9** Charles Haughey elected P.M. of Ireland after gaining support of left. **16** President Brezhnev announced unilateral freeze on deployment of Soviet missiles in Europe. **18** Group of Argentinians in South Georgia to dismantle whaling station raised Argentinian flag. **19** Cricketers playing in unofficial tour of South Africa banned from playing for England for 3 years. **23** Coup in Guatemala City. **24** After bloodless coup, Bangladesh under martial law for third time since independence.

April 2 Argentina invaded Falkland Islands: emergency Cabinet meeting, and humiliation for Foreign and Defence Secretaries. **3** Special Saturday sitting of Commons to discuss crisis. **5** Lord Carrington and 2 other Foreign Office ministers resigned; Francis Pym appointed Foreign Secretary; Fleet set sail from Portsmouth for the Falklands. **6** UK banned all Argentinian imports. **7** Defence Secretary announced 200-mile naval blockade of Falklands. **12** Start of British naval blockade of Falklands. **15** 5 Muslims executed for assassination of President Sadat. **25** British troops recaptured South Georgia; Israel handed over Sinai to Egypt. **28** Britain announced air blockade of Falklands.

May 1 British aircraft bombed Port Stanley airport, followed by naval bombardment. **2** Argentine cruiser *General Belgrano* sunk after British attack. **4** British destroyer *HMS Sheffield* hit by Exocet missile and abandoned after fire: 20 men lost. **7** Britain extended total exclusion zone to within 12 nautical miles of Argentine coastline; UN peace proposals under discussion by both sides. **9** British boarding party took over Argentine trawler *Narwal* believed to have been spying on fleet. **11** Navy frigate attacked Argentine vessel between 2 main Falkland islands; MPs rejected return of death penalty by 357 votes to 195 in free vote. **12** *QE2* sailed to join task force; 2 Argentine Skyhawk jets shot down. **15** British commando raid on Argentine airstrip at Pebble Island. **18** Decision on farm prices taken by EEC on majority vote: Britain criticised unprecedented breaking of Luxembourg compromise. **21** British forces estab-

A.D

lished a bridgehead at San Carlos: 5 warships hit, *HMS Ardent* sunk with loss of 22 lives, 21 soldiers killed when Sea King helicopter crashed. **24** *HMS Antelope* sunk after fire; De Lorean car company in Belfast to suspend production. **25** *HMS Coventry* and Cunard container ship *Atlantic Conveyor* destroyed. **27** British task force began to move forward from San Carlos bridgehead. **28** Goose Green and Darwin captured by paratroops; Pope arrived in Britain at start of 6-day visit. **30** Marines captured Douglas and Teal Island.

June 3 British dropped leaflets on Port Stanley urging surrender; Israeli ambassador shot in London. **4** Israeli aircraft bombed Palestinian quarters of Beirut in retaliation. **6** British took Bluff Cove and Fitzroy; Death of 2 British climbers on Everest reported. **7** Argentine raids on *Sir Tristram* and *Sir Galahad* off Bluff Cove. **11** *QE2* returned to Southampton with survivors from 3 British warships. **14** Ceasefire agreed in Falklands as British troops reached outskirts of Port Stanley. **17** General Galtieri deposed as President of Argentina. **21** Birth of Prince William of Wales. **22** John Hinckley acquitted of attempted assassination of President Reagan by virtue of insanity. **23** Labour National Executive voted for action against Militant Tendency. **25** Alexander Haig replaced as US Secretary of State by George Shultz; Former Governor of Falklands returned to Stanley.

July 1 General Reynaldo Bignone installed as President of Argentina. **2** Roy Jenkins elected leader of SDP. **7** Church of England rejected proposals for covenanting with 3 Free Churches. **9** Boeing 727 crashed into residential suburb of New Orleans: 153 dead. **13** Gerard Tuite gaoled in Dublin for bomb offences committed in Britain. **20** IRA bomb explosions in Hyde Park and Regent's Park killed 11 and injured 50. **26** End of hire purchase restrictions announced.

August 4 Arthritis drug Opren suspended after allegations about side effects; Israeli tanks invaded West Beirut. **12** Further ceasefire in Lebanon forced on Israel by President Reagan. **14** Barclays Bank branches opened on Saturday for the first time in 13 years. **17** Mutiny in Seychelles put down within 24 hours; US and China agreed on common policy towards Taiwan; Ruth First, prominent member of African National Congress killed by letter bomb in South Africa. **21** Evacuation of PLO fighters from Beirut began.

September 11 48 killed in helicopter crash near Mannheim. **14** Princess Grace of Monaco died following road accident; Lebanese leader Bashire Gemayel killed by bomb in East Beirut; Britain and Argentina ended financial sanctions. **15** Israeli troops crossed ceasefire line to bomb West Beirut. **17** Hundreds of Palestinians massacred in refugee camps in West Beirut: widespread international condemnation. **19** Swedish Social Democrats won general election. **23** Shirley Williams elected President of SDP.

October 1 Helmut Kohl, leader of Christian Democrats, became Chancellor of West Germany after defeating Helmut Schmidt in no confidence vote. **2** Bomb explosion in centre of Tehran killed at least 60. **8** Polish government dissolved Solidarity, Eastern Europe's first trade union. **11** Tudor warship *Mary Rose* finally raised; Strike in Gdansk against ban on Solidarity. **21** Election for Ulster Assembly: SDLP won 14 seats and Sinn Fein 5 and both parties said they would not take up seats. **28** Socialists came to power in Spain. **31** Thames barrier raised for first time.

November 1 Opening of Channel 4 television. **4** Irish government collapsed after no confidence vote. **10** Over 1,000 Soviet troops and Afghans killed in crash in tunnel north of Kabul; Geoffrey Prime gaoled for 35 years for spying; Death of Leonid Brezhnev, Soviet leader. **11** Massive explosion at Israeli military HQ in Tyre: 89 dead; First session of Ulster Assembly. **12** Yuri Andropov became new Soviet leader. **24** El Al, Israeli national airline, put into liquidation. **25** Irish general election: neither main party had overall majority—coalition of Fine Gael and Labour formed.

December 6 Bomb killed 16 and injured 66 at

A.D.

Droppin Well bar in Ballykelly: INLA claimed responsibility. **8** £31m to be given in government aid to Falklands. **10** 2 Russian cosmonauts landed after record 211 days in space. **12** 30,000 women ringed perimeter of Greenham Common missile base in anti-nuclear protest. **15** Government defeated by 15 votes on proposed new immigration rules; Gibraltar's frontier with Spain opened to pedestrians after 13 years. **21** New Soviet leader Yuri Andropov offered to reduce medium range nuclear weapons by two-thirds if NATO gave up Pershing and Cruise missiles: proposal rejected by Western leaders. **30** Martial Law suspended in Poland.

1983

January 11 Opening of public inquiry into proposed pressurised water reactor at Sizewell. **17** Start of breakfast TV in Britain. **25** EEC agreement on common fishing policy after 7 years. **27** New High Court judgement allowed GLC to cut fares. **31** Law came into force about wearing of seat belts.

February 8 Publication of report on Beirut massacre: Defence Minister Sharon later forced to resign whilst remaining in cabinet. **9** 1981 Derby winner Shergar stolen from stable in County Kildare. **13** Queen started 4-week tour of Jamaica, Mexico, US and Canada. **23** Labour NEC voted to expel 5 members of Militant Tendency.

March 1 Launch of new BL car, the Maestro. **5** Labour Party won decisive victory in Australian general election. **6** Chancellor Helmut Kohl's Christian Democrats won clear victory in West German general election. **8** Miners voted against strike action over pit closures. **14** Tadworth Hospital for children saved from closure. **18** Start of Prince and Princess of Wales' tour of Australia and New Zealand. **22** Chaim Herzog elected president of Israel in preference to PM's candidate. **28** Ian MacGregor appointed chairman of NCB. **31** 3 Russians expelled from Britain for alleged espionage.

April 4 White senator and 2 others killed by dissidents in Zimbabwe. **6** UK passport issued to Ian Smith, ex-PM of Rhodesia. **10** Relatives of Falklands casualties attended service at San Carlos. **12** British-made film Gandhi won 8 Oscars. **18** Many killed in bombing of US embassy in West Beirut; Government agreed to phasing out of lead in petrol. **21** New £1 coin came into circulation. **24** Austria's Chancellor, Dr Bruno Kreisky, resigned after 13 years in office. **25** Socialists failed to gain absolute majority in Portuguese general election. **26** 8 famine relief workers kidnapped in Ethiopia by Tigré People's Liberation Front. **28** High Court judge refused to declare Exit guide to euthanasia illegal.

May 1 Police broke up demonstrations in 20 Polish cities. **6** West German government pronounced that so-called Hitler diaries published in Stern magazine were a forgery. **8** US Secretary of State left Middle East after 2 weeks without peace deal. **13** Parliament dissolved: George Thomas retired as Speaker. **16** London police began fitting wheel clamps to illegally parked cars. **17** Israeli-Lebanon agreement signed on troop withdrawal: Syria imposed blockade in protest. **18** State of Emergency in Sri Lanka after election violence. **19** Missing barrels of Dioxin from chemical plant at Seveso found in Northern France. **20** Bomb exploded in centre of Pretoria, S. Africa; Roof-top protest at Albany gaol: ended 6 days later. **23** Retaliatory S. African raids on Maputo, Mozambique. **24** Huge bomb damaged Andersonstown police station in Belfast. **30** End of Williamsburg summit of 7 industrialised nations: reaffirmation of commitment to fight inflation.

June 9 Election Day: Conservatives had majority of 144; Foreign relief workers freed after 6 weeks as captives of Tigré liberation group in Ethiopia. **13** Roy Jenkins resigned as leader of SDP: David Owen succeeded without election; Pioneer 10 spacecraft became first man-made object to travel beyond solar system. **14** Government 'Fortress Falklands' policy endorsed by all-party Commons defence committee. **15** Mr. Bernard Weatherill elected Speaker. **16** Mr Andropov elected President of USSR. **18** At

A.D

European summit £450m budget rebate granted to Britain. **22** State opening of Parliament. **24** Syria expelled Yasser Arafat, PLO leader.

July 3 Home of former Ulster MP Gerry Fitt burnt out by IRA. **6** Chancellor announced £500m cuts in state spending. **13** Commons decisively rejected return of death penalty. **15** 6 killed by suitcase bomb at Orly airport: Armenian extremists responsible; Backbench MPs agreed to pay increases of 5½%. **16** BA helicopter crashed near Scillies with loss of 20 lives. **19** Government agreed to stop OFT inquiry into restrictive practices of Stock Exchange. **21** Polish authorities ended Martial Law. **25** Riots in Colombo against minority Tamil community. **26** Curfew in Hebron after renewed violence; High Court ruling that under-16s were entitled to contraceptive advice without parental consent.

August 1 12 injured in oil rig explosion in Forties field. **3** BR announced plans to close 114 miles of track; Settlement of Financial Times dispute that had halted production for 9 weeks. **4** Mr. Bettino Craxi became Italy's first socialist Prime Minister since 1946. **5** Explosion in Lebanese mosque killed 19 people. **8** Military coup in Guatemala. **11** Chad town of Faya-Largeau fell to Libyan troops. **14** French troops took up positions in north-east Chad. **15** Joshua Nkomo returned to Zimbabwe to claim seat in parliament. **21** Philippine opposition leader shot dead at Manila airport; 7 killed and over 50 injured in train crash in Irish Republic. **29** 2 US marines from international peace-keeping force killed in Beirut. **31** South Korean airliner reported missing off coast of Japan: USSR accused of shooting it down and later admitted it.

September 4 Israeli army withdrew from Chouf mountains above Beirut. **8** Rocket attack on Managua airport, Nicaragua. **12** 63 killed in South African mine disaster. **15** Cabinet announced pay target of 3% in public sector; PM Begin of Israel formally resigned amid speculation about his health. **17** US shelled artillery positions in Lebanon. **18** St. Kitts and Nevis became independent. **23** Air crash near Abu Dhabi: all 112 on board killed. **25** 38 IRA prisoners escaped from Maze Prison: prison officer stabbed to death. **26** Lebanese cabinet resigned; Australia II beat Liberty in America's Cup.

October 2 Neil Kinnock elected leader of Labour Party and Roy Hattersley deputy. **7** Government plans announced for abolition of GLC and 6 metropolitan counties. **9** South Korean deputy PM and Foreign Minister among 19 killed by bomb explosion in Rangoon. **10** Mr Yitzhak Shamir's new Israeli government took office. **14** Cecil Parkinson resigned from cabinet. **19** PM of Grenada, Maurice Bishop shot by troops: army commander General Hudson Austin took control. **23** Suicide bombers killed 229 US marines and 58 French paratroops in Beirut. **25** US troops invaded Grenada together with troops from 6 Caribbean states: Britain opposed to invasion. **27** Last outpost of Grenadan resistance, Fort Frederick, fell to US: Governor-General Sir Paul Scoon returned to island; European Parliament to freeze Britain's promised EEC rebate of £450m. **30** Earthquake in eastern Turkey: at least 226 killed; Raul Alfonsin, Radical Party leader won Argentine general election.

November 3 White minority in South Africa gave 2:1 endorsement to plan to give limited representation to Asians and Coloureds. **4** Dennis Nilsen sentenced to 8 life sentences for 15 killings; 60 people killed in suicide bomb attack on Israeli headquarters in Tyre; 2 RUC men killed by bomb at Ulster Polytechnic. **6** Conservative Motherland Party won election in Turkey. **10** The Queen and Duke of Edinburgh began state visit to Kenya. **12** Gerry Adams, MP for West Belfast became leader of Irish Republican movement. **14** First cruise missiles arrived at Greenham Common. **15** Turkish Cypriots declared UDI under Rauf Denktash. **16** PLO leader Yasser Arafat driven back to Tripoli. **18** Sextuplets born in Liverpool; Enthronement of Archbishop of York, Dr John Habgood. **20** 3 killed and 7 injured in terrorist attack in Darkley Gospel Hall in Northern Ireland. **21** Unionist Party

A.D.

withdrew from Northern Ireland Assembly in protest. **23** Soviet Union walked out of Geneva disarmament talks. **24** 6 Israelis released by PLO in return for 4,700 PLO prisoners. **26** 2-day Fleet St. newspaper strike in support of Warrington NGA; £26m gold bullion stolen from Heathrow. **27** Columbian jumbo jet crash near Madrid: 181 killed. **28** European space lab blasted off from Cape Canaveral.

December 5 14 killed in car bomb explosion in Beirut's Moslem area. **6** First heart-lung transplant operation in Britain: patient died after 2 weeks; European summit ended in total failure. **7** 2 Spanish airliners crashed in fog on runway at Madrid airport: 92 killed; Official Unionist, Mr Edgar Graham shot dead at Queen's University, Belfast. **8** US announced lifting of ban on arms sales to Argentina. **10** Bomb explosion at Woolwich RA barracks. **13** Bomb found and detonated in Kensington High St. **15** NGA industrial action called off; European Parliament blocked Britain's EEC rebate. **17** Massive bomb explosion outside Harrods: 6 killed and many injured: IRA stated bomb was 'unauthorised'; 83 died in disco fire in Madrid. **20** Britoil's cancellation of oil rig order led to crisis in Scott Lithgow yard on Clyde. **20** Yasser Arafat and 4,000 guerrillas left Tripoli by sea. **25** Small bomb exploded in Oxford St. **27** Pope met his assailant in prison; Collapse of deal between BSC and US Steel Corporation over Ravenscraig plant. **31** Military coup in Nigeria: Maj.-Gen. Mohammed Buhari new leader.

1984

January 9 Share prices exceeded 800 on FT index. **11** 2 lorry drivers hijacked by French farmers in protest against foreign meat imports. **13** Civil disturbances in Hong Kong. **17** 13 Tories voted against government and 20 abstained in second reading of Rates Bill. **20** £1m diamonds stolen from Christie's. **23** Further Tory revolt over government proposals to curb rate rises; 17 drowned when *Radiant Med* sank in English Channel. **25** Government announced ban on union membership at GCHQ. **26** Maze prison governor resigned after critical Hennessy report on escape of IRA prisoners. **29** Spanish general murdered by Basque terrorists in Madrid.

February 1 General Kiessling reinstated as German NATO commander. **3** Indian diplomat Ravindra Mhatre kidnapped in Birmingham and later found dead. **5** Lebanese cabinet resigned following 4 days of bitter fighting between army and Shi'ite Moslems. **8** British contingent of multi-national force in Lebanon airlifted to *Reliant*. **9** Death of President Andropov of Russia: succeeded by Konstantin Chernenko; Mr Harold Macmillan awarded earldom on his 90th birthday. **15** Druze and Shi'ite militiamen pushed Lebanese army out of southern approaches to Beirut. **20** Italian peace-keeping contingent left Beirut. **24** French lorry drivers lifted roadblocks which had been crippling traffic in France. **26** All but 100 US marines withdrawn from Beirut. **29** Pierre Trudeau announced resignation as Canadian PM.

March 6 NCB announced loss of 20,000 jobs in mining industry and closure of 21 pits; Deputy prison governor at Maze, William McConnell, shot dead outside home. **12** First day of miners' strike against pit closures. **14** Gerry Adams, MP for West Belfast, injured in assassination attempt. **15** Massive £5m silver robbery at Woburn Abbey. **20** Collapse of EEC summit: Britain blamed for intransigence. **23** Sarah Tisdall, Foreign Office clerk, gaoled for 6 months for leaking documents to *The Guardian*: widespread protests. **25** France began withdrawing peace-keeping force from Beirut. **26** Queen in Jordan for 4-day visit: unprecedented security after bomb explosion. **28** Jardine Matheson to withdraw from Hong Kong; British diplomat shot dead in Athens; Government approved sale of Scott Lithgow shipyard to Trafalgar House. **30** Rugby Union team to go to South Africa.

April 3 Coup in Guinea following death (8 days earlier) of President Sekou Touré. **4** Women evicted by bailiffs at Greenham Common. **5** BBC1 blacked

A.D

out by strike; ILEA to be replaced by directly elected body, not board of nominees. **8** Daughter of RC magistrate killed in IRA trap: woman later charged with murder. **10** Fire destroyed Falkland Islands' only hospital: 8 died; Shuttle crew succeeded in retrieving Solar Max satellite for repair. **11** Konstantin Chernenko approved as President of Supreme Soviet. **13** 5 airmen and 2 soldiers from Cyprus charged under Official Secrets Act. **16** Michael Bettaney gaoled for 23 years after conviction on espionage charges. **17** WPC Yvonne Fletcher shot dead outside Libyan embassy: embassy under siege. **22** Britain broke off diplomatic relations with Libya. **26** British diplomatic families arrived home from Libya. **27** End of siege with deportation of 30 Libyans and return of British ambassador and diplomats from Tripoli.

May 2 47 rescued after ditching of Chinook helicopter in North Sea; NCB announced deal to sell 175,000 tonnes of coke to American steel works. **7** Napoleon Duarté, Christian Democratic candidate claimed victory in Salvadorean presidential election. **8** Russians announced boycott of Olympic Games: followed later by other Warsaw Pact countries; Commandos attacked Gadafy barracks in Tripoli. **10** Verdict of unlawful killing at inquest into death of WPC Yvonne Fletcher outside Libyan embassy. **13** 16 held hostage by rebels in Angola since February freed. **18** 4 members of security forces killed by IRA. **23** Horrific explosion at underground pumping station in Lancs killed 15 people; Talks between NCB and NUM abandoned after 65 minutes. **24** Increase in tension in Gulf war: tanker ablaze.

June 1 President Reagan in Ireland for 3-day visit: Fresh disturbances in Punjab; PM Botha of South Africa in talks with Mrs Thatcher at Chequers amidst protests by anti-apartheid movement. **5** US announced increase in military role in Gulf with dispatch of Awacs. **6** Sikh fanatics in Golden Temple of Amritsar surrendered to Indian army: leader found dead. **14** Elections to European Parliament: substantial gains by Labour although Tories kept majority. **15** 4 killed in explosions in oil tanker at Milford Haven. **16** John Turner elected leader of Canadian Liberal Party and thus PM. **20** Education Secretary announced plans for new GCSE to replace O level and CSE in 1986. **22** Reports of massive explosion in Soviet Union naval base at Severomorsk. **26** Agreement reached over EEC budget: Britain settled for 66% rebate; West German Economics Minister resigned after corruption charges.

July 2 2,000 short-term prisoners released under new parole procedures. **5** Abducted Nigerian exile, Umaru Dikko found in crate at Stansted. **6** David Jenkins installed as Bishop of Durham. **9** Roof of York Minster destroyed by fire. **12** Robert Maxwell acquired Mirror Group Newspapers. **13** Labour Party won general election in New Zealand. **16** High Court ruled that government ban on unions at GCHQ was illegal; Lords finally voted to abolish GLC and other metropolitan authority elections. **17** Resignation of French government. **21** Amnesty for 652 political prisoners in Poland. **23** General election in Israel: inconclusive result. **25** Soviet cosmonaut became first woman to walk in space. **29** Opening of Olympic Games in Los Angeles. **31** Air France Boeing hijacked; surrendered on 2 August after blowing up flight deck.

August 2 Bomb exploded at Madras airport. **5** Leader of Israeli Labour Party, Mr Shimon Peres asked to form coalition government. **16** De Lorean cleared of drugs charges in USA. **19** 11 killed in veteran plane crash in Staffs. **21** Widespread arrests in South Africa on eve of coloured elections which were won by Labour Party. **26** Start of outbreak of salmonella poisoning at Stanley Royde hospital in Wakefield: 26 died. **31** TUC general council agreed to back pit strike; 2 Britons detained in Libya released; Bomb explosion at Kabul airport.

September 3 29 killed in rioting in black townships in Transvaal. **4** Erich Honecker, East German PM cancelled visit to West Germany; Conservatives won enormous victory in Canadian general election: Mr Brian Mulroney became PM. **5** Israeli government of national unity agreed; TUC voted to rejoin Neddy. **13** MoD official Clive

A.D.

Ponting charged under Official Secrets Act; 6 political fugitives took refuge in British Consulate in Durban. 15 Birth of Prince Henry to Prince and Princess of Wales. 20 US embassy in Beirut attacked by suicide bombers: 20 killed. 26 Sino-British declaration on future of Hong Kong signed in Peking: capitalist system to be maintained until at least 2047.

October 1 Bank of England rescued leading bullion dealer Johnson Matthey; Sikh Golden Temple returned to civilian hands. 10 European Parliament paid Britain rebate frozen for 10 months. 12 IRA bomb explosion at Grand Hotel, Brighton: 4 killed, Norman Tebbit and John Wakeham injured. 23 350 blacks arrested in SA Vaal townships after 24 hours of violence; Military blamed for murder of Philippines opposition leader. 24 Salvadorean opposition leader died in helicopter crash. 25 High Court ordered sequestration of NUM assets; Ethiopian government and Red Cross launched concerted attempt to airlift emergency food supplies. 30 EEC announced £34m aid for Ethiopia; Kidnapped Polish priest, Father Popieluszko found dead. 31 PM of India, Mrs Indira Gandhi assassinated by Sikh members of bodyguard: 12 hours later her son Rajiv was sworn in as PM; ACAS talks between NUM and NCB broke down again.

November 4 Daniel Ortega elected President of Nicaragua. 5 Irish court froze NUM assets as drift back to work continued. 6 President Reagan won second term of office: Senate with smaller Republican majority and House of Representatives controlled by Democrats. 9 2 Britons to face spying charges in Libya. 15 C of E voted to begin process to allow ordination of women; Edward du Cann replaced as chairman of Tory backbench committee after 12 years by Cranley Onslow; Proposals for new pay structure for teachers announced by employers. 19 Anglo-Irish summit ended without any significant agreement; Over 600 killed in gas explosion in Mexico City. 22 Law Lords upheld ban on unions at GCHQ; Foreign Secretary announced cuts in BBC external services, British Council and withdrawal from UNESCO. 26 President Chernenko promised Labour leader that no missiles would be targetted on Britain if Labour scrapped independent deterrent. 27 British deputy high commissioner in Bombay, Mr Percy Norris murdered. 30 Taxi driver taking miner to work killed after concrete post dropped from bridge; High Court appointed receiver to control NUM funds.

December 1 Labour Party returned with reduced majority in Australian general election. 3 Leakage of poisonous gas from pesticides factory in Bhopal, India: at least 2,500 killed and thousands blinded; British Telecom shares made massive gains in first day's trading. 4 2 killed and 77 injured in collision between Inter-City express and fuel train in Salford; Kuwait airliner hijacked to Tehran: 2 killed and passengers tortured but finally freed on 9 Dec. after action by security forces; Herbert Blaize became PM of Grenada after Nationalist Party won 14 out of 15 seats. 10 Inspector recommended immediate expansion of Stansted airport; South African authorities freed 11 anti-apartheid campaigners and re-arrested 6 of them. 11 Patrick Jenkin announced statutory rate limits for 18 high-spending councils; Fog crash on M25 killed 11 motorists. 12 Anti-apartheid demonstrators left British consulate in Durban: 2 arrested at once. 18 Environment Secretary told local authorities to cut capital spending by at least £1 billion next year: Tory backbench revolt. 19 Ted Hughes appointed Poet Laureate. 20 Appeal Court ruled that under-16s should not be given contraceptive advice without parental consent; Oil tanker on derailed train exploded in Summit tunnel under Pennines. 23 PM returned from talks with President Reagan on limiting 'Star Wars' weaponry. 28 Results of Indian general election gave Rajiv Gandhi massive majority.

THE END OF THE COLD WAR:
THE NEW RUSSIA

1985

January 3 News released of airlift of over 12,000

A.D

Ethiopian Jews to Israel. 8 US Treasury Secretary, Donald Regan and White House Chief-of-Staff, James Baker to change posts. 11 3 US soldiers killed in fire in Pershing missile in Heilbronn. 15 Civilian became President of Brazil after elections. 17 Commons suspended for 20 minutes after leftwing protests over miners' strike. 20 36 killed by Tamil separatist bomb on Sri Lankan train. 23 House of Lords debate televised live for first time. 29 Oxford University refused PM an honorary degree. 30 Larry Whitty elected general secretary of Labour Party; Tory revolt over plan to extend Stansted airport. 31 Labour censure motion on handling of economy.

February 4 Border between Spain and Gibraltar re-opened. 5 Release of 4 Britons held hostage in Libya. 7 4 members of Polish secret police gaoled for murder of Polish priest. 10 9 killed in motorway pile up in snow. 11 Clive Ponting acquitted of breaching the Official Secrets Act; 20 servicemen from RAF band killed in bus collision in W. Germany. 18 Deaths in rioting at Crossroads shanty town, South Africa. 19 Arrest of leading anti-apartheid leaders in South Africa after continuing violence. 20 PM spoke to joint session of US Congress. 25 Increase in number of miners returning to work after failure of TUC initiative; Pound reached record low against dollar; General election in Pakistan. 26 Statement from chairman of US Federal Reserve led to recovery of sterling. 28 9 police killed in IRA mortar bomb attack on Newry police station.

March 3 Miners agreed to call off strike without an agreement. 4 New Zealand PM re-affirmed his country's ban on nuclear weapons after visit to Britain; 15 killed in bombing of Shi'ite mosque in Lebanon. 7 2 Belfast men sentenced to life imprisonment for bombings in London; Sizewell inquiry ended after 26 months. 8 Car bomb killed 80 in Beirut. 10 Lebanese car bomb killed 12 Israeli soldiers in retaliation; Death of President Chernenko of Soviet Union: Mikhail Gorbachev named as successor. 11 Israelis killed 34 Shi'ite Muslims in further reprisals. 12 Geneva arms control talks began. 14 3 Britons freed by Angolan rebels. 15 Belgian government gave go-ahead for deployment of cruise missiles. 21 SA police shot dead 19 blacks in Uitenhage on 25th anniversary of Sharpeville massacre. 29 Political crisis in Greece after election of president.

April 6 President Numeiri of Sudan deposed in military coup. 11 24 killed by Tamil bomb at Colombo shortly before arrival of British PM in Sri Lanka. 18 2 Russians expelled from Britain: later expulsions of Britons from Russia in retaliation. 24 3rd stage of Israeli withdrawal from Lebanon began. 30 Britain's first black bishop, Venerable Wilfred Wood appointed.

May 1 US banned all trade with Nicaragua; Ethiopia's largest famine relief camp forcibly cleared by troops; President Reagan arrived in Germany at start of controversial tour of Europe. 3 Epidemic in Stafford identified as Legionnaires' disease: 30 dead. 6 4 schoolboys drowned by wave at Land's End. 8 Commemoration of 40th anniversary of VE day. 10 President Reagan agreed to freeze in defence spending. 11 Fire at Bradford City FC left 55 dead and many others seriously injured; Violence at Birmingham halted match. 12 Demonstrations against Pope in Holland; Prince Andrew opened new £276m Falklands airport. 13 Government suffered fourth defeat in Lords over GLC abolition bill. 15 Sri Lankan Tamil terrorists shot dead more than 146 people. 16 2 miners gaoled for life for murder of taxi driver during miners' strike: later reduced to manslaughter. 20 3 Israeli prisoners exchanged for 1,150 Palestinians and Lebanese held by Israel. 22 Massive car bomb devasted residential area of E. Beirut in week of renewed violence. 24 Tidal wave swamped islands off coast of Bangladesh: thousands drowned or made homeless. 26 33 killed when 2 oil tankers exploded and caught fire in Bay of Algeciras. 29 38 killed after wall collapse in soccer violence at Heysel stadium, Brussels before Liverpool v. Juventus match: British teams later banned indefinitely from European competition.

A.D.

June 2 Socialist Party won absolute majority in Greek general election. **5** Government approved development of Stansted as London's third airport. **6** Worldwide ban on English football teams imposed by Fifa. **7** 700 passengers evacuated from holed British ferry *Norland*. **10** President Reagan announced continued adherence to unratified Salt II; Israel announced completion of withdrawal from Lebanon. **11** 4 Soviet spies exchanged for 25 Western agents. **12** Mr Ron Todd won re-run election for general secretary of TGWU; Shi'ite Moslem gunmen blew up Jordanian aircraft cockpit after releasing hijack passengers and crew. **13** John Paul Getty Jnr offered £50m to the National Gallery. **17** Government gave go-ahead for closer links between Honda and BL. **19** Bomb explosion in departure hall at Frankfurt airport: 3 killed; Car bomb in Tripoli killed 60. **23** Air India Boeing crashed in Irish Sea killing all 329 on board; Bomb found in Rubens Hotel near Buckingham Palace successfully defused.

July 2 Mr Andrei Gromyko became President of USSR and Mr Eduard Shevardnadze, Foreign Minister; Church of England general synod approved ordination of women as deacons. **3** Israel released 300 Lebanese prisoners from detention. **7** Robert Mugabe won 63 out of 79 seats in Zimbabwe election. **8** Britain lifted ban on trade with Argentina. **9** Violence in Kwa Thema township near Johannesburg; 2 suicide bombers killed 15 in South Lebanon. **10** 2 explosions sank Greenpeace campaign ship *Rainbow Warrior* in Auckland, NZ. **13** President Reagan underwent operation to remove cancerous growth from his intestines; Live Aid pop concert in Britain and America raised more than £50m for famine victims in Africa. **19** 260 died in dam collapse in tourist resort of Stava, Italy; Spain agreed to new extradition treaty with Britain. **21** South African goverment declared State of Emergency after increasing unrest in black townships. **26** Transport Secretary announced routing of Okehampton bypass through Dartmoor National Park. **27** Milton Obote of Uganda overthrown in military coup.

August 2 TriStar crash at Dallas-Fort Worth killed 133. **11** Death toll of 65 in 6 day's rioting in Durban townships. **12** Japanese Boeing 747 crashed near Tokyo: 524 killed, 4 survived. **17** 54 killed by car bomb in Christian East Beirut. **19** 29 killed in retaliation in Muslim area: led to escalation of violence with another 200 killed. **20** Moderate Sikh leader Sant Harchand Singh Longowal shot dead by extremists in Punjab. **22** 54 died and 83 escaped when Boeing 737 burst into flames at Manchester airport. **23** Guinness took over control of Arthur Bell and Son, whisky maker. **27** Nigeria's military government overthrown in coup.

September 1 South Africa announced suspension of repayments on foriegn debt in order to protect the rand; Riots in Cork prison destroyed much of the building. **4** Arjun Dass of Indian Congress Party shot dead by Sikh extremists. **9** President Reagan announced limited sanctions against SA; Riots in Handsworth area of Birmingham: large scale disturbances, looting and arson. **11** President P. W. Botha to restore SA citizenship to nearly 8m blacks in tribal 'homelands'. **12** Britain expelled 25 Russians after defection of KGB double agent, Oleg Gordievsky. **14** Russia expelled 25 diplomats in retaliation: on subsequent days a further 6 from each side were expelled. **17** Defection of secretary of Chancellor Kohl to East Berlin. **9** Massive earthquake in Mexico: more than 4,700 killed and 30,000 injured. **20** French Defence Minister Mr Charles Hernu resigned over *Rainbow Warrior* affair: PM later admitted Hernu had ordered sinking. **25** Sikh party won landslide victory in elections to Punjab assembly. **28** Violent rioting in Brixton following shooting of Mrs Cherry Groce by police inspector.

October 1 Tension in Toxteth area of Liverpool; Israeli bombers launched air raid on PLO guerrilla headquarters in Tunisia: 60 killed. **6** Policeman killed in riots on Broadwater Farm estate in Tottenham: followed collapse and death of black woman while police searched her home; Portuguese general election returned minority centre right government. **7** Italian cruise ship *Achille*

A.D

Lauro hijacked by PLO group: 1 passenger killed, remainder released on 9 October. **11** US F-14 fighters hijacked 4 *Achille Lauro* terrorists to Sicily as they were being flown to Tunis; Queen began tour of Caribbean in Belize. **13** Belgian general election: centre right coalition had slightly increased majority. **17** Italian coalition collapsed after row over *Achille Lauro* kidnapping. **18** Miners in Notts and South Derbyshire voted to leave NUM and join Union of Democratic Mineworkers. **20** Commonwealth leaders at Nassau summit agreed measures to be taken against South Africa: ban on imports of krugerrands and government funded trade missions. **24** French commandos seized Greenpeace protest yacht *Vega*; Trading in tin suspended on London Metal Exchange. **25** South Africa State of Emergency extended to cover Cape Town and 7 surrounding areas. **27** Prince and Princess of Wales began 10-day Australian tour; Armed gang stole Monet's painting *Impression, Sunrise* and 8 other paintings from Paris gallery.

November 1 Netherlands government to proceed with deployment of cruise missiles. **2** South African government banned television coverage of riots and imposed restrictions on newspaper reporters. **4** 'Voluntary' entrance charge introduced at Victoria and Albert museum. **7** Siege of Bogota's Supreme Court by Colombian left-wing guerrillas ended with death of more than 90. **11** Report on Land's End drowning tragedy censured head for failure to lead trip adequately. **13** Israeli PM sacked Likud Minister of Trade, Ariel Sharon; High Court ruled Bradford Council did have right to suspend head, Ray Honeyford despite opposition of governors. **14** Eruption of long-dormant volcano in W. Colombia caused landslide: 20,000 feared dead in Armero; NUM apologised in court to end sequestration of assets. **15** Agreement on Ulster signed by PM and Dr Garret Fitzgerald: Republic given right to formal participation in Ulster affairs: Treasury Minister Ian Gow resigned in protest. **19** Start of summit meeting between President Reagan and Mr Gorbachev: news black-out imposed. **20** Commons voted against televising of proceedings. **21** Summit ended in harmony but with few concrete proposals: acceleration of arms control negotiations, opening of consulates and increased trade and cultural exchanges; Irish parliament approved Anglo-Irish accord; 13 killed in further unrest in South Africa. **24** 60 killed when Egyptian commandos in Malta stormed hijacked Boeing. **27** Anglo-Irish agreement approved in Commons by massive majority of 473 to 47: 2 Unionist MPs resigned. **28** City of London police announced discovery of fraud against Johnson Matthey Bank in 1981.

December 3 Publication of Anglican report *Faith in the City* highly critical of government policy; Blom-Cooper Report criticised many of those involved in death of Jasmine Beckford: 3 council employees subsequently dismissed; Common Market summit marathon ended with agreement on trade barriers and reforms. **5** Britain announced decision to withdraw from Unesco. **6** Britain signed agreement to participate in US strategic defence initiative (SDI). **9** In Argentina 2 junta members were sentenced to life imprisonment but ex-President Galtieri acquitted on human rights charges; OPEC ended controls on oil production. **13** Westland helicopters announced it had agreed to a deal with US and Italian consortium: Defence Secretary against deal. **20** Nigerian coup failed. **25** Eruption of Mount Etna. **27** Terrorist attacks at Rome and Vienna airports directed at Israeli check-in desks: 19 killed. **30** 550 extra soldiers flown to Ulster; Military rule ended in Pakistan.

1986

January 5 Westland to recommend US rescue plan to shareholders in preference to European option. **7** President Reagan broke off economic and commercial links with Libya: Britain refused to join sanctions. **9** Michael Heseltine resigned over Westland affair and accused Prime Minister of stifling debate: George Younger became Defence Secretary. **12** Lazard, financial advisers to Westland failed to buy out Alan Bristow the largest shareholder. **13** Leon Brittan forced to apologise

A.D.

to the Commons for concealing the existence of letter about Westland: planned meeting of shareholders postponed. **15** Government majority of 153 at end of Westland debate. **17** Westland shareholders blocked US deal; Royal yacht *Britannia* evacuated Britons and others from Aden. **19** Rebel forces claimed victory in Aden. **20** Anglo-French agreement on twin tunnel Channel rail link; Chief Jonathan overthrown in Lesotho. **22** 3 Sikhs sentenced to death in India for part in assassination of Mrs Indira Gandhi. **23** PM statement to Commons admitted leak of letter had been authorised by No 10 and DTI; Further 2,000 refugees rescued from S. Yemen by British, French and Soviet ships. **24** Leon Brittan resigned after criticism over leaks; Ulster by-election caused by mass resignation of MPs: 14 seats retained by Unionists, 1 won by SDLP. **26** Rupert Murdoch printed *Sunday Times* and *News of the World* at Wapping despite strike action by print unions. **27** Thatcher statement on Westland affair resulted in government majority. **28** *Challenger* shuttle crashed during take-off: all 7 on board killed. **29** Yoweri Museveni sworn in as new President of Uganda.

February 6 Cabinet vetoed Ford take-over of Austin-Rover. **7** Jean-Claude Duvalier left Haiti for French exile. **8** New Haitian military rulers attempted to restore order after looting and violence against Tontons Macoutes. **11** Anatoly Shcharansky and 3 others freed by Soviet Union in return for 5 Eastern bloc agents. **12** Control of Westland finally passed to Sikorsky-Fiat after shareholders' vote. **15** President Marcos proclaimed victor in Philippines amid protests of illegality. **16** 700 saved after wreck of Soviet cruise liner off New Zealand; Mario Soares won Portuguese presidential election. **25** Mrs Corazon Aquino assumed power in Philippines as Marcos fled. **26** Rioting in Cairo left 107 dead; European Court ruled that retirement age should be the same for men and women; Admission charges to be imposed at 3 further national museums. **28** Olof Palme, Swedish PM assassinated; President Aquino freed over 400 political prisoners.

March 2 Queen signed proclamation giving Australia legal independence. **3** End of teachers' strike: NUT to continue ban on extra activities. **4** South African PM announced lifting of State of Emergency; First issue of *Today* published. **12** Spanish referendum voted to stay in NATO; Ingvar Carlsson elected PM of Sweden. **16** Move to right in French general election: Jacques Chirac later appointed Prime Minister; 75% of Swiss voters voted against joining UN. **17** 176 foreign hostages in Angola handed over to Red Cross. **18** Budget Day: standard rate income tax reduced to 29%, 11p on cigarettes and 7·5p on petrol. **19** Engagement of Prince Andrew and Miss Sarah Ferguson. **20** President Reagan defeated in House of Representatives on aid to Contras in Nicaragua. **22** US conducted nuclear test beneath Nevada desert. **23** Floods damaged priceless treasures at Victoria and Albert museum. **24** US fleet destroyed missile battery on Gulf of Sidra. **31** Loyalist riots in Portadown, Co. Armagh; GLC and 6 Metropolitan councils abolished.

April 5 Bomb in Berlin disco killed US soldier and a civilian. **7** Sinclair home computers sold to Amstrad Electronics. **8** *HMS Coventry* launched at night in face of union protests. **13** Rising tension between US and Libya; RC Bishop of Tripoli abducted in Benghazi. **15** US bombed Benghazi and Tripoli in retaliation for Libyan terrorism: planes came from British bases, widespread international protest; Government defeated by 14 votes on Second Reading of Shops Bill, **17** 2 British hostages killed in Lebanon in retaliation for government support for US. **18** Guinness succeeded in take-over of Distillers. **20** British residents in W. Beirut moved into E. Beirut. **21** 60th birthday of the Queen; EEC foreign ministers agreed restrictions on Libyans based in Europe. **23** King Juan Carlos addressed both Houses of Parliament. **24** Death of Duchess of Windsor. **26** Major nuclear power accident at Chernobyl in Soviet Union reported: caused 19 deaths and sent cloud of radioactivity over Scandinavia. **30** Police invaded Sikh Golden Temple at Amritsar and seized extremists who had earlier proclaimed independent state; Colonel Gadaffi ordered expulsion of 19 Britons in retaliation for British expulsions.

A.D

May 1 Night of violence in prisons as officers took industrial action: 841 gaol places destroyed in fires. **2** Minority Labour government in Norway after resignation of centre right PM; Prison officers suspended industrial action for talks with Home Office. **3** Fierce clashes between police and pickets at Wapping. **4** Rocket salvo fired at palace where Tokyo economic summit was being held; Afghan leader Babrak Karmal resigned. **5** Tokyo summit agreed relentless campaign against terrorism and co-ordinated course for economies. **7** Bangladesh parliamentary election; Iraqi planes set on fire Tehran's main oil refinery. **10** Britain ordered expulsion of 3 Syrians suspected of being involved in terrorism. **11** Syria expelled 3 British diplomats in retaliation. **12** Libya expelled 36 diplomats from 7 West European countries. **13** Prison officers' dispute resolved. **16** Ex-President Galtieri and 2 others gaoled for negligence in conduct of Falklands war. **18** Sri Lankan army launched attack against Tamil guerrillas. **19** South African commando attacks on Zimbabwe, Zambia and Botswana. **25** 7 killed by South African police in weekend of violence. **30** NATO divided over US threat to scrap SALT II arms treaty.

June 4 Riots in Mexico City after victory in opening World Cup game. **6** Chief Constable of W. Yorks to replace suspended Mr John Stalker in N. Ireland inquiry. **8** Dr Kurt Waldheim elected President of Austria: widespread international criticism. **9** Chancellor resigned in protest; Publication of report on *Challenger* disaster: Nasa blamed for over-reaching itself. **10** Patrick Magee found guilty of bombing of Grand Hotel in Brighton; Bob Geldof given honorary knighthood. **11** 5 members of IRA, including Magee found guilty of planning bombing of London and 12 coastal resorts. **12** New State of Emergency declared for whole of South Africa: Mrs Thatcher under pressure from Commonwealth to impose sanctions; Derek Hatton, deputy leader of Liverpool Council expelled from Labour Party; Lonrho rescued *Today* by gaining 35% share in company. **20** South African parliament approved bill allowing 180-day detention without trial; Ban on sheep movement in Cumbria and North Wales because of build-up of radiation levels: extended to Scotland on 24 June. **22** Spanish general election: victory for Socialists. **23** Social Services Secretary announced extension of invalid care allowance to married women; 13 killed in M4 crash. **24** Oliver Tambo, President of ANC met Secretary of State, Lynda Chalker; Britain awarded substantial Star Wars contracts; Democratic Unionists ejected from sit-in at Stormont following dissolution of Northern Ireland Assembly the previous day. **25** 16 Sinhalese died in land-mine attacks by Tamils; Further crackdown on press reporting in South Africa. **26** 13 injured in bombing of El Al airliner at Madrid. **27** EEC summit called for release of Mandela and recognition of ANC: Sir Geoffrey Howe to undertake peace mission; Government of Signor Craxi in Italy resigned; International Court of Justice ruled US support of Contras in Nicaragua illegal. **30** Greater Manchester Police Authority formally suspended Mr John Stalker.

July 1 Militant candidate John Macreadie elected General Secretary of CPSA; South African pass laws abolished. **4** 2,000 miners in South Africa forced closure of diamond mines by strike action. **6** Liberal Democratic Party won Japanese general election with increased majority. **8** BSC showed profit for first time in 17 years. **14** 9 Civil Guards killed in Madrid by Eta bomb. **17** US Senate approved new extradition treaty with UK. **22** President Reagan refused to yield on South Africa sanctions; 31 died in Tamil violence in Sri Lanka; Commons voted by majority of one to ban corporal punishment in schools. **23** Prince Andrew named Duke of York on day of marriage to Miss Sarah Ferguson. **24** Royal Ordnance to be sold by tender to private sector; Opening of Commonwealth Games in Edinburgh: 32 nations absent. **25** Appeal Court imposed blanket ban on publications by former MI5 officer, Peter Wright; Turks and Caicos Islands' Chief Minister and 2 members of government sacked. **28** Coalition government in Thailand after general election; Car bomb killed 32 in E. Beirut. **29** Retaliatory bomb in W. Beirut killed 25; Howe mission to South Africa ended in failure; 2,500 jobs lost with closure of British Aerospace in Weybridge.

A.D.
August 1 New Italian government formed under Socialist Bettino Craxi. **4** OPEC agreed to slash oil output. **5** Australia, Canada and India to lead Commonwealth action on sanctions against South Africa; South Africa to impose levy on goods passing through to neighbouring black countries. **7** Security forces alert in Ulster after loyalist mob crossed border into south: Peter Robinson MP arrested and later fined £15,000. **14** Opposition leader Benazir Bhutto arrested in Pakistan: released 8 September. **18** Mr Gorbachev announced further unilateral extension of freeze on nuclear testing. **21** Report on Chernobyl disaster blamed chain of human errors. **25** 1,500 killed in Cameroon in gas escape from volcanic crater. **27** Death toll in Soweto riots rose to 21. **31** 89 killed after mid-air collision near Los Angeles.

September 1 Soviet cruise liner sank after collision with cargo ship: more than 400 died. **3** South Africa clamped down on press before Soweto funerals. **5** Hijack of PanAm jet at Karachi ended with panic after storming of plane by commandos: 18 hostages died. **6** 21 killed in bombing of synagogue in Turkey. **8** New Chairman of British Coal imposed pay deal on NUM. **11** Meeting between President Mubarak and PM Shimon Peres in Alexandria. **13** Earthquake devastated the southern Greek town of Kalamata. **16** Underground fire in Kinross gold mine, Transvaal killed 177; Common Market Foreign Ministers agreed truncated package of sanctions against South Africa: dissent from Britain and Germany. **22** 35 nations reached agreement on European security; monitoring and notification of all troop movements.

October 2 US Senate over-ruled Presidential veto and imposed sanctions towards South Africa; Assassination attempt on Mr Rajiv Gandhi in New Delhi. **5** Dr Yuri Orlov arrived in New York after release from Siberia. **7** Launch of new national daily *The Independent*; Education Secretary announced setting up of 20 state-funded city technology colleges. **10** TSB shares opened on Stock Market; Earthquake in El Salvador left 1,000 dead and 10,000 injured. **12** Summit talks between Reagan and Gorbachev collapsed over Star Wars programme; Queen arrived in Peking at start of 7-day visit to China. **19** President Samora Machel of Mozambique killed in plane crash in South Africa: succeeded by Joaquim Chissano. **20** Likud leader Mr Yitzhak Shamir took over as Israeli PM. **24** Nazar Hindawi found guilty of El-Al bomb attempt: Britain broke off diplomatic relations with Syria. **25** Military Governor of San Sebastian killed by Eta bomb. **26** Jeffrey Archer resigned as deputy chairman of Tory Party after rumours of a scandal. **27** 'Big Bang' day in City: shambles as computer failed. **29** Britain to establish 150-mile fishery protection zone round Falklands; Final section of M25 opened. **30** Sheikh Yamani sacked as oil minister of Saudi Arabia. **31** Prison officer held hostage in Edinburgh gaol released after 3 days: siege ended on 2 November.

November 2 US hostage David Jacobsen freed in Beirut. **4** Sweeping victory for Democrats in US Senate and House of Representatives elections. **6** 45 oil rig men killed in Shetlands helicopter crash. **10** EEC (except Greece) backed sanctions against Syria. **13** Peterhead prison siege ended with release of hostage and destruction by fire of part of prison; President Reagan admitted US arms sales to Iran. **18** Share prices fell on Wall Street after insider-dealing scandal over Ivan Boesky. **23** President Aquino sacked Defence Minister after foiling coup attempt. **24** Barclays Bank pulled out of South Africa. **25** Derek Hatton finally resigned as deputy leader of Liverpool City Council; US National Security Adviser, John Poindexter resigned and Col. Oliver North was sacked after further revelations about sale of arms to Contras in Nicaragua; UN General Assembly adopted Argentinian resolution calling for negotiation over Falklands. **27** Syrian diplomats expelled from West Germany after court ruled that there was Syrian participation in Berlin bombing. **30** Sikh terrorists killed 24 Hindus in bus ambush.

December 1 Government appointed 2 DTI inspectors to investigate affairs of Guinness. **2** President Reagan appointed special prosecutor to look into Iran-Contra scandal; Mr Frank Carlucci appointed

A.D
National Security Adviser. **4** Start of riots in Paris against higher education proposals: proposals withdrawn 7 December; 14 found guilty in Grenada of murder of Maurice Bishop. **8** British Gas shares opened trading at 50p and rose to 62.5p. **9** Key witnesses in Irangate scandal refused to testify; European interior ministers reached agreement on measures against terrorism. **11** South Africa introduced further curbs on press; Israeli planes bombed Palestinian targets NE of Tripoli: at least 15 killed. **15** Over 150 killed in violence between rival Pakistani groups in Karachi over 2 days; Change of government in Trinidad and Tobago after general election. **16** EEC farm ministers agreed to CAP reforms. **18** EEC fishing ministers agreed to reductions in North Sea quotas. **19** John Stalker announced intention to retire from Greater Manchester police force. **23** Dr Andrei Sakharov returned to Moscow from exile. **25** Iraqi aircraft hijacked: crashlanded in Saudi Arabia with loss of 60 lives. **29** Sweeping new powers in South Africa to counter protests in schools and universities.

1987

January 3 49 killed in Brazilian airliner crash in Ivory Coast. **5** Barlinnie gaol taken over by prisoners: 3 prison officers later taken hostage and released after 5 days. **6** Continuing industrial trouble in France: power cuts and halving of bus and metro services. **8** BA privatisation launched. **12** Start of big freeze: record-breaking low temperatures and heavy snowfall; Prince Edward resigned from Royal Marines. **13** Government announced payment of £5 to all on supplementary benefit as freeze continued; Rate Support Grant settlement: cuts of up to 30% imposed on 20 local authorities. **14** Guinness board sacked Mr Ernest Saunders and asked 2 other close associates to resign; Government announced TV licence fee to be linked to retail price index. **16** Hu Yaobang resigned as General Secretary of the Chinese Communist Party; Start of industrial action at BT. **20** 2 further directors at Morgan Grenfell resigned over Guinness scandal; European Court of Human Rights dismissed case of GCHQ workers; Sir Henry Plumb elected President of European Parliament; Terry Waite, Archbishop of Canterbury's special envoy disappeared in Beirut. **21** Heron Corporation repaid £5.6m to Guinness after admitting unlawful operation. **22** Crisis in Philippines as troops killed 12 demonstrators. **23** Argyll group acquired Safeway stores; 187 anti-nuclear demonstrators arrested outside MoD. **24** 300 injured in clashes outside Wapping print works; 3 American and one Indian professor abducted from Beirut University College. **25** Chancellor Kohl's centre-right coalition returned to power in German election with loss of 5% of previous vote. **27** Philippine coup attempt by armed forces dissidents; Mr Gorbachev offered Soviet people right to choose from different candidates in elections and criticised Brezhnev era. **28** US air and naval forces moved within striking distance of the Gulf and all Americans ordered to leave Lebanon; Lord Young announced new job training programme of £206m. **29** Resignation of Mr Alasdair Milne as Director-General of BBC.

February 2 Archbishop of Canterbury attacked government tax cuts policy; 80% voted yes in Philippines referendum on new constitution; Resignation of Director of CIA, William Casey. **3** US exploded nuclear bomb below Nevada desert. **5** Sogat executive voted to end backing for Wapping dispute: followed by NGA next day. **6** BA shares 11 times over-subscribed. **9** Car bomb killed 15 in a Muslim district of Beirut; Attempt at suicide by Robert McFarlane, former US National Security Adviser. **10** 140 political prisoners released from Soviet prison camps. **12** Peaceful human rights demonstration in Moscow brutally broken up; DPP excluded police from investigations into Guinness affair; 6 new Tory peers and 5 Labour announced; Oxfam and Save the Children launched appeal for Mozambique. **13** Rocket fire halted relief convoy to refugees in camp in southern Beirut; following day some relief to other camps. **17** Irish general election: Charles Haughey's Fianna Fail failed to get overall majority. **18** Soviet Union freed Dr Anotoly Koryagin; Dr Josef Begun freed later in week. **19** Leyland's truck-making business sold to DAF: 2,200 jobs to go; After 5 days' vicious street-

A.D.

fighting in Beirut, Druze routed Shi'ites: at least 100 died. **21** French police arrested senior members of *Action Directe*. **22** 6 leading non-Communist finance ministers agreed deal to stabilise falling dollar; 4,000 Syrian troops moved into West Beirut to enforce the peace. **23** High Court ruled in Leeds that Bradford City FC and West Yorks CC were legally responsible for fire at football ground. **24** Launch of 2 London evening papers: *London Daily News* and *Evening News*. **25** National breast cancer screening service to be launched; High Court lifted injunction against journalist Duncan Campbell. **26** Tower Commission indicted "chaos" at White House over foreign policy; Church of England took decisive step towards the ordination of women as priests; Mr Michael Checkland chosen as Director General of BBC; Soviet Union ended 19-month moratorium on nuclear testing. **27** Don Regan resigned as White House chief-of-staff; Howard Baker appointed; 7 servicemen killed in Chinook crash in Falklands.

March 2 Education Secretary imposed modified pay deal on teachers after Royal Assent to bill. **4** President Reagan admitted that Iran arms initiative had "deteriorated" into arms-for-hostages deal and that "it was a mistake". **6** Townsend Thoresen ferry capsized outside Zeebrugge: many rescued but 188 dead; Briton Derrick Gregory sentenced to death in Malaysia for drug trafficking. **10** Charles Haughey elected PM of Irish Republic on casting vote of Speaker. **11** 4 Sicilian Mafia members gaoled in Britain on drugs smuggling charges; Dr Garrett Fitzgerald resigned as leader of Irish Fine Gael Party. **12** Government approved building of PWR nuclear power station at Sizewell; Liverpool Labour rate rebels lost legal battle to keep seats on Council. **13** Judge ruled in favour of publication of Wright memoirs in Australia: British government later appealed; High Court judge ruled that Abbeystead pumping station disaster caused by negligence. **14** Roy Jenkins elected Chancellor of Oxford University. **18** Saudi Arabian hostage freed in West Beirut after 66 days. **19** 3 men convicted and sentenced to life imprisonment for murder of PC Blakelock on Broadwater Farm estate. **20** Terrorists in Rome killed Director-General of Italian Space and Air Armaments Division. **23** Willy Brandt resigned as leader of German SDP: succeeded by Hans-Jochen Vogel; Bomb injured 31 at BAOR headquarters at Reindallen. **27** 12 killed in violent storms in Britain: Severn Bridge closed for only second time in 21 years.

April 1 House of Commons rejected motion calling for return of capital punishment by 112 majority. **2** BAe to buy Royal Ordnance factories for £190m. **3** Myra Hindley confessed to 2 further murders. **5** Prison officer taken hostage by Loyalists at Magilligan Prison, Co. Londonderry; 6 lorries laden with food and clothes drove into Bourj al-Barajneh refugee camp after lifting of blockade. **6** Shatila camp relieved and PLO claimed agreement over Lebanese camps. **7** *Herald of Free Enterprise* righted outside Zeebrugge harbour. **8** Further 104 bodies found in wreckage; Conservative MP, Keith Best, who made multiple applications for BT shares to resign at general election: later fined; Harvey Proctor, MP charged with gross indecency. **10** Second MP who made multiple applications for shares to stand down. **13** 9 trains set alight in Soweto, SA; High Court judges blocked extradition of soccer fans to Belgium. **14** Syrian troops moved to Sidon in extension of military presence in Southern Lebanon. **17** 107 killed in Tamil bus ambush in Sri Lanka; President Reagan announced 100% tariffs against imports of Japanese electrical goods. **19** President Alfonsin personally confronted leaders of military rebellion. **21** Bomb in bus station in Colombo, Sri Lanka killed 150 people. **22** 6 black railway workers shot dead by SA security forces. **23** Second day of Sri Lankan air raids on Tamil bases in retaliation for bomb attack. **24** Natal Supreme Court overturned press restrictions in South Africa. **25** Lord Justice Gibson and Lady Gibson assassinated by car bomb in Ulster. **27** US barred President Kurt Waldheim from future entry to US as private citizen; Egyptian government to close all PLO offices in Egypt. **29** South African police raided black trade union headquarters; Scottish engineer, Robert Maxwell, returned to

A.D

Britain after 6 years in Libyan gaol; Westland to axe 1,900 jobs in West country.

May 1 Government abandoned plan to dump nuclear waste in 4 areas. **3** Wright memoirs serialised in US and Canada. **5** First day of Congressional hearing into Irangate affair. **6** South Africa whites-only election: 1m blacks went on strike in protest, National Party won with improved majority; **8** 9 IRA gunmen killed in gun battle with police and soldiers in Co. Armagh; 4 Chelsea fans convicted of organising campaign of soccer violence. **9** 183 killed in Polish air crash. **12** Nationalist PM sworn in in Malta after control seized from Labour after 16 years. **13** Further 1,155 staff to be laid off by Westland in Yeovil. **14** Coup led by Lieutenant-Colonel Sitiveni Rabuka in Fiji. **15** NATO disagreement over double zero option: Germany out of step with Britain. **17** 37 Americans on *USS Stark* killed by Iraqi Exocet. **20** 3 South African policemen killed by car bomb in Johannesburg; Racial violence in Fiji in continuing crisis. **21** Fijian Council of Chiefs and Governor-General failed to break deadlock. **24** 12 killed in Sri Lankan bombing of Tamil villages in Jaffna peninsula. **25** More than 100 killed in communal violence in N. Indian city of Meerut. **26** US authorised Kuwaiti tankers in Gulf to fly US flag; Sri Lankan government launched offensive to recapture Jaffna Peninsula. **29** British diplomat, Edward Chaplin released in Tehran after being held hostage for 24 hours; German airman flew across Russia and landed in Red Square; South African commandos attacked targets near centre of Mozambique's capital, Maputo. **30** Dismissal of 2 Soviet military commanders after Red Square landing.

June 1 Murder of Lebanese PM, Mr Rashid Karami. **2** High Court judge dismissed charges against 3 newspapers over allegations of unlawful conduct by MI5 officers; Dr Alan Greenspan to be Chairman of US Federal Reserve Board in place of Mr Paul Volcker; 30 Buddhist monks killed by Tamils. **3** Indian fleet turned back after Sri Lankan navy prevented delivery of relief supplies to Jaffna Tamils; *Sunday Today* ceased publication and editor of *News on Sunday* dismissed. **7** The Queen refused to receive deposed Fijian PM. **10** Customs officials at Ramsgate and Dover walked out on indefinite strike. **11** General election: Conservatives elected for 3rd term with majority of 101; President Reagan withdrew sales of missiles to Saudi Arabia. **12** Birthday honours: Queen gave title of Princess Royal to Princess Anne; Cabinet appointments: Michael Havers as Lord Chancellor, David Waddington as Chief Whip, Cecil Parkinson as Energy Secretary, Norman Tebbit to backbenches; Sikh terrorists killed 14 in New Delhi. **15** Italian general election: Christian Democrats remained largest party; PM announced junior ministerial appointments: 13 ministers left government. **16** 11th anniversary of Soweto uprising marked by strike of black workers. **17** British Gas reduced prices by 4%; Coup in Sharjah (UAE); American journalist kidnapped in West Beirut. **19** Car bomb in Barcelona killed 17 people. **20** 31 killed in guerrilla attack on village in E. Turkey. **21** 16 held in Spain after major drugs operation; Cocaine with street value of £9m seized in Harley Street, London. **22** 2 of missing 9 American hostages said to have been put on trial in Iran as spies. **25** John Fleming, extradited from US over Brinks Mat gold bullion raid, freed by magistrate after 10 months in custody. **27** OPEC agreed nominal 16.6m barrel per day ceiling on output; Continuing controversy over sexual abuse of children in Cleveland. **29** Korean leader capitulated to weeks of popular protest: direct presidential elections to be held; EEC revolt among poorer members over budget cuts at summit in Brussels. **30** PM refused to fall in line with draft conclusions at summit; Rupert Murdoch took over *Today* newspaper.

July 1 Chancellor ordered cut-backs in operation of National Economic Development Office; Moors murderers' victim's body found at Saddleworth. **2** British Coal promised 9,200 jobs in exchange for new flexible working practices. **3** Klaus Barbie found guilty of crimes against humanity committed as Gestapo chief, and sentenced to life imprisonment; Short Bros. shut down production in Belfast after Loyalist picket. **4** Fresh violence in Seoul after

A.D.

student died: the following day, 177 political prisoners released. **6** 36 passengers killed in attack on bus in Punjab by Sikh extremists. **7** Further 34 shot in bus attack in Haryana. **8** Miners voted against flexible working at annual conference; Oliver North admitted White House had misled Congress. **9** 2 armed robbers shot dead by police in Plumstead. **10** Record damages of £1m awarded to student for doctor's error. **12** *Sunday Times* published extracts from Wright's memoirs; IRA gunman opened fire on Loyalist crowd. **13** Law Lords allowed extradition of 20 Liverpool fans to Belgium over Heysel stadium riot; Labour Party won Australian general election for third time. **14** 72 died in 4 bomb explosions in Karachi. **15** Admiral Poindexter insisted that he did not tell President Reagan of arms sales to Contras; 44 killed in mud slide in French Alps. **17** France and Iran cut diplomatic relations. **20** Social Democratic Party won Portuguese general election; UN Security Council called for ceasefire between Iran and Iraq. **21** Bulgaria's military attaché ordered to leave Britain because of suspected espionage. **22** Judge lifted High Court injunction on publication of Wright memoirs; Mr Gorbachev signalled concession on US-Soviet arms negotiations; Palestinian, Naji Al-Ali shot outside offices of Middle Eastern newspaper in London. **23** Shultz told Irangate inquiry that he offered to resign 3 times after being kept in the dark. **24** Zeebrugge inquiry report published: 3 crew members blamed and disciplined, company accused of 'disease of sloppiness'; Jeffrey Archer awarded record libel damages of £500,000 against *Star* newspaper; Lebanese hijacked Air Afrique jet *en route* from Rome to Paris: French passenger killed and man overpowered in violent struggle; Robert Maxwell closed *London Daily News* after 5 months; American flagged tanker *Bridgeton* damaged by mine in Gulf. **26** Over 1,000 reported dead in Greek heat wave: State of Emergency declared. **29** Indo-Sri Lankan peace accord signed after rioting in Colombo; US dispatched mine-sweeping helicopters to Gulf; Former head of Chernobyl and 2 aides sentenced to labour camp. **30** Poll tax to be phased in over 4 years; Law Lords re-imposed injunctions against newspapers publishing *Spycatcher* excerpts; Britain refused minesweeping aid for Gulf; Norman Tebbit made CH and 19 life peers created in dissolution honours; 3,000 Indian troops air-lifted to Jaffna peninsula in Sri Lanka. **31** President Reagan had further cancerous growth removed from nose; 402 killed in rioting at Mecca.

August 6 Dr David Owen resigned as leader of SDP after 57% of party voted to open merger talks with Liberals. **8** Chad army recaptured northern town of Aouzou: Libyans responded by bombing. **10** Captain Simon Haywood gaoled for 5 years for drug smuggling in Uppsala, Sweden; US tanker hit mine in Gulf; South African NUM claimed strike of 340,000 miners had put 44 mines out of action. **11** Secretary for Defence announced minesweepers were to be sent to Gulf, reversing earlier decision. **12** President Reagan accepted responsibility for Iran-Contra affair but denied knowledge of diversion of funds. **14** BA announced £500m order for 11 American Boeings. **16** 154 killed in air crash in Detroit. **17** Suicide of Rudolf Hess reported; MoD withdrew contract for RN vessels at Scott Lithgow. **18** Charles Glass, US journalist, escaped from kidnappers in Beirut after 2 months; President of Sri Lanka escaped attempt on his life. **19** Gunman, Michael Ryan massacred 16 in Hungerford. **20** 3,400 jobs to go at Devonport dockyard after privatisation. **22** Thousands delayed at British airports as result of Spanish air traffic controllers' strike. **24** Rudolf Hess buried secretly to avoid demonstrations at funeral. **25** Japan to provide largest sum of money to build Channel Tunnel; Coastguards failed to gain sufficient majority for strike action. **26** Chancellor Kohl announced German willingness to scrap Pershings if super-power agreement in Geneva. **27** President Aquino crushed 5th coup attempt in 18 months in Philippines. **28** Barcelona air traffic controllers called off further strike action. **29** Hostilities broke out again in Gulf after 6 week lull; Robert Maclennan appointed new SDP leader. **30** Black miners called off strike in South Africa after 16,000 had been sacked; 3 arrested near Northern Ireland Secretary's home: later charged with conspiracy to

A.D

murder Tom King. **31** SDP conference voted against David Owen and for merger proposals; Notting Hill carnival ended: man killed on Sunday and riots on Monday evening; Explosion in South African gold mine killed 62.

September 2 Home Secretary ordered extradition of 26 Liverpool fans to Belgium; Trial of Mathias Rust who landed light plane in Red Square began in Moscow: ended with 4-year labour camp sentence. **3** Parents in Dewsbury began protest against allocation of children to primary school; Monsoon in Bangladesh left 24m homeless. **4** UN Security Council unanimously endorsed Secretary-General's peace plan for Iran/Iraq war: Iran attacked Kuwait with Silkworm missile. **5** 8 killed in M6 motorway crash; 40 killed in Israeli air strike on Palestinian refugee camp. **6** Miners' leaders voted for overtime ban; Chad destroyed Libyan air base. **7** TUC voted for 6-month breathing space over no-strike deals; Lebanese kidnappers released West German hostage; Leaders of East and West Germany met for first time on West German soil. **8** Left gained votes in Danish general election. **9** Sir George Jefferson resigned as chairman of BT; Liverpool fans extradited to Belgium; Iraq launched string of air raids on Iran. **12** Voting in New Caledonia showed overwhelming majority in favour of remaining part of France. **17** Liberals voted at party conference to open merger negotiations with SDP. **18** President Reagan announced imminent arms control deal and superpower summit with Mr Gorbachev; Launch of report calling for independent tests for drugs in sport. **20** Cannabis with street value of £4m seized in Essex; Arab League Foreign Ministers agreed to hold Arab summit on Gulf situation. **21** British-flagged ship attacked and set on fire in Gulf. **22** US helicopters attacked mine-laying Iranian vessel; Iran accused US of lying about attacks in Gulf; Home Secretary announced prohibition on semi-automatic rifles. **23** Home Secretary refused to sell further arms to Iran. **25** 2nd coup by Brigadier Sitiveni Rabuka in Fiji. **28** Ken Livingstone won seat on Labour National Executive: Conference voted to select candidates by electoral college. **29** Coroner's jury returned verdict of unlawful killing on victims of Hungerford massacre; Australian federal judge lifted ban on publication of *Spycatcher*; US senators voted for trade ban against Iran.

October 1 7 died in Los Angeles earthquake; 6 killed in riot in Lhasa, Tibet: Buddhists claimed misrule by China; 5th foreign tanker in 3 days attacked by Iranians in Gulf. **3** End of siege at Peterhead gaol: prison officer held hostage since Monday freed by police. **4** Officer taken hostage at Perth gaol: freed several days later. **5** 10 Tamil Tigers committed suicide with cyanide in Sri Lankan army custody: in following 3 days 160 killed in breakdown of ceasefire. **6** Leader of Fiji's coup formally declared a republic. **8** China ordered foreign journalists to leave Tibet; Inquest jury found that Zeebrugge victims were unlawfully killed; Sir Jack Lyons, millionaire business consultant charged with theft of £3.25m from Guiness; Further clash between US and Iranian forces in Gulf. **11** Indian troops moved to take control of Jaffna peninsula from Tamil Tigers. **13** Multi-millionaire, Gerald Ronson arrested on charges of theft; 160 civilians reported killed in fighting round Jaffna; Opening of Commonwealth conference in Vancouver; Iran killed 32 children in attack on Baghdad. **15** Queen stepped down as monarch of Fiji as Governor-General resigned; Coup in Burkina Faso as President killed; American-protected supertanker, the *Sungari*, hit by Iranian Silkworm missile. **16** Hurricane in southern Britain: 19 killed and trees and property devastated by winds, Stock Exchange suspended and public transport disrupted. **17** UNESCO leader Amadou M'Bow stepped down: Federico Mayer of Spain elected in his place; Indian army finally crushed rebel Tamil fighters in Jaffna: 400 Tigers and 120 troops killed in one week. **18** Torrential rain in Wales and Cumbria led to widespread flooding. **19** 4 drowned when bridge collapsed as train crossed near Llandeilo; Black Monday with crash of shares in London and New York: £50 billion wiped off City stock values and by end of week nearly £102 billion. **20** 9 killed as American fighter crashed on to Indianapolis hotel; 3 children sheltered by screens for first time in child

A.D.

abuse case. **22** Iran attacked Kuwait's key offshore oil loading terminal. **23** Lester Piggott began 3-year prison sentence for tax evasion. **26** Lord Havers resigned as Lord Chancellor: succeeded by Lord Mackay. **27** Gilbert McNamee gaoled for 25 years for conspiracy to cause explosions, including Hyde Park attack in 1982. **28** 12 killed in motorway accident on M61. **29** Government announced rescue package for BP shares; 278 killed in rebel ambush in Mozambique. **30** *Evening News* closed. **31** Customs seized 150 tons of arms on *Eksund* off Brittany coast: 5 Irishmen later charged with transporting arms for terrorist purposes.

November 1 Deng Xiaoping stepped down from Chinese politburo together with 8 other veterans: replaced by Zhao Ziyang. **2** Mr Peter Brooke appointed chairman of Tory Party. **3** Chancellor's autumn statement: hints of tax cuts next year, extra money for public spending; Energy Secretary announced rise in electricity prices. **5** Kidnapped Dublin dentist, John O'Grady, freed after shootout between police and kidnappers; Govan Mbeki, former chairman of ANC, released by South African government after 23 years in gaol; Resignation of Caspar Weinberger as US Defence Secretary: succeeded by Frank Carlucci. **7** President Bourguiba removed from office in Tunisia. **8** 11 killed in Remembrance Day bomb at Enniskillen: widespread condemnation. **9** Bomb exploded in suburb of Colombo, Sri Lanka, killing 32. **10** Government called halt to deployment of cruise missiles in Britain. **11** Customs seized £51m cocaine in Southampton; Boris Yeltsin, reformist leader in Moscow, sacked; Arab leaders ended summit with declaration of support for Iraq; Captain Simon Hayward lost appeal in Sweden against 5-year sentence for drug trafficking. **13** Police inquiry ordered into Zeebrugge ferry disaster; Anglo-French Channel Tunnel group won support from City for £770m share offer. **15** Violence in South Korean election rally. **17** Prince and Princess of Wales in Enniskillen; Domestic rates to be abolished in one fell swoop (except in London) and not as preferred by Treasury. **18** 31 died in escalator fire at Kings Cross station; Congress accused President Reagan 'of failing in his constitutional duty' in Iran-Contra affair. **19** Extreme loyalist politician, George Seawright shot: died 2 weeks later. **20** Queen and Prince Philip's ruby wedding; President Reagan agreed to $75bn cuts in budget; *News on Sunday* ceased publication after 7 months. **24** US and USSR reached historic agreement to scrap intermediate range nuclear weapons; LRT extended no-smoking ban to all underground areas. **25** Health Minister announced new charges for NHS dental and eye checks. **26** 16 whites murdered in Zimbabwe mission. **27** Dessie O'Hare re-captured and companion shot dead in border trap; Beirut kidnappers freed 2 French journalists. **28** South African Boeing 747 crashed into Indian Ocean: 160 dead. **29** Haiti's free elections called off after riots; Iranian terrorist freed in Paris as part of hostage deal; Cuban prisoners released 26 hostages after 8 days; Korean aircraft crashed in Burma with 116 dead. **30** Poles rejected General Jaruzelski's plans for economic and political reform; BT to lose monopoly in public phone boxes; Iranian intelligence agent exchanged for French consul in Iran.

December 2 Home Secretary announced stringent controls on firearms and shotguns; Spain and Britain reached agreement in principle on joint use of Gibraltar airport. **3** Government obtained injunction to prevent BBC from broadcasting programme on secret service. **5** EEC summit on food surplus and budget ended in failure. **6** Demonstrations in Moscow by Jews as Mr Gorbachev left for summit. **7** Dr Gareth Bennett who attacked Archbishop in preface to Crockford's committed suicide; British-built aircraft crashed in California after reports of gunfire. **8** INF treaty signed by President Reagan and Mr Gorbachev in Washington. **9** Sir Joshua Hassan resigned as Gibraltar's chief minister. **10** Conclusion of summit: progress on further arms' reduction, further summit next year; 2 prisoners freed in helicopter swoop at Gartree. **11** 12 killed by Eta bomb in Saragossa; 63 killed, mainly children, when coach collided with train in Cairo. **13** Belgian

A.D

general election: opposition socialist parties made substantial gains. **14** Nissan to invest £216m in Sunderland car factory. **16** Korean presidential election: Roh Tae Woo won, amidst accusations of rigging. **17** Poll tax vote: 17 Tory backbenchers voted against government; President Husack of Czechoslovakia stepped down to be succeeded by Milos Jakes. **18** Ivan Boesky gaoled for 3 years for insider dealing. **20** 2,000 drowned after ferry collided with tanker south of Manila. **21** BA finally won battle for control of BCal; 3 Israeli soldiers shot dead in West Bank after 12 days of unrest when at least 22 Palestinians detained and 1,000 arrested. **22** Deputy leader of UDA, John McMichael killed. **29** Soviet cosmonaut, Yuri Romanenko, returned to earth after nearly 11 months in space; £12bn wiped off share values in London as market opened after Christmas; *Sun* newspaper broke embargo and published honours list early. **31** Robert Mugabe sworn in as executive President of Zimbabwe with Joshua Nkomo as one of two Vice-Presidents.

1988

January 2 Israeli air raids on guerrillas in southern Lebanon: 21 killed. **3** Mrs Thatcher became longest serving PM this century. **4** Deaths of 3 people in Malvern from meningitis over holiday reported; Large purchases of dollars by Japanese and German banks halted slide in US currency. **5** Northern Ireland judge resigned over curtailment of his police protection. **7** Night nurses in Manchester went on strike over cuts in pay for unsocial hours: government later withdrew proposal; Death of actor, Trevor Howard. **8** Further crash in Wall Street: Dow fell by 140.59 points. **10** Viscount Whitelaw resigned as Leader of House of Lords owing to ill health: replaced by Lord Belstead; NUM recommended return to work in Yorks pit strike; Israel sent more troops to Gaza strip. **11** Start of work to rule in Leeds area blood transfusion service: agreement reached on 14 Feb.; Government responded to pressure from fire chiefs: flammable furniture foams to be banned; John Hughes, MP for Coventry NE, banned from Commons for 5 days for protesting during prayers; Death of Sir Con O'Neill; Secret talks in Belfast between leaders of SDLP and Sinn Fein. **12** Government majority of only 47 over freezing of child benefit; Director-General of MI5 to be Mr Patrick Walker. **13** Steel-Maclennan policy document rejected by party members and eventually withdrawn; Death of South African politician Connie Mulder and Taiwanese President, Chiang Ching-kuo. **15** About 70 Tories refused 3-line whip, and 20 voted for private member's bill reforming 1911 Official Secrets Act; Clashes between Israeli soldiers and Palestinians around Temple Mount mosque, Jerusalem; Death of Sean MacBride, winner of Lenin and Nobel peace prizes. **16** Rebellion by army leader Lt.-Col. Rico in Argentina: later surrendered to government forces. **17** General election in Haiti: Leslie Manigat declared winner 7 days later amid protests of illegalities; Agreement reached between SDP and Liberal negotiators on policy for merged party. **18** Start of High Court hearing on *Spycatcher*. **19** 3 new national commercial radio networks announced by Home Secretary; Christopher Nolan, paralysed Irish writer, won Whitbread prize. **21** End of siege of refugee camps in Lebanon. **22** 2 large bombs exploded in Afghan city of Jalalabad killing at least 5 during funeral of Pathan leader; Alton bill to reduce upper limit on abortions won clear majority in Commons. **24** Arthur Scargill re-elected President of NUM with 53.8% vote; Liberals voted for merger with SDP. **25** Attorney-General announced no RUC prosecutions over shoot-to-kill policy: extreme anger in Dublin. **26** Death of Raymond Williams. **27** Cleveland doctors at centre of child abuse controversy to be moved to new jobs; Gunmen kidnapped West German in Beirut. **28** Court of Appeal rejected appeal of 6 Irishmen serving life sentences for Birmingham pub bombings; Irish police found explosives and arms on Atlantic beach; Death of spy, Klaus Fuchs. **29** 12 seamen drowned after sinking of cargo ship; Anglo-French summit ended with little agreement. **30** 12 Palestinians suffered bullet wounds from Israeli troops; **31** SDP voted for merger.

A.D.

February 1 2 Palestinian protesters shot and killed in clash with Israelis; Bank of England ordered ½% rise in base rate; Caspar Weinberger given honorary knighthood. **2** Gunmen shot alleged French secret service agent in East Beirut; 3 women protesters abseiled into Lords in Clause 28 protest. **3** Day of action by nurses over state of NHS; British Coal started fresh round of pit closures. **4** House of Representatives voted against President Reagan's package of aid for Contras; NUS ferry strike called off after 3 days in face of High Court proceedings to have assets seized; Abolition of ILEA in 1990 announced. **5** 2 UN relief workers kidnapped in Lebanon; Comic Relief day raised £6.75m. **7** Worst weekend of violence in West Bank and Gaza strip since start of uprising in December; Death of novelist and critic, Marghanita Laski. **8** Start of first strike for 10 years at Ford plants; Mr Gorbachev announced withdrawal from Afghanistan in mid-May; International commission stated that Kurt Waldheim was aware of wartime atrocities. **9** Commons voted by majority of 54 to allow television experiment; 6 killed in 100 mph gales. **10** Court of Appeal dismissed government attempt to impose blanket ban on security disclosures; South African government foiled coup in Bophuthatswana; Publication of government plans for 1997 hand-over of Hong Kong. **12** 2 Palestinian boys shot dead in Nablus. **13** EEC summit decision on farm prices after hard bargaining. **14** 3 PLO officials killed in bomb explosion in Limassol. **16** Home Secretary announced Prevention of Terrorism Act to be made permanent; TVam sacked 229 technicians who had been on strike since November; IRA terrorist gaoled for life for shooting PC Tibble in 1975. **17** 2 further inquiries to be held into RUC to reconsider whether 11 officers should be disciplined; US Marine, Lt.-Col. William Higgins kidnapped in S. Lebanon. **18** PM announced radical changes in Civil Service; Ford workers voted for return to work after 2-year pay deal of 14%; Appeal Court ruled design engineers to blame for Abbeystead disaster of 1984. **19** Bomb outside bank in Namibia killed at least 14. **20** 78 killed and thousands homeless after storms in Rio de Janeiro. **21** Strike of manual workers at Land Rover; Cyprus presidential election: George Vassiliou elected; Aidan McAnespie shot dead by soldier at checkpoint in County Tyrone. **22** Death of pianist, Solomon. **23** Reports of demonstrations in Soviet republic of Armenia; Chancellor cleared sale of Britoil to BP. **24** New ban on 17 opposition organisations in South Africa; IRA booby trap in Belfast city centre: 2 part-time soldiers killed; Report into hurricane in October criticised Met. Office for relying too much on computers; British businessman, John Smith, freed in Iraq after serving 8 years of life sentence. **25** Publication of government plans to re-structure electricity industry; President Delvalle of Panama forced General Noriega to step down. **25** National Assembly ordered Delvalle to step down instead and replaced him with former education minister; World outrage at film of Israeli soldiers beating 2 Arabs; Russian police and paratroops flown to Armenian capital, Yerevan; Britons held in Belgium on manslaughter charges bailed. **27** Death of Basil Boothroyd. **29** Record trade deficit reported for January; Announcement of 20p rise in prescription charges to £2.60; 2 IRA men killed near Crossmaglen when bomb they were loading exploded; Archbishop Tutu and other church leaders detained as police halted Cape Town protest; New outburst of attacks on cities in Iran and Iraq: following day 17 missiles directed at Tehran.

March 1 BAe disclosed plans to buy Rover; ILEA agreed to £93m spending cuts; Russian tanks patrolled Azerbaijani city of Sumga'it: Soviets admitted 31 had died in disturbances. **2** Nato summit agreed to maintain 'effective and up-to-date' nuclear and conventional forces; Far right Conservative Party in South Africa won decisive victories in 2 by-elections. **3** Following votes in favour by both parties, the Liberals and SDP formed the Social and Liberal Democratic Party; Bangladeshi elections held. **4** Oxfam official, Peter Coleridge, seized in Lebanon: released 8 March; Sikh massacre in Punjab killed 40. **6** 3 members of IRA shot dead in Gibraltar after plan uncovered to detonate bomb in town centre. **8** Vice-

A.D

President Bush won 'Super Tuesday' elections; Sir Nicholas Goodison to leave Stock Exchange to become chairman of TSB; Missing car belonging to Gibraltar bombers found in Marbella loaded with explosives. **9** Government made council lease-back deals illegal; 4 killed in attempted hijack of Aeroflot airliner. **10** Hugh Lindsay, friend of Prince Charles killed by avalanche: Prince escaped unharmed; Lord Spens charged in Guinness affair. **11** Mr Andy Tyrie deposed as leader of UDA after 15 years. **13** Avalanche at St Anton in Austria killed 10; Disagreement between PM and Chancellor over value of pound; Church leaders in South Africa refused to 'turn back from road of confrontation'; Briton, James Abra, freed from prison in Libya. **14** Man shot and killed by army in Belfast: coffins of Gibraltar bombers piped through streets of Dundalk; Fighting flared again in Gulf war; NHS day of action; Israeli army imposed indefinite nightly curfew in Gaza and West Bank. **15** Budget day: 2p off standard rate, slashing of top rate to 40%, independent taxation of married women from 1990, tax on company cars doubled: uproar, suspension of sitting and expulsion of Scottish Nationalist MP. **16** Loyalist gunman, Michael Stone, killed 3 at IRA funeral: 68 injured; Seamen at Dover voted to continue 6-week-old strike; Street protests in Panama City after unsuccessful coup attempt; Admiral Poindexter and Lt.-Col. North indicted on criminal charges arising from Irangate: North left the Marines 2 days later. **17** Sharpeville six won one month stay of execution only hours before hanging; ½% cut in interest rates; Ford abandoned scheme for plant at Dundee because unions failed to agree on single union deal; President Reagan sent 3,000 troops to Honduras. **18** Death of gardener, Percy Thrower; Panamanian government declared State of Emergency; Gas prices to rise 6% from 1 April. **19** 2 British soldiers beaten and shot dead by mob in vicinity of Republican funeral. **20** Israeli soldier shot and killed by Palestinians in Bethlehem: 200 Palestinians arrested by Israeli troops. Irish Republic lifted 2-month ban on cross-border meetings of police chiefs; Death of test-tube baby pioneer, Patrick Steptoe. **23** BBC handed over film of IRA funeral after threats under Prevention of Terrorism Act. **24** Anglo-Irish ministerial meeting in attempt to reassert control; Stockbroker Anthony Parnes granted bail in Guinness case. **25** Government agreed to fundamental review of administration of justice in Northern Ireland; Fresh Soviet curbs on Armenian protest. **27** Surprise victory by Jesse Jackson in Democratic vote in Michigan. **28** Government inquiry into restrictive labour practices in TV industry; Israel declared occupied territories a "closed military area"; Richard Gephardt withdrew from Democratic race; RCN voted to maintain union no-strike policy; South African commandos killed 4 in Gaberone, Botswana; American troops began withdrawal from Honduras. **29** Rover to be sold to BAe for £150m; Ian Botham sacked from Queensland cricket team; In test case judge ruled that whooping cough vaccine not responsible for permanent brain damage; Senator Robert Dole withdrew from Republican presidential race; Head of ANC assassinated in Paris. **30** 2 army camps opened as temporary gaols in attempt to ease over-crowding; Leyland bus sold to Volvo.

April 1 Chaos at Dover because of ferry strikes. **2** 6 Palestinians killed in sharp rise in death toll in Israel. **3** Secretary of State Shultz in Israel to discuss peace settlement; Bishop of Durham called government social policy "wicked" in Easter interview. **4** 4 Berkshire schoolboys killed on Austrian mountain; 3,000 Indian troops moved to Indo-Pakistan frontier. **5** Kuwait Airways 747 hijacked to Mashad. **6** 32 of the hostages released; Start of 60-day ceasefire between Sandanista government and Contras; Israeli teenage girl shot by security guard. **7** 22 Britons released from hijack plane; ANC lawyer, Albie Sachs, injured by car bomb in Mozambique. **8** Hijack aircraft left Mashad and landed in Larnaca after refused permission to land in Beirut; Base rate cut to 8%. **9** Kuwaiti hostage killed by hijackers. **10** At least 80 killed in Islamabad and Rawalpindi as arsenal fire led to explosions; Sandy Lyle won US Masters golf championship. **11** Second hostage killed; New social security measures came into force amidst

A.D.

protests. **12** Hijacked aircraft flew from Larnaca to Algiers after 12 captives set free; Publication of Road Traffic Law Review report proposing higher penalties for dangerous and drunken driving; Ernest Saunders and 5 others remanded on Guinness charges; Death of Alan Paton. **13** Landing error at Gatwick brought 2 planes close to head-on collision; Emergency debate on social security reforms: Dave Nellist MP suspended for 5 days; ILEA parents' postal ballot rejected by large majority government plans; Dessie O'Hare sent to prison for 40 years in Dublin for kidnapping of dentist. **14** Death of John Stonehouse; Accord signed in Geneva on withdrawal from Afghanistan; Elderly hostage freed in Algiers; Another near miss over Watford on approach to Heathrow; 5 killed in car bomb outside US servicemen's club in Naples. **15** Death of actor, Kenneth Williams; Murder of PLO military commander Abu Jihad. **16** International Amateur Athletic Federation recommended 1-year suspension for Zola Budd; Serious rioting in West Bank and Gaza: at least 14 Palestinians shot dead. **17** London marathon won by Henryk Jorgensen; Start of Iraqi attack which re-captured Faw peninsula. **18** Tory revolt against poll tax: majority cut to only 25; Escalating violence in Gulf: 2 Iranian oil platforms destroyed; John Demjanjuk found guilty of operating death chambers at Treblinka: later sentenced to death. **19** Teachers to get 4·75% pay rise. **20** Hostages freed in Algiers: hijackers went free amidst international protests. **21** Lord Hailsham and Viscount Leverhulme appointed to Order of Garter; Nurses pay rise of average 15%; Top salaries review body awarded 7·45% to judges and 5·4% to others; President Botha hinted at new power-sharing agreement in South Africa. **22** Rioting on New Caledonia by Kanak militants: gendarmes taken hostage. **23** Death of Lord Ramsey, former Archbishop of Canterbury. **25** 37 Tories rebelled in Commons against poll tax; Fire at Shropshire army depot released asbestos into the air. **27** £100m concession to social security rebels: John Moore announced changes in Commons; Bomb exploded in Afghan capital Kabul, killing 6; Kanak separatists in New Caledonia took 6 new hostages; Entry charges to be introduced at Science Museum. **28** IBA refused government requests to postpone documentary on shooting of IRA terrorists in Gibraltar; Death of Lord Brockway; Law Lords gave servicemen right to sue government for damages over atmospheric nuclear tests 30 years ago. **29** Ferry dispute confrontation as 2 P and O ferries sailed for Dover with crews who had broken with NUS; Pilot landed Boeing after explosion over Hawaii which ripped roof; Death of actor, Andrew Cruikshank. **30** 37 killed by Tamils in weekend attacks on buses.

May 1 Prison officer held captive in Perth gaol: released after 17 hours; 3 British servicemen killed by IRA in Netherlands. **2** Israeli troops moved into Lebanon to round up Palestinian guerrillas: withdrew 2 days later; Start of sit-in at Gdansk shipyard. **3** Bomb found in British forces car at Bielefeld, West Germany; High Court sequestrated £2·8m NUS funds and fined them £150,000. **4** 3 French hostages freed in Lebanon: Chirac accused of election stunt. **5** Polish authorities cleared strikers from Gdansk shipyard; Hostages in New Caledonia freed: 17 killed in shoot-out and further election stunt accusations; BBC screened programme in N. Ireland on Gibraltar shootings; Local elections: Labour net gains of 106, SLD losses of 63. **6** Alton abortion bill killed off when time ran out; 405 runs scored by Graeme Hick at Taunton; 2 RAF men killed in Chinook crash at Hanover air show; *Rainbow Warrior* saboteur freed from detention on S. Pacific island. **8** President Mitterrand re-elected by 54% to 46%: Chirac later forced to resign as PM and replaced by Michel Rocard. **9** Dover and Calais blocked by angry lorry drivers demanding end to strike; Zola Budd to leave athletics and return to South Africa. **10** Danish general election: almost the same coalition elected as before; Polish workers called off 9-day dispute at Gdansk. **11** Death of spy, Kim Philby reported in Moscow. **12** New French government named: posts mainly to socialists; NUS executive called off secondary picketing of Sealink and lorry drivers lifted blockade of Channel ports; Peers voted against conditions for opting out in Education Reform

A.D

Bill; 4 priests arrested at Golden Temple by anti-terrorist police. **13** Sharp rise in pound after disagreements in Cabinet over exchange rates. **14** Wimbledon beat Liverpool 1–0 in FA Cup final. **15** 3 killed by gunmen in Catholic bar in Belfast; 4 Britons killed in terrorist attack on Khartoum hotel. **16** Sir William Rees-Mogg appointed Chairman of new Broadcasting Standards Council; Soviet troops began withdrawal from Afghanistan. **17** Interest rates cut to 7.5%; Commandos stormed Golden Temple; Lords voted for abolition of ILEA. **18** Death of Sir Brandon Rhys Williams MP; Second trial of soccer fans halted after suspicion of police evidence. **19** Peers voted to enshrine academic freedom in new bill; Labour Party withdrew whip from Ron Brown after mace-throwing incident. **20** Inflation higher for second month: rose to 3.9%. **22** James Kadar deposed as party leader in Hungary; Pieter Jacobs, coloured South African MP shot dead leaving church near Johannesburg. **23** Government won vote on poll tax in Lords after second largest attendance this century; Man killed in fire in engine room of Sealink ferry. **24** Education Secretary announced plan to allow unqualified teachers in schools; NHS lottery scrapped after DPP said organisers would face police proceedings; Louis Blom-Cooper appointed Chairman of Press Council. **25** Government refused to refer proposed take-over of Rowntrees by Nestlé to Monopolies Commission; General Noriega of Panama rejected deal with US. **26** Plans for reforms in Russia published; Suchard launched counter-bid for Rowntree. **27** Syrian troops moved into Shi'ite southern suburbs of Beirut. **29** Summit talks began in Moscow: INF treaty signed by President Reagan and Mr Gorbachev.

June 1 Car bomb in East Beirut killed 16. **2** Mine disaster in Borken, West Germany: 57 killed but 6 rescued several days later; Base lending rate rose by ·5%. **3** 4 killed in mine explosion in Johannesburg. **5** 68 killed after explosion on Soviet train in Arzamas; Disappointing result for socialists in first round of French elections; Neil Kinnock in speech signalled move away from unilateralist stance. **6** 26 escaped from Haverigg prison: all but 3 recaptured; Lester Piggott stripped of OBE; Base rate increased to 8·5%; 1·9m workers joined first day of 3-day strike in South Africa. **7** Commons voted by majority of 123 against capital punishment; Government announced sale of Girobank by auction; Higginson proposals on A level instantly rejected by Government; Michael Dukakis won final 4 primaries. **8** Talks at Foreign Office on mutual compensation for damage in British and Iranian embassies; Death of broadcaster, Russell Harty. **9** Mike Gatting stripped of English cricket captaincy: John Emburey later appointed. **10** Michael Meacher lost libel action against *The Observer*; Sir William Rees-Mogg became life peer in birthday honours; MoD announced 3,300 redundancies at Royal Naval Dockyard at Plymouth; Celebrations in Moscow of millenium of Christianity in Russia; South Africa widened curbs on press in renewal of emergency powers. **11** 10-hour anti-apartheid concert at Wembley in honour of Nelson Mandela's 70th birthday. **12** Weekend of riots involving English soccer fans in Germany for European championships; Communists held balance of power in French general election. **13** Irish court refused extradition of Patrick McVeigh wanted in connection with IRA bombing campaign in London; Start of 2-day general strike in Armenia. **14** Resignation of Howard Baker, White House Chief-of-Staff; 2 killed at ICI explosive works in Penrhyndeudraeth; Resignation of Denzil Davies as Labour's defence spokesman. **15** 6 soldiers killed by IRA bomb at Lisburn fun-run; Financier Peter Clowes charged with perverting course of justice over collapse of Barlow-Clowes investment empire. **16** Government announced that it would legislate to curb football hooliganism; Government rejected demands for selective detention in Northern Ireland; John Goulding resigned as Secretary of National Communications Union after allegations about his private life. **17** Viraj Mendis lost his appeal against deportation to Sri Lanka; Expulsion of Iranian diplomat and PLO official from Britain; 2 Belfast men convicted of plotting bombing campaign in Britain: gaoled for total of

A.D.

37 years; Inflation rate rose to 4·2% in May. **18** Arrest of suspected IRA terrorist in Toronto on eve of summit of seven largest market economies; Mrs Marie Wilks murdered on M50. **19** Haitian coup: civilian leader exiled. **20** TUC agreed on new code of practice banning no-strike deals. **21** Summit communiqué attempted to calm nervous financial markets; Government told BBC that it could go ahead with series *My country right or wrong*, banned by court injunction; European Court ruled that Britain should not exempt construction industry and other businesses including charities from VAT. **22** Third increase of base rate in June to 9%; Sir John Hermon to retire after 10 years as head of RUC; TUC voted to suspend EETPU. **23** Rowntree finally agreed to £2·55 billion take-over by Nestlé; IRA shot down army helicopter in Crossmaglen; EEC agreed farm prices freeze for 1988–89; Turkish landslide in village of Catak; Government report showed poll tax as costly to collect as rates; Death of judge, Dame Elizabeth Lane. **24** Surge in dollar following Toronto summit; Kings Cross inquiry concluded management was to blame. **26** 4 killed in crash of A320 airbus at air show in eastern France. **27** 57 killed in train crash at Gare de Lyon, Paris; Record £1·2 billion current account deficit for May announced; £1m damages for widow of man killed in road accident; Swiss report blamed skiing group for accident but cleared Prince Charles of personal blame. **28** Monet sold for record price of £14·3 mn; Mr Gorbachev opened historic conference of Communist Party with reforming speech; Bank rate raised again for 4th time in June to 9·5%; 14-year-old girl injured after IRA bombed school bus in Fermanagh. **29** Government announced proposals for reform of Official Secrets Act: public interest no longer an excuse. **30** Law Lords ruling on equal pay plugged legal loopholes; Archbishop Lefebvre, rebel RC, declared 'formally schismatic' for consecrating bishops.

July 1 Mr Gorbachev gained approval at conference for his democratising proposals. **2** Steffi Graf won Wimbledon. **3** *USS Vincennes* shot down Iranian airbus 'by accident' killing 290 civilians. **4** Interest rates returned to 10%; Stefan Edberg defeated Boris Becker in postponed men's final at Wimbledon. **5** US Attorney Edwin Meese to resign post; C of E general synod voted to prepare for ordination of women as priests; Former Catholic priest held in Brussels over IRA arms procurement; Spanish coroner ruled that SAS soldiers could be screened but must be visible to judge and lawyers. **6** Explosion on North Sea oil rig Piper Alpha killed 170; Publication of report on Cleveland child abuse cases: criticism of agencies involved; Troops broke up 2-day occupation of airport in Armenian capital of Yerevan. **7** 2 civilians killed in bomb attack at Belfast swimming pool: following day soldier killed by booby-trap bomb at same complex; Metropolitan Police paid £75,000 to family of Blair Peach killed during demonstration. **8** Britain to supply £6 billion arms to Saudi Arabia; Death of Jimmy Edwards; Train plunged in lake in south India: 100 killed. **9** Death of Barbara Woodhouse. **10** Death of Noel Barber. **11** 9 killed in terrorist attack on *City of Poros* off Athens; Government ordered 3 frigates from Yarrow Shipbuilders on Clyde; Death of Baroness Wooton. **12** Kirklees council offered out-of-court settlement to Dewsbury parents; Execution of Sharpeville Six suspended indefinitely in South Africa; Michael Dukakis chose Lloyd Benson as running mate rather than Jesse Jackson; Armenian majority in Soviet Nagorno-Karabakh voted to leave Azerbaijan. **13** Oil helicopter ditched 20 miles off Shetland: all passengers rescued; Berkeley power station to close next March; Bombing of army barracks in Duisburg, West Germany; Marre committee report showed split over proposals to allow solicitors to appear in Crown Court jury trials. **14** Last-minute agreement over BAe's take-over of Rover; Chris Cowdrey appointed third English cricket captain; Tories won Kensington by-election with greatly reduced majority. **15** Pound dropped sharply against dollar in response to rise in British inflation rate; Chaos at airports because of action by European air traffic controllers;

A.D

Another helicopter ditched in North Sea after technical failure. **16** Riot in Lindholme prison. **17** Kinnocks detained at gunpoint by Zimbabwean soldiers at airport. **18** Rover announced closure of 2 factories with loss of 4,900 jobs after sale to BAe; Iran accepted unconditionally UN terms for ceasefire with Iraq; Further rise in interest rates to 10·5%. **19** Government defeated in Lords on eye and dental charges; 56 prisoners in roof-top protest at Longriggend gaol in Scotland; Soviet team arrived at Greenham Common for nuclear missile check. **20** Mountbatten's killer, Thomas McMahon, fired a shot in court escape attempt in Dublin; South Africa, Angola and Cuba announced agreement in principle to end Angolan war. **21** Inquest verdict of unlawful killing when train plunged in river in Wales in October 1987; Mortgage rate rose to 11·5%; Government published proposal to ban local government officials from political activity; Energy Secretary announced cuts in nuclear research and development; Michael Dukakis accepted nomination as Democratic candidate for President. **22** Disclosure that patients at Exeter hospital had been receiving 25% overdose of gamma rays; PM announced replacement of Lord Cockfield as EEC Commissioner by Leon Brittan. **23** 3 members of family killed by IRA landmine intended for Justice Higgins. **24** First jet landed at City airport in Docklands to demonstrate noise levels. **25** Kenneth Clarke became new Secretary of State for Health, John Moore Secretary of State for Social Security and Tony Newton joined Cabinet as Chancellor of Duchy of Lancaster at DTI; South African student, David Bruce gaoled for 6 years for refusing national service; General Ne Win retired as leader of ruling Socialist Party in Burma after 26 years; Gulf peace talks opened at UN. **27** Massive balance of payments deficit of over £1 billion for second month; British pole vaulter, Jeff Gutteridge banned from competition for life for taking drugs; 8·5% pay rise for police officers. **28** Paddy Ashdown elected leader of SLD with 71·9% of vote and Ian Wrigglesworth elected President; Winnie Mandela's home in Soweto destroyed by fire. **29** Police seized copies of *Cry Freedom* in South Africa on day Publications Board gave approval to it; Bruce Millan MP to be Labour nominee as EEC Commissioner. **31** Special envoy of Archbishop of Canterbury completed 3-day meeting with Christian leaders in Beirut.

August 1 Bomb at Inglis barracks in north London killed soldier; Strike of officers at Holloway gaol; Lambeth compromise on women bishops adopted. **2** South Africa put forward proposals for Angolan ceasefire and withdrawal of troops from Namibia; 3 separate attacks by IRA on security forces in Northern Ireland. **3** 143 white South Africans defied military call up; Martial law declared in Rangoon; West German pilot Mathias Rust freed in Moscow. **4** 2 building workers killed by IRA as they left work at police station. **5** Bomb exploded at British army base in Ratingen, West Germany; Trial of Col. Oliver North postponed until after election. **6** Main traffic control computer at West Drayton broke down causing long delays; Train crash at Gare de l'Est, Paris: Chairman of SNCF resigned. **8** South Africa and Angola announced cessation of hostilities; Iran and Iraq pledged to lay down arms following announcement of ceasefire; Bomb exploded near George Shultz in Bolivia; Birth of Princess of York; First convoy of Soviet troops withdrew from Kabul; ·5% rise in interest rates. **9** 2 Tornado jets crashed over Cumbria. **11** Start of renewed industrial action by nurses; 6,000 seals dead in North Sea: later attributed to canine distemper; Iran offered to help secure release of British hostages in Lebanon; Disastrous floods in Sudan. **12** British soldier shot dead at traffic lights in Ostend; Burmese leader, Sein Lwin resigned after week-long uprising with more than 1,000 deaths; 3 merchant bankers sacked for insider trading. **15** Riot police blocked march of South Korean students to rally with North Korean students at border. **16** Senator Dan Quayle surprise choice as Republican Vice-Presidential candidate; Hostages taken by bank robbers in West Germany: incident ended 54 hours later with 1 policeman and 2 hostages dead.

A.D.

17 President Zia of Pakistan killed as aircraft exploded: American ambassador and a dozen military officers also killed; Death of Lord Silkin; New wave of strikes in Poland. **18** Horizon Travel taken over by Thomson Travel Holdings. **19** Death of Sir Frederick Ashton; Burmese Attorney-General Maung Maung appointed President. **20** Coachload of British soldiers blown up in Northern Ireland by explosive device left at roadside: 8 killed. **21** Report of massacre of 24,000 in Burundi; 500 killed in earthquake in India and Nepal; Arrests in Moscow after demonstration on anniversary of Warsaw Pact invasion of Czechoslovakia: protests in Prague too. **22** Start of all-day opening in pubs in England and Wales; Bomb killed RN officer in Belfast; Talks between North and South Korea ended in deadlock. **23** 500,000 in peaceful march in Burma against socialist government. **24** IRA announced new campaign of city centre bombings; Greek and Turkish communities in Cyprus agreed to resume talks on re-unification. **25** Record £2·2 billion balance of payments deficit: interest rates up to 12%; Controversial film *The last temptation of Christ* passed by censors; Heart of Lisbon gutted by fire. **26** 1,000 Burmese killed in prison riot. **28** 66 killed in Ramstein air disaster when low flying jets crashed in mid-air: West Germany responded by banning military aircraft from air displays. **29** Graham Gooch chosen to captain England in India despite South African connections; Notting Hill carnival passed off without major incident; *Karin B* with toxic waste on board off Britain: following day told that cargo would not be allowed entry. **30** 3 IRA members shot dead in County Tyrone. **31** 24-hour strike by Post Office workers: followed by further action; 2 civilians killed in IRA booby-trap; 2 IRA suspects held at West German border; Nelson Mandela moved to private clinic with TB; Bomb wrecked HQ of South African Council of Churches; Lech Walesa called for end of strikes in Poland; Anti-Pinochet riots in Chile: following day return of exiles announced.

September 1 Guerrilla rockets exploded at Kabul airport. **2** Thousands of Kurds fled to Turkey to escape fighting. **3** Singapore general election: Lee Kuan Yew's party won all but one seats. **4** Two-thirds of Bangladesh under water after 20m left homeless by floods; Archbishop Tutu called for boycott of municipal elections. **5** Opening of inquest into Gibraltar shooting of 3 IRA members by SAS; Postal system came to halt as result of strike action; Brezhnev's son-in-law on trial in Moscow on bribes charge; EETPU expelled from TUC. **6** Kurdish rebel leader appealed to UN to intervene to stop genocide; RUC discovered massive Loyalist gun-making factory in Co. Down. **7** 2 cosmonauts stranded in space finally succeeded in landing; Peter Palumbo to be new Chairman of Arts Council; TUC voted to veto E.T. programme. **9** Burmese opposition forces led by U Nu formed provisional government. **11** Gunman shot at 3 youths and then killed himself in Walsall; Sportaid Race against Time. **12** IRA stepped up campaign of violence: bomb in Belfast city centre and attack on home of head of NI civil service; Britain expelled Cuban ambassador and 3rd secretary after shooting incident in central London; Barclays raised mortgage rate to 13%; West German hostage freed by kidnappers in Beirut; Deal reached to end postal strike. **13** Hurricane Gilbert devastated Jamaica before moving on to Mexico; 3 anti-apartheid activists escaped from custody in South Africa and took refuge in US consulate. **14** South African troops stormed bus in Maseru as pilgrims to Papal mass were held hostage: some hostages and gunmen killed. **17** Olympic Games opened in Seoul. **18** Further coup in Burma: General Saw Maung took power: Coup in Haiti. **19** PM of Poland resigned. **20** Building Society mortgage rate rose to 12.75%; Mrs Thatcher rejected idea of United States of Europe; Argentina's Foreign Minister, Dante Caputo elected President of UN General Assembly. **21** Curfew in Nagorny Karabakh after fresh disturbances; Birth of baby to Benazir Bhutto. **22** 3 Czech diplomats expelled from London for spying; Fire on oil rig, *Ocean Odyssey*: 1 crewman killed; Christian PM appointed in Lebanon by President Gemayal at end of 6-year

A.D

term: constitutional chaos ensued; Exiles returning to Chile for first time since 1973. **24** Ben Johnson won Olympic gold medal and world record in 100m: later stripped of both after failing drugs test; Rev Barbara Harris elected first woman bishop of Anglican communion. **26** SLD voted to be known as Democrats. **27** Balance of payments deficit £1.3bn; PM called for action to protect the environment. **29** 2 British competitors failed drugs test: Linford Christie later cleared but Kerrith Brown lost medal; Dismissal proceedings started against 14 union members at GCHQ; Nobel peace prize awarded to UN peacekeeping forces; Space shuttle *Discovery* launched; First report on Piper Alpha disaster blamed human error. **30** Sweeping changes in Soviet leadership: Andrei Gromyko left presidency, Yegor Ligachev demoted and next day Gorbachev became President; 60 killed when gunmen opened fire in Hyderabad, Pakistan: death toll rose to 300 in succeeding days; Jury in Gibraltar decided that 3 IRA terrorists were 'lawfully killed'; Britain and Iran agreed to resume diplomatic relations.

October 1 English hockey team won gold medal at Olympics: Britain won 12 gold medals in total. **2** Kinnock and Hattersley won leadership election in Labour Party; Resurgence of nationalism in Estonia: founding of Estonian Popular Front. **3** Death of Sir Alec Issigonis and Franz Josef Strauss; Indian academic released by kidnappers in Beirut. **4** IRA killed senior officer in Northern Ireland prison service; Kuwait ordered to reduce shareholding in BP. **5** Result of Chilean plebiscite: Pinochet defeated with 54.68% against him; Dramatic fall in oil prices as OFT announced enquiry into cost of petrol. **6** Kinnock defeated in key defence debate: vote for unilateralism; State of Emergency in Algiers after 3 days of rioting against austerity measures. **7** BAe announced closure of 2 Royal Ordnance armaments factories; Sarah Keays won temporary injunction banning publication of Norman Tebbit's autobiography. **9** Mass Serbian protests continued in Yugoslavia; BBC announced plans for 5th radio channel. **10** Czech PM resigned: new federal government later formed with 10 new members. **11** Ian Paisley interrupted Pope's speech to European Parliament; Inquest jury found verdicts of accidental deaths in Kings Cross fire. **12** Home Office announced decision to test electronic tagging system. **13** Law Lords declared media did have right to publish extracts from *Spycatcher*; Turin Shroud shown to be fake dating from medieval times; Extra £138m available to settle nurses pay dispute; Egyptian novelist Naguib Mahfouz won Nobel literature prize. **14** PM spoke of commitment to community at party conference; Inflation at highest level for 3 years. **15** UDA killed leading member Jim Craig after feud. **16** Agreement reached between SA rugby chief and outlawed ANC on multi-racial rugby. **17** Queen on official visit to Spain; Controversy over terms of sale of Royal Ordnance and Rover groups to BAe; Ugandan aircraft crashed at Rome airport: 31 killed, 21 survivors; Sir James Black joint winner of Nobel prize for medicine; First day of Heysel riot trial ended in confusion. **18** 4 trade unionists sacked from GCHQ; Kurds accused Iraq of using poison gas. **19** Home Secretary announced prohibition on broadcast interviews with groups supporting violence in Northern Ireland; Monopolies Commission report accused British Gas of discrimination in pricing and supply of gas; 164 people killed in 2 separate air crashes in India; Ravi Tikkoo withdrew from negotiations to purchase Harland and Wolff. **20** Criminals' right of silence to be abolished in Ulster; Serbian rage at humiliation of leader Siobodan Milosevic at communist Central Committee. **21** Cruise liner *Jupiter* sank outside Piraeus after collision with freighter: British pupil and teacher killed, freighter captain later charged with manslaughter. **22** Havoc in Nicaragua as Hurricane Joan struck. **25** Typhoon Ruby hit Philippines: estimated 300 killed in sinking of ferry *Dona Marilyn*; Peter Carey won Booker prize for *Oscar and Lucinda*. **26** South African municipal elections: boycott by black voters, inconclusive outcome for extreme right-wing. **27**

A.D.

Government announced freezing of child benefit for second year; 3 Irish terrorists found guilty of conspiracy to murder Tom King and other prominent people. **28** Police in Prague crushed rally to mark 70th anniversary of Czech independence. **30** Woman and 3 children killed in petrol bomb attack on bus near Jericho. **31** Polish government announced closure of Gdansk shipyard on eve of visit by Mrs Thatcher to Poland; General Galtieri sentenced to 12 years for mishandling Falklands War.

November 1 Tory majority only 8 on proposal to introduce charges for eye tests; Chancellor's autumn statement: extra £2bn for NHS; Israeli general election: leaders of Labour and Likud only reached agreement on forming a government on 19 December. **2** First vote in favour of opting out of local authority control recorded at Skegness grammar school. **3** Indian troops crushed coup involving mercenaries in Maldives. **4** Mrs Thatcher met Lech Walesa after urging reform in Poland; Soviet Union suspended withdrawal from Afghanistan; Lord Chancellor disciplined by Free Presbyterian church for attending Catholic funeral. **5** Indians captured Maldives mercenary ship after 4 hostages killed. **6** New Caledonian referendum left future in doubt after only 37% voted. **7** Home Secretary published broadcasting White Paper: increased choice of channels with new Channel 5; Strike in support of GCHQ union members joined by some 90,000 civil servants. **8** George Bush won US presidential election; Lords failed to stop charges for dental and eye checks; Salman Rushdie won Whitbread prize with *The Satanic Verses*. **9** White Paper proposed student loans; Israeli troops killed boy of 3. **10** Sir Keith Bright and Dr Ridley resigned following Kings Cross inquiry report critical of carelessness with safety; Scottish Nationalists won Govan by-election with record swing; Hungary legalised opposition political parties for first time since 1948; Britain and Iran signed agreement for full resumption of diplomatic relations. **11** President of West German Bundestag had to resign after apparently anti-semitic speech; Czech police broke up meeting of dissidents in Prague. **13** Car crashed into Remembrance parade in Birmingham. **14** Agreement reached to end civil war in Sudan: approved by government on 1 December. **15** Publication of proposals for English in the national curriculum. **16** Death of composer, Antal Dorati. **17** Benazir Bhutto's party emerged as largest group in Pakistan national assembly; Britain expelled 3 Iraqi embassy staff for spying; Death of Baroness Lee. **20** Albanians demonstrated in Kosova over forced resignation of 2 of their leaders. **21** Canadian general election: Brian Mulrooney won with reduced majority. **22** Queen's speech: plans to put security services on statutory footing, privatisation of water and electricity, children's bill; Agreement reached with Occidental Petroleum for £100m Piper Alpha pay-out; Ethnic clashes in 2 Azerbaijani centres: State of Emergency declared. **23** British Steel shares to go on sale at 125p; South African Appeal Court rejected plea by Sharpeville Six, but President Botha granted reprieve. **24** Extra payments for pensioners over 75 announced by Secretary of State for Social Security; Police clashed with students in Westminster protest over student loans. **25** Belgium released IRA suspect, Patrick Ryan to Ireland without allowing extradition to Britain; Base rates rose to 13%. **27** US government banned PLO leader from United States. **28** Picasso sold for £20·9m. **30** Benazir Bhutto became PM of Pakistan; Britain abstained in vote in UN deploring US ban on PLO leader.

December 2 Start of EC summit in Rhodes: Mrs Thatcher snubbed Irish PM and confronted Belgian PM over Ryan extradition; Soviet plane hijacked to Israel: hijackers later sent back to Soviet Union; South African editor, Mr Sisulu, released but placed under severe restrictions. **4** Argentinian army mutineers agreed to surrender: army chief resigned later in month; Edwina Currie, junior Health Minister claimed most British eggs were infected by salmonella: resigned

A.D

on 16 December after storm of protest. **6** 2 Shadow ministers resigned in revolt over Prevention of Terrorism Bill; Morgan Grenfell announced 450 redundancies in City. **7** Sunderland shipyard to be closed; Soviet leader, in US for visit, announced plans to cut armed forces by 10%; Yasser Arafat stated for first time that Palestinians recognised Israel's existence; Nelson Mandela moved to 'safe house' within confines of gaol; Earthquake in Armenia left thousands killed or homeless: Mr Gorbachev abandoned overseas trip. **9** Israeli officer killed in raid on Palestinian bases in Lebanon; George Davis sacked as chairman of Next. **12** Clapham rail crash: 34 killed as 2 trains collided; Athlete David Jenkins gaoled for 7 years in California on drugs charges. **13** Irish authorities refused to extradite Patrick Ryan; Yasser Arafat called on Israeli leaders to come to Geneva to discuss peace; Death of MP, Brynmor John. **14** General strike in Spain in protest against economic policies; US declared willingness to talk with PLO. **15** Epping Forest by-election: seat held by Tories with greatly reduced majority; UN voted in favour of setting up international conference on Middle East. **16** 4 Palestinians shot dead by Israeli troops near Nablus; First formal meeting between US and PLO in Tunis. **17** *The Post* closed after only 33 editions. **19** Sri Lankan presidential election: PM declared victor, but opponents rejected poll result; Ministry of Agriculture outlined government proposals for helping egg producers. **20** Fire destroyed Plymouth department store: incendiary devices found in 8 other stores; Government announced Vickers to develop tank in preference to American firm; State of Emergency in Sudan. **21** Pan Am jumbo jet crashed on Lockerbie: 270 aboard and 11 residents killed, later found to be result of terrorist bomb; Terrorist bomb factory found by chance in south London flat; Changes in Politburo in Poland to strengthen Jaruzelski's position. **22** South Africa, Cuba and Angola signed accord to bring independence to Namibia, withdrawal of Cuban troops and end to South African assistance to Unita in Angola; Israeli PM, Yitzhak Shamir won vote of confidence for coalition; UK temporarily declined to comply with EC terrorist ruling on suspects' access to court within 4 days. **23** YTS scheme had 29,000 places unfilled. **26** Violence in Andhra Pradesh, India after politician killed whilst on hunger strike: curfew later imposed. **27** Briton Nicholas Nicola back in Britain after 2 years in Tehran gaol; Japanese cabinet re-shuffled after allegations of financial scandal. **28** 18-year-old boy shot dead in Nablus. **29** NatWest and Woolwich announced further mortgage rises; 2 French girls released from Lebanon by Abu Nidal after 14 months; Rajiv Gandhi began first working visit to Pakistan by Indian PM for 28 years; Sudan government cancelled price rises which had led to demonstrations. **30** President Reagan and President-elect Bush subpoenaed to testify at trial of Oliver North; Yugoslav government resigned after parliament rejected budget; Knighthood for Leon Brittan and several company chairmen; Brezhnev's son-in-law gaoled for 12 years for taking bribes.

1989

January 1 51 drowned when ferry capsized off Rio de Janeiro. **2** Reports of continuing racial conflict between African students and Chinese in Beijing. **3** BP bought back £2·4bn shares from Kuwait; Edwina Currie refused to give evidence to Commons select committee. **4** US navy jets shot down 2 Libyan MiGs over Mediterranean: Americans claimed self-defence, Libyans aggression. **5** Secretary of State for Health called for cuts in junior hospital doctors hours to maximum 84 per week; US and Britain agreed in principle to attend human rights conference in Moscow. **6** Andrei Sakharov nominated for election to new Soviet parliament; 2 Sikhs executed in India for murder of Indira Gandhi; Further rises in mortgage rates; Chase Manhattan Bank sacked 135 staff in the City; Rupert Murdoch gained control of Collins. **7** Death of

A.D.

Emperor Hirohito of Japan. **8** Boeing 737 crashed on M1 motorway embankment near Kegworth, Leics: 47 killed, 82 injured; USSR announced that chemical weapons would be unilaterally destroyed. **9** Massive increases in long-distance commuter fares on BR. **10** Czechoslovakia agreed to stop exporting Semtex explosives. **11** British airlines ordered to check warning systems on all Boeing 737s; UN triple veto blocked Security Council resolution deploring shooting down of MiG jets; Great Ormond St. appeal reached £42m target a year early; End of conference on chemical warfare in Paris: 149 signed accord not to use weapons and eventually to eliminate them. **12** Energy Secretary apologised to Commons for giving incorrect figure for electricity privatisation; Continued battle in electronics industry: matter referred to Monopolies Commission and competition authorities in Brussels; Death of Ray Moore; End of 5-year emergency in Sri Lanka. **13** General Electric and GEC to join forces in Europe; 10 miners rescued after roof collapse near Sheffield; Announcement of sacking of Daniel Barenboim as director of Bastille opera. **15** Police broke up demonstrations in Prague; 102 killed in train crash in Bangladesh; Economic measures announced in Brazil to counteract 100% inflation; Death of cricketer, Wilf Slack. **16** Staff walk out from Social Security offices in London after plans announced for move out of capital; Guildford bombing convictions to be re-examined by Appeal Court; Uproar in South African court after heavy sentences passed on 3 ANC leaders: prosecutor gave Nazi salute. **17** Publication of plan to issue football fans with ID cards; High Court instructed Trade Secretary to refer Al Fayed take-over to Monopolies Commission: Appeal Court later overturned decision; 52 killed in level crossing accident in Sri Lanka; 5 children killed and 52 injured by gunman in California. **18** Manchester church stormed to remove Viraj Mendis: deported to Sri Lanka on 20 Jan. after appeal to High Court failed; After all-night meeting in Poland, General Jaruzelski paved way for legalisation of Solidarity; President Botha suffered stroke. **19** Attempt to buy out GEC by consortium failed; Moscow to withdraw some tactical nuclear weapons from Europe. **20** Nagorny Karabakh placed under direct control from Moscow; Engine fell off Boeing 737 near Fort O'Hare, Chicago; President Bush sworn in as 41st President of US; Death of Field Marshal Lord Harding. **21** Another Boeing landed safely at Heathrow after technical problems; Home Secretary re-affirmed commitment to immigration laws. **22** News of sale of kidneys by Turkish men to private London hospital; Russians airlifted food to Kabul to avoid famine. **23** Earthquake in Soviet Tajikistan: 2 villages buried in landslide; Death of Salvador Dali; Guerrillas seized army barracks in Argentina: army regained control after fierce fighting and 38 deaths. **24** Whitbread award won by Paul Sayer; ICC agreed on penalties for cricketers with South African links. **25** Death of Lord Basnett, former union leader; Publication of Green Paper on reform of English legal profession; 6 Tory MPs voted against government during committee stage of Official Secrets Bill; Edwina Currie admitted mistake in warning that led to controversy over salmonella in eggs. **26** Windlesham report cleared *Death on the Rock* documentary of main criticisms; PM rejected findings; Inquiry into death of 4 boys in Austria suggested that 'teachers may have been complacent'; Alan Coren sacked as editor of *The Listener*. **27** Britain along with other countries announced closure of embassy in Kabul. **28** Death of Panchen Lama in Tibet. **29** Wandsworth prison officers suspended from duty: police moved into prison; Far right won seats in West Berlin local elections. **30** Foreign Secretary confirmed cuts of 800 troops in Gibraltar; Government defeated in Lords amendment to Companies Bill; Public spending held unchanged at £167bn. **31** Publication of White Paper on future of NHS: more market-orientated service proposed; Anatoly Sharansky nominated as Israeli ambassador to UN.

February 1 UK Civil Aviation Authority ordered

A.D

checks on Boeings, following similar checks in US. **2** P. W. Botha resigned as leader of National Party in South Africa: succeeded by Education Minister, F. W. de Klerk. **3** Coup in Paraguay: Alfredo Stroessner deposed after 35 years: replaced by General Andres Rodriguez; In test case, 3 judges approved sterilisation of mentally handicapped woman. **5** Launch of Sky television. **6** BT closed down 11 chat lines after complaints; Plans announced to improve London Underground safety. **7** Wandsworth prison officers voted for return to work after 9-day strike. **8** Edwina Currie appeared before Commons Select Committee after previously refusing; 145 killed in Boeing crash in Azores. **9** General election in Jamaica: Michael Manley re-elected after period in opposition; Chief executive of Westminster to retire with golden handshake. **10** Government advised pregnant women and the sick not to eat soft cheeses; 5 granite figures at least 3,000 years old found at Luxor. **12** 5 died in disturbances in Pakistan over Salman Rushdie's book, *The Satanic Verses*; Belfast solicitor who represented alleged terrorists shot dead; Trial of Oliver North delayed. **13** Tory rebellion against government in guillotine motion on Official Secrets Bill; 90 mph winds in Scotland caused damage. **14** Ayatollah Khomeini ordered execution of Salman Rushdie for blasphemy: Rushdie goes into hiding; Sinn Fein councillor shot dead in Northern Ireland; Paul Vanden Boeynants, former Belgian PM, released after one month on payment of £1m kidnap ransom. **15** Parliamentary elections in Sri Lanka; Last Russian soldier left Afghanistan. **16** Police announced that Lockerbie bomb was in cassette player; Public employee pay rises announced. **18** State of Emergency declared in Kabul; Salman Rushdie issued apology for causing offence to Islam. **19** Reports in Ireland that wanted IRA suspect Patrick Ryan had left the country. **20** 3 bombs destroyed large parts of army barracks at Tern Hill, Salop: sentries interrupted IRA bombers and prevented injuries; ANC called on Winnie Mandela to disband her bodyguards; Government defeated in Lords over football ID cards scheme. **21** Britain expelled Iranian chargé in Rushdie row; Czechs gaoled leading playwright, Vaclav Havel; 2 of Winnie Mandela's bodyguards charged with murder of 14-year-old black activist. **22** Death of MP Sir Raymond Gower; Secrets Bill debate ended in uproar on point of order; Israeli PM and Soviet Foreign Minister agreed to strengthen links between their countries; First 2 schools given go-ahead to opt out of local authority control. **23** Hugh Annesley of Metropolitan Police to be new RUC Chief Constable; Tory majority cut to only 2,600 and SDP in second place in Richmond by-election: Labour won Pontypridd with Welsh Nationalists in second place. **24** Funeral of Emperor Hirohito; 8 killed in Bombay anti-Rushdie protests; 16 sucked out of Boeing at 22,000 feet when cargo doors blew out. **26** John Tower pledged on TV to give up alcohol if he became Defence Secretary; 9 killed in Spain in storms. **27** Kosovo's Communist Party leader forced to resign after strikes and student protests in Yugoslav province; David Owen rejected SLD's call for by-election pact. **28** Hereford Cathedral dropped plans to sell *Mappa Mundi*; Government refused to help Hammersmith and Fulham Council over £60m losses in money market dealings; Government announced extra £5m for 20,000 widows; Civil rights suspended in Venezuela after riots against austerity measures.

March 1 Trade gap widened again, but no increase in base rates; Curfew in Kosovo imposed; Likud won sweeping victories in Israeli municipal elections; Sabotage forced Spanish state airline to ground many flights; All-party committee accused government ministers of misjudgement in salmonella row; South Africa promised to release 300 detainees. **2** EC agreed to ban CFCs by 2000; President Botha ruled out early general election; Britain rejected Iranian offer of talks over Rushdie affair; Last union member left GCHQ. **3** Czech spy gaoled in Britain for 10 years; Michael Stone sentenced to life in Belfast for Milltown cemetery murders. **4** 5 killed in Purley train crash. **5** 11 killed and 100 injured when Chinese

A.D.

troops opened fire on separatist protesters in Tibetan capital Lhasa; Start of Saving the Ozone Layer conference in London; New Government in Sudan moved towards peace talks with liberation army. **6** Arms and explosives found hidden near Scarborough; Rail crash in Glasgow: 2 killed. **7** China imposed martial law in Lhasa; Iran cut ties with Britain; Ted Dexter appointed chairman of the England cricket selectors; 3 Protestants shot dead by IRA in Coagh. **8** Britons advised to leave Lebanon following the severing of diplomatic relations; 2 soldiers killed in Northern Ireland by bomb under army vehicle; British Rail announced channel link route: tunnelling to protect homes in SE London and Kent. **9** US Senate rejected nomination of John Tower as Defence Secretary: Dick Cheney later chosen instead; Polish government and Solidarity union agreed package of electoral reforms; Prescription charges to rise to £2·80; Police seized drugs worth £75m in two operations. **10** Car bomb explosion in San Diego: wife of captain of *USS Vincennes* escaped unhurt; Comic Relief day; Judge gaoled woman who refused to give evidence against man accused of attacking her. **12** Christian Democrats had heavy losses in municipal elections in Hesse, West Germany. **13** Manchester Airport disaster report: widespread safety recommendations; National Party in South Africa backed party leader, F. W. de Klerk to replace P. W. Botha as President; Publication of Elton report on discipline in schools. **14** Budget day: changes in National Insurance, cheaper lead-free petrol, abolition of earnings rule for pensioners; Search began in Channel for containers of poison lost after sinking of Panamanian ship. **15** South African Foreign Minister visited PM in Britain whilst Soviet Union stated opposition to escalation of revolutionary violence in southern Africa; Hungarian demonstrations to mark anniversary of 1848 revolution. **16** Greek Cabinet resigned, prior to reshuffle to restore confidence in government; Transport Minister denied charges of lying over Lockerbie warnings. **17** Court of Appeal upheld convictions in Carl Bridgewater case; Massive car bomb explosion outside bakery in Beirut: 12 killed. **19** *Death on the Rock* won BAFTA award for documentary; Election day in El Salvador: clashes between troops and guerrillas, right-wing Arena Party defeated ruling Christian Democrats. **20** 2 senior RUC officers ambushed and shot dead by IRA on South Armagh border; EC ambassadors to be allowed to return to Iran. **21** Monopolies and Mergers Commission recommended measures to break brewers' tied house monopoly; Government blocked £1·6bn bid by Elders for Scottish and Newcastle Breweries. **22** Van packed with explosives blew up in Peterborough, killing a fireman; Man found guilty of plot to smuggle £100m cocaine into Britain; Government support for management and employee buyout of Harland and Wolff announced. **23** Death of Labour MP, Robert McTaggart; Explosion and fire aboard N. Sea oil platform Brae B. **24** President Bush announced agreement with Congress over provision of aid to Contras; *Exxon Valdez* supertanker ran aground in Alaska and spilt 12m gallons oil; Further unrest in Yugoslav province of Kosovo; 27 rescued after cable car accident at Alton Towers. **26** Soviet general election: many senior officials defeated, landslide victory in Moscow for rebel, Boris Yeltsin; Floods in central Australia after worst rain for 130 years. **27** Mrs Thatcher in Africa for tour. **28** Remains of Piper Alpha consigned to bottom of sea; 21 killed in Kosovo riots; Possible successor to Ayatollah Khomeini, Ayatollah Montazeri withdrew. **29** 2 armed youths hijacked plane from Prague to West Germany: surrendered to army; Muslim cleric in Belgium killed over Rushdie remarks; Turkish opposition MP shot dead in parliament building. **30** Court halted special edition of *The Observer* on Al-Fayed deal report; Tribunal ruled in favour of man denied job because of Rasta dreadlocks; 4-day prison siege in Guatemala, in which 10 people died, ended in surrender; Berkeley power station switched off after 27 years. **31** UN special representative, Mr Ahtisaari of Finland arrived in Namibia to prepare for free elections; BMA launched campaign against health reforms;

A.D

Lonrho refused to return copies of DTI report on Al-Fayed appeal; *Valdez* captain sacked after being found to have drunk more than legal limit before running aground; Shell followed Texaco to announce price rises.

April 2 Heavy casualties in weekend of fighting between Swapo guerrillas and South African troops: Namibian accord threatened; President Gorbachev in Ireland en route for Cuba; Haitian coup foiled: unrest continued and State of Emergency declared 5 April; 7 leading industrial nations agreed plan to ease Third World debt problems. **3** 2 killed in petrol attack at Soho amusement arcade; UN blamed for Namibian fighting; Lord Young insisted that publication of Harrods take-over report would hamper police enquiries. **4** Soviet Union to let scientist, Georgi Samoilovich, come to West for cancer treatment. **5** Solidarity to be legalised and elections to be held in Poland; President Gorbachev arrived in Britain for 3-day visit; Swapo rejected South African terms for ending Namibian fighting; Unofficial tube strike caused chaos to London traffic; David Gower appointed England captain for the summer. **6** President Botha announced retirement at end of term and dissolution of parliament towards end of May; Government announced plans to abolish National Dock Labour Scheme. **7** Soviet nuclear submarine sank near Spitzbergen after fire: 42 died; Queen accepted invitation to visit Soviet Union. **8** Death of two horses in Grand National led to criticism of safety of the race; Second coup in Haiti put down. **9** At least 16 killed in demonstrations in Georgia; Agreement signed by Angola, South Africa and Cuba to end fighting in Namibia: Swapo forces to be removed to Angola. **10** Mr Shevardnadze sent to Georgia as curfew imposed in Tbilisi; Law Lords accused Lonrho of possible contempt after receiving copies of *Observer* report on Harrods take-over. **11** 90% vote in favour of Abbey National becoming a public limited company. **12** Hungarian reshuffle: hardliners removed in favour of reformist wing; Bomb at Warrenpoint: woman killed, many injured; Death of boxer Sugar Ray Robinson. **13** Israeli police shot dead Palestinians in border incident; Bomb explosion in Trincomalee, Sri Lanka: over 45 killed; Judges postponed meeting planned for Monday which would have disrupted courts; Re-shuffle of German Cabinet as Chancellor Kohl attempted to save post; Alleged IRA man, Paul Kane, extradited from Irish Republic. **14** Georgia's Communist Party leader, Prime Minister and President resigned. **15** 95 Liverpool supporters crushed to death at Hillsborough in soccer disaster; Death of Hu Yaobang in China started period of student rioting in Beijing. **16** Spanish ambassador to Lebanon and 2 members of his family killed in shell attack in Beirut. **17** Lord Justice Taylor to head inquiry into Hillsborough disaster: government in favour of all-seat stadia; Petrol prices to rise again; Bosch to build plant in South Wales; Solidarity given legal status in Polish court hearing. **18** Toyota to build car factory near Derby; Prime Minister to visit Soviet Union in 1990; Explosion on Cormorant Alpha platform led to shut-down of 25% North Sea oil production. **19** 47 sailors died after explosion in gun turret aboard US ship *Iowa* off Puerto Rico; Death of novelist Daphne Du Maurier. **20** Alliance and Leicester made £130m offer for Girobank; Anti-government riots in Jordan after price rises; Transport Union gave go-ahead for ballot over dock strike; Unofficial underground strike brought chaos to London; Government to delay football membership card legislation until summer. **21** Monopolies and Mergers Commission gave conditional clearance of GEC/Siemens takeover bid for Plessey; 3 Ulster Loyalists arrested in Paris after reportedly selling missile plans to South African agent: France later expelled 3 South African diplomats. **22** Silence observed at all football matches in memory of Hillsborough dead. **23** Weekend riots in China in continuing violence following death of deposed Hu Yaobang; Illegal rally by Democratic Union in Moscow during which 47 were arrested; D. Wakihuru of Japan won London Marathon. **25** Japanese PM, Noboru Takeshita resigned in

A.D.

wake of corruption scandal: followed by suicide of his secretary; President Gorbachev purged Politburo of 110 members; London 01 phone code to be replaced in 1990. **26** Bangladesh tornado killed at least 700 people; Blackmailer involved in sabotaging baby food: public warned of danger; 2 Palestinian children shot dead in occupied territories. **27** Massive student protest in Beijing; Chancellor Kohl called for Nato/Warsaw Pact negotiations on reduction of short-range missiles. **28** 14 Liverpool fans sentenced to 3 years for part in Heysel riots; Awards for psychological injury granted to Zeebrugge survivors. **30** Man killed and 13 injured by gunman in Monkseaton, Whitley Bay: man later charged with murder.

May 1 Riots and roof-top protests at Risley remand centre: ended 3 days later with promise of inquiry; May day riots in Turkey and Prague; Civil rights activist, David Webster, shot dead in Pretoria. **2** Dutch government fell after split between coalition partners over anti-pollution measures; Danish police discovered arms cache in terrorists' flat: link with Lockerbie suspected; Ruling party won Paraguay general election, but allegations of fraud. **3** President Botha apologised to Britain over Northern Ireland arms deal affair. **4** Agreement reached between government and GPs on new contract; High Court blocked underground strike on legal grounds; Labour won Vale of Glamorgan by-election with swing of 12·5%; Oliver North found guilty on three counts. **5** Death threats made by Iranian Speaker Rafsanjani against Americans, French and British: security at airports strengthened; Britain expelled 3 South African diplomats in Northern Ireland arms deal affair. **7** Panamanian general election: President Noriega's candidate alleged to have won, but independent allegations of fraud; 3 killed and 150 injured in worst weekend of violence in Gaza. **8** Land-mine in Northern Ireland: one of IRA attackers shot by farmer; 2 naval men killed in air crash at Portland; 3 newspapers fined over publication of *Spycatcher* extracts whilst other papers were banned; Mrs Thatcher met President Ortega of Nicaragua in London. **9** High Court halted distribution of Poll Tax leaflet: later refused to make ban permanent; Labour national executive backed change of defence policy from unilateralism. **10** Opposition candidate in Panama beaten by military in escalating violence following election: next day President Bush ordered further 2,000 troops to Panama; Government troops broke out of besieged city of Jalalabad in Afghanistan; President Gorbachev offered unilateral cuts in Soviet short-range nuclear weapons: mixed reception from Nato countries. **13** Briton, Jack Mann, kidnapped in Beirut. **14** Argentine presidential election won by Peronist candidate, Carlos Menem; Protest against developers burying site of Rose Theatre in Southwark: delay granted for one month. **15** Chaos in London with bus and tube strike and Southern Region overtime ban; President Gorbachev's arrival in China coincided with start of massive student protest in Beijing; Government defeated in Lords over EC drinking water standards. **16** Coup foiled in Ethiopian capital of Addis Ababa; Muslim moderate, Sheikh Khaled assassinated in Beirut. **17** Over a million marched in streets of Beijing; EC proposals for Social Charter to be opposed by Britain: Britain allowed to zero-rate VAT on food and children's clothes; Labour Party imposed Kinnock loyalist candidate for Vauxhall by-election; Mohammed Hamadei sentenced for life for hijack of aircraft and murder of hostages in 1985; Church of Ireland voted for ordination of women. **18** Government announced £12bn road-building programme; Law Lords ruled against Lonrho over publication of DTI report on Al-Fayed take-over; BMA launched advertising campaign against NHS plans; General Noriega agreed to share control of armed forces in Panama. **19** Britain expelled Soviet diplomats: 2 days later Soviet Union expelled a similar number of Britons, followed by further tit-for-tat expulsions. **20** Chinese PM imposed martial law: no response to orders from military. **22** Gurkha brigade to be reduced by up to 50%; Debts from water authorities to be written off by government. **24** Base rate increase to 14%; 18 charged after

A.D.

drugs raid in Wolverhampton. **25** Chinese PM Li Peng defended imposition of martial law; General Election in Irish Republic announced for 15 June; UK expelled 4 Czech diplomats; Czechs retaliated by expelling same number; Lord Chancellor disciplined by Free Presbyterian Church for attending RC funeral: Lord Chancellor resigned from church. **26** Defeat for Boris Yeltsin in Supreme Soviet election: seat later found for him by resignation of Siberian deputy; Reformist leader in China, Zhao Ziyang, placed under house arrest: students voted to continue sit-in in Tiananmen Square; 14 black men in South Africa sentenced to death for murder of white policeman. **27** Violence in Muslim protests in Parliament Square against Salman Rushdie. **28** Nato leaders arrived in Brussels for 40th anniversary summit. **29** Troops ordered to surround Beijing as hardliners attempted to impose will on party. **30** NATO summit ended in compromise on short-range missiles and cuts in conventional forces; Riots in Argentina over high inflation: 4 killed and later State of Emergency declared. **31** President Bush arrived in London for visit; Japanese Foreign Minister, Sosuko Uno to become leader of ruling Liberal Democratic Party and Prime Minister; Jim Wright resigned as Speaker of House of Representatives: succeeded by Thomas Foley.

June 1 2 gaoled for life in Belfast for murder of 2 army corporals. **2** Soldiers attempted to encircle Tiananmen Square: shots fired and massacre took place in which hundreds were killed; Rose Theatre to be preserved for public viewing. **3** *Mappa Mundi* share issue failed; Death of Ayatollah Khomenei; successor as spiritual leader Ali Khamenei. **4** Two trains blown up in Russia after gas pipeline explosion: 460 killed; Polish elections: Solidarity won overwhelming victory; Clashes in Uzbekistan: nearly 80 killed in attacks on minority community. **5** Government suffered second Lords defeat on Electricity Bill; Hong Kong markets crashed by 22% due to lack of confidence in colony's future. **6** Religious frenzy caused problems at Ayatollah Khomenei's funeral; Spain to join EMS. **7** Appeal Court banned national dock strike; Soviet PM announced plans to halve arms spending by 1995. **8** Peter Palumbo won approval for development of Mansion House site in City of London. **9** EC agreed to cut exhaust emissions in small cars by two-thirds by end of 1992; Hardliners back in control in China: Deng Xiaoping spoke on television; South Africa re-imposed State of Emergency in preparation for election. **11** Chinese authorities detained hundreds of leaders of pro-democracy movement. **12** Decisive vote for industrial action by British Rail and London Underground; Outbreak of botulism: traced to hazelnut yogurt; Ben Johnson admitted taking drugs knowing they were banned; MPs gave final approval to televising of Commons; 2,000 refugees arrived in Turkey to join more than 10,000 deported in three weeks by Bulgaria; 12 Boeing 737s grounded in Britain by CAA for safety reasons. **13** Home Secretary announced measures to protect broadcasting standards following deregulation. **14** China ordered 2 American journalists to leave after dissident given protection at US embassy; Queen bestowed honorary knighthood on Ronald Reagan. **15** Labour won European election with 45 seats to 32 for Tories: Greens in third place; Labour won Vauxhall and Glasgow Central by-elections with big swings; Inflation rose to 8·3%; China sentenced 3 to death for setting fire to a train during unrest: executed a week later; Nicholas Ridley refused to schedule Rose Theatre as ancient monument; Irish election saw swing to left and indecisive result. **16** Stephen Hawking made Companion of Honour. **18** Greek elections: New Democracy Party defeated Socialists. **19** Bombs at Osnabruck barracks found in time to avoid carnage; Education Secretary announced plans for top-up loans for students. **20** Curfew imposed in Kazakhstan town of Novy Ozen in wake of rioting; Turkey called on UN to end deportation of Turks from Bulgaria. **21** London crippled by bus, train and underground strikes: national rail strike; Civil servants voted to end Passport Office strike. **22** Manslaughter summons against 7 P & O employees and against P & O itself over Zeebrugge; Ceasefire agreed after 14-year civil war in Angola; 7 more executions in

A.D.

Beijing despite international protests; Lords defeated Social Security Bill clauses on child benefit: voted for rises from 1990. **23** West Midlands Serious Crimes squad to be disbanded after allegations of fabricated confessions; Spectacular 3,000-year-old hoard of weapons found in bog near Peterborough. **24** Zhao Ziyang sacked as General Secretary and expelled from Politburo in China. **25** Sikh gunmen killed 24 right-wing Hindus in Punjab. **26** 24 killed in explosion on Shanghai train; Third accident in three months to Soviet submarine. **27** Death of A. J. Ayer, the philosopher; EC leaders agreed on steps towards economic and monetary union; TGWU voted against Kinnock approach to defence. **28** Public transport strike crippled London again. **29** Irish PM resigned after defeat in Dail; Cuba's Interior Minister sacked after drug-trafficking scandal. **30** Raoul Alfonsin resigned as President of Argentina in preparation for early hand-over to Carlos Menem; Military coup in Sudan.

July 2 Soldier killed by car bomb in residential area of Hanover; Hostile reception for Geoffrey Howe in Hong Kong; Death of Andrei Gromyko. **3** Royal Mail announced restoration of Sunday collection in some areas and increase in postal rates. **4** Howe left Hong Kong giving British passport holders no guarantee for the future; Soviet MiG fighter flew across 3 West European countries without a pilot before crashing on a house; Toyota to build £140m engine plant at Shotton; President Gorbachev in Paris on official visit. **5** Oliver North given fine and suspended sentence. **6** Death of Janos Kadar, Hungarian leader; 14 Israelis killed in bus after a Palestinian seized the wheel. **7** Dock workers voted in favour of national strike. **8** News reported of Mandela/Botha meeting on 5 July. **9** President Bush in Warsaw at start of Iron Curtain tour of Poland and Hungary; Boris Becker and Steffi Graf won Wimbledon titles for West Germany. **10** Death of comedian Tommy Trinder; Government agreed to compromise on public house proposals. **11** Death of Lord Olivier; Sir James Goldsmith launched £13·4bn take-over for BAT Industries. **12** Charles Haughey re-elected Irish PM at head of coalition; Department of Health warning to pregnant women over listeria in paté; French farm worker killed 14 in shotgun rampage; South African government issued statement by Nelson Mandela over his talks with President Botha. **13** Honda to take 20% share in Rover and build assembly plant in Swindon; Bicentenary celebrations opened in Paris shared by 39 world leaders; Isosceles claimed victory in take-over battle for Gateway; Report on death of baby Doreen Mason critical of Southwark Social Services department. **14** Seven nation economic summit in Paris: agreement reached on importance of maintaining economic expansion. **16** Death of Herbert von Karajan; 11 killed in battles over Georgian university quotas and unrest in Siberia after week-long miners' strike: later spread to other regions. **17** 6 Iranian army officers executed for plotting to overthrow Islamic Republic; BR offer of 10% accepted by train drivers but rejected by NUR: ten days later agreed after two further one-day strikes. **18** 5 IRA members arrested in Paris charged with explosives and conspiracy offences; State of Emergency in western Georgia; W. H. Smith paid £42m for Waterstones. **19** DC10 crashed in Iowa with 298 aboard: 186 survivors walked from crash; Safety net rules on community charge changed in attempts to calm Tory MPs' fears; White Paper outlined radical plans for legal profession despite opposition from lawyers; General Jaruzelski elected executive president of Poland. **20** Publication of government report on NatWest's investment division: chairman Lord Boardman and 3 senior colleagues resigned. **21** Ken Dodd cleared of tax charges; Water supplies cut off in large area of London for 6 days; Burmese opposition leader placed under house arrest. **23** Japan's ruling party defeated in upper house elections: PM later resigned; President Gorbachev appealed to striking miners to return to work; Italy's 49th post-war government sworn in under Giulio Andreotti; Riots at detention centre in Hong Kong: police injured large number of boat people. **24** Massive cabinet re-shuffle: Geoffrey Howe became deputy PM and Leader of

A.D.

House of Commons, John Major Foreign Secretary, Kenneth Baker party Chairman, Chris Patten Secretary of State for Environment. **25** 16 shop stewards at Tilbury sacked because of strike action; Risley to close as remand centre. **26** 3 died in 2 separate outbreaks of salmonella poisoning. **27** Drug addict, Chester Petterson convicted of murder of Olaf Palme; White Paper published on food safety; Soviet parliament approved plans for Estonia and Lithuania to take control of their own trade, industry and natural resources. **28** Israelis kidnapped Abdul Obeid, leading Hizbollah sheikh in Lebanon. **29** India began to withdraw peacekeeping troops from Sri Lanka. **30** Press Council criticised press coverage of Hillsborough disaster. **31** Lebanese terrorists released videotape showing hanging of US hostage Lt-Col William Higgins, executed in reprisal for Israel's kidnapping of Sheikh Obeid: further executions threatened including that of Joseph Cicippio; Many dockers returned to work under threat of dismissal; BBC went ahead with screening of programme championing Salman Rushdie's *Satanic Verses* despite plea from Archbishop of Canterbury and outrage of British Muslims; Further outbreaks of salmonella in N of England: 400 victims.

August 1 TGWU called off dock strike: later 2,300 defied instructions to return to work; First Cruise missiles left Greenham Common in first phase of decommissioning; Government appealed to 16 cricketers to boycott rebel tour of S Africa: threat to 1990 Commonwealth Games. **2** Black patients presented themselves at 'whites-only' hospitals in S Africa in first stage of peaceful anti-apartheid protest directed at medical services; Polish Communist leaders forced appointment of Interior Minister C Kiszczak as PM; Argentina lifted trade ban with Britain. **3** Joseph Cicippio reprieved an hour before his pro-Iranian captors' death sentence due to be carried out; Lebanese terrorist killed when his bomb exploded prematurely in Paddington hotel; Midland Bank showed £531m loss after setting aside Third World debts. **4** Interim report blamed S Yorkshire police for Hillsborough disaster: lack of crowd control; Indian troops massacred 50 civilians in Sri Lanka in retribution for landmine attack by Tamil Tiger guerrillas; Evidence of efficacy of AZT as anti-Aids drug. **5** Hungarian opposition parties defeated ruling Communists in by-elections. **6** Lebanese kidnappers demanded release of Sheikh Obeid and 450 others in exchange for Joseph Cicippio; Britain's male athletes won European Cup for first time. **7** Toshiki Kaifu the new leader of Japan's ruling Liberal Democratic party; Central American leaders issued plan to disband remaining 12,000 Nicaraguan Contra guerrillas; Pirates in S China Sea slaughtered 70 Vietnamese boat people, bringing total known dead this year to 271. **8** Commonwealth Foreign Ministers meeting in Sydney were split over sanctions against S Africa; 2 black cricketers withdrew from rebel tour of S Africa; Geoffrey Palmer, new PM of New Zealand, pledged to keep his country nuclear-free. **9** Liverpool and Tilbury docks, followed by Bristol, banned unloading of toxic waste from Canada; ship returned to Canada; Acas formula accepted by both sides in London tube dispute, ending weeks of disruption; Russian workers in Estonia went on strike over restrictive voting and language laws passed by Estonian parliament; Over 100 dead in Mexican rail disaster when bridge collapsed. **10** China announced further arrests of student leaders in hiding since events of Tiananmen Square; Commons Select Committee report attacked proposed health service changes. **12** Unrest in Ulster over period of days covering 20th anniversary of deployment of British troops: behaviour of foreign press criticised and one US photographer arrested; Oliver Tambo, acting President of ANC, flown to London for treatment following a stroke. **13** At least 80, mostly civilians, reported dead in inconclusive 4-day battle for control of Beirut, between Christian-led troops and Syrian forces with Lebanese allies; Numbers of would-be refugees from Eastern-bloc countries rose dramatically, inspired by political and ethnic unrest and economic deprivation; Hot air balloon disaster near Alice Springs: 13 dead. **14** 3 weeks

A.D.

before general election, President Botha of S Africa resigned, bringing a long and acrimonious leadership struggle to an end: Mr Frederik de Klerk appointed acting President; Gen C Kiszczak resigned as Polish PM after less than 2 weeks: unable to form government; Further deaths in ethnic violence in Nagorno-Karabakh. **15** Iranian and Syrian foreign ministers hosted conference in Damascus enrolling virtually all Muslim militia in Lebanon against Gen Aoun's Christian army; 15 prisoners and 5 hostages including Australian woman missionary killed when troops ended jail siege in Davao, Philippines. **16** UN call for ceasefire in Beirut honoured by both sides: many fled city; Many injured in India in disturbances on 42nd anniversary of Independence; Water shortages in many parts of England and Wales following months of drought. **17** Tamil militants in Sri Lanka killed 24 Indian soldiers in retaliation against massacre on August 4. **18** Britain and Argentina agreed to immediate upgrading of diplomatic communications; Inflation fell by 0·1 points to 8·2%. **18** Presidential candidate and judge murdered in Colombian drugs war; 150 tonnes of crude oil leaked from Shell pipeline in Mersey estuary, threatening thousands of migratory birds: massive clean-up operation followed. **20** *Marchioness* pleasure boat sunk in Thames collision: 51 dead; George Adamson, conservationist and "lion man", murdered by Kenyan bandits; Archbishop Desmond Tutu led 200 blacks onto Cape "whites-only" beach in peaceful protest. **21** 320 arrested in Prague as Czechoslovakians demonstrated on 21st anniversary of Soviet invasion; Turkey closed border with Bulgaria after 300,000 ethnic Turks had fled Bulgarian oppression in previous 2 months. **23** Over 1m people formed human chain between capitals of Estonia, Latvia and Lithuania in demonstration for independence on 50th anniversary of Soviet annexation; July trade deficit of £2·06bn announced: second largest on record. **24** Enormous majority in Polish parliament appointed first non-Communist PM for 45 years, Solidarity's Tadeusz Mazowiecki; Dow Jones Industrial Average closed at 2,734·64, an all-time high. **25** Voyager spacecraft passed Neptune 12 years after launch: 2 previously unknown moons discovered; Colombian drug barons declared war on government: banks bombed and political HQs dynamited: US announced financial aid to Colombia against drug cartels. **27** Colombia's Justice Minister Monica de Grief resigned after threats from cocaine barons; Moldavians rallied in capital Kishinev to demand official status for their language. **28** Talks between F. W. de Klerk and Kenneth Kaunda at Livingstone, Zambia. **29** Iranian parliament endorsed President Rafsanjani's 22-man cabinet after 3-day debate. **30** Loyalist paramilitaries in N Ireland alleged security forces had provided them with information on Republican suspects; 11 Indians died in violence during national anti-government strike. **31** Cholera epidemic among Vietnamese boat people in Hong Kong refugee camps; Official announcement of separation between Princess Anne and Captain Mark Phillips.

September 1 US broke off diplomatic relations with Panama as Pres Noriega installed new puppet government; Many E German refugees in Hungary hoping to escape to West; Archbishop Desmond Tutu and 35 others arrested in Cape Town on protest march to security police HQ. **2** Kremlin conservatives demanded action to curb nationalism in republics of Soviet Union; 2 off-duty British soldiers injured by IRA gunmen in Munster. **3** Neil and Glenys Kinnock escaped injury in multiple car accident in Dublin; Boeing 737 crashed in Amazon Basin jungle: later 41 survivors of 54 on board were rescued; 50th anniversary of outbreak of World War II commemorated throughout Europe. **4** Death of Georges Simenon, novelist. **5** Pres Bush appeared on nationwide tv to outline anti-drug strategy at home and in Colombia. **6** S African General Election took place amid strikes and violent protests by 3m voteless blacks: de Klerk's National Party retained power with a tiny majority: Democratic Party made significant gains: later allegations of 23 deaths during clashes; Scenes of hooliganism in Stockholm at

A.D.

Sweden v England World Cup match: many arrests. **7** Polish PM Mazowiecki named cabinet of 6 Solidarity and 4 Communist ministers; German-born wife of British soldier shot dead in Dortmund: later IRA admitted mistaken identity. **8** Scottish Conservatives' president resigned after disclosure of sexual misdemeanours. **10** 151 drowned in Romanian pleasureboat collision on Danube. **11** Hungary opened border allowing more than 6,000 E German refugees to escape to the West: later E German government protested officially to Hungary; S African police banned use of whip in crowd control. **12** Senior white official of Swapo assassinated in Windhoek. **13** 20,000 in peaceful anti-apartheid protest in Cape Town after legal permission granted by Mr de Klerk; Islamic Party of Great Britain launched to contest elections; British Muslims' attitude to new party divided. **14** Rapturous crowds welcomed Sam Nujoma, president of Swapo, on his return to Namibia after 30 years' exile; RUC admitted loss of confidential documents identifying IRA suspects; BP announced 1,700 job losses in reorganisation, mainly in Scotland. **15** Pakistan to rejoin Commonwealth after 16 years; Hooliganism in Greece by Welsh soccer fans; Announcement of fall in inflation rate from 8·2% to 7·8% in August; St Leger called off after course subsided. **16** Azerbaijani parliament demanded end to direct rule from Moscow and return of Nagorno-Karabakh to Azerbaijani rule: blockade of rail link to Armenia continued. **17** Hurricane Hugo caused widespread damage and loss of life in Caribbean: later US troops moved into devastated Puerto Rico to quell violence and looting; 2 tankers collided and caught fire near Humber estuary: large clean-up operation to prevent pollution disaster in N Sea; In Lvov 100,000-strong rally called for Ukrainian independence and reinstatement of Ukrainian Catholic church; Leading defence contractor Ferranti International feared possible fraud during 1987 takeover: future uncertain; Spanish police arrested 26 Eta terrorists after motorway shootout. **18** Hungary announced transition to Western-style democracy and first free elections for 40 years, in agreement between Communist Party and opposition groups. **19** French DC10 crashed in Sahara with no survivors: Islamic Jihad guerrillas claimed to have planted bomb; Vietnamese army began withdrawal from Cambodia to be completed within a week; Mrs Thatcher began 4-day visit to Japan. **20** F. W. de Klerk sworn in as S Africa's President and promised further reforms; 5 leading conservatives, opponents of Gorbachev's policies, ousted from Soviet Politburo; Britain to be prosecuted by EC over polluted drinking water; Ceasefire between Indian troops and Tamil guerrillas in Sri Lanka. **22** 10 young bandsmen killed when IRA bomb exploded at Royal Marines School of Music, Deal, Kent; Hurricane Hugo caused devastation and 8 deaths in Charleston, S Carolina. **23** Mrs Thatcher met Pres Gorbachev for talks in Moscow. **24** European golfers retained Ryder Cup in drawn match. **25** In speech to the UN, Pres Bush proposed moves towards complete ban on chemical weapons over next 10 years; Pres Gorbachev gave ultimatum to feuding trans-Caucasian states. **26** £2bn current account deficit announced: although £ initially stable, it fell sharply on foreign exchange over subsequent days; John Major, Foreign Secretary, in maiden speech to UN announced details of British aid to Colombia in drugs war; Helen Suzman created Honorary DBE for services to British/S African relations. **28** Death of ex-Pres Marcos of Philippines in exile in Hawaii. **29** Delay of 6 months announced in privatisation plans for electricity industry; Police carried out huge anti-drugs raid on Broadwater Farm estate, N London; Archbishop Runcie of Canterbury began 4-day visit to Vatican for ecumenical discussions.

October 1 7,000 E German refugees arrived in W Germany after escaping through embassies in Prague and Warsaw. **2** A further 3,000 E Germans sought refuge in W German embassy in Prague awaiting transport to West: demonstrations calling for reform in many E German cities: later E Germany closed borders; Deepening crisis over funding of Channel Tunnel: costs had risen by 50% to £7bn. **3** Unsuccessful coup attempt by

A.D.

junior army officers against Pres Noriega of Panama; later evidence of a bloodbath emerged and USA admitted standing by to support coup if successful. **4** Trains carrying E German refugees to W Germany from Prague became focus of violent demonstrations along route: worst riots in Dresden; Revelation that Sotheby's had lent Australian entrepreneur Alan Bond £15m, half the purchase price of Van Gogh's *Irises*, world's most expensive painting; Chris Patten, Environment Minister, halted plans for new town at Foxley Wood in Hampshire countryside; University of Zimbabwe closed by government after students clashed violently with police in protest against arrest of 2 left-wing student leaders. **5** Base lending rate rose 1 point to 15%, highest for 8 years; Dalai Lama awarded 1989 Nobel peace prize; Labour Party conference rejected moves towards proportional representation voting system; Kurdish refugees in London detention centre set fire to themselves and 1 died; Jim Bakker, US TV evangelist, found guilty of $815m swindle on devotees: later jailed for 45 years. **6** Pres Gorbachev arrived in E Berlin at height of political crisis on visit to commemorate 40th anniversary of E Germany; Soviet army moved in supplies by train to end Azerbaijan's blockade of Armenia. **7** Pres Menem of Argentina pardoned 200 army officers accused of human rights abuses and members of junta which conducted Falklands War; Greek coalition government resigned in leadup to November elections; Pope began visit to S Korea and Indonesia. **8** All foreign journalists expelled from E Berlin; Senior RUC officer murdered by car bomb in Lisburn; Claudio Abbado named as new conductor of Berlin Philharmonic Orchestra. **9** Continuing demonstrations in E Germany: 50,000 in Leipzig demanded legalisation of New Forum opposition party; Pressure on Government to withdraw opposition to full membership of European Monetary System; £ continued to fall steeply: Halifax Building Society announced 1% rise in mortgage rate to 14·5%; Soviet parliament overwhelmingly approved laws giving workers right to strike but outlawing stoppages in key economic sectors. **9** Queen began visit to Singapore and Malaysia. **11** Remains of Globe Theatre discovered in Southwark: owners of site promised preservation. **12** Appeal Court in Stockholm overturned Christer Petterson's conviction for murder of Olof Palme; Eire's DPP announced that Fr Patrick Ryan would not face prosecution on terrorism charges. **13** Announcement that inflation rate rose to 7·6% in September; Dramatic fall on New York Stock Market aroused fears of worldwide crash. **15** Great rejoicing as ANC's Walter Sisulu released after 25 years in S African jails, together with 7 other political prisoners; Violence followed arrest of hundreds of militant Sind nationalists in Pakistan; Reconciliation talks in Cairo between Libya's Col Gaddafi and Egypt's Pres Mubarrak after 16 years of cool relations. **16** In Leipzig 120,000 people demonstrated for political reform and press freedom in E Germany's largest protest for 36 years: meanwhile exodus of refugees via Hungary continued; Global Stock Market disaster averted as world governments urged calm; Leaders of 20m Middle Eastern Kurds resolved to press for observer status at UN; Indian troops began phased withdrawal from Sri Lanka; Jan Syse became Norwegian PM, heading centre-right coalition, after Labour's Gro Harlem Bruntland resigned; Convention on International Trade in Endangered Species (CITES), meeting in Lausanne, agreed worldwide ban on ivory trade in bid to save African elephant. **17** Earthquake in San Francisco measuring 7·1 on Richter scale left many dead and injured, and caused widespread damage to buildings, bridges and freeways: second-worst quake in US history; Austrian Pres Kurt Waldheim cleared of criminal involvement in World War II executions. **18** Erich Honecker forced by recent unrest to resign as E German leader: succeeded by Egon Krenz, former security chief; Opening of Commonwealth Prime Ministers' Conference in Malaysia by HM Queen. **19** "Guildford Four" released from jail after quashing of their convictions for pub bomb murders in 1974: judicial inquiry ordered; Formal end to hostilities between Britain and Argentina. **20** Camilo Jose Cela, Spanish writer, awarded Nobel prize for

A.D.

literature; Home Office report found Wandsworth Prison seriously inadequate. **21** Mrs Thatcher under pressure to dismiss her personal economic adviser Sir Alan Walters after renewed rift with Chancellor of Exchequer Nigel Lawson; After 89 hours, a man was rescued from ruins of collapsed freeway in San Francisco: final earthquake toll much lower than originally anticipated; Honduran Boeing 727 crashed in mountains near Tegucigalpa: 131 dead. **22** Commonwealth Prime Ministers' Conference published agreement on continuing sanctions against S Africa: followed immediately by statement from Mrs Thatcher expressing reservations: outrage from other Commonwealth leaders; Lebanon's Muslim and Christian leaders accepted Arab League plan aimed at bringing lasting peace to their country: plan rejected by Christian army chief Gen Aoun; Syria apologised to Turkey for accidentally shooting down civilian survey plane in Turkish air space, killing 5 occupants; Huge explosion and fire at plastics plant in Pasadena, Texas: 22 dead; 15th conference of parties to Antarctic Treaty ended in Paris with progress towards preservation of Antarctic as last great wilderness on earth. **23** Ever-increasing numbers of protesters on streets of E Germany: continuing flood of refugees; Acting Pres Szuros proclaimed new Hungarian Republic on 33rd anniversary of 1956 uprising; Soviet Foreign Minister Shevardnadze admitted breach of 1972 Anti-Ballistic Missile Treaty and condemned Soviet intervention in Afghanistan; Reports of severe earthquakes in N China causing serious damage and loss of life; University of Zimbabwe reopened for examinations under tight controls. **24** 10% of E German parliament refused to vote for Egon Krenz as Head of State, the first time any MPs had opposed Communist choice; Supreme Soviet voted to end quota system guaranteeing Communist Party seats in parliament; Government gave go-ahead for Manchester Metrolink railway with £55m grant; Edwina Currie admitted mistakes in "salmonella in eggs" affair during previous December. **25** Announcement that 40,000 boat people in Hong Kong refugee camps were to be forcibly repatriated to Vietnam; Pres Mitterrand in speech to European Parliament called for renegotiation of Treaty of Rome to give greater power to Community institutions; Child Benefit to remain frozen for 3rd consecutive year; Pres Gorbachev arrived in Finland on 3-day visit; Levels of radon radioactive gas found to be higher and more widespread in Britain than hitherto believed; Challenge to Vietnamese-backed Cambodian government by Khmer Rouge guerrillas: areas near Thai border overrun. **26** Nigel Lawson resigned as Chancellor of Exchequer after Mrs Thatcher repeatedly refused to dismiss Sir Alan Walters as her personal economic adviser: John Major became new Chancellor, Douglas Hurd Foreign Secretary and David Waddington Home Secretary: Walters also obliged to resign; Off-duty RAF corporal and 6-month-old daughter shot dead by IRA in Wildenrath, W Germany; Pres Gorbachev endorsed freedom of Eastern bloc countries to determine their own futures; Kasuo Ishiguro won Booker prize for *The Remains of the Day*. **27** E Germany announced amnesty for those convicted of attempting to escape to west; Announcement of formation of Prince of Wales' Summer School on Architecture for August 1990. **29** Huge rally in Soweto peacefully celebrated release of Walter Sisulu and ANC veterans; Spanish General Election showed swing to left but PM Gonzales retained power by small majority; Powerful earthquake in Algiers killed at least 30. **30** 5 days of demonstrations in Tbilisi calling for UN investigation of "illegal annexation" of Georgia by USSR. **31** Turgut Ozal became President of Turkey; High speed rail link to Channel Tunnel delayed due to government's refusal of financial help; New York's Rockefeller Center sold to Japanese corporation.

November 1 Pakistan's PM Benazir Bhutto survived motion of no confidence in her government: opposition pledged to continue offensive against her; Nicaraguan government ended 19-month ceasefire against Contras. **3** Jaguar cars agreed to £1.6bn takeover by Ford; John Gummer, Agriculture Minister, announced plans

A.D.

for Food Safety Directorate; Disclosure of gross pollution of Amazon due to use of mercury by Brazilian gold miners. **3** Egon Krenz sacked 5 hardliners from E German Politburo; Peter Brooke, N Ireland Secretary, caused major stir by refusal to rule out talks with Sinn Fein; Large bomb safely defused outside Londonderry Police HQ; Privatisation of water industry to cost taxpayer £1.3bn; Fossilised reptile skull 100m years old discovered in N Queensland. **4** Prince and Princess of Wales began tour of Indonesia and Hong Kong. **5** Lebanon's Muslim PM Selim el-Hoss resigned after parliament elected Syrian-backed moderate Rene Moawad as President; 250 dead as Typhoon Gay swept across Gulf of Thailand; New wave of violence in Sri Lanka between rival Tamil groups, Sinhalese extremists and security forces: at least 60 dead. **6** *Private Eye* magazine and Sonia Sutcliffe, estranged wife of "Yorkshire Ripper", settled long-running libel action out of court with £160,000 payment; Inconclusive Greek General Election left caretaker PM Grivas still in power until new administration could be formed. **7** US agreed to repay Iranian assets frozen after seizure of its embassy in Tehran in 1979; Principle of ordination of women accepted by General Synod of Church of England; Thousands of gallons of milk from W of England herds discarded after cattle ate feed imported from Netherlands contaminated with lead. **8** Following resignation of cabinet, E German Politburo also resigned in face of continuing demands for political reforms: Hans Modrow named as new PM; Ambulance workers' dispute had escalated to a point where army ambulances were dealing with emergency calls in London; Harwich-Hamburg ferry collided with container vessel off Bremerhaven: 3 died; In speech to UN Mrs Thatcher pledged £100m to preserve world's rainforests. **9** E Germany opened all borders to west: within 24 hours demolition of Berlin Wall began with creation of many new crossing points; Deng Xiaopeng handed over chairmanship of Central Military Commission to successor Jiang Zemin; Jordan's Islamic Party unexpectedly won 34 seats in parliamentary elections; Nuclear power stations withdrawn from planned privatisation of electricity industry. **10** After 35 years, Bulgarian Communist leader Todor Zhivkov removed from power and replaced by Foreign Minister Peter Mladenov. **11** Leftist guerrillas in El Salvador launched offensive against government with simultaneous attacks throughout country: many dead and injured. **12** In Namibian General Election Swapo won 57% of votes, ensuring government after independence: later they conferred with runners-up Democratic Turnhalle Alliance to draft national constitution; 2m E Germans visited the west over the weekend; Troops in Moldavia enforced ban on public meetings after riots on anniversary of October Revolution; *Mappa Mundi* to remain in Hereford in £3m deal. **13** IRA bomb trap for senior British army chief failed when placed under wrong car and spotted by workman; Lech Walesa received Presidential Medal of Freedom from Pres Bush at White House ceremony: during 5-day visit to USA he addressed both Houses of Congress; Prince Franz Josef II of Liechtenstein, Europe's longest-reigning Head of State, died. **14** Czechoslovakia opened borders to west; Italian Communist Party renounced name and planned to join Socialist International. **15** In Chancellor of Exchequer's autumn statement John Major said inflation likely to remain at 7% until mid-1990: announcement of extra cash for NHS, education and homeless; Tornadoes killed 26 in Eastern USA. **16** Bulgaria's new leader Mladenov purged 10 senior hardline Communist Party officials and won agreement to his election as Head of State: later came out in favour of free elections; 6 Jesuit priests murdered in El Salvador, allegedly by left-wing guerrillas, although a right-wing death squad also implicated; Former captain in S African security police alleged existence of terror network set up by government to organise assassinations, bombings and kidnappings: later Pres de Klerk set up an investigation. **17** Huge anti-government demonstration in Prague ended in deaths and injuries when police used violence and gas to disperse crowds; E German parliament accepted PM Modrow's plan for a democratic socialist society with more market-orientated economy, less bureaucracy, educational reform and end to Ministry of State Security; Romania sealed border with Hungary, highlighting increasing isolation within eastern bloc; Pres de Klerk announced immediate desegregation of S African beaches. **18** EC leaders met for dinner-summit in Paris to discuss developments in E Europe: agreement reached on aid for Poland and Hungary and future trade talks with E Germany; later Mrs Thatcher expressed deepening disagreement with EC partners over monetary union; IRA bombs killed 3 soldiers in S Down and severely injured an army sergeant in Colchester; Salvadorean government warned Catholic church leaders to leave country as safety could not be guaranteed. **20** Huge anti-Communist demonstrations in Prague and Brno passed off peacefully; E Germany's first free elections announced for late 1990; Sir Anthony Meyer, MP for Clwyd NW announced he would stand against Mrs Thatcher in Conservative Party leadership elections; California astronomers announced discovery of quasar in Ursa Major, the most distant known object in universe. **21** Queen's speech at State Opening of Parliament: NHS plan to give doctors budgets: launch of 5th TV channel: polluters to face strict controls: legal code governing embryo research: law to sack "wildcat" strike leaders; Televising of proceedings in House of Commons began; Czechoslovak PM Ladislav Adamec received delegation including opposition leaders, as ever-larger demonstrations continued in Prague; Moscow's hardline Communist Party chief ousted. **22** Pres Moawad of Lebanon killed in massive bomb explosion in W Beirut: 23 others killed: Christian Gen Aoun's faction immediately blamed; India's General Election marred by violence and 23 deaths: allegations of fraud. **23** Alexander Dubcek appeared in Prague after 21 years to address crowd of 300,000, including industrial workers, demonstrating for democracy and reform; Last S African troops withdrew from Namibia after 74 years of armed occupation; Britain's current account deficit shrank by £74m to £1.54bn; New Greek government sworn in headed by Xenophon Zolotas and supported by all 3 main parties. **24** Communist Party leader Milos Jakes and entire Czechoslovak Politburo resigned; Lebanese deputies meeting in Syrian-controlled E Lebanon elected Elias Hrawi as President; Mrs Thatcher in talks with Pres Bush at Camp David concerning future of NATO and troop levels in Europe; Mass anonymous testing for HIV virus announced for 1990 in Britain; South African government named 4 newly-designated multi-racial suburbs. **25** Helen Sharman, a food scientist, and Timothy Mace, freefall parachute champion, named as first British astronauts. **26** 500,000 people in opposition rally in Prague assured by PM Adamec of Communist Party's serious intention to reform and change; Rioting and hunger strikes in Hong Kong camps by boat people; Swiss voters rejected draft law to abolish army. **27** General strike in Czechoslovakia organised by Civic Forum, newly-formed opposition party, called for free elections and permanent changes: country brought to standstill for 2 hours; In referendum on presidency, Hungarians voted against elections and in favour of parliamentary nomination; All British newspapers carried text of newly-agreed code of practice, covering freedom of speech and respect for privacy; IRA for second time penetrated Shorts aircraft manufacturers in Belfast and destroyed a plane; Colombian passenger jet crashed near Bogota after 2 explosions on board: 109 killed; Pres Abdallah of Comoros Islands assassinated: European mercenaries in control. **28** Czechoslovak government bowed to demand that Communist supremacy should be abolished and promised new government acceptable to Civic Forum; Soviet parliament restored Azerbaijan's powers over disputed territory of Nagorno-Karabakh; Romanian gymnast Nadia Comaneci disappeared, apparently in attempt to flee country: later she was granted political asylum in USA. **29** Indian PM Rajiv Gandhi resigned, but immediately and unanimously re-elected leader of Congress Party; Renewed famine threatened 4m people in N Ethiopia: civil war delayed aid appeals and action by relief agencies; Pres Gorbachev began state visit to Rome; Yugoslav

A.D.

states of Serbia and Slovenia severed relations. **30** Erich Honecker stripped of immunity from prosecution: criminal investigations launched into misuse of office; Nicholas Ridley, Trade and Industry Secretary, admitted previously withheld details of £38m inducement plan to clinch sale of Rover to British Aerospace in 1988; Alfred Herrhausen, chief executive of Deutsche Bank, murdered by Red Army Faction guerrillas' bomb in Frankfurt; N Yorkshire police agreed to pay compensation of more than £50m to relatives of Hillsborough victims; Lord Aldington won £1.5m libel damages over allegations of involvement in World War II atrocities.

December 1 Pope John Paul II and Pres Gorbachev met at Vatican: agreement to restore official relations: Soviet pledge on religious freedom and invitation to Pope to visit Moscow; Coup attempt against Pres Aquino of Philippines thwarted with help from US war planes stationed there; Czechoslovakia began demolition of Iron Curtain along border with Austria: visa requirements suspended on both sides; E German Communist Party voted away constitutional right to monopoly of power; Armenian parliament voted to unite with Nagorno-Karabakh and declared themselves a single republic. **2** V. P. Singh sworn in as PM of India, with 30 days to prove his coalition had support of parliament. **3** At end of 2-day summit in stormy weather in Malta, Pres Bush and Pres Gorbachev declared end of Cold War: progress towards economic co-operation and new arms control agreement; Czechoslovak opposition, frustrated by limited reforms to date, called fresh anti-government demonstrations; Entire E German Politburo forced to resign by party reformers; Sweeping victory for Labour in Queensland state elections after 30 years of ultra-conservatism. **4** Pres Bush addressed NATO leaders speaking of EC members' obligation to become integrated and to encourage reform in E Europe; Soviet Union and Warsaw Pact countries admitted culpability in events of "Prague Spring" of 1968; 200,000 marched in Leipzig for end to Communist supremacy and corruption. **5** Mrs Thatcher won emphatic victory in Conservative Party leadership ballot, although 60 MPs failed to back her; Former E German leader Erich Honecker placed under house arrest: security police chiefs and chief public prosecutor resigned: public outrage at revelation of luxurious lifestyle of former leaders: in several cities crowds entered public buildings to prevent destruction of evidence of corruption and crime; Flu epidemic in Britain. **6** Egon Krenz resigned as Head of State 3 days after being ousted as Communist Party chief; Pres Aquino declared state of emergency in Philippines; 40 killed in bomb blast at Bogota's police HQ; Britain backed Australian plan to install UN caretaker administration in Phnom Penh pending free elections. **7** Czech PM Adamec resigned: Pres Husak named Marion Calfa as acting PM: former leader Jakes expelled from Communist Party with Prague party leader Stepan; Leaders of E German opposition groups, churches and Communist-led coalition parties met in round table talks: call for free elections early in 1990 and abolition of Stasi secret police; Indian PM Singh made positive gestures towards healing religious divisions, including appointment of first-ever Muslim Home Minister; Lithuanian parliament abolished article of constitution guaranteeing Communist supremacy. **8** Bulgarian Communist leaders purged further party chiefs; Outlawed Jammu and Kashmir Liberationists kidnapped daughter of Indian Home Minister Sayeed: 5 days later she was released in exchange for 5 imprisoned activists. **9** Last 400 rebel troops surrendered in Philippines with threat of further coup failing immediate reforms; 2-day EC summit in Strasburg endorsed principle of self-determination for German peoples and agreed on aid to E bloc countries working towards democracy. **10** End of 42 years of Communist rule in Czechoslovakia: Pres Husak resigned after swearing in new government with non-Communist majority; Central Committee Plenum met in Moscow: later revelations that Pres Gorbachev had been forced by concerted onslaught from hostile conservative elements to threaten resignation; 50,000 Bulgarians demonstrated in Sofia in support of new

A.D.

opposition coalition, Union of Democratic Forces, and demanded end to Communist monopoly of power; Gregor Gysi named as E Germany's new Communist Party chief, with diminished powers. **11** Thousands in Leipzig demonstration called for German reunification; Principle of German confederation supported by both main W German political parties; Ambassadors of the 4 World War II allies met in Berlin to discuss closer links between various sectors of divided city; Bulgarian Communist leader Mladenov promised free elections within 6 months and end to constitutional guarantee of Communist supremacy. **12** First boat people to be forcibly repatriated arrived in Vietnam; First moves towards creation of European Bank; MPs in free vote backed legislation for prosecution of World War II criminals living in Britain; Billionaire US hotel owner Leona Helmsley sentenced to 4 years jail and $7m fine for tax evasion. **13** Nelson Mandela had meeting with Pres de Klerk: further talks planned; Former Bulgarian leader Todor Zhivkov expelled from Communist Party and immunity from prosecution withdrawn: investigation began into alleged offences including embezzlement; Ukrainian Catholic Church recognised by state authorities; 2 soldiers killed in IRA attack on Co. Fermanagh border checkpoint. **14** Death of Andrei Sakharov, Soviet nuclear physicist and human rights activist: 4 days later he was buried with huge national display of mourning; E German cabinet announced disbanding of Stasi; Demonstration in Romanian city of Brasov demanding freedom and better standard of living dispersed violently; Christian Democrat Patricio Aylwin elected President of Chile after 16 years of Gen Pinochet's dictatorship; Conservative backbenchers warned government that they would oppose bill to allow 40,000 Hong Kong Chinese families into Britain before colony was returned to China in 1997. **15** Pres Noriega announced state of war between Panama and USA; UN General Assembly voted unanimously for first time to condemn S Africa's apartheid system; Leading Colombian drug baron killed in gun battle with police; British Muslims upheld death sentence on Salman Rushdie. **16** Protest in Timisoara, Romania, against eviction of ethnic Hungarian priest, turned into huge demonstration against Pres Ceausescu: it continued next day and was broken up with bloodshed by military police and Securitate (State Secret Police): over following days news of death toll of hundreds gradually leaked out; US marine shot dead in Panama City. **17** Brazil's 82m voters elected a new President for first time in 29 years: Fernando Collor de Mello won by several million votes. **18** Despite Romanian unrest, Pres Ceausescu left on state visit to Iran; Eduard Shevardnadze, Soviet Foreign Minister, signed historic trade and economic agreement with EC. **19** Further bloodshed in Romania as rebellion against Ceausescu's regime continued: fighting in Bucharest, Timisoara and other cities: borders closed: reports of many hundreds dead and injured, factories ablaze and curfews broken: universal condemnation of bloodshed by international community; Eduard Shevardnadze made historic visit to NATO HQ in Brussels: later had 2 hours of talks with Mrs Thatcher in London; Soviet parliament approved by huge majority the government's programme to rescue ailing economy; Lithuanian Communist Party Congress opened with call for re-establishment of democratic and independent statehood, and creation of independent national Communist Party; Chancellor Kohl visited E Germany for first time and spoke of reunification to enthusiastic crowds: plans for further talks on economic, environmental and social cooperation; Government agreed to pay out unprecedented £150m to investors in collapsed Barlow Clowes investment empire. **20** US troops invaded Panama to protect US citizens and the Canal Zone Treaty, and to bring Gen Noriega to justice in US on drugs charges: 19 US soldiers died in initial fighting, and 59 Panamanians: many injured: many Panamanians taken prisoner but Noriega disappeared: $1m reward offered for his capture: new President Guillermo Endara sworn in: condemnation of US action from USSR but support from Mrs Thatcher; Pres Ceausescu returned to Bucharest and spoke on TV blaming external agitators and hooligans, and declared state of

A.D.

emergency: troops in Timisoara surrendered; High Street banks withdrew from government's proposed student loan scheme; Tamil Tigers renounced violence and proposed reforming as political democratic socialist party. **21** Pres Ceausescu addressed rally in Bucharest which after jeering broke up in street fighting, injuries and deaths: troops fired on civilians although some summarily executed for refusing to do so: unrest continued throughout Romania; Details of new government announced in Panama: fighting petered out apart from isolated resistance from Noriega's supporters: looting in streets: new radio station replaced the old government station destroyed by US troops; 28 killed in Australia's worst-ever road accident on Pacific Highway, N.S.W.: second serious crash in 2 months on this highway. **22** Nicolae and Elena Ceausescu fled Central Committee building in Bucharest by helicopter while huge crowds including the army celebrated in the streets: government resigned: soon afterwards Securitate forces loyal to the dictator opened fire: many killed and public buildings ablaze: battle for control of TV station and airport: later Ceausescu reported arrested; New pedestrian way in Berlin Wall opened at Brandenburg Gate by Chancellor Kohl and Hans Modrow amid wild rejoicing; Hungarian MPs voted themselves out of existence removing last obstacle to free elections in early 1990; Death of Samuel Becket, Anglo-Irish writer, in Paris; Interim Pres Djohar of Comoros Is announced French troops would stay for 2 years to train security forces: European mercenaries who seized power 3 weeks ago deported. **23** 2 days of savage fighting in Bucharest and other Romanian cities as Securitate diehards refused to surrender: desperate shortage of medical supplies: Romanian embassies abroad pledged allegiance to new regime; Food aid necessary to alleviate catastrophic famine in Ethiopia previously underestimated: Ethiopian government decided to allow relief operation to cross rebel-held territory. **24** Manuel Noriega took refuge in Papal Nunciature in Panama City, which was immediately surrounded by US troops. **25** Nicolae Ceausescu and his wife Elena, her husband's deputy, tried by a military court on charges of genocide and executed by firing squad at barracks outside Bucharest. **26** Ion Iliescu, former Central Committee secretary named as Pres of National Salvation Front government and Romania's provisional leader: new Vice-Pres Dumitru Mazilu announced end to former plan to demolish villages and create agroindustrial complexes: worldwide support for new regime; US troops ringing Papal Nunciature in Panama City shot out light bulbs in courtyard and played loud rock music in psychological warfare: 9 of Noriega's former colleagues emerged and surrendered: Vatican rejected US demand to hand over Noriega. **27** Romania's new rulers promised democratic free elections in April 1990 and speedy end to food shortages: ultimatum to Securitate remnants to lay down arms: a warren of secret tunnels for use of Securitate discovered under Bucharest with caches of food and arms: later in day crowds in Bucharest called for end to Communist Party. **28** Alexander Dubcek elected chairman of Czechoslovakian Federal Assembly, and next day playwright and human rights activist Vaclav Havel sworn in as President, each to hold office until free elections in 1990; Occasional gunfire on Romania's streets, but generally calm: members of Ceausescu family all under arrest: former dictator's brother found hanged; Thousands of Bulgarian Muslims demonstrated in Sofia against official persecution and for right to use Muslim names: later in day others joined protests, demanding political pluralism, speedy democratisation and access to media; Lithuania formally launched Soviet Union's first multiparty system; Latvia abolished Communist Party's power monopoly; Earthquake centred on Newcastle NSW, measuring 5.5 on Richter scale, killed 11: first-recorded earthquake deaths in Australia. **29** Vietnamese boat people fought with Hong Kong riot police in protest against forcible repatriation: at least 1 dead and many injured; Petre Roman named as Romanian PM: Gen Milea, previously reported a suicide victim, now said to have been shot for refusing to order troops to fire on unarmed civilians; Bulgar-

A.D.

ian Muslims granted religious and cultural freedom. **30** Pres Ortega of Nicaragua expelled 20 US diplomats after US troops allegedly ransacked Nicaraguan ambassador's residence in Panama.

1990

January 1 Interim Pres Iliescu announced abolition of Communist Party in Romania and end of Securitate; French marine experts in Morocco to help after huge oil slick from crippled Iranian tanker threatened fishing grounds and bird life in Atlantic; Militant Sikh students organised general strike throughout Punjab after disappearance of newly-elected Sikh MP; David Dinkins became 1st black Mayor of New York; **2** Riots along 80 miles of border between Soviet Azerbaijan and Iran: official Iranian complaint: unrest in disputed territory of Nagorno-Karabakh; Loyalist killed by car bomb in E Belfast. **3** Manuel Noriega left Papal Nunciature in Panama City and surrendered to US troops; KGB rushed troop reinforcements to Azerbaijan after 7,500 Muslim Azeris demanding open borders with Iran besieged its entire 490-mile length burning guardposts and ripping up fences; Norman Fowler resigned as Employment Secretary: Michael Howard took his place. **4** Manuel Noriega in court in Florida on drug-trafficking charges refused to plead, claiming to be political prisoner captured during illegal invasion: held in secret location pending trial; Pres Gorbachev told Lithuanian Communist Party chiefs that they might split from Soviet Communist Party and pursue Lithuanian independence unhindered; Erich Honecker released from house arrest; E German opposition parties combined in campaign to defeat Communists in May elections; Pakistan's worst-ever rail disaster: 225 dead: later fears of sabotage; Heatwave in Australia: temperatures reached 47 °C. **5** Local Communist chief resigned in Azerbaijan: demonstrations in capital Baku: foreign journalists banned; Strikes and protests in Bulgaria against new religious freedoms for Muslims: later said to have been organised by hardline Communist cells. **7** Demonstration along River Araks at Nakhichevan on Soviet-Iran border continued, calling for unification between Muslims in Iran and Azerbaijan; Khmer Rouge started fires in 3-day attack on Battambang, Cambodia's 2nd city: later Phnom Penh claimed to have repulsed them. **8** E German opposition groups broke off talks with government because of uncertainties concerning secret police; Members of Securitate went on trial in Romania; Indications of imminent release of Nelson Mandela; Deal between syndicate of 200 world banks to save Channel Tunnel project. **9** Soldiers in clashes with civilians in Stepanakert, chief city of Nagorno-Karabakh: grenades and missiles said to have been smuggled into disputed territory from Armenia: bridges linking Azerbaijan with Azeri-inhabited areas of Nagorno-Karabakh blown up; 7 killed and many injured in clash near Johannesburg between striking and non-striking rail workers: strikers claimed police failed to intervene; E German Environment Minister resigned, drawing attention to vast pollution crisis costing huge sums to correct; Leaders of Czechoslovakia, Poland and Hungary called for radical reform of Comecon to fit into world economic structure; Romania sought full diplomatic relations with EC; Danny Morrison, Sinn Fein Vice President, on serious terrorist charges, including conspiracy to murder. **10** Ford union leaders rejected 10.2% pay offer: blow to government's inflation policy; Brazilian government reversed promise to protect Yanomami tribe in Amazon rainforests from lawless white gold miners; tribal territory reduced by 70%; Government to spend £12m on research into "mad cow disease" BSE. **11** Pres Gorbachev began 3-day visit to Lithuania during which he confirmed possibility of Lithuania's secession from USSR, and said that draft laws on secession mechanism were being drawn up by Moscow: afterwards 250,000 rallied for independence in Vilnius; Armenian parliament voted itself the right to veto Soviet laws: Azerbaijani nationalists blockaded public buildings in Caspian Sea city of Lenkoran; Mr Modrow defended government plan

A.D.

to form new internal security agency before May elections: crowds formed human chain round parliament building in protest, and workers staged 1-hour strike and protest march: 150,000 demonstrated against plan in Leipzig; Albanian exiles rallied in Athens to protest against violation of human rights by Tirana regime, after reports of protest in NW Albanian town of Shkoder violently suppressed; 27 dead in dispute between striking and non-striking S African rail workers: senior political figures in anti-apartheid movement stepped in to mediate. **12** Chinese authorities lifted martial law in Beijing and removed troops from Tiananmen Square to which public readmitted: some visitors signalled brief protest before police intervened; Romania banned Communism: in response to angry crowd, Pres Iliescu promised confiscated funds to be redistributed among new parties, and referendum on capital punishment; Albanian authorities reported to have declared state of emergency; Scientists found evidence of global warming: 1980s warmest recorded decade. **13** More than 25 Armenians dead in riots in Baku; fighting in Azerbaijan city of Shaumyan; 3 criminals shot dead by plainclothes soldiers in Belfast: no IRA connection proved: renewal of "shoot to kill" allegations. **14** Armenian nationalist leaders declared "total mobilisation" against Azerbaijan; more troops dispatched by Moscow: bloodshed continued, many dead; 50,000 rallied in Sofia calling for immediate end to Communist monopoly of power and control of media; Archbishop of Canterbury began week-long visit to Africa to investigate most effective aid to Ethiopian famine victims. **15** State of emergency declared in Nagorno-Karabakh: 11,000 troops sent to join 4,000 already in Azerbaijan to halt ethnic violence: many Armenians evacuated from Baku by ship across Caspian Sea, others by rail and air; Thousands of angry E Germans stormed former Stasi HQ; Lithuanian Communist Party leader A Brazaukas elected President by Supreme Soviet in endorsement of his stance independent of Moscow; Albanian leader R Alia rejected rumours of unrest; Romania's interim National Salvation Front government admitted mistake in bowing to angry crowd's demand for abolition of Communist Party: referendum announced instead; Bulgarian parliament abolished Communist monopoly of power. **16** Pogrom by Azeris against Armenians at its height: at least 70 dead: roads and airports blocked by Azeri nationalists to hinder troop movements: demonstrators defying ban rallied to demand resignation of republic's Communist leaders; Cambodia accepted in principle a peace plan to divide country into zones held by Phnom Penh government and resistance under UN supervision, pending elections; Irish government taking up 6-month Presidency of EC pledged to press for more powers for MEPs. **17** Alexander Dubcek addressed European Parliament, calling for support for Soviet reforms; Marion Calfa, Czechoslovakian PM resigned from Communist Party; Reports of 50,000 dead in Somali civil war in past 19 months. **18** 20,000 rallied in Baku demanding government's resignation and end to Soviet power: general strike declared: Popular Front in Azerbaijan claimed reunification of Azeris as main goal, and continued bitter opposition to state of emergency; Gorbachev condemned conservative critics in Kremlin of his policies in Azerbaijan: Armenians attacked Azeris in Nakhichevan, Azeri enclave on Iranian border; Arrest warrant issued in Bulgaria for former leader Todor Zhivkov on grounds of incitement to racial hatred and embezzlement; China released 573 "repentant" rebels held since May: many thousands feared to be still in jail or secretly executed; Romania's interim government cancelled decrees on death penalty and Communist Party status, and cancelled announced referenda: Communist wealth to be appropriated by State. **19** Protests in N Caucasian towns against call-up of reservists to maintain order in Azerbaijan; Iran warned USSR against use of force to "suppress Azeri Islamic zeal": leader of Armenian Independence Movement killed by Azeris in Nakhichevan fighting; Mayor Marion Barry of Washington arrested on drugs charges but did not offer resignation; Protesters in Johannesburg at arrival of rebel cricket tour dispersed by tear gas and police dogs. **20**

A.D.

Azerbaijani Communist Party leader Vesirov sacked and replaced by Azeri: Pres Gorbachev appealed to Azerbaijani and Armenian citizens on TV: later Soviet troops moved in by sea and air to take control of Baku: bloody fighting and many deaths; Indian government assumed direct rule over rebellious Muslim-dominated Jammu and Kashmir state: troops opened fire on demonstrators defying curfew, killing 30. **21** Nakhichevan made unilateral declaration of independence, calling for international aid: reports of pontoon bridge across River Araks and illegal crossings into N Iran for arms; armed Iranians reported in Nakhichevan; For 4th consecutive week crowds demonstrated in Ulan Bator in temperatures of $-30°$ for political reform and perestroika; E German Communist Party expelled Egon Krenz: Dresden's Mayor and Deputy Party chairman resigned from Party calling for dissolution: mass demonstrations for end of Communist Party continued throughout country; 300 mile human chain across Ukraine calling for independence; Commonwealth Games opened in Auckland. **22** Mass funerals in Baku of 60 people killed in weekend's fighting: vast crowds of mourners in streets: Azerbaijan parliament joined Popular Front in declaring state of emergency null and void; Yugoslavia's Communist Party voted to abolish Party's monopoly of power. **23** GEC bought Ferranti Defence Systems 24 hours after Ferranti won £1·6bn contract for European Fighter Aircraft; Continuing protests in S Africa over rebel cricket tour; Romania's National Salvation Front decided to turn itself into political party and contest May elections; USSR agreed to withdraw troops from Hungary as soon as possible after 45 years. **24** Soviet navy opened fire on ships blockading port of Baku: Azeri Popular Front agreed to attend peace talks in Riga with Armenian National Front; Ethnic Albanians in Yugoslav province of Kosovo rioted against Serbian rule, calling for free elections; E German PM Modrow pleaded for loyalty from opposition parties, who promised cooperation: Christian Democratic Union later left coalition with demand that Modrow should resign from Communist Party. **25** Hurricane-force winds battered S of England: 46 died: 3m trees lost; Azeri nationalists agreed to ceasefire on Armenia/Nakhichevan border, but fighting continued in Baku: 10,000 ethnic Azeris demonstrated in Turkish town of Igdir against Soviet intervention in Azerbaijan; Thousands of Indian troops arrived in Srinagar, capital of Kashmir state, to keep peace and prevent Muslim separatist revolt; Daughter born to Pakistan's PM Benazir Bhutto, world's first-ever head of government to have a child while in office. **26** Announcement of December trade gap of £1·12bn: 1989 deficit was all-time record at £20·31bn; BBC announced cuts amounting to saving of £75m; Romanian Vice Pres Mazilu resigned accusing National Salvation Front of Stalinist methods; Demonstrations in Pakistan's Azad Kashmir in support of Indian Kashmiri independence. **27** Famine threatened Angola after failure of rains and persistent raids by Unita's anti-government guerrillas. **28** Serbian province of Kosovo near to anarchy after continued fighting between ethnic Albanians and riot police; Demonstration in Bucharest against National Salvation Front's decision to participate in elections ended in violence; Soviet forces regained power in Nakhichevan and town of Lenkoran: January death toll now at 200; IRA bomb killed boy during "Bloody Sunday" anniversary march. **29** Erich Honecker left hospital after cancer surgery and was immediately arrested: later he was released on grounds of ill-health, pending investigations into corruption; Further confrontations in Romania between government and opposition parties' supporters; Polish Communist Party renamed itself the Social Democracy of the Republic of Poland; Publication of report on Hillsborough disaster: football clubs faced £130m bill for improved safety: government abandoned proposed identity card scheme. **30** Many thousands joined rallies throughout Britain in support of ambulance workers in the 21st week of pay dispute; Fighting broke out again between rival Christian factions in Beirut; Riots and police violence continued to accompany rebel cricket tour in S Africa; Pres Gorbachev acknowledged

A.D.

likelihood of German reunification; 2 Welsh weightlifters disqualified at Commonwealth Games for drugtaking. 31 Pres Bush in annual State of the Nation address proposed reduction of US and Soviet troop levels in Europe to 195,000; More ethnic Albanians dead in Kosovo as riots continued: federal troops and tanks ordered in by Yugoslav government to keep peace; First McDonald's hamburger restaurant opened in USSR, in Moscow's Pushkin Square.

February 1 Hans Modrow outlined proposal for German reunification: later dismissed by Chancellor Kohl until after free elections had taken place in E Germany; Bulgaria's Communist government resigned to make way for broad-based coalition: Party congress met to choose new leaders; Labour led Conservatives by 15·5% in opinion polls; 9 Iranians deported from UK in connection with death sentence on Salman Rushdie. 2 Pres F W de Klerk announced 30-year ban on ANC lifted: death sentences suspended, and political prisoners released: Nelson Mandela's unconditional release imminent: speech widely welcomed in S Africa and internationally; Gen Aoun, having lost a large part of the Lebanese Christian enclave to Phalangist opponents, laid siege to densely-populated Christian area of E Beirut, in attempt to consolidate his remaining military power and ignoring appeals for ceasefire: many deaths; 4 leading members of Ceausescu's regime jailed for life in Romania for ordering slaughter of civilians during December revolution; Tear gas and tanks used by troops to disperse rioting ethnic Albanians in Kosovo. 3 Romania's National Salvation Front dissolved, after agreeing to form new provisional Council of National Unity (CNU) with 29 opposition parties pending May 20 elections. 4 More than 100,000 gathered in Moscow on eve of Communist Party plenum to demand steps towards genuine multiparty democracy; Machine gun and grenade attack on tourist bus carrying Israelis near Ismalia: 9 dead, many wounded; Slovene Communist Party abolished itself, ending hopes of reconciliation with Yugoslavia's Federal Communist Party: reconstituted as Party of Democratic Renewal; Storms and flooding lasting several days in Britain and N Europe caused destruction and loss of life. 5 S African police continued to use violence against peaceful and legal marches, despite Pres de Klerk's declaration of 2 Feb; 8 ministers from opposition parties joined Mr Modrow's government in temporary Government of National Responsibility; Indian troops opened fire on 4,000 Pakistanis who crossed border into Kashmir state to protest against Indian rule: several dead; Announcement that Wrens were to serve on Royal Navy warships at sea. 6 Fighting in Lebanon between Phalangists and Gen Aoun's army continued: death toll at least 300; Chancellor Kohl called for urgent talks with E Germany in view of E Germany's grave economic position and continuing exodus of refugees. 7 Soviet Communist Party plenum, extended to third day, amended Article 6 of constitution to abolish monopoly rule: call for genuine Presidential system of government; Gun battles in Karachi between Pakistani security forces and anti-government protesters: 64 dead, many wounded. 9 US and USSR announced 80% cut in chemical weapons; Iranian leader Khamenei reaffirmed year-old death sentence against Salman Rushdie: later leading British Muslims condemned the action; John Gotti, reputedly America's leading Mafia boss, acquitted on all charges after highly publicised trial. 11 Nelson Mandela freed from jail after 27 years, proclaiming himself still totally committed to struggle against white minority rule in S Africa: he addressed crowds in centre of Cape Town: worldwide rejoicing at his release; Returning from Moscow, Chancellor Kohl claimed Soviet support for his German reunification plan. 12 Nelson Mandela speaking in first press conference since release, in Archbishop Tutu's Cape Town garden, assured white population of respect for their rights; Ethnic and anti-Soviet riots in Dushanbe, capital of Tajikistan Soviet Central Asian republic; state of emergency declared: 40 dead; India accused Pakistan of fermenting Muslim rebellion in Kashmir: PM Benazir Bhutto refuted accusation: fighting continued: at least 85 dead in

A.D.

previous 3 weeks; Labour's Carmen Lawrence took power in W Australia, as first-ever woman state premier in Australian history; Ariel Sharon, leader of Israel's hardliners, resigned from PM Shamir's cabinet, leaving government in disarray. 13 Pravda published radical document outlining policies to be put before summer Communist Party Congress: surrender of power monopoly, creation of federal structure allowing republics to secede, transfer of executive power to government under the president, and reform of economy; Nelson Mandela returned home to Soweto and addressed 100,000 at City Soccer Stadium, attacking "thuggery" in townships and calling for negotiations demonstrating goodwill towards whites; Rebel cricket tour of S Africa abandoned; Conference of World War II allies and E and W Germany agreed formula for German reunification. 14 Indian Airlines airbus crashed in Bangalore, killing 97; Continuous fighting in Tajikistan, many casualties: Dushanbe airport attacked: women wearing non-Muslim dress or with short hair attacked and raped; Rioting in Hong Kong's boat people camps; Mortgages at all-time high as Abbey National Building Society raised standard lending rate to 15·4% 15 Pres Bush in "drug summit" in Cartagena with Presidents of Bolivia, Colombia and Peru; to discuss common anti-drug strategy; 20,000 right-wingers rallied in Pretoria against release of Nelson Mandela and in support of apartheid: meanwhile US civil rights leader Jesse Jackson visited Mandela in Soweto; Sweden's Social Democrat government resigned after defeat of economic austerity package; Definite link established for first time between exposure to radiation at Sellafield and leukaemia in children of men working there; 20,000 students marched in London against proposed introduction of student loans. 16 Romania's Defence Minister Militaru resigned after allegations of links with Ceausescu regime; More than 200,000 rallied for independence on Lithuania's national day, many young people protesting against compulsory service in Soviet army. 17 Czechoslovakia's Communist Party expelled 22 former leaders including former Pres Husak; Fidel Castro announced reorganisation of Cuban Communist Party. 18 Foundation of Mongolian Democratic Party, the country's first opposition party: immediate call for trials of officials responsible for economic mismanagement and for mass resignations of Communist leaders. 19 Financial crisis threatening Channel Tunnel resolved by appointment of leading US executive to run project; 8,000 Romanian miners rallied to support provisional government whose HQ was earlier ransacked by angry crowds; 5 killed in Nepal when police opened fire on strikers calling for multi-party democracy. 20 At EC conference in Dublin, Foreign Secretary Douglas Hurd announced British government's intention of lifting sanctions against S Africa, following Mandela's release: White House later refuted claim that US supported this decision; Bomb exploded in army vehicle in Leicester, injuring 3. 21 Polish PM Mazowiecki insisted on Polish–German treaty on Oder-Neisse border before German reunification, to eliminate any ambiguities: Chancellor Kohl later agreed to this; Vietnam, in talks with Britain agreed to an increase in rate of voluntary repatriation of boat people, but continued to block forcible repatriation; Cambodian resistance and Phnom Penh government signed joint communique in first step towards uniting warring factions: later resistance leader Prince Sihanouk returned to Cambodia, urging many thousands of refugees to follow; Romania's National Peasant Party called on government to put an end to "terrorism" after alleged assassination of an official. 22 Iranian newspaper urged unconditional release of 18 hostages held by pro-Iranian Shias in Lebanon, to end growing international isolation of Tehran regime: later this call reiterated by Sheikh Fadlallah, spiritual leader of Hizbollah, the group believed to be holding the hostages; Former Pres Reagan admitted ordering covert action to supply arms to Nicaraguan Contra guerrillas, but denied authorisation of illegal activities. 23 6-month-long ambulance dispute settled after 20 hours of talks, with basic pay increase of 17.6% but no long-term pay mechanism agreed: not all ambulance staff pleased with deal: crews on strike on Merseyside and in

A.D.

London; Ceasefire between Christian forces in Lebanon collapsed; 500,000 Muslims marched peacefully in Srinagar for Kashmir independence; Anti-government riots in Nairobi following funeral of Foreign Minister Ouko, whom demonstrators believed murdered; Ingvar Carlsson to head new Swedish government. **24** Syrian gunboat shelled Cyprus-Jounieh ferry off Lebanese coast; PM Benazir Bhutto dismissed Chief Minister of Sind province after month of ethnic violence. **25** In Moscow, 150,000 marched in pro-democracy demonstration: other demonstrations in Byelorussia, Russian Republic and Ukraine; In Lithuanian General Election, Communist Party suffered crushing defeat as Popular Front was returned with mandate for swift progress towards independence; Exiled ethnic Albanian leader from Kosovo assassinated in Brussels; 200,000 Bulgarians marched in anti-Communist demonstration, urging more speedy reforms. **26** Week of further severe storms in Britain: 2,000 evacuated from Towyn, Clwyd, due to severe flooding on N Wales coast; In Nicaraguan General Election, Pres Ortega's Sandinista government defeated by Violeta Chamorro's 14-party coalition National Opposition Union (UNO): vote monitored by 2,000 international observers: later Daniel Ortega visited Mrs Chamorro to offer peace and reconciliation; 400 arrested in Nepal as activists protested against 30 years of repression by system forbidding political parties. **27** Soviet parliament approved establishment of an executive presidency, giving Pres Gorbachev increased powers to lead country through current critical period; 80 Conservative MPs signed letter declaring themselves unable to support bill giving 225,000 Hong Kong citizens right to settle in Britain after 1997; 60 killed in N Indian state of Bihar during state assembly elections; Nelson Mandela in Zambia on first foreign visit since release. **28** January trade deficit of £1·88bn announced; Mrs Chamorro ordered immediate demobilisation of Contra guerrillas after Daniel Ortega declared unilateral halt to Sandinista military action; State elections in India rejected Congress Party, casting doubt on Rajiv Gandhi's future as party leader; Collapse of Cambodian peace talks in Jakarta.

March 1 70 dead as rival Christians fought for control of E Beirut: Vaclav Havel visiting Moscow secured agreement for 75,000 Soviet troops to quit Czechoslovakia by July; Ethiopian government announced plans to airlift food to interior of famine-stricken Eritrea; Prescription charges to rise by 9% to £3.05; Cambridge University astronomers discovered previously-unsuspected galaxy orbiting our own at distance of 300,000 light years. **2** 2-day ANC executive committee meeting in Lusaka announced election of Nelson Mandela as Deputy President and transfer of HQ to Johannesburg: immediate contacts sought with Pretoria government to discuss obstacles to negotiations; Indian authorities imposed indefinite curfew in Kashmir after troops killed 60 independence demonstrators; Soviet troops to be withdrawn from Mongolia over next 2 years; General Strike called by pro-democracy movement in Nepal: The Queen present at inauguration of Glasgow as "European City of Culture 1990". **4** Army officers in bloodless coup in independent homeland of Ciskei overthrew Pres-for Life Lennox Sebe: later S African troops sent in at request of coup leaders to maintain law and order; Township violence in S Africa: police shootings; Peter Walker, Welsh Secretary, to resign for family and business reasons; National Union of Mineworkers in financial scandal with renewed allegations of cash received from USSR and Libya during 1984–5 pit strike: Arthur Scargill issued denial: NUM executive and later Neil Kinnock called for independent inquiry; Rebel Philippine governor with 600 armed supporters in hotel siege: 16 dead. **5** Chris Patten, Environment Secretary, announced dumping of sewage at sea to end by 1999; Ethnic unrest in Uzbekistan: 10 dead. **6** Unsuccessful coup attempt led by Afghan Defence Minister against Pres Najibullah: Kabul under curfew after bombing raids and street fighting; Results from Soviet regional and local elections showed big gains for nationalists and radicals; Soviet parliament passed law sanctioning private property for the

A.D.

first time since Lenin's New Economic Policy of 1920s. **7** Dept of Trade & Industry report revealed gross deception practised by Al-Fayed brothers in their 1985 Harrods take-over; Revelation that Czechoslovakia's sales of Semtex explosive, said to have ceased in 1982, in fact continued until 1989; Libya alleged to hold huge stocks; at conference on N Sea attended by EC Environment Ministers, Britain severely attacked for negligence. **8** Farzad Bazoft, Iranian-born journalist on *Observer* newspaper, tried in Baghdad on espionage charges with nurse Daphne Parrish, and sentenced to death; Afghan opposition forces formed Revolutionary Council to continue war against Pres Najibullah; S African troops intervened on behalf of Pres Mangope of Bophuthatswana after huge demonstrations calling for his resignation and reincorporation of the homeland into S Africa: 14 dead and hundreds injured in gunfire. **9** In the week that many local councils met to set Community Charge rates, demonstrations throughout England, leading in some cases to violent confrontation with police and many arrests: violence denounced by all party leaders; Violence in S African townships, principally Katlehong, among rival black groups: many dead and injured; First formal steps towards German reunification when senior E and W German Foreign Office officials met. **10** Haiti's leader, Lt-Col Prosper Avril resigned after weeks of unrest. **11** Lithuania's Supreme Council proclaimed independence from USSR: earlier Vytautas Landsbergis, leader of Nationalist movement Sajudis, named Chairman of newly-elected parliament: reinstatement of national anthem and flag of pre-war independent Lithuania; Israel's PM Shamir blocked cabinet vote on US Middle East peace plan. **12** Mongolian Communist Party leader Zhambyn Batmunk resigned. **13** Full Soviet parliament approved Pres Gorbachev's plan for a powerful executive presidency, and voted an end to guaranteed Communist monopoly of power; Irish Supreme Court ruled against extradition of 2 convicted IRA terrorists, previously escaped from Maze prison; Ambulance workers voted for pay deal ending 6-month dispute, but pursued pay formula demand; Invisible earnings in last quarter of 1989 £713m in deficit; Haiti's first-ever woman President Ertha Pascal-Trouillot inaugurated, pending internationally-monitored autumn elections. **14** David Hunt announced as new Welsh Secretary; Tamil rebels in virtual control of NE Sri Lanka. **15** Execution of Farzad Bazoft in Baghdad, despite pleas for clemency from many world leaders: British Ambassador to Iraq recalled: anti-British demonstrations followed; PM Shamir lost vote of confidence in Knesset, first Israeli PM in history to do so; Mongolia's new Communist leaders promised first free elections for 69 years. **16** Director of WHO $100m AIDS programme resigned after row over methods of fighting disease: later his deputy also resigned. **17** Kremlin hardliner Yegor Ligachev attacked erosion of Communist Party status and Pres Gorbachev's new powers; Scotland won Grand Slam for third time in rugby history. **18** Right-wing Alliance for Germany won E German General Election in vote of confidence for Chancellor Kohl: invitation to Social Democrats and Alliance of Free Democrats to join coalition frostily received; Huge supplies of arms to Afghan mujaheddin aroused fears of fresh offensive. **20** Budget day: raising of limits for income support and poll tax benefit aroused complaint in Scotland where poll tax already established for one year: income tax allowances raised: alcohol and tobacco up: duty on petrol up, increasing differential in favour of unleaded petrol: injection of £100m into football over 5 years to improve ground safety: range of measures to help small savers: company car charges raised; Benazir Bhutto at huge rally in Lahore pledged support for Kashmiri separatists; Imelda Marcos on trial in New York charged with embezzlement and racketeering involving huge sums from Philippine treasury; Marks & Spencer staff got 26% wage rise following Sainsbury's 20%: Tesco followed suit. **21** Invoking new powers, Pres Gorbachev ordered tightening of KGB border controls and temporary ban on firearms in Lithuania: Soviet military presence increased; Fresh but limited policy enquiry announced into

A.D.
1974 "Birmingham Six" pub bombings case; 400 new E German MPs to be investigated for Stasi links; Namibian Independence celebrated; Pres Vaclav Havel on State Visit to London; China to increase military spending. **22** Sylvia Heal won Mid-Staffs by-election for Labour with 21% swing; Government obliged to announce ex gratia payment of £4m to Scottish poll tax payers after Budget gaffe; Pres Gorbachev issued 2-day ultimatum to Lithuania to disband alleged unofficial militia formed to protect the republic; After 4 successive days of anti-Hungarian demonstrations in Tirgu Mures, interim Pres Iliescu promised Transylvania would remain part of Romania; February current account deficit of £1.4bn announced, a £600m reduction. **23** Birth of Princess Eugenie of York by caesarian section; Kremlin barred journalists from Lithuania: Pres Bush appealed for peaceful settlement; Mongolian MPs abolished Communist monopoly of power; February inflation figure of 7.5% announced. **24** PM Bob Hawke's Labour Party won Australian General Election, the first-ever party leader to win a 4th term in office: Andrew Peacock resigned as Liberal leader. **25** Inconclusive Hungarian General Election necessitated second vote in April; 87 dead in fire in unlicenced New York disco: later a Cuban refugee charged with arson: crackdown on similar premises promised; Estonian Communist Party voted to split from Soviet Party; Archbishop of Canterbury announced retirement in January 1991. **26** 8 killed and hundreds injured in fighting in Johannesburg townships; Attempt to form new E German government faltered when Ibrahim Böhme, leader of SPD, stepped down after allegations of Stasi links; Anglo-Soviet Juno space mission threatened by cash crisis; Launch of campaign to protect Britain's threatened peat bogs. **27** Soviet troops occupied independent Communist Party HQ in Vilnius and rounded up deserters from Soviet army: foreign citizens ordered to leave; Proposed new roads to ease London's traffic axed in policy reversal; Actress Glenda Jackson nominated as Labour Party candidate at next General Election. **28** Heathrow customs officials foiled alleged plan to smuggle to Iraq 40 triggering devices for nuclear bombs: 4 arrested and senior Iraqi Airways representative deported; Luke Rittner, Secretary-General of Arts Council, resigned over government decision to devolve many of its powers to the regions; Viscount Linley awarded libel damages against *Today* newspaper in first such case brought by member of Royal family; Maoist guerrillas decreed general strike in Lima in campaign to sabotage Peru's Presidential and congressional elections: assassinations and car bombings caused deaths and injuries. **29** Norman Tebbit announced his candidacy against Michael Heseltine as Conservative Party leader if vacancy arose; Chancellor Kohl's 3-day visit to Britain highlighted differences between him and Mrs Thatcher. **30** Estonian parliament voted to suspend Soviet constitution on its territory and proclaimed start of transitional period to independence; Nelson Mandela called off talks with Inkatha leader Chief Buthelezi, after 50 deaths and thousands made homeless in recent Natal fighting; Deaths reported as trans-Caucasian violence flared again. **31** Massive anti-Community Charge demonstration in London ended in violence: hundreds arrested, many injured including 65 police: cars and shops wrecked: anarchists and extremists blamed.

April 1 Riot at Strangeways Prison, Manchester: 1,000 prisoners took over and wrecked entire jail, setting fire to some blocks: rooftop protests against overcrowding and inhumane conditions: attacks on sexual offenders: prisoners who did not take part or later surrendered moved to other already overcrowded prisons throughout country; E German dismay at W German Bundesbank proposal for 2 Ostmarks: 1 Deutschmark exchange rate. **2** Pres Hussein of Iraq denied construction of nuclear weapons and threatened Israel with chemical warfare; Earth tremor registering 5.2 on Richter scale centred on Wrexham: effects felt from London to Dublin and Lancashire; Brother of ex-Pres Ceausescu tried for murder in Bucharest. **3** Pres Gorbachev's close advisers in talks with Lithuanian delegates in Moscow: Soviet parliament passed law defining complex secession

A.D.
procedure; Bomb planted by Sikh separatists killed 32 and injured 50 in Punjab; SPD in negotiations to form E German coalition government. **4** 3 doctors found guilty by General Medical Council in "kidneys for sale" case: one struck from register; Colombia cocaine war escalated with 30 dead. **5** Inaugural session of E Germany's first democratically-elected parliament: Frau Sabine Bergmann-Pohl elected Volkskammer President and acting Head of State; Pres de Klerk and Nelson Mandela agreed date for government/ANC talks: investigation into police brutality promised; Judicial enquiry announced into Strangeways riot and continuing occupation: prison officer who had been on duty at start of riot died; Hospital waiting lists had risen by 30,000. **6** Troops fired on pro-democracy demonstrators as political turmoil continued in Nepal: many dead and injured in past week: run on banks and strikes: curfew imposed: later King Birendra dismissed cabinet and brought in new moderate PM; Irish Supreme Court refused to extradite former Republican MP Owen Carron to N Ireland. **7** Fire on Oslo/Frederikshavn car ferry *Scandinavian Star*: 168 dead: arson suspected; John Poindexter found guilty on 5 Irangate charges; Huge pro-democracy demonstration in Tblisi commemorating last year's massacre; Moderate Latvian Communist Party leader replaced by hardliner after one-third of delegates walked out of session. **8** Further riots in several British prisons: prisoner dead at Dartmoor in burnt-out cell; Second round of Hungarian General Elections won by traditionalist Hungarian Democratic Forum (MDF); King Birendra lifted 30-year ban on political parties in Nepal and promised amended multiparty constitution; Britain's Nick Faldo became only the second-ever golfer successfully to defend US Masters title. **9** Fire on Pembroke/Rosslare ferry: 1 dead, 32 taken to hospital: arson suspected: later a man died during fire on Brittany Ferries' *Reine Mathilde* in English Channel; 4 UDR soldiers killed by huge IRA bomb near Downpatrick; Pres Mugabe of Zimbabwe named new government after easy election victory; World Ministerial Drugs Conference opened in London. **10** 3 hostages, French Jacqueline Valente, Belgian Fernand Houtekins and 2-year-old daughter released by Abu Nidal's Palestinian terrorists, after intervention by Col Gaddafi: thought to be in return for French sale of Mirage fighter-bombers to Libya; Britain persuaded Commonwealth and other allies to grant thousands of passports to Hong Kong citizens; Escalating Kurdish rebel insurgency in SE Turkey; Constantine Mitsotakis, leader of conservative New Democracy party, named as new Greek PM; Lech Walesa announced intention of standing as Poland's President; Prison officer held hostage for 24 hours by prisoners at Shotts jail, Lanarkshire. **11** Teesside Customs & Excise officers detained consignment of steel cylinders bound for Iraq, on suspicion of their being parts of 40m gun barrel, and not for petrochemical industry as alleged; Pres de Klerk met Nelson Mandela and ANC representatives in Cape Town, first such meeting since founding of ANC in 1912; Irish Taoiseach Charles Haughey in Belfast as Pres of EC to address Institute of Directors amid tight security; Mother Teresa resigned as head of Missionaries of Charity religious order: PM of Yugoslavia's Kosovo province and 6 other ethnic Albanian ministers resigned. **12** Christian Democrat Lothar de Maziere appointed E German PM; Ex-King Michael prevented by interim Romanian government from returning to Bucharest on private Easter visit; Militant Zionists held disputed Greek Orthodox building in Jerusalem: Christian protesters gassed by police: later Palestinian demonstrators entered Church of Holy Sepulchre; Increase in annual rate of inflation to 9.5%: inflation rate up from 7.5% to 8.1% in year to March. **13** Pres Bush and Mrs Thatcher met for talks in Bermuda; USSR admitted responsibility for death of 15,000 Poles in 1940, including Katyn massacre; Pres Gorbachev issued ultimatum to Lithuania to annul acts of parliament since March 11 or face economic blockade; New Nepalese interim government formed by opposition parties approved by King Birendra; 3 Baltic states agreed common market programme. **14** Armenian nationalists besieged KGB HQ in Yerevan: 1

A.D.

dead. **15** Nelson Mandela admitted torture of ANC dissidents had occurred in the past but had been stamped out; Guerrilla revolt in NE Liberia: many deaths reported; The Pope offered Vatican mediation between Lithuania and USSR. **16** At Wembley rock concert to celebrate his release, Nelson Mandela insisted on continuing sanctions; 3 prisoners suffering from food poisoning surrendered at Strangeways. **17** National Union of Teachers voted to strike if Poll Tax "capping" led to redundancies: leaders disowned decision; King Birendra invited opposition parties to form interim government after dissolving parliament and accepting resignation of his nominated PM; 100 dead in fire on overcrowded train near N Indian town of Patna. **18** Secretary of State for Trade & Industry confirmed that steel tubes seized on Teesside were part of "supergun" for Iraq: row erupted with allegations of government's previous knowledge and negligence; Oil and later gas supplies to Lithuania from USSR cut off; 11 children and 4 adults killed when incendiary grenade hit Beirut school bus: Christian factions blamed each other; Right-wing coalition formed Slovenian government, first non-Communist government in Yugoslav republic since World War II. **19** "Supergun" identified as £4m ballistics test-bed providing Iraq with technological ability to upset Middle East military balance: Brussels-based Space Research Corporation which designed installation wound up; Government bill to give passports to 50,000 Hong Kong families reached committee stage despite backbench revolt; India and Pakistan on brink of war over Kashmiri nationalism; Pres de Klerk announced rescinding of 2 laws central to apartheid; Ceasefire and disarmament agreement between Nicaraguan Sandinistas and Contras. **20** Lorries carrying "supergun" parts for Iraq seized by customs officers in Greece and Turkey; Food deliveries diverted from Lithuania by USSR: Soviet troops stormed printing works of independent Lithuanian Communist Party, beating up workers. **21** The Pope on 2-day visit to Czechoslovakia. **22** US hostage Robert Polhill, Beirut University professor, released by Islamic Jihad guerrillas after 39 months; Attempted coup against Nigerian Pres Babangida; Channel Tunnel costs rose to £7·5bn; First-ever death in London

A.D.

Marathon when runner collapsed from heart attack. **23** MPs voted in favour of continued human embryo research; 100 young inmates rioted at Pucklechurch Remand Centre near Bristol, causing £1m-worth of damage; E Germany welcomed W German offer of more generous exchange rate for currency union; Renewed violent demonstrations in Kathmandu: 6 dead, many injured; Right-wing victory for Croatian HDZ party threatened Yugoslavia's future. **25** Specially-trained prison officers entered Strangeways jail and last 6 prisoners surrendered after 3½-week siege; MPs voted to reduce upper time limit for abortion to 24 weeks; Assassination attempt on W German Social Democrat leader Oskar Lafontaine by schizophrenic woman; Foreign Ministers of India and Pakistan met in New York and agreed to avoid confrontation; Trade deficit reached £2·18bn, second-worst figure on record; Pres Ozal, Mrs Thatcher and Australian PM Bob Hawke in Turkey to commemorate 75th anniversary of Gallipoli landings. **26** Labour leader Shimon Peres unable to form new Israeli government: later Pres Herzog asked Likud's Yitzhak Shamir to make attempt; Floods in Australia: an area the size of W Europe under water in Queensland/NSW outback. **27** Appeal Court freed 3 people imprisoned for 1988 conspiracy to murder Tom King, then N Ireland Secretary: they were subsequently deported; S Africa's Communist Party leader Joe Slovo returned home after 30 years' exile; Jerusalem's Christian churches closed for 24 hours in protest against occupation of hospice by Orthodox Jews. **28** EC summit in Dublin discussed steps towards European union: Mrs Thatcher expressed British concern for status of Royal family and Parliament. **29** Scotland's Stephen Hendry youngest-ever world snooker champion. **30** US hostage Frank Reed freed in W Beirut after 3½ years; 10 killed when RAF Shackleton crashed in Outer Hebrides; Confusion over future of Poll Tax: Mrs Thatcher to chair reviewing Cabinet committee; China lifted martial law in Tibet after 14 months; Anti-government protesters occupied centre of Bucharest for 9 days: 5 opposition parties threatened to boycott first elections since overthrow of Ceaucescu on grounds that NSF taking unfair advantage and threatening the opposition.

PROMINENT PEOPLE

Glimpses of some of the famous people in the history of the world. See also Section E for composers; Section M for prominent English poets and novelists; and Section D for a Who's Who in British politics.

B2

PROMINENT PEOPLE

A

Abel, Sir Frederick (1826–1902). English military chemist, an authority on explosives. He and his friend James Dewar patented the propellant cordite (*see* Section L).

Abelard, Peter (1079–1142), one of the founders of scholastic moral theology, b. at Pallet (Palais) near Nantes. He lectured in Paris, where he was sought by students, though persecuted for alleged heresy. His main achievement was to discuss where others asserted. His love for Héloïse, a woman of learning, ended in tragic separation and in a famous correspondence.

Abercrombie, Sir Patrick (1879–1957), architect and town-planner. He was consulted on the re-planning of Plymouth, Hull, Bath and other cities and produced a plan for Greater London, 1943.

Acton, 1st Baron (John Emerich Edward Dalberg Acton) (1834–1902), English historian. He planned the *Cambridge Modern History*.

Adam, Robert (1728–92), architect, one of four Scottish brothers. He developed a character-istic style in planning and decoration and his achievements in interior design include Hare-wood House, Yorks.; Osterley Park, Middlesex; Syon House, Middlesex; Kedleston Hall, Derbyshire; Luton Hoo, Bedfordshire; and Kenwood. *See* Neo-Classical Style, Section L.

Adams, John (1735–1826), succeeded Washington as president of the U.S.A. He was the first of the republic's ambassadors to England.

Adams, John Couch (1819–92), English mathe-matician and astronomer. He shared credit for the discovery of the planet Neptune (1846) with the French astronomer Leverrier, working independently.

Adams, Samuel (1722–1803), American revolution-ary statesman, b. Boston. He advocated "no taxation without representation" as early as 1765; promoted the "Boston tea-party"; and in 1776 signed the Declaration of Independence.

Adams, William (*c.* 1564–1620), navigator, b. Gillingham, Kent; the first Englishman to visit Japan. He found favour with the shogun Ieyasu, and an English and Dutch trading settlement was established till 1616.

Addams, Jane (1860–1935), American sociologist who founded Hull House, Chicago, in 1889.

Addison, Joseph (1672–1719), writer and Whig politician. He contributed to the *Tatler*, and was co-founder with Steele of the *Spectator*.

Adelard of Bath (*c.* 1090–*c.* 1150), English mathe-matician who translated into Latin the *Arith-metic* of Al-Kwarizmi and so introduced the Arabic numerals to the West (*see* L7).

Adenauer, Konrad (1876–1967), chancellor of the West German Federal Republic, 1949–63; founder and chairman of the Christian Democra-tic Party, 1945–66. To a defeated Germany he gave stable constitutional government and a place in the Western alliance. He promoted reconciliation with France but resisted accom-modation with Russia.

Adler, Alfred (1870–1937), Austrian psychiatrist, founder of the school of individual psychology. An earlier pupil of Freud, he broke away in 1911, rejecting the emphasis on sex, regarding man's main problem as a struggle for power to com-pensate for feelings of inferiority. *See* Adlerian psychology, Section J.

Adrian, 1st Baron (Edgar Douglas Adrian) (1889–1977), English physiologist. He shared with Sherrington the 1932 Nobel Prize for medicine for work on the electrical nature of the nerve impulse, Pres. Royal Society 1950–5; Pres. British Association 1954; Chancellor Leicester Univ. 1958–71; Chancellor Cambridge Univ. 1967–75; O.M. 1942.

Adrian IV (Nicholas Breakspear) (d. 1159), pope 1154–50, the only English pope, b. near St. Albans. He crowned Frederick Barbarossa Holy Roman Emperor. Granted overlordship of Ireland to Henry II.

Aeschylus (524–456 B.C.), founder of Greek tragic drama. Of the many plays he wrote, only seven have come down to us, including *The Seven against Thebes*, *Prometheus Bound*, and a trilogy on Orestes.

Aesop (? 6th cent. B.C.), semi-legendary fabulist, originally a slave. The fables attributed to him probably have many origins.

Agassiz, Louis (1807–73), Swiss-American em-bryologist, author of *Lectures on Comparative Embryology*, intended for laymen, *Researches on Fossil Fishes*, and *Studies on Glaciers*. He was an opponent of Darwinian evolution.

Agricola, Gnaeus Julius (37–93), Roman governor of Britain, who subdued the country except for the Scottish highlands. His son-in-law Tacitus wrote his life.

Agrippa, Marcus Vipsanius (63–12 B.C.), Roman general.

Ahmad Khan, Sir Syed (1817–98), Indian educa-tionist and social reformer who founded what is now the Aligarh Muslim University.

Airy, Sir George Biddell (1801–92), English mathe-matician who was astronomer royal for over 40 years, 1835–81. He set up a magnetic observatory at Greenwich.

Akbar, Jalal-ud-din Mohammed (1542–1605), Mogul emperor of India, son of Humayun. He extended the imperial power over much of India, stabilised the administration, promoted commerce and learning; and, though a Muslim, respected Hindu culture and tolerated Christian missions. His reign saw a flowering of Mogul culture.

Akhenaten, the name adopted by the heretic pharaoh **Amenhotep IV** (d. 1362 B.C.), who in-troduced a short-lived but influential religious and artistic reformation. He sought to convert his people from their polytheistic beliefs to a more compassionate religion based on the one supreme sun-god Aten (hence his name). His pacifism caused the temporary loss of most of Egypt's overseas territories. His wife was Nefertiti and he was succeeded by Tutankha-mun, who gave in to the conservative forces of the priesthood.

Alanbrooke, 1st Viscount (Alan Francis Brooke) (1883–1963), British field-marshal; chief of the imperial general staff 1941–46. Sir Arthur Bryant's *The Turn of the Tide* and *Triumph in the West* are based on his war diaries.

Alarcón, Pedro Antonio de (1833–91), Spanish novelist. His short story, *El Sombrero de tres picos* (The Three-Cornered Hat) became the subject of Falla's ballet and of Hugo Wolf's opera *Der Corregidor*.

Alaric I (376–410), Visigothic chief who, as first auxiliary to the Roman emperor Theodosius, later attacked the empire and sacked Rome in 410.

Alban, St. (d. *c.* 303), proto-martyr of Britain, con-verted by a priest to whom he had given shelter. He suffered under Diocletian at Verulam (now St. Albans), where in the 8th cent. King Offa of Mercia founded the abbey of that name.

Albert, Prince Consort (1819–61), son of the Duke of Saxe-Coburg-Gotha, married Queen Victoria in 1840. He helped the queen with political duties, projected the international exhibition of 1851, and in 1861 in a dispute with the United States advised a conciliatory attitude which averted war. He died of typhoid fever and is commemorated by the Albert Memorial in Kensington Gardens.

Albertus Magnus (Albert the Great) (1206–80), Dominican scholastic philosopher, b. Swabia. His interest in nature as an independent obser-ver marked the awakening of the scientific spirit. Among his pupils was Thomas Aquinas.

Alcibiades (*c.* 450–404 B.C.), Athenian general and statesman. Pupil and friend of Socrates, he was an egoist whose career brought Athens disaster. He was murdered in Phrygia.

Alcott, Louisa May (1832–88), American author of books for girls, notably *Little Women*.

Alcuin (735–804), English scholar, who settled on the Continent and helped Charlemagne with the promotion of education.

Aldred (d. 1069), Saxon archbishop of York who crowned William the Conqueror.

Aldrich, Henry (1647–1710), English composer of church music, theologian and architect. He designed Peckwater quadrangle at Christ Church, the chapel of Trinity College, and All Saints' Church, Oxford, and wrote the "Bonny Christ Church bells."

Alekhine, Alexander (1892–1946), world chess champion, 1927–35, 1937–46. He was born in Moscow but later became a French citizen.

Alembert, Jean le Rond d' (1717–83), French mathematician and philosopher, one of the encyclopaedists, a leading representative of the Enlightenment.

Alexander of Tunis, Earl (Harold Leofric George Alexander) (1891–1969), British field-marshal, b. Ireland. Directed retreat at Dunkirk 1940, and Burma 1942; C.-in-C. Allied Armies in Italy 1943–4; Supreme Allied Commander, Mediterranean 1944–5, Governor-general of Canada 1946–52.

Alexander II (1818–81), reforming Tsar of Russia, succeeded his father Nicholas in 1855. In 1861 he emancipated the serfs and in 1865 established provincial elective assemblies. Later his government became reactionary; he was assassinated by Nihilists; the pogroms followed.

Alexander the Great (356–323 B.C.), Greek conqueror. Educated by Aristotle, he succeeded his father Philip as king of Macedon in 336 B.C. He led the Greek states against Persia; and, crossing the Hellespont, he defeated Darius and sacked Persepolis. He captured Egypt and founded Alexandria. He penetrated to India. D. at Babylon.

Alexandra, Queen (1844–1925), daughter of Christian IX of Denmark, married the Prince of Wales (afterwards Edward VII) 1863.

Alfieri, Vittorio, Count (1749–1803), Italian poet and dramatist.

Alfonso the Wise (1221–84), king of León and Castile, known for his code of laws and his planetary tables. He caused the first general history of Spain to be written. Dethroned 1282.

Alfred the Great (849–99), king of Wessex who became a national figure. From the outset he had to repel Danish invaders. After years of effort he won the battle of Ethandun (Edington), and subsequently, probably in 886, made peace with Guthrum, leaving to the Danes the north and east. He built ships, was an able administrator, and promoted education, his own translations from the Latin being part of the earliest English literature.

Al-Kwarizimi (fl. c. 830), Persian mathematician said to have given algebra its name.

Allenby, 1st Viscount (Edmund Henry Hynman Allenby) (1861–1936), British general. He served on the Western front 1914–16, commanded in Palestine 1917–18, capturing Jerusalem on 9 December 1917.

Allende, Salvador (1908–73), Chilean radical leader, a Marxist democrat, who won the presidency 1970. He tried to bring social reform by democratic means but met his death resisting the military coup in which it is alleged the American CIA played a role.

Alleyne, Edward (1566–1626), actor and founder of Dulwich College.

Al-Mamun (1813–33), caliph of Baghdad, son of Harun-al-Rashid. He built an observatory at Baghdad where observations were long recorded.

Ampère, André Marie (1775–1836), French physicist who propounded the theory that magnetism is the result of molecular electric currents. The unit of electric current is named after him.

Amundsen, Roald (1872–1928), Norwegian explorer, the first to navigate the north-west passage and to reach the south pole. Sailing in the fishing smack *Gjoa*, he made the north-west passage in 3 years, 1903–6, and in 1911 sailed to the Antarctic in the *Fram*, reaching the pole on 14 December 1911, a month before his English rival Scott. His attempt to rescue Nobile after

his crash in the airship *Italia* cost him his life.

Anacreon (c. 569–475 B.C.), Greek lyric poet.

Anaxagoras (488–428 B.C.), Ionian philosopher who came to Athens about 464 B.C. and inspired Pericles and the poet Euripides with his love of science. His rational theories outraged religious opinion.

Anaximander (611–547 B.C.), Miletan philosopher, pupil of Thales, the first among the Greeks to make geographical maps, and to speculate on the origin of the heavenly bodies. He introduced the sundial from Babylon or Egypt.

Anaximenes (b. c. 570 B.C.), the last of the Miletan school founded by Thales. For him the primal substance was air. He was the first to see the differences between substances in quantitative terms.

Andersen, Hans Christian (1805–75), Danish writer, especially of fairy tales such as *The Little Mermaid* and *The Ugly Duckling*.

Anderson, Elizabeth Garrett (1836–1917), one of the first English women to enter the medical profession. She practised in London for many years and later became mayor of Aldeburgh, her native town, the first woman to hold the office of mayor. Sister of **Millicent Garrett Fawcett**.

Andrea del Sarto (1487–1531), Italian painter, b. Florence, the son of a tailor. Known as the "faultless painter," his chief works are the frescoes of the Annunziata at Florence and his Holy Families. He died of the plague.

Andrée, Salomon August (1854–97), Swedish explorer who attempted in 1897 to reach the north pole by balloon. In 1930 a Norwegian scientific expedition discovered the remains of the Andrée expedition on White Island.

Andrew, St., one of the apostles of Jesus, brother of Simon Peter, whose festival is observed on 30 November. He became the patron saint of Scotland in the 8th cent.

Andrewes, Sir Christopher (1896–1988), British medical researcher. Prominent virologist. Helped discover the common cold virus. Director, World Influenza Centre until 1961.

Andropov, Yuri Vladimirovich (1914–84), Russian statesman. Counsellor, subsequently Ambassador, to Hungary, 1953–7. Chairman, State Security Committee (K.G.B.), 1967–82. Succeeded Brezhnev as Secretary-General of C.P.S.U., 1982; State President, 1983–84.

Angelico, Fra (1387–1455), Italian painter. An exquisite colourist, Fra Giovanni (his Dominican name) painted especially religious frescoes, mainly at Florence and Rome.

Ångström, Anders Jöns (1814–74), Swedish physicist who studied heat, magnetism, and spectroscopy; hence the ångström unit used for measuring the wavelength of light.

Anne, Queen (1665–1714), Queen of Gt. Britain and Ireland. A daughter of James II, she succeeded William III in 1702. The act of union with Scotland was passed in 1707. A well-intentioned woman without marked ability, she was influenced by favourites, at first by the Duchess of Marlborough, but in the main she was guided by Tory and high church principles (she established Queen Anne's Bounty to improve church finances). Her reign was notable for literary output (Swift, Pope, Addison, Steele, Defoe), developments in science (Newton), architecture (Wren, Vanbrugh), and for the Duke of Marlborough's victories in war.

Anouilh, Jean (1910–87), French dramatist, whose plays with various settings—classical, historical and contemporary—include *Eurydice, Antigone, The Lark, Becket, The Fighting Cock*.

Anselm, St. (1033–1109), Italian scholar who succeeded Lanfranc as archbishop of Canterbury.

Anson, 1st Baron (George Anson) (1697–1762), English admiral who sailed round the world 1740–44, his squadron being reduced during the voyage from seven ships to one. An account was compiled by his chaplain.

Antoninus Pius (86–161), Roman emperor, successor of Hadrian. In his reign, which was peaceful, the Antonine wall built between the Forth and the Clyde was built to protect Britain from northern attack.

Antonius Marcus (Mark Antony) (c. 83–30 B.C.), Roman triumvir. He supported Caesar, and after the latter's death was opposed by Brutus and Cassius, and defeated by Octavian; committed suicide. His association with the Egyptian queen Cleopatra is the subject of Shakespeare's play.

Antony, St. (c. 251–356), early promoter of the monastic life. B. in Upper Egypt, he retired into the desert, where he was tempted, but attracted disciples and founded a monastery. Took part in the Council of Nicaea 325. (From his supposed help against erysipelas derives its name of St. Antony's fire.)

Apelles, 4th cent. B.C., Greek painter whose chief paintings, which have not survived, were of Alexander the Great holding a thunderbolt and of Aphrodite rising from the sea.

Apollinaire, Guillaume (Wilhelm Apollinaris Kostrowitzi) (1880–1918), French poet representative of the restless and experimental period in the arts before the first world war. He invented the term *surrealism* (*see* **Section L**). B. Rome of Polish extraction.

Apollonius of Perga (fl. 220 B.C.), Greek mathematician of the Alexandrian school, remembered for his conic sections; introduced the terms *ellipse, parabola*, and *hyperbola*.

Apollonius Rhodius (fl. 250 B.C.), scholar and poet of Alexandria and Rhodes, librarian at Alexandria. His epic *Argonautica* is about the Argonaut heroes.

Appert, Nicholas (1752–1841), sometimes known as François Appert, invented the method of preserving animal and vegetable foods by means of hermetically sealed cans or tins, and paved the way for the creation of a vast world industry.

Appleton, Sir Edward Victor (1892–1965), English physicist, best known as the discoverer of the ionised region of the upper atmosphere which became known as the Appleton layer. His researches led to the development of radar. Nobel prizewinner 1947.

Aquinas, Thomas, St. (c. 1225–74), scholastic philosopher and Dominican friar of Italian birth, whose philosophico-theological system (called Thomism) is still accepted by Catholic ecclesiastics. He understood Aristotle well and interpreted his thought in accord with Christian teaching. His most important works are *Summa contra Gentiles* and *Summa theologica*. *See also* **God and Man, Section J**.

Arago, Dominique François Jean (1786–1853), French astronomer and physicist, remembered for his discoveries in electromagnetism and optics.

Archimedes (287–212 B.C.), Greek mathematician, b. Syracuse, son of an astronomer; remembered for his contributions to pure mathematics, mechanics, and hydrostatics, notably the Archimedean screw for raising water, the conception of specific gravity, the doctrine of levers, and the measurement of curved areas. Not less than his scientific knowledge was his practical skill. He was killed by the Romans in the siege of Syracuse.

Argand, Aimé (1755–1803), Swiss physician, inventor of the lamp bearing his name, which was the first to admit a current of air to increase the power of the flame, by use of a chimney glass and circular wick.

Ariosto, Ludovico (1474–1533), Italian poet, author of *Orlando Furioso*.

Aristides (d. c. 468 B.C.), Athenian general and statesman, called "the just"; fought at Marathon.

Aristippus (c. 435–356 B.C.), founder of the Cyrenaic school of philosophy. He taught that man should aim at pleasure, but held that the pleasant was identical with the good.

Aristophanes (c. 444–c. 385 B.C.), Greek dramatist and comic poet, who satirised Athenian life. Among his plays are *The Clouds* and *The Birds*.

Aristotle (384–322 B.C.), Greek philosopher, pupil of Plato, after whose death in 347 he left Athens to become tutor to the young prince Alexander of Macedon. Subsequently at Athens he established his famous school in the garden known as the *Lyceum*, where he lectured in the *peripatos* (cloister) which gave his school of philosophy its name *Peripatetic*. He took the whole field of knowledge as his subject, giving it unity, and providing a philosophy which held its own for 2,000 years.

Arkwright, Sir Richard (1732–92), English inventor. A native of Preston, and originally a barber, he experimented with cotton-spinning machines. His "water frame" (run by water power), patented in 1769, was an early step in the industrial revolution. In 1790 he made use of Boulton and Watt's steam-engine. Rioters sacked one of his mills in 1779.

Armstrong, Neil (b. 1930), American astronaut, the first man to set foot on the moon, 21 July 1969.

Arne, Thomas Augustine (1710–78), English composer, remembered for *Rule, Britannia!* (from a masque called *Alfred*), and for Shakespearean songs such as *Where the Bee Sucks*. He also wrote operas (women singers appeared in *Judith* in 1761) and oratorios.

Arnold, Thomas (1795–1842), English headmaster, whose influence at Rugby (1828–42) gave it a high position among public schools.

Arrhenius, Svante August (1859–1927), Swedish chemist, one of the founders of modern physical chemistry. Received 1903 Nobel prize for originating the theory of electrolytic dissociation (ionisation).

Artaxerxes, the name borne by several ancient Persian kings. The first Artaxerxes, son of Xerxes, reigned 464–424 B.C.; he was succeeded by Darius II 424–404 B.C., who was followed by Artaxerxes II, who reigned until 358 B.C. Artaxerxes III, the last to bear the name, was a cruel and treacherous man and was poisoned in 338 B.C.

Arthur (c. 500), fabled Celtic warrior, whose feats, although referred to in passing in early Celtic writings, were first narrated in Geoffrey of Monmouth's *Historia* (c. 1135). In mediaeval times his legend developed an extensive literature, woven together by Sir Thomas Malory in his *Morte d'Arthur*, printed in 1485. Excavations have recently been carried out at South Cadbury, Somerset, the supposed site of his seat, Camelot.

Arundel, Thomas (1353–1414), archbishop of Canterbury 1396, and for a time lord chancellor. An enemy of heresy, he persecuted the Lollards.

Aske, Robert, (c. 1500–37), leader of the Pilgrimage of Grace 1536, directed against the Henrician Reformation; executed 1537.

Asoka (c. 269–232 B.C.), Indian emperor and upholder of Buddhism. At first he expanded his empire by conquest, but on being converted to Buddhism rejected war and aimed at the good of his people. He sent Buddhist missionaries as far as Sri Lanka and Syria. Art flourished, and many rock inscriptions commemorate his doings.

Asquith, Herbert Henry, 1st Earl of Oxford and Asquith (1852–1928), Liberal prime minister 1908–16, having previously served under Gladstone. His government enacted social reforms including old-age pensions (1908) and unemployment insurance (1911), but as a war minister he had to give way to Lloyd George. He resigned leadership of his party in 1926. His daughter Violet (1887–1969), an eloquent speaker, was created a life peeress in 1964.

Asser, a Welsh monk of the 9th cent., traditionally author of a life of King Alfred.

Astor, John Jacob (1763–1848), founder of the millionaire family, was a native of Heidelberg, emigrated to America, and made a fortune by trading in fur.

Astor, Viscountess (Nancy Witcher Astor, *née* Langhorne) (1879–1964), the first woman M.P. to take her seat in the House of Commons, an American by birth, wife of the 2nd Viscount Astor.

Atatürk, Kemal (1881–1938), builder of modern Turkey. A fine soldier, he defended the Dardanelles against the British in 1915 and drove the Greeks out of Turkey in 1922. President of the Turkish Republic, and virtually dictator, 1923–38.

Athanasius, St. (296–373), upholder of the doctrine of the Trinity against Arius, who denied the divinity of Christ. He was bishop of Alexandria. He is not now thought the author of the creed which bears his name.

Athelstan (895–940), grandson of Alfred the Great, was crowned king of England in 925, and was the first ruler of all England.

Attila (406–53), invading king of the Huns from Asia. He defeated the Roman Emperor Theodosius, and entered Gaul, but was defeated in 451 near Châlons-sur-Marne.

Attlee, 1st Earl (Clement Richard Attlee) (1883–1967), Labour prime minister 1945–51, having served as deputy to Churchill 1942–5. Called to the Bar in 1905, he lectured at the London School of Economics 1913–23, was mayor of

Stepney 1919, and parliamentary leader of his party 1935–55. His government helped to create a welfare society and granted independence to India. His writings include an autobiography, *As it Happened*, and *Empire into Commonwealth*.

Auchinleck, Sir Claude John Eyre (1884–1981), British field-marshal; G.O.C. North Norway 1940; C.-in-C. India 1941, 1943–7; Middle East 1941–2.

Auden, Wystan Hugh (1907–73), poet, b. in England and naturalised an American. Succeeded C. Day Lewis as professor of poetry at Oxford 1956–61.

Auer, Leopold (1845–1930), Hungarian violinist and teacher; Mischa Elman and Jascha Heifetz were among his pupils.

Augustine of Canterbury, St. (d. *c*. 605), first archbishop of Canterbury. He was sent from Rome in 597 by Gregory the Great to convert the English peoples.

Augustus, Caius Octavianus (63 B.C.–A.D. 14), first Roman emperor. Great-nephew of Julius Caesar, he was for 12 years triumvir with Mark Antony and Lepidus; then reigned alone. His reign was notable for peace, and for writers like Horace and Virgil; hence Augustan age for a great period in literature (the title Augustus was given him by the Senate).

Aurelius, Marcus Antonius. *See* Marcus Aurelius Antoninus.

Auriol, Vincent (1884–1966), French politician. He voted against surrender in 1940, was interned and escaped to London in 1943. President of the Fourth Republic 1947–54.

Aurangzeb (1618–1707), Mogul emperor of India. Son of Shah Jehan, he obtained power by acting against his father and brothers. In his long reign the Mogul empire reached its fullest extent; but he estranged Hindus and Sikhs; and when he died his authority was in dispute and the Mogul empire broke up.

Austen, Jane (1775–1817), author of *Emma*, *Mansfield Park*, *Northanger Abbey*, *Persuasion*, *Pride and Prejudice*, and *Sense and Sensibility*. Though confining herself to the personal relations of the English middle classes, she combined artistry, accuracy, imaginative power, satiric humour, sense, and genuine feeling with the ability to create a range of living characters. She spent the first 25 years of her life at her father's Hampshire rectory. She was unmarried.

Austin, 1st Baron (Herbert Austin) (1886–1941), English motor manufacturer, pioneer of the small car—the 7-horsepower car—which he put on the market in 1921.

Avenzoar (Ibn Zuhr) (*c*. 1090–1162), Arab physician, b. Seville. His chief work was the *Tasir*.

Averroës (Ibn Rushd) (1126–98), Arab philosopher, b. Córdova. He believed in the eternity of the world (not as a single act of creation as demanded by the current theology of Islam, Christianity and Judaism, but as a continuous process) and in the eternity of a universal intelligence, indivisible but shared in by all. He expounded Aristotle to his countrymen, but his teaching was modified by Neoplatonism. He was a friend of Avenzoar.

Avicenna (Ali ibn-Sina) (980–1037), Arab philosopher and physician, of Bukhara, whose influence on mediaeval Europe was chiefly through his *Canon of Medicine*, in which he attempted to systematise all the medical knowledge up to his time.

Avogadro, Amedeo (1776–1856), Italian physicist, remembered for his hypothesis, since known as Avogadro's Law, that equal volumes of gases under identical conditions of temperature and pressure contain the same number of molecules.

Avon, Earl of. *See* Eden, Anthony.

Ayrton, William Edward (1847–1908), English electrical engineer, inventor of a number of electrical measuring instruments. His first wife, **Matilda Chaplin Ayrton** (1846–83), was one of the first woman doctors, and his second wife, **Hertha Ayrton** (1854–1923), became known for her scientific work on the electric arc and sand ripples and for her work for woman suffrage.

Ayub Khan, Mohammed (1907–74), Pakistani military leader; president of Pakistan, 1958–69.

Azikiwe, Nnamdi (b. 1904), Nigerian statesman; president of Nigeria, 1963–6.

B

Babbage, Charles (1801–71), British mathematician. He designed an analytical engine, the forerunner of the modern digital computer.

Baber, Babar or Babur (Zahir ud-din Mohammed) (1483–1530), founder of the Mogul dynasty which ruled northern India for nearly three centuries; a descendant of Tamerlane.

Bach, Johann Sebastian (1685–1750), composer. B. at Eisenach, Germany, he was successively violinist, church organist, and chief court musician. It was as organist at the Thomaskirche, Leipzig, that he composed the St. Matthew and the St. John Passion and the B minor Mass. His work was in the school of the contrapuntal style (especially the fugue and the chorale); after his day it lost favour, but during the last century it has gained ground continually.

Bach, Karl Philipp Emmanuel (1714–88), 3rd son of the above, and one of the first experimenters in the symphonic and sonata forms.

Backhaus, Wilhelm (1884–1969), German pianist, gifted in interpreting classical and romantic concertos.

Bacon, Francis, Lord Verulam (1561–1626), English philosopher. He threw over Aristotelian deductive logic for the inductive method (*see* **Baconian method, Section J**); remembered for the impulse his writings gave to the foundation of the Royal Society (*c*. 1662). His chief work is the *Novum Organum*. His career as statesman under Elizabeth and James I was brought to an end by charges of corruption.

Bacon, Roger (*c*. 1219/20–94), founder of English philosophy, advocate of the value of observation and experiment in science. He first studied arts at Oxford but when he returned from lecturing in Paris he devoted himself to experimental science, especially alchemy and optics. He became a Franciscan friar in 1257. After his death he acquired a reputation for necromancy which was undeserved.

Baden-Powell, 1st Baron (Robert Stephenson Smyth Baden-Powell) (1857–1941), founder of Boy Scouts (1908) and Girl Guides (1910) to promote good citizenship in the rising generation; Chief Scout of the World 1921–41. As a young cavalry officer in the South African war he defended Mafeking.

Baer, Karl Ernst von (1792–1876), German naturalist, b. Estonia, founder of the science of embryology. He discovered the mammalian ovum (1827). An opponent of Darwin's theory.

Baffin, William (1584–1622), British navigator and explorer who in 1616 discovered the bay which separates the north-east coast of Canada from Greenland, which bears his name.

Bagehot, Walter (1826–77), English economist and journalist, editor of *The Economist*. Among his works are *The English Constitution*, *Physics and Politics*, and *Lombard Street*.

Baird, John Logie (1888–1946), Scottish television pioneer, inventor of the televisor and the noctovisor.

Baker, Sir Benjamin (1840–1907), English civil engineer. With Sir John Fowler he built the Forth bridge and the London Metropolitan railway. He designed the vessel which brought Cleopatra's Needle to London. In Egypt he was consulting engineer for the Aswan dam.

Baker, Sir Herbert (1862–1946), English architect who designed the Bank of England, Rhodes House, Oxford, and, with Sir E. Lutyens, New Delhi.

Bakst, Léon (1868–1924), Russian painter who designed scenery and costumes for Diaghilev's ballets.

Baldwin of Bewdley, 1st Earl (Stanley Baldwin) (1867–1947), Conservative prime minister, 1923–4, 1924–9, and 1935–7. His handling of the crisis over Edward VIII's proposed marriage ended with the king's abdication.

Balewa, Sir Abubakar Tafawa (1912–66), federal prime minister of Nigeria, 1960–6; murdered during the crisis of January 1966.

Balfour, 1st Earl (Arthur James Balfour) (1848–1930), statesman and writer. He was Conservative prime minister 1902–5. As foreign secretary under Lloyd George, he was responsible for a declaration on Palestine.

Ball, John (d. 1381), English priest and a leader of the Peasants' Revolt, after which he was executed. The couplet *When Adam delved, and Eve span, Who was then the gentleman?* is attributed to him.

Balliol, John de (d. 1269), founder of Balliol College, Oxford; a regent for Scotland; sided with Henry III against his barons.

Balliol, John de (1249–1315), king of Scotland. Son of the above, he claimed the throne against Robert Bruce and was chosen by the arbitrator, Edward I of England, whose overlordship he acknowledged. Later, on renouncing homage, he was taken captive and d. in retirement. His son Edward Balliol (d. 1363) obtained the kingdom for a time, acknowledging Edward III of England and surrendering Lothian; but retired on an annuity, 1356.

Balzac, Honoré de (1799–1850), French novelist of wide influence, and author of over eighty novels to which he gave the covering title of *La Comédie Humaine*, depicting the appetites and passions of the new social class born of the revolution and Napoleon.

Bancroft, Sir Squire (1841–1926), Victorian actor-manager.

Bandaranaike, Solomon West Ridgway Dias (1899–1959), socialist prime minister of Ceylon from 1956 until his assassination in 1959. His widow, **Mrs Sirimavo Bandaranaike** (b. 1916) became the world's first woman premier, 1960–5, 1970–7.

Banks, Sir Joseph (1743–1820), an amateur scientist of wealth who accompanied Captain Cook on his expedition to the Pacific 1768–76. He left botanical collections to the British Museum.

Banting, Sir Frederick Grant (1891–1941), Canadian physician who with C. H. Best discovered insulin.

Bantock, Sir Granville (1868–1946), composer of songs, orchestral and choral music.

Barbarossa (Ital. = red beard), surname of two brothers who were Barbary pirates: **Uruz** (*c.* 1474–1518), was killed by Spaniards, and **Khaireddin** (*c.* 1483–1546) conquered Tunis for the Turks and died in Constantinople.

Barbirolli, Sir John (1899–1970), conductor of the Hallé Orchestra 1943–70; succeeded Toscanini as conductor of the New York Philharmonic Symphony Orchestra 1937–42.

Barbusse, Henri (1874–1935), French writer, author of the war novel *Le Feu*, which portrays in a starkly vivid way the experience of the common soldier.

Barham, Richard Harris (1788–1845), English humorist, author of *The Ingoldsby Legends*, written under his pen-name of Thomas Ingoldsby. His best-known poem is *The Jackdaw of Rheims*.

Barnardo, Thomas John (1845–1905), founder of homes for orphan-waifs; devoted himself to the protection, education, and advancement of destitute children.

Barrie, Sir James Matthew (1860–1937), Scottish author and dramatist. His novels include *A Window in Thrums*. Among his plays are *Dear Brutus*, *The Admirable Crichton*, and *Peter Pan* which gained great popularity with children.

Barrow, Isaac (1630–77), divine and mathematician, tutor of Sir Isaac Newton.

Barry, Sir Charles (1795–1860), architect of the houses of parliament at Westminster, the details of which were contributed by his assistant A. W. Pugin.

Barth, Karl (1886–1968), Swiss theologian, described by the late Pope John as a Protestant St. Thomas Aquinas.

Bartók, Bela (1881–1945), Hungarian composer. From an early age he was deeply interested in folk-song which inspired his researches into Hungarian and Rumanian peasant music. He left for America in 1940, where he lived precariously and apparently unhappily until the end of the war made a return possible, regrettably too late. *See* **Section E**.

Bartolommeo, Fra (di Paolo) (1475–1517), Italian painter. At first influenced by Savonarola, he later resumed painting. Some of his best work is at Lucca.

Bartolozzi, Francesco (1725–1815), Italian engraver, who settled in England and became a founder-member of the Royal Academy; noted for his stipple engravings.

Bashkirtseva, Maria Konstantinovna (1859–84), a Russian girl, achieved eminence as a painter in Paris, author of a famous diary.

Bassi, Agostino (1773–1856), Italian amateur microscopist who first suggested that infectious diseases might be caused by the invasion of the body by micro-organisms.

Batten, Jean Gardiner (b. 1909), New Zealand airwoman who flew solo from England to Australia in 1934.

Baudelaire, Charles Pierre (1821–67), French poet of originality and sensitivity, best known for his *Les Fleurs du Mal*. His life was darkened by poverty and ill-health. He was also a talented draughtsman.

Bax, Sir Arnold (1883–1953), composer of piano compositions, songs, and chamber works.

Baxter, Richard (1615–91), noncomformist divine, b. Shropshire; author of many books on theology; imprisoned after the Restoration by Judge Jeffreys.

Bayard, Pierre de Terrail, Seigneur de (*c.* 1474–1524), French knight, known as the "chevalier sans peur et sans reproche." He fought in campaigns against Italy and fell at the battle of Romagnano.

Bayle, Pierre (1647–1706), French philosopher, author of the *Dictionnaire historique et critique* (1697). His sceptical views influenced Voltaire and the encyclopedists of the 18th cent.

Baylis, Lilian Mary (1874–1937), manager of the Old Vic theatre from 1898 and of Sadler's Wells from 1931.

Beardsley, Aubrey Vincent (1872–98), black-and-white artist, who published much work, some of it controversial (as in the *Yellow Book*).

Beatles, The (Paul McCartney (b. 1942), John Lennon (1940–80), George Harrison (b. 1943), Ringo Starr (b. 1940)), a Liverpool pop group whose highly original and melodic songs held the attention of youth all over the world, especially during the period 1963–5 when they were in their prime. They parted in 1971 and went their separate ways. Lennon was shot dead in New York in 1980.

Beatty, 1st Earl (David Beatty) (1871–1936), British admiral; succeeded Jellicoe as commander of the Grand Fleet 1916–19. Commanding the British battlecruisers, he fought the German fleet on 28 August 1914 in the Heligoland Bight, and on 31 May 1916 off Jutland.

Beaufort, Sir Francis (1774–1857), hydrographer of the navy, who introduced the wind scale (1805) which bears his name. *See* **Section Z**.

Beaumont, Francis (1584–1616), and **Fletcher, John** (1579–1625), joint authors of many plays, including *The Maid's Tragedy* and *Philaster*.

Beaverbrook, 1st Baron (William Maxwell Aitken) (1879–1964), British newspaper owner and politician, a Canadian by birth. He gave energetic service as minister of aircraft production 1940–1. He controlled the *Daily Express*, *Sunday Express*, and *Evening Standard*, which sponsored his political campaigns.

Becket, Thomas (1118?–70), saint and martyr. An able chancellor, 1155–62, on becoming archbishop of Canterbury he made the position of the church his first care; and, coming into conflict with Henry II, was murdered in Canterbury cathedral. His shrine became a place of pilgrimage.

Beckett, Samuel (1906–89), Anglo-Irish dramatist and novelist, b. Dublin. Plays include *Waiting for Godot*, *Endgame*, *Krapp's Last Tape*, *Happy Days*, *Not I*; novels include *The Nouvelles* (3 stories), the trilogy: *Molloy*, *Malone Dies*, *The Unnamable*, and *How It Is*. His work expresses man's isolation, bewilderment and suffering. Nobel Prize for Literature, 1969.

Becquerel, Antoine Henri (1852–1908), French physicist who in 1896 discovered radioactivity in uranium. Shared with the Curies the 1903 Nobel prize in physics.

Bede, the Venerable (673–735), English historian and scholar; lived at Jarrow. His chief work is his *Ecclesiastical History* to 731.

Beecham, Sir Thomas (1879–1961), English conductor and impresario. Founded the London Philharmonic Orchestra in 1931; introduced into England the operas of Richard Strauss, Russian operas, and the Diaghilev ballet; championed the music of Delius.

Beecher, Henry Ward (1813–87), American preacher whose church was at Brooklyn.

Beerbohm, Sir Max (1872–1956), critic and caricaturist, master of irony and satire. His works include *Zuleika Dobson* and *A Christmas Garland*, and he contributed to the *Saturday Review*.

Beethoven, Ludwig van (1770–1827), composer. B. at Bonn (his father being a tenor singer at the Elector's court), at 17 he went to Vienna, was recognised by Mozart, and eventually settled there; he never married; gradually he became deaf. In the development from simplicity to complexity of musical treatment, he stands midway between Mozart and Wagner; but in him were uniquely combined the power to feel and the mastery of musical resources necessary to express his feelings. Between the years 1805 and 1808 he composed some of his greatest works: the oratorio *Mount of Olives*, the opera *Fidelio*, and the *Pastoral* and *Eroica* symphonies besides a number of concertos, sonatas, and songs. The symphonies, nine in number, rank as the greatest ever written. See **Section E**.

Begin, Menachem (b. 1913), b. Poland; active in Zionist movement since youth; leader of Israeli *Likud* party; prime minister 1977–83. Made peace with Egypt (1979) but failed to solve Palestinian problem; took Israel into war in Lebanon (1982) which led to the end of his premiership and to renewed conflict in that country. Nobel Peace Prize 1978. See **Section C**.

Behring, Emil von (1854–1917), German bacteriologist, founder of the science of immunology. Nobel prizewinner 1901.

Behring, Vitus (1680–1741), Danish navigator who entered the Russian service and in 1728 discovered the strait which bears his name.

Belisarius (505–65), Roman general under Justinian who fought against the Vandals.

Bell, Alexander Graham (1847–1922), inventor, b. Edinburgh, emigrated to Canada in 1870, later becoming an American citizen. In 1876 he exhibited an invention which was developed into the telephone. He devoted attention to the education of deaf-mutes.

Bell, Gertrude Margaret Lowthian (1868–1926), the "uncrowned queen of Arabia," was a traveller in the Middle East; her knowledge proved of service to the British government in the first world war.

Bellini, family of Venetian painters: **Jacopo** (c. 1400–70) and his two sons, **Gentile** (1429–1507), whose works include the *Adoration of the Magi* (National Gallery); and **Giovanni** (c. 1429–1516), brother-in-law of Mantegna, and teacher of Giorgione and Titian.

Belloc, Hilaire (1870–1953), versatile writer whose works include *The Bad Child's Book of Beasts*, *The Path to Rome*, *Hills and the Sea*, *Cautionary Tales*, and historical studies of Danton, Robespierre, and Richelieu. B. in France, he became a British subject in 1902.

Bellow, Saul (b. 1915), American novelist and short-story writer, author of *Adventures of Augie March*, *Henderson the Rain King*, *Herzog*, *Mr. Sammler's Planet* and *Humboldt's Gift*. Nobel prizewinner 1976.

Belzoni, Giovanni Battista (1778–1823), Egyptologist. B. at Padua, he settled in England in 1803. His first interest was in hydraulics, and for this purpose he went to Egypt to Mehemet Ali. There he explored Thebes, Abu Simbel, and one of the pyramids, sending some sculptures to the British Museum.

Benavente y Martinez, Jacinto (1866–1954), Spanish dramatist, whose plays include *Los Intereses Creados* (Bonds of Interest). Nobel prizewinner 1922.

Benedict, St. (c. 480–c. 550), patriarch of western monasticism. B. at Nursia, and at first a hermit at Subiaco, he attracted numerous followers and grouped them in twelve monasteries. Later he went to Monte Cassino, where he formulated the Benedictine rule, of wide application in Western Christendom.

Beneš, Eduard (1884–1948), Czechoslovak statesman; co-founder with Thomas Masaryk of the Czech Republic after the break-up of the Austro-Hungarian monarchy (1918).

Ben Gurion, David (1886–1973), Zionist leader. He helped organise the Jewish Legion in 1918, and was prominently connected with the Labour movement in Palestine in between the world wars. Prime minister of Israel 1948–63.

Bennett, (Enoch) Arnold (1867–1931), English author, who wrote of the pottery towns where

he was brought up. His novels include *Clayhanger* and *Hilda Lessways*.

Bennett, James Gordon (1841–1918), proprietor of the *New York Herald*. He sent out Stanley on an expedition to find Livingstone.

Bennett, Sir William Sterndale (1816–75), English composer, pianist and teacher, best known for his oratorio *The Woman of Samaria*, songs and piano pieces. Founded the Bach Society.

Bentham, Jeremy (1748–1832), utilitarian philosopher and writer on jurisprudence. His main works are *Government* and *Principles of Morals and Legislation*.

Bentley, Richard (1662–1742), classical scholar who did pioneer work in textual criticism.

Benz, Karl (1844–1929), German engineer whose motor car produced in 1885 was one of the first to be driven by an internal combustion engine.

Beresford, 1st Viscount (William Carr Beresford) (1768–1854), British general. He fought under Wellington in the Peninsular War and reorganised the Portuguese army.

Berg, Alban (1885–1935), Austrian composer whose best-known work is the three-act opera *Wozzeck*, based upon a drama by Büchner, which has become a modern classic.

Bergson, Henri Louis (1859–1941). French philosopher, exponent of the theory of creative evolution and the life force. Nobel prizewinner 1927. See **Vitalism, Section J**.

Bériot, Charles Auguste de (1802–70), Belgian violinist, whose wife was the operatic contralto Malibran. His son, **Charles Wilfrid de Bériot** (1833–1914) was a pianist and the teacher of Ravel.

Berkeley, George (1685–1753), idealist philosopher and critic of Locke. His spiritual outlook led him to believe that reality exists only in the eye of God, that it is undiscoverable by science, though it can be revealed by religion. His chief work is *Alciphron*. He was a master of prose. Of Irish birth, he became bishop of Cloyne.

Berlin, Irving (1888–1989), American composer of popular songs, b. Russia; pioneer of both ragtime and jazz music. Celebrated his 100th birthday, 1988.

Berlin, Sir Isaiah (b. 1909), British philosopher, b. Riga; Chichele Prof. of Social and Political Theory at Oxford 1957–67. His works include *Karl Marx*, *The Hedgehog and the Fox*, and *The Age of Enlightenment*. O.M. (1971).

Berlioz, Hector (1803–69), composer. B. near Grenoble, the son of a doctor, his romantic sensibility, taste for the grand (as in his *Requiem*), and response to literary influence made him a prime figure in the French romantic movement. His works include the symphony *Romeo and Juliet*, and the operas *Benvenuto Cellini* and *Beatrice and Benedict*. See **Section E**.

Bernadotte, Count Folke (1895–1948), nephew of the late King Gustav of Sweden. U.N. mediator for Palestine 1947. Assassinated by Jewish terrorists.

Bernadotte, Jean Baptiste (1764–1844), a French commander who served under Napoleon, and in 1810 was chosen heir to the throne of Sweden. In 1818 he succeeded as Charles XIV.

Bernal, John Desmond (1901–71), physicist, b. Ireland. Prof. of Physics, Birkbeck College, Univ. of London, 1937–63; Prof of Crystallography, 1963–8. Author of *The Social Functions of Science*, *Science in History*, *The Origin of Life*. Lenin peace prize 1953.

Bernard, Claude (1813–78), French physiologist whose discoveries though not of immediate application paved the way for the work of Pavlov and Hopkins.

Bernard of Menthon (923–1008), patron saint of mountaineers. He founded Alpine hospices in the passes that bear his name.

Bernard, St. (1090–1153), abbot of Clairvaux, which became a chief centre of the Cistercian order. This order aimed at seclusion and austerity, and practised manual work. His writings had wide influence in Europe.

Bernhardt, Sarah (1844–1923), French tragedienne, b. Paris, daughter of Dutch jewess. She became a member of the Comédie Française after the siege of Paris. Her first performance in London was in 1879. Her successes included *Phèdre*, *La Dame aux Camélias*, *Fédora*, *Théodora*, and *La Tosca*, and she produced and played in Racine and Molière.

Berthelot, Marcellin Pierre Eugène (1827–1907), French chemist and politician. He was the first to produce organic compounds synthetically.

Berzelius, Jöns Jakob (1779–1848), Swedish chemist, founder of electrochemical theory. His work was mainly concerned with the exact determination of atomic and molecular weights and he devised the system of chemical symbols in use today.

Bessemer, Sir Henry (1813–98), inventor of the process of converting cast-iron direct into steel. This revolutionised steel manufacture, reducing the cost of production and extending its use.

Best, Charles Herbert (1899–1978), Canadian physiologist, who with F. G. Banting discovered the use of insulin in the treatment of diabetes.

Betjeman, Sir John (1906–84), English poet, author and broadcaster; Poet Laureate from 1972 until his death in May 1984.

Bevan, Aneurin (1897–1960), British socialist politician, architect of the National Health Service which came into operation in 1948.

Beveridge, 1st Baron (William Henry Beveridge) (1879–1963), British economist who drew up the Beveridge Plan (1942), which formed the basis of the present social security services.

Bevin, Ernest (1881–1951), British trade union leader, who later became a forceful foreign secretary. He was assistant general secretary of the Dockers Union (his masterly advocacy of the London dockers' case in 1920 earned him the title of "the dockers' K.C."), later general secretary of the Transport and General Workers Union; Minister of Labour 1940–5, and Foreign Secretary 1945–51.

Beyle, Marie Henri. *See* Stendhal.

Bhave, Vinova (b. 1895), Indian reformer, leader of the Sarvodaya movement. A follower of Gandhi, in 1951 he began a walking mission to persuade landlords to help landless peasants.

Bichat, Marie François Xavier (1771–1802), French physiologist whose study of tissues founded modern histology. His theory was that life is "the sum of the forces that restrict death."

Biddle, John (1615–62), unitarian. He taught in Gloucester: was several times imprisoned for his controversial writings; and died of fever contracted in prison.

Binyon, Laurence (1869–1943), poet, art critic, and orientalist, who worked at the British Museum 1893–1933.

Birch, Samuel John Lamorna (1869–1955), English landscape painter in watercolour, known for his Cornish and Australian studies.

Birkbeck, George (1776–1841), founder of mechanics' institutes, first at Glasgow, later in London (the Birkbeck Institution developed into Birkbeck College, London University).

Birkenhead, 1st Earl of (Frederick Edwin Smith) (1872–1930), English lawyer and politician; lord chancellor 1919–22; secretary for India 1924–8.

Bishop, Sir Henry Rowley (1786–1855), English composer who wrote *Home, sweet Home*, glees, and operas.

Bismarck, Otto Eduard Leopold von, Prince Bismarck, Duke of Lauenburg (1815–98), Prusso-German diplomat and statesman, chief architect of the German empire. He was of Junker family. As Prussian ambassador at St. Petersburg (1859–62) and at Paris (1862), he learned to assess the European situation. He was recalled to Berlin by the king to become chief Prussian minister; and when the house of representatives would not pass a military bill he closed the house. He used a dispute over Schleswig-Holstein to bring about the defeat of Austria at Königgratz in 1866; and he provoked the Franco-Prussian war of 1870–1 when France was defeated at Sedan. Germany then became united under the military leadership of Prussia, with the king as emperor, instead of by the slower processes of democracy. He presided over the Berlin Congress of European powers in 1878. In 1884 he began a colonial policy. His authoritarian system, in spite of its inherent defects, was at least based on cautious and accurate assessment of power politics. This factor was not understood by William II, who succeeded as emperor in 1888, and dismissed the "iron chancellor" in 1890.

Bizet, Georges (1838–75), properly **Alexandre César Léopold**, French composer, chiefly remembered for his opera *Carmen*.

Björnson, Björnstjerne (1832–1910), Norwegian poet, dramatist and novelist. His work provides an image of Norwegian life from the period of the sagas (*Kong Sverre*) to contemporary problems (*Over Aevne*).

Black, Sir James (b. 1924), Eminent British scientist. Discovered life-saving drug used to prevent heart attacks. Awarded Nobel Prize for Medicine, 1988.

Black, Joseph (1728–90), Scottish chemist. A professor first at Glasgow, later at Edinburgh, he was the first to undertake a detailed study of a chemical reaction. He laid the foundation of the quantitative science of heat and his dis-covery of latent heat was applied by Watt in improving his steam-engine.

Blackett of Chelsea, Baron (Patrick Maynard Stuart Blackett) (1897–1974), British physicist whose work on nuclear and cosmic ray physics gained him a Nobel prize in 1948; author of *Military and Political Consequences of Atomic Energy* (1948), *Lectures on Rock Magnetism* (1956), *Studies of War* (1962). Pres. British Assoc. 1956; Pres. Royal Society 1966–70; O.M. 1967.

Blackmore, Richard Doddridge (1825–1900), English novelist and author of *Lorna Doone*.

Blackstone, Sir William (1723–80), English judge. His *Commentaries on the Laws of England* is a classic.

Blackwood, Algernon (1869–1951), English novelist and writer of short stories.

Blackwood, William (1776–1834), originator of *Blackwood's Magazine*.

Blair, Robert (1699–1746), Scottish poet, author of *The Grave*.

Blake, Robert (1599–1657), Parliamentary general and an admiral in the Cromwellian navy in the Dutch and Spanish wars.

Blake, William (1757–1827), English poet, mystic, and artist, son of a hosier in Carnaby market, Soho. A solitary and deeply religious man, he had a hatred of materialism. He produced his own books, engraving on copper plates both the text of his poems and the illustrations. His *Book of Job* is a masterpiece in line-engraving in metal, his poems range from the mystical and almost incomprehensible to the delightfully simple *Songs of Innocence*. He has been called "the great teacher of the modern western world." His art is in many ways reminiscent of that of the Spanish painter Goya.

Blanqui, Louis Auguste (1805–81), French revolutionary leader, master of insurrection. He invented the term "dictatorship of the proletariat," and his social theories, stressing the class struggle, influenced Marx. Active in 1830, 1848, and 1871, he spent 37 years in prison.

Blériot, Louis (1872–1936), French airman; the first to fly the English Channel from Calais to Dover, on 25 July 1909.

Bligh, William (1754–1817), sailor, b. Plymouth. He accompanied Cook 1772–4, and discovered bread-fruit; but was in 1789 cast adrift from *The Bounty* by his mutinous crew. As governor of New South Wales (1806) he fought to suppress the rum traffic.

Blind, Karl (1826–1907), German agitator, b. Mannheim. He was active in the German risings of 1848, and imprisoned; but escaped and settled in England, remaining in touch with men like Mazzini and Louis Blanc.

Bliss, Sir Arthur (1891–1975), English composer; succeeded Sir Arnold Bax as Master of the Queen's Musick 1953.

Bloch, Ernest (1880–1959), composer, whose music is characterised by Jewish and oriental themes. B. in Geneva, he became a naturalised American.

Blondin, Charles (1824–97), French rope performer, who crossed the Niagara Falls on a tight-rope.

Blücher, Gebhard Leberecht von (1742–1819), Prussian general. He fought against Napoleon, especially at Lützen and Leipzig; and he completed Wellington's victory at Waterloo by his timely arrival.

Blum, Léon (1872–1950), French statesman, leader of the French Socialist Party. His efforts strengthened the growth of the Popular Front and the campaign against appeasement of Hitler. He held office only briefly and was interned in Germany 1940–5.

Blumlein, Alan Dower (1903–42), British electronics engineer and inventor, chiefly remembered for his fundamental work on stereophony.

Blunden, Edmund Charles (1896–1974), English poet and critic; professor of poetry at Oxford 1966–8.

Blunt, Wilfrid Scawen (1840–1922), English poet and political writer who championed Egyptian, Indian, and Irish independence; imprisoned in 1888 for activities in the Irish Land League.

Boadicea (Boudicca), queen of the Iceni in eastern Britain, who fought against the Roman invaders, but was defeated in A.D. 61 and killed herself. Archaeologists in 1982 tentatively identified her palace at Gallows Hill, Thetford, Norfolk.

Boccaccio, Giovanni (1313–75), Italian author, father of the novel. He is chiefly known for his *Decameron* (set in the neighbourhood of Florence during the plague), and for his life of Dante.

Boccherini, Luigi (1743–1805), Italian cellist and composer of chamber music.

Bode, Johann Ehlert (1747–1826), German astronomer remembered for his theoretical calculation (known as Bode's law) of the proportionate distances of the planets from the sun.

Boethius (480–524), Roman scientific writer who translated the logical works of Aristotle and provided the dark ages with some elementary mathematical treatises.

Bohr, Niels Henrik David (1885–1962), Danish nuclear physicist whose researches into the structure of the atom gave him great authority in the world of theoretical physics. With Rutherford he applied the quantum theory to the study of atomic processes. Nobel prizewinner 1922.

Boieldieu, François Adrien (1775–1834), French composer especially of operas, including *La Dame blanche*.

Boileau-Despréaux, Nicolas (1636–1711), French literary critic and poet, best known for his *Satires*.

Boito, Arrigo (1842–1918), Italian poet and composer; he wrote the libretti of *Otello* and *Falstaff* for Verdi.

Boleyn, Anne (1507–36), queen of Henry VIII and mother of Queen Elizabeth. She was maid-in-waiting to Catherine of Aragon and her successor when Catherine's marriage was annulled. She failed to produce a male heir and was beheaded on a charge of adultery.

Bolivar, Simón (1783–1830), South American revolutionist, called the Liberator, b. Carácas. He led independence movements in the northwest of South America against Spanish rule, aiming at a South American federation. He founded Grand Colombia (now Venezuela, Colombia, Panama, Ecuador). Revered as a Latin-American hero.

Bonaventura, St. (1221–74), Franciscan theologian, b. Orvieto. His mystical theory of knowledge was in the Augustinian tradition.

Bondfield, Margaret Grace (1873–1953), as minister of Labour, 1929–31, she was the first woman to enter the cabinet and become a privy councillor.

Bondi, Sir Hermann (b. 1919), British mathematician and astronomer, b. Vienna: chief scientist to Min. of Defence, 1971–7.

Bone, Sir Muirhead (1876–1953), architectural draughtsman and etcher, b. Glasgow; excelled in dry-point and drawings of intricate scaffolding; official war artist in both world wars.

Bonheur, Rose (1822–99), French painter of animals.

Boniface, St. (680–754), apostle of Germany. B. at Crediton, Devon, his name being Wynfrith, he became a Benedictine monk, and went as missionary to Friesland, securing papal approval. He founded Fulda Abbey and became archbishop of Mainz, but was martyred.

Bonnard, Pierre (1867–1947), French painter of landscapes, still life, and nudes, a colourist and skilled draughtsman.

Booth, Edwin Thomas (1833–93), American Shakespearean actor, brother of John Wilkes Booth who assassinated President Lincoln.

Booth, William (1829–1912), founder and first general of the Salvation Army, b. Nottingham. In 1865, with the help of his wife, Catherine Booth, he began mission work in the East End of London, which led to the creation in 1878 of the Salvation Army on military lines. It developed branches in many parts of the world. His son Bramwell (d. 1929) and his daughter Evangeline were among his successors. *See also* **Salvation Army, Section J.**

Borges, Jorge Luis (1899–1986), Argentine poet, critic, and short story writer. Some of his work has been translated into English, including *A Personal Anthology* and *Labyrinths*.

Borgia, Caesar (1476–1507), Italian general. The son of Pope Alexander VI, at 17 he was suspected of murdering his brother. He became captain-general of the church, and made himself master of Romagna, the Marches, and Umbria. Banished by Pope Julius II he met his death fighting in Spain.

Borlaug, Norman Ernest (b. 1914), American wheat scientist, responsible for the "green revolution" (*see* **Section L**) which is transforming the agricultural prospects of the less-developed countries of the world. Nobel prize for peace 1970.

Borodin, Alexander Porfyrievich (1833–87), Russian composer who taught chemistry and founded a school of medicine for women. In a busy professional life he wrote two symphonies, two string quartets, the symphonic sketch *In the Steppes of Central Asia* and the opera *Prince Igor. See* **Section E.**

Borrow, George Henry (1803–81), English author, for many years agent for the British and Foreign Bible Society; in the course of his wanderings he studied gypsy life and wrote of his experiences in *Lavengro*, *Romany Rye*, *Bible in Spain*.

Bose, Subhas Chandra (1897–1945), Indian nationalist leader; killed in a plane crash.

Boswell, James (1740–95), Scottish author of *The Life of Dr. Johnson*, with whom he spent some years in intimacy. His own journals and letters recently published form an extensive literary collection.

Botha, Louis (1862–1919), South African soldier and statesman. In command of Transvaal forces 1899–1902 in the Boer war, he became prime minister of the Transvaal in 1907, and first premier of the Union of South Africa in 1910. In the 1914–18 war he conquered territory then under German rule.

Bottesini, Giovanni (1821–89), Italian double-bass player.

Botticelli, Sandro (c. 1445–1510), Italian painter. He worked under Fra Lippo Lippi, and was influenced by Savonarola. His art is delicate and poetic. His *Birth of Venus* is in the Uffizi Gallery, Florence, and his *Mars and Venus* in the National Gallery. He illustrated Dante's *Inferno*.

Bottomley, Horatio (1860–1933), English politician, journalist, and notorious financier, who died in poverty after serving a prison sentence for fraud.

Botvinnik, Mikhail (b. 1911), Russian chess player: world champion 1948–57, 1958–60, 1961–3. Retired 1965.

Boughton, Rutland (1878–1960), English composer of the opera *The Immortal Hour*, and writer on the history and philosophy of music.

Boult, Sir Adrian (1889–1983), conductor of the London Philharmonic Orchestra 1950–7, and of the B.B.C. Symphony Orchestra 1930–50. Musical Director B.B.C. 1930–42.

Boulton, Matthew (1728–1809), engineer who in partnership with James Watt manufactured steam-engines at his Soho works near Birmingham. He also minted a new copper coinage for Great Britain.

Bowdler, Thomas (1754–1825), issued for family reading expurgated editions of Shakespeare and Gibbon, hence the term "bowdlerise."

Boyce, William (1710–79), London organist and composer, who also collected the works of English church composers. He was master of the orchestra of George III.

Boyd Orr, 1st Baron (John Boyd Orr) (1880–1971), British physiologist and nutritional expert. Director-general World Food and Agriculture Organisation 1945–8. Chancellor Glasgow Univ. 1946. Nobel prizewinner 1949.

Boyle, Robert (1627–91), English scientist who with Robert Hooke laid the foundations of the modern sciences of chemistry and physics. He established the law which states that the volume of a gas varies inversely as the pressure upon it, provided temperature is constant. His chief work is the *Sceptical Chymist* (1661).

Bradley, Omar Nelson (1893–1981), American general. In the second world war he commanded in Tunis, Sicily, and Normandy.

Bradman, Sir Donald George (b. 1908), Australian cricketer who captained Australia in test matches against England 1936–48.

Bragg, Sir William Henry (1862–1942), English physicist. He held the chair of physics at Adelaide, Leeds, and London, and was professor of chemistry at the Royal Institution 1923–42. Pres. Royal Society 1935–40.

Bragg, Sir William Lawrence (1890–1971), son of the above. He succeeded Rutherford at the Cavendish laboratory, Cambridge, 1938–53. Dir. Royal Institution 1954–66. Shared with his father the 1915 Nobel prize for their fundamental work on X-rays and crystal structure.

Brahe, Tycho (1546–1601), Danish astronomer. At his island observatory at Uraniborg, provided by his sovereign, he carried out systematic observations which enabled Kepler to work out his planetary laws.

Brahms, Johannes (1833–97), composer. B. in Hamburg (son of a double-bass player). He was a friend of the Schumanns. *See* **Section E.**

Braille, Louis (1809–52), French educationist, who, as teacher of the blind, perfected his system of reading and writing for the blind. As the result of an accident when he was three years old he was himself blind.

Bramah, Joseph (1749–1814), English inventor of the safety-lock and hydraulic press which bear his name. He also invented the modern water-closet (1778) and a machine for printing the serial numbers on bank-notes.

Brandes, Georg Morris Cohen (1842–1927), Danish literary critic who exerted a vitalising influence on literature and art.

Brandt, Willy (b. 1913), first social democratic chancellor of the Federal Republic of Germany, 1969–74. His main achievements have been the Moscow and Warsaw treaties (1972) the treaty between E. and W. Germany (1973) which recognised their sovereign existence and the Brandt Report setting out a world development programme. Resigned party leadership, March 1987. *See* **Section C, Part II.**

Brangwyn, Sir Frank (1867–1956), artist of Welsh extraction, b. Bruges; first worked for William Morris making cartoons for textiles; he excelled in murals and in etching.

Breakspear, Nicholas. *See* **Adrian IV.**

Brecht, Bertolt (1898–1956), German dramatist and poet, b. Augsburg, whose brilliant experimental theatre was characteristic of the period in Germany between the two world wars. A Marxist, he left Nazi Germany in 1933 and returned after the war to direct the Berliner Ensemble in E. Berlin and develop his influential techniques of production. His plays include *The Threepenny Opera* (with music by Kurt Weill), *Mother Courage* and *The Caucasian Chalk Circle.* He may be regarded as the most original and vigorous dramatist and producer of this century.

Brennan, Louis (1853–1932), inventor, b. Ireland. His inventions include a gyro-directed torpedo and a mono-rail locomotive.

Breton, André (1896–1966), French poet, founder of the surrealist literary movement in France and a close friend of Apollinaire.

Brewster, Sir David (1781–1868), Scottish physicist, noted for his research into the polarisation of light; invented the kaleidoscope. He helped to found the British Association for the Advancement of Science.

Brezhnev, Leonid Ilyich (1906–82), succeeded Khrushchev as First Secretary of the Soviet Communist Party in 1964. Under his leadership the Soviet Union achieved strategic parity with the United States, society became more stable, education and living standards steadily improved, though the economy was put under strain with expectations not matching performance.

Bridges, Robert (1844–1930), poet laureate 1913–30. His *Testament of Beauty* (1929) has been called "a compendium of the wisdom, learning and experience of an artistic spirit."

Bridgewater, 3rd Duke of (Francis Egerton) (1736–1803), founder of British inland navigation by his canal, to the design of James Brindley *(q.v.)* from Manchester to his coal mines at Worsley, later extended to join the Mersey at Runcorn.

Bridie, James (pseudonym of Osborne Henry Mavor) (1888–1951), Scottish author and dramatist. The first of his many successful plays was *The Anatomist,* produced in 1931. Other plays include *Tobias and the Angel, Jonah and the Whale, Mr. Bolfrey, Dr. Angelus.*

Bright, Sir Charles Tilston (1832–88), English telegraph engineer who supervised the laying of the British telegraph network and the Atlantic cables (1856–8).

Bright, John (1811–89), radical Quaker statesman and orator, b. Rochdale; friend of Cobden, with whom he promoted the movement for free trade.

Brindley, James (1716–72), English canal builder, b. Derbyshire, of poor parents, apprenticed as a millwright. He was employed by the Duke of Bridgewater *(q.v.)* and designed and constructed the Bridgewater canal, carrying it over the R. Irwell by an aqueduct, the first of its kind. He also built the Grand Trunk canal linking the Mersey with the Trent.

Britten, Baron (Edward Benjamin Britten) (1913–76), English composer, closely associated with the Aldeburgh festival. O.M. 1965. *See* **Section E.**

Broca, Paul (1824–80), French pathologist, anthropologist and pioneer in neuro-surgery. He localised the seat of speech in the brain and originated methods for measuring brain and skull ratios.

Broch, Hermann (1886–1951), Austrian novelist, author of the trilogy *The Sleepwalkers.* Lived in U.S.A. after 1938.

Broglie, prominent family of Piedmontese origin; **Victor Maurice** (1647–1727), and **François Marie** (1671–1745) were marshals of France; **Louis Victor, Prince de Broglie** (b. 1892) received the Nobel prize for his work on quantum mechanics, and his brother **Maurice, Duc de Broglie** (1875–1960), also a physicist, is noted for his work on the ionisation of gases, radioactivity, and X-rays.

Brontë, Charlotte (1816–55), forceful novelist, daughter of an Anglican clergyman of Irish descent, incumbent of Haworth, Yorkshire. She published under a pseudonym *Jane Eyre,* which was at once successful and was followed by *Shirley* and *Villette.* Her sister **Emily** (1818–48) wrote poetry and also *Wuthering Heights;* and **Anne** (1820–49) wrote *Agnes Grey.*

Brooke, Rupert (1887–1915), English poet who died during the first world war, whose works, though few, showed promise and include the poems *Grantchester* and *The Soldier.*

Brougham and Vaux, 1st Baron (Henry Peter Brougham) (1778–1868), English legal reformer; advocate of Queen Caroline against George IV; helped to found London university.

Brown, Sir Arthur Whitten (1886–1948), together with Sir John Alcock (d. 1919) in 1919 made the first transatlantic flight, crossing from Newfoundland to Ireland in 16 hr. 12 min.

Brown, John (1800–59), American abolitionist. His action in inciting Negro slaves to rebel in 1859 led to the civil war. He was hanged after failing to hold the U.S. arsenal at Harper's Ferry which he had captured. Known as "Old Brown of Osawatomie" and regarded as a martyr.

Browne, Charles Farrer (1834–67), American humorist who wrote under the pseudonym of Artemus Ward.

Browne, Hablot Knight (1815–82), English artist, the "Phiz" of many book illustrations, including Dickens's *Pickwick Papers.*

Browne, Sir Thomas (1605–82), author of *Religio Medici* and *Urne-Buriall,* was born in London and practised in Norwich as a physician.

Browning, Elizabeth Barrett (1806–61), English poet. Owing to an injury in childhood, she spent her youth lying on her back, but her meeting with Robert Browning, whom she married, brought a remarkable recovery. In her lifetime her works were more read than those of her husband. They include *Cry of the Children, Sonnets from the Portuguese,* and *Aurora Leigh.*

Browning, Robert (1812–89), English poet. Because of his involved style his reputation grew only slowly. In *Strafford* and *The Blot on the 'Scutcheon* he attempted drama also. He married Elizabeth Barrett and lived mainly abroad. His works include *Dramatis Personae* and *The Ring and The Book.*

Bruce, Robert (1274–1329), Scottish national leader against Edward I and Edward II of England. Crowned king in 1306, after years of struggle he defeated Edward II at Bannockburn in 1314.

Bruce, William Spiers (1867–1921), Scottish polar explorer who led the Scottish national antarctic expedition in the *Scotia* 1902–4 and set up a meteorological station on the South Orkneys.

Bruch, Max (1838–1920), German composer and conductor, best known for his G minor violin concerto.

Bruckner, Anton (1824–96), Austrian composer and organist. *See* Section E.

Brummell, George Bryan (1778–1840), "Beau Brummell," fashion leader and friend of the Prince Regent (George IV).

Brunel, Isambard Kingdom (1806–59), English civil engineer, son of **Sir Marc Isambard Brunel** (1769–1849), whom he assisted in building the Thames (Rotherhithe) tunnel. He was engineer of the Great Western Railway and built the ocean liners, the *Great Western*, the *Great Britain* (brought back from the Falkland Is. to Bristol in 1970), and the *Great Eastern*. His other works include the Clifton suspension bridge over the R. Avon at Bristol and the Royal Albert bridge over the R. Tamar at Saltash.

Brunelleschi, Filippo (1377–1446), Italian architect, b. Florence; he adapted the ideals of the Roman period. His work in Florence includes the Pitti Palace, the churches of San Lorenzo and San Spirito, and the cathedral dome.

Bruno, Giordano (1548–1600), Italian philosopher. A Dominican friar, he came to favour the astronomical views of Copernicus and was burnt at the stake.

Bruno, St. (*c.* 1032–1101), German monk, founder in 1084 of the Carthusian order at La Grande Chartreuse in the French Alps.

Brutus, Marcus Junius (85–42 B.C.), conspirator against Julius Caesar; later committed suicide.

Buchanan, George (1506–82), Scottish humanist who spent most of his life in France lecturing and writing Latin poems, plays, and treatises.

Buchner, Eduard (1860–1917), German chemist, remembered for his work on the chemistry of fermentation. Nobel prizewinner 1907.

Büchner, Georg (1813–37), German dramatist. Dying at 24, his limited output (principally *Dantons Tod* and the fragment *Wozzeck*) is marked by power and maturity.

Buckle, Henry Thomas (1821–62), author of *The History of Civilisation in England.*

Buddha. *See* Gautama, Siddhartha.

Budge, Sir Ernest Alfred Wallis (1857–1934), archaeologist who conducted excavations in Mesopotamia and Egypt.

Buffon, Georges-Louis Leclerc, Comte de (1707–88), French naturalist, author of the *Histoire naturelle* (44 vols., 1749–1804).

Bulganin, Nikolai Alexandrovich (1895–1975), Soviet prime minister 1955–8; defence minister 1947–9, 1953–5. Retired 1960.

Bull, John (*c.* 1562–1628), English composer; possibly composer of *God save the Queen.*

Bülow, Hans Guido von (1830–94), German pianist and conductor. He married Liszt's daughter Cosima, who later left him to marry Wagner.

Bunsen, Robert Wilhelm (1811–99), German chemist, discoverer of the metals caesium and rubidium, and inventor of the Bunsen burner, battery, and pump. Made important observations in spectrum analysis.

Bunyan, John (1628–88), was originally a travelling tinker and is believed to have served in the Parliamentary army. He joined an Independent church in Bedford in 1655 and became a popular preacher. After the Restoration he was thrown into prison, and there wrote *The Pilgrim's Progress.* Of his 60 works, the best known after *Pilgrim's Progress* are *The Holy War, Grace Abounding,* and *Mr. Badman.*

Burckhardt, Jacob Christoph (1818–97), Swiss historian, author of *The Civilisation of the Renaissance in Italy.*

Burghley, 1st Baron (William Cecil) (1520–98), English statesman. After holding office under her two predecessors, he was Queen Elizabeth I's secretary of state, 1558–72, and lord high treasurer, 1572–98.

Burke, Edmund (1729–97), Whig writer and political philosopher. B. in Dublin, he became secretary to Lord Rockingham and entered parliament in 1765. He advocated the emancipation (though not the independence) of the American colonies; and better administration in India; but was against the French revolution.

Burnett, Gilbert (1643–1715) bishop of Salisbury, b. Edinburgh. He wrote a *History of his Own Times,* which deals with many events of which he had personal knowledge.

Burnet, Sir John James (1859–1938), architect, b. Glasgow. The north front of the British Museum (King Edward's galleries) is his most important work in London.

Burney, Fanny (Madame D'Arblay) (1752–1840), originator of the simple novel of home life. Daughter of the organist, Dr. Burney, she published *Evelina* in 1778, and this brought her into court and literary society. She also wrote *Cecilia* and *Camilla.*

Burns, Robert (1759–96), Scottish poet. The son of a cottar, his first poems published in 1786 were at once successful, and he bought a farm. The farm failed, but he had a post as exciseman, and continued to write simply with tenderness and humour. Among his best-known poems are *Auld Lang Syne, Scots wa hae, Comin' through the rye,* and *The Banks of Doon.*

Burton, Sir Richard Francis (1821–90), British explorer and orientalist, who made a pilgrimage to Mecca and Medina in 1853 disguised as a Moslem. He explored Central Africa and translated the *Arabian Nights* (16 vols.).

Burton, Robert (1577–1640), English cleric and scholar, author of *The Anatomy of Melancholy.*

Bush, George Herbert Walker (1924–). American politician. Vice-president of America, 1981–89. Elected 41st President, succeeding Ronald Reagan, November 1988. Inaugurated, January 1989. First Vice-President to be elected President since Martin van Buren in 1836. Ordered US invasion of Panama, December 1989. *See also* Section C.

Busoni, Ferruccio Benvenuto (1866–1920), pianist and composer of three operas (the last *Dr. Faust,* unfinished at his death), much orchestral and chamber music, and works for the piano. B. in Empoli, he lived in Germany. *See* Section E.

Butler, Joseph (1692–1752), English bishop, remembered for his *Analogy of Religion,* published in 1736 in reply to deistic attacks.

Butler, Nicholas Murray (1862–1947), American educationist who shared with the sociologist Jane Addams the 1931 Nobel peace prize.

Butler, Baron (Richard Austen Butler) (1902–82), Conservative M.P. for Saffron Walden 1929–65. Brought in Education Act 1944; helped secure Conservative acceptance of the welfare state; held high office 1951–64. "Butskellism" applied to Conservative social and economic policies of the '50s. Described by Sir Harold Wilson as the best prime minister we never had. Life peerage 1965.

Butler, Samuel (1612–80), English verse-satirist; author of the poem *Hudibras* against the Puritans.

Butler, Samuel (1835–1902), English novelist and satirist, author of *Erewhon* and its sequel *Erewhon Revisited.* Other works include *The Fair Haven, Life and Habit,* and *Evolution Old and New,* in which he attacked Darwinism. His autobiographical novel *The Way of All Flesh* and his *Notebooks* were published after his death. He exhibited regularly at the Academy and was also a musician.

Butt, Clara (1872–1936), English contralto; made her début in London in 1892.

Buxton, Sir Thomas Fowell (1786–1845), English social reformer; succeeded Wilberforce as leader of the anti-slavery group in parliament.

Buys Ballot, Christoph Henrich Diedrich (1817–90), Dutch meteorologist who formulated the law which bears his name (an observer with back to wind in northern hemisphere has lower pressure to left; in southern hemisphere to right).

Byrd, Richard Evelyn (1888–1957), American rear-admiral, explorer and aviator. He flew over the north pole, 1926; and in 1929 made the first flight over the south pole. He made other expeditions in 1925, 1933–5, 1939 and 1946.

Byrd, William (1543–1623), English composer of church music, sacred choral music, string music, vocal and instrumental music; and a founder of the school of English madrigalists. He was organist of Lincoln cathedral at 20 and later of Queen Elizabeth's chapel royal. See **Section E.**

Byron, 6th Baron (George Gordon Byron) (1788–1824), English romantic poet who influenced European literature and thought. At 20 he published *Hours of Idleness*, which was violently attacked by the *Edinburgh Review*. This provoked his retaliatory *English Bards and Scotch Reviewers*, which caused a sensation. His *Childe Harold's Pilgrimage* appeared in 1812. His married life was unhappy. He went to help the Greeks in their struggle for independence and died at Missolonghi.

C

Cable, George Washington (1844–1925), American author and social critic, b. New Oreleans, whose writings reflect the colour problems of his day: *Ole Creol Days, The Silent South.*

Cabot, John (1425–*c.* 1500), Genoese explorer who settled in Bristol and sailed westwards under letters-patent from Henry VII of England in 1497. Discovered Newfoundland and Nova Scotia, believing them to be part of Asia, and may have reached the mainland of America before Columbus did. His son:

Cabot, Sebastian (1474–1557), was born in Venice, and in 1509 in search of a north-west passage to Asia sailed as far as Hudson Bay. Entered Spanish service in 1512, and spent several years exploring the Plate and Paraná rivers. Re-entered English service in 1548 and organised expedition to seek a north-east passage to India, which resulted in trade with Russia. English claim to North America is founded on the voyages of the Cabots.

Cabral, Pedro Alvarez (*c.* 1467–*c.* 1520), Portuguese navigator, friend of Vasco da Gama, discovered Brazil, which he named "Terra da Santa Cruz."

Cadbury, George (1839–1922), liberal Quaker philanthropist of Cadbury Bros., mainly responsible for the pioneer garden city of Bournville.

Cadogan, Sir Alexander (1884–1968), English diplomat. He helped to draft the charter of the United Nations organisation and became Gt. Britain's representative on the Security Council.

Caedmon, the first English Christian poet, lived in the 7th cent. and, according to Bede, was first a cowherd and later a monk at Whitby. His poetry was based on the scriptures.

Caesar, Caius Julius (*c.* 101–44 B.C.), Roman general and writer. Under the declining republic, he was assigned in 61 the province of Gaul; in the course of pacifying it he invaded Britain (55 B.C.). Opposition in Rome to his career, mainly from Pompey, provoked him in 49 to the defiance of crossing the Rubicon with his army. He defeated Pompey, whom he pursued to Egypt, where he established Cleopatra as queen. At Rome he became dictator, and his reforms include the Julian calendar. He was murdered in 44. His career paved the way for Rome becoming an empire under his nephew Octavian.

Calderón de la Barca, Pedro (1600–81), Spanish dramatist, representative of contemporary Spanish thought, who also wrote court spectacles for Philip IV. Among his best-known works are *La Vida es Sueño* and *El divino Orfeo.*

Callaghan, Lord (Sir James Callaghan) (b. 1912), Labour's fourth prime minister, 1976–9; parliamentary leader of the Labour Party, April 1976, following Sir Harold Wilson's resignation: elected for South Cardiff 1950–87; served as Chancellor of the Exchequer, Home Secretary, and Foreign Secretary in the Labour administrations, 1964–70, 1974–76. Succeeded by Foot as leader, 1980. Retired from Parliament, 1987. Order of the Garter, 1987.

Calvin, John (1509–64), French Protestant reformer and theologian. B. in Picardy, he broke with the Roman Catholic church about 1533, and subsequently settled in Geneva, where from 1541 he established a theocratic regime of strict morality. His theology was published in his *Institutes*; while, like Luther, he accepted justification by faith without works, he also believed in predestination. His doctrines spread on the continent, in Scotland and to some extent in England. See **Section J.**

Câmara, Helder Pessoa (b. 1908), Brazilian archbishop of Recife; critic of the economic imperialism of multinational companies and courageous campaigner for social reform.

Camden, William (1551–1623), English antiquary and historian. His *Britannia* appeared in 1586.

Cameron, Sir David Young (1865–1945), Scottish etcher and landscape painter.

Cameron, Richard (1648–80), Scottish preacher who revolted in defence of the Solemn League and Covenant and was killed at Airds Moss (Ayrshire).

Cameron, Verney Lovett (1844–94), English explorer, the first to cross the African continent from east to west. He surveyed Lake Tanganyika and in 1872 went out to find Livingstone.

Camillus, Marcus Furius (4th cent. B.C.), Roman general. When the Gauls attacked in 387 B.C., he was made dictator and defeated them.

Camões, Luis Vaz de (1624–80), Portuguese poet, author of *Os Lusiadas*, an epic of Portuguese history and discovery.

Campbell, Colin, 1st Baron Clyde (1792–1863), Scottish general who was commander-in-chief in India during the Mutiny.

Campbell, Sir Malcolm (1885–1948), racing driver who held the land-speed record of 301 mile/h (1935) and water-speed record of 141·7 mile/h (1939). His son **Donald** held the water-speed record of 276·33 mile/h (1964); killed in 1967 at Coniston.

Campbell, Mrs. Patrick (Beatrice Stella Tanner) (1865–1940), English actress of beauty and wit, friend of G. B. Shaw.

Campbell, Thomas (1777–1844), Scottish poet, who at 22 published *The Pleasures of Hope*. His war poems include *Ye Mariners of England* and *The Battle of the Baltic*. He was one of the founders of University College, London.

Campbell-Bannerman, Sir Henry (1836–1908), Liberal statesman, prime minister 1905–8. His ministry included Asquith, Lloyd George, and Churchill.

Camus, Albert (1913–60), French existentialist philosopher and writer, native of Algeria. Pre-occupied with the themes of the Stranger and the Absurd, the works for which he is particularly remembered are the philosophical essay *Le Mythe de Sisyphe*, the plays *Caligula* and *The Price of Justice*, and the novel *L'Etranger*. Nobel prize 1957. Killed in car crash.

Canaletto (Antonio Canal) (1697–1768), Italian artist. B. at Venice, he painted views of his city. From 1746 to 1756 he worked mainly in London. Some of his work is in the National Gallery, and there is a collection at Windsor.

Canning, George (1770–1827), English statesman. He was an advocate of Catholic emancipation, and was the first to recognise the free states of South America.

Cannizzaro, Stanislao (1826–1910), Italian chemist who carried forward the work of Avogadro in distinguishing between molecular and atomic weights.

Canova, Antonio (1757–1822), Italian sculptor. B. at Venice, he infused grace into the classical style.

Canton, John (1718–72), English physicist and schoolmaster, the first to verify in England Franklin's experiments on the identity of lightning with electricity. He was the first to demonstrate that water is compressible and produced a new phosphorescent body (Canton's phosphorus) by calcining oyster shells with sulphur.

Canute (*c.* 994–1035), king of the English, Danes and Norwegians. The son of a Danish king, after some years of fighting he established himself as king of England and ruled with wisdom and firmness.

Capablanca, José Raoul (1888–1942), Cuban chess player, world champion from 1921 to 1927 when he was beaten by Alekhine.

Caractacus or **Caradoc,** a king in west Britain, who resisted the Romans in the first century. After capture he was freed by the emperor Claudius.

Carey, William (1761–1834), first Baptist missionary to India. An Oriental scholar, he published 24 translations of the scriptures.

Carissimi, Giacomo (1604–74), Italian composer, b. near Rome. He introduced more instrumental variety into the cantata and oratorio, and brought the recitative to perfection. His *Jephtha* is still in print, and there are collections of his works at Paris and Oxford. *See* **Section E.**

Carlyle, Thomas (1795–1881), Scottish author. Of peasant stock, he went to Edinburgh university, but later lived mainly in England where he lectured. He married Jane Welsh. His individual views pervade his historical writing. His best-known works include *Sartor Resartus, Heroes and Hero Worship, Cromwell's Letters and Speeches,* and the *French Revolution.*

Carnegie, Andrew (1835–1919), philanthropist b. Dunfermline; emigrated to America 1848; after early struggles established the Carnegie iron works. He made munificent gifts to Free Libraries and other educational work.

Carnot, Lazare Nicolas Marguerite (1753–1823), French military engineer, prominent in the French revolutionary wars, 1792–1802. His son, **Sadi Carnot** (1796–1832), was a physicist and engineer who worked on the motive power of heat, establishing the principle that heat and work are reversible conditions.

Caroline, Queen (1768–1821), was married to George IV when he was Prince of Wales. They soon separated, but when he became king in 1820, she tried to assert her position. The question came before parliament. In spite of some public sympathy she was unsuccessful.

Carrel, Alexis (1873–1944), American surgeon who won the Nobel prize in 1912 for his success in suturing blood vessels in transfusion and in transplantation of organs. A Frenchman by birth, he returned to France in 1939.

Carroll, Lewis. *See* **Dodgson, Charles Lutwidge.**

Carson, Baron (Edward Henry Carson) (1854–1935), Irish barrister, solicitor-general for Ireland 1892; attorney general 1915; first lord of the admiralty 1916–17; member of the war cabinet 1917–18. He led a semi-militant organisation against Home Rule.

Carson, Rachel (1907–64), American biologist, remembered for *The Silent Spring.*

Carter, Howard (1873–1939), Egyptologist who was associated with Lord Carnarvon in discovering in 1922 the Tomb of Tutankhamun.

Carter, James Earl (b. 1924), American Democratic President 1977–81; former Governor of Georgia. His main achievements were the treaty between Israel and Egypt, the Panama Canal treaty, Salt II (though not ratified) and the settling of the release of American hostages held captive in Iran.

Cartier, Jacques (1494–1557), French navigator, b. St. Malo, who explored Canada, especially the gulf and river of St. Lawrence.

Cartwright, Edmund (1743–1823), English inventor of the power-loom, and also of a wool-combing machine, important steps in the weaving side of the textile revolution.

Cartwright, John (1740–1824), brother of the above; reformer and agitator against slavery.

Caruso, Enrico (1873–1921), Italian tenor, b. Naples.

Carver, George Washington (1864–1943), American Negro agricultural chemist of world repute.

Casabianca, Louis de (*c.* 1752–98), captain of the French flagship *L'Orient* at the Battle of the Nile. He and his ten-year-old-son died together in the burning ship.

Casals, Pablo (1876–1973), Spanish cellist and conductor, son of an organist, b. Vendrell, Tarragona. He exiled himself from Spain in 1938 as a protest against dictatorship.

Casanova de Seinfalt, Giacomo (1725–98), Italian adventurer, author of licentious memoirs.

Cassini, French family of Italian origin, distinguished for work in astronomy and geography. Through four generations (1671–1793) they were heads of the Paris Observatory.

Cassius, Caius Longinus, Roman general who opposed the dictatorship of Julius Caesar, and took part in his murder. He died in 42 B.C. after being defeated by Mark Antony.

Castlereagh, Viscount (Robert Stewart Castlereagh) (1769–1822), British minister of war and foreign secretary, who took a leading part in the Napoleonic wars. He was however unpopular and committed suicide.

Castro, Fidel (b. 1927), Cuban revolutionary. After two unsuccessful attempts he succeeded in 1959 in overthrowing a police-state. He has

initiated reforms in agriculture, industry, and education, and repulsed American economic dominance. His acceptance of Russian support led to the "missiles crisis" of 1962.

Catchpool, E. St. John (1890–1971), first secretary of the English Youth Hostels Association, 1930–50; president, International Federation, 1938–50.

Catherine, St. (4th cent.). Traditionally a virgin martyr in Alexandria, though not mentioned before the 10th cent. Legend represents her as tied to a wheel.

Catherine de' Medici (1519–89), Italian-born wife of Henry II and mother of three French kings (she was regent for Charles IX). Her antagonism to the Protestants may have led to the massacre of St. Bartholomew's day. She was able, and appreciated art and literature, but was unscrupulous and cruel.

Catherine of Aragon (1485–1536), first wife of Henry VIII of England, was daughter of Ferdinand and Isabella of Spain, and mother of Mary Tudor. After the Pope had refused to release Henry VIII from the marriage an English declaration of nullity was obtained (thus precipitating a movement towards the Reformation).

Catherine the Great (1729–96), Empress Catherine II of Russia. Daughter of a German prince, she married in 1745 the future Peter III, a weakling, later deposed and murdered. Intelligent, cultivated, autocratic, she proved a capable ruler for a time but was hampered and opposed by the landed interests and, despite plans for reform, her reign was marked by imperialist expansion and extension of serfdom.

Cato, Marcus Porcius (234–149 B.C.), Roman statesman and writer. His tenure of office as censor was characterised by austerity and conservatism. He advocated opposition to Carthage. His writings deal with agriculture and history.

Catullus, Caius Valerius (*c.* 84–54 B.C.), Roman poet who wrote lyrics to Lesbia. His poems show sincere feeling and also Greek influence.

Cavell, Edith Louisa (1865–1915), English nurse who cared for friend and foe in Brussels in 1914–15, but was executed by the Germans for helping Allied fugitives to escape.

Cavendish, Henry (1731–1810), English scientist, a contemporary of Black, Priestley, Scheele, and Lavoisier, remembered for his investigations into the nature of gases. He discovered hydrogen and the chemical composition of water. The Cavendish Laboratory is named after him.

Cavour, Camilio Benso di (1810–61), Italian statesman, who, as premier of Sardinia, helped to bring about the unification of Italy.

Caxton, William (1422–91), the first English printer and publisher, a man of wide-ranging abilities. He probably learnt the art of printing at Cologne (1471–2), setting up his own printing press at Westminster (1476). He printed Chaucer's *Canterbury Tales,* Malory's *Le Morte d'Arthur* and Aesop's *Fables.* He was an accomplished linguist.

Cecil of Chelwood, 1st Viscount (Robert Cecil) (1864–1958), English politician who helped draft the Charter of the League of Nations. Nobel prize for peace 1937.

Cecilia, St. (2nd or 3rd cent.), patron saint of music. She is often represented playing the organ.

Cellini, Benvenuto (1500–71), Italian sculptor and goldsmith. B. at Florence, he worked for some years in Rome. His bronze statue *Perseus* with *the head of Medusa* is at Florence. His life was adventurous and he wrote an *Autobiography* which is revealing of himself and his time.

Celsius, Anders (1701–44), Swedish physicist and astronomer who invented the centigrade thermometer.

Ceresole, Pierre (1879–1945), Swiss founder of International Voluntary Service. He was by profession a teacher of engineering, and his pacifism led him to become a Quaker.

Cervantes, Saavedra Miguel de (1547–1616), Spanish novelist and dramatist, b. at Alcalá de Henares. He was injured at the battle of Lepanto, and thereafter struggled to earn a livelihood from literature. His *Don Quixote* describes the adventures of a poor gentleman, confused in mind, who on his horse Rosinante with his squire Sancho Panza seeks adventures; it satirised chivalry, but is also a permanent criticism of life. Of his plays only two survive.

Cézanne, Paul (1839–1906), French painter, b. in Aix-en-Provence, the son of a wealthy banker and tradesman. He developed a highly original style, using colour and tone in such a way as to increase the impression of depth. He said that he wanted "to make of Impressionism something solid and durable, like the art of the Museums." Like Giotto, six hundred years before, he more than any other artist determined the course European painting was to take. *La Veille au Chapelet* and *Les Grandes Baigneuses* are in the National Gallery. He was a friend of Zola.

Chadwick, Sir Edwin (1800–90), English social reformer whose most important work was as Secretary of the Poor Law Board.

Chadwick, Sir James (1891–1974), English physicist, one of Rutherford's collaborators in the field of atomic research. Discovered the neutron in 1932, one of the main steps in the discovery of the fission process which led to the production of the atom bomb.

Chagall, Marc (1889–1985), Russian painter, b. at Vitebsk; the forerunner of surrealism.

Chamberlain, Joseph (1836–1914), English statesman. He began with municipal work in Birmingham. At first a Liberal under Gladstone, he became Conservative. He opposed Home Rule for Ireland, and was the first advocate of a partial return to protection.

Chamberlain, Neville (1869–1940), son of Joseph. He was prime minister 1937–40, when he appeased Hitler by the Munich agreement, 1938.

Chambers, Sir William (1726–96), British architect, b. Stockholm. He rebuilt Somerset House and designed the pagoda in Kew Gardens.

Champlain, Samuel de (1567–1635), French navigator who founded Quebec (1608), and discovered the lake known by his name.

Champollion, Jean François (1790–1832), French egyptologist, who found the key to the decipherment of hieroglyphics from the Rosetta stone **(L106)**.

Chantrey, Sir Francis Legatt (1781–1841), English sculptor who left a fortune to the Royal Academy for the purchase of works of British art.

Chaplin, Sir Charles Spencer (1889–1977), first international screen star, with more than 50 years' achievement. B. in London, his mother was a music-hall singer and he made his début at five. In 1910 he went to the United States; and with the Keystone Company in Los Angeles (1914–15) he made films in which his early hardships are reflected in humour and sadness. His films include *Shoulder Arms, The Kid, The Gold Rush, City Lights, The Great Dictator, Modern Times,* and *Limelight. Autobiography* (1964).

Chapman, George (1559–1634), Elizabethan poet, dramatist, and translator of the *Iliad* and *Odyssey*. His best-known play is *Bussy d'Ambois*.

Chapman, Sydney (1888–1970), English mathematician and geophysicist, noted for his work on the kinetic theory of gases, geomagnetism, and solar and ionospheric physics. He was president of the special committee of the I.G.Y., 1957–8. An upper layer of the atmosphere and a crater on the moon are named after him.

Charcot, Jean Baptiste (1867–1936), French explorer, who in 1903–5 and 1908–10 commanded expeditions to the south polar regions. Charcot Island in the Antarctic is named after him.

Chardin, Jean Baptiste Siméon (1699–1779), French painter of still life and domestic scenes.

Chares (*c.* 300 B.C.), Greek worker in bronze from Rhodes, sculptor of the Colossus of Rhodes, one of the seven wonders of the world.

Charlemagne (742–814), Charles the Great. From being King of the Franks, he came to govern an empire comprising Gaul, Italy, and large parts of Spain and Germany, and was crowned Emperor by the Pope in Rome on Christmas Day, A.D. 800. His revival of the Western Empire was the foundation of the Holy Roman Empire *(q.v.)*.

Charles, Jacques Alexandre César (1746–1823), French physicist, the first to use hydrogen gas in balloons and who anticipated Gay-Lussac's law on the expansion of gases.

Charles Edward (Stuart) (1720–88), the Young Pretender (*i.e.,* claimant of the English throne), grandson of James II, led an unsuccessful rising in 1745 and died in exile.

Charles (Philip Arthur George) (b. 1948), Prince of Wales, Duke of Cornwall and Rothesay, eldest son of Queen Elizabeth II; married Lady Diana Spencer, daughter of 8th Earl Spencer, 1981.

Charles I (1600–49), King of England, Scotland, and Ireland, succeeded his father James I in 1625. Personally sincere, and having an appreciation of art, he was yet ill-fitted to cope with the political problems of his time. His marriage with the French princess Henrietta Maria was unpopular. He supported Archbishop Laud's strict Anglicanism, and he also attempted to rule without parliament. Defeated in the Civil War which broke out in 1642, he spun out negotiations for a settlement till he was beheaded in 1649.

Charles II (1630–85), King of England, Scotland, and Ireland, son of Charles I; after the Civil War escaped to France, and returned in 1660 when the monarchy was restored. His religious sympathies were Roman Catholic and his personal life was amorous; but in political matters he was shrewd and realistic, and contrived not to "go on his travels" again. He promoted the development of the navy, but had to accept the laws enforcing religious conformity imposed by parliament.

Charles V (1500–58), Hapsburg ruler, succeeded his grandfather, Maximilian I, as emperor of the Holy Roman Empire, and as heir to Ferdinand and Isabella succeeded to the Spanish crown. His rivalry with Francis I of France led to prolonged war. He crushed a revolt of peasants in 1525. He presided in 1521 at the Diet before which Luther appeared, after which religious struggle continued in Germany till the Augsburg settlement of 1555. In that year he retired to a monastery in Spain.

Charles XII of Sweden (1682–1718), a brave but rash and ambitious general. He repelled Russian attacks at Narva in 1700, but subsequently pursuing military adventure he was defeated by Peter the Great at Poltava in 1709; and on invading Norway was killed.

Chateaubriand, François René, Vicomte de (1768–1848), French writer and diplomat. In a varied career he was at first an emigré, and later served as diplomat under both Napoleon and Louis XVIII. He was a friend of Mme. Recamier. His writings include *Mémoires d'outre-tombe*.

Chatham, 1st Earl of (William Pitt) (1708–78), English statesman and orator. His energetic conduct of the Seven Years War was an important contribution to English victory and to acquisitions in Canada and India at the peace (1763), though by then he was out of office. In the dispute with the American colonies he upheld their right to resist imposed taxation, and collapsed while making a last speech on this dispute.

Chatterton, Thomas (1752–70), English poet who tried to pass off his writings as newly discovered ancient manuscripts. Killed himself at the age of 17.

Chaucer, Geoffrey (1340?–1400), English poet. His main work, *The Canterbury Tales*, gives a vivid picture of contemporary life.

Chekhov, Anton (1860–1904), Russian dramatist and short-story writer, whose plays include *The Cherry Orchard, Uncle Vanya,* and *The Three Sisters*. His stories include *The Steppe, The Sleepyhead, The Post, The Student,* and *The Bishop*. He was of humble origin and while a student at Moscow supported his family by writing humorous sketches and tales.

Chernenko, Konstantin Ustinovich (1911–85) Soviet politician. Succeeded Andropov (q.v.) as General Secretary of the Communist Party, February 1984. Long career as bureaucrat, serving the Praesidium of the Supreme Soviet. Widely regarded as a protégé of Brezhnev, his ineffectual rule lasted a mere 13 months.

Cherubini, Luigi (1760–1842), Italian-born musician, director of the Paris Conservatoire.

Chesterfield, 4th Earl of (Philip Dormer Stanhope) (1694–1773), English statesman, whose *Letters* to his natural son, Philip Stanhope, are full of grace, wit, and worldly wisdom.

Chesterton, Gilbert Keith (1874–1936), English essayist, novelist and poet, who also wrote studies of Charles Dickens and Robert Browning. His works include *The Napoleon of Notting Hill* and *The Ballad of the White Horse*.

Chevalier, Albert (1861–1923), English music-hall comedian known for his coster sketches.

Chiang Kai-shek (1887–1975), Chinese general. He at first fought for Sun Yat-sen. After the latter's death (1925), as commander of the

Kuomintang army, he attempted to unite China; but (involved as he was with business interests) he was more anxious to defeat the Communists than to repel the Japanese adventure in Manchuria in 1931. He was unable to establish peace and a stable, progressive régime; and in 1949 retired to Formosa after military defeat by the Communists. His widow is Mayling Soong.

Chichester, Sir Francis (1902–72), English seaman, who sailed his *Gipsy Moth IV* into Sydney harbour in 1966 after a 107-day voyage from Plymouth, and back again round the Horn.

Chippendale, Thomas (1718–79), designer of furniture, b. Otley, Yorks, son of a joiner. His designs are shown in *The Gentleman and Cabinet Maker's Director*, 1754.

Chirico, Giorgio de (1888–1978), painter associated with the surrealist school, born in Greece of Italian parents.

Chomsky, Noam (b. 1928), American theoretical linguist, professor of Linguistics, Massachusetts Institute of Technology; inventor of transformational grammar.

Chopin, Frédéric François (1810–49), Polish pianist and composer, son of a French father and Polish mother. He has been called "the poet of the piano" because of the originality and delicacy of his playing. He enjoyed Paris intellectual and musical society, was a friend of George Sand, and played in numerous concerts all over Europe. He died of consumption. *See* **Section E.**

Chou En-lai (1898–1976), Chinese revolutionary statesman, administrator and diplomat. He organised revolt in Shanghai 1927, later formed close partnership with Mao Tse-tung, took part in the "long march" 1934–5, becoming prime minister of the new China in 1949. Headed the Chinese delegation to the Geneva Conference of 1954.

Chrysostom, St. John (c. 347–407), preacher. Chrysostom means golden-mouthed. First at Antioch, and later as patriarch of Constantinople, he was an eloquent teacher; but by outspokenness he lost the Empress Eudoxia's favour and died from ill-treatment.

Chulalongkorn, Phra Paramindr Maha (1853–1910), Siamese reforming monarch.

Churchill, Lord Randolph Henry Spencer (1849–95), Conservative politician, who held brief office only. He was father of Winston Churchill.

Churchill, Sir Winston Leonard Spencer (1874–1965), British statesman and author, son of the last-named. He entered parliament in 1900. He served as a junior officer with the British forces abroad; and during the Boer War he acted as war correspondent. He held the following ministerial posts; Under-Secretary for the Colonies 1905–8; President of the Board of Trade 1908–10; Home Secretary 1910–11; First Lord of the Admiralty 1911–15, 1939–40; Chancellor of the Duchy of Lancaster 1915; Minister of Munitions 1917; Minister of War 1918–21; Minister of Air 1919–21; Secretary of State for the Colonies 1921–2; Chancellor of the Exchequer 1924–9; Prime Minister and Minister of Defence 1940–5; Prime Minister 1951–5. He was rector or chancellor of three universities. Cast in the heroic mould, he lived a full life. His main achievement was as leader of the British people in the second world war. His writings include a biography of his ancestor, Marlborough, and histories of the first and second world wars. He exhibited at the Royal Academy. Hon. American citizenship conferred 1963.

Cibber, Colley (1671–1757), a London actor and dramatist. His best comedies are *The Careless Husband* and *Love's Last Shift*. He wrote an autobiography.

Cicero, Marcus Tullius (106–43 B.C.), Roman orator and philosopher, many of whose letters and speeches survive. He held political office but was killed by the troops of the triumvirate.

Cid (El Campeador) (c. 1035–99), name given to the Spanish knight Rodrigo Diaz, a soldier of fortune who fought against Moors and Christians alike. Myth made him a national hero of knightly and Christian virtue.

Cierva, Juan de la (1895–1936), Spanish engineer who invented the autogiro.

Cimabue, Giovanni (Cenni di Pepo) (1240–1302), early Florentine painter. His only certain work is the St. John in Pisa cathedral.

Cimarosa, Domenico (1749–1801), Italian composer. His best-known opera is *Il Matrimonio Segreto*. He held revolutionary views.

Cimon (c. 512–449 B.C.), Athenian statesman and general, son of Miltiades. He defeated the Persian fleet at the mouth of the Eurymedon in 468. He worked for cooperation with other states, including Sparta.

Cipriani, Giambattista (1727–85), Italian painter of historical subjects who worked in London; a founder member of the Royal Academy.

Clair, René (1898–1981), French film producer, whose early films, full of wit and satire, include *Sous les Toits de Paris* and *A Nous la Liberté*.

Clare, John (1793–1864), Northamptonshire labourer who became a poet. *Poems Descriptive of Rural Life and Scenery*, and *The Village Minstrel* were among his publications. He died in the county lunatic asylum.

Clarendon, 1st Earl of (Edward Hyde) (1609–74), English statesman and historian. He was for some years chancellor to Charles II, and his daughter married the future James II, but he fell and died in exile. He wrote a *History of the Rebellion*.

Clark, Baron (Kenneth McKenzie Clark) (1903–83), English art historian. He was director of the National Gallery 1934–45, Slade professor of fine arts at Oxford 1946–50, and chairman of the Arts Council 1953–60. Life peer 1969. Chanc. York University 1969. O.M. 1976.

Clarkson, Thomas (1760–1846) devoted his life to the abolition of slavery and shares with Wilberforce credit for the passing of the Act of 1807 abolishing the British slave trade.

Claude Lorrain (Gelée) (1600–82), French landscape painter. B. near Nancy, he settled in Rome. A close student of nature, he excelled in depicting sunrise or sunset, and founded a "picturesque" tradition.

Claudius (10 B.C.–A.D. 54), Roman emperor. After the murder of Caligula, he was proclaimed emperor almost accidentally by the Praetorian Guard. He was a sensible administrator. In his time the empire was extended to include Britain, Thrace, and Mauretania. He was probably poisoned by his wife Agrippina.

Clausewitz, Karl von (1780–1831), German military expert whose *Vom Kriege*, expounding his theories on war, dominated Prussia in the 19th cent.

Clemenceau, Georges (1841–1929), French statesman of radical views; twice premier, 1906–9, 1917–20. He was a defender of Dreyfus. In old age he presided at the peace conference of 1919, where he was hostile to Germany ("the Tiger").

Cleopatra (69–30 B.C.), daughter of Ptolemy XI, the sixth queen of Egypt by that name, a brilliant, ambitious woman. In 51 she became joint sovereign with her younger brother Ptolemy XII. She was banished to Syria, but, obtaining the help of Caesar, regained the kingdom. She and Caesar became lovers, and in 47 she bore him a son Caesarion (later Ptolemy XIV). After Caesar's murder she returned to Egypt. She met the triumvir Mark Antony and bore him twins; he deserted his wife and broke with his brother-in-law Octavian (later Augustus). Antony and Cleopatra were, however, defeated in 31 B.C.; Antony fell upon his sword, and Cleopatra killed herself with an asp bite. Her life inspired Shakespeare's *Antony and Cleopatra* and Shaw's *Caesar and Cleopatra*.

Clive, 1st Baron (Robert Clive) (1725–74), English general who helped to lay the foundations of English power in India. B. near Market Drayton, he entered the service of the East India Company. He contemplated suicide, but Anglo-French rivalry, culminating in the Seven Years War, gave scope for his military powers in the siege of Arcot and the battle of Plassey. As a governor he showed administrative capacity. In his later life he was unpopular which led to his suicide.

Clovis (c. 465–511), Merovingian king of the Franks and a convert to Christianity. He defeated the Burgundians and West Goths, and fixed his court at Paris.

Clyde, Lord. *See* **Campbell, Colin.**

Cobbett, William (1763–1835), English controversialist. He is chiefly known for his *Rural Rides*, but also published a weekly *Political Register* from 1802.

Cobden, Richard (1804–65), English advocate of free trade. The son of a Sussex farmer, he led agitation against the laws restricting import of corn, and they were repealed in 1846. He was impoverished by his public work and was helped by subscription.

Cochrane, Thomas, 10th Earl of Dundonald (1775–1860), British seaman, who crippled a French fleet in Biscay (1809), aided the liberation of Chile and Peru from Spanish rule (1819–22), of Brazil from Portuguese rule (1823–5), and assisted the Greeks in their struggle to throw off the Turkish yoke (1827).

Cockcroft, Sir John Douglas (1897–1967), Cambridge nuclear physicist who shared with E. T. S. Walton the 1951 Nobel prize. They had worked together at Cambridge in the historic "atom-splitting" experiments beginning with the transmutation of lithium into boron. He was directly involved in Britain's first nuclear power programmes.

Cockerell, Christopher (b. 1910), English inventor of the hovercraft, which works on the aircushioning principle. *See* **Hovercraft, Section L.**

Cocteau, Jean (1891–1963), French writer and artist in widely varied forms of art.

Cody, Samuel Franklin (1861–1913), American aviator, the first man to fly in Britain (1,390 ft. on 16 Oct. 1908). He became a British subject in 1909. Killed while flying.

Cody, William Frederick (1846–1917), American showman, known as "Buffalo Bill," whose Wild West Show toured America and Europe.

Coggan, Donald (b. 1909), enthroned 101st archbishop of Canterbury, January 1975; archbishop of York 1961–74; Canterbury 1975–80.

Cohn, Ferdinand Julius (1828–98), German botanist, founder of the science of bacteriology.

Coke, Sir Edward (1552–1634), English legal author, judge, and rival of Francis Bacon. His legal works are his *Reports* and *Institutes.*

Colbert, Jean Baptiste (1619–83), French statesman under Louis XIV, who fostered new industries, encouraged commerce, reformed the finances and established the navy on a sound basis. A patron of literature, science, and art.

Cole, George Douglas Howard (1889–1959), English economist and political journalist, professor of social and political theory at Oxford, 1944–57. Among his writings are *The Intelligent Man's Guide through World Chaos,* and *A History of Socialist Thought* (5 vols.).

Coleridge, Samuel Taylor (1772–1834), English poet, critic, and friend of Wordsworth, with whom he published *Lyrical Ballads.* His poems include *The Ancient Mariner, Christabel,* and *Kubla Khan.* His literary criticism is still valuable.

Coleridge-Taylor, Samuel (1875–1912), English composer, the son of a West African doctor practising in London and an Englishwoman. He is best known for his Hiawatha trilogy.

Colet, John (c. 1467–1519), English humanist and divine, founded St. Paul's School (1512). As scholar and friend of Erasmus he helped to bring the new learning to England.

Colette (Sidonie Gabrielle Claudine Colette) (1873–1954), French author of the *Claudine* stories, *Chéri* and *La Fin de Chéri.*

Collier, John (1850–1934), English painter noted for his "problem" pictures.

Collingwood, 1st Baron (Cuthbert Collingwood) (1750–1810), British admiral whose ship, the *Royal Sovereign,* led the fleet to battle at Trafalgar, and who on Nelson's death assumed command.

Collingwood, Robin George (1889–1943), English philosopher, historian, and archaeologist, associated with Oxford from 1908 to 1941. His philosophical thought is best studied in *Speculum Mentis, Essay on Philosophical Method, Idea of Nature,* and *Idea of History.*

Collins, Michael (1890–1922), Irish politician and Sinn Fein leader. He successfully organised guerrilla warfare, and mainly negotiated the treaty with Britain in 1921, but was killed in a Republican ambush on his return.

Collins, William (1788–1847), English landscape and figure painter.

Collins, William Wilkie (1824–89), son of the above; one of the first English novelists to

deal with the detection of crime. *The Woman in White* appeared in 1860.

Colt, Samuel (1814–62), of Hartford, Connecticut, invented the revolver in 1835. It was used in the war with Mexico.

Columba, St. (521–97), founder of the monastery of Iona, b. Ireland. From the island shrine he made missionary journeys to the Highlands of Scotland.

Columbanus, St. (c. 540–615), Irish abbot who founded a number of monasteries in continental Europe. *See* **Monasticism, Section J.**

Columbus, Christopher (c. 1451–1506), Italian navigator, b. Genoa, who, prevailing upon Ferdinand and Isabella of Spain to bear the expense of an expedition, in 1492 discovered the Bahamas, Cuba, and other West Indian islands. In 1498 he landed on the lowlands of S. America.

Comenius, John Amos (1592–1670), Czech educationist and pastor, advocate of the "direct" method of teaching languages, of the use of pictures in education, and of equality of educational opportunity for girls.

Compton, Arthur Holly (1892–1962), American physicist whose work on X-rays established what is known as the Compton effect (1923). While professor of physics at the university of Chicago (1923–45) he helped to develop the atomic bomb. Nobel prizewinner 1927.

Compton, Karl Taylor (1887–1954), scientist-administrator, brother of the above. Pres. Massachusetts Institute of Technology 1930–48.

Compton-Burnett, Dame Ivy (1884–1969), English novelist whose books deal with family relationships and include *Pastors and Masters, Men and Wives, A House and Its Head, Manservant and Maidservant.*

Comte, August (1798–1857), French philosopher, founder of positivism. *See* **Positivism, Section J.**

Condé, Louis, Prince de (1621–86), French general who defeated Spain at Rocroi in 1643.

Confucius or K'ung Fu-tse (c. 551–478 B.C.), Chinese philosopher, founder of the system of cosmology, politics, and ethics known as Confucianism. He was not concerned with the supernatural, but appealed to reason and taught love and respect of one's fellows, superiority to ambition, charity, forgiveness, and repentance. *See* **Confucianism, Section J.**

Congreve, William (1670–1729). Restoration dramatist, whose witty plays include *The Way of the World* and *Love for Love.*

Conrad, Joseph (1857–1924), English novelist of Polish birth, whose parents were exiled to Russia for political reasons. He became master mariner in the British merchant service, and began to write novels after he left the sea in 1884. His novels include *Almayer's Folly, Lord Jim, Nostromo.*

Conscience, Hendrik Henri (1812–83), Flemish novelist who wrote *The Lion of Flanders.*

Constable, John (1776–1837), English landscape painter, b. East Bergholt, Suffolk. Unlike his contemporary Turner, who journeyed over the Continent with his sketchbook, he found his scenes within a few miles of his home. His work was more popular in France than in England at the time and affected the Barbizon school and Delacroix. Examples of his work are in the National Gallery (including *The Hay Wain, Flatford Mill,* and *The Cornfield*), the Victoria and Albert, and the Tate (*The Valley Farm*).

Constant, Jean Joseph Benjamin (1845–1902), French painter of portraits and Oriental subjects.

Constantine (274–338), called "the Great," the first Christian Roman emperor. He was proclaimed at York by the army in 306. He stabilised the empire after a period of decline, and founded a new capital at Constantinople. A Christian council was held under his auspices at Nicaea in 325, and he was baptised on his death-bed.

Cook, James (1728–79), English navigator, son of an agricultural labourer. He entered the Royal Navy and gained a high reputation for his scientific skill. He made voyages of discovery to New Zealand and Australia in the ships under his command, *Endeavour, Resolution,* and *Adventure.* He anchored at Botany Bay in 1770 on his first voyage and gave it that name because of the interesting plants found on its shores. He also surveyed the Newfoundland coast. In an attempt to find the north-west passage he was murdered at Hawaii.

Cooper, Sir Astley Paston (1768–1841), English surgeon and author of medical textbooks.

Cooper, James Fenimore (1789–1851), American novelist, who produced stirring stories of adventure, among them *The Spy*, *The Last of the Mohicans*, *The Pathfinder*, and *The Deerslayer*.

Cooper, Samuel (1609–72), English miniaturist, represented with his brother Alexander (d. 1660) in the Victoria and Albert Museum. Among his miniatures is a portrait of Cromwell.

Copernicus, Nicolas (1478–1543), founder of modern astronomy, b. at Torun in Poland. He studied at Cracow and at a number of Italian universities before settling at Frauenburg in 1512 where he became canon of the cathedral. More of a student than a practical astronomer, he spent most of his private life seeking a new theory of the heavenly bodies. In his *On the Revolution of the Celestial Orbs*, published after his death, he broke with the past and put forward the novel theory that the planets, including the earth, revolve round the sun.

Coppée, François Joachim (1842–1908), French poet, novelist and dramatist.

Coquelin, Benoit Constant (1841–1909), and **Coquelin, Ernest** (1848–1909), (Coquelin aîné et cadet), brothers, were leading lights of the French theatre.

Corelli, Arcangelo (1653–1713), Italian composer and violinist, who established the form of the concerto grosso. *See* **Section E.**

Corneille, Pierre (1606–84), French dramatist, who ranks with Racine as a master of classical tragedy. *Le Cid*, *Polyeucte*, and *Le Menteur* marked a new era in French dramatic production.

Cornwallis, 1st Marquess (Charles Cornwallis) (1738–1805), British general who commanded the British forces which surrendered to the Americans at Yorktown in 1781, thus ending the war of independence. He was twice governor-general of India.

Corot, Jean Baptiste (1796–1875), French landscape painter.

Correggio, Antonio Allegri da (1494–1534), Italian painter, b. Correggio. His style anticipates the baroque. His *Ecce Homo* is in the National Gallery.

Cortés, Hernando (1488–1547), Spanish adventurer, b. Medellin, Estremadura, who captured Mexico for Spain, crushing an ancient civilisation.

Coulton, George Gordon (1858–1947), scholar and historian of the Middle Ages. In his *Five Centuries of Religion* he sets forth his interpretation of monastic history in England from the Conquest to the Reformation.

Couperin, a family of French musicians who were organists at St. Gervais, Paris, from about 1650 till 1826. **François Couperin** (1668–1783), called "Couperin the Great," is the best known today for his harpsichord music.

Cousin, Victor (1792–1867), French educationist and philosopher, founder of the eclectic school.

Cousins, Samuel (1801–87), English mezzotint engraver of plates after Reynolds, Millais, Landseer, and Hogarth.

Cousteau, Jacques-Yves (b. 1910), French underwater explorer, pioneer of aqualung diving.

Couve de Murville, Maurice (b. 1907), French diplomat; General de Gaulle's foreign minister 1958–68.

Coverdale, Miles (1488–1568), one of the early English reformers, b. Yorkshire, later to become bishop of Exeter. He assisted Tyndale in translating the Pentateuch and completed his own translation of the Bible in 1535. The Psalms still used in the Prayer Book and many of the phrases in the authorised version of 1611 are from his translation.

Cowper, William (1731–1800), English religious poet. His work is characterised by simplicity and tenderness. His best-known poems are *John Gilpin* and *The Task*.

Cox, David (1783–1859), English landscape painter. A collection of his works is in the Birmingham Gallery and the Tate Gallery.

Crabbe, George (1754–1832), English narrative poet of grim humour; author of *The Village* and *The Borough*.

Craig, Edward Gordon (1872–1966), son of Ellen Terry, producer and author of books on stagecraft.

Cranmer, Thomas (1489–1556), archbishop of Canterbury under Henry VIII, and Edward VI; an ardent promoter of the Reformation. On Mary's accession he at first consented to return to the old faith, but when called upon to make public avowal of his recantation, refused, and was burnt at the stake. His contributions were the English Bible and Book of Common Prayer.

Crichton, James (1560–82), Scottish adventurer who for his scholarly accomplishments was called "the admirable Crichton." He was killed in a brawl.

Cripps, Sir Stafford (1889–1952), British Labour statesman. A successful barrister, he relinquished practice for public work. As chancellor of the exchequer in post-war Britain, his programme was one of austerity, but his able exposition and single-minded purpose won him general support. Ill-health terminated his career.

Crispi, Francesco (1819–1901), Italian statesman, who aided Garibaldi and was later premier.

Crispin, St. (c. 285), martyr with his brother. By tradition they were Roman and became shoemakers, hence patron saints of shoemaking.

Croce, Benedetto (1886–1952), Italian philosopher and critic. His philosophy is expounded in the four volumes of *Filosofia dello Spirito* (which has been translated into English). He founded and edited *La Critica* in 1908, a review of literature, history, and philosophy. He was strongly opposed to fascism.

Croesus (d. c. 546 B.C.), last king of Lydia, reputed to be of immense wealth. Conquered and condemned to death by Cyrus, he was reprieved when Cyrus heard him recall Solon's saying "Call no man happy till he is dead."

Crome, John (1769–1821), English landscape painter, b. Norwich.

Cromer, 1st Earl of (Evelyn Baring) (1841–1917), British diplomat who, as British comptroller-general in Egypt from 1883 to 1907, did much to maintain order, improve the finances, and promote development. His *Modern Egypt* appeared in 1908.

Crompton, Samuel (1753–1827), English inventor of the spinning-mule (1779), which substituted machinery for hand work. He was b. near Bolton, a farmer's son, and benefited little by his invention.

Cromwell, Oliver (1599–1658), Protector of the commonwealth of England, Scotland, and Ireland. B. at Huntingdon, he represented Huntingdon in parliament. When civil war broke out, he served under the Earl of Essex; and then reorganised the parliamentary army, winning victories at Marston Moor and Naseby. Tortuous negotiations with Charles I could not be brought to an end, and he promoted the king's trial and execution in 1649. He defeated the Scots at Dunbar. When continued difficulties beset government he became Protector in 1653, but was soon obliged to govern by major-generals. His handling of Ireland enhanced the difficulties of that country. An able general and a strong character, he was personally tolerant (an Independent), sincere and devout; but he found himself in the revolutionary's dilemma—that there is no easy exit from a revolutionary situation; thus paradoxically he provoked English aversion to military rule.

Cromwell, Richard (1626–1712), son of the above, and his successor in the protectorate.

Cromwell, Thomas (1485–1540), English statesman, who succeeded Wolsey in the service of Henry VIII, and carried out the dissolution of the monasteries, but on his fall from favour he was executed.

Crookes, Sir William (1832–1919), English physicist who discovered the element thallium (1861) and invented the Crookes tube (1874) which was used by J. J. Thomson and others in their researches into the conduction of electricity in gases. He was also an authority on sanitation.

Cruikshank, George (1792–1878), caricaturist and book illustrator, whose work includes illustrations to *Grimm's Fairy Tales*, and *Oliver Twist*. Collections of his work are in the British Museum and the Victoria and Albert Museum.

Cummings, Bruce Frederick (1889–1919), English

zoologist and won fame as author of *Journal of a Disappointed Man*.

Cunard, Sir Samuel (1787–1865), founder of the Cunard line of steam ships. He was born in Nova Scotia, of a Welsh family of Quakers.

Cunningham of Hyndhope, 1st Viscount (Andrew Browne Cunningham) (1883–1963). British admiral in two world wars, b. Edinburgh. He served as commander-in-chief, Mediterranean, 1939–42 and Feb.–Oct. 1943; naval commander-in-chief for the Allied assault on North Africa 1942; first sea lord 1943–6.

Curie, Marie Sklodowska (1867–1934), first great woman scientist, b. Poland. Her father was a professor of physics at Warsaw. She came to Paris to study at the Sorbonne and married **Pierre Curie** (1859–1906), professor of physics. Thus began a fruitful collaborative career that led to the discovery of radium for which they shared the 1903 Nobel prize for physics. In 1911 Mme. Curie received the Nobel prize for chemistry. Pierre Curie was killed in an accident. *See also* **Joliot-Curie**.

Curzon of Kedleston, 1st Marquess (George Nathaniel Curzon) (1859–1925), statesman and administrator; viceroy of India 1898–1905; member of Lloyd George's war cabinet 1916–18; foreign secretary 1919–24.

Cuthbert, St. (*c.* 635–87), Celtic monk who became prior of Old Melrose (on the Tweed) and later of Lindisfarne. For a time he lived in seclusion on one of the Farne islands. The story of his life we owe to Bede.

Cuvier, Georges (1769–1832), French naturalist, noted for his system of classification of animals and his studies in comparative anatomy. His *La Règne Animal* (1819) became a standard work.

Cuyp, Albert (1620–91), Dutch landscape painter of sea and river views.

Cyprian, St. (d. 258), bishop of Carthage, and early Christian writer who was martyred.

Cyrus (559–529 B.C.), Persian emperor. He founded the Achaemenid line, having defeated the Medes. By conquering Lydia and Babylonia, he controlled Asia Minor. He was a wise and tolerant ruler, allowing the Jews to rebuild their temple.

D

Daguerre, Louis Jacques Mandé (1789–1851), French photographic pioneer, who invented the daguerrotype process. *See* **Section L**.

Daimler, Gottlieb (1834–1900), German inventor, with N. A. Otto of Cologne, of the Otto gas engine. The Mercédès car, exhibited at Paris in 1900, was named after the daughter of Emile Jellinek, Austrian banker and car enthusiast.

Dalai Lama, *see* **Section L.**

Dale, Sir Henry Hallett (1875–1968), English physiologist. He shared the 1936 Nobel prize for medicine for his work on the chemical transmission of nerve impulses.

Dalhousie, 1st Marquess of (James Andrew Broun Ramsay) (1812–60), governor-general of India. He annexed the Punjab and later other states; opened the civil service to Indians and acted against suttee.

Dalton, John (1766–1844), English chemist and mathematician, a Quaker teacher of Manchester. In 1808 in the first number of his *New System of Chemical Philosophy* (1808–27) the modern chemical atomic theory was first propounded by him. According to this the atoms of the chemical elements are qualitatively different from one another.

Damien, Father (1840–89), Belgian missionary priest, originally named Joseph de Veuster, who, witnessing the sufferings of the lepers confined on the Hawaiian island of Molokai, obtained permission to take charge, and remained there until he himself died of leprosy.

Damocles, 5th cent. B.C., Syracusan flatterer who pronounced the tyrant Dionysius the happiest of men. To illustrate the uncertainty of life, Dionysius invited him to a banquet, where a naked sword hung over his head by a hair. Hence the expression "Sword of Damocles" to mean impending danger or threat.

Damrosch, Walter Johannes (1862–1950), American conductor and composer, b. Breslau, Prussia. He promoted musical development

in the U.S., especially while conductor of the New York Symphony Society which his father, Leopold Damrosch (1832–1885) had founded in 1878.

D'Annunzio, Gabriele (1863–1938), Italian poet, dramatist and nationalist. In 1919 he led a raid on Fiume and seized it, but was eventually forced to surrender. His bodyguard wore the black shirt which was to be the uniform of the Fascists.

Dante Alighieri (1265–1321), Italian poet, a figure of world literature. He was b. at Florence in a troubled period. Though he saw her but once or twice, he loved a lady whom he called Beatrice, who is believed to have been Bice Portinari who married Simone di Bardi; she died in 1290, after which Dante wrote his *Vita Nuova*. His next work *Convivio* was philosophical. He joined the party of the Bianchi, attained municipal office, but was imprisoned and in 1301 fled. His *Divina Commedia* is a description of hell, purgatory, and heaven, a work of moral edification, replete with symbolism. He d. at Ravenna.

Danton, Georges Jacques (1759–94), French revolutionary. To his eloquent lead in 1792 was largely due the defeat of the foreign forces attempting to quell the revolution. He was a member of the committee of public safety, and sought to modify the extremists, but was displaced by Robespierre and was subsequently executed.

D'Arblay. *See* **Burney.**

Darby, Abraham (1677–1717), member of the Quaker family of ironmasters of Coalbrookdale, Shropshire, who paved the way for the industrial revolution by developing iron metallurgy. His grandson **Abraham** (1750–91) built the first cast-iron bridge (1779) over the Severn at Coalbrookdale.

Darius I (548–486 B.C.), Persian king and founder of Persepolis. He extended the borders of the Persian empire beyond the Indus, and reorganised it into satrapies. He declared "God's plan for the earth is not turmoil but peace, prosperity and good government." On clashing with the Greeks, however, he was defeated at Marathon. **Darius II** was a natural son of Artaxerxes I and d. 405 B.C. **Darius III** (d. 331 B.C.) was the last of the Persian kings, and was defeated by Alexander and assassinated.

Darling, Grace Horsley (1815–42), English heroine who by putting off in a small boat from the lighthouse on one of the Farne islands, of which her father was keeper, saved the shipwrecked crew of the *Forfarshire*.

Darnley, Henry Stewart, Lord (1545–67), second husband of Mary, Queen of Scots (1565). He plotted the murder of her secretary Rizzio, and was subsequently himself murdered. Through his son James I he is the ancestor of the Stuart monarchs.

Darwin, Charles Robert (1809–82), English naturalist, b. Shrewsbury, one of the pioneers of experimental biology. After returning from his formative voyage round the world as naturalist on the *Beagle* (1831–6), he spent nearly twenty years building up evidence for his theory of evolution before publishing it in *The Origin of Species* (1859). In it he argued that the evolution of present-day morphology had been built up by the gradual and opportunistic mechanism of natural selection. His ideas though welcomed by biologists aroused bitter controversy.

Daudet, Alphonse (1840–97), French writer who covered a wide range and whose works include *Lettres de mon Moulin*, *Robert Helmont*, and *Tartarin de Tarascon*.

David I (1084–1153), King of Scotland. As uncle of Matilda, daughter of Henry I of England, he supported her claim to the English crown, but was defeated. In Scotland he promoted unity and development.

David II (1324–71), King of Scotland. He was son of Robert Bruce. In invading England he was captured at Neville's Cross, 1346.

David, Sir Edgeworth (1848–1934), Australian geologist who accompanied Shackleton's antarctic expedition, 1907–9, leading the party that reached the south magnetic pole.

David, Jacques Louis (1748–1825), French painter of classical subjects and an ardent republican.

David, St., patron saint of Wales who lived in south Wales in the 6th cent.

Davidson, 1st Baron (Randall Thomas Davidson) (1848–1930), archbishop of Canterbury, 1903–28.

Davies, Sir Walford (1869–1941), English organist, composer, and broadcaster on music.

Davies, William Henry (1871–1940), Welsh poet. He spent some years tramping in both England and America, and his work shows knowledge of and love for nature. He wrote *Autobiography of a Super-tramp*.

Da Vinci. *See* Leonardo.

Davis, Jefferson (1808–89), American civil war leader. B. in Kentucky, he was made president of the Confederate States when the civil war broke out. After the war he was tried for treason, but discharged. He wrote *The Rise and Fall of the Confederate Government*.

Davis, John (c. 1550–1605), Elizabethan explorer and discoverer of Davis's Strait, the channel between the Atlantic and Arctic oceans on the west of Greenland. Invented the backstaff, or Davis's quadrant.

Davitt, Michael (1846–1906), Irish nationalist. The son of a peasant who later came to England, he joined the Fenians, and in 1870 was sentenced to penal servitude. On his release he helped to found the Land League in 1879; was again imprisoned; and wrote *Leaves from a Prison Diary*. He was subsequently returned to parliament.

Davy, Sir Humphry (1778–1829), English chemist, b. Penzance. Much of his work found practical application, e.g., the miner's safety lamp which still bears his name. His *Elements of Agricultural Chemistry* (1813) contains the first use in English of the word "element." He took Michael Faraday as his assistant at the Royal Institution.

Dawber, Sir Guy (1861–1938), English architect. As chairman of the Council for the Preservation of Rural England, he did much to bring about the restoration of buildings throughout the country.

Day Lewis, Cecil (1904–72), poet and critic; professor of poetry at Oxford from 1951–6. He succeeded Masefield as poet laureate in 1968.

Debussy, Claude Achille (1862–1918), composer and leader of the French Impressionist school in music. Among his works are *Suite bergamasque*, containing the popular *Clair de lune*; *L'après-midi d'un Faune*, inspired by the poem of Mallarmé, and *La Mer*. He also wrote an opera *Pelléas et Mélisande* based on Maeterlinck's drama. *See also* Section E.

Defoe, Daniel (1660–1731), English political writer; also author of *Robinson Crusoe, Moll Flanders*, and a *Tour of Gt. Britain*. His *Shortest Way with Dissenters* brought him imprisonment.

De Forest, Lee (1873–1961), American inventor who was the first to use alternating-current transmission, and improved the thermionic valve detector by which wireless and sound films were made possible.

Degas, Edgar (1834–1917), French impressionist painter and sculptor, son of a banker. He painted subjects from everyday life—dancers, café life, the racecourse.

De Gasperi, Alcide (1881–1954), Italian politician who founded the Christian Democrat Party.

de Gaulle. *See* Gaulle, Charles de.

De Havilland, Sir Geoffrey (1882–1965), pioneer of civil and military aviation in Britain; designer of the famous Moth machines. His son was killed in 1946 while testing a plane.

Delacroix, Ferdinand Victor Eugène (1798–1863), French painter of the Romantic school.

De la Mare, Walter John (1873–1956), English poet and novelist whose work has a characteristic charm. Much of it was written for children.

Delane, John Thadeus (1817–79), editor of *The Times*, 1841–77, who did much to establish that paper's standing.

Delaroche, Paul (1797–1856), French historical painter.

Delibes, Clément Philibert Léo (1836–91), French composer of much graceful music, including operas, of which *Lakmé* is the best known, and ballets, among them *Coppélia*.

Delius, Frederick (1862–1934), English composer of German parentage. His music, highly idiosyncratic in idiom, was more readily re-

ceived in Germany than in England until promoted by Sir Thomas Beecham. *See* Section E.

Democritus (c. 470–c. 400 B.C.), one of the first scientific thinkers, pupil of Leucippus (fl. c. 440 B.C.). He took an atomic view of matter, denied the existence of mind as a separate entity, and counted happiness and inner tranquility as important moral principles. His attitude was not shared by his contemporary, Socrates, nor by Plato and Aristotle, but was accepted by Epicurus. The atomic theory thus passed into the background for many centuries.

Demosthenes (384–322 B.C.), Greek orator who, by his *Philippics*, roused the Athenians to resist the growing power of Philip of Macedon.

Deng Xiaoping (b. 1904), Chinese politician, b. Szechwan; rehabilitated at Eleventh Party Congress (1977); effective leader of China in 1980s, target of May 1989 student revolt.

De Quincey, Thomas (1785–1859), English essayist and critic; friend of Wordsworth and Southey. He wrote *Confessions of an English Opium-eater*.

De Reszke, Jean (1853–1925) and **De Reszke, Edouard** (1856–1917), Polish operatic singers, the first a tenor, the second a baritone.

Derwentwater, 3rd Earl of (James Radcliffe) (1689–1716), leader of the English Jacobite movement for placing the pretender on the throne. He was defeated at Preston in 1715 and beheaded.

Descartes, René (1596–1650), French mathematician, pioneer of modern philosophy. Unconvinced by scholastic tradition and theological dogma, he sought to get back to why anything can be said to be true, which turned out to be a fruitful line of thought. The basis of his Cartesian philosophy is summed up in his own words, *Cogito, ergo sum* (I think, therefore I am).

Desmoulins, Camille (1760–94), French revolutionary. He represented Paris in the National Convention, and wrote witty and sarcastic pamphlets and periodicals. He was an ally of Danton.

Deutscher, Isaac (1907–67), Marxist historian, biographer of Stalin and Trotsky. B. in Poland, he joined the outlawed Polish Communist Party but was expelled for his anti-Stalinist views. In 1939 he came to London.

De Valéra, Eamon (1882–1975), Irish statesman, b. New York, son of a Spanish father and an Irish mother. He was imprisoned for his part in the Easter rising of 1916. He opposed the treaty of 1921; and in 1926, when the republican Fianna Fáil was founded, he became its president. Fianna Fáil won the election of 1932, and he then became president of the Executive Council, 1932–7; prime minister, 1937–48, 1951–4, 1957–9; president of the republic, 1959–73. He promoted Irish neutrality in the second world war, encouraged the use of the Irish language, and in spite of early intransigence his leadership was moderate.

de Valois, Dame Ninette (b. 1898), Irish-born ballet dancer and choreographer. She toured Europe with Diaghilev, 1923–5, and in 1931 founded the Sadler's Wells Ballet School (now Royal Ballet School), of which she became director. *Autobiography* (1957).

Dewar, Sir James (1842–1923), chemist and physicist, a native of Kincardine. He succeeded in liquefying hydrogen, and invented the vacuum flask. The explosive cordite was the joint invention of himself and Sir Frederick Abel.

Dewey, John (1859–1952), American philosopher, psychologist, and educationist. A follower of William James, he was an exponent of pragmatism.

De Witt, Jan (1625–72), Dutch republican statesman, who carried on war with England and later negotiated the Triple Alliance, but was overthrown by the Orange Party and murdered.

Diaghilev, Sergei Pavlovich (1872–1929), Russian ballet impresario and founder of the Russian ballet. Among those associated with him are Anna Pavlova, Vaslav Nijinsky, Tamara Karsavina, Leonide Massine, Michel Fokine, the choreographer, L. N. Bakst, the painter, and Igor Stravinsky, the composer.

Dickens, Charles (1812–70), popular English novelist of the 19th cent., with enormous output and capacity for vivid story-telling. Of humble origin, he was extremely successful.

His best-known works are perhaps *Pickwick Papers*, *Oliver Twist*, *A Christmas Carol* (this influenced the observance of Christmas), *Dombey and Son*, *David Copperfield*, *Little Dorrit*, and *Great Expectations*. He gave public readings from his works.

Dickinson, Emily (1830–86), American poet whose writing has a mystic quality. She lived a cloistered life and published almost nothing in her lifetime.

Dickinson, Goldsworthy Lowes (1863–1932), English author, an interpreter and upholder of the Greek view of life.

Diderot, Denis (1713–84), French man of letters, critic of art and literature, and editor of the *Encyclopédie* (1713–84) to which many writers of the Englightenment contributed.

Diemen, Anthony van (1593–1645), Dutch promoter of exploration. As governor-general in the Far East, he promoted Dutch trade and influence; and despatched Abel Tasman, who in 1642 discovered New Zealand and Van Diemen's Land (now Tasmania).

Diesel, Rudolf (1858–1913), German engineer, inventor of an internal combustion engine which he patented in 1893. *See also* L31.

Diocletian (245–313), Roman emperor and persecutor of Christianity. He divided the empire under a system of joint rule; later abdicated; and built a palace in Dalmatia.

Diogenes (412–322 B.C.), Greek cynic philosopher who lived in a tub and told Alexander to get out of his sunshine. He sought virtue and moral freedom in liberation from desire.

Dionysius the elder and younger, tyrants of Syracuse in the 4th cent. B.C.

Dirac, Paul Adrien Maurice (1902–84), English physicist who shared with Erwin Schrödinger the 1933 Nobel prize for their work in developing Heisenberg's theory of quantum mechanics. Order of Merit (1973).

Disney, Walter Elias (1901–66), American film cartoonist, creator of Mickey Mouse. He is known for his *Silly Symphonies*, *Snow White and the Seven Dwarfs*, and *Pinocchio*.

Disraeli, Benjamin, Earl of Beaconsfield (1804–81), British statesman and novelist who helped to form modern Conservatism in England. The son of Isaac (*q.v.*), he published his first novel at 21, and later *Coningsby* and *Sibyl*, which helped to rouse the social conscience. He entered parliament in 1837 and was prime minister 1868 and 1874–80, when he arranged the purchase of shares in the Suez canal. He was rival of Gladstone and friend of Queen Victoria.

D'Israeli, Isaac (1766–1848), father of Benjamin (*q.v.*) and author of *Curiosities of Literature*.

Dobson, Austin (1840–1921), English writer of light verse and of 18th cent. biography.

Dodgson, Charles Lutwidge (1832–98), English writer. Under the pseudonym Lewis Carroll, he wrote poems and books for children, including *Alice's Adventures in Wonderland*. In private life he was a lecturer in mathematics at Oxford.

Dolci, Carlo (1616–86), one of the last Florentine painters.

Dolci, Danilo (b. 1924), Italian social reformer who since 1952 has dedicated himself to the rehabilitation of the people of Sicily in their desperate poverty.

Dominic, St. (1170–1221), founder of the Friars Preachers or Black Friars. B. in Castile, he and his followers sought to teach the gospel. In 1216 they were formed into an order and vowed to poverty. The order spread through Europe.

Domitian (Titus Flavius Domitianus) (A.D. 51–96), Roman emperor, son of Vespasian. He ruled despotically, aroused the hatred of the senate, and was assassinated as a result of a palace conspiracy.

Donatello (Donato di Niccolò) (*c.* 1386–1466), Italian sculptor, b. Florence, son of Niccolò di Betto di Bardo. He was the founder of modern sculpture, producing statues independent of a background, designed to stand in the open to be viewed from all angles. Among his masterpieces are the statues of *St. George* and *David* (in the Bargello, Florence) and his equestrian *Gattamelata* in Padua, the first bronze horse to be cast in the Renaissance.

Donizetti, Gaetano (1797–1848), Italian composer. The best known of his sixty operas are *Lucia*

di Lammermoor, *La Fille du Régiment*, and *Don Pasquale*. *See* **Section E.**

Donne, John (1572–1631), English metaphysical poet and preacher (dean of St. Paul's). His poems and sermons marked by passion, wit, and profundity of thought have received full publicity only in the present century. His writings include *Elegies*, *Satires*, *Songs and Sonnets*, *Problems and Paradoxes* and the *Holy Sonnets*.

Doré, Gustave (1833–83), French artist who painted scriptural subjects and illustrated Dante, Milton, and Tennyson.

Dostoyevsky, Feodor Mikhailovich (1821–81), Russian novelist, b. Moscow. As a result of his revolutionary activity he was sent to hard labour in Siberia. In his books, which include *Crime and Punishment*, *The Brothers Karamazov*, *The Idiot*, and *The Possessed*, he explored the dark places of the human spirit to a degree not previously attempted.

Douglas of Kirtleside, 1st Baron (William Sholto Douglas) (1893–1969), British airman; commanded Fighter command, 1940–2, Coastal command, 1944–5. A Labour peer.

Douglas, Norman (1868–1952), novelist and travel writer. A Scot, born in Austria, he made his home on the Mediterranean. His works include *South Wind*.

Doulton, Sir Henry (1820–97), English potter and the inventor of Doulton ware.

Dowden, Edward (1843–1913), English literary critic and Shakespearean scholar.

Dowding, 1st Baron (Hugh Caswell Tremenheere Dowding) (1882–1970), British airman; commanded Fighter command during the Battle of Britain period (1940).

Dowland, John (*c.* 1563–1626), English composer of songs with lute accompaniment. His son Robert succeeded him as Court lutenist to Charles I.

Doyle, Sir Arthur Conan (1859–1930), British writer, b. Edinburgh, creator of the detective Sherlock Holmes and his friend and foil, Dr. Watson. He was trained as a doctor but gave up his medical practice in 1890 to devote himself to writing.

Doyle, Richard (1824–83), humorous artist on the staff of *Punch*.

D'Oyly Carte, Richard (1844–1901), English theatrical manager, who built the Savoy theatre and there produced Gilbert and Sullivan operas.

Drake, Sir Francis (*c.* 1540–96), English seaman. In 1577–80 he sailed round the world in the *Golden Hind*. In 1587 he destroyed a number of Spanish ships in Cadiz harbour; and under Lord Howard he helped to defeat the Spanish Armada in 1588.

Draper, John William (1811–82), American chemist, b. near Liverpool. He was the first, using Daguerre's process, to take a successful photograph of the human face (1840), and of the moon.

Dreiser, Theodore (1871–1935), American novelist of austere realism. Author of *An American Tragedy*.

Dreyfus, Alfred (1859–1935), French victim of injustice. Of Jewish parentage, in 1894 he was accused of divulging secrets to a foreign power, and was sentenced by a military secret tribunal to imprisonment for life on Devil's Island in French Guiana. At a new trial in 1899 he was again found guilty. Efforts continued to be made on his behalf, and in 1906 he was entirely exonerated, restored to his rank in the army, and made a Chevalier of the Legion of Honour.

Drinkwater, John (1882–1937), English poet and playwright. His plays include *Abraham Lincoln*, and *Oliver Cromwell*.

Drummond, William, (1585–1649), Scottish poet and Royalist pamphleteer. He was laird of Hawthornden.

Drury, Alfred (1857–1944), English sculptor, especially of statues of Queen Victoria at Bradford and Portsmouth.

Dryden, John (1631–1700), prolific English poet and dramatist, who also wrote political satire (*Absalom and Achitophel*). He was hostile to the revolution of 1688, and thereafter mainly translated classical writers, including Virgil.

Du Barry, Marie Jean Bécu, Comtesse (1746–93), mistress of Louis XV of France and guillotined by the revolutionary tribunal.

Dubček, Alexander (b. 1921), Czech communist leader. First Secretary, Slovak Communist Party, 1968-69. His reform programme (the 'Prague Spring') prompted the Russian invasion of August 1968. Restored to public life, 1989, becoming Chairman of the Parliament.

Du Chaillu, Paul Belloni (1835–1903), traveller in Africa, who in 1861 and 1867 published accounts of his explorations. A French-American.

Dufferin and Ava, 1st Marquess of (Frederick Temple Hamilton-Temple Blackwood) (1826–1902), British diplomat, writer, and governor-general of Canada and viceroy of India.

Dulles, John Foster (1888–1959), U.S. Secretary of State in the Republican administration 1953–9. His foreign policy was inflexibly opposed to negotiations with Russia and to U.S. recognition of China, during a period when the Cold War was still a potent factor.

Dumas, Alexandre (1802–70), French romantic novelist, among whose many works are *The Three Musketeers*, *The Count of Monte Cristo*, and *The Black Tulip*.

Dumas, Alexandre (1824–95), French dramatist, son of the above; author of *La Dame aux Camélias*.

Du Maurier, George (1834–96), contributor to *Punch* and author of *Trilby*.

Dummett, Professor Michael (b. 1925), English philosopher. Succeeded Ayer as Wykeham Professor of Logic at Oxford University. Author of *Logical Basis of Metaphysics* (1990). Anti-racist.

Dundee, 1st Viscount (John Graham of Claverhouse), (1648–89), Scottish soldier ("Bonnie Dundee"). Employed to suppress the covenanters, he was defeated at Drumclog, but victorious at Bothwell Brig. At the revolution of 1688 he supported James II, and was killed in the (victorious) battle of Killiecrankie.

Dundonald, Earl of. *See* **Cochrane, Thomas.**

Duns Scotus, John (*c.* 1265–1308), Scottish scholastic philosopher, b. at Maxton near Roxburgh, opponent of Thomas Aquinas. He joined the Franciscans, studied and taught at Oxford and Paris, and probably d. at Cologne. He challenged the harmony of faith and reason.

Dunstable, John (*c.* 1380–1453), the earliest English composer known by name. He was a contemporary of the Netherlands composers Dufay and Binchois. *See* **Section E.**

Dunstan, St. (908–88), reforming archbishop of Canterbury. He lived through seven reigns from Athelstan to Ethelred, and was adviser especially to Edgar. Under him Glastonbury Abbey became a centre of religious teaching.

Dupleix, Joseph François (1697–1763), French governor in India. He extended French influence and power in the Carnatic, but his plans were frustrated by his English opponent, Clive. He was recalled in 1754 and died in poverty.

Dürer, Albrecht (1471–1528), German painter and engraver. B. at Nuremberg, he was (like his Italian contemporary, Leonardo) a man of intellectual curiosity and scientific insight. His best work is in his copper engravings, woodcuts, and drawings; the former include *The Knight*, *Melancholia*, and *St. Jerome in his Study*. He was the friend of Luther and Melanchthon.

Durham, Earl of (John George Lambton) (1792–1840), governor-general of Canada after the disturbances of 1837, and in 1839 presented to parliament the *Durham Report*, which laid down the principle of colonial self-government.

Duse, Elenora (1861–1924), Italian tragedienne.

Duval, Claude (1643–70), notorious highwayman who came to England from Normandy and was eventually hanged at Tyburn.

Dvořák, Antonin (1841–1904), Czech composer whose music is rich in folk-song melodies of his native Bohemia. In 1884 he conducted his *Stabat Mater* in London. His *New World* symphony was composed in New York, where he was head of the National Conservatoire (1892-5). *See* **Section E.**

Dyson, Sir Frank Watson (1868–1939), English astronomer who was astronomer royal 1910-33, and astronomer royal for Scotland 1905–10.

Dyson, Sir George (1883–1964), English composer and writer. In *The New Music* he analysed the technique of modern schools of composition. He composed several choral works such as *The Canterbury Pilgrims* and *Nebuchadnezzar*, which still remain popular.

E

Earhart, Amelia (1898–1937), American air pioneer. First woman to fly the Atlantic alone. Disappeared in 1937 during a Pacific flight.

Eastlake, Sir Charles Lock (1793–1865), English painter of historical and religious works.

Eastman, George (1854–1932), American inventor of the roll photographic film and the Kodak camera.

Eck, Johann von (1486–1543), German Catholic theologian and opponent of Luther.

Eddington, Sir Arthur Stanley (1882–1944), English astronomer (Greenwich observatory 1906–13; Cambridge observatory 1914–44). His works include *The Nature of the Physical World*.

Eddy, Mrs Mary Baker (1821–1910), American founder of the Church of Christ Scientist. Her *Science and Health with Key to the Scriptures* was published in 1875. *See* **Christian Science, Section J.**

Edelinck, Gerard (1640–1707), Flemish engraver, b. Antwerp, the first to reproduce in print the colour, as well as the form, of a picture.

Eden, Robert Anthony, 1st Earl of Avon (1897–1977), British statesman. He entered parliament in 1923; became foreign secretary in 1935 (resigning in 1938 over Chamberlain's negotiation with Mussolini and rebuff to President Roosevelt); deputy prime minister in 1951; succeeded Sir Winston Churchill in 1955. His Suez policy divided the country. He resigned for health reasons in 1957. Earldom 1961.

Edgar (943–75), King of England 959–75. He was advised by Archbishop Dunstan.

Edgar Atheling (*c.* 1060–*c.* 1130), was the lawful heir of Edward the Confessor, but in the Norman invasion could not maintain his claim.

Edgeworth, Maria (1767–1849), Irish novelist, whose stories include *Castle Rackrent*, *The Absentee*, and *Belinda*.

Edinburgh, Duke of (Philip Mountbatten) (b. 1921), consort of Queen Elizabeth II. He relinquished his right of accession to the thrones of Greece and Denmark on his naturalisation in 1947 when he took the name of Mountbatten. He is the great-great-grandson of Queen Victoria, grandson of Admiral Prince Louis of Battenberg, and nephew of the late Earl Mountbatten of Burma.

Edison, Thomas Alva (1847–1931), American inventor of the transmitter and receiver for the automatic telegraph; the phonograph; the incandescent lamp (shared with the British inventor Swan); and many devices for the electrical distribution of light and power. From being a newsboy on the railway and later a telegraph clerk, he became a master at applying scientific principles to practical ends. He set up a laboratory at Menlo Park, New Jersey.

Edmund II (Ironside) (*c.* 990–1016), the son of Ethelred, king of the English, made a compact with Canute to divide England, but soon afterwards died.

Edward the Confessor (*c.* 1004–1066), English king who preceded the Norman Conquest and founded Westminster Abbey. He was canonised in 1161.

Edward the Elder (*c.* 870–*c.* 924), son of Alfred, succeeded him as king of the West Saxons in 899. He overcame the Danes and reoccupied the northern counties.

Edward I (1239–1307), King of England, succeeded his father Henry in 1272. Able and energetic, his legislation influenced the development of the land law, and he summoned parliamentary assemblies. A soldier, he conquered Wales, building castles, but could not maintain his hold on Scotland.

Edward II (1284–1327), succeeded his father Edward I as king of England in 1307 and was defeated by the Scots at Bannockburn. Weak and inept, he was murdered in 1327.

Edward III (1312–77), succeeded his father Edward II as king of England in 1327. Popular and ambitious for military glory, he began the Hundred Years War with France. He fostered the woollen industry. Latterly he became senile.

Edward IV (1442–83), able but dissolute Yorkist leader whose reign (1461-70, 1471-83) brought about a revival in the power of the monarchy, in

English sea power, and in foreign trade (in which he himself took part). Spent 1470–71, in exile. Began rebuilding of St. George's chapel, Windsor. Patron of Caxton.

Edward V (1470–83), succeeded his father Edward IV at the age of 12 and was a pawn in the quarrels of baronial relatives. He and his brother were shut up in the Tower by his uncle, Richard, Duke of Gloucester, and there probably murdered, though exact proof has not been established.

Edward VI (1537–53), succeeded his father, Henry VIII, as king of England when in his tenth year. He was delicate and studious, and his government was carried on successively by the Dukes of Somerset and Northumberland; while under Archbishop Cranmer the prayer book was issued. He was induced to name Lady Jane Grey his successor.

Edward VII (1841–1910), King of Gr. Britain and Ireland. The son of Queen Victoria, he married Princess Alexandra of Denmark in 1863, and succeeded his mother in 1901. Interested mainly in social life and in international contacts, he visited India in 1875 and travelled much in Europe.

Edward VIII (1894–1972), King of Gt. Britain, succeeded his father George V 1936, and abdicated later that year because of disagreement over his proposed marriage. He was created Duke of Windsor, and was governor of the Bahamas 1940–45. The Duchess of Windsor died in 1986 in Paris.

Ehrlich, Paul (1854–1915), German bacteriologist, who at Frankfort-on-Main carried out work in immunology. He discovered salvarsan for the treatment of syphilis. Nobel prizewinner 1908.

Eiffel, Alexandre Gustave (1832–1923), French engineer, one of the first to employ compressed air caissons in bridge building. Among his works are the Eiffel Tower (1887–9) and the Panama Canal locks.

Einstein, Albert (1879–1955), mathematical physicist whose theory of relativity superseded Newton's theory of gravitation. He was born in Ulm of Jewish parents, lived for many years in Switzerland, and held a succession of professorial chairs at Zurich, Prague, and Berlin. In 1921 he was awarded the Nobel prize for his work in quantum theory. He was driven by the Nazis to seek asylum in America and became professor at the Institute of Advanced Study at Princeton 1933–45. In August 1939 at the request of a group of scientists he wrote to President Roosevelt warning of the danger of uranium research in Germany and stressing the urgency of investigating the possible use of atomic energy in bombs. *See* **Relativity, Section F, Part II.**

Eisenhower, Dwight David (1890–1969), American general and statesman. He was C.-in-C. Allied Forces, N. Africa, 1942–3; and and in the European theatre of operations, 1943–5; and was Republican President, 1953–61.

Eisenstein, Sergei Mikhailovich (1898–1948), Russian film director of *The Battleship Potemkin*, *Alexander Nevsky*, and *Ivan the Terrible*.

Eleanor (1246–90), Queen of Edward I. After her death in 1290 the king had memorial crosses erected at the twelve places where her body rested on its way from Grantham to Westminster.

Elgar, Sir Edward (1857–1934), English composer, specially of choral-orchestral works for festivals. His oratorios include *The Kingdom*, *The Apostles*, and *The Dream of Gerontius*; he also wrote the *Enigma Variations*, and the tone-poem *Falstaff*. *See* **Section E.**

Elgin, 7th Earl of (Thomas Bruce) (1766–1841), British diplomat who, with the object of saving them, conveyed some sculptures from the Parthenon in Athens to the British Museum.

Eliot, George (1819–80), pen-name of Mary Anne (later Marion) Evans, b. Warwickshire. Her novels include *Adam Bede*, *The Mill on the Floss*, *Silas Marner*, *Middlemarch*, and *Daniel Deronda*. Her works show deep insight. She lived with the writer George Lewes from 1854 until his death 25 years later. (Although Lewes had been deserted by his wife it was not then possible to obtain a divorce.) She brought up his three children.

Eliot, Thomas Stearns (1888–1965), poet and critic. He was born in St. Louis, Missouri,

and became a British subject in 1927. His poems include *Prufrock and Other Observations*, *The Waste Land*, *The Hollow Men*, *Ash Wednesday*, *Four Quartets*; his verse dramas *Murder in the Cathedral* and *The Family Reunion*. He described himself as "classical in literature, royalist in politics, and Anglo-Catholic in religion". He was a Nobel prizewinner 1948.

Elizabeth (b. 1900), Queen Consort of George VI, daughter of the 14th Earl of Strathmore. Before her marriage in 1923 she was Lady Elizabeth Angela Marguerite Bowes-Lyon.

Elizabeth I (1533–1603), Queen of England, daughter of Henry VIII, succeeded her sister Mary in 1558. Politically and intellectually able and firm, though personally vain and capricious, she chose to serve her able men such as William Cecil; and her long reign was one of stability, victory over the Spanish, and adventure in the New World; while the Church of England was established, and literary output prepared the way for Shakespeare; it was however marred by the execution of Mary, Queen of Scots.

Elizabeth II (Elizabeth Alexandra Mary of Windsor) (b. 1926), Queen of Gt. Britain and N. Ireland, ascended the throne Feb. 1952 on the death of her father George VI. Her Consort, Prince Philip, Duke of Edinburgh, is the son of Prince Andrew of Greece and a descendant of the Danish royal family. They have four children: Charles, Prince of Wales (b. 1948), Princess Anne (b. 1950), Prince Andrew (b. 1960), and Prince Edward (b. 1964). Princess Anne was styled the Princess Royal in June 1987.

Ellis, Havelock (1859–1939), English writer whose *Studies in the Psychology of Sex* was influential in changing the public attitude towards sex. His books were first published in America.

Emerson, Ralph Waldo (1803–82), American poet and essayist, b. Boston, member of the transcendentalist group of thinkers. Among his best-known poems are *Woodnotes*, *Threnody*, *Terminus*, *Brahma*, *The Problem*.

Emin Pasha, the name adopted by **Eduard Schnitzer** (1840–92), a German explorer associated with Gen. Charles Gordon in the Sudan as a medical officer; and governor of the Equatorial Province 1878–89, when he was menaced by the Mahdi and rescued by Stanley. He had contributed greatly to African studies.

Emmet, Robert (1778–1803), Irish patriot, led the rising of 1803, was betrayed, and executed.

Empedocles (c. 500–c. 430 B.C.), Greek philosopher, b. Agrigentum in Sicily, founder of a school of medicine which regarded the heart as the seat of life, an idea which passed to Aristotle, as did his idea that all matter was composed of four elements: earth, air, fire, and water.

Engels, Friedrich (1820–95), German socialist, son of a wealthy textile manufacturer, lifelong friend of Karl Marx, with whom he collaborated in writing the *Communist Manifesto* of 1848. Through him Marx acquired his knowledge of English labour conditions.

Epicurus of Samos (342–270 B.C.), refounded the atomic view of matter put forward by Democritus, and held that peace of mind comes through freedom from fear, the two main sources of which he regarded as religion and fear of death. The Epicureans were a rival sect to the Peripatetics and Stoics.

Epstein, Sir Jacob (1880–1959), sculptor, b. New York of Russian–Polish parents. His work includes *Rima*, in Hyde Park; *Day* and *Night* on the building of London Underground headquarters; *Genesis*, exhibited in 1931; *Lazarus*, in New College, Oxford; the *Madonna and Child* group in Cavendish Square, London; the figure of *Christ in Majesty* in aluminium in Llandaff cathedral; a sculpture for the T.U.C. headquarters in London; and a bronze group for Coventry cathedral.

Erasmus, Desiderius (1466–1536), Dutch Renaissance humanist, who spent several years in England and was the friend of Dean Colet and Sir Thomas More. He aimed at ecclesiastical reform from within and scorned the old scholastic teaching. He thus prepared the way for Luther. His *Praise of Folly* continues to be widely read.

Erhard, Ludwig (1897–1977), German economist and politician; succeeded Adenauer as Chancellor of the West German Federal Republic, 1963–7.

Essex, 2nd Earl of (Robert Devereux) (1566–1601), favourite of Queen Elizabeth I in her old age. Unsuccessful as governor-general of Ireland, he returned to England against the Queen's wish; plotted; and was executed.

Ethelbert, King of Kent at the close of the 6th cent., accepted Christianity on the mission of St. Augustine.

Ethelred II (c. 968–1016), King of England. Unable to organise resistance against the Danish raids, he was called the Unready (from Old Eng. uraed = without counsel).

Etty, William (1787–1849), English artist of historical and classical subjects.

Eucken, Rudolf Christoph (1846–1926), German philosopher of activism, which puts personal ethical effort above intellectual idealism. Nobel prizewinner 1908.

Euclid, Greek mathematician of the 3rd cent. B.C. Famous for his *Elements*.

Euler, Leonhard (1707–83), Swiss mathematician, remembered especially for his work in optics and on the calculus of variations. He was called by Catherine I to St. Petersburg, where he was professor, 1730–41, and by Frederick the Great to Berlin, 1741–66. He became blind but continued his work.

Euripides (480–406 B.C.), Greek tragic dramatist, who is known to have written about 80 plays of which 18 are preserved, including *Alcestis, Medea, Iphigenia,* and *Orestes.* He displayed a sceptical attitude towards the myths.

Eusebius (264–340), ecclesiastical historian. His *Ecclesiastical History* gives the history of the Christian church to 324. He also wrote a general history, *Chronicon.*

Evans, Sir Arthur John (1851–1941), English archaeologist, known for his excavations at Knossos in Crete and his discovery of the pre-Phoenician script.

Evans, Dame Edith Mary (1888–1976), versatile English actress who made her first appearance as Cressida in *Troilus and Cressida* in 1912.

Evelyn, John (1620–1706), cultured English diarist who gives brilliant portraits of contemporaries. A book collector and librarian who wrote *Sylva,* a manual of arboriculture. His magnificent library was sold by Christies in 1977.

Eyck, Jan van (c. 1389–1441), Flemish painter, whose best-known work is the altarpiece in Ghent cathedral. His brother Hubert (c. 1370–1426) is associated with him.

F

Fabius, the name of an ancient Roman family who over many generations played an important part in early Roman history. **Quintus Fabius Maximus Verrucosus** (d. 203 B.C.) saved Rome from Hannibal by strategic evasion of battle; hence his name *Cunctator* (delayer), and the term Fabian policy.

Fabre, Jean Henri Casimir (1823–1915), French naturalist, whose study of the habits of insects were delightfully recorded in his *Souvenirs entomologiques.*

Faed, name of two Scottish genre painters, **Thomas** (1826–1900), and **John** (1819–1902). A third brother, **James,** engraved their works.

Fahrenheit, Gabriel Daniel (1686–1736), German physicist, b. Danzig. He introduced c. 1715 the mercury thermometer and fixed thermometric standards.

Fairbairn, Sir William (1789–1874), Scottish engineer. In 1817 he took the lead in using iron in shipbuilding.

Fairfax, 3rd Baron (Thomas Fairfax) (1612–71), parliamentary general in the English civil war, and victor of Marston Moor. In 1650 he withdrew into private life.

Falconer, Hugh (1806–65), British botanist and palaeontologist, b. Forres, Scot.; physician to East India Co.; introduced tea into India.

Falla, Manuel (1876–1946), Spanish composer whose music is highly individual with a strong folk-song element. *See* **Section E.**

Faraday, Michael (1791–1867), English experimental physicist, founder of the science of electro-magnetism. He was the son of a Yorkshire blacksmith and at 13 became apprenticed to a bookseller in London. In 1813 he became laboratory assistant to Sir Humphry Davy at the Royal Institution, succeeding him as professor of chemistry in 1833. He set himself the problem of finding the connections between the forces of light, heat, electricity, and magnetism and his discoveries, translated by Maxwell (*q.v.*) into a single mathematical theory of electromagnetism, led to the modern developments in physics and electronics. He inaugurated the Christmas lectures for juvenile audiences at the Royal Institution.

Farman, Henri (1874–1958), French aviator, one of the pioneers of aviation, and a designer and builder of aeroplanes.

Farouk I (1920–65), King of Egypt, 1936–52. He was forced to abdicate as a result of the military coup of 1952.

Farrar, Frederick William (1831–1903), English clergyman, author of the schoolboy story *Eric.*

Faulkner, William (1897–1962), American novelist, whose series of novels, *The Sound and the Fury, As I Lay Dying, Light in August, Sanctuary,* depict the American South. Nobel prizewinner 1949.

Fauré, Gabriel Urbain (1845–1924), French composer and teacher. His works include chamber music, nocturnes, and barcarolles for piano, an opera *Pénélope,* some exquisite songs, and *Requiem.* Ravel was among his pupils.

Fawcett, Millicent Garrett (1847–1929), educational reformer and leader of the movement for women's suffrage; one of the founders of Newnham College, Cambridge. She was the wife of the blind Liberal politician and economist, **Henry Fawcett** (1833–84) and sister of **Elizabeth Garrett Anderson.**

Fawkes, Guy (1570–1606), a Yorkshire catholic, who with Catesby and other conspirators planned the Gunpowder Plot. Though warned, he persisted and was captured and hanged.

Fénelon, François de Salignac de la Mothe (1651–1715), archbishop of Cambrai and author of *Telemachus.*

Ferdinand II of Aragon (1452–1516), who married Isabella of Castile, and with her reigned over Spain, saw the Moors expelled from Spain, equipped Columbus for the discoveries that led to Spain's vast colonial possessions, and instituted the Inquisition.

Ferguson, James (1710–76), Scottish astronomer who, from being a shepherd-boy, educated himself in astronomy, mathematics, and portrait painting.

Fermi, Enrico (1901–54), Italian nuclear physicist whose research contributed to the harnessing of atomic energy and the development of the atomic bomb. Nobel prizewinner 1938.

Fichte, Johann Gottlieb (1762–1814), German philosopher of the nationalistic Romantic school who prepared the way for modern totalitarianism.

Field, John (1782–1837), Irish composer of nocturnes, pupil of Clementi and teacher of Glinka. His work served as a model for Chopin.

Fielding, Henry (1707–54), English novelist, author of *Tom Jones, Joseph Andrews,* and *Amelia,* as well as plays.

Fildes, Sir Luke (1844–1927), English painter and woodcut-designer.

Finsen, Niels Ryberg (1860–1904), Danish physician who established an institute for light therapy and invented the Finsen ultra-violet lamp. Nobel prizewinner 1903.

Firdausi, *pen-name of* **Abu'l Kasim Mansur** (940–1020), Persian poet, author of the epic *Shah-Nama* or Book of Kings.

Fisher of Lambeth, Baron (Geoffrey Francis Fisher) (1887–1972), archbishop of Canterbury, 1945–61; Headmaster of Repton School, 1914–32.

Fisher, Herbert Albert Laurens (1865–1940), English historian and educational reformer; author of *A History of Europe.*

Fisher, Sir Ronald Aylmer (1890–1962), British scientist who revolutionised both genetics and the philosophy of experimentation by founding the modern corpus of mathematical statistics.

FitzGerald, Edward (1809–83), English poet who translated the *Rubáiyát* of Omar Khayyám (1859).

Fitzroy, Robert (1805–65), British meteorologist, who introduced the system of storm warnings which were the beginning of weather forecasts.

Flammarion, Camille (1842–1925), French astronomer, noted for his popular lectures and books which include *L'Astronomie Populaire*.

Flamsteed, John (1646–1719), the first English astronomer royal, for whom Charles II built an observatory at Greenwich (1675) where he worked for 44 years.

Flaubert, Gustave (1821–80), French novelist, and creator of *Madame Bovary*. Other works were *Salammbô, L'Education sentimentale*, and *Bouvard et Pécuchet*.

Flaxman, John (1755–1826), English sculptor, b. York, employed as modeller by Josiah Wedgwood. He then took to monumental sculpture.

Flecker, James Elroy (1884–1915), English poet whose works include *Golden Journey to Samarkand, Hassan* (staged in London, 1923), and *Don Juan*, as well as many lyrics.

Fleming, Sir Alexander (1881–1955), Scottish bacteriologist who discovered the antibacterial enzyme lysozyme in 1922 and penicillin in 1928. Full recognition came during the war when Florey separated the drug now used from the original penicillin. Awarded Nobel prize jointly with Florey and Chain, 1945.

Fleming, Sir Ambrose (1849–1945), British scientist whose invention of the radio valve in 1904 revolutionised radio telegraphy and solved problems of radio-telephony. This eventually made possible high quality sound transmission, and thus led to broadcasting and television.

Fletcher, John (1579–1625), English dramatist who collaborated with Francis Beaumont (*q.v.*) in writing many pieces for the stage.

Flinders, Matthew (1774–1814), English navigator and explorer who made discoveries in and around Australia. He sailed through Bass Strait, so called in honour of his surgeon.

Florey, Baron (Howard Walter Florey) (1898–1968), British pathologist, b. Australia. Shared 1945 Nobel prize with Fleming and Chain for work on penicillin.

Foch, Ferdinand (1851–1929), French general, b. Tarbes. In the first world war he halted the German advance at the Marne (1914), and was engaged in the battles of Ypres (1914 and 1915) and the Somme (1916). In 1918 he became supreme commander of the British, French, and American armies and dictated the terms of Allied victory.

Fokine, Michel (1880–1944), Russian dancer, choreographer to Diaghilev's company, and creator of *Les Sylphides, Prince Igor, Scheherazade, Firebird*, and *The Spectre of the Rose.*

Fokker, Anthony (1890–1939), Dutch aircraft engineer, b. Java. The Fokker factory in Germany made warplanes for the Germans in the first world war.

Fonteyn, Dame Margot (Mme. Roberto de Arias) (b. 1919), prima ballerina of the Royal Ballet and acclaimed foremost English dancer.

Foot, Michael (b. 1913), British journalist and politician; leader of the Labour Party 1980–83; pubs. inc. biography of Aneurin Bevan. *See* Sections C & D.

Ford, Gerald R. (b. 1913), American Republican President 1974–7; automatically succeeded Richard Nixon when he resigned.

Ford, Henry (1863–1947), founder of Ford Motor Company (1903), of which he was president until 1919, when he was succeeded by his son, Edsel B. Ford (1893–1943). He was the pioneer of the cheap motor car.

Forester, Cecil Scott (1899–1966), English novelist, author of the *Captain Hornblower* series.

Forster, Edward Morgan (1879–1970), English novelist, author of *The Longest Journey, A Room with a View, Howards End, A Passage to India*. O.M. 1969.

Foscari, Francesco (c. 1372–1457), Doge of Venice and victor over Milan.

Fourier, Charles (1772–1837), French socialist who propounded a system of associated enterprise which although utopian stimulated social reform.

Fourier, Jean Baptiste Joseph (1768–1830), French mathematical physicist. He played an active part in politics, holding administrative posts in Egypt and Isère, yet finding time for his own research, especially on the flow of heat.

Fowler, Sir John (1817–98), was the engineer of the first underground railway (the London Metro-

politan) and with his partner Sir Benjamin Baker, of the Forth bridge.

Fox, Charles James (1749–1806), English Whig statesman. Son of the 1st Lord Holland, he entered parliament at 19. He held office only for brief periods between 1770 and 1806, but he upheld the liberal causes of the day (American independence, the French revolution, and parliamentary reform), and was one of the impeachers of Warren Hastings.

Fox, George (1624–91), founder of the Society of Friends, son of a weaver of Fenny Drayton, Leicestershire.

Foxe, John (1516–87), English martyrologist, author of *History of the Acts and Monuments of the Church* (better known as *Foxe's Book of Martyrs*).

Frampton, Sir George James (1860–1928), English sculptor of the Peter Pan statue in Kensington Gardens and the Edith Cavell memorial.

France, Anatole (1844–1924), French writer, especially of short stories. Nobel prize 1921.

Francis I (1494–1547), King of France. Brilliant but ambitious and adventurous, he fostered learning and art, and met Henry VIII at the Field of the Cloth of Gold. His rivalry with the Emperor Charles V involved France in prolonged war, especially in Italy (he was captured at Pavia, 1525). He persecuted the Protestants.

Francis of Assisi, St. (1181/2–1226), founder of the Franciscan Order. Son of a wealthy cloth merchant, in 1208 he turned from a life of pleasure to poverty and the complete observance of Christ's teaching. He and his friars went about preaching the gospel by word and example, and the brotherhood increased rapidly. He was canonised in 1228.

Francis, Sir Philip (1740–1818), English politician, reputed author of the *Letters of Junius*.

Franck, César Auguste (1822–90), composer and organist, b. at Liège in Belgium. *See* Section E.

Franco, Francisco (1892–1975), Spanish general and dictator. He led the Fascist rebellion against the Republican government (1936) and with German and Italian help ended the civil war (1939), after which he ruled Spain with utter ruthlessness.

Franklin, Benjamin (1706–90), American statesman. B. at Boston, he was at first a printer and journalist. He then took an interest in electricity, explained lightning as of electrical origin, and invented the lightning conductor. He was active in promoting the Declaration of Independence in 1773; he negotiated French support; and helped to frame the American constitution.

Franklin, Sir John (1786–1847), English Arctic explorer. His expedition in the *Erebus* and the *Terror* to find the north-west passage ended disastrously, and all attempts to find survivors failed.

Franks, Baron (Oliver Shewell Franks) (b. 1905), British academic, diplomat and banker; British ambassador to U.S.A. 1948–52; provost of Worcester College, Oxford 1962–76; chosen to head Falklands inquiry 1982. O.M. 1977.

Fraunhofer, Joseph von (1787–1826), optical instrument-maker of Munich, the first to map the dark lines of the solar spectrum named after him.

Frazer, Sir James George (1854–1941), Scottish anthropologist, author of *The Golden Bough.*

Frederick I (c. 1123–90). Holy Roman Emperor, nicknamed Barbarossa. A strong personality, he sought to impose his will on the city-states of northern Italy and the papacy, and was defeated at Legnano in 1176 but was more successful with a conciliatory policy (1183). He had also to contend with opposition at home. He died on the third crusade.

Frederick II (1194–1250), Holy Roman Emperor, grandson of the above, and son of the heiress of Sicily. Brilliant and enlightened, he attracted to his court in Sicily Jewish, Mohammedan, and Christian scholars; founded the university of Naples; was a patron of the medical school of Salerno; wrote a treatise on falconry; and commissioned a code of laws. Politically he was less successful, having trouble with the Lombard cities, and being involved with the papacy especially as regards his delay in going on crusade; but after negotiations with the sultan of Egypt he actually was crowned king of Jerusalem.

Frederick II (the Great) (1712–86), King of Prussia. Having inherited from his father a well-drilled army, in 1740 he seized Silesia from Austria, and retained it through the resulting war and the Seven Years war. He also took part in the partition of Poland. An able administrator and and outstanding general he made Prussia powerful and strengthened its military tradition. He corresponded with Voltaire and he also played the flute.

French, Sir John, 1st Earl of Ypres (1852–1925), first British commander-in-chief in the first world war; replaced by Sir Douglas Haig in 1915.

Freud, Sigmund (1856–1939), psychiatrist and founder of psychoanalysis; b. Moravia, studied medicine in Vienna, where he lived until 1938 when the Nazi invasion of Austria sent him into exile in London where he died. His theories of the mind, based on years of investigation, illumined the way we think about ourselves, and had immense influence upon modern thought. *See* **Psychoanalysis, Section J.**

Friese-Greene, William (1855–1921), English inventor of the cinematograph. His first film was shown in 1890. He died in poverty.

Frobisher, Sir Martin (1535–94), first British navigator to seek the north-west passage from the Atlantic to the Pacific through the Arctic seas. He is commemorated in Frobisher's Strait. He also fought against the Spanish Armada.

Froebel, Friedrich Wilhelm August (1782–1852), German educational reformer, founder of the Kindergarten system.

Froissart, Jean (1337–1410), French author of *Chronicles* covering the history of Western Europe from 1307 to 1400, one of the chief sources for the history of the first half of the Hundred Years war.

Frost, Robert (1874–1963), American poet, author of *Stopping by Woods on a Snowy Evening, Birches, The Death of the Hired Man, After Apple-Picking.*

Froude, James Anthony (1818–94), English historian and biographer of Carlyle.

Fry, Christopher (b. 1907), English poet and dramatist of Quaker family; author of *The Lady's Not for Burning, Venus Observed, The Dark is Light Enough, Curtmantle, A Yard of Sun* and the religious play *A Sleep of Prisoners.*

Fry, Elizabeth (1780–1845), English prison reformer. She lived at Norwich and belonged to the Society of Friends.

Fry, Roger (1866–1934), English art critic and painter; introduced the work of Cézanne and the post-impressionists into England; author of *Vision and Design.*

Fuchs, Leonhard (1501–66), German naturalist whose compendium of medicinal plants was for long a standard work. He was professor of medicine at Tübingen and the genus *Fuchsia* is named after him.

Fuchs, Sir Vivian Ernest (b. 1908), British geologist and explorer; leader of the British Commonwealth Trans-Antarctic Expedition 1957–8, the first to cross the Antarctic continent.

Fuller, Thomas (1608–61), English antiquarian and divine, author of *Worthies of England* and a *Church History of Britain.*

Fulton, Robert (1765–1815), American engineer who experimented in the application of steam to navigation, and in 1807 launched the *Clermont* on the Hudson.

Furniss, Harry (1854–1925), caricaturist, b. Wexford. He came to London as a young man, served on the staff of *Punch* and illustrated the works of Dickens and Thackeray.

G

Gade, Niels Vilhelm (1817–90), Danish composer. While studying at Leipzig he met Mendelssohn, whom he succeeded as conductor of the Gewandhaus orchestra.

Gagarin, Yuri Alexeyevich (1934–68), Soviet cosmonaut, the first man to be launched into space and brought safely back (12 April 1961). His flight was made in the front portion of a multi-

stage rocket which made a single circuit of the earth in 108 min. Killed in an air crash.

Gainsborough, Thomas (1727–88), English landscape and portrait painter, b. at Sudbury in Suffolk. His portraits are marked by informality and grace.

Gaiseric or Genseric (c. 390–477), king of the Vandals, the ablest of the barbarian invaders of the Roman empire. He led his people from Spain into Africa, took Carthage, gained control of the Mediterranean and sacked Rome in 455.

Gaitskell, Hugh Todd Naylor (1906–63), Labour politician and economist. He represented Leeds South from 1945; was chancellor of the exchequer 1950–1; and leader of the Labour opposition 1955–63.

Galbraith, John Kenneth (b. 1908), American university professor of economics, b. Canada; author of *The Affluent Society* (1958), *The Liberal Hour* (1960), *The New Industrial State* (1967), *The Age of Uncertainty* (1977). He was ambassador to India 1961–3.

Galdós, Benito Pérez. *See* **Pérez Galdós.**

Galen, Claudius (131–201), physician, b. Pergamum (Asia Minor) of Greek parents. He systematised medical knowledge with his idea of purposive creation by the will of God; and thus discouraged original investigation. Many of his treatises survive, and his influence lasted for more than a thousand years.

Galileo (1564–1642), Italian scientist whose experimental-mathematical methods in the pursuit of scientific truth laid the foundations of modern science. He became professor of mathematics at Pisa university when he was 25 and lectured at Padua for 18 years. He made a number of fundamental discoveries, *e.g.*, in regard to the hydrostatic balance, thermometer, telescope, and foreshadowed Newton's laws of motion. He detected the four major satellites of Jupiter, the ring of Saturn, and the spots of the sun. He supported the superiority of the Copernican over the Ptolemaic theory, and was put under house arrest for so doing. He died the year Newton was born.

Galsworthy, John (1867–1933), English novelist and playwright, author of *The Forsyte Saga*, a series of novels dealing with the history of an upper middle-class family. Nobel prizewinner 1932.

Galton, Sir Francis (1822–1911), founder of eugenics, cousin of Darwin. His early work *Meteorographica* (1863), contains the basis of the modern weather chart. He was an early advocate of using finger-prints for rapid identification, and was one of the first to apply mathematics to biological problems.

Galvani, Luigi (1737–98), Italian physician and physiologist, whose experiments at Bologna demonstrated the principle of animal electricity.

Gama, Vasco da (c. 1460–1524), Portuguese navigator who discovered the sea route to India in 1498 by rounding the Cape of Good Hope.

Gandhi, Indira (1917–84), daughter of Nehru, succeeded Shastri in 1966 to become India's first woman prime minister. She suffered a defeat at the polls in 1977 but was spectacularly successful in 1980. Assassinated 1984. Succeeded by her son, **Rajiv Gandhi.** *See* **Section C, Part II.**

Gandhi, Mohandás Karamchand (Mahatma) (1869–1948), Indian patriot, social reformer and moral teacher. From 1893 to 1914 he lived in South Africa opposing discrimination against Indians. In the movement for Indian independence after 1914 he dominated Congress, instituted civil disobedience, and advocated non-violence; and he sought to free India from caste. After independence he strove to promote the co-operation of all Indians but was assassinated on his way to a prayer meeting. His teaching of non-violence has had great influence.

Garbo, Greta (1905–90), Swedish film actress of poetical quality. Her films included *Queen Christina* and *Ninotchka.*

García, Manuel de Popolo Vincente (1775–1832), Spanish tenor, composer, and singing master. His son **Manuel Patricio Rodriguez** (1805–1906) was tutor to Jenny Lind. Both his daughters (Mme. Malibran and Mme. Viardot) were operatic singers, and his grandson and great-grandson baritones.

Garcia Lorca, Federico. *See* **Lorca.**

Gardiner, Samuel Rawson (1890–1902), English historian of the Stuart period.

Garibaldi, Giuseppe (1807–82), Italian soldier and patriot, who with Mazzini and Cavour created a united Italy. In 1834 he was condemned to death for helping in a republican plot to seize Genoa, but escaped to S. America. He returned in 1848 to fight for Mazzini but was again forced to flee. In 1851 he returned and gave his support to Cavour, taking part in the Austrian war of 1859. In 1860 with a thousand volunteers he freed Sicily, took Naples, and handed over the Two Sicilies to Victor Emmanuel who was proclaimed king.

Garrick, David (1717–79), English actor and theatrical manager. Brought up at Lichfield, he was taught by Samuel Johnson.

Garrison, William Lloyd (1805–79), American philanthropist who worked to end slavery.

Gaskell, Mrs. Elizabeth Cleghorn (1810–65), English novelist, author of *Mary Barton*, *Cranford*, and a *Life of Charlotte Brontë*. She was brought up by an aunt in the little Cheshire town of Knutsford.

Gaulle, Charles de (1890–1970), French general and statesman, son of a headmaster of a Jesuit school; first president of the Fifth Republic 1959–69. He fought in the first world war until his capture in 1916. In the second world war he refused to surrender (1940) and raised and led the Free French forces, with headquarters in England. He came to political power in 1958; allowed Algerian independence in 1962 in face of an army and civilian revolt, initiated closer ties with West Germany (Franco-German treaty 1963), recognised Communist China, withdrew from NATO, building his own nuclear force, vetoed Britain's entry into the Common Market (1963 and 1967); and based his government on personal prestige and use of the referendum in place of parliamentary approval. He was taken by surprise by the rising of students and workers in 1968 and resigned after losing the referendum in 1969.

Gauss, Karl Friedrich (1777–1855), German mathematician. He spent most of his life at the university of Göttingen where he set up the first special observatory for terrestrial magnetism. He made major contributions to astronomy, mathematics, and physics. The unit of magnetic induction is named after him.

Gautama, Siddhartha (Buddha, the enlightened) (c. 563–c.483 B.C.). B. near Benares, a rajah's son, he gave himself up to the religious life and attracted many disciples. Concerned with man's sorrow and suffering, he planned a movement which could be universally shared, in which kindness to others, including animals, took a leading part. His teaching is summarised in the "four noble truths" and the "eightfold path" (*see* **Buddhism, Section J**). After his death his teaching spread (with the help of the King Asoka) over much of India and through eastern Asia as far as Japan, and developed varying schools of thought. Buddhism is tolerant and also maintains that the good of the part is that of the whole; hence it is wrong to harm another or take life.

Gautier, Théophile (1811–72), French poet and novelist, author of *Mademoiselle de Maupin*.

Gay, John (1685–1732), English poet, author of *The Beggar's Opera* (set to music by Pepusch) and *Polly*.

Gay-Lussac, Joseph Louis (1778–1850), French chemist, who showed that when gases combine their relative volumes bear a simple numerical relation to each other and to the volume of their product, if gaseous (1808), *e.g.*, one volume of oxygen combines with two volumes of hydrogen to form two volumes of water vapour.

Ged, William (1690–1749), Scottish printer who patented stereotyping.

Geddes, Sir Patrick (1854–1932), Scottish biologist and a pioneer in town and regional planning, who invented the term conurbation.

Geikie, Sir Archibald (1835–1924), Scottish geologist. His brother James specialised in glacial geology.

Genghis Khan (1162–1227), Mongol conqueror. After years of struggle to make good his succession to his father, he overran the greater part of Asia bringing devastation wherever he went.

Geoffrey of Monmouth (1100–54), chronicler, b. Monmouth, later bishop of St. Asaph. His chronicle drew on his creative imagination.

George I (1660–1727), became King of Great Britain in 1714 as descendant of James I. His chief minister was Sir Robert Walpole. Himself personally undistinguished, his reign saw political development; and in spite of the Jacobite threat (rising in 1715) it began a period of dynastic stability.

George II (1683–1760), son of the above, succeeded in 1727, and survived a more serious Jacobite rising in 1745. His long reign helped the development of constitutional government, for he kept within the limitations of his powers and capacity; and it saw the extension of English power in India and North America.

George III (1738–1820), grandson of George II reigned 1760–1820. Sincere and well-intentioned, but not politically able, he suffered from mental illness due to intermittent porphyria. His reign saw a clash with John Wilkes, the rise of Methodism, and agrarian and industrial revolution; also the loss of the American colonies, the extension and the questioning of English power in India (Warren Hastings), and prolonged French wars.

George IV (1762–1830), eldest son of George III, reigned 1820–30, having become Prince Regent in 1812. Styled "the first gentleman of Europe," he is remembered for his interest in art and architecture. His married life was unfortunate, and the monarchy was at a low ebb; while his reign was a time of distress and of demand for reform.

George V (1865–1936), was the second son of Edward VII and Queen Alexandra. His elder brother died in 1892 and, in 1901, on his father's accession, he became heir to the throne. He joined the Navy as a cadet in 1877. In 1893 he married Princess Mary of Teck. He succeeded in 1910 and discharged his office conscientiously. In 1932 he began the royal broadcast on Christmas Day and in 1935 celebrated his silver jubilee. His reign included the Kaiser's war, the emergence of the Irish Free State, and the first Labour government.

George VI (1895–1952), second son of George V, was called to the throne in 1936 on the abdication of his elder brother, Edward VIII. His personal qualities gained wide respect. His reign was marked by Hitler's war and rapid social change.

George, Henry (1839–97), American political economist whose "single tax" on land values as a means of solving economic problems is expounded in his *Progress and Poverty* (1879).

George, St., patron saint of England, adopted by Edward III. He is believed to have been martyred by Diocletian at Nicomedia in 303 (and not, as believed by Gibbon, to be confused with George of Cappadocia). The story of his fight with the dragon is of late date.

Gershwin, George (1898–1937). American jazz pianist and song-writer, composer of *Rhapsody in Blue* and the Negro folk-opera *Porgy and Bess*.

Gesner, Conrad (1516–65), Swiss naturalist, b. Zurich. His magnificently illustrated volumes describe animal and vegetable kingdoms.

Ghiberti, Lorenzo (1378–1455), Florentine sculptor whose bronze doors, beautifying the baptistry in Florence, were described by Michelangelo as fit for the gates of paradise.

Ghirlandaio, Domenico (1449–94), Florentine painter. Most of his frescoes are in Florence, including the cycle of the life of the Virgin and the Baptist in S. Maria Novella. Michelangelo began his apprenticeship in his workshop.

Giacometti, Alberto (1901–66), Swiss sculptor and painter, who worked mainly in Paris and produced abstract symbolic constructions.

Giap, Vo Nguyen (1912–86), Vietnamese general who defeated the French at Dien Bien Phu (1954) and withstood American intervention in the Vietnam war which followed; replaced in 1980 as defence minister. Retired in 1982.

Gibbon, Edward (1737–94), English historian of the *Decline and Fall of the Roman Empire*.

Gibbons, Grinling (1648–1720), English woodcarver and sculptor, b. Rotterdam, was brought to the notice of Charles II by Evelyn, the diarist. The choir stalls of St. Paul's and the carving in the Wren library at Trinity College, Cambridge, are his work.

Gibbons, Orlando (1583–1625), English composer

of church music. *See also* **Section E.**

Gide, André (1869–1951), French writer of many short novels in which he gives expression to his struggle to escape from his protestant upbringing (*Strait is the Gate, The Counterfeiters*). In his memoir *Si le grain ne meurt* he tells the story of his life up to his marriage. The narratives of his journeys in Africa led to a reform in French colonial policy.

Gielgud, Sir John (b. 1904), English actor and producer, grand-nephew of Ellen Terry, to whom, the Hamlet of his generation, the present popularity of Shakespeare is largely due.

Gigli, Beniamino (1890–1957), Italian operatic tenor.

Gilbert, Sir Alfred (1854–1934), English sculptor and goldsmith. His sculptures include *Eros* in Piccadilly Circus.

Gilbert, Sir Humphrey (1537–83), English navigator. He was knighted by Queen Elizabeth for service in Ireland. In 1583 he discovered Newfoundland, but was drowned the same year.

Gilbert, William (1540–1603), English physician to Queen Elizabeth. His book *On the Magnet*, published in Latin in 1600, was the first major original contribution to science published in England.

Gilbert, Sir William Schwenck (1836–1911), English humorist and librettist, of the Gilbert and Sullivan light operas. First known as author of the *Bab Ballads*, from 1871 he collaborated with Sir Arthur Sullivan, his wit and satire finding appropriate accompaniment in Sullivan's music. Their operas include *H.M.S. Pinafore, Patience, Iolanthe, The Mikado, The Gondoliers*, and *The Yeomen of the Guard*.

Gill, Eric (1882–1940), English sculptor and engraver, whose works include the *Stations of the Cross* (Westminster Cathedral), *Prospero and Ariel* (Broadcasting House), *Christ Driving the Money-changers from the Temple* (Leeds University). He also worked as a designer for printing (Gill Sans type), and the George VI stamps were his designs.

Gillray, James (1757–1815), English caricaturist who produced over a thousand political cartoons.

Giotto di Bondone (1267–1337), Florentine artist. A pupil of Cimabue, he continued the development away from Byzantine tradition towards greater naturalism. His frescoes survive in the churches of Assisi, Padua, and Florence. He designed the western front of the cathedral at Florence and the campanile.

Gissing, George Robert (1857–1903), English novelist whose works deal with the degrading effect of poverty. The best known is *New Grub Street*.

Giulio Romano or **Giulio Pippi** (*c.* 1492–1546). Italian artist, was a pupil of Raphael. He was also an engineer and architect.

Gladstone, William Ewart (1809–98), English Liberal statesman. B. at Liverpool, he entered parliament in 1832 as a Tory and held office under Peel. From 1852 he served several terms as chancellor of the exchequer and was Liberal prime minister 1868–74, when his legislation included the education act of 1870, the ballot act, the disestablishment of the Church of Ireland and an Irish land act. In 1874 when Disraeli came to power, he temporarily withdrew, but made a come-back in 1879 with his Mid-Lothian campaign. He was again prime minister 1880–5, 1886 and 1892–4; he carried a parliamentary reform act, and advocated home rule for Ireland but was not able to carry it. He was also a classical scholar and a writer on church matters.

Glazunov, Alexander Constantinovich (1865–1936), Russian composer, pupil of Rimsky-Korsakov. The first of his eight symphonies was composed when he was 16.

Glendower, Owen (*c.* 1350–*c.* 1416), Welsh chief, who conducted guerrilla warfare on the English border, and figures in Shakespeare's *Henry IV*.

Glinka, Mikhail Ivanovich (1804–57), Russian composer, first of the national school, best known for his operas, *A Life for the Tsar*, and *Russlan and Ludmilla*, based on a poem by Pushkin. *See* **Section E.**

Gluck, Christoph Wilibald (1714–87), German composer, important in the development of opera.

He studied in Prague, Vienna and Italy, and his first operas were in the Italian tradition; but with *Orfeo ed Euridice* (1762) his style became more dramatic. There followed *Alceste, Armide*, and *Iphigénie en Tauride*. *See* **Section E.**

Godfrey of Bouillon (*c.* 1061–1100), Crusader on the first crusade. On capturing Jerusalem declined title of "king", preferring that of protector of the Holy Sepulchre.

Godiva, Lady (1040–80), English benefactress. According to tradition, she obtained from her husband Leofric, Earl of Chester, concessions for the people of Coventry by riding naked through the town.

Godwin, Earl of the West Saxons (d. 1053), was the father of Edith, wife of King Edward the Confessor, and of Harold, last Saxon king.

Godwin William (1756–1836), English political writer and philosopher, author of *Political Justice* (which criticised many contemporary institutions) and a novel *Caleb Williams*. He married **Mary Wollstonecraft** (1759–97), author of *A Vindication of the Rights of Women*; and their daughter, **Mary Wollstonecraft Godwin** (1797–1851) wrote *Frankenstein* and married Shelley.

Goethe, Johann Wolfgang von (1749–1832), German poet and thinker. B. at Frankfurt-on-Main, his first notable work was a romantic play, *Götz von Berlichingen*, followed by a novel *Werthers Leiden*. In 1776 he became privy councillor to the Duke of Weimar, whom he served for many years. He had wide-ranging interests, and made discoveries in anatomy and in botany. Among his later writings are the play *Iphigenie* and the novel *Wilhelm Meister*. His best-known work however is *Faust*.

Gogol, Nikolai Vasilievich (1809–52), Russian novelist and dramatist. His comedy, *The Government Inspector*, satirised provincial bureaucracy; and his novel, *Dead Souls*, deals with malpractice in the supposed purchase of dead serfs.

Goldsmith, Oliver (1728–74), Irish poet, dramatist and novelist. The son of a poor curate, he came to London in 1756, and eventually joined the circle of Dr. Johnson. He is best known for his novel *The Vicar of Wakefield* and his play *She Stoops to Conquer*.

Goncourt, Edmond Louis Antoine Huot de (1822–96) and **Jules Alfred Huot de** (1830–70), French brothers, remembered for their *Journal des Goncourts*, an intimate account of Parisian society.

Góngora y Argote, Luis de (1561–1627), Spanish poet, b. Córdova. In *Polifemo* and *Soledades* he attempted to express the core of poetry in new experimental forms.

Goodyear, Charles (1800–60), American inventor who discovered the art of vulcanising rubber.

Goossens, Sir Eugene (1893–1962), English conductor and composer of Belgian descent. His compositions include the operas *Judith* and *Don Juan de Mañara*; brother of Léon, oboe virtuoso, and of Sidonie and Marie Goossens, harpists.

Gorbachev, Mikhail (b. 1931). Soviet politician. Succeeded Chernenko (*q.v.*) as General Secretary of the Communist Party, 1985. His accession marked the end of the "old-guard" leadership. Identified with policies of *glasnost* (openness) and *perestroika* (restructuring). President of the USSR since 1988, becoming first Executive President, 1990. He has presided over revolutionary changes both in Eastern Europe and Russia, but faces a growing political crisis over economic reforms and the rise of his rival, Boris Yeltsin. *See* **Section C, Part II.**

Gordon, Charles George (1833–85), Scottish soldier. After service in the Crimea and China, in 1873 he was made governor of the Equatorial provinces of Egypt; and he was a notable governor of the Sudan, 1877–80. When a rising was led by the Mahdi, he was sent out in 1884 to the garrisons in rebel territory and was killed at Khartoum.

Gordon, Lord George (1751–93), agitator, led No-Popery riots in London in 1780.

Gorky, Maxim (Alexey Maximovich Peshkov) 1868–1936), Russian writer. From the age of ten he worked at many trades from scullion on a Volga steamboat to railway guard, while learning to write: see *My Childhood*. His early work was romantic. He spent many years abroad, but returned in 1928, a supporter of the Soviet regime. His later work is marked by social realism.

Gosse, Sir Edmund (1849–1928), English poet and critic, known for his literary studies of the 17th and 18th centuries; and for his memoir *Father and Son*.

Gounod, Charles François (1818–93), French composer, known for his operas *Faust* and *Roméo et Juliette*, though his lyrical gifts are shown in earlier works, such as *Le Médicin malgré lui* and *Mireille*.

Gower, John (1325–1408), English poet of the time of Chaucer, author of *Confessio Amantis*.

Goya y Lucientes, Francisco José (1746–1828), Spanish painter and etcher b. nr. Saragossa. He became court painter to Charles III in 1786. His portraits are painted with ruthless realism; his series of satirical etchings (*Los Caprichos* and the *Disasters of War*) expose man's inhumanity and express his hatred of the cruelty and reaction of his day. His work can best be seen in Madrid.

Grace, William Gilbert (1848–1915). English cricketer who scored 54,896 runs, including 126 centuries, and took 2,876 wickets. Scored 1,000 runs in May 1895; and three times made over 300 runs in an innings.

Grahame, Kenneth (1859–1932), Scottish writer of books for children, including *The Golden Age*, *Dream Days*, and *Wind in the Willows*.

Grahame-White, Claude (1879–1959), aviator and engineer, the first Englishman to gain an aviator's certificate, 1909.

Grant, Ulysses Simpson (1822–85), American general of the civil war, and president of the United States from 1869 to 1876.

Granville-Barker, Harley (1877–1946), English dramatist, actor, and producer, who promoted the plays of Ibsen, Shaw, and other serious writers. His own works include *The Voysey Inheritance*.

Grattan, Henry (1746–1820), Irish statesman, who struggled for Irish legislative independence and for Catholic emancipation (though himself a Protestant) and parliamentary reform; but unsuccessfully.

Graves, Robert Ranke (1895–1985), English writer, author of *Goodbye to All That*, written after the first world war; and of *I Claudius* and *Claudius the God*; besides poetry.

Gray, Thomas (1716–71), English poet, author of *Elegy written in a Country Churchyard* and *Ode on a Distant Prospect of Eton College*.

Greeley, Horace (1811–72), American newspaper editor, founder of the New York *Tribune* (1841).

Green, John Richard (1837–83), English historian, author of *Short History of the English People*.

Greenaway, Kate (1846–1901), English artist of children, especially for book illustrations.

Greene, Graham (b. 1904), English novelist and journalist, whose novels (*The Power and the Glory*, *The Heart of the Matter*, *The End of the Affair*, *The Quiet American*, *Our Man in Havana*, *A Burnt-out Case*, *The Comedians*, *The Honorary Consul*), like his plays (*The Complaisant Lover*) and films (*Fallen Idol*, *The Third Man*) deal with moral problems in a modern setting. O.M. (1986).

Gregory, St. (*c*. 240–332), converted King Tiridates of Armenia and was thus founder of the Armenian church.

Gregory I (the Great), St. (*c*. 540–604), Pope 590–604, was the last great Latin Father and the forerunner of scholasticism. The main founder of the temporal power and the political influence of the papacy, he also maintained the spiritual claims of Rome, enforcing discipline, encouraging monasticism, defining doctrine, and adding to the music, liturgy, and canons of the Church. It was he who sent Augustine on a mission to England.

Gregory VII (Hildebrand) (*c*. 1020–85), Pope 1073–85. He strove for papal omnipotence within the church and for a high standard in the priesthood (especially by stamping out simony and clerical marriage). He also upheld the papacy against the Holy Roman Empire, and the emperor Henry IV did penance for three days in the snow at Canossa; but he had not quite the vision of Gregory I of an ideal theocracy embracing all states.

Gregory XIII (1502–85), Pope 1572–85; introduced the Gregorian calendar.

Gregory, James (1638–75), Scottish mathematician. He invented a reflecting telescope and was the first to show how the distance of the sun could be deduced by observations of the passage of Venus across the disc of the sun. Successive generations of the family reached distinction.

Grenville, Sir Richard (1541–91), English sea captain, who with his one ship engaged a fleet of Spanish war vessels off Flores in 1591, an exploit celebrated in Tennyson's ballad *The Revenge*.

Gresham, Sir Thomas (1519–79), English financier and founder of the Royal Exchange. Son of a Lord Mayor of London, he was an astute moneyfinder for four successive sovereigns, including Queen Elizabeth I. "Gresham's Law" is the statement that bad money drives out good.

Greuze, Jean Baptiste (1725–1805), French artist, known especially for his studies of girls. His *Girl with Doves* is in the Wallace Collection.

Grey, 2nd Earl (Charles Grey) (1764–1845), British Whig statesman under whose premiership were passed the Reform Bill of 1832, a bill abolishing slavery throughout the Empire (1833), and the Poor Law Amendment Act, 1834.

Grey, Lady Jane (1537–54), Queen of England for a few days. The daughter of the Duke of Suffolk, she was put forward as queen by protestant leaders on the death of her cousin, Edward VI; but overcome by the legal claimant, Mary Tudor, and executed.

Grieg, Edvard Hagerup (1843–1907), Norwegian composer, b. Bergen. He presented the characteristics of his country's music with strong accentuation. He is best known for his incidental music to *Peer Gynt*.

Griffin, Bernard William (1899–1956), Roman catholic archbishop of Westminster from 1944 until his death.

Griffith, Arthur (1872–1922), the first president of the Irish Free State, 1921; founder of the *Sinn Fein* movement.

Griffith, David Wark (1880–1948), American film producer, who introduced the close-up, and the flash-back, and developed leading actors. His films include *Birth of a Nation*, and *Broken Blossoms*.

Grimm, the brothers Jakob Ludwig Karl (1785–1863), and **Wilhelm Karl** (1786–1859), German philologists and folk-lorists, best known for their *Fairy Tales*. Jakob published a notable philological dictionary, *Deutsche Grammatik*. The brothers also projected the vast *Deutsches Wörtebuch* which was completed by German scholars in 1961.

Grimthorpe, 1st Baron (Edmund Beckett Denison) (1816–1905), horologist who invented the double three-legged escapement for the clock at Westminster, familiarly known as "Big Ben" (the name of the bell). For long known as Sir Edmund Beckett.

Gromyko, Andrei Andrecvich (1909–89), Russian diplomat and statesman. President, USSR, July 1985–88, Foreign Minister, 1957–85; first deputy prime minister, 1983; Ambassador to Britain 1952–3.

Grossmith, George (1847–1912), English actor. With his brother, **Weedon Grossmith**, he wrote *Diary of a Nobody*. His son, **George Grossmith** (1874–1935) was a comedian and introduced revue and cabaret entertainment into England.

Grote, George (1794–1871), English historian, author of a *History of Greece*.

Grotius (Huig van Groot) (1583–1645), Dutch jurist, the founder of international law. He was condemned to life imprisonment for religious reasons, but escaped to Paris, where he wrote *De Jure Belli et Pacis*.

Grouchy, Emmanuel, Marquis de (1766–1847), French general, who served under Napoleon; after Waterloo led defeated army back to Paris.

Grove, Sir George (1820–1900), English musicologist, author of *Dictionary of Music and Musicians*. By profession he was a civil engineer.

Guedalla, Philip (1889–1944), English historian, author of *The Second Empire*, *Palmerston*, and *The Hundred Days*.

Guevara, Ernesto "Che" (1928–67), revolutionary hero, b. Argentina. He took part in the Cuban guerrilla war and became a minister in the Cuban government 1959–65. He was killed while leading a band of guerrillas against American-trained Bolivian troops. ("Che" is Argentine for "chum".)

Guido Reni (1575–1642), Italian painter of the Bolognese school whose works are characteristic of the Italian baroque of his period and include the *Aurora* fresco in the Rospigliosi palace at Rome, and *Crucifixion of St. Peter* (Vatican).

Gustavus Adolphus (1594–1632), King of Sweden, the "Lion of the North." After a campaign in Poland he entered the Thirty Years' war in support of Swedish interests and Protestant distress, won the battle of Breitenfeld in 1631 and was killed in action the next year.

Gutenberg, Johann (*c.* 1400–68), German printer, b. Mainz, the first European to print with movable types cast in moulds. The earliest book printed by him was the Mazarin Bible (*see* **L76**).

Guy, Thomas (1644–1724), English philanthropist. A printer, he made money by speculation; and in 1722 founded Guy's Hospital in Southwark.

Gwyn, Nell (*c.* 1650–87), English actress and mistress of Charles II by whom she had two sons (one to become Duke of St. Albans). Of Hereford origin, she sold oranges in London and became a comedienne at Drury Lane.

H

Haakon VII (1872–1957), King of Norway, 1905 to 1957. He resisted the Nazi occupation.

Habgood, John Stapylton (b. 1927), Archbishop of York since 1983. Formerly Bishop of Durham, 1973–83.

Hadley, George (1685–1768). He developed Halley's theory of the trade winds by taking into account the effect of the earth's rotation and the displacement of air by tropical heat (1735).

Hadrian (76–138), Roman emperor. An able general, he suppressed revolts, and he was also a lover of the arts. He visited Britain *c.* A.D. 121 and built a protective wall between Wallsend-on-Tyne and Bowness-on-Solway.

Hafiz, pseudonym of **Shams ad-Din Mohammed** (d. *c.* 1388), Persian lyrical poet. His principal work is the *Divan*, a collection of short sonnets called *ghazals*. The sobriquet *Hafiz*, meaning one who remembers, is applied to anyone who has learned the Koran by heart.

Hahn, Otto (1879–1968), German chemist and physicist, chief discoverer of uranium fission, the phenomenon on which nuclear power and the atom bomb are based.

Hahnemann, Samuel Christian Friedrich (1755–1843), German physician who founded homoeopathy (treatment of disease by small doses of drugs that in health produce similar symptoms).

Haig, Douglas, 1st Earl of Bermersyde (1861–1928), British field-marshal, b. Edinburgh. He replaced French as commander-in-chief in France, 1915–19, leading the offensive in August 1918; and after the war presided over the British Legion.

Haile Selassie I (1891–1975), Emperor of Ethiopia 1930–74. He spent the years of the Italian occupation 1936–41 in England. Deposed 1974.

Hakluyt, Richard (1553–1616), English writer on maritime discovery. B. in Herefordshire, he spent some time in Paris. From 1582 (when *Divers Voyages* appeared), he devoted his life to collecting and publishing accounts of English navigators, thus giving further impetus to discovery.

Haldane, John Burdon Sanderson (1892–1964), biologist and geneticist, noted not only for his work in mathematical evolutionary theory but for explaining science to the layman. He emigrated to India in 1957. He was the son of **John Scott Haldane** (1860–1936), b. Edinburgh, who studied the effect of industrial occupations upon health.

Haldane, 1st Viscount (Richard Burdon Haldane) (1856–1928). British Liberal statesman. As war minister in 1905 he reorganised the army and founded the Territorials.

Hale, George Ellery (1868–1935), American astronomer, after whom is named the 200-inch reflecting telescope on Mount Palomar.

Halévy, Ludovic (1834–1903), French playwright, who collaborated with Henri Meilhac in writing libretti for Offenbach and Bizet.

Halifax, 1st Earl of (Edward Frederick Lindley Wood) (1881–1959), British Conservative politician; foreign secretary during the period of appeasement of Germany; as Lord Irwin, viceroy of India 1926–31.

Halifax, 1st Marquess of (George Savile) (1633–95),

English politician of changeable views, who wrote *Character of a Trimmer.*

Hallam, Henry (1777–1859), English historian, best known for his *Constitutional History.* He was father of Arthur Hallam, friend of Tennyson.

Hallé, Sir Charles (1819–95), German-born pianist and conductor, who settled in Manchester and organised an orchestra of high-class talent. He married the violinist Wilhelmine Neruda.

Halley, Edmond (1656–1742), English astronomer royal 1720–42. He published observations on the planets and comets, being the first to predict the return of a comet (*see* **Section L**). He furthered Newton's work on gravitation, setting aside his own researches. He made the first magnetic survey of the oceans from the naval vessel *Paramour,* 1698–1700. His meteorological observations led to his publication of the first map of the winds of the globe (1686).

Hals, Frans (*c.* 1580–1666), Dutch portrait painter, b. at Mechlin. He is best known for his *Laughing Cavalier* in the Wallace Collection, and for portraits in the Louvre and at Amsterdam.

Hamilton, Alexander (1755–1804), American statesman and economist. With Madison and Jay he wrote the *Federalist* (1787). As secretary of the Treasury (1789–95) he put Washington's government on a firm financial footing and planned a national bank. He was the leader of the Federalists, a party hostile to Jefferson. He was killed in a duel.

Hamilton, Emma, Lady (*née* **Lyon**) (*c.* 1765–1815), a beauty of humble birth who, after several liaisons, was married in 1791 to Sir William Hamilton, British ambassador at Naples. There she met Nelson, and later bore him a child, Horatia.

Hammarskjöld, Dag (1905–61), world statesman. After an academic and political career in Sweden, in 1953 he became secretary-general of the United Nations, and aimed at extending its influence for peace, especially by initiating a U.N. emergency force in the Middle East. He was killed in an air crash while attempting to mediate in a dispute between Zaire and the secessionist province of Katanga. Posthumous Nobel peace prize.

Hammond, John Lawrence (1872–1949), English historian of social and industrial history, whose works (with his wife Barbara) include *The Town Labourer* and *The Village Labourer.*

Hampden, John (1594–1643), English parliamentarian and civil war leader. He refused to pay Charles I's ship money in 1636. When civil war broke out, he raised a regiment and was killed on Chalgrove Field.

Hamsun, Knut, pen-name of Knut Pedersen (1859–1952), Norwegian author who in his youth struggled for existence, visited America twice and earned his living by casual labour. *The Growth of the Soil* won him the Nobel prize in 1920. Other great novels are *Hunger* and *Mysteries.*

Handel, George Frederick (1685–1759), German composer, son of a barber-surgeon to the Duke of Saxony; b. Halle, the same year as Bach; spent much of his life in England composing operas and oratorios. His operas, of which there are over 40, include *Atalanta, Berenice* and *Serse,* and his oratorios, of which there are 32, include *Saul, Israel in Egypt, Samson, Messiah, Judas Maccabaeus,* and *Jephtha.* Eight years before he died he became blind and relied upon his old friend and copyist John Christopher Smith to commit his music to paper. *See* **Section E.**

Hannibal (247–182 B.C.), Carthaginian general. He fought two wars against Rome. In the first he conquered southern Spain. In the second he overran Gaul, crossed the Alps, and defeated the Romans in successive battles, especially at Cannae. Thereafter his forces were worn down by Roman delaying tactics; he was defeated by Scipio at Zama and later poisoned himself.

Harcourt, Sir William Vernon (1827–1904), Liberal politician who revised death duties.

Hardicanute (1019–42), son of Canute, and last Danish king of England.

Hardie, James Keir (1856–1915), Scottish Labour leader, one of the founders of the Labour party. He first worked in a coal-pit; in 1882 became a journalist; and in 1892 was the first socialist to be elected to the House of Commons (for

West Ham – South). He edited the *Labour Leader* 1887–1904. He was the first chairman of the parliamentary Labour party, 1906. A pacifist, he opposed the Boer war.

Hardy, Thomas (1840–1928), English novelist and poet, was trained as an architect and practised for some time, but became known in 1871 with *Desperate Remedies*. In 1874 his *Far from the Madding Crowd* was published. Following that came a series of novels, including *The Trumpet-Major*, *The Mayor of Casterbridge*, *Tess of the D'Urbervilles*, and *Jude the Obscure*. In 1908 he completed a dramatic poem, *The Dynasts*, whose central figure is Napoleon. His underlying theme is man's struggle against neutral forces, and he depicts the Wessex countryside.

Hargreaves, James (1720–78), English inventor, b. Blackburn. His spinning-jenny was invented in 1764 and became widely used, though his own was broken by spinners in 1768 and his invention brought him no profit.

Harkness, Edward Stephen (1874–1940), American banker and philanthropist, who in 1930 founded the Pilgrim Trust in Gt. Britain.

Harley, Robert, 1st Earl of Oxford and Mortimer (1661–1724), English statesman and collector of MSS. He held office under Queen Anne, and brought a European war to an end with the treaty of Utrecht. After the Hanoverian succession he lived in retirement, and formed the MSS. collection, now in the British Museum, which bears his name.

Harold II (1022–66), last Saxon king of England, was son of Earl Godwin. He was chosen king in succession to Edward the Confessor. He had at once to meet a dual invasion. He defeated the Norwegian king at Stamford Bridge; but was himself defeated by William of Normandy at the battle of Hastings (fought at Battle 1066).

Harriman, William Averell (1891–1986), American public official. He was adviser to President Roosevelt and later presidents especially on Marshall Aid and foreign affairs.

Harris, Joel Chandler (1848–1908), American author, creator of Uncle Remus and Brer Rabbit in Negro folk-tales.

Harrison, Frederick (1831–1923), English philosopher and lawyer, author of *The Meaning of History* and *The Philosophy of Common Sense*. He was president of the Positivist committee. *See* **Positivism, Section J.**

Harrison, John (1693–1776), "Longitude Harrison," English inventor of the chronometer, b. near Pontefract, Yorkshire, the son of a carpenter.

Harty, Sir Hamilton (1880–1941), composer and for some years conductor of the Hallé orchestra; b. County Down.

Harun ar-Rashid (Aaron the Upright) (763–809), 5th Abbasid caliph of Baghdad. His court was a centre for art and learning, but he governed mainly through his vizier until the latter lost favour and was executed in 803. The *Arabian Nights* associated with him are stories collected several centuries later.

Harvey, William (1578–1657), English physician and discoverer of the circulation of the blood. B. at Folkestone, he studied at Padua while Galileo was there, and was physician to James I and Charles I. His treatise on circulation was published in Latin in 1628.

Hastings, Warren (1732–1818), English administrator in India. As governor-general of Bengal for the East India Company he revised the finances and administration and put down disorder. On his return to England he was impeached for alleged corruption, and, though acquitted, lost his fortune in his own defence. Later however he received a grant from the company.

Hauptmann, Gerhart (1862–1946), German dramatist and novelist. B. in Silesia, he lived at first in Berlin and later abroad. His play *The Weavers* deals with a revolt of 1844 and has a collective hero. Other works include *Die versunkene Glocke*, *Der arme Heinrich*, and *Rose Bernd*. Nobel prizewinner 1912.

Havelock, Sir Henry (1795–1857), British general who helped to put down the Indian mutiny.

Hawke, 1st Baron (Edward Hawke) (1705–81), English admiral, who in 1759 defeated the French at Quiberon in a tremendous storm.

Hawking, Stephen William (b. 1942), British theoretical physicist. Lucasian Professor of Mathematics, Cambridge University, since 1979. Author

of *300 Years of Gravitation* (1987) and *A Brief History of Time* (1988). Awarded C.B.E., 1982. Companion of Honour (1989). Sufferer from motor neurone disease.

Hawkins, Sir John (1532–95), English sailor and slave-trader. In 1562 he was the first Englishman to traffic in slaves. He helped to defeat the Spanish Armada in 1588.

Hawthorne, Nathaniel (1804–64), American author. His works include *The Marble Faun*, *The Scarlet Letter*, *The House of the Seven Gables*.

Haydn, Franz Joseph (1732–1809), Austrian composer, belongs to the classical period of Bach, Handel, and Mozart. He has been given the title "father of the symphony." Much of his life was spent as musical director to the princely Hungarian house of Esterhazy. In 1791 and again in 1794 he visited London, where he conducted his Salomon symphonies. His two great oratorios, *The Creation* and *The Seasons*, were written in old age. *See* **Section E.**

Hazlitt, William (1778–1830), English essayist and critic. His writings include *The Characters of Shakespeare's Plays*, *Table Talk*, and *The Spirit of the Age*. His grandson **William Carew Hazlitt** (1834–1913) was a bibliographer and writer.

Hearst, William Randolph 1863–1951), American newspaper proprietor who built up a large newspaper empire.

Heath, Edward (b. 1916), British statesman, leader of the Conservative Party 1965–75; prime minister 1970–4; leader of the opposition 1965–70, 1974–5. In 1973 his Government took Britain into the EEC. In the contest for the leadership held in 1975 he was defeated by Mrs. Thatcher.

Hedin, Sven Anders (1865–1952), Swedish explorer of Central Asia; wrote *My Life as Explorer*.

Heenan, John Carmel (1905–76). English Roman Catholic prelate, archbishop of Westminster 1963–76; member of Sacred College (1965–76).

Hegel, Georg Wilhelm Friedrich (1770–1831), German idealist philosopher, b. Stuttgart, whose name is associated with the dialectic method of reasoning with its sequence of thesis —antithesis—synthesis. He studied theology at Tübingen with his friend Schelling. He taught philosophy at Jena, Nuremberg, Heidelberg, and Berlin. He produced an abstract philosophical system which was influenced by his early interest in mysticism and his Prussian patriotism. His doctrines were very influential in the 19th cent. and led to modern totalitarianism. He died of cholera. *See* **Dialectical Materialism, Section J.**

Heidenstam, Verner von (1859–1940), Swedish author and poet, leader of a new romantic movement. Nobel prizewinner 1916.

Heifetz, Jascha (b. 1901), Russian-born violinist, a U.S. citizen. He was the first musician to win a reputation in England by gramophone records before a personal appearance.

Heine, Heinrich (1797–1856), German lyric poet, b. Düsseldorf of Jewish parents. He lived mostly in Paris. His poems show profound beauty and subtlety of thought, but the satire and sometimes bitterness of his writings excited antagonism.

Heisenberg, Werner (1901–76), German physicist, noted for his theory of quantum mechanics and the Uncertainty Principle. Nobel prizewinner 1932.

Helmholtz, Herman von (1821–94), German physicist and physiologist. He published his *Erhaltung der Kraft* (Conservation of Energy) in 1847, the same year that Joule gave the first clear exposition of the principle of energy. His pupil Heinrich Hertz discovered electromagnetic radiation in accordance with Maxwell's theory.

Heloïse (c. 1101–64), beloved of Abelard (*q.v.*). Her letters to him are extant.

Hemingway, Ernest (1898–1961), American novelist of new technique and wide influence. His works include *A Farewell to Arms*, *Death in the Afternoon*, *For Whom the Bell Tolls*, *The Old Man and the Sea*. He committed suicide. Nobel prizewinner 1954.

Henderson, Arthur (1863–1935), British Labour politician, b. Glasgow. He worked mainly for disarmament. President, World Disarmament Conference, 1932–5. Nobel peace prize 1934.

Henrietta Maria (1609–69), the daughter of Henry IV of France and wife of Charles I.

Henry, Joseph (1797–1878), American physicist and schoolteacher who independently of Faraday discovered the principle of the induced current. The weather-reporting system he set up at the Smithsonian Institution led to the creation of the U.S. Weather Bureau.

Henry I (1068–1135), King of England. The youngest son of William the Conqueror, he ascended the throne during the absence on crusade of his elder brother Robert of Normandy. His long reign brought order and progress, not entirely destroyed by the anarchy under his successor Stephen.

Henry II (1133–89), King of England. He was son of Matilda, daugher of Henry I, and Geoffrey Plantagenet, count of Anjou; and his lands stretched to the Pyrenees. He was a strong ruler to whom we largely owe the establishment of the common law system and permanent administrative reforms. His conflict with the Church brought about the murder of his archbishop Becket.

Henry III (1207–72), King of England, succeeded his father John in 1216. Himself devout and simple, his long reign was troubled by a partly factious baronial opposition.

Henry IV (1367–1413), grandson of Edward III and heir to the Duchy of Lancaster, became king of England in 1399. More solid and practical than his cousin Richard II, whom he had supplanted, he consolidated the government.

Henry V (1387–1422), son of Henry IV, succeeded his father as king of England in 1413. A successful commander, he renewed the French war and won the battle of Agincourt, but died young.

Henry VI (1421–71), son of Henry V, succeeded his father as king of England in 1422 as a baby. Gentle and retiring, he inherited a losing war with France. He founded Eton, and King's College, Cambridge. The Yorkist line claimed the crown from his (the Lancastrian) line, and the Wars of the Roses led to his deposition and death. Ruled 1422–61, 1470–71.

Henry VII (1457–1509) succeeded Richard III as king of England after defeating him in 1485. The first Tudor king, he was firm and shrewd, even avaricious; he built Henry VII's Chapel in Westminster Abbey, and encouraged John Cabot to sail to North America.

Henry VIII (1491–1547), King of England, succeeded his father Henry VII in 1509. A prince of the Renaissance, skilled in music and sports, he loved the sea and built up the navy. His minister Cardinal Wolsey fell when Henry, seeking divorce to obtain a legal heir, rejected papal supremacy and dissolved the monasteries. Ruthless and ostentatious, he executed Sir Thomas More, spent his father's accumulation, and in spite of six marriages left a delicate son to succeed.

Henry IV of France (Henry of Navarre) (1553–1610). Prior to becoming king, he was the leader of the Huguenots; and although on being crowned he became a Catholic, he protected the Protestants by the Edict of Nantes. He then became a national king, but was later assassinated by Ravaillac, a religious fanatic.

Henry the Navigator (1394–1460), Portuguese promoter of discovery, son of John I. His sailors discovered Madeira and the Azores.

Henschel, Sir George (1850–1934), singer, composer, and conductor. B. in Breslau, he became a naturalised Englishman in 1890. Founder and conductor of the London Symphony Concerts (1886).

Hepplewhite, George (d. 1786), English cabinet-maker whose name is identified with the style which followed the Chippendale period.

Heraclitus of Ephesus (c. 540–475 B.C.), Greek philosopher. His discovery of a changing world (he lived in an age of social revolution when the ancient tribal aristocracy was beginning to give way to democracy) influenced the philosophies of Parmenides, Democritus, Plato, and Aristotle, and later, of Hegel.

Herbert, George (1593–1633), the most purely devotional of English poets.

Hereward the Wake, the last Saxon leader to hold out against the Normans. His base in the fens was captured in 1071 but he escaped. His exploits were written up by Kingsley.

Herod the Great (c. 73–4 B.C.). At first governor of Galilee under the Romans, he obtained the title of king of Judaea in 31 B.C. The massacre of the Innocents reported in St. Matthew (though not corroborated in any contemporary history) is in keeping with his historical character.

Herodotus (c. 485–425 B.C.), Greek historian, called by Cicero, the father of history. He travelled widely collecting historical evidence.

Herrick, Robert (1591–1674), English lyric poet. His poems include *Gather ye Rose Buds*, *Cherry Ripe*, and *Oberon's Feast*.

Herriot, Édouard (1872–1957), French Radical-Socialist statesman. A scholar, mayor of Lyons for more than a generation, three times prime minister, he resisted the German occupation, and was president of the National Assembly 1947–54.

Herschel, Sir John (1792–1871), British astronomer who continued his father's researches and also pioneered photography, a term introduced by him. One of his twelve children introduced fingerprints into criminology.

Herschel, Sir William (1738–1822), German-born astronomer who came to England from Hanover as a musician; father of the above. Unrivalled as an observer, and with telescopes of his own making he investigated the distribution of stars in the Milky Way and concluded that some of the nebulae he could see were separate star systems outside our own. He discovered the planet Uranus in 1781. His sister, **Caroline Lucretia** (1750–1848), compiled a catalogue of the clusters and nebulae discovered by him.

Hertz, Heinrich Rudolf (1857–95), German physicist, whose laboratory experiments confirmed Maxwell's electromagnetic theory of waves and yielded information about their behaviour.

Herzl, Theodor (1860–1904), founder of modern political Zionism, was b. Budapest. He convened a congress at Basle in 1897.

Hesiod (fl. c. 735 B.C.), Greek poet, author of *Work and Days*, which tells of life in the country.

Hill, Octavia (1838–1912), English social reformer concerned with the housing conditions of the poor, a pioneer in slum clearance in London; founder (with Sir Robert Hunter and Canon Rawnsley) of the National Trust.

Hill, Sir Rowland (1795–1879), originator of the penny postal system. He was secretary to the Postmaster-General 1846–54, then chief secretary to the Post Office until 1864.

Hindemith, Paul (1895–1963), German composer and viola player. He is associated with the movement in *Gebrauchsmusik*, which regarded music as a social expression. He incurred Nazi hostility and his later life was spent abroad. His numerous works include chamber works, songs, operas, ballet music, symphonies, and the oratorio *Das Umaufhörliche*. See **Section E.**

Hindenburg, Paul von (1847–1934), German field-marshal. In 1914 he defeated the Russians at Tannenberg. In his old age a national hero, he was president of the German Reich, 1925–34.

Hinshelwood, Sir Cyril Norman (1897–1967), English chemist. He shared with Prof. Semenov of Russia the 1956 Nobel prize for chemistry for researches into the mechanism of chemical reactions. Pres. Royal Society, 1955–60.

Hinton of Bankside, Baron (Christopher Hinton) (1901–83), as managing director of the industrial group of the U.K. Atomic Energy Authority he played an important part in the building of Calder Hall. O.M. 1976.

Hippocrates of Chios (fl. c. 430 B.C.), Greek mathematician, the first to compile a work on the elements of geometry.

Hippocrates of Cos (fl. c. 430 B.C.), Greek physician, whose writings are lost, but who is believed to have established medical schools in Athens and elsewhere, and to have contributed towards a scientific separation of medicine from superstition. Traditionally he is the embodiment of the ideal physician.

Hirohito, Emperor of Japan (1901–89), acceded to the throne in 1926. In 1946 he renounced his legendary divinity. Much controversy surrounds his role in Japanese aggression in the 1930s and his part in the Second World War. Succeeded by his son, **Akihito**, the 125th Emperor.

Hitler, Adolf (1889–1945), German dictator, founder of National Socialism, b. in Austria, son of a customs official. He was in Vienna for 5 years with no regular work before going to Munich in

1913; enlisted in Bavarian infantry at outbreak of the Kaiser's war. At the end of the war conditions in Germany favoured the growth of a fascist movement and under his leadership the National Socialist (Nazi) party climbed to power. He became Reich chancellor in 1933 and on the death of Hindenburg in 1934 Führer; and commander-in-chief Wehrmacht 1935. Under his regime working class movements were ruthlessly destroyed; all opponents—communists, socialists, Jews—were persecuted and murdered. By terrorism and propaganda the German state was welded into a powerful machine for aggression. There followed the occupation of the Rhineland (1936), the annexation of Austria and Czechoslovakia (1938–9), the invasion of Poland and declaration of war by Great Britain and France (1939), the invasion of Russia (1941). Final defeat came in 1945; on 30 April he committed suicide as the Russian troops closed in on Berlin.

Hobbes, Thomas (1588–1679), English philosopher who published *Leviathan* in 1651. He favoured strong government and supported the supremacy of the state, but his arguments aroused antagonism even among royalists. He was a child of his age in his enthusiasm for scientific enquiry.

Hobhouse, Leonard Trelawney (1864–1929), English sociologist. His books include *The Theory of Knowledge*, *Morals in Evolution*, and *Development and Purpose*.

Ho Chi-minh (1892–1969), leader of the Vietnam revolutionary nationalist party of Indo-China, which struggled for independence from France during and after the second world war. His main purpose was to weld together the nationalistic and communistic elements in Vietnam. As president of North Vietnam he fought to extend his control over South Vietnam, defying the United States.

Hodgkin, Sir Alan (b. 1914), British biophysicist working in the field of nerve impulse conduction. During the second world war he worked on the development of radar. Pres. Royal Society, 1970–75. Nobel prizewinner, 1970; Chancellor Univ. of Leicester (1971), O.M. 1973.

Hodgkin, Dorothy Crowfoot (b. 1910), the third woman to win the Nobel prize in chemistry, awarded in 1964 for her X-ray analysis to elucidate the structure of complex molecules, notably penicillin and vitamin B-12. She and her team at the Dept. of Molecular Biophysics at Oxford succeeded in 1969 in determining the crystalline structure of insulin. O.M. (1965).

Hofbauer, Imre (d. 1990), Hungarian-born artist, whose brilliance was portrayed in his compassionate studies of the down-trodden.

Hogarth, William (1697–1764), English engraver and painter, who satirised his time with character, humour, and power, especially in his *Harlot's Progress*, *Rake's Progress*, *Marriage à la Mode*, *Industry and Idleness*, and *The March to Finchley*.

Hogg, Quintin (1845–1903), educationist and philanthropist who purchased the old Polytechnic Institution in 1882 and turned it into a popular college providing education at moderate rates. His grandson, **Lord Hailsham**, was lord chancellor in the 1970–4, 1979–83, 1983–87, Conservative administrations.

Hokusai, Katsushika (1760–1849), Japanese artist of the Ukiyo-e (popular school). He excelled in landscapes.

Holbein, Hans, the elder (c. 1465–1524), German painter, b. Augsburg, father of:

Holbein, Hans, the younger (1497–1543), German painter, b. Augsburg; settled in London 1532. He won the favour of Henry VIII, for whom he painted many portraits. He is also known for his series *The Dance of Death*.

Holden, Charles (1875–1960), British architect, designer of public buildings, including British Medical Asscn. Building, London; Underground Head Offices; Univ. of London Senate House.

Holden, Sir Isaac (1807–97), British inventor of woolcombing machinery.

Hölderlin, Johann Christian Friedrich (1770–1843), German poet, friend of Hegel. His works include the novel *Hyperion* and the elegy *Menon's Laments for Diotima*. In his middle years his mind became unhinged.

Holford, Baron (William Graham Holford) (1907–75), British architect and town-planner; planned post-war redevelopment of City of London, including precincts of St. Paul's.

Holmes, Oliver Wendell (1809–94), American author. His writings include *Autocrat of the Breakfast Table*, *The Professor of the Breakfast Table*, and *The Poet at the Breakfast Table*.

Holst, Gustave Theodore (1874–1934), British composer of Swedish descent whose compositions include *The Planets* suite, *The Hymn of Jesus*, an opera *The Perfect Fool*, and a choral symphony. He was outstanding as a teacher. See **Section E**.

Holyoake, George Jacob (1817–1906), English social reformer and secularist. He wrote a history of the co-operative movement.

Holyoake, Keith Jacka (1904–83), New Zealand politician; prime minister 1960–72.

Homer (c. 700 B.C.), epic poet. He is supposed to have been a Greek who lived at Chios or Smyrna, and has been regarded as the author of the *Iliad* and the *Odyssey*, though this is tradition rather than ascertained fact.

Hood, 1st Viscount (Samuel Hood) (1724–1816), British admiral who in 1793 was in command of the Mediterranean fleet and occupied Toulon.

Hood, Thomas (1799–1845), English poet. His poems include *The Song of the Shirt*, *The Dream of Eugene Aram* and *The Bridge of Sighs*. He was also a humorist and punster.

Hooke, Robert (1635–1703), English physicist. His inventions include the balance spring of watches. He was also an architect and drew up a plan for rebuilding London after the Great Fire. His *Diary* is published.

Hooker, Richard (1554–1600), English theologian, author of *Ecclesiastical Polity*. He was Master of the Temple, 1585–91. For his choice of words he was known as "Judicious Hooker".

Hopkins, Sir Frederick Gowland (1861–1947), English biochemist, pioneer in biochemical and nutritional research. He first drew attention to the substances later known as vitamins. Pres. Royal Society 1930–5. Nobel prize 1929.

Hopkins, Gerard Manley (1844–89), English poet of religious experience and of a style new in his day.

Hopkins, Harry (1890–1946), Franklin Roosevelt's personal assistant at foreign conferences, and in the New Deal and Lend-Lease.

Hopkinson, John (1849–98), English engineer. By developing the theory of alternating current and of the magnetic current in dynamos he paved the way to the common use of electricity.

Hoppner, John (1758–1810), English portrait painter, b. Whitechapel, of German parents.

Horace (Quintus Horatius Flaccus) (65–8 B.C.), Roman satirist and poet, son of a Greek freedman. He wrote *Satires*, *Epodes*, *Odes*, and *Epistles*. He fought on the republican side at Philippi, but lived to become poet laureate to Augustus.

Horniman, Annie Elizabeth Fredericka (1860–1937), founder of the modern repertory system in England. Her father F. J. Horniman founded the Horniman Museum.

Houdini, Harry (Erich Weiss) (1874–1926), American illusionist, son of a Hungarian rabbi. Famed for his escapes from handcuffs.

Housman, Alfred Edward (1859–1936), English poet, author of *A Shropshire Lad*; he was also a classical scholar. His brother Laurence (1865–1959) was a playwright and wrote *Little Plays of St. Francis* and *Victoria Regina*.

Howard, John (1726–90), English prison reformer. Imprisoned in France in wartime, he subsequently investigated English prisons, securing reforms; and later also continental prisons, dying in Russia of gaol fever.

Howard of Effingham, 2nd Baron (Charles Howard) (1536–1624), afterwards Earl of Nottingham; commanded the fleet which defeated the Spanish Armada (1588), and took part in the capture of Cadiz (1596).

Howe, Elias (1819–67), American inventor of the sewing machine.

Howe, Sir Geoffrey, *see* **Section D.**

Howe, Julia Ward (1819–1910), American suffragette, author of *Mine eyes have seen the glory*.

Howe, 1st Earl (Richard Howe) (1726–99), British admiral whose victories over the French in two wars included that off Ushant on 1 June 1794 ("the glorious first of June").

Hua-Guofeng (b. 1922), b. Hunan, succeeded Mao Tse-tung as Chairman of the Chinese Communist Party, 1976–81. *See* **Section C, Part II.**

Hubble, Edwin Powell (1889–1953), American astronomer, noted for his work on extragalactic nebulae. With the 100-inch telescope on Mount Wilson he detected the Cepheid variables.

Hudson, Henry (d. 1611), English navigator credited with the discovery of the Hudson river and Hudson Bay, where mutineers turned him adrift to die. He was on a voyage to find a passage by the north pole to Japan and China.

Hudson, William Henry (1841–1922), naturalist, b. Buenos Aires of American parents, naturalised in England (1900). His books include *The Purple Land, Green Mansions,* and *Far Away and Long Ago.* Hyde Park bird sanctuary was established in his memory.

Huggins, Sir William (1824–1910), British astronomer who pioneered in spectroscopic photography.

Hughes, Ted (b. 1930), English poet. Succeeded Sir John Betjeman as Poet Laureate (*see* **L97**) in December 1984. Best known for his poetry of wild animals.

Hughes, Thomas (1822–96), English novelist, author of *Tom Brown's Schooldays,* which is based on Rugby school.

Hugo, Victor Marie (1802–85), French poet, dramatist, and novelist, who headed the Romantic movement in France in the early 19th cent. His dramas include *Hernani, Lucrèce Borgia, Ruy Blas,* and *Le Roi s'amuse.* Of his novels *Notre Dame* belongs to his early period, *Les Misérables, Les Travailleurs de la mer,* and *L'Homme qui rit* were written while he was living in exile in Guernsey.

Humboldt, Friedrich Heinrich Alexander, Baron von (1769–1859), German naturalist and explorer whose researches are recorded in *Voyage de Humboldt et Bonpland* (23 vols., 1805–34), and *Kosmos* (5 vols., 1845–62).

Hume, David (1711–76), Scottish philosopher who developed the empiricism of Locke into the scepticism inherent in it. His main works are *Treatise of Human Nature* and *Dialogues Concerning Natural Religion.* He also wrote a *History of England.*

Hunt, Holman (1827–1910), English artist, one of the founders of the Pre-Raphaelite movement. His best-known picture is *The Light of the World.*

Hunt, Baron (John Hunt) (b. 1910), leader of the 1953 British Everest Expedition when Tenzing and Hillary reached the summit.

Hunt, Leigh (1784–1859), English poet and essayist. In 1813 he was fined and imprisoned for libelling the Prince Regent in *The Examiner.* He was a friend of Keats and Shelley.

Hus, Jan (1369–1415), Bohemian religious reformer. Strongly influenced by Wyclif, he urged reform both of abuses in the church and of doctrine. Sentenced to death or recantation, he suffered martyrdom on 6 July 1415. His death caused a civil war which lasted many years.

Hutton, James (1726–97), an Edinburgh doctor who founded modern geological theory.

Huxley, Aldous (1894–1963), English novelist, author of *Brave New World.*

Huxley, Sir Julian (1887–1975), biologist and writer, grandson of T. H. Huxley and brother of Aldous; director of the London Zoo 1935–42; first director general of Unesco 1946–8; one of the founders of the international Union for the Conservation of Nature and of the World Wild Life Fund.

Huxley, Thomas Henry (1825–95), English biologist, b. Ealing. He acted as assistant-surgeon on H.M.S. *Rattlesnake* and during the voyage (1846–50) studied marine organisms. After the publication of Darwin's *Origin of Species* he became an ardent evolutionist and gave the first recognisably modern lecture on the origin of life to the British Association in 1870. He coined the term "agnostic" to distinguish a person who does not know whether God exists or not from the atheist who asserts there is no God. By his popular lectures and vigorous writings, *e.g., Man's Place in Nature,* he made a real attempt to interest the public in the importance of science.

Huygens, Christian (1629–95), Dutch mathematician, physicist, and astronomer, son of the poet **Constantijn Huygens** (1596–1687); discovered the rings of Saturn, invented the pendulum clock, and developed the wave theory of light in opposition to Newton's corpuscular theory.

Hyde, Douglas (1860–1949), Irish scholar, historian, poet, and folk-lorist; first president of Eire in the 1937 constitution, 1938–45.

Hypatia of Alexandria, the only woman mathematician of antiquity. She excited the enmity of Christian fanatics. Murdered in A.D. 415.

I

Ibsen, Henrik Johan (1828–1906), Norwegian playwright and poet, who dealt with social and psychological problems and revolutionised the European theatre. His chief works are *Ghosts, The Wild Duck, The Master Builder, A Doll's House, Hedda Gabler* and the poetic drama, *Peer Gynt.*

Ingres, Jean Auguste Dominique (1780–1867), French historical and classical painter. His paintings include *La grande odalisque* in the Louvre.

Innocent III (*c.* 1160–1216), Pope 1198–1216. He asserted the power and moral force of the papacy over the Emperor Otto IV, Philip II of France, and John of England. He launched the fourth crusade, encouraged the crusade against the Albigensian heretics, and held the 4th Lateran council. His pontificate marks the zenith of the mediaeval papacy.

Inönü, Ismet (1884–1973), Turkish soldier and statesman; premier, 1923–38; president 1938–50 and 1961–5.

Ionesco, Eugene (b. 1912), French playwright of the Absurd, b. Romania, whose influential plays include *The Bald Prima Donna, The Chairs,* and *Rhinoceros.*

Iqbal, Sir Muhammad (1877–1938), poet-philosopher, b. Slalkot (Pakistan). He wrote both poetry and prose in Urdu, Persian, and English, and his work is marked by mystic nationalism.

Ireland, John (1879–1962), English composer, popularly known for his setting of Masefield's *Sea Fever,* but also a composer of chamber music and sonatas for pianoforte and violin.

Irving, Sir Henry (1838–1905), English actor. At the Lyceum theatre from 1871, later with Ellen Terry, he gave notable Shakespearean performances, especially as Shylock and Malvolio.

Irving, Washington (1783–1859), American essayist, whose works include *Tales of a Traveller* and *The Sketch Book,* also biographies.

Isabella of Castile (1451–1504), reigned jointly with her husband, Ferdinand II of Aragon, over a united Spain, from which the Moors and the Jews were expelled. During their reign the New World was discovered.

Ismail Pasha (1830–95), grandson of Mehemet Ali, was Khedive of Egypt, and became virtually independent of the Sultan. Under him the Suez canal was made, but his financial recklessness led to Anglo-French control and to his own abdication.

Ismay, 1st Baron (Hastings Lionel Ismay) (1887–1965), British general who was chief of staff to Sir Winston Churchill in the second world war, and later the first secretary-general of NATO.

Ito, Hirobumi, Prince (1841–1909), Japanese statesman, four times premier, who helped to modernise his country. He was assassinated.

Ivan the Great (1410–1505) brought the scattered provinces of Muscovy under one control and put an end to Tartar rule.

Ivan the Terrible (1530–84), crowned as first Tsar of Russia in 1547, was an autocratic ruler who consolidated and expanded Russia.

J

Jackson, Andrew (1767–1845), American general who was twice president of the United States.

Jackson, Reverend Jesse Louis (1941–   ). American clergyman and civil leader. Sought Democratic nomination, 1984 and 1988. Radical black politics.

Jackson, Thomas Jonathan (1824–63), "Stonewall Jackson," was general on the Southern side in the American Civil War; killed at Chancellorsville.

Jacobs, William Wymark (1863–1943), English

novelist, b. London, author of humorous sea and other stories.

Jacquard, Joseph Marie (1752–1834), French inventor whose loom provided an effective method of weaving designs.

Jahangir (1569–1627), 3rd Mogul emperor and patron of art.

James I (1566–1625), King of England (1603–25) and, as James VI, King of Scotland (1567–1625). He was the son of Mary Stuart and succeeded to the English throne on the death of Elizabeth I. His reign saw the Gunpowder Plot of 1605 and the publication of the Authorised Version of the Bible, but it also marked an increasingly critical attitude of the Puritans towards the established church. Described as "the wisest fool in Christendom."

James II (1633–1701), King of England and, as James VII, King of Scotland (1685–8), was the younger son of Charles I. Personally honest, and an able admiral, he lacked political understanding; and when, having put down Monmouth's rebellion, he tried and failed to obtain better conditions for his fellow Roman Catholics, he was obliged in 1688 to flee the country.

James, Cyril Lionel Robert (1901–89), Trinidadian historian, literary critic, political theorist and activist. Also a cricket writer. Author of *Nkrumah and the Ghana Revolution* (1977) and *Spheres of Existence* (1980).

James, Henry (1843–1916), American novelist. He lived mainly in England. His work, noted for intellectual subtlety and characterisation, includes *The American, Daisy Miller, The Portrait of a Lady, What Maisie Knew,* and *The Spoils of Poynton.*

James, William (1842–1910), American psychologist and philosopher, brother of Henry. He was a protagonist of the theory of pragmatism developed by his friend C. S. Peirce, and invented the doctrine which he called "radical empiricism." His major works are *The Principles of Psychology, The Will to Believe,* and *The Meaning of Truth.*

Janáček, Leoš (1854–1928), Czech composer and conductor, and student of folk music, b. in Moravia, son of a village schoolmaster, creator of a national style. His best-known opera is *Jenufa. See* **Section E.**

Jefferies, Richard (1848–87), English naturalist of poetic perception, b. in Wiltshire, author of *Gamekeeper at Home* and *The Life of the Fields.*

Jefferson, Thomas (1743–1826), American president, 1801–9. He created the Republican Party, by which the federalists, led by Hamilton, were overthrown, and helped to draft the Declaration of Independence. He tried unsuccessfully to bring an end to slavery.

Jeffreys, 1st Baron (George Jeffreys) (1648–89), English judge who held the "bloody assize" after Monmouth's unsuccessful rebellion. In 1686 he was sent to the Tower and there died.

Jellicoe, 1st Earl (John Rushworth Jellicoe) (1859–1935), British admiral. He fought the uncertain battle of Jutland in 1916, after which the German fleet remained in harbour.

Jenkins, Lord (Roy Jenkins) (b. 1920), British politician, b. Wales; Pres. EEC Commission 1977–80; served as Labour's Home Sec. 1965–7; Chanc. of Exchequer 1967–70. Elected M.P. for Glasgow Hillhead for Social Democrats (1982), having previously contested Warrington. Leader, SDP 1982–June 1983. Elected Chanc., Oxford University, 1987–. Defeated in 1987 General Election.

Jenner, Edward (1749–1823), English physician, b. in Gloucs., pupil of John Hunter. His discovery of vaccination against smallpox (1798) helped to lay the foundations of modern immunology.

Jerome, Jerome Klapka (1859–1927), English humorous writer, author of *Three Men in a Boat.*

Jerome, St. (*c.* 331–420), scholar, whose translation of the Bible into Latin (the Vulgate) became for centuries the standard use.

Jesus Christ (*c.* 4 B.C.–A.D. 30), founder of Christianity, the son of Mary whose husband was Joseph, was born in a critical period of Jewish history. His home was at Nazareth in Galilee, but virtually nothing is known about his early life. When he was about 30 he began the mission which he believed to have been entrusted to him, proclaiming the Kingdom of God was at hand. His teaching is summarised in the Sermon on the Mount, and its main theme is love, especially for the poor and downtrodden. He was later

crucified. The main source of his life is the New Testament. The title "Christ" comes from the Greek word *christos* = anointed, which is the Greek translation of the Hebrew title *Messiah.* Modern dating has amended the probable year of his birth.

Jiménez, Juan Ramón (1881–1958), Spanish lyric poet. Nobel prizewinner 1956.

Jinnah, Mohammed Ali (1876–1948), Pakistani statesman. B. at Karachi, he became president of the Muslim League, and succeeded in 1947 in establishing the Dominion of Pakistan, becoming its first governor-general.

Joachim, Joseph (1831–1907), Hungarian violinist and composer.

Joan of Arc, St. (Jeanne d'Arc) (1412–31), French patriot, called the Maid of Orleans; of peasant parentage (she was b. at Domrémy), she believed herself called to save France from English domination; and by her efforts Charles VII was crowned at Rheims in 1429. Captured by the English, she was burned as a heretic; but canonised in 1920.

Joffre, Joseph Jacques Césaire (1852–1931), French general. He was commander-in-chief of the French army in the 1914–18 war.

John, St., the Baptist (executed A.D. 28), the forerunner of Jesus Christ.

John, St., the Evangelist, one of the twelve apostles of Jesus Christ, a Galilean fisherman, son of Zebedee and brother of James; traditionally author of the fourth Gospel.

John (1167–1216), youngest son of Henry II, was King of England from 1199. Able but erratic and arbitrary, he lost Normandy. Baronial opposition to him, under the influence of Archbishop Stephen Langton, acquired a national character, and in 1215 he was obliged to seal Magna Carta (*see* **Section L**).

John of Gaunt (1340–99). Duke of Lancaster, son of Edward III and father of Henry IV.

John XXIII (1881–1963), elected Pope in 1958, succeeding Pius XII, was formerly Cardinal Angelo Giuseppe Roncalli, patriarch of Venice. He sought to bring the Church closer to modern needs and to promote Christian unity. His teaching is given in his encyclicals, *Mater et Magistra* and *Pacem in Terris.*

John Paul II, (b. 1920), succeeded Pope John Paul I after his sudden death in 1978; formerly Cardinal Karol Wojtyla, archbishop of Cracow; first Pope to come from Poland. Assassination attempt made 1981. Historic meeting with Gorbachev, 1989.

John, Augustus (1878–1961), British painter and etcher, b. in Wales; noted for his portraits, *e.g.,* Lloyd George, Bernard Shaw, T. E. Lawrence.

Johnson, Amy (1904–41), was the first woman aviator to fly solo from England to Australia. She lost her life serving in the Air Transport Auxiliary in the second world war.

Johnson, Lyndon Baines (1908–73), President of the United States, 1963–9. He became president on Kennedy's assassination and followed a progressive policy at home, but his achievements were clouded by the war in Vietnam.

Johnson, Samuel (1709–84), English lexicographer and man of letters, b. at Lichfield. His *Dictionary* was published in 1755, and was followed by *Rasselas, The Idler* (a periodical), and *Lives of the Poets.* He was a focus of London literary life of his day, and his biographer, James Boswell, has vividly portrayed his circle.

Joliot-Curie, Jean Frédéric (1900–58), and his wife Irène (1896–1956), French scientists who discovered artificial radioactivity. Nobel prizewinners 1935. Joliot-Curie was one of the discoverers of nuclear fission. Irène was the daughter of Pierre and Marie Curie. Both were communists, and both died from cancer caused by their work.

Jones, Ernest Charles (1819–69), English Chartist leader and poet.

Jones, Sir Harold Spencer (1890–1960), British astronomer royal, 1935–55. His major research was to determine the mean distance of the earth from the sun, 93,004,000 miles.

Jones, Inigo (1573–1652), architect of the English renaissance who studied in Italy and inspired the use of Palladian forms in England. His buildings include the banqueting hall in Whitehall and the queen's house at Greenwich. He also designed furniture and introduced the proscenium arch and movable scenery on the English stage.

Jonson, Ben (1573–1637), English poet and dramatist. His plays include *Every Man in his Humour*, *Volpone*, and *The Alchemist*; and his poems *Drink to me only with thine Eyes*. He also produced court masques.

Josephine, Empress (1763–1814), wife of Napoleon I, *née* de la Pagerie, she was previously married to the Vicomte de Beauharnais. She was divorced from Napoleon in 1809.

Josephus, Flavius (38–*c.* 100), Jewish historian, author of *History of the Jewish War*.

Joule, James Prescott (1818–89), English physicist, pupil of Dalton, who researched on electro-magnetism and determined the mechanical equivalent of heat. *See* **Section L.**

Jowett, Benjamin (1817–93), English scholar. He translated Plato's *Dialogues*, and he was an influential Master of Balliol College, Oxford.

Jowitt, Earl (William Allen Jowitt) (1885–1957), British Labour politician and lord chancellor. He wrote *The Strange Case of Alger Hiss*.

Joyce, James (1882–1941), Irish author, b. Dublin. His *Ulysses* gives a microscopic picture of a day in the life of two Irishmen, and flouted the conventions of his day. Other works include *Portrait of the Artist* and *Finnegans Wake*. He spent most of his life on the Continent.

Juin, Alphonse (1888–1967), French general who took part in the Allied invasion of Tunisia and the Italian campaign in the second world war.

Julian the Apostate (331–63), Roman emperor who tried to restore paganism in the empire. He was killed in war against Persia.

Jung, Carl Gustav (1875–1961), Swiss psychiatrist. A former pupil of Freud, he later formulated his own system of analytical psychology. *See* **Section J.**

Junot, Andoche (1771–1813), French general defeated by Wellington in the Peninsular War.

Jusserand, Jean Jules (1855–1932), French author and diplomat, who wrote on English literature and wayfaring life in the Middle Ages.

Justinian I (483–565), Roman emperor in the East. He and his wife Theodora beautified Constantinople, and his general Belisarius was successful in war. He codified Roman law.

Juvenal (60–140), Roman poet and Stoic, remembered for his *Satires*.

K

Kafka, Franz (1883–1924), German-speaking Jewish writer, b. Prague, whose introspective work, the bulk of which was not published till after his early death from tuberculosis, has had a notable influence on later schools, especially the surrealists. It includes the three novels *The Trial*, *The Castle*, and *America*, and some short stories.

Kālidāsa (*c.* A.D. 400), chief figure in classic Sanskrit literature. No facts are known about his life and date, but certain evidence places him in the 5th cent. Seven of his works survive: two lyrics, *Ritu-samhara* (The Seasons), and *Megha-dūta* (Cloud Messenger); two epics, *Raghu-vamsa* (Dynasty of Raghu) and *Kumara-sambhava* (Birth of the War-god); and three dramas, *Śakūntalā*, *Mālavikāgnimitra*, and *Vikramorvaśīya*.

Kant, Immanuel (1724–1804), German philosopher, author of *Critique of Pure Reason* (1781), *Critique of Practical Reason* (1788), and *Critique of Judgement* (1790). He came from a Pietist family of Königsberg, where he lectured, but the Prussian government forbade his lectures as anti-Lutheran. He was influenced by the writings of his neighbour Hamann (*see* **Romanticism, Section J**) and by Rousseau and Hume, and his own work was of immense influence in shaping future liberal thought. He believed in the freedom of man to make his own decisions and considered the exploitation of man as the worst evil. In *Perpetual Peace* he advocated a world federation of states.

Kapitza, Pyotr (1894–1984), Russian physicist who worked on atomic research with Rutherford at the Cavendish Laboratory, Cambridge, and returned to Russia in 1935. Member of the Soviet Academy of Sciences and Fellow of the Royal Society. Nobel Prize for Physics, 1978.

Kauffman, Angelica (1741–1807), Anglo-Swiss

painter, a foundation member of the Royal Academy and the first woman R.A.

Kaulbach, Wilhelm von (1805–74), German painter who illustrated the works of Goethe and Schiller.

Kaunda, Kenneth (b. 1924), African leader of international standing, son of Christian missionaries. He has been president of Zambia since independence in 1964.

Kean, Charles John (1811–68), English actor-manager, son of Edmund. He married Ellen Tree and in the 1850s played with her in spectacular revivals at the Princess's Theatre, London.

Kean, Edmund (1787–1833), English tragic actor. He made his name as Shylock.

Keats, John (1795–1821), English poet who in his short life produced poems notable for richness of imagination and beauty of thought. They include *Odes*, *Isabella*, and *The Eve of St. Agnes*.

Keble, John (1792–1866), English clergyman associated with the Tractarian movement and author of *The Christian Year*. *See* **Tractarianism, Section J**.

Keller, Helen Adams (1880–1968), American author and lecturer who overcame great physical handicaps (blind and deaf before the age of two) to live an active and useful life.

Kelvin of Largs, 1st Baron (William Thomson) (1824–1907), British mathematician and physicist, b. Belfast, known for his work on heat and thermodynamics, and contributions to electrical science and submarine telegraphy. In the domain of heat he stands to Joule as Maxwell stands to Faraday in the history of electrical science, both bringing pre-eminently mathematical minds to bear on the results of experimental discoveries. He introduced the Kelvin or Absolute scale of temperature and was one of the original members of the Order of Merit.

Kemble, Fanny (1809–93), English actress. She came of a noted theatrical family, her father and uncle respectively being the actors Charles Kemble and John Philip Kemble, and her aunt, Mrs. Siddons.

Kempenfelt, Richard (1718–82), English admiral, who sank with his ship the *Royal George* together with 600 of the ship's company off Spithead through a shifting of the guns which caused it to capsize.

Kempis, Thomas à (1380–1471), name by which the German mystic Thomas Hammerken was known, was a monk of the Augustinian order, whose life was mainly spent at a monastery near Zwolle. He was the author of *The Imitation of Christ*.

Kennedy, John Fitzgerald (1917–63), President of the U.S.A., 1961–3, the youngest and the first Roman Catholic to be elected; son of a financier. He had world-wide pre-eminence and gave the American people a sense of purpose to meet the challenges of a scientific age. He opposed racial discrimination and initiated a new era of East–West relations; but his foreign policy sowed the seeds of the Vietnam war. He and his brother Robert were assassinated, the latter while campaigning for the presidency in 1968.

Kent, William (1684–1748), English painter, furniture designer, landscape gardener, and architect, protégé of Lord Burlington, whose buildings include the great hall at Holkham and the Horse Guards, Whitehall.

Kenyatta, Jomo (1893–1978), African leader who became president of Kenya in 1964.

Kepler, Johann (1571–1630), German astronomer and mystic, for a short time assistant to Tycho Brahe whose measurements he used in working out his laws of planetary motion, which are: 1. Planets move round the sun not in circles, but in ellipses, the sun being one of the foci. 2. A planet moves not uniformly but in such a way that a line drawn from it to the sun sweeps out equal areas of the ellipse in equal times. 3. The squares of the period of revolution round the sun are proportional to the cubes of the distances. The explanation of these laws was given by Newton; they dealt a death-blow to Aristotelian cosmology.

Keyes, 1st Baron (Roger John Brownlow Keyes) (1872–1945), British admiral who led the raid on Zeebrugge in 1918.

Keynes, 1st Baron (John Maynard Keynes) (1883–

1946), British economist, who was a Treasury representative at the Versailles peace conference, and published his views in *The Economic Consequences of the Peace.* His *Treatise on Money* (1930) and *The General Theory of Employment, Interest and Money* (1936) influenced economic thought all over the world.

Khomeini, Ayatollah (1900–89), Iranian religious leader. After 16 years in exile, returned to Iran in 1979 after the overthrow of the Shah. Architect of Islamic Republic of Iran. Virulently anti-Western. Waged costly, futile war with Iraq.

Khrushchev, Nikita Sergeyevich (1894–1971), Russian statesman who became leader of the Soviet Union soon after the death of Stalin; first secretary of the Soviet Communist Party, 1953–64; prime minister, 1958–64. After the harsh years of the Stalinist régime he pursued a policy of relaxation both in home and foreign affairs. Relations with America improved but those with China became strained. In 1964 his posts were taken over by Leonid Brezhnev (first secretary) and Alexei Kosygin (prime minister).

Kierkegaard, Sören (1813–55), Danish philosopher and religious thinker, whose views have influenced contemporary existentialism. His main work is *Either-Or.*

King, Martin Luther (1929–68), American clergyman and Negro integration leader; awarded the 1964 Nobel peace prize for his consistent support of the principle of non-violence in the coloured people's struggle for civil rights. Assassinated at Memphis, Tennessee.

King, Mackenzie (1874–1950), prime minister of Canada, 1921–5, 1926–30, and 1935–48.

Kingsley, Charles (1819–75), English clergyman and novelist, author of *Hypatia, Westward Ho!, Hereward the Wake* and *The Water Babies.*

Kinnock, Neil, *see* **Section D.**

Kipling, Rudyard (1865–1936), British writer, b. Bombay. His vivid work portrays contemporary British rule in India and includes *The Light that Failed, Stalky and Co., Kim,* and the *Barrack Room Ballads.* Among his books for children are the *Just So Stories, Puck of Pook's Hill* and the *Jungle Books.* Nobel prize 1907.

Kirchhoff, Gustav Robert (1824–87), German mathematical physicist, who with R. W. Bunsen discovered that in the gaseous state each chemical substance emits its own characteristic spectrum (1859). He was able to explain Fraunhofer's map of the solar spectrum. Using the spectroscope, he and Bunsen discovered the elements caesium and rubidium.

Kissinger, Henry (b. 1923), American Secretary of State 1973–7 and special adviser on national security affairs to Richard Nixon; inventor of shuttle-service diplomacy. Shared Nobel peace prize for 1973 with Le Duc Tho.

Kitchener of Khartoum, 1st Earl (Horatio Herbert Kitchener) (1850–1916), English general. In 1898 he won back the Sudan for Egypt by his victory at Omdurman. He served in the South African war; and in the first world war he was secretary of war, 1914–16. He was drowned on his way to Russia.

Klee, Paul (1879–1940), Swiss artist, whose paintings, in a restless, experimental period, are small-scale, delicate dream-world fantasies of poetical content.

Klemperer, Otto (1885–1973), German-born conductor, renowned as interpreter of the Beethoven symphonies. Expelled by the Nazis he became an American citizen and returned to Europe in 1946. He had been principal conductor of the Philharmonia Orchestra since 1959.

Kneller, Sir Godfrey (1646–1723), portrait painter, b. at Lübeck, who settled in England and was patronised by English sovereigns from Charles II to George I.

Knox, John (1514–72), Scottish reformer, b. near Haddington. While in exile at Geneva he was influenced by Calvin. On return to Scotland he was a leader of the reforming party against Mary, Queen of Scots. He wrote a *History of the Reformation in Scotland.*

Koch, Robert (1843–1910), German bacteriologist who discovered the bacillus of tuberculosis, and worked on cholera and cattle diseases.

Kodály, Zoltán (1882–1967), Hungarian composer and teacher. He worked with Bartok in the collection of folk-tunes. *See* **Section E.**

Kohl, Helmut (b. 1930), Chancellor of the Federal Republic of Germany. *See* **Section C, Part II.**

Kokoschka, Oskar (1886–1980), Austrian portrait and landscape painter, who, after teaching in Dresden, in 1938 settled in England.

Korolyov, Sergei (1907–66), Russian space scientist, who designed the world's first earth satellite, the first manned spaceship and the first moon rocket.

Kosciusko, Tadeusz (1746–1817), Polish patriot. After experience gained in America in the War of Independence, he led his countrymen against Russia in 1792 and 1794 in opposition to the partition of Poland.

Kossuth, Louis (1802–94), Hungarian patriot, who in 1848 led a rising of his countrymen against the Hapsburg dynasty, but had to flee to Turkey and later to England.

Kosygin, Alexei Nikolayevich (1904–80), succeeded Nikita Khrushchev as chairman of the Council of Ministers of the U.S.S.R. (prime minister) in 1964; key technocrat and economic organiser; resigned on health grounds, 1980.

Krebs, Sir Hans (1900–81), British biochemist, b. Germany. Taught at Cambridge and Sheffield and became Professor of Biology at Oxford in 1954. Nobel prize 1953.

Kreisler, Fritz (1875–1962), Austrian violinist, who composed violin music and an operetta. He became an American citizen in 1943.

Krenek, Ernst (b. 1900), Austrian composer of partly Czech descent, whose compositions cover a wide range, including the jazz opera *Jonny spielt auf.* He settled in America in 1938.

Kropotkin, Peter, Prince (1842–1921), Russian anarchist, geographer and explorer, who was imprisoned for favouring the political action of a working men's association, but escaped to England. He wrote on socialistic and geographical subjects. Returned to Russia in 1917.

Kruger, Stephanus Johannes Paulus (1825–1904), Boer leader, who in 1881 was appointed head of the provisional government against Britain, and later president. When the war of 1899–1902 turned against the Boers, he vainly sought help in Europe.

Krupp, Alfred (1812–87), founder of the German gun factories at Essen. He installed in a disused factory left him by his father a new steam-engine from England, began to make cast steel, and from 1844 specialised in armaments. The firm's factories made the Big Bertha guns which shelled Paris in 1918. His great-grandson Alfried (b. 1907) was tried as a war criminal in 1948.

Krylov, Ivan Andreyevich (1768–1844), Russian writer of fables who has been called the Russian La Fontaine.

Kubelik, Jan (1880–1940), Czech violinist who at the age of 12 played in public. His son **Rafael** (b. 1914) was musical director of the Royal Opera House, Covent Garden, 1955–8.

Kublai Khan (1216–94), grandson of Genghis Khan, was the first Mongol emperor of China. He extended the Mongol empire by conquest, and lived in unparalleled splendour. His court was described by Marco Polo and is the subject of a poem by Coleridge.

L

La Fayette, Marie Joseph Paul Roch Yves Gilbert du Motier, Marquis de (1757–1834), French soldier and statesman. He fought for the colonists in the American War of Independence; and in the 1789 French revolution he proposed a declaration of rights and was commander of the National Guard till his moderation made him unpopular. When the monarchy was restored he was an opposition leader, and took part in the revolution of 1830.

La Fontaine, Jean de (1621–95), French poet and fabulist, b. in Champagne, a friend of Molière, Boileau, and Racine, all brilliant writers of the reign of Louis XIV.

Lagerlöf, Selma (1858–1940), Swedish novelist and first woman member of the Swedish Academy, Nobel prizewinner 1909.

Lagrange, Joseph Louis, Comte (1736–1813), French mathematician, of Turin and Paris, whose interest in astronomy led him to distinguish two types of disturbance of members of the solar system, the periodic and the secular. He was called by Frederick the Great to Berlin to succeed Euler.

Lalande, Joseph Jerome LeFrançais de (1732–1807), French astronomer, author of *Traité d'astronomie*.

Lamarck, Jean Baptiste Pierre Antoine de Monet de (1744–1829), French biologist whose explanation of evolution was that new organs are brought into being by the needs of the organism in adapting to its environment and that the new characters acquired during its life-time can be passed on to the offspring through heredity, resulting in evolutionary change. See **F30**.

Lamb, Charles (1775–1834), English essayist, b. London. A clerk in the East India Office, he devoted his life to his sister Mary, who was of unstable mind. He is chiefly known for his *Essays of Elia*, and his letters, which have a blend of humour and tenderness.

Lambert, Constant (1905–51), English composer and critic, and conductor of Sadler's Wells ballet. His *Rio Grande* is in jazz idiom.

Landor, Walter Savage (1775–1864), English writer, b. Warwick, remembered for his *Imaginary Conversations* and poems.

Landseer, Sir Edwin (1802–73), English animal painter, b. London. He painted the *Monarch of the Glen* and designed the lions in Trafalgar Square.

Lane, Edward William (1801–76), English Arabic scholar, translator of the *Arabian Nights*.

Lanfranc (c. 1005–89), ecclesiastic. B. at Pavia, he became a prior in Normandy, and in 1070 archbishop of Canterbury, in which office he was energetic.

Lang, Andrew (1844–1912), Scottish man of letters, whose output includes *Myth, Ritual and Religion*, poems, fairy-tales, and fiction.

Lang, 1st Baron (Cosmo Gordon Lang) (1864–1945), was archbishop of Canterbury, 1928–42.

Langland, William (1330?–1400?), English poet, probably educated at Malvern, author of *The Vision of Piers the Plowman*.

Langton, Stephen (1151–1228), archbishop of Canterbury, and adviser to the insurgent barons who induced King John to grant Magna Carta.

Lansbury, George (1859–1940), British Labour politician, founder of the *Daily Herald*. He improved London's amenities.

Lâo Tsze (old philosopher) (c. 600 B.C.), traditional founder of Taoism in China. See **Section J**.

Laplace, Pierre Simon, Marquis de (1749–1827), French mathematician and astronomer, author of *Celestial Mechanics* (1799–1825). He advanced the hypothesis that the solar system had condensed out of a vast rotating gaseous nebula.

La Rochefoucauld, François, Duc de (1613–80), French writer, author of *Reflections and Moral Maxims*.

Lasker, Emanuel (1868–1941), German chess player, world champion, 1894–1921.

Lassalle, Ferdinand (1825–64), German socialist who took part in the revolutionary movement of 1848 and organised workers to press for political rights.

Lassus, Orlandus (Lasso, Orlando di) (c. 1532–94), Flemish composer and choirmaster, contemporary of Palestrina, writer of *chansons*, madrigals, and sacred music. See **Section E**.

Latimer, Hugh (c. 1485–1555), English Protestant martyr, became bishop of Worcester in 1535, and was executed under Queen Mary.

Laud, William (1573–1645), archbishop of Canterbury and adviser to Charles I. His attempt to get conformity for his high church policy made him unpopular and he was impeached and beheaded.

Lauder, Sir Harry (1870–1950), Scottish comic singer of wide popularity. He also wrote *Roamin' in the Gloamin'*.

Laval, Pierre (1883–1945), French politician who collaborated with the German occupation in the second world war and was subsequently tried and executed.

Lavoisier, Antoine Laurent (1743–94), French chemist, b. Paris, was the first to establish the fact that combustion is a form of chemical action. We owe the word *oxygen* to him. He

perished in the French Revolution.

Law, Andrew Bonar (1858–1923), Conservative politician, prime minister 1922–3.

Lawrence, David Herbert (1885–1930), English poet and novelist, b. Notts., a miner's son. He tried to interpret emotion on a deeper level of consciousness. His works, which have had wide influence, include *The White Peacock*, *Sons and Lovers*, *The Rainbow*, *Women in Love*, and *Lady Chatterley's Lover*; his plays had to wait half a century before coming to the stage in the 1960s.

Lawrence, Sir Thomas (1769–1830), English portrait painter.

Lawrence, Thomas Edward (1888–1935) (Lawrence of Arabia), British soldier who led the Arabs against the Turks in the war of 1914–18, and wrote *The Seven Pillars of Wisdom*.

Leacock, Stephen (1869–1944), Canadian humorist.

Leavis, Frank Raymond (1895–1978), British critic, who edited *Scrutiny*, 1932–63, and whose works include *The Great Tradition*, *D. H. Lawrence, Novelist*, and *"Anna Karenina" and Other Essays*.

Lecky, William Edward Hartpole (1838–1903), Irish historian, author of *England in the Eighteenth Century*.

Leclerc, Jacques Philippe (Philippe, Comte de Hautecloque) (1902–47), French general. He led a Free French force in Africa in the second world war and liberated Paris in 1944. He died in a plane crash.

Le Corbusier (1887–1965), pseudonym of Charles Édouard Jeanneret, Swiss architect, whose books and work (especially his Unité d'Habitation at Marseilles and the Punjab capital at Chandigarh) have influenced town-planning.

Le Duc Tho (b. 1911), member of the Politburo of the N. Vietnamese Workers' Party who was his country's chief negotiator at the Vietnam truce talks 1970–3. He would not accept the 1973 Nobel peace prize awarded jointly with Dr. Kissinger until peace had "really been restored in S. Vietnam."

Lee of Fareham, 1st Viscount (Arthur Hamilton Lee) (1868–1947), British politician who presented Chequers Court to the nation as prime minister's residence.

Lee, Robert Edward (1807–70), American Confederate general in the Civil War, who made the surrender at Appomattox.

Lee, Sir Sidney (1859–1926), English critic, and joint editor of the *Dictionary of National Biography*.

Leech, John (1817–64), humorist artist, b. London, of Irish descent, contributed to *Punch*.

Lehár, Franz (1870–1948), Hungarian composer. Among his most popular operettas are *The Merry Widow* and *The Count of Luxembourg*.

Leibnitz, Gottfried Wilhelm (1646–1716), German philosopher and mathematician, who invented the differential and integral calculus (1684) independently of Newton whose previous work on the same subject was not published until 1687. It was Leibnitz's nomenclature that was universally adopted.

Leicester, Earl of (Robert Dudley) (1533–88), English soldier, commanded English troops in the Netherlands, 1585–7, without much success, and in 1588 commanded forces assembled against the Armada. He was husband of Amy Robsart.

Leif Ericsson (fl. 1000), discover of Vinland on the north-east coast of America; b. Iceland, son of the Norse explorer, Eric the Red, who colonised Greenland.

Leighton, 1st Baron (Robert Leighton) (1830–96), English painter of wide popularity, whose works include *Paolo and Francesca*. He was also a sculptor.

Lely, Sir Peter (Pieter van der Faes) (1618–80), Dutch painter who settled in London and painted court portraits.

Lenin (Vladimir Ilyich Ulyanov) (1870–1924), Russian revolutionary leader and statesman. From 1893 to 1917 he worked underground in Russia and abroad for the revolutionary cause. During this time the Social-Democratic party was formed; within it developed an uncompromising revolutionary group, the Bolsheviks, and of this group Lenin was the leading spirit. In April 1917 he and his fellow exiles returned; after the November revolution he headed the new government having to face both war and anarchy. In 1921 his "new economic policy" somewhat modified the intensive drive towards planned industrial development. He was born in Simbirsk (now Ulyanovsk) on the middle Volga, the son of the local inspector of education. His body lies embalmed in Red Square, Moscow.

Leonardo da Vinci (1452–1519), Italian artist and man of science, son of a Florentine lawyer and a peasant. He described himself (when applying to Lodovico Sforza, Duke of Milan, for the post of city planner) as painter, architect, philosopher, poet, composer, sculptor, athlete, mathematician, inventor, and anatomist. His artistic output is small in quantity, and he is best known for his *Last Supper* in the refectory of Santa Maria delle Grazie in Milan and his *Mona Lisa* in the Louvre. He recorded his scientific work in unpublished notebooks written from right to left in mirror writing. The anatomy of the body (himself carrying out dissections), the growth of the child in the womb, the laws of waves and currents, and the laws of flight, all were studied by this astonishing man who believed nothing but had to see for himself. Although he was much admired, few people in his time had any notion of his universal genius.

Leoncavallo, Ruggiero (1858–1919), Italian composer of the opera *Pagliacci*.

Leonidas was king of Sparta at the time of the invasion of Greece by Xerxes (480 B.C.), and led the defence of the pass of Thermopylae, where he fell.

Lermontov, Mikhail Yurevich (1814–41), Russian poet and novelist, exiled to the Caucasus for a revolutionary poem addressed to Tsar Nicholas I on the death of Pushkin. He has been called the poet of the Caucasus. His novel *A Hero of Our Time* was written at St. Petersburg. He lost his life in a duel.

Le Sage, Alain René (1668–1747), French author, b. in Brittany, who wrote *Gil Blas* and *Le Diable Boiteux*. He was also a dramatist and his plays include *Turcaret*.

Lesseps, Ferdinand, Vicomte de (1805–94), French engineer who while serving as vice-consul at Alexandria conceived a scheme for a canal across the Suez isthmus; the work was completed in 1869. He also projected the original Panama canal scheme, which failed.

Lessing, Gotthold Ephraim (1729–81), German philosopher, dramatist, and critic, noted for his critical work *Laokoon* and his play *Minna von Barnhelm*.

Leucippus (fl. 440 B.C.), Greek philosopher, founder with Democritus of atomism, a theory of matter more nearly that of modern science than any put forward in ancient times. One of his sayings survives: "Naught occurs at random, but everything for a reason and of necessity."

Leverhulme, 1st Viscount (William Hesketh Lever) (1851–1925), British industrialist and philanthropist. He founded Lever Bros. which later became Unilever Ltd., and was a practical exponent of industrial partnership. He gave Lancaster House to the nation.

Leverrier, Urbain Jean Joseph (1811–77), French astronomer who, working independently of J. C. Adams of Cambridge, anticipated the existence of the planet Neptune which was later revealed by telescopic search.

Lévi-Strauss, Claude (b. 1908), French social anthropologist, b. Belgium, exponent of the theory of symbolic structures. He has written works on anthropology, religion, myths and language. The fourth and final vol. of his *Introduction to a Science of Mythology* about the myths and rituals of American Indians was published in 1981.

Lewis, Sinclair (1885–1951), American writer of novels satirising small-town life and philistinism. His works include *Main Street, Babbitt* and *Elmer Gantry*. Nobel prizewinner 1931.

Liaquat Ali Khan (1895–1951), leader of the Moslem League (1946) and first premier of Pakistan in 1947. He was assassinated.

Lie, Trygve (1896–1968), Norwegian politician who became secretary-general of the United Nations, 1946–52.

Li Hung Chang (1823–1901), Chinese statesman, who though enlightened, was unable to secure

much modernisation and had to cede Formosa to Japan in 1895.

Lilburne, John (1614–57), English agitator and pamphleteer, leader of the Levellers in the Civil War period.

Linacre, Thomas (c. 1460–1524), English humanist and physician, who translated Galen's works and founded the College of Physicians.

Lincoln, Abraham (1809–65), American president. Born in Kentucky, he became a lawyer and was returned to Congress from Illinois in 1846. He was a leader of the Republican party which was formed in 1856 to oppose slavery. He became president in 1861, in which year the Confederate States proposed to withdraw from the Union, and war broke out. The phrase "government of the people, by the people, for the people" comes from his Gettysburg speech of 1863. He was assassinated in 1865.

Lind, Jenny (1820–87), Swedish singer, popular in Europe, and known as the Swedish nightingale. She founded musical scholarships.

Linnaeus (1707–78), Swedish botanist, remembered for his system of defining living things by two Latin names, the first being its *genus*, and the second its *species*. His method is expounded in *Philosophia Botanica* (1751). In 1757 he was ennobled as Karl von Linné. He studied, taught and died at Uppsala.

Lippi, Fra Filippo (1406–69), Italian artist, b. Florence. Frescoes in Prato cathedral are his main work. His son **Filippino** (1457–1504) finished Masaccio's frescoes in the Carmine, Florence, and executed others, for instance in Santa Maria Novella.

Lippmann, Gabriel (1845–1921), French physicist who invented a capillary electrometer and was a pioneer in colour photography. Nobel prizewinner 1908.

Lippmann, Walter (1889–1974), American journalist of influence, writing for the New York *Herald Tribune*, 1931–62.

Lipton, Sir Thomas Johnstone (1850–1931), Scottish business man and philanthropist. B. Glasgow, he emigrated to America, but returned to Scotland and established extensive chainstores for groceries. He unsuccessfully competed in yachting for the America's Cup.

Lister, Baron (Joseph Lister) (1827–1912), English surgeon, son of **J. J. Lister** (1786–1869), an amateur microscopist. He founded antiseptic surgery (1865) which greatly reduced mortality in hospitals.

Liszt, Franz (1811–86), Hungarian pianist and composer. His daughter Cosima became the wife of Hans von Bülow and later of Wagner. *See* Section E.

Litvinov, Maxim (1876–1952), Russian diplomat, of revolutionary origin, who first as ambassador in London, then as commissar for foreign affairs, and 1941–3 ambassador to the U.S., gained respect and understanding for his country.

Livingstone, David (1813–73), Scottish explorer in Africa. He discovered the course of the Zambesi, the Victoria Falls and Lake Nyasa (now Lake Malawi), and roused opinion against the slave trade. At one time believed lost, he was found by Stanley (*q.v.*) on 10 Nov. 1871.

Lloyd-George of Dwyfor, 1st Earl (David Lloyd George) (1863–1945), Liberal statesman of Welsh origin. He was M.P. for Caernarvon, 1890–1944; and as chancellor of the exchequer he introduced social insurance, 1908–11. The war of 1914–18 obliged him to become a war premier (superseding Asquith), and he was subsequently one of the main figures at the peace conference. In 1921 he conceded the Irish Free State. His daughter, **Lady Megan Lloyd George**, was M.P. for many years, latterly for the Labour Party.

Locke, John (1632–1704), English liberal philosopher and founder of empiricism, the doctrine that all knowledge is derived from experience. His chief work in theoretical philosophy, *Essay Concerning Human Understanding*, was written just before the revolution of 1688 and published in 1690. Other writings include *Letters on Toleration, Treatises on Government*, and *Education*.

Lombroso, Cesare (1836–1909), Italian criminologist, whose *L'uomo delinquente* maintained the existence of a criminal type distinguishable from the normal.

Lomonosov, Mikhail Vasilievich (1711–65),

Russian philologist and poet who systematised Russian grammar and orthography.

London, Jack (1876–1916), American author of adventure tales such as *Call of the Wild*.

Longfellow, Henry Wadsworth (1807–82), American poet, popular in his lifetime, author of *The Golden Legend* and *Hiawatha*.

Lope de Vega Carpio, Félix (1562–1635), Spanish writer of immense output. First a ballad-writer, he took to play-writing and founded the Spanish drama. The number of his plays is said to have been 1,500, the earlier ones historical, the later ones dealing with everyday life; but most are lost.

Lorca, Federico García (1899–1936), Spanish poet and dramatist of Andalusia. Among his works are *Llanto por Ignacio Sánchez Mejías*, an unforgettable lament on the death of a bull-fighter, and *Canción de Jinete* with its haunting refrain, "Cordoba, far away and alone." He was brutally murdered by Franco sympathisers at the outbreak of the civil war.

Louis IX (1214–70), St. Louis, King of France. Of saintly character (as described in Joinville's *Memoirs*), he also carried out practical reforms. He died on crusade.

Louis XIV (1638–1715), King of France. A despotic ruler, builder of Versailles, he also dominated the Europe of his day; but he sowed the seeds of future trouble for France by his exhausting wars. He revoked the Edict of Nantes which had given religious freedom to the Huguenots since 1598. His reign, however, was a great period for literature.

Louis XV (1710–74), King of France. Extravagant and self-indulgent, his reign marked a declining period for the monarchy, but produced some fine art.

Louis XVI (1754–93), King of France. Well-meaning but incapable, this king saw the outbreak of the French revolution of 1789, in which he and his queen Marie Antoinette were executed.

Louis, Joe (Joseph Louis Barrow) (1914–81), American Negro boxer, who became world heavyweight champion in 1936, successfully defending his title 26 times.

Low, Archibald Montgomery (1888–1956), British scientist who worked in varied fields, including wireless, television, and anti-aircraft and anti-tank apparatus.

Low, Sir David (1891–1963), British cartoonist, b. New Zealand, associated with the *Evening Standard* and later the *Guardian*; creator of Colonel Blimp.

Lowell, Robert (1917–77), American poet, author of the verse play *The Old Glory*, and *Life Studies*, an autobiographical volume in verse and prose.

Loyola, St. Ignatius (1491–1556), Spanish founder of the Jesuits, a missionary order working directly under the Pope.

Lucretius (99–55 B.C.), Roman poet, author of *De rerum natura*, a long philosophical poem advocating moral truth without religious belief.

Ludendorff, Erich (1865–1937), German general who directed German strategy in the first world war.

Lugard, 1st Baron (Frederick John Dealtry Lugard) (1858–1945), British colonial administrator in Africa, especially Nigeria, and exponent of the system of indirect rule through native chiefs.

Lukács, Georg (1885–1971), Hungarian writer, Marxist thinker and literary critic. His ideas are expounded in *History and Class Consciousness* (1923), *Studies in European Realism* (1946, Eng. tr. 1950), *The Historical Novel* (1955, Eng. tr. 1962).

Luther, Martin (1483–1546), German Protestant reformer. After spending time in a monastery, he was ordained priest (1507), and lectured at Wittenberg university. In 1517 he protested against the sale of indulgences; and when summoned before the Diet of Worms made a memorable defence. He was protected by the Elector of Saxony, and translated the Bible. German Protestantism culminated in the Augsburg confession (1530). *See also* **Lutheranism, Section J.**

Luthuli, Albert (1899–1967), African non-violent resistance leader, an ex-Zulu chief. Killed in train accident. Nobel prize for peace 1960.

Lutyens, Sir Edwin Landseer (1869–1944), English architect both of country houses and public buildings; designed the cenotaph, Whitehall; city plan and viceroy's house, New Delhi, British Embassy, Washington and Liverpool Roman catholic cathedral.

Lyell, Sir Charles (1797–1875), Scottish geologist, whose *Principles of Geology* (1830–33) postulated gradual geological change and helped to shape Darwin's ideas. His terminology—Pliocene (*Greek* = more recent), Miocene (less recent) and Eocene (dawn)—is still in use.

Lysenko, Trofim (1898–1976), Russian biologist who maintained that environmental experiences can change heredity somewhat in the manner suggested by Lamarck. After the death of Stalin his novel theories were severely criticised.

Lytton, 1st Baron (Edward George Earle Lytton Bulwer-Lytton) (1803–73), English novelist and playwright, author of *The Last Days of Pompeii*.

M

Macadam, John Loudon (1756–1836), Scottish inventor of the "macadamising" system of road repair.

MacArthur, Douglas (1880–1964), American general. He defended the Philippines against the Japanese in the second world war, and was relieved of his command in 1951 in the Korean war.

Macaulay of Rothley, 1st Baron (Thomas Babington Macaulay) (1800–59), English historian, poet and Indian civil servant. His poems include *Lays of Ancient Rome*. In India he reformed the education system.

Macaulay, Zachary (1768–1838), anti-slavery agitator, father of the above.

Macbeth (d. 1057), Scottish king, married Gruoch, granddaughter of Kenneth, king of Alban. He was mormaer of Moray, succeeding Duncan in 1040 after killing him in fair fight. His reign of seventeen years was prosperous, but he was killed by Duncan's son, Malcolm, in 1057. Shakespeare's play is based on the inaccurate *Chronicle* of Holinshed.

MacDiarmid, Hugh (1892–1978), pseudonym of Christopher Murray Grieve, Scottish poet, leader of the Scottish literary renaissance; author of *A Drunk Man Looks at the Thistle*.

Macdonald, Flora (1722–90), Scottish Jacobite heroine who saved the life of Prince Charles Edward after the defeat at Culloden Moor in 1746.

Macdonald, Sir John Alexander (1815–91), Canadian statesman, first prime minister of the Dominion of Canada.

MacDonald, James Ramsay (1866–1937), Labour politician of Scottish origin, premier 1924 and 1929–31; also of a coalition 1931–5. His action over the financial crisis of 1931 divided his party.

MacDonald, Malcolm (1901–81), son of above, held positions overseas in the Commonwealth, the last as special representative in Africa.

Machiavelli, Niccolò (1467–1527), Florentine Renaissance diplomat and theorist of the modern state. His book *The Prince* (1513), dedicated to Lorenzo, Duke of Urbino, is concerned with the reality of politics—what rulers must do to retain power. His *Discourses* is more republican and liberal.

Mackail, John William (1859–1945), British classical scholar, translator of the *Odyssey*.

Mackenzie, Sir Compton (1883–1972), British writer, whose works include *Carnival, Sinister Street*, and a monumental autobiography.

McLuhan, Herbert Marshall (1911–80), Canadian author of a number of books on contemporary communications, including *The Gutenberg Galaxy, The Mechanical Bride. See* **Section J.**

Macmillan, Harold (1894–1986), British Conservative statesman, prime minister 1957–63; During his premiership came the crises of the Berlin Wall and the Cuban missiles (in which his personal diplomacy played an influential role), de Gaulle's veto to our entry into Europe, the signing of the Partial Test-Ban Treaty and his "wind of change" speech which hailed African independence. Chancellor of Oxford University (1960–86), O.M. 1976. Created Earl of Stockton, 1984.

McMillan, Margaret (1860–1931), Scottish educational reformer, b. New York, and pioneer of open-air nursery schools.

Macneice, Louis (1907–63), British poet, playwright, and translator.

Macready, William Charles (1793–1873), British actor and manager, especially associated with Shakespearean roles.

Maeterlinck, Maurice (1862–1949), Belgian man of letters, whose plays include *La Princesse Maleine*, *Pelléas et Mélisande*, and *L'Oiseau Bleu*. Nobel prizewinner 1911. He also did scientific work on bees.

Magellan, Ferdinand (*c.* 1480–1521), Portuguese navigator, and commander of the first expedition (1519) to sail round the world.

Mahler, Gustav (1860–1911), Austrian composer and conductor; a writer of symphonies and songs, a classical romantic, much influenced by Anton Bruckner and Wagner. *See* **Section E.**

Mahavira, Vardhamana Jnatriputra (6th cent. B.C.), Indian historical (as opposed to legendary) founder of Jainism, which teaches the sacredness of all life. *See* **Jainism, Section J.**

Maintenon, Françoise d'Aubigné, Marquise de (1635–1719), second wife of Louis XIV. Her first husband was the poet Scarron.

Makarios III (1913–77), Greek Orthodox archbishop and Cypriot national leader. Deported by the British to the Seychelles in 1956, he returned in 1957. First President of Cyprus.

Malibran, Marie Félicité (1808–36), Spanish mezzo-soprano.

Malik, Yakov Alexandrovich (1906–80), Soviet diplomat; permanent representative at U.N. 1949–52, 1967–76; ambassador to Britain 1953–60; deputy foreign minister 1960–7.

Malory, Sir Thomas (*c.* 1430–71), English writer. From earlier sources and legends of King Arthur and the Knights of the Round Table, he compiled the *Morte d'Arthur* printed by Caxton in 1485.

Malraux, André (1895–1976), French novelist and politician. His works include *La Condition humaine*, *L'Espoir*, and *Psychologie de l'art* (tr. in 2 vols., *Museum without Walls*, and *The Creative Act*). Served under de Gaulle.

Malthus, Thomas Robert (1766–1834), English clergyman and economist who in his gloomy essay *The Principle of Population* contended that population tends to increase faster than the means of subsistence and that its growth could only be checked by moral restraint or by disease and war. *See* **Malthusianism, Section J.**

Mandela, Nelson Rolihlahia (b. 1918), South African lawyer and politician; son of chief of Tembu tribe; imprisoned on political grounds 1964–90. The symbolic father figure of black nationalism. His release from prison in February 1990 transformed the political scene in South Africa. Elected Deputy President, ANC, March 1990. *See* **Section C, Part II.**

Manet, Edouard (1832–83), French painter. His Impressionist pictures include *Olympia* and *Un bar aux Folies-Bergères* (the latter at the Courtauld).

Mann, Thomas (1875–1955), German writer who won world recognition at the age of 25 with his novel *Buddenbrooks*. His liberal humanistic outlook had developed sufficiently by 1930 for him to expose national socialism. He left Germany in 1933 to live in Switzerland, then settled in the U.S. Other works are *The Magic Mountain*, and the *Joseph* tetralogy. Nobel prizewinner 1929.

Mann, Tom (1856–1941), British Labour leader for more than fifty years.

Manning, Henry Edward (1808–92), English cardinal; archbishop of Westminster 1865–92. He was an Anglican churchman before he entered the church of Rome.

Mansfield, Katherine (Kathleen Beauchamp) (1890–1923), short-story writer, b. Wellington, New Zealand, whose work was influenced by the short stories of Chekhov. Her second husband was John Middleton Murry, literary critic.

Manson, Sir Patrick (1844–1922), Scottish physician, the first to formulate the hypothesis that the malarial parasite was transmitted by the mosquito. His joint work with Sir Ronald Ross rendered habitable vast areas of the earth hitherto closed.

Manuzio, Aldo Pio (1450–1515), Italian printer, founder of the Aldine press in Venice, which for just over a century issued books famed for their beautiful type and bindings.

Manzoni, Alessandro (1785–1873), Italian novelist

and poet, b. Milan, whose historical novel *I Promessi Sposi* (The Betrothed) won European reputation.

Mao Tse-tung (1893–1976), Chinese national and Communist leader. B. in Hunan, of rural origin. As a young man he worked as assistant librarian at Peking University. He understood how to win peasant support for a national and progressive movement. Attacked by Chiang Kai-shek, he led his followers by the "long march" to N.W. China, whence later they issued to defeat both Japanese and Chiang and proclaim a People's Republic in 1949, and later to promote the "great leap forward" of 1958–9 (the commune movement). He stood for an egalitarian democratic society, unbureaucratic, with revolutionary momentum. He was much to the fore in the "cultural revolution" from 1965 to 1969. *See* **Section C, Part II, and Maoism, Section J.**

Marat, Jean Paul (1743–93), French revolution leader, largely responsible for the reign of terror, and assassinated by Charlotte Corday.

Marconi, Guglielmo Marchese (1874–1937), Italian inventor and electrical engineer who developed the use of radio waves as a practical means of communication. In 1895 he sent long-wave signals over a distance of a mile, and in 1901 received in Newfoundland the first transatlantic signals sent out by his station in Cornwall, thus making the discovery that radio waves can bend around the spherically-shaped earth. Nobel prizewinner 1909.

Marcus Aurelius Antoninus (121–180 A.D.), Roman emperor and Stoic philosopher of lofty character, whose *Meditations* are still read.

Marcuse, Herbert (1898–1979), political philosopher. B. Berlin, he emigrated to the U.S. during the Nazi regime. A critic of Western industrial society, he saw the international student protest movement as the catalyst of revolutionary change.

Maria Theresa (1717–80), Empress, daughter of the Hapsburg Charles VI. Able and of strong character, she fought unsuccessfully to save Silesia from Prussian annexation. She promoted reforms in her dominions. She married the Duke of Lorraine and had 16 children.

Marie Antoinette (1755–93), Queen of France, was daughter of the above and wife of Louis XVI; accused of treason, she and her husband were beheaded in the French revolution.

Marie Louise (1791–1847), daughter of Francis I of Austria, became the wife of Napoleon and bore him a son (Napoleon II).

Marius, Caius (157–86 B.C.), Roman general who defended Gaul from invasion; later civil war forced him to flee from Rome, and on his return he took terrible revenge.

Mark Antony. *See* **Antonius, Marcus.**

Marlborough, 1st Duke of (John Churchill) (1650–1722), English general, victor of Blenheim, Ramillies, Oudenarde and Malplaquet. His wife, Sarah Jennings, was a favourite of Queen Anne.

Marlowe, Christopher (1564–93), English dramatist and precursor of Shakespeare. His plays include *Dr. Faustus*, *Tamburlaine the Great*, *Edward II*, and *The Jew of Malta*. His early death was due to a tavern brawl.

Marryat, Frederick (1792–1848), English author of sea and adventure stories, including *Peter Simple*, *Mr. Midshipman Easy*, and *Masterman Ready*. A captain in the Royal Navy.

Marshall, George Catlett (1880–1959), American general. U.S. chief of staff 1939–45; originated the Marshall Aid plan for European reconstruction. Nobel prize for peace 1953.

Martial, Marcus Valerius (*c.* 40–104), Roman poet, b. in Spain, remembered for his epigrams.

Marvell, Andrew (1620–78), English poet and political writer. He was Milton's assistant and wrote mainly during the commonwealth.

Marx, Karl (1818–83), German founder of modern international communism, b. Trier of Jewish parentage. He studied law, philosophy and history at the universities of Bonn and Berlin, and later took up the study of economics. In conjunction with his friend Engels he wrote the *Communist Manifesto* of 1848 for the Communist League of which he was the leader. Because of his revolutionary activities he was forced to leave the continent and in 1849 settled in London. Here, mainly while living at 28 Dean Street, Soho, he wrote *Das Kapital*, a deep analysis of the economic laws that govern modern society. In 1864 he helped to found the first International. He ranks as one of the most original and influential thinkers of modern times. He was buried at Highgate cemetery. *See* Marxism, Section J.

Mary I (1516–58), Queen of England, was daughter of Henry VIII and Catherine of Aragon. A Roman Catholic, she reversed the religious changes made by her father and brother, and about 300 Protestants were put to death. She married Philip of Spain.

Mary II (1662–94), Queen of England with her husband the Dutch William III. As daughter of James II, she was invited to succeed after the revolution of 1688 and expelled her father.

Mary Stuart, Queen of Scots (1542–87), daughter of James V of Scotland and Mary of Guise, she laid claim to the English succession. She was imprisoned in England by Elizabeth and beheaded. Her husbands were the dauphin of France (d. 1560), Lord Stanley Darnley (murdered 1567) and Bothwell.

Masaryk, Jan Garrigue (1886–1948), Czech diplomat. The son of Thomas, he was Czech minister in London 1925–38, and foreign secretary while his government was in exile in London and after it returned to Prague, 1940–8.

Masaryk, Thomas Garrigue (1850–1937), Czech statesman and independence leader. He was the first president of Czechoslovakia, 1918–35.

Mascagni, Pietro (1863–1945), Italian composer of *Cavalleria Rusticana*.

Masefield, John (1878–1967), English poet. His best-known works are *Salt-Water Ballads* (as a boy he ran away to sea), and *Reynard the Fox*. He became poet laureate in 1930.

Maskelyne, John Nevil (1839–1917), English illusionist. He also exposed spiritualistic frauds.

Massenet, Jules Emile Frédéric (1842–1912), French composer of songs, orchestral suites, oratorios, and operas, among them *Manon* and *Thaïs*.

Massine, Léonide (1896–1979), Russian dancer, one of Diaghilev's choreographers. In 1944 he became a U.S. citizen.

Masters, Edgar Lee (1869–1950), American poet remembered for his *Spoon River Anthology*.

Matisse, Henri (1869–1954), French painter, member of a group known as *Les Fauves* (the wild beasts) for their use of violent colour and colour variation to express form and relief. A number of his paintings are in the Moscow Museum of Western Art.

Matsys (**Massys**), **Quentin** (1466–1530), Flemish painter, b. Louvain, settled Antwerp; he worked at a time when Italian influence was gaining ground. His *Money-changer, and his Wife* is in the Louvre.

Maugham, William Somerset (1874–1965), British writer, b. Paris. He practised as a doctor till the success of *Liza of Lambeth* (1897) followed by *Of Human Bondage*. He was a master of the short story and his work reflects his travels in the East. In both world wars he served as a British agent.

Maupassant, Guy de (1850–93), French writer whose novels and short stories show penetrating realism. His stories include *Boule de Suif*, *Le Maison Tellier*, and *La Parure* (The Necklace).

Mauriac, François (1885–1970), French writer whose novels deal with moral problems and include *Le Baiser au Lépreux* and the play *Asmodée*. Nobel prizewinner 1952.

Maurois, André (**Emile Herzog**) (1885–1967), French writer whose works include lives of Shelley and Disraeli.

Maxim, Sir Hiram Stevens (1840–1916), American inventor of the automatic quick-firing gun.

Maxton, James (1885–1946), Scottish Labour politician and pacifist; entered parliament 1922; chairman of I.L.P. 1926–31, 1934–9.

Maxwell, James Clerk (1831–79), Scottish physicist. He wrote his first scientific paper at 15, and after teaching in Aberdeen and London became first Cavendish professor of experimental physics at Cambridge. His mathematical mind, working on the discoveries of Faraday and others, gave physics a celebrated set of equations for the basic laws of electricity and magnetism. His work revolutionised fundamental physics.

Mazarin, Jules (1602–61), cardinal and minister of France was b. in Italy. In spite of opposition from the nobles, he continued Richelieu's work of building up a strong monarchy.

Mazeppa, Ivan Stepanovich (1644–1709), Cossack nobleman, b. Ukraine (then part of Poland, before E. Ukraine passed to Russia, 1667). He fought unsuccessfully for independence allying himself with Charles XII of Sweden against Peter I of Russia (Poltava, 1709). According to legend he was punished for intrigue by being tied to the back of a wild horse and sent into the steppes. Byron wrote a poem about him.

Mazzini, Giuseppe (1805–72), Italian patriot. B. Genoa, he advocated a free and united Italy, and from Marseilles he published a journal, *Young Italy*. Expelled from the Continent, he took refuge in London in 1837. In 1848 he returned to Italy, and became dictator of the short-lived Roman republic, which was put down by French forces. His contribution to Italian unity was that of preparing the way.

Mechnikov, Ilya (1845–1916), Russian biologist who discovered that by "phagocytosis" certain white blood cells are capable of ingesting harmful substances such as bacteria (*see* Diseases of the Blood, Section P). For his work on immunity he shared the 1908 Nobel prize for medicine.

Medawar, Sir Peter Brien (1915–87), British zoologist, author of *The Art of the Soluble* and *The Future of Man*; president of the British Association 1969. Nobel prizewinner 1960. O.M. 1981.

Medici, Florentine family of merchants and bankers who were politically powerful and who patronised the arts. **Cosimo the Elder** (1389–1464) was for over 30 years virtual ruler of Florence. His grandson, **Lorenzo the Magnificent** (1449–92), poet, friend of artists and scholars, governed with munificence. His grandson, **Lorenzo**, was father of **Catherine de' Medici**, Queen of France (*q.v.*). A later **Cosimo** (1519–74) was an able Duke of Florence and then Grand-Duke of Tuscany, which title the Medicis held until 1737.

Méhul, Etienne Nicolas (1763–1817), French operatic composer. *Joseph* is his masterpiece.

Meir, Golda (1898–1978), leading member of the Israeli Labour Party, her premiership included the Six Day and Yom Kippur wars.

Meitner, Lise (1878–1969), co-worker of Otto Hahn (*q.v.*) who interpreted his results (1939) as a fission process.

Melanchthon, Philip (1497–1560), German religious reformer, who assisted Luther, and wrote the first Protestant theological work, *Loci communes*. He drew up the Augsburg confession (1530).

Melba, Nellie (Helen Porter Mitchell) (1861–1931), Australian soprano of international repute, b. near Melbourne.

Melbourne, 2nd Viscount (William Lamb) (1779–1848), English Whig statesman, was premier at the accession of Queen Victoria.

Mendel, Gregor Johann (1822–84), Austrian botanist. After entering the Augustinian monastery at Brünn he became abbot and taught natural history in the school. His main interest was the study of inheritance, and his elaborate observations of the common garden pea resulted in the law of heredity which bears his name. His hypothesis was published in 1866 but no attention was given to it until 1900. *See* Section F, Part IV.

Mendeleyev, Dmitri Ivanovich (1834–1907), Russian chemist, first to discover the critical temperatures. He formulated the periodic law of atomic weights (1869) and drew up the periodic table (*see* Section F), predicting the properties of elements which might fill the gaps. Element 101 is named after him.

Mendelssohn-Bartholdy, Felix (1809–47), German composer, grandson of Moses Mendelssohn, philosopher. He belongs with Chopin and Schumann to the early 19th cent. classic-romantic school, and his music has delicacy and melodic beauty. He was conductor of the Gewandhaus concerts at Leipzig for a time and often visited England. *See* Section E.

Mendès-France, Pierre (1907–82), French politician, premier 1954–5, but defeated on his North African policy. He was a critic of de Gaulle.

Menuhin, Sir Yehudi (b. 1916), world-famous violinist, b. New York of Russian Jewish parentage. He first appeared as soloist at the age of seven and has international repute. Founded a School for musically gifted children. Acquired British citizenship, 1985. Awarded Order of Merit, 1987.

Menzies, Sir Robert Gordon (1894–1978), Australian Liberal statesman, P.M. 1939–41, 1949–66.

Mercator, Gerhardus (Gerhard Kremer) (1512–94), Flemish geographer who pioneered the making of accurate navigational maps. He worked out the map which bears his name in which meridians and parallels of latitude cross each other at right angles, enabling compass bearings to be drawn as straight lines.

Meredith, George (1828–1909), English writer, b. Portsmouth. His novels include *The Ordeal of Richard Feverel*, *The Egoist*, *Evan Harrington*, *Diana of the Crossways*, and *The Amazing Marriage*. His poetry has had renewed attention; the main works are *Modern Love* and *Poems and Lyrics of the Joy of Earth*.

Mesmer, Friedrich Anton (1733–1815), Austrian founder of mesmerism, or animal magnetism. *See* **Mesmerism, Section J**.

Mestrovič, Ivan (1883–1962), Yugoslav sculptor of international repute. He designed the temple at Kossovo. He later lived in England, and examples of his work are in London museums.

Metastasio, Pietro (Pietro Bonaventura Trapassi) (1698–1782), Italian librettist who lived in Vienna and provided texts for Gluck, Handel, Haydn, and Mozart.

Michelangelo (Michelagniolo Buonarroti) (1475–1564), Italian painter, sculptor and poet. Of a poor but genteel Tuscan family, his first interest in sculpture came through his nurse, wife of a stone-cutter. He was apprenticed to Domenico Ghirlandaio. Like Leonardo, he studied anatomy, but instead of spreading his talents over a wide field, he became obsessed with the problem of how to represent the human body. In him, classical idealism, mediaeval religious belief, and renaissance energy met. Perhaps his most impressive work is the ceiling of the Sistine Chapel (a surface of about 6,000 square feet), the *Last Judgement* behind the chapel altar, his marble *Pieta* (St. Peter's) the statue of *David* (Academy, Florence), the great figure of *Moses* (San Pietro in Vincoli, Rome), and the four allegorical figures *Day*, *Night*, *Dawn*, *Twilight* (intended for the tombs of the Medici family at San Lorenzo, Florence).

Michelet, Jules (1798–1874), French historian who wrote a history of France in 24 vols. and of the revolution in 7 vols.

Michelson, Albert Abraham (1852–1931), American physicist, b. Poland. He collaborated with E. W. Morley in an experiment to determine ether drift, the negative result of which was important for Einstein. Nobel prizewinner 1907.

Mickiewicz, Adam (1798–1855), Polish revolutionary poet, author of *The Ancestors* and *Pan Tadeusz*.

Mill, John Stuart (1806–73), English philosopher. A member of Bentham's utilitarian school, he later modified some of its tenets. His main work is *On Liberty*, which advocates social as well as political freedom and warns against the tyranny of the majority. *The Subjection of Women* supported women's rights. He also wrote *Principles of Political Economy*. He was godfather to Bertrand Russell.

Millais, Sir John Everett (1829–96), English artist, b. Southampton; in his earlier years a pre-Raphaelite (*Ophelia*). Later works include *The Boyhood of Raleigh* and *Bubbles*. He married Mrs. Ruskin after the annulment of her marriage.

Millet, Jean François (1814–75), French painter of rural life, sometimes in sombre mood; his works include *The Angelus*.

Millikan, Robert Andrews (1868–1954), American physicist, who determined the charge on the electron and discovered cosmic rays. Nobel prizewinner 1923.

Milne, Alan Alexander (1882–1956), English humorist and poet whose work for children is still widely read.

Milner, 1st Viscount (Alfred Milner) (1854–1925), British administrator, especially in South Africa; author of *England in Egypt*.

Miltiades (d. 489 B.C.), one of the leaders of the Athenian army against the Persians at Marathon.

Milton, John (1608–74), English poet, author of *Paradise Lost*. B. in London, he wrote while still at Cambridge *L'Allegro*, *Il Penseroso*,

Comus, and *Lycidas*. The Civil War diverted his energies for years to the parliamentary and political struggle, but during this period he defended in *Aereopagitica* the freedom of the press. After he had become blind he wrote *Paradise Lost* and a sonnet *On His Blindness*.

Minot, George Richards (1885–1950), who with W. P. Murphy discovered the curative properties of liver in pernicious anaemia. Shared Nobel prize 1934.

Mirabeau, Gabriel, Honoré Victor Riquetti, Comte de (1749–91), French revolutionary leader. His writings and speeches contributed to the revolution of 1789.

Mistral, Frédéric (1830–1914), French poet, and founder of a Provençal renaissance. His works include *Lou Trésor dóu Félibrige* and a Provençal dictionary. Nobel prizewinner 1904.

Mitchell, Reginald Joseph (1895–1937), British aircraft designer. Famous for developing the *Spitfire*.

Mithridates (*c.* 132–63 B.C.), King of Pontus, in Asia Minor; after early successes against the Romans was defeated by Pompey.

Modigliani, Amedeo (1884–1920), Italian painter and sculptor, b. Livorno. His portraits and figure studies tend to elongation and simplification. He lived mainly in Paris.

Moffatt, James (1870–1944), Scottish divine who translated the Bible into modern English.

Mohammed (570–632), the founder of Islam, the religion of the Moslems, received the revelation of the Koran (their sacred book), and the command to preach, at the age of 40. By his constant proclamation that there was only One God he gathered around him a loyal following, but aroused the hostility of other Meccans, who worshipped idols. The Moslems were forced to flee to Medina in 622, but grew in strength sufficiently to return to Mecca eight years later, and establish the Kaaba as the goal of the pilgrimage in Islam. Mohammed always described himself as only the messenger of God, making it clear that he did not bring a new religion. *See* **Islam, Section J**.

Molière (Jean Baptiste Poquelin) (1622–73), French playwright. B. in Paris, he gained experience as a strolling player, and subsequently in Paris, partly in the king's service; he wrote an unsurpassed series of plays varying from farce as in *Les Précieuses ridicules* to high comedy. Among his plays are *Tartuffe*, *Le Misanthrope*, and *Le Bourgeois gentilhomme*.

Molotov, Vyacheslav Mikhailovich (1890–1986), Russian diplomat. He succeeded Litvinov as commissar for foreign affairs, 1939–49, and was chief representative of the Soviet Union at numerous post-war conferences. Expelled from the Communist Party 1964.

Moltke, Helmuth, Count von (1800–91), Prussian general and chief of staff (1858–88) during the period when Prussia successfully united Germany.

Mond, Ludwig (1838–1909), German chemist who in 1867 settled in England as an alkali manufacturer and in partnership with John Brunner successfully manufactured soda by the Solvay process.

Monet, Claude (1840–1926), French painter, leader of the Impressionists, the term being derived in 1874 from his landscape *Impression soleil levant*. He liked painting a subject in the open air at different times of day to show variation in light.

Monier-Williams, Sir Monier (1819–99), English Sanskrit scholar whose works include grammars, dictionaries, and editions of the *Sâkuntalá*.

Monk, George, 1st Duke of Albemarle (1608–69), English general and admiral, whose reputation and moderation were mainly responsible for the return of Charles II in 1660.

Monmouth, Duke of (James Scott) (1649–85), English pretender, natural son of Charles II; centre of anti-Catholic feeling against succession of Duke of York (later James II). His troops, mostly peasants, were routed at Sedgemoor (1685) by John Churchill (later Duke of Marlborough). Beheaded on Tower Hill.

Monnet, Jean (1888–1979), French political economist, "father of the Common Market." He drafted the Monnet plan for French economic recovery (1947) and the plan for the establishment of the European Coal and Steel Community, of which he was president 1952–5.

Monroe, James (1758–1831), president of the U.S. He negotiated the purchase of Louisiana from France in 1803 and propounded the doctrine that the American continent should not be colonised by a European power. (At that time however the U.S. could not have enforced it.)

Montagu, Lady Mary Wortley (1689–1762), English writer. From Constantinople where her husband was ambassador she wrote *Letters* of which a complete edition was published 1965–7. She introduced England to the idea of inoculation against smallpox.

Montaigne, Michel de (1533–92), French essayist of enquiring, sceptical and tolerant mind.

Montcalm, Louis Joseph, Marquis de (1712–59), French general, who unsuccessfully commanded the French at Quebec against Wolfe.

Montesquieu, Charles-Louis de Secondat, Baron de la Brède et de (1689–1755), French philosopher. His works include *Lettres persanes*, a satire on contemporary life; and *De l'esprit des lois* giving his political philosophy. The latter was based largely, but to some extent mistakenly, on English practice, and its influence led the U.S. constitution to separate the executive (President) from the legislature (Congress).

Montessori, Maria (1870–1952), Italian educationist, who developed an educational system based on spontaneity.

Monteverdi, Claudio (1567–1643), Italian composer who pioneered in opera. His chief dramatic work is *Orfeo* (1607). *See* **Section E.**

Montezuma II (1466–1520), Aztec emperor of Mexico when the Spanish under Cortés invaded.

Montfort, Simon de, Earl of Leicester (*c.* 1208–65), English statesman. He led the barons in revolt against the ineffective rule of Henry III, but he differed from other rebels in that he summoned a parliamentary assembly to which for the first time representatives came from the towns. He was killed at Evesham.

Montgolfier, the name of two brothers, **Joseph Michel** (1740–1810) and **Jacques Etienne** (1745–99), French aeronauts who constructed the first practical balloon, which flew 6 miles.

Montgomery of Alamein, 1st Viscount (Bernard Law Montgomery) (1887–1976), British field-marshal; commanded 8th Army in North Africa, Sicily, and Italy, 1942–4; commander-in-chief, British Group of Armies and Allied Armies in Northern France, 1944. He served as Deputy Supreme Allied Commander Europe (NATO), 1951–8. Memoirs published in 1958.

Montrose, Marquess of (James Graham) (1612–50), Scottish general. In the Civil War he raised the Highland clansmen for Charles I and won the battles of Tippermuir, Inverlochy, and Kilsyth; but was finally defeated and executed. He was also a poet.

Moody, Dwight Lyman (1837–99), American revivalist preacher, associated with Ira D. Sankey, the "American singing pilgrim."

Moore, George (1852–1933), Irish novelist, author of *Confessions of a Young Man, Esther Waters,* and *Evelyn Innes.*

Moore, Henry (1898–1986), English sculptor in semi-abstract style, son of a Yorkshire coalminer. Examples of his work are to be seen all over the world, in the Tate Gallery, St. Matthew's Church, Northampton, the Unesco building in Paris, in Kensington Gardens and on the site in Chicago where the world's first nuclear reactor was built (1942).

Moore, Sir John (1761–1809), British general, who trained the infantry for the Spanish Peninsular campaigns and conducted a brilliant retreat to Corunna, where he was mortally wounded after defeating the French under Soult.

Moore, Thomas (1779–1852), Irish poet, author of *Irish Melodies, Lalla Rookh,* and *The Epicurean* (novel). He also wrote a life of Byron.

More, Sir Thomas (1478–1535), English writer and statesman. In 1529 he succeeded Wolsey as lord chancellor, but on his refusal to recognise Henry VIII as head of the church he was executed. His *Utopia* describes an ideal state. He was canonised 1935.

Morgan, Sir Henry (*c.* 1635–88), Welsh buccaneer who operated in the Caribbean against the Spaniards, capturing and plundering Panama in 1671. Knighted by Charles II and made deputy-governor of Jamaica.

Morgan, John Pierpont (1837–1913), American financier who built the family fortunes into a vast industrial empire.

Morland, George (1763–1804), English painter of rural life.

Morley, 1st Viscount (John Morley) (1838–1923), English biographer and Liberal politician. He held political office, but is mainly remembered for his life of Gladstone. He also wrote on Voltaire, Rousseau, Burke, and Cobden.

Morley, Thomas (*c.* 1557–1603), English composer of madrigals, noted also for his settings of some of Shakespeare's songs. He was a pupil of Byrd, organist of St. Paul's cathedral, and wrote *Plaine and Easie Introduction to Practicall Music* (1597) which was used for 200 years.

Morris, William (1834–96), English poet and craftsman. His hatred of 19th-cent. ugliness, his belief in human equality, and in freedom and happiness for all, combined to make him a socialist, and he accomplished much for the improvement of domestic decoration. He was a popular lecturer, founded the Socialist League and the Kelmscott Press.

Morrison of Lambeth, Baron (Herbert Morrison) (1888–1965), British Labour statesman. From being an errand-boy, he rose to become leader of the London County Council. During the war he was Home Secretary, and he was deputy prime minister, 1945–51.

Morse, Samuel Finley Breeze (1791–1872), American pioneer in electromagnetic telegraphy and inventor of the dot-and-dash code that bears his name. He was originally an artist.

Mountbatten of Burma, 1st Earl (Louis Mountbatten) (1900–79), British admiral and statesman. In the second world war he became chief of combined operations in 1942. As last viceroy of India, he carried through the transfer of power to Indian hands in 1947 and was the first governor-general of the dominion. He became first sea lord in 1955 and was chief of defence staff 1959–65. His assassination by Irish extremists evoked world-wide horror.

Mozart, Wolfgang Amadeus (1756–91), Austrian composer. B. Salzburg, he began his career at four and toured Europe at six. In 1781 he settled in Vienna, where he became a friend of Haydn and where his best music was written. His genius lies in the effortless outpouring of all forms of music, in the ever-flowing melodies, in the consistent beauty and symmetry of his compositions, and in the exactness of his method. Among the loveliest and grandest works in instrumental music are his three great symphonies in E. flat, G minor, and C (called the "Jupiter"), all written in six weeks in 1788. Three of the greatest operas in musical history are his *Marriage of Figaro* (1786), *Don Giovanni* (1787), and *The Magic Flute* (1791). His last composition, written under the shadow of death, was the *Requiem Mass,* a work of tragic beauty. *See* **Section E.**

Mugabe, Robert Gabriel (b. 1924), first prime minister of independent Zimbabwe after his election victory in March 1980.

Müller, Sir Ferdinand (1825–96), German-born botanist who emigrated to Australia, where he was director of the Melbourne Botanical Gardens, 1857–73, and whence he introduced the eucalyptus into Europe.

Mumford, Lewis (b. 1895), American writer on town-planning and social problems. His works include a tetralogy: *Technics and Civilisation, The Culture of Cities, The Condition of Man,* and *The Conduct of Life; The Myth of the Machine,* and *The Urban Prospect.*

Munnings, Sir Alfred (1878–1959), English painter, especially of horses and sporting subjects.

Murdock, William (1754–1839), Scottish engineer and inventor, the first to make practical use of coal gas as an illuminating agent (introduced at the Soho works, Birmingham, 1800).

Murillo, Bartolomé Esteban (1617–82), Spanish painter, b. Seville, where he founded an Academy. His early works, such as *Two Peasant Boys* (Dulwich) show peasant and street life; his later paintings are religious, *e.g.,* the *Immaculate Conception* in the Prado.

Murray, Gilbert (1866–1957), classical scholar of Australian birth who settled in England. A teacher of Greek at the universities of Glasgow and Oxford, he translated Greek drama so as to bring it within the reach of the general public. His interest in the classics was begun by an English master's enthusiasm at his country school at Mittagong, New South Wales. He was a strong internationalist.

Mussolini, Benito (1883–1945), Fascist dictator of Italy 1922–43. From 1935 an aggressive foreign policy (Abyssinia and Spain) was at first successful, and in June 1940 he entered the war on the side of Hitler. Defeat in North Africa and the invasion of Sicily caused the collapse of his government. He was shot dead by partisans while trying to escape to Switzerland.

Mussorgsky, Modest Petrovich (1839–81), Russian composer whose masterpiece is the opera *Boris Godunov* after the play by Pushkin. His piano suite *Pictures at an Exhibition* was orchestrated by Ravel. See **Section E.**

N

Naipaul, Sir Vidiadhur Surajprasad (b. 1932), Trinidadian novelist and writer, whose novels include *A House for Mr Biswas* (1961). He was awarded the Booker Prize for *In a Free State* (1971) and was knighted in 1990. *See also* **Section M.**

Nanak (1469–1538), Indian guru or teacher, who tried to put an end to religious strife, teaching that "God is one, whether he be Allah or Rama." See **Sikhism, Section J.**

Nansen, Fridtjof (1861–1930), Norwegian explorer. In 1893 his north polar expedition reached the highest latitude till then attained—86° 14′. He published an account called *Farthest North.* He was active in Russian famine relief, 1921. Nobel peace prize 1922.

Napier, John (1550–1617), Scottish mathematician, b. Edinburgh, invented logarithms (published 1614) and the modern notation of fractions, improvements in the methods of mathematical expression which helped to advance cosmology and physics.

Napoleon I (**Bonaparte**) (1769–1821), French emperor and general, of Corsican birth (Ajaccio). Trained in French military schools, he became prominent in the early years of the revolution, with uncertainty at home and war abroad. In 1796 he became commander of the army in Italy and defeated the Austrians, so that France obtained control of Lombardy. He then led an expedition to Egypt but Nelson destroyed his fleet. After further Italian victories, he made a *coup d'état* in 1799, and in 1804 became emperor. Against continuing European opposition, he defeated the Austrians at Austerlitz, and his power in Europe was such that he made his brothers Joseph, Louis, and Jerome kings of Naples, Holland, and Westphalia; but in Spain he provoked the Peninsular War, and his armies were gradually driven back by the Spanish, helped by Wellington; while his invasion of Russia in 1812 ended in a disastrous retreat from Moscow; and in 1814 the Allies forced him to abdicate and retire to Elba. He emerged again in 1815 to be defeated at Waterloo and exiled to St. Helena. His government at home was firm and promoted some reforms (*e.g.*, legal codification), but the country was weakened by his wars. In Europe, in spite of the suffering caused by war, there was some spread of French revolutionary ideas, and equally a reaction against them on the part of authority. The imperial idea lingered in France, and Napoleon's remains were brought to Paris in 1840. He married first Josephine Beauharnais and second Marie Louise of Austria. Marie Louise was the mother of **Napoleon II** (1811–32).

Napoleon III (1808–73), son of Napoleon I's brother Louis. He returned to France in the revolution of 1848, and in 1851 came to power by a *coup d'état.* In his reign Paris was remodelled. His foreign policy was adventurous (the Crimean war, intervention in Mexico, war against Austria and Italy); but when he was manoeuvred by Bismarck into the Franco-Prussian war and defeated at Sedan he lost his throne and retired to England. His wife was Eugénie de Montijo.

Nash, John (1752–1835), English architect who planned Regent Street, laid out Regent's Park, enlarged Buckingham Palace, and designed Marble Arch and the Brighton Pavilion.

Nash, Paul (1889–1946), English painter and designer, official war artist in both world wars. Best-known pictures are *The Menin Road* of 1918 and *Totes Meer* of 1941.

Nash, Walter (1882–1968), New Zealand Labour politician; prime minister 1957–60.

Nasmyth, James (1808–90), Scottish inventor of the steam-hammer, which became indispensable in all large iron and engineering works.

Nasser, Gamal Abdel (1918–70), leader of modern Egypt and of the Arab world. He led the 1954 coup that deposed General Neguib. He became president of the Egyptian Republic in 1956 and of the United Arab Republic in 1958. His nationalisation of the Suez Canal in 1956 precipitated a short-lived attack by Britain and France, Israeli–Arab hostility led to the June war of 1967. He carried out reforms to bring his people out of feudal backwardness, including the building (with Russian help and finance) of the Aswan High Dam.

Needham, Joseph (b. 1900), British biochemist, historian of science, orientalist, author of the monumental work of scholarship *Science and Civilisation in China* (7 vols., 1954–).

Nehru, Pandit Jawaharlal (1889–1964), Indian national leader and statesman, first prime minister and minister of foreign affairs when India became independent in 1947. He studied at Harrow and Cambridge, and was for many years a leading member of the Congress Party, during which time he was frequently imprisoned for political activity. He played a part in the final negotiations for independence. Under his leadership India made major advances. In world affairs his influence was for peace and non-alignment. His daughter **Indira Gandhi,** became India's first woman prime minister in 1966.

Nelson, 1st Viscount (Horatio Nelson) (1758–1805), English admiral. Son of a Norfolk clergyman, he went to sea at 12 and became a captain in 1793. In the French revolutionary wars he lost his right eye in 1794 and his right arm in 1797. Rear-admiral in 1797, he defeated the French at Aboukir Bay in 1798. He was also at the bombardment of Copenhagen in 1801. In 1805 he destroyed the French fleet at Trafalgar, in which battle he was killed. His daring and decision made him a notable commander. He loved Emma Hamilton.

Nenni, Pietro (1891–1980), Italian socialist politician. He became secretary-general of his party in 1944, and was deputy prime minister, 1963–8.

Nernst, Walther Hermann (1864–1941), German scientist who established the third law of thermodynamics that dealt with the behaviour of matter at temperatures approaching absolute zero. Nobel prizewinner 1920.

Nero, Claudius Caesar (A.D. 37–68), Roman emperor, the adopted son of Claudius. He was weak and licentious and persecuted Christians. In his reign occurred the fire of Rome.

Newcomen, Thomas (1663–1729), English inventor, one of the first to put a steam-engine into practical operation. In 1705 he patented his invention, the pumping-engine used in Cornish mines until the adoption of Watt's engine.

Newman, Ernest (1868–1959), English music critic, whose chief work is the *Life of Richard Wagner.*

Newman, John Henry (1801–90), English priest and writer, who became a cardinal of the Roman church in 1879, and was a founder of the Oxford Movement. (*See* **J52**) He is best remembered by his *Apologia pro Vita Sua* in which he described the development of his religious thought. He wrote *Lead, kindly Light,* set to music 30 years later by J. B. Dykes, and *The Dream of Gerontius,* set to music of Elgar. The centenary of his death (1990) was marked by moves for his canonisation.

Newton, Sir Isaac (1642–1727), English scientist, b. Woolsthorpe, Lincs. (the year Galileo died). He studied at Cambridge but was at home during the plague years 1665 and 1666 when he busied himself with problems concerned with optics and gravitation. Through his tutor Isaac Barrow he was appointed to the Lucasian chair of mathematics at Cambridge in 1669 and remained there until 1696 when he was appointed Warden, and later Master of the Mint. He was a secret Unitarian and did not marry. His three great discoveries were to show that white light could be separated into a sequence of coloured components forming the visible spectrum; to use the calculus (invented by him independently of Leibnitz) to investigate the forces of nature in a quantitative way; and to show by his theory of gravitation (for which Copernicus, Kepler and Galileo had prepared the way) that the universe was regulated by simple mathematical laws. His vision was set forth in the *Philosophiae Naturalis Principia Mathematica* of 1687, usually called the *Principia*. It was not until 200 years later that Einstein showed there could be another theory of celestial mechanics.

Ney, Michel (1769–1815), French general who served under Napoleon, especially at Jena, Borodino, and Waterloo.

Nicholas II (1868–1918), last emperor and Tsar of Russia, son of Alexander III. His reign was marked by an unsuccessful war with Japan (1904–5), and by the 1914–18 war. Ineffective and lacking ability, he set up a Duma in 1906 too late for real reform. Revolution broke out in 1917 and he and his family were shot in July 1918.

Nicholson, Sir William (1872–1949), English artist known for his portraits and woodcuts. His son, **Ben Nicholson, O.M.**, (1894–1981) was noted for his abstract paintings.

Nicolson, Sir Harold (1886–1968), English diplomat, author, and critic. His works include *King George V*; and *Diaries and Letters*. His wife was the novelist **Victoria Sackville-West** (1892–1962).

Niemöller, Martin (1892–1984), German Lutheran pastor who opposed the Nazi regime and was confined in a concentration camp. He was president of the World Council of Churches in 1961.

Nietzsche, Friedrich Wilhelm (1844–1900), German philosopher, in his younger years influenced by Wagner and Schopenhauer. His teaching that only the strong ought to survive and his doctrine of the superman are expounded in *Thus spake Zarathustra*, *Beyond Good and Evil* and *The Will to Power*.

Nightingale, Florence (1820–1910), English nurse and pioneer of hospital reform, who during the Crimean war organised in face of considerable official opposition a nursing service to relieve the sufferings of the British soldiers, who called her "the lady with the lamp." Her system was adopted and developed in all parts of the world.

Nijinsky, Vaslav (1892–1950), Russian dancer, one of the company which included Pavlova, Karsavina and Fokine, brought by Diaghilev to Paris and London before the 1914–18 war. In *Les Sylphides*, *Spectre de la Rose* and *L'Après-midi d'un Faune* he won a supreme place among male dancers.

Nikisch, Arthur (1855–1922), Hungarian conductor of the Boston Symphony Orchestra, 1889–93. He was piano-accompanist to the Lieder singer, Elena Gerhardt.

Nimitz, Chester William (1885–1966), American admiral, commanded in the Pacific 1941–5; chief of naval operations 1945–7.

Nixon, Richard Milhous (b. 1913), Republican president (for two terms) of the U.S., 1969–74. In foreign affairs he negotiated the withdrawal of American troops from S. Vietnam and began a process of reconciliation with China and détente with the Soviet Union. But at home the Watergate conspiracies brought disgrace and an end to his presidency. His resignation in August 1974 rendered the impeachment process unnecessary; he accepted the pardon offered by his successor, President Ford. *See* **The United States, Section C, Part II**.

Nkrumah, Kwame (1909–72), Ghanaian leader, first premier of Ghana when his country achieved independence in 1957. Promoted the Pan-African movement; but unsound finance and dictatorial methods led to his overthrow in 1966.

Nobel, Alfred Bernhard (1833–96), Swedish inventor and philanthropist. An engineer and chemist who discovered dynamite, he amassed a fortune from the manufacture of explosives; and bequeathed a fund for annual prizes to those who had contributed most to the benefit of mankind in the fields of physics, chemistry, medicine, literature and peace.

Nolan, Sir Sidney Robert (b. 1917), Australian artist and set designer. O.M. 1983.

North, Frederick (1732–92), favourite minister of George III who held the premiership from 1770

to 1782. (He held the courtesy title of Lord North from 1752.) The stubborn policies of George III led to the American war of independence.

Northcliffe, 1st Viscount (Alfred Charles Harmsworth) (1865–1922), British journalist and newspaper proprietor, b. near Dublin. He began *Answers* in 1888 with his brother Harold, (later Lord Rothermere). In 1894 they bought the *Evening News*, and in 1896 the *Daily Mail*. In 1908 he took over *The Times*.

Northumberland, John Dudley, Duke of (1502–53), English politician who attempted to secure for his daughter-in-law Lady Jane Grey the succession to the throne after Edward VI.

Nostradamus or **Michel de Notre Dame** (1503–66), French astrologer and physician, known for his prophecies in *Centuries*.

Novalis, the pseudonym of Baron Friedrich von Hardenberg (1772–1801), German romantic poet and novelist, whose chief work is the unfinished *Heinrich von Ofterdingen*.

Nuffield, 1st Viscount (William Richard Morris) (1877–1963), British motor-car manufacturer and philanthropist, and until he retired in 1952 chairman of Morris Motors Ltd. He provided large sums for the advancement of medicine in the university of Oxford, for Nuffield College, and in 1943 established the Nuffield Foundation, endowing it with £10 million.

Nyerere, Julius (b. 1922), Tanzanian leader. He became first premier of Tanganyika when it became independent in 1961; and president in 1962. In 1964 he negotiated its union with Zanzibar.

O

Oates, Lawrence Edward (1880–1912), English antarctic explorer. He joined Scott's expedition of 1910, and was one of the five to reach the south pole; but on the return journey, being crippled by frost-bite, he walked out into the blizzard to die.

Oates, Titus (1649–1705), English informer and agitator against Roman catholics.

O'Casey, Sean (1880–1964), Irish dramatist whose plays include *Juno and the Paycock*, *The Silver Tassie*, *Red Roses for Me*, and *Oak Leaves and Lavender*.

Occam (**Ockham**), **William of** (c. 1270–1349), English scholar and philosopher and one of the most original thinkers of all time. He belonged to the Order of Franciscans, violently opposed the temporal power of the Pope, espoused the cause of nominalism and laid the foundations of modern theories of government and theological scepticism. *See* **Occam's razor, Section J**.

O'Connell, Daniel (1775–1847), Irish national leader. A barrister, he formed the Catholic Association in 1823 to fight elections; his followers aimed at the repeal of the Act of Union with England, and formed a Repeal Association in 1840; but the formation of the Young Ireland party, the potato famine, and ill-health undermined his position and he died in exile.

O'Connor, Feargus (1794–1855), working-class leader in England, of Irish birth. He presented the Chartist petition in 1848.

O'Connor, Thomas Power (1848–1929), Irish nationalist and journalist, sat in parliament 1880–1929 and founded the *Star*.

Oersted, Hans Christian (1777–1851), Danish physicist who discovered the connection between electricity and magnetism.

Offa (d. 796), king of Mercia (mid-England), was the leading English king of his day, and built a defensive dyke (**L90**) from the Dee to the Wye.

Offenbach, Jacques (1819–80), German–Jewish composer, b. Cologne, settled at Paris, and is mainly known for his light operas, especially *Tales of Hoffmann*.

Ohm, Georg Simon (1787–1854), German physicist, professor at Munich, who in 1826 formulated the law of electric current, known as Ohm's law, one of the foundation stones in electrical science. *See* **Section L**.

Olivier, Baron (Laurence Kerr Olivier) (1907–89), British actor and director, especially in Shakespearean roles. He also produced, directed, and played in films, including *Henry V*, *Hamlet*, and *Richard III*, and in television drama. In

1962 he was appointed director of the National Theatre (which opened in 1976) and in 1970 received a life peerage. O.M. 1981.

Oman, Sir Charles William (1860–1946), English historian, especially of mediaeval warfare and of the Peninsular War. He also wrote memoirs.

Omar ibn al Khattab (581–644), adviser to Mahomet, succeeded Abu Bakr as 2nd caliph. In his reign Islam became an imperial power. He died at the hands of a foreign slave.

Omar Khayyám (c. 1050–1123), Persian poet and mathematician, called Khayyám (tent-maker) because of his father's occupation. His fame as a scientist has been eclipsed by his *Rubaiyat*, made known to English readers by Edward FitzGerald in 1859.

O'Neill, Eugene Gladstone (1888–1953), American playwright who, after spending his adventurous youth in sailing, gold-prospecting, and journalism, first won success in 1914 with the one-act play, *Thirst*. His later plays include *Anna Christie*, *Strange Interlude*, *Mourning Becomes Electra*, *The Iceman Cometh*. Nobel prizewinner 1936.

Oppenheimer, J. Robert (1904–67), American physicist who was director of atomic-energy research at Los Alamos, New Mexico, 1942–5, when the atomic bomb was developed but in 1949 he opposed work on the hydrogen bomb on moral grounds.

Orchardson, Sir William Quiller (1835–1910), Scottish painter, b. Edinburgh, best known for his *Napoleon I on board H.M.S. Bellerophon* and *Ophelia*.

Origen (c. 185–254), Christian philosopher and Biblical scholar, who taught at Alexandria and Caesarea, and was imprisoned and tortured in the persecution of Decius, 250

Orpen, Sir William (1878–1931), British painter of portraits, conversation pieces, and pictures of the 1914–18 war.

Ortega y Gasset, José (1883–1955), Spanish philosopher and essayist, known for his *Tema de Nuestro Tiempo* and *La Rebelión de Las Masas*.

Orwell, George (Eric Arthur Blair) (1903–50), English satirist, b. India, author of *Animal Farm* and *Nineteen Eighty-Four*.

Osler, Sir William (1849–1919), Canadian physician and medical historian, authority on diseases of the blood and spleen.

Ossietzky, Carl von (1889–1938), German pacifist leader after the first world war; sent by Hitler to a concentration camp. Nobel peace prize 1935.

Oswald, St (c. 605–42), won the Northumbrian throne by battle in 633 and introduced Christianity there.

Otto I (the Great) (912–73), founder of the Holy Roman Empire (he was crowned king of the Germans in 936 and emperor at Rome in 962). The son of Henry I of Germany, he built up a strong position in Italy (as regards the papacy) and in Germany where he established the East Mark (Austria).

Otto, Nikolaus August (1832–91). German engineer who built a gas engine (1878) using the four-stroke cycle that bears his name.

Ouida (Maria Louise Ramé) (1839–1908), English novelist of French extraction, whose romantic stories include *Under Two Flags*.

Ovid (43 B.C.–A.D. 18), Latin poet (Publius Ovidius Naso), chiefly remembered for his *Art of Love* and *Metamorphoses*. He died in exile.

Owen, David, *see* Section D.

Owen, Robert (1771–1858), Welsh pioneer socialist, b. Montgomeryshire. As manager, and later owner, of New Lanark cotton mills he tried to put his philanthropic views into effect; other communities on co-operative lines were founded in Hampshire and in America (New Harmony, Indiana) but although unsuccessful they were influential in many directions. He challenged the doctrine of *laissez-faire*, inaugurated socialism and the co-operative movement, and foresaw the problems of industrial development.

P

Pachmann, Vladimir de (1848–1933), Russian pianist gifted in the playing of Chopin.

Paderewski, Ignace Jan (1860–1941), Polish pianist and nationalist. He represented his country at Versailles and was the first premier of a reconstituted Poland. He died in exile in the

second world war.

Paganini, Niccolo (1782–1840), Italian violinist and virtuoso who revolutionised violin technique.

Paine, Thomas (1737–1809), political writer, b. Norfolk, son of a Quaker. Spent 1774–87 in America supporting the revolutionary cause. On his return to England wrote *The Rights of Man* in reply to Burke's *Reflections* on the French revolution which led to his prosecution and flight to France where he entered French politics and wrote *The Age of Reason*, advocating deism. His last years were spent in America but this time in obscurity.

Palestrina, Giovanni Pierluigi da (c. 1525–94), Italian composer of unaccompanied church music and madrigals. *See* Section E.

Palgrave, Sir Francis (1788–1861), English historian and archivist, an early editor of record series. His son **Francis Turner Palgrave** (1824–97) was a poet and critic and edited *The Golden Treasury*; while another son, **William Gifford Palgrave** (1826–88) was a traveller and diplomat.

Palissy, Bernard (c. 1510–89), French potter who discovered the art of producing white enamel, after which he set up a porcelain factory in Paris which was patronised by royalty.

Palladio, Andrea (1508–80), Italian architect, b. Padua, whose style was modelled on ancient Roman architecture (symmetrical planning and harmonic proportions) and had wide influence; author of *I Quattro Libri dell' Architettura*.

Palmer, Samuel (1805–81), English landscape painter and etcher, follower of Blake whom he met in 1824. *Bright Cloud* and *In a Shoreham Garden* are in the Victoria and Albert Museum.

Palmerston, 3rd Viscount (Henry John Temple) (1784–1865), English Whig statesman. At first a Tory, he was later Whig foreign secretary for many years, and prime minister 1855 and 1859–65. His vigorous foreign policy wherever possible took the lead and bluntly asserted English rights.

Pancras, St. (d. 304), patron saint of children, was (according to tradition) baptised in Rome where he was put to death at the age of fourteen in the persecution under Diocletian.

Pandit, Vijaya Lakshmi (b. 1900), sister of Nehru, was India's first High Commissioner to the United Kingdom. Envoy to the U.S. (1949–51), and the first woman to be elected president of the U.N. General Assembly (1954).

Panizzi, Sir Anthony (1797–1879), Italian bibliographer and nationalist. Taking refuge in England after 1821, he became in 1856 chief librarian of the British Museum, undertook a new catalogue and designed the reading room.

Pankhurst, Emmeline (1858–1928), English suffragette who, with her daughters Christabel and Sylvia, worked for women's suffrage, organising the Women's Social and Political Union.

Papin, Denis (1647–1714), French physicist and inventor. He invented the condensing pump, and was a pioneer in the development of the steam-engine. Not being a mechanic, he made all his experiments by means of models.

Paracelsus (Theophrastus Bombastus von Hohenhelm) (1493–1541), Swiss physician whose speculations though muddled served to reform medical thought. He criticised the established authorities, Galen and Aristotle, and experimented and made new chemical compounds. His earliest printed work was *Practica* (1529).

Park, Mungo (1771–1806), Scottish explorer in west Africa, where he lost his life. He wrote *Travels in the Interior of Africa* (1799).

Parker of Waddington, Baron (Hubert Lister Parker) (1900–72) Lord Chief Justice of England 1958–70.

Parker, Joseph (1830–1902), English Congregational preacher, especially at what later became the City Temple.

Parnell, Charles Stewart (1846–91), Irish national leader. To draw attention to Ireland's problems, he used obstruction in parliament. He was president of the Land League but was not implicated in crimes committed by some members. His party supported Gladstone, who became converted to Home Rule. His citation in divorce proceedings brought his political career to an end.

Parry, Sir William Edward (1790–1855), English explorer and naval commander in the Arctic, where he was sent to protect fisheries and also tried to reach the north pole.

Parsons, Sir Charles Algernon (1854–1931),

English inventor of the steam-turbine, who built the first turbine-driven steamship in 1897.

Pascal, Blaise (1623–62), Frenchman of varied gifts, b. at Clermont-Ferrand. At first a mathematician, he patented a calculating machine. His *Lettres provinciales* influenced Voltaire. In 1654 he turned to religion, and his incomplete religious writings were published posthumously as *Pensées*. *See* **Jansenism, J28(2)**.

Pasternak, Boris Leonidovich (1890–1960), Russian poet and writer. B. Moscow, he published his first poems in 1931. For some years his time was spent in translating foreign literature, but in 1958 his novel *Dr. Zhivago*, which describes the Russian revolution and is in the Russian narrative tradition, was published abroad, though banned in the Soviet Union. He was awarded a Nobel prize but obliged to decline it. The centenary of his birth in 1990 witnessed a rehabilitation in Russia which he had never known during his lifetime.

Pasteur, Louis (1822–95), French chemist, b. at Dôle in the Jura, whose work was inspired by an interest in the chemistry of life. His researches on fermentation led to the science of bacteriology and his investigations into infectious diseases and their prevention to the science of immunology. The pathological-bacteriological import of his researches came about mainly through his disciples (Lister, Roux, and others) and not directly, though all founded on his early non-medical investigations on organisms of fermentation, etc., which were of great importance in industry, and fundamentally. He spent most of his life as director of scientific studies at the Ecole Normale at Paris. The Institute Pasteur was founded in 1888.

Patmore, Coventry (1823–96), English poet. *The Angel in the House* deals with domesticity. Later he became a Roman catholic, and *The Unknown Eros* is characterised by erotic mysticism.

Patrick, St. (*c.* 389–*c.* 461), apostle of Ireland, was born in Britain or Gaul, and after some time on the continent (taken thither after his capture by pirates) went as missionary to Ireland, where after years of teaching and a visit to Rome he fixed his see at Armagh. He wrote *Confessions*.

Patti, Adelina (1843–1919), coloratura soprano, b. in Madrid of Italian parents, and of international repute.

Paul, St. (*c.* A.D. 10–64), Jew to whom was mainly due the extension of Christianity in Europe. B. Tarsus (in Asia Minor), he was a Pharisee, and became converted about A.D. 37. His missionary journeys took him to the Roman provinces of Asia, Macedonia, and Greece (Rome had already had Christian teaching); and his epistles form nearly half the New Testament and were written before the gospels. He helped to develop both the organisation of the early church and its teaching. The date order of his epistles is to some extent conjectural. It is believed that he was executed in Rome. His Hebrew name was Saul.

Paul VI (Giovanni Battista Montini) (1897–1978), elected Pope in 1963 on the death of John XXIII. He was formerly archbishop of Milan. His encyclical *Humanae Vitae* (1968) condemned contraception.

Pauli, Wolfgang (1900–58), Austrian-born physicist who first predicted theoretically the existence of neutrinos. Nobel prize 1945.

Pavlov, Ivan Petrovich (1849–1936), Russian physiologist, known for his scientific experimental work on animal behaviour, particularly conditioned reflexes and the relation between psychological stress and brain function. Nobel prizewinner 1904.

Pavlova, Anna (1882–1931), Russian ballerina, b. St. Petersburg, excelling in the roles of *Giselle* and the *Dying Swan*.

Peabody, George (1795–1869), American philanthropist, a successful merchant who lived mainly in London. He gave large sums to promote education and slum clearance.

Peacock, Thomas Love (1785–1866), English novelist, b. Weymouth. His work, which is mainly satirical, includes *Headlong Hall* and *Nightmare Abbey*.

Pearson, Lester Bowles (1897–1972), Canadian politician served as minister for external affairs 1948–57, and prime minister 1963–8. He supported the United Nations. Nobel peace prize 1957.

Peary, Robert Edwin (1856–1920), American arctic explorer, discoverer of the north pole (1909).

Peel, Sir Robert (1788–1850), English Conservative statesman, b. in Lancashire, son of a manufacturer. He first held office in 1811. With Wellington he enacted toleration for Roman catholics in 1829. As home secretary he reorganised London police. He developed a new policy of Conservatism, and in 1846, largely as a result of the Irish famine, he repealed the corn laws. He died from a riding accident.

Peirce, Charles Sanders (1839–1914), American physicist and philosopher of original mind, founder of the theory of pragmatism later developed by his friend William James. *See* **J49**.

Penfield, Wilder Graves (1891–1976), Canadian brain surgeon, author of *The Cerebral Cortex of Man, Epilepsy and the Functional Anatomy of the Human Brain*. O.M.

Penn, William (1644–1718), English Quaker and founder of Pennsylvania. The son of Admiral William Penn, he persisted in becoming a Quaker, and on receiving for his father's services a crown grant in North America he founded there Pennsylvania. He wrote *No Cross, No Crown*.

Penney, Baron (William George Penney) (b. 1909), British scientist. His nuclear research team at A.E.A. developed the advanced gas-cooled reactor (A.G.R.) chosen for the Dungeness "B" and Hinkley Point "B" power stations.

Pepys, Samuel (1633–1703), English diarist and naval administrator. His diary, 1660–69, was kept in cipher and not deciphered till 1825. It gives vivid personal details and covers the plague and fire of London. (The first complete version of the diary was issued in 1970.)

Pereda, José Maria de (1833–1906), Spanish regional novelist (around his native Santander).

Pérez Galdós, Benito (1843–1920), Spanish novelist and dramatist, who has been compared to Balzac for his close study and portrayal of all social classes, especially in the series of 46 short historical novels *Episodios nacionales*. His longer novels, *Novelas españolas contemporáneas*, some of which are translated, number 31.

Pergolesi, Giovanni Battista (1710–36), Italian composer, best known for his humorous opera *La Serva Padrona* and his *Stabat Mater*.

Pericles (*c.* 490–429 B.C.), Athenian statesman, general, and orator, who raised Athens to the point of its fullest prosperity, and greatest beauty, with the Parthenon, Erechtheum, and other buildings; but he died in the plague which followed the outbreak of the Peloponnesian war.

Perkin, Sir William Henry (1838–1907), English chemist, b. London, who while seeking to make a substitute for quinine discovered in 1856 the first artificial aniline dye, mauve. His son, **W. H. Perkin** (1860–1929) was an organic chemist of note.

Perrin, Francis (b. 1901), French scientist and socialist; succeeded Joliot-Curie as High Commr. of Atomic Energy, 1951; professor of Atomic Physics, Collège de France, 1946, Nobel prizewinner 1926.

Persius Flaccus Aulus (A.D. 34–62), Roman satirist and Stoic philosopher.

Perugino, Pietro (1446–1524), Italian artist. He worked in the Sistine Chapel at Rome and he taught Raphael.

Pestalozzi, Johann Heinrich (1746–1827), Swiss educational reformer whose theories laid the foundation of modern primary education. His teaching methods were far in advance of his time. He wrote *How Gertrude Educates Her Children*.

Pétain, Henri Philippe (1856–1951), French general and later collaborator. In the first world war he was in command at Verdun, and between the wars he sponsored the Maginot line. In the second world war, when French resistance collapsed, he came to terms with Germany and headed an administration at Vichy. After the war he was sentenced to life imprisonment.

Peter I, the Great (1672–1725), emperor of Russia. Son of Alexei, he succeeded his brother after some difficulty. He reorganised the army, and, after coming to Deptford to learn shipbuilding, he created a navy. To some extent he western-ised Russian social life, and created a new capital at St. Petersburg (1703). In war with Charles XII of Sweden he was at first defeated, but later victorious at Poltava (1709). He married a peasant, Catherine, who succeeded him.

Peter the Hermit (c. 1050–1115), French monk who preached the First Crusade, originated by pope Urban II at the council of Clermont. He went on the crusade himself, but gave up at Antioch.

Petrarch, Francesco (1304–78), Italian poet, son of a Florentine exile. He is chiefly remembered for his poems *To Laura*, but he was also a scholar who paved the way for the Renaissance.

Petrie, Sir Flinders (1853–1942), British egyptolo-gist. He excavated in Britain (1875–90), Egypt (1880–1924), and Palestine (1927–38). See his *Seventy Years of Archaeology*.

Phidias (5th cent. B.C.), Greek sculptor especially in gold, ivory and bronze, worked at Athens for Pericles. No certain examples of his work are extant, but the Elgin marbles in the British Museum may be from his designs.

Philip II of France (1165–1223), son of Louis VII. He went on the Third Crusade with Richard I of England, but in France is mainly remembered for firm government, the recovery of Normandy from England, and the beautifying of Paris.

Philip II of Macedonia (382–336 B.C.), a successful commander, made his the leading military king-dom in Greece and was father of Alexander the Great.

Philip II of Spain (1527–98), succeeded his father Charles V in Spain and the Netherlands, also in Spanish interests overseas. In the Nether-lands his strict Roman catholic policy provoked a revolt which ended in 1579 in the independence of the United Provinces. He married Mary Tudor of England; and after her death sent the ill-fated Armada against Elizabeth in 1588.

Philip V of Spain (1683–1746), first Bourbon king, succeeded his great-uncle Charles II and was grandson of Louis XIV. His accession provoked European war.

Phillip, Arthur (1738–1814), first governor of New South Wales. Under his command the first fleet of 717 convicts set sail from Britain to Australia, and with the founding of Sydney in 1788 colonisation of the whole country began.

Phillips, Stephen (1868–1915), English poet who wrote verse dramas, including *Paolo and Fran-cesca*.

Piast, first Polish dynasty in Poland until the 14th cent. and until the 17th cent. in Silesia.

Piazzi, Giuseppe (1746–1826), Italian astronomer who discovered Ceres, the first of the asteroids to be seen by man.

Picasso, Pablo Ruiz (1881–1973) Spanish painter, b. Málaga; received his early training in Catalonia and settled in Paris in 1903. He and Braque were the originators of Cubism (c. 1909). His influence over contemporary art is comparable with that exercised by Cézanne (q.v.) over the artists of his time. Perhaps the best-known single work is his mural *Guernica*, painted at the time of the Spanish civil war, expressing the artist's loathing of fascism and the horrors of war. His genius also found scope in sculpture, ceramics, and the graphic arts, and he designed décor and costumes for the ballet.

Piccard, Auguste (1884–1962), Swiss physicist, noted for balloon ascents into the stratosphere and for submarine research. In 1960 his son Jacques made a descent of over 7 miles in the Marianas trench in the western Pacific in a bathyscaphe designed and built by his father.

Pilsudski, Joseph (1867–1935), Polish soldier and statesman who in 1919 attempted by force to restore Poland's 1772 frontiers but was driven back. From 1926 he was dictator.

Pindar (522–443 B.C.), Greek lyric poet.

Pinero, Sir Arthur Wing (1855–1934), English dramatist whose plays include *Dandy Dick*, *The Second Mrs. Tanqueray* and *Mid-Channel*.

Pirandello, Luigi (1867–1936), Italian dramatist and novelist whose plays include *Six Characters in Search of an Author*. Nobel prizewinner 1934.

Pissarro, Camille (1830–1903), French impression-ist painter of landscapes; studied under Corot.

Pitman, Sir Isaac (1813–97), b. Trowbridge, English inventor of a system of phonographic shorthand.

Pitt, William (1759–1806), English statesman. Younger son of the Earl of Chatham, (q.v.) he entered parliament at 21 and became prime minister at 24 in 1783 when parties were divided and the American war had been lost. He rose to the position, and held office with scarcely a break till his death. An able finance minister, he intro-duced reforms, and would have gone further, but Napoleon's meteoric rise obliged him to lead European allies in a long struggle against France. He died worn out by his efforts.

Pius XII (1876–1958), elected pope 1939. As Eugenio Pacelli, he was papal nuncio in Ger-many and later papal secretary of state. It has been argued that, as pope in wartime, he could have taken a stronger line against Nazi war crimes.

Pizarro, Francisco (c. 1478–1541), Spanish adven-turer, b. Trujillo. After Columbus's dis-coveries, he conquered Peru for Spain, over-throwing the Inca empire. He was murdered by his men.

Planck, Max (1857–1947), German mathematical physicist, b. Kiel, whose main work was on ther-modynamics. In 1900 he invented a mathe-matical formula to account for some properties of the thermal radiation from a hot body which has since played an important role in physics. Nobel prizewinner 1918. See **Quantum theory, Section L.**

Plato (427–347 B.C.), Athenian philosopher, pupil of Socrates, teacher of Aristotle. He founded a school at Athens under the name of the Acade-my, where he taught philosophy and mathe-matics. His great work is his *Dialogues*, which includes the *Republic*, the longest and most celebrated. His known writings have come down to us and constitute one of the most influential bodies of work in history. *See also* **Mind and Matter, Section J.**

Playfair, 1st Baron (Lyon Playfair) (1818–98), a far-sighted Victorian who stood for the greater recognition of science in national life. He for-sook his profession as professor of chemistry at Edinburgh to enter parliament. Pres. British Association 1885.

Plimsoll, Samuel (1824–98), English social re-former, b. Bristol. He realised the evil of overloading unseaworthy ships, and as M.P. for Derby he procured the passing of the Merchant Shipping Act, 1876 which imposed a line (the Plimsoll Mark) above which no ship must sink while loading.

Pliny the Elder (A.D. 23–79), Roman naturalist, author of a *Natural History*. He died of fumes and exhaustion while investigating the eruption of Vesuvius. His nephew, **Pliny the Younger** (A.D. 62–113), wrote *Letters* notable for their charm and the insight they give into Roman life.

Plotinus (c. 203–c. 262), Greek philosopher, was the founder of Neoplatonism, which had con-siderable influence on early Christian thought. *See also* **God and Man, Section J.**

Plutarch (c. 46–120), Greek biographer, whose *Lives* portray 46 leading historical figures (in pairs, a Greek and a Roman whose careers were similar). Although based on myth his *Life of Lycurgus* about life in Sparta had a profound influence on later writers, e.g., Rousseau and the romantic philosophers. He was educated at Athens but visited Rome.

Poe, Edgar Allan (1809–49), American poet and story-writer, b. Boston, Mass. His poems include *The Raven*, *To Helen*, and *Annabel Lee*, and his stories, often weird and fantastic, include *Tales of the Grotesque and Arabesque*.

Poincaré, Raymond Nicolas (1860–1934), French statesman. He was president 1913–20, and as prime minister occupied the Ruhr in 1923.

Pole, Reginald (1500–58), archbishop of Canter-bury, cardinal of the Roman church and antag-onist of the reformation. He opposed Henry VIII's divorce and went abroad in 1532, writing *De Unitate Ecclesiastica*; as a result of which his mother, Countess of Salisbury, and other relatives were executed. Under Queen Mary Tudor he became archbishop and died the year she did.

Pollard, Albert Frederick (1869–1948), English historian, especially of the Tudor period, and first director of the Institute of Historical Research.

Polo, Marco (1256–1323), Venetian traveller, who made journeys through China, India, and other eastern countries, visiting the court of Kubla Khan, and leaving an account of his travels.

Pompadour, Jeanne Antoine Poisson, Marquise de (1721–64), mistress of Louis XV of France. She exercised disastrous political influence.

Pompey (106–48 B.C.), Roman commander, who cleared the Mediterranean of pirates, and became triumvir with Caesar and Crassus.

Pompidou, Georges Jean Raymond (1911–74), French administrator and politician who succeeded de Gaulle as president 1969.

Pope, Alexander (1688–1744), English poet, b. London, of a Roman catholic family, and largely self-educated. His brilliant satire was frequently directed against his contemporaries. He is especially remembered for *The Rape of the Lock*, *The Dunciad*, *Essay on Criticism*, and *Essay on Man*.

Popper, Sir Karl (b. 1902), British philosopher of science, b. Vienna; author of *The Open Society and Its Enemies* (1945), *Conjectures and Refutations* (1963), *Objective Knowledge* (1972). He rejects the doctrine that all knowledge starts from perception or sensation and holds that it grows through conjecture and refutation. C.H. (1982).

Pound, Ezra Loomis (1885–1972), American poet and writer on varied subjects, a controversial figure. Noted for his translations of Provençal, Latin, Chinese, French, and Italian poets.

Poussin, Nicolas (1593–1665), French painter. He lived in Rome 1624–40, 1642–65. His *Golden Calf* is in the National Gallery.

Powys, John Cowper (1872–1964), English writer, best known for his novel *Wolf Solent* and his essays *The Meaning of Culture* and *A Philosophy of Solitude*. His brothers, **Theodore Francis** (1875–1953) and **Llewelyn** (1884–1939) were also original writers.

Prasad, Rajendra (1884–1963), Indian statesman, first president of the Republic of India, 1950–62.

Praxiteles (4th cent. B.C.), Greek sculptor, whose main surviving work is *Hermes carrying Dionysus*.

Preece, Sir William Henry (1834–1913), Welsh electrical engineer, associated with the expansion of wireless telegraphy and telephony in the United Kingdom. He was connected with Marconi and introduced the block system.

Prichard, James Cowles (1786–1848), English ethnologist who perceived that people should be studied as a whole. His works include *Researches into the Physical History of Mankind* and *The Natural History of Man*. He practised medicine.

Priestley, John Boynton (1894–1984), English critic, novelist, and playwright, b. Bradford. His works include the novels *The Good Companions*, *Angel Pavement*, and the plays *Dangerous Corner*, *Time and the Conways*, *I Have Been Here Before*, and *The Linden Tree*. O.M. 1977.

Priestley, Joseph (1733–1804), English chemist who worked on gases, and shared with Scheele the discovery of oxygen. A presbyterian minister, he was for his time an advanced thinker. In 1794 he settled in America.

Prior, Matthew (1664–1721), English poet. In early life he was a diplomat. He was a neat epigrammatist and writer of occasional pieces. His works include *The City Mouse and Country Mouse* and *Four Dialogues of the Dead*.

Prokofiev, Serge Sergeyevich (1891–1953), Russian composer, whose music has a strong folk-song element, rich in melody and invention. He has written operas; *The Love of Three Oranges*, *The Betrothal in a Nunnery*, *War and Peace*; ballets: *Romeo and Juliet*, *Cinderella*; symphonies, chamber music, and the music for Eisenstein's films *Alexander Nevsky*, *Ivan the Terrible*.

Protagoras (c. 480–411 B.C.), Greek philosopher, chief of the Sophists, noted for his scepticism and disbelief in objective truth, and for his doctrine that "man is the measure of all things."

Proudhon, Pierre Joseph (1809–65), French socialist. In 1840 he propounded the view that property is theft. His main work is *Système des contradictions économiques* (1846). He was frequently in prison.

Proust, Marcel (1871–1922), French psychological novelist, author of a series of novels best known

under the title of *A la recherche du temps perdu*. His works have been admirably translated into English by C. K. Scott Moncrieff.

Ptolemy of Alexandria (Claudius Ptolemaeus) (fl. A.D. 140), astronomer and founder of scientific cartography. In the *Almagest* he attempted a mathematical presentation of the paths along which the planets appear to move in the heavens. His other great work was his *Geographical Outline*.

Puccini, Giacomo (1858–1924), Italian composer, b. Lucca, whose operas include *Manon Lescaut*, *La Bohème*, *Tosca*, *Madam Butterfly*, and *Turandot* (completed by a friend).

Pupin, Michael Idvorsky (1858–1935), physicist and inventor (telephony and X-rays), b. Idvor, Hungary (now in Yugoslavia); went to America penniless 1874 to become professor of electromechanics at Columbia University.

Purcell, Henry (1659–95), English composer, b. Westminster, son of a court musician. He became organist of the chapel royal and composer to Charles II. His best works are vocal and choral. See **Section E**.

Pusey, Edward Bouverie (1800–82), English theologian, a leader of the Oxford or Tractarian movement with Keble and at first also with Newman, till the latter became Roman catholic. The movement aimed at revival.

Pushkin, Alexander (1799–1837), Russian writer, b. Moscow, whose place in Russian literature ranks with Shakespeare's in English. He wrote in many forms—lyrical poetry and narrative verse, drama, folk-tales and short stories. Musicians have used his works as plots for operas—the fairy romance *Russlan and Ludmilla* was dramatised by Glinka; the verse novel *Eugene Onegin* and the short story *The Queen of Spades* were adapted by Tchaikovsky, and the tragic drama *Boris Godunov* formed the subject of Mussorgsky's opera. Like Lermontov, who too was exiled, he was inspired by the wild beauty of the Caucasus. He was killed in a duel defending his wife's honour.

Pym, John (1584–1643), English parliamentary leader in opposition to Charles I. He promoted the impeachment of the king's advisers, Strafford and Laud. A collateral descendant is Mr. Francis Pym, Conservative Foreign Secretary, 1982–June 1983.

Pythagoras (c. 582–500 B.C.), Greek philosopher, b. on the island of Samos, off the Turkish mainland, which he left c. 530 to settle at Croton, a Greek city in southern Italy. He was a mystic and mathematician, and founded a brotherhood who saw in numbers the key to the understanding of the universe.

Q

Quasimodo, Salvatore (1901–68), Italian poet of humanity and liberal views whose works include *La vita non e sogno*. Nobel prizewinner 1959.

Quesnay, François (1694–1774), French economist, founder of the physiocratic school who believed in *laissez-faire* and influenced the thought of Adam Smith. See **Physiocrats, Section J**.

Quiller-Couch, Sir Arthur Thomas (1863–1944), English man of letters, b. Bodmin, known as "Q." He edited the *Oxford Book of English Verse* and his works include *From a Cornish Window*.

R

Rabelais, François (c. 1495–1553), French satirist. At first in religious orders, he later studied medicine and practised at Lyons. His works, mainly published under a pseudonym, are full of riotous mirth, wit and wisdom. The main ones are *Gargantua* and *Pantagruel*.

Rachel, Élisa (Élisa Felix) (1821–58), Alsatian-Jewish tragic actress. Her chief triumph was in Racine's *Phèdre*.

Rachmaninov, Sergey Vasilyevich (1873–1943), Russian composer and pianist, b. Nijni-Novgorod (now Gorki), best known for his piano music, especially his *Prelude*. After the Russian revolution he settled in America. See **Section E**.

Racine, Jean (1639–99), French tragic poet whose dramas include *Andromaque*, *Iphigénie* and *Phèdre*. An orphan, he was brought up by grandparents who sent him to Port Royal school where he acquired a love of the classics. In Paris he became a friend of Molière, whose company acted his first play, and of Boileau, with whom he became joint historiographer to Louis XIV. *Esther* and *Athalie* were written for Madame de Maintenon's schoolgirls.

Rackham, Arthur (1867–1939), English artist and book-illustrator, especially of fairy tales.

Radhakrishnan, Sir Sarvepalli (1888–1975), Indian philosopher and statesman, vice-president of India 1952–62, president 1962–7. He was at one time a professor at Oxford.

Raffles, Sir Thomas Stamford (1781–1826), English colonial administrator who founded a settlement at Singapore in 1819. He was also a naturalist, and founded the London Zoo.

Raikes, Robert (1735–1811), English educational pioneer, whose lead in the teaching of children at Gloucester on Sundays led to an extensive Sunday School movement.

Raleigh, Sir Walter (1552–1618), adventurer and writer. He found favour at the court of Elizabeth I, helped to put down the Irish rebellion of 1580, and in 1584 began the colonisation of Virginia, introducing potatoes and tobacco to the British Isles. At the accession of James I he lost favour and was sent to the Tower, where he wrote his *History of the World*. Released in 1615 to lead an expedition to the Orinoco, he was executed when it failed.

Raman, Sir Chandrasekhara Venkata (1888–1970), Indian physicist whose main work has been in spectroscopy. For his research on the diffusion of light and discovery of the "Raman effect" he was awarded the 1930 Nobel prize.

Rameau, Jean Philippe (1683–1764), French composer and church organist whose works on musical theory influenced musical development.

Ramón y Cajal, Santiago (1852–1934), Spanish histologist who made discoveries in the structure of the nervous system. Shared 1906 Nobel prize.

Ramphal, Sir Shridath 'Sonny' (b. 1928), Guyanese statesman. Secretary-General of the Commonwealth, 1975 to 1990. Foreign Minister, Guyana, 1972 to 1975. First black Chancellor of a British university (Warwick, since 1989).

Ramsay, Sir William (1852–1916), Scottish chemist, and discoverer with Lord Rayleigh of argon. Later he discovered helium and other inert gases, which he called neon, krypton, and xenon. Nobel prizewinner 1904.

Ramsey, Arthur Michael (1904–88), archbishop of Canterbury, 1961–74. His previous career was: professor of divinity at Cambridge 1950–2; bishop of Durham 1952–6; archbishop of York 1956–61. Widely travelled, he worked hard for church unity.

Ranke, Leopold von (1795–1886), German historian, one of the first to base his work on methodical research. His chief work is a *History of the Popes*.

Raphael (Raffaello Santi) (1483–1520) of Urbino was the youngest of the three great artists of the High Renaissance. He was taught at Perugia by Perugino, and then at Florence he came under the influence of Leonardo and Michelangelo. Raphael's Madonnas, remarkable for their simplicity and grace, include the *Madonna of the Grand Duke* (Palazzo Pitti), the *Sistine Madonna* (Dresden) the *Madonna with the Goldfinch* (Uffizi), the *Madonna of Foligno* (Vatican), and the *Ansidei Madonna* (National Gallery). He painted the frescoes on the walls of the Stanza della Segnatura in the Vatican, and designed 10 cartoons for tapestries for the Sistine Chapel. After the death of Bramante he was appointed architect in charge of the rebuilding of St. Peter's.

Rasputin, Grigori Yefimovich (1871–1916), Russian peasant from Siberia, a cunning adventurer who at the court of Nicholas II exerted a malign influence over the Tsarina through his apparent ability to improve the health of the sickly Tsarevich Alexis. He was murdered by a group of nobles.

Rathbone, Eleanor (1872–1946), social reformer who championed women's pensions and in her book *The Disinherited Family* set out the case for family allowances.

Ravel, Maurice (1875–1937), French composer, pupil of Fauré, one of the leaders of the impressionist movement.

Rawlinson, Sir Henry Creswicke (1810–95), English diplomat and archaeologist. He made Assyrian collections now in the British Museum and translated the Behistun inscription of the Persian king Darius. He also wrote on cuneiform inscriptions and on Assyrian history.

Ray, John (1627–1705), English naturalist. A blacksmith's son, he went to Cambridge, travelled in Europe, and produced a classification of plants. He also wrote on zoology.

Rayleigh, 3rd Baron (John William Strutt) (1842–1919), English mathematician and physicist. He studied sound and the wave theory of light; and with Sir William Ramsay discovered argon. Nobel prizewinner 1904.

Read, Sir Herbert (1893–1968), English poet and art critic. His writings include *Collected Poems*, *The Meaning of Art*, and an autobiography, *Annals of Innocence and Experience*.

Reade, Charles (1814–84), English novelist. His chief work is *The Cloister and the Hearth*. He also wrote *Peg Woffington*, *It is Never too Late to Mend*, and *Griffith Gaunt*, aimed at social abuses.

Reagan, Ronald (b. 1911). U.S. President, 1981–89; former T.V. and film star, 1937–66. Governor of California, 1967–74. Won Republican victory, 1980. Re-elected in landslide victory, 1984. His popularity remained, helping ensure the election of **George Bush** (*q.v.*) as his successor. Awarded Order of the Bath, June 1989, by the Queen. *See* Section C, Part II.

Réaumur, René Antoine Ferchault de (1683–1757), French naturalist who invented a thermometer of eighty degrees, using alcohol.

Récamier, Jeanne Françoise (*née* Bernard) (1777–1849), French beauty and holder of a noted salon. Her husband was a banker.

Regnault, Henry Victor (1810–78), French chemist and physicist, who worked on gases, latent heat, and steam-engines.

Reith, 1st Baron (John Charles Walsham Reith) (1889–1971), Scottish civil engineer, first director-general of the B.B.C. 1927–38

Rembrandt (Rembrandt Harmenszoon van Rijn) (1606–69), Dutch painter and etcher, b. Leiden, a miller's son, one of the most individual and prolific artists of any period. His output includes portraits, landscapes, large groups, etchings, and drawings. He settled in Amsterdam establishing his reputation with *The Anatomy Lesson*, painted in 1632. In 1634 he married Saskia, a burgomaster's daughter. *The Night Watch* was painted in 1642; it was not well received and Saskia died the same year, leaving the infant Titus. The path from relative wealth to lonely old age is depicted in his self-portraits. Caring little for convention or formal beauty, his work is characterised by bold realism and spiritual beauty, by vitality and simplicity. His understanding of the play of colour and the effects of light can give his pictures a mystical beauty, as in the atmospheric painting *The Mill*. His figures, even for religious pictures, were taken from real life, the Jews in the etching *Christ Healing* from the Jewish quarter where he lived. He met the misfortunes of later life by withdrawing from society, but it was then that he produced his greatest works.

Renan, Ernest (1823–92), French writer who, though not accepting the orthodox viewpoint, wrote on religious themes, especially a *Life of Jesus*.

Reni, Guido. *See* Guido Reni.

Rennie, John (1761–1821), Scottish civil engineer who built the old Waterloo and Southwark bridges and designed the granite London bridge which stood until recently. He also designed docks at London, Liverpool, Leith, Dublin, and Hull; constructed Plymouth breakwater; made canals and drained fens.

Renoir, Pierre Auguste (1841–1919), French impressionist painter, b. Limoges. His works include portraits, still-life, landscapes, and groups, including *La Loge*, *Les Parapluies*, *La première Sortie*, *La Place Pigalle*. He was later crippled with arthritis.

Reuter, Paul Julius, Freiherr von (1816–99), German pioneer of telegraphic press service, who in 1851 fixed his headquarters in London.

Reymont, Vladislav Stanislav (1868–1925), Polish novelist, author of *The Peasants*. Nobel prize-winner 1924.

Reynolds, Sir Joshua (1723–92), English portrait painter, b. Plympton, Devon. His portraits, which include *Mrs. Siddons*, are remarkable for expressiveness and colour and he was a sympathetic painter of children. He was first president of the R.A. from 1768 till his death.

Rhodes, Cecil John (1853–1902), English empire-builder. B. at Bishop's Stortford, he went to South Africa for health reasons and there prospered at the diamond mines. He became prime minister of what was then Cape Colony and secured British extension in what is now Zimbabwe and Zambia. He withdrew from politics after the failure of the ill-advised Jameson Raid of 1896 into the Transvaal. He bequeathed large sums to found scholarships at Oxford for overseas students.

Ricardo, David (1772–1823), English political economist of Jewish descent. By occupation a London stockbroker, he wrote a useful work, *Principles of Political Economy*.

Richard I (1157–99), succeeded his father Henry II as king of England in 1189. A patron of troubadours and a soldier (Lion-heart), he went on the third Crusade and took Acre, but could not recover Jerusalem from Saladin. On his return journey across Europe he was imprisoned and ransomed. He was killed in war with France.

Richard II (1367–1400), son of the Black Prince, succeeded his grandfather Edward III as king of England in 1377. Artistic and able, but erratic and egocentric, he personally at the age of fourteen met the Peasants' Revolt in 1381, making untenable promises. Latterly his rule became increasingly arbitrary, and he was deposed and imprisoned in 1399.

Richard III (1452–85), King of England (1483–5), younger brother of the Yorkist, Edward IV, is believed to have murdered his two nephews in the Tower. He was defeated and killed at Bosworth by the invading Earl of Richmond, who as Henry VII brought to an end the Wars of the Roses, Richard's character is disputed, but he was able and might have been a successful ruler.

Richardson, Sir Albert Edward (1880–1964), British architect, author of *Georgian Architecture*.

Richardson, Sir Owen Willans (1879–1959), English physicist who worked on thermionics, or emission of electricity from hot bodies. Nobel prizewinner 1928.

Richardson, Sir Ralph David (1902–83), English actor who worked at the Old Vic, on the West End stage, and at Stratford-on-Avon, and appeared in films, including *South Riding, Anna Karenina*, and *The Fallen Idol*.

Richardson, Samuel (1689–1761), English author of *Pamela, Clarissa*, and *The History of Sir Charles Grandison*, exercised considerable influence on the development of the novel.

Richelieu, Armand Jean du Plessis, Duc de (1585–1642), French statesman, cardinal of the Roman church. As minister to Louis XIII from 1624 till his death, he built up the power of the French crown at home in central government, and by his military preparedness and active foreign policy gave France a lead in Europe.

Ridley, Nicholas (1500–55), English Protestant martyr, bishop of Rochester and later of London, was burnt with Latimer under Queen Mary Tudor.

Rienzi, Cola di (1313–54), Italian patriot, b. Rome, led a popular rising in 1347 and for seven months reigned as tribune, but had to flee, was imprisoned, and eventually murdered.

Rilke, Rainer Maria (1872–1926), German lyric poet, b. Prague. His work, marked by beauty of style, culminated in the *Duino Elegies* and *Sonnets to Orpheus*, both written in 1922, which gave a new musicality to German verse. His visits to Russia in 1899 and 1900 and his admiration for Rodin (who had been his wife's teacher) influenced his artistic career.

Rimbaud, Jean Nicolas Arthur (1854–91), French poet, b. Charleville, on the Meuse. In his brief poetic career (4 years from about the age of 16) he prepared the way for symbolism (*Bateau ivre, Les Illuminations*) and anticipated Freud (*Les déserts de l'amour*). He became in-

timate with Verlaine and at 18 had completed his memoirs. *Une saison en enfer*. He died at Marseilles.

Rimsky-Korsakov, Nikolai Andreyevich (1844–1908), Russian composer whose works include the operas *The Maid of Pskov, The Snow Maiden, Le Coq d'or*, and the symphonic suite *Scheherezade*. He was a brilliant orchestrator and re-scored many works, including Borodin's *Prince Igor*.

Rizzio, David (1533?–66), Italian musician and secretary of Mary, Queen of Scots. He was murdered in her presence at Holyrood by her jealous husband, Darnley.

Robbia, Luca Della (1400–82), Florentine sculptor who introduced enamelled terra-cotta work.

Roberts of Kandahar, 1st Earl (Frederick Sleigh Roberts) (1832–1914), British general. He took part in the suppression of the Indian Mutiny, in the Afghan war (relieving Kandahar), and when put in command in South Africa in the Boer War he relieved Kimberley and advanced to Pretoria.

Robertson, Sir William (1860–1933), the only British soldier to rise from private to field-marshal. His son, **Brian Hubert, 1st Baron** (1896–1974) served in both world wars and was chairman of the British Transport Commission, 1953–61.

Robeson, Paul (1898–1976), American Negro singer, b. Princeton, especially remembered for his singing of Negro spirituals, and his appearance in works ranging from *Showboat* to *Othello*.

Robespierre, Maximilien Marie Isidoire de (1758–94), French revolutionary. A country advocate, b. Arras, he was in 1789 elected to the States General and in 1792 to the Convention. He became a leader of the Jacobins, the more extreme party which came to power under stress of war and after the king's execution in 1793. In this crisis, the Committee of Public Safety, of which he was a member and which used his reputation as a cloak, sent many to the guillotine. He opposed the cult of Reason and inaugurated the worship of the Supreme Being. In the reaction from the reign of terror he was denounced, tried to escape, but was guillotined.

Robinson, William Heath (1872–1944), English cartoonist and book-illustrator, especially known for his fantastically humorous drawings of machines.

Rob Roy (Robert McGregor) (1671–1734), Scottish freebooter who helped the poor at the expense of the rich, and played a lone hand in the troubled times of the Jacobite rising of 1715.

Robsart, Amy (1532–60), English victim (it is believed) of murder. The wife of Robert Dudley, Earl of Leicester, she was found dead at Cumnor Place. Her death was used by Scott in *Kenilworth*.

Rockefeller, John Davison (1839–1937), American philanthropist, b. Richford, N.Y. He settled in Cleveland, Ohio, and with his brother William founded the Standard Oil Company, making a fortune. His philanthropic enterprises are carried on by the Rockefeller Foundation. **Nelson Rockefeller** (1908–79), Gov. of New York 1958–73, Vice-Pres. of the United States 1974–7, was his grandson.

Rodin, Auguste (1841–1917), French sculptor, b. Paris. His best-known works include *Le Penseur, Les Bourgeois de Calais*, the statues of Balzac and Victor Hugo, and *La Porte d'Enfer*, a huge bronze door for the Musée des Arts Décoratifs, which was unfinished at his death.

Rodney, 1st Baron (George Rodney) (1719–92), English admiral, who served in the Seven Years War and the War of American Independence; in the latter war he defeated the French fleet under de Grasse.

Roland de la Platière, Manon Jeanne (1754–93), a leading figure in the French revolution. Her husband **Jean Marie** (1734–93), belonged to the more moderate or Girondist party, and when threatened escaped; but she was imprisoned and executed. She wrote *Letters* and *Memoirs*.

Rolland, Romain (1866–1944), French author, whose main work is a ten-volume novel, *Jean-Christophe*, the biography of a German musician, based on the life of Beethoven, and a study of contemporary French and German civilisation. Nobel prizewinner 1915.

Romilly, Sir Samuel (1757–1818), English lawyer

and law-reformer, who aimed at mitigating the severity of the criminal law.

Rommel, Erwin (1891–1944), German Field-Marshal. He took part in the 1940 invasion of France, and was later successful in commanding the Afrika Korps till 1944. He committed suicide. His son **Manfred** was awarded the C.B.E. in 1990 for services to Anglo-German Friendship.

Romney, George (1734–1802), English artist, b. in Lancashire. He painted chiefly portraits, especially of Lady Hamilton, and lived mainly in London, but returned to Kendal to die.

Röntgen, Wilhelm Konrad von (1845–1923), German scientist who in 1895 discovered X-rays. Nobel prizewinner 1901.

Roosevelt, Franklin Delano (1882–1945), American statesman, a distant cousin of Theodore Roosevelt. During the first world war he held office under Wilson, and though stricken with poliomyelitis in 1921 continued his political career, becoming governor of New York in 1929 and U.S. president in 1933 (the first to hold office for more than two terms), till his death. A Democrat, he met the economic crisis of 1933 with a policy for a "New Deal" (*see* **Sec. L**). He strove in vain to ward off war. Towards other American countries his attitude was that of "good neighbour." After Pearl Harbor, he energetically prosecuted the war, holding meetings with Churchill and Stalin, and adopting a "lend-lease" policy for arms. He kept contact with his people by "fireside talks." His wife **Eleanor** (1884–1962) was a public figure in her own right.

Roosevelt, Theodore (1858–1919), American president. Popular because of his exploits in the Spanish-American war, he was appointed Republican vice-president in 1900, becoming president when McKinley was assassinated, and was re-elected 1905. He promoted the regulation of trusts; and his promotion of peace between Russia and Japan gained the Nobel prize, 1906.

Rops, Félicien (1833–98), Belgian artist, known for his often satirical lithographs and etchings.

Ross, Sir James Clark (1800–62), Scottish explorer of polar regions, who accompanied his uncle Sir John, and himself discovered the north magnetic pole in 1831. He commanded the *Erebus* and *Terror* to the antarctic (1839–43), where his discoveries included the Ross ice barrier.

Ross, Sir John (1777–1856), Scottish explorer of polar regions, uncle of the above. He searched for the north-west passage and discovered Boothia peninsula.

Ross, Sir Ronald (1857–1932), British physician, b. India, who discovered the malaria parasite. Nobel prizewinner 1902.

Rossetti, Dante Gabriel (1828–82), English poet and painter, son of **Gabriele** (1783–1852), an exiled Italian author who settled in London in 1842. With Millais, Holman Hunt and others he formed the Pre-Raphaelite brotherhood which returned to pre-Renaissance art forms. His model was often his wife, Elizabeth Siddal. His poems include *The Blessed Damozel*. His sister **Christina Georgina** (1830–94) wrote poetry, including *Goblin Market*.

Rossini, Gioacchino Antonio (1792–1868), Italian operatic composer. *See* **Section E**.

Rostand, Edmond (1868–1918), French dramatist, whose *Cyrano de Bergerac* created a sensation in 1898.

Rothenstein, Sir William (1872–1945), English portrait painter. His son, **Sir John** (b. 1901), is an art historian and until 1964 was director of the Tate Gallery.

Rothschild, Meyer Amschel (1743–1812), German financier, founder of a banking family, b. Frankfurt. His five sons controlled branches at Frankfurt, Vienna, Naples, Paris and London (**Nathan Meyer**, 1777–1836). Nathan's son, **Lionel** (1808–79), was the first Jewish member of the House of Commons.

Roubiliac, Louis François (1695–1762), French sculptor who settled in London and carved a statue of Handel for Vauxhall gardens and one of Newton for Trinity College, Cambridge.

Rouget de Lisle, Claude Joseph (1760–1836), French poet, author of words and music of the *Marseillaise*, revolutionary and national anthem.

Rousseau, Henri (1844–1910), influential French

"Sunday" painter, called "Le Douanier" because he was a customs official; self-taught, he was for long unrecognised as an artist of considerable talent and originality; he used the botanical gardens for his jungle scenes.

Rousseau, Jean-Jacques (1712–78), French political philosopher and educationist, b. Geneva, herald of the romantic movement. After a hard childhood he met Mme. de Warens who for some years befriended him. In 1741 he went to Paris where he met Diderot and contributed articles on music and political economy to the *Encyclopédie*. *La Nouvelle Héloïse* appeared in 1760, *Emile*, and *Le Contrat Social* in 1762. *Emile* is a treatise on education according to "natural" principles and *Le Contrat Social*, his main work, sets forth his political theory. It begins, "Man is born free and everywhere he is in chains." Both books offended the authorities and he had to flee, spending some time in England. Later he was able to return to France. His views on conduct and government did much to stimulate the movement leading to the French Revolution.

Rubens, Sir Peter Paul (1577–1640), Flemish painter. B. in exile, his family returned to Antwerp in 1587. He studied in Italy and visited Spain. His range was wide, his compositions vigorous, and he was a remarkable colourist. *Peace and War*, *The Rape of the Sabines*, and *The Felt Hat* are in the National Gallery.

Rubinstein, Anton Grigorovich (1829–94), Russian pianist and composer, who helped to found the conservatoire at St. Petersburg (Leningrad); as did his brother **Nicholas** (1835–81) at Moscow.

Rücker, Sir Arthur (1848–1915), English physicist, who made two magnetic surveys of the British Isles, 1886, and 1891.

Ruisdael, Jacob van (*c.* 1628–82), Dutch painter of landscapes, b. Haarlem. Several of his works are in the National Gallery, including *Coast of Scheveningen* and *Landscape with ruins*. He was also a fine etcher.

Runcie, Robert (b. 1921), 102nd Archbishop of Canterbury, 1980–91. Bishop of St. Albans, 1970–80; Principal of Cuddesdon College, Oxford 1960–69. Historic first official visit to the Vatican 1989. Announced resignation decision, March 1990.

Rupert, Prince (1619–82), general, son of Frederick of Bohemia and his wife Elizabeth, daughter of James I of England. He commanded the Royalist cavalry in the English civil war, but was too impetuous for lasting success.

Rusk, David Dean (b. 1909), American politician, who has held various posts especially in connection with foreign affairs; a former Rhodes scholar.

Ruskin, John (1819–1900), English author and art critic, b. London. His *Modern Painters* in 5 volumes was issued over a period of years, the first volume having a strong defence of Turner. He helped to establish the Pre-Raphaelites. Other notable works include *The Seven Lamps of Architecture*, *The Stones of Venice* and *Praeterita*. *Unto this Last* develops his views on social problems, and he tried to use his wealth for education and for non-profitmaking enterprises. Ruskin College at Oxford, the first residential college for working people, is named after him. In 1848 he married Euphemia Gray, but in 1854 she obtained a decree of nullity and later married Millais.

Russell, 3rd Earl (Bertrand Arthur William Russell) (1872–1970), English philosopher, mathematician, and essayist, celebrated for his work in the field of logic and the theory of knowledge, and remembered for his moral courage, belief in human reason and his championship of liberal ideas. He published more than 60 books, including *The Principles of Mathematics* (1903). *Principia Mathematica* (in collaboration with A. N. Whitehead; 3 vols., 1910–13), *The Problem of Philosophy* (1912), *Mysticism and Logic* (1918), *The Analysis of Mind* (1921), *An Inquiry into Meaning and Truth* (1940), *History of Western Philosophy* (1945), and a number on ethics and social questions. His *Autobiography* (3 vols.) appeared 1967–9. He was the grandson of Lord John Russell and John Stuart Mill was his godfather. Nobel prize for literature 1950; O.M. 1949.

Russell, 1st Earl (John Russell), (1792–1878), English statesman, third son of the 6th Duke of Bedford. He had a large share in carrying the parliamentary reform bill of 1832. He was Whig prime minister 1846–52 and 1865–6. He was also a historian and biographer.

Russell of Killowen, 1st Baron (Charles Russell), (1832–1900) British lawyer, b. Ireland; lord chief justice 1894–1900. He defended Parnell.

Rutherford, 1st Baron (Ernest Rutherford) (1871–1937), British physicist, b. New Zealand, eminent in the field of atomic research. His experiments were conducted at Manchester and Cambridge and attracted young scientists from all over the world. In 1911 he announced his nuclear theory of the atom and in 1918 succeeded in splitting the atom. His work prepared the way for future nuclear research.

Ruysdael, Jacob van. See **Ruisdale.**

Ruyter, Michiel Adrianszoon de (1607–76), Dutch admiral who ranks with Nelson. He fought against England and in 1667 caused alarm by sailing up the Medway as far as Rochester and up the Thames as far as Gravesend. He was mortally wounded at Messina.

S

Sachs, Hans (1494–1576), German poet, b. Nuremberg. A shoemaker, he wrote over 6,000 pieces, some dealing with everyday life, many (including *Die Wittenbergische Nachtigall*) inspired by the Reformation.

Sachs, Julius von (1832–97), German botanist, founder of experimental plant physiology. He demonstrated that chlorophyll is formed in chloroplasts only in light.

Sadat, Mohammed Anwar El (1919–81), Egyptian statesman, President of Egypt 1970–81. His visit to Israel in Nov. 1977 was a bold and courageous move which led to the Camp David peace treaty with Israel. Assassinated 1981.

Sádi or **Saadi** (Muslih Addin) (c. 1184–1292), Persian poet, b. Shiraz, best known for his *Gulistan* (Flower Garden).

Sainte-Beuve, Charles Augustin (1804–69), French critic, b. Boulogne. He studied medicine, abandoning it for journalism, and after attempting to write poetry, turned to literary criticism. His work reveals the wide range of his intellectual experience and includes *Causeries du lundi* and *Histoire de Port-Royal*.

Saint-Just, Antoine (1767–94), French revolutionary, a follower of Robespierre.

St. Laurent, Louis Stephen (1882–1973), Canadian politician, prime minister 1948–57.

Saint-Saëns, Charles Camille (1835–1921), French composer, for 20 years organist at the Madeleine. His compositions include symphonic and chamber music and the opera *Samson et Dalila*, which was produced by Liszt at Weimar in 1877. *See* Section E.

Saint-Simon, Claude, Comte de (1760–1825), French socialist, who in his *L'Industrie* and *Nouveau christianisme* prepared the way for much later thought.

Saintsbury, George Edward (1845–1933), English critic and literary historian.

Sakharov, Andrei Dimitrievich (1921–89), Soviet nuclear physicist and human rights campaigner. Nobel prizewinner 1975.

Sala, George Augustus (1828–95), English journalist who contributed to *Household Words* and was a notable foreign correspondent.

Saladin (el Melik an-Nasir Salah ed-Din) (1137–93), sultan of Egypt and Syria and founder of a dynasty, who in 1187 defeated the Christians near Tiberias and took Jerusalem. This gave rise to the unsuccessful Third Crusade, in which Richard I of England joined. His great qualities were admired by his opponents, and his administration left many tangible signs in such matters as roads and canals.

Salazar, Antonio d'Oliveira (1889–1970), Portuguese dictator, having first been premier in 1932, a new constitution being adopted in 1933. He gave Portugal stability, but refused to bow to nationalism in Portuguese Africa and India.

Salimbene de Adamo (1221–c. 1228), mediaeval chronicler, b. Parma, whose vivid description of life in the 13th cent. is embodied in his *Cronica.*

Salisbury, 3rd Marquess (Robert Arthur Talbot Gascoyne-Cecil (1830–1903), English Conservative

statesman, prime minister 1885–6, 1886–92, 1895–1902, mainly remembered for his conduct of foreign affairs during a critical period, culminating in the Boer War. His grandson, **Robert Arthur, 5th Marquess** (1893–1972), led the Conservative opposition in the House of Lords.

Samuel, 1st Viscount (Herbert Samuel) (1870–1963), British Liberal statesman of Jewish parentage. He published philosophical works, including *Practical Ethics.*

Sand, George (1804–76), pseudonym of the French writer Armandine Lucie Dupin. Her publications are extensive and varied, and include the novel *Mauprat*, rural studies, and an autobiography *Histoire de ma vie*. She was associated with Alfred de Musset and Chopin.

Sandow, Eugene (1867–1925), German "strong man" who opened an Institute of Health in London.

Sanger, Frederick (b. 1918), British scientist noted for his work on the chemical structure of the protein insulin. Nobel prizewinner 1958, and 1980. O.M. (1986).

Sankey, Ira David (1840–1908), American evangelist and composer, associated with Moody.

San Martin, José de (1778–1850), South American national leader in securing independence from Spanish rule to his native Argentina, Chile and Peru.

Santayana, George (1863–1952), American philosopher and poet, b. Madrid, of Spanish parentage. He was professor of philosophy at Harvard, 1907–12. His books include *The Sense of Beauty, The Life of Reason*, and *The Realms of Being.*

Santos-Dumont, Alberto (1873–1932), Brazilian aeronaut who in 1898 flew a cylindrical balloon with a gasoline engine. In 1909 he built a monoplane.

Sappho of Lesbos (fl. early 6th cent. B.C.), Greek poetess, of whose love poems few remain.

Sardou, Victorien (1831–1908), French dramatist popular in his day. Sarah Bernhardt created famous parts in *Fédora, Théodora* and *La Tosca*; *Robespierre* and *Dante* were written for Irving.

Sargent, John Singer (1856–1922), American painter, b. Florence, who worked mainly in England, especially on portraits.

Sargent, Sir Malcolm (1895–1967), popular British conductor, who conducted the Promenade Concerts from 1950 till his death, and succeeded Sir Adrian Boult as conductor of the B.B.C. Symphony Orchestra, 1950–7.

Sartre, Jean-Paul (1905–80), French existentialist philosopher, left-wing intellectual, dramatist, essayist and novelist. His major philosophical work is *L'Etre et le Néant* and his plays include *Les Mouches, Huis Clos, Crime passionel, La Putain respectueuse*, and *Les Séquestrés d'Altona*. He was awarded (though he declined it) the 1964 Nobel prize.

Sassoon, Siegfried (1886–1967), English poet and writer with a hatred of war. He is mainly known for *The Memoirs of a Foxhunting Man*, the first part of the *Memoirs of George Sherston.*

Savonarola, Girolamo (1452–98), Florentine preacher and reformer, a Dominican friar, who denounced vice and corruption not only in society but also in the Church itself, especially attacking Pope Alexander VI. He was excommunicated, imprisoned, and with two of his companions, hanged and burned. His passion for reform made him impatient of opposition and incapable of compromise, yet he was a notable figure and commands the respect of later ages. George Eliot's *Romola* portrays him.

Scarlatti, Alessandro (1659–1725), Italian musician who founded the Neapolitan school of opera. He composed over 100 operas, 200 masses, and over 700 cantatas and oratorios. His son **Domenico** (1685–1757) was a harpsichord virtuoso whose work influenced the evolution of the sonata. The chief years of his life were spent at the Spanish court in Madrid. *See* Section E.

Scheele, Carl Wilhelm (1742–86), Swedish chemist, discoverer of many chemical substances, including oxygen (c. 1773—but published in 1777 after the publication of Priestley's studies).

Schiaparelli, Giovanni Virginio (1835–1910), Italian astronomer, noted for having observed certain dark markings on the surface of the planet Mars which he called canals (recent close-range photographs show none).

Schiller, Johann Christoph Friedrich von (1759–1805), German dramatist and poet, b. Marbach in Württemberg, began life as a military surgeon. His play *The Robbers* with a revolutionary theme was successful in 1782 in Mannheim. After a stay at Dresden, where he wrote *Don Carlos*, and at Jena, where he wrote a history of the Thirty Years War, he became the friend of Goethe and removed to Weimar, where he wrote *Wallenstein, Mary Stuart, The Maid of Orleans* and *William Tell*. He is a leading figure in the European romantic movement.

Schirrmann, Richard (1874–1961), German originator of youth hostels. A schoolmaster, in 1907 he converted his schoolroom during holidays to a dormitory. The Verband für deutsche Jugendherbergen was founded in 1913, and the International Youth Hostels Federation in 1932, with Schirrmann as first president.

Schlegel, Friedrich von (1772–1829), German critic, b. Hanover, prominent among the founders of German ·omanticism, whose revolutionary and germinating ideas influenced early 19th-cent. thought. His brother, **August Wilhelm** (1767–1845), made remarkable translations of Shakespeare (which established Shakespeare in Germany), Dante, Calderón, and Camões.

Schliemann, Heinrich (1822–90), German archaeologist, who conducted excavations at Troy and Mycenae. He has been the subject of numerous biographies mostly based on his own writings which are now viewed with some scepticism.

Schmidt, Helmuth (b. 1918), German social democrat (SPD) statesman; succeeded Brandt as Chancellor of the West German Federal Republic 1974–83. *See* **Section C , Part II**.

Schnabel, Artur (1882–1951), American pianist of Austrian birth, regarded as a leading exponent of Beethoven's pianoforte sonatas.

Schoenberg, Arnold (1874–1951), Austrian composer of Jewish parentage who in 1933 was exiled by the Nazi regime and settled in America, teaching at Boston and Los Angeles. Among his works are the choral orchestral *Gurre-Lieder* and *Pierrot Lunaire*, a cycle of 21 poems for voice and chamber music. *See* **Section E**.

Schopenhauer, Arthur (1788–1860), German philosopher, b. Danzig, important historically for his pessimism, and his doctrine that will is superior to knowledge. His chief work is *The World as Will and Idea*. He regarded his contemporary Hegel as a charlatan.

Schubert, Franz Peter (1797–1828), Austrian composer, b. Vienna, the son of a schoolmaster, and a contemporary of Beethoven. He wrote not only symphonies, sonatas, string quartets, choral music and masses, but also over 600 songs of unsurpassed lyrical beauty. He might almost be called the creator of the German *Lied* as known today.

Schumann, Robert Alexander (1810–56), composer of the early 19th cent. German romantic school. He wrote much chamber music, four symphonies, a piano concerto, and choral music, but it is his early piano pieces and songs that give constant delight. His wife **Clara** (1819–96) was one of the outstanding pianists of her time.

Schweitzer, Albert (1875–1965), Alsatian medical missionary, theologian, musician and philosopher, b. at Kaysersberg. After publishing learned works, he resigned a promising European career to found at Lambaréné in French Equatorial Africa a hospital to fight leprosy and sleeping sickness and made it a centre of service to Africans. His funds were raised by periodic organ recitals in Europe. His motivation was not patronage but atonement. Nobel peace prize 1952. O.M. 1955.

Scipio, Publius Cornelius (237–183 B.C.), Roman general in the second Punic War, known as Scipio Africanus the elder. **Scipio Africanus the younger** (185–129 B.C.) was an adoptive relative and an implacable opponent of Carthage (destroyed 146).

Scott, Charles Prestwich (1846–1931), English newspaper editor. Under his editorship (1872–1929) the *Manchester Guardian* (now *The Guardian*) became a leading journal.

Scott, Sir George Gilbert (1811–78), English architect in the Gothic revival. He restored many churches and designed the Albert Memorial and the Martyrs' Memorial at Oxford.

Scott, Sir Giles Gilbert (1880–1960), English architect, grandson of above, designed the Anglican cathedral at Liverpool and planned the new Waterloo Bridge.

Scott, Robert Falcon (1868–1912), English antarctic explorer. He led two expeditions; one 1901–4 which discovered King Edward VII Land; and another 1910–12 which reached the south pole and found the Amundsen records; but while returning the party was overtaken by blizzards and perished 11 miles from their base. *See also* **Antarctic exploration, L7.** His son, **Sir Peter Scott** (1909–89), was an artist, ornithologist and pioneer conservationist.

Scott, Sir Walter (1771–1832), Scottish novelist and poet, b. Edinburgh. He was educated for the law, but came to know and love the Border country and his interests were literary; and in 1802–3 he issued a collection of ballads, *Border Minstrelsy*. Poems such as *Marmion* and *The Lady of the Lake* followed. His novels appeared anonymously, beginning with *Waverley* in 1814; and continuing with *Guy Mannering*, *The Antiquary, Old Mortality, Rob Roy*, and *The Heart of Midlothian*. From 1819 he turned also to English history, with *Ivanhoe* and *Kenilworth*. In 1826 he became bankrupt, largely as the fault of his publishing partner.

Scott-Paine, Hubert (1891–1954), pioneer in the design and construction of aircraft and sea-craft.

Scriabin, Alexander (1872–1915), Russian composer and pianist, who relied to some extent on extra-musical factors such as religion, and in *Prometheus* tried to unite music and philosophy. *See* **Section E.**

Seeley, Sir John Robert (1834–95), English historian, author of a life of Christ, *Ecce Homo*.

Segovia, Andrés (1894–1987), Spanish concert-guitarist. He adapted works by Bach, Haydn, Mozart etc. to the guitar.

Selfridge, Harry Gordon (1858–1947), American-born merchant who in 1909 opened a new style of department store in Oxford Street.

Semmelweis, Ignaz Philipp (1818–65), Hungarian obstetrician, a pioneer in the use of antiseptic methods, thus reducing the incidence of puerperal fever.

Seneca, Lucius Annaeus (c. 4 B.C.–A.D. 65), Roman stoic philosopher who was a tutor to Nero, but lost favour and was sentenced to take his own life.

Senefelder, Alois (1772–1834), Bavarian inventor of lithography about 1796.

Severus, Lucius Septimius (146–211), Roman emperor, and a successful general. On a visit to Britain he suppressed a revolt, repaired Hadrian's Wall, and died at York.

Sévigné, Marie de Rabutin-Chantai, Marquise de (1626–96), French woman of letters. Her letters to her daughter Françoise written in an unaffected elegance of style give a moving picture of fashionable society in 17th cent. France.

Sgambati, Giovanni (1841–1914), Italian pianist (pupil of Liszt), composer and teacher, who revived interest in classical instrumental music in an age of opera.

Shackleton, Sir Ernest Henry (1874–1922), British explorer, who made four antarctic expeditions; that of 1909 reached within 100 miles of the south pole. He died on his last expedition.

Shaftesbury, 7th Earl of (Anthony Ashley Cooper) (1801–85), English philanthropist largely responsible for legislation reducing the misery of the industrial revolution. He was for 40 years chairman of the Ragged Schools Union.

Shakespeare, William (1564–1616), England's greatest poet and dramatist, b. Stratford-on-Avon. Little is known of his career up to his eighteenth year, when he married Anne Hathaway. He came to London at the height of the English renaissance and soon became connected with the Globe theatre as actor and playwright. Thirty-eight plays comprise the Shakespeare canon. Thirty-six were printed in the First Folio of 1623 (the first collected edition of his dramatic works), of which eighteen had been published during his lifetime in the so-called Quartos. *Love's Labour's Lost* and *The Comedy of Errors* seem to have been among the earliest, being followed by *The Two Gentlemen of Verona*, and *Romeo and Juliet*. Then followed *Henry VI, Richard III, Richard II, Titus Andronicus, The Taming of the Shrew, King John, The*

Merchant of Venice, A Midsummer Night's Dream, All's Well that Ends Well, Henry IV, The Merry Wives of Windsor, Henry V, Much Ado about Nothing, As You Like It, Twelfth Night. Then came some of his greatest plays, *Julius Caesar, Hamlet, Troilus and Cressida, Othello, Measure for Measure, Macbeth, King Lear, Timon of Athens, Pericles, Antony and Cleopatra, Coriolanus, Cymbeline, A Winter's Tale, The Tempest, Henry VIII,* and *The Two Noble Kinsmen.* In mastery of language, in understanding of character, in dramatic perception, and in skill in the use of ritual he has never been surpassed. Fresh interpretation of his work continues.

Sharp, Granville (1735–1813), English abolitionist of slavery, and founder of the colony of Sierra Leone.

Shastri, Shri Lal Bahadur (1904–66), Indian politician who became prime minister of India after the death of Nehru in 1964. He died of a heart attack at the end of the Soviet-sponsored Tashkent talks.

Shaw, George Bernard (1856–1950), Irish dramatist who conquered England by his wit and exposure of hypocrisy, cant, and national weaknesses, and whose individual opinions found expression in musical criticism, socialist pamphlets and plays. His plays include *Man and Superman, Heartbreak House, Back to Methuselah, Saint Joan, The Apple Cart,* and *Buoyant Billions,* and most have important prefaces. In 1884 he joined the newly-born Fabian Society. Nobel prizewinner 1925.

Shelley, Percy Bysshe (1792–1822), English poet, b. Horsham. He was a master of language and of literary form, and a passionate advocate of freedom and of new thought. Sent down from Oxford for his pamphlet *The Necessity of Atheism,* he came under the influence of William Godwin; and, after his first marriage came to an unhappy end, married the latter's daughter, Mary Wollstonecraft, herself a writer. In the same year began his friendship with Byron. His works include *The Revolt of Islam,* The *Masque of Anarchy* (an indictment of Castlereagh), *The Cenci* (a play on evil), and *Prometheus Unbound,* besides lyrics such as *To a Skylark* and *Ode to the West Wind.* He was accidentally drowned while sailing near Spezzia.

Sheppard, Hugh Richard (Dick) (1880–1937), Anglican divine and pacifist. He made St. Martin-in-the-Fields a centre of social service and also founded the Peace Pledge Union.

Sheraton, Thomas (1751–1806), English cabinet-maker, b. Stockton, whose *Cabinetmaker's Book* promoted neo-classical designs.

Sheridan, Richard Brinsley (1751–1816), British dramatist, b. Dublin. He was a brilliant writer of comedies, especially *The Rivals, The Duenna, The School for Scandal,* and *The Critic.* He acquired and rebuilt Drury Lane theatre, which reopened in 1794, but was burnt down in 1809; and this, with his lack of business sense, brought him to poverty, in spite of his friends' efforts to help him. He was also in parliament where he made some notable speeches.

Sherman, William Tecumseh (1820–91), American general, who served especially in the Civil War. He took part in the battles of Bull Run and Shiloh, was appointed in 1864 to the command of the southwest, and with 65,000 men marched across Georgia to the sea. In 1865 he accepted Johnston's surrender.

Sherrington, Sir Charles Scott (1857–1952), English scientist, an authority on the physiology of the nervous system. His research led to advances in brain surgery. His principal work is *Integration Action of the Nervous System* (1906). Shared with E. D. Adrian the 1932 Nobel prize.

Shirley, James (1596–1666), English dramatist. His tragedies include *The Traitor,* and his comedies *Hyde Park.* His death was hastened by the Great Fire.

Sholokhov, Mikhail Aleksandrovich (1905–84), Russian novelist, author of *And Quiet Flows the Don.* Nobel prizewinner 1965.

Shostakovich, Dimitri (1906–75), Russian composer whose music is complex, profound, and deeply significant of the Soviet age in which he lived. His works include operas, ballets, symphonies, chamber music, and music for films. Hero of Soviet Labour 1966. *See* **Section E.**

Sibelius, Jean (1865–1957), Finnish composer imbued with national feeling. His works include seven symphonies, a violin concerto, and several tone poems, notably *Finlandia,* and some based on the Finnish poem *Kalevala. See* **Section E.**

Sickert, Walter Richard (1860–1942), British artist, b. Munich. He was influenced by Degas, and has himself influenced later painters. His *Ennui* is in the Tate Gallery.

Siddons, Sarah (1755–1831), English actress especially in tragic parts. She was daughter of the manager Roger Kemble and her reputation was almost unbounded.

Sidgwick, Henry (1838–1900), English philosopher who wrote *Methods of Ethics,* and who also promoted women's education, especially in the foundation of Newnham and Girton colleges at Cambridge.

Sidney, Sir Philip (1554–86), English poet and writer, best remembered for his *Arcadia, Apologie for Poetrie,* and *Astrophel and Stella,* all published after his death. He was killed at the battle of Zutphen, where he passed a cup of water to another, saying "Thy necessity is greater than mine."

Siemens, Sir William (1823–83), German-born electrical engineer who settled in England and constructed many overland and submarine telegraphs. He was brother of **Werner von Siemens,** founder of the firm of Siemens-Halske.

Sienkiewicz, Henryk (1846–1916), Polish novelist and short-story writer; best known of his historical novels is *Quo Vadis?* Nobel prizewinner 1905.

Sikorski, Vladislav (1881–1943), Polish general and statesman, prime minister of the Polish government in exile (1939) and commander-in-chief of the Polish forces. Killed in an aircraft accident at Gibraltar.

Simpson, Sir James Young (1811–70), Scottish obstetrician who initiated the use of chloroform in childbirth.

Sinclair, Upton (1878–1968), American novelist whose documentary novel *The Jungle* on the Chicago slaughter yards caused a sensation in 1906.

Singer, Isaac Merritt (1811–75), American mechanical engineer who improved early forms of the sewing-machine and patented a single-thread and chain-stitch machine.

Sisley, Alfred (1839–99), French impressionist painter of English origin, who painted some enchanting landscapes, such as *Meadows in Spring* in the Tate Gallery. He was influenced by Corot and Manet.

Sitwell, Edith (1887–1964), English poet, a great experimenter in verse forms. *Gold Coast Customs, Façade* (set to music by William Walton) and *Still Falls the Rain* are probably best known. She had two brothers, **Osbert** (1892–1969) and **Sacheverell** (b. 1897), both poets and critics.

Slim, 1st Viscount (William Slim) (1891–1970), British general. He commanded the 14th Army in Burma, was chief of the Imperial General Staff 1948–52, and governor-general of Australia 1953–60.

Sloane, Sir Hans (1660–1753), British collector, b. Ireland. He practised in London as a physician. His library of 50,000 volumes and his collection of MSS. and botanical specimens were offered under his will to the nation and formed the beginning of the British Museum.

Slowacki, Julius (1809–49), Polish romantic poet, a revolutionary, he lived in exile in Paris. His work includes the poetic dramas *Kordian, Balladyna* and *Lilli Weneda,* written in the style of Shakespeare; and the unfinished poem *King Spirit* which reveals his later mystical tendencies.

Smeaton, John (1724–92), English engineer; he rebuilt Eddystone lighthouse (1756–59), improved Newcomen's steam-engine, and did important work on bridges, harbours, and canals. He also invented an improved blowing apparatus for iron-smelting.

Smetana, Bedřich (1824–84), Czech composer, creator of a national style. He was principal conductor of the Prague National Theatre, for which he wrote most of his operas, including *The Bartered Bride* and *The Kiss.* Best known of his other compositions are the cycle of symphonic poems *My Country* and the string quartets *From My Life*. He became totally deaf in 1874, suffered a mental breakdown, and died in an asylum. *See* **Section E**.

Smiles, Samuel (1812–1904), Scottish writer, *b.* Haddington, in early life a medical practitioner, remembered for *Self Help* (1859), and his biographies of engineers of the industrial revolution.

Smith, Adam (1723–90), Scottish economist, b. Kirkcaldy. In Edinburgh he published *Moral Sentiments*. Later he moved to London, and his *Wealth of Nations* (1776) is the first serious work in political economy.

Smith, Sir Grafton Eliot (1871–1937), Australian anatomist who did research on the structure of the mammalian brain. His works include *The Evolution of Man*.

Smith, John (1580–1631), English adventurer who in 1605 went on a colonising expedition to Virginia and was saved from death by the Red Indian Pocahontas.

Smith, Joseph (1805–44), American founder of the Mormons. He claimed that the *Book of Mormon* was revealed to him. In 1838 feeling against the Mormons culminated in a rising and Smith was murdered. He was succeeded by Brigham Young. *See* **Mormonism, Section J.**

Smith, Sydney (1771–1845), Anglican divine and journalist, who founded the *Edinburgh Review* and supported Catholic emancipation.

Smith, William (1760–1839), English surveyor and canal-maker, the first to map the rock strata of England and to identify the fossils peculiar to each layer.

Smith, Sir William Alexander (1854–1914), Scottish founder of the Boys' Brigade (1883), the oldest national organisation for boys in Britain.

Smith, William Robertson (1846–94), Scottish biblical scholar whose "Bible" contribution to the 9th edition of *The Encyclopaedia Britannica* resulted in an unsuccessful prosecution for heresy.

Smollett, Tobias George (1721–71), Scottish novelist whose work is characterised by satire and coarse humour. His main novels are *Roderick Random*, *Peregrine Pickle*, and *Humphrey Clinker*.

Smuts, Jan Christian (1870–1950), South African statesman and soldier. B. in Cape Colony, during the Boer War he fought on the Boer side. He was premier of the Union 1919–24, 1939–48, and worked for cooperation within the Commonwealth and in the world, but his party was defeated in 1948 by the Nationalists under Malan.

Smyth, Ethel Mary (1858–1944), English composer and suffragette. Her main works are operas (*The Wreckers* and *The Boatswain's Mate*) and a *Mass in D*. She studied at the Leipzig Conservatory.

Snow, Baron (Charles Percy Snow) (1905–80), English physicist and novelist, author of the essay *The Two Cultures of the Scientific Revolution*, and a sequence of novels *Strangers and Brothers* (11 vols.).

Snyders, Frans (1597–1657), Flemish still-life and animal painter who studied under Breughel.

Soane, Sir John (1753–1837), English architect who designed the Bank of England. He left the nation his house and library in Lincoln's Inn Fields (Soane Museum).

Sobers, Sir Garfield (b. 1936), West Indies and Nottinghamshire cricketer who ranks as one of the greatest all-rounders. Knighted 1975.

Socinus or **Sozzini Laelius** (1525–62), Italian founder of the sect of Socinians, with his nephew **Faustus** (1539–1604). Their teachings resemble those of Unitarians.

Socrates (470–399 B.C.), Greek philosopher and intellectual leader, was the son of a sculptor of Athens. He distinguished himself in three campaigns (Potidaea, Delium, and Amphipolis). Returning to Athens, he devoted himself to study and intellectual enquiry, attracting many followers; through these, especially Xenophon and Plato, we know of his teachings, for he wrote nothing. In 399 B.C. he was charged with impiety and with corrupting the young, found guilty, and accordingly died by drinking hemlock; *see* Plato's *Apology*, *Crito*, and *Phaedo*.

Soddy, Frederick (1877–1956), English chemist, who in Glasgow about 1912 laid the foundation of the isotope theory, before the physicists became prominent in that field. Nobel prizewinner 1921.

Solon (638–558 B.C.), Athenian lawgiver, who in a time of economic distress cancelled outstanding debts, and introduced some democratic changes.

Solzhenitsyn, Alexander Isayevich (b. 1918), Russian novelist, b. Rostov-on-Don; author of *One Day in the Life of Ivan Denisovich*, a documentary novel depicting life in one of Stalin's prison camps where he spent many years of his life. He was expelled from the Soviet Writers' Union in 1969, and from his country in 1974. Nobel prizewinner 1970.

Somerset, Duke of (**Edward Seymour**) (1506–52), lord protector of England in the time of the young Edward VI, but he fell from power and was executed.

Sophocles (495–406 B.C.), Athenian dramatist, who was awarded the prize over Aeschylus in 468. Of over a hundred plays of his, the only extant ones are *Oedipus the King*, *Oedipus at Colonus Antigone*, *Electra*, *Trachiniae*, *Ajax*, *Philoctetes*.

Sorel, Georges (1847–1922), French advocate of revolutionary syndicalism, author of *Reflections on Violence* (1905). The irrational aspects of his philosophy (derived from Bergson) appealed to Mussolini and the Fascists.

Soult, Nicolas Jean de Dieu (1769–1851), French general who fought under Napoleon in Switzerland and Italy, at Austerlitz, and in the Peninsular War.

Sousa, John Philip (1854–1932), American bandmaster and composer of some stirring marches.

Southey, Robert (1774–1843), English poet and historian. In 1803 he settled near Coleridge at Keswick, and in 1813 became poet laureate. His best work was in prose: histories of Brazil and of the Peninsular War; lives of Nelson Wesley, and others.

Southwell, Robert (1561–95), English poet and Jesuit martyr, beatified 1920. His poems include *The Burning Babe*.

Spaak, Paul Henri (1899–1972), Belgian statesman, first president of the U.N. General Assembly in 1946, and of the Assembly of the Council of Europe, 1949–51; secretary-general of NATO, 1957–61.

Spartacus (d. 71 B.C.), Thracian rebel. A Roman slave and gladiator in Capua, he escaped and headed a slave insurrection, routing several Roman armies, but was defeated and killed by Crassus.

Speke, John Hanning (1827–64), British explorer. In 1858 he discovered the Victoria Nyanza; and in 1860 with J. A. Grant traced the Nile flowing out of it.

Spence, Sir Basil Urwin (1907–76), Scottish architect, mainly known for the new Coventry cathedral, and for Hampstead civic centre. He also brought a new approach to university buildings. O.M. 1962.

Spencer, Herbert (1820–1903), English philosopher. B. Derby, he was at first a civil engineer, then a journalist (sub-editor of the *Economist*), when he wrote *Social Statics*. He coined the phrase (1852) "the survival of the fittest" and his *Principles of Psychology* (1855), published four years before Darwin's *Origin of Species*, expounded doctrines of evolution. His ten-volume *Synthetic Philosophy* was issued over a period of thirty years.

Spencer, Sir Stanley (1891–1959), English artist of visionary power. His two pictures of the *Resurrection* are in the Tate Gallery. He also painted *Cookham regatta*.

Spengler, Oswald (1880–1936), German historicist who held that every culture is destined to a waxing and waning life cycle and that the West European culture was entering its period of decline. His principal work is *The Decline of the West*. His views prepared the way for national socialism.

Spenser, Edmund (1552–99), English poet, b. London and educated at Cambridge. His *Shepheards Calendar* appeared in 1579. In 1580 he went to Ireland as the lord deputy's secretary, and later acquired Kilcolman castle, where he wrote most of his main work, *The Faerie Queene*. His castle was burnt in an insurrection in 1598, when he returned to London. He is called "the poet's poet."

Spinoza, Baruch (1632–77), Dutch philosopher, b. Amsterdam, whose parents came to Holland from Portugal to escape the Inquisition. An independent thinker, his criticism of the Scriptures led to his being excommunicated from the synagogue. He supported himself by grinding and polishing lenses. He owed much to Descartes but was mainly concerned with religion and virtue. His philosophical theories are set out in the *Ethics* which was published posthumously. In the light of modern science his metaphysic cannot be accepted but his moral teaching has enduring validity.

Spofforth, Reginald (1770–1827), English writer of glees, including *Hail, Smiling Morn*.

Spurgeon, Charles Haddon (1834–92), English Baptist who preached at the vast Metropolitan Tabernacle, London, from 1861 (burnt down 1898).

Staël, Anne Louise, Baronne de Staël-Holstein (1766–1817), French writer. Daughter of the finance minister, Necker, she married the Swedish ambassador, and kept a salon. Her *Lettres sur Rousseau* appeared in 1788. After the revolution she lived partly abroad, partly in France, and after a visit to Italy wrote her novel *Corinne* (1807).

Stalin (Joseph Vissarionovich Djugashvili) (1879–1953), Soviet statesman who for nearly 30 years was leader of the Russian people. He originally studied at Tiflis for the priesthood, but became an active revolutionary and took part in the civil war after 1917. After Lenin's death, he ousted Trotsky and became the outstanding figure. He modernised agriculture on socialist lines by ruthless means, and his series of five-year plans from 1929 made Russia an industrial power. On the German invasion in 1941 he assumed military leadership; and later attended Allied war conferences. After his death some of his methods and the "personality cult" were denounced by Khrushchev, and this had far-reaching results in other Communist countries. In his attack on "official" Marxism, George Lukács says Stalin "turned Marxism on its head" by making it into theories and strategies which fitted his own tactics of the day.

Stanford, Sir Charles Villiers (1852–1924), Irish composer of instrumental, choral, operatic, and other music.

Stanley, Sir Henry Morton (1841–1904), British explorer, b. Denbigh. He fought for the Confederates in the American Civil War. He then became a correspondent for the *New York Herald*, was commissioned to find Livingstone, and did so in 1871 at Ujiji, and with him explored Lake Tanganyika. In 1879 he founded the Congo Free State under the Belgian king. His works include *Through the Dark Continent* and an *Autobiography*.

Stark, Freya Madeline (b. 1893), British writer and explorer of the Arab world.

Steel, Sir David *see* Section D.

Steele, Sir Richard (1672–1729), British essayist, b. Dublin. He founded the *Tatler* (1709–11), to which Addison also contributed, and later the *Spectator* (1711–12) and the *Guardian* (1713).

Steen, Jan (1626–79), Dutch genre painter, b. Leiden, son of a brewer. *The Music Lesson* and *Skittle Alley* are in the National Gallery, the *Lute Player* in the Wallace collection.

Steer, Philip Wilson (1860–1942), English painter, especially of landscapes and of portraits.

Stefansson, Vilhjalmur (1879–1962), Canadian arctic explorer of Icelandic parentage; his publications include *Unsolved Mysteries of the Arctic*.

Stein, Sir Aurel (1862–1943), British archaeologist, b. Budapest. He held archaeological posts under the Indian government and explored Chinese Turkestan.

Stendhal, pseudonym of Marie Henri Beyle (1783–1842), French novelist, b. Grenoble. He was with Napoleon's army in the Russian campaign of 1812, spent several years in Italy, and after the revolution of 1830 was appointed consul at Trieste, and afterwards at Civitavecchia. In his plots he recreates historical and social events with imaginative realism and delineates character with searching psychological insight. His main works are *Le Rouge et le Noir*, and *La Chartreuse de Parme*.

Stephen (1105–54), usurped the crown of England from Henry I's daughter in 1135; and, after anarchy, retained it till his death.

Stephen, Sir Leslie (1832–1904), English writer, critic, and biographer. He edited the *Cornhill Magazine* (1871–82), and the *Dictionary of National Biography* (1882–91), and was the father of Virginia Woolf.

Stephenson, George (1781–1848), English engineer; a locomotive designer, b. at Wylam near Newcastle, a colliery fireman's son. As enginewright at Killingworth colliery he made his first locomotive in 1814 to haul coal from mines. He and his son Robert built the *Locomotion* for the Stockton and Darlington Railway (1825), the first locomotive for a public railway. His *Rocket* at 30 miles an hour won the prize of £500 in 1829 offered by the Liverpool and Manchester Railway. He also discovered the principle on which the miners' safety lamp was based. First president of the Institution of Mechanical Engineers.

Stephenson, Robert (1803–59), English engineer, son of the above, engineered railway lines in England and abroad, and built many bridges including the Menai and Conway tubular bridges.

Sterne, Laurence (1713–68), English novelist and humorist. His main works are *Tristram Shandy* and *A Sentimental Journey*. He led a wandering and unconventional life, dying in poverty. His work helped to develop the novel.

Stevenson, Adlai (1900–65), American politician, an efficient governor of Illinois, 1949–53; ambassador to the U.N., 1960–5, and unsuccessful presidential challenger to Eisenhower 1952 and 1956.

Stevenson, Robert (1772–1850), Scottish engineer and builder of lighthouses, who invented "intermittent" and "flashing" lights.

Stevenson, Robert Louis (1850–94), Scottish author, b. Edinburgh. He suffered from ill-health and eventually settled in Samoa. His main works are *Travels with a Donkey*, *Treasure Island*, *Kidnapped*, *Dr. Jekyll and Mr. Hyde*, and *The Master of Ballantrae*.

Stinnes, Hugo (1870–1924), German industrialist who built up a huge coalmining, iron and steel, and transport business, and later entered politics.

Stockton, Earl of. *See* **Macmillan, Harold**

Stoker, Bram (Abraham Stoker) (1847–1912), Irish author of the horror story *Dracula* and *Personal Reminiscences of Henry Irving*.

Stokes, Sir George Gabriel (1819–1903), Irish mathematician and physicist to whom is due the modern theory of viscous fluids and the discovery that rays beyond the violet end of the spectrum (the ultra-violet rays) produce fluorescence in certain substances.

Stopes, Marie Carmichael (1880–1958), English pioneer advocate of birth control. Her *Married Love* appeared in 1918, and she pioneered birth control clinics.

Stowe, Harriet Beecher (1811–96), American author of *Uncle Tom's Cabin* (1852), written to expose slavery.

Strachey, John St. Loe (1901–63), English Labour politician and writer. He held office under Attlee, 1945–51.

Stradivari, Antonio (1644–1737), Italian maker of violins, b. Cremona, first in his art.

Strafford, 1st Earl of (Thomas Wentworth) (1593–1641), English statesman. He supported Charles I with a "thorough" policy, both as president of the north and as lord deputy in Ireland, where he introduced flax. His efficiency made him a special target when parliament met, and he was impeached and executed.

Strauss, David Friedrich (1808–74), German theologian, whose *Life of Jesus* attempted to prove that the gospels are based on myths.

Strauss, family of Viennese musicians. **Johann Strauss** (1804–49), the elder, was a composer of dance music, who with Joseph Lanner established the Viennese waltz tradition. His son, **Johann Strauss** (1825–99), the younger, although not so good a violinist or conductor as his father, was the composer of over 400 waltzes, which include *The Blue Danube* and *Tales from the Vienna Woods*. Two of his brothers, **Josef Strauss** (1827–70) and **Eduard Strauss** (1835–1916) were also composers and conductors.

Strauss, Richard (1864–1949), German composer and conductor, the son of a horn player in the opera orchestra at Munich. He succeeded von Bülow as court musical director at Meiningen. His works include the operas *Salome*, *Elektra*, and *Der Rosenkavalier*, the symphonic poems *Don Juan*, *Till Eulenspiegel*, and *Don Quixote*, and many songs. *See* **Section E.**

Stravinsky, Igor (1882–1971), Russian composer and conductor, pupil of Rimsky-Korsakov. His ballets *The Fire Bird* (1910). *Petrushka*

(1911), representative of his early romantic style, and the revolutionary *The Rite of Spring*, which caused a furore in 1913, were written for the ballet impresario Diaghilev. He adopted a neo-classical style in later works, for example, in the ballets *Pulcinella* and *Apollo Musagetes* and the opera-oratorio *Oedipus Rex*. He brought new vigour and freedom to rhythm and younger composers have been much influenced by his music. He became a French citizen in 1934 and a U.S. citizen in 1945. *See* **Section E.**

Strindberg, Johan August (1840–1912), Swedish writer of intense creative energy. His work is subjective and reflects his personal conflicts. He married three times but never happily. He produced some 55 plays as well as novels, stories, poems, and critical essays. *Lucky Peter, Gustav Adolf, Till Damascus, The Father, Miss Julie* are some of his plays.

Suckling, Sir John (1609–42), English poet, author of *Why so pale and wan?* He invented cribbage.

Sudermann, Hermann (1857–1928), German writer of plays and novels, including *Frau Sorge* (translated as Dame Care).

Sulaiman the Magnificent (1494–1566), sultan of Turkey, conqueror, and patron of art and learning, who dominated the eastern Mediterranean but failed to capture Malta.

Sullivan, Sir Arthur Seymour (1842–1900), Irish composer, mainly known for the music he wrote for light operas with W. S. Gilbert as librettist, especially *The Pirates of Penzance, Patience, The Mikado, The Yeomen of the Guard* and *The Gondoliers*. He also wrote sacred music which was popular at the time. He and a friend discovered Schubert's lost *Rosamunde* music.

Sully, Maximilien de Béthune, Duc de (1560–1641), French statesman, finance minister to Henry IV. He also left *Memoirs*.

Sun Yat Sen (1867–1925), Chinese revolutionary, idealist and humanitarian. He graduated in medicine at Hong Kong, but after a rising failed in 1895 he lived abroad, planning further attempts, which succeeded in 1911 when the Manchus were overthrown and he became president. He soon resigned in favour of Yuan Shih-kai.

Sutherland, Graham Vivian (1903–80), British artist. He painted the 80th birthday portrait of Sir Winston Churchill for parliament, and designed the tapestry for Coventry cathedral. O.M. 1960.

Swan, Sir Joseph Wilson (1829–1914), British scientist who shares with Edison the invention of the incandescent electric lamp. He also invented a number of printing processes.

Swedenborg, Emanuel (1689–1772), Swedish author of *Arcana Coelestia, The Apocalypse Revealed, Four Preliminary Doctrines,* and *The True Christian Religion*. He claimed that his soul had been permitted to travel into hell, purgatory, and heaven. His works became the scriptures of the sect named Swedenborgians.

Sweelinck, Jan Pieterszoon (1562–1621), Dutch organist and composer of sacred music. In his fugues he made independent use of the pedals, and prepared the wày for Bach. *See* **Section E.**

Swift, Jonathan (1667–1745), English satirist, b. Dublin of English parents. He crossed to England in 1688 to become secretary to Sir William Temple, and took Anglican orders, but did not obtain promotion. His *Tale of a Tub* and *The Battle of the Books* appeared in 1704. At first active in Whig politics, he became Tory in 1710, writing powerful tracts such as *Conduct of the Allies* (1711). In 1714 he retired to Ireland as Dean of St. Patrick's. His devoted women friends followed him—Hester Johnson (d. 1728), the Stella of his *Journal*, and Esther Vanhomrigh (d. 1723), the Vanessa of his poetry. Here he wrote his best work, including *Gulliver's Travels* (1726) and *The Drapier's Letters*.

Swinburne, Algernon Charles (1837–1909), English poet and critic. He first won attention with a play, *Atalanta in Calydon*, in 1865, followed by *Poems and Ballads*. Later followed *Songs before Sunrise, Bothwell,* and *Mary Stuart*. His criticism includes an essay on Blake.

Swithin, St. (d. 862), English saint, bishop of Winchester. Violent rain for 40 days fell in 971 when his body was to be removed to the

new cathedral; hence the superstition as to rain on 15 July.

Syme, Sir Ronald (1903–89), Camden Professor of Ancient History at Oxford, 1949–70; an authority on Tacitus. O.M. 1976.

Symonds, John Addington (1840–93), English author who wrote on the Italian Renaissance.

Synge, John Millington (1871–1909), Irish poet and playwright, author of *Riders to the Sea* and *The Playboy of the Western World*. He was a director of the Abbey Theatre.

T

Tacitus, Gaius Cornelius (*c.* 55–120), Roman historian. His chief works are a life of his father-in-law Agricola, and his *Histories* and *Annals*.

Tagore, Sir Rabindranath (1861–1941), Indian poet and philosopher who tried to blend east and west. His works include the play *Chitra*. Nobel prize 1913 (first Asian recipient).

Talbot, William Henry Fox (1800–77), English pioneer of photography which he developed independently of Daguerre. He also deciphered the cuneiform inscriptions at Nineveh.

Talleyrand-Périgord, Charles Maurice de (1754–1838), French politician and diplomat, led a mission to England in 1792 and was foreign minister from 1797 until 1807. He represented France at the Congress of Vienna.

Tallis, Thomas (*c.* 1510–85), English musician, with Byrd joint organist to the chapel royal under Elizabeth. He composed some of the finest of our church music.

Tamerlane (Timur the Lame) (1336–1405), Mongol conqueror. Ruler of Samarkand, he conquered Iran, Transcaucasia, Iraq, Armenia, and Georgia, and invaded India and Syria. He defeated the Turks at Angora, but died marching towards China. A ruthless conqueror, he was also a patron of literature and the arts. The line of rulers descended from him are the Timurids. He is the subject of a play by Marlowe.

Tarquinius: two kings of Rome came from this Etruscan family; **Lucius the Elder** (d. 578 B.C.); and **Lucius Superbus,** or the proud, (d. 510 B.C.) whose tyranny provoked a successful rising and brought an end to the monarchy.

Tartini, Giuseppe (1692–1770), Italian violinist, who wrote *Trillo del Diavolo*. He discovered the "third sound" resulting from two notes sounded together, a scientific explanation of which was later given by Helmholtz.

Tasman, Abel Janszoon (1603–59), Dutch navigator despatched by Van Diemen. He discovered Tasmania or Van Diemen's Land, and New Zealand, in 1642.

Tasso, Torquato (1544–95), Italian epic poet, b. Sorrento, author of *Gerusalemme Liberata*. He also wrote plays, *Aminta* and *Torrismondo*.

Tawney, Richard Henry (1880–1962), British historian, b. Calcutta, pioneer of adult education, and leader of socialist thought—the first critic of the affluent society. His works include *The Acquisitive Society, Equality, Religion and the Rise of Capitalism*.

Taylor, Sir Geoffrey Ingram (1886–1975), British scientist, noted for his work on aerodynamics, hydrodynamics, and the structure of metals. O.M. 1969.

Taylor, Jeremy (1613–67), English divine, b. Cambridge, author of many religious works, of which the chief are *Holy Living* and *Holy Dying*.

Tchaikovsky, Peter Ilyich (1840–93), Russian composer. His music is melodious and emotional and he excelled in several branches of composition. Among his works are the operas *Eugene Onegin* and *The Queen of Spades* (both from stories by Pushkin), symphonies, including the *Little Russian* and the *Pathétique*, ballets, including *Swan Lake, The Sleeping Beauty,* and *The Nutcracker*, the fantasies *Romeo and Juliet,* and *Francesca da Rimini*, the piano concerto in B flat minor, the violin concerto in D, and numerous songs. *See* **Section E.**

Tedder, 1st Baron (Arthur William Tedder) (1890–1967), British air marshal. From 1940 he reorganised the Middle East Air Force and later became deputy supreme commander under

Eisenhower for the invasion of Europe. He wrote an autobiography.

Teilhard de Chardin, Pierre (1881–1955), French palæontologist and religious philosopher. He went on palæontological expeditions in Asia, but his research did not conform to Jesuit orthodoxy, and his main works were published posthumously, *The Phenomenon of Man* and *Le Milieu Divin.*

Telemann, Georg Philipp (1681–1767), German composer, b. Magdeburg. His vitality and originality of form are appreciated today after a long period of neglect.

Telford, Thomas (1757–1834), Scottish engineer, originally a stonemason. He built bridges (two over the Severn and the Menai suspension bridge), canals (the Ellesmere and Caledonian canals), roads, and docks.

Tell, William, legendary Swiss patriot, reputedly required by the Austrian governor Gessler to shoot an apple from his son's head, and the subject of a play by Schiller. The story is late, but the Swiss confederation did first arise in the 14th cent. with Schwyz, Uri, and Unterwalden.

Temple, Frederick (1821–1902), English divine. He was headmaster of Rugby, 1857–69, and archbishop of Canterbury, 1897–1902.

Temple, William (1881–1944), English ecclesiastic, son of above, was a leading moral force in social matters and a worker for ecumenism. He was headmaster of Repton, 1910–14, and became archbishop of Canterbury in 1942.

Temple, Sir William (1628–99), English diplomat and writer, was instrumental in bringing about the marriage of Princess Mary with William of Orange. Swift was his secretary.

Templewood, 1st Viscount (Samuel John Gurney Hoare) (1880–1959), British Conservative politician. He piloted the India Act through the Commons while secretary for India, 1931–5; and as foreign secretary he negotiated an abortive pact with Laval.

Teniers, David, the elder (1582–1649), and **the younger** (1610–94), Flemish painters of rural life and landscape. The elder lived at Antwerp and the younger at Brussels.

Tenniel, Sir John (1820–1914), English book illustrator, especially for *Alice in Wonderland* and *Punch.*

Tennyson, 1st Baron (Alfred Tennyson) (1809–92), English poet-laureate, b. Somersby, Lincs. A master of language, his publications extended over 60 years, mirroring much of his age. *In Memoriam* reflects his grief for his friend Arthur Hallam. Apart from his lyrics, his longer works include *The Princess, Maud, Idylls of the King*, and *Enoch Arden.* Interest in his work is returning.

Terence, Publius Terentius Afer (c. 184–159 B.C.), a Latin poet and dramatist, an African (Berber), who rose from the position of a slave.

Teresa, St. (1515–82), influential Spanish religious reformer and writer, b. Avila, a woman of boundless energy and spiritual strength. She entered the Carmelite order about 1534, established a reformed order in 1562 (St. Joseph's, Avila), and also founded, with the help of St. John of the Cross, houses for friars. Her writings which rank high in mystical literature include *The Way of Perfection* and *The Interior Castle.*

Terry, Ellen Alice (Mrs. James Carew) (1848–1928), English actress, especially in Shakespearean parts with Sir Henry Irving, and in the plays of her friend Bernard Shaw.

Tertullian Quintus (c. 160–220), Carthaginian theologian whose works, especially *Apologeticum*, have profoundly influenced Christian thought.

Tesla, Nikola (1856–1943), Yugoslav physicist and inventor; went to America 1883; pioneer in high-tension electricity.

Tettrazzini, Luisa (1871–1940), Italian soprano, especially successful in *Lucia di Lammermoor.*

Tetzel, John (c. 1465–1519), German Dominican preacher, whose sale of indulgences for St. Peter's building fund provoked Luther.

Thackeray, William Makepeace (1811–63), English novelist, b. Calcutta, author of *Vanity Fair, Pendennis, Esmond, The Newcomes, The Virginians, Philip*, and *Lovel the Widower.* He edited the *Cornhill Magazine* from the first number in 1860, his most notable contributions being *Roundabout Papers.* He also wrote *Yellow-*

plush Papers, The Book of Snobs, and *The Four Georges* (lectures given in the United States).

Thales of Miletus (c. 624–565 B.C.), earliest of the Greek scientists, he created a sensation by his prediction of an eclipse of the sun, which was visible at Miletus in 585 B.C. He looked upon water as the basis of all material things, and in his mathematical work was the first to enunciate natural laws. *See also* **God and Man, Section J.**

Thant, Sithu U (1909–74), Burmese diplomat; secretary-general of the U.N. 1962–1972.

Thatcher, Margaret Hilda (b. 1925), leader of the Conservative Party 1975– ; prime minister, 1979– ; first woman to lead a western democracy; secured landslide victory, June 1983; M.P. (Finchley), 1959– . Historic third successive election victory, June 1987. On 3 Jan 1988 became longest serving P.M. since Asquith. By 1990 she faced increasing unpopularity. *See* **Section C, Part I.**

Themistocles (c. 523–458 B.C.), Athenian soldier and statesman. He fortified the harbour of Piraeus and created a navy, defeating the Persians at Salamis in 480 B.C. He prepared the way for later greatness, but fell from power and died in exile.

Theocritus (c. 310–250 B.C.), Greek poet, especially of pastoral subjects. His short poems came to be called *Idylls.*

Theodoric the Great (455–526), King of the East Goths, who conquered Italy. Himself an Arian, he practised toleration, and his long reign was peaceful and prosperous.

Theodosius the Great (346–95), Roman emperor of the East (the Empire being divided in 364). He was baptised as a Trinitarian, issuing edicts against the Arians, and after a judicial massacre at Thessalonica he did penance to (St.) Ambrose.

Theophrastus (c. 372–287 B.C.), Greek philosopher, who succeeded Aristotle as teacher at Athens and inherited his library. He is best known for his botanical works and his *Characters* (moral studies).

Thibaud, Jacques (1880–1953), French violinist, killed in an air crash.

Thierry, Augustin (1795–1856), French historian, known for his *History of the Norman Conquest.*

Thiers, Louis Adolphe (1797–1877), French statesman and historian. After a varied political career, he became president in 1871, helping to revive France after defeat. He wrote a history of the Revolution.

Thomas, Dylan (1914–53), Welsh poet, whose highly individual *Eighteen Poems* (1934) brought him instant recognition. There followed *Twenty-five Poems* and *Deaths and Entrances. Under Milk Wood*, a play for voices, has more general appeal.

Thompson, Sir D'Arcy Wentworth (1860–1948), Scottish zoologist whose *On Growth and Form* (1917), written in lucid and elegant style, has influenced biological science.

Thomson, Sir George Paget (1892–1975), English physicist, son of Sir J. J. Thomson; author of *The Atom, Theory and Practice of Electron Diffraction, The Inspiration of Science.* Nobel prizewinner 1937.

Thomson, James (1700–48), Scottish poet who wrote *The Seasons* and *The Castle of Indolence.*

Thomson, James (1834–82), poet and essayist, b. near Glasgow, who wrote *The City Of Dreadful Night.*

Thomson, Sir Joseph John (1856–1940), English physicist and mathematician, leader of a group of researchers at the Cavendish laboratory, Cambridge. He established in 1897 that cathode-rays were moving particles whose speed and specific charge could be measured. He called them corpuscles but the name was changed to electrons. This work was followed up by the study of positive rays which led to the discovery of isotopes, the existence of which had earlier been suggested by Soddy. Nobel prizewinner 1906.

Thoreau, Henry David (1817–62), American essayist and nature-lover, who rebelled against society and lived for a time in a solitary hut. His chief work is *Walden.* He was a friend of Emerson.

Thorez, Maurice (1900–64), French communist leader from 1930 and especially after the second world war.

Thorndike, Dame Sybil (1882–1976), English actress. She made her début in 1904, and played in Greek tragedies, in the plays of Shakespeare and Shaw, and in Grand Guignol. Her husband was Sir Lewis Casson.

Thornycroft, Sir William Hamo (1850–1925), English sculptor, whose works include a statue of General Gordon in Trafalgar Square.

Thorpe, Sir Thomas Edward (1845–1925), English chemist who researched in inorganic chemistry and with his friend Arthur Rücker made a magnetic survey of the British Isles.

Thorwaldsen, Bertel (1770–1844), Danish sculptor whose works include the Cambridge statue of Byron.

Thucydides (c. 460–399 B.C.), Greek historian, especially of the Peloponnesian War in which he himself fought. He was not merely a chronicler, but saw the significance of events and tried to give an impartial account. The speeches attributed by him to leaders include the beautiful funeral oration of Pericles.

Tiberius, Claudius (42 B.C.–A.D. 37), Roman emperor who succeeded Augustus. His early reign was successful but his later years were marked by tragedy and perhaps insanity. He is the Tiberius of Luke 3.1.

Tillett, Benjamin (1860–1943), English trade-union leader, especially of a dockers' strike in 1889 and a transport-workers' strike in 1911.

Tillotson, John (1630–94), English divine, a noted preacher who became archbishop of Canterbury in 1691.

Tindal, Matthew (1655–1733), English deist, author of *Christianity as old as the Creation*.

Tintoretto (1518–94), Venetian painter whose aim it was to unite the colouring of Titian with the drawing of Michelangelo. His numerous paintings, mostly of religious subjects, were executed with great speed, some of them on enormous canvases. His *Origin of the Milky Way* is in the National Gallery. His name was Jacopo Robusti, and he was called Il Tintoretto (little dyer) after his father's trade.

Tippett, Sir Michael Kemp (b. 1905), English composer whose works include the operas *The Midsummer Marriage*, *King Priam*, and *Knot Garden*, and the song-cycles *Boyhood's End* and *The Heart's Assurance*. O.M. 1983. *See* **Section E.**

Titian (Tiziano Vecelli) (c. 1487–1576), Venetian painter. He studied under the Bellinis and was influenced by Giorgione, for example, in his frescoes at Padua. His mature style is one of dynamic composition and full colour, as in his *Bacchus and Ariadne* (National Gallery). Among his principal works are *Sacred and Profane Love* (Borghese Gallery, Rome), and some in the Prado, Madrid.

Tito (Josip Broz) (1892–1980), Yugoslav leader, b. Kumrovec. In 1941 he organised partisan forces against the Axis invaders, liberated his country, and carried through a communist revolution. In 1945 he became the first communist prime minister and in 1953 president. He successfully pursued an independent line for his country. Order of Lenin (1972).

Titus (A.D. 39–81), Roman emperor, son of Vespasian, brought the Jewish war to a close with the capture of Jerusalem. He completed the Colosseum.

Tizard, Sir Henry Thomas (1885–1959), English scientist and administrator. He was chairman of the Scientific Survey of Air Defence (later known as the Tizard Committee) that encouraged the birth of radar before the second world war and turned it into a successful defence weapon. He was chief scientific adviser to the government, 1947–52.

Tocqueville, Alexis, Comte de (1805–59), French liberal politician and historian, author of *Democracy in America*, still relevant reading.

Todd, 1st Baron (Alexander Robertus Todd) (b. 1907), Scottish biochemist, noted for his work on the structure of nucleic acids. Nobel prizewinner 1957; Pres. Royal Society 1975. Chancellor Univ. of Strathclyde. O.M. 1977.

Tolstoy, Leo Nikolayevich, Count (1828–1910), Russian writer and philosopher, b. Yasnaya Polyana. Of noble family, he entered the army and fought in the Crimean War. Beginning with simple, natural accounts of his early life (*Childhood* and *Boyhood*), he proceeded to articles on the war, and so eventually to perhaps his best work, the long novel *War and Peace*, followed by *Anna Karenina*. Increasingly pre-

occupied with social problems, he freed his serfs before this was done officially, and refused to take advantage of his wealth. His later works include *The Kreutzer Sonata* and *Resurrection*. By many he was regarded as a moral teacher.

Tooke, John Horne (1736–1812), English politician and pamphleteer, was a supporter of Wilkes and later of Pitt. He was tried for high treason, but was acquitted.

Torquemada, Tomas de (1420–98), first inquisitor-general of Spain.

Torricelli, Evangelista (1608–47), Italian physicist, pupil of Galileo. He invented the barometer and improved both microscope and telescope.

Toscanini, Arturo (1867–1957), Italian conductor, b. Parma. He had a remarkable musical memory, and was at the same time exacting and self-effacing. He spent the second world war in exile.

Toulouse-Lautrec, Henri de (1864–1901), French painter, whose pictures portray with stark realism certain aspects of Parisian life in the nineties, especially the *Moulin Rouge* series. Many are in the Musée Lautrec at Albi.

Tovey, Sir Donald Francis (1875–1940), English pianist and composer. His compositions include chamber music, a piano concerto, and an opera *The Bride of Dionysus*; and his writings *Essays in Musical Analysis*.

Toynbee, Arnold (1852–83), English historian and social reformer. The settlement Toynbee Hall was founded in his memory.

Toynbee, Arnold Joseph (1889–1975), nephew of above, English historian, known mainly for his 10-volume *A Study of History*, an analysis of many civilisations. He was for 30 years director of the Institute of International Affairs.

Traherne, Thomas (c. 1636–74), English religious poet, b. Hereford; author also of *Centuries of Meditations*.

Trajan (c. 53–117), Roman emperor, was a successful general and firm administrator. He was born in Spain.

Tree, Sir Herbert Beerbohm (1853–1917), English actor-manager of the Haymarket theatre until 1897 when he built His Majesty's theatre. Sir Max Beerbohm was his half-brother.

Trenchard, 1st Viscount (Hugh Montague Trenchard) (1873–1956), British air-marshal. He served with the Royal Flying Corps in the first world war and became the first air marshal of the R.A.F. He was largely responsible for the R.A.F. college at Cranwell and was also concerned in establishing Hendon police college.

Trent, 1st Baron (Jesse Boot) (1850–1931), British drug manufacturer, b. Nottingham. He built up the largest pharmaceutical retail trade in the world, and was a benefactor of Nottingham and its university.

Trevelyan, George Macaulay (1876–1962), English historian, known for his *History of England* and *English Social History*.

Trevelyan, Sir George Otto (1838–1928), English liberal politician, father of above. He wrote a life of his uncle Lord Macaulay.

Trevithick, Richard (1771–1833), English mining engineer and inventor, b. near Redruth, Cornwall. His most important invention was a high-pressure steam-engine (1801) and he is commonly acknowledged as the inventor of the steam locomotive for railways.

Trollope, Anthony (1815–82), English novelist. His early life was a struggle, the family being supported by his mother's writings. His own career was in the post office, but by strict industry he produced many novels especially portraying clerical life (the *Barchester* series) and political life (the *Phineas Finn* series).

Trotsky, Leo (Lev Davidovich Bronstein) (1879–1940), Russian revolutionary, b. of Jewish parents in the Ukraine, one of the leaders of the Bolshevik revolution. As commissar of foreign affairs under Lenin he led the Russian delegation at the Brest-Litovsk conference. He differed from Stalin on policy, believing in "permanent revolution," according to which socialism could not be achieved in Russia without revolutions elsewhere, and was dismissed from office in 1925 and expelled from the Communist party in 1927. In 1929 he took up exile in Mexico where he was assassinated.

Trudeau, Pierre Eliott (b. 1919), Liberal prime minister of Canada 1968–79, 1980–84.

Truman, Harry F. (1884–1972), U.S. President, 1945–53. He inherited the presidency on Roosevelt's death in 1945 when he took the decision to drop the first atom bomb, and he won the election of 1948. He intervened in Korea, dismissed General MacArthur, and aimed at raising standards in underdeveloped countries.

Tulsi Das (1532–1623), Indian poet whose master piece *Ram-Charit-Mānas* (popularly known as the *Ramayana* and based on the Sanskrit epic of Vālmiki) is venerated by all Hindus as the Bible is in the West.

Turenne, Henri de la Tour d'Auvergne, Vicomte de (1611–75), French commander who was successful in the Thirty Years' War.

Turgenev, Ivan Sergeyvich (1818–83), Russian novelist, friend of Gogol and Tolstoy, who spent part of his life in exile. His works include *Fathers and Children, Smoke,* and *Virgin Soil.*

Turner, Joseph Mallord William (1775–1851), English landscape painter, b. London, a barber's son. He entered the Royal Academy and was at first a topographical watercolourist. Later he turned to oil and became a master of light and colour, achieving magical effects, especially in depicting the reflection of light in water. His works include *Crossing the Brook, Dido building Carthage, The Fighting Temeraire, Rain, Steam and Speed.* He also made thousands of colour studies. He encountered violent criticism as his style became more abstract which led to Ruskin's passionate defence of him in *Modern Painters.* He bequeathed his work to the nation.

Tussaud, Marie (1761–1850), Swiss modeller in wax who learnt from her uncle in Paris, married a Frenchman, and later came to England where she set up a permanent exhibition.

Tutankhamen (d. *c.* 1340 B.C.), Egyptian pharaoh of the 18th dynasty, son-in-law of Akhenaten, whose tomb was discovered by Howard Carter in 1922, with the mummy and gold sarcophagus intact. He died when he was 18.

Tutu, Desmond Mpilo (b. 1931), South African churchman. Archbishop of Cape Town since 1986. Nobel Peace Prize, 1984. Outstanding opponent of apartheid.

Twain, Mark (Samuel Langhorne Clemens) (1835–1910), American humorist. His *Innocents Abroad* was the result of a trip to Europe. His works include *A Tramp Abroad, Tom Sawyer, Huckleberry Finn,* and *Pudd'nhead Wilson.*

Tweedsmuir, 1st Baron (John Buchan) (1875–1940), Scottish author of biographies, historical novels, and adventure stories, including *Montrose* and *Thirty-nine Steps.* He was governor-general of Canada 1935–40.

Tyler, Wat (d. 1381), English peasant leader. He was chosen leader of the Peasants' Revolt of 1381 (due to various causes), and parleyed at Smithfield with the young king Richard II, but was killed.

Tyndale, William (*c.* 1494–1536), English religious reformer, translator of the Bible. He had to go abroad, where he visited Luther and his New Testament was printed at Worms. When copies entered England they were suppressed by the bishops (1526). His Pentateuch was printed at Antwerp, but he did not complete the Old Testament. He was betrayed, arrested, and executed. Unlike Wyclif, who worked from Latin texts, he translated mainly from the original Hebrew and Greek and his work was later to become the basis of the Authorised Version of the Bible.

Tyndall, John (1829–93), Irish physicist whose wide interests led him to research on heat, light, and sound, and on bacteria-free air and sterilisation. He discovered why the sky is blue (Tyndall effect) and pioneered popular scientific writing, *e.g., Heat as a Mode of Motion.*

U

Unamuno, Miguel de (1864–1936), Spanish philosopher, poet, essayist, and novelist, author of *El Sentimiento Trágico de la Vida* (The Tragic Sense of Life).

Ulanova, Galina (b. 1910), Russian ballerina, who made her début in 1928.

Undset, Sigrid (1882–1949), Norwegian novelist, daughter of an antiquary, author of *Jenny, Kristin Lavransdatter,* and *Olav Audunsson.* Nobel prizewinner 1928.

Unwin, Sir Raymond (1863–1940), English architect of the first garden city at Letchworth.

Ursula, St., said in late legend to have been killed by Huns at Cologne with many companions while on pilgrimage. It took rise from a 4th cent. inscription which simply referred to virgin martyrs.

Usher or **Ussher, James** (1581–1656), Irish divine who in 1625 became archbishop of Armagh, and whose writings include a long-accepted chronology, which placed the creation at 4004 B.C.

V

Valentine, St., was a christian martyr of the reign of the emperor Claudius II (d. A.D. 270). The custom of sending valentines may be connected with the pagan festival of Lupercalia.

Valéry, Paul (1871–1945), French poet and essayist, strongly influenced by the symbolist leader, Mallarmé. His poems include *La jeune Parque, Charmes,* and *Le cimetière marin.*

Vanbrugh, Sir John (1664–1726), English architect and playwright. His buildings include Blenheim Palace and his plays *The Provok'd Wife.*

Vancouver, George (1758–98), British navigator who served under Captain Cook, also doing survey work, and who sailed round Vancouver island.

Vanderbilt, Cornelius (1794–1877), American merchant and railway speculator who amassed a fortune and founded a university at Nashville. His son, **William Henry Vanderbilt** (1821–85), inherited and added to it.

Van Dyck, Sir Anthony (1599–1641), Flemish painter, b. Antwerp. He studied under Rubens, travelled in Italy, and then settled in England with an annuity from Charles I. He excelled in portraits, especially of Charles I and Henrietta Maria, and of their court.

Vane, Sir Henry (1613–62), English parliamentary leader during the civil war period, though not involved in the execution of Charles I. He was executed in 1662.

Van Gogh, Vincent (1853–90), Dutch painter of some of the most colourful pictures ever created. With passionate intensity of feeling he painted without pause whatever he found around him—landscapes, still life, portraits; his was a truly personal art. His life was one of pain, sorrow, and often despair, and in the end he committed suicide.

Vauban, Sebastien de Prestre de (1633–1707), French military engineer, whose skill in siege works (*e.g.,* at Maestricht 1673) was a factor in the expansive wars of Louis XIV. He protected France with fortresses and also invented the socket bayonet.

Vaughan Williams, Ralph (1872–1958), English composer, b. Gloucestershire. After Charterhouse and Cambridge he studied music in Berlin under Max Bruch and, later in Paris, under Ravel. He wrote nine symphonies besides a number of choral and orchestral works, operas (including *Hugh the Drover, Riders to the Sea*), ballets, chamber music, and songs. He showed great interest in folk tunes. *See* Section E.

Velasquez, Diego (*c.* 1460–1524), Spanish conquistador, first governor of Cuba.

Velasquez, Diego Rodriguez de Silva y (1599–1660), Spanish painter, b. Seville, especially of portraits at the court of Philip IV, and also of classical and historical subjects. He made two visits to Italy (1629–31, 1649–51), studying the Venetian painters, especially Titian, which hastened the development of his style. Among his masterpieces are *The Maids of Honour, The Tapestry Weavers* (both in the Prado), the Rokeby Venus and a portrait of Philip IV (both in the National Gallery), the landscape views from the Villa Medici (Prado) and *Juan de Pareja* (sold in London in 1970 for £2·25 million).

Venizelos, Eleutherios (1864–1936), Greek statesman, b. Crete. He became prime minister in 1910 and held this office intermittently. He promoted the Balkan League (1912), forced the king's abdication (1917), and brought Greece into the war on the Allied side, securing territorial concessions at the peace conference, but his expansionist policy in Turkish Asia failed.

Verdi, Giuseppe (1813–1901), Italian composer, b. near Busseto in the province of Parma. His early works include *Nabucco*, *Ernani*, *I Due Foscari*, and *Macbeth*; a middle period is represented by *Rigoletto*, *Il Trovatore*, *La Traviata*, *Un Ballo in Maschera*, and *Don Carlos*; to the last period of his life belong *Aida*, *Otello*, and *Falstaff* (produced when he was 80). See **Section E.**

Verlaine, Paul (1844–96), French poet, one of the first of the symbolists, also known for his memoirs and confessions. His works include *Poèmes saturniens*, *Fêtes galantes*, *Sagesse*, and *Romances sans paroles*. He was imprisoned for two years in Belgium for shooting and wounding his friend Rimbaud. He died in poverty in Paris.

Vermeer, Jan (1632–75), Dutch painter, b. Delft. His main paintings are of domestic interiors, which he makes into works of art, as in *Lady at the Virginals* (National Gallery). His reputation has grown during the last century.

Verne, Jules (1828–1905), French writer of science fiction, including *Five Weeks in a Balloon*, *Twenty Thousand Leagues Under the Sea*, *Round the World in Eighty Days*.

Vernier, Pierre (1580–1637), French inventor of the small sliding scale which enables readings on a graduated scale to be taken to a fraction of a division.

Veronese, Paolo (1528–88), Italian painter of the Venetian school, whose works include *Marriage Feast at Cana in Galilee*, *The Feast in the House of Simon*, and *The Presentation of the Family of Darius to Alexander*, *His Adoration of the Magi* is in the National Gallery.

Veronica, St., legendary woman who was said to hand her kerchief to Christ on the way to Calvary, to wipe his brow, and his impression was left on the kerchief. In its present form her legend dates from the 14th cent.

Verwoerd, Hendrik Frensch (1901–66), South African politician, b. Amsterdam, exponent of the policy of apartheid; prime minister 1958–66. He was assassinated.

Vespasian, Titus Flavius (A.D. 9–79), Roman emperor. He was sent by Nero to put down the Jews and was proclaimed by the legions. He began the Colosseum.

Vespucci, Amerigo (1451–1512), Florentine explorer, naturalised in Spain, contractor at Seville for Columbus. He later explored Venezuela. The use of his name for the continent arose through a mistake.

Vico, Giambattista (1688–1744), Italian philosopher of history and of culture, b. Naples. His ideas were developed in his *Scienza nuova* (science of history) but it was not until our own day that his originality as a thinker was fully recognised.

Victor Emmanuel II (1820–78), first king of Italy. King of Sardinia, he was proclaimed king of Italy in 1861 after the Austrians had been defeated and Garibaldi had succeeded in the south. Rome was added in 1870.

Victoria (1819–1901), Queen of the United Kingdom of Gt. Britain and Ireland and Empress of India, was granddaughter of George III and succeeded an uncle in 1837. In 1840 she married Prince Albert of Saxe-Coburg-Gotha, who died in 1861. Conscientious, hard-working, and of strict moral standards, she had by the end of a long life (jubilees 1887 and 1897) won the affection and respect of her subjects in a unique degree. Her reign saw industrial expansion, growing humanitarianism, literary output, and in the main prolonged peace; and by its close the British empire and British world power had reached their highest point.

Villeneuve, Pierre de (1763–1806), French admiral defeated by Nelson at Trafalgar and captured along with his ship, the *Bucentaure*.

Villon, François (1431–?1463), French poet, b. Paris, who lived at a turbulent time at the close of the Hundred Years' War. After fatally stabbing a man in 1455 he joined the *Conquillards*, a criminal organisation. They had a secret language (the *jargon*) and it was for them that he composed his ballads. His extant works consist of the *Petit Testament* (1456),

originally called *Le Lais*, and the *Grand Testament* (1461), masterpieces of mediaeval verse.

Virgil (Publius Vergilius Maro) (70–19 B.C.), Roman epic poet, b. at Andes near Mantua, he went to Rome to obtain redress for the military confiscation of his farm. He was patronised by Maecenas, and wrote his pastoral *Eclogues*, followed by his *Georgics*. His best-known work, the *Aeneid*, deals with the wanderings of Aeneas after the fall of Troy till his establishment of a kingdom in Italy.

Vivaldi, Antonio (c. 1675–1743), Venetian composer, violin master at the Ospedale della Pieta. His output of orchestral works was prolific and Bach arranged some of his violin pieces for the harpsichord. See **Section E.**

Volta, Alessandro (1745–1827), Italian physicist of Pavia, who, working on the results of Galvani, invented the voltaic pile, the first instrument for producing an electric current. It provided a new means for the decomposition of certain substances. His name was given to the volt, the unit of electrical potential difference.

Voltaire (François Marie Arouet) (1694–1778), French philosopher and writer. His first essays offended the authorities, and he spent the years 1726–9 in England, where he wrote some of his dramas. Returning to France, he published his *Philosophical Letters*, which aroused the enmity of the priesthood. At this juncture, the Marquise du Châtelet offered him the asylum of her castle of Cirey, and for the next 15 years he made this his home, writing there his *Discourses of Man*, *Essay on the Morals and Spirit of Nations*, *Age of Louis XIV*, etc. The marquise was a mathematician and taught him some science, thus helping him in his interpretation of Newton's *Principia*. To Voltaire we owe the story of the falling apple, also the dictum that Admiral Byng was shot "pour encourager les autres." In challenging accepted beliefs and traditions he prepared the way for the French revolution.

Vondel, Joost van don (1587–1679), Dutch poet who lived at Amsterdam. Most of his dramas are on biblical subjects, and the two most famous are *Jephtha* and *Lucifer*.

Voroshilov, Klimentiv Efremovich (1881–1969), Soviet general who commanded the Leningrad defences in 1941. U.S.S.R. president, 1953–60.

Vyshinsky, Andrei Yanuarievich (1883–1954), Soviet jurist and diplomat; conducted the prosecution of the Moscow treason trials, 1936–8.

W

Wade, George (1673–1748), English general and military engineer who, after the rising of 1715, pacified the Scottish highlands, constructing military roads and bridges. In the 1745 rising Prince Charles' forces evaded him.

Wagner, Richard (1813–83), German composer, b. Leipzig. He achieved a new type of musical expression in his operas by the complete union of music and drama. He made use of the *Leitmotif* and was his own librettist. His originality and modernism aroused a good deal of opposition, and he was exiled for some years. But he was supported by loyal friends, including Liszt, the young King Ludwig of Bavaria, and the philosopher Nietzsche. He began the music of the *Ring des Nibelungen* in 1853, but it was not until 1876 that the whole of the drama (Rheingold, Valkyrie, Siegfried, Götterdämmerung) was performed at Bayreuth under the conductor Hans Richter. Other operas are *The Flying Dutchman*, *Rienzi*, *Tannhäuser*, *Lohengrin*, *Tristan und Isolde*, *Die Meistersinger von Nürnberg*, and *Parsifal*, a religious drama. He married Liszt's daughter Cosima.

Waldheim, Kurt (b. 1918), Austrian diplomat; succeeded U Thant as secretary-general of the United Nations. Held office, 1972–81. Elected President of Austria, 1986, amid controversy over his record in the Second World War.

Walesa, Lech (b. 1943), Polish trade unionist. Shipyard worker in Gdansk. Leader of *Solidarity*. Awarded 1983 Nobel Peace Prize.

Waley, Arthur (1889–1966), English orientalist, known for his translations of Chinese and Japanese poetry and prose, being the first to bring the literature of those countries to the western world.

Walker, George (1618–90), hero of the siege of Londonderry in 1688, who kept the besiegers at bay for 105 days.

Wallace, Alfred Russel (1823–1913), British naturalist, b. Usk, Monmouth, joint author with Darwin of the theory of natural selection. In 1858, while down with illness in the Moluccas, he sent a draft of his theory to Darwin in England who was amazed to find that it closely agreed with his own theory of evolution which he was on the point of publishing. The result was a reading of a joint paper to the Linnean Society.

Wallace, Edgar (1875–1932), English novelist and playwright, known for his detective thrillers.

Wallace, Sir Richard (1818–90), English art collector and philanthropist. His adopted son's wife bequeathed his collection to the nation (Wallace Collection, Manchester Square, London).

Wallace, Sir William (c. 1274–1305), Scottish patriot. He withstood Edward I, at first successfully, but was defeated at Falkirk and executed.

Wallenstein, Albrecht von (1583–1634), German soldier and statesman during the Thirty Years War. An able administrator of his own estates, he sought the unity of Germany, but was distrusted and eventually assassinated.

Waller, Edmund (1606–87), English poet of polished simplicity, author of *Go, lovely rose*. He was able to agree with both parliamentarians and royalists.

Wallis, Sir Barnes Neville (1887–1979), British scientist and inventor whose many designs include the R100 airship, the Wellington bomber, the swing-wing aircraft, and the "bouncing bomb" that breached the Ruhr dams in 1943.

Walpole, Horace, 4th Earl of Orford (1717–97), younger son of Sir Robert Walpole, English writer, chiefly remembered for his *Letters*, his *Castle of Otranto*, and his "Gothic" house at Strawberry Hill.

Walpole, Sir Hugh Seymour (1884–1941), English novelist, b. New Zealand. His works include *Fortitude*, *The Dark Forest*, and *The Herries Chronicle*.

Walpole, Sir Robert, 1st Earl of Orford (1676–1745), English Whig statesman, who came to office soon after the Hanoverian succession and is considered the first prime minister—a good finance minister, a peace minister, and a "house of commons man."

Walter, Bruno (1876–1962), German-American conductor, especially of Haydn, Mozart, and Mahler.

Walter, John (1776–1847), English newspaper editor. Under him *The Times*, founded by his father **John Walter** (1739–1812), attained a leading position.

Walton, Izaak (1593–1683), English writer, especially remembered for *The Compleat Angler*. He also wrote biographies of Donne, Hooker, and George Herbert.

Walton, Sir William Turner (1902–83), English composer, whose works include concertos for string instruments, two symphonies, two coronation marches, *Façade* (setting to Edith Sitwell's poem), and an oratorio, *Belshazzar's Feast*. O.M. 1967.

Warbeck, Perkin (1474–99), Flemish impostor, b. Tournai, who claimed to be the younger son of Edward IV with French and Scottish backing, but failed and was executed.

Warwick, Earl of (Richard Neville) (c. 1428–71), "the kingmaker." At first on the Yorkist side in the Wars of the Roses, he proclaimed Edward IV king; but later changed sides and restored the Lancastrian Henry VI. He was killed at Barnet.

Washington, Booker Taliaferro (1858–1915), American Negro educationist, author of *Up from Slavery*. He became principal of Tuskegee Institute, Alabama.

Washington, George (1732–99), first U.S. president. B. in Virginia, of a family which originated from Northamptonshire, he served against the French in the Seven Years War. When the dispute between the British government and the Americans over taxation came to a head, he proved a successful general, and Cornwallis's surrender to him at Yorktown in 1781 virtually ended the war. In 1787 he presided over the Philadelphia convention which formulated the constitution, and was president 1789–97.

Watson, John Broadus (1878–1958), American psychologist, an exponent of behaviourism. *See* **Behaviourism, Section J.**

Watson-Watt, Sir Robert (1892–1973), Scottish physicist, who played a major part in the development of radar.

Watt, James (1736–1819), Scottish engineer and inventor, b. Greenock. He made important improvements to Newcomen's steam-engine by inventing a separate condenser (applying Black's discoveries (1761–4) on latent heat) and other devices based on scientific knowledge of the properties of steam. He was given support by Matthew Boulton, a capitalist, and settled down in Birmingham with him. He defined one horse-power as the rate at which work is done when 33,000 lb are raised one foot in one minute. He also constructed a press for copying manuscripts. The watt as a unit of power is named after him.

Watteau, Jean Antoine (1684–1721), French painter. He painted pastoral idylls in court dress. His works include *Embarquement pour Cythère* in the Louvre.

Watts, Isaac (1674–1748), English hymn-writer, author of *O God, our help in ages past*.

Watts-Dunton, Walter Theodore (1836–1914), English poet and critic, friend of Swinburne whom he looked after until his death in 1909.

Waugh, Evelyn (1902–66), English satirical writer, author of *Vile Bodies, The Loved One, Brideshead Revisited, Life of Edmund Campion, The Ordeal of Gilbert Pinfold*, and an autobiography, *A Little Learning*.

Wavell, 1st Earl (Archibald Percival Wavell) (1883–1950), British general. He served in the first great war on Allenby's staff and in the second he commanded in the Middle East 1939–41, defeating the Italians; and in India 1941–3. He was viceroy of India 1943–7.

Webb, Matthew (1848–83), English swimmer, the first to swim the English Channel (1875).

Webb, Sidney James, Baron Passfield (1859–1947), and his wife **Beatrice**, *née* Potter (1858–1943), English social reformers and historians. They combined careful investigation of social problems (their books include *History of Trade Unionism* and *English Local Government*) with work for the future; they were members of the Fabian Society, launched the *New Statesman*, and helped to set up the London School of Economics. He held office in Labour governments.

Weber, Carl Maria Friedrich Ernst von (1786–1826), German composer, who laid the foundation of German romantic opera. His reputation rests principally on his three operas, *Der Freischütz, Euryanthe*, and *Oberon*. He was also an able pianist, conductor, and musical director. *See* **Section E.**

Webster, Daniel (1782–1852), American statesman and orator. He held office more than once and negotiated the Ashburton Treaty which settled the Maine-Canada boundary.

Webster, Noah (1758–1843), American lexicographer, who published an *American dictionary of the English language*.

Wedgwood, Dame Cicely Veronica (b. 1910) English historian, author of *William the Silent, Thomas Wentworth, The Thirty Years' War, The King's Peace, The Trial of Charles I*; a member of the Staffordshire pottery family. O.M. 1969.

Wedgwood, Josiah (1730–95), English potter, who at his Etruria works near Hanley produced from a new ware (patented 1763) pottery to classical designs by Flaxman, and gave pottery a new impetus.

Weill, Kurt (1900–50), German composer of satirical, surrealist operas, including *Die Dreigroschenoper* and *Mahagonny* (librettist Brecht). His wife, the Venetian actress Lotte Lenya (d. 1981) will be remembered for her singing of the Brecht songs and the interpretation of her husband's works. They left Europe for the United States in 1935.

Weingartner, Felix (1863–1942), Austrian conductor, also a composer and writer of a text book on conducting.

Weismann, August (1834–1914), German biologist. He worked on the question of individual variability in evolution, stressing the continuity of

B 64

the germ plasm and rejecting the idea of inheritance of acquired characteristics.

Weizmann, Chaim (1874–1952), Israeli leader, b. Pinsk. He came to England in 1903 and taught biochemistry at Manchester. He helped to secure the Balfour Declaration (1917), promising a Jewish national home, and was for many years president of the Zionists. In 1948 he became first president of Israel.

Wellesley, Marquess (Richard Colley Wellesley) (1760–1842), British administrator. He was a successful governor-general of India, and was brother of the Duke of Wellington.

Wellington, 1st Duke of (Arthur Wellesley) (1769–1852), British general. B. in Ireland, he joined the army and gained experience in India. In the Peninsular War he successfully wore down and drove out the invading French. When Napoleon escaped from Elba, Wellington defeated him at Waterloo. Thereafter he took some part in politics as a Tory, but in the last resort was capable of accepting change.

Wells, Herbert George (1866–1946), English author. B. London, he was at first a teacher. He believed in progress through science, and became one of the most influential writers of his time. His long series of books includes romances of the Jules Verne variety (*The Time Machine*, *The Island of Dr. Moreau*, *The Invisible Man*), sociological autobiography (*Love and Mr. Lewisham*, *Kipps*, *Tono-Bungay*, *The History of Mr. Polly*, *Mr. Britling Sees it Through*), and popular education (*Outline of History*, *The Science of Life*, *The Work*, *Wealth and Happiness of Mankind*, *The Shape of Things to Come*, *The Fate of Homo Sapiens*). He was an early and successful educator of the common man. He was also a founder member of the Fabian Society.

Wesley, Charles (1707–88), English hymnwriter. He was the companion of his brother John, and wrote over 5,500 hymns, including *Love divine* and *Jesu, lover of my soul*.

Wesley, John (1703–91), English evangelist and founder of Methodism (at first a nickname applied to friends of himself and his brother), b. at Epworth. After a trip to Georgia and after encountering Moravian influence, he began to teach on tour, covering in over 50 years more than 200,000 miles and preaching over 40,000 sermons. He made religion a live force to many ignorant folk of humble station who could only be reached by a new and direct challenge. He made a feature of the Sunday school and increased the use of music (the brothers' first hymnbook appeared in 1739). He did not plan separation from the Anglican church, though it was implicit in his ordination of a missionary, and it took place after his death. *See also* **Methodism, Section J.**

Westermarck, Edward Alexander (1862–1939), Finnish sociologist. His works include *History of Human Marriage*, *Origin and Development of the Moral Ideas*, and *The Oedipus Complex*.

Westinghouse, George (1846–1914), American engineer who invented an air-brake for railways (1868) called by his name, and pioneered the use of high tension alternating current for the transmission of electric power.

Westmacott, Sir Richard (1775–1856), English sculptor of Achilles in Hyde Park.

Wharton, Edith (1862–1937), American novelist and friend of Henry James. Her works include *House of Mirth* and *Custom of the Country*.

Whately, Richard (1787–1863), English archbishop of Dublin. He wrote treatises on *Rhetoric* and *Logic*.

Wheatstone, Sir Charles (1802–75), English physicist, one of the first to recognise Ohm's law. In 1837 he (with W. F. Cooke) patented an electric telegraph. He also introduced the microphone.

Wheeler, Sir Charles (1892–1974), English sculptor, especially on buildings. His autobiography is *High Relief*. P.R.A., 1956–66.

Whistler, James Abbott McNeill (1834–1903), American artist. B. at Lowell, he studied in Paris and settled in England. He reacted against the conventions of his day, and Ruskin's uncomprehending criticism of his work resulted in a lawsuit. Among his main works are studies of the Thames, and a portrait of his mother, now in the Louvre.

White, Sir George Stuart (1835–1912), British general who defended Ladysmith in the South African War.

White, Patrick (b. 1912), Australian novelist whose books include *The Aunt's Story*, *Riders in the Chariot*, *The Solid Mandala* and *The Eye of the Storm*. Nobel prize 1973.

Whitefield, George (1714–70), English evangelist, b. Gloucester. He was at first associated with the Wesleys, but differed from them on predestination. His supporters built him a "Tabernacle" in London, and he had other chapels elsewhere, but founded no lasting sect.

Whitgift, John (1530–1604), archbishop of Canterbury in the time of Elizabeth I (from 1583). His policy helped to clarify and strengthen the Anglican church.

Whitman, Walt (1819–92), American poet, b. Long Island. He led a wandering life and did hospital work in the Civil War. He aimed at forming a new and free American outlook. His works include *Leaves of Grass*, *Drum Taps*, and *Democratic Vistas*.

Whittier, John Greenleaf (1807–92), American Quaker poet, b. Haverhill, Mass. He wrote against slavery (*Justice and Expediency*), turning to poetry after the Civil War, especially remembered for *Snow-bound*.

Whittington, Richard (c. 1358–1423), English merchant. Son of a Gloucestershire knight, he became a London mercer and was mayor of London 1398, 1406, 1419. The cat legend is part of European folklore.

Whittle, Sir Frank (b. 1907), pioneer in the field of jet propulsion. The first flights of Gloster jet propelled aeroplanes with Whittle engines took place in May 1941. O.M. (1986).

Whymper, Edward (1840–1911), English woodengraver and mountaineer. He was the first to climb the Matterhorn.

Widgery, Baron (John Passmore Widgery) (1911–81), Lord Chief Justice of England 1971–80.

Wilberforce, William (1759–1833), English philanthropist, b. Hull. He was the parliamentary leader of the campaign against the slave trade, abolished in 1807. He then worked against slavery itself, but that further step was only taken in the year of his death.

Wilcox, Ella Wheeler (1855–1919), American writer of romantic sentimental verse.

Wilde, Oscar Fingall (1854–1900), Irish author and dramatist, son of a Dublin surgeon and leader of the cult of art for art's sake. His works include poems, fairy-tales, short stories, and witty comedies—*Lady Windermere's Fan*, *A Woman of No Importance*, *An Ideal Husband*, and *The Importance of Being Earnest*. In a libel action he was convicted of homosexual practices and imprisoned for two years, when he wrote *The Ballad of Reading Gaol*.

Wilder, Thornton Niven (1897–1975), American author and playwright. Among his books are *The Bridge of San Luis Rey* and *Ides of March*.

Wilkes, John (1727–97), English politician. A Whig, he violently attacked George III in his paper the *North Briton*, and as a result of unsuccessful proceedings against him, general warrants were determined illegal. He was again in trouble for obscene libel; his defiance of authority brought him popularity, and he was four times re-elected to parliament but refused his seat, until his opponents gave way. His motives were mixed, but he helped to establish freedom of the press.

Willcocks, Sir William (1852–1932), British engineer, b. India, who carried out irrigation works in India, Egypt, South Africa, and Mesopotamia. He built the Aswan dam (1898–1902).

Willett, William (1856–1915), English advocate of "daylight savings," adopted after his death.

William I of England (1027–87), the "Conqueror," Duke of Normandy, claimed the English throne as successor to Edward the Confessor, and defeated Harold II at Hastings in 1066. An able commander and a firm ruler, he crushed Saxon resistance, especially in the north, transferred most of the land to his Norman followers, and drew England into closer relations with the continent, as did his archbishop Lanfranc. He ordered the Domesday survey.

William II of England (1056–1100), the Conqueror's son, surnamed Rufus, succeeded in 1087. Capricious and self-indulgent, his reign was troubled, and he was shot (by accident or design) while hunting in the New Forest.

William III of England (1650–1702), King of England, Scotland, and Ireland (1689–1702), son of William II of Orange and Mary, daughter of Charles I. He married Mary, daughter of the Duke of York (later James II) while stadtholder of Holland. In 1688, when James had fled the country, he was invited to succeed and he and Mary became joint king and queen. The revolution of 1688 brought to England tolerance of Protestant worship, but William was mainly concerned with war against France, brought to an end in 1697.

William IV of England (1765–1837), third son of George III, succeeded his brother George IV in 1830; called the "sailor king." The reform bill of 1832 and other reform measures were carried without obstruction from him.

William I of Germany (1797–1888), King of Prussia and first German emperor. He succeeded to the throne in 1861 and continued resistance to reform, appointing Bismarck as chief minister, and supporting him through the Austro-Prussian and Franco-Prussian wars. His personal character was simple and unassuming.

William II of Germany, the Kaiser (1859–1941), King of Prussia and German emperor from 1888, was grandson of William I and of Queen Victoria. He was intelligent but impetuous, and believed in military power. He dismissed Bismarck. In 1914 his support of Austria helped to precipitate European war, and the resulting defeat brought his abdication, after which he lived in retirement at Doorn in Holland.

William the Silent (1533–1584), Dutch national leader. Prince of Orange, he led the revolt of the Protestant Netherlands against the rule of the Spanish Philip II. The union of the northern provinces was accomplished in 1579, and Spanish rule was renounced by 1584, in which year William was assassinated.

Williams, Sir George (1821–1905), founder of the Young Men's Christian Association.

Williamson, Malcolm (b. 1931), Australian composer, pianist and organist; succeeded Sir Arthur Bliss as Master of the Queen's Musick.

Wilson, Edmund (1895–1972), American critic, author of *Axel's Castle* (1931), *The Triple Thinkers* (1938), *The Wound and the Bow* (1941), *To the Finland Station* (1940), *The Shores of Light* (1952), *The Dead Sea Scrolls* (1955).

Wilson of Rievaulx, Lord (Sir Harold Wilson) (b. 1916), British statesman, leader parl. Labour Party 1963–76; prime minister 1964–6, 1966–70, 1974–6. Entered parliament 1945 as member for Ormskirk; elected for Huyton 1950–83. Returned three times, in 1964 and a decade later, to head a government facing a formidable balance-of-payments deficit. Resigned March 1976. Founder of the Open University.

Wilson, Richard (1714–82), British landscape painter, b. Montgomeryshire. Admired by Turner and Constable.

Wilson, Thomas Woodrow (1856–1924), American statesman. He was U.S. president 1913–21, brought America into the first world war and advocated the League of Nations, but was not a successful negotiator at the peace conference and could not carry his country into the League. His administration introduced prohibition and women's suffrage.

Wingate, Orde Charles (1903–44), leader of the Chindit forces engaged behind the Japanese lines in Burma during the second world war.

Winifred, St., the 7th cent. patron saint of North Wales, said in late legend to have been killed by her rejected suitor, Prince Caradoc, but restored by her uncle.

Wiseman, Nicholas Patrick (1802–65), cardinal, b. in Spain of an Irish family. In 1850 on the restoration in England of the Roman Catholic hierarchy he became first archbishop of Westminster, and reorganised and developed his church in Great Britain.

Wittgenstein, Ludwig Josef Johann (1889–1951), Austrian linguistic philosopher whose main works were the *Tractatus Logico-Philosophicus* of his early period, much admired by Russell, and the *Philosophical Investigations*.

Wodehouse, Pelham Grenville (1881–1975), English humorist, creator of Jeeves in the Bertie Wooster stories. He became a U.S. citizen.

Wolf, Friedrich August (1759–1824), German classical scholar, a founder of scientific classical philology.

Wolf, Hugo (1860–1903), Austrian song-writer. In his settings of over 300 German lyrics, including many of Mörike and Goethe, he achieved complete union of poetry and music. See **Section E**.

Wolfe, James (1727–59), British general, b. Westerham. He showed early promise in the Seven Years' War, and was given command of the expedition against Quebec, which in spite of its strong position he captured, but lost his life.

Wolsey, Thomas (c. 1475–1530), English cardinal. A butcher's son at Ipswich, he entered the church, becoming archbishop of York and cardinal, while in the same year (1515) he became Henry VIII's lord chancellor. But in spite of his ability he was unable to secure papal sanction for the king's divorce from Catherine of Aragon, and fell from power and died. He was the last of the great ecclesiastical statesmen of the Middle Ages.

Wood, Sir Henry Joseph (1869–1944), English conductor, founder of the Promenade Concerts which he conducted from 1895 till his death.

Woodcock, George (1904–79), English trade union leader. T.U.C. general secretary 1960–69; first chairman of the Commission on Industrial Relations, 1969–71.

Woodsworth, James Shaver (1874–1942), Canadian politician, parliamentary leader of the Co-operative Commonwealth Federation.

Woodville, Elizabeth (1437–91), wife of Edward IV. Her daughter Elizabeth married Henry VII.

Woolf, Virginia (1882–1941), English writer, daughter of Sir Leslie Stephen and wife of Leonard Woolf with whom she founded the Hogarth Press. Her works develop the stream-of-consciousness technique and include *To the Lighthouse*, *Mrs. Dalloway*, *The Waves*, *A Room of One's Own*.

Woolley, Sir Richard van der Riet (b. 1906), succeeded Sir Harold Spencer Jones as astronomer royal (England), 1956–72.

Wootton of Abinger, Baroness (Barbara Frances Wootton) (b. 1897), English social scientist; chairman Metropolitan Juvenile Courts 1946–62; deputy speaker of the House of Lords 1966–70. Her works include *Social Science and Social Pathology*, *Crime and the Criminal Law*, and an autobiography *In a world I never made*.

Wordsworth, William (1770–1850), English poet, b. Cockermouth. He went to Cambridge, and in 1798 with Coleridge issued *Lyrical Ballads*, a return to simplicity in English poetry. He settled at Grasmere with his sister Dorothy (1771–1855), to whose insight his poems owe much. Among his best works are his sonnets and his *Ode on the Intimations of Immortality*, besides his *Prelude*.

Wren, Sir Christopher (1632–1723), English architect, b. Wiltshire. After the great fire (1666) he prepared an abortive plan for rebuilding London, but did in fact rebuild St. Paul's and more than fifty other city churches, including St. Stephen, Walbrook, and St. Mary-le-Bow. Other works include Chelsea Hospital, portions of Greenwich Hospital, the Sheldonian theatre, Oxford, and Queen's College library, Oxford. He had wide scientific interests (he was professor of mathematics at Gresham College, London, and professor of astronomy at Oxford) and helped to found the Royal Society.

Wright, Frank Lloyd (1869–1959), American architect, initiator of horizontal strip and all-glass design. His influence has spread over the world. His buildings include the Imperial Hotel, Tokyo, and the Guggenheim Museum, New York.

Wright, Orville (1871–1948), American airman who with his brother Wilbur (1867–1912) in 1903 was the first to make a controlled sustained flight in a powered heavier-than-air machine, flying a length of 852 ft. at Kitty Hawk, N.C.

Wyatt, James (1746–1813), English architect who built Fonthill Abbey.

Wyatt, Sir Thomas (1503–42), English poet who introduced the sonnet from Italy. He was also a diplomat.

Wyatt, Sir Thomas the younger (c. 1520–54), son of above, unsuccessfully led a revolt against Queen Mary on behalf of Lady Jane Grey.

B66

Wycherley, William (1640–1715), English dramatist of the Restoration period. A master of satiric comedy, his plays include *Love in a Wood*, *The Plain Dealer*, and (the best known) *The Country Wife*.

Wyclif, John (*c.* 1320–84), English religious reformer. He taught at Oxford, later becoming rector of Lutterworth. He insisted on inward religion and attacked those practices which he thought had become mechanical. His followers, called Lollards, were suppressed, partly for political reasons. The Wyclif Bible, the first and literal translation of the Latin Vulgate into English, was mainly the work of his academic followers at Oxford.

Wykeham, William of (1324–1404), English churchman. He held office under Edward III and became bishop of Winchester in 1367. He founded New College, Oxford, and Winchester School, and improved Winchester cathedral.

Wyllie, William Lionel (1851–1931), English marine painter of *The Thames Below London Bridge*.

Wyspianski, Stanislav (1869–1907), Polish poet, dramatist and painter. His plays *The Wedding*, *Liberation*, and *November Night* treat of national themes.

X

Xavier, St. Francis (1506–52), "apostle of the Indies," b. at Xavero in the Basque country. He was associated with Loyola in founding the Jesuits, and undertook missionary journeys to Goa, Ceylon, and Japan. He died while planning another to China.

Xenophon (444–359 B.C.), Athenian general and historian. He commanded Greek mercenaries under the Persian Cyrus, and on the latter's death safely marched the Ten Thousand home through hostile country. His chief works are the *Anabasis*, the *Hellenica*, and *Cyropaedia*.

Xerxes (*c.* 519–465 B.C.), King of Persia, was son of the first Darius. In 481 B.C. he started on an expedition against Greece when, according to Herodotus, he had a combined army and navy of over two and a half million men. He defeated the Spartans at Thermopylae, but his fleet was overcome at Salamis. He reigned from 485 to 465 B.C. and met his death by assassination.

Ximénes de Cisneros, Francisco (1436–1517), Spanish statesman and churchman. He became cardinal in 1507; carried out monastic reforms; and directed preparation of a polyglot bible, the *Complutensian*; but as inquisitor-general he was fanatical against heresy. He was adviser to Queen Isabella; in 1506 regent for Queen Juana; and himself directed an expedition to conquer Oran and extirpate piracy.

Y

Yeats, William Butler (1865–1939), Irish lyric poet and playwright, b. near Dublin, a leader of the Irish literary revival. His plays were performed in the Abbey Theatre (which with **Lady Gregory** (1852–1932) he helped to found), and include *Cathleen Ni Houlihan*, *The Hour Glass*, and *Deidre*. A complete edition of the *Collected Poems* appeared in 1950.

Yonge, Charlotte Mary (1823–1901), English novelist. Influenced by Keble, she wrote novels which faithfully reflect some aspects of Victorian life; one such is *The Daisy Chain*. She also wrote historical fiction such as *The Dove in the Eagle's Nest*.

Young, Brigham (1801–77), American Mormon leader, and president in 1844 after the founder's death. He was a main founder of Salt Lake City. He practised polygamy. *See also* **Mormonism, Section J.**

Young, Francis Brett (1884–1954), English novelist, author of *My Brother Jonathan* and *Dr. Bradley remembers*.

Young, James (1811–83), Scottish chemist, b. Glasgow, whose experiments led to the manufacture of paraffin oil and solid paraffin on a large scale.

Young, Thomas (1773–1829), English physicist, physician and Egyptologist, b. Somerset, of a

Quaker family. He established the wave theory of light and its essential principle of interference, put forward a theory of colour vision, and was the first to describe astigmatism of the eye. He was also largely responsible for deciphering the inscriptions on the Rosetta stone.

Younghusband, Sir Francis Edward (1863–1942), English explorer and religious leader. He explored Manchuria and Tibet, and wrote on India and Central Asia. He founded the World Congress of Faiths in 1936 (*see* **Section J).**

Ypres, 1st Earl of. *See* **French.**

Ysayë, Eugène (1858–1929), Belgian violinist and conductor, noted chiefly for his playing of the works of Bach and César Franck.

Yukawa, Hideki (b. 1907), Japanese physicist, who received the 1949 Nobel prize for predicting (1935) the existence of the meson.

Z

Zadkiel (angel in rabbinical lore), pseudonym of two astrologers: **William Lilly** (1602–81) and **Richard James Morrison** (1794–1874).

Zadkine, Ossip (b. 1890), Russian sculptor in France, who makes play with light on concave surfaces. His works include *Orpheus* and the public monument *The Destruction of Rotterdam*.

Zaharoff, Sir Basil (1849–1936), armaments magnate and financier, b. Anatolia of Greek parents. He was influential in the first world war.

Zamenhof, Ludwig Lazarus (1859–1917), Polish-Jew who invented Esperanto. He was by profession an oculist.

Zeno of Citium (?342–270 B.C.), philosopher, founder of the Stoic system. He left Cyprus to teach in Athens.

Zeppelin, Ferdinand, Count von (1838–1917), German inventor of the dirigible airship, 1897–1900. It was used in the first world war.

Zeromski, Stefan (1864–1925), Polish novelist, author of *The Homeless*, *The Ashes*, *The Fight with Satan*.

Zhukov, Georgi Konstantinovich (1896–1974), Soviet general, who led the defence of Moscow and Stalingrad and lifted the siege of Leningrad in the second world war, and accepted the German surrender in 1945. He continued to be active till 1957.

Zhukovsky, Vasily Andreyevich (1783–1852), Russian poet and translator of German and English poets. For many years he was tutor to the future Tsar Alexander II.

Zola, Emile Edouard (1840–1902), French novelist, b. Paris, of Italian descent. His series, *Les Rougon-Macquart*, portrays in a score of volumes (the best known of which are perhaps *L'Assommoir*, *Nana* and *Germinal*) the fortunes of one family in many aspects and in realistic manner. He had the moral courage to champion Dreyfus.

Zorn, Anders Leonhard (1860–1920), Swedish sculptor, etcher, and painter.

Zoroaster (Zarathustra) (fl. 6th cent. B.C.), Persian founder of the Parsee religion. He was a monotheist, and saw the world as a struggle between good (Ahura Mazda) and evil (Ahriman). *See* **Zoroastrianism, Section J.**

Zoshchenko, Mikhail (1895–1958), Russian writer of humorous short stories, which include *The Woman who could not Read and other Tales* and *The Wonderful Dog and other Stories*.

Zosimus (fl. *c.* 300), the first known alchemist. He lived in Alexandria.

Zuccarelli, Francesco (1702–88), Italian artist of fanciful landscapes. He spent many years in London and was elected a founder member of the R.A. (1768).

Zuckermann, Baron (Solly Zuckermann) (b. 1904), British biologist; chief scientific adviser to British governments; 1940–71. His publications include *Scientists and War* and *The Frontiers of Public and Private Science*. O.M. 1968.

Zwingli, Ulrich (1484–1531), Swiss religious reformer. He taught mainly at Zurich, where he issued a list of reformed doctrines, less extreme than those of Calvin.

Zwirner, Ernst Friedrich (1802–61), German architect who restored Cologne cathedral.

BACKGROUND TO PUBLIC AFFAIRS

This section is in three parts. The first provides an up-to-date chronicle and analysis of recent changes in Britain, intended to put into perspective current political events. The second part provides a wide-ranging guide to events and movements elsewhere in the world. The third section consists of a series of special topics, including in this edition a background analysis of the upheavals in Russia, the dramatic developments in Germany and the record of the Bush administration in the United States.

TABLE OF CONTENTS

BACKGROUND TO PUBLIC AFFAIRS

This section is in three parts. The first outlines the political history of the United Kingdom since 1970. The second part provides a wide-ranging guide to events elsewhere in the world and takes stock of the changing patterns in international relations. The third section contains special topics on particular themes. The reader is invited to turn to Section D for further key facts and figures relating to the British political system.

I. SURVEY OF THE BRITISH POLITICAL SCENE

BRITISH POLITICAL EVENTS 1970–90

The Political Situation in 1970.

The Labour Party, which had been in office for almost six years under the leadership of Harold Wilson, approachee the General Election of June 1970 with confidence. After some traumatic years both economically and politically, the Government's popularity appeared to have been restored. The outcome, however, was a 4·7% swing to the Conservatives and their return to power, led by Edward Heath, with an overall majority of 30.

A New Style of Government.

Initially, the new Government made some radical changes in policy:
(1) *Reorganisation of the Machinery of Government,* including the creation of two new giant departments (Environment, and Trade and Industry) and a new advisory unit, the Central Policy Review Staff. Between 1970 and 1974 the Government also passed legislation reforming the structure of local government (implemented in England and Wales in 1974 and Scotland in 1975), the National Health Service (implemented in 1974) and the water industry (implemented in 1974).
(2) *Cuts in Public Expenditure.*—The Conservatives believed that government was intervening too much in the life of the nation and that too high a proportion of the nation's resources were committed to public expenditure. Following a major review of government activities, the Chancellor of the Exchequer announced that the Government planned to be more selective in its approach to the social services and to withdraw generally in its relations with private industry.
(3) *Reform of Industrial Relations.*—One of the major issues of the Conservative election campaign had been the need to take stronger action to reform industrial relations. The Government published its proposals in October 1970 and, after a long and bitter parliamentary battle, the Industrial Relations Act became law in 1971. The provisions of the Act came into force during 1972. The Act was strongly opposed by an overwhelming majority of the trade unions, most of whom refused to register, as they were required by the Act in order to receive certain benefits it conferred, and initially they decided to boycott the institutions created by the Act, in particular the National Industrial Relations Court. However, following a number of controversial decisions, most unions decided that they should at least appear in order to defend themselves.

Industrial Unrest.

The first two and a half years of the Government's life were marked by widespread outbreaks of industrial unrest. This was the result of a number of factors. First, the Government's policy of confrontation as a means of limiting wage inflation led to a number of prolonged disputes, for instance, in the docks, in the electricity power industry and by local authority manual workers. Trade union opposition to the Industrial Relations Act produced a number of one-day stoppages and unofficial strikes of longer duration. These prob-

lems were aggravated by persistently high levels of unemployment especially in certain regions. Finally, after 1972, there was industrial action in protest against the Government's prices and incomes policy. In 1972 there were three serious disputes, involving the miners, the railwaymen and the dockworkers.

The Government's About-Turn.

1972 was not a happy year for the Government. We have already seen that it was a year of confrontation with the trade unions. It was also a year in which the pressure of circumstances, especially the problems of unemployment and inflation, forced the Government to abandon many of the initiatives it had started in 1970 and to adopt policies similar to those which it had attacked so vehemently when it had been in Opposition. This was particularly the case in three fields:
(1) *Regional Policy.*—Faced with the twin problems of low levels of industrial investment and persistent unemployment in the regions, the Chancellor of the Exchequer announced in his 1972 Budget that the Government was substantially increasing government assistance to private industry and that, in the development areas, investment grants were to be reintroduced.
(2) *Consumer Protection.*—Although in 1970 the Government had brought about the demise of the Consumer Council, by 1972 it had come round to the view that some form of statutory consumer protection was necessary. Consequently, a new office, that of Director-General of Fair Trading, was created in 1973 and a new committee established to protect the interests of consumers.
(3) *Prices and Incomes Policy.*—Despite its strong opposition to the Labour Government's prices and incomes legislation and its initial refusal even to contemplate such a policy, the continuing problem of inflation placed the Government under increasing pressure to introduce some kind of prices and incomes policy. During the autumn tripartite talks were held between the Government, the TUC and the CBI in the search for voluntary agreement on prices and incomes restraint, but these broke down at the beginning of November. Consequently, the Government came to the conclusion, albeit reluctantly, that they would have to introduce legislation to give effect to their proposals. A 90-day standstill was imposed on wages and salaries, dividends, rates and rents, and prices and charges for goods and services were similarly frozen. Provision was made for firms which claimed that their costs had risen so much for it to be impracticable for them to be absorbed to apply to the Government for permission to increase prices. The prices of fresh food and of imported raw materials were excluded from the freeze.

Entry into Europe.

Negotiations with the EEC started immediately after the General Election of 1970. After a long series of talks in Brussels and a summit meeting between President Pompidou and Mr. Heath in Paris in May 1971, a formula was found to which Britain and the Six could agree. On this basis the House of Commons took the decision in principle to join the EEC on 18 October 1971, when the Conservative Government, opposed by some of its back-benchers but supported by 69 Labour pro-marketeers and five of the Liberals, had a majority of 112. Legislation to give effect to this decision was passed after a long parliamentary struggle in September 1972. Thus, twelve years after the first application had been made, Britain joined the Common Market on 1 January 1973.

Phases Two and Three.

The standstill on prices and incomes was extended until the end of April 1973 when it was replaced by the second phase of the Government's counter-inflation policy. Under Phase Two wage increases were limited to £1 per week plus 4%, with an overall ceiling of £250 per annum. Prices and dividends continued to be controlled as during the standstill. To enforce these controls the Government created two new statutory bodies, the Pay Board and the Price Commission. Phase Two was opposed by the TUC, which decided not to nominate members to serve on the new controlling bodies nor to co-operate in the implementation of the Government's policy. During the summer of 1973 bilateral talks took place between the Government and both the CBI and the TUC as to what measures should succeed Phase Two in November 1973. In October the Government published its plans in a Green Paper, and these were put into practice with a few modifications. On prices the basis of control was unchanged, but there was some tightening of the regulations. On incomes, however, a more complex formula was introduced permitting a choice between a 7% increase, with a maximum of £350 per year, or an increase of £2·25 per week. In addition, higher increases could be awarded by the Pay Board on various grounds such as the removal of anomalies or the necessity of working "unsocial" hours. New Year's Day was also declared to be a public holiday.

The Oil Crisis.

The implementation of Phase Two took place against a rapidly changing economic situation. In the aftermath of the Arab–Israeli war of October 1973, problems arose in the supply of oil, on which Britain depends for 50% of her energy. First, the Arab oil producers decided to boycott some countries and to restrict supplies to most others. British imports were cut by 15%. Second, all the oil exporting countries decided to increase the price of crude oil dramatically. Shortage of petrol produced panic among many motorists leading to long queues and even violent scenes at some garages. The Government took the precaution of issuing ration coupons but managed to avoid introducing rationing, relying instead on voluntary restraint.

Deepening Economic Crisis.

The increased cost of oil imports and the reduction in supplies adversely affected both the balance of payments and industrial output. The economic situation was further weakened by the decision of the National Union of Mineworkers (NUM) in November 1973 to implement a ban on overtime and weekend working in support of a pay claim in excess of Phase Three. The rapidly deteriorating fuel situation was aggravated by an out-of-hours working ban by electricity power engineers which limited the ability of the Central Electricity Generating Board to cope with shortages at various power stations. Consequently on 13 November the Government declared a State of Emergency. Orders were enacted restricting space heating by electricity, except in the home and certain other places, and prohibiting the use of electricity for advertising, displays or floodlighting. The position worsened still further following the decision of the Amalgamated Society of Locomotive Engineers and Firemen (ASLEF) to ban Sunday, overtime and rest-day working. This had the effect of disrupting the delivery of coal to power stations as well as causing a considerable amount of inconvenience to passengers, especially in the South-East. The Government refused to make an offer to the miners outside the terms of Stage Three and was therefore compelled to introduce a package of tougher measures to deal with the crisis. Most important, as from 1 January, electricity was only provided to in-dustry on three specified days per week. In addition a 50 mile/h speed limit was introduced on all roads, a maximum heating limit was imposed on all commercial premises and offices and television was required to close down at 10.30 p.m. each evening. The Chancellor of the Exchequer also announced large cuts in public expenditure and tighter controls on consumer credit.

Miners' Strike and the February 1974 Election.

Following an overwhelming vote in a pithead ballot, the NUM decided to intensify its industrial action by calling a national strike as from 10 February. Before the strike began, however, the Prime Minister announced that he had asked the Queen to dissolve Parliament so as to hold a general election on 28 February. For the Government, the main issue of the election was the attempt by a trade union to use its industrial strength to defeat the policy of the elected government. The Labour Party, however, attempted to widen the campaign to include the Government's general record since 1970. There was also general interest in the performance of the Liberals following a series of dramatic by-election successes in 1972 and 1973.

Minority Labour Government.

At the dissolution, Mr. Heath had had an overall majority of 16 in the House of Commons. As the results came in on election night it was clear that he was going to lose this and that the result was going to be very close. Eventually the result was as follows:

Labour	301
Conservative	296
Liberal	14
Others	24

In this situation Mr. Heath did not offer his resignation immediately but entered into discussions with Mr. Jeremy Thorpe, the Leader of the Liberals, to see if the basis existed for the formation of a coalition. No agreement, however, was reached and Mr. Heath resigned on 4 March. The Queen then asked Mr. Wilson to form a government which he agreed to do without obtaining the support of any other parties. Immediate steps were taken to settle the miners' dispute and to end the three-day working week.

The Social Contract.

Although leading a minority government, Mr. Wilson knew that the other parties would be reluctant to force another election immediately. The Government was therefore able to make a start in implementing its programme. Most of its domestic policies were included in the *Social Contract*, a package of measures agreed between the Labour Party and the Trades Union Congress in 1973. Most important were the measures to control inflation. In return for the abolition of the Pay Board and all associated statutory controls on pay, which occurred in July 1974, the trade unions agreed voluntarily to restrain wage increases. Other measures included the repeal of the Industrial Relations Act 1971, the introduction of food subsidies, the strengthening of price controls and increased payments to old-age pensioners.

October 1974 Election.

Despite the Government's success in exploiting its parliamentary position, it was clear that it would seek a new mandate from the electorate at an early opportunity. Following the publication of a large number of statements of policy during the summer, the Prime Minister sought a dissolution of Parliament for polling to take place on 10 October. The Labour Party remained ahead in the opinion polls throughout the campaign and this was confirmed in the results, but its margin was rather smaller than predicted. Labour only obtained a majority of three over all other parties. However its position was in fact considerably stronger than this because of the fragmented nature of the opposition.

Conservative Leadership.

Although many Conservatives were critical of Mr. Heath's leadership, his support was not tested immediately after the February election because of the proximity of another general election. However, after the October election Mr. Heath decided to establish a committee, under the chairmanship of Lord Home, to review the procedure for electing the leader of the Conservative Party. It proposed a number of changes which were adopted for the election, held in February 1975. In the first ballot, Mrs. Margaret Thatcher defeated Mr. Heath but failed to win the required majority. Mr. Heath then withdrew, announcing his intention of returning to the backbenches, and in the second ballot Mrs. Thatcher secured an overall majority.

European Renegotiation.

The Government was committed to seek a fundamental renegotiation of the terms of entry into the European Economic Community and to consult the British people as to whether the new terms should be accepted. In April 1974 Mr. Callaghan outlined to the Council of Ministers the terms which Britain wished to change, the most important of which were the contribution to the Community budget, the effects of the Common Agricultural Policy, the need to safeguard the interests of the Commonwealth and developing countries and the promotion of regional development. After concluding successful negotiations on most of these points the Cabinet voted to recommend continued membership and this view was endorsed by 67·2% of those who voted in a referendum held in June 1975.

Counter-Inflation Programme.

Despite the agreement of the trade unions voluntarily to restrain wage increases, the rate of inflation accelerated so much that by the middle of 1975 it had reached 25% per annum. In July 1975, the Government was therefore compelled to introduce a limit of £6 a week on pay settlements for people earning up to £8,500 a year, with no increase for those earning more. This policy remained voluntary but the Government announced that employers who increased pay by more than the limit would have not only the excess but the whole pay increase disallowed for the approval of price increases under the Price Code and it warned that if the limits were exceeded it would have to seek statutory powers of enforcement. The Government also undertook to maintain strict price controls and to continue and extend the payment of food subsidies.

Rising Unemployment.

The measures taken by the Government to reduce the rate of inflation, implemented during a serious world-wide recession, led to a sharp rise in unemployment such that in January 1976 1·3 million were out of work. Various steps were taken to provide additional employment but, short of major reflationary measures which were ruled out on other grounds, there was little that the Government could do. Preparations were made, however, to facilitate the development of the economy when conditions permitted. In November 1975 the Government published a new industrial strategy designed to ensure that assistance was given to those sectors of the economy with good prospects. Its difficulties, however, were highlighted in the following month when it had to launch a major rescue to avert the closure of Chrysler car production in Great Britain. Earlier in the year the Government had purchased 95% of the shares of British Leyland as part of a package of measures of financial support.

Pay and Prices.

Although the £6 limit, which was observed without exception, succeeded in reducing the rate of inflation, it was clear that further pay restraint was needed. In his 1976 Budget the Chancellor announced various tax reliefs conditional upon agreement being reached on a voluntary pay limit for another year. Such an agreement was made in May with a new limit curbing average wage increases to 4½% in the year starting in August 1976. Price controls were also maintained, but there was some relaxation to encourage industrial investment.

Resignation of Harold Wilson.

In March 1976 Harold Wilson, to everyone's surprise, announced his intention of resigning as Prime Minister. Six candidates were nominated to succeed him and, after three ballots, James Cal-

laghan was declared the winner, defeating Michael Foot by 39 votes, and he became Prime Minister on 5 April. A number of changes were made in the Cabinet and four senior ministers, including Ted Short and Barbara Castle, retired. Ted Short remained Deputy Leader of the Labour Party until October when he was succeeded by Michael Foot. Harold Wilson, who remained an M.P., received a knighthood from the Queen in recognition of his services to the country as the longest-serving Prime Minister this century.

Cuts in Public Expenditure.

During 1976 a vigorous campaign was mounted in favour of cuts in public expenditure. Concern that the Government was borrowing excessively to finance this spending also led to weakness of sterling on the foreign exchange markets. In July, to avert a further fall in the value of sterling, substantial cuts were announced in the Government's spending plans for 1977–8 and interest rates were raised to record levels. These measures were not sufficient, however, to prevent a dramatic slide in the £ during the autumn which forced the Government to seek a $3,900 million loan from the International Monetary Fund. To obtain this assistance, further cuts in public expenditure, amounting to £3,000 m. over the next two years, and increases in taxation were imposed in December. The Government also introduced new and tighter "cash limits" over public spending.

Lords v. Commons.

Despite these economic problems, the Government proceeded with one of the largest legislative programmes ever introduced in a single session. Most of it was also controversial, and strong opposition was encountered in the House of Commons, where the Government's small majority was frequently threatened, and in the House of Lords. The Lords attempted to make major changes in six bills, but the conflict eventually centred around two bills: the Dock Work Regulation Bill and the Aircraft and Shipbuilding Industries Bill. The former was returned to the Commons with its main provision transformed by the Lords, but the defection of two of its own backbenchers prevented the Government restoring its original proposal. Disagreement over the latter was not resolved by the time Parliament was prorogued and the bill to nationalise the aerospace and shipbuilding industries therefore had to be reintroduced at the beginning of the 1976–7 session. It became law in March 1977 but only after the Government had made substantial concessions.

Devolution.

In October 1974 the Scottish National Party secured 30·4% of the Scottish vote, winning 11 seats, and Plaid Cymru won 10·8% of the Welsh vote, winning 3 seats. The SNP also came second in 42 constituencies, 35 of them held by Labour. These successes brought the question of devolution to the centre of political debate and the Government announced its intention of setting up assemblies in Scotland and Wales. Both parties were split on this issue. Traditionally the Labour Party, and particularly its Scottish members, had opposed devolution, but with a few prominent exceptions in both Scotland and Wales, the Party supported the Government's proposals. The Conservatives had supported the creation of a Scottish assembly since the late 1960s, but in 1976 decided officially to oppose the Government's plans. A number of senior Conservatives, however, dissented from this apparent change of policy. In December 1976 the Scotland and Wales Bill was given a Second Reading by a majority of 45, the Government having secured the votes of most Labour MPs by promising to hold referendums before bringing the assemblies into existence. To get the Bill through its Committee Stage, which had to be taken on the floor of the House of Commons, the Government had to introduce a "guillotine" motion, but this was defeated by 29 votes in February 1977, with back-bench Labour rebels joining Conservatives and Liberals.

Lib/Lab Pact.

By-election losses meant that by 1977 the Government had lost its overall majority. Its failure to make progress with the devolution bill also meant that it could no longer count upon the support of the Nationalists. In this situation, the Conservatives in March 1977 put down a motion of no confidence in the Government. Faced with the prospect of defeat, the Government entered into an agreement with the Liberal Party, initially until the summer. It therefore succeeded in defeating the Conservative motion with a comfortable majority of 24. In July the agreement was renewed for the next session of Parliament provided that the Government maintained the fight against inflation. Under its terms both parties retained their independence for electoral purposes and in the House of Commons, but the Liberals agreed to support the Government in return for formal consultations on government policy and some specific undertakings on subjects such as direct elections to the European Parliament and devolution.

Stage Three.

One of the reasons behind Liberal support for the Government was their belief that it would be able to agree a further year of pay restraint with the TUC. Negotiations took place during the early part of the summer but the TUC refused to agree to a limit on settlements, believing that there should be an immediate return to free collective bargaining subject only to an undertaking that settlements should last for twelve months. The Government, however, announced unilaterally in July 1977 its own pay guidelines which stated that the general level of settlements should be such that the nation's earnings would increase during 1977–8 by no more than 10%. In contrast to the first two years of pay policy, these guidelines led to a considerable number of industrial disputes. Most serious was the nine-week strike of firemen between November 1977 and January 1978 during which fire services were provided by the armed forces.

Political Tension.

1977 saw violent scenes in various parts of Britain. One problem was the rise of the National Front, a party calling among other things for a halt to immigration and the repatriation of many coloured residents. Its activities in holding marches and demonstrations, particularly in areas with large coloured populations, were opposed by many groups and resulted in clashes between its supporters and those of the extreme left, for instance in Lewisham and in Birmingham during August. There were also violent scenes in north London outside the Grunwick film-processing factory as the trade union movement organised a mass picket in connection with the firm's refusal to recognise the right of its employees to belong to a trade union.

Foreign Affairs.

For the first six months of 1977 it was Britain's turn to hold the Presidency of the EEC. This burden, along with many others, was one of the causes of the sudden death of the Foreign Secretary, Anthony Crosland, in February 1977. He was succeeded by one of his junior ministers, Dr. David Owen, who at the age of 37 was the youngest person in this office since Sir Anthony Eden in the 1930s. One of the first problems he had to face was the situation in Rhodesia. Following the breakdown of constitutional talks, held between October and December 1976 in Geneva, intensive diplomatic activity led to the publication of joint Anglo-American settlement proposals in September 1977. At the same time Ian Smith, the Rhodesian Prime Minister, also announced his intention of seeking an internal settlement with moderate African leaders.

Brighter Economic News.

The harsh economic measures taken by the Government in 1976 produced results more quickly than had been expected, and by the end of 1977 most indicators pointed to a dramatic change in the financial outlook. The balance of payments in the last part of the year was in surplus on both visible and invisible accounts; the pound was strong in relation to most other currencies and there had been massive increases in

Britain's reserves; and the rate of inflation was falling steadily and was expected to be in single figures in the spring of 1978. However, unemployment remained at the very high level of 1·4 million and the growth in industrial output was still sluggish. None the less, the Chancellor of the Exchequer was able to cut taxes on two occasions during 1977 and interest rates fell progressively from their record levels of the previous year. One cause of this economic recovery was North Sea oil. The first oil was brought ashore in 1975, and by the end of 1977 50% of the country's needs were being met from this source.

Devolution: The Second Attempt.

The defeat of its guillotine motion in February 1977 prevented the Government from proceeding with its plans for Scottish and Welsh devolution in the remaining months of that session. However, suitably modified to win Liberal support, the legislation was reintroduced in November 1977, this time in the form of separate bills for Scotland and Wales. With Liberal and Nationalist support, the Government had no difficulty in obtaining a guillotine motion, but the bills still had a lengthy and stormy passage through Parliament in the face of determined opposition from the Conservatives, a number of Labour backbenchers and from members of the House of Lords. They eventually received the Royal Assent in July 1978 but with a number of amendments that had been opposed by the Government. Most important, the schemes were to be implemented only if they were endorsed by 40% of the Scottish and Welsh electorates in the referendums which the Government had decided to hold.

Rhodesia: The Internal Settlement.

Events in Rhodesia continued to play an important part in British politics during 1978. In March, Rhodesian premier Ian Smith signed an internal agreement with three moderate African leaders on the formation of a transitional government to prepare for elections and majority rule by the end of the year. This development was welcomed by the British Government only as a first step towards a settlement as it did not include the leaders of the other African group, the Patriotic Front. The Government therefore continued to press for an all-party conference based on the latest Anglo-American proposals. Two unsuccessful attempts were made to bring all the parties to the conference-table, the first by a civil servant in June, the other in December by Cledwyn Hughes, a Labour MP and close friend of the Prime Minister. Rhodesia also caused a major political storm with the publication of a report by Mr. Thomas Bingham, QC, revealing that BP and Shell had, through their subsidiaries and various swap agreements, been breaking oil sanctions. Amidst allegations that both the Wilson and the Heath Governments had been aware of this, the Government decided to institute a further inquiry to be conducted by 7 Members of Parliament under the chairmanship of a law lord.

Strains within the EEC.

Despite the vote in 1975 in favour of continued membership of the EEC, the Government, under pressure from within the Labour Party, maintained its lukewarm attitude towards many developments in the Community. Problems in various member-countries, and especially in Britain, prevented the first elections to the European Parliament being held as planned during 1978. However, the necessary legislation was passed in February 1978 and the first elections were fixed for June 1979. On other important issues, notably agriculture and fishing, the Government antagonised other member-countries by the tough line it adopted in negotiations. Further strains occurred towards the end of 1978 when it decided not to join the new European Monetary System (EMS), designed by France and Germany to promote greater economic and financial integration, on the grounds that it would damage the British economy and impair the freedom of action of British ministers.

Ending of the Lib/Lab Pact.

The poor performances of Liberal candidates in by-elections during 1977 led to mounting pressure on Liberal MPs to end their agreement to support the Government. An attempt to persuade them to do this immediately was rejected at a special conference in January 1978, but four months later Liberal MPs decided not to renew the agreement at the end of the parliamentary session. As there was no prospect of any other party entering into a formal pact with the Government, politicians and commentators were almost unanimous in predicting an autumn general election. The Government's prospects of success also looked rosier than they had for some time. The economic situation had continued to improve and in his April Budget the Chancellor of the Exchequer had been able to make substantial reductions in personal taxation. This had been reflected in a number of good by-election results for Labour, particularly in Scotland. However, to everyone's surprise, the Prime Minister announced at the beginning of September that the Government intended to soldier on. Attention therefore turned to the problems of maintaining the fight against inflation and to the Government's tactics for survival in the Commons.

Stage Four: The Winter of Discontent.

Although the average increase in earnings during Stage Three was 5% higher than the Government's norm, this was much better than had been expected in view of TUC opposition to the pay policy, and was one factor in the fall in the rate of inflation to about 8%. Encouraged by its success, the Government announced that, in the 1978–9 pay round, settlements should not exceed 5%, excluding self-financing productivity deals and with a few exceptions such as the firemen, police, armed forces and the very low-paid. Stage Four was, however, overwhelmingly rejected by both the TUC and the Labour Party at their annual conferences. The first major confrontation occurred at Ford's, where a nine-week strike was settled only with an offer of 17%. The tough line adopted initially by Ford management was influenced by the Government's threat of sanctions if the pay guidelines were broken. However, in December, Parliament refused to endorse this course of action, thus weakening the Government's ability to enforce its pay policy. It was not long before other groups secured increases in excess of the norm: among them were staff at the BBC, who had threatened to strike over the Christmas holiday, and petrol tanker drivers, whose unofficial action caused acute shortages in many parts of the country. 1979 opened with various serious industrial disputes. An official strike of lorry drivers severely interrupted the provision of essential supplies for industry, agriculture and the retail trade. At the same time the railway drivers and many manual workers in the public sector held one-day strikes in support of their pay claims. The impact of these strikes was reinforced by the worst winter for 16 years.

No Confidence in the Government.

Until March 1979 the Government was able to survive in the House of Commons by securing the support, on different occasions, of either Ulster Unionist or Nationalist MPs. The support of the former was gained by the introduction of a bill to increase the number of parliamentary constituencies in Northern Ireland from 12 to 17. The latter were wooed by the Government's decision to hold the devolution referendums on 1 March 1979. However, once the constituencies bill was on the statute-book there were no further concessions the Government was willing to offer the Unionists; and the result of the devolution referendums effectively put an end to its marriage with the Nationalists. In Wales the Government's proposals were rejected by 80% of those who voted; in Scotland they were supported by the barest of majorities and by only a third of those entitled to vote. The Government was pressed by the Nationalists to proceed with its Scottish proposals and to attempt to overturn the requirement that they should be endorsed by 40% of the Scottish electorate, but it was unwilling to do this for fear of provoking a sizeable rebellion in its own ranks. In these circumstances the Scottish Nationalists indicated that they would no longer support the Government and in a vote of confidence held on 28 March the Government was defeated by one vote, thus precipitating an immediate dissolution of Parliament.

The 1979 General Election.

Polling day was fixed for 3 May, coinciding with local government elections in most of England and Wales. The campaign was overshadowed by the murder on 30 March of Airey Neave, Opposition spokesman on Northern Ireland and one of Mrs. Thatcher's closest advisers, when a bomb planted in his car by Irish extremists exploded in the House of Commons car park. This led to a tightening of security with fewer meetings and other public appearances by leading politicians. Television thus played an even more dominant role than in recent elections with the main focus being on the party leaders. Generally it was a very quiet campaign disrupted only by various incidents involving supporters and opponents of the National Front, the most serious of which was at Southall where one person was killed and over 300 arrested. The Conservatives started the campaign with an overwhelming lead in the opinion polls, largely reflecting the winter's industrial troubles. During the campaign the gap between the parties narrowed but the Conservative lead was maintained and it was confirmed by the actual results. There was a swing of 5·2% to the Conservatives, sufficient to give them an overall majority of 44 in the House of Commons. There were, however, significant regional variations. The swing to the Conservatives was largest in southern England, it was smaller in the north, and in Scotland there was a very small swing to Labour. The most dramatic change in Scotland was the collapse of support for the Nationalists whose share of the vote was almost halved and they lost 9 of their 11 seats. The performance of the Liberals was patchy. Overall their vote fell by 1 million and they lost 3 seats but some of their MPs, including their leader David Steel, greatly increased their majorities. The National Front did very badly, all its candidates losing their deposits and securing only 0·6% of the poll. Among the casualties of the election were Shirley Williams, Labour's Education Minister, Teddy Taylor, the Conservative spokesman on Scotland, and Jeremy Thorpe, former leader of the Liberal Party.

Mrs. Thatcher's Government.

Mrs. Thatcher's arrival at 10 Downing Street attracted great interest, not only because she was the first woman Prime Minister of a Western state, but also because of the radical policies she had advocated in Opposition. Some of her closest associates were appointed to senior posts in the Cabinet, particularly on the economic side (for instance Sir Geoffrey Howe as Chancellor of the Exchequer and Sir Keith Joseph as Industry Secretary) but the Cabinet also included many who had been closely identified with the approach of her predecessor, Edward Heath. Among them were William Whitelaw (Home Secretary), Lord Carrington (Foreign Secretary), James Prior (Employment Secretary) and Peter Walker (Minister of Agriculture). However, even though he had campaigned energetically for the Conservatives during the election, no place was found in the Government for Edward Heath himself.

A Radical Programme.

The Queen's Speech for the first session of the new Parliament (lasting from May 1979 until October 1980) was an ambitious one both in its scale and in the magnitude of the changes it proposed. Among the most important measures were: the abolition of statutory price controls; changes in the law on picketing and the closed shop; repeal of the devolution legislation; granting council tenants a statutory right to purchase their homes; denationalisation of the nationalised airline and freight and aerospace industries and a reduction generally in the powers of state intervention in industry; and repeal of the requirement that local authorities introduce comprehensive education. Legislation giving effect to most of these changes was introduced in the autumn of 1979 and, although the congestion of the Parliamentary timetable led to some problems, the Government's comfortable majority ensured that it reached the statute-book by the end of the session.

Taxation and Public Spending.

During the election campaign the Conservatives attracted widespread support with their promises to cut direct taxation and eliminate wasteful public spending. Although many commentators thought that the economic situation would preclude fulfilment of public expectations immediately, the Chancellor confounded such scepticism by cutting the standard rate of income tax from 33% to 30%, with even greater reductions at higher levels, in his first Budget in June 1979. To finance these cuts he announced, as expected, reductions in public spending but he also had to increase VAT by 7% and petrol duty by 10p a gallon and to raise interest rates. These changes, however, added to the inflationary pressure already in the economy and in November the Chancellor had to raise interest rates to record levels and to make additional cuts in public spending affecting all sectors except for the armed forces and the police. These cuts were reflected in the withdrawal of some services, increased charges for others, reductions in staffing and in the winding-up of various government agencies.

The Labour Party Constitution.

As in the past, Labour's electoral defeat was followed by internal dissent, on this occasion centred upon those parts of the Party's constitution dealing with the powers of Party members to control their leaders. In October 1979, the Party Conference endorsed two changes in the constitution, requiring sitting MPs to be re-selected during the life of each Parliament and giving the final say on the election manifesto to the National Executive Committee. These decisions were referred to the committee of inquiry it also agreed to establish into the Party's organisation. Disagreement over the composition of this committee delayed the start of its work until January 1980. James Callaghan was re-elected Leader of the Party shortly after the General Election and most of the members of the outgoing Cabinet were elected to the Shadow Cabinet; one notable absentee was Tony Benn who chose to return to the backbenches in order to have greater freedom to speak on a wide range of issues.

Europe: A Fresh Start?

The campaign for the first direct elections to the European Parliament attracted little public interest, particularly as it came immediately after the General Election, and this was reflected in a very low turnout on polling day, 7 June. The result was a further victory for the Conservatives who won 60 of the 78 British seats. The new Government promised that it would be more positive than its predecessor in its attitude towards the EEC but it soon found itself in conflict with all its partners over its demand that Britain's net contribution to the EEC Budget be reduced by £1,000 million. Britain was also alone in calling for a tough response, including a boycott of the Moscow Olympics, to the Soviet invasion of Afghanistan in January 1980. Finally there were rows with particular countries, for example with France over the latter's refusal to permit imports of British lamb and with Germany over Britain's policy on North Sea oil.

Rhodesia: Return to Legality.

Elections, under the terms of the internal settlement, were held in Rhodesia in April 1979, leading to the formation in June of a coalition government led by Bishop Abel Muzorewa. Contrary to expectations, the Conservative Government did not recognise this government and continued to seek all-party agreement. The turning point occurred during the Commonwealth Conference at Lusaka in August 1979 where agreement was reached on the basic elements of a settlement. This led to three months of difficult negotiations in London, under the chairmanship of the Foreign Secretary, Lord Carrington, which culminated in the signing of a ceasefire and the lifting of sanctions in December 1979. Under its terms, a Cabinet Minister, Lord Soames, was appointed Governor for the period leading up to independence which was to be achieved following elections in February 1980. These elections, supervised by British and Commonwealth officials, resulted in a landslide victory for one of the Patriotic Front leaders, Robert

Mugabe. Following the formation of a coalition government, including two whites, independence was officially achieved in April 1980, Zimbabwe becoming the 43rd member of the Commonwealth.

Trade Unions and the Law.

One consequence of the Government's tough economic policies was an increase in unemployment. In the public sector the Government's plans to cut jobs and its reluctance to support industries in financial difficulty caused widespread alarm among the trade unions. However, an early collision between the Government and the unions was not expected, partly because of the refusal of the Employment Secretary, James Prior, to be stampeded into tough action against the unions, and partly because of the reluctance of the unions to take on the Government so soon after it had received a mandate in an election in which public dislike of union power had played a major part. However, these predictions were confounded by a crisis at British Steel. The world recession and the strict limits placed by the Government on its financial support for the industry forced British Steel to announce major redundancies, with dramatic implications for the level of employment in places such as Corby and Port Talbot. British Steel was also unable to offer its employees wage increases corresponding to the rate of inflation. Tension on both issues culminated in January 1980 in the first national steel strike for over 50 years.

Growing World Tension.

The Government, and Mrs. Thatcher in particular, acquired a reputation for taking a tough stance on international issues. Its determination to resist Soviet aggression led it to allow American Cruise missiles to be stationed in Britain and to decide to replace Polaris with Trident missiles as Britain's strategic nuclear deterrent (decisions that were opposed by a revived Campaign for Nuclear Dis-armament). Its attempt to organise a boycott of the Moscow Olympics in protest at the Soviet invasion of Afghanistan had only limited success and its strong recommendation against participation was heeded by only a minority of British sportsmen. Relations with Europe, however, became more cordial, assisted by the settlement, albeit on terms less favourable than the Prime Minister had hoped, of the dispute over Britain's contribution to the EEC budget. EEC governments acted in concert on various issues such as the Middle East and the American hostages in Iran. The problems of Iran spread dramatically to London at the end of April when seven gunmen seized the Iranian Embassy, taking 24 people hostage. Under the full view of TV cameras, the siege was successfully ended by the SAS a few days later.

Leadership of the Labour Party.

Constitutional questions dominated the Labour Party throughout 1980 and into 1981. At the 1980 Annual Conference the earlier decision to require re-selection of sitting MPs was confirmed but the plan to give the National Executive Committee the final say on the election manifesto was reversed. The most controversial decision, however, was to take the election of the Party leader out of the hands of the Parliamentary Labour Party alone and to set up an electoral college consisting of Labour MPs, the constituency parties and the affiliated trade unions. No agreement could be reached in October on the precise composition of such a college and a special conference was convened for this purpose in January 1981. In the midst of all this uncertainty, James Callaghan announced his retirement. The election of his successor therefore took place under the old system and, on the second ballot, the PLP elected Michael Foot by a margin of ten votes over Denis Healey. Denis Healey was subsequently elected Deputy Leader.

Deepening Recession.

The Government's counter-inflation policies, implemented at a time of worldwide recession, had a severe effect upon levels of output and employment. Industry was especially hard hit by the record interest rates and by the strength of the pound. Although inflation did fall steadily, public attention switched increasingly to unemployment which early in 1981 reached 2½ million. The Government came under bitter attack from the trade unions, although the 13-week steel strike was ended without major concessions and the TUC's Day of Action in May 1980 met with only limited success, and more woundingly from the CBI and some prominent Conservative backbenchers. These problems led ministers to relax their policy of non-intervention in industry and large amounts of money were pumped into some of the major lossmakers such as British Leyland and British Steel. Despite accusations that it was making U-turns, the Government insisted that its overall economic strategy was unchanged. Confirmation of this was provided by the Chancellor of the Exchequer. Although interest rates were lowered in November 1980 and March 1981, offsetting action was taken to restrict monetary growth. In the Budget in March substantial increases in personal taxation were imposed and windfall taxes were applied to the profits of the banks and oil companies.

The Birth of the Social Democratic Party.

During 1980 various leading members of the Labour Party became increasingly critical of its decisions on its constitution and on policy (such as the support at the Annual Conference for unilateral nuclear disarmament and withdrawal from the EEC). Led by Shirley Williams, David Owen and William Rodgers (popularly known as the Gang of Three), their disillusionment was heightened by the Special Conference at Wembley in January 1981 which not only reaffirmed the decision to establish an electoral college but also decided that its composition should be: trade unions 40%, constituency parties 30% and Labour MPs 30%. A week later, the Gang of Four (having been joined by Roy Jenkins on his retirement as President of the EEC Commission) published the Limehouse Declaration announcing the formation of a Council for Social Democracy. Initially this was not a separate party but only a group to campaign for moderate left-wing policies, but in March 1981 12 Labour MPs (including David Owen and William Rodgers) resigned the Party Whip and announced that they would not be seeking re-election as Labour MPs.

On 26 March 1981, to a fanfare of publicity, the Social Democratic Party was formally launched. In the House of Commons the SDP consisted initially of 14 MPs (13 ex-Labour and 1 ex-Conservative). One of its first decisions was to negotiate an electoral alliance with the Liberals.

Healey versus Benn.

In April 1981 Tony Benn announced his intention of standing against Denis Healey for the Deputy Leadership of the Labour Party, thereby bringing into play for the first time the new procedures which had been agreed at the Wembley conference at the beginning of the year. In a bruising six months of campaigning, Benn and Healey were joined by a third candidate, John Silkin, who offered himself as a conciliator between the Party's left and right wings. At the electoral college, held the day before the Annual Conference in Brighton in October, Silkin was eliminated in the first ballot and in a photofinish, in which the abstention of a number of MPs who had supported Silkin was decisive, Healey defeated Benn by the narrowest of margins. The ensuing conference produced further victories for the parliamentary leadership, notably in the election of the National Executive Committee and on the control of the Party's election manifesto. Although there was growing pressure from within the Party for a truce, symbolised by a meeting of the NEC and trade union leaders at Bishops Stortford in January 1982, Michael Foot's problems were by no means solved. Tension persisted between Tony Benn, who failed to secure election to the Shadow Cabinet in November, and his parliamentary colleagues. Under pressure from MPs, the NEC instituted an inquiry into the influence in the constituency parties of a Trotskyite group, the Militant Tendency.

"Wets" versus "Dries".

The Chancellor's tough Budget in March 1981 brought to the surface the tensions that had existed for some time within the Government and the Conservative Party generally. In an attempt to reassert her authority, Mrs. Thatcher undertook a major ministerial reshuffle in September. Among those dismissed was one of her most outspoken critics (who became widely known as "wets"), Sir Ian Gilmour, and another, James Prior, was switched from the Department of Employment to the Northern Ireland Office. Most of those who were promoted were loyal colleagues of the Prime Minister. Particularly significant were the appointments of Norman Tebbit as Secretary of State for Employment, charged with the task of introducing new legal curbs upon the trade unions, and of Nigel Lawson as Secretary of State for Energy who lost no time in announcing the Government's intention of privatising important parts of the state-owned North Sea oil and gas industries. The reshuffle, however, failed to silence the Prime Minister's critics within the Cabinet. After a lengthy battle, they succeeded in forcing the Chancellor of the Exchequer to make some relaxations in his plans for public spending in 1982–3 although he insisted upon recouping part of the cost in increased employee national insurance contributions. Their determination to press for a more radical change in economic strategy was strengthened by the continuing rise in the level of unemployment, which in January 1982 passed the 3 million mark, and by the financial problems of many companies which resulted in a record number of bankruptcies.

Social Unrest.

The Government's economic policies were alleged to be one of the contributory factors behind the ugly street violence which broke out in Brixton in April 1981 and in various cities, notably Liverpool, Manchester and London, three months later. Following the Brixton riots, the Government appointed a distinguished judge, Lord Scarman, to inquire into their causes. His report, completed in November, concluded that there had been a breakdown of confidence between the coloured community and the police against a background of urban deprivation, racial disadvantage and a rising level of street crime. The Liverpool riots prompted the Prime Minister to send a top-level task force, led by a Cabinet minister, Michael Heseltine, to investigate the area's problems and to find ways of overcoming them. Unemployment continued to keep down the number of industrial disputes. The Government became embroiled, however, in a major dispute with its own employees. Incensed by the Government's failure to honour its agreement that civil service pay should be fixed on the basis of fair comparison with equivalent work in the private sector, civil servants began a series of selective strikes in March which lasted for 21 weeks and had a major impact upon the work of the Government, for instance seriously disrupting the collection of tax revenue.

The Liberal/SDP Alliance.

Labour's continuing problems and the Government's economic record provided fertile ground for the launching of the Liberal/SDP Alliance. Its first real test (although it was formally endorsed by the Liberal Assembly only in September) occurred at a parliamentary by-election in Warrington in July 1981 where, in a safe Labour seat of a kind generally considered to be unpromising for the SDP, Roy Jenkins almost succeeded in overturning the Labour majority. Three months later, a Liberal, who had lost his deposit in the 1979 General Election, won the Conservative marginal seat of Croydon North West. Most dramatic of all, however, was Shirley Williams' victory in the safe Conservative seat of Crosby in late November. She thus became the first MP to be elected under the SDP's colours but the 24th member of its parliamentary group, nine further Labour MPs having transferred their allegiance since the inauguration of the Party in March. The SDP did not contest the county council elections in May but it won many local by-elections and, as a result of the defection of a majority of the Labour councillors in Islington, it took control of its first council. At the end of 1981 the opinion polls predicted a decisive victory for the Alliance were there to be an immediate general election. However, its popularity began to decline during the first few months of 1982 as the SDP (by then the third largest party in the House of Commons with 27 MPs) began to finalise its constitution and policy programme and as strains emerged in its alliance with the Liberals over the distribution of seats for the next general election. Nonetheless its momentum was maintained by Roy Jenkins' victory in the Glasgow, Hillhead by-election in March 1982, although in the May local elections it secured very few successes.

The Falkland Islands Crisis.

The Argentinian invasion of the Falkland Islands, British colonial territory in the South Atlantic, at the beginning of April 1982 provoked a major political crisis in Britain. At a special session of Parliament, the first to be held on a Saturday since the Suez crisis of 1956, there was almost universal condemnation of the Government's failure to take action to defend the Falklands against Argentinian aggression. Both the Foreign Secretary, Lord Carrington, and the Defence Secretary, John Nott, offered their resignations to the Prime Minister but only the former resigned (to be replaced by Francis Pym), along with two of his ministerial colleagues at the Foreign Office. Amidst great patriotic fervour, the Government despatched a major naval task force to re-take the islands. As it sailed on its long voyage to the South Atlantic, the United States Secretary of State, Alexander Haig, shuttled back and forth between London and Buenos Aires in an attempt to find a diplomatic solution to the crisis.

War in the South Atlantic.

A month after the task force had set out, military action commenced with British aircraft bombing Port Stanley airfield and clashes in the air and at sea. Following further unsuccessful efforts to reach a negotiated settlement, this time by the Secretary-General of the United Nations, British troops landed on East Falkland and, after 3½ weeks of bitter fighting, they encircled Port Stanley and secured the surrender of the Argentinian forces. During the conflict, over 1,000 lives were lost (255 British and 720 Argentinian). Fearing further Argentinian aggression, the Government had to make arrangements for a large permanent garrison on the islands. It also established a top-level committee of inquiry, under the chairmanship of Lord Franks, to investigate the events leading up to the crisis.

The Peace Movement.

The achievements of the task force resulted in strong public support for the armed forces and there were scenes of great jubilation on their return to this country. In other respects too defence attracted considerable public attention. The Campaign for Nuclear Disarmament organised a number of major demonstrations against the Government's nuclear weapons policy and peace camps were established at some of the bases where Cruise missiles were due to be sited in the autumn of 1983, such as Greenham Common near Newbury. Unilateral nuclear disarmament was adopted by the Labour Party as official policy at its 1982 Conference and it was recommended by a committee of the Church of England, although early in 1983 this recommendation was rejected by the Church's Synod in favour of multilateral disarmament, but with the proviso that Britain should never be the first to use nuclear weapons. To counter the arguments of the peace movement, Mrs. Thatcher appointed one of the Government's most effective orators, Michael Heseltine, to be Secretary of State for Defence in January 1983, replacing John Nott who some months earlier had announced his intention of retiring from politics at the next general election.

The Difficulties of the Opposition.

In some respects 1982 was an easier year for the leadership of the Labour Party. Michael Foot and Denis Healey were re-elected as Leader and Deputy Leader unopposed and they increased their control over the National Executive Committee. However, the Party's problems were by no means resolved. At a time of national crisis and patriotic fervour the task of Opposition leader is never easy and this was one factor contributing to a steady decline in the popularity of Mr. Foot among the electorate. His difficulties were exacerbated by continuing rows within the Party. Following receipt of the report into the activities of the Militant Tendency, it was decided to require all groups that wished to operate within the Party to register and to meet certain conditions laid down by the NEC. In the opinion of

the NEC, Militant failed to satisfy these conditions but action to expel its leaders was delayed by legal complications. These and other problems were reflected in the Party's electoral popularity. In October 1982 it narrowly succeeded in winning the Conservative marginal seat of Birmingham, Northfield, but in February 1983 it suffered the crushing blow of losing Bermondsey, one of the safest Labour seats in the country. This setback was to some extent offset by the retention of the marginal seat of Darlington a month later.

The 1983 General Election.

Throughout most of 1982 the Government, and Mrs. Thatcher in particular, enjoyed a commanding lead in the opinion polls. This was a remarkable achievement for a government in the fourth year of its existence, particularly in view of the continuing upward trend in unemployment, and it largely reflected public approval of the Government's handling of the Falklands crisis (and it was exonerated by the Franks Committee for not having averted the Argentinian invasion). From early 1983 onwards the continuing Conservative lead in the opinion polls fuelled speculation about an early general election. The Prime Minister, who could easily have dampened such speculation, did not do so. Instead, having seen an analysis of the municipal election results in May, she decided on a snap poll on 9 June.

Potentially, the election could have been of exceptional interest. For the first time since the 1920s it was a three-horse race, with the Liberal/SDP Alliance contesting every seat in mainland Britain. The constituency map had also been extensively redrawn since 1979, with many well-known MPs having to fight new constituencies. In practice, however, it produced few excitements. The commanding lead of the Conservatives was never challenged during the campaign and interest therefore focused upon the contest between Labour and the Alliance for second place. Labour's difficulties were aggravated, in what was an increasingly presidential-style campaign, by unfavourable comparisons drawn by most voters between Mr. Foot and Mrs. Thatcher.

A Decisive Conservative Victory.

From the very first result there was no doubt about the outcome of the election. With the Labour vote in retreat everywhere and with the Alliance polling well but failing to secure a real breakthrough, the Conservatives coasted to a decisive victory, winning an overall majority of 144, only two short of the massive majority won by Labour in the landslide of 1945. (For the full results, see **D3–4**.) In terms of votes, however, the Conservative share of the vote (43%) had *fallen* since 1979. What had happened was that the Conservatives had won a large number of seats because the opposition was divided, with the Alliance eating seriously into the Labour vote. Labour's share of the vote (28%) was the lowest since the early 1920s and it held only two seats in southern England outside London. Elsewhere it managed to hold on to seats and, with 209 MPs, was easily the second largest party. The Alliance polled almost as many votes as Labour (26%) but because its vote was less concentrated it won many fewer seats (only 23), and had to be content with coming second in as many as 313 constituencies. The result was a particular disappointment for the SDP, most of whose leading members, apart from Roy Jenkins and David Owen, were defeated. Other prominent casualties in the election included Tony Benn, Albert Booth, Joan Lestor and David Ennals, all former Labour Ministers.

Mrs. Thatcher's Second Term.

Strengthened by her success at the polls, Mrs. Thatcher made various ministerial changes designed to increase her dominance over the Cabinet. She sacked Francis Pym, who had been Foreign Secretary since the start of the Falklands crisis but with whom she had never enjoyed an easy relationship, and replaced him with Sir Geoffrey Howe, who had been her loyal Chancellor of the Exchequer since 1979. In his place, she promoted Nigel Lawson, a keen supporter of her economic policies. As a reward for his work as Party Chairman, she appointed Cecil Parkinson to head a new department, combining

Trade and Industry. William Whitelaw left the Home Office but remained Deputy Prime Minister and was elevated to the House of Lords as a Viscount. This was the first hereditary peerage to be conferred since 1964. (However, neither he nor the second such peer, the former Speaker, George Thomas, had male heirs; the hereditary principle was to be fully restored only in 1984 when an earldom was conferred upon Harold Macmillan on the occasion of his 90th birthday.) Victory at the polls, however, did not assure Mrs. Thatcher of an easy time. On various issues, including reductions in NHS manpower, control of local authorities, fuel prices and housing benefits, there was open criticism from Conservative backbenchers, sometimes about the substance of what the Government was doing, and often about its presentation. The most serious embarrassment concerned the personal life of Cecil Parkinson. The disclosure that his former secretary was expecting his child did not lead to his immediate resignation. However, further revelations during the Party Conference, which but for this would have been a victory celebration, made his departure from the Government inevitable and resulted in the appointment of Norman Tebbit to replace him (he had earlier handed over the Party Chairmanship to John Selwyn Gummer).

New Opposition Leaders.

Shortly after the General Election, both Michael Foot and Denis Healey announced their intention of standing down as Leader and Deputy Leader of the Labour Party at the Party Conference in October 1983. Four candidates stood for the leadership, but early in the campaign it soon emerged that left-winger, Neil Kinnock, would be the easy winner over Roy Hattersley, the leading "moderate" candidate. Interest therefore focused upon the contest for the deputy leadership where, although there were again four candidates, the race was between Hattersley (both he and Kinnock had agreed to stand for both offices and to serve under the other) and Michael Meacher, the standard bearer for the left in the absence of Tony Benn. Although there were close decisions in a number of trade unions, Hattersley emerged as a comfortable winner, thus giving the Party the so-called "dream ticket" of balanced leadership which many supporters believed was essential if it was to rebuild its electoral support. That this was going to be a lengthy process was acknowledged in the choice of a leader aged only 41. A similar development occurred also in the SDP where David Owen, aged 45, was elected unopposed to replace Roy Jenkins as leader.

The Cruise Missile Debate.

Failure to reach a negotiated arms control agreement on intermediate-range missiles led the Government to proceed with the deployment of US Cruise missiles in Britain. This decision was endorsed by the House of Commons in October 1983 which also rejected a proposal for a dual-key control system, designed to ensure that the missiles could be used only with the consent of the British Government. This decision, and that of the German Parliament to commence deployment of Pershing II missiles, resulted in a Soviet walkout from the arms control talks at Geneva. The first Cruise missiles arrived in Britain at Greenham Common, near Newbury, in November and were operational by Christmas. Demonstrations against these developments continued throughout the year and were fuelled by tensions in the Anglo-American alliance over the US invasion in October 1983 of the Caribbean island of Grenada, an independent member of the Commonwealth, despite the serious reservations of the British Government. Sir Geoffrey Howe's handling of this crisis and of the decision early in 1984 to ban trade unions from the Government Communications Centre at Cheltenham (GCHQ) was widely criticised. At the same time, however, there were signs that Western leaders' attitudes towards the Warsaw Pact were softening, symbolised by Mrs. Thatcher's visit to Hungary in February 1984, her first visit to a Communist country, by her decision to travel to Moscow for the funerals of Presidents Andropov and Chernenko, and by her warmth towards the new Soviet leader, Mr. Gorbachev, on his accession to office in March 1985.

Implementing its Manifesto.

The Queen's Speech for the first session of the new Parliament contained few surprises. Various measures, such as the privatisation of British Telecom and bills on data protection and police powers, had been introduced in the last Parliament but had been lost as a result of the early dissolution; others, including the abolition of the Greater London Council and the metropolitan county councils, the creation of a quango to run London Transport, and new curbs on local authorities, had featured prominently in the Conservative Manifesto. The Government also proceeded with its plans further to regulate the activities of trade unions, introducing legislation requiring the periodic election of union officials, and the holding of secret ballots before strike action and to decide whether to maintain a fund for financing political objectives. The prospect of a further five years of Conservative rule injected a new realism in most union leaders and this, coupled with a less strident tone on the part of ministers following Tom King's appointment to replace Norman Tebbit as Secretary for State for Employment, led to concessions on the last of these proposals. Industrial relations problems, however, remained in the public eye, especially in the printing industry where there were a number of serious disputes, including a confrontation between the National Graphical Association and a Warrington newspaper publisher which led to protracted litigation and in the mining industry, where a bitter battle against pit closures developed.

Privatisation.

Privatisation—limiting the role of the state and extending the operation of market forces—was one of the hallmarks of the Government. It embarked upon the biggest change in the boundary between the public and private sectors since 1945. It encouraged the contracting out to private firms of work that previously was undertaken by public bodies (e.g. local authority cleansing and refuse collection services, NHS cleaning, laundry and catering); it relaxed statutory monopoly powers and licensing arrangements in various sectors (e.g. buses and telecommunications); and it sold all or part of a number of public enterprises. During its first term these included selling a majority stake in British Aerospace, in the oil-producing side of the British National Oil Corporation—Britoil—and in Cable and Wireless. These were dwarfed by the sales of just over 50% of British Telecom in November 1984 and of almost all the shares in British Gas – the largest ever flotation of a company – two years later. Other sales during its second term included Jaguar, the Trustee Savings Bank and British Airways and, during 1987, the Government disposed of its remaining shareholding in BP and sold British Airports.

Miners' Strike.

In March 1984 the National Coal Board (NCB) announced plans to close various pits to eliminate excess capacity. This exacerbated tensions that already existed in the industry and rapidly escalated into a national strike. Given the history of relations since the early 1970s between the miners and the Conservatives, a major confrontation seemed inevitable. But few predicted its length or bitterness. The NCB, whose chairman Ian MacGregor had earlier established a reputation for toughness at British Steel, with the full backing of the Government, was determined not to surrender; its attitude was matched by that of the striking miners, led by Arthur Scargill, who were driven on by the feeling that they were defending the very existence of their communities. The NUM, however, failed to bring the economy to its knees as it had done in 1972–4. Not only was it unsuccessful in attracting effective support from the rest of the trade union movement, it also was itself divided, with about one third of its members, especially in the prosperous Nottinghamshire coalfield, refusing to join the strike. The Government too went to some lengths to ensure that alternative sources of fuel were available. The NUM's attempts to prevent working miners getting to work led to violent scenes between pickets and the large numbers of police who were deployed, often in riot gear, to restrain them. Eventually, after various abortive rounds of negotiation, striking miners, many of whom were suffering severe financial hardship, started to trickle back to work and, after almost exactly a year, the NUM decided to end the strike without reaching an agreement with the NCB. Quite apart from the damage that it did to the economy, the strike imposed major strains upon both the TUC and the Labour Party. The Labour leadership sought to distance itself from the more extreme statements and behaviour of Arthur Scargill and his followers while supporting the miners' case. It was criticised, however, for not giving more wholehearted support by the left wing of the Party, whose ranks in Parliament had been strengthened in March 1984 by the victory of Tony Benn in a by-election at Chesterfield.

Brighton Bombing.

The Conservative Party Conference in October 1984 at Brighton was overshadowed by a bomb explosion at the Grand Hotel where most of the Cabinet was staying. Mrs. Thatcher herself had a narrow escape and, among those seriously injured were Norman Tebbit and the Chief Whip. Responsibility was claimed by the IRA. A month earlier, Jim Prior had resigned as Secretary of State for Northern Ireland, choosing to return to the back-benches, thus removing from the Cabinet yet another critic of the Government's economic strategy. Ministers continued to be embarrassed by back-bench revolts on various issues but the Government's majority in the Commons was never endangered. In the Lords, however, it was forced to amend its plans, for example over the cancellation of the GLC and metropolitan county elections in 1986. One Opposition backbencher, Tam Dalyell, had his persistence in probing the Government's account of the sinking of the Argentinian ship, the General Belgrano, during the Falklands crisis rewarded when a leak by a senior civil servant in the Ministry of Defence, Clive Ponting, revealed inconsistencies. Controversially, the Attorney-General decided to prosecute Mr. Ponting under the widely discredited Official Secrets Act and when, contrary to all expectations, he was acquitted a major political row erupted.

Close to Dollar Parity.

The damage inflicted on the economy by the miners' strike (estimated by the Chancellor of the Exchequer to have cost £2¾ billion) was one of the factors behind a slide in the exchange rate. Miscalculations by the Government, however, also contributed to the rapid decline in the dollar value of sterling. Faced with the imminent possibility of parity between the pound and the dollar, the Chancellor was forced to re-introduce minimum lending rate and to force up interest rates. This eventually succeeded in calming the nerves of the money markets. But it had an adverse effect on the prospects of economic revival. The Government was widely attacked for its failure to take direct action to alleviate the problem of unemployment not only by the Opposition but also by some of the most senior members of its own Party and by prominent members of the Church of England. One such critic was the Earl of Stockton, formerly Harold Macmillan, who took advantage of the first televised debate from the House of Lords in January 1985 to reach a wide audience for his views.

Getting the Message Across.

By the summer of 1985, the Government's popularity was at a low ebb. Continuing record levels of unemployment, cuts in many public services, and long-running industrial disputes (the year-long miners' strike was followed by an equally protracted teachers' dispute), all contributed to the worst by-election defeat for the Conservatives for many years at Brecon and Radnor in July. In an attempt to improve the Government's standing, Mrs. Thatcher made a number of important changes in the Cabinet in September. As Party Chairman she appointed her close ally, Norman Tebbit (and to assist him in getting the Government's message across she recruited best-selling author, Jeffrey Archer, as his deputy). In the sensitive area of law and order she shifted Douglas Hurd from Northern Ireland to the Home Office. His predecessor, Leon Brittan, who was generally regarded as a poor performer on TV and who had been widely criticised for putting pressure on the BBC to cancel a programme on political extremism in Northern Ireland, replaced Norman Tebbit as Secretary of State for Trade and Industry. For a

few months these changes seemed to have been successful, even though the new Home Secretary was immediately embroiled in controversy over the outbreak of rioting in Handsworth in Birmingham and in Brixton and Tottenham in London and over the tactics adopted by the police in attempting to restore order.

Stronger Labour Leadership.

Although Labour did well in the county council elections in May 1985, it continued to share the spoils of the Government's unpopularity with the Alliance which succeeded in breaking the two-party hold on most of the counties in England and in winning the Brecon and Radnor by-election. The strains within the Labour movement caused by the miners' strike persisted as a result of the creation of a breakaway union, the Union of Democratic Miners, which successfully challenged the National Union of Mineworkers in parts of the country. In addition, the Labour leadership was challenged to support various left-wing Labour controlled local authorities in their defiance of the new financial curbs that had been imposed by the Government. At the Party's Annual Conference, Neil Kinnock answered those who had criticised him for lack of leadership by making a vigorous attack both upon Arthur Scargill and upon hard left Labour councillors, particularly in Liverpool. His stand won him support among Labour M.P.s and in the opinion polls but it did not resolve the problems facing the Labour Party. The NEC launched an inquiry into the running of the Liverpool District Party which early in 1986 recommended action which could lead to the expulsion of various leading members. Labour councillors in Liverpool and Lambeth were also confronted with bankruptcy and disqualification following court action initiated by the District Auditor over their delay in setting a rate. They and other Labour councillors facing similar penalties pressed the Labour leadership to indemnify them on Labour's return to power.

The Westland Saga.

The Government's calmed nerves were soon disturbed by an extraordinary internal battle over the fate of a West Country helicopter manufacturer, Westland plc. Throughout the Christmas recess an unusually public row simmered between two Cabinet ministers over the merits of two alternative solutions to the financial problems of the company. The Defence Secretary, Michael Heseltine, campaigned hard for a European solution whereas the Trade and Industry Secretary, Leon Brittan, with the backing of the Prime Minister, favoured leaving the decision to the company's shareholders which in effect meant that the company would be bailed out by the American firm, Sikorsky. The first casualty was Michael Heseltine who walked dramatically out of a Cabinet meeting, refusing to accept the Prime Minister's attempt to shackle his campaign. The next fortnight saw intense political controversy, fuelled by allegations first over different versions of a meeting between Leon Brittan and the chief executive of Westland and then over the unprecedented leaking of a letter to Michael Heseltine from the Solicitor-General. Although he retained the support of the Prime Minister, Leon Brittan's position became untenable and he followed his adversary onto the backbenches. Westland continued to dominate the headlines for some weeks but the focus of attention switched to the company itself and its shareholders, who eventually backed the American option. The Government, however, was immediately involved in a new political row over the future of the state-owned car firm, British Leyland, when it was disclosed that discussions had reached an advanced stage over the sale of different parts of the company to General Motors and Ford. The Government was forced to break off its negotiations with Ford over Austin-Rover and this change of course further dented the Government's reputation.

Anglo-Irish Agreement.

Westland and British Leyland were not the only sources of trouble for the Government in the early months of 1986. In November 1985, Mrs. Thatcher and the Irish premier, Dr. Fitzgerald, signed an

Anglo-Irish Agreement. Both Governments affirmed the status of Ulster as part of the UK so long as this was the wish of the majority of its people; and they set up an inter-governmental conference to enable the Irish Government to comment on certain aspects of Northern Irish affairs, and to foster improved cross-border cooperation, particularly on security, establishing an inter-governmental conference to discuss issues of common interest This provoked the resignation of all the Unionist M.P.s in protest at what they saw as the first step towards a united Ireland and their stand attracted the support of a number of senior Conservative M.P.s, one of whom, Ian Gow, who earlier had been one of Mrs. Thatcher's closest aides, resigned from the Government. All but one of the Unionists were re-elected in by-elections held in January 1986. The Government's refusal to abandon the Agreement, however, led to a one-day strike in the province in February and to further acts of defiance.

A World Leader.

After six years in office, Mrs. Thatcher had become one of the most experienced political leaders in the world. She enjoyed a very close relationship with President Reagan, demonstrating her support by allowing US aircraft based in Britain to be used in a reprisal attack on centres of terrorism in Libya in April 1986 and by refusing to join international criticism of Reagan over the sale of arms to Iran in exchange for hostages (the so-called Irangate Affair). On other issues too Mrs. Thatcher took an independent line. Although condemning apartheid in South Africa, she refused to support the call for economic sanctions. In an attempt to maintain unity, a Commonwealth Eminent Persons Group, which included the former Conservative Chancellor, Lord Barber, was sent on a mission to South Africa to investigate means of promoting peaceful political change. Despite its negative conclusions, published in 1986, Mrs. Thatcher persuaded her EEC colleagues to send Sir Geoffrey Howe on a further mission. Its failure resulted in a Commonwealth decision to take various economic measures against South Africa but the British Government agreed only to impose voluntary bans upon new investment and the promotion of tourism and, in conjunction with the EEC, to stop imports of iron and steel.

Big Bang in the City.

Westland was not the only cause of unusual public attention on the business world. A rash of company mergers and takeovers gave rise to extensive advertising campaigns as rival bidders sought to influence shareholders' votes. The battle over the future of the Distillers Company was particularly bitter. However, the eventual victor, Guinness, was widely criticised when a number of undertakings given at the time of the takeover were not honoured and, following disclosure of improprieties during the course of the bid, its chief executive, Ernest Saunders, and a number of his advisers were forced to resign. This affair, coupled with the radical changes that occurred in the City of London in October 1986, led to pressure on the Government to introduce tighter regulation of the financial markets. The so-called 'Big Bang' opened up membership of the Stock Exchange and extended competition in share dealing and in financial services generally. One consequence was a rapid growth in foreign involvement in the City with new firms offering extremely high salaries to attract key staff. Although the Government did introduce some new statutory controls, it stuck to its view that self-regulation was more likely to be effective.

Election Speculation.

The Government also benefited from the spectacularly successful publicity generated by Mrs. Thatcher's visit to the Soviet Union in April 1987. This confirmation of her stature as a world figure contrasted sharply with the reception accorded to Mr. Kinnock by President Reagan when he visited Washington to explain Labour's non-nuclear defence strategy.

The 1987 General Election.

A good performance by the Conservatives in the local elections in May 1987 led Mrs. Thatcher to seek an immediate dissolution of Parliament with polling day on 11 June. More than ever before, the style of the campaign was determined by the media. Every TV and radio station provided near-saturation coverage and the parties responded by seeking to exploit all the time and space offered to them. The result was an almost presidential campaign with a succession of 'photo-opportunities' of the party leaders. Unlike 1983, the Labour Party was in much better shape to mount this kind of campaign, making full use of the relative youth and informality of its leader, Neil Kinnock. However, the three weeks of the campaign were remarkably uneventful with no incident seriously disrupting the stage management of the party managers. Nor did all the money and effort expended by the parties appear to have much effect upon public opinion. With only one hiccough, the Conservatives' lead in the opinion polls remained secure. Labour's position improved by a few points but it was almost entirely at the expense of the Alliance.

Third Conservative Victory.

At the eve of the poll the only uncertainty concerned the size of the Conservative majority and the impact that tactical voting might have in some marginal constituencies. From the first declared result in Torbay, it was clear that the majority was going to be larger than most commentators had predicted and that the Alliance in particular was not going to benefit from tactical voting on a scale comparable with that seen in recent by-elections. The final outcome was an overall majority for the Conservatives of 101 over all other parties, a fall of only 43 from its landslide in 1983. They gained 12 seats, and lost 29; Labour gained 26, mainly in Scotland and the North of England, and lost 6; and the Alliance gained 3 and lost 8. Nationally, there had been a swing of 2.5% from Conservative to Labour since 1983 but this figure hides the extent of Labour's success in Scotland (where it won 50 out of the 72 seats) and Wales, and its poor showing in London (where it lost 3 seats) and the South East. As never before, the political map of Britain was divided, with the Conservatives overwhelmingly predominant south of a line from the Wash to the Severn, and Labour strengthening its hold on the urban areas in the North. For details of the Election result, *see* **D3–4.**

Mrs. Thatcher's New Cabinet.

The election hattrick – Mrs. Thatcher was the first Prime Minister since Lord Liverpool in 1827 to win three successive election victories – was a personal triumph for the Prime Minister. Relatively few changes were made in the Cabinet but their effect was to strengthen still further her position. Out went John Biffen, who had criticised Mrs. Thatcher's style and some of her policies; following strains during the campaign between Downing Street and party headquarters, Norman Tebbit also left the Cabinet at his own request, but he retained the Chairmanship of the Party until the Autumn. Lord Young, who had played an increasingly influential role during the Election, was promoted, Cecil Parkinson was brought back after nearly four years on the backbenches following his personal difficulties, and most of the newcomers, such as John Moore and John Major, were close personal supporters of the Prime Minister.

Strains in the Alliance.

The Election result was especially disappointing for the Alliance. Far from breaking the mould of two-party politics, its overall vote fell, it suffered a net loss of 5 seats including some of its leading M.P.s, and it failed to win almost any of the marginal seats it had targeted. On the other hand it had still gained 23% of the votes cast. Reflecting on this performance over the weekend after polling day, David Steel called for the 'democratic fusion' of the two wings of the Alliance into a single united party. His initiative set in train many months of protracted and increasingly bitter negotiations. On the Liberal side, the overwhelming majority of the Party accepted the case for merger albeit tinged for many with regret at the passing of the party which traced its origins to the eighteenth century. The SDP however split in two. Its leader, David Owen, supported by two of his Parliamentary colleagues, mounted a powerful campaign against merger; the other two M.P.s, one of whom—Robert Maclennan—was elected leader after the SDP voted to open negotiations with the Liberals, and prominent members such as Shirley Williams and Roy Jenkins took the opposite view. During the first few months of 1988, the negotiations were concluded and the outcome ratified by both parties. The new party, the Social and Liberal Democrats (SLD), was launched in March 1988. Initially it had joint leadership—David Steel and Robert Maclennan—but in July 1988 Paddy Ashdown was elected leader, defeating Alan Beith.

The Next Moves Forward.

Far from running out of steam, the Government embarked upon a radical programme for its third term of office. Its initial agenda, following closely its election manifesto, included the abolition of domestic rates and their replacement by a flat-rate community charge, or poll tax as its critics preferred to claim; privatisation of the electricity supply, steel and water industries; far-reaching reform of education, including giving schools the right to opt out of local authority control and the abolition of the Inner London Education Authority; introduction of radical changes in the social security system; and further reforms of housing, immigration control and industrial relations. With its substantial majority, the Government's prospects were set fair. However, its standing and self-confidence suffered a severe blow from almost the only area of government in which radical changes had not been introduced since 1979: the National Health Service. Throughout the Autumn public attention focused relentlessly upon the financial difficulties being experienced by many health authorities, especially in large cities, which were leading to closed wards and postponement of operations. The Government's defence of its record, based largely on statistics which demonstrated substantial increases in overall spending on the NHS, failed to carry weight against a barrage of individual instances of breakdown in services. To make matters worse, the Secretary of State for Social Services, John Moore, was away on extended sick-leave. In an attempt to regain the initiative, the Prime Minister launched in January 1988 a fundamental review of the NHS.

Tax-cutting Budget.

The Government's difficulties with the NHS had a damaging effect upon Conservative morale and worked wonders for the Opposition. After many unrewarding years, Labour had found an issue on which the Government was vulnerable and its case attracted strong public support. In other areas however the Government continued to ride high. In his 1988 Budget the Chancellor was able to achieve his goal of reducing the standard rate of income tax by a further 2p to 25p, and of introducing various major tax reforms. His approach was criticised by his opponents on two grounds. It was argued first that priority should have been given to increasing public spending, particularly on the NHS, rather than to cutting taxes, and second that the principal beneficiaries of the Budget were the well-off. This charge was fuelled a month later when changes in social security benefits hit many low earners. One change in particular, relating to housing benefit, led to such pressure on Conservative backbenchers that the Government was compelled to revise its decision. Ministers also faced a difficult few months in securing the passage of controversial legislation on the community charge and educational reform through the House of Lords. Its task there was exacerbated by the retirement through ill-health early in 1988 of Viscount Whitelaw whose popularity and experience had proved invaluable in the past both in Cabinet discussions and in Parliamentary business. On the other hand, the Government still enjoyed the exceptional good fortune of a divided and ineffective Opposition. Despite its better showing in Parliament, the Labour leadership was distracted for much of 1988 by a challenge which under the protracted electoral college system took six months to resolve; and the Social and Liberal Democrats had the daunting task of rebuilding their support in competition with David Owen's Social Democratic Party.

Mid-term Difficulties.

By the end of 1988, Nigel Lawson's tax-cutting Budget was looking ill-advised. Booming consumer spending had led to the recurrence of two all too familiar problems: inflation and a trade deficit. Inflation, the Government's own touchstone of economic success, rose steadily, reaching almost 8% by March 1989. The balance of payments deficit at the turn of the year broke all previous records. Virtually alone, the Chancellor remained confident that these were merely temporary and minor hiccoughs in the country's economic recovery which could be overcome by the single weapon of increasing interest rates. In other respects too the Government was experiencing mid-term difficulties. It faced an uphill task in convincing the public of the merits of major measures such as the introduction of the community charge, or poll tax, and privatisation of water and electricity. Its reputation for competence also began to look tarnished. Increasing public concern about food safety was highlighted in angry exchanges between the Ministry of Agriculture and the Department of Health over salmonella in eggs which led to the resignation of the outspoken junior Health Minister, Edwina Currie; and a run of transport disasters turned an unusual and unflattering spotlight on the performance of the Secretary of State for Transport, Paul Channon. Most damaging of all, the Government's problems over the NHS persisted. In mid-1988, Mrs. Thatcher split the DHSS, appointing Kenneth Clarke to take a high profile in Health, and relegating the hapless John Moore to Social Security. The benefits of this change were soured by bitterness over the handling of nurse regrading and by continuing uncertainty over the outcome of the Prime Minister's Review. The eventual White Paper, published in January 1989, heralded far-reaching changes and was greeted by almost universal opposition, spearheaded by the doctors.

A Divided Opposition.

Despite all these problems, the Conservatives' lead in the opinion polls did not disappear immediately. In part this reflected the electoral collapse of the Centre. The SLD and the SDP seemed intent upon destroying each other, not only splitting the former Alliance share of the vote—thereby enabling the Conservatives to scrape home in the Richmond by-election in February 1989—but also reducing their combined support as they no longer appeared a credible alternative. Labour benefited also from their disarray but, after three successive election defeats, it had its own problems of credibility. Following the 1987 Election, Neil Kinnock initiated a fundamental review of all aspects of Labour policy. Although he beat off easily the challenge to his position from Tony Benn at the 1988 Conference, his attempts to present a new image were dented by continuing difficulties over defence policy which highlighted the role of the trade unions in the Party's affairs. Labour's problems were compounded by the loss of the safe seat of Glasgow Govan to the Scottish National Party in November 1988.

A Decade in Office.

May 1989 marked the tenth anniversary of Mrs. Thatcher's accession to office. Throughout the decade she had dominated British politics to an extent unequalled in recent history. Within the Conservative Party her critics, with just one or two exceptions, had either retired or sat impotent on the backbenches. Radical changes had been implemented in almost every area of government, frequently against bitter opposition, and the Prime Minister often seemed to set the agenda and dictate the solution regardless of the issue—exchange rate policy, football hooliganism, and the environment to name just three recent examples. Abroad too she had outlasted most of her allies and adversaries. The former, led by President Reagan, feted her as a leading world statesman; and even those who disagreed accorded her considerable respect. However fate allowed little time for celebration. In June the Conservatives were defeated in the elections for the European Parliament, a result attributed to Mrs Thatcher's negative attitude towards Europe. In an attempt to restore her fortunes, the following month the Prime Minister undertook a more radical reshuffle than had been expected. In particular she moved a reluctant Sir Geoffrey Howe from the Foreign Office to the Leadership of the House of Commons with the courtesy title of Deputy Prime Minister. The handling of the negotiations with her most senior colleague, and her apparently cavalier treatment of a number of others tarnished her reputation. Nor did the promotion of John Major to Foreign Secretary inspire confidence. His inexperience in this field and his closeness to Mrs Thatcher signalled Downing Street's determination to control foreign policy. In the Autumn matters were no easier for the Prime Minister. Continuing tension between the Chancellor, Nigel Lawson, and her personal economic adviser, Sir Alan Walters, led to the Chancellor's abrupt resignation in October. To fill the gap, John Major was moved to the Treasury and Mrs Thatcher had to appoint a much more independently minded Douglas Hurd to the Foreign Office. Finally she had to face the indignity of a challenge to her position as Conservative leader from a backbench critic, Sir Anthony Meyer. Although not a credible challenger, he nonetheless attracted 33 votes and there were also about 25 abstentions.

Delors Plan and the Social Charter.

Always a determined defender of UK interests within the EEC, Mrs Thatcher took every opportunity of challenging the moves towards greater integration and a shift of power from national capitals to Brussels. She angered European opinion by refusing to reappoint Lord Cockfield as one of the British members of the European Commission and delivered a swingeing attack on the aspirations of many continental Europeans at a ceremony at the College of Europe in Bruges. During 1989 Britain became increasingly out of step with its partners. On monetary integration there were differences of view between the Prime Minister on the one hand and her Chancellor and Foreign Secretary on the other. At the Madrid Summit in June they obtained her reluctant acquiescence in the first stage of the Delors Plan (prepared by the President of the Commission, Jacques Delors) including Britain's acceptance in principle to join the exchange rate mechanism (ERM) of the European Monetary System (EMS). However, Britain alone opposed stages 2 and 3 of the Plan, leading to monetary union and a single currency. Britain was also isolated in its opposition to the Social Charter, a wide-ranging statement of rights on employment, including pay, working hours, leave and free time, social benefits, vocational training, equal opportunities, worker consultation and participation, which Mrs Thatcher argued would impose excessive burdens on industry and introduce undesirable state control.

Out of Line or Ahead of Time?

On other overseas issues Britain was becoming increasingly isolated. The special relationship with the USA became weaker with the retirement in January 1989 of Mrs Thatcher's close personal friend Ronald Reagan, and his replacement as President by George Bush who appeared to be closer to a number of other European leaders. On the question of sanctions against South Africa, Mrs Thatcher was at odds with both the Commonwealth, producing her own communique at the Heads of Government conference in Kuala Lumpur in October 1989, and the EEC. Britain welcomed the reforms introduced by the new State President of South Africa, F. W. de Klerk, and the release of Nelson Mandela in February 1990 after 27 years in detention. In the Government's view, these steps called for a positive response through a progressive relaxation of sanctions lest they provoked a white backlash; its partners argued that pressure required to be maintained to ensure the dismantling of apartheid and the ending of the state of emergency.

Elsewhere, however, Mrs Thatcher claimed to be ahead of her colleagues. She had been one of the first world leaders to recognise the significance of Gorbachev's rise to power; and the changes that swept the Soviet Union and Eastern Europe during the second half of 1989 were heralded as part of the same process of freeing people from the shackles of state control and socialism that she had introduced

in Britain. In contrast, the return to repression in China cast doubt on China's promises regarding Hong Kong and, faced with a "haemorrhage of talent", the Government had—despite criticism from its own supporters—to grant full British citizenship to about 50,000 leaders of the colony and their families. The Government also attracted international criticism over its decision to repatriate those Vietnamese boat people who did not qualify for refugee status. On a happier note, diplomatic relations were restored with Argentina, eight years after the Falklands War.

Return to Two-Party Politics.

The early months of 1989 saw an upturn in the Labour Party's fortunes. Neil Kinnock began to score some Parliamentary victories over the Prime Minister; there was a general view among commentators that Labour's frontbench team matched and probably outshone their counterparts; and the White Paper on the NHS provided an issue on which they were able to lead public opinion. This was reflected in two victories at the polls: the Vale of Glamorgan by-election in May and the Euroelections in June. At the Party Conference in October, Mr Kinnock completed his transformation of the Party's image by winning overwhelming endorsement of the outcome of the policy reviews. Throughout the Autumn, Labour maintained a firm lead in the opinion polls and, in February 1990, this had stretched to around 15% and Neil Kinnock was rated above Mrs Thatcher. The Government's difficulties remained unabated. Despite unprecedently high interest rates, inflation showed little sign of falling; public doubts about its handling of the NHS were compounded by a six-month pay dispute with ambulancemen; and April 1990 heralded the introduction of the poll tax in England and Wales. British politics appeared to have returned to its familiar two-party character. Both the SLD—restyled as Liberal Democrats following a poll of members—and the SDP remained in the doldrums, suffering the discomfort of losing third place in the Euro-elections to the Greens. Their 15% share of the vote reflected a marked increase in environmental concern which affected all parties. This prompted Mrs Thatcher to replace Nicholas Ridley as Environment Secretary with a more environmentally friendly Chris Patten and to introduce a "Green" Bill in the 1989–90 session. This was not the only move towards "softening" the Government's image, prompted in part by the introduction of TV cameras into the House of Commons in November 1989.

Conservatives in Disarray.

The unpopularity of the poll tax surpassed the worst fears of those Conservatives who had opposed its introduction. As local councils declared the initial level of tax, in almost every case—Tory and Labour controlled—well in excess of the Government's estimate, they were met by strong protest. Nor did the violence of some of the demonstrations, especially at a rally in London, rebound on the Government's critics. By April 1990 Labour's lead in the polls was over 20%, and the Prime Minister's personal popularity had plummetted. With the prospect also of double-figure inflation, backbench jitters prompted renewed speculation about a further challenge to her leadership in the Autumn. Although scrupulously loyal in public, Michael Heseltine's candidature lacked only its formal announcement; Norman Tebbit began to mobilise the right of the Party; and the results of the local elections were awaited with unusual interest, although in the event Conservative losses were not as heavy as feared. In particular, the Conservatives polled unexpectedly well in such London boroughs as Ealing.

Major Government Decisions, May 1979–June 1990.

Economic Affairs

Reduction in standard rate of income tax to 30% in 1979 (offset by increase in VAT to 15%) to 29% in 1986, to 27% in 1987, and to 25% in 1988.

Abolition of exchange controls

Reform of system of monetary control, including abolition of Minimum Lending Rate (re-introduced as temporary crisis measure in 1985).

Introduction of various schemes to reduce unemployment including major new Youth Training Scheme

Abolition of hire purchase controls

Education

Strengthening of position of parents on school governing bodies and in choosing schools for their children

Introduction of Assisted Places Scheme to give financial support to enable certain pupils to attend independent schools

Decision to replace O Level and CSE with a new examination as from 1988

Imposition of settlement of teachers' dispute involving abolition of negotiating machinery

Establishment of national curriculum

Provision for schools to opt out of local authority control

Abolition of Inner London Education Authority in 1990

Introduction of student loans supplementing maintenance grants

Foreign Affairs and Defence

Independence granted to Zimbabwe

Decision to permit US Cruise missiles to be stationed in Britain from 1983 until the INF Treaty in 1988

Decision to replace Polaris with US Trident missiles

Defeat of Argentinian invasion of Falkland Islands and decision to create a large permanent garrison there in 1982; resumption of diplomatic relations in 1990

Agreement with China over future of Hong Kong after expiry of British lease in 1997

Introduction of majority voting on certain issues in EEC Council of Ministers

Housing

Establishment of a charter for public sector tenants, including the right to buy their homes

Reform of law relating to private rented sector

Industrial Relations

Provision for public funds to be used to pay for secret union ballots

Changes in the law relating to the closed shop, picketing, unfair dismissal, trade union immunities, strike ballots, and election of union officials

Industry

Strengthening of Office of Fair Trading and Mono-

polies and Mergers Commission, including power to investigate misuse of monopoly by nationalised industries

Privatisation of public enterprises, including denationalisation of British Aerospace, Cable & Wireless, Britoil, British Telecom, British Gas, British Airways, British Steel, water and electricity industries; introduction of competition into the bus and telecommunications industries

Creation of enterprise zones with special tax relief and industrial benefits, and of 10 urban development corporations

Changes in law relating to building societies and financial services

Abolition of Dock Labour Scheme

National Health Service

Ending of withdrawal of private beds from NHS hospitals

Reorganisation of NHS, including replacement of area health authorities with a larger number of district health authorities

Major reform of NHS, set out in NHS and Community Care Act 1990

Social Security

End of index-linking of short-term social security benefits

Introduction of new sickness benefit arrangements

Major reform of social security system, including new income support system (replacing supplementary benefits), family credit and social fund

Other Decisions

Changes in the financial relationship between central and local government, strengthening central control with a new system of grants and restrictions on the powers of local authorities to levy rates

Abolition of domestic rates and their replacement by a community charge (poll tax) in 1989 in Scotland, 1990 in England and Wales

Abolition of Greater London Council and metropolitan county councils

Extension of franchise to British citizens resident abroad, and of postal voting to holidaymakers, increase in deposit at parliamentary elections

Redefinition of British citizenship and nationality and changes in the provisions relating to right of abode in the UK

Establishment of Channel 4 and Welsh language channel in 1982; Broadcasting Act in 1990 leading to Channel 5 and further changes in 1990s

New rules governing unauthorised disclosure of official information

Anglo-French decision to build Channel Tunnel

Establishment of Crown Prosecution Service in England and Wales; reform of legal profession

II. THE CHANGING WORLD SCENE

WESTERN EUROPE

FRANCE

France under Mitterrand.

M. Francois Mitterrand was elected President of France when he defeated the incumbent President, Giscard d'Estaing, in the second ballot of the elections on 10 May 1981. Mitterrand thus became the first socialist President of the Fifth Republic—indeed, the first socialist President since M. Vincent Auriol who was head of state from 1947 to 1954. Mitterrand strengthened his political position very considerably a few weeks later when, in elections which he had called for the National Assembly, the Socialist Party (PS) achieved an absolute majority for the first time in the party's history. Not since the huge Gaullist victories in 1968 had the governing party had an absolute majority in the National Assembly. President Mitterrand followed this by bringing four Communist Party (PCF) ministers into the government headed by Pierre Mauroy on 23 June. Communists had not tasted government power since 1947, but their situation

in 1981 was one of profound weakness, not strength.

The first ballot left Mitterrand in a stronger electoral position than Giscard, and with distinct tactical advantages. The fall-off in total right-wing support on the first ballot in comparison with 1974 meant that Giscard had ground to make up. But in addition, the Communist Party managed a first ballot performance of only 15·3%. For the PCF, this was an unmitigated disaster and caused a good deal of muttering and speculation about the future of Marchais as leader of the Party. But Mitterrand had broken free of the PCF's clutches and did not have the problem of staving off Communist demands for participation in any future Socialist government as the price of PCF support for Mitterrand in the second ballot. Mitterrand's position was sufficiently strong to allow him to dictate the terms of any possible future participation. Giscard's claim that a PS victory would lead either to "socialist disorder or communist order", which would have been a potent message had the PCF ran strongly on the first ballot, therefore carried little weight. In any case, opinion polls indicated that 84% of the PCF vote would go to Mitterrand in the next ballot. And, partly because of the disunity on the right, about 18% of Chirac's first-ballot vote would also go to Mitterrand. The socialist leader also picked up most of the left minor parties' votes.

So Francois Mitterrand won a remarkable victory, with a plurality of 1·066 million votes. He was inaugurated as the fourth President of the Fifth Republic at the Elysee Palace on 21 May. In his inaugural address, President Mitterrand pledged himself to build a union of socialism and liberty, declaring himself in a grand way to be "President of all the French people". Immediately after the ceremony, President Mitterrand named Pierre Mauroy as Prime Minister. Mauroy was a long-time confidant of the President, Mayor of Lille, and a member of the national secretariat of the PS.

The Assembly Elections.

The PS completely dominated the run-up to the Assembly elections which the new President called. The two rounds on 14 and 21 June left the Socialists with a large overall majority over all the other parties. Remarkably, in the space of just two months, the Right had lost all that they had had.

Even so, Mitterrand had a surprisingly long honeymoon period which lasted at least into the first months of 1982. Even then, it was clear that the left would be returned to power if elections were held. And the decline of the Communists continued unabated. Although Marchais retained his hold on the leadership of the PCF at the 24th Congress of the Communist Party in the early weeks of 1982, the Party's standing in the opinion polls fell to only a little over 10%. This was less than half the voting support which it received at the end of the 1960s when Marchais first rose to the top of the PCF ladder. And the PCF was also caught on the horns of a dilemma in deciding when to break with the Socialist government and resign the seats which it held under Mauroy.

Mitterrand's Domestic Programme.

The Government had its difficulties, however. In January 1982, the Constitutional Council rejected parts of the law providing for nationalisation—a key part of Mitterrand's domestic programme. And in four by-elections on 17 January, the socialists were beaten by three Gaullists and one Giscardien. Some middle-class voters deserted the PS because they were disillusioned with the rapid pace of change whilst some left-wingers abstained because of what they viewed as the government's excessively moderate stance. These pressures were reflected within the socialist party, but they were for the most part successfully contained and did not seriously hamper the government's freedom of action. However, the Left suffered further serious reverses in the local elections of March 1982, with the Communists rather than the Socialists emerging as the main losers.

Mitterrand Under Pressure.

As 1982 progressed, the Mitterrand administration came under increasing pressure, most particularly on the economic front. With inflation soaring, with a sorry under constant pressure and with government borrowing also rapidly mounting, Mitterrand entered 1983 with a crisis on his hands. It looked as if the local elections would be a first major humiliation.

However, after suffering significant reverses in the first round of municipal elections on 6 March 1983, the Left recovered strongly in the second round a week later. So marked was the recovery that the pro-socialist daily newspaper Le Matin headlined its lead story on the Monday after the second round "The Miracle."

The Left lost control of 31 major towns, many fewer than the 61 the Right lost in the 1977 municipal elections. The Opposition parties won just 49·6% of the vote in the second round; Jacques Chirac could therefore credibly claim success for the Right. But the extent of the success was certainly less than had been widely anticipated just two days before the second round of voting, and Chirac just failed in his objective to claim that the Opposition parties now constituted a majority in France.

But the local election reprieve was short-lived. With the franc still sinking, in March 1983 Mitterrand acted. The Cabinet was re-shuffled and a crisis economic package was hurriedly introduced. It comprised a 1% levy on taxable income and a special duty on cigarettes, other tobaccos and spirits. Later in 1983, as the difficulty which President Mitterrand would have in meeting his target of keeping the government deficit down to 3% of GNP became apparent, the pressure grew to cut government spending and increase taxes still further. After intense debate within the cabinet, the country and the socialist party, the highest marginal rate of tax was increased to 70% and the 1% levy retained for a further year.

With workers voicing their discontent, and a regime of austerity under the direction of Finance Minister Jacques Delors, it was therefore all the more striking that the socialist party should have remained united. The party's triennial conference took place in a cordial atmosphere, largely free from the rancorous exchanges that might have been expected in a party which continues to be deeply factionalised. The key to tranquillity lay in Lionel Jospin's, the party secretary, success in keeping the leaders of most of the union groups in line behind the policies of financial rigour pursued by Mitterrand and Delors.

Mitterrand's support in the party was not reflected in the country where his approval rating fell to one-third, the lowest recorded for a Fifth Republic President. Indeed, it was this weakness which persuaded some of his opponents to still their criticisms at the congress for fear of damaging the President's position and that of the party further. For so long as the socialist party remained reasonably united, the Communist Party's freedom of manoeuvre continued to be very limited, and its standing in the country seemed likely to continue to decline.

The Communist Withdrawal.

On 19 July 1984, the Communists withdrew their four members from the government. The stresses and strains induced by the government's austerity programme (riguer). Thus the union of the left of which M. Mitterrand was the author broke apart as politicians of all parties fixed their gaze anxiously on the forthcoming assembly elections in 1986 in which the socialists run the risk of doing particularly badly—thereby greatly complicating the French President's calculations for the rest of his term as he considers the prospect of struggling with the problems of constructing a parliamentary majority. The Communist Party's problems continued and even intensified—indeed, their falling fortunes as registered in the opinion polls took on the character of a fundamental decline. Their support in the 1984 elections to the European Assembly fell to just 11%—less than half its level in 1979.

The Advent of Fabius.

In government, the twin themes of "industrial modernisation" and "liberalism" came to dominate Mitterrand's speeches and the political agenda. Their impact was sharpened by announcements on 14 July of tax cuts for 1985, and the resignation of M. Pierre Mauroy's cabinet on the following day. Mr. Laurent Fabius, just 37 years old, was named as Mauroy's successor. He had a deserved reputation for being a brilliant technocrat, tactically adept, and completely devoted to the changing policies pursued by Mitterrand since 1981 without allowing support for them to damage him politically. With Mitterrand's personal popularity at a low ebb, Fabius's tactical skills were to be much needed to win support for the socialists in 1986.

The 1986 Election.

There was never any doubt that the PS would lose; the major issue was the size of the defeat. In the event, the result was a remarkably good one for the PS, which surpassed its target of 30% of the poll and proclaimed itself still the major political force in France. The collapse of the PCF vote to below 10% also represented a personal triumph for Mitterrand, whose strategy since 1972 has been to establish the PS as the major party on the Left. Calls from within the PCF for a democratic debate on the

Party's worst election performance since 1932 suggest that Marchais may shortly be replaced as PCF leader. The conventional Right lost votes to the FN, which did better than predicted, particularly in the South where it won over 20% of the vote. With its 35 seats, the FN could become an embarrassing source of unsolicited support for the RPR-UDF government.

List	% vote	Seats
Extreme Left	1·53	—
PCF	9·78	35
PS	31·04	206
MRG/Centre Left	1·61	9
Ecologists	1·21	—
Regionalists	0·10	—
RPR	11·21	76
UDF	8·31	53
Union RPR-UDF	21·46	147
Other Right	3·90	14
FN	9·65	35
Other Extreme Right	0·08	—

Electorate: 37,162,020; votes cast: 29,094,929 (78·29%)

(Source: Ministry of Interior results, Le Monde, 20 March 1986) *

The Politics of Cohabitation.

Cohabitation worked with remarkable ease and smoothness for several months, but was disrupted by student rebellion, labour unrest, terrorism, and a currency crisis. As events helped prise cohabitation apart, public opinion polls recorded diminishing enthusiasm for the arrangement. Although not universally shared, this sentiment was exploited by Raymond Barre who argued that effective government was impossible under such circumstances. There was much to this charge, despite the long-standing yearning among the electorate for consensual government: since the power to dissolve Parliament, to declare a national emergency, and call for a referendum, are vested in the presidency, Jacques Chirac was obliged to play his role whilst handicapped. These were powers which, even under cohabitation, could not be shared - a constitutional provision which Mitterrand was able to exploit to Chirac's discomfiture, to Barre's advantage on the right, and his own on the left. By the Spring of 1987, Chirac's standing in the opinion polls showed him to be the weakest of the major presidential candidates on the right, and Barre to be the strongest. On the left, Mitterrand indicated in the autumn of 1986 that he was disinclined to stand again for the presidency, but in a way that allowed him the freedom to reconsider if his chances appeared encouragingly good or if he judged that he would take the blame for the defeat of the left if he were not to stand.

Industrial Disruption.

In January 1987, the Constitutional Council declared unconstitutional the government's chosen method of forcing flexible working legislation through parliament in the previous month, further embarrassing Chirac after an exceptionally rocky six months, and straining yet further the government's relations with the unions. These had come under considerable pressure following a rash of public sector strikes. With the exception of the Communist-led CGT's cynical attempt to widen the labour discontent which it had not anticipated, the pressure for strikes in support of pay claims arose from militant grass-roots groups in the railways and the electricity generating industry. By the middle of January, the momentum of the disorganised strikers had begun to fade and a return to work ensued without substantial pay increases having been conceded but, in the railways, with reform of the pay structure having been postponed.

Unlike in 1968, the unrest was on this occasion incoherent, ill-organised, and presented no significant threat to the régime. Yet it exacted a political price: Chirac emerged from it much weakened, and showed himself unable to press ahead with his full programme of economic reform (of which the flexible working legislation struck down by the Constitutional Council was one part), reform of the universities (where he sought to improve standards by making them more selective), and new nationality-cum-immigration measures designed to placate right-wing voters. Chirac's chances of defeating Barre in 1988 for the right-wing presidential candidacy were thereby damaged, and made worse by rising imports and a weak export performance, and continuing upward pressure on labour costs.

The 1988 Elections.

Political debate in France in the closing months of 1987 was dominated by the forthcoming 1988 presidential elections as the major political parties concentrated on the selection of candidates and campaign planning. The neo-Gaullist government's privatisation programme suffered a setback following the October international stock market collapse which wiped 10% off share values and prompted the Finance Minister, Edouard Balladur to announce a 'pause' in the government's ambitious privatisation programme. Prime Minister Jacques Chirac was also faced with the problem of continued violent opposition from Kanak separatists in the overseas territory of New Caledonia after most indigenous Kanaks boycotted the September referendum on the issue of the island's independence in which 59% of the electorate voted overwhelmingly (by 98·30% of votes cast) to remain French.

Foreign policy developments in this period were designed to boost the right-wing Prime Minister's chances in the forthcoming presidential contest. On 27 November 1987 two of the five French hostages held in Lebanon, Jean-Louis Normandin and Roger Auque, were released in West Beirut. Despite the government's denials of any deals having been done just two days later, charges against the Iranian embassy official, Wahid Gordji, suspected by French police of terrorist related offences were dropped. His immediate departure for Karachi prompted criticism from the British Prime Minister,

FIRST BALLOT		SECOND BALLOT	
Registered Voters: 38,128,507		Registered Voters: 38,168,869	
Valid Votes Cast: 30,406,038		Valid Votes Cast: 30,923,249	
CANDIDATE	% VALID VOTES	CANDIDATE	% VALID VOTES
Francois Mitterrand (PS)	34·09	Francois Mitterrand (PS)	54·02
Jacques Chirac (RPR)	19·94	Jacques Chirac (RPR)	45·98
Raymond Barre (UDF)	16·54		
Jean-Marie Le Pen (FN)	14·39		
André Lajoinie (PCF)	6·76		
Pierre Juquin (Ind. Communist)	2·10		
Arlette Laguiller (LO)	1·99		
Pierre Boussel (Workers' Party)	0·38		
Antoine Waechter (Ecol.)	3·78		

Abbreviations: Ecol. = Ecologist; FN = Front National; LO = Lutte Ouvrière; PCF = Parti Communiste Francais; PS = Parti Socialiste; RPR = Rassemblement pour la République; UDF = Union pour la Démocratie Française.

Source: Official Results published by the Constitutional Court quoted in 'L'Election Presidentielle 1988', Le Figaro/Etudes Politiques 1988.

Margaret Thatcher and the US President, Ronald Reagan both of whom reproached the French government for doing deals with terrorists. These allegations were repeated in January 1988 following the arrest in Paris of some 20 members of the Iranian anti-Khomeini *Mujaheddin* organisation and deportation from France to Gabon of 15 Iranians and ethnic Kurds despite the fact that several of those deported had refugee status. In the same month, Major Alain Marfart, one of the two secret agents responsible for blowing up the Greenpeace ship *Rainbow Warrior* was repatriated to France from New Zealand, allegedly for medical treatment. Finally, in January 1988 Erich Honecker became the first East German Head of State to make a state visit to France, having separate meetings with the Socialist President, François Mitterrand and the Prime Minister, Jacques Chirac.

The 1988 French Presidential Elections.

The presidential elections of May 1988 brought to an end two years of 'cohabitation' between the Socialist President, Francois Mitterrand and the neo-Gaullist Prime Minister, Jacques Chirac. Of the nine candidates who stood in the first round on 24 April only the two best-placed candidates, Mitterrand and Chirac, went through to the run-off ballot a fortnight later. In this second poll the outgoing Socialist President defeated his right-wing rival by 54·02 to 45·98 per cent of the votes cast thereby becoming the first French President to be re-elected for a second seven year term of office by popular vote. Mitterrand's re-election was not a decisive victory for socialism. His election programme contained few left-wing proposals; his success reflected his ability to attract centrist votes. This fact, together with the continued decline of the Communist Party vote and the impressive performance of the neo-fascist candidate, Jean-Marie Le Pen confirmed the extent to which French politics has shifted to the Right since 1981.

The Battle on the Right.

The first to enter the presidential contest as early as April 1987 was Jean-Marie Le Pen, leader of the neo-fascist FN. Le Pen's campaign focussed upon the alleged threat to French identity and *sécurité* (law and order) posed by coloured immigrants. His anti-immigrant, nationalist programme promised to stop clandestine immigration, strengthen traditional family values and defend the French nation. The two 'system' right-wing candidates were next to enter the race; the neo-Gaullist Prime Minister, Jacques Chirac announced his candidacy in January 1988 followed two weeks later by the economist and former Prime Minister, Raymond Barre. Though formally an independent candidate, the latter enjoyed the support of the centrist UDF government coalition Party. The campaign for the first ballot was dominated by the battle between these two candidates for a place in the second round. Chirac campaigned on his government's major achievements in the last two years—low inflation (reduced from 8% to 7·5% since 1986), privatisation and anti-terrorist successes—promising tax cuts for business, budget austerity and (in an attempt to stem the flow of votes to Le Pen) tougher immigration controls. Barre—who had refused to participate in the cohabitation arrangement—criticised Chirac's rapid policy changes since 1986 and close party ties, but had little new to offer in the way of policies. The main difference between the two programmes was Barre's greater commitment to European integration. The most popular right-wing politician in France through 1987, he trailed behind Chirac from the outset. As the campaign progressed it became apparent that Barre was hampered by his somewhat staid image, poor media coverage and lack of strong party support.

In the event, both candidates did less well than predicted in the first ballot. While Barre lost ground to the Socialist candidate, François Mitterrand, Chirac lost votes to Jean-Marie Le Pen who polled 14·39% of the vote. As expected, Le Pen did well in the Mediterranean bastions established by the FN since 1981 (obtaining 28% of the vote in Marseilles). More disturbing was the extent to which the FN candidate attracted high levels of support generally east of the line Le Havre–Valence–Perpignan obtaining 18% of the votes in the Rhone, 19·8% in

Seine–Saint-Denis, 19·9% in the Moselle, 21·7% in the Haut-Rhin and 26·4% in the Bouches-du Rhone. This shock result for the racist FN candidate, who last September dismissed the holocaust as a 'small detail', was in part a protest vote, a gesture facilitated by the double ballot system. However, it also reflected the extent to which anti-immigrant sentiments are now widespread throughout France, particularly among blue collar workers, small businessmen and the self-employed in areas of relatively high levels of unemployment and/or immigration.

The Left: Mitterrand's Appeal to the Centre.

The decline of the PCF continued with the official candidate, André Lajoinie obtaining the Party's worst election result since 1932. Juquin, a former PCF member critical of the Party's orthodox line was expelled from the Party in October 1987 after announcing his opposition to the official candidate. His respectable performance as an independent red-green Communist candidate confirmed the deep divisions within the French Communist movement. The principal candidate on the left, François Mitterrand was the last to enter the presidential contest, finally declaring his candidacy in de Gaulle fashion on 22 March 1988. His silence was a strategic one. By refusing to enter the political fray earlier he was able—as the incumbent President—to prolong his publicly popular image as 'father of the nation' acting in the interest of the whole of France (and at the age of 71 conserve his energies for the second round). His delayed entry into the campaign also gave Chirac sufficient time to crush the centrist Barre who would have posed a greater challenge to Mitterrand on the second round. There was little socialist about Mitterrand's programme which emphasised his commitment to European integration and stressed the need for economic modernisation, comprehensive welfare provision and increased educational investment. Significantly, Mitterrand also promised to reduce the seven year presidential term to five years. Whereas in 1981 Mitterrand's presidential campaign had been closely linked to the Socialist Party and left-wing policies, this time his appeal was a personal one intended to mobilise both left and right-wing voters.

The Second Ballot.

Confident of left-wing support in the second round Mitterrand—with the election slogan 'a united France'—pitched his campaign firmly at the centre. His speeches focussed upon the need for all French people to unite to defend the traditional values of the Republic; a thinly veiled reference to Le Pen. Chirac meanwhile attempted to secure votes from both centrists who had voted for Barre and supporters of Jean-Marie Le Pen. The task proved an impossible one. Many UDF voters were repulsed by Chirac's crude appeal to FN voters and—in the absence of a clear lead from Le Pen—some 20% of those who had voted for Le Pen switched their allegiance to Mitterrand in the second ballot. While Mitterrand serenely awaited the second ballot Chirac embarked upon a frenetic campaign, shamelessly attempting to improve his miserable standing in the polls by arranging the release of French hostages from the Lebanon, ordering military attacks on New Caledonian separatists and securing the return to France of Dominique Prieur, the secret agent imprisoned in New Zealand for bombing the Greenpeace ship, *Rainbow Warrior*.

The voters were unimpressed; Mitterrand won a landslide victory on 8 May winning over 50% of the votes cast in all but 19 of the 96 metropolitan departments. His victory was Gaullien; national and personal in character. Elected with centrist support, Mitterrand confirmed his opening to the centre by appointing Michel Rocard, leader of the social-democratic wing of the PS as Prime Minister and asking him to form a centre-left coalition government. Despite long negotiations with leading UDF politicians including the former UDF President, Giscard d'Estaing, Rocard was unable to form a government which was acceptable to the right-wing Parliament. Just one week after his re-election President Mitterrand therefore dissolved the National Assembly in order to seek a Socialist parliamentary majority. The legislative elections were held on 5 and 12 June.

The June Legislative Elections.

These elections, called a week after President Mitterrand's re-election on 8 May 1988 were held under the double ballot, single member constituency electoral system. Re-elected with centrist support, Mitterrand continued his policy of *ouverture* towards the centre during the election campaign in an attempt to divide the "system" Right. However, the two principal right-wing parties, the neo-Gaullist RPR (*Rassemblement pour la République*) and the more centrist UDF (*Union pour le Démocratie Française*) which had supported rival candidates in the presidential election hurriedly formed a new electoral alliance, the URC and agreed to support a joint candidate in each constituency. Early polls forecast a large overall majority for the President's Socialist Party together with the marginalisation or even the elimination of both the PCF and FN (both of which had benefited from proportional representation in 1986).

The polls proved only partially correct. As predicted, the FN lost all but one of its 33 seats (including that belonging to the FN leader Jean-Marie Le Pen in Marseilles). The PCF's electoral fortunes meanwhile revived and (partly because of PS backing for PCF candidates on the second round) the Party retained 27 of its 33 seats. The biggest surprise was the failure of the PS to obtain an overall majority. Several factors help to explain this result. The PS was the party most affected by the record abstention level in the first round—complacency and election fatigue kept many voters away from the polls. Secondly, the PS election message to voters was ambiguous: appeals to voters to give the President a stable parliamentary majority (and electoral deals with the PCF) were combined with Mitterrand's public statements in favour of an opening to the centre. Finally, while many centrists and Communists had been willing to support Mitterrand in the presidential contest they refused to vote for a Socialist Party candidate in the parliamentary elections. Lacking an overall parliamentary majority the Socialists must now either form an alliance with the Communists or—and this seems more likely— seek the support of centrist politicians in a centre-left governing coalition.

In the important municipal elections of March 1989, the Socialists gained control of several cities, including Avignon, Dunkirk, Mulhouse, Orleans, and Strasbourg. The right and centre-right parties lost ground, weakened by the attractions of the National Front for some of their supporters. The decline of the Communist Party continued, most notably in Amiens where they lost power after eighteen years in control, whilst the Greens continued to make a firm impression. Their electoral challenge fuelled the determination of President Mitterrand and Prime Minister Rocard to establish their own ecological credentials with the public.

Recent Events.

French politics in the second half of 1989 and the early months of 1990 were marked to a striking degree by the contending for advantage on both the right and the left by candidates for the Presidency since it seemed improbable that Mitterrand would choose to seek a third term upon the expiry of his second in 1995.

On the left, no politician possessed Mitterrand's weight and popularity which enabled him to chart his own course with relative freedom on the foundation of strict party discipline. At the biennial congress of the French Socialist Party in March 1990 at Rennes, Laurent Fabius (Mitterrand's second Prime Minister) beat a group led jointly by Pierre Mauroy (Mitterrand's first Prime Minister, and currently the Party's first secretary) and Lionel Jospin (Education Minister, and formerly first secretary of the party), into second place and Michel Rocard, the leading social democratic figure on the right of the party (and Mitterrand's current Prime Minister), into third for the post of party secretary. The contest was superficially bound up with ideological dispute but in fact had more to do with personal politicking with a view to the presidential election in 1995 (or before in the event that Mitterrand chose to retire early), than with substantive differences over policy. Whilst Rocard's position continued to be somewhat distinctive,

there was little ideological distance between Mauroy and Fabius but much animus.

On the right, the three major figures of the 1970s and 1980s, Giscard d'Estaing, Jacques Chirac, and Raymond Barre, came under increasing pressure from new contenders for power. All three senior figures were in any case handicapped by Mitterrand's crushing of Chirac in the 1988 presidential elections, and by his having pursued a conservative economic policy with conspicuous success since 1983.

THE TWO GERMANYS.

Adenauer and West Germany.

The Federal Republic of Germany, founded in 1949, had as its first Chancellor Dr. Konrad Adenauer until his retirement in 1963 at the age of 86. His Christian Democrat government produced conditions of stability and confidence in which Germany rebuilt her shattered prosperity and a viable parliamentary democracy. His work in building a special relationship with France, culminating in a treaty of friendship, was a dramatic contrast to the long tradition of enmity towards France. But while he succeeded in building his country into the Western community he remained intransigent over German reunification within the boundaries of 1937, stressing West Germany's right to speak for the whole of Germany, including the Soviet Zone. The two states drifted steadily apart, and a seal was set on their division by East Germany's building of the Berlin Wall in 1961.

Erhard and Kiesinger.

Adenauer's successor Dr. Erhard had the prestige of having as economics minister been the main architect of West Germany's "economic miracle." As Chancellor from 1963 to 1966 he was a loyal supporter of the Atlantic Alliance— indeed it was held that he encouraged ties with the United States at the expense of the Franco-German friendship treaty, which had not lived up to the hopes reposed in it. This partly accounted for the enmity of the Bavarian wing of the Christian Democrats called the Christian Social Union (CSU), the party of Franz-Josef Strauss.

In 1966 a governmental crisis caused by the resignation of the junior partners in the coalition, the Free Democrats (FDP), led to the formation under Dr Kiesinger of a Grand Coalition in which the Social Democrats (SPD) joined the CDU and so had their first taste of government on the national level since the Federal Republic's foundation. This helped to establish the SPD in the eyes of the electorate as a potential governing party.

The End of Christian Democratic Rule, 1969.

In the general election of September 1969 the SPD made significant gains in both votes and seats. Despite widespread publicity the extreme right-ring NPD (often referred to as Neo-Nazis) failed to qualify for any seats since it polled less than the necessary 5 per cent of the total votes. It is now virtually defunct. Thus the three-party system remained. Although the CDU was still the largest party, the SPD and FDP leaders agreed to form a coalition government with Herr Brandt, the SPD leader, as Chancellor and Herr Scheel the FDP leader, as Foreign Minister.

Herr Brandt's achievement in reaching the Chancellorship was considerable, in view of his unpopularity in some quarters for having fled to Norway during the war and taken out Norwegian citizenship. However he had built up his reputation as Mayor of West Berlin.

Herr Brandt's Ostpolitik.

The Brandt Government's main achievements were in the field of foreign policy. A radical development in 1970 was the two meetings between Chancellor Brandt and the East German Prime Minister, Herr Stoph. These showed that Herr Brandt had accepted the existence of two separate states within the German nation (although this fell short of East Germany's demand for complete recognition by Bonn). A treaty signed by West Germany and the Soviet Union in Moscow on 12 August stated that the borders of all European countries are inviolable, including that between the Federal and the Democratic Republics. Bonn implies that frontiers can still be changed by mutual agreement.

Bonn insisted that the ratification of the Moscow treaty and of the Warsaw treaty recognising the Oder-Neisse Line and normalising relations between West Germany and Poland depended on a satisfactory outcome of the Four-Power talks on Berlin. At last in September 1971 an agreement was signed by which the Soviet Union in turn accepted the realities which matter to the West. It recognised the rights of the Allies in Berlin and the city's special relations with the Federal Republic, which had been constantly disputed, especially by the East Germans. The free flow of traffic to and from Berlin, formerly unregulated and therefore a favourite object of disruption and escalation of tension, is now covered by an agreement for which the Soviet Union, rather than East Germany, can be held responsible. The representation abroad of West Berlin by the Federal Republic is now legally based. West Berliners can again visit the eastern part of the city and the GDR. The details of transit were left to be filled in by East and West Germany, and after the Russians had overcome East German recalcitrance the first treaty between the two German states was signed on 20 December 1971. The Brandt Government immediately initiated the ratification of the Moscow and Warsaw treaties, which was eventually achieved in May 1972 after prolonged antagonism from the opposition CDU and some former government supporters. Bonn stressed that the treaties were not an anticipation of a Peace Treaty and formed no legal basis for the existing frontiers, but this view was rejected by the USSR and Poland.

The way was now open for general agreements on traffic and for a general treaty between East and West Germany signed on 21 December 1972, which recognised the existence of two virtually sovereign German states. Though a shock for those who clung to the illusion of German unity, the treaty marked a new realism which promised greater contact between the two states and was therefore welcomed by a majority of Germans. The concessions extorted from the East Germans as a condition of signing the treaty considerably increased the numbers of West Germans and Berliners able to visit the East. The advantages gained by the GDR in terms of confirmation of its statehood and of the division of Germany for the foreseeable future are evident from the flood of countries (including Britain and France) which have recognised it since the signature of the treaty. It was quickly followed by the admission of the two German states to the United Nations. However the limits of détente were shown up by highly restrictive interpretations of the agreements by East Germany. In pursuance of the Basic Treaty, Permanent Missions were opened in Bonn and East Berlin in May 1974.

1973 also saw the conclusion of a treaty normalising relations between West Germany and Czechoslovakia, long delayed by the Czech attempt to have the Munich Agreement of 1938 declared invalid "ab initio". In 1975 agreements were signed between West Germany and Poland on the granting of credits to Poland, the payment of claims arising from the Second World War and the resettlement of ethnic Germans living in Poland. This was criticised as paying for emigration by the Opposition who blocked it with their majority in the Upper house.

The SPD/FDP Coalition.

In April 1972 a government crisis was brought about by defection from the government coalition mainly on the question of its Ostpolitik. This led to an early election in November 1972 as a result of which Chancellor Brandt's government was triumphantly returned to power. For the first time, the SPD became the largest party in the Bundestag.

The 1980 Elections.

In the General Elections to the lower house of Parliament, the Bundestag, on 5 October, the coalition of the SPD/FDP retained power, increasing its overall majority by winning 271 of the 497 seats. The SPD improved its parliamentary strength only slightly, but the junior partners in the coalition, the FDP, made significant gains, with 10·6% of the vote. The FDP won an additional 14 seats, giving it a total of 53. Indeed, the FDP did well in all 10 *Länder*; equally, the CDU/CSU lost ground everywhere. Support for the Ecological Party, *Die Grünen*, fell away in the election from the high levels it had achieved earlier in the year.

Schmidt's government depended upon the continuing support of the FDP under the tactically astute leadership of Herr Genscher who continued to hold the post of Foreign Minister in the coalition government. The tensions within the government were heightened by protracted negotiations over policies to counter the sharply rising trend of unemployment. But although West Germany was, by the late winter of 1981–2, in deep economic recession with unemployment climbing towards two million, an economic recovery package was eventually agreed upon and Herr Schmidt easily won a re-sounding vote of confidence in the Bundestag. The respite was to be short-lived and West Germany was soon to change political direction.

Background to the 1983 Elections.

On Sunday 6 March 1983, general elections took place in West Germany. Generally acknowledged as the most important in German post-war history, they were caused by the CDU Chancellor, Helmut Kohl, deliberately losing a vote of confidence in the Bundestag. Kohl had succeeded Helmut Schmidt as Chancellor after Hans-Dietrich Genscher, the leader of the FDP, had withdrawn from the governing coalition and changed his Party's allegiance to the CDU. After the SPD/FDP government fell, Schmidt stepped down as leader of the Social Democrats. Hans Jochen Vogel, a former Justice Minister, succeeded him.

The elections resulted in a substantial victory for the CDU/CSU. When the final votes were counted, they were only a shade away from gaining an overall majority. Despite the public odium heaped upon Herr Genscher for having deserted Herr Schmidt's coalition, the FDP won nearly 7% of the votes, thereby renewing their eligibility to sit in Parliament. The Greens, too, cleared the 5% hurdle, with 5·6 of the vote.

The results of the elections were greeted with scarcely-concealed relief by West Germany's allies, fearful of the consequences of a government being returned in Bonn which refused to fulfil the NATO "twin-track" agreement of December 1979. Had the SPD depended upon support from the Greens, NATO's cohesion and policy would have been under serious strain; hence Moscow's uninvited and clumsy interventions during the campaign on behalf of the SPD, and the general pleasure in the west at the result.

Helmut Kohl, in his first year after the General Election, did not make a significant impact upon European politics or upon outstanding German domestic problems. He failed in particular to establish a comparably warm and productive relationship with the French President, Francois Mitterrand, as his predecessor had done with Giscard. The absence of leadership from the two most important West European leaders was keenly felt in the European Community, which drifted deeper towards budgetary crisis and political lethargy during 1983.

The Deployment of American Missiles.

1983 was a year dominated in Europe by the question of the deployment of new American intermediate-range nuclear missiles; few important foreign policy questions for the major European powers were unaffected by it. With the question of inter-German relations, and the future political status and condition of each German state, still perhaps the central issue in European politics, the impact of the missile deployment upon it was intensively discussed throughout the year.

In fact, whilst the tension between East and West caused by the missile question did not leave inter-German relations unscathed, they did emerge relatively undamaged. There was no general freeze on relations with the deployment of the Pershing II weapons in West Germany from November onwards. In part, this is due to the advantage which the Soviet Union saw in retaining a channel to other Western countries through West Germany at a time of general political difficulty. But the economic relationship between the two Germanys was too strong for a complete clamp-down on political contact to be possible; that is strengthened by East Germany's external debt of $13 billion, much of which is owed to West German banks.

Herr Josef Strauss, the leader of the CSU, visited East Germany in June 1983 in an attempt, he claimed, to prepare the ground for a loan of DM1 billion from the west to the east, and guaranteed by the West German government, in July. Other West German politicians, including Herr von Weizsacker, the Mayor of West Berlin, visited East Germany in the course of the year, and Herr Kohl's government in Bonn was receptive to later enquiries from the East for further loans, the conditions of which would tie both countries closer both financially and industrially.

West Germany derived little discernible advantage from these continuing financial subventions to her neighbour. Hopes that the doubling of the hard currency exchange fee by the East in 1980 would be revoked, or at least reduced, were dashed; similarly, the dismantling of some of the East German automatic firing devices along the border reported by the western press in the late summer later proved to be only partly true. Many of the devices had been modernised; those that had been removed affected only twenty miles of the border. But Herr Kohl, anxious to portray himself to the electorate as a pan-German statesman in the tradition of Brandt and Schmidt, would perhaps be grateful that the anticipated deterioration in relations in the event of the Bundestag's approval of the American Cruise and Pershing II deployment had not been realised.

The incidents of East Germans squatting in West German embassies in Eastern Europe in 1984 came at an unfortunate time for both Germanies. The incidents themselves created political problems for East Germany in her relations with Moscow, and for the West German government in her domestic political circumstances where conservative critics are always glad of an opportunity for criticising East German government policies, and West German governments for being insufficiently vigorous in response.

Cancellation of the Honecker Visit.

The embarrassment was highlighted in the summer of 1984 by the impending visit of Herr Honecker to West Germany for talks with Herr Kohl. As the first-ever visit of an East German leader to West Germany, the visit took on considerable symbolic political importance of the mutual desire of Berlin and Bonn to allow themselves a degree of insulation from the wider freeze which characterised East–West relations. However, on 4 September, Herr Honecker announced that the trip would not take place. The intensity of Soviet opposition proved too much for Honecker to absorb or deflect, despite the attempts of the East German party newspaper, *Neues Deutschland* before the cancellation to trumpet the merits of closer cooperation, and then afterwards to blame the change in plans on West German conservative sniping at Herr Kohl for his handling of the affair. But the cancellation is unlikely to do long-term damage to relations between the two Germanies, as is indicated by Honecker's ability to grant record numbers of exit visas to East Germans in 1984, despite Moscow's restraining hand.

Developments in West Germany

The spy scandals of August 1985 which did so little to alter the course of relations between the two Germanies nonetheless added to the growing woes of Chancellor Kohl's government. Whilst in the early months of 1986, defeat for the Christian Democrat-led coalition in the 1987 elections still seemed improbable, the possibility was actively discussed. The

causes of the change were clear enough: Chancellor Kohl's leadership of his Cabinet colleagues was uncertain, and the defection of Joachim Tiedge did nothing to enhance the government's standing within Germany or among her international partners.

Elections in Schleswig-Holstein in early March 1986 confirmed the declining popularity of the CDU and the FDP. The CDU lost its absolute majority, and saw its share of the vote fall by nearly 6% to 44%, whilst the FDP slumped to a mere 4·4% of the vote. The SPD's share of the poll rose to over 40% and took control of the state's four largest cities. *Die Grünen* won a substantially increased vote, securing 7·4% of the poll.

Further, Hans-Jochen Vogel, long considered by CDU opponents to be a relatively easy opponent in the 1987 elections, relinquished the leadership of the SPD in favour of Johannes Rau, the charismatic premier of North Rhine-Westphalia. His favourable image with voters was reflected in high public opinion poll ratings (just as Chancellor Kohl's own ratings began to fall below 50%) and was supplemented by revised policies designed to appeal both to traditional SDP voters and to deflect the brunt of the electoral threat posed by *Die Grünen*.

The 1987 Elections.

The West German electorate went to the polls on 25 January 1987, and confirmed the coalition led by Helmut Kohl in office, albeit with a reduced share of the vote. Herr Kohl's partners in the coalition, the Free Democrats led by Hans-Dietrich Genscher, emerged strengthened from the elections; their share of the vote increased from 7·0% in 1983 to 9·1% in 1987.

	CDU/ CSU	FDP	SPD	Die Grünen	Others
% share of the vote	44·3	9·1	37·0	8·3	1·3
Seats in the Bundestag	223	46	186	42	—

The FDP's performance was especially reassuring to a party which just five years earlier had appeared to be teetering on the edge of electoral obliteration following its switch from support for Helmut Schmidt's SPD to Herr Kohl's CDU/CSU. Analysis of poll returns indicated that about 800,000 former CDU/CSU supporters defected to the FDP, many of them displeased by the vigour of Herr Franz Josef Strauss's attacks upon the FDP leader, and convinced that they demonstrated the need for moderate ballast in the Federal Government. Bolstered by his own strong performance during the campaign, Herr Genscher remained in the post of Foreign Minister following the election.

Die Grünen's performance left the party justly satisfied, having gained a million votes – almost all of them from voters who had supported the SPD in 1983. Whilst the SPD's vote did not suffer as greatly as some commentators had anticipated, it was still the party's worse result since the 1961 ideological divisions within the party, and deep disagreement over the question of a possible coalition with Die Grünen caused some on the left of the party to campaign with less than complete enthusiasm, and consequently weakened the party's credibility.

The dominant conservative grouping within the government, CDU/CSU, did very much less well than had been expected despite the considerable advantage afforded it by a large trade surplus, negative inflation and steady economic growth. Their 44·3% share of the vote was the party's poorest performance since 1949, although still better than all but one of the SPD's shares since 1949.

The election campaign was dull, thereby emulating the tone of Chancellor Kohl's leadership. Kohl's approach to government posed few electoral problems in a setting of economic strength, but seemed less likely to suffice for the more difficult and challenging circumstances posed by the strength of the D-Mark and the resultant pressure on Germany's traditional export markets. His campaign slogan of *Weiter so, Deutschland* ('More of the same') reflected the Chancellor's innate caution and disinclination to translate Germany's economic strength into political leadership, either within Europe or in relations with the United States.

The FDP's new strength was reflected in the apportionment of Cabinet places following Herr Kohl's reelection as Chancellor by the Bundestag on 12 March 1987. In addition to its control of the Foreign, Economics and Justice ministries, the Party now took the education portfolio. The change was largely symbolic since West Germany's federal structure devolves most education responsibilities to the states. Herr Franz Josef Strauss opted not to accept a Cabinet portfolio but instead to remain Prime Minister of Bavaria, itself an indication that Strauss may privately have judged the new government to have a short life.

The INF Treaty.

The Intermediate Nuclear Force Treaty negotiated by the Soviet Union and the United States in December 1987 had considerable implications for West Germany. The modernisation of NATO's intermediate missiles had taken place in part as a result of the anxiety of Helmut Schmidt (then Chancellor) about the weakening of the linkage between conventional forces and the American strategic deterrent. The successful eliminination of the Soviet Union's SS20s, the United State's Cruise, and Pershing IIs, and Germany's own Pershing Is, nonetheless caused most German politicians to look either for cuts in short-range weapons (as Herr Genscher, the FDP Foreign Minister sought) or their complete withdrawal (as the SPD wished). Chancellor Kohl successfully resisted the attempts of the United States and Britain at the NATO summit in early March 1988 to declare the Organisation's willingness to modernise short-range weapons wherever necessary. German sensitivity on the matter was scarcely surprising: any nuclear exchange involving short-range weapons would take place for the most part on German soil.

The Coalition under Pressure.

Pressure on the governing coalition grew in the early months of 1988. The CDU lost ground in the opinions polls, falling to just 40% (the same as the SPD) in early March, whilst the FDP (buoyed by Herr Genscher's popularity) moved ahead to 12%. Worse still for Chancellor Kohl, his CDU appeared likely to do badly in state elections in the Spring, just as it had done in 1987. Herr Strauss, frustrated by his powerlessness, criticised Herr Stoltenberg, the West German finance minister, for deciding to tax the incomes of churches and charities, and for raising taxes on petrol and tobacco in an attempt to cut the burgeoning West German budget deficit. The real objects of Herr Strauss's attack were Foreign Minister Genscher and Chancellor Kohl, both of whom held jobs which he had spent his life seeking; its probable consequence was the further weakening of the CDU. Chancellor Kohl's difficulty was that he was torn between on the one hand attempting to appeal to centrist voters who had been wooed by the SPD and Die Grünen, and on the other of trying to retain the coalitional support of Bavarian conservatives. Some of the latter, especially farmers disaffected by West German concessions in the EC, began to drift away from the CSU towards extreme right-wing parties.

Political Developments in 1988.

The intermediate-range nuclear question having been settled by the INF Treaty between the United States and the Soviet Union, short-range nuclear modernisation emerged in 1988 as a politically embarrassing question for the West German government. Whereas Britain and the United States were firmly committed to modernising American Lance missiles in West Germany, the German government sought to postpone a decision. In public, Herr Kohl and Herr Genscher argued that to modernise the missiles without delay would be an inappropriate move at a time when negotiations on conventional forces were proceeding well. Privately, both Kohl and Genscher were concerned at the impact a decision to modernise would have on German public opinion, and upon their respective parties' prospects at the Federal elections in 1990.

A left-led coalition formed of the SPD and Die Grunen was formed in early March 1989 to govern West Berlin. The move was significant for coming less than two years before national elections. If the coalition was successful, both parties within it could

employ it to attempt to defeat Helmut Kohl's CDU-led government. If it failed, Kohl would himself have an opportunity to embarrass his opponents.

The Berlin elections were also notable for revealing the strength of the Republicans, an extreme right-wing party which derives its popularity from unremitting hostility to foreigners and which won 7·5% of the vote and eleven seats on the City Council. The Republicans' electoral prospects are rosier in the wake of the death in 1988 of Franz-Josef Strauss, the ebullient and powerful leader of the right-wing CSU. With Strauss gone, the Republicans offer a new vehicle for right-wing protest outside the political mainstream of the four major parties. Another outlet exists in the shape of the National Democrats, the much older neo-Nazi party, which secured 6·6% of the vote in local elections in Frankfurt in March.

Chancellor Kohl's position within the CDU and the CDU-FDP alliance which he led accordingly came under scrutiny in the months after the poor results in Berlin and in other local elections. Criticism focussed upon his seeming inability to respond to the challenges posed from the right, and to the implications that this had for the vulnerability of the CDU's electoral base. As the national elections approached in December 1990, so Kohl's room for manoeuvre lessened, and the possibility of a new national coalition of the SPD, the FDP, and the Greens emerging after the poll, grew. The Greens are more plausible coalition partners for the FDP and the SDP now that the Fundis, the hard-line faction within the Party, have been overcome by the more pragmatic faction of Realos who led the move to coalition with the SPD in Berlin.

Developments in East Germany.

Between 7 and 11 September 1987, Herr Honecker, the East German party leader, paid his first official visit to West Germany. The fact that the visit went ahead at all was a mark of the improved condition of relations between the United States and the Soviet Union; when the visit was first planned, three years before, the Russians vetoed the proposal. The visit was in itself remarkably unspectacular: the agreements signed during the visit were relatively insignificant and had in any case been well-flagged in advance. Nonetheless, the occasion marked an extraordinary shift since Chancellor Willy Brandt struggled against intense domestic opposition in the early 1970s to establish his policy of Ostpolitik. This was reflected in increased trade, a decrease in tensions generally, and a marked increase in visits among friends and families across the border. Early in 1988, it appeared likely that Chancellor Kohl would visit East Germany later in the year, and possibly include a visit to East Berlin – an especially sensitive matter in view of the two countries' wholly different views of the city's status.

Figures released by the West German government in January 1988 showed that many East Germans used the additional travel permits granted by the East German government to enter West Germany and stay. Some 1·29 million travel permits were issued to persons under pensionable age in 1987; of these, as many as 12,000 stayed in the West – double the number of escapees in the same year. The issue posed a dilemma for the East German authorities: if travel restrictions were increased, discontent in the East was likely to rise, and escape attempts might well become more common. On the other hand, a more liberal policy towards travel permits clearly carried the risk that many (especially the young, and professional persons who could earn more in the West) would not return.

Honecker Soldiers On.

As her Eastern European neighbours adapted to perestroika in the Soviet Union in different ways, the East German Communist Party showed no sign in 1988 and early 1989 of shifting from its self-assigned path of rigid adherence to the command economy which, in contrast to the experience elsewhere in Comecon countries, had brought about considerable economic success for East Germany. The waning of state repression in Hungary, Poland, and the Soviet Union similarly had little effect upon politics in East Germany. Yet the authorities in East Berlin had to contend with the continuing exposure of the population to currents of western opinion and news through West German television. The East German population were hence well aware of the primacy which western analysts and journalists accorded Soviet economic and political developments. Equally, they knew well that the reforms within several Comecon member states aroused at best cold indifference among Erich Honecker and his colleagues, and more commonly their ill-concealed scorn.

Recent Developments.

For an analysis of the dramatic recent events in Germany, and the prospects for reunification, see Special Topics C85–86.

ITALY.

Background to the 1987 Elections.

Mr. Craxi handed in the resignation of the government he led to the Italian President, Mr. Francesco Cossiga on 25 February 1987. Hints of an election (not required under Italy's constitution until June 1988) had been in the air for some months, and Craxi's shrewdly-timed resignation did nothing to dispel them. His last months in office had been made awkward by Christian Democratic impatience with his evident political success and high standing both at home and abroad.

His successor was the veteran Christian Democrat Mr. Giulio Andreotti who had been Prime Minister on five previous occasions and at the time of Craxi's resignation was serving as Foreign Minister. Now he found himself dependent upon the backing of Mr. Craxi's Socialist Party; Craxi therefore had the luxury of being able to withdraw support from the new government at the moment when he judged that it would bring him electoral reward. The results of this political shrewdness were seen in the June 1987 election. Craxi's Socialists won 94 seats in the Chamber (up from 73), whilst the Communists fell from 198 to 177 (losing support also to the anti-nuclear Greens, with 13 seats). Otherwise, little changed. The Christian Democrats (with 234 seats) remained the largest party.

The June 1987 Election Aftermath.

The major issue in the election of 14 June 1987 was that of the environment. Its prominence was symbolised by the emergence of the Green list to secure 2·5% of the vote; all the major parties attempted to accommodate themselves to the new prominence of environmental questions. Whilst the election did nothing to settle Italy's underlying political difficulties, the results confirmed the continuing decline of the Communist Party whose vote fell from 29·9% to 26·6%. They also marked a slight improvement in the Christian Democratic vote from 32·9% to 34·3%, and a continuing growth in the Socialist Party's vote from 11·4% to 14·3%. In the light of the growing convergence between the Socialists, Social Democrats, and Radicals, there began to emerge the possibility of a Socialist-led left majority. For the time being, however, the Christian Democrats and the Socialists were condemned to live together in government.

The Goria Government.

The new government was led by Giovanni Goria who was, at the age of 44, Italy's youngest-ever Prime Minister. He had since 1982 been Treasury Minister. That valuable experience notwithstanding, he was surrounded in government by senior politicians (many of them from his own Christian Democratic Party) whose interest in the survival of his administration was less than complete.

Goria's coalition lasted just six months. He offered his resignation to the Italian President on 10 February 1988 having sustained a parliamentary defeat over his budget. The defeat which caused him to resign was the seventeenth in the space of just three weeks. The cause of his downfall was factionalism within the Christian Democrats, made possible by party colleagues taking advantage of parliamentary procedures permitting secret votes to oppose the budget. Such party infighting had never before been so intense as to cause an Italian govern-

ment to lose a vote on the Ministry of Finance's administrative budget, but it found its focus in 1988 on dissatisfaction with Mr. Goria and a widespread determination to be rid of him (albeit under the cover of secret voting). There was, however, no consensus on who should succeed Goria as party leader.

Eventually the choice was Giriaco De Mita. Mr. De Mita's government encountered severe difficulties before it was a year old: his factious party proved exceptionally difficult to control, and Bettino Craxi continued to be in the powerful position of determining how long the government would last.

De Mita did succeed in winning one minor and one major reform in the course of the year. The minor reform was of the office of Prime Minister which in theory enables the holder to take a much more prominent and decisive role in government. The major reform was of the secret vote in the Italian Parliament, long a means whereby governments could be privately voted out of office by Deputies. It was abolished on 13 October 1988. The margin was small. All of the opposition parties abstained, and the absolute majority of the Camera (the lower house) required for the measure to pass was achieved with just seven votes to spare. Even so, the measure before the Camera was the product of much haggling and negotiation in the three weeks before the vote took place: the Communist Party and others ensured that the secret vote was retained on numerous matters, including civil rights, the rights of linguistic minorities and, unsurprisingly, on parliamentary rules. The reform offered no assurance that the system of institutionalised factionalism in Italy would end, merely that one of the key supports for the destructive conduct of party politics in secret was weakened.

The underlying economic problems remained severe. The external deficit for the year October 1987—October 1988 was \$9·8 billion, and the fiscal deficit remained stubbornly high. Tackling the problem of chaotic public finances remains the central policy difficulty for Italian governments. Unfortunately, Italian party politics continues to offer powerful incentives for opposition politicians to place party and factional manoeuvring above the national interest.

De Mita retained the two posts of Christian Democrat Party Secretary and Prime Minister until February 1989 when his nominal party colleagues, divided by intense factional infighting, deprived him of the Party Secretaryship. Opponents had lost patience with De Mita's assiduous rewarding of his followers.

In May 1989, however, the 13-month-old Centre-Left coalition of Sr. De Mita collapsed after a bitter attack by the Socialists.

Recent Events.

De Mita was replaced by Andreotti. Factional struggles within the Christian Democratic Party and the customary manoeuvering for advantage between the partners in the governing coalition in advance of regional elections in May 1990 threatened the continued existence of Mr. Giulio Andreotti's government. The Prime Minister's attempts in his first six months in office to secure his position involved him (as it has done other Italian Prime Ministers) in dispensing patronage to some and denying it to others. Mr. de Mita, having lost his job as secretary of the Christian Democratic Party in February 1989 and having resigned as Prime Minister on 20 May, found that he and the members of his faction within the Party did poorly. De Mita and his colleagues, already discontented with parts of the coalition government's programme, resigned from their party posts in protest.

The calculations of Mr. Craxi loomed as large as ever in estimations of the remaining life of the government. He saw an opportunity for the Socialist Party to make gains at the expense of the Communist Party, embroiled in travails of its own centring on the changing of its name, the abandonment of revolutionary objectives, and the acceptance of a social market economy. The reformist programme was that of Achille Occhetto, the party's leader, but it was bitterly opposed by the party's left wing, comprising approximately 35% of the delegates at the special Party Congress called to consider the matter.

PORTUGAL.

Results of the 1983 Elections.

Amidst political chaos, the government of Mr. Balsemao resigned in December 1982 after a period of disagreement between Centre Democrats and Social Democrats, the two main parties in the coalition. Balsemao had proved a weak leader of the governing alliance. He failed to push vital economic reforms through Parliament and, as President Eanes noted, perversely resigned at the moment when a change in Portugal's constitution gave him the powers to initiate the reforms. Eanes announced on 23 January 1983 that he was dissolving Parliament in an attempt to solve the impasse created by the break-up of Balsemao's coalition. The results of the election proved inconclusive. The Socialists under Soares emerged as the largest single party, but well short of an overall majority. Whilst it was clear that Soares would return to office, it was not clear how, or with whom, he would govern.

The Return of Soares.

Dr. Soares eventually formed a coalition government with the Social Democrats on 4 June. A joint statement issued by the two parties said that the coalition agreement heralded "a majority government based on the principles of democratic socialism ready to tackle the nation's problems through reform, modernisation and social justice."

The government, the sixth since 1976, was formed of a Cabinet comprising nine socialists, seven social democrats and one independent, the Finance Minister, Sr. Ernani Lopes. Soares had campaigned on the platform of an austerity programme designed to improve the country's weak economy. The assembly passed the government's programme on 24 June; it took steps to reduce Portugal's deficit on external trade, to stabilise the currency, and to allow for the introduction of private capital into certain sectors, including banking and insurance, which had been nationalised after the 1974 revolution. Negotiations to prepare for Portugal's accession to the EEC were to be continued. Government subsidies on food were removed, resulting in large and sudden price rises. Just prior to the passage of these measures, the escudo had again been devalued—this time by 12%.

As in Spain, Portuguese politics centred in 1984, as increasingly in years past, around an almost unchallenged Prime Minister. Mario Soares's authority was symbolised by his arrest of an armed group led by Lt.-Col. Otelo, a veteran of the 1974 revolution and his pressing through Parliament (in the same week) an anti-terrorist statute which will effectively suspend civil liberties and due process for those suspected of terrorist offences.

The October 1985 Elections.

1985 and the first two months of 1986 provided sharp changes in the direction of Portuguese politics. In May 1985, Mr Cavaco Silva won the leadership of the Social Democratic Party and promptly withdrew his party from the government coalition led by Mario Soares, thereby precipitating a general election. In the election held on 6 October, the Social Democrats won 88 of the 250 seats in the Portuguese parliament. The Socialists saw their representation fall from 101 to 57, whilst the newly-formed Democratic Renewal Party, composed of President Eanes's followers, won 45 seats. The right-wing Centre Democrats slumped badly, securing just 22 seats. The Communists and their allies also failed to make any significant impression, winning 6 fewer seats than in the 1983 election to give a total of 38.

Forming a government took several weeks: on 29 October, President Eanes asked Mr. Silva to form an administration. This he did with the consent, if not quite the enthusiastic support, of the two smaller right-wing parties. This shift of fortunes for the Portuguese left owed much to the electoral unpopularity of the deflation which the socialist-led government had pursued between 1982 and 1985 in an attempt (which proved mostly successful) to control the country's problems of inflation and balance of payments deficit. It was no surprise when opinion polls in early January showed Mario Soares's presidential candidacy to be in deep trouble with a rating of 17%. Running against Mr. Freitas do Amaral, Soares lost the first round and then unexpectedly secured victory with just 51·3% of the vote in the second round of balloting. The success or otherwise of Portugal's continuing economic recovery would depend on whether political stability could be built on the shaky foundations which the general and presidential elections had provided.

Constancio elected Socialist Leader.

Following Mario Soare's election as president, the Socialist Party chose Vitor Constancio as its new leader in preference to Jaime Gama who had appeared to be the front-runner for the post. Constancio is an intellectually impressive economist, a former Governor of the country's central bank, and a social democrat in all but name. On taking office, Constancio urged his party colleagues to follow the example set by Prime Minister Gonzalez of Spain in the development and presentation of policy in preparation for a challenge for power at the polls.

Anibal Cavaco Silva, the prime minister, was chosen as leader of the Social Democratic Party, and was subsequently successful in strengthening his political position by winning a vote of confidence for the minority government he led.

Portugal was struck in the winter of 1987/8 by a series of strikes. Employees of the Post Office (including the telephone service) the national airline, and the railways all took one-day strikes following a strike lasting three weeks by public transport workers in Lisbon during January 1988.

SPAIN.

The 1977 Election.

On 15 June 1977 the first free parliamentary elections for 41 years were held in Spain. This was a decisive step on the road from dictatorship to democracy, and in July the new two-chamber parliament replaced the old Cortes of General Franco. The strongest group was the "Union of the Democratic Centre" led by Sr. Suárez, who formed a minority government. The Socialist Workers' Party (PSOE) came a strong second, the Communist Party a weak third. The first task of the new government and parliament was the drawing up of a new democratic constitution. On 28 July Spain submitted its application to join the EEC. A serious economic crisis had been inherited from the last years of the Franco regime and the transitional period. But the most crucial issue for the future of the Spanish state was the regional problem. This applied not only to the Basque country, where the militant separatist organisation ETA had stepped up its terrorist activities. Both there and in Catalonia systems of "pre-autonomy" in anticipation of the new constitution were introduced in late 1977, setting Spain on the road from a strictly centralist to a federal state. Initiatives for more autonomy were taken in other Spanish regions also. However during 1978 there was growing disappointment in Catalonia and the Basque Country about the extent of the powers actually granted to them. The wave of ETA murders in the Basque Country brought fears that they might damage the process of democratisation and the lack of success of the security forces led to growing impatience in the navy and elsewhere. In July brutal and unprovoked police action, apparently in revenge for the government's decision to allow the Basques to form their own police force, increased the traditional ill-feeling against them in the Basque Country. Although the main Basque parties at last publicly denounced terror and violence, the large circle of ETA sympathisers and the Koordinadora Abertzale Sozialista which acts as ETA's political wing put forward demands amounting virtually to independence. In December 1978 EEC membership was accepted in principle, with negotiations to start in 1979 and accession planned for 1983.

The New Constitution.

Spain's new democratic constitution was adopted by both houses of parliament by an overwhelming majority in the autumn of 1978 and approved, despite substantial abstentions in the Basque provinces, by 87·87% of the votes in a referendum on 6 December. The King signed the new constitution on 27 December, thus becoming a constitutional monarch. The Cortes was then dissolved and elections called for 1 March 1979 followed by the long overdue local elections on 3 April. Prime Minister Suárez's aim in the elections was to reduce the dependence of his Union of the Democratic Centre, which had only 165 of the 350 seats in the old parliament, on the votes of small autonomy parties and its consequent vulnerability to blackmail over the coming of autonomy. However, although the UDC made slight gains, in common with the Socialist Workers' Party and the Communists, and the right-wing Democratic Coalition suffered severe losses, Sr. Suárez still fell short of an absolute majority. Thus the regionalist groupings still held the balance of power. The gains of the Socialist Workers' Party were much less than had been expected, and in May Sr. Felipe González resigned as its General Secretary after being defeated in an attempt to reduce the party's Marxist orientation.

In July 1979, following skilful negotiations by the leaders of the Basque Nationalist Party, an autonomy statute was adopted providing the Basque Country with its own legislature and judiciary and wide-ranging powers including the sensitive areas of police, education and taxation.

Early in 1981, under pressure from the conservative element in his party, Sr. Suárez resigned. As Parliament debated his successor, a military *coup* was attempted on 23 February 1981. The resolute action of the King prevented the army joining this rash coup attempt which rapidly collapsed.

The 1982 Socialist Victory.

In national elections on 28 October 1982, nearly 80% of Spanish voters went to the polls and handed a solid victory to the Socialist Party. Its leader, the 40-year-old Felipe Gonzalez, became Prime Minister.

The Socialists won 201 of the 350 seats in the lower house, the Congress, and 134 of the 205 seats in the Senate. The right-wing Popular Alliance won almost all the other seats; 105 in the Congress and 53 in the Senate; the centre, extremist and minor parties were effectively eliminated. The divided Centre Party was especially badly mauled; in February of 1983, it broke apart. The Prime Minister, Calvo Sotelo, and all but two of the ministers in the Centre Government which he had led, were defeated at the polls.

For the Socialist Party, it was an enormously significant victory; for Spain, the peaceful transfer of power to a left of centre political party held yet greater significance. The Socialist Party had only existed legally for six years after a 40-year ban under Franco's rule. When a socialist victory at the polls seemed likely, commentators in Spain and elsewhere wondered aloud whether the brooding military machine, smarting at their exclusion from political power and at Spain's transition to a modern liberal democracy, would stay their hand. They did so, and Spain's experiment with democracy prospered.

The Socialists' policy consisted of economic growth, improvements in education, and social reform. The last ingredient posed problems for the government in its early months, and seemed likely to continue to do so: Gonzalez's declared intention to introduce a bill permitting abortion in strictly limited circumstances provoked great controversy. The easing of the law was insufficient to placate many Spaniards, including the 300,000 Spanish women who have illegal abortions every year, anxious for a more rapid move towards the European norm; yet it was too great for the Church and millions of traditional conservative Spanish voters. There was no political advantage to Gonzalez in confronting the issue, nor any easy way of avoiding it.

The Ascendancy of Gonzalez.

In 1984, Mr. Gonzalez surmounted the political challenge to his administration's authority posed by wide differences of views on education and defence policy. The education question in many ways resembled that in France: the government pushed through parliament in the Spring a law which requires those private schools in receipt of state

subsidies to accept pupils without regard to the religious views of their parents or lose their subsidies. For many Catholics, the prospect of losing either control over their schools or state support for them was unacceptable, and national demonstrations ensued, culminating in a huge march on Madrid on 18 November. But the government, determined to improve Spain's inadequate education system, survived the challenge to the law and to its partial secularisation of Spanish society.

A month later, Gonzalez was overwhelmingly re-elected as the leader of the Spanish Socialist Party, having made his commitment to Spain's continued membership of NATO abundantly clear. The pledge to hold a referendum on the issue would, he said, be met in February 1986. But he made clear his determination to work for a vote of approval, whilst opponents to NATO within the party were hampered by the widespread acknowledgement that he was irreplaceable as Party Leader and Prime Minister.

NATO and EEC membership.

The debate about NATO membership continued throughout 1985, peaking in the weeks before the referendum on 12 March 1986 which delivered a majority of 52%–39% in favour of retaining NATO membership. The result was a surprise for many left-wing voters unhappy with the prospect of remaining in an alliance dominated by the United States whilst right-wing voters had been urged by Manuel Fraga to abstain.

EEC membership was a less contentious matter altogether: Spain joined, with Portugal, on 1 January 1986, just a decade after the end of dictatorship. In that time, Spain had moved some way to becoming a modern secular European society, benefitting from remarkable political stability and (a stubbornly high unemployment level apart) relative economic success. To mark the tenth anniversary of his enthronement, King Juan Carlos unveiled in November 1985 a memorial in memory of all Spain's military dead. It was a characteristically shrewd gesture of reconciliation from the King, supremely skilled in the binding of Spain's internal political wounds, conducted before veterans of both sides from the civil war.

By the international language of economic progress, too, Spain had recorded striking successes in the ten years of her democracy. Under Mr. Soares's premiership, inflation, taxation, and wage rises were all reduced sharply – but by employing economic and financial policies of a distinctly conservative kind. More striking still, economic growth was maintained at a steady, if sluggish rate, and Spain's external trade balance moved into surplus.

The result of the referendum on NATO membership might have been different had Spanish voters known at the time what they learned in October of 1986: Felipe Gonzalez's government indicated to NATO that it would do its best to ensure that it played a full part in cooperating with NATO partners. Whilst there was no clear indication that Spain would join the integrated military command, Gonzalez appeared in private to be willing to entertain a far closer relationship than he had indicated in public.

The June 1986 Election.

As most observers anticipated, the General Election in Spain held on 22 June 1986 resulted in a clear victory for the party of the incumbent Prime Minister, Felipe Gonzalez, albeit with a smaller majority than in 1982. The outcome was in many ways remarkable for a Socialist leader who had practised monetarist economic policies and under whom unemployment had risen by 800,000 (the amount by which in 1982 he had pledged himself to reduce it). However, the improved standing of the regionalist parties and of the small groupings to the Socialist Party's left were reminders (if the Prime Minister needed them) of the persistence of the Catalan and, more seriously, the Basque questions, and of the unpopularity of his economic policies with the left of Spanish politics. The full results were:

United Left (Communist-dominated)   7
Left Basque Regionalists   2
Herri Batasuna (ETA supporters)   5

Socialists	184
Popular Coalition	105
Social and Democratic Centre	19
Catalan Regionalists	18
Basque Nationalists	6
Sundry regionalists	4

One consequence of the elections was the resignation of Manuel Fraga from the presidency of the Popular Alliance in December 1986. The new leader, Antonio Hernandez Mancha, was elected in early February by an overwhelming 71% of the vote at a specially-convened party conference. Just 35 years old, Sr. Mancha lacked a parliamentary seat at the time of his election, and so had to look elsewhere in the party for a leader in the *Cortes*. Compared to Adolfo Suarez, buoyed by the performance of his Social and Democratic Centre Party's performance in the June elections, he had little experience and much ground to make up if a serious challenge was to be presented to the Socialist Party's successful blend of cautious centrism. As it happened, the government's control of events was in any case coming under some pressure by early 1987: protests by students (echoing those the previous year in France) against the rules for entrance to university ran the risk of acting as a catalyst for more general left-wing, and especially labour, protest against the government's economic policies in general, and the very high rate of unemployment among young people in particular.

By early 1988, the unemployment rate stood at 3 million—some 20% of the working age population, and there was little prospect that the figure might be reduced significantly. The rate of creation of new jobs was sufficient only to absorb new entrants into the labour market. Disaffection among the voters manifested itself in poor local election results in 1987, and within the trade unions in the resignation of Nicolas Redondo, the leader of the UGT, the national trade union federation, from his parliamentary seat. The proximate cause of Mr. Redondo's resignation was a quarrel with the government over public sector pay, but this followed a period of general disagreement over the government's policy of wage restraint and continued pressure on levels of public spending. As the PSOE changed its character from a working-class socialist party to a middle-class centrist organisation, relations between it and the UGT had inevitably become somewhat distant. Indeed, it was precisely this distance which permitted Mr. Gonzalez sufficient freedom to keep tight control of pay and public spending.

The 1988 Party Congress.

At the Party Congress in January 1988, Mr. Gonzalez and his lieutenants such as the Deputy Prime Minister, Alfonso Guerra, easily overcame the dissent within the trade unions and from the few left-wingers prepared to state publicly their opposition to the Prime Minister's policies of high economic growth, the attraction of capital to Spain, and of a firm if not uncritical partnership with NATO and the EC. The policies won the overwhelming approval of Congress. The left had nowhere to turn: there was in early 1988 no more prospect of a credible challenge being mounted to Gonzalez's leadership from among their ranks, or from among assorted regional interests discontented with central control of policy and politics, than there was of a united centre or right-wing opposition emerging in the foreseeable future. Although the PSOE's public opinion poll rating fell to 40% at the beginning of the year, Mr. Gonzalez was his party's most powerful asset with voters and immune from serious challenge from within his own party or from another.

Mr. Gonzalez had more reason to regard labour discontent with some alarm. The UGT, fresh from its leader's break with Mr. Gonzalez in the previous October, reached a policy agreement in February 1988 with the Communist-dominated union, *Comisiones Obreras*. The immediate significance of the agreement was that labour unrest would probably grow. In the longer term, the trial separation of the UGT from the PSOE might well become a divorce, with damaging consequences for the Socialist government's standing.

Trade Union Problems.

Relations   between   the   Spanish   Socialist

government of Felipe Gonzalez and the socialist UGT trade union federation led by Nicolas Redondo worsened markedly during 1988 and early 1989. The main point of contention was social welfare policy which is very much less generous in Spain than in most other advanced Western European countries. Welfare policy is of particular importance in Spain because of the politically awkward combination of a nominally socialist government and the very high unemployment rate of 18·5%. Less than one-third of Spain's unemployed qualify for unemployment benefit; pledges made by the government in 1984 to raise the proportion to about half have not been met. The government's spending projections accord welfare spending no higher priority for the next four years. In these circumstances, the high expectations which the unions had of Mr. Gonzalez's administration following the increases in welfare benefits in his first year as Prime Minister have been dashed. The unions' response has been to overturn the corporatist arrangement between government, employers and unions to determine the level of national pay settlements.

The October 1989 Election.

The Prime Minister of Spain, Felipe Gonzalez, called an election for 20 October 1989, eight months before he was obliged to do so. High unemployment and a widening trade deficit apart, the economic achievements of the government he led were sufficiently impressive for him to seize the opportunity. Opportunism was precisely the charge levelled against the Prime Minister by his opponents in the conservative People's Party (led by a former member of Franco's government, Manuel Fraga) and the Social and Democratic Centre (led by the last Francoist Prime Minister, Adolfo Suarez). There was much truth to it, The Socialist government had benefitted from a weak and divided opposition, and had paid little regard to the needs of the unemployed. The conservative and centrist opposition parties were tainted by reason of the association of their senior members with the old fascist regime; their support was accordingly limited.

The result of the election was to confirm the dominance of the Socialist Party. It remained by far the largest party with 176 seats, though with a majority of only one, and lost support on its left to the United Left with 17 seats, dominated by the Communist Party who tapped the discontent with the Socialists' parsimonious welfare policy, and its toleration of high unemployment. The People's Party benefitted from its running a new candidate for Prime Minister: Jose Maria Aznar who, unlike Fraga, was entirely untainted by links to Francoism. They won 106 seats but, as the People's Party gained, so the CDS under Suarez lost ground sharply with its total of seats falling to just 14.

EASTERN MEDITERRANEAN

GREECE.

The June 1985 Election.

In the approach to the June 1985 legislative elections, political manoeuvring centred around the office of President. Having publicly backed the candidacy of the incumbent Constantine Karamanlis, Prime Minister Papandreou withdrew his support when he judged that to do so might placate the left-wing members of his party dissatisfied with the lack of substantive achievement in economic or foreign policy since PASOK's victory in 1981.

The ploy worked. Papandreou's nominee for President, Christos Sartzetakis, won election to the presidency on the third ballot. Having satisfied his left wing, Papandreou campaigned by attempting to draw the starkest contrast between his own party and the New Democracy opposition, and declining to rest his case on the slender achievements of his administration.

The parliamentary elections resulted in a surprising win for PASOK, with 45.8% of the vote, and 161 seats in the 300 seat legislature. The New Democracy Party won less than 41% of the vote, and 126 seats. The Communist Party were denied the place in government for which they had hoped by the defection of communist voters to the socialist party, fearful of a victory by the right.

Papandreou's gradual modification of his commitment to withdraw Greece from NATO became complete on 23 January 1987 when he informed parliament that Greece would remain within the Alliance, and that he would entertain proposals for keeping an American military presence within the country if a suitable agreement could be negotiated. Having already ratified by decree the Single European Act (a measure to which all member governments of the European Community had subscribed and which provided for modifications in the Community's procedures) in order to avoid the possibility of its defeat at the hands of parliament, Papandreou claimed (in clear contradiction of his previous stand on the matter) that NATO membership afforded Greece protection against Turkish military threats, and that there was a price at which he would countenance the renewal of the American bases agreement as being in Greece's national interest.

Papandreou's Political Difficulties.

None of this did the Prime Minister any good with the left wing of his own party, deeply disillusioned with his trimming of what had once been an unequivocal set of commitments. Given the deep unpopularity with his left wing of the austerity programme over which he presided, his apparent willingness to bargain with the Americans was somewhat surprising since anti-Americanism might have proved a unifying rallying call in a country and party divided over rising unemployment and financial retrenchment. But Papandreou found himself under pressure not just from the left, but the right too: local elections in October 1986 resulted in voters defecting from PASOK to the Communists and the conservative New Democracy party: the country's three largest cities, Athens, Salonica and Piraeus, were all won by New Democracy. Meanwhile early 1987 saw increased tension with Turkey over the Aegean.

Improved Relations with Turkey.

Relations with Turkey underwent a marked improvement with the reelection to power of Turgut Ozal, the Turkish Prime Minister in his country's November 1987 election. The cautious diplomatic soundings between the two states, frozen into immobilism since 1981, was linked to glimmerings of a possible solution to the problem of divided Cyprus with the election there in February 1988 of George Vassiliou, a prominent businessman but who enjoyed Communist support. Greek Cypriots in particular took careful note of the distinctly warm meeting between the Greek and Turkish Prime Ministers in Davos, Switzerland, at the end of January.

The two heads of government agreed to meet regularly in the future and to establish two working groups. One would explore avenues of economic cooperation, and the other consider how progress might best be made on the fundamental disputes between Greece and Turkey: mineral exploitation rights in the Aegean, Turkey's application to join the EC, and Cyprus. Greece's opposition to Turkey's European ambitions was and is negotiable, especially in the light of the considerable potential that exists for an expansion of trade between the two countries.

Although at an early stage, the warming of relations with Turkey was evidently more than a fluctuation in the general freeze. The foreign ministers met during a conference of Balkan nations in Belgrade in late February, partly in order to prepare the way for a further meeting between the two Prime Ministers at the NATO summit in Brussels in early March.

Scandal and Disarray.

The Greek government fell into disarray in 1988 and 1989 as a result of a financial scandal. Mr. George Koskotas, owner of the Bank of Crete, was charged with embezzling government assets on deposit at the Bank. Having bought the Bank in 1984, Koskotas built up the Bank, acquired companies, and a personal fortune in the years that

followed. Advisers from PASOK, and Mr. Papandreou's government, assisted him in his commercial decisions.

In the face of the government's sluggishness in investigating how he managed to acquire so large a fortune with such speed, the Bank of Greece took the lead in investigating Mr. Koskotas's affairs as a result of which charges were laid against him. Koskotas subsequently left Greece for the United States (in violation of an order confining him to Greece).

Mr. Papandreou's attempt to pass the affair off as an American conspiracy to topple the PASOK government was not widely believed. The embroilment of several ministers in the matter damaged the government's credibility and its electoral hopes, as was shown by the parliamentary debate on a motion of no-confidence on 13 March. Although the government survived the vote, three PASOK members abstained—an action for which they were stripped of their party membership.

In an attempt to prevent the electoral disaster which threatened to engulf his party at the June elections, Papandreou and his colleagues introduced a bill to modify the electoral system. The most likely outcome seemed to be that the smaller parties (not least the Communists) would gain at the expense of PASOK, and, as Papandreou clearly intended, the conservative New Democracy opposition party which had benefited from the discomfiture of PASOK.

Electoral Stalemate.

The election of 18 June resulted in a stalemate. The largest party was Constantine Mitsotakis's New Democracy with 145 seats, 6 short of an overall majority but PASOK's securing of 125 seats and 39% of the vote was very much better than any but its most ardent supporters could have hoped for three months earlier (although the seat total was assisted considerably by Papandreou's modification of the electoral system in order to limit the damage done to his party).

After much haggling, there emerged the most improbable coalition of the conservative New Democracy, and the Marxists and quasi-Marxists of the Alliance of the Left and Progress (a grouping of neo-Stalinists and Euro-Communists). The government, led by Tzannis Tzannetakis of New Democracy, set itself a limited agenda by which it sought to address the scandals afflicting Papandreou and his former government, and the question of the political bias of state television (which had once again been prominent during the election campaign). This having been done, Tzannetakis declared that a further election would be held in the autumn.

The second election came no nearer to producing a result. PASOK gained three seats, the Communist alliance (partly because of the unpopularity among many of its supporters of its coalition with the conservatives) lost seven, and New Democracy gained three. Papandreou's resilient leadership of the Socialists was, under the circumstances, remarkable, and the stability of the Party's vote astonishing. The coalition government which emerged from the second stalemated election of 1989 was even broader than the first: it included PASOK in addition to the two other main parties. The government was led by Xenophon Zolotas whose political task of maintaining political stability until yet another general election on 8 April 1990 was made the greater by the growing crisis in public finance. The International Monetary Fund estimated in early 1990 that Greece's public sector borrowing requirement was likely to exceed 22% of GNP. Dire forecasts of this sort increased the pressure for tax reform and for cuts in public spending. The April 1990 elections finally ended the stalemate with a narrow victory for New Democracy.

TURKEY.

The 1983 Election.

A general election took place on 6 November 1983, but was only a qualified expression of democracy: just three of the country's political parties were permitted to participate. The high turnout of 92%

was cited by both President Evren and Mr. Turgut Ozal, the leader of the victorious and conservative Motherland Party, as evidence of the enthusiasm for the restoration of democratic elections. Enthusiasm was unquestionably buttressed, however, by the compulsion to vote on pain of a fine.

President Evren and the Generals had thrown their support in the election to Turgut Sunalp's Nationalist Democracy Party (NDP). But Ozal's accomplished performances on television in the campaign, together with his emphasis upon his ability to accelerate Turkey's economic development propelled him to an overall majority over the lacklustre Sunalp and the left of centre populist party led by Mr. Nedet Calp. To the surprise of many observers, Calp's party emerged as the second largest party in Parliament.

Ozal quickly made good his relations with President Evren, who had earlier dismissed the Motherland Party leader as a "confidence trickster" and assembled a small Cabinet composed, like himself, overwhelmingly of businessmen who shared his free-market philosophy and determination to attract inward investment and promote stronger trading ties with the Arab states. Such an approach carried high risks; failure to secure the substantial economic progress he promised during the election could quickly deprive Ozal of much of his political support.

Ozal made a further promise during his campaign which attracted little attention in the West at the time; he assured voters that he would support northern Cyprus with substantial aid if elected. After his victory, he went further and said that he would support the Turkish Cypriots if they declared independence. On 15 November, the leader of the Turkish Cypriots, Raoul Denktash, announced the birth of the "Turkish Republic of Northern Cyprus". Although officially welcomed by the new government in Ankara, Denktash's move embarrassed many senior politicians and officials in Turkey and bought immediate, but ineffective, condemnation from Greece and Turkey's NATO allies.

Reshaping Turkish Politics.

1985 saw a reshaping of the party political map in Turkey, and changes in leadership. Two of the new parties lie to the left of Turkey's political centre, and two to the right. The Social Democratic Populist Party is a moderately left-wing amalgamation of two old parties, and won early popularity in the opinion polls. The former Prime Minister's wife, Mrs. Ecevit, led an incipient grouping to the left of this moderate party's left. Although the left-wing vote was thereby split just two ways instead of three, a disunited opposition to the Prime Minister was not unwelcome to him.

The Prime Minister had two main opponents on the right. The first was Mr. Ulku Soylemezoglu, elected leader of the National Democracy Party in succession to Mr. Turgut Sunalp in July 1985; the other continued to be Mr Demirel, the main figure in the True Path Party. Like Mr. Ecevit, Demirel was officially banned from politics until 1992 but continued to make his influence felt.

In February 1986, Mr. Turgut Ozal, the Turkish Prime Minister, visited Britain in an attempt to press his case for closer links with the EEC, and for increased investment in Turkey's economy. The occasion offered the enticing prospect to British defence contractors, eager to export to Turkey, but the Ankara government's continued systematic abuse of human rights (confirmed by all independent reports) lessened the chances of major changes in European policies towards Turkey.

Eleven by-elections held in Turkey on 28 September 1986 confirmed the reemergence of Suleiman Demirel as a major force in Turkish politics. His party, the 'True Path', won four of the seats and almost a quarter of the votes, whilst Turgut Ozal's 'Motherland' party slipped from the 45% which it won in the general election of three years before to slightly less than one-third of the votes. The Prime Minister's monetarist economic programme had done nothing for his standing in the country; middle-class voters deserted his party in droves following the failure of the government to reduce the rate of inflation from 45% in 1985. Left-wing parties did poorly; the new "Democratic Left" party formed by Bulent Ecevit won 8·6%, and the Social Democrat-Populist party 22·8%. The recurrent tendency of Turkish parties to form around personalities rather than issues made for particular difficulties in the campaign: Ecevit and Demirel involved themselves fully despite having been banned from active politics by President Evren following the 1980 coup.

Turkey and the EEC.

The Turkish government's attempts to establish closer economic relations with the European Community as a prelude to full membership met with predictable opposition from Greece. Opposition arose from Turkey's recognition of and support for the supposedly independent state of northern Cyprus (which Turkey is the only country to recognise), and what Greece continues to declare to be a military threat from its neighbour. Turkey fuelled Greek fears by conducting amphibious exercises in the Aegean in the summer of 1986. Greek opposition, and the fears expressed by other EEC members of the consequences for their own labour markets, caused the Community to withdraw its commitment to open its borders to Turkish migrant workers from 1 December. Frustrated abroad, President Evren warned in January 1987 that the growing strength of Islam threatened the secularist tradition of Kemalism. The claim was not an idle one, especially since the fundamentalist government in Iran ('Turkey's neighbour) had an interest in fostering Islamic discontent.

The 1987 Elections.

In elections on 29 November 1987, Mr. Turgut Ozal won a substantial parliamentary majority. Not needing to call the elections until the autumn of 1988, Mr. Ozal caught his opponents on the hop by declaring early. The Motherland Party which he led secured 292 seats in the new 450 seat Parliament, giving him an overwhelming lead over his nearest challenger, Mr. Erdal Inonu's Social Democratic People's Party with 99 seats, and former Prime Minister Suleiman Demirel's True Path Party with just 59 seats. Four other parties did not secure the 10% of the vote required to win parliamentary representation—among them, former Prime Minister Bulent Ecevit's Party. Ozal's huge parliamentary majority owed much to new voting regulations designed to squeeze out minority parties, especially Islamic ones.

The Motherland Party's victory owed virtually everything to the sound political judgment of Ozal who in his timing of the referendum in the Spring of 1987, and the election in the autumn, had outmanoeuvred old opponents such as Ecevit and Demirel and proved too experienced for newcomers such as Inonu. Coalition governments in the 1970s had caused persisting instability in Turkish politics, and precipitated the 1980 coup; the Motherland Party's dominance offered the prospect that the military might continue to keep their distance. Just as significantly, the election gave Ozal a mandate to press ahead with his plan to build a modern European economy in Turkey with growth rates of seven per cent *per annum* with, if possible, much lower inflation rates than the 25—40% which have been common in Turkey in recent years. Whether this could be achieved whilst fending off the rising challenge of the Islamic right, and surmounting incipient balance of payments crises was unclear.

Growing Political Difficulties.

Turkish politics took on a less stable cast in early 1989 as Prime Minister Ozal's government suffered heavy losses in local elections. The Social Democratic Party came first with 28% of the vote, followed by Suleiman Demirel's True Path Party with 26%. Although the Prime Minister was not bound to call a general election until 1992, the Motherland Party's 22% of the vote, and defeat in Ankara, Istanbul and Izmir, weakened the government's legitimacy and Ozal's personal authority.

The Motherland Party's poor showing was worse than most of its senior members had forecast. More importantly, it was sufficiently calamitous to make it unlikely that, coupled with undefeated inflation and public discontent with Mr. Ozal's nepotism, he will be able to survive to the end of his constitutional term. The solidity and coherence of his own factious party in the National Assembly is bound to come under pressure from within as well as from without.

The election results presented a further difficulty, for the constitution requires that a new President be elected by the National Assembly upon the expiration of the seven-year term of President Kenan Evren in November 1989. That event now assumes much greater political importance, for the opposition parties and the military are in no doubt as to the symbolic and substantive significance of the Turkish presidency. The Prime Minister will accordingly come under intense pressure to find a compromise candidate whose election by the Assembly (in which the Motherland Party continues to have, though scarcely to enjoy, a majority) will still opposition rather than inflame it.

The Bulgarian Exodus.

The exodus of ethnic Turks from Bulgaria under that country's old Communist regime swelled in 1989 to 3,000 per day. Their circumstances in Bulgaria were desperate. The Bulgarian Communist authorites had offered them a choice between "forced assimilation" into Bulgarian culture with a concomitant elimination of Turkish names and culture, or expulsion. As in the case of migrants from East to West Germany, the recipient state faced grave difficulties in accepting the large number of refugees in question. On 21 August, having accepted 300,000 Turks from Bulgaria, Mr. Ozal's government severely restricted the flow by imposing strict entry visa requirements. The incident had placed Ozal in a most difficult position. In the short-term, he was bound to accept the refugees for reasons of ethnic solidarity, and the defence of human rights, but in the longer-term the additional pressures on the Turkish labour and housing markets were intolerable. Bound as he was to take the responsibility for drastically reducing the flow across the border, he nonetheless exposed himself to political criticism from the leaders of other parties who sought to exploit the issue.

Ozal as President.

Ozal announced in October that he would run for the Presidency, which he duly won. His successor as Prime Minister was Akbulut whose first months in office were marked by much manoeuvering for advantage within the party. Akbulut's hold on power was far from secure: a full challenge to his leadership remains entirely possible, and may come from Mehmet Kececiler, a leading Moslem member of the government. The atmosphere of discontent and instability was heightened in the first three months of 1990 by a resurgence of politically-motivated killings which aroused fears of a new wave of terrorist activity. Behind the scenes, Turgut Ozal continued to exercise immense influence over the Party which had served as the vehicle for his career. The Motherland Party nonetheless enjoyed little popular support, and its prospects in the General Election, to be held by the autumn of 1992 at the latest, were poor.

THE SOVIET UNION

A Turning Point in Soviet History.

Stalin died in 1953 and the struggle for succession then continued for five years. A triumvirate of successors, Malenkov, Molotov, and Beria had decided to give the post of party chief to Khrushchev, then a relatively harmless outsider, or so he was deemed by them. Beria, the all powerful police chief, was executed as a spy in 1953, Malenkov was forced to give up the premiership in 1954 and three years later both he and Molotov were expelled from the Central Committee. Khrushchev thereupon emerged with supreme powers.

In 1961 Khrushchev publicly and dramatically completed the process which he had begun in 1956, of finally rejecting the cult of Stalin. Destalinisation brought the scaling down of the secret police; the rebuilding of the administrative apparatus; and a new theory that war was not inevitable. But the Stalinist concept of the "monolithic" party was little changed.

Khrushchev was abruptly removed from power in October 1964 and replaced by Brezhnev and Kosygin.

The Collective Leadership.

A meeting of the Supreme Soviet in 1965 confirmed the principle of collective leadership, with Kosygin as Premier and Brezhnev General Secretary. The Brezhnev era has seen no re-Stalinisation as originally forecast, but there has been a retrenchment of the restrictive power of the establishment which had been disturbed by Khrushchev. Critics of Brezhnev, included the conservative Pyotr Shelest and Voronov, were dropped from the Politburo and subsequently all the most important ministers including Andrei Gromyko (Foreign Secretary) and Marshal Grechko (Defence Minister) were brought into the Politburo. Tension between the party and state machinery was thus eased. In April 1975 Shelepin, at 56 the youngest member of the Politburo, was ousted. At the 25th Party Congress in February 1976, Brezhnev appeared fully in control and in May he was promoted to Marshal of the Soviet Union following the death of Marshal Grechko. Under Brezhnev and his successors, the old order ruled in Russia. This changed with the advent of Gorbachev in 1985.

The Advent of Gorbachev.

In his first year in office, Gorbachev moved quickly and deliberately to consolidate his power base, and succeeded to a degree which astonished many observers. The widely-held view that the power of General Secretaries is weak at the beginning of their period in office was not confirmed by Gorbachev's skilful political display during his first year.

Preparing for the Party Congress in February 1986, he promoted four of his supporters to the Politburo, and quickly eased out Grigori Romanov, his main rival for the post of General Secretary, Nikolai Tikhonov retired as Prime Minister, and Andrei Gromyko left the post of Foreign Minister which he had occupied for more than thirty years, to become President. Gromyko's successor was Edward Shevardnadze, a loyal supporter of Gorbachev but whose inexperience in foreign affairs allowed Gorbachev to exercise strong influence in the field. Tikhonov's successor as Prime Minister was Nikolai Ryzhkov who shared Gorbachev's enthusiasm for radical organisational reform as part of a policy to revitalise the Soviet economy. Ryzhkov lacked the power-base of Yegor Ligachev, who gained bases in both the Central Committee and the Politburo. Ligachev assumed responsibility for ideology, and in pursuing Gorbachev's campaign to reshape party membership, showed himself strikingly orthodox in his views. Economic reform was combined, in varying degrees, with ideological conservatism. The veteran Moscow party head, Viktor Grishin, was replaced in December 1985 by Boris Yeltsin.

Elsewhere, the party's Central Committee membership changed considerably at the Party Congress, having already seen three new secretaries and seven departmental heads installed within the first eight months of Gorbachev's leadership. A reshuffle on 6 March saw five newcomers in the secretariat (one of whom was Anatoly Dobrynin, Soviet ambassador to Washington since John Kennedy's presidency), the replacement of two candidate members of the Politburo, and the promotion of Lev Zaikov, a central committee member with responsibilities for defence, to full membership.

At the regional level, Gorbachev ruthlessly pursued a policy of replacing entrenched party leaders with his own people; the reforms which Andropov initiated, but which ground to a halt under Chernenko's fitful leadership, were now restarted. By early 1986, few senior party members who had been supporters of Brezhnev remained in place.

Continuing Economic Difficulties.

The central difficulty with which Gorbachev and his allies had to contend was the Soviet Union's continuing poor economic performance. The rate of growth in the first half of the 1980s was half that of the 1970s which itself was half the rate of the 1960s. Without a significant improvement, the prospects of maintaining defence programmes and investing in consumer goods industries were slight. In fact, the target which Gorbachev set in late 1985 for the rest of the century was modest, envisaging an average growth rate of less than 5%. As with changes of political leadership, the pattern set in the first year was clear: he set out to achieve it by introducing high-technology into Soviet industry.

1987 illustrated again the political threat posed by incipient nationalisms within the Soviet Union to central control from Moscow. There are altogether some one hundred different nationalities within the country. Whilst Russians comprise some 60% of the population, the proportion is falling because of the higher birth rates among Asian nationalities. On 6 July, and again from 23 to 26 July, some 100 Tartar protesters demonstrated in Moscow's Red Square against the government's refusal to allow them to return to the Crimea (from where they had been expelled towards the end of the Second World War following the collaboration of some of their number with the Nazis) and grant them the status of an autonomous republic. The demonstration itself served as a vivid and public reminder that nationalist tensions are rarely far from the surface of Soviet politics; the government's decision to permit it, and President Gromyko's subsequent agreement to meet those involved, marked a distinctively open approach by the government to certain categories of protest.

Disturbances in the Baltic.

Within a month of the protest by the Crimean Tartars, disturbances occurred in the Baltic states of Estonia, Latvia and Lithuania. The peoples of these Baltic states had suffered as much from the various cruelties of Nazi and Stalinist occupation, as the Crimean Tartars. In a further parallel with the July demonstration in Red Square, the authorities did not attempt to stop demonstrations in Vilnius, Riga, and Tallinn, the capitals of Lithuania, Latvia, and Estonia respectively. The protests in Riga centred on the gradual 'Russification' of the Republic since Soviet occupation, and on a demand that the secret protocol to the Ribbentrop–Molotov Pact in 1939 by which Hitler acquiesced in Stalin's occupation of the three Baltic Republics be published. Despite the dangerous implications such publication had for the official view of Stalin's regime, Gorbachev permitted the demonstrations to proceed. Difficult as the nationalities question was for Gorbachev (an ethnic Russian who had spent his entire working life in Russia) and his senior colleagues (the great majority of whom were Russian) simple repression was not a plausible option.

The dilemma was sharpened in February 1988 when large demonstrations took place in Armenia calling for the redrawing of boundaries with neighbouring Azerbaijan. The protest had a particularly powerful significance because it enjoyed support from Communist Party officials in the Republic who supported demands for the return to (mostly Christian) Armenia of the Naborno–Karabakh region in (Shi'ite Moslem) Azerbaijan. The region was part of Armenia before the Revolution in 1917; 95% of the population are Armenians. Gorbachev appealed for calm, offering the prospect of discussions to address the Armenians' grievances. The disquiet which he and his senior colleagues felt owed as much to the implications of the individual dispute for the general problem of whether to encourage the merging of nationalities or to permit them free expression and development. Within a week, the problem broadened: rioting took place in the city of Sumgait in Azerbaijan on 28 February in what may have been a response to Armenian territorial demands. *Glasnost* added to the leadership's difficulty for it had contributed to an atmosphere in which the highly political questions of national aspiration and resentment could be discussed with a degree of freedom.

At a meeting of the Communist Party's Central Committee on 21 October 1987, Mr. Boris Yeltsin attacked Yegor Ligachev for conservative resistance to Gorbachev's programme of *perestroika*. On 11 November, Yeltsin was dismissed from his job as head of the Moscow Party organisation. At the Central Committee meeting in Moscow in February 1988, Yeltsin duly lost his place on the Politburo. The outcome weakened Gorbachev: Yeltsin's decision to articulate his enthusiastic support for *perestroika* by openly venting his anger upon Yegor Ligachev (the powerful Party Secretary in charge of ideology) and others who were less supportive was

politically unwise, yet his substantive purposes were the same as those of the General Secretary. By obstructing Yeltsin in Moscow, and precipitating his outburst in the Central Committee, senior conservatives served notice that Gorbachev's campaign for reform would not be easily won.

Gorbachev continued to appeal over the heads of conservative party officials by speaking direct to the public. In early January 1988, he met a number of Soviet journalists and argued that an acceleration and deepening of the drive to "democratisation" would be the main focus of an extraordinary party conference to be held in Moscow in the summer. With the Yeltsin affair still in his and his listeners' minds, he dismissed both conservative and radical critics:

"We are frequently criticised—by some people from the right and others from the left. To stop now would be disastrous. If we take fright and stop the processes we have begun, it would have the most serious consequences, because we simply could not raise our people to such a massive task a second time."

Foreign Policy Developments.

In foreign affairs, Gorbachev moved to stabilise relations with western Europe and the United States by agreeing to the elimination of all intermediate nuclear missiles from Europe, and sought to extricate the Soviet Union from its costly and painful embroilment in Afghanistan by announcing in early 1988 a date for withdrawal. At a major summit meeting in Washington in December 1987, President Reagan and General Secretary Gorbachev signed the Intermediate Nuclear Forces Treaty. It provided for the withdrawal and destruction of all land-based nuclear missiles in Europe with ranges of between 500 and 5,500 kilometres. Included in this category were the American Pershing IIs and Cruise missiles, and Soviet SS-20. The Treaty was marked by extremely tight and detailed provisions for verification by each side of the removal of its weapons systems, and of their destruction. In contrast to previous Treaties dealing with strategic systems, the INF Treaty provided for "on-site" verification—teams of inspectors from each side ensuring compliance with the Treaty's clauses detailing precisely how the missiles were to be dismantled and destroyed.

The Treaty marked a significant shift in Soviet policy. This was true not just with regard to Soviet acceptance of on-site verification, but with respect to the strategy that underpinned it. The dominant thrust in thinking among Gorbachev's senior foreign policy advisers and colleagues by the summer and autumn of 1987 was that Soviet security could be achieved at lower cost by intensified diplomacy rather than by an endless expansion in weaponry. Whilst there was no prospect that Soviet defence spending would fall significantly, Gorbachev was acutely conscious of the need to restrain defence spending if there were to be any prospect of securing the domestic objectives of higher consumer spending. To that end, the successful conclusion of the INF Treaty was publicly treated by Gorbachev as a welcome interim step on the path of agreeing major cuts in strategic weaponry. In the late winter and early Spring of 1988, Secretary of State George Schultz and Foreign Minister Eduard Shevardnadze attempted to clear a path through disagreements between the two sides on their respective Star Wars programmes.

For the latest developments in Russia's growing political ferment, *see* Special Topic C82–85.

EASTERN EUROPE

POLAND.

In the mid-1980s Polish politics had a thoroughly peculiar cast. Following a rebellion led by the Solidarity trade union organisation in 1980 which threatened to challenge the legitimacy of Communist Party rule in the country, martial law was imposed by General Jaruzelski, the Soviet Union's chosen instrument for the restoration of authority and order. Unfortunately for Poland, the gradual return to 'normality' was painful politically and economically. The new regime was, initially, sharply repressive; economically, it brought no improvement on the sluggish backwardness which had long been Poland's lot. Not least among the difficulties which the government faced was that of dealing with the immensely powerful Roman Catholic church; although Jaruzelski had shown that direct threats to the state could be contained, the economy proved resistant to reform attempts. By 1988, the state enjoyed little more legitimacy in the eyes of most Poles than it had done at the time of the imposition of Martial Law in December 1981.

The 1987 Referendum.

In 1987, the government attempted to demonstrate its legitimacy by seeking direct support for reform measures. On 29 November, Poles had what is by Eastern European standards the decidedly unusual experience of participating in a referendum. Even more unusually, the results were not fixed by the state. Two questions were asked of Polish voters: did they approve of radical economic reforms, and were they in favour of greater democracy? The implications of the economic changes were considerable, and adverse in the short-term. Inflation, which was 25% before the referendum, had been expected to double if the referendum had gone Jaruzelski's way: the prices of some foods would have doubled whilst some rents and fuels would have trebled.

Neither Solidarity nor the Catholic Church supported the government's proposals. Jerzy Urban, the government's spokesman, announced that of the 27 million people entitled to vote, 67% took part of whom 66% favoured the first, and 69% the second. Unfortunately for the Polish government, this meant that less than half of those entitled to vote supported either proposal; the terms which the government itself set for the referendum required that the result could be binding only if more than 50% supported the questions on the ballot paper.

The referendum, a remarkable event in itself, marked an attempt by General Jaruzelski's regime to secure popular backing for the economic liberalisation which he had long favoured (even though a number of his colleagues did not). To that extent, the failure to secure majority national support for change was a rebuff to him and an excuse for more cautious ministers to avoid reform.

At a meeting of the Polish Communist Party's Central Committee the following month, conservatives failed to exploit the passing damage caused to Jaruzelski's policies of cautious economic and political reform: the leadership kept control of the agenda, and succeeded in securing the promotion to the Politburo of Mczyslaw Rakowski, a liberal reformer. Yet the direction and pace of both economic reform (aimed at increasing the role of the private sector and reducing the scale of direct government interference in the economy), and political liberalisation (intended to increase participation in decision-making) remained uncertain. Lacking a mandate which a referendum victory would have provided, the government announced more modest (though still substantial) increases in the price of food in 1988 of 40%, partially compensated by wage rises half as great.

By the Spring of 1989, it was becoming evident that the changes in Polish politics amounted to a revolution. In essence, the PUWP, the Communist Party, had lost its political monopoly, and the economy moved from being overwhelmingly dominated by the state to being mixed.

Poland's economic problems are two-fold: she labours under a huge foreign debt—some $23 billion, most of it owed to western banks, inflation is roaring ahead at 60% per annum, and economic growth is sluggish. The first of these problems can be addressed only by the combination of a reinvigorated economy, and further assistance from the West. Western governments are, however, insisting that any further help be conditional upon Poland moving towards a liberalised polity and economy. The second of these, involving extensive privatisation and the introduction of market reforms generally, is taken both within Poland and without to be a prerequisite for internal economic regeneration.

The difficulty of leading Poland in such times was apparent when the Prime Minister, Zbigniew Messner, resigned in September. It was explicitly acknowledged by his replacement in the post, Mieczslaw Rakowski. The authority of the government had indeed diminished greatly during the 1980s, underminded further by the crumbling of the legitimacy of the PUWP.

Indeed, the PUWP's monopoly of political power has now ended, symbolised by the round-table talks between Solidarity and the government, and the move towards qualified parliamentary elections in the summer of 1989. For agreeing to talks with the government which began on 6 February 1989, Lech Walesa, Solidarity's leader, was subjected to considerable criticism within the disparate movement, more suited to being a vehicle of protest than a coherent influence upon a weak government. Walesa travelled round Poland in an attempt to still protests from Solidarity members. The main element of the deal between Solidarity and the government was the recognition of both Solidarity and the independent students' union in return for an acceptance of the government's restrictive conditions for elections to the new Parliament.

Under the proposed agreement, a two-chamber parliament would be established, presided over by a powerful executive president. The lower house would be controlled by the PUWP and its allies, whilst the Senate, or upper house, would be determined by relatively free elections.

The New Poland.

Poland marked in 1989 a less complete break with the past than either Czechoslovakia or Hungary but one which was still a significant further shift away from totalitarianism. The elections of June 1989 marked a stunning rebuff to the Communist Party (PUWP) but the restrictive rules under which the elections took place ensured that the old order could not be completely and immediately swept away. The election resulted in 160 out of 161 Solidarity candidates being victorious, giving it almost all of the 35% of the seats in the Sejm for which it had been permitted to compete. It became apparent by August 1989 that the new Prime Minister, General Kiszczak, would be unable to form a government.

Tadeusz Mazowiecki emerged as the country's first non-Communist leader in forty years. Mazowiecki, a 63 year old lawyer, is a former editor of a Catholic monthly journal, and of Solidarity's weekly newspaper in 1981. He led a government where the defence and interior ministries are in Communist hands, the fellow-travelling Peasants and Democrat parties had four and two ministries respectively, and Solidarity took the remaining six. The Peasants Party is a misnomer since the party enjoys scarcely any support from peasants; Rural Solidarity is the main political force among Poland's farmers but it played little role in the formation of the government. Its composition reflected Mr. Lech Walesa's judgement of what was prudent under the circumstances. Walesa had taken charge of the task of forming a government only after Solidarity's negotiations with the two small parties collapsed.

In early 1990, the Polish Communist Party (the PUWP) dissolved itself, to be replaced by two parties: the Social Democratic Party of the Polish Republic (which inherited most of the PUWP's physical assets) and the Union of Social Democrats. The first is led by Alex Kwasniewski who disarmingly observed that only a "crazy" person would have wanted the post. The second is headed by Tadeusz Fiszbach, formerly the PUWP leader in Gdansk.

CZECHOSLOVAKIA.

In January 1968, in a significant move, a Slovak, Alexander Dubček, was elected to replace Novotný as Party Secretary (Novotný was later replaced as President by General Svoboda), and the era opened which has since been dubbed "the Prague Spring", when an attempt was made to give Socialism "a human face". Wide-ranging reforms were mooted in the Action Programme issued in April, but the Communist Party did not envisage relinquishing its commanding position in society. Fears that this was happening, however, led the USSR first to press for the abandonment of the Programme in a number of talks with the Czechoslovak leadership between May and August, and ultimately, in concert with the other Warsaw Pact powers except Romania, to occupy Czechoslovakia on 21 August in accordance with the "Brezhnev Doctrine" of "limited sovereignty". Soviet efforts to set up a puppet government at first met with no success. The projected federalisation of the country into the twin republics of the Czech Lands and Slovakia went ahead in October, although plans for a similar federalisation of the Party were vetoed. Gradually, however, Dubček and his team were ousted from positions of influence, and Gustav Husák, a partisan of "normalisation", took over as Party Secretary in April 1969. Czechoslovakia repudiated its condemnation of the Warsaw Pact invasion in October 1969 and consented to the stationing of Soviet troops. Pro-Dubček personnel were hounded from the Party and their jobs (Dubček himself becoming a forestry official) and most of the reforms were abandoned. In May 1970 Czechoslovakia signed a 20-year treaty of friendship with the USSR. In December 1973 West Germany and Czechoslovakia signed a treaty annulling the Munich Agreement, thus normalising their relations.

Czechoslovakia under Jakes.

Gustav Husak, the man chosen by the Soviet leadership to succeed Alexander Dubcek following the Soviet invasion of Czechoslovakia in 1968 presided over a repressive regime. As elsewhere in Eastern Europe, the convulsive changes in Soviet policy and politics had economic and political consequences for Czechoslovakia with which the leadership found it difficult to deal. Husak eventually resigned from the party leadership on 17 December 1987, and was succeeded not by Lubomir Strougal (who had advocated economic reform with especial enthusiasm) but by Milos Jakes. In a lifetime of working within the Party, Jakes had acquired little reputation for being a reformer. Sixty-five years old upon taking over from Husak, Jakes nonetheless had the skills of political flexibility to be expected of a party *apparatchik* in a country with a painfully difficult postwar history, overcoming the conservative Vasil Bilak and the more vigorous reformer, Lubomir Strougal.

Jakes permitted a degree of press criticism by a thoroughly sceptical public of party policy to be voiced, and indicated that the Soviet reforms could serve as a model for Czechoslovakia. His tactical position was difficult. He was simultaneously obliged to welcome Soviet reforms whilst denying that *perestroika and glasnost* bore a close resemblance to the policies of Alexander Dubcek, the Slovak leader whose own reforms had been ended by the Soviet-led invasion of 1968. On 4 December 1987, an article published in *Rude Pravo* acknowledged the similarities between the restructuring attempted in Czechoslovakia in 1968, and those of the Soviet leadership twenty years later, but argued that the Czech reforms had been "... abused by revisionist and right-oriented groups existing then within the party and outside it." This interpretation was disingenuous, and fuelled internal debate among intellectuals who were less cowed than in previous years by the threat of state repression.

Economic Problems.

The difficulties which Jakes faced in giving shape and justification to economic reform were enhanced by the publication in *L'Unita*, the Italian Communist Party newspaper, of an 18,000 word interview with Dubcek in January 1988 in which the former leader explicitly drew parallels between Gorbachev's reforms and his own. The timing of the interview was deliberate for it marked the twentieth anniversary of the election of Dubcek by the "January plenum". Jan Fojtik, the Central Committee Secretary for Ideology reacted with evident fury to Dubcek's interview claiming that he "... could hardly believe his eyes, and the arrogance of our right-wing forces, some of whom have begun to give us lessons on restructuring." Within days of Dubcek's observations being published, Prime Minister Strougal added to Jakes's problems by giving an interview to a group of West German journalists in which he criticised all of Czechoslovakia's leaders for having failed to carry out economic reforms essential to prevent the country's relative decline. Confirming his reputation as an

avid reformer, Strougal went further, arguing for a "pluralism of interests" within the party. Such incaution seemed unlikely to advance his political career under Jakes's more studied leadership. By early March, rumours abounded in Prague that Strougal's political career was drawing to a close.

Greater Political Diversity.

1988 brought a greater diversity to East European politics than at any time since the imposition of Communist rule by Soviet force in the years after the war. As Hungary and Poland represented the liberalising end of the spectrum, so Czechoslovakia represented the conservative, Stalinist end.

Czechoslovak economic policy was as conservative as Poland's and the Soviet Union's was radical. Its human rights policies remained brutally repressive, and in the starkest contradiction with its agreement at the Conference on Security and Cooperation to improve human rights. In January 1989, police arrested eight human rights activists on charges connected with their peaceful marking of the 20th anniversary of the suicide of Jan Palach, a student who burned himself to death in a protest against the Soviet invasion of his country. Attempts by the demonstrators to lay flowers at the site of his suicide were stopped by the police; the demonstrators were charged with a number of offences including "hooliganism". Among those arrested, tried, and found guilty was Vaclav Haval, the internationally-known playwright, and co-founder of Charter 77, the Czechoslovak human rights monitoring organisation. Haval was sentenced to nine months in prison for "incitement".

In October 1989, Vaclav Havel was a prisoner of a Communist-run Czechoslovakia; on 29 December, he was sworn in as the newly-democratic Czechoslovakia's President. Alexander Dubcek, the country's leader during the "Prague Spring" of 1968 which was ended by the Soviet invasion in the August of that year and who lived in internal exile for most of the twenty-two years that followed, was elected chairman of the federal assembly in Prague on 27 December 1989. Full elections are due to take place in June 1990 to a new federal assembly which will be charged with the task of electing a new president.

Democratic Revolution.

Czechoslovakia's democratic revolution was slow to arrive. A large demonstration in Prague on 17 November 1989, brutally treated by police in baton-charges, spawned others on succeeding nights in other Czech and Slovak cities. Too late for their own good, the Prime Minister, Ladislav Adamec and the Communist Party secretary, Milos Jakes, made small concessions to those demonstrating for Czechoslovakian reforms as far-reaching as those in Poland and Hungary. Within a fortnight, Communist power in Czechoslovakia collapsed and Civic Forum, the opposition peacefully led by the inspirational Vaclav Havel, emerged as the dominant political force. On 10 December, what was left of the Communist leadership accepted the formation of a government in which they were a minority. The new foreign minister was Jiri Dienstbier, a founder of Charter 77, the human rights group and spokesman for Civic Forum. Other ministers were also drawn from the ranks of dissidents, until recently marginalised (many of them imprisoned) by the old communist regime.

HUNGARY.

Hungary under Grosz.

In June 1987, Karoly Grosz was appointed Hungary's new Prime Minister in succession to Gyorgy Lazar. His economic inheritance was less than happy: the net hard currency debt rose in 1987 to $9·1 bn., making Hungary the most heavily indebted nation *per capita* in Eastern Europe.

Within three months, Grosz grasped the nettle, announcing plans to introduce an income tax, and a Value Added Tax. Despite increases (on basic pay, but not on bonuses) to employees of state firms, the tax reforms were officially forecast to result in retail price increases of 14–15%, and real wage cuts of 8–10%; the actual consequences were privately thought by economists to be more severe, a judgment which received a measure of confirmation with the actual rise in prices of more than half the country's goods and services on 1 January 1988 of 16.2%. Later in January, the government announced that most of the remaining controls on consumer prices would be abolished by the Spring. Reductions in company taxes were also implemented in the package of reforms, collectively designed to shift the burden of taxation from companies to individuals and to make more apparent which companies were profitable and which not.

The reforms were important (if politically and economically risky) in themselves, but significant, too, for the question of the succession to Janos Kadar, the Hungarian Party leader. Grosz faced much hostility as a result of the tax measures, but equally won admiration for the candour with which he justified their introduction—the product of a careful calculation for the consequences upon his chances of succeeding Kadar.

A special party conference in May 1988 relegated Mr. Kadar to the post of Party President and promoted Mr. Grosz to the post of Party General Secretary which for the time being he declared it his intention to hold in conjunction with the post of Prime Minister. Large numbers of members of the Central Committee were dropped and replaced by technocratic reformers, whilst eight of the 13 members of the old Politburo lost their positions.

Growing Political Debate.

Politics in Hungary moved further in the year to the Spring of 1989 than at any time since the Communist takeover in 1948. What had been unthinkable even three years after Gorbachev's accession to power in 1985 was suddenly commonplace. Two developments were of particular importance.

The first was the grappling within the party leadership over the interpretation of the 1956 uprising (in particular, whether it constituted a "counter-revolution" as the official line had always had it, or a "popular uprising", as most ordinary Hungarians had always known it to have been). Discussion was facilitated by much laxer censorship. Whilst expression was less than completely free, its bounds had by early 1989 expanded greatly.

The second was the central question of the very survival of the Communist Party in its accustomed hegemonic form. In November 1988, the Justice Minister, Mr. Kulcsar, announced that the law would be changed in order to acknowledge the possible emergence of a multi-party system. The new law on association, passed in January, permitted any group of ten or more persons to form a political party. A Central Committee meeting in February determined that Hungary's move towards a multi-party system would gather pace. Unlike in some other parts of Eastern Europe, many senior members of the Hungarian Communist Party viewed the prospect of change with confidence. This was reflected in the omission from the new draft constitution published in March 1989 of any reference to the Party's leading role.

They did so in part because despite its economic difficulties, Hungary had already begun to adapt to the politics of legitimate opposition—the Romanian government's oppression of Hungarian minorities gave some opposition groups an issue around which they could easily coalesce without threatening the government, whilst environmental issues prompted the establishment of several environmental groups. However, haltingly, a civil society began to grow in Hungary—exemplified by the proliferation of unofficial political groups, and by the official trade unions' assertion of greater autonomy from the authorities. As one-party rule faltered, trade unions ignored their members' actual desires and aspirations at their peril.

Dissolution of the Communist Party.

At its congress in October 1989, the Hungarian Communist Party dissolved itself, reforming as the Hungarian Socialist Party to be led by Tezso Nyers.

The proclaimed programme of the new party was that of commitment to a multi-party system (an accommodation to a fast-developing reality) and a social market economy. The move was prompted by the Communist Party's poor performance in by-elections held during the summer and early autumn, and by fears within the party about its likely fate in the general election to be held in March 1990.

The elections took place in two stages, with an absolute majority of the vote required for election. Voters had the task of voting for individual constituency candidates and for nationwide party lists; of the 386 seats in the parliament, 176 came from constituencies and the remaining 110 from party lists. In the first round of voting, the Hungarian Socialist Party fared poorly, falling to fourth place by gaining just under 11% of the vote for the party lists. Just ahead of it was the rural conservative Independent Smallholders' Party.

The two major parties after the first round were the conservative Hungarian Democratic Forum, and the liberal Alliance of Free Democrats. It seemed improbable that the second round of voting would result in either of them having an overall majority. A coalition between them, or between one of them and one or more small parties, would therefore be necessary for the formation of a government. The Democratic Forum's most likely coalition partner would be the Christian Democratic People's Party whereas the Alliance's would be the slightly larger Federation of Young Democrats.

In the second round of voting, the Democratic Forum secured 165 of the 386 seats; the Smallholders Party 43, and the Christian Democratic People's Party 21. A coalition of these three would give a total of 228 seats, and an overall majority of 72. Opposition parties include 92 Free Democrats, and 33 Socialists. The President of the Hungarian Democratic Forum and the country's probable Prime Minister, Jozsef Antall, declared after his party's success that Hungary's first priority would be to seek membership of the European Community.

ROMANIA.

In internal affairs rigid and orthodox, Romania began to develop an independent foreign policy in Gheorghiu-Dej's last years, and Ceaucescu continued this trend, maintaining friendly relations with China and Israel, becoming the first Soviet bloc country to recognise West Germany, and objecting to the Soviet invasion of Czechoslovakia. There are no Soviet troops in Romania. Although a full member of Comecon, Romania has blocked plans to integrate the Communist countries' economies for fear of becoming a second-class supplier of raw materials to the more industrialised members. Instead the Romanians are aiming for economic independence by pushing ahead with a massive industrialisation programme of their own.

1985 showed that Ceaucescu's much-vaunted independence from Moscow was only as strong as Romania's economy allowed. The signs of weakness, publicly evident in the crisis in the power-supply industry in the winter of 1984, were reinforced in the autumn of 1985 when Ceaucescu imposed military regulations on power station workers. In a demonstration of his dissatisfaction (and an implicit recognition of his dramatic policy failure) a deputy prime minister and two energy ministers were sacked. Romania's inefficient industries had for years drained her oil reserves; oil imports rose from almost zero in the mid-seventies to about 60 billion lei in 1985. Coal production, too, slumped alarmingly below both planning targets and industry's requirements, exacerbating the country's economic difficulties, especially in export sectors.

Romania's economy lurched from bad to worse in 1986, unrelieved by any lightening of the Stalinist gloom which Nicolae Ceaucescu's regime symbolised and enforced. In order to lessen pressure on the government, defence spending was reduced by 5%, a move which was sanctioned in a patently ludicrous "referendum" which gained the support of 100% of those who voted, and 99.99% of the country's voting-age population.

No management could obscure the harsh reality of the country's desperate economic plight. Fuel shortages were particularly severe in the winter of 86/87; private households were instructed to reduce electricity and gas consumption by 20% in February and March; offices, schools and theatres were required to reduce consumption by up to 30%.

Romania under Ceaucescu.

In the summer of 1987, the Soviet Communist Party's General Secretary, Mikhail Gorbachev, paid an official visit to Bucharest but the occasion fuelled rather than stilled growing exasperation among Romania's nominal allies in Eastern Europe with the isolationist policies of Ceaucescu, and their palpable embarrassment at Romania's catastrophic economic failure. The country appeared incapable of reform for so long as Ceaucescu remained in power; his grip on office appeared sufficiently firm to ward off challenges to his rule but woefully inadequate for the country's needs. Ceaucescu persisted with his policy of paying off the country's external debt, and weathered the effective collapse of the Romanian economy which it occasioned.

Economic collapse was paid for politically by government ministers, eighteen of whom Ceaucescu dismissed in five hectic weeks during the early autumn. In early December, Alexandru Babe, the Finance Minister was sacked for "failing to fulfil his job obligations" in having negotiated interest rates which Ceaucescu deemed too high on loans from the World Bank. As with the earlier dismissal of Iaon Avram, the country's energy minister, for failing to solve the energy crisis, the discredited policy was in fact Ceaucescu's own. Rotating and dismissing ministers offered no solution to Romania's economic crisis, only a palliative to his own growing political difficulties. These were given added point by disturbances at Brasov and Timisoara in November 1987 when several thousand workers marched in protest at reductions in incomes, and shortages of food and fuel. In most of the country, bread was rationed to 300 grams per day, and sugar to five hundred grams per month; in practice, many items of food are simply unobtainable. Leaders of the demonstration were subsequently arrested, and dissent crushed by Tudor Postelnicu, newly appointed as Minister of the Interior.

Addressing the national conference of the Romanian Communist Party in Bucharest in December, Ceaucescu made no reference to the protests of workers at Brasov, but claimed that more food would be directed to domestic consumption in 1988 rather than to the export market where it had contributed to debt repayments. Ceaucescu eschewed the rhetoric of *glasnost* and *perestroika* increasingly common elsewhere in Eastern Europe.

The Revolution in Romania.

Having watched the rapid progress of the democratic revolutions in Eastern Europe with as a great a horror as others experienced exhilaration, President Ceaucescu's own brutal Stalinist regime collapsed within the space of a few days in December 1989. Within five weeks of the opening of the choreographed Communist Party Congress in Bucharest, Ceaucescu was overthrown. After a 'trial' by a kangaroo court, he and his wife were shot on Christmas Day.

The revolution began with demonstrations in Timisoara which were ended bloodily by troops on 17 December. Attempting to bolster his support by a rally in Bucharest on 21 December, troops again opened fire—but this time on demonstrators who defied Ceaucescu by openly denouncing him. The army's loyalty to Ceaucescu quickly evaporated, and he was obliged to leave the headquarters of the Communist Party by helicopter in order to escape the wrath of the crowds at its doors.

The revolution was bloody. During the three days between the capture of Ceaucescu and his wife Elena and their execution, the *Securitate* secret police fought a rearguard action against the army and the people. The number of persons killed is unknown, but probably not more than 2,000. Unsurprisingly, politics in Romania were unsettled afterwards. Preparations were made for elections in May but there was a good deal of criticism of the Council for National Salvation for containing mostly reform-minded communists rather than anti-communists. The slowness with which members of the *Securitate* were brought to trial also aroused popular wrath but it is in the nature of revolutions that not all of those associated with the *ancien régime* can be held to account. The outcome of the 1990 election was a big victory for the National Salvation Front.

YUGOSLAVIA.

Yugoslavia after Tito.

In the years following Tito's death, successive Yugoslav leaders struggled with the consuming problems of economic crisis, corruption in public life, and the profound difficulty of governing a country composed of eight provinces each of which enjoyed substantial autonomy from the weak centre, Belgrade.

The inflation rate continued to rise in Yugoslavia during 1987, reaching more than 170% by the end of the year, whilst the total foreign debt amounted to some $20 billion. Faced with the huge servicing charges that resulted (consuming some 50% of foreign earnings), the government finally turned in desperation to the International Monetary Fund (IMF) for assistance—a source which Prime Minister Branko Mikulic had rebuffed as recently as May 1986—but which in late 1987 presented the only plausible option. The government had defaulted in July 1987 on payments of $250 million, an event which prompted urgent discussions among commercial bankers and official creditors of how the country's financial weakness might be overcome.

The IMF's traditional prescription for circumstances of this kind seemed likely to worsen rather than alleviate the problem of unemployment, made especially difficult politically by its varying rates among the eight provinces. In Slovenia and Croatia, for example, unemployment is low and economic activity high; in the rural provinces of Macedonia and Kosovo, unemployment varied between 20 and 40%. These sharp differences in economic experience among the provinces were reflected in parliamentary attitudes towards Prime Minister Mikulic's package of economic measures designed to deal with the problem: opposition came mostly from the poorer provinces. With real incomes falling and prices rising rapidly, the government was not well placed to exert its will either over provincial governments, or over workers whose discontent was increasingly apparent.

The Crisis in Kosovo.

By the beginning of 1989, Yugoslavia's inflation rate had risen to 250%, its rate of unemployment to 15%, and its external debt to $22 billion. Its many factions had little in common with each other than their passports (of which many wished to divest themselves) and, as the old year ended, the government of Mr. Branko Mikulic resigned.

Such a combination of circumstances would test the resolve of a country with a resilient political structure and organisation. Yugoslavia failed that examination. The country was throughout 1988 and early 1989 rent by strife centering upon the person and political ambitions of Slobodan Milosevic, the leader of the Communist Party in Serbia. Mr. Milosevic was concerned in particular to keep the mostly Albanian province of Kosovo in line by defending the rights of minority Serbs within it. Kosovo's Albanians are wholly opposed to an increase in Serbian influence over the affairs of their province which since 1974 has enjoyed almost as much autonomy from Serbia as the six federal republics of Yugoslavia. More than 1,000 Kosovo miners staged a hunger strike in February 1989 with the aim of forcing the removal of senior officials of the Communist Party in Kosovo whom most of the Albanians there regarded as Mr. Milosevic's placement. Whilst the Yugoslavian federation as a whole rejected the demands of the discontented Kosovo Albanians, the striking miners enjoyed support from the northern republics of Slovenia and Croatia whose own relations with Serbia became increasingly strained throughout 1988. The combination of extreme discontents among the peoples of the Republics, and economic failure in the federation as a whole, induced severe political weakness.

For long one of the most liberal Eastern European

communist states, Yugoslavia's political progress towards a western-style democracy was decidedly less smooth in 1989 and early 1990 than processes elsewhere. The explanation for the difference lies with the peculiarly fractured character of Yugoslavia, and the intensity with which nationalist passions are fought out. There is no simple or single path from communist autocracy to capitalist democracy in Yugoslavia because so many political forces pull in different directions.

The Collapse of Communism.

The Communist Party had by the Spring of 1990 effectively crumbled away. At its congress in January 1990, the Slovenian delegation withdrew following attempts by Serbia to weaken plans for the introduction of multi-party democracy and the translation of the Yugoslav Communist party into a more thoroughly devolved federation. (The Slovenian and Croatian parties had already decided to move towards a multi-party system Slovenia's parliament declared the Republic independent in early March 1990. Prime Minister Markovic struggled to keep the country together, conscious always of the threat presented by Milosevic's assertion of nationalist values in general, and of Serbian nationalist power over Kosovo in particular. In Kosovo, under direct rule from Serbia, Milosevic sent in troops to quell demonstrations calling for an end to the state of emergency. At least 25 ethnic Albanians were killed in the unrest.

In economic policy, Milosevic enjoyed greater success. The nettle of full currency convertibility was grasped, a wage and price freeze implemented, and tight monetary controls implemented. 10,000 old dinars were made equivalent to one new dinar which was given a fixed exchange rate of seven per Deutschmark. Hyperinflation disappeared as a result, but unemployment and insolvency suddenly became serious threats as the inescapable accompaniment to a market-based system.

THE MIDDLE EAST

ISRAEL.

Israel was established as an independent sovereign republic by proclamation on 14 May 1948. Arab hostility to the emergence of a Jewish state led to armed conflict, in which, due to her enemy's lack of unity, Israel gained more territory than originally allocated under the partition plan for Palestine. The Arab states' continued refusal to recognise Israel's right to exist brought new wars in 1956, 1967 and 1973, at the end of which Israel was still in possession of territory formerly belonging to Egypt, Jordan and Syria.

The Camp David Agreement.

General elections held in Israel in May 1977 resulted in the replacement of the long-standing Labour government by the right-wing alliance, the Likud bloc, led by Menachem Begin. There was a dramatic breakthrough in the search for peace in November 1977 when President Sadat of Egypt visited Jerusalem to address the Knesset, the Israeli parliament, on the subject of a Middle East settlement. In September 1978 Prime Minister Begin and President Sadat met for talks under the chairmanship of President Carter at Camp David, Maryland. A framework for peace was agreed and on 26 March 1979 a treaty was signed in Washington. In return for the normalisation of relations with Egypt, Israel agreed to withdraw from the Sinai peninsula, occupied in the Six-Day War of 1967. The withdrawal was completed in April 1982.

The 1982 Invasion of the Lebanon.

Mr. Begin called a general election in June 1981, in which Israel's economic problems and her relations with her neighbours were the main issues. Mr. Begin's decision to launch an air strike against Iraq's Osirak nuclear plant shortly before the election was bitterly debated. At the polls both the Likud and Labour parties gained seats at the expense of the smaller groups. Mr. Begin ended with a one-seat advantage in the Knesset over Labour,

and, after protracted negotiations with the smaller parties, he was able to form a new government in August 1981.

Mr. Begin now pursued more aggressive policies towards the occupied territories and neighbouring Arab states. In December 1981 Israeli law was extended to the Golan Heights, conquered from Syria in the 1967 war, in effect annexing the territory. Even the United States voted for the unanimous UN Security Council Resolution condemning this action. Then in June 1982 Mr. Begin launched a full-scale invasion of the Lebanon in order to stop the Palestinian guerrillas using the country as a base for attacks on Israel.

Beirut was surrounded and the PLO guerrillas forced to evacuate. However, as casualties mounted, Israel found it more difficult to extricate her army of occupation from Lebanon then it had been to send it in. A treaty signed in May 1983 with the United States and President Gemayel of Lebanon proved to be a dead-letter when the Syrians refused to accept it.

The General Election of 1984.

The ailing Mr. Begin resigned in September 1983. The Foreign Minister, Mr. Shamir, formed the new government and with hyper-inflation running at over 500% per annum, introduced an urgent package of austerity measures. Labour unrest grew and Mr. Shamir's government narrowly survived a no-confidence motion in the Knesset in January 1984.

General elections were held in July 1984. The result was inconclusive, with the smaller groups doing well at the expense of the two main parties. Labour won 44 seats as against the ruling Likud's 41 seats, with thirteen other parties securing representation. As leader of the largest group in the Knesset, Labour's Shimon Peres was invited to attempt to form a government by President Herzog. After several weeks of negotiation, a national unity government was formed in September 1984, with Mr Peres as Prime Minister and Mr Shamir as Deputy Prime Minister for the first 25 months, then reversing roles for the second.

In January 1985 Mr Peres' government announced its decision to carry out a unilateral withdrawal from occupied Lebanon. Over six hundred Israelis had died in Lebanon since the ill-fated invasion of 1982. Mr. Peres now sought to make progress towards a settlement of the Palestinian problem. In October 1985 he had talks with President Reagan, in which he said Israel was ready for unconditional talks with Jordan and might make 'territorial compromises' in the search for peace. In an address to the UN General Assembly Mr. Peres announced that Israel was willing to end the state of war with Jordan and negotiate with a Jordanian-Palestinian delegation within the framework of an international forum under the auspices of the UN Security Council.

A no-confidence motion in the Knesset was defeated in October 1985, but divisions began to emerge within the coalition government. In November Mr. Peres demanded the resignation of his most outspoken critic, Mr. Sharon, the Trade and Industry Minister, if he did not apologise for violent attacks on the policy of seeking to open peace talks with King Hussein. Mr. Peres finally agreed to accept a form of apology, or 'clarification', from Mr. Sharon.

Although Israel sought a Palestinian settlement under Jordanian auspices, there was no acceptance of participation by the PLO. A number of violent incidents in 1985 helped to harden this position. In September one British and two Arab gunmen killed three Israelis on board a yacht in Larnaca harbour, Cyprus, after demanding the release of certain Palestinians held in Israel. In retaliation in October Israeli planes bombed the headquarters of the PLO near Tunis, killing some sixty people. Then at the end of December guerrillas attacked El Al Israel Airlines' passengers at Rome and Vienna airports. In turn on 4 February 1986 the Israelis forced down a Libyan executive jet which was thought to be carrying Palestinian guerrilla leaders, but was found to have only Syrian and Lebanese politicians on board. Later in February the Israelis were quick to applaud when King Hussein announced his repudiation of the PLO as a partner in the search for a Middle East peace settlement.

As laid down in the national unity government agreement of 1984, Mr. Peres resigned in October 1986 and Mr. Shamir took over from him as Prime Minister. Mr. Peres became Deputy Prime Minister and Foreign Minister. A brief delay in the change-over was caused by arguments over Likud's wish to bring Mr. Yitzhak Modai, former finance minister, back into the cabinet. He had resigned after publicly criticising Mr. Peres' economic policy and the Labour Party objected to his return. President Herzog had to step in to bring about a compromise by which Mr. Modai was included as a minister with-out portfolio.

Relations with Egypt.

In September 1986 Mr. Peres met President Mub-arrak for talks in Alexandria, the first for five years. Mr. Peres announced his support in principle for an international conference under UN auspices to dis-cuss a general Middle East settlement and the two leaders declared that 1987 would be a "year of peace".

In February 1987 Mr. Peres, now Foreign Minis-ter, flew to Cairo to continue discussions on the possibility of a preparatory conference before direct Arab-Israeli negotiations. Mr. Shamir, how-ever, said that he strongly opposed such a confe-rence, and the issue seemed likely to impose great strains on the continuation of the coalition government.

Violence in the Occupied Territories.

In December 1987 violence erupted amongst the 1·5 million Palestinians in the occupied West Bank and Gaza Strip areas. Anti-Israeli strikes, de-monstrations and riots were met by mass arrests, beatings and expulsions. There was international condemnation of the Israeli policy of beating de-monstrators graphically shown on television around the world, but the Israeli government also came under pressure to take even firmer action against Jewish settlers in the occupied areas.

In April 1988 an Israeli special service unit assas-sinated the PLO military commander, Abu Jihad, who was believed to be masterminding the Pal-estinian unrest. But violence continued and when the 40th anniversary of the creation of the state of Israel was celebrated later in April some 170 Palestinians and 2 Israelis had died in the unrest.

The General Election of 1988.

General elections for the 120-member Knesset took place on 1 November 1988. The result was again inconclusive, with both Labour and Likud losing seats to the smaller parties. Likud won 39 seats to Labour's 38. The religious parties secured a record number of eighteen seats, compared with twelve in 1984. Mr. Shamir began negotiations for the support of the ultra-orthodox parties, but these became bogged down over their demands for the enforcement of religious laws and a narrowing of the definition of who was a Jew.

Mr. Shamir also had talks with the Labour Party, until at the end of November Labour's political bureau voted to break them off. But President Herzog called on Mr. Shamir to form a wide and stable government, and finally, on 19 December, Likud and Labour reached agreement on the formation of another national unity coalition. Mr. Shamir was to continue as Prime Minister, while Mr. Peres took over the Finance Ministry, indicating Labour's intention of concentrating on the economy, rather than on the problems of foreign affairs and the Palestinian question.

The Continuing Intifada.

How Israel should respond to the continuing intifada in the occupied territories threatened the coalition's survival from the outset. Meetings in February 1989 between Labour MPs and West Bank Palestinian leaders were approved by Finance Minister Shimon Peres, Labour's leader, but attacked by the Prime Minister, Mr Shamir. Behind this disagreement lay the question of whether or not Israel should eventually talk with the PLO. In March the US government called on Israel and the PLO to reduce tensions in the occupied territories and acknowledged the PLO's growing political status. Mr Arens, the Israeli Foreign Minister, reiterated his determination not to talk with the PLO.

Visiting the United States in April, Mr Shamir offered elections to Palestinians in the occupied territories leading to eventual autonomy as part of a wider Arab-Israeli settlement. Despite opposition from some members of his own Likud party, Mr Shamir gained cabinet approval for the proposal on 14 May. US Secretary of State James Baker's advice on 22 May that Israel should begin dialogue with the Palestinians was condemned by Mr Shamir as "useless". By July continuing opposition from Likud forced Mr Shamir to modify his proposals. No elections would take place until the intifada ended; no East Jerusalem resident could stand in the elections (ruling out the candidacy of influential PLO figures); and Israel would not tolerate the creation of a Palestinian state. The PLO claimed these conditions "closed the door" to any agreement while Mr Peres said he refused to "accept the dictates of Mr Shamir". Labour now seemed prepared to abandon the coalition, its leaders recommending this on 20 July. Collapse was averted when Mr Shamir confirmed the elections proposal still stood without mentioning the new conditions.

On 18 September Egyptian President Mubarrak presented a 10 point peace plan to Israeli Defence Minister Mr Rabin in Cairo. His suggestion that Israeli representatives should meet a Palestinian delegation in Cairo for preliminary talks on election arrangements provoked further division within the coalition. The proposal was increasingly pressed by US Secretary of State James Baker. On 6 October the 12-strong inner cabinet divided evenly on discussions with Palestinians, the six Likud members voting against and Labour voting for.

The violence of the intifada had meanwhile intensified, with over 500 Palestinians and 22 Israelis reported killed by June. There was growing polarisation between Jewish and Arab communities, particularly on the West Bank where Jewish vigilantes were arming to attack Arab areas. When on 18 June a Jewish settler was stabbed to death in the West Bank fellow settlers denounced Mr Shamir for not acting firmly enough against the uprising. Pro-Arafat moderates in the underground Unified Leadership orchestrating the intifada faced militant pressure to take up arms.

The March 1990 Crisis.

US pressure for talks to begin in Cairo brought Israel's political crisis to a head. The cabinet attempted to hold off collapse by postponing a decision on 7 March 1990. But on 13 March Mr Shamir dismissed Labour leader Mr Peres and the remaining Labour ministers resigned. Mr Shamir's government lost a Knesset confidence vote by 60–55 on 15 March and Israel faced the prospect of a Labour-led coalition or a general election.

EGYPT.

From Independence to Revolution.

Britain ended its protectorate over Egypt in Feb-ruary 1922 and recognised the country as an independent state. The Sultan, Fuad, took the title of King of Egypt. In July 1952 a group of young soldiers, the 'Free Officers', secured the abdication of King Farouk in favour of his infant son, who became King Fuad II. However, in June 1953 Gen-eral Neguib, head of the military junta, deposed the young king and Egypt became a republic. General Neguib became President and Prime Minister, with the leader of the Free Officers, Colonel Nasser, as Deputy Prime Minister. A power struggle between Neguib and Nasser ensued, which resulted in victory for the latter in November 1954.

From Nasser to Sadat.

Nasser's period as president saw two Israeli in-vasions of Egyptian territory: in 1956, when British and French troops also attacked the Suez canal, and in June 1967. The Six-Day War of 1967 re-sulted in a disastrous defeat for Egypt and left the Sinai peninsula in Israeli hands. Nasser began the difficult task of reconstruction, but died in Septem-ber 1970. He was succeeded by the Vice-President, Anwar Sadat.

In October 1973 President Sadat launched a surprise Egyptian attack across the Suez Canal on the Israeli occupying forces in the Sinai. The Yom Kippur War did much to restore Egypt's prestige and to foster serious attempts to seek a permanent peace. There was a dramatic development in November 1977 when President Sadat visited Jerusalem to address the Israeli parliament, the Knesset, on the subject of a Middle East peace settlement. In September 1978 a summit meeting took place between the United States' President, Jimmy Carter, Mr Begin of Israel and President Sadat at Camp David in Maryland. A treaty was signed on 26 March 1979 normalising relations between Egypt and Israel, with Egypt agreeing to recognise Israel in return for the restoration of the Sinai. Egypt was ostracised by the Arab world as a result of the decision to come to terms with Israel.

Sadat's Domestic Problems.

President Sadat's domestic problems mounted at the start of the 1980s. Inflation and unemployment rose whilst the government continued the economically unsound policy of paying out huge subsidies on a range of goods to prevent a recurrence of the serious riots over food and petrol price increases which took place in 1977. Economic discontent was compounded by the growth of Islamic radicalism in Egypt. In September 1981 President Sadat arrested over 1,500 Islamic militants, left-wingers and other opponents of his regime. But on 6 October Sadat was assassinated by Islamic fundamentalists while watching a military parade in Cairo.

Mubarak in Power.

President Sadat was succeeded by the Vice-President Mubarak, a former commander of the Egyptian air force, who had been vice-president since 1975. Mubarak broadly continued his predecessor's policies. Crucially the change of leadership did not delay the completion of the planned Israeli withdrawal from the remainder of occupied Sinai in April 1982. Mubarak effected a reconciliation with the Palestine Liberation Organisation when he met Yasser Arafat in December 1983, and relations with Jordan, broken off after Egypt's peace with Israel, were restored in September 1984. However, the failure to deal with the economic inequalities in Egyptian society and the demands of Islamic militants resulted in outbreaks of violence. In February 1986 a mutiny by paramilitary police conscripts led to more general rioting which had to be suppressed by the army.

Egypt's Domestic Problems.

In October 1986 Egypt went to the polls to elect members for the Majlis al-Shura, the consultative upper house of parliament. The opposition parties called for a boycott in protest at the voting system by which the party winning over 50% of the votes in each province won all the seats. The result was an overwhelming victory for President Mubarak's National Democratic Party.

In November 1986 Dr Ali Lutfi, who had been Prime Minister since September 1985, resigned and Mr Atef Sedki, a little-known economic specialist, took his place. His cabinet included ten new ministers. The governmental changes heralded an era of even greater economic retrenchment and austerity. Egypt faced tremendous economic and social problems, with its population growing at the rate of more than one million a year and foreign debts of £35,000 million. Demands by the International Monetary Fund for the reduction of government subsidies on basic food and fuel prices required a change in the fundamental socialist principles of the Egyptian government handed down from President Nasser.

The 1987 Election.

With President Mubarrak's period in office due to expire in October 1987, the Egyptian Supreme Court had ruled the existing parliament unconstitutional because no independent candidates had been allowed to contest the 1984 elections. In order to remove any doubts about the legitimacy of the

People's Assembly before it considered his re-election, President Mubarrak called an election for April 1987.

In the run-up to the elections there were outbreaks of sectarian violence in February 1987 between Christians and Muslims in the southern cities of Sohag and Beni Suef. When the elections came the Muslim Brotherhood, the party of Egypt's Islamic fundamentalist movement, although officially banned, ran in alliance with the Labour and Liberal parties. The elections resulted in the expected overwhelming victory for the National Democratic Party, but the main opposition parties —the rightwing Wafd and the Muslim Brotherhood—succeeded in winning seats. This was not unwelcome to President Mubarrak, who hoped to bring opposition groups within the parliamentary framework and thereby involve them in the difficult decisions needed on Egypt's economy. A significant feature of the elections was that the Muslim Brotherhood, in alliance with the Labour and Liberal parties, won sixty seats, overtaking the Wafd party as the main opposition group.

In July 1987 President Mubarrak was nominated by parliament for a second 6-year term. He was supported by the opposition Islamic Alliance on condition that progress was made towards applying Islamic law in Egypt. A referendum in October confirmed Mr Mubarrak as president by 97 per cent of votes cast.

Egypt and the Arab World.

During 1987 there were signs that Egypt's isolation, caused by the peace with Israel, was coming to an end. Egypt's support for Iraq and the Gulf states in the Iran–Iraq war was bringing about a change. The Arab summit at Amman in November 1987 agreed that relations with Egypt were a matter for individual states. A number of Arab countries, including Saudi Arabia, Morocco and Iraq, proceeded to restore full diplomatic relations with Egypt. Improvements in relations with other Arab states continued with a visit to Cairo by King Fahd of Saudi Arabia on 27 March 1989. President Mubarrak sought Saudi financial aid for his country's weak economy. How crucial this might be was suggested by a United States threat on 8 March to withhold a promised $230 million unless Egypt undertook economic reforms proposed by the International Monetary Fund. Egypt warned of the dangers an austerity programme posed to domestic order. On 7 April 1,500 Moslem fundamentalists who sought to make Egypt an Islamic state were arrested following riots at the beginning of Ramadan.

Egypt's return to the Arab fold was confirmed by President Mubarrak's attendance at the Arab League conference in Casablanca in May, the first attended by Egypt since 1979. In October, following the re-opening of the border with Libya and restoration of travel links, President Mubarrak met Col. Gaddafi, announcing after that the two states had "no differences on Arab issues". At the centre of this activity was the Egyptian role in Arab-Israeli peace efforts. President Mubarrak discussed the issue with Soviet foreign minister Sheverdnadze in Cairo on 20 February and with President Bush in Tokyo three days later, pressing the US to support Egypt's proposal for an international peace conference. Egypt announced a 10-point peace programme in July and on 18 September Israeli defence minister Rabin visited Cairo to discuss its terms, including possible Israel-PLO talks. The Israeli coalition cabinet rejected the proposals on 6 October, despite President Mubarrak having gained the US government's support on a visit to Washington on 2 October.

JORDAN AND THE PALESTINIANS.

The Creation of Jordan.

Britain recognised Transjordan as an independent state by a treaty signed in London on 22 March 1946. On 25 May 1946 Amir Abdullah assumed the title of King and in June the name of the country was changed to the Hashemite Kingdom of Jordan. Following the war with Israel in 1948 a considerable enclave of territory on the West Bank of the River Jordan remained in Jordanian hands and this was formally annexed in 1950. King Abdullah was assassinated in 1951 and in 1952 his son, King Talal, was found to be suffering from mental illness. He was therefore deposed by parliament and succeeded by his son, Hussein.

The Palestinian Problem.

In June 1967 King Hussein led the country into the Six-Day War with Israel and suffered the loss of all his territory west of the River Jordan. There was a fresh influx of Palestinian refugees from the lands occupied by Israel. These came under the wing of the Palestine Liberation Organisation (PLO), which had been formed in 1964 and included the al-Fatah guerrilla group, headed by Yasser Arafat. In 1968 Mr. Arafat became chairman of the PLO. Relations between the Palestinians and King Hussein deteriorated as the guerrillas came to represent a serious challenge to his authority. Civil war broke out in 1970 and the guerrillas were driven from the country by the Jordanian army in 1971. However, in 1974 at an Arab summit conference in Rabat King Hussein reluctantly endorsed a resolution naming the PLO as the sole legitimate representative of the Palestinian people and affirmed their right to an independent state as their homeland.

The Reagan Plan.

In September 1982 President Reagan put forward a new set of proposals for the Israeli-occupied West Bank to be constituted as a homeland for the Palestinians in association with Jordan. However, when in April 1983 King Hussein reached agreement with Mr. Arafat on the role Jordan might play in the negotiations, this was rejected by the PLO executive committee. A rebellion against Mr. Arafat's leadership by a Syrian-backed PLO faction broke out. Mr. Arafat and his supporters, driven out of Beirut by the Israelis in August 1982, were now besieged in Tripoli. The Arafat loyalists were eventually evacuated in Greek ships flying the UN flag in December 1983.

The Hussein Initiative.

In January 1984 King Hussein took the initiative in seeking a solution of the Palestinian problem by recalling the Jordanian national assembly which had not met since 1976, because elections could not be held on the West Bank. Instead deputies were now nominated to represent the Israeli-occupied territory. However, Mr. Arafat again grew in importance in November 1984 when he succeeded in assembling a quorum for the 17th Palestine National Council in Amman.

The Arafat–Hussein Accord.

In February 1985 Mr. Arafat and King Hussein reached agreement on a common approach to negotiations, advocating an international peace conference and calling for the creation of a Palestinian state in confederation with Jordan. However, the search for a settlement was complicated by an Israeli air raid on the PLO headquarters south of Tunis on 1 October 1985, followed by the hijacking of the Italian cruise ship *Achille Lauro* off the Egyptian coast by Palestinian guerrillas on 7 October. On 14 October Britain's Foreign Secretary, Sir Geoffrey Howe, cancelled a planned meeting with representatives of Jordan and the PLO when the latter refused to agree to a statement opposing terrorism and supporting a territorial settlement based on UN Security Council Resolutions 242 and 338 (which implied an acceptance of Israel's right to exist).

Mr. Arafat held further talks with King Hussein at the end of October 1985, but the relationship between the two parties was uneasy as a result of the *Achille Lauro* incident and the rapprochement which had just taken place between Jordan and Syria. (Syria supported the anti-Arafat dissidents within the PLO.) In November 1985 Mr. Arafat travelled on to Egypt for talks with Mr. Mubarrak. These led to Mr Arafat's issuing of the 'Cairo declaration', in which he announced his opposition to international terrorism, but maintained the right of the Palestinians to continue the armed struggle in the occupied territories. However, the response of PLO dissidents was the hijacking of an Egyptian Boeing 737 en route from Athens to Cairo on 23

November and attacks on El Al Israel Airlines' passengers at Rome and Vienna airports on 27 December. The Israelis retaliated on 4 February 1986 by forcing down a Libyan executive jet which was thought to be carrying Palestinian guerrilla leaders, but was found to have only Syrian and Lebanese politicans on board.

Rift between King Hussein and Mr. Arafat.

King Hussein and Mr. Arafat met for further talks in February 1986. The previous October the Americans and Israelis had accepted the idea of an international conference on the Palestinian problem and in January 1986 Jordan appeared to have achieved a breakthrough when the Americans agreed that the PLO should be invited to attend once it had renounced terrorism and accepted Resolutions 242 and 338. But Mr. Arafat still insisted on prior American approval for the Palestinians' right of self-determination within a Jordanian-Palestinian confederation. Finally on 19 February 1986 King Hussein announced his repudiation of the PLO as a partner in the search for a Middle East peace settlement, accusing its leadership of bad faith. He planned to strengthen the West Bank representation in the national assembly, thereby paving the way for a revival of Jordan's claim to represent the Palestinians, rather than the PLO.

The PLO's Problems.

In July 1986 Jordan announced that it was closing down all twenty-five offices of Mr. Arafat's Fatah wing of the PLO. Mr. Arafat's deputy, Mr. Khalil al-Wazir, the military commander of Fatah, was also ordered to leave. Meanwhile there was growing friction between the PLO based in Tunisia and the government of that country. In October 1986 Mr. Arafat announced that his remaining military command posts in Tunisia would be moved to Iraq and North Yemen.

The PLO remained deeply divided at the beginning of 1987. In March, however, agreement was reached in Tunis for the calling of a Palestine National Council in Algiers the following month. In order to achieve Palestinian unity, Mr. Arafat agreed officially to abrogate the joint peace strategy with Jordan and to downgrade relations with Egypt. This led to the return to the fold of the hardline Popular Front for the Liberation of Palestine under Dr. Habash, who said that Amal's war on the Palestinian camps in Lebanon had also prompted a desire for reconciliation. Although a few non-Syrian groups boycotted the National Council, it marked a significant point in the re-establishment of a united Palestinian movement with Yasser Arafat at its head, despite calls for a collective leadership.

Following the assassination by Israeli agents of the PLO military leader, Abu Jihad, at his Tunis home in April 1988, the president of Syria met Mr. Yasser Arafat for talks in Damascus aimed at mending their five-year-old rift.

The Declaration of Independence.

The Palestinian uprising or *Intifada* against Israeli rule on the West Bank led to a reappraisal by King Hussein of his role in Palestinian affairs. At the Arab summit conference in Algiers in June 1988, he announced that he no longer aspired to represent the Palestinians in a Middle East peace settlement. At the end of July Jordan terminated its West Bank development plan, and announced that the payment of civil servants' salaries and the representation in the lower house of the Jordanian parliament for the West Bank would be ended.

On 15 November 1988 the parliament of the PLO meeting in Algiers issued a declaration of Palestinian independence. Algeria and many other countries recognised the new Palestinian state, which had announced its acceptance of the key UN Security Council Resolutions 242 and 338, recognising Israel's right to exist.

Mr. Arafat's intention of addressing the UN General Assembly in New York at the beginning of December was blocked by the United States' refusal to grant him an entry visa. The General Assembly therefore convened in Geneva, and on 13 December Mr. Arafat presented to it the resolutions adopted in Algiers in November. At first the United States rejected the idea of opening a dialogue with the PLO, but the following day Mr. Arafat held a news conference at which he made an even stronger renunciation of terrorism. As a result the United States announced that its ambassador to Tunisia, Mr. Robert Pelletreau, would meet the PLO for talks. This move was strongly attacked by Israel, which did not accept the PLO's new-found moderation as being genuine.

King Hussein met Egyptian President Mubarrak and PLO chairman Yasir Arafat on 25 March 1989 to unify their position on Arab-Israeli negotiations. In discussions with US leaders in April King Hussein appeared to support Israeli proposals for elections in the occupied Gaza Strip and West Bank. But on 21 April King Hussein abandoned his visit to Washington to meet a growing domestic crisis.

The 1989 Elections.

Price increases of 15–50% imposed under an economic austerity programme to gain a World Bank loan provoked riots in southern Jordan on 18 April. Demonstrators, ten of whom were killed, called for the prime minister's resignation. As rioting spread, King Hussein replaced Mr Al-Rifai with Mr bin Shaker and promised general elections, the first for 22 years. The elections, held on 8 November, were a setback for King Hussein. Of 80 seats in a new lower house, 20 were won by the Moslem Brotherhood and a further 12 by other pro-Islamic candidates, making fundamentalists the largest single group. Arab Nationalists took seven seats and radical left candidates four. Denied the conservative majority he had sought, King Hussein announced that reform would continue but dismissed suggestions that he intended to create a constitutional monarchy.

LEBANON.

Origins of the Conflict.

Tensions between the Christian and Moslem communities in the Lebanon were exacerbated by an influx of Palestinian guerrillas expelled from Jordan in 1970, and this resulted in full-scale civil war in 1975. Since then there has been great loss of life and economic disruption. Intervention by Syria and other neighbours, forming the Arab 'deterrent force', brought only a brief respite in 1976. Palestinian raids led to an invasion of the south of the country by Israeli forces between March and June 1978.

The Israeli Invasion of 1982.

Attempts to establish a workable basis for government in Lebanon repeatedly foundered amid fresh outbreaks of fighting between rival Christian and Moslem militias. Following the attempted assassination of the Israeli ambassador in London, Shlomo Argov, Israel launched a full-scale invasion of the Lebanon on 6 June 1982, aimed at driving out the Palestinians. Beirut was besieged and after tense negotiations Palestinian guerrillas were evacuated from the capital at the end of August.

The Lebanese president, Mr. Sarkis, retired in July 1982 and a Christian Phalangist Party militia leader, Bashir Gemayel, was elected to succeed him. However, he was assassinated almost immediately by a bomb explosion at the Phalangist headquarters. His elder brother, Amin Gemayel, a more moderate figure, was elected in his place. The start of his presidency was marred when on 17 September 1982 massacres of several hundred Palestinian civilians were carried out by Christian militiamen who entered the Chatilla and Sabra refugee camps in Beirut.

Negotiations took place to try to end the Israeli occupation of southern Lebanon. An American-sponsored agreement between President Gemayel and the Israelis in May 1983 proved to be a dead-letter when the Syrians refused to accept continuing Israeli influence in a buffer zone in the south of Lebanon. However, in January 1985 Israel announced that it had unilaterally decided on a three-stage withdrawal from Lebanon which was completed later in the year. As a postscript to the episode, an American Trans World Airlines Boeing 707 was hijacked in June en route from Athens to Rome by Lebanese Shia Moslems demanding the release of prisoners taken by the Israelis as they withdrew. The aircraft was forced to fly to Beirut and the passengers taken to various locations in the city. After secret negotiations, Israel began to release the detainees and the hostages were set free.

Syria's Peace Plan.

Israel's withdrawal did not solve the problems of Lebanon's internal strife. Syrian efforts at mediation led to the signing in December 1985 of a new peace pact by Syria's vice-president and leaders of Christian, Druze and Shi'ite militias. This set out a plan for a cease-fire, followed by constitutional reforms reducing the power of the Christian-held presidency, with Syria policing the settlement. However, President Gemayel was not a party to the negotiations and when he visited the Syrian capital, Damascus, in January 1986, he refused to support the agreement. The pact collapsed when the Christian signatory, Elie Hobeika, was overthrown by pro-Gemayel Phalangist Party fighters and rebels in his own Lebanese Forces militia, and peace between the warring factions in the Lebanon seemed as far away as ever.

War of the Camps.

The disintegration of Lebanon continued during 1986. The most serious conflict arose from attacks by the Shi'ite militia Amal on the Palestinian refugee camps with a view to preventing a revival of the military strength of Mr. Arafat's party in them. Heavy fighting took place round the Beirut camps in May 1986, but Syria mediated a truce in June and sent some 500 observers to police the cease-fire with the Lebanese army.

In October 1986 Palestinian fighters took the offensive in the Sidon area in an attempt to secure the lifting of the siege of Rashidiyeh camp. In November the Palestinians captured the Amal stronghold of Maghdoush. By December the Shatila and Bourj Barajneh camps in Beirut were closely besieged by Amal and the Shi'ite Sixth Brigade of the Lebanese Army.

As anarchy seemed imminent in February 1987, Syria took the gamble of sending some 4,000 troops and armoured units into West Beirut to clear the militias off the streets. Order was restored, but the war of the camps continued, as the pro-Syrian Amal militiamen were allowed to carry on their efforts to starve the 12,000 Palestinians in Bourj Barajneh and 4,000 in Shatila into submission. Finally at the beginning of April 1987 Syria called a halt and an agreement was reached to end the blockade of food and medical supplies to the camps. The camps war had claimed up to 3,000 Palestinian lives since it began in mid-1985. The ending of the sieges left Amal deeply divided and Syria's influence with the Palestinians at a low ebb.

The Hostage Situation.

The plight of foreign nationals kidnapped and held prisoner in Lebanon came to the forefront of world attention in 1986 with the revelations that the United States had arranged arms shipments to Tehran in order that the Iranians would use their influence to secure the release of Americans held hostage in Beirut.

In July 1986 Reverend Lawrence Jenco, former head of the Catholic Relief Services Office in Beirut, was released after nineteen months' captivity. Then in November Islamic Jihad, which was demanding the release of seventeen convicted terrorists imprisoned in Kuwait, set free American hospital director, David Jacobsen. His release had been secured through the mediation of Terry Waite, the Archbishop of Canterbury's personal envoy, whose efforts on behalf of hostages in Libya, Iran and the Lebanon dated back to 1980. In January 1987 Terry Waite returned to Beirut in order to negotiate the release of two other American hostages, Tom Sutherland and Terry Anderson, but he himself was detained by Islamic Jihad.

On 1 June 1987 the Prime Minister, Mr Rashid Karami, was assassinated by a bomb planted in his army helicopter. The explosion was the work of the pro-Israeli Lebanese Forces, seeking to discredit President Gemayel and the Lebanese Army. Selim Hoss, the Minister of Labour and Education, took over as acting Prime Minister.

Attempts were made in 1987 to conclude a peace agreement between the Amal militia, led by Mr. Nabih Berri, and the PLO in Lebanon. Eventually in January 1988 Mr. Berri ordered the lifting of the sieges of three Palestinian refugee camps as a gesture of support for the unrest in the Israeli-occupied territories.

Fighting flared up in February 1988 between Amal, which was backed by Syria, and the Hezbollah, supported by Iran. This followed the abduction by Hezbollah of a US Marine, Lt.-Col. William Higgins, attached to the UN peace-keeping force. In April 1988, after a week's heavy fighting, Amal completed its military recovery of southern Lebanon, disarming the last pocket of pro-Iranian gunmen. The conflict between Amal and Hezbollah then switched to Beirut itself. At the end of May, after negotiations with Iran, the Syrians sent troops into the Hezbollah-controlled southern suburbs in order to end the fighting.

The Disintegration of Lebanon.

President Gemayel's six-year term of office was due to expire in September 1988. The National Assembly twice failed to obtain a quorum to elect a successor. Syria supported the candidacy of the former president, Suleiman Franjieh, but this was rejected by the Christians, and no other acceptable candidate could be found. When President Gemayel stepped down, his final act was to appoint a military government headed by the Maronite Christian army commander, General Michel Aoun. However, there was also the alternative government of the Syrian-backed cabinet, under the acting Prime Minister, Dr Selim Hoss.

In October 1988 the Lebanese parliament failed to elect a new speaker to replace Mr. Hussein Husseini, and the elections were postponed indefinitely. By the end of the year Lebanon was therefore left with no president, a paralysed legislature and two rival prime ministers. Violent feuds within, as well as between, the military forces of the two communities in Lebanon continued. In January 1989 bitter fighting took place between the pro-Syrian Amal and the pro-Iranian Hezbollah Shi'ite militias. Syria stepped in, and a peace agreement was signed in Damascus. Then in February there were serious clashes between the Christian units of the Lebanese Army, loyal to General Aoun, and the Lebanese Forces militiamen, under Mr. Somir Geagea. Mr. Geagea was opposed to General Aoun's participation in the talks held in Tunis and Kuwait between leaders of the main communities in Lebanon under the sponsorship of the Arab League, in the hope of preventing the complete partition of the country.

The February fighting ended with a Lebanese Army victory over the Lebanese Forces militia, strengthening General Aoun's position. In March General Aoun's army and its Christian militia allies clashed with Syrian troops and Moslem militias as he attempted to extend his authority into Moslem West Beirut. Artillery duels, which by the summer had killed 700 and driven thousands from the city, continued into May despite Arab League truce attempts. On 16 May 22 people were killed by a car bomb in West Beirut, including Sheikh Hassan Khalid, the Sunni Moslem leader and an advocate of national reconciliation.

Ceasefire Attempts.

Arab League truce efforts were initially successful in June. But on 13 August Syrian troops and Moslem militia forces mounted an assault on Christian positions above Beirut. General Aoun acknowledged a UN cease fire call but insisted he would continue to resist the 40,000 Syrian troops in the Lebanon. On 23 September he accepted an Arab League call for an end to Iraqi arms supplies to Christian forces and of Syrian to Moslems. Both states promised to honour the embargo.

From 30 September to 4 October 63 of Lebanon's remaining MPs met in Saudi Arabia to agree a permanent peace settlement under an Arab League committee drawn from Algeria, Morocco and Saudi Arabia. The Arab League proposals included a shift of powers from the Christian president to the Moslem prime minister, a larger parliament divided equally between Christians and Moslems, and the withdrawal of Syrian forces two years after the

formation of a national unity government. There were initial disagreements over the timetable for Syrian withdrawal but on 24 October the MPs approved the peace plan. It was, however, condemned by both Christian and Moslem militia forces in Lebanon. General Aoun insisted on a firmer guarantee of Syrian withdrawal but West Beirut premier Selim al-Hoss described the plan as Lebanon's final hope.

The Assassination of Moawad.

On 5 November the Lebanon parliament ratified the Arab League plan and elected Rene Moawad, a Maronite Christian with Syrian approval, as president. General Aoun rejected both, saying parliament had violated the constitution. President Moawad reappointed Mr al-Hoss as Lebanese prime minister on 13 November. But on 22 November President Moawad was assassinated in a bomb explosion. Responsibility for the murder was unclear and there were mutual accusations. Elias Hrawi, like Moawad a Maronite Christian, became president. General Aoun refused to recognise him and was dismissed as army commander on 28 November, a dismissal few of his supporters accepted.

In January 1990, while continuing his fight against the Syrian-backed Moslem militias, General Aoun re-opened an unsuccessful battle with the Christian Lebanon Forces in East Beirut. But by March his position had shifted and he announced that not only was conflict over but that he favoured peace talks involving "our Syrian brothers".

IRAN.
The Islamic Revolution.

The Islamic revolution headed by Ayatollah Khomeini drove the Shah into exile in January 1979. Dr. Mehdi Bazargan became Prime Minister but real power lay in the hands of Khomeini and the Revolutionary Council which was mainly composed of senior Shi'ite Muslim clergy. A referendum in March 1979 resulted in an overwhelming vote in favour of Iran becoming an Islamic republic. Conflict inside Iran grew as left-wing groups clashed with Muslim extremists, and guerrillas from minority groups such as the Kurds sought autonomy.

The American Hostages.

On 4 November 1979 the American embassy in Tehran was occupied by militant students and its staff held hostage against the return of the Shah to stand trial in Iran. Dr. Bazargan resigned and in elections held in January 1980 Dr. Bani-Sadr became president with over 70% of the votes. He soon came into conflict with the Islamic Republic Party. The issue of the American hostages occupied the centre of the stage as President Carter launched a military rescue attempt in April. The mission was aborted and eight American servicemen were killed as they were being evacuated. The fifty-two hostages were eventually released on 20 January 1981, the same day as Ronald Reagan was sworn in as American President, following Algerian mediation over the political and financial obstacles.

In September 1980 President Saddam Hussein of Iraq, hoping to take advantage of the turmoil in Iran, abrogated the Algiers Pact of 1975 by which his country had been forced to accept joint control of the important Shatt al-Arab waterway, and invaded Iran. Despite initial Iraqi gains, any hopes of an Israeli-style *blitzkrieg* victory soon proved to be misplaced as the offensive bogged down. A turning point in the conflict came in the autumn of 1981 as the Iranians counter-attacked and raised the siege of Abadan. The rashness of President Hussein's decision to attack revolutionary Iran was now clear.

Iran began a new offensive in March 1982. By June almost all Iraqi troops had withdrawn from Iranian territory, and in July the Iranians mounted a counter-invasion of Iraq. This was checked, but fighting continued despite calls for a cease-fire.

In 1983 and 1984 Iran launched a number of major offensives, but the military situation on land remained deadlocked. Repeated air attacks by both sides on international shipping in the Gulf represented a significant escalation of the conflict. During 1984 67 vessels, ranging from supertankers to small supply ships, were damaged by the warring states.

Downfall of Dr. Bani-Sadr.

The power struggle between secular and religious political forces culminated in Dr. Bani-Sadr's dismissal from office by Ayatollah Khomeini on 22 June 1981. Violence in Tehran increased. At the end of June seventy-two leading officials were killed in an explosion at the headquarters of the Islamic Republican Party and in August an explosion at the Prime Minister's offices killed both Prime Minister and President. During July and August the Iranian authorities retaliated by executing over six hundred opponents of the regime.

Executions continued during 1982, including that of Sadeq Qotbzadeh, the former Foreign Minister, in September after he had been found guilty of attempting to overthrow the government. The search for a successor when Ayatollah Khomeini dies took a step forward in December 1982 when an Assembly of Experts was elected to decide on a new leader or a leadership council of three or five men to succeed Khomeini as the dominant force in Iran.

Action against opponents of the revolution continued in 1983 with the outlawing of the communist Tudeh Party in May. At the same time 18 Soviet diplomats were expelled from Iran for interfering in internal political affairs. Iran's relations with the USSR were as bad as those with the USA.

The Emergence of Ayatollah Montazeri.

On the domestic front in August 1985 Ali Khameini, who had become President of Iran in October 1981, was re-elected for a further four-year term with a large majority. Then in November 1985 it was announced that the Assembly of Experts had nominated Ayatollah Hussein Ali Montazeri to succeed Ayatollah Khomeini when he dies or retires. The conservative minority in the ruling Islamic republican party was said to have favoured a leadership council, but no candidates of equal weight to Ayatollah Montazeri were put forward.

Developments in the Iran–Iraq War 1985–87.

Iran's war with Iraq continued during 1985, with Iraq on the defensive and each side launching air attacks on enemy cities. In June 1985 Iraq announced the suspension of such attacks, but Iran rejected all conciliatory gestures. In February 1986 Iranian troops overran the former oil port of Faw, but the military situation remained deadlocked.

In January 1987, after months of preparation, Iran launched its biggest offensive of the war on the southern front, codenamed Karbala-5. Its aim was the capture of Basra, which could be used as the base for a rival government of Iraq, even if its fall did not lead to the immediate collapse of President Hoddam Hussein's regime. The Iranians advanced against Iraq's elaborate defences, suffering enormous casualties, but penetrating to within ten miles of Basra, which brought the city well within artillery range.

Iraq retaliated with air attacks on Tehran and more than thirty other Iranian cities. In fresh fighting in April 1987 Iran consolidated the gains of Karbala-5 east of Basra, and launched a new offensive round Qasr al-Shireen, a key defensive position in the central sector, north-west of Baghdad. Both sides in the war had more than a million men under arms, but Iran, with its population of 45 million compared to Iraq's 14 million, was better able to bear the huge economic and human cost of the war. Meanwhile, the accidental Iraqi Exocet attack in May 1987 on the American frigate *USS Stark* in the Gulf (with the loss of 37 American lives) served to show the danger of the conflict escalating.

American Involvement in the Gulf.

In May 1987 the United States agreed to reflag eleven Kuwaiti tankers and to provide them with escorts in the Gulf. When the escorting began in July the Kuwaiti supertanker, the *Bridgetown*, struck a mine despite its American protectors. In September and October U.S. helicopters attacked Iranian gunboats, and later in October, following an Iranian missile attack on a U.S.-flagged Kuwaiti supertanker, *Sea Island City*, U.S. warships de-

stroyed two Iranian oil platforms. Conflict continued in 1988 and in April a U.S. frigate, *Samuel B. Roberts*, hit a mine while on escort duty. In response the Americans attacked two Iranian oil platforms and sank an Iranian patrol boat.

The End of the Gulf War.

In July 1987 the UN Security Council called on Iran and Iraq to stop fighting. Iraq observed the cease-fire, but Iran refused to do so until its adversary was branded as the aggressor. Iraq therefore resumed heavy attacks on Iranian cities. In April 1988 the Iraqis mounted an unexpected land offensive and regained the southern end of the Faw peninsula occupied by the Iranians in 1986.

In May the Iraqis drove the Iranians from the marshlands east of Basra, and during June recaptured all the territory lost since 1984. At the beginning of June Ayatollah Khomeini appointed Mr. Rafsanjani, the speaker of the Iranian parliament, as acting commander-in-chief, with orders to streamline the country's war machine. But in July Iraq launched further offensives, advancing twenty-five miles into Iran. On 3 July the US cruiser *Vincennes* shot down an Iranian Airbus after mistaking it for an attacking aircraft, and 300 lives were lost.

On 18 July 1988 Iran · suddenly accepted UN Resolution 598, calling for a cease-fire in the Gulf War. Speaker Rafsanjani announced the decision, which Ayatollah Khomeini two days later described as "more deadly than taking poison". Iraq was suspicious of Iran's sincerity, but the UN Secretary-General, Mr. Perez de Cuellar, succeeded in negotiating a cease-fire with effect from 20 August. A UN observer group was established to monitor the truce, and talks between Iran and Iraq on finding a permanent peace settlement began.

Relations with Britain.

In the autumn of 1988, improving relations between Iran and Britain led to the reopening, after eight years, of the British Embassy in Tehran in November. Although diplomatic relations had never been formally broken off, the normalisation of relations offered an improved prospect of freeing the British citizens detained in Iran and by Iranian-backed groups in Lebanon. However, in February 1989 Ayatollah Khomeini denounced as blasphemous to Islam the book *The Satanic Verses* by the British author, Salman Rushdie, and called for his execution. An expression of regret by Mr. Rushdie was rejected. As a result Britain withdrew its diplomats from Iran, and asked Iran's representatives to leave Britain. In March Iran broke off all diplomatic relations with Britain.

Death of Ayatollah Khomeini.

On 4 June 1989, the ailing Ayatollah Khomeini died. By his creation of the Islamic Republic of Iran he had earned his place in history, but the nature and policy of the government that would follow were uncertain.

President Ali Khamenei was immediately appointed supreme religious leader in succession to Ayatollah Khomenei. But the confidence of *Majlis* (parliament) speaker Ali Akbar Hashemi Rafsanjani of his own success in the forthcoming presidential elections suggested a possible future moderation in Iranian policies. He called for improved relations with the Soviet Union and visited Moscow on 20–23 June. Rumours that the late Ayatollah Khomeini's son, Ahman Khomeini, would seek the presidency with radical support proved ill-founded. On 28 July Rafsanjani took 94·5% of the vote against only token opposition. Constitutional changes extending presidential powers and abolishing the office of prime minister were approved by 97·4%.

The Advent of Rafsanjani.

Taking office on 3 August, President Rafsanjani offered help in the Lebanon hostages crisis, signifying a moderation of Iran's attitude towards the United States. Ayatollah Khameini's immediate attack on the US and his rejection of the possibility of negotiations demonstrated continuing divisions within the government. But President Rafsanjani's nomination of a cabinet with a large sprinkling of economic pragmatists, and its acceptance by the *Majlis* on 29 August, implied a growing mood in favour of reform and away from radicalism. On 6 November the US released $567 million Iranian assets frozen since 1979. Although President Rafsanjani had said only a few days earlier that it was too soon to begin discussions with the United States, this did suggest an underlying easing of relations.

IRAQ AND SYRIA.

Iraq and Syria were both governed by left-wing revolutionary Arab regimes during the 1970s. Both dealt severely with their internal opponents and Iraq in particular (where the Iranian Ayatollah Khomeini had spent almost thirteen years in exile at Najaf) was strongly hostile to the Islamic upsurge. But in Syria, fierce antagonisms between the country's Sunni majority and its Shi'ite minority—represented by President Hafiz Assad himself—revived. During the summer of 1979 there were serious incidents of violence between Sunni and Shi'ite Syrians, including the massacre of 60 cadet officers. This reflected Sunni Shi'ite conflicts immediately to Syria's north in Eastern Turkey where 120 people were murdered in the town of Kahramanmaras in riots in December 1978. In 1980, Iraq went to war with Iran whilst relations between Syria and Jordan grew increasingly tense. A rapprochement took place between Jordan and Syria in October 1985 when, in the context of negotiations over the Palestinian problem, they agreed to reject 'partial and unilateral' peace settlements with Israel and to exchange ambassadors after a four-year diplomatic freeze. President Assad and King Hussein held talks in Damascus at the end of December 1985—their first meeting since 1979—and President Assad paid a return visit to Amman in May 1986.

SAUDI ARABIA.

Saudi Arabia—whose royal family enforced the strict tenets of the puritanical Wahabbi sect of Islam—began the 1970s as one of the principal backers of Islamic revivalism. It ended it as a country alarmed at the spread of Islamic militancy. In March 1975 King Faisal was assassinated by a mentally deranged member of the royal family and was succeeded by his half-brother Prince Khaled. King Khaled pursued policies of careful modernisation and moderation with regard to oil pricing. The worst moment in his reign came in November 1979 when a gang of Islamic fanatics seized the Great Mosque in Mecca and held it for two weeks, threatening the position of the House of Saud as guardians of Islam's holy places.

King Khaled died of a heart attack on 13 June 1982 and was succeeded by his brother, Prince Fahd. Prince Fahd had been associated with the progressive, pro-American faction in the royal family and his succession to the throne did not bring any great changes in Saudi Arabian policy.

In October 1986 Sheikh Yamani, the Minister for Petroleum and Natural Resources since 1962, was removed from his post. His direction of Saudi oil policy, which had won him an international reputation, was often controversial, whilst his prominent role was resented by some Saudis, especially those with royal connections. He was replaced by Mr. Hisham Nazer as acting oil minister.

Relations with Iran.

Despite a ban on political demonstrations in Mecca, Iranian pilgrims organised marches in the holy city in July 1987. More than 400 people, mainly Iranians, died when Saudi security forces dispersed the demonstrators.

In April 1988 Iranian attacks on Saudi and neutral oil tankers in the Gulf and threats of fresh disorders in Mecca led the Saudi Arabians to break off all diplomatic relations with Iran.

SOUTH YEMEN.

Post-Independence Problems.

After a protracted guerrilla war against the British colonial rulers, the People's Republic of South Yemen became independent on 30 November 1967. The country's name was changed to the People's Democratic Republic of South Yemen in 1970. In 1969 President Qahtan Al-Shayabi, who had conducted the independence negotiations, was ousted in a bloodless coup by more radical members of his party. This was the first of a series of internal conflicts, based on personal, tribal and doctrinal differences, which has divided the government of the South Yemen since independence.

The new president, Salem Rubayi Ali was himself deposed and shot in 1978 and Abdel Fattah Ismail became head of state. In 1980 he was forced into exile in the Soviet Union, which had developed close relations with South Yemen in the 1970s, and the prime minister, Ali Nasser Mohammed, assumed the presidency.

The 1986 Coup.

Abdel Fattah Ismail returned from Moscow in 1985 and was brought back into the political bureau of the Yemeni Socialist Party. This led, however, to renewed conflict within the party, since Abdel Fattah Ismail took a hard-line Marxist stance, whereas President Ali Nasser Mohammed adopted a more pragmatic approach, for example, to relations with South Yemen's conservative neighbours. Bloodshed broke out in January 1986, either as a result of an attempted coup or pre-emptive action by the President. Thousands died in extensive fighting in and around Aden, and an international rescue of foreign nationals took place, in which the royal yacht Britannia participated. President Ali Nasser Mohammed was forced to flee the country and the prime minister, Haider Attas, who had been appointed in February 1985, took over as the country's interim head. The upheaval had a serious effect on Soviet interests in South Yemen—Russia's most important military facility in the Middle East—as over 6,000 of its 'advisers' had to be taken to safety from the fighting.

During 1986 considerable effort and resources had to be devoted to repairing the damage done by the January fighting, and to the purchase of replacement equipment for the armed forces. In November 1986 Haider Attas was formally elected President for a five-year term by the Supreme People's Council.

Merger Proposals.

On 30 November 1989 the northern Yemen Arab Republic and the southern People's Democratic Republic of Yemen agreed to merge within a year. The traditionalist Yemen Arab Republic was established after a military coup in 1962. The People's Democratic Republic, the former British colony of Aden, achieved independence in 1967 after a National Liberation Front led a guerrilla war and had turned almost at once to the Soviet Union for support. President Haidar Abu Bakr Saleh took power in 1986 following a civil war between rival left-wing factions. The new state would have a combined population of 12 million and its capital was to be Sana'a in the north. Its leader was expected to be the northern President Ali Abdullah Saleh. The only internal opposition to the merger came from the Moslem Brotherhood, whose leader Sheikh Zindani said the proposed constitution conflicted with Islamic Law. Neighbouring Saudi Arabia too expressed opposition.

Withdrawal of Soviet Aid.

Unity appeared one means of confronting severe economic problems in both parts of Yemen. The People's Democratic Republic could no longer depend on aid as the Soviet Union withdrew from its overseas commitments. The ruling Socialist Party promised increasing democratisation at its February 1990 congress. Foreign Minister Dr Abdul el-Aziz Aldally announced that by the end of April there would be greater press freedom and an increased role for the private sector in the economy.

SOUTH ASIA

INDIA SINCE 1984.

Mrs. Gandhi's Assassination.

Mrs. Gandhi was assassinated on 31 October 1984

by two Sikh members of her bodyguard. Rioting followed as Hindu mobs took revenge on Sikhs and some 3,000 people died. Mrs Gandhi was succeeded as Prime Minister by her son, Rajiv. He continued with the planned elections in December 1984 and, in the aftermath of his mother's death, his party won 401 of the 508 seats in parliament. Rajiv Gandhi announced that he would embark on a programme of communal reconciliation and economic reform. Earlier in the month India had experienced one of the world's worst environmental disasters. On 3 December over forty tons of poisonous methyl isocyanate leaked from the Union Carbide pesticides factory at Bhopal, capital of Madhya Pradesh state. Some 2,500 people died and as many as 200,000 were injured.

Moves towards Reconciliation in 1985.

Outbreaks of violence led to the introduction in May 1985 of the Terrorist and Disruptive Activities (Prevention) Bill. But Mr. Gandhi remained faithful to the path of reconciliation rather than confrontation. In July he signed an accord with the president of the Sikh Akali Dal party, Sant Harchand Singh Longowal, affording greater political and religious autonomy to the Punjab. Sant Longowal was murdered by Sikh extremists in August, but new elections for the state assembly and representatives in the national parliament went ahead in September. The Akali Dal emerged victorious in both polls. Presidential rule in the Punjab, imposed in October 1983, was finally lifted on 29 September when Surjit Singh Barnala, leader of the Akali Dal, was sworn in as chief minister.

Turning to the problems of Assam, Mr. Gandhi announced an agreement in August regarding the protection of Assamese linguistic and cultural identity against the immigrants from Bangladesh. Illegal immigrants who entered Assam between January 1966 and March 1971 were to be disenfranchised for ten years, while any who had arrived after 1971 were to be expelled. The state assembly returned in the violently-disputed 1983 elections was dissolved and new elections were held in December 1985. These resulted in a win for the Asom Gana Parishad, a party formed only two months before by Assamese students.

Congress Party Problems.

Although opposition victories in the Punjab and Assam had promoted national reconciliation, they had left the Congress Party in a state of disarray. By the end of 1985 Mr. Gandhi's party was out of power in nine out of the twenty-two states and union territories. In January 1986 he announced a thorough shake-up of the party's leadership in an effort to regain the ground lost to regional parties.

Despite the agreement of July 1985, unrest continued in the Punjab, particularly when Mrs. Gandhi's three Sikh assassins were sentenced to death in January 1986. In addition, a border dispute led to delays in handing over Chandigarh, the capital city the Punjab shared with neighbouring Haryana, to the Sikh state, a measure which had formed part of the July 1985 accord.

Violence by Sikh extremists continued during 1986. In August Sikh gunmen killed the former army chief of staff, General Arun Vaidya, who had helped plan the assault on the Golden Temple. In February 1987 Mr. Barnala, chief minister of the Punjab, was excommunicated by the high priests of the Golden Temple, but his Akali Dal party continued to support him against the militants.

Mid-term elections for the upper house of the Indian parliament, for which members are chosen by the state assemblies, were held in June 1986. They left the Congress Party dominant, with 148 of the 244 seats. Nevertheless in November 1986 Mr. Kamlapati Tripathi, the 82-year-old executive president of the Congress Party, resigned at Mr. Gandhi's request, along with other senior officials, to make way for a reorganisation of the party.

Mr. Gandhi's Problems.

The Congress Party had an opportunity to boost its image in the state elections held in March 1987 in West Bengal, Kerala and Jammu and Kashmir.

Despite energetic campaigning by Mr. Gandhi, however, the Communist-led Left Front in West Bengal increased its majority in winning a further five-year term. In Kerala the United Democratic Front, which included the Congress Party, was pushed out of office by the Left Democratic Front. Only in Jammu and Kashmir, where the Congress Party was fighting as the junior partner in alliance with the National Conference Movement, was the challenge from opposition groups, including Muslim fundamentalists, beaten off. The overall poor performance of the Congress Party was seen as a severe personal blow to Mr. Gandhi.

A further problem for Mr. Gandhi in March 1987 was the complaint by the head of state, President Zail Singh, that he was not being kept fully informed of developments at home and abroad. President Zail seemed to represent a widespread feeling against Mr. Gandhi's arrogant manner and 'playboy' image. Nearly all the opposition members walked out of the lower house when the Speaker refused to allow a debate on the constitutional position of the presidency. Mr. Gandhi took steps to defuse the crisis by making a conciliatory visit to the presidential palace for talks with Zail Singh at the end of March.

The rift between Mr. Gandhi and the President was smoothed over. In July 1987 a new president, Mr. Ramaswany Venkataraman, was sworn in.

There was no let up for Mr. Gandhi in the second half of 1987, with the defeat of the Congress Party in the state poll in Haryana in June, government corruption scandals involving defence contracts and continuing violence by Sikh militants in the Punjab.

A United Opposition.

In August 1988 a grouping of opposition parties was formed to coordinate an electoral programme under the chairmanship of Mr. N. T. Rama Rao, chief minister of the southern state of Andhra Pradesh. And in October three opposition parties merged into the new Janata Dal (People's Party) under the leadership of Mr. V. P. Singh, the former Finance and Defence Minister, who had made allegations of governmental corruption in his resignation in 1987.

There was speculation that these moves towards opposition unity might prompt Mr. Gandhi to go to the country sooner rather than later in the elections due in 1989. In December 1988 Mr. Gandhi paid a successful visit to China, and an agreement was reached on setting up a joint working group to tackle border problems. Also in December Mr. Gandhi had talks with Miss Bhutto of Pakistan at the fourth annual summit of the South Asian Association for Regional Cooperation at Islamabad. In the first agreement between India and Pakistan for sixteen years, the leaders signed an undertaking not to attack each other's nuclear installations. Such foreign policy successes seemed to strengthen Mr. Gandhi's position.

In January 1989, however, Mr. Gandhi suffered a personal humiliation when the Congress Party was heavily defeated in elections for the Tamil Nadu state assembly, despite his interventions in the election campaign. Although the Congress Party had not held power in Tamil Nadu since 1967, the scale of the defeat seemed to rule out an early national poll. Following the Tamil Nadu election, Congress Party rebels in at least four states defied Mr. Gandhi's authority and threatened to disrupt the Congress-ruled state governments. Mr. Gandhi recalled his mother's most powerful aide, Mr. R. K. Dhawan, to his cabinet in an effort to regain control of the situation.

Mr Dhawan's appointment as Mr Gandhi's adviser threatened to be potentially embarrassing when, on 27 March 1989, a report released to Parliament alleged Mr Dhawan's involvement in the assassination of Mrs Gandhi. Home Affairs Minister B. Singh said this aspect of the report, which dated from 1986, had been investigated by police who were satisfied Mr Dhawan was not involved. This was, however, the least of the problems confronting Mr Gandhi in what would prove to be an election year. An opinion poll in February had suggested that, should the opposition to Mr Gandhi be capable of building a united front at an election, his Congress (I) party would lose office. Behind this lay an air of corruption around his administration, particularly in relation to a $1·3 billion arms purchase from the Swedish Bofors Company.

The Bofors Scandal.

On 18 July a report criticised the government for corruption in the Bofors deal. Mr Gandhi himself was not, at this stage, accused of any personal involvement. The opposition demanded he test his authority with immediate elections. Mr Gandhi refused. Leaders of twelve opposition parties protested by taking all their 106 members out of the 545-member lower house of parliament. In August the opposition called a one day general strike against government corruption. The action—in which 11 people were killed and 350 injured—gathered significant support in the six states controlled by opposition parties but was less effective in the sixteen Congress ruled states.

By early September media attention had moved to Mr Gandhi's personal role in the Bofors affair. A former army chief of staff alleged Mr Gandhi had been actively involved in covering up the bribes scandal. A newspaper published part of a hitherto secret 1987 Swedish report revealing conclusively that Bofors had paid $100 million in illegal commissions to smooth the path of its contract with the Indian government. Allegations of a direct link between Gandhi and these commissions followed.

The November 1989 Elections.

On 17 October a beleaguered Mr Gandhi, his position clearly undermined by the scandal, announced that parliamentary elections would be held in November, two months earlier than constitutionally necessary. Four days previously his government had lost two important votes in the upper house on local government changes. Congress failed to win the necessary two-thirds majority on both occasions, the first time an Indian government had suffered what amounted to humiliation since 1952. In addition, from September the government was faced with violent clashes between Hindus and Moslems in Kota, Badain and Indore. 170 were killed in two weeks of rioting in Bihar state.

Mr Gandhi faced a united opposition. Five regional organisations rallied in a National Front under Janata Dal, the People's Party. Its manifesto issued on 20 October denounced government corruption and promised increased autonomy for state governments. Congress in its manifesto proposed legislation to improve the position of women and, to encourage rural support, the creation of self-governing village councils.

The November campaign proved to be the bloodiest since independence, with 120 deaths. Turnout for the 525 house seats contested was a little under 60%. Congress took 192 seats, a dramatic decline from the 415 it had won in 1984. Much of its lost support was in the hitherto traditionally loyal north. An allied party in the south won a further 11 seats. For the opposition, Janata Dal and two smaller associated parties took a total of 144 seats; the right-wing Hindu BJP (the Indian People's Party), 88; and four left-wing parties, 51. Though Congress remained the largest single party it was well short of a majority.

The New Prime Minister.

National Front leader Vishwanath Pratap Singh became Prime Minister on 2 December, heading a minority government supported by the BJP and four left-wing parties. He promised an investigation into the Bofors scandal, a freedom of information act, and encouragement for agriculture and small-scale industry. In announcing his cabinet Mr Singh broke with tradition by appointing a Moslem, Mohammed Sayeed, as home affairs minister. Mr Gandhi's Congress party suffered further defeats in state elections held in March 1990, losing control of a number of traditionally Congress northern and central states. The most striking successes came for the right-wing BJP, suggesting that Mr Singh would face increasing demands from the BJP for its support.

SRI LANKA.

Ceylon became a self-governing member of the British Commonwealth by the Ceylon Independence Act 1947, which came into force on 4 February 1948. A new constitution was adopted in 1972 and the country was renamed the Republic of Sri Lanka. In 1977 the National State Assembly approved a constitutional amendment introducing a presidential form of government and the Prime Minister, Junius Jayawardene, became the first Executive President on 4 February 1978. In presidential elections held on 20 October 1982 President Jayawardene was returned to office for a further six years. In November 1982 the Assembly, dominated by President Jayawardene's United National Party, voted to extend for a six-year period its term which would have expired in August 1983. This was approved by a national referendum on 20 December 1982.

Communal Violence after 1983.

There has been a long history of tension and outbreaks of violence between the majority Sinhalese Buddhist population and the Tamil Hindu minority. Parliamentary and local elections in May 1983 resulted in a landslide victory for the United National Party, but they were accompanied by bomb blasts attributed to separatist guerrillas, the Tamil Tigers. The deaths of 13 soldiers in a guerrilla ambush near Jaffna in July led to serious communal violence in the capital Colombo which spread rapidly. Some 20,000 Tamils were made homeless and many were evacuated from Colombo to the area of Jaffna where the main Tamil population is located. Over 400 people were killed in the rioting. A law was passed requiring all MPs to take an oath denouncing separatism, and the Tamil United Liberation Front boycotted the National Assembly in protest.

In January 1984 President Jayawardene convened all-party "amity talks", which were attended by the Tamil United Liberation Front. However, the Tamil politicians could not accept less than regional autonomy, and so, in the absence of such a political settlement, violence continued during 1984. Guerrilla attacks provoked army reprisals which further alienated the Tamil population. Sri Lanka's relations with India were strained by accusations that the guerrillas were being trained in the southern Indian state of Tamil Nadu. In November the government announced a series of wide-ranging emergency regulations, including the formation of a prohibited zone on Sri Lanka's northern coast where all movement was to be strictly controlled.

Search for a Settlement.

Following talks in New Delhi between President Jayawardene and Rajiv Gandhi in June 1985, the Sri Lankan government announced a three-month cease-fire and in July began talks with Tamil separatists in the remote capital of Bhutan, Thimbu. However, the talks broke down in August when reports were received of new killings of Tamils in Sri Lanka.

In Spring 1986 the government put forward a new peace plan, based on substantial devolution of powers to all nine of Sri Lanka's provinces. Discussions opened between President Jayawardene and a range of political parties in the Summer of 1986, but there were disputes over the powers of the provincial councils and the government's refusal to consider the idea of a merger between the predominantly Tamil eastern and northern provinces. In July 1986 representatives of the five main guerrilla groups, based in India, rejected the devolution proposals and renewed their demand for a Tamil homeland.

India's Mediation Role.

Violence continued in Sri Lanka throughout 1986 between government forces and Tamil guerrillas, and also between the rival liberation groups, the Tamil Tigers and the Eelam People's Revolutionary Liberation Front. In November 1986 Indian police took action against the guerrilla groups in Tamil Nadu, confiscating their weapons and putting the leaders under house arrest. India supported a scheme for a "close association" between Sri Lanka's northern province and a truncated eastern province, which could be represented as a Tamil homeland, and President Jayawardene accepted this idea in December.

However, in February 1987 Mr. Gandhi withdrew his commitment to act as a mediator unless the government ended military operations in the north and lifted its fuel embargo on Jaffna. He resumed this role, however, in March, although the conditions had not been fully met. At the beginning of April the Tamil Tigers' Jaffna commander, Kittu, was seriously wounded in an ambush by members of the rival Tamil Eelam Liberation Organisation, and in retaliation the Tigers massacred over a hundred of their opponents. Indian hopes of promoting a peaceful settlement were rendered even more remote in April 1987 by two outrages perpetrated by Tamil extremists: a massacre of bus passengers near Trincomalee and a car bomb explosion in Colombo, in both of which over a hundred people died.

India–Sri Lanka Accord.

In May 1987 the Sri Lankan army launched a new offensive against rebels in the Jaffna peninsula. The Indian government protested, and after failing to get permission to send in relief supplies by sea to the civilian population, it carried out unauthorised air drops. Negotiations now progressed rapidly and on 29 July 1987 the Indian and Sri Lankan governments signed an accord to end the four years of bloodshed. A single north-eastern province was to be created from the two existing mainly Tamil provinces. The Sri Lankan army was to return to barracks and the Tamil rebels were to surrender their weapons to an Indian peace-keeping force.

Riots by the Sinhalese majority against the accord took place in Colombo, and in August President Jayawardene narrowly escaped assassination when hand-grenades were thrown into a parliamentary committee room. In December 1987 the chairman of the ruling United National Party was shot dead by a member of the extremist left-wing Sinhalese JVP, which rejected the accord with India.

But the peace accord was also under threat from the other side. The Tamil Tigers rejected the proposals for a federal solution rather than an independent Tamil homeland. They resumed their campaign of violence and the Indian army was forced to take action in October. After two weeks' heavy fighting the army gained control over the Jaffna peninsula. By the beginning of 1988 the Indian peace-keeping force had grown to over 40,000 men.

Presidential and Parliamentary Elections.

In accordance with his agreement with India, in his last months as president Mr. Jayawardene issued a proclamation in September 1988 merging the northern and eastern provinces of Sri Lanka. In November elections were held for the new devolved provincial council. There was no poll in the northern area, where Indian-backed groups were allocated the seats. But in the east there was a 60 per cent turn-out of voters despite Tamil Tiger calls for a boycott. The Indian-backed Eelam People's Revolutionary Liberation Front won 40 of the 71 seats, with 17 going to the Sri Lankan Muslim Congress and 13 to the Eelam National Democratic Liberation Front. Threats from the JVP led to a Sinhalese boycott of the elections, and the United National Party (UNP) won only one seat. The EPRLF set about establishing a cabinet to run the Tamil-dominated areas.

In December 1988 Sri Lanka went to the polls to elect a successor to Mr. Jayawardene as president. The main candidates were Mrs. Bandaranaike, the head of the Sri Lanka Freedom Party, who was the world's first woman prime minister when she formed the government of Sri Lanka in 1960; and Mr. Premadasa, leader of the UNP. Despite his background—he was born in the slums of Colombo, rather than to the high caste which normally provides Sri Lanka's leaders—Mr. Premadasa had been appointed prime minister in 1978 when Mr. Jayawardene assumed the presidency. The elections were marred by considerable violence, mainly from the JVP, including some thirty deaths on polling day. The turn-out was 55 per cent, and Mr. Premadasa secured 50·4 per cent of votes cast. This was just sufficient to avoid a count of the second preference votes cast by supporters of the third candidate, representing the leftist People's Party, and Mr. Premadasa was declared president.

After his victory President Premadasa ordered an end to the five-year state of emergency, and the release of 2,500 people detained under the emergency regulations. In February 1989 the first parliamentary elections for twelve years were held. Some 64 per cent of voters went to the polls. The result was a victory for the ruling UNP, which took 125 of the 225 seats. A new system of proportional representation meant that the Sri Lanka Freedom Party won 67 seats. There were 39 deaths on polling day.

Problems Facing Premadasa.

President Premadasa in his first year of office faced two main issues: communal violence which threatened to break Sri Lanka in two, and the presence of a 45,000 strong Indian peacekeeping force. On 3 May India announced it would withdraw 20,000 troops by the end of July, the remainder leaving by the end of 1989. On 11 May President Premadasa opened discussions with the leaders of the "Liberation Tigers", the largest of the Tamil guerrilla groups. By late June the government and the Tigers had negotiated a ceasefire, though a Tamil spokesman stressed that demands for a separate homeland would continue. President Premadasa now faced threats from the Sinhalese People's Liberation Front (JVP). Strikes and violence organised by the JVP forced a renewal of the state of emergency on 20 June. His attempts to restore peace by convening a meeting 21 of Sri Lanka's 27 political parties seemed in vain, not least because of the JVP's refusal to attend. The JVP's founder and leader, Rohana Wijeweera, was shot in security force custody in November. An enquiry was ordered into the circumstances of the shooting.

Proclamation of Independent Eelam.

A further conference called by President Premadasa on 14 February 1990 took place against a more orderly background. In the Tamil north the Tigers had renounced armed action in favour of forming a political party to contest elections. The government had ridden the worst of JVP guerrilla attempts at its overthrow. President Premadasa proposed reforms to promote communal harmony and promised an early end to the state of emergency. But on 1 March the chief minister of the Tamil provinces, Anamalai Varatharaja Perumal declared the area to be an independent state of Eelam. Mr Perumal fled to India shortly after but Sri Lanka still faced the possibility of permanent division.

PAKISTAN.

Civil War.

As a result of the elections in December 1970, Sheikh Mujibur Rahman of the Awami League obtained a majority in the East and Mr. Bhutto or the People's Party triumphed in the west. Due to the greater population of the East, the Awami League commanded an overall majority, and insisted on a constitution which would give East Pakistan wide-ranging autonomy. Mr. Bhutto opposed this and Civil War erupted on 26 March 1971 following the outlawing of the Awami League and the declaration of E. Pakistan as the independent republic of Bangladesh. The opposition was quickly suppressed, but involved the loss of thousands of innocent lives and created a severe refugee problem as many fled to India. Widespread disease and the cyclone disaster of November 1970 threatened a major famine in E. Pakistan.

Support for the Bangladesh guerrillas (Mukti Bahini) was provided by India and war broke out between India and Pakistan in late 1971 following Mrs. Gandhi's demand for the withdrawal of Pakistani troops from Bangladesh. Bitter fighting occurred in both E. and W. Pakistan which was ended by Yahya Khan's acceptance of India's unilateral offer of a cease-fire.

The Aftermath.

On 20 December 1971 President Yahya Khan resigned and was replaced by Mr. Bhutto who released Sheikh Mujibur Rahman the following January. At the same time Pakistan left the

Commonwealth as other members were about to recognise Bangladesh. (In April 1972 Bangladesh was admitted in place of Pakistan.) Peace negotiations with India were initiated to deal mainly with withdrawal from areas conquered in 1971 and the exchange of prisoners. The latter was only achieved after Pakistani recognition of Bangladesh. Diplomatic relations with India were finally re-established in May 1976. Internal problems within Pakistan arose with conflict in the provinces of Sindh and Baluchistan and have continued since then. Mr. Bhutto gradually introduced economic reform but throughout 1975 and 1976 unrest in the provinces and the outlawing of the Awami League led to approval of a declaration of a state of emergency. Elections were held in March 1977. Amid accusations of election malpractice, Mr. Bhutto claimed victory. Widespread unrest followed, with organised opposition to Mr. Bhutto being answered by the arrest of leading opposition politicians. Martial law was imposed in the major cities. The opposition Pakistani National Alliance continued to demand the resignation of Mr. Bhutto and the holding of new elections. Finally, agreement was reached on new elections to be held in October, though there was still disagreement on measures for ensuring fairness. But on 5 July the army under General Mohammed Zia ul-Haq took over power, and Mr. Bhutto and other leading politicians were arrested. The General declared that his only aim was the holding of free and fair elections. These were fixed for October, and the politicians were released at the end of July. However, the expected return to democracy did not materialise.

The Execution of Bhutto.

In March 1978 Mr. Bhutto was condemned to death for implication in the murder of a political opponent. He was eventually executed on 4 April 1979. For a short time General Zia pursued a policy of conciliation, but in October 1979 he cancelled elections planned for the following month and banned all political activities and strikes.

Opposition nevertheless continued during 1980 to his regime and in February 1981 nine political parties formed an alliance known as the Movement for the Restoration of Democracy which called for the holding of elections and the lifting of martial law. However, the movement collapsed after a Pakistani airliner was hijacked in March by members of an underground organisation headed by Murtaza Bhutto, son of the executed Prime Minister.

The Policy of Islamisation.

Public outrage gave General Zia the excuse for carrying out mass arrests of his opponents, including Mr Bhutto's wife and daughter. On 24 March he promulgated an interim constitution to remain in effect until martial law could be lifted. In 1982 General Zia continued his drive to make Islamisation reach every aspect of life in Pakistan and to foster national feeling by such measures as ordering the greater use of Urdu and national dress. In August 1983 President Zia announced his plan to hold elections in March 1985, but martial law would remain in force until then and only approved candidates would be allowed to stand. Proposed constitutional changes would also increase the powers of the President. The Movement for the Restoration of Democracy announced a campaign of civil disobedience, but dozens of its members were arrested in a pre-emptive move by the military government.

In December 1984, General Zia held a referendum on his policy of Islamisation. According to official figures 60% of the population voted and 98% of these approved the policy. General Zia declared that he was therefore endorsed as president for a further five years. Shortly before the elections the government imposed strict regulations on the press, forbidding publication of the views of the opposition who were in any case barred from competing.

Elections were held at the end of February 1985. Although they were boycotted by the Movement for the Restoration of Democracy, a turnout of 53 per cent was reported. The People's Party, formerly led by Mr Bhutto, was the largest group in the new National Assembly, and five of the nine federal ministers who stood for election were defeated. Shortly after the elections, however, General Zia

announced wide-ranging constitutional amendments reducing the authority of the Prime Minister and increasing his own. In March 1985 the suspended 1973 constitution was restored and the new parliament assembled.

The End of Martial Law.

General Zia announced that he was lifting martial law on 30 December 1985. Military courts were abolished and trials transferred to civilian courts, though not before many pending cases had been rushed through in December. The response of the opposition was sceptical, particularly as General Zia retained the power of veto over political parties, which have to apply for registration and submit their political programmes to an Election Commission in order to be legalised.

In April 1986 Miss Benazir Bhutto returned to Pakistan from London. She was arrested in Karachi in August after addressing an independence day rally banned by the government of Prime Minister Junejo. Police opened fire on protesters in succeeding days and some twenty people were killed. Miss Bhutto and other opposition activists were released in September 1986, but faced the problem of how to challenge Mr. Junejo's government without provoking the army.

In November 1986 outbreaks of communal violence in Karachi, capital of Sind province, gave the opposition a stick with which to beat the government. Poor conditions in the rapidly growing slums exacerbated ethnic tensions and led to serious rioting. The disorders were linked to army and police operations to stamp out arms and drugs dealing and to drive large numbers of Afghan refugees from the city into camps outside.

In January 1987 the governor of Sind province, Mr. Jehandad Khan, resigned and the army enforced a strict curfew in Karachi. President Zia came under mounting pressure to curb the strength of the Afghan Mujaheddin guerrillas in Pakistan, and to seek a peace settlement in Afghanistan as a matter of urgency.

After lengthy negotiations Pakistan and Afghanistan signed a peace agreement in April 1988, which it was hoped would lead to the return home of the three million Afghan refugees in Pakistan.

Dismissal of Mr. Junejo.

However, General Zia was more hesitant about the peace agreement than his prime minister, Mr. Junejo. Growing differences between the two men led President Zia in May 1988 to take the surprise step of dissolving parliament, dismissing Mr. Junejo and ordering new elections. He blamed the government's failure to carry forward his programme of Islamisation. In July General Zia announced that the elections would take place in November, but on a non-party basis.

The Death of President Zia.

On 17 August 1988 President Zia was killed when his C-130 transport aircraft exploded a few minutes after taking off from Bahawalpur, seventy miles from the Indian border. All those on board were killed, including the US ambassador to Pakistan, Mr. Arnold Raphel. The subsequent enquiry ruled out an accident or a missile attack, leaving sabotage—perhaps by Afghan agents or disaffected elements in the army—as the most likely cause.

A state of emergency was declared, and the chairman of the Senate, Mr. Ghulam Ishaq Khan, became acting president, with a council of military and civilian leaders. He announced that the elections would go ahead as planned in November, and supported a decision by the Supreme Court in October, setting aside President Zia's order that they could not be contested by political parties.

The Triumph of Miss Bhutto.

Voting in the national elections took place on 16 November 1988. Miss Bhutto's Pakistan People's Party (PPP) won 95 of the 207 elected Muslim seats in the National Assembly, plus a further twelve when indirect elections took place for the twenty seats reserved for women. Her main opponents, the Islamic Democratic Alliance, won 54 seats. The next largest party was the Mohajir Qaumi

Movement (MQM), with thirteen seats, representing the Urdu-speaking population of Sind who had come as refugees after partition. Two weeks of uncertainty followed the elections. This came to an end when Miss Bhutto reached an understanding with the leader of the MQM, Mr. Altaf Hussein. When the National Assembly met, President Ishaq Khan named Miss Bhutto as prime minister.

In December 1988 Miss Bhutto won a vote of confidence in the National Assembly by 148 votes to 55. Miss Bhutto supported the election of President Ishaq Khan for a five-year term, and he received 348 votes compared with his nearest rival's 91. In appointing her cabinet Miss Bhutto kept personal control of the defence and finance ministries, so that she would be responsible for relations with the army and the country's economy, her two main potential problem areas in 1989.

Throughout 1989 Miss Bhutto's authority appeared increasingly vulnerable. Islamic fundamentalist leaders claimed her position as prime minister violated the teachings of the Koran and demanded her replacement by a man. Her Pakistan People's Party suffered a setback in national and provincial by-elections fought in January. Its main opponents, the Islamic Democratic Alliance, took seven of the 13 National Assembly places contested and three of the seven provincial legislature seats. Miss Bhutto's party won four and three respectively, with independents taking the remainder. The PPP did, however, retain its position as the National Assembly's largest party.

Bhutto under Pressure.

In March Miss Bhutto moved to strengthen her position by attempting to oust Nawaz Sharif, chief minister of the Punjab, Pakistan's largest and wealthiest state, and her leading political rival. He easily won a vote of no confidence and by early 1990 appeared, with some success, to be ruling Punjab as a virtually autonomous state. Miss Bhutto followed this by appointing her mother as, in effect, deputy prime minister and, in May, dismissing the chief of the Inter Services Intelligence Directorate in an effort to retain control over the military. There were, nonetheless, reports—unconfirmed by the government—of an attempted military coup in September.

Allegations of Corruption.

Miss Bhutto's administration came under increasing criticism for inefficiency, corruption—with rumours touching her closest family—and a failure to fulfill any of its election promises. In November, shortly after Pakistan had rejoined the Commonwealth, the Islamic Democratic Alliance forced a confidence vote in the National Assembly. The ensuing 107 votes against Miss Bhutto were only 12 short of the 119 necessary to drive her from office. Miss Bhutto responded by reshuffling her cabinet. Ghulam Mustafa Jatoi, the IDA leader, proclaimed the result the "beginning of the end" for Miss Bhutto.

In early 1990 tension between Pakistan and India resumed over the disputed Kashmir region. In July 1989 Indian prime minister Mr Gandhi had visited Miss Bhutto to improve relations. But soon after his successor, Mr Singh, had taken office Indian troops were firing on Moslem demonstrators in Kashmir.

AFGHANISTAN.

The last King of Afghanistan, Zahir Shah, was deposed in a coup on 17 July 1973. A republic was created with General Muhammad Daud as President. A new constitution was approved by a special National Assembly in February 1977 and Daud was elected President for a six-year term. However, he began to crack down on his opponents and in April 1978 there were massive demonstrations in the capital, Kabul, after the death of the left-wing leader Mir Ali Khaibar. On 27 April a military coup took place, in which Daud and his family were killed.

The leaders of the People's Democratic Party of Afghanistan (PDPA) were released from prison and put in power by the military. The head of the PDPA, Nur Muhammad Taraki, became President of the Revolutionary Council and Prime Minister. The PDPA introduced major land reforms, but en-

countered opposition from tribal and religious groups. A power-struggle developed within the PDPA between the Khalq and Parcham factions. The government looked increasingly to the USSR for aid, and in November 1978 a new Afghan–Russian Treaty of Friendship and Co-operation was signed.

The Soviet Invasion.

In September 1979 Taraki was ousted by Hafizullah Amin, but on 27 December 1979 Soviet forces invaded Afghanistan and installed a new regime under Babrak Karmal. The USSR justified the invasion on the grounds that it was at the invitation of the Afghan government to prevent interference by outside powers, but on 14 January 1980 an emergency session of the UN General Assembly called for a Russian withdrawal.

A campaign against the Russian occupying forces and the Afghan army has been waged by the Mujaheddin guerrillas since the invasion. Although President Karmal attempted to conciliate opposition groups, his regime has failed to win the support of the mass of the people on whom the guerrillas depend. It has also failed to achieve international recognition. The United Nations has been working for an agreement involving the withdrawal of Russian troops, to which Pakistan and Iran would be parties. In June 1982 peace negotiations began at Geneva in which the UN representative, Diego Cordovez, acted as intermediary between the Afghan and Pakistani foreign ministers. The UN-sponsored talks continued in 1985, but no solution was found to the problems created by the Russian invasion, including the presence of over four million Afghan refugees in Pakistan and Iran. At the start of 1986 there were still some 100,000 Soviet troops in Afghanistan, at least 9,000 having already died there. In October 1985 the American Congress had approved 300 million dollars of clandestine military aid to the Mujaheddin guerrillas over the next two years.

Resignation of Babrak Karmal.

President Karmal paid a private visit to the Soviet Union for medical reasons in March 1986. When he returned to Kabul in May he announced that he was standing down as general-secretary of the ruling People's Democratic Party. Major-General Mohammad Najibollah, the head of the secret police, was elected in his place. In November 1986 Mr. Karmal resigned his other offices as president of the revolutionary council and chairman of its praesidium. He was succeeded by Haji Mohammad Chamkari.

In January 1987 Dr. Najibollah announced that the government would observe a six-months' ceasefire and pursue a policy of national reconciliation. However, the Mujaheddin rejected the cease-fire and continued the armed struggle against Soviet and government forces. UN-sponsored talks at Geneva resumed early in 1987. The scale of American aid to Pakistan gave the United States considerable influence on the policy of President Zia, who might otherwise have welcomed an end to the war so that Afghan refugees could return home. Furthermore the Soviet army was unlikely to withdraw from Afghanistan while the United States was supplying arms to the Mujaheddin, so the American attitude to a long-term settlement was crucial.

The Soviet Withdrawal.

Despite the failure of Dr. Najibollah's proposals for a coalition government, the Soviet Union reduced the proposed timescale for the withdrawal of its troops to only ten months. This led to the signing of an accord in Geneva on 14 April 1988 by which Pakistan and Afghanistan agreed to non-interference in each other's affairs. The Soviet Union undertook to begin the withdrawal of its 115,000 troops from Afghanistan on 15 May. Half would be removed by mid-August and the remainder by mid-February 1989 at the latest. The United States and the Soviet Union signed formal guarantees as to the observance of the agreements. However, they reserved the right to go on supplying arms respectively to the Mujaheddin guerrillas and the Afghan army, so an immediate end to the civil war could not be anticipated. The first Russian troops duly began withdrawing in May 1988.

As laid down in the Geneva accord, half the Soviet troops in Afghanistan had left by mid-August 1988. But Soviet attempts to establish a government which would endure in Afghanistan after their departure made little progress, as they found it was easier to persuade their allies of the need for compromise than the rebels. In August Mr. Shevardnadze, the Soviet Foreign Minister, visited Afghanistan, and in October Mr. Yuli Vorontsov, deputy foreign minister, was sent as ambassador to Kabul. At a plenary meeting of the central committee of the ruling People's Democratic Party in October, a purge took place of party members who opposed the policy of making peace with the rebels. Dr Najibullah announced that reconciliation with the Mujaheddin was his main aim.

The Call for a Ceasefire.

In December Mr. Gorbachev called for a ceasefire, an end to all arms supplies, an international conference to guarantee the neutrality and demilitarisation of Afghanistan and the dispatch of a UN force to Kabul. Mr. Vorontsov took the unprecedented step of holding talks in Saudi Arabia with representatives of the Mujaheddin, and with Iranian-backed rebels in Tehran. He also met the ex-King of Afghanistan, Zahir Shah, in Rome. Mr. Shevardnadze, too, had talks with rebel leaders in Islamabad in an unsuccessful attempt to persuade them to allow the People's Democratic Party to participate in a new government of national unity.

The withdrawal of Soviet troops was completed on schedule on 15 February 1989. The last soldier to cross the "Friendship Bridge" between Afghanistan and the USSR was the Soviet commander, Lt.-Gen. Boris Gromov. Official figures for Soviet casualties during the nine-year intervention in Afghanistan were 15,000 killed and 37,000 wounded. Shortly after the final Soviet departures, President Najibullah declared a state of emergency, dismissed a quarter of his cabinet and created a supreme military council to direct the country's affairs.

As rebel forces closed in on Kabul, however, their political leaders were having great difficulty reaching agreement on the establishment of a rival government-in-exile. A council or *shura* of more than four hundred Mujaheddin leaders convened in Islamabad in February 1989. Arguments took place from the outset between fundamentalists and moderates, with the composition of the *shura* itself becoming a contentious issue. Finally, at the end of February, an election was held, and the *shura*, by one vote, chose a moderate, Professor Mujadidi, as president of the government-in-exile. In second place was a fundamentalist, Professor Sayyaf, and he was named a prime minister. However, until the Mujaheddin guerillas actually controlled a major city in Afghanistan, which could form a base for the new government, it was unlikely to gain international recognition.

The opposition's real power lay with rebel commanders on the ground in Afghanistan rather than with exile politicians whose authority could be only nominal. The fate of a government no longer underpinned by the Soviet military presence depended on how far these guerrilla commanders could act in unity. This was soon to be put to the test. On 18 February 1989 President Najibullah declared a state of emergency. Two days later Prime Minister Mohammed Hassan Sharq resigned, a supreme military council taking the majority of government functions with Soltan Ali Keshtmand as chairman of the council of ministers executive committee.

The Jalalabad Offensive.

With Soviet troops gone, on 6 March rebel forces launched an offensive on the strategically important eastern city of Jalalabad, 180 miles from the capital Kabul. Both Pakistan and the United States denied allegations that they had encouraged this attack. By 24 March the battle had become a stalemate, with the rebels held 1½ miles outside the city, largely as a result of superior government airpower. The crisis did, however, encourage the Soviet Union to resume arms shipments to the Afghan government. On 28 March—and again in May—President Najibullah offered guerrilla commanders local autonomy in their own areas if they stopped fighting. He was, presumably, staking his regime's survival

on divisions within the forces opposing him. By early July government forces were on the offensive at Jalalabad and broke the siege. In the same month 30 Afghan Islamic fundamentalist rebel leaders were reported killed by rival guerrillas. By August—with the unifying factor of Soviet occupation removed—rebel forces appeared to be splintering into rival ethnic and social groupings. An estimated 70–80 died in inter-guerrilla fighting in the south and 300 in the north of the country. Nevertheless, the rebels deployed their forces effectively enough to threaten the eastern city of Khosi at the end of August. The US government—having itself increased arms supplies to anti government forces in the summer—alleged that Soviet military advisers remained in Afghanistan and were operating SCUD surface to surface missiles. But by early 1990 improved US-Soviet relations made it plain to both powers that co-operation between the two was essential if Afghanistan was to find stability.

Unsuccessful Coup Attempt, 1990.

Peace overtures to the Mujaheddin guerrillas by President Najibullah opened divisions within the ruling People's Democratic Party which led in March 1990 to an unsuccessful coup attempt by defence minister General Shah Nawaz Tanai, who fled to Pakistan. The attempt, in which Kabul was bombed and there were heavy casualties, appeared to have weakened President Najibullah's position.

BANGLADESH.

After the release of Sheikh Mujibur Rahman in 1972, plans were announced to make Bangladesh a parliamentary democracy and to carry out large-scale nationalisation. In March 1973 the Awami League won all but 7 seats in the general elections. However, rising food prices, corruption among leading members of the Awami League and national disasters created widespread unrest. In 1975 a state of emergency was declared, fundamental civil rights were suspended and the parliamentary government was replaced by a presidential one party system under President Mujib. A series of radical reforms ensued causing resentment and opposition particularly from the army and in August 1975 the President and his family were killed in a military coup. After further coups power passed to the hands of President Sayem and the chiefs of the armed services. Although steps were taken to restore normal conditions to Bangladesh and the ban on political parties was lifted in August 1976, the general elections planned for 1977 were later postponed indefinitely. In April 1977 President Sayem designated Major-General Zia ur-Rahman, the Chief Martial Law Administrator, as his successor and himself resigned. The latter released political prisoners and announced general elections for December 1978. Islam was officially made a basic principle of the state. On 30 May President Zia ur-Rahman's position was confirmed by referendum. An attempted coup in October 1977 led to the banning of several political parties and the founding of a new government-sponsored National Democratic Party. In presidential elections held in June 1978 General Zia ur-Rahman was overwhelmingly successful, reaping the benefits of his achievements in restoring order, eliminating corruption and safeguarding food supplies. He formed a new cabinet with representatives of the parties which had supported him.

The 1979 Elections.

In late 1978 the removal of most restrictions on political parties was followed by an announcement by the President that all "undemocratic provisions" of the 1975 constitutional amendment establishing presidential government had been repealed. The new Parliament was to be a sovereign body; a Prime Minister was to be appointed who commanded its confidence; and there was to be no Presidential power to veto legislation. When elections were finally held in February 1979 the Bangladesh Nationalist Party, uniting the supporters of President Zia, won a massive victory, mainly because the opposition parties were divided among themselves. President Zia then lifted martial law.

Assassination of President Zia, 1981.

President Zia was assassinated at Chittagong on 30 May 1981 during a military insurrection allegedly led by Major-General Manzur who was himself killed as the coup collapsed on 1 June. Vice-President Abdus Sattar took over as President. However, in March 1982 the army chief, Lt.-Gen. Hossain Mohammed Ershad seized power in a bloodless coup. He said that the army had taken over to save the country from social, economic and political bankruptcy. Lt.-Gen. Ershad consolidated his position during the remainder of 1982.

At the beginning of November 1983 a general strike and protest marches took place in defiance of martial law. Shortly before the arrival of Queen Elizabeth II on a state visit to Bangladesh on 14 November, Lt-Gen. Ershad announced that presidential elections would be held in May 1984 and parliamentary elections in November; free political activity would be permitted immediately. However, the two opposition alliances demanded that the parliamentary elections should be held first. When violence broke out, Lt-Gen. Ershad reimposed the ban on political activity on 28 November.

Ershad as President.

In December he announced that he was assuming the presidency. The elections were again postponed for the duration of 1984 and set instead for April 1985. The opposition alliances feared that the elections would be rigged in favour of General Ershad's Jatiya Party, and called for the lifting of martial law and the formation of a caretaker government before they took place. In December 1984 they launched a full-scale civil disobedience campaign to back these demands.

General Ershad responded by reimposing martial law early in March 1985 and cancelling the planned elections. Instead in late March a referendum was held which was claimed to have given General Ershad's rule an overwhelming vote of confidence. Rural sub-district elections went ahead in May despite a boycott organised by the main opposition parties. The universities, which had been shut down in March, were allowed to re-open in July, and in October the ban on political activity was partially lifted. Political parties were permitted to re-open their offices, but street demonstrations remained illegal.

The long-awaited parliamentary elections were held in May 1986, amid widespread violence and accusations of vote-rigging. The outcome was a comfortable majority for the pro-government Jatiya Party, whilst the leader of the opposition Awami League, Sheikh Hasina Wajed, denounced the elections as a fraud.

In July 1986 Mr. Mizanur Rahman Chowdhury was appointed prime minister at the head of a civilian cabinet. The Awami League, which had won 76 seats, boycotted the opening session of parliament in protest at the continuation of martial law.

Presidential Election Results 1986.

In the second stage of General Ershad's plan to restore Bangladesh to democracy, presidential elections were held in October 1986. General Ershad had resigned as army chief of staff in August and accepted nomination as the Jatiya Party candidate. The Bangladesh National Party, at the head of a seven-party alliance, boycotted the presidential elections as it had the parliamentary ones. In the presidential poll General Ershad was declared to have been elected with 83·6% of the votes cast and he was sworn in for a five-year term.

In November 1986 a bill indemnifying all actions of the martial law administration passed through parliament with a two-thirds majority and martial law was then lifted. At the end of November President Ershad appointed an expanded civilian cabinet in an effort to boost public support for the new government.

Continuing Unrest.

However, President Ershad also sought to strengthen military influence in politics by giving the army a formal role in local government. In July 1987 parliament adopted a controversial bill allowing the army to be represented on the country's district councils. This provoked strikes and violent demonstrations. In August President Ershad called for further discussion on the bill and the unrest subsided amid torrential rains and the worst floods for forty years.

There were widespread anti-government protests in Dhaka in November. Some 2,000 activists were arrested and a nationwide state of emergency was declared. Parliament was dissolved, but when elections were held in March 1988 the opposition parties organised an effective boycott. The state of emergency imposed in November 1987 was lifted in April 1988.

Natural Disasters.

In August 1988 devastating floods caused by torrential monsoon rains destroyed or damaged over eight million homes and ten thousand miles of roads. In September President Ershad said that 53 of Bangladesh's 64 districts were flooded. Then in November a cyclone, the worst for twenty years, accompanied by tidal waves, left at least 2,000 dead and a further 200,000 homeless.

In February 1989 President Ershad returned from a visit to Britain with a promised £15 million in aid to be confronted by a wave of natural disasters. In April a tornado and heavy rains in central Bangladesh caused 1,000 deaths and destroyed over 20 villages. There was a cholera epidemic in May and in the same month a drought which, apart from the April storm, had lasted since February threatened to halve the summer harvest. In August Bangladesh suffered two weeks of torrential rain, with 100,000 forced from their homes and at least 150 deaths.

On 25 June Islamic fundamentalist demonstrators attacked a Canadian owned shoe company in Tongi protesting that the sole pattern on sandals resembled the Arabic characters for Allah. Rioting spread to two other cities. On the same day tribal council elections were held in the Chittagong hills region, despite threats of disruption by local separatist guerrillas. In August Vice President Nurul Islam was dismissed on the grounds of incompetence, to be replaced by prime minister Moudud Ahmed. Kazi Zafar Ahmed became prime minister.

THE FAR EAST

CHINA.

On 1 October 1949, after the Communists had gained complete control of the Chinese mainland and the Nationalist forces of Chiang Kai-shek had retreated to Taiwan, the Chinese People's Republic was proclaimed under Chairman Mao Tse-tung. It claims sovereignty over one fifth of mankind, with a population of over 1,100 million (1990 est.).

China after Mao.

On 9 September 1976 after leading China since 1949, Chairman Mao died at the age of 82. He was succeeded by Hua Guofeng, who before he replaced Chou En-lai had been a security minister for one year and had previously only been known as an agricultural specialist in the southern province of Hunan. In the months after Mao's death, a vicious poster campaign was mounted against Jiang Qing (Mao's widow) and three others, Wang Hongwen, Zhang Chungqiao and Yao Wenyuan—known as the "gang of four". All four were arrested and the allegations against them included their planning to persuade the armed militia to take over the army and causing unrest by their backing of the Shanghai radicals.

Hua's colleagues were close associates of Chou En-lai and he appeared to have the support of the army. During 1977 Deng Xiaoping, who had been dismissed from his government and party posts in April 1976, was fully rehabilitated. Meanwhile, after a series of national conferences of practically all branches of the economy, new guidelines for a more pragmatic economic policy were worked out on the lines of Chou En-lai's basic programmes as previously pursued by Deng Xiaoping.

China's Change of Course.

China's change of course internally and externally was confirmed in 1978. While the Russians were still regarded as the main enemy, partly from a historically-based nationalist hostility, reconciliation was pursued with the West. This culminated in the establishment of diplomatic relations with the USA in December. China was clearly opening up to the world in search of the benefits of modernisation and looking especially to collaboration with Western Europe. At the same time internal liberalisation brought a new emphasis on democracy and equality before the law. Henceforth the courts were to decide without interference from the Party and the State, while the people's communes in the country, the managers of industrial plants, workers and peasants were to be freed from central tutelage. All this was intended to release new energies for the new modernisation programme masterminded by Deng Xiaoping, which aims to turn China from a developing country into a leading industrial nation by the end of the century. But it was not clear how the new developments were to be kept in line with the dictatorship of the proletariat and a communist-planned economy. Demonstrations for more freedom and civil rights seemed to provide a foretaste of future problems at the beginning of 1979, and later there were riots by young people in Shanghai. The result was an abrupt end to the freedom of expression at the Wall of Democracy in Beijing, which had been tolerated only so long as it did not question the system itself. This was accompanied by a dampening of the initial euphoria of economic reform and industrialisation plans. China appeared to have suffered economically more than had been assumed from the periods of chaos under Mao. The latter's teaching was no longer treated as sacred, and on the 30th anniversary of the foundation of the People's Republic the Cultural Revolution was denounced as a dreadful disaster.

Meanwhile, the limits of Chinese foreign policy were also becoming evident. The punitive expedition launched against Vietnam in early 1979 did not succeed in removing Vietnamese pressure from Cambodia. The propaganda attacks on the Soviet Union were reduced and the first serious talks on détente took place. But these did not get very far, and China's links with the West remained more important, as was shown by the visits of Deng Xiaoping to the USA and Hua Guofeng to Western Europe in the autumn. The Soviet invasion of Afghanistan at the end of 1979 brought increased co-operation between China and the United States.

The Trial of the "Gang of Four".

China's change of course and Deng Xiaoping's rise culminated in 1980 with two events. The first of these was the Fifth Plenary Session of the Communist Party Central Committee in February. Some of Deng's leading opponents were removed while his supporters were promoted. The rehabilitation of Liu Shaoqi, the most prominent victim of the Cultural Revolution, was a further denunciation of that phenomenon.

The show trial of Jiang Qing and the other members of the "gang of four" led to the passing of a suspended death sentence on Mao's widow in January 1981. This was commuted to life imprisonment in January 1983. Although the official Chinese press said that this should not be taken as implicit condemnation of her late husband, in June 1981 Hu Yaobang succeeded Hua Guofeng as Communist Party Chairman marking a further shift away from Mao's policies.

In external affairs, China's relations with America and the West grew firmer, as did they also with Japan.

New Party and State Constitutions, 1982.

In September 1982 a new constitution for the Communist Party was approved. This abolished the posts of Chairman and Vice-Chairman in a move to transfer power back to the party bureaucracy. Hu Yaobang had held the post of general-secretary, as well as that of Chairman, so retained his leading position, and it remained to be seen how far a more collective form of leadership would emerge. In December 1982 a new constitution for China as a whole was approved by the National People's Congress, which included increased powers for the Prime Minister, Zhao Ziyang.

Deng Xiaoping's Policies.

In June 1983 the National People's Congress met and elected the veteran politician Li Xiannian to the newly-revived post of President, with General Ulanhu as Vice-President. Deng Xiaoping was chosen as chairman of the new State Military Commission. He already headed the Communist Party's committee in charge of military affairs and therefore had both party and state control of the army in his own hands to ensure that expenditure on national defence would be kept in check.

China's Modernisation Drive.

Deng Xiaoping's national drive towards modernisation continued during 1984, despite opposition from some die-hard Maoists. In the countryside the emphasis on the collective was reversed, with the relaxation of production quotas and central price controls leading to a considerable rise in agricultural production. In industry, factories were allowed to keep their own profits and managers to exercise greater responsibility. The armed forces were also urged to support modernisation, including the opening of more ports to foreign business and investment. In May 1984 Prime Minister Zhao Ziyang undertook a six-country tour of western Europe intended to secure additional sources for new technology.

Slowing down of Reform.

The modernisation programme and reforms in the Communist Party continued in 1985. The 'rectification campaign' against corrupt officials, launched in 1983, proceeded, and it was announced in November that party members in the countryside were to have their credentials re-examined in order to root out any remaining Maoist tendencies. Younger men were introduced into the upper echelons of the party; for example, at a meeting of the Communist Party Central Committee in September 1985 ten members of the politburo were retired.

There was, however, a greater degree of caution about Deng Xiaoping's modernisation policies. In July 1985 the leadership launched a campaign to reassert party control and the number of cities open to foreign investment was greatly reduced. The five-year plan published in September announced that, although the reduction in state control of production would continue, the pace of reform would be slowed down to curb the consumer boom. It promised a better standard of living, but higher rents and fuel and shopping bills.

Fall of Hu Yaobang.

In 1986 the Chinese leadership launched a new propaganda campaign on the need for changes in the country's political structure, including the possibility of greater "democracy". However, matters soon got out of hand, as expectations were aroused beyond anything envisaged by the leadership. In December 1986 students demanding greater freedom and democracy took to the streets in Shanghai and Beijing. Government attempts to ban such demonstrations were ignored by the students, who burned copies of the *Peking Daily* in protest at the increasingly hostile official coverage of their activities.

The student demonstrations provoked a conservative backlash, which had immediate repercussions on the struggle over the succession to Deng Xiaoping prior to the key party congress in October 1987. On 16 January 1987 the party general-secretary, Hu Yaobang, was forced to resign. The speed of Mr. Hu's downfall suggested that Deng Xiaoping had come under heavy pressure to sacrifice his protégé from conservatives who were prepared to support his economic reforms only if there was firm control of political ideology.

Hu Yaobang was succeeded by premier Zhao Ziyang. The purge continued in February 1987 when the propaganda chief, Zhu Houze, a close associate of Mr. Hu, lost his job. In March Mr. Zhao said in his opening speech to the National People's Congress that economic reform would continue in China, but that the spread of bourgeois liberalisation had been checked. Mr Zhao was now seen as a possible successor to Deng Xiaoping.

Agreement on Macao.

In March 1987 representatives of China and Portugal met in Beijing to initial a document relating to the return of Macao, the last remnant of the Portuguese colonial empire. In an agreement along the same lines as that relating to Hong Kong, the Portuguese undertook to leave Macao, a colony since 1557, on 20 December 1999. This was an important step for the Chinese towards the reunification of their country. Taiwan remained as the main target for peaceful reintegration before the year 2000.

The Old Guard Retires.

The 13th Party Congress was held in Beijing in October 1987. At its conclusion eight senior politicians followed Deng Xiaoping's lead in stepping down from the Politburo. This marked the victory of Mr. Deng in his long struggle to rejuvenate the party's aged leadership and ensure the continuation of economic reform. The new 17-member Politburo was composed overwhelmingly of youngish technocrats. The average age of the new 5-member Standing Committee was sixty-three.

Zhao Ziyang was confirmed as general secretary. He resigned as premier and was succeeded by Li Peng, a cautious reformer. In March 1988 Mr. Zhao made a speech to the party Central Committee in which he said that greater speed was now needed in transforming China's social and economic system.

By the summer of 1988, however, economic deregulation and the ending of price controls were causing problems. In the six months following the lifting of price controls, some prices rose by sixty per cent, and inflation reached a record twenty per cent. There was increased industrial unrest, panic buying and runs on banks. As a result the brakes were applied at a conference of the party's central committee in September 1988. Its decision to freeze price reforms for two years was a victory for Li Peng and the conservatives over Zhao Ziyang. By the spring of 1989 Zhao Ziyang's future, as well as that of his economic reform policy, looked uncertain.

Deng Xiaoping continued his policy of developing contacts with the wider world in 1988 and 1989. Relations with the Soviet Union improved, and talks were held in preparation for the first Sino-Soviet summit for thirty years. In November 1988 China signed a border treaty with the Soviet satellite state of Mongolia, and in December Mr. Gandhi visited Peking for the first Sino-Indian summit since the 1962 border war.

The 1989 Student Rising.

In the spring of 1989 the Communist government faced a serious challenge to its authority, triggered by the death on 15 April of Hu Yaobang, the disgraced former party general-secretary. Beijing University students demanding his rehabilitation staged a sit-in outside the Great Hall of the People. On the day of his funeral, 22 April, there were demonstrations in a dozen major cities. Deng Xiaoping warned of possible bloodshed. But on 27 April a march by 100,000 students in Beijing calling for democracy and attacking party corruption passed off peacefully. On 4 May 300,000 demonstrators filled Tiananmen Square, signifying growing popular support. Students began a hunger strike in the square on 13 May, demanding political reforms of the kind being enacted in the Soviet Union, their presence disrupting a visit by Mr Gorbachev on 15 May.

The hunger strikers called for a televised dialogue with the government as, on 17 May, a million people marched in Beijing, others demonstrated in 20 cities, and workers announced they would strike in support of the students. Divisions opened in the party hierarchy, with Zhao Ziyang apparently favouring dialogue while the Prime Minister, Li Peng, announced that martial law would come into force on 20 May. The people of Beijing massed in the square to prevent the troops entering.

Massacre in Tiananmen Square.

As the students in the square perceptibly tired hardliners within the party prevailed. On 4 June thousands of troops and scores of tanks moved in, staging a bloody massacre in which 2,500 were

initially reported killed. With the world watching the carnage on television, China appeared on the brink of chaos. Sporadic clashes continued in Beijing and in cities throughout China over the next two days. There were reports that the 38th Army, which had refused to enforce the martial law decree, was facing the 27th Army and a clash seemed possible.

But on 8 June Li Peng appeared on television and praised the troops who had put down the protesters. The following day the party leadership, minus Zhao Ziyang, presented a united front on television. The official government media called on citizens to inform on "counter-revolutionary" dissidents. Arrests of activists now began alongside a government propaganda campaign to minimise the extent of casualties in the Tiananmen Square massacre. By 21 June 1,500 activists had been arrested, including Guo Haifong, a prominent student leader. All independent student and workers organisations were ordered to disband. As the arrests continued protesters received heavy punishment and nine were executed publicly in Shanghai.

Purge of Student Sympathisers.

The party now began a purge of what it saw as its own unreliable elements. Several leading officials were ousted at a Central Committee meeting on 24 June, including Zhao Ziyang, who was dismissed for "counter-revolutionary rebellion" and replaced by Jiang Zemin. Many lower level party members were expelled for having supported the democracy movement. In a keynote speech on 28 June Deng Xiaoping denounced the protesters, praised the army, and warned of "evil influences from the West".

By July unofficial reports claimed 10,000 had been arrested and the government itself admitted 2,500. Through the summer arrests, prison sentences and executions continued. The party did, however, acknowledge the legitimacy of some of the protesters' complaints. The party Politburo announced a programme to combat government and party corruption on 28 July. On 6 September Li Peng pointed to inflation, party corruption and inequalities in wealth as justifiable grievances, though he rejected the wider demands raised in the summer demonstrations.

The 40th anniversary of Communist rule was celebrated in Tiananmen Square on 1 October with parades behind a heavy security cordon.

Background of Economic Discontent.

Although the dramatic events of the summer had passed and resistance crushed, the government faced economic problems that might provoke a renewal of discontent and unrest. An austerity programme introduced in September 1988 to combat inflation of over 30% had resulted in falling living standards and rising unemployment. Articles in the party and army press implied that troops would be used again if the party felt itself to be in danger. With unconfirmed reports that 1,500 officers and soldiers faced courts martial for mutiny in the protests, the party conducted a campaign of ideological indoctrination to guarantee the army's loyalty.

Rise of Jiang Zemin.

At the meeting of China's parliament, the National People's Congress, in March 1990, there was an easing of the austerity programme. Deng Xiaoping resigned on 22 March as chairman of the State Military Commission, handing its leadership to Jiang Zemin. Although the party leadership appeared to be attempting to distance itself from the Tiananmen Square massacre, Li Peng declared on 20 March that "socialist China will stand firm as a rock" and dissent would be punished. The party was determined that China would not follow the path of the Soviet Union and Eastern Europe.

HONG KONG.

Historical Background.

Hong Kong was first occupied by the British as a trading post in January 1841 and China's cession of the island to Britain was confirmed by the Treaty of Nanking in 1842. South Kowloon and Stonecutters Island were ceded by China in the Treaty of Peking in 1860, and in 1898 the New Territories, which consist of the area north of Kowloon and other islands around Hong Kong, were leased to Britain for 99 years. Hong Kong was occupied by the Japanese from 1941 to 1945. The approaching expiry of the lease on the New Territories led to the initiation of diplomatic discussions between Britain and China on the future of Hong Kong in 1979 with a visit by Sir Murray MacLehose, governor of Hong Kong, to Beijing. Mrs. Thatcher herself visited Beijing in 1982. Britain had initially taken the line that the 19th century "unequal treaties", as the Chinese termed them, were not invalid, but it was forced to concede that sovereignty over Hong Kong would have to be surrendered.

The 1984 Agreement.

A new phase in the negotiations began in July 1983 and by December Britain had also given up its proposal for retaining an administrative role in Hong Kong after 1997. Deng Xiaoping insisted that an agreement should be reached by September 1984, and on 26 September the Sino-British declaration on the future of Hong Kong was initialled in Beijing. China will resume the exercise of sovereignty from 1 July 1997. Except in foreign and defence affairs, however, the Hong Kong Special Administrative Region will have a considerable degree of autonomy, and for at least fifty years the social and economic system and "life-style" of Hong Kong will remain unchanged.

In 1985 the British colonial administration began to give way to a form of representative government. In September indirect elections were held for 24 seats to represent professionals, local councils and special interest groups on the new 56-seat Legislative Council. The remaining seats were filled by government officials and appointees. The first session of the Council was held at the end of October.

The Chinese National People's Congress formally approved the 1984 agreement on the future of Hong Kong in April 1985, but the Chinese government was unhappy about the introduction of democracy into the colony. China stressed that in 1997 sovereignty passes to her and not to the people of Hong Kong, whose form of government would finally be decided by Beijing. In December 1985 a senior Chinese official, Mr Ji Pengfei, visited Hong Kong but pointedly did not formally meet the Legislative Council.

In October 1986 Queen Elizabeth II paid a successful visit to Hong Kong after her tour of China. Following the death of the governor, Sir Edward Youde, Sir David Wilson was appointed to be his successor in January 1987.

China's Attitude to Democratisation.

In January 1987 the important step was taken of promoting a group of Hong Kong citizens to senior civil service posts to emphasise the role of the local population in the last phase of British rule. At the same time the government was working on a Green Paper discussing the options for representative government. In March 1987 an independent body was established to sound out public opinion in Hong Kong on political reform.

Hong Kong had continued to enjoy an economic boom in 1986, but uncertainty about the future was evident in the increasing number of citizens emigrating (some 10,000 to Canada during the year) or applying for second passports. Anxiety increased after Hu Yaobang was brought down by conservative forces in China in January 1987. Although the Chinese government assured Hong Kong that nothing had changed, a more decidedly frosty reception was expected for the Green Paper's proposals on democratisation.

A Green Paper on representative institutions was published by the government of Hong Kong in May 1987. It emphasised that there were now divided opinions over the desirability of direct elections in the immediate future. After consultations the White Paper published in February 1988 ruled out direct elections, albeit for only 10 of the 56 seats on the Legislative Council, until 1991.

Voting again took place in September 1988 for the 24 seats on the Legislative Council representing professionals, local councils and special interest groups. Some 61,000 of the 98,000 eligible registered to vote, but there was no contest in many constituencies, and only 17,000 voters actually had a choice of candidates.

The Basic Law.

Prospects for the development of truly democratic government in Hong Kong did not look particularly encouraging following a meeting in January 1989 of representatives drafting the Basic Law relating to the territory's administration after 1997. The draft was generally conservative. It proposed that the chief executive of the Hong Kong Special Administrative Region should be chosen by an electoral college for the first three five-year terms of office. Only after fifteen years would a referendum be held to decide whether the chief executive should be elected by universal suffrage.

The convulsions in China, led by mass student protests, once again cast major doubts on future stability in Hong Kong itself.

Repercussions of Tiananmen Square.

The 1989 upheavals in China had immediate repercussions in Hong Kong, which faced absorption by its Communist neighbour in 1997. Hong Kong stock market prices fell by 22% on 5 June as troops moved against protesters in Beijing. There were two days of protests by hundreds of thousands of demonstrators and a general strike on 7 June.

Refusal of Passport Rights.

On 5 June Mrs Thatcher said events in Beijing could not alter Britain's obligation to cede Hong Kong. She refused to guarantee refuge to the 3·25 million of Hong Kong's 5·7 million citizens who had a right to British passports. On 2 July the Foreign Secretary, Sir Geoffrey Howe, faced angry crowds in the colony as he repeated that Britain could accommodate only a few who had been "of service" to the UK. His successor, John Major, reiterated Britain's position on 27 September. The intention was to persuade individuals essential to Hong Kong's stability to remain at least till 1997.

Recent Events.

Early in 1990 Britain promised legislation to allow entry to 50,000 selected citizens and their families after 1997 should China threaten their liberties. Britain also promised a bill of rights and a Basic Law to establish democratic government. But as negotiations with China on the Basic Law continued, 1,000 people a day were leaving Hong Kong by February 1990. China refused to accept proposals that Hong Kong's 60 strong legislative council should have half its members directly elected by universal suffrage by 1997 and be fully elected by 2003, insisting initially on 18 and agreeing in March to 20. The attempt to draft a bill of rights appeared stalemated by the difficulty of reconciling local demands for legally guaranteed human rights after 1997 with China's suspicion of any such legislation.

JAPAN.

The June 1980 Election.

On 16 May 1980, the first successful no confidence motion since 1953 was carried against the government. The general election was scheduled for 22 June, but Mr. Ohira died on 12 June and the campaign was seriously affected. However, the LDP was able to regain its majority in both Houses, winning 284 of the 511 seats in the Lower House.

Mr. Ohira's successor was Mr. Zenko Suzuki, who formed a government on 17 July. Mr. Suzuki's government included representatives of all the rival factions in the LDP, and it was hoped that they would unite in a programme of consensus and compromise. Although one of the major aims was to establish closer trading links with China, many of the contracts agreed in 1978 were suspended following the change in emphasis in Chinese economic policy away from steel and other heavy industrial production.

Mr. Suzuki Steps Down.

Despite the hopes for unity, growing discord in the LDP over economic policies led Mr. Suzuki to announce on 12 October 1982 that he would not seek re-election when his two-year term of office ended. On 24 November Mr. Yasuhiro Nakasone was elected President of the LDP and confirmed as Prime Minister by the Upper and Lower Houses two days later. Mr. Nakasone announced that his government would give priority to improving trade and security relations with the United States, but a visit to America by the Prime Minister in January 1983 showed that the two countries were still some way from an agreement on American exports to Japan.

The December 1983 Election.

On 12 October 1983 the former Prime Minister, Mr. Tanaka, was sentenced to four years in prison for taking bribes to help the sales of the Lockheed Aircraft Corporation. He was released on bail and refused to resign his parliamentary seat. The issue of political morality therefore dominated the general election called by Mr. Nakasone for 18 December 1983. The LDP failed to gain an overall majority, winning only 250 seats, and now had to rely on the votes of one of the independent parties. Mr. Tanaka regained his seat with an increased majority and his faction comprised about a quarter of the LDP's parliamentary strength. Although Mr. Tanaka had proved an electoral handicap to the LDP, Mr. Nakasone was therefore dependent on his support.

Mr. Nakasone's Election Triumph 1986.

In June 1986 Mr. Nakasone called an election for the House of Representatives to coincide with the partial elections due for the House of Councillors. The Lower House's four-year term was not due to expire until December 1987, but Nr. Nakasone was gambling on restoring the ground lost in the 1983 election. He also hoped to boost his chances of getting the LDP to change its rules so that he could stand for a third term as party leader when his current one expired in October 1987.

Voting took place on 6 July 1986. Mr. Nakasone and the LDP won a landslide victory in the elections, in which 71·4% of the nation's 87 million registered voters participated. The LDP increased its seats in the Lower House from 250 to 304, with the Socialist Party winning 85 and Komeito 56. In the Upper House LDP representation increased from 131 to 143 seats. Mr. Nakasone no longer needed to rely on the votes of the New Liberal Club to stay in office.

Mr. Nakasone's Problems.

However, after this great success Mr. Nakasone ran into difficulties over his plans to bring in a 5% sales tax and a 20% tax on interest from small savings. There was widespread hostility to these measures, including from within the LDP, and a number of popular demonstrations took place. The opposition, in a rare show of unity, boycotted the Diet at the beginning of February 1987, halting the progress of the proposals, which formed part of the budget.

In March 1987 the degree of government unpopularity was shown by the overwhelming victory in a by-election in the constituency of Iwate-ken for the Japan Socialist Party, which had not won the seat since 1962. Mr. Nakasone also came under pressure from demands by the United States, and also Britain, in March 1987 for the opening of Japan's domestic market to greater foreign competition. However, Mr. Nakasone could not politically afford to do other than resist such international pressure, in order to show the electorate and his party that he remained a strong leader.

In April 1987 results in local elections, widely seen as a form of referendum on Mr. Nakasone's leadership and his controversial tax proposals, preserved the status quo in all thirteen governorships. However, Mr. Nakasone's personal popularity rating had sunk to around 25% from a high of more than 50% only six months previously.

Japan under Takeshita.

In October 1987 Mr. Noburo Takeshita was chosen to succeed Mr. Nakasone. He was, in fact, nominated by Mr. Nakasone when the rival claimants could not reach agreement. Mr. Takeshita, who headed the largest grouping of Liberal Democractic Party MPs in the Diet, succeeded as President of the party and Prime Minister in November.

The Death of Emperor Hirohito.

In September 1988 Emperor Hirohito, aged 87, fell critically ill. His eldest son, Crown Prince Akihito, who was born in 1933, formally assumed all his father's duties. Emperor Hirohito died of duodenal cancer on 7 January 1989, the world's longest reigning monarch, having spent five years as regent and sixty-two as emperor. He had been worshipped as a god until 1 January 1946, on which date he renounced his divinity as part of the democratic reforms imposed on Japan by the Americans after the Second World War. The extent of Hirohito's involvement in and responsibility for Japan's policies leading up to and during the war in the Far East were much debated after his death.

The Recruit Cosmos Scandal.

In December 1988 Prime Minister Takeshita succeeded in securing the passage of some sweeping tax reforms, and then in his first reshuffle since taking office, he brought fifteen new faces into his cabinet. One motive for the changes was that the old cabinet was tainted by the scandal involving the information and property company, Recruit Cosmos, which had been shown to have offered cheap shares to members of parliament and civil servants. Those who lost their jobs included the Finance Minister, Mr. Kiichi Miyazawa.

However, within days of the reshuffle, the newly-appointed Minister of Justice, Mr. Takashi Hasegawa, had to resign after admitting that he had accepted monthly political contributions from Recruit Cosmos since 1976. And in January 1989, Mr. Harada, the minister responsible for the country's Economic Planning Agency, resigned after he too was shown to have been involved. In February the Tokyo public prosecutors arrested the founder and former chairman of Recruit Cosmos, Mr. Hiromasa Ezoe, on bribery charges. Pressure increased on Mr. Takeshita, who was himself implicated in the scandal, to resign. The crisis reached a climax when, on 25 April, Takeshita announced he was to resign. He was eventually succeeded by the Foreign Secretary, Sosuke Uno.

The Resignation of Uno.

After two days in office Mr Uno was faced with revelations of his extramarital affairs with geishas since the 1960s. The political impact was immediate. On 25 June the Socialist Party overwhelmingly defeated an LDP candidate in a by-election. In the Tokyo municipal elections a week later LDP representation fell from 63 to 43 seats while the Socialists, using a "madonna strategy" to win female votes, increased their seats from 12 to 36. On 23 July the LDP lost its majority in elections for the 252 seat Diet upper house for the first time since 1955. Although the Recruit Cosmos and sex scandals had played a part in the result, the LDP was also weakened by the introduction of a 3% sales tax and rural discontent at increasing agricultural imports. The Socialists, under the leadership of Takako Doi, the first woman to lead a major Japanese party, had significantly moderated their position. Mr Uno, nevertheless, accepted the defeat as his personal responsibility and resigned after 69 days in office.

The Advent of Toshiki Kaifu.

Toshiki Kaifu became prime minister on 9 August. Inexperienced in economic and foreign affairs, he was seen as a caretaker figurehead behind whom LDP faction leaders would wield real authority. The growing female role in politics was acknowledged by his appointment of two women cabinet members. On 1 October the LDP was successful at a by-election for an upper house seat, taking 51% of the vote, the Socialists winning 43%. It was clear, however, that LDP political dominance had ended and that a two-party system had re-emerged in Japan, with the Socialists as a national opposition.

The February 1990 Elections.

But at the general election on 18 February 1990 the Socialists failed to capitalise on a year of scandals. 73·27% of the 90 million eligible voters turned out. The LDP, with over 25 million votes, took almost 50% of the popular vote, while the Socialists gained a little under 25%. The Socialists had expanded at the expense of rival opposition parties rather than taking votes from the LDP. The LDP returned with 275 MPs but support from 15 of the 21 independents elected put their new parliamentary strength at 290, only five short of the pre-election position. The Socialists won 136 seats. Although Mr Kaifu's personal position in the LDP now seemed secure he faced an opposition majority in the Upper House.

KOREA.

Political Repression.

The 1970s saw increasing political repression in South Korea. After President Park had narrowly defeated an Opposition rival in the 1971 elections, the authoritarian Yushin Constitution was introduced. This approved a procedure for election of the President by electoral college in place of direct elections and established a system whereby one-third of the seats in the National Assembly were reserved for Government nominees. This new constitution provoked bitter opposition, which in turn gave rise to further repression. Martial law was declared in 1972, and in 1974 an emergency decree was passed banning all dissident movements. The following year the notorious "Emergency Measure No. 9" prohibited public criticism of the constitution and the Government. This followed an assassination attempt on the President, in which his wife was killed, and the discovery of the first of a series of North Korean tunnels under the Demilitarised Zone.

President Carter took office in 1977 committed to a substantial reduction of US forces in Korea. Relations with the United States were further soured by the "Koreagate" scandal, in which it was revealed that South Korean agents had paid substantial sums to American Congressmen in return for political support. However, after a reassessment of the build-up of North Korean military strength the phased withdrawal of US troops was frozen in 1978. When he visited Seoul in the summer of 1979 President Carter publicly criticised the repression practised by President Park's regime but reconfirmed the American commitment to maintain South Korea's integrity.

Although President Park was re-elected for another six-year term by electoral college in 1978, the elections to the National Assembly in December of that year brought severe losses for the pro-Government Democratic Republican Party and corresponding gains for the opposition New Democratic Party and independents. The following spring the newly-elected leader of the New Democrats, Kim Young-sam, began to make public demands for constitutional reform. The Government reacted by procuring a court decision declaring Mr Kim's election as leader of the New Democratic Party invalid, and in early October 1979 he was expelled from the National Assembly on nine charges of damaging the national interest. The result was dramatic. The members of the New Democratic Party resigned en masse from the Assembly and serious rioting broke out in Pusan.

The Assassination of President Park.

It was against this background that President Park Chung-hee was assassinated in late October 1979. It was believed that his murder might have resulted from a dispute between the different security services about responsibility for the breakdown of internal security. But few believed the offical version that the assassin, Kim Jae-kyu, and his five fellow-conspirators had acted on their own initiative. The General Chief of Staff was suspected of being implicated, but this could not be proved, and the military initially remained in the background. Under the new President, Choi Kyu-hah, there was an initial period of liberalisation with the release of political prisoners. In December, however, the military hawks and the

supporters of ex-President Park seemed to gain the upper hand, and the style of government became more authoritarian.

The Imposition of Martial Law.

Then on 17 May 1980, following widespread civil unrest, martial law was extended throughout South Korea, with many political leaders being arrested and all political activity being banned. This led to a popular uprising in the Kwangju district which was violently suppressed by the Army, and on 31 May a Special Committee for National Security Measures was set up. This committee was controlled by the army and it carried out a massive political purge, which included the resignation of President Choi Kyu Hah on 16 August, who was succeeded by the Head of the Army Security Command, General Chun Doo Hwan on 27 August.

The problems in South Korea were intimately bound up with the country's grave economic position, but they were also exacerbated by the heavy-handedness of the military. This was shown not only in their suppression of the Kwangju uprising, but also in the execution of Kim Jae Kyu and the others who assassinated President Park, in secret on 24 May, and also the sentencing to death of the leading dissident Kim Dae Jung on 17 September, which brought the South Korean authorities into conflict with both the Carter Administration and the Japanese government. The sentence was later commuted. President Chun was re-elected for a seven-year term in February 1981 by a popularly-elected electoral college. His Democratic Justice Party gained a majority in the National Assembly after elections in March.

International Disasters.

In 1983 South Korea was involved in two serious international incidents. On 1 September a South Korean Boeing 747 civil airliner on a flight from New York to Seoul was shot down over Soviet airspace by a Russian fighter. The 240 passengers and 29 crew on board were killed. After some delay, the Soviet Union admitted responsibility but claimed that the plane was spying. Then on 9 October 21 people, including 4 Korean cabinet ministers, were killed in a bomb explosion in Rangoon, Burma. It was alleged that North Korean agents had intended to assassinate President Chun but the bomb had exploded prematurely before he arrived at the Martyr's Mausoleum.

The 1985 Elections.

There was an 84% turnout of voters in the elections held in February 1985. President Chun's ruling Democratic Justice Party maintained its position with 148 seats in the National Assembly, but the moderate opposition group, the Democratic Korea Party, gained only 35 seats, compared with 83 in 1981. It was supplanted by the newly-formed, more radical New Korea Democratic Party (NKDP), sponsored by the main opposition leader, Kim Dae Jung, and his Movement for the Restoration of Democracy. Kim Dae Jung returned from exile in the United States five days before the elections, though he was immediately placed under house-arrest. The NKDP won 67 seats, doing particularly well in the cities. The elections improved the international respectability of President Chun's regime abroad, but at home it showed that, despite considerable economic progress, the country was looking for more genuine democracy in its system of government. Nevertheless, in the autumn of 1985 it seemed that President Chun was again cracking down on the opposition, particularly on student dissent.

Background to 1987 Riots.

During 1986 President Chun's regime in South Korea came under sustained pressure from the opposition to change the constitution to allow direct presidential elections. A new opposition alliance, the National Liaison Organisation for Democratisation, was formed in Seoul in March 1986. A student demonstration on the campus of Seoul National University, in support of a campaign to organise a petition with 10 million signatures, was broken up by police using tear-gas on 7 March.

In April President Chun announced his willingness to amend the constitution, probably with an eye to securing domestic harmony before the 1988 Olympics. A new select committee of the National Assembly was established in June 1986 to draft constitutional amendments. It failed to reach agreement, however, and unrest grew. An attempted opposition demonstration in November was prevented by a massive police presence on the streets of Seoul.

Then in an abrupt reversal of policy in April 1987, President Chun announced that there would be no constitutional reform before he stepped down in February 1988. An electoral college of some 5,300 people was to vote on a presidential successor late in 1987. President Chun said that there was not sufficient time for major constitutional reform. The result was extensive rioting in June 1987, so serious that the future stability of the government seemed at stake as well as the 1988 Olympic Games.

The Presidential Elections.

In June 1987 the Chairman of the Democratic Justice Party, Mr Roh Tae Woo, was nominated as the party's presidential candidate. He announced his support for the principle of direct elections for the presidency and President Chun was obliged to accept. South Korea's first direct presidential election for sixteen years therefore took place in December 1987.

The fact that both the main opposition candidates decided to stand split the anti-government vote and Mr. Roh was elected president. On a turnout of 89·2 per cent, the official figures gave Mr. Roh 8·3 million votes, Kim Young Sam 6·3 million, Kim Dae Jung 6·1 million and others 2·3 million. Mr. Roh's gamble had paid off.

The Olympic Games.

Mr. Roh took over as president in February 1988 in succession to Mr Chun who soon afterwards resigned from all public offices amid charges of corruption against his regime. On President Roh's inauguration day there were clashes between police and students accusing him of electoral fraud, but onlookers did not support the protesters as they might have done the previous year.

In February 1988 Kim Young Sam resigned as head of his party so that the rift with Kim Dae Jung would not lead to another victory for President Roh Tae Woo in the forthcoming parliamentary elections. In these, held in April 1988, President Roh's Democratic Justice Party lost its overall majority in the National Assembly.

The Olympic Games took place as planned from 17 September to 2 October 1988. Some 10,000 athletes took part in the games, which were boycotted by only seven countries in support of North Korea's demands to co-host the event. Although the issue of drug-taking by athletes cast a shadow across the Olympic ideal, from an organisational and security point of view the games were a great success for South Korea.

In the aftermath of the games, President Roh declared his willingness to attend a summit meeting with North Korea. In October he addressed the UN General Assembly, and proposed the holding of an international conference on the problems of north-east Asia.

Continued Opposition Protests.

At home opposition protests centred on President Roh's refusal to prosecute the former president on corruption charges, although in September Mr. Chun's brother was sentenced to seven years in prison for such offences. In December 1988 President Roh carried out a major cabinet reshuffle, replacing 21 out of 25 ministers. Six ministers left from ex-President Chun's regime were dismissed, leaving only one in a minor post. President Roh appointed Mr. Kang Young-hoon as prime minister. A retired general, he was nevertheless not in favour of military involvement in politics in South Korea, and he had been sacked and imprisoned for opposing the 1961 coup.

Improved Relations with North Korea.

As 1989 opened relations between the two parts

of Korea appeared to be easing. In February South Korean industrialists agreed with a North Korean bank to develop a tourist site in North Korea, the first business agreement since partition, while the first trade deal took place when South Korea bought 20,000 tons of coal from the north. But on 2 March talks to arrange a meeting between the northern and southern premiers collapsed when the south rejected the north's demand for cancellation of planned US/South Korean military exercises. Further preliminary talks were cancelled by the north in April in protest against the arrest of a South Korean opposition leader for illegally visiting North Korea.

In June, however, Kim Young Sam, leader of the South Korean opposition Reunification Democratic Party met Ho Dam, a member of the North Korean Politburo, for discussions in Moscow. The meeting was approved by both governments and demonstrated a new conciliatory attitude on North Korean President Kim Il Sung's part. But when on 11 September President Roh Tae Woo announced a unification plan it was dismissed by the North Korean press. President Roh had proposed the initial creation of a "Korean Commonwealth" and unified National Assembly by August 1990, the 45th anniversary of partition.

Roh Strengthens His Position.

Domestically, President Roh took steps to counter threats to his own position. On 20 March he postponed indefinitely a referendum promised since 1987 to test support for his rule. Though opinion polls suggested President Roh had the backing of over 50% of South Koreans, he feared the referendum might cause "confusion and violence". At the end of the month he dismissed the commander of South Korea's military academy following the officer's criticisms of the government. This, and the promotion of 49 generals, was seen as an attempt by the president to strengthen his control over the armed forces. Faced by student protests and strikes, on 22 March President Roh authorised the police to open fire in self-protection against rioters. An estimated 37,000 students battled with police in the streets on 19 April, the anniversary of the 1960 uprising against President Syngman Rhee. Over 6,500 arrests were made to prevent May Day rallies and on 3 May six police were killed in clashes with Pusan University students. President Roh threatened "emergency measures".

In June the South Korean government imposed a 10% limit on price and wage increases to curb inflation and promote exports. A month later President Roh reshuffled the 24 strong cabinet and dismissed the head of the country's intelligence agency.

VIETNAM.

Neither War nor Peace.

March 1973 marked the end of an era of US military presence in Vietnam. Soon Saigon was alleging large-scale infiltration of troops and munitions into S. Vietnam. The attempts of the International Commission of Control and Supervision to enforce the cease-fire were proving largely ineffective. Talks between the S. Vietnamese Government and the Provisional Revolutionary Government on a political settlement remained fruitless: President Thieu would have no truck with anything approaching coalition government, and the Communists therefore refused to agree to elections. Then in January 1974 the increasingly offensive role of the Communist forces prompted President Thieu to put his troops on a war footing again.

Communist Victory.

In March and April 1975 as a result of increasing Vietcong pressure, South Vietnamese forces were withdrawn from the Central Highlands in order to strengthen the defence of more strategic towns. After the decisive battle of Xuan Loc in April 1975 and with Saigon encircled, President Thieu resigned. By the beginning of May the Communists had triumphed. During the latter half of

1975 an estimated 230,000 refugees left S. Vietnam. On 21 January 1976 the Military Management Committee handed over government to the People's Revolutionary Committee. Following the elections in April of a National Assembly for all Vietnam, the reunification of the country was proclaimed for the first time since 1859. A government for the Socialist Republic of Vietnam was formed by Mr Phan van Dong.

During 1978 relations with China steadily worsened owing to discrimination against the Chinese in Vietnam and the expulsion or flight of large numbers of them to China. This, combined with territorial disputes, led to border clashes. In these circumstances the Vietnamese signature of a treaty of friendship with the Soviet Union in November was particularly significant. Meanwhile many ships overladen with Vietnamese refugees tried to land in Malaysia, Hong Kong and elsewhere, often without success. The plight of these "Boat People" gave rise to international humanitarian action to save the lives of as many as possible; it also brought a worldwide loss of prestige for the Vietnamese Government. This and the serious economic situation induced Hanoi in 1979 to mitigate its clumsy integration policies in South Vietnam and abate its campaign against private trade.

The China-Vietnam Conflict.

Vietnam was punished for its military interference in Cambodia by China, whose army launched an invasion across the frontier in February 1979. Bitter fighting took place, with Chinese forces penetrating several miles across the border. Both sides suffered heavy casualties and the Chinese withdrew their forces in March. The Soviet Union stepped up its military and economic aid to Vietnam, which found itself bogged down in a familiar war of attrition in Kampuchea. Conflict on the border with China, including heavy bouts of shelling, continued during 1984 and early 1985.

Leadership Changes in 1986.

Sweeping changes in the leadership of Vietnam took place at the end of 1986, marking the end of an era in the country's politics. As a foretaste, Mr. Tran Phuong, a deputy premier, was dismissed in January 1986 at the request of the National Assembly, after the failure of his attempts to reform prices, wages and the currency the previous autumn. In July 1986 the secretary-general of the Communist Party, Mr. Le Duan, died and was succeeded by Mr. Truong Chinh, who was also chairman of the State Council. This proved to be a temporary measure as there was growing concern that the existing leadership had failed to bring about the much-needed revival of the country's economy in the decade since the war ended.

In December 1986 the sixth congress of the Communist Party convened in Hanoi. On 17 December the retirement was announced of the country's three veteran leaders: Mr. Truong Chinh, chairman and party general-secretary, Mr. Pham Van Dong, the prime minister, and Mr. Le Duc Tho, senior politburo member and party organiser. (The three were later designated "comrade advisers".) The following day Mr. Nguyen Van Linh, a noted economic reformer, was elected general-secretary.

Before his resignation Mr. Truong Chinh had endorsed a major shift in the country's economic direction, with priority being moved away from heavy industry to the encouragement of small-scale production in export-orientated industries, greater decentralisation and the growth of private business. Mr. Nguyen Van Linh's election confirmed the change to a more pragmatic management of the country's political and economic affairs. In February 1987 thirteen ministers were dismissed in a major reshuffle intended to instil new vigour and efficiency throughout the government.

Elections were held in April 1987 and when the National Assembly met in June, Mr. Pham Hung was appointed as Prime Minister and Mr. Vo Chi Cong as President.

Withdrawal from Cambodia.

On 5 April 1989 Vietnam announced that 45,000 troops would withdraw unconditionally from Cambodia by 30 September, ending an occupation lasting over ten years in which over 25,000 had been killed and 55,000 seriously wounded. Vietnam proposed the formation of an international commission to monitor both the withdrawal and an end to foreign arming of anti-Cambodian government guerrillas. The last troops left on 26 September. But within a month several thousand had returned in the guise of "advisors", as Vietnam admitted in February 1990, to assist a Cambodian regime still vulnerable to guerrilla attack.

Vietnam made attempts in 1989 to improve relations with the United States. As a token of good will Vietnam returned the bodies in April and June of a number of US troops killed in the war, though the government denied claims that Vietnam continued to hold American prisoners. Vietnam also allowed 10,000 former political prisoners and their families to emigrate to the United States.

The Modernisation of the Economy.

Domestically, the communist party took steps to modernise the economy and to confront growing popular dissatisfaction symbolised by the thousands of "boat people" fleeing Vietnam. On 6 March 1989 party secretary-general Nguyen Van Linh appointed Pham Van Kai, a leading advocate of economic reform, to the post of state planning minister. In December 1989 the Politburo, recognising the fate of European communist governments, made moves to encourage internal party democracy, wider debate and a more pragmatic approach. Open attacks on party privileges and corruption appeared in the press. Party secretary Nguyen Van Linh was expected to resign at a central committee plenum to be held in March 1990.

LAOS.

The war in Laos officially ended on 21 February 1973 with a standstill cease-fire agreement (leaving the Pathet Lao in control of two-thirds of the country). The formation of a coalition government was agreed after some US pressure on the rightists in the Vientiane Government.

In May 1975 after local fighting and left-wing demonstrations in Vientiane the right-wing ministers resigned and fled. Army units mutinied against right-wing officers and southern Laos was occupied by Pathet Lao forces. The American protégé Souvanna Phouma remained at the head of the coalition government until December when his half-brother Prince Souphanouvong proclaimed a People's Democratic Republic with a government headed by Mr Kaysone Phomvihan. Since 1975 the government has given Laos a much-needed period of peace and brought a degree of unity to this mountainous, ethnically-diverse country.

In October 1986 Prince Souphanouvong resigned as head of state due to illness and was succeeded by Phoumi Vongvichit as acting head.

The first elections since the communists took power in 1975 were held on 26 March 1989. There were 121 candidates for 79 seats in the Supreme People's Assembly but only 47% of the electorate voted.

KAMPUCHEA (CAMBODIA).

In Cambodia President Lon Nol proclaimed a state of emergency in March 1973: Prince Sihanouk's predominantly Communist forces had virtually cut off all supply routes to the capital Phnom Penh. The Republican Government was saved only by greatly intensified US bombing. However, by dramatically cutting off all funds the US Congress forced an end to bombing raids on Cambodia by 15 August. Heavy fighting followed with the Sihanoukists just failing to take Kom-pong.

During 1974 the authority of the Lon Nol régime ceased to extend beyond Phnom Penh, Battambang and a few other centres. Increasing diplomatic recognition of the exiled Sihanouk régime followed. Lon Nol left the country in March 1975 and in April came surrender to the victorious Khmer Rouge Army.

All foreigners were swiftly expelled from Cambodia (renamed Kampuchea), and although information was scanty, apparently the whole population of Phnom Penh was sent to work in the fields to increase food production.

The victors were an uneasy alliance between the royalist followers of the exiled Prince Sihanouk and the Marxist Khmer Rouges. Prince Sihanouk remained as head of state with Penn Nouth as Prime Minister. After returning to Cambodia from Peking in September 1975 Sihanouk left soon afterwards on extensive travels. Elections were held on 30 March 1976 and the Prince resigned in April. Penn Nouth's Government was followed by a new Cabinet under Mr. Pol Pot. In the early months of 1976 the entire population was mobilised in order to reconstruct the economy, but reports reached the West of massive killings verging on genocide.

Conflict with Vietnam.

From September 1977 onwards several border clashes occurred between Vietnam and Cambodia and in late 1978 Hanoi appeared to have escalated the conflict into a concerted invasion. Although the Soviet Union supplied arms and aid to Vietnam, and China to Cambodia, this conflict between communists was in fact a revival of the traditional enmity between the two neighbours. The Vietnamese, much the stronger in numbers and in arms, appear to have held back, preferring to seek dominant influence rather than open conquest. However, on 4 January 1979 Radio Phnom Penh claimed that invading Vietnamese troops were advancing into Kampuchea in eight separate thrusts, supported by heavy artillery and air bombardments. The government of Pol Pot, previously noted for its isolationism, repeatedly demanded an urgent meeting of the UN Security Council to halt the Vietnamese advance. Prince Sihanouk, having a better international reputation than Pol Pot, was sent to New York to plead the Cambodian case before the UN. The Chinese made it clear that they would not intervene militarily, no doubt because of the threat of confrontation with the Soviet Union. Phnom Penh fell on 8 January, though fighting continued in the provinces. The Vietnamese still denied having intervened, but their role in installing the "Cambodian Liberation Front for National Renewal" was clearly decisive.

Starvation and Guerrilla Warfare.

The forces of Pol Pot continued to resist by guerrilla warfare in the jungle and the mountains, tacitly tolerated by the Thais and supported by the Chinese. In September 1979 the United Nations voted to allow the Pol Pot régime to keep its seat in the General Assembly, and not the government of Heng Samrin installed by the Vietnamese—even though Pol Pot was a fugitive and had been condemned to death for genocide. Meanwhile it became clear that vast numbers of Cambodians were literally dying of starvation while the Government cynically looked on. Hundreds of thousands managed to cross the border and fill ever more refugee camps in Thailand. A major international effort was launched to get food and supplies to the population, but despite the Phnom Penh government's agreement to open the Mekong River for supplies the political will to overcome the communications problem was clearly lacking. At the end of December 1979 the Khmer Rouges replaced the notorious Pol Pot as head of government by the former head of state Khieu Samphan. But this meant no real change, since the latter was also a fanatical revolutionary and Pol Pot remained commander-in-chief of the guerrilla force, estimated at some 30,000, which controlled about one-fifth of the country. Thus the announcements about respect for property, human rights and religion were no more than a transparent attempt to halt the loss of support in the West which had set in since the UN resolution in September. Meanwhile the negotiations took place and the starvation continued.

Fighting between the Heng Samrin government and the Khmer Rouge forces continued throughout 1980, but gradually the former extended its control over most of the country.

Anti-Vietnamese Coalition Formed.

Groups opposed to the Vietnam-backed regime of Heng Samrin formed a coalition in Kuala Lumpur,

Malaysia, on 22 June 1982, and announced the establishment of a rival government on Kampuchean territory held by guerrillas on 9 July. This consisted of Khieu Samphan, Khmer Rouge Prime Minister, Prince Norodom Sihanouk and Son Sann, head of the Khmer People's National Liberation Front. The coalition sought international support, but in a counter-move Vietnam announced partial troop withdrawals from Kampuchea. By mid-1984 there were still some 150,000 Vietnamese troops in the country. These forces began a major offensive in November 1984, overrunning many guerrilla bases near the Thai border. During 1985 Vietnam indicated that it expected all its troops to be withdrawn from Kampuchea by 1990, by which time the Heng Samrin government would be able to maintain itself unaided.

The security situation remained deadlocked during 1986. Anti-government guerrillas, numbering over 50,000, continued to receive training from China, sanctuary in Thailand and money from the West, but for the first time Kampuchean troops took over front-line duties from the Vietnamese. In December 1986 new ministers were appointed to the foreign affairs, defence and planning portfolios in an effort to put new life into the government. Major efforts were expected in 1987 to secure international recognition for the Heng Samrin regime.

Prince Sihanouk Steps Down.

In May 1987 Prince Sihanouk announced that he was taking a year off from leading the Kampuchean anti-government coalition after attacks on his followers by the Khmer Rouge. However, in December 1987 he nevertheless took part in talks with the Vietnamese Prime Minister, Hun Sen, near Paris. A joint communiqué at the end of the talks affirmed their desire to bring about peace through elections held under international supervision and a phased withdrawal of Vietnamese troops.

Further talks took place in January 1988. Then Prince Sihanouk declared that there would be no further meetings as he had irrevocably resigned as president of the Coalition Government of Democratic Kampuchea. He blamed criticism of his role in the peace negotiations by his prime minister, Son Sann, for his resignation.

In May 1988 Vietnam confirmed that it would withdraw 50,000 troops from Kampuchea by the end of the year, and all its forces by December 1990.

The Jakarta Informal Talks.

Diplomatic activity during 1988 was directed towards trying to reach agreement on how a new government might be chosen by the people of Kampuchea. In July informal talks began near Jakarta in Indonesia between Prime Minister Hun Sen, leaders of the three resistance factions, the Vietnamese Foreign Minister, Nguyen Co Thach, and representatives of other south-east Asian countries.

In August 1988 China and the Soviet Union had talks on the future of Kampuchea in Beijing, and a return round of talks took place in Moscow in December. An agreement between China and the Soviet Union, leading to pressure being brought to bear by them on their respective protégés, would be likely to bring a settlement closer. During a visit to Bangkok in November, the Chinese Prime Minister, Li Peng, said that China did not support the return of Pol Pot and the Khmer Rouge to exclusive power in Kampuchea, but a government representing the Hun Sen regime and the three resistance groups under Prince Sihanouk.

The informal talks in Jakarta resumed in February 1989, but rapidly became deadlocked over the refusal of Mr. Hun Sen to make way for an interim government to oversee the Vietnamese withdrawal and new elections. Mr. Hun Sen stated that if a political settlement was reached, the Vietnamese withdrawal would be completed by September 1989. The Vietnamese Foreign Minister again confirmed that all his country's troops would leave by December 1990, whether a settlement was reached or not.

New Resistance Grouping.

Prince Sihanouk resumed his role as president of the anti-government coalition on 11 February 1989 and announced the formation of a "National

Resistance of Cambodia" with the communist Khmer Rouge and the non-communist Khmer People's National Liberation Front (KPNLF) on 14 March. He met Cambodian premier Hun Sen in Jakarta on 2–3 May but little resulted because of the latter's insistence that Sihanouk—whom he offered the position of head of state (Kampuchea renamed itself Cambodia on 30 April) after the Vietnamese withdrawal—should break with the Khmer Rouge, the largest anti-government group. A 19 nation peace conference in Paris between 30 July and 30 August similarly broke down over conflicting views on the future role of the Khmer Rouge in Cambodia. On 27 August Prince Sihanouk resigned as leader of the guerrilla coalition and it appeared that civil war would follow the Vietnamese withdrawal.

The Vietnamese Withdrawal.

Vietnam withdrew the final 26,000 of its troops between 21–26 September. Immediate clashes began between Cambodian government and Khmer Rouge forces. Prime minister Hun Sen called on Prince Sihanouk to break with the Khmer Rouge and join in a national government of reconciliation. Meanwhile, KPNLF forces captured five towns in north-west Cambodia in an offensive from 30 September to 4 October. The greatest blow to the government came with the loss to the Khmer Rouge on 23 October of Pailin, a mining town and a crucial source of revenue. Vietnam at once sent military "advisers" to aid the government, as the ambassador in Phnom Penh admitted in February 1990.

In January 1990 the United Nations Security Council approved a peace plan involving a UN presence in Cambodia and the formation of a Supreme National Council to supervise elections. By February the military situation was moving in the government's favour, with the recapture of KPNLF occupied territory. Prince Sihanouk agreed with Hun Sen to work towards national unity. Son Sann, the KPNLF leader said however that an alliance of his forces, Prince Sihanouk and the government against the Khmer Rouge was unlikely. Nevertheless, as Prince Sihanouk returned from an 11 years exile, it seemed the country was moving towards a peace settlement. But talks in February 1990 collapsed when Khmer Rouge representatives objected to references to their "genocide" in a conference statement which announced agreement had been reached on most major issues.

THE PHILIPPINES.

The Downfall of Marcos.

Unrest continued in the Philippines throughout 1985, with greatly increased guerrilla activity by the communist-inspired New People's Army in the countryside. This situation and pressure from the Philippines' most important ally, the United States, led President Marcos to seek a new mandate by calling elections for February 1986, although his six-year term of office did not end until 1987. In December 1985 it was announced that the opposition to President Marcos would be led by Benigno Aquino's widow, Corazon Aquino, under the banner of the United Nationalist Democratic Organisation (UNIDO). The head of UNIDO, Salvador Laurel, withdrew as a presidential candidate and put himself forward as Mrs Aquino's vice-presidential running mate.

Polling took place on 7 February 1986, amidst violence and widespread evidence of intimidation and ballot-rigging, reported both by foreign observers and the citizen watchdog group, the National Movement for Free Elections (Namfrel). Mrs. Aquino took the lead in Namfrel's tally, but official vote-counting proceeded slowly, giving rise to fresh charges of fraud. On 15 February the National Assembly, dominated by Mr Marcos' New Society Movement, declared that Mr. Marcos had won by 1·5 million votes. Mrs. Aquino announced a campaign of civil disobedience and President Reagan, who had initially blamed both sides for malpractices, now said that the actions of Mr. Marcos' supporters rendered the result of the election invalid.

The Advent of Aquino.

Events moved swiftly when the Defence Minister, Juan Ponce Enrile, and the head of the Philippines Constabulary, Lt.-General Fidel Ramos, resigned, claiming they faced imminent arrest, and transferred their allegiance to Mrs. Aquino. In a display of 'people power', thousands of Mrs. Aquino's supporters blocked the way to troops loyal to Mr. Marcos. On 25 February both Mr. Marcos and Mrs. Aquino held presidential inauguration ceremonies, but later in the day Mr. Marcos finally accepted that the time had come to stand down and allowed himself and his family to be evacuated from the American Clark Air Base. Mrs. Aquino thus became the new President of the Philippines, with Mr. Laurel as her Prime Minister and Foreign Minister.

Unsuccessful Coup Attempts.

Mrs. Aquino faced a series of coup attempts during the second half of 1986. In July 1986 Arturo Tolentino, who had been Mr. Marcos' running mate, was proclaimed "acting president" by Mrs. Aquino's opponents, but the rebellion quietly collapsed. The most serious threat came in November from Mr. Enrile, who had for some time been challenging Mrs. Aquino's authority. However, in his capacity as chief of staff of the armed forces, General Fidel Ramos issued a directive that Defence Minister Enrile's orders were not to be obeyed. On 23 November Mr. Enrile was replaced as Defence Minister by his deputy, General Rafael Ileto. A third attempt to overthrow Mrs. Aquino came in January 1987 when rebel soldiers seized two broadcasting stations, but they were persuaded to surrender after two days.

The New Constitution 1987.

On 2 February 1987 a referendum was held to endorse the new constitution for the Philippines, drafted by a 47-member commission during 1986. The result of the plebiscite was announced as showing 76 per cent of votes in favour of the draft. It confirmed Mrs. Aquino in power until 1992, but limited the presidential right to declare martial law. On the debit side the cease-fire with the NPA collapsed in February 1987, but to counter this the general election of May 1987 produced a convincing vote for the policies of the Aquino government and a blow to the extremists.

Continuing Political Uncertainties.

A fifth coup attempt against Mrs. Aquino's government was put down in August 1987, but there were over fifty dead. The leader of the coup, Colonel Honasan, was arrested in December, but escaped from his prison ship in Manila Bay in April 1988 and threatened to mount a new rebellion.

Mrs. Aquino also had problems with her ministerial team. In September 1987 the Vice-President, Salvador Laurel, resigned from his post as Foreign Affairs secretary, saying that the government contained people sympathetic to the communists. Then at the end of January 1988 the Defence Minister, Rafael Ileto, resigned, and was replaced by Mrs. Aquino's staunch supporter, the Chief of Staff, General Fidel Ramos.

Mrs. Aquino's estrangement from Vice-President Laurel was confirmed when he called on her to resign and hold immediate elections in August 1988. He announced he had agreed to head the newly-formed Union for National Action, a grouping of right-wing politicians.

The divisions between President Aquino and Vice President Laurel intensified in February 1989 when Mr Laurel flew to Honolulu to visit ex-President Marcos in hospital and appealed for him to be allowed to return to Manila on compassionate grounds. On 9 March Mr Laurel joined another of Mrs Aquino's opponents, Juan Ponce Enrile, in reviving the Nacionalista Party which had been prominent in Philippines politics in the 1950s and 60s. Mrs Aquino remained determined that Mr Marcos would not return, alive or dead. On 28 September he died in Honolulu, where he was buried on 15 October.

Continuing Guerrilla Activity.

Another of the political problems confronting Mrs

Aquino was continuing communist guerrilla activity. A US military adviser was killed in April. Economically, the government was successful in gaining foreign aid. The IMF agreed a three-year $1·3 billion aid package. In July a World Bank conference promised increased assistance from the US, Japan and Europe. This was followed in August by foreign bankers' agreement to reduce the Philippines $28 billion debt.

The December 1989 Coup Attempt.

Mrs Aquino's position, however, remained precarious and in December she faced the sixth and most threatening coup attempt since taking office. Led by former Col. Gregorio Honasan, 2,000 troops moved against the government on 1 December, occupying Manila's financial district and a military airport. Honasan charged Mrs Aquino with incompetence, corruption and an inability to defeat communist guerrillas. Vice President Laurel declared his support for the rebels and called on her to resign. US air support enabled Mrs Aquino to quell the rising at a cost of 119 killed and 448 wounded. Fears that another attempt might soon follow prompted the Senate to grant Mrs Aquino emergency powers for six months on 14 December.

Mrs Aquino now entered into conflict with the United States, a move at odds with her recent dependence on American air support. In February 1990 the US Congress withdrew $96 million from a promised $481 million payment for military bases in the Philippines. Mrs Aquino refused to meet the US Secretary of Defense when he visited Manila for talks, while government officials threatened not to renew the treaty allowing the US to occupy the bases when it expired in 1991. Mrs Aquino's hold on power appeared increasingly fragile despite attempts to assert her authority by ordering the arrest in March 1990 of Juan Ponce Enrile for complicity in the December coup attempt and of former colonel Rodolfo Guinaldo.

INDONESIA.

Independence under Sukarno.

Indonesia proclaimed its independence from the Netherlands in August 1945, though it was not until 27 December 1949 that the Dutch formally recognised the transfer of power. Dr. Sukarno became the country's first president. In 1957 he introduced a type of authoritarian rule known as 'guided democracy', in which the elected parliament was replaced by an appointed legislature. Sukarno laid great stress on fostering unity, using opposition to imperialism and neo-colonialism—as in the 'confrontation' with Malaysia (1963–66)—to stimulate national sentiment.

The Overthrow of Sukarno.

Following an abortive coup in September 1965, the Indonesian Communist Party was charged with plotting to destroy the power of the army. The party was banned and thousands of its members were killed. In March 1966 the army, led by General Suharto, assumed emergency powers. The following February Sukarno handed over all power to General Suharto, who was elected President by the People's Consultative Assembly in March 1968. He was re-elected in 1973, 1978 and 1983.

The Army's Role.

President Suharto introduced his 'New Order', in which the army became the dominant factor in Indonesian political life. The army regards itself as a force for stability, occupying as it does the centre ground between the communists on the left and the Islamic fundamentalists on the right. In 1983 President Suharto brought in a large number of younger men to top military posts so that there would be continuity in the army's political role.

The Indonesian army is also involved in military operations to counter separatist insurgencies in East Timor and Irian Jaya. In the former case, when Portugal withdrew from East Timor in 1975 Indonesia brutally intervened to prevent the Fretilin movement taking power. In July 1976 East Timor was formally integrated into Indonesia. Neither Portugal nor the U.N. recognised this illegal annexation. There is also conflict in Irian Jaya, which was incorporated into Indonesia in 1963. Renewed fighting in 1984 led to the flight of over 11,000 refugees to Papua New Guinea. In mid-1986 East Timor was the scene of fresh conflict as government troops mounted a campaign to capture the Fretilin leader, Sha Na Na.

The Status of Islam.

Alongside the military there is an impressive government political apparatus centred on the official party, Golkar. It has won all three elections since President Suharto came to power. In 1982 it won 64 per cent of the total votes and two-thirds of the parliamentary seats. Although the Muslims supported the army take-over in the mid-1960s, they have still been denied any real power.

Indonesia has the world's largest Islamic population, with 90 per cent of its 160 million inhabitants belonging to the Muslim faith. However, President Suharto rejects any thought of its becoming an Islamic state. This is made easier by the fact that only a small proportion of the population are orthodox Muslims. In 1972 four Muslim parties were forced to merge into the United Development Party (PPP), but this remains deeply divided.

However, President Suharto has to take care not to alienate grass-roots Islamic sentiment by pressing too strongly the official state ideology, "Pancasila", the tenets of which are belief in God, humanitarianism, national unity, social justice and democracy. In August 1984 Suharto assured the congress of the P.P.P. that Pancasila was not intended to create a one-party state or reduce religious freedom, but there were riots and bombings in the capital, Jakarta, in September. These were blamed on militant Muslims and had to be suppressed by the army.

Nevertheless in the mid-1980s Indonesia enjoyed a far greater degree of political stability than many other developing countries. It had also made reasonable economic progress, although it had felt the effects of the world recession and the fall in the price of oil, which provided 60% of the country's income. Inflation and unemployment rose steadily during 1986.

The Influence of Pancasila.

In 1985 parliament passed a bill laying down that all mass organisations, including political parties, should accept Pancasila. In December 1986, after eighteen months' negotiation with the government, Indonesia's ten million Protestants were allowed freedom of religious expression and required to accept Pancasila only in "social life, the nation and the state". The Catholic church pressed for a similar concession.

A general election was held in Indonesia in April 1987. In the run-up to the polls the Muslim PPP was gravely handicapped by a split between its parliamentary leader, Mr. Soedardji, and its general chairman, Mr. Jaelani Naro, and also by the fact that it could only campaign on the basis of Pancasila, not Islamic principles. As expected Golkar won a landslide victory in the elections, increasing its share of the vote from 64 to 73%.

In March 1988 President Suharto was appointed to a fifth 5-year term in office by a special session of the People's Consultative Assembly, the upper house of parliament. His nominee for the post of vice-president, Secretary of State Sudharmono, was elected by the acclamation of the National Assembly after President Suharto had persuaded Mr. Naro not to contest the nomination in the interests of consensus politics. Later in the year, however, Vice-President Sudharmono, who was unpopular with the military, was voted out of office as party chairman by Golkar's National Congress.

There was some relaxation during 1988 of the strict military control of movement in and out of East Timor. Following a visit from President Suharto, in November eight of the thirteen regions in East Timor were reported to be open to Indonesians, although foreigners still required permits.

Rapprochement with China.

In February 1989 Indonesia suffered its most serious religious violence for five years when 30 people were killed in clashes between troops and Moslem rebels in Lampung province, southern Sumatra. But on 23 February diplomatic relations with China broken in 1967 were restored at a meeting between President Suharto and the Chinese foreign minister. Indonesia had alleged Chinese involvement in a 1965 coup attempt. China now pledged never to interfere in Indonesian internal affairs.

AFRICA

ETHIOPIA.

Ethiopia's New Constitution.

A new constitution for Ethiopia was published in June 1986, by which the country would become a People's Democratic Republic with an elected national assembly. In February 1987 a countrywide plebiscite of Ethiopia's twelve million registered voters approved the new form of government.

Voting took place in June 1987 for members of the new 835-seat national Shengo or parliament. In September 1987 the Shengo unanimously elected Colonel Mengistu, who had ruled Ethiopia since the overthrow of Haile Selassie, as the country's first President.

New Famine Threat.

The failure of the 1987 harvest brought fears of a major new famine and calls for international relief aid. There was also an upsurge of fighting by the country's separatist movements early in 1988. The Eritrean and Tigrean guerrillas announced that they had resumed co-operation broken off in 1985. The Ethiopian army airlifted troops from the Somali border to counter guerrilla successes. In May 1988 a state of emergency was imposed in Eritrea and Tigre. In June the Tigrean guerrillas withdrew into the mountains, leaving the towns to be reoccupied by the Ethiopian army.

In April 1988 Somalia and Ethiopia restored full diplomatic relations, agreeing to refrain from interfering in each other's affairs, and to pull back military forces at least nine miles from their border. There were signs during 1988 of a relaxation in the Ethiopian government's hard-line socialist management of the economy. Private traders were given a bigger role in grain marketing, and in October plans were announced to boost private investment and reform taxes. In May 1989 an attempted army coup was rigorously suppressed in Addis Ababa.

The Coup Aftermath.

Although President Mengistu had survived the coup, it weakened his position significantly. In April 1989 the USSR had threatened to end arms supplies unless he opened negotiations with the Eritrean and Tigrean rebels. On 5 June Mengistu announced to the Shengo his government's willingness to enter into unconditional talks. After some hesitation, the EPLF—in control of most of Eritrea—and the TPLF—whose forces completely dominated Tigre—accepted the offer.

Peace Negotiations.

Ethiopian and EPLF representatives met in Atlanta under the auspices of former US President Carter in September. The talks adjourned on 19 September with both agreeing to open formal peace negotiations in November. The TPLF had accepted President Carter's offer to mediate in discussions in Addis Ababa but on 31 August President Mengistu accused the TPLF of launching an unprovoked offensive. The TPLF inflicted heavy casualties on the government in an advance into Welo province between 3–18 October and stood within 200 miles of Addis Ababa, threatening the road from the capital to the Red Sea port of Assab.

In addition to the war, Eritrea was suffering a drought which would reportedly reduce the harvest by 85%. The United Nations called for relief to avert a famine putting 1.5 million people in Eritrea at risk together with a further 200,000 in Tigre by March 1990.

The Eritrean Offensive.

In February 1990 the Eritreans captured the Red Sea port of Massawa, a devastating psychological blow to Ethiopian government forces. The Oromo Liberation Front—Oromos made up half of Ethiopia's 47 million population—had driven government troops out of the Asosa region of western Wallagga province. While the EPLF fought for secession, the TPLF sought the overthrow of President Mengistu and formed an Ethiopian People's Revolutionary Democratic Front to unite the opposition to his regime. As famine took hold, President Mengistu's government appeared to be facing a final battle for survival.

TUNISIA.

Overthrow of Bourguiba.

In October 1987 a new Prime Minister was appointed, Mr. Zine el Abdin ben Ali. The following month he organised a bloodless palace coup which removed President Bourguiba from office on the grounds of senility. Mr. ben Ali promised greater political and press freedom and several hundred political detainees were released. In May 1988 President ben Ali pardoned the leader of the Islamic Tendency Movement, and announced a general amnesty for political prisoners in July. However, a new law forbade the existence of parties based on religion.

Constitutional Reforms.

In July 1988 President ben Ali introduced a series of constitutional reforms. The most important was the abolition of the presidency for life, instituted by Mr. Bourguiba. Tenure was to be restricted to three five-year terms, with an upper age limit of seventy. The minimum age for parliamentary candidates was reduced from 28 to 25.

At the end of July the President carried out a major reshuffle of his cabinet, replacing Mr Bourguiba's men with younger technocrats. At a three-day conference of the ruling party President ben Ali pledged to establish a multi-party political system. But despite calls for greater democracy in the party, more than half the members of the central committee were appointed by the President, rather than elected.

LIBYA.

The Fall of King Idris.

Libya became an independent state on 24 December 1951 under King Idris of the Libyan Sanussi dynasty. He was overthrown by a small group of junior army officers on 1 September 1969. A twelve-member Revolutionary Command Council was established as Libya's supreme authority, with Colonel Moammar Gaddafi as its chairman. Although the coup had been primarily anti-royalist, the revolutionaries announced that they sought to establish "freedom, socialism and unity", ridding Libya of colonialism and economic and social backwardness.

The Jamahiriya.

Colonel Gaddafi was born in 1942, the only son of semi-nomadic parents. His revolutionary thinking was greatly influenced by President Nasser of Egypt, with strong elements of puritanism and pan-Arabism in its make-up. In 1977 his regime implemented a new system of government involving popular participation in the political processes. A form of direct democracy, the Jamahiriya (state of the masses), was introduced and the official name of the country was changed to the Socialist People's Libyan Arab Jamahiriya. At local level authority is vested in 186 Basic and 25 Municipal People's Congresses, which appoint Popular Committees to execute policy. Officials from the Congresses and Committees form at national level the General People's Congress, a body of some 1,000 delegates which normally meets for about a week twice a year.

Gaddafi's Policies.

Under the new system Colonel Gaddafi holds no

formal post, but his position as leader of the revolution and his personal popularity confer great power on him within Libya. Internationally Libya's standing is the result of its role as one of the world's major oil producers. It has enormous oil reserves, estimated at over 25,000 million barrels. Revenue from oil has been used to improve the standard of living of the small population (about 3·5 million), financing civil engineering and irrigation projects. In 1984 a 120-mile pipeline to recover water from under the desert was completed at a cost of 11 billion dollars.

Oil revenue has also been used for large-scale arms buying, as militarism, with conscription and popular militias, has become a feature of Libyan life. Colonel Gaddafi has ensured Libya a place in the world's headlines over the past fifteen years by virtue of his radical and idiosyncratic foreign policy. This has seen Libyan military involvement in the affairs of neighbouring Chad and support for international terrorism.

Britain and Libya.

Britain broke off diplomatic relations with Libya in April 1984 as a result of the shooting of a policewoman, Yvonne Fletcher, from the Libyan embassy in London during an anti-Gaddafi demonstration. Following terrorist attacks at Rome and Vienna airports in December 1985, President Reagan announced a total break in economic relations with Libya and ordered all Americans to leave the country. Although Colonel Gaddafi, whom President Reagan described as "flakey" or unbalanced, denied that there were guerrilla bases in his country, the Americans continued to argue that if their European allies joined in bringing pressure to bear on Libya, this would significantly reduce terrorist activity world-wide.

American Air Strikes.

Tension steadily increased between Libya and the United States in the Spring of 1986. In March American naval exercises in the Gulf of Sirte (claimed by Colonel Gaddafi as Libyan territorial waters) led to clashes in which Libyan patrol boats and a missile site were hit. Matters came to a head when on 2 April a bomb went off in the passenger cabin of a T.W.A. jetliner over Greece, killing four Americans, and on 5 April a second device exploded in a West Berlin night club, killing two and injuring some 230. The Americans claimed that they had indisputable evidence of Libyan involvement in the latter attack. In retaliation during the night of 14/ 15 April American bombers from two carriers in the Mediterranean and four US bases in Britain struck at three targets in the Tripoli area and two near Benghazi. There were many civilian casualties, including two of Colonel Gaddafi's sons and his adopted daughter.

Gaddafi's New Stance.

During 1988 Colonel Gaddafi showed signs of a new flexibility in his policies. In April the free movement of goods between Libya and Tunisia was established in agreement with President ben Ali, and in May Colonel Gaddafi offered to make peace with Chad. In September, during celebrations of the Libyan revolution, he announced new economic policies modifying centralised state ownership, admitted that the war with Chad had been a mistake and urged his opponents in exile to return to Libya. Meanwhile, however, American anger grew at the disclosure of Russian delivery of bombers – supersonic Su-24Ds – to Libya.

Tension with the United States.

Tension between Libya and the United States took a more dramatic turn when on 4 January 1989 two US Navy fighters shot down two Libyan MiGs over the Mediterranean. The US claimed self defence while Libya described the action as pre-meditated. The clash coincided with US charges that Libya had constructed a chemical weapons plant in Rabta. Col. Gaddafi insisted it was a pharmaceutical factory. (The plant was severely damaged by an apparently deliberate fire in March 1990.) On 22 February US Naval Intelligence alleged Libya was attempting to develop nuclear weapons.

There were, however, signs that Col. Gaddafi was attempting to moderate both his domestic and foreign stance. A lessening of state controls and a shift to a more market oriented economy encouraged definite improvements in Libyan citizens' lives. Col. Gaddafi acknowledged the legitimacy of complaints against his internal security forces. But it was in the international arena that Libya appeared to be taking decisive, if occasionally erratic, steps to end its isolation.

Relations with Chad and Egypt.

Gaddafi suggested in January 1989 that he and President-elect Bush—whom he later described as "wise and mature"—should discuss the issues dividing Libya and the US. There were reports that Libya had reduced funding of terrorist movements. On 17 February Libya became a founder member with Algeria, Mauritania, Morocco and Tunisia of the Arab Mahgreb Union, a North African common market. Commemoration of the 20th anniversary of Col. Gaddafi's rule opened on 31 August with a treaty ending Libya's war with Chad. His speech at the celebration, although containing a denunciation of Israel, was relatively mild in tone. Having re-opened the border with Egypt and restored air links, Col. Gaddafi drove to meet Egyptian President Mubarrak on 16 October, a visit the President returned the following day. They agreed to co-operate on a range of agricultural and transport matters and announced that Egypt and Libya had no differences over Arab issues. A week later Col. Gaddafi called for improved relations with the United States based on "mutual respect and common interests".

CHAD.

Chad has been in a state of civil war for most of its history since independence in 1960, originally as a result of a guerrilla campaign waged against the government by the Chad Liberation Front (FROLINAT), backed by Libya. In 1978 the Chad head of state, General Malloum, who had come to power in a military coup in 1975, announced a cease-fire with FROLINAT. In August 1978 the former rebel leader, Hissène Habré, become Prime Minister.

However, relations between the Prime Minister and President Malloum worsened. Fighting was renewed between their supporters in February 1979 and central government in Chad broke down as Habré's forces took over part of the capital, Ndjamena. Negotiations resumed and on 21 August 1979 the eleven factions fighting in Chad signed a peace agreement in Lagos, Nigeria. A Goverment of National Unity was set up with the Toubou leader, Goukouni Oueddi, as head of state and Hissène Habré as Defence Minister.

This too broke down in renewed civil strife in March 1980 and there was increasing Libyan involvement on behalf of President Oueddei. President Gaddafi sent some 4,000 Libyan troops and at least thirty Russian-built tanks to fight for the President. Although at one point in November 1980 Hissène Habré's forces controlled two-thirds of Ndjamena, he was forced to agree to a cease-fire in December.

Libyan Intervention.

President Gaddafi's intervention in Chad greatly disturbed neighbouring African states who saw the Libyan presence there as a threat to their own security. However, in November 1981 President Gaddafi announced that he had ordered the withdrawal of all Libyan soldiers from Chad. In December the Organisation of African Unity sent a 3,000-strong peace-keeping force to Chad to replace the Libyan troops. The OAU plan for a ceasefire, negotiations and new presidential elections was rejected by President Oueddei in February 1982.

Alienated by President Oueddei's refusal to negotiate, the OAU peace-keeping force remained neutral when Hissène Habré's forces retook the Chad capital on 7 June 1982. President Oueddei was driven into exile in Cameroon, and Hissène Habré established his own government in Ndjamena.

There was renewed fighting in June 1983 as Mr. Oueddei's Libyan-backed forces advanced into Chad and captured the strategically important town of Faya-Largeau. President Habré appealed to France, and in August French troops took up front-line positions in northern Chad to prevent any further rebel advances. Fighting subsided, and the 10th Franco-African summit meeting at Vittel in France in October 1983 rejected a partition of Chad and called for reconciliation between the warring groups. However, in January 1984 negotiations between the factions held in Addis Ababa broke down when President Habré withdrew from the talks. Reconciliation talks later took place in Brazzaville, capital of the Congo, in October 1984, but made little progress.

French Troops Withdrawn.

In September 1984 it was announced that France and Libya had agreed to a mutual withdrawal of their forces from Chad, to be completed by mid-November. The French contingent flew out, but there was strong evidence of a continuing Libyan presence in the north of the country. The government of Chad issued an official complaint to the UN Security Council in June 1985. Despite attempts by Mali and Morocco to mediate a settlement, the country remained divided and continued to suffer the hardships of drought and famine.

Libyan Forces Defeated.

Towards the end of 1986 critical new developments occurred in the civil war. In a dispute with his Libyan allies, Mr. Goukouni Oueddi was wounded and became a prisoner in Tripoli. His men then agreed a truce with President Habré in October, and joined government troops in heavy fighting against the Libyans.

At the beginning of 1987 President Habré's forces crossed the demarcation line into Libyan-controlled Chad and captured the garrison town of Fada. In March 1987 the Chadian army mounted a surprise attack on the main Libyan air base at Duadi Doum, routing the 4,000-strong defending force, which lost over 1,200 dead. Deprived of the use of their two-mile aluminium plate runway at Duadi Doum, Libyan troops began to evacuate their last important base in Northern Chad at Faya-Largeau. The area of Chad still occupied by Libya was reduced to the narrow Aouzou strip of disputed border territory. In August 1987 Chadian troops actually captured the town of Aouzou, driving the Libyan army out of the border strip. The Libyans counter-attacked successfully and a cease-fire was agreed in September.

Peace with Libya.

In May 1988 Colonel Gaddafi recognized President Habré's government, and declared his wish to end the dispute between the two countries. Talks were held in Libreville in Gabon in July, and in October Libya and Chad re-established diplomatic relations, marking the end of the war.

A move towards a more formal peace agreement with Libya came on 20 July 1989 when President Habre met Colonel Gaddafi in Mali. At the end of August the Chad and Libyan Foreign Ministers announced in Algiers that both countries had pledged to settle their differences over the disputed Aouzou Strip diplomatically. If political agreement proved impossible within a year the issue was to be taken to the International Court at The Hague.

SUDAN.

Return to Civilian Rule.

A general election was held in April 1986 to establish a civilian government at the end of the agreed transitional period of military rule. In the south of the country voting took place in only 31 of the 68 constituencies due to the military situation. Of the 264 deputies elected to the Constituent Assembly, the People's Party (Umma) won 99 seats and the Democratic Unionist Party won 63. These two parties decided to form a broad-based government. In May 1986 a five-member Supreme Council was sworn in as collective head of state and the Constituent Assembly elected Dr. Sadiq el-Mahdi, the Umma leader, as Prime Minister.

State of Emergency.

Following a wave of demonstrations against the government, power cuts and intensified civil war in the south, a state of emergency was declared in July 1987. In August the coalition government collapsed when the Democratic Unionist Party suspended its alliance with Umma.

In April 1988 Dr Sadiq el-Mahdi was re-elected Prime Minister by the Constituent Assembly. He formed a new national unity government in May, together with the Democratic Unionist Party and the National Islamic Front. The latter's participation made it more difficult to see the southern rebels' demand for the removal of Islamic law, the Sharia, being met. A new version of the Sharia was, in fact, introduced in parliament in September 1988. Although the south was to be exempt from stoning, flogging and amputation as punishments, twenty-two deputies of the opposition Union of Sudanese African Parties walked out in protest.

On top of Sudan's political problems, 1988 brought a series of natural disasters. Sudan had to appeal for United Nations' help as the country was affected by drought and locusts. Then in August the heaviest rains for fifty years led to massive flooding, with many dead and over a million homeless.

The Search for Peace.

Attempts to bring an end to the civil war continued, and in November 1988 the Democratic Unionist Party concluded a peace agreement of their own with the SPLA leader, Garang, involving a cease-fire and a freeze on Sharia legislation. But this led to a new political crisis, when Dr Sadiq el-Mahdi proposed convening a constitutional conference, but refused to acknowledge the DUP's peace agreement. At the end of December 1988 the DUP again withdrew from the coalition government.

Meanwhile industrial and social unrest continued to grow in Sudan. The government agreed wage rises of up to 500 per cent for public sector workers in December, but at the same time attempted to introduce price rises, including a 600 per cent increase in the cost of sugar. In the demonstrations that followed, police opened fire to disperse the crowds, and an emergency cabinet meeting rescinded the price increases.

At the end of February 1989 the country's Defence Minister resigned, and senior army officers issued an ultimatum to the government, calling for political and economic change, including the formation of a broad-based cabinet. In his initial reply Dr el-Mahdi said his government was working on a new plan to end the civil war.

Major SPLA Successes.

The army's demand came against a background of increasing SPLA military success in southern Sudan, with the capture of a number of major towns. Facing opposition from the army and an alliance of political parties and trade unions, the cabinet resigned on 12 March and Dr el-Mahdi formed a more broadly-based government supported by all but the National Islamic Front. He promised peace talks with the SPLA and accepted a UN proposal for a one month cease-fire from 1 April to enable relief supplies to reach southern Sudan. His government had been accused of preventing aid reaching the south as part of its campaign against the SPLA.

The June 1989 Coup.

These moves did not, however, assist in Dr el-Mahdi's political survival. On 30 June his government was overthrown in a coup led by Gen. Omar Hassan Ahmed al-Bashir. A 15-man military revolutionary council declared a state of emergency, abolished the constitution and banned political activity. Officials and cabinet members, including Dr el-Mahdi, were arrested. The junta promised an "honourable peace" with the SPLA, and that the contentious issue of Sharia, or Islamic law, which had provoked the SPLA rebellion, would be put to a national referendum.

NIGERIA.

The Overthrow of Buhari.

By mid-1985 it was clear that the Buhari regime had failed to deal with the country's economic problems—unemployment, inflation and an over-dependence on oil revenues. There were also accusations of bias towards northerners, failure to deal even-handedly with former officials and excessive repression. On 27 August 1985 Maj-Gen. Buhari's government was overthrown in a bloodless military coup and Maj-Gen. Ibraham Babangida took control as head of a new Armed Forces Ruling Council. A National Council of Ministers was appointed in September, with twelve military and ten civilian members.

The new government promised greater flexibility and a more liberal approach to dealing with the country's problems. In October 1985 Maj-Gen. Babangida announced that the country would be under a fifteen-month economic "state of emergency", aimed at improving productivity and national self-reliance.

Tensions within Nigerian society led to student demonstrations in June 1986, in which at least twenty people died. Restrictions on visiting student hostels for the opposite sex were resented as an attempt by the north to impose Islamic custom on the whole country. After complaints by the Christian south Maj-Gen Babangida set up a national commission to re-examine the decision that Nigeria should join the Islamic Conference organisation.

Falling oil prices during 1986 continued to make Nigeria's path to economic recovery a difficult one. On 1 January 1987 Maj-Gen Babangida announced the end of the economic "state of emergency", but urged the need for continuing austerity.

In July 1987 Nigeria's military rulers announced that the return to civilian government would be postponed from 1990 to 1992. The transitionary period would begin with local elections and end with two-party elections for the presidency and federal legislature in 1992. The local elections, involving some 13,000 candidates, took place in December 1987, and were followed by widespread complaints of incompetent administration by the National Electoral Commission.

Continuing Austerity.

At the beginning of 1989 the Nigerian government launched a new austerity budget, designed to channel investment and scarce resources into agriculture and small-scale industry, in order to continue the process of reducing Nigerian dependence on oil revenues.

President Babaniga continued his economic reforms by easing restrictions on foreign investment in January 1989. A 40% limit on foreign ownership of enterprises imposed in the 1970s was raised to 100%, except in banking and insurance, mining and oil prospecting. The intention was to encourage investment and assist in the government's privatisation programme. Within days the IMF approved $620 million credit to aid Nigerian development. Economic and political liberalisation appeared to be running parallel when in May Mr Babaniga lifted a five year ban on political activity.

Anti-Government Demonstrations.

But there was clearly intense discontent with the austerity programme's effects. On 24 May—shortly after he had returned from Britain with the promise of £60 million in aid—students mounted demonstrations against the alleged corruption of Mr Babaniga and his government. These spread across nine states, were joined by non-students protesting against the government's economic policies, and became increasingly violent. Cars and buildings were burnt amidst widespread looting and the police and army were authorised to shoot rioters. The official death toll was 22 but unofficial figures suggested over 100 were killed. The government closed all universities, renewed its ban on political activity and arrested hundreds. As the unrest waned Mr Babaniga announced an easing of his economic reforms, but a failed coup attempt by junior officers early in 1990 demonstrated his political problems.

GHANA.

Independence and Military Coups.

Ghana became independent from Britain on 6 March 1957. The country was led by Dr. Kwame Nkrumah, who became president when Ghana was declared a republic in 1960. Ghana became a one-party state in 1964. Nkrumah's government became increasingly autocratic and extravagant, and this led to his overthrow in a military coup while he was on a state visit to China in February 1966. Military rule continued until elections were held in August 1969, which were won by the Progress Party led by Dr. Kofi Busia. In turn he was deposed by the army under General Acheampong in January 1972.

Jerry Rawlings in Power.

Plans were made for a return to civilian rule, but shortly before the elections in 1979 General Acheampong and the Supreme Military Council were overthrown in a coup staged by junior officers led by Flight-Lieutenant Jerry Rawlings. An Armed Forces Revolutionary Council took power, and in an anti-corruption drive, executed senior officers, including General Acheampong. The scheduled elections took place and resulted in a victory for Dr. Hilla Limann and the People's National Party. In December 1981, however, Rawlings staged a second coup, which dismissed parliament, suspended the constitution and banned political parties. A defence council chaired by Flight-Lieutenant Rawlings ruled by decree.

In 1987 Jerry Rawlings was still a popular and respected figure, but his regime had critics from both the left and the right. A National Commission for Democracy, set up in June 1984, had been consulting groups throughout Ghana, but its progress was slow. Ghanaians were reported to be frustrated that they had no say in the running of the country, whilst Jerry Rawlings seemed to have no clear plans for Ghana's long-term future.

KENYA.

Background to Current Events.

Kenya became independent from Britain on 12 December 1963, with Jomo Kenyatta as prime minister and first president when the country became a republic in December 1964. President Kenyatta died in August 1978 and was succeeded by the vice-president, Daniel Arap Moi.

The first half of the 1980s saw a growing concentration of power in the hands of President Moi. In June 1982 the National Assembly declared Kenya officially a one-party state, with the Kenya African National Union (KANU) as the only permitted party. An attempted coup against President Moi was suppressed in August 1982.

In December 1986 the National Assembly voted overwhelmingly for a further increase in presidential power, so that Arap Moi could now dismiss the Attorney-General and Auditor-General without reference to a Commonwealth tribunal as had previously been required. In 1987 President Moi's regime not only faced domestic opposition from those on both the right and the left who objected to his autocratic rule, but it also came under international pressure because of accusations of the abuse of human rights. In March 1987 President Moi cut short a visit to the United States when President Reagan voiced criticisms of the routine use of torture in Kenya.

Nevertheless, in August 1988 the National Assembly unanimously passed a bill to amend the constitution, and give the President and the police wider powers. President Moi was given authority to dismiss High Court and Appeal Court judges, as well as members of the public service commission which supervises the civil service, without consulting a tribunal. The police could detain for up to fourteen days before bringing to court anyone suspected of a capital offence.

In late April 1989 President Moi ordered the closure of the *Financial Review*, a weekly business magazine, for attacks on his government. In June Kenya's largest newspaper, the *Daily Nation*, was banned from reporting parliament after publishing criticisms of President Moi. But, alongside these moves, President Moi ordered the release of a number of political detainees and announced an amnesty for political opponents living in exile.

In May Vice President Josephat Karanja faced a parliamentary vote of no confidence, accused of corruption and of accepting Ugandan money to undermine President Moi's position. Despite his denials he was forced to resign his office—to be replaced by Finance Minister George Saitoti—and his post as deputy president of the Kenya African National Union.

Political Problems Mount.

A greater political problem was posed for President Moi by the death—whether by murder or suicide was unclear—of his Foreign Minister Robert Ouko in February 1990. In July and August 1989 Kenya had suffered a spate of murders of foreigners by bandits. This threatened the country's tourist trade, the main source of foreign exchange. Mr Ouko's death had potentially more dramatic repercussions. A member of the Luo tribe, Mr Ouko was seen as a loyal supporter of President Moi, who belonged to the Kalenjin tribe. Suggestions that Mr Ouko had been too loyal implied continuing underlying tribal conflicts and raised questions about what lay behind his death. At his funeral in Nairobi on 24 February Luo students, having already expressed doubts about government explanations, clashed with police and demanded to see Mr Ouko's body. The government promised a full enquiry into his death.

UGANDA.

Uganda under Amin.

Uganda became independent from Britain on 9 October 1962. In January 1971 the President, Dr. Milton Obote, was overthrown during his absence at the Singapore Commonwealth Conference in a military coup led by General Idi Amin. Britain at first welcomed Amin's rise to power, but it soon became clear that a violation of human rights on a massive scale was taking place in Uganda against potential opponents of his regime.

From the outset the judiciary and police had most of their powers removed in favour of the armed forces. Then in 1972 Amin ordered all Asians with British passports to leave Uganda within ninety days and more than 40,000 were expelled. He was created president for life in June 1976, the same month in which he suffered the humiliation of having an Israeli task force rescue the passengers from an Air France airbus who were being held hostage at Entebbe airport. Britain severed diplomatic relations with Uganda in August 1976. Amin's reign of terror continued amidst reports of massacres and atrocities, including the murder of the Anglican Archbishop of Uganda in February 1977.

In 1978 Uganda invaded Tanzania and made a number of bombing raids. This proved Amin's undoing since previously his African neighbours had been restrained from intervening against him by a fear of creating a precedent by breaking the sacred principle of respect for the arbitrarily drawn colonial frontiers of Africa. By early 1979 Tanzanian forces and Ugandans in exile were advancing through southern Uganda and Amin's troops were mutinying or deserting in large numbers. In April came the fall of Kampala, ending Amin's 8-year brutal rule of terror. He himself was believed to have escaped abroad.

The Return of Obote.

Following the coup against Amin, Professor Yusuf Lule was chosen as a neutral President, although in June he was replaced by Mr. Godfrey Binaisa. This created an unstable security situation, which was worsened in May 1980 when Mr. Binaisa was replaced by Mr. Paulo Muwanga, Chairman of the Military Commission of the Uganda National Liberation Front. Mr. Binaisa had been trying to prevent the return of former President Milton Obote, but the attitude of Tanzania was again decisive. President Nyerere supported Mr. Muwanga, whilst insisting on elections being held. Mr. Obote returned to Uganda in May 1981 and in the ensuing elections his Uganda Peoples Congress won a majority amid charges of ballot-rigging. The remaining Tanzanian troops were withdrawn from Uganda in June.

The Overthrow of Obote.

Violence persisted in Uganda between government forces and guerrillas of the National Resistance Army (NRA), led by the former defence minister, Yoweri Museveni. There were also widespread army atrocities against the civilian population. The turmoil in Uganda came to a head in July 1985 when dissension developed within the army between members of the Langi and Acholi tribes over sharing the burden of the campaign against the NRA. On 27 July Mr. Obote was overthrown and a military council formed, led by the army chief, General Tito Okello.

Museveni Comes to Power.

Negotiations with the NRA began in Nairobi and in December 1985 General Okello and Mr. Museveni reached agreement on a power-sharing government, with the latter taking the position of deputy head. However, continuing violence and indiscipline by the army in Kampala led Mr. Museveni to delay implementing the agreement. Finally, in January 1986 the NRA occupied the capital, General Okello was deposed and Mr. Museveni was sworn in as the new president. As his forces consolidated their hold on the country, President Museveni said in his inauguration address that his priorities would be the promotion of democracy and safeguarding personal security against human rights violations.

President Museveni faced enormous economic problems in seeking to re-establish sound government in Uganda. The period since General Amin's take-over in 1971 had seen the Ugandan economy shrink by over 11 per cent and food production fall by 64 per cent. By 1986 inflation was running at over 200 per cent a year. President Museveni's priority, however, was the security situation. His troops carried out successful operations against rebel bands in the north, killing over 350 in one battle at Corner Kilak in January 1987. With the security situation under control, but inflation still officially running at 120 per cent, Uganda in July 1988 announced a 60 per cent devaluation of the Ugandan shilling and some 100–150 per cent price increases.

President Museveni's National Resistance Movement brought some stability to Uganda. There were, however, rumours in January 1989 that Idi Amin Dada was contemplating a return to Uganda from exile when he was reported to have entered neighbouring Zaire on a false passport. President Museveni demanded Zaire hand him over to be tried for crimes committed while he was in power but Amin returned to exile in Saudi Arabia within days.

The Policy of National Reconciliation.

Throughout 1989 the National Resistance Movement continued a policy of national reconciliation following the long drawn-out turmoil of Uganda's recent past. A congressional commission toured the country inviting proposals for a new constitution from local "resistance committees", many of which were made up of peasants who had been active in the armed struggle against former President Obote. Devolved decision making gave the committees a degree of local autonomy. Political stability encouraged efforts at economic diversification to reduce Ugandan dependence on coffee production. Coffee had accounted for 95% of the country's foreign earnings and by early 1990 it was at a record low price on world markets. Indian owned sugar estates were re-opened and attempts made to create more broadly based agricultural and industrial sectors. At the beginning of 1990 President Museveni announced that his four year old transitional government would be extended for a further five years. But Uganda People's Front armed resistance to the government continued in north-eastern Uganda, led by a former minister in Mr Obote's government.

SOUTH AFRICA.

The Implementation of Apartheid.

The Afrikaans-led Nationalist Party has been in power since 1948. In 1961 after a referendum they made South Africa a republic.

The theory of the government's policy of "apartheid", which owes much to the late Prime Minister, Dr. Verwoerd, looks forward to the eventual partition of South Africa as the only viable alternative to integration, which most Afrikaners regard as racial suicide. In practice, however, the government's policies are adapted to making a rigid caste system based on colour compatible with industrialisation and economic growth. Hence the increasing emphasis on the migrant labour system. Africans are brought to work in industry and returned to the Reserves at the end of their contracts.

The government is unable to impose the taxes on White voters that genuine separate development would require. The Bantustans are therefore likely to remain overcrowded Labour reserves, and millions of Africans will always live and work in the "White areas".

The implementation of apartheid legislation covering employment, housing and education after 1948 led to increasing African unrest, organised especially by the African National Congress (ANC). In 1959 the Pan-Africanist Congress (PAC) broke from the ANC, and began to organise anti-pass law demonstrations. In March 1960 such a demonstration took place at the police station in the African township of Sharpeville. The police opened fire, killing 69 Africans and wounding over 180. The government declared a state of emergency and began mass arrests of African leaders. Strikes and mass marches of Africans continued for another week and the government then banned the ANC and PAC under the Suppression of Communism Act. Some African leaders went underground and organised a campaign of sabotage. But the security forces were able to infiltrate the organisations and in 1963 Nelson Mandela, the outstanding African leader, was captured with others and brought to trial. He was sentenced to life imprisonment.

Unrest among the Africans broke out again in 1973 with widespread strikes in Natal. In 1976 the worst riots since Sharpeville occurred in Soweto. The immediate cause was opposition to the compulsory use of Afrikaans as the medium of instruction in schools. The riots continued throughout the summer and spread to other areas. In 1976 independence was granted to the Transkei, a Bantu homeland, and in 1977 Bophutatswana became the second "Bantustan", followed by Venda in 1979. However, these states have not received international recognition.

Growing Repression in South Africa.

During 1977 the South African Government was faced with challenges to the apartheid system from various quarters. The Roman Catholic church opened its schools to all races and its Bishops' Conference published a 21-point programme for improving the situation of the Blacks. Several large American firms announced their intention of ending racial segregation in their South African branches. And the European Community also laid down guidelines for firms operating in South Africa which required equality for Black workers. The reaction was mixed. In the spring, the threat of compulsory press censorship produced an agreement on voluntary self-censorship by the press. On the other hand, White political leaders in Natal announced in July that they wanted to investigate the possibility of an autonomous multi-racial government in the province. The following month plans were made for a new South African Constitution whereby significant rights and participation would be extended to the Coloureds and the Indians but not to the Blacks, on the ground that they were covered by the Bantustan policy.

Tension and violence increased following the deaths in prison of numerous Black activists who had been imprisoned without trial. Major riots were triggered off by the death of Steve Biko, the most popular Black leader, in whose case there were contradictions in the explanations given by the Minister of Justice and an inquiry showed severe head-wounds. In October the police raided 17 Black nationalist organisations and the Christian Institute, which was hostile to the régime: all were banned. This action represented a short-sighted snapping of the last threads of understanding between the races. Coming in the wake of steadily worsening relations between the United States and

South Africa, it probably indicated that the latter had given up the attempt to placate Western opinion. General elections held on 30 November, in which Mr. Vorster's National Party won its greatest ever electoral victory with 135 seats out of 165, also suggested that Black unrest and world indignation over developments in South Africa had produced a dangerous attitude of defiance among Whites.

Mulder and the Resignation of Vorster.

In the autumn of 1978 Mr. Vorster moved to the less strenuous office of President. He was succeeded as Prime Minister by Pieter Willem Botha. The latter was given a difficult start by the uncovering of a scandal at the Information Ministry, where it emerged that public money had disappeared into a secret fund to finance shady activities and propaganda. Leading politicians were implicated, the former Information Minister Connie Mulder had to resign and the government suffered a serious loss of popularity. Significantly this scandal rocked the government much more than the Soweto riots, since which little seemed to have changed. By mid-1979 the "Muldergate" scandal had implicated the very highest echelons of the South African Government. President Vorster resigned in June after the report of the commission of inquiry set up by the Government concluded that he must bear joint responsibility for continued irregularities of which he had been aware while Prime Minister. He was succeeded by Mr. Marais Viljoen, who had previously been President of the Senate. A traditional conservative, he was seen by some as a possible bridgebuilder between the Government and those groups which were hostile to Mr. Botha's reform plans, which were further strengthened by the government reorganisation of 26 August, 1980, with reformist ministers being placed in three key positions, including defence and education. However, Botha's plans continued to cause dismay in certain sections of his party. The election called by Botha for April 1981, though resulting in an easy victory for the ruling party, saw significant defections both to the extreme-right and to the progressives.

Plans for Constitutional Reform.

A bill to give a limited parliamentary voice to Asians and coloureds (but not blacks) was introduced on 5 May 1983. It proposed a three chamber parliament, with separate assemblies for whites, coloureds (mixed race) and Indians. Each race would exercise control over its own domestic affairs, while dealing in common with matters such as defence. An executive President, elected by an electoral college of the three chambers, would decide what were "common" affairs. Despite opposition from the Conservative Party, the bill was approved by parliament on 9 September 1983 by 119 votes to 35. In a referendum in November, two-thirds of the white population voted in favour of the new constitution.

The New Constitution.

Elections to the new assemblies for coloureds and Indians were held in August 1984. Violence occurred during the elections as the multi-racial United Democratic Front campaigned for a boycott. In the poll for the coloured House of Representatives there was a 30% turn-out of registered voters (some 60% of those eligible had registered) and the Labour Party won 76 of the 80 seats; for the Indian House of Delegates there was a 20% turn-out (80% had registered) and the two biggest groups were the National People's Party with 18 seats and Solidarity with 17 in the 40-seat House. The revised constitution came into effect in September and P. W. Botha was elected to the post of executive President by an electoral college of the three assemblies. President Botha's new cabinet included one coloured and one Indian member, although neither had executive portfolios.

South Africa's position in the international community initially appeared to be improving at the beginning of 1984. In February and March, South African pressure led her neighbours, Mozambique and Angola, both facing grave economic and internal security problems, to come to terms in the Nkomati and Lusaka accords.

Growing Violence and Repression.

However, South Africa's efforts to improve her standing in the world in spite of apartheid were offset by rioting in black townships in September over rent increases (later suspended), continuing sabotage attacks by ANC guerrillas and the award of the Nobel Peace Prize to the anti-apartheid campaigner, Desmond Tutu, who was installed as the first black Bishop of Johannesburg in February 1985. Moreover, the full implementation of the Nkomati and Lusaka accords to bring peace to the region was still not accomplished at the beginning of 1985. During spring 1985 continued unrest, especially in the Eastern Cape black townships led to severe police repression. It was reported that between 3 September 1984 and 9 July 1985 there were 443 deaths in the townships. Finally on 20 July a state of emergency was proclaimed in 36 areas of the country. When violence continued the government imposed strict regulations on the reporting of the unrest in November 1985.

Hopes of radical changes in the system of apartheid were disappointed in August 1985 when President Botha, in a much-heralded speech to the Natal Congress of his National Party, attacked his country's critics rather than announcing reforms. As a result South Africa's foreign exchanges had to be closed for a week when the rand hit a record low against the dollar. In September the government announced a four-month freeze on foreign debt capital repayments.

President Botha adopted a more conciliatory stance in September when he proposed a restoration of South African citizenship to the five million blacks who had been assigned to the homelands in the 1970s but were still living in South Africa; he suggested negotiations regarding the five million actually in the homelands. However, he received a setback in terms of his own white support in October when the ultra-rightwing Herstigte Nasionale Party captured the parliamentary seat of Sasolburg in the Orange Free State, the first in its sixteen-year existence.

International Pressure.

Lack of progress on reform and the violent repression of unrest in the black townships led to increased international pressure on South Africa in the autumn of 1985. The EEC approved a modest package of sanctions and President Reagan imposed American trade restrictions in September, though the latter were intended to forestall more extensive sanctions under consideration by Congress. A meeting of Commonwealth leaders at Nassau in October also agreed, despite British reluctance, on limited measures, such as a ban on the import of Krugerrands.

After the negative effects of his speech in August 1985, President Botha attempted to make a fresh start in his address at the opening of parliament in January 1986. He said that South Africa had outgrown the apartheid system and that he intended to establish a national statutory council, including black representatives, to find answers to the country's problems. But the genuineness of white South Africa's desire for reform remained in doubt.

In his January 1986 speech President Botha referred to the release of Nelson Mandela, the leader of the outlawed African National Congress serving a life sentence for sabotage. He linked Mr. Mandela's release to that of Soviet dissidents and Captain Wynand du Toit, a South African commando captured in 1985 by the Angolans. However, Mr. Mandela had earlier rejected President Botha's offer to set him free if he renounced violence as a political instrument, and in February 1986 his wife, Winnie Mandela, said he would only accept freedom if he was released in South Africa and not sent into exile. The first major conference of the African National Congress for sixteen years had been held in June 1985 in Kabwe in Zambia and agreed to intensify the people's war against apartheid.

South Africa Goes it Alone.

In 1986 South Africa's rejection of outside interference in its future became more stark. During the second visit by the Commonwealth "eminent persons group" in May 1986, the South African defence forces launched raids on ANC targets in Zambia,

Zimbabwe and Botswana. The Commonwealth delegation left in protest at what could only be seen as the deliberate wrecking of their mediation efforts. In July 1986 Sir Geoffrey Howe undertook a mission to southern Africa in his capacity as president of the Council of the European Communities, but President Botha bluntly rejected proposals for negotiations with the ANC.

In turn the international community took further steps to express its disapproval of South Africa's policies. In the United States in September 1986 President Reagan vetoed a bill providing for new economic measures against South Africa, but both the House of Representatives and the Senate voted in favour by the two-third's majority necessary to override the veto. In November 1986 a number of American, Canadian and British firms, including Barclays Bank and Kodak Eastman, withdrew from their business dealings in South Africa.

Violence continued at a high level during 1986 (an estimated 1,300 people died during the year), and brought new repressive measures. A nationwide state of emergency was declared in June, just before the tenth anniversary of the Soweto uprising. Then in December 1986 sweeping new curbs were imposed on the media, including a ban on reporting any opposition activity without prior authorisation. In the lead-up to the white-only elections in May 1987, the South African government introduced restrictions on all forms of protest intended to secure the release of detainees in April. The government's brake on the reform programme, together with the failure of the right-wing Conservative Party and Herstigte Nasional Party to reach an electoral pact, helped to defuse the electoral threat to Mr. Botha's National Party from the right. A commando raid by South African forces on alleged ANC targets across the Zambian border in Livingstone at the end of April was also seen as a vote-catching exercise by Mr. Botha's government.

The May 1987 Elections.

The results of the election constituted a landslide victory for the ruling National Party. South Africa's whites lurched to the right, returning the National Party with 123 of the 166 seats. The ultra-right Conservative Party, with 26% of the vote won 22 seats, becoming the official opposition in place of the weakened Progressive Federal Party. Only one independent (Wynand Malan, in Randburg) was victorious. Dennis Worrall, South Africa's former Ambassador in London, missed victory by 39 votes. All in all, the outcome was one of despair for those seeking peaceful change in South Africa.

The Right-Wing Challenge to Botha.

The election results strongly suggested that the main threat to the political authority of Mr. Botha and the National Party came from the right-wing rather than the liberal opposition. To keep that threat at bay Mr. Botha continued to crack down on the opponents of the apartheid system. In February 1988 Mr. Botha introduced a ban on all the activities of seventeen anti-apartheid groups and the Congress of South African Trades Unions was restricted to a non-political role only. Nevertheless the National Party suffered a series of defeats in by-elections at the hands of the Conservative Party in the spring of 1988.

In October 1988 the struggle between the Conservative Party and the National Party focussed on the local government elections. For the first time all races went to the polls, though the eight hundred municipal councillors were segregated by race. In the white elections the National Party did well enough to suggest that the swing to the right was slowing down. The National Party won Johannesburg, as well as gaining ground in Natal.

The Conservatives had their successes, however. They took a large majority of urban and rural seats in the Transvaal, though Pretoria itself narrowly remained loyal to the National Party. In November the Conservative Party resolved to restore apartheid in the municipalities it controlled. In the black elections only 344,000 of the 1,500,000 registered voters (from a total black population of 26 million) turned out to vote. Only half the seats for black councillors were contested, and there were no candidates in more than a hundred wards.

South Africa's International Standing.

Pressure on South Africa to change its apartheid policies continued in 1988. In August the United States' House of Representatives voted to impose further economic sanctions. But there were also moves by South Africa to improve its international image. In August a cease-fire was arranged in Angola, and in December 1988 an agreement on Namibian independence was reached. In September and October President Botha visited Mozambique, Malawi and Zaire for talks with their leaders.

At home, when Nelson Mandela was admitted to hospital suffering from tuberculosis, it gave the government the opportunity to announce in November 1988 that he would be kept under close house arrest, but not returned to prison. Also in November, the "Sharpeville Six" were reprieved from hanging for their alleged part in the death of a Sharpeville councillor in 1984, another issue which had stirred world opinion.

Mr Botha's Future.

In January 1989 73-year old President Botha suffered a mild stroke. During his recovery the Minister of Constitutional Affairs, Mr. Heunis, was sworn in as acting president. In February Mr. Botha stood down as leader of the National Party and the Transvaal leader, Mr. F. W. de Clerk was elected in his place. Although Mr. Botha at first insisted that he had no plans for early retirement, in early May he announced a general election to be held on 6 September. The Botha era was effectively over.

Recent Events.

See **Special Topic, C86–88** for the dramatic background to the release of Nelson Mandela in early 1990 and the reforms of President de Klerk.

NAMIBIA.

Namibia, formerly South-West Africa, was colonised by Germany in 1884. It was captured by South African troops in 1915 and mandated to South Africa by the League of Nations at the end of the First World War. After the Second World War the status of the area became a matter of dispute as South Africa sought to integrate Namibia into its territory. In 1966 the UN General Assembly resolved that the South African mandate should be revoked on the grounds that South Africa was extending apartheid to the territory. In the same year guerrillas belonging to the South-West Africa People's Organisation (SWAPO), founded in 1960, launched an armed liberation struggle against the South African armed forces. In 1971 the United Nations recognised SWAPO as the sole authentic representative of the Namibian people. South Africa pursued plans of its own for a constitutional settlement involving independence for Namibia, in the 1970s and 1980s, but these were generally unacceptable to SWAPO and the United Nations.

Agreement on Namibian Independence.

In May 1988 delegations representing Angola, South Africa and Cuba met in London for talks on Namibian independence, with the United States acting as mediator. After a number of rounds of talks in Brazzaville and New York, an agreement was reached in Geneva in August for a cease-fire in Angola.

The main stumbling block to a settlement in Namibia was the South African demand for the withdrawal of Cuban troops from Angola. A timetable was eventually agreed in talks in Geneva in November 1988. The following month at the UN headquarters in New York, an accord was signed by South Africa, Cuba and Angola for the transition of Namibia to independence to begin in April 1989, and a second agreement for the withdrawal of all Cuban forces from Angola by July 1991. The Namibian independence accord entailed the establishment of a UN Transition Assistance Group to oversee Namibia's seven-month progress through free elections to independence, while a smaller force would monitor the Cuban troop withdrawals. The incursion of SWAPO fighters into Namibia threatened this accord. SWAPO leader Sam Nujoma ordered the guerrillas to withdraw from Namibia, which they did at the end of April after 263 had died in clashes with South African forces.

But tension increased in the run up to the November elections. A formally disbanded South African led paramilitary police unit was accused of intimidating blacks to weaken their support for SWAPO. On 12 September a leading white SWAPO member was murdered in Windhoek, apparently by a white terrorist group. But the South African administrator repealed apartheid legislation in Namibia and agreed on amnesty for returning exiles. Mr Nujoma returned from his 30-year exile and urged the country's 85,000 whites to assist actively in the independence process.

Electoral Success for SWAPO.

SWAPO was successful at the November elections, though not to the extent its leaders might have wished. The organisation's manifesto proposed a mixed economy with none of the large-scale nationalisation previously advocated. When the results were announced on 14 November SWAPO had taken 53% of the vote and won 41 of the 72 Constituent Assembly seats being contested. The main opposition party, the Democratic Turnhalle Alliance, won 21 seats with 28% of the vote. Two smaller parties, the United Democratic Front and Action Christian National, gained four and three seats respectively. SWAPO's disappointment lay in being denied the two thirds majority which would have allowed a decisive say in formulating Namibia's post-independence constitution. Mr Nujoma promised SWAPO co-operation with other parties, though his eventual objective was a one-party state.

He was unanimously elected the country's first President by the Constituent Assembly on 16 February 1990, to be sworn in by the UN secretary general when Namibia gained independence in March.

ZIMBABWE.

In order to preserve white minority rule in Rhodesia, the Prime Minister, Ian Smith, made a "unilateral declaration of independence" from Britain in November 1965. Britain imposed trade sanctions and an oil embargo, but Mr. Smith was able to rely on South Africa for support. Rhodesia declared itself a republic in March 1970. A guerrilla campaign waged against Mr. Smith's regime by black nationalists grew in intensity. The two main liberation movements, the Zimbabwe African People's Union (ZAPU), under Joshua Nkomo, and the Zimbabwe African National Union (ZANU), led by Robert Mugabe, formed the Patriotic Front alliance in October 1976.

In October 1976 a conference on Rhodesia was held at Geneva, involving Mr. Smith and a range of Rhodesian African leaders, but no settlement was reached. Instead Mr. Smith pursued negotiations with moderate Africans inside Rhodesia led by Bishop Muzorewa, and in March 1978 concluded an agreement for a new constitution with them. However, this was unacceptable to the Patriotic Front and was rejected by Britain and the UN.

At the Commonwealth Conference in Lusaka in August 1979 arrangements were made for fresh constitutional talks to be held at Lancaster House in London and these took place from September to December 1979. A cease-fire was agreed, together with terms for a new constitution, fresh elections and legal independence for Zimbabwe. Voting for the twenty white seats in the legislative assembly took place in February 1980, all of them going to Ian Smith's Rhodesian Front, and voting for the black seats followed in March.

Mugabe's Sweeping Victory.

The elections for the 80 Black seats in the 100-member House of Assembly produced a sweeping victory for Mugabe. His ZANU (PF) Party won 57 seats and 63% of the vote. Nkomo's Party won a disappointing 20 seats, while Bishop Muzorewa's United African National Council won only a humiliating 8% of the vote and a mere 3 seats. On 17 April 1980, Zimbabwe became an independent Republic with Mugabe as Prime Minister of a coalition which included Nkomo. The Rev. Canaan Banana became the first President.

Mugabe's early period of office was made difficult by murder charges being brought against one of his Cabinet ministers, Mr. Edgar Tekere, who was subsequently acquitted. However, he was later dismissed in a Cabinet reshuffle which also saw the demotion of Joshua Nkomo. The latter's followers, who along with many whites were worried by Mugabe's assumption of control of the news media, took part in violent clashes with Mugabe supporters, and there were many casualties before order was restored. The disarming of guerrilla groups was largely completed by May 1981. In the previous month Salisbury, the capital of Zimbabwe, had been renamed Harare.

Dismissal and Exile of Mr Nkomo.

The political outlook in Zimbabwe changed considerably in February 1982 when secret stockpiles of weapons were found on farms belonging to Nkomo. He denied he had been planning a coup, but he and three other ZAPU officials were dismissed from the cabinet by Mugabe. ZAPU retained a token presence in the government but the coalition was a dead letter. Nkomo's dismissal passed off initially without bloodshed. However, later in 1982, a new threat to Zimbabwe's stability occurred. Outbreaks of violence took place in Matabeleland following harsh repressive action by the North Korean-trained Fifth Army Brigade against supporters of Nkomo. This reached a head in March 1983 when Nkomo himself fled, first to Botswana and then on to exile in London.

Nkomo returned in August 1983 when the government made moves to strip him of his parliamentary seat. However, Mugabe took another step towards making Zimbabwe a one-party state in October 1983 when he arrested Bishop Muzorewa on the grounds of his being a threat to Zimbabwe's security. Bishop Muzorewa was freed in September 1984.

Relations with Britain and America.

Zimbabwe's relations with Britain were soured in 1983 by the trial of six white air force officers begun in May for complicity in the sabotage of 13 military aircraft at Thornhill Air Base in July 1982. Evidence that their confessions had been obtained by torture led to the acquittal of the six men on 31 August, but they were immediately redetained by the government. Three were released in September, but the others were not released until 23 December. Then at the close of 1983 the United States announced that it had cut its $75 m of aid to Zimbabwe by $35 m after Zimbabwe had co-sponsored a UN resolution condemning the American invasion of Grenada and abstained in a Security Council vote condemning the Russian shooting down of a South Korean airliner.

Towards a One-Party State.

In August 1984 ZANU held its second national congress (the first was in 1964) in Harare, which consolidated Mr. Mugabe's position in the party and government and ZANU's national authority. Some six thousand ZANU delegates attended the five-day conference. Mr. Mugabe was made First Secretary and President of the party, and a new fifteen-member political bureau, chosen by him, was created to exercise supreme power. The congress called for the creation of the post of executive president for Zimbabwe, and also endorsed a resolution calling for the creation of a one-party state, though the timing of this would respect the Lancaster House constitution. In November, Mr. Mugabe dismissed the two remaining ZAPU ministers from his cabinet, after blaming ZAPU for the death of a member of the ZANU central committee, thus ending all co-operation between ZANU and ZAPU.

Elections were held in mid-1985. At the end of June, elections for the 20 seats reserved for whites in the House of Assembly resulted in 15 being won by Ian Smith's Conservative Alliance of Zimbabwe, to the displeasure of Mr. Mugabe's supporters. Elections for the remaining seats were held at the beginning of July. ZANU won a landslide victory with 64 seats, but Mr. Nkomo's ZAPU secured all 15 seats in Matabeleland. The country therefore seemed to be more divided than ever on racial and tribal lines.

When Mr. Mugabe announced a new cabinet after the elections, Mr. Anderson was the only white and non-ZANU member. A number of senior members of ZAPU were detained in August, but nevertheless talks in September 1985 between ZANU and ZAPU delegations reached broad agreement on a merger between the two parties.

ZANU-ZAPU Relations.

In April 1987, however, on the eve of the seventh anniversary of independence, Mr. Mugabe suddenly announced the suspension of unity talks between ZANU and ZAPU, on the grounds that they had been deadlocked too long and were serving no useful purpose. Mr. Nkomo said that this was only a temporary setback, but it reflected the difficulty of securing agreement within ZANU to the sharing of power with ZAPU and the Ndebele minority which it represented.

There were renewed attacks by dissidents in May 1987 and in June the government banned ZAPU from holding meetings or rallies. Although Mr. Nkomo denied that his party was connected with the violence, all ZAPU offices were closed in September.

ZANU-ZAPU Merger.

In June 1987 the government announced that it planned to abolish separate white representation in parliament. Seven years after the Lancaster House settlement it was possible to enact this with seventy votes in favour rather than one hundred as was previously the case. The departing whites were replaced by the nominees of all races chosen by the eighty black MPs.

Despite events earlier in the year Mr. Mugabe and Mr. Nkomo finally reached agreement on the merger of the two parties in December 1987. Mr. Mugabe became the party's first secretary and president, while Mr. Nkomo became one of the two vice-presidents. On the last day of 1987 President Banana retired and Mr. Mugabe became Zimbabwe's first executive President. In January 1988 an expanded cabinet was sworn in, with Mr. Nkomo nominated to oversee several ministries concerned with rural development. Two other ZAPU members and a white MP were also given cabinet posts. In April 1988 special meetings of ZAPU and ZANU endorsed the merger of the two parties. Mr. Nkomo was appointed the party's interim second vice-president.

Investigation into Corruption.

The road to a one party state did not run as smoothly as Mr Mugabe might have hoped. In March and April 1989 his government was shaken by a scandal involving senior members. In November 1988 Mr Mugabe had appointed an investigation commission under Justice Sandura to examine press allegations of ministerial involvement in corrupt dealing in state manufactured automobiles. Before the results of the inquiry were made public six of Mr Mugabe's associates resigned, including his defence minister. The most senior of them, Mr Maurice Nyagumbo, committed suicide on 20 April. Sandura, reporting on 13 April, called for the prosecution of former and present ministers and of two MPs. A junior minister was later given nine months for perjury, a sentence personally quashed by Mr Mugabe.

The affair added little to the popularity of a government held responsible for the unemployment of a million of Zimbabwe's nine million citizens.

Economic Problems in Zimbabwe.

Mr Mugabe concentrated on Zimbabwe's pressing economic problems in a speech on 18 April, the ninth anniversary of the country's independence. Growth since 1980, he said, had been inadequate and he proposed to remedy this by creating a more market oriented economy, encouraging foreign investment, and reducing administrative interference in business. Mr Mugabe insisted, however, that his ambition for Zimbabwe remained socialism.

But Edgar Tekere, a former close ally in the independence struggle expelled from ZANU-PF in 1988 for alleging government corruption and for his opposition to a one-party state, favoured a more thorough-going capitalist economy combined with multi-party democracy. He announced on 30 April the formation of a new party, the Zimbabwe Unity Movement (ZUM).

The Zimbabwe Unity Movement.

Mr Mugabe described the new party as "the joke of the year" but his government nevertheless banned ZUM demonstrations and public meetings and there were rumours of assassination attempts on Mr Tekere. The move to a one-party state continued. At a ZANU-PF "Victory Congress" early in 1990 Mr Mugabe shook hands with the leaders of PF-ZAPU, the largest opposition party, and said the two tribal based parties had pledged to work closely together. At the same time he renewed the state of emergency first introduced by the Smith regime in 1965, to protests from the churches and human rights groups. Mr Mugabe's position appeared strengthened by the results of the March 1990 elections. He was returned as President with 78% of the votes cast, Mr Tekere winning 16%. In the contest for the new single chamber parliament ZANU-PF took 116 of the 120 seats and ZUM only two. But only 54% of Zimbabwe's 4·8 million eligible voters turned out (the figure had been 95% in previous elections) and apathy was deepest among the urban working-class. There were also charges of ballot rigging. Nevertheless, Zimbabwe was expected to become a one party state in 1990.

MOZAMBIQUE.

A transitional government was installed in September 1974 made up of Frelimo (Front for the Liberation of Mozambique) and Portuguese elements and full independence was scheduled for July 1975. However, the agreement led to serious racial unrest with white extremists attempting to proclaim UDI and thereby provoking a Black backlash. Nevertheless independence was granted on schedule. The Marxistoriented government under President Machel produced plans to revolutionise the state machine and improve the economy. In December an attempt to overthrow President Machel was crushed. Relations with Portugal deteriorated and in February 1976 the capital Lourenço Marques was renamed Maputo.

Growing Internal Resistance.

President Machel continued to face internal opposition from the so-called Mozambique National Resistance Movement which carried out widespread sabotage and terrorist attacks. The rebels were supported by South Africa as a lever to force the Mozambique government to withdraw its backing for the African National Congress, the militant black nationalist organisation banned in South Africa. In January 1981 South African forces carried out a commando raid in a suburb of Maputo against three houses occupied by the ANC. Guerrilla warfare continued throughout 1982–3. Following a car bomb explosion in Pretoria, the South African Air Force mounted a raid on Maputo on 23 May 1983, killing five people. Representatives of Mozambique and South Africa met for talks on security problems and economic co-operation in January 1984.

The Nkomati Accord.

These talks resulted in the signing of a non-aggression pact, the Nkomati accord, by Mozambique and South Africa in March 1984. A joint commission was set up to monitor the working of the accord. After a series of negotiations, the South African foreign minister, Pik Botha, announced in Pretoria in October that the government of Mozambique and the MNRM had agreed in principle to a cease-fire. However, guerrilla warfare continued into 1985 and President Machel accused South Africa of not curbing MNRM attacks, although Mozambique had expelled many ANC members. During talks in September 1985 President Machel was able to confront the South Africans with documents captured at the MNRM headquarters at Gorongosa, proving their continuing support for the guerrillas.

By mid-1986 Mozambique was in a state of semi-paralysis as the MNRM concentrated on striking at transportation targets. Eighty per cent of the countryside was controlled by the MNRM, although no major towns. Raids on Maputo itself had been halted by a successful ambush by government troops in March 1986. In September 1986 Mr. Veloso, Minister of Co-operation, appealed for international aid to bring relief to some four million Mozambicans in danger of starvation.

Death of President Machel.

Tragedy struck on 19 October 1986 when President Machel was killed as his plane crashed returning from Zambia, where he had been taking part in a conference with the leaders of Angola, Zambia and Zaïre. The aircraft, a Soviet Tupolev-134A3 jet, struck the ground a short distance inside South Africa. Despite suspicions of some form of sabotage, an enquiry blamed bad weather and pilot error for the accident.

Samora Machel had been president of Frelimo since 1970, following the murder of the movement's founder, Eduardo Mondlane, and president of Mozambique since independence in 1975. He was a charismatic leader, who enjoyed great personal popularity although his Marxist policies were not always successful. As his successor, the central committee of Frelimo elected the Foreign Minister, Mr. Joaquim Chissano, to be president of the party and thus of the country. Mr. Chissano, a close political associate of Mr. Machel though in some respects a more moderate figure, was sworn in as head of state in November 1986.

Mozambique under Chissano.

Mozambique under Mr. Chissano now faced both the ravages of war and the threat of starvation. In December 1986 Tanzanian troops were brought in to join the Zimbabwean contingent which had been assisting the Mozambique army against the MNRM since 1982. By April 1987 eight of Mozambique's ten provinces were officially on the famine danger list.

During 1988 Mozambique remained heavily dependent on foreign aid, especially from the USSR. Putting into effect an IMF-inspired economic recovery programme led in April 1988 to the removal of food subsidies, and a seven-fold increase in the price of rice. In November 1988, as an economy measure, Tanzania recalled its troops assisting the Mozambique army, but Zimbabwean forces remained to defend road and rail links, and the oil pipeline to Zimbabwe from the port of Beira.

On 19 July 1989 South African President de Klerk, making his first visit to a black African state, met President Chissano in Maputo, the Mozambique capital. President de Klerk urged the Renamo rebels to stop fighting and to assist in the search for peace. He said South Africa was no longer providing aid to Renamo guerrillas.

ANGOLA.

Independence from Portugal.

Negotiations for Angolan independence from Portugal in 1974 were complicated by the presence of three rival independence movements: People's Movement for the Liberation of Angola (MPLA), National Union for the Total Independence of Angola (UNITA) and National Front for the Liberation of Angola (FNLA). However, agreement was reached that Angola should become independent on 11 November 1975.

The Civil War.

But fighting continued, particularly between the FNLA and the Marxist MPLA, despite a truce agreement in March and became increasingly intense. During the summer of 1975 the MPLA gradually took over sole control of the capital Luanda, and UNITA joined the FNLA in operations against the MPLA. The latter held a central strip from the coast to the border with Zaïre, while UNITA held most of the South, and FNLA the rest of the South and the northern provinces.

In the months before independence there was a massive departure of European settlers, leaving appalling economic problems for Angola. Meanwhile there was increasing evidence of the Soviet Union supplying the MPLA with arms. Several thousand Cuban soldiers also appeared on the MPLA side. The FNLA received support from China and initially from the USA via Zaïre. In November two separate Angolan Republics were proclaimed with rival governments being set up, by the MPLA in Luanda and by FNLA and UNITA in Huambo (formerly Nova Lisboa).

Full-scale civil war now developed. With Soviet and Cuban support, the MPLA first brought the North under control pushing the FNLA back into Zaïre. UNITA forces in the South were attacked and the South African forces which had advanced several hundred miles into Angola withdrew to patrol a 30-mile wide strip along the border. In February 1976, following the capture of Huambo, an MPLA victory was declared. UNITA forces under Dr. Jonas Savimbi and the FNLA under Mr. Holden Roberto continued guerrilla activities throughout 1976 while the MPLA attempted to bring the country back to normal. Periodic UNITA success kept President Neto dependent on the Cubans, with whom a series of agreements on co-operation had been concluded.

In September 1979 President Neto died. Though Moscow's protégé, he kept the Russians and Cubans at a distance after gaining power and won the respect of neighbouring, and even of Western, states. Dr. José Eduardo dos Santos was elected to succeed him.

The Lusaka Accord.

Frequent raids into Angola were mounted by South African forces hunting for South West Africa People's Organisation (SWAPO) guerrillas. A major incursion was launched in December 1983. This was followed, however, by a South African announcement of a one-month truce in February 1984. After talks in the Zambian capital, Lusaka, an accord was signed by Angola and South Africa on 16 February 1984. The cease-fire was extended, and, in return for a South African withdrawal, Angola agreed to curb SWAPO operations into Namibia.

It was not until April 1985 that South African troops officially withdrew from Angolan territory and then fresh incursions took place in June and September. The latter came just as government forces were attempting to mount a major offensive against UNITA. The South African government admitted it was still supporting the rebels and would continue to do so until all foreign troops had been withdrawn from Angola.

The Angolan government faced fresh problems as the American Congress voted in mid-1985 to repeal the 1976 Clark amendment banning aid to the UNITA guerrillas. In July 1985 Angola announced the suspension of all contacts with the United States.

Relations with the West.

American support for UNITA, at a time when the Angolan economy was already suffering from the effects of falling oil prices, forced the Angolan government to turn to the Soviet Union for increased aid. In June 1986 the air force commander, General Carreira, was dismissed after advocating that Angola should buy military equipment from the West as well as from the Soviet bloc.

However, this proved to be a brief hiatus in Angola's movement towards a rapprochement with the West. In December 1986 the Foreign Minister, Alfonso van Dunen, visited Portugal for talks, and in Spring 1987 Angola resumed its contacts with the United States over the future of southern Africa.

South African Involvement.

Conflict continued in Angola during 1987, and in November South Africa admitted that its defence forces were as heavily engaged in support of UNITA as at any time since 1985. The UN Security Council passed a resolution condemning South Africa for its interference in Angolan affairs.

Talks regarding a cease-fire, independence for Namibia and the withdrawal of Cuban troops from Angola began in the Spring of 1988 between Angola, South Africa and Cuba, with the United

States acting as mediator. In August 1988 an agreement for a cease-fire in Angola was reached in Geneva, and South African troops withdrew from Angola by the end of the month. A formal cease-fire was signed at Ruacana, near the border between Angola and Namibia.

Negotiations continued, and led in December 1988 to the signing at the UN headquarters in New York of an agreement for the start of Namibia's transition to independence to begin in April 1989, and also for a complete withdrawal of Cuban forces from Angola by 1 July 1991. The first contingent of about 3,000 Cuban troops left in January 1989, three months before the deadline for the start of the Cuban disengagement.

On 14 February 1989 Jonas Savimbi suspended UNITA's annual offensive against the MPLA which had opened on 8 February. This was at the request of Ivory Coast President Houphouet-Boigny who was attempting to mediate an end to the civil war. The MPLA had offered an amnesty for UNITA guerrillas and their integration into Angola's one party state, provided Mr Savimbi was excluded. On 13 March UNITA announced his willingness to withdraw during a two year government of national reconciliation provided he could contest later elections. But President dos Santos denounced Mr Savimbi as a war criminal.

The June Cease-Fire.

However, on 22 June President dos Santos and Mr Savimbi met at an African summit in Zaire and announced a cease-fire commencing on 23 June, followed by peace negotiations. Their agreement was encouraged by the Soviet Union's reluctance to continue arming the MPLA and the US view that UNITA was less important now Cuban forces were withdrawing. Peace talks in Zaire on 28–29 June were temporarily suspended on 30 June when both sides accused each other of breaking the truce. A second round was held from 16–22 July. The cease-fire ended again at the end of August, with mutual recriminations, but Mr Savimbi agreed to allow another month for negotiations to recommence. In Washington on 5 October, Mr Savimbi accepted President Bush's urging to renew the cease-fire.

Membership of IMF.

Meanwhile, Angola became a member of the International Monetary Fund and the World Bank on 19 September, despite US opposition. Finance Minister Augusto Teixeira de Matos argued that his government was instituting reforms to create a more market oriented economy. He said Angola would require aid to rebuild the war-damaged infrastructure.

THE UNITED STATES

Reagan's First Months.

Ronald Reagan's first year in office demonstrated that the political skills which he had nurtured as Governor of California, and refined in his bids for the Presidency, had not deserted him. The November 1980 elections were thought to have given him a clear mandate both for his domestic economic policies and his foreign policy. The latter rested on a huge expansion of the defence budget to meet Soviet military expansion. Reagan drew heavily on the stock of political capital provided by his election victory and the Republican advances in Congress to cut severely spending on social, welfare and educational programmes in an attempt to reduce the growing Federal deficit. But, like President Carter before him, Reagan discovered by the end of his first year as President that eliminating, or even substantially reducing the Federal deficit was far from easy.

Indeed, the deficit grew substantially under the triple pressures of the cut in taxes (which Reagan skilfully piloted through Congress), the effect of the deepening recession on the total tax revenues, and the heavy increases in defence spending. By early 1982, Reagan's sure touch in front of the television cameras, and his ardent wooing of Congress (which was in any case ideologically predisposed to support him) no longer seemed sufficient to meet the mounting doubts about his fiscal and monetary policies. Interest rates remained stubbornly high, propped up by the Federal deficit, and the rate of unemployment increased. Reagan's own budget for 1982 projected a deficit of between $90 and $100bn. The Congressional Budget Office was more pessimistic, forecasting a deficit of $160bn for 1984, the year of the next Presidential elections. But there were political pressures building up in the short term, too. The approach of the mid-term elections in 1982 caused Republican Congressmen and Senators to look hesitantly at their electorate's views before supporting the President's domestic strategy.

But if doubts were raised about Reagan's policies, he continued to show deft political touches. Perhaps the most striking was his nomination of Judge Sandra Day O'Connor to be an Associate Justice of the Supreme Court. Mrs. O'Connor took the place of Justice Potter Steward who had sat on the Court for 23 years. She was an active Republican from Arizona, and an excellent jurist, but clearly not associated with the extreme right-wing of the Republican Party. The Moral Majority and other extreme groups opposed her confirmation by the Senate because of her somewhat liberal views on abortion. The Senate none the less confirmed her nomination by 99 votes to 0. President Reagan thus distanced himself from the far-right of his Party, appeased liberal and women's groups by selecting a woman, but still succeeded in selecting a moderately conservative nominee with an impeccable legal, and unassailable political, record.

1982 Congressional Elections.

The mid-term Congressional elections in November 1982 produced the customary swing to the party in opposition: the Democrats made net gains of 24 seats in the House of Representatives and seven state Governorships, but failed to alter the party balance in the Senate. The outcome was a mild rebuff to President Reagan. It would certainly make life more difficult for him on Capitol Hill. But there was no widespread revolt against the President's brand of Republicanism. High levels of unemployment and a sluggish economy had led some commentators to predict a larger swing to the Democrats.

Significantly, the New Right, who were thought so important a component of Reagan's coalition in 1980, did badly. Whereas several senior liberal Democrats had been successfully targetted for defeat in 1980 by conservative political action committees, hardly any of those similarly arraigned in 1982 were defeated.

If the Republicans were weakened by disappointment among their 1980 supporters at the lack of economic progress, the Democrats were badly handicapped by the widespread feeling that they had no coherent policy alternative to offer. Furthermore, President Reagan proved tactically more adept than many Democrats had expected and he distanced himself from his most conservative supporters.

The 1984 Presidential Elections.

Reagan's tactical adroitness was to be seen again in the 1984 Presidential elections. Ronald Reagan capitalised upon divisions in the Democratic Party and exploited his own formidable gifts of communication to capture the presidency for a second term in the November 1984 elections.

Mondale secured the Democratic nomination at a high political cost; the mauling he had received in the primaries from Senator Gary Hart, and the mostly effective and wholly novel campaign of Jesse Jackson, weakened the Party in the approach to November. Jackson's supporters (mostly black) were much less enthusiastic about supporting a white male candidate in the presidential election than they had been in backing Jackson in the primaries. Ninety per cent of those blacks who voted supported Mondale, but many abstained. A significant proportion of Hart's primary supporters switched their general election support not to Mondale but to Reagan; defections from registered Democratic voters to Reagan were high, and strikingly so among young white professionals. Such advantage as Mondale had hoped for by having Congresswoman Geraldine Ferraro on the ticket as his running-mate was dissipated by her own insipid television performances and by the whiff of scandal surrounding Mrs. Ferraro's husband's business activities.

Reagan's victory over Mondale was huge. As a percentage of the popular vote, it was not quite as large as that secured by Lyndon Johnson in his victory over Barry Goldwater in 1964, but it approached it. Reagan improved on the size of Johnson's victory in the Electoral College: he won everywhere except in Minnesota (Mondale's home state) and Washington, DC, which, with a majority black population went decisively for the democratic candidate.

The Congressional Elections.

The implications of Reagan's victory could not be considered except in the context of the congressional election results. Although Reagan's victory at the presidential level was entirely decisive, he did not have the advantage of a large intake of Republicans in the congressional elections. The Republicans lost two seats in the Senate and gained fewer than they had anticipated in the House. By the time of Reagan's inauguration in January 1985, it seemed probable that his support in Congress would be insufficient to deliver the conservative ideological majority which he had exploited to such effect in 1981. Furthermore, Democratic control of the House, as political observers in Washington noted, was certain to be strengthened at the time of the mid-term elections in 1986 and the Republicans would very probably lose control of the Senate at the same time.

The change in circumstances between 1981 and 1985 was neatly illustrated by the rebuff delivered to the president in January 1985 when Senator Robert Dole, the new Republican Majority Leader in the Senate, announced that Mr. Reagan's budget proposals had no chance of adoption by congress. Dole emphasised that congress would take the initiative in creating a budget, and hence in attempting to deal with the major political question of the day, the large, and growing, budget deficit.

Divisions among the Democrats.

As during the election campaign, so in the early weeks of Mr. Reagan's new term: the Democrats could provide no clear alternative because they were divided among themselves. The old liberal remedies of the 1950s and 1960s had less appeal to many Democratic supporters (especially those who had backed Senator Hart's candidacy in 1984) than formerly, and to a growing proportion of Democratic sympathisers lacked intellectual or political plausibility. The task for the Democratic nominee in 1988 was bound to be great. Even with the considerable burden of a large budget deficit and high interest rates, the Republicans had good reason in early 1985 for believing that the Republican presidential ascendancy would continue beyond 1988, probable congressional losses in 1986 notwithstanding.

Background to 1986 Elections.

The approach of the 1986 elections complicated politicians' calculations about both domestic and foreign policy. The budget deficit and the consequential problems of the growing trade deficit and high real interest rates provided the economic context for policy-making during 1985 and the first few months of 1986; the cautious moves towards a new round of arms control talks with the Soviet Union dominated foreign policy considerations.

The budget deficit of approximately $200,000 billion in the 1986 fiscal year did little to damage President Reagan's standing in the opinion polls. His political finesse lay in using the deficit which his tax cuts and defence spending increases of 1981 had produced to reshape the political agenda more decisively than any president since Lyndon Johnson. The size of the deficit made a coherent political response by the Democratic opposition in congress and among the ranks of contenders for the presidency exceedingly difficult; they could propose no new spending programmes without exposing themselves to charges of irresponsibility from the president and his party allies. The discussions within congress and between congress and the president about measures to reduce the deficit resulted in a bizarre piece of legislation, the Gramm-Rudman-Hollings Act, which brought automatic spending cuts into play in the event of president and congress failing to agree upon their size and location. The problem had become so great that politicians of all ideological stripes were simultaneously anxious to condemn the size of the deficit, whilst evading responsibility for cutting it.

In foreign affairs, the summit meeting between President Reagan and Mikhail Gorbachev, the new General Secretary of the Soviet Communist Party, at Geneva signalled the end of the rhetorical hostilities and political immobilism which had characterised superpower relations since the Soviet invasion of Afghanistan six years before.

The 1986 Mid-Term Elections.

The extent of the defeats for the Republican Party at the November 1986 mid-term elections surprised many of those who had accustomed themselves to the likelihood of a Republican majority in presidential elections gradually showing itself in congressional elections as Republican strength in the southern states grew. In fact, the Republican Party lost control of the Senate, and lost further ground in the House, thereby leaving the Democrats in control of both Houses of Congress for the remaining two years of President Reagan's term, an outcome which President Reagan had striven hard to prevent in his campaign appearances for a succession of Republican Senators and Congressmen and which he had declared prior to the election would cripple his presidency. The final outcome in the Senate was a 55–45 majority for the Democrats, and a Democratic advantage of 275–160 in the House. Whereas in 1980 (when the Senators running for re-election in 1986 had last been up for election), the Republicans had won most of the close races, they now lost most of them.

With their majorities, the Democrats took all of the committee chairmanships in each chamber, together with a majority on each committee of their own party. Since there is no neat correspondence between party and ideology in the United States, this did not automatically mean that President Reagan had no chance of giving a legislative or political lead in the remainder of his term; equally, it reduced the prospects that he would be successful in constructing a coalition on Capitol Hill in support of proposals he might make in areas of policy such as the Strategic Defence Initiative, further aid to the Contra guerrillas fighting against the Nicaraguan government, and additional cuts in funding for remaining domestic welfare and education programmes.

The Irangate Crisis.

As the significance of the mid-term elections was being digested, and the implications for policy and politics discussed, the President found himself thrown into the midst of a scandal of devastating proportions. Irangate, as the matter quickly, awkwardly and unimaginatively became known, had to do with deals sanctioned by President Reagan to sell arms to Iran notionally in an attempt to open lines of communication with the Khomeini regime. In fact, the deals were explicitly designed to persuade the Iranians to require the Shi'ite militia in south Beirut to release American hostages, a thoroughly uncertain and shady arrangement. Worse, it flew in the face of President Reagan's repeated declarations that the United States would under no circumstances deal with the Iranian regime or other sponsors of terrorism. At the same time that the President was authorising a devastating air-strike against Tripoli, the capital of Libya, in the spring of 1986 in order to galvanise support at home and (as he and his advisers had hoped) to kill Colonel Gadaffi, he and his most senior advisers on the National Security Council were engaged in complicated barter arrangements with the Iranians and, to make matters still more unattractive, to launder the receipts in payment for arms to be used by Contra guerillas in Nicaragua (in violation of the controls which Congress had lawfully placed upon central American policy).

The Tower Commission.

As the central fact of the deal became known in November 1986, America's influence in the Middle East sharply declined; with the gradual leaking of details in the subsequent months (and especially

with the revelations in the report of a three-man official Commission headed by former Senator John Tower), a number of Reagan's senior staff resigned and the President's personal influence over Congress and his standing in the country fell precipitously. Having for so long adroitly overcome the tendency to political paralysis which had befallen so many of his recent predecessors, a poorly-considered policy now weakened him severely.

Especially damaging to the President was the clear message of the Tower Commission's report that the proper means for the consideration and implementation of covert foreign policy actions were eschewed. The departments with prime responsibility (State, Defence, and CIA) were ignored, Congress was kept in the dark, and the operation was run out of the White House itself by senior National Security Council staff with the approval, but weak and uncertain supervision of the President himself. Whilst the authors of the Report were highly critical of the National Security Council staff, and of the autocratic Chief of Staff Mr. Donald Regan (who resigned following its publication), they properly emphasised that the NSC system was designed to serve the needs of the President and could not do so unless the President led it. President Reagan's determination to release the hostages from the Lebanon, and his persisting tendency to delegate authority to key advisers led to a failure to subject the policy to periodic review. Such reviews should have been employed to satisfy the President both as to its legality and effectiveness.

In fact, the arms transfers, conducted with the aid of the Israelis, were a violation of U.S. law, and a disastrous failure. Anxious to protect themselves from what they (correctly) deemed likely to be a serious failure of policy, the Secretaries of Defence, George Shultz and Caspar Weinberger distanced themselves from its implementation. In the words of the report, Shultz ". . . specifically requested that he be informed only as necessary to perform his job." William Casey, the Director of the CIA until his resignation following an operation to remove a brain tumour in December 1986, failed to make clear to the President that the operation carried grave risks both for the President and the country, and also failed to press for operational responsibility for the operation to be transferred to the Agency (where it properly belonged) from the offices of National Security Council staff.

The Key Resignations.

Following the resignations of Vice-Admiral Poindexter, the President's National Security Adviser, and of Donald Regan, the President's Chief of Staff and their replacement by Mr. Frank Carlucci and former Senator Howard Baker, a measure of order was restored to the operation of the White House staff, and a degree of political and administrative coherence to the administration. Presidential power is nonetheless a fragile commodity, won with difficulty and easily (often irreparably) damaged. Whilst his Presidency was not necessarily fatally wounded, it was in the Spring of 1987 certain that the continuing investigations of the Independent Counsel, Lawrence Walsh, and the two Congressional Select Committees would keep the matter before the public throughout 1987. President Reagan seemed likely to be able to protect his political interests only insofar as he took full account of congressional preferences, particularly on such matters as arms control where a measure of agreement on intermediate range nuclear weapons offered him a relatively painless means of restoring some of the lustre to his faded administration.

From Reagan to Bush.

The last year of the Reagan administration was dominated by the 1988 Presidential election. Although Reagan's popularity remained high, his authority was diminished. For an analysis of the 1988 election and the first years of the Bush administration, *see* **Special Topic C81–82.**

CANADA

The Quebec Referendum.

In a referendum held on 20 May 1980, the people of Quebec voted against the proposal of the *Parti*

Québecois Government to negotiate a much looser form of political association with the rest of Canada. In an 84% turnout, the vote against negotiation of political secession was almost 60%. Thus Quebec Premier René Lévesque's drive for the independence of Quebec was effectively ended. But the need for constitutional reform was generally acknowledged, and discussions were set in motion on the question within days of the "no" vote in the referendum.

The Patriation Issue.

Canadian politics in 1981 and early 1982 centred on the question of whether the constitution would be patriated or not. For some time, it seemed unlikely that Pierre Trudeau would manage to arrive at a constitutional settlement which satisfied the fears and concerns of the provinces and of the Indians. Many British M.P.s made it clear that, whatever Trudeau's wishes, they could not support the passage of a new Canada Act, and the patriation of the Canadian constitution on terms which the Provinces rejected. Eventually, however, a settlement was arrived at which, with the exception of Quebec and the Indian National Brotherhood (themselves only a minority of the Canadians), carried with it the broad support of Canadians. In early 1982 the Canada Bill came before the House of Commons in London and duly completed its passage.

The Trudeau Succession.

Party leadership was the prominent issue in Canadian politics during 1982 and the first few months of 1983. It seemed certain to continue to be so for some time. Pierre Trudeau continually affirmed his intention to step down from the Liberal leadership, to make way for a new face to lead the Party into the elections due by early 1985 at the latest. Meanwhile, Joe Clark had gradually lost his hold on the Conservative Party, and then lost the leadership on 11 June 1983 to Mr. Brian Mulroney. Mulroney makes a substantial living as a lawyer in Montreal, but lacks political experience and knowledge. Like Prime Minister Trudeau, Mulroney is from Quebec and speaks perfect French; that was a major advantage to him in the Conservative Party's drive to gain a hold in Quebec province, long a bastion of liberal strength—indeed, increasingly, the major source of liberal strength in Canada.

Pierre Trudeau visited European capitals during the latter part of 1983 as part of his campaign to bring about a disarmament conference of the five major nuclear powers; he tried to see President Andropov on the same quest. Neither of the superpowers did more than give a cautious welcome to Trudeau's proposal; Britain and France showed still less interest. Senor Perez de Cuellar, the Secretary-General of the United Nations, supported the initiative, but it seemed unlikely to gather more substantial support in the absence of warmer political relations between East and West. Then, in early 1984, Trudeau at last announced that he was standing down as Prime Minister, to be succeeded by John Turner.

The 1984 Election.

The Canadian elections of September 1984 produced a remarkable change in fortunes for the two major political parties: the Conservatives won 211 of the 282 seats in the House of Commons, whilst the Liberals, who had been in power for more than twenty of the preceding twenty-one years and for much of the century before that, won just 40 seats. Although in the weeks before the election a Conservative victory had been expected, its scale was a surprise to almost all.

Comparisons were naturally drawn with Mr. Diefenbaker's victory in 1958. But the differences between the two are considerable, and emphasise the extraordinary nature of the Conservatives' success in 1984. Diefenbaker struck an alliance with Quebec Prime Minister, M. Duplessis, in 1958 which caused 50 Union Nationale seats to be added to the Conservatives' own strength. Twenty-seven years on, the Conservatives themselves captured 58 seats in the province of Quebec—an astonishing political achievement. Those 58 actually outnumber the Conservatives' total in the four western provinces

of the country which, in recent years have been the heartland of Canadian Conservative strength. The resulting geographical shift of party strength within the party may yet cause its leader political and tactical problems of a wholly unanticipated kind.

The Conservative victory in Canada, and particularly in Quebec, owed much to the distinctive leadership provided by Mr. Brian Mulroney. A rich Montreal lawyer and business executive, Mulroney displayed a remarkable campaigning ability in both English and French putting Mr. John Turner, who had suceeded Pierre Trudeau as Liberal Party leader and Prime Minister in June, in the political shade. Turner appeared both indecisive and slow in comparison with the dynamic Mulroney.

Unsurprisingly given his corporate background, Mulroney's policy appeal rested on the Conservatives' proclaimed intention to attract substantial inward investment in order to revive the economy and reduce the unemployment level which on election day stood at 11%. This found much favour with the Reagan administration in Washington, anxious to reduce the tension between the United States and Canada which Trudeau's economic nationalism had partly caused.

Progressive Conservatives in Power.

Canada's first year under the Progressive Conservatives brought no radical changes of policy. The prudent reluctance of Canadian governments to force policies upon reluctant minorities in this sensitive federal system was thus again revealed. The nationalist sentiment which had informed Pierre Trudeau's energy policy after 1979, and the Liberal government's pursuit of increased Canadian ownership of industry, had abated thus allowing Mr. Mulroney and his colleagues to adopt a different course. His administration's aim was one of attracting inward investment in Canada. This pragmatic approach fitted well with the traditions and necessities of Canadian politics, and informed the policy of privatisation of loss-making firms.

The sheer difficulty of governing such a huge country with disparate ethnic and political cultures made Mr. Mulroney's task difficult. But his administration also encountered difficulties of a kind which could not so easily be explained away. The fisheries minister resigned after a scandal, and the communications minister became involved in a dispute over his election expenses. The two incidents, coupled with the strikingly incompetent government response to the failure of two Alberta banks, suggested that Mr. Mulroney and his colleagues would take some while to adjust to the subtleties and magnitude of governing the federation.

The November 1988 Elections.

In a campaign which turned on the parties' contrasting policies toward one issue, the free-trade agreement between Canada and the United States, Brian Mulroney's Progressive Conservatives won 43% of the vote in the Canadian General Election of 21 November 1988, and an overall majority in the House of Commons. The immediate consequence was that the Prime Minister pressed the free-trade legislation (which had been delayed by the election) on the legislature and the agreement quickly became accomplished fact.

The Progressive Conservatives won 170 seats, the Liberals 82, and the New Democrats 43. As so often in Canadian elections, the parties' share of the vote varied widely across the country. In contrast to previous elections, however, the Liberals' stronghold of Quebec Province fell to Mr. Mulroney's colleagues who won 58 of its 75 seats (in 1980, the year of the Quebec Party's huge advance, they had won must one).

Although Mr. Mulroney's defence of the Free-Trade agreement, and the Liberal leader Mr. John Turner's attacks upon it, served to give a sharp focus to the campaign, public opinion of it shifted considerably in the weeks before the election. That the Agreement involves some risk for Canada is clear: as it opens up the markets of her huge neighbour to the south, so it carries the implicit threat that capital and job opportunities will move south, imperilling Canada's economic security. The voters, on balance, saw greater attraction in the possibility of the former than in the risk of the latter.

The Meech Lake Accord.

By early 1990, the terms of the Meech Lake Accord had become the focus of intense political disagreement which threatened the stability of the federation. The Accord had been negotiated in 1987 by Prime Minister Mulroney and the premiers of the ten provinces in an attempt to make the constitution acceptable to the people of Quebec. Among the concessions made to Quebec in the Accord were the recognition of French in Quebec and English elsewhere as the dominant languages; a requirement that amendments to the constitution win the support of the federal government and all ten provinces; greater influence for the provinces in the appointment of Supreme Court justices and members of the Senate; the granting of authority to Quebec to control foreign immigration into the province; and restrictions on federal programmes and spending authority.

In order to become law, the Accord must win the approval of all provincial legislatures by 23 June 1990. New Brunswick, Manitoba, and Newfoundland are declining to grant their approval. If the Accord is not supported, separatist pressure within Quebec will grow. If the Accord should eventually win the backing of the provinces, its devolution of powers to all provinces is still likely to weaken the Canadian federation. The federal–provincial balance is a highly contentious matter, not only within Quebec but in other provinces, too. This is especially so with respect to language rights of English-speaking towns and cities in Ontario but more generally with regard to the capacity of the federal government to formulate national policy. Neither the Conservative nor the Liberal Parties find themselves on one side or the other of the issue: the Liberal Party in particular is deeply divided on Meech Lake and its implications. Internal party divisions make the resolution of the problem all the more difficult as Canada's economic problems mount, and the unpopularity of Mr. Mulroney's administration deepens.

LATIN AMERICA

MEXICO.

The Institutional Revolutionary Party (PRI) has dominated Mexican political life since 1929 but in recent years has maintained its grip on power by the strength of its bureaucratic structure, its control of patronage and if need be selective interference in electoral contests rather than through popular support. Indeed political inertia within an alienated electorate and the absence of an effective opposition have often benefitted the PRI. However, the Presidential Election of 1988 proved a real challenge to PRI hegemony for several reasons. The right wing opposition group PAN had steadily built up its organisation and support particularly in rural areas. More especially, the centre-left National Democratic Front (FDN) emerged as a real alternative having developed considerable support in Mexico City and other urban areas and offered the charismatic Cuauhtemoc Cardenas, son of the popular Lazaro Cardenas (President 1934–40), as its Presidential Candidate.

Unresolved structural economic problems, the enormous foreign debt and difficulties in the crucial relationship with the US had bedevilled the De La Madrid administration and diluted further PRI support prompting fissures to appear within the party leadership. Some PRI stalwarts, disillusioned with the candidacy of Carlos Salinas, saw a need to stiffen campaign tactics. On the eve of the election Xavier Ovando (FDN electoral campaign organiser) and his assistant were shot dead in Mexico City and campaign documents stolen. There were numerous attempts to invalidate proposed FDN poll invigilators.

Early urban results in the July Presidential contest were disastrous for the PRI and produced a controversial breakdown of the electoral computer and an indefinite delay whilst the votes were counted. This did not prevent the PRI from announcing an overwhelming victory despite angry protests from all three opposition candidates. In August as the opposition called for new elections the PRI-dominated Electoral College declared Carlos Salinas the victor although no voter break-down was given for half the constituencies. In the half of polling stations where figures were released Cardenas received 39% of the vote, Salinas 34% and Clouthier 22%. For the official result to be correct Salinas had to obtain 67% of the votes in the undisclosed stations! In many isolated rural areas there was a 100% turnout for the PRI. Cardenas is still popularly believed to have been the real victor but at least his campaign was a significant dent in the PRI's suffocating monopoly of Mexican political life. In difficult electoral circumstances opposition groups still managed to win 48% of seats in the Chamber of Deputies.

A contrite Carlos Salinas promised to rule for all Mexicans and to open up Mexico's political life. November state elections in Tabasco told another story. Registration of FDN voters was deliberately delayed, there were ballot rigging allegations against the PRI in nearly half of the electoral districts, the theft of ballot boxes, a police crackdown on FDN rallies and the murder of a trade union leader and others sympathetic to the FDN. In a state where Cardenas had won over 60 electoral districts in July the PRI quickly claimed victory and over 80% of the vote with the FDN only winning in 10 districts.

Although in an election for governor in Baja California in July 1989 the PRI conceded its first defeat in 60 years to the right-wing PAN there was ample evidence in 1989 that the ruling party was prepared to maintain its position by electoral fraud. In July state legislature elections in Michoacan, an FDN stronghold, the PRI was victorious due to the padding of electoral rolls, the intimidation of opposition supporters and the annulling of voting in districts won by the FDN due to "irregularities". In Juarez in July 1989 the electoral fraud of 1986 was repeated whilst in December 1989 electoral fraud in favour of the PRI in local elections in Sinaloa produced riots.

Ironically, one of the successes of President Salinas' first year was a drive against corruption in other spheres of public life. In January the head of the Petroleum Workers Union was arrested and charged with systematic corruption. In February over one hundred people including Eduardo Legorreta, of a powerful business family, were arrested on charges of insider dealing or embezzlement during the 1987 stock-market crash. In Sinaloa state over 1,000 police including 13 commanders were dismissed in an operation against a prominent 'cocaine baron' in April.

The Economic Outlook.

In July the Salinas administration successfully renegotiated Mexico's enormous foreign debt following protracted talks with the IMF, the World Bank and Commercial Bank creditors. Inflation in 1989 was brought down to 25% pa but the administration's policies have only brought a breathing space. Fickle middle class support may quickly evaporate whilst industrial unrest was widespread amongst the opposition's most powerful supporters in 1989. The importance of new loans to the Mexican economy and the continued discounting of the existing debt can be well illustrated by President Salinas' tour of European nations in January 1990. Salinas is concerned that Europe and Japan will divert loan capital earmarked for Mexico to the transforming Eastern European governments. The PRI administration's Six Year Economic Plan and Mexico's economic outlook are dependent upon the availability of fresh loans otherwise the pressure of servicing debt repayments will produce a timebomb under the Salinas Presidency, which may ultimately threaten the PRI's political monopoly.

EL SALVADOR.

In 1979 a "young officer's" coup ousted the repressive regime of General Romero but in January 1980 civilian junta members resigned ushering in "*Romerismo sin Romero*". A State of Siege declared in March 1980 completed political polarisation and was the prelude to increased official violence well symbolised by the murder of human rights campaigner, Archbishop Romero. Over 75,000 people, mainly peasants, have been killed in the ten years of subsequent civil strife, mostly at the hands of the security forces and the right-wing death squads.

Greater unity amongst opposition groups has been generated by the conflict. On a political level the pluralist Revolutionary Democratic Front (FDR) has gained experience by its numerous international negotiations whilst armed opposition united into the "Farabundo Marti Liberation Front" (FMLN) which, like the "Sandinistas", takes its name from a national patriot of the 1930s.

Since 1981 a protracted war has ebbed and flowed with heavy fighting in Chalatenago and Morazan. Guerrilla successes and the failure of the army's "big sweep" policy cost the Defence Minister his post in 1983. Subsequent heavy army losses in September 1983 prompted increased US aid and a change of strategy whereby certain rural areas were declared "free-fire" zones subjected to bombing and military attack in an effort to reduce civilian support for the guerrillas.

US military aid has been crucial to the survival of the Salvadorean regime, rising from $10 million in 1981 to a level of over $125 million p.a. since 1986 sustaining the expansion of the security forces from 17,000 in 1981 to over 60,000 men. The armed forces have increasingly become the dominant prop to the existing political system. A military career is seen as the best means of economic advancement with US aid funds guaranteeing high pensions for the officer class, substantial property purchases and a burgeoning role for the army within the Salvadorean economy. US economic aid continues to run at over $1m a day and constitutes 80% of the Salvadorean government's budget. This financial lifeline could not obscure government economic mismanagement and failed to save the ailing Christian Democratic government of President Duarte. In 1988, with Duarte suffering from a terminal illness, the demoralised Christian Democrats split over their choice of a Presidential candidate causing a further desertion of middle class support to the right-wing Arena party.

Arena revamped its image with Major D'Aubuisson, aware of his dubious international image, moving into the background whilst a presentable businessman, Freddy Cristiani, acts as party frontman. An Amnesty International report of October 1988 stressed the increased activity of the "death squads" since October 1987 and noted the substantial involvement in terror of the Treasury Police. Many disaffected Army Officers give crucial support to the hard-line faction in Arena. The FMLN followed up an October 1988 offensive with a major peace initiative in January 1989. The change in the balance of forces within El Salvador ensured the rejection of these proposals, the election of an Arena government and sharpened polarisation in the civil conflict in 1989.

The Arena Victory.

In a low poll, disrupted in some areas by guerrilla activity, Arena swept to victory in the executive and legislature elections of March 1989 as the middle classes deserted the weakened centre ground for the hardened certainties of the right. Although Freddy Cristiani was inaugurated President in May 1989 subsequent events have demonstrated that he is unable to control either hardliners in Arena or powerful forces within the military leadership. Roberto D'Aubuisson remains the dominant figure in the Arena movement, six of the eight member Executive Commission of the government are his supporters whilst Cristiani was forced to accept Francisco "Chico" Merino as Vice-President and Interior Minister. Merino is D'Aubuisson's nominee and has close links with the "civilian intelligence network" (death squads). In August 1989 the UN Human Rights Commission condemned the escalation of human rights abuses since Arena took power. In 1989 political murders doubled and illegal detentions were four times higher than those of 1988.

The FMLN Offensive.

An FMLN offer of a ceasefire and a dialogue with the government was answered by elements in the army bombing the offices of the National Federation of Salvadorean Workers in October. Talks were suspended and in November the FMLN undertook its largest offensive in the capital whilst being active in all 14 provinces of El Salvador. For the first time the guerrillas took and held positions in

the NE of the capital in San Roman, Zazamil and Soyapango. Following jet, rocket and artillery attacks by government forces on these working class districts the FMLN temporarily seized the Sheraton Hotel. A second guerrilla offensive commenced in the SW of the capital at the end of November. Over 2,000 people were killed during this bitter fighting in the capital whilst the army used the guerrilla offensive as an excuse to vent their frustration against the "civilian left" demonstrating that President Cristiani is not in control of the armed forces or the shadowy elements of Arena.

The murder in November 1989 of six Jesuit priests, prominent teachers at the Central American University, and their cook and her 15 year old daughter by members of the elite Atlacati battalion was a new milestone in the record of official terror. A forthcoming US Congressional review of aid to El Salvador, and one officer's leaking of names, forced President Cristiani in January 1990 to arrest Colonel Armando Aviles, 3 lieutenants and 4 soldiers for the Jesuit murders. Everyone in El Salvador knows that these men are merely the "material authors" whilst the "intellectual authors" remain in high positions in the army and elsewhere. The death squad murder of a prominent moderate MNR politician, Hector Oqueli, after his abduction in Guatemala in January 1990 symbolises the intense polarisation of Salvadorean politics and the intransigence of Arena's hardline elements.

NICARAGUA.

For recent events in Nicaragua, and the 1990 elections, *see* **Special Topic, C86.**

PANAMA.

The Historical Background.

In 1901 the US negotiated the Hay–Pauncefote Treaty with the British (abrogating the Clayton–Bulwer Treaty of 1850) allowing single US control and defence of any canal it constructed and facilitating negotiations with Philippe Bunau-Varilla's New Panama Canal Company, which represented the remaining interests of the ill-fated De Lesseps project. The US government then attempted to negotiate a new Canal Treaty with Colombia prior to purchase of existing Canal interests. When in August 1903 the Colombian Senate unanimously rejected US proposals sections of the Panamanian urban elite, linked to Canal interests, organised the cession of Panama from Colombia in November 1903. The USS *Nashville* symbolically appeared at the Atlantic port of Colon. Bunau-Varilla became the first Panamanian ambassador to the US and drafted the Canal Treaty which guaranteed US rights in the canal area "to the entire exclusion of the exercise by the Republic of Panama of any such sovereign rights, power and authority". The Panamanian elite then cooperated with the US to disband the Panamanian army in 1904 removing the only institution that could hinder the domination of Panama by a narrow urban elite linked to Canal Zone and ultimately US interests.

These arrangements have not only constrained the development of political life but have defined the major socio-political conflicts. Two key issues became central to Panamanian politics. The nationalist question of Panamanian rather than US control over the Canal Zone and the conflict between the small white *zonista* urban middle class who dominate Panamanian life and the black urban poor and rural masses largely denied access to politics.

Political Background.

In the 1930s the National Police became a political force under the leadership of Jose Antonio Remon. In the 1950s due to Cold War considerations and in the 1960s in the wake of the Cuban Revolution the US encouraged the growth and development of the National Guard. Ironically, as an institution the National Guard developed as a counterweight to the traditional elite in the political structure and in the charismatic nationalism of General Omar Torrijos eventually allowed some access to the politically marginalised majority of Panamanians. Torrijos took power in 1968, ousting the repressive regime of Lopez Arias. In 1977, whilst retaining the leadership of the National Guard, he vacated the Presidency in favour of Aristedes Royo but the existence of two power sources prompted fierce conflict when the unifying influence of Torrijos was lost in an unfortunate plane crash in 1981. Political infighting resulted in the ousting of President Aristides Royo in 1982 and confirmed National Guard leadership as the "de facto" centre of power.

From 1983 General Manuel Antonio Noriega dominated Panamanian politics. Washington recognised the situation and sought to influence the National Guard Commander indirectly through CIA recruitment. However, the style of Noriega's rule gradually infuriated a succession of US administrations. In 1987 allegations of corruption and increasing opposition to Noriega's rule by the Panamanian middle class gave the US government the opportunity to denounce Noriega. The General's stubborn and embarrassing refusal to step down ultimately precipitated the US invasion of December 1989.

Background to Noriega's Downfall.

Noriega's downfall began in June 1987 when Colonel Roberto Diaz (a retired deputy military commander) accused the General of murder and corruption and the Catholic Church added its voice to opposition demands for civilian rule. In the subsequent demonstrations against the government a State of Emergency was declared, suspending the rights of assembly and free speech. Increased US opposition in the diplomatic and economic spheres seemed to be the primary concern for the Noriega government in 1987 for the Panamanian economy is heavily interlocked with US finance. In July 1987 the US closed its consular section in Panama City and in December a US Senate committee recommended that Congress wind down all military and economic aid to Panama.

In retrospect Noriega's indictment (in absentia) on drugs charges by a Florida court in February 1988 was the beginning of the end for the General's government and ultimately provided a justification (to the US electorate rather than to the international community) for military intervention. In March Noriega was forced to put down an attempted coup whilst in May he annulled elections and his supporters attacked protesting opposition leaders. In October troops loyal to Noriega crushed a junior officers coup. Crucially, the Bush administration was criticised in the US for inactivity during the fighting.

The American Invasion.

In December 1989 General Noriega carried brinkmanship too far by instigating the National Assembly to declare Panama "in a state of war" with the US. After a substantial build-up of its forces in Panama the US ousted the Noriega regime by force on 20 December 1989. For all his excesses General Noriega inherited the nationalist and populist legacy of Torrijos, explaining the extent of military support for Noriega and the quality of the "Dignity Brigades" which harassed the occupying forces and surprised US military intelligence. The US army installed Guillermo Endara as President and his government has yet to show to many Panamanians that it is more than another group of "middlemen for the Gringos".

The Invasion Aftermath.

The Panamanian invasion won the Bush administration much domestic acclaim but the "Monroe bigstick" was greeted with dismay in Latin America whilst it was contrasted by the international community to current Soviet policy in Eastern Europe. In Panama itself the number of civilian casualties and destruction of property in the invasion may create a backlash against the US if substantial aid does not materialise promptly whilst the US policy objectives in Colombia and Nicaragua may be harmed. The surrender of General Noriega to the US authorities and his imprisonment in Miami in January 1990 may

appear more of a liability than a victory to the US administration in the long run. The trial of General Noriega threatens to open up a kaleidoscope of issues in International and Criminal Law. As an opening shot in February the General's lawyers pushed for prisoner of war status for their client. An interminable trial in the international spotlight may embarrass the Bush Presidency as George Bush was in charge of the CIA when Noriega was recruited.

SOUTH AMERICA

ARGENTINA.

A chaotic Peronist government was removed in 1976 by a military coup and Argentina was ruled until late 1983 by a series of military dictatorships which used State of Siege legislation to justify mass arrests, torture and political repression during which over 15,000 people "disappeared". National attention was diverted from worsening economic and social conditions by the initially successful invasion of the Falklands (Malvinas) in April 1982. The shock of subsequent defeats and public disillusionment redoubled the stress on the political framework of dictatorship. Faced by internal military bickering over the defeat and renewed pressure for civilian rule Galtieri's successor, General Bignone was eventually forced to bow to popular demands for an election.

The candidate of a deeply factionalised Peronist movement was well beaten by the leader of the Radical Party, Raul Alfonsin in the subsequent electoral contest of October 1983. President Alfonsin assumed power in December 1983 to the delight of a relieved populace but within six years three thorny problems had broken his government. Difficulties relating to the aftermath of the 'Malvinas' fiasco, the political consequences of judicial procedures against military personnel responsible for 'disappearances' during the dictatorship and above all the deeprooted structural problems in the economy combined to overwhelm the administration.

Alfonsin Loses Support.

Investigation into human rights offences committed by the military dictatorship were never fully carried through. Although in 1985 the leader of the original junta General Videla and Admiral Massera were sentenced to life imprisonment and in 1988 the Federal Appeal Court confirmed the twelve year sentence on General Galtieri and sentences on the other two junta members held responsible for the 'Malvinas' fiasco, civilian confidence in the administration and the military courts evaporated when the notorious Lieutenant Astiz was freed with no case to answer. Alfonsin lost credibility and popular support when, under pressure from an impatient military leadership, he rushed a 'final point' bill through Congress in December 1986 designed to prevent further prosecution of 'dirty war' criminals after February 1987. In January 1987 an armed forces supreme council absolved 15 admirals of human rights offences at the notorious Naval 'Mechanics School' further disheartening those seeking justice for 'los desaparecidos'. Economic difficulties in rescheduling Argentina's $55 billion foreign debt and in tackling rampant domestic inflation forced Alfonsin to introduce an austerity plan and reform of state enterprises in 1985. Further economic deterioration led to a second austerity plan in July 1987 which merely provided ammunition to a revived Peronist movement and alienated the military administrators of the state industrial conglomerates. Sweeping Peronist gains in Congressional elections in September 1987 and a worsening economic crisis in 1988 pointed to inevitable defeat for the Radical Party government in the Presidential Election of May 1989. Although unable to solve Argentina's deepseated economic problems or to prevent the military's re-entry into national political life the Alfonsin administration survived attempted insurrections by opponents within the armed forces in April 1987 and January 1988 and the occupation of the Tablada army camp in January 1989 and staggered on until June 1989 to oversee elections and the transfer of power to a new civilian government.

THE CHANGING WORLD SCENE

power in the Workers Confederation (CUT). It seems unlikely that Collor will be able to persuade a house facing re-election in October 1990 to pass policies introducing stringent austerity measures and selling off large portions of the public sector.

CHILE.

In September 1973 a military junta headed by General Augusto Pinochet seized power ousting the civilian government in a bloody coup. Thousands of supporters of Popular Unity were killed including President Allende himself. State of Siege legislation was augmented by a series of decrees which established a complete framework of state repression. In September 1980 a farcical referendum, held under State of Emergency provisions with all political parties banned and no use of electoral registers, adopted a new constitution which appointed President Pinochet for a renewable eight year term with highly centralised executive power.

However, the regime's political strait-jacket failed to suffocate opposition totally. The collapse of the monetarist economic "miracle", with unemployment rising to over 25% of the workforce, added to the social frustration building up against the junta. Political opposition has slowly gained in confidence since the popular demonstrations associated with the tenth anniversary of the coup. In November 1984 Pinochet reintroduced State of Siege provisions, a prelude to further intimidation of the opposition. In August 1985 impatience with Pinochet's intransigence at last overcame inter-party differences, unifying groups across the political spectrum into the Democratic Alliance of the centre-left Popular Democratic Alliance and the centre-left Popular Democratic Movement. The activity of the Manuel Rodriguez Popular Front (FPMR), associated with the illegal Communist Party, also increasingly irritated the regime.

Pinochet's partial lifting of State of Emergency restrictions in January 1987 and legalisation of some political parties in March were seen by many as merely a temporary relaxation of authoritarian dictatorship in order to appease international opinion. An Amnesty International report stressed continued "death squad" activity and official intimidation continued into 1988 with 1,500 people being arrested in the run up to the crucial October plebiscite. This referendum on the reselection of General Pinochet as a sole candidate for the Presidency until 1997 provided a perfect rallying point for all opposition to the regime. The unity of diverse opposition groups was maintained in 1988 and formed the basis of the successful "No" vote campaign against Pinochet. In the October plebiscite the opposition obtained 55% of the vote against the junta's 43% despite a massive media and public spending drive launched to bolster Pinochet's image.

Growing Political Difficulties.

Pinochet's cabinet resigned twice in October 1988 following this defeat but the General stressed his determination to fulfil his constitutional term until March 1990. The new Minister of the Interior initially cancelled talks with the opposition planned for January 1989 but then granted an audience with Patricio Aylwin, Christian Democratic leader and spokesman for the 17 party alliance. Although a dialogue continued with the regime until July 1989 over possible constitutional reform such negotiations increasingly took second place to the opposition's campaign for victory in the forthcoming Presidential Election. The opposition alliance agreed upon a single Presidential candidate: Patricio Aylwin.

Hernan Buchi, a former Finance Minister in the Pinochet regime, agreed to stand in July 1989 and was later accepted as the single candidate for both the National Renewal and the Independent Democratic Union (the right wing pro-Pinochet parties). Inevitably, Buchi was seen as a civilian "stand-in" for Pinochet whilst his electoral programme of high spending state economic policies was at odds with the economic austerity he had so recently supervised. Pinochet's "Economic Miracle" had turned sour and its victims even in the centre-right were not impressed by Buchi's tainted

campaign. The opening of the economy to market forces had increased and diversified exports but had also increased unemployment after "shake-out" recessions in 1975 and 1982. UN statistics reveal that although 20% of Chileans now enjoy greater affluence nearly 60% of the population live below a stringent poverty line whilst Chile is the only nation on the continent to see its nutritional standards decline from those attained twenty years ago. Opposition victory was sealed by the growing defection of disillusioned conservatives to the independent far right candidate, businessman Francisco Errazuriz.

The 1989 Elections.

In the Presidential Election of December 1989 Patricio Aylwin emerged as a comfortable victor receiving 55% of the vote compared to the 29% received by Hernan Buchi and 15% for Francisco Errazuriz. In Congress the opposition won 72 of the 120 seats (the Christian Democrats are the largest party with 48 deputies) and in the Senate won 22 seats but the government retains a majority due to the Constitutional and Electoral "arrangements" which grant the regime an additional 10 nominees in the Upper House. In a December meeting with the President-Elect, General Pinochet stressed his determination to continue as Commander in Chief of the Armed Forces neatly emphasising the unresolved contradictions in Chilean politics.

The civilian government which assumed office in March 1990 faced many intractable political problems. Although comfortable victors the opposition did not obtain the necessary two thirds majority to initiate immediate constitutional reform and it may well be difficult for Aylwin to maintain multi-party unity in government. The need to re-integrate the powerful trade union and left-wing party forces into political life and to meet the rising expectations of the Chilean people for democracy may yet be hampered by government expediency in the face of entrenched military power. Similarly, pressure for investigating Human Rights abuses during military rule may only produce embarrassing compromises (as in Alfonsin's Argentina) for through the powerful National Security Council the Chilean Armed Forces still maintain a constitutional supervisory role in the nation's politics.

COLOMBIA.

In August 1989 the murder by the "drugs mafia" of the Liberal Party Presidential candidate scandalised even a Colombian people conditioned to political violence and assassination. Over 50,000 people attended the funeral of the popular Senator Luis Carlos Galan who was a known opponent of the drug cartels and their growing prominence within the Colombian economic elite. In 1987 the Colombian Supreme Court under pressure declared a 1980 extradition treaty with the US illegal on a technicality removing the main fear of the Medellin cartel leadership. The murder of Galan, a police chief and prominent judge in forty eight hours forced President Virgilio Barco to initiate an offensive against the drug interests, declaring a State of Siege and introducing extradition by decree so encouraging the US government to re-submit a list of the most wanted drug barons. However, only minor figures in the Medellin cartel were extradited on charges of money laundering whilst the pressure upon Justice Minister, Monica de Grieff increased after her visit to Washington reflecting the high level of intimidation the drugs organisations can bring upon the judiciary and other organs of the state.

The Drugs War.

Indeed, the "extraditables" launched a policy of terror, bombing the offices of both major political parties, the secret police building and a civilian airliner. Although the number two in the Medellin organisation, Gonzalo Rodriguez Gacha—"the Mexican"—was killed with his son and bodyguards in a shootout with elite police in December, President Barco still seems to have started a war he cannot win. The drug organisations are so entrenched that national institutions are compromised and drug interests overlap in influence with the landowning elite, the hard-line military and the death squads. This is particularly true in the Magdalena Medio where death squads cooperate with the army ostensibly against guerrilla groups but really to safeguard the whole "zone of operations" for the drug cartels. Pablo Escobar remains leader of the Medellín cartel but individuals are no longer crucial for after ten years of cocaine trade the organisations control many legitimate companies and in part have supplanted the traditional elite, for "drug dollars" are the engine of the economy at a time when the nation's major export, coffee, is fetching the lowest prices in real terms since the 1920s.

President Barco, whilst accepting the offer of helicopters and other hardware in the Bush anti-drug initiative, has stressed that the $7·8 billion allocated to the total US programme is inadequate whilst the prices of traditional exports like coffee (the alternatives to "harvesting drugs") are kept down by US pressure in the International Commodity Organisations and the US does little to stem the demand end of the cocaine trade. Furthermore, US banks have laundered over $100 billion in drug receipts.

AUSTRALASIA

AUSTRALIA AND NEW ZEALAND.

The General Elections of 1984.

General elections took place in both Australia and New Zealand in 1984. In New Zealand the election in July resulted in a defeat for the government of Sir Robert Muldoon. In an 86% poll, the Labour Party under David Lange won 56 seats to the National Party's 37. The Social Credit Party won 2 seats. In November Sir Robert Muldoon was replaced as leader of the National Party by James McLay.

In Australia, in the election held in December, the Labour Party under Bob Hawke was returned to office but with a reduced majority. Contrary to all opinion poll forecasts, there was a 1·5% swing to the Liberal-Country opposition coalition led by Andrew Peacock, and the government's majority was reduced. The unexpected electoral rebuff damaged Mr. Hawke's standing in the country and his party.

Mr. Hawke's position improved, however, during 1985. In South Australia's state elections in December 1985 the Liberal Party, led by John Howard, who had succeeded Andrew Peacock as leader of the party in September, did badly at the polls. The party's policies of privatisation and the deregulation of housing interest rates and the labour market suggested radical change, whilst Mr. Hawke, whose August budget emphasised economic and social responsibility, seemed to offer greater stability.

Crisis in the ANZUS Pact.

The Pacific Security Treaty, better known as the ANZUS pact, was signed by Australia, New Zealand and the United States in 1951. The American Navy patrols the Pacific with its Fifth Fleet based at Honolulu, and requires port facilities in Australia and New Zealand. However, doubt was cast on the working of the Pact by New Zealand's new Labour government's policy of declaring the country a nuclear-free zone. This led Mr. Lange to refuse port facilities to an American destroyer, USS *Buchanan*, which could have been carrying nuclear weapons. The United States raised the possibility of ending New Zealand's preferential treatment in trade and security matters, and Bob Hawke condemned Mr. Lange's stance. However, in February 1985 pressure from the left-wing of his party caused Mr. Hawke to withdraw an earlier offer of refuelling facilities for American aircraft monitoring two proposed MX missile tests in the south Pacific. At the beginning of 1985 the future of defence co-operation in the Pacific was thus called into question. In February a meeting of ANZUS communications officials in Sydney was cancelled and in March Mr. Hawke

announced the indefinite suspension of the ANZUS council meeting scheduled for July.

The Rainbow Warrior Affair.

France continued its nuclear test programme at its Mururoa site in the Pacific during 1985. On 10 July two explosions in Auckland harbour sank the Greenpeace flagship, Rainbow Warrior, which was to have led a flotilla attempting to disrupt the French tests. One crew member, Fernando Pereiro, was killed. In September the French Prime Minister, Laurent Fabius, admitted that France had ordered the sinking. The French Defence Minister, Charles Hernu, and the head of the foreign intelligence service, Admiral Pierre Lacoste, were both replaced. In November 1985 two French agents were convicted of manslaughter and sentenced to ten years in prison in Auckland.

At the 16th Annual Conference of the South Pacific forum in August 1985 an agreement was reached declaring the south Pacific a nuclear-free zone. The thirteen members of the forum called on France to adhere to the pact, but President Mitterrand's visit to the Pacific test site in September indicated that there was little chance of her doing so.

New Zealand and the ANZUS Pact.

The future of the ANZUS pact looked increasingly uncertain in 1986. In August 1986 after a meeting in San Francisco between American and Australian ministers it was announced that the United States was suspending its security obligations towards New Zealand. Then in February 1987 the United States declared that it would not renew the logistic support agreement by which New Zealand received cut-price military equipment, when it expired in June.

Australian Domestic Affairs.

On 2 March 1986 during her visit to Australia, Queen Elizabeth signed into law the Australia Act which gave Australia full legal independence from the United Kingdom. For example, the right of appeal from Australian courts to the Privy Council in London was abolished. The Queen remained the sovereign of Australia.

The main problem confronting Mr. Hawke was the state of the Australian economy, with its huge trade deficit, rising foreign debt and high interest rates. In June 1986 he warned that it would be necessary to accept lower living standards and cuts in real wages. In August a tough budget was brought in which cut 3,000 million Australian dollars off government spending and added 1,400 million dollars in new taxes.

The 1987 and 1990 Elections.

Elections were held in both Australia and New Zealand in 1987. In Australia the election in July resulted in a decisive win for the Labour Government. Despite a slight national swing against him, Mr. Hawke increased his representation in the House of Representatives from 82 to 86 seats. The result meant that he was able to lead the country into the celebration of the bicentenary of the birth of Australia in 1988.

In New Zealand a general election was held in August 1987. David Lange's government won 58 out of 97 seats and increased its overall majority in a slightly enlarged parliament, despite a 3 per cent swing to the opposition National Party.

At the March 1990 elections in Australia Mr Hawke sought a fourth term as Labour prime minister. His opponent was Mr Andrew Peacock, the Liberal leader who headed a Liberal–National Party coalition. Australia had an unprecedented external debt, high interest rates, dire balance of payments problems, and business collapses. Mr Hawke was nonetheless re-elected, albeit with a narrow majority, but it was clear that he would be leading a country moving into serious economic recession and a period of rising unemployment.

III. SPECIAL TOPICS

THE BUSH ADMINISTRATION

The 1988 Election.

In the election of 8 November 1988, George Bush was elected the 41st President of the United States. His percentage of the popular vote was 54%, but in the electoral college (where the outcome is actually decided) he won with a lopsided majority. This is explained by the effect of the rule by which a small victory in a state gives the winner all of that state's electoral college vote. This transformed tiny popular margins in California, Illinois, and Pennsylvania into complete victories. Mr. Bush won all of the largest states except for New York, and secured a total of 426 electoral college votes to Governor Dukakis's 112.

The Electoral Map.

The ten states which Mr. Dukakis won were all in the north: Massachusetts, New York, Rhode Island, and West Virginia in the north-east; Iowa, Minnesota (the only state won by Walter Mondale in 1984) and Wisconsin in the mid-west; and Oregon and Washington in the Pacific north-west. Dukakis also won the District of Columbia, which has been safely and overwhelmingly Democratic since the District's voters were first enfranchised in Presidental elections in 1964. Bush won everywhere else. In some major states, such as California and Illinois, he did so with the tiniest pluralities; in the south, and the mountain states, he won with the greatest of ease. However, Bush's margins in the farming belt were noticeably smaller than Reagan's had been in 1980 and 1984—the crisis in American farming harmed the Republican ticket. Two of the nation's fastest-growing states, Florida and Texas, went solidly for Bush; the south was in general his strongest region.

In formulating his new administration, President Bush erred on the side of caution. For the major foreign policy posts, he selected people from the ranks of the Republican establishment. James Baker was named as the new Secretary of State, an old associate of Mr. Bush, his campaign manager for the 1970 Senate campaign in Texas, and for the Republican Presidential nomination in 1980, President Ford's campaign manager in 1976, and President Reagan's Chief of Staff in his first term between 1981 and 1985. Reagan then nominated Mr. Baker to be Secretary of the Treasury which post he held until resigning to run Mr. Bush's campaign for the Presidency.

The Tower Controversy.

For the post of Secretary of Defense, Mr. Bush nominated former Senator John Tower who had been the first Republican elected to the Senate from Texas since Reconstruction and then rose in that body to become Chairman of the Senate Armed Services Committee during President Reagan's first term when the Republicans enjoyed a six-year period as the majority party. Tower was therefore accustomed to authorizing the expenditure of large, and rapidly-rising, sums of money on major weapons systems in the defence build-up which President Reagan sponsored. He did not run for reelection to the Senate in 1986, but turned instead to earning large fees from defence contractors lobbying the United States government. His nomination encountered great difficulty when the nature and extent of these lobbying activities became known, and with the discovery by the FBI in the customary security checks of Tower's having led an exceedingly active social life in the wake of his two divorces.

When the vote on his nomination was finally taken by the Senate Armed Services Committee in late February 1989, its Chairman, Senator Sam Nunn, announced that the revelations about Tower's drinking habits were such that he would oppose confirmation. Such is Senator Nunn's standing in the Committee (and, indeed, in the Senate as a whole) that his decision prompted other Senators on the Committee to oppose him. The Committee vote was 11–9 against confirmation—an astonishing rebuff to a new President.

Despite the Committee's vote against Tower, the nomination was sent to the floor of the Senate for a full vote to take place. There, with all the Republican Senators supporting the nominee of their party's President, and all Democrats voting against, Senator Tower's nomination was rejected by 53 votes to 47. It was the first occasion in American history that a President in his first term had had a nominee to his Cabinet rejected.

Major Appointments.

For the post of National Security Adviser, President Bush selected Brent Scowcroft, who had held the same post under President Ford and who more recently was a member of the Presidential Commission charged with the investigation of the Iran-Contra affair.

The Directorship of the CIA did not change with Bush's Presidency. William Webster, Director of the FBI from 1978 until 1987 when President Reagan appointed him CIA Director, continued in his post despite pressure from within the intelligence community to have him replaced.

In economic policy, President Bush asked Nicholas Brady to continue on in his post as Secretary of the Treasury. Brady had been appointed by President Reagan when James Baker resigned to run Mr. Bush's campaign for the Presidency in the summer of 1988. For the key post of Director of the Office of Management and Budget, Mr. Bush nominated Mr. Nicholas Darman. Darman had worked in senior staff positions in the Reagan White House, and is widely respected for his financial expertise and political skill. Such assets were essential if Mr. Bush was to have any chance of reducing the huge fiscal deficit without reneging on his campaign promise not to raise income taxes. The deficit remained the central problem in American government. It quickly became evident that Alan Greenspan, the Chairman of the Federal Reserve Bank, was willing to risk a minor recession in the economy if that should prove necessary to defeat incipient inflationary pressures.

Domestic Policies.

In domestic affairs, Bush's appointments revealed two characteristics: a mostly sound political judgment (not always evident elsewhere in the early months of his administration), and his implicit espousal of a Republicanism of a more centrist kind than President Reagan's. Dr Louis Sullivan, the black head of the Morehouse School of Medicine in Atlanta, was named as the new Secretary of Health and Human Services. After causing a flurry of opposition among right-to-life campaigners on the Republican right when it appeared that his views on abortion were more liberal than the President's own, he was confirmed by the Senate. William K. Reilly, the President of the World Wildlife Fund, was named as the new Administrator of the Environmental Protection Agency.

In the White House, John Sununu was named Chief of Staff.

Financial Scandals.

In the summer of 1989, both the Speaker and the Majority Whip of the House of Representatives, Jim Wright, resigned following financial scandals. The former Majority Leader of the House, Tom Foley, was elected by his colleagues to succeed Wright. Richard Gephardt (who had been a contender for the Democratic nomination for the Presidency in 1988) was elected Majority Leader.

The intensity of the partisan battle in Congressional politics in the spring and summer of 1989 reflected in part the intense political frustration felt by House Republicans at their exclusion from power since 1955, a condition made more severe by their domination of the White House for all but twelve of those years.

The skill with which Mr. Foley and his colleagues lead their party will do much to determine the Democrats' prospects of achieving unity in advance of the 1990 mid-term Congressional elections and the 1992 Presidential contest. Their task is made politically more demanding by the intractability of the fiscal deficit, and the rise of environmental and regulatory issues on the political agenda.

Congressional Leadership Crisis.

As the growing crisis in the Congressional leadership came to dominate politics in Washington during the first half of 1989, the passivity of President Bush's administration was especially apparent in the second. Indeed, the President's first fifteen months in office were quiescent, and major problems of public policy lay effectively unaddressed. In his single major economic initiative, the proposal to reduce capital gains tax, the President failed when the Senate rejected the move. His greatest opportunity for dealing with them passed with the close of the first session of his first Congress in December 1989. Unlike President Reagan, Mr. Bush did not exploit the window of opportunity in his first year to establish clear priorities for his administration, and to urge Congressional action upon them. By the comparable point in his first term, Reagan had signed all of his major legislation on the economy and defence into law.

The President's weak legislative record was nonetheless combined in the early months of 1990 with widespread democratic revolution abroad from Nicaragua to South Africa and to Eastern Europe, and with extraordinarily high public approval ratings for the President from the American public. Not since President Kennedy's first year has an American President enjoyed such great approval from the American public. Bush has set out deliberately to redefine the nature of the Presidency, to keep public expectations low, and to ensure that his few foreign initiatives (such as the invasion of Panama in December 1989) were marked with quick and overwhelming success.

The President's comparative inactivity with respect to domestic policy in his first year is not to be traced to ideological rigidity on his part (unlike his predecessor, President Bush does not attempt to make political capital from opposition to government as such) but to the tight fiscal handicap under which the United States labours. The greatly enlarged internal deficit during the 1980s has left little scope for expensive remedial federal action in social, educational, environmental or urban policy.

The Domestic Agenda.

Notionally, President Bush has a domestic agenda on which he has established three main objectives: firstly, to reform the educational system and raise educational standards; secondly, to control and reduce the incidence of demand for and supply of illegal drugs; thirdly, to initiate a new policy for the environment. In each case, the President's policy proposals have been modest in scope and involve small net additions to federal spending. A consequence is that governments below the federal level are assuming increasing importance in policy and politics. For example, the states themselves, together in many cases with counties and local governments beneath them, have economic development offices (and in the case of many states, have such offices in foreign countries). Such offices are important points of contact with the private sector and foreign governments. To them is the task of developing attractive packages for the relocation of industries from elsewhere, the location of new facilities or, in certain cases, to persuade existing companies not to move (by, for example, declaring existing facilities to be part of an enterprise zone). In education policy, in the regulation of finance and the environment, the states and local governments are becoming of increasing importance.

Conclusion.

The President's political success for the remainder of his first term and in the 1992 Presidential election will be contingent more upon domestic than foreign policy. That in turn will require him to deliver continued economic growth (upon which his hopes of reducing the fiscal deficit depend) and some measurable success in addressing the policy problems which he has identified and others (such as crumbling urban infrastructure, homelessness, and declining American international competitiveness in some high technologies) which he has not but which political opponents will.

POLITICAL CRISIS IN RUSSIA

During 1988 and early 1989, Mikhail Gorbachev succeeded in extricating himself from Afghanistan, the costly engagement into which Leonid Brezhnev had pitched the Soviet Union nine years earlier.

As a military engagement on her south-west frontier was liquidated, so a diplomatic opening with her major neighbour to the south proceeded apace. Preparations were made during the latter part of 1988 for a full meeting between Mr. Gorbachev and Mr. Deng Xiaoping on 15 May in Beijing, thereby setting the seal on careful preparation firstly by officials, and then by foreign ministers, to heal the rift between the two powers.

Elsewhere, the Soviet Union set an extraordinarily fast diplomatic pace. In a major speech to the General Assembly of the United Nations in December 1988, Gorbachev announced that he had decided to reduce the Soviet armed forces by 500,000, and in Eastern Europe and the western part of the Soviet Union, to cut the numbers of tanks by 10,000, combat aircraft by 800, and guns by 8,500. In addition to announcing unilateral force reductions, Gorbachev also addressed himself to questions of environmental pollution and third world debt. The tone of his speech could scarcely have been in sharper contrast to that of his predecessors in the Soviet leadership.

In later months, the Soviet Union kept the diplomatic initiative by offering in early March to reduce the numbers of troops, tanks, and aircraft on both sides in Europe to between 10 and 15% below NATO's current levels. Once again, the Soviet Union's opening position at these new conventional force reduction negotiations marked a radical departure from its previous stance. It was also strikingly close to much western thinking.

If in foreign policy Gorbachev made his mark with flair and altered policy with relative ease, the several outbreaks of nationalist unrest, and the sluggishness of the economy, posed him grave problems at home. In Armenia, Azerbaijan, Moldavia, and the Baltic Republics, nationalist sentiments flared. The dispute between Armenia and Azerbaijan continued in fitfully violent form, eventually requiring the introduction of the Army to restore a measure of order. Even the devastation wreaked by an appallingly destructive earthquake in Armenia in December 1988 (and which caused Mikhail Gorbachev to return home from his trip to the United States) did not effect a halt to the violence. In the Baltic Republics, protest took a more constructive form. All three Baltic Republics (Estonia, Latvia, and Lithuania) saw the formation during the year of popular front movements to represent nationalist feelings, undimmed by nearly fifty years' forced incorporation into the Soviet Union. They were also captivated by Gorbachev's policies of *perestroika* and *glasnost*, being close to the prosperous economies of Scandinavia and having national memories of comparable wealth in the first forty years of the century.

The Limitations of Perestroika.

Perestroika did not in 1988 and early 1989 have the results which Mr. Gorbachev and his allies sought. The deeply-engrained features of the central command economy which liberalisation was designed to overcome were as apparent in 1989 as they had been at the time of Gorbachev's accession four years earlier. Soviet economists and politicians openly acknowledged the existence of a large fiscal deficit (estimated at 11% of GNP). Other indicators were apparent to Soviet consumers: prices, stable for years under the mismanagement *perestroika* was designed to end, were in 1988 rising by more than 6% per annum. Worse still, the shortages of food and consumer goods grew more severe.

The central difficulty was the inconsistent (not to say chaotic) application of price reforms. Without a consistent price mechanism, economic success in the shape of freely-available consumer goods, faster economic growth, and the more efficient use of labour, would (not least in the opinion of many Soviet economists) prove illusory. Nationalist pressures burst through into public Soviet politics during 1988. In Georgia, well-established nationalist sentiment took on a sharper form in the autumn of 1988 when a proposal to construct a large hydro-electric scheme met with vigorous opposition on the grounds that it would flood sites of special significance in the Republic. That event sparked a wave of protests which lent weight to the secessionist movement in Georgia.

Dramatic Change in Russia.

The revolutions which engulfed Eastern Europe in 1989 did not sweep through the Soviet Union to the same extent or with comparably great change but the country nonetheless changed irrevocably. The gathering changes of *perestroika* and *glasnost* in the latter half of the 1980s issued in 1989 and early 1990 four juddering instances of democratic change:

(i) the leading role of the Communist Party was ended through the renunciation of Article Six of the programme of the CPSU;

(ii) in place of the Communist Party's single line came the multiple and at times anarchic lines of the new parliamentary system;

(iii) an executive presidency was created with wide-ranging powers over the machinery of central government, and

(iv) an entirely new legal system began to be established in order that those in authority govern whilst subject to the law.

(i) Astonishingly, the leading role of the Communist Party was abolished in February 1990 by the virtually unanimous vote of the Central Committee of the Party at its plenary session. Boris Yeltsin was the person to oppose the motion. A vote at the Congress of People's Deputies meeting in March 1990 to abolish Articles 6 and 7 of the Constitution which had enshrined the leading role of the Party was passed overwhelmingly. A multiparty system was certain to result from this momentous change in place of the faction-ridden Communist Party. By mid-March 1990, it seemed entirely possible that the Party would split, perhaps even before the Party Congress took place in July.

(ii) The elected Congress of People's Deputies has quickly come to assume a prominence and substantive importance in Soviet political life which would have been inconceivable immediately prior to its birth in the Spring of 1989. Its proceedings are televised, debates are frequently contentious, and it offers real obstacles to executive and party power (despite the fact that nearly 90% of its 2,250 deputies are members of the Communist Party). It has a life of its own, is developing procedural rules and institutional interests of its own. But it is also a reflection of the extraordinary vigour with which political debate now occurs within the Soviet Union, and of the diversity of opinions expressed. In December 1989, its autonomy and standing was further enhanced by an amendment to the constitution which abolished the procedure whereby one-third of the members of the Congress were indirectly elected by the Communist Party and other social organisations. If the Communist Party was not to be destroyed by this process, it was certain to be weakened dramatically. Indeed, the Congress at its March 1990 meeting voted to delete all references to the Communist Party from the Constitution, albeit by less than the two-thirds vote required to make it mandatory.

(iii) At its extraordinary session in March 1990, the Congress of People's Deputies voted by 1817 to 133 with 61 abstentions to create the office of executive presidency for which Mr. Gorbachev had argued and to which he was later elected by 1,329 to 495 with 176 abstentions and spoiled papers. In the first instance, the election was by the Congress (which dissatisfied many radicals); in the future, it was to be by popular vote.

The significance of the move lay in its independence from the Communist Party, giving the holder of the office autonomy from the organisation which had lain at the centre of Soviet political life since the revolution. The sweeping powers accorded the presidency in Gorbachev's original proposal alarmed many parliamentarians who feared that it would overwhelm the Congress; the powers finally approved by Congress, though still considerable, were more limited than those Gorbachev had sought. The new Presidential power of veto of legislation passed by the Congress will be subject to an override by a two-thirds vote of each chamber of the Supreme Soviet whilst a declaration of a state of emergency can be made without the consent of the Republic affected by the declaration only if the Supreme Soviet agrees by a two-thirds majority to his doing so.

Although the new presidency on balance marked a qualification of the process of democratisation, there was by the Spring of 1990 no doubt that Gorbachev and his allies were bent upon a much more radical democratisation of the Soviet Union than had seemed possible twelve months earlier. The elections that took place between December 1989 and June 1990 to local government and to the Supreme Soviets of the Republics resulted in remarkable rebuffs to Communist Parties in many parts of the country, including that in Leningrad.

(iv) The creation of a body of law which constrains public officials and makes provision for holding them accountable marks a fundamental change in Soviet politics. Hitherto, the law has been an instrument employed by the Party and by state agencies to bolster their power. Law is now being transformed from its former role of licensing power to limiting it. This change is itself an outgrowth of the stuttering but powerful democratisation of Soviet society, of widely-shared discontent with the unaccountability of state agencies, and of the impulses to the creation of a civil society.

Constitutional Reform.

Constitutional reform is part of this change to a state itself subject to the rule of law. The old document has in the space of eighteen months already been the subject of radical amendment: the establishment of the Congress of People's Deputies was itself the product of a constitutional amendment in December 1988, whilst the creation of the executive Presidency in March 1990 resulted from debate at the extraordinary session of the Congress in that same month. Progress towards a full-scale revision of the constitution is nonetheless slow, retarded by the continuing debates about private property, the rules governing relations between the centre and the periphery, and the nature of the civil society to be built. Since the constitution will in part be an expression of these political decisions and social movements which are themselves in a state of flux, it is scarcely surprising that a completely new document, called for in December 1988, has still to emerge.

Fundamental Economic Problems.

Whilst these political changes surged through the Soviet Republics, the economic system showed no sign of responding favourably to the treatment of *perestroika*. On the contrary, the supply of goods in the shops deteriorated, and economic growth remained stubbornly slow. The Soviet economy is in profound crisis. For seventy years the economy has been directed to the maintenance of external and internal security objectives. In peace and war, the insatiable demands of the Soviet military (and the "heavy industry" which in large part services it) have crippled the economy, stifled creativity, and partly concealed the inefficiency and corruption which characterise it. The transition from a command economy directed to military production to a market-based consumer economy will in the short term add to, not detract from, the problems of shortages, inflation, and general crisis. Many goods are unobtainable. Where they are produced, they often do not make their way to the shops but are sidetracked into the black market where profits (and prices) are high.

Thus it is that crisis plans to increase the volume of consumer goods produced (yet another was announced in 1989 by the Chairman of Gosplan) have so little effect: even if production increases, the products are generally siphoned off from the official, rouble-based, economy. The reason is plain enough: the rouble is worthless. Despite its ten-fold devaluation in 1989, there is little incentive to work harder for roubles since it is a currency which carries little weight even within the Soviet Union. This has immense significance for savers as well as would-be spenders: the huge volume of rouble-denominated savings are, in fact, virtually worthless. In effect, there are now two economies in the country: the first, based on the roubles, is the official version where goods are scarce, incentives negligible, productivity lamentably poor by international standards, and corruption rife; the second is based on foreign currencies (often the US dollar) and barter. It is against this background that

Gorbachev made his dramatic call in May 1990 for a drastic reform of the economy.

The Failure of Perestroika.

Perestroika has not succeeded. The most liberal economists among Mr. Gorbachev's critics declare that the main reason for its failure lies with its partial character: the full disciplines of a market in labour, of a convertible currency, of the free movement of capital, of full private ownership, of privatisation, is, they claim, necessary for the Soviet Union to break out of the spiral of economic decline. Conservative critics make the sharply contrasting claim that Mr Gorbachev's policies have made an unsatisfactory economic condition infinitely worse, and pregnant with political danger. It is certainly the case that fundamental economic reform rather than the tinkering indicated by the introduction of cooperatives, or the tokenism suggested by the opening of a McDonald's hamburger restaurant early in 1990 would involve far greater economic dislocation and the pain would rise massively, increasing the political pressure on the leadership which undertook such reform.

Yet Gorbachev and his allies are caught most uncomfortably between conservative opponents in the party and the bureaucracy who decry reform (in large part because they have profited so richly from the corruption and inefficiencies of the command system), radical critics who proclaim the virtues of the free-market without having to take responsibility for the political repercussions which would result from its introduction, and the mass of the people who, unused to the disciplines of the market and discontented with the gross inefficiencies of the command system, are unwilling to accept increasing misery and privation and have little left to sacrifice. A continuation of the present melange of reformist policies offers little consolation to Gorbachev or hope to the Soviet people. His short-term failure in turn adds to the political pressures upon him and his reformist allies, decreases his political leverage and legitimacy, and adds to the sense of failure which is generally acknowledged and expressed.

Inflation and Indebtedness.

Inflation and foreign indebtedness, both long regarded by many foreign observers as of trivial importance, are major problems: Prime Minister Ryzhkov has himself said that more than half of the Soviet Union's hard-currency earnings are used to service foreign debt; some Soviet spokesmen calculate that inflation is running at 10%, and the fiscal deficit is 11% of Gross Domestic Product. The current policy is to monetize the debt—that is, to finance it by increasing the money supply. It is no more than a palliative and has the serious long-term cost of increasing inflationary pressures. The seriousness of the fiscal deficit is now generally acknowledged by Soviet economists. Its proximate causes are agreed to be a combination of declining government revenues both from the falling price of oil on world markets, and the fall in revenues as a result of the government's campaign against alcohol consumption.

Managing the transition from the command economy is therefore proving exceptionally testing—not just in economic terms, but in the political, too. However, whilst it is clear from what condition the economy has moved, it is not apparent to what condition it is now changing. There is not yet a full consensus within either the elite or among the mass of the people behind a complete shift to a full market system. The disorder caused by the piecemeal breakup of the old system is the first priority on his daily agenda; establishing long-range objectives and forming the means to achieve them is under these highly-pressured circumstances formidably difficult. Nonetheless, Gorbachev's election to the executive presidency gave him very much greater freedom in setting the agenda for economic policy, and a sharp shift towards a full market economy appeared certain after Gorbachev himself declared at the March 1990 Congress the need to "... get down to creating a full-blooded domestic market".

Rising Nationalist Pressures.

Nationalist pressures underwent a quantum leap upwards from the Spring of 1989 onwards culminating with the declaration of independence by the Republic of Lithuania and the certainty that similar movements would establish themselves elsewhere. The cohesion of the Soviet Union was beginning to be called into the most serious question as Republics on its western borders edged away from Moscow and Republics on the southern borders fell victim to racial and ethnic discontent and conflict. In Latvia and Estonia, Georgia and the Ukraine, nationalist pressures also intensified.

The Baltic Republics: Lithuanian Independence.

The process of national assertion was in 1989 and early 1990 most pronounced in the Baltic Republics. In Latvia, Lithuania, and Estonia a multi-party system emerged by the end of 1989, and the process of establishing economic independence from Moscow was relatively advanced. Full independence for all three was only a matter of time but Lithuania was the first of the three to establish it formally. Members of the Republic's Supreme Council (the successor to its Supreme Soviet) voted on 11 March 1990 by 124–0 in favour of the declaration of independence, with just six abstentions. On the same day, the Supreme Council elected a non-Communist, Vytautas Landsbergis, as the newly-independent Republic's first President. That there existed a most important distinction between the declaration of secession and its accomplishment was plain to the would-be secessionists and to the Politburo in Moscow. Gorbachev together with both his allies and his opponents responded calmly to the developments. Whilst excluding a resort to force, Gorbachev insisted that secession would be bought only at a high price and that the Lithuanians would be required to pay in hard currency for the industrial development and infrastructural investment in the Republic.

Estonia.

Unlike in Lithuania, where nationalist pressures for independence were channelled through the existing parliamentary body by the existing Communist Party, Estonians formed an entirely new Congress which declared firstly that the annexation of their country by the Soviet Union in 1940 had been illegal, and secondly affirmed its independence. As in Lithuania, Estonian parliamentarians demanded the end to the presence of Soviet troops, and then turned to the immensely difficult question of whether and how to establish a new currency. As for the other Baltic Republics, this was an especially severe policy problem: if the currency was to be hard and convertible with western currencies, it would have profoundly damaging consequences in the short term for Estonia's trade with the Soviet Union. If a soft, non-convertible currency, an independent Estonia would fail to reap the longer-term advantages of extensive and growing trade with the west and especially with Scandinavia, Poland, and Germany who would be its most obvious trading partners. Independence movements in Estonia and Latvia were bolstered by the victories of nationalist movements in elections in March 1990.

Georgia.

In Georgia, too, the Republic's parliament began a similar process—declaring the means by which Georgia joined the Union illegal. The reawakening of independence sentiment in Georgia can be traced to a single dramatic event: the massacre by Soviet troops on 9 April 1989 of some twenty peaceful demonstrators in Lenin Square in the Republic's capital, Tbilisi. Among the lethal methods used to repress demonstrators were sharpened shovels and a mixture of CN and CS gases. The combination of the crudely repressive measures to contain the unrest and the political failure of the Republic's authorities in having lost the confidence of the people caused the local party leadership to be replaced, and weakened conservatives in Moscow who had supported the call for the decisive use of force.

The Ukraine.

In the Ukraine, Belorussia, and Russia, nationalist sentiment grew stronger throughout 1989. In the Ukraine, a significant self-styled popular front movement pressed for independence whilst in Russia an assortment of Russian nationalist groupings gave voice to varied discontents, many of them rooted in old Russian antagonisms and resentments against other ethnic groups. In the first three months of 1990 alone, twelve regional party secretaries in the three Slav Republics lost their posts.

Foreign Policy Changes.

Faced with multiple secessionist pressures within the Soviet Union and chronic economic crises, it is remarkable that a complete transformation in foreign policy should have taken place. Beyond Europe's borders, the old policy of fomenting revolution in foreign countries to the advantage of the USSR was abandoned; the old orthodoxy that class was the most significant international division was similarly jettisoned. Within Europe, the USSR's hold over the states which had so recently comprised its "clients" within the Warsaw Treaty Organisation weakened throughout the first nine months of 1989, and then fell away. The logic of the abandonment of the Brezhnev doctrine, by which the USSR had asserted (and invoked) the right to intervene in the affairs of its Eastern European neighbours when their internal developments conflicted with its own, had quickly worked itself out. Having denied itself the use of the military instrument to control its unruly nominal sister states, the Soviet Union lacked leverage over them. Reformist movements within their borders accordingly asserted their rights sure in the knowledge that the superpower to the east would not intervene.

The conservative communist establishments in the Warsaw Pact responded in different ways but all knew that the guarantee until recently afforded them by Soviet armed forces was, suddenly, removed. That was a major factor in their downfall in Czechoslovakia, Hungary, and East Germany. Following the end of Communist rule in Czechoslovakia and Hungary, the new governments quickly negotiated agreements with the Soviet authorities for the removal of all their occupying forces. The withdrawal of Soviet forces from Hungary began in March 1990 with a deadline for a full and final departure by June 1991.

Improved US Relations.

Partly as a result of the ending of the Brezhnev doctrine but also because of the Soviet Union's decisive shift to market economics and democratic politics, relations with the United States improved dramatically. President Bush was anxious not to embarrass the Soviet leader in his reform policies, and in any case benefitted from a quite remarkable weakening in the USSR's negotiating position. This had particular importance for negotiations between the superpowers on the strategic nuclear balance, and on the disposition of conventional forces in central Europe. The essential truth of Soviet-American arms negotiations, that their progress depended primarily upon the state of political relations between them, was borne out by the speed with which agreement was secured in both strategic and conventional negotiations.

Not for the first time in Soviet history, the difficulty lies not so much in fomenting political change as in controlling it. It is wholly improbable that when he took office five years ago Mr. Gorbachev could have had anything approaching the current scale of political and economic change in mind. It is certain that he did not envisage anything approaching the contemporary chaos as being a product of the changes he initiated in his first year. Predicting the course of Soviet politics and policy has never been as difficult in the postwar era as it has now become. A continuing series of lurches towards a free-market economy (albeit one hedged around with restrictions on foreign ownership) in a country shorn of its Baltic and southern Asian Republics, with a shrunken military presence, in a more fluid and challenging Europe and Asia, seems the most likely general course. But it is possible that the adjustment to the utter failure of the Soviet economic and political model, both at home and abroad, may occasion a severe con-

servative reaction within Russia with the gravest consequences, or an uncontrolled radicalism under Yeltsin, newly-elected President of the Russian Federation.

THE FUTURE OF GERMANY

From 1990, discussion of German politics can no longer be easily divided into East and West. The East German Communist regime collapsed in late 1989, as waves of East Germans took advantage of the ending of travel restrictions between Hungary and Austria to leave their crumbling country. As the regime disappeared by Christmas 1989, the East German state had begun its own process of disappearance by Easter 1990. The official celebrations attending the 40th anniversary of the East German state were marked by the attendance of Mikhail Gorbachev whose policies had done so much to undermine Communist rule in eastern Europe, and by mass unrest in Leipzig, Dresden, and East Berlin. In the space of a few weeks, the remaining shreds of legitimacy attaching to Herr Honecker's administration fell away. His successor was Egon Krenz, who had the distinct political disadvantage of having had responsibility for internal security and of rigging the municipal elections in May 1989. He lasted but a few weeks until his replacement by Hans Modrow, the reformist Mayor of Dresden.

The End of the Berlin Wall.

On 9 November, the Berlin Wall was breached. In the ten months preceding that momentous event, 200,000 East Germans had left for the West; in the week that followed it, 3 million East Germans followed (most of them simply to visit and return). The regime fell away from beneath its leaders; on 3 December, the Politburo and Central Committee resigned. Politicians who had only weeks before exercised absolute power now found themselves under investigation for corruption and abuse of power.

Formation of New Parties.

New parties sprang up, and old ones which for forty years had been quiescent allies of the ruling Communist Party now broke free, finding independent voices. Elections were set for 18 March 1990. In the three months between the effective collapse of Communism and the elections, West and East German politics became inextricably linked. Two states, with two economic systems, remained. But the one nation now looked to a fusing of its nationhood with statehood, and the calculations of German voters on both sides of the disappearing border were made with unity in mind. As the elections approached, so the timetable for unity shortened. Foreign politicians gradually accommodated themselves to the prospect of unity. Mikhail Gorbachev and Margaret Thatcher had as late as December 1989 been powerfully antipathetic to German unity, they were forced by the extraordinary speed of events to acquiesce in its inevitability. From early 1990 onwards, discussion proceeded not about whether unity would take place but about the circumstances under which it would occur, and with what speed.

These circumstantial considerations were several and of immense importance, not just for a reunited Germany but for Europe as a whole and for the two superpowers. Firstly was the question of whether the two parts of a reunited Germany would retain membership of NATO and the Warsaw Pact; secondly was the related question of whether United States and Soviet troops would remain in the two parts; thirdly was the wider question of the effects of German unification on the power balance in central Europe; fourthly was the problem of the relationship between the eastern part of Germany and the European Community; fifthly was the problem of the integration of the East German financial and economic system into West Germany.

Underpinning the military and political questions was the realisation that the *raison d'etre* of NATO was fast disappearing with the shrinking of Soviet power and the evident fact that the Warsaw Pact had effectively ceased to exist by February of 1990. The economic questions focussed on the transition in the eastern part of Germany from the Ostmark to the Deutschmark and the rate at which the exchange should take place.

The March 1990 Elections.

The election on 18 March took place between three main groupings: the Alliance for Germany which was a coalition of three conservative parties favouring rapid reunification, immediate introduction of the Deutschmark to the east on the basis of a one-for-one exchange rate, and a free-market economy; the Social Democratic Party which favoured a more gradual approach to unity and a social market economy; and the Democratic Socialist Party, the successor to the discredited Communist Party. The campaign was dominated by West German political parties and the leading West German politicians, and resulted in a landslide victory for the conservative Alliance for Germany. This result had not seemed remotely likely as recently as two weeks before polling day but the East German CDU's commitment to rapid reunification and a market economy swung the day. The new East German Prime Minister, Lothar de Maizière, was faced with the remarkable task of overseeing the process of the elimination of the East German state and its absorption into a new Federal Republic.

NICARAGUA AT THE CROSSROADS

In June 1979 popular resistance led by the Sandinista National Liberation Army (FSLN)—an organisation named after Augusto Cesar Sandino, a national hero murdered by the Somoza family in the 1920s—forced Anastasio "Tachito" Somoza out of power. He was the last member of a "dynasty" of dictators which had dominated Nicaragua since the 1920s and by manipulating a system of extortion and graft had accumulated a fortune of over $500 million. In the bitter conflict against the dictatorship 40,000 people died and a further 750,000 were made homeless. In July 1979 the Sandinista government was formed to tackle the massive problems of economic reconstruction but throughout the 1980s scarce resources were diverted to defence by a niggling insurgency which has caused increased economic dislocation.

Initially, armed opposition came only from ex-Somoza National Guard operating in the border areas but between 1982 and 1986 the situation worsened as heavily armed US backed "contra" guerrillas operated against the Sandinistas from bases in Honduras ultimately sparking a brief border conflict between the Nicaraguan and Honduran armies. Although the "contras" never mounted a determined military campaign liable to topple the Sandinistas their insurgency has had a variety of crucially debilitating effects upon the Nicaraguan economy.

Economic Crisis.

Heightened popular mobilisation and heavy expenditure upon defence within Nicaragua have produced labour shortages and financial constraints which have been exacerbated by the US trade embargo (enforced by the Reagan administration in May 1985). The lack of spare parts for the electricity, oil and telephone systems has caused the greatest economic disruption prompting a series of austerity measures to ensure the supply of industrial goods and, increasingly, agricultural produce. The "contra" insurgency has cost the agricultural sector $530 million in lost production and prompted a rural exodus to Managua which has doubled the city's population to 900,000 since 1979. A dual economy has developed and a parallel market for basic consumer goods has deteriorated into a black market (the "bisnes") which has mushroomed in the last five years severely hampering the government's ability to control the supply of goods and labour in the economy. Continued devaluation of the national currency (the "cordoba") failed to counter declining economic performance. The hurricane that hit Nicaragua in October 1988 left 300,000 homeless and flattened the coastal town of Bluefields worsening economic dislocation. Throughout 1989 there was a continued shortage of foreign exchange whilst the US embargo remained intact.

Relentless US hostility has been the crucial

pressure upon a nation psychologically under siege since 1982 when a state of emergency was first declared. In July 1983 US warships simulated a blockade of Nicaragua. A subsequent US military build up in the Honduran and Costa Rican border areas with Nicaragua intimated invasion preparations. Joint military manoeuvres by US and Honduran forces, culminating with the rapid deployment of 3,200 US combat troops to Honduras in March 1988, have sustained the pressure upon the Sandinista government.

The Arias initiative, which produced the "Guatemalan Pact" of August 1987, offered some temporary hope of a political solution to the entrenched conflict. A Sandinista initiative in January 1988 was followed by abortive talks with the "contras" in February in Guatemala and then in March, when "contra" uncertainty increased about continued US funding, producing the "Sapoa" truce. This agreement, named after the Nicaraguan border town where the two sides met produced an all too shaky ceasefire. The "contras" increasingly appeared to be a spent force but as a part of a massive campaign of destabilisation they precipitated considerable economic and social dislocation ultimately eroding civilian support for the Sandinista war effort.

A UN and OAS commission stressed in October 1989 that "contra" demobilisation was seriously behind schedule and that a force of 3,000 had re-infiltrated Nicaraguan territory. President Ortega decided to resume hostilities against these "contra" forces in a Sandinista offensive of November 1989. With elections only four months away in a nation weary of war this decision may have alienated civilian support for the Sandinistas. Conscription became as important an issue as falling Gross Domestic Product in the electoral campaign.

The National Opposition Union (UNO), an alliance of 14 disparate political factions, chose the editor of "La Prensa" Violeta Chamorro as its candidate for the Presidential Election of February 1990. Although right-wing business elements disliked the choice of Virgilio Godoy (an ex-Sandinista Minister) as her running mate Chamorro's campaign was well financed by the US administration and called for peace whilst criticising the Sandinista's economic shortcomings. The US government promised to lift sanctions if Chamorro was elected.

The Fall of the Sandinistas.

In January 1990 the electoral campaign hotted up with "La Prensa" attempting to smear Ortega and the Sandinista paper "Barricada" showing old photographs of UNO candidates in National Guard uniforms. Opinion polls (by US companies) in January predicted a comfortable Sandinista victory in a clean and fair election but in the February contest Violeta Barrios de Chamorro won 55·2% of the votes cast to 40·8% for Daniel Ortega. Both leaders appealed for calm and to undertake an orderly transfer of government when the new President assumed power on 25 April 1990. It remains to be seen whether Mrs Chamorro can hold together her fractious 14 party coalition in government and rule for all Nicaraguans. The Sandinistas (FSLN) are still the single largest party in the Assembly with 38 seats as against the 52 obtained by the 14 party alliance. The FSLN also controls a myriad of trade union and base organisations and is prominent in the revolutionary army. Daniel Ortega and Violeta Chamorro have held a series of talks aiming at compromise but the FSLN sees itself as the guardian of the achievements of the revolution in agrarian reform, health programmes and education. Ortega called for the immediate demobilising of the "contras" whilst Chamorro wishes to install a civilian Minister of Defence above a Sandinista leader of the army. US promises of economic aid and an end to sanctions remain unimplemented at present and may be tied to the new government's commitment to re-privatising the economy and ending Sandinista programmes.

FOCUS ON SOUTH AFRICA

End of the Botha Era.

The summer of 1989 saw the last days of the Botha era, but the President had a final card to play. On 5 July he invited African National Congress leader Mr. Nelson Mandela to his Cape

Town office for discussions. This clearly signalled the imminence of Mr. Mandela's release. The exiled ANC leadership described the gesture as a "public relations exercise". The far-right white opposition denounced it as a step towards black majority rule. On 14 August President Botha resigned following a bitter Cabinet argument over a projected visit to Zambia by Mr. de Klerk. The following day Mr. de Klerk was sworn in as acting President. He declared that South Africa was "on the threshold of a new era".

As a general election approached the anti-apartheid movement mounted a nationwide civil disobedience campaign against the state of emergency from 2–23 August. The campaign was led by the Mass Democratic Movement, a coalition including the multiracial United Democratic Front, the black trade unions and churches. The government response to an apparently increasingly unified opposition was to begin re-arresting activists. The MDM marked the September elections with a general strike supported by hundreds of thousands. Unofficial reports claimed police killed 25 and wounded 100.

The 1989 General Election.

The 6 September election tested the white electorate's reactions to the ruling National Party's reforms. In June the NP had unveiled a five-year action plan promising South Africa's 23 million blacks access to 'democratic participation' but denying them real power. NP representation fell from 123 seats to 93, the party failing for the first time to win at least 50% of white votes. The right-wing Conservative Party's seats increased from 22 to 39. The reformist Democratic Party's support rose from 21 seats to 33. Though the NP lost ground to the right, the left President de Klerk claimed a 'clear mandate' for change.

Release of Political Prisoners.

President de Klerk's next step was to announce the release of eight leading political prisoners, all of whom had been jailed for life with Mr Mandela, and the most prominent of whom was Mr Walter Sisulu. The move followed discussions between government officials and Mr Mandela, a recognition of his stature as South Africa's black leader. The announcement was made on 10 October, a week before a Commonwealth Conference at which demands were expected for firmer financial sanctions against South Africa.

On 11 October President de Klerk met three black clergy, including Archbishop Desmond Tutu, for "talks about talks". He was presented with demands his government should meet if talks were to become negotiations. The state of emergency was to be lifted, restrictions on political activity ended, banned organisations legalised, all detainees without trial released, and prisoners facing death sentences reprieved. All apartheid legislation should then be repealed within six months. President de Klerk complained that the extent of the reforms he had made did not seem to be appreciated.

The de facto unbanning of the ANC was almost immediate. Mr Sisulu held a technically illegal press conference on the morning of his release and the police interfered with neither this nor later celebratory rallies. In November President de Klerk announced a series of practical if limited changes including an end to segregated beaches and a moderation of the Group Areas Act, a cornerstone of apartheid. He re-asserted the primacy of parliament and civil administration over the security forces by dismantling the National Security Management System which had operated as a shadow government under the state of emergency.

South Africa was entering a decisive period. On 13 December President de Klerk followed his predecessor by meeting Mr Mandela. Fears were expressed by some black activists that Mr Mandela might be compromising himself in private talks of this kind. Although he was to say that no negotiations took place these fears were to take on a greater significance. Events now moved rapidly. On 2 February 1990 President de Klerk declared at the opening of parliament, "The time for talking has arrived." To the apparent surprise of his supporters

and of his white and black opponents he delivered five concessions. Over 60 banned organisations were legalised, including the ANC, the Pan-Africanist Congress, the Communist Party, the UDF and the Azanian People's Organisation. There was to be a moratorium on hangings, The Separate Amenities Act would be repealed. Detention without trial would be limited to six months. Finally, Mr Mandela would be unconditionally released.

Response to Reforms.

The response of the black movements was mixed. The ANC called for an "urgent review" of the new situation. The UDF, the leading force behind the liberation struggle, praised the President's "boldness" but insisted that little had changed while apartheid remained. The PAC, led by Mr Zephania Mothopeng, was more blunt, calling the changes "irrelevant and meaningless". President de Klerk faced equally vehement criticism from his right. The Conservative Party leader Dr Andres Treurnicht demanded a general election. The neo-Nazi *Afrikaner Weerstandsbewegin* leader Mr Eugene Terre'Blanche accused the President of handing power to the ANC and the Communists.

There could be no doubting what had brought white South Africa to this position: the revolt in the black townships which had begun in 1983; and international sanctions following in its wake. Military repression, it was clear, would ultimately fail to contain let alone crush the revolt. Sanctions were weakening the South African economy, denying it new investment, draining the country's foreign reserves, and increasing unemployment, particularly among blacks.

The Release of Mandela.

Mr Mandela was freed on 11 February. His 25 years in prison had become a symbol to the world of white repression; now his release symbolised the hope of change. At a welcoming rally Mr Mandela described President de Klerk as a "man of integrity". He declared, however, that the armed struggle would continue as long as its cause—apartheid—remained. He appealed for a continuation of sanctions against South Africa. But Mr Mandela now faced his test as a politician rather than an inspirational symbol.

Since 1988 Natal province had been undergoing a virtual civil war between the Zulu national Inkatha movement and the ANC/UDF in which over 2,500 had died in bitter political and criminal violence. Chief Mangosuthu Buthelezi, the chief minister of the Kwazulu homeland, was competing for political control with the ANC and its allies. Mr Mandela was seen as the only leader with the stature to end the fighting, a continuation of which, he said, would "endanger the peace process in the whole of the country." A conference of Inkatha, the ANC and the UDF was planned for 2 April to negotiate an end to the daily toll of deaths. But Mr Mandela's agreement to the meeting without consulting local opinion was criticised by Natal ANC activists. On 30 March the meeting was cancelled by the ANC, a move which revealed the split within the ANC. Wider divisions within the anti-apartheid movement were opening up. In March the ANC announced plans to create a broad black coalition to negotiate with the government. The PAC leadership in exile rejected this, declaring that "no basis for genuine negotiations" existed. The "settler regime", it said, would never negotiate its own demise. Fears were expressed on 14 March by Mr Joe Modise—the commander of the ANC's military wing—that the ANC was being rushed into premature negotiations with the government. Nevertheless, it was announced on 16 March that "talks about talks" between President de Klerk and the ANC would begin on 11 April. The government was preparing a "constitutional model" to present at eventual negotiations.

But on 26 March police—claiming that demonstrators were shouting "Kill the Boers"—fired on a black march in Sebokeng, a town near Johannesburg, killing 11 and wounding 450. Mr Mandela was initially reluctant to allow this to prevent the planned talks but widespread anger in the black community forced their abandonment.

Mr Mandela, admitting that differences within the ANC existed but unwilling to go into detail, met President de Klerk on 5 April for personal discussions. As a result ANC-government talks began on 2 May 1990.

South Africa in the 20th Century.

1899–1902	Boer War against Britain. Boer republics become British colonies.
1910	Union of South Africa proclaimed.
1912	African National Congress formed.
1913	Black protests against Native Land Act.
1919	First militant black action against pass laws.
1944	Nelson Mandela organises ANC Youth League.
1948	Afrikaner National Party government elected committed to apartheid.
1949	ANC adopts militant Programme of Action.
1950	Black National Day of Protest, 26 June.
1950s	Dr H. F. Verwoerd formulates Grand Apartheid.
1952	8,000 jailed in black civil disobedience campaign.
1955	Freedom Congress formulates Freedom Charter.
1956	Nelson Mandela, Oliver Tambo and 154 others charged with treason.
1958	African nationalist Pan-Africanist Congress splits from ANC.
1960	69 killed at Sharpeville Massacre protesting against Pass Laws. ANC and Communist Party banned.
1961	ANC joins with Communist Party to form Umkhonto we Sizwe and begins armed struggle.
1964	Nelson Mandela jailed for life at Rivonia treason trial.
1976	Soweto uprising against white domination.
1977	Guerrilla campaign in South Africa begins.
1989	President Botha resigns. Replaced by President de Klerk.
1990	ANC and other black organisations legalised. Nelson Mandela freed.

POLITICAL COMPENDIUM

This compendium provides a compact reference work of key facts and figures for an understanding of modern British politics. Readers will also find that the preceding section, *Background to Public Affairs*, complements this part of the book.

TABLE OF CONTENTS

POLITICAL COMPENDIUM

A. THE MONARCHY

The Queen is a constitutional monarch. In law she is the head of the executive, an integral part of the legislature, head of the judiciary, commander-in-chief of the armed forces and temporal head of the Church of England. In practice, the Queen's role is purely formal; she reigns, but she does not rule. In all important respects she acts only on the advice of her ministers. However, she still plays an important role symbolically as Head of State and Head of the Commonwealth.

Monarchs since 1900

1837–1901	Victoria
1901–1910	Edward VII
1910–1936	George V
1936	Edward VIII
1936–1952	George VI
1952	Elizabeth II

B. GENERAL ELECTIONS

For electoral purposes the United Kingdom is divided into 650 constituencies (an increase of fifteen since 1979) each returning one M.P. to the House of Commons. All British subjects and citizens of the Irish Republic are entitled to vote provided they are 18 years old and over and are included on the electoral register which is compiled annually. The only exceptions are members of the House of Lords and those incapacitated through insanity or imprisonment. Anyone who is entitled to vote and aged at least 21 may stand as a candidate, the only exceptions being undischarged bankrupts, clergymen in the established church and the holders of certain other public offices. All candidates have to pay a deposit of £500 (recently increased from £150), which is forfeited unless they receive 5 % of the votes cast. In each constituency the winning candidate has only to obtain a simple majority.

General elections must be held every five years,

General Elections since 1918

VOTES CAST (thousands)

	Conservative	Labour	Liberal*	Communist	Plaid Cymru	SNP	Others
1918	4,166	2,546	2,753	—	—	—	1,296
1922	5,500	4,241	4,189	34	—	—	462
1923	5,538	4,438	4,311	39	—	—	260
1924	8,039	5,489	2,928	55	—	—	126
1929	8,656	8,390	5,309	51	1	—	243
1931	12,320	6,991	1,509	75	2	21	293
1935	11,810	8,465	1,422	27	3	30	273
1945	9,988	11,995	2,248	103	16	31	752
1950	12,503	13,267	2,622	92	18	10	290
1951	13,745	13,949	731	22	11	7	177
1955	13,312	12,405	722	33	45	12	313
1959	13,750	12,216	1,639	31	78	22	125
1964	12,023	12,206	3,093	46	70	64	168
1966	11,418	13,095	2,328	62	61	128	171
1970	13,145	12,198	2,117	38	175	307	384
1974 (Feb.)	11,910	11,646	6,059	33	171	632	958
1974 (Oct.)	10,501	11,457	5,347	17	166	840	897
1979	13,698	11,532	4,314	17	133	504	1,024
1983	12,991	8,437	7,775	12	125	331	952
1987	13,761	10,030	7,340	6	124	417	859

* 1983 and 1987 figures for Liberals include the SDP total.

The Speaker has been regarded as a candidate of the party he represented before appointment.

SEATS WON

	Conservative	Labour	Liberal*	Communist	Plaid Cymru	SNP	Others (GB)	Others (NI)	Total
1918	383	73	161	0	0	0	9	81	707
1922	344	142	115	1	0	0	10	3	615
1923	258	191	158	0	0	0	5	3	615
1924	412	151	40	1	0	0	10	1	615
1929	260	287	59	0	0	0	6	3	615
1931	521	52	37	0	0	0	3	2	615
1935	429	154	21	1	0	0	8	2	615
1945	213	393	12	2	0	0	16	4	640
1950	299	315	9	0	0	0	0	2	625
1951	321	295	6	0	0	0	0	3	625
1955	345	277	6	0	0	0	0	2	630
1959	365	258	6	0	0	0	1	0	630
1964	304	317	9	0	0	0	0	0	630
1966	253	364	12	0	0	0	0	1	630
1970	330	288	6	0	0	1	1	4	630
1974 (Feb.)	297	301	14	0	2	7	2	12	635
1974 (Oct.)	277	319	13	0	3	11	0	12	635
1979	339	269	11	0	2	2	0	12	635
1983	397	209	23	0	2	2	0	17	650
1987	376	229	22	0	3	3	0	17	650

Others (NI): Ireland in 1918, Northern Ireland only 1922–79. Ulster Unionists regarded as Conservatives 1922–70.

The Speaker has been regarded as an M.P. of the party he represented before appointment.

* 1983 and 1987 figures for Liberals include SDP M.P.s.

By-Elections 1945–90

Parliament	Government	No. of By-elections	Changes	Con. +	Con. −	Lab. +	Lab. −	Lib./All.* +	Lib./All.* −	Others +	Others −
1945–50	Lab.	52	3	3	—	—	—	—	—	—	3
1950–51	Lab.	16	0	—	—	—	—	—	—	—	—
1951–55	Con.	48	1	1	—	—	1	—	—	—	—
1955–59	Con.	52	6	1	4	4	—	1	1	—	1
1959–64	Con.	62	9	2	7	6	2	1	—	—	—
1964–66	Lab.	13	2	1	1	—	1	1	—	—	—
1966–70	Lab.	38	16	12	1	—	15	1	—	3	—
1970–74	Con.	30	8	—	5	1	3	5	—	2	—
1974	Lab.	1	0	—	—	—	—	—	—	—	—
1974–79	Lab.	30	7	6	—	—	7	1	—	—	—
1979–83	Con.	20	6	1	4	1	1	4	1	—	—
1983–87	Con.	31†	6	—	4	1	1	4	—	1	1
1987–	Con.	11	3	—	2	2	1	—	—	1	—

* Liberal 1945–79; Alliance (Liberal and SDP) after 1979.
† Includes 15 by-elections held in Northern Ireland in January 1986 following Unionist resignations in protest at Anglo-Irish Agreement.

Composition of House of Commons, May 1990

Conservative	372
Labour	227
Social and Liberal Democrat	19
Ulster Unionist	9
Scottish National	4
Independent Social Democrat	3
Plaid Cymru	3
Social and Democratic Labour (NI)	3
Ulster Democratic Unionist	3
Others	3
Speaker and deputies	4
	650

The House of Commons currently includes 43 women M.P.s.

but may occur more frequently either because no government can command a majority in the House of Commons or at the request of the Prime Minister. If a seat falls vacant between general elections a by-election is held on a date usually chosen by the party which previously held the seat. Elections are generally held on Thursdays.

TURNOUT AND PARTY SHARE OF VOTES CAST

Turnout (%)		Share of Poll (%)		
		Conservative	Labour	Liberal
1918	59	39	24	26
1922	71	38	30	29
1923	71	38	31	30
1924	77	48	33	18
1929	76	38	37	23
1931	76	59	32	7
1935	71	54	39	6
1945	73	40	48	9
1950	84	44	46	9
1951	83	48	49	3
1955	77	50	46	3
1959	79	49	44	6
1964	77	43	44	11
1966	76	42	48	9
1970	72	46	43	8
1974 (Feb.)	78	38	37	19
1974 (Oct.)	73	36	39	18
1979	76	44	37	14
1983	73	42	28	26*
1987	75	42	31	23*

* includes SDP figures.

C. POLITICAL PARTIES

To understand the operation of the British system of government it is essential to appreciate the importance of the party system. Since the seventeenth century two parties have usually been predominant, at different times Tories and Whigs, Conservatives and Liberals, and since the 1930s Conservatives and Labour. Parties exist to form governments, and the path to this goal lies in the House of Commons, for

the party which obtains a majority of seats has the right to have its leaders form the government. The other party forms Her Majesty's Opposition.

To this end parties in this country have been highly disciplined organisations. The opposition accepts that, unless the government's majority is very small, it is unlikely to defeat it in the Commons, and it thus sees its role as one of criticising government policy and setting forth an alternative programme.

Party Leaders

The Conservative Party leader is elected by the members of its parliamentary party. The Labour Party leader is elected by an electoral college in which affiliated trade unions have 40% of the votes, constituency parties 30% and the Parliamentary Labour Party 30%. The Social and Liberal Democrat, and Social Democrat leaders are elected by party members nationally.

Present Leaders (June 1990)

Conservative	Mrs. Margaret Thatcher
Labour	Mr. Neil Kinnock
Social and Liberal Democrat	Mr. Paddy Ashdown
Social Democrat	Dr. David Owen
Plaid Cymru	Mr. Dafydd Elis Thomas
Scottish National	Mrs. Margaret Ewing
Ulster Unionist	Mr. James Molyneaux

Past Leaders

Conservative Party Leaders

1900–2	Marquis of Salisbury
1902–11	A. Balfour
1911–21	A. Bonar Law
1921–22	A. Chamberlain
1922–23	A. Bonar Law
1923–37	S. Baldwin
1937–40	N. Chamberlain
1940–55	(Sir) W. Churchill
1955–57	Sir A. Eden
1957–63	H. Macmillan
1963–65	Sir A. Douglas-Home
1965–75	E. Heath
1975–	Mrs. M. Thatcher

Labour Party Leaders

1906–8	J. K. Hardie
1908–10	A. Henderson
1910–11	G. Barnes
1911–14	J. R. MacDonald
1914–17	A. Henderson
1917–21	W. Adamson
1921–22	J. Clynes
1922–31	J. R. MacDonald
1931–32	A. Henderson
1932–35	G. Lansbury
1935–55	C. Attlee
1955–63	H. Gaitskell
1963–76	H. Wilson
1976–80	J. Callaghan
1980–83	M. Foot
1983–	N. Kinnock

Liberal Party Leaders

1900–8	Sir H. Campbell-Bannerman
1908–26	H. Asquith
1926–31	D. Lloyd George
1931–35	Sir H. Samuel
1935–45	Sir A. Sinclair
1945–56	C. Davies
1956–67	J. Grimond
1967–76	J. Thorpe
1976–88	D. Steel

Social and Liberal Democratic Party Leaders

1988–	P. Ashdown

Social Democratic Party Leaders

1981–3	R. Jenkins
1983–7	D. Owen
1987–8	R. Maclennan
1988–	D. Owen

Party Officers

Conservative Party

Chairman of the Party Organisation
(appointed by the Leader of the Party)

1959–61	R. Butler
1961–63	I. Macleod
1963	I. Macleod ⎫
	Lord Poole ⎭
1963–65	Viscount Blakenham
1965–67	E. du Cann
1967–70	A. Barber
1970–72	P. Thomas
1972–74	Lord Carrington
1974–75	W. Whitelaw
1975–81	Lord Thorneycroft
1981–83	C. Parkinson
1983–85	J. Selwyn Gummer
1985–87	N. Tebbit
1987–89	P. Brooke
1989–	K. Baker

Chairman of Conservative (Private) Members'
Committee (or the 1922 Committee)

1955–64	J. Morrison
1964–66	Sir W. Anstruther-Gray
1966–70	Sir A. Harvey
1970–72	Sir H. Legge-Bourke
1972–84	E. du Cann
1984–	C. Onslow

Labour Party

General Secretary

1944–62	M. Phillips
1962–68	A. Williams
1968–72	Sir H. Nicholas
1972–82	R. Hayward
1982–85	J. Mortimer
1985–	L. Whitty

Chairman of the Labour Party (elected annually
by the National Executive Committee)

1984–85	A. Hadden
1985–86	N. Hough
1986–87	S. Tierney
1987–88	N. Kinnock
1988–89	D. Skinner
1989–90	J. Richardson

Chairman of the Parliamentary Labour Party

1970–74	D. Houghton
1974	I. Mikardo
1974–79	C. Hughes
1979–81	F. Willey
1981–87	J. Dormand
1988–	S. Orme

Liberal Party

Head of Liberal Party Organisation

1960–61	D. Robinson
1961–65	P. Kemmis
1965–66	T. Beaumont
1966–70	P. Chitnis
1970–76	E. Wheeler
1976–83	W. N. Hugh Jones
1983–85	J. Spiller
1986–88	A. Ellis

Social and Liberal Democratic Party—Chief Executive: G. Elson.

Scottish National Party—National Secretary: J. Swinney.

Plaid Cymru—General Secretary: D. Williams.

National Front—Chairman of National Directorate: I. Anderson.

Communist Party of Great Britain—Secretary: N. Temple.

Green Party—Co-Chairs: N Anderson, D. Batchelor, C. Lucas. General Manager: J. Bishop.

D. PARLIAMENT

Parliament consists of the Queen, the House of Lords and the House of Commons. Over the centuries the balance between the three parts of the legislature has changed such that the Queen's role is now only formal and the House of Commons has established paramountcy over the House of Lords. Because of the party system the initiative in government lies not in Parliament but in the Cabinet. But Parliament, and especially the Commons, has important functions to play not only as the assembly to which the government is ultimately responsible but also in legitimising legislation, voting money and in acting as a body in which complaints may be raised.

House of Lords

Composition. The House of Lords comprises about 1,200 peers, made up in 1990 as follows:

Hereditary Peers	785
Life Peers	365
Lords of Appeal	9
Archbishops and bishops	26

No new hereditary peers were created between 1964 and 1983. Since then, there have been 3: Viscounts Tonypandy (George Thomas) and Whitelaw, and the Earl of Stockton (Harold Macmillan who died in December 1986). Less than 300 peers attend more than one-third of the Lords' proceedings. Figures of party strengths in the Lords are not easy to obtain, but one source identified 447 Conservatives, 125 Labour, 60 Social and Liberal Democrats, and 26 Social Democrats in 1988.

Functions.

(1) Legislation. Some bills on subjects which are not matters of partisan controversy are initiated in the Lords. It also examines in detail many bills which originated in the Commons, but its part is limited by the Parliament Acts, under which it cannot require the Commons to agree to amendments nor delay a bill indefinitely.

(2) Debate. The Lords provides a forum for men and women, distinguished in most fields of national life, to discuss issues of importance free from the reins of party discipline.

(3) Court of appeal. The Lords is the highest court of appeal. Only the law lords take part in its legal proceedings.

House of Commons

Composition. The House of Commons comprises 650 M.P.s (an increase of fifteen since 1979) elected to represent single-member constituencies (523 in England, 72 in Scotland, 38 in Wales and 17 in Northern Ireland). Its proceedings are presided over by the Speaker, who is elected by M.P.s at the beginning of each session. The present Speaker is Mr. Bernard Weatherill.

M.P.s sit on parallel rows of seats, known as benches, with those who support the government on one side of the chamber and the rest on the other side. Members of the government and the spokesmen of the Opposition are known as "frontbenchers"; other M.P.s are "backbenchers".

Functions.

(1) Legislation. There are two types of legislation—*public acts*, most of which are introduced by the government, but which can also be introduced by individual M.P.s, and *private acts*, which confer special powers on bodies such as local authorities in excess of the general law and which are subject to special procedures.

All public legislation must pass through the following stages before becoming law:

First Reading. The bill is formally introduced.

Second Reading. The general principles of the bill are debated and voted.

Committee Stage. Each clause of the bill is debated and voted.

Report Stage. The bill is considered as it was reported by the committee, and it is decided whether to make further changes in individual clauses.

Third Reading. The bill, as amended, is debated and a final vote taken.

The Other House. The bill has to pass through the same stages in the other House of Parliament.

Royal Assent. The Queen gives her assent to the bill which becomes law as an Act of Parliament.

(2) Scrutiny of government activities. There are a number of opportunities for the opposition and the government's own back-benchers to criticise government policy. They can question ministers on the floor of the House; they can table motions for debate and speak in debates initiated by the government; and they can take part in one of the select committees set up to scrutinise government activity.

Committees. The House of Commons uses committees to assist it in its work in various ways. They are of two types:

Standing Committees. A standing committee is a miniature of the House itself, reflecting its party composition, and consists of between 20 and 50 M.P.s. Its function is to examine the Committee Stage of legislation. Usually seven or eight such committees are needed.

Select Committees. A select committee is a body with special powers and privileges to which the House has delegated its authority for the purpose of discovering information, examining witnesses, sifting evidence and drawing up conclusions which are then reported to the House. A few select committees are established *ad hoc*, but the majority are semi-permanent, although the House can always wind them up at any time.

Since 1979, there have been 13 or 14 select com-

E. HER MAJESTY'S GOVERNMENT
The Cabinet (1 June 1990)

Prime Minister, First Lord of the Treasury and Minister for the Civil Service	Mrs. Margaret Thatcher
Lord President of the Council and Leader of the House of Commons	Sir Geoffrey Howe
Lord Chancellor	Lord Mackay
Secretary of State for Commonwealth and Foreign Affairs	Mr. Douglas Hurd
Chancellor of the Exchequer	Mr. John Major
Secretary of State for the Home Department	Mr. David Waddington
Secretary of State for Defence	Mr. Tom King
Secretary of State for Trade and Industry and President of the Board of Trade	Mr. Nicholas Ridley
Chancellor of the Duchy of Lancaster	Mr Kenneth Baker
Secretary of State for Health	Mr. Kenneth Clarke
Secretary of State for Education and Science	Mr. John MacGregor
Secretary of State for Scotland	Mr. Malcolm Rifkind
Secretary of State for Transport	Mr. Cecil Parkinson
Secretary of State for Energy	Mr. John Wakeham
Lord Privy Seal and Leader of the House of Lords	Lord Belstead
Secretary of State for Social Security	Mr. Anthony Newton
Secretary of State for the Environment	Mr. Christopher Patten
Secretary of State for Northern Ireland	Mr. Peter Brooke
Minister of Agriculture, Fisheries and Food	Mr. John Gummer
Chief Secretary to the Treasury	Mr. Norman Lamont
Secretary of State for Employment	Mr. Michael Howard
Secretary of State for Wales	Mr David Hunt

Ministers not in the Cabinet

Agriculture, Fisheries and Food, Minister of State	Baroness Trumpington
Defence, Minister of State for Defence Procurement	Mr. Alan Clark
Minister of State for the Armed Forces	Mr. Archibald Hamilton
Education and Science, Minister of State	Mrs. Angela Rumbold
Employment, Minister of State	Mr. Tim Eggar
Energy, Minister of State	Mr. Peter Morrison
Environment, Minister for Housing and Planning	Mr. Michael Spicer
Minister for Environment and Countryside	Mr. David Trippier
Minister for Local Government and Inner Cities	Mr. Michael Portillo
Foreign and Commonwealth Office, Ministers of State	Mr. William Waldegrave
	Lord Brabazon
	Mr. Francis Maude
Minister for Overseas Development	Mrs. Lynda Chalker
Health, Minister for Health	Mrs. Virginia Bottomley
Home Office, Ministers of State	Mr. John Patten
	Mr. David Mellor
	Earl Ferrers
Northern Ireland Office, Minister of State	Mr. John Cope
Privy Council Office, Minister of State, and Minister for the Arts	Mr. Richard Luce
Scottish Office, Ministers of State	Mr. Ian Lang
	Lord Sanderson
Social Security, Minister of State	Mr. Nicholas Scott
Trade and Industry	
Minister for Industry and Enterprise	Mr. Douglas Hogg
Minister for Trade	Lord Trefgarne
Transport, Minister for Public Transport	Mr. Roger Freeman
Welsh Office, Minister of State	Mr. Wyn Roberts
Treasury, Paymaster General	Earl of Caithness
Financial Secretary	Mr. Peter Lilley
Parliamentary Secretary, Treasury (Chief Whip)	Mr. Tim Renton
Attorney-General	Sir Patrick Mayhew
Lord Advocate	Lord Fraser
Solicitor-General	Sir Nicholas Lyell
Solicitor-General for Scotland	Mr. Alan Rodger

Principal Ministers 1900–45

	Prime Minister	Chancellor of the Exchequer	Foreign Secretary	Home Secretary	Leader of the House of Commons
1900–2	Marquis of Salisbury	Sir M. Hicks-Beach	Marquis of Salisbury Marquis of Lansdowne	Sir M. White-Ridley C. Ritchie	A. Balfour
1902–5	A. Balfour	C. Ritchie A. Chamberlain	Marquis of Lansdowne	A. Akers-Douglas	A. Balfour
1905–8	Sir H. Campbell-Bannerman	H. Asquith	Sir E. Grey	H. Gladstone	Sir H. Campbell-Bannerman
1908–16	H. Asquith	D. Lloyd George R. McKenna	Sir E. Grey	H. Gladstone W. Churchill R. McKenna Sir J. Simon Sir H. Samuel	H. Asquith
1916–22	D. Lloyd George	A. Bonar Law A. Chamberlain Sir R. Horne	A. Balfour Earl Curzon	Sir G. Cave E. Shortt	A. Bonar Law A. Chamberlain
1922–23	A. Bonar Law	S. Baldwin	Earl Curzon	W. Bridgeman	A. Bonar Law
1923–24	S. Baldwin	N. Chamberlain	Earl Curzon	W. Bridgeman	S. Baldwin
1924	J. R. MacDonald	P. Snowden	J. R. MacDonald	A. Henderson	J. R. MacDonald
1924–29	S. Baldwin	W. Churchill	(Sir) A. Chamberlain	Sir W. Joynson-Hicks	S. Baldwin
1929–35	J. R. MacDonald	P. Snowden N. Chamberlain	A. Henderson Marquis of Reading Sir J. Simon	J. Clynes Sir H. Samuel Sir J. Gilmour	J. R. MacDonald
1935–37	S. Baldwin	N. Chamberlain	Sir S. Hoare A. Eden	Sir J. Simon	S. Baldwin
1937–40	N. Chamberlain	Sir J. Simon	A. Eden Viscount Halifax	Sir S. Hoare Sir J. Anderson	N. Chamberlain
1940–45	W. Churchill	Sir K. Wood Sir J. Anderson	A. Eden	H. Morrison Sir D. Somervell	C. Attlee Sir S. Cripps A. Eden

Principal Ministers 1945–90

Prime Minister	Chancellor of the Exchequer	Foreign Secretary	Home Secretary	Leader of the House of Commons
1945–51 C. Attlee	H. Dalton Sir S. Cripps H. Gaitskell	E. Bevin H. Morrison	C. Ede	H. Morrison C. Ede
1951–55 Sir W. Churchill	R. Butler	Sir A. Eden	Sir D. Maxwell-Fyfe G. Lloyd George	H. Crookshank
1955–57 Sir A. Eden	R. Butler H. Macmillan	H. Macmillan S. Lloyd	G. Lloyd George	R. Butler
1957–63 H. Macmillan	P. Thorneycroft D. Heathcoat Amory S. Lloyd R. Maudling	S. Lloyd Earl of Home	R. Butler H. Brooke	R. Butler I. Macleod
1963–64 Sir A. Douglas-Home	R. Maudling	R. Butler	H. Brooke	S. Lloyd
1964–70 H. Wilson	J. Callaghan R. Jenkins	P. Gordon Walker M. Stewart G. Brown M. Stewart	Sir F. Soskice R. Jenkins J. Callaghan	H. Bowden R. Crossman F. Peart
1970–74 E. Heath	I. Macleod A. Barber	Sir A. Douglas-Home	R. Maudling R. Carr	W. Whitelaw R. Carr J. Prior
1974–76 H. Wilson	D. Healey	J. Callaghan	R. Jenkins	E. Short
1976–79 J. Callaghan	D. Healey	A. Crosland D. Owen	R. Jenkins M. Rees	M. Foot
1979– Mrs. M. Thatcher	Sir G. Howe N. Lawson J. Major	Lord Carrington F. Pym Sir G. Howe J. Major D. Hurd	W. Whitelaw L. Brittan D. Hurd D. Waddington	N. St John-Stevas F. Pym J. Biffen J. Wakeham Sir G. Howe

mittees, each one scrutinising the work of one or two government departments (e.g. Agriculture, Foreign Affairs, Treasury and Civil Service); and various others including the following: European Legislation, Members' Interests, Parliamentary Commissioner for Administration, Privileges, Public Accounts, and Statutory Instruments.

Central Government

The executive work of central government is performed by the Prime Minister and the other ministers of the Crown. The power of executive action is not given to a government department as a corporate body but to the minister individually, who is responsible for the exercise of his duties legally to the Queen and politically to Parliament. For this reason, all ministers must be members of either the Commons or the Lords.

At the head of the government structure is the Cabinet, which consists of the leading members of the majority party in the Commons, selected by the Prime Minister. Most Cabinet ministers are the heads of government departments, which are staffed by civil servants, but there are usually some without departmental responsibilities. Although legally ministers are individually responsible for the exercise of government powers, politically it is accepted that the Cabinet is collectively responsible for government policy. It thus acts as one man, and a minister who disagrees with the Cabinet must either resign or remain silent.

Size of the Government 1945–90

	Cabinet Ministers	Non-Cabinet Ministers	Junior Ministers	Total
1945	20	20	49	89
1950	18	22	44	84
1960	20	23	45	88
1965	23	33	55	111
1970	17	26	41	84
1975	24	31	54	109
1990	22	33	51	106

F. HER MAJESTY'S OPPOSITION

The leader of the largest party opposed to the government is designated Leader of Her Majesty's Opposition and receives an official salary. The leading spokesmen of the Opposition meet together as a committee and are generally known as the Shadow Cabinet. A Conservative Shadow

Cabinet, officially known as the Leader's Consultative Committee, is selected by the leader of the party. Labour Shadow Cabinets, officially known as the Parliamentary Committee, are elected by the Parliamentary Labour Party, but the leader retains the right to invite members to take charge of particular subjects.

G. OTHER EXECUTIVE BODIES

A large number of semi-autonomous agencies have been established to carry out functions on behalf of the government, usually because a particular function is considered to be unsuitable for a normal government department. In this category are bodies such as the British Broadcasting Corporation and the Commission for Racial Equality which need to be insulated from the political process, and the nationalised industries, most of which are managed by public corporations so as to secure managerial flexibility. Some public control over these bodies is maintained by means of various powers which ministers possess.

National Health Service

The National Health Service was created in 1948. Overall responsibility for the NHS rests with the Secretary of State for Social Services and the Secretaries of State for Scotland and Wales. Managerial and operational responsibility, however, is delegated to various health authorities appointed by central government in consultation with local authorities and the health service professions. In England there are two tiers of authorities: 14 Regional Health Authorities and 190 District Health Authorities. In Scotland and Wales the Scottish and Welsh Offices act as the regional tier and there are 15 Health Boards and 9 Health Authorities respectively.

H. THE CIVIL SERVICE

The civil service is the body of permanent officials who, working in the various departments, administer the policy of central government. It consists of some 567,000 people (2·5% of the working population), of whom 499,000 are non-industrial civil servants and the rest industrial workers in places such as the ordnance factories and naval dockyards. Over 80% of the civil service work outside Greater London, mainly in the regional and local offices of departments such as Health and Social Security, Employment and the Inland Revenue.

The political head of each department is a minister, but, as he often has no previous experience of the field to which he is appointed and his tenure of office may be fairly short-lived, great

Labour's Shadow Cabinet (June 1990)

Parliamentary Committee* (elected 1989)

Leader of the Opposition	Mr. Neil Kinnock
Deputy Leader, Home Affairs	Mr. Roy Hattersley
Opposition Chief Whip	Mr. Derek Foster
Chairman of the Parliamentary Labour Party	Mr. Stan Orme
Trade and Industry	Mr. Gordon Brown
Treasury and Economic Affairs	Mr. John Smith
Health	Mr. Robin Cook
Employment	Mr. Tony Blair
Foreign and Commonwealth Affairs	Mr. Gerald Kaufman
Children	Ms. Joan Lester
Women	Ms. Jo Richardson
Leader of the House of Commons and Campaigns Coordinator	Dr. John Cunningham
Environment	Mr. Bryan Gould
Energy	Mr. Frank Dobson
Transport	Mr. John Prescott
Social Security	Mr. Michael Meacher
Agriculture, Food and Rural Affairs	Dr. David Clark
Development and Co-operation	Ms. Ann Clwyd
Scotland	Mr. Donald Dewar
Wales	Mr. Barry Jones
Chief Secretary to the Treasury	Ms. Margaret Beckett
Education	Mr. Jack Straw

Others

Defence and Disarmament and Arms Control	Mr. Martin O'Neill
Northern Ireland	Mr. Kevin McNamara
Arts	Mr. Mark Fisher
Disabled People	Mr. Alf Morris
Legal Affairs	Mr. John Morris
Science and Technology	Dr. Jeremy Bray

*The Parliamentary Committee also includes three Labour Peers: Lord Cledwyn (Leader), Lord Ponsonby (Chief Whip), and Lord Dean.

Major Nationalised Industries

	Chairman
British Railways Board	Mr Robert Reid
British Coal	Sir Robert Haslam
Post Office	Sir Bryan Nicholson

Other Public Bodies

	Chairman
Arts Council	Mr. Peter Palumbo
Bank of England	Mr. Robin Leigh-Pemberton
Advisory Conciliation and Arbitration Service	Mr. Douglas Smith
British Broadcasting Corporation	Mr. Marmaduke Hussey
Civil Aviation Authority	Mr. Christopher Tugendhat
Commission for Racial Equality	Mr. Michael Day
Equal Opportunities Commission	Mrs. Joanna Foster
Independent Television Commission	Mr. George Russell
Health and Safety Commission	Dr. John Cullen
London Regional Transport	Mr. Wilfred Newton
Monopolies and Mergers Commission	Mr. Sydney Lipworth
National Consumer Council	Lady Wilcox
Polytechnics and Colleges Funding Council	Sir Ron Dearing
Radio Authority	Lord Chalfont
Universities Funding Council	Lord Chilver

responsibility falls on the shoulders of the permanent civil servants in his department. Civil servants remain largely anonymous and their relationship with their minister is a confidential one. They are non-political in the sense that they serve all political parties impartially.

Civil Service Numbers

	Total	Industrial	Non-Industrial
1914	779,000	497,000	282,000
1938	581,000	204,000	377,000
1950	972,000	397,000	575,000
1960	996,000	359,000	637,000
1970	702,000	209,000	493,000
1979	732,000	166,000	566,000
1989	567,000	68,000	499,000

Note: The drop in numbers between 1960 and 1970 is the result of the exclusion of Post Office staff, who ceased to be civil servants in 1969. Otherwise the size of the civil service grew by more than 50,000 between 1960 and 1970.

Senior Civil Servants

Head of the Home Civil Service

1945–56	Sir E. Bridges
1956–63	Sir N. Brook
1963–68	Sir L. Helsby
1968–74	Sir W. Armstrong
1974–78	Sir D. Allen
1978–81	Sir I. Bancroft
1981–83	{ Sir R. Armstrong / Sir D. Wass }
1983–88	Sir R. Armstrong
1988–	Sir R. Butler

Head of the Diplomatic Service

1945–46	Sir A. Cadogan
1946–49	Sir O. Sargent
1949–53	Sir W. Strang
1953–57	Sir I. Kirkpatrick
1957–62	Sir F. Hoyer Millar
1962–65	Sir H. Caccia
1965–68	Sir S. Garner
1968–69	Sir P. Gore-Booth
1969–73	Sir D. Greenhill
1973–75	Sir T. Brimelow
1975–82	Sir M. Palliser
1982–86	Sir A. Acland
1986–	Sir P. Wright

Permanent Secretary to the Treasury

1945–56	Sir E. Bridges
1956–60	{ Sir N. Brook / Sir R. Makins }
1960–62	{ Sir N. Brook / Sir F. Lee }
1962–63	{ Sir N. Brook / Sir W. Armstrong }
1963–68	{ Sir L. Helsby / (Sir) W. Armstrong }
1968	{ Sir W. Armstrong / Sir D. Allen }

1968–74	Sir D. Allen
1974–83	Sir D. Wass
1983–	Sir P. Middleton

Secretary to the Cabinet

1938–47	Sir E. Bridges
1947–63	Sir N. Brook
1963–73	Sir B. Trend
1973–79	Sir J. Hunt
1979–88	Sir R. Armstrong
1988–	Sir R. Butler

Other Public Servants

The civil service constitutes only 11% of the public service. The remainder work as follows:

Local Government	42%
National Health Service	17%
Nationalised industries and other public bodies	24%
Armed Forces	6%

In all there are 5.6 million employees in the public sector (about 25% of the total working population).

I. LOCAL GOVERNMENT

Local government in the United Kingdom is the creation of Parliament. Its structure is laid down by Parliament, and local authorities may only exercise those powers which Parliament either commands or permits them to exercise. Their functions include responsibility for all education services, except the universities, most personal welfare services, housing, public health, environmental planning, traffic management and transport, in each case subject to some central government control.

The structure of local government varies in different parts of the country. In non-metropolitan England (often known as the shire counties), Scotland and Wales there is a two-tier system. In London and the six metropolitan areas there has been, since April 1986 (when the Greater London Council and the metropolitan county councils were abolished), a single-tier system with a few special bodies undertaking county-wide functions.

Next Elections

England
County Councils 1993
Metropolitan District Councils, 1991 (when a third of each council retires)
Non-metropolitan District Councils, 1991 in districts in which a third of the council retire each year, and in districts in which the whole council retires every four years
London Borough Councils, 1994

Wales
County Councils, 1993
District Councils, 1991

Scotland
Regional (and Islands) Councils, 1994
District Councils, 1992

First-tier Authorities

ENGLAND	Name	Population in 1987	Political control in 1990	Number of districts	Administrative capital
Non-Metropolitan Counties	Avon	951,000	NOM.	6	Bristol
	Bedfordshire	526,000	NOM.	4	Bedford
	Berkshire	741,000	Con.	6	Reading
	Buckinghamshire	621,000	Con.	5	Aylesbury
	Cambridgeshire	642,000	Con.	6	Cambridge
	Cheshire	952,000	NOM.	8	Chester
	Cleveland	555,000	Lab.	4	Middlesbrough
	Cornwall	453,000	NOM.	6	Truro
	Cumbria	487,000	NOM.	6	Carlisle
	Derbyshire	919,000	Lab.	9	Matlock
	Devon	1,010,000	Con.	10	Exeter
	Dorset	649,000	Con.	8	Dorchester
	Durham	599,000	Lab.	8	Durham
	East Sussex	698,000	Con.	7	Lewes
	Essex	1,522,000	Con.	14	Chelmsford
	Gloucestershire	522,000	NOM.	6	Gloucester
	Hampshire	1,537,000	Con.	13	Winchester
	Hereford and Worcester	665,000	Con.	9	Worcester
	Hertfordshire	987,000	Con.	10	Hertford
	Humberside	847,000	Lab.	9	Hull
	Isle of Wight	127,000	Dem.	2	Newport
	Kent	1,511,000	Con.	14	Maidstone
	Lancashire	1,381,000	Lab.	14	Preston
	Leicestershire	879,000	NOM.	9	Leicester
	Lincolnshire	575,000	Con.	7	Lincoln
	Norfolk	736,000	Con.	7	Norwich
	Northamptonshire	562,000	Con.	7	Northampton
	Northumberland	301,000	Lab.	6	Newcastle-upon-Tyne
	North Yorkshire	706,000	NOM.	8	Northallerton
	Nottinghamshire	1,008,000	Lab.	8	Nottingham
	Oxfordshire	578,000	NOM.	5	Oxford
	Shropshire	397,000	NOM.	6	Shrewsbury
	Somerset	452,000	Con.	5	Taunton
	Staffordshire	1,028,000	Lab.	9	Stafford
	Suffolk	635,000	Con.	7	Ipswich
	Surrey	1,000,000	Con.	11	Kingston-upon-Thames
	Warwickshire	484,000	Con.	5	Warwick
	West Sussex	700,000	Con.	7	Chichester
	Wiltshire	551,000	NOM.	5	Trowbridge
WALES					
Counties	Clwyd	403,000	Lab.	6	Mold
	Dyfed	577,000	NOM.	6	Carmarthen
	Gwent	443,000	Lab.	5	Cwmbran
	Gwynedd	236,000	Ind.	5	Caernarfon
	Mid Glamorgan	535,000	Lab.	6	Cardiff
	Powys	113,000	Ind.	3	Llandrindod Wells
	South Glamorgan	399,000	Lab.	2	Cardiff
	West Glamorgan	363,000	Lab.	4	Swansea
SCOTLAND					
Regions	Borders	103,000	Ind.	4	Newtown St. Boswells
	Central	272,000	Lab.	3	Stirling
	Dumfries and Galloway	147,000	Ind.	4	Dumfries
	Fife	345,000	Lab.	3	Cupar
	Grampian	503,000	NOM.	5	Aberdeen
	Highland	202,000	Ind.	8	Inverness
	Lothian	741,000	Lab.	4	Edinburgh
	Strathclyde	2,333,000	Lab.	19	Glasgow
	Tayside	394,000	NOM.	3	Dundee
Islands Councils	Orkney	19,000	NP.	—	Kirkwall
	Shetland	23,000	NP.	—	Lerwick
	Western Isles	21,000	NP.	—	Stornoway

NOM.—No overall majority.   NP.—Non-party

Second-tier Authorities

	Number	Range of population	Party Control
England Non-Metropolitan District Councils	296	24,000—416,000	Con. 120, Lab. 66, SLD. 5, Other 22, NOM 83.
Wales District Councils	37	20,000—282,000	Con. 2, Lab. 17, Other 9, NOM 9.
Scotland District Councils	53	9,000—856,000	Con. 3, Lab. 24, SLD 2, Other 14 NOM 10.

NOM—No overall majority.   NP—Non-party.

Metropolitan Councils in England

	Name	Population in 1987	Political control in 1990
London	Barking & Dagenham	148,000	Lab.
	Barnet	305,000	Con.
	Bexley	221,000	Con.
	Brent	257,000	NOM.
	Bromley	298,000	Con.
	Camden	185,000	Lab.
	Croydon	319,000	Con.
	Ealing	297,000	Con.
	Enfield	262,000	Con.
	Greenwich	217,000	Lab.
	Hackney	187,000	Lab.
	Hammersmith and Fulham	151,000	Lab.
	Haringey	194,000	Lab.
	Harrow	200,000	Con.
	Havering	237,000	NOM.
	Hillingdon	231,000	Con.
	Hounslow	194,000	Lab.
	Islington	169,000	Lab.
	Kensington and Chelsea	133,000	Con.
	Kingston-on-Thames	132,000	Con.
	Lambeth	243,000	Lab.
	Lewisham	232,000	Lab.
	Merton	164,000	Lab.
	Newham	207,000	Lab.
	Redbridge	230,000	Con.
	Richmond-on-Thames	163,000	SLD.
	Southwark	217,000	Lab.
	Sutton	169,000	SLD.
	Tower Hamlets	159,000	SLD.
	Waltham Forest	215,000	Lab.
	Wandsworth	258,000	Con.
	Westminster	173,000	Con.
Greater Manchester	Bolton	262,000	Lab.
	Bury	174,000	Lab.
	Manchester	450,000	Lab.
	Oldham	220,000	Lab.
	Rochdale	207,000	Lab.
	Salford	238,000	Lab.
	Stockport	291,000	NOM.
	Tameside	216,000	Lab.
	Trafford	216,000	Con.
	Wigan	307,000	Lab.
Merseyside	Knowsley	162,000	Lab.
	Liverpool	476,000	Lab.
	St. Helens	187,000	Lab.
	Sefton	297,000	NOM.
	Wirral	335,000	NOM.
South Yorkshire	Barnsley	222,000	Lab.
	Doncaster	290,000	Lab.
	Rotherham	252,000	Lab.
	Sheffield	532,000	Lab.
Tyne & Wear	Gateshead	207,000	Lab.
	Newcastle-upon-Tyne	283,000	Lab.
	North Tyneside	193,000	Lab.
	South Tyneside	156,000	Lab.
	Sunderland	297,000	Lab.
West Midlands	Birmingham	998,000	Lab.
	Coventry	309,000	Lab.
	Dudley	303,000	Lab.
	Sandwell	298,000	Lab.
	Solihull	204,000	Con.
	Walsall	262,000	Lab.
	Wolverhampton	251,000	Lab.
West Yorkshire	Bradford	463,000	Lab.
	Calderdale	195,000	Lab.
	Kirklees	376,000	Lab.
	Leeds	709,000	Lab.
	Wakefield	310,000	Lab.

Local Government Structure (showing numbers of authorities of each type)

	England			Wales	Scotland	
1st Tier	Metropolitan District Councils 36	Non-Metropolitan County Councils 39	London Borough Councils* 32	County Councils 8	Regional Councils 9	Islands Councils 3
2nd Tier		Non-Metropolitan District Councils 296		District Councils 37	District Councils 53	
3rd Tier	Parish Councils 221	Parish Councils 8,919		Community Councils	Community Councils	Community Councils

*Excluding the City of London.

Table derived from J. Stanyer and B. C. Smith, *Administering Britain* (Martin Robertson, 1980), p. 119.

Local Government—Division of Functions

Service	England and Wales			Scotland
	Metropolitan areas	Non-Metropolitan areas	Greater London	
Education	District	County	Borough[1]	Region
Personal social services	District	County	Borough	Region
Police and fire services	Joint boards[2]	County	Home Secretary/Joint Board[2]	Region
Planning	District	Shared	Borough	Shared
Highways	District[3]	Shared	Borough[3]	Shared
Environmental Health	District	District	Borough	District
Housing	District	District	Borough	District

Notes:

1. In Inner London a special body, the Inner London Education Authority (ILEA), ran the education service until its abolition in 1990.

2. Joint boards are composed of borough and district councillors, appointed by the councils within the metropolitan area or Greater London.

3. In the metropolitan areas except London, passenger transport services are run by joint boards; London Regional Transport has, since 1984, been appointed by central government.

J. REDRESS OF GRIEVANCES

In the first instance most citizens who are aggrieved by the decision of a public body take up their complaint with the body concerned, either personally or in writing. If this does not satisfy them they have a number of options which vary according to the type of body and the nature of their complaint.

Central Government

1. *M.P.s.* M.P.s may be contacted by letter, and many of them hold regular surgeries in their constituencies. On receipt of a complaint they can write to the minister in charge of the department concerned or ask a question in Parliament. If the complainant alleges maladministration (*e.g.*, arbitrary action, undue delay) this can be referred to the *Parliamentary Commissioner for Administration* (usually known as the Ombudsman) who is empowered to investigate complaints and report his findings to Parliament.

2. *Tribunals and inquiries.* In certain areas of government (*e.g.*, social security), special tribunals exist to adjudicate on disputes between citizens and government. In others (*e.g.*, planning) an inquiry can be set up. In both cases the machinery is less formal and more flexible than the ordinary courts.

3. *Courts of law.* On certain restricted matters (*e.g.*, that a public body has acted outside its lawful powers), citizens have recourse to the ordinary courts.

Local Government

1. *Councillors.* Local councillors can be contacted in the same way as M.P.s. They can also refer complaints of maladministration to a *Commissioner for Local Administration* (or local Ombudsman). There are five commissioners, three in England and one each in Scotland and Wales, each investigating complaints in a particular part of the country.

2. *Tribunals and inquiries* (as above).

3. *Courts of law* (as above).

Other Public Bodies

1. *National Health Service.* Each health authority has its own complaints procedure subject to a national code of practice. Complaints, other than those involving the exercise of clinical judgement, may be taken to the *Health Service Commissioner.* Special procedures exist for complaints against doctors.

2. *Nationalised Industries.* Each industry has a consumer council which exists both to take up individual complaints and to represent the views of consumers to the board of management for the industry (*e.g.*, The Post Office Users National Council, the Transport Users Consultative Committees). In four former nationalised industries, privatised during the 1980s – telecommunications, gas, water and electricity – independent regulatory bodies have been created to ensure the companies do not abuse monopoly power and to deal with consumers' complaints. Special arrangements apply to broadcasting (*see* **D14**).

Parliamentary Commissioner for Administration
(and Health Service Commissioner since 1973)

1967–71	Sir Edmund Compton
1971–76	Sir Alan Marre
1976–78	Sir Idwal Pugh
1979–85	Sir Cecil Clothier
1985–90	Sir Anthony Barrowclough
1990–	Mr. Willian Reid

Commissioner for Local Administration in England

Dr. D. C. M. Yardley

Office of Gas Supply (OFGAS)

Mr. J. McKinnon (Director-General)

Office of Telecommunications (OFTEL)

Sir B. Carsberg (Director-General)

Office of Water Services

Mr. I. C. R. Byatt (Director-General)

Office of Electricity Regulation

Professor S. Littlechild (Director-General)

K. PRESSURE GROUPS

Large numbers of groups exist to exert pressure on government by direct consultation with ministers and civil servants, lobbying Parliament and general publicity campaigns. Some exist to defend interests such as labour, business or consumers; others promote particular causes such as the prevention of cruelty to children or the banning of blood sports. Of great importance in contemporary politics are the groups representing labour and business.

Trade Unions

About 40% of the working population belong to a trade union. The 10 largest unions are:

Transport and General Workers' Union
Amalgamated Engineering Union
General, Municipal, Boilermakers' and Allied Trades Union
National and Local Government Officers Association
National Union of Public Employees
Manufacturing, Science, Finance Union
Union of Shop, Distributive and Allied Workers
Electrical, Electronic, Telecommunication and Plumbing Union
Union of Construction, Allied Trades and Technicians
Confederation of Health Service Employees.

Union	Members	Principal Officer
TGWU	1,312,000	R. Todd
GMBATU	800,000	J. Edmonds
AEU	794,000	W. Jordan
NALGO	755,000	A. Jinkinson
MSF	653,000	K. Gill
NUPE	635,000	R. Bickerstaffe
USDAW	400,000	S. Tierney
EETPU	330,000	E. Hammond
UCATT	255,000	A. Williams
COHSE	220,000	H. MacKenzie

83 trade unions, representing over 80% of total union membership, are affiliated to the *Trades Union Congress*, which is the federal body of the trade union movement, representing its views to government and others, and giving assistance on questions relating to particular trades and industries.

TUC General Secretaries since 1946

1946–60	(Sir) V. Tewson
1960–70	G. Woodcock
1970–74	V. Feather
1974–84	L. Murray
1984–	N. Willis

Business

The peak organisation representing British business is the *Confederation of British Industry*, formed in 1965. Its members comprise (1983) over 11,000 individual enterprises (mainly in the private sector but also including most nationalised industries) and over 200 representative organisations (employers' organisations, trade associations etc.).

Director-Generals of the CBI

1965–69	J. Davies
1969–76	(Sir) C. Adamson
1976–80	(Sir) J. Methven
1980–87	(Sir) T. Beckett
1987–	J. Banham

Business is also represented by large numbers of associations which promote the interests of individual industries and sectors (*e.g.*, the Society of Motor Manufacturers and Traders, the Retail Consortium, the Association of Independent Businesses).

Other major groups

	Principal Officer
Campaign for Nuclear Disarmament	M. Beresford
Consumers Association	J. Beishon
European Movement	P. Luff
Friends of the Earth	D. Gee
National Society for the Prevention of Cruelty to Children	C. Brown
Royal Society for the Prevention of Accidents	E. Hooper
Royal Society for the Prevention of Cruelty to Animals	A. Richmond
Royal Society for the Protection of Birds	I. Prestt
Shelter (National Campaign for the Homeless)	S. McKechnie

Some of the largest groups (*e.g.* the Automobile Association, the National Federation of Women's Institutes) exist primarily to provide services for their members but also exert pressure upon government on issues within their field of interest.

L. THE MEDIA

1. Principal Newspapers

The principal national dailies, with their proprietors and circulation, are set out on **D15**.

There are also a number of provincial morning daily newspapers in England (*e.g.*, *The Birmingham Post and Gazette*, *The Liverpool Daily Post*, *The Yorkshire Post*). Scotland has five morning dailies, of which the most important are *The Scotsman*, *The Glasgow Herald* and *The Daily Record*. Wales has one, *The Western Mail*, and Northern Ireland two, *The News-Letter* and *Irish News*.

A voluntary Press Council exists to consider complaints against the Press and to promote standards.
Chairman, 1989– Mr. Louis Blom-Cooper

2. Broadcasting

British Broadcasting Corporation

Established in 1926 as a public service body and financed by licence fees paid by all owners of TV sets. It is directed by a board of governors appointed by the government.

Services: Radio—4 national networks; 36 local radio stations. TV—2 channels.

Chairman of the Board of Governors, 1986–
Mr. Marmaduke Hussey

Director-General, 1987– Mr. Michael Checkland

Independent Broadcasting Authority

Established in 1954 to license programme contracting companies and to regulate their output. In 1972 its functions were extended to include local sound broadcasting. Independent broadcasting is financed by advertising revenue.

Services: TV—One channel, operated by 15 regional companies, and a second (Channel 4) run by two organisations (one for England and Scotland, the other for Wales). A common news service is provided for all the companies by Independent Television News Ltd. Radio 47 local radio stations.

Chairman of IBA, 1988–90 Mr. George Russell

As part of a major reorganisation of broadcasting, the IBA is to be split on 1 January 1991 into two bodies (*see* **D18**):

Independent Television Commission
Chairman, 1991– Mr. George Russell

Radio Authority
Chairman, 1991– Lord Chalfont

Editorially all broadcasting authorities are expected to show political balance. Two bodies exist to deal with complaints and standards:

Broadcasting Complaints Commission – to adjudicate on complaints of unjust or unfair treatment in sound or TV programmes.
Chairman, 1987– Lady Anglesey

Broadcasting Standards Council – to establish a code on the portrayal of sex and violence and standards of taste and decency.
Chairman, 1988– Lord Rees-Mogg.

Paper	Proprietors	Circulation in 1989 (millions)	General political stance
National Dailies			
Daily Express	United Newspapers	1·6	Right
Daily Mail	Associated Newspapers	1·8	Right
Daily Mirror	Pergamon Press	3·2	Left
Daily Star	United Newspapers	0·9	Right
Daily Telegraph	Telegraph Newspaper Trust	1·1	Right
Financial Times	Pearson Longman	0·2	Right
Guardian	Guardian and Manchester Evening News	0·4	Centre
Independent	Newspaper Publishing	0·4	Ind.
Morning Star	Morning Star Co-op Society	0·03	Comm.
Sun	News International	4·2	Right
The Times	News International	0·4	Right
Today	Lonrho International	0·6	Right
National Sundays			
Independent on Sunday	Newspaper Publishing	n/a	Ind.
Mail on Sunday	Associated Newspapers	2·0	Right
News of the World	News International	5·3	Right
Observer	Lonrho Group	0·7	Centre
Sunday Correspondent	Sunday Correspondent	n/a	Ind.
Sunday Express	United Newspapers	2·0	Right
Sunday Mirror	Pergamon Press	3·0	Left
Sunday People	Pergamon Press	2·7	Left
Sunday Telegraph	Telegraph Newspaper Trust	0·7	Right
Sunday Times	News International	1·3	Right
London Evening			
London Standard	Associated Newspapers	0·5	Right

M. SCOTLAND, WALES AND NORTHERN IRELAND

The structure of government in Scotland, Wales and Northern Ireland differs from that in England.

Scotland

Most central government functions in Scotland are the responsibility of a single department, the Scottish Office, based in Edinburgh and represented in the Cabinet by the Secretary of State for Scotland. On many matters special Scottish legislation is enacted by Parliament and administrative structure (*e.g.* the local government system—*see* **D13**) and practice (*e.g.* the educational system) differ from that in England.

Wales

The Welsh Office, based in Cardiff and represented in the Cabinet by the Secretary of State for Wales, performs many central government functions in Wales but its responsibilities are narrower than its Scottish counterpart. In other respects too government in Wales resembles more closely that in England.

Northern Ireland

From 1921 until 1972 Northern Ireland was governed under the scheme of devolution embodied in the Government of Northern Ireland Act 1920. This created the Northern Ireland Parliament, generally known as Stormont after its eventual location. Executive powers were formally vested in the Governor of Northern Ireland, but were in effect performed by a Prime Minister and small cabinet, responsible to Stormont.

The recent troubles in the province led the UK Government in 1972 to suspend the Government of Northern Ireland Act. Since then, apart from a period of four months in 1974, Northern Ireland has been ruled direct from Westminster, the powers of government being vested in the Secretary of State for Northern Ireland. Most local government functions in the province are performed either by the Secretary of State or by special boards. There are, however, 26 elected district councils with limited functions, mainly in the environmental field. Under the terms of the Anglo-Irish agreement, signed in November 1985, the Republic of Ireland has been granted consultative status on certain issues.

N. BRITAIN IN EUROPE

Since joining the European Economic Community in 1973, the United Kingdom has participated in the principal Community institutions as follows:

Council of Ministers

The Council of Ministers is the main decision-making body within the Community, consisting of representatives of the 12 member states, each government delegating one of its ministers according to the business under discussion. The principal U.K. delegate is the Secretary of State for Foreign and Commonwealth Affairs (Sir Geoffrey Howe).

Commission

The Commission heads a large bureaucracy in Brussels which submits proposals to the Council of Ministers, implements its decisions, and has powers of its own to promote the Community's interests. It consists of 17 members, appointed by agreement among the member states for 4-year renewable terms. Members are pledged to independence of national interests.

President of the Commission: Mr. Jacques Delors (France)

U.K. members:
Sir Leon Brittan (responsible for competition policy and financial institutions).
Mr. Bruce Millan (responsible for regional policy).

European Parliament

Apart from general powers of supervision and consultation, the Parliament, which meets in Luxembourg and Strasbourg, can dismiss the Commission and has some control over the Community Budget. Until 1979 it consisted of members nominated by the national parliaments of the member states. The first direct elections were held in June 1979, the second in June 1984, and the third in June 1989. The next elections will be in 1994.

U.K. Seats Won			
	1979	1984	1989
Conservative	60	45	32
Labour	17	32	45
Scottish Nationalist	1	1	1
Democratic Unionist	1	1	1
Official Unionist	1	1	1
Social Democratic and Labour	1	1	1

U.K. Party Leaders:
Conservative   Mr. Christopher Prout
Labour   Mr. Glyn Ford

European Court of Justice

The European Court is responsible for interpreting and applying the Community treaties. Its decisions are binding in the member countries. It consists of nine judges, appointed by the member governments for 6-year renewable terms.

U.K. members: Sir Gordon Slynn, Professor Francis Jacobs

O. BRITAIN AND THE U.N.

Britain was one of the founding members of the United Nations Organization which was created in 1945. The U.N. now has 160 member states. Its principal organs, with headquarters in New York, are:

the General Assembly in which each member state has one vote and which normally meets once a year in September;
the Security Council which has five permanent members (China, France, U.K., U.S.A., U.S.S.R.) and ten non-permanent members elected for a two-year term.

Also linked with the U.N. are various international organizations, including the International Court of Justice (based in the Hague), the International Labour Organization (based in Geneva), the Food and Agriculture Organization (based in Rome), the UN Educational, Scientific and Cultural Organization (based in Paris) and the World Health Organization (based in Geneva).

U.N. Secretary-General: Mr. Javier Perez de Cuellar (Peru).
U.K. Permanent Representative to the U.N. and Representative on the Security Council: Sir David Hannay.

P. WHO'S WHO IN BRITISH POLITICS
(for M.P.s, present constituency only is indicated)

Ashdown, Paddy, b. 1941; M.P. (Lib.) 1983–8, (SLD) since 1988 (Yeovil); Leader, Social and Liberal Democratic Party since 1988.

Baker, Kenneth, b. 1934; M.P. (Con.) since 1968 (Mole Valley); Secretary of State for the Environment 1985–6, for Education and Science 1986–9, Chancellor of Duchy of Lancaster since 1989; Chairman of the Conservative Party since 1989.

Banham, John, b. 1940; McKinsey & Co. 1969–83; Controller, Audit Commission for Local Authorities in England and Wales 1983–7; Director-General, Confederation of British Industry since 1987.

Beith, Alan, b. 1943; M.P. (Lib.) 1973–88, (SLD) since 1988 (Berwick); Deputy Leader, Liberal Party 1985–8; contender for leadership of SLD, 1988.

Belstead, Lord, b. 1932; Member of House of Lords since 1958; Minister of State in various Departments 1982–8; Lord Privy Seal and Leader of the House of Lords since 1988.

Benn, Anthony Wedgwood, b. 1925; M.P. (Lab.) 1950–83 (except for short period between father's death and renunciation of the family peerage) and since 1984 (Chesterfield); Minister of Technology 1966–70, Secretary of State for Industry 1974–5 and for Energy 1975–9; Member Labour Party NEC 1959–60 and since 1962.

Biffen, John, b. 1930; M.P. (Con.) since 1961 (Shropshire North); Chief Secretary to the Treasury 1979–81, Secretary of State for Trade 1981–2; Leader of the House of Commons 1982–7, also Lord President of the Council 1982–3, and Lord Privy Seal 1983–7.

Blair, Tony, b. 1953; M.P. (Lab.) since 1983 (Sedgefield); Shadow spokesman on employment since 1989.

Brittan, Sir Leon, b. 1939; M.P. (Con.) since Feb.

1974 (Richmond); Minister of State, Home Office 1979–81, Chief Secretary to the Treasury 1981–3, Secretary of State for Home Department 1983–5, and for Trade and Industry 1985–6 (resigned over Westland affair); EEC Commissioner since 1989.

Brown, Gordon, b. 1951; M.P. (Lab.) since 1983 (Dunfermline East); Shadow spokesman on trade and industry since 1989.

Butler, Sir Robin, b. 1938; entered civil service in 1961, Treasury 1961–9, 1975–82 and 1985–7, Principal Private Secretary to Prime Minister 1982–5, Secretary to the Cabinet and Head of the Home Civil Service since 1988.

Callaghan, Lord, b. 1912; M.P. (Lab.) 1945–87 (Cardiff South and Penarth); Chancellor of the Exchequer 1964–7, Home Secretary 1967–70, Foreign Secretary 1974–6, Prime Minister 1976–9; Leader of Labour Party 1976–80.

Carrington, Lord, b. 1919; Member of House of Lords since 1938; Leader of Opposition in the Lords 1964–70 and 1974–9; Secretary of State for Defence 1970–4, for Energy 1974, and for Foreign and Commonwealth Affairs, 1979-82; Secretary-General of NATO 1984–8; Chairman Conservative Party Organisation 1972–4.

Cook, Robin, b. 1946; M.P. (Lab.) since 1974 (Livingston); Shadow spokesman on health and social security since 1987; Member, Labour Party NEC since 1988.

Cunningham, John, b. 1939; M.P. (Lab.) since 1970 (Copeland); Shadow Leader of the House of Commons since 1989.

Dobson, Frank, b. 1940; M.P. (Lab.) since 1979 (Holborn and St. Pancras); Shadow spokesman on energy since 1989.

Donaldson, Sir John, b. 1920; Barrister since 1946, QC 1961; High Court Judge 1966–79, President, National Industrial Relations Court 1971–4; Lord Justice of Appeal 1979–82; Master of the Rolls since 1982.

Edmonds, John, b. 1944; National Industrial Officer, General and Municipal Workers Union (later General, Municipal, Boilermakers and Allied Trades Union) 1972–85, General Secretary since 1985.

Foot, Michael, b. 1913; M.P. (Lab.) 1945–55 and since 1960 (Blaenau Gwent); Secretary of State for Employment 1974–6, Lord President of the Council and Leader of the Commons 1976–9; Member Labour Party NEC 1971–83, Deputy Leader 1976–80, Leader, 1980–3.

Fowler, Norman, b. 1938; M.P. (Con.) since 1970 (Sutton Coldfield); Secretary of State for Transport 1979–81, for Social Services 1981–7 and for Employment 1987–90.

Gould, Bryan, b. 1939; M.P. (Lab.) 1974–9 and since 1983 (Dagenham); Shadow spokesman on the environment since 1989; Member, Labour Party NEC since 1988.

Hattersley, Roy, b. 1932; M.P. (Lab.) since 1964 (Birmingham Sparkbrook); Secretary of State for Prices and Consumer Protection 1976–9; Shadow Home Secretary since 1987; Member Labour Party NEC and Deputy Leader since 1983.

Healey, Denis, b. 1917; M.P. (Lab.) since 1952 (Leeds East); Secretary of State for Defence 1964–70, Chancellor of the Exchequer 1974–9; Member Labour Party NEC 1970–5 and 1980–3, Deputy Leader 1980–3.

Heath, Edward, b. 1916; M.P. (Con.) since 1950 (Old Bexley and Sidcup); Chief Whip 1955–9, Minister of Labour 1959–60, Lord Privy Seal 1960–3, Secretary of State for Industry, Trade and Regional Development 1963–4, Prime Minister 1970–4; Leader of the Opposition 1965–70 and 1974–5; Leader Conservative Party 1965–75.

Heseltine, Michael, b. 1933; M.P. (Con.) since 1966 (Henley); Secretary of State for the Environment

1979–83 and for Defence 1983–6 (resigned over Westland affair).

Howe, Sir Geoffrey, b. 1926; M.P. (Con.) 1964–6 and since 1970 (Surrey East); Solicitor-General 1970–2, Minister for Trade and Consumer Affairs 1972–4, Chancellor of the Exchequer 1979–83, Secretary of State for Foreign and Commonwealth Affairs 1983–9, and Leader of the House of Commons (and Deputy Prime Minister) since 1989.

Hurd, Douglas, b. 1930; M.P. (Con.) since 1974 (Witney); Minister of State, Foreign Office 1979–83, Home Office 1983–4, Secretary of State for Northern Ireland 1984–5, for Home Department 1985–9, and for Foreign and Commonwealth Affairs since 1989.

Jenkins, Lord, b. 1920; M.P. (Lab.) 1948–76, (SDP) 1982–7 (Glasgow Hillhead); Home Secretary 1965–7 and 1974–6, Chancellor of the Exchequer 1967–70; Deputy Leader of Labour Party 1970–2; President, EEC Commission 1977–80; co-founder of Social Democratic Party 1981 and Leader, 1982–3.

Kaufman, Gerald, b. 1930; M.P. (Lab.) since 1970 (Manchester Gorton); Minister of State, Department of Industry 1975–9; Shadow Foreign Secretary, 1987–.

King, Tom, b. 1933; M.P. (Con.) since 1970 (Bridgwater); Minister for Local Government 1979–83, Secretary of State for the Environment Jan.–June 1983, for Transport June–Oct. 1983, for Employment 1983–5, for Northern Ireland 1985–9, and for Defence since 1989.

Kinnock, Neil, b. 1942; M.P. (Lab.) since 1970 (Islwyn); Leader of the Opposition since 1983; Member Labour Party NEC since 1978, Leader since 1983.

Lane, Lord, b. 1918; Member of House of Lords since 1979; Barrister since 1946, QC 1962; High Court Judge 1966–74, Lord Justice of Appeal 1974–9, Lord of Appeal 1979–80, Lord Chief Justice since 1980.

Lawson, Nigel, b. 1932; M.P. (Con.) since Feb. 1974 (Blaby); Editor, *The Spectator*, 1966–70; Financial Secretary to the Treasury 1979–81, Secretary of State for Energy 1981–3, Chancellor of the Exchequer 1983–9.

Mackay, Lord, b. 1927; Member of House of Lords since 1979; Advocate since 1955, QC 1965; Lord Advocate 1979–84; Lord of Appeal 1985–7; Lord Chancellor since 1987.

Major, John, b. 1943; M.P. (Con.) since 1979 (Huntingdon); Chief Secretary to the Treasury 1987–9, Secretary of State for Foreign and Commonwealth Affairs 1989, Chancellor of the Exchequer since 1989.

Meacher, Michael, b. 1939; M.P. (Lab.) since 1970 (Oldham West); Shadow spokesman on social security since 1989; Member Labour Party NEC 1983–8.

Middleton, Sir Peter, b. 1934; entered civil service in 1960, Treasury since 1960, Deputy Secretary 1980–3, Permanent Secretary since 1983.

Orme, Stanley, b. 1923; M.P. (Lab.) since 1964 (Salford East); Minister for Social Security 1976–9; Chairman, PLP since 1987.

Owen, David, b. 1938; M.P. (Lab.) 1966–81, (SDP, Ind. Soc. Dem. after 1990) since 1981 (Plymouth Devonport); Secretary of State for Foreign and Commonwealth Affairs 1977–9; co-founder of Social Democratic Party 1981 and Leader 1983–7 and from 1988 until its dissolution in 1990.

Paisley, Rev. Ian, b. 1926; M.P. (Protestant Unionist 1970–4, Democratic Unionist since 1974) since 1970 (Antrim North); M.E.P. since 1979; member of Stormont 1970–2, NI Assembly 1973–5, NI Constitutional Convention 1975–6, NI Assembly since 1982.

Prescott, John, b. 1938; M.P. (Lab.) since 1970 (Hull East); Shadow spokesman on transport since 1988.

Prior, Lord, b. 1927; M.P. (Con.) 1959–87 (Waveney); Minister of Agriculture 1970–2, Lord President of the Council and Leader of the Commons 1972–4, Secretary of State for Employment 1979–81 and for Northern Ireland 1981–4.

Prout, Christopher, b. 1942; M.E.P. (Con.) since 1979 (Shropshire and Stafford); Chief Whip, European Democratic Group 1983–7, Leader since 1987.

Ridley, Nicholas, b. 1929; M.P. (Con.) since 1959 (Cirencester and Tewkesbury); Secretary of State for Transport 1983–6, for the Environment 1986–9, and for Trade and Industry since 1989.

Smith, John, b. 1938; M.P. (Lab.) since 1970 (Monklands East); Secretary of State for Trade 1978–9; Shadow Chancellor since 1987.

Steel, Sir David, b. 1938; M.P. (Lib.) since 1965 (Tweeddale, Etterick and Lauderdale); Leader Liberal Party 1976–88; Acting Joint Leader, Social and Liberal Democratic Party 1988.

Tebbit, Norman, b. 1931; M.P. (Con.) since 1970 (Chingford); Secretary of State for Employment 1981–3, for Trade and Industry 1983–5, Chancellor of the Duchy of Lancaster 1985–7; Chairman, Conservative Party Organisation 1985–7.

Thatcher, Margaret, b. 1925; M.P. (Con.) since 1959 (Finchley); Secretary of State for Education and Science 1970–4, Prime Minister since 1979; Leader of the Conservative Party since 1975.

Todd, Ron, b. 1927; Ford Motor Co. 1954–66; full-time official of Transport and General Workers' Union since 1966, National Organiser 1978–85, General Secretary since 1985.

Waddington, David, b. 1929; M.P. (Con.) since 1979 (Ribble Valley); Government Chief Whip 1987–9, Home Secretary since 1989.

Walker, Peter, b. 1932; M.P. (Con.) since 1961 (Worcester); Secretary of State for the Environment 1970–2 and for Trade and Industry 1972–4, Minister of Agriculture 1979–83, Secretary of State for Energy 1983–7 and for Wales 1987–90.

Weatherill, Bernard, b. 1920; M.P. (Con.) since 1964 (Croydon North East); Conservative Party Whip 1970–9; Deputy Speaker 1979–83, Speaker since 1983.

Whitelaw, Viscount, b. 1918; M.P. (Con.) 1955–83; Lord President of the Council and Leader of the Commons 1970–2, Secretary of State for Northern Ireland 1972–3, for Employment 1973–4 and Home Secretary 1979–83, Lord President of the Council and Leader of the House of Lords 1983–8; Chairman Conservative Party Organisation 1974–5.

Williams, Shirley, b. 1930; M.P. (Lab.) 1964–79, (SDP) 1981–3; Secretary of State for Prices and Consumer Protection 1974–6 and for Education and Science 1976–9; Member Labour Party NEC 1970–81; co-founder of Social Democratic Party 1981 and President 1982–8; joined Social and Liberal Democratic Party 1988.

Willis, Norman, b. 1933; official of Trades Union Congress since 1959, Deputy General Secretary 1977–84, General Secretary since 1984.

Wilson, Lord, b. 1916; M.P. (Lab.) 1945–83; President of Board of Trade 1947–51; Prime Minister 1964–70 and 1974–6; Leader of Labour Party 1963–76.

Wright, Sir Patrick, b. 1931; entered Diplomatic Service in 1955, Deputy Under Secretary, Foreign and Commonwealth Office 1982–4, Ambassador to Saudi Arabia 1984–6, Permanent Under Secretary since 1986.

Younger, George, b. 1931; M.P. (Con.) since 1964 (Ayr); Secretary of State for Scotland 1979–86 and for Defence 1986–9.

Q. GLOSSARY OF POLITICAL PLACES AND TERMS

Political Places

Cathays Park	Location of Welsh Office in Cardiff
Chequers	Country house of Prime Ministers in Buckinghamshire
Congress House	Headquarters of TUC in London
Downing Street	The heart of government: No. 10 is the Prime Minister's official residence; No. 11, that of the Chancellor of the Exchequer; and No. 12, the offices of the Government Chief Whip
Fleet Street	Traditional home of the main national newspapers (most of which have now moved elsewhere)
St. Andrew's House	Location of the Scottish Office in Edinburgh
Smith Square	Location of Conservative Party headquarters (formerly Labour Party also)
Stormont	Location of Northern Ireland Parliament until 1972; now NI Assembly and Northern Ireland Office
Transport House	Former headquarters of Labour Party (shared with Transport and General Workers' Union) in Smith Square
Walworth Road	Current headquarters of Labour Party

Political Terms

Backbencher	An M.P. who is neither a member of the Government nor an official Opposition spokesman
Chiltern Hundreds	A fictional office of profit under the Crown, acceptance of which requires an M.P. to vacate his seat (*i.e.* the means by which an M.P. can resign)
Crossbencher	A member of the House of Lords who does not take a Party whip (see below)
Father of the House	M.P. with the longest *continuous* service in the Commons.
Frontbencher	An M.P. who is a member of the Government or an official Opposition spokesman
Guillotine	A means of curtailing debate on parliamentary legislation
Hansard	The official report of debates in both houses of Parliament
Hung Parliament	A Parliament in which no party has an overall majority (also known as a balanced Parliament)
PLP	Parliamentary Labour Party
PR	Proportional representation (an alternative electoral system favoured by the SLD and SDP)
Shadow Cabinet	The official Opposition's counterpart to the Cabinet (hence Shadow Chancellor etc)

Tactical voting	Voting behaviour determined by calculation of which party has the best chance of winning in a particular constituency
Tories	Abbreviation for Conservatives
Whips	Name given to the party managers in Parliament and to the written instructions they issue to M.P.s, the urgency of which is denoted by the number of times they are underlined (*e.g.* three-lined whip = extremely important)
1922 Committee	Conservative backbenchers' committee

R. MAJOR LEGISLATION 1989–90

Broadcasting Bill introduces greater competition in broadcasting, strengthens the oversight of programme standards, and reforms the independent TV and radio system. It establishes in 1993 a new independent national TV service (Channel 5), three new national commercial radio stations, and provides for many local radio and TV channels. It breaks up the Independent Broadcasting Authority into two bodies: the Independent Television Commission and the Radio Authority, which come into existence in January 1991.

Court and Legal Services Bill introduces greater competition in legal and related matters, and reforms the civil court system. It extends the right of solicitors to plead cases in the higher courts, ·and allows banks, building societies and insurance companies to provide conveyancing and probate services. It transfers large numbers of civil cases from the High Court to the county courts; and strengthens the complaints system against lawyers.

Education (Student Loans) Bill empowers the provision, in addition to maintenance grants, of interest-free top-up loans for full-time higher education students as from Autumn 1990.

Environmental Protection Bill tightens existing controls over pollution, waste disposal, litter, radiological and biological hazards; and replaces the nature Conservancy Council with seperate councils for England, Scotland and Wales.

British Nationality (Hong Kong) Bill grants full British citizenship to a limited number of people and their dependents in Hong Kong (up to a maximum of 50,000 households, an estimated 225,000 people).

Human Fertilization and Embryology Bill institutes a legal framework for scientific research on human embryos up to 14 days after fertilisation, and reduces the legal time limit for abortions from 28 to 24 weeks.

NHS and Community Care Bill implements the reforms set out in two White Papers 'Working for Patients' and 'Caring for People', including provision for self-governing NHS Trusts, GP Practice Funds, indicative drug budgets, and a competitive market within the NHS; and the transfer of responsibility and funding for care in the community to local authorities.

THE
WORLD OF
MUSIC

The art of music as it has developed in the Western world,
with a glossary of musical terms
and an index to composers. A
Special Topic in this edition celebrates the music of Mozart on the
occasion of the bicentenary of his
death.

TABLE OF CONTENTS

THE WORLD OF MUSIC

In writing this section no special knowledge on the part of the reader is assumed; it is for those who want to know about the history of music, how different styles evolved, and how one composer influenced another. It is a background to music as the science section is a background to science, and just as the latter cannot show the reader the colours of the spectrum but only tell of Newton's experiments and of the relationship between colour and wavelength, so in this section we can only describe man's achievements in the world of sound. But knowing something about a composer, his work, and when he lived can help to bring fuller understanding and enjoyment when listening to his music.

The section is in four parts:

I. **Historical Narrative and Discussion**
II. **Glossary of Musical Terms**
III. **Index to Composers**
IV. **Special Topic**

I. HISTORICAL NARRATIVE AND DISCUSSION

The history of music, like that of any people or art, is not one of uninterrupted progress towards some ideal perfection. For five centuries or more music in the West has achieved peaks of accomplishment in one style or another before society has dictated or composers have felt the need for something new and different. Thus Wagner's music-drama *Parsifal*, lasting five hours, is not necessarily a more rewarding work than what Monteverdi achieved in *Orfeo* 250 years earlier. More complex yes, more rewarding—well, that is for the listener to judge.

We must keep this in mind when considering the development of music from a starting point of, say, Gregorian chant down to the complicated structures of a Schoenberg in our own day. In this development there is no true dividing line between one period and another, nor must simplifying terms such as "classical" or "romantic" be taken too literally.

The earliest history of Western music as we know it today is closely bound up with the Church, for music had to be provided for services. The earliest Christian music was influenced by Greek songs, few of which unfortunately have survived, and by the music of synagogues, where the art of chanting originated. The modal system of the ancient Greeks was highly organised. The earliest Greek scale was from A to A and the four descending notes A,G,F,E became the basis of their musical theory, and it is from them that Western music learned to call notes after the letters of the alphabet. A scale can begin on any note and always includes two semitones upon which much of the character of a melody depends.

The Greek modes were based on the white notes only; the Dorian, Phrygian, Lydian, and Mixolydian began respectively on E,D,C, and B. Their character was thus decided by the position of the semitones, and they formed the basis, often corrupted, of the mediaeval modes. This system was transmitted through Latin writers such as Boethius and Cassiodorus, and through Arabic writers. The eight Church modes were not established until the 8th or 9th cent. Their four plagal modes, as they are called, started in each case, for technical reasons, a fourth below the authentic modes.

By the end of the 6th cent. Gregorian chant had developed so far that some sort of permanent record was required. *Neumes*, signs placed over the Latin text, were the earliest attempt at musical notation. Gradually lines came into use until a four-line stave was established, probably in the 11th and 12th cent., and with them clef signs, although the treble clef as we know it today did not appear until the 13th cent.

And what is this music—plainchant—like? It is an unaccompanied, single line of melody, which, when we have become used to its "antique" flavour is heard to have a wide range of spiritual and emotional expression, not excluding word painting. The texts used came from the Liturgy. These beautiful, extended lines of flowing, flexible melody can still be heard on Sundays in Roman Catholic cathedrals and churches.

Polyphony is Born.

The 10th cent. saw the appearance of a book called *Musica Enchiriadis* (whose authorship is disputed) which introduced theories about unison singing in which the melody is doubled at the fourth or fifth. Organum, or diaphony, is used to describe this method of writing, a term which confusingly could also be used for a kind of singing where melismatic melody was heard over a drone note on the organ. Rules came into fashion defining which intervals were allowed and which parts of the church services could be sung in more than one part. By the time of Guido d'Arezzo (c. 990–1050), a Benedictine monk who helped advance notation, a contrary motion was permitted as the cadence was approached, another technical advance. Gradually the voices became more and more independent, and the third, so long considered a discord, came into use. Pérotin, of Notre Dame, was the first composer to write for three and four voices, and he and his great predecessor Léonin were the great masters of early polyphony. The proximity and spikiness of Pérotin's harmony is almost modern-sounding, and as with Gregorian chant, once we have adjusted ourselves to the sound, this music can be a rewarding experience.

Early Secular Music.

In mediaeval France, towards the end of the 11th cent., there developed what has become known as the age of the troubadours, poet-musicians. They were the successors to the *jongleurs*, or jugglers, and minstrels about whom we know little as practically none of their music has survived. The troubadours hymned the beauty of spring and of ladies. Contemporary with them in Germany were the Minnesingers. Their songs were mostly set in three modes. Adam de la Halle (d. 1287), because so much of his music survives, is perhaps the best known of the troubadours. He was a notable composer of *rondels*, an early form of round, of which the English *Sumer is icumen in*, written by a monk of Reading c. 1226, is a fine example. In that modes were used, the troubadours' music remained definitely akin to that of ecclesiastical hymns, although there is an undoubted feeling of our modern major scale in some of the songs.

Ars Nova and Early Renaissance.

The term *ars nova* derives partly from writings of Philippe de Vitry (1291–1361) who codified the rules of the old and the new music in a valuable treatise. This *new art* represented a freeing of music from organum and rhythmic modes, and an increase in the shape and form of melodic line. France was the centre of music during the 14th cent. and apart from Philippe de Vitry the leading composer was Guillaume de Machaut (1300–77), who wrote many secular works as well as a polyphonic setting of the Mass. His music is notable for its vigour and tenderness as well as for its technical expertise. Meanwhile in 14th-cent. Italy a quite separate branch of *ars nova* was developing. Imitation and canon were to be noted in the music of Italian composers, and vocal forms such as the Ballata, Madrigal (which often included instrumental accompaniment) and Caccia (a two-voice hunting song in canon) were common. The greatest Italian composer of this period was the blind organist and lutenist Francesco di Landini (*c.* 1325–97). Italian pieces of the time, as compared with their French counterparts, are notable for their sensual rather than their intellectual qualities, a difference—it has been noted—between The Southern and The Northern New Art.

England was less affected by *ars nova*, but surviving music shows the influence of the Continent. Not until the 15th cent. did she begin to make a significant contribution to the history of music. Both John Dunstable (*c.* 1380–1453), who was no less eminent as a mathematician and an astronomer than as a musician, and his contemporary Lional Power advanced the technique of music by their method of composition (use of the triad, for instance) and mellifluous style. Their musicianship was much appreciated on the Continent. Dunstable depended less upon the use of *cantus firmus*—a fixed melody—and increased the use of free composition.

After Dunstable the next great figure in European music was Guillaume Dufay (*c.* 1400–74), the most celebrated composer of the Burgundian school. His music is distinguished for its blend of flowing melody, cleverly wrought counterpoint and tender expressiveness. Much travelled, Dufay was a man of catholic outlook. Together with Dunstable and the Burgundian Gilles Binchols he bridged the gap between 14th cent. *ars nova* and the fully developed polyphony of the 15th cent.

Composers of the 14th and 15th cents. also showed an interest in secular music, and many of their songs (those of Binchois particularly) have been preserved.

The results of Dufay's good work can be heard in the flowering of the Franco-Netherland school later in the 15th cent. Its two most notable representatives are Ockeghem (*c.* 1420–95) and his pupil Josquin des Prés (*c.* 1450–1521), who carried musical expressiveness even further than Dufay; their work can also be grand and majestic. Indeed Josquin's wide range, from the humorous to the dignified, partially accounts for his justly deserved high reputation. He was a master of counterpoint but tempered his mechanical ingenuity with imaginative insight.

Throughout the Renaissance choral music was breaking away, as we have seen, from its earlier bonds. The mediaeval tradition of having the *cantus firmus* in the tenor went by the board; the use of dissonance, when only two voices were used in mediaeval times, was abandoned in favour of euphony; and all the voices, democratically, came to share the musical lines. Composers also began to respect their texts; where words were previously fitted to the music, the reverse was now the case. In Josquin's music, indeed, we have the first attempts at symbolism: matching verbal ideas with musical ones. The importance of this musical renaissance has been realised only over the past thirty years. At last the Renaissance composers are coming to be seen not merely as historical figures relevant only in so far as their work culminated in the great classical composers,

but as masters in their own right, whose music should be nearly as familiar to us as is that of a Mozart or a Beethoven.

With the exception of Dufay, little is known of the lives of the musicians so far mentioned. Most of them were in the service of royal or ducal households where they were in charge of the chapel choir, or else they worked in or around the great cathedrals, teaching at choir-schools. They were well rewarded for their services and their social position was probably high.

During recent years there has been an appreciable revival of interest in mediaeval music. Numerous ensembles have emerged with their own ideas about how it should be performed—an indication that it is alive and not just part of the history of music. It can communicate just as well as the music of later eras.

The Sixteenth Century.

By the 16th cent. music in England was a steadily expanding art and much encouraged. Music-making in the home was becoming quite the fashion in social circles. The Chapels Royal remained the chief musical centres but the music was changing with the development of new secular forms so that it was not so much religious as a part of life. Composers began their lives as choirboys and received a thoroughgoing education, both theoretical and practical.

Carrying on from where Josquin and his contemporaries left off, Palestrina in Italy, Victoria in Spain, Lassus in the Netherlands, and Byrd in England brought the polyphonic style to its zenith. At the same time came the rise of the madrigalists, first in Italy, then in the Netherlands; and then the beginnings of instrumental music as it came to be known in the succeeding centuries.

The vocal composers began to use chordal (homophonic) as well as contrapuntal (polyphonic) methods of writing—examples are Victoria's *Ave Verum Corpus* and Palestrina's *Stabat Mater*—but polyphony was still the fullest most magnificent instrument of composition, as for instance in Byrd's *O Quam Gloriosum* which shows an eager response to the mood and to the inflection of the words in a kind of vocal orchestration. A feature of all these composers' music, but more especially that of Victoria (*c.* 1535–1611) and Palestrina (1525–94), is its serene simplicity and fervour of utterance. Palestrina was perhaps more spacious in his effects, Victoria the more passionate. How well we can imagine—and sometimes hear—their music resounding down the naves of the great cathedrals of Europe.

The music of Lassus (*c.* 1532–94) is distinguished both in sheer amount and in vitality. His mastery in the field of motets was unrivalled, encompassing a wide range of subject and mood. He and his fellow Flemish composers, Willaert, de Monte and Arcadelt, were also expert in the Madrigal, a form popular in Italy and England as well. The Madrigal was a contrapuntal setting of a poem, usually not longer than twelve lines, in five or six parts. The subject (of the poetry) was usually amorous or pastoral. It was a short-lived, but highly prolific vogue. Orlando Gibbons (1583–1625), Thomas Weelkes (*c.* 1573–1623), and John Wilbye (1574–1638) were the most prominent English exponents.

Instrumental Music.

By the end of the 14th cent. instrumental music began to become something more than mere anonymous dance tunes or primitive organ music. Instruments often accompanied voices, or even replaced them, so that the recorder, lute, viol and spinet indoors, and sackbuts and shawms outdoors, had already been developed by the time instrumental music came to be written down. Gradually a distinction grew up between what was appropriate to the voice and what was suitable for instruments, Byrd, Gibbons, and Giles Farnaby in England, the great blind keyboard player, Cabezón (1510–66) in Spain, and Frescobaldi (1583–1643) in Italy produced valuable instrumental works. Perhaps the *Parthenia* and the *Fitzwilliam Virginal Book*, collections of Early English Keyboard music, give as fair a representative idea as any of the development of instrumental form at this time.

In chamber music musicians often played collections of dance tunes strung together to make a whole; or they chose fantasies (or "fancies"), where a composer altered a tune as he wished. Then there were sets of variations on a ground, that is a simple tune played over and over again on a bass viol.

As far as brass instruments are concerned, they were often used on festive occasions in spacious halls or in cathedrals. The Venetian composer Andrea Gabrieli (c. 1510–86) was the first to combine voice and instruments and his nephew Giovanni Gabrieli (1557–1612) carried the process further to produce sacred symphonies, often using antiphonal effects.

Drama in Music.

Not until the end of the 16th cent. did anyone begin to think about combining drama and music, and so "invent" the new art we know today as opera. A group of artistic intelligentsia met together in Florence and conceived the idea of reviving the ancient declamation of Greek tragedy. They took Greek mythological subjects, cast them in dramatic form, and set them to music, not in the choral polyphonic style of the Madrigal, but with single voices declaiming dialogue in music. The earliest examples of what was called *Dramma per Musica* were Peri's *Dafne* in 1597 (now lost) and his *Euridice*, in which he co-operated with Caccini. The new style came to its full flowering with the appearance of Monteverdi (1567–1643), whose genius would surely have shone in any age.

Monteverdi's first opera, *Orfeo*, produced in 1607, is a landmark of dramatic expression, and it is nothing less than a catastrophe that so many of his later operas have been lost. His *Orfeo* provides the basic ground work for the operas of the next two centuries: recitative, accompanied recitative, and aria. His last opera *L'Incoronazione di Poppea*, written when he was at the great age (for those days) of 75, succeeds in its aim of creating a free, fluid form, slipping easily from recitative to arioso and even aria without the strict, closed forms that were to be used in the 17th and 18th cent. He focuses attention to an almost unbelievable extent on character rather than situation. He creates real people with all their faults and foibles—the kittenish, sexually attractive Poppaea, the power-drunk, infatuated Nero, the noble Seneca, and the dignified, rejected empress Octavia. As recent productions have shown these characters leap from the musical page as if they had just been created, each unerringly delineated in musical terms. Only the vocal line, the continuo, and the very incomplete instrumental ritornelli parts have been preserved, but in sensitive, knowledgeable hands tonal variety in the shape of wind and string parts can be added, as we know certain instruments were available to the composer.

Monteverdi's successors were Cavalli (1602–76), Cesti (1623–69) and Stradella (1642–82), who gave the solo voice more and more prominence encouraged by the advent of the castrati's brilliant voices. These artificially created singers had a vogue and popularity similar to "pop" singers of today, fêted wherever they appeared. The aria became more extended and ornate, and dramatic verisimilitude gradually but inexorably took second place to vocal display. An aria was nearly always in *da capo* form, the first section being repeated after a contrasting middle one.

Sixteenth- and Seventeenth-century Church Music.

Of course, the invention of a new dramatic style affected church music too. The concentration on

the vertical aspect of music (homophony) as opposed to the horizontal (polyphony) led to the increasing importance of the voice in religious music. In Italy, it is true, there was the late-flowering, great madrigalist Carlo Gesualdo (1560–1614), whose harmonic daring still astonishes us today, but by 1600 the cantata was coming to replace older forms in church music. In its simplest form this was a story told in accompanied recitative, Giacomo Carissimi (c. 1604–74) was one of the first significant composers of this new form. He too was in on the birth of the oratorio, whose forerunner was the *sacra rappresentazione* (mystery or miracle play) of early 16th-cent. Florence. Then in the mid-16th cent. St. Philip Neri brought in elements from popular plays on sacred subjects in his services in Rome, designed to hold the attention of youth—rather as certain parsons have tried with "pop" services today. Emilio del Cavalieri (c. 1550–1602) and Carissimi developed the form adding arias and choral movements, omitting actual representation. Alessandro Scarlatti (1660–1725), whose oratorios bear a close resemblance to his operas, brought oratorio to its zenith in Italy.

Heinrich Schütz (1585–1672), Bach's great predecessor, was the founder of German church music. His historical place has never been called into question but only in recent times have the intrinsic merits of his own music come to be recognised. He studied with Giovanni Gabrieli in his youth and later came under the influence of Monteverdi, so it was not surprising that he brought Italian ideas across the Alps to Germany and wrote the first German opera *Daphne*, now sadly lost. He also introduced his country to the Italian declamatory style and to the new kind of concertato instrumental writing. But his dramatic religious works were his greatest contribution to musical development. He wrote with a devout intensity, bringing to life the scriptural texts by closely allying his urgent music to the words. His three settings of the Passions—Matthew, Luke, and John—paved the way for Bach's even more remarkable works in this genre. Two contemporaries of Schütz, Johann Herman Schein (1586–1630) and Samuel Scheidt (1587–1654), were both important figures in German Reformation music.

Lully, Purcell, and Seventeenth-century Opera.

France resisted the tide of Italian opera, although paradoxically it was an Italian, Jean-Baptiste Lully (c. 1632–87), who charted the different course of French opera which was from the beginning associated with the court ballet. His musical monopoly during the reign of Louis XIV was put to good use. In his thirteen operas the libretto, usually on classical, allegorical themes, plays a vital part in the composition, which is therefore less clearly divided between recitative and aria than in Italian opera. The orchestration and the ballets assume greater importance than in the traditional Italian form. It was, in short, a more realistic, less stylised art.

In England, opera developed out of the entertainment known as the Masque, a succession of dances, accompanied by voices and instruments and often incorporated in a drama or spectacle. Henry Lawes's (1596–1662) setting of Milton's *Comus* is probably the most famous of these entertainments. The *Venus and Adonis* of John Blow (1649–1708) can be called the first English opera because here the music is gradually gaining the ascendancy over the spoken word. However, it was Purcell (c. 1659–95), Blow's pupil, with *Dido and Aeneas*, who really gave dramatic life to the new medium by giving his characters a true musical personality that was subtler than anything the mere spoken word could achieve. The grief-laden lament of the dying Dido "When I am laid in earth" has an expressive power, achieved by extraordinarily bold harmonic effects, never before and seldom since achieved. The opera was in fact written for a young ladies' boarding school. Purcell followed it with several outstanding semi-operas—such as *The Fairy Queen* (to Dryden's text). His untimely death at the age of 36 probably robbed us of several full-length operas—and perhaps a consequence of this was that English music after him did not develop as it should have done.

His verse anthems and much of his instrumental music, especially the Fantasias, are also rich in imaginative mastery through his original use of harmony and counterpoint. However, a large number of his pieces were written for a specific occasion and many of the odes are set to impossibly trite texts. At least his genius was partly acknowledged in his own day, and he was appointed organist in Westminster Abbey where he was buried with due pomp. He is said to have died through catching cold when locked out of his own house at night.

Vivaldi and the Rise of Instrumental Music.

Out of the dance suites popular in the 16th cent. and the beginning of the 17th (known in Italy as the *Sonata da Camera*) developed the concerto. This began as two groups of instrumentalists compared and contrasted with each other as in Giovanni Gabrieli's *Sonata piano e forte*. With Arcangelo Corelli (1653–1713) the concerto grosso took a more definite shape, alternating a solo group of instruments with the main body of strings in three or more contrasting movements. Guiseppe Torelli (1658–1709), Francesco Geminiani (1687–1762) and Tommaso Albinoni (1671–1750) were other notable contributors to the form, but none of the composers so far mentioned has today achieved the popularity of the priest Antonio Vivaldi (*c.* 1678–1741), himself a violinist, who had at his disposal the orchestra at the Ospedale della Pieta in Venice. The young women at this music school also contributed the vocal side of the concerts there of which there are many descriptions. One says: "They sing like angels, play the violin, flute, organ, oboe, cello, bassoon—in short no instrument is large enough to frighten them … I swear nothing is so charming than to see a young and pretty nun, dressed in white, a sprig of pomegranate blossom behind one ear, leading the orchestra, and beating time with all the grace and precision imaginable." For this body, Vivaldi wrote about 500 concertos which maintain a remarkably even quality, but "The Four Seasons" are perhaps the most felicitous.

Meanwhile organ music was advancing rapidly in technique. Girolamo Frescobaldi (1583–1643) and Jan Pieterszoon Sweelinck (1562–1621) wrote works that provided the foundation of the Italian and Northern German schools of organ music. Their ricercares gradually developed into the fugue, a vein so richly mined by Bach. Among their successors the most notable figure before Bach was Johann Pachelbel (1653–1706).

Other keyboard music, especially for the harpsichord, was the particular province of France; and Jean-Philippe Rameau (1683–1764) and François Couperin (1668–1733) were both masters of keyboard style and harmonic invention. They wrote many pieces of subtle charm and exquisite craftsmanship.

Bach (1685–1750).

The two giant figures of Bach and Handel bestride the first half of the 18th cent. Their differences are perhaps greater than their similarities. Bach wrote essentially for himself (although of course, he had to satisfy his employers at Cöthen and Leipzig) while Handel was composing to please his wide public. Bach was a provincial, always remaining in central Germany; Handel was widely travelled. Bach was devoutly religious, almost ascetic; Handel was more a man of the world. They never met.

To summarise Bach's vast output in a short space is virtually impossible. One can only try to distil the flavour of his music. He brought the art of polyphony to the highest pitch of mastery that has ever been achieved or is ever likely to be achieved. In his famous "Forty-Eight" and "the Art of the Fugue" he explored all the fugal permutations of the major and minor keys. At the same time his music rose above technical brilliance to achieve, especially in his organ music,

the two Passions, many of the church cantatas, and the B minor Mass, intense emotional and expressive power. The cantatas, from his Leipzig appointment (1723) onwards, were integrated into the services. They consisted usually of a chorus based on a Lutheran hymn tune, recitatives, several extended arias, and a concluding chorus usually a straightforward version of the hymn tune in which the congregation joined. There are some two hundred of these works and they contain a wealth of comparatively unknown and sometimes even unrecognised beauties. The St. John and the St. Matthew Passion extend these procedures to a grand scale, an Evangelist telling the new Testament story in vivid recitative, the chorus taking the part of the crowd, soloists pondering in arias on the meaning of the Gospel, and Jesus's words being sung by a bass. Anyone who has heard either of these works well performed cannot help but dismiss from his mind any idea of Bach as a mere dry-as-dust musical mathematician. In the St. Matthew Passion, every suggestion in the text that can possibly be illustrated by a musical equivalent is so illustrated. The Old Testament Pharasaic law is represented by strict musical forms such as the canon; Christ's sayings are given noble arioso life; and the arias reflect truly the New Testament's compassionate message. Technically the work is a marvel; expressively it is eloquent. The B minor Mass, although it contains borrowings from many of his own works, still stands as a satisfying monumental whole in which Bach's choral writing achieved a new richness, the adaptations being in accord with their new setting.

Bach's instrumental music, especially the violin concertos and the unaccompanied works for violin and cello, not only show the immense range of his powers but also contain many of his deeper thoughts, whereas the orchestral suites and the Brandenburg concertos are more extrovert, particularly the rhythmically exuberant fast movements.

Bach closes an era—that of the later contrapuntalists—by achieving the *ne plus ultra* in fugal composition; his last, incomplete work, The Art of the Fugue, is evidence of that. In recent years there has been a trend towards playing Bach's music on original instruments of his time (or replicas) and singing it with appropriately sized, sometimes all-male choirs.

Handel (1685–1759).

During his lifetime Handel was far more widely recognised as a great composer than Bach, and his music, unlike Bach's, maintained its place in popular esteem until the re-discovery of Bach and the dominance of the symphony placed Handel somewhat in the background.

During the latter part of the 19th cent. Handel's name was mainly associated with mammoth, anachronistic performances of a small sample of his oratorios at the Crystal Palace and elsewhere in England. In his lifetime these works, and all his other pieces in the genre, were sung by a small choir who were outnumbered by the instrumental players. Over the past few years authentic-sized performances of his oratorios and a revival of interest in his operas have revealed the real Handel, unknown to our grandparents.

The operas were neglected partly because the vocal prowess they required—and which the castrati so brilliantly supplied—was no longer available and because their dramatic life, at least according to 19th- and early 20th-cent. tenets, hardly existed. Now it is realised that this neglect has deprived us of an unending stream of glorious melody and of much daring harmony. But perhaps it is in the hitherto disregarded oratorios, such as *Semele*, that Handel's innate dramatic sense and musical range are to be heard gloriously fulfilled, and the pastoral serenade *Acis and Galatea* is surely one of the most delightful scores ever composed.

Handel was a colourful, imaginative orchestrator, and this can be heard both in his accompaniment to vocal music and in his concerti grossi, op. 3 and 6, the earlier set exploiting a diversity of interesting string and wind combination. In his writing he was at home in a polyphonic or homophonic style as his superb choruses show. His organ concertos, of which he was the "inventor" (to quote a contemporary source), were often played between the acts of his oratorios. They are alternately expressive and exuberant pieces calling for some virtuosity from the player. His occasional works, such as the Water Music and Fireworks Music show his ingenuity in extending the range of the typical 17th cent. suite to serve a particular occasion.

Handel's working life was mostly spent in England where his Italian operas were acclaimed. In the years between his arrival here in 1711 and 1722 he wrote nearly thirty operas. It was only when the public tired of these and his reputation slumped that he turned to oratorio with equal success.

Bach and Handel between them crowned the age of polyphony that had lasted for two hundred years or more. After them, it is hardly surprising that composers began looking for a new style, already anticipated in the music of Rameau and particularly Dominico Scarlatti (1685–1737), whose harpsichord sonatas foreshadowed the classical sonata form that was to dominate music for the next two hundred years. The change in musical style about 1750 was partly the result of a change in musical patronage. Bach was the last great composer to earn his living through being employed by the church. The new patrons were the nobility who liked to have a composer on hand to write for the various evening entertainments of the time. For this purpose the princes and dukes had their own orchestras and their own small opera houses. The music required had to be elegant, formal, galant. Haydn was exceptionally fortunate in having an employer, Prince Nicholas of Esterhazy, who allowed him to write more or less as he wished so that he was able to develop symphonic form into something more than a pleasing way of passing an evening.

The early symphonists, culminating in Haydn, broke away from Bach's contrapuntal treatment of the orchestra. Instruments now came to be treated in a more colourful manner according to their particular timbre. The court of Mannheim had an orchestra of a standard unheard hitherto, and Johann Stamitz (1717–57) and his son Karl (1745–1801) influenced the great composers who were to follow in their footsteps. The composition of their orchestra was flexible, oboes, flutes, and horns often being added to the standard string section. Bach's son Carl Philipp Emanuel (1714–88) added to and developed symphonic and sonata form, especially as regards keys and subjects.

Haydn and Mozart.

These two figures dominate the second half of the 18th cent. as Bach and Handel do the first. In a brief space only a general picture can be presented of their huge output and influence. Of Haydn's 104 symphonies (there may even be others) nearly all are worthy of study and hearing. The craftsmanship is always remarkable, the invention ever new. Indeed without Haydn's harmonic daring or his melodic ingenuity, the even greater symphonic thought of Beethoven would have been impossible: Haydn laid the groundwork on which his successor built towering edifices. A work such as the 93rd symphony in D is typical of his mature style with its searching introduction, powerfully wrought, earnestly argued first movement, beautiful Largo and resourceful bustling finale. Haydn did not fight shy of contrapuntal writing: the development section of this symphony's first movement and the finale are evidence of that, but it was only as an integral part of a predominantly homophonic technique.

Mozart's symphonies are not so different in form from Haydn's but—and this must be a subjective judgment—he put more emotional feeling into his. Nobody could listen to the heart-

searching first movement of his 40th symphony without being deeply moved. It was in his final three works in the medium that Mozart brought his symphonic art to perfection, and these obviously had an effect on Haydn's later symphonies written after them. For passion and tenderness contained within a classical form these late symphonies, and many other of Mozart's works, have yet to be surpassed.

Haydn, who has been rightly termed "the Father of the Symphony", was also the founder of the string quartet—perhaps the most perfect, because the most exactly balanced, form of musical expression. The four instruments—two violins, viola, and cello—discuss, argue, commune with each other over the whole gamut of feeling. In his quartets Haydn's mastery of structure is even more amazing than in his symphonies. Mozart's quartets (especially the six devoted to Haydn) and even more his quintets achieve miracles of beauty in sound, nowhere more so than in the first movement of the G minor (his most personal key) quintet. The two late piano quartets show how the piano can be ideally combined with strings. His clarinet quintet is also a masterly work.

Haydn did not leave any concertos of consequence. Mozart's, especially those for piano, are among his greatest works. As a brilliant clavier player himself, he showed a consummate skill in writing for the keyboard. Although the instrument he knew was slightly less advanced than the piano today, his concertos call for virtuosity in execution, yet they are as searching in emotional content as the late symphonies and quartets. Indeed the C major concerto (K. 467) and the C minor (K. 491) may be said to hold the quintessential Mozart. As well as twenty (mature) piano concertos, Mozart wrote six for the violin, four for the horn, and eighteen others, but none of these, delightful as they are, can be placed in quite the same class.

Of their church music, Haydn's sixteen masses and his oratorios—The Creation and The Seasons (both late works)—are perhaps more worthy of attention than Mozart's various masses, but we must not forget Mozart's final work—the Requiem or the serene late Motet Ave Verum Corpus.

Eighteenth-century Opera.

Mozart—for many the first great opera composer—did not, of course, create his masterpieces out of nothing. In France, Lully was followed by Rameau (1683–1764), who carried on his tradition of using classical themes but developed a more flexible style of recitative and greatly increased vividness of expression. But it was Gluck (1714–87) who more than anyone broke out of the straitjacket of the now ossified Italian form of opera—dominated by the singer—and showed just what could be achieved in moving human terms. Drama in music really came of age with his Orfeo e Euridice (1762), Alceste (1767) and Iphigénie en Tauride (1779). His simplicity and poignancy of expression were not lost on Mozart.

Meanwhile in Germany a kind of opera called Singspiel appeared during the 18th cent. Breaking away from classical themes, mundane stories were told in dialogue and music.

Until quite recently Haydn's operas were dismissed as unworthy representations of his genius but, chiefly through the enlightening efforts of the Haydn scholar, H. C. Robbins Landon, some of his fifteen surviving works in the medium have been successfully revived. They have proved to be perfectly viable for the stage and, especially in the ensembles, full of that delightful invention to be found in the rest of his opus, if on a less fully developed scale. Still as musical drama they inevitably fall far short of Mozart's achievements, for the younger composer seems to have had an instinctive feeling for the stage. Into his operas he poured his most intense, personal music. He vividly portrays the foibles, desires, loves, and aspirations of mankind.

The earlier, immature stage pieces of his youth led to such works as Lucio Silla (1772) and La

Finta Giardiniera (1775) with their first glimpses of the glories to come. His first indubitably great opera is *Idomeneo* (1781). Despite its unpromisingly static plot, *Idomeneo* reveals Mozart's stature through its ability to breathe new life into a conventional *opera seria* form. Though influenced by Gluck it is yet more human and touching in its musical expression. To succeed this Mozart wrote a much more frivolous piece *Die Entführung aus dem Serail*. Stemming from the *Singspiel* tradition, it none the less creates real-life characters who have much charming music to sing.

After three lesser pieces Mozart embarked on his four masterpieces—*Le Nozze di Figaro* (1786), *Don Giovanni* (1787), *Cosi fan tutte* (1790), and *Die Zauberflote* (1791).

Figaro, as well as being a delightful comedy, explores more fully than any previous opera situation and character, which find expression in beautiful arias and in two finales of symphonic proportion. In *Don Giovanni*, less satisfactory as a dramatic structure, the range of musical characterisation and insight into human motives is widened still further. *Cosi* lyrically but humorously expresses the follies of love. Mozart could not help but love his characters and his music for them is at one and the same time amusing and heartfelt, *Die Zauberflöte*—The Magic Flute—displays Mozart's deep-felt concern for his fellow men and for truth in an opera of great spiritual strength. Nor has opera any more loveable personality than the birdcatcher Papageno. Mozart's final opera *La Clemenza di Tito*, extolling imperial magnanimity, has never achieved the success or popularity of his other maturer stage works, though it contains much excellent music, and has recently been revived with honour in several opera houses.

Beethoven.

Mozart was the last major composer to depend, to any large extent, on private patronage for his living, and even he left the service of the Archbishop of Salzburg because he could not stand the restrictions imposed on his freedom. Henceforth composers would have to stand on their own two feet with all the advantages (liberty) and disadvantages (lack of security) that implied. Beethoven (1770–1827) was the first such composer of importance.

Although his work is usually divided into three periods, that division is somewhat too arbitrary, for no other composer in history, with the possible exception of Wagner, has shown such a continual development of his genius. Coming at just the right moment in musical history, he crowned the achievements of Haydn and Mozart with music of the utmost profundity of thought and feeling that looks back to its classical heritage and forward to the romantic movement of the 19th cent. His influence on musical thinking and writing is incalculable.

His first period shows his strong melodic gifts and the beginning of his individuality in developing form and structure to suit his own ends and match his particular genius. Unusual keys are explored, unusual harmonic procedures employed. With the "Eroica" (his third symphony) he established his position as a great composer. The unity of purpose he here achieved within a long and diverse structure is truly staggering, even today. In the first movement alone the formal invention and cogency went far beyond what even Mozart had achieved in his "Jupiter" symphony, and the second movement—a vast funeral March —has an overwhelmingly tragic emotional content. But the "Eroica" was followed by six equally great symphonies, each one as varied, as inventive, as unified as the others. The ninth symphony is significant both for its length and its finale. Here Beethoven crowns three superb instrumental movements with a choral movement that, as well as summing up all that has gone before, expresses in music the joy in existence more ecstatically than any other work.

The burning intensity of Beethoven's genius is just as evident in his chamber music. His quartets are the product of a revolutionary age in which the social graces and formal restraint of the 18th cent. were thrown off in a search for a more personal mode of expression. The early op. 18 set, and the Razoumovsky quartets, op. 59, go even beyond the range of Haydn's and Mozart's works in the medium but it was in his late quartets, his final musical testament, that Beethoven refined and distilled his art for posterity. No words can possibly describe their unique quality, but any and every chance should be taken to make their acquaintance; the effort required will be more than amply rewarded.

The early piano concertos do not reach quite that level of attainment, but the last three, together with the violin concerto, are on a par with the finest of the symphonies and quartets, as well as being considerable tests of the performers' technique. The Triple Concerto for piano, violin, and cello is an unusual and rewarding work.

Beethoven's grandest choral work—and one of the most noble in existence—is the Mass in D (*Missa Solemnis*). Its vast scale and sublime utterance often defeat performers, but when it is successfully done there is no more spiritually uplifting experience for the listener, except perhaps Beethoven's only opera, *Fidelio*. This simple escape story was transformed by Beethoven's creative fire into a universal symbol of liberty, the composer identifying himself with the struggle for freedom from tyranny and release from darkness.

Beethoven lived in a period of war and revolution. A passionate believer in the brotherhood of man and in liberty, he was shocked to find his ideals thrown over by revolutionaries-turned-dictators. His own tragedy of deafness, which came upon him at the moment of his triumph, nearly submerged him, but in the end he won through and produced the string of masterpieces from the "Eroica" onwards. Hope springing from despair, love from hatred, victory over defeat, these are the unquenchable legacies left by Beethoven.

The Romantic Movement.

Inevitably, the Romantic movement in literature that burst forth about 1800 was bound to have its counterpart in music. And so it was. Breaking the classical bonds, composers such as Schubert, Schumann, Liszt, and Berlioz sought a new freedom in musical expression. Form became of less importance than content; and that content often had literary connections. For their purposes a larger orchestra was needed and supplied, but the miniature, the song especially, because of its very personal connotation, was also a favourite form.

Schubert (1797–1828)—described by Liszt as "the most poetic of musicians"—is perhaps the greatest lyrical genius in musical history. In him the Viennese tradition and influence of Haydn, Mozart, and Beethoven reached its zenith. The song was always Schubert's starting point, so it is hardly surprising that his reputation as a song writer has never been impaired but in his symphonic and instrumental works too it is always his inexhaustible fund of melody that first calls for attention. Nobody could listen to his "Trout" quintet, for piano and strings, his octet, his fifth symphony, or his song cycle *Die Schöne Müllerin* without being enchanted and invigorated by the sheer tunefulness of the music. But there is much more to Schubert than this: his understanding of the possibilities of harmonic change, his grasp of orchestral coloration (in the great C major symphony, for instance), his free use of sonata structure.

Although Mozart, Haydn, and Beethoven had all contributed to the song as an art form, it was with Schubert that it achieved its first full flowering. If he had written nothing but his songs, his place in the musical firmament would be assured. With his *Erlkönig* in 1815 the German *Lied* came of age and from then until the end of his life he wrote more than six hundred songs, hardly a dud among them. Whether it is the charm of *Heiden-röslein*, the drama of *Der Doppelgänger* or the numbed intensity of the *Winterreise* cycle, Schubert unerringly went to the heart of a poet's meaning; indeed he often raised poor verses to an inspired level by his settings. And for the first time the pianist shares a place of equal importance with the singer.

There is only room to mention one or two other composers, some of them wrongly neglected, who were roughly contemporaries of Beethoven and Schubert: the Czech Dussek (1760–1812), who like Beethoven bridges the classical–romantic gulf, Boccherini (1743–1805), the two Italian opera composers Cimarosa (1749–1801) and Paisiello (1740–1816), the Frenchman Méhul (1763–1817) and the German Hummel (1778–1837).

Weber (1786–1826) lacked Beethoven's energy and constructive powers and Schubert's sheer lyrical profundity, but he is an important figure, especially in the field of opera, where his *Der Freischütz* and *Oberon* led the way to a more flexible, dramatically realistic form of opera. His vivid imagination exactly fitted the new romantic mood abroad. The sheer beauty in the melodic shape of his music is also not to be denied. His instrumental works are attractive but insubstantial.

Mendelssohn and Schumann.

Mendelssohn (1809–47) was the civilised craftsman among the Romantic composers. A boy genius—many of his finest works were written before he was twenty—he maintained the importance of classical form while imbuing it with his own affectionate brand of poetic sensibility. His third and fourth symphonies—the "Scottish" and "The Italian"—(and possibly the fifth "The Reformation"), his string quartets (some of which go deeper than the rest of his music), octet, violin concerto, first piano concerto, and of course, the incidental music to "A Midsummer Night's Dream" represent his tidy yet effervescent style at its most winning.

Schumann (1810–56) is less easy to categorise. His early romantic flame was burnt out by some flaw in his intellectual and/or emotional make-up, and his inspiration seems to have declined in later years. No matter, by then he had given us the marvellous song cycles of 1840, an ever fresh piano concerto, many fine piano solos, including the mercurial, popular *Carnaval* and four symphonies, which, if not structurally perfect, contain much lovely music. The joys and sorrows of love and the feeling for natural beauty are all perfectly mirrored in these charming, lyrical works, and in the genial piano quintet.

Romantic Giants.

Berlioz (1803–69) and Liszt (1811–86) are the two most typical representative composers of the Romantic era. Both have always been controversial figures, with ardent advocates and opponents either unduly enthusiastic or unfairly derogatory. Berlioz might be termed the perfect painter in music. With an uncanny mastery of orchestral sound he could conjure up the countryside, the supernatural and the historical with the utmost ease. He based his music on the "direct reaction to feeling" and a desire to illustrate literature by musical means. That his technical expertise was not always the equal of his undoubted genius, can be heard in many of his larger works such as the dramatic cantata *The Damnation of Faust* and the dramatic symphony *Romeo and Juliet*, yet most people are willing to overlook the occasional vulgarity for the ineffable beauty of his many fine pages, but brutal cuts in his music, such as are often made in, for instance, his epic opera *The Trojans* only have the effect of reducing the stature of his works. We must accept him, warts and all. Anyone who has seen the two parts of *The Trojans*, presented complete in one evening at Covent Garden, will realise that Berlioz knew what he was about.

His output is not quantitatively large but includes several monumental works, as well as *The Trojans*, The *Requiem* ("Grand Messe des Morts") requires a tenor solo, huge chorus and orchestra, and brass bands, although Berlioz uses these forces fastidiously. The *Symphonie funèbre et triomphale* calls in its original form, for choir brass, and strings. But Berlioz was just as happy writing on a smaller scale as his exquisite song cycle, to words of Théophile Gautier, *Nuits d'Été*, shows. Gautier perhaps summed up better than anyone Berlioz's singular talent: "In that renaissance of the 1830s Berlioz represents the romantic musical idea, the breaking up of old moulds, the substitution of new forms for unvaried square rhythms, a complex and competent richness of orchestration, truth of local colour, unexpected effects in sound, tumultuous and Shakespearian depth of passion, amorous or melancholy dreaminess, longings and questionings of the soul, infinite and mysterious sentiments not to be rendered in words, and that something more than all which escapes language but may be divined in music."

During his lifetime Liszt was fêted and honoured not only by his musical colleagues but by the world at large, which idolised him and his piano. Then his reputation took a plunge from which it has only recently recovered. To be sure much of his early music is glitter and gloss, but his symphonies and tone poems—especially the Faust Symphony, the Dante Symphony (both, of course, inspired by literature), and *Orpheus* and *Prometheus*—and his late piano works show that he was an extraordinary harmonic innovator. The piano sonata in B minor brings his romantic, wilful temperament within a reasonably stable, pianistic form, and as such is a landmark in the repertory of the instrument. Liszt's output was prodigious, but the inquiring listener should explore the more original of his compositions already mentioned to form a true picture of his fertile genius.

Chopin.

Chopin (1810–49) was the master of the keyboard, par excellence. His development of the technical and expressive capabilities of the piano is unique in musical history. His inventive powers were poured out with nervous passionate energy and in a highly individual style through twenty astonishing, possibly agonised years of creative activity before his early death. A Chopin melody, limpid, transparent, singing, can be recognised easily by anyone, but his style gradually developed into something more subtle, more satisfying than pure melody. He took the greatest care of every detail so that any alteration, however small, upsets the perfect balance of his work. His poetic sensibility can be found in any of his works; for his constructive ability we must turn to the Ballades, the B minor Sonata, and the Barcarolle, while the Preludes and Studies blend technical powers and emotional expressiveness in ideal proportions.

Nineteenth-century Opera.

After Mozart's operas and Beethoven's *Fidelio* the medium might have been expected to decline. Instead it took on a new, if different, lease of life that culminated in Verdi's extraordinary output.

Rossini (1792–1868) created a world of exuberant high spirits in his operatic works that are as cheerful and heart-warming today as they were a hundred or more years ago.

He always worked in and around the lyric theatres of Italy and between 1810 and 1830 poured out a stream of works, not all of which can be expected to be masterpieces. However, *Il Barbiere di Siviglia*, *L'Italiana in Algieri*, *La Cenerentola* and *Le Comte Ory* will always delight audiences as long as opera houses exist. Although these works are difficult to sing really well, their vitality and charm can never be submerged even by poor voices or indifferent staging.

His German contemporaries were critical of his confidence and frivolity, but his works show a consistency of invention and an irresistible tune-fulness that anyone might envy. In recent years, there has also been a renewed interest in his more serious operas—*Otello* (1816), *La Gazza Ladra* (1817), *Semiramide* (1823), *La Siège de Corinthe* (1820), and *Guillaume Tell* (1829)—which were certainly surpassed in dramatic power by his successors but which nevertheless are not to be despised or neglected.

William Tell, to give it its most popular title, was his last work for the stage although he lived on for nearly forty years in retirement in Paris, scene of many of his greatest successes. There he enjoyed good living, dispensing *bons mots*, and occasionally composing trifles. An exception is the unpretentious *Petite Messe Solennelle*, written originally for soloists, chorus, a harmonium, and two pianos. Rossini later orchestrated it, but he would not allow it to be performed during his life-time. The first public performance was on 28 February 1869, as near as possible to the 78th anniversary of the composer's birth on Leap Year Day 1792.

In contrast to the mercurial Rossini, Vincenzo Bellini (1801–85) was an exquisite, romantic figure dealing with exquisite, romantic stories, an operatic equivalent to Chopin, who much admired him. His delicate, sinuous vocal line (in the arias) and brilliant acrobatics in the final sections (caba-lettas) require singers of the utmost accomplish-ment to do them justice, although his music is never as florid as Rossini's. His most typical and popular works are probably *La Sonnambula* (1831), *Norma* (1831) and *I Puritani* (1835). The first is a tender, homely country story, the second an almost heroic lyrical drama of sacrifice, and the third a rather unsatisfactory historical story re-deemed by its appealing music. In our own day singers of the calibre of Maria Callas, Joan Sutherland, Guiletta Simionato, and Marilyn Horne have brought Bellini's operas a popularity almost equal to that they enjoyed at the time they were written.

Gaetano Donizetti (1797–1848) was an even more prolific operatic composer than Rossini. He wrote at least 75 works, mostly for the Italian stage, several of which, such as *Alfredo il Grande* or *Emilia di Liverpool*, are never likely to be re-vived, but during the past few years, with the renewed interest in what are called the *Ottocento* operas, many of his serious operas have been resuscitated and found as enjoyable in perfor-mance as his more frequently heard comedies.

He was a well-grounded musician and although his invention is often criticised for being too tied to the conventions of his day performances often belie his reputation, his dramatic instinct proving sure. *Lucia di Lammermoor*, because of the chances it offers to a coloratura soprano with tragic pretensions, has always held the stage and of late, *Lucrezia Borgia*, *Anna Bolena*, *La Favorita*, and *Poliuto* have all been successfully revived. Of his lighter works, the comedies *L'Elizir d'Amore* and *Don Pasquale* have never declined in popularity. One of his last works was *Linda di Chamounix* (1842) which he wrote for Vienna where it aroused such enthusiasm that the Emperor appointed him Court Composer and Master of the Imperial Chapel.

French Opera.

The taste in Paris was for more and more lavish productions. Following Spontini (1774–1851), whose works were comparatively austere, came Halévy (1799–1862) and Giacomo Meyerbeer (1791–1864) whose operas contain all the ingre-dients that came to be expected of "Grand Opera"—spectacle, huge ensembles, showpieces for the soloists, and extended, if superfluous ballet. Drawing from Italian, German, and French tradi-tions Meyerbeer's works contained everything the public wanted, yet today they are seldom re-vived, perhaps because his creative powers were essentially derivative, yet when they *are* given, operas like *Les Huguenots*, *Le Prophète*, and *L'Africaine* still have the power to fascinate and his influence on his successors, notably Wagner, was considerable.

Verdi.

Italian opera in the 19th cent. culminated in the works of Giuseppe Verdi (1813–1901), who rose from a peasant background to become his coun-try's most noted composer, as well as something of a natural hero during the period of the Risorgi-mento. His earliest works, indeed, often roused his hearers to patriotic fervour. For instance, *Nabucco* (1841), with its theme of an oppressed people seeking deliverance, was treated as a symbol of the Italians' fight for freedom.

Musically, Verdi developed out of all recognition during the course of his long career. The con-tinuously flowing structure of his last two operas *Otello* and *Falstaff* is very far removed from the start-stop formulas, inherited from his predeces-sors, of his first works, yet even then they are touched, in harmonic subtleties, orchestral felicities, and a sense of drama, by a spark of genius, a burning inspiration that sets him apart from all other operatic composers. *Ernani* (1844), *I due Foscari* (1844), and *Luisa Miller* (1849) all have foretastes of glories to come even if as a whole they are flawed dramas, and these "galley years", as Verdi him-self later described them, gave him the essential know-how to produce his later, greater operas, as well as establishing him incontrovertibly as the most popular Italian composer of the time.

However, it was with *Rigoletto* (1851), *Il Trovatore* (1853), and *La Traviata* (1853) that Verdi first really staked his claim to immortality. In these pieces his increasing dramatic mastery is married to a wonderful flow of lyrical melody, at the same time controlled by a fine musical sensibility. They were followed by four operas—*Simon Boccanegra* (1857), *Un Ballo in Maschera* (1858), *La Forza del Destino* (1862), and *Macbeth* (revised version, 1865)—in which Verdi overcame complexities of story line by his continually developing musical powers. This period is crowned by *Don Carlos* (written for the Paris Opéra, 1867) a masterly exercise in combining private and public situations in a single, grand, and characterful work. In some respects Verdi never surpassed the subtlety of his writing in this opera. *Aïda* (1871) carried on the process but the characterisation in this ever-popular piece is less refined than in *Don Carlos*, if the grandeur of the design is more spectacular.

The success of *Otello* (1887) owes nearly as much to the skill of Boito whose literary ability com-bined with musical knowledge (he was himself a composer) presented Verdi with an ideal libretto for his seamless music in which the drama moves inevitably to its tragic end. Recitative, aria, ensemble are fused in a single, swiftly moving music-drama, which in its very different way equals that of Wagner. *Falstaff* (1893) achieves the same success in the field of comic opera, a brilliant, mercurial ending to a distinguished career. If Verdi had written only these two final masterpieces his place in musical history would have been assured.

Brahms.

Brahms (1833–97) has justly been described as "a romantic spirit controlled by a classical intellect," for while complying with most of the formal regulations of sonata form he imbued them with an emotional content that accorded with his time. Indeed Schumann declared that he was the "one man who would be singled out to make articulate in an ideal way the highest expression of our time."

Perhaps in his chamber music will be found the quintessence of his art. The piano and clarinet quintets, the two string sextets, the horn trio, and the violin sonatas alike are designed on a large scale yet the expression remains intimate, the design and structure clear.

The symphonies and concertos, though, remain his most popular works; they are part of the solid repertory of every orchestra and most piano and violin players in the world. Their high serious-ness, constant lyrical beauty, and control of form are deeply satisfying. They do not provide the extremes of passion and excitement provided by his contemporaries, but their study provides continuous absorption and delight. The double concerto for violin and cello deserves a mention as a unique work in music.

Brahms wrote more than two hundred songs in which the desire for melodic beauty takes precedence over the words and meaning. Many are set to poor poetry, but hidden away are still some unexplored treasures, and the Four Serious Songs, at least, are tragic masterpieces. In a lighter vein the two sets of *Liebeslieder Walzer* for four voices are irresistible. The choral Requiem, too, is a fine work.

Bruckner.

In recent years Bruckner's reputation *vis-à-vis* his great contemporary Brahms has been enhanced in England. The old conception of him as a naïve Austrian unable to grasp the fundamentals of symphonic architecture has died hard, and the prevailing popularity of his grandest works is at last gaining him his rightful place in the 19th cent. firmament. The nine symphonies and the masses are his chief claim to immortality. They contain melodies of unforgettable beauty, symphonic paragraphs of unparalleled grandeur, and an appreciation of formal development that, though different, is equally as valid as that of Brahms. The movements of his symphonies are long and he often pauses, as if for breath and to admire the scenery, before he reaches the climactic peak of his musical journey. His idiom is best approached by a newcomer to his work through the fourth and seventh symphonies as they are perhaps the easiest to understand, but the fifth, sixth, eighth, and ninth (unfinished) are just as beautiful—and cogently argued—once one has acquired the knack, so to speak, of listening to his music. Most of these works are now to be heard in their original form, stripped of the veneer of "improvements" suggested to the diffident composer by his friends.

The masses, which translate Bruckner's symphonic ideas to the choral plain, and Bruckner's delightful string quintet are worth investigating.

Wagner.

Praised only this side of idolatry by his admirers, unmercifully criticised by his detractors, Richard Wagner (1813–83) is perhaps the most controversial composer in musical history. And so it was bound to be with such a revolutionary figure, whose writings, other than his music, contain, to say the least, dubious theories and whose operas, composed to his own libretti, broke the bonds of the form as known until his time. He regarded music-drama as a fusion of all the arts—music, literature, painting—in one unity. With *The Ring of the Nibelungs* he achieved his purpose; no other work of art has ever tried to encompass the whole of existence. Today, and surely forever, musicians, philosophers, and writers will argue over its meaning, and each age will reinterpret it according to its own lights.

But before he reached this pinnacle of achievement, Wagner gradually transformed opera—through *Rienzi, The Flying Dutchman, Tannhäuser,* and *Lohengrin*—so that a new mould was fashioned to take what he wanted to pour into it. He introduced the *Leitmotiv,* a musical theme that could be associated with a particular person, situation, or idea, each time it occurred. Slowly he developed the musical form so that the drama could unfold continuously without breaks for arias. By the time he began to write *Tristan and Isolde* and *Die Meistersinger,* he had perfected his methods and had he never undertaken *The Ring* that tragedy and that comedy would have assured him his place in the musical firmament. Indeed, *Die Meistersinger* is considered a masterpiece even by those who are not willing or prepared to accept the rest of the Wagnerian ethos.

The length and complexity of these operas, and of *Parsifal,* a work of unique beauty in spite of certain *longueurs,* means that it is almost essential to prepare oneself by homework, with libretti and records, before attempting to assimilate them in the opera house. The added effort is well worth while for the ultimate musical satisfaction they bring because Wagner was more than an operatic reformer; he opened up a new harmonic language (especially in the use of chromaticism) that was logically to develop into the atonality of the 20th cent.

Wolf.

As Wagner was the culmination of the 19th cent. symphonic and operatic tradition, so Hugo Wolf (1860–1903) summed up, if he did not surpass, the achievements in song-writing of Schubert, Schumann, and Loewe (1796–1869).

Wolf was a lonely, pathetic man. He lived much of his life in poverty, and eventually lost his reason and died of an incurable disease. These circumstances account perhaps for his almost feverish bursts of creative activity, which were also the outward sign of his burning genius. His greatest contributions to the art of *Lieder* were his extraordinary insight into the poet's meaning and the harmonic means by which he heightened the expression of the words. He raised the importance of the piano part even higher than had Schumann, and in some of his songs the vocal part takes the form of a free declamation over a repeated idea in the piano. However, in the main the vocal and piano parts are interwoven with great subtlety, and he unerringly matched the very varied moods of the poems he chose to set. His greatest creative period was between early 1888 and early 1890 when songs poured from his pen daily—more than 50 settings of the German poet Mörike, 20 of Eichendorff, more than 50 of Goethe, and more than 40 of Heyse and Geibel (the Spanish Song-book). Later he composed songs from Heyse's Italian Song-book and the three Michelangelo sonnets. And the range of his creative understanding was wide, taking in the almost wild passion of the Spanish songs, the humanity and humour of the Italian love-songs, the titanic power of *Prometheus* (Goethe), the varying moods of the Mörike book, and the intangible power of the Michelangelo sonnets. There are almost inexhaustible riches here for the inquiring mind to discover. Outside *Lieder,* Wolf's output is small, but it includes a sadly neglected opera, *Der Corregidor,* the Italian Serenade for string quartet (alternatively for small orchestra) and a tone poem *Penthesilea.*

Ernest Newman, his greatest champion, summed up his work most aptly: "Wolf practically never repeats himself in the songs; every character is drawn from the living model. It is a positively Shakespearian imagination that is at work—Protean in its creativeness, inexhaustibly fecund and always functioning from the inside of the character or the scene, not merely making an inventory from the outside."

National Movements.

During the course of the 19th cent., alongside the emergence of national political identity, came the rise of nationalism in music, fertilising traditional Western—that is basically German—musical forms with folk material. Of these groups the Russian is certainly the most important, if not the most vital.

Glinka (1804–57) was the first important Russian composer of the national school and, although his two operas *A Life for the Tsar* (sometimes called *Ivan Susanin*) and *Russlan and Ludmilla* are strongly influenced by Italian models, they do introduce Russian song and harmony into the texture. He undoubtedly influenced Borodin (1833–87), Cui (1835–1918), Balakireff (1837–1910), Mussorgsky (1839–81) and Rimsky-Korsakov (1844–1908)—the so-called "Five" of 19th-cent. Russian music. However, each was very much of an individualist too. Borodin was a lecturer in chemistry who wrote in his spare time. His two symphonies, two string quartets led up to his most notable work, the opera *Prince Igor*, left incomplete at his death. Balakireff, friend and adviser to the rest of the group, wrote little himself, but his orchestral works and the piano fantasia, *Islamey*, are worthy of investigation.

Modest Mussorgsky (1839–81) is today seen as the most important and inspired of "The Five." More than the others he used Russian song and Russian speech as the basis of his operas in which he portrayed the lives and destinies of his own people. Although his capacities were seriously impaired by an uncongenial job, poverty, and drinking, he produced two great operas, *Boris Godunov* and *Khovanshchina*, and another *Sorochintsy Fair* that is immensely enjoyable. *Boris* should be given in its original, with spare orchestration, but more often than not it is heard in Rimsky-Korsakov's more elaborate revision. In any case the opera exists in various versions, none of them necessarily the right one; what is important is to hear it in one or the other because of its great portrayal of Boris's personality set against the background of the Russian people, unforgettably presented in choral outbursts. *Khovanshchina* was completed by Rimsky-Korsakov, *Sorochintsy Fair* by Tcherepnin (although other versions also exist). Mussorgsky's songs explore a new vein of naturalistic vocal declamation. Each of the four *Songs and Dances of Death* is a miniature drama worthy of Wolf, although of course in a quite other idiom. The *Nursery* songs miraculously conjure up a child's world as seen from a child's point of view. Many of the individual songs, the *Sunless* cycle too, should be investigated.

Rimsky-Korsakov (1844–1908) is perhaps a less attractive figure because so much of his music seems heartless or merely decorative, but this judgment is probably made on the strength of hearing *Shéhérazade* and the *Capriccio Espagnol* a few too many times. Such of his 15 operas as are played evince a (literally) fantastic mind and lyrical vein, and it is a pity that *Sadko*, *The Snow Maiden*, and *The Tsar's Bride*, at least, are not heard more often.

Tchaikovsky.

Peter Ilyich Tchaikovsky (1840–93) is a more universally admired figure than any of "The Five" and his music is indubitably closer to the mainstream than theirs in that it adheres more nearly to Western European forms. His popularity is due to his unhesitating appeal to the emotions and to his tender, often pathetic melodic expression. His lyrical gift is stronger than his sense of architecture, as he himself admitted. Yet his later symphonies—the fourth, fifth, and sixth (the *Pathétique*)—are all cogently enough argued and invigorating, as can be heard in the hands of a conductor willing to emphasise their formal power rather than their tendency towards sentimentality; the orchestral craftsmanship is also superb. The three piano concertos and the violin concerto offer rare opportunities for virtuoso display within a reasonably dramatic structure and his various overtures are always exciting to hear.

The three ballets—*The Sleeping Beauty*, *Swan Lake*, and *Nutcracker* show Tchaikovsky's skill on a smaller and perhaps more congenial scale, but only two of his operas—*Eugene Onegin* and *The Queen of Spades*—survive in regular performance. They demonstrate his ability to delineate character and his always eloquent melodic invention. His songs often felicitously capture a passing mood or emotion.

Bohemia (Czechoslovakia).

The Czech national school is dominated by two composers—Smetana (1824–84) and Dvořák (1841–1904). In his own country Smetana holds a unique position as the father of his country's music—which is remarkable when you consider that he lived in a country that was then under Austrian rule and never spoke the Czech language perfectly. Yet his music is filled with the spirit

of Czech history and national life, and many of his operas, his most important contribution, deal purely with national subjects. The reawakening of interest in things national, after Austria's defeat by Italy in 1859, led to the establishment of a Provisional Theatre in 1862 and Smetana's first opera *The Brandenburgers in Bohemia* was produced there in 1866, but its success was eclipsed by the enormous popularity of *The Bartered Bride*, which appeared the same year. Its melodic charm, lively characterisation and cosy humour have carried it round the world and it is the one Smetana opera to be in the repertory of most opera houses. However, his next opera *Dalibor* (1868) is considered by some authorities as his masterpiece. It is conceived on a heroic scale, and frequently rises to great dramatic heights. His later operas include *Libuše* (1872) a solemn festival tableau, *The Two Widows* (1874), a delightful comedy, *The Kiss* (1876), *The Secret* (1878), and *The Devil's Wall* (1882).

His main orchestral work *Má Vlast* (My Country), written between 1874 and 1879, is a cycle of six symphonic poems nobly depicting the life and legends of his country. He composed only three mature chamber works—an elegiac piano trio, written in 1855 in memory of the death of his eldest daughter, and two string quartets, both autobiographical. The first in E minor (1876)—"From My Life"—tells of his youth and aspirations until a terrible, screeching E in *altissimo* describes the onset of deafness; the second in D minor, sadly neglected, was described by the composer as an attempt to explain the "whirlwind of music in the head of one, who has lost his hearing," and was probably influenced by Beethoven's later music.

Dvořák combined a fecund melodic gift with an intelligent grasp of structure. His symphonies and chamber music are mostly written in classical form, yet the works are imbued with a spontaneity and freshness that have not lost one whit of their charm over the years.

He wrote nine symphonies and, although only the last three or four are regularly performed, they are mostly mature works, several of which, for instance No. 7 in D minor (formerly known as No. 2) reach a tragic grandeur at times. They are all orchestrated in a masterly way and are full of delightful detail. Dvořák wanted to show that a Brahms could come out of Bohemia—and he succeeded in doing so while maintaining a definitely individual flavour, strongly influenced by natural rhythms.

He wrote three concertos, one each for piano, violin, and cello. The earlier ones are interesting without being quite in the first flight of the composer's output, but the cello concerto of 1895 is perhaps the composer's crowning achievement—warm, mellifluous, romantic.

He wrote chamber music throughout his long creative life. Some of the early works are weak and derivative, but the later string quartets, the "Dumky" trio, and the piano quartet and quintet are expressive and full of unforced invention. Dvořák felt himself somewhat hampered when setting words, nevertheless his *Stabat Mater* and *Te Deum* are both deeply felt choral works and he wrote songs throughout his career, many of them very fine indeed. He wrote ten operas, but only *Rusalka* (1901) has gained a foothold outside Czechoslovakia.

Janáček.

The Moravian composer Leoš Janáček (1858–1928) spent most of his life in Brno as a working musician. His music has recently come to be recognised as some of the most original written in the past hundred years. His operas, in which he closely followed the inflection of the speech of his native land, are his finest works. Over the score of his last opera, *From the House of the Dead*, he wrote the words "In every human being there is a divine spark", and it is this deep love of humanity that permeates all his works. Of his operas *Kátya Kabanová* (1921) and *The Cunning Little Vixen*

(1924), the *Makropoulos Affair* (1926), and *From the House of the Dead* (adapted from a Dostoyevsky novel, 1928) are the most important and they have all been produced in Britain in recent years. His original genius is self-evident in all of them.

Among his orchestral works *Taras Bulba* and *Sinfonietta* should be noted, and his two string quartets, very difficult to play, should be better known. The song cycle, *Diary of one who has disappeared*, for tenor, contralto, and three female voices with piano, and the Glagolithic Mass contain music of much expressive beauty.

Hungary.

The Hungarian musical outburst came somewhat later than that of other countries. Its great figure is Bela Bartók (1881–1945) who, as well as being a national figure, has proved an influential composer in the whole of 20th-cent. music. His mind was full of folk music, but it was transmuted by his strongly personal style and powerful intellect into something highly original. His music is tense and volatile but this restlessness is sometimes relieved by a kind of other-wordly, ethereal lyricism, as in the lovely slow movements of his quartets.

Bartók was affected as much by the musical innovations of Debussy and Stravinsky (see below) as by East European, notably Magyar, folk music and many of his works are an attempt to meld the two.

The most important part of his output is undoubtedly his string quartets which cover most of his creative life. To this intimate form he confided his personal innermost thoughts and in it conducted his most far-reaching musical experiments, thereby extending its boundaries beyond anything previously known. As with Beethoven's late quartets many of Bartok's rely on organic or cyclic development while remaining just within the laws of classical form. As Mosco Carner puts it, "For profundity of thought, imaginative power, logic of structure, diversity of formal details, and enlargement of the technical scope, they stand unrivalled in the field of modern chamber music."

The most important of his orchestral works are the three piano concertos, of which the first two are harsh and uncompromising, and fiendishly difficult to play, while the third, written in 1945, is mellower and more diatonic. The second violin concerto (1937–8) shows the various elements of Bartók's style in full flower, by turns exuberant, passionate, and brilliant. The *Music for Strings, Percussion and Celesta* (1937) is remarkable for its strange sonorities and its fascinating texture. The *Concerto for Orchestra* (1944) is more immediately appealing and again shows the composer in complete command of a large canvas. Of the piano works *Mikrokosmos* (1935) and the sonata for two pianos and percussion (1937) are worth investigating.

His chief stage pieces are *The Miraculous Mandarin* (1919), a harsh, cruel ballet which drew appropriately dramatic music from the composer, and the opera *Duke Bluebeard's Castle* (1911), a luscious, original score that makes one regret that he wrote no more operas later in his career.

Kodály (1882–1967) was from early years closely associated with Bartók and with him collected Hungarian folk melodies using many of them in his music. He worked in many forms and the more important of his works are the *Peacock Variations* for orchestra, the choral *Psalmus Hungaricus* and *Te Deum*, The *Dances of Galánta*, and the opera *Háry János*, and the sonatas for cello and for unaccompanied cello.

Sibelius, Nielsen and Grieg.

Among Scandinavian composers the Finn Jean Sibelius (1865–1957) and the Dane Carl Nielsen (1865–1931) are outstanding. Sibelius is a lone northern figure ploughing his own furrow

oblivious or, at any rate, ignoring the unusual developments that were taking place in Central Europe, yet his seven symphonies are strong as granite, honest, rugged works that will undoubtedly stand the test of time. They are not by any means all similar in mood, or even form. The first is very much influenced by Tchaikovsky and Borodin, the second and third show a more personal style developing, the fourth is terse and tragic, the fifth lyrical, bright, and lucid; the sixth is perhaps most typically Sibelian in its evocation of primeval nature, and the seventh—in one continuous movement—is a more purely abstract piece, notable for its structural logic and the grandness of its themes. The violin concerto is the most easily understood of the composer's main works and has a grateful part for the soloist.

The tone poems *The Swan of Tuonela, Pohjola's Daughter, En Saga, Night Ride and Sunrise, The Bard*, and *Tapiola* uncannily evoke the icy words of the legends of the far north, and the primeval forces of nature. Sibelius's one string quartet *Voces Intimae* and many of his songs are worth hearing too. His music, reviled in some quarters during the 1950s, has since been restored to favour, and seems to be enjoyed again by critics and the general public alike.

Carl Nielsen (1965–1931) is another individualist. His six symphonies, like Sibelius's seven, are the most important part of his output, but whereas Sibelius was dealing with a huge, uninhabited northern landscape, Nielsen is more friendly and serene in his music, which is seldom forbidding, always inventive, throwing a new light, through unusual ideas about harmony, structure and tonality, on traditional forms. He also wrote highly individual concertos for the flute and clarinet, four string quartets and two operas— the dramatic, rather Brahmsian *Saul and David* (1902) and a delightful comedy, *Maskarade* (1906), full of lyrical music.

The Norwegian composer Edvard Grieg (1843–1907) was essentially a miniaturist whose range of feeling was not wide but whose music is always gentle and appealing. His most notable works are the romantic piano concerto, the atmospheric incidental music to Ibsen's play *Peer Gynt*, the charming Lyric Suite, and the small piano pieces. Not an important composer, then, but always an attractive one.

Elgar and the English Revival.

After the death of Purcell there is hardly a name in English music worth speaking of until the 19th cent. when Hubert Parry (1848–1918) and Charles Villiers Stanford (1852–1924), actually an Irishman, led a revival. Their music is seldom heard today, but their pioneer work paved the way for Edward Elgar (1857–1934). Although all were influenced by Brahms they nevertheless managed to establish a new English tradition that has been carried on in our own day. Elgar's symphonies are laid out on a grand, leisurely scale and they are both eloquent and exhilarating. His violin concerto has an elegiac slow movement as has the glorious cello concerto and both contain many fine opportunities for the soloist. The cello concerto is as appealing a work as any by Elgar expressing his innermost thoughts. His *Enigma Variations* are a series of portraits in sound of his friends, but there is another overall theme to go with them that has never been identified. This has not prevented the work from becoming Elgar's most popular, not surprisingly when one considers its charm and melodiousness. Three other orchestral pieces that should not be neglected are his symphonic study *Falstaff*, a many-sided musical picture of the Fat Knight, and the overtures *Cockaigne*, a happy evocation of London, and *In the South*, inspired by a visit to Italy. His three late chamber works, written when he was 61, are reticent, economic pieces that remove any misconception of Elgar as a bombastic composer. His songs are mostly feeble, but the oratorios, notably *The Dream of Gerontius*, show the composer's ability to control a large canvas. The composer himself wrote over the score of *Gerontius*,

"This is the best of me"—a verdict with which we can readily agree.

French Music.

César Franck (1822–90) was the main figure in mid-19th-cent. musical France and his influence spread even wider than his music of which only the D minor Symphony, the Symphonic Variations for piano and orchestra, the piano quintet, and the violin sonata are likely to be encountered today. The leading French opera composers of that time were Gounod (1818–93), Bizet (1838–75) and Massenet (1842–1912). Gounod's *Faust*, Bizet's *Carmen* (composed just before his untimely death when he caught cold after a swim) and Massenet's *Manon* all retain a deserved place in the repertory; each is a well-judged mini-drama unafraid of romantic ardour and forceful, histrionic strokes. Some of Massenet's other numerous operas, such as *Werther* and *Don Quichotte*, have enjoyed a revival in recent years.

Concurrently with similar movements in French painting and poetry came the French Impressionist composers at the end of the 19th cent. Their leader—and one of the great seminal forces of modern music—was Claude Debussy (1862–1918). His aim was to capture a mood or sensation, and he did that by more or less inventing a fresh system of harmony using a whole-tone scale, unusual chords, and by creating in the orchestra new, highly personal textures—there is no mistaking the Debussy idiom once you have heard at least one piece by him. His impressionistic style did not lead him, however, to abandon form as some have suggested, and his main works are just as closely organised as those by classical German composers. His music is sensuous and poetic yet nearly always structurally satisfying as well.

His reputation, at least with the general musical public, rests largely on his orchestral music, a few piano pieces and his only opera *Pelléas et Mélisande*. *La Mer* is a scintillating evocation of the sea in all its moods; *Nocturnes*, *Images*, and *Prélude à l'Après-midi d'un Faune* exactly suggest different places, times, moods—the "Iberia" and "Gigues" sections of *Images*, calling to mind respectively the spirit of Spain and the flickering light of a rainy English night. *Pelléas*, based on a Symbolist drama by Maeterlinck, tells a story of love, jealousy, and murder in predominantly restrained yet emotionally loaded terms. It is an elusive original work that has no predecessor or successor. Intensely atmospheric, rivetingly beautiful, it weaves an irresistible spell over the listener.

Debussy's chamber music is unjustly neglected. His string quartet (1893) was one of the first works in which he displayed his new and strange world of sound, and the three late sonatas, one for violin, one for cello, and the third for flute, viola, and harp are elliptical, compressed pieces which seem to be questing disjointedly into new regions of sound. His songs too, are worthy of investigation, and his piano music, especially the twenty-four Preludes and some of the shorter pieces, contain some of his most imaginative and original ideas and thoughts.

Gabriel Fauré (1845–1924) is a difficult figure to place. He lived through all kinds of musical revolutions yet they seemed to affect the character of his work very little. He has never been, and is never likely to be, a widely known or popular composer, yet his music has a reticence and delicacy that is very appealing. Despite his dreamy, retiring art he was not a recluse, but a very sociable man.

He was content with forms as he found them, but he imbued them with a very personal, human style. Perhaps his art is best heard in his songs. They are not overtly passionate or dramatic but the long, sinuous melodies and subtle harmonies are exquisitely wrought. Of the song-cycles, *La Bonne Chanson*, *Cinq Mélodies* (Verlaine), *Le Chanson d'Eve*, and *L'Horizon Chimérique* are best known. The last written in 1922, when the composer was seventy-seven, is a beautiful setting of words by a soldier killed in the first World War. There are also many remarkable single songs, many of them settings of poems by Verlaine. His opera *Pénélope*, based on the classical heroine, is unjustly neglected.

He wrote few orchestral pieces, but the *Ballade* for piano and orchestra and the *Pavane* are among his most typical and delicate compositions, and his outstanding piano music, modelled on Chopin's, includes Nocturnes, Impromptus, and Barcarolles. His chamber music covers more than half a century from the violin sonata of 1876 to the string quartet written the year he died. In that period he composed two piano quartets, two piano quintets, another violin sonata and two cello sonatas, the later works failing to show quite the unforced lyrical grace of the earlier ones. Perhaps Fauré is best approached with the first piano quartet, a charming, easily assimilated work, and the beautiful choral *Requiem*.

Saint-Saëns (1835–1921), an accomplished, cultivated musician, has had a "bad press" but his craftsmanship, as displayed in his symphonies, concertos, and *Samson et Dalila* (one among his 12 operas) is not to be despised.

Henri Duparc (1844–1933), despite a very long life, is known today only for a group of songs he wrote before he was forty. They are among the most emotionally direct yet tasteful melodies ever written. Paul Dukas (1865–1935) is another figure off the beaten track, as it were. He, too, is known only for a handful of compositions. He was strongly influenced by Vincent d'Indy (1851–1931) and the school who strongly opposed Debussy's new ideas, yet he could not help but come under Debussy's spell. Dukas's one great work is his opera *Ariane et Barbe-Bleue*, the text adapted from a Maeterlinck play written with the composer in mind.

Maurice Ravel (1875–1937), a pupil of Fauré, followed in Debussy's footsteps, although his later pieces were more ascetic. Indeed, he was one of the most fastidious of composers, always seeking, and often finding, artistic perfection. The works he wrote before 1918 are definitely of the Impressionist School and it would be difficult to imagine more beautiful sounds than are to be found in the ballet *Daphnis et Chloé*, in the song-cycle *Shéhérazade*, and the piano fantasy *Gaspard de la Nuit*. His first style was summed up in the A minor piano trio (1915). In his later music Ravel was struggling, not always successfully, to keep up with new developments such as jazz and atonality. The piano concerto, for instance, shows very strongly the influence of jazz.

Outstanding orchestral works of his, other than *Daphnis* are *Rapsodie espagnole* (1907), *La Valse* (1920), a sumptuous evocation of the Vienna waltz, and the ever-popular *Boléro*. Two chamber works, besides the trio, are masterpieces—the string quartet (1902–3) and the Introduction and Allegro for Harp, String Quartet, Flute, and Clarinet. This Septet composed in 1906, ravishes the senses with magical sound.

Ravel's piano pieces are perhaps his most notable contribution to music, combining an extraordinary feeling for the instrument's technical possibilities with the sensibility of a Chopin, and in this field *Jeux d'eau*, *Miroirs*, and *Ma Mère l'Oye*, all written just after the turn of the century, come very close to the perfection of *Gaspard de la Nuit*. His songs show his unusual appreciation of the need to fuse poetic and musical values, and he set exotic poems for preference. His output in this field includes the cycle *Histoires naturelles* (1906), acutely observed settings of five poems about birds and animals; *Cinq Mélodies populaires grecques* (1907), charming settings of Greek folk songs; *Trois Poèmes de Mallarmé* (1913); and *Chansons madécasses* (1926), suitably exotic settings of three poems by an 18th-cent. Creole poet called Parny. Finally in 1932 came *Don Quichotte à Dulcinée*, three poems by Paul Morand, Ravel's last composition.

Ravel wrote two operas—the slight but moderately amusing *L'Heure espagnole* (1907), nicely orchestrated in a faintly and appropriately Spanish style and *L'Enfant et les Sortilèges* (1925) to a story by Colette, a delicious fantasy about a naughty child who gets his due punishment for tormenting animals and destroying furniture.

French music after Debussy and Ravel was dominated by the slighter composers known as *Les Six*, the most important of whom were Arthur Honegger (1892–1955, Swiss born), Darius Milhaud (1892–1974) and Francis Poulenc (1890–1963). Each has contributed music of some wit and charm to the repertory. They were influenced by Erik Satie (1866–1925), an eccentric but interesting figure who wrote works with odd titles such as *Three Pear Shaped Pieces.* His music is entirely unsentimental, often ironic.

Spain.

Felipe Pedrell (1841–1922) has been aptly described as the midwife of Spanish nationalist music. As a musicologist and teacher he strongly influenced the two main composers of the school, Manuel de Falla (1876–1946) and Enrique Granados (1867–1916). Falla's output was not large and most of it was written around the years of the first world war. The pre-war years were spent in Paris where Falla came under the influence of Debussy. However his style is individual and evokes all the passion and gaiety of his native land. Perhaps his most typical works are in two ballets *Love the Magician* (1915) and *The Three-Cornered Hat* (1919). The opera *La Vida Breve* (1905) despite its weak libretto also has much appeal. The vivacity and smouldering passion at the heart of the country's character is conjured up by the *Seven Popular Songs* (1914) and the *Nights in the Gardens of Spain* (1916) for piano and orchestra. His later works, especially the harpsichord concerto of 1926, show Falla tending towards a less ebullient, more restrained style. The second opera, *Master Peter's Puppet Show* (1923) is a miniaturist work, refined and intense. His third opera *Atlantida*, left unfinished at his death, was completed by his pupil Ernesto Halffter and first staged in 1962.

Granados was perhaps a more restrictedly Spanish composer than Falla, but his music is unfailingly attractive and deserves to be better known. The opera *Goyescas* (1916) is most famous for the second interlude and opening of Act III—*La Maja y el Ruiseñor* (The Lover and the Nightingale), a haunting, sinuous melody for soprano, generally heard in its original form as a piano solo.

The chief claim to fame of Albéniz (1860–1909) is *Ibéria*, masterly descriptive pieces for piano. Many of his other piano works are now more well known in the form of very effective guitar arrangements. Turina (1882–1949), attempted a more cosmopolitan style, but his most often heard music is typically Spanish.

The Late German Romantics.

While composers such as Debussy, Sibelius, Stravinsky and Schoenberg (see below for the latter pair) were striking out along new paths, Richard Strauss (1864–1949) continued in the trend of 19th-cent. German composers; he was the tradition's last great figure. At least two of his operas—*Salome* and *Elektra*—were considered shocking at the time, but today we can hear that they are essentially big-scale, romantic works—natural successors to Wagner's—however startling the harmonies may once have seemed.

If Strauss did not achieve the granite intellectual greatness of Beethoven or Wagner, there is no denying his melodic genius and powers of fertile invention which overlaid the streak of vulgarity and inflation in his musical make-up. His first outstanding achievement was in the field of the symphonic poem, where he carried the work of composers such as Liszt and Berlioz to its logical conclusion. Starting with *Don Juan* in 1888 and ending with *Sinfonia Domestica* in 1903 he wrote a series of kaleidoscopic works, full of enormous vitality, endless melody, and fascinating orchestration. The most easily assimilated—and the most popular—are *Don Juan* and *Till Eulenspiegel* but some of the longer works, notably *Also Sprach Zarathustra* (based on Nietzsche's

prose poem) and *Don Quixote* (based, of course, on Cervantes's great work) will reward the persistent, inquiring mind with long hours of enthralled listening. Other works sound somewhat dated in their bombastic over-confidence, though Strauss's skill in composition seldom flagged at this stage of his long creative career. The symphonic poems all tell something of a story usually based on a literary source, but it is not essential to the enjoyment of the music to know what this is, although it may be helpful.

Strauss's reputation is even more solidly based on his fifteen operas, the earliest of which *Guntram* was first performed in 1894, the last, *Capriccio*, in 1942. During these years the essentials of Strauss's style changed little, though it became very much more refined as the years passed. His first operatic period ended with the violent, sensual tragedies *Salome* (1905) and *Elektra* (1909), the latter being his first collaboration with his chief librettist, Hugo von Hofmannsthal. Then came their unique *Der Rosenkavalier* (1911), which filters the charm and the decadence of 18th-cent. Vienna through early 20th-cent. eyes. This was followed by *Ariadne auf Naxos* (1912). Originally intended to be given after Molière's *Le Bourgeois Gentilhomme*, it was later presented (1916) without the play but with an amusing Prologue, written by von Hofmannsthal. *Die Frau ohne Schatten* is the most grandiose result of the Strauss–Hofmannsthal partnership. It is a complex psychological allegory, but Strauss's contribution is not on as consistently lofty a level as is his librettist's. *Intermezzo* (1924), which has a libretto by Strauss himself, is a largely autobiographical domestic comedy, which has lately gained in reputation as a compact, charming piece. With *Die Aegyptische Helena* (1928), an opera on a mythical theme, and *Arabella* (1933), another sensuous Viennese comedy, the Strauss–Hofmannsthal collaboration ended on account of the librettist's death. Strauss then wrote *Die Schweigsame Frau* (1935) to a libretto by Stefan Zweig, based on a play by Ben Jonson, and *Friedenstag* (1938), *Daphne* (1938)—a beautiful opera—and *Die Liebe der Danae* (written 1938–40) with Josef Gregor as librettist. His swan-song was *Capriccio*, a dramatisation of the old argument about the relative importance of words and music in opera. The libretto is by the conductor Clemens Krauss and the opera, a serene, melodious work, was a fit end to a great operatic career.

However, Strauss went on composing till nearly the end of his life, adding a group of late orchestral pieces to his already large catalogue of works. The *Metamorphosen* for 23 solo string instruments, is probably the best of these. During his long creative career he wrote numerous songs, many of them, such as *Morgen, Wiegenlied* and *Ruhe, meine Seele* of surpassing beauty.

Other notable figures in German music at this time were Max Reger (1873–1916), a somewhat ponderous but highly accomplished composer who, in a quarter of a century of creative life, wrote more than 150 works, of which his sets of variations, his piano concerto, and chamber music are probably the most impressive. Hans Pfitzner (1869–1949), another German traditionalist, is chiefly remembered today for his opera *Palestrina*, about events, now known to be spurious, in the life of the 16th-cent. Italian composer.

Twentieth-century Music.

Gustav Mahler (1860–1911), the Austrian Jewish composer, is one of the most important figures in 20th-cent. music. In a sense he bridges the gulf between the late Romantics, who were tending more and more towards chromaticism and away from established key relationships, and the atonalists, who abandoned the key system entirely. His detractors maintain that his inflation of allegedly banal Viennese beer-house music to unheard-of lengths rules him out of court as a serious writer. His admirers would claim that his music encompasses the whole of life in enormous, valid structures. The truth, if truth there be, perhaps lies somewhere in between: if his material does not always justify the length of his symphonies, and if there are occasional imperfections and *longueurs*, these shortcomings are worth enduring for the sake of the depth of utterance, the humanity and the poetry of the great pages. He admitted himself that "I cannot do without trivialities," but it is out of these impurities that he forged his titanic victories.

His music is undoubtedly best approached through his songs, where the words force him to discipline his wide-ranging vision. *Lieder eines fahrenden Gesellen* (1884), to his own words, *Kindertotenlieder* (1901–4), to poems by Rückert, and some individual songs perfectly relate words to music, and are all of a poignant loveliness. Similarly *Das Lied von der Erde* (1908), especially the last of the six songs, is a touching farewell to the world, nobly expressed.

The ten symphonies, however, are Mahler's most impressive legacy to posterity. They are almost impossible to characterise briefly so vast are they in terms of both length and variety. The first, fourth and ninth are probably the easiest to grasp but the fifth, sixth and seventh, despite flaws, contain some of his most awe-inspiring conceptions. The second and third, both of which use soloists and chorus, are revolutionary in orchestration and structure; they both try, inevitably without complete success, to carry out the composer's dictum, "a symphony should be like the world—it must contain everything." The eighth is even more gargantuan, but as in all Mahler's work size does not mean loss of clarity or an overloading of the structure. Part one—a mighty choral invocation—is a visionary setting of the mediaeval hymn *Veni Creator Spiritus*. Part two, which incorporates adagio, scherzo, and finale in one, is a setting of the final scene of Goethe's *Faust*. Until recently all of Mahler's unfinished tenth symphony that was ever performed was the Adagio, but the musicologist and Mahler scholar, the late Deryck Cooke, provided a performing version of the symphony to critical and popular acclaim during the 1960s and thus added a noble, and also optimistic epilogue to the Mahler opus. The debate over the quality of Mahler's music is likely to continue; one fact, however, that cannot be gain-said is his popularity with an ever-increasing audience, largely made up of young people. There must be something in his uncertainty and intense self-inquiry that accords with the mood of the youthful mind.

Schoenberg and the Second Viennese School.

Arnold Schoenberg (1874–1951) revolutionised Western music by his twelve-note method—a system which uses all the notes of the chromatic scale "and denies the supremacy of a tonal centre," as Schoenberg himself puts it. This serial technique of composition, as it is commonly called, naturally sounds strange to an ear acclimatised to music written, as it were, with a home base, but Schoenberg and his disciples Berg and Webern showed that the system could produce works that were something more than mere intellectual exercises. None of the more recent advances in music would have been possible, even thinkable, without Schoenberg's pioneer work.

Schoenberg always considered himself as much a composer as a theorist or teacher, and his works are supposed to appeal as much to the emotions as to the intellect, although to be understood they do, of course, require the listener's concentrated attention. To appreciate how his ideas developed it is necessary to hear first his pre-atonal music, such as the *Gurrelieder* (1900–1) and *Verklärte Nacht* (1899), in which he carried Wagnerian chromaticism to extreme lengths. The *Gurrelieder*, in particular, is a luxuriant, overblown work that shows the Wagnerian idiom in an advanced stage of decay, in spite of many beautiful pages of music. In his succeeding works the feeling of tonality began to disappear until in the Three Piano Pieces (opus 11), of 1909, he finally rejected tonality, although the new 12-note scheme is not yet evident; traces of the old order can still be heard. The succeeding works were mostly short, highly compressed, and very expressive. Schoenberg was reaching out for a new system,

which would "justify the dissonant character of these harmonies and determine their successions." By 1923 he had formulated his 12-note system and the Five Piano Pieces (opus 23), and the Serenade (opus 24) of that year, can thus be considered the first works that used a note-row as the fundamental basis of their composition. Between 1910 and 1915, however, the Russian composer Alexander Skryabin (1872–1915) had attempted to define a new method of composition of his own employing the "mystic chord" of ascending fourths, but his scheme proved comparatively abortive when compared with Schoenberg's. Josef Hauer (1883–1959) also developed a 12-note system which he propounded in 1919 and he always considered himself, rather than Schoenberg, as the true founder of the system. He later worked out a system of tropes (*i.e.*, half-series of six notes).

To return to Schoenberg, in later works he shows much more freedom and assurance in the use of his system. The wind quintet (1924), the Variations for Orchestra, opus 31 (1927–8), the third (1926), and fourth (1936) string quartets, and the string trio (1946) are modern classics of their kind; they require concentrated listening and a degree of understanding of the unfamiliar style of composition. The set of songs with piano *Das Buch der hängenden Gärten* (opus 15), written in 1908, *Pierrot Lunaire*, opus 21 (1912) and the Four Songs, opus 22 (1913–14) provide a kind of bridge between tonality and atonality that the adventurous mind should cross. The monodrama *Erwartung* (1909) is another fascinating work, but perhaps the unfinished *Moses and Aaron* (1932) is Schoenberg's masterpiece as its production at Covent Garden in 1965 showed. Here, for certain, the composer matched his obvious intellectual capacities with an evident emotional content and managed to combine *Sprechgesang* (speech-song) and singing with a real degree of success.

It is only in recent years that Schoenberg's music has had a real chance to make its mark through the essential prerequisite of frequent performance. If his idiom now seems approachable, and a reasonably natural outcome of late 19th-cent. developments, it is perhaps because other, more recent composers have extended the boundaries of sound much further.

Schoenberg's two most respected disciples were Anton Webern (1883–1945) and Alban Berg (1885–1935). Webern's output is small, reaching only to opus 31, and many of his works are very brief. They are exquisitely precise, and delicate almost to a fault. He was trying to distil the essence of each note and in so doing carried the 12-note system to its most extreme and cerebral limit. His music has often been described as pointillist in the sense that one note is entirely separated from the next, there being little discernible melody. Beyond Webern's music, there is indeed the sound of nothingness, and he was rightly described during his lifetime as the "composer of the *pianissimo espressivo*". In his later works, Webern tended towards a strict, and often ingenious use of form and the Variations for Orchestra of 1940 are a good example of this and of his delicacy of orchestration. Webern's influence has perhaps been greater than the impact of his own music, even though he has had no direct successor.

Berg's music is much more accessible. Like Webern his total output was not large, but nearly all his works are substantial additions to the repertory. He is also the directest link between Mahler and the second Viennese School, as Mahler's music influenced him strongly. He studied with Schoenberg from 1904 to 1910. His music is more intense, more lyrical, and less attenuated in sound than Schoenberg's or Webern's. His humanity and abiding compassion can be heard most strongly in his finest opera *Wozzeck* (1925) and his violin concerto (1935), written as an elegy on the death of Manon Gropius, a beautiful 18-year-old girl. Both works are very carefully designed yet formal considerations are never allowed to submerge feeling, and the note-row is fully integrated into the structure.

Both *Wozzeck* and the unfinished but rewarding

Lulu are concerned with society's outcasts who are treated with great tenderness in both operas. The later work is entirely dodecaphonic, all the opera's episodes being based on a theme associated with Lulu. Between these operas Berg wrote the highly complex Chamber Concerto for piano, violin, and thirteen wind instruments (1925) and the expressive Lyric Suite (1926). Among his other works the Seven Early Songs (1908–9) and the concert aria *Der Wein* (1929) are notable.

Stravinsky.

Igor Stravinsky (1882–1971) was another vital figure in 20th-cent. music. If his influence has been in quite another and perhaps less drastic direction than Schoenberg's it is hardly less important. Indeed, future musical historians may consider his achievement the more significant. He has been compared with the painter Picasso in his almost hectic desire to keep up with the times, yet, although he wrote in a number of very different styles over a period of fifty years, every work of his is stamped with his own definitive musical personality. His most revolutionary and seminal work is undoubtedly *The Rite of Spring* (written for the ballet impresario Diaghilev), which caused a furore when it first appeared in 1913, and although it no longer shocks, the rhythmical energy, the fierce angular thematic material, and the sheer virtuosity of the orchestration will always have the power to excite new audiences. Before *The Rite* Stravinsky had written two ballets for Diaghilev—*The Firebird* and *Petrushka*—that are no less filled with vitality and new, albeit not so violent, sounds. During the next thirty years Stravinsky wrote a series of ballet works, gradually becoming more austere and refined in composition. *Apollo* (1928) and *Orpheus* (1947) belong among his most attractive scores.

Stravinsky did not confine himself in stage works to the ballet. *The Nightingale* (1914) is a charming, early opera; *The Soldiers Tale* (1918) is a witty combination of narration, mime, and dance; *Les Noces* (1923) is a concise, original choreographic cantata for soloists and chorus; *Oedipus Rex* (1927) is a dignified version of the Sophocles play, which can be staged or given on the concert platform; either way it is a moving experience. *Perséphone* (1934), a melodrama for reciter, tenor, chorus, and orchestra is an appealling, lucid score. After the war his most important stage work by far was *The Rake's Progress* (1951), with a libretto by W. H. Auden and Chester Kallman. This fascinating opera is deliberately based on 18th-cent. forms and the music itself is neo-classical, always attractive, sometimes haunting.

Stravinsky was no laggard in writing for the concert-platform either. The finest of his orchestral pieces are probably the fervent choral *Symphony of Psalms* (1930), the violin concerto (1931) and the aggressive compact Symphony in Three Movements (1945). Of his chamber music the octet (1923), a duo concertant (1932), and septet (1952) are probably the most important, but no piece, even the dryest and most pedantic, is without redeeming features.

Stravinsky is often thought of as an aloof, detached figure. He has been castigated for his lack of lyrical warmth. But in spite of his own professed desire to drain his music of specific emotion, craftsmanship and originality, often with a strange other-worldly beauty added, are unmistakably there throughout his many scores. Quirky and annoying he may be, dull never.

Busoni and Puccini.

Italian music in the early part of the century was dominated by two very different composers— Ferruccio Busoni (1866–1924) and Giacomo Puccini (1858–1924). Busoni is a difficult figure to place. His austere, intellectual power is never called in question, but he seldom, it ever, succeeded

in translating his technical prowess into altogether successful compositions. We can admire the strength, honesty, and often beauty of such works as his huge piano concerto (1903–4), *Fantasia Contrappuntistica* (1912)—for piano solo—and his unfinished opera *Doktor Faust* without ever capitulating to them entirely. None the less, it has to be admitted that those who have studied his music closely have always fallen completely under his spell. In style his music is anti-Romantic and often neo-Classical yet he was an ardent admirer of Liszt and more especially of Liszt's realisation of the possibilities of the pianoforte. Busoni, himself a great pianist, carried on where Liszt had left off in his own piano music, in which form and expression often find their perfect balance. *Doktor Faust* is undoubtedly his most important opera but *Die Brautwahl* (1908–10) and *Turandot* (1917) have many points of interest too.

Puccini's *Turandot*—his last opera—is a much grander version of the same Gozzi fable and the culmination of this great opera composer's work. His achievement is at an almost directly opposite pole to Busoni's. Not for him the severity or intellectuality of his contemporary. He sought and found an almost ideal fusion of straight-forward lyricism and dramatic truth. His music unerringly follows the pathos and passion of the stories he sets and all his characters "live" as human beings. That, and his abundant flow of easy, soaring melody, are the reasons for his immense popular success, unequalled by any other 20th-cent. composer. Whether it is the pathetic Mimi (*La Bohème*—1896) and Cio-Cio-San, (*Madam Butterfly*—1904), the evil Scarpia (*Tosca* —1900), the cunning Schicchi (*Gianni Schicchi*— 1918), the ardent Rodolfo (*La Bohème*) and Cavaradossi (*Tosca*), or the ice-cold Turandot (*Turandot*—1926). Puccini's musical characterisation is unfailing. And he backs his *verismo* vocal writing with an orchestral tissue that faithfully reflects the milieu of each opera, for instance, Japanese for *Butterfly*, Chinese for *Turandot*, while never losing his particular brand of Italian warmth. His orchestration is always subtle and luminous.

Other Italian composers who wrote operas in the *versimo* style of Puccini were Leoncavallo (1858– 1919), Mascagni (1865–1945), and Giordano (1867– 1948). Mascagni's *Cavalleria Rusticana* and Leoncavallo's *Pagliacci* have formed an inseparable bill and a regular part of the repertory in most opera houses.

Prokofiev, Shostakovich, and Rachmaninov.

Sergey Prokofiev (1891–1953) spent part of his creative life in his native Russia, part of it (1918– 34) abroad, mostly in Paris. His early music, apart from the popular Classical Symphony (1916– 17) tended to be acid and harsh, but on his return to Russia his style, though still frequently satirical, became warmer, more Romantic. The third piano concerto (1917) and the second symphony (1924) are good examples of the former period, the ballets *Romeo and Juliet* (1935) and *Cinderella* (1941–4) and the fifth (1944) and sixth (1946) symphonies of the latter. His music gives the impression of immense rhythmical energy, as in the outer movements of several of his nine piano sonatas, but this fierce drive is often leavened by the soft, wistful lights of his slow movements. His second string quartet (1941), perhaps, presents all the elements of his music in the kindest light.

His strong leaning towards fantasy and mordant parody is felt in his earlier operas *The Love of the Three Oranges* (1921) and *The Fiery Angel* (1922–5). Towards the end of his life much of Prokofiev's music fell into official disfavour.

Dmitri Shostakovich (1906–75) also suffered from attacks on his style. He had to conform to Stalin's requirements for writing music, but he survived and continued to produce music of universal appeal, as, for example, his later string quartets. Like Prokofiev, his music falls into two very distinct styles: one humorous and spiky, the other intense, very personal and often large-scale in its implications. Not all his symphonies reach the expressive depths of numbers one, five, six, eight, ten and fourteen, but they all have reward-ing passages, and his violin and cello concertos are of high quality. He also wrote fifteen string quartets, a piano quintet (an attractive piece) and two operas: the satirical *The Nose* (1930) and *Katrina Ismailova* (1934, revised 1959), originally known as "Lady Macbeth of Mtsensk."

Although Sergey Rachmaninov (1873–1943) was born in Russia, he left his home country in 1918, disliking the Soviet régime, and lived mostly in Switzerland and the United States. His music is chiefly notable for its Romanticism, nostalgic melody, nervous energy and, in the piano works, its opportunities for displays of virtuosity. The first three piano concertos, the third symphony, the piano preludes, and the Rhapsody on a theme of Paganini, are his most typical and attractive works, and many of his songs are touching and beautiful. He wrote three operas.

Weill and Hindemith.

Kurt Weill (1900–50) is chiefly known for his socio-politically pointed operas, such as *Die Dreigros-chenoper* (1929), *Mahagonny* (1929), *Der Jasager* (1930) and *Happy End* (1929), all effective works on the stage, and for his particular brand of brittle, yet fundamentally romantic music. His influence on later composers has been considerable.

Paul Hindemith (1895–1963) in his later years wrote in a strictly tonal, often neo-classical idiom, after being one of the most advanced intellectuals of his time. As well as many chamber and orchestral works, he wrote three formidable operas: *Die Har-monie der Welt, Cardillac* and *Mathis der Maler.*

Ives and Copland.

Charles Ives (1874–1954) is generally recognised as the first American composer of major stature. Most of his works were composed before about 1920, while he was pursuing a successful career in insurance. Ives' music is noted for its thorough-going electri-cism and his refusal to be bound by rules and con-ventions. His work anticipates many 20th century techniques, such as polytonality and polyrhythm, which he seems to have arrived at independently of others. Folk song, hymn tunes, dance music and the sound of the brass band all appear in his composi-tions, many of which are evocative of his New Eng-land background (*e.g. Three Places in New England,* the *Holidays Symphony,* the *Concord* Sonata). It was not until the 1930s that Ives began to achieve re-cognition, but his influence on later American com-posers can hardly be exaggerated.

Aaron Copland (b. 1900) is a composer who has absorbed a variety of influences—from his Jewish background, contemporary Europe, American folk music and jazz, Latin American music—while writ-ing music which is instantly recognisable as his own in its clean textures and taut rhythms. Early works such as the Piano Concerto (1927) show the use of jazz styles, while the Piano Variations (1930) com-bine inventiveness and technical discipline in a tough, concentrated and highly dissonant piece. A move towards a simpler, more immediately appeal-ing idiom is evident in pieces like *El Salón México* (1936), and the ballets *Billy the Kid* (1938), *Rodeo* (1938) and *Appalachian Spring* (1944) and the Third Symphony (1946). These works remain Copland's most popular and frequently performed pieces. A number of works from the 1950s and 1960s experi-ment with serial techniques, while retaining his individual voice.

Vaughan Williams, Holst and Delius.

The twentieth century revival of music in Eng-land owes much to Ralph Vaughan Williams (1872–1958) and Gustav Holst (1874–1934). The English folk song revival, associated with Cecil Sharp, was in full swing during their formative years, and both composers produced arrangements of folk songs as well as assimilating the folk idiom into their own styles. The influence of 16th century polyphony is also strong in Vaughan Williams' music, the most obvious example being the *Fantasia on a Theme by Thomas Tallis* (1909). Vaughan Williams' strongest works (*e.g.* the first, fourth, fifth and sixth sym-

phonies, the ballet *Job,* the choral *Dona Nobis Pacem*) show his characteristic alternation of the forceful and the contemplative.

Holst was a more enigmatic figure. Only his suite *The Planets* and the choral work *The Hymn of Jesus* have established themselves in the regular re-pertory, but his bold harmonic experiments and the austerity, even mysticism, of his style as heard in the opera *Savitri* and the orchestral piece *Egdon Heath* are perhaps more typical of this meditative, original composer.

Frederick Delius (1862–1934) was the major Eng-lish composer to fall under the sway of French im-pressionism, though his English (north country) background, his friendship with Grieg, and the time he spent in America all contributed to the formation of his musical style. He lived in France from 1888 onwards. His most important works are the atmo-spheric tone-poems for orchestra, such as *Brigg Fair,* the vocal and orchestral *A Mass of Life, Sea Drift* and *Appalachia,* and the opera *A Village Romeo and Juliet.*

Walton, Britten and Tippett.

Sir William Walton (1902–83) became known as an *enfant terrible* with the witty and irreverent *Façade* (1923) for speaker and chamber orchestra (with words by Edith Sitwell). The poetic Viola Concerto (1929) shows another side of his musical character. His First Symphony (1934–5) is an arresting, dramatic score and the colourful oratorio *Bel-shazzar's Feast* (1931) is a landmark in choral music. Walton's rhythms show the influence of jazz and of Stravinsky but he is generally felt to be a quintes-sentially English composer. An Elgarian element is clear in such occasional pieces as the coronation marches *Crown Imperial* (1937) and *Orb and Sceptre* (1953).

Benjamin Britten (1913–76) did as much as anyone to establish English music on the forefront of the international stage. Much of his music seems to have an immediate appeal to large audiences and certainly his many stage works earned him quite exceptional prestige both at home and abroad. *Peter Grimes* (1945), *Billy Budd* (1951), *Gloriana* (1953), *A Midsummer Night's Dream* (1960) all show his mastery of stage technique and the first two are also moving human documents. On a smaller scale he has achieved as much with his chamber operas—*The Rape of Lucretia* (1946), *Albert Herring* (1947), *The Turn of the Screw* (1954)—and the three Parables for Church Performance—*Curlew River* (1964), *The Burning Fiery Furnace* (1966) and *The Prodigal Son* (1968). His operatic output was crowned by *Death in Venice* (1973). If he had written nothing else, these dramatic works would have marked him out as a composer of outstanding imaginative gifts. In addition to these, numbering the choral works cul-minating in the *War Requiem* (1962), the various song cycles written, like so much else, for his friend Peter Pears, the *Serenade* for tenor, horn and strings, *Nocturne* for tenor and orchestra, the three *Canticles,* and the *Spring Symphony* are further evi-dence of both his intense emotional commitment and his technical skill. Despite the strong influence of such composers as Purcell, Schubert, Verdi, Mahler and Berg, his style is entirely his own; his musical personality combines, it has been said, "a deep nostalgia for the innocence of childhood, a mercurial sense of humour and a passionate sympa-thy with the victims of prejudice and mis-understanding."

This last quality is also evident in the emotional make up of Sir Michael Tippett (b. 1905), as ex-pressed in such works as the oratorio *A Child of our Time* (1941) one of his earliest successes, which shows both his compassion and his ability to write on a large scale. This and the Concerto for Double String Orchestra (1939) remain his most popular works. Tippett has been open to a wide range of in-fluences, both musical (from English Madrigals, Monteverdi and Beethoven to Negro spirituals and jazz) and non-musical (*e.g.* the ideas of Jung). His early style—often richly lyrical and affirmative of the continued power of tonality—reached its culmi-nation in his allegorical opera *The Midsummer Mar-riage* (1952), the Piano Concerto (1955) and the Second Symphony (1957). A new style, spare and incisive, with structure arising from the juxtaposition of contrasting ideas rather than from a process of development, is evident in his second opera, *King Priam* (1961) and its offshoots, the Second Piano Sonata (1962) and the Concerto for Orchestra (1963). The mystical, ecstatic *The Vision of St. Augustine* (1965), a complex, difficult but rewarding work, is one of his finest from this period. The opera *The Knot Garden* (1970) exemplifies again Tippett's concern with human relationships and the need for self-knowledge. Tippett has never ceased to explore and experiment; his inspiration now seems as fresh as ever. His most recent works, *The Mask of Time*—a huge choral piece—and the Fourth Piano Sonata (1984) have something of the quality of summarising statements about the musical and non-musical concerns of a lifetime.

Olivier Messiaen and Elliott Carter.

Amongst the many schools and groups of composers in the twentieth century, two major figures stand apart, Olivier Messiaen and Elliott Carter. Both born in 1908, each is an individualist of great influence and stature who has pursued his own path to a personal style of composition.

A devout Catholic, Messiaen views himself as a theological composer and music as a medium for a profound communication, celebration and contemplation of the love and mystery of God. Few of his works are liturgical but most have religious and doctrinal themes, for example *La Nativité du Seigneur* (1935) for organ and *Vingt Regards sur l'Enfant-Jésus* (1944) for piano. Messiaen was inspired to compose by hearing the music of Debussy. This influence can be particularly seen in Messiaen's flexible rhythms, sensitive scoring and use of timbre. Indeed, he identifies sounds with colours and views composition as painting. The other major early influence was that of the East, particularly Indian music. Messiaen often uses Hindu rhythmic patterns alongside Greek poetic metres, plainsong and other medieval techniques and Stravinskian devices. The sum of these can be seen in *Quatuor pour le fin du temps* for violin, clarinet, cello and piano which he composed in a prisoner of war camp in 1940. A very complex work, it reflects the primacy Messiaen gives to rhythmic control. Its overwhelming impression however is of lush and exotic sounds and textures. Similarly, the vibrant colours and rhythms of the massive *Turangalila-symphonie* (1946–8) for orchestra effectively realise the ideas of life and vitality embodied in the Sanskrit title.

After *Turangalila*, Messiaen adopted a less luxurious style. It was works such as the *Livre d'orgue* (1951) which profoundly influenced many young composers of post-war years in the use of systematic transformations of rhythm and dynamics using a system of modes in a quasi-serial fashion. For Messiaen it is the seven harmonic modes, inspired by Debussy, Liszt and the Russian "Five", which are perhaps more important because they give his music its unique sound quality.

The 1950s saw the integration of the final element crucial to Messiaen's music; birdsong. A keen ornithologist, he collected and accurately notated the songs of many birds for incorporation into compositions. *Catalogue d'oiseaux* (1951–8) is a collection of thirteen piano pieces featuring French bird songs. For Messiaen birdsong represented, "the true lost face of music", and it provided a source of inspiration for many of his major post-war works. Since 1960, his style has become simpler and less complex to the ear. To encounter the many elements of his music one can do little better than to listen to *La Transfiguration de Notre Seigneur Jésus-Christ* (1963–9) for one hundred voices, seven instrumental soloists and a large orchestra. Its subject is the mystery of God, his relationship with man and nature as a revelation of God. Messiaen draws upon all his compositional techniques in a spellbinding and overwhelming work that is a profound affirmation of faith. It is fitting that his most recent work is a vast opera (1973–83), *St François d'Assise* about the saint who is best known for his great spirituality and for gaining inspiration and insight from nature.

Carter's reputation is based on a small number of works. He has concentrated on problems of language and structure in a dramatic context unlike Messiaen's preoccupations with colour and the communication of religious truths. Carter's early works reflect a variety of influences: Stravinsky, Hindemith and the English Virginalists. He con-

sciously aimed at a simple, lyrical, accessible style, for example, in the ballet, *Pocahontas* (1938–9) and *Holiday Overture* (1944). During those war years however there occurred a change of direction. The Piano Sonata (1945–6) saw the start of a compositional style where instruments were endowed with personalities who act as protagonists in a drama. His ideas crystallised in the *String Quartet No. 1* (1950–1) after an absorbing study of the music of Ives, Cowell and African and Oriental music. It led to the use of very complex rhythmic relationships and a very tightly-knit pitch structure that could be traced back to a simple and small source, in this case a four-note chord. After this Carter refined his portrayal of his dramatis personae such that in *String Quartet No. 2* (1959) his players each have a separate personality defined by melodic material, gestures and rhythms. They converse, argue and enact that work's dramatic programme. *String Quartet No. 3* (1971) marked a shift in approach. Although the players were still "personalities", the work relied heavily on the use of contrast between strict and flexible writing between members of two duos. The *Symphony of Three Orchestras* (1975–7) and *Triple Duo* (1983) continue to explore the possibilities of simultaneous presentation of independent and sometimes unrelated processes. Carter's music makes rewarding, though not always easy, listening.

MUSIC SINCE 1945—THE AVANT GARDE

Serialism.

The early post-war years saw a renewed interest in "twelve-note techniques" otherwise known as "serialism". Composers like Stravinsky and Dallapiccola (1904–75), who had shunned serialism in earlier years, began to experiment and absorb serial techniques into their musical style. Stravinsky, for example, in works such as *Threni* (1957–8) explored ideas of varied repetition both of small ideas and large sections, in a serial context. A clear example to listen to is the fifteen-minute *Requiem Canticles* (1964–6). During the progression from its Prelude to Postlude, one can hear the piece subtly develop. The succeeding movements, and phrases within movements, slightly alter that which has gone before, evolving into something fresh.

This period also saw the emergence of a new generation of composers, keen to jettison the past and begin anew. Serialism was a favoured tool, its revival stemming from Paris, where Webern's pupil René Leibowitz was teaching, and the USA where Schoenberg had fled from Nazi Germany. The American Milton Babbitt (b. 1916) was much concerned with codifying serial techniques. His younger European contemporaries Pierre Boulez (b. 1925) and Karlheinz Stockhausen (b. 1928) sought to increase the number of musical elements that could be controlled by a predetermined method. They sought to emulate the rigorous methods of Webern, hoping to control not only pitch, but also rhythm, timbre and intensity of attack. In doing so they hoped to create an impersonal, emotionally restrained music.

Attention went first to controlling rhythm. Forerunners of this control can be seen in movement three of Berg's *Lyric Suite* and in Webern's Op.30 Variations. However, the catalyst came from Messiaen. He inspired his pupil Boulez to explore the possibilities of rhythmic and dynamic serialism in his Second Piano Sonata (1951). The performance of Messiaen's *Modes de valeurs et d'intensités* (1949) at the Darmstadt Summer School proved decisive for Stockhausen. Although not serial, the piece established scales of pitch, length of note (duration), loudness and attack. The 1950s were to see this potential for serialism taken to extremes. Boulez reached "total serialism" in *Structures Ia* for piano. However, having attained it he soon became frustrated with its restrictions. Some of the more fantastic and exotic elements of earlier works were allowed to reappear. *Le Marteau sans Maître* (1952–4) for mezzo-soprano and six instruments is a masterly setting of three surreal poems by René Char, with instrumental interludes. For the listener it is the contrasts of timbres, of flexible and regular pulsing rhythms, of sound and silence that are spellbinding. The virtuosic serial workings are hidden.

Stockhausen reached total serialism in *Kreuzspiel*

(1951) for oboe, bass clarinet, piano and percussion. Each note's pitch, length, dynamic and timbre are part of a predetermined plan. All are concerned with "Kreuzspiel" or "crossplay". Its various processes reverse or change over throughout so that at the end we have returned full circle. The effect is of clear-cut lines where each note is weighted. However, despite the intention of the composer, the effect is not unemotional, especially with the insistent throbbing of the percussion, and the piece builds to a series of climaxes before dying away. *Punkte* (points) (1952) for orchestra finds each note being treated as an isolated point of sound. It illustrates some of the problems of total serialism; often very difficult to play, it can be monotonous or lack focal points, appearing to be random rather than rigorously controlled. Stockhausen therefore transferred his attention to using not points but bursts of sound and moved towards possibly his most significant contribution to music, "moment form". There, different aspects of a note, chord or sound are suspended in eternity for contemplation and re-examination. Works became longer, slower and had a greater emphasis on colour and the effects of spatial separation, both between sounds and between their sources. *Carré* (1959–60) uses four orchestras between which chords move and evolve. Stockhausen wrote "you can confidently stop listening for a moment . . . each moment can stand on its own and at the same time is related to all the other moments". Although unifying principles in pitch content *etc.* might be present, "strict" serialism had been gently left behind, until *Mantra* (1970). This work for two pianos, percussion and two electronic ring modulators is totally based on a thirteen-note row, the mantra, with a different duration, mode of attack and dynamic for each note. These permeate the whole piece. For example, each of the thirteen sections is dominated by one of the thirteen types of attack. The work's climax is the coda where the 156 versions of the mantra used are rushed through in a few minutes. The work is important, not only as marking a return to serialism and notated music, but also in its rediscovery of melody—something unthinkable twenty years earlier.

Mathematics and Music.

The younger generation of composers have often used mathematical systems for composing which are not necessarily serial. A good example is Sir Peter Maxwell Davies (b. 1934). The use of durational ratios, ciphers and magic squares features prominently in his work, partly reflecting his interest in medieval music. A magic square is a number square where the sum of any line is the same. This becomes the basis for a composition by assigning notes to the numbers—a technique that Davies has often used since the mid-1970s. For example, in *Ave Maris Stella* (1975), each of the nine movements uses a different transformation of the square and follows a characteristic route through the square. The work is governed by the square at all levels: it even determines the precise length of each movement. Far from being a mathematical exercise however the piece shows masterly control which is particularly revealed in its drama and the beauty of its colours.

Mathematical processes of a different type have been taken up by the Greek, Xenakis (b. 1922), possibly because of his original training as an engineer and architect in France. His rejection of serialism led to the use of "stochastic" principles, derived from the mathematical laws governing probability. He also applied mathematical set theory to composition. The use of these ideas however is not audible. In *Nomos Alpha* (1965) for solo cello, for example, it is the use of contrasts, of texture, dynamic, register and timbre which give shape and form for the listener.

Chance.

Although for many serialism represented the way of reviving music after the excesses of romanticism, some looked beyond Europe to the East. John Cage (b. 1912) found inspiration there, studying Zen Buddhism in the early 1950s. By using the "chance operations" of the Chinese *I Ching* (Book of Changes) Cage brought a new radical approach to Western music. *Music of Changes* (1951) for piano is fully notated but its content is the result of operations where chance has a role. The use of "indeterminacy" or "chance" gave the performer an active role in determining the course of a piece. This might come about by providing "graphic notation"—an artist's impression of what the piece might sound like. Thus Earle Brown's *December 1952* is a visual design to be realised on any instrument as the performer sees fit. Alternatively the composer could give the performer control over the order of sections or their content. *Twenty-five pages* (1953) by Brown is for one to twenty-five pianos. Each person has twenty-five pages and may arrange them in any order before commencing. Thus music was no longer to be necessarily a progression of fixed and immutable steps to an endpoint. This and other traditional assumptions about music were challenged in Cage's most well-known outrage, *4′ 33″*. The performer does not play any notes at all. The music consists of the sounds in the environment that occur during a period of four minutes and thirty-three seconds.

In 1957, both Stockhausen and Boulez took to chance having realised that total control was an impossibility. The more rigorous the control of musical elements, the more impossible it became to realise it accurately. Stockhausen's first experiment with chance techniques was Piano Piece XI which is a single page with nineteen fragments of music. They may be played in any order but the tempo, dynamic and attack must be that shown at the end of the previous fragment. After one fragment has been played three times the work ends. Boulez's Third Piano Sonata was less free. There the choices are in the nature of varying routes through the piece. Boulez saw his music as using a form of control that is not random but akin to throwing a dice. Limited choices in the combination of instruments and their choice of lines form the basis of *Pli selon pli* (1957–65) for soprano and orchestra, offering Boulez a way "to fix the infinite".

For Stockhausen, chance has been a way to encourage performer participation and the development of "intuitive music-making". In *Prozession* (1967) for example, performers react to what is going on guided by plus or minus signs in the score which denote whether the response should be positive or negative. It has worked well in combination with the ideas behind moment form. *Stimmung* (1968) is a 45 minute meditation on one chord whose parts and overtones emerge and merge into the whole, punctuated by erotic poems, magic numbers and words which are delivered in response to chance operations. The culmination of these ideas may be seen in *Aus den Sieben Tagen* (1968) where the score for each of the seven movements is a short poem.

Use of indeterminacy does not necessarily have to be so extreme. For György Ligeti (b. 1923) and Witold Lutoslawski (b. 1913) use of controlled chance techniques has provided a way for composing atonal music without embracing serialism. During 1955–60 Lutoslawski evolved a harmonic language which used twelve-note chords for expression and colour. In 1960 he heard a performance of Cage's Piano Concerto and realised that he could use chance techniques to add a rhythmic freedom and new types of texture to his music. The exact combination of sounds at any given moment is often a matter of chance but the overall effect is planned. Textures are created by the constant repetition of small melodic ideas and simple rhythms in different parts, creating a kaleidoscope of sound, and by lines of counterpoint set off against each other, often sliding from one note to another blurring the transition between chords. The music of Lutoslawski is a fine example of the use of chance as a tool in compositions which still have strong links to tradition. The direction and drama of works such as *Mi-Parti* (1976) and his Third Symphony (1983) are firmly in the composer's hands, relying heavily on his skilful sense of harmonic movement, use of colour and proportion. Only small rhythmic details are left to chance.

Ligeti has also made use of textures created by chance operations. The contrast of such sections with fixed areas has been a way of creating large structures as in his *Requiem* (1963–5). The idea of clocks and clouds underlies several of his works of the late 1960s and 1970s: in the Double Concerto for flute, harp and orchestra (1972) we hear the transition from dense clusters or clouds of notes to regular clock-like single notes. Chance techniques have been an important element in creating these.

Electronic Music.

An important part of the post-war struggle with musical language has been the development of electronic means to generate, manipulate and record sounds. Its pioneer was the Frenchman Edgard Varèse (1883–1965). Before the war he had been an independent and radical composer much concerned with the exploration of new sounds. This had led to an emphasis on the exploitation of percussion effects in works such as *Intégrales* (1924–5) and *Ionisation* (1933). The following work *Ecuatorial* (1934) explored further, using primitive electrically generated sounds produced by two Ondes Martenot. However the catalyst for further development was the invention of the tape recorder which provided an easy means to store sounds that could then be rearranged by cutting and rejoining the tape in different ways. Varèse explored these possibilities in *Déserts* (1949–54) which alternated recorded and instrumental sounds in an atmospheric work which really seems to conjure up the aridity and emptiness of the desert. Recorded sound offered the possibility of creating illusions of aural space by technical manipulation and by judicious positioning and control of loudspeakers. This is a fundamental part of Varèse's great masterpiece, *Poème Electronique* (1958) which used soprano, chorus, bells, organs and artificial sounds. Its spatial effects were achieved by using many loudspeakers positioned around a specially designed pavilion at the 1958 Brussels Exhibition.

Generally, electronic music-making required a studio and the 1950s saw the setting up of important studios in Paris and Cologne. In Paris Pierre Schaeffer (b. 1910) pioneered "musique concrète" which used altered and rearranged natural sounds, for example, the sound of a steam train, to create a musical piece. At Cologne where Stockhausen worked, the emphasis was on creating new synthetic sounds.

Electronic music had the potential to generate complex, accurate serial structures through precise electronic operations. Boulez's studies in this however did not satisfy him and he neglected the medium until 1970 when he became Director of IRCAM (*Institut de Recherche et de Coordination Acoustique/Musique*). Stockhausen however found electronic music an ideal medium to create a musical unity far beyond that of serialism; pitch, timbre, rhythm and form could be seen as different aspects of the same thing—vibration. He did not restrict himself to pure synthetic sounds and in 1955–6 created perhaps his most well-known electronic work, *Gesang der Jünglinge*. This combines synthetic sounds with a recorded boy's voice to portray the three boys in the fiery furnace from the Book of Daniel.

With *Kontakte* (1958–60) for piano, percussion and tape, Stockhausen began an exploration of the interplay between live performers and electronic sound which still preoccupies him today. The work explores "contact" between real and artificial sounds and between the elements of music. Compared to pure electronic music, the presence of the live performers made it easier to listen to, providing a visual focus and making each performance unique. The next step was to create "live" electronic music where performers created their electronic sounds on stage. Cage had already begun this in 1960 with *Cartridge Music*. Unlike Stockhausen's first attempt, *Mikrophonie I* (1964–5), *Cartridge Music* gives much freedom to the performer in creating the electronic effects. A desire to create a world music led to one of the most vast electronic works to date, *Hymnen* (1966–7), a two-hour work for quadraphonic tape or tapes, soloists and optional symphony orchestra. Stockhausen constructed it out of national anthems from all over the world. Inspired by the occult *Urantian Book*, he became more ambitious still, seeking a galactic music. *Sirius* (1977) for four soloists and electronic music deals with the arrival on earth of four visitors from the star Sirius.

In America, developments have followed a different course. There, the use of computer synthesised sounds has been the main interest because of the computer's superior control and accuracy. It has allowed the continuation of abstract composition where complicated operations are achieved simply and effectively. Computer synthesis can also be applied to existing material. For example, *Chronometer* (1971) by Harrison Birtwistle (b. 1934) (an English composer working at that time in New York) is based on clock sounds.

Minimalism.

The transformation of existing material on tape has been a crucial part of an American movement dating from the 1960s known as 'Minimalism'. Its chief exponents are Steve Reich (b. 1936), Philip Glass (b. 1937), Terry Riley (b. 1935) and La Monte Young (b. 1935). Minimal music uses material which is limited in pitch, rhythm and timbres; the elements are subjected to simple transformations relying heavily on repetition. Of great importance are the subtle evolution from one idea to another as repetitions are modified, and the use of "phasing" techniques. Phasing is the effect of altering the rate of repetition between parts repeating the same material so that it is no longer synchronised. The effect of works such as *Drumming* (1971) by Reich may appear long and non-dramatic. However, the listener is not expected to concentrate all the time but to become aware of a piece's various elements and processes. The music's patterns will change as the listener's attention shifts from one aspect to another. As in moment form, minimalist works owe much to Indian concepts of time as a circular rather than linear phenomenon. In recent years, the minimalists have developed their style and there are greater differences between the four. Philip Glass has written four operas, *Einstein on the Beach* (1975), *Satyagraha* (1980), *Akhnaten* (1983) and *The Making of the Representative for Planet 8* (1986) while recent works by Reich such as *Desert Music* (1983) are less monochrome, exploiting bright sound colours and far from minimal forces.

Music Theatre.

During the early post-war years many composers were grappling with the tools of composition. Only more "traditional" writers such as Britten, Tippett and Hans Werner Henze (b. 1926) were engaged in writing opera. By 1970 however, most composers were including elements of theatre in their work even if they were not necessarily engaged in writing full-scale operas.

One of the major composers of "traditional" opera has been Henze. His first three operas draw heavily on the past. For example, *Boulevard Solitude* (1952) updates the story of Manon, a nineteenth-century favourite. After moving to Italy in 1953, Henze's stance appeared more traditional still as lyrical elements became more dominant in contrast to the abstract athematic style of contemporaries such as Stockhausen. Increasingly Henze's operas began to reflect his preoccupation with socialism. The *Bassarids* (1966), for example, examines through a mythological guise the precipitation of social upheaval and disruption. The oratorio *Das Floss der "Medusa"* (1968) is dedicated to Che Guevara and provoked such struggles between police and left-wing students at its premiere that Henze went to Cuba for a year. There he was inspired to write *El Cimarrón* (1969–70), a vocal monologue portraying a Cuban runaway slave accompanied by flute, guitar and percussion. For a while, Henze continued to reject the traditional opera format because of its bourgeois overtones, preferring a more intimate, chamber style. But in 1976 Henze returned to opera with *We come to the River*. It reflected a renewal of Italianate lyricism, the exploitation of opera's full potential and a less overt political message.

Luigi Nono (b. 1924) also exploited theatre for political ends, beginning with *Intolleranza* (1960). However he found greater resource than Henze in contemporary developments, taking full advantage of the opportunities offered by electronics. *Contrappunto dialettico della mente* (1967–8) includes the sounds of political demonstrations. Like Henze, Nono also returned to the opera house after a long break from large-scale opera with *Al gran sole carico d'amore* (1972–4), which consolidated the techniques he had developed in the previous decade.

"Theatre" became a dominant characteristic in the works of Luciano Berio (b. 1925). One of his most famous works is *Circles* (1960) for female voice, harp and percussion. The virtuosic technique used there and in other works was inspired by the phenomenal vocal elasticity of his then wife, Cathy Berberian. 'Circles' are depicted at many different levels in the work's structure and content. More importantly, these are underlined by the singer moving about the stage during the performance. Berio's next few works became overtly political, culminating in *Laborintus II* (1965) which was intended as an attack on capitalism via a musical collage and extracts from Dante's *Inferno*. Many of Berio's larger scale works since *Laborintus II* have been theatrical in their virtuosity and instrumental technique. For example, *Sequenza IV* (1965) demands a pianist with very agile feet. This type of dramatic gesture is much seen in Stockhausen's work, particularly those written for his own music ensemble, for example, *Solo* (1966). Since *Alphabet für Liege* (1972) his work has become increasingly theatrical and from 1978, Stockhausen has been working on an opera project *Licht*. Twenty years earlier, such a project would have been unthinkable.

The small-scale synthesis of text, music and gesture characteristic of Berio has greatly influenced British work in music theatre, notably the work of Sir Peter Maxwell Davies and Sir Harrison Birtwistle. Davies' work is very powerful particularly through its use of parody and wild use of outrageous gesture. *Vesalii Icones* (1969) uses a naked male dancer portraying parts of the Stations of the Cross and scenes from the anatomy text by Vesalius. It is a good example of parody, particularly of what Davies views as nineteenth-century grossness—it includes a vile distortion of a Victorian hymn tune which turns into a foxtrot, both played on a honky-tonk piano. Many of his works feature a single vocal soloist, with instrumental back up, who plays the part of a crazed, obsessive individual. For example, *Eight Songs for a Mad King* (1969) features the instrumentalists in giant bird cages who must suffer the mad ravings of George III played by the singer.

Davies has written two full-scale operas to date, *Taverner* (1962–8) and *The Martyrdom of St. Magnus* (1976) and is currently working on a third, *Resurrection*. *Taverner* deals with two fundamental preoccupations of Davies—the nature of faith and betrayal—and uses both musical and dramatic parody to convey its message. *St. Magnus* was written after Davies moved to Orkney. It reflects a change in style, uses only a small orchestra and is for production "in the round".

Birtwistle's first major dramatic work was a chamber opera, *Punch and Judy* (1966) which uses grotesque and violent gestures. However, while Davies' roots may lie with early Schoenberg, Birtwistle has found inspiration in the clear-cut lines and ritualism of Stravinsky. Possibly his most significant work to date is *The Mask of Orpheus* (1973–5 and 1981–3). This deals with Birtwistle's central

dramatic concern, the conflicts between the individual ego and the collective unconscious. An important aspect of the work is the use of electronics, developed at IRCAM to create atmospheric "auras", for example, "cloud" music, and six mime interludes. Crucially, Apollo gives utterance to his commands through electronic fragments which vary in length from a second to almost a minute.

The Contemporary Music Scene.

While earlier sections have already covered part of the 1980s, little mention has been made of some younger composers. It is difficult to stand back from the music of the present, but here is a brief survey of some British composers working now who deserve attention.

Brian Ferneyhough (b. 1943) is continuing to expand the chamber music repertoire using traditional structures as a framework for music in which micro-tones play an increasingly important part. He is currently working on a seven-part cycle of chamber works of which three are complete; *Superscripto* for solo piccolo (1981), *Carceri d'Invenzione I* (1982) and *Carceri d'Invenzione II* (1985) for chamber orchestra (II with solo flute). Robin Holloway (b. 1943) has also been active in composing smaller scale works, often lyrical, of which recent examples are his *Viola Concerto* (1985) and the bleak *Ballad* for harp and chamber orchestra (1985). Nigel Osborne (b. 1948) has used electronic and non-Western music in his work, gravitating recently towards vocal works. 1986 saw the premiere of his theatre piece, *Hells Angels*. Other recent operas are *Where the Wild Things Are* (1984) and *Higglety, Pigglety Pop!* (1985) by Oliver Knussen (b. 1952) which attracted acclaim for a young composer already noted for his symphonies, vocal and chamber work. Tim Souster (b. 1943) has been active in composing and promoting electronic music of all types, some influenced by rock music. A recent example is his *Quartet with Tape* (1985). Meanwhile choral music is flourishing with new works by Paul Patterson (b. 1947) which often involve new types of notation and vocal technique, and several ritualistic works by John Tavener (b. 1948), inspired by his Eastern Orthodox faith. For example *Doxa* (1982) sets a single word from the Eastern liturgy. A meteoric rise to fame has been achieved by George Benjamin (b. 1960) starting with *Ringed by the Flat Horizon* (1980) written while still at Cambridge.

The contemporary scene is varied, exciting and constantly changing. It is well worth exploring both for itself and because it speaks to us as the music of our time.

II. GLOSSARY OF MUSICAL TERMS

A. Note of scale, commonly used for tuning instruments.

Absolute Music. Music without any literary descriptive or other kind of reference.

A Capella. Literally "in the church style." Unaccompanied.

Accelerando. Quickening of the pace.

Accidental. The sign which alters the pitch of a note; ♯ (sharp) raises and a ♭ (flat) lowers note by one semitone, ✕ (double sharp) and ♭♭ (double flat) alter by two semitones.

Accompaniment. Instrumental or piano part forming background to a solo voice or instrument that has the melody.

Ad lib. (L. *ad libitum*). Direction on music that strict time need not be observed.

Adagio. A slow movement or piece.

Aeolian mode. One of the scales in mediaeval music, represented by the white keys of the piano from A to A.

Air. A simple tune for voice or instrument.

Alberti Bass. Characteristic 18th century keyboard figuration derived by splitting chord(s) of an accompanying part. Tradition credits Alberti as its inventor.

Allegretto. Not quite so fast as *Allegro*.

Allegro. Fast, but not too fast.

Alto. An unusually high type of male voice; also the vocal part sung by women and boys with a low range.

Ambrosian Chant. Plainsong introduced into church music by St. Ambrose, bishop of Milan (d. 397), and differing from Gregorian chant.

Andante. At a walking pace, not so slow as *Adagio* nor as fast as *Allegretto*.

Animato. Lively.

Answer. Entry in a fugue or invention which imitates or "answers" the theme at a different pitch.

Anthem. Composition for use in church during a service by a choir with or without soloists.

Antiphonal. Using groups of instruments or singers placed apart.

Appoggiatura. An ornament consisting of a short note just above or below a note forming part of a chord.

Arabesque. Usually a short piece, highly decorated.

Arco. Direction for string instruments to play with bow.

Aria. Vocal solo, usually in opera or oratorio, often in three sections with the third part being a repeat of the first. An *Arietta* is a shorter, lighter kind of aria.

Arioso. In the style of an aria; halfway between aria and recitative.

Arpeggio. Notes of a chord played in a broken, spread-out manner, as on a harp.

Ars antiqua. The old mediaeval music, based on organum and plainsong, before the introduction of *Ars nova* in 14th cent.

Ars Nova. New style of composition in 14th century France and Italy. It has greater variety in rhythm and independence in part-writing.

Atonal. Not in any key; hence *Atonality*.

Aubade. Morning song.

Augmentation. The enlargement of a melody by lengthening the musical value of its notes.

Ayre. Old spelling of *air*.

B. Note of scale, represented in Germany by *H*.

Bagatelle. A short, generally light piece of music. Beethoven wrote 26 Bagatelles.

Ballad. Either a narrative song or an 18th-cent. drawing-room song.

Ballade. A substantial and dramatic work, often for piano. Notable examples are by Chopin and Brahms.

Ballet. Stage entertainment requiring intrumental accompaniment; originated at French court in 16th and 17th cent.

Bar. A metrical division of music; the perpendicular line in musical notation to indicate this.

Barcarolle. A boating-song, in particular one associated with Venetian gondoliers.

Baritone. A male voice, between tenor and bass.

Baroque. A term applied, loosely, to music written in the 17th and 18th cent., roughly corresponding to baroque in architecture.

Bass. The lowest male voice; lowest part of a composition.

Bass Drum. Largest of the drum family, placed upright and struck on the side.

Bassoon. The lowest of the woodwind instruments, uses double reed.

Beat. Music's rhythmic pulse.

Bel canto. Literally "beautiful singing"—in the old Italian style with pure tone and exact phrasing.

Berceuse. Cradle song.

Binary. A piece in two sections is said to be binary in form. The balance is obtained by a second phrase (or section) answering the first.

Bitonality. Use of two keys at once.

Bow. Stick with horsehair stretched across it for playing string instruments.

Brass. Used as a collective noun for all brass or metal instruments.

Breve. Note, rarely used nowadays, with time value of two semibreves.

Bridge. Wood support over which strings are stretched on a violin, cello, guitar, etc.

Buffo(a). Comic, as in *buffo bass* or *opera buffa*.

C. Note of scale.

Cabaletta. Final, quick section of an aria or duet.

Cadence. A closing phrase of a composition or a passage, coming to rest on tonic (key note).

Cadenza. Solo vocal or instrumental passage, either written or improvised, giving soloist chance to display technical skill to audience.

Calando. Becoming quieter and slower.

Canon. A piece or section of music resulting from one line of music being repeated imitatively in the other parts which enter in succession.

Cantabile. Song-like, therefore flowing and expressive.

Cantata. Vocal work for chorus and/or choir.

Cantilena. Sustained, smooth melodic line.

Cantus firmus. Literally "fixed song." Basic melody from 14th to 17th cent., around which other voices wove contrapuntal parts.

Canzonet. Light songs written in England *c.* 1600.

Carillon. A set of bells in tower of church, played from a keyboard below.

Carol. Christmas song.

Castrato. Artificially-created male soprano and alto, fashionable in 17th and 18th cent. (The castration of vocally gifted boys prevailed in Italy until the 19th cent.)

Catch. A part-song like a round, in vogue in England from 16th to 19th cent.

Cavatina. An operatic song in one section, or a slow song-like instrumental movement.

Celesta. Keyboard instrument with metal bars struck by hammers.

Cello. Four-stringed instrument, played with bow, with a bass range. Comes between viola and double bass in string family.

Cembalo. Originally the Italian name for the dulcimer, but sometimes applied to the harpsichord.

Chaconne. Vocal or instrumental piece with unvaried bass.

Chamber Music. Music originally intended to be played in a room for three or more players.

Chanson. Type of part-song current in France from 14th to 16th cent.

Chant. Singing of psalms, masses, etc., in plainsong to Latin words in church.

Choir. Body of singers, used either in church or at concerts.

Chorales. German hymn tunes, often made use of by Bach.

Chord. Any combination of notes heard together. *See also* Triad.

Chording. Spacing of intervals in a chord.

Chorus. Substantial body of singers, usually singing in four parts.

Chromatic. Using a scale of nothing but semitones.

Clarinet. Woodwind instrument with single reed in use since mid-18th cent.

Clavichord. Keyboard instrument having strings struck by metal tangents, much in use during 17th and 18th cent. as solo instrument.

Clavier. Used in German (*Klavier*) for piano, in England for any stringed keyboard instrument.

Clef. Sign in stave that fixes place of each note.

Coda. Closing section of movement in Sonata form.

Coloratura. Term to denote florid singing.

Common chord. See Triad.

Common Time. Four crotchets to the bar, 4/4 time.

Compass. Range of notes covered by voice or instruments.

Composition. Piece of music, originated by a composer's own imagination; act of writing such a piece.

Compound Time. Metre where beats are sub-divided into threes rather than twos.

Con Brio. With dash.

Concert. Public performance of any music.

Concertato. Writing for several solo instruments to be played together.

Concerto. Work for one or more solo instruments and orchestra.

Concerto grosso. Orchestral work common in 17th and 18th cent. with prominent parts for small groups of instruments.

Concord. Opposite of discord, *i.e.,* notes that when sounded together satisfy the ear. (Conventional term in that its application varies according to the age in which one lives.)

Conduct. To direct a concert with a baton.

Consecutive. Progression of harmonic intervals of like kind.

Consonance. Like Concord.

Continuo. Bass line in 17th and 18th century music. Played by a bass instrument and keyboard, the latter improvising on the indicated harmonies.

Contralto. A woman's voice with a low range.

Counterpoint. Simultaneous combination of two or more melodies to create a satisfying musical texture. Where one melody is added to another, one is called the other's counterpoint. The adjective of counterpoint is contrapuntal.

Counter-tenor. Another name for male alto.

Courante. A dance in triple time.

Crescendo. Getting louder.

Crook. Detachable section of tubing on brass instruments that change the tuning.

Crotchet. Note that equals two quavers in time value.

Cycle. Set of works, especially songs, intended to be sung as group.

Cyclic form. Form of work in two or more movements in which the same musical themes recur.

Cymbal. Percussion instrument; two plates struck against each other.

D. Note of scale.

Da Capo (abbr. D.C.). A *Da Capo* aria is one in which the whole first section is repeated after a contrasting middle section.

Descant. Additional part (sometimes improvised) sung against a melody.

Development. Working-out section of movement in sonata form. *See* Sonata.

Diatonic. Opposite of chromatic; using proper notes of a major or minor scale.

Diminished. Lessened version of perfect interval, e.g., semitone less than a perfect fifth is a diminished fifth.

Diminuendo. Lessening.

Diminution. Reducing a phrase of melody by shortening time value of notes.

Discord. Opposite of concord, *i.e.,* notes that sounded together produce a clash of harmonies.

Dissonance. Like discord.

Divertimento. A piece, usually orchestral, in several movements; like a suite.

Dodecaphonic. Pertaining to 12-note method of composition.

Dominant. Fifth note of major or minor scale above tonic (key) note.

Dorian Mode. One of the scales in mediaeval music, represented by the white keys on the piano from D to D.

Dot. Placed over note indicates staccato; placed after note indicates time value to be increased by half.

Double bar. Two upright lines marking the end of a composition or a section of it.

Double bass. Largest and lowest instrument of violin family; played with bow.

Drone bass. Unvarying sustained bass, similar to the permanent bass note of a bagpipe.

Drum. Variety of percussion instruments on which sound is produced by hitting a skin stretched tightly over a hollow cylinder or hemisphere.

Duet. Combination of two performers; composition for such a combination.

Duple Time. Metre in which there are two beats to a bar.

Dynamics. Gradations of loudness or softness in music.

E. Note of scale.

Electronic. Term used to describe use of electronic sounds in music.

Encore. Request from audience for repeat of work, or extra item in a programme.

English horn (*Cor anglais*). Woodwind instrument with double reed of oboe family.

Enharmonic. Refers to use of different letter names for the same note, *e.g.* F and E♯. Often exploited to achieve modulation between distantly related keys.

Ensemble. Teamwork in performance; item in opera for several singers with or without chorus; a group of performers of no fixed number.

Episode. Section in composition usually divorced from main argument.

Exposition. Setting out of thematic material in a sonata-form composition.

Expression marks. Indication by composer of how he wants his music performed.

F. Note of scale.

False relation. A clash of harmony produced when two notes, such as A natural and A flat, are played simultaneously or immediately following one another.

Falsetto. The kind of singing by male voices above normal register and sounding like an unbroken voice.

Fanfare. Flourish of trumpets.

Fantasy. A piece suggesting free play of composer's imagination, or a piece based on known tunes (folk, operatic, etc.).

Fermata. Pause indicated by sign ⌒ prolonging note beyond its normal length.

Fifth. Interval taking five steps in the scale. A perfect fifth (say, C to G) includes three whole tones and a semitone; a diminished fifth is a semitone less, an augmented fifth a semitone more.

Figure. A short phrase, especially one that is repeated.

Fingering. Use of fingers to play instrument, or the indication above notes to show what fingers should be used.

Flat. Term indicating a lowering of pitch by a semitone, or to describe a performer playing under the note.

Florid. Term used to describe decorative passages.

Flute. Woodwind instrument, blown sideways. It is played through a hole, not a reed. Nowadays, sometimes made of metal.

Folksong. Traditional tune, often in different versions, handed down aurally from generation to generation.

Form. Course or layout of a composition, especially when in various sections.

Fourth. Interval taking four steps in scale. A perfect fourth (say, C to F) includes two whole tones and a semitone. If either note is sharpened or flattened the result is an augmented or a diminished fourth.

Fugato. In the manner of a fugue.

Fugue. Contrapuntal composition for various parts based on one or more subjects treated imitatively but not strictly.

G. Note of scale.

Galant. Used to designate elegant style of 18th-cent. music.

Galliard. Lively dance dating back to 15th cent. or before.

Gavotte. Dance in 4/4 time, beginning on third beat in bar.

Giusto. Strict, proper.

Glee. Short part-song.

Glissando. Rapid sliding scales up and down piano or other instruments.

Glockenspiel. Percussion instrument consisting of tuned steel bars and played with two hammers or keyboard.

Grace note. See Ornament.

Grave. In slow tempo.

Grazioso. Gracefully.

Gregorian Chant. Plainsong collected and supervised mainly by Pope Gregory (d. 604).

Ground Bass. A bass part that is repeated throughout a piece with varying material on top.

Guitar. Plucked string instrument of Spanish origin, having six strings of three-octave compass.

H. German note-symbol for *B.*

Harmony. Simultaneous sounding of notes so as to make musical sense.

Harp. Plucked string instrument of ancient origin, the strings stretched parallel across its frame. The basic scale of C flat major is altered by a set of pedals.

Harpsichord. Keyboard stringed instrument played by means of keyboard similar to a piano but producing its notes by a plucking, rather than a striking action.

Homophonic. Opposite of polyphonic, *i.e.*, indicated parts move together in a composition, a single melody being accompanied by block chords, as distinct from the contrapuntal movement of different melodies.

Horn. Brass instrument with coiled tubes. Valves introduced in 19th cent. made full chromatic use of instrument possible.

Hymn. Song of praise, especially in church.

Imitation. Repetition, exactly, or at least recognisably, of a previously heard figure.

Impromptu. A short, seemingly improvised piece of music, especially by Schubert or Chopin.

Improvise. To perform according to fancy or imagination, sometimes on a given theme.

In alt. The octave above the treble clef; *in altissimo,* octave above that.

Instrumentation. Writing music for particular instruments, using the composer's knowledge of what sounds well on different instruments.

Interlude. Piece played between two sections of a composition.

Intermezzo. Formerly meant interlude, now often used for pieces played between acts of operas.

Interval. Distance in pitch between notes.

Ionian mode. One of the scales in mediaeval music, represented on piano by white keys between C and C, identical therefore to modern C major scale.

Isorhythmic. Medieval technique using repetitions of a rhythm but with different notes. Much used in 15th century motets.

Jig. Old dance usually in 6/8 or 12/8 time.

Kettledrum (It. pl. *Timpani*). Drum with skin drawn over a cauldron-shaped receptacle, can be tuned to definite pitch by turning handles on rim, thus tightening or relaxing skin.

Key. Lever by means of which piano, organ, etc., produces note; classification, in relatively modern times, of notes of a scale. Any piece of music in major or minor is in the *key* of its tonic or keynote.

Keyboard. Term used to describe instruments with a continuous row of keys.

Key-signature. Indication on written music, usually at the beginning of each line, of the number of flats or sharps in the key of a composition.

Kitchen Department. Humorous term for percussion section of an orchestra.

Lament. Musical piece of sad or deathly significance.

Largamente. Spaciously.

Largo. Slow.

Leading-motive (Ger. *Leitmotiv*). Short theme, suggesting person, idea, or image, quoted throughout composition to indicate that person, etc.

Legato. In a smooth style (of performance, etc.).

Lento. Slow.

Libretto. Text of an opera.

Lied (pl. *Lieder*). Song, with special reference to songs by Schubert, Schumann, Brahms, and Wolf.

Lute. String instrument plucked with fingers, used in 15th- and 16th-cent. music especially.

Lydian mode. One of the scales in mediaeval music, represented by white keys of piano between F and F.

Lyre. Ancient Greek plucked string instrument.

Madrigal. Contrapuntal composition for several voices, especially prominent from 15th to 17th cent.

Maestoso. Stately.

Major. One of the two main scales of the tonal system with semitones between the third and fourth, and the seventh and eighth notes. Identical with 16th-cent. Ionian mode.

Mandolin(e). Plucked string instrument of Italian origin.

Manual. A keyboard for the hands, used mostly in connection with the organ.

Master of the King's (or Queen's) Musick. Title of British court appointment, with no precise duties.

Melisma. Group of notes sung to a single syllable.

Mélodie. Literally a melody or tune; has come to mean a French song (cf. German *Lied*).

Metronome. Small machine in use since the beginning of the 18th cent., to determine the pace of any composition by the beats of the music, *e.g.*, = 60 at the head of the music indicates sixty crotchets to the minute.

Mezzo, Mezza. (It. = "half") *Mezza voce* means using the half voice (a tone between normal singing and whispering). *Mezzo-soprano*, voice between soprano and contralto.

Minim. Note that equals two crotchets in time value.

Minor. One of the two main scales of the tonal system (cf. major), identical with 16th-cent. Aeolian mode. It has two forms—the harmonic and melodic, the former having a sharpened seventh note, the latter having the sixth and seventh note not sharpened.

Minuet. Originally French 18th-cent. dance in triple time, then the usual third movement in symphonic form (with a contrasting trio section) until succeeded by scherzo.

Mixolydian mode. One of the mediaeval scales represented by the white keys on the piano from G to G.

Modes. Scales prevalent in the Middle Ages. *See* Aeolian, Dorian, Ionian, Lydian, Mixolydian, Phrygian.

Modulate. Changing from key to key in a composition, not directly but according to musical "grammar".

Molto. Much, very; thus *allegro molto*.

Motet. Sacred, polyphonic vocal composition. More loosely, any choral composition for use in church but not set to words of the liturgy.

Motive, motif. Short, easily recognised melodic figure.

Motto. Short, well-defined theme recurring throughout a composition, cf. *Idée fixe* in Berlioz's *Symphonie Fantastique*.

Movement. Separate sections of a large-scale composition, each in its own form.

Music drama. Term used to describe Wagner's, and sometimes other large-scale operas.

Mutes. Devices used to damp the sound of various instruments.

Natural (of a note or key). Not sharp or flat.

Neoclassical. Clear-cut style, originating during 1920s, that uses 17th and 18th century forms and styles. It constituted a reaction to the excesses of romanticism.

Ninth. Interval taking nine steps, *e.g.*, from C upwards an octave and a whole tone to D.

Nocturne. Literally a "night-piece" hence usually of lyrical character.

Nonet. Composition for nine instruments.

Notation. Act of writing down music.

Note. Single sound of specified pitch and duration; symbol to represent this.

Obbligato. Instrumental part having a special or essential rôle in a piece.

Oboe. Woodwind instrument with double reed, descended from hautboy; as such, in use since 16th cent., in modern form since 18th cent.

Octave. Interval taking eight steps of scale, with top and bottom notes having same "name"; C to C is an octave.

Octet. Composition for eight instruments or voices.

Ondes Martenot. Belongs to a class of melodic instruments in which the tone is produced by electrical vibrations controlled by the movement of the hands not touching the instrument.

Opera. Musical work for the stage with singing characters, originated *c.* 1600 in Italy.

Opera buffa (It.), *Opéra bouffe* (Fr.). Comic opera (in the English sense), *not* to be confused with *Opéra comique* (Fr.) which is opera with spoken dialogue and need not be humorous.

Opera seria. Chief operatic form of 17th and 18th cent., usually set to very formal librettos, concerning gods or heroes of ancient history.

Operetta. Lighter type of opera.

Opus (abbr. *Op.*). With number following *opus* indicates order of a composer's composition.

Oratorio. Vocal work, usually for soloists and choir with instrumental accompaniment, generally with setting of a religious text.

Orchestra. Term to designate large, or largish, body of instrumentalists originated in 17th cent.

Orchestration. Art of setting out work for instruments of an orchestra. To be distinguished from *Instrumentation* (q.v.).

Organ. Elaborate keyboard instrument in which air is blown through pipes by bellows to sound notes. Tone is altered by selection of various stops and, since the 16th cent., a pedal keyboard has also been incorporated.

Organum. In mediaeval music a part sung as an accompaniment below or above the melody of plainsong, usually at the interval of a fourth or fifth; also, loosely, this method of singing in parts.

Ornament. Notes that are added to a given melody by composer or performer as an embellishment.

Overture. Instrumental introduction or prelude to larger work, usually opera. Concert overtures are simply that: *i.e.*, work to be played at start of a concert.

Part. Music of one performer in an ensemble; single strand in a composition.

Part-song. Vocal composition in several parts.

Passacaglia. Composition in which a tune is constantly repeated, usually in the bass.

Passage. Section of a composition.

Passion. Musical setting of the New Testament story of Christ's trial and crucifixion.

Pastiche. Piece deliberately written in another composer's style.

Pavan(e). Moderately paced dance dating from 16th cent. or earlier.

Pedal. Held note in bass of composition.

Pentatonic. Scale of five consecutive notes, *e.g.*, the black keys of the piano.

Percussion. Collective title for instruments of the orchestra that are sounded by being struck by hand or stick.

Phrygian Mode. One of the scales of mediaeval music, represented by the white keys on piano from E to E.

Piano. Soft, abbr. *p*; *pp = pianissimo*, very soft; instrument, invented in 18th cent., having strings struck by hammer, as opposed to the earlier harpsichord where they are plucked. The modern piano has 88 keys and can be either "upright" (vertical) or "grand" (horizontal).

Pianoforte. Almost obsolete full Italian name for the piano.

Pitch. Exact height or depth of a particular musical sound or note.

Pizzicato. Direction for stringed instruments, that the strings should be plucked instead of bowed.

Plainchant, Plainsong. Mediaeval church music

consisting of single line of melody without harmony or definite rhythm.

Polka. Dance in 2/4 time originating in 19th cent. Bohemia.

Polonaise. Polish dance generally in 3/4 time.

Polyphony. Combination of two or more musical lines as in *counterpoint*.

Polytonality. Simultaneous use of several keys.

Postlude. Closing piece, opposite of Prelude.

Prelude. Introductory piece.

Presto. Very fast. *Prestissimo.* Still faster.

Progression. Movement from one chord to next to make musical sense.

Quartet. Work written for four instruments or voices; group to play or sing such a work.

Quaver. Note that equals two semiquavers or half a crotchet.

Quintet. Work written for five instruments or voices; group to play or sing such a work.

Rallentando. Slowing down.

Recapitulation. Section of composition that repeats original material in something like its original form.

Recitative. Term used for declamation in singing written in ordinary notation but allowing rhythmical licence.

Recorder. Woodwind instrument, forerunner of flute.

Reed. Vibrating tongue of woodwind instruments.

Register. Set of organ pipes controlled by a particular stop; used in reference to different ranges of instrument or voice (*e.g.*, chest register).

Relative. Term used to indicate common key signature of a major and minor key.

Répétiteur. Member of opera house's musical staff who coaches singers in their parts.

Rest. Notation of pauses for instrument in composition, having a definite length like a note.

Retrograde. Term used to describe a melody played backwards.

Rhapsody. Work of no definite kind with a degree of romantic content.

Rhythm. Everything concerned with the time of music (*i.e.*, beats, accent, metre, etc.) as opposed to the pitch side.

Ritornello. Passage, usually instrumental, that recurs in a piece.

Romance, Romanza. Title for piece of vague song-like character.

Romantic. Term used vaguely to describe music of 19th cent. that has other than purely musical source of inspiration.

Rondo. Form in which one section keeps on recurring.

Rubato. Manner of performing a piece without keeping strictly to time.

Sackbut. Early English name for trombone.

Saxophone. Classified as wind instrument, although made of brass, because it uses a reed.

Scale. Progression of adjoining notes upwards or downwards.

Scherzo. Literally "a joke". Often used as a light movement in the middle of a sonata type work.

Score. Copy of any music written in several parts.

Second. Interval taking two steps in scale, *e.g.*, C to D flat, or to D.

Semibreve. Note that equals two minims or half a breve.

Semiquaver. Note that equals half a quaver.

Semitone. Smallest interval commonly used in Western music.

Septet. Composition for seven instruments or voices.

Sequence. Repetition of phrase at a higher or lower pitch.

Serenade. Usually an evening song or instrumental work.

Seventh. Interval taking seven steps in the scale.

Sextet. Composition for six instruments or voices.

Sharp. Term indicating a raising of pitch by a semitone.

Shawm. Primitive woodwind instrument, forerunner of oboe.

Simple time. Division of music into two or four beats.

Sinfonietta. Small symphony.

Sixth. Interval taking six steps in the scale.

Solo. Piece or part of a piece for one performer playing or singing alone.

Sonata. Term to denote a musical form and a type of composition. In *sonata form* a composition is divided into exposition, development and recapitulation. A *sonata* is a piece, usually for one or more players following that form.

Song. Any short vocal composition.

Soprano. Highest female voice.

Sostenuto. Sustained, broadly.

Sotto voce. Whispered, scarcely audible, applied to vocal as well as instrumental music.

Spinet. A small keyboard instrument belonging to the harpsichord (*q.v.*) family.

Sprechgesang. (Ger. Speech-song.) Vocal utterance somewhere between speech and song.

Staccato. Perform music in short, detached manner.

Staff. Horizontal lines on which music is usually written.

Stop. Lever by which organ registration can be altered.

String(s). Strands of gut or metal set in vibration to produce musical sounds on string or keyboard instruments. Plural refers to violins, violas, cellos, and basses of orchestra.

Study. Instrumental piece, usually one used for technical exercise or to display technical skills, but often having artistic merits as well (*e.g.*, Chopin's).

Subject(s). Theme or group of notes that forms principal idea or ideas in composition.

Suite. Common name for piece in several movements.

Symphony. Orchestral work of serious purpose usually in four movements, occasionally given name (*e.g.*, Beethoven's "Choral" symphony).

Syncopation. Displacement of musical accent.

Tempo. Pace, speed of music.

Tenor. Highest normal male voice.

Ternary. A piece in three sections is said to be in ternary form. The balance is obtained by repeating the first phrase or section (though it need not be exact or complete) after a second of equal importance.

Tessitura. Compass into which voice or instrument comfortably falls.

Theme. Same as *subject* but can also be used for a whole musical statement as in "theme and variations."

Third. Interval taking three steps in scale.

Time. Rhythmical division of music.

Timpani. See Kettledrum.

Toccata. Instrumental piece usually needing rapid, brilliant execution.

Tonality. Key, or feeling for a definite key.

Tone. Quality of musical sound; interval of two semitones.

Tonic Sol-fa. System of musical notation to simplify sight-reading.

Transcribe. Arrange piece for different medium, instrument, or voice than that originally intended.

Transition. Passage that joins two themes or sections of a composition.

Transpose. To move a musical idea, theme or piece to a different key from its original.

Treble. Highest part in vocal composition; high boy's voice.

Triad. Three note chord. Usually consists of a note and those a third and fifth above.

Trio. Work written for three instruments or voices; group to play or sing such a work.

Trombone. Brass instrument with slide adjusting length of tube.

Trumpet. Metal instrument of considerable antiquity; modern version has three valves to make it into a chromatic instrument.

Tuba. Deepest-toned brass instrument with three or four valves.

Twelve-note. Technique of composition using full chromatic scale with each note having equal importance. Notes are placed in particular order as the thematic basis of works.

Unison. Two notes sung or played together at same pitch.

Valve. Mechanism, invented in early 19th cent. to add to brass instruments allowing them to play full chromatic scale.

Variation. Varied passage of original theme. Such variations may be closely allied to or depart widely from the theme.

Verismo. Term to describe Italian operas written in "realist" style at the turn of this century.

Vibrato. Rapid fluctuation in pitch of voice or instrument. Exaggerated it is referred to as a "wobble" (of singers) or tremolo.

Viol. String instrument of various sizes in vogue until end of 17th cent.

Viola. Tenor instrument of violin family.

Violin. Musical four-string instrument, played with bow, of violin family, which superseded viol at beginning of 18th cent.

Virginals. English keyboard instrument, similar to harpsichord of 17th and 18th cent.

Vivace. Lively.

Voluntary. Organ piece for church use, but not during service.

Waltz. Dance in triple time, fashionable in 19th cent.

Whole-tone scale. Scale progressing by whole tones. Only two are possible, one beginning on C, the other on C sharp.

Xylophone. Percussion instrument with series of wood bars tuned in a chromatic scale and played with sticks.

Zither. String instrument laid on knees and plucked. Common in Central-European folk music.

III. INDEX TO COMPOSERS

IV. SPECIAL TOPIC

THE MUSIC OF MOZART

"Before God and as an honest man, I tell you that your son is the greatest composer known to me either in person or by name." Haydn made this famous comment to Mozart's father in 1785 on hearing three of the six string quartets which Mozart later dedicated to him. Two hundred years after Mozart's death we live in a culture which is rightly distrustful of absolute value-judgements, and whose musical perspective has been extended in both time and space. The 19th and 20th centuries have produced composers of extraordinary stature, and we can now look back through the centuries before Mozart and appreciate a wealth of music of the highest quality (even the music of J. S. Bach was scarcely known in the later 18th century except to *cognoscenti*). We are now increasingly aware that Europe does not possess the only valid musical culture: recognition of the technical and expressive qualities (and the variety) of non-Western music introduces a necessary relativism into our judgements and assumptions. And yet, with all these qualifications, we do not consider Haydn's comment inappropriate. Musicians and music-lovers go back time and again to Mozart's music and find it constantly refreshing, intellectually and emotionally; we respond to both his greatness and his humanity.

Mozart's Life

Wolfgang Amadeus Mozart was born in 1756 in Salzburg. His father was Leopold Mozart (1719–1787), a violinist in the employment of the Prince-Archbishop of Salzburg and the author of an important treatise on violin-playing. Wolfgang's outstanding musical gifts became evident very early: at the age of six he was a keyboard virtuoso and had begun composing. A good deal of his childhood and adolescence was spent touring Europe as a performer. In 1762 with his father and sister Maria Anna ("Nannerl") he visited Munich and Vienna; between 1763 and 1766 the three of them undertook a tour of Germany, Paris and London (in the course of which they played before French and English royalty, and Wolfgang met J. C. Bach, a composer whose Italianate style greatly influenced him). Visits to Italy took place in 1769–71, 1771 and 1772; his operas *Mitridate* (1770) and *Lucio Silla* (1772) were successfully premiered in Milan. He returned to Vienna in 1773 and to Munich in 1774–75.

The years from 1775 to 1777 were spent in Salzburg, where Mozart like his father was employed by the Archbishop. He was an important figure in the musical life of the town, but his horizons were not those of a provincial musician. He went on a European tour in 1777–79, this time with his mother, hoping to find a post worthy of his ability, but nothing was forthcoming. They visited Munich, Mannheim (an important musical centre) and Paris, where his mother died; Mozart thereupon returned unwillingly to Salzburg, where he took up a post (arranged by his father) as court organist. His opera *Idomeneo*, commissioned by the Elector of Bavaria, was premiered in Munich in 1781; in March Mozart returned thence to Vienna where the Archbishop was at the time resident. Relations between Mozart and his employer were not good: Mozart felt restricted and resentful of his status as a servant; the Archbishop took a poor view of his constant requests for leave. The situation culminated in the famous incident of May 1781 when Mozart offered his resignation and after an argument with the Archbishop was literally thrown out.

Mozart spent the final decade of his life as a freelance musician in Vienna. This should not be seen as a romantic artist's bid for freedom—he would have welcomed a worthwhile court appointment, and he did accept a poorly paid and undemanding post at the imperial court in 1787. It was during this last decade that Mozart's genius flowered to the full, despite professional disappointments and the financial problems which plagued him.

Significant dates in his personal life are 1782, when he married, 1785, when he became a free-mason, and 1787, when his father died (an event which commentators of a Freudian cast of mind have associated with the composition in that year of the opera *Don Giovanni*). Outstanding musical achievements were the great series of piano concertos, many of them composed between 1784 and 1786 for Mozart himself to play; the two German operas *Die Entführung aus dem Serail* (1782) and *Die Zauberflöte* (1791)—the latter full of masonic symbolism—and the three Italian operas *Le Nozze di Figaro* (1786), *Don Giovanni* (1787)—a remarkable combination of serious and comic—and *Così fan tutte* (1790); chamber music, notably string quartets and quintets; and symphonies—the "Prague" Symphony of 1786 and the three written in 1788.

In 1789 Mozart visited Leipzig and Berlin; in Leipzig he was able to study music by J. S. Bach, some of whose works he had already got to know in 1782. In July 1791 he received an anonymous commission to compose a requiem; illness prevented its completion, and Mozart died early on 5 December 1791. The cause of his death has been variously ascribed to kidney failure and to rheumatic fever; there seems to be no evidence to support the idea that he was poisoned by the court composer Salieri. His burial in a pauper's grave was less unusual than romantic mythology would have it; likewise, contrary to popular belief, the weather at his funeral was mild.

The Music

If we seek to characterise Mozart's greatness in one word, that word must be "universality"; and this can be appreciated under three related aspects. Firstly, he absorbed and synthesised the various styles current at the time. From an early age his travels had given him first-hand contact with the whole world of European music; and he was able not only to write music to suit a particular national taste—as in the "Paris" Symphony of 1778—but to transcend national styles in a musical language of richness and flexibility. His absorption of influences extends also to music of the past—to the late baroque music of Handel and Bach which so excited him when he encountered it, and which left its mark in, for example, Donna Elvira's forceful aria "Ah fuggi il traditor" from *Don Giovanni* and the chorale of the Armed Men from *Die Zauberflöte*.

Secondly Mozart was a master of all the major musical genres of his time. The supreme exponent of opera and concerto in the classical period, he also composed some of the greatest symphonies, instrumental and chamber works of that or any era; and, while his output of church music written for Salzburg is often at the level of brilliance rather than depth, there are two powerful later sacred works, both unfinished: the C minor Mass, composed on the occasion of his marriage, and taking in an astonishing variety of musical styles, and the awe-inspiring Requiem.

Thirdly, the emotional and expressive range of Mozart's music is extraordinary. If the qualities of melodiousness, formal balance and technical perfection are still those popularly associated with Mozart, it is worth remembering that in his time his music was often thought to be over-complex, over-emotional and "difficult"—indeed, there are passages which still strike us now as strange and "advanced", like the opening of the C major String Quartet K.465. Frequently in Mozart an apparently serene or light-hearted surface only partly conceals disturbed emotional depths, and an unexpected turn of phrase or harmony may cast an expressive or dramatic shadow over the prevailing mood. Emotional ambiguity is characteristic of Mozart, as are shifts of mood, sometimes direct, often subtle. His operatic music, of course, offers many instances: consider, for example, the beginning of the duet between Susanna and the Count in Act III of *Le Nozze di Figaro* ("Crudel, perchè"), with its subtle reflection of the text, or on a larger scale the sextet from Act II of *Don Giovanni* ("Sola, sola in bujo loco") in which the action moves forward and the different characters express their feelings and reactions all within a convincing musical continuity. But the orchestral and instrumental music—so often imbued with the same dramatic sense as the operas—is equally rich in such qualities: the first movement of the Symphony No. 41 offers a variety of moods and a wealth of ideas which would be bewildering were they not held together in a strong structural framework. It is, of course, this marriage of form and content which makes Mozart essentially a classical composer. Form is not imposed but is organic to the individual work; emotion, however strong, is controlled, and the effect is all the more powerful as a consequence.

Tragedy and Humour

There is a serious, intense and passionate side to Mozart's musical character; there is tragedy and deep melancholy. These aspects come to the fore in the great minor key works: in G minor, the Symphony No. 40 and the String Quintet K.516; in D minor, the String Quartet K.421, the Piano Concerto No. 20, and parts of *Don Giovanni* and the Requiem; in C minor, the Wind Serenade K.388, the Fantasia and Sonata for piano, K.457 and 475, and the Piano Concerto No. 24. There is also good humour, wit, a sense of fun, and *joie de vivre*. The D minor Piano Concerto, an intense and sometimes brooding work, ends by sweeping aside the minor mode with a genial major key transformation of one of its themes. The finale of the Symphony No. 41 contains in its coda an exuberant demonstration of contrapuntal skill when five themes from earlier in the movement are combined. Many passages from the operas—Leporello's "catalogue" aria in *Don Giovanni*, in which he lists his master's amorous conquests; the famous "Non più andrai" from *Le Nozze di Figaro*, sending the page-boy Cherubino off to the army; the music for Papageno and Papagena in *Die Zauberflöte*, to mention only three very different examples—show Mozart's sharp yet understanding humour; while the final pages of, for instance, *Figaro* and *Die Zauberflöte* are guaranteed to send the audience away with a sense of delight and well-being. But these operas contain much more than comedy—a whole gamut of emotions and reactions is explored, and the overwhelming impression, despite the artificialities and complications of plot, are of "truth to life", achieved through Mozart's superb musical characterisation.

Mastery of Instrumentation

An aspect of Mozart's music which should not go unremarked is the actual sound of it. One expects, of course, a mastery of orchestration, and this is everywhere in evidence, in the symphonies, concertos and operas. There is great resourcefulness in, for example, the combination and interplay of wind instruments, strings and piano in works like the two C major piano concertos (Nos. 21 and 25)—the slow movement of the first of these being particularly beautiful and justly popular. Mozart's orchestral writing is full of interesting and imaginative touches, such as the clarinet duet (exploiting the different registers of the instruments) in the third movement of the Symphony No. 39. (Mozart was the first great composer fully to appreciate the possibilities of the clarinet, which was a compara-

tively new instrument at the time; his friendship with the clarinettist Anton Stadler resulted in the first masterpieces for the instrument, namely the Trio for clarinet, viola and piano, the Quintet for clarinet and strings and the Clarinet Concerto.) The combination of voices with muted strings is used to ravishing effect in the famous *terzettino* 'Soave sia il vento' from *Così fan tutte*. In the field of chamber music the medium of the string quintet held a special appeal for Mozart and he exploited its effects to the full. The slow movement of the G minor Quintet, with muted strings in textures that are at times fragmented and bleak and at times rich and sonorous, is particularly remarkable; while the brief passage in the middle of the slow movement of the D major Quintet K.593, featuring the violins in duet, with accompanying violas and pizzicato cello, is haunting for its sheer beauty of sound. In recent years the trend towards performing classical music on period instruments has gathered pace, and to hear Mozart's keyboard concertos, for example, played on a fortepiano such as they were written for, with an orchestra of "authentic" instruments, rather than on a modern concert grand pianoforte with a modern symphony orchestra, is to gain fresh insight into the keenness of Mozart's ear and the way in which the music matches the medium.

Technical Skill

Finally, any appreciation of Mozart's music must take account of his formidable technical skill. This shows itself in, for instance, the apparently effortless incorporation of contrapuntal complexities (the finales of the Symphony No. 41 and the G major String Quartet K.387, the canonic minuet in the C minor Wind Serenade), and the inventiveness with which a single musical idea is exploited and developed—a technique which he partly learned from Haydn and which is exemplified in the six quartets dedicated to the senior composer (works which, interestingly, Mozart described as being "the fruit of long and arduous toil"). The appreciation of technique should add to, not detract from, the listener's response to the music, for in Mozart technique and expression are indivisible.

Summary

Mozart offers something for all tastes and all levels of musical sophistication and knowledge. He wrote appealing melodies, easily memorable and very singable; he created complex and fascinating musical structures. Throughout we are aware, whether in a simple song or in the most elaborate of concerto movements, of his complete mastery in handling the raw materials of music. Despite his comparative lack of worldly success he was esteemed by musicians in his lifetime and certain works achieved popular acclaim. Esteem and popularity have never been lacking since. The list of composers who have revered Mozart and, often, responded creatively to him is long and varied: it includes such names as Schumann, Chopin, Wagner, Tchaikovsky, Mahler, R. Strauss, Ravel, Stravinsky and Britten. It is true that his standing has fluctuated in the 200 years since his death. Perhaps more of his music is more widely known now than ever before, and partly for this reason, because we are better able to see him whole, his status as one of the handful of absolutely central figures in Western music seems secure now and for the foreseeable future.

THE WORLD OF SCIENCE

A contemporary picture of scientific discovery, designed to explain some of the most important ideas in astronomy, physics, chemistry, biology, physical and social anthropology, and to give some account of recent research in various fields. Also included is a variety of useful scientific tables.

TABLE OF CONTENTS

THE WORLD OF SCIENCE

In Parts I, II, and III the inanimate universe is described. This is the domain of cosmology, astronomy, geology, physics, and chemistry. There are already many interesting links which join this realm to that of the living and make it difficult to say where the boundary lies. Nevertheless it is still convenient to accord to the biological and social sciences two separate chapters, IV and V. In Part VI provides some useful scientific tables.

I. ASTRONOMY AND COSMOLOGY—THE NATURE OF THE UNIVERSE

The universe includes everything from the smallest sub-atomic particle to the mightiest supercluster of galaxies. The scientific view of the universe (not the only view but the one we are concerned with here) is a remarkable achievement of the human mind, and it is worth considering at the outset what a "scientific view" is, and what is remarkable about it.

A scientific view of something is always an intimate mixture of theories and observed facts, and not an inert mixture but a seething and growing one. The theories are broad general ideas together with arguments based on them. The arguments are designed to show that, if the general ideas are accepted, then this, or the other thing ought to be observed. If this, that, or the other actually are observed, then the theory is a good one; if not, then the theoreticians have to think again. Thus theoretical ideas and arguments are continually subjected to the severe test of comparison with the facts, and scientists are proud of the rigour with which this is done. On the other hand, theories often suggest new things to look for, *i.e.*, theories lead to predictions. These predictions are frequently successful, and scientists are entitled to be proud of that too. But it follows that no theory is immutable; any scientific view of any subject may, in principle, be invalidated at any time by the discovery of new facts, though some theories are so soundly based that overthrow does not seem imminent.

A remarkable aspect of the scientific view of the universe is that the same principles are supposed to operate throughout the whole vastness of space. Thus the matter and radiation in stars are not different from the matter and radiation on earth, and their laws of behaviour are the same. Therefore theories hard won by studies in terrestrial physics and chemistry laboratories are applied at once to the whole cosmos. Astronomy and cosmology are spectacular extensions of ordinary mechanics and physics.

LOOKING AT THE UNIVERSE

The universe is observable because signals from it reach us and some manage to penetrate our atmosphere.

First, there are waves of visible light together with invisible rays of somewhat longer (infra-red) and somewhat shorter (ultra-violet) wavelengths. These waves show us the bright astronomical objects and, to make use of them, astronomers have constructed telescopes of great power and precision backed up with cameras, spectroscopes, and numerous auxiliaries. The biggest telescope in the world is the 6 m reflector at Mt. Pastukhov in the northern Caucasus (USSR). The earth's atmosphere acts as a distorting and only partially transparent curtain and the erection of telescopes on satellites is beginning to extend optical telescope performance significantly.

Secondly, there are radio waves of much longer wavelength than light. Radiotelescopes are sensi-

tive radio receivers with specialised aerial systems. The scientific stature of modern radioastronomy was emphasised by the award in 1974 of the Nobel Physics Prize to two Cambridge radioastronomers, Ryle and Hewish.

Other types of radiation reach the earth from outer space. Cosmic radiation consists of fundamental particles, including protons (**F16**) of extremely high energy, moving at velocities very close to that of light. These particles can be detected by Geiger counters and by their tracks on photographic plates. X-rays and neutrinos (**F16**) are also generated by certain interesting classes of astronomical objects (**F5**). With the recent advent of satellite-borne detectors and apparatus buried in deep mines, new facets of cosmic-ray astronomy, X-ray astronomy, and neutrino astronomy are now rapidly deepening our knowledge of the nature of the universe and of the violent processes by which galaxies as well as individual stars and planetary systems evolve (**F6, F7**).

Great Distances and Large Numbers

To visualise the immense scale of the universe is almost as much a problem for the scientist as for the layman. The conventional shorthand is to express 1,000 as 10^3; 1,000,000 as 10^6. On this scale the earth is $1 \cdot 496 \times 10^8$ km away from the sun. Concorde, for example, the world's fastest airliner, took about $3\frac{1}{2}$ hours to travel 5,000 km from London to New York. The "Viking" spacecraft in 1976 took just over a year to travel the 200 million km to Mars. These distances, however, are minute by comparison with the distance even to the nearest star, Proxima Centauri, some 4×10^{13} km away. This distance is more conveniently expressed in terms of the travel time of light itself. With a velocity of nearly 300,000 km per second, in a year light travels about $9 \cdot 46 \times 10^{12}$ km. The distance to Proxima Centauri is therefore $4 \cdot 2$ light years. Even this distance, enormous on our terrestrial scale, is a small cosmic distance. The diameter of our galaxy is about 10^5 light years, while the most distant objects yet observed are an incredible $1 \cdot 2 \times 10^{10}$ light years distant.

PLANETS, STARS AND GALAXIES

The Solar System

The earth is the third, counting outward of nine planets revolving in nearly circular orbits round the sun. Some of their particulars are given in the Table (**F8**). The sun and its planets are the main bodies of the solar system. Mainly between the orbits of Mars and Jupiter revolve numerous small bodies—the minor planets or asteroids, the largest of which, Ceres, is only 800 km in diameter. Apart from these, the solar system is tenuously populated with particles varying in size from about a micron (10^{-6} m) to hundreds of metres in diameter. Some of these objects collide with the earth's atmosphere. The smaller fragments (micro-meteors) are too small to be visible. Large particles (meteors), about 1 mm up to tens of cm, cause the phenomena known as "shooting stars" when they burn up at about 100 km altitude. Even larger chunks, of rocky or iron composition, cause the rare and brilliant fireballs, some of which survive their high-speed flight through the earth's atmosphere and may later be recovered. Such objects (meteorites) are very important, providing examples of extra-terrestrial rocks, and thus giving the composition of some of the most primitive material left in the solar system. Collisions with very large meteorites (or small asteroids) are now, fortunately, very rare. However, the large meteorite crater in Arizona is one recent reminder that such collisions still occur, although much less frequently now than earlier in the history of the planetary system. The surfaces of Mercury, the Moon, Mars, and Venus still show the scars from collisions with a multitude of objects of up to tens of km in diameter.

Comets are fascinating objects which, from time to time, provide a spectacular sight. More than 700 comets have been observed so far, and about six new ones are discovered each year. At the heart of every comet is a small nucleus. In 1986 the Giotto space probe revealed that Halley's comet has a potato-shaped nucleus measuring 15 km by 10 km. This nucleus consists of ices of various gases, chiefly water, interspersed with dust particles. In their highly elliptical orbits comets spend most of their life at great distances from the sun, where the temperature is very low because of the feeble solar radiation, so that all the "icy" materials are solid. Periodically, when each comet returns to the inner parts of the solar system, the increasing solar radiation heats the surface layers, evaporating the volatile ices, which carry the surface dust away from the comet nucleus. After this heating and evaporation process, the ultra-violet component of sunlight further breaks down the parent "icy" molecules, a process known as photo-dissociation, and many molecules become ionised. Solar-radiation pressure, acting on the dust constituents, and the solar wind acting on the ionised constituents, form the gigantic cometary tails which may reach 2×10^8 km in length—larger than the radius of the earth's orbit. *See also* **L28.**

The sun itself is a dense, roughly spherical mass of glowing matter, 1,392,000 km across. Its heat is so intense that the atoms are split into separated electrons and nuclei (**F11**) and matter in such a state is called plasma. At the sun's centre the temperature has the unimaginable value of about 13 million degrees Centigrade (a coal fire is about 800°C). Under such conditions the atomic nuclei frequently collide with one another at great speeds and reactions occur between them. The sun consists largely of hydrogen and, in the very hot plasma, the nuclei of hydrogen atoms interact by a series of reactions whose net result is to turn hydrogen into helium. This is a process which releases energy just as burning does, only these nuclear processes are incomparably more energetic than ordinary burning. In fact, the energy released is great enough to be the source of all the light and heat which the sun has been pouring into space for thousands of millions of years.

Emerging from the sun and streaming past the earth is a "solar wind" of fast-moving electrons and protons (**F11**) whose motion is closely linked with the behaviour of an extensive magnetic field based on the sun. Thus, the region round the sun and extending far into space past the earth is full of complex, fluctuating particle streams and magnetic fields which interact with planetary atmospheres causing, among other things, auroras and magnetic storms.

Stars

In colour, brightness, age, and size the sun is typical of vast numbers of other stars. Only from the human point of view is there anything special about the sun—it is near enough to give us life. Even the possession of a system of revolving planets is not, according to some modern views, very unusual.

No star can radiate energy at the rate the sun does without undergoing internal changes in the course of time. Consequently stars evolve and old processes in them give rise to new. The exact nature of stellar evolution—so far as it is at present understood—would be too complex to describe here in any detail. It involves expansion and contraction, changes of temperature, changes of colour, and changes in chemical compositon as the nuclear processes gradually generate new chemical elements by reactions such as the conversion of hydrogen to helium, helium to neon, neon to magnesium, and so on. The speed of evolution changes from time to time, but is in any case very slow compared with the pace of terrestrial life; nothing very dramatic may occur for hundreds of millions of years. Evidence for the various phases of evolution is therefore obtained by studying many stars, each at a different stage of its life. Thus astronomers recognise many types with charmingly descriptive names, such as supergiants, blue giants, sub-giants, red, white and brown dwarfs.

The path of stellar evolution may be marked by various explosive events. One of these, which occurs in sufficiently large stars, is an enormous explosion in which a substantial amount of the star is blown away into space in the form of high-speed streams of gas. For about a fortnight, such an exploding star may radiate energy 200 million times as fast as the sun. Japanese and Chinese (but not Western) astronomers recorded such an occurrence in A.D. 1054, and the exploding gases, now called the Crab nebula, can still be seen in powerful telescopes and form a cloud six or seven light-years across. While it lasts, the explosion shows up as an abnormally bright star and is called a *supernova*. In late February 1987 a spectacular supernova occurred in our nearby galaxy the Large Magellanic Cloud. At a distance of only $1\cdot7 \times 10^5$ light years this supernova was the closest to the Earth for over 300 years. Many exciting findings are expected.

Groups of Stars

It is not surprising that ancient peoples saw pictures in the sky. The constellations, however, are not physically connected groups of stars but just happen to be patterns visible from earth. A conspicuous exception to this is the Milky Way, which a telescope resolves into many millions of separate stars. If we could view the Milky Way from a vast distance and see it as a whole we should observe a rather flat wheel of stars with spiral arms something like the sparks of a rotating Catherine wheel. This system of stars is physically connected by gravitational forces and moves through space as a whole; it is called a *galaxy*.

The galaxy is about 10^9 light-years across and contains roughly 10^{11} stars. An inconspicuous one of these stars near the edge of the wheel is our sun; the prominent stars in our night sky are members of the galaxy that happen to be rather near us. Sirius, the brightest, is only $8\cdot6$ light-years away, a trivial distance, astronomically speaking.

The galaxy does not contain stars only, there are also clouds of gas and dust, particularly in the plane of the galaxy. Much of the gas is hydrogen, and its detection is difficult. However, gaseous hydrogen gives out radio waves with a wavelength of 21 cm. Radio telescopes are just the instruments to receive these, and workers in Holland, America, and Australia detected the gas clouds by this means. In 1952 they found that the hydrogen clouds lie in the spiral arms of the galaxy, and this is some of the strongest evidence for the spiral form.

Another important feature of the galactic scene is the weak but enormously extensive magnetic field. This is believed to have an intimate connection with the spiral structure.

Around the spiral arms, and forming part of the galaxy, are numerous globular clusters of stars. These are roughly spherical, abnormally densely packed, collections of stars with many thousands of members. Because of its form and density, a globular cluster may be assumed to have been formed in one process, not star by star. Thus all its stars are the same age. This is of great interest to astronomers, because they can study differences between stars of similar age but different sizes.

Galaxies

One might be forgiven for assuming that such a vast system as the galaxy is in fact the universe; but this is not so. In the constellation of Andromeda is a famous object which, on close examination, turns out to be another galaxy of size and structure similar to our own. Its distance is given in the table (**F8**). The Milky Way, the Andromeda nebula, and a few other smaller galaxies form a cluster of galaxies called the Local Group. It is indeed a fact that the universe is populated with *groups*, *clusters* and *superclusters*, of *galaxies*. A cluster may contain two or three galaxies, but some contain thousands.

Some recent developments

By about 1920 it was known that there were at least half a million galaxies, and with the advent of the 2·54 m. Mt. Wilson telescope this number rose to 10^8 and has now been increased further by larger telescopes which can see out to distances greater than 10^{10} light years. Through the powerful telescopes the nearer galaxies reveal their inner structures. Photographs of galaxies are among the most beautiful and fascinating photographs ever taken, and readers who have never seen one should hasten to the nearest illustrated astronomy book. Most galaxies have a spiral or elliptical structure but about 2 per cent have peculiar wisps and appendages. Some galaxies are strong emitters of radio waves. A recently discovered type of galaxy is the starburst galaxy. This is an otherwise normal galaxy in which huge numbers of stars are forming in a small volume at its centre.

The Expanding Universe

Two discoveries about galaxies are of the utmost importance. One is that, by and large, clusters of galaxies are uniformly distributed through the universe. The other is that the distant galaxies are receding from us.

How is this known? Many readers may be familiar with the Doppler effect first discovered in 1842. Suppose a stationary body emits waves of any kind and we measure their wavelength, finding it to be L cm. Now suppose the body approaches us; the waves are thereby crowded together in the intervening space and the wavelength appears less than L; if the body recedes the wavelength appears greater than L. The Austrian physicist, J. Doppler (1803–53), discovered the well-known change of pitch of a train whistle as it approaches and passes us. The same principle applies to the light. Every atom emits light of definite wavelengths which appear in a spectroscope as a series of coloured lines—a different series for each atom. If the atom is in a receding body all the lines have slightly longer wavelengths than usual, and the amount of the change depends uniquely on the speed. Longer wavelengths mean that the light is redder than usual, so that a light from a receding body shows what is called a "red shift". The speed of recession can be calculated from the amount of red shift.

It was the American astronomer, V. M. Slipher, who first showed (in 1914) that some galaxies emitted light with a red shift. In the 1920s and 1930s the famous astronomer E. Hubble (1889–1953) measured both the distances and red shift of many galaxies and proved what is now known as Hubble's Law about which there is now some controversy. This states that the speed of recession of galaxies is proportional to their distance from us. This does not apply to our neighbours in the Local Group, we and they are keeping together. Hubble's Law has been tested and found to hold for the farthest detectable galaxies; they are about 7×10^9 light-years away and are receding with a speed approaching that of light.

The expansion of the universe does not imply that the Local Group is the centre of the universe —from any other viewpoint in the universe Hubble's Law would also be valid, and the distant galaxies would, similarly, all appear to be rapidly receding.

One possible implication of this most exciting scientific discovery is that, if the galaxies have always been receding, at an early time they must have been closer together. We can calculate that about 10^{10} years ago all the matter of the universe could have been densely packed. The truth or otherwise of this hypothesis is the most fundamental question of cosmology, and its testing still drives the quest to explore the universe, by larger and more sensitive telescopes, to the greatest possible distances.

Quasars, Pulsars and Black Holes

In November 1962 Australian radio astronomers located a strong radio emitter with sufficient precision for the Mt. Palomar optical astronomers to identify it on photographs and examine the nature of its light. The red shift was so great that the object must be exceedingly distant; on the other hand it looked star-like, much smaller than a galaxy. By the beginning of 1967 over a hundred of these objects had been discovered and other characteristics established, such as strong ultraviolet radiation and inconstancy, in some cases, of the rate at which radiation is emitted. Not all of these so-called quasars are strong radio emitters; some show all the other characteristics except radio emission. It has been estimated that the "quiet" kind are about a hundred times more numerous than the radio kind. One great problem here is: how can such relatively small objects generate such inconceivably great amounts of energy that they appear bright at such huge distances? Recent observations suggest that quasars are only the central visible part of an otherwise undetected galaxy. There may also be a massive black hole near the quasar centre.

Late in 1967, while investigating quasars, Cambridge radio astronomers discovered pulsars, a new type of heavenly body. Their characteristic is the emission of regular pulses of radio waves every second or so. A pulsar in the Crab nebula has a repetition rate even faster—about 1/30 sec—and it follows that pulsars must be very small bodies little if at all bigger than the Earth.

The existence of such small bodies raises again the problem of the ultimate fate of evolving stars. Much depends on their mass because this determines how strong the inward pull of gravity is. For a star to be at least temporarily stable the inward pull must be balanced by an outward pressure. In the sun this is the pressure of the burning hydrogen (**F6**) and the resulting average density is about 1·4 times that of water (**Table, F8**). In some stars the inward pressure is so great that collapse proceeds until it is balanced by a different type of outward pressure that sets in when electrons and atomic nuclei are forced into proximity. Stars so formed are the "white dwarfs". They are millions of times denser than the sun—"a matchbox of their matter would weigh a ton"— and they are very small though not small enough to be pulsars. The latter are now generally thought to be a million times denser even than white dwarfs and to consist largely of tightly packed neutrons (*see* **F11**). Such bodies are called neutron stars.

Could the tendency of a massive star to fall inwards ever be so great that no outward pressure known to physics would suffice to balance it? Apparently it could! Many astrophysicists now hold on theoretical grounds that such a gravitational collapse could create a high density object whose gravitational field would be too strong to allow anything—including light waves—ever to leave the body. Such hypothetical objects are called "black holes" because, light and other signals being unable to emerge from them, their matter has literally disappeared from view. Black holes could be detected by the disturbance their gravitational attraction causes to neighbouring visible stars and also because atoms attracted by the black hole should emit intense X-rays before falling so far in that they too disappear into the black hole. Both of these detection methods have led some astronomers to conjecture (by 1973) that there is a black hole in the constellation Cygnus. There is another promising candidate for a black hole in the Large Magellanic Cloud. The theory of gravitational collapse raises profound and unresolved problems about our physical concepts.

Very recently, it has been conjectured that black holes, formed by the "death" of individual stars, and perhaps even on a massive scale at the centre of large and dense galaxies, have been responsible for "devouring" a very significant proportion of the total mass of the universe. Since this "devoured" mass is invisible by direct observation, we may have considerably underestimated the average density, and thus the total gravitational field of the universe.

THE ORIGIN AND DEVELOPMENT OF THE UNIVERSE

Scientists can only attempt to explain the universe by relating its observable structure to the features predicted by alternative theories of its origin and development. The time span of all our observations of the Cosmos so small by comparison with the lifetime of the universe (more than 10^{10} years). Also, contrary to many other scientific disciplines, it is impossible to repeat the "experiment", under controlled conditions. We must, therefore, explore the evolution of the universe by using the fact that light from the most distant galaxies has taken about 10^{10} years to reach us, thus providing us with a crucial, if tantalisingly remote and thus indistinct, view of the universe at a much earlier epoch.

Several models of the universe have been based on Einstein's theory of General Relativity (**F17**). Einstein's equations may be solved to predict the evolution of the universe. However, there is a spectrum of solutions which vary from a continuous and indefinite expansion at the present rate to an eventual slowing and subsequent contraction to a dense state, again in the distant future, which hints at a "pulsating" universe.

The Steady-State Theory

As an alternative to the Evolutionary theory, Bondi, Gold, and Hoyle (1948) suggested the so-called "Steady-State" theory. This theory has no initial dense state or "origin" and, on a large scale, the density of galaxies and stars is always as at present. To permit this possibility, they proposed that matter—hydrogen atoms—is continuously created throughout space at a rate sufficient to compensate for the present observed expansion of the universe. Thus the average density of matter would always remain constant.

The Formation of Galaxies and Stars

On any theory of the universe, some explanation has to be found for the existence of clusters of galaxies. In all theories galaxies condense out from dispersed masses of gas, principally hydrogen.

It is believed on theoretical grounds each galaxy could not condense into one enormous star but must form many fragments which shrink separately into clusters of stars. In these clusters many stars, perhaps hundreds or thousands or even millions, are born. A small cluster, visible to the naked eye, is the Pleiades. The Orion nebula, visible as a hazy blob of glowing gas in the sword of Orion, is the scene of much star-forming activity at present. However, the best evidence yet for witnessing the birth of a star comes from observations by the Infrared Astronomical Satellite (IRAS). Deep within a gas and dust cloud called the Ophiuchus dark nebula, matter is falling inward in a manner predicted by contemporary theories of star formation. At the centre of this collapsing cloud there seems to be an embryonic star perhaps only 30,000 years old.

According to the Evolutionary theory the "initial dense state" consisted of very hot plasma in a state of overall expansion. The expanding plasma was both cooling and swirling about. The random swirling produces irregularities in the distribution of the hot gas—here it would be rather denser, there rather less dense. If a sufficiently large mass of denser gas happened to occur, then the gravitational attraction between its own particles would hold it together and

maintain its permanent identity, even though the rest of the gas continued to swirl and expand. Such a large mass would gradually condense into fragments to become a cluster of galaxies.

The Changing Scene

The 1960s witnessed revolutionary developments in both observational and theoretical astronomy. For example, it now seems agreed that remote sources of radio waves are more abundant the weaker their intensity. This strongly suggests that they are more abundant at greater distances. Thus the universe is not *uniform* as the original steady-state theory prescribed. Since greater distances correspond to earlier times, any extra abundance of objects observed at the greater distance means that the universe was denser in its younger days than now. This favours an evolutionary theory of the universe.

The same theory requires that the initial dense state of the universe—aptly christened "the primaeval fireball"—should contain intense electromagnetic radiation with a distribution of wavelengths characteristic of the high temperature. As the fireball, *i.e.*, the universe, expanded over a period of about 10^{10} years it cooled, and one feature of this process is that the wavelengths of the radiation increase and their distribution becomes characteristic of a much lower temperature. In fact, the wavelengths should now be concentrated about 1 mm to 1 cm (corresponding to about $-270°$ C) and the radiation should approach the earth uniformly from all directions. Radiation just like this was detected in the 1960s by extremely sensitive instruments both at ground-based observatories and flown from balloon payloads high in the earth's atmosphere—above most of the water vapour and other constituents which interfere with such delicate observations. This "microwave background" radiation appears to be "cosmological", and thus supports strongly the evolutionary or "Big Bang" theory as opposed to the "Steady-State" theory, which cannot rationally explain the radiation.

The Formation of the Chemical Elements

A stable nucleus is one that lasts indefinitely because it is not radioactive. There are 274 known kinds of stable atomic nuclei and little likelihood of any more being found. These nuclei are the isotopes (**F12**) of 81 different chemical elements; the other elements, including, for example, uranium and radium are always radioactive. Some elements are rare, others abundant. The most common ones on earth are oxygen, silicon, aluminium, and iron. However, the earth is rather atypical. It is especially deficient in hydrogen, because the gravitational attraction of our small planet was not strong enough to prevent this very light gas from escaping into space.

It is possible to examine the chemical constituents of meteorites and to infer the composition of the sun and other stars from the spectrum of the light they emit. By such means, the conclusion has been reached that 93% of the atoms in our galaxy are hydrogen, 7% are helium; all the other elements together account for about one in a thousand atoms. A glance at the Table of Elements (*see* end of Sec.) will show that hydrogen and helium are two of the lightest elements: they are in fact the two simplest. The problem is to explain how the heavier chemical elements appear in the universe at all. It is here that a fascinating combination of astronomy and nuclear physics is required.

We have already referred to the fact that the energy radiated from the sun originates in nuclear reactions which turn hydrogen into helium. Why is energy given out? To answer this question we note that nuclei are made up of protons and neutrons (**F11**). These particles attract one another strongly—that is why a nucleus holds together. To separate the particles, energy would have to be supplied to overcome the attractive forces. This amount of energy is called *binding energy* (**F11**) and is a definite quantity for every kind of nucleus. Conversely, when the particles are brought together to form a nucleus the binding energy is *released* in the form of radiations and heat. Different nuclei consist of different numbers of particles, therefore the relevant quantity to consider is the *binding energy per particle*. Let us call this B. Then if elements of *high* B are formed out of those of *low* B there is a *release* of energy. *See also* **Nuclear Energy, L88.**

Now B is small (relatively) for light elements like lithium, helium, and carbon; it rises to a maximum for elements of middling atomic weight like iron; it falls again for really heavy elements like lead, bismuth, and uranium. Consequently, energy is released by forming middleweight elements either by splitting up heavy nuclei ("nuclear fission") or by joining up light ones ("nuclear fusion"). *See also* **L88.**

It is the latter process, fusion, that is going on in stars. The fusion processes can be studied in physics laboratories by using large accelerating machines to hurl nuclei at one another to make them coalesce. In stars the necessary high velocity of impact occurs because the plasma is so hot. Gradually the hydrogen is turned into helium, and helium into heavier and heavier elements. This supplies the energy that the stars radiate and simultaneously generates the chemical elements.

The Heaviest Elements

The very heavy elements present a problem. To form them from middleweight elements, energy has to be *supplied*. Since there is plenty of energy inside a star, a certain small number of heavy nuclei will indeed form, but they will continually undergo fission again under the prevailing intense conditions. How do they ever get away to form cool ordinary elements, like lead and bismuth, in the earth? One view links them with the highly explosive supernovae, to which we have already referred (**F4(2)**). If the heavy elements occur in these stars the force of the explosion disperses them into cool outer space before they have time to undergo the fission that would otherwise have been their fate. The heavy elements are thus seen as the dust and debris of stellar catastrophes. The view is in line with the steady-state theory, because supernovae are always occurring and keeping up the supply of heavy elements. In the evolutionary theory some of the generation of elements is supposed to go on in the very early stages of the initial dense state and to continue in the stars that evolve in the fullness of time. It cannot be claimed that the origin of the chemical elements is completely known, but we have said enough to show that there are plausible theories. Time and more facts will choose between them.

The Formation of the Planets

Precisely how the planetary system was formed is still not understood in detail. From extremely precise observations of the movements of some nearby stars, it seems certain that other planetary systems occur among our stellar neighbours. By inference, it is thus probable that among certain classes of stars, planetary systems are very common throughout the universe.

Two other facts are crucial for any theory of planetary system formation. First, all the planetary orbits lie nearly in the plane perpendicular to the axis of rotation of the sun. The planets' rotations about the sun are all in the same direction and their axes of rotation, with two exceptions (Venus and Uranus), are close to the polar axis of their orbit planes, and in the same sense as their orbital rotation about the sun. Secondly, there is a very strong inverse correlation between planetary distance from the sun and the planet's mean density, particularly if the correct allowance is made for the effects of gravitional compression in the deep interiors of planets (greater in large than in small planets).

Rather than theories which would place planetary formation as either the random collection of

pre-formed planets by the sun in its path through the galaxy or as the consequence of a very near encounter between our sun and another star, it is now generally believed that the origin of the planetary system (and most of the satellites, etc.) was a direct consequence of the process which originally formed the sun.

As the primaeval solar nebula contracted, to conserve angular momentum, its rotation rate increased, and a diffuse equatorial disk of dust and gas formed. In the cold outer region (10–20° K) of this disk, all materials except helium and possibly hydrogen could readily condense on dust particles. Near the centre the temperature was higher, increasingly so as the proto-sun heated up, initially by the energy released by its gravitational contraction and, later, by the thermonuclear processes (**F4(1)**).

The Process of Accretion

Within this rotating and swirling disk of gas and dust, the process of accretion proceeded. Low-velocity collision between dust particles from time to time allowed larger particles to be created, composed of a mixture of the heavier elements and also the "icy" materials, particularly so in the colder outer regions where more of the "ices" were in a frozen state. Virtually our only information on the composition of such particles comes from detailed study of meteorites and from spectroscopic observation of comets. Eventually rocks of the size of centimetres, metres, and even kilometres were built up in this way. The build-up, controlled by low-velocity collisions, particularly of "sticky" materials, and also by electrostatic charges, was, at all times, however, moderated by occasional destructive high-velocity collisions. The relatively high viscosity of the dust and gas mixture throughout the disk must have been very important in producing a relatively uniform, rotational motion throughout the disk.

When "rocks" a few kilometres in size had been created new factors became important. Gravitational forces firstly increased the capacity of the larger "rocks" to accrete additional dust and smaller particles and, secondly, allowed some retention of material after even high-velocity collisions which would have destroyed smaller pieces.

The next stage is possibly the most difficult to model. Within a relatively uniform disk containing large numbers of rocks up to a few kilometres in diameter mixed within the residual dust and a large amount of gas, and extending to well outside Pluto's orbit, a small number of massive planets were formed. Some debris now remains as the comets and asteroids; however this debris and all the major planets, including the massive Jupiter, represent in total only a very small percentage of the original material of the solar nebula which was not condensed to form the sun.

It would appear that relatively quickly, during a period of 10^7 or 10^8 years, the large numbers of kilometre-sized objects, by collision and mutual gravitational attraction, formed the nuclei of the present planets and probably, in most cases, their major satellites also, in orbits relatively similar to their present ones. The planet-building process was most efficient at distances from the sun corresponding to the present orbits of Jupiter or Saturn, a compromise between temperature decreasing with distance from the sun, allowing a greater percentage of the total material to be solid and thus available for accretion, and density of material being greater closer to the sun.

The Jovian Planets

The outer or "Jovian" planets must have grown quickly, sweeping up hydrogen and helium gas as well as solid particles. Closer to the sun, the "icy" materials, still mainly in gaseous form, could not contribute very significantly to the initial accretion process, so that only smaller planets could form. Owing to their smaller mass, gravitational field and thus lower "escape velocity," they were only able to accrete a small proportion of the heavier gas present within the inner part of the solar system. Thus, at present, these

THE SOLAR SYSTEM

	Mean distance from Sun (millions of km)	Diameter km	Period of Revolution	Average density (water = 1)	Number of Satellites
Sun	—	1,392,000			—
Mercury	57·9	4,880	88 days	5·4	0
Venus	108·2	12,104	224·7 days	5·2	0
Earth	149·6	12,756	365·26 days	5·5	1
Mars	227·9	6,787	687 days	3·9	2
Jupiter	778·3	142,800	11·86 years	1·3	16
Saturn	1,427	120,000	29·46 years	0·7	17
Uranus	2,869·6	52,400	84·01 years	1·2	15
Neptune	4,496·6	48,600	164·8 years	1·7	2
Pluto	5,900	2,400	247·7 years	0·6	1

Note: Chiron, an object recently discovered orbiting the sun between Saturn and Uranus has not been given "planet" status due to its small size.

"terrestrial" planets are much denser than the outer "Jovian" planets, much smaller in size, and contain very little hydrogen or helium. The planet-building process was probably ended by two factors: the gravitational disruptive effect of the planets already formed and the enhanced "solar wind" of the young sun, which swept much of the residual dust and gas out of the solar system.

Before the process was complete, however, the gravitational energy released by the material falling onto the proto-planets plus the radioactive heating of short-lived isotopes present at the time of planetary formation were responsible for melting most of the bodies of the planets and probably all the larger satellites and asteroids. This process allowed gravitational segregation of denser and lighter materials within the planets, and the production of the core, mantle and crustal regions of each of the terrestrial planets. Long after the dust and gas were driven from the solar system and the planet surfaces cooled and solidified, the residual larger rocks and asteroids, of which enormous numbers were originally still present, continued to be swept up by each of the planets. The record of this violent stage of the solar system's development can still be seen in the saturation cratering observed on the Moon, Mercury, and Mars.

In the past two decades, direct space exploration, using automated space probes (and manned spacecraft in the case of the Moon) has enormously increased our knowledge of the solar system. Notable have been the Mars "Viking" project, the Venus probes, the later Pioneer probes with Pioneer 11 flying on from Jupiter to Saturn, and the Voyagers 1 and 2, the latter visiting no less than four planets, ending with Neptune in 1989. The five space probes to Halley's comet in 1986 were also a huge success. Important discoveries have continued to be made by ground-based telescopes such as a new ring system of Uranus, the object Chiron, and the radar investigation of the terrain of Venus. Future space missions such as the Galileo probe to Jupiter, the Ulysses probe over the poles of the Sun, and the Hubble Space Telescope promise exciting new results.

THE EARTH

Structure

The earth has the shape of a slightly flattened sphere, with an equatorial radius of 6,378 km and a polar radius 21 km less. Its mass can be calculated from Newton's Law of Gravitation and from measurements of the acceleration due to gravity, and is $5·97 \times 10^{24}$ kg. The average density follows from these two figures and is about 5·5 grams per cubic centimetre. This is nearly twice the density of typical rocks at the surface, so there must be very much denser material somewhere inside, and the earth must have a definite internal structure.

This structure can be investigated using shock waves from earthquakes or large explosions. These are received at recording stations at different distances from their source, having penetrated to varying depths within the earth, and their relative times of arrival and characteristic forms enable the deep structure to be worked out. This consists of three main units, a core at the centre with a radius about half that of the earth, the mantle outside this, and the thin crust, about 35 km thick under the continents and 5 km thick under the oceans, forming a skin surrounding the mantle.

The composition of these three units can be deduced by observation and inference. For example, meteorites which arrive at the earth's surface from other parts of the solar system consist of three main types, composed of iron-nickel alloy, stony silicates, and a mixture of iron and silicates. Could these have originated from the break-up of some planet like the earth? If so, then perhaps the core of the earth is made up of iron-nickel alloy and the mantle of magnesium-rich silicates. Experiments on the physical properties of these materials at high pressures show strong similarities with the measured properties of the earth's interior. In addition, rocks composed of magnesium-rich silicates are found at the earth's surface in places where material seems to have come from great depth, such as in the debris from volcanic explosions. These may be direct samples of the earth's mantle.

Core, Mantle and Crust

By these arguments, and by many others, a picture can be built up of the internal structure of the earth. The core is composed of iron-nickel

SOME ASTRONOMICAL DISTANCES

(1 light-year = $9·46 \times 10^{12}$ km).

Object	Distance from Earth (light-years)	Velocity of recession (km per second)	Object	Distance from Earth (light-years)	Velocity of recession (km per second)
Sun	$1·6 \times 10^{-5}$	—	Andromeda Galaxy	$1·5 \times 10^6$	—
Nearest star (Proxima Centauri) . .	4·2	—	Galaxy in Virgo .	$7·5 \times 10^7$	1,200
Brightest star (Sirius) .	8·6	—	Galaxy in Gt. Bear	10^9	14,900
Pleiades	340	—	Galaxy in Corona Borealis . .	$1·3 \times 10^9$	21,600
Centre of Milky Way .	$2·6 \times 10^4$	—	Galaxy in Bootes .	$4·5 \times 10^9$	39,300
Magellanic clouds (the nearest galaxies) .	$1·7 \times 10^5$	—	Very remote quasi-stellar object .	$\sim 1·2 \times 10^{10}$	$\sim 280,000$

alloy. It is liquid at the outside, but contains a solid inner core of radius about one-fifth of that of the earth. Convection currents flowing in the liquid part give rise to the earth's magnetic field. Outside this the mantle is solid, and is made up mainly of magnesium–iron silicates of various kinds. By studying its physical properties through earthquake wave observations, the mantle may be divided into several zones, of which the most important is the asthenosphere. This is the part of the mantle between 70 and 300 km depth in which volcanic lavas are formed. In this region the mantle is everywhere quite near to the temperature at which it begins to melt, and is thus rather soft compared with the rest of the mantle. The presence of a soft asthenosphere accounts for many of the surface features of the earth, mountain belts and ocean basins, that make it so very different from cratered planets such as the Moon and Mars.

The sharp boundary between mantle and crust is called the Mohorovicic Discontinuity. Above it, the crust is different under continents and oceans. The thick continental crust has a composition that can broadly be called granitic, while the thin oceanic crust is poorer in silicon, sodium, and potassium and richer in calcium, iron, and magnesium. The continental crust has been built up over thousands of millions of years by welding together mountain belts of different ages, while the oceanic crust is made up of basalt lavas and is nowhere older than 250 million years.

Rocks

Rocks are naturally occurring pieces of the solid earth. If you take a rock and break it up into grains, then separate the grains into different heaps of like grains, each heap will consist of grains of the same *mineral*. For example, the kind of rock called granite can be divided into glassy grains of the mineral quartz, milky white or pink grains of the mineral feldspar, shiny black flakes of the mineral biotite, and shiny colourless flakes of the mineral muscovite. Both biotite and muscovite belong to the mica group of minerals. Each different mineral has a well-defined composition or range of composition, and a definite and characteristic arrangement of the atoms that compose it. There are several thousand known kinds of minerals, but only fifty or so are at all common.

There are three main kinds of rock; igneous rocks, formed by the solidification of molten lava; sedimentary rocks, formed from material laid down under gravity on the earth's surface; and metamorphic rocks, formed by heating or reheating of either of the other kind of rock. Each of these broad groups may be further subdivided. When *igneous rocks* solidify deep inside the earth, they cool slowly and large crystals have time to form. Coarse-grained igneous rocks such as granites are known as plutonic igneous rocks. Conversely the rapidly cooled fine-grained igneous rocks that form the volcanic lavas, such as basalts and rhyolites, are called volcanic igneous rocks. *Sedimentary rocks* can be divided into three kinds: Clastic sediments are those formed from mechanically abraded and transported fragments of pre-existing rocks and include sandstone, mudstone, and clay. Organic sediments are those composed, as are most limestones, of fragments of organically produced material such as shells, wood, and bone. Chemical sediments are formed by direct chemical action and include, most typically, salt deposits formed by evaporation of sea water. *Metamorphic rocks* are more difficult to subdivide. They are usually classified on the basis of their original composition and/or the maximum pressure and temperature to which they have been subjected. Chemical reactions in metamorphic rocks give rise to successions of minerals as the pressure and temperature change, so that examination of a metamorphic rock will often allow one to say how deeply it was buried and how hot it was.

Age of Rocks

There are two distinct ways of estimating the age of rocks. The first gives the *relative age*. It is based on the principle that in a sequence of sediments, older rocks lie underneath and younger ones above, that igneous rocks are younger than the rocks they intrude, and that folded rocks are formed earlier than the earth movements that fold them. Correlation of a sequence of rocks in one place with those in another is made by fossil faunas and floras. Thus a complete scale of relative ages can be built up, stretching back to the first rocks containing fossils (see the table in Part IV). The *age in years* can, on the other hand, be measured by using radioactive elements (Part II) contained in rocks. If the amount of a radioactive element present is measured, and the amount of the product of radioactive decay can also be found, then, using the known rates of decay, the time since the product started to accumulate (defined for this purpose as the age in years) can be measured. This method is particularly useful for studying rocks that do not contain fossils (igneous and metamorphic rocks, or those too old to contain fossils). By similar methods, the *age of the earth* can be obtained. This turns out to be about $4 \cdot 6 \times 10^9$ years. The rocks containing the first fossils are $2 \cdot 5 - 3 \times 10^9$ years old, while organised life in abundance first appeared about $0 \cdot 6 \times 10^9$ years ago.

The Continents and the Ocean Floor

The outer part of the earth, namely, the asthenosphere and the solid mantle and crust overlying it, the lithosphere, is in a state of restless movement, and it is this movement that gives rise to the formation of oceans, continents, and mountain belts. The surface of the earth can be divided into a number of rigid plates of lithosphere, which move apart, or together, or slide past one another. Some of these plates are very large, such as the one which contains all of North America, all of South America, and about half of the Atlantic Ocean. Others are no more than a few thousand square kilometres in size. But they are all moving about relative to one another like ice floes in pack-ice. Where two plates move apart, hot material rises from the asthenosphere to fill the gap, partly melts, and gives rise to a chain of volcanoes and a thin volcanic crust. This is how ocean basins form and grow larger. In the Atlantic, the Mid-Atlantic Ridge marks the line along which plates are moving apart, and where new ocean is being formed. Long narrow pieces of ocean such as the Red Sea and the Gulf of California mark where a continent has just begun to split apart, and a new ocean is forming. Where two plates slide past one another, a great tear fault results. Such a fault is the San Andreas fault which runs from the Gulf of California to San Francisco. Jerky movement on this fault gave rise to the great San Francisco earthquake of 1906 and could give rise to another earthquake there at any time.

Where two plates move together, the result depends on the nature of the crust forming the plates. If at least one of the plates is oceanic, the oceanic crust dips down into the mantle and slides away to great depths until it eventually merges with the asthenosphere. Along this dipping sheet of crust, strong earthquakes occur and frictional heating of the sheet leads to melting and the production of quantities of lava. Examples of such boundaries are the Andes, where the Pacific Ocean bed dips beneath South America, and Indonesia, where the Indian Ocean bed dips below Asia. When both plates are continental, on the other hand, the crust is too thick and buoyant to slide into the mantle, and a collision results, giving rise to a fold mountain chain. Eventually the movement grinds to a halt, the plates weld together, and the fold mountains become dormant. The Himalayas were formed in this way from the recent collision of India and Asia. The evidence that has led to these conclusions is too complex to summarise here. It comes from a study of rock magnetism, earthquakes, the flow of heat from inside the earth and even from the shapes of the continents, that must match across the oceans by which they have been split apart. Confirmation has come from a series of holes drilled in the ocean which has shown how the crust becomes younger towards the centres of the oceans.

Rates of movement of plates have been calculated, ranging from a few millimetres a year to ten centimetres a year. The faster movements can be measured directly on the ground by such simple techniques as looking at the displacement of railway lines, walls, and roads, but the slower ones, and those beneath the oceans must be measured by more indirect geophysical methods. The mechanism by which this movement takes place is still unknown. Are the plates pulled by their sinking edges, or pushed by their rising edges, or moved by some other means? But it cannot be doubted that the movement does happen, and that it holds the key to the development of the earth's crust since the time it was first formed.

The Rest

There is a lot more to the study of the earth than has been possible to set down here. The oceans, the atmosphere, and the rocks of the crust all interact with one another in their development in a complex way. The surface of the earth has gradually changed as life has evolved over thousands of millions of years and ice ages have come and gone, changing the surface again and again. Just as important is the economic potential of the earth, on which we depend for all of our energy and all raw materials. This section has given the basic framework within which such further investigations are carried out, to help the reader understand as he reads more widely.

II. PHYSICS—THE FUNDAMENTAL SCIENCE OF MATTER

WHAT PHYSICS IS ABOUT

Anyone compelled by curiosity or professional interest to look into contemporary journals of pure physics research is soon struck by the fact that the old test-book division of physics into "heat, light, sound, electricity, and magnetism" has become very blurred.

Two different, though complementary, sections can be distinguished. First, there is the physics concerned with the properties of matter in bulk, with solids, liquids, and gases, and with those odd but very important substances, such as paints, plastic solutions, and jelly-like material, which are neither properly solid nor liquid. In this vast domain of physics questions like this are asked: Why is iron magnetic, copper not? What happens when solids melt? Why do some liquids flow more easily than others? Why do some bodies conduct electricity well, others badly, some not at all? During the last century, particularly the last few decades, it has become clear that such questions can be answered only by raising and solving others first. In particular, we must ask: (i) Of what nature are the invisible particles of which matter is composed? and (ii) How are those particles arranged in bulk matter?

The first of these two questions has generated the second major category of modern physics: this is the physics of particles and of the forces that particles exert on each other. In this field which represents science at its most fundamental questions like this are asked: If matter is composed of small units or particles, what are they like? How many kinds of particle are there? Do the particles possess mass? electric charge? magnetism? How do the particles influence each other? How can their motion be described and predicted?

The discussion which follows has been divided into two main parts (1) Particles and Forces, and (2) The Properties of Matter in Bulk, with part (1) describing the microscopic structure of matter and part (2) its macroscopic properties.

PARTICLES AND FORCES

Aristotle to Newton

The inference that matter should be composed of small particles or atoms originated, it is true, in classical times. The atomic idea was an attempt to solve the age-old problem of matter and its peculiar properties. The ancients had provided themselves with two solutions to the problem of matter:

(i) The theory of the four elements (earth, water, fire, air), from which all different forms of matter were composed by selecting different ratios of the four ingredients. This approach had been used by traditional philosophy and was adopted by Aristotle.

(ii) The theory of atomism which postulated the existence of atoms and empty space.

Atomism remained very much in the background in the development of Western Science and persisted even longer in the Arab world. The idea that matter is composed of "small units" was in reality forced into the mental development of mankind by the repeated application of the process of dimension halving. By the time of Newton atomism had come to the fore and Newton considered that God had made the Universe from "small indivisible grains" of matter. Nevertheless, the search for the "philosopher's stone" was still, in the seventeenth century, the main pursuit of many scientists, but the new chemistry of the seventeenth century made use of atomistic concepts. Newton's physics was a mechanics concerning particles in a vacuum and when Boyle described his gas law (i.e., Pressure × Volume is constant at a fixed temperature) he visualised matter as composed of particles with specific qualitative properties. It was, of course, the advance of experimental techniques which enabled scientists to test ideas and theories on the nature of matter.

Dalton and Atomic Theory

The modern view of atomism need be traced no farther than the beginning of the nineteenth century when Dalton and his contemporaries were studying the laws of chemical combination using precise weighing techniques. By that time the distinctions between elements, compounds, and mixtures were already made. Compounds and mixtures are substances which can be separated into smaller amounts of chemically distinguishable constituents. Elements (see end of Sec.) cannot be so divided. In a mixture the components may be mixed in any proportion and sorted out again by non-chemical means. In a compound the elements are combined in fixed proportions by weight. This last fact gives the clue to atomic theory.

Dalton pointed out that the fixed combining weights of elements could easily be explained if the elements consisted of atoms which combined in simple numerical ratios, e.g., 1 atom of element A with one of B, or one of B with two of C, and so on. For instance, 35·5 g of chlorine combine with 23·0 g of sodium to make 58·5 g of ordinary salt. If we assume one atom of chlorine links with one of sodium, then the atoms themselves must have weights in the ratio 35·5 to 23·0. This turns out to be consistent with the combining weights of chlorine and sodium in all other compounds in which they both take part. Sometimes two elements combine in several different proportions by weight. But this is easily explained by assuming that the atoms link up in a variety of ways e.g., one iron atom with one oxygen, or two irons with three oxygens, or three irons with four oxygens. Then the three different combining proportions arise from the three different numbers of atoms, using in each case the same ratio of oxygen atom weight to iron atom weight.

Atomic Weight

Over the century and a half since Dalton, these ideas have been repeatedly tested by chemical experiments No. one now doubts that every chemical element has atoms of characteristic weight. The atomic weight or more properly the relative atomic mass, of an element is by international agreement expressed relative to one isotope (*see* below) of carbon, namely carbon-12 which is given the relative mass of twelve. These numbers are only ratios; the real weight of one single oxygen atom is $2 \cdot 7 \times 10^{-23}$ g.

Valency

That the combinations of atoms in definite proportions was necessary to produce compounds, or more correctly molecules, was known from 1808. The reason why only one atom of sodium and one of chlorine was required to produce one molecule of salt was unknown. Further the seemingly odd combinations of two atoms of hydrogen (H) with one of oxygen (O) to give water (H_2O), while only one atom of hydrogen could combine with chlorine to give hydrogen chloride (HCl) could not be explained. This situation was not resolved until around 1860, when the chemical formulae of many molecules were known. It was then discovered that homologies existed in the elements, for example the series Na, K, Rb, Cs, or Fl, Cl, Br, I, and this culminated in the Periodic Table of the elements (see end Sec.). The valency of an atom was determined by its position in the periodic table and determined by the number of electrons (see below) which the atom has orbiting its nucleus. Atoms combined to form molecules in a manner which maintained the number of "valence" electrons in a stable grouping of 2, 8, or 18 (*see* **F24**). For example, sodium has one valence electron and chlorine seven, therefore the combination NaCl gives the stable grouping of eight; hydrogen has one and oxygen six, hence it requires two atoms of hydrogen and one of oxygen to give one stable molecule, H_2O. Other more complicated molecular structures and types of bonding between atoms are dealt with in the chemistry section. This discovery of particles smaller than the atom itself was necessary to fully comprehend the nature of valency in atomic combinations.

J. J. Thomson and the Electron

Matter is electrically uncharged in its normal state, but there exist many well-known ways of producing electric charges and currents—rubbing amber, or rotating dynamos, for example. It is therefore necessary to have some theory of electricity linked to the theory of matter. The fundamental experiment in this field was made by J. J. Thomson when, in 1897, he discovered the electron.

If you take two metal electrodes sealed inside a glass vessel and if the pressure of the air is reduced from atmospheric pressure, 76 cm of mercury, to 1 mm of mercury by mechanical pumping and then a high voltage, several kilo-volts, is applied to the electrodes, the negative electrode emits a "radiation" which causes the walls of the tube to glow. The rays are called *cathode rays*. The discovery of the electron is essentially a clarification of the nature of cathode rays. Thomson showed that they were streams of particles with mass and negative electric charge and a general behaviour unlike any other atomic particle known at that time. The importance of this discovery for the world of science cannot be overestimated, and its technical progeny are in every home and factory in X-ray machines, television tubes, and all electronic devices.

Rutherford–Bohr Atom

Since the electrons emerge from matter, they are presumably parts of atoms. The relation between the negative electrons and the positively charged constituents of matter was elucidated by the great experimenter Rutherford and the great theoretician Bohr. Their work, just before the First World War, showed that the positive charge, together with almost all the mass, is concentrated in the central core or nucleus of the atom about which the very light-weight electrons revolve. The diameter of an atom is about 10^{-8} cm, roughly one three-hundred-millionth part of an inch. The central nucleus has a diameter about 10,000 times smaller still. The nucleus and the electrons hold together because of the electric attraction between them.

The positive charge of the nucleus is responsible for holding the electron in the region of space around the nucleus. The electrostatic Coulomb force, if left on its own would quickly attract the electrons into the nucleus but since the electrons move in orbits, circular and elliptical, they experience an outward centrifugal force which balances the inward electrostatic force. The mechanism is similar to that which holds the earth in orbit around the sun, only here a gravitational force replaces the effect of the Coulomb force. Modern theories of the electronic structure of atoms are quantum mechanical (*see* below).

At this stage work could, and did, go on separately along several different lines:

(i) Electrons could be studied on their own. Nowadays the handling of beams of electrons of all sizes and intensities has become a major branch of technology.

(ii) The nucleus could be treated as a special problem, and this led to the mid-century flowering of nuclear physics, to the atomic bomb, and to nuclear power.

(iii) The behaviour of electrons in the atom could be analysed; this is the great domain of atomic physics which spreads into many other sciences as well.

Volumes have been written about each of these three fields, but we can spare only a few lines for each.

The Electron

Electrons are expelled from solids by light, heat, electric fields, and other influences. It has therefore been possible to study beams of electrons on their own *in vacuo*. Electrons inside matter, either as constituents, or temporarily in transit, can also be observed by their innumerable effects. These observations all show the particles to be indistinguishable one from another; all electrons are the same wherever they come from. They have a definite mass ($9 \cdot 11 \times 10^{-28}$ g), a negative electric charge, a magnetic moment, and a "spin" (intrinsic rotatory motion). No one has ever subdivided an electron or obtained an electric charge smaller than that on one electron. The electronic charge is therefore used as a basic unit of charge in atomic physics. The electron has come to be the best known of all the "fundamental particles." It is now used in research as probe for studying the structure of matter, for which it is ideally suited, since it is very much smaller than an atom. A whole field of electron-scattering research which studies the nature and structure of solids, liquids, and gases is being actively conducted in many laboratories.

The Nucleus

The early research programmes in nuclear physics were greatly facilitated by the occurrence in nature of certain unstable (radioactive) nuclei which emit fast-moving fragments. The latter can be used as projectiles to aim at other nuclei as targets; the resulting impacts yield much valuable information. This technique still dominates nuclear physics, though nowadays the projectiles are artificially accelerated by one or other of the large costly machines designed for the purpose.

The most important early discovery was that the nucleus consists of two types of fundamental particle—the positively charged *proton* and the electrically neutral *neutron*. These two are of nearly equal mass (about 1,800 times that of the electron), and like electrons, have a magnetic moment and spin. The proton charge is equal to the electron charge, though opposite in sign. Consider a moderately complex nucleus like that of iron. This usually has 30 neutrons and 26 protons. Its atomic weight therefore depends on the total number of neutrons plus protons, but the total charge depends only on the number of protons—called the *atomic number*. The latter is denoted by Z while the total number of neutrons plus protons is called the *mass number* and denoted by M. A species of nucleus with given values of Z and M is called a *nuclide*. Z is also the number of electrons in the atom, since the atom as a whole is electrically neutral. The atomic number determines the chemical nature of the atom (see below), so that by altering the number of *neutrons* in a nucleus we do not change the chemical species. It is therefore possible to find—and nowadays to make—nuclei of the same element which nevertheless differ slightly in weight because they have different numbers of neutrons. These are called *isotopes*. Iron isotopes are known with 26, 27, 28, 29, 30, 31, 32, and 33 neutrons, but all have 26 protons. Thus a set of isotopes consists of the various nuclides that have the same Z but different M's.

When the atomic properties of isotopes are measured it is found that small, hyperfine differences in the motions of the electrons around the respective nuclei exist. These result from the different total spin of the isotopes and its effect on the orbiting electrons. This influence of atomic properties by nuclear effects is important in that it provides a link between different fields of research.

Stable Nuclides

The protons and neutrons in a nucleus are bound together by strong forces called *nuclear forces*. In many cases, the forces are so strong that no particles ever escape and the nucleus preserves its identity. There are two hundred and seventy-four different combinations of neutrons and protons of this kind, and they are called the *stable nuclides*. The earth is largely composed of such stable nuclides, because any unstable ones have, in the course of time, spontaneously broken up into stable residues.

Nevertheless, there are some unstable nuclei left on earth. They give rise to the phenomenon of radioactivity which was discovered by Becquerel in 1893.

Unstable Nuclides: Radioactivity

Becquerel found that certain chemicals containing uranium gave off rays capable of blackening a photographic plate, and shortly afterwards Marie and Pierre Curie discovered more substances, including radium, which produce similar but stronger effects. By now, about fifty chemical elements having radioactive properties are known to exist on earth, some, like radium, being strongly radioactive, others, like potassium, being so weak that the radiations are difficult to detect. These are called the *natural radioactive nuclides*.

The main facts about radioactivity are as follows: it is a *nuclear* phenomenon and (with minor exceptions) proceeds quite independently of whatever the electrons in the atom may be doing. Thus, the radioactivity of an atom is not affected by the chemical combination of the atom with other atoms, nor by ordinary physical influences like temperature and pressure. The radioactivity consists of the emission by the substance of certain kinds of rays. The early workers, Rutherford being the giant among them, distinguished three kinds of rays labelled a, β, and γ. These are described below. Whatever kind of ray is examined, it is found that the radiation from a given sample decreases gradually with time according to a definite law which states that the intensity of radiation decreases by half every T seconds. The number T, called the half-life, is constant for each radioactive material, but varies enormously from substance to substance. For instance, radium decreases its activity by a half every 1,622 years, whereas the half-life of one of the polonium isotopes is about 0.3×10^{-6} sec.

a-, β-, and γ-rays

The three most well-known types of radioactive emission are quite distinct from one another.

(i) a-rays or a-particles consist of two protons and two neutrons bound together. They are ejected from the radioactive nucleus with one of several well-defined speeds. These speeds are high, often of the order 10^9 cm per sec. Two protons and two neutrons are the constituents of the nucleus of helium, and a-particles are thus fast-moving helium nuclei.

(ii) β-rays are moving electrons. They may emerge from their parent nucleus with any speed from zero to a definite maximum. The maximum speed often approaches that of light, and is different for each isotope. The electron has a

positively charged counterpart, the positron (see below), and β-rays are sometimes positrons. To distinguish the two cases, the symbols β^- and β^+ are used. The naturally occurring β-radiations are almost all β^-.

(iii) γ-rays travel with the speed of light because they are in fact electromagnetic waves differing from light only in the extreme shortness of their wavelength. They have no electric charge.

It is unusual, though not unheard of, for the same radioactive substance to emit both a- and β-rays. On the other hand, γ-rays frequently accompany either a- or β-rays.

γ-rays pass through matter easily; in fact, they are extra penetrating X-rays. a-rays can be stopped by thin sheets of tissue paper. a-rays brought to rest pick up a pair of electrons from the surrounding matter and become neutral helium atoms, and helium gas from this source is consequently found imprisoned in certain radioactive rocks. β-rays are intermediate in penetrating power between a- and γ-rays.

We must now try to interpret these observations.

Radioactive Disintegration

A nucleus is a collection of neutrons and protons interacting with each other and possessing collectively a certain amount of energy. Just as some human organisations lose their coherence if they accept too many members, so nuclei can remain stable only if (i) the total number of particles is not too great, and (ii) neutrons and protons are there in suitable proportions. Radioactive nuclei are the ones for which either or both these conditions do not hold. Sooner or later such nuclei eject a fragment, thus getting rid of some energy they cannot contain. This is called a *radioactive disintegration*, and the fragments are the a-, β-, and γ-rays. a-emission relieves a nucleus of two neutrons and two protons and some energy; γ-emission simply carries off excess energy without altering the number or kind of particles left behind. β-emission is more complicated. There are no electrons normally present in a nucleus, but they are suddenly created and explosively emitted if a neutron changes into a proton; positive electrons are similarly generated if a proton changes into a neutron. β-emission is therefore a mechanism for changing the ratio of protons to neutrons without altering the total number of particles.

Both a- and β-emission change the Z of a nucleus, and the product, or daughter nucleus, is a different chemical element. a-emission also changes the M. It might happen that the daughter nucleus is unstable, in which case it too will disintegrate. Successive generations are produced until a stable one is reached. Part of such a family tree is shown below. The symbols above the arrows show the kind of rays emitted at each stage, the figures are the mass numbers, M, and the names and symbols of chemical elements can be found at the end of the Section.

$$\mathrm{U}^{238} \xrightarrow{a} \mathrm{Th}^{234} \xrightarrow{\beta} \mathrm{Pa}^{234} \xrightarrow{\beta} \mathrm{U}^{234} \xrightarrow{a} \mathrm{Th}^{230} \xrightarrow{a}$$

$$\mathrm{Ra}^{226} \xrightarrow{a} \mathrm{Rn}^{222} \xrightarrow{a} \mathrm{Po}^{218} \xrightarrow{a} \mathrm{Pb}^{214} \xrightarrow{\beta} \mathrm{Bi}^{214} \xrightarrow{\beta}$$

$$\mathrm{Po}^{214} \xrightarrow{a} \mathrm{Pb}^{210} \xrightarrow{\beta} \mathrm{Bi}^{210} \xrightarrow{\beta} \mathrm{Po}^{210} \xrightarrow{a} \mathrm{Pb}^{206}$$

(Pb^{206} is stable lead).

This family exists naturally on earth, because the head of the family, U^{238}, has so long a half-life (4.5×10^9 years) that there has not yet been time enough since its formation for it to have disappeared.

Artificial Radioactivity

Nowadays many new radioactive isotopes can be man-made. All that is required is to alter the M or Z (or both) of a stable isotope to a value which is incompatible with stability. The means for doing this is *bombardment*, i.e., stable nuclei are exposed to the impacts of atomic particles such as streams of protons from an accelerator, neutrons in an atomic reactor, or simply the a-particles from another radioactive substance.

The new material is called an *artificially radio-active isotope*. Artificial radioactivity is not different in kind from that of the naturally radio-active substances, but the half-lives are usually on the short side. Indeed, the isotopes in question would exist in nature but for the fact that their short half-lives ensured their disappearance from the earth long ago.

Suppose a piece of copper is exposed to the intense neutron radiation in an atomic reactor at Harwell.

The more abundant of the two stable isotopes of ordinary copper has thirty-four neutrons and twenty-nine protons (*i.e.*, $Z = 29$, $M = 63$). In the reactor many (not all) of these nuclei absorb a neutron, giving an unstable copper nucleus with $Z = 29$, $M = 64$. When removed from the reactor the specimen is observed to be radioactive with a half-life of $12\cdot8$ hours. It is somewhat unusual in that it gives out both β^- and β^+ rays. Some nuclei emit electrons, leaving a daughter nucleus with one more positive charge than copper, *i.e.*, a zinc nucleus ($Z = 30$, $M = 64$). One neutron has become a proton, and the re-sulting zinc nucleus is stable. The others emit positrons, leaving behind a nucleus in which a proton has been turned into a neutron ($Z = 28$, $M = 64$); this is a stable nickel nucleus. The overall process is one example of the artificial transmutation of the chemical elements which is now a commonplace of nuclear physics. It was first discovered by Irene and Frederick Joliot-Curie in 1934.

Lack of a Complete Theory

Consider now a collection of, say, one million radioactive nuclei of the same kind. It is im-possible to tell exactly when any one of them will disintegrate; it is a matter of chance which ones break up first. All we know is that, after a time equal to the half-life, only a half a million will survive unchanged. In general, the more excess energy a nucleus has, the more likely it is to break up, and therefore the shorter the half-life of that particular nuclear species. In principle, to cal-culate the half-life theoretically, one would have to have a reliable theory of nuclear forces and energies. This is still being sought after, so it is probably fair to say that while the laws of behaviour of radioactive isotopes are well and accurately known, the *explanation* of this behaviour in terms of the properties of protons and neutrons is by no means complete.

Nuclear Fission—Chain Reaction

A discovery important not just for nuclear physics but for the whole of mankind was made by Hahn and Strassman in 1939. This was the dis-covery of nuclear fission in uranium. One of the natural isotopes of uranium is an unstable one, U^{235}, with 143 neutrons and 92 protons. It norm-ally shows its instability by emitting a- and γ-rays. If uranium is bombarded with neutrons, some U^{235} nuclei temporarily gain an extra neutron, which makes them even less stable. This they show by splitting into two roughly equal parts, called fission fragments, together with two or three neutrons. There are two highly important things about this disintegration. One is that the two or three neutrons can promote further disintegrations in other uranium nuclei, and the process can therefore be self-propagating: it is then called a *chain re-action*. The other is that the total mass of the fission products is less than that of the original nucleus. This mass difference does not disappear without trace; it turns into energy according to a formula referred to in a paragraph below (**F18(1)**).

Nuclear Fusion

The ability of two light nuclei to combine and form a heavier nucleus is called fusion. A reac-tion of this nature does not form a chain process but proceeds in singly induced reactions. A typical fusion reaction is the formation of a helium nucleus (mass 3) from two deuterium nuclei which are made to collide at an energy of 60 keV (speed of $2\cdot410^6$ m/s)

i.e., $^2D_1 + {}^2D_1 \rightarrow {}^3He_2$ $(0\cdot82$ meV$) + n(2\cdot45$ meV$)$

where the $^3He_2$ particle has kinetic energy of $0\cdot82$ meV and the free neutron has free kinetic energy of $2\cdot45$ meV. This type of reaction is exo-energetic, the additional kinetic energy coming from the tighter binding of the nucleus in ^{3}He than in the two separate deuterium nuclei. The energy released in this form of nuclear reaction is much more than that in a fission process and is respon-sible for the emitted energy of the sun which burns hydrogen to form helium.

Applications of Nuclear Reactions

The world has two uses for the energy released in nuclear reactions:

    (1) nuclear weapons;
    (2) nuclear power plants.

The only nuclear bombs to be used in anger employed the fission chain reaction proceeding at a rapid rate which quickly becomes uncontrollable and produces a tremendous explosion. The second generation of nuclear warhead uses the fusion reaction, which is initiated by a fission-reacting detonator to produce an even more des-tructive blast. The third generation of nuclear warhead uses the large flux of very energetic neutrons to kill biological material, but the blast effect is essentially zero, hence attacks with neutron bombs leave most non-biological material and structures intact.

In the second application the nuclear fission process is controlled to provide a constant source of energy to drive turbines which produce elec-tricity.

Both uses represent epoch-making technical achievements, but mankind has yet to show itself capable of bearing sanely the burden of respon-sibility which nuclear physicists have laid upon it. One thing is certain: the discoveries will not cease. Already, other fissionable elements have been made and used; new chemical elements have been created; nuclear plants ("atomic piles") have stimulated great demands for new materials that will stand the heat and radiation inside the reactor, and this promotes research in other fields of science; irradiation inside an atomic pile gives new, and potentially useful properties to old materials; nuclear power drives ships and submarines. It is difficult to write even briefly about contemporary nuclear physics without feel-ing keenly the ambiguity of its powerful promises.

Atoms

A nucleus surrounded by its full complement of electrons is an electrically neutral system called an atom. Neither the atom as a whole, nor its nucleus, counts as a "fundamental particle" because either can be subdivided into more elementary parts, thus:

atom $\longrightarrow$ electrons + nucleus $\longrightarrow$ electrons + neutrons + protons

The chemical identity of the atoms of a given element, which was Dalton's key idea, depends entirely on the number and motion of the elec-trons. For example, the simplest element, hydrogen, has one proton for a nucleus, and one electron. The latter is comparatively easily detached or disturbed by the electric forces exerted by neighbouring atoms, consequently hydrogen is reactive chemically, *i.e.*, it readily lends its electron to build chemical structures with other equally co-operative elements. The second element, helium, has a nucleus of two protons and two neutrons; outside are two electrons in a particularly stable arrangement. Both electrons orbit the nucleus in the same spacial orbit, but with their spin directions oppo-site and at 90° to the plane through the nucleus and the electrons. This pair of electrons is so difficult to disarrange that the special name of closed shells has been coined to cover such cases. The fact that two electrons can be present in the same orbit is only possible if their spins are anti-parallel (Pauli Exclusion Principle). In the case of a stable group of eight electrons they arrange themselves in groups of two and their spins antiparallel. Helium with its closed shell will not react chemically, whereas hydrogen, which has an open shell of only one electron, will react very quickly with other atoms.

As the nuclear charge increases, different electron arrangements of greater or lesser stability succeed one another, with every so often a closed shell corresponding to one of the chemically inert gases neon, argon, xenon, krypton.

Such considerations, pursued in sufficient detail, enable atomic physics to account for all the differences and similarities among the chemical elements and, in principle at least, for all other facts of chemistry as well.

Ions

Changes in the atomic properties of an atom are accomplished by altering the position of any electron from one orbit to another. In the limit when an electron is completely removed from the atom, leaving it positively charged, the atom is said to be ionised and is called a positive ion. An atom can be singly or multiply ionised up to a level equal to the number of electrons existing in the neutral atom. In addition, atoms can, through distortion of the existing electrons, accept an additional electron and become negative ions. These can be formed in a resonance scattering process and exist only for life-times of only 10^{-14}s or be formed by chemical reactions. The roles played by negative and positive ions in the upper atmosphere of the earth and stellar atmospheres have been of special interest to atomic physicists since the 1930s.

Maxwell and Electromagnetic Waves

Atoms are held together by the electric attraction of the nucleus for the electrons. Finer details of atomic behaviour depend on the magnetic moments of the particles. Any moving charged particle gives rise to magnetic effects, and in the dynamo a coil moving in a magnet produces an electric current. It can be seen therefore that electric and magnetic phenomena are intimately linked. Any region of space subject to electric and magnetic influences is called an *electromagnetic field*.

In 1862, before the discovery of the electron, Maxwell, while still in his twenties, had perfected a general theory of the electro-magnetic field. This theory today still describes correctly almost all electro-magnetic phenomena. The elegance of this theory is difficult to appreciate, but it alone was the only theory of pre-twentieth century physics which satisfied the prerequisites of Einstein's relativity theory (1905), *i.e.*, inherent in its structure was the concept of relativistic invariance. *Inter alia*, he proved that disturbances in the electric and magnetic conditions at one place could be propagated to another place through empty space, with a definite velocity, just as sound waves are propagated through air. Such electromagnetic disturbances in transit are called *electromagnetic waves*, and their velocity turned out experimentally to be the same as that of light and radio waves—which was a decisive argument to show that both of these phenomena are themselves electro-magnetic waves.

Einstein and Photons

In the years between about 1900 and 1920 this view was upset by Planck, Einstein, Millikan, and others, who focused attention on phenomena (radiant heat, photoelectricity) in which light behaves like a stream of particles and not at all like waves. A wave and a particle are two quite different things, as anyone will admit after a moment's contemplation of, say, the ripples on a pond and a floating tennis ball. The acute question was: is light like waves or particles?

Theoretical physicists have devised means of having it both ways. To say that light behaves as particles means that the waves of the electromagnetic field cannot have their energy subdivided indefinitely. For waves of a given frequency, there is a certain irreducible quantity of energy that must be involved whenever light interacts with anything. This quantity is the product hv where v is the frequency and h is a constant named after Planck. Each such unit

is called a *quantum of the electromagnetic field* or a *photon* and is counted as one of the fundamental particles. Frequencies and wavelengths vary widely. Typical wavelengths are: radio—hundreds or thousands of metres; radar—a few centimetres; visible light—5×10^{-5} cm; X-rays—10^{-8} cm.

De Broglie and Particles

Since it seemed possible to attribute particle properties to electro-magnetic waves, then why not associate wave properties with particles. If an electron (mass m) is travelling with a velocity of v cm/s, then De Broglie (1923) suggested that its characteristic wavelength would be given by the relation $mv \ \lambda = h$; for example if $v = 10^8$ cm/s, $m = 9 \times 10^{-28}$ g, $h = 6 \cdot 610^{-27}$ erg-seconds, then $\lambda = 7{,}500$ Å, which is the same wavelength as red light. This proposal was confirmed in 1927 by Davisson and Germer when they showed that electrons could produce diffraction, a property until then only associated with light. These wave-like properties are now known to exist for all particles, and we now consider a particle with momentum mv to behave like a wave of wavelength $\lambda = h/mv$.

De Broglie made his revolutionary assertion in his doctoral thesis, and his examiners were so uneasy about the validity of the hypothesis that they were prepared to fail the young man in his examination. Happily for De Broglie, Einstein was visiting that particular university and he was asked his opinion of the idea; his reply ensured success for De Broglie and saved the examiners from future embarrassment.

Molecules

Electrical attractions and interactions of various kinds can cause atoms to combine with each other or themselves to form molecules. Two similar atoms, say hydrogen, combining to form the homonuclear diatomic molecule H_2, while two different atoms, hydrogen and chlorine, will form a heteronuclear diatomic molecule HCl. Molecules have a wide range of complexity, from simple pairs of atoms to highly intricate spirals and chains composed of thousands of atoms. The biological basis of all life is, of course, molecular in both origin and function.

Excited Atoms

Like nuclei, atoms, when given excess energy (insufficient to ionise them), will absorb the energy in one of the electrons, which is then displaced from its equilibrium state to a state (or orbit) of higher energy. It will remain there for typically 10^{-8} seconds before returning to its equilibrium position with the excess energy being emitted as light. The time an atom remains in its excited state can exceed 10^{-8} seconds; lifetimes of $0 \cdot 1$ second are known, and these metastable states are prevented by the atomic properties of the atom from decaying quickly to their equilibrium states. The colour of the light emitted is characteristic of the atom involved, with the more energetic transitions giving blue light while the less energetic transitions give red light. Hence the emitted colour (or wavelength) of the light can be used as a tool for chemical identification and study of the various transition probabilities in atoms.

Herein lies the explanation of innumerable natural and technical phenomena, such as the colours of glowing gases whether they exist in the sun and stars, in aurora, or in street-lamps and neon signs. Herein also lies the reason for the importance of spectroscopy, which is the study of the characteristic radiation from excited states for spectroscopy is not only a useful tool for the chemical identification of substances ("spectroscopic analysis") but was one of the main routes along which twentieth-century physicists broke through to a knowledge of the inner nature of the atom.

Forces in Nature

Nature uses four, possibly five, apparently different forces to make one particle interact with another. The weakest force is **gravity** which although present at all particle interactions, is insignificant in atomic and nuclear interactions. Gravity controls the mass distribution in the universe and the force has an infinite range of interaction.

The **electric force** which also has an infinite range of interaction is much stronger than the gravitational force and is responsible for the binding forces inside atoms by the attraction of nuclei for electrons.

Inside the nucleus two types of interaction take place which require different forces for their existence:

(1) the forces which hold neutrons and protons together in the nucleus and this is the **strong force,** and

(2) the **weak force** which controls the changes in charge state of nucleons, *e.g.*, the β-decay process when a neutron in a nucleus changes into a proton with the ejection of an electron is controlled by the weak force.

Both these nuclear forces are short-range with their radius of influence approximately 10^{-13} cm, with the weak force acting on all matter and the strong force acting on nucleons only. In today's parlance the strong force will act only on particles which are single multiples of quarks (see later). Since quarks exist (or more precisely, since their existence has been deduced), then it is necessary to have a force through which they can interact.

The fifth force of the universe is postulated to be the **colour force** which operates only on quark particles and has a mode of interaction which prevents a normal range restriction being placed on it. The proton, *i.e.*, the nucleus of atomic hydrogen, is composed of three quarks which move about freely within the shell of the proton; only when one quark tries to escape across the boundary of the proton does it experience the colour force which rebinds into the proton. Before we discuss further the interactions of these forces we must describe the range of particles which exist in physics.

Elementary Particles

When considering the word elementary in this context the reader should be wary of thinking that it implies some degree of absoluteness. The elementary mass of any particular particle is always highly qualified and subject to change. When a particle is discovered physicists measure its properties, *i.e.*, mass, electric charge, and spin, and determine which of the five forces to which it is subject. In addition, its life-time must be determined to see if the particle is stable or only a transient particle which will break up into other particles. The life-times of unstable particles are extremely short, ranging from 10^{-17}s to 10^{-21}s, and it is debatable if a particle which lasts only for 10^{-21}s should be called a particle. Generally now such short-lived particles are called resonances which are produced in an interaction which is only a step to the final product.

The rudimentary classification of particles is into four groups:

(1) photons
(2) leptons
(3) mesons
(4) baryons

All particles have an anti-particle which has the same mass but opposite charge as the real particle, the only exception being the photon, which is its own anti-particle and forms a group on its own. The leptons (electron, muon, and neutrino) form a stable group of particles and do not react to the strong or colour forces. This group of particles, and the photon, are perhaps the most fundamental of all particles. The mesons are unstable particles and (as will be seen later) exist only to act as a means which enables nucleons to interact with each other. They are subjected to the strong nuclear force. All particles heavier than the proton are called baryons, every one of them, except the proton, is unstable in some degree, and a vast number of them are known. Only a few are listed in the Table on page **F16.**

Mesons and baryons are collectively called hadrons. All of these unstable particles have been detected either in the cosmic flux falling on the earth or produced in the very high energy accelerating machines in Europe, the USA, and the USSR.

Strangeness

Some particles have long life-times $\sim 10^{-9}$ s, which is much larger than that encountered normally. Particles which possessed these long life-times were called "strange". Strangeness describes not a new property of matter but a different quality of matter which persists long enough to enable that particle to engage in strong nuclear-force interactions. Hence strangeness does not persist indefinitely. The decay of a strange particle into other particles with the abolition of strangeness proceeds via the weak nuclear force. The strange (and doubly strange) particles form highly symmetrised shapes when combined with non-strange particles. The pattern itself does not explain anything, but the underlying theory, known as Group Theory, does indicate by symmetry arguments which particle should be necessary to form a complete group. This mathematical procedure had a resounding success in 1964 when it predicted the existence of a triply strange particle known as "omega minus". The organisation of particles according to their properties of mass, spin, and strangeness in groups is now only an organisation exercise, and it will not tell us anything about the composition of nucleons.

Interactions of Particles

The method by which atomic, nuclear, and sub-nuclear particles interact is via the exchange of energy which can be considered as a particle exchange. The interaction between electric charges proceeds by the exchange of photons. For example, two charges feel each other by one charge emitting a photon which interacts with the second charge. Since the electric force has infinite range, its force-carrying particle has zero mass. The same criteria apply in the gravitational force, where the graviton is the particle which carries the force effect between particles of matter. Since the weak, strong, and colour forces are short-range, then their force-carrying particles have finite masses. The weak force is transmitted by W and Z particles and the strong force can be considered as transmitted by mesons. The quarks interact via the colour force, which is carried by gluons (mass at present unknown), which also feel the force themselves. The colour force does not distinguish between or acknowledge the existence of strangeness and charm.

A theory which combines the electric and weak forces into a single interaction has predicted the masses of the W and Z particles to be around 80 and 90 Gev respectively. In early 1983 experimental evidence was found by international groups at *CERN* for the existence of the W particle with the predicted mass thereby giving considerable support to this theory. A long term aim is to unify all the known forces of nature into a single interaction.

Quarks

The stability of the leptons contrasts sharply with the instability of the hadrons (excepting the proton), and this as well as other things had led physicists to consider that all hadrons were composed from different combinations of yet undiscovered particles. Gellmann has postulated the existence of three particles from which the nucleons, mesons, and hence all hadrons are composed. These "new" particles are attributed with fractional electric charges of $+\frac{2}{3}$, $-\frac{1}{3}$, and $-\frac{1}{3}$ of the electron charge. The particles were called quarks. The name quark was taken from the novel *Finnegans Wake* by James Joyce, the meaning of which is obscure, which is perhaps appropriate, but as students of Joyce will know, quark means "non sense", and other interpretations as to its meaning, such as the "sound of seagulls" or "quarts" are wrong. The three

SOME MEMBERS OF THE ATOMIC FAMILY

The numbers in brackets after the name denote first the electric charge and second, the mass. The charge on an electron is counted as -1 unit and the electron mass as $+1$ unit. Thus $(+1,207)$ means the particle has a positive charge of 1 unit and a mass 207 times that of the electron.

The mass energy of an electron is 0·51 MeV, hence conversion to mass energies can be made by multiplying the given mass by 0·51. Thus the muon has a mass energy of 106 MeV. Note: the letter M is used to denote quantities of millions and the letter G to denote quantities of thousand of millions.

Photon (0, 0)	A quantum of electromagnetic radiation, e.g., light, X-rays, γ-rays. The concept was introduced by M. Planck in 1900 when he described the emission of light as taking place in "packets" rather than in a steady stream. The energy of a photon is proportional to the frequency of the radiation and inversely proportional to the wavelength.
	Leptons
Electron $(-1, 1)$	Discovered by J. J. Thomson in 1897. The number of orbital electrons in an atom determines its chemical properties. Actual rest mass = 9.1×10^{-28} g. Emitted as β-rays by some radioactive nuclei. A stable particle.
Positron $(+1, 1)$	Positive counterpart or, "anti-particle", to the electron. Predicted theoretically by P. A. M. Dirac in 1928 and first discovered in cosmic rays by C. D. Anderson in 1932. Emitted as β-rays by some radioactive nuclei. When positrons and electrons collide they usually annihilate each other and turn into γ-rays; consequently, positrons only last about 10^{-10} sec. within ordinary matter, but are stable in isolation.
Neutrino (0, 0) and Anti-neutrino (0, 0)	These particles travel with the speed of light and are distinguished from one another by the relation of their spin to their direction of motion. A neutrino is emitted with the positron during positive β-decay; and an anti-neutrino with the electron during negative β-decay. Their interaction with matter is extremely slight. First postulated by Pauli in 1933 and detected in 1956. π-meson decay also produces neutrinos and anti-neutrinos but in 1962 it was proved experimentally that these are a different species. Thus there are two kinds of neutrino each with an anti-neutrino. All these particles are distinguished from photons by having different spin.
Muon $(\pm 1, 207)$	Similar to, but heavier than, the electron and positron; disintegrates into electron (or positron if positive) + neutrino + anti-neutrino.
	Mesons
Pion $(\pm 1, 273)$ or $(0, 264)$	The π-meson. Charged pions decay either into muons and neutrinos or into electrons and neutrinos. Neutral pions decay into γ-rays, into "positron-electron pairs", or both. Pions are intimately connected with nuclear forces, i.e., with the "strong" interaction.
Kaon $(\pm 1, 966)$ or $(0, 974)$	The K-mesons. These decay in many different ways producing other mesons, electrons, and neutrinos.
	Baryons
Proton $(+1, 1836·1)$	The positively-charged constituent of nuclei; the hydrogen nucleus is one proton. Fast-moving protons occur in cosmic rays. Does not spontaneously disintegrate.
Anti-proton $(-1, 1836·1)$	Negative anti-particle of the proton. Its existence was long suspected. Artificially produced and detected for the first time in 1955. Will react with the proton to produce pions or kaons.
Neutron (0, 1838·6)	Discovered by J. Chadwick in 1932. The neutral constituent of nuclei. When free it spontaneously disintegrates into a proton, an electron, and an anti-neutrino, after an average lifetime of about 18 minutes. Passes through matter much more easily than charged particles.
Anti-neutron (0, 1838·6)	The anti-particle of the neutron from which it is distinguished by properties connected with its magnetic moment and spin. Will react with neutron to produce pions or kaons.
Lambda Particle (0, 2183)	Discovered in 1947. Decays into proton plus pion.
Sigma Particle (0 or ± 1; about 2330)	Various modes of disintegration, producing neutrons, protons, mesons and lambda particles.
Omega Particle $(\pm 1, 3272)$	Predicted by recent theory and discovered at Brookhaven, New York, in 1964.
Psi Particle (0, about 6100)	Discovered independently by two laboratories in the USA 1974. Still under intensive study.

quarks were called up, down, and strange and have the properties given in the Table below:

Name	charge	spin	mass-energy (MeV)
up	$+\frac{2}{3}$	$\frac{1}{2}$	336
down	$-\frac{1}{3}$	$\frac{1}{2}$	338
strange	$-\frac{1}{3}$	$\frac{1}{2}$	540

These particles interact with each other via the colour force. Hence it can be seen that by taking different combinations of quarks, different hadrons can be built up. For example, the proton is two up quarks and one down, the neutron is two down and one up. The simplicity of this system can be appreciated, but the only experimental evidence to support the existence of quarks is indirect. No one has yet isolated a single quark! Many scientists are seeking ways to produce and detect them, but as yet (1982) no claims have stood the test of scrutiny. Of course as well as the three quarks up, down, and strange, there are the corresponding anti-quarks.

The K-mesons, for example, are composed of a quark and an anti-quark either with the spins of the two quarks aligned parallel to give a net spin of one, or aligned antiparallel to give a net spin of zero. The charges $+1$, -1, and 0 are simply determined by selecting the correct combination of up and down quarks.

Charm

In the quest to unite the weak and electric forces, theoreticians were forced to introduce yet another new particle into the quark family. This was a charmed quark with charge $+\frac{2}{3}$. The four members of the quark family seemed now to be symmetrical with the four members of the lepton group (electron, muon, and two neutrinos). Since the charmed quark had charge $+\frac{2}{3}$ and mass of 1,500 MeV, it could simply replace the up quark as a building brick in nucleons to produce charmed matter. For example, by replacing the up quark in a proton and a meson by a charmed quark we get a charmed proton and a charmed meson. The first experimental evidence of the existence of charm was obtained by the high-energy physics group at University College, London, working at CERN laboratory, when they established the existence of "a neutral current interaction" in neutrino scattering experiments. Although "naked" charm has never been detected, charmed mesons (masses of 1,865 and 2,020) have been detected by the SPEAR laboratory in USA and charmed anti-protons have also been detected with masses of 2,260 MeV. The experimentally determined masses are in sufficient agreement with theory to confirm the existence of the charmed quark. If a charmed quark combined with an anti-charmed quark it would form a particle of mass 3,000 MeV (3 GeV), and this has been given the name of the Gipsy particle. Several laboratories in 1976 reported the possible existence of a particle of this mass energy, and called it either a J particle or psi particle. The uncertainty has now been resolved and the existence of the Gipsy has been confirmed. It can exist in an excited state of 3·7 GeV, from which it decays by gamma-ray emission to a value of 3·1 GeV, the predicted value. It can further change its spin state and decay to a mass energy value of 2·8 GeV. The building bricks of matter now seemed complete!

Quarks and Pre-Quarks (Preons)

The final picture of the structure of matter is not yet complete, and indeed theorists have added two further quarks to the family of four called truth and beauty, although to date (1982) no experimental evidence of their existence is available. It is further postulated that even the quarks are composed of only two different particles called preons. All of this is only theoretical, and we must wait for the definite isolation of a single quark to settle the matter.

QUANTUM THEORY AND RELATIVITY
Quantum Theory

In our discussion of the nature of the various particles in physics we have alluded to them as being classified with well-defined sizes and weights. Of course, once we consider the physics of matter on a scale which is smaller than that of our every-day comprehension, then the classical physics of Newton is insufficient and we must use quantum physics. In the atomic region of reality we are again faced with the problem of indivisibility where the Greeks stopped their thinking and called the smallest particles of the universe atoms. Today we know that each separate particle is composed of a definite amount of energy, and the larger the particle, i.e., the more energy it is composed of, the easier it is to detect. We also know that the exchange of force between nucleons is carried by particles and that this inchangeability between mass and energy is a reality of quantum theory. To see this more fully we must realise that quantum theory rests on the theory of measurement! If a particle, of any type or structure, is composed of an amount of energy ΔE, then it is necessary to make measurements on it for a certain minimum time before it is detected. This minimum time Δt is given by the equation $\Delta E \times \Delta t \geqslant \hbar$, where $\hbar$ is Planck's constant divided by 2π; hence it can be seen that the smaller ΔE, then the longer a measurement must be made to detect the particle. Correspondingly, the time of measurement itself introduces an uncertainty, ΔE, in the energy of the particle. As well as the parameters ΔE and Δt, a particular physical event can be expressed in terms of its momentum p and position q, and these can also be expressed in a relationship as $\Delta p \times \Delta q \geqslant \hbar$. Hence one can ask at what position in space, q, is a particular particle with momentum p? Or what exactly is the wavelength of a wave? It may be thought that the first question cannot reasonably be asked of a wave nor the second of a particle, but bearing in mind the dual roles of particles and waves discussed earlier, then these questions can be interchanged. We know that electrons behave both as particles and waves. Since electrons have something in common with both, one question cannot be answered precisely for electrons without ignoring the other; alternatively, both questions can be given an imprecise answer. As the wavelength of electrons is intimately connected with their speed, one has to accept an accurate knowledge of the speed (wavelength) and ignorance of position, or the converse, or inaccurate knowledge of both. This is the famous Heisenberg Uncertainty Principle. Quantum theory is a set of mathematical rules for calculating the behaviour of fundamental particles in accordance with the Uncertainty Principle. In spite of its equivocalsounding name, the principle has led to an enormous increase in the accuracy with which physical phenomena can be described and predicted. Quantum theory includes all that previous theories did and more.

Quantum theory grew up in the same epoch as the Theory of Relativity. Heroic attempts have been made to combine the two, but with only partial success so far. Relativity is concerned with all motion and all physical laws, but its characteristic manifestations occur only when something is moving with nearly the velocity of light. Quantum theory is likewise all-embracing, but its typical phenomena almost always occur when something on the minute atomic scale is in question. Co. Consequently, the vast majority of everyday mechanics needs no more than the classical theory laid down by Newton, which is neither relativistic nor quantum.

Relativity

Historically, relativity grew out of attempts to measure the speed with which the earth moved through that hypothetical medium called the ether, which was supposed at that time to be the bearer of light waves. To take a simple analogy: sound waves travel through still air with a certain definite speed, v. If you move through the air with speed v' towards oncoming sound waves, they will pass you at the speed $v + v'$. Michelson and Morley, in their celebrated experiment of 1887, failed to find the corresponding behaviour on the part of light. This is so important an experiment that it has been repeated, and repeatedly discussed ever since. In Octobe58 the latest and most accurate confirmation of the Michelson–Morley result was announced. It seems as if light always travels with the same speed relative to an observer, however fast he moves relative to anything else. Einstein put it this way: two observers moving with any constant velocity relative to each other will always agree that light travels past them at the same speed; this speed is denoted by c, and is approximately 186,000 miles per second.

It should be remembered that the limiting value of the velocity of light in relativity is a postulate introduced by Einstein not a conclusion which the theory provides. There may exist forms of matter which can travel faster than light!

Nevertheless, the postulate that the maximum velocity encountered in the universe is c, logically developed, leads to remarkable conclusions. For instance: if you walk from tail to nose of an aircraft at 4 m.p.h. and the plane is receding from me at 300 m.p.h., then you recede from me at 304 m.p.h. "Common sense", Newton, and Einstein would all agree on this. But if you could walk at $0.25c$ and the plane moved at $0.5c$, the Newtonian mechanics would give your recession speed as $0.75c$, whereas Einsteinian relativity would give about $0.67c$. Although at the everyday speed of 300 m.p.h., the disagreement, though present in principle, is absolutely negligible, at speeds near that of light it becomes very pronounced. Many experiments show that the relativity answer is right.

Equivalence of Mass and Energy

The most famous consequence of relativity theory from which we derive most benefit is the knowledge that mass can be converted into energy. The amount of energy, E, which can be derived from a given mass, m, of any type of material is given by the celebrated equation $E = mc^2$. If we take one gram of ash and convert it into the free energy of which it is composed we would get 10^8 kilowatts of power, sufficient to heat 15 houses for a year. The heat provided by the material which produced the ash is equivalent to that obtained from burning a single match. The massive energy released by $E = mc^2$ has been demonstrated in the power of nuclear weapons, but this energy has also been put to peaceful uses in nuclear-powered electricity generating stations.

In fundamental particle physics the masses of particles were always expressed in units of mass energy using $E = mc^2$ as the conversion equation. This is a matter of convenience from the realisation that mass is simply a condensed form of energy. The mesons which are the force-exchanging particles in the strong interaction have a mass energy of approximately 130 MeV, which is equivalent to a real mass of only 210^{-28} grams. The energy of the sun is provided by the conversion of real mass into light energy through thermonuclear fusion processes.

Mass and Rest Mass

The concept of mass is not a simple idea to grasp, for as we have seen, the mass of a body which is at rest is equivalent to its inherent latent energy. Further complications and interpretations arise when the body starts moving and its mass is no longer necessarily a constant quantity.

A stationary body can be observed to have a mass called its *rest mass*. If the body moves, it has energy of motion and therefore, according to Einstein's mass–energy equation, it increases its mass. Mass thus depends on speed, but in such a way that there is very little change unless the speed approaches that of light. Many experiments on atomic particles demonstrate this. The interesting question now arises: do all fundamental particles have rest mass? or do some have mass derived solely from their energy? The answer appears to be that photons and neutrinos have no rest mass; all other particles have. The Table on **F16** gives their rest masses.

Special Theory of Relativity

The mathematical development of Einstein's ideas, leading to the conclusions just referred to, constitutes the Special Theory of Relativity.

Stated more generally, the theory raises the question whether two observers in uniform relative motion could ever detect, as a result of their relative speed, any difference in the physical laws governing matter, motion, and light. To this, Special Relativity answers: No. The detailed theory involves special consideration of the results the two observers would obtain when measuring (i) the spatial distance, and (ii) the time interval, between the same two events. It turns out that they would not agree on these two points. They would agree, however, on the value of a certain quantity made up jointly of the spatial distance and the time interval in a somewhat complex combination. The intimate mixture of space and time in this quantity has led to the treatment of the three space dimensions and time on an equivalent footing. Hence the frequent references to time as the "fourth dimension". Minkowski devised an extremely elegant presentation of relativity theory by using an extension of ordinary geometry to four dimensions. A line drawn in his four-dimensional space represents the path of a particle in space and time, *i.e.*, the whole history of the particle. Thus the movement of particles in the ordinary world is turned into the geometry of lines in Minkowski's four-dimensional world of "space–time".

General Relativity and Gravitation

In 1915, 10 years after the publication of the Special Theory of Relativity, Einstein published his theory of General Relativity. This apparently innocuous extension of the ideas of special relativity to include accelerated relative motion opened up new and difficult fields of mathematical complexity which, when solved, enabled Einstein to include gravitation in the theory. In discussing the physics of atomic, nuclear, and subnuclear particles, we did not include the effect of the gravitational force, since in relation to the Electric, Weak, Strong, and Colour forces it is extremely small and can be neglected in the discussion of the structure of matter but not in the discussion of astronomical problems and the movements of large-scale electrically uncharged bodies.

It has been usual, ever since Newton, to say that two bodies of mass m_1 and m_2, separated by a distance r attract one another with a force proportional to $m_1 m_2 / r^2$. This is Newton's inverse square law of gravitation which explains the movements of planets and comets and the falling to earth of an apple from a tree.

The apple's fall is accelerated, and we observe this by noting its position relative to certain marks fixed with respect to us, and by timing it with some sort of clock. This system of location in space and time may be called our "frame of reference". We therefore assert that, in our frame of reference, the apple falls down with an acceleration which Newton saw no alternative but to attribute to a thing called gravitational attraction. Galileo had shown that *all* bodies fall with the same acceleration at all points, and we can now rephrase this by saying that in our frame of reference there is a constant gravitational attraction or *uniform gravitational field*. (This last statement and Galileo's demonstration only refer strictly to points fairly near the earth's surface; at greater distances the gravitational field decreases and is therefore not uniform.)

Now suppose a collection of falling bodies is observed by us and an intelligent creature, designated C, inhabits one of them. C has his own frame of reference fixed relative to him and we have ours fixed relative to us. In C's frame neither his own body, nor any of the others, is accelerated, and therefore he has no reason to suppose a gravitational force is acting on them. We have, therefore, the following situation:

    (i) in our frame, fixed relative to us, we find all the bodies falling subject to a gravitational pull;

    (ii) in C's frame, undergoing accelerated fall relative to us, no gravitational field is apparent to C.

It looks, therefore, as if one has only to choose the correct frame of reference for the measurements in order to remove the need for any assumptions about the existence of gravitational fields. This is a simple illustration of the connection between gravitation and frames of reference for the measurement of space and time. Einstein's General Theory of Relativity extends this to cover non-uniform gravitational fields and shows that what Newton taught us to call the gravitational field of material bodies is better thought of as a peculiarity of the space and time in the neighbourhood of such bodies. Since space–time, as we mentioned above, can be expressed in geometrical terms, Einstein has transformed the theory of gravitation into an exercise (a difficult one) in the geometry of space–time. Other physicists, in Einstein's tradition, are trying to turn *all* physics into geometry, but no one knows whether this is really feasible.

All this abstruse work is much more than a demonstration of mathematical power and elegance. Observable phenomena which fall outside the scope of Newton's theory of gravitation are accounted for by relativity. One is the small but definite discrepancy between the actual orbit of the planet Mercury and the predictions of Newton's theory. Another is the effect of a gravitational field on the wavelength of light emitted by atoms. Similar atoms in different places in a gravitational field emit radiations with slightly different wavelengths. For example, the light from an atom in the intense field of a star should have slightly longer wavelength than the corresponding light from an atom on earth. This effect has always proved very difficult to detect with certainty. However, Einstein's prediction was verified with moderate accuracy in 1960 by a very subtle method which was purely terrestrial in its operation. The atoms being compared were placed at the top and bottom of a water tower and the difference in their emission was detected by means that belong rather to nuclear physics than to astronomy.

Quantum Theory and Relativity Combined

The atomic family table refers to "antiparticles". The theory which first introduced such things in 1934 is due to the Cambridge physicist Dirac and was epoch-making. Dirac conceived an equation to describe the motion of electrons subject to the laws of both quantum theory and relativity. His achievement was thus to synthesise these two great ideas. The spin of the electron was originally a supposition that helped to make sense of spectroscopic observations of light emitted from atoms. Dirac's equation made spin a logical consequence of the union of relativity and quantum theory. Perhaps even more important was the brilliant inference that the equation for the electron implied the existence of another particle having the same mass and spin but with a positive instead of a negative electric charge. This object is called the electron's antiparticle and is now well known as a positron. Every particle is now believed to imply an antiparticle, so it is conceivable that the universe could have been (but isn't) an anti-universe, *i.e.*, all the electrons and protons might have been positrons and antiprotons and so on. The laws of physics would still have been applicable, however.

The gravitational force has an infinite range and therefore its force-carrying particles must travel at the speed of light. The graviton is the name of the particle which transmits the gravitational force between bodies with mass. To date (1983) no experiment has detected the existence of gravitons which are the postulated quanta of gravitational waves. There is an exact analogy between photons, the quanta of electro-magnetic radiation, and gravitons.

Conservation Laws

If charged particles interact, then it is found that the amount of electric charge existing after the reaction is the same as that which existed before the event. This is called the law of conservation of charge. Many other conservation laws exist in physics, *e.g.*, conservation of mass energy, angular momentum, linear momentum, and other more abstruse conservation laws exist in particle physics, *e.g.*, conservation of baryons, leptons, strangeness, isotopic spin, and parity. The last three conservation laws listed have been found to have a limited jurisdiction, and the violation of parity in the weak interaction was a great surprise to physicists.

Any reader who looks in a mirror knows that the left- and right-hand sides of his face are interchanged in the image. Fortunately mirrors do not also turn the image upside down, but, if they did, the face would then have undergone what is called "a parity transformation". A screwdriver driving a right-handed screw downwards becomes, on parity transformation, a screwdriver driving a left-handed screw upwards. The law of conservation of parity is a way of asserting that any physical process that goes on in the world could equally well go on—obeying the same laws—in a parity transformed world. There is nothing left-handed that does not in principle have a right-handed counterpart.

For many years this belief was strongly held. It came as something of a shock when, in 1957, after theoretical proposals by Lee and Yang in America, Wu and co-workers proved that parity was not always conserved. To understand Wu's experiment, we must recall that nuclei can have intrinsic spin. Suppose the axis of spin were downwards into the page and the rotation were suitable for driving an ordinary screw into the page. Then Wu showed that beta-rays from such a nucleus are emitted *preferentially upwards, i.e.*, against the direction of travel of the screw. The parity transformed version of this would have the beta-rays preferentially emitted in the same direction as the travel of the screw and, if parity is conserved, this process would happen too. But it does not. If the beta-rays in the experiment had been emitted in equal numbers up and down, then the parity transformed version would have had this feature too, and thus parity would have been conserved.

Modern research on elementary particles is greatly concerned to find out which types of process obey which conservation laws. The parity surprise is only one of the stimulating shocks that this type of work is heir to.

Conclusion

Over a century's development of the atomic ideas has brought a progressive, if jerky, increase in the mathematical precision of the theories. In some fields of particle physics, observations to one part in a million, or even better, can be explained, to that level of accuracy, by the existing theories. At the same time, however, the theories have lost visual definition. An atom as an invisible but none the less solid billiard ball was easy enough; so was a light wave conceived like a sound wave in air. Even after Rutherford, an atom consisting of a miniature solar system merely exchanged the solid billiard ball for a system of revolving billiard balls and was no great obstacle to visualisation. But since quantum theory and the Uncertainty Principle, every unambiguous visualisation of fundamental wave-particles leaves out half the picture, and although the electrons are in the atom, we can no longer represent them in definite orbits. The moral seems to be that visualisation is unnecessary, or at best a partial aid to thought.

THE PROPERTIES OF MATTER IN BULK

One of the most obvious and at the same time most wonderful things about the properties of matter is their great variety. Think of air, diamond, mercury, rubber, snow, gold, pitch, asbestos.... Even the differences of state of the same chemical substance are remarkable enough, ice, water, and steam, for example. One of the aims of physics is to reach an understanding of all these different properties by explaining them in terms of the behaviour of the particles discussed in the previous section (**F10–19**). The widespread success with which this imposing programme has been carried out indicates the maturity of physics. It is difficult to think of any major property of matter in bulk for which there is not some attempted theoretical explanation, though future physicists will no doubt regard some present-day theories as rudimentary or incorrect.

Physics, Statistics, and Thermodynamics

Take a number equal to the population of London, multiply it by itself, and multiply the product by another million. The answer is about the number of molecules in 1 cubic centimetre of ordinary air. They are constantly moving about and colliding with one another. Even if the nature of the molecules and their laws of motion were perfectly understood, it would clearly be impracticable to calculate the exact paths described by each particle of so vast an assembly. This difficulty brought into being a whole branch of physics concerned with calculating the overall or average properties of large numbers of particles. Just as statisticians will provide the average height, income, expectation of life, and so on, of the population of London, without knowing everything about every individual, so statistical physicists can work out average properties of molecules or atoms in large groups. This important branch of physics is called *Statistical Mechanics*. It was founded in the nineteenth century by Maxwell, Boltzmann, and Gibbs and is still being actively developed.

Consider now all the molecules in 1 cubic centimetre of air contained in a small box. They are continually bombarding the walls of the box and bouncing off. This hail of impacts (it is actually about 10^{23} impacts per square centimetre per second) is the cause of the pressure which the gas exerts against the walls of the box. Now suppose we pump air in until there is twice as much as before, though the box is still the same size and at the same temperature. This means that the density of the gas (*i.e.*, the mass of 1 unit of volume) has doubled. We should now expect twice as many impacts per second on the walls as before, and consequently twice the pressure. We therefore arrive at a conclusion that, if the volume and temperature are constant, the pressure of a gas is proportional to its density. This is one of the simplest statistical arguments that can be checked against observation; in fact, it stands the test very well.

Heat, Temperature, and Energy

The proviso about the temperature remaining the same is an important one for the following reason. In the nineteenth century there was much discussion about the nature of heat. To Joule we owe the now well-established view that heat is equivalent to mechanical work. In one of his experiments, in the 1840s, the work necessary to rotate paddle wheels against the resistance of water in a tank generated heat that caused a slight rise in the temperature of the water. Joule found out exactly how much work was equivalent to a given quantity of heat. However, one can do other things with work besides generate heat; in particular, work creates motion, as when one pushes a car. Bodies in motion possess a special form of energy, called kinetic energy, which is equal to the work done in accelerating them from a state of rest. We have, then, three closely connected ideas: work, heat, and kinetic energy. Now according to the views of the nineteenth century, which are still accepted, any heat given to a gas simply increases the kinetic energy of its molecules; the hotter the gas, the faster its molecules are moving. If, therefore, the gas in our box is allowed to get hotter, there is an increase in molecular speed, and the impacts on the walls become correspondingly more violent. But this means the pressure increases, so we have another law: if the density remains the same, the pressure increases if the temperature does.

Laws of Thermodynamics

Such considerations as these have been pursued with great elaboration and subtlety. The notions of heat, temperature, energy, and work—familiar but vague in everyday life—have been given precise definitions, and the relations between them have been enshrined in the Laws of Thermodynamics. Enshrined is perhaps a suitable word, because these laws are so soundly and widely based on experimental results that they have greater prestige than any others in physics. If any proposed physical law comes in conflict with thermodynamics then so much the worse for that law—it has to be revised. It is sometimes asserted that no one is properly educated who does not understand the Second Law of thermodynamics. We cannot, therefore, leave this section without at least stating the two best known thermodynamic laws:

First Law: *If any physical system is given a quantity of heat, and if the system performs some work, then the energy of the system increases by an amount equal to the excess of heat given over work done.* This law asserts that heat, energy, and work are convertible one into the other, and that all such transactions balance exactly. This is one form of a principle accepted as fundamental in all science, *viz.*, the Principle of the Conservation of Energy, according to which energy can never be created or destroyed, but only changed from one form to another.

Second Law: *It is impossible to make an engine which will continuously take heat from a heat source and, by itself, turn it all into an equivalent amount of mechanical work.* In fact, all engines which produce work from heat—steam engines for example—always use only a fraction of the heat they take in and give up the rest to some relatively cool part of the machine. The Second Law makes this obligatory on all work-from-heat devices. This statement of the Second Law has an engineering ring about and, indeed, it arose from the work of the nineteenth-century French engineer Carnot. Nevertheless, it can be rephrased in terms of the concept of entropy, and has been applied with unbroken success to all fields of science involving the transfer of heat and allied matters. It sets a definite limit to the kinds of physical and chemical process that can be conceived to take place. Nothing has been known to contravene it.

The States of Matter

The molecular motion in gases has been referred to in the previous section. Tacitly it was assumed that each molecule acted independently of all others, except that collisions occurred between them. In reality, molecules exert attractive forces on one another and, if a gas is cooled so that molecular movements become relatively sluggish, a time comes when the attractive forces succeed in drawing the molecules close together to form a liquid. This process is called condensation.

The molecules in a liquid are packed tightly together and they impede each other's movements. On the other hand, movement still persists, and the molecules struggle about like people in a milling crowd. Besides wandering about, the molecules vibrate. These motions represent the energy contained in the liquid.

The fact that the molecules, though irregularly packed, can still slip past one another and move from place to place, explains the essential property of liquids that distinguishes them from solids—ability to flow. As a matter of fact, although the rather vague assertion that in a liquid molecules are irregularly packed would be generally accepted, there is no agreed opinion on what the irregularity is actually like. Indeed, not only the precise structure of liquids, but the theory of liquids in general, is fraught with such considerable mathematical difficulties that the liquid state is much less well understood than the solid or gaseous.

Most solids are crystals. The popular idea of a crystal is of something which has a more or less regular geometrical form with faces that shut in the light—like snowflakes or gems. However, crystallinity really depends on a regular inner pattern of the atoms, and may or may not show itself on the visible surface. A lump of lead, for example, is crystalline, despite its appearance.

The actual arrangement of the atoms in a crystal can be extremely complex. Some are quite simple, however. The largest model of a crystal structure must surely be the 400-ft. "Atomium" building in the 1958 Brussels Exhibition. This consisted of eight balls, representing atoms, situated at the corners of a cube, and one more ball exactly in the middle. Imagine this repeated in all directions so that every ball is the centre of a cube whose corners are the eight neighbouring balls. This is known to crystallographers and physicists as the "body-centred cubic structure"; it is the actual arrangement of atoms in iron, sodium, chromium, and some other metals. If every ball, instead of being the centre of a cube, were the centre of a regular tetrahedron (a solid figure with four equal triangular faces), and had its four neighbours at the corners of the tetrahedron, then we should have the "diamond structure". This is how the carbon atoms are arranged in diamonds.

In crystals the atoms are locked into a regular ordered structure by attractive forces which give the solid its rigidity and prevent it from flowing. The atoms are so close together that any attempt to press them closer involves crushing or distorting the atoms—a process they resist strongly. This explains why solids (and liquids too) are so difficult to compress. Gases can easily be compressed because there is so much space between the molecules.

The distinction between solid and liquid is not so sharp as is commonly supposed. A lump of dough will not bounce, but is plastic; a steel ball-bearing is very elastic and bounces excellently, but one cannot mould it in the fingers. Neither dough nor steel qualifies for description as a liquid. There are, however, substances which can be moulded like plasticine into a ball that will then bounce very well on the floor like an elastic solid, and finally, if left on a flat table, will spread into a pool and drip off the edge like a liquid. There is no point in trying to force such things into rigid categories. One may say instead that for short, sharp impacts the material behaves like an elastic solid, but under long-sustained forces it flows like a liquid. The properties of these, and many other anomalous materials, are increasingly engaging the attention of those who study the science of flow—*rheology*. It is interesting to see how many familiar and important materials exhibit peculiar rheological behaviour—paint, dough, ball-pen ink, cheese, unset cement, and solutions of nylon and other plastics are only a few examples.

Inside a Crystalline Solid

We now return to our wallpaper analogy of crystal structure and give some free play to our visual imagination.

Suppose we have walls papered with a regular pattern of, say, roses, fuchsias, and green leaves. These represent the different kinds of atoms in the solid. Careful observation shows that the whole pattern is shimmering. The flowers and leaves are not stationary, but are undergoing slight random oscillations about their proper positions. In a crystal these movements are called thermal vibrations, and are never absent. The hotter the crystal, the more the vibration, and at a high enough temperature the vibrations become so great that the atoms get right out of position and the pattern disappears altogether, *i.e.*, the crystal melts. Thermal vibrations are essential to the theory of solids, and are responsible for numerous physical properties.

Next we note something extraordinary about some of the papered walls. On these the paper has been hung in irregular patches fitted together like a not very well-made jig-saw puzzle. Lines of roses which should be vertical are horizontal in some patches, oblique in others. This represents the situation in most ordinary solids, for they consist of many small pieces of crystal irregularly packed together. Such material is called *polycrystalline*, and the small pieces are *crystal grains*. Crystal grains may be almost any size, sometimes visible to the naked eye, as often on galvanised iron.

However, on one wall, we see excellent regularity and no obvious patches at all. The physicist would call this a *single crystal*, and several techniques exist for preparing them. Natural single crystals can be found, and there are some beautiful large single crystals of rock salt. But on examining the single crystal wall closely, we find a number of places where the paperhanger has failed to make adjacent pieces register perfectly—there is a slight disjointedness. This occurs in real single crystals, and the line along which the structure fails to register is called a *dislocation*. These are much studied by physicists because of their bearing on the mechanical properties of solids, on the yielding of metals under strong stress, for instance.

This by no means exhausts the possibilities of the wallpaper analogy; several other phenomena can be found. For example, in a place where there should be a fuchsia there is actually a daffodil—something completely foreign to the pattern. Or perhaps a small wrongly shaped leaf is jammed between the proper leaves in a place that should really be blank. These represent chemical impurity atoms. The first is called *substitutional*, because it occupies the position of an atom that should be there, the second is called *interstitial*, because it does not. Substitutional impurities of indium metal, deliberately added to the semi-conductor silicon, make possible the manufacture of transistors (*see* **Section L**). Some steels derive their valuable properties from interstitial carbon atoms within the iron pattern.

What physicists call a vacancy would occur if a flower or leaf were simply missing. Remembering that all the atoms are vibrating, we should not be surprised if occasionally an atom jumps into a neighbouring vacancy if there happens to be one, *i.e.*, the atom and the vacancy change places. Later this may occur again. In the course of time, a rose which was near the ceiling may make its way to the floor by jumping into vacant rose positions when they occur near enough. This process, which the physicist calls *diffusion*, is also analogous to the game in which numbers or letters can be moved about in a flat box because there is one vacant space to permit adjustment. The more vacancies there are in a crystal, the faster diffusion occurs. It is, in fact, very slow in solids, but is nevertheless evidence that apparently quiescent materials are really internally active.

Metals, Electricity, and Heat

There is ample evidence that inside metals there are large numbers of free electrons. To illuminate this statement let us take sodium metal as an example. One single sodium atom has a nucleus with eleven protons; there are therefore eleven electrons in the atom. The outermost one is easily detached, leaving a positively charged sodium ion behind. We may think of these ions arranged in the three-dimensional pattern characteristic of sodium crystals. It is the same as the iron structure previously described. The detached electrons, one per atom, occupy the spaces in between. The usual metaphor is that the structure of ions is permeated by a "gas" of electrons. Like all visualisations of fundamental particles, this must be taken as a rough approximation. The important point is that the electrons in the gas are not bound to individual atoms but may wander freely about the crystal, hindered only by the collisions they make with the vibrating ions.

This is the picture as it appeared to physicists of the first decade of this century, and we can explain many properties of metals with it. Naturally the theory has developed greatly since then, thanks to the great work of Lorentz, Sommerfeld, and Bloch; it now relies heavily on quantum theory, but it is surprising how little violence is done to modern ideas by the simple picture we are using.

The free electrons move randomly in all directions at thousands of miles per hour. If the metal is connected across a battery it experiences an electric field. Electrons are negatively charged particles, and are therefore attracted to the electrically positive end of the metal. They can move through the metal because they are free; this flow is not possible to those electrons which remain bound to the ions. The function of the battery is to keep the flow going and, for as long as it is going, it is the electric current.

The flow of electrons is not unimpeded. They

constantly collide with the ions and are deflected from the path of flow. This hindrance is what the electrician calls *electrical resistance*. The electric force, due to the battery or a dynamo, accelerates the electrons, thus giving them extra energy; but they lose this to the ions at collisions because the ions recoil and vibrate more than before. The net effect of innumerable collisions is to increase the thermal vibrations of the ions, *i.e.*, to make the metal hotter. This is the explanation of the fact well known to every user of electric irons; that electric current heats the conductor. If a strong current is passed through a wire, the heating is so great the wire glows, as in electric-light bulbs, or melts and breaks, as in blown fuses.

If one end of a metal rod is heated we soon feel the heat at the other end; metals are excellent thermal conductors. This is because the mobile free electrons carry the heat energy down the rod, passing it on to the ions by colliding with them. Substances without free electrons cannot do this, nor can they conduct electricity well; we have, in the free electrons, an explanation of the fact that the good electrical conductors are the good heat conductors. For technical purposes, it would be useful to have electrical insulators that would conduct heat well, and *vice versa*; but this is almost a contradiction in terms, and one can only compromise.

Non-conductors and Semi-conductors

There are some elements, and numerous compounds in which all the electrons are so tightly bound to their parent atoms that free electron flow is impossible. These materials are electrical and thermal insulators.

Let us return to our sodium atom. It readily loses its outer electron, forming a positive ion. The ion is very stable; indeed, its electron arrangement resembles the "closed shell" belonging to the inert gas neon. The chlorine atom, on the other hand, would have a very stable structure, resembling the inert gas argon, if only it could be given one extra electron to complete the closed shell. If the outer sodium electron were given to a chlorine atom we should have two stable ions, one positive and one negative. These would then attract each other and form a compound. This is just how common salt, sodium chloride, is formed, and its crystals consist of a regular network of alternate sodium and chlorine ions. As all the electrons are bound to ions, it is not surprising that salt will not conduct electricity or heat to any appreciable extent. Not all insulating compounds are built on this pattern, but all have structures which bind the electrons tightly.

We have seen (**F20**) that Nature does not permit a hard-and-fast distinction between solids and liquids; nor does she between conductors and insulators. Over a hundred years ago, Faraday knew of substances which would conduct electricity, but rather badly. A common one is the graphite in pencils. Others are the elements selenium, germanium, and silicon, and a considerable number of compounds. Such substances are called semi-conductors.

Semi-conductors conduct badly because they have so few free electrons, many thousands of times fewer than metals. In very cold germanium—say, 200 degrees below freezing—all the electrons are tightly bound to atoms and the substance is an insulator. It differs from normal insulators in that, on warming it, the gradually increasing thermal vibration of the crystal detaches some of the electrons, for they are only moderately tightly bound. The warmer the crystal becomes, the more of its electrons become detached and the better it conducts electricity. By about the temperature of boiling water, there are so many freed electrons that conduction is moderately good, though less good than in metals. This is basic semi-conductor behaviour. Because transistors were made of germanium, and because they are of such great technical importance, more knowledge has accumulated about germanium than about any other material. *See also* **Transistor, Section L** and **Section V**.

Magnetism

The most important thing about magnetism is that it is inseparably connected with electricity. Oersted showed this in July 1820, when he deflected a magnetic compass needle by passing an electric current through a wire near it. Since then, many experiments have shown that wherever a current flows there will certainly be a magnetic field in the surrounding space. The laws of this are very well known now—they are the Maxwell equations previously referred to (**F14**). However, most people first meet magnetism when, as children, they pick up pins with a magnet. Where is the electricity here? and what is a magnet?

The explanation of magnetism exemplifies beautifully the technique of explaining the bulk properties of matter in terms of fundamental particles. In the atoms the electrons are moving, and a moving electric charge constitutes an electric current. Therefore each moving electron is a tiny source of magnetism. It does not immediately follow that every atom is a source of magnetism because it might—and often does—happen that the magnetic effect of different electrons in the atom cancel out. In helium atoms, for example, the two electrons have equal but opposed magnetic effects. Nevertheless, some atoms and ions have a net effect called their *magnetic moment*. This simply means they behave like tiny magnets. Crystals containing such atoms will be magnetic, though the magnetism is much weaker than in ordinary magnets because the different atoms largely annul one another's effects. In a very limited number of crystals, however, the magnetic ions act on one another in a special way which forces all the atomic magnets to point in the same direction. The total effect of many co-operating atoms is very strong and the crystal becomes what we normally call a magnet. Iron acts like this, so do cobalt and nickel, the rarer elements gadolinium and dysprosium, and a fair number of alloys. On the whole, this behaviour, which is called *ferromagnetism*, is very rare. The reason for the co-operation of all the atomic magnets is not explained to everyone's satisfaction yet, though the key idea was given by Heisenberg in 1928.

In the section dealing with the electron it was pointed out that every electron has an *intrinsic* magnetic moment. This is in addition to any effect simply due to the electron's motion round a nucleus. The net effects of ions are therefore partly due to the intrinsic magnetism of electrons. In the ferromagnetic metals the latter is by far the most important contribution. Thus we pick up pins, and benefit from magnets in other ways, because innumerable fundamental particles act in co-operation for reasons that are still somewhat obscure. It is interesting to ask whether the electrons responsible for magnetism are the same free electrons that allow the metals to conduct electricity. It is thought not.

We are accustomed to think of magnets as metallic. Actually the magnet originally discovered by the Chinese was the mineral lodestone, which is a non-metallic oxide of iron. Nowadays a number of non-metallic magnets are made. They are called *ferrites*, and some are insulators and some are semi-conductors. The combination of magnetism and insulation is technically very valuable in radio, radar, and other applications. The explanation of ferrite behaviour is related to that of metallic ferromagnetism, but is not the same.

Conclusion

The aim of the second part of this account of physics is to show how our conception of fundamental particles allows us to build theories of the properties of matter. This very aim shows that the two "major divisions" of physics referred to at the beginning (**F10**) are divided only in the way that labour is divided by co-operating workers to lighten the task. For the task of physics is a very great one—no less than to explain the behaviour of matter; and since the universe, living and inanimate, is made of matter, physics must necessarily underlie all the other sciences.

F23

III. THE WORLD OF THE CHEMISTS

WHAT CHEMISTRY IS ABOUT

Chemistry is the scientific study of the preparation, composition and architecture of chemical compounds, and of the modes and mechanisms of their transformations or reactions. Natural (and other) processes can be classified as *physical*, in which no chemical reactions occur, for example water running down a hill, and *chemical* if changes occur in the chemical compounds involved. Common examples are the burning of fuel, whether in a biological cell, an internal combustion engine, or a lowly domestic grate. Biological changes at the molecular level in plants and animals generally consist of many chemical reactions, as do some geological changes in rocks and deposits. Chemistry therefore is rooted in physics and interpenetrates biology (biochemistry) and geology (geochemistry). Some of the main sub-divisions of chemistry are delineated in the Table. Chemists not only aim to discover new reactions by trial and error, but by seeking to understand chemical change aspire to design new compounds and reactions. New reactions can be used to produce useful physical *effects* in new ways—like light from the cold chemical candle (chemiluminescence) as the firefly does, and electricity from more efficient batteries and from fuel cells—or to produce new *synthetic products*. These can be faithful copies of compounds like penicillin which have been discovered first in nature, or completely new, invented, compounds like the sulphonamide drugs.

This research activity, which is mainly centred in the Universities, is the basis of a large chemical industry, one of the major manufacturing industries. Other branches which deal with more restrictive topics or use combinations of the above for specific goals have names which are self-explanatory, for example:—analytical chemistry, colloid chemistry, pharmaceutical chemistry, chemistry of dyes, petroleum chemistry, polymer chemistry, environmental chemistry, medicinal chemistry.

Main Divisions of Chemistry

	Elements, Compounds and reactions involved	*Examples*
Organic Chemistry	Carbon in combination mainly with H, O, N.	Natural products Carbohydrates Steroids Proteins
Inorganic Chemistry	All elements and compounds not covered in organic chemistry. Minerals and salts.	Inorganic polymers (*e.g.*, silicones) Transition metal complexes Organometallic compounds
Physical Chemistry	Mathematical and physical descriptions of organic and inorganic compounds and reactions.	Electrochemistry Chemical thermodynamics Molecular spectroscopy Photochemistry
Biochemistry	The chemistry of biological systems	Enzymes Biosynthesis.

ELEMENTS AND COMPOUNDS

Elements

The reader will find a description of the formation of chemical elements in Part I (**F6**). They are listed alphabetically in the Table of Elements (with their chemical symbols) and in order of atomic number (*see* **F11**) in the Periodic Table. Other details may be found in Section L. They vary widely in natural abundance terrestrially. In the earth's crust the most abundant elements are oxygen (O), silicon (Si), aluminium (Al), and iron (Fe). Our familiarity with them varies too, not only because of the rarity of some (thulium, Tm, and radium, Ra) but because we meet some only in combination with other elements and not in their elemental state, for example, fluorine (F) in fluorides. The most familiar non-metallic elements besides oxygen and nitrogen in their gaseous molecular states (O_2 and N_2) are probably carbon (C), as graphite (or diamond!) and sulphur (S). Among the metallic elements most people know aluminium (Al), tin (Sn) and lead (Pb) from the main groups of the Periodic Table, and the transition metals: iron (Fe), chromium (Cr), nickel (Ni) as well as copper (Cu) and the precious metals silver (Ag), gold (Au) and platinum (Pt). Increasingly familiar because of their use in semi-conductors are the metalloids silicon (Si) and germanium (Ge).

Compounds

Most terrestrial matter as we know it can be classified in terms of the chemical compounds it contains, *i.e.*, is a mixture of compounds. Each compound consists of chemical elements in combination, the relative amount of each being characteristic and definite (Law of Constant Composition). Compounds vary not only in the number of elements combined but also in their proportions: carbon dioxide has twice as much oxygen per carbon as carbon monoxide (*see* atoms and molecules).

The properties of a compound can be, and normally are, very different from the properties of the elements it contains, a fact not commonly recognised in the popular imagination, witness phrases like—"it's good for you, it's got iron in it". This does not mean that elemental metallic iron is present but rather that some seemingly beneficial compound of iron is present. The ambiguity is that although iron is essential to human life in the form of haemoglobin in the blood, it also can form highly poisonous compounds. Similarly arsenic (As), although notoriously poisonous as the element and in some of its compounds, was nevertheless contained in one of the first chemotherapeutic drugs ever produced, salvarsan. The point can be further illustrated by sodium chloride, a water-soluble white crystalline solid, which is a compound of the very reactive metal sodium (capable of reacting violently with water), and of chlorine (known as a poisonous green gas). Similarly diamond (a particular elemental form, or allotrope, of carbon) is one of the hardest known substances but may be combined with hydrogen (the highly inflammable gas which can combine with oxygen to give water), to give thousands of different derivatives which include benzene (a liquid), methane (a gas) and various hydrocarbon waxes and polishes.

ATOMS AND MOLECULES

Atoms vary in weight, structure and size from one element to the next (*see* **Part II, F10**). Molecules are made from whole numbers of atoms in combination. A particular molecule is characterised by the number of atoms of each of its constituent elements. It has a characteristic weight called its *molecular weight* (the sum of the weights of the atoms in it), and a characteristic three dimensional structure (*see below*).

An aggregate of molecules of the same type is a chemical compound, so that the molecule is to a compound as the atom is to an element.

The Mole

It is frequently very useful to know when the amounts of two compounds are the same, not in terms of their masses but in terms of the number of molecules each contains, since chemical reactions occur at the molecular level and involve small relative numbers of molecules of the reacting species at each step. Avogadro (*see* **B5**) suggested that equal volumes of gases under identical conditions contained equal molecular numbers (*see* **L12**) and it followed that if the weights of two substances were in the ratio of their relative molecular masses (molecular weights) then they too contained equal numbers of molecules. The approximate molecular weights of water (H_2O) and ethanol or ethylalcohol (C_2H_5OH) are 18 and 46 respectively and so 18 g of water for example contain the same number of molecules as 46 g of ethanol.

The amount of substance referred to in each case is called 1 mole. For any compound the weight of 1 mole is equal to the gramme molecular weight. Molecular weights (or relative molecular masses) are now referred to the carbon-12 atomic scale (*see* **F10**). The modern definition of the mole therefore is that it is the amount of substance which contains the same number of elementary particles as there are atoms in twelve grammes of carbon-12. This number, called Avogadro's number, is $6 \cdot 022\ 169 \times 10^{23}$.

Molecular Structure and Isomers

Modern spectroscopic and diffraction methods have enabled the details of molecular structures to be accurately determined not only with respect to the distances between atoms (normally in the range 1–5 Å, *i.e.*, 100–150 pm for adjacent atoms) and the angles which define the structure, but also with respect to the various internal motions (vibrations and rotations).

Sometimes two (or more) different compounds have the same molecular weight (and are called, therefore, *isomers*) but have different molecular structures in which the same atoms are arranged in different relative positions, and hence have different properties. If two isomeric structures are related as left and right hands are related, the isomers are stereoisomers of a particular class called enantiomers. An example is glucose. Even such subtle variation as this produces differences in properties which can be crucial in biological function or drug metabolism.

A familiar simple example of *structural* isomers are ethylalcohol (or ethanol) and dimethyl ether of formula C_2H_6O. They each can be represented by the structural formulae

$$CH_3-CH_2-OH \text{ and } \begin{matrix} CH_3 \diagdown \\ \qquad O \\ CH_3 \diagup \end{matrix}$$

in which the lines represent some of the *covalent chemical bonds* (*see below*). It is these interatomic forces which hold the atoms in specific spatial arrangements. Some examples are shown in Fig. 1.

CHEMICAL BONDING

The number of possible arrangements of a given set of atoms is limited since each type of atom (each element) is capable of forming only a limited number of bonds, equal to its *valency*. The valency varies from element to element; hydrogen has a valency of one (exceptionally two); oxygen, two; nitrogen, three; and carbon four (hence the molecular formulae H_2, H_2O, NH_3 and CH_4 for hydrogen, water, ammonia and methane respectively).

In some compounds two atoms may be joined by a *multiple bond* so that the valency number may be reached. Examples are the double and triple bonds in ethylene (ethene) and acetylene (ethyne respectively):

$$CH_2 = CH_2 \text{ and } CH \equiv CH$$

The modern theory of chemical bonding is electronic. Bonds are formed:

(i) by the sharing of electrons in pairs between two bonded atoms (*covalent* bonding); or

(ii) by the transfer of an electron from one atom to another to form oppositely charged ions (*ionic* bonding).

The ionic situation is electrically *polar* whereas pure covalent bonds have no polarity. If, however, the shared electrons are not shared equally between the bound atoms some effective electron transfer occurs and the bond has some polar character. Covalent bonds between *dissimilar* atoms are generally polar. If one of the two atoms provides *both* the shared electrons, the polarity is particularly high and the bond is called *dative covalent*.

VALENCIES OF THE ELEMENTS

Electronic Theory of Valency

These ideas of the chemical bond lead to a ready explanation of the valencies of the elements (which are periodic if the elements are arranged in order of atomic number) when combined with knowledge of the electronic structure of atoms.

In the original Bohr theory the electrons of atoms move in well defined orbits arranged in shells. The known elements use seven shells, and each element has its unique number of electrons equal to the atomic number, Z ranging from 1 in hydrogen to 103 in lawrencium. Each element also has its unique arrangement of its electrons in these shells. The build-up of electrons in the above sequence follows well-defined rules. The resulting electron configuration of the elements is an important starting point for a discussion of valency. The shells each have a limited capacity and the numbers of electrons that can be accommodated in the first four labelled 1, 2, 3, 4 (or sometimes K, L, M, N) are 2, 8, 18, 32 respectively. Each of these shells has sub-shells of which there are four main types designated s, p, d and f which can contain 2, 6, 10 and 14 electrons respectively. If all the orbits in a shell have electrons actually present in them the shell is filled or closed and this confers on the shell an unusual stability or inertness. Conversely, unfilled shells lead to activity and the electrons in the incompletely filled shells largely determine the chemical and physical properties of the element and are responsible for the combination of atoms to form molecules. These electrons are referred to as *valence electrons*. The inner shell, *i.e.*, the one nearest the nucleus, can accommodate only two electrons (the element helium has just that number) and the next two shells can hold eight each. Large atoms, *e.g.*, lead, radium, have many filled shells and, subject to special exceptions, the general rule is that the inner shells are the filled ones and the outer shell may be incomplete. Elements which have equal numbers of electrons in their outer shell resemble each other and come in the same Group of the Periodic Table. Thus the elements with complete electronic shells are chemically unreactive gases, *e.g.*, argon and neon (minor constituents of the atmosphere). Elements with just one electron in the outer shell are highly reactive metals, *e.g.*, sodium and potassium which lose this electron readily to give monopositive ions, *e.g.*, Na^+. These elements are called electropositive. Contrariwise elements with just one electron too few are electronegative and readily gain one electron either by sharing, or by capture (to form anions, *e.g.*, Cl^-).

More generally, at least for the light elements of Periods 2 and 3 of the Periodic Table, the valence of an element is given by the Group Number, N, *i.e.*, the number of valence electrons which must be lost by the electropositive metals, or by $8-N$, the number of electrons which electronegative elements need to gain.

The covalence of an electronegative element is increased by one if it loses one electron to form a positive ion, and decreased by one if it gains an electron. Thus nitrogen with a covalence 3 can give either N^+ which can form 4 covalent bonds (in the ammonium ion, NH_4^+) or the N^- ion with

Valence Electrons (N) and Valency (V)

N = 1	2	3	4	5	6	7	8
V = 1	2	3	4	3	2	1	0
Hydrogen							Helium
Sodium	Magnesium	Aluminium	Carbon	Nitrogen	Oxygen	Flourine	Neon
Potassium	Calcium	Gallium	Silicon	Phosphorus	Sulphur	Chlorine	Argon
			Germanium	Arsenic		Bromine	
			Tin			Iodine	
	Barium		Lead				

←————————Metals————————→ ←————————————————→ Non-metals:
Positive ions   Covalent   Negative ions
                     compounds   or covalent compounds

a covalency of 2 (*e.g.*, NH_2^-). Similarly oxygen can give H_3O^+, the hydroxonium ion (the acid principle in water), H_2O (water itself), and OH^- (the hydroxyl ion).

IONIC BONDS, SALTS AND ACIDS

These bonds are normally formed between electropositive elements (at the left of the Periodic Table, *e.g.*, sodium and potassium) and electronegative elements (at the right of the Periodic Table, *e.g.*, oxygen, fluorine, chlorine). The ionic charge may be determined from the valency: Na^+, Mg^{++}, Al^{+++}; $O^=$, Cl^-.

Ions may contain a number of atoms, as shown by many of the common anions: hydroxyl, OH^-; nitrate, NO_3^-; sulphate, $SO_4^=$; carbonate $CO_3^=$. Ionic solids formed from a metal ion and one of these anions are called *salts* and are derived from the parent *acid* (acid ion or ions): HNO_3, nitric acid; H_2SO_4, sulphuric acid. Sulphuric acid can form two series of salts, one called *normal* based upon the $SO_4^=$ ion and a second (called acid salts since they contain a hydrogen) based upon the HSO_4^- ion. Phosphoric acid, H_3PO_4, has three series of salts. A substance which reacts with an acid to form a salt and water as the only products is called a *base*. An example is sodium hydroxide, NaOH (caustic soda). The Lewis definitions of acid and base are given below.

The ionic forces are less directional in character than covalent bonds are, but in solids the ions are in regular fixed arrangements (*see* Part II). Each anion is surrounded by cations and is attracted to them by electrostatic Coulomb forces. These are of long range and so the anion is attracted not only to the closest cations. Additionally each cation is surrounded by anions so that the bonding is not localised. The whole solid therefore is like a giant molecule and is not easily broken down by melting. This contrasts with covalent compounds in which the forces between molecules are small, the main attractions being within the molecule.

The structures adopted depend upon the relative numbers of the anions and cations (which are determined by ionic charges) and by the relative ionic sizes, which have been deduced from X-ray diffraction measurements.

COVALENT BONDS

In the simple theory the shared electron pairs are localised between two atoms. Multiple bonds result when there are more pairs shared. The multiplicity (or *bond order*) is then integral. The theory may be extended by admitting that an electron pair may be shared between more than two atoms in *delocalised bonding* which can then give rise to fractional bond orders. The best example is benzene (and graphite) where nine pairs of electrons are shared between six carbon-carbon bonds giving a bond order of 1·5.

Modern Theories

Modern theories of valency make use of the concepts of quantum mechanics (*see* **F17**) in which each of the well-defined electron orbits of the Bohr theory is replaced by the idea of the electron cloud with a spatial electron density and distribution. Each of these electron clouds (now called an orbital) has a definite shape depending upon the type of electrons. The orbitals of s electrons are of spherical shape with a density that falls off with the distance from the nucleus. The peak density occurs at the old Bohr radius. Electrons of the p type have orbitals with double lobes giving the figure of eight or dumbell shape. There are three such orbitals in every shell except the first and they are arranged mutually at right angles. Each one can contain two electrons giving a total of six. The d orbitals are five in number. Each again can contain two electrons giving a total of ten. Four of these d orbitals have shapes like four-leaf clovers, whereas the fifth has two lobes, rather like the p orbitals but with the addition of a torus or doughnut. The shapes of the f orbitals are even more complicated. It is the shape of these orbitals and their relative spatial arrangement which gives the covalent bond its directional character. The idea of electron sharing between two atoms becomes the notion of overlap of an orbital on one atom with an orbital on another to give a bonding *molecular orbital* which can contain the pair of shared electrons. The bond energy is a maximum when this overlap is optimum and this occurs when the atoms are in certain definite positions thus giving the molecule its own characteristic shape.

Molecular shape

For elements from the second row of the Periodic Table the number of electrons in the valence shell can be eight arranged in four pairs of orbitals (one 2s and three 2p orbitals). These orbitals can be combined or *hybridised* to give the basic tetrahedral shape (*see* Fig. 1). Each of these can overlap with say an orbital of a hydrogen atom (the 1s) to give a bonding orbital which can accommodate two electrons. Alternatively each orbital can, if the atom has enough electrons, contain two non-bonding electrons called a *lone pair*. The basic molecular shapes of methane (CH_4), ammonia (NH_3), and water (H_2O) may then be rationalised as in Fig. 1.

The bond angle in methane is the tetrahedral angle (109° 28′). The angles in ammonia (107° 18′) and water (104° 30′) are smaller probably because the lone pair orbital is slightly more repulsive than the bonding orbital is. This closes down the angles between the bonds.

The lone pairs may be used to bind the hydrogen ions from acids to give tetrahedral NH_4^+ and pyramidal H_3O^+. It is the lone pairs therefore which give ammonia and water their basicity. In the modern concept of acids and bases due to Lewis, a base is an electron donor and an acid becomes an electron acceptor. This definition of an acid includes the older idea of it as a hydrogen ion producer in that the hydrogen ion is an electron acceptor but it is more general—a Lewis acid need not be a protic acid.

Bond Lengths

Many covalent bond distances have been measured

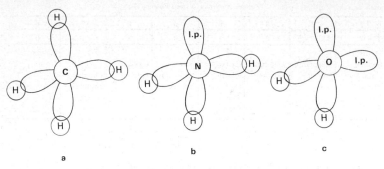

Fig. 1. The spatial arrangements of the atoms and orbitals in (a) methane (CH_4), (b) ammonia (NH_3) and (c) water (H_2O). The basic shape is tetrahedral and the hybridised orbitals are lone pair orbitals (l.p.) and bonding orbitals.

and each may be apportioned between the bound atoms to give a self-consistent set of covalent bond-radii for each element which can be used in predictions of molecular structures. These radii vary inversely with the bond order involved. Thus the carbon-carbon bond length varies from 154 pm (*i.e.*, 10^{12}m) for $C-C$ to 135 pm for $C=C$.

Bond Energies

Bonds differ in their strength depending upon the atoms and the bond order. A double bond between two given atoms is stronger than a single bond but generally not as strong as two single bonds. Thus "unsaturated" compounds, which contain multiple bonds, will tend to form "saturated" compounds containing only single bonds since the energetics are favourable.

Functional Groups

Compounds may be further classified according to certain persistent groups of atoms which have a residual valency and can combine with other groups. Thus the methyl group (CH_3) related to methane (CH_4) by the removal of a hydrogen atom can combine with other atoms or groups of valency one: methyl chloride (chloromathane), CH_3Cl; methyl alcohol (methanol), CH_3OH; dimethyl ether, CH_3OCH_3. Common functional groups are shown in the table.

CHEMICAL ENERGETICS

Chemical reactions are accompanied by energy changes which can be utilised as heat (in fires) or mechanical work (in explosions or rockets), or to produce electric current in batteries. Chemical compounds can therefore be said to store energy and to possess "internal energy". The energy can be thought of as being stored in the chemical bonds. The energy change (at constant volume) in a reaction is then a result of changes (denoted ΔU) in the nett internal energy of the reactants and products by the law of the conservation of energy. If the conditions are those of constant pressure, the energy change is due to overall changes in a closely related properly called enthalpy (ΔH).

It was at one time thought that reactions would proceed only if energy was given out (*exothermic* processes). Although this is now known to be true at the lowest temperature, in other cases a second consideration, the entropy term, needs to be considered, as the existence of *endothermic* changes confirms. A new "energy" term defined to contain the entropy consideration and called the Gibbs Free Energy, G, may then be used. Natural or "spontaneous" processes are accompanied by a decrease in the nett value of G, and systems tend to assume whichever state has the lowest value of G.

Chemical Equilibrium

Certain chemical changes, like physical changes

Some Classes of Simple Organic Compounds

Name	General Description and Formula	Examples
Alkanes (or paraffins)	"Saturated" hydrocarbons of the general formula C_nH_{2n+2} Contain single bonds only	methane (CH_4) butane (C_4H_{10})
Alkenes (olefins)	"Unsaturated" hydrocarbons of general formula C_nH_{2n} Contain double bonds	ethylene (C_2H_4) styrene ($C_6H_5.C_2H_3$)
Alkynes (acetylenes)	"Unsaturated" hydrocarbon of general formula C_nH_{2n-2} Contain triple bonds	acetylene (C_2H_2)
Enols (alcohols)	Contain the OH group, bound for example to an alkyl group $C_nH_{2n+1}OH$	methylalcohol (CH_3OH) ethylalcohol (C_2H_5OH)
Ketones	Contain the $C=O$ group $C_nH_{2n+1})_2C=O$	acetone ($CH_3)_2CO$
Aldehydes	Contain the CHO group	formaldehyde (HCHO) acetaldehyde (CH_3CHO)
Aromatic hydrocarbons	Ring compounds with reactions similiar to the proto- type, benzene (C_6H_6)	napthalene ($C_{10}H_8$) anthracene ($C_{14}H_{10}$)
Phenyl compounds	Derivatives of the phenyl group, C_6H_5	phenol (C_6H_5OH) aniline ($C_6H_5NH_2$)
Heterocyclic compounds	Ring compounds containing mainly carbon atoms and one or more other atoms, *e.g.*, nitrogen	pyridine (C_5H_5N) thiophene (C_4H_4S)

such as raising and lowering weights, or freezing and melting water, may be easily reversed. The forward and backward reactions which are proceeding continuously can then be made to balance out, given enough time, and the system is said to be in equilibrium.

Suppose that X and Y when mixed are partially converted to Z and an equilibrium mixture is obtained under certain defined conditions. The relative amounts $[X]$, $[Y]$, etc., are then definite and governed by the equilibrium constant defined as

$$K = \frac{[Z]}{[X][Y]}$$

Putting it in another way, if we know K we can predict the relative amounts of products and reactants, i.e., the extent to which the reaction proceeds. K in turn depends upon the change in Gibbs Free Energy for the reaction:

$$\Delta G = - RT \ln K$$

where R is the gas constant, and T the absolute temperature, and ln denotes the natural logarithm.

The efficiency of a reaction therefore can be predicted theoretically since values for ΔG can frequently be calculated from tabulated values of ΔH and ΔS. Such studies constitute *chemical thermodynamics*, the branch of thermodynamics (see **F20**) applied to chemical reactions. It is an essential consideration in industrial processes.

Bond Enthalpies

The enthalpy (**L40**) of a molecule can be thought of as the sum of the enthalpies associated with each covalent bond, for each of which there is a characteristic value. Determination and tabulation of these bond energies helps in the prediction of enthalpy changes in new reactions involving covalent molecules. Similarly for ionic solids.

THE SPEED OF REACTIONS—CATALYSIS

A good analogy to illustrate the difference between chemical thermodynamics and kinetics is the downhill flow of water. The water will seek the lowest point where it has the lowest potential energy, and in an analogous way a reaction will try to proceed to the state with the lowest Gibbs Free Energy. However, the speed of both water flow and reaction will depend upon a large number of factors, particularly the available *pathway* (or reaction mechanism). Indeed water at the top of a mountain or in a domestic bath may not flow down at all if a suitable path is blocked say by a hillock (or bath plug). The unblocking may involve the expenditure of energy, for example to lift the water over the dam (or pull out the plug). In reactions this type of energy is called the *activation energy*. It can be supplied in a number of ways (see below) such as heating. Sometimes it is small and (thankfully) at other times it is large enough that thermodynamically feasible reactions do not occur at all quickly. Each of us is, in fact, *thermodynamically* unstable with respect to our combustion products, mainly CO_2 and H_2O, i.e., we should burn (!), but fortunately we are *kinetically stable*.

A *catalyst* is a substance which will provide an alternative reaction pathway of low activation energy, i.e., it can speed up a reaction, without itself being consumed in the process. The analogy for the water flow would be a tunnel through the hillock. Catalysts are very important industrially, for example, in the manufacture of sulphuric acid (using platinised asbestos or vanadium pentoxide), in the Haber process for ammonia used for fertilisers (iron derivatives), and in the "cracking" of crude oil to give lighter oils (aluminium oxide). Natural catalysts are called *enzymes* (see **F31(2)**).

CLASSIFICATION OF REACTIONS

Chemical change can be brought about by a variety of techniques used separately or together:

mixing of single substances
heating single substances or mixtures
electrolysing solutions
exposure to light or radiation
addition of catalysts.

The changes can be classified according to the results produced:

Dissociation—breakdown into simpler substances or ions
Addition—in which one type of molecule or ion is added to another
Polymerisation—reaction of a substance (monomer) with itself to produce larger molecules of the same composition (polymer)
Substitution—in which one particular group in a molecule is replaced by another
Elimination—in which one particular group in a molecule is lost
Exchange—in which two groups are mutually substituted one by the other
Oxidation—removal of electrons (increase of oxidation number), e.g., Fe^{++} ferrous ion is oxidised to ferric, Fe^{+++}
Reduction—the converse of oxidation

More significantly modern classifications are based upon the precise *molecular mechanism* employed. Examples are

Nucleophilic attack—where an electron-rich reagent attacks a position of low electron density in a molecule
Electrophilic attack—where an electron-depleted reagent—an electrophile (for example, a positive ion)—attacks a position of high electron density
Bimolecular reaction—one which involves two molecules unlike a monomolecular reaction which involves only one in each step

Precise descriptions can be built up: substitution, nucleophilic, bimolecular.

ELECTROLYTES, ELECTROLYSIS AND ELECTROCHEMICAL CELLS

Electrolytic Solutions

Ionic solids can dissolve in some solvents especially if each has a high dielectric constant to cut down the force of attraction between oppositely charged ions. The process can be assisted by solvation of the ions and also by the entropy changes which favour the less ordered state of affairs—the liquid rather than the ordered solid.

Electrolysis

The oppositely charged ions are capable of independent movement and the application of an electric potential from an external battery or source of direct current to electrodes in the solution will cause the ions to move. The positive ions (cations) will move to the negatively charged electrode (the cathode) and the negatively charged ions (anions) to the positively charged anode. At the electrodes chemical changes occur and ions may be converted to uncharged species and deposited: for example, sodium ions (Na^+) to sodium metal, Na. This process is referred to as electrolysis. Faraday discovered two laws of electrolysis: (i) the amount of any substance deposited (or dissolved) is proportional to the amount of electricity used; (ii) the relative amounts of substances deposited by the same quantity of electricity are in the ratio of their *equivalent weights*.

For any ion discharged below a certain value of the applied voltage the *discharge voltage* is small. In an electrolyte containing many different ionic species therefore, each ionic discharge will occur only as the appropriate potential is reached. For solutions of acids, hydrogen (formed from H^+ ions) is discharged at the cathode, and oxygen (formed from OH^- ions) at the anode. Electrolysis is important commercially for the refining of metals, electroplating, and in the production of many basic chemicals.

Electrochemical Cells

Ever since 1800 when Volta produced an electric battery consisting of alternate plates of silver and zinc separated by cloth impregnated with salt, the search for new batteries has been continuous. In each new battery a different chemical process is harnessed to produce electrical energy. The battery must not only be feasible according to the laws of thermodynamics, but must be practicable and cheap for widespread consumer use.

The voltages developed in any battery can be predicted from a knowledge of the two processes occurring: one at the cathode and the other at the anode. Voltages can be ascribed to each of these "half cells" according to the chemical reaction which occurs and the condition used, for example concentrations of the reactants (the so-called "standard electrode potentials"). The voltage of any combination of two half cells is the sum of the half-cell voltages. Furthermore each of these voltages is related to the change in the Gibbs Free Energy for its reaction and can, in theory, therefore be predicted thermodynamically.

CHEMISTRY IN MODERN LIFE

Chemistry plays a crucial role in modern life, not least in the third world, as well as in the more developed nations. In the U.K. chemistry has been studied, developed and put to practical use as well as anywhere in the world in modern times. It is no accident that the largest specialised scientific society in the U.K. is the Royal Society of Chemistry (R.S.C.) which has 40,000 members, and that its forerunner, The Chemical Society, lays claim to being the oldest in the world. The high quality of chemical science at the crucial level of basic research is indicated by the remarkable frequency with which the Nobel Prize in Chemistry has come to the U.K. The success is not confined to academic activity but, surely as a consequence, it extends to the economic life of the nation.

The U.K. chemical industry is among the largest in the world and one of the most successful. In national statistics it is included in the manufacturing sector alongside other sectors which have a high chemical component such as petroleum and petroleum products. Its output covers a very wide range. Firstly there are the so called "basic chemicals", such as sulphuric acid, which are utilised in the manufacturing processes of other sectors.

In agriculture chemicals are not only important in the form of bulk products such as fertilizer, without which modern agriculture could not operate efficiently, but also for the 'finer' chemicals such as herbicides and insecticides. Manufactured synthetic polymers and plastics are omnipresent in modern life, for example in architecture and building as well as in many familiar household products and uses. The list here is long and includes moulded casings for televisions and other electronic and electrical products, kitchen utensils, all forms of coverings from paints and varnishes to fabrics. Then there are the "fine" chemicals: cosmetics and pharmaceuticals, ranging from vanity products to the birth control pill and life-saving synthetic drugs. Petroleum products from oil cover an extremely wide range. Petroleum is a most valuable "feed stock" for other products and in this use it is arguably more unique and precious than as a fuel or energy source.

The economic statistics are impressive. The U.K. chemical industry accounts for 9% of manufacturing industry's "gross value added" output. The chemical industry provides for 6% of the employment in the manufacturing industry as well as directly supporting several hundred thousand additional jobs throughout the economy. Over the last decade the industry has accounted for 15% of industry's new capital spending. In 1984 for example the gross fixed capital investment in chemical and allied industry was £804m in comparison with £663m in food, £230m in metals and £672m in vehicles. It exports around 40% of its output. Comparative figures for the value of exports in 1984 are chemicals £6929m, food £2748m, petroleum and products £12,525m. Most importantly it is also profitable. In 1984 it achieved a net positive balance of payments surplus of £1.8 billion in contrast with a deficit of £6.9 billion for the rest of the British manufacturing industry.

Nevertheless, chemistry has had as bad a press recently as other basic physical sciences have had, with the consequence that young people turned away at the turn of the decade from studying the sciences. In the popular mind, chemistry has become associated with pollution resulting from the manufacturing, use and misuse of synthetic chemicals, as well as industrial accidents. Indeed, the word "chemical" has been used increasingly in a pejorative way, even in informed broadcasting and reportage. Thus chemical fertilizers (meaning synthetic fertilizers) are distinguished falsely from organic fertilizers. This sort of practice ignores the fact that we ourselves consist of, use, rely on, are surrounded by naturally occurring chemicals, organic and inorganic, as well as the useful man-made synthetics.

The word *chemist* fares no better. Whereas the terms physicist, biologist, mathematician and scientist are generally used unambiguously, the word chemist is commonly used for the pharmacist or apothecary, at least in the U.K. if not generally in the rest of the world.

IV. BIOLOGY—THE SCIENCE OF LIFE

WHAT BIOLOGY IS ABOUT

Biology embraces the study of all living things which exist on earth at the present time and also the recognisable remains of those that are extinct. Living things or organisms range from the apparently simple micro-organisms such as viruses and bacteria to the largest animals and plants.

Living Processes

The enormous variation and complexity of living processes make the task of understanding and defining life a very difficult one. Every living organism undergoes continual physical and chemical changes which, in spite of their diversity, are referred to as the metabolism of the organism. Metabolism involves the processing of food materials, the production of waste products, and all the intermediate stages between these whereby energy and matter are provided for the operation, maintenance, and growth of the organism. These reactions are under very exact chemical or nervous control at every stage and can be slowed down or speeded up as the need arises. Thus the organism can react to changes in the environment in which it lives, adjusting its activities in relation to the external changes. Finally, organisms can reproduce either in an identical or very slightly modified form. In this process new individuals are produced and the species continues to survive. Differences between offspring and parents can, under certain circumstances, act cumulatively over many generations and so form the basis of evolutionary change in which new species of organism are ultimately formed.

Molecular Biology

It has been evident for many years that the most fundamental aspects of these living processes occur in basic structural units known as cells. The study of living processes at the molecular and cell level has been given a tremendous impetus in recent years by the advent of new techniques which enable microscopic and submicroscopic parts of cell to be examined. Physicists, chemists, and mathematicians have found themselves working alongside biologists in this field and several of the very notable advances have been made by physical scientists. Molecular biology is a term frequently used in describing this rapidly expanding and fascinating field of research.

EVOLUTION

Introduction.—The idea that species of living organisms could change over long periods of time was considered by some Greek writers and, much later, by the Frenchmen Buffon and Lamarck at the end of the 18th cent. Further, the work of the 18th cent. geologists such as James Hutton and William Smith provided a basis without which the major contribution of Darwin, the great 19th cent. naturalist, would have been impossible. Hutton showed that the earth's surface had undergone prolonged upheavals and volcanic eruptions with consequent changes in sea level. This implied that the earth was much older than had previously been supposed. Smith developed a method of dating the geological strata by means of the fossils found in them and demonstrated that widely different types of animals and plants existed at different periods of the earth's history. Later in this section (**F47–8**) a general picture is presented of the evolution of organisms from the simple to the complex and from the aquatic to the terrestrial environment.

These discoveries were in conflict with the Biblical account in the book of Genesis and, although various attempts were made to explain them away or discredit them, it became abundantly clear that through millions of years life has been continually changing, with new species constantly arising and many dying out.

The Evidence for Evolution

1. *The Geological Record.*—It has already been pointed out that successively younger rocks contain fossil remains of different and relatively more complex organisms. The spore-bearing plants preceded the gymnosperms and the angiosperms arose much later. Similarly in the vertebrate series the fish appeared before the amphibia which were followed by the reptiles and later by the air breathing, warm-blooded birds and mammals. On a more restricted level the evolution of the horse has been worked out in great detail from the small Eohippus which was about a foot high and had four digits on the forefeet and three on the hind-feet to the large one-toed animal living today. However, such complete series are rare and the geological record is very incomplete. There are a number of gaps, particularly between the major groups of organisms. No satisfactory fossil evidence is known of the ancestors of the angiosperms (**F43**) so perhaps they did not grow in conditions which favoured their preservation as fossils. On the other hand, Archæopteryx provides an indisputable link between the reptiles and the birds.

Although we talk about the age of fishes, the age of reptiles and so on it must be emphasised that these are the periods during which particular groups were abundant or even dominant. Each group probably originated many millions of years before it became widespread. Further, some groups, such as the giant reptiles and the seed-ferns, died out completely whereas others, the fishes and true ferns for example, are still common today although many fishes and ferns that exist today are very different from those of the Devonian and Carboniferous periods (**F48**). On the other hand some species, for example the Maidenhair tree, have remained unaltered for many millions of years.

2. *Geographical Distribution.*—Nearly all the marsupials or pouched mammals are found in the Australian continent which was cut off from the mainland about 60 million years ago. All the fossil evidence indicates that at that time the eutherian or placental mammals did not yet exist. The marsupials are the only naturally occurring mammals in Australia (**F37(1)**) but since the isolation of the continent the group has given rise to a large number of species very similar in appearance to those which evolved elsewhere in the world among the eutherian mammals. There are marsupials which look like wolves, dogs, cats and squirrels; yet they have no close biological relationships to these animals. Further, some marsupials such as the kangaroos have evolved which are unlike any other creatures in the rest of the world. Quite clearly the isolation of Australia so long ago has resulted in the evolution of these distinct types, just as Darwin found in the Galapagos islands where each has its own distinct flora and fauna which differ also from those of the S. American mainland.

3. *Anatomy.*—The comparative study of the development and mature structure of the mammalian body provides much evidence that all the species have evolved from a single ancestral stock.

Although the arm of an ape, the leg of a dog, the flipper of a whale and the wing of a a bat appear very different externally they are all built on the same skeletal plan. It would be difficult to explain such similarities unless they had all evolved from a common type. There is also evidence that the early development of an animal recapitulates its biological history to a certain extent. For example, the gill slits found in fish are formed during the early stages in the development of a mammal although later they disappear. Finally, apparently useless vestigial structures sometimes occur which would be inexplicable unless regarded in the light of an evolutionary history. In man a small appendix and vestiges of a third eyelid occur but these are functionless although in other animals such structures are well developed and functional, e.g., the appendix in the rabbit.

4. *Human Selection.*—During his brief history on earth modern man has continually selected and bred animals and plants for his own use. We have only to look at the various breeds of dogs which have been developed from a single wild type to see that under certain circumstances great structural divergence can occur in a species even in a relatively short time.

The Darwinian Theory of Evolution.—Darwin amassed a great deal of information such as that outlined above which convinced him that evolution of life had taken place over millions of years. His was the first real attempt to collect all the evidence scientifically and no other satisfactory alternative explanation of all the facts he presented has been proposed. Perhaps even more important was his attempt to explain *how* evolution had actually occurred. He published his theory after many years of work in his book *The Origin of Species by Means of Natural Selection* in 1859. Some of his ideas have since been modified owing to our increased knowledge of genetics but they are so important that it is worth-while recounting the main points of his theory.

1. *The Struggle for Existence.*—It is clear that in nature there is a severe struggle for existence in all animals and plants. Over a period of time the number of individuals of a species in a given community does not vary greatly. This implies that the number of progeny which survive to become mature breeding individuals more or less replaces the number of mature ones that die. Generally speaking the reproductive output of a species is much greater than this. For example, a single large foxglove plant may produce half a million seeds each one of which is potentially capable of giving rise to a new individual. Obviously nearly all the progeny die before reaching maturity and the chance of any single one surviving is very remote.

2. *Variation.*—The individuals of any generation of human beings obviously differ from one another and such differences are found in other organisms. It is clear that they vary considerably in structure, colour, activity and so on. Darwin also pointed out that generally these variations were passed on from one generation to the next, for example, the children of tall parents tend to grow tall.

3. *Survival of the Fittest.*—If there is an intense struggle for existence in their natural environment among individuals of a species having different characteristics, those which are best "fitted" to a given set of conditions are most likely to survive to maturity. These will reproduce and the features which enabled them to survive will be passed on to their offspring. This process is liable to continue and a species will become better adapted to its environment.

4. *Natural Selection.*—Over a long period of time the environment of a given species is never stable but will change in various ways. As it does so the characters which best fit the individuals to the changed environment will be selected (not consciously of course) and the species will change. The environment may change only in part of the range of the species and thus lead to divergence and the production of a new species alongside the old one.

Darwin and Lamarck.—Darwin pictured evolution as a slow continuous process with natural selection operating on the small inheritable variations found between the individuals of a species which were undergoing intense competition. This neglects the important effect of the environment on the growth and structure of the individual. It is obvious that external conditions will affect the development of an organism, for example the effect of various soil conditions on the growth of a plant or the amount of food material available to an animal. Lamarck maintained that the characters acquired by an individual owing to the effect of its environment could be passed on to its offspring. Undoubtedly characters are acquired by the individual during its growth but in spite of many attempts to prove otherwise no experiments have been done which prove conclusively that these are inherited by the offspring. Thus Lamarck's theory that evolution has occurred by the inheritance of acquired characters is not generally acceptable today.

Neodarwinism

Darwinism received something of a setback during the early years of modern genetics. There did not seem to be much in common between the large mutations studied by geneticists and the small continuous variations which Darwin thought were the basic material upon which selection acted. With time, it became evident that not all mutations are large in their effects and that much of the continuous variation which occurs does indeed have a genetic basis. Mathematicians such as J. B. S. Haldane and Sewall Wright showed that even very small selective advantages would cause genes to spread throughout populations as the generations passed by. Experiments and observations on natural populations showed that evolution—seen as progressive, adaptive genetic change—does indeed occur today. For example, the proportion of dark-coloured moths has greatly increased in many areas where smoke pollution occurs, as a result of predation by birds on the now more obvious light forms. Again, many pest insects have evolved genetic resistance to the insecticides used to attack them.

GENETICS

Mendelism

Genetics is the study of the mechanisms of the hereditary process. Modern genetics began with the experiments of Gregor Mendel, an Austrian monk in 1865. He studied the inheritance of different factors in peas by crossing different strains and counting the numbers of plants with different characters in the succeeding generations.

In one experiment Mendel crossed peas with round seeds with peas having wrinkled seeds. All of the offspring (known as the "first filial" or F1 generation) had round seeds. Mendel allowed these plants to pollinate themselves, and then measured the characteristics of their offspring (the F2 generation). There were 5,474 round-seeded plants and 1,850 wrinkled-seeded plants in the F2 generation, a ratio of very nearly three to one. The character of roundness can be described as being "dominant" over the "recessive" character of wrinkledness.

In order to explain his results Mendel suggested that the characters of roundness and wrinkledness were determined by particulate factors (now called *genes*), and that each plant possessed two genes for each feature. Suppose the gene for roundness is *A* and that for wrinkledness is *a*. Then the parental plants in Mendel's experiment will be represented by *AA* (round seeds) and *aa* (wrinkled seeds). The gametes (the ovules and the sperm nuclei of the pollen grains) will be *A* and *a* respectively. When these combine to form the F1 generation they will produce plants with the genetic constitution *Aa*. Both male and female gametes of the F1 generation are then of the two types *A* and *a*, and these can combine, on self-pollination, in four different ways:

F1	male gamete	female gamete	F2
	A	*A*	*AA*
	A	*a*	*Aa*
Aa	*a*	*A*	
	a	*a*	*aa*

The individuals of the F2 generation will thus have genetic constitutions of *AA*, *Aa* and *aa* in the approximate proportions 1:2:1. Since both *AA* and *Aa* individuals have round seeds, the ratio of round-seeded plants to wrinkled-seeded plants will be about three to one, which indeed it is.

Mendel's results were ignored for many years until their rediscovery at the beginning of this century. Mendelian ratios were then found to govern inheritance in a large number of other cases, such as coat colour in rabbits and cattle, and white eyes and other characteristics in the fruit fly *Drosophila*. In other cases characteristics are governed by more than one set of genes so the simple mathematical relationships are obscured. This occurs in quantitative features, such as yield in crop plants and weight in animals.

Chromosome Theory

The chromosomes are dark-staining filaments which, as we shall see later, can be observed in the nucleus at cell division. Their behaviour was described in the nineteenth century, but it was not clear what their function was. After the rediscovery of Mendel's work, Sutton suggested that the genes are carried on chromosomes, since the observed behaviour of the chromosomes corresponded very well with the theoretical behaviour of Mendel's factors.

Further evidence for the chromosome theory of inheritance came from study of the phenomenon known as sex-linkage, in which the expression of a gene depends upon the sex of the individual in which it is found. Haemophilia in man, for example, is a hereditary disease which is normally found only in males, although it is clear that females can act as carriers (Queen Victoria was one, since one of her sons, three of her grandsons and seven of her greatgrandsons were haemophiliacs). Cytological study shows that there is one pair of chromosomes which differ in the two sexes. In the female (in man and most animals) the two chromosomes of this pair are similar and are known as the X chromosomes. In the male one of these is replaced by a much smaller Y chromosome. Hence recessive genes which are found on only one X chromosome are expressed in the male, since there is no other dominant gene present. A female haemophiliac would have haemophilia genes on both X chromosomes; this could only arise from a carrier mother and a haemophiliac father, a very rare occurrence.

In recent years it has become clear that chromosomes are composed largely of the DNA molecules of the cell nucleus, to be discussed later (**F33–4**). And since it has become evident that genes are DNA molecules, we now have a firm chemical basis for the assumption that genes are carried on chromosomes. Genetics has thus to some extent become a branch of molecular biology.

Mutations

Sometimes a DNA molecule may not replicate itself exactly during the process of cell division. When this happens the gene which it constitutes has changed its character so as to produce a difference of effect when expressed in the individual organism. Such a change is known as a gene mutation. It seems likely, for example, that Queen Victoria's haemophilia gene arose as a mutation in herself or in her mother. Mutations, as we shall see, are of vital importance in providing the genetic variation upon which evolutionary selection can act.

The frequency with which mutations occur is increased by certain chemicals and by ionising radiation. Hence the need for caution in exposing the body to X-rays and to radioactive materials, and the concern over the possible genetic effects of radioactive waste from power stations and from military testing programmes.

THE CELL

Cells were first seen in 1665 by Robert Hooke when he looked at a piece of cork under his primitive microscope. It was not until 1839, however, that Schlieden and Schwann produced the cell doctrine which visualised the cell as both the structural and functional unit of living organisation. Exceptions may be found to the cell doctrine. For example, some protozoa, algae, and fungi show very complex internal organisation but are not divided into cells; they are usually called acellular organisms. The viruses also constitute a difficulty since in many ways they are intermediate between living and dead matter. They are absolutely dependent on cells of other organisms for their continued existence. Outside living cells they are inert molecules which may take a crystalline form. Inside a host cell, however, they become disease-producing parasites which multiply and show many of the other properties of living organisms. They are minute and lack the complex organisation usually associated with cells. Notwithstanding their somewhat ambiguous position, the viruses are often treated as though they were single cells or parts of cells and their extreme simplicity has made them ideal material for many types of research at this level. The bacteria also lack some of the properties of cells but the differences are not so clearly defined as they are in the case of viruses.

Structure and Function of Cells

Though the constituent cells of a multicellular organism are usually specialised to perform particular functions, they have a great many features in common. The cell is often said to be made up of a substance called protoplasm, a term for the fundamental material of life which dates from the 19th cent. Protoplasm has two main constituents, the cytoplasm and the nucleus, and is bounded on the outside by a cell or plasma membrane. Plant cells generally have an additional wall composed primarily of cellulose and used for support. The nucleus is the controlling centre of the cell and has rather limited metabolic capabilities. The cytoplasm contains various subunits which operate to produce energy and new cell structure during the normal metabolism of the cell.

Cells take up the raw materials for metabolism through the cell membrane from extracellular fluid which surrounds them. The nutrients include carbohydrates, fats, proteins, minerals, vitamins, and water. Fats and carbohydrates are important principally as sources of energy, though both types of compound are found in permanent cell structure. Proteins are complex substances of high molecular weight which contain nitrogen in addition to the carbon, hydrogen, and oxygen found in the other compounds. They are of fundamental importance in the structure and function of the cell and are built up of a number of simple nitrogen-containing organic molecules called amino acids. There are twenty amino acids occurring commonly in nature so that the number of possible combinations in large protein molecules is quite clearly enormous. A group of proteins whose significance is well established are the enzymes which are the catalysts of chemical reactions in living cells. Each enzyme will control and speed up a specific reaction even though it is present in very small amounts and is usually unchanged at the end of the process. A large number of inorganic mineral salts are essential for cells to function normally. Some, such as sodium, potassium, and calcium salts, are needed in considerable quantity; others are required only in trace amounts and these include iron, copper, and manganese. The trace elements are usually important constituents of enzyme systems. Vitamins are also necessary in very small amounts and it seems reasonable to conclude that their function is also a catalytic one in parts of some enzyme systems.

I. CYTOPLASM

For a long time cytoplasm was thought to be a homogeneous and structureless substrate in which enzymes occurred as part of a general colloidal system. With the refinement of techniques such as electron microscopy and ultracentrifugation, more and more identifiable components have been found within the cytoplasm. It now seems certain that the material other than these recognisable particles is not a structureless matrix but a highly organised and variable complex.

Mitochondria and Oxidation

Mitochondria vary in shape from cylindrical rods to spheres and in size from 0·2 to 3·0 microns. When seen in the living cell they are in constant motion. The whole structure is enclosed within a thin double membrane, the inner layer of which is thrown into folds extending across the central cavity of the mitochondrion and dividing it into small chambers. The function of mitochondria is to provide energy for the reactions of the rest of the cell. Almost the whole machinery for the oxidation of foodstuffs is to be found in the mitochondria. Slight damage to the mitochondrion will render it unable to carry out a complete cycle of oxidative processes. Destruction of parts of the double membrane system prevents the production of energy-rich phosphate bonds in adenosine triphosphate (ATP) in which energy is stored and transported about the cell.

Chloroplasts and Photosynthesis

Chloroplasts are particles found in cells in the green parts of plants, in fact they contain the green pigment which is called chlorophyll. They are involved in the process known as photosynthesis in which energy absorbed from light is used to synthesise carbohydrates from carbon dioxide and water, oxygen being formed as a by-product.

Chloroplasts are disc-shaped or flat ellipsoids from 2 to 20 microns across, possessing a complex structure which in many ways is reminiscent of that found in mitochondria. A typical double membrane surrounds the structure and the inside is made up very largely of a stack of discs consisting of paired membranes connected at their ends to form closed systems. This seems to be a further development of the type of lamellated structure seen dividing the central cavity of a mitochondrion. The chlorophylls and other pigments, such as the orange yellow carotenoids, seem to be arranged in layers a single molecule thick in the chloroplast discs so that they are maximally exposed to light.

The importance of this process whereby plants can make use of the energy in sunlight to fix carbon dioxide and produce carbohydrates is quite clear. The whole animal population of the world, including man, is dependent on plants for food since even the meat-eating carnivores prey upon herbivores. Although scientists continue to make efforts to produce adequate food materials from simple compounds, there is still no better machinery known for doing this than the plant cell. Man is dependent on photosynthesis not only for his supplies of food but also for much of his fuel, since much of the combustible material removed from the earth is of plant origin.

Endoplasmic Reticulum, Ribosomes, and Protein Synthesis.

A network of elaborate and oriented double membranes existing within parts of the cytoplasm can be seen in the electron microscope. In the space between the pairs of double membranes small granules are visible, either free in the space or attached to a membrane. The whole system is called the endoplasmic reticulum. When the cell is homogenised and centrifuged the endoplasmic reticulum appears as the microsomal fraction. Biochemical analysis after separation of the membranous from the granular components reveals that the former is composed largely of phospholipids and cholesterol, which are compounds closely related to fats, and the latter of ribonucleic acid (RNA).

Nucleic Acids

The term nucleic acid covers a class of substances, usually of great complexity, built up from smaller units called nucleotides. Each nucleotide consists of a base, united to a sugar, in turn united to phosphoric acid. Nucleotides are joined together in a linear fashion by means of the phosphoric acid residues to form a chain from which the bases project at right angles. Two types of sugar are found in naturally occurring nucleic acids and these are the ribose of RNA and the deoxyribose of desoxyribonucleic acids (DNA). We shall return to the latter when the nucleus is considered. Four nitrogen-containing bases occur in nucleic acids and in RNA—adenine, cytosine, guanine, and uracil. In DNA the uracil is replaced by thymine.

Protein Synthesis

There is good evidence that RNA is manufactured exclusively within the nucleus and subsequently moves out into the cytoplasm. Some of it, called ribosomal RNA, unites with protein to form the granules, or ribosomes, of the endoplasmic reticulum. Another form, called messenger RNA, also migrates from the nucleus to be associated with ribosomes but does not become incorporated into their permanent structure. It is also well established that the ribosomes are closely linked with protein synthesis in the cell because radioactive amino acids, when fed to an animal, are always found first in the ribosomes before any other cell structure. The specificiation for a particular protein is not carried on the ribosome which is merely the factory for making these complex molecules. It is thought that messenger RNA carries instructions from the nucleus which specify exactly the protein to be synthesised at a ribosome. This is done by means of a code in which a "triplet" of three nucleotide bases codes one amino acid (Fig. 1). Thus on a long molecule of RNA, three adjacent uracil bases would specify an amino acid called phenylalanine. If these were followed on the RNA molecule by one uracil and two guanines then the amino acid tryptophan would be specified and this would be joined to the phenylalanine. In this way complex protein molecules can be built up according to instructions emanating from the nucleus for each of the 20 different amino acids.

This system is responsible for building and maintaining much of the organisation of the cytoplasm. All the enzymes, for example catalysing every reaction within the cell will be specified and built up on the appropriate RNA template. The understanding of protein synthesis is of fundamental importance to the whole of biology and has particular significance in studies on cancer where cell growth becomes abnormal.

The Golgi Apparatus

The characteristic features of the Golgi apparatus are numbers of large vacuoles or spaces bordered by closely packed layers of double membranes. The latter look very much like the

FIG. 1. This shows a portion of a molecule of messenger RNA, associated with a ribosome and synthesising a protein. Adenine specifies Uracil (U), Cytosine specifies Guanine (G), Thymine specifies Adenine (A), and Guanine specifies Cytosine (C). The ribosome is moving down the messenger RNA strand "reading" the triplet code. Amino acid 4, which is phenylalanine specified by UUU, has just been joined to three other amino acids and its carrier RNA released to the cytoplasm. Amino acid 5, tryptophan specified by UGG, is attached to its carrier RNA and in position ready to be joined to the protein chain by the ribosome. Amino acid 6, methionine specified by UAG is attached to its carrier RNA but has not been brought into position on the messenger RNA strand. Other amino acids and carrier RNA molecules exist free in the cytoplasm and have not yet associated.

membranes of the endoplasmic reticulum but do not have the ribosome particles along their edge. They are therefore known as "smooth" membranes in contrast to the "rough" membranes of endoplasmic reticulum. The function of the Golgi apparatus may be associated with secretory activity of the cell.

Cell Membrane

Though the cell membrane plays a most vital part in regulating what can enter and leave the cell, it remains rather poorly understood. It is thought to consist of a double layer of lipid molecules with a layer of protein probably outside the lipid. Fairly large molecules seem to be able to penetrate the membrane in relation to their fat solubility, which would support the hypothesis of its lipid framework. Small molecules and ions appear to penetrate in relation to their size, the smaller ones getting through more readily than the larger. This suggests that pores of a certain size exist in the membrane.

The cell membrane has mechanisms which can move ions and other substances against concentration differences either into or out of the cell. A fine microelectrode can be pushed into a cell and the electrical potential of the inside determined with respect to the outside. In all the cells studied so far there is a potential difference across the membrane which is produced by the non-uniform distribution on either side of ions, particularly those of sodium, potassium, and chloride.

Though these potentials have been studied in animal and plant cells generally, they are best known from the work on nerve cells where sudden changes in the membrane potential are the basis of nerve impulses. The basic process which produces the nerve impulse in any region of the nerve fibre has been shown to be a sudden increase in permeability of the membrane to sodium ions in that region. Transmission from one nerve cell to the next takes place at a special region called a synapse and when an impulse reaches this region it causes the release of a small amount of chemical transmitter substance which diffuses to the membrane of the adjacent cell. There it combines with the membrane in such a way as to change its permeability to ions and so produce a response in the second cell. A number of transmitter substances have now been identified and many of them are related chemically to tranquillisers and other drugs affecting the nervous system.

II. NUCLEUS

The main regions of the nucleus are the surrounding nuclear membrane, a mass of material known as chromatin, and a small sphere called the nucleolus. The nuclear membrane is a double structure very much like the membranes of the cell surface and endoplasmic reticulum. Suggestions have been made that these membranes are continuous at some regions within the cell. The status of chromatin was in doubt for many years. Light microscope studies reveal very little structure in the nucleus until the time when the cell is preparing for, and undergoing, division or mitosis. At this time a number of discrete double strands, the chromosomes, are revealed by virtue of their chromatin content—the material stains heavily with basic dyes.

Cell Division

During division the chromosomes behave in regular and recognisable sequence. In the first stage called prophase they appear and at the same time the nuclear membrane breaks down. Next, in metaphase, the chromosomes become arranged across the equator of a spindle-shaped collection of fibrils which appears in the area formerly outlined by the nucleus. Then follows anaphase in which the two threads of each chromosome, the chromatids, move to opposite poles of the spindle. Finally in the last stage, telophase, nuclear membranes are formed round the two separate collections of chromosome material and the cytoplasm itself divides into two. Thus two cells are formed each containing the same number of chromosomes as the parent and the cells enter a period of rest, or interphase, between divisions. During interphase the chromatin material disappears.

Genes

These are the elements which contain all hereditary information and the medium whereby hereditary features are transmitted from one cell to the next, either in the same organism or from parents to offspring via the fertilised egg. Experiments indicated that the same genes always occupy the same position on chromosomes and this really demands a structural continuity through the life of the cell. The chromosomes undoubtedly persist, but it is still not certain why or how they change so as to become visible during division. One suggestion has been that the nucleic acids of which they are very largely made up condense during the period of prophase. In the resting nucleus the chromosomes may be much more swollen and occupy much of the nucleus.

The problem that has attracted the most attention and is possibly the most fundamental that biology has to offer is that of the nature of the genes. The important material of the genes is known to be deoxyribonucleic acid (DNA), made up of nucleotides as is RNA, though in this case the bases are adenine, cytosine, guanine, and thymine. The DNA molecule is large and complex. Two long chains of nucleotides are known to coil round in a double helix with the pairs of bases on each helix directed towards one another and linked by means of hydrogen bonds (Fig. 2). Furthermore, if adenine is the base on one chain, thymine must be its partner on the other and similarly guanine can link only with cytosine. Because of this pairing off of bases there is sufficient information in a single chain of nucleotides to resynthesise the double helix once more. Thus if we examine a section of a single strand of the helix and find bases in the order adenine, thymine, guanine, adenine, cytosine, we can predict that in similar positions on the other strand we shall find thymine, adenine, cytosine, thymine, guanine. The capacity of one half of a DNA molecule to specify the other half exactly, enables the system to be self-replicating in a way that is essential in a hereditary transmitter and fits in well with what is known of chromosome behaviour during cell division.

Transmission of Genetic Information

Long before the structure and significance of the DNA molecules was known, geneticists were finding that alterations in a gene, known as a mutation, usually affected a particular chemical reaction and this in turn caused the changes seen in the organism as a whole. The effect was due to the failure to synthesise a necessary enzyme and so the hypothesis "one gene = one enzyme"

gathered currency. This view has now been extended to include proteins other than enzymes and it is now certain that specific genes control the synthesis of specific proteins. The DNA of the genes transmits the instructions about protein synthesis to the ribosomes via messenger RNA. In the nucleus, messenger RNA is made with specific base sequences in its molecule by using DNA as the template; thus a group of three adjacent adenine bases in DNA would produce a group of three adjacent uracil bases in the synthesised RNA and this would lead to the specification of phenylalanine at the ribosome as we have seen. Only one of the two strands in the DNA double helix participates in the production of RNA.

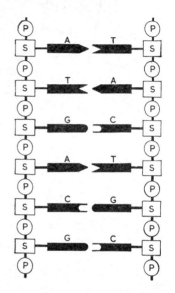

Fig. 2. A portion of a DNA molecule showing how it is made up of two strands of nucleotides. Each nucleotide consists of a base, which may be Adenine (A), Thymine (T), Guanine (G), or Cytosine (C), united to the Pentose Sugar, Desoxyribose (S), in turn joined to Phosphoric Acid (P). The nucleotides are linked through the phosphoric acid groups. The two strands are held together by hydrogen bonds between bases, adenine linking only with thymine, and guanine only with cyto-sine. They are twisted round each other so that the molecule is in the form of a double helix.

The processes involved in nuclear control and the transmission of information from cell to cell is summarised in the aphorism "DNA makes RNA and RNA makes protein." The system of carrying that information in the base sequences of DNA molecules has become known as the "genetic code." A remarkable landmark in the study of DNA occurred when, towards the end of 1967, Kornberg and his colleagues managed to synthesise a virus DNA in a test tube. The synthesised molecules proved to be capable of infecting bacteria in the same way that the naturally occurring virus would. The DNA was synthesised using an extracted virus DNA molecule as template and attaching nucleotides by means of appropriate enzymes. The newly made molecules were then separated from the template. It can hardly be claimed that this is the creation of life in a test tube since the template was extracted from a living virus. The experiment suggests many possibilities in experimental modification of the genetic constitution of an organism with all the far-reaching ethical consequences.

MULTICELLULAR ORGANISATION

It is axiomatic, if evolutionary theory is accepted, that in the course of very long periods of time there has been a general change in multicellular organisation from the simple aggregation of cells with little individual differentiation, to the highly specialised and differentiated cells and tissues seen in complex animals and plants.

Furthermore the complex organisation must be built up in the lifetime of each animal or plant from the single-celled stage of the fertilised egg. The essential problems in development are: (1) how is the smooth succession of shape changes produced during cell division so that an appropriate and recognisable end product is reached?; (2) how do the cells *differentiate* during this temporal sequence so that those which form part of the eye, say, are different from those of liver and blood?

Method of Development

There are some important differences in the method of development in animals and plants. In animals there tends to be a relatively short period during which the basic structure is produced and after which growth, repair, and replacement may cause adjustment rather than major change. In higher plants, on the other hand, the apical regions of both roots and shoots remain in a permanently embryonic state and add material, which then differentiates, in a continuous process throughout the life of the plant. In spite of these differences—and in any case there are many exceptions—the two main problems in development are essentially similar in both animals and plants.

A great deal of work has been done on animal development since this takes place in a fairly stereotyped way during a short period of time. The fertilised egg of an animal divides in such a way as to form a hollow ball of cells, the blastula, which folds in on itself to produce a two-layered sac, the gastrula. A third layer, the mesoderm, is now added between the two layers, known as ectoderm on the outside, and endoderm on the inside. At this stage much of the animal's basic structure is established. Many aspects of this orderly sequence can be explained in terms of specific adhesive properties of cells, so that a cell will stick to others of the same type but not to unrelated types. Other mechanical properties such as elasticity, particularly in surface layers, are important in maintaining shape and producing appropriate changes during processes when one layer is folded in on another. Why cells should have the different physical properties necessary to produce an integrated whole embryo is not known, but certainly it cannot be thought that every cell has an absolutely fixed constitution and therefore a predetermined role in development. Large parts of developing embryos can be removed in early stages and their places taken by remaining cells so that intact organisms are still produced.

Formation of Specialised Tissues

This is essentially a problem in the regulation of gene activity since we know that each cell division produces daughter cells which are genetically identical. It seems likely therefore that instructions are carried on the chromosomes to cope with all requirements of the organism, but that in specialised cells only a small fraction of this full potential is realised. For a long time embryologists have known that egg cytoplasm shows regional differences which make identical nuclei behave differently, and it is thought that regional cytoplasm can in some way control gene activity. Techniques for the transplantation of nuclei in developing frog embryos have been perfected and it has been possible to put a nucleus from an intestinal cell of a tadpole into an enucleate egg. The egg will go on to develop normally even though its nucleus came from a fully specialised cell derived from endoderm. The embryo will form blood and muscle from the mesodermal layer and all the other components of an organism, under the influence of a nucleus which normally would have produced none of these things. One can conclude that all the genes are present, even in the nuclei of specialised cells, but that they have to be placed in a suitable cytoplasmic environment in order to be activated. Similar nuclear transplantation experiments indicate that genes can be "turned off" as well as "turned on" by an appropriate cytoplasmic environment, even though the nuclei come from cells which are so specialised as to stop dividing. The components of cytoplasm which control gene activity are still quite unknown.

A study of cell differentiation and the development of multicellular organisation leads us to the view that, important though the nucleus and its genes are in controlling cell activity, an integrated organism is the result of complex interactions between its constituent cells and between the cytoplasm of those cells and their nuclei.

THE CLASSIFICATION OF ORGANISMS

It was clear to the biologists of the 17th cent. that animals and plants could be fitted into different groups or species. John Ray, a leading biologist of the day, defined a species as a group of individuals capable of interbreeding within the group. This criterion, with its corollary that a species is reproductively isolated from organisms outside the group, has survived more or less unchanged to the present day. The early workers also saw that some species were very similar to one another while others were obviously dissimilar. Systems of classification based on the similarities and differences were drawn up so that all organisms could be fitted into an orderly scheme and species could be given names in accordance with the scheme. The most famous collector and classifier was the Swede, Linnaeus, who established his reputation in the 1730s. A very large number of animals and plants are known by the names given to them by Linnaeus.

Systematics, as this type of study is called, acquired a new significance after Darwin and the Theory of Evolution. The most satisfactory classification became one which reflected the evolution of the organisms classified, a so-called natural classification. It is not always easy to produce because ancestral types tend to become extinct and the problem then becomes one of reconstructing a whole branching system when only the ends of the branches are known. A great deal of the work on systematics has, of necessity, to be done on museum specimens which may be fossils or material preserved in some way by the collectors. The biological criterion of reproductive isolation cannot be used to define a species when the only available representatives are in a preserved state. In this case the scientist must resort to an assessment of structural differences in an attempt to decide whether two organisms are of different species. In recent years computer techniques have been used to compare large numbers of structural differences between groups of animals or plants, as well as physiological and biochemical characteristics. All these techniques have led to the realisation that even the species cannot be regarded as a static point in an evolutionary pattern. Some species die out and others arise as conditions in the environment slowly change.

When the systematist shifts his attention to the higher levels of classification the problems are just as great as at the species level. Different species having features in common may be grouped together into genera, genera into families, families into orders, orders into classes, and classes into phyla. The dividing lines between different groups at all levels is always difficult and in the final analysis somewhat arbitrary since at these levels we do not have any biological criterion such as exists for the species. The evolutionary status of the larger groups is also poorly defined. Many are now recognised to be polyphyletic, which is to say that there are several main evolutionary lines running right through the group.

THE ANIMAL KINGDOM

The animal kingdom is divided into about 24 large groups or phyla though the number varies between different classifications. Ten of the more important phyla are listed below.

1. Protozoa.—Microscopic, unicellular forms of great variety. Some may have more than one nucleus and others form colonies. Many are able to swim by waving hair-like flagella or cilia. Others move by putting out extensions of the body or pseudopodia into which the rest of the body then flows. Protozoa are found in the sea, in fresh water and in the soil. Some are parasitic and cause important diseases in animals and man such as sleeping sickness and malaria.

2. Porifera.—Sponges. Very primitive, multi-cellular animals whose cells display considerable independence of one another. Largely marine. The body which may become branched and plant-like is supported by a framework of spicules and fibres. The bath sponge is the fibrous skeleton of certain species.

3. Coelenterates.—Hydra, jellyfish, sea anemones, corals. Simple animals which have a body only two cells thick surrounding a gut cavity with a single opening to the outside. Largely marine. Many are colonial. Coral reefs are formed from the calcareous skeletons of these animals.

4. Platyhelminths.—Flatworms, which are free living in water, and liver flukes and tapeworms, which are parasitic. A third, solid block of cells, the mesoderm, has been developed between the two layers of cells seen in the coelenterates. A simple gut may be developed and the reproductive system is complex especially in the parasitic forms.

5. Nematodes.—Roundworms. The body is smooth and pointed at each end. Some of the most numerous and widespread of all animals. Free living in all environments and parasitic in practically all groups of plants and animals. At the same level of complexity as the Platyhelminths.

6. Annelids.—Segmented worms such as earthworms, marine worms and leeches. A system of spaces, the body cavity, is developed in the mesoderm so that movements of the main body of the animal and movements of the gut become more or less independent. Digestive, excretory, circulatory, nervous and reproductive systems are all well developed.

7. Arthropods.—A very large, diverse and important group of animals which includes crustaceans such as crabs, shrimps and water fleas; myriapods, such as centipedes and millepedes; insects; and arachnids, such as spiders and scorpions. The arthropods show many of the developments seen in annelids and in addition they possess a jointed, hard exoskeleton. Paired appendages grow out from the segments of the body and form antennae, mouth parts, walking legs, etc. The muscles within the skeleton are able to exert a fine control over the movement of the appendage. In order to grow these animals have to shed the exoskeleton periodically.

8. Molluscs.—Mussels, clams, oysters, squids, octopods and snails. Complex body form but somewhat different from annelid-arthropod type. Unsegmented body protected by shell which is variously developed in different types. It forms two valves in mussels and oysters, a spiral structure in snails, is reduced and internal in squids and completely lost in octopods.

9. Echinoderms.—Starfish, brittle stars, sea cucumbers, sea urchins, and sea lilies. All marine and all radially symmetrical, usually with five radii. Completely unlike the other advanced, major groups. Circulatory, excretory and nervous systems differently developed. Locomotion and feeding by means of hundreds of tube feet projecting from under surface.

10. Chordates.—Sea squirts, Amphioxus, fish, amphibia, reptiles, birds and mammals. Segmented animals which at some stage in their life have gill slits leading from pharynx to the outside and a supporting notochord from which, in all chordates except sea squirts and Amphioxus, is developed a vertebral column or backbone. Those animals with a backbone are commonly referred to as vertebrates, *all* those without as invertebrates. These are obviously names of convenience having no phylogenetic significance since they lump together totally unrelated phyla in one case and align these with a part of a single phylum in the other. The vertebrates have been investigated more completely than any other animals because of their direct structural and functional relationship with man himself. There are five well defined classes which are listed below. The first vertebrates were the fish and from them came the amphibia. The amphibia gave rise to the reptiles and both birds and mammals evolved from different reptilian stock.

(a) Fish

Cold blooded, aquatic animals breathing by means of gills. Sharks, rays and dogfish belong to a group known as the elasmobranchs characterised by a skeleton made of cartilage. Bony fish, most of them in a group called the teleosts, include almost all the fresh water fish and the common marine fish such as cod, mackerel, plaice, herring, etc.

(b) Amphibia

Cold blooded, more or less terrestrial animals which have to return to water to breed. Five fingered limbs are developed in place of the fins of fish. The egg hatches into a tadpole larva which is aquatic and breathes by gills. At metamorphosis the larva changes into the terrestrial adult which possesses lungs. Some amphibia such as the axolotl may become sexually mature as a larva and so never metamorphose into the adult. The class includes newts, salamanders, frogs and toads.

(c) Reptiles

Cold blooded and terrestrial. These animals do not return to water to breed because they have an egg with a relatively impermeable shell containing the food and water requirements of the developing embryo. There is no larval stage. Present day reptiles such as lizards, snakes and crocodiles are all that remains of a tremendous radiation of dinosaur-like creatures which occurred in the Mesozoic (**F48**).

(d) Birds

Warm blooded and adapted for aerial life. The characteristic feathers are both to insulate the body against heat loss and to provide the airfoil surfaces necessary for flight. The birds are an astonishingly uniform group and show less diversity of structure than much lower classification categories (*e.g.*, the teleosts) in other classes. The relationships of the 8,000 or more species of bird are difficult to establish because of this uniformity. It is clear that the flightless forms such as the ostrich are primitive and that the penguins are also in a separate category but the typical modern birds are classified in a large number of rather arbitrary orders. About half of all the known species are placed in one enormous order called the Passeriformes or perching birds.

(e) Mammals

Warm blooded animals which have been successful in a tremendous variety of habitats. Mammals are insulated from the environment by the characteristically hairy and waterproofed skin. They are, with two exceptions, viviparous which means that their young are born alive and in typical mammals at an advanced stage of development. In the marsupials of Australia the young are born at an early stage and transferred to a pouch where they develop further. The two exceptions referred to are primitive monotreme mammals known as the duck-billed platypus and spiny ant-eater and these animals lay eggs. The young of mammals are suckled by means of the milk producing mammary glands. The mammals include aquatic whales and dolphins, hoofed ungulates, flesh eating carnivores, rodents and insectivores, the aerial bats, and the tree climbing primates to which man himself belongs.

THE PHYSIOLOGY OF ANIMALS

In multicellular animals cells are of various types, constituting distinct tissues and organs which perform special functions in the body. Although each cell has its own complex metabolism there must be coordination between cells forming special tissues and between the tissues which form the whole organism in order for the body to function efficiently. The study of these functional interrelationships at the tissue and organism level of organisation is the province of the physiologist.

1. Movement, Fibrils and Skeletons

(a) **Muscles.**—The prime movers in almost all animal movement are large protein molecules in the form of microscopic fibrillar threads. In some way not yet fully understood these fibrils can convert the chemical energy stored in the high energy phosphate bonds of ATP into mechanical energy. In the long, thin cells forming the muscles of animals, it has been discovered that there are two sets of fibrils, one formed of a protein called myosin, the other of actin, arranged in a regular, interdigitating fashion. When the muscle contracts the fibrils slide past one another so that, although the fibrils themselves do not change in length, the muscle as a whole develops tension and shortens. Fine bridges extend from the myosin fibrils to attach on to the actin and it is here that the conversion of chemical to mechanical energy goes on.

(b) **Skeletons.**—In order for muscles to work effectively it is necessary for them to operate in some sort of skeletal system. Contraction but not relaxation is an active process; muscles must be arranged in antagonistic pairs so that one muscle can extend the other. A skeleton also provides a system of levers so that the muscles can do work against the environment in an efficient manner. A simple type of skeleton found in fairly primitive animals is the hydrostatic system of coelenterates and worms. Here the animal can be thought of as a fluid-filled bag or tube which can change shape but whose volume remains constant. By contraction of circular muscles the tube will become long and thin and conversely contraction of longitudinal muscles makes the tube short and fat. Examination of an earthworm will demonstrate how alternating waves of activity of this type passing from head to tail can move the animal over the ground. The earthworm shows an advance over

the simplest systems because the hydrostatic tube is broken up into small units by the segmentation of the body. This makes local responses possible. The next advance to be seen is the development in animals such as arthropods and vertebrates of a firm skeleton to which muscles are directly attached. The skeleton can then be used to support the body and to engage the environment. It seems to matter little whether an endoskeleton (vertebrates) or exoskeleton (arthropods) is developed since in both cases a tremendous radiation of fins for swimming, legs for walking and wings for flying can be seen. However in other respects these two types of skeleton show significant differences. The exoskeleton for example offers more protection than the endoskeleton while apparently setting an upper size limit. All the really big animals have endoskeletons.

(c) **Filia.**—Fibrillar systems are also seen in the hair-like cilia which project from the surface of some cells. Cilia are important in a number of ways. They are the organelles of movement in many Protozoa, they are used to produce water currents past the bodies of some aquatic animals, and they are of great importance in moving fluid within the body of almost all animals. They beat in a regular fashion, the effective stroke being accomplished with the cilium held straight out from the surface and the recovery stroke with the cilium flexed at the base.

2. Feeding

All animals require complex organic substances, proteins, fats and carbohydrates, together with small amounts of salts and vitamins. These materials are obtained by eating the dead bodies of plants and other animals. They are taken into the alimentary canal and there broken down or digested by enzymes into simpler, soluble amino acids, sugars and fatty acids. These substances are absorbed and distributed to various parts of the body where they are used in cell metabolism (**F31–2**) or stored for future use. Many animals, called macrophagous feeders, take in relatively large masses of food. Some such as frogs and snakes swallow their food whole, but many break it up first. Arthropods have modified appendages arranged round the mouth for cutting, some molluscs have a rasp-like radula with which to scrape off particles, and many mammals break up their food with jaws and teeth. The teeth are usually well adapted to the type of food. Carnivores have large, sharp canines, premolars and molars with which to tear the flesh of the prey, fish-eating seals have small peg-like teeth to grip the fish and herbivorous ungulates have flat grinding teeth with which they break up hard plant material.

In contrast, microphagous feeders collect small particles of food material from the environment by continuous filtration. In bivalve molluscs and many marine worms water currents are produced by beating cilia. Food is trapped within the confined space through which the water flows by means of a plentiful supply of sticky mucus in the filtering region. Some crustacea use fine hairs to sieve off food material, often from water currents created by the swimming movements. The most startling of filter feeders is the whalebone whale. As the whale swims forward a stream of water flows in at the front of the mouth and out at the sides via sheets of whalebone which filter off the organisms on which the animal feeds. Though macrophagy seems to favour the attainment of larger size there are exceptions! Another type of particulate feeding is seen in those animals which eat deposits of detritus as do many worms. Finally some animals take in only soluble food materials. These fluid feeders include internal parasites like the tapeworm which absorb substances over the surface of the body, and insects such as the aphid with sucking mouth parts.

3. Respiration. Gills, Lungs and Tracheae

All living cells respire and remain alive only if supplied with oxygen. In a multicellular body, however, many cells are remote from the oxygen of the environment and the need arises for an efficient respiratory system by which oxygen can be taken up and carbon dioxide released. In addition a circulatory system is necessary to transport the oxygen to and from the respiring cells.

(a) Simple Gas Exchange Systems

Animals such as protozoa do not need special structure for gas exchange. Diffusion over the whole body surface ensures an adequate supply of oxygen. Much larger animals such as earthworms also find it possible to rely on diffusion alone, partly because their consumption of oxygen is fairly low, and partly because their bodies are permeable all over. For various reasons most animals restrict the permeability of the outer layers of the body and under these conditions special respiratory areas have to be developed.

(b) Gas Exchange in Water

Aquatic animals, except those such as whales breathing at the surface, have to obtain their oxygen from the supplies which are dissolved in the water. This presents several problems because water is a dense medium, there is not a lot of oxygen in solution, and its diffusion rate is low. For these reasons there is a surprisingly functional uniformity in gill systems and they are very different from lungs. Gills are fine, finger-like processes with a good blood supply which are held out in a water stream. The water current is brought very close to the gill filaments so that the length of diffusion pathway for oxygen is minimal. There is a "counter current" flow of water and blood so that the water containing most oxygen comes into contact with the blood just leaving the gill. This ensures that most of the oxygen can be transferred from water to blood through the thin gill cells. The efficiency of "counter current" systems is well known to the engineer but they were invented by aquatic animals long before they were by man. These features can be seen in the gills of molluscs, crustacea and fish. The pumping devices which maintain the water currents also operate economically. Flow is maintained in crustacea by appendages modified to form beating paddles, in many molluscs by ciliary movement, and in fish by the operation of a double pump in mouth and opercular cavities. In almost all cases there is a continuous current over the gills, the water coming in one way and going out another. Thus the animal avoids reversing the flow with the consequent waste of energy in accelerating and decelerating a large mass of water. Fish, for example, take water in at the mouth and force it out through the gill slits (sharks) or operculum (teleosts).

(c) Gas Exchange in Air

Air breathing animals do not encounter these problems since the medium is less dense, contains a great deal (20%) of oxygen and diffusion rates are high. Lungs are therefore in the form of sacs whose walls are well supplied with blood. The area of the walls may be increased by folding so that the lung becomes spongy and full of minute air spaces called alveoli where the gas exchange goes on. Only the main airways receive fresh air as the lung expands; oxygen is renewed in the alveoli by diffusion. Ventilation of the lung is accomplished by a tidal flow of air in and out of the same tubular opening known as the trachea. The actual ventilating mechanism varies in different animals. In the amphibia for example air is forced into the lungs when the floor of the mouth is raised with the mouth and nostrils shut. The lungs are emptied by elastic recoil and by lowering the floor of the mouth. Higher vertebrates use a costal pump which changes the volume of chest and lungs by movements of the ribs. This change in volume is further assisted in mammals by the diaphragm, a sheet of muscle which lies beneath the lungs and separates thorax and abdomen. In many animals sound producing organs are associated with the lungs and trachea. The larynx is a vocal organ in frogs, some lizards, and most notably mammals. In birds voice production takes place in the syrinx situated further down at the base of the trachea.

A completely different gas exchanging system is seen in insects. Branching tubes, known as tracheae, run throughout the body and carry oxygen directly to the cells without the intervention of a blood system. The tracheae communicate with the outside world via a series of holes called spiracles. Although the main tubes may be actively ventilated, diffusion in the system accounts for a large part of the movement of oxygen between the outside world and cells.

4. Circulation

In the larger animals a transport system is necessary to convey materials about the body and in many, but not all, it is in the form of a blood system. Blood systems are of two types, closed and open.

(a) Open Systems

In an open circulatory system blood is pumped from the heart into a few major arteries but these very quickly give way to large tissue spaces or sinuses so that the tissues and organs of the body are directly bathed in blood. Blood flows slowly from the sinuses back to the heart. Both mollusc and arthropods possess an open system.

(b) Closed Systems

In a closed system blood is pumped round the body in a branching network of arteries and comes into contact with tissues and cells via very thin walled vessels called capillaries. Substances diffuse into and out of the blood through capillary walls. From capillaries, blood enters the veins and so returns to the heart. Blood flow in the tubes of a closed system is much more brisk and blood pressures tend to be higher than in an open system. In annelids the closed system is fairly simple with a vessel above the gut in which blood moves forward connecting to one below in which blood moves backwards. The blood is pumped by peristaltic contraction of the vessels and this system must be regarded as the precursor of a localised pump. Simple hearts are in fact seen in some annelids.

In vertebrates a well defined heart is always present, situated ventrally at the level of the forelimbs. In fish there is a single auricle and ventricle and the latter pumps blood directly to the gills. From the gills the blood is collected into a dorsal aorta which then branches to serve the rest of the body. Associated with the development of lungs and loss of gills in the tetrapods, we see a progressive modification of this simple pattern. The most posterior gill vessel is taken over as the lung or pulmonary artery and slowly a completely separate circuit evolves. This involves the division of the single heart into right and left sides, the former pumping blood to the lungs and the latter to the body. In the birds and mammals where the division is complete the system can be seen to be functionally satisfactory. Blood flows along the following route: left auricle to left ventricle, to body, to right auricle, to right ventricle, to lungs, to left auricle, and so on. Thus blood charged with oxygen in the lungs returns to the heart before being pumped to the body.

(c) Function of the Blood

Most of the materials transported by the blood such as nutrients, waste materials and hormones are carried in solution in the plasma. The respiratory gases, oxygen and carbon dioxide, are present in greater quantity than would be possible if they were in simple solution. Carbon dioxide is carried in the form of bicarbonate and oxygen combines with blood pigment. The best known blood pigment is haemoglobin which is found in a variety of animals and gives the red colour to blood. When oxygen is present in high concentration, as it is in the lungs, combination occurs to give oxyhaemoglobin. If the concentration of oxygen is low, as it is in the tissues, dissociation occurs and oxygen is given off leaving reduced haemoglobin. Carbon monoxide will combine more readily than oxygen with haemoglobin so that in carbon monoxide poisoning the blood cannot transport oxygen. The haemoglobin of vertebrates is contained in high concentration in red blood corpuscles. The amount of haemoglobin and, hence, oxygen carried is greater than if the pigment is not in corpuscles. In mammals the oxygen carrying capacity of blood is thirty times that of a similar quantity of water. Other blood pigments are the blue haemocyanin found in crustacea and molluscs, and the violet haemerythrin found in some worms. Also present in the blood are various types of white corpuscle which are part of the defence mechanism of the body and ingest invading bacteria. Special blood proteins such as fibrinogen, causing clot formation, and antibodies effective against foreign substances occur in the plasma.

5. Excretion, Ionic Regulation and Kidney Tubules

As the chemical reactions included under the term metabolism proceed, so numerous waste products accumulate. The most important of these are compounds containing nitrogen, such as ammonia, urea and uric acid, arising from the use of protein as an energy source. In terrestrial animals they are removed from the blood by the kidney. The basic unit of a kidney is the tubule; in worms these tubules are not concentrated into a solid kidney but occur, a pair in every segment, right down the body. The kidney tubule begins with an end sac, corpuscle or funnel which is closely associated with the body cavity or the blood system. Fluid is filtered from the body cavity or blood into the corpuscle whence it passes to the tubule proper. During passage down the tubule, useful materials are reabsorbed through the tubule cells into the blood whereas unwanted materials remain and pass to the outside world.

Although it is usual to think of kidney function being primarily one of nitrogenous excretion, it is quite common to find that in aquatic animals the kidneys are hardly used for this purpose. In these animals the tubules are primarily concerned in regulating the salt and water levels in the body, nitrogenous wastes being eliminated by diffusion through any permeable surface. In fresh water for example all animals have osmotic problems since the body fluids have a much greater osmotic pressure than the environment. Water tends to enter the body and salts tend to leave. Fresh water animals produce large quantities of very dilute urine, filtering off a lot of blood plasma into the tubules but reabsorbing all wanted materials including the invaluable salts. Fresh water crustacea, molluscs and fish all possess tubules of different morphology which show very similar functional properties.

Different environmental conditions impose different demands on the osmotic and ionic regulating machinery. In very dry conditions, such as in deserts, it is obviously of advantage to reabsorb as much water from the tubule as possible. All animals do this but it is interesting that only birds and mammals have discovered the secret of so concentrating the urine that its salt concentration is higher than that in the blood. This is done by means of a hairpin-like loop in the tubule called the Loop of Henle, another example of a counter current device.

6. Co-ordinating Systems

Overall co-ordination of the animal's body, so that it functions as a whole and reacts appropriately to environmental changes, is largely the province of two systems, one chemical or hormonal, the other nervous. In one respect these are systems for homeostasis, that is for preserving the *status quo*, in spite of considerable environmental fluctuation. Paradoxically they can also initiate change as, for example, one can see in the daily repertoire of complicated behaviour patterns produced by almost any animal.

(a) Nervous Systems

(i) *Sensory Information*

Before appropriate reactions can be produced to any stimulus it is necessary to measure its intensity, position, duration and, most important, character. This is done by sense organs which are usually specialised to receive stimuli of a single modality or character. Thus photoreceptors detect light, mechanoreceptors detect mechanical disturbance and chemoreceptors detect specific chemicals. In all cases the sense organs produce a message about the stimulus in the form of nerve impulses (*see* **F33**—Cell Membrane) which travel up the nerve from the sense organ to the rest of the nervous system. Change of stimulus intensity is usually signalled as a change in frequency of nerve impulses. The position of the sense organ which is active indicates the position of the stimulus within or without the body. The duration of the repeated discharge of nerve impulses indicates the duration of the stimulus.

(ii) *Simple Networks*

The simplest type of nervous system is the network of interconnected nerve cells (neurones) found in the coelenterates. Branching processes of the nerve cells communicate with neighbouring processes at special regions called synapses (**F33**). Quite complicated behaviour is possible even with this relatively simple system. If a sea anemone is prodded violently it will close up equally violently, showing that activity has spread throughout the network. If it is tickled gently it will respond with local contractions around the site of stimulation. The movements of feeding and locomotion are very delicately performed at appropriate times.

(iii) *Central Nervous Systems*

In the majority of animals all the nerve cells tend to become collected into a solid mass of tissue referred to as a central nervous system (C.N.S.). Within the mass the nerve cells are interconnected via synapses in the same way as in a nerve net. The connexions with sense organs and muscles are made via long processes called axons. Numbers of axons are usually bound together with connective tissue to form a nerve trunk. In annelids and arthropods the C.N.S. is seen as a ventral cord lying beneath the gut with a swelling or ganglion in each segment of the body. In molluscs, the ganglia are usually more closely grouped around the oesophagus, with the possible provision of a pair of ganglia further back in the viscera. Vertebrates possess a dorsal nerve cord which is uniform in diameter and not ganglionated, though nerves emerge from it in a segmental fashion. The segmental nerves arise in two separate bundles or roots. The dorsal root is made up entirely of sensory nerves conveying information to the C.N.S. The ventral root consists of motor nerves which convey nerve impulses to the muscles of limbs and alimentary canal together with other effector organs such as glands.

(iv) *Reflexes*

A reflex, in which stimulation of a sense organ or sensory nerve results in the almost immediate contraction of a muscle, is the simplest type of C.N.S. activity. Reflexes have been studied in all animals but the best known ones can be seen in frogs, cats, dogs, and sometimes humans. The very simplest is the stretch reflex, in which a stretched muscle is made to contract by activity coming into the C.N.S. from stretch receptors in the muscle. The activity is relayed directly to the motor neurones of the muscle concerned, making them active and thus causing the muscle to contract. This reflex is monosynaptic, *i.e.* there is only the single synaptic connexion between sensory nerve and motor neurone. The knee jerk in humans is a stretch reflex, the stretch being caused by hitting the muscle tendon as it passes over the knee. Much of the recent work on reflexes has been done on this simple system, notably by Eccles. The flexor reflex, which is seen as the sudden withdrawal of a limb from any painful stimulus, is more complicated. Although the stimuli may vary, the withdrawal response is always accomplished by contraction of flexor muscles which bring the limb in towards the body. The reflex is polysynaptic, *i.e.* several intermediate neurones connect the sensory nerves through to the motor neurones. More complicated still is the scratch reflex in which an animal is made to scratch its flank in response to an irritation or tickling in that region. This reflex demonstrates some of the more involved properties of the C.N.S. For example a dog will continue to scratch for a time after the tickling has stopped, so that the C.N.S. must continue to be active in the absence of sensory stimulation. This has been called after-discharge.

(v) *The Brain*

The C.N.S. functions in a more complicated way than is suggested by study of the reflexes and most of these higher activities are co-ordinated by the brain. A greater condensation of neurones is seen at the front end of the C.N.S. of all animals because of the larger numbers of sense organs in that region. Brains, which become the dominant part of the C.N.S., can be seen in arthropods, molluscs and vertebrates. The close association with sense organs is illustrated by the vertebrate brain which is divided into three regions: (*a*) forebrain (nose), (*b*) midbrain (eye) and (*c*) hindbrain (ear and taste). However, the brain is much more than a relay station for these stimulus modalities and it receives information from other parts of the body via the spinal cord. All this information is correlated and activity patterns initiated and transmitted to appropriate regions. In lower vertebrates, the roof of the midbrain (the optic tectum) is the important correlation centre and its effectiveness has been well established in studies on instinct and learning in fish. Another region of the brain of importance in all vertebrates is a dorsal upgrowth of the hindbrain called the cerebellum. This is a motor co-ordinating centre which ensures that all activities are performed in a smooth and well balanced way by the muscles and limbs of the body. In reptiles, the forebrain begins to take over the correlation role and in mammals this development reaches its peak in the cerebral cortex. In man the cortex overshadows the rest of the brain and contains some 1,000,000,000 neurones. It is easy to see the magnitude of the problem of understanding a system of this complexity. The bee's brain with far, far fewer cells can initiate complicated behaviour such as the hive dances. The possibilities offered by the human cortex seem vastly greater, though they are often realised in ways which give cause for concern. At the moment it would be quite impossible to build a computer with the properties of the human brain. To do this in the future would depend on major advances in computer technology and even greater advances in the knowledge of central nervous systems.

(b) Hormonal Regulation

Many aspects of an animal's metabolism are regulated, not by the nervous system, but by specific chemical signals known as hormones which are circulated in the blood stream. Growth, carbohydrate metabolism, salt balance, activity of ovaries and testes and their associated structures, and colour change are all regulated in some way by hormones. The substances are secreted by endocrine glands or ductless glands as they are often called. The important endocrine glands in vertebrates are the thyroid, parathyroid, adrenal, pancreas, the sex glands, and the pituitary.

In the past the endocrine and nervous systems were regarded as exerting an independent control in slightly different functional areas of the body. It is clear now that the integration of the two systems is much greater than was formerly envisaged and in vertebrates is accomplished through the pituitary gland. Secretions of this gland regulate almost all other endocrine glands and the secretions of the pituitary are either produced in the C.N.S. with which it is directly connected or are controlled by C.N.S. secretions. An astonishing, parallel development of other neurosecretory systems, such as those of the pituitary, has been found in a variety of animals and in all types the neurosecretory organ complex is the dominant endocrine gland of the body. In crustacea the so-called X organ complex found within the eyestalk, and in insects neurosecretory cells connecting to the corpora cardiaca glands, occupy the functional position of the vertebrate pituitary. They all regulate growth, metabolism and reproductive physiology, either directly or through the medication of other endocrine glands.

7. Animal Behaviour

In discussing the nervous system we have already dealt with simple mechanisms such as the reflex. Very much more complicated are the instinctive and learned patterns of behaviour which are studied by animal psychologists and ethologists such as Lorenz and Tinbergen.

(a) Instinct

Instinct is inborn behaviour which does not have to be learnt and is usually performed in a stereotyped way. For example a gull will retrieve an egg taken out of its nest by shovelling it back with the underside of its beak. The gull will never replace an egg in its nest in any other way, for example by using a wing or leg, and once it has begun a retrieval it will usually continue the movements back to the nest even though the egg is taken away. An instinctive behaviour pattern is triggered off by a particular stimulus or "releaser" which may be a very small part of the total environment. A male stickleback will attack a very crude model with a red belly but will not attack an exact model without it. The red underside appears to be a much more important stimulus than general shape. A particular instinctive pattern cannot always be elicited and the reaction of an animal very largely depends on when the behaviour was last produced. The longer the time that elapses, the easier it is to trigger off the instinctive pattern until eventually it may appear in the absence of an appropriate set of environmental circumstances.

(b) Learning

Learning is that behaviour acquired during the organism's lifetime as a result of experience. Evidence of learning has been seen in many animals from worms upwards though, as might be expected, the more complicated types of learning are found only in those animals with elaborate nervous systems. A simple type of learning is seen when an animal, upon repeated exposure to a stimulus, gradually decreases the normal response which is usually one of flight, until eventually the response may disappear completely. This process is called habituation. More complex are the conditioned reflexes, which were first discovered by Pavlov. In these an animal can in some way connect a conditioned stimulus such as a bell, with an unconditioned stimulus such as meat, so that eventually it salivates when the bell is rung. Trial and error learning of the type needed to be successful in running a maze is more complicated still. In this there is a retrospective element because the reward at the end of the maze comes after all the responses. Many animals can run mazes but the white rat has been extensively used in experiments of this nature and there is a huge literature on this one animal. A final category of learning can be called insight learning; in this an animal shows evidence of resolving a new problem without trial and error. This type of learning involves the perception of relations between different parts of the environment and though there may be examples in arthropods and molluscs the clearest evidence of it is seen in the behaviour of birds and mammals.

8. Reproduction

A single animal may live for a short or long time, but eventually it dies, and the continuance of the species is dependent upon reproduction. Some protozoa, such as *Amoeba*, reproduce asexually by the simple division of the cell to produce two new individuals. Asexual reproduction also occurs in some coelenterates, such as jelly-fish, in which there is an alternation of sexual and asexual generations. However, the vast majority of animals only reproduce sexually.

This involves the fusion of two cells, the gametes, produced by adult individuals, and each zygote thus formed develops into an individual of the next generation. The gametes are of two kinds, the large, spherical, immobile ova produced by the female gonad or ovary and the much smaller motile sperms produced by the male gonad or testis. The motility of the sperms helps them to reach the passive ovum, which contains food reserves to support the early development of the embryo.

Worms.—The flat worms, particularly parasitic forms, have complicated life cycles, and many are hermaphrodite, *i.e.*, each individual has both male and female organs. Cross-fertilisation usually occurs, the sperms from one worm being introduced into the female duct of another. The round worms are unisexual, and internal fertilisation also occurs. Of the annelids the polychaete worms are unisexual, but the ova and sperms are shed into the sea, where fertilisation takes place. However, *Lumbricus* and the leeches are hermaphrodite, cross-fertilisation takes place and the eggs are laid in cocoons.

Arthropods.—Many crustacea are unisexual, though the sedentary barnacles are hermaphrodite. Internal fertilisation may occur, but in the crabs and crayfish pairing takes place and the sperms are deposited on the tail of the female. When the eggs are shed they become fertilised and remain attached to the abdominal appendages. Most crustacea have motile larval stages into which the eggs first develop. In *Daphnia*, the water-flea, parthenogenesis sometimes occurs, *i.e.*, the eggs develop without being fertilised. The sexes are separate in the arachnida and there are usually no larval stages except in the primitive king-crabs. The insects are also unisexual, and the fertilised eggs are laid after copulation. In some, *e.g.*, dragon-flies, an immature nymph similar to the adult is formed, but in flies, beetles, moths, and many others the egg hatches into a larval form. This then develops into a pupa, from which the final adult or imago is produced. In the social ant's nest the workers are sterile females with large heads, reduced eyes, and no wings. The males and queens are winged, and insemination of the latter occurs during the "nuptial" flight.

Molluscs and Echinoderms.—Most lamellibranchs are unisexual, although some species of scallops and oysters are hermaphrodite. There are motile larval forms, and in the swan mussel, *Anodonta*, the larvae develop in the mantle cavity of the parent and when liberated become attached to the gills or fins of fish, where they remain parasitic for some time. Some gastropods are unisexual, but the slugs and snails are hermaphrodite. In the latter cross-fertilisation occurs, the two approaching snails being stimulated to copulate by firing small sharp darts of calcium carbonate into each other. The echinoderms are unisexual, and fertilisation takes place in the sea. The egg first develops into a ciliated larval form.

Vertebrates.—The sexes are always separate in the vertebrates. In some cartilaginous fish, *e.g.*, dogfish, internal fertilisation occurs and the eggs are laid in protective sacs. In contrast, the bony fish shed ova and sperms into the water, where fertilisation takes place. Although pairing may take place in amphibia, fertilisation occurs in water, and there is usually an aquatic larval stage. The reptiles, birds, and mammals are independent of water for fertilisation, as copulation takes place and the sperms from the male are introduced directly into the female. Most reptiles and all birds lay eggs with hard shells. Development of the embryo in marsupial mammals begins in the female uterus, but is continued in a ventral pouch which surrounds the teat of the mammary gland. In the two living species of monotreme mammals the eggs are incubated in a similar pouch. Finally, in the eutherian mammals the embryo develops in the female uterus and is born at an advanced stage.

Diversity of Sexual Reproduction.—This brief survey will give some idea of the diversity of sexual reproduction in animals. External fertilisation is very much a matter of chance, and large numbers of gametes are produced which offset the great losses of gametes and embryos that this method involves. Internal fertilisation is more certain, and is also independent of external water—an important factor in land animals. In vertebrates particularly there is increase in the care of the young by the parents, involving the development of characters of behaviour as well as those of structure. Some fish lay their eggs in holes or nests which are protected by the male. Similarly, a few frogs build nests, while others carry the eggs about. The eggs of birds require a constant high temperature for their development, and they are usually incubated by the parents. After hatching the young are fed and guarded by the parents until they can leave the nest and fend for themselves. In the eutherian mammals the embryos are attached to the uterus wall by the placenta, *via* which food materials pass from the mother. The period of gestation is long, and after birth the young are supplied with milk from the mother until they are weaned and can feed themselves. Another feature in mammals is the period of "childhood" during which they play and learn and are protected and fed by their parents. The internal fertilisation, internal development, and care and protection of the young after birth which is so conspicuous in the higher vertebrates results in the reduction of losses during the vulnerable embryonic and young stages, and in consequence relatively few progeny are produced by a pair of individuals.

THE PLANT KINGDOM

There are various ways in which the main classes of the plant kingdom can be grouped, but a simple, up-to-date arrangement is given in the chart. Vascular plants are often known as the *Tracheophyta* because they all possess woody conducting elements. These are absent in non-vascular plants, and the bacteria, fungi, and algæ are often called *Thallophyta*, *i.e.*, they have a relatively simple plant body or thallus. Many of the bryophytes also possess a thallus, but in some there is a stem bearing leaves, although a true vascular system is absent. Many thallophytes are aquatic, whereas the tracheophytes are mostly land plants in which the development of woody tissues can be related to the attainment of the land habit as the plant kingdom evolved. However, the chart should not be taken as indicating the evolutionary relationships of the various groups. It is more a convenient arrangement which reflects the relative complexity of the plant body.

1. Bacteria.—This is a vast group of minute organisms of very simple structure. They are spherical or rod shaped and may exist as separate cells, some species being motile, or as long chains or irregular masses. Their minute size makes the elucidation of their structure very difficult. There is a wall of complex composition, and cytoplasm which contains glycogen and fat. Electron-microscope studies have revealed the presence of structures which appear to consist of nuclear material. Multiplication is by simple division, which may take place very rapidly. For example, *Bacillus subtilis* can divide every 20 minutes, so that in 8 hours a single cell may give rise to 16 millions. Recent research indicates that a sexual process may also occur. Bacteria can survive unfavourable conditions by producing a resistant spore within the cell. They do not possess chlorophyll, though a few are pigmented. Most obtain their food already formed, and are thus either saprophytes or parasites. The saprophytic bacteria occupy a vital position in the living world. They are responsible for most of the decay of dead organic matter, and it has been truly said that without them the surface of the earth would soon become completely covered with the dead bodies of animals and plants. Bacteria also play a vital part in the circulation of nitrogen in nature. By breaking down organic material, ammonia is released and ammonium carbonate is formed in the soil. This is oxidised by other bacteria to form nitrates, which can be absorbed by plants again. Yet other bacteria can "fix" atmospheric nitrogen, and one species, *Rhizobium leguminosum*, occurs in the root nodules of the pea plant. Such plants are often grown on poor soils and ploughed in, thus improving the fertility of the soil. The parasitic bacteria are also of great importance, as they are responsible for many diseases of plants, animals, and man.

2. Fungi.—This is a large group of plants, none of which contain chlorophyll. Hence, like the bacteria, they are either parasites on other living plants and animals or saprophytes which live on dead organic matter. Some are unicellular aquatic plants, but many have a body called a mycelium composed of many branched threads or hyphæ. In the higher fungi (*e.g.*, toadstools, bracket fungi, and puff-balls) complex reproductive structures are formed. All fungi produce spores. In the aquatic species these may be motile, but the majority form minute, airborne spores. The spore output is often very great, and a single mushroom may produce, 1,800 million spores. Some fungi are serious diseases of crop plants, such as potato blight and wheat rust.

3. Algae.—These are essentially aquatic plants which contain chlorophyll. They range from microscopic forms to the large seaweeds. The green algae (Chlorophyceae) live mostly in fresh water and may be unicellular, motile or non-motile, or filamentous, though a few found in tropical seas are more complex. The brown algae (Phaeophyceae) are mostly seaweeds which possess a brown pigment, fucoxanthin, which masks the green chlorophyll. They include the bladder-wracks (*Fucus*) and kelps (*Laminaria*) of our coasts and the seaweeds which form dense floating masses over hundreds of square miles of the Sargasso Sea. Other groups are the red algae (Rhodophyceae), mostly seaweeds of delicate form, the unicellular motile diatoms (Bacillariophyceae), and the blue-green algae (Cyanophyceae). All algae possess unicellular reproductive organs. Various types of life cycle occur, the most complex being found in the red algae.

4. Bryophyta.—These are the liverworts (Hepaticae) and the mosses (*Muscineae*). They are all small plants characterised by a sharply defined life-cycle. This consists of an alternation of generations, the "plant" being a gametophyte bearing sex organs. The latter are multicellular, the female archegonium containing a single stationary ovum and the male antheridium producing many motile sperms. The latter are released and swim in water to the archegonium, where fertilisation takes place. After this a sporophyte is formed which is always dependent on the gametophyte and never becomes free living. The sporophyte usually consists of an absorbing foot buried in the tissue of the gametophyte and a stalk or seta bearing at the top a single sporangium. In many mosses this is a complex structure with hygroscopic teeth which move apart only when dry, thus releasing the minute spores only when conditions are suitable for their dissemination in the air. The bryophytes are of little economic importance, and may be looked upon as an evolutionary side-line. However, they occupy suitable "niches" in many plant communities, and species of the bog-moss *Sphagnum* cover large areas where rainfall is high.

5. Psilopsida.—This is a small group of primitive, vascular, spore-bearing plants. Its only living representatives are two rare genera of the Southern Hemisphere. However, a number of fossil forms are known from the Devonian period. The best known are those found in the chert at Rhynie in Scotland. The plants are excellently preserved, and their internal structure can be easily seen. They were probably marsh plants with prostrate and erect leafless stems, although *Asteroxylon* had simple leaves.

6. Sphenopsida.—The only living members of this group are about twenty-five species of horse-tails (*Equisetum*). In the Carboniferous period many tree forms existed (*e.g.*, *Calamites*), the remains of which are very common in coal deposits.

7. Lycopsida.—In the Carboniferous period the tree clubmosses were also prominent members of the forests (*e.g.*, *Lepidodendron*). They often reached 30m in height, were branched or unbranched, and had large simple leaves. They also had extensive root systems. The only living members belong to a few genera of small herbaceous clubmosses, such as *Lycopodium* and *Selaginella*. Like the true mosses, they have an alternation of generations, but the elaborate plant with stem, leaves, and roots is the sporophyte, and the gametophyte is very small. In *Lycopodium* only one kind of spore is produced, and the resultant gametophyte is bisexual. *Selaginella* produces numerous small microspores which give rise to the very reduced male gametophytes and motile sperms and the few large megaspores which produce the female gametophytes. The latter are formed within the megaspore wall, which splits to allow the sperms to reach the small archegonia.

8. Filicinae.—These are the true ferns, which in some classifications are put with the horsetails and clubmosses in the Pteridophyta or vascular cryptogams (*i.e.*, vascular plants without seeds). The ferns have a long fossil history, and remains very similar to the living Royal ferns (*Osmunda*) are known from the Carboniferous. The ferns are widespread and particularly abundant in tropical forests. The majority are herbaceous perennial plants, but a few are aquatic, and there are some tree ferns, which may reach 6 m in height. Most ferns possess a stem bearing roots and large leaves or fronds. The plant is the sporophyte and produces numerous spores in sporangia borne on the fronds. Each spore gives rise to a minute green free-living gametophyte known as the prothallus, which bears the archegonia and antheridia. After fertilisation a young sporophyte develops, which at first draws nourishment from the prothallus. Thus, as in the Bryophyta, external water is essential for the motile sperms to swim in, and there is a clearly defined alternation of generations, but the sporophyte is a complex independent plant, and the gametophyte is reduced though free-living.

9. Gymnospermae.—These were the dominant land plants in the Mesozoic era, although fossil remains are found as far back as the Devonian. The living members still form large forests in the North Temperate regions. They are mostly tall evergreen trees with roots, stems, and small leaves. The conifers include the pines (*Pinus*), larches (*Larix*), and yews (*Taxus*). The cycads are a relic group of tropical plants with thick, unbranched trunks and large fern-like leaves. The maiden-hair tree of Japan (*Ginkgo biloba*) has also had a long geological history. Another interesting Gymnosperm is *Metasequoia*, a genus well known to palaeobotanists. In 1948 a few living specimens were found in a remote area of China. Seeds were collected and plants are now being grown in botanical gardens all over the world. The Gymnosperms are characterised by the production of "naked" seeds, which are usually born on cones. The male pollen grains, which are equivalent to the microspores of *Selaginella*, are carried by wind to the ovule of the female cone. The pollen germinates and the pollen tube carries the male gametes to the reduced archegonia borne on the female prothallus, which, unlike those of the ferns, is retained within the ovule on the parent plant. After fertilisation an embryo is formed, the prothallus becomes the food store or endosperm, and the outer part of the ovule becomes the seed coat. The cycads and *Ginkgo* retain a primitive feature in that the male gametes are motile and they swim to the archegonia from the pollen tube.

10. Angiospermae.—The apparent sudden rise of the Angiosperms in the Cretaceous period is still the "abominable mystery" it was to Darwin. Various suggestions have been put forward, but nothing definite is known about the origin of the group. The Angiosperms or flowering plants are now the dominant group over most of the land surface of the earth, and at least 250,000 species are known. Apart from the natural vegetation, the majority of our crop and garden plants are Angiosperms. They occur in every type of habitat and range in form from gigantic trees to minute plants, such as the duck-weeds. Some are climbers, others succulents, and a number have reverted to the aquatic habit. Although most possess chlorophyll, a few are partial (*e.g.*, Mistletoe) or complete parasites (*e.g.*, Dodder).

Flower, Fruit and Seeds.—The diagnostic feature of the group is the production of seeds, which are completely enclosed within the female part of the flower, the ovary. Basically a flower is a short reproductive shoot which bears several whorls of lateral organs. At the base are several, often green, protective sepals forming the calyx, and above this are the often brightly coloured petals of the corolla. Within this are the stamens of the androecium or male part of the flower. Centrally is the female gynoecium of one or more carpels containing the ovules. The parts of the flower may be free, as in the buttercup, or fused together. In many species the petals are fused (sympetalous), the stamens are borne on the corolla (epipetalous), and the carpels are fused to form a compound gynoecium (syncarpous). The stamens possess anthers, which produce pollen grains. These are shed and carried by insects or wind to the receptive stigmas of the carpels. Each produces a tube which grows down the style to the ovary and enters an ovule. The ovule is a complex structure containing an ovum and a primary endosperm nucleus. Two male nuclei are discharged from the pollen tube, one fuses with the ovum and the other fuses with the primary endosperm nucleus. After this "double fertilisation" an embryo is formed which is embedded in the nutritive endosperm and the outer tissues of the ovule form the seed coat or testa. The ovary of the carpel develops into the fruit containing the seeds. Fruits are of various kinds, being either dehiscent and opening when mature to release the seeds or indehiscent, with a succulent or dry wall. The indehiscent fruits are shed as a whole, and often contain only a single seed. Seeds and fruits show great variation in structure, and often have adaptations assisting dispersal. Some have hairs or wings which aid wind dispersal, whereas others have hooks or are sticky and are transported by animals. Some have flotation devices and may be carried a great distance from the parent plant by water. Seeds vary in size from the microscopic seeds of orchids to those of the double coconut, which may weigh 15 kg. Only about 10% of the weight of a seed is water, and the embryo, although alive, is dormant. The bulk of

a seed consists of stored food material, commonly fats or starch and proteins, which may be contained in the endosperm surrounding the embryo, although in some species the endosperm is absorbed during seed development and the food is stored in the one or two swollen seed leaves or cotyledons of the embryo.

Classification of Flowering Plants.—John Ray (1627–1705) was the first botanist to recognise the two great divisions of the Angiosperms—the dicotyledons with two seed leaves and the monocotyledons with only one. This primary division of the flowering plants has stood the test of time and is still recognised. Other differences are also found between the two groups. The dicotyledons usually have net-veined leaves and the floral parts are in fours or fives, whereas the monocotyledons usually have leaves with parallel veins and the floral parts are in threes.

THE PHYSIOLOGY OF PLANTS

Some of the fundamental differences between animals and plants can be ascribed to the ways in which the two groups of living organisms satisfy their requirements for food material. In a simple way at least, an animal can be thought of as a mobile gastro-intestinal tract which is highly specialised to search out and receive food in convenient, concentrated packets. In typical land plants, however, a quite different organisation exists because the organic nutrition is based on the process of photosynthesis in which carbon dioxide from the air is combined with water from the soil to form simple carbohydrates. An expanded foliage system is necessary to absorb carbon dioxide and to expose the photosynthetic pigment, chlorophyll, to sunlight. Similarly, an expanded root system is needed to absorb the other ingredients of nutrition, water and mineral salts, from the soil.

The work of the plant physiologist is devoted to understanding the functional relationships between these two expanded systems of root and shoot. The production of carbohydrates by photosynthesis has already been discussed (**F32**).

The Spread of Roots

In addition, the physiologist is concerned with the progressive elaboration of root and shoot as the plant grows. Plants show much less specialisation of their cells into discrete tissues and organs than do animals and they also retain special areas, at root and shoot tips for example, where new cells are added to the structure throughout the life of the plant. In some cases whole plants can be regenerated from very few cells taken almost anywhere from a growing plant body. The orderly regulation of growth and differentiation is thus a basic property of much plant tissue.

1. Movement of Solutes and Water

The movement of water and inorganic solutes in a plant is primarily upwards from the roots where they are absorbed, to the leaves or growing regions where evaporation of water or the use of both water and salts occurs. Water and inorganic ions permeate freely through the cell walls and air spaces of the more peripheral cells of the roots. Equilibrium is established between the insides of cells in this region and the water and salts outside, water tending to enter by osmosis and the salts by diffusion or active transport. Increase in cell volume which would be caused by continual influx of materials is, of course, restricted by the inextensible cell wall. In the centre of the root is a region packed with the specialised conducting tissues called xylem and phloem. These form continuous channels through the root and into the shoot and clearly serve for the conduction of water and substances in solution. In the root this central region is separated from the more peripheral tissue by a single layer of cells, the endodermis. The endodermal layer can actively pump water and salts from the outer regions through into the longitudinal conducting strands of, in this case, the xylem. Evidence for this pumping activity can be seen in the exudation of liquid from the base of a plant stem cut close to ground level. In some cases pressures of 8 to 10 atmospheres have been generated in roots as a result of the pumping action of the endodermal cells.

Water is also moved up a plant by forces generated in the leaves. Constant evaporation from the walls of leaf cells, both on the surface and within the substance of the leaf, causes loss of water from the plant. The process is called transpiration and, within limits, the plant can control transpiration rate by regulating the ease with which water-saturated air passes to the exterior through perforations in the leaf surface called stomata. The diameter of these apertures can be regulated by movements of guard cells surrounding the stomatal openings. Loss of water from the leaf cells is made good by withdrawing more water from the xylem elements within the leaves and stem of the plant. Cohesive forces between water molecules prevent the continuous water columns within the xylem from breaking. The net result is that water is drawn up the stem as transpiration occurs in the leaves. Considerable suction pressures have been measured by suitable manometer systems attached to the cut stems of actively transpiring plants. In addition materials such as dyes or radioactive isotopes have been followed as they move up the conducting xylem vessels at rates which can usually be related to the rate of transpiration.

2. Movement of Organic Substances

The organic substances, whose site of manufacture is primarily in the leaves, have to be distributed to the rest of the plant body. It is thought that a second conducting tissue, the phloem, is mainly responsible for the distribution of these materials in solution. Ploem is found as a layer of tissue to the outside of the xylem vessels in a plant stem. It consists of conducting cells which are rather different from those of the xylem, which serve, as we have seen, mainly in the transport of water and salts. Whereas xylem tissues are composed of dead cells whose cell walls form effective longitudinal conducting channels, phloem is made up mainly of living cells. Elements called sieve tubes are the most important conducting cells in phloem and, during the initial stages of differentiation, a sieve tube has a full complement of cytoplasm and cell organelles. Later differentiation sees the protoplasmic structures break down, but even in mature sieve tubes protoplasmic strands join through the perforated ends of adjacent cells and may extend longitudinally through the conducting elements.

Ringing experiments in which a complete ring of phloem is cut from the outside of a plant, provide evidence of the tissue's function in longitudinal conduction of carbohydrates. Sugars accumulate above such a ring but not below it. Samples of fluid taken from sieve tubes have also revealed high concentrations of carbohydrates in the sap. The method used to obtain such samples is very ingenious. Several aphids (insects such as green fly) are known which parasitise the phloem translocation channels of plants. The aphid is allowed to insert its stylet tip into the phloem vessels and is then anaesthetised and cut off the inserted stylet. Sap exudes from the stylet stump and can be collected and analysed.

3. Growth

Growth is usually, but not always, thought of as involving increase of size as measured by length, volume, or weight. In these terms any unit in a plant, whether root, shoot or fruit would follow a sigmoid growth curve with growth starting slowly, then speeding up, before finally slowing down at maturity leading on to death. Growth may also be considered as an increase in the number of cells, an increase in substances such as water, protein or DNA in the growing system, or an increase in complexity of organisation.

The organisation of growth, no matter how it is measured, presents a number of interesting problems. In the first divisions of a fertilised egg, all cells divide. Very soon this property becomes localised, polarity is established, and the young embryo develops a shoot tip and a root tip. These have then become discrete regions of cell division. The cells behind them cease active division, enlarge by developing large vacuoles and form mature plant tissue. A circular strand of dividing tissue, called the cambium, is left in the stem between differentiated xylem and phloem. The cambium is responsible for growth in girth. The acquisition of polarity has far-reaching consequences, for the behaviour of a shoot tip is very different from that of a root. The shoot tip, for example, gives rise to leaf cells with photosynthesising chloroplasts and it grows upwards away from gravity and towards light. The root tip gives rise to cells which absorb salt and water, and it grows towards gravity and away from light.

Quite a lot is known about the mechanisms which regulate growth by cell enlargement in the regions behind the actively dividing tips. Cell enlargement is achieved by the secretion of water and solutes to form a substantial vacuole within the cell, thus causing an overall increase of volume and expansion of the cell wall. The degree of enlargement is affected by external stimuli such as light and gravity, producing the differential growth patterns seen when plants orientate to these stimuli. Substances, called plant hormones or auxins, are now known to be produced at the growing apex and to move back causing vacuole formation in the actively elongating region. The distribution of auxin is affected by light or gravity so that the plant will turn towards or away from the stimulus. Indoleacetic acid is the active growth substance occurring naturally in many plants. Several man-made substances are also effective and are widely used as weedkillers. Evidence is also accumulating to show that a group of substances exists in plants to control cell division, just as auxins regulate cell enlargement.

ECOLOGY—THE STUDY OF LIVING ORGANISMS IN THEIR ENVIRONMENT

The important branch of biology which deals with the relationship between living organisms and their environment must now be considered. Living organisms and the physical environment in which they exist form what is termed an ecosystem. Obviously it would be possible to regard the whole world as a giant ecosystem, though for purposes of study it would be extremely unrewarding and impractical. A pond, a rocky or sandy shore, a forest, and a peat bog are examples of ecosystems on a somewhat smaller scale, possessing different properties and containing populations of animals and plants that are different both in number of individuals and in species represented. The ecologist seeks to understand why a particular species is present in certain numbers in an ecosystem in terms of that species' interaction with all other living organisms (biotic factors) and with the physical (abiotic) factors of the ecosystem.

1. Abiotic Factors

All living organisms will show ranges of tolerance for abiotic factors such as temperature, humidity, salinity, oxygen levels, amount of light, etc. Clearly, if any factor in the environment moves outside the range of tolerance of a species, it becomes limiting for that particular species which is then excluded from the environment. Within the range of tolerance there will be an optimum value for each abiotic factor at which a species will survive best.

There is not a firm line separating suitable and unsuitable environments, but rather a steady shift from optimum values into conditions in which an organism finds it more and more difficult to survive.

One of the most important abiotic factors in an environment is the nature of the substrate upon or within which an organism moves and settles.

(a) **The Terrestrial Environment.**—Soil is the commonest substrate for terrestrial organisms. Particle sizes, ranging from the coarsest gravel soils, through sands and silts to the finely textured clays, have extensive effects on the flora and fauna of any area. Coarsely textured soils are obviously penetrated most easily both by roots and by soil animals. Soils of this type also allow the rapid movement of water and soil gases, but they have the serious disadvantage of poor water retention. The level at which water saturation occurs is known as the water table and is an important abiotic factor. The terrestrial environment tends on the whole to dehydrate organisms and there is always a marked dependence on water supplies.

Soil characteristics also vary with depth. A vertical section through any soil is referred to as its profile and has considerable bearing on the ecosystems in which the soil is involved. The layers, or horizons, of a soil profile vary enormously from one soil to another. Below a surface layer of organic debris one can, in general terms, distinguish a layer of soil from which substances have been leached (A horizon), soil containing the leached-out substances from the layer above (B horizon), the weathered parent material (C horizon), and finally the parent rock or some other stratum beneath the soil (D horizon).

Humus

Humus, which is formed from animal and plant remains and is located in the lower parts of the A profile, is of great importance in providing food for soil organisms and chemical elements such as nitrogen, phosphorus, and calcium for plant growth. It is also important in maintaining good soil structure and, though inorganic fertilisers can supply chemical elements, they have little or no effect on structure. Soil requires careful cultivation, and structure is easily disturbed by such things as heavy farm machinery, which can lead to the creation of impermeable layers with the disastrous exclusion of oxygen and oxygen-consuming organisms.

(b) **The Aquatic Environments.**—Marine and freshwater environments together cover more than 75 per cent of the earth's surface and, since they can be occupied throughout their entire depth, offer a much greater volume of living space than does the land. There is only a slight difference between the density of water and of living tissues, so that the bodies of aquatic organisms are very largely supported by the environment and do not need strong woody stems or powerfully muscled limbs to hold them up. Water has a high specific heat, which means that large amounts of heat are needed to raise its temperature. The result is that aquatic environments tend to show much smaller fluctuations in temperature than the terrestrial ones. In general, the larger the volume of water the smaller are the fluctuations in temperature, and so the fauna and flora of the oceans will not show wide temperature tolerance, whereas that of small pools will, but in neither case will the tolerance be so great as that shown by many terrestrial forms. Oxygen and carbon dioxide concentrations are very different in water and in air and are also variable from one aquatic environment to another, making them suitable for the support of different fauna and flora.

An important difference between the sea and freshwater is seen when their salt concentrations are determined.

Osmotic and ionic regulation

Organisms living in fresh or in sea water face quite dissimilar problems in osmotic and ionic regulation. Life evolved originally in the sea and the salt concentration in the blood of marine molluscs, crustaceans, and echinoderms, for example, is about the same as in sea water itself. Marine organisms have, on several occasions in the course of their evolution, moved into freshwater. Representatives of the worms, crustaceans, molluscs, and vertebrates have all independently invaded this very dilute habitat. What is more, all these animals show approximately the same types of modification to cope with the change. Their outer layers, in the main, become impermeable and the salt concentration of their blood is reduced considerably and to a spectacularly low level in the freshwater mussel. The kidneys become enlarged and produce a large volume of dilute urine. By these means freshwater animals can cut down loss of their salts (*see* **F39**). It is interesting that all terrestrial vertebrates, including the mammals have retained a salt concentration in their blood of about half the seawater level and this is partly attributable to their freshwater ancestry. The ultimate development of salinity tolerance is seen in such animals as the salmon and eel which move from fresh to salt water and back again during their life cycle.

2. Biotic Factors

(a) **Associations between Organisms.**—No organism can be considered to be independent of any other organism in an ecosystem but in some cases close associations of various types can be developed between different species or different members of the same species.

Commensalism is an association which benefits one member but has little effect on the other. Small organisms can live within the protective covering offered by a larger individual, as, for example, commensal crabs living within the shell of some species of oyster.

Symbiosis is a somewhat closer association in which both members benefit, as do certain species of green algae and the coelenterates in whose body tissues they live. The algae are protected and the coelenterates benefit from the food produced by the photosynthetic plant. Some symbiotic organisms are unable to survive outside the association. The lichens which are associations of algae and fungi, are examples of this type of symbiosis, as are some of the food-processing micro-organisms together with the animals in whose intestinal tracts they live.

Social animals. In some cases animals of the same species form social groups in which cooperative effort and division of labour makes them more successful in exploiting a particular environment. Social development is most obvious among certain insects such as termites, ants, wasps, and bees, and among the vertebrates. Social organisation in these groups may lead to the development of different behaviour patterns and ultimately, as in ants and bees, for example, to the evolution of a variety of structural modifications so that different castes are recognisable.

Parasitism. Not all associations are of mutual benefit and when one organism becomes sufficiently specialised so that it can live successfully on materials extracted from another, the latter is always adversely affected. Parasites, by causing disease in, and sometimes the death of, the host, can influence population growth and size. Important groups are bacteria, protozoa, fungi, nematodes (roundworms), and platyhelminths (tapeworms and liver flukes). Viruses are also important disease-producing agents which are incapable of an independent existence outside the cells of the host and utilise the host cell's metabolic pathways directly to synthesise new virus material.

Control of Parasites

Many parasites (and other pests which may disturb the comfort and health of man) can now be controlled to some extent, and, for a variety of reasons, such control procedures have extensive effects on the ecosystems involved. The regulation of some bacterial parasites by means of antibiotics, and control of the insect vectors of organisms such as the malaria parasite by means of insecticides, have both been important factors in the increase in human population. Though the beneficial effects of pest control of all types are clear, the process is not without its difficulties and dangers. Indiscriminate use of many chemical agents has led to the development of resistant strains. In any group of organisms, some will naturally be more resistant to a pesticide or antibiotic than others and these will be the survivors of any treatment that is less than totally effective. They will form the breeding stock for subsequent generations and so progressively more and more resistant types will evolve. Thus, there are now many strains of bacteria resistant to penicillin and other antibiotics. Even more alarming is the recent discovery that this resistance can be transferred in an infective way between bacteria of different species. Another complication associated with chemical control is that the agent concerned frequently affects a wide spectrum of organisms, including those that are in no sense injurious to man or his crops. Thus DDT kills bees and other pollinating insects unless its application to a crop is very precisely timed. In addition, the accumulation of quantities of chlorinated hydrocarbons such as DDT in the environment is known to have an injurious effect on organisms other than insects. Because these chemicals are broken down very slowly they now form a serious problem in environmental pollution.

Predation. A less direct association than that between parasite and host is the one which exists between predators and the prey which they capture and kill. However, interactions in both parasitism and predation have features in common particularly those affecting population numbers.

(b) **The Food Factor.**—Plants are the ultimate source of organic food for all animals. The most important food plants are those capable of photosynthesis (**F32**) in which organic material is synthesised from carbon dioxide and water, using radiant energy from the sun to drive the reaction.

Food Chains. Plants are eaten by herbivores which in turn are eaten by carnivores. It is possible to see many such sequences, called food chains, in all ecosystems. For example, in the open sea, green algae are the important photosynthetic organisms; these are eaten by a small crustacean, *Calanus*, which in turn forms a large part of the diet of the herring. Feeding relationships are usually of much greater complexity than is suggested by a simple food chain. Thus, *Calanus* represents about 20 per cent of the herring's diet but it is also eaten by many other marine animals as well. For example, it forms about 70 per cent of the total diet of larval sand eels. The larval eels are eaten in turn by the herring and may form 40 per cent of its diet. Because an animal's diet is usually quite varied and one species of animal or plant may be part of the food of a wide range of different animals, interactions are set up which are referred to as food webs. However, for general comparative purposes it is possible to disregard the detail of species and to group together all organisms with similar food habits. When this is done a relationship known as pyramid of numbers often appears in which organisms at the base of a food chain (the primary producers) are extremely abundant, while those at the apex (the final consumers) are relatively few in number.

Productivity. The validity of using numbers of individuals in such an analysis is often open to question, especially when ecosystems are to be compared. For example, a comparison between numbers of herring and numbers of whales as final consumers in two pyramidal systems is not very informative. This difficulty is partially overcome by using estimates of the total weight (biomass) of organisms at each level rather than their number. Even this has disadvantages because determinations of biomass give a measure of the amount of material present at any one time (the standing crop) but give no indication of the amount of material being produced or the rate of its production (the productivity). In some parts of the sea, for example, the biomass of small animals forming the zooplankton is greater than that of the plant life or phytoplankton on which it depends for food. This seems to contravene the pyramid concept. However, the rate of production of new material by the phytoplankton is very much greater than by the zooplankton so that, if taken over a year, the total amount of plant material produced would far exceed the total production of animal material. Productivity is a concept of great practical and theoretical importance. It may be determined in terms of the actual organic material produced in an area over a set period of time or, more usefully, in terms of the amounts of energy transferred and stored at each food level, again over a set period of time.

Photosynthetic efficiency

Under natural conditions only 1 to 5 per cent of the light falling on a plant is converted by its photosynthetic system into chemical energy contained in the material of its tissues. Similarly herbivores which consume plants will pass on to their predators only some 10 per cent of the energy contained in the plant material they eat. These low values for photosynthetic efficiency and ecological efficiency respectively are due to the fact that most of the energy appears as heat during the metabolic reactions needed to sustain life and only a small amount is incorporated into new tissue. It is easy to see that the form of a pyramid of numbers can be explained in terms of low ecological efficiency, as can the observation that a food chain rarely has more than five links. The loss of energy at each stage must mean that each succeeding stage becomes smaller and smaller in number and that the number of stages is severely limited.

Human Population and Food. The present very large increase in human population and the predicted rise from 4,124 million in 1977 to 6,000 million in the year 2000 has led to a pressing need for the controlled exploitation of food resources in the world. Consideration of the processes of energy transfer suggests that man should be mainly herbivorous. They also suggest that present agricultural crops, with the possible exception of sugar cane, do not achieve as high a primary productivity as that encountered in some natural ecosystems. Crops rarely achieve complete plant cover of the land throughout the growing season so as to trap the maximum amount of sunlight. It would be necessary to mix crops to do this effectively and there would then be complicated harvesting problems.

If man remains an omnivore, as he almost certainly will, then his domestic food animals will continue to be herbivorous as they are at present, though whether they will be the same herbivores is less easy to predict. Beef cattle raised on grassland convert only 4 per cent of the energy in the plants of their environment into similar chemical energy in their tissues. At the present time intensive farming practices are being employed to improve conversion, usually by harvesting plant material, processing it, and bringing it to the animals which are housed in special buildings. This cuts down on the wastage of plant food because it can be grown under better conditions and less of it is consumed by animals other than the cattle. Careful breeding and the limitation of the period over which livestock is raised to that of maximum growth efficiency have also contributed to conversions of some 35 per cent, achieved in the case of broiler chickens and calves. The moral problems raised by these methods and the circumstances which make them necessary give rise to widespread concern.

Fish are also an important part of man's diet. Many populations have been overfished so that returns have gone down in spite of intensified fishing effort. The fisheries scientist is concerned to discover the limit at which the maximum number of fish can be taken without depleting the population year by year. Research is also going on into possible methods of enclosing and farming areas of the sea or estuaries.

Population Dynamics

Study of the numbers of organisms in a population, together with their change and regulation, forms a branch of the subject of considerable practical importance known as population dynamics.

Numbers of animals and plants tend to increase up to the capacity of the environment. The rate of increase will be determined by the balance between reproduction rate and mortality. As Malthus appreciated, adults of any organism tend to replace themselves by a greater number of progeny and, in the absence of losses by mortality and other factors, there is a vast potential for increase in all populations. If an organism doubles its number in a year, there will be a 1,000-fold increase in 10 years, and a 10 million-fold increase in 20 years. Increase of this type soon leads to shortages and overcrowding so that mortality goes up, the net rate of increase diminishes, and finally an equilibrium is reached with no further increase in number. The change with the passage of time follows and S-shaped curve. At equilibrium, the numbers are kept at a steady level by factors such as competition for food, refuge, or space.

Human population is increasing rapidly at the present time, mainly because of the fall in deathrate. Food production is also increasing, but in some areas the world supply and requirement are so evenly matched that drought or war are inevitably followed by a famine. Though the human population has not yet reached the stage of equilibrium, it is clear that ultimately it must be subject to forces of regulation similar to those that control populations of other organisms. Birthrate cannot exceed death-rate indefinitely in any living organism. By limiting the size of families it is possible for man to achieve a population equilibrium at levels lower than those at which regulative factors such as famine or aggression must begin to operate. Rational control of birth-rate seems to offer the best chance of averting a global population disaster.

THE GEOLOGICAL RECORD

The various stages in the history of the earth can be read by the geologists in the strata or layers of rock laid down since the planet began to solidify, and it is in these rocks, too, that the record of life upon earth may be traced.

No Life Rocks.—The earliest rocks in the record are known as the Azoic (no life) rocks, because they show no trace of living things, and these layers are of such thickness that they occupy more than half of the whole record. That is to say, for more than half the earth's history nothing living existed upon any part of the globe. For millions of years the surface of our planet was nothing but bare rock without soil or sand, swept by hot winds exceeding in violence the wildest tornadoes of today, and drenched by torrential downpours of tropical rain which, as we have seen elsewhere, gradually tore away the surface to form sandy sediments at the bottom of the seas. In such ancient rocks pushed above the surface by later upheavals we can still trace the marks of primeval oceans as they rippled upon the barren shores or of raindrops which left their imprint perhaps 1,500 million years ago.

Primitive Sea-life.—As we move upwards through the strata, however, traces of life begin to appear and steadily increase as we come to the more recent levels. The earliest signs appear in what is known as the Early Palaeozoic Age (or by some writers as the Proterozoic Age), when we find the fossilised remains of small shellfish, seaweeds, and trilobites—the latter were creatures somewhat like the plant-lice of modern times. All these primitive animals and plants lived in the shallow tidal waters of ancient seas; for as yet life had not invaded either the dry land or the deep oceans. It is, of course, clear that these creatures of Early Palaeozoic times were not the first living things; they were merely the first creatures capable of leaving fossilised remains, and without doubt must have had more primitive ancestors—amoebic-like forms, jellyfish, bacteria, and so on whose bodies were too soft to leave any traces in the record of the rocks.

The Age of Fishes.—Towards the end of the Early Palaeozoic Era, in what we now know as the Silurian period, there arose a new form of life: the first backboned animals, primitive fishes somewhat similar to the sharks of today; and in the division of the Upper Palaeozoic Era known as the Devonian, they had come to multiply so greatly that this is frequently described as the Age of Fishes.

First Land Animals and Plants.—It is from this time, too, that we find traces of animal and plant life upon the dry land. Both animals and plants had acute problems to solve before it became possible for them to live out of water; for both animals and plants had hitherto been supported by the surrounding water and respired by removing oxygen dissolved in the water. In land animals this problem was solved by a long series of adaptations from gills to lungs. Plants were able to invade the land because of the evolution of an impermeable outer cuticle which prevented water loss and also the development of woody tissues which provided support and a water-conducting system for the whole plant body.

Amphibia and Spore-bearing Trees.—The first type of vertebrates (backboned animals) to live upon dry land was the group of amphibia in the Carboniferous Age, which is today represented by the newts, frogs, toads, and salamanders. In all these forms the eggs give rise to a tadpole stage with gills which lives for some time entirely in water. Later the gills give place to a primitive form of lung which enables the animal to live upon land. Even so, amphibia want to remain more or less to swampy or marshy land, and without a damp environment they would dry up and shrivel to death. The most abundant forms of plant life in the Carboniferous period were the tree-like horsetails, clubmosses, and ferns, the fossilised tissues of which are found in the coal measures and are burned as household coal. But these plants also, as in the case of the amphibia, could exist only amongst the swamps and marshes, and life, although it had freed itself from the necessity of existence in the waters of the earth, still had to return to the water in order to reproduce itself. The highlands and the deeper waters of the planet were still empty of living things. Although the Carboniferous period had been a period of warmth and abundance, the Palaeozoic Era came to an end with a long cycle of dry and bitterly cold ages. Such long-term climatic changes were due, it is now supposed, to such factors as changes in the earth's orbit, the shifting of its axis of rotation, changes in the shape of the land masses, and so on. Long before the Ice Ages of more recent times, there are records in the rocks of alternating periods of warmth and cold as far back as the Azoic and Early Palaeozoic Eras. This long cold spell at the close of the Palaeozoic era came to an end about 220 million years ago, and was succeeded by a long era of widely spread warm conditions—the Mesozoic Era, the so-called Age of Reptiles.

The Mesozoic Era.—The reptiles first appeared in the Permian, but it was during the Mesozoic era that they became the dominant group of animals. The giant reptiles included the stegosaurus, the gigantosaurus, the diplodocus, and many other kinds which were far larger than any land animals living today. Some, for example the diplodocus, were 100 ft. long, although they were vegetarian in habit and were preyed upon by other almost equally huge flesh-eating reptiles. Some species, such as the plesiosaurs and ichthyosaurs, became secondarily aquatic, while the pterodactyl possessed wings with which it could glide and perhaps fly short distances. However, they all differed from the amphibia in that they had hard, dry skins, their lungs were more efficient, fertilisation was internal due to the development of copulatory organs, and they laid eggs with hard, protective shells.

It was also during the Mesozoic era that the warm-blooded birds arose. The birds, like the reptiles, lay eggs with hard shells, and they have several internal features found in the reptiles. The fossil bird Archaeopteryx, three specimens of which have been found in Germany, lived in the Jurassic period. Although it was obviously a bird, it retained many reptilian features. Earliest mammals are recognised in rocks of the late Palaeozoic but in the Mesozoic considerable evolution of the group took place. The fossil Trituberculata which are also found in the Jurassic, are believed to be related to forms from which both the marsupial and placental mammals arose. Although insects were present as far back as the Carboniferous, it was in the Mesozoic that many of the groups we know today first appeared.

Great changes also took place in the plant cover of the land during this era. The spore-bearing giant horsetails and tree clubmosses declined and were replaced by gymnosperms—trees bearing naked seeds. One large group of these, the cycadeoids, has become extinct, but the conifers and a few of the once abundant cycads still remain. The flowering plants or angiosperms also made their appearance, and towards the end of the Cretaceous their evolution was extremely rapid. In fact, many of the fossil leaves found in rocks of Cretaceous age are indistinguishable from those of some present-day flowering plants.

A New Era.—But, perhaps 150 million years later, all this seemingly everlasting warmth and sunshine, the lush tropical life, the giant reptiles who had ruled the world, were wiped out by a new period of bitter cold which only the hardy species could survive. A new Era known as the Caenozoic was beginning, ushered in by a period of upheaval and volcanic activity, following which the map of the world came to resemble more closely the picture we know today. The old period may have lasted several million years, and the main species to survive it were those which had come into existence towards the end of the Mesozoic Era, the seed-bearing flowering plants, the birds, and the mammals. The once all-powerful reptiles from this time onwards are represented only by the comparatively few and relatively small reptilian species of today: the snakes, lizards, crocodiles, and alligators. It was at this time, too, that, long after the creation of the mountains of Scotland and Norway (the so-called Caledonian revolution), or even of the Appalachian mountains (the Appalachian revolution), there arose the great masses of the Alps, the Himalayas, the Rocky Mountains, and the Andes. These are the mountain chains of the most recent, the Caenozoic revolution. Initially, as we have seen, the climate of the Caenozoic Era was cold, but the weather grew generally warmer until a new period of abundance was reached, only to be followed at the end of the Pliocene by a period of glacial ages generally known as the First, Second, Third, and Fourth Ice Ages.

CHRONICLE OF EVENTS

4,500,000,000	Formation of Earth's crust.
3,500,000,000	Earliest evidence of life – fossil blue-green algae.
600,000,000	Earliest fossil evidence of invertebrates.
450,000,000	First jawless fishes appear in fossil record. First land plants.
400,000,000	First bony fishes appear. Early seed plants. First amphibians. First insects.
350,000,000	Earliest reptiles in fossil record.
270,000,000	First conifers; coal seams laid down.
220,000,000	Dinosaurs appear in fossil record; First fossil evidence of mammals (*Megazostrodon*).
135,000,000	Evolution of flowering plants; First bird in fossil record (*Archaeopteryx*). Dinosaur extinction begins (ends 65,000,000 years ago).

V. SCIENCES OF MAN

PHYSICAL ANTHROPOLOGY

MAN'S PLACE IN NATURE

In the broadest terms of scientific classification, humans are part of the *animal kingdom*—that is to say they are multicellular organisms which feed by ingesting complex organic substances and are capable of independent movement. More than one million animal species have been described (and the actual number may be nearer 10 million). Each belongs to one of the many phyla (singular *phylum*, meaning tribe or stock) into which the animal kingdom is divided. Humans belong to the phylum chordata, *subphylum* vertebrata, which includes all animals with a spinal cord enclosed within a vertebral column, and with a skull enclosing the brain.

Each phylum is divided into a number of *classes*, among which humans are classified as four-limbed vertebrates of the class mammalia: warmblooded animals with mammary glands which secrete milk for the nourishment of young, skin with hair or fur, a body cavity divided by a muscular diaphragm which assists respiration, three ear bones and seven neck vertebrae.

There are about 4,500 species of mammal, classified in three *subclasses*: the *prototheria*, which is a group of oviparous (egg-laying) mammals consisting solely of the duckbill platypus and spiny anteaters of Australia and New Guinea; the *metatheria*, represented by about 260 species of viviparous (live-bearing) marsupials whose young are born in a very immature state and carried by their mother in an external pouch for some time after birth; and the *eutheria*, which are mammals with a placenta permitting substantial development of the young before birth.

The great majority of mammals belong to the eutheria—including humans. The subclass itself is divided into *orders*, numbering 16 in all, which range from the insectivora (shrews, moles, hedgehogs *etc*) and pholidota (pangolins), to the proboscidea (elephants) and cetacea (whales). Lemurs, monkeys, apes and humans are grouped together in the primate order; all are tree-dwellers (or descendants thereof) whose distinctive similarities are their fingers, flat nails, and reduced sense of smell.

The primate order is split into three *suborders*: the prosimii, represented by the living lemurs, lorises and galagos; the tarsoidea (the living tarsiers); and the anthropoidea (monkeys, apes and humans). The anthropoidea order is divided into two *infraorders*: the platyrrhini, meaning flat-nosed and comprising the New World monkeys of central and south America; and the catarrhini (thin-nosed), which are the Old World monkeys, the gibbons, the apes, and humans.

The catarrhini infraorder divides into two *superfamilies*: the cercopithecoidea (Old World monkeys), and the hominoidea (gibbons, apes and humans); and the hominoid superfamily splits into three *families*: the hylobatiae (gibbons); the pongidae (apes), and the hominidae (humans). The hylobatids and pongids are distinguished by long arms and short legs, reflecting a predominantly arboreal way of life, while the principal distinguishing features of the hominid family are an habitual upright posture and bipedal gait, and a large brain.

Each zoological family is a group of related genera (sing. *genus*, meaning race, origin); a genus is a collection of closely related *species* (meaning kind, or sort), and a species is a group of individuals which are capable of breeding among themselves. There are several genera and numerous species of the hylobatid and pongid primate families alive today, but only one living species of hominid: modern humans – *Homo sapiens*.

It will be seen from the above that the relationships which form the basic structure of zoological classification set every species in the context of a greater whole—genus, family, order, and so on. *Homo sapiens* is no exception. Man is not the endproduct of the entire evolutionary process, as is commonly supposed. On the contrary, man's place in nature is at the end of a relatively short line radiating from among the millions which have evolved since life on Earth began more than 3·5 billion years ago.

The origin of the primates

The primates are essentially tropical animals. With the exception of humans, virtually all living species are arboreal, and 80 per cent of them are found in the tropical rain forests. Their most distinctive characteristic is the very general and unspecialised nature of their anatomical structure, and the highly specialised and adaptable nature of their behaviour. While other mammals evolved specialised physical characteristics (the giraffe's long neck, for example), the primates have retained the basic structure of the ancestral mammalian form and have instead adapted their behaviour to suit prevailing circumstances. The human hand is a case in point—it has the same number of bones operated by the same arrangement of muscles as the arboreal primates possessed 45 million years ago, yet the human hand serves a much greater variety of uses.

The fossil evidence indicates that primates have existed for at least 70 million years. They were one of the groups of placental mammals which survived the mass-extinction event which closed the Cretaceous period of geological time, about 65 million years ago. The dinosaurs were among those which disappeared with that event, and their passing marks the end of the epoch known as the Age of the Reptiles. Some reptiles survived, of course, but with the declining prominence of the dinosaurs the mammals flourished, heralding the Age of the Mammals with a burst of adaptive radiation which eventually took them into every ecological niche which the dinosaurs had previously occupied.

The early mammals had lived in the shadow of the dinosaurs for more than 100 million years before the Age of the Reptiles came to a close. They were small (typically about 10 cm long), and occupied parts of the environment that the large reptiles could not reach—the nocturnal world, for instance, (a temporal dimension in which the cold-blooded reptiles could not function), and rocky crags, holes and forest undergrowth. Here they evolved a high degree of sensory perception. Sight, sound, touch and smell assisted their capture of the invertebrate prey upon which they largely subsisted; integration of cerebral and physical equipment was crucial, and while the later evolution of the dinosaurs was concerned primarily with physical structure, that of the early mammals was concerned with the development of brain and behaviour. This equipped them well for the radiation which followed.

Of the various habitats available to the mammals as the Age of the Reptiles drew to a close, the ancestors of the primates took to the trees. Here they found a rich and varied diet—leaves, buds, fruit, insects, birds' eggs and nestlings—but also a suite of new demands. Life in the trees called for a shift in the emphasis of the mammals' environmental awareness. While the nose had probably been the most important organ of ground-dwelling mammals, the eyes were more crucial in the trees.

Because a tree is a spatially restricted environment, an arboreal animal needs to be particularly aware of its whereabouts. It must know if a potential predator is in the same tree, and if a fruit is at the end of a safe branch. It must be able to see clearly and judge distances accurately as it moves through the branches. These requirements favoured the evolution of stereoscopic vision, which was further enhanced by the advent of colour vision.

Life in the branches also called for greater agility. An ability to flex the paws and grasp things was advantageous; digits evolved into fingers, claws into fingernails. Front limbs became principally a means of holding on, while the rear limbs served as a means of propulsion and also of static support.

Thus the animals could leap safely about the trees, and also could sit with the spine erect, the head turning with a perceptive eye, the ears twitching.

It can be supposed that the attributes favouring an arboreal existence also promoted yet more cerebral development. A large brain relative to body size evolved; accommodating a larger brain required some restructuring of the skull, which in turn was affected by the masticatory demands of the foods which the animals ate—fruit, leaves, insects, meat. Such an omnivorous diet calls for neither the specialised canines and slicing teeth of the carnivores, nor the grinding molars of the herbivores. The ancestral set of general all-purpose teeth was retained. The jaws broadened and shortened, the face flattened, the eyes looked forward and the expanding brain took up more and more room at the back of the skull. These interactive and interdependent features evolved over millions of years, a mosaic of cause and effect from which evolved the order of mammals known as the primates.

In basic zoological terms, the primates which evolved from the early arboreal mammals are distinguished from all other placental mammals by the fact that they have retained the four kinds of teeth found in ancestral mammals (incisors, canines, premolars and molars); they can hold things between finger and thumb, they have frontally directed eyes and have a large brain, relative to body size. They are represented today by 193 living species, all but one of which are covered with hair.

Hominid ancestry

The broadest categories of the primate order were also the earliest to have existed in evolutionary time, and the divisions were created principally by the geographic isolation resulting from the breakup of Gondwanaland, the supercontinent on which the primates had originated. Thus, the tarsier suborder became confined to the islands of Indonesia and the Philippines, and the prosimian suborder is best represented today by the lemurs of Madagascar, where the infraorder has been isolated for close on 60 million years. Another infraorder of prosimian, represented by the pottos, lorises and bushbabies, remained on continental Africa and Asia, and has found isolation in a nocturnal way of life as other primates adopted a diurnal lifestyle.

Isolation similarly split the anthropoid suborder when the landmass of South America broke away from Gondwanaland about 40 million years ago, carrying with it the primate stock which evolved into the platyrrhines—the New World monkeys. Subsequently, the catarrhine stock left on Gondwanaland split into its two main groups, probably along the lines of diverging dietary preferences. One group adopted a mainly herbivorous diet and gave rise to the Old World monkeys or cercopithecoids (represented today by the baboons and the colobines), while the other retained a more omnivorous diet and produced the hominoids (gibbons, apes and humans).

The precise dates at which these splits occurred are uncertain, but the fossil evidence suggests that the hominoid line is at least 30 million years old. A putative ancestor from that time has been found in the Fayum, south west of Cairo. The land is arid desert now, but 30 million years ago it was tropical rain forest and swampland, laced with broad meandering rivers. Scientists excavating fossil beds in the region have recovered the remains of a creature which is described formally as *Aegyptopithecus zeuxis*, though it is more colloquially known as the "dawn ape". Jaws and teeth, a skull and the skeletal parts of several individuals suggest that *Aegyptopithecus* was diverse and very generalised in its physical form. Experts have reconstructed from the fossil evidence a picture of a small arboreal primate, about the size of a domestic cat, with a sinuous back, long limbs, and all four feet capable of both grasping branches and conveying food to the mouth. The eyes looked forward, indicating stereoscopic vision, and the brain was larger in proportion to bodyweight than that of any other mammal then alive.

The descendants of *Aegyptopithecus* and its kind appear to have been very successful in evolutionary terms. More than 50 species are known from the fossil record, and hence palaeoanthropologists are inclined to refer to the Miocene (the geological period extending from 26 million to 8 million years ago) as the Age of the Ape. One of these species, *Proconsul africanus*, is believed to represent the evolutionary line which led to the modern apes and humans.

First described from a nearly complete face and partial skull discovered by Mary Leakey on Kenya's Rusinga Island, Lake Victoria, in 1948, *Proconsul* was a tree-dwelling animal about the size of a baboon which roamed East Africa about 18 million years ago, sometime after the monkey and ape lines had diverged. More remains were recovered during the 1970s, enabling scientists to reconstruct a skeleton that was essentially 75 percent complete. The result showed an unexpected mixture of characteristics. *Proconsul* had a backbone resembling that of the gibbon, shoulder and elbow joints like those of the chimpanzee, and the wrists of a monkey. Overall, *Proconsul* is quite unlike any living ape, but could be ancestral.

Around 17 million years ago, the African continental plate butted up against Europe, raising high mountains and creating a landbridge across which many African animals migrated into Eurasia for the first time. Among them were apes whose fossil remains have also been proposed as candidates for the ancestry of the ape and human lines. *Dryopithecus* was found in Greece, *Ramapithecus* and *Sivapithecus* in the Siwalik Hills of northern Pakistan. The fossil evidence was fragmentary, but for many years *Ramapithecus*, dating from 14 million to 7 million years ago, was almost universally accepted as the earliest known ancestor of the human line. During the early 1980s, however, the discovery of more complete ramapithecine remains showed that it and the sivapithecines are more likely to represent ancestors of the orang-utan on their evolutionary and migratory journey to the south-east Asian islands where they are found today. Consensus opinion now rates the dryopithecines as close cousins headed for extinction, and regards Africa as the cradle of mankind.

The emergence of mankind

The question of human origins has intrigued every generation. The biblical story of creation provided a longstanding and widely-accepted explanation, to which Charles Darwin (see **B18**) added a biological dimension with the publication of *The origin of species* in 1859. The controversy aroused by Darwin centred very largely around the mistaken idea that the theory of evolution implied that humans were descendants of the apes. This mistake is still encountered with surprising frequency, even though Darwin's original work and the many studies conducted since then all make the evolutionary proposition quite clear: humans are not descended from the apes, the two branches evolved simultaneously from a common ancestor which existed sometime in the past.

Among evolutionists, the question of human origins is basically a question of when the divergence of the ape and human lines occurred, and what the common ancestor looked like. For the greater part of the time since Darwin's day it has been assumed that the answers to these questions would be supplied by the fossil remains of the ancestral forms which might be recovered from geological deposits of ever-greater antiquity—if only those fossils could be found. Thus began the search for the missing link, as it became popularly known. By the 1960s the results of these fossil hunts had provided the basis for a widely-accepted scenario in which humans had evolved from *Ramapithecus* on a line which had split from the apes some 30 million years ago. Since the 1960s, however, this fossil-based scenario has been displaced by one based on biochemistry which puts the human/ape split at just 5 million years ago.

Instead of studying fossil bones, biochemists have used the genetic material (DNA—deoxyribonucleic acid) of related living species to measure the amount of time which has passed since they diverged from a common ancestor. This work is based on three findings: first, DNA accumulates random mutations and changes over time which are evident in the protein structure of all individuals of a species. Second, as two lineages diverge from a common ancestor, each lineage accumulates changes in its DNA which are different from those of the other. Third, the accumulation of changes tends to occur at a regular, almost clocklike rate through time. Clearly, the greater the differences, the longer the divergence, and biochemists have thus been able to put a timescale on the divergence of the apes and humans. The orang-utan split away from the African hominoid stock about 12 million years ago, and the gorilla lineage diverged from the common ancestor of apes and humans about 8 million years ago. The chimpanzee and human lineages were the most recent to diverge from the common ancestor, their split having occurred about 5 million years ago.

Origin of the hominid lineage

In one sense the facts of human origins can be reduced to a series of dates at which humans and related species diverged from their common ancestors. But an intriguing question remains even then: what caused the splits; why did the species diverge from their common ancestor?

A species is the result of reproductive isolation. If the individual members of a viable breeding population reproduce only among themselves for any length of time, the genetic changes which accumulate with each generation will eventually produce a closely-related population which is significantly different from both its ancestral stock and the other descendants of that stock. If the process continues long enough a discrete species will have evolved, one which can only produce fertile offspring among its own kind. It can be supposed with some certainty that the reasons for the isolation which provoked speciation lay in the prevailing ecological circumstances of the time. Food supply would have been a primary factor, and this would have been susceptible to other factors such as climatic variation, the incursion of competing animals, climatic changes, or simply the pressures of a growing population.

Any one or a combination of these ecological factors could have moved a viable breeding population of individuals into reproduction isolation where they might evolve into a discrete species. Migration is the most obvious course by which such isolation could have been achieved—but not the only one. Exploiting an alternative food resource, or adopting different social strategies could have achieved a similar degree of isolation even in close proximity with the ancestral population.

Precisely why the gorilla, chimpanzee and human lineages diverged between 8 million and 5 million years ago is not known. It may have been a consequence of the major climatic fluctuations which occurred during that time, when the overall pattern ranged from hot and dry to wet and very cold. The tropical forests retreated to the equatorial region, woodlands became dominant and grasslands proliferated. And with the changes in vegetation the composition of resident animal populations changed too. Many species became extinct, particularly among the browsers, while the grazers became more numerous. Doubtless the common ancestor of apes and humans was also affected by these developments, but the only certainties are that divergence and speciation occurred during that time, and that the distinctive characteristics of the living species can be considered as adaptations which proved advantageous to a reproductively isolated population.

The distinctive characteristics of humans are the adaptation to a terrestrial way of life and bipedal locomotion; the much reduced face and jaws, and the greatly enlarged brain. In evolutionary terms, bipedalism was the crucial development, and it has been suggested that this was a consequence of the climatic changes which reduced the forest area and thereby increased competition for its resources. Under pressure from other arboreal primates, the human ancestor found a niche on the savannah. Whatever the case, bipedalism offered extensive evolutionary advantages. This was not because bipedalism itself is a particularly effective means of locomotion but rather because it freed forelimbs from locomotor functions and made them available for other purposes. One of the most important of these was the use of tools, and subsequently toolmaking. When the ancestral hominids first colonised the terrestrial habitat they had few inbuilt defence mechanisms and the ability to use stones, sticks and bones to ward off predators must have been of considerable survival value (as has

been observed among present-day chimpanzees when they take to the ground). Initially used for defence, tools eventually were used in attack, heralding the adoption of a hunting mode of life. Toolmaking is also thought to have been one of the practices which favoured the development of language, and, since toolmaking called for fine manipulative skills, hand and brain evolved together; particularly those parts of the brain concerned with precise motor control and tactile sensation.

Another consequence of freeing the forelimbs through bipedalism was that carrying became so much easier. Thus food and other items could be carried over considerable distances and this facilitated the establishment of a home base. Perhaps even more important, the human infant could be carried in its mother's arms and held close to her body, allowing a much closer and more intimate relationship between mother and child than is possible in other animals. In terms of its physical development, the human infant is born in a very immature state; in part because of the limitations to the size of the birth canal imposed by the demands of bipedalism. It is therefore long dependent on parental care. This raises problems in a society where pregnant women and nursing mothers become dependent upon the group for food. Social bonds were forged in response, and it has been argued that the evolution of the particular form of reproductive cycle found in humans, in which the female is receptive to the male throughout most of her menstrual cycle should be seen as a means of ensuring that a male will be willing to assume responsibility for females and offspring.

THE FOSSIL EVIDENCE OF HUMAN EVOLUTION

A fundamental premise of palaeoanthropology (the study of man in times past) rests on the contention that unequivocal evidence of human evolution would be found in fossils of known antiquity linking modern man to extinct ancestor. Ideally, the fossils should comprise a series of complete skeletons from a precisely dated sequence of time: this would enable scientists to trace the evolutionary development of humans with complete certainty. But the arbitrary nature of the fossilization process virtually eliminates all chance that such an ideal could ever be achieved or even approached. Far from ideal, palaeoanthropology has had to work with a slowly accumulating collection of diverse and often very fragmentary specimens ever since it became an established discipline in the mid-19th century. In the first fifty years only five specimens were discovered; another twenty-five years passed before a dozen were known, and even today the significant specimens could all be accommodated on a billiard table. The fossils have come from Europe, the Far East and Africa; they span over 3 million years, but as clues to the process of human evolution during that time they represent a minute fraction of mankind's potential ancestry. It has been calculated that ten skulls from East Turkana in Kenya (an exceptional collection covering 1 million years), for example, represent only one individual in every 100 million.

The shortage of evidence is compounded by other problems. Uncertainties concerning age, for instance, mean that differing features which may represent evolutionary change over time cannot be placed in chronological order. And many fossils are so broken, distorted or incomplete that unequivocal interpretation of their significance is rarely possible. In such cases, different authorities may emphasize the importance of different features with equal validity, and the points distinguishing their interpretations may be so slight that each depends as much upon the proponent's beliefs about the course of human evolution as upon the evidence being presented.

Beliefs have always been an important component of palaeoanthropological debate, and for many years they centred around the question of the order in which humans had acquired the characteristics which distinguish them from other primates. Which came first—the restructuring of the jaw and speech? The erect posture and bipedal gait? The enlargement of the brain? Two broad groupings developed in the science—one believing that enlargement of the brain had been the prime mover; the other contending that bipedalism had led the way—and as each new fossil was discovered it was immediately assessed according to those propositions. Neanderthal Man (1857) was initially dismissed as non-human on the basis of the shape and proportions of its brain; Java Man (1891) was promoted as small-brained but bipedal and dubbed *Homo erectus* because a thighbone was found in the same deposit as the skull; Piltdown Man (1912) was a forgery which found widespread acceptance because its large brain and apelike jaw confirmed the beliefs of prominent authorities; *Australopithecus* (1925) was rejected as a candidate for human ancestry because its small brain did not match the expectations of the day.

Subsequent discoveries, including fossils and a trail of fossilized footprints, have shown that hominids were fully bipedal more than 3.6 million years ago, though the configuration of skull and jaw remained distinctly apelike for some time thereafter, while brainsize did not begin to approach modern proportions until 1.5 million years ago.

Finding the fossils

Fossils (from the latin *fossilis*, meaning dug up) are the end products of a process in which organisms are buried and infiltrated by minerals which replace them, molecule by molecule, until, where organic material existed before, stone remains, exactly preserving the form of the original. Fossils have been the source of virtually all that is known about the evolution of life—from the oldest known forms (microscopic fossil algae dating back to 3.5 billion years) to modern times.

For an organism to become fossilized it must first of all be entrapped in a suitable material, away from the attention of scavengers and decomposers. Aquatic organisms comprise by far the greatest number of fossils, not only because they have been more numerous throughout the history of life, but also because the seabed or lake bottom favours fossilization. Terrestrial organisms are less commonly found as fossils (most are consumed or decomposed by other creatures soon after death), and hominid fossils are among the rarest of all.

Palaeoanthropologists wishing to find the fossil remains of early humans are limited by two major factors. First, humans evolved in the comparatively recent past and were not numerous until recent times—which means that the total number available for fossilization must always have been relatively small. Second, their way of life and the terrain they occupied were unlikely to favour the fossilization of their remains, and there are few places in the world where fossil beds of a suitable age and composition are exposed.

In scouring the world for potential fossil deposits, palaeoanthropologists have found ancient caves to be a most productive source of fossils (and not only of hominids). Whether originally used as shelters, or as dens to which predators such as leopards or hyenas may have retreated with their victims, bones left in the cave did not decay, but were fossilized as debris and rockfalls filled the caves. The first hominid fossils ever known to science were discovered at cave sites in Europe—Cannstadt in Germany (c.1700); Koestritz, Upper Saxony (1820); Kent's Cavern, Devon (1829); Engis in Belgium (1833), Gibraltar (before 1848), Neanderthal in Germany (1857). Several of the discoveries made before Darwin published his theory of evolution in 1859 received little notice at the time of discovery; some were lost. Investigations moved to the Far East at the end of the 19th century, where *Homo erectus* was recovered from riverbed deposits in Java (1891), and again in cave deposits near Peking during the 1920s.

Cave sites in South Africa have also proved to be a good source of hominid fossils. Alerted in the 1920s by quarrymen exploiting the lime-rich infills of ancient cave systems in the dolomitic hills, palaeoanthropologists have since recovered a number of important fossils from these sites.

The famed fossil sites of East Africa are predominantly volcanic in origin; the ash settling from eruptions associated with the formation of the Rift Valley having created conditions that were particularly suitable for the fossilization of bone. At Olduvai Gorge in Tanzania, where an ancient lake basin was inundated by successive eruptions of ash

and subsequently drained by geological faulting, a river has sliced through the deposits to reveal much evidence of the hominids who frequented the area from at least 2 million years ago. Volcanic eruptions similarly preserved the 3.6 million year old footprint trail at Laetoli, near Olduvai.

As at Olduvai, volcanic activity and a lakeside environment were also responsible for the preservation of hominid fossils dating from 3.1 million years ago which have been found in the Afar depression of Ethiopia, and those dating from 1.8 million years ago found in the Koobi Fora region of the Lake Turkana basin, northern Kenya.

Hominid fossil sites may be discovered by chance or by a geological survey which deliberately sets out to locate cave sites or sedimentary beds of an age and situation which renders them likely to contain hominid remains. In cave sites the fossils are nearly always embedded in a hard calcrete matrix from which they are removed by careful preparation after the rock has been removed from the cave. Open sedimentary beds often extend over many hundreds of square kilometres and spedific sites worthy of excavation are usually identified by foot surveys leading to the discovery of fossil bone eroding from the side of a watercourse, or a steep slope cutting into the fossil deposits.

If fossil material is lying exposed on the surface, the site will be marked out with pegs and line in a grid of one-metre squares and the exact position of each fossil fragment will be recorded before it is removed. Each square is then excavated to a precise depth and the soil sieved as it is removed; the precise location of every fossil (or artifact, such as stone tools) is recorded as the excavations proceed. Meanwhile, geochronologists take samples from specific levels of the excavation for laboratory analysis which will give a sequence of dates for the deposit. Thus the final result of the excavation will be a collection of fossils and artifacts accompanied by precise information on their location and date. Such meticulous attention to detail enables palaeoanthropologists to assess the use of a site through time, and the developments (if any) which its users underwent during that period.

Assessing the age of hominid fossils

The age of a fossil is of paramount importance to the palaeoanthropologist in the assessment of its evolutionary significance. Until the late 1950s scientists could do no more than assess the age of their finds in *relative* terms, that is according to the kinds of other fossil animals found in the same deposit or sequence of deposits. The fossil record as a whole gives a broad picture of the order in which various animal forms have evolved and become extinct through the course of geological time. Hominid fossils are not found among the remains of dinosaurs, for instance, so must be younger; on the other hand, they must be older than any extinct animals (such as hyenas and pigs) which may be found in deposits overlaying the hominid beds.

Relative dating was always of limited use to palaeoanthropologists since human evolution occurred in a recent and extremely brief period of geological time (if the whole of Earth history was condensed into 24 hours, man would have existed for little more than one minute). The sequence of arrivals and extinctions identified in the fossil record is on a broad scale and therefore unable to give the resolution needed for meaningful assessment of hominid evolution through time. Estimates of the fossils' age in years were made from time to time, but they were rough estimates based on guesses of how fast evolution proceeds, and of the rate at which sedimentary deposits accumulate. Most underestimated the actual ages which were given when developments during the 1950s, enabled geochronologists to give an *absolute* date for hominid fossil deposits.

Several methods of absolute dating have been applied to the study of fossil man:

Radiometric dating is based on the principle that a radioactive "parent" element decays into a stable "daughter" element at a constant rate. Once the rate of decay is known, the age of a sample can be calculated from the ratio of parent to daughter elements which it contains. It should be noted that it is not the fossils themselves that are dated, but the deposits in which they are found. The cave sites of South Africa and elsewhere are devoid of materials suitable for radiometric dating, but the volcanic beds of East Africa have proved especially informative in this respect because they contain the minerals necessary for the *potassium-argon* dating method, which measures the ratio of the radioactive isotope of potassium, K-40, to its decay product, the gas argon 40. Potassium-argon is used for the absolute dating of deposits between 230,000 and 26 million years old, which makes it particularly suited to the needs of palaeoanthropologists.

Fission-track dating is a method in which the age of a specimen is assessed from the tracks made by the fission of uranium atoms within them. The density and number of tracks already present in the specimen are compared with those produced when the specimen is exposed to neutron radiation in the laboratory. This comparison provides the basis for an estimate of age.

Radiocarbon dating: the radioisotope carbon-14 accumulates in living tissue, but begins to decay after death. The rate of decay is known, and so the proportion of carbon-14 remaining in a specimen is a measure of the time which has passed since the organism ceased to live. After about 50,000 years, however, so little carbon-14 remains that dating becomes impossible. This limited timespan makes the methods of little use to palaeoanthropologists, but it has proved immensely useful for the dating of wood and other organic materials.

Thermoluminescence: with the passage of time, certain substances accumulate energy in the form of electrons trapped at defects in the crystal lattice of their constituent minerals. When the materials are heated this energy is given off as a "puff" of light (thermoluminescence, or TL); the intensity of that light is a measure of how long the energy had been accumulating in the material, and this can be set against a known timescale to give an estimate of the material's age. The method has been particularly useful in dating archaeological finds such as pottery, where it is certain that the firing process reset the material's TL clock to zero when the pot was made, but it has also been used to date flints that were dropped in early man's campfires. These go back to 100,000 years ago.

Geomagnetic dating (also known as *palaeomagnetic dating*): makes use of the fact that the Earth's magnetic field has changed direction many times in its history. When metals are deposited in sediments they align with the prevailing magnetic field, which is then effectively "fossilized" as the sediments harden. The record of these directional changes through geological time establishes a sequence of broad time-segments which can be used for dating deposits directly, or as a check of other methods.

THE FOSSIL LINEAGE

From the earliest days of palaeoanthropological research, investigators have tended to consider the fossils in chronological order (on either the relative or the absolute timescale), from oldest to youngest, and to describe the differences between them as progressive evolutionary changes which have led, ultimately, to modern man. So long as the number of hominid fossils remained small, and the temporal distance between them large, this attractively simple scheme remained valid, inculcating a general readiness to believe that human evolution had been a straightforward single-line affair, unwaveringly directed towards its ultimate expression: *Homo sapiens sapiens* and contentious only in the matter of which human attributes were acquired first—restructuring of the jaw, the bipedal gait, or the large brain?

Straightforward and attractive, yes, but contradicting the evidence of evolution in many other mammalian lineages. The fossil remains of pigs, horses, and antelopes, for example, display a tremendous amount of variation, not only through the geological sequence, but also at any given point on it, indicating that their evolution had been more of a radiation than a single line, with extinctions and proliferations of species occurring at many points in their evolutionary histories. Indeed, the frequency of extinction and speciation found in the fossil record of most organisms whose remains have been found in large quantities suggests that such patterns are the rule. Why should humans be the exception?

The answer emerging from the tremendous

advances made in palaeoanthropological research over the past twenty years is that they are not. Though the total number of fossil hominids is small (as was the total number of hominids available to be fossilized, especially when compared with the size of living pig, antelope and horse populations), it shows that there have been extinctions and speciations during the course of human evolution too.

The fossil hominids discovered so far date from over 3.5 million years ago to less than 30,000. This survey presents them in a series of broad groupings which represents both a chronological sequence and a presumed evolutionary progression, but it should be noted that the relationship of one fossil to another is not always a matter of universal agreement. A brief account of the discovery and initial description of each is given, together with some discussion of evolutionary status and affinities.

The australopithecines

The oldest known group of hominids, dating from 3.7 to 1.6 million years ago, most authorities now accept four species—*Australopithecus afarensis*, *A. africanus*, *A. boisei* and *A. robustus*. The taxon was created in 1925 by Raymond Dart (1893–1988), professor of anatomy at the Witwatersrand University in South Africa, to accommodate a fossil skull which had been sent to him following its discovery during blasting activities at a lime quarry near Taung, in the northern Cape Province. The specimen comprised the greater part of a juvenile skull, together with an endocast of the right half of the brain (formed by the petrifaction of sediments which had filled the cranium after death). The face was complete and undistorted, with large rounded orbits, flattened nasal bones and a forward jutting jaw. Though the overall configuration of the specimen was essentially apelike, Dart noted several features which in his view made it more likely to represent the hominid lineage. The dental arcade was parabolic (it is more U-shaped in the apes); the erupting permanent teeth had a hominid cusp pattern; the braincase displayed certain hominid characteristics, and the foramen magnum (the hole in the base of the skull through which the spinal cord joins the brain) was set well forward beneath the skull, indicating that the head had been held erect at the top of the spine as in humans, and implying that the creature had been bipedal. In apes the foramen magnum is more to the rear of the skull and the head is slung forward, as befits their quadrupedal gait.

When Dart published his conclusions he claimed that his *Australopithecus africanus* (the southern ape of Africa) represented an early stage of human evolution. The claim was rejected, principally because it contradicted prevailing views. No evidence of early man had been found in Africa until then, and consensus opinion held that man had evolved in Asia or Europe, where the known fossils had been found. Furthermore, *A. africanus* had a small brain and a jaw of hominid configuration, which directly contradicted the faked Piltdown skull then still reinforcing the contention that a large brain and ape-like jaw would have characterised the earliest human ancestors. The leading authorities of the day dismissed *Australopithecus* as an ape, and therefore nothing to do with human evolution.

More than a decade later, in 1936, a retired Scots medical doctor and palaeontologist, Robert Broom (1866–1951), decided to look for more specimens of *Australopithecus* and re-investigate the matter of its relationship to human evolution. Broom was then 69. By the time he died in 1951 at the age of 84, he and his associates had recovered numerous australopithecine fossils from cave sites at Sterkfontein, Swartkrans and Kromdraai near Pretoria, in the Transvaal. Broom's findings confirmed Dart's assertion that the australopithecines were good candidates for the ancestry of man. Though Broom tended to create a new taxon for each of his finds, it soon emerged that two species were represented: the lightly-built *A. africanus*, which includes the Taung specimen and is often referred to as the *gracile* australopithecine; and the heavily-built *A. robustus*, the *robust* australopithecines. Mean brain size is estimated to have been 450 cc for *A. africanus*; 500 cc for *A. robustus*.

Dating the South African fossils has always been a problem, due to the confused geology of the infills and a lack of materials suitable for dating. The current consensus view suggests a date of about one million years ago, though some authorities claim that two million could be nearer the mark.

In 1959 Louis Leakey (1903–72) and his wife, Mary (1913–), recovered an almost complete skull, lacking the mandible, from deposits at Olduvai Gorge in Tanzania subsequently dated at 1.7 million years by the potassium-argon method. Though the skull showed definite affinities with the robust australopithecines from South Africa, it was thought to differ sufficiently to merit the creation of a new genus: *Zinjanthropus* (East African man), with the species name *boisei* honouring a benefactor. Subsequently the generic distinction has been dismissed and the specimen is now known as *Australopithecus boisei*.

Since 1969 teams under the direction of National Museums of Kenya Director, Richard Leakey (1944–), have recovered numerous australopithecine fossils with both gracile and robust affinities from 1.4 to 1.8 million year old deposits at East Turkana, northern Kenya. In 1985, the same team recovered a robust australopithecine skull from 2.5 million year old deposits on the west shore of Lake Turkana.

Between 1973 and 1977 joint French and American expeditions recovered large numbers of gracile australopithecine fossils from deposits dated at 2.6 to 3.3 million years ago in the Afar depression region of north-eastern Ethiopia. The fossils proved to be remarkably similar to others found at Laetoli, near Olduvai Gorge, by Mary Leakey in 1974–5 which were dated at 3.6 million years ago. In publishing the Afar findings, Donald Johanson, (1943–) and his co-authors concluded that the Afar and Laetoli material represented a single species which was sufficiently distinct from existing species to merit the creation of a new taxon: *Australopithecus afarensis*. Mary Leakey objected to this conclusion.

The fossil hominids discovered at Laetoli came from the same age deposit as a trail of fossilised footprints, and this circumstantial evidence invites the inference that the trail was made by those same hominids—*A. afarensis*. Evidence has been adduced for and against, but the issue remains contentious.

The affinities of the australopithecines

The South African discoveries established the australopithecines as viable candidates for the early ancestry of man, while fossils from East Africa and Ethiopia have shown that the species were widely dispersed through Africa between 3.7 and 1.6 million years ago. The distinction between the robust and gracile species is considered to represent differences in diet, the heavier teeth and facial build of the robust australopithecines reflecting the masticatory demands of an herbivorous diet while the lightly-built gracile australopithecines were adapted to a less demanding omnivorous diet. This distinction is presumed to represent a dietary specialization which led the robust australopithecines away from the ancestral australopithecine stock and ultimately to extinction, while the gracile line continued and thus represents the earliest known stage of hominid evolution.

Several schemes of australopithecine phylogeny (the evolutionary history of the group) have been proposed, their suggestions as to the manner by which the australopithecines evolved among themselves and ultimately into *Homo* differing principally on the questions of whether or not *A. afarensis* is accepted as a valid species, and whether the Afar and Laetoli fossils represent a single species or two distinct species. But despite their differences, no scheme denies that the australopithecines represent a pre-human phase of hominid evolution during which considerable advances were made in the development of the upright stance and bipedalism, and in the modification of the dentition, while expansion of the brain proceeded slowly; and all agree that the next stage of human evolution as presently understood is represented by *Homo habilis*.

HOMO HABILIS

The taxon was created by Louis Leakey and his co-authors in a 1964 *Nature* paper describing hominid remains excavated at Olduvai Gorge in 1961 from deposits dated at 1.7 million years by the potassium-argon method. The fossils comprised a lower mandible, skull fragments, and a group of handbones. They were found in association with stone tools, and this was a persuasive factor in the authors' decision to assign the fossils to the genus *Homo*, since no tools had ever been found incontrovertibly associated with the australopithecines and it was generally considered that man by definition was a toolmaker. Hence the name, *Homo habilis*, colloquially translated as "handy man".

Further remains of *Homo habilis* were found at Olduvai in succeeding years, including teeth, limb bones and a badly crushed and distorted skull. Richard Leakey's team at East Turkana discovered the skull known as 1470 (from its museum accession number KNM-ER 1470), which is informally described as *Homo habilis*, as are sundry other finds from East Turkana. Remains assigned to *Homo habilis* have also been recovered from excavations at the Swartkrans and Sterkfontein cave sites in South Africa, and at deposits in the Omo river basin in southern Ethiopia. In 1986, a new survey of the Olduvai Gorge deposits (led by Donald Johanson), recovered numerous fragments of skull, jaw and limb representing a single individual, which was subsequently assigned to *Homo habilis*.

The fossil evidence of *Homo habilis* recovered to date gives the species wide distribution through Africa, and a timespan dating from 2.1 to 1.8 million years ago. The species' mean brainsize is estimated to have been 750 cc.

The affinities of *Homo habilis*

Though the significance of the fossils was widely acknowledged, and the association of stone tools as a definition of man not questioned, *Homo habilis* did not find universal acceptance when the species was first proposed in 1964. All agreed that stone tools and an enlarged brain represented a significant step in the human direction, but some critics felt that the Olduvai material was insufficient evidence upon which to found a new species; others felt that if the material were to be assigned to a new species it should be within the genus *Australopithecus*, not *Homo*. The specimen certainly possessed a blend of gracile australopithecine and *Homo* characteristics which might be supposed to present an intermediatory stage between the two, but critics observed that in the then prevailing state of knowledge there was insufficient temporal and morphological space for a new species between *Australopithecus* and *Homo erectus* (the latter is generally accepted as the immediate antecedent of modern humans, *see below*). Louis Leakey, however, firmly believed that both *Australopithecus* and *Homo erectus* were aberrant offshoots from the hominid line which became extinct, and his promotion of *Homo habilis* as the oldest representative of the human line must be seen in the light of this belief.

The status of *Homo habilis* itself has not been much clarified in the quarter century since it was first described. Two main issues have arisen: First, the discovery of *Homo erectus* fossils from 1.6 million year deposits at East Turkana indicates that *Homo habilis* was one of at least three hominid species alive at that time (the other was *A. robustus*), which questions its status as an ancestor of *H. erectus*. Second, the *Homo habilis* fossils discovered at Olduvai in 1986 by Johanson and his team show a considerable degree of affinity with the *Australopithecus afarensis* material dating from more than 3.5 million years ago, which suggests that the ancestral form remained unchanged for a very long time, and that the *Homo* characteristics evident in later specimens of *H. habilis* must have evolved very quickly.

The evidence suggests that *Homo habilis* is still more of an idea in an evolutionary scheme than a well-defined example of anatomical fact linking one species to another. Only more evidence and rigorous analysis of early hominid variation will resolve the question of its status.

HOMO ERECTUS

The most widespread and longest-surviving of the fossil hominids. Remains have been found in north and east Africa, Europe, Indonesia and China. The fossils date from 1.6 million years ago (West

Turkana) to less than 300,000 years (China). Mean brain size ranges from 900 cc in early specimens to 1100 cc in late specimens.

The first known specimens were described by Eugene Dubois (1858–1940) in 1894 and included a calotte (the cranial vault) and a complete femur (thighbone) excavated from sedimentary deposits comprising freshwater sandstones, conglomerates and volcanic material at a bend of the Solo river in Central Java, Indonesia. The cranial capacity was relatively small (900 cc) while the femur was entirely human, and this combination led Dubois to assign the fossils to a new species: *Pithecanthropus erectus*, meaning erect ape-man, while the specimen became popularly known as Java Man. When fossils of similar configuration were found in China (Peking Man) both the Java and Peking material was assigned to the taxon *Homo* with sub-specific distinctions made for the Java (*Homo erectus javensis*) and Peking material (*Homo erectus pekinensis*). Subsequently, sub-specific distinctions were dropped and the taxon became known as *Homo erectus*.

Remains displaying *Homo erectus* characteristics have been recovered in Europe from sites in Germany (both East and West), Hungary, Greece, and France, and in 1960 a skull found at Olduvai Gorge extended the range of the species to Africa. Subsequently, further remains were found in Morocco and Algeria, in the Omo river basin of Ethiopia, and the Lake Turkana basin, northern Kenya.

In 1985 a virtually complete *Homo erectus* skeleton was found in deposits on the western side of Lake Turkana dated at 1.6 million years old. The remarkable preservation of the specimen is thought to be the result of the body having sunk quickly into lake silts after death. The skeleton is immature, its development matching that of a modern 12 year old. Estimates based on its limb size and modern growth rates suggest that the individual would have stood 1.68 m tall as an adult. Cranial capacity is as yet undetermined, but clearly relatively low. The forehead is low and recedes, as does the chin.

The affinities of *Homo erectus*

Though *Homo erectus* is well positioned in time to be both a descendent of earlier hominid forms and an ancestor of modern humans, several questions arise from its distribution and physical characteristics. Some authorities argue that the Asian and African forms are so distinct that the latter should not be assigned to *Homo erectus*. Others have suggested that the species represents a side branch of human evolution which became extinct, and its co-existence with *Homo habilis* at East Turkana indeed could be seen as reason for dismissing it from the human line.

There is also continuing debate on whether the relatively incomplete material from Europe represents the "true" *Homo erectus* or a group that should be more closely aligned to modern humans. This in turn raises the question of the *Homo erectus/Homo sapiens* transition: was this a gradual change, as some authorities see demonstrated in the Omo material? Or was there a long period of stasis followed by abrupt change, as the differences between the African and Asian fossils seem to indicate?

ARCHAIC HOMO SAPIENS

A term applied to specimens which might be said to exemplify the *Homo erectus/Homo sapiens* transition mentioned above, and also integral to the proposition that modern man evolved in Africa in the relatively recent past (*see* **F72**). The definitive specimen (Rhodesia Man) was found in the course of mining operations at Kabwe, Zambia in 1921, and comprises a complete cranium, teeth and skeletal fragments. Recent appraisal of the site and associated finds has suggested that the remains date from at least 125,000 years ago. Cranial capacity is 1280 cc, indicating an enlarged brain. Numerous other specimens assigned to the group have come from more than 30 sites spanning Africa from north to south and covering a timespan ranging from 500,000 to 30,000 years ago. Some display features characteristic of the ancestral hominids, others are entirely modern. An age of about 100,000 years has been given to comparable forms known from Qafzeh in Israel, but all other

evidence of anatomically modern man known from outside Africa is significantly younger. This is seen as indicating that modern man originated in Africa and migrated from the continent to populate the rest of the world not more than 200,000 years ago.

NEANDERTHAL MAN

The first specimen was discovered by quarrymen clearing a cave in the Neander valley, near Dusseldorf in 1857. Following its classification as a distinct species in 1864, *Homo neanderthalensis* soon became symbolic of the popular view of early man as an inferior and degenerate version of modern man. Based at first on a shortage of evidence and a determination to believe in the purity of the human line, this misconception was later reinforced by the distinguished palaeontologist Marcellin Boule (1861–1942) in a series of reports on Neanderthal remains found in cave sites at La Chapelle-aux-Saints and La Ferrassie between 1908–1912. Boule interpreted skeletal deformities as indicative of an habitual slouching gait and concluded that Neanderthal Man was every bit as degenerate as had been popularly supposed. Subsequent studies have shown that the deformities were the result of arthritis and that the Neanderthals were a sturdy and successful race, well-adapted to the environmental conditions of their time.

Discoveries of Neanderthal fossils at Engis in Belgium (1832), and Gibraltar (before 1848) predated the original find, and further remains have been found in Europe, Iraq and Israel. Bone structure and stout muscular attachments indicate that the Neanderthals were generally short and thick-set, with large feet and hands and a body form similar to that of modern cold-adapted people. Average brain size was over 1400 cc (some 10 percent larger than modern human, relative to body size) and exceeded 1700 cc in some large males. Dating of the fossil sites indicates that the Neanderthals lived from about 130,000 to 35,000 years ago. Thus they appear to have been a well-adapted and successful group of hunters and gatherers who ranged across Europe with the advance and retreat of the Ice Age.

The affinities of *Homo neanderthalensis*

Anatomical characteristics evident in both the Neanderthals and *Homo erectus* indicate that the two shared a common ancestry and possibly even a direct line of descent, but their relationship to modern man is far less clear. There are common characteristics, but much more that is different between the two forms. Moreover, it is generally felt that the proximity of the dates at which the Neanderthals disappeared and the modern humans became prevalent leave too little time for evolution to have effected the change from one to the other. After 100,000 years of unchallenged existence, the Neanderthals disappeared between 35,000 and 30,000 years ago. Only the remains of people anatomically indistinguishable from modern humans have been recovered from more recent sites.

This transition from Neanderthal to anatomically modern man poses what has become known as the "Neanderthal Problem": what happened to the Neanderthals in Europe? Only one of three explanations could apply: either the Neanderthals themselves were transformed into modern humans by a very rapid process of evolution, or they were overrun and replaced by modern humans who moved into Europe from some other point of origination, or they interbred with modern human immigrants and their distinctive characteristics were lost in the process. All three explanations have had their advocates. Argument and counter-argument have been pursued at length since the turn of the century, but genetic research (see below) indicating that modern humans originated in Africa and left the continent relatively recently strongly suggests that replacement was probably responsible for the disappearance of the Neanderthals. This need not have been a violent process. Some interbreeding also could have been involved, and the principal factor could have been better adaptation, perhaps of a behavioural or social nature. It has been suggested, for instance, that speech and enhanced social communication could have given the modern humans adaptive advantages in the changing, post-Ice Age climate of Europe which increased their reproductive rate and population growth while

Neanderthal numbers declined to the point of extinction.

HOMO SAPIENS SAPIENS

Fossil remains of anatomically modern humans are known from sites in Europe, Africa, the Near East, Asia and Australia. The first and most famous to be found was Cro-Magnon Man, unearthed in the Dordogne region of France in 1868 and dating from about 40,000 years ago. Fragmentary fossils of a wholly modern form recovered from a cave at the Klasie's river mouth in South Africa date back to more than 100,000 years ago, while those from the Mungo site in Australia are from 32,000 years ago. On present knowledge, these two finds represent the greatest time-depth and geographic dispersal of early modern humans.

The dispersal of modern humans appears to have been rapid between 30,000 and 20,000 and became especially so with the domestication of animals and crop plants from about 10,000 years ago. Migration into the Americas was delayed until a landbridge across the Bering Straits opened through glacial ice about 18,000 years ago, but excavations have shown that modern humans were well-established in north America soon thereafter and had spread as far south as the Chilean Andes by 12,000 years ago.

The spread and proliferation of anatomically modern humans is inextricably linked with the development of technological skills, art, and circumstantial evidence of social interaction. While the Neanderthals employed a stone tool technology little improved from earlier forms, the anatomically modern humans introduced the flint-flaking techniques by which a greater variety of tools were made. Personal adornment and careful burial of the dead were features of their lifestyle not evident among the Neanderthals, and cave paintings speak eloquently of their perceptive talents.

THE STUDY OF SOCIAL ANTHROPOLOGY

Social anthropology is concerned with the way men live as members of ordered societies. It has been described as a branch of sociology, or as the sociology of the simpler peoples. Neither description is wholly correct. A social anthropologist seeks to identify the *structure* of the society he studies and the *processes* of social interaction within it. His method is direct contact—what has been called "participant observation." Therefore he must deal with a unit small enough to be manageable with this technique. Nation-states, such as sociologists commonly work among, are too large. Most social anthropologists have done their work in what we call "small-scale" societies; that is, peoples who lacked such media of communication as writing or money, let alone mechanical means of transport, until these were brought to them from Europe. A social anthropologist may choose to work in some section of a society that possesses those techniques—in the ancient countries of the East or in Europe or America. In that case he confines himself to a microcosm such as a village or a factory. When he is writing of societies alien to his own and that of most of his readers he is obliged to describe their *culture* as well as their social relationships, since without such a description his readers would not be able to picture, or even understand, the social rules that are his main subject of study; this would be superfluous for a sociologist taking modern machine society for granted. Culture has been called the raw material out of which the anthropologist makes his analysis of social structure. It is the sum total of standardised ways of behaving, of lore and technique, of belief and symbolism, characteristic of any given society. The founders of social anthropology in Britain were B. Malinowski and A. R. Radcliffe-Brown.

The Notion of Roles

All the world, as Shakespeare said, is a stage, and this is a key metaphor for social anthropologists. Every individual does indeed play many parts, not consecutively but all together; for every social relationship carries with it the expectation of society that the parties to it will behave in approved ways. Father and children, ruler and subject, buyer and seller, husband and wife; every one of these words is the name of a *role* to be played by the person it describes. The playing of roles involves the recognition of claims and obligations as well as appropriate modes of behaviour in personal contacts. All these rules are called *norms*; when they are concerned with rights and obligations they are *jural norms*. A social norm is what people think ought to happen; unlike a statistical norm, it may or may not be what happens in the majority of cases.

Kinship and Marriage

In societies of simple technology most roles are *ascribed*; that is, the parts people will play in life are given them at birth by the fact of their parentage and of the group of which this makes them members. In other words, the most important principle of organisation is *kinship*. W. H. R. Rivers called this "the social recognition of biological ties." The ties in question can be called genealogical; they all derive from the recognition of common ancestry. Such ties may be fictitious, as when a child is adopted. But in the vast majority of cases the relationships that are recognised are actually biological.

No man can recognise for social purposes all the individuals with whom he has a common ancestor somewhere in the past, or even know of their existence; their number increases with every generation. In every society a selection is made, from the whole universe of genealogically related persons, of certain categories towards which an individual recognises specific obligations and on whom he can make specific claims. Such *corporate groups* of kin have a permanent existence; they recruit new members in each generation in accordance with recognised rules. Kin groups are concerned largely with the transmission of property, and for this and other purposes they recognise the common authority of a senior man; they are also religious groups, performing together rituals directed to their common ancestors.

The common patrimony of a kin group normally consists in land or livestock; in societies of more advanced technology it may be a boat, as in Hong Kong, or even, as in Japan, a family business. It may have non-material resources too, such as the right to supply chiefs or priests for the society as a whole; this may be put conversely as the right to hold political or religious office. Those who share a common patrimony have a common interest in preserving and increasing it. Wrongs done by their members to outsiders are compensated from their collective resources, and they have joint responsibility for seeking compensation if one of their own members is injured, particularly in the case of homicide.

Descent

Kin groups may be recruited according to a number of principles. A principle widely followed in small-scale societies is that of *unilineal descent*; that is, group membership is derived from one parent only, either the father (*patrilineal* or *agnatic*) or the mother (*matrilineal*). Property is *administered* by men in either system, but in the matrilineal system it is *inherited* from the mother; hence its control passes from a man to the sons of his sisters. In a unilineal system every individual recognises kin linked to him through the parent from whom he does not trace his descent; this is the principle of *complementary filiation*. The complementary kin are *matrilateral* where the descent rule is patrilineal, *patrilateral* where it is matrilineal. A unilineal descent group is called a *lineage*.

Descent can also be traced *cognatically*; that is, all descendants of a common ancestral pair may be recognised as forming one *kindred*. In such a system there is no permanent group patrimony; people inherit a share of the property of both their parents, and this is often conferred upon them when they marry, while their parents are still living. Or all the inhabitants of a village may share rights in its rice-fields or fishing ponds; a man chooses among what kin he will live, but he can have rights in one village only. In such a system there are no continuing groups defined by descent; the permanent group is territorial, consisting of the inhabitants of the village.

Marriage

Kinship status is defined by legitimate birth, and this in its turn by legal marriage. There are always rules against marriage with specified categories of kin, though these are not necessarily near kin. Some societies consider that the ideal marriage is that between the children of a brother and a sister; if such marriages are repeated through the generations they create a permanent link between two lineages. Marriage between members of the same lineage is nearly always forbidden; this is expressed in the term *lineage exogamy*. The general effect of the prohibitions is to spread widely through a society the links created by marriage, links that impose an obligation of friendship on groups that without them would be mutually hostile.

In a matrilineal system women bear children for their own lineage; it is expected that they should be fathered by a man who has married their mother according to the approval procedure, but a child's lineage membership is not affected by the marriage of its mother. But in a patrilineal society wives must be brought from outside to bear children for the group. Associated with this fact is the payment of *bridewealth*, which used to be mistakenly interpreted as the purchase of wives. This payment is what fixes the status of a woman's children; all those she bears while the bridewealth is with her lineage are reckoned as the children of the man on whose behalf it was paid, even if he is dead and she is living with another partner. In a matrilineal society the making of gifts is part of the marriage procedure, but they are of slight economic value in comparison with bridewealth. The difference is correlated with the difference in what the husband acquires by the marriage; in both cases he gains the right to his wife's domestic services and sexual fidelity, but where bridewealth is paid he can also count her children as his descendants and call on their labour when he needs it.

In societies where most roles are ascribed by the fact of birth, marriage is the most important field in which there is freedom of choice. But the choice is commonly exercised not by the couple but by their lineage seniors, who are more concerned with alliances between lineages than with the personal feelings of the pair. *Polygamy*, or the simultaneous marriage of a man to more than one woman, is permitted in lineage-based societies; indeed it is the ideal, though only a minority of men attain it. One reason why it is valued is that it enables a man who has the resources necessary for successive bridewealth payments to build up a network of alliances.

Authority Systems

Every society has some arrangements for the maintenance of order, in the sense that force may be used against those who infringe legitimate rights. In every society theft, adultery, and homicide are treated as offences. Where no individual has authority to punish these on behalf of the community, *self-help* is the approved course. Lineage membership is significant here; a man who is wronged will go with his kin to seek redress (for a theft or adultery) or vengeance (for the homicide of a kinsman). Vengeance can be bought off by the payment of compensation; but because the taking of life is a serious matter in the most turbulent of societies, there must also be a solemn reconciliation, with a sacrifice to the ancestral spirits, between the lineages of killer and victim. The recognition of an appropriate method of dealing with injuries has been described as "the rule of law" in its simplest form.

Within a lineage the senior man is expected to settle quarrels, and the ancestral spirits are believed to punish with sickness juniors who do not listen to him. When quarrels break out between members of different lineages, their elders may meet and seek a solution. Where there is no hereditary authority individuals may attain positions of leadership in virtue of their powers of mediation by persuasion.

In addition to the maintenance of rights, most societies require at some time arrangements for the organisation of collective activities. It is possible for there to be no ascribed role of organ-

iser; in such a case leadership is a matter of competition. Competitive leadership in economic activities is characteristic particularly of the very small societies of New Guinea. What is needed here is not only powers of persuasion but resources to reward the participants. The very important principle, to be discussed later, that every gift ought at some time to be returned, is the basis of their position. A man who can put others in his debt can call upon their labour. It may take a long time to build up the necessary resources for acknowledged leadership, and leadership may be lost to a rival and is not necessarily passed to an heir.

Responsibility both for law and order and for collective activities may be shared on recognised principles among the whole adult male population. This is done where society is organised on the basis of *age*, a system widely found in east and west Africa. In such a system all adult men pass through a series of stages at each of which appropriate tasks are allotted to them. In its simplest form the division is made into "warriors" and "elders". This principle may be complicated in various ways, but the essence of it is that men in their prime are responsible for activities requiring physical strength, impetuosity, and courage, while their elders have the task of mediating in disputes, discussing public affairs, and performing sacrifices to the ancestors. Men in the warrior grade are the fighting force, and may also have the police functions of summoning disputants and witnesses before the elders, and seizing property from a man who has been adjudged to pay compensation and does not do so voluntarily. Sometimes specific public works are allotted to them, such as rounding up stray cattle or clearing weeds from paths or springs. It is also possible for community responsibilities to be shared in more complicated ways, as for example among the Yakö of Nigeria, where the adherents of particular religious cults are believed to call on the spirit which they worship to punish persons guilty of particular offences.

Where there are hereditary chiefs, both public works and the maintenance of law and order are the responsibility of the chief and his subordinate officials. Resources are accumulated for public purposes by the collection of tribute, and labour is obtained for public works by the recognition of the principle that persons in authority can claim the labour of those subject to them. Expectations are attached to the role of chief as to any other. Chiefs are expected to dispense justice fairly, to be generous to the poor, to reward loyalty, and to be successful in war, and they are reminded of these expectations in the course of the elaborate rituals performed at their accession. The prosperity of the whole land is commonly held to be bound up with the health of the chief and the favourable attitude towards him of supernatural beings. He may be obliged to obey all kinds of ritual restrictions to this end; for example it was believed of the ruler of Ruanda, in east Africa, that he must not bend his knee lest the country be conquered. Chiefs are either themselves responsible for the performance of ritual on behalf of the whole populace or must maintain priests to do this.

Social anthropologists have recently turned their attention to the process of competition for the commanding roles which any society offers. Some would claim to have discarded the idea of structure altogether in favour of that of process; yet the structure must be taken into account as the set of rules in accordance with which the game is played. There are societies where it is the rule that on the death of a chief his sons must fight for the succession, to test who is the strongest and has the largest following. There are others where the rule of succession may seem to be clear, and yet there can always be dispute as to who fits it best. Sometimes people pursue the struggle for power by accusing their rivals of witchcraft; sometimes by massing their followers behind them in a show of strength before which their adversaries retire; the first is the method of the Ndembu in western Zambia, the second that of the Pathans in the Swat Valley in Pakistan. Such confrontations occur at moments of crisis, but the process of building up support is going on all the time. The study of these processes is among the most interesting new developments in social anthropology.

Economic Systems

The typical methods of subsistence in societies of simple technology are food-gathering (hunting and collecting roots and berries), herding, and agriculture. The domestication of animals and plants came relatively late in man's history; without it there could have been no permanent settlement, no cities, no civilisation. But the life of those food-gatherers who still exist is not a hard one; they can get an adequate diet in a very short working week. The three modes of subsistence should not be thought of as forming a historical series; moreover, there are many varieties of each, depending on the nature of the environment and the techniques used.

We shall never know what brought about the "agricultural revolution" or why the greater number of our ancestors chose the harder, but more productive, life of cultivators. This may have been somehow made necessary by the pressure of population in certain areas. Nor shall we know when and how trade and exchange began. We can reject the argument of Adam Smith that people first provided themselves with enough to eat and then began to exchange the products of specialists for surplus food. Exchanges are made among and between peoples who suffer from periodic famines, and the objects which are most valued are not exchanged for food.

These exchanges are not conducted, however, through the medium of a currency which enables people to calculate the relative value of goods of different kinds, as does money in a commercial society. Certain goods can be exchanged only for certain others—in the highlands of New Guinea, for example, shells and the plumes of rare birds. This has led to much controversy on the question whether primitive peoples can be said to have money. Of course, if money is defined as a universal medium of exchange, they do not. But some modern anthropologists find that too strict a definition, and prefer to say that, whereas modern currencies are "general-purpose money," societies of simple technology have different kinds of "special-purpose money"—strings of shells, hoe-blades, iron bars and the like, which are used only in a limited range of transactions.

It is certainly true, however, that money of this kind cannot be made the means of very exact calculations of profit and loss. It is often assumed that where there is no such common medium of exchange people do not make any economic calculations, and dispose of their property in ways that are the reverse of business-like. The principal reason why this assumption is made is the great importance attached to the making of gifts. The essential difference between a gift and a commercial exchange is that no return is stipulated. In the commercial world goods are sold, services hired, at a price, and anyone who fails to pay has broken a contract and is liable to be punished. The obligation to return a gift is a moral one. Moreover, to compete in the giving of gifts seems at first sight the very opposite of competition in the acquisition of wealth. But in most societies people who have a surplus of wealth like to have a reputation for generosity; only in the affluent world of machine production people feel the need to have many more material possessions before they begin to think in terms of surplus.

The exchange of gifts plays a particularly large part in the societies of Melanesia, where men form partnerships for the express purpose of giving and receiving valuable objects, and earn prestige at least as much by giving as by receiving. This exchange of valuables, mostly shell ornaments, is so important that it has a name in the language of each society. The first such exchange system to be described by an anthropologist was the *kula* of the Trobriand Islands, observed by Malinowski. An important man had a partner in an island on either side of his own home; from one he received armbands and returned necklaces, from the other he received necklaces and returned armbands. These objects did not become part of a store of wealth for any man; nobody could hold one long before it was time to pass it on to his partner. To receive his gift a man sailed by canoe to his partner's home; he was there welcomed peaceably,

and while he was making his formal visit the crew were bartering their goods on the shore with the local populace. Thus the *kula* partnership had the nature of a political alliance; it was a means of maintaining peaceful relations between populations which would otherwise have been hostile.

In the highland area of New Guinea identical objects are exchanged, so that the relative value of amounts given and received can be calculated. In some parts the ideal is that a return gift should be twice the original one. Naturally it is no small achievement to carry on a prolonged series of exchanges at such a rate. Very few men manage it, and those who do are the acknowledged leaders of their community. For each large gift he has made a man wears a little bamboo stick hung round his neck; thus his munificence is publicly proclaimed. A new partnership is initiated by making the minimum gift. Men make these partnerships with others not bound to them by kinship, notably with their relatives by marriage. Each partnership extends the range within which a man can count on friendly treatment. So widespread is the idea that gifts should be repaid, and services rewarded, after some delay, and at the discretion of the man making the return, that where the highland people have taken to growing coffee for sale, the large-scale planters do not pay wages but employ young men for planting who get their return by coming to them later for help in difficulties. Of course the young men would stop giving their work if they judged that the return was not adequate.

Gift-giving, then, is an investment, but not one that produces a direct material return. One anthropologist, R. F. Salisbury, has called it an investment in power. The second classic example of the uneconomic use of goods is the *potlatch* practised by the Kwakiutl and kindred tribes of the northwest coast of America. This was a public distribution of goods at which the recipients had to be given their gifts in strict order of rank. The giver earned prestige and power by the scale of his gifts, by his knowledge of the correct rank order, and by the famous deeds (*potlatches* and others) which he was able to claim as feats of himself and his ancestors. Rivals for precedence would assert their claim by vying with each other in the amounts they distributed. The Kwakiutl way of avenging an insult was what has been called the "rivalry gesture." The man who thought he had been insulted actually destroyed valuable property by throwing it on a fire, or into the sea, and his enemy had to match him in destruction or be humiliated.

Certainly this is not turning resources to material advantage. No more is the giving of a very expensive dinner-party in London or New York. But equally certainly, it is not done without calculation. In the affluent society people display their superior affluence because this demonstrates their prestige rating, just as in the *potlatch*; and they keep on good terms, through the hospitality they offer, with people from whom they may later seek a return in professional dealings, rather as in the Melanesian gift-exchanges. In fact a substantial proportion of the incomes of people in European societies who are by no means affluent goes into the making of gifts—to parents, to kin, to friends, to persons who have helped one or given one hospitality; gifts which are given as a matter of moral obligation. The difference between the uses to which resources are put in societies of simple and of complex technology is one only of degree. The proportion that is devoted to securing non-material advantages is higher in the small-scale societies, and so is the proportion of gift-giving to commercial exchange. In gift-giving there is no bargaining, but there is a clear expectation of return. The initiation of new social relationships by the making of gifts is not by any means confined to New Guinea. Bride-wealth which legitimises children is the most widespread example. Pastoral peoples in East Africa also make gifts of stock to selected friends in distant parts. The friend on his home ground is a sponsor for his partner, and he is expected to make return gifts from time to time, and may be asked for a beast if his partner is in difficulties. One could think of such an arrangement as a type of insurance.

A small number of social anthropologists have

specialised in the study of the economic systems of small-scale societies, and have asked whether the concepts devised for the analysis of monetary economies—such notions, for example, as capital and credit—can be applied to people who gain their livelihood directly from the resources of their immediate environment. Starting from the assumption that there is always some choice in the allocation of resources, they have observed how these choices are actually made in the societies where they have worked. They have asked how the value of such goods as are obtained by barter is measured; how labour is obtained, how directed and how rewarded for such enterprises as the building of a canoe or a temple, which call for the co-operation of large numbers. They have examined the use of media of exchange, asking how far any of these fulfil the functions that we associate with money.

The general conclusion of these studies is that peoples of simple technology are perfectly capable of rational calculation in the allocation of their resources, even though their calculations are rough by comparison with those of the entrepreneur in an industrial society. They know what to regard as an adequate return when they are bartering goods. They withhold goods from consumption when they are planning an enterprise; that is to say, a man who proposes to initiate such an activity as canoe-building, arranges to be able to feed his labour force.

Religion

At a time when people questioned whether "primitive" societies could be said to have religion, E. B. Tylor offered as a "minimum" definition of religion "the belief in spiritual beings." All societies of simple technology have such beliefs, and think that unseen personalised beings influence the course of nature by direct intervention, causing rain to fall if they are pleased with the actions of men and withholding it if they are angry, sending sickness as a punishment and so forth. In the great majority of such societies the most important spirits to be worshipped are those of dead ancestors. But there may also be a belief in gods responsible for particular aspects of the world, to whom offerings are made for protection or success in their special fields. Many preliterate peoples believe in a "high god" from whom all other spirits derive their power, and one school of anthropology sees this as evidence of an original state of higher religious consciousness from which man has declined; but this view is not widely held.

Rituals involving groups of people are commonly performed on occasions when changes of status are to be signalised. A child becomes a member of society not by being born, but at a naming or showing ceremony. A youth or girl becomes adult at initiation. Marriage, which makes a couple into potential parents and links their kin groups, is another such ritual.

In funerary rites the dead person is made into an ancestor, and his heir adopts his social personality and his responsibilities. The accession of a man to political office is surrounded by ritual, and chiefs frequently observe annual rites at the time of harvest, when it is the season, not the person, that is changing. These are *confirmatory* rituals, designed to keep society and the world on an even course. When something goes wrong, a drought or epidemic or an individual sickness, *piacular* rituals are performed to make peace with the spirits responsible for the disaster.

An essential aspect of many of these religions is the belief in witchcraft—that is that it is possible for humans to harm others merely by hating them. Witchcraft supplies an explanation of an undeserved misfortune. Diviners employ a multitude of techniques (which anthropologists rather inaccurately call oracles) to detect whether a disaster is a merited punishment or is due to witchcraft.

Every small-scale society has its myths—stories which tell how the word as people know it came to be. Sometimes their ritual re-enacts the myth; often the myth tells how the ritual was first performed and thereby gives a reason for its continuance. Then there are myths telling how death and evil came into the world. Some myths lend authority to the existing social order, and

particularly to the claims of ruling groups, by telling how the social structure was divinely ordained. Under the influence of the French anthropologist Lévi-Strauss, many anthropologists are beginning to see both myths and the symbolism of ritual as man's earliest attempt to order intellectually the world of his experience.

The existence of ultra-human beings on whom the affairs of men depended was universally taken for granted until a very short time ago. As long as this belief was held, the established order in any society was supported by the tenets of religion. But there are also revolutionary religions. In recent years anthropologists have been inspired by the many new religions that have arisen in developing territories to give more attention to this side of the subject. Notably in Melanesia, a succession of prophets have appeared with a message announcing the imminent coming of an ideal world from which all hardships would be banished, including the subjection of the indigenous peoples to colonial rulers. These events turned the attention of anthropologists, along with sociologists and historians, to the study of similar movements in the past, and we now have a considerable body of literature on such subjects as "the religions of the oppressed."

Closer study of traditional religions from this point of view has shown that they also often include symbolic reversals as part of their regular ritual. The high are brought low and the humble exalted. In his ritual installation a chief may be beaten and abused by his subjects, or a rite that confirms his authority may include a simulated rebellion. Women may assume for a day the garb and authority of men. There is a temporary suspension of the rules and cultural forms which differentiate the members of the ritual congregation. This may go as far as "ritual licence", in which actions that at other times are offences liable to punishment, notably sexual promiscuity, are permitted and must not be made a reason for quarrels. Or it may be simply that the participants are masked, stripped naked, or dressed identically. Such rituals affirm their common membership, or communitas, as it has been called, and where they express not merely unity and equality, but the reversal of high and low, they remind the powerful that they must not abuse their power. Rites of this kind form a phase in complex rituals. They are followed by a re-affirmation of the accepted order in its ideal form, where hierarchical relations maintain order without promoting injustice. This theory would interpret the new "subversive" religions as the response to situations in which the injustices of the powerful have gone too far for the re-assertion of communitas to be possible.

Social Change

No doubt all the societies that anthropologists have studied have been gradually changing throughout the centuries when their history was not recorded. But they experienced nothing like the rapidity of the changes that came to them when they were brought under the rule of European nations and introduced to mass production and a money economy. The effect of this has been in essence to widen the range of choice in the relationships that people can form. A man may choose to be dependent on an employer rather than on work in co-operation with his kin or village mates. He is more likely to rise in the world by going to school and getting a city job than by earning the respect of the villagers or the approval of a chief. Small-scale societies are now becoming merged in larger ones and the close ties of the isolated village are loosened. In the newly created industrial areas new specialised associations are formed to pursue professional and other interests. The social insurance that kinship provided is lacking, and it has not as yet been replaced by what the state offers in the highly industrialised societies. The minority that has whole-heartedly adopted the values of the industrialised world now produces the political rulers of new states. They are impatient to carry the majority along the same road, but there are profound conflicts of value between them and the still largely illiterate masses.

The first studies of this type of social change

were mainly interested in the effects of intrusive influence on traditional institutions in rural areas. Later, attention was turned to social relationships in the cities which have come into being, or greatly increased in size and population, as a result of the development of commerce and industry. Recent work is largely concerned with the extent to which immigrants to the cities preserve their sense of a distinctive home origin. Immigrant populations which have abandoned all their traditional customs often preserve a strong sense of a common identity which differentiates them from their neighbours, and sometimes they even create a myth of the possession of "special customs" that has no foundation in fact. This sense of a particularly close relationship between people from the same place of origin is called *ethnicity*. It has been argued that when the members of an *ethnic group* are in a privileged position they appeal to the sense of ethnicity to close the ranks against outsiders. The less fortunate might be more likely to unite on a non-ethnic basis to improve their position. Divisions based on ethnicity cut across those based on social class. This is a field in which the interests of social anthropologists and sociologists overlap. The conclusions drawn from studies in African cities could be, and no doubt will be, tested against work among immigrant populations in Europe and America.

Recent Trends in Social Anthropology

Structural Anthropology, as it has been developed in France by Lévi-Strauss, has the aim of establishing the universal characteristics of cultural, that is rule-governed, human behaviour, as opposed to the natural, instinctive behaviour of non-human species. Lévi-Strauss finds the distinguishing feature of man in communication by symbols, and holds that the way in which symbols are constructed reflects the structure of the human brain. As he uses the term social structure, it means the system of symbols by which a given society comprehends the world of its experience.

According to Lévi-Strauss communication is an exchange, and for him all exchange is communication. The prohibition of incest, which represents to him man's first move from natural to cultural life, obliges men to exchange their sisters, giving them to other men as wives. Then they exchange goods for goods or services. But for Lévi-Strauss the most important exchange is that of messages, and his central interest is in the codes in which the messages are embodied. Every code is an arbitrary set of symbols, the meaning of which depends on the way in which they are related. A code is based on a logical structure, so that social structure is the structure of a socially accepted code. It should be noted that the existence of the structure is not demonstrated independently of the code, but deduced from it, while the nature of the code is deduced from the supposed nature of the structure.

For the principles of structure Lévi-Strauss turns to the linguists, notably Roman Jakobson, according to whom all speech-sounds can be analysed into pairs of opposites; it is by recognising these opposites that children learn to speak and to distinguish meaning. Lévi-Strauss argues that the structure of the human brain leads men to classify the objects of their experience into opposites, then finding mediating terms to link the opposites. The recognition of differences is in his view the basis of classification, more important than the recognition of similarities. In totemism, a phenomenon which many anthropologists have tried to explain, awareness of differences between social groups is expressed by associating them with different animals. Exogamous descent groups, the groups which exchange sisters, are commonly called by the names of animal species. Each group has its totem animal, and they often believe that they must not eat this animal. The rules attached to these animal names form a code which can be decoded as: "We, Elephants, are different from them, Lions", not because either group is *like* elephants or lions, but because the groups differ as species differ. Any contrasting species would do; there is no intrinsic relation between Elephants and elephants just as there is none between the sounds of a word and its

meaning. Totemism, then, is an arbitrary code to express the principles on which a society is organised.

Lévi-Strauss' most massive work is devoted to the interpretation of myth. In his view the material of myth comes from the unconscious. He has made an extensive study of the myths of Amerindian peoples, and has found that stories in which the incidents are superficially dissimilar lead to the same conclusion (convey the same message), and on the way deal with oppositions (or contradictions) between rules or necessary facts of life and human wishes. The episodes of myths are the symbols of the code, and they can be combined in many different ways, but always according to an underlying, unconscious logic (structure). To explain this logic he draws comparisons with music and with mathematics. A musical note has no meaning in itself, only as an element in a melody or a chord. A musical composition plays with modifications or transformations of themes or harmonies, and just as a theme can be transposed into a different key, so a message can be conveyed in images that may refer to the objects of all the different senses; sight (light and darkness), taste (cooking—the first volume of his great book on myths is called *The Raw and the Cooked*), hearing (noise and silence) and so on. Note that all these codes are concerned with contrasts. From mathematics Lévi-Strauss takes the idea of a system of algebraic signs which can be combined in many permutations. Ultimately the theory of myth tells us that the important socially prescribed relations between persons of different status can be represented as relations between animal species, between kinds of food, between kinds of sound and silence, smells and tastes, aspects of landscape or any of these in combination.

According to Lévi-Strauss, although the deep structure of thought is unconscious, the classification of observed phenomena is conscious, and is the first activity of the human mind. Hence he rejects the view that peoples of simple technology are interested in natural phenomena only in so far as these have practical uses.

Cognitive Anthropology was first taken up as a special field in America, where its pioneers were Ward Goodenough, Charles E. Frake and Harold Conklin. It has much in common with the structuralism of Lévi-Strauss, but its practitioners are not interested in myths, and the majority make less extensive claims than he does. Some of them do believe that studies of the way in which different peoples classify the objects of their experience should lead to the discovery of universal cognitive principles, but they do not seek to reduce all categories to binary oppositions; rather they talk of *contrast sets*.

Studies in cognitive anthropology began with the examination of kinship terms by the method known as *componential analysis*. Instead of asking what relatives are grouped together under a designation found in English kinship, such as "father" or "brother", cognitive anthropologists looked for the essential *components* of any kin term, and found these to be sex, generation, and lineal or non-lineal relationship to the speaker or the person referred to by the term. This method was considered to give a truer picture of the principles according to which people group their relatives.

Cognitive anthropology has also been directed to other *domains* of experience, that is fields to which a distinguishable vocabulary is observed to apply; for example, to the classification of colours or of disease, but most of all to that of flora and fauna, or folk taxonomy, as this is called. These studies elucidate not only the principles according to which people group and distinguish the objects of their environment but also the factual knowledge they have of them.

Marxist anthropology has developed along with a general revival of interest in Marxist theory largely inspired by the new interpretation of Marxism introduced by the French writer Louis Althusser, not himself an anthropologist. The leading anthropological theorist in this field is Maurice Godelier, also in France. Like Lévi-Strauss, Marxists look for the unperceived structural laws on which all society rests, but they look in another direction. They find their answer in the *relations of production*, that is in the manner in which production is organised, and in particular the distribution of the resources which make production possible. They apply to the study of pre-capitalist societies the analysis which Marx himself made of capitalism, and seek to place the primitive and peasant societies of today, and also some vanished societies of which there are records, in their place in a line of developing social formations, each a transformation of its predecessor. Thus Marxist anthropology is in a sense an historical study, and can be contrasted with functional analysis in which societies are taken as they are when the observer sees them and treated, as Malinowski put it, as "going concerns". A functionalist study asks what keeps a society going; hence Marxists regard such studies as essentially conservative.

For Marxists a *social formation* is a combination of the forces of production and the relations of production. The forces of production consist in labour power and technical knowledge, and in the way production is organised. The relations of production are the relations between those who control the means of production—land or machines —and those who supply their labour power. Those who control the means of production are able to determine what share of the product shall go to the workers, and invariably they take more than a fair share. The state exists to practise this *extraction of surplus value*, as it is technically called. Accepted religious beliefs and other systems of ideas are not, as Lévi-Strauss and the cognitive anthropologists would have it, attempts to organise experience; they are delusions which conceal from the workers the way in which they are exploited. One social formation gives way to another when its *internal contradictions*—conflicts, incompatibilities—become too acute to be contained within the existing system. All aspects of a society are linked to the relations of production. Hence Marxist anthropologists do not admit the validity of cross-cultural comparisons between different institutions, such as kinship, economics, politics or religion, and argue that only social formations can be compared.

Thus they have given much more attention than earlier anthropologists to societies of hunters and gatherers, where nobody is dependent on others for the weapons that are the sole means of production. As soon as the means of production are appropriated by one section of society, the opposition of classes is observed. This change took place in the Neolithic period, when the invention of agriculture led to the recognition of rights in land. Even in those systems in which land is regarded as the common property of a group, the senior man or men who control its use are in a position to exploit their juniors, so that there are class divisions among kinsmen. It is also sometimes argued that where people believe that specialists in magic can influence the weather, or promote the growth of crops as the Trobriand magicians observed by Malinowski do, their knowledge is indispensable to production, and so they, too, make the workers dependent on them and can exploit them.

Marxist anthropologists make use of the ethnographic work of Malinowski and his pupils, who looked, as Malinowski had taught them, for the importance of reciprocity in exchange. Lévi-Strauss also discusses this in his theory of the exchange of women as the basis of kinship systems. But Marxists are concerned with inequalities rather than reciprocities in exchange, inequalities that those who own the means of production can impose. Thus they would not agree with Malinowski's followers, that there is any reciprocity in a state between rulers and ruled, that subjects pay tribute and rulers make their return both by maintaining order and in direct economic terms by the redistribution of wealth.

The study of **ecology** combines the work of anthropologists with that of human geographers and many natural scientists. It is associated with the name of the American anthropologist Julian Steward. Ecologists study the relations between society, technology and environment. They differ from the biologists who invented the term "ecology" in that they examine man's modification of his environment as well as his adaptation to it. Early ecological work concentrated on food-gathering populations who modify their environment very little, but it was soon extended to societies of pastoralists and cultivators.

Ecological studies have practical implications in various directions. They throw light on the success or failure of policies that are intended to raise standards of living, for example by persuading or compelling nomad pastoralists to become settled cultivators. A type of enforced change which has become widespread is the resettlement of populations whose homes have been flooded by the damming of rivers for hydro-electric projects; here the alteration in the environment is sudden and dramatic, quite unlike the effects of the unplanned changes of the past. It is usually accompanied by attempts to create a new environment that will make higher standards of living available, through housing schemes, new educational facilities, the introduction of new crops or farming methods, and so on. The proliferation of such schemes has been said to provide the anthropologist with a "laboratory situation" in which both policies and reactions can be compared. By combining ecological with medical studies it is possible to consider the prevalence of malnutrition or parasitic diseases in relation not only to the non-human environment but also to social groupings and norms which render certain populations, and particular categories within such populations, more vulnerable than others to these health hazards.

Another meeting-ground between anthropology and the natural sciences is in the new interest of sociologists in **ethology**, the study of the evolution of social behaviour. The classical exponents of this study have been Tinbergen in Holland and Lorenz in Austria. Close observation of the interaction between individuals and groups among non-human species has led many ethologists to conclude that animal populations may appropriately be regarded as societies. They hope to learn what tendencies among humans are genetically determined and so may not be amenable to deliberate attempts at social change. A subdivision of this study, human ethology, concentrates on minute details of behaviour with the aim of identifying gestures, facial expressions and the like that are found in all cultures, and so may be supposed to spring from affective systems common to all humanity. Yet a narrower subdivision is child ethology. Some anthropologists believe that these studies offer the key to the question What is Man? What are the characteristics that distinguish him from other animals, and how in fact did natural selection enable him to develop them?

These studies are still in their infancy, and in their present state they are vulnerable to some dangers. It is difficult, perhaps impossible, to use in the description of behaviour language which does not assume that what is described is social, the very question that the ethologists are asking. The assumption may be made unconsciously, but if it is consciously recognised it is possible to guard against it. The language used may also lead to the attribution to non-human animals of reactions that are specifically human (*anthropomorphism*). Zoologists may too readily assume that all human behaviour can be reduced to those reactions which are transmitted in our evolutionary heredity, forgetting that the processes of social conditioning are much more elaborate in man than in other animals. Anthropologists on their side may be too ready to seek the kind of interpretation of non-human behaviour that supports their *a priori* idea of the nature of man, *e.g.*, whether he is essentially aggressive or pacific, competitive or co-operative.

DEVELOPMENT ANTHROPOLOGY

Introduction

The word development became a technical term in colonial administration with the implementation in the British territories of the Colonial

Development and Welfare Act of 1940. With the passing of this measure Britain abandoned the principle that colonial territories should be self-supporting, and made available from British revenues grants for projects expected to improve the standard of living of the local populations. "Welfare" implied the expansion of social services: "development" was investment calculated to increase productivity. After the Second World War a similar policy was introduced in France, and as former colonial territories became independent the United States and the United Nations also contributed funds for their development; the United Nations proclaimed a "development decade" in 1960. The motives behind these policies were various; governments sought to extend their political influence, their trading relations and opportunities for their nationals, but a humanitarian element was also present. The development of resources had always been the aim of colonial powers, but now the emphasis was on the development of peoples.

The Problems of Development

In a sense anthropologists have been interested in problems of development from the time when, under the influence of Malinowski, British anthropologists turned from the reconstruction of the past to what he called "the anthropology of the changing African". African was taken as the type because it was the International African Institute, supported by large American grants, which supplied the bulk of the funds made available for research in anthropology in the period between the two world wars. Malinowski's pupils observed the effects that European penetration had had on African and other populations, and tended to concentrate on those which had been adverse. For a time they deplored economic development altogether, but they came to realise that the changes introduced by colonial rule were irreversible. They also had to recognise the fact that Western science and technology could and should be used for the benefit of non-Western peoples, particularly to raise standards of health and nutrition. Their attention was now focused on small-scale innovations with these aims, such as had of course always been attempted under colonial rule. The "community development" projects which had some vogue in West Africa in the period just before independence aimed at making much improvements through the efforts of the people expected to benefit from them, with some assistance from governments. Independent India adopted a community development policy which involved the division of the whole country into development areas under officials of the central government. Since the improvements sought were of a kind that any anthropologist would approve, it now became our task to explain the indifference or resistance which they so often encountered. Some also looked critically at the explanations in terms of "peasant conservatism" that were offered by people who were interested in development but not versed in anthropological theory.

The Awareness of Poverty

The interest in development which was manifested after the Second World War arose from a new awareness of the poverty of many millions of people in those newly independent countries that began to be called "under-developed", and later from the recognition that population was increasing faster than natural resources. These poorer countries were contrasted with the highly industrialised ones, which were assumed to be "developed", and it was further assumed that their problem was simply that too little capital had been invested in industry. Hence external finance was offered for development programmes which aimed at rapid industrialisation, and the next assumption made was that this would increase national productivity, as it often did, and thus would automatically raise standards of living. It proved, however, to do little to alleviate the poverty of the peasant majorities of the populations concerned.

Food Production

Attention then turned to the possibility of increasing food production and peasant incomes along with it, by introducing more efficient methods of farming. Since most anthropologists have worked among rural populations, it is here that they might be expected to have something to contribute, and that their advice has in fact sometimes been sought. An anthropologist may, for example, be appointed as a member of a UN development team; or a private company may engage one as consultant, as was done when copper was discovered on the island of Bougainville and the inhabitants were not satisfied with the compensation they were offered for the expropriation of their land. Sometimes one has been asked to comment on an elaborate multiple project such as the damming of a river for a hydro-electric scheme and the resettlement of the people whose homes would be flooded, and has been able to indicate situations that would have to be taken into account and persuade the planners to work to a slower timetable.

But more often anthropologists have come to the scene after a plan has been carried through, and have been able to see the various ways in which the results have differed from what was expected, and sometimes reasons why it has failed altogether—if, for example, a farm project does not attract or hold settlers.

The Colson–Scudder Survey

A well-known example of a study which was begun before the change that was planned and continued after it, is that made by Elizabeth Colson and the ecologist Thayer Scudder of the 56,000 Gwembe Tonga who were moved from their homes when the Kariba Dam was built on the Zambezi River. They made a detailed study of the Gwembe social organisation and adaptation to the environment in their traditional homes, and returned when the move was still a recent drama in most people's lives, and at intervals in later years. Their final study contrasted the adaptation to the move made by two village communities whose home environments had been very different and who had been moved to new sites only a few miles apart.

In their study of the resettlement process they called attention to the hardships that had been caused by requirements of technicians which were allowed to override consideration for human values. The height of the dam was raised after the preparations for resettlement had begun, so that the area to which many people had agreed to move was flooded and they had to be sent elsewhere. Those who had furthest to go had to be moved *en bloc* in a single day because the Public Works Department could only release the number of lorries needed for one day. New sites were not provided with water in time for the move, as had been promised.

This list of grievances illustrates both a failure to co-ordinate the activities of different technical departments of government and a lack of imaginative sympathy. But it also indicates that the agents of change must work within the limits of their technical resources. It would have been quite impracticable in this case, for example, for Public Works to transport several thousand people over 100 miles by a shuttle service, picking up families or even whole villages as and when they were ready to move. After all, the Kariba Dam had not been conceived as an operation to benefit the Gwembe Tonga. Anyone who is convinced that a project must go through can argue that the people who are affected will settle down after a temporary upset; and in a sense they do, as they come to take their new circumstances for granted.

Nevertheless, if those in authority think it important not to impose unnecessary hardships on those who are subject to their decisions, this detailed account of an exercise which is likely to be repeated in some form where dams are built, populations moved from disaster areas, refugees settled and so on, is a record to which they can look to see what mistakes they might avoid.

The Weinrich Study

A comparable study is that made by Dr. A. H. K. Weinrich (Sister Mary Aquina) of the African response to the various policies pursued by the government of Rhodesia (before independence) with the aim of improving African farming. Certain areas of land were earmarked for purchase by Africans who were required to show that they were efficient farmers. Others were irrigated and offered on lease to farmers who had to follow a closely controlled programme of work. The largest proportion of the area of land allotted to African occupation was "tribal trust land", where, after an attempt to enforce fixed standards of cultivation, the authorities fell back on the educational work of missionaries and extension officers. Dr. Weinrich investigated communities holding land in each of these three ways, and concluded that no great improvement in cultivation could be observed in any, except in the case of a minority of men and women who had followed courses of training to qualify as "master farmers". Her own conclusions were drastic: that *all* rights to agricultural land, including those of Europeans, should be conditional on efficient cultivation, and that every African cultivator should be held individually responsible for a specified area of land. Much more attention should be given to the education of peasant farmers in place of attempts at coercion, and farming communities should be given a say in the management of their own affairs. At the time when her findings were published, Zimbabwe had not achieved independence but whatever the type of government, it will have to deal with the problems that she has analysed.

These two examples are of action taken in territories where policy was dominated by European settler interests. Few such territories remain today, and it is the professed aim of the rulers of all the new states to seek the welfare of the indigenous populations. In such a context an anthropologist could be in a stronger position. If his views were asked in advance, he might be able to say that an apparently beneficial scheme would not really be so; or that it would need to overcome specific difficulties arising from existing power structures or modes of co-operation; or that the benefits would be lost if they were not accompanied by technical instruction (for instance, in the control of irrigated water supplies or the maintenance of pumps).

A difficulty in organising co-operation between anthropologists and development agents lies in the different time-scales with which they work. An anthropologist does not expect to speak with confidence about the people he studies until he has worked with them for at least a year. No doubt a development plan takes a year to complete, but once it has been adopted it is expected to be put into operation as soon as possible. Time-tables are drawn up, and even if deadlines are seldom met, there must be an attempt to meet them. In any event, decisions have to be taken at the moment when problems arise. Occasionally an anthropologist has actually been put in charge of a small-scale project and has had to face this dilemma.

Some would say, then, that the studies made after the event to explain failure or disappointment form the most valuable contribution of social anthropology; they are there as warnings or lessons for future planners, provided the planners will read them—but this is a risky assumption. Others would say that development agents should learn the elements of social anthropology as part of their training, and if they did, "village level" or "rural development" workers would certainly be more sensitive to the reception of their activities by villagers.

Intermediate Technology

Where there are the best prospects for fruitful co-operation is in the introduction of small-scale improvements such as are sometimes called "intermediate technology". Such improvements can sometimes be made by people who have made no academic study of anthropology at all, if they have enough local knowledge. It was an anthropologist working with a WHO team who pointed out that apparently simple additions to children's diet were far beyond the means of urban workers in Jakarta, but it was a doctor in India who discovered how to make existing food sources far more nutritious.

A field that anthropologists are only now beginning to enter is that of the traditional contribution of women to the farm and household economy. The exhortations and demonstrations of agronomists have commonly been directed to men, and men have been persuaded—sometimes—that methods involving harder work will bring in higher returns; it is not often noticed that the women may be doing the harder work while the men get the price of the crop. A move is now being made to train women for anthropological fieldwork among their own compatriots. They will have the general knowledge of social structure that must be the basis of any research, but they will concentrate their attention on women and on those aspects of co-operation in the household that have generally been taken for granted in the past. What are the chores that occupy a woman's day and how could they be lightened by the adoption of simple labour-saving devices? What are their ideas on the health and feeding of children and on the treatment, or recourse for aid, in sickness? How much independence of decision do they have, and in what contexts? One outcome of these studies is expected to be a fuller understanding of women's attitudes towards child-bearing and their receptiveness or resistance to the idea of family planning which is now beginning to be considered so urgently important in heavily populated countries.

The Anthropology of Development

A distinction has been drawn between "development anthropology", that is anthropology in the service of development and "the anthropology of development", or the study of interactions between all persons concerned in development, those who intend to bring benefits as well as the supposed beneficiaries. Studies of the latter type would depart from that focus on the reaction of intended beneficiaries which has been the main interest of anthropologists up to now, and would examine not only the motives of development planners but the interactions between the representatives of different interests engaged in planning. In the two African examples cited here, the benefit of the peasant cultivators was not the primary aim; the Kariba Dam was intended to provide electric power for industry, the various Rhodesian land policies, as Dr. Weinrich repeatedly emphasises, to enable an African population to subsist within limits set by the interests of a European one. Other plans are forced on governments by one crisis or another. But in addition, closer analysis would show how the competing interests of different technical agencies may influence the content of any development scheme and will certainly influence the allocation of resources within it. Governments are not the only empire-builders; divisions within them also seek to extend their power, and every expert thinks the most important benefits are those that depend on his own expertise (anthropologists are no exception). The most effective study of this kind that has been made is the work not of an anthropologist but of a political scientist, Robert Chambers, who followed in detail the history of the Mwea land settlement that was initiated in Kenya just before independence. He, however, was not solely interested in description as opposed to prescription; he travelled through Africa looking at settlement schemes, and concluded that the most important prerequisite for success was to keep government provision to the minimum and rely on self-help. But, brilliant as his analysis of the planning process is, it does not tell anyone how to plan better. It just throws light on human weakness and suggests the impossibility of making a perfect plan. A good many anthropologists would hope to offer more, even if they had to confine themselves to limited aspects of a plan.

VI. SCIENTIFIC TABLES
TABLE OF ELEMENTS

Element (Symbol)	Atomic Number	Atomic Weight	Valency	Element (Symbol)	Atomic Number	Atomic Weight	Valency
actinium (Ac)* . .	89	227		molybdenum			
aluminium (Al) . .	13	26·9815	3	(Mo).	42	95·94	3, 4, 6
americium (Am)* .	95	243	3, 4, 5, 6				
antimony (Sb). . .	51	121·75	3, 5	neodymium (Nd)	60	144·24	3
argon (Ar)	18	39·944	0	neon (Ne).	10	20·17	0
arsenic (As)	33	74·9216	3, 5	neptunium (Np)*	93	237	4, 5, 6
astatine (At)* . . .	85	210	1, 3, 5, 7	nickel (Ni)	28	58·71	2, 3
				niobium (Nn) . .	41	92·906	3, 5
barium (Ba)	56	137·34	2	nitrogen (N) . . .	7	14·0067	3, 5
berkelium (Bk)*. .	97	247	3, 4	nobelium (No)*	102	254	
beryllium (Be). . .	4	9·0122	2				
bismuth (Bi). . . .	83	208·980	3, 5	osmium (Os) . . .	76	190·2	2, 3, 4, 8
boron (B).	5	10·811	3	oxygen (O).	8	15·9994	2
bromine (Br). . . .	35	79·904	1, 3, 5, 7				
				palladium (Pd) .	46	106·4	2, 4, 6
cadmium (Cd) . . .	48	112·40	2	phosphorus (P) .	15	30·9378	3, 5
calcium (Ca)	20	40·08	2	platinum (Pt) . .	78	195·09	2, 4
californium (Cf)* .	98	251		plutonium (Pu)*	94	244	3, 4, 5, 6
carbon (C)	6	12·0111	2, 4	polonium (Po)* . .	84	210	
cerium (Ce).	58	140·12	3, 4	potassium (K) . .	19	39·102	1
caesium (Cs)	55	132·905	1	praseodymium			
chlorine (Cl)	17	35·453	1, 3, 5, 7	(Pr)	59	140·907	3
chromium (Cr). . .	24	51·996	2, 3, 6	promethium			
cobalt (Co)	27	58·9332	2, 3	(Pm)*.	61	145	3
copper (Cu)	29	63·546	1, 2	protactinium			
curium (Cm)* . . .	96	247	3	(Pa)*	91	231	
				radium (Ra)* . .	88	226	2
dysprosium (Dy)	66	162·50	3	radon (Rn)* . . .	86	222	0
				rhenium (Re) . .	75	186·2	
einsteinium (Es)* .	99	254		rhodium (Rh) . .	45	102·905	3
erbium (Er)	68	167·26	3	rubidium (Rb). .	37	85·47	1
europium (Eu). . .	63	151·96	2, 3	ruthenium (Ru) .	44	101·07	3, 4, 6, 8
				samarium (Sm) .	62	150·35	2, 3
fermium (Fm)* . .	100	253		scandium (Sc) . .	21	44·956	3
fluorine (F).	9	18·9984	1	selenium (Se) . .	34	78·96	2, 4, 6
francium (Fr)*. . .	87	223	1	silicon (Si)	14	28·086	4
				silver (Ag)	47	107·870	1
gadolinium (Gd) .	64	157·25	3	sodium (Na) . . .	11	22·9898	1
gallium (Ga)	31	69·72	2, 3	strontium (Sr) . .	38	87·62	2
germanium (Ge). .	32	72·59	4	sulphur (S). . . .	16	32·064	2, 4, 6
gold (Au)	79	196·967	1, 3				
				tantalum (Ta) . .	73	180·947	5
hafnium (Hf) . . .	72	178·49	4	technetium (Tc)*	43	99	6, 7
helium (He)	2	4·0026	0	tellurium (Te) . .	52	127·60	2, 4, 6
holmium (Ho) . . .	67	164·930	3	terbium (Tb). . .	65	158·925	3
hydrogen (H) . . .	1	1·00797	1	thallium (Tl) . . .	81	204·37	1, 3
				thorium (Th). . .	90	232·038	4
indium (In)	49	114·82	3	thulium (Tm) . .	69	168·934	3
iodine (I)	53	126·904	1, 3, 5, 7	tin (Sn)	50	118·69	2, 4
iridium (Ir).	77	192·2	3, 4	titanium (Ti). . .	22	47·90	3, 4
iron (Fe)	26	55·847	2, 3	tungsten (see wolfram)			
krypton (Kr) . . .	36	83·8	0	uranium (U) . . .	92	238·03	4, 6
lanthanum (La). .	57	138·01	3	vanadium (V) . .	23	50·942	3, 5
lawrencium (Lr)*	103	257					
lead (Pb)	82	207·19	2, 4	wolfram (W) . . .	74	183·85	6
lithium (Li)	3	6·941	1				
lutetium (Lu) . . .	71	174·97	3	xenon (Xe). . . .	54	131·30	0
magnesium (Mg)	12	24·305	2	ytterbium (Yb) .	70	173·04	2, 3
manganese (Mn)	25	54·9380	2, 3, 4, 6, 7	yttrium (Y) . . .	39	88·905	3
mendeleevium							
(Md)*.	101	256		zinc (Zn)	30	65·37	2
mercury (Hg) . . .	80	200·59	1, 2	zirconium (Zr). .	40	91·22	4

* In the cases of these elements, which are very rare or not found in nature, but have been artificially prepared, atomic weight in the chemical sense is meaningless; the integral mass of the most stable isotope known is given.

Note: In 1961 the isotope of carbon-12 replaced oxygen as a standard, the weight of its atom being taken as 12. This change of standard has meant a slight adjustment in atomic weights from the old chemical scale.

The new elements with an atomic number higher than that of uranium 238 (element 92) are termed Transuranics.

GAS LAWS

The Perfect or Ideal Gas Law: $pV = nRT$
where n is the number of moles in volume V at pressure p and absolute temperature T, and R is a universal constant.

Van der Waals' equation: $\left(p + \dfrac{a}{V^2}\right)(V - b) = nRT$

where a and b are constants, different for each gas.

PERIODIC TABLE

PERIODIC TABLE OF THE ELEMENTS

Key to Chart

Atomic Number → 5
Symbol → B
Atomic Weight → 10.811

GROUP / Period ↓	1A (Alkali metals)	2A (Alkaline earth metals)	3B	4B	5B	6B	7B	8	8	8	1B (Noble metals)	2B	3A	4A	5A	6A	7A	0 (Inert gases)
1	1 **H** 1·00797																	2 **He** 4·0028
2	3 Li 6·941	4 Be 9·0122											5 **B** 10·811	6 **C** 12·0111	7 **N** 14·0067	8 **O** 15·9994	9 **F** 18·9984	10 **Ne** 20·179
3	11 Na 22·9898	12 Mg 24·305		Transition metals									13 Al 26·9815	14 *Si* 28·086	15 **P** 30·9738	16 **S** 32·064	17 **Cl** 35·453	18 **Ar** 39·948
4	19 K 39·103	20 Ca 40·08	21 Sc 44·9559	22 Ti 47·90	23 V 50·942	24 Cr 51·996	25 Mn 54·938	26 Fe 55·847	27 Co 58·933	28 Ni 58·71	29 Cu 63·546	30 Zn 65·37	31 Ga 69·72	32 *Ge* 72·59	33 *As* 74·9216	34 *Se* 78·96	35 **Br** 79·904	36 **Kr** 83·80
5	37 Rb 85·4678	38 Sr 87·62	39 Y 88·9059	40 Zr 91·22	41 Nb 92·9064	42 Mo 95·94	43 Tc 99	44 Ru 101·07	45 Rh 102·905	46 Pd 106·4	47 Ag 107·870	48 Cd 112·40	49 In 114·82	50 Sn 118·69	51 *Sb* 121·75	52 *Te* 127·60	53 **I** 126·904	54 **Xe** 131·30
6	55 Cs 132·905	56 Ba 137·34	57 La* 138·91	72 Hf 178·49	73 Ta 180·947	74 W 183·85	75 Re 186·2	76 Os 190·2	77 Ir 192·2	78 Pt 195·09	79 Au 196·967	80 Hg 200·59	81 Tl 204·37	82 Pb 207·19	83 Bi 208·980	84 Po 210	85 **At** 210	86 **Rn** 222
7	87 Fr 223	88 Ra 226	89 Ac† 227															71 Lu 174·97

*Lanthanides (see **L72**)

58 Ce 140·12	59 *Pr* 140·907	60 *Nd* 144·24	61 Pm 145	62 Sm 150·35	63 Eu 151·96	64 Gd 157·25	65 Tb 158·925	66 Dy 162·50	67 Ho 164·930	68 Er 167·26	69 Tm 168·934	70 Yb 173·04	71 Lu 174·97

† Actinides (see **L3**)

90 Th 232·038	91 *Pa* 231	92 U 238·03	93 Np 237	94 Pu 244	95 Am 243	96 Cm 247	97 Bk 247	98 Cf 251	99 Es 254	100 Fm 253	101 Md 256	102 No 254	103 Lr 257

Roman type—metals
Italic type——semiconductors
Bold type—non-metals

These designations refer to the normal materials usually at room temperature. Processes like heating or compressing can turn metals into insulators and vice versa.

Note: It may be possible by artificial methods such as bombardment by other nuclei to produce elements with atomic numbers greater than 103. However all the very heavy elements are unstable and decay spontaneously into lighter elements. Because the lifetime of such elements is short no element with an atomic number greater than Uranium (92) occurs naturally on earth.

MEASURES, UNITS AND METROLOGY

Before any quantity can be measured one must decide on the *units* used for measurement. For example, a 2 lb loaf of bread when weighed in ounces will give 32, *i.e.* 2 × 16. This is because there are 16 oz in a pound. It would be incorrect to say the weight of the loaf is 2 or 32. We say it is 2 lb or 32 oz and we can convert from one unit to another by knowing the ratio of their sizes.

If a standard pound is kept somewhere this can be used to calibrate other standard weights using accurate scales. These in turn can be used to calibrate other weights which in turn can be compared with the loaf with scales in order to weigh the bread. Nowadays, for scientific purposes, weights are compared with that of the *international prototype kilogram* (**L70**), kept at Sèvres in France. For a long time the length of an object was obtained by making a comparison, direct or indirect, with the standard metre if using the metric system or the standard yard if using the Imperial system. The standard metre was the length between two notches on a metal rod, kept at a controlled temperature, at Sèvres. Time is measured in seconds, which at one time was defined as a certain fraction of the tropical year.

Definitions of this kind are unsatisfactory for two reasons. First, the tropical year is not constant and even the most carefully kept metal rods are liable to change their dimensions over a long period of time. Secondly, it is not always convenient to do a comparison with an object kept in France. Nowadays every effort is made to define units in terms of some fundamental property of matter which is reproducible everywhere and does not require comparison with one particular object. The second is now defined using an atomic clock and can be measured to an accuracy of 1 part in 10^{12}. Variations in the rotation of the earth are far greater than this. The metre is nowadays defined in terms of the distance light travels in one second (**L82**). Although the kilogram could likewise be defined in terms of some fundamental property of matter, such as insisting the mass of an electron is 9.1083×10^{-31} kilogram, this quantity is only known to about 2 parts in 10^6. Comparisons with the standard kilogram can lead to an accuracy of the order 10^{-9}, so at present this definition of the kilogram stands.

The scientist nowadays mainly uses the S.I. system of units. SI is short for "Système International d'Unités" and it is a system of metric units now coming into international use through the agency of such bodies as the General Conference of the International Bureau of Weights and Measures and the International Organisation for Standardisation (ISO) in whose work Britain participates. Information about SI units is available in booklets published by the British Standards Institution, Sales Branch, 101–113 Pentonville Road, London, N.1.

Definitions of the Base Units

The system uses the seven *base quantities* listed below:

Quantity	Name of unit	Symbol of unit
Length	metre	m
Mass	kilogram	kg
Time	second	s
Electric current	ampere	A
Thermodynamic temperature	kelvin	K
Luminous intensity	candela	cd
Amount of substance	mole	mol

The seven S.I. base units are defined as follows:

The *metre* is the length travelled by light in a vacuum in 1/299 792 458 sec (**L82**).

The *kilogram* is the mass of the international prototype of the kilogram (**L70**). Scientists use the word "mass" where the layman would say "weight". Strictly speaking, weight is not a base quantity and is a measure of *force*.

The *second* is the duration of 9 192 631 770 periods of the radiation corresponding to the transition between the two hyperfine levels of the ground state of the caesium-133 atom (see **Clock L26**).

The *ampère* is that constant current which, if maintained in two straight parallel conductors of infinite length, of negligible circular cross-section, and placed 1 metre apart in vacuum, would produce between these conductors a force equal to 2×10^{-7} newton per metre of length.

The *Kelvin*, unit of thermodynamic temperature, is 1/273·16 of the thermodynamic temperature of the triple point of water (see **Absolute Temperature L3**).

The *Candela* is the luminous intensity, in the perpendicular direction, of a surface of 1/600 000 square metre of a black body at the temperature of freezing plantinum under a pressure of 101 325 newtons per square metre. Luminous intensity is a property of a *source* and is the amount of luminous flux (light) it throws out per steradian.

TABLE I

Quantity	Name of SI unit	Symbol	SI unit in terms of base units or derived units
frequency	hertz	Hz	$1\ Hz = 1\ s^{-1}$
volume	stere	st	$1\ st = 1\ m^3$
density	kilogram per cubic metre		$kg\ m^{-3}$
velocity	metre per second		$m\ s^{-1}$
force	newton	N	$1\ N = 1\ kg\ m\ s^{-2}$
pressure, stress	pascal	Pa	$1\ Pa = 1\ N\ m^{-2}$
viscosity (dynamic)	pascal second		$Pa\ s$
work, energy, quantity of heat	joule	J	$1\ J = 1\ N\ m$
power	watt	W	$1\ W = 1\ J\ s^{-1}$
quantity of electricity	coulomb	C	$1\ C = 1\ A\ s$
electric potential, EMF	volt	V	$1\ V = 1\ W\ A^{-1}$
electric field	volt per metre		$V\ m^{-1}$
electric capacitance	farad	F	$1\ F = 1\ C\ V^{-1}$
electric resistance	ohm	Ω	$1\ \Omega = 1\ V\ A^{-1}$
electric conductance	siemens	S	$1\ S = 1\ \Omega^{-1}$
magnetic flux	weber	Wb	$1\ Wb = 1\ V\ s$
magnetic flux density	tesla	T	$1\ T = 1\ Wb\ m^{-2}$
inductance	henry	H	$1\ H = 1\ V\ s\ A^{-1}$
magnetic field	ampère per metre		$A\ m^{-1}$
luminous flux	lumen	lm	$1\ lm = 1\ cd\ sr$
luminance	candela per square metre		$cd\ m^{-2}$
illuminance	lux	lx	$1\ lx = 1\ lm\ m^{-2}$
heat flux density, irradiance	watt per square metre		$W\ m^{-2}$
heat capacity	joule per kelvin		$J\ K^{-1}$
specific heat capacity	joule per kelvin per kilogram		$J\ kg^{-1}\ K^{-1}$
thermal conductivity	watt per metre per kelvin		$W\ m^{-1}\ K^{-1}$

The *mole* is the amount of substance of a system which contains as many elementary entities as there are atoms in 0·012 kilogram of carbon 12. Since this number is approximately 6·022 17 × 10²³ a mole of hydrogen molecules, for example, is approximately this number of hydrogen molecules.

In addition to the base units, two SI *supplementary units* are listed below:

Quantity	Name of unit	Symbol of unit
Plane angle	radian	rad
Solid angle	steradian	sr

They are defined as follows:

The *radian* is the plane angle between two radii of a circle which cut off on the circumference an arc equal in length to the radius.

The *steradian* is the solid angle which, having its vertex in the centre of a sphere, cuts off an area of the surface of the sphere equal to that of a square with sides of length equal to the radius of the sphere.

Derived Units

Most quantities that occur in nature are *derived quantities* and are measured in *derived units*. Speed is a derived quantity which can be measured in metres/sec, so that the units of speed involve the definition of two base units, *i.e.* metres and seconds. It is said that speed has the dimensions of [length]/[time], also written $[L]/[T]^{-1}$, since the metre is a measure of length and the second is a measure of time. In any equation in science the dimensions of both sides must always be the same and this is often a useful check of whether the equation is correct. If a mile = 1609·3 metre and an hour = 3600 sec, one mile/hr = 1609·3/3600 m s⁻¹. Conversions between any unit and any other unit which measures the same quantity can be similarly obtained.

Table I gives a list of some important derived quantities that occur in nature and in the fourth column the SI unit that is used to measure it. Some of these derived units have a name (usually that of a famous scientist) and a symbol which are given in the second and third columns. Thus for example, the SI unit of force is a kilogram metre sec⁻², but this unit is also given the name of a newton. A force of 5 kg m s⁻² is 5 newton, which is sometimes written "5N".

Multiples and Fractions of Units

Within the SI system there are special prefixes for forming multiples and sub-multiples of its units.

Factor by which the unit is multiplied	Prefix	Symbol
10¹²	tera	T
10⁹	giga	G
10⁶	mega	M
10³	kilo	k
10²	hecto	h
10	deca	da
10⁻¹	deci	d
10⁻²	centi	c
10⁻³	milli	m
10⁻⁶	micro	μ
10⁻⁹	nano	n
10⁻¹²	pico	p
10⁻¹⁵	femto	f
10⁻¹⁸	atto	a

Examples: one thousandth of a metre is one millimetre (1 mm); one million volts is one megavolt (1 MV). These prefixes are *recommended* but other multiples and sub-multiples will be used when convenient, *e.g.*, the centimetre (cm), the cubic decimetre (dm³).

The following is a selection of special points to note:

    (i) The name litre now means 1 cubic decimetre or 10⁻³m³ and is a measure of volume.

    (ii) Days, hours, and minutes are still used to measure time, though some scientists may prefer to use kiloseconds, etc.

    (iii) The SI unit of plane angle is the radian (rad), but degrees, minutes and seconds are still used as well. $1° = \dfrac{\pi}{180}$ rad.; 1 rad $= 57·295\ 78° = 57°\ 7'\ 44·81''$

    (iv) A Celsius temperature, say 15 degrees, is written 15°C; note that 15C would mean 15 coulombs.

The Imperial System of Units

The SI system is not the only system of units in use today, although it is the one most favoured by scientists. The Imperial system is widely used in the U.K. and other English speaking countries and some Imperial weights and measures are given below:

Length.

1 nail	= 2¼ in	
1 link	= 7·92 in	
12 in	= 1 ft	
3 ft	= 1 yd	
22 yd	= 1 chain	
10 chains	= 1 furlong	
8 furlongs	= 1 mile = 1760 yd = 5280 ft	

Area.

1210 yd²	= 1 rood
4 roods	= 1 acre = 4840 yd²
640 acres	= 1 mile²

Volume.

1728 in³ = 1 ft³
27 ft³ = 1 yd³

Capacity.

4 gills	= 1 pint
2 pints	= 1 quart
4 quarts	= 1 gallon
2 gallons	= 1 peck
4 pecks	= 1 bushel
8 bushels	= 1 quarter
36 bushels	= 1 chaldron
1 gal	= 277·274 in³

Weight (Avoirdupois).
(System used in commerce)

1 dram	= 27·343 75 grains
16 drams	= 1 oz = 437·5 grains
16 oz	= 1 lb = 7000 grains
14 lb	= 1 stone
28 lb	= 1 quarter
4 quarters	= 1 cwt = 112 lb
20 cwt	= ton = 2240 lb

Troy Weight.

1 pennyweight	= 24 grains
480 grains	= 1 ounce

The only unit of troy weight which is legal for use in trade in Britain is the ounce Troy, and weighings of precious metal are made in multiples and decimals of this unit.

The term *carat* is not a unit of weight for precious metals, but is used to denote the quality of gold plate, etc., and is a figure indicating the number of 24ths of pure gold in the alloy, *e.g.*, a 9 carat gold ring consists of nine parts of pure gold and fifteen parts of base metals.

Nautical Measures.

1 nautical mile = 6080 ft = 1853·18 m
1 knot = 1 nautical mile per hour = 1·151 mile/h

Note.—In future the international nautical mile of 1852 m will be used.

Note.—The British Pharmaceutical Code and the

British National Formulary—the official works of medicinal reference—no longer contain the apothecaries' units of measurement since medicine is now measured in metric units. Prescriptions are in 5 millilitre (*ml*) units; medicine bottles are in six sizes from 50 to 500 m*l*.

Selected Conversions between Units

Length

1 inch	= 2·54 cm
1 foot	= 30·48 cm
1 yard	= 0·9144 m
1 mile	= 1609·344 m
1 fathom	= 6 feet
1 nautical mile	= 1852 m
1 fermi	= 1 fm (femtometre)
1 X unit	= 0·1002 pm (picometre)
1 angstrom	= 100 pm
1 micron	= 1 μ m
1 astronomical unit	= 149·6 Gm
1 light year	= 9460·70 Tm
1 parsec	= 30,857 Tm
	= 3·26 light years

For Angstrom, Light year, Parsec, Astronomical Unit *see* **Section L.**

Area.

1 hectare (ha)	= 10^4 m2 = 2·471 acre
1 acre	= 0·404686 ha
1 acre	= 4840 yd² which is approximately 70 yards square
1 mile²	= 258·999 ha = 2·58999 km²
1 barn	= 10^{28} m² (measure of nuclear cross-section)

Volume.

1 litre (l)	= 0.001 m³
1 gallon UK	= 4.546 092 l
1 gallon UK is the volume of 10 lb water at 62° F	
1 pint	= 0.568 l which is approximately 4/7 l
1 gallon US	= 0.8327 gallon UK

Mass and Weight

1 oz	= 0·02835 kg
1 lb	= 0·453 592 37 kg
1 cwt	= 50·80 kg
1 ton	= 2240 lb = 1016 kg = 1·016 tonne
1 tonne	= 1000 kg

Angle

		degree	minute	second	radian	revolution
1 degree	=	1	60	3600	$1·745 \times 10^{-2}$	$2·778 \times 10^{-3}$
1 minute	=	$1·667 \times 10^{-2}$	1	60	$2·909 \times 10^{-4}$	$4·630 \times 10^{-5}$
1 second	=	$2·778 \times 10^{-4}$	$1·667 \times 10^{-2}$	1	$4·848 \times 10^{-6}$	$7·716 \times 10^{-7}$
1 radian	=	57·30	3438	$2·063 \times 10^5$	1	0·1592
1 revolution	=	360	$2·16 \times 10^4$	$1·296 \times 10^6$	6·283	1

1 rt angle = 90°   1 grade = 0·01 rt angle

Time

		second	minute	hour	solar day	year
1 second	=	1	$1·667 \times 10^{-2}$	$2·778 \times 10^{-4}$	$1·157 \times 10^{-5}$	$3·169 \times 10^{-8}$
1 minute	=	60	1	$1·667 \times 10^{-2}$	$6·944 \times 10^{-4}$	$1·901 \times 10^{-6}$
1 hour	=	3600	60	1	$4·167 \times 10^{-2}$	$1·141 \times 10^{-4}$
1 solar day	=	86400	1440	24	1	$2·738 \times 10^{-3}$
1 year	=	$3·156 \times 10^7$	525,900	8766	365·24	1

Force

		newton	dyne	poundal	kg force	pound force
1 newton	=	1	10^5	7·233	0·1020	0·2248
1 dyne	=	10^{-5}	1	$7·233 \times 10^{-5}$	$1·020 \times 10^{-6}$	$2·248 \times 10^{-6}$
1 poundal	=	0·1383	13830	1	0·01410	0·03108
1 kg force	=	9·807	980700	70·93	1	2·205
1 lb force	=	4·448	$4·448 \times 10^5$	32·17	0·4536	1

Energy, Work, Heat

		joule	kW . hr	ft lb	calory	B.t.u
1 joule	=	1	$2·778 \times 10^{-7}$	0·7376	0·2389	$9·478 \times 10^{-4}$
1 kW. hr	=	$3·600 \times 10^6$	1	$2·655 \times 10^6$	$8·598 \times 10^5$	3412
1 ft lb	=	1·356	$3·766 \times 10^{-7}$	1	0·3238	$1·285 \times 10^{-3}$
1 calory	=	4·187	$1·163 \times 10^{-6}$	3·088	1	$3·968 \times 10^{-3}$
1 B.t.u.	=	1055	$2·931 \times 10^{-4}$	778·2	252	1

1 kW. hr (kilowatt hour) is 1 unit (Board of Trade unit) as measured by the electricity meter.
   1 B.t.u. is a British thermal unit and is the amount of heat required to raise the temperature of 1 lb of water by 1° Fahrenheit.
   1 Therm is 100 000 B.t.u. and is equivalent to the heat generated by 29·3 units of electricity.
   1 calorie is the heat required to raise the temperature of 1 gm of water by 1° C. The calorie as used by weightwatchers is actually 1000 calories as defined above.
   1 erg is 10^{-7} joule.
   1 electron volt (eV) is $1·6 \times 10^{-19}$ joule.

Pressure

	pascal	millibar	atmosphere	torr	lb/sq in
1 pascal	= 1	0·01	$9·869 \times 10^{-6}$	$7·501 \times 10^{-3}$	$1·450 \times 10^{-4}$
1 millibar	= 100	1	$9·869 \times 10^{-4}$	0·7501	0·01450
1 atmosphere	= 101 300	1013	1	760	14·7
1 torr	= 133·3	1·333	$1·316 \times 10^{-3}$	1	0·01934
1 lb/sq in	= 6895	68·95	0·06805	51·72	1

1 pascal = 1 newton/sq metre = 10 dyne/sq cm
1 torr is the pressure due to 1 mm of mercury.
By atmosphere is meant "standard atmosphere" which is 760 mm or 29·92 inches of mercury.

Temperature

The Celsius scale is the same as the Centigrade scale. To convert from degrees Fahrenheit (°F) to degrees Celsius (°C), subtract 32 from the temperature in Fahrenheit and multiply by 5/9. To convert from Celsius to Fahrenheit multiply the temperature in Celsius by 9/5 and add 32. Applying this rule we obtain:

0° C = 32° F	20° C = 68° F
5° C = 41° F	25° C = 77° F
10° C = 50° F	30° C = 86° F
15° C = 59° F	35° C = 95° F

37° C (normal body temperature) is 98·6 ° F, − 40° C = − 40° F.

The absolute zero temperature (lowest possible temperature) is − 273·15° C.
To convert from ° C to degrees Kelvin (° K) add 273·15 to the temperature in Celsius so that the absolute zero is 0° K.
To obtain the temperature according to the Rankine scale add 459·69 to the temperature in Fahrenheit. 0° Rankine is the absolute zero.

The c.g.s System in Electromagnetism

The centimetre gram second (c.g.s.) system of units is favoured by some scientists (notably theoretical physicists). There are in fact two sets of c.g.s. units: electrostatic units (e.s.u.) and electromagnetic units (e.m.u.). Electrostatic units are sometimes given the prefix *stat* and electromagnetic units sometimes given the prefix *ab*. Thus voltage can be measured in statvolts (e.s.u.) or abvolts (e.m.u.) as well as in volts (S.I.).

These two systems do not normally treat charge or current as base quantities as the S.I. system does but as derived quantities. In the electrostatic system the unit of electric charge, the statcoulomb is defined so that one statcoulomb of charge placed at a distance of 1 cm from another statcoulomb of electric charge in a vacuum repels it with a force of 1 dyne. In the electromagnetic system the abampere is such that if two parallel wires in a vacuum 1 cm apart both carry a current of 1 abampere the force between them is 2 dynes per cm length of wire. Also the force between two magnetic poles of unit strength one centimetre apart in a vacuum is one dyne. These two systems usually treat permittivity and permeability as dimensionless quantities, unlike the S.I. system.

In the table below $c = 2·997 \ 925 \times 10^{10}$ and is the speed of light in cm s^{-1}.
The symbol "$\simeq$" means "is approximately equal to".
Thus $c \simeq 3 \times 10^{10}$ cm s^{-1}.

Quantity	S.I. Unit		e.m.u.	e.s.u.
Current	ampere	A	1 abampere = 10A	1 statampere = 1 abamp/c 1 amp $\simeq 3 \times 10^9$ statamp
Charge	coulomb	C	1 abcoulomb = 10 C	1 statcoulomb = 1 abcoulomb/c
EMF	volt	V	1 abvolt = 10^{-8} V	1 statvolt = c abvolt $\simeq$ 300 V
Capacitance	farad	F	1 abfarad = 10^9 F	1 statfarad = 1 abfarad $\times$ c^{-2} 1 F $\simeq 9 \times 10^{11}$ statfarad
Permittivity	F m^{-1}			1 e.s.u./1 S.I.U. = $10^{11}/(4\pi c^2)$. Since the permittivity of a vacuum in e.s.u. is 1 this is equivalent to saying the permittivity of a vacuum in S.I. units = $10^{11}/(4\pi c^2) \simeq 1/(36\pi \times 10^9$.
Magnetic field	A m^{-1}		1 oersted (e.m.u.) = $10^3/(4\pi)$ Am^{-1}	
Magnetic flux density	tesla	T	1 gauss (e.m.u.) = 10^{-4} tesla. 1 gauss is equivalent to a magnetic field of 1 oersted in a vacuum	
Magnetic flux	weber	Wb	1 maxwell (e.m.u.) = 10^{-8} Wb	
Inductance (self or mutual)	henry	H	1 abhenry = 10^{-9}H	
Permeability	H m^{-1}		1 e.m.u./1 S.I.U. = $4\pi \times 10^{-7}$. Since the permeability of a vacuum in e.m.u. is 1, this equivalent to saying the permeability of a vacuum in SI units = $4\pi \times 10^{-7}$.	

Units Related To Radioactivity

Radioactivity is the spontaneous disintegration of atomic nuclei to form lighter nuclei and to simultaneously emit fast moving particles. These particles are usually either a particles, electrons, neutrons, X rays or γ rays, the latter two being photons. These particles constitute radiation and can have a profound effect on the materials through which they pass, $e.g.$ causing cancer in humans. Units are required to define the amount of radioactivity, exposure to radiation, absorbed dose of radiation and effective absorbed dose of radiation by human tissue.

The SI unit of radioactivity is the *bequerel* (Bq), which is the number of disintegrations per second. It is a measure of the amount of radioactive material present.

The emitted particles cause ionisation in a substance through which they pass. If this substance is a gas an electric field can be used to collect the ionised particles at electrodes before they recombine and enable the amount of ionisation produced to be measured. The number of SI units of exposure to radiation is the number of coulombs of electricity that would be produced in a kilogram of dry air by the radiation. The SI unit of exposure to radiation is the *coulomb* per kilogram.

Since the particles are fast moving they have energy. If they are absorbed by the medium through which they pass this energy is transmitted to the medium. The number of SI units of absorbed dose of radiation is the number of joules produced in a kilogram of this medium. The SI unit of absorbed dose of radiation is called the *gray* (Gy).

Some of the absorbed particles have more effect on human tissue than others. Each type of particle has a factor and the effective absorbed dose of radiation is the absorbed dose times the quality factor (g.v.) which is a weighted sum of the quality factors for each of the component particles. For a particles q.v. = 20, for neutrons q.v. = 10, for electrons, X rays and γ rays q.v. = 1. The SI unit of effective absorbed radiation dose is called the Sievert (Sv).

$$\text{Number of Sv} = \text{Number of Gy} \times \text{q.v.}$$

Non SI units are also used to measure these quantities. The conversions are as follows:

1 Curie (Ci) $= 3.7 \times 10^{10}$ Bg,
1 Roentgen (R) $= 2.58 \times 10^{-4}$ C kg^{-1}
1 rad $= 10^{-2}$ Gy
1 Roentgen Equivalent Man (REM) $= 10^{-2}$ Sv

Quantity units	Name of SI unit	Symbol	SI unit in terms of base or derived
Radioactivity, disintegrations per second	becquerel	Bq	s^{-1}
Exposure to radiation	coulomb/kilogram		C kg^{-1}
Absorbed dose of radiation, joule/kilogram	gray	Gy	J kg^{-1}
Effective radiation dose absorbed by tissue	sievert	Sv	J kg^{-1}

BACKGROUND TO ECONOMIC EVENTS

The aim of this section is to help the ordinary reader to follow economic events as they happen, and to understand the controversies that accompany them. Special Topics in this edition look at the economic consequences of German reunification and the European Monetary System.

TABLE OF CONTENTS

BACKGROUND TO
ECONOMIC EVENTS

This section is divided into five parts. Part I gives a brief description of the most important problems of economic policy. Part II is concerned with a more detailed survey of the British economy and the way in which it operates. In the course of this survey, the specialised terms used by economists are explained, and the attempt is made to present an intelligible summary of the information, facts and figures relevant to an understanding of economic events. There are five main sub-sections: International Trade and Payments; Employment, Production, and Industry; Incomes, Wages, and Prices; Money, Banking, and Finance; and Economic Aspects of the Public Services. Part III outlines the main economic problems faced by the less developed countries, and the economic policies of Britain and other developed countries towards the less developed world. Some suggestions for further reading are given at the end of Parts II and III. Part IV is written as shortly before publication as possible, and contains a survey of recent developments in the British economy. Part V examines subjects of particular topicality.

I. CENTRAL PROBLEMS OF ECONOMIC POLICY

Why Economists Disagree.

On many of the most important issues Economics is in a state of disarray. Economic problems are in general as serious as they have ever been, yet the economics profession is more divided now than ever on the diagnosis of the problems and on the prescriptions for economic policy. Why is this the case?

It is important to distinguish between *positive* and *normative* economics, *i.e.*, between consideration of how the economy actually works and of how it ought to be made to work. Even if economists were unanimous in their understanding of the economy, different economists might nevertheless prescribe conflicting policies because they made different moral or political judgements. For instance, macroeconomic policy prescriptions might depend crucially on the relative strength of one's dislike for the two evils, inflation and unemployment. But disagreement among economists is not only about goals and objectives. In macroeconomics, the "Keynesian consensus" which held sway in the 1950s and 1960s gave way in the 1970s and 1980s to a variety of different schools of thought. This development reflected changes in the economy and the emergence of new and more pressing economic problems: a rise in the rates of inflation and unemployment and a fall in the rate of economic growth. The accepted analysis and prescriptions were found wanting. At the simplest level, the disputing schools divide into the *New Keynesians*, on the one hand, and the *Monetarists*, or *New Classical* school, on the other.

The two major political parties in Britain have, in the 1980s, been committed to extreme and radically different approaches to the solution of Britain's economic problems. The Conservative Government, in office since 1979, has placed its faith in *laissez faire* economics, in the efficient operation of market forces, and in Monetarist policies. The Labour Party does not accept that the uncontrolled play of market forces would be beneficial, and it has favoured Keynesian reflation and a major expansion of state activity and state control. In part, these different approaches are based on differences in economic analysis. For instance, the parties might disagree on what would be the consequences of import controls, or of incomes policy, or of running a budget deficit, or of reducing unemployment benefits. However, much of the disagreement is really based on differences in objectives, or on ideological considerations. Policies based on ideology or slogans can be dangerous. A great disservice is done by those who claim to have simple answers to what in reality are complex problems.

Economic relationships are complicated and changeable, and normally difficult to measure. Economists cannot conduct rigorous experiments in the way that natural scientists do. Everything is happening at once in an economy, and the influence of any one variable is not easy to isolate, even with the use of sophisticated statistical techniques. This is another reason why economists disagree, and why they should always bear in mind the limitations of their knowledge.

Are Economists Useful?

Given their disagreements and the limitations of their knowledge, can economists perform a useful function? In the 1985 Reith Lectures, concerned with the influence of economic ideas on economic policy, David Henderson complained about the influence of what he called *do-it-yourself economics*. Over wide areas of policy the judgements of politicians and their officials, as also public opinion in general, are guided by beliefs and perceptions about the workings of the economy which owe little or nothing to the economics profession. The amateurs have not been driven from the field, and they are often in control of policy.

According to Henderson, do-it-yourself economics is based on peoples' intuitions and tends to be interventionist: politicians like to be active and to be seen to be active. These intuitions rarely extend beyond the immediate effects of the intervention, whereas professional economists analyse the less obvious, indirect and often unintended effects of interventions, which take place through the response of market forces. To give a simple example, rent controls appear to tackle the ill-effects of housing shortage but, by deterring investment in housing, they may exacerbate the shortage. Or mortgage interest tax relief may be electorally popular, but the economist's approach is to trace its consequences through to the end of the chain—higher house prices, losers as well as gainers, and less resources for non-housing. The professional approach is generally more quantitative than that of the amateur. Economists *can* often be useful, but their advice is ignored more frequently by policy-makers than that of, say, lawyers or engineers.

The Objectives of Economic Policy.

The central issues of economic policy concern certain desirable objectives. One important objective is the avoidance of unemployment. Between the wars, mass unemployment was Britain's most urgent problem: unemployment caused waste, hardship and poverty. After 1945, the maintenance of full employment was accepted as a primary objective of economic policy by all political parties. Until the late 1960s less than 2 per cent of the labour force was unemployed.

Unemployment can be either *cyclical* or *structural*. Cyclical unemployment, arising from a lack of demand in the economy, can be tackled by Government measures to increase total spending in the economy. Structural unemployment arises from a misallocation of resources. In the 1970s and 1980s structural unemployment grew as redundancies

rocketed in the increasingly uncompetitive manufacturing sector, *e.g.*, motor and engineering industries, and in declining industries such as steel and
coal. Moreover, cyclical unemployment grew as
world economic recession set in and deflationary
policies were introduced at home.

With the emergence during the last decade of new
and greater problems of inflation, the commitment
to full employment first faltered and then was withdrawn. The concern that has daunted Governments
in recent years is that expansionary policies to eliminate cyclical unemployment might fuel a spiral of
inflation. Between 1983 and 1987 unemployment
exceeded the figure of 3 million, or 11 per cent of
the labour force.

A second objective of economic policy has been
the cure of inflation. Between 1960 and 1970 retail
prices increased on average by 4·4 per cent per
annum; between 1970 and 1980 the inflation rate
averaged no less than 14 per cent per annum; and
between 1980 and 1989 by 5·7 per cent per annum.
Inflation can be harmful in various ways. It is associated with an arbitrary redistribution of purchasing power. Prices rise for everyone but some groups
in society are better able to protect themselves
against inflation. The feeling that particular groups
are falling behind is a source of much unrest and
discontent. Moreover, the general economic uncertainty that inflation brings can become a threat to
economic prosperity.

Two main explanations have been advanced to
account for inflation. The first stresses the role of
excess demand or spending power in the economy—
of too much money chasing too few goods. Such
demand-pull theories are put forward by Monetarists, who point to increases in the money supply in
generating demand, and by Keynesians who recommend restrictive monetary and fiscal policies
to curb excess demand, when it arises. The second
explanation stresses the role of excessive increases in costs, *e.g.*, wage costs or imported
raw material costs, in raising prices. Such *cost-push*
theories imply, for instance, that policies are
needed to restrain the power of trade unions to
raise wages. Neither explanation precludes the
other: both demand-pull and cost-push factors are
likely to have contributed—with different
strengths at different times—to inflation. Moreover, adherents of both views recognise that, once
expectations of continued inflation become entrenched, these expectations themselves sustain and
fuel the inflation.

A third objective of economic policy is the fostering of economic growth. Successive British Governments in the post-war period have tried to raise the
growth rate—the most important long run determinant of the standard of living. Britain's living
standards have until recently been rising: output per
head of population increased annually by 2 per cent
between 1960 and 1970, by 1·5 per cent between
1970 and 1980 and by 2·6 per cent per annum between 1980 and 1989. Nevertheless, the British
growth rate compares unfavourably with that
achieved by most other industrial countries.

The determinants of economic growth are not well
understood, but most economists would agree that
in order to raise the growth rate it is necessary to
encourage the community to save, and businessmen
to invest, a higher proportion of the national
income. In a fully employed economy the source of
increased output is higher productivity, *i.e.*, output
per worker. There is a danger, however, that higher
productivity growth will be achieved at the
expense of employment, as has largely been the case
in Britain since 1980.

A constraint on the achievement of the above
objectives has been the need to maintain balance
in international payments. The British balance of
payments position has been precarious, so that unfavourable turns of events have precipitated economic crises. Indeed, concern about the balance of
payments so dominated economic policy-making at

times during the post-war period that improvement
in the balance of payments became a major objective of policy. The objective has normally been to
achieve a surplus in order to pay off international
debts, build up external assets by investing abroad,
and provide development aid to less developed
countries.

The expansion in the late 1970s of North Sea oil
production, and the resulting confidence of foreign
investors, transformed the British balance of payments. But this created new problems, particularly
the adverse effect of the ensuing high exchange rate
on manufacturing, our traditional export sector and
an important employer of labour.

The Inter-relationship of Economic Problems.

The achievement of each of the objectives briefly
described above is extremely complex. The difficulties are further aggravated by the fact that
the problems are inter-related in such a way that
measures which are helpful for one objective can
make others more difficult to achieve. For example, a reduction of purchasing power might be
considered helpful in the control of inflation,
and might ease balance of payments problems by
reducing—or slowing down the increase of—imports. But it could also lead to an increase in unemployment, and to a slowing down in the rate of
growth of the economy. Many economic commentators now hold that it is no longer possible to
keep unemployment down to the levels of the
1950s and 1960s without unleashing cumulative
inflation, and that the control of inflation must
now have the highest priority. This must be the
rationale for the economic policies of the Conservative Government in office since 1979, as it
has paid little heed to the short run effects of its
policies on unemployment and economic growth. In
1980 the Government faced an inflation rate of 18
per cent and an unemployment rate of 6 per cent.
By 1987 it had got inflation down, to below 4 per
cent, but unemployment had risen to 11 per cent.

There are other examples of a conflict in policy
objectives. For instance, while the advent in the
1970s of a floating exchange rate helps to correct
the balance of payments, a depreciating pound can
in turn fuel inflation. If import controls were
introduced to protect the manufacturing sector,
this in turn would be liable to harm developing
countries.

The Worsening Economic Climate.

In the mid-1970s, after 30 years of rapid
growth and unprecedented prosperity for the
major Western economies, the prospects for continued growth became much less favourable.
This resulted partly from the acceleration of
inflation in many countries, bringing with it
insecurity and militancy in industrial relations.
However, the main cause was the remarkable
increase in the price of oil in 1973 and again in
1979, a fuel on which the Western economies had
become heavily dependent. This produced a strong
burst of inflation; and, because much of the oil
revenue accruing to producers could not be spent,
gave rise to an unprecedented balance of payments
problem and severe world recession. There was a
danger that, through a lack of international co-
ordination and of business confidence and through
misplaced attempts by countries to cure their
immediate economic problems by means of deflation, mass unemployment on the scale of the 1930s
would again appear. The international infecti-
ousness of high interest rates, economic recession
and rapid inflation made it hard for any one
country to avoid these ills. In the changing situation both the problems of economic policy and
the inter-relationships between them became more
difficult.

II. SURVEY OF THE BRITISH ECONOMY

1. INTERNATIONAL TRADE AND PAYMENTS

International Trade.
(i) Imports and Exports.

In 1988 the United Kingdom bought from abroad goods to the value of £106 billion (thousand million), or about £1,850 per head. Food accounted for 10 per cent of this total, raw materials and fuels another 11 per cent, and semi-manufactured goods bought for further processing 27 per cent. The biggest item was finished manufactures, which accounted for just over half of the total. This category of imports had increased sharply over a couple of decades. In 1968 finished manufactures were only a fifth and and non-manufactures were over half of total imports. All this can be seen in the table, which compares 1968 with the most recent year, 1988.

There are three main determinants of the level of British imports. One is the competitiveness of British with foreign producers. Britain imports those commodities which—at the ruling exchange rate between the pound and foreign currencies—can be bought more cheaply from foreign than from home producers. Secondly, the level of imports depends on the extent to which free trade is prevented by tariffs on imported goods or by other devices. Thirdly, as total incomes in the economy expand, there is a general increase in the demand for goods and services including imports. There-fore imports can be expected to vary with the total incomes in the country, known as the *national income*.

UNITED KINGDOM IMPORTS AND EXPORTS

Imports of goods (c.i.f.)	£ millon		Percentage of total	
	1968	1988	1968	1988
Food, drink, and tobacco	1.900	10,590	24	10
Basic materials	1,207	5,991	15	6
Fuels and lubri-cants	902	5,058	11	5
Semi-manu-factures	2,119	28,898	27	27
Finished manu-factures	1,653	54,465	21	51
TOTAL*	7,900	106,413	100	100
Exports of goods (f.o.b.)				
Food, drink, and tobacco	430	5,537	7	7
Basic materials	232	2,121	4	3
Fuels and lubri-cants	168	5,818	3	7
Engineering products	2,657	31,886	41	39
Other manu-factured goods	2,756	34,150	43	43
TOTAL*	6,442	81,476	100	100

*The column figures do not add up exactly to the totals because the latter include unclassified inputs.

Whereas in 1968 imports amounted to 23 per cent of national income, in 1988 the proportion was 31 per cent. One reason for this rise is the liberalisation of trade among the industrialised countries during the post-war period, and the tendency for trade in manufactures among these countries to increase. An example is the formation of the *European Economic Community* in 1956 and Britain's entry to it in January 1973. Another reason is the great

increase in the price of oil which occurred in the 1970s. Britain's oil import bill rose from £880 million in 1968 to £5·6 billion in 1976. Since then, however, North Sea oil has transformed the oil picture. Imports have fallen in volume, although they still amounted to nearly £5.1 billion in 1988, and exports have risen, to a peak of £16·7 billion in 1985 and to £5.8 billion in 1988. For most of the 1980's Britain was a net exporter of oil.

Since the exports of one country must be the imports of another, the same factors in reverse, foreign competitiveness, access to foreign markets, and the level of foreign incomes determine the level of British exports. In 1988 these amounted to over £81 billion of which no less than 82 per cent were manufactures. In 1968 it was true to say that Britain gained from trade by exporting manufac-tures, in which she had a *comparative advantage*, in return for food and raw materials, which she was not suited to produce. This is still partly true; but increasingly—with the growth of trade and specialisa-tion among the major economies—Britain gains from trade by exporting those manufactures in which her producers specialise and importing other manufactures. Among the main manufacturing exports are cars and commercial vehicles, tractors, aircraft and aircraft engines, finished steel, various forms of machinery, woollen fabrics, man-made fibres, and chemicals; among the main manu-factured imports are wood products, aluminium, newsprint, cars, and aircraft. With the expansion of British oil production, the pattern of trade con-tinued to show rapid change.

(ii) The Terms of Trade.

The value of trade increased more than twenty-fold between 1968 and 1988. This increase can be separated into two components, price and volume, of which price has been the more important. The ratio of the average price of exports to that of imports is known as the *terms of trade*; and a rise in the price of exports relative to imports indicates an improvement in the terms of trade. Thus, when we note in the table that the terms of trade deteriorated by some 11 per cent between 1968 and 1978 we mean that 11 per cent more exports by volume would have been needed in 1978 to buy the same amount of imports as in 1968. This deterioration reflected the commodity boom and the oil price increase which occurred in the 1970s.

VISIBLE TRADE: VOLUME AND PRICES

	1970 = 100	
	1968	1988
Value		
Imports	19	227
Exports	18	230
Volume		
Imports	68	170
Exports	57	139
Price		
Imports	27	168
Exports	30	170
Terms of trade	111	101

(iii) The Volume of Trade.

Superficially it would appear that any improve-ment in the terms of trade raises the value of British exports relative to imports. However, this is not always true: faster inflation in Britain, leading to a more rapid increase in export prices, would harm rather than help the balance of pay-ments. If the prices of our export goods rise faster than the prices of our competitors' in overseas markets it becomes progressively more difficult to sell our exports. Conversely, inflation in Britain makes it progressively more difficult to compete with imports. Growth in the volume of imports exceeded that in exports during the period 1968–88. The trade balance may well be harmed by a rise in the price of imported primary products (as it was in the first decade); but the balance of trade in manufactures is worsened by an improvement in their terms of trade.

In the post-war period there was a considerable fall in Britain's share of world exports; from 20 per cent of exports of manufactures in 1954 to 12 per cent in 1967, the year of sterling devaluation, and to the figure of 8 per cent in 1984. Britain's main competitors in export markets—and particularly Germany and Japan, with 18 and 20 per cent respectively in 1984—were more successful in expanding their exports. Britain's competitive position in manufacturing has been persistently eroded over the years.

The Balance of Payments.

A detailed examination of recent movements in the British *balance of payments* is made in **Part IV.**

(i) The Balance of Visible Trade.

The *balance of (visible) trade* is the difference between exports and imports of goods. It is said to be in *surplus* if exports exceed imports and in *deficit* if imports exceed exports. In estimating the balance of trade it is important that imports and exports be valued on the same basis. The normal method in the trade returns is to measure imports *c.i.f.* (cost, insurance, and freight) and exports *f.o.b.* (free on board). In other words import prices are shown to include the cost of transporting them to Britain, and exports are valued at the prices when loaded in British ports. Our table shows both imports and exports *f.o.b.*

Britain's visible balance is normally in deficit. The trade balance in 1983 was relatively small. On the other hand, the year 1987 produced the largest deficit ever recorded. In that year Britain's trade was heavily in deficit to her EC partners, to the rest of Western Europe and to Japan.

BALANCE OF PAYMENTS OF THE
UNITED KINGDOM, 1983 AND 1987
(£ million)

	1983	1987
Exports (f.o.b.) .	60,698	79,422
Imports (f.o.b.) .	61,773	89,584
Visible balance .	− 1,075	− 10,162
Invisible balance .	4,907	7,458
of which:		
services . .	3,721	5,638
interest profits and dividends .	2,847	5,523
transfers .	− 1,661	− 3,503
Current balance .	3,832	− 2,504
UK investment overseas .	− 12,610	− 8,909
Overseas investment in UK .	5,274	16,758
Net transactions of UK banks .	2,788	2,525
Other financial transactions .	− 369	599
Drawings on (+) or additions to (−) reserves .	607	− 12,012
Net transactions in assets and liabilities	− 4,310	− 1,039
Balancing item .	478	3,543

(ii) Patterns of British Trade.

West Germany and the United States are Britain's largest trading partners, each with over 11 per cent of total British trade (exports plus imports)

in 1987, followed by France, the Netherlands, Italy and Belgium. Britain's EC partners as a group accounted for no less than 51 per cent of her trade, and the rest of Western Europe for 12 per cent. The oil exporting countries as a group accounted for 4 per cent, and other less developed countries for 10 per cent of British trade in that year.

PATTERNS OF BRITISH TRADE, 1987

	British exports to: (£ billion)	British imports from: (£ billion)	Exports plus imports (as a percentage of the total)
European Community	39·4	49·6	51·2
of which:			
France	7·8	8·3	9·3
Netherlands	5·9	7·1	7·5
Belgium	3·9	4·4	4·8
Germany	9·4	15·8	14·5
Italy	4·1	5·2	5·3
Ireland	3·8	3·5	4·2
Denmark	1·2	1·9	1·8
Rest of Western Europe	7·6	12·9	11·8
of which:			
Norway	1·2	3·3	2·6
Sweden	2·3	3·0	3·0
Spain	2·2	2·1	2·5
Switzerland	1·8	3·3	2·9
United States	11·0	9·1	11·6
Canada	1·9	1·6	2·0
Japan	1·5	5·5	4·0
Australia	1·2	0·7	1·1
South Africa	0·9	0·7	0·9
Oil exporting countries	5·2	1·7	4.0
of which:			
Saudia Arabia	2·0	0·4	1·4
Nigeria	0·5	0·2	0·4
Other developing countries	8·5	9·3	10·2
of which:			
India	1·1	0·5	0·9
Hong Kong	1·0	1·5	1·4
South Korea	0·4	0·9	0·7
Centrally planned economies	1·5	2·1	2·0
of which:			
USSR	0·5	0·9	0·8
TOTAL	79·9	94·0	100·0

(iii) The Balance on Current Account.

The chronic deficit in the balance of visible trade has in normal years been offset by a surplus in the *balance of invisible trade.* This relates to international transactions in services as opposed to goods. The main components are: receipts from non-residents *less* payments to non-residents for services such as shipping, civil aviation, tourism, insurance, and financial services; receipts from foreign governments in respect of military bases in the country *less* payments by this country in respect of military bases abroad; receipts of gifts and grants made to this country, *less* gifts and grants made by this country; all receipts of interest, dividends, and profits earned on overseas investment *less* interest dividends, and profits paid out of foreign investment in this country.

The *balance on current account* is the sum of the balances on visible and invisible trade. We see that in 1983 there was a surplus and 1987 a deficit.

(iv) Capital Flow.

It is not sufficient simply to avoid deficits on current account. It has been the Government's objective to earn a surplus in order to finance investment abroad at times to repay foreign debts previously incurred and to build up reserves of gold and foreign exchange.

The capital account of the balance of payments

contains net private investment abroad (being the difference between investment abroad by United Kingdom residents and investment by foreigners in the United Kingdom). There are also large, short-term capital flows, sometimes referred to as *monetary movements.* These include bank lending and borrowing—trade credits, changes in sterling reserves held by foreign governments, and Euro-dollar transactions. Such funds can be highly volatile, moving out of a currency if there is a risk of its depreciation and into it if there is a chance of appreciation or if other currencies are suspect. Therefore, monetary movements often accentuate a surplus or deficit in the other items of the balance of payments. They are also dependent on relative rates of interest at home and abroad, being attracted to financial centres which offer high interest rates.

(v) Foreign Exchange Reserves.

A deficit on current plus capital account can be financed through an increase in liabilities, *i.e.* by government borrowing from abroad, or by a reduction in assets, *e.g.*, a depletion of the official gold and foreign-exchange reserves. The official reserves are used to finance payments abroad which cannot be financed in any other way: they are a last line of defence in international trade.

The current account surplus of 1983 was outweighed by a capital account deficit. The combined deficit was financed by drawing on the official reserves. By contrast, the current account deficit of 1987 was overshadowed by a net capital inflow, associated with high interest rates. The official reserves increased by no less than £12 billion.

The book-keeping identity of international payments and receipts requires that the flow of goods and services on current account should be precisely offset by the total *net transactions in assets and liabilities.* However, not all such transactions can be accurately recorded. In both years there was an unrecorded capital inflow, known as the *balancing item.* In 1987 the balancing item was so large (£3·5 billion) that it actually exceeded the current account deficit.

Correcting a Deficit.

If an imbalance in international payments persists, the deficit cannot be met indefinitely from official financing. At some stage the Government must take action to remove the deficit. What action can it take? There are a number of alternatives available, each with its advantages and disadvantages, and economic opinion is by no means unanimous on the choice of policy. Let us consider each of these alternatives in turn.

(i) Variation of the Exchange Rate.

The *exchange rate* is the ruling official rate of exchange of pounds for dollars or other currencies. It determines the value of British goods in relation to foreign goods. Under the post-war Bretton Woods arrangements (*see* **G9**), Britain and other countries maintained a constant value of their currencies in terms of gold, permitting only very minor fluctuations of the exchange rate about its par value. However, persistent balance of payments deficits or surpluses caused occasional adjustments of the official exchange rate, the response to persistent deficit being *devaluation* and to persistent surplus *upvaluation.* In 1972 the major countries adopted a system of fluctuating exchange rates. However, exchange rates are not permitted to fluctuate entirely freely, *i.e.*, so that the market supply and demand for foreign exchange are continuously equated. While the monetary authorities permit the foreign-exchange market to influence the exchange rate, they are prepared to intervene in the national interest to intervene in the market (by buying or selling their currency) and so to keep the exchange rate within bounds. Given some flexibility in the exchange rate, a tendency for a deficit to arise is thus met by a *depreciation* of sterling, and an incipient surplus by *appreciation.*

If the pound depreciates in terms of other currencies, British exports (which are paid for in pounds) become cheaper to foreigners and British imports

(paid for by purchasing foreign currency) become more expensive to holders of pounds. In this way a fall in the value of the pound can improve the British balance of payments position by encouraging exports and discouraging imports.

But there are certain disadvantages attached to depreciation. The prospect of depreciation results in a speculative outflow of capital funds: and one fall may be taken as a sign that there will be a further fall in the future. Moreover, the rise in the price of imports of raw materials and consumption goods results in higher costs and prices and then in wage demands to maintain the British standard of living. It is possible that inflation will in this way neutralise the beneficial effects of depreciation.

The probable effect of a depreciation in Britain is initially to *worsen* the balance of trade, because the sterling price of imports is likely to be raised by more than that of exports. After about six months the effect of the depreciation on quantities —curbing imports and expanding the volume of exports—dominates, and the balance of trade improves. However, the improvement is maintained only if fiscal and monetary or incomes policies can prevent the fall in sterling from feeding through to domestic prices and costs and so both neutralising the gain in competitiveness and exacerbating inflation.

The pound was devalued in 1949, when an official exchange rate of £1 = $2·8 was established, and again in 1967, to a rate of £1 = $2·4. After the devaluation of the dollar in December 1971, the exchange rate with dollars became £1 = $2·6. After June 1972 the value of sterling in relation to other currencies was allowed to *float.* With widespread floating, an *effective exchange rate* is now calculated, which shows the value of sterling in relation to a bundle of other currencies, with each currency receiving a weight according to the extent of trade with Britain. This rate fluctuated from month to month, but with a strong downward tendency until 1977, followed by a recovery until 1980 due mainly to the advent of North Sea oil, and a subsequent fall interrupted only in 1987. With the exchange rate equal to 100 in 1975, the weighted average value of sterling moved as follows:

1972	1977	1980	1981	1982	1983
123·5	81·2	96·1	95·3	90·7	83·3

1984	1985	1986	1987	1988	1989
78·8	78·4	71·7	70·6	74·9	65·0

(ii) Exchange Controls and Convertibility.

A currency is fully *convertible* if it can be freely exchanged for any other currency at the ruling rates of exchange. Exchange controls impose restrictions on convertibility. In the early post-war period there was a world-wide shortage of dollars: if sterling had been convertible, there would have been a rush to obtain dollars, with the consequence that Britain's reserves would soon have been exhausted.

Exchange controls on residents can be enforced by requiring that earnings of foreign currencies (*e.g.*, the proceeds from the sale of exports) be handed over to the exchange control authority in return for domestic currency; and by permitting the exchange of domestic for foreign currency (*e.g.*, to enable the purchase of imports) only for transactions approved by the exchange control authority. By restricting convertibility the Government can make it more difficult for funds to move into or out of the country.

Foreign exchange control has become a less feasible policy as a result of the revolution in information technology. The explosion in the way in which funds can be transferred and intermediation of all kinds can take place makes such controls increasingly impractical for any reasonably sophisticated economy (*see* **Part IV**).

(iii) Import Controls and Tariffs.

Import controls impose limitations on the quantity or value of goods which are permitted to enter a country; tariffs are duties levied on imported goods so that the price of those goods to consumers in a country is higher than the price received by the foreigners supplying the goods.

In the early post-war years. Britain maintained strict import controls over a wide range of goods. These were gradually dismantled during the 1950s.

All countries impose tariffs. Some tariffs are primarily intended to raise revenue for the Government, and others are primarily intended to protect home industries by raising the price of competing goods from abroad. The rights of countries to raise tariffs, or to operate tariffs in a discriminatory way (*i.e.*, to offer lower tariffs on goods from some sources than on similar goods from other sources), are closely circumscribed by the rules of the *General Agreement on Tariffs and Trade* (GATT). The object of the GATT is to work towards free trade, especially through a reduction in tariffs. The disadvantage of introducing import controls or tariffs to correct a deficit in the balance of payments is that the benefits of free trade are lost. Moreover, there is always the possibility of retaliation by trading partners. Yet, import controls or tariffs may well be preferable to another measure which has been used to correct a deficit, deflation.

Britain's powers to impose tariffs and quotas on imports were greatly circumscribed in 1973 by her accession to the European Economic Community, since this requires free trade within the Community and a common external tariff.

(iv) Deflation.

Until the late 1970s the U.K. balance of payments was far from secure. As a result, domestic economic policies were much influenced by balance of payments considerations. Devaluation was turned to only as a last resort. The movement in the 1950s and 1960s was towards greater freedom of trade. By ruling out devaluation and trade restrictions, the authorities had to fall back on *deflation* of the economy to correct periodic deficits. In other words, the Government took measures to discourage demand and so cut back incomes and employment. By reducing demand in general, the authorities secured a fall in demand for imports. However, it was necessary to cut back national income by many times the ensuing fall in imports. Deflation is a painful method of correcting a deficit: not only does it have a direct effect on the level of incomes and employment, but it is also liable to slow down the rate of growth of the economy. This can happen because deflation can weaken the incentive to expand productive capacity by investing.

(v) International Trade Flows.

We can divide the world into four trading groups: the industrial countries (mainly OECD), the oil-producing developing countries (OPEC), the other developing countries, and the communist countries. In 1985 the industrial countries accounted for 66 per cent of total world exports, 48 per cent being exports to countries within that group, 4 per cent to oil producers, 13 per cent to developing countries, and 3 per cent to communist countries. Over two-thirds of the industrial countries' exports were manufactured products. The oil exports of the oil producers amounted to 18 per cent of world exports, 12 per cent going to the industrial countries. 55 per cent of the exports of the other developing countries were primary products. Their exports amounted to 16 per cent of the world total, most going to the industrial countries. The communist group exported 9 per cent of the world total, half of which was traded within the group. Of the total world exports, 56 per cent were manufactures, 20 per cent fuels and 22 per cent primary products.

The International Monetary System.

(i) International Liquidity.

Imbalance in payments between countries is financed by transfers of gold or foreign-exchange reserves. These reserves are known as *international liquidity*. Their basic characteristic is general acceptability: they can perform their function only if they retain the confidence of those engaged in international transactions. In addition, countries in difficulty can finance international payments by means of their drawing rights on the International Monetary Fund (IMF). Each of these will be described below.

The amount of international liquidity required depends on various factors. One is the proneness of the international economy to sharp changes in the balance of payments among countries: high and variable rates of inflation and fluctuations in the oil price since the early 1970s have strengthened the need for liquidity. A second factor, having the same effect, is the remarkable increase that has occurred in international flows of short-term funds. Offsetting these, however, is the greater flexibility of exchange rates in recent years: the need for international liquidity would in principle be eliminated in a world of completely freely fluctuating exchange rates.

(ii) The International Monetary Fund.

The *International Monetary Fund* was set up at Bretton Woods in 1944 with the object of working towards free trade at stable exchange rates. Under the original agreement establishing the Fund, members agreed to make their currencies convertible into other currencies and gold at fixed rates of exchange, and agreed not to impose exchange or import controls without the permission of the Fund.

The function of the Fund is to make foreign-exchange resources available to members which run into balance of payments difficulties. Each member country has a deposit (called its quota), paid partly in gold and partly in its own currency, with the Fund. The size of the deposit is fixed in relation to the country's share in world trade. In return, it is granted certain automatic drawing rights, which entitle it to borrow foreign currencies from the Fund. The Fund has power to make larger loans, and to grant standby credits to be drawn on if required. Before the Fund will make such loans and credits available it has to be satisfied that the borrowing country is taking appropriate action to correct the balance-of-payments disequilibrium.

(iii) Gold.

Gold played a central role in the international monetary system during the 1950s and 1960s. Central banks were prepared to buy and sell gold at a fixed price in terms of their currencies, and gold was exchanged among them in settlement of imbalances. The price of gold was held for many years at $35 per fine ounce. However, this fixed price in the face of rising costs of gold production meant that gold supply could not increase rapidly enough to provide the international liquidity needed to finance expanding world trade.

It was not clear, however, that an increased price of gold was the best solution to this problem. First, it would help those countries most which needed help least—those with large gold reserves. It would represent a victory for gold hoarders and speculators, and so act as a stimulus to further hoarding and speculation in the future; the United States had no incentive to help in particular the gold-producing countries Russia and South Africa; and finally, it would represent a sheer waste of economic resources: gold had no intrinsic value. The *demonetisation* of gold is described in **Part IV.**

(iv) An International Currency?

The domestic currency of the United Kingdom is not backed by gold: on a ten-pound note the Governor of the Bank of England promises to pay the bearer on demand the sum of ten pounds—merely another note! Yet, within Britain, there is complete confidence in the currency, because it is generally acceptable and so convertible into goods and services. Just as gold no longer backs the domestic currency, there is no need for gold in settlement of international payments. All we need is a generally acceptable international currency, *i.e.*, one in which all countries have confidence.

Such a currency could be created by an international authority constituted for this purpose; and it could be made available to deficit countries, which could then pay their creditors in the new currency. In this way the shortage of international liquidity could be made good, and indeed gold—Keynes' "barbarous relic"—could be supplanted. There are various difficulties with such a scheme. It involves some loss of national autonomy and the vesting of considerable power in the international authority issuing the paper currency. Decisions have to be made as to which countries should receive the new currency, and in what quantities. And there is a fear that it will enable reckless governments to pursue inflationary policies without the discipline imposed by shortage of reserves, and that their inflation will be infectious.

The very limited steps towards the creation of an international currency—the issue by the IMF of small quantities of *special drawing rights* —are described in **Part IV.**

(v) Foreign Exchange Reserves.

Two national currencies have been widely used in settlement of international payments: the pound and the dollar. The pound performed this function after the First World War, but the dollar became the main reserve currency after the Second World War. Surplus countries are prepared to hold short-term debt in foreign currencies—so earning a rate of interest—confident that their future trading deficits can be financed by payment of these currencies. They can perform their function only if there is confidence that they can be converted into other currencies and hence into goods and services at current exchange rates.

The United States ran a large and persistent payments deficit during the 1950s and 1960s, made possible by the willingness of the creditor countries to build up their dollar balances. Indeed, this increase in dollar balances was the main source of new international liquidity during that period. But there is necessarily a limit to such a process. The weakness in the U.S. balance of payments in fact added to the problem of international liquidity. The deficits produced periodic fears that the dollar would be devalued; and this resulted in speculation against the dollar, and contributed to the breakdown of the Bretton Woods system. The problems which have beset the dollar in recent years are explained in **Part IV.**

(vi) The Sterling Balances.

Governments and individuals may hold balances in sterling (*e.g.,* Treasury bills, Government stocks, and bank accounts) for many reasons. Some countries reckon to keep a high proportion of their reserves in the form of sterling balances. It is convenient to hold sterling to finance trading transactions because sterling is widely acceptable in settlement of trading debts. It is profitable to hold sterling if the rate of interest paid on balances in London is higher than that paid in other financial centres, provided that the interest-rate differential is not offset by an expectation that sterling will be depreciated in terms of other currencies.

Near the end of 1988, the sterling balances totalled £73 billion—more than the official reserves, which stood at £50 billion. £15 billion was held by central banks, with the oil-exporting countries accounting for a third of this.

An increase in the sterling balances enables Britain to finance an adverse balance of payments without reducing her foreign exchange reserves or depreciating sterling. Conversely, a reduction in sterling balances can impose a drain on reserves even if there is no adverse balance. Since short term capital flows depend not only on the interest rate in London relative to other countries but also on expected movements in the exchange rate, the authorities cannot be confident that interest rate policy will suffice to finance a persistent balance of payments deficit.

(vii) The Eurocurrency Market.

The Eurocurrency market is a market for bank deposits which are denominated in foreign currencies. It derives its name from the fact that most of the banks which accept these foreign currency deposits are in Europe (including Britain) and most of the deposits are denominated in U.S. dollars. The Eurodollar market has grown at remarkable speed since the 1960s. The reason for that growth was the profitability of Eurodollar transactions. Banks found that, particularly if only large units of money were handled, they could

profitably borrow funds in country A and lend in country B, while paying interest rates higher than those paid in country A and charging rates lower than those charged in country B. Its growth was helped by the continuous deficit in the United States balance of payments, since this meant that banks and institutions received dollars which they were willing to hold and lend. OPEC funds obtained from their trade surpluses after 1973 tended to make their way into the market (as *petro-dollars*).

London and Tokyo are the largest international banking centres in the world, each accounting for nearly a quarter of the lending market. In late 1988 the external liabilities of UK banks totalled $930 billion. Such large balances can create problems for the regulation of economic activity. Movements in the market affect interest rates, credit and exchange rates in different countries, and they can thwart domestic monetary policies.

2. EMPLOYMENT, PRODUCTION, AND INDUSTRY

Population.

In 1989 the population of the United Kingdom was estimated to be 57·1 million—50·4 m. in England and Wales, 5·1 m. in Scotland, and 1·6 m. in Northern Ireland. Since 1971 the population has increased by only 2 per cent. This slow increase is accounted for by the birth rate (the number of live births per 100 people) of 1·4 exceeding the crude death rate of 1·2. Partially offsetting this is the fact that more people migrated from the United Kingdom than have migrated to this country.

The official estimate of the population of the United Kingdom in the year 2031 is 61·2 million. But prediction of future trends is difficult. For instance, it depends on immigration and emigration policies, the effect of improving medical services on the average length of life, trends in the age at which people marry, advances in techniques of birth control, and attitudes towards desirable family size. This projection is based on the belief that there will be a continued small outward migration from Britain, and that the birth rate will slightly exceed the death rate.

The Labour Force.

Of the total population only some are of *working age, i.e.,* between the minimum school leaving age of 16 (15 before 1973) and retiring age—65 years for men and 60 for women. Of course, not all those of working age do work and not all those above working age have retired. In 1989 the labour force was 27·8 million. Of males aged between 16 and 64, 87 per cent were in the labour force compared with 72 per cent of females. The labour force is defined to include not only those who are gainfully employed (as employees or self-employed) but also the unemployed who are looking for work and those on work related government training programmes. Students and housewives are excluded unless they do some work for cash. One feature of the past decade or so has been a slight fall in the proportion of adult males going out to work, a fall which is expected to continue. It is caused by an increasing number of students and others undergoing full-time training and by more people retiring early. Those factors also affected the proportion of women going out to work, but they have been more than offset by a rising participation of married women, particularly in part-time work. This trend is again expected to continue. A particularly worrying demographic development is the decline in the number of school-leavers available to enter the labour market. This will persist until the middle of the 1990s, and will require a major adjustment in the hiring policies of many employers.

Most of the labour force work for wages and salaries as employees. Of the total for the United Kingdom in September 1989 of 27·8 million, 3·0 m. were employers or self-employed. 0·3 m. were in the Forces, 22·5 m. were employees and 1·9 m. were recorded as unemployed. So less than half the population who are at work have to produce not only for themselves but also for the rest of the population who are either not in the labour force or who are unemployed.

The table shows the industries in which people work. As an economy develops there is a tendency for employment in the primary sector to decline as the production industries expand. As an economy gets richer still, the proportion of income spent on services increases, and employment in the service sector consequently rises whilst the proportion of the workforce in production industries declines. Thus, in 1955 services accounted for only 36 per cent of total employment; whereas by 1989 the proportion had risen to 69 per cent.

Employment and Unemployment.

In 1989 an average of 1,798,700 persons—6·4 per cent of the working population—were unemployed in the U.K. This figure excludes school-leavers. In most post-war years until the late 1960's the average was lower than 1·5 per cent. Even in January 1959, the worst month of the 1950s, the rate rose to less than 3 per cent, and in February 1963—an exceptional month owing to weather—to less than 4 per cent. These contrast with an average figure in 1937, the best year of the 1930s, of 11 per cent, and with a figure of 22 per cent at the bottom of the slump in 1932. The low unemployment of the post-war years was not maintained from the late 1960s. Unemployment grew to reach almost one million in early 1972. It then started to fall back with the general economic recovery, only to start rising again from late 1974 as the economy moved back into recession. Unemployment peaked in 1986, since when it has fallen

Until the late 1960s 1–1·5 per cent unemployment was somewhere near the practicable minimum; for some unemployment is more or less inevitable. A seasonal rise in unemployment in the winter must be expected, e.g., in seaside towns, and for this reason unemployment in January is half a per cent or so higher than in June. Moreover, some unemployment is bound to be involved in job-changing and as the demands of industries change. Finally there is a core of people who are simply unemployable. "Full employment" means that there should be about as many jobs vacant as there are workers looking for jobs. A large excess of vacancies is evidence of inflationary pressure in the labour market, for it means that the employers needing workers to meet the demands for their products will have to compete with each other by bidding up wages.

Most commentators feel that the practicable minimum level of unemployment has increased since the late 1960s. By this they mean that any attempt to reduce unemployment further, by injecting monetary demand, would be likely to cause increasing inflation. Many possible reasons have been advanced for the increase in this "non-accelerating inflation rate of unemployment". One explanation is that as the fixed costs (like National Insurance contributions) of employing workers went up, so employers were more careful to economise on labour. Another possible explanation is that workers who were unemployed took longer to find a new job, because they may have drawn redundancy pay (since the Redundancy Payments Act of 1965) or they may have drawn earnings-related unemployment benefit, the earnings-related supplement having been introduced in 1966 (but withdrawn in 1982). A more general argument was that the level of social security benefits as a whole was too high, causing people to demand an unrealistically high wage before accepting a job. Whilst the above factors, particularly the burden of National Insurance contributions, may well have played a role at times, it is unlikely that they have been persistently important. Many of the unemployed have skills which are redundant in an economy where the structure of industry is changing. Hence there may be an excess demand for some skills even when many people are without work—indeed this is the case at present. As well as skill mismatch of this sort, there may be geographical mismatch—that is the distribution of the population may not coincide with the distribution of job vacancies. This is one interpretation of Mr. Tebbit's famous exhortation: "Get on your bike!" However, labour immobility is likely to have been exacerbated in recent years by a growing disparity in housing costs. In any case, there is grave disagreement amongst observers about the importance of such mismatch explanations. No-one denies that there is a severe degree of mismatch in the British economy; the doubt concerns whether it has increased. Similar disagreement attends the claim

Agriculture, forestry, and fishing	305
Coal, oil and natural gas extraction and processing	159
Electricity, gas, other energy and water supply	294
Manufacturing industries	5,139
Construction	1,043
Wholesale distribution and repairs	1,194
Retail distribution	2,153
Hotels and catering	1,099
Transport	888
Postal services and telecommunications	440
Banking, finance and insurance	2,640
Public administration	1,920
Education	1,629
Medical and other health services	1,278
Other services	1,652
GRAND TOTAL	22,044

that technological advance, reducing the need for labour, is a major factor. Interestingly many industrialists would put this as a prime explanation. Most economists would be inclined to disagree with them. They would put greater stress on a too rapid growth of real wages (that is wages compared to prices), causing employers to try to produce a given amount of output with smaller quantities of labour. Many put a large share of the blame for this on the shoulders of trade unions. Also of great importance is the stance of the Government. If trade unions push up wages, employers may respond by putting up prices; unions then push up wages again in an attempt to obtain an increase in their living standards. Thus a wage-price spiral may cause increasing inflation. Governments concerned about inflation may therefore be forced to run the economy at lower levels of demand. There is evidence that the wage-price spiral has worsened, thereby necessitating harsher government action and higher unemployment at full employment.

Whatever the relative importance of these explanations, there is little doubt that the major cause of the rise in unemployment in the early 1980s was deficiency of aggregate demand for British goods. This in turn is was partly the consequence of restrictive government policies, and partly of our loss of international competitiveness. There is, however, dispute as to how much of this reduction in demand was necessary to stabilise inflation. Equally there are those who believe that even if it was necessary in the above sense, it contributed to increasing the non-accelerating inflation rate of unemployment. This was because some of the workers who lost their jobs became hard to re-employ. Partly this was because of the effect of joblessness on their attitudes and skills, and partly because of the perceptions of employers as to their worth. It may also have been difficult for the unemployed to "compete" with the employed by "bidding down" wages, since the latter may have great bargaining power vis a vis their employers for whom their departure would have represented a major waste of training expenditure.

To some extent official unemployment figures are misleading, in that certain individuals may not record themselves as being out of work and will thus appear to drop out of the working population. Until 1982 the official unemployment figure was calculated on the number registered as available for work. Registration was a prerequisite for claiming unemployment benefit. Individuals not eligible for such benefits—particularly married women—often did not register as unemployed even if they still wished to work. Their only incentive for doing so was if they felt that the authorities would help them find a job. Further, the count did not include those who were temporarily stopped or working short time. Since late 1982 the official unemployment figures have been calculated according to the number actually claiming benefit, for which registering as available for work is no longer essential. Those under 18 are now not included in the unemployment figures, as they are assumed to be on a training scheme, to have a job, or to have remained in full-time education. The above are not

UNEMPLOYMENT AND VACANCIES
(United Kingdom, thousands)

	Unemploy-ment.† (Annual Average)	Vacancies. (Annual Average)	Unemploy-ment as a percentage of total labour force
1932*	2,829	n.a.	22·1
1937*	1,482	n.a.	10·9
1970	602	188	2·4
1972	826	147	3·3
1974	591	298	2·3
1976	1,229	122	4·7
1978	1,299	210	4·9
1980	1,561	136	5·8
1982	2,793	114	10·5
1984	3,047	150	11·2
1986	3,185	189	11·5
1988	2,370	248	8·4
1989	1,799	219	6·4

* Figures relate only to population insured against unemployment.
† Excluding school-leavers. From 1971 figures are based on claimants at unemployment benefit offices. Prior to 1971 they were based on registrations at employment offices.

the only changes that have been introduced in the last few years in the way that unemployment is measured. For example, older workers tend not to get included in the count, whilst many believe that the special employment measures (*see* **G15–16**) artificially deflate the unemployment figure. A combination of the changes in the way unemployment has been calculated, and the rapid expansion of demand in the second half of the decade, has meant that recorded unemployment fell steadily between the middle of 1986 to the end of 1989, from a peak of over 3·25 million to 1·6 million.

Regional Unemployment.

Extreme variations in regional unemployment were not a general feature of the post-war period: until recently only in Northern Ireland was unemployment persistently very high. Between 1954 and 1989 unemployment there ranged between 5 and 19 per cent. Nevertheless, regional inequalities exist and were magnified in absolute terms during the 1980s.

In 1989 the proportion of all workers unemployed in the U.K. was 6·4 per cent. But the table shows a lower proportion was unemployed in the South East, East Anglia, the East Midlands and the South West, and that there was a much higher proportion unemployed in the North, North West, Wales, Scotland, and Northern Ireland. Even within the more fortunate regions there are pockets of high unemployment. These are concentrated particularly in the inner areas of large cities, but also elsewhere. For example, in the South-East, Clacton had an unemployment rate of 10·7 per cent in early 1990, whilst in the South West, Redruth had 12·7 per cent. This does not compare, however, with the 28·4 per cent rate in Strabane, Northern Ireland.

One of the main reasons for the regional pattern of unemployment used to be that certain industries and services, in which big changes have been taking place, tended to be grouped in specific regions. Most of our early industrial centres had to be established close to coal, iron ore, and adequate water supplies. But employment in many long-established industries has recently been declining. Such industries include textiles, mining and quarrying, shipbuilding, and agriculture. On the other hand new and growing industries, and their related head offices, were concentrated in Greater London, the South East, and the Midlands. The growth of services, too, has centred on the areas where industry is booming and population is increasing. In the absence of government intervention, the process would tend to become cumulative, and regional inequalities would grow rather than diminish. The 1970s saw an interesting change. The West Midlands, tradi-

PERCENTAGE OF WORKERS
UNEMPLOYED, BY REGIONS

	Annual average* 1965	Annual average* 1989
North	2·4	9·9
Yorkshire and Humberside	1·0	7·6
East Midlands	0·8	5·6
East Anglia	1·2	3·7
South East	0·8	4·0
South West	1·5	4·6
Wales	2·5	7·7
West Midlands	0·6	6·5
North West	1·5	8·5
Scotland	2·8	9·4
Northern Ireland	5·9	15·0

* Excluding school-leavers.

tionally after the South-East, the most prosperous area of the country, was severely hit by the particular impact of the recession on engineering, and appeared as one of the regions with higher than average unemployment. This persisted until 1987, when the West Midlands began to benefit from the ripple effect of the boom in the South East and as firms began to relocate some of their activities from the crowded South-East to areas where the labour market was less tight. By 1989 unemployment in the West Midlands was in line with the national average. In contrast other areas of high unemployment saw little or no improvement in their relative position during the period of strong economic growth 1986–1988, the worst affected regions remaining Northern Ireland, Scotland, the North and North-West. This may be linked to an additional factor—the relative concentration of unemployment in inner city areas in particular regions. Unemployment in the inner cities has grown more rapidly than elsewhere since the 1960s, and seems to be the result of limited growth of firms there together with only a slow emergence of new enterprise. It is thought that this largely reflects physical limits to expansion.

Regional Planning.

There are essentially two ways of tackling the problem of regional imbalances; taking jobs to the people or bringing people to the jobs. In so far as the latter alternative is chosen, the Government should encourage the mobility of labour, *e.g.*, through retraining schemes or rehousing subsidies. However, the migration of population may damage community life in the denuded areas, and cause congestion, housing shortages, and overcrowding in the booming regions. The Government can create employment opportunities in the relatively depressed regions in various ways. It can try to induce expanding industries to set up new plants in these regions by offering tax incentives or grants; it can authorise additional expenditure on public works—*e.g.*, by accelerating road-building programmes—to provide additional employment; it can place orders for the goods it needs—*e.g.*, defence contracts—where work is required. It can also use physical controls on expansion in the better-off areas; between 1947 and 1981 factory building over a particular size, which was changed from time to time, required the granting of an *Industrial Development Certificate*.

(i) Labour's Policy.

On taking office in October 1964, the Labour Government made regional planning the responsibility of its Department of Economic Affairs. Britain was divided into eight regions, with the intention of producing a plan for each region.

Fiscal incentives to locate industry in the depressed regions were given, *e.g.*, the cash grants provided in 1966 for new plants and machinery in manufacturing were at twice the national rate in the Development Areas. Buildings also received cash grants in Development Areas, in Intermediate Areas (where regional depression existed but in not such an acute form), and in Special Development Areas (where depression was most acute). By contrast, office building in London and some other cities was strictly limited. To encourage the mobility of labour, the Government introduced redundancy compensation and achieved some expansion in both public and private training facilities. In 1967 regional differentials in the selective employment tax were also introduced. This was known as the Regional Employment Premium.

(ii) Policy in the 1970s.

In 1970 the incentive to invest in the Development Areas was affected by the Conservative Government's replacement of cash grants (except on buildings) by a system of initial allowances against tax. Whereas cash grants had been 40 per cent of investment in plant and machinery in Development Areas and 20 per cent in other areas, there was now a 100 per cent initial allowance in Development Areas and 60 per cent initial allowances in other areas. The system of initial allowances is explained on **G**15.

Early in 1972 unemployment rates in Northern Ireland, Scotland, Wales and Northern England had reached high levels. The Government introduced 100 per cent allowances throughout the country on all investment in plant and machinery; the preferential treatment of investment in Development Areas was therefore ended. Instead *regional development grants*, in the form of cash payments towards investment in plant, machinery and buildings, were introduced. The Government also proposed in four years to triple expenditure on retraining facilities, and to pay a worker who had undergone retraining a housing grant if he moved house to take a new job; and also a grant to any worker in an assisted area who moved house to take a new job. It should be remembered, however, that strong measures were necessary merely to replace the Labour Government's system of cash grants, and the Regional Employment Premium which it was planned to phase out in 1974. Though, in the event, REP was retained by the incoming Labour Government, it was finally replaced by more selective measures in 1977.

(iii) Conservative Policy.

In July 1979, the new Conservative Government announced some changes to be introduced over the 1979–83 period. The extent of the assisted areas would be gradually reduced, so as to cover 25 per cent instead of 40 per cent of the employed population and some areas were "down-graded". Industrial Development Certificate procedures were abolished in 1981. By the end of 1984 there were only two types of assisted areas in Britain—development and intermediate.

In 1983 the Government introduced a Green Paper on regional policy. The suggestion was for a tighter and more selective approach, with aid being directed more at job creation, at small firms and at the services. But even this non-interventionist Government concluded that "wage adjustments and labour mobility cannot be relied upon to correct regional imbalance in employment opportunities". However, the real value of expenditure on all regional incentives is currently less than half the levels of the early 1970's, although spending on both employment schemes and urban aid has increased.

In 1981 the Government also set up two Urban Development Corporations (UDCs), one in London's Docklands and the other in Merseyside. The aim of the UDCs was to reclaim and develop derelict land for housing, commercial and recreational purposes. In the period to mid-1989 the London Docklands UDC had received over £500 million in Government aid and had secured almost £7 billion in private sector funding commitments. The London Docklands is to be the site for one of the largest single office developments in Europe. In 1987 a further five UDCs were established in Manchester, Teesside, Tyne and Wear, the Black Country and Cardiff. Three more were set up in 1989, including one in Bristol and there are now eleven UDCs, with a total budget of £439 million in the financial year 1990–91. In 1985 the Government also announced an Action For Cities programme to improve co-operation between Government departments, private enterprise and local authorities in order to rejuvenate derelict inner city areas.

Though regional problems remain, studies have shown that IDC's, financial incentives and REP, but particularly cash grants, have to a limited extent mitigated them. However, it was felt by many that the instruments were too blunt and insufficiently selective. It was also felt that in a slack labour market, regional policy was more likely to re-allocate a given number of jobs rather than increase them in net terms. Alongside regional policy, therefore, were introduced measures on inner city decay (a problem even in non-assisted areas such as the South East), rural development and derelict land. In his March 1980 Budget the Chancellor announced proposals to establish about half a dozen "Enterprise Zones". These were small sites (of no more than 500 acres) with problems of economic and physical decay. The Zones were an experiment to test how far industrial and commercial activity could be encouraged by the removal of certain fiscal burdens, and by the removal or streamlined administration of statutory or administrative controls. Currently there are 26 such zones. An additional measure, announced in the 1983 Budget, was the establishment of a number of 'freeports' which would enjoy similar relief from fiscal burdens, in particular local authority rates. By early 1985 there were 6 of these.

The experiment with freeports has proved to be somewhat unsuccessful. Of the six established only two have achieved any real measure of progress. Two, in Belfast and Cardiff, never opened while one in Prestwick ceased trading after two years. A fourth in Birmingham was drastically scaled down in early 1989. Only the freeports in Southampton and Liverpool have lived up to their initial expectations, though in some cases these were much too ambitious. The planned abolition of fiscal barriers within the EC after 1992 in any case removes much of the rationale for freeports and they are likely to disappear over the next few years.

The present Government's distrust of general regional assistance was confirmed by its decision in 1988 to abolish automatic regional grants. All assistance for the regions is now selective. The new philosophy is that the "market" will eventually erode the disparity in regional performance, as regional variations in pay encourage a redistribution in regional employment. There is little evidence that such a mechanism is at work and experiments with UDCs and freeports are unlikely to have more than a marginal impact in reducing regional inequality.

National Income.

Gross domestic income (GDI) is the sum total of incomes received for the services of labour, land, or capital in a country. Gross domestic product (GDP) is the money value of all the goods and services produced in the country. So as to avoid double-counting, only the *value added* at each stage of production is included: firms' purchases of goods and services from other firms are excluded. The revenue from selling the GDP is either paid out to the hired factors of production—labour, land, and capital—or retained in the form of profits. Therefore, provided it is calculated net of taxes on goods produced, GDP must equal GDI. To estimate gross national income (GNI) from GDI it is necessary to add the net income—such as profits and interest—received from abroad. If an allowance is made for wear and tear of the nation's capital equipment, *i.e.*, for *capital consumption*, we arrive at net national income, better known as the *national income*.

In 1989 the gross national income of the United Kingdom was £511,867 million, implying a national income per head of £9,091. In 1955 the corresponding figure had been £338 per head. However, only part of the increase in value was due to an increase in the quantity of goods and services produced; some of the increase simply reflected a rise in prices. It is important to calculate changes in the volume of output—known as *real output*—as well as changes in its value. Real output is calculated by the statistical device of constructing an index number. This is done by calculating the volume of goods and services provided in each year and then valuing these goods and services at the prices found in one particular year. Thus between 1955 and 1989 the money value of gross national product per head rose by 2,829 per cent, whereas real per capita incomes increased by only about 164 per cent, and the difference represented a rise in prices.

AN INTERNATIONAL GROWTH LEAGUE TABLE

	Percentage change per annum, 1960 to 1980				
	Output	Employment	Output per head	Fixed investment as percentage of GDP, average, 1960-80	GNP per head, 1980 $
Japan	7·7	1·1	6·5	32·5	9,890
France	4·6	0·5	4·1	22·7	11,730
W. Germany	3·7	0·1	3·8	23·9	13,590
Italy	4·4	0·2	4·3	20·8	6,480
U.S.A.	3·5	2·0	1·5	18·2	11,360
U.K.	2·3	0·1	2·2	18·3	7,920

The Quality of Life.

In real terms national income per head rose by about 164 per cent between 1955 and 1989, or by 2·3 per cent per annum. National income per head is an indicator of the standard of living. However, this measure is necessarily a crude one. For instance, it cannot take into account new and better products, e.g., television, man-made fibres, faster flight, long-playing records, or the lowly plastic bucket; nor does it indicate changes in the distribution of income between rich and poor; nor in the length of the working week.

Data of national income per head may also conceal important changes in the "quality of life", e.g., in our physical environment. This is affected by such things as traffic congestion, noise, water- and air-pollution. Between 1961 and 1988 the number of private cars on British roads tripled, from 6·3 million to 20·4 million; the number of motor vehicles of all types more than doubled over the same period. Movement of civil aircraft over Britain doubled during the 1960s and has doubled again since 1970. The air in our cities became less polluted by smoke, sulphur dioxide and lead, though there were greater emissions of carbon monoxide. The number of our rivers, canals and estuaries which were grossly polluted remained significant, whilst complaints about noise were noticeably higher in the 1980s than before. In recent years environmental concerns have moved increasingly from national to international trusts. In particular the issue of global warming has become important. This is in part the consequence of emissions of carbon dioxide and carbon monoxide destroying the ozone layer. Noteworthy is that consumption—cars and aerosols, for example—as well as production contributes to this problem.

Industrial Production.

It is fairly easy to measure output in the main manufacturing industries, and in many of the other industries producing goods. It is much more difficult to do so for the service industries: the output of a doctor or a teacher is not easily measured. So each month the Central Statistical Office calculates the *index of industrial production* covering the main production industries. Industrial production is thus an early indicator of economic trends (*see* **Part IV**), but it is prone to fluctuate more than the other components of GDP.

Manufacturing industry accounts for about 70 per cent of industrial production. Within manufacturing the following industries have expanded rapidly since World War II—chemicals, including drugs, plastics, cosmetics and detergents, coal and petroleum products, including oil refining, and instrument and electrical engineering. The slowest growing manufacturing industries are textiles, clothing, leather and shipbuilding, which are losing their markets to cheaper competitors. Those industries in which demand has stagnated tend to be the industries in which output per employee, i.e., productivity, has stagnated.

International Comparisons.

In the 1960s and 1970s Britain's GDP grew less rapidly than that of almost any other major Western country. The British economy was also characterised by a relatively slow growth of output per head, *i.e.*, productivity. Britain fell behind many of the European countries in terms of income per head. Some comparisons with other countries are made in the table. However, these may be misleading because incomes are converted into pounds at official exchange rates, and these need not reflect relative costs of living.

Many explanations of Britain's poor performance were suggested, and there is by no means agreement on this matter among economists. It was argued that the U.K.—like the U.S.A.—had a highly advanced economy in which there was a relatively high demand for services; and that it was difficult to raise productivity in the large services sector. Another argument was that Britain used to be hampered by its slowly growing labour force, which restricted growth not only in output but also in output per man. The reason given was that an expanding labour force needed to be equipped with additional plant and machinery so that its capital equipment tended to be newer on average than that used by a static labour force, and thus more up-to-date and efficient.

Some commentators put the blame on the inefficiency of our business management; some on our educational system, biased towards the humanities, and on our relatively poor training performance; some on the social milieu which looked down on money-making as a career; some on over-manning and other restrictive practices of trade unions. A good deal of attention has also been paid to the proportion of output which different countries devoted to *investment*, *i.e.*, expenditure on commodities—such as plant and machinery—for use in future production. These investment ratios are shown in the table. With the exception of the U.S.A., all countries had investment ratios considerably higher than in the U.K., with correspondingly higher growth rates of output and productivity. Since investment in dwellings contributes very little to growth, it may be appropriate to exclude this: however, similar results are obtained. This leads to the hypothesis that Britain's growth rate could have been raised if a higher proportion of output had been devoted to investment, particularly in plant and machinery.

The performance of the British economy in the mid- to late 1980s was much better relative to other countries than was the case in the 1970s. Growth in total output averaged more than 2·1 per cent per annum compared to a European average of 1·9 per cent in the decade as a whole. Productivity grew by an average 2·4 per cent per year from 1980. **Part IV** includes a discussion of possible reasons for the UK's relatively better economic performance in the mid to late 1980s. Sceptics who believed that there had been no real underlying improvement are now being proved at least partly correct. The period of rapid growth 1986–88 finally ended because it resulted in the UK's traditional constraints of high inflation and balance of payments weakness. The policy tightening invoked to cope with these will certainly keep growth well below the European average in the period 1989–92.

Investment.

In 1989 gross investment in capital assets amounted to £98,634 million in the United Kingdom. This was 19 per cent of GNP. The net addition to the nation's stock of capital assets was only 30 per cent of total investment, the rest being needed to offset the wastage of assets already in use, *i.e.*, to make good the *capital consumption*.

There are four main kinds of investment: plant and machinery, vehicles, dwellings, and other new buildings and works. In 1988 the four categories accounted for 42·9, 10·0, 18·2 and 28·8 per cent respectively. Investment may also be analysed by the purpose for which it is used. Social services such as education and health take a surprisingly small proportion of total investment. Distribution and other service industries and public corporations take a large proportion: investment in oil, electricity, gas and water alone accounts for over 10 per cent of total non-dwelling investment. It is clear that some sectors of the economy are more capital-intensive than others. Manufacturing investment accounts for 17 per cent of the total. This is small in relation to the contribution of manufacturing to output, and has declined in recent years. Manufacturing investment fell more than any other form of investment in the recession at the beginning of the 1980s. However, many of the fast-growing manufacturing industries—*e.g.*, chemicals and electronics—use much machinery and equipment per unit of output produced. These capital-intensive plants cannot pay unless they are worked at near full capacity. With the growing capitalisation of industry it is increasingly necessary to introduce shift work.

Increasing Investment.

Historically, the proportion of total output invested—the *investment ratio*—has been lower in Britain than in other countries with faster growth rates of out-put and productivity; and there is reason to believe that a higher proportion would have improved the growth rate to a certain extent. This was seen in the mid 1980s when a sharp acceleration in productivity growth was associated with a recovery of investment (particularly in manufacturing) from the very depressed levels of the early 1980s. But in a fully employed economy it is not possible to increase investment expenditures without curtailing other forms of expenditure, notably private and public consumption. This curtailment would have to be brought about by increasing taxation or encouraging people to save or by pruning public services. Yet the very act of restricting private consumption may induce private firms to *reduce* their investment expenditures. For society as a whole, increasing investment involves a choice between the loss in current consumption and the ensuing gain in future consumption. Of course not all consumption expenditure is equally important to the standard of living: some would agree that if British defence expenditure was pruned to permit more investment, there would be no loss to set against the future gain.

In 1989 85·4 per cent of total investment in the United Kingdom was carried out in the private sector, 9·1 per cent by public authorities and 5·5 per cent by the public corporations. The Government has more control over investment in the public sector than in the private sector. Governments do possess various policy measures by which to influence private investment (*see also* Part IV) but private investment is volatile and highly dependent on businessmen's expectations, especially their expectations about the future growth of their markets. It is no easy matter to raise the British investment ratio. Even in the sustained growth of the mid and late 1980s, investment rates were particularly high only for two or three years.

The Finance of Investment.

Any business is allowed to charge as a cost the depreciation of its assets. Normal depreciation allowances used to be based on the original cost of the asset and on its expected useful life. In a time of price inflation depreciation allowances calculated in this way will not provide sufficient finance to permit the replacement of assets at higher prices, and accountants have been slowly moving towards the concept of depreciation allowances being based on replacement costs.

Governments have, however, adopted certain fiscal devices to encourage replacement and net investment. Soon after the war initial allowances were introduced. Under this system firms were permitted to charge against profits in the first year of its life 20, or at times 40, per cent of the cost of any new equipment, and the system amounted to a loan of the tax saved in the first year, repaid over the life of the asset. In 1954 initial allowances for machinery were replaced by a system of investment allowances, under which a firm could charge against profits 20 per cent of the cost of any new machine, with the difference that all ordinary depreciation allowances were still chargeable. So the investment allowance was a grant, not a loan, of the saved tax. In 1966, initial and investment allowances on new plant and machinery in three sectors—manufacturing, mining, and shipping—were replaced by cash grants. Other plant and machinery and industrial building received higher initial allowances. In 1970 the Conservative Government reintroduced initial allowances in place of investment grants but in 1972 tried to encourage investment by granting free depreciation; *i.e.* 100 per cent allowance in the first year. The details of capital allowances changed from time to time over the following decade, but in the 1984 Budget a more radical change was announced. By 1986 first year allowances would be scrapped, to be replaced by an annual allowance of 25 per cent and lower rates of corporation tax. In 1988/9 the Corporation Tax rate was reduced to 35 per cent, with a lower rate for small companies.

The Corporation Tax Rate was left unchanged at 35 per cent in the March 1989 and 1990 Budgets although the rate at which smaller companies start paying the lower rates was increased by more than would have been necessary to compensate for the rate of inflation. As with income tax, the Government has stated that it would like to reduce the burden of corporate taxation as and when economic conditions permit.

Apart from Government help, companies rely mainly on retained profits, which are often larger, taking companies as a whole, than their net investment. Other sources of company finance are borrowing in financial markets and the issue of company shares. As compared to many other countries, in Britain a relatively high proportion of external investment funds are raised by equity issue rather than by direct borrowing. Much public investment must be financed by the Treasury, except for relatively small amounts raised by public corporations on the financial markets. The 1979 Conservative Government announced its intention to seek private capital for some investment projects, *e.g.* roadbuilding. The Government also maintained a new stress on helping small firms. This had been given particular impetus by the report of the Wilson Committee and by differentially favourable tax treatment in recent Budgets. The 1989 Enterprise Initiative continued this theme of assistance to small firms—by, for example, state-funded consultancy help. Traditionally investment measures are concerned with reducing the cost of capital. Many people believe that investment could be increased more effectively if more steps were taken to encourage a high and stable demand for output.

Labour Subsidies.

Initially Government subsidies were employed primarily as incentives for investment, particularly in a regional context. A 1972 Act, however, gave wide powers to the Government to offer financial assistance in almost any form to almost any enterprise, provided the assistance was "in the public interest". The Labour Government in 1974 greatly increased subsidisation, aimed chiefly at maintaining employment. These subsidies consisted chiefly of direct assistance to industries both within and outside the assisted areas and labour subsidies in the form of temporary employment and job creation schemes, aimed particularly at young people. Thus there was a new emphasis on subsidies which cheapened the cost of labour. Some of the schemes, like the Temporary Employment Subsidy, were pure subsidies in this sense. Others combined the subsidy element with measures to increase either the mobility or training of workers, the Youth Opportunities Programme, for instance. The new Conservative Government cut back on such schemes soon after its election in 1979, but did continue an emphasis on training, particularly with the Youth

Training Scheme, which was significantly extended in 1986.

Two other major subsidies were introduced. The Community Programme encouraged sponsoring agencies or individuals to set up projects of community value to utilise unemployed labour. The Government provided a cash grant for each person employed, and paid their wage which was supposed to be equivalent to the going rate for the job in the area. A second subsidy was the Enterprise Allowance Scheme, which provided a small weekly payment to help the unemployed set up their own business. Until 1985 the Government had a fourth scheme called the Young Workers' Scheme, which paid employers to take on youths, in order to help them gain work experience.

In 1986 and 1987 the Government shifted to more overt job subsidies, including the Job Start Scheme whereby a worker taking a job paying less than a specified minimum was paid the balance by the State. Other schemes were however phased out, including the New Workers Scheme (designed to encourage the young to accept low-paid employment) and the Job Release Scheme (which subsidised early retirement). Job-Sharing schemes however remained in place.

By 1989 all training schemes for unemployed adults had been amalgamated under an umbrella Employment Training Scheme which offers full-time training with an employer for all those who have been unemployed for at least six months. The scheme is available for up to a year and pays a training allowance of between £12 and £14 per week in excess of benefit entitlement. Assistance is also given with travelling expenses. The Job Restart Scheme is still provided for those who have been unemployed for more than two years.

Training.

An emphasis on training is an important part of the Government's supply strategy for the labour market, as set out in the 1985 White Paper on unemployment, *The Challenge to the Nation*. There had long been criticism of the British training effort. It was said that the school system was ill attuned to the needs of industry, that not enough young people continued with education or full-time training after the minimum school-leaving age. The old apprenticeship system was justly accused of being too rigid and of forming skills often inappropriate to changing technology. Financing of industrial training was thought to be insufficient. There was inadequate provision for the retraining of adults—so necessary if sufficient occupational flexibility was to be assured in a changing world.

In some respects matters had been getting worse. The recession of the early 1980s, for example, decimated training recruitment. Most of the old Industrial Training Boards were disappearing, without adequate substitutes being found. Yet at the same time, official thinking on training became more sophisticated after the mid 1970s. The present Government has issued many documents on the subject, perhaps the most significant being *The New Training Initiative* (1981) and *Training for Employment* (1987).

Despite the enthusiasm, in substantive terms little has been done on adult training and on the financing of training. Most emphasis has been put on youth training, and on the educational system, through projects like the Technical and Vocational Education Initiative. The precise worth of these policies has yet to be seen. The cynic might argue that measures such as the YTS are a cosmetic to cover up unemployment. A more measured commentator would have to agree that it is hard to discern how much is cosmetic and how much is real. In stressing the desirability of employers financing a higher proportion of training expenditure, there is a potential inconsistency in Government attitudes. Unless an employer can guarantee that an employee stays with him for the whole of his working life, then that employer's return from the training is lower than society's return. Therefore, there is a strong argument for a proportion of training costs being financed by the Government. Nevertheless, progress has been made. The school curriculum has been made more vocationally directed. The 1988 Education Act introduces a National Curriculum which, along with the recent switch from "O" Levels to GCSE, is intended to improve the vocational orientation of secondary education.

More generally, the National Council for Vocational Qualifications will, by 1991, have introduced a standard set of national qualifications to replace the myriad presently available. Some YTS schemes are excellent whilst some industries are developing better alternatives to the old apprenticeship system, the Construction Industry Training Board, for instance.

The 1988 Employment Act incorporated all the Employment Training Schemes under the Employment Training Initiative. The scheme is workplace-based and is supported by a significant number of large employers. The scheme has been designed to provide job-specific training over twelve months, and cost the government around £1·4 billion in 1989. Despite support from many employers, the scheme has been criticised widely in the Trade Union movement where it is regarded as another means of attracting cheap labour and, like the Job Restart Scheme, artificially reducing the official unemployment register. It is too early to say if Employment Training is actually improving job prospects for the long-term unemployed; there is some doubt about the quality of training being offered by some of the firms participating in the scheme.

As well as introducing the Employment Training Scheme, the 1988 Employment Act also brought substantial changes in structure of responsibility for adult training. At the local level, training is to be overseen by a network of Training and Enterprise Councils (TECs). These will each cover a local labour market with a working population of approximately 250,000. Each TEC will be an independent company, with two-thirds of its board being comprised of local employers. The reason for majority representation for businesses in TECs is that local industry should have the best insight into local skills needs. One difficulty is that the government has laid down fairly rigid rules about the seniority of the businessmen serving on TECs and this is causing recruitment difficulties in some areas. It is doubtful whether increased employer involvement in TECs will, in itself, make any difference to Britain's poor record in the area of skills training compared to other countries (particularly Japan and Germany). A deficiency in education and training is now widely blamed for the UK's bad industrial record and for the emergence of skills shortages at relatively high levels of unemployment. TECs will operate on contract to the government and will be set performance targets. The government has set up a National Training Task Force, its main purpose being to assist in the establishment and development of TECs.

Monopoly and Competition.

A trend to increasing size and increasing capitalisation has been going on now for many decades, and in the process it has changed the face of British industry. In the early 19th century the typical firm was the owner-managed textile mill. Then in the 1860s and 1870s came the discovery of cheap methods of making steel, with the consequential immense growth in the engineering industries. Most of the chemical industry is still newer, and there are many entirely 20th century industries such as aircraft and electronics.

In the capital-intensive industries the big firm predominates. In some it has become almost a monopoly; in others the pattern is of a few firms, all large. In 1990 the top British companies included oil firms (British Petroleum and Shell), tobacco firms (British American Tobacco and Imperial Tobacco), chemical firms (Imperial Chemical Industries and Unilever) and one in the motor industry (the Rover Group) although the latter has now been incorporated into the defence company British Aerospace. There is evidence that the extent of *concentration* of British industry—according to measures such as the proportion of the output of an industry produced by the largest three firms—has increased since 1945. Concentration increased particularly rapidly in the 1960s. There are two possible reasons for such an increase. The first is the natural growth of already large firms; the second is because of merger activity. This latter factor has been the more important in Britain. Although evidence is scanty, there is some suggestion that for a while in the mid 1970s, concentration stopped increasing, and it may even have fallen a little. Since 1986 there has been an increase in merger activity.

Competition goes on, but it has changed its form. Competition used to be largely by price. Now it is largely by advertising and by variations in the quality and other features of the product—detergents and motor cars being good examples. In many industries, groups of firms producing similar products entered into agreements which had the effect of restricting competition, for example through schemes for price-fixing. The effect was to increase the price to the consumer and to reduce the amount of output available. Some authorities have estimated that the total "welfare" loss because of this was relatively small, and have argued that our major concern should be over the dangers of large corporations having substantial political power because of their size, and over their using this power to force the Government into unwise decisions about, for example, subsidising inefficient management.

Domestic monopolies are also limited by foreign competition, and by the discipline of "potential cross entry"—that is, the possibility that a powerful firm may be attracted into a new sector by the sight of very high profits. The British industrial scene has nevertheless changed substantially, not only with the emergence of very large and powerful domestic firms, but also with the extensive presence of foreign-owned multinationals. Finally, however, it is worth remembering the words of the Nobel Prize winning economist, Sir John Hicks, that the greatest return to a monopolistic existence is a quiet life. In other words, firms will try not to make "too large" profits for fear of attracting new competition. An interesting question, however, is how far the stock market "disciplines" firms into maximising their profits. If they do not, the argument goes, dividends will be low, investors will sell their shares whose price will be driven down, thus rendering the firm liable to be taken over.

Regulation of Competition and Monopoly.

(i) Restrictive Practices Court.

The Restrictive Trade Practices Acts of 1956 and 1968 outlawed many of the main forms of restrictive agreements preventing competition. Collective price-fixing was declared to be illegal unless an industry could show that the practice brought substantial benefit to the public. Collective price-fixing was the system under which a central association for the industry laid down minimum prices at which members might sell. Usually such a system was backed by arrangements for collective boycotts, under which members of the association would refuse to sell goods to wholesalers or retailers who broke the rules. Collective boycotts were also found in industries without collective price-fixing, one common purpose being to make sure that retailers did not sell a manufacturer's products below his recommended price. This form of collective resale price maintenance was also outlawed by the Acts.

Under the Acts any restrictive agreements of several specified kinds had to be registered with the Registrar of Restrictive Practices. He then had to decide whether there was a *prima facie* case for the discontinuation of the agreement, and, if he thought there was, the case was referred to a Restrictive Practices Court, containing both judicial and lay members. For an agreement to be upheld, the agreeing parties had to prove to the Court that the agreement conferred some substantial benefit on the public which out-weighed any injury it did to the public. A 1976 Act extended this legislation to cover service agreements. The 1989 Enterprise Act proposed more effective laws and penalties against anti-competitive cartels.

(ii) Resale Prices Act.

The Act of 1956 permitted individual manufacturers to enforce *resale price maintenance* (r.p.m.) for their own products. Few suppliers would want the publicity of enforcing r.p.m. through the courts, but they could still put some commercial pressure on price-cutters, e.g., by offering less favourable terms or by refusing them supplies. The Resale Prices Act of 1964 prohibited all methods of enforcing minimum resale prices. However, goods which had been registered in due time with the Registrar of Restrictive Practices or had been approved by the Restrictive Practices Court, were exempted,

temporarily in the former case and permanently in the latter. For r.p.m. to be approved by the Court, it had to be shown that some ensuing benefit to customers (e.g., of increased quality or more retail outlets) outweighed any detriment. It was also lawful to withhold supplies to retailers selling goods at a loss to attract customers.

As a result of the Act r.p.m. has ceased to be a common practice, and has largely been replaced by "recommended" retail prices, which are in effect maximum prices. This practice has been investigated by the Monopolies Commission, which found that it was not always against the public interest.

(iii) The Monopolies Commission.

The Restrictive Practices Acts left untouched those industries in which one firm is dominant: these remained the responsibility of the Monopolies Commission. This is an independent administrative tribunal, established in 1948, with powers to investigate and decide whether a monopoly (defined in terms of market share) is contrary to the "public interest."

The Monopolies and Mergers Act of 1965 strengthened control over monopolies and mergers. With regard to monopolies, the Government wished to provide itself with legal powers of enforcement: previously monopolies had been expected to comply voluntarily with the findings of the Monopolies Commission. The Act also permitted the Government to refer a merger or a proposed merger to the Monopolies Commission in cases where the merger would lead to monopoly (defined as control of at least one third of the market) or would increase the power of an existing monopoly, or where the value of the assets taken over exceeded £5 million. The 1965 Act was repealed in 1973 and replaced by the Fair Trading Act. The rules governing referral to the Monopolies Commission were changed in this later Act. Since 1989, the decision to refer a merger to the Monopolies Commission, and the criteria by which the commision examines the public interest, have become less rigidly defined. Considerations of formal market share are probably less important than for example, the existance of barriers to entry.

In interpreting the public interest, the Monopolies Commission has criticised monopolies for various practices, e.g., if they attempt to deter entry to the industry, or earn abnormally high profit rates, or show weakness in research and innovation. The Commission has a difficult task in attempting to protect the consumers' interests, and also to avoid inhibiting the growth of firms, since evidence suggests that it is often the large firms which are able to compete effectively abroad.

(iv) The Fair Trading Act.

The 1973 Fair Trading Act placed the previously dispersed responsibilities for overseeing competition policies in the hands of a civil servant—the Director General of Fair Trading. The Monopolies Acts of 1948 and 1965 were repealed and replaced by rather more comprehensive rules. Monopoly was now defined as control of one quarter of the market instead of one third. For the first time local monopolies were made subject to control. Also "complex monopolies" were made subject to investigation—that is situations where no one firm had 25 per cent of the market, but where several of them collaborated to restrict competition. The Director General of Fair Trading—as well as the Department of Trade and Industry—was enabled to refer monopoly situations to the Monopolies Commission; though it was still only the Department which could make references on mergers. Additionally the Director General took over the functions of the Registrar of Restrictive Practices and responsibility for general consumer protection, and set up a new body to assist in that aim—the Consumer Protection Advisory Committee.

In 1978 the Labour Government published a review of its general policy which recommended a more neutral policy towards mergers and that greater stress should be put on the importance of competition.

In 1980 the new Conservative Government introduced a Competition Act which strengthened the powers of the authorities to deal with practices which limited competition in both the public and private sectors. Procedures were also speeded up considerably. There was a new power to refer nationalised industries and other public bodies for investigation of their efficiency, costs, services to consumers, and possible abuse of monopoly position. Perhaps the most celebrated case of applying the authorities' new legislation involves the UK Stock Exchange. In return for a pledge from the Government not to prosecute, the Stock Exchange abolished the restrictive practices which governed entry into the stockbroking profession, and separate the broking from the market-making function in the stock market—the so-called "Big Bang" in the City of London. Also relevant are EC provisions, Articles 85 and 86, which relate to anti-competitive practices which affect trade between member states.

(v) The Enterprise Act.

A 1988 Enterprise White Paper proposed changes to competition policy. Some of which were enacted in the course of 1989. Henceforth the main reason for referring mergers will be their likely effect on competition. Though "public interest" referrals will remain, the Government will intervene only rarely. Generally, it was claimed, the "market" would look after the public interest. When judging the impact of a merger on competition, due regard will be given to foreign competition and also to potential entrants. The latter represents a particular fashion among modern industrial economists, who argue that many apparently monopolistic or oligopolistic industries may in fact be constrained to behave in a relatively competitive manner by the possibility that other firms might be attracted into their sector by high profits. Accordingly Monopolies Commission hearings are increasingly concerned with the existence or otherwise of "barriers to entry". The Act is also designed to speed up Monopolies Commission hearings, and to have a procedure of legal undertakings about the competitive effects of mergers, which might obviate the need for a full Commission investigation. Mergers policy is not, however, without its critics many of whom believe that the criteria for referral are now too lax, particularly compared to general practice in Europe. One example was the decision not to refer Nestlé's bid for Rowntree.

(vi) Industrial Structure.

Mergers may lead to monopoly and to the abuse of monopoly power. But it would be wrong to presume that mergers are always bad: mergers—by facilitating research and other economies of large-scale production—may increase industrial efficiency. For this reason the *Industrial Reorganisation Corporation* (IRC) was set up in 1966 under Government auspices. Its functions were to promote industrial reorganisation in the interests of industrial efficiency, *e.g.*, by enabling industries to achieve economies of scale or by reorganising inefficiently managed firms. It assisted firms in agreed regroupings and could intervene to encourage a particular takeover which, in its estimation, was in the public interest. However its objective in making loans was to "prod" and not to "prop" inefficient firms. It supported mergers in electronics, trawling, nuclear power, mechanical engineering, and other industries. In 1970 the Conservative Government decided to wind up the IRC. However, some of the proposed functions of the National Enterprise Board, set up in 1975, were similar to those performed by the IRC (*see* **Part IV**). The 1979 Conservative Government initially streamlined the NEB, and subsequently amalgamated it with the National Research and Development Corporation to form the British Technology Group.

Nationalised Industries.

After the extensive privatisation of industries and utilities undertaken during the last ten years, the Nationalised Industries now account for only 5 per cent of British production. In many cases—*e.g.*, the railways and postal services—these remaining state industries are natural monopolies, in which the provision of competing services could be wasteful, although the present government seems determined to privatise even those industries where there appears to be a natural monopoly.

With the exception of steel—denationalised 1951–53 and re-nationalised in 1967—nationalisation was for a long time not extended into manufacturing industry. The post-1974 Labour Government nationalised the shipbuilding and aerospace industries, and established the British National Oil Corporation and the National Enterprise Board with wide powers to take holdings in private industry. Under the 1979 Conservative Government the post-war trend towards greater public ownership of industry was reversed (*see* **Part IV**).

A 1967 White Paper dictated that as well as achieving specified financial targets, nationalised industries should earn a target rate of return on their investments and price according to the marginal cost of a service. With respect to investment, the initial rate of return was set at 8 per cent, and was subsequently raised to 10 per cent.

With respect to marginal cost pricing, a hypothetical example will illustrate the principle. Once all electricity production and transmission equipment have been installed the cost incurred in supplying additional electricity is low; thus consumers are charged a low price per unit of electricity consumed and, to avoid a financial loss, the Electricity Boards make a standing charge to help cover overheads. It is government policy that subsidies can be made for some services which are justified on social grounds, *e.g.*, grants to British Rail to continue unremunerative rail services, although these are due to be phased out over the next few years and have been halved in real terms since 1982. Cross-subsidisation of non-commercial services by commercial services within a nationalised industry is discouraged.

A new White Paper in 1978 changed the emphasis of government policy. Although the TDR and the principle of marginal cost pricing were retained, primary emphasis was moved from efficient decisions at the margin to a reasonable average performance, in terms of return on capital.

The present Government has challenged the whole concept of running publicly-owned industries even where a natural monopoly quite clearly exists. Industries remaining under state control have also been unable to raise sufficient outside investment capital because of the imposition of strict External Financing Limits. Public sector monopolies such as British Gas and British Telecom which have been returned to the private sector have also been accused of operating against the public interest. For this reason, future privatisations of monopoly industries are being conducted in such a manner that a degree of competition can be demonstrated, *e.g.* between the electricity producers and distributors in the forthcoming privatisation of the electricity industry. The Government is also seeking to introduce competition in the provision of public services. For example, local authorities are now obliged to put services such as refuse collection out to public tender. Following the 1988 Education Act schools can effectively compete for pupils and when planned health reforms are enacted hospitals will be essentially competing for patients referred through general practitioners.

3. INCOMES, WAGES, AND PRICES

Personal Income.

National income is a measure of the total income accruing to the residents in a country in return for services rendered (*see* **G13**). It therefore consists of the sum of wages, salaries, profits, and rents having allowed for depreciation. But not all this income accrues to persons, *e.g.*, companies do not distribute all their profits to shareholders and some nationalised industries earn profits. This is part of national income but not of *personal income*. On the other hand, some personal incomes are not payments for services rendered. Such incomes are called *transfer incomes* to emphasise that their payment does not add to the national income, but only transfers income from one agent to another. Included in this category are retirement pensions, child benefit and student grants. In the United Kingdom in 1988 central and local government made transfer payments to the personal sector of £59·5 billion.

Personal Disposable Income.

Not all personal income is available for spending.

In 1988 the State took 12·9 per cent of personal income in *direct taxation*, and 8·3 per cent went as Social Security contributions, which being compulsory are in effect a form of tax. Another 2 per cent went in contributions to pension schemes. The remaining 76·8 per cent of personal income—called *personal disposable income*—was available for spending. However, not all disposable income need be spent on consumer goods and services; income can instead be saved. There are many possible motives for saving, *e.g.*, to meet future contingencies, for a future purchase such as a house or car, for retirement, or for the income to be derived from saving. Saving as a fraction of personal disposable income fluctuated from 7 to 10 per cent between 1960 and 1971. By 1975 it had reached 12·8 per cent. It remained high thereafter, and peaked at 15·1 in 1980. Since then it has generally fallen, and was only 2·4 per cent in 1988 although it recovered to a level above 5% in 1989. Many explanations of this varying savings ratio have been advanced—it seems to be higher, the higher is the rate of inflation. In recent years the fall in savings has also been related to rapid growth in the value of personal sector wealth, particularly in housing.

Types of Personal Income.

The table shows the sources of household income. In 1988, the share of income from employment was 59 per cent. This rose considerably in the post Second World War period. The share of salaries grew relative to that of wages, not because average salaries rose faster than average wages but because the number of salaried workers expanded rapidly. With the development of the Welfare State there was an increase in the percentage of incomes derived from public grants—pensions, social security payments, student grants, *etc.*

SOURCES OF HOUSEHOLD INCOME,
1978 AND 1988

(As percentage of total)

	1978	1988
Wages and salaries	66	59
Self employment	9	10
Investments and rents	5	8
Annuities and pensions (other than social security benefits)	5	8
Social security benefits	12	12
Other sources	3	4

Over the post-war period as a whole, the share of self-employment income and incomes from property fell while that from wages and salaries and from social security benefits tended to rise. Over the past ten years, however, income from self-employment has begun to increase a little, in line with a larger share of the self-employed in the labour force. The share of income from annuities and pensions is also tending to grow along with the expansion of privately-funded occupational pension schemes. This will be encouraged further by incentives to transfer out of the state pension scheme into private pension plans.

Inequality of Income.

In 1986, the top 20 per cent of income receivers (defined as households rather than individuals), received 51·0 per cent of total income, whilst the bottom 20 per cent obtained only 0·3 per cent. Thus Britain is far from being an egalitarian

WEALTH OF INDIVIDUALS IN BRITAIN,
1987

Percentage of wealth owned by:	
Most wealthy 1 percent of population	18
,, ,, 5 ,, ,, ,, ,,	36
,, ,, 10 ,, ,, ,, ,,	50
,, ,, 25 ,, ,, ,, ,,	74
,, ,, 50 ,, ,, ,, ,,	93

society, but discrepancies have narrowed since before the war, though with a subsequent widening in the last decade.

Taxes on income are of course progressive, rising as income increases. This progressivity has been sharply reduced by the 1988 Budget and, although no further changes were announced in the 1989 or 1990 Budgets, policy is to reduce higher marginal tax rates still further in future years. The table (**G20**) shows the shares of disposable income. This is original income minus direct taxes and plus cash benefits. We can see that both are redistributive. In 1986 the share of the top 20 per cent fell to 41·6 per cent after allowing for these two items, whilst the share of the bottom 20 per cent rose to 7·4 per cent. Allowing for the effects of indirect taxation and benefits in kind produces final income. As the table shows, these two latter effects tend to be offsetting, but in 1986 meant that the top 20 per cent lost 2·1 per cent and the bottom fifth gained the same.

Thus the direct tax burden somewhat squeezes the distribution of incomes. But until the mid 1970s the narrowing dispersion of incomes before tax was of greater importance in making Britain rather more egalitarian than taxation policy. Since the late 1970s, however, inequality of pre-tax incomes has increased, whilst the tax system has not become significantly more redistributive.

Income and Spending Power.

In various ways figures for incomes alone underestimate the degree of inequality in British society. First, incomes are incomes as defined for income tax purposes. Any allowed expenses are excluded; and for the self-employed and the higher ranks of management the expense allowance now adds substantially to spending power. Second, if one buys an asset which then rises in value one gains extra spending power. Such capital gains can be very important to the wealthy in periods of boom in ordinary share prices, land prices and house prices—as experienced in Britain in the 1950s and 1960s. Yet only in 1965 did capital gains become taxable and even then the rate of tax on capital gains was low in relation to the rate on additional income. The 1988 Budget applied the same rate of tax as on incomes, though capital gains still attracted a larger initial tax-free allowance.

Inequality of Wealth.

Spending power depends not only on income and capital gains but also on the sheer amount of capital owned. Data on the ownership of capital in Britain have to be estimated indirectly from information arising in connection with the payment of death duties, supplemented by information from capital transfer tax (from 1986 inheritance tax) returns and therefore cannot always be relied upon. An alternative method is to estimate the stock of wealth by working back from information on investment income, but this approach is also prone to error. It appears from the table that the most wealthy 1 per cent of the population own 18 per cent of all wealth, whilst 50 per cent of all wealth is owned by the richest 10 per cent. Even more strikingly, the poorer half of the population own only 7 per cent of total wealth. It should be emphasised, however, that the data refer to *individuals* rather than to *households*: this can give a misleading impression if, for example, the assets of married couples are generally registered in the name of one of the marriage partners rather than as jointly-owned assets. Nevertheless, it is fair to conclude from the data that the disparity of wealth is considerably greater than that of income. Moreover, there is a natural tendency for the inequality of wealth to grow because the higher income groups tend to save a higher proportion of their income and so to accumulate capital more readily. The Government by capital transfer tax tried but largely failed to neutralise this tendency. Between 1971 and 1987 the share of the wealthiest 1 per cent fell from 31 to 18 per cent of total wealth. But this represents a minor change, particularly since much of what the top 1 per cent has lost has been redistributed to the rest of the top decile.

The capital transfer tax (CTT) was introduced in 1974. Until then only transfers of wealth on death or shortly before death were taxable. The CTT had

DISTRIBUTION OF ORIGINAL, DISPOSABLE AND FINAL HOUSEHOLD INCOME

	Quintile groups of households				
	Bottom Fifth	Next Fifth	Middle Fifth	Next Fifth	Top Fifth
Original Income					
1976	0·8	9·4	18·8	26·6	44·4
1981	0·6	8·1	18·0	26·9	46·4
1983	0·3	6·7	17·7	27·2	48·0
1987	0·3	5·7	16·4	26·9	51·0
Disposable Income					
1976	7·0	12·6	18·2	24·1	38·1
1981	6·7	12·1	17·7	24·1	39·4
1983	6·9	11·9	17·6	24·0	39·6
1987	7·4	10·9	16·3	28·8	41·6
Final Income					
1976	7·4	12·7	18·0	24·0	37·9
1981	7·1	12·4	17·9	24·0	38·6
1983	6·9	12·2	17·6	24·0	39·3
1987	9·5	11·8	16·1	23·2	39·5

GROSS WEEKLY EARNINGS, GREAT BRITAIN

(Average earnings, adults, April 1989)

	Manual	Non-Manual
Men . . .	£217·8	£323·6
Women . . .	£134·9	£195·0

many loopholes, but did something to redistribute wealth. The 1986 Budget effectively abolished CTT for gifts *inter vivos*, the tax (renamed inheritance tax) applying on death or transfers made in the 7 years preceding death.

Wages and Salaries.

In 1988 59 per cent of personal income was paid in the form of wages and salaries. The distinction between the two is very much a matter of convention; many salary-earners now earn less than wage-earners, and a more important division is between those salary-earners who are paid monthly and the rest. Even though monthly paid staff do not now earn more than wage-earners, they may still in effect be better off; for they generally work shorter hours, are more likely to be covered by private superannuation schemes, and work in better conditions. The table shows the earnings of manual and non-manual workers.

Earnings by Occupation.

Different occupations command different pay, as the table shows. The figures are of average earnings. The structure of pay reflects in part the amount of responsibility which the different jobs entail. The differentials reflect also the ease of entry into various occupations. This in turn depends on the degree of specialised knowledge, skill or talent required, and in a few cases it depends on the extent to which artificial barriers to entry have created scarcity. The structure of pay is also influenced, of course, by the degree of organisation and bargaining strength of workers in different occupations. Finally, the relative strengths of demand for different types of worker is important, as is the force of custom.

Within the manual occupations the difference between skilled, semi-skilled and unskilled pay narrowed over the post-war years. This was most marked during the war, in the years immediately after the war and between 1970 and 1976 when skilled workers were often granted the same flat rate advances as unskilled. The last few years may well be seeing a reversal of such narrowing and indeed further widening; but as yet it is too early to make a full assessment.

Occupational differentials have been a major source of industrial strife in some industries. In engineering, for instance, there has been continued conflict between unions with membership largely

AVERAGE GROSS WEEKLY EARNINGS OF FULL-TIME ADULT MALE EMPLOYEES, BY SELECTED OCCUPATIONS, APRIL 1989

	£ per week
Medical practitioner . .	588·2
Finance, insurance specialist .	571·6
Office manager . . .	388·6
Accountant	370·7
Scientist	361·7
Teacher in further education .	342·6
Production manager . .	340·4
Engineer, civil or structural .	337·2
Policeman (below Sergeant) .	308·1
Primary teacher . . .	298·9
Electrician	271·1
Train driver	261·6
Maintenance fitter . . .	257·3
Telephone fitter . . .	252·0
Plumber	232·8
Heavy goods driver . .	231·2
Postman	214·6
Bricklayer	195·7
General clerk . . .	187·4
Painter, decorator . . .	184·6
Dustman	183·7
Unskilled building worker . .	176·2
Butcher	164·4
Hospital porter . . .	157·1
General farm worker . . .	150·4
Total workers . . .	269·5
of which: Manual . . .	217·8
Non-manual . .	323·6

among the skilled and those with membership largely among the less skilled, over what forms demands for wage increases should take. On the railways there has been similar strife. Because of the importance placed on occupational differentials in collective bargaining there exist powerful rigidities in the structure of earnings in Britain.

Earnings by Industry.

Even within the manual occupations there are significant differences in earnings among industries. These are associated with the bargaining strength of different groups of workers, with the prosperity of the industry, and with the average skill levels required in production. Manufacturing industries as a whole pay relatively well. Public administration (including local government, road-men and the like) is a low-wage sector.

Earnings by Sex.

The table also shows very significant earnings differences within each industry between men and women. There are two possible reasons why women are paid less than men. One is that they

AVERAGE WEEKLY EARNINGS OF
MANUAL WORKERS IN CERTAIN
INDUSTRIES (£)
(April 1989)

	Men	Women
Mineral oil refining . .	359·5	—†
Printing and publishing .	263·7	169·4
Motor vehicles . . .	256·7	172·2
Chemicals	242·4	153·7
Textiles	188·9	125·2
*All manufacturing** .	*230·6*	*138·2*
Transport and		
communication . .	230·7	181·5
Public administration .	182·8	147·0
Retail distribution . .	181·5	125·1
*All industries** . .	*217·8*	*134·9*

*Including industries not listed.
†Too small a number of women in this category to
be recorded.

are crowded into lower-paying occupations. The
second is that they may have lower pay than men
within the same occupation. Either form of disadvantage could be the result of discrimination or
of women possessing inferior productive characteristics. In practice it is a very difficult distinction to
make. Equal opportunities and equal pay legislation
attempts to reduce discrimination. The Equal Pay
Act (1970) obliged a firm to pay men and women,
who are doing the same job, the same wage by the
end of 1975. In 1972 women in manual occupations
had median earnings which were about half those of
men. By 1978 this figure had risen to over 60 per
cent, though by the early 1980s this improvement
had slowed down, and was only 61·9 per cent in
1989. Women in non-manual occupations had
median earnings which were just over 60 per cent of
their male counterparts'. These changes are explained by the impact of the Act, by flat rate general
increases agreed under incomes policies, and by
trade union bargaining policy under inflation.
There have been renewed initiatives against sexual
discrimination. In particular, in 1984 an amendment to the Equal Pay Act insisted that as well as
paying men and women doing the same job the
same rate of pay, parity of pay should also apply to
jobs of equal value. The Equal Opportunities
Commission has issued a Code of Practice which
suggests positive actions which employers might
take to improve the lot of women in employment.
Recently this has contributed to a catch-up for
women in areas of the retail trade.

Overtime and short-time.

The earnings of any individual worker depend
on many factors, and are usually well above the
basic wage rate payable for a *standard working
week*. They include overtime earnings; and overtime working is common for men. In most weeks in
the 1970s about 1–2 million operatives in manufacturing—about a third of the total—worked overtime to the extent of 8 to 9 hours. In early 1990
capacity pressures in industry meant that 39 per
cent of operatives worked an average of 9·9 hours
overtime each. Nor is overtime confined to male
manual employment; it is found, for example, in
office work and even in some of the professions like
medicine and accountancy. The working week is
composed of standard hours and overtime hours.
Its length has diminished since before the war,
although the standard week has been more significantly reduced.

In most industries, for manual workers it was cut
from 48 to 44 hours soon after the war. A 42-hour
week was introduced between 1960 and 1962, and
there was a movement towards a 40-hour standard
working-week in the late 1960s. More recently there
have been pressures from unions, notably in
engineering industries, to reduce the standard week
below 40 hours, and indeed this has happened in
many sectors. In much of the chemical industry, for
example, it is often as low as 35 hours. The
standard working week tends to be slightly less for
white collar workers than for manual workers.

Short-time, the working of less than the standard
week, has not been common since the war. It has
been important in particular industries at particular
times; but at the beginning of 1990 it was far
smaller than overtime. Then 13,000 operatives in
manufacturing were on an average short-time of
11·5 hours a week—a total 0·15 million hours lost as
against 16·1 million hours of overtime in the same
week. It is disappointing that, in the past three
years, much of the extra demand for goods has been
met from higher overtime rather than more
employment. This may reflect continued caution
among firms about longer-term prospects for UK
manufacturing, particularly when interest rates are
being maintained at very high levels.

Earnings and Rates.

Overtime is not, however, the main reason why
earnings exceed minimum wage-rates; for most
workers earn very much more than the minimum
in the standard working-week. One reason is
payment by results, the system of payment under
which the worker's wage depends partly on output
or performance. A common form is still the piecework system, under which pieceworkers are paid a
fixed low rate per hour for each hour worked plus
a fixed piecework price for each operation performed; but increasingly employers tend to prefer,
as a more effective incentive, some scheme under
which the bonus payment is related to the output
or some other measure of the performance of a larger
group or to that of a whole factory. With such incentive schemes, earnings rise as productivity rises,
and, as usually such workers also participate in
advances in wage-rates negotiated between employers and unions, the gap between earnings and wage-
rates tends to widen for them. So workers not paid
on incentive systems press for similar advances for
themselves, and in times of booming trade get them
under a wide variety of names and forms—merit
payments, lieu rates, compensation bonuses *etc*.
Merit-related pay is becoming increasingly fashionable, particularly in white-collar work. An example
of such a scheme would be that each employee is
given a cost of living increase each year plus an
additional amount based on merit, as judged by an
annual assessment. This principle has been extended
further in some large firms, where employees receive
performance-related bonuses according to whether
or not they have met pre-determined objectives or
targets. These are usually, but not exclusively,
based on sales performance. Some trade unionists
regard this as a potentially severe threat to collective
negotiations about pay.

Wage Negotiation.

In Britain there were 10·3 million trade union
members in 323 unions at the end of 1988. Most of
these unions are very small, 234 having less than
2,500 members, but 21 have a membership of over
100,000. The main job of unions is collective
bargaining with employers, and in most industries
most employers also belong to associations which
bargain collectively on their behalf. Some big firms,
however, prefer to remain outside the associations,
and strike their own bargain with the unions. Before
the war many firms tried to encourage the formation
of Company Unions, *i.e.*, of unions confined to employees of a single firm; but this is now uncommon.
In some lowly paid trades minimum wages are fixed
by Wages Councils set up by the Department of
Employment: and representatives of the workers
and employers, and independent members, meet
together to reach agreement on the settlement to be
recommended to the Minister. But over most of industry the aim of collective bargaining is to reach
voluntary agreement, and the Department of
Employment intervenes only when no agreement
is reached. In 1974 the Labour Government set up
the *Advisory Conciliation and Arbitration Service*
(A.C.A.S.) to provide independent mediation and
arbitration services.

The usual pattern of negotiation is like this.
First, the union puts in a claim for an all-round
increase, usually much larger than it expects to
get. Then after a time the employers reply, often
offering a much smaller increase, and sometimes
none at all. They then argue round a table until
either they reach agreement or they definitely fail
to reach agreement. If the latter happens the next
step varies considerably from industry to industry.

WAGES AND PRICES
(1955 = 100)

	Weekly earnings	Index of retail prices	Real earnings
1955 . . .	100	100	100
1960 . . .	130	114	114
1965 . . .	175	136	129
1970 . . .	250	169	148
1975 . . .	540	313	173
1980 . . .	997	611	163
1985 . . .	1,537	865	178
1989 . . .	2,120	1,054	201

INDEX OF RETAIL PRICES
(1956 = 100)

	1956 Weight*.	1989 Weight*.	Monthly average index.						
			1960	1965	1970	1975	1980	1985	1989
Food . . .	350	154	105	121	152	313	601	790	921
Drink . . .	71	83	97	125	153	239	463	729	879
Tobacco . . .	80	36	108	140	162	250	491	901	1,163
Housing . . .	87	175	128	162	206	368	790	1,326	1,982
Fuel and light .	55	54	116	148	188	359	763	1,216	1,332
Household goods .	66	71	97	107	129	212	366	427	467
Clothing and footwear	106	73	103	112	130	220	359	390	454
Transport and vehicles	68	151	116	132	163	311	624	848	949
Services . . .	58	107	116	148	202	379	735	1,067	1,305
Other goods . .	59	47	112	136	178	315	629	891	1,007
Meals bought outside the home	—	49	—	—	160	209	458	653	889
All items . . .	*1000*	*1000*	*109*	*130*	*163*	*301*	*589*	*834*	*1,013*

* *i.e.*, proportionate importance of items in total expenditure in 1956 and in 1987.

Many industries have their own "conciliation" machinery, in which outsiders try to help the two sides to reach agreement. Some, though not many, also have their own "arbitration" machinery, in which outsiders can recommend a solution of the dispute, which is sometimes binding and sometimes not. It depends on what the two sides have agreed on in advance. Many industries have no machinery of their own and until 1974 depended on the general facilities the Minister responsible could offer. Since then they have relied on the services of A.C.A.S. Just as neither unions nor employers were obliged to call in the Minister, so now they are under no obligation to call in A.C.A.S.; the unions may opt to put pressure on the employers immediately either by strike action, or by banning overtime or piecework, or by other action.

After the Second World War plant bargaining developed as an increasingly important supplement to industry-wide bargaining in many sectors of the economy. Initially this was largely informal bargaining, with shop-stewards (unpaid lay trade union officials at the plant level) negotiating with management about, for example, special rates for working new machines. It is this which to a large degree was responsible for the growing gap between wage rates and earnings. The Donovan Commission, which was set up to inquire into the state of industrial relations and which reported in 1968, also saw it as a major cause of many of Britain's industrial relations problems, such as a high level of strike activity. Realising that it was impossible to put the clock back, the Commission recommended that plant bargaining procedures should be formalised, giving, for instance, proper channels for the resolution of wage disputes. Since then there has indeed been an increase in *formal* plant negotiations, with many plants now setting their own wage rates and using national agreements purely as a minimum benchmark. This development has probably improved the climate of industrial relations. Recently some, especially in manufacturing, companies concerned about the administrative cost as well as about the leapfrogging effects of plant agreements, have moved to single company bargains. As yet it is too early to discern whether this will be an extensive or permanent development, particularly when the Government is encouraging the development of local pay bargaining to reflect different demand pressures in different areas. However, it is safe to say that today Britain has two systems of industrial relations. In large companies, especially in manufacturing, there is single employer bargaining whether this be at the establishment or company level. In small organisations, especially outside manufacturing, multi-employer industry-wide bargaining is still surprisingly important.

Such developments, however, have done little to increase the Government's power to control wages directly or to impose agreements—if anything quite the reverse. Indeed, the past few years have seen increasing evidence that more decentralised bargaining was resulting in upward pressure on real wages—contributing to the beginnings of a wage/price spiral in 1989 and 1990. Attempts to introduce compulsion in wage-determination are described in **Part IV**.

Strikes.

The strike is the unions' weapon of last resort. Most unions maintain strike funds in order to support their members when they call them out on strike; but these funds are small, and strike pay is usually very much below normal wages. So unions cannot afford to call strikes irresponsibly, and major official strikes are relatively uncommon. Nevertheless, the big strikes are important; for the success or failure of one big strike can affect the results of all the other collective bargaining under way at the time.

Most strikes are neither large nor official. An official strike is one called by a union, usually by decision of the national executive, and is typically the result of collective bargaining about wages. But unofficial strikes called by local leaders are often about other matters. Few of the big unofficial strikes which plagued the docks were about wages; rather they reflected job insecurity and the poor state of labour relations in that industry. Much the same may be said about the continual strikes in ship-building, many of them caused by demarcation disputes concerning which jobs should be done by which type of skilled worker. Other strike-prone industries are mining and vehicles. In most industries there are very few strikes, and they tend to be concentrated in the larger plants.

From the mid-1950s the number of strikes in Britain tended to increase, except in coal mining. In 1969 and 1970 there was a huge jump in both the number of stoppages and working days lost. After that industrial disputes fell to a more normal level, and indeed by the early 1980s were at an historically very low intensity. Partly this reflected the impact of high unemployment, but may also have represented a more permanent improvement in Britain's strike record. When unemployment fell sharply in 1988 and 1989, the number of strikes did not increase disturbingly. However, in spite of a succession of transport strikes in the summer of 1989, and an ambulance dispute later in the year, working days lost in 1989 numbered just over 4 million, only a little above the average of the previous four years. But is Britain particularly strike prone compared with other countries? Making allowances for the size of their labour forces, Sweden and West Germany have fewer strikes and lose fewer working days than Britain. The United States has less strikes, but the ones they have are very large, and thus they lose more working days than the U.K. The strike records of Australia and France are most comparable with the U.K.'s.

In its Industrial Relations Act of 1971 the Conservative Government laid down new laws for the regulation of industrial relations and for the curbing of strikes. However, the Act was repealed by the incoming Labour Government in 1974, which itself brought in several new pieces of legislation, including the Trade Unions and Labour Relations Act, the Employment Protection Act, and the Trade Unions and Labour Relations (Amendment) Act. As well as increasing legal protection for the individual employee and extending trade union immunities and rights, this legislation was concerned to improve industrial relations practice. The belief behind the legislation was that this could be done by machinery which ensured, for example, that employers formally recognised unions for collective bargaining purposes and that unions had greater access to information to enable them to negotiate about issues (such as a firm's investment plans) which previously ignorance had precluded them from doing.

With the election of a Conservative Government in 1979, the direction of legislation altered again. The 1980 Employment Act introduced measures to moderate the closed shop, provide funds for secret union ballots about important issues such as industrial action, and to limit picketing to only the establishments at which strikes were taking place. A further Act in 1982 intensified pressure on the unions. In particular it introduced further measures against existing closed shops and increased the liability of unions for the actions of their members. In 1984 came the Trade Union Act concerned with union democracy. In this unions were denied immunity if strikes took place without ballots, voting members of union executives had to be elected, and periodic ballots on the political use of union funds were required. In 1988 a further piece of legislation was passed by Parliament, which, inter alia, made it illegal for unions to discipline members who refused to obey a strike call, even a legal one. Such legislative developments are likely to reduce unions' ability to call and prosecute strikes, and possibly also will diminish the scope for local union leaders to have a decisive impact on strike decisions. The process continues. A new Employment Bill, which was before Parliament in early 1990, proposed to effectively outlaw pre-entry closed shops and secondary industrial action. Its proposals would also lead to unofficial strikes being more costly to the union.

Prices and Real Incomes.

The aim of a trade union is to get for its members a higher standard of living, and its success depends on the extent to which wage advances exceed the rise in the cost of living. Prices rose very rapidly (by over 30 per cent) between 1949 and 1953, and earnings only just kept ahead in this period. But after that *real earnings* (*i.e.*, the command which money earnings have over goods and services) rose steadily until the early 1970s. Since then real earnings have increased more spasmodically (*see* **Part IV**).

Price Changes.

In the calculation of real wages it is usual to make use of the *index of retail prices*, commonly called the cost-of-living index. The index is calculated monthly by the Department of Employment, and it naturally has an influence on the course of wage negotiations.

The table (**G22**) shows how consumers allocate their expenditure among different commodities in Britain, and how the prices of these commodities have moved over time. About 18 per cent of expenditure in 1989 was on food; and housing, fuel and light between them accounted for 22·9 per cent. Drink and tobacco represented 11·9 per cent; and expenditure on transport and vehicles no less than 15·1 per cent. Comparing the allocation of expenditure in 1956 and in 1989, we see in particular the growing importance of housing and transport and vehicles and the declining importance of food in household budgets. As people grow richer they choose to spend less of their income on food.

Price changes have not been the same for all types of goods. For instance, between 1956 and 1989, when the total index rose by 1,013 per cent, housing went up by 1,982 per cent and fuel and light by 1,332 per cent; but the prices of drink, and especially clothing and durable household goods rose less than the average.

The general retail price index is calculated by weighting each of the commodity price indexes by the proportionate importance of that commodity in total expenditure in a particular year, and then summing all the indexes, *i.e.*, the general index is a *weighted average* of its constituent indexes. A different pattern of expenditure would mean a different set of weights, and hence a different cost-of-living index. For instance, the poor—and particularly pensioners—spend a higher proportion on the basic necessities; food, fuel and light, and housing. It is possible that the cost-of-living rose more for the poor than for the rich over these years.

The cost-of-living index has not risen evenly in Britain. There were spurts of rapid inflation in the periods 1950–52 and 1954–56, followed by a decade of relatively little inflation (averaging under 3 per cent per annum). After 1967, however, the rate of inflation accelerated, rising progressively from 2·5 per cent per annum between 1966 and 1967 to 7·0 per cent between 1971 and 1972. For more recent developments *see* **Part IV**.

The Causes of Inflation.

(i) Import Prices.

Prices charged in the shops are determined by a great many factors, over many of which the Government has little or no control. First among these is the price of imports. Prices of imported food and raw materials are determined in the world markets, in which Britain is only one of many purchasers. Prices in raw material and food markets can fluctuate wildly. Big increases in commodity prices occurred during the Korean war, in the early 1970's and in 1979 (*see* **Part IV**). The sharp increases in the prices of primary commodities contributed to British inflation at these and other times, but for most of the post-war period the rise in import prices has been less rapid than domestic inflation even allowing for unfavourable exchange rate movements which push up the price of imports in sterling terms.

The source of domestic inflation has to be looked for in the tendency of wages and salaries, or profits, or other incomes to rise faster than real output; and this one or other of them has done in almost every year since the war.

(ii) Demand-Pull Inflation.

An explanation of domestically generated inflation is that it arises not so much from increased costs as from demand pressures increasing prices and profits. If there is an increase in aggregate demand for goods and services in the economy, how does the economy respond? If it is operating at less than full employment, producers are able to expand their production to meet the additional demand. But if full employment has already been achieved, it is the price level and not production which rises. Given an excess demand for goods and services, there is competitive bidding for the limited supplies and producers are able to sell at higher prices. A more sophisticated version of this argument recognises that full employment cannot be precisely defined: rather, there are degrees of less or more unemployment. Bottlenecks appear in different firms and industries at different stages; so that any increase in demand is met by an increase in both prices and production. But the lower the rate of unemployment, the more does the response take the form of price increases.

A variant of the demand-pull theory is the so-called *quantity theory of money*, in which inflation is seen as a response to an increase in the supply of money; there is too much money chasing too few goods. The theory dates back at least to David Hume, but it was generally discredited as a result of the writings of Maynard Keynes in the 1930s. However, it was revived by Milton Friedman and has received some measure of acceptance among economists, especially in the United States.

The evidence for the demand-pull theory of inflation in Britain is very slight, at least in more recent times and especially since the mid-1960s. No doubt there are times at which demand contributes to inflation in the economy as a whole or in particular sectors. Thus, for instance, the great shortages during and immediately after the war would no doubt have generated rapid demand inflation had it not been for rationing and price controls; and the spurt of inflation between 1954 and 1956 was associated with a very high pressure of demand. On the other hand, inflation has occurred even in periods of relatively high unemployment. Moreover, the method by which most firms price their products is on the basis of their costs; so that most prices are not directly sensitive to the pressure of demand. A more plausible mechanism by which demand might influence prices indirectly is through its effect on wages. In fact, there has been a lively debate as to the extent to which wages are influenced by the pressure of demand as opposed to being relatively independent of it. There is, however, general agreement that wages are the main driving force behind prices.

(iii) Wages and Inflation.

When a trade union negotiates a wage increase for all or most employees in an industry, firms will immediately consider whether they should increase their prices to cover their increased wage-costs. As it is common practice for firms to fix the selling prices of their products by first calculating the direct cost of labour and of materials, and then adding on a percentage to cover overhead costs and profits, they will tend to want to raise their prices not only to cover the cost of the wage advance, but also to cover their percentage addition. Moreover, in deciding whether or not their customers will stand for such increases, firms will be influenced by the knowledge that their competitors have to pay the increased wages too, and will probably therefore be raising their prices. So industry-wide wage advances—and changes in costs of materials—are particularly likely to be passed on to the consumer; and, as wage-earners are also consumers, to generate further demands for wage advances to cover the increased prices.

Once this spiral gets going, it is very hard to stop it. In general, the requirement is that wage earnings should not rise faster than productivity (output per man). But as in some industries productivity is very slow to rise, and as it would be unfair and impracticable to exclude their workers from participating in any general rise in the standard of living, this requirement means that in industries with a rapid growth of productivity wage advances should be kept well below the rate of rise of productivity. For two reasons this is rather difficult. First, rising productivity often raises the wages of some workers in these industries automatically, because they are paid by results or through some incentive scheme. The rise of wages from this source takes the form of a tendency on the part of earnings in these industries to rise faster than wage-rates; but that does not mean that all employees benefit, or that the unions in these industries will not press for the same rate of increase in wage-rates as is achieved in the slowly-growing industries. Second, employers in the rapidly-growing industries have far less reason to resist demands for wage increases than those in slowly-growing industries. Indeed, they are quite likely to bid up wages in order to get the labour they need, rather than to try to hold down wages.

There are therefore major problems in preventing a faster rise in wages than in productivity, with its consequence of rising prices. And once a wage-price spiral has started, the problems become more acute because unions and employers become accustomed to substantial annual advances in money wages. A main source of continuing price inflation has been the tendency of money wages to continue to advance at a rate that was appropriate when the cost-of-living was going up sharply, but ceased to be appropriate in later years.

(iv) The Phillips Curve.

Even if wage behaviour is primarily responsible for inflation, the pressure of demand may still be important. If unemployment is low or falling rapidly, and unfilled vacancies high, there is competitive bidding among employers to obtain or retain their workers. Moreover, with the economy booming the bargaining strength of trade unions increases: employers are more willing to concede wage demands. These possibilities have led economists to postulate—and indeed to measure—the so-called *Phillips Curve* relationship: the lower the level of unemployment, the faster the rate of increase in money wages. Such a relationship has been found to exist in the British economy over some periods. But it is dangerous to postulate "general laws" in economics: inflation accelerated despite high and growing unemployment. Clearly, changes in the cost-of-living, expectations for the future, Government policies and the degree of militancy of trade unionists can all have a significant influence on wage behaviour; and the level of demand may at times be relatively unimportant.

There are many schools of thought attempting to explain developments since the late 1960s, but it is possible to discern two general approaches. The first is that trade unions behave reactively. In other words, they respond in their wage demands to their expectations about prices and Government policies. A restrictive monetary policy might help moderate inflation, in that it might directly reduce prices and it might affect expectations. The second school of thought is that unions, as well as responding to their perception of the events they face, act in a more initiatory way—to fulfil, for example, aspirations (developed perhaps over a long period of time) about what their real earnings, and therefore their share of the national cake, should be. In striving to realise these aspirations, they may be relatively unaffected by concern over rising unemployment. A likely explanation is that unions felt unconcerned about relatively minor variations in the unemployment rate, safe in the knowledge that Government was committed to the maintenance of full employment. In the mid-1970s such a commitment was quite explicitly abandoned. That, together with the experience of very high unemployment in the 1980s might, it was argued, tighten the demand constraint in more prosperous future times. No longer, it was argued, would unions be able to count on being "protected from the consequences of their own actions". Many economists, therefore, were surprised at the persistence of quite high wage inflation during the very high unemployment of the mid-1980s. Their attempts to explain this are described in **Part IV**.

The Effects of Inflation.

British Governments have been concerned about inflation mainly because of its effects on British competitiveness, and hence on the balance of payments. If our costs rise relative to competitors' costs, British exporters find it more difficult to compete in foreign markets if they raise their prices; and if they keep prices down in order to compete, this implies their having to accept lower profit margins on exports than on sales in the home market, and so discourages exporting. Alternatively, this lack of competitiveness might be reflected in falling exchange rates. This by itself is not necessarily a bad thing, but the danger is that it can start a spiral. An initial depreciation causes price inflation to increase at home, which causes further wage increases, which leads to further depreciation, and so on. The result could be hyperinflation. This clearly has a major efficiency cost, since it will cause people to economise on the use of money in conducting their transactions.

Inflation can have other harmful consequences. It often produces a redistribution of income, with the strong gaining at the expense of the weak, *i.e.*, the poorly organised workers and the pensioners. In inflationary conditions income gains can appear to result not so much from work or sacrifice as from ingenuity and speculation and the exercise of economic and political power. Inflation can breed insecurity and industrial unrest. Among businessmen it increases uncertainty, reduces investment and hence growth. Finally, it causes a redistribution of income away from lenders to borrowers unless interst rates remain positive in real terms, as they are at present. What is clear is that the costs of inflation are significantly greater the more unanticipated it is.

Government Policy against Inflation.

There are several possible methods of attack on the inflationary spiral of wages and prices. Their usefulness will depend on the causes of the inflation.

One policy appropriate to most inflations, and also helpful to other objectives of economic policy, is to achieve a faster rate of productivity growth. The faster the growth of average productivity the faster can average incomes rise without an increase in average prices. Comprehensive and detailed government control of wages except as an emergency policy was thought for a long time to be impractical for political and institutional reasons, as was comprehensive and detailed control of prices. Experience suggested that such detailed policy, except as a temporary general "freeze", would be very difficult to operate and, if successful, would involve a major loss of flexibility in the economy. At the other extreme, general exhortations to unions to exercise restraint on wages, and to manufacturers to exercise restraint on prices, were thought to have little effect. After 1974 more people began to think that a semi-permanent incomes policy might in fact be a viable policy tool. This is discussed in **Part IV.**

The Government can attempt to regulate inflation by controlling purchasing power through its monetary and fiscal policies, the nature of which will be examined below. There is a danger that curbing demand also curbs the growth of output and productivity in the economy; so conflicting with other objectives of economic policy. Moreover, there is no certainty that inflation is sensitive to the rate of unemployment over the politically acceptable range of unemployment.

4. MONEY, BANKING AND FINANCE
Economic Objectives and Demand Management.

The various economic objectives—full employment, balance of payments equilibrium, the control of inflation, *etc.*—which, as mentioned in **Part I,** have been shared by all post-war British Governments, are all to a greater or a lesser extent dependent for their attainment upon the type of *demand management* policy pursued by the government. By this is meant the policy, or set of policies, with which the government seeks to regulate the total level of expenditure on goods and services. The latter is the sum of consumption and investment expenditure by both the private sector (firms and consumers) and the public sector (the government and the nationalised industries). If the resulting level of aggregate demand for output is greater than the amount which can be produced with the economy's resources the result will be shortages leading to inflation and/or an increased demand for imports. If the level of demand is not high enough, on the other hand, the result will be a waste of resources, *i.e.*, workers will be unemployed and capital equipment will be underutilised. Hence it is crucial for the government to keep the pressure of demand at an appropriate level by regulating the various types of expenditure making up the total.

Fiscal and Monetary Policy.

One way in which the government can attempt to regulate demand is by fiscal policy, *i.e.*, the regulation of taxes and public expenditure (*see* **Part IV**). If the government believes, for example,

that the level of demand is too high, it may seek to reduce it by raising taxes whilst leaving public expenditure unchanged, thereby reducing its *budget deficit* (*i.e.*, the excess of public spending over tax revenue). Since the private sector's expenditure plans are financed partly out of its after-tax income and partly out of borrowing, an increase in taxes will generally reduce private sector expenditure, so that total expenditure then falls if public expenditure is held constant. Conversely, the government can cut taxes or increase public spending if it wants to expand the economy by increasing total expenditure.

However, fiscal policy of this type is not independent of *monetary policy, i.e.*, the regulation of interest rates or the stock of money in the economy. For example, if the government increases public spending it has to pay for the various resources which this involves. The finance may come from additional taxes, but if the government does not raise taxes the extra expenditure then has to be paid for in one of two ways: either the government increases its borrowing from the private sector by issuing government stock in return for money to pay for public expenditure; or the government prints new money for this purpose. In the latter case the supply of money is increased; in the former case interest rates will generally be increased, since the private sector will probably require higher interest rates if it is to be induced to lend extra funds to the government.

Economic Controversies.

Changes in the government's "fiscal stance" (*i.e.*, the size of its budget deficit) necessarily involve monetary changes in the form of interest rate and/or money supply changes. The operation of monetary and fiscal policies has been a long-standing area of controversy among economists, although the nature of the disagreements has tended to alter somewhat over time. One traditional controversy has been between "Keynesian" and "monetarist" economists. The former take their lead from the English economist J. M. Keynes, whose most well-known work was published in the 1930s, whilst the pioneer of monetarism, in a series of books and articles in the 1950s and 1960s, was Milton Friedman of Chicago University. Keynesian ideas dominated economic policy making in Britain and elsewhere from the end of the second world war up to the late 1960s. Since the mid-1970s policy making has been predominantly monetarist, though by the mid-1980s some Keynesian elements appeared to be re-surfacing. These various phases of policy making are described in more detail later, after the main principles of monetary and fiscal policies, and the sources of economic controversy, have been considered.

The Keynesian approach had a clear view about both the aims and the methods of macroeconomic policy making. The main aim was to achieve and maintain high levels of output and employment—Keynes's ideas were developed primarily in reaction to the mass unemployment of the inter-war period—and the main policy instrument for this purpose was fiscal policy. Keynesians argued that suitable choices of tax rates and of levels of public spending could maintain demand at a level high enough to secure continuous full employment. They also advocated that fiscal policy should be *fine tuned, i.e.* that tax and spending decisions should be frequently reviewed and amended in the light of short term changes in economic conditions. In this way it was argued that economic fluctuations could be largely avoided, in effect by operating fiscal policy counter-cyclically—adopting a more expansionary policy stance if unemployment showed signs of rising, and *vice versa*. During the 1950s and 1960s Keynesians largely downgraded the role of monetary policy, which was seen as an unreliable and possibly an ineffective means of regulating demand. Some Keynesians argued that the appropriate monetary policy was to manipulate the supply of money in order to stabilise interest rates.

From the mid-1950s onwards, Milton Friedman and others began to dispute both the aims and the methods of Keynesian policy makers. They had several important criticisms. First, they argued that on the basis of evidence from America, Britain, and elsewhere, the money supply was the main determinant of the level of economic activity, contrary to Keynesian ideas. Secondly, they were suspicious of fine tuning, arguing that frequent policy changes could destabilise rather than stabilise the economy. Thirdly, they questioned the policy aim of giving over-riding priority to the level of employment, arguing that this potentially conflicted with other aims such as the balance of payments and the control of inflation. Monetarists therefore urged governments to pay much more attention to controlling the money supply, and to a wider range of policy objectives.

From the mid-1970s to the mid-1980s monetarist prescriptions were broadly followed. The experience led to modifications in the traditional attitudes of both groups of economists, and some of the traditional disagreements have been partially resolved. However, there is still a considerable range of views amongst economists about both the aims and the methods of macroeconomic policy making.

The Definition of "Money".

Money plays a central role in any modern economy: without it, all but the simplest buying and selling transactions would become difficult or impossible, since people would then have to use barter. In a barter economy goods are traded directly, so that anyone wishing to obtain, say, food has to pay for it by providing the food producer with some good or service which he requires. The obvious difficulty is that this relies on a "double coincidence" of wants: if the prospective food purchaser cannot supply anything which the food producer wants, the transaction cannot take place. Hence barter only works well in very simple economies with a limited range of goods and with a high degree of self sufficiency. It cannot operate in an economy with a significant range of goods and services, and with specialisation of production. In these circumstances money is the essential oil which lubricates the economic process: an individual can buy a range of goods with the money earned from his job, instead of having to trade products directly.

Although most people probably have a clear idea of what they understand by "money", it is in fact an extremely difficult concept to define with precision. Economists tend to define it as anything which is readily acceptable as a means of payment. Evidently "money" in this sense constitutes "cash"—banknotes and coins—and also current account bank deposits, since possession of the latter allows the drawing of cheques which, normally, are a universally acceptable means of payment. The total of cash and current account deposits at any given time is one possible definition of the supply of money existing at that time: it is known as "M1", and also as the "narrowly-defined" money supply, since an alternative definition—known as "M3"—embraces other types of bank accounts (deposit accounts, foreign currency accounts, and public sector accounts) as well as the components of M1. The argument in favour of M3 is that cheques can in practice be drawn on the additional types of account which it includes and that these accounts should therefore be classed as "money" when the latter is defined as a means of payment.

The competing claims of M1 and M3 as the appropriate definition of money were recognised when monetary targets were adopted as an important part of economic policy making in Britain in the late 1970s (*see Part IV*). Separate targets were set for the growth of M1 and M3, and for a time it was not clear which was regarded as more important by policy-makers. In the early 1980s, however, *sterling M3 (i.e.* excluding the foreign currency components of M3) was regarded as the main target, and in 1984 M1 was abandoned as a formal policy target. It was replaced by M0, the so-called "monetary base", defined as notes and coins in circulation plus banks' deposits held at the Bank of England. The argument in favour of M0 was that a growing proportion of M1 was made up of interest-bearing deposits and that it therefore increasingly represented peoples' savings decisions; hence it no longer provided a good guide to the amount of money available to finance current demands for goods and services. In contrast, because notes and coins constituted about 90 per cent of M0, the latter was a reliable indicator of current demand pressure.

Whatever the merits of M0 as an indicator of demand pressure, it should be noted that it does not correspond to the definition of "money" as a means of payment because it excludes all current and deposit bank accounts, essentially on the grounds that holders of such accounts might choose to regard them as vehicles for savings rather than for financing current spending. It therefore narrows the definition of money beyond the "narrowly defined" M1 by including only those elements for which there is no plausible demand other than as a means of payment.

Liquidity.

In contrast, many people have criticised even the "wide" definition of money, M3, on the grounds that it excludes accounts at institutions other than banks. This is potentially important since total deposits with the banks are less than total deposits with non-bank institutions. If the government controls M1 (or M3) as a means of controlling aggregate demand, its policy may be circumvented if, say, people run down building society accounts in order to increase their current expenditure. Many Keynesians regard this as a crucial objection to the idea of controlling aggregate demand by controlling the money supply (whether M1 or M3). They argue that what matters for the control of aggregate demand is not "money" but the economy's stock of *liquid assets, i.e.*, assets which can readily be converted into "money", and hence into potential expenditure on current output. This argument has led to attention being given to wider measures of monetary aggregates than either M1 or M3. Two wider measures now receive considerable attention from policy makers. M4 equals M3 plus building society accounts, and M5 equals M4 plus money market instruments such as Treasury Bills.

The traditional argument for concentrating on measures like M1 or M3 rather than on wider measures of liquidity was that building society accounts, and similar assets, could not be used directly as means of payment: it was necessary first to withdraw cash from a building society account before making a purchase. However, during the 1980s this changed rapidly, as the banks and the building societies began to compete much more closely. On the one hand, the banks moved increasingly into the home loans business in an attempt to capture some of the traditional business of the building societies. Conversely, the building societies sought to take some of the banks' traditional business by offering accounts providing facilities close to those of current accounts at the banks. Towards the end of the 1980s most of the main building societies were issuing cheque books to account holders, and such cheques were becoming more widely acceptable as a means of payment. Hence for most practical purposes it was becoming increasingly difficult not to include building society accounts in any standard definition of "money" as a means of payment. This emphasises the difficulty of defining "money", and also illustrates the point that the appropriate boundaries between what does and does not constitute "money" are not immovable: as the financial sector of the economy alters, so does the appropriate definition.

The building societies altered in other ways, widening their range of financial and housing services to the point at which the larger societies were more appropriately viewed as financial conglomerates—firms offering a full range of financial services—than in terms of their traditional role as lenders for house purchase. This trend was accentuated in 1989 when the second largest society, the Abbey National, took steps to convert itself from a mutual society—the traditional arrangement for building societies, whereby they are owned by their members—to a public company, quoted on the Stock Market, and so owned by shareholders. Members voted in favour of the proposal, making the Abbey National much more like a bank and much less like a traditional building society.

The Choice of Targets.

The fact that "money" can be defined in so many different ways, each having some plausible justification, poses an obvious problem for monetarists: if it is important to control the money supply, which measure is the one to be controlled? This is of some practical importance since the various monetary aggregates often grow at very different rates. In 1972 and 1973, for example, M3 grew much more

Annual growth rates,
December 1987–December 1988
£

MO	M1	M3	M4	M5
6·8	14·4	20·8	17·6	16·7

THE NATIONAL DEBT IN SELECTED YEARS

	The National Debt (£bn.)	The National Debt as a percentage of national income
1900	0·6	31·9
1914	0·7	25·6
1921	7·6	147·7
1938	7·8	150·6
1946	23·0	259·6
1975	46·4	49·0
1988	171·0	38·0
1989	164·1	32·0

rapidly than M1; in 1975 and 1977 the position was reversed. Over the longer term, moreover, M1 has been steadily falling in size relative to M3: the ratio of M1 to M3 was about 2/3 in 1963 but less than 1/2 in the early 1980s. Similar variations also occur as between the various other possible measures of money supply and liquidity. The table illustrates the range of growth rates of the various measures in 1987–88. These variations in the growth of different monetary aggregates were one reason why monetary targets lost favour with the British government in the mid-1980s (see **G31**, and **Part IV**).

The Liquidity Spectrum.

By definition "money" is completely liquid. Building society accounts are clearly highly liquid assets. Other types of financial assets—e.g., long-dated government stock, known as gilt-edged securities—are less liquid, since although the owner of such assets can easily exchange them for money, he cannot confidently predict the price at which he can do so. For example, he may have to sell at a time when the market price of government stock is unusually low, so that he realises relatively little money from the sale. Thus "liquidity" refers not only to the speed with which assets can be sold, but also to the predictability of the amount of money which the sale will realise. In practice, there is a liquidity spectrum, i.e., a whole range of different types of asset, each possessing a different degree of liquidity. The spectrum includes not only financial assets but also real assets—houses, capital equipment, etc.—the latter being highly illiquid, e.g., selling a house takes a long time, involves high transactions costs, and the sale price is unpredictable.

Liquidity and Expenditure.

There is a traditional difference between Keynesians and monetarists about the working of the liquidity spectrum. Keynesians believe that firms and consumers regard "money" and non-money liquid assets as good alternatives to one another in as much as both provide security, predictability, etc. That is, there is on the Keynesian view a high degree of substitutability between money and other liquid financial assets; and, in contrast, a relatively low degree of substitutability between money and real assets. Monetarists, on the other hand, assume the reverse: relatively high substitutability between money and real assets, relatively low substitutability between money and other financial assets. These different assumptions imply different effects if the government increases the money supply. Monetarists argue that much of the extra money is spent directly on real assets, i.e., there is a strong effect upon aggregate demand for real output. Keynesians argue, in contrast, that much of the extra money is spent on acquiring other financial assets, i.e., the direct effect upon aggregate demand for real output is relatively low. This is not the end of the matter in the Keynesian viewpoint, however; for the increase in demand for financial assets will tend to push up their prices where these are determined in the markets, as in the case of gilt-edged securities, and this will tend to lower interest rates. (This happens because gilt-edged securities pay a fixed sum of money each year as interest; hence their proportional interest rate falls as their price rises, and this tends to push down interest rates elsewhere.) When interest rates fall this increases aggregate demand for real output because borrowing—which, as noted above, finances part of private expenditure—now becomes more attractive. Hence an increase in the money supply eventually increases demand for real output in the Keynesian approach; however, the mechanism is less direct than the monetarist one, and the size of the eventual increase in demand is likely to be smaller if, as many Keynesians argue, the demand for output is not very responsive to changes in interest rates.

This Keynesian view of liquidity helps to explain the traditional scepticism of many economists towards policies of monetary control. If "money" and various forms of "near money" are in practice very close substitutes for one another, attempts by the government to control the money supply may be self defeating, because whatever the precise definition of "money" which is used, some liquid assets will be excluded, and the financial sector may then negate the effects of the controls by shifting towards greater use of other assets, not included in the definition and therefore not subject to control. This problem is often known as "Goodhart's Law", named after Charles Goodhart, formerly an economic adviser at the Bank of England. Goodhart's Law states that as soon as the government attempts to regulate any particular set of financial assets, these become unreliable as indicators of economic trends. The basic reason is that financial institutions can relatively easily devise new types of financial assets, and this allows them to negate the effects of controls on particular types of assets, based on particular definitions of the money supply. There is very little which the government can do to prevent it. The persistent failure by the government to achieve its monetary targets during the 1980s, and the wide divergences in different monetary series, led many economists, including those sympathetic in principle to the idea of monetary control, to question its practical usefulness.

The National Debt and Government Borrowing.

The National Debt is a measure of the total indebtedness of the government, excluding local authorities. The accompanying table shows how it has varied over time. Although the absolute size of the National Debt has risen steadily, this simply reflects inflation: as a proportion of national income the National Debt has fluctuated, rising sharply after each of the two World Wars—both of which saw borrowing on a massive scale by the government to finance the war effort—but falling slowly but steadily for 20 years up to 1975. From 1975 to the mid-1980s the proportion altered little; since then it has fallen sharply.

The government borrows in several different ways. First, the issue of new bank-notes is a form of borrowing: as seen above it can be used to finance a budget deficit. Second, it borrows from foreign governments (see **G9**). Third, it borrows from companies through tax reserve certificates, whereby company taxes are paid at the later date when the taxes become legally due. Fourth, it borrows from private individuals through the various forms of national savings, e.g., Post Office accounts.

These four types of borrowing result in non-marketable debt, i.e., an individual who has a Post Office account cannot sell it in the market to another individual. Two other types of borrowing—gilt-edged securities and Treasury Bills—result in marketable debt, i.e., an individual who owns gilt-edged securities can sell them in the market to someone else. In practice, most gilt-edged and all Treasury Bills are held by institutions—banks, discount houses, etc.—rather than by private individuals. However, whereas Treasury Bills, representing short-term (usually three months) loans to the government are liquid assets (i.e., they can quickly be cashed at a predictable price), gilt-edged are illiquid. They represent promises to repay a certain sum of money at a specified date, e.g., government stock outstanding in 1985 had an average remaining life of 10·4 years, with significant redemptions due in each of the next five years. Occasionally stock is issued without a repayment date. Owners of such stock are in effect promised a fixed annual interest payment for ever. At any time prior to repayment gilt-edged can be traded, and there is a large market for such trading in which the market price (as opposed to the fixed repayment price) varies widely.

Interest Rates and Debt Financing.

As already seen, such variations in gilt-edged market prices cause changes in interest rates on all financial assets. Aside from the effects on aggregate demand, interest rate changes themselves have a large impact upon the financing of the National Debt, and hence upon overall public expenditure. For example, if restrictions on the growth of the money supply cause interest rates to rise, this increases the interest charges which the government has to pay on its existing debts. Furthermore, the accompanying fall in the market price of government stock may cause potential buyers of new issues of stock to anticipate further falls (i.e., further increases in interest rates), in which case they will be reluctant to purchase the stock—and the government will be unable to finance its budget deficit—unless and until these further changes occur. When they do, the interest charges on the National Debt are further in-creased; and the market may still be unsettled, expecting yet further changes.

It is problems of this sort which lead many Keynesians to advocate a policy of promoting stable (or at least slowly changing) interest rates—an "orderly market" for financial assets—rather than a predetermined growth rate of the money supply. Monetarists object on the grounds that the government cannot in practice stabilise interest rates in this manner. They argue that although the government may be able to stabilise or even reduce interest rates in the short run by a rapid expansion of the money supply, this expansion will itself *increase* interest rates in the longer run. This is because, on the monetarist approach, the monetary expansion increases demand for real output, which in turn generally increases the rate of inflation. If this causes people to expect a higher future rate of inflation, gilt-edged stock then becomes less attractive to investors because of the associated decline in the anticipated real value of its fixed interest payments. The demand for gilt-edged stock therefore falls, which pushes its price down and thus its effective interest rate up. This continues until the effective interest rate has risen sufficiently to offset the higher expected inflation. Interest rates elsewhere tend to get bid up at the same time, since banks, building societies, etc., have to protect their own reserves.

Monetarists therefore distinguish between the *nominal* interest rate, i.e., the current money value of the interest rate, and the *real* interest rate, i.e., the nominal rate minus the expected rate of price inflation on real output. They argue that firms and consumers are concerned about the real, not the nominal, interest rate; in this case nominal rates must inevitably rise if inflation increases—which it will do, on the monetarist argument, if the government, in pursuing a Keynesian policy of stabilising interest rates, over-expands the money supply. Hence the monetarists produce a paradox; a monetary policy which seeks to hold interest rates down may instead cause them to rise.

The Trend of Interest Rates in Britain.

It is difficult to deny that some element of the monetarist view of interest rates has operated in the post-war period, especially in more recent years. The accompanying table shows the course of (nominal) interest rates and yields on certain types of financial assets since the war. It can be seen that with the exception of the yield on Ordinary Shares—which is considered later—all rates showed a trend increase until the early 1980s. Since inflation and therefore, in all probability, inflationary expectations have shown a similar trend, the rise in nominal interest rates is broadly consistent with the monetarist position. Furthermore, there was a tendency for all rates to rise in 1975–6, decline in 1977–8, and rise again in 1979–80. Infla-

tion and therefore, presumably, inflation expectations followed a similar pattern. It can be seen that from the early 1980s onwards the previous trend was reversed, with nominal rates showing a clear downward trend from the peak levels reached in 1979–81. Again this is broadly what monetarist analysis would predict: inflation has fallen sharply since 1980, and nominal interest rates would be expected to fall also.

One point to note from the table is that *nominal* interest rates can be very misleading as a guide to *real* interest rates which, as explained above, are equal to nominal rates minus the expected rate of inflation. In the 1970s nominal rates were very high but for most of the time the rate of inflation was even higher, so that real interest rates were negative. This was particularly marked in 1975–76, when nominal rates reached a then record high level of around 16 per cent. At the time, however, inflation was running at around 25 per cent, implying real interest rates of around minus 9 per cent—a record *low* level. The same has applied in reverse in the 1980s. Nominal interest rates fell to lower levels than in the 1970s, but inflation fell faster, so that by 1986 nominal interest rates of around 12 per cent coexisted with inflation of around 5 per cent, implying real interest rates of plus 7 per cent—a record *high* level. Thus changes in nominal interest rates cannot be taken as a good guide to changes in the real cost of borrowing.

International Influences on Interest Rates.

Another substantial complication in considering interest rates concerns the relationship between interest rates in Britain and in other countries. The removal of exchange controls in 1979, and the much greater degree of competition and openness in foreign exchange markets which emerged in the 1980s, mean that changes in interest rates in other countries, especially the United States, have come to play a major role in determining British rates. Institutions such as pension funds, insurance companies, and large industrial companies which have substantial amounts of money to invest are now easily able to move money between alternative assets in different currencies. Consequently, if interest rates in the United States rise above those in Britain there will normally be a large movement of funds out of assets such as British government bonds, denominated in sterling, and into dollar assets in the United States in order to take advantage of the higher rates of return. The same applies if interest rates rise in other important financial centres such as Tokyo. Since selling of sterling assets implies a reduced demand for sterling and increased demand for other currencies, this tends to push down the exchange rate of sterling against other currencies. If the British government is reluctant to see a fall in the exchange rate it will then be forced to allow a rise in British interest rates in order to prevent it.

This problem played an important part in British economic policy at several times in the 1980s. The government wished to prevent rapid falls in the exchange rate because of the importance which it attached to reducing inflation: if the exchange rate falls this pushes inflation up because of the resulting rise in the sterling price of imported goods. Hence British interest rates in the 1980s were to a significant extent outside the control of the British government, depending instead on events in the world economy. The very large budget deficit of the United States tended to keep its interest rates at high levels, and this went a long way towards explaining why British interest rates remained high even when inflation fell substantially. Of course, the government could have chosen to allow interest rates to fall, but only at the cost of abandoning a key part of its economic policy, namely the commitment to low inflation.

The Commercial Banks.

If the government does adopt monetary targets, its main need is to find ways of influencing the behaviour of the commercial banks, known in England as the clearing banks. For as seen above, the main component of the money supply is the deposits of the clearing banks, regardless of whether M1 or M3 is the chosen definition.

In Britain there are four main banks with one

PERCENTAGE YIELD ON FINANCIAL
ASSETS
(Range during period)

	Trea- sury Bill rate	Long- dated govern- ment stock	Indus- trial ordin- ary shares divi- dend yield
1945–50	½	2–3	3¼–5¼
1951–60	1–6¼	3¼–6	4¼–7
1961–70	3¼–8	5–10	4–6
1971–78	5¼–14¼	7½–17½	3–12
1979–81	11–17	11–16	4½–8
1982–85	8½–14	10–13½	5–7½
1986–87	8–12	8½–11	3–4½
1988	7–13	9–9½	4–4½

or more branches in every town. Each of them
earns profits by borrowing at low or zero rates of
interest—anyone holding a bank account is in
effect making a loan to his bank—and lending out
part of the resulting funds at higher interest rates.
In normal circumstances—*i.e.*, unless there is a run
on the banks—not all deposits will be withdrawn
at once; therefore the banks need keep only a
small proportion of their deposits in the form of
cash. This proportion is known as the *cash ratio*
and until 1971 the Bank of England required it to
be at least 8 per cent. Also, between 1951 and
1971 the Bank of England requested that the
banks held liquid assets—Treasury Bills, commercial bills, and money at call and short notice as
well as cash—equal to at least 30 per cent of deposits. This was known as the *liquidity ratio*.

The commercial banks can "create" money
because of their ability to accept deposits far in
excess of their cash and liquid asset holdings; as
economists would say, because they operate under
a *fractional reserve system*. If a bank provides an
overdraft facility to a customer who then draws
cheques on the facility, the recipients of these
cheques pay the proceeds into their bank accounts
which are thereby enlarged; and this represents
an increase in the money supply, since the enlarged accounts can be used to finance additional
transactions. Thus any increase in the banks'
cash and liquid asset holdings allows them to
expand loans, overdrafts, etc.—and thereby the
money supply—by a multiple amount.

Controlling the Commercial Banks.

The government can control the money supply by
controlling the components of banks' cash and
liquid asset holdings. A reduction in the latter can
be engineered by *open market operations*, which
involve the Bank of England's selling more gilt-
edged than it otherwise would; this reduces the
banks' liquidity, since, as already seen, gilt-edged
are not regarded as liquid assets, so that their purchase involves a drain of liquidity from the banks.
At the same time, as already seen, it will generally
involve a rise in interest rates.

In 1971 the government introduced a new
policy, *Competition and Credit Control*, which redefined the liquidity ratio and lowered it to 12½ per
cent, this being the banks' required ratio between
what were defined as *eligible reserve assets* and *eligible liabilities*. The former comprised balances with
the Bank of England, Treasury Bills, some commercial bills and local authority bills, and gilt-edged
stock with less than one year to maturity. Eligible
liabilities are, after various minor adjustments,
sterling deposits.

The 1971 changes put far less stress on direct
controls and placed the emphasis of policy upon
controlling credit through the redefined reserve
ratio. It also imposed this reserve ratio on *all*
banks—not just on the clearing banks, as had
previously been the case—and also on Finance
Houses. There were two reasons for this widening of
controls. First, it was felt unfair to the clearing
banks to subject them to controls which did not
apply to potential competitors. Second, it was seen

as a means of rationalising, and obtaining greater
control over, an increasingly complicated market for
credit: in the previous two decades institutions other
than clearing banks had grown in importance as
sources of credit, and it had become increasingly
anomalous not to seek to influence the whole of the
market.

Current controls.

In 1981 further changes in monetary control
techniques were made. In August the reserve
assets ratio was abolished. Instead, the banks
undertook to keep an average of 6 per cent, and
never normally less than 4 per cent, of their eligible
liabilities as secured money with members of the
London Discount Market Association and/or with
money brokers and gilt-edged jobbers. They were
also required to keep cash balances equal to ½ per
cent of eligible liabilities in non-interest bearing
accounts at the Bank of England. At the same
time the Government abolished *Minimum Lending
Rate*. It intended instead to set short term interest
rates within an undisclosed band, thus abandoning its previous ability to influence the general
level of interest rates by announcing a change in
MLR. The main idea behind these changes was to
attempt to introduce a greater role for market forces
in the determination of interest rates.

The Stock Exchange.

Whilst short-term credit is mostly provided by
banks and Finance Houses, long-term borrowing
by companies is undertaken through the Stock
Exchange. Firms in the private sector of the
economy issue three main types of security on the
Stock Exchange. *Debenture Stock* is simply a
fixed-interest loan. *Preference Stock* is a fixed-
interest loan with provisions for waiving the interest if no profits are earned. The most important type, representing the great majority of holdings, are *Ordinary Shares*. The owner of an
Ordinary Share is, legally, a part-owner of the
company concerned, with a right to participate
in any net profits which it makes (though he has
no legal right to any particular level of dividend
or interest payment).

In contrast to government stock, a significant
proportion of Ordinary Shares is owned by private
individuals. However, an increasing proportion is
owned by insurance companies and pension funds,
which have grown in importance as private superannuation schemes have become more widespread.
It is likely that the market for Ordinary Shares,
like that for government stock, will eventually be
completely dominated by such large institutional
investors.

The attraction of Ordinary Shares to the investor wanting an outlet for his savings is that because
they represent a part ownership of the firm concerned, their prices and dividends are likely to rise
as the value of the firm increases. This is so
whether the firm's value increases in real terms,
because it is expanding, or simply in money terms,
because of general inflation. Thus Ordinary
Shares generally represent a reasonable "hedge"
against inflation—unlike fixed-interest securities
such as gilt-edged. It is for this reason that, as
seen in the earlier table, the dividend yield on
Ordinary Shares does not tend to rise with inflation: the demand for Ordinary Shares does
not necessarily fall if inflation increases, so
that their prices and yields are not affected in
the same way as those of gilt-edged and other
fixed-interest securities by changes in inflation
rates.

The Big Bang.

In October 1986 several major changes occurred
in the organisation of the Stock Exchange. These
had been under active discussion and planning for
several years, but because they were all formally
introduced simultaneously, they became known
as the *Big Bang*. The main changes consisted of
alterations in the structure and ownership of firms
operating in the stock market, removal of
restrictions on charging for financial services, and
new forms of regulation of activity.

Traditionally, stock market firms had been
divided into "jobbers" and "brokers". The former

were responsible for the trading of shares on the floor of the stock market, whilst the latter dealt with clients and provided business for the jobbing firms—clients wishing to buy or sell shares were not allowed to deal directly with jobbers. The market imposed what was known as the "single capacity" restriction: no firm was allowed to be both a jobber and a broker. It also imposed strict limits on the ownership of all member firms: they were required either to be partnerships, or to be limited companies with a maximum limit on the amount of capital which could be owned by non-member firms (*i.e.* firms not actually operating in the market). In addition, the market operated fixed minimum commission rates on share deals.

Although this structure had worked well in earlier years, during the 1970s and 1980s it started to become increasingly inappropriate. The main catalyst for change was the growing *internationalisation of financial markets* (*see* **G56–7**). This was the result of several forces. Technological developments were making it very easy for financial firms to obtain virtually instant information, at very low cost, about assets in any currency and any country. Simultaneously, firms needing finance, especially the large multinationals operating throughout the world, were becoming increasingly willing to consider finance from any source. In addition, the abolition of UK exchange controls in 1979 meant that UK financial institutions rapidly acquired a much more diversified range of assets and interests, and needed to deal regularly in markets throughout the world, and also to compete within the UK against foreign based financial firms. Their ability to do so was heavily constrained by the traditional arrangements: minimum commission requirements restricted competition, the single capacity arrangement was unwieldy, and the limits on outside capital ownership meant that most of the firms were undercapitalised in terms of the scale of risks which they needed to run in global operations.

The Big Bang swept away most of the old restrictions. It allowed "single capacity" firms to operate, ended minimum commission rates, and removed restrictions on the entry and the ownership of firms. The main result was a series of mergers between and takeovers of old-established stock market firms. After Big Bang, most of the firms operating in the market were merely parts of, or subsidiaries of, much larger financial conglomerates, many of them foreign owned. These large firms felt that they could raise their overall profitability by operating in the UK stock market, though for many of them this was only one part of a large range of financial activities. Big Bang effectively recognised that the London stock market, like other stock exchanges around the world, could no longer be organised so as to supply finance for solely UK-based firms: instead, it was now a part of a global market for finance.

It was recognised that these new arrangements would need *regulation*, to protect the interests, and retain the confidence, of clients. The 1986 Financial Services Act provided the framework. This gave the Trade and Industry Minister the power to authorise firms as "fit and proper" to operate in the stock market, and in other financial contexts such as insurance services. In practice this power was largely delegated, in the first instance to the *Securities and Investments Board* (SIB), whose members were appointed by the Bank of England and the government.

Monetary Policy in Britain.

(i) The Keynesian Era.

Until 1968 British monetary policy was in practice strongly Keynesian in the sense described earlier. That is, the government was mainly concerned with attempting to stabilise interest rates in order to facilitate the management of the National Debt. For although successive governments several times embarked on a policy designed to reduce the rate of growth of the money supply by squeezing banks' liquidity, each such phase of policy was ended when the government concerned found itself unable to countenance the resulting rise in interest rates. This occurred when the banks sought to replenish their liquid assets by selling their gilt-edged holdings, particularly those nearing maturity; the banks preferred to do this rather than call in advances, since the latter were generally more profitable. In practice, it was

usually the Bank of England which bought the gilt-edged being unloaded by the banks, thereby undoing the effects of its own monetary squeeze.

In effect, therefore, the Bank of England's priority was to support gilt-edged prices and keep interest rates down, without worrying too much about money supply. Such a policy is often called "permissive" monetary policy.

(ii) The Monetarist Revival.

Keynesian ideas began to come under increasingly strong intellectual challenge from monetarists in the 1960s, and this has been reflected in the gradual change of policy to a predominantly monetarist stance. The first hint of this came in 1968, when the Chancellor of the Exchequer, expressed in a "Letter of Intent" to Britain's creditor, the International Monetary Fund, the intention of controlling the growth of the money supply in order to control aggregate demand and thereby help to push the balance of payments into surplus following the 1967 devaluation. The fact that an explicitly monetarist approach was thus made the centre-piece of policy for the first time reflected not only the growing intellectual influence of such ideas in Britain, but also (and probably more importantly) their influence in the I.M.F., which has traditionally favoured the setting of monetary targets.

This trend towards monetarism appeared to have been strengthened by the 1971 measures described earlier: these removed support from the gilt-edged market in order to focus attention upon the control of money and credit. In practice, however, these measures were followed in 1972–73 by a vast expansion of the money supply —M3 rose at an annual rate of nearly 30 per cent—which was the reverse of the policy advocated by monetarists (or indeed by most Keynesians). Other measures adopted at this time—moral suasion in an attempt to limit lending for property development; subsidies to building societies to hold down their interest rates—were also incompatible with the monetarist view that the market should operate freely within a framework of monetary control. Thus in the period 1972–73 policy may have become more monetarist in form, but it was certainly not monetarist in substance.

In the second half of the 1970s, however, monetarist ideas became increasingly the dominant influence upon policy making. This happened in two stages. The first occurred in the autumn of 1976 when Britain applied to the I.M.F. for large credit facilities. One of the requirements which the I.M.F. imposed as a condition of granting these facilities was that the Government should lay down, and stick to annual *monetary targets*, *i.e.*, target annual growth rates in sterling M3. Successive governments adopted this approach for the next ten years.

The adoption of monetary targets in turn meant that the *public sector borrowing requirement* (p.s.b.r.) became a target, rather than a consequence, of policy. The p.s.b.r. is the combined deficit of the central government, local authorities and public corporations. It has to be financed by a combination of borrowing (from the private sector or from abroad) and increasing the money supply. Since domestic borrowing will push up interest rates, any government which has a monetary target and which is also unwilling to tolerate rises beyond a certain point in interest rates, will be compelled to limit the size of the p.s.b.r. This has to be done by a combination of tax rises and cuts in public spending. Thus targets for monetary growth carry implications for the government's tax and expenditure policies.

The second, and decisive, stage in the growth of monetarist influence was the election of a Conservative government in May 1979. The new government came into office committed to a monetarist approach to economic policy; several of its leading members declared themselves converts, to a greater or lesser extent, to the teachings of Professor Friedman, and rejected the Keynesianism of earlier post-war years.

Early in its term of office, therefore, the new government published its medium-term financial strategy, designed to operate over the period 1980–84. It aimed to secure steady cuts from year to year over this period in both the monetary growth rate, and the p.s.b.r. as a proportion of national income. The government took the view that the scale of past government borrowing had contributed a great deal to the rapid inflation rates of the 1970s. Whether or not this was true, however, the actual burden of public debt had tended to fall during this period, as the accompanying table shows. Although total public sector indebtedness rose during the 1970s, this simply reflected inflation; indebtedness as a percentage of national income fell quite sharply. This was because the nominal interest rates paid by the government on its borrowing were below the inflation rate. Consequently, the government was effectively borrowing at negative rates of interest. Ironically, net indebtedness as a proportion of national income has tended to rise, albeit slowly, in the early 1980s, though it has since fallen sharply.

A further important contribution to the growth of monetarist influence at the end of the 1970s was that many of the most influential people in financial markets—the policy-makers of large institutional investors; academic economists with good connections in the City; financial journalists —had become monetarists. In this sense the "financial markets became monetarist". This caused some changes in their working, most of which had the effect of making interest rates more sensitive to short run variations in monetary policy. For reasons discussed in **Part IV**, this tended to make it more difficult for governments to adopt non-monetarist policies, even if they had wanted to. **Part IV** also provides a much more detailed account of policy making and the growth of monetarism during the 1970s and 1980s.

(iii) Doubts about Monetarism.

By the end of 1981 the experience since 1976, and more especially since 1979, had begun to erode support for monetarist ideas, at least in their simple form. One area of doubt concerned the actual ability of the government to control money supply, however defined; this led to the 1981 changes in monetary control techniques mentioned above. A second argument revived the traditional Keynesian emphasis upon wider measures of liquidity: some economists, led by Nobel prize winner Professor James Meade, argued that the government should abandon monetary targets and instead set targets for the growth of *money national income*—the volume of output multiplied by its average price level—and should use a variety of fiscal instruments for this purpose, with monetary policy being used mainly to influence interest rates and the exchange rate. A third criticism of monetarism, also associated with Professor Meade and consistently advanced by another Nobel prize-winner, James Tobin of Yale University, and also many politicians, was that deflation had mainly reduced output and employment rather than inflation, and that this would always be the case unless the government returned to some form of *incomes policy*. However, most monetarists remained hostile to the idea of incomes policy, and this therefore remained an intensely controversial question. These issues are considered further in **Part IV**.

(iv) The Demise of Monetary Targeting.

In the course of the 1980s these criticisms gathered force. Despite its clear commitment to steady reductions in the growth rate of the money supply as a central part of its anti-inflation policy, Mrs. Thatcher's government persistently failed to achieve its monetary targets. Moreover its main target—£M3—became very volatile and, apparently, increasingly unreliable as a guide to underlying economic trends. In 1985–86, for example, £M3 grew very rapidly, suggesting that monetary policy was becoming lax, at just the time when real interest rates reached a record high level (which has traditionally been seen as an indication of tight monetary policy). By the middle of the 1980s it was clear that the government was attaching steadily less weight to formal monetary targets, and the 1987 Budget announced the end of £M3 as a target. This was certainly a substantial change from the period 1979–83, when £M3 was over-

whelmingly the main policy instrument of macro-economic policy.

(v) New Controversies.

This modification of the Government's views was matched by changes in the views of many Keynesian economists. The traditional Keynesian view that money does not matter, which as discussed above dominated policy making for some twenty years after 1945, had been discarded by almost all the government's critics (some of whom pointed out Keynes himself had never argued that money was unimportant). Most economists accepted that there was sufficient evidence from the experience of the British economy in recent years to indicate that excessive expansion of the money supply was bound to lead to rises in inflation and nominal interest rates and was therefore harmful. In a sense, therefore, some of the traditional disputes between monetarists and Keynesians, which had persisted to the end of the 1970s, seemed to be coming to an end. Many monetarists accepted that simple monetary targeting was not sufficient; nearly all Keynesians accepted the need to prevent excessive monetary expansion.

New areas of controversy had partly replaced some of these traditional disagreements. For example, as the public sector borrowing requirement was reduced and eventually eliminated, giving way to a budget surplus during the 1987–8 financial year, there was much discussion on how this surplus should be used. Options included cutting tax rates, raising public spending, or repaying some of the accumulated National Debt. The Government, and many erstwhile monetarists, tended to favour the tax cutting option; many erstwhile Keynesians favoured increased public spending. However, this disagreement had little to do with traditional disputes about fiscal and monetary policies, and much more to do with alternative views about how best to stimulate the supply side of the economy. The Government argued that lower taxes would stimulate enterprise; those favouring higher spending argued that the rate of return on, for example, investment in education and training, would be very high. Hence traditional arguments about how best to regulate the *demand* side of the economy were increasingly being replaced by disputes about how to regulate the *supply* side—though many of the protagonists remained the same.

(vi) Confusion in Policy Making.

The abandonment of monetary targetting in the second half of the 1980s coincided with what, in retrospect, appears to have been a considerable loss of cohesion in economic policy making. Up to the mid-1980s the Thatcher governments, despite the various criticisms mentioned, had maintained a consistent approach to policy, with the defeat of inflation always the main priority and the use of monetary targets within the Medium Term Financial Strategy the main policy instrument. In the second half of the decade neither of these features was so clear cut. Whilst the Government continued to maintain that control of inflation was still the main priority, its actions suggested some modification. Similarly, whilst it continued to argue that monetary control was vital, in practice it seemed relatively unconcerned at evidence that various monetary indicators suggested a danger of rapidly rising inflation.

Two episodes of policy making in particular illustrated these apparent changes. In 1986, £M3 exceeded its target by a large amount. The Government's response, as already mentioned, was to abandon £M3 as a target in the following year, thus ignoring the potential inflationary implications. This policy was justified by the Chancellor at the time on the grounds that £M3 had become too volatile to be a useful policy indicator. In effect Mr. Lawson was invoking Goodhart's Law. Whilst this had some intellectual justification, it is difficult to believe that the Government would have responded in the same way as in the early 1980s. A second, similar policy episode occurred in 1988. By this time the Government was using M0 as its only formal monetary indicator. However, at the same time the Government had become increasingly preoccupied with exchange rate targets, and at the

THE COST OF PUBLIC SERVICES
(£ million)

Expenditure.	1978	1988	Percentage increase 1978–88	Percentage of total 1988
Defence	7,594	19,738	160	11·1
Education	9,154	22,543	146	12·7
Health	7,833	22,960	193	13·0
Social Security benefits	17,908	54,448	204	31·0
Housing and community amenities	5,997	7,957	33	4·5
Agriculture, forestry and fishing	1,121	2,338	109	1·3
Transport and communication	2,685	4,096	53	2·3
Public order and safety	2,433	8,277	240	4·7
General public services	3,070	7,610	148	4·3
Other expenditure	14,584	27,282	87	15·3
Total expenditure	72,379	177,249	145	100·0

time the Chancellor was seeking to prevent the exchange rate of the pound from rising above three D-marks. To achieve this aim he was prepared to accept increases in M0 above the target range. Hence the Government in effect abandoned its monetary target in favour of an exchange rate target.

This emphasis on exchange rate targetting had emerged partly in response to pressure from companies engaged in large amounts of international trade, for whom volatile and unpredictable exchange rates had become an increasingly important problem. These firms argued in favour of policies aimed at stabilising exchange rates so as to make trading conditions more predictable. Many economists and policy makers were sympathetic to this view. However, economists emphasised that a policy of fixing or controlling the exchange rate was incompatible with one of monetary targetting. If the Government fixes the exchange rate it then has to allow the money supply to vary by whatever amounts are required to maintain the exchange rate target. However, it seemed that this point was not clearly grasped by the British Government, with the result that the clarity which had characterised policy making in the early 1980s was lost. After 1987 it became increasingly difficult to be sure about either the aims or the methods of policy making. This perception of confusion caused a gradual erosion of confidence in the Government by the financial markets.

Towards the end of the 1980s the confusion was deepened by a growing internal disagreement within the Government about whether or not Britain should become a full member of the European Monetary System (EMS) by joining its Exchange Rate Mechanism (ERM) (*see* **G59**). This important disagreement over a central aspect of policy making further eroded confidence. A crisis point was reached in October 1989 when Mr. Lawson resigned. Most observers regarded it as inevitable that Britain would enter the ERM eventually, but until this point was reached it seemed certain that the guiding principles of policy making would remain unclear.

5. ECONOMIC ASPECTS OF THE PUBLIC SERVICES

The Cost of Public Services.

In 1988, total public expenditure was £177,249 million, about £3,121 per head. Of this total, 72% was spent by central government, and the remainder by local authorities and the investment programmes of the remaining nationalised industries. Total public expenditure increased about seventeenfold in the period 1960–87, and rose as a proportion of GNP from 34% to a peak of more than 50 per cent in 1983, before declining again to 46 per cent in the period 1983–87.

Central Government collects in revenue considerably more than it spends itself, but transfers funds to the local authorities, to the National Insurance Fund, and to the nationalised industries. The expenditure of the public sector as a whole has generally exceeded its revenue, the difference being met by net borrowing. However, the buoyancy of privatisation receipts and the process of "real fiscal

drag"—where tax allowances keep pace with inflation but not the rise in earnings so that tax payments as a percentage of earned incomes go up—have enabled the government to post surpluses in the past three fiscal years. These amounted to £3.6 billion in 1987–88, £14·4 billion in 1988–89 and £7.0 billion in 1989–90.

A breakdown of public expenditure is shown in the above table. Not all categories of public expenditure have expanded at the same rate. Over the period from 1977, for example, expenditure on public order and safety, social security, defence and health increased faster than the total; expenditure on housing, community amenities, education and transport and agriculture fell behind the total.

Council Housing.

Expenditure on council housing (net of sales) amounted to 0·5 per cent of public expenditure in 1988. Housing expenditure consists of two quite different items. There is the capital cost of building new council houses or of improvement grants and the like. This is financed out of borrowing by local authorities, both from the Government and from the market, and through the proceeds of sales of existing council houses to tenants. There is also a recurrent cost, in the form of subsidies on council housing. This subsidy amounted to £476 million in 1988, representing a significant cut in real terms from an annual cost of around £640 million in 1982 and 1983. This represents the difference between the cost of housing, including the cost of borrowing, and rents received.

Up to 1957 the Government contracted to pay a flat subsidy per year on every council house built. From 1957, government subsidies were no longer paid on new council houses, but in 1961 were reintroduced, in a form intended to encourage councils to charge higher rents on their existing houses. The Labour Government substantially increased the subsidy in 1967.

The 1972 Housing Finance Act made major changes to the system of council housing finance. Councils were required to charge "fair rents"—the likely market rent for a dwelling if supply and demand for rented accommodation were in balance. The Government also financed a rent rebate scheme whereby people in need, both council tenants and private tenants, could claim a rebate according to a formula based on family size and income. A slum clearance subsidy was also paid to councils and—to encourage housebuilding—a "rising costs" subsidy whereby the additional costs resulting from council house building were subsidised. The system of "fair rents" was ended by the Housing Rents and Subsidies Act of 1975. Under this Act most Government help went to new building, the acquisition of land and housing and improving the stock of council housing. This Act was replaced by the 1980 Housing Act. Since then, council house subsidies have been substantially reduced. Central government now calculates the amount by which it will finance housing subsidies on the assumption that local authorities charge council house tenants a "fair" or "market" rent. The result is that council rents have risen substantially in real terms. At the same time, private ownership has been encouraged *e.g.* through the sale of council houses. Between 1980 and 1988, more than 1·4 million council houses are estimated to have been sold. The Housing Act of 1988 further eroded the role of local authorities in the provision of housing by allowing public sector tenants to change their landlord if the authority in question was deemed to be unsatisfactory. Housing Action Trusts are being set up to take over responsibility for local authority housing in designated areas.

The Housing Market.

Government housing policy must be seen in terms of the housing market as a whole. In 1988 there were 22·5 million dwellings in the United Kingdom, 65 per cent being owner-occupied, 25 per cent council houses, and the other 10 per cent privately rented. The importance of owner-occupation has grown and that of private renting has declined: in 1960 they had accounted for 42 per cent and 32 per cent of the total respectively. Of the privately rented accommodation today, around one third is military and company owned property let free to employees. On an international comparison, the private rented sector in the early 1980s, as a percentage of total housing stock, was about 60 per cent in Switzerland, 50 per cent in Holland, 40 per cent in the USA, and 18 per cent in France. It should also be noted that the pattern of tenure varies quite significantly across different parts of the U.K.—owner occupation ranges from 45 per cent in Scotland to 73 per cent in South-West England.

The switch to owner-occupation in the U.K. is largely the result of Government policy. Rent controls meant that there was little incentive to build houses for renting, nor even to maintain existing rented houses, although the 1988 Housing Act was intended to remove some of the disincentives to private rental. On the other hand, Government has given considerable tax advantages to owner-occupiers. Owner-occupied houses are exempt from the capital gains tax introduced in 1964, and owner-occupiers can also obtain tax relief on mortgage-interest payments on a principal of up to £30,000. Until August 1988 unmarried owner-occupiers could claim tax relief on multiples of £30,000, depending on the number sharing. Relief is now restricted to £30,000 per property. Since the abolition of the Schedule A tax in 1961—whereby owner-occupiers paid tax on the rental income imputed to their houses—this tax relief on interest payments must be justified as an inducement to home-ownership; but it is also a considerable subsidy to owner-occupiers, who tend to be the relatively well-off. The trend towards owner-occupation was further encouraged by the 1980 Housing Act which gave local authority and new town tenants a legal right to buy their homes.

The year 1953 was a peak for public sector housebuilding in the United Kingdom when 262,000 council dwellings were completed. There was a trough in 1961 (122,000), a peak in 1967 (211,000) and a subsequent fall to 113,000 in 1973. Since the mid 1970s there has been a steady decline in the construction of public dwellings. In 1988 only 15,983 new houses were completed. By contrast, the number of private dwellings completed rose steadily from 65,000 in 1953 to a peak of 226,000 in 1968. Thereafter the number fell back to an annual average of slightly less than 200,000 in the early 1970s, and still further to an average of about 120,000 in the early 1980's, rising again in 1983 to about 150,000, and to 161,000 in 1988. The total number of dwellings completed reached a peak of 436,000 in 1968, and fell to 279,000 in 1974. Since then, the best year has been 1976 (338,000), the worst 1982 (159,000), while 293,264 dwellings were completed in 1988.

Over the 15 years 1955–70 the rate of inflation in the price of modern existing houses averaged 5 per cent per annum: somewhat faster than the rise in the cost of living. After 1970 there was a great surge in house prices: between December 1970 and December 1972 the average rise was no less than 30 per cent per annum. There are various reasons for this remarkable inflation. Partly it reflected the rapid acceleration of general inflation; in such times it is sensible to hold one's wealth in the form of assets which will appreciate in value. It also reflected the decline in house-building after 1968, and a slowing-down in the rate at which building land became available. The precise timing of the inflation

resulted from the sudden and large increase in the availability of building society mortgages. And as the inflation grew, so optimistic expectations helped to raise house prices still further. By 1974 the rate of increase had slowed down considerably. It slowed even further in 1975 and 1976. In 1978 and 1979 prices started to accelerate again, slackening off in 1980, only to start accelerating again at the end of 1982. This rise was sustained through to 1988, but 1989 and early 1990 saw falls in house prices, particularly in areas such as the South East and East Anglia where house price inflation had accelerated rapidly in the previous two years. By the first quarter of 1990 the housing market slowdown was evident in all regions, and national house price inflation was zero.

In 1988 the number of dwellings exceeded the number of households by just under one million. Yet the picture is not as rosy as this implies. The regional distribution of supply and demand was not equally spread. The measured number of households understates the number of "units" needing accommodation—a married couple, for example, living in someone else's house. Such concealed units are thought to number 800,000. Much accommodation is substandard in some way or other—a 1981 survey of dwellings in England and Wales indicated that about 11 per cent of the housing stock was unfit for habitation. The above factors, together with personal financial and social problems, mean that a worrying number of people are homeless. Thus in 1988 local authorities were dealing with 116,100 households which were homeless or in danger of being so.

Education.

Educational expenditure accounted for 12·7 per cent of public expenditure in 1988. It had increased rapidly over the previous 25 years for two reasons. First the number of full-time pupils had grown. Second the more expensive sectors—secondary schools and universities—expanded most rapidly. For example, in 1988 there were 3·7 million students in secondary schools as opposed to 3·2 million in 1961, although the 1988 figure was well below the comparable total for 1981 of 4·6 million. This reflects changing demographics. Falling birth rates meant that the secondary school population reached a peak in the mid-to-late 1970s, since when it has fallen—a fall which is projected to continue until the early 1990s. Higher education has also started to see the impact of these declining birth rates. Even so, there were 626,900 students in higher education in 1987/88, compared with a total of 456,800 in 1970/71.

In December 1972 the Conservative Government published a White Paper setting out plans for the expansion of education over the following decade. More emphasis was to be placed on nursery schooling for the 3- and 4-year-olds: within 10 years it would be available to all children whose parents wanted them to attend. There would be a school building programme to replace old school buildings. Teacher training would be expanded to reduce pupil-teacher ratios further. Higher education would be expanded less rapidly than in the previous decade, and the emphasis would be placed on polytechnics and other non-university colleges. Unfortunately many of these plans were thwarted, largely as a result of cut-backs in total public expenditure. It is, however, generally recognised that education can be an economic investment for the future just as much as capital formation in, say, machinery or roads. There is a "private return" on "investment in education", which takes the form of higher earnings over the lifetime of the person educated; and there is a "social return" on public resources devoted to education being the greater contribution to the national product which trained and educated people can make. Although many of the 1972 White Paper plans were not implemented, both the 1974 Labour and 1979 Conservative Governments considered longer term policies for education. The key theme of a consultative White Paper in 1977 was the need to attune school curricula to the employment needs of school-leavers, and to encourage stronger ties between schools and industry. This has been a recurrent theme. Questions about longer term educational requirements were initially subsumed under the present Conservative Government by debate on the relative merits of private and public sector education. There was also a renewed emphasis on making the later years of school education more directly related to labour market requirements, represented, for example, by the increased involvement in the mid 1980s of the Manpower Services Commission, and later the Training Commission, in school programmes, such as the Technical and Vocational Education Initiative.

In 1985 in a White Paper entitled "The Development of Higher Education into the 1990s", the Government also considered ways of improving the contribution of higher education to economic performance. Thus the links between full-time education and job training are being intensified.

Such themes were continued in the Education Reform Act, passed in the 1988 Parliamentary session. It proposed the introduction of a National Curriculum, the establishment of City Technical Colleges and giving business greater representation on the new University Funding Council than it had had on the University Grants Committee. Many of the provisions of the 1988 Education Reform Act remain highly controversial, particularly those which relate to the National Curriculum and what is perceived to be over-rigid prescription of its content. By early 1990 it was still unclear if the government would adhere to its commitment to formal testing at ages 7 and 11. Many commentators see the Act as increasing central government's control over education—for example, LEAs are to lose control of the larger Colleges of Further Education and of Polytechnics. At the same time the Act emphasised the theme of intensified competition in the provision of education. Schools would have to compete for pupils and universities for funding.

Social Security.

In 1988 the Social Security system underwent considerable change. In what follows we first describe the old system, before turning to the new.

There were two forms of social security: *National Insurance* and *Supplementary Benefits*. The former was non-means tested. They were designed to be exactly what the name indicated—insurance for when an individual met circumstances implying a loss of income, be that circumstance old age, unemployment or sickness. By contrast the latter were means tested, and were designed to keep people out of poverty. As such under the original Beveridge scheme, they were meant to be a safety net for the unfortunate few. The majority were to be covered by the insurance element. Formidable financing difficulties meant that this ideal was never achieved, and supplementary benefits attained an unwanted prominence in the British social security system.

(i) National Insurance.

Under this scheme employees received rights to unemployment benefit, sickness benefit, retirement pensions, widows' benefits, injury and disablement benefits, *etc.* In 1989, 9·7 million pensioners received National Insurance pensions. For those below pensionable age, the major national insurance benefit available (under both the old social security system and the new one described in part (v) below) is unemployment benefit. This was paid to 0·6 million recipients in 1989. Weekly rates are laid down for each benefit, *e.g.*, in April 1990 a rate of £37·35 was paid to a single person receiving unemployment benefit. The basic rate was increased according to the number of dependants. In 1966 an earnings-related supplement was introduced for benefits paid to persons between 18 and 65 (men) or 60 (women): the supplement being related to earnings in the previous tax year. The maximum total benefit, including increases for dependants, amounted to 85 per cent of earnings. This, together with tax rebates, meant a higher income out of work for a very few people. In the March 1980 Budget, the Chancellor announced that from 1982 the earnings-related unemployment supplement would be withdrawn, whilst unemployment benefit would become taxable.

By far the most important benefit is the retirement pension, paid as of right to contributors on retirement. Individuals may increase their rate of pension by staying on at work after the minimum retiring age of 65 for men and 60 for women. In

April 1990 basic retirement pensions were £46·90 per week for single persons and £75·10 for a married couple.

Social Security benefits were up-dated in November each year, to account for inflation in the year to the previous May. Under the Government's social security reforms (*see* **G35**), in 1986 the uprating took place in July, and in subsequent years in April.

(ii) The Financing of National Insurance.

The main source of finance for National Insurance payments is the National Insurance Fund. These funds are built up largely from the compulsory weekly National Insurance contributions which most of the adult population have to pay. For employees, both employer and employee pay a contribution. The self-employed also pay contributions of smaller size than the sum of the employer's and employee's contribution, but they are not entitled to unemployment benefit. Weekly contributions include a contribution to the cost of the National Health Service. As a result of the 1985 and 1989 Budgets, employers' and employees' national insurance contributions were cut for the lowest paid workers, in order to increase the incentives to work and to hire more labour. At the same time, while a maximum earnings limit for employees' contributions remains, the upper-earnings limit on employer's contributions has been abolished. In the 1989 Budget the structure of National Insurance payments was altered. Previously, the rate went from zero to more than 9 per cent once an individual hit the lower earnings limit. This meant that someone moving just above the lower limit for National Insurance contributions could face a marginal tax rate in excess of more than 100 per cent which was clearly a major disincentive. Although such traps have by no means been eradicated, National Insurance contributions are now on a graduated scale rising from 2 per cent to the maximum 9·25 per cent.

The National Insurance Scheme is an odd mixture of insurance and tax. The levels of contributions, when the scheme started in 1948, were fixed on the actuarial principle that contributions by or on behalf of an individual plus a specified State contribution should on average suffice to pay for the benefits to which he was entitled. But the scheme did not allow for inflation and a rising standard of living. In particular a succession of increases granted in the rate of pensions has put an end to this actuarial probity. Instead the principle became established that the rate of contributions in each year, together with a transfer from the Government, should equal the total benefits paid out in that year. Expenditure on non-contributory benefits is covered by general revenues.

(iii) Reform of Pensions.

There are almost ten million pensioners in Britain. Up to a quarter these are kept out of poverty only by receiving income support: it is estimated that another 10 per cent are entitled to a supplementary pension, but do not draw it. Many of the remainder find their living standards considerably reduced from when they were working. This is because the existing state retirement pension is inadequate. There are some occupational pension schemes which offer a better income, but these are still rather restricted in their coverage, being available to many more non-manual than manual workers. Like personal savings, many of them also tend to have only limited safeguards against inflation unless they are index-linked. In an era of rapidly rising prices, the pensioner is at a particular disadvantage. Widows form the poorest groups among them, with over half of them needing to draw a supplementary pension.

A scheme for graduated pensions was introduced for employees in 1961. Under the scheme there were two kinds of employees—*ordinary* and *contracted-out*. In the case of contracted-out workers, their employer (on whom the decision whether to contract out rested) had to institute a private superannuation scheme that gave at least as favourable terms as the new State scheme, including the provision that rights under the scheme should be transferable up to the limits of the State scheme. Transferability was the guarantee that the individual did not lose his pension rights when he changed his job. In practise transferability was never really achieved.

In 1969 the Labour Government made proposals in a White Paper to replace the National Insurance Scheme by a new scheme of superannuation and social insurance, in which both contributions and benefits would be related to the earnings of the individual. It argued that the existing scheme failed to provide security in old age. The new earnings-related contributions would be mostly higher than contributions under the existing scheme, especially among higher earners; and in return higher pensions and other benefits would be paid.

An important feature of the proposed scheme was that benefits were to take into account both changes in prices and in general living standards. Thus, for instance, a contributor who received earnings equal to the national average throughout his working life would receive a pension calculated on the national average earnings at the time he reached pension age, not on the money he received over his working life. Some two-thirds of employed men were contracted-out, *i.e.*, in occupational pensions schemes, in 1970. The Government intended that these schemes should continue to exist together with the State scheme, and it proposed to allow for partial contracting out of the State scheme.

These plans lapsed with the change of Government in 1970. The Conservative Government announced its proposals for reform in a White Paper published in 1971. It considered that the costs of earnings-related benefits would be too great; instead it favoured earnings-related contributions for basically flat-rate pensions. In addition it wished to encourage contracting out, so that almost all employees would also be members of a private occupational pension scheme, in which pensions would be related to past contributions. The Government recognised that it would have to ensure that occupational pension rights were transferable between jobs. Like the previous Government, it envisaged a legal guarantee that State pensions would be revised every two years. It also envisaged that the share which the State provides from taxation for National Insurance—about 18 per cent of contributions in 1970—would be maintained. Again the plan lapsed.

Meanwhile the Government had become aware of the need for a frequent adjustment of pension rates in an era of high inflation. In early 1975 the full pension entitlement was £10 for a single person and £16 for a married couple. In April 1990 the rates stood at £46·90 for a single person and £75·10 for a married couple. The difficulty of funding an adequate state pension when the number of pensioners is rising relative to the size of the workforce has led to a withdrawal from the goals for pensions laid down in the 1970s. These goals were for a two-tier pension. The bottom tier was a common flat-rate for everyone. The top tier was earnings-related—that is, a fixed proportion of the pensioner's previous earnings. Because of the flat-rate element, a low earner would be able to expect a pension which was a higher percentage of his working income than that obtained by a higher earner. Contributions to the scheme would be earnings related. The pensions would be fully protected against inflation, and women would enter the scheme on the same footing as men. There was an obvious emphasis on the need to protect women from poverty in retirement, after the death of the husband. There would be a maximum pension entitlement and a maximum contribution. For this reason among others, the Government planned to encourage new and improved occupational schemes, to exist alongside the state scheme. It was hoped that the scheme would come to full maturity by 1998, this long delay reflecting the formidable difficulties in financing the plan. In the meantime fully earnings-related contributions started in 1975, and minor earnings-related benefit in 1979. These replaced flat-rate National Insurance payments and graduated pension contributions.

A renewed concern in the early 1980s was with a particular aspect of occupational pensions—their transferability from job to job. Someone who left an occupational scheme had the choice of either leaving his pension rights at his old employer, and receiving a deferred pension at retirement age, usually unadjusted for inflation between his depar-

ture and retirement; or, if his old and new employers both agreed, transferring the fund, from which effectively the pension is paid, to his new employer, usually at great loss to himself. The Government is attempting to introduce the full transferability of pension rights from job to job—at least for those who have been with an employer for more than two years. In changes introduced in 1988, employees were given the right to opt out of SERPS or of an employer's own scheme, and set up their own private pension plan. Unfortunately most employers appeared willing to pay only the minimum contribution. At the same time, a worker who left for another job after 2 years (instead as previously after 5 years) would be able to preserve his pension rights (with some protection for inflation) or have them transferred to a new scheme if the scheme was willing to accept them. The extent of take-up of personal pension schemes can be gauged by the cost to the Government in foregone National Insurance contributions as individuals contract out of the state pension scheme. National Insurance rebates to those taking out personal pensions amounted to £1·75 billion in 1989–90.

(iv) Poverty in Britain.

Despite the existence of National Insurance there were many people in Britain whose income fell below that which the Government regarded as adequate. These people were supported from Government revenues by means of *supplementary benefits*, before 1966 known as *National Assistance*. It was a fault of the National Insurance Scheme that so many have required this assistance. In 1989 more than 2 million pensioners received income support, with many more getting help with rent and rates. Of families whose head was in work, 285,000 received additional Family Credit, whilst well over half of the male unemployed were wholly dependent on additional state support. Anyone who is out of work for more than a year loses entitlement to unemployment benefit and becomes reliant on supplementary payments through what was the supplementary systen and is now income support (*see* (v) *below*). Despite these provisions at least 1·4 million households were below the official poverty line, of whom probably about 25 per cent were over pension age. A major fault with the supplementary benefits scheme was that they could not be paid to those in employment whose earnings were below the benefit level, and if such persons became unemployed they could claim benefits only up to their normal earnings level. The *Family Income Supplement* was introduced in 1971 to alleviate hardship amongst low earners, but it has been estimated that only half of those eligible claimed F.I.S. The take-up of new Family Credit payment, is expected to have been even lower. As for Supplementary Benefit, it was estimated that only three quarters of those entitled to it were in fact making claims.

(v) The Reform of Social Security.

In 1985 the Government issued a White Paper detailing reforms of the whole social security system. The basis of dissatisfaction was three-fold. First, the system was a complex and costly one to run. Second, it worked in such a way as to help some who, on official definitions of poverty, did not need assistance; whilst, conversely, it failed to provide it for some who did. Third, it created unemployment benefit traps, supplementary benefit traps and poverty traps. These imply that people who are unemployed or employed on low pay might be deterred from taking employment or taking jobs with higher pay, because the combined effects of the tax and benefit system mean that the consequential increase in their net income is negligible. Behind their proposed reforms was the concern about future financing difficulties, and a wish to make the system simpler. The main elements of the new system were introduced in April 1988.

On pensions, it was originally proposed to retain basic pensions, but to abolish earnings related pensions (SERPS). Instead, greater stress was to be placed on occupational pension schemes. Substantial political pressures caused a change of mind, and SERPS was retained, albeit in modified form.

SOURCES OF PUBLIC REVENUE

Revenue.	1978. £m	1988. £m	Percentage increase 1978–88.	Percentage of total revenue 1988.
Taxes on income	*37,725*	*92,809*	*184*	*47·8*
of which paid by:				
personal sector	19,460	48,655	150	25·0
companies	3,526	12,873	265	6·6
national insurance contributions	10,101	31,686	214	16·3
Taxes on capital	*808*	*4,760*	*489*	*2·4*
of which:				
capital gains tax	416	3,662	780	1·9
Taxes on expenditure	*13,723*	*50,661*	*269*	*26·1*
of which levied on:				
alcohol	2,236	4,509	102	2·3
tobacco	2,153	4,919	128	2·5
Rates	*5,660*	*18,417*	*5,660*	*9·5*
Other revenues	*9,479*	*27,627*	*192*	*14·2*
Total revenue	62,395	194,319	211	100·0
Net borrowing	−8,144	12,084		
Total expenditure	70,539	182,235		

Universal child benefit was retained. But for low earnings families, FIS was replaced by *Family Credit*, paid through the pay packet. As compared to FIS it allows a smoother tapering of payments as original income increases. For those not in work, supplementary benefits were replaced by *"income support"*, which is intended to be simpler and to involve a smaller range of payments. Benefits are at a lower rate for the under-25s and at a higher rate for pensioners. An additional sum is paid for each dependent child, as it is for single parents and the long-term sick and disabled. Beyond these, there are no additional payments. There is, however, a new *Social Fund* "to provide for exceptional circumstances and emergencies", payments from which are rationed through a system of strict budget limits for each Social Security Office Recipients of income support are still entitled to free school meals and free welfare foods, unlike those getting family credit. There is also a new simplified scheme for housing benefits. Unemployment benefit, the maternity allowance (in revised form) and sickness benefit remain, but maternity and death grants have been abolished. Substantial changes have been made in provisions for widowhood.

The Government's catchphrase for these reforms has been "the twin pillars": state help combined with encouragement for private provision. Returning to the three major complaints about the previous system, certainly the revised one is cheaper to administer. It probably will target the benefits more accurately. It may also have alleviated the worst traps, but in substantially improving the lot of some in this respect, it has worsened it for more. Indeed, the new scheme is not a major departure, and falls far short of the more radical proposals of (for example) the Institute for Fiscal Studies, who propose a combined tax and benefit credit system.

Public Revenue.

In the table above we show the sources of revenue. No less than 48·0 per cent of the total public revenue in 1988 came from taxes on income; almost half of this being personal income tax. Taxation of profits amounted to only 6·6 per cent of total public revenue. Taxes on expenditure and rates accounted for almost 36 per cent of the total. Two commodities in particular were heavily taxed: alcoholic drink and tobacco. Together they accounted for almost 6 per cent of public revenue. These commodities are singled out partly for social reasons and partly because—in economists' jargon—the demand for them is *inelastic*; *i.e.*, the public reduces its consumption of drink and tobacco only slightly in response to a rise in their price. Indirect taxation—taking the form of excise duties and purchase taxes (value added tax after 1973)—used to be spread very unevenly over the different sorts of expenditure. The introduction of Value Added Tax in 1973 tended to even out the incidence of indirect taxes on different goods and

services, though tobacco, drink and motoring continued to be hit heavily.

Until 1989 in Scotland, and 1990 in England and Wales, the major method of collecting local taxes was through rates. A rateable value was assessed for each commercial or domestic property, corresponding roughly to its size, imputed rental value, and amenities. Each year, the appropriate local authority decided at what rate in the pound to tax this rateable value. On the dates mentioned above, the government substantially altered the local tax system in an ostensible effort to broaden the tax base for the domestic element. Instead of local taxes being paid on the basis of property ownership, each adult pays a flat rate charge or poll tax. Although some minor adjustment is made for personal circumstances, the tax is highly regressive and its introduction has been very controversial. Part but not all of the objections relate to the government's under-estimate of the burden of local government revenue which would fall on the personal sector. Local authorities can no longer levy rates on the business sector—these are charged uniformly by central government and the proceeds are then distributed to local authorities on some notional calculation of need.

The Budget.

Each year in the Spring the Chancellor of the Exchequer announces his Budget for the coming fiscal year. The most important and most difficult task in drawing up the Budget is to decide on the size of deficit to aim for. The deficit is the excess of public expenditure over public revenue; and it has to be financed by borrowing or by printing money. A large deficit is normally reflationary; sometimes that may be required to get the economy out of recession. A small deficit—and even more, a surplus—is deflationary, and is a means of holding a demand-pull inflation in check.

In 1970 there was a small surplus, and thus the net borrowing requirement was negative. After that the borrowing requirement became large and positive, peaking in the recessionary years 1979–82. Since then, more favourable economic circumstances and the one-off receipts from major privatisations have enabled the public sector accounts to swing into surplus. In 1988/89 this surplus or Public Sector Debt Repayment (PSDR) was £14·3 billion (3·5 per cent of GDP) although it fell to £8 billion in 1989/90. The reason for the virtual halving of the PSDR between 1988–89 and 1989–90 was a combination of slower economic growth, difficulties with the privatisation programme, and a significant increase in government expenditure. The last of these was largely due to much higher public sector pay awards. However, a large surplus is not itself indicative of a very tight fiscal policy, any more than a deficit automatically implies an expansionary stance. To assess the true fiscal stance, one must adjust the surplus/deficit for the effects of inflation, privatisation receipts, and the stage of the economic cycle, *i.e.* the level of unemployment.

The calculation of the precise deficit or surplus needed is a chancy business; for the level that is required depends on the amount of saving and on the amount of spending out of credit that people intend to do—and this is not easily predictable. It also depends on the change in the foreign balance. Nor can the Chancellor be sure his figures are right: estimating next year's revenue, and even next year's expenditure, by the Government is difficult enough, but he needs to estimate also the likely trends of private income and expenditure, without really reliable information as to what they were in the past year. This has been particularly evident in the past two years, when official economic statistics have been subject to massive error and subsequent revision, and the Chancellor's Budget forecasts for the year ahead have proved wildly inaccurate. One good example is provided by his 1988 Budget forecast for the balance of payments. In March 1988 the official forecast for the current account deficit in the year ahead was £4 billion—in the event the deficit was almost four times larger at £14·7 billion.

The introduction of advance *cash limits* on a large proportion of expenditure in 1976 was meant to give the Government greater control over projected spending. Prior to that the general rule had been to estimate public expenditure for the following year on the basis of its volume. If inflation was higher than predicted, then the tendency was to preserve volume by increasing the value of expenditure. Cash limits altered this, and in 1982 cash planning institutionalised this change. A large proportion of government spending was fixed in value terms, and if inflation exceeded the predicted rate, then volume suffered.

In spite of such problems, fiscal policy—running large deficits when economic activity is low, and small ones or surpluses when it seems to be excessively high—is the most important action through which the economy can be kept on an even keel. Monetary policy may help; but the Budget decision of the Chancellor on changes in taxation and public expenditure is the key one.

6. SOURCES OF STATISTICS: SOME SUGGESTIONS FOR FURTHER READING

The non-specialist will find that most of the sta-tistics he needs are given in the *Annual Abstract of Statistics*, published every year by Her Majesty's Stationery Office. This comprehensive document includes figures on population, social conditions, education, labour, production, trade and balance of payments, national income and expenditure, wages and prices, and many other topics. For more up-to-date information, reference should be made to the *Monthly Digest of Statistics* which has a similar coverage and gives month-by-month figures. A selection of the more important series, presented in a manner which can more easily be understood by the layman, is given in another Stationery Office publication, *Economic Trends*, also issued monthly.

Fuller information on labour problems is given in the *Department of Employment Gazette*, on trade in *British Business*, and on financial matters in the *Bank of England Quarterly Bulletin*. These three periodicals include discussions on the statistics presented. *Social and Cultural Trends* contains articles and detailed statistics on social, cultural and economic conditions in Britain.

For an analysis of developments in the economy see the *National Institute Economic Review*, a private publication issued by the National Institute for Economic and Social Research. To explain economic events and policy, the Treasury publishes a monthly *Economic Progress Report*. The quarterly *Oxford Review of Economic Policy* (Oxford University Press) contains up-to-date articles on aspects of the economy.

For a comprehensive and systematic introduction to the British economy the reader is referred to A. R. Prest and D. J. Coppock, *The U.K. Economy: a Survey of Applied Economics* (Weidenfeld and Nicolson). Other introductory texts include J. Black, *The Economics of Modern Britain* (Martin Robertson), M. Stewart, *Keynes and After* (Penguin), and D. Morris (ed), *The Economic System in the UK* (Oxford).

Interesting books on particular topics include J. Vickers and G. Yarrow, *Privatization: An Economic Analysis* (MIT) and A. B. Atkinson, *The Economics of Inequality* (Oxford). A sourcebook on the EEC is *The Economy of the European Community* (Office for Official Publications of the European Communities). A recent view of the international debt crisis is given by H. Lever and C. Huhne, *Debt and Danger* (Penguin).

III.   THE LESS DEVELOPED ECONOMIES

Income Levels.

Two-thirds of the world's population live in dire poverty—a poverty which can scarcely be imagined by those accustomed to the standards of living attained in the relatively few developed countries of the world. The orders of world inequality may be seen from the table comparing annual gross national products per capita by region, converted into pounds sterling at official exchange rates. These figures are only very approximate because exchange rates are misleading indicators of purchasing power and because the averages conceal considerable income inequalities within some regions and countries. Nevertheless, it is clear that poverty is widespread in the world. The alleviation of this poverty is widely recognised as the most important economic—and indeed political—task of the remainder of the twentieth century. The 37 low-income developing countries referred to in the table have an average income per capita under £200 per annum, and contain 2,400 million people; over 2,100 million in 12 Asian countries and 200 million in 25 African countries.

According to a World Bank estimate, a third of the population of all developing countries in 1980 had a calorie intake below 90 per cent of the requirement laid down by the Food and Agricultural Organisation and the World Health Organisation; this meant that they did not get enough calories for an active working life. A sixth (340 million) had a calorie intake below 80 per cent: they did not get enough calories to prevent stunted growth and serious health risks. The areas particularly affected were South Asia and sub-Saharan Africa.

What is a Less Developed Country?

There are no less than 140 countries comprising the so-called "Third World," known variously as "less developed" or "developing" or "under-developed" or "poor" countries. There is a great diversity among them, and yet they have a number of features in common. Foremost is their poverty, but even poverty is not universal: some of the oil-producing countries such as Saudi Arabia, Kuwait and Libya have achieved very high levels of income per capita while retaining many of the other characteristics of less developed countries.

Most of the developing countries are primarily agricultural economies, with the bulk of the population engaged in *subsistence agriculture*. For many millions of peasant farmers the primary objective is to produce enough food for their family to subsist. India is a classic example, with no less than 70 per cent of its 760 million people dependent on agriculture for a living. Most less developed countries have only a small industrial sector as yet: it is rare for the output of the manufacturing sector to exceed 20 per cent of the gross domestic product. The main exceptions to this rule are the successful exporters of labour-intensive manufacturing goods, such as Hong Kong, Singapore, Taiwan and South Korea. Many of the less developed countries lack the necessary ingredients for successful industrialisation—capital, skills and entrepreneurship.

The developing countries vary enormously in size—from the teeming masses of India and China to scores of countries with less than a million people, including Bahrain, Botswana, Fiji, Gabon, Mauritius and many West Indian islands.

GROSS NATIONAL PRODUCT PER CAPITA
BY GROUPS OF COUNTRY AND SELECTED
COUNTRIES, 1987

	(£ p.a.)
37 low-income developing countries	177
of which: Bangladesh	98
India	183
Sri Lanka	244
Tanzania	110
China	177
59 middle-income developing countries	1,104
of which: Egypt	415
Thailand	518
Brazil	1,232
Mexico	1,116
19 industrialised countries	8,945
of which: Spain	3,665
U.K.	6,354
W. Germany	8,780
U.S.A.	11,299
4 high-income oil exporters	4,805
of which: Saudi Arabia	3,780

The development problems and possibilities facing
large and small countries are very different. The
small size of most developing economies forces
them to concentrate on the production of one or
two primary products for world markets. Their
high degree of specialisation and heavy dependence on exports and imports makes these economies dangerously vulnerable to the vagaries of
world trade and the world economy.

Enough has been said to show that, apart
from their poverty, the less developed countries
have other economic characteristics and problems in common. However, it is dangerous to
generalise because there are also important differences. In particular, they vary in their degree
of development and in their potential for development. A semi-industrialised, urbanised country
such as Argentina has little in common with an
utterly backward country such as Chad, and the
economic prospects for an oil-rich country such as
Indonesia are far brighter than for a country with
few natural resources such as Tanzania.

Population Growth.

Many underdeveloped countries are experiencing an unprecedented population explosion:
annual rates of increase of between 2 and 3 per
cent—which double population in as little as 35
and 24 years respectively—are common. This is a
phenomenon of the last four decades. Death
rates have fallen sharply in response to improved
health services and modern methods of control,
e.g., the eradication of malaria through DDT

POPULATION SIZE, GROWTH AND
DENSITY BY REGION

	Popula-tion 1986 (m).	Growth rate 1980–85 (% p.a.).	Density 1986 (per sq km).
North America	266	0·9	12
Europe . .	493	0·3	100
U.S.S.R. . .	281	1·0	13
Oceania . .	25	1·5	3
Africa . .	572	2·9	19
Latin America .	414	2·3	20
East Asia . .	1,264	1·2	107
South Asia .	1,601	2·2	101
World Total	4,917	1·7	36

spraying. On the other hand, birth rates have been
kept up by such factors as tradition, social
prestige, religion, the need for security in old age
and a lack of facilities for family planning.

The table indicates that over half the world's
population lives in Asia, and that the developed
regions account for under a third of the total.
Apart from Australasia (into which immigration
is high) the developed countries show slower rates
of population growth than Africa, Latin America
and Asia. The figures of population density may
easily be misleading, since they take no account
of the nature of the area, *e.g.*, deserts are
included. But it is clear that Asia is more densely
populated than Africa or Latin America.

Life Expectancy.

Although death rates have fallen in the
developing countries, especially infant mortality,
life expectancy is generally low in the poorest
countries. Thus, for instance, the expectation of life
at birth in 1987 was below 50 years in many
countries of Africa, including Angola, Ethiopia,
Niger and Sierra Leone, and some in Asia, including
Laos and Nepal. Life in these countries is all too
short.

Life expectancy is related to income per head. In
most of the developed countries life expectancy at
birth is about 76 years, being 75 in the United
Kingdom, West Germany and the United
States and 78 in Japan in 1987. However, the
average length of life depends also on the quantity
and quality of medical provision and the degree of
income inequality about the mean: life expectancy
exceeded 60 years in some of the poorest countries,
including China and Sri Lanka. Life expectancy is
an important but neglected indicator of the
"quality of life".

The Population Problem.

In many developing countries there is population pressure on the land, and many people want
more land for farming. Population density is a
hindrance in agricultural economies, but not
necessarily in industrial economies: because it is
industrialised and has accumulated much capital,
Europe can support at a high standard of living a
population more concentrated even than that of
Asia.

As a result of rapid population growth the
pressure of population on the land has increased.
The consequences have been far more serious in
countries such as Bangladesh (with a population
density of 700 people per square kilometre in 1986)
or India (233 per sq km) than in Zambia (9 per sq
km) or Brazil (16 per sq km). In those countries with abundant land the expanding population
can spread into unused areas; but as land becomes
increasingly scarce, less and less productive land
must be brought into cultivation and soil erosion
and loss of fertility become major problems. A
substantial increase in output is required to prevent a fall in per capita income as population
grows, and an even greater increase is required if
living standards are to be improved. Between
1975 and 1986 food production in the developing countries as a group increased by 37 per cent
and per capita food production rose by only 5 per
cent.

Even in those countries with plenty of land a
rapid increase in population can have harmful
effects. For instance, it diverts scarce investment
resources away from directly productive investments such as factories and irrigation projects
so as to meet the needs of the expanding population for more schools, hospitals, housing, cities
and other public services.

Family Planning Programmes.

In many African and Latin American countries
the rate of population growth appears to be constant or even rising, but in parts of Asia there are
signs that the growth rate has peaked and is now
declining. The different experiences may reflect differences in government policies: in 1980 a quarter
of less developed countries had no official family
planning programme. The success stories include
India, where in 1985, 35 per cent of married women
used contraceptives and the birth rate fell from 4·5

to 3·3 per cent per annum between 1965 and 1985, Colombia (63 per cent contraceptive use and a fall from 4·5 to 2·7 per cent) and South Korea (70 per cent contraceptive use and a fall from 3·5 to 2·1 per cent). The successful cases show what can be done, but private incentives and attitudes still favour large families in many poor societies: simply providing facilities for family planning may not be enough.

Problems of Agriculture.

There are many millions of peasant farmers throughout the Third World eking out a subsistence from the soil. The margin between what can be produced and what is required to support life is narrow: the failure of crops because of drought, floods or pests can lead to famine unless food is quickly supplied from outside the area affected. For instance, relief action by the international community was too slow to prevent the drought which struck the Sahel area of Africa in 1973 and 1974 from claiming some 100,000 lives, endangering future income by destroying seeds and livestock, and breaking up rural communities. Relief was again slow and patchy in response to the more widespread and severe African famines of 1984 and 1985.

Agricultural production may be held back by a shortage of land, or by the use of primitive tools and methods of cultivation (which may in turn be due to a lack of farming knowledge and skills or to a lack of funds for investment in land improvement or equipment), or by an unjust system of land tenure which deprives the farmer of incentive to raise his production. Perhaps all these problems must be tackled simultaneously.

The Green Revolution.

A technology is being introduced which can increase the yields from foodgrains by 50 per cent or more in tropical areas. This new technology is commonly thought to have caused a *green revolution*. It consists of new high-yielding seeds, largely for wheat and rice. Not only are the yields per acre higher but also shorter cropping cycles permit multiple cropping. The new technology economises on land and, being labour-intensive, provides more farm employment. The introduction of high-yielding cereals is probably the most decisive single factor in the emergence of India and Pakistan into the ranks of solid economic achievers.

However, we cannot assume that it is going to solve the problem of foodgrain shortage in the underdeveloped countries. As yet, the new seeds are less resistant to drought, floods and disease. To be effective, they require substantial inputs of fertiliser and of water; in many areas expensive irrigation will be essential to their success. Moreover, the fact that fertiliser and water are complementary inputs has meant that the green revolution has caught on—and been encouraged by governments—among the larger, more prosperous farmers in the better-watered, more prosperous regions. This is true of, *e.g.*, Mexico, Pakistan and the Philippines. Unless governments ensure that the benefits of the green revolution are widely spread, the effect might even be to harm small peasant farmers by increasing the competition from large farmers.

Land Reform.

There are many forms of land tenure in less developed countries. In black Africa communal or tribal ownership of land is common, with members of the community or tribe receiving rights to use the land individually. In parts of Asia and Latin America, there is private ownership of land, which—particularly where the land is densely populated—has often led to great inequality of land ownership. In some cases land tenure is characterised by absentee landlords and share-cropping tenants. The development of large estates produces a class of landless labourers.

The need for land reform varies according to the circumstances. In most cases the main argument is for greater social justice. In some cases it may be possible also to expand production by redistributing land more evenly or by giving land to share-cropping tenants and so improving their incentives. On the other hand, large farmers may have access to technology, skills and capital which small farmers lack: there is a danger that greater equity will be achieved only at the expense of efficiency. Hence the need to ensure that land reform is accompanied by a package of measures, *e.g.*, education, training and advice, and credit for fertiliser, tools and land improvements. Few governments have succeeded in implementing serious land reform programmes. The main reason is that the system of land tenure in a country often reflects the balance of political power: land reform invariably faces political opposition from entrenched interests. By the same token, a successful land reform may alter the balance of political power so as to facilitate broad-based development.

Exports of Primary Products.

Almost all developing countries export primary products (foodstuffs, industrial raw materials or minerals) and import manufactured goods, especially the capital goods (plant, machinery and vehicles) required for development. This international division of labour has recently operated to the disadvantage of the developing countries. The world demand for their primary products has increased only very slowly. This is because people spend just a small part of their additional income on food (*e.g.*, tea, coffee, cocoa), because synthetic substitutes have been developed for many raw materials (*e.g.*, rubber, cotton, jute), because developed countries protect their own agriculture (*e.g.*, sugar) and because demand in the developed countries has moved towards commodities with low raw material content (*e.g.*, from heavy industries to services).

In consequence, the general trend has been for the prices of primary products to fall in relation to those of manufactured goods. This was an important cause of the improvement in Britain's terms of trade (*see* **G6**). The reverse of the coin was a deterioration in the terms of trade of many developing countries, *i.e.*, they could now buy fewer imports for a given quantity of exports. Primary commodities exported by developing countries actually decreased in price on average by 10 per cent over the period 1957–70. Most poor countries benefited from the soaring prices of various commodities in world markets during 1972 and 1973. These were years of world economic boom, food shortage and speculative purchasing of primary commodities. However, the non-oil-producing developing countries suffered as a result of the oil prices rise after October 1973. The subsequent world recession depressed primary commodity prices, and inflation in developed countries increased the price of manufactured imports (*see* **Part IV**). When fuels are excluded, the terms of trade of the developing countries with the developed countries fell by 4 per cent between 1970 and 1980.

Unsatisfactory prices of primary commodities have contributed to the shortage of foreign exchange which restricts investment expenditure in many less developed countries. This was particularly marked in the early 1980s. World recession and tardy growth depressed primary product prices and sales. The purchasing power of exports from the developing countries fell by 17 per cent between 1980 and 1987: oil-exporting countries and African countries were the most badly affected.

Economic Instability.

The prices of various primary products tend to fluctuate violently from one year to another. Many developing economies depend heavily on the exports of one or two commodities. For instance, coffee is the most important product in Brazil, cotton in Egypt, copper in Zambia, sugar in Cuba, cocoa in Ghana and rice in Burma. Fluctuations in the world price of its main export cause instability in the export revenues of a country, and this in turn can produce fluctuations in income throughout its domestic economy.

Even the oil-producing developing countries, whose problems are in many ways quite different, have faced problems of economic instability. The governments of these countries have had to decide how best to use their vastly increased oil revenues so as to promote economic and social development without overturning their societies. Recent political

URBAN POPULATION AS A PERCENTAGE
OF TOTAL POPULATION IN SELECTED
DEVELOPING COUNTRIES, 1965 AND 1985

	1965	1985
37 low-income developing countries	17	22
of which: Ethiopia	8	15
China	18	22
Tanzania	6	14
Ghana	26	32
59 middle-income developing countries	37	48
of which: Nigeria	15	30
Peru	52	68
Brazil	37	54
Iran	37	54
Jamaica	38	53
4 high-income oil exporters	40	73
of which: Libya	29	60

events in Iran were closely related to the economic
boom which oil produced. The effects of political
instability in Saudi Arabia on the world economy
would be incalculable.

Problems of Industrialisation.

In those underdeveloped countries where there
is population pressure on the land, alternative
employment has to be created in industry or
services. Even in countries with a surplus of
land, if there is heavy dependence on one or two
primary products, industrialisation provides a
means of diversifying the economy.

But industrialisation is not an easy course.
Because the margin between agricultural production and food consumption is narrow, the surplus
from the agricultural sector exchangeable for the
products of other sectors e.g., industry and
services—is small; i.e., the demand for the goods
and services produced by other sectors is low. A
second constraint on industrialisation is imposed
by competition from abroad; new industries in
an underdeveloped country have to compete with
established industries in developed countries,
which have the advantage of experience, a trained
labour force and markets big enough for them to
reap all the potential economies of large-scale
production.

Industrialisation Strategies.

One means of overcoming the small size of
market is to export manufactures to the developed
countries. Developing countries with cheap
labour are likely to have a comparative advantage
in the manufacture of relatively labour-intensive
commodities. A number of less developed countries have had remarkable success in following
this strategy. Among their successful activities are
textiles, clothing and labour-intensive components
of electronic equipment. However, the developed
countries often impose protective tariffs. Another
form of manufacturing is the processing of primary
products before exporting them. Here developing
countries sometimes face the problem that tariffs
are higher on the processed than on the
unprocessed products.

A means of overcoming competition from the
industries of the developed countries is by nur-
turing an infant industrial sector behind tariff
walls—which is how the United States and Germany developed their industries in the face of
British competition in the nineteenth century.
A number of developing countries have adopted
this strategy. However, it has its drawbacks.
Sometimes the "infants" never grow up, and
vested interests press for continued protection.
Import-substituted industrialisation often means
that raw materials or semi-processed goods are
imported for local processing. There is a danger
that fluctuations in export proceeds will periodically curtail imports of necessary intermediate
goods. The under-utilisation of capital in the

manufacturing sector because of foreign exchange
shortages has frequently occurred in countries
such as India, Pakistan, Tanzania and Ghana.

The Newly Industrialising Countries.

The remarkable success of a handful of developing
countries—the *newly industrialising countries*
(NICs)—in exporting manufactured goods raises the
questions: why were they successful, and can others
do the same?

South Korea is perhaps the most successful of the
NICs. After a period in which government pursued
a policy of industrialisation through import substitution, the policy was changed in the 1960s to one
of promoting exports of labour intensive manufactures. This was achieved by devaluing the currency
in order to encourage export industries in which
the country would have a competitive advantage,
and liberalising imports to discourage inefficient
industrial production. In 1962 South Korea
exported manufactures worth $10 million; in 1986
their value was $32,000 million. Between 1962 and
1982 the proportion of the labour force employed
in industry rose from 10 to 30 per cent, manufacturing production rose by 17 per cent per annum,
and GNP per capita rose by 7 per cent per annum.
The labour-intensive nature of industrialisation,
as well as its speed, helped to alleviate poverty
through the market: first employment and later, as
labour became less abundant, also real wages rose
rapidly.

South Korea benefited from its trading relationships with Japan and its close ties with the
United States in finding markets for its products. It
has a well educated labour force: 95 per cent of the
relevant age group in 1986 were enrolled in secondary school, which is higher than any other developing country. Industrialisation may also have
benefited from stable autocratic government and a
beleaguered sense of national purpose. In part the
Korean success represents the harnessing of cheap
labour in almost free trade conditions for exporters.
However, the government also played an active
role, e.g. it both generated high savings and successfully directed savings into the favoured sectors.
It will take much more than policies of *laissez faire*
for other developing countries to be able to emulate
South Korea. Moreover, since the world market for
labour-intensive products is limited, only a minority
of developing countries can take the Korean path.
The most successful NICs—known as the "Gang
of Four"—are Hong Kong, South Korea, Taiwan
and Singapore. As a group they exported manufactures worth $155 billion in 1986—more than either
Britain or France.

Outward-Oriented Industrialisation Policies.

The success of the NICs has led many policy
advisers to press for more outward-oriented industrialisation policies. The policy advice is gradually
to dismantle the system of protection of import-
substituting industries and to devalue the currency
in order to provide incentives to export manufactures. It is argued that competition in world
markets will act as a spur to domestic efficiency
and help to divorce economic activities from
domestic political processes.

The traditional view has been that few developing countries could succeed in breaking into world
markets for manufactures. However, despite the
resurgence of protectionism in the 1980s (*see* **G52**),
potential access to the markets of industrialised
countries is better than it used to be, and broadly-
based progress has been made. In 1965 manufactures accounted for 19 per cent of the exports of the
developing countries, but in 1987 for 56 per cent. If
the NICs constitute the "first division", a "second
division" of countries has expanded manufacturing exports rapidly, including India, China, Pakistan, the Philippines, Thailand, Turkey, Malaysia,
Brazil and Morocco. In 1987 manufacturing accounted for a quarter of the exports of low-income
developing countries (excluding China and India),
for 10 per cent in the case of the oil-exporters, and
for half of the total in the case of the middle-income,
non-oil exporting developing countries.

Unemployment and Underemployment.

Unemployment and underemployment occur on

a very considerable scale in both the rural and the urban areas of developing countries. Consider first the rural case. Because farm work is normally shared, underemployment—disguised unemployment—is more common than open unemployment. People work for only a part of the day or year. Where land is scarce, underemployment is chronic: people would like to work more if only they had more land. Unless the yield from the land can be raised, growth in population causes greater underemployment and reduces income per head on the land. Where land is abundant, underemployment is a seasonal phenomenon. People are fully employed in the busy season—harvesting and planting—but underemployed at other times of the year.

In the towns open unemployment is common with people queueing for *modern sector* jobs at the labour exchanges and at the factory gates. Rates of urban open unemployment in excess of 10 per cent are frequently recorded, *e.g.*, in Ghana, Colombia, Puerto Rico, Trinidad, Sri Lanka and the Philippines. Few developing countries can afford unemployment benefits, so that job-seekers remain openly unemployed only until their savings are used up or support by their relations is withdrawn. Then they have to scrape out a subsistence in the urban *traditional sector* while waiting and hoping for something better. Underemployment is rife in the easily entered traditional sector activities such as petty trading, hawking, beer brewing, fetching and carrying. A shoeshiner may be on the streets for ten hours a day but have only a couple of customers. The more people enter these activities, the further average income per worker is depressed. In many less developed countries this self-employment in the traditional sector accounts for the majority of urban workers.

Migration to the Cities.

Urbanisation is proceeding at an unprecedented pace in much of the Third World. Over the decade 1970–80 the total urban population of the developing countries as a whole grew by 50 per cent and over the period 1980–87 by 50 per cent again. The table (*see* **G40**) illustrates the pace of urbanisation in a number of developing countries.

Rural people are being drawn to the cities at a rate well in excess of the capacity of the cities to absorb them productively. The reason for this migration might be economic or social. The economic explanation runs in terms of an income differential between the urban and the rural areas. Relatively unskilled wages in the modern sector of the economy—often governed by minimum wage legislation or trade union bargaining—can be well above the incomes to be derived from peasant agriculture. People go to the town in search of modern sector wage jobs, although they may actually end up underemployed in the low-income traditional sector. Rural–urban migration may be a social phenomenon: rural people are attracted by the facilities and "bright lights" of the cities. The recent expansion of education in many countries may also play a part, since a high proportion of the migrants are school leavers.

Whatever the reasons the consequences are socially harmful and politically explosive. Shanty towns and slums proliferate in the cities and their outskirts; poverty, disease and crime flourish.

In 1950 there were only two urban agglomerations in the world with more than 10 million inhabitants, New York and London. On present trends, there will be by the year 2000 some 25 such cities, of which 20 will be in the third world and the largest will be Mexico City with a forecast population of 31 million.

Employment Creation.

As recognition has grown that unemployment, in its open and disguised forms, is both high and rising in many of the developing countries, so the objective of creating productive employment has received higher priority. For various reasons the growth of modern sector employment has been tardy and has lagged behind the growth of output. One reason is that the modern sector normally uses capital equipment and technology which is imported from the developed countries. This means that, even in countries with cheap and abundant labour, the most profitable techniques of production are often highly capital-intensive, so that the amount of scarce investment funds required to equip a worker is high. Hence the case for developing an *intermediate technology* which is both profitable and suited to the needs of the underdeveloped countries.

There is some danger that the establishment of capital-intensive factories may actually harm existing labour-intensive production. For instance, sandals can be made by small cobblers using local leather (or old car tyres) or by a large plant using imported plastic materials: a new factory employing a few machine operators might displace many more traditional craftsmen who have no alternative employment opportunities.

Governments, by encouraging or discouraging particular forms and areas of investment, have the power to influence the growth of employment. In the rural areas the encouragment and organisation of labour-intensive developmental or community projects can assist in harnessing the one abundant resource which almost all developing countries possess: unskilled labour.

Educated Manpower.

Many underdeveloped countries are faced with the dual problem of unskilled labour surpluses and scarcities of skilled and educated manpower. The problem is particularly acute in some of the recently independent countries of Africa. To give an extreme example: at the time of its independence in 1964, Zambia had only 100 Zambian university graduates and 1,200 secondary school graduates in a population of 3·5 million. In such countries the great shortage of educated and skilled people enables them to earn high incomes—with the result that there is a very unequal distribution of income. And even in countries where surpluses have developed, the existence of an international market for professional people such as doctors and engineers helps to keep up their earnings: these countries suffer from a "brain drain" to the developed world.

In sub-Saharan Africa in 1980 64 per cent of children of the relevant age were at primary school, 14 per cent at secondary school and only one per cent in higher education; fewer than a third of adults were literate. The provision of education on this meagre scale nevertheless took up 16 per cent of government budgets. A reason for the expensiveness of education is the cost of scarce teachers: a primary school teacher's salary averaged 7 times the GNP per capita in Africa. In such circumstances it is not easy to meet the demand for universal primary education; especially if the sort of education provided does not enable those who receive it to become better farmers. The demand for education is generally strong and unsatisfied in Africa; often it is perceived as the passport to a good urban job.

Educational Policies.

Economic development is not just a matter of capital accumulation: it requires also an increase in educated manpower. Not only more knowledge but also new habits and attitudes—*e.g.*, attitudes towards risk-taking, hard work and thrift. Education—of the right sort and with suitable content—is generally acknowledged to be important for development, although the benefits of education cannot be quantified at all satisfactorily.

The table shows enrolment ratios (the percentage of children in the relevant age-group who are enrolled in education) at the primary, secondary and higher educational levels for selected developing countries in 1985. There is a strong tendency for enrolment ratios to increase with the income per head of a country. Educational provision remains extremely low in most of the low-income developing countries, particularly beyond the primary level. On the other hand, there are developing countries whose problem is now surplus rather than shortage of educated manpower. Such cases are common in Asia, e.g. India and the Philippines.

The table also shows that enrolment ratios in-

EDUCATIONAL ENROLMENT RATIOS IN
DEVELOPING COUNTRIES, 1965 AND 1985

	Primary		Secondary		Tertiary	
	1965	1986	1965	1986	1965	1986
China	89	129	24	42	0	2
India	74	92	27	35	5	9
37 low-income developing countries	44	76	9	25	1	4
of which:						
Ethiopia	11	36	2	12	0	1
Tanzania	32	69	2	3	0	0
Sri Lanka	93	103	35	66	2	4
Pakistan	40	44	12	18	2	5
58 middle-income developing countries	85	104	22	54	5	18
of which:						
Egypt	75	86	26	66	7	21
Brazil	108	105	16	36	2	11
South Korea	101	94	35	95	6	33
Philippines	113	106	41	68	19	38

Note: A figure of zero indicates that it is closer to 0
than to 1 per cent, and a figure greater than 100 is
possible because of the difficulties of choosing the
appropriate age-group.

creased rapidly in many countries between 1965 and
1983. The high financial returns accruing to the
educated have generated powerful pressures for the
expansion of state education, to which governments
have often acceded. Rapid expansion in quantity
has frequently been accompanied by a decline in
quality of education. In the Philippines, for instance, where a higher proportion are in tertiary
education than is the case in Britain (38 per cent as
against 22 per cent), most are in institutions of poor
quality.

Some governments have found that it is easier to
expand an educational system than it is to expand
an economy, and shortages have given way to surpluses. The response to surplus may take various
forms: unemployment of the educated, or displacement of the less educated from their jobs, so pushing
the unemployment down the educational ladder, or
pressures on government to create unnecessary jobs
for the educated in the public service. In this last
case—true of Egypt—scarce resources are doubly
wasted.

Economic Aid.

The gap between living standards in the developing areas of the world and in the areas already
developed has tended to widen in recent years. In
the 1950s real income per capita rose in the
developed countries by 2·7 per cent per annum on
average, and in the less developed countries by 2·3
per cent per annum. It was through a growing
world recognition of the situation that the 1960s
were designated "The United Nations Development
Decade." But between 1960 and 1970 these rates of
growth widened to 3·8 and 3·0 per cent per annum
respectively. World inequalities continued to
increase in the 1970s. A World Bank estimate for
the 1970s has the annual average per capita growth
of developing countries (2·8 per cent) exceeding
that of developed countries (2·4 per cent). However,
when developing were divided into 33
low-income and 63 middle-income countries (the
dividing line being per capita income of £180 in
1980) the low-income group was found to average
less than 2 per cent per annum.

Over the period of world economic recession and
subsequent tardy recovery, 1980–87, GNP per
capita in the industrialised countries grew by 2·1 per
cent per annum whereas the developing countries
managed only 0·7 per cent per annum. This masked
wide variation in performance: GNP per capita in
sub-Saharan Africa fell annually by 1·1 per cent and
in Latin America by 0·9 per cent, whereas it rose by
4·1 per cent in the developing countries of Asia.

The main industrial countries—organised as a
17-member *Development Assistance Committee*
(DAC)—have provided economic aid to the developing countries. The total net flow of economic assistance from the DAC countries was $70
billion in 1987. Roughly $23 billion of this was net
private investment and $42 billion official aid from
governments. A quarter of the net *official development assistance* (ODA) was contributed by the
United States; the other principal donors were
Japan, France, West Germany, Italy and
Britain in that order. Net private investment
is volatile and cannot be relied upon.

The DAC nations have accepted three aid targets.
One is that the net flow of private and official
resources combined should exceed 1 per cent of each
country's gross national product. In 1987, 2 out of
18 countries achieved this percentage. The second
target is that net ODA should exceed 0·7 per cent of
GNP; 5 countries managed this in 1987. The third
target, more generally achieved, concerns the
"grant element"—the extent to which ODA contains an element of grant as opposed to commercial
loans. In 1987 it averaged 87 per cent of total ODA.

After the first oil crisis of 1973 many of the
developing countries were in greater need of
assistance but slower economic growth in the
developed countries made the provision of aid more
difficult. The flow of resources from the DAC
countries to the developing countries continued to
grow but, expressed as a proportion of GNP, it fell
from 0·79 to 0·55 per cent between 1973 and 1987.
Net ODA was the same proportion of GNP (0·35
per cent) in the two years. In real terms the flow of
ODA rose by 3·5 per cent per annum over the
period.

Forms of Aid.

Aid to the developing countries takes many
forms, it serves many purposes and it is required for
many reasons. Less developed countries need aid to
provide finance for development projects; to
provide foreign exchange with which imports for
development purposes can be bought; and to
provide the trained manpower and technical
knowledge they lack. The motives of the donor are
not always humanitarian. "Aid" can take a
military form; it can be used to prop up an
incompetent or unjust government, or to buy
support in the cold war. Nor is aid always beneficial
to the recipient country. It may be wasted on ill-
conceived or prestige projects, or cause the
government simply to relax its own efforts.
Sometimes schools or hospitals are built with aid
but there is a lack of local revenues with which to
staff and run these institutions. Concern over
donor's motives and instances of waste have led
some people to react against aid-giving. However,
the correct remedy is not to cut off aid but rather to
prevent its misuse.

Donor governments may finance specific projects, or they may contribute to the general pool
of funds available for expenditure by the governments of underdeveloped countries. But financial
aid is not always enough. Many developing
countries need technical assistance in planning
their development, to ensure that development
possibilities are exploited and that scarce resources are used to best advantage. Hence the
many schemes for providing experts by individual
countries and by the technical agencies of the
United Nations, such as the Food and Agriculture
Organisation (FAO), the World Health Organisation (WHO), the International Labour Organisation
(ILO), the United Nations Educational, Scientific
and Cultural Organisation (UNESCO), and so on.
Hence also the schemes for educating and training
people from the developing countries.

Foreign Private Investment.

One possible form of aid is private investment
by firms from developed countries. These investments—setting up branch factories, for example—
are concentrated in those projects which appear
profitable to the investor. However, it is a
characteristic of underdevelopment that there are
few openings for profitable investment. Most of
the U.K. private investment overseas, for example, has been concentrated in relatively highly
developed countries of the world. Private investment cannot be relied upon to provide an adequate
flow of resources.

Indeed, it has been questioned whether private

FINANCIAL FLOWS FROM BRITAIN TO DEVELOPING COUNTRIES, 1970–1988

	Net total flows, official and private.		Net official development assistance.		
	£m.	% of GNP.	£m.	% of GNP.	Constant prices 1970 = 100
1970	520	1·02	186	0·36	100
1975	2,920	2·82	404	0·39	106
1980	5,253	2·29	797	0·35	119
1985	1,871	0·53	1,180	0·33	117
1988	1,657	0·36	1,485	0·32	128

investment constitutes aid to less developed countries at all. Its opponents argue that the benefits are often small or even negative: foreign-owned firms repatriate high profits and avoid tax by means of royalty payments to the parent company or unrealistic pricing of their transactions with the parent company; and these firms deter local enterprise. Supporters of foreign investment point to the high political risks which necessitate high profits in order to attract investors to developing countries, and question whether resources are available for any alternative path to development. A form of compromise which has become common in the Third World is a partnership arrangement between multinational companies and the host country's government.

British Aid.

The table above shows how British assistance to developing countries has grown over the years, and how it has measured up to the international aid targets now accepted by the British Government. The first target is that the total net financial flow to developing countries should exceed 1 per cent of GNP. The large but fluctuating flows of private capital meant that this target was achieved in some of the years. The second target is for a net official development assistance (ODA) in excess of 0·7 per cent of GNP. We see that British ODA as a percentage of GNP was only half of the officially accepted target in each of the selected years. The table also shows that ODA has grown in value; in 1987 it equalled £26 per head of British population. However, if we allow for inflation by expressing official aid in real terms, we see that the volume of aid has risen little.

Government aid may be divided into multilateral aid and bilateral aid. Multilateral aid is given through the medium of the international development institutions: bilateral aid is given directly to the developing countries. Multilateral aid constituted 40 per cent of total British aid in 1988. Some 92 per cent of British ODA in 1988 took the form of grants, and the rest was loans. Most of the loans were fairly "soft" with long maturities and low rates of interest. Roughly half of bilateral financial aid is formally tied to the purchase of British goods and services. Other aid is not tied formally, and may be used directly to finance local expenditure; but when it is used to finance imports directly, it has to be spent on British goods if these are available on competitive terms. Most multilateral aid is untied. The tying of aid tends to raise the costs to developing countries; but it also enables countries with precarious foreign balances to be more generous.

Aid takes the form not only of financial but also of technical assistance. Government expenditure on technical assistance amounted to 40 per cent of bilateral aid in 1988. At the end of 1988 British technical assistance personnel overseas totalled 1,760, and there were also many volunteers recruited by voluntary agencies; including 1,400 teachers, 500 agricultural experts and 350 doctors and medical workers. Kenya, Botswana, Malawi, Zambia, Tanzania, Zimbabwe and the Solomon Islands all had more than 100 British experts and volunteers working in them.

In 1988 British aid financed some 7,000 people (measured in man-years) from developing countries to receive education or training in Britain. Sixty per cent of these were from the Commonwealth and half were from Africa south of the Sahara. Kenya

(with 455 people), Malawi (399), Nigeria (269), Zambia (302), Bangladesh (323), India (484) and China (721) were the largest beneficiaries.

All British official aid is channelled and co-ordinated by the Overseas Development Administration. In addition there are various private associations concerned with promoting development, such as Oxfam, War on Want and World Development Movement.

Who Receives Most Aid?

In 1987–88 the countries which received the largest shares of British ODA were India (6·0 per cent), Bangladesh (2·8 per cent), Kenya (2·7 per cent) and Tanzania (2·0 per cent). This contrasts with the pattern for the DAC countries' ODA as a whole: Indonesia (3·7 per cent), Egypt (3·4 per cent), India (2·9 per cent), Israel (2·8 per cent) and China (2·2 per cent). On the whole, it helps to be a small country. British aid per head of recipient population in 1988 was greatest to the small micro-states such as Belize, Vanuatu, Anguilla, Grenada and the Solomon Islands. Because of India's size, British aid per capita to that country was actually below average. The importance of Egypt and Israel as aid-recipients reflects United States foreign policy towards the Middle East.

The World Bank.

The International Bank for Reconstruction and Development (IBRD) known as the *International Bank* or as the *World Bank*, is an agency of the United Nations established in 1945. It has the primary function of making funds available to assist developing countries. Member nations agreed to subscribe quotas—fixed in much the same way as the quotas for the IMF—to the Bank. In fact, only a small proportion of the quotas has been called up by the Bank; the major part of the Bank's resources are borrowed—on the security of the remainder of the quotas—in financial centres.

Usually, loans are made to finance specific projects of investment in underdeveloped countries; and the Bank will normally make a loan only if it is satisfied that the investment will yield a revenue sufficient to enable the payment of interest on the loan, and the repayment of the sum lent. In 1988 the Bank made loans to the value of $14·5 billion. Thus a sizeable amount of lending is channelled through the Bank, but it is clear that some projects of great value to underdeveloped countries cannot be financed in this way, because they would not yield returns quickly or large enough to meet the Bank's requirements for interest and repayment. Accordingly, the *International Development Association* has the power to make loans at low rates of interest and with more generous repayment conditions. The IDA contributes towards the development of education and agriculture ($4·4 billion in 1986).

UNCTAD.

In 1964 the first United Nations Conference on Trade and Development (UNCTAD) was held. For the first time the poorer nations of the world—77 were represented—came together to act as a pressure group on trading matters. The Conference made the following recommendations. Developing countries should be given free access to world markets for their manufactures and semi-manufactures by the elimination of quotas and tariffs. International *commodity agreements* should be made for each major primary commodity in world trade, to stabilise commodity prices. Compensation schemes—whereby countries are compensated for the declining prices of their primary products—were recommended for consideration. The Conference also resolved that the developed countries should aim to provide at least 1 per cent of their national income as aid for the underdeveloped countries.

Subsequent sessions of the Conference have been held at four-year intervals. Little positive action has resulted from what have at times been political tournaments. However, UNCTAD has helped to modify international thinking. The developed countries have accepted more firmly the principle of discrimination in favour of developing countries, and the notion that aid should reach a target level.

Stabilising Export Earnings.

Two international facilities exist to help stabilise the export earnings of developing countries. One is the IMF's *Compensatory Financing Facility* (CFF). A country in balance of payments difficulty is eligible to draw up to 100 per cent of its quota with the IMF if exports fall below a defined trend for reasons generally beyond its control. In 1988 the scheme was extended to become the *Compensatory and Contingence Financing Facility* (CCFF), by providing also for contingency funding to help developing countries deal with external shocks to their economies.

The other facility is the EEC's *Stabex scheme*. It covers the 58 African, Caribbean and Pacific countries that are members of the Lomé agreement. Under the second Lomé agreement 44 primary products are eligible for support. These countries receive grants (if one of the 35 *least* developed countries) or interest-free loans if export earnings from a qualifying product fall below average earnings over the four preceding years by a certain percentage.

Thirdly, there is the UNCTAD *Common Fund*—agreed to in principle but still to be set up. The idea is that a central fund will finance buffer stocks under separate international commodity agreements, and will thereby stabilise commodity prices. Many countries ratified the agreement for establishing a Common Fund although their pledged contribution fell short of the capital required for its launching.

The Impact of the Oil Price Rise.

In October 1973, during the Arab–Israeli war, the members of the Organisation of Petroleum Exporting Countries (OPEC) cut supplies of oil and increased their prices drastically. The price of oil subsequently rose fourfold above its initial level. By acting as a cartel to control supplies the OPEC countries were able to maintain the higher prices without surpluses accumulating and a competitive price war breaking out. The impact on all countries was great; indeed, on a number of less developed countries it was disastrous.

The bout of inflation in the industrial countries resulting from the oil crisis meant that the developing countries also had to pay more for their other imports. They were further hit by the world recession generated by the oil crisis, because the resultant fall in world demand produced a slump in the prices of primary commodities. The developing countries had to cut back on the volume of their imports, to the detriment of development programmes. However, they were partly cushioned by the emergency loans provided through the *oil facility* scheme introduced by the IMF.

Of course, a number of less developed countries benefited from the oil price increases. These included the five oil countries (Saudi Arabia, Kuwait, Qatar, Abu Dhabi and Libya) whose levels of income per capita now exceeded those in the industrial countries. Their use of the new revenues was limited by the ability of their economies to absorb them: for that reason they continued to need technical assistance. Other, less wealthy, oil-producing countries—including Iran, Iraq, Venezuela, Indonesia and Nigeria—have much larger populations and more absorptive capacity. They had an opportunity to transform their economies with the oil revenues.

Growing Indebtedness.

The external indebtedness of the developing countries grew alarmingly in the years after 1973. In nominal terms debt grew at 20 per cent per annum. Debt servicing obligations increased from $10 billion in 1971 to $162 billion in 1989. For non-oil developing countries as a whole, external debt amounted to 31 per cent of GDP in 1989, and debt service payments to 17 per cent of their exports. World inflation tempers the story in two ways. First, the increase in indebtedness was much less rapid in real than in nominal terms. Secondly, with interest rates being low in the mid-1970s, inflation meant that real rates of interest on much developing country debt were actually negative. Nevertheless, many developing countries failed to adjust fully to the worsened economic and trading conditions after 1973.

The Tokyo Round.

A round of multilateral trade negotiations was completed in Tokyo in 1979. It provided a legal basis within GATT for preferential treatment for developing countries, and offered them some trade liberalisation. The industrialised countries agreed to reduce tariffs generally, and by an average of 25 per cent for industrial and 7 per cent for agricultural products conventionally exported by developing countries. The extent to which developing countries actually gain, however, depends on whether developed countries make use of the *safeguard clause* which permits emergency protection on the grounds of serious injury to domestic industry: safeguard measures have frequently been invoked against imports from developing countries. Nevertheless, the prospects for success of export-based industrialisation in developing countries (*see* **G**39) were improved.

Food Policies.

In the last couple of decades food production in the developing countries has done little more than keep pace with the growth of population: between 1970 and 1980 food production per capita fell by 0·2 per cent per annum in the 41 least developed countries and rose by only 0·5 per cent per annum in all developing countries as a group. The corresponding figures for the period 1980–1987 were even more dismal: −0·7 and +0·2 per cent respectively. Many developing countries have become net food importers, and this trend is likely to continue. In 1987 food imports represented no less than 14 per cent of the total merchandise imports of the 37 low-income developing countries and 10 per cent in the case of the 58 middle-income developing countries.

The years 1972–74 were ones of poor harvests in various parts of the developed and developing world. Famines occurred in the Sahel area of Africa, in Bangladesh and in parts of India. In response to vast imports of grain by the Soviet Union and many other countries, world grain stocks were reduced to very low levels and the price of grain rocketed. In response to the World Food Conference of 1974, most of the DAC donor countries decided to increase very substantially their aid to agriculture in the recipient countries. An International Emergency Food Reserve was established in 1976 and has been built up, and an IMF Food Facility was set up in 1981 to provide financial assistance to offset fluctuations in countries' food import bills. Total bilateral and multilateral ODA earmarked for agriculture grew rapidly after 1973.

The Causes of Famine.

Famine is by no means always simply the result of a fall in food production which affects all people in the area uniformly. In the 1974 Bangladesh famine and the recent Ethiopian famines, those who suffered most were respectively the landless, who normally exchange labour for food, and pastoralists, who normally exchange cattle for food grains. The landless, losing their source of earnings because farmers no longer hired labourers, and pastoralists, seeing the prices of their emaciated beasts fall as more and more were marketed, could no longer buy food: these were the people who starved.

Inequality Within Countries.

The growth performance of the less developed countries taken together—growth of GNP per capita of 2·3 per cent per annum in the 1950s, 3·0 per cent per annum in the 1960s and 3·1 per cent per annum in the 1970s—is good by the standards of the past. However, in some less developed countries these growth rates have been achieved without any apparent improvement in the lot of the masses.

The majority of the people are engaged in agriculture in the rural areas, whereas much of the development has taken place in industry and services in the urban areas. A minority of people have benefited—industrialists, bureaucrats, educated and skilled workers, organised labour in the modern sector of the economy—but the poor living in the urban slums, often in open or disguised unemployment, and the enormous numbers in the rural areas have been little affected by development. In many countries the fruits of development have not been widely spread. It is a growing criticism that development policies have been biased towards industry and towards the cities, and that rural people in agriculture have been neglected. This outcome may be a reflection of the uneven distribution of political power within a developing country.

Increasingly, the growth of GNP per capita as a goal of development has been questioned, both within the less developed countries and among national and international aid agencies. Both recipient and donor governments have recently shown a greater concern for poverty, employment creation and social equity. Many donors have modified their aid policies to try to reach the poor. Of course, this redirection coincides to a considerable extent with the increased concern for agricultural development.

Basic Needs.

A direction in which international thinking has moved is towards the acceptance of a *Basic Needs* strategy of development. Essentially the aim is to alleviate absolute poverty, *i.e.*, to meet minimum standards of food, shelter, clothing and safe drinking water, and to satisfy certain other basic human needs. It is proposed that these standards be reached not so much by means of welfare transfers as by enabling the poor to help themselves through productive employment. The minimum standards are inevitably subjective, there are economic and political obstacles to the fulfilment of basic needs, and the approach does not translate easily into specific policies. Nevertheless, the basic needs strategy may have an impact on the priorities both of aid agencies and of recipient governments.

Inequality Among Countries.

Not all less developed countries have fared equally well in recent years. In particular there appears to be a tendency for disparities among less developed countries to widen. The countries which have performed well tend to be semi-industrialised and able to respond to opportunities for exporting manufactures to the developed countries, or to be well endowed with mineral or oil resources. Growth success stories include Brazil, Colombia, South Korea, Taiwan, Mexico and Singapore. Some of these are on the way to becoming self-reliant economically: they are known as the *newly industrialising countries* (NICs). The poorest countries—31 of which were designated the *least developed countries* (LDCs)—are experiencing the greatest difficulty in escaping from the vicious circle of poverty. A growing recognition of their problem has led the DAC countries to reallocate aid in favour of the least developed countries, and to offer aid on more concessionary terms to these countries.

We see in the table that it is the poorest areas of Sub-Saharan Africa and South Asia that have fared least well. East Asia has fared best, assisted by an exceptionally high growth rate in China. Setting China and India on one side, we see that, when countries are grouped by income level, the growth of income per head rises with the level of income per head.

Revision of British Aid Policies.

The revision of DAC aid policies mentioned above also occurred in the British aid programme. In the mid-1970s the British Government began to direct more of its aid towards the poorest developing countries, and all future ODA to them was to take the form of outright grants. Aid for family planning was stepped up. Increasing weight was placed on rural development and the expansion of agricultural production, in particular on helping the poor in rural areas, *e.g.*, small farmers and landless labourers. The proportion of net bilateral ODA disbursed which went to the poorest 50 countries was 70 per cent in 1988. The British Government has cancelled much of the debt owed to it by the poorest countries in recent years. British food aid and disaster relief increased sharply in the 1980s.

The Brandt Report.

In 1980 the independent commission on international development issues, under the chairmanship of Willy Brandt, published its report on relations between the North and the South. It regarded such relations as *the* great social challenge of our time, and saw its task as being to bring understanding and to change attitudes in the rich countries of the North, and to contribute to the development of "worldwide moral values". However, Brandt also appealed to the self-interests of the North: it was in the North's long run interests that poverty and hunger should not linger and spread in the countries of the South.

The commission made various general recommendations, *e.g.*, that priority be given to the poorest countries and to the elimination of hunger. Its most challenging proposal was that all countries except the poorest should contribute development finance on an automatic sliding scale related to national income—a sort of international progressive income tax. Recognising that the obstacles to action are frequently political, it recommended greater power-sharing between North and South in international economic bodies.

Public Attitudes to Aid.

A recurring theme is the need to build public support for development efforts: aid is widely seen as having no political constituency. An opinion poll carried out in Britain in 1983 at the Government's request showed that 60 per cent of respondents were in favour of British aid to the poorest countries; a similar figure had been found in 1969. The proportion of respondents who wanted aid to be increased rose from 16 to 37 per cent once they were told what the aid level was in relation to other expenditures.

Aid to Africa.

Of all the less developed regions, Africa has done least well in recent years. For instance, food production per capita in the developing countries of Africa was 10 per cent lower in 1980 than it had been 10 years before. In 1981 the World Bank undertook a study of the problem at the request of African governments. The ensuing report argued for a near doubling of external aid for these countries, even though they were already dependent on aid: aid to the sub-Saharan region was almost 40 per cent of its total imports and over half its total investment in 1981. The report also argued for policy changes by their governments, if a further fall in living standards was to be averted. The policy changes recommended generally involved less state intervention in the economy and more rein to individual incentives and to the market. The report also recognised the constraint on development imposed by a lack of trained manpower and of good management.

One problem will not be easy to deal with: the lack of political stability widely found in Africa, and in other parts of the Third World, is inimical to economic development. Violent changes of government are common, and there were in 1980 some 3 million African refugees who had fled from their own to neighbouring countries. The main "culprits" were Ethiopia, Angola, Rwanda, Burundi, Equatorial Guinea, Uganda and Chad.

LEVEL OF INCOME PER HEAD 1987 AND GROWTH OF INCOME PER HEAD 1965–1987,
GROUPED BY REGION AND BY INCOME LEVEL

Group		Income per head ($)	Growth of income per head (% p.a.)
By region	Sub-Saharan Africa	330	0·6
	South Asia	290	1·8
	East Asia	470	5·1
	Latin America	1,790	2·1
By income level	India	300	1·8
	China	290	5·2
	Other low income countries	280	1·5
	Lower middle income countries	1,200	2·2
	Upper middle income countries	2,700	2·9
All developing countries		700	2·3

Crisis and Response in Africa.

In 1983 and 1984 drought drove millions of Africans deeper into poverty. With the recurring drought and dismal statistics came vivid photographs of human suffering, conveying to the world an image of continent-wide disaster. The drought particularly affected countries in south eastern Africa, such as Mozambique, and the Sahel belt below the Sahara, *e.g.*, Ethiopia, Sudan, and Chad. In 1983 cereal imports amounted to over a third of cereal production in two dozen affected African countries

A number of African governments had by 1984 accepted the need for measures to stimulate agricultural production, such as the raising of prices paid to producers for their crops and a transfer of investment priorities towards agriculture. Aid donors also responded to the crisis, giving short term assistance in the form of food aid and longer term assistance in the form of increased development aid. Sub-Saharan Africa received 30 per cent of ODA in 1984 compared with 25 per cent in 1975. In 1985, widespread rains made possible a one-third increase in Sub-Saharan cereal production. With the immediate problem eased, most African countries were able to shift their attention from hunger to rehabilitation and development.

The Prospects for African Development.

Africa has become the area that presents the greatest economic problem. Income per head in Sub-Saharan Africa fell sharply in the 1980s, by 2·8 per cent per annum between 1980 and 1987. There are various reasons not associated with natural phenomena. First, population growth has continued to rise and now stands at 3·1 per cent per annum. Second, the terms of trade of the region deteriorated by almost 25 per cent between 1979 and 1987. Third, Africa's long term debt is now as large as its GNP, making the region the most heavily indebted of all. Debt service obligations were 47 per cent of export revenues in 1988, but only about half were actually paid, so that arrears accumulated. Both the level and the efficiency of investment have fallen.

With the World Bank forecasting a further fall in living standards in the early 1990s, Africa is set to become the focus of aid donors' attention. Some of Africa's problems are within the control of their governments, and aid agencies have increasingly made their aid to African countries conditional on the reform of economic policies. This is likely to involve a strategy requiring less government intervention, less top-down planning and more grass-roots development, and emphasising the development of institutional and human capacities to provide the enabling environment for economic growth.

Economic Reform in China.

China is an enormous and important country about which little was known during the period of isolation until the late 1970s. In 1987 it had a population of 1,070 million people and an income per head of $290 per annum (to be compared with India's 800 million people and income per head of $300).

Prior to 1978 China's economy was characterised by state ownership, centralised planning and collective farming. In that year a process of economic reform was commenced. The state now tried to control economic activity by regulating the market rather than by directly controlling individual production units. In agriculture, the system of peoples' communes was dismantled, land was leased by the state to farming households, and markets for produce were recreated. Managers of state industrial enterprises were given more responsibility and incentives and, because China lacks modern technology, joint ventures with foreign multinational companies were set up. Small private businesses were encouraged.

The economy responded well to these reforms. It achieved a remarkably high rate of economic growth—10 per cent per annum—between 1980 and 1987, and food production grew at 7 per cent per annum. The big question facing China in 1990 was: can growth at such a pace be sustained or will it be halted by the political convulsions sparked off by mass student protests in Beijing?

The Second Oil Price Rise.

In the wake of the second sharp increase in the price of oil in 1979, the world economy went into a prolonged recession. With growth in the volume of world trade falling to zero in 1981 and becoming negative in 1982, the growth in GDP of the oil-importing developing countries fell to below 2 per cent per annum, and their exports fell in value between 1980 and 1983. Over this period their current account deficits represented a quarter of their total value of exports. Many developing countries were squeezed between stagnating foreign exchange earnings and heavy foreign exchange commitments. This precipitated two problems: a *debt crisis* for certain heavily indebted developing countries and the need for *stabilization policies* among a broader group of developing countries.

The Debt Crisis.

The debt position deteriorated at the turn of the decade. Most developing countries had to go further into debt in response to the renewed increase in the oil price. With nominal interest rates now very high and real rates positive, the burden of debt servicing become more onerous. The table shows how the external debts of developing countries increased between 1980 and 1983. In 1983 private bank claims on developing countries amounted to $417 billion. It was the more successful developing countries which had attracted private funds: Brazil and Mexico together accounted for some 40 per cent of this total.

A measure of the strain on developing countries is given by the ratio of debt to annual foreign exchange earnings from exports. The table shows that this rose from 82 to 133 per cent, and that debt servicing (annual interest and amortization payments) rose from 13 to 18 per cent of exports, between 1980 and 1983. Countries with particularly high percentages included some newly industrialising countries with large oil imports whose export markets had contracted (*e.g.* Brazil and Korea), some low-income countries whose export prices fell in the world recession (*e.g.* Bolivia and Zaire) and some oil exporting countries whose export earnings

EXTERNAL DEBT OF
DEVELOPING COUNTRIES, 1980–1989

	1980	1983	1986	1989
Total debt				
($ billion)	633	894	1,103	1,194
(per cent of exports)	82	133	169	126
Debt service				
($ billion)	103	119	145	175
(per cent of exports)	13	18	22	17

collapsed (*e.g.* Mexico and Nigeria). The danger of default posed by the debt crisis was widely feared.

Increasing Indebtedness.

Of greatest benefit to the indebted nations would be a strong and sustained recovery of the world economy. In the event, world economic recovery—averaging 3·5 per cent per annum between 1983 and 1989—proved too tardy to solve the debt crisis. Part of the problem was the persistently high level of world interest rates and a deterioration in primary commodity markets. Expressed in real terms (*i.e.* deflated by export unit values for manufactures of industrial countries) non-oil primary commodity prices fell by a third between mid-1984 and mid-1986.

Indebtedness increased every year between 1983 and 1989. The table shows that in 1989 the total external debt of developing countries was no less than $1,194 billion, half of it owed to private banks, and that the ratio of debt servicing to exports was 17 per cent. At the end of 1986 Mexico had external debt of $97 billion, Brazil $106 bn., Argentina $50 bn., Venezuela $33 bn., South Korea $31 bn., Indonesia $45 bn., Philippines $24 bn. and Nigeria $26 bn. In 1987 debt service represented no less than 27 per cent of exports in Brazil, 30 per cent in Mexico and 45 per cent in Argentina.

Solutions to the Debt Crisis.

Countries became increasingly dependent on new loans to service the old, and private banks were reluctant to provide these. In all the major cases a rescheduling of debt repayments was arranged, usually in conjunction with IMF programmes. However, in 1987 the formal procedures for managing debt problems were overtaken by informal actions. Brazil suspended debt service payments to private creditors, and a number of other Latin American and several smaller African countries accumulated arrears of interest to private creditors. In the wake of action by Citicorp, the largest US bank, the mounting arrears caused Western banks to raise their balance sheet provisions against loans to the problem debtors, writing the cost off against profits. Relations between creditors and debtors deteriorated.

Various proposals have been made for debt relief. One ambitious proposal, with the potential to solve the debt crisis, would be the creation of an international agency to take over claims from private banks, buying the debt at a discount. The debt could then be restructured to pass on the benefit of the discount to the debtors. The credit risk would thus pass from the private banks to the agency and its official shareholders.

Meanwhile, the problem continues although in relation to GDP and exports, the peak year was 1986. For creditors it represents a threat to the international financial system. For debtors, it represents economic hardship, a collapse of investment expenditures and increasing social and political problems. Between 1980 and 1988 real per capita income in the two groups most distressed by debt—the heavily indebted middle-income countries and the low-income sub-Saharan countries—fell by 10 per cent and by 5 per cent respectively.

Accelerating Inflation.

The serious macroeconomic strains which most developing countries experienced in the 1980s gave rise to accelerating inflation in many cases. Whereas the annual rate of inflation over the period 1980–1987 in OECD countries averaged 5 per cent, in

developing countries it averaged 44 per cent. This average was of course much influenced by the hyperinflations in a few countries (Bolivia 600 per cent per annum, Brazil 170 per cent, Argentina 300 per cent, Israel 160 per cent and Nicaragua 90 per cent) but high inflation was a pervasive phenomenon. It was a response—sometimes acting as a safety valve—to such problems as foreign exchange shortage, loss of government revenue, food shortage, debt servicing, and tardy growth of real incomes. Once established, inflation could feed on itself by changing expectations and behaviour, and it became very difficult to eliminate.

The IMF and Stabilization Policies.

Many developing countries ran into serious balance of payments problems in the 1980s. The current account deficit of the developing countries taken as a whole, at $41 billion in 1986, was equivalent to 6 per cent of exports. Many sought temporary financial assistance from the International Monetary Fund (*see* **G9**).

As a condition of its larger loans the IMF generally requires a country to accept a series of *stabilization* measures. The typical stabilization package contains the following policies: a devaluation to assist the balance of payments, monetary and credit restrictions and reduced government budget deficits to reduce demand and curb inflation, and, more generally, the elimination of restrictions such as import controls and interest rate regulations in order to harness market forces.

The wisdom of such a package in a developing country is much disputed among economists. It is most obviously the correct remedy when the problem is one of general excess demand in the economy. However, when the problem arises from an extraneous shock, such as a fall in the world price of a major export or a rise in the price of imported oil, the IMF's remedies may prove to be inappropriate. Credit restrictions and cuts in government spending may depress the economy, reducing output and employment. This may temporarily alleviate the immediate problems of inflation and balance of payments deficit, but the effect on long run economic growth may be negative.

It is for these reasons that critics accuse the IMF of doctrinairely and narrowly focussing on monetary variables and ignoring structural problems and developmental objectives. The IMF, on the other hand, often sees itself as a handy scapegoat for unpopular measures made inescapable by domestic economic mismanagement.

Environmental Issues.

To be economically sustainable development must also be environmentally sustainable. Much of the population increase in the 1990s will occur in environmentally fragile regions of the world. Desertification, deforestation, soil depletion through over-use of fragile land, and pollution are issues of growing concern.

Environmental degradation can contribute to famine (as in Ethiopia) and to devastating flooding (as in Bangladesh). Population pressures, poverty, inadequate systems of land tenure and the growing need for fuelwood lead to the cutting or burning of forests and the clearing of new land. This can be a problem of global as well as national dimensions on account of its effects on the global climate. Problems of pollution have become critical in many of the large urban agglomerations of the Third World.

Environmental dangers are greater in poor countries which can little afford to invest in environmental protection and resource management. In 1989 the OECD nations agreed to give greater emphasis to environmental improvements in their aid policies.

Some Suggestions for Further Reading.

For an introduction to the subject the reader is referred to Jagdish Bhagwati, *The Economics of Underdeveloped Countries* (World University Library). Ian Little, in *Economic Development* (Basic Books) assesses the development record and the way in which ideas and policies have evolved. On Asia the reader may wish to dip into three volumes of Gunnar Myrdal entitled *Asian Drama: An*

Enquiry into the Poverty of Nations (Allen Lane, The Penguin Press). On South America there is Celso Furtado, *Economic Development of Latin America* (Cambridge University Press). On Africa there is the World Bank's 1989 report, *Sub-Saharan Africa. From Crisis to Subtainable Growth.* Michael Lipton's book *Why Poor People Stay Poor* (Temple Smith) throws light on the "urban bias" in development policies.

The Overseas Development Administration has compiled a handbook of *British Aid Statistics* (H.M.S.O.), The World Bank produces an annual *World Development Report.* The Organisation for Economic Co-operation and Development, comprising all the major non-communist developed countries, publishes an Annual Review of aid and development entitled *Development Cooperation* (O.E.C.D.). The report of the Brandt Commission is available in paperback as *North–South: a Programme for Survival* (Pan Books).

An interesting quarterly publication of the I.M.F. and the World Bank, *Finance and Development*, is available free of charge; applications should be sent to *Finance and Development*, I.M.F. Building, Washington, D.C. 20431, U.S.A.

IV. RECENT DEVELOPMENTS IN THE BRITISH ECONOMY

1. INTERNATIONAL DEVELOPMENTS

The Balance of Payments.

The balance of payments problem has dominated events in the British economy until recent years and may do so again. It is therefore important to analyse the balance of payments in some detail; to understand why the balance of payments has been a problem; and to see its effects on economic policy. The balance of payments and its components are explained in detail on **G6–8**. The balance of payments in each year from 1980 to 1988 is shown in the table on **G49**.

The 1970s.

The competitive position of the United Kingdom was weakened after 1971 by an inflation more rapid than in other countries and also by the dollar devaluation of 1971. There were sharp increases in demand for such consumer goods as cars and colour television sets—no doubt set off by the abolition of hire-purchase restrictions in 1971—and the inability of domestic producers to expand their production correspondingly both constrained exports and accelerated imports. The trade balance deteriorated from a surplus in 1971 to a record deficit in 1972. There was a large outflow of short-term funds in mid-1972, which culminated in a sterling crisis and a floating of the pound in June. That was the first time that sterling had been allowed to float since a period in the 1930s, and it represented a contravention of the increasingly criticised Bretton Woods system (*see* **G9**). The pound then floated downwards after June, from about $2·60 = £1 to an average value of roughly $2·40 during 1973, and $2·20 in 1975. The downward slide continued, and in March 1976 the pound fell below $2·00 for the first time.

The falling value of the pound was of no immediate assistance to the balance of payments: experience suggests that the improvement occurs only after a lag of a year or two. In the meantime the depreciation pushed up the domestic price of imports of raw materials and foodstuffs, so raising both the costs of production and the cost of living. The downward floating of the pound made a counter-inflation policy both more difficult and more important.

Inflation in Commodity Markets.

The current account of the balance of payments deteriorated sharply in 1973, to reach a deficit of £1·0 billion. The import bill soared, increasing by no less than 41 per cent. Import volume increased by 14 per cent, reflecting the rapid upsurge of the economy. More important was the higher price of imports: this period witnessed a remarkable inflation in the prices of various primary products in world markets. To give some examples, between the first quarter of 1972 and the last quarter of 1973 average price increases in major world markets were as follows: cocoa 173 per cent, copper 115 per cent, cotton 127 per cent, rubber 123 per cent, wool 138 per cent and zinc 308 per cent.

This unprecedented jump in primary commodity prices stemmed from the sharp and well-synchronised expansion of the major industrial economies during 1972 and 1973, and it was assisted by some speculative buying as a hedge against inflation. Commodity prices generally reached their peak in the second quarter of 1974.

The Oil Crisis.

An event of great importance to Britain and to other industrial countries was the decision of the Arab oil-producing states, taken in October 1973, to restrict oil supplies and to raise oil prices. The restriction of supplies was initiated as a short-run political weapon in the Arab–Israeli conflict; but it revealed a potential for obtaining higher prices which had not previously been exploited by the *Organisation of Petroleum Exporting Countries* (OPEC). In the past the world demand for oil had grown very rapidly—by about 8 per cent per annum between 1960 and 1973—but it had been successfully met by expansion of production. A slower growth of oil supply in relation to demand produced scarcity and a rocketing of price. Alternative sources of energy could not be developed—and thus the demand for oil could not be curtailed or even its growth retarded—for some years. However, maintenance of high prices depended on the ability of the OPEC group to restrict oil supplies to the market despite the incentive of each individual country to take advantage of the high prices by expanding its sales. Comparing 1974 with 1973, the price of oil imported into Britain almost trebled.

Oil and the Balance-of-Payments.

Largely because of higher import prices Britain's current balance deteriorated sharply in 1974, when Britain recorded her worst ever current account deficit; no less than £3·3 billion; in fact the additional oil bill amounted to £2·8 billion.

In the wake of the oil crisis the world economy duly moved into severe recession. To this the British economy was no exception: real GDP stagnated in 1974 and fell in 1975. The world recession made it difficult for OPEC to raise oil prices still further; and the already depressed state of world demand caused the prices of primary commodities actually to fall. Britain therefore benefited from improvement in the terms of trade.

In 1976 the world economy began to emerge from its severe recession. This helped the British current account, but the deficit in total currency flow rose to no less than £3·8 billion. To understand the reason we must examine the way in which the oil deficits have been financed, and movements of the exchange rate.

Financing the Deficit.

In 1974 the oil exporting countries financed the largest part of the current account deficit by adding to their sterling balances. The reduced deficit of 1975 actually posed a greater problem of financing, because the oil producers were less willing to accumulate balances in sterling. Britain's foreign exchange reserves fell, and to protect them interest rates were kept high in London. However, during 1975 the rate of inflation in Britain was some 15 per cent above the average for the OECD countries: it became clear that sterling would have to be depreciated further. Speculative outflows of funds forced the authorities to intervene strongly in the foreign exchange market by selling foreign exchange.

THE UK BALANCE OF PAYMENTS 1981–89 (£ BILLION)

	1981	1982	1983	1984	1985	1986	1987	1988	1989
Exports (f.o.b.) . . .	50·7	55·3	60·7	70·3	78·0	72·7	79·4	80·6	92·5
Imports (f.o.b.) . . .	47·3	53·1	61·8	74·8	80·3	81·4	89·6	101·4	115·6
Visible balance . . .	3·4	2·2	−1·1	−4·6	−2·3	−8·7	−10·2	−20·8	−23·1
Invisible balance . . .	3·6	2·5	4·9	6·6	5·7	8·5	7·4	6·2	2·3
Current balance . . .	6·9	4·7	3·8	2·0	3·3	−0·2	−2·5	−14·6	−20·9
UK investment overseas .	−10·5	−11·7	−12·6	−15·9	−28·1	−36·8	−8·9	−24·9	−56·9
Overseas investment in UK	3·3	3·3	5·3	1·2	11·3	12·6	16·8	12·0	27·9
Other capital transactions .	−2·6	4·7	2·4	6·1	9·5	12·9	3·1	18·0	27·9
Official reserves * . .	2·4	1·4	0·6	0·9	−1·8	−2·9	−12·0	−2·8	5·4
Net capital transactions .	−7·4	−2·3	−4·3	−7·7	−9·1	−14·2	−1·0	2·3	4·3
Allocation of SDRs . .	0·2								
Balancing item . . .	0·3	−2·4	0·4	5·6	5·7	14·4	3·5	12·3	16·5

* A positive sign denotes drawings on and a negative sign additions to the reserves.

THE UK BALANCE OF TRADE IN OIL, 1974–1989 (£ BILLION)

1974	1975	1976	1977	1978	1979
−3·8	−3·4	−4·4	−3·3	−2·6	−1·6

1980	1981	1982	1983	1984	1985
−0·7	+1·9	+3·3	+5·4	+5·5	+5·5

1986	1987	1988	1989
+1·8	+4·0	+2·1	+0·8

Despite the agreement of a $5·3 billion standby credit facility made available to the Bank of England by the "Group of Ten" countries, which was announced in June 1976, the exchange rate slid to a low point of $1·57 in October, and the Bank of England's minimum lending rate (*see* **G29**) was raised to the unprecedented level of 15 per cent. The Government applied to the IMF to draw on the United Kingdom's credit tranche of $3·9 billion. The successful conclusion of these negotiations in January 1977, and the borrowing of more than £1 billion from the IMF, helped to restore confidence. However, the terms of the agreement involved some loss of control over domestic affairs: in his Letter of Intent to the IMF, the Chancellor agreed to restrictions on the rate of *domestic credit expansion* (DCE) and on the *public sector borrowing requirement* (PSBR).

There was a need to protect the British economy against the massive fluctuations in the sterling balances (*see* **G10**). The IMF agreement was followed by the successful negotiation of a "safety net" for the officially held sterling balances. The new facility, for an amount of $3 billion, was to operate with the support of various major central banks. Under the scheme, the British Government was able to draw on the credit facility in respect of net reductions in the official sterling holdings.

North Sea Oil.

The table shows how the "oil deficit" in the balance of payments, huge in 1974, gradually declined as North Sea oil production expanded, disappeared in the course of 1980, and was transformed into an "oil surplus", becoming as large as £5·5 billion in the mid-1980s, and then declining.

The future course of the British balance of payments depends considerably on the value of British oil production. The sharp build-up in production from almost nil in 1975 had arrived at about 100 million tonnes in 1980, roughly equal to U.K. net consumption of oil. Oil continues to be both exported and imported because of differences in quality: the United Kingdom exports a higher quality than it imports. British production of petroleum and natural gas amounted to 7 per cent of GDP in the peak year, 1984. The value of North Sea oil to Britain in the future depends on many imponderables, including the price of oil itself. This depends on the ability of the OPEC cartel to survive and on the growth of the world economy in relation to the supply (influenced by the development

of new fields such as the North Sea, Alaska and Mexico, and by the political stability of major producers such as Iran and Saudi Arabia).

The exploitation of North Sea oil has been a mixed blessing. Through its strengthening of the balance of payments and consequent raising of the exchange rate, it has harmed the manufacturing sector. The problems of structural adjustment, of which rising unemployment was a symptom, brought a social cost. The precise extent to which manufacturing suffered as a result of North Sea oil has been debated among economists. Some economists attribute much of the slump in manufacturing—by 10 per cent between early 1979 and early 1982—to the 25 per cent rise in the exchange rate over the same period; others put most of the blame on the Government's deflationary monetary and fiscal policies. It is generally agreed, however, that if it had not been for North Sea oil, Britain in the post-1973 era would have had to devote additional resources to the production of manufactures for export simply to pay for more expensive oil.

Recovery in the Late 1970s.

Pressure on sterling beginning in 1977 was met in part by the willingness of the monetary authorities to let the exchange rate rise. From its lowest level of £1 = $1·58 in October 1976, it rose steadily to reach a peak of $2·44 in October 1980. The heavy balance of payments deficit of the United States and speculation against the dollar was partly responsible. However, sterling rose steeply against other currencies as well. This was partly due to North Sea oil production, its direct effect on the balance of payments and its indirect effect on foreign confidence in the British economy. Also important were the high interest rates engendered by the government's restrictive monetary policy and the low level of demand for imports caused by the recession in the domestic economy.

Balance of Payments Surplus in the 1980s.

With the economy slumping in 1980, the trade balance moved into surplus for the first time in many years. In 1981 the trade balance was in even greater surplus, reflecting the growth of North Sea oil revenues and the deeper recession in the UK than abroad, and the current account exceeded £6 billion.

The appreciation of sterling helped to curb domestic inflation by keeping down the sterling price of imports (an imported good selling for $1 could now be bought for fewer pence). However, it also had a harmful effect on the manufacturing sector and on competitiveness (an exported good costing £1 would now have to be sold at a higher dollar price to cover costs). The trade surplus remained high, however, because of oil, and the current account surplus was £5 billion. The current account surplus fell to £4 billion in 1983, and the trade balance moved into deficit despite an increase in the oil surplus of over £2 billion. Net trade in manufactures deteriorated by over £4·5 billion. This reflected a lagged adjustment to the unfavourable competitiveness of British products. The worsening trade balance made domestic recovery more difficult.

Decline in the Exchange Rate.

The effective weighted exchange rate of sterling against the currencies of Britain's trading partners (with 1975 = 100) peaked at just over 100 in late 1980. The fall in 1981 was mainly due to a depreciation against the dollar, in turn attributable to the tight monetary policy and high interest rates prevailing in the United States. The effective rate was stable at 90 during much of 1982 but in November it began to fall. Despite the strength of the balance of payments, the relatively low British inflation rate and Bank of England intervention to support sterling, the pound dropped to an effective exchange rate of below 80 by March 1983.

The 1982–3 depreciation of sterling was due to two main factors. First, expectations were aroused that the authorities might attempt to improve British competitiveness in the run-up to a General Election, and the publication of the Labour Party's economic programme calling for "a substantial drop in the exchange rate" unsettled the market. Secondly, the fall in the world price of oil and the rumoured break-up of OPEC generated speculation against sterling.

Repayments of Debts.

The United Kingdom incurred large overseas debts to finance balance of payments deficits in the years 1973–77. In consequence, the total official foreign borrowing outstanding, which (excluding $5 billion of long-term post-war debts) had been negligible at the end of 1972, rose to over $18 billion at the end of 1977. By then, however, the recovery in the balance of payments and the flight from the dollar enabled the British Government to begin early repayments. At the end of 1984 the total was down to $11 billion.

The End of Exchange Controls.

In October 1979 the Conservative Government announced the immediate lifting of all remaining exchange control restrictions. Exchange controls had been in force in the United Kingdom for more than 40 years, but the tightness and effect of these controls had varied considerably over time. The announcement meant that it was now possible for residents to obtain foreign exchange for outward portfolio investment or the purchase of holiday homes abroad without the payment of a premium, and to acquire unrestricted access to foreign exchange for direct investment abroad.

The effect was to induce a capital outflow which helped to keep the exchange rate from rising further. There was a strong outflow of portfolio investment: in 1980 the outflow was £3·3 billion, and it rose in the subsequent years to a peak of £23·1 billion in 1986. However, this was probably not against the national interest: the alternative methods of financing the massive current account surpluses—a buildup of foreign exchange reserves or a further appreciation of the exchange rate—were less attractive.

Sterling See-Saw.

Sterling fell sharply in 1984, mainly as a result of the appreciation of the dollar against all currencies. From an average of £1 = $1.52 in 1983 and a value of $1.46 in March 1984, the pound collapsed to $1.22 in October and to a low of $1.05 in March 1985. However, sterling depreciated against other currencies as well. The trade-weighted exchange rate index fell from 81 in March 1984 to 76 in October and to a floor of 71 in March 1985.

The reason for the particular weakness of sterling appeared to be market fears about oil. There were doubts about the level of official oil prices, which had been raised by the appreciation of the dollar, and about the sustainability of OPEC pricing and output arrangements. Because Britain is a net oil exporter these jitters depressed sterling. There may also have been concern in the foreign exchange markets about the coal miners' strike and its possible repercussions on the balance of payments and the economy.

The flight of capital from sterling to the dollar and the collapse of sterling forced the Government to take undesired corrective action. Between December and March, the authorities intervened to make a series of three interest rate increases, totally 4·5 per cent. In March the treasury bill rate reached 14 per cent, well above the US rate of 9 per cent.

The depreciation of sterling helped to improve British trade competitiveness. Although changes in competitiveness affect trade only with a significant lag, a continued improvement in the trade balance could be expected for that reason. Indeed, exports increased in volume by over 10 per cent in 1984, assisted also by economic expansion in other industrial countries. However, imports rose even more rapidly, and the trade deficit deteriorated sharply, to over £4 billion, while the surplus on current account fell to £2 billion. The trade balance was adversely affected by the coal miners' strike, which brought about a reduction in net oil exports and an increase in net coal imports.

In 1985 the trade deficit fell to $2 billion and the current account surplus rose to £3·3 billion, mainly because the miners' strike ended in March. The effects of the improved competitiveness of 1984 were still being felt. Sterling see-sawed in 1985 but rose on average, partly because of the fall of the dollar (*see* **G55**) and partly because high interest rates attracted funds from abroad.

Is a Lower Oil Price Good for Britain?

The market price of oil collapsed early in 1986 (*see* **G54**). Was this a matter for concern, Britain being a net oil exporter? There were advantages as well as disadvantages, and Britain may on balance have been a beneficiary.

The obvious ill-effects are on the balance of payments and on North Sea oil tax revenues. The Government estimated that, if the price were $15 a barrel, oil would yield it £6 billion in 1986–7 instead of the £11·5 billion of 1985–6; and that each fall of one dollar in the price per barrel would reduce its revenue by £400 million. Moreover, if the pound came under speculative pressure it might be necessary to maintain high domestic interest rates, with adverse effects on investment and spending.

Some fall in sterling would be beneficial. The depreciation required by the worsened balance of payments on current account would improve competitiveness, expand manufacturing and reduce unemployment. The loss of tax revenue from a fall of one dollar in the price per barrel could be offset by a six per cent depreciation of the pound against the dollar. The expansion of the economy would also increase tax revenue, and should not cause inflation because the lower oil price would not tend to neutralise any inflationary pressures. Most important, the boost to economic growth in oil-importing countries and to world trade would be good for Britain.

Deteriorating Balance of Payments 1986–89.

The British trade balance deteriorated sharply in 1986, the deficit increasing to £8·7 billion; and the current account surplus became a small deficit. The trade deficit was £10·2 billion in 1987 and the current account deficit rose to £2·5 billion. The deterioration reflected the sharp fall in oil prices in 1986 as well as an increased deficit on trade in manufactures. The volume of manufactured exports was 11 per cent higher in 1987 than in 1985, but equivalent imports were 16 per cent higher. This was mainly due to the faster growth in domestic demand in the United Kingdom than overseas. The effective exchange rate see-sawed, falling by 15 per cent during 1986 (as the yen and the deutschmark appreciated) but rising by 10 per cent during 1987 (as the dollar depreciated).

The overall balance of payments was protected by relatively high interest rates in London. In 1987 the short term rate of interest (9·2 per cent) exceeded the average for the U.S., Japan, Germany and France by 3·5 percentage points. This interest rate differential and the movement of international funds out of the depreciating dollar explain why the UK official reserves increased rapidly—despite the deterioration in the current account—from $15·5 billion at the start of 1986 to $51·7 billion at the start of 1989.

Forecasts of the British current account in 1988 suggested that there would be a substantial deficit. And yet the problem which the authorities faced was one of a short-term capital inflow—out of New York and into London with its high interest rates. The inflow threatened to appreciate sterling at a time when the current account justified a depreciation.

The policy dilemma which this posed led to a re-

UK IMPORT PENETRATION AND
EXPORT SALES RATIOS IN
MANUFACTURING, 1975 AND 1987

	Imports as a percentage of home demand	
	1975	1987
Chemicals	23	38
Mechanical engineering	26	38
Electrical and electronic engineering	25	49
Office machinery and data processing equipment	71	93
Motor vehicles	26	48
Instrument engineering	47	58
Food, drink and tobacco	18	18
Textiles	22	47
Clothing and footwear	21	39
Paper, printing and publishing	20	22
Total manufacturing *	23	35

	Exports as a percentage of manufacturers' sales	
	1975	1987
Chemicals	32	32
Mechanical engineering	43	42
Electrical and electronic engineering	33	43
Office machinery and data processing equipment	69	91
Motor vehicles	43	34
Instrument engineering	48	52
Food, drink and tobacco	8	12
Textiles	22	32
Clothing and footwear	11	21
Paper, printing and publishing	9	11
Total manufacturing *	24	30

* Includes some industries not listed.

markable public conflict between the Prime Minister and the Chancellor of the Exchequer at the time of the 1988 Budget: the former favoured a free market outcome and the latter stabilisation of the pound through official intervention. The Prime Minister was right in the sense that the authorities now have limited power to control the exchange rate in the face of huge capital flows. The Chancellor was right in the sense that the market, left to itself, is unlikely to produce the outcome that the balance of trade and the economy require. Both could be accused of exacerbating the problem through the Government's reliance on monetary and therefore on high interest rate policy.

The balance of payments deteriorated very sharply in 1988, much more sharply than the official forecasts. The trade deficit rose to £20·8 billion and the current account to £14·6 billion (compared with a forecast of some £4 billion). What went wrong? The deterioration was in the visible rather than the invisible balance. The oil surplus fell to £2·1 billion, because of the fall in both the price and production of oil, but the main culprit was an increased volume of manufactured imports—up by no less than 19 per cent on 1987. This reflected the growth of demand in the British economy—GDP was up by 4·7 per cent. Despite this increase in production, demand outpaced available domestic capacity (*see* **G63**) and the excess demand was diverted to imports. The exchange rate also played a part. Sterling appreciated against a basket of currencies by 13 per cent between December 1986 and March 1988, reflecting the relatively high interest rates in London. This loss of competitiveness contributed to the rise in the trade deficit in 1988.

In 1989 the trade deficit was £21 billion and the current account deficit £15 billion. Most of the £5 billion deterioration over 1988 took place in the oil balance (due to temporary production problems) and the invisible balance (associated with high British interest rates). With the high cost of credit causing a fall in expenditure on investment and

consumer durables and in stockholding by firms, it was forecast that output in the economy would grow slowly in 1990, perhaps by 1·5 per cent per annum. This would help to improve the current account in 1990 but the deficit was nevertheless likely to exceed £10 billion.

A Policy Contradiction.

In 1988 British interest rates were raised in order to curb demand and reduce inflation. For instance, over the course of the year the Treasury bill rate rose from 8·5 to 13·0 per cent. Again, in 1989, the Chancellor expressed his willingness to raise interest rates as his main means of controlling inflation. Yet this policy would exacerbate the balance of payments problem. High interest rates would attract funds from abroad and appreciate the pound at a time when an improvement in manufacturing competitiveness was needed. The heavy reliance placed by the Government on the manipulation of interest rates thus posed a policy contradiction. On the one hand, a higher interest rate was needed to curb inflation; on the other hand, it had the effect of curbing trade competitiveness.

A danger inherent in the policies pursued by the Conservative Government is that they would fail to solve, and indeed contribute to, a serious structural problem. Between 1975 and 1988 employment in manufacturing fell by 2·3 million jobs, from 7·5 to 5·2 million. Monetary and interest rate policies and concern about inflation could keep the exchange rate at a level too high for the manufacturing sector to be competitive: they would thus contribute to the *de-industrialization* of Britain.

The Effects of Entry to the EMS.

In 1990 it became increasingly likely that Britain would soon become a full member of the *European Monetary System* (EMS). This would have important implications for the conduct of economic policy. Greater co-ordination of monetary policy with the rest of Europe would be required. The Bank of England would have to be given more independent responsibility and the setting of interest rates would be less subject to political control. There would be less scope for exchange rate realignment. With interest rates and exchange rates no longer available as instruments to control the domestic economy, fiscal policy would become more important. The prospects for the UK economy would be more closely linked to the rest of Europe.

In the long run the wage and price inflation rate and the interest rate in Britain would be brought into line with those of Europe. However, the tendency for the British economy to generate excessive wage pressure remains firmly-rooted. Should the United Kingdom enter the EMS with higher inflation and interest rates, the transitional problems could be severe (*see* **G59**).

The Competitiveness of Manufactured Products.

In which products has British manufacturing been losing competitiveness and in which has it been gaining? This question can be answered by examining the degree of import penetration (imports expressed as a percentage of home demand) and the export sales ratio (manufacturers' exports as a percentage of their sales), and their movements over time. These are shown in the table for selected industries for the years 1975 and 1987. The first thing to note is that the import share and the export share were very similar in 1975, and that both rose over the next decade, the former more rapidly than the latter. This trend reflects the general increase in trade among nations, associated with the decline in trade barriers, the growth in importance of multinational companies and the United Kingdom's entry into the European Economic Community. In most of the industries listed both the import share and the export share increased. Nevertheless, the high exchange rate in the wake of North Sea oil and high interest rates weakened the competitive position of British manufactures: import share has increased more than export share in most industries, and especially in motor vehicles, textiles, clothing and footwear.

Britain's traditional manufacturing strengths were in all forms of engineering, chemicals and vehicles. Some of these sectors came under pressure. In the case of vehicles, for instance, the export share fell from 43 to 34 per cent, but the import share rose sharply, from 26 to 48 per cent. There are more foreign cars on the roads in every country, but the international competitiveness of British car and truck production has nevertheless declined. The demise of the British motor cycle industry is an example of this trend. Britain improved or maintained her competitive position in food and drink, office machinery and paper, printing and publishing.

The growing industries in a manufacturing sector which otherwise stagnated in recent years were pharmaceuticals, plastic products, scientific instruments, electronics and computers. It is high-technology, growth industries such as these that offer the best prospects for exporting in the 1990s. Using as the classifying criterion expenditure on *R and D* by different industries, it is found that high-technology industries increased production at 2·8 per cent per annum, compared with an overall manufacturing decline of 1·1 per cent per annum, during the period 1975–85. In 1985, when there was a trade deficit of £2·1 billion, this category of industries achieved a trade surplus of £1·1 billion.

Should Imports be Controlled?

In the wake of the oil crisis of 1973, pressure was brought to bear on the British Government to ease the balance of payments and unemployment problems by imposing import duties or quotas. The Government rejected controls on manufactured goods: they would infringe treaty obligations to the GATT and the EEC, and might lead to retaliation and the danger of an international trade war. That remained the policy of the Labour Government, and also of the Conservative Government returned in 1979. However, the competitive squeeze on the manufacturing sector and the rise in unemployment, and support for import controls by the Labour Party while in opposition, meant that import controls continued to be a live political issue in the 1980s, but it became less and less relevent as European integration proceeded and as unemployment began to fall.

The economics profession, as on so many issues, is by no means in agreement on the relative merits of depreciation and import controls for remedying a balance of payments deficit. The protagonists of import controls point to their scope for selectivity, *e.g.*, permitting concentration on manufactures and excluding raw materials and food, to the possibility of using price increases in the sheltered industries, and to the avoidance of financial crises which would result from the prospect of depreciation. The imposition of tariffs could ensure that the benefits of any price increases accrued to the Government, which could then use the tariff revenues to subsidise commodities important to wage-earners' living standards. Those who would rely on exchange rates, on the other hand, argue that import controls are more likely to provoke retaliation by other countries, that controls breed inefficiency in production, that selective controls need to be very substantial to have the same impact as depreciation, and that controls may have to be progressively intensified.

Foreign Investment.

One of the more successful items in the UK balance of payments has been net interest, profit, and dividends from private sources. After the freeing of controls on direct investment abroad in 1979, UK direct investment overseas rose sharply, from £5·9 billion in 1979 to £15·2 billion in 1988. This was accompanied by corresponding increases in interest, dividends and profit from abroad, which contributed to the net surplus on invisibles in the current account (by £5·6 billion in 1988).

The Rise of Multinational Companies.

The remarkable expansion since 1960 of international investment, both by foreign companies in the United Kingdom and by British companies abroad, reflects the growing importance of *multinational companies* in the world economy. Some 165 multinationals account for 80 per cent of British private investment abroad. The multi-

nationals tend to dominate the world markets for technologically advanced products. They account for no less than 60 per cent of trade in manufactures in the developed world. Their financial and market power, their global investment strategies, and their ability to avoid national taxation pose a challenge to the economic sovereignty of national governments.

Multinationals in Britain.

Just as many British companies operate abroad, so many foreign companies have subsidiaries and affiliates in Britain. Some household names—including the oil companies Esso, Mobil and Texaco, the motor companies Ford, Vauxhall and Nissan, the electrical companies Phillips and Hoover, and new technology companies like I.B.M., Kodak and Rank Xerox—are foreign-based. Events such as the takeover of Westland helicopters and the possible sale of British Leyland in 1986, and Nestlés' takeover of Rowntree in 1988, brought the issue of foreign ownership into public debate.

Opponents of foreign takeovers may be motivated by crude nationalism or by a concern that production would become internationally more footloose. Although particular cases may require scrutiny, the liberal policies which British Governments have adopted towards both inward and outward foreign investment make sense. Countries which cut themselves off from the technological and other skills of multinational companies would find it difficult to compete internationally in the long run.

The International Economic System.

The international monetary system and international liquidity are explained on **G9–10**. The main problem facing the international economic system during the 1960s was an increasing shortage of international liquidity in the face of expanding world trade. This threatened the continuation of free trade. In the 1970s the focus moved to the problems of world inflation and to the international imbalance caused by the increased price of oil, and the resultant threat to economic growth. We trace the issues and events as they unfolded.

Recycling of Funds.

The main function of the IMF has been to provide deficit countries with loans, to be repaid over a certain period (*see* **G9–10**). The amount of these credit facilities has been increased over time, but the level has remained low in relation to needs, and the IMF facility has therefore been supplemented in various ways. For instance, the main trading countries—the *Group of Ten*—undertake (subject to some control by lending countries over the use of the funds) to make available substantial loans to the IMF for re-lending to countries of the Group suffering an outflow of short-term funds.

The Group of Ten has played an important role in coping with the flows of funds which have grown vastly in scale in the 1970s and 1980s. Increasingly, however, a Group of Seven—Canada, France, Germany, Italy, Japan, the United Kingdom and the United States—have assumed the role of international economic co-ordination and co-operation.

Special Drawing Rights.

In 1967 the members of the IMF agreed in principle to a scheme according *special drawing rights* (SDRs) to member countries, and in 1970 the scheme came into operation. SDRs were distributed to all members in proportion to their quotas with the IMF. They are generally accepted as a means of payment. Thus a deficit country can use its SDRs to buy the currency of the countries with which it has a deficit, and the surplus countries, in accumulating SDRs, earn a rate of interest on them. This is a movement towards an international paper currency, since the SDRs, unlike IMF loans, do not have to be repaid: they are a permanent addition to international reserves. Allocations were made in 1970–2, and again in 1979–81. The scheme was launched on a scale which is minute in relation to the size of the problem: the value of SDRs amounted to 20·0 billion, or 3·3 per cent of total world reserves, at the end of 1989. The IMF, in its statistics, now values all reserves in terms of SDRs.

The Gold and Dollar Crises.

The United States ran a large and persistent payments deficit in the 1950s and 1960s. This was initially financed through the willingness of foreigners to run up dollar balances. However, distrust of the dollar grew, and since many speculators expected the devaluation of the dollar in terms of gold to be followed by a corresponding devaluation of other currencies, there was a growing demand for gold. The central bankers gathered for a crisis meeting in 1968, and decided to introduce two markets for gold, with private transactions taking place in the free market at a price determined by supply and demand, and transactions among central banks taking place in the official market at the official gold price.

In 1970 the deficit in the United States balance of payments rose to a record level. This was financed by creditor countries increasing their dollar balances. If the United States failed to reduce its deficit, the creditor countries would either have to go on financing American deficits by accumulating dollars or allow their currencies to appreciate in terms of the dollar. In 1971, in response to speculative capital movements mainly to West Germany, the *deutschmark* was allowed to float upwards, *i.e.*, the authorities allowed its price to rise above the official ceiling. But massive speculation against the dollar continued and the United States Government suspended the convertibility of dollars into gold. Currencies of the major trading countries were then allowed to float upwards against the dollar by varying amounts.

Introduction of Flexible Exchange Rates.

The Smithsonian Agreement of December 1971 set the seal on the biggest realignment of exchange rates for nearly a quarter of a century. After negotiations among the Group of Ten it was agreed that the United States would devalue the dollar against gold if other countries would revalue upwards or at least not devalue. The U.S. balance of payments on current account deteriorated and speculation against the dollar broke out early in 1973. The dollar was devalued by 10 per cent and the EC countries agreed that their currencies would float jointly against the dollar, but with the currencies of Britain, Ireland and Italy—then in balance of payments difficulties—temporarily floating independently.

The international monetary system had entered a new era of flexible exchange rates. The Bretton Woods system, which had operated throughout the post-war period, had come to an end. No longer would countries be required to maintain fixed exchange rates subject only to periodic realignment in response to fundamental disequilibrium in their balance of payments. Although governments might wish to intervene to stop their currencies changing too rapidly and too far, most chose to unpeg their currencies.

The system had broken down because it could no longer perform its function. The imbalance between the United States and the other major countries was the immediate cause of the breakdown. Perhaps the more basic reasons, however, were the growing shortage of international reserves, the growing volume of internationally mobile short-term funds, and the more rapid and divergent national rates of inflation.

The First Oil Crisis.

In 1973 the oil-producing countries exported oil worth $27 billion and their surplus on current account was $13 billion. Their surplus for 1974 was estimated at $59 billion. This surplus involved a corresponding deficit for the oil-importing countries as a group. Such a transformation in the international balance of payments was unprecedented in its scale and speed. It involved a massive transfer of purchasing power from consumers to producers of oil. Since only a small part of the additional oil revenue was spent, this had a severe deflationary effect on the world economy. This effect was not remedied, and it was even compounded by the restrictive monetary and fiscal policies introduced by many of the major countries to stem their oil-induced inflation and balance of payments deficits.

The oil-producing countries had to invest their surplus funds abroad, so that there was a corresponding surplus on the capital account of the oil importing group of countries. However, the current account deficit of each individual country was not offset by a corresponding capital inflow. These funds were highly mobile between recipient countries, thus introducing considerable instability in the currency flows of the western oil consumers.

The Response to Oil Deficits.

Many governments took restrictive measures to combat both domestic inflation and their balance of payments deficits. In 1974 and 1975 the industrial countries experienced the worst economic recession of the post-war period. For instance, the level of industrial production in the OECD group of countries was 10 per cent lower at the end of 1975 than it had been at the end of 1973. The leaders of the six major non-communist countries held a summit meeting in France and agreed to various forms of economic co-ordination and co-operation, *e.g.*, rejecting protectionism, retaliatory beggar-my-neighbour trade policies.

Financing the Oil Deficits.

The OPEC group ran huge trade surpluses in 1974 and 1975. The U.S. and U.K. attracted some of the OPEC funds, but many countries, including the less developed countries, could not attract funds. Yet the less developed countries sustained large deficits in the wake of the oil price increase. Their needs were met in part through the IMF's *oil facility*: a loan fund intended to help countries cope with their oil deficits. In 1976 the IMF agreed to give all its member countries a temporary increase in borrowing rights of 45 per cent. The deposits made by oil-producers in western banks gave these banks an opportunity to lend on a much enlarged scale. Private lending to developing countries increased greatly; this sowed the seeds of the debt crisis of the 1980s (*see* **G54**). Some developing countries took temporary measures—such as import quotas—to conserve foreign exchange.

These various methods of financing oil deficits provided a temporary accommodation but they did not obviate the need for a long-run correction of the new imbalance in world trade and payments.

The Second Oil Crisis.

The price of oil doubled over the course of 1979, rising from $13 to $25 a barrel. This was due to the halving of Iranian oil production after the revolution in Iran, and to a scramble for oil stocks by the consuming countries. In 1980, assisted by the outbreak of war between Iran and Iraq, the OPEC oil price averaged $32 a barrel.

These factors combined to cause an actual fall in industrial production in OECD countries during 1980; their GDP rose on average by only one per cent. The higher oil price led again to higher inflation (13 per cent in 1980) and an increased balance of payments deficit ($58 billion) in the industrialised countries. Unusually, Japan and West Germany were running the biggest deficits, Britain being cushioned by her domestic oil supplies.

The high inflation rates ensured that nominal interest rates would be high in the major countries, but one of the consequences of the restrictive monetary policies generally being pursued was to raise interest rates in real terms as well. For instance, the Eurodollar rate in London—over 17 per cent in late 1980 and early 1981—was well above inflation rates at that time. Both the restrictive policies and the high interest rates which they generated had a depressing effect on the major economies: OECD output again rose by only one per cent during 1981.

World Oil Prices.

The table shows how average world prices of oil have moved since 1973, both in nominal terms and in real terms (nominal prices being deflated by the price of world exports of manufactures). The two great increases occurred in 1973-4 and 1979-80; both involved a more than doubling of the purchasing power of oil. Despite the apparent glut of 1985, the oil price was in real terms well over four times the level of 1973; even with the collapse of OPEC in 1986, it was on a par with the 1974-5 level.

WORLD PRICE AND PRODUCTION OF OIL,
1973–1989

	Price (OPEC average)		Production (billion barrels)	
	Nominal ($ per barrel)	Real (1973 = 100)	OPEC	World
1973	3·5	100	11·3	21·2
1974	9·6	228	11·2	21·2
1975	10·7	225	9·9	20·1
1976	11·9	249	11·3	21·9
1977	12·8	249	11·4	22·6
1978	13·1	222	10·9	23·1
1979	19·0	283	11·3	24·0
1980	31·9	428	9·8	23·1
1981	35·9	512	8·2	21·6
1982	34·4	502	6·9	20·6
1983	29·9	456	6·3	20·6
1984	28·6	451	6·3	21·1
1985	28·0	442	5·8	20·8
1986	15·6	220	6·7	21·9
1987	17·1	218	6·5	21·8
1988	13·5	159	7·3	22·6
1989	16·5	181	8·1	23·3

The Collapse of OPEC.

The year 1982 was characterised by oil price cutting below the OPEC reference price of $34 a barrel. In part this reflected the weakness of world demand, and in part the waning position of OPEC in the market. The OPEC countries tried to stabilise the market by agreeing both to curb production and to reduce the OPEC price. The new reference price was set at $29 a barrel. This was held for more than two years: the average OPEC price stayed at about $28 a barrel until the end of 1985.

The table shows the world production of crude oil (including communist production of 5·3 billion barrels) in 1985 was at the same level (21 billion barrels) as it had been in 1974. However, OPEC production was down to below 6 billion barrels. In particular, Saudi Arabia, which alone had produced over 3 billion barrels in 1974, was producing only half that amount a decade later. In 1974 OPEC had produced more than half of world production; now it produced only a third.

Meeting in January 1985 the OPEC members agreed to cut production down to their new, lower quotas. However, world production actually rose during 1985, whereas world demand failed to increase. Saudi Arabia was unwilling to continue withholding production so that other members—such as expansionist Libya, war-torn Iran and Iraq and heavily indebted Nigeria—could exceed their quotas: Saudi production expanded rapidly from September onwards. At its December meeting, OPEC decided on a new strategy: it would threaten a price war against outside producers in order to persuade them to curb production. It was hoped that Britain, as a high-cost producer, would be one of the countries amenable to such pressure, but the British Government responded that it had neither the power nor the purpose to limit North Sea production. A fall in the oil price would have benefits as well as costs for Britain (see **G50**).

The oil-dependent OPEC economies were generally more vulnerable to a fall in the oil price than the producers outside the cartel. OPEC's bluff was therefore called. With world production continuing at 52 million barrels a day (mbd), equivalent to 19·0 billion barrels a year, and world demand at 46 mbd (16.8 billion barrels a year), market forces took over. The spot price of oil collapsed, from just under $30 a barrel at the beginning of December to $10 a barrel at the beginning of April 1986. The cartel had fallen apart.

The OPEC members, meeting in December 1986, set themselves the objective of lifting the price of oil to $18 a barrel. They agreed to new quotas which, if adhered to, would reduce non-communist world production, then running at 17 billion barrels per annum. The initial results were favourable: in March 1987 the average OPEC oil price exceeded $17 a barrel. However, the strains within the organization proved to be too great and in October 1988 the OPEC price fell short of $12 a barrel. Demand for oil by the industrial countries started

to grow more rapidly, and Saudi Arabia reduced its production below quota. As a result, the price of oil began to rise and had reached $18 by February 1990. There was no sign, however, that a return to the world oil crises of 1973–4 and 1979–80 was in the offing.

World Recession, 1982.

Weaknesses in the world economy which had been apparent for almost a decade reached an alarming crescendo in 1982, as the world recession deepened. Industrial production in the OECD countries fell by 4 per cent during 1982 and real GNP by half a per cent. Unemployment reached the remarkable level of 8·5 per cent, representing over 30 million workers, in the 24 OECD countries. Yet inflation was still running at an annual rate of about 8 per cent, and interest rates were generally still in double figures.

The New Protectionism.

The rise in unemployment led to intensified protectionist measures in many countries, aimed at preserving jobs by keeping out imports, whether from other industrial countries or from developing countries. An example of this was the curbs placed by various countries on imports from Japan of cars and other "threatening" products such as television sets and videos. By 1982 the restrictions affected virtually all Japanese exports of cars to industrial countries. Another example was the import restrictions imposed by the United States—complaining of European subsidies of steel production—on steel from the EEC. The Multifibre Agreement—which authorises countries to restrict imports of textiles—was extended for 5 years in 1981 and for another 5 years in 1986. These restrictions commonly take the form of bilateral export restraint agreements.

Western Europe and America have found increasing difficulty in competing in two areas: labour-intensive manufactures, such as textiles and clothing, and certain engineering products, such as cars and consumer electronics. The competiton has come from low-wage countries, in the former case, and from Japan, in the latter. In 1986 Japan had a current account surplus of over $80 billion, and the United States ran a huge trade deficit (over $50 billion) with Japan. Despite the economic recovery in industrial countries, there were considerable pressures for more protection, particularly against Japan, and governments brought concurrent pressure on Japan to open its markets to Western goods. An example of these pressures was the threat made by the British Government to Japan in April 1987 that Japanese financial institutions might be excluded from the city of London if obstacles were maintained against British exports to the Japanese market. In the same month the United States imposed 100 per cent tariffs on some Japanese electronic goods.

Not all developments were in the direction of protectionism, however. In September 1986 representatives of 92 nations agreed to stage a new round of multilateral trade negotiations, to be called the Uruguay Round in succession to the Tokyo Round (see **G44**). The negotiations, which were expected to last 4 years, were intended to halt and reverse protectionism.

Crisis in the Banking System.

Between 1979 and 1982, the non-oil developing countries suffered a 21 per cent worsening of their terms of trade, reflecting the rise in the oil price and the drop in world demand for other primary products. This group of countries thus continued to maintain a large current account deficit. They were in general not prepared to take the harsh measures needed to control their deficits, so long as they could obtain finance from somewhere. Although this response of the poor countries was understandable, it contributed to the growing problem of international indebtedness (see **G47**).

The difficulties experienced by the international banks were partly beyond their control, being due, for instance, to the rise in interest rates produced by restrictive monetary policies, and partly to their own lack of caution. Perhaps they were too much swayed by the competitive pressures to make loans from the additional deposits coming from the OPEC surplus, and complacently confident that

CURRENT ACCOUNT OF MAJOR ECON-
OMIES,
1986–1989 ($ billion)

	1986	1987	1988	1989
United States	− 133	− 144	− 125	− 125
Japan	86	87	79	72
Europe	53	37	13	8
of which:				
West Germany	39	45	49	53
United Kingdom	0	− 6	− 26	− 31

"the authorities" would rescue banks which got
into difficulties.

The Mexican debt crisis of late 1982 brought out
the precariousness of the international banking
system. After that, one substantial debtor country
after another sought debt rescheduling or a standstill on repayments of principal. Stop-gap credits
had to be cobbled together, and in addition the IMF
emergency lending facility was enlarged, and agreement was reached to expand the IMF quota resources by about half.

The debt crisis was eased as the world economy
recovered during 1984. At the London summit
meeting of the seven major industrial countries in
June, it was agreed to extend the rescheduling of
debts in cases where debtor countries were themselves making successful adjustment efforts. Substantive agreements with Argentina and the Philippines took shape, and a multi-year rescheduling of
Mexico's debt was agreed in principle. Both Mexico
and Brazil, the two largest troubled debtors,
achieved great improvements in their balance of
payments. The atmosphere of foreboding was less
in evidence, but risks undoubtedly remained and the
total amount of debt continued to rise.

World Recovery, 1983–89.

The world economy began to recover in 1983. The
inflation rate continued to fall, however, averaging
5 per cent over the year, so making it less likely that
world recovery would be pinched in the bud by
fears of renewed inflation. In 1984 the increase in
GDP of the industrial countries averaged no less
than 5·0 per cent, the United States leading with a
remarkable 6·8 per cent. Reflecting the considerable
slack in the international economy, inflation did
not accelerate in response to the recovery but
actually fell slightly, to 4·2 per cent.

The promising start to world recovery gave way
to slower growth. The industrial countries managed
only 3·4 per cent growth in 1985, 2·6 per cent in
1986 and 3·5 per cent in 1987. One consolation was
that OECD inflation also fell, reaching 2·9 per
cent in 1987 and 1988, the lowest level for many
years.

The Rise of the Dollar.

The United States recovery occurred despite a
rising dollar. The effective exchange rate of the
dollar against other currencies rose by 20 per cent
in the 15 months up to March 1985. The reason for
this appreciation is rather a puzzle. It was
certainly not due to the strength of the current
account. On the contrary, with rapid economic
recovery the record American current account
deficit of $35 billion in 1983 gave way to one of $80
billion in 1984. Rather, the relentless rise of the
dollar has to be explained mainly in terms of
developments in financial markets. Interest rates in
the United States were high, and well above those
in other countries. This was due to the strength of
economic expansion and the consequent demand for
funds, and to the vast Federal Government budget
deficit which, on account of the restrictive monetary
policy, was financed by debt issue. These high rates
of interest, together with the anticipated profitability of the booming economy and the widespread
sentiment that the dollar would continue to rise,
attracted funds from abroad. By 1985 the loss of
funds to the United States was putting authorities
in other countries under pressure to raise interest
rates in a way not required by domestic considerations.

The U.S. Trade and Budget Deficits.

With investment harmed by the high interest rate
and export industries harmed by the high exchange
rate, the United States economy slowed down
sharply after 1984. This was an important reason
why world economic growth fell back in those
years. However, the long-expected depreciation of
the dollar eventually came in March 1985: it had
fallen 20 per cent against other currencies by the
end of the year. It continued to fall, by 14 per cent
against other currencies during 1986 and by 12 per
cent during 1987. By the end of 1989 the dollar was
only 56 per cent of its 1985 peak value.

The extent of international imbalance in current
accounts is shown in the table. The huge U.S. deficit,
offset by the growing Japanese and West German
surpluses, did not respond to the depreciation of the
dollar, both because of the time-lags involved and
because of the continuing Federal budget deficit.
The latter deficit declined from a peak in 1983 of
5·6 per cent of GNP but remained huge, being 2·8
per cent in 1989.

World Financial Crisis, 1987.

The structural imbalances in the world economy
came home to roost in the global financial crisis of
October 1987. The most fundamental cause was a
loss of confidence in the economic policies of the U.S.
Government. No significant action had been taken
to reduce the Federal budget deficit—action which
would be needed to eliminate the trade deficit. Nor
was there willingness on the part of the surplus
countries, in particular Germany, to stimulate their
economies sufficiently to help the United States out
of its predicament.

The budget deficit and tight monetary policy increased U.S. interest rates in 1987. This posed a
threat to equity prices, which had risen during the
year on a speculative wave. Both in February—the
Louvre Accord—and again in September, the
governments of the Group of Seven agreed to co-
operate in stabilising exchange rates and protecting
the dollar against speculative depreciation. However, market operators became increasingly sceptical that the dollar could be supported in the face
of the US trade deficit. In October the markets
panicked, share prices plummeted and, as funds left
the US, the dollar depreciated sharply. Stock exchanges around the world followed the New York
lead.

Prospects for the World Economy.

The financial crisis led to fears that it would
cause world-wide economic recession if business
confidence was shaken and investment dried up.
As a precaution, governments in various countries
responded to the deflationary impetus by adopting
more expansionary fiscal and monetary policies,
hoping thereby to lower interest rates. While the
United States continued to run large budget and
trade deficits, however, the danger to the world
economy would not disappear: the crisis of market
confidence in US economic policies could recur.

In other respects, conditions in 1988 were favourable for faster world economic growth: world inflation was lower than it had been for many years, and
oil and primary commodity prices were low. These
propitious factors prevailed: the world economy
grew more rapidly (by 4·0 per cent) in 1988 than it
had done since 1984. Moreover, this was achieved
without an acceleration of inflation.

It was the prospect of inflation accelerating which
caused most governments—including those of the
United States and the United Kingdom—to raise
interest rates during 1988. As inflationary pressure
built up (rising from 3·3 to 4·5 per cent in the
industrial countries between 1988 and 1989) economic growth was curbed. In 1989 growth of the
industrial economies was 3·5 per cent and in the
world as a whole 3·1 per cent. It was forecast that in
both cases growth would fall below 3 per cent in
1990.

The Economic Performance of Japan.

Japan's economy has outpaced all the major
industrial economies in recent years. Over the
period 1965–1987 annual growth of real income per
head was no less than 4·2 per cent. Even in the
1980s it was 3·2 per cent, whereas inflation was only

1·4 per cent per annum. After the recession of the early 1980s the current account surplus was consistently above 2 per cent of GNP, partly offset by an outflow of long term capital, and the yen continued to appreciate in value (*see below*). The Tokyo stock market rose inexorably—by over fourfold between 1982 and 1989.

By 1987 Japan's national income per capita (expressed in purchasing power parity) was 6 per cent higher than Britain's, and its total GNP was 60 per cent that of the United States. Japan, with its population of 122 million, had become an economic superpower. Its success is bound up with the hard work and thriftiness of its people.

In 1990 signs emerged that Japanese economic confidence and expectations were faltering. Despite a continuing current account surplus, the yen depreciated: it fell 17 per cent over the twelve months to April 1990. The Nikkei share index fell by 27 per cent in the first three months of 1990, and interest rates were raised sharply. It is not clear why confidence was lost. Commentators attributed the crisis to rising inflation and a deteriorating trade balance, but inflation was only 2 per cent per annum and the current account still in huge surplus. Perhaps the high level of share prices in relation to company profits strengthened the incentive to move capital abroad, and this realisation triggered the fall in the yen and in shares and the rise in interest rates. The long run prospects for the Japanese economy remained good, however, despite the financial crisis of 1990.

SDRs and Gold.

Originally the SDR (*see* **G52**) was valued in terms of the dollar, and then in terms of gold but in 1974 the IMF introduced a new system of valuation based on the value of a group of 17 major currencies in specified proportions. The number of currencies was reduced to 5 in 1981. These are the dollar, the mark, the franc, the yen and the pound.

The rapid inflation and great uncertainty in the world economy in the 1970s contributed to the speculative demand for gold; this raised its price many times over in the free market. The price of gold rose during 1978, assisted by speculation against the dollar and fears of another oil price increase. Political events in the Middle East caused further speculation during 1979, and the instability after the Soviet invasion of Afghanistan catapulted the gold price to $700 in September 1980. Gold flourishes in times of uncertainty and expected inflation. The price of gold subsequently declined as inflation rates began to diminish and as real rates of interest rose.

LONDON GOLD PRICE, 1976–1989
(U.S. $ per fine ounce, end-year)

1976	135	1984	308
1978	226	1985	330
1979	524	1986	391
1980	590	1987	487
1981	398	1988	411
1982	444	1989	410
1983	410		

Exchange Rate Arrangements.

Towards the end of 1989 the following exchange rate arrangements were in operation. Eighteen cur-

EXCHANGE RATES, 1985* AND 1990†

	Exchange rate against sterling, 1990 (£1 =)	Index of effective exchange rate, 1990 (1985 = 100)
Sterling	1·00	86·0
U.S. dollars	1·61	67·3
French franc	9·33	103·5
Italian lira	2,045·56	99·9
Deutschmark	2·73	119·6
Japanese yen	231·88	130·7

* 1975 average. † Start of year.

rencies, including the dollar, the pound and the yen, were independently floating. Another 24 currencies had "managed floats", *i.e.*, floating subject to a policy of periodic government intervention. Eight members of the EEC other than Britain maintained a co-operation arrangement to float together under the European Monetary System. Most developing countries pegged their currencies to those of major trading partners, 33 to the dollar, 14 to the French franc, 7 to the SDR, and 32 to some currency composite of their own choice.

Experience of Exchange-rate Flexibility.

One of the advantages claimed for greater flexibility in exchange rates is that it diminishes the need for international liquidity. Variations in exchange rates should reduce the size of imbalances and therefore the resources required to tide over deficits.

However, it is not clear from recent experience that greater exchange-rate flexibility can produce equilibrium in international payments. It seems that the balance of payments takes a long time—perhaps two or three years—to adjust to a depreciation of the exchange rate. In the meantime there might be wage increases to compensate for the increase in the cost of living brought about by the depreciation, which in turn tend to neutralise the depreciation. For instance, the table indicates that, between 1985 and January 1990 the pound had depreciated against a basket of other currencies by 14 per cent and the lira had stayed the same, the mark had appreciated by 20 per cent and the yen by 31 per cent. Yet because of their different rates of inflation, the signs were that the competitiveness of British goods was no stronger than it had been in 1985. A worrying feature of the flexible exchange rate system is that it not only permits but also generates a far wider spread of inflation rates among the major countries.

The Integration of Financial Markets.

There is a growing worldwide integration of financial markets. Financial intermediation has become a footloose industry with only limited ties to particular national markets or stock exchanges. Borrowers and lenders in different countries are brought together often by intermediaries based in a third country. The major currencies are traded in most financial centres and dealing continues around the clock. There are now over 250 companies whose equity is traded around the world.

Much of this change is due to technological innovations in communications. The declining cost of communication has meant that arbitrage is now possible at only very small price differentials, and companies throughout the world are alive to the advantages of scanning money and currency markets on a worldwide basis to meet their requirements at least cost. The consequent competitive pressures have meant that those markets have become more integrated.

Volatility of the Foreign Exchanges.

The movements in the 1970s towards greater flexibility of exchange rates and increased international liquidity helped to correct international imbalances. But there were various reasons for believing that they would not provide a permanent solution. Reasons have been given above for questioning whether exchange-rate flexibility can cope with the international imbalances of the 1980s. Moreover, the amount of short-term funds and the scope for speculation with them is greater than ever. The surpluses of the OPEC countries—with their *increase* in funds totalling $350 billion in the seven years 1974–80–present a considerable problem. In September 1989 the OPEC countries had a stock of external financial assets of $180 billion, of which $57 billion was held in the United Kingdom, mainly in Eurocurrency bank deposits. International companies, with structures that span the remaining exchange control barriers, have accumulated vast sums which they move about in search of security and profit.

The burgeoning and integration of financial markets epitomised by the growth of the Eurocurrency market (*see* **G10**), make control of short term capital flows very difficult and give rise to the possibility of exaggerated and destabilising movements in international exchange rates. For instance, the large differences in interest rates between financial centres in the 1980s, arising because of different inflation rates and monetary policies, stimulated huge and destabilising capital flows across the exchanges. The ensuing exchange rate fluctuations were detrimental to both private and public decision-taking. Exchange rates have become more responsive to expectations about currency revaluation and to interest rate arbitrage than to underlying current account imbalances.

Towards Greater Stability of Exchange Rates?

The early 1980s was a period in which governments made a virtue out of their reduced control over financial markets, and appeared to throw themselves on the mercies of the market. It also coincided with a world-wide shift in the political climate away from a belief in the efficiency of central control towards a greater reliance on the allocative forces of competition. Fairly "clean" floating of currencies (with little central bank intervention) was adopted, and exchange rate policies were not pursued. By the late 1980s, the inadequacies of this system—the volatility and economic irrationality of the behaviour of currencies—were more apparent, and the portents were that governments would attempt to intervene more vigorously in order to achieve greater exchange rate stability.

In 1987 the governments of the major economies moved towards a policy of stabilising exchange rates. In the *Louvre Accord* it was agreed to aim for particular exchange rates, which would be maintained within bands. In part this was because the major surplus countries were anxious to protect their export sectors from the consequences of further exchange rate appreciation, while the US wished to avoid the inflationary consequences of further depreciation. When confidence in the dollar was lost, however, the markets demonstrated the impotence of politicians in the face of powerful economic forces.

The European Community.

The *European Community* (EC), otherwise known as the Common Market, was set up by the Treaty of Rome, ratified in 1958. It consisted of six full members—Belgium, France, Holland, Italy, Luxembourg, and Western Germany. Britain had participated in the negotiations which led up to its formation, and had argued in favour of a looser "free trade area" without a common external tariff, and excluding trade in agricultural products. No compromise acceptable to the Six was found, and Britain joined with six other European countries—Austria, Denmark, Norway, Portugal, Sweden, and Switzerland—in forming the *European Free Trade Area* (EFTA).

Economic Arrangements of the EC.

The EC forms a common market with no tariffs or trade controls within it and a Common External Tariff (CET). There is a Common Agricultural Policy (CAP), which is maintained by a system of variable import levies setting *threshold prices* on

GDP PER HEAD OF EC MEMBER
COUNTRIES, 1987 (Average = 100) *

Belgium	101
Denmark	114
German Federal Republic	114
Greece	54
France	110
Ireland	64
Italy	104
Luxembourg	125
Netherlands	105
Portugal	53
Spain	74
United Kingdom	105

* Comparisons are based on purchasing power parities.

imports of agricultural products from outside the Community, and by means of *intervention prices* at which agricultural products of the Community are purchased. The EC has a large Budget required mainly for supporting the CAP, *i.e.*, for subsidising Common Market farmers. There is free movement of both goods and labour within the Community, and a certain degree of fiscal harmonisation.

Accession to the Community 1973.

The United Kingdom acceded as a full member of the EC on 1 January 1973. Two of Britain's EFTA partners—Ireland and Denmark—joined on the same date, so forming an expanded Community of nine countries. Economic ties with the Community strengthened. In 1972 trade with the original six members of the EC accounted for about 23 per cent of total British trade, trade with the EFTA partners about 13 per cent, and with the Commonwealth 19 per cent. After accession, trade with the EC expanded sharply and the proportion of trade with the former EFTA countries and the Commonwealth fell. Excluding trade with the oil-exporting countries, British trade with the original EC countries rose from 25 per cent of the total in 1972 to 30 per cent in 1974. In 1988 no less than 52 per cent of British trade was with the EC.

The EC Budget.

It is in the British interest that the CAP—with its heavy support of Common Market farmers—be reformed. Community funds are available to protect farmers by buying excess food and building up stocks of food if the free market price falls below the intervention price. As a result "food mountains" have developed.

The British contribution to the EC Budget was initially small. The average annual *net* contribution (payments *less* benefits) was £27 million in the period 1973–5. Britain gained from "monetary compensation amounts," *i.e.*, refunds associated with the difference between the values of the pound in the foreign exchange markets and the *green pound*. The green pound is the agreed exchange rate between the pound and the other Community currencies which is used in calculating contributions to the Budget.

Britain's net contribution to the EC budget rose to about £1 billion in 1980, *i.e.* about 60 per cent of the total net contributions to the Community budget. Yet Britain's GNP per head was then the third lowest of the Nine. The high level of Britain's net contribution reflects her heavy dependence on imported food: she has only a small agricultural sector whereas most of the Community budget is used for farm support.

Negotiating Britain's Budget Contribution.

The British Government determined to negotiate a reduction in its contribution. After much bitter wrangling, the EC governments agreed on a formula to limit the U.K.'s net contribution in 1980 and 1981. Further talks were necessary for 1982 and 1983. The Government went so far as to veto CAP farm price rises as a lever to obtain a higher budget rebate, but this was overruled by an unprecedented majority decision. Total refunds negotiated for the four-year period 1980–83 amounted to more than £2·5 billion.

These negotiations were *ad hoc*: the British Government also pressed for new financial arrangements for the Community, based on more equitable principles. Since two-thirds of the budget goes to finance the CAP, a permanent solution satisfactory to Britain would involve changes in the CAP itself. British interests would be served by a relative decline in CAP expenditure, and by country contributions being calculated as a percentage of GDP, that percentage rising as a country's GDP per head rose in relation to mean GDP per head of the Community.

Negotiations on refunds to the United Kingdom were successfully concluded at Fontainebleau in 1984. The agreement made automatic arrangements for the future. The United Kingdom would receive a refund each year equal to two-thirds of the difference between its share of VAT payments to the Community (each country paid VAT to the Community at the rate of 1·4 per cent of value added) and its share in expenditure from the Community budget. The British Government appeared satisfied with the deal.

Reforming the Budget.

In 1984, perhaps for the first time in the history of the CAP, EC farm ministers agreed to cut subsidies and freeze prices. The system of open-ended guarantees was to be largely discontinued in an effort to halt the growth of agricultural surpluses. For instance, the production of milk was subjected to restricted quotas, with adverse effects for British dairy farmers. Another aspect of the agricultural agreement was the decision to phase out the monetary compensation amounts, i.e., the border taxes which iron out the effects of national currency fluctuations. Despite this talk, by July 1986 the surplus food stocks had reached new levels in all cases except beef. In 1987 the President of the Commission declared that the objective should be to bring farm price intervention back to its original role of short term market stabilization.

The basic problem was that the ceiling of 1·4 per cent of value added had become insufficient to finance Community expenditure, given the increase in farm subsidies and the accession arrangements for Spain and Portugal: VAT at 1·6 per cent was needed to balance the 1987 budget. Radical reform of the financial arrangements was still required.

Agricultural Protectionism.

There is good cause for the reform of agricultural policies not just in the EC but in the OECD countries generally. Agriculture is heavily supported in all the major economies—probably more so in Japan and the US than in the EC. A study of 7 major countries found that government assistance to agriculture exceeded one third of the value of their agricultural output. Half of this assistance came from tax-payers' pockets (subsidies) and half from consumers' pockets (higher prices).

This inefficient use of the world's resources is expensive to non-farming people in the rich countries and harmful to people of the poor countries. Negotiations in the multilateral forum of the GATT (see **G9**) are needed to reduce agricultural protection in the OECD countries, but reform of the CAP need not wait on GATT negotiations.

Prospects for Economic Union.

In 1970 the Commission of the European Economic Community published the *Werner Plan*, a report on the establishment of economic and monetary union of the EC. The plan aimed at transferring the principal economic decisions from the national to the Community level, and at establishing within the Community complete freedom of movement of goods, services, persons and capital, with fixed and constant rates of exchange between national currencies or, preferably, a common currency. A centre of decision for economic policy would be established and made responsible to a European parliament.

These ideas have far-reaching economic and political implications, since they involve a considerable reduction of national sovereignty. For instance, the loss of power to correct balance of payments deficits by means of trade controls or variation in the exchange rate implies either that the deficit country's currency should be generally acceptable to its creditors (so that the country within the Community—like a region within a country—simply cannot have a balance of payments problem), or the country must resort to deflation. And even if there is a common currency, it is very likely that resources will concentrate in some regions of the Community to the neglect of the other regions, possibly those far from the main centres of production and consumption. Complete mobility of resources is likely to produce a regional problem within the Community just as it can produce a regional problem within a country. But the Community may not, to the same extent as a country, possess the political power and determination required to remedy the problem. It is not surprising that the Werner Plan has been pursued in only

limited respects and that its eventual implementation is uncertain; economic union cannot precede political union.

Regional differences within the Community increased with the joining of Greece in 1981, and of Spain and Portugal in 1986. The Community now united 330 million Europeans, but there were large differences in their incomes. Its population was almost as large as that of the US and Japan combined, and its output was similar to that of the US.

The Single European Act.

The Single European Act was introduced in 1986 to amend the Treaty of Rome. Its intention was to establish a free internal market in the Community by the end of 1992. This was defined as an area without frontiers in which the free movement of goods, persons, services and capital is ensured. The single market will involve the end of exchange controls, common financial services and technical standards, and mutual recognition of professional qualifications. The legislation is concerned to remove barriers—barriers that increase costs, impede entry to markets, or distort markets. Thus, for instance, it outlaws delays at customs posts, form-filling, the need to conform to different national rules and regulations, and national restrictions on purchases by governments and on professional practice.

The Act circumscribed the powers of member countries to impose a veto in all but sensitive issues. It also made provision for what is called "cohesion", which means reducing the gap between rich and poor regions of the Community. The Act should be seen as a very small step in the direction of a federal Europe.

Towards Monetary Union.

It was on the issue of monetary union that the first major economic problem for Britain arose after entry. In conformity with the Werner Plan, the Community agreed in March 1973 to fix the exchange rates between member currencies and to float them together against the dollar. This arrangement was known as the *snake in the tunnel*. Britain and Italy—then in balance of payments difficulties—decided to float independently.

There is a danger that the right to vary exchange rates be withdrawn from member countries without there being uniformity in other policies. If there is to be a monetary union, there should also be uniformity in other economic policies, even industrial relations and incomes policies! For if inflation is more rapid in Britain than in her partner countries, and if Britain is prevented from adjusting the exchange rates or imposing import restrictions against her partners to correct the ensuing balance of payments deficit, the Government might see no alternative but to deflate the economy: stagnation could ensue.

In October 1987 the European Commission adopted proposals for the complete liberalisation of capital movements in the Community. Controls were to be removed from July 1990 for most member countries. The liberalization should lead to the development of Community-wide financial and banking services, and the increased competition should make them cheaper.

The European Monetary System.

A modification of the snake, the *European Monetary System* (EMS) was introduced in 1979. A currency is permitted to float within a 2¼ per cent band on either side of the par rate between the currency and any other member's currency. Central bank intervention is required to keep the currency within the band. The participating currencies are defined in *European Currency Units* (ECUs), issued against the deposit of 20 per cent of national gold and foreign exchange reserves and used to settle intervention debts. There is a system of central bank "swaps" and short- and medium-term credit.

For some, the EMS is the response to a growing disillusionment with the operation of floating exchange rates and a strong desire to move towards greater exchange rate stability among close trading partners. For others, the EMS represents an early step on the path to European monetary union. The restriction on national sovereignty under the EMS is not large: it probably means that exchange rate adjustments will be in discrete steps rather than by continuous and perhaps erratic floating.

The difference in inflation rates among countries in the EMS necessitated periodic currency realignments, in October 1981, June 1982, March 1983, April 1986 and January 1987. In each case the deutschmark was upvalued relative to the French franc: the combined result of these realignments was that the franc fell by 38 per cent against the mark. In September 1989 one ECU (representing a weighted bundle of EC currencies) was worth 68 pence.

Should Britain Join the EMS?

Early in 1988 four EC countries had not entered the EMS: Britain, Greece, Spain and Portugal. Britain had resisted the blandishments of EMS members to join them. This was partly because of the large and unpredictable flows of funds in and out of sterling on account of London's role as a financial centre. However, the main reason was that, Britain being a net oil exporter, the British balance of payments is likely to move inversely to that of other EC countries as the world price of oil fluctuates. With the oil price falling sharply in 1986, Britain needed the power to permit a depreciation of sterling in order to maintain balance in payments. Despite the even sharper depreciation of the dollar, sterling depreciated by no less than 11 per cent against a basket of other currencies between the end of 1985 and the end of 1986, and by 16 per cent against the deutschmark.

Nevertheless, events were pushing Britain towards full membership of the EMS, involving entry to the *Exchange Rate Mechanism* (ERM). The ERM requires member countries to keep their exchange rates fixed within narrow bands and to adopt domestic monetary policies to achieve this target. Entry to the ERM was supported by most industrialists because exchange rate stability would reduce the uncertainty they faced in exporting and importing. In April 1989 a cabinet division emerged over entry to the ERM. The Chancellor of the Exchequer was in favour but the Prime Minister was against, mainly because it would involve loss of control over monetary policy. This disagreement was one of the factors that led to Nigel Lawson's resignation as Chancellor in October. The new Chancellor, John Major, also made it clear that he favoured entry, so the issue did not go away.

Towards EMU.

The President of the European Community, Jacques Delors, was firmly in favour of economic and monetary union (EMU) of the Community. The Delors report on EMU was presented to the European Council's meeting in Madrid in June 1989. Its conclusions were in many ways similar to those of the Werner report. They envisaged a three-stage process of movement towards EMU. Stage one would consolidate the single market. Stage two would see the setting up of a European System of Central Banks (ESCB), but responsibility for policy would remain with national authorities. Stage three would involve an irrevocable locking of exchange rates, the creation of a single Community currency, binding constraints on national budgets, and a transfer of responsibility for monetary policy to the ESCB. The ESCB would also decide on exchange rate policy and manage all official reserves.

The British Response to Delors.

The British Government was unhappy both about the pace and ultimate form of EMU. Addressing the EC summit in Madrid in June 1989, the Prime Minister set terms for British entry to the ERM: there should first be liberalisation of financial markets, agreement on competition policy, an end to exchange controls, and completion of a single market. These conditions represented the first of Delors' three stages. In addition, the Prime Minister wanted British inflation to be closer to the European average (between 1988 and 1989 British inflation was 7·8 per cent whereas the Community average was 5·1 per cent).

In November the Treasury published proposals for an evolutionary approach to EMU, as an

alternative to the Delors plan. It proposed that, when stage one was complete, there should be a number of piecemeal measures to strengthen market competition and encourage integration, *e.g.* encouragement of private ECUs and the removal of restrictions on the use of Community currencies. The British Government was against binding rules on the size of budget deficits: budgetary policies should be left to national authorities. It proposed a multi-currency system which, through competition among monetary authorities, it expected to lead to convergence of inflation rates. It was concerned that Delors would take the control of monetary policy away from national governments while leaving those governments answerable to their electorates for policies over which they would have no control.

Price Differentials within the EC.

The EC is supposed to be a common market. Why, then, does a £9,000 car in Britain cost £6,000 in Belgium? A study showed that if the price of a car was 100 in the United Kingdom, it sold net-of-tax for 82 in Ireland, 72 in France, 70 in West Germany and 66 in the "Benelux" countries. It has become profitable for specialist companies to arrange for British customers to go and buy their cars in other countries; but this occurs only on a small scale.

There are various possible explanations for the price differences. One is that prices are set by the degree of Japanese penetration, which is greatest in the Benelux countries. More plausible is the view that price differences result from collusive policies on the part of manufacturers, assisted by the difficulty of buying a car in one country for use in another and the "drive on the left" rule in Britain. It is possible that the British government did not discourage the collusion—*e.g.* by not making transfers simpler—because of the adverse effect that would have on the ailing domestic car producer, British Leyland; but the policy implies a hidden subsidy not only to BL but also to foreign manufacturers, paid by British car buyers. Price differences of this sort should be reduced with the advent of a free internal market by 1992.

2. INTERNAL DEVELOPMENTS

Trends in Post-war Economic Policy.

Since the end of the Second World War in 1945, economic policy making in Britain can be loosely divided into several phases: the *Keynesian era* from 1945 to the mid-1960s, the era of *doubts about Keynesianism* from the mid-1960s to 1976, and since 1976 the *monetarist era*. Many economists would add a fourth phase, an era of *doubts about monetarism*, dating from the early 1980s. It should be emphasised that this division of the post-war period into these various phases is intended to provide only a very rough guide to broad trends in policy making. Further discussion of some

POSTWAR BRITISH ECONOMIC
EXPERIENCE

	Average annual rates of:		
	Unemployment	Inflation	Growth of Gross National Product
1945–64	1·9	3·4	2·4
1965–69	2·1	4·3	2·5
1970–74	3·0	11·0	1·6
1975–79	5·5	14·1	1·7
1980	6·4	18·1	− 2·5
1981	9·9	11·9	− 1·4
1982	11·5	8·7	1·9
1983	12·3	4·6	3·0
1984	12·7	5·0	2·1
1985	13·1	6·1	3·4
1986	13·2	3·5	3·0
1987	10·4	3·3	4·2
1988	8·3	4·9	4·5
1989	6·5	7·7	2·5

of these trends, and of the contrast between Keynesian and monetarist policies is to be found in **Part II.**

Doubts About Keynesianism.

Worries about the balance of payments and inflation started to become widespread in the 1960s and led to the emergence of serious doubts about Keynesian policies, despite their success in preventing a return to high unemployment. The critics arued that policy-makers tended to stimulate demand too much, leading to shortages of goods which in turn produced both balance of payments and inflation problems. These doubts received powerful intellectual support from the growing number of monetarist economists led by Professor Milton Friedman (*see also* **Part II**). The monetarists argued that there were limits to the ability of governments to lower unemployment by stimulating demand, and that attempts to go beyond these limits would lead not just to inflation but to progressively *rising* inflation—in rather the same way that users of stimulant drugs often find that their bodies eventually adapt to a particular level of use so that higher levels are thereafter needed in order to maintain the same degree of stimulation.

This idea that Keynesian expansion risked ever-worsening inflation found an increasingly sympathetic audience from the late 1960s onwards, for as the table shows, it was just at that time that Britain (and most other industrialised countries) experienced a sharp rise in inflation. In an attempt to combat this the British Government allowed unemployment to rise sharply in 1970 and 1971. This represented the first time since the war that any British Government had given top priority for any significant time to an objective other than the Keynesian one of maintaining low unemployment.

The policy was reversed at the beginning of 1972 when the Government decided that unemployment levels had become unacceptably high. However, the subsequent expansion proved to be ill-judged. Demand was expanded far beyond the ability of domestic output to meet it, leading inevitably to balance of payments and inflation problems. At the same time the effects on unemployment were disappointing. This experience significantly strengthened support for the monetarist critique of Keynesian policy-making: it seemed that the latter was now producing inflation and import problems without even achieving the desired result of low unemployment. Morevoer, although with the benefit of hindsight it is clear that the expansion was ill-judged—it was delayed too long, and then proceeded too rapidly—this was not clear at the time: in 1972 most economic forecasters broadly approved the strategy. This seemed to confirm another monetarist objection to Keynesian policy, namely its reliance upon short run forecasts as a basis for *fine tuning* the economy, *i.e.*, making frequent adjustments to monetary and fiscal policies in the light of such forecasts. Monetarists argued that such forecasts were too inaccurate to provide a basis for detailed policy adjustments, and that fine tuning should therefore be abandoned. They advocated instead *fixed rule* policies, in which the main lines of monetary and fiscal policies are laid down for 4 to 5 years in advance, and are therefore not substantially altered in response to short term events.

Problems of the 1970s.

In retrospect it is clear that many of the problems which emerged in the early and mid-1970s were not only the product of over-expansionary Keynesian policies but also reflected several adverse changes in the world economy, all dating from the beginning of the 1970s, which were outside the control of the British government. These included a significant slowdown in the growth of world trade; a sharp rise in world-wide inflation; the emergence of negative real interest rates in most countries; and—perhaps the most dramatic—a vast rise in the international price of oil. Over the decade as a whole real unit energy costs rose drastically (*see* **G54**).

In such an unfavourable world economic climate the British economy was bound to experience problems. The 1970s became the decade of *stagflation*—a combination of both inflation and stagnation (and thus unemployment). Britain was by no means the only country to experience such problems. In all the main industrial economies, higher energy costs reduced the profitability of most parts of the manufacturing sector which in turn reduced its output and employment. Nearly all countries also shared in the general rise in world-wide inflation. Hence Britain's problems in the 1970s were by no means unique. However, Britain fared worse than most, and mistakes by successive British governments were partly to blame.

The Monetarist Era.

In the autumn of 1976 a loss of international confidence in the government's economic policy led to speculation against the pound and to a sharp fall in its international value. The government had to apply to the International Monetary Fund for a loan. The latter was granted, but only on condition that the government introduced *monetary targets*, i.e. specified annual growth rates of the money supply. The emergence of monetarism in Britain really dates from this time.

The introduction of monetary targets meant that government spending could no longer be financed by unlimited monetary expansion, and thus forced the government to choose between cutting public spending, raising taxes, or increasing its borrowing (and therefore rising interest rates). The Labour government found all these options unpalatable, but at the 1979 General Election it lost power, and was replaced with a Conservative Government led by Margaret Thatcher, with Sir Geoffrey Howe as Chancellor.

Monetarism in Action, 1979–1983.

In some respects the new Government's economic policy was little more than a continuation of the Labour Government's policy since 1976. The centrepiece of economic policy was the *Medium Term Financial Strategy*, which involved laying down targets for monetary growth and the p.s.b.r. for 3 to 4 years ahead, and which thus embraced the 'fixed rule' monetarist idea discussed earlier. This policy was not substantially different in principle from that followed between 1976 and 1979.

Economic policy nonetheless differed in some important respects from that of the previous Labour Government, and indeed of all previous Governments since 1945. To begin with, it was clear that Mrs. Thatcher and Sir Geoffrey Howe were enthusiastic supporters of monetarism, whereas the feeling that existed that the previous Labour Government had only reluctantly embraced monetary targets and that it would change course if the opportunity arose. This was evidenced by attitudes towards unemployment. Within months of Mrs. Thatcher's accession to power unemployment began to rise at an unprecedented rate, far exceeding the rate of rise under Labour, though this had itself been much higher than anything previously seen since 1945. However, whereas the Labour Government had clearly been dismayed by the rise, the Conservative Government seemed to take a different view, arguing that the rise was necessary if inflation was to be reduced, that there was little that the Government could or should do to prevent it, and that the main responsibility for the rise lay with the trade unions who, it was argued, could prevent it by accepting smaller pay increases.

As much as anything, therefore, the change brought about by Mrs. Thatcher's Government was a change of attitudes towards economic policy, with the Keynesian priority of low unemployment finally giving way to the monetarist priority of low inflation. The two years 1980 and 1981 saw the sharpest recession for 50 years, with substantial falls in output and huge rises in unemployment. The gains, in terms of lower inflation, appeared from 1982 onwards, by which time it was clear that the "inflation psychology" of the 1970s—in which people had come to regard high and rising inflation rates as the normal state of affairs—had been broken: by 1982 few people anticipated a return to high inflation.

The Government introduced two other important

THE PUBLIC SECTOR
BORROWING REQUIREMENT

	£billion	as a percentage of gross domestic product
1979–80	9·9	4·8
1980–81	13·2	5·6
1981–82	8·8	3·4
1982–83	9·2	3·2
1983–84	9·8	3·2
1984–85	10·2	3·2
1985–86	5·8	1·8
1986–87	2·5	0·6
1987–88	− 3·0	− 0·7
1988–89	− 14·0	− 3·0
1989–90	− 7·6	− 1·7

A negative sign indicates a public sector surplus

changes in economic policy. One was its refusal to countenance the sort of formal incomes policy to which every Government since the early 1960s had been forced to turn in attempts to control inflation. The Conservatives argued that the evidence showed such policies to be at best short term expedients, failing to secure lasting reductions in inflation.

The other main economic policy change was the Government's long term commitment to securing reductions in public spending, in taxes, and in the p.s.b.r. These objectives—like the opposition to formal incomes policy—reflected its conviction that Government intervention was in general harmful to the economy, and that long term economic gains would follow if the extent of such intervention could be reduced. The table shows that the aim of a reduced p.s.b.r. was indeed achieved by 1982–83. However, this aim was controversial. In part, criticism reflected the view that the p.s.b.r. is not an appropriate policy target since it is unpredictable in the short run: it is, in effect, simply the difference between two very large magnitudes, namely total public spending and total public sector receipts, and small proportionate variations in either can therefore produce large proportionate variations in the p.s.b.r. More fundamentally, Keynesians objected to cuts in the p.s.b.r. on the grounds that a recession should be combated by raising, not lowering, public sector borrowing. The crucial point came in 1981, when with unemployment rising very fast and output falling the Chancellor rejected Keynesian arguments for additional borrowing and moved in the opposite direction, producing a very tough monetarist Budget which increases taxes in order to maintain the Government's borrowing targets.

One of the main effects of the government's economic policy was a very sharp rise in the exchange rate between 1979 and 1981. This reflected two things. The first was North Sea oil (*see* **G49**) and the second was the government's tough monetary policies, which pushed up interest rates in Britain and therefore attracted investment funds into Britain, increasing the demand for sterling and so raising its exchange value. The rise in the exchange rate was the principal cause of the fall in output and rise in unemployment between 1979 and 1982. It eroded the competitiveness of tradable goods produced in Britain compared with those produced in other countries and this reduced exports and increased imports. The economy's manufacturing sector—the traditional tradable sector of the British economy—was particularly hard hit and indeed virtually all the job losses during the period were from manufacturing and construction firms.

In 1983 the Prime Minister called a General Election. The economic policies pursued since 1979 were a principal issue in the campaign. The Government lost some support compared with the 1979 election but nevertheless secured a vastly increased Parliamentary majority: this contradictory result reflected the split in the opposition vote between Labour and the Alliance.

The Second Conservative Government.

After the election Mr Lawson, the new Chancellor, confirmed that the basis of the Government's macro-

economic policies was unchanged: it remained committed to controlling the public sector borrowing requirement, to securing further reductions in inflation, and if possible to cutting both taxes and public expenditure. However, an important new aspect of government policy soon appeared: the *privatisation* of large parts of the public sector. Indeed, this emerged as the most distinctive feature of the second Conservative Government.

The Privatisation Policy.

The Government committed itself to selling shares in existing public enterprises to the private sector. The Government had two motives for this policy. First, it anticipated raising some £2 billion per year through such sales, and this was intended to help finance the p.s.b.r. Secondly, it argued that most economic activity was more efficiently carried out by the private sector, and that privatisation would therefore ultimately raise the economy's overall level of efficiency and productivity.

Both these arguments were strongly attacked. Critics pointed out that there was no evidence from international comparisons of different countries to support the view that the size of the public sector had any appreciable effect upon economic performance. There was also widespread criticism of the way in which the government chose to incorporate privatisation into its macroeconomic policy. Officially, money raised by selling off state assets was counted as negative public spending. Hence it had the effect of reducing official measures of the public sector borrowing requirement, since it reduced the official measure of total public spending. However, there was virtual unanimity among independent commentators that this could not be taken seriously, and that sales of public sector assets should be seen as a means of *financing* the p.s.b.r. rather than as something which reduced its size.

This point assumed considerable importance as the scale of privatisation expanded during Mrs. Thatcher's second term of office. In 1983–84 privatisation sales were worth approximately £2 billion, rising to £3 billion in 1984–85 and to £5 billion in 1985–86, with projections of further annual sales of £5 billion up to 1990. By the time of the 1987 Budget, this meant that the value of privatisation sales was virtually equal to the official size of the p.s.b.r. The critics argued that in reality the p.s.b.r. was thus double its official size, with privatisation sales financing half.

Economic Policy in the Mid-1980s.

The rapid rise in unemployment which had characterised Mrs. Thatcher's first term of office was not repeated in her second. The unemployment total reached 3 million and thereafter showed little trend in either direction until 1986, when it began to fall. However, the picture was confused by the increasing emphasis placed on *special employment measures*. The most important of these was the *Youth Training Scheme* which began in 1983. This aimed to provide one year's training and work experience to all 16 or 17 year olds; in 1986 it was extended to two years. Those taken on by firms operating the scheme were not counted in the unemployment statistics. Another important scheme was the *Community Programme*, which provided the long-term unemployed (those out of work for over a year) with the chance to undertake useful community work. The table shows the numbers involved in such schemes and their rapid rise after 1983. If none of the schemes had been in operation most of those involved would instead have been counted as unemployed, so that the official unemployment total would have been in the region of 600,000 higher in each year since 1983.

Inflation did not continue the sharp fall of 1980–83 but after 1983 stabilised in the region of 3 to 5 per cent, and the government could not succeed in lowering it further. Indeed there seemed to be little indication that it attached a high priority to doing so, though it continued to attach a very high priority to preventing any increase. One reason why it proved impossible to lower inflation further was that the growth of wages and salaries also stabilised at around 7 to 8 per cent per annum. With labour costs thus continuing to rise relatively

NUMBERS IN SPECIAL EMPLOYMENT SCHEMES ('000s)

	1983	1985	1987
Youth Training Scheme	0	357	417
Community Programmes	24	151	221
Enterprise Allowance	0	49	96
Other Schemes	294	10	42
TOTAL	318	671	776

rapidly, it was impossible to reduce price inflation. Indeed, throughout the second Conservative government, the growth of earnings considerably outstripped the growth of prices, so that people in work experienced significant improvements in their real living standards despite continued high unemployment.

Two possible reasons were advanced for this. One argued that it is *rising* unemployment, rather than a high *level* of unemployment, which threatens the job security of people in work, and that if unemployment is high but not significantly increasing—as in 1986—this has little effect on workers with jobs. Another explanation focused on the very large number of long-term unemployed—those out of work for over a year—and argued that many of these people were so discouraged by repeated failures to find work that they tended to search less hard for jobs, so putting less competitive pressure on those already in work.

Changes in Taxation.

The Chancellor introduced several types of tax change over the course of the Parliament. One was a reform of company taxation in which most tax reliefs and allowances on investment were phased out, and simultaneously the rate of Corporation Tax was sharply reduced. The aim was to increase post-tax company profits, whilst leaving individual firms free to decide on the best and most efficient way of using these profits, free from tax incentives which tended to make some types of investment more profitable than others. This fitted into the government's general philosophy of leaving as many decisions as possible to private markets, with a minimum of direct government intervention.

Another major change was in personal taxation. When Mrs. Thatcher had first been elected in 1979, reductions in income tax had been one of her main aims. However, apart from the reduction of tax rates in Sir Geoffrey Howe's first Budget in 1979, little had been done by 1983. In her second government this objective was given a fresh priority, and over the course of the Parliament the Chancellor succeeded in cutting the standard rate of income tax from 30 to 27 per cent, and also in raising the tax thresholds by more than the rate of inflation. Hence the government succeeded in reducing the burden of income tax. At the same time other tax burdens—indirect taxes, and National Insurance contributions—were still substantially higher than in 1979. Hence it remained true for most people that their total tax burden was higher by the end of Mrs. Thatcher's second government than it had been when she was first elected. Only those earning more than around four times the national average had obtained a reduction in their overall tax burdens.

Another important change in personal taxation was the introduction of tax incentives for firms and employees who agreed to systems of *profit related pay* (PRP). The idea of such schemes is that a proportion of employees' wage and salary payments should be related to the size of their employer's profits, automatically rising or falling according to the success of the firm. The Chancellor announced in his 1986 Budget that employees would be entitled to tax relief on half of their PRP up to a limit of either 20 per cent of their income or £3,000, whichever was lower. For employees who took up their full entitlement under the scheme the tax gain would be very large. The Chancellor was prepared to introduce such concessions because he believed that PRP would bring important benefits to the economy. One reason was his belief that by giving employees a stake in the profitability of their firms it would encourage harder

and more productive work. Perhaps more important, the Chancellor argued that PRP schemes might combat unemployment by making pay more flexible: if profits fell in a recession, so would wages, and this would cause less jobs to be lost than if wages and therefore labour costs were rigid. However, critics argued that evidence from firms which already operated some form of PRP did not support the view that it increased their efficiency.

Expanding Share Ownership.

Another theme which emerged during Mrs. Thatcher's second term was the aim of *expanding share ownership*—encouraging a larger proportion of the population directly to own shares quoted on the Stock Market. (This is distinct from indirect ownership accumulated through contributions to pension funds, already a widespread feature of the economy). There were three methods by which the spread of share ownership was encouraged. The first was through the privatisation of previously state-owned assets, which was achieved by the government selling shares in newly-privatised companies to the general public. The second involved tax incentives encouraging the growth of employee share option schemes (ESOPs), under which employees could be paid bonuses or other parts of their remuneration in the form of issues of shares in their own company. Thirdly, the government gave incentives to encourage individuals to take out Personal Equity Plans, under which up to £200 per month could be paid into a fund to purchase shares, with the resulting dividend and capital gain income all being tax free.

The evidence indicated that the aim of wider share ownership was successfully achieved during Mrs. Thatcher's second term of office. By the end of 1987 over 20 per cent of all adults—around 9 million people—owned shares in at least one company, compared with 7 per cent when Mrs. Thatcher took office in 1979. It was clear that privatisation and ESOP schemes had been the main causes of this widening: about 4 million people owned shares in at least one privatised company, and about 1·5 million owned shares of the company in which they worked.

Mrs. Thatcher's Third Term.

In June 1987 a General Election returned the government to power with only a small reduction in its Parliamentary majority, and with little change in its degree of popular support. Whilst the government had a number of proposals for radical changes, these were mostly in the field of social policy: in economic policy the emphasis was on continuity.

The remainder of 1987 saw a continuation of the themes of the previous few years. It was a year of very rapid economic growth, in which those in work saw significant increases in their real incomes, the latter being the main source of the continuing boom in consumer spending. The main potential problem was the deficit on the current account of the balance of payments. An additional and dramatic problem was the Stock Market crash in October, which was matched in other stock exchanges throughout the world (*see* **G55**). This partly reflected the fact that share prices had risen very fast in the first half of the year—by around 45 per cent in Britain—and as a result had reached unsustainable levels. The world-wide collapse of share prices also reflected general unease about the imbalance in the world economy resulting from the continuing large budget and trade deficits in the United States. Initially it was feared that the crash would lead to a recession, or at least a sharp fall in growth, in Britain. However, by the beginning of 1988 it seemed that the volatility of share prices in 1987 might not have any marked effect upon the rest of the economy.

The 1988 Budget.

Most attention in the March Budget was focused on changes in income tax. The basic rate of tax was cut from 27 per cent to 25 per cent, and the higher rates on relatively high incomes were slashed from a range of from 40 to 60 per cent to a new single rate of 40 per cent. Also, the main tax allowances were raised by roughly double the amount needed to compensate for inflation over the previous year.

The cut in the basic rate of tax had been widely anticipated before the Budget, and fulfilled a long-standing commitment by the Chancellor, who made a new commitment to reduce the standard rate further, to 20 per cent, as soon as possible. However, it was the reduction in the higher rates of tax which attracted the most attention. Mr. Lawson's main argument was that Britain's previous top rate of 60 per cent was higher than in many competing countries, that cuts were needed to restore comparability, and that high tax rates destroyed incentives, initiative and enterprise. Critics argued that the cuts in top rates were unfair, since they would bring disproportionate benefits to people already earning very high incomes. Another objection was the lack of evidence that cuts in top rates (or indeed in income tax rates generally) would make much difference to incentives and enterprise. Various studies by economists suggest that tax cuts tend to have little overall effect on work effort: some people work harder because of the increased earnings opportunities, but others work less hard because when taxes are cut they can still earn as much as before with less work. The evidence suggests that in many circumstances these two opposing effects approximately cancel one another out. A third objection was that the cuts had gone further than needed to attain comparability with other countries: the new rates treated high income earners in Britain more generously than in most comparable countries.

The Chancellor sought to end "tax penalties on marriage" whereby couples could find their tax bill higher if they were married than if they lived together as two single people. The main item here was his decision to limit tax relief on mortgages for house purchase to one set of reliefs per property, thus ending the system in which two or more single people could each claim tax relief towards the joint purchase of a house, whilst a married couple could claim only once.

One area in which taxation was sharply increased concerned company cars. The amounts employees provided with a company car would have to pay in tax were doubled, and there was a suggestion of further rises in future years. The Chancellor's argument was that this would more fairly reflect the benefit provided by the use of a company car. In addition, he argued that when tax rates in general were being reduced, the case for paying employees in kind rather than in cash became weaker, and should not be encouraged by the tax system.

The most noteworthy feature of the Chancellor's general policy stance was the projection of a public sector *surplus* of £3 billion for 1988–89. This matched the eventual surplus of just over £3 billion for 1987–88. These surpluses attracted much attention because the public sector had previously run a deficit in almost every year since the early 1950s. The main reason for the move into a sizeable surplus was the very rapid rate of economic growth during 1987: the growth of incomes boosted the government's tax revenues. A second, and partly associated, reason was the fall in unemployment during 1987, which reduced public spending on unemployment and other benefits. This surplus for 1987–88 was also somewhat misleading: as mentioned earlier, official measures of the public sector deficit or surplus count receipts from privatisation sales as negative public spending, whereas in reality they are clearly methods of financing spending. Allowing for this altered the surplus for 1987–88 to a deficit equal to approximately 0·5 per cent of national income. Even with this alteration, however, it was clear that the overall fiscal position was stronger than for many years.

Economic Boom, 1988.

The public disagreement between Mr. Lawson and Mrs. Thatcher early in 1988 revealed the Government's policy dilemma (*see* **G51**). When the markets started to push up the value of the pound against the West German mark, Mr. Lawson wanted to intervene to prevent a rise beyond his target, whilst Mrs. Thatcher appeared to rule this out when she said that it was impossible for any government to "buck the market". Although this argument was superficially about a technical aspect of policy, underlying it was a more important disagreement about the appropriate policy objectives for the third Thatcher government. Rises in the value of the pound against the mark and other currencies help to reduce the rate of domestic inflation because they reduce the cost of imported

goods. By opposing attempts to limit the rise in the pound, therefore, Mrs. Thatcher was signalling a continued commitment to her original 1979 policy priority of securing continued reductions in inflation towards the eventual target of stable prices. However, higher exchange rates also tend to reduce domestic economic growth because they reduce the profitability of exports and of domestically-produced import substitutes. By opposing a rise in the exchange rate, therefore, Mr. Lawson was signalling a commitment to a continuation of the relatively rapid rate of economic growth.

The majority of economists tended to favour the Chancellor's view, on the grounds that there were few economic arguments for expecting the economy to benefit significantly from a further reduction of inflation below its current rate of around 4 per cent. On the other hand, many economists were also worried about signs of "overheating" in the economy. Three symptoms were shortages of many types of labour, rapid rises in house prices, and a growing current account balance of payments deficit. Consequently, even some economists who saw little advantage in further reductions in inflation urged the Chancellor to consider some tightening of his policy stance if such symptoms showed any signs of worsening.

In a sense this represented a partial return to a Keynesian attitude to policy making, with the emphasis on adjusting policy instruments according to short term shifts in the balance of aggregate demand and supply. The fact that the Chancellor seemed to be thinking partly in these terms indicated the extent to which the government had moved away from its initial strict adherence to medium term targets, and the primacy of low inflation as a policy objective.

Fears of economic overheating turned out to be fully justified as 1988 proceeded, as the various symptoms rapidly became unmistakeable. The most worrying of these was a huge deficit on the current account of the balance of payments. Over the year as a whole the deficit amounted to £14·5 billion. Another symptom was a sharp rise in the inflation rate, from around 4 per cent at the start of the year to 6·5 per cent by the end. A third (and more welcome) symptom was a continued rapid fall in unemployment, by approximately 530,000 during the year.

The main source of overheating was a sharp rise in both consumption and investment demand. During the year consumption increased by 6·5 per cent and investment by around 12 per cent. The rapid rise in investment was one reason why the Chancellor appeared, for much of the year, to be relatively unconcerned about the balance of payments deficit. He argued that private companies were optimistic about the future, and that they were therefore seeking to expand their productive capacity; hence much of the rapid rise in demand represented the potential for further economic growth in the future, and some of the balance of trade deficit could be attributed to companies importing stocks, equipment, and other essential inputs to sustain future growth.

However, Mr. Lawson's critics pointed to the rapid rise in consumer demand as evidence that the spending spree was getting out of hand, arguing that such rapid rises in consumption were unsustainable, and that the Chancellor's overall fiscal and monetary stance was too expansionary. They pointed to the cuts in taxes in the 1988 Budget, to cuts in interest rates during late 1987 and early 1988, and to a growth of "narrow" money well above its target range (and a still more rapid rise in broader definitions of money). The combination of all these policies, the critics argued, was fuelling a rapid consumer boom, which was further exacerbated by the increasingly easy availability of credit to finance almost every component of consumer expenditure.

By the summer the evidence of an unsustainable consumer boom was becoming undeniable, and the Chancellor was forced to alter course. His response was a series of increases in interest rates: in the second half of the year these gradually rose from around 8 per cent to over 13 per cent. The main idea was that this would raise the cost of interest payments for people with mortgages for house purchase. This would reduce the amount of income they had available for other purchases, and so would slow down the growth of consumer demand. Initially the rises in interest rates appeared to be having little effect, but by the end of the year there was some evidence of a slowdown.

In retrospect it seems clear that some policy misjudgments occurred during 1987 and 1988, leading to too rapid an upswing. In part this probably represented a pessimistic view about the effects of the stock market crash of October 1987. At the time many commentators had predicted that this would lead to a large fall in demand, reflecting the fall in the value of share holdings. However, with the benefit of hindsight the crash did little more than correct the very large rise in share prices over the previous year, thus restoring share prices towards a longer run trend level. Hence in attempting to correct for the feared effects of the crash, especially with interest rate cuts, the Government probably over-reacted.

The unexpectedly rapid growth of demand caused national output also to rise very rapidly, by some 4·5 per cent. This in turn produced a remarkable fiscal outcome, with a huge surplus of tax revenue over public spending. The surplus totalled some £14 billion in the 1988–89 tax year, and represented a dramatic change from the experience of virtually the whole of the post-war period.

The 1989 Budget.

However, this large budget surplus presented Mr. Lawson with a problem as he planned his 1989 Budget. On the one hand, he had not planned to accumulate such a large surplus, and since the Government remained committed to lower taxes as a policy aim, he was tempted to reduce the surplus by cutting income tax rates and raising tax allowances. On the other hand, the problems of overheating, and the Government's equally strong commitment to preventing a rise in inflation, made him reluctant to raise taxes. In the event he decided to make minimal changes in taxes, and instead to devote most of the surplus to repaying part of the accumulated National Debt. (For this reason the budget surplus rapidly became known as the *public sector debt repayment* (PSDR), replacing the earlier and more familiar acronym PSBR.)

In a sense the Chancellor was embarrassed by the large PSDR. Because of problems of overheating he felt unable to use it for the tax cuts which, in other circumstances, he would have favoured. Some of his critics argued that this justified their earlier criticisms of the tax cuts in the 1988 Budget. They had argued then that this would fuel a consumer boom, met mainly by imports, and had instead advocated increased public spending on the infrastructure and on education, health, and training: compared with tax cuts, such spending increases would have improved the efficiency of the economy whilst avoiding a sharp rise in imports.

Mr. Lawson emphasised that the Government had no plans to continue to make large repayments of debt in future years. At the end of 1988 the total value of the National Debt stood at £171 billion, equal to 38 per cent of national income. With the planned repayment during the year these figures would fall, by the end of the financial year, to £157 billion, 32 per cent of national income—a lower proportion than at any time since the first world war. The Chancellor's plans for the next five years involved continued repayments, but on a steadily smaller scale, moving eventually to his aim of a balanced budget.

The other main projections in the Budget foreshadowed slower economic growth, and a continued commitment to counter-inflationary pressures. Growth was expected to be around 2·5 per cent during 1989—little more than half the rate during 1988—and inflation was expected to peak at around 8 per cent, but then to fall back to 5·5 per cent by the year end (though many other forecasters thought that this was too optimistic). A target range of 1 to 5 per cent was set for M0, the same as in the previous year. The current account of the balance of payments was expected to remain in deficit during 1989 at approximately the same level as in 1988, but then to improve in 1990: this reflected mainly the prediction of a sharp fall in imports as growth slowed down.

Overall, the Chancellor's aim in the Budget was clearly to seek to restore the credibility of his commitment to resist inflationary pressures. To this end he emphasised that he would not hesitate to raise interest rates further if necessary.

The Chancellor raised the main income tax allowances in line with the rise in prices over the past year, but made no changes in income tax rates. However, there were significant changes in the system of National Insurance payments (which for most practical purposes represent an additional component of income tax). Previously the National Insurance system had been organised in a way which provided disincentives for low paid individuals to seek better paid jobs. Under the old system, anyone earning less than £75 per week paid no National Insurance, but if his income rose above £75 he then had to make payments of 5 per cent of his *entire* earnings, not just on the excess. A similar disincentive existed at £115, above which the rate rose to 9 per cent on all earnings. This system meant that many low-paid workers found themselves worse off if they crossed over one of the thresholds. The new system proposed that people earning less than £43 per week would pay nothing, whilst above £43 they would pay at a rate of 2 per cent on the first £43 and 9 per cent on the rest (up to a maximum of £325). Thus the disincentive of crossing a threshold was significantly reduced.

This change was generally welcomed, as was another proposal: the abolition of the "earnings rule" for pensioners. This had penalised people beyond retirement age who wished to continue working, by reducing the pension by a proportion of their earnings. One of the Chancellor's motives in abolishing this system was probably the growing perception that demographic changes, involving a declining number of school leavers, threatened many parts of industry with labour shortages. One way of offsetting this would be to encourage older workers to continue in employment, perhaps on a part time basis.

During the rest of 1989, the economic situation deteriorated sharply. Inflation continued to edge inexorably upwards, reaching approximately 7 per cent by the year-end. The current account deficit also mounted alarmingly. In response to these trends the Government increased interest rates in a series of steps. By the year-end interest rates were at record levels, being in the range 15 to 20 per cent, depending on the type of borrowing. The large gap between this level of interest rates and the inflation rate meant that real interest rates were also at a record high level. The Government argued that this was the only way to reduce the pressure of demand, which in turn was required if inflation and the current account deficit were to be reduced. Some critics said that a preferable alternative would be to reverse some of the income tax cuts in the 1988 Budget. However, the Government's ideological position meant that it was not prepared to consider increases in income tax.

By the end of the year, therefore, the government was under considerable pressure, both economically and politically. The main reason for its difficulties stemmed from mistakes and misjudgements in policy-making over the period 1986–1988. Also, there seemed to be some evidence that the Government's overall policy objectives had lost clarity. These issues are described in more detail in **Part II**.

Evaluating the 1980s.

These immediate difficulties obviously detracted from the Government's overall economic record. However, at the end of a decade throughout which Conservative governments under Mrs. Thatcher had been in power, it was possible to form some longer term judgements about the performance of the economy over the decade, and by inference about the policies pursued by the Government. At one extreme, leading members of the Government repeatedly asserted that they had achieved an "economic miracle". At the other extreme, some of their critics in the Labour party described the 1980s in Britain as "the decade which the locusts ate".

One way of assessing economic performance is by comparisons with other similar economies. The accompanying tables give details of some important aspects of economic performance in Britain and various other industrialised economies. In terms of productivity growth, Britain's performance was better than in the mid and late 1970s, but less good than during the late 1960s and early 1970s. There was no clear pattern of either improvement or worsening in comparison with the record of other industrialised countries.

At first sight the British record on inflation appears to be more clear cut. Over the period from 1979 to 1988 Britain achieved by far the largest

PRODUCTIVITY GROWTH PER EMPLOYEE
(% per year)

	1966–73	1973–79	1979–83	1983–88
Britain	3·2	1·2	2·1	2·0
Other EEC	4·2	2·2	1·2	2·2
USA	1·2	0·0	0·2	1·3
Japan	7·9	2·9	2·4	3·4
Sweden	2·8	0·5	0·9	1·9
OECD average	3·5	1·5	1·3	1·9

UNEMPLOYMENT AND INFLATION RATES,
1979 AND 1988

	Unemployment		Inflation	
	1979	1988	1979	1988
Britain	4·7	8·5	13·2	5·6
Other EEC	4·7	8·7	8·9	3·1
USA	5·8	5·6	8·8	3·3
Japan	2·1	2·5	1·5	1·8
Sweden	2·1	1·7	8·3	5·8
OECD average	5·4	7·5	8·3	3·5

reduction in inflation of any of the major industrialised economies. On the other hand, there
was also more room for improvement, since Britain
started from a much higher initial level of inflation;
and by 1988 British inflation was still nearly the
highest in the industrial world. Moreover, the table
conceals the fact that by 1988 Britain's inflation
was worsening.

The British record on unemployment over the
period was poor. The large rise in unemployment
was matched by other EEC countries but was a
good deal bigger than in the rest of the industrialised
world. On the other hand, the pattern here is the
reverse of that for inflation: the table conceals the
fact that British unemployment trends were improving, relative to other industrialised countries, at the
end of the period.

Overall, therefore, trends in productivity, growth,
inflation, and unemployment—often viewed as the
major indicators of economic success—show a
mixed picture. They do not provide support for
extreme views about either a miraculous or a
disastrous decade.

Economic Inequality.

A feature of the 1980s which many saw as
unsatisfactory was a large increase in economic
inequality. This had several causes. One was a
widening in the dispersal of pre-tax earnings.
Another was disproportionate cuts in the rates of
tax levied on high incomes, particularly a a result of
the tax changes made in the 1988 Budget. The
combined effect of these two trends was that those
in the top 10 per cent of income earners saw their
real after tax earnings rise, on average, by 73 per
cent from 1979 to 1988, whilst for those in the
bottom 10 per cent the average rise was only 13 per
cent. A third source of rising inequality was the
growth in people unable to earn at all, including the
long term unemployed and single parents unable to
work because of family responsibilities. People in
these categories, and some others including those
retired people who were without occupational
pensions or other income sources, and who were
therefore dependent on the state pension, saw their
incomes fall compared with those in regular
employment. This partly reflected the Government's decision to index state benefits to retail
prices rather than to average earnings.

All these changes, and others affecting capital
and inheritance taxes, had the effect of widening
inequality during the 1980s, after several decades
during which it had narrowed. Since there is little
reason, or evidence, to suggest that greater inequality improves economic efficiency, many people
argued that these changes should be seen as an
unfavourable aspect of economic performance
during the decade.

Industrial Relations and Working Practices.

An area in which the Government claimed great

success during the 1980s was improved labour
relations. Compared with the 1960s and 1970s, the
1980s saw a large reduction in the amount of
industrial conflict, measured either in terms of the
total numbers of strikes or in terms of days lost
through strikes. The Government argued that this
was mainly the result of its various pieces of
legislation during the 1980s, aimed at imposing
clearer legal restraints on unions' ability to take
strike action.

The Government also argued that a new, more
constructive, spirit in management-employee relationships had fostered productivity gains. The
figures for productivity growth in the table above
are averages for the whole economy, and conceal a
significantly better performance in some parts of
the manufacturing sector. It was this improvement
in industrial efficiency which Government supporters often claimed as its most significant
achievement. The sources of this improvement were
not wholly clear, but it certainly did not reflect
investment in either productive equipment or
research and development—the record on both of
these was poor throughout the decade. Many
commentators argued that the main source was
changes in working practices, themselves the result
partly of greater determination by management to
overcome union resistance to change, and partly a
forced response to the very deep recession of the
early 1980s—when many companies were faced
with a stark choice between improved efficiency or
bankruptcy. Some research seemed to support this
view: the biggest gains in productivity were often
found in companies which had faced the greatest
pressure for change, and which were also heavily
unionised.

At the same time, it was not clear to what extent
the Government's legislation on union activity and
strike behaviour had established a *permanent*
change in industrial relations. For one thing, the
reduction in strike activity during the 1980s was
matched in nearly all other countries. Indeed,
Britain's record in relation to other countries was
not discernibly better in the 1980s than in the
1970s. Another reason for doubt was the upsurge in
strikes during 1988 and 1989 as the level of
unemployment fell sharply, and many labour
markets experienced significant labour shortages.
In some of these disputes, it seemed that the unions
were actually strengthened by the effects of the
Government's legislation, which required them to
obtain majority approval for strike action in ballots
of their members. Having obtained a majority,
their bargaining power with employers, and also
their degree of public support, appeared to be
enhanced. Hence it was far from clear that the
Government's industrial relations legislation,
mainly passed during the recession of the early
1980s, would continue to work effectively in
conditions of lower unemployment.

The Supply Side.

Another important feature of the economy during
the decade was the emphasis put on the *supply
side*. This contrasted with earlier decades during
which the influence of Keynesian ideas had led to
emphasis on policies to manipulate aggregate
demand in order to regulate economic activity. In
the 1980s demand management was mainly seen
instead as subordinate to the aim of controlling
inflation, and the Thatcher Governments argued
that the key to improved economic performance lay
in policies to improve the supply side. Their main
methods were cuts in direct taxes, reform of the
trade unions, and privatisation and deregulation.

It was a measure of the extent to which economic
and political thinking changed during the course of

the decade that most of the Government's critics increasingly came to accept the new emphasis on the supply side. Discussion instead began to focus upon the appropriate supply side policies. Many critics argued that the Government's policies were at best only marginally relevant to the most important supply side weaknesses in the British economy, which had to do with low levels of educational and training attainments. A series of detailed studies showed that, in a variety of industrial and service sectors, British labour productivity levels were very low in comparison with those in other countries, especially West Germany, France, and Japan. These large differences in productivity levels continued to show up even where employees were using similar types of productive equipment in both countries. The implication seemed to be that British employees' education and training were inferior, so preventing them from operating as effectively as their foreign counterparts—in the language of economics, Britain's *human capital* was inadequate. Related studies suggested reasons, by showing persistently lower educational achievements by British school-children compared with children in other countries, persistently lower participation rates in higher education, and persistently lower investment in training and retraining.

In response to these findings, the Government could argue that it was taking a variety of actions. Its 1988 Education Act had introduced a national curriculum, with attainment targets designed to ensure that all children reached and were assessed on clearly identified educational target levels. It was aiming for a large increase in the number of students in higher education by the end of the century. In the training field, it had introduced the Youth Training Scheme and similar initiatives.

The critics accepted the principles behind many of these initiatives, but questioned the details. It was argued that the introduction of the national curriculum risked being undermined by a growing crisis of teacher shortages. This appeared to be mainly the result of uncompetitively low salaries for teachers. Critics argued that a Government which proclaimed its belief in market forces was refusing to let them operate in determining teachers' pay. Somewhat similar problems also threatened the aim of expanding higher education. As for industrial training, critics argued that greater Government intervention, perhaps through tax incentives, was needed to induce private employers to take it more seriously and invest more in it.

The Shifting Debate.

The area of debate about economic policy had thus shifted drastically over the decade. What was certain, however, was that the British economy still had some deep-seated problems, especially relating to the quality of its human capital resources. There were doubts among some of the critics that these problems could be solved by the Thatcher Government, since their solution seemed to require significant increases in public spending, something to which the Government remained ideologically opposed. Similar problems were becoming evident in parts of Britain's transport system. For example, increasing congestion in London, and to a lesser extent in other major cities, threatened to become a significant obstacle to continued economic growth in these centres. Similarly, British business began to perceive the need for much improved transport links, especially high speed rail links, with continental Europe in the approach to the Single European Market of 1992. Again, however, alleviating congestion and improving rail networks seemed to require additional public spending. Some critics pointed out that Britain provided less public investment in transport infrastructure than its major trading partners in the European Community.

Hence, after a decade during which Mrs. Thatcher's Governments had consistently given priority to attempting to reduce levels of public spending in the economy, there remained serious arguments about the balance of public and private spending, and about the extent to which the country's supply side problems could be met without significant public sector intervention.

The 1990 Budget.

The first Budget of the new decade was prepared in the context of the most unfavourable economic circumstances since the 1981 Budget. With inflation rising, interest rates at record levels in both real and nominal terms, the current account of the balance of payments in a large deficit, and output growth slowing sufficiently to threaten a rise in unemployment, the new Chancellor, John Major, was faced with a series of awkward choices. On the one hand, he wanted to avoid deflating the economy too heavily, which would risk plunging it into a deep recession. On the other hand, he also needed to be sufficiently tough to reassure financial markets about his determination to lower inflation and cut the current account deficit. This need for toughness also provided a paradox, however. Financial markets were starting to take seriously the chance that the Government would lose the next General Election, and there was some suggestion that an unduly tough Budget would also alarm the markets by increasing the Government's unpopularity with voters, and so making its chances of defeat higher. This in turn might cause the exchange rate to fall and so put upward pressure on interest rates. Hence the Chancellor found himself in the unfortunate position of fearing that either too soft or too tough a budget might upset the financial markets.

Faced with these awkward conflicting pressures, the Chancellor opted for a cautious Budget in terms of its predicted effect on the overall economy, though it also contained some important changes in the structure of taxation. The predicted net effect of the various tax changes was an increase in tax revenue of some £430 million in the tax year 1990–91, and just under £1 billion in the following year. This increase, small in proportion to the Government's overall levels of tax revenue, meant that its fiscal stance was set to remain broadly unchanged compared with the previous year. Hence the Government rejected the possibility of significantly tightening its fiscal policy, for example by an increase in income tax rates, as part of its policy to reduce the inflation rate and the current account balance of payments deficit. Instead the Government remained committed to monetary policy as its main instrument for these purposes. It set a target for growth in M0—"narrow money"—during 1990–91 of 5 per cent. However, with inflation running at between 8 and 9 per cent, and predicted to rise towards 10 per cent in the coming months, a target for M0 of only 5 per cent implied a restrictive monetary stance, and so signalled the Government's determination to maintain high interest rates until inflation started to fall.

The size of the budget surplus for 1989–90 was expected to be around £7 billion. This was only about half of the level which had been forecast at the time of the 1989 Budget. The main sources of this large reduction were lower than expected revenue from privatisation, extra spending by local authorities, and the effect of the growth of personal pension plans: individuals choosing to opt out of corporate pension schemes and instead establish their own individual pension plans were entitled to rebates on National Insurance payments, thus reducing the Government's tax revenue in the short run. The Chancellor announced that the target surplus for the coming year would also be £7 billion. The budget surplus for 1989–90, like that for 1988–89, was used to repay part of the National Debt.

The Details.

Income tax rates were unchanged in the Budget, and the main personal tax allowances were raised in line with inflation, though the starting point behind which higher rate tax was paid remained unchanged. The main excise duties were also raised broadly in line with inflation, apart from vehicle excise duty which remained unchanged for the fifth consecutive year. Other changes related to income tax included a further sharp rise, by 20 per cent, in the tax on company cars. This continued the policy of seeking to phase out incentives for firms to pay employees in kind rather than in money.

This last principle was, however, ignored in the decision to introduce income tax relief to parents whose employers provided them with subsidised nursery care for their children. This decision, which had been widely anticipated before the Budget, represented the government's response to the growing concern by many employers about the difficulty of attracting and retaining female employees. This concern had been much intensified by demographic changes. The number of school leavers had started to fall sharply, and was expected to remain at a much lower level than hitherto for at least the next five years. Many employers who had traditionally recruited heavily amongst school leavers, such as the commercial banks and the National Health Service, perceived that this would cause them major difficulties unless they could find an alternative source of recruitment. Recruiting and retaining married women with children was one possibility, and such employers had therefore started to put pressure on the Government to use the tax system so as to help with the child care costs which this would involve.

Perhaps the most important change in the structure of taxation was the move to fully independent taxation for married couples. This change was introduced primarily because the previous system was generally viewed as inappropriate to modern circumstances in which the majority of wives were in either full time or part time employment, with their own independent incomes. However, by making it easier for married couples to reduce their overall tax liabilities by rearranging their ownership of interest producing assets, the scheme was expected to reduce total tax revenue, and hence implied some loosening of the fiscal stance.

Another tax change was the abolition of composite rate tax (CRT). Under the CRT scheme, banks and building societies deducted tax at a rate of 22 per cent from all interest payments to their depositors, regardless of whether or not individual depositors were liable for tax. This was widely seen as unfair, particularly to people such as pensioners who in many cases had incomes too low to pay tax, but nonetheless had CRT deducted from any interest paid on their savings.

The abolition of CRT was also linked to the introduction of independent taxation for married couples. Under independent taxation, wives without a job would still have a tax allowance, and would thus be entitled to receive interest income up to the value of the allowance without incurring any tax liability. Hence married couples in which the wife had no job would benefit by transferring interest bearing assets into the wife's name, which would allow them to avoid paying tax on the resulting income.

The Chancellor introduced another new scheme of tax-exempt special savings accounts (which he labelled TESSA). Under this scheme, each adult would be entitled to one TESSA at a bank or building society, and the interest income paid on savings in the TESSA would be tax-free provided that the capital remained untouched for a five-year period. Up to £9,000 could be paid into such an account over the five-year period.

The Chancellor had two main objectives in introducing this scheme. One was to extend the principle of the Personal Equity Plans (PEPs) which the Government had introduced in 1987. PEPs provided a scheme for investment in equity shares or unit trusts which was free of capital gains tax: a similar scheme was now available for people who preferred to save in a building society or similar form of account rather than by buying shares or unit trusts. The second objective was to try to encourage personal saving. One of the major problems which emerged during the 1980s was a marked decline in the personal savings ratio—the proportion of their incomes which private individuals save. Simultaneously there was an increase in the average amount of borrowing. The net effect was that the private sector moved into a position in which, in aggregate, it was spending in excess of its income. This private sector deficit, in turn, was the source of the current account balance of payments deficit, and to offset its effects the Government was forced to continue to run a large public sector surplus. By seeking to encourage more saving, the Chancellor hoped to reduce the extent of the private sector deficit. However, critics argued that his policy might not have this result. Tax incentives for particular types of asset, they argued, might cause a rearrangement of financial assets—towards the new TESSA scheme—rather than a significant net increase in saving.

The main test for the Budget was the reaction of world financial markets. The markets were looking for reassurance that the Government was seriously committed to cutting the inflation rate and the current account deficit. Early signs suggested that judgement was being reserved. The main thrust of government policy was not via the Budget but via high interest rates. One significant worry was the existence of pressures in the world economy for further increases in interest rates, especially in Japan and in West Germany—the latter mainly in response to the effects of the coming reunification with East Germany—which would almost certainly force another rise in British interest rates.

Prospects for Economic Growth.

The post-war economy has seen boom-periods and recessions, but generally speaking, until the mid 1980's the UK has tended to lag behind most other industrial countries in terms of economic growth (*see* **G14**). During this period various governments have adopted policies aimed at stimulating economic growth. Prior to Mrs Thatcher's Conservative government, which came to power in 1979, most of these measures were based on demand management policies. An early example of such policies was the National Plan introduced by the Labour government in 1965. The plan aimed for a growth rate of 4 per cent per annum but was abandoned after only a year when the economy was faced with a balance of payments crisis. Most policies aimed at expanding growth through stimulating demand have failed because of unforeseen supply-side bottlenecks. The Conservative government under Mrs. Thatcher has exhibited a major reversal in political judgement by persuading voters to reward government for long-term supply-side economic policies, although, the evidence that the UK has undergone a "supply-side" revolution under Mrs. Thatcher's stewardship is mixed.

(i) Pressures on the Industrial Sector.

In common with other industrialised economies, the UK has seen a major shift in the structure or composition of the economy. This involved a significant reduction in the productive base of the economy, specifically the manufacturing sector, and a greater dependence on the service sector. This process is known as de-industrialisation. To illustrate the shift it is useful to look at the structure of the labour force. Between 1960 and 1989 the total number of persons employed in the UK remained fairly constant. Within this total, however, employment in manufacturing fell by 38% whilst in the service sector it increased by 51%. This larger non-industrial sector imposes extra demands on industrial production. Capital goods for investment in services have to be provided from the output of the industrial sector, whilst industrial production is also needed for consumers employed in the services and elsewhere. Thus less is left over for investment in industry itself and for industrial exports. This has meant an inadequate growth of industrial capacity. Consequently when governments have attempted to stimulate the economy, bottlenecks quickly develop and imports of consumer goods increase rapidly. The result is balance of payments difficulties, which are only partially alleviated by increasing exports of services like insurance, and force the government into taking deflationary action. This vicious circle could only be broken by an upsurge in industrial investment, which until the last few years was prevented by declining profitability.

Some commentators have argued that the problem was a direct result of the growth in public sector employment in the 1960s and 1970s. This had to be paid for either by workers or private employers, and trade unions made sure that it was the employers; if, for example, income tax was raised, this was passed on in successful wage demands. The result was declining profitability. This analysis is at best speculative. It is not, for example, at all evident that public sector employment has grown nearly as rapidly as implied. In certain activities such as local government there was a very rapid growth, but overall the ratio of public sector to total employment increased only modestly—from 23·9 per cent in 1961 to 27·2 per cent in 1974. Similarly over the same period public sector spending on goods and services increased only from 21·5 per cent to 26·8 per cent of gross domestic product. It was argued that such figures understated the true change: the spending figures are in constant prices; in current money terms the change was more striking because of the *relative price effect*, *i.e.*, items like teachers' and civil servants' salaries rising faster than the general price level. The figures also exclude transfers from people who produce to those who do not, such as pensioners, though this may be justifiable since such *transfer payments* do not represent final claims on resources by the public sector. It was argued that the claim of the public sector on output which could be sold increased by almost 50 per cent between 1961 and 1974 thus reducing the resources available for industrial investment. The present Conservative government, subscribing to this view, has been committed to reducing the share of public expenditure in GDP, believing that this is necessary to reduce taxes on both persons and companies. This, they believe, would restore work and profit incentives, although there is scant evidence in support of this view. Since 1979 the share of public expenditure has in fact fallen only slightly mainly because of much greater demands on the social security system. If the arguments mentioned above gain force, then it is possible that the whole method of providing health care, education etc. will be called into question. This would be particularly sad if, as some of the points made above suggest, it is based on fallacious economic reasoning.

This is only one school of thought among those economists who are concerned that Britain is becoming *de-industrialised*. Another group of economists, also concerned with de-industrialisation, rejects the argument that it is the consequence of the expansion of the public sector. They stress the inability of British industry to maintain its share of world trade in manufactures, a share which fell from almost 13 per cent in the early 1970s, to about 8 per cent in 1989. The forces causing this failure cannot be arrested by a once-and-for-all devaluation. On the demand side the conditions for an expansion of British exports are unfavourable; an important reason for this being that Britain tends to specialise in products for which demand tends to rise relatively slowly in response to increases in the standard of living. On the supply side, it is argued, there is a vicious circle of declining market share, declining profits and investment and declining competitive power. Some members of this group then point to the need for demand expansion, in order to stimulate output growth, and ultimately, higher productivity growth, which is the key to international competitiveness. The problem in Britain, though, appears to be in stimulating supply in an effective manner. Yet other economists have argued that Britain's industrial structure, similar as it is to that of Germany, cannot account for our problems. Rather it is that Britain has narrowed the technological gap between herself and the US—for a long time the technical leader—more slowly than have her major competitors, thus failing to exploit the opportunities for unusually rapid growth. Recently particular stress has been put on Britain's supply-side faults leading to non-price competitiveness. Particularly emphasised are flaws in education and training at all levels—often dubbed as low quality-low skill equilibrium.

Whatever disagreement exists about causes, there is basic agreement that Britain does have an industrial problem. Not least is the question of which new activities—be they in industry and services—will replace those activities in which we were once strong but no longer are. A recent House of Lords Select Committee documented the decline of manufacturing, accelerated as it was by the general recession after 1979. To many it was too messianic in tone, both in regard to its view of the inevitability of manufacturing's demise and the lack of new activities to take its place. Be that as it may, it is worrying that Britain still lags in international competitiveness.

(ii) The National Enterprise Board.

In 1975 the Labour Government introduced an *Industry Act*. Underlying this Act was the feeling that private enterprise, on its own, had not done enough to stimulate a high rate of growth. The Act aimed to remedy this by setting up the *National Enterprise Board*. Its functions were to assist the establishment, development or maintenance of any industrial enterprise or industry, to extend public ownership into profitable areas of manufacturing, to promote industrial democracy in undertakings controlled by it, and to hold and manage the securities of any other property in public ownership. The Board's borrowing capability was very modest in relation to the market value of the share capital of major British firms. Funds for aid could also be dispensed by the Board. Both the Minister for Industry and the Treasury had a responsibility to ensure that the Board earned an "adequate" return on capital employed.

Critics argued both that the Act was doctrinaire socialism and that it was not proved that such state intervention would have more favourable effects than the workings of free private enterprise.

Even before the NEB was effectively operational, state acquisitions in the private sector had proceeded apace. Normally the Government had provided help to ailing companies on condition of taking a shareholding, under the provisions of the Conservatives' 1972 Industry Act. State holdings in eight companies were handed over to the NEB at its inception. These companies were British Leyland, Rolls-Royce, Cambridge Instruments, Ferranti, Herbert, Brown-Boveri-Kent, Dunford and Elliott, and ICL. The NEB acquired shareholdings in another twenty-eight companies by early 1978.

When the Conservatives won the 1979 General Election there was some expectation that the National Enterprise Board would be abolished. Though this did not happen immediately, it soon became plain that the new Government did not intend to allow the Board any role other than that of overseeing a limited number of companies in need of temporary assistance. Subsequently the NEB was merged with the National Research and Development Corporation to form the British Technology Group. BTG's aims are noticeably different from those of the NEB. The aim of BTG is, primarily, to promote the development of new technology, often from public sector institutions such as polytechnics and universities, into commercial products. In order to assist the transfer of technology BTG can also provide finance, either through equity or project finance. Currently, BTG has a portfolio of 6,788 British patents and patent applications, 537 licencees in Britain and overseas, 495 development projects at universities and other public institutions, and 170 projects with industrial companies. 86 per cent of BTG's income is provided by its own licensing activities.

(iii) Privatisation.

Soon after taking office, the new Conservative Government announced its intention to sell off a portion of official holdings in several sectors—British Airways, British Aerospace, shipbuilding, freight and British Petroleum. The Government believes that reform of the nationalised industries is a key element in providing the framework for economic recovery, arguing that exposure to market forces through privatisation and competition is the best way to improve industrial performance. Since 1979, 19 state-owned companies have been privatised, yielding the Government some £23·0 billion in revenues. Companies that have been privatised include British Gas, British Telecom, British Steel Corporation, Cable and Wireless, the National Freight Consortium, Amersham International, The Rover Group, Jaguar, Enterprise Oil, Britoil, Associated British Ports, Rolls-Royce, Royal Ordnance, BAA, nearly all the National Bus Company subsidiaries the British Shipbuilders' warship-building yards and most recently the regional water and sewage companies in England and Wales. Legislation, under the Electricity Act 1989, provides for the privatisation of the electricity supply industry in Great Britain. The Central Electricity Generating Board (CEGB), formerly responsible for the generation and distribution of electricity throughout Great Britain has been split into three companies: Power Gen which now owns 30 per cent of all non-nuclear electricity generation, National Power, comprising the remainder of the CEGB's generating capacity, and a national grid company owned by the 12 existing area electricity boards.

One major effect of the privatisation program has been an increase in share ownership. In 1979 only 7 per cent of the population were shareholders; by early 1989 this had increased to over 20 per cent. Although there has also been a fashion for privatisation abroad, the process has been more intense in Britain than in any other country. Going alongside this programme, were programmes of "liberalisation" and of "franchising". By the former is meant the policy of allowing and encouraging competition in previously uncompetitive or regulated markets—for example, telecommunications and road passenger transport. By the latter is meant the process by which state establishments (e.g. hospitals) "put out" certain functions, which had previously been performed "in-house", to private companies (e.g. catering). This spread of sub-contracting, however, extends far beyond publicly provided activities.

(iv) An Approach to Industrial Strategy.

In 1975 a White Paper, entitled *An Approach to Industrial Strategy*, set out the Government's general views on planning for growth. The strategy was based on the fact that despite Britain's overall poor performance, some sectors had done very well. There was therefore a need to identify specific problems which had held back particular industries as well as a need to identify general problems. Some 40 sectoral working parties were established and were composed of representatives of management, workers and the Government. Their task was to analyse their own industry in detail and to agree a programme of action designed to improve competitive performance, and to make Britain a high-output, high-wage economy. Specifically they were asked to consider the following: how to get more out of existing investment and manpower in order to improve productivity; how to increase the level and quality of investment; how to improve non-price competitiveness; how to ensure that their sectors concentrate on the "correct" export markets; how to provide a sufficient supply of skilled workers. In 1978 the working parties presented their first reports. They were full of suggestions, particularly on how to improve export performance. The planning provisions of the 1975 Industry Act were abandoned by the Conservative Government, but the NEDC Sector Working Parties continue to operate, though they were subsequently re-titled Economic Development Councils. It is difficult to quantify their precise effects upon sectoral performance.

One area where the 1975 Industry Act had practical consequences was in the introduction of schemes of financial assistance to industry. By mid-1978 these schemes had run their course in six sectors and were working in eight others (including paper and board, electronic components, wool textiles, non-ferrous foundries, instrumentation and automation, and footwear). Other sectors have received funds since then. The assistance has been directed towards increases in productivity (e.g. by re-equipment), or to increases in product relevance to export markets, to improving non-price competitiveness and to improving marketing. In addition there is a selective investment scheme (before that the accelerated projects scheme) to provide funds for particular projects, there is an export market entry guarantee scheme to cover the risks of entering new markets, and there has been substantial training expenditure. Nevertheless, the crucial question remains not just whether the performance of particular sectors can be improved, but whether it can be ensured that Britain produces the right mix of products to meet the threat to employment and to our trading balance of both technological change and foreign competition. On these issues, the present Government believes firmly that if Britain is to succeed, the impetus is most likely to come from risk-taking individual entrepreneurs, and companies. This, together with the encouragement of small companies, was very much the focus of the Government's 1988 Enterprise White Paper. In January 1988 the Department of Trade and Industry launched its Enterprise Initiative specifically to help small businesses. A total provision of £80 million was made available for 1989/90 to help small independent businesses with consultancy costs for advice on design, quality, manufacturing

systems, business planning, and financial and information systems.

(v) British Oil Production.

The discovery of oil and gas in the UK Continental Shelf in the 1960s had major implications for the UK's long-term growth prospects. The main benefit so far has been to "cushion" our trade deficit as revenues from oil exports and a reduced dependence on imported oil have helped to offset a gradual deterioration in the balance on non-oil goods. The other side of the coin, however, is that after the first oil price shock in 1973 many oil producers' exchange rates became overvalued as the price of oil rose and also more volatile as exchange rates were influenced by expectations of future oil price movements. The UK, along with other oil producing nations suffered as a higher exchange rate eroded competitiveness and exacerbated the deterioration in the trade balance. Linked to this is the idea of Dutch disease which suggests that the loss of competitiveness resulting from petrocurrency status accelerates the process of de-industrialisation. Problems such as these were specific to the oil producing countries, but the repercussions of two oil price hikes, in 1973 and 1979, were felt world-wide.

The UK became self-sufficient in oil in 1981 and production of both gas and oil reached a peak in 1985 and 1986. A gradual decline is expected from now on but, given the uncertainties in estimating the amount of oil and gas remaining in recoverable reserves, it is difficult to predict when the UK's oil will run out. Using official estimates of the maximum possible amount of oil remaining in discovered reserves, the UK could carry on producing at current rates of extraction for another 17 years. However, the viability of producing oil from such reserves depends on many economic factors not least of which is the price of oil itself. Following the oil price collapse in 1986, the prospects for future production weakened, since the incentive for further exploration and development diminished. The subsequent recovery of prices in 1987 weakened but did not fully allay the concern.

Meanwhile the Government tried to ensure that the state got a substantial share of the returns from offshore oil extraction. A major worry was the large degree of foreign ownership of the oil companies involved in the operations. A specific oil tax was initially proposed in the 1974 Oil Taxation Bill and implemented, in a modified form, in the 1975 Oil Taxation Act. Petroleum Revenue Tax (PRT) was introduced at 45 per cent and royalties at 12·5 per cent. Corporation tax was to be deducted from the residue at the standard rate. It was envisaged that this would allow the oil companies an adequate return on capital. A ring fence around a company's oil extraction activities prohibited losses made outside the North Sea being used to offset North Sea profits for corporation tax purposes. Concern had been expressed that such a tax system would discourage exploitation of the "marginal fields", that is the smaller oil-fields which might not justify the huge initial expenditure needed to make them productive. Several safeguards were, therefore, proposed. No petroleum revenue tax would be levied until a field had earned back 175 per cent of its capital outlay. Fields returning less than 30 per cent on investment after paying p.r.t. would have the tax refunded. There was also to be discretionary provision to return all or part of the 12½ per cent royalties. The Government reiterated its intention to press for 51 per cent state participation in the oil-fields, which it proceeded to do through the agency of the British National Oil Corporation. Since its inception in 1975 the UK offshore taxation system has undergone many modifications. In August 1978 the rate of PRT was increased to 30 per cent while the PRT capital uplift was raised to 175 per cent from 135 per cent. In 1980 the PRT rate was once again increased, this time to 70 per cent. In March 1981, a fourth tax—Supplementary Petroleum Duty (SPD)—was introduced and was charged at 20 per cent of the landed value of gross revenues less an allowance equivalent to 0·5 million tonnes of oil per six-month period. In March 1982 SPD was replaced by Advance Petroleum Revenue Tax, identical to SPD save for the time of charges. The taxation system was becoming increasingly onerous for the oil companies and, as concern grew about the viability of developing marginal North Sea fields, modifications to the tax regime had to be made to ease the fiscal burden on oil. The main change was that a distinction was made between the tax treatment of the established Southern Basin fields and newer higher cost fields granted development approval after April 1982. For the latter group the PRT allowance was doubled to 1 million tonnes and royalty payments were abolished. In addition, APRT was abolished from January 1987. In March 1988 the PRT allowance for the more profitable Southern Basin fields was reduced to 100,000 tonnes.

In March 1978 the Government published a White Paper, *The Challenge of North Sea Oil*. In this it was estimated that by the mid-1980s North Sea Oil would increase national income by £6 billion per year and improve the balance of payments to the tune of £8 billion per year. Perhaps a more crucial aspect of the White Paper was that the annual benefit to government revenue was expected to be £4 billion. This estimate has, however, on occasions proved wide of the mark, largely because of fluctuations in the exchange rate and in the dollar price of oil. Revenue was £4·9 billion in 1986–7, £4·7 billion in 1987–8, £3·2 billion in 1988–9 and was expected to be £2·3 billion in 1989–90.

The most crucial issue however was how the extra revenue was to be used. The 1978 White Paper designated four priorities: more resources for industrial investment; funds for energy conservation and new energy investment; the reduction of the level of personal taxation; the improvement of certain essential services. It was clear that the Government believed that North Sea oil provided it with an opportunity to stimulate sustained growth, and the first two of the four priorities were obviously designed with this in mind. However, the election of a Conservative Government in 1979 signalled a change of emphasis.

In the 1980 Budget it was implied that henceforth the oil tax revenue would be used almost exclusively to reduce the size of the public sector borrowing requirement and the scale of personal and corporate taxation. In the previous year proposals were published to reduce BNOC's role. Its preferential position in future licensing was ended, as were special access to official finance through the National Oil Account and its statutory role as adviser to the Government. Effectively its role in exploration and production activities was abandoned. In early 1985, the Conservative government announced that BNOC was to be abolished, and that oil prices would be much more closely related to market developments. The authorities' other main energy worry was the fast rate of extraction of North Sea gas.

(vi) A Productivity Breakthrough?

One cause of our poor relative growth rates in this post-war period was lower productivity increases than achieved in other countries: and as in other countries this growth slowed down in the 1970s. Between 1963 and 1973, the average annual growth of output per person employed was 3 per cent in the whole economy and 4·2 per cent in manufacturing. Productivity fell between 1973 and 1975, in the wake of the first oil-price shock. Between then and 1979, it grew at an average of 2·5 per cent per annum in the economy as a whole and at 2·1 per cent in manufacturing. Indeed but for North Sea oil, this performance would have looked even worse. Capital scrapping appears to have been an important contributory factor. With the second oil crisis and recession productivity declined in 1980. Since 1980, productivity growth has averaged 5·1 per cent in manufacturing and 2·3 per cent in the economy as a whole.

Many commentators have described the experience of the 1980s as a "productivity breakthrough". Certainly the U.K.'s performance has improved significantly relative to that of its major competitors. A number of possible explanations have been advanced for this. Some argue that it is largely explained by a rapid shedding of labour, others that it is a reflection of reduced union power and of a greater realism amongst both managers and workers. This, it is contended, led to a substantial improvement in working practices. Yet others believe that it was a statistical effect, stemming from record company bankruptcies and liquidations in the early 1980s. The productivity figures quoted are averages; and if, as seems a fair assumption, it

was generally the less efficient companies which went bankrupt, then their departure from the scene would have increased the average measure, without the performance of the remaining firms having really improved at all. A final possibility is that we were witnessing the impact of new technology.

Which mixture of explanations is correct is important for deciding whether the productivity breakthrough of the 1980s was a once-and-for-all phenomenon, whether it presaged a longer run improvement in our productivity performance, or indeed whether the gains which had been made were likely to be lost at some future date. The recovery of productivity probably had much to do with the end of capital scrapping, whilst undoubtedly the rapid shedding of labour and the statistical effects of bankruptcy were important. These suggest a once and for all improvement. Nevertheless there is evidence that working practices and management techniques continue to improve.

On balance, it seems reasonable to hope for a return to the productivity performance of the late 1960s. Certainly, for once, Britain's recent performance compares favourably with that of its major competitors.

Inflation.

(i) Wages and Prices.

Between 1970 and 1989 inflation averaged 10·2 per cent a year. In other words by 1989, prices were 522 per cent higher than they had been in 1970. Only a part of this increase can be attributed to an increase in import prices. During the same period average earnings rose by 12·5 per cent a year whilst, due to a poor productivity performance, unit labour costs (wages and salaries per unit of output) rose by over 10 per cent. These increased costs were passed on to the consumer in the form of higher prices. Thus real earnings only increased by some 2 per cent a year. The table shows annual average prices, earnings, real earnings and also real disposable income (*i.e.* the purchasing power of total personal incomes after income tax), all as indices based on 1970 = 100.

(ii) The Growing Inflation.

Between the late 1960s and the mid 1970s there was a growing rate of inflation. Between 1969 and 1970 retail prices rose by 6 per cent, between 1970 and 1971 by 9½ per cent, between 1971 and 1972 by 7 per cent, between 1972 and 1973 by 9 per cent, between 1973 and 1974 by 16 per cent and between 1974 and 1975 by 24 per cent. The increase in average weekly earnings also accelerated.

RETAIL PRICES, AVERAGE EARNINGS,
REAL AVERAGE EARNINGS AND REAL
DISPOSABLE INCOMES
1970 = 100

	Retail prices	Average earnings	Real average earnings	Real disposable incomes
1970	100·0	100·0	100·0	100·0
1971	109·4	111·5	101·9	101·3
1972	117·2	124·6	106·3	109·8
1973	128·0	141·8	110·8	116·4
1974	148·5	167·2	112·6	115·6
1975	184·4	211·5	114·7	116·2
1976	214·9	245·9	114·4	115·8
1977	249·0	268·9	108·0	113·3
1978	269·6	303·3	112·5	121·8
1979	305·8	350·0	114·5	128·7
1980	360·7	422·1	117·0	130·7
1981	403·6	476·2	118·0	129·8
1982	438·3	521·3	118·9	129·6
1983	458·4	564·8	123·2	132·5
1984	481·2	599·2	124·5	135·4
1985	510·5	649·2	127·2	139·4
1986	527·9	700·8	132·8	145·3
1987	549·8	754·9	137·3	149·9
1988	576·7	819·7	142·1	157·7
1989	621·7	894·3	143·8	165·3

RISE IN CONSUMER PRICES, PER CENT PER ANNUM

	1959–1984	1984–1985	1985–1986	1986–1987	1987–1988	1988–1989
U.S.	5·1	3·6	1·9	3·7	4·1	4·8
Japan . . .	6·4	2·0	0·8	0·0	0·7	2·3
France . . .	7·0	5·8	2·5	3·3	2·7	3·7
W.Germany .	3·8	2·2	0·2	0·3	1·2	2·8
Italy	9·6	9·2	5·8	4·7	5·0	6·3
U.K.	8·1	6·1	3·4	4·2	4·9	7·8

* Annual average.

(iii) The Attack on Inflation.

1975 saw an even higher rate of inflation than 1974. Average weekly earnings rose by nearly 27 per cent. Productivity fell and prices rose by about 24 per cent. Import prices made a smaller contribution to inflation than in the previous two years. Real earnings rose by 2 per cent, implying a further drop in the share of profits in domestic income. But through 1975 inflation moderated. Average earnings increases started to slow down in the second quarter, and wholesale and retail prices followed with a lag. By the third quarter they were all increasing at about 15 per cent. The slowdown of average earnings in fact started before the imposition of the £6 limit, and it has been suggested that this was caused by growing unemployment. Such an effect was, however, small compared with the direct impact of the £6 rule.

Domestic inflation moderated still further in 1976, retail prices being 16 per cent higher than in 1975. The main contributor to this was the deceleration in the rate of increase in labour costs. Average weekly earnings were 15 per cent higher than in 1975. Real earnings were therefore slightly lower than in the previous year, implying some recovery in the share of profits in domestic income. By far the largest influence on the deceleration of wage inflation was the voluntary incomes policy, first the £6 limit and from August its successor, which aimed at a 4½ per cent increase in basic wage rates. However, in the last few months of the year price inflation showed a small increase. This upturn is explained by the sharp fall in the value of the pound during the year putting up the cost of raw materials and fuel purchased by British industry.

Retail prices were nearly 16 per cent higher in 1977 than in 1976, whilst earnings were only 10 per cent higher. Real earnings, therefore, fell by nearly 5 per cent, and this meant some further recovery in the share of profits in national income. Real disposable income fell by the smaller amount of 1½ per cent, because of the reduction of taxes in the April and October budgets. Productivity improved hardly at all during the year, and so the earnings increases meant a similar increase in labour costs per unit of output, these costs feeding through to prices.

There was a considerable contrast between the two halves of 1977. In the year to July 1977 prices rose at the rate of about 17 per cent, inflation being exacerbated by the depreciation of sterling in 1976, and further fed by the delayed impact of earnings increases of 14 per cent during Stage I of incomes policy, which ended in July 1976. Since by early 1977 Stage II of the incomes policy was holding earnings increases down to 10 per cent, real personal income was badly squeezed in the first half of the year. These lower increases in earnings together with the appreciation of sterling had their effect on retail prices in the second half of the year. By early 1978 price inflation had fallen below 10 per cent. At the same time earnings had begun to increase at the rate of about 15 per cent per annum. This, together with the 1977 tax cuts, meant an appreciable recovery in real personal income.

Thus by early 1978 price inflation had fallen back into single figures, and it continued to fall steadily until the middle of the year. From then inflation started to increase again, so that by the spring of 1979 was going back into double figures.

Stage III of the incomes policy, which ran for the year ending July 1978, was looser than Stage II, and was accompanied by earnings increases of nearly 15 per cent. This was beginning to feed through to prices by the middle of 1978, and was the cause of the acceleration of inflation. By early 1979 earnings were rising at an annual rate of 14 per cent, and this despite continued low rates of increase of import prices and a renewed squeeze on profits, implied a likely further increase in price inflation. Real personal disposable income continued its recovery of late 1977. With earnings rising faster than prices and with only a modest increase in direct tax payments, r.p.d.i. improved substantially during 1978.

In early 1979, then, price inflation was starting to increase slowly but was still within single figures (at annual rates). Two important wage settlements following strikes—the lorry drivers and local authority manual workers—set the pace for a higher rate of increase of earnings. By the end of 1979 they were rising at nearly 20 per cent per annum compared to about 14 per cent a year earlier. In December 1979 retail prices were going up at a rate of 17 per cent per annum. An increase in indirect taxation contributed 3 per cent to price inflation. But pay remained the main force driving prices. The Conservative Government was elected in May 1979 with the defeat of inflation a central plank of its economic policy. Despite a deflationary fiscal and monetary policy, retail prices continued to rise, reaching a year on year increase of over 20 per cent in the second quarter of 1980. Much of this was due to the effects of higher indirect taxes and continued wage pressure, and was despite an appreciation in the value of sterling. Towards the end of 1980 the rate of inflation began to fall. This was partly a consequence of the recession, both at home and abroad, making it difficult for firms to mark up over costs. Real wages rose, albeit slowly, implying a further squeeze on profits.

Inflation continued to fall in 1981, as pressure on wages eased and the recession became deeper. The year on year increase in retail prices was 12 per cent. Real personal disposable income fell by 2 per cent mainly because of the Chancellor's failure to index income tax allowances and bands in the 1981 Budget. The squeeze on disposable incomes continued into 1982 as the real burden of taxation rose further.

The fall in inflation continued in 1982 and into 1983, when the annual rates were 8·6 per cent and 4·6 per cent respectively. This was despite a declining effective exchange rate. The recession and international competition were important influences making British industrialists very wary of putting up prices. At the same time earnings inflation was falling, being 9·4 per cent in 1982 and 8·4 per cent in 1983, whilst productivity was still increasing very strongly.

Since 1983 price inflation has remained low, successive year-on-year figures until 1987 being 5·0 per cent, 6·1 per cent, 3·4 per cent and 4·2 per cent. The main cause of these slight variations was the course of oil prices. During 1987 inflation altered little. A strong pound, low world inflation and a resurgence of strong productivity growth all played their part. Inflation reached a low point of 3·3 per cent at the beginning of 1988, helped by a strong exchange rate. However, it soon became clear that inflationary pressures were emerging in the economy, largely as a result of excessive demand, but the trend was exacerbated by rising interest rates and sustained earnings growth. In early 1989, inflation averaged 7·8 per cent and concerns over accelerating growth in labour costs forced the Government to maintain a tight monetary stance.

Ironically, higher interest rates feed through into higher retail prices via their effect on mortgage rates. This effect was seen clearly in 1989, when interest rate rises early in the year pushed inflation to a peak of 8·3 per cent in the spring. A period of unchanged interest rate levels allowed retail price inflation to fall back to 7·1 per cent in the early autumn, before another interest rate rise in October (this time to defend a weak pound) pushed inflation back to above 8 per cent in early 1990. Wage bargainers base their assessment of changed living costs on movements in retail prices, so an anti-inflationary policy based solely on the use of high interest rates may, perversely, create just the right conditions for a wage-price spiral.

More seriously, 1989 also saw a steady rise in underlying inflation. If one strips out the effect of mortgage interest rate changes, retail price inflation accelerated from under 5 per cent in early 1989 to 6·3 per cent in March 1990. This shows that inflationary pressures were building up quite in-dependently of interest rate rises. One source of pressure was higher unit labour costs as earnings growth accelerated and productivity performance deteriorated. A second source was the exchange rate; between February 1989 and the end of the year the pound fell by around 15 per cent against the deutschemark and by 10 per cent against the US dollar. This clearly put up import prices.

The introduction of the poll tax (*see* **G36**) will have raised retail price inflation by 1 percentage point. Combined with excise duty changes an-nounced in the March 1990 Budget, the poll tax will have forced inflation up towards 9·5 per cent in the summer of 1990. Such an inauspicious background to the start of the 1990–91 pay round raises a serious possibility of a return to the wage-price spirals of the 1970s.

The growth in earnings is a particular cause for concern: between 1980 and the end of the decade, our earnings were rising faster than those of most other OECD countries. Thus, despite improved productivity performance, wage costs per unit of output also increased faster than those of our major competitors. In other words, they did even better on these critical variables than we did.

In this context, a remarkable fact is that throughout the early 1980s, when unemployment was rising, the real earnings of those in work continued to increase, as did real personal disposable earnings, which also incorporates the income of those not working. In early 1990 earnings inflation showed little sign of slowing down, running as it was at 9·5 per cent. The unemployed have not bid down pay. Rather it has been forced up by high company profits, skill shortages, and the needs of employers—to attract good workers and to motivate their existing employees.

Incomes Policy.

Britain's cost competitive position in world trade has deteriorated over the medium term in relation to that of her main rivals; this is one major reason for her recurrent balance of payments difficulties. The British share in total world exports of manu-factures fell from 17·7 per cent to 12·3 per cent between 1959 and 1967. It fell further to 10·0 per cent by 1972 and to 8·6 per cent in 1976. Thereafter it recovered back to approximately its 1972 level, only to fall back again in the early 1990s. In 1989 it stood at just over 8 per cent. There are essentially two methods of remedying this situation. Either there must be a depreciation of the pound in terms of other currencies, or we must have a policy to limit the increase in British costs; either by increasing productivity growth or by limiting pay rises. Up to 1967 the Government concentrated on the latter alternative, either by restrictive budg-etary policies or by *incomes policy*. In 1967 the pound was devalued, and from 1972 it was allowed to float, though the Government from time to time stepped in to prevent it floating freely. However, for many years it was generally believed that an incomes policy was still needed if any depreciation was to be successful, and if harshly restrictive monetary and fiscal policies were to be avoided.

Other harmful effects of inflation are discussed in **Part II.**

(i) The Pay Pause.

In July 1961 the Chancellor of the Exchequer called for a "pause" in wages, salaries, and dividend payments. Exhortations for restraint had been a familiar feature of ministerial statements for many years, but on this occasion the Government soon made it clear that it intended to use such power as

it had to influence the amount and timing of wage and salary awards. It had the power to decide when the pay awards recommended by the Wages Coun-cils—which fix minimum wages in some low paid industries—should be implemented. The Govern-ment's power is strongest over workers which it directly or indirectly employs, *e.g.*, civil servants, and teachers. Their pay awards were cut back. The Government also had a limited influence on awards made in nationalised industries.

The "pay pause" came to an end in April 1962. It was envisaged as a temporary policy, and its effects are difficult to assess. It certainly post-poned some wage awards which would otherwise have been made, and it may have contributed to a stiffening of employer resistance to wage claims. But because the pause affected some groups of people more severely than others, this form of incomes policy was seen to be dis-criminatory.

(ii) The National Incomes Commission.

In February 1962 the Government issued a White Paper which outlined its incomes policy for the period after the pause. It stated that "the objective must be to keep the rate of increase in incomes within the long-term rate of growth of national production." The Government stressed that most of the arguments which had in the past been advanced in justification of wages and salary claims—*e.g.*, increases in the cost of living, trends in productivity or profits in particular industries, and comparisons with levels or trends in other employments—should be given less weight; and that "general economic considerations"—*i.e.*, the increases which the economy can afford given the prospective rate of increase in national production—should be given more weight.

Late in 1962 the Government set up the *National Incomes Commission* (NIC). However, the powers of this body were limited. It had, for example, no power to cancel or modify a wage agreement on which it reported. NIC produced only 4 reports, and was wound up after the change of Government.

(iii) The National Board for Prices and Incomes.

In October 1964 the Labour Government's new Department of Economic Affairs was made re-sponsible for achieving an incomes policy. The lessons of the past had been learned; the Govern-ment recognised that a successful incomes policy would require the support of both sides of in-dustry. Its first objective was to achieve a "Joint Statement of Intent on Productivity, Prices and Incomes"; this was signed in Decem-ber 1964. In this document the T.U.C. and the employers' organisations undertook to co-operate with the Government in producing an effective machinery for the implementing of an incomes policy.

It was Government policy that growth in earn-ings per employee should equal the planned growth in national output per employee of 3–3½ per cent per annum. Thus, in those industries (*e.g.*, engineering) in which productivity growth ex-ceeded this "norm", earnings should rise less rapidly than productivity, and in those industries in which productivity growth fell short of the norm, earnings could rise more rapidly than productivity. Growth in earnings per employee should exceed the norm only in exceptional cases; *i.e.*, as a reward for increasing productivity by eliminating re-strictive working practices; if necessary to transfer labour from one industry to another; if earnings were too low to maintain a reasonable standard of living; or if a group of workers had fallen seriously out of line with earnings for similar work.

To make specific recommendations on the basis of this policy, the Government set up a *National Board for Prices and Incomes*. The Board produced over 150 reports. There was no statutory authority to enforce its recommendations: reliance was placed on voluntary methods and the power of persuasion and public opinion. However, in late 1965 the Government introduced a compulsory "Early Warning" system, whereby it was notified in ad-vance of any intended increase in incomes or in cer-tain prices. As a result, the Government and the Board had time to consider increases before they were put into effect.

(iv) The Prices and Incomes Standstill.

A voluntary incomes policy is very difficult to implement, since it depends on co-operation among Government, workers, and employers; moreover, co-operation among representatives at the top may be undermined by "wage-drift" at the factory level. Thus the annual average of weekly wage-rates rose by 5 percentage points between 1965 and 1966. In fact all of this increase took place in the period before July 1966. Clearly the voluntary incomes policy was meeting with little success.

Therefore, as part of the July measures taken to deal with the balance of payments problem, the Government introduced a "prices and incomes standstill." Increases in prices and incomes were as far as possible to be avoided altogether until the end of 1966. Increases already negotiated but not yet implemented were deferred for 6 months. The first half of 1967 was a period of "severe restraint." Any price increases were carefully examined, and the norm for income increases was zero. Any increase in earnings had to be justified by one of the four conditions for exception, referred to above. To enforce its "freeze" the Government took the unprecedented step of asking Parliament for reserve powers (including penalties for offenders), which were to be used only if the need should arise. For the most part, there was a voluntary observation of the standstill; but from October 1966 the Government found it necessary to exercise its powers of compulsion in a few cases. These powers lapsed in August 1967.

There then followed a year in which there was to be a "nil norm" except where increases in incomes could be justified by one of the four exceptional criteria. The Government could no longer legally enforce its policy, but it did retain the power to delay price and pay increases. Whereas the Government succeeded in slowing down the rise in wages and prices during the year in which it took compulsory powers, in the second half of 1967 weekly wage rates rose at an annual rate of 6 per cent. The advantage gained from the previous restraint was reduced but not entirely lost.

(v) Incomes Policy after Devaluation.

Incomes policy was made both more difficult and more important by the devaluation of the pound: more difficult in that devaluation involved a cut in the standard of living, and more important in that it was important that the trading benefit from devaluation should not be neutralised by inflation.

In April 1968 the Government published a White Paper outlining its policy for the period until the end of 1969. Wage increases had still to be justified by the four criteria, and there was a "ceiling" of 3½ per cent per annum except for "productivity agreements" and low-paid workers. Price increases were permitted only as a result of unavoidable increases in costs per unit of output, and price reductions were required when these fell. The Government intended to rely on the voluntary cooperation of unions and employers over pay; but it decided to lengthen its delaying powers for pay and price increases up to 12 months, and take powers to enforce price reductions recommended by the Board.

Between November 1967 and November 1968 the retail price index rose by over 5 per cent, mainly due to the effect of devaluation on import prices. In the face of this rise in the cost of living the incomes policy met with firm resistance. In practice the ceiling of 3½ per cent per annum rapidly became the normal increase. In the first year after devaluation average earnings rose by 7·5 per cent. Workers were thus able to protect themselves against price inflation and to increase slightly their real incomes.

During 1969 the process of wage and price inflation accelerated. In December the Government published a White Paper on its incomes policy for the period after 1969. It laid down a norm for wage increases of 2·5 to 4·5 per cent per annum: increases were to exceed the upper limit only in exceptional circumstances. Comparisons with other workers were not to be used, except in the case of public servants (e.g., teachers and nurses) whose productivity could not easily be measured. The Government's powers to delay the implementation of proposed wage and price increases were reduced. However, the incomes policy laid down in the White Paper was tempered by the imminence of a General Election and the recent cost of living increases; and it did not prevent a "wage explosion" occurring in 1970.

(vi) Conservative Policy.

On taking office in June 1970 the Conservative Government eschewed its predecessor's approach to incomes policy and disbanded the National Board for Prices and Incomes. To curb the inflation it maintained the economy in recession and squeezed company liquidity, hoping in this way to weaken wage pressures and strengthen the resistances of employers. In addition it attempted to resist demands for wage increases in the public sector, at the cost of prolonged strikes, e.g., in electricity supply, postal services and coal mining. In the former two cases it met with some success; in the case of the coal miners' strike early in 1972 the Government was unable to enforce its policy. In any event this form of incomes policy—like the "pay pause" of 1961—was both partial and discriminatory. The Government also intervened to curb price rises in the nationalised industries, e.g., postal charges and steel prices. The main initiative on prices came from the Confederation of British Industry (CBI): in July 1971, it asked its members to avoid price increases over the next twelve months or to limit them to 5 per cent or less in unavoidable costs. Over 170 leading British companies agreed to comply.

The Government measures were by no means a sure remedy for the inflation spiral. Moreover, even its apparent strategy of deterring wage demands by maintaining high unemployment was dropped in the reflationary budget of 1972. The Government appeared to be placing its faith in its Industrial Relations Act to solve the problem of wage inflation in the long run.

(vii) The Pay and Price Standstill.

In 1972 wage demands became more difficult to contain because of the increase in the cost-of-living resulting from the effective devaluation of the pound in June and the rise in world food prices during the year. There was a marked increase in the number and seriousness of strikes (see **G21**). The principal cause was a sharp rise in disagreements over pay claims. In the six months between the first and third quarters of 1972 average weekly earnings rose by no less than 7 per cent. It was inevitable that the Government would intervene. The expectation of an impending freeze encouraged further wage and price increases, especially after the CBI's period of voluntary restraint had elapsed.

The Government first tried to achieve a tri-partite voluntary agreement with the CBI and the TUC. After this attempt had failed, in November the Conservative Government reversed its previous policy and introduced a statutory Prices and Pay standstill. In effect there was a standstill on all prices of goods and services other than imports and fresh foods, a standstill on rents, on dividends, and on all wages and salaries including those previously negotiated but not yet in operation. Offenders were liable to be fined.

(viii) The Price Commission and the Pay Board.

In early 1973 the Government formulated its policy for after the standstill in a series of documents, culminating in a Price and Pay Code. Two new agencies—a *Price Commission* and a *Pay Board*—were established to regulate prices, dividends, rent, and pay in accordance with the Price and Pay Code.

In Stage Two of the policy—lasting from the end of the pay standstill on 31 March until the autumn—the following criteria on pay applied. The total annual pay increase for any group of employees should not exceed £1 a week plus 4 per cent of the current pay bill excluding overtime. There was flexibility for negotiation of increases within a group: emphasis was to be on the lower paid and the maximum allowable increase was £250 a year. Exceptions to the limit were made for, *e.g.*, movement towards equal pay between the sexes, personal increments and promotion, and some improved pension benefits. The Pay Board had to be notified of all settlements involving less than 1,000 employees but settlements involving more than 1,000 employees required its prior approval. It became an offence to strike or threaten to strike to force an employer to contravene an order of the Pay Board.

Prices in Stage Two could be increased only to take account of *allowable* cost increases, and were to reflect only the percentage increases in these costs per unit of output since 1 October 1972. Moreover to allow for productivity growth, firms were permitted to pass on as price increases only a fraction of the increase in the wage costs allowed by the Code. Prices were also limited by the requirement that net profit margins should not exceed the average percentage level of the best two of the last five years. Exceptions were made for companies which could show that without higher profits their investment would be held back. Large firms had to give prior notice of price increases to the Price Commission, medium sized firms had to report regularly on prices, and small firms had to keep price records. Imports, fresh foods, auctioned goods, secondhand goods and interest charges were among the exemptions from the controls. Dividends could not be raised by more than 5 per cent over the previous year.

One of the problems facing the policy was the continued sharp rise in world food prices after the standstill was declared. This made public acceptance of the Government policy more difficult to achieve.

(ix) Stage Three.

Stage Three of the counter-inflation policy was introduced in October 1973. Price controls were similar to those under Stage Two. Wage increases negotiated for any group of workers were statutorily limited to an average of either £2·25 a week per head, or if preferred, 7 per cent per head, with a limit of £350 a year on the amount to be received by any one individual. However, further increases were permitted beyond these limits, to deal with certain specific matters: changes in pay structures, better use of manpower, efficiency schemes, "unsocial" hours, and progress towards equal pay for women. A novel aspect of the pay policy was the *threshold agreement* to safeguard against increases in the cost of living. It was possible for wage negotiators to bargain for a pay increase of up to 40p a week, payable if the retail price index reached 7 per cent above its level at the beginning of Stage Three, with up to another 40p a week for each percentage point it rose thereafter until the end of Stage Three in November 1974. It was claimed that these agreements were responsible for a large part of the wage and price inflation of 1974. Indeed in a purely statistical sense this was correct. The threshold was triggered eleven times, which meant an extra £4.40 per week for anyone under the scheme. It was estimated that 10 million workers were covered by such arrangements by October 1974. The idea behind thresholds was that unions, when negotiating wage increases, might have unduly pessimistic expectations about inflation. By introducing automatic compensation, such expectations would be taken out of the bargaining situation. Without this compensation, it might be argued, many groups would have refused to settle under Stage Three terms, and their pay increases would have been just as large or even larger than the ones which they actually obtained.

(x) The Miners' Strike.

Over 6 million workers had settled under the Stage Three provisions by the end of February 1974. The National Union of Mine-workers, however, feeling strongly that their relative pay had fallen and recognising their new bargaining powers resulting from the oil crisis, refused to settle under Stage Three. A national overtime ban was begun in November which in January 1974 became a national strike. In November the Government declared a State of Emergency and in January introduced a three-day week for industry in order to conserve coal and electricity (which depended on coal). It was unwilling to waive the Stage Three legislation in the miners' case, despite a declaration by the Trade Union Congress that its member unions would not invoke a settlement of the miners' dispute in support of their own claims. The Government referred the NUM claim to the Pay Board, for the Board to determine whether the miners constituted a special case which justified a further increase in their relative pay. The Government then called a General Election. The Pay Board reported just after the election, and recommended that an additional increase be paid, on the grounds that the long-run contraction of the industry would in future be reversed and that higher relative pay would be necessary to recruit and retain sufficient mine-workers. The incoming Labour Government settled with the miners on terms very similar to those recommended by the Pay Board.

(xi) The Social Contract.

The Labour Party came to power pledged to deal firmly with prices but to abandon statutory wage controls. It took early action on house rents and food prices, by means of controls and subsidies. The Pay Board was abolished and the policy of compulsory wage restraint thus finally ended in July 1974. The Price Code and the Price Commission were, however, retained.

During the February 1974 general election campaign an agreement between the TUC and the Labour Party was announced. This became known as the *social contract*, and formed the backbone of the Labour Government's attempts to stem wage inflation. The hope was that, in return for the repeal of the Industrial Relations Act, the introduction of a measure of industrial democracy and various other concessions, the TUC would be able to persuade its members to co-operate in a programme of voluntary wage restraint. In this way it was hoped to avoid the strains caused by formal incomes policies, which have always appeared to trade unionists to leave them without any role to play. Under a voluntary system they could still do their job—that is bargain about wage rates. The terms of the contract were that there should be a twelve-month interval between wage settlements; and that negotiated increases should be confined either to compensating for price increases since the last settlement, or for anticipated future price increases before the next settlement. It is hardly surprising that most negotiators took the latter option. An attempt by the TUC to exclude this had failed.

(xii) Voluntary Restraint.

By early 1975 it was evident that this policy had failed. Some wage settlements were of the order of 30 per cent. In July 1975 the Government announced that there would be a limit of £6 per week on pay increases, £6 representing 10% of average earnings. There were to be no exceptions to this, and those earning more than £8,500 a year were to get nothing at all. The Government had the prior agreement of the TUC, which agreed to try to persuade its members to comply. The policy was voluntary to the extent that there were no legal sanctions against individual unions, but in another sense there were very powerful sanctions. These operated through the Price Code. No firms could pass on in prices any part of a pay settlement above the limit.

The £6 limit was due to lapse in July 1976, and the April 1976 Budget gave the first indications of a possible successor. The Chancellor announced that he would make cuts in the effective amount of tax paid by private individuals, if he could secure trade union agreement to a second year of pay restraint. This would allow an increase in take-home pay with the employers bearing less than half the cost. Therefore prices would rise more slowly and our competitive position deteriorate more slowly than if the whole increase had been achieved by putting up money wages. There were, however, those who felt that the integrity of Parliament was threatened by making taxation decisions conditional on trade union agreement. Be that as it may, agreement was reached with the TUC. From August 1976 more severe limits on pay operated than under the £6 limit. For those earning less than £50 a week, wage increases were limited to £2.50; for those earning between

£50 and £80 the limit was 5 per cent, whilst those earning more than £80 could get no more than a £4 per week increase. Average earnings at that time were about £75 per week, and the implied overall limit was about 4½ per cent.

There is no doubt that this pay policy was successful in holding down earnings. During the £6 policy, earnings rose by 14 per cent—a dramatic fall from the near- 30 per cent rise in the previous year. An all-round increase of £6 would have meant a 10 per cent rise. Another 2 per cent can be explained by the implementation of agreements made before August 1975, by moves towards equal pay, and by increased overtime earnings. This leaves only 2 per cent unaccounted for. Some of this "slippage" was no doubt evasion of the limits. There is no reason to think that there was any greater slippage from the 4½ per cent policy, and during the year of its operation (until August 1977) earnings rose by only 9 per cent. It is unclear whether the success of the policy was due as much to the threat of Price Code sanctions and to the recession in the economy as to the voluntary co-operation of the trade unions.

The 4½ per cent policy was due to lapse at the end of July 1977, and in the March 1977 Budget the Chancellor again offered the prospect of tax cuts if trade union agreement to a new stage could be reached. In the event the TUC agreed to continue its support for the 12-month rule, whereby no union should attempt more than one settlement in a year. It could not, however, agree to a limit of a specific amount. In return the Government gave a modest reduction in income tax, and introduced a "voluntary" policy of its own. This new Stage III policy was to last until the end of July 1978 and aimed for a national earnings increase of no more than 10 per cent during this time. No specific limit was to be put on individual negotiations, but the Government reserved the right to impose sanctions on firms whose settlements appeared inconsistent with the national target. These sanctions might be exercised through the Price Commission's controls on profit margins (though it was expected that these would lapse in July 1978), through public purchasing policy and the placing of contracts, and through consideration of industrial assistance. The Government did stress, however, the possibility that larger increases could be obtained by self-financing productivity deals.

By the spring of 1978 it seemed that earnings increases during this stage of policy would turn out to be as high as 14 per cent. The Government was reasonably successful in holding the public sector down to near 10 per cent, though there were some costly productivity deals, particularly in coal mining. But the main problem was in the private sector. Though the majority of wage-rate increases were at about 10 per cent, earnings drift together with consolidation of the previous two years' increases in rates worked out for overtime, piece rates or shiftwork were pushing earnings increases way above 10 per cent. In addition, productivity deals were incorporated in about 30 per cent of agreements, in each case adding between 6 per cent and 10 per cent to pay. It is unclear how many of these deals involved genuine cost saving, or how sanctions discouraged false deals of this sort.

In the early summer the Government announced its plans for the 1978-79 pay round. Its objective was to limit the growth in national earnings to around 5 per cent, and it was soon clear that its tactics were very similar to those it had employed in support of its 10 per cent target during the 1977–78 pay round: seeking to keep as many groups of workers as possible to settlements at or very near to the target figure by direct negotiations in the public sector and by the renewed threat of sanctions in the private sector; allowing additional increases for self-financing productivity deals; and using promises of additional increases in subsequent pay rounds in order to induce groups regarding themselves as "special cases" to settle for 5 per cent in the current round.

(xiii) Conflict with the Unions.

A serious problem, however, was the TUC's hostility to the policy. Although the TUC had not supported the Government's 10 per cent target of the previous year, it had in practice helped the Government by putting pressure on unions to settle for increases which were not too obviously out of line with its policy. This time the TUC was not prepared to do this. Its reluctance stemmed partly from the opposition of some union leaders to continued pay controls but much more from the view that even if official union policy was to observe the 5 per cent guide-lines, the frustration apparently felt by many workers after three years of pay controls would lead to widespread unofficial strikes which would undermine union leaders' authority.

The Government therefore had to enforce its policy without TUC help. In the early autumn of 1978 it seemed to be having some success as several groups settled for not much more than the limit, but the policy was severely undermined by a two-month strike at Ford's which ended with a settlement of around 17 per cent. Subsequently Parliament refused to support the Government's proposed use of sanctions against Ford and other firms breaching the guidelines, so that the Government was left without any effective incomes policy in the private sector. As a result other groups of workers felt free to ignore the guidelines: the most spectacular breach of the policy being an increase of over 20 per cent for road haulage drivers after a disruptive strike in January 1979.

Such settlements in the private sector naturally made public sector workers unwilling to accept 5 per cent increases. The Government therefore offered 9 per cent more to most groups. However, this did not satisfy some of the lower-paid, public sector employees, particularly ambulance drivers and manual workers in hospitals and local authorities. They mounted a series of strikes, some of which—withdrawal of emergency ambulance services and disruption of hospitals—caused widespread concern and led to a growing public debate about the extent and the use of trade union power.

To deal with these problems the Government set up a new body, the Comparability Commission, to review the pay of those public sector workers who claimed that they had fallen behind comparable groups in the private sector: health and local authority workers were among the first to have their pay referred to the Commission.

(xiv) Reluctant Union Acquiescence.

The new Conservative Government, which took office in May 1979, allowed the work of the Comparability Commission to continue until the end of 1980. Otherwise it eschewed a formal incomes policy. Its strategy to control earnings inflation consisted of two strands. The first was to use cash limits in the public sector and a tight monetary policy in the private. This might moderate settlements. If it did not, it was argued, it would at least make unions aware that high settlements had an unemployment cost. The second strand of policy was to reform the structure of bargaining, so as to redistribute the balance of power between union and employer. By the early autumn of 1980, the Government had moved in the direction of declaring specific limits in the public sector. Whilst they were managing to keep their settlements low in public services, they were less successful in nationalised industries. It was certainly hard to argue that pay inflation in the public sector as a whole was noticeably less than in the recession-hit private sector.

There was a muted union reaction to this policy. Though 1979 saw the largest number of working days lost through strikes in any year since 1926, by early 1981 working days lost, like the number of stoppages, were at a very low level, and thereafter on both measures, industrial strife remained very low. By early 1982 the Government's policies were having some measure of success. In the nationalised industries even the miners were held to just over 9 per cent. In the civil service, the government launched a sustained attack on automatic comparability-based pay determination, arguing that market forces should play a role. Thus grades—like computer staff—for whom demand was high were offered greater pay increases than others, whilst new entrants—of whom there was excess supply—were offered no pay increases at all. The Megaw Committee, the Government hoped, would permanently revise methods of pay determination in the Civil

Service. In the weaker tax-dependent sections of the public sector—*e.g.* teachers—the Government was ruthless in enforcing very low pay settlements.

Meanwhile the recession kept settlements in the private sector at low levels. Through 1982 and into 1983 there was a further gradual reduction in pay inflation. In 1984 the policy was under some—albeit not serious—threat. There was evidence that the Government was finding it more difficult to hold the line in the public sector—a number of comparability deals were threatening. In the private sector, better economic fortunes were starting to result in some pay pressures. 1985 saw a continuation of these tensions in the public sector. Apart from the miners' strike, the Government faced severe difficulties from the civil servants and teachers. Yet, though it failed to hold public sector pay down to the 3 per cent cash limit, it was still managing to impose significantly lower settlements than in the private sector. In 1986 and 1987, however, pay in the public sector rose as rapidly as in private employment—by about 7 and 8 per cent respectively. In 1988 and 1989 earnings inflation started to edge up again as strong corporate profits and expectations of higher price inflation encouraged high pay demands. The Government was very eager to limit the extent of earnings increases and tried through high interest rates and a strong exchange rate to dissuade employers from conceding to what it considered to be excessive pay awards. In the public sector the Government faced severe opposition from several sectors. During the summer of 1989, British Rail and London Underground workers staged a series of one day strikes causing considerable disruption to businesses in central London, whose employees needed to commute. This was followed by a prolonged strike by the Ambulance service, who withdrew all but emergency services. The Government's policy throughout these disputes was to keep its distance from the negotiations and leave the discussions to the management and unions, presumably in an attempt to deflect criticism away from the Government at a time of increasing dissatisfaction with the Conservative Government and Mrs. Thatcher.

Earnings inflation continued to accelerate and the threat of a return to the wage-price spirals of the 1970s was of concern to commentators, who were questioning just how fundamentally the labour market has been reformed.

(xv) Making the Labour Market Work.

Incomes policies are often criticised on two grounds. The first is that, at best, they work for only a short time. The second is that they cause distortions in relative pay and prices. Hindsight might tell us that their success is no more short-run than is the impact of savage budgetary policies. It might also tell us that

whatever allocative inefficiencies are involved, such inefficiencies are minor when compared with the vast waste of resources and personal anguish caused by very high levels of unemployment.

The Conservative Government seemed to believe that structural reform of the labour market was the only real alternative to incomes policies of the conventional kind. If there were features of the labour market which tended to produce inflationary pressures, better, it was argued, to root these out at source rather than tinker with them as an incomes policy would do. Thus the emphasis on trade union reform and on the recession producing permanent changes in attitudes. This concern also explains the emphasis on reducing the real value of social security benefits as a percentage of income in work. Thereby people would have a greater incentive to work and to demand reasonable wage settlements. This approach was confirmed in the 1985 White Paper, *The Challenge to the Nation.* Three desiderata were mentioned: individuals pricing themselves into jobs; flexibility in the face of change; freedom from regulation. In this spirit, the Government reformed Wages Councils in 1986, in particular totally removing juveniles from their orbit. It also further weakened employment protection legislation. Whether this "strategy" will work or not is a vital, but undecided, question. Certainly the UK's failure to improve more significantly its relative unit labour cost performance casts some shadows of doubt. Yet many who are sceptical, now accept that our labour market problems are so deep-seated as to require structural action. They do not regard conventional incomes policies as sufficient. Rather they are seeking more permanent policies of this kind. Amongst an array of suggestions are three which have received much attention. The first is a tax-based incomes policy, which imposes, as part of the tax system, penalties on companies who pay over a declared maximum. The second involves various ideas of compulsory arbitration, in the hope that such arbitration can be arranged to moderate pay outcomes. The third, and most radical, involves changing the system of pay, such that a significant component takes the form of a profit share. The hope is that this would make it easier to obtain pay reductions in a recession, and moderate individual pay increases as the economy expands. The 1987 Budget introduced tax incentives for profit-related pay schemes. However, after an initially enthusiastic response interest in such schemes appeared to dwindle and the Chancellor felt obliged to increase the tax attractiveness of profit-related pay schemes in his 1989 Budget. Nevertheless, these schemes are largely untested in Britain, and they have many faults. But further productive thought along these lines is essential, if any Government is going to be able to safely run the economy at higher levels of demand.

V. SPECIAL TOPICS

ECONOMIC CONSEQUENCES OF GERMAN REUNIFICATION

The Background.

The dramatic events in Eastern Europe in 1989 have already reshaped the political character of the continent. During the next decade a fundamental restructuring of the Eastern European economies will take place with major consequences for Western Europe. In no area is this more the case than with East and West Germany. The removal of the Honecker and Krenz governments has already led to East Germany turning more to the West for economic support and partnership. Indeed it was the economic attractions of West Germany that encouraged the heavy migration of labour from East Germany in the autumn of 1989 that, in turn, ignited the calls for reform that rapidly led to the overthrow of the communist government. With closer ties between East and West Germany, probably culminating in a reunification, taking place at the same time that the members of the European Community are moving towards a "single European market" (which will be completed in 1992) it is inevitable that the 1990s will witness major changes to European economic life. This prospect had an immediate effect on the financial

markets in late 1989. The Deutsch Mark gained in value sharply reflecting the general view that West Germany had most to gain from the changes in Eastern Europe in general and East Germany in particular. World stock markets rallied in the hope that the opening up of East European economies would boost trade and profits for the West.

The Speed Factor.

The consideration of how extensive the economic changes will be poses the question of whether and how soon the two Germanies could become reunified. Despite the revolution in East Germany an early full reunification originally seemed unlikely despite the linguistic, historical, cultural and financial links and despite a clamour for reunification from groups in both countries. In November 1989 Chancellor Kohl of West Germany prepared a 10 point plan for the means of achieving a federation between West and East Germany. The plan received substantial backing in the Bundestag. A major pre-condition set by Kohl and shared by West German financial and industrial institutions was completely free elections in East Germany which subsequently took place in March 1990. The initial response to this initiative within East

THE GERMAN ECONOMIES IN 1988

	West Germany	East Germany
Gross National Product (DM bn)	2,121	268
Exports (DM bn)	568	90
Imports (DM bn)	440	87
Population (million)	61.1	16.7
GNP per capita (DM)	35,000	16,000

Source: Bundesbank Publications.

DISTRIBUTION OF FOREIGN TRADE IN 1987

(%)	East Germany	West Germany
Comecon	67	4
West Germany	7	—
East Germany	—	1
The European Community	6	53
Other	20	42
	100	100

Sources: EIU; Bundesbank Publications.

THE STRUCTURE OF THE ECONOMY IN 1985

% of Total GNP	East Germany	West Germany
Agriculture and Forestry	8	2
Manufacturing and Energy	70	35
Construction	6	5
Transportation and Distribution	4	15
Retail and Service Sector	9	26
Others	3	17
	100	100

Note: Sectors not exactly comparable.
Sources: EIU; Bundesbank Publications.

Germany seemed to indicate, however, that the desire for reunification was far from overwhelming. The major new political force in East Germany, the New Forum Party, indicated that they wished to maintain some form of socialist state, which appeared to preclude an early reunification with capitalist West Germany. These views were shared by the government of Hans Modrow who succeeded Egon Krenz as Prime Minister in December 1989. The Soviet President Gorbachev, who has been instrumental in encouraging change in Eastern Europe, originally stated that he saw no need for German reunification. On a visit to East Germany in January 1990 he did, however, moderate this view by indicating that he had no objections to a carefully planned move towards reunification within the context of an overall European agreement on security and military alliances. This change of stance by Gorbachev triggered a snowballing of opinion in favour of an early full reunification in both Germanies, with regular demonstrations in East German cities proving that the public was not prepared to endure a gradual or diluted approach to unification with West Germany. Claims made early in 1990 that the East German economy was on the verge of collapse further reinforced the view that reunification was a necessity. The most likely outcome at this stage therefore seems to be an early move towards a form of federation between the two Germanies subsequently leading to a full reunification. *See* **C85–6**, for more on the political background.

The Two Germanies.

East and West Germany currently have dramatically different economies. West Germany is the most powerful European economy with living standards amongst the highest in the world. The currency (Deutsch Mark) is strong, dominating the European Exchange Rate Mechanism (ERM), and there is a substantial surplus on foreign trade. Along with Japan, West Germany has been a blueprint for a successful capitalist economy over the past quarter of a century. East Germany by

contrast was, until the demise of the Krenz government, one of the most centrally and rigidly controlled economies in the communist bloc. All companies were state owned. Despite possessing some successful manufacturing sectors, lack of access to hard currency and with it modern technologies has stunted economic growth. Foreign trade has been largely with the rest of Comecon, the trading block which incorporates East European countries. Gross National Product per head is no more than one half that in West Germany—and probably significantly less than one half if a realistic exchange rate between the Deutsch Mark and East Germany's Ost Mark is used in making comparisons. The East German economy is much more heavily based on agriculture and less heavily based on the retail and service sectors than West Germany.

With or without reunification it is inevitable that the two German economies will change radically in the 1990s. The likely features include:

(i) The Migration of Labour.

In 1989 around 300,000 people migrated from East to West Germany, with the majority moving in the weeks before the political revolution in October and November. With the changed political climate in East Germany and the prospect of free elections and economic change the flow from East to West can be expected to diminish slightly despite the opening up of the Berlin Wall and the East German border. Even if full reunification takes place, however, the greater potential earnings will still result in a drift of labour towards the West. The boost to West Germany's labour supply that East to West migration will bring should be helpful to their economy in the near term since unemployment is currently falling and job vacancies are rising rapidly. With the help of retraining the influx of labour could help to reduce some of West Germany's skill shortages. Obviously higher public expenditure will be required as a result of the migration and in 1989 an addition to government spending of DM8 billion was announced for the construction of housing. The Federal Labour Office has also stated that up to DM6 billion will need to be spent during 1990/1 on retraining the new workers. There has been some concern in some quarters that the migrant labour will keep down wage levels. These fears are probably unfounded since only a proportion of the migrants are in a position to compete for jobs at the moment and, in addition, the unions should be able to prevent any undercutting of existing wage levels. The more likely prospect is that, even ahead of reunification, wages in East Germany will rise from their current level of around 40 per cent to perhaps 70 per cent of West German rates.

(ii) A Boom for West German Industry?

It appears inevitable that the closer links between East and West Germany will further strengthen German industry in the 1990s. It has been forecast that the higher public expenditure and private sector investment will boost annual growth in West Germany by 1%. The growth in demand for consumer goods both from migrants to West Germany and from East Germans now allowed greater access to foreign goods augurs well for West German output and profits. In particular it is estimated that East Germans spend close to 100% of their net income whilst West Germans spend 60%, and save 40%. Consequently the potential demand for goods from an East Germany growing in affluence is substantial and some forecasts put the boost to consumption expenditure as high as DM20 billion over the period 1989–1992. It is for these reasons that the West German stock market rose rapidly in the weeks after the opening up of the Berlin Wall. In his plans for a move towards federation with East Germany Chancellor Kohl offered to help develop their infrastructure including housing, telecommunications and transport networks. This again offers West German industry an incentive for expansion although the scale of East Germany's requirements will necessitate involvement from other European Community countries. Some major West German companies, including Mercedes and Daimler-Benz, have already started to extend their operations into East Germany. The prospect of reunification makes it inevitable that others will follow quickly.

(iii) The Wider Impact on the West German Economy.

The impact of immigration and economic expansion will inevitably have knock on effects on other aspects of the West German economy. Higher public expenditure will put pressure on the West German government's budget and this prospect has already depressed bond prices. The likelihood is, however, that this will be partly counterbalanced by the higher tax revenues resulting from the increased level of economic activity. Inflationary pressures in West Germany seem likely to increase in the early 1990s due to higher expenditure and these fears have led to forecasts that West German interest rates must rise. This in turn could lead to a realignment of currencies within the European Exchange Rate Mechanism (ERM). This is because other European economies fearing a recession will be reluctant to follow any West German rate increases. In this situation the Deutsche Mark will appreciate in value and a new alignment against other ERM currencies will have to be determined. In addition a reduction in the size of the West German balance of payments surplus of up to DM10 billion per annum is likely in the short term due to the outward investment to East Germany and the enhanced demand for imports deriving from the migrants to the West.

Even ahead of a reunification, however, the major financial problem that has to be addressed is a currency union between East and West Germany. No move towards a proper economic reunification of Germany can occur until the relationship between the strong West German Deutsche Mark and the ailing East German Ost Mark is resolved. In February 1990 West Germany's Chancellor Kohl suggested that currency union should be achieved simply by extending the Deutsche Mark to all German territory—although the exact rate at which Deutsche Marks would replace Ost Marks was unclear. This proposal was initially opposed by Karl Pohl, the President of the Bundesbank, who believed such a scheme would undermine monetary controls and greatly increase inflation. Certainly a straight currency union based on a one-for-one conversion between the two Marks (which is what was proposed, effective from July 1990) will be inflationary. The alternative was to have an exchange rate which reflects the strength of the two currencies, yet this could be as high as 8 Ost Marks for 1 Deutsche Mark and would automatically devalue sharply the capital and savings of East Germans. A possible solution to the problem put forward by the European Commission was to have a transitional currency the "DM-East". This could be issued by the Bundesbank and, for an interim period, it would have limited convertibility and an exchange rate fixed to take account of the productivity gap between the two economies.

The problems with currency union highlight the fact that there are potential pitfalls for West Germany to set against the substantial opportunities arising from moves towards reunification. It has been estimated that the overall cost of transfers to East Germany, including unemployment benefits, wage adjustments and infrastructural investments, could be as high as 5 per cent of West Germany's gross national product. Reunification will not be an inexpensive exercise for West Germany.

(iv) The Impact on the Rest of the European Community.

It is difficult to evaluate at this stage the likely impact of the developments in the two Germanies on the rest of the European Community particularly as the impact of the move to a single market in 1992 will be having its own restructuring effects on the economies of member countries. There seems certain to be a role for the financial institutions of European Community members through the need to fund the estimated DM500 billion of expenditure needed to restructure the East German economy. Discussions have already begun about the establishment of a "European Bank for Reconstruction and Development" to perform a role akin to the World Bank by channelling long term finance from the West to Eastern Europe. The scale of the problems should, however, not be underestimated. One report in 1990 claimed that DM210 billion alone was required to eradicate the major pollution problems in East Germany created by unfettered industrial expansion in the 1970s and 1980s.

Certainly the greater contact with Western Europe will shift the volume of East Germany's foreign trade from Comecon to the European Community. Indeed there were some suggestions in early 1990 that, if reunification did not take place, East Germany might apply for membership of the European Community in its own right. There are however fears that the shift in capital and trade to Eastern Europe will be at the expense of expenditure elsewhere in the Community, with the southern European Community economies (Greece, Spain and Portugal) deemed to be most at risk from such shifts and the resultant geographical relocation of economic activity.

In January 1990 the United Kingdom took the lead in announcing enhanced economic aid to Eastern Europe, including East Germany. The package of measures introduced by the Foreign Secretary, Douglas Hurd, included financial support for retraining, for developing journalistic and parliamentary activities and for extending foreign trade links. The granting of this aid was made dependent upon adequate progress being made in the recipient countries towards full democracy.

Even countries outside Europe—particularly Japan and the USA can be expected to play an investing role in East Germany and the rest of Eastern Europe. The United States is planning to open up export controls on the sales of high technology products to the Eastern bloc. Japan has already made major investments in Eastern Europe in industrial and service industries. Clearly Japan shares the view of the financial markets which see East Germany and the rest of Eastern Europe as having the potential for the fastest economic growth for any region in the world in the 1990s.

The economic and political developments of the past year together with the prospect of reunification have inevitably raised the expectations of East

Germans for higher living standards. It is important though that such expectations do not outpace the growth in output and productivity. Indeed early in 1990 Prime Minister Modrow warned that the prevailing demands for wage and benefits increases amounted to DM40 billion—twice the existing size of the budget deficit.

The revolution in East Germany and the likely moves towards a reunification therefore present major opportunities and several policy dilemmas for West Germany and Western Europe as a whole. Time alone will tell if the excitement and expectations arising in the Germanies from the prospect of reunification are matched by the economic achievements of a united Germany.

THE EUROPEAN MONETARY SYSTEM

The Background.

The issue of full membership of the European Monetary System (EMS) for the United Kingdom came to a head in 1989 following the publication of the Delors Report on the economic and monetary union of European Community (EC) member countries and the Madrid Summit where the Report's proposals were discussed. The issue exposed sharp differences of opinion within the Cabinet with the Prime Minister, Margaret Thatcher expressing strong reservations about the contents of the Delors Report whilst Sir Geoffrey Howe and Nigel Lawson favoured full membership of the EMS and its "Exchange Rate Mechanism" (ERM). The debate was given added colour by the opposition of the Prime Minister's personal economic adviser, Sir Alan Walters, to the EMS. These differences of opinion were central to Nigel Lawson's decision to resign from the Chancellorship in October 1989. Political commentators have also claimed that the earlier removal of Sir Geoffrey Howe from the Foreign Office was in part caused by his differences of opinion over the EMS and European Community policy generally with the Prime Minister. Despite Margaret Thatcher's misgivings it appears that full membership of the EMS is only a matter of time, with the United Kingdom likely to be within the Exchange Rate Mechanism by the end of 1992. This special article explores the history of the EMS and the causes of the United Kingdom's reluctance to become a full member in the 1980s. The potential costs and benefits of membership together with the prospects for extended economic and monetary union within the European Community are also examined.

(a) The EMS: An Attempt to Control Exchange Rate Movements.

The European Monetary System was established in 1979 by the majority of the European Community members in an attempt to regulate and stabilise fluctuations in the movement of European currencies. The move reflected a desire to move away from the extreme volatility in exchange rates which had been a feature of the 1970s. Member countries currencies were aligned against each other at agreed "bilateral central rates". Any divergence from these central rates beyond a defined amount was to be countered by obligatory currency intervention by the member countries. Thus a currency gaining in value and threatening to exceed the maximum limit would be sold in the foreign currency markets by the member countries' central banks; by contrast a weakening member currency would be bought. The proponents of the EMS argued that the exchange rate stability created would provide the financial climate for encouraging trade since businesses would be fairly certain about the future level of member countries currencies. In addition the absence of extreme movements in exchange rates was seen as freeing member countries from the consequences of either a rapidly falling currency (which adds to inflation by pushing up the cost of imports) or an appreciating currency (which pushes up unemployment by making exports uncompetitive). Indeed a managed exchange rate system was seen as a major stepping stone towards economic and monetary union in the European Community by providing a stable currency framework.

The United Kingdom decided however not to become a full member of the EMS. The decision reflected doubts about technical aspects of the

Exchange Rate Mechanism and wider member states. In 1979 the new Conservative Government was adopting monetarist policies in the management of the economy and this precluded full entry since monetarists argue that exchange rates should be allowed to float freely to find their own level based upon the strengths of economies (particularly relative inflation rates). In addition the Government was keen to use the exchange rate to support its economic policy aims. In particular a high exchange rate policy was seen as a means of reducing inflation by cutting import costs and reducing economic activity through its depressing effect on export industries. It was argued that the experiences of the 1950s and 1960s proved that it was impossible to hold exchange rates at fixed, or semi-fixed, levels for any length of time since economies grow at different rates and experience varying levels of inflation with the inevitable knock-on consequences for the health of the currency. Indeed the experiences of the EMS since 1979 support this view: there have been regular realignments of the member countries' currencies, the most recent being in January 1987 with a new realignment likely before the end of 1990. The longest period between realignments has been three years (1983–1986). The regular need for intervention to maintain the periodic alignments has arguably diverted the attention of the member countries from other aspects of domestic economic policy during the 1980s and denied full freedom in determining policy. Concern was also expressed at the time of the launch of the EMS about how the mechanism would lead to the Deutsche Mark, and hence West Germany's Bundesbank, becoming dominant. This has been borne out by events with movements in West German interest rates usually triggering identical movements across Europe—indeed without such parallel adjustments the exchange rate alignments in the ERM would be threatened by the currency levels of the high interest rate members appreciating. In 1987 an attempt was made by the then French Finance Minister Balladur to reduce the relative power of the Bundesbank within the ERM. The move was largely unsuccessful due to the opposition of the Bundesbank although the Basle-Nyborg agreement in September 1987 did extend the role of the European Currency Unit (ECU) at the expense of the Deutsche Mark without affecting the latter's pre-eminence.

The fear of a loss of economic sovereignty to the European Community is general and West Germany in particular therefore strengthened the resolve of the opponents to full EMS membership in 1979. A decade later the stance of the Government was to change.

(b) The EMS: The U.K.'s change of heart in the 1980s.

British sentiment about membership of the EMS became more favourable during the 1980s. The extreme volatility of Sterling during the decade encouraged the view that a fixed exchange rate mechanism would reduce uncertainties for firms engaged in international trade. The relatively low rates of interest and low rates of inflation which were enjoyed by many of the member countries during the 1980s were attributed, by some commentators, to the EMS. It was argued that through bilateral intervention in the foreign exchange markets the need for high interest rates to defend weak currencies in the system was avoided. Some economists indeed began to see full membership of the EMS as a panacea for all sorts of economic problems including slow growth and price inflation. Throughout the decade there was regular speculation that the United Kingdom was on the verge of full membership of the EMS with such speculation usually being accompanied by sharp rises in the prices of stocks and shares. Yet the change of heart of the Government towards the EMS was not really attributable to a belief that full membership would perform miracles for the economy. It was, in fact, more due to wider economic and political changes that were occurring in Europe during the decade. The European Community was expanding with the entry of Spain and Portugal and with this came an expansion in the membership of the ERM, with the Spanish Peseta joining in 1989 on a transitional basis ahead of full participation. The System at the start of 1990 thus comprised the Dutch Guilder, the Belgian Franc, the Deutsche Mark, the Danish Krone and the French Franc, all obliged to remain within 2.25 per cent of their bilateral central rates, and the Italian Lira and Spanish Peseta operating with a 6 per cent band. With such extensive participation, with the U.K.'s growing trading links with other Community members and with the move towards a single European Market devoid of trade barriers within the Community in 1992 it simply became unrealistic to ignore the EMS and the relationship of the British Pound to the currencies of the member countries. Indeed in the recognition of this Nigel Lawson, when Chancellor between 1983 and 1989, increasingly adopted an unofficial target level (of 3 DM) and target range for the Sterling exchange rate against the Deutsche Mark using intervention in the exchange rate markets and interest rate movements (particularly in 1988 and 1989) to sustain them. In this way the UK arguably became a surrogate member of the EMS in the late 1980s. The acceptance of this strategy by the Chancellor was made easier by the move away from monetarist strategies by the Government in the mid-1980s since managed exchange rates have no place within strict monetary policy. By 1989 it seemed that the only barrier to full entry into the EMS was the attitude of the Prime Minister who remained unconvinced of the merits and wary of the longer term initiatives in the European Community for monetary union. Her position on the issue was reinforced by the return of Sir Alan Walters, a fierce opponent of the EMS, as her personal economic adviser in 1989.

(c) The EMS: The Delors Report and the 1989 Madrid Summit.

Two major developments in 1989 eventually brought the UK closer to full membership of the EMS. In April the Delors Report was published (M. Delors being the President of the EEC Commission). The report laid down a three staged approach towards full economic and monetary union in the European Community.

Stage 1 All European Community currencies to be within the EMS. The elimination of all foreign exchange controls (the UK abolished such controls in 1979). The removal of trade barriers and the "co-ordination" of fiscal policy within the European Community;

Stage 2 The establishment of a European System of Central Banks (ESCB). The development of a Community wide monetary policy. The introduction of precise rules for Community and national fiscal policies. Realignments within the EMS only to be undertaken in exceptional circumstances;

Stage 3 Exchange rates within the EMS to become irrevocably fixed. The ESCB to assume responsibility for the formulation and implementation of monetary and exchange rate policy. Community wide fiscal policy to be binding on member states.

The adoption of Stages 2 and 3 would require amendments to existing European Community legislation and the Treaty of Rome.

At the subsequent Madrid Summit the Prime Minister was strongly critical of the content of stages two and three stating that such supranationalism would eliminate the ability of member countries to determine their own economic policies. However, with the encouragement of the then Foreign Secretary Sir Geoffrey Howe, she committed the UK to stage one of the plan. Exactly when and on what terms the UK is to become a full EMS member was however unclear and was hardly

helped by the subsequent removal of Howe from the post of Foreign Secretary and the resignation of Lawson from the Chancellorship, since it was these two senior cabinet members who were pushing most keenly for EMS entry. The Prime Minister's position at the start of 1990 was that entry would take place when the time was right and when other EMS members, principally France and Italy, abolished their exchange controls. This probably means no later than 1992 when the single European Market will be established, with the exact timing depending upon when UK interest rates and inflation have fallen to levels comparable with other EMS members and when an agreeable target parity rate for the Pound against the Deutsche Mark has been determined.

Although Delors "stage one" was due to begin for member countries of the EMS in July 1990 stages two and three are due to be discussed at an Inter-Governmental Conference on the steps to full union in December 1990. The UK seems set to remain opposed in principle to stages two and three and has already forwarded alternative ideas including competition within the European Community between the central banks and currencies of the EMS members. Such counter notions have, to date, got fairly short shrift from the other major members of the European Community who seem intent upon embarking upon the road towards economic, monetary and fiscal union regardless of whether the UK is a fellow traveller.

(d) The EMS: A Panacea for the UK Economy?

As and when full membership of the EMS is taken up by the UK, it will be interesting to see how the economy responds to a fixed exchange rate system. It has been argued and it is tempting to believe, that just because many EMS members have achieved steady growth with low inflation and low interest rates over the past decade then these benefits will be automatically conferred on the UK via a convergence towards European inflation and interest rates after full entry. The reality is likely to be different and lessons may be learned from Spain's experience after joining in 1989. Because of Spain's relatively high interest rates capital flowed into the country after EMS entry leading to a rise in the value of the Peseta to the point where the upper 6 per cent band was in danger of being exceeded. The obvious reaction was to use cuts in interest rates and foreign exchange intervention to reduce the Peseta's level. Both of these policies were however inflationary at a time when inflation in Spain was already accelerating. Consequently Spain reluctantly considered a sharp tightening of fiscal policy to neutralise the impact of the expansionary monetary policies required by the ERM. Such an outcome is hardly reassuring for the UK whose full entry into the exchange rate mechanism could also result in an inflow of capital and lower interest rates in the short term and the need for a tighter fiscal policy to control the inflationary consequences in the longer term.

Full membership of the EMS seems only a matter of time for the UK regardless of the debate about the likely economic effects. Many commentators are suggesting that entry will take place in the run up to the next general election, since a move into the ERM will probably allow UK interest rates to fall quickly. The long term benefits of entry seem however greatly in doubt since, as Avinash Persaud of UBS Phillips and Drew says, "like fools' gold, the glitter of the EMS quickly fades once exposed to an impartial assessment".

MONEY
MATTERS

This popular section, specially devised for readers of Pears, provides
a concise yet authoritative introduction to the complex problems
of money, investment and taxation.
This edition includes details of the
1990 Budget as well as a description
of the new system of Independent
Taxation for married couples and
the Community Charge (Poll
Tax).

TABLE OF CONTENTS

MONEY MATTERS

I. MONEY

1. SPENDING

Planning a Budget.

Most of us need some form of financial planning. Wages and salaries are usually paid in regular weekly or monthly instalments. The flow of expenditure, on the other hand, is normally much less even. Bills often seem to get lonely and like to arrive in batches. The way to deal with this problem is to work out an annual budget consisting of your major expenditures. An example is given in Table 1.

TABLE 1. *An Example of an Annual Budget*

	£
Rates or Poll Tax	700
Mortgage or rent	2,000
House and contents insurance	200
Gas	200
Electricity	200
Telephone	200
Road tax	100
Car insurance	200
Television rental and licence	200
Life assurance	100
Holidays	1,000
Christmas expenses	500
Annual subscriptions	100
Clothing	400
Season ticket	—
	6,100
Allowance for price increases (say 5% of 6,100)	305
Estimated total bills	6,405
Monthly average	533·75

List the amounts you spent last year under each of the headings. As prices are likely to continue to rise, it is worth adding on a little extra to be on the safe side. In the example, average price increases of 5 per cent are allowed for. It is also sensible to add a small amount for unforeseen expenditure. Having calculated your estimated total bills for the forthcoming year, you can then calculate how much money has to be reserved each month or each week for these items. In the example, this works out at £533·75 per month, or £123·17 per week on average.

Preparing a budget like this has a number of advantages. First of all, by planning in this way you can save money. For example, it is cheaper to pay car tax once a year rather than every six months. Annual season tickets are cheaper than monthly or quarterly ones. Also, it is usually cheaper to pay your insurance premiums in one go, rather than by instalments. A second advantage is that you have a clear idea of your major expenses, so you know how much money there is left over for day-to-day expenses. Thirdly, because the money can be put aside when you are paid, the cash is usually ready when the bills come in.

It is also possible to arrange this through a bank with a budget account. What happens is that you calculate your monthly expenses as above. The bank then transfers that amount each month from your current account (more on this below)

to a separate budget account. A separate cheque book is provided for this account. When the bills come in, you simply write out a cheque for them. Using a bank in this way does have an advantage in that you can overdraw on the budget account if a lot of bills come in early in the year. The bank will, however, expect the account to run mainly in credit. There is also a charge for this service.

2. SPENDING ECONOMICALLY

Many forms of expenditure are almost unavoidable. The Community Charge and rent or mortgage payments cannot usually be altered unless you move home. Nevertheless, in many other areas savings can be made.

As a general guide, the Consumers' Association publishes a monthly magazine *Which?* This provides a great deal of information about the price and quality of different products. Information about subscriptions to this magazine can be obtained from *Which?*, Subscription Department, PO Box 44, Hertford SG14 1SH. Alternatively, it is available at libraries.

Food.

There are several points to remember when buying food. First of all, larger shops often sell goods at lower prices than smaller shops. As most people know, supermarkets often sell their own brands of many products. "Own brands" are, on average, cheaper than the brands of leading manufacturers. For example, on items such as peas, baked beans, soup and soap powder, own brands can be up to 15 per cent cheaper. On some lines, such as washing-up liquid, the savings can be even greater. There is no reason to suppose that own brands are inferior. They are commonly produced in the same place as the branded products. Often, the only difference is the packaging—and the price.

Other savings can be made with stores' special offers. Things like washing powder and toothpaste will be needed sooner or later; so it can make sense to buy these items when an offer is on, rather than waiting until you have run out.

When comparing prices, it is worth bearing in mind that the quantity varies as well. It is, therefore, better to compare the *unit cost* of products. This is the cost per ounce or pound. Packaging can easily make something look larger than it actually is.

Domestic Appliances.

Like food, the price of domestic appliances varies. Much of the variation depends on the number of extras. For example, a basic gas or electric cooker costs something in the region of £300. Such a cooker would serve a family quite adequately. If, however, you want a model with extras, then the cost can be £800 or more. A second important factor is where the appliance is sold. The price of the same model can vary considerably from place to place, so it is very worthwhile shopping around. There may also be a delivery charge. Discount warehouses are usually the cheapest place to buy appliances. The sales can also make a substantial difference to the price. Most appliances are likely to be cheaper in both winter and summer sales. Fridges are often particularly good bargains in winter sales, for obvious reasons. There is nothing inferior about domestic appliances sold in sales. Traders usually want to clear their premises for new lines. They also realise that January and the summer would otherwise be very lean times for them.

A particular question often arises as to whether to rent or to buy a television set. The advantages of renting are that repairs and service calls are included in the rent. If the set breaks down it is also likely to be repaired more quickly than if you owned a set. And if it cannot be fixed straight-away the rental company will provide a substitute until the original is repaired. On the other hand, it is generally true that it is cheaper to buy in the long run. This is true even if you buy the set on hire purchase. And if you decide to dispose of the set, you can always sell it. (Provided, of course, that any HP payments have been completed.)

Cars.

Cars are very expensive to buy and to run. It is quite common for the annual cost of running a car (including the drop in its secondhand value) to exceed £3,000. So it is worth thinking care-fully about whether or not to buy a car. It may be cheaper to use taxis. They also have the advantage of removing any worries about parking, maintenance and drunken driving.

If you do decide to buy a car, the initial invest-ment can be greatly reduced by buying a second-hand car. The value of most cars drops con-siderably in their first year. There are other advantages in buying second hand. A used car will have been run in and the teething troubles ironed out. However, if the car is more than three years old it must have an MOT (Ministry of Transport) test every year. The test is now very tough, so cars should be checked carefully before purchase.

If you do not get a guarantee from a reputable dealer you should consider having it examined by the A.A. or the R.A.C. They charge a fee for the service, but it may avoid a purchase you later regret. Alternatively, if faults are discovered it may enable you to negotiate a lower price.

Before setting out to buy a secondhand car it is sensible to study the market. Car price guides are widely available. They provide useful infor-mation on cars of different ages and condition. The two major sources of secondhand cars are professional dealers and private sellers. You are unlikely to get a bargain if you buy from a dealer, since they are very familiar with the value of used cars. If you buy privately you avoid the mark-up of the dealer, and so can expect to pay less. Even if you buy a new car, it can pay to ask for a dis-count, especially if you are paying cash. Dealers receive a sizeable discount on new cars. You may be able to persuade one to pass some of it on to you. Whatever sort of car you buy, new or old, you should give it a test drive. Even new cars are not immune from faults.

3. BORROWING

Under certain circumstances, it can be advan-tageous to borrow money. The biggest example in many peoples' lives is buying a house with the aid of a mortgage (*see* **H11**). On a much smaller scale most goods can be bought with the aid of credit. This does enable you to enjoy something without having to wait while you accumulate the cash to buy it outright. As prices rise, you may also be able to buy goods more cheaply through buying straightaway. And you save money buy-ing things like season tickets annually. But there are some disadvantages with borrowing. Some people might find easy credit too much of a tempt-ation and spend more than they can afford.

In addition, borrowing usually costs money. How much it costs depends on where the loan comes from. At the cheapest end of the scale are first mortgages. At the beginning of 1990 mortgage interest rates varied around 14·5 per cent and overdraft rates varied from 16 to around 22 per cent. At the other end of the scale are second

mortgages, some hire-purchase arrangements and check trading. The rates of interest at the top end can be 30 per cent per year or even more. There are many sources of credit, so only the main ones will be discussed here.

Banks.

Banks offer three main types of loan: over-drafts, ordinary loans and personal loans. In recent years they have also increased their lending for house purchase. An overdraft is simply an agree-ment with your bank manager allowing you to overdraw on your account up to an agreed figure. There is no formal arrangement about the timing of repayments, though the agreement will normally be for a specified period. Ordinary and personal loans, on the other hand, are repaid on a regular basis.

Credit Cards.

Banks also provide credit cards. Barclays Bank operate *Barclaycard* which is also associated with the *Visa* credit card system. The four other main banks, Lloyds, Midland, National Westminister and The Royal Bank of Scotland have their own credit card—*Access*. The Trustee Savings Banks issue their *Trustcard*. In addition, in the last few years a number of other financial institutions have issued their own credit cards. Credit cards are very simple to use. When you buy something on credit the retailer makes out a sales voucher which you check and sign. The retailer then gives you a copy. You can also draw cash from a bank displaying the appropriate sign. Every month you are sent a statement showing how much you owe. You then have to repay a certain minimum amount. If you wish to pay more, or clear all the debt completely, you can.

Most credit cards can be obtained without charge, but Lloyds and Barclays Banks have now set an annual fee. Others may follow. Normally no interest is charged if the full amount is repaid within 25 days of the date of the statement. If only part payment is made then the period of free credit is from the date of the purchase until the date of the statement. After that interest is charged on a daily basis on the outstanding balance. The arrangements for amounts drawn in cash differ. Barclaycard and Trustcard have a 1·5 per cent handling charge, but the 25 days free credit is still allowed. Access does not impose a handling charge, but charge interest from the date the cash was drawn.

The rate of interest charged has fluctuated in recent years between 1·5 and 2·25 per cent. These rates are equivalent to rates of interest as follows:

Rate per month %	Equivalent rate per year %
1·50	19·5
1·75	23·1
2·00	26·8
2·25	30·6

However, if the interest-free period is taken into account the annual rate of interest is lower. How much lower depends on when you made the pur-chase. If the purchase was made just before the statement you may only get about 30 to 35 days free credit in all. If, however, the purchase was made, say, three weeks before the statement, you would get up to 56 days free credit. If the retailer is slow in sending details of the purchase to the credit card centre the interest-free period may be even longer. For this reason, it can be useful to have two credit cards. If your statement dates differ, you can then use the card with the statement date furthest away. Credit cards can also be used overseas.

If you lose a credit card, or have it stolen, you should inform the credit centre at once. You are liable if anyone dishonestly obtains goods with the card until the credit card centre is told of the loss of the card. However, provided the card-holder acts in good faith, Access, Barclaycard and Trustcard limit this liability to £25.

Other Cards.

There are several other cards. Two of the main ones are *American Express* and *Diners Club*. They have longer free credit periods than Access

Barclaycard and Trustcard, but they are accepted by fewer outlets in Britain. They also charge for the card itself.

Hire Purchase.

The rates of interest on hire-purchase agreements are generally higher than those charged on bank or credit-card loans. To see this clearly, we should describe two ways of quoting interest rates. Salesmen sometimes quote "flat" rates of interest. This refers to the difference between the cash price and the cost if bought on credit. For example, suppose you could buy a cooker for £500 cash, or £625 payable in monthly instalments for one year. The extra cost of buying on credit is £125. This gives an annual flat rate of interest of 25 per cent on the £500 borrowed. But this is not the real rate of interest. The reason is that from the first month some of the capital has been repaid. In fact, the average amount borrowed throughout the year is just over £250. The true rate of interest on the balance outstanding (rather than the original loan) is over 40 per cent in this example. This calculation is known as the APR or annual percentage rate.

Insurance Companies.

If you have an insurance policy you may be able to borrow money from the insurance company on the strength of it. The policy would have to have a cash-in, or surrender value. The interest charged on such loans is often lower than other rates.

4. SAVING

There are several reasons why people save. They include the need to meet unforeseen expenditures, to provide for retirement or simply to buy large items such as a car. It is normally cheaper to pay cash rather than to buy on hire purchase. Although many people save only when they have money left over from their various outgoings, it is better to plan savings. That is, budget your income and expenditure and to regard savings as part of your regular outgoings. This allows capital to be built up on a regular basis.

Before deciding where to invest these savings there are factors that you should consider. The first is whether to invest for short or long periods of time. It is generally true that long-term savings attract a higher rate of interest. However, there are usually financial penalties or constraints that will restrict your ability to draw on the money when required. This loss of *liquidity* is important, since you may require money immediately to meet unforeseen expenditures.

You must also consider how taxation affects the income from your investments. This is considered in the section on taxation. Nevertheless, it is important to establish the tax position of different investments. For instance, the rates of interest offered by building societies are free of income tax at the basic rate. These rates may appear low in comparison with other rates, but if you are paying tax at the basic rate they can be quite advantageous. If you do not pay tax, then there are normally better investments, since you cannot claim back the tax already paid by the building society. From 6 April 1985 this system of taxing interest has been extended to banks, but National Savings still offer a range of investments which are either tax free, or taxable but tax is not deducted at source. However the goverment has announced that this system will be changed on 6 April 1991 so that non-taxpayers will no longer pay tax on bank and building society accounts from that date.

Another consideration is the rate at which prices are increasing; that is the rate of inflation. The saver is particularly concerned with what goods or services money will buy in the future. The important rate of return of an investment is not the nominal or money rate of interest but the real rate of interest. If, for example, an investment offers a return of 7 per cent per annum and the rate of inflation is 5 per cent per annum, the real rate of interest is 2 per cent per annum. The individual requires 5 per cent per annum merely to maintain the purchasing power of his capital.

The real rate of interest is very important during periods of inflation because it may well be negative. For example, if the nominal rate of interest

is 7 per cent per annum and the rate of inflation rises again, to say, 10 per cent per annum the real rate of interest is minus 3 per cent per annum. This means that when the saver withdraws money in the future, it will not buy the same quantity of goods or services it would have when the investments were made.

Having considered these general points, we can now look at the specific forms of investment open to the saver.

National Savings.

These are schemes provided by the Government. They include The National Savings Bank, Savings Certificates, Premium Bonds and the Save-As-You-Earn Scheme.

The National Savings Bank.

This was formerly known as the Post Office Savings Bank. There are over 20,000 post offices in the U.K. where you can deposit or withdraw money. There are two types of account available:

Ordinary Accounts.

Ordinary accounts can be opened with as little as £5. They can also be opened for young children, but withdrawals are not normally allowed until the child reaches seven years of age.

Interest is calculated on each complete £1 deposited for a full calendar month. The money begins to earn interest from the first day of the month after it is deposited. It does not earn interest on the month in which it is withdrawn. You should therefore try to deposit money towards the end of the month and withdraw at the beginning of the month. There are two rates of interest. In 1990 these are 2·5 per cent and 5 per cent. The higher rate applies to balances of £500 or more, and the lower rate to other balances. The interest is added on 31 December of each year, and the first £70 is tax free. The maximum amount normally allowed in an account is £10,000.

Up to £100 a day can be drawn on demand from your account. The bank book will be retained for checking if the withdrawal exceeds £50. If you require more than £100 you will have to allow a few days before you get your money. This is because you must apply in writing. Greater flexibility in withdrawing money can be achieved by having more than one account. For example, if you have two accounts you can draw up to £200 on demand. If you have a 'Regular Customer Account', you can withdraw up to £250 a day at your chosen post office and still retain your bank book. The £250 can also be drawn in Thomas Cook travellers cheques. A person qualifies for a Regular Customer Account if he or she has used the chosen post office for at least six months.

Ordinary accounts also have a 'Paybill' service. This allows you to pay bills directly from your account. You can pay one or more at a time provided their total value is not over £250. This service covers bills which can normally be paid through the Post Office, such as electricity, gas, rates and the TV licence.

The advantage of the system is its accessibility, since there are post offices in almost every town and village, and they are open six days a week. It is cheap, since there are no bank charges and money earns interest. Also, money is available on demand.

So, National Savings accounts are a good place to keep small amounts of money to meet unforeseen expenditures. On the other hand, the services offered are still limited, when compared with banks for example.

Investmenmt Accounts.

Like ordinary accounts, anyone over the age of seven can open an account. Children under seven can have one opened on their behalf. The minimum sum required to open an account is £5. The rate of interest is higher than an ordinary account and is liable to tax, but tax is not withheld at source. The upper limit on deposits was £100,000 up to 31 December 1989. From 1 January 1990 the upper limit is £25,000. However, existing holdings of more than £25,000 are not affected, though no further deposits may be made over the new limit. In 1984 the method of calculating interest on investment accounts was changed. Previously interest had been calculated in the same way as for ordinary accounts. From 1 January 1984 interest is calculated on a daily basis. This means that interest is earned on each whole pound for every day it is in the account. The interest is automatically credited on 31 December each year. The current rate of interest is displayed at post offices.

There is no limit on the amount of money that can be withdrawn. However, notice of one month is required. Investment accounts are better than ordinary accounts for long-term savers, although higher rates of interest can be obtained elsewhere. The rate of interest is more attractive to non-tax payers when compared with the rates offered by building societies and banks, which are tax paid.

National Savings Certificates.

There have been thirty-four issues of fixed interest Savings Certificates, but only one is on sale at any particular time. At the time of writing, the 34th Issue was on sale. The minimum investment is £25, and an individual can invest up to £1,000. However there are special facilities for people cashing in earlier Issues of Certificates, which they have held for at least five years, and are reinvesting in the 34th Issue. If they do this, they may hold up to £10,000 of 'Reinvestment Certificates' of the 34th Issue in addition to any purchases made within the general £1,000 limit. This £1,000 (or £11,000) may be held in addition to any holdings of other National Savings Certificates. Instead of earning interest in the usual way, the value of the Certificates rises at an accelerating rate. As shown in Table 2, the increase in value of the 34th Issue over five years is equivalent to a compound interest rate of 7·5 per cent per annum.

TABLE 2. *The rates of interest on the 34th Issue of Savings Certificates*

Minimum Period held	Rate of interest (per annum from date of purchase)
1 year	6·00%
2 years	6·25%
3 years	6·50%
4 years	7·00%
5 years	7·50%

This is free of both income tax and capital gains tax. If allowance is made for the basic rate of income tax, 7·5 per cent is equivalent to 10 per cent gross. So, for example, after five years a £25 Certificate would become worth £35·89, and Certificates to the value of £1,000 would become worth £1,435·63. Interest is earned for each completed period of three months. No interest is earned on Certificates cashed in the first year except for the 34th Issue Reinvestment Certificates mentioned above.

You need not cash in Certificates when they reach maturity. In most cases, however, it will pay to do so. The General Extension Rate, the rate of interest currently paid on matured Certificates, is now well below most interest rates. Again anyone can hold certificates, including children under seven.

Index-linked National Savings Certificates.

These were originally known as 'granny bonds' because when index-linked certificates were first issued they were only available to people over a certain age. This restriction no longer applies and the version currently available is the Fourth Issue. Provided the certificates are held for at least a year, their value is linked to increases in prices. Interest is also paid and the rate increases every year, from 3 per cent after the first year up to a maximum of 6 per cent after five years. If the certificates are held for five years the overall return is 4·04 per cent. (This is in addition to the increase in their value to match inflation and, once the interest is added to the capital, it is index-linked as well.) The repayments are also tax free.

The certificates are available in units of £25. You may buy up to £5,000 of the Fourth Issue in addition to any holdings you may have from previous issues.

The Yearly Plan.

This scheme is designed for regular investment. The saver agrees to make monthly payments by standing order for one year. The payments must be at least £20 per month and higher amounts in multiples of £5 up to a maximum of £200. At the end of the first year a Yearly Plan Certificate is issued to the value of the payments and the interest they have earned so far. The maximum rate of interest is earned if the Certificate is then held for four full years.

Once a plan has been taken out, the rate of interest in force at the time is guaranteed for five years. The payments can be continued beyond the first year if desired. The saver simply continues his payments and each extra year's payments gain another certificate. The returns on the Yearly Plan scheme are tax free.

Premium Savings Bonds.

Premium Bonds are one of the most popular forms of national savings. No interest is earned as such on the bonds. Instead, you have a regular chance to win a cash prize each week and month. The monthly prize fund is set by calculating one month's interest at the rate of 6·5 per cent per year on all bonds eligible for the draw.

All the prizes are tax free. However, before a bond is included in the draw it has to be held for three calendar months following the month in which it was bought. The winning numbers are generated by ERNIE (Electronic Random Number Indicator Equipment). The winning numbers are drawn entirely at random so that each bond has an equal chance of winning.

The size of the prizes varies from £50 to £250,000. Prizewinners are notified by post, so it is important to notify the Bonds and Stock Office of any change of address. The numbers of prize-winning bonds are published in the London Gazette Supplement which can be consulted at major post offices. In addition most daily newspapers publish the numbers of bonds which have won the larger prizes. If you fail to claim a prize at the time of the draw, this can be done later.

Premium Bonds can be bought at post offices, and banks. Any person over the age of 16 can buy bonds. A parent or guardian can buy bonds on behalf of their children in multiples of £10. For individuals aged 16 or over the mimimum initial purchase is now £100 and the maximum holding is £10,000. The bonds can be cashed by completing a withdrawal form available at post offices. Although bondholders can always realise the amount they invested originally, it should be remembered that there is no interest and as inflation continues, the real value of Premium Bonds falls.

Capital Bonds.

Capital bonds are for people who wish to put some money away for a period of five years. They are available in multiples of £100 and there is no maximum limit on the amount that can be held. On each anniversary of the purchase interest is added and the rate of interest increases each year. The amount of interest is guaranteed over the period. At current rates a £100 bond would be worth £105·50 at the end of the first year rising to £176·24 at the end of five years. The bonds are repayable in full at the end of this period with all the interest due.

Although the interest is paid at the end of the five years, for income tax payers the interest is taxable each year. No further interest is earned after five years. Early repayment can be made after three months' notice is given but no interest is payable for repayments made in the first year.

Income Bonds.

These bonds provide a regular income from capital. The minimum investment is £2,000. Extra amounts can be invested in multiples of £1,000. The maximum holding was £100,000 up 31 December 1989 and £25,000 since then. Existing holdings over £25,000 are not affected but no further purchases may be made over the new limit. The interest is paid on the fifth of each month and tax is not withheld at source. Repayments may be obtained by giving three months' notice, but if repayment is made in the first year the bond will earn only half the published rate of interest. The interest rate is adjusted from time to time and full details are available at post offices.

Building Societies.

There are many building societies in the United Kingdom. Some of these are national, others local. All building societies are 'mutual' organisations set up for the benefit of their investing and borrowing members. However, the former Abbey National Building Society has converted itself into a public limited company and other societies may follow. There is no difference in the security of your money as between the small and large societies. If you want to be absolutely sure, you should choose one that has Trustee Status and is a member of the Building Societies Association.

For many years the interest rates quoted by building societies have been tax paid at the basic rate but non-taxpayers have not been allowed to claim the tax back. However the system is to be changed so that from 6 April 1991 non-taxpayers will no longer have to suffer tax on the interest. Interest rates tend to be higher for regular savings and the longer you are prepared to commit your money. The most popular way of saving with a building society has been through a share account. These earn a higher rate of interest than deposit accounts, usually 0·25 per cent more. This is because, in the unlikely situation of a building society failure, deposit account holders have a prior claim on the assets of the society. Interest is calculated daily and credited half-yearly.

Building societies now offer a wide variety of investments, in addition to share accounts. These do differ between different building societies and go by names such as higher interest accounts, term shares, capital bonds, bonus accounts and subscription shares. It is therefore worth shopping around to find those that are nearest your requirements. A final consideration is that those who have invested in a building society may get preferential treatment when it comes to getting a mortgage.

Banks.

Banks offer two main types of account, current and deposit. Current accounts are for everyday transactions and are discussed later (**H8**). Deposit accounts are more suitable for savings.

The rates of interest offered on deposit accounts do tend to change more quickly than those offered by other schemes. This is because the deposit rate is based on each bank's base rate which change as interest rates generally change. The deposit rate is usually between 4½ and 3 per cent below the base rate. The current rate offered by the various banks is usually on display at the bank branches. Interest is calculated on a daily basis. The interest is taxable, but in the past tax has not been deducted at source. However, from 6 April 1985, bank interest has been paid in the same way as building society interest. There is no minimum or maximum amount that can be deposited. Although seven days notice of withdrawal is technically required, in practice you can withdraw fairly substantial sums on demand. If you do, you will usually lose seven days interest. You can only withdraw money at the branch at which you have an account. If you want ready access to your savings, deposit accounts can be attractive for small amounts of money. But you should look at the rates offered by National Savings, and Building Societies before choosing a deposit account with a bank.

Tax Exempt Special Savings Schemes (TESSAs).

In his Budget in March 1990, the Chancellor of the Exchequer announced that a new method of planned savings would be introduced in January 1991 after consultations with the banks and building societies. This will take the form of Tax Exempt Special Savings Schemes or "TESSAs" and the interest will be free of income tax. The proposal is that anyone over 18 will be able to open one TESSA. He or she will be able to put up to £3,000 into a TESSA in the first year and then up to £1,800 a year up to a maximum of £9,000 over five years. Interest may be withdrawn during this period but only up to the "net of tax" level.

At the end of the five years the saver will receive a bonus consisting of the money which would otherwise have gone in tax, provided that the capital has remained untouched. Capital can be withdrawn at any time but this would lead to the loss of all tax advantages. After five years the account will cease to be tax exempt and any further interest arising will be taxable in the usual way.

Personal Equity Plans.

Personal equity plans (PEPs) were introduced on 1 January 1987 to provide a tax incentive for investing in shares. Individuals over 18 can invest up to £6,000 a year in a PEP (though there is a limit of £3,000 for investment in unit trusts and investment trusts). A person can take out only one PEP in any one year. A husband and wife may have one each, whether or not they are assessed for tax together. All income and capital gains on investments in a PEP are free of tax. Originally, to qualify for tax relief, investments had to be retained for at least one full calendar year but this requirement was abolished in 1989.

PEPs are available from banks and investment companies. The plans have the advantage of permitting tax-free investment in shares, which is particularly beneficial for taxpayers subject to the higher rate of income tax and also to those paying capital gains tax. Obviously this benefit does not extend to non-taxpayers. As with any investment in shares there is the risk that share prices might fall. For this reason, it is sensible to view PEPs as a long term investment. Finally, in considering the tax benefits, you should take account of the charges made by the plan managers.

Gilt Edged Securities.

As well as raising taxes to finance its expenditure, the Government borrows from the general public. It does this by issuing gilt-edged stock. There are basically two types of stock, redeemable and irredeemable. Redeemable or dated stocks are those that the Government has agreed to repurchase on a certain date. Usually, two dates are given. This means that the Government cannot redeem them before the first date, but it must redeem them on or before the last date. Each stock has a *par* or face value of £100. This is the amount that will be repaid on redemption. An example of a redeemable stock is the 8¼ per cent Treasury Stock 1987–1990. Stocks that the Government is not committed to redeem are called irredeemable or undated stocks. The 2½ per cent consol introduced after the Second World War is an example.

The cost of buying or selling securities will depend on whether you go through a stockbroker or through the Department for National Savings, Bonds and Stock Office. It is cheaper to use the National Savings Stock Office, although you can only deal in stocks that are on the National Stock Register. There is no limit to the total amount you may hold. Application forms may be obtained from Post Offices.

The interest or *coupon rate* on a stock is normally paid half-yearly. Some pay quarterly, which is particularly useful for old-age pensioners, for example. This is based on the nominal or par value. For example, the 8¼ per cent Treasury Stocks pays £8·25 per year. However, the price that you pay for the stock will probably be less than par. The effective rate of interest or *running yield* will therefore be greater than 8¼ per cent.

Prices of stocks fluctuate so that their yield keeps in line with interest rates generally. This presents the possibility of a capital gain or loss. However, it is generally true that as the stock approaches redemption, the closer the price will be to par, and the smaller the capital gain. The further away redemption is, the lower the price of the stock, and hence the greater will be the capital gain if the stock is held to redemption. Government securities are a very marketable investment. They can be sold quickly if need be. Also, stocks are free of capital-gains tax if in your possession for more than one year. For larger sums of money, gilt-edged stock provides a good alternative to local authority loans.

Shares.

For the more adventurous, there is the possibility of investing in shares on the stock market. Since share prices can fall as well as rise, it is advisable to "spread your risk." This means that you must have a varied and balanced collection of shares in your portfolio. To do this will require a lot of capital and knowledge of the market. So it is best to seek professional advice from a stockbroker or your bank manager. People with more limited means will be better advised to participate indirectly in the stock market by holding units in a unit trust.

Unit Trusts.

Unit trusts sell 'units' to investors and use the proceeds to buy shares. This allows the investor to spread the risk of his investment over all the shares the trust owns. Unit trusts are run by professional managers who can be expected to know more than many investors about the merits of different securities. The value of the units of a trust are worked out each day in line with the value of the fund's stock market investments. Two prices are quoted. The 'offer' price is the price at which investors can buy units. The 'bid' price is the price at which the managers will repurchase units. The offer price is higher than the bid price and the difference contributes towards the cost of running the trust. In addition, there is usually a small half-yearly or yearly charge. Units can be bought and sold directly from the managers.

Investment Trusts.

Investment trusts are companies which invest in securities. Like unit trusts they enable investors to spread their investment risk. However, unlike unit trusts they have a fixed share capital. The shares in investment trusts are bought and sold in the same way as those of other companies, but some investment trusts also have savings schemes which can be taken out directly with the managers.

Life Assurance as Saving.

Life assurance policies provide an alternative method of saving regular amounts for long periods of time. The various policies are considered in the section on insurance.

5. BANKS

Most people are familiar with the high street banks. These are the clearing banks and are known as the Big Four. They are the National Westminster, Midland, Barclays and Lloyds. In addition, there are a number of smaller banks, such as the Royal Bank of Scotland and the Co-operative Bank. There are also the Girobank and the Trustee Savings Bank. Banks offer a variety of services, and we begin by considering current accounts.

Current Accounts.

A current account is a safe and easy way of making and receiving payments. Opening an account is straightforward. You simply go into the local branch of the bank of your choice and tell the cashier or enquiries clerk that you want to open an account. The bank will want samples of your signature, and you will have to fill in a form giving your name and address. Finally, it will require you to give two references. These could be your employer and a friend with a bank account. To pay further amounts into your account, you simply fill in a form provided by the bank.

Making Payments.

With a current account you will receive a cheque book. This is used in making cash withdrawals from the bank or in making payments without using cash. A cheque is not money. It is merely a written instruction to the bank to pay an amount out of your account, to the person(s) named on the cheque. Cash can be obtained from your local branch. If you require cash from another you must make special arrangements or use a cheque card.

Cheque Cards.

Most retailers are reluctant to accept an unsupported cheque. This is because they do not know if you have sufficient money in your account for the bank to honour the cheque. And, of course, the cheque book may have been stolen. This problem is overcome by a cheque card. The card guarantees that the bank will honour cheques up to £50 or sometimes more regardless of the state of the customer's account. You have to be a reliable and well-established customer before your bank will give you a cheque card. A cheque drawn on a cheque card cannot be stopped or cancelled.

Cash Cards.

A major problem with people who work is access to the banks. Most banks are only open between 9.30 a.m. and 3.30 p.m. from Monday to Friday though some are open on Saturdays. The major banks have various schemes whereby sums of money can be automatically dispensed outside the branch, usually twenty-four hours a day. The problem is that not all branches have these installed.

Standing Orders.

There are other ways of making payments apart from cheques. If asked, the bank will automatically make regular payments from your account. These "standing orders" are useful for paying such things as insurance premiums, subscriptions and mortgage repayments.

Direct Debiting.

Direct debits are slightly different from standing orders. In both cases you give your bank a written instruction to meet payments as they fall due. However, with direct debiting the recipient approaches your bank which then deducts the payment from your account. This can be convenient where the amount varies. The recipient has to tell you beforehand of the date and amount of payment.

Borrowing from your Bank.

You can borrow from your bank by either having an overdraft or a personal loan. An overdraft simply means that your current account is allowed to go from credit to debit, up to a limit agreed with the bank manager. With a personal loan you recieve a lump sum and pay it back in fixed instalments.

Banks prefer to lend money by means of a loan rather than an overdraft. The interest on loans tends to be higher than that charged on an overdraft, but by being overdrawn you might incur higher bank charges. In addition to the services mentioned, banks provide a whole range of other services. These include deposit accounts (considered in the section on Saving), travel facilities, advice on investment, insurance and taxation, safe custody of items and many more. For further information on the additional services banks offer, contact your nearest branch.

Girobank.

The National Giro was set up by the Government to provide a low-cost current-account bank service. When Giro started it was considerably cheaper to run compared with a current account at a bank. However, the difference is now small. Giro can be opened via the post or through the 20,000 Post Offices in the U.K. These are generally open six days a week. You therefore have access to your account for more days and for longer hours than you do with the commercial banks.

The Trustee Savings Bank.

The Trustee Savings Bank has gradually taken on the identity of a clearing bank. It offers cheque accounts which are similar to current accounts. The Trustee Savings Bank also issues its own "Trustcard". This can be used both as a credit card and as a cheque guarantee card for cheques up to £50.

The Trustee Savings Bank also has many other services similar to those offered by the other banks. These include deposit accounts, term deposits, personal loans, unit trusts and the selling of Government stocks at low rates of commission. It thus offers a very competitive alternative to the clearing banks.

6. INSURANCE

Insurance is a contract to pay a premium in return for which the insurer will pay compensation in certain eventualities, for example, fire or theft. In effect, insurance is a means of sharing certain risks. The traditional forms of insurance are general insurance and life assurance. The latter is usually called "assurance" because the cover is given against the occurrence of an event which is inevitable.

Life Assurance.

Life assurance provides a capital sum to your estate in the event of your death. Some policies also combine a savings element so that you receive a lump sum if you survive the period. These are called endowment policies. As a general point, it is just as important that you do not overburden yourself with life assurance as it is to have some form of cover. If you have to give up or surrender your policy before it matures there are usually severe financial penalties. There are three basic types of life assurance: term assurance, whole-life assurance and endowment assurance. All forms of life assurance used to attract tax relief. However, this was changed in the Budget of 13 March 1984 so that the tax relief does not apply to policies taken out after that date.

Term Assurance.

This type of policy provides life assurance for a fixed period of time. Should you die during the term of the policy your estate will receive the sum assured. However, if you survive the period you receive nothing. There are variations on the basic type of term policy. A *decreasing term* policy, for example, is often necessary if you have a mortgage. The sum assured decreases as you pay off the mortgage.

Other types of policies include level and convertible term policies. With *level term* policies the sum assured remains fixed throughout the term of the policy A *convertible term* policy has the additional option of being able to convert it to another kind of policy later on, if you so desire. Term policies provide the cheapest form of life cover.

Whole-Life Assurance.

With this type of policy you are normally required to pay the premiums for the whole of your life-time. Like term assurance, the sum assured is paid out to your estate only on your death. Whole-life policies can either be with or without profits. A with-profits policy will be more expensive, since the sum received on your death will be the sum assured plus a share in the profits made by the company. Having to keep up the premiums after your retirement can be a problem, so *limited payment* policies are available. Premiums are paid until you reach a specific age, although life cover continues until your death. The premiums will be higher than for a straight whole-life policy.

Endowment Assurance.

Both whole-life and term policies provide benefit only on your death. With an endowment policy, benefit is still provided should you die before the maturity date of the policy. But if you survive this period you will receive the sum assured. Like whole-life policies, these policies can be with or without profits. Although the more expensive, with-profits endowment policies are the most popular form of life assurance in this country. However, the proportion of the premium used to provide death cover is small. This is because the chances of dying before the maturity date are usually low. Thus, the bulk of the premiums is used by the company to build up the capital sum on maturity.

Endowment policies are often used in conjunction with loans for house purchase, school fees and for providing for retirement. As well as with-profits investment policies, life assurance companies offer other investment policies. These include equity linked contracts, property bonds and policies linked to building societies. With equity contracts the bulk of the premium is used to purchase units in a unit trust. Property bonds are very similar, except the investment is in property.

General Insurance.

As mentioned earlier, this provides cover for an eventuality that may never happen. The types of general insurance considered here are for house and possessions, motor vehicles, sickness and medical insurance.

Insuring your House.

If you are buying a house on a mortgage the building society will insist that it is insured. The sum that you will have to insure your house for may be more than what you paid for it. This is because the insurance value will be related to the cost of rebuilding the house. It is therefore important to adjust the amount for which the house is insured periodically to keep pace with inflation. Alternatively, you can take out policies which are "index-linked." Although most policies give the same kind of cover, there is no standard house insurance. So you should check to see if your policy covers all eventualities. This is particularly important if your area is prone to such events as flooding or subsidence.

Insuring your Possessions.

Unless you have a combined policy, the contents of your home and other possessions will not be covered by your house insurance. In the past insurance companies have reimbursed the purchase cost of articles, less a charge for wear-and-tear. However, you can get policies that do not make this deduction.

House and Possessions.

If you are a tenant living in rented accommodation you should only buy policies that cover the contents of the house and leave the landlord to buy insurance for the buildings. For owner-occupiers, it is best to buy a combined policy of house and possessions. This has the advantage that it will be generally cheaper than buying two separate policies.

Motor Insurance.

Motor insurance is compulsory by law. However, only a basic minimum is compulsory, and many people prefer to take out more comprehensive policies. Insurance companies offer two main types of policy; third party and comprehensive insurance.

Third-Party Motor Insurance.

The additional cover provided by this type of policy is the cost of repairing the other driver's car. Also, if you incur legal costs in dealing with a claim, these will be reimbursed if your insurer approves your actions. Since third-party insurance does not cover damage to your car, it is only suitable if your car is fairly old. "Third party, fire and theft" will cover you if your car is burnt out or stolen, but not if it is damaged in an accident.

Comprehensive Motor Insurance.

If your car is relatively new and hence more valuable, then you should consider a comprehensive policy. The most important additional benefit of such a policy is cover for loss or accidental damage to your car.

Sickness and Medical Insurance.

If you consider the benefits provided by the National Insurance schemes and the National Health Service to be inadequate, you can take out insurance that provides for you when ill. There are several schemes. *Hospital risk insurance* provides a sum only for the period you are in hospital. You may consider it best to have a *permanent health insurance*. This provides cover for the total period you are ill. In addition to providing an income for yourself when ill, there are schemes that provide for private medical treatment. The most well-known is the British United Provident Association (B.U.P.A.).

Buying Insurance.

Because of the bewildering variety of policies available it is often best to seek professional advice when buying insurance. This can be obtained from an insurance broker or your bank manager.

7. BUYING A HOUSE

Buying a house is very often preferable to renting a home. Your own house provides you and your family with a secure home. A house is also one of the soundest investments available to most people. The general tendency is for house prices to rise, and it is unusual for someone to lose money on a house, if they own it for a number a years. In addition, a house can be a very useful asset. For example, if you wish to move elsewhere the house can always be sold and the proceeds used to buy a home elsewhere. A house can be particularly valuable on retirement. With the mortgage paid off the retired owner can choose from a number of possible courses of action. He or she could continue living in it rent free. If the house proved too large for retirement part of it could always be let out to provide some additional income. Alternatively, the owner could move to a smaller home and the difference in the value of the two houses would provide a useful capital sum.

For many people there is no satisfactory alternative to buying a home. Most people are unlikely to be offered council accommodation. Furthermore, a home owner is likely to find it much easier to move than a council tenant. Councils are often reluctant or unable to offer new accommodation when their tenants wish to move; whereas an owner occupier can always sell his house and buy another elsewhere.

Accommodation rented privately also has its disadvantages. Reasonably priced rented accommodation is often difficult to find. Tenants sometimes pay nearly as much, or even more, in rent than they would have to pay for a mortgage on similar property. And mortgage interest normally attracts tax relief whereas rent does not. Finally, rents are likely to rise as inflation continues. Mortgage repayments on the other hand, although they fluctuate from time to time, are related to the original loan and not to the current value of the property.

The basic drawback of buying a house is the cost of buying and selling. The costs can include solicitor's and surveyor's fees and (in the case of selling) an estate agent's fee. Normally there will be the costs of fitting out a new home—the cost of curtains is one example. These costs clearly mean that it is not advantageous to buy a home if you expect to move in the near future.

An obstacle for many people is cash. One hundred per cent mortgages are uncommon, and the buyer has to find the difference between the mortgage offered and the price of the house. There are also the other fees mentioned above. The position may be illustrated with an example. Mr. and Mrs. Smith agree to buy a house for £50,000. The Smiths' building society is prepared to lend them 95 per cent of the value of the property. In this case, the loan would be £47,500 which leaves the Smiths £2,500 to find. On top of the £2,500, the Smiths have to pay a valuation fee to the building society of, say, £100. The valuation fee is related to the value of the property so that the higher the value, the higher the fee. If the price of the house exceeds £30,000 stamp duty also has to be paid. The rate of the stamp duty is currently 1 per cent of the value of the house. Note that duty is levied on the total price of the house, and not just the excess over £30,000. So, for example, the stamp duty on a £50,000 house would be £500. The Smiths also decide to have a professional survey of the house done in order to see if there are any defects in the property. The surveyor's fee depends on how detailed the buyer wishes the survey to be. In this example the fee is £200. Finally, the Smiths receive a solicitor's bill for £350. The solicitor's charge will depend partly on the value of the house, and partly on how much work the solicitor has to do to transfer the house from the seller to the buyer.

In this example, therefore, the Smiths need at least £3,650 of their own money. Frequently the amount of money needed will be greater than this. For example, if the Smiths' mortgage were limited to 90 per cent of the value of the house they may have had to find at least £6,150.

Cost of the house	£50,000
Mortgage	£47,500
	2,500
Valuation fee	100
Survey fee	200
Solicitor's fee	350
Stamp duty	500
	£3,650

It should also be borne in mind that more money is needed to furnish the house. A first-time buyer needs almost everything from curtains to a cooker, and from doormats to a dinner service. Not all of these things need to be bought straight away of course. Nevertheless, some items, such as something to sleep on, and to eat off, will be needed almost immediately.

So it can be seen that, unless one is likely to move in the near future, buying a house can be a sensible decision. The key thing is to save up a reasonable sum of money towards the various costs. The next step is choosing a home.

Choosing a House.

Given the price of houses, selecting your future home is clearly not a decision to be rushed. Possibly the first thing to do is to work out how much you can afford to pay. If you need a mortgage, building societies and other lenders will give you a rough indication of the maximum amount they will lend. They cannot give a precise figure, however, because the amount a society will lend depends not only on your income but also the house itself. There is more on this below. The next stage is to decide where you would like to live. If you are not familiar with the area it pays to spend time studying a map in detail. That way you soon get an idea of the proximity of each area to your work, to the nearest shopping centre and so on. It is also worth thinking carefully about the type of house you want. You may, of course, be influenced by what is available. Nevertheless, if you have a fairly clear idea of what you want a lot of time can be saved by eliminating houses that are obviously unsuitable. Features to think about include whether you want a house, bungalow or flat; the number of bedrooms you require and whether you want a large, medium or small garden.

The next move is to find out as much as possible about the current state of the home market. Estate agents are always delighted to deluge prospective home buyers with details of many properties. Many of them might be unsuitable for you, but they will begin to give you an idea of the value of different houses. You may also change your mind about the sort of house you want. Estate agents are not the only source of information about houses for sale. Houses are often advertised privately, usually in the local newspaper. And because the seller will be saving hundreds of pounds in estate agent's fees, you might be able to buy a house advertised privately for a bit less than it it were handled by an agent.

There are several other considerations that should be borne in mind. For example, if you are likely to have to move within a few years you may wish to buy a house which is relatively easy to resell. Such a house might be a fairly modern three-bedroomed semi-detached house which is close to shops and schools: rather than a "character" property in a remote area.

Buying a House.

The process of buying a house should not be rushed either. In fact, at this stage it is well to have two or three properties in mind. This reduces the disappointment should you fail to get your first choice. It also puts you in a better bargaining position over the price of the house. There is nothing sacred about the asking price.

Sellers will often ask for a bit more than they think they will probably get. So, depending on the state of the market, it can often pay to offer less than the advertised price.

When a price is agreed, make it "subject to contract." Neither party is formally bound to the agreement until the contracts are actually signed. Before that happens there are a number of things to be done. First of all you will probably want a solicitor. It is not absolutely necessary to use a solicitor, but unless you are familiar with the procedure it is usually advisable to do so. If you need a mortgage the next thing to do is to give full details of the house you intend to buy to your building society or bank manager. He will then arrange to have the property surveyed and valued. The purpose of this is to safeguard the building society's money by making sure that the house is a good investment. When the building society is ready it will inform you how much it is prepared to lend on the house. Your solicitor should then be instructed to complete the remaining formalities.

As soon as the solicitors are satisfied about the technicalities of the purchase the next stage is the signing and exchange of contracts. The contract is usually prepared in duplicate with one copy to be signed by the buyer and one by the seller. The buyer is normally expected to pay a deposit of 10 per cent of the purchase price when contracts are exchanged. The exchange of contracts legally commits both parties to the purchase. This commitment stands regardless of what happens thereafter. This is why it is important for you or your solicitor or both to find out as much as possible about the property before the contract is signed. The contract will contain a number of details, including the date on which the deal will be completed. The date is usually a few weeks ahead and allows both parties to make final arrangements before the house is actually handed over. On the completion date the balance of the purchase money is paid, and the purchaser can take possession of the house.

The length of time between finding a house of your choice and taking possession can vary considerably. It depends on the number of complications involved. If everything goes well it would probably take between eight and ten weeks to buy the house. Such is the process of buying a home. However for many people the major consideration is the mortgage. It is therefore worth describing mortgages in greater detail.

Mortgages.

A "mortgage" is a technical term meaning that certain rights over one's property are given to someone else as security for a loan. In other words, if you buy a house with a loan you give a mortgage as security. In everyday usage, however, a mortgage refers just to the loan, even though the property is still used as security. Even if you can afford to pay cash, it is often worthwhile buying a house with the aid of a mortgage. There are several reasons for this. First of all, if the house is to be your main residence the mortgage interest on the first £30,000 borrowed qualifies for tax relief. Secondly, as inflation continues the value of money declines, and so the real value of the mortgage also declines. As a result, the mortgage repayments will not tend to rise in line with inflation.

It is true that interest rates fluctuate and that when they rise your mortgage repayments will rise as well. But sooner or later the rate of interest will fall again. In the meantime, higher interest payments are mitigated by higher tax relief. In addition, when interest rates rise it is sometimes possible to extend the repayment period, rather than increase the monthly repayments. The most common types of mortgage are repayment mortgages and endowment mortgages.

Repayment Mortgages.

Repayment mortgages are usually the most straightforward. They are repaid in equal monthly instalments. Each payment consists partly of interest and partly of a repayment of capital. In the early years the repayments consist almost entirely of interest. As the loan is paid off, the interest element declines.

It should be noted that in April 1983 the method of giving tax relief on mortgages changed. Previously the taxpayers received the relief directly through a reduction in their tax payments. Now, for most mortgages, the Inland Revenue gives the relief directly to the lenders and the borrowers pay the lenders less instead. With these arrangements there is no longer a need for the old "option mortgage" scheme, which has now been discontinued. Loans within that scheme have been incorporated into the new arrangements.

Endowment Mortgages.

An "endowment mortgage" is a mortgage linked to an insurance policy. When the policy matures it pays off the mortgage. In the meantime you only pay interest on the loan. If you die before the end of the agreement the insurance policy would pay off the mortgage. Endowment mortgages usually cost more than repayment mortgages because of the premium for the insurance policy. However, there is the advantage that as with other insurance policies, it is possible to have a "with-profits" element in an endowment policy. This costs more, but it means that the insurance company not only guarantees to provide a minimum sum but also adds "bonuses" each year. The size of the bonus depends on the investment position of the company. When the policy matures the pay-out (including bonuses) will cover the mortgage and leave you with a substantial sum as well.

Where to Get a Mortgage.

The majority of mortgages are supplied by building societies and in recent years banks have become an important source of mortgages. Some insurance companies also provide mortgages, but this is only a minor source of loans. Some employers, such as banks and building societies, will provide their employees with loans at favourable rates.

Getting a Mortgage.

The first thing to do is to plan ahead. As we have seen, you will probably need to put up a substantial sum of money of your own, so you should start saving as soon as possible. It can be advantageous to save by investing in a building society. When mortgage funds are in short supply societies are likely to consider their own investors before casual applicants. Building societies have fairly strong preferences about the sort of property they are prepared to lend on. For example, they are often very reluctant to lend on older property. Many building societies are also reluctant to lend on flats. Nevertheless, the lending policies of building societies differ, so if you are turned down by one society, try another. It can also help to ask people who are likely to have close contacts with building societies. Estate agents, your solicitor or bank manager may each be able to suggest a possible source.

How Much Can Be Borrowed?

The final question to be dealt with in this section is how much an individual will be allowed to borrow. As stated above, this partly depends on the value of the house concerned. But it also depends on the financial status of the borrower. Building societies have to safeguard their investors' money. Societies are careful not to lend more to anyone than they are likely to be able to repay. A person with a secure career may therefore be treated more favourably than a person whose future earnings are uncertain. Again, different societies have different policies. None the less, it is very rare for building societies to lend more than two and a half or three times your annual income. Most building societies will also take a spouse's income into account, but for a smaller proportion.

For example, suppose you went to a building society which was prepared to lend up to two and a half times your annual earnings plus an amount equal to your spouse's annual income. If you earn £20,000 and your spouse £10,000, the society would then be prepared to lend you up to £60,000:

Your income	£20,000	Maximum loan	£50,000
Spouse's income	£10,000	Maximum loan	£10,000
		Combined Limit	£60,000

The extent to which your spouse's income is taken into account depends on the lender.

II. TAXES

Taxation permeates almost every aspect of financial life. In addition, the entire subject is exceedingly complex, and the tax system is altered or amended at least once a year. All that will be attempted here, therefore, is a description of some of the most common situations faced by taxpayers. If your circumstances are more complicated you should consult your tax office, or take professional advice, or both.

For reasons which are largely historical, taxes are often divided into *direct* and *indirect* taxes. Direct taxes are paid to the Inland Revenue. There are four main types of direct taxation:

1. Income tax
2. Capital gains tax
3. Inheritance tax (formerly Capital transfer tax)
4. Corporation tax

It could also be argued that National Insurance Contributions are a form of tax and they are also described below.

Indirect taxes are collected mainly by the Customs and Excise. They include:

1. Value added tax
2. Customs and excise duties
3. Car tax
4. Stamp duties

Stamp duties are, however, the responsibility of the Inland Revenue.

In terms of the amount of revenue raised, income tax is by far the most important tax. It is also the tax most likely to affect the average taxpayer directly.

8. INCOME TAX

If you are resident in the United Kingdom tax is levied on your income whether it originates in the UK or from overseas. Even if you are not resident, tax is still levied on any income you have which originates in the UK. Tax is charged for each year of assessment; that is the year from 6 April to the following 5 April.

Income Subject to Tax.

Most types of income are taxable, including the following:

Income from employment. This includes wages, bonuses, commission, tips and benefits in kind, such as the private use of the company's car.

Income from self-employment, business, professions and vocations.

Interest, dividends and annuities.

Rent.

Pensions.

Income not Subject to Tax.

A few types of income are not subject to tax. The main groups are:

The first £70 of interest per person received from ordinary deposit accounts in the National Savings Bank.

Interest on National Savings Certificates and increases in the value of Index-Linked National Insurance Certificates. Also, interest from the Save-As-You-Earn scheme is exempt.

Sickness benefit (but not statutory sick pay), family credit, attendance allowance, mobility allowance, maternity benefit, death grant and child benefit, invalidity benefit and non-contributory invalidity pension.

Educational grants and awards.

Compensation for loss of employment—up to £30,000.

War widows' pensions.

Wound and disability pensions.

Any wins from gambling, including Premium Bond prizes.

The capital element of annuity payments.

Allowances and Rates of Tax.

As most people know, there are allowances which may be deducted before tax is levied on the remainder of a person's income. The allowances for 1989/90 and 1990/91 are shown in Table 3. The table this year is complicated by the introduction of Independent Taxation for married couples on 6 April 1990 and this is explained more fully in a Special Topic later (*see* **H19–20**). However it should be noted that the married allowances are now given in addition to the personal allowance and the age allowance is reduced if total income exceeds a certain limit (£12,300 for 1990/91). The age allowance is reduced by £1 for every £2 that limit is exceeded until it reaches the normal single or married allowance. The widow's bereavement allowance applies only to the tax year in which the

TABLE 3. *Allowances Against Gross Income in 1989–90 and 1990–91*

	1989–90	1990–91
	£	£
Personal allowance (formerly single allowance)	2,785	3,005
Married allowance	4,375	1,720
Wife's earned income allowance	2,785	0
Additional personal allowance	1,590	1,720
Widow's bereavement allowance	1,590	1,720
Age allowances		
Personal allowance age 65–74	3,400	3,670
Personal allowance age 75 and over	3,540	3,820
Married couple age 65–74	5,385	2,145
Married couple age 75 and over	5,565	2,185
Blind person's allowance (each)	540	1,080

Note: The new system of Independent Taxation for married couples is described in more detail in a Special Topic (*see* **H19–20**).

husband died, and the tax year following the bereavement. After these allowances have been deducted from gross income, the remaining taxable income is subject to the basic rate of tax of 25 per cent on the first £20,700 (in 1989/90) and the higher rate of tax of 40 per cent on the excess. Finally the dependant relative allowance, the housekeeper allowance and the sons or daughters services allowance were all abolished as from 6 April 1988.

Investment Income Surcharge.

Investment income surcharge was abolished in 1984. Before April 1984, it was levied on investment income in addition to the normal rates of income tax. For 1983/84 it was levied at a rate of 15 per cent on investment income over £7,100.

9. ASSESSMENT AND COLLECTION

The administration of income tax is the responsibility of the Inland Revenue. In practice, the job is divided into two parts: assessment and collection. The "assessments" for tax are the responsibility of inspectors of taxes in over 700 tax offices spread throughout the country. When an individual's tax has been assessed the information is then passed to a collector of taxes who actually sends out the bill. If you receive a tax bill which you think is wrong you should contact the inspector. The collector has no power to amend the bill, his job is simply to collect the amounts decided between you and the inspector.

The Tax Schedules.

For historical reasons, income is divided into six groups known as "schedules." These are:

1. *Schedule A:* Income from property.

2. *Schedule B:* Income from commercial woodlands. Schedule B was finally abolished in 1988.

3. *Schedule C:* Certain interest and annuities paid out of public revenue.

4. *Schedule D:* Income from trades, businesses and professions. Also included are interest, rents and income not covered by other schedules.

5. *Schedule E:* This is the schedule that affects most people as it covers wages and salaries. It also deals with pensions.

6. *Schedule F:* Dividends and other distributions made by companies.

Pay-As-You-Earn.

By far the largest schedule is Schedule E. Nearly all Schedule E income is taxed through the Pay-As-You-Earn (PAYE) system. PAYE is the method used to deduct tax from wages, salaries and some pensions. In order to keep the deductions as accurate as possible, PAYE is operated on a cumulative basis. This means that your earnings, tax paid and so on are accumulated throughout the tax year. This is how it works. At the beginning, or before the start of the tax year, your tax-free allowances are added up. The total is then converted into a code number. For example, if your allowances came to £4,000 and you are married, then your code number would be 400H. The H suffix denotes that you are entitled to the married allowance. (The H stands for the "higher" allowance.) If you are single or a working wife the suffix would be L (representing the "lower" single person's allowance). If there are special circumstances, for example if you had a second job, the suffix would probably be T. There are also special suffixes for pensioners. The main ones are P for single people, and V for married pensioners. If your current code number is different from the previous one the tax office will send you a "Notice of Coding." This will show the allowances the tax has taken into account and how your code number has been calculated. If you do not receive a notice of coding you may

request one. You should always check to see that you have received your full entitlement to allowances. Your code number is also sent to your employer so he knows how much tax to deduct from your earnings. It is worth noting that the higher your code, the lower the tax deducted from your pay.

It may be of interest to work through a simple example of PAYE operating. Suppose that a person's allowances for the year amount to £5,200, and the appropriate code is issued to his employer. The principle is that the annual allowances are divided by the number of pay periods in the year. If an individual is paid weekly, therefore, his allowances are divided by 52. In our example the individual would be granted £100 worth of allowances each week. This weekly allowance is then accumulated as the tax year progresses. Hence in, say, week 26 of the tax year the individual would be entitled to £2,600 worth of allowances. At the same time, the PAYE system accumulates the amount of earnings received. This enables the amount of tax to be deducted to be calculated accurately. Suppose the individual in our example earned £140 in Week 1 of the tax year. The employer knows from the code number that the person's allowances for that week amount to £100. The employer then deducts this £100 from the £140 gross pay, which leaves £40 of "taxable pay". The next stage is to calculate the tax due on the £40.

To assist him in this process, the employer has two sets of tax tables. The first table converts code numbers into weekly or monthly allowances. After these allowances have been deducted from gross pay the second set of tables is used to calculate the tax due on the remaining pay. In the example, there is £40 of taxable pay, so with a tax rate of, say, 30 per cent, £12 would be deducted in tax. Suppose that the wage in the second week was also £140. Because of the cumulative feature, the value of the allowances would now be £200. (£100 for the second week, plus £100 for the first week). Cumulative pay would now be £280. After deducting the allowances, taxable pay is now £80. The second set of tables would now show a total of £24 due in tax. However, £12 ("cumulative tax paid") was deducted in week 1. The amount of tax due in week 2, therefore, is a further £12 (£24 minus the £12 deducted in week 1). This process then continues for the rest of the tax year.

PAYE has a number of advantages. These include accurate deductions of tax. The system can also repay tax during the year if the employee's pay falls substantially. Repayments occur when the value of the allowances accumulates faster than gross pay. The system does not always work in this way. For example, suppose you fail to send your tax return back to the tax office. You may find that you are then put on the Emergency Code (E). This code only gives you allowances equal to the single person's allowance, so if you are entitled to more you will have too much tax deducted. This, of course, provides you with an incentive to sort out your tax affairs with the Inland Revenue. In addition, a taxpayer who becomes unemployed will not normally receive any rebate due until after either he or she ceases to claim unemployment or supplementary benefit, or the end of the tax year. Also, rebates cannot usually be paid while a person is on strike.

Sometimes you may find that you have been put on what is known as a "week 1" basis. This means that tax is being deducted from your pay on a *non-cumulative* basis. In other words, every week is treated as though it were the first week of the tax year. One of the main results of the "week 1" basis is that it prevents tax repayments being made automatically if, say, your income falls through unemployment.

How to Check your Code Number.

As you can see from the above explanation, your code number is the factor that determines the amount of tax that is deducted from your pay. You can check your code number by examining your Notice of Coding. You should compare the allowances and expenses you claimed on your tax return with the ones listed on the Notice. One item which might appear on the Notice of Coding is "Tax unpaid for earlier years." This is to enable the tax office to collect outstanding tax by lowering the value of your code. The tax will then be collected slowly over the tax year rather than in one lump sum.

Appeals.

When your tax for the year is assessed you will be sent a Notice of Assessment. This is often not considered necessary if you are taxed under PAYE and your tax situation is straightforward, though you can still ask for one.

If you receive a Notice of Assessment which you think is wrong you must appeal within 30 days of the date appearing on the Notice. Appeals made after 30 days are normally allowed only if you can provide a satisfactory explanation such as being in hospital or abroad, and can show that the appeal was made without unreasonable delay. Most appeals are settled directly with the inspector. If you and the inspector cannot agree, then the case goes before the Commissioners of Income Tax. There are two types of Commissioners: the General Commissioners and the Special Commissioners. The General Commissioners are unpaid and recruited from members of the public. They sit with a clerk who provides advice on tax law. The Special Commissioners are professional civil servants who are experts in tax matters. It is often said that if your appeal is based on common sense, rather than the intricacies of tax law, you may do better to go to the General Commissioners. Each party pays its own costs for hearings before the Commissioners. If, however, the case is taken on to the High Court, or further, the loser usually pays the costs.

10. HOW TO COMPLETE A TAX RETURN

There are several types of tax return including:

1. *Form P1*. This form is mainly for people who earn a salary or a wage and do not have complicated tax problems. For example, if your main source of income is your job, and you have small amounts of interest from your savings but no other income you will probably receive form P1. (The "P" prefix, incidentally, stands for "Pay-As-You-Earn.")

The form P1 is simpler than some of the other forms and a completely redesigned version was introduced in 1984. Most people who receive form P1 do not get one every year. When this happens, the reason is that the tax office is pretty sure that it has enough information to ensure you pay the right amount of tax without having to fill in a return every year. But, remember, it is your responsibility to tell the tax office if your tax liability changes as a result of a change in your circumstances.

For example, if you become entitled to a new allowance because, say, you get married, you should tell the inspector. Nobody else will. Alternatively, if you begin to receive a new source of income you should also tell the inspector. He may well find out anyway. For instance, banks must inform the Inland Revenue of the interest they pay to depositors. Concealing income can lead to demands for back tax plus interest. You may also be liable to penalties.

2. *Form 11P*. This form is designed for people with more complicated circumstances. For example, if you have a job and some other outside earnings you will probably be sent form 11P.

3. *Form 11*. This form is mainly for the self-employed.

General Points.

It is very worthwhile keeping a tax file containing all the information relevant to your tax affairs. The whole process of completing a tax return is much simpler if you keep all the relevant documents close together. These documents include items such as: P60 (from your employer); dividend advice slips; receipts for expenses. You may also be asked by the inspector to submit detailed records supporting expense claims. A second point is to keep a copy of your return. This photocopy is perhaps the best method of doing this. Alternatively, you can keep a separate record of what you put in the return as you go along.

Keeping a copy of your return has two advantages. First of all it will help you deal with any questions the inspector may have about your return. Secondly, it will enable you to complete your next return more easily. The tax office usually compares your latest tax return with your previous one to see if you have forgotten something. So it is better if you spot any omissions first. If you get into difficulties with your return, you can always telephone or write to the tax office whose address appears on the front of the form. If you wish to call personally, most tax offices are open for public enquiries between 10 am and 4 pm. But remember to take your tax file with you. It does not matter if you wish to make a personal call and your tax office is hundreds of miles away. This is often the case with Londoners and people who work for large nationwide companies. You can always call at a local office and in London there are special PAYE enquiry offices. (Their addresses are in the telephone directory.) Most enquiries can be handled without recourse to your official file. If the file is needed, the Inland Revenue can arrange to have it sent to a local office.

The Return Itself.

As stated above, there are four main types of return, and there are some other variations. Most returns cover two years. They ask for details of your income and capital gains in the previous tax year, and have room for claims for allowances in the current year. Whichever return you receive you should always read the accompanying notes. The different returns sometimes ask different questions and are set out in a different way, but most include the following areas:

INCOME.

Employments or Offices.

If you are an employee, you will receive a form P60 from your employer after 5 April each year. The P60 will show your total earnings and tax deducted under PAYE. It will do this even if you changed your job during the year. You should enter the total figure on the return, plus any bonuses, tips and so on. You should also enter any earnings from spare-time jobs. The same information should be entered for your wife.

The tax treatment of overseas earnings is unusually complicated—even by income-tax standards! If you are going to work abroad you should enquire about the tax implications. One place to start is with the Inland Revenue's explanatory leaflets.

Trade, Profession or Vocation.

Any profits you make from self-employment should be entered here. This section covers both partnerships and sole traders. The figure required is your net profit for your accounting year which ended in the twelve months to 5 April 1986. The figure should be supported by a statement of account. If you do not know what your profits are when you complete the return you should write "per accounts to be submitted." Your accounts should then be sent to the Inspector as soon as possible.

Social Security Pensions and Benefits.

Certain pensions and social security benefits are tax-free and do not have to be entered on the tax return. Further details of these are given in the notes accompanying the return. All other pensions and social security benefits must be entered. "Retirement pension or old person's pension" refers to the state retirement pension. If you are approaching retirement you should inform the tax office. This will help the Revenue make sure that your tax affairs are kept up to date when you retire. Otherwise, it is possible that you many pay too much (or too little) tax until your affairs are sorted out.

Other Pensions.

If a pension is paid by a former employer it will usually be taxed through the PAYE system. At the end of the tax year, therefore, you should receive a form P60 showing the gross pension paid during the year. This section also covers pensions from abroad. Normally overseas pensions are taxed on a preceding year basis. In other words, your current tax bill will be based on the pension you received during the previous tax year.

Property.

Rent can be treated in one of two ways. If the accommodation is furnished *and* the rent covers services such as meals and cleaning the income will be treated as *earned* income. If the accommodation is unfurnished *or* it is furnished and the rent does not cover services the rent will be treated as *investment* income. The figures required are those for total income, expenses and net income. It is only the last of these, the net income, that is taxable, and included in the taxpayer's total income. The details of property income should be presented in a separate statement.

The expenses that may be claimed include:

Rates.

Repairs and maintenance.

Insurance for the structure and its contents (but not insurance against loss of rent).

Costs of providing services to tenants.

Wear and tear for furniture and fittings. The allowance is usually 10 per cent of the rent receivable.

Management expenses. This includes items such as agents' commission for letting the property or collecting the rent.

Dividends from United Kingdom Companies, etc.

Because dividends from UK companies and distributions from unit trusts are accompanied by a "tax credit," you do not have to pay basic-rate tax on them. However, you still have to enter the dividends and tax credits from each company or unit trust, in case you are liable to higher-rate tax or are entitled to a rebate. The necessary information will be shown on your dividend slips. If you do not have enough room, make out a separate list and submit it with the return. The totals should be entered on the return itself. One point should be made about unit trusts. Part of the first distribution you receive will be called *equalisation*. This is part of your capital, and *so should not* be entered on the return.

Other Dividends, etc.

This section requires you to enter the gross (before tax) amount of income from each source. Where tax has already been deducted from foreign income you should give the details.

Interest not Taxed before Receipt.

The first £70 of interest received from ordinary (but *not* investment) accounts with the National Savings Banks is exempt from tax. Your husband or wife is also entitled to a £70 exemption. You should still enter the total amounts of interest from both ordinary and investment accounts. Also enter interest from National Savings Income and Deposit bonds, British Government stocks bought on the National Savings Stock Register and any other taxable interest which you recieve without tax being deducted at source.

Untaxed Income from Abroad.

This section refers only to unearned income from overseas. (Foreign earnings, business income and pensions are dealt with in earlier sections.) You should enter the total amounts involved, whether or not they were actually remitted to the UK. You may deduct expenses incurred. If the income has already been taxed overseas you may be entitled to relief. Details are given in the Inland Revenue's booklet IR6.

Interest from UK Banks and Building Societies.

Bank and Building society interest is "tax paid"—but this only saves you from tax at the basic rate. If you are liable to higher rates of tax you will have to pay more tax on the interest. The Inland Revenue will calculate the additional amount of tax payable. For this purpose, the interest payment will be *grossed up* to include tax at the basic rate.

Any Other Profits or Income.

As you can guess, this section is for any source of income not covered elsewhere.

Alterations in Untaxed Income, etc.

The Inspector needs to know about changes in your untaxed income and your outgoings so that he can, if necessary, adjust your code number. This will enable your deductions of tax to be kept up to date. Such a change may, of course, also affect an assessment on other income.

OUTGOINGS.

Expenses in Employment.

The basic rule covering claims for employment expenses is that they must be incurred wholly, exclusively and necessarily in the performance of the duties of that employment. The rule is usually applied quite strictly. Thus, for example, travel expenses to and from work are not normally allowable because they are not incurred *in the performance* of the duties of the employment. Travelling expenses may be allowed, but only if incurred in the course of the employment.

Nevertheless, there are several types of expenditure which may be claimed. They include subscriptions to professional bodies, tools and some types of industrial clothing. Trade Unions often agree a fixed allowance with the tax office, but you can still claim for actual expenses if they exceed the agreed figure.

Interest on Loans.

Tax relief on interest paid is now very limited. Loans from a building society, bank or a local authority for the purchase of your main residence qualify for relief. You do not have to enter the amount of interest paid to these organisations, as they will inform the tax office themeslves. The only thing you need to do is to enter the name of the building society, bank or local authority and your account number. Bank overdrafts do not qualify for tax relief. Nor do loans obtained with credit cards.

Capital Gains.

You should give details of the assets you have bought and sold during the tax year. Capital gains tax and how to calculate your gain or loss are discussed in greater detail in a separate section below.

Allowances.

Unlike the income part of the return, which refers to income received in the previous year, the allowances section refers to your entitlement in the current year. Compared to some aspects of income tax, the allowances are relatively straightforward. You should be able to establish your entitlement by reading the official notes carefully. If not, ask at the tax office.

11. CAPITAL GAINS TAX

When you dispose of an asset or possession you may make a capital gains or a capital loss. An asset is property of any kind. It includes both property in the United Kingdom and property overseas. You are considered to have disposed of an asset if you sell it, lose it, exchange it or give it away. However, the transfer of a possession between a husband and wife who are not separated is not considered to be a disposal.

Tax-free Gains.

The following assets are exempt from capital gains tax:

Your home (but see below).

Personal possessions, household goods and other chattels, provided that each item is worth £6,000 or less at the time of the disposal. A set of goods, for example a pair of vases, is counted as one item. (*Chattels* means tangible, movable property.)

Animals, private cars, caravans and boats. Also other chattels which are wasting assets; that is assets expected to last 50 years or less.

Life assurance policies.

National Savings Certificates, British Savings Bonds and Save-As-You-Earn.

British government stocks if owned for more than one year or inherited. This exemption has been extended to corporate bonds (*e.g.* debentures) which are issued after 13 March 1984 and which are held for at least twelve months.

British money.

Foreign currency obtained for personal or family expenditure.

Winnings from betting or from Premium Bonds.

Gifts to charities.

Gifts to certain institutions such as the National Trust and the British Museum.

Your Own Home.

When you sell your house any capital gains you make will normally be exempt from tax. From 1980/81 onwards this exemption also applies (within certain limits) if you let part of your home. However, there are a number of circumstances in which you may get only partial exemption. For example, if you use part of your home for business you may not be allowed full exemption from capital gains tax. These circumstances are described in more detail in the Inland Revenue leaflet CGT4, *Capital Gains Tax—Owner-occupied houses.* You should enter any gains from the disposal of your house on your tax return in case they are not wholly exempt.

Capital Losses.

Your capital gains can be reduced by deducting allowable losses. An allowable capital loss is usually one which would have been taxable if it had been a gain. For example, a loss on an item which is exempt, such as your car, would *not* be considered an allowable loss. If your losses exceed your gains in the tax year you can carry the balance forward to set against gains in future years. You can also deduct allowable expenditure from your capital gains (or add them to your capital losses). Allowable expenditure includes the costs of acquiring or disposing of an asset; for example, commission, conveyancing costs and advertising. It also includes expenditure which increases the value of the asset, such as improvements to property.

Working Out Your Gain.

Normally your capital gain (or loss) is the amount you receive when disposing of the asset *minus* the original amount you paid for it. If you give the asset away, the market value at the time of disposal is used instead. The same method is used if you were originally given the asset, or if you inherited it.

Shares.

If you buy batches of the same share at different prices the cost of each share is considered to be the average cost. For example, suppose you purchase 100 shares in a company for £200. Three months later you buy a further 100 of the same shares for £300. You would then have a total of 200 shares which cost you £500. The average cost is, therefore, £2·50 per share. When you come to sell all or some of these shares the calculation of your gain or loss will be based on this average cost.

The Rates of Capital Gains Tax.

From its introduction in 1965 to 1988, capital gains tax was levied at a flat rate of 30 per cent. From 6 April 1988 capital gains will be charged at an individual's highest income tax rate—either 25 or 40 per cent. However the tax is only applied to an individual's gains over £5,000 during the year and gains accruing prior to April 1982 are exempt.

12. INHERITANCE TAX
(Formerly CAPITAL TRANSFER TAX)

Inheritance tax emerged from the remains of the previous capital transfer tax in March 1986. Capital transfer tax applied to transfers of capital made both during life and on a person's death. However, since its introduction in 1975 the scope of the tax had been steadily reduced so that the number of people actually paying capital transfer tax fell from 61,000 in 1976/77 to 28,000 by 1982/83.

Capital transfer tax had replaced the old estate duty which was imposed on property passing at death, and gifts made within 7 years before death. The position has now turned full circle because, essentially, inheritance tax, like the old estate duty, is levied on transfers between individuals made on the death of the donor, or up to 7 years before his or her death.

The Tax.

Inheritance tax is payable on transfers made on or after 18 March 1986 on transfers made at death or in the years preceding death. Certain gifts, most of which are listed below, are exempt from tax. All other gifts which are not exempt and which are made within 7 years of death are taxable as soon as the total amount of taxable transfers exceeds the threshold for tax (£128,000 from 6 April 1990).

Furthermore, there are rules, similar to those operated under estate duty, which apply where the donor continues to enjoy some benefit from a gift even after it has been 'given away'. For example, this might apply where a person gives his or her home to the children, but continues to live in it. If this happens, for the purpose of inheritance tax, the gift will normally be treated as if it had been given on the date such enjoyment finally ceases.

The method of valuing assets largely continues on from the previous capital transfer tax and estate duty. Assets are usually valued at the price they would fetch on the open market at the time of the transfer.

The value of the estate on death will be taxed as the top slice of cumulative transfers in the 7 years before death. (For capital transfer tax the cumulation period was 10 years.)

From 6 April 1990 the tax is levied at a single rate of 40 per cent on transfers over the £128,000 threshold. However, where gifts are made between individuals more than 3 years before the death of the donor the rate of tax is reduced by the relevant percentage given in Table 4. Different rules apply to gifts into and out of trust, discretionary trust charges and gifts involving companies.

TABLE 4. *Relief for Lifetime Transfers*

Years between gift and death	Percentage of full charge
0–3	100
3–4	80
4–5	60
5–6	40
6–7	20
Over 7	0

Exempt Transfers.

Certain transfers are eligible for exemption in much the same way as they were under capital transfer tax, including the following:

Transfers up to £3,000 in any one year (unused relief may be carried forward for one year only).

Small gifts of up to £250 to any one recipient in any tax year.

Gifts made as part of normal expenditure.

Marriage gifts as follows:

Parents	£5,000 each
Grandparents	£2,500 each
Bride and groom	£2,500 to each other
Other people	£1,000 each

Transfers between husband and wife if the recipient is domiciled in the United Kingdom.

Gifts to charities and political parties. A 'political party' is defined for this purpose as one with two M.P.s, or one M.P. and not less than 150,000 votes for its candidates at the last general election.

Gifts for national purposes, *etc.* For example, gifts to the National Trust, National Gallery, universities and museums are exempt.

Other Relief.

There is also some relief for business assets, agricultural land and shares which represent a controlling interest in a company. In addition, a certain amount of relief is available for minority shareholdings in unquoted companies.

Administration and Collection.

The responsibility for the administration of inheritance tax lies with the Inland Revenue, and the procedures for assessment, appeals and penalties are similar to those for income tax. As with the previous capital transfer tax, the responsibility for dealing with Inland Revenue enquiries about transfers made before death lies with the personal representatives of the deceased. Where a person's death creates tax liability on gifts previously made, the main responsibility for the tax falls on the recipient, but with recourse to the donor's estate if necessary.

13. VALUE ADDED TAX

Value Added Tax (VAT) was introduced in the United Kingdom on 1 April 1973, and replaced the old Purchase Tax and Selective Employment Tax. One of the main reasons for changing the system was to harmonise the UK's indirect tax system with those of the other members of the Common Market, each of which now has some kind of value added tax.

As its name suggests, VAT is levied on the goods and services you buy. In the budget of June 1979, the standard and higher rates of VAT were amalgamated into a single rate of 15 per cent. The government, however, has the power to vary the rates of VAT by up to a quarter during the year in the interests of economic management. Some goods and services are "zero-rated" and others are "exempted" from VAT, a distinction which is explained shortly.

Anyone who has a business with a turnover of £23,600 per year or more must register with the Customs and Excise. In some circumstances it can be advantageous to register even if you have a business with a turnover below this level (*see* "Registration" below).

How VAT Works.

VAT is payable at every stage of production when goods and services are supplied either to another business or to the final consumer. VAT is also payable on imported goods (and some important services). The tax is charged by the supplier, who then pays it over to the Customs and Excise. For example, a simple VAT invoice for a good would show:

	£
Goods supplied	100
VAT at 15%	15
	——
Total payable	£115

When a business calculates how much VAT is payable to the Customs and Excise it can deduct any VAT it has been *charged* on the goods and services it has purchased itself. For instance, suppose a firm buys some wood for £100 (plus £15 VAT) which it turns into furniture and sells for £200 (plus £30 VAT). The tax position would then be as follows:

	£	£
Receipts for furniture	200	
VAT charged to customer		30
Cost of wood	100	
VAT charged by supplier		15
VAT payable to Customs & Excise		£15

The final customer is charged £30 VAT and the Customs and Excise receives £30 in VAT (£15 from the furniture maker and £15 from the wood supplier).

In principle, each business pays tax on only the *value* it has *added* to its output. In our example above, the firm took £100 worth of wood and turned it into £200 worth of furniture. It could be said, therefore, that the firm has increased the value of the wood by £100. Accordingly, £15 VAT is payable to the Customs and Excise. Since each firm is taxed on its "value added," and charges the tax to its customer, the eventual VAT bill is related to the final value of the product and is paid by the final customer.

The way VAT is operated can be further illustrated by tracing the production of a good from the raw material stage through to the sale to the final customer. This is done in the Table on page **H18**.

Zero-rated Supplies.

Goods and services that are "zero-rated" are in principle subject to VAT, but the rate applying to them is zero. This means that while VAT is not charged on these goods, businesses can still recover VAT paid on their own purchases. The effect of this arrangement is that zero-rated goods and services should be entirely free of VAT. For example, exports are relieved of VAT in this way.

Goods and services which are zero-rated may be summarised as follows:

Food—but not items such as pet foods, ice cream, soft drinks, alcoholic drinks, "meals out," and hot takeaway food and drink.

Water—except distilled water and bottled water.

Books—including newspapers, periodicals, music and maps (stationery is taxable).

Talking books and wireless sets for the blind.

News services. News services supplied to newspapers.

Fuel and Power—but not petrol and petrol substitutes.

Construction—of buildings.

Transport—except taxis, hired cars and boats and aircraft used for recreation.

Caravans—provided they are too large to be used as trailers on the roads. Houseboats are also zero-rated.

Gold and banknotes—but not gold coins or jewellery.

Drugs, medicines, medical and surgical appliances—provided they are purchased on a prescription.

Exports.

Charities.

Clothing and Footwear—for young children, industrial protective clothing and crash helmets.

Exempt Supplies.

Exempt goods and services are not subject to VAT, even in principle. A business cannot take

	Basic Price £	VAT £	Amount Received by Customs and Excise (C & E) £
Manufacturer imports raw materials	1,000	150	
Manufacturer pays VAT to C & E			+ 150
Manufacturer sells goods to wholesaler	2,000	300	
Manufacturer pays VAT to C & E			+ 150 (£300 minus £150)
Wholesaler sells goods to retailers	3,000	450	
Wholesaler pays VAT to C & E			+ 150 (£450 minus £300)
Retailers sell goods to customers	5,000	750	
Retailers pay VAT to C & E			+ 300 (£750 minus £450)
Customers pay	5,000 plus 750 VAT		
			────
Customs and Excise receive total			£750
			────

any credit for VAT paid on the supplies used to produce exempt goods. Exemption is therefore less advantageous than zero-rating, but if a good falls into both categories it is zero-rated. Exempt items include:

Land.
Insurance including brokers' services.
Postal services, but not telephones and telex.
Betting, gaming and lotteries.
Finance such as banking.
Education—including incidental services.
Health.
Burial and cremation services.
Trade Unions and Professional Bodies
Sports Competitions.

The Tax Point.

The tax point is the date on which liability to VAT arises. There are rigid rules for fixing the tax point. This is to prevent businesses from gaining an unfair advantage from manipulating the date of transactions, either to delay the payment of VAT, or to take advantage of changes in the rates of tax.

Basically the tax point is the date when goods are despatched or made available to the customer. There are, however, two main exceptions to this. First, if an invoice is issued within 14 days of this time, the date of the invoice becomes the tax point. Secondly, if payment is made in advance, the date of payment becomes the tax point. It is also possible for particular businesses to make special arrangements with the Customs and Excise regarding the tax point.

Registration.

As already stated, anyone who has a business which has a taxable turnover of £25,400 or more a year must register with the Customs and Excise. For this purpose a "business" means any trade, profession or vocation. This includes partnerships, one-man businesses and free-lance work. It also includes clubs and associations such as sports clubs, but it does not include trade unions.

Businesses with a turnover of less than £25,400 a year are not liable to register, but it might be in their interests to do so. Where a trader pays more VAT for his supplies than he receives from his customers, he may be entitled to a rebate. This is most likely to happen where a business makes or supplies mainly items that are zero-rated or exported, but it may also happen with a new business. Rebates can be claimed only by registered traders.

To register for VAT, you simply contact the local VAT office (the address will be in the local telephone directory under "Customs and Excise"). You will then be sent form VAT 1, which you will have to complete and return. If a person wishes to de-register he may do so if he can satisfy the Customs and Excise that his taxable turnover (including the VAT) of all his business activities in the next 12 months will be £25,400 or less. You can also, of course, de-register if you sell, cease trading or retire from your business.

VAT Records.

Businesses which are not exempt from VAT are required to keep certain records of their purchases

and sales and the VAT relating to them. Furthermore, a *tax account* must be kept. This should contain a summary of the VAT totals from the main records and also VAT payments made to the Customs, or any repayments received.

Most businesses also have to issue *tax invoices* when making sales. Exceptions are retail businesses and sales of zero-rated goods and services. A tax invoice has to include the business's VAT registration number, the invoice number, the tax point and the tax charged.

Returns and Payment.

Traders registered for VAT have to make a return every three months. Some traders who are likely to receive rebates may be allowed to submit returns every month. The return must be made within 30 days of the end of the period to which it relates, and any VAT due should be paid at the same time.

Essentially, the return requires the trader to calculate the value of his sales and the VAT charged thereon. He must also add up all the purchases of his business and the VAT paid on these inputs. The basic calculation will then look something like this:

Total sales for the period	£10,000	
VAT received		£1,500
Total inputs (purchases) for the period	£8,000	
VAT paid		£1,200
		────
Balance payable to the Customs & Excise		£300
		────

Appeals.

There are independent VAT tribunals to deal with appeals over a wide range of issues. This includes whether or not a trader should be registered and, if so, what the effective date of registration is; the amount of VAT payable; the amount of credit that can be taken for VAT paid on a business's purchases; and the value of goods and services supplied. From the tribunal there is an appeal to the High Court and from there to the Court of Appeal on a point of law (but not questions of fact). In Scotland such appeals go to the Court of Session. There are time limits for submitting appeals, and the procedure for appealing to the VAT Tribunals is described in a booklet available from the local VAT office.

Retailers.

Retailers are in a special position because they are usually unable to record each sale separately. Retailers are not required to issue tax invoices unless asked by customers, and there are several special schemes for calculating the amount of VAT payable. Retailers usually charge a price which is inclusive of VAT, and the amount of VAT can be calculated by using the appropriate fractions. With the rate of 15 per cent the relevant fraction is 3/23rds of the gross price. For example, the amount of VAT payable on an article with a gross price of £46 would be £46 × 3/23 = £6.

Bad Debts.

Where goods or services have been supplied by

a trader and VAT paid to the Customs and Excise, but the purchaser then fails to pay, relief can be obtained for the VAT paid. The relief is subject to certain conditions. First of all, the purchaser must be insolvent and the insolvency must have occurred after 1 October 1978. Secondly, the seller must obtain an acknowledgement of a claim for debt from the person acting in the insolvency, for example, the liquidator. Thirdly, the claim must not include the amount of VAT included in the debt, and the price of the goods must not have been greater than the market value. The relief takes the form of a refund of the VAT originally paid on the bad debt.

Further Information.

The Customs and Excise provide a series of detailed leaflets which cover all aspects of VAT, and which are available free of charge from any VAT office.

14. NATIONAL INSURANCE CONTRIBUTIONS.

There are four classes of National Insurance. Class 1 relates to employees, Classes 2 and 4 to the self-employed and Class 3 is voluntary.

The Class 1 contribution is paid partly by the employee and partly by the employer. Employees pay contributions of 2 per cent of their earnings up to the 'lower earnings limit' (£46 a week in 1990/91) and 9 per cent of earnings between the lower earnings limit and the 'upper earnings limit' (£350 a week in 1990/91). Employees contracted out of the state earnings related pension scheme pay a lower rate of contribution on earnings between the lower and upper earnings limits. No further contributions are required on earnings over the upper earnings limit and employees with earnings below the lower earnings do not pay any Class 1 contributions at all. A similar contribution is required from employers except that there is no upper earnings limit on the employer's contributions.

Class 2 contributions are payable by the self-employed and are levied at a flat rate of £4·45 in 1990/91. This contribution is payable if earnings from self-employment exceed a minimum amount which is £2,600 for 1990/91. The self-employed are also liable to Class 4 contributions which are related to the level of their profits. For the year 1990/91 the rate of contribution was 6·3 per cent of profits between £5,450 and £18,200, though from 1985/86, 50 per cent of this contribution receives relief from income tax. Finally Class 3 contributions are payable at a flat rate of £4·45 in 1990/91.

III. SPECIAL TOPICS

INDEPENDENT TAXATION
(for Married Couples)

Introduction.

Before April 1990 part of the UK law relating to income tax stated that 'A woman's income chargeable to income tax shall ... [for any year] during which she is a married woman living with her husband be deemed for income tax purposes to be his income and not to be her income'. Legally the husband was responsible for completing tax returns relating to both his own and his wife's income, and paying the tax on both their incomes. Although there were provisions for separate assessment and the separate taxation of a wife's earned income, all of this was swept away with the introduction of independent taxation on 6 April 1990.

The Main Changes.

Under the new system, husbands and wives are taxed independently on their own incomes and they are each responsible for their own tax affairs. If they wish, they may have complete privacy in relation to their financial circumstances. It will no longer be the case that some married couples pay more income tax than if they were single.

The system of personal allowances has also been changed. The former single person's allowance, the married man's allowance, the wife's earned income allowance and the age allowance have been replaced by a new personal allowance and a married couple's allowance. Essentially the new personal allowance replaces the old single person's allowance but it is now given to everyone resident in the United Kingdom, whether they are married or not. The new married couple's allowance is rather different in that it is given *in addition to* not instead of the personal allowance. It is therefore given at a lower level and in Table 3 (*see earlier*, **H12**), the 'married allowance' shows a fall from £4,375 to £1,720 for 1990/91. For the same reason Table 3 shows that the levels of allowance given to married taxpayers over certain ages are lower for 1990/91. However, the overall result, together with the transitional arrangements mentioned below, is that married couples should not be any worse off as a result of the introduction of independent taxation. Indeed many will be better off.

The new personal allowance may be set against any source of income. This means, for instance, that a married woman can now use this allowance against her investment income and any state retirement pension based on her husband's National Insurance contributions. Furthermore, from 6 April

1991 the composite rate tax arrangement will be abolished so that non-taxpayers will no longer have to suffer tax on bank and building society interest. This means that from April 1991 a married woman with income below the level of her personal allowance will no longer have to pay tax on any such interest she receives.

The amount of the personal allowance is £3,005 in 1990/91 for individuals aged under 65. There are higher levels for taxpayers aged 65 and over if their incomes do not exceed a certain limit (£12,300 in 1990/91). For taxpayers aged from 65 to 74 the allowance is worth £3,670 and for those aged 75 and over the value is £3,820 in 1990/91. If a taxpayer's income exceeds the income limit, the value of his or her higher allowance is reduced by £1 for every £2 the income exceeds the limit. However the allowance cannot be reduced below the basic amount available to a person aged below 65. The higher allowances are first given in the tax year when an individual reaches the age of 65 or 75.

The new married couple's allowance is available to a man who is living with his wife for any part of the year and is given in addition to his personal allowance. It cannot be claimed if the couple have separated. If the husband has insufficient income to take full advantage of the married couple's allowance, he can ask the tax office to transfer any unused part to his wife to be set against her income. If the husband's income is more than his allowances added together he cannot transfer any of the married couple's allowance to his wife.

Current Rates.

For 1990/91 the basic level of the married couple's allowance is £1,720. Like the new personal allowance, there are two higher rates which are given if the husband or wife are 65 or over or 75 or more. If either or both of them are 65 or over, the married couple's allowance is £2,145 and if 75 or over, £2,185 in 1990/91. If the *husband's* income exceeds the income limit (£12,300 in 1990/91), the higher allowance is reduced by £1 for every £2 the income exceeds the limit until it reaches the level of the allowance available to those under 65.

The blind person's allowance (£1,080 in 1990/91) is granted to registered blind people. If a husband and wife are both registered blind they can each claim a blind person's allowance. If a married blind person has insufficient income to take full advantage of the allowance, he or she may transfer the unused part of the allowance to their spouse.

If a married couple have a mortgage on their only or main residence and the loan is in both names the relief is usually divided equally between husband and wife. If the loan is in one of the names, then that person usually gets all the tax relief. For most couples these rules allow the maximum amount of relief available. However, the couple can jointly choose to share the tax relief in any way they like so that, for example, even if the loan is in the husband's name the wife can have all the relief. This decision is known as an 'allocation of interest election' and should be made on a special form available from the tax office. It can be advantageous to make such an election where, for instance, one but not both of the partners is liable to income tax at the higher rate. The upper limit for relief continues in 1990/91 at £30,000 per residence.

For capital gains tax, from 6 April 1990 a husband and wife are taxed independently on any capital gains they may have and each is entitled to a separate exempt amount (of £5,000 in 1990/91).

Transitional Arrangements.

If no special arrangements had been made some couples' entitlement to allowances could have been reduced in 1990/91 as a result of the introduction of independent taxation. This could have happened, for example, where the husband had a low income and the wife was the main income earner. The effect of the transitional rules ensures that such couples need not suffer a fall in their allowances only as a result of independent taxation and further details are given in the Inland Revenue's leaflets IR81 and IR82 which are among those listed below. These leaflets provide further details on a number of aspects of independent taxation and are available from tax offices.

IR80: Independent Taxation—A guide for Married Couples
IR81: Independent Taxation—A guide for Pensioners
IR82: Independent Taxation—A guide for Husbands on a low income
IR86: Independent Taxation—A guide to Mortgage Interest Relief for Married Couples
IR90: Independent Taxation—A guide to Tax Allowances and Reliefs
IR91: Independent Taxation—A guide for Widows and Widowers

THE COMMUNITY CHARGE
(POLL TAX)

The community charge, or poll tax as it is widely known, was introduced in Scotland in April 1989 and in England and Wales in April 1990. It replaced the system of domestic rates which had formed an important source of finance for local authorities, but which had been criticised for many years. Business rates continue to be charged on property other than domestic property. However, under the new system, business rates are charged at the same rate poundage throughout the country. This rate is set annually by the Government and cannot rise by more than the rate of inflation. The proceeds of business rates go into a central fund which is then distributed to individual authorities.

To administer the community charge, local authorities have a Community Charge Registration Officer. He or she is responsible for setting up and maintaining a register of adults subject to the charge. Each person is responsible for informing the Registration Officer of any changes in their circumstances which may affect their entry on the register.

There are three types of community charge. The *personal community charge* is payable by everyone over 18 unless they are exempted. The *standard community charge* may be levied on a person who has a 'second' home. The *collective community charge* relates to certain accommodation inhabited mostly by short-term residents.

The Personal Community Charge.

The personal community charge is the main form of the community charge and is payable by most adults though some may be entitled to community charge benefit which is described later. Each year local authorities will set the level of the personal community charge in their areas. Every adult at each address should receive his or her own bill for the community charge, though husbands and wives, and those living as husband and wife, could be liable for the debts of their partners. Chargepayers are also able to pay in monthly instalments

if they wish. When people move between areas during the course of the year the proportion of the community charge they pay each council is related to the proportion of the time spent living in each area.

Students who are following a full-time course of education have to pay only 20 per cent of the full community charge and are not eligible for community charge benefit. The charge which applies to them during the course (including vacations) is that relating to their term-time address.

The Standard Community Charge.

The standard community charge may be levied if a person has a second home which no one else uses as their only or main residence. The level of the standard community charge is set by the local authority but it must not exceed twice the amount of its personal community charge. An exemption may be granted where a person has domestic property which is empty for up to three months. This might apply, for instance, where a person has moved but not yet sold their previous home. If the second home is used by someone else as their main residence, they will pay the personal community charge in the normal way and no standard charge is then payable.

The Collective Community Charge.

This charge is payable by landlords of some lodging houses and bed and breakfast hotels and certain other premises where residents normally stay for only short periods and it would be difficult to register and collect the personal community charge from them. The Registration Officer is responsible for deciding whether most of the residents of an establishment fall into this category and therefore whether or not the collective charge should be applied. The collective community charge will not apply to hotels where most of the guests have a permanent address and therefore should be registered for and pay a personal community charge. Such hotels will be subject to the business rate in the same way as any other business.

Community Charge Benefit.

Community charge benefit can be given to people who have to pay a personal community charge or collective community charge contributions if they have a low income and their savings do not exceed a certain level. It can be given for up to 80 per cent of the community charge bill and the actual amount will depend on each person's circumstances. It cannot be used for water charges or for the standard community charge on second homes. The community charge benefit scheme is run by local councils. Claims should be made on forms available from the local council. Alternatively, people who claim income support may claim community charge benefit (and housing benefit) at the same time. Claims should be made as soon as possible as community charge benefit cannot *normally* be backdated.

Exemptions.

Although the great majority of adults are liable to the community charge, some people are exempt if they meet certain conditions. These include resident hospital patients and individuals who are being cared for in residential care homes and hostels providing a high level of care. Also exempt are individuals who are severely mentally handicapped, nearly all monks and nuns and also 18 year olds who are still at school and for whom child benefit is payable. People who are homeless and sleep rough are automatically exempt. Prisoners do not have to pay the personal community charge while they are in prison unless they are in prison for not paying a fine or the community charge.

Appeals.

Appeals against the level of the community charge cannot be made, though a person can ask for the level of any community charge benefit granted to be looked at again. However, there are some aspects of the administration of the charge which might form the basis for an appeal, for example if your entry on the register is wrong.

STUDENT FINANCIAL ASSISTANCE

Introduction.

If you wish to undertake a course of full-time study (defined as taking at least 21 hours per week) at an establishment of Further or Higher Education (Universities, Polytechnics, Colleges of H.E. and F.E.) you may be eligible to receive financial assistance. At present this is by means of a Local Education Authority award or "grant"; these are given according to strict criteria laid down by Regulations passed by Parliament. However, the proposals outlined in the Education (Student Loans) Bill make it clear that arrangements should be amended with effect from 1990-91. There is much controversy, as well as practical problems, concerning the introduction of student loans. The situation at present (June 1990) remains very fluid. Currently, the awards automatically pay your course fees and will also contribute towards your "maintenance costs" (your day to day costs of living), although the amount of the award given may vary considerably, it being calculated according to the aforesaid criteria. There are two types of award, "Mandatory" and "Discretionary".

Mandatory Awards.

These are available for "designated" courses run in the United Kingdom. These are normally full-time or sandwich courses leading to the following qualifications:

  (i)   a University or CNAA first degree;
  (ii)   the Diploma of Higher Education;
  (iii) BTEC Higher National Diploma awards;
  (iv) other qualifications deemed comparable to a first degree course;
  (v)   a University Certificate or Diploma lasting at least three years;
  (vi) initial teacher training, including PGCE's and Art-Teachers' Certificate or Diploma;
  (vii) Part-time initial teacher training courses designated for grant purposes;
  (viii) certain degree level qualifications, provided jointly by a United Kingdom and an overseas establishment.

Discretionary Awards.

These awards relate to all courses not covered by Mandatory awards (as shown in the list above). They may also be given to individuals who have previously undertaken some period of full-time study. Each Local Education Authority decides its own policy, which may be subject to annual review. The awards fall into a number of categories, which are largely determined by the course 'grading' structure used, known as the Burnham scale. In a number of cases Local Education Authorities will not give any discretionary awards to provide assistance for any courses running outside their boundaries.

(i) *Major Awards* may be given to some students following ADVANCED courses not included in the Mandatory scheme. Generally, these include courses where GCE "A" levels, or equivalent, are an entry requirement, and refers to courses at Burnham grades 1, 2, and 3. A number of "Foundation" courses also fall into this category.

(ii) *Intermediate Awards* may be awarded to follow a NON-ADVANCED course if you fulfil one or more of the requirements to be regarded as an "*Independent*" student, namely:

* you have before or during the course, attained the age of 25 (you may become "Independent" during the course of study).
* you have, irrespective of age, been self-supporting for an aggregate of 3 years or more before the first year of study.
* you have been married for over 3 years before the start of the course (this applies even if you have subsequently divorced).

Again, policy may vary from one Local Education Authority to another, so always check in advance.

Eligibility for Awards.

Whilst the majority of full-time students are able to apply for some sort of financial assistance, there are various restrictions for both Mandatory and Discretionary awards. These regulations are complex and only brief general guidelines can be given here. For more detailed information write to the Awards Section of your Local Education Authority (*see below*).

a. Correct Local Education Authority (LEA): You should apply for an award to the LEA in which you are permanently resident as at 30 June in the summer immediately prior to the autumn in which your course starts. For courses starting in the spring term the qualifying date will be 31 October, and the last day in February applies for the summer term. You should not apply to more than one LEA.

If you have not remained at the same address for any length of time and do not have a permanent home at the relevant dates, you may still be able to receive financial assistance from an LEA. You should give as much detail as possible, in particular your places of residence during the last 2 years, on the form which can be supplied by the Awards Section of any LEA, and from these details it can be surmised which LEA can give you an award.

b. Residence: You will not normally receive an award if you were born outside the United Kingdom and either have not been "ordinarily resident" in the British Islands (United Kingdom, Channel Islands and Eire) throughout the 3 years immediately preceding the start of your course, or if the purpose for your residence during part of this period has been wholly or partially to receive full-time education.

You may still be eligible if you have been absent because you, or your family were *temporarily* employed abroad for this period. There are also special provisions for refugees and for migrant workers from member states of the EC.

c. Previous study: You will not normally receive financial assistance if you are following a second course which is at the same academic level as previously attended, *e.g.* a 3 year teacher training course, after a degree. Generally this applies whether or not the previous course was passed or failed, although transfer between courses, prior to completion, may enable you to retain your eligibility for a grant, which may be given for the duration of the new course less the period attended on the previous course. Individual LEAs may have different practices and policies in these discretionary cases, so it is advisable to check your grant position with the Awards Section before taking any decision.

When to apply.

You should not wait to gain admission to a course or for the results of any qualifying examination before applying for an award but should submit an application as soon as possible, normally for your first choice, which could be done approximately six months before you hope to start the course. Generally applications are dealt with in the order in which they are received. Individual LEAs may have different procedures regarding closing dates for applications and the timing of making decisions on applications, so it is best to contact the Awards Section of your LEA to ascertain their timetable prior to making an application.

Level of Financial Assistance.

The level of grants to be distributed by LEAs is agreed annually by Parliament. All grants are means tested and take into account income you may receive during the academic year. In most cases the income of your parents is also taken into account unless you can be classified as "Independent" (*see above*). If an "Independent" student is married, then the income of the student's spouse will be taken into account. The Regulations regarding the calculation of "residual" income (gross income less certain allowances; approximately a 10% reduction) for the purposes of assessing the level of contribution are extremely complex and you are advised to contact your LEA for further details. Your LEA will assess your "maintenance requirements" and your "resources", and subtract one from the other: whatever is left is your net grant.

The standard rates of grant for the academic year 1990–91 are:

£2265—if you are living in a hall of residence or in lodgings and studying at an establishment outside London.

£2845—as above but attending an establishment within London.

£1795—if you are living at your parents' home. LEAs also reserve the right to award this grant to those who could live at home and travel to college daily but prefer to live away from the parental home. This does not apply to married students or to those with "Independent" status.

Student Loans.

The Education (Student Loans) Act which passed through Parliament in 1990 indicates substantial changes in the system of financial assistance for students whereby grants from LEAs, and contributions from parents, are supplemented by top-up loans to students. These will be adopted from the beginning of the 1990 session. Full details have yet to be agreed, and still await Parliamentary approval, but certain general characteristics of such an arrangement can be identified as follows:

a. Eligibility: Non-means tested loans will be offered to all full-time students up to the age of 50 at recognised educational institutions who are enrolled on degree level or equivalent courses, and who are eligible for a Mandatory award. Those who receive Discretionary awards are ineligible for these loans, but the special Access Funds (*see later*) are available to these students.

b. Application procedure: To apply for a loan you will need the special loan form, obtainable from the newly-created Student Loans Company in Glasgow (your LEA should have details on this). Upon receipt of your form your eligibility will be considered and, if it is agreed, you will receive a lump sum of money rather than termly payments as per grants.

c. Level of loan: There will be 3 levels of loan—(i) for students living in the parental home in London; (ii) for students living away from home in London; (iii) for students away from home outside London. Precise details have yet to be agreed, but the suggested maximum values of loans for the 3 levels identified above are: (i) £330 (ii) £460 (iii) £420. Values would fall in the final year of study because there are only 9 months of study to (i) £240 (ii) £340 (iii) £310. Mandatory grants will remain frozen at current rates while loans will be reassessed annually until both are of equal proportions. You will also be barred from claiming income support, housing benefit and unemployment benefit; the restrictions will not apply to spouses and all other benefits are unaffected, as are any parental contributions.

d. Repayments: The rate of interest on the loan will be tied to the Retail Price Index and repayments (commencing normally in the April following the end of the course), will be deferred when the graduate's income is low (less than 85% of national average earnings). Although there could be consultation over the repayment period, it is proposed that this should be 5 years, payable in monthly instalments by Direct Debit, with agreement to write off all debts at the age of 50 providing there has been no history of evasion.

e. Access Funds: In addition, institutions will be required to make bids for the allocation of £5 million for 3 special Access funds which will be available to students through their institution to provide further support for those facing special hardship. This includes those on discretionary awards and those supporting themselves, postgraduates who will not be eligible for top-up loans, and students over 19 and in Further Education.

CLASSICAL MYTHOLOGY

The purpose of this section is to give brief accounts of the myths and legends of Greece and Rome in an easily referable form. Great artists and writers throughout the ages have enriched their work by reference to these ancient tales of the classical world and some knowledge of them is indispensable to the full appreciation of our art and literature.

INTRODUCTION TO
CLASSICAL MYTHOLOGY

A

Abas. In Greek mythology either (1) the son of Celeus and Metanira. His mockery of Demeter (q.v.) as she drank resulted in his being turned into a lizard, or
(2) the twelfth king of Argolis who owned a magic shield from which he derived authority. He was the father of Acrisius (q.v.) and Proetus (q.v.).

Abderus. The friend of Heracles (q.v.) in whose care Heracles left the mares of Diomedes (q.v.). The horses ate him and Heracles founded Abdera, a coastal town in Thrace, in his honour.

Absyrtus (or **Apsyrtus**). Half brother of the sorceress Medea (q.v.). When Aëtes pursued Jason (q.v.) and Medea, in order to recover the golden fleece, Medea slew the boy, cut his corpse into pieces and tossed the pieces into the sea. Because Aëtes stopped his ship to collect the pieces of his son for burial Jason and Medea were able to escape.

Abyla. See "Pillars of Hercules".

Acamas. Son of Theseus (q.v.) and Phaedra (q.v.), brother of Demophon (q.v.). He went to Troy (q.v.) with Diomedes (q.v.) to demand the return of Helen (q.v.). He and his brother also rescued their grandmother Aethra, who had been Helen's slave, when Troy fell.

Acastus. Son of Pelias King of Iolcos and one of the Argonauts (q.v.). When Medea (q.v.) caused his father's death he banished her and Jason (q.v.). Showed hospitality to Peleus (q.v.) but suspecting him of advances towards his wife he left Peleus to die at the hands of the Centaurs (q.v.). Later Peleus returned to slay the couple. Acastus was the father of Laodamia (q.v.).

Acestes. In Roman mythology a chieftain of Trojan descent who had settled in Sicily prior to the arrival of Aeneas (q.v.).

Achelous. A great river god, the son of Oceanus (q.v.) and Tethys (q.v.). By defeating Achelous Heracles (q.v.) won the hand of Deianeira (q.v.) daughter of Oeneus (q.v.).

Acheron. A real river of Epirus flowing into the Ionian Sea. Part of it runs underground which may account for its position in Greek mythology. Here it is the "river of grief" which flows in the underworld of the dead.

Achilles. A Greek warrior who is the principal character of the *Iliad*. The son of Peleus (q.v.) King of the Myrmidones in Phthia in Thessaly and Thetis (q.v.) one of the Nereids (q.v.). As a baby his mother dipped him in the Styx (q.v.) making him invulnerable save for his heel, by which she held him. He was educated in the arts of war and hunting, and in morality, by Cheiron (q.v.). His mother, knowing that he would die at Troy (q.v.) tried to prevent him joining the Greek expedition there by disguising him as a girl and sending him to the court of Lycomedes, King of Scyros. Here Lycomedes' daughter Deidamia, bore him a son, Neoptolemus (q.v.). Odysseus (q.v.) learned of this subterfuge and visited Lycomedes' court disguised as a merchant. While the king's daughters and the disguised Achilles were surveying his wares he suddenly produced swords which Achilles eagerly clasped, thus revealing himself. Achilles proved himself the most formidable warrior at Troy. At Tenedos on the way to Troy he killed King Tenes and his father Cyncus and by raiding Aeneas' (q.v.) cattle prompted him to join the Trojan forces. In the tenth year of the war Achilles quarrelled with Agamemnon (q.v.) over the captive girl Briseis and withdrew from the fighting. However he loaned his armour to Patroclus, his cousin and friend who was slain by Hector (q.v.). His death prompted Achilles to cease sulking in his tent and to return to the fray. Thetis gave him new armour made by Hephaestus (q.v.) and wearing this he slew Hector. He also killed Penthesilea (q.v.) and the Greek Thersites

(q.v.). After killing Memnon (q.v.) Achilles was shot in his vulnerable ankle at a battle near the Scaean gate (q.v.) Odysseus and Ajax (q.v.) recovered his body and argued over his armour.

Acis. In later Greek legend the young son of Faunus (q.v.) and a river nymph. He loved the sea-nymph Galatea (q.v.) and was killed by his jealous rival Polyphemus (q.v.). According to Sicilian tradition he was then turned into the river of the same name which runs out at the foot of Mount Etna. This tradition first appears in the writing of Theocritus (q.v.) and later in Ovid's (q.v.) "Metamorphoses". It inspired paintings by Poussin and Claude and the opera *Acis and Galatea* by Handel.

Acrisius. Son of Abas (q.v.), twin brother of Proetus (q.v.) and King of Argos. Warned by an oracle that the son of his daughter Danaë (q.v.) would kill him he had her locked up in a brazen tower. But this was to no avail because Zeus (q.v.) visited her and fathered Perseus (q.v.), Acrisius then cast mother and son adrift on the sea, locked in a chest. Years later Perseus returned to Argos causing Acrisius to flee to Larissa. However Perseus, visiting Larissa to take part in the games, accidentally killed him with a discus.

Acropolis. In general terms a high citadel found in all Greek cities. The best known acropolis is that at Athens which was first inhabited around 2000 B.C. From time immemorial it was dedicated to Athene (q.v.).

Actaeon. Mythical huntsman and grandson of Cadmus (q.v.) of Thebes. Artemis (q.v.) turned him into a stag, torn to pieces by his own hounds because he inadvertently spied her bathing. The story is recounted in Ovid's (q.v.) "Metamorphoses" and recalled in the works of Titian, Veronese, Poussin, Rembrandt, Gainsborough and Parmigiano.

Admetus. King of Pherae in Thessaly and husband of the beautiful Alcestis (q.v.). Apollo (q.v.) offered to allow Admetus to avoid death if one of his family would die in his place. Alcestis offered herself but according to legend either Persephone (q.v.) refused the self-sacrifice or Heracles (q.v.) rescued Alcestis from Hades (q.v.). This forms the theme of one of Euripides' best known plays and Gluck's opera *Alceste* (in which Apollo not Heracles saves her).

Adonis. A Syrian deity associated with the mystery of vegetation. He was a beautiful Cypriot youth, the son of Myrrha and her father. For this incest Myrrha was turned into a tree. Nine months later Adonis was born from the bark of the tree, taken up by Aphrodite (q.v.) and placed in the care of Persephone (q.v.). He spent alternate parts of the year with Persephone and Aphrodite who loved him. He was killed by a boar sent by Artemis (q.v.). Shakespeare's *Venus and Adonis* is based on Ovid's (q.v.) version of the tale while Shelley's elegy on the death of Keats, *Adonais*, derives its title from Bion's *Lament for Adonis*. Adonis was painted by Titian, Veronese and Poussin.

Adrastus. Son of Talaus and King of Argos. An oracle told him that his offspring would be a lion and a boar and in accordance with this he gave his daughter Argia to Polynices (q.v.) and her sister to Tydeus (q.v.) who bore images of these animals on their shields. He attempted to restore Polynices to his throne at Thebes (see **Seven against Thebes**). He survived this adventure—some say due to his magic horse Arion (q.v.)—and led a second expedition (of the Epigoni, q.v.) against Thebes, dying of grief when he heard that his son Aegialeus had fallen in the attack.

Aeacides. The descendants of Aeacus (q.v.).

Aeacus. Son of Zeus and Aegina and King of the Myrmidones. The Myrmidones were originally ants, transformed into men by Zeus at the request of Aeacus. He aided Poseidon (q.v.) and Apollo (q.v.) in the construction of the walls of Troy. He had two sons, Peleus (q.v.) and Telamon (q.v.) by his wife Endeis. He was also the father of Phocus (*q.v.*) by a Nereid. Aeacus later exiled Peleus (future father of Achilles) for the murder of Phocus. A model of virtue and piety, Aeacus was made one of the three judges of the Underworld.

Aeaea. In the Odyssey the island home of Circe (*q.v.*).

Aedon. In Greek mythology the wife of Zethus, king of Thebes. She was jealous of Niobe, wife of Zethus' brother Amphion (*q.v.*). In trying to murder Niobe's son she killed her own son Itylus by mistake. In pity Zeus (*q.v.*) turned her into a nightingale whose song still mourns Itylus.

Aegaeon. Alternative name for Briareus (*q.v.*).

Aegeus. King of Athens and father of Theseus (*q.v.*) by Aethra (*q.v.*) daughter of Pittheus king of Troezen. She brought Theseus up secretly at her father's court, during which time Aegeus married Medea (*q.v.*). When Theseus finally returned to his father's court Medea fled. Before Theseus went to slay the Minotaur (*q.v.*) he and Aegeus agreed that he would hoist a white sail when returning to Athens to signal his success. On returning Theseus forgot to do this and Aegeus seeing a black sail on his son's ship supposed him dead and, in grief threw himself into the sea, henceforth called the Aegean.

Aegisthus. The son of Thyestes (*q.v.*) by his daughter Pelopia. Pelopia exposed the baby but it was rescued by her husband Atreus (*q.v.*) who believed it to be his own son. Atreus was king of Mycenae and when Thyestes, an enemy, returned in later years he ordered Aegisthus to kill him. But father and son recognised each other and Aegisthus killed Atreus. Thyestes became king of Mycenae but Atreus had had two sons by Aerope, Menelaus (*q.v.*) and Agamemnon (*q.v.*). Agamemnon expelled Thyestes and reclaimed his father's throne. While Agamemnon was at Troy (*q.v.*) Aegisthus seduced his wife Clytemnestra (*q.v.*) and helped her murder him on his return. These two murderers of Agamemnon now ruled Mycenae. But at the urging of his sister Electra (*q.v.*) (whom Aegisthus would have liked to kill and whom he forced to marry a peasant) Agamemnon's son Orestes (*q.v.*) and his friend Pylades (*q.v.*) returned from exile in Phocis and with Electra's help avenged their father, slaying Aegisthus and Clytemnestra.

Aeneas. The Trojan hero regarded by the Romans as their ancestor. The son of Anchises (*q.v.*) and Aphrodite (*q.v.*). Led the survivors of the Trojan War to Italy. The lover of Dido. *See under* **Aeneid**.

Aeneid. Virgil's (*q.v.*) unfinished epic poem. In 12 volumes, it is written to honour Rome, to increase the prestige of Augustus (by recalling the deeds of his supposed ancestor) and to foretell prosperity to come. It describes Aeneas' (*q.v.*) wanderings after Troy fell, recounting his stay in Carthage and love for Dido (*q.v.*) the funeral games of his father Anchises (*q.v.*) in Sicily, a journey to the Underworld to visit his dead father's spirit and his arrival at the mouth of the Tiber where he landed on the Latin shore. Here he fought wars with the Latins and their allies before finally defeating Turnus the Rutulian prince and uniting the races by marrying Lavinia the Latin princess. He founded Lavinium, named in her honour.

Aeolian Isles. The present Aeolian Isles are off the North East of Sicily, forming part of the Liparia group. They are mentioned in the *Odyssey*.

Aeolus. In Greek mythology (1) the son of Helen and ruler of Thessaly, believed to be the brother of Dorus and Xuthus (*q.v.*) and the ancestor of the Aeolians or Aeolic Greeks, *i.e.* those inhabiting Aeolis.

(2) The son of Poseidon (*q.v.*) and ruler of the Aeolian isles (*q.v.*). Zeus (*q.v.*) made him guardian of the winds. He gave Odysseus (*q.v.*) a bag of winds which his men let loose and which blew the ship off course.

Aeschylus. *See* **B2.**

Aetolus. Legendary conqueror of Aetolia. The son of Endymion (*q.v.*) king of Elis, he was banished across the Corinthian Gulf after accidentally killing Apis in a chariot race.

Agamemnon. Son of Atreus (*q.v.*) and Aerope, brother of Menelaus (*q.v.*) and king of Mycenae. He married Helen's (*q.v.*) half-sister Clytemnestra (*q.v.*) and commanded the Greek forces at Troy (*q.v.*). Before the Greek fleet could leave Aulis to sail for Troy he had to sacrifice his daughter Iphigenia (*q.v.*). At Troy he quarrelled with Achilles (*q.v.*) when he seized Briseis from Achilles. He did this because Apollo (*q.v.*) had forced him to return Chryseis to her father, the Trojan Chryses (*q.v.*).

On his return to Mycenae he was murdered by Aegisthus (*q.v.*) and Clytemnestra. Clytemnestra attacked him with an axe while he was bathing. This occurred despite the warning given to Agamemnon by Cassandra (*q.v.*) whom he had brought back from Troy as his mistress. He was avenged by his children Orestes (*q.v.*) and Electra (*q.v.*). The story inspired Aeschylus' (*q.v.*) trilogy *Orestia*.

Aganippe. A fountain at the foot of Mt. Helicon, sacred to the Muses (*q.v.*) who are sometimes called Aganippides. It inspired those who drank from it. The fountain of Hippocrene, also sacred to the Muses, was known as Aganippis.

Agathyrsans. In the *Aeneid* (*q.v.*) a tribe in Thrace.

Aglaia. "The bright one": one of the Graces (*q.v.*).

Aides or Aidoneus. Hades (*q.v.*).

Ajax. (Greek Aias) In Greek legend two Ajaxes appear. The first was the son of King Telamon of Salamis. He killed Teuthras King of Teuthrania, an ally of Troy (*q.v.*) and took his daughter Tecmessa. At Troy he fought all day with Hector (*q.v.*) and at the end of the duel they exchanged gifts, Hector giving him a sword. With Menelaus (*q.v.*) he rescued the body of Patroclus (*q.v.*) and with Odysseus (*q.v.*) killed Glaucus and rescued the body of Achilles. Homer (*q.v.*) says the pair quarrelled over the armour and that Odysseus killed him. Later, when Odysseus summoned the spirits of the dead Ajax held aloof. But Sophocles (*q.v.*) in his *Ajax* calls on another tradition in which Ajax, disappointed at not being given the Palladium (*q.v.*) of Troy when the city fell, went mad, killing the Greek sheep under the delusion they were his rivals before impaling himself on the sword Hector had given him. The other Ajax was the son of Oileus, king of the Locrians. He was courageous but blasphemous. When Troy was sacked he dragged Cassandra (*q.v.*) from the altar of Athene (*q.v.*) where she sought refuge and gave her to Agamemnon (*q.v.*). On his return to Greece Poseidon (*q.v.*) saved him from shipwreck in a storm sent by Athene. Taking shelter on a rock he boasted himself more powerful than the goddess. She commanded Poseidon to crack the reef with his trident and Ajax drowned.

Alba Longa. The Latin city founded by Ascanius (*q.v.*) in the Alban Hills. In fact, as well as legend, Alba was the mother city of Rome which was probably founded as one of her western outposts. Alba was capital of the Latin League, a confederation of Latin states, but was eventually supplanted by Rome.

Alcaeus. *See* **Alcmene.**

Alcestis. Daughter of Pelias (*q.v.*) and the only one of his daughters not to follow Medea's (*q.v.*) advice and boil him alive. Married Admetus (*q.v.*) and was devoted to him.

Alcides. Another name for Heracles (*q.v.*) whose grandfather was reputed to be Alcaeus.

Alcinous. King of the mythical Phaeacians of the isle of Scheria. A grandson of Poseidon (*q.v.*), he married Arete his own sister. Father of the beautiful Nausicaa (*q.v.*). He entertained Odysseus and gave him a ship. He was also said to have entertained the Argonauts and refused to return Medea to her father. Scheria has been identified with Corfu.

Alcmaeon. In myth the son of Amphiaraus (*q.v.*) and Eriphyle (*q.v.*). One of the Epigoni (*q.v.*).

Alcmene. The wife of Amphitrion (*q.v.*) son of Alcaeus. Her brothers had been slain by the Taphians and she would not consummate her marriage until Amphitrion avenged them. While he was away warring with the Taphians Zeus (*q.v.*) appeared in his likeness and fathered Heracles (*q.v.*) upon her. Hermes (*q.v.*) was ordered to delay the dawn in order that Zeus might take his time—an amusing situation which has appealed to Plautus, Molière and Dryden. Later that night the real Amphitrion returned and fathered Iphicles (*q.v.*). In his *Amphitryon 38* Jean Giraudoux claims 37 versions of the tale have preceded him. On the death of Amphitrion Alcmene married Rhadamanthus (*q.v.*).

Alcyone or Halcyone. (1) Leader of the Pleiades (*q.v.*), daughter of Atlas (*q.v.*) and Pleione.

(2) The daughter of Aeolus (*q.v.*) and wife of Ceyx. When Ceyx was lost at sea she drowned herself in sorrow. The sympathetic gods turned the pair to kingfishers which supposedly bred during the winter solstice. Then Aeolus forbids the wind to blow leaving the Aegean calm while they build and sit on their nest. This is the time of year

called the "Halcyon days". The story is told in Ovid's (q.v.) "Metamorphoses" and Chaucer's "Book of the Duchess".

Alecto. One of the Erinnyes (q.v.).

Alexander the Great. See **B3**

Amalthea. The she-goat which nursed the infant Zeus in the Dictaean cave in Crete. As a reward she was placed among the stars as Capricorn while one of her horns which had broken off became the Cornucopia, or horn of plenty.

Amazons. Mythical race of female warriors at one time believed by the Greeks to live in Thrace or Asia Minor. As the Greeks' knowledge of the world grew, so the homeland of the Amazons was held to be more distant. In the *Iliad* (q.v.) Priam (q.v.) is said to have warred with them, though they came to the aid of Troy (q.v.). Achilles (q.v.) slew their queen Penthesilea (q.v.). Heracles (q.v.) fought with them and seized the girdle of the queen Hippolyte (q.v.) while Theseus (q.v.) carried off either Hippolyte or Antiope (q.v.). Theseus' act caused the Amazons to invade Attica but Theseus defeated them in the streets of Athens. In antiquity it was thought they amputated their right breast (Greek *mazos*) in order to hold a bow better.

Ambrosia. The food of the Olympians which gave immortality.

Ammon. The Egyptian god Amun was known to the Greeks from the 7th century B.C. when they came into contact with his cult at the Siwa oasis. They identified him with Zeus. Alexander the Great consulted the oracle of Zeus and Ammon was recognised as the son of Zeus by the priests of the oracle. A legend grew up that Alexander was begotten by Ammon in the form of a snake.

Amphiaraus. See **Seven Against Thebes.**

Amphion. Twin brother of Zethus, sons of Zeus (q.v.) and Antiope (q.v.). Antiope was married to Lycus King of Thebes who divorced her. She was cruelly treated by his second wife Dirce. The twins were raised by herdsmen on Mt. Cithaeron. When they reached manhood they avenged their mother by killing Zethus and tying Dirce to the horns of a wild bull. The fountain into which her body was thrown henceforth bore her name. The twins now took possession of Thebes and built the fortifications below the Cadmea. Amphion, who had been given a lyre by Hermes (q.v.) played so skilfully that the stones moved into place of their own accord. They ruled jointly, Zethus marrying Thebe who gave her name to the city, and Amphion marrying Niobe (q.v.).

Amphitrion. Son of Alcaeus, husband of Alcmene (q.v.) and father of Iphicles (q.v.). Foster father of Heracles (q.v.). When Heracles killed his teacher Linus with Linus' own lyre, Amphitrion sent him away to keep cattle. Later Amphitrion was killed helping Heracles defeat the Minyans.

Amphitrite. The daughter of Nereus (q.v.) leader of the Nereids (q.v.). Persuaded by Delphinos to accept Poseidon (q.v.) (Delphinos was rewarded by having his image placed amongst the stars as the Dolphin). By Poseidon she was mother of Triton (q.v.). Her hatred of Scylla (q.v.), Poseidon's daughter by another, led her to turn Scylla into a monster with six barking heads and twelve feet.

Amphitroniades. Another name for Heracles (q.v.) whose putative father was Amphitrion (q.v.).

Amyclae. One of the most sacred sites in the Peloponnese, a sanctuary a few miles from Sparta consecrated to Hyacinthus (q.v.).

Anchises. A cousin of Priam (q.v.). For his piety he was allowed to sleep with Aphrodite (q.v.) who bore him Aeneas. When Troy (q.v.) fell Aeneas carried his father (now blind) to safety through the Dardanian gate of the city. He died in Sicily and was buried at Eryx. In the *Aeneid* (q.v.) he appears among the blessed spirits of the dead to foretell Rome's greatness. *Aeneas carrying his Father* is an early work of Bernini.

Ancus Martius. The legendary fourth king of Rome who succeeded Tullus Hostilius. A grandson of Numa Pompilius (q.v.) he ruled from 640 to 616 B.C. He was very religious but also succeeded in defeating the Latins. He was succeeded by Tarquin the Elder.

Andromache. A Trojan princess, wife of Hector (q.v.) and by him mother of Astyanax. When Troy fell her son was thrown from the city walls, despite her spirited defence of him with a pestle. She was carried off to Epirus by Neoptolemus (q.v.) and here married his brother in law Hellenus and

became joint ruler. She also had a son by Neoptolemus and was threatened by his jealous wife Hermione (see Racine's *Andromaque*). Her days were ended at Pergamum, the city founded by her and Neoptolemus' son, Molossus. In historic times the Molossi claimed descent from Molossus and Neoptolemus.

Andromeda. See **Cassiopeia.**

Antaeus. A Libyan giant, son of Poseidon (q.v.) and Ge (q.v.). An invincible wrestler until Heracles (q.v.), realising he drew his strength from his mother, held him in the air and squeezed him to death. He is featured in a painting by Pollaiuolo in Florence.

Antenor. The wisest of the Trojans. Priam (q.v.) sent him to reclaim Hesione from Telamon after Heracles (q.v.) sacked Troy (q.v.). He advised the Trojans to return Helen (q.v.) to Menelaus (q.v.) but they refused. His hatred for Deiphobus (q.v.) led him to help the Greeks steal the Palladium (q.v.). The husband of Theano and father of Laocoön (q.v.). After Troy fell he and his wife went to Italy and founded either Venice or Padua.

Antigone. Daughter of Oedipus (q.v.) and Jocasta (q.v.) she accompanied her father into exile (recalled in Sophocles' *Oedipus at Colonus*). After his death she returned to Thebes where her brother Eteocles (q.v.) and Polynices (q.v.) were warring on each other. Both perished in battle and her uncle Creon (q.v.) seized power. Because Polynices had fought against his own country Creon refused him burial. Antigone defied Creon and buried her brother with full rites and was imprisoned in a cave for doing so. Here she hung herself, and her betrothed, Creon's son Haemon, committed suicide in despair. The story and the ethical principles it raises are the basis of Sophocles' *Antigone*. In his work of the same name Anouilh reconsiders the arguments involved.

Antilochus. Son of Nestor (q.v.) a valiant Greek warrior at Troy (q.v.). Too young to sail from Aulis when the expedition began he arrived later. Slain by Memnon (q.v.) while defending his father.

Antinous. See **Odysseus.**

Antiope. (1) An Amazon, sister of Hippolyte (q.v.). According to some legends she was carried off by Theseus (q.v.), perhaps with the aid of Heracles (q.v.) and bore him Hippolytus (q.v.).

(2) A Theban princess who bore Amphion (q.v.) and Zethus to Zeus (q.v.) who visited her in the form of a satyr (q.v.). Her father exposed the children on Mt. Cithaeron. She was badly treated and imprisoned by Lycus and his wife Dirce (Lycus was either her husband, who divorced her to marry Dirce, or her uncle). She was later freed and avenged by her twin sons. Titian, Correggio and Watteau have all painted Zeus visiting Antiope as a satyr.

Aphaia. A goddess worshipped in Aegina and identified with the Cretan Britomartis.

Aphrodite. The goddess of love, desire and procreation, known to the Romans as Venus. She sprang from the seed of Uranus (q.v.), rising naked from the sea at Paphos in Cyprus. However, Homer (q.v.) holds her to be the daughter of Zeus (q.v.) and Dione, and makes her the wife of Hephaestus (q.v.). She was not faithful to Hephaestus, but bore children by Ares (q.v.), Poseidon (q.v.), Dionysus (q.v.), and Hermes (q.v.), She loved the mortals Adonis (q.v.) and Anchises (q.v.) by whom she bore Aeneas (q.v.), and tempted Paris (q.v.) to desert Oenone. It was to her that Paris gave the golden apple of discord, she being the "fairest" goddess. In return she promised him the most beautiful woman in the world. Around her waist she wore a magic girdle which made her beautiful and irresistibly desirable.

Apis. The sacred bull of Memphis which the Egyptians worshipped as a god.

Apollo. Son of Zeus (q.v.) and the mortal Leto; twin brother of Artemis (q.v.). As a child he killed the she-dragon Python on Mt. Parnassus and took over her role as the oracle at Delphi. Hence he was sometimes known as the Pythian or as Loxias "the Ambiguous". He was also a symbol of light and was known as Phoebus or "shining". Apart from being god of prophecy he was a god of song and music, having been given the lyre by Hermes (q.v.). He was the leader of the Muses (q.v.) and was sometimes called Musagetes. He could be a destroyer (he is always portrayed with bow and arrows) and sent plagues amongst the Greeks at Troy, but was also protective against evil and was father of Asclepius (q.v.). When Zeus slew Asclepius he retaliated by slaying the Cyclopes (q.v.)

and was punished by being sent as a servant to Admetus (q.v.) of Pherae in Thessaly. Prior to this Zeus had sent him as a bondsman to King Laomedan whom he helped to build the walls of Troy. This was punishment for his part in a conspiracy (led by Hera, Poseidon and himself) against Zeus. He loved Hestia (q.v.) but also seduced the nymph Dryope and attempted to seduce Daphne. When Daphne protested she was turned into a laurel tree. Amongst mortal women he at one time loved Cassandra (q.v.). With his sister Artemis he shot the giant Tityus, whom the jealous Hera sent to violate Leto; it was he who shot the vulture which tormented Prometheus and he also helped Paris (q.v.) shoot Achilles (q.v.). He was identified with the sun-god by later writers but in Homer (q.v.) he and Helios (q.v.) are quite distinct.

Arachne. A Lydian maiden who competed with Athene (q.v.) at a weaving contest. When she won the angry goddess forced her to hang herself before turning her into a spider and her weaving into a cobweb.

Arcadia. Green but mountainous region, isolated in the centre of the Peloponnese. Its inhabitants were primitive shepherds and peasants.

Arcas. The son of Zeus (q.v.) and Callisto (q.v.) who gave his name to Arcadia (q.v.).

Ares. The son of Zeus (q.v.) and Hera (q.v.) and the god of war. Associated with Mars, by the Romans. He was disliked by all the gods save Hades (q.v.) and Eris (q.v.) because of his love of battle for its own sake. He loved Aphrodite (q.v.), and Hephaestus (q.v.) once caught the pair in an invisible net exposing them to the ridicule of the other gods. The father of Penthesilea (q.v.) by Otrere. He was once defeated by Heracles (q.v.), was wounded by Diomedes (q.v.) and imprisoned for 13 months (till Hermes (q.v.) released him) in a brazen vessel by the Aloeidae (q.v.). Athene (q.v.) got the better of him on several occasions. He once stood trial on the site of the Areopagus.

Arethusa. A river and a river goddess of southern Greece. She was pursued under the sea to Sicily by the river god Alpheus. In Sicily she was identified with Artemis and a cult of Artemis Arethusa flourished at Syracuse.

Argo. A fifty-oared ship built for Jason (q.v.) by Argus. In its prow Athene (q.v.) fitted an oracular beam.

Argonauts. The heroes who sailed with Jason (q.v.) in the Argo (q.v.) to fetch the golden fleece from Colchis. Their ranks included Heracles (q.v.), Orpheus (q.v.) Castor and Polydeuces (q.v.) Echion, Idas (q.v.) and Lynceus (q.v.). The voyage was an adventurous one and after dallying at Lemnos they passed through the Hellespont and reached Mysia. Here Hylas (q.v.) was lost and Heracles stayed to look for him. At some point the Sirens (q.v.) were passed with the help of Orpheus (q.v.) and at Bebrycos Polydeuces (see **Castor**) slew Amycus. In Thrace they rid Phineus (q.v.) of the Harpies (q.v.) and in return were told how to navigate the Symplegades (q.v.).

Argus. (1) The builder of the Argo (q.v.).
(2) A hundred-eyed giant set by Hera (q.v.) to watch Io (q.v.).
(3) The faithful hound of Odysseus (q.v.).

Ariadne. The daughter of Minos (q.v.) and Pasiphae (q.v.). She helped Theseus (q.v.) but he abandoned her at Naxos when Dionysus (q.v.) fell in love with her. He married her and gave her a crown of seven stars which became a constellation after her death.

Arimaspi. A mythical people of the Scythian steppes said to be neighbours of the Hyperboreans. They had one eye and constantly fought a group of griffins for the gold they guarded. Herodotus (q.v.) tells of a poem by Aristeas, a priest of Hyperborean Apollo, about them. Aristeas is clearly a *shaman*, able to separate body and soul and to be in two places at once. Aeschylus (q.v.) refers to them when describing Io's (q.v.) wanderings.

Arion. A fabulous horse, the offspring of Demeter (q.v.) and Zeus (q.v.). Demeter had taken the form of a mare and Zeus raped her in the form of a horse. She also gave birth to the nymph Despoena and possibly Persephone (q.v.) at the same time as Arion. It saved Adrastus (q.v.) at the siege of Thebes.

Aristaeus. The son of Apollo (q.v.) and a Lapith (see Lapithae) girl Cyrene. A minor deity, the protector of cattle, fruit trees and bee-keepers. Virgil (q.v.) makes Cyrene a nymph and says that Aristaeus fell in love with Eurydice who died of a snake bite she received while fleeing from him. In punishment all his bees were killed. Cyrene sought the advice of Proteus (q.v.) and Aristaeus made sacrifices of cattle to placate the nymphs. Nine days later he found fresh swarms in the carcasses.

Aristophanes. See **B4**.

Artemis. The daughter of Zeus (q.v.) and Leto (q.v.) twin sister of Apollo (q.v.). Her Roman counterpart was Diana. She was often conflated with Hecate (q.v.) and Selene (q.v.), the moon goddess. A goddess of the chase and protectoress of children and young animals. She was also treated as a mother or earth goddess in the Asian tradition and was worshipped orgiastically at Ephesus. She was generally portrayed with a bow and arrow, made by Hephaestus (q.v.) and like Apollo could spread the plague and death. With her arrows she punished impiety (e.g. Niobe). A virgin who sternly protected her own chastity, she was known to punish unchastity in others e.g. Callisto (q.v.).

Ascanius. The son of Aeneas (q.v.) and Creusa, who escaped from Troy (q.v.) with his father. Another tradition makes his mother the Latin princess Lavinia. He succeeded his father as king and made Alba Longa (q.v.) his capital.

Asclepius or **Aesculapius.** The son of Apollo (q.v.) and Coronis, a god of healing whose worship spread to Rome after a plague in 293 B.C. He was taught healing by Cheiron the centaur (q.v.). Once he brought a dead man back to life and Zeus (q.v.) punished him, killing him with a thunderbolt. At Apollo's request he was placed among the stars.

Asopus. A river god, the son of Oceanus (q.v.) and Tethys (q.v.). The father of Evadne, Euboea and Aegina.

Astraeus. A Titan (q.v.) and by Eos the father of the beneficent winds. According to other traditions he also fathered the stars.

Astyanax. The son of Hector (q.v.) and Andromache (q.v.). He was a sensitive child frightened by the plume of his father's helmet. When Troy (q.v.) fell Andromache struggled to protect him but Neoptolemus (q.v.) threw him from the city walls. Another tradition says she took him to Neoptolemus' court in Epirus.

Atalanta. The Boeotian Atalanta was the daughter of Schoeneus and wife of Hippomenes, the Arcadian Atalanta, the daughter of Iasus and Clymene and wife of Milanion. Similar tales were told of her in both traditions. She was exposed by her father and suckled by a bear sent by Artemis (q.v.) with whom she was sometimes identified. She became a famous huntress and hunted the Calydonian Boar (q.v.). Though vowed to virginity she bore Meleager (q.v.) a son. She refused to marry any suitor except he who beat her in a foot race. Hippomenes (or Milanion) did this by placing three golden apples, gifts from Aphrodite (q.v.) in her path, causing her to stop and collect them.

Athamas. The son of Aeolus and king of Orchomenus in Boeotia. He loved Ino (q.v.) who bore him Learchus and Melicertes, but Hera (q.v.) forced him to marry Nephele who bore him Phrixus and Helle (q.v.). Hera drove him mad because he sheltered Dionysus (q.v.) and he killed Learchus. Ino flung herself into the sea with Melicertes and both became sea deities. Ino became Leucothea and Melicertes became Palaemon. Athamas fled to Thessaly.

Athene or **Athena.** Identified with Minerva by the Romans. The daughter of Zeus (q.v.) and Metis (q.v.). Though it was foretold she would be a girl, an oracle said that if Metis bore another child it would be a son who would depose Zeus. He then swallowed Metis and later suffered a terrible headache near Lake Triton. Hermes (q.v.) knew the cause and persuaded Hephaestus (q.v.) to cleave Zeus' skull. Out sprang Athene fully armed. She was the goddess of wisdom and patron of arts and crafts, a protectress of agriculture and also a warrior. Moreover, she was a virgin (see Pallas). She disputed possession of Athens with Poseidon (q.v.); he offered the city the horse, Athene the olive which was judged to be the better gift. Henceforth she was patron of the city which was a centre of her cult. Her epithet "glaucopis" meant "bright-eyed" or "owl-faced" and in the *Odyssey* (q.v.) she assumed the form of a bird. Athenian coins bore an owl and the saying "Owls to Athens" meant the same as "Coals to Newcastle". She was worshipped on the Acropolis. A defender of all heroes who worked for the good of mankind, e.g. Heracles (q.v.).

Atlantiades. Another name for Hermes (q.v.) whose mother Maia was the daughter of Atlas (q.v.).

Atlantis. A legendary island said to be to the west of the Pillars of Hercules (*q.v.*). Its inhabitants, once powerful and virtuous, became wealthy and degenerate and were conquered by the Athenians. Later the island sank beneath the ocean in a day and a night. It may be that the island Plato speaks of in *Timaeus* was part of Crete or some other island which suffered when a volcano on Suntorini (ancient Thera) erupted.

Atlas. A Titan (*q.v.*) the son of Iapetus and Clymene and brother of Prometheus (*q.v.*) and Epimetheus. For his part in the Titanomachia (*q.v.*) he was condemned to carry the sky on his shoulders and stood holding it far to the west of the Pillars of Hercules (*q.v.*). For a brief time Heracles (*q.v.*) shouldered his burden. It is said Perseus (*q.v.*) turned him to stone with Medusa's (*q.v.*) head and he was identified with Mt. Atlas in North-West Africa. The father of Calypso (*q.v.*) and the Pleiades (*q.v.*).

Atreus. *See* **Thyestes.**

Attis. A god of vegetation whose cult originated in Phrygia and involved a festival of death and resurrection in the Spring. A consort of Cybele (*q.v.*) according to one tradition he castrated himself in a religious frenzy and became head of her college of eunuch priests.

Augias. A king of Elis with more sheep and cattle than any other man. Heracles (*q.v.*) was given the task of cleansing his filthy stables which had not been cleared for many years. Heracles promised to cleanse them in a day in return for one tenth of the cattle. He did so by diverting the rivers Peneius and Alphaeus through them but Augias refused to pay him. Heracles later invaded Elis, killed Augias, his sons and their allies the Moliones and destroyed the city of Pylus which had also helped Augias. One tradition says he spared Augias.

Aurora. The Roman goddess of the dawn, associated with the Greek Eos (*q.v.*).

Autolycus. The son of Hermes (*q.v.*) and Chione, father of Anticleia and thus grandfather of Odysseus (*q.v.*). Also grandfather of Sinon (*q.v.*). He was renowned for trickery, cunning and theft.

Aventine. One of the hills of Rome and the southernmost. It was close to the Tiber, was outside the pomerium and was associated with the "plebians".

Avernus, Lake. The modern Lago di Averno near Naples, thought to be an entrance to the Underworld. This is how Aeneas (*q.v.*) was told to enter Hades (*q.v.*). Agrippa linked it with the Lucrine Lake while building the harbour of Portus Julius.

B

Bacchae. The female followers of the cult of Bacchus or Dionysus whose worship was characterised by wine-induced frenzies of a mystic nature. At the height of such frenzies they believed themselves to be at one with the god. Also known as Bacchantes, Maenads and Thyiads.

Bacchoi. Male equivalent of the Bacchae.

Bacchus. Latin name for Dionysus (*q.v.*).

Bassaris. A Bacchante (*See* **Bacchae**).

Baucis. *See* **Philemon.**

Bellerophon. Son of Glaucus (*q.v.*) King of Corinth. He killed one Bellerus and fled to Tiryns where Anteia, wife of the King Proetus falsely accused him of trying to seduce her. Proetus sent him to his father-in-law Iobates with a letter requesting Iobates to kill the bearer of it. Reluctant to kill a guest Iobates sent him to kill the Chimaera (*q.v.*). Capturing Pegasus (*q.v.*) with a golden bridle given to him by Athene (*q.v.*) he was able to accomplish the task. He was then sent to fight the Amazons (*q.v.*) and again triumphed. On his return to Tiryns he survived an ambush set by Iobates and finally persuaded the king of his innocence. Iobates made him his heir. One tradition says Bellerophon presumed to rise to Olympus on Pegasus but Zeus sent a gadfly which stung the horse. Pegasus threw Bellerophon to earth but itself entered Olympus.

Belus. One of Poseidon's (*q.v.*) sons and father of Danaus (*q.v.*), Cepheus (*q.v.*) and Aegyptus.

Biton and Cleobis. Sons of a priestess of Hera (*q.v.*) in Argos who drew their mother's chariot several miles to the goddess's temple when no oxen could be found. Their mother asked Hera to bestow on them the best of gifts for mortals, and they died in their sleep in the temple.

Boeotia. Region of northern Greece; the capital city was Thebes.

Bona Dea. A Roman fertility goddess. Only women worshipped her. Cicero (*q.v.*) recounts an occasion when his opponent Clodius (*q.v.*), disguised as a woman, entered an annual nocturnal ceremony of her worshippers over which the chief magistrate's wife presided.

Boreas. The Roman Aquilo; the north wind in Greek mythology. Son of Astraeus (*q.v.*) and Eos (*q.v.*) and brother of the other beneficent winds Zephyrus (*q.v.*), Notus (*q.v.*) and Eurus (*q.v.*). A friend of Athens who destroyed Xerxes' (*q.v.*) fleet. He carried off Oreithyia, daughter of Erechtheus king of Athens who bore him two sons Zetes (*q.v.*) and Calais (*q.v.*) and two daughters, Chione and Cleopatra, wife of Phineus.

Brauron. Site on the east coast of Attica. Centre of a cult of Artemis (*q.v.*). It was believed the locals had killed a she-bear, an animal sacred to the goddess, and that she demanded they worship her on the site, and that girls between the ages of 7 and 11 serve her and live in her temple. Also believed to be the burial place of Iphigenia (*q.v.*) after her sacrifice at Aulis.

Briareus or **Aegaeon.** One of the Hecatoncheires (*q.v.*).

Briseis. *See* **Achilles.**

Brontes. One of the Cyclopes (*q.v.*).

Brutus, Lucius Junius. According to a Roman tradition accepted by Livy (*q.v.*) the liberator of Rome from the Etruscan kings following the rape of Lucretia (*q.v.*). Also the first Roman consul in 509 B.C. He ordered the execution of his own sons when they became involved in a conspiracy to restore the monarchy.

C

Cacus. In Roman tradition this fire-breathing giant and his sister Caca were children of Vulcan (*q.v.*) who lived on the Palatine hill (*q.v.*), although Virgil in book 8 of the *Aeneid* (*q.v.*) makes it the Aventine (*q.v.*). Virgil tells how Cacus stole the cattle of Geryon (*q.v.*) from Hercules (*q.v.*) who pursued Cacus back to his cave, tracking him by the cattle's mooing. There he slew Cacus. This event has been portrayed in a painting by Poussin and a statue by Bandinelli in the Signoria, Florence.

Cadmus. Son of Agenor, king of Phoenicia and grandson of Poseidon (*q.v.*). When Zeus (*q.v.*) carried off his sister Europa (*q.v.*) he went to look for her but was told by the Delphic oracle (*see* Apollo) to relinquish the search and to follow a magical cow. Where the cow lay down he was to found a city. The place where it sank became the site of the Cadmea, the citadel of Thebes. Here Cadmus slew the dragon guarding the spring of Ares and on her advice sowed its teeth. The Sparti (*q.v.*) sprang up. Cadmus married Harmonia (*q.v.*) and their wedding was attended by the gods. Their children included Autonoe, Ino, Semele (*q.v.*) Agave Polydoros (*q.v.*) and Illyrius. In old age Cadmus, who had introduced the use of letters to Greece from Phoenicia, gave up his throne to his grandson Pentheus and went to reign in Illyria. Later he and Harmonia were received into Elysium (*q.v.*) in the form of serpents.

Caeneus. Originally the nymph Caenis turned into a man at her own request by Poseidon (*q.v.*). Accompanied the Argonauts (*q.v.*) and hunted the Calydonian Boar (*q.v.*). Invulnerable to normal blows he was killed by the Centaurs (*q.v.*) in their battle with the Lapithae (*q.v.*) when they buried him beneath a pile of trees. His soul left the body as a bird and in the Underworld again became female.

Calais. Twin brother of Zetes. Winged sons of Boreas (*q.v.*) and Oreithyia, they accompanied the Argonauts (*q.v.*) and drove off the Harpies (*q.v.*), tormenting Phineus (*q.v.*) husband of their sister Cleopatra.

Calchas. A renegade Trojan seer who helped the Greeks at Troy (*q.v.*). He foretold that Troy would not fall without Achilles' (*q.v.*) presence and that the sacrifice of Iphigenia (*q.v.*) was necessary to secure a favourable wind. It was he who advised Agamemnon to return the girl Chryseis to her father the Trojan priest Chryses. This caused Agamemnon to seize Briseis and sparked the quarrel with Achilles. Calchas later died of grief when surpassed in prophecy by Mopsus, a mysterious mythical figure who was also said to have sailed with the Argonauts (q.v.).

Calipe. See **Pillars of Hercules.**

Calliope. See **Muses.**

Callirhoë. Daughter of the river god Achelous (q.v.) and wife of Alcmaeon (q.v.). Alcmaeon gave her the necklace and robe of Harmonia (q.v.).

Callisto. Daughter of Lycaon (q.v.). One of Artemis' (q.v.) huntresses. She bore Arcas (q.v.) to Zeus (q.v.) who sought to conceal their affair from Hera (q.v.) by turning Callisto into a bear. Realising the ruse Hera had the bear hunted down but Zeus saved her and placed her amongst the stars as Arctos. Others say that Artemis turned her into a bear and Arcas hunted her. In this version Callisto became the Great Bear constellation and Arcas the Little Bear.

Calydonian Boar. A savage boar which Artemis (q.v.) sent to ravage Calydon because its king, Oeneus (q.v.) had not offered her proper sacrifice (see also Atalanta and Meleager). Pausanias (q.v.) tells of a story of long tusks found at Tegea, seen by Augustus and taken to Rome.

Calypso. A nymph of Ogygia who tended Odysseus (q.v.) there for eight years until Zeus (q.v.) ordered her to send him home to Ithaca. The name means "hidden" and she may have been a death goddess. At one point she offers the hero eternal youth, but he refuses, preferring real life. She bore him two sons.

Camilla. The Roman equivalent of an Amazon (q.v.)—a female warrior.

Capaneus. See **"Seven Against Thebes".**

Capricorn. See **Amalthea.**

Cassandra. Daughter of Priam (q.v.) and Hecuba and twin of Helenus. She was given the gift of prophecy by Apollo (q.v.) but when she disappointed him he decreed that no one would ever believe her prophecies. Several times her important warnings went unheeded, e.g. against Paris (q.v.) going to Sparta, and against the wooden horse (q.v.). She was taken as a slave by Agamemnon (q.v.) when Troy (q.v.) fell and became his mistress. She was murdered with him by Clytemnestra (q.v.).

Cassiopeia. The wife of Cepheus and mother of Andromeda. Her boast that Andromeda was more beautiful than the Nereids (q.v.) caused Poseidon (q.v.) to send a monster to ravage the kingdom. Only the sacrifice of Andromeda could prevent this. Perseus (q.v.), who found her chained naked to a rock by the sea, offered to save her if she would become his wife. Cepheus and Cassiopeia agreed to this and Perseus slew the beast. Her parents then attempted to renege on their promise, claiming Andromeda was promised to another. At her wedding to Perseus the other suitor and his followers attempted to seize the bride but Perseus turned them all to stone with the head of Medusa (q.v.). The images of Cepheus and Cassiopeia were set amongst the stars by Poseidon.

Castalian Spring. Sacred spring on Mt. Parnassus, near the site of the Delphic oracle. Here the young girl Castalia drowned herself to avoid Apollo's (q.v.) advances.

Castalides. A name for the Muses (q.v.).

Castor and Polydeuces. (Latin **"Pollux"**) The "Dioscuri". The twin "Sons of Zeus", brothers of Helen (q.v.) and the sons of Leda (q.v.), the wife of Tyndareus of Sparta. One tradition says that they were born from an egg, like Helen, after Zeus had visited Leda in the form of a swan. Others say only Polydeuces was Zeus' son and that Castor being the son of Tyndareus was a mere mortal. Castor was a famous horse tamer and Polydeuces a great boxer. Sailing with the Argonauts (q.v.) Polydeuces slew Amycus son of Poseidon (q.v.) who lived on the isle of Bebrycos. Amycus was a renowned boxer who killed travellers by challenging them to a boxing match. They also hunted the Calydonian boar (q.v.). The Dioscuri fought a mortal battle with their cousins the twins Idas and Lynceus Zeus then killed Idas but Polydeuces begged to die with his brother. However Zeus decided they should live alternate days with the gods and under the earth. Their image was placed amongst the stars as Gemini. Poseidon gave them power over the wind and waves and they became protectors of seafarers. They were said to have appeared on horseback to help the Romans against the Latins in the battle of Lake Regillus in 484 B.C., after which their cult was adopted at Rome.

Centaurs. A race of savage creatures, half-man, half-horse which inhabited the woodlands and mountains, particularly those of Thessaly. They were the offspring of Ixion and a cloud. In Homer (q.v.) the centaurs appear as representatives of primitive desires, fighting, drinking and womanising, but later they are only portrayed as turning to violence when drunk. When they tried to abduct Deidamia (q.v.) from her wedding, they became involved in a famous battle with their neighbours the Lapithae (q.v.).

Centimani. See **Hecatoncheires.**

Cephalus. Husband of Procris who was carried off by Eos (q.v.). Eos released him but Procris, suspicious of the time he spent hunting, followed him into the woods. Hearing him praying for a breeze she supposed it to be his mistress (the Roman equivalent of Eos was Aurora, the Latin for breeze aura). Moving closer she was struck by his spear, which never missed, and killed. The story is told by Hesiod and Ovid and inspired paintings by Poussin and Claude.

Cepheus. King of Tegea and one of the Argonauts (q.v.). He and most of his 20 sons were killed helping Heracles (q.v.) fight Hippocoon.

Cerberus. A huge and savage dog, the offspring of Echidne (q.v.) and Typhon (q.v.) which guarded the entrance to Hades (q.v.). He is usually said to have had three heads, but Hesiod gives him fifty. His back was covered with serpents' heads and he had a snake for a tail. Heracles (q.v.) dragged him from the Underworld; Orpheus (q.v.) charmed him with music when seeking Eurydice while Aeneas (q.v.) drugged him with a cake of honey and narcotics, hence "a sop to Cerberus".

Cercyon. A son of Hephaestus (q.v.) reigning near Eleusis. Here he challenged all travellers to a wrestling match and killed them, until he challenged Theseus (q.v.) and was killed himself.

Ceres. Ancient Italian corn-goddess worshipped in a temple on the Aventine. Games and a spring festival, the Ceriala, were held in her honour. She was associated with Demeter (q.v.) from an early date and her daughter Proserpina with Persephone (q.v.).

Ceryneian Hind. A creature with brazen feet and golden antlers. One of Heracles' (q.v.) tasks was to catch it alive. He pursued it for a year and caught it without shedding blood by pinning its forelegs together with an arrow.

Chalybes. Mythical inhabitants of north Asia Minor said by some traditions to have invented iron working.

Chaos. In Greek creation myth Chaos was the infinite space existing before creation. From Chaos sprang Ge (q.v.), the Earth.

Charities. Also called the Gratiae or Graces by the Romans. They were originally divinities of nature. In the Iliad (q.v.) only one Charity is personified, Charis, wife of Hephaestus (q.v.). Later the three Graces appear, Aglaia, Thalia and Euphrosyne, friends of the Muses (q.v.) with whom they inhabited Mt. Olympus.

Charon. The surly ferryman who transported the dead across the Styx (q.v.) to Hades (q.v.). He only transported them if they had received the correct funeral rite and if their relatives had placed a small coin, his fare, under the tongues. However Heracles (q.v.) forced his passage and Orpheus (q.v.) charmed his with his lyre. Amongst the Etruscans (q.v.), as in modern Greek folklore, he was regarded as a synonym or figure of death. Virgil (q.v.) portrays him with unkempt white hair and eyes of fire in the 6th book of the Aeneid.

Charybdis and Scylla. Two monsters guarding the Straits of Messina. Charybdis swallowed the sea and vessels on it, three times a day, regurgitating what she swallowed each time. Opposite was Scylla, the daughter of Poseidon (q.v.) by a mortal, whom the jealous Amphitrite (q.v.) turned into a monster with six barking heads and twelve feet. Odysseus (q.v.) was forced to pass between the two evils and the equally undesirable choice between the pair has become proverbial.

Cheiron. Also called Chiron. A centaur (q.v.). A son of Cronus (q.v.) and Philyra, hence he is sometimes referred to as Philyrides. Unlike his fellow centaurs a wise and kindly being who learnt music, medicine, hunting and prophecy from Apollo (q.v.) and Artemis (q.v.). This learning he imparted to numerous heroes including Achilles (q.v.), the Dioscuri (q.v.), Jason (q.v.) and Peleus (q.v.). An immortal, he was accidentally wounded by the poisoned arrow of his friend Heracles (q.v.). In pain he longed for death. By surrendering his immortality he was relieved of life and suffering and placed among the stars as Sagittarius.

Chimeira. A monster with a lion's head, goat's body and a serpent for a tail. It could breathe fire. The offspring of Echidne (q.v.) and Typhon (q.v.), though some say it was begot by the Sphinx (q.v.) and Orthrus (q.v.). It was killed by Bellerophon (q.v.) while ravaging Lycia. The beast gave us the word "chimera" or fanciful notion.

Chryseis. (Cressida) Daughter of the Trojan seer and priest of Apollo (q.v.). Chryseis was captured by Agamemnon (q.v.) who refused to ransom her. Apollo then sent a plague on the Greek camp and when Calchas (q.v.) explained the cause Agamemnon released her. He then seized Briseis thus causing the quarrel with Achilles (q.v.). The medieval *Roman de Troie* tells how Troilus loved her, but she left him for Diomedes (q.v.). This is the basis of Chaucer's *Troilus and Criseyde* and Shakespeare's *Troilus and Cressida*.

Chrysippus. The son of Pelops (q.v.), murdered by his half-brother Atreus (q.v.) and Thyestes (q.v.) at the instigation of his step-mother Hippodameia (q.v.).

Chthonius. *See* Spartii.

Circe The daughter of Helios (q.v.) and Perse. A sorceress living on the island of Aeaea (Virgil (q.v.) identifies it with Circeii in Campania (q.v.)). She turned Odysseus' (q.v.) men into swine but he resisted by use of the herb "moly" given to him by Hermes (q.v.). Having forced her to restore his men he stayed a year with her and she advised him on his trip to the Underworld and return to Ithaca. She had a son, Telegonus by him and later married his son by Penelope (q.v.), Telemachus (q.v.). In the *Argonautica* of Apollonius of Rhodes she purifies Jason (q.v.) and Medea (q.v.) of murder on their return from Colchis. She was worshipped in Campania in the form of Feronia.

Cisseus. Father of Hecabe (q.v.).

Claros. Site of a shrine and oracle of Apollo (q.v.) to the south of Smyrna.

Cleobis. *See* Biton.

Clio. *See* Muses.

Cloacina. Ancient Roman divinity of "purification", later identified with Venus.

Cloelia. A Roman girl, legendary for having escaped from Porsenna (q.v.) when taken hostage and swimming back to Rome across the Tiber.

Clotho. One of the Fates (q.v.). She pulled the limbs of Pelops (q.v.) from the cauldron in which they were to be boiled, thus enabling his restoration to life.

Clytemnestra. Daughter of Tyndareus (q.v.) and a half-sister of Helen (q.v.) and Castor and Polydeuces (q.v.). Wife of Agamemnon (q.v.) by whom she bore Orestes (q.v.), Iphigenia (q.v.) and Electra (q.v.). While Agamemnon was at Troy (q.v.) she began an affair with Aegisthus (q.v.) and on his return the pair murdered him. She was killed by Orestes. Her murder of Agamemnon should be seen in the context of his infidelity with Cassandra (q.v.) and others and his sacrifice of Iphigenia. This is how Strauss views the matter in his opera *Elektra*.

Cocles. The "one-eyed", a nickname of Horatius (q.v.) who kept the bridge across the Tiber.

Cocytus. The river of wailing in Hades (q.v.).

Coeus. One of the Titans (q.v.).

Cornelia. Mother of the "Gracchi", daughter of Scipio Africanus and a model of what Romans of the Republic thought a matron should be. On the deaths of her sons she withdrew to Misenum and her home became a centre of culture. She appears in Plutarch's (q.v.) *Lives* of her sons and he tells us that when a visitor asked to see her jewels she presented her sons saying "These are my jewels".

Coronis. Thessalian princess made pregnant by Apollo (q.v.) but who fell in love with an Arcadian youth. Learning of this from a crow, Apollo sent Artemis (q.v.) to kill her. The unborn child was snatched from her and given to Cheiron (q.v.) to rear. The child was Asclepius (q.v.).

Corybantes. Priests of Rhea (q.v.) or Cybele (q.v.) in Phrygia and Asia Minor. Known for their dancing and performance of wild rites to the sound of drums and cymbals.

Corydon. Common Arcadian shepherd's name but in Virgil's (q.v.) second *Eclogue* the shepherd

Corydon laments his "faithless Alexis". From this Corydon has become a symbol of homosexual love.

Creon. A "ruler" or "prince" and the name often given to subsidiary characters in Greek legend, e.g. the brother of Jocasta (q.v.) who succeeds Oedipus (q.v.). *See also* **Jason.**

Cretan Bull. A magnificent white bull sent by Poseidon (q.v.) to Minos (q.v.) for sacrifice. Minos' wife Pasiphaë (q.v.) so admired the bull she had Daedalus (q.v.) construct a hollow cow for her to get inside. She then mated with the bull and later bore the Minotaur (q.v.). Minos also admired the bull and rather than sacrifice it, substituted another bull. The original bull escaped to ravage Crete until captured by Heracles (q.v.) and taken to Eurystheus (q.v.). Eurystheus freed it and it ravaged Greece until captured by Theseus (q.v.) at Marathon (q.v.) and sacrificed to Athene (q.v.).

Creusa. Feminine equivalent of Creon. The most famous is the daughter of Priam (q.v.), first wife of Aeneas (q.v.) and mother of Ascanius. She was lost in the escape from Troy (q.v.) when the city fell. When Aeneas looked for her he met only her ghost who bid him go forward to meet his destiny.

Croesus. Last king of Lydia who in the mid-6th century B.C. amassed a great fortune. His wealth is proverbial. Regarded as a model of piety for his gold offerings to Apollo (q.v.) at Delphi (q.v.). He met Solon and tried to persuade him to admit that Croesus was the happiest of men. Solon refused, saying that no man could be considered happy till his life had ended. The Delphic oracle told him that a great empire would fall if he invaded Persia. His own did. The Persian king Cyrus ordered him to be burnt alive but he called on Solon's name and told Cyrus of Solon's sayings. Cyrus pardoned him and made him an adviser. A later tradition says Apollo saved him and carried him to the land of the Hyperboreans.

Crommyum, Sow of. Wild sow slain by Theseus (q.v.).

Cronus. The son of Uranus (q.v.) and Ge (q.v.). The youngest of the twelve Titans (q.v.). When Ge stirred the Titans to revolt against Uranus she gave Cronus a flint sickle with which he castrated his father. Having deposed Uranus, Cronus reigned supreme and consigned the Cyclopes (q.v.) and the Hecatoncheires (q.v.) to Tartarus (q.v.). He married his sister Rhea (q.v.) and by her was father of Hestia (q.v.), Demeter (q.v.), Hera (q.v.), Poseidon (q.v.), Hades (q.v.) and Zeus (q.v.). Mindful of a curse by Uranus and Ge that he too be deposed by his own son, he swallowed each child at birth. But Rhea gave him a stone to swallow instead of Zeus and later gave him an emetic forcing him to regurgitate his other children. They now joined Zeus in a war on Cronus and the Titans. The Cyclopes aided them and gave Zeus the thunderbolt, Poseidon the trident and Hades a helmet of darkness or invisibility. Cronus was defeated and the Titans were consigned to Tartarus.

Cupid or **Amor.** Roman god of love, identified with the Greek Eros (q.v.).

Curetes. Priests of Rhea (q.v.) who drowned the cries of the infant Zeus (q.v.) as he lay in the Dictaean Cave by the clashing of their weapons. This prevented Cronus (q.v.) finding and devouring him. They were half-divine and in later times were conflated with the Corybantes (q.v.) who were also believed to be half-divine. All became part of Dionysus' ritual.

Cybele. The mother goddess of Phrygia where she and her lover Attis (q.v.) were worshipped in orgiastic rites and purification ceremonies including bathing in the blood of a sacrificed bull. Her symbol was a black stone and this was brought to Rome from Pessinus in 204 B.C. However it was only during the reign of Claudius that Roman citizens were allowed to serve as her priests and the oriental eunuchs serving her cult were always frowned upon. Her worship is described by Lucretius (q.v.) in book 2 and Catullus in his *Attis*. The artists of the classical world portray her with a crown of towers, a libation dish and tambourine, flanked by lions to show her control of wild nature.

Cyclopes. Generally known to the Greeks as one-eyed giants living in a distant country, perhaps Sicily. In Homer (q.v.) the Cyclops Polyphemus is a man-eating son of Poseidon (q.v.), made drunk and blinded by Odysseus (q.v.) and his men whom he had captured and meant to eat. Hesiod (q.v.) refers to three Cyclops but describes them as Titans (q.v.). The three (Brontes, Steropes and Arges) were sons of Ge (q.v.) and Uranus (q.v.) who made weapons for Zeus (q.v.), Poseidon and Hades (q.v.) (see Cronus). Other traditions make them skilled craftsmen helping Hephaestus (q.v.) at his Sicilian forge. They were also builders of cities including Athens and the walls of Tiryns.

Cyllenius. Another name for Hermes (q.v.) who was said to have been born on Mt. Cyllene in southern Greece.

Cyncus. "The Swan", a mythical king of Liguria who loved Phaeton (q.v.) and was turned into a swan.

Cynthia. A name given to Artemis (q.v.). She and Apollo (q.v.) were thought to have been born on Mt. Cynthus in Delos and were thus referred to as Cynthia and Cynthus.

Cyrene. In myth the mother of Aristaeus (q.v.) by Apollo (q.v.) who carried her to Libya where she gave her name to the city of Cyrene.

Cythera. An island off the south-east coast of Greece noted for its sanctuary of Aphrodite (q.v.). She was thus referred to as "the Cytherean".

D

Dactyli. Greek equivalent of the Roman Chalybes (q.v.) the mythical beings who lived on Mt. Ida in northern Asia Minor and invented iron-working.

Daedalus. Mythical Athenian craftsman. His jealousy of his nephew Perdix or Talos, who was said to have invented the saw, caused him to throw Perdix from Athene's (q.v.) temple on the Acropolis (q.v.). Having thus committed murder he fled to Crete. Here he arranged the liaison between Pasiphaë (q.v.) and the Cretan Bull (q.v.) which produced the Minotaur (q.v.). Then, to conceal what had transpired from Minos (q.v.) he built the famous labyrinth to hide the Minotaur. When Minos discovered the truth he imprisoned Daedalus and his son Icarus in the labyrinth. Pasiphaë released them and Daedalus invented wings which, when attached to their shoulders by wax, enabled him and his son to fly. However Icarus flew too near to the sun, the wax melted, and he fell to his doom in the Icarian sea. Daedalus reached Cumae and then went to Sicily. Here King Cocalus welcomed him and when Minos arrived in pursuit Cocalus' daughters helped Daedalus kill him. In Sicily Daedalus was credited with many wonderful buildings including a honeycomb of gold for Aphrodite's (q.v.) temple on Mt. Eryx. His name has become synonymous with ingenuity and skill, hence "Daedal" and "daedalian" in the English language.

Damocles. Member of the court of Dionysius I, tyrant of Syracuse. Cicero tells how the tyrant had him eat a sumptuous dinner while a sword was suspended by a hair over his head. This illustrated the luxurious but precarious life style of the tyrant and "the sword of Damocles" has become proverbial.

Danaë. A princess of Argos, daughter of King Acrisius (q.v.). An oracle told the king that Danaë's son would kill him so he imprisoned her in a brazen tower. Zeus (q.v.) visited her in a shower of gold and fathered Perseus (q.v.). Acrisius cast them adrift in a box and they came to Seriphos. They were found by the fisherman Dictys and taken to the king Polydectes. He wished to marry Danaë and so, to get Perseus out of the way, sent him to fetch the head of Medusa (q.v.). Danaë was saved from Polydectes' advances when Perseus returned and, showing the head, turned him to stone.

Danai. A general name used by Homer for the Greeks assembled at Troy. It was meant to perpetuate the memory of a common ancestor, Danaus (q.v.).

Danaus. A king of Libya and the father of 50 daughters, the "Danaides". His brother Aegyptus, who had 50 sons, wanted a mass marriage, but Danaus fled with his daughters to Argos where he became king. Eventually Aegyptus' sons followed and demanded the "Danaides". Danaus agreed but gave each daughter a weapon with which they slew their husbands on the wedding night. All, that is, save Hypermestra who spared Lynceus. Lynceus killed Danaus and became king of Argos. In the Underworld the Danaides were condemned to carry water in sieves for ever. The story is told by Pindar (q.v.) and the Danaides form the chorus in Aeschylos' (q.v.) Suppliants.

Daphne. The daughter of the river god Peneus or Ladon. A nymph pursued by Apollo (q.v.). To escape him she prayed either to her father or to the Earth to be turned into a laurel tree, which she was. Apollo made himself a laurel wreath as consolation and it became the prize at the Pythian Games held in his honour.

Daphnis. The son of Hermes (q.v.) and a nymph. She abandoned the infant but he was raised by Sicilian shepherds. Pan (q.v.) taught him the pipes and he was the originator of pastoral poetry. Later he was unfaithful to a nymph who loved him and in revenge she blinded him. His father ordered forth the fountain of Daphnis near Syracuse in his honour.

Dardanus. The son of Zeus (q.v.) and the Pleiad (q.v.) Electra. He founded Dardania on land given to him by Teucer. He was grandfather of Tros, great grandfather of Ilus (q.v.) and Ganymede (q.v.). Hence an ancestor of the Trojans who were sometimes called Dardanids, Dardans or Dardonians. Roman legend sometimes envisages him migrating to Dardania from Italy.

Deianeira. The daughter of Oeneus, king of Calydon and the wife of Heracles (q.v.) who won her hand by defeating the river god Achelous (q.v.). She bore him a son Hyllus. After accidentally killing Eunomus, Heracles took her and Hyllus into voluntary exile. When they came to cross the River Evenus the centaur (q.v.) Nessus offered to transport her on his back. However he tried to rape her and was killed by Heracles. As he lay dying he told her to take his blood as it was a charm which would keep Heracles in love with her. Later Heracles won Iole, daughter of Eurytus King of Oechalia, in an archery contest. When Eurytus refused to surrender Iole Heracles invaded Oechalia and defeated him. He then ordered Deianeira to send him a white shirt which he was to wear at a thanksgiving sacrifice to Zeus (q.v.). Deianeira, jealous of Iole, dipped the shirt in the blood of Nessus. But the blood was poisonous and when Heracles donned the shirt it burned his body and attempts to pull it off tore pieces of flesh from the hero. In agony he ordered Hyllus to build a funeral pyre on which he would find quick death and release from the pain. He also had Hyllus marry Iola. Deianeira, horrified at the result of her action, hanged herself. The story forms the plot of Sophocles' Women of Trachis.

Deidamia. The maiden who fell in love with Achilles (q.v.) and bore him Neoptolemus (q.v.).

Deiphobus. See Helen and Helenus.

Delis, Delius. Epithets of Artemis (q.v.) and Apollo (q.v.) who were born on Delos (q.v.).

Delos. Site of the important Ionian shrine of Apollo (q.v.). Here he was known as Phoebus ("the shining") or Lycius. When the jealous Hera (q.v.) pursued Leto (q.v.) she sought asylum where she could give birth to Apollo, her son by Zeus (q.v.). Delos, which was so poor it could lose nothing to Hera's wrath, accepted her.

Delphi. Site of Apollo's (q.v.) Dorian shrine and the most famous centre of his worship. Here he took his prophetic role having replaced Python. The oracle, located near the Castalian spring, was supposed to contain the omphalos or navel store of the Earth. A priestess, the Pythia, sat on a tripod chewing the intoxicating laurel leaf and voicing his utterances. Intoxicating vapours also issued from a chasm in the shrine. In this role Apollo was known as Loxias "the Ambiguous". (See Croesus). The priests of the shrine were not incorruptible and were known to take sides, e.g. with Sparta against Athens and with Philip of Macedon against Greece. The oracle had greatest influence during the period of overseas colonisation when its advice on location of colonies was always sought. The oracle encouraged Rome to defy Hannibal but was looted by Sulla. Nero visited it and Hadrian tried in vain to revive its prestige. Its decline came with the advance of Christianity and the growing interest in astrology as a means of prophecy. The temples at Delphi were sacked by Alaric in A.D. 396. Apollo's temple with its inscribed maxims "Know thyself" and "Nothing in excess" had stood on the highest point of Mt. Parnassus and had housed the sepulchre of Bacchus (q.v.) who was also worshipped at Delphi.

Demeter. The counterpart of the Roman Ceres, a

Greek corn-goddess responsible for the fertility of the earth. The daughter of Cronus (q.v.) and Rhea (q.v.) she became mother of Persephone (q.v.) or Kore ("the maiden") by her brother Zeus (q.v.). A 7th century B.C. Homeric *Hymn to Demeter* tells how Hades (q.v.) carried off Persephone from Eleusis twelve miles from Athens (Ovid says she was taken while gathering poppies in Sicily). Demeter scoured the earth for her until Helios (q.v.) told her what had occurred. She then shunned Olympus (q.v.) and wandered the earth, forbidding it to bring forth fruit and therefore threatening famine. Zeus finally agreed that Persephone could leave Hades provided she had not eaten in the Underworld. Hades agreed to let her go but tempted her into eating a pomegranate. She thus had to spend half a year with him in the Underworld and half with Demeter. Demeter again made the earth fertile but turned Ascalaphus, who had seen and reported Persephone eating the pomegranate, into an owl. She punished those who had been unkind to her during her wandering (see **Abas**) but rewarded those who had treated her hospitably. She taught Triptolemus, another son of Celeus (q.v.) the art of agriculture and gave him an ear of corn whose virtues he revealed to his fellow men. The Eleusian Festival was held in Demeter's honour from the 6th century B.C. and there was an annual procession from Eleusis to Athens. Those who spoke Greek were initiated into the mysteries of her cult. The Thesmophoria, a celebration of the foundation of laws, was held in her honour in many cities.

Demophon (1) The son of Theseus (q.v.) and Phaedra (q.v.) brother of Acamas (q.v.). He helped rescue his grandmother Aethra who had been Helen's (q.v.) slave, when Troy (q.v.) fell. Phyllis, a Thracian princess, loved him and committed suicide when he left her to visit Athens. She was then transformed into a tree.

(2) The son of Celeus and Metaneira. Demeter (q.v.) tried to reward the pair for their kindness to her by making Demophon immortal. To achieve this he had to be suspended above a fire, but Metaneira cried out thus breaking the spell and he perished.

Deucalion. The son of Prometheus (q.v.), husband of Pyrrha and father of Hellen. He was thus the ancestor of the Greeks. When Zeus (q.v.) decided to flood the earth in order to destroy mankind they escaped in an ark which finally made land on Mt. Parnassus. The couple prayed to Themis (q.v.) that mankind be restored and were told to scatter their mother's bones behind them. They took this to mean stones, the skeleton of Mother Earth. The rocks Deucalion scattered became men; those Pyrrha scattered became women.

Diana. Italian goddess of woods, women, childbirth and later, by association with the Greek Artemis (q.v.), the moon. Her cult was originally centred on the volcanic Lake Nemi at Aricia. The lake was known as Diana's mirror. The priest here, known as the rex, was always a runaway slave who had murdered his predecessor. A temple of Diana, said to have been founded by Servius Tullius also stood on the Aventine.

Dictaean Cave. A cave on Mt. Dicte in Crete, the reputed childhood home of Zeus (q.v.). Hence he was known as Dictaeus.

Dictys. (1) The sailor who found Perseus (q.v.) and his mother Danaë (q.v.) adrift at sea in a chest.

(2) A Cretan said to have accompanied Idomeneus (q.v.) to the Trojan war. His diary of the war was supposedly buried near Cnossos and found in the reign of Nero.

Dido. A daughter of the king of Tyre originally called Elissa. Her husband Sychaeus was murdered but with a few followers she escaped to Libya and founded Carthage (**K31**). Local legend said she burnt herself on a funeral pyre to avoid marrying Iarbas, a native king. The Roman version, given in the *Aeneid* takes Aeneas (q.v.) to Carthage where Dido's unrequited love for him results in her death. Aeneas abandons her to fulfil his destiny as ancestor of Rome.

Didyma. A great sanctuary of Apollo (q.v.) at Miletus.

Dindyma. Mountain in Asia Minor and a centre of the Cybele's (q.v.) cult.

Diomedes. (1) A king of the Bistones in Thrace who possessed man-eating mares. A labour of Heracles (q.v.) was to bring them to Eurystheus (q.v.). This he did by stealing them and beating off

his pursuers. But while he was busy fighting, the mares devoured his friend Abderus. Heracles founded the city of Abdera in his honour. Eurystheus freed the horses on Mt. Olympus (q.v.) where wild beasts devoured them.

(2) The son of Tydeus, king of Argos. One of the Epigoni (q.v.). He also went to Troy (q.v.) and was a companion of Odysseus (q.v.). With Odysseus he sailed to fetch Achilles (q.v.) and later Neoptolemus (q.v.). He encouraged Agamemnon (q.v.) to sacrifice Iphigenia (q.v.) and helped Odysseus capture the Trojan spy Dolon. He wounded Aeneas (q.v.) and Aphrodite (q.v.) as she saved the Trojan. He also wounded Ares. He returned from Troy to find his wife had been unfaithful and went to settle in Daunia in Italy. Here he married Euippe, daughter of king Daunus. He was buried on one of the Diomedan islands.

Dionysus. The Roman Bacchus. Also called Bromius "the Boisterous". The son of Zeus (q.v.) and Semele, a mortal, Zeus visited her in the guise of a mortal but when she was six months pregnant the jealous Hera (q.v.) came to her as an old woman. She advised Semele to demand her lover appear in his true form. Zeus unwillingly agreed to do so and Semele was consumed by fire. The unborn child was sewn up in Zeus' thigh to be born as Dionysus. The child was given into the care of Athamas and Ino. He was disguised as a girl but Hera learned the truth and drove Athamas mad, causing him to kill his own son. Hermes (q.v.) then took Dionysus to Mt. Nysa in India where he was raised by nymphs. Zeus placed their images in the stars as the Hyades. Here he was taught the use of the vine by his tutor Silenus and his satyrs and here he invented wine. As an adult he journeyed through India, Egypt, Syria and Asia accompanied by a wild following of Maenads or Bacchae and Satyrs. As he went he founded cities and taught cultivation of the vine. When he reached Thrace, Lycurgus, king of the Edones, opposed him but was driven mad by Rhea (q.v.) and slew his own son. His people then had him torn apart by horses. King Pentheus of Thebes also opposed Dionysus and was torn apart by crazed Bacchae whose ranks included his mother and sisters. Entranced they took him for a wild animal. Sailing to Naxos Dionysus was captured by pirates for sale as a slave. He became a lion and turned the oars to serpents. Ivy grew on the mast. The terrified pirates jumped overboard and became dolphins. At Naxos he married Ariadne (q.v.) whom Theseus (q.v.) had deserted. He was eventually received into Olympus as a god, replacing Hestia (q.v.). He fetched his mother to Olympus from the Underworld and she was henceforth known as Thyone. Dionysus was the god of wine and intoxicating herbs like ivy and laurel. He was also the god of tillage and law giving. He was worshipped at Delphi (q.v.) and in the spring festival, the Great Dionysia. In Rome the mysteries of his cult were a closely guarded secret. His followers worshipped him in communal wine-induced frenzies and the ritual involved sacrifice of animals, flagellation and a mystical marriage of novices with the god.

Dioscuri. See **Castor and Polydeuces.**

Dirce. See **Antiope.**

Dis or **Orcus.** Hades (q.v.).

Dodona. Site of an oracle of Zeus (q.v.) in north west Greece near modern Janina. It was associated with the union of Zeus and Dione, a minor goddess. The oracle centred on an oak and messages were transmitted by the rustling branches and cooing of pigeons nesting in it. The priests were "Selloi" who slept on the ground and walked barefoot. It was visited by Croesus (q.v.) and Alexander the Great offered the sanctuary a large sum of money.

Dryope. The daughter of King Dryops. Apollo (q.v.) seduced her and she was carried off by the Hamadryads (nymphs of trees).

E

Echidne. A mythical creature, half-woman, half-serpent. Mother by Typhon (q.v.) of the Chimaera (q.v.), Sphinx (q.v.), Cerberus (q.v.), Hydra (q.v.), Nemean Lion, Orthrus (q.v.), and Ladon. Slain by Argus.

Echion. A son of Hermes (q.v.). An Argonaut (q.v.) who took part in the hunt of the Calydonian boar (q.v.).

Echo. A nymph who occupied Hera's (q.v.) attention by incessant talk while Zeus (q.v.) enjoyed himself with the other nymphs. In punishment Hera deprived her of the power of speech except to repeat the words of others. Echo loved Narcissus who refused her. Heart-broken she pined away to nothing, only her voice remaining. Artemis (q.v.) punished Narcissus for his heartlessness by making him fall in love with his own reflection. Desparingly he committed suicide and was turned into a flower.

Egeria. An Italian goddess or nymph whose worship was connected with that of Diana (q.v.). She was associated with water. It was believed she advised Numa Pompilius (q.v.) especially on religious matters and Livy tells us they met in a sacred grove near Rome.

Eileithyia. A goddess of childbirth whom the Greeks associated with Artemis (q.v.) and the Romans with Juno (q.v.).

Elatus. The father of Caeneus and one of the Lapithae (q.v.).

Electra. (1) A Pleiad (q.v.).
(2) The daughter of Agamemnon (q.v.) and Clytemnestra (q.v.). Treated as a slave by her mother and Aegisthus (q.v.) she later helped her brother Orestes (q.v.) and his friend Pylades (q.v.) avenge their father and married Pylades. This is the basis of Euripedes' *Electra* and Strauss's *Elektra*. Freud gave the name "Electra complex" to female fixation on the father, the opposite of the "Oedipus complex".

Electryon. The son of Perseus (q.v.) and Andromeda (q.v.). King of Mycenae and father of Alcmene (q.v.) wife of Amphitrion (q.v.).

Eleusis. A sacred site twelve miles west of Athens facing Salamis. Here Celeus received Demeter (q.v.). Games and an oracle were found there. A cult involving "Mysteries" was centred there and administered by two families, the Eumolpidae and Kerykes. Ceremonies were held twice a year in Spring and Autumn and initiation to the mysteries, of which we know little, was open to all men, Greek or not, free or slave, who had not committed murder.

Elissa. *See* **Dido.**

Elpenor. One of Odysseus' (q.v.) crew who fell off the roof of Circe's (q.v.) palace while sleep-walking and broke his neck. When Odysseus visited the Underworld his shade begged for cremation and a burial mound in which his oar was to be planted.

Elysium. A blessed abode of the dead, placed by Homer near the Underworld but not in Hades (q.v.). The virtuous went here after death. It was a land of warmth never knowing cold or snow. Later it was associated with "Fortunate Isles" holding "Elysian Fields" which were believed to be far to the west, beyond the Pillars of Hercules (q.v.).

Empusae. Daughters of Hecate (q.v.). They were demons with the haunches of an ass who wore brazen slippers. Able to turn themselves into cows, bitches or young maidens, as the latter they lay with young men and sucked their blood as they slept.

Enceladus. A son of Ge (q.v.). One of 24 giants (q.v.) with serpents' tails whom Alcyoneus led in an assault on Olympus (q.v.). Buried under Mt. Etna in Sicily as a punishment.

Endymion. Either a shepherd of Caria or an Aeolian youth who became king of Elis. As he slept in a cave Selene (q.v.) the moon saw him and descended to kiss him. Captivated by his looks she made him fall into a dreamless everlasting sleep so that she could always gaze upon him. His son Aetolus conquered Aetolia.

Enipeus. A river god, beloved of Tyro (q.v.).

Eos. The goddess of the dawn, the Romans identified her with Aurora (q.v.). The daughter of Hyperion (q.v.) and Theira and sister of Helios (q.v.). She drove the chariot of Helios each morning to announce his arrival and traversed the sky with him as Hemera before landing in the west as Hespera. The wife of Astraeus and by him mother of the stars and all the winds save the east. She carried off several handsome youths including Orion (q.v.). Cephalus (q.v.), and Tithonus to whom she bore Memnon (q.v.). She requested Zeus (q.v.) to make Tithonus immortal but forgot to ask for eternal youth and as he aged he shrank to a cicada.

Epaphus. The son of Zeus (q.v.) and Io who ruled Egypt and was said by some to be the sacred bull of Egypt, Apis (q.v.).

Epeius. A cowardly son of Panopeus who built the Trojan Horse.

Ephialtes. One of the 24 giants (q.v.) led by Alcyoneus. (*See also* **Otus**).

Epidaurus. Site of a famous sanctuary of Asclepius (q.v.) built in the 6th century B.C. Here pilgrims could see the tomb of the god.

Epigoni. Descendants of the "Seven against Thebes" (q.v.) who also attacked the city ten years after their fathers had done so. They were assembled by Adrastus (q.v.) and their ranks included his own son Aegialeus, Diomedes son of Tydeus, Sthenelus son of Capaneus and Eradne and Therseander. Like his father Polynices (q.v.) Therseander bribed Eriphyle (q.v.) into persuading Alcmaeon into joining the assault on Thebes. Aegialeus died at the walls of the city but the Theban prophet Teiresias advised the citizens to leave the city at night as he had foreseen the Argives (i.e. the Epigoni), capturing an empty city. He died next morning drinking from the well of Tilphussa. Adrastus died of grief hearing of his son's death while the remaining Epigoni were left holding an empty city. Alcmaeon went home to take revenge on Eriphyle (q.v.).

Erebos. A deep chasm in the Underworld.

Erebus. "Darkness", the son of Chaos (q.v.) and father of Aether and Hemera by "Night", his sister. Some traditions hold that the Fates (q.v.) were daughters of Erebus and Night and that they held sway even over Zeus (q.v.).

Erechtheus. Son of Pandion and grandson of Erichthonius (q.v.) with whom he is sometimes confused or identified. Both were reared by Athene (q.v.) and were associated with serpents. Both were mythical kings of Athens. When the Eleusians led by Eumolpus, a son of Poseidon (q.v.), invaded Athens, Erechtheus was told by an oracle to sacrifice his daughter Otonia. He did so and her sisters Protogonia and Panora also sacrificed themselves. He slew Eumolpus and was slain by lightning from either Poseidon or Zeus (q.v.).

Erichthonius. A son of Hephaestus (q.v.) by Athene (q.v.). The child was concealed in a chest by the normally chaste Athene and entrusted to the daughters of Cecrops of Athens who were forbidden to open it. However they did so and finding a serpent inside went mad and leaped to their death from the Acropolis (q.v.). Erichthonius eventually succeeded Cecrops as King of Athens and was grandfather of Erechtheus. It was said Erichthonius was the founder of the Panathenaean games in honour of Athene and that he was the first man to harness a team of four horses to a single chariot.

Eridanus. An Italian river god, later thought to be the River Po.

Erigone. The daughter of Icarius. Led to her father's grave by his faithful pet hound Maera, she hanged herself from the tree beneath which he lay.

Erinnyes. Three daughters of Mother Earth whom she conceived by the blood of Uranus (q.v.) when Cronus (q.v.) castrated him. They personified the conscience and were powerful divinities who punished crimes of sacrilege, especially matricide. They pursued Alcmaeon (q.v.) and drove Orestes (q.v.) mad and into exile. These winged creatures had serpent hair and lived in the Underworld. Their names were Alecto, Magaera and Tisiphone. Orestes was acquitted by Athene (q.v.) of matricide following his defence by Apollo (q.v.). To pacify the Erinnyes Athene gave them a grotto at Athens where they received libations and sacrifices. Henceforth they were euphemistically referred to as the Eumenides or "kindly ones".

Eriphyle. The sister of Adrastus (q.v.) and wife of the seer Amphiarus. Mother of Alcmaeon (q.v.). Polynices (q.v.) bribed her into persuading Amphiarus into joining the Seven Against Thebes (q.v.) despite the seer's prophecy that only Adrastus would survive their expedition. She received the necklace of Harmonia (q.v.) for this. Later Thersander bribed her with the magic robe of Harmonia into persuading Alcmaeon to join the Epigoni (q.v.). On returning from Thebes Alcmaeon slew her for her selfish deceit.

Eris. A female divinity personifying Quarrels and Strife for the Greeks.

Eros. The Greek god of love, identified with the Roman Cupid (q.v.) or Amor. A son of Aphrodite (q.v.), whom he often accompanied, by either her father Zeus (q.v.) or Hermes (q.v.). His half-brother was Anteros, son of Aphrodite and Ares (q.v.) who personified mutual love. It was only from the 4th century B.C. onwards that he came to be represented as a winged boy firing arrows of love which could wound both men and gods. (See **Psyche**).

Erymanthian Boar. A giant wild boar from Mt. Erymanthus which was ravaging the region of Psophis until captured by Heracles (q.v.). Whilst performing this task he was given wine made by Dionysus (q.v.) by the centaur Pholus. A dispute broke out with other centaurs, eager as ever for their share of the drink, and in the resulting battle Heracles accidentally wounded his friend Cheiron (q.v.). He caught and chained the boar in a snow drift and delivered it to Eurystheus (q.v.) before going to join the Argonauts (q.v.).

Erysichthon. Son of Triopas. He was punished with an insatiable hunger by the goddess Demeter (q.v.) for felling trees in one of her sacred groves.

Eryx. Mythical Sicilian hero. A son of Venus (q.v.) and a renowned boxer. The mountain near modern Trapani is named after him.

Eteocles. See **Seven Against Thebes**.

Etruscans. See **L41**.

Eumneus. Born of royal birth but given to Phoenician slave traders, Eumneus' story is told in Book 15 of the Odyssey. He became Odysseus' (q.v.) faithful swineherd.

Eumolpus. "The good singer", son of Poseidon (q.v.) and Chione. Chione threw him into the sea at birth but Poseidon saved him and he was raised at the court of King Tegyrius of Thrace before becoming a priest of Demeter (q.v.) and Persephone (q.v.) at Eleusis. Here he initiated Heracles (q.v.) into the mysteries and taught the hero the lyre. He later made war on Athens and was slain by Erechtheus (q.v.). His descendants became hereditary priests of the Eleusian mysteries.

Euphorbus. Son of Panthous, a Trojan who wounded Patroclus (q.v.) before he was slain by Hector (q.v.).

Euphrosyne. One of the Charities or Graces (q.v.).

Euripides. See **B23**.

Europa. Daughter of Agenor and Telephassa and a grand-daughter of Poseidon (q.v.). While she was on the sea-shore Zeus (q.v.) appeared in the form of a white bull and when she jumped on his back carried her off to Crete where he fathered three sons on her, Minos (q.v.), Rhadamanthus (q.v.) and Sarpedon (q.v.). The Cretan king married her and adopted the children. Zeus gave her a necklace fashioned by Hephaestus (q.v.) which rendered the wearer irresistibly beautiful.

Eurystheus. A grandson of Perseus (q.v.). He was conceived shortly after Heracles (q.v.) but when Zeus (q.v.) boasted that Heracles would rule the House of Perseus, Hera (q.v.) in her jealousy extracted a promise from Zeus that the next son born to the House of Perseus would be its ruler. She then delayed the birth of Heracles until after that of Eurystheus. Later, after Heracles had slain his children in a fit of madness he was told by the oracle to serve Eurystheus in order to be cleansed of guilt. Eurystheus, a cowardly and contemptible creature, set him twelve labours. After Heracles' death he decided to expel the Heracleidae (q.v.) or descendants of Heracles from Greece but they sheltered at Athens. Eurystheus attacked the city but was resisted by Theseus (q.v.), Iolaus (q.v.) and Hyllus (q.v.). An oracle demanded the sacrifice of one of Heracles' children and Macaria slew herself. Eurystheus was then defeated and slain by Alcmene.

Eurus. The South-East wind, son of Astraeus (q.v.) and Eos.

Euryale. One of the Gorgons (q.v.).

Eurydice. The wife of Orpheus (q.v.). She died from a snake bite and Orpheus followed her to the Underworld. Hades (q.v.) delighted by Orpheus' lyre playing allowed him to take her back to life provided he did not look back. Unfortunately at the gates of the Underworld the anxious Orpheus could no longer resist the temptation to gaze on her beauty nor acquiesce in her accusations of indifference. He turned round to see her and she was lost to him.

Eurytus. See **Deianeira**.

Euterpe. Muse of music and lyric poetry.

Evadne. The daughter of Iphis and wife of Capaneus who killed herself on the funeral pyre of the Seven against Thebes (q.v.).

Evander. A mythical king of Arcadia who settled in Italy on the future site of Rome.

Evenus. The father of Marpessa. When Idas carried her off he drowned himself in the river which henceforth bore his name.

F

Fates. The personifications of impersonal destiny who sometimes seem to control even Zeus (q.v.), at others merely to perform his will. The concept developed of three Moirae (Latin Parcae) daughters of Zeus and Themis (q.v.), or of Erebus (q.v.) and Night. The first, Clotho, spans the thread of life, Lachesis who measured it, and Atropus who cut it. With Hermes (q.v.) they composed the Alphabet.

Faunus. An Italian god of the flocks, herds and wild countryside, later identified with Pan (q.v.). In this context he was half-human, half-goat and lived in Arcadia (q.v.). He had a shrine on the Palatine Hill. He is sometimes regarded not as one god but as numerous spirits of the woods or "fauns".

Faustulus. A kindly shepherd who, with his wife Acca Larentia, raised Romulus (q.v.) and Remus (q.v.). His name relates to Faunus (q.v.) and his wife's to Lares (q.v.) respectively the pastoral god of Latium and the tutelary deities of the Roman home. Up to Cicero's time Romans proudly pointed to a hut on the Palatine which was said to be that where Faustulus raised Romulus but, embarrassingly, a hut with similar claims also stood on the Capitol.

Fidius. Dius Fidius was a name for Jupiter (q.v.) as guarantor of Good Faith.

Flora. Italian goddess of flowers and the spring, worshipped at Rome from the mid 3rd century B.C. Ovid tells us the April festival in her honour, "Ludi Florales" was one of drunken boisterousness. As an earth nymph called Chloris she was pursued by Zephyr (q.v.) and changed into Flora whose breath spread flowers across the fields. The scene has been a subject for Botticelli, Titian and Poussin.

Fortuna. Roman goddess identified with Tyche (q.v.).

Fortunate Isles. See **Elysium**.

G

Gaea or Ge. The "Earth" who sprang from Chaos (q.v.). She was mother of Uranus (q.v.), the heavens, and Pontus the sea. By Uranus she was mother of the Hecatoncheires (q.v.), the Cyclopes (q.v.), the Titans (q.v.) and Themis (q.v.). When Uranus condemned the Cyclopes to Tartarus (q.v.) she instigated rebellion by the Titans and gave Cronus (q.v.) the flint sickle with which he castrated Uranus. From the blood which fell on her she bore Erinnyes (q.v.) and from the blood which fell into the sea came Aphrodite (q.v.). By Tartarus she was mother of Typhon (q.v.). She gave Hera (q.v.) a tree of golden apples which was guarded by the Hesperides (q.v.). The Romans identified her with their own earth goddess Tellus.

Gaetulians. A mythical savage tribe which the Romans placed in North Africa.

Galatea. (1) A sea nymph who loved the Sicilian shepherd Acis (q.v.). She was pursued by the Cyclops Polyphemus and to escape him threw herself into the sea off Sicily. She turned Acis into a river.

(2) See **Pygmalion**.

Ganymede. The most handsome of youths, the son of Tros (q.v.) and Callirhoë. Zeus (q.v.) loved the youth and taking the form of an eagle carried him off to become cup-bearer of the gods, leaving Tros two white horses in compensation. A subject for Correggio, Rubens, and Rembrandt.

Garamantians. Mythical North African tribe appearing in the Aenead (q.v.).

Ge. See **Gaea**.

Geryon. A three-bodied monster living on the island of Erythia far to the west of the known world.

Here he kept cattle guarded by Eurytion, son of Ares (q.v.) and Orthrus (q.v.). Heracles (q.v.) was sent to steal the cattle by Eurystheus (q.v.) and on his way to Erythia erected the "Pillars of Hercules" (q.v.), before sailing, on a boat provided by Helios (q.v.), to the island. He overcame Eurytion, Orthrus and Geryon and fetched the cattle to Eurystheus.

Giants (Gigantes). (1) The sons of Ge (q.v.) and Uranus (q.v.), twenty-four giants with serpents' tails who, to avenge the imprisonment of their brothers the Titans (q.v.), attacked the gods on Mt. Olympus (q.v.). Their leader was Alcyoneus and their ranks included Porphyrion, Ephialtes, Pallas, Minas, Enceladus and Polybotes. The gods finally triumphed due to the help of Heracles (q.v.) and the giants were buried under various volcanoes in punishment.

(2) In another version two giants, Ephialtes and Otus, the sons of Iphimedeia and Poseidon (q.v.), but called the Aloeidae after the name of Iphimedeia's husband Aloeus, attacked Olympus. At an early age the two imprisoned Ares (q.v.), then swearing to rape Hera (q.v.) and Artemis (q.v.) they stacked Mt. Pelion on top of Mt. Ossa in order to climb to the heavens. But Artemis lured them to Naxos and disguised as a doe leapt between them and they slew each other by accident. In Hades (q.v.) they were tied by vipers to a pillar back to back.

Glauce. Or Creusa, daughter of Creon. For her Jason (q.v.) forsook Medea (q.v.) and in revenge the sorceress sent Glauce a garment which enveloped her in flames and also killed Creon.

Glaucus. (1) King of Corinth, son of Sisyphus and Merope and father of Bellerophon (q.v.). He fed his horses on human flesh but Aphrodite (q.v.) caused them to devour Glaucus himself because he mocked her.

(2) His great-grandson, the grandson of Bellerophon who fought for the Trojans and was slain by Ajax (q.v.).

(3) The son of Minos (q.v.) and Pasiphaë (q.v.) who was drowned in a barrel of honey. The seer Polyides found the corpse and was entombed with the boy for failing to restore him. Both were saved when a serpent revealed a magic herb which resurrected Glaucus.

(4) A Boeotian fisherman who pursued Scylla (q.v.) and was turned into a sea god on eating a magic herb.

Golden Age. A concept of Hesiod's who lists four ages of man in his *Works and Days*: golden, silver, bronze and iron. Horace, Virgil, and Ovid also refer to it. A tranquil time when Cronus (q.v.) ruled as the ideal king.

Golden Bough. A gift Aeneas (q.v.) had to take to Proserpina (q.v.) before he could enter the Underworld. Also associated with the cult of Diana (q.v.) at Aricia where a runaway slave had to break the bough from a sacred tree before killing the priest and taking his place. Subject of a painting by J. W. M. Turner.

Gordian Knot. Gordius was a peasant who was acclaimed king of Phrygia by the inhabitants when he appeared in a wagon. An oracle had prophesied that the new king would appear thus. In thanksgiving he dedicated the cart to Zeus (q.v.) in the acropolis of Gordium. An oracle prophesied that he who untied the complex knot joining the yoke and pole would rule all Asia. It was eventually severed by Alexander the Great.

Gorgons or **Gorgones.** Three beautiful sisters, Medusa (q.v.), Stheno and Euryale, daughters of Phorcys and Ceto. Medusa slept with Poseidon (q.v.) in a temple of Athene (q.v.) and was transformed into a winged monster with serpent hair and brazen claws by the goddess as punishment. She could turn those who looked on her to stone. The Gorgons were sisters of the Graeae (q.v.). *See also* Perseus.

Graces (also **Gratiae**). *See* **Charities.**

Graeae. Sisters of the Gorgons (q.v.) who lived on Mt. Atlas. The three old women possessed only one eye and one tooth which they shared, passing them from one to the other. Perseus (q.v.) stole the eye and thus forced them to reveal the whereabouts of Medusa (q.v.) and also of the Stygian nymphs who gave him the winged sandals, magic wallet and helmet of Hades which Hermes (q.v.) said he needed in order to slay Medusa.

Gyes or **Gyges.** One of the Hecatoncheires (q.v.).

H

Hades. (1) The son of Cronus (q.v.) and Rhea (q.v.) brother of Zeus (q.v.) and Poseidon (q.v.). The Cyclopes (q.v.) gave him a helmet of darkness which made him invisible. When he and his brothers threw lots for their kingdoms Hades won the Underworld, home of the dead. His name was later extended to his realm itself. He was one of the few gods to like Ares (q.v.) and Hermes (q.v.) was his herald, conducting the shades of the dead to the Underworld. Because his name was too dread to mention he was often called "Pluto" (q.v.). No favours were expected of him so no temples were dedicated to him. He abducted Persephone (q.v.) and also chased the nymph Minthe (whom the jealous Persephone turned into a mint plant) and Leuce, who was turned into the white poplar.

(2) His realm, the Underworld, land of the dead. Its deepest reaches were called Tartarus (q.v.). Hades and Persephone ruled over it. Persephone was accompanied by Hecate (q.v.). There were five rivers in Hades, the Styx, Acheron, river of woe, Phlegethon, river of flame, Lethe, river of forgetfulness and Cocytus river of wailing. Three judges Minos (q.v.), Aeacus (q.v.) and Rhadamanthus (q.v.) decided on what would happen to souls, sending the evil for punishment, the virtuous to Elysium (q.v.) and those who had led indifferent lives to the drab asphodel fields.

Harmonia. The daughter of Ares (q.v.) and Aphrodite (q.v.) and the wife of Cadmus (q.v.). The gods attended their wedding and Aphrodite gave her the necklace which Zeus (q.v.) had given to Europa (q.v.). It had been made by Hephaestus (q.v.) and conferred irresistible beauty on the wearer. Athene (q.v.) gave her a robe which conferred divine dignity on its possessor. The couple had three children, Autonoe, Ino and Semele (q.v.). After Cadmus had resigned his throne to Pentheus (q.v.) the couple left Thebes and were eventually, in the form of serpents, received in Elysia (q.v.). The necklace and robe were later used to bribe Eriphyle.

Harpalyce. A mythical princess of Thrace, a fierce warrior and huntress.

Harpies (Greek "snatchers"). Originally spirits of the wind, in Homer they appear to carry people off to their death. Later they are portrayed as winged monsters with women's heads and claws, sent by the gods to torment mortals. They snatched and carried off people for their food.

Hebe. A personification of the Greek word for youth, the daughter of Zeus (q.v.) and Hera (q.v.). She was cupbearer to the gods until replaced by Ganymede (q.v.). Her Roman counterpart was Juventas (q.v.). She married Heracles (q.v.) after his apotheosis.

Hecabe or **Hecuba.** The second wife of Priam (q.v.) who bore him 19 sons including Hector (q.v.) and Paris (q.v.). By Apollo (q.v.) the mother of Troilus (q.v.). Taken as a slave by Odysseus (q.v.) when Troy (q.v.) fell. Priam had entrusted their youngest son Polydorus, plus much gold, to Polymester, king of the Thracian Chersonese. He had murdered Polydorus and thrown his body into the sea. When Odysseus took her to the Thracian Chersonese she found the body, killed Polymester and his two sons, and escaped in the form of a bitch, Maera.

Hecate. An ancient goddess, later closely associated with Artemis (q.v.). Originally she was venerated by women, she was powerful in Heaven, Earth and the Underworld. But primarily she was seen as a goddess of the Underworld and companion of Persephone (q.v.). She was represented holding torches and accompanied by wolves. She was most formidable at the full moon with which she was associated. A practitioner of sorcery her image was worshipped at crossroads where she was portrayed with three heads or three bodies.

Hecatoncheires. The sons of Ge (q.v.) and Uranus (q.v.), three 100-handed giants called Cottus, Gyes or Gyges and Briareus or Aegaeon.

Hector. The eldest son of Priam (q.v.), Trojan hero of the Trojan War. Husband of Andromache (q.v.) and father of Astynax. He fought the great Ajax (q.v.) until nightfall when the two exchanged gifts. He slew Patroclus and in turn was slain by Achilles (q.v.) who dragged his body round the walls of Troy (q.v.). Priam begged for the corpse and his funeral is the closing scene of Homer's *Iliad*. A chivalrous warrior.

Helen. The daughter of Leda (*q.v.*) by Zeus (*q.v.*), hatched from an egg, and the sister of Clytemnestra (*q.v.*), Castor and Polydeuces (*q.v.*) (known as the Dioscuri). She was raised at the court of Leda's husband, Tyndareus of Sparta. As a child she was abducted by Theseus (*q.v.*) and Pirithous (*q.v.*) but being too young to marry, was left with Theseus' mother Aethra. The Dioscuri rescued her and Aethra became her slave. The most beautiful of women she had many suitors who swore to defend her chosen husband, Menelaus (*q.v.*). She was taken by Paris (*q.v.*) to Troy (*q.v.*) thus causing the Trojan war (*q.v.*) and "launching a thousand ships" (of the Greeks who went to reclaim her). When Paris died Helenus (*q.v.*) and Deiphobus quarrelled for her, the latter forcibly marrying her. By then she was homesick for Sparta and when Odysseus (*q.v.*) entered Troy in disguise told him so and gave him information useful to the Greek cause. When Troy fell Deiphobus was killed and mangled by Odysseus and Menelaus, but when Menelaus chased her, sword drawn, to punish her, she calmed him by baring her breast. In the *Odyssey* she was reconciled to Menelaus and became a domesticated and faithful wife. She bore him a daughter, Hermione. It appears that Helen may have been a pre-Greek goddess associated with birds and trees. Various tales are told of her. Stesichorus says that only her phantom went to Troy: the real Helen went to Egypt. Another legend says that at her death she was carried off to live eternally with Achilles (*q.v.*) on a "white isle". Others suggest that her mother was not Leda but Nemesis (*q.v.*).

Helenus. The son of Priam (*q.v.*) and Hecabe (*q.v.*), twin of Cassandra (*q.v.*) and a prophet. He quarrelled with his brother Deiphobus over Helen (*q.v.*) and when the latter forcibly married her fled Troy (*q.v.*) and was captured by Odysseus (*q.v.*). Calchas (*q.v.*) had said that only Helenus knew the secret oracles of how Troy would fall. He told Odysseus that the city would be taken in the summer if a bone of Pelops (*q.v.*) were brought to the Greeks, if Neoptolemus (*q.v.*) joined them, and if the Palladium (*q.v.*) were stolen. These things were done. After the war he was taken by Neoptolemus and prophesied a safe route home for him. When Neoptolemus settled in Epirus he gave part of the kingdom to Helenus who married Andromache (*q.v.*).

Helicon. A mountain in Boeotia (*q.v.*) sacred to Apollo (*q.v.*) and inhabited by the Muses (*q.v.*) who were thus called respectively Heliconiades and Heliconides.

Helios. The Roman "Sol". A Titan (*q.v.*) later identified with Hyperion and Apollo (*q.v.*), though some traditions make him the son of Hyperion and Theia. A sun-god, his chariot was drawn across the sky each day by four horses and at night he returned to the east floating on the stream of Ocean, which surrounded the earth, in a large cup. The husband of Rhode by whom he had seven sons and a daughter, Pasiphaë. He was father of Phaeton (*q.v.*) by Clymene and of Circe (*q.v.*) by Perse. He reputedly saw all, but missed Odysseus' (*q.v.*) men stealing his cattle. When he shone too brightly Odysseus (*q.v.*) fired an arrow at him. Admiring the hero's boldness he lent him his cup or boat with which to travel to Erythia. It was he who told Demeter (*q.v.*) that Hades (*q.v.*) had abducted Persephone (*q.v.*).

Hellas, Hellenes, Hellenism. The Greeks of the classical period termed themselves Hellenes and their country Hellas (in contrast to Homer's "Achaeans"). They traced their common descent from Hellen (*q.v.*) an eponymous hero. In modern times Hellenism refers to the culture flourishing in Greece, the Aegean isles, the Ionian coast of Asia Minor and Magna Graecia between the first Olympiad in 776 B.C. and the death of Alexander the Great in 323 B.C.

Hellen. Eponymous ancestor of the Greeks or Hellenes (*q.v.*), the son of Pyrrha and Deucalion (*q.v.*). His sons were Aeolus, Dorus and Xuthus.

Hephaestus. One of the Olympian gods, the son of Zeus (*q.v.*) and Hera (*q.v.*). The god of fire and metal work, known to the Romans as Vulcan (*q.v.*). He was hated by Hera because he was lame and she threw him down from Olympus and he landed in the sea where Thetis (*q.v.*) and Eurynome cared for him. Nine years later Hera

accepted him back but Zeus, angry with him for taking Hera's side in a quarrel, again cast him down. He was a day falling and landed on Lemnos. On returning to Olympus he sought to keep the peace between Zeus and Hera. The other gods always laughed at his lameness. His workshop was said to be on Olympus or else in Sicily, where the Cyclopes (*q.v.*) helped him in his labours. He made palaces for all the gods, the necklace of Harmonia (*q.v.*), the armour of Achilles (*q.v.*) and a wide variety of other wonderful articles. He was married either to Charis or to Aphrodite (*q.v.*) who deceived him with Ares (*q.v.*).

Hera. The Roman Juno, daughter of Cronus (*q.v.*) and Rhea (*q.v.*), sister and wife of Zeus (*q.v.*). A pre-Hellenic goddess, originally having power over all living things and vegetable life, she gradually lost these functions and eventually was only the goddess of marriage and childbirth. She was the mother of Ares (*q.v.*), Hephaestus (*q.v.*), Hebe (*q.v.*) and Ilythia (*q.v.*) by Zeus. Her virginity was renewed annually by bathing in a magical spring near Argos. Though she was the goddess of marital fidelity she had difficulty controlling the amorous adventures of her own husband (who had wooed her in the form of a cuckoo) and was violently jealous of his many affairs and cruel to her rivals and their offspring, *e.g.* Semele, Leto, Alcmene and Heracles. She once led a conspiracy against Zeus in which Poseidon (*q.v.*) and Apollo (*q.v.*) participated. Zeus was enchained and when he was freed he punished her by suspending her from the sky by the wrists with an anvil on each ankle. She helped Jason (*q.v.*) but was opposed to the Trojans because Paris (*q.v.*) did not give her the apple of discord. Her name means simply "lady".

Heracleidae. The children of Heracles (*q.v.*). Eurystheus (*q.v.*) attempted to expel them from Greece but failed.

Heracles. A hero who later became a god, a figure popular all over Greece and in Italy where the Romans knew him as Hercules. The son of Alcmene (*q.v.*) and Zeus (*q.v.*) and half-brother of Iphicles (*q.v.*). Alcmene fearing Hera's (*q.v.*) jealousy exposed him but by mistake Hera nursed him. After he had been returned to his mother Hera sent two snakes to kill him in his cradle, but he strangled them. He was taught to fight by Castor (*q.v.*), to play the lyre by Eumalpus, to wrestle by Autolycus (*q.v.*) and the art of archery by Eurytus. Linus also tried to teach him to play the lyre but, when he censured his awkward pupil, Heracles killed him with his own instrument. Amphitrion (*q.v.*) then sent him to keep cattle. At the age of 18, after a 50-day chase, he killed a huge lion on Mt. Cithaeron because it had been ravaging the herds of Amphitrion and Thespius. He did this with a wild olive club and later wore the pelt everywhere, though some other sources say he wore the pelt of the Nemean lion. In reward Thespius gave him his 50 daughters. At Thebes he defeated the Minyan heralds of Orchomenus who had come to demand tribute. Creon, king of Thebes, rewarded him by giving him his daughter Megara or Megera who bore him several children. His half-brother Iphicles married Creon's youngest daughter. Hera now made him mad and he killed his own children and two of Iphicles'. At Delphi the Pythia (*q.v.*), calling him Heracles for the first time, sent him to serve, for 12 years, his wretched cousin Eurystheus (*q.v.*) in order to purify himself of the murder. At the end of that time he would become immortal. With his nephew Iolaus (*q.v.*) as companion he embarked on 12 labours set by Eurystheus. These were to fetch the pelt of the Nemean lion, to kill the Hydra of Lerna (*q.v.*), to capture alive the Ceryneian Hind (*q.v.*), to capture alive the Erymanthian Boar (*q.v.*), to cleanse the stables of Augias (*q.v.*), to drive off the Stymphalian Birds (*q.v.*), to capture the Cretan Bull (*q.v.*), to fetch the horses of Diomedes (*q.v.*), to fetch the girdle of Hippolyte (*q.v.*), to steal the cattle of Geryon (*q.v.*), to fetch the golden apples of the Hesperides (*q.v.*) and to bring back Cerberus (*q.v.*). After capturing the Erymanthian Boar he had joined the Argonauts (*q.v.*) but his squire Hylas was spirited off by the Naiads (*q.v.*) while fetching water at Cios in Mysia and Heracles left the expedition to search for him. Having completed his service for Eurystheus he returned to Thebes and here gave Megara to Iolaus. But Hera again drove him mad and he killed Megara and her children. Some traditions say he also killed himself and his family. He now desired to marry Iole daughter of his friend Eurytus of Oechalia and won her in an archery contest. But Eurytus refused to surrender her because Heracles had slain his own children. The incident ended in Heracles killing Iphitus (*q.v.*) but he later seized Iole. To purify himself of this murder he went to serve Omphale (*q.v.*). After serving her he and Telamon saved Hesione, daughter of Laomedon (*q.v.*) and sacked Troy (*q.v.*). Heracles gave Hesione to Telamon and ransomed Priam (*q.v.*). Next he made war on Augias and Neleus (*q.v.*) and then on Hippocoon who had helped Neleus. In this he was assisted by Cepheus (*q.v.*) and he restored Tyndareus (*q.v.*). At this time he seduced the priestess Auge, daughter of Aleus king of Tegea, who bore him a son, Telephus. Now he married Deianeira (*q.v.*) who inadvertently caused his death. As Heracles ascended his funeral pyre, to be burned alive he gave his bow and quiver to Philoctetes (*q.v.*) who kindled the flame but thunderbolts demolished the pyre and he was carried on a cloud to Olympus. Here he was reconciled to Hera and married Hebe (*q.v.*), himself becoming an immortal. Numerous other legends concerning Heracles exist. We are told he rescued Alcestis (*q.v.*), helped the gods defeat the Giants (*q.v.*), defeated Antaeus (*q.v.*) and, when the Delphic Oracle would not give him an answer seized the sacred tripod and struggled with Apollo (*q.v.*) for it. Xenophon tells us that before beginning his adventures Heracles was confronted by two beautiful women, one offering a life of ease, the other of service to mankind and he had to choose between the two. Other writers tell of him having to choose between two roads offering similar alternatives to the women. From a mighty and boisterous hero the picture of Heracles gradually developed into a morality tale of selfless service and fortitude eventually rewarded and for this reason the Stoic philosophers of Rome idealised him.

Hercules. *See* **Heracles**.

Hermaphroditus. The son of Hermes (*q.v.*) and Aphrodite (*q.v.*) who refused the advances of the nymph Salmacis. Her request that their bodies be joined in one was then granted by the gods. The name gives us the word "hermaphrodite", a being with the characteristics of both sexes.

Hermes. The Roman Mercury. Originally a god of fertility. The son of Zeus (*q.v.*) and Maia, daughter of Atlas (*q.v.*). He was born on Mt. Cyllene (hence he was sometimes referred to as Cyllenius). While still hours old he left the cradle and stole Apollo's (*q.v.*) cattle. He invented the lyre by stringing a tortoise shell with cow-gut and gave it to Apollo. This calmed Apollo's wrath and the two became friends. Zeus made him messenger of the gods and gave him his winged sandals (the Alipes), broad-brimmed hat (the Petasus) and herald's staff (caduceus) originally entwined with two white ribbons, later represented as entwined snakes. He conducted the souls of the dead to Hades (*q.v.*) and in this role was known as Psychopompus. The patron of travellers, traders and thieves and the father of Autolycus the thief, by Chione, and of Echion herald of the Argonauts (*q.v.*). He was the father of Pan (*q.v.*) by Penelope (*q.v.*) and a companion of the Muses (*q.v.*). He helped the Fates compose the alphabet, invented the musical scale, weights and measures and olive cultivation. A god of dice games. As herald he was eloquent and in *Acts* ch. XIV St. Paul, who spoke in tongues more than any man, is mistaken for him.

Hermione. The daughter of Helen (*q.v.*) and Menelaus (*q.v.*). Betrothed by Tyndareus (*q.v.*) to Orestes (*q.v.*) but given to Neoptolemus (*q.v.*) by Menelaus.

Hero. A priestess of Aphrodite (*q.v.*) at Sestos. Her lover Leander (*q.v.*) used to swim the Hellespont each night to see her but drowned when a storm extinguished the light she used to guide him. She then drowned herself. The subject of a play by Marlowe and paintings by Rubens and Turner.

Herodotus. *See* **B31**.

Heroes. To the Greeks a hero was the son of a mortal or divinity who was essentially superior to other men. They were venerated and received sacrifices because they were believed to help the living. Thus Theseus (*q.v.*) was supposed to have helped the Athenians at Marathon. "Heroic poetry" was epic poetry, telling of their deeds.

Hesiod. *See* **B31**.

Hesperides. "The daughters of evening" who lived in a land at the end of the world, far to the west. These maidens guarded a tree belonging to Hera (*q.v.*) which bore golden apples. They were assisted by a dragon, Ladon. Ge (*q.v.*) had given the tree to Hera on her wedding day. On the advice of Prometheus (*q.v.*) Heracles (*q.v.*) (who had been sent to get the apples by Eurystheus (*q.v.*)) persuaded Atlas (*q.v.*) to fetch three apples while he shouldered Atlas' burden. Atlas then refused to take the sky back on his shoulders but Heracles tricked him into doing so. On his return journey Heracles slew Antaeus (*q.v.*). Eurystheus gave the apples back to Heracles and he passed them to Athene to return to the Hesperides.

Hesperus. The evening star, the Greek form of the Latin vesper or evening.

Hestia. The sister of Zeus (*q.v.*) and Hera (*q.v.*), the goddess of the hearth worshipped by every family. Though Poseidon (*q.v.*) and Apollo (*q.v.*) tried to seduce her she swore to Zeus always to remain a virgin. The Romans worshipped her counterpart, the goddess Vesta (*q.v.*).

Hippodamia. (1) The daughter of Oenomaus, king of Elis. An oracle said he would die at the hands of his son-in-law so he challenged all her suitors to a chariot race. Victory meant they could marry Hippodamia, defeat meant death. His horses were the gifts of his father Ares (*q.v.*). However Pelops (*q.v.*) engineered his death and married Hippodamia.

(2) The wife of Pirithous (*q.v.*). When a drunken centaur (*q.v.*) abducted her on her wedding day the battle between the Lapithae (*q.v.*) and Centaurs occurred.

Hippolyte. A queen of the Amazons (*q.v.*) and sister of Antiope. Heracles (*q.v.*) had to fetch her golden girdle for Eurystheus. At first he was well received but Hera (*q.v.*) stirred the Amazons against him and in the fight he slew Hippolyte and took the girdle. Returning home he saved Laomedon's (*q.v.*) daughter Hesione. Another legend says Theseus (*q.v.*) abducted Hippolyte who bore him the son Hippolytus (*q.v.*).

Hippolytus. The son of Theseus (*q.v.*) and the Amazon Hippolyte (*q.v.*) or her sister Antiope (*q.v.*). When Theseus married again to Phaedra (*q.v.*), sister of Ariadne (*q.v.*), Phaedra fell in love with her stepson and committed suicide when he refused her. She left a note falsely accusing Hippolytus. Theseus prayed to Poseidon (*q.v.*) who was under an obligation to him, that Hippolytus would die the same day. Poseidon then sent a sea-monster which scared the youth's horses and he was dragged to death behind his chariot.

Homer. *See* **B32**.

Horae. The "hours", three daughters of Zeus (*q.v.*) and Themis (*q.v.*) and tutelary goddesses of nature and the seasons. They were bound to the soil and promoted fertility. Thus they were important and are involved in solemn oaths. However they rarely appear except in attendance on other gods and have no "adventures".

Horatii. Three Roman brothers whose tale is told by Livy. In the mid 7th century B.C. while Rome was ruled by Tullus Hostilius the city of Alba Longa (*q.v.*) was destroyed and its population transferred to Rome. According to legend the Horatii challenged the three Alban champions, the Curatii, to a sword battle. Two Horatii were killed but the third slew all the Curatii. On returning to Rome he met his sister, who had been engaged to one of the Curatii, weeping. He stabbed her to death. After ceremonies of expiation Tullus acquitted him of murder.

Horatius Cocles. Another of the Horatii family, the "one-eyed" (Cocles). In the 6th century B.C. he held the Etruscans at bay on the wooden Sublican bridge into Rome until it was pulled down beneath him. He then swam the Tiber to safety. The subject of a *Lay* by Macaulay.

Hyacinthus. A Peloponnesian youth loved by Apollo (*q.v.*) who was killed when the jealous Zephyrus (*q.v.*) diverted a discus to hit him. From his blood sprang the "hyacinth" flower. He had a shrine at Amyclae in Laconia and a three-day festival, the Hyacinthia, was held in his honour at Sparta.

Hyades. Nymphs who cared for Dionysus (*q.v.*) as a child on Mt. Nysa. Zeus (*q.v.*) placed their images in the sky as the "rain stars", part of the constellation of Taurus which rises at midnight in the rainy season.

Hydra of Lerna. The "water snake", offspring of Echidne (*q.v.*) and Typhon (*q.v.*) and raised by

Hera (*q.v.*). It was a monster with the body of a dog and 9 serpent heads. Heracles (*q.v.*) was sent to kill it by Eurystheus (*q.v.*). It lived at the source of the River Amymone in the swamp of Lerna. As Heracles lopped off a head two more grew. He also had to crush a giant crab which Hera placed among the signs of the zodiac. Finally he crushed the Hydra's heads with his club and Iolaus (*q.v.*) burned them to stop them regrowing. He dipped his arrows in the beast's blood thereby making them poisonous.

Hygeia. The wife or daughter of Asclepius (*q.v.*), a goddess of health.

Hylas. *See* **Heracles.**

Hyllus. The son of Heracles (*q.v.*) and Deianeira (*q.v.*). He conducted Heracles to his funeral pyre. Either he or Iolaus (*q.v.*) defeated Eurystheus (*q.v.*). Eventually he was slain by Echemus, king of Tegea.

Hymen. God of weddings.

Hyperboreans. A mythical race living far to the north, behind Boreas (*q.v.*) *i.e.* at the place where the north wind originates. Apollo (*q.v.*) spent time with them before going to Delphi and spent the winter months with them. A Hyperborean soothsayer, Olen, installed Apollo's oracle at Delphi. Their land was supposed to have perpetual sunshine and was a land of plenty, an earthly paradise where men lived in peace and ease on the fruits of the earth. Herodotus (**B31**) tells us that one of their priests, Aburis, travelled the world on a golden arrow and never needed to eat. He places their land in Southern Russia.

Hypenor. One of the Spartii (*q.v.*).

Hyperion. A Titan (*q.v.*) and sun-god, father of Helios (*q.v.*), Selene (*q.v.*) and Eos (*q.v.*), the sun, moon and dawn. In Keats' poem he is the last of the old gods to be deposed, the young Apollo (*q.v.*) taking his place.

Hypermestra. *See* **Danaus.**

Hypnus. The god of sleep.

I

Iacchus. Alternative name for Dionysus (*q.v.*) used in the Eleusian mysteries where he was regarded as the son of Zeus (*q.v.*) and Demeter (*q.v.*), not Semele (*q.v.*).

Iapetus. A Titan (*q.v.*), father of Prometheus (*q.v.*), Atlas (*q.v.*) and Epimetheus.

Iasion. Or Iasius or Iasus, the son of Zeus (*q.v.*) and Electra (*q.v.*), lover of Demeter (*q.v.*) who bore him a son Pluton. Zeus in his jealousy slew him with a thunderbolt.

Icarius. Father of Erigone. An Athenian to whom Dionysus (*q.v.*) taught cultivation of the vine and who gave wine to a band of shepherds. Mistaking drunkenness for witchcraft they slew him.

Icarus. *See* **Daedalus.**

Idaea. A nymph, mother of Teucer (*q.v.*) by Scamander (*q.v.*) of Crete.

Idas. The twin of Lynceus and a son of Poseidon (*q.v.*). He abducted Marpessa in a chariot given to him by Poseidon and fought Apollo (*q.v.*) for possession of her. Given the choice by Zeus (*q.v.*) she chose Idas. He and Lynceus took part in the voyage of the Argonauts (*q.v.*) and the hunt of the Calydonian boar (*q.v.*) and were killed in battle with their cousins the Dioscuri (*q.v.*).

Idomeneus. King of Crete who contributed 100 ships to the expedition against Troy (*q.v.*). Virgil adds that on his return from Troy he was caught in a storm and vowed to sacrifice the first person he met to Poseidon (*q.v.*) in return for safe passage. This proved to be his son and the sacrifice brought a pestilence on Crete. Idomeneus was banished to Calabria in Italy.

Ilia. A priestess of Vesta (*q.v.*) also called Rhea Silvia. The mother of Romulus (*q.v.*) and Remus.

Iliad. Homer's epic poem on the siege of Troy (*q.v.*). Although it hints at earlier and later events it covers only a period of weeks in the tenth year of the war, recounting Achilles' (*q.v.*) quarrel with Agamemnon (*q.v.*), the death of Patroclus (*q.v.*) and the death of Hector (*q.v.*). It ends with Achilles returning Hector's (*q.v.*) body to Priam (*q.v.*). Although many gods and heroes appear, Achilles and Hector are the main protagonists.

Ilioneus. An old and venerated Trojan who accompanied Aeneas (*q.v.*).

Ilithyiae. Daughters of Hera (*q.v.*) who helped women

in childbirth. Later only one goddess, Ilithyia, is mentioned in this connection.

Ilus. (1) The son of Tros (*q.v.*) and father of Laomedon (*q.v.*). An ancestor of the Trojans.
(2) Original name of Ascanius (*q.v.*) son of Aeneas (*q.v.*) and Creusa.

Inachus. The first king of Argos, son of Oceanus (*q.v.*) and Tethys. A river was named after him.

Ino. Daughter of Cadmus (*q.v.*) and Harmonia (*q.v.*), sister of Autonoe, Agave, Polydoras, Illyrus and Semele. She helped to rear Dionysus (*q.v.*) and her husband Athamas (*q.v.*) was punished for it by Hera (*q.v.*) who drove him into madness and the murder of his own children. Ino, Autonoe and Agave were Bacchae (*q.v.*) and they slew Pentheus, the son of Agave and heir to Cadmus, for opposing the worship of Dionysus. Ino committed suicide (*see* **Athamas**) and became a sea deity.

Io. The daughter of Inachus. Zeus (*q.v.*) loved her and turned her into a white heifer to deceive the jealous Hera (*q.v.*). He did not succeed in this and Hera set the hundred-eyed Argus to watch the heifer. But Hermes (*q.v.*) at Zeus' command cut off his head and placed his eyes in the tail of the peacock. He also sent a gadfly whose sting caused Io to wander the earth till she reached Egypt. On her wanderings she gave her name to the Ionian sea and to the Bosphorus ("ford of the cow"). In Egypt Zeus restored her to human form and she bore him a son, Epaphus, an ancestor of Danaus (*q.v.*).

Iobates. *See* **Bellerophon.**

Iolaus. Son of Iphicles (*q.v.*) and nephew of Heracles (*q.v.*) to whom he was charioteer and constant companion. He helped Heracles kill the Hydra (*q.v.*) and perform his other labours and in return Heracles gave him his wife Megara. He also sent Iolaus as the leader of his sons by the daughters of Thespius to settle in Sardinia.

Iolcus. The kingdom of Jason's (*q.v.*) father Aeson, usurped by his half brothers Pelias and Neleus.

Iole. *See* **Deianeira.**

Ion. The son of Xuthus and Creusa, brother of Achaeus. In Euripides' play *Ion* he is the son of Creusa and Apollo (*q.v.*) who is carried off to Delphi (*q.v.*), as a baby but is eventually restored to Creusa and adopted by Xuthus. The eponymous ancestor of the Ionian Greeks.

Iphicles. (1) One of the Argonauts (*q.v.*).
(2) The son of Amphitrion (*q.v.*) and Alcmene (*q.v.*) a night younger than Heracles (*q.v.*). The father of Iolaus (*q.v.*). He married the youngest daughter of Creon of Thebes when Heracles married Megara.

Iphigenia. The daughter of Agamemnon (*q.v.*) and Clytemnestra (*q.v.*), sacrificed by her father at Aulis to get a favourable wind for the Greek fleet sailing to Troy (*q.v.*). Euripides cites another tradition in which Artemis (*q.v.*) substituted a doe for Iphigenia at the last moment and carried her off to Tauris. Later Orestes (*q.v.*) found Iphigenia on the Tauric Chersonese and brought her home to Greece.

Iphitus. A son of Eurytus who argued that his father should deliver Iole (*see* **Deianeira**) to Heracles (*q.v.*). But in a rage Heracles slew him and though purified for the murder was told by an oracle to sell himself into slavery and give the proceeds to Iphitus' family.

Irene. The daughter of Zeus (*q.v.*) and Themis (*q.v.*), goddess of peace and one of the Horae (*q.v.*). The Romans identified her with Pax.

Iris. The personification of the rainbow and, in later myth, a messenger of the gods, particularly Hera (*q.v.*).

Isis. An Egyptian goddess, wife of Osiris and mother of Horus. In Hellenistic times she became one of the most important deities of the Mediterranean world, her cult arriving in Rome by the time of Augustus. Here the features of her worship, Egyptian priests, processions, initiation ceremonies etc. were described by Apuleius in his *Golden Ass*. One of her temples is preserved at Pompeii.

Ismene. The daughter of Oedipus (*q.v.*) and Jocasta (*q.v.*). She followed her father and her sister Antigone (*q.v.*) into exile.

Issa. The daughter of Macareus and his sister Canace, beloved by Apollo (*q.v.*).

Isthmian Games. Quadrennial games held at Corinth in honour of Poseidon (*q.v.*).

Ithaca. The island home of Odysseus (*q.v.*), one of the Ionian islands.

Itys, Itylus. *See* **Procne.**

Iulus. A name used for Ascanius (*q.v.*) by Virgil to indicate the descent of the Julian clan from Aeneas (*q.v.*).

J

Janus. A god of beginnings or new ventures, worshipped at Rome. He had a flamen (sacred priest) and was very important but the origin and nature of his worship is obscure. He had two faces and may represent the assimilation of an eastern god and an Etruscan (*see* **L41**) deity. Also associated with doorways and thresholds.

Jason. Son of Aeson, rightful king of Iolcus who was usurped by his half-brothers, Pelias and Neleus. The infant Jason was smuggled out of Iolcus and reared by Cheiron (*q.v.*) while Pelias expelled Neleus and ruled alone. When Jason returned to claim his birthright Pelias sent him to fetch the Golden Fleece from Colchis. This was the fleece of the ram on which Phrixus (*q.v.*) had escaped and which he had given to Aëtes, king of Colchis. Its presence was the cause of Colchis' prosperity and it hung from an oak tree in the grove of Ares (*q.v.*) where a dragon guarded it. After numerous adventures Jason and his Argonauts (*q.v.*) arrived at Colchis and Aëtes promised Jason the fleece if he could yoke two fire-breathing bulls with brazen feet made by Hephaestus (*q.v.*), and sow the grove of Ares with dragons' teeth left by Cadmus of Thebes (*q.v.*). Medea (*q.v.*) the sorceress gave him a fire-proof lotion which allowed him to complete the task and when her father Aëtes refused to give up the fleece, charmed the dragon to sleep while Jason stole it. Pursued by Aëtes the couple escaped when Medea murdered her half-brother Absyrtus and dropped pieces of his corpse into the sea, causing Aëtes to stop and collect them. They were purified of the murder by Circe (*q.v.*). At Iolchus Pelias had forced Aeson to commit suicide and in revenge Medea persuaded Pelias' daughters to boil their father alive pretending it would restore his youth. The couple were banished because of this and went to Corinth. Here Jason abandoned Medea for Glauce (*q.v.*) whom Medea killed. Jason took his own life though one tradition holds he was killed by the falling prow of the Argo (*q.v.*).

Jocasta. Daughter of Menoeceus, wife of Laius king of Thebes and mother of Oedipus (*q.v.*). When her unwitting incest with Oedipus brought a plague on Thebes Menoeceus sacrificed himself in answer to an oracle demanding the life of one of the Sparti (*q.v.*) *i.e.* a descendant of the "sown men". Jocasta hanged herself when she learned the truth of her marriage to Oedipus.

Jove. Alternative name for Jupiter (*q.v.*).

Juno. Italian goddess of womanhood and childbirth, associated by the Romans with the Greek Hera (*q.v.*) and regarded as the consort of Jupiter (*q.v.*).

Jupiter. Originally an Italian sky-god, later regarded by the Romans as *Dies Pater*—"Father Day", god of the day. Later still identified with Zeus (*q.v.*). His cult was introduced to Rome by the Etruscans and the temple to Jupiter Optimus Maximus (Best and Most High) stood on the Capitol. His *flamen*, the *flamen* Dialis was the most important of the college. He was guarantor of the *imperium* and city of Rome and triumphs were an act of Jupiter worship. Worshipped in various capacities as *Stator* (he who founds or maintains), *Teretrius* (he who strikes), *Ultor* ("Avenger") and *Tonans* ("Thunderer").

Juturna. (1) An Italian goddess of springs and streams.

(2) The sister of Turnus (*q.v.*).

Juventas. Italian goddess identified with Hebe (*q.v.*).

L

Labdacus. Mythical king of Thebes; a descendant of Cadmus (*q.v.*) and an ancestor of Oedipus (*q.v.*).

Lachesis. One of the Fates (*q.v.*).

Laelaps. A fleet-footed hound given to Procris by Cephalus (*q.v.*).

Laertes. The king of Ithaca, father of Odysseus (*q.v.*)

by Anticleia, daughter of the thief Autolycus. While Odysseus was at Troy (*q.v.*) Penelope's (*q.v.*) suitors forced him to retire to the country.

Laestrygones. A race of giant cannibals ruled by Lamus. At Telepylos, their capital city, Odysseus (*q.v.*) lost all but one of his twelve ships to them. Homer says their summer nights were so short that shepherds going out with their flocks in the morning met those returning at sunset. Traditionally located in eastern Sicily or at Formiae in central Italy.

Laius. *See* **Oedipus.**

Lamia. One of the Empusae (*q.v.*), daughter of Belus.

Lamus. *See* **Laestrygones.**

Laocoön. A Trojan prophet, son of Antenor and a priest of Apollo (*q.v.*) and Poseidon (*q.v.*). He warned the Trojans against the Wooden Horse (*q.v.*) and flung a spear at it. However he had angered Apollo by breaking his vows of celibacy and the god now sent two sea serpents which crushed him and his two sons. A famous group of statues depicting the scene, carved in Rhodes *c.* 25 B.C., now stands in the Vatican museum. The Trojans disastrously drew the wrong conclusion *viz.* that his death was punishment for striking the horse.

Laodamia. The daughter of Acastus and wife of Protesilaus of Thessaly, the first Greek ashore at Troy (*q.v.*) though he knew from an oracle the first Greek to land would die. Homer says he left his wife mourning and his house unfinished but Catullus, Virgil and Ovid follow another tradition in which she begged the gods that Protesilaus might return to life for three hours. When he died a second time she committed suicide. Wordsworth's poem *Laodamia* takes the tale as its subject.

Laodice. (1) A daughter of Priam (*q.v.*), sister of Cassandra (*q.v.*) and wife of Helicaon. When Troy (*q.v.*) fell the earth swallowed her.

(2) Alternative name for Electra (*q.v.*), Agamemnon's (*q.v.*) daughter.

Laomedon. The son of Ilus (*q.v.*), king of Troy (*q.v.*) and father of Hesione and Priam (*q.v.*). Apollo (*q.v.*) and Poseidon (*q.v.*) helped him build the walls of Troy and he refused to pay them. Poseidon then sent a sea monster to devour Hesione but Heracles (*q.v.*) saved her. Laomedon then refused to pay Heracles the agreed white horses left by Zeus (*q.v.*) in exchange for Ganymede (*q.v.*). Heracles and Telamon then sacked Troy and slew Laomedon and all his sons save Priam (*q.v.*).

Lapis Niger. Black marble paving in the Roman Forum said to cover the tomb of Romulus (*q.v.*).

Lapithae or **Lapiths.** Mythical tribe of Thessaly, governed by Pirithous, son of Ixion (*q.v.*) and thus half-brothers to the Centaurs (*q.v.*). At the wedding of Pirithous and Hippodamia, attended by Theseus (*q.v.*) a centaur tried to abduct the bride and a famous battle between the Lapithae and Centaurs ensued. It is described by Ovid and is depicted in the Parthenon and the frieze of Apollo's (*q.v.*) temple at Bassae. It is also the subject of a sculptured frieze by Michelangelo.

Lares. Originally fertility gods, worshipped by the Romans privately in the home and semi-publicly at crossroads. They were represented as youths with handfuls of fruit who wandered the farmstead incessantly whirling round and round. They kept away maleficent demons and ensured the prosperity of the family home. Each month they received offerings of oat cakes, milk, honey and flowers. Generally associated with the Penates, the spirits who guarded the household stores. Together the guardians of the hearth and home.

Larissa. A city in Thessaly near modern Volos. Reputed birthplace of Achilles (*q.v.*) hence his nickname "the Larissaen".

Lars Porsenna. Legendary Etruscan chief whom Livy tells us besieged Rome on behalf of the exiled Tarquinius Superbus. Lars means "overlord" and he is probably a symbol of Etruscan suzerainty over Rome. (*See* **Horatius Cocles**).

Latinus. Eponymous king of the Latini or Latins in Italy. Hesiod makes him the son of Odysseus (*q.v.*) and Circe (*q.v.*). Virgil makes him the son of Faunus (*q.v.*). Livy and Virgil portray him as opposing the settlement of Aeneas (*q.v.*) and the Trojans in Italy but then agreeing Aeneas should marry his daughter Lavinia. He next helps Aeneas fight Turnus king of the Rutuli, to whom Lavinia had been promised. Livy says he died in battle and Aeneas became king of the Latins; Virgil that he survived to celebrate the marriage and uniting of Latins and Trojans.

Leander. Mythical youth who drowned while swimming to meet Hero (q.v.).

Leda. Daughter of Thestius and wife of Tyndareus king of Sparta. Seduced by Zeus (q.v.) in the form of a swan she gave birth to two eggs, from one of which hatched Helen (q.v.) and Polydeuces (q.v.) from the other, Castor (q.v.) and Clytemnestra (q.v.). One tradition says that Helen was the daughter of Nemesis (q.v.) who left the egg for Leda to incubate.

Lemnos. A small island at the mouth of the Hellespont, home at one time of a primitive people known to the Greeks as the Pelasgi. Hephaestus (q.v.) was said to have landed on the island when Zeus (q.v.) hurled him out of heaven and supposedly had a forge here.

Lethe. "Forgetfulness", one of the rivers of the Underworld whose waters induced amnesia in those who drank of them. Virgil holds that here souls forgot their past prior to reincarnation and Ovid says that it flowed round the "cave of sleep".

Leto. Known to the Romans as Latona. The daughter of the Titans (q.v.) Coeus and Phoebe and the mother of Apollo (q.v.) and Artemis (q.v.) by Zeus (q.v.). While she carried the unborn gods the jealous Hera (q.v.) forced her to wander the earth until she finally gave birth to them at Ortygia, henceforth called Delos (q.v.). Hera sent the giant Tityus (q.v.) to rape her but her children slew him with their arrows. See also **Niobe.**

Leuce. A nymph loved by Hades (q.v.) who turned her into a white poplar tree.

Leucippus. (1) King of Messenia whose daughters Hilaera and Phoebe were abducted by the Dioscuri (q.v.) and whose brothers Idas (q.v.) and Lynceus (q.v.) fought to save them.

(2) The son of Oenomaus who loved Artemis (q.v.) To be near her he disguised himself as a nymph but when Apollo (q.v.) advised the nymphs to bathe naked he was discovered and torn to pieces by them.

Leucothea. Originally Ino, daughter of Cadmus (q.v.) and wife of Athamas who helped Zeus (q.v.) save Dionysus (q.v.) at the death of Semele (q.v.). In revenge Hera (q.v.) drove her mad and she leapt into the foaming sea to become the sea deity Leucothea—"the white goddess". In this role she helped Odysseus (q.v.) land on Scheria. Her son was Palaemon, a minor sea god.

Liber Pater. An ancient Italian god of the vine, early identified with Bacchus (q.v.) by the Romans.

Lichas. The herald of Heracles (q.v.) who took the shirt of Deineira (q.v.) to him. In his agony Heracles took him by the ankle, swung him round three times and threw him into the Euboean Sea where he became a rock of human shape which henceforth bore his name.

Linus. (1) The son of Psamathe of Argos and Apollo (q.v.). Fearful lest her father learn of her liaison with the god she exposed the baby who was reared by shepherds but later killed by her father's hounds. When her distress revealed her secret her father condemned her to death but Apollo sent a plague to the city which only abated when the Argives propitiated mother and son with dirges called *linoi.*

(2) The son of a Muse who was so gifted musically that the jealous Apollo killed him.

(3) Heracles' (q.v.) music tutor whom Heracles slew in a rage with his own lyre.

Lotophagi. ("The Lotus eaters"). A mythical people living on lotus fruit which induced trances and forgetfulness and made the eater lose any desire to return home. They gave the fruit to Odysseus' (q.v.) men. Herodotus placed them in western Libya, possibly the island of Jerba.

Luceres. One of the original three tribes into which Rome was divided and which were believed to date back to Romulus (q.v.). The other tribes were the Ramnes and Tities.

Lucifer. The "light bringer", the name given to the planet Venus which can be seen before dawn. In the evening sky the Greeks called it Hesperus.

Lucretia. Wife of Tarquinius Collatinus whose rape by Sextus, son of Tarquinius Superbus led her to stab herself in shame. Junius Brutus then swore by her spirit to expel the Tarquins which he did. The story is told by Livy and Ovid and inspired Shakespeare's poem *The Rape of Lucrece* and Brit-

ten's opera *The Rape of Lucretia.* A subject also for Titian, Botticelli, Tintoretto and Veronese.

Lucretius. *See* **B39.**

Lycaon. A mythical character who tricked Zeus (q.v.) by feeding him human flesh. Zeus killed him and all his sons save Nyctinus by lightning or turned them into wolves, hence Lycanthropy.

Lycomedes. The king of Scyros who murdered Theseus (q.v.). It was to his court that Thetis (q.v.) sent Achilles (q.v.), and Lycomedes' daughter Deidamia bore Achilles his son Neoptolemus (q.v.).

Lycurgus (1) Mythical king of Thrace who was made blind and mad for opposing the worship of Dionysus (q.v.).

(2) Mythical founder of the Spartan constitution and military regime, first mentioned by Herodotus and subject of a *Life* by Plutarch. Some traditions say the Pythia at Delphi gave him the constitution, others that he devised it while in Crete. In Sparta he was worshipped as a god.

Lynceus. (1) *See* **Danaus.**

(2) Twin of Idas (q.v.) noted for his keen eyesight.

Lyrnessus. City near Troy (q.v.) sacked by Achilles (q.v.).

M

Macareus. *See* **Issa.**

Macaria. *See* **Eurystheus.**

Machaon. The son of Asclepius the physician (q.v.).

Maenads. *See* **Bacchae.**

Maia. The daughter of Atlas (q.v.) and Pleione, eldest of the Pleiades (q.v.) and the most beautiful. By Zeus (q.v.) the mother of Hermes (q.v.). The Romans identified her with spring and as a nature goddess gave her name to the month of May.

Manes. "The good ones", the Roman name for the spirits of the dead, regarded as a collective divinity, *Di Manes.* On certain days they could leave the Underworld and were capable of great mischief. Thus they demanded propitiatory ceremonies at funerals and on set days when the head of the house, the *paterfamilias,* would go into the night and cast boiled beans to them. The Roman poets applied the term also to the gods of the Underworld and to the Underworld itself.

Marpessa. *See* **Idas.** The daughter of the river god Evenus.

Mars. Roman god of war, at one time also associated with agriculture. Later completely identified with Ares (q.v.).

Marsyas. A Phrygian, in some traditions a silenus (q.v.), who found the flute invented and discarded by Athene (q.v.). He challenged Apollo (q.v.) to a music contest, judged by the Muses (q.v.). Apollo won and had him flayed alive. The tears of the woodland spirits and animals which wept for him formed the river Meander.

Medea. The niece of Circe (q.v.) and daughter of Aëtes of Colchis some say by Hecate (q.v.). She loved Jason (q.v.) and helped him steal the Golden Fleece, murdering her half-brother in their escape. Having cut a goat in pieces, boiled them and pulled forth a lamb she persuaded the daughters of Pelias to boil him, causing his death. When Jason left her for Glauce (q.v.) she caused her death and slew her sons by Jason. She then escaped in a chariot drawn by winged serpents to Athens. Here she married Aegeus (q.v.). When Theseus (q.v.) returned she tried to poison him to secure the succession of her own son Medus (q.v.) but Aegeus recognised Theseus and saved him. She fled to wander the earth: some say she returned to Colchis and was reconciled to her father, others that she went to Asia Minor where her son gave his name to the Medes. She became an immortal.

Medus. Son of Medea (q.v.) and Aegeus (q.v.) eponymous ancestor of the Medes.

Medusa. *See* **Gorgons.** Slain and beheaded by Perseus (q.v.) as she slept. From her corpse sprang forth the fully grown Pegasus (q.v.) and the warrior Chrysaor.

Megaeia. One of the Erinnyes (q.v.).

Megara or **Megaera.** The eldest daughter of Creon of Thebes. Wife of Heracles (q.v.) and bore him several children. Later married Iolaus (q.v.) though one tradition says Eurystheus tried to kill her and Heracles instead killed Eurystheus. In revenge Hera (q.v.) drove Heracles mad and he killed Megara and his children.

Melampus. Son of Amythaon, a seer who introduced the worship of Dionysus (q.v.) to Greece. He and his brother Bias cured the women of Argos (including the daughter of the king, Proctus) of madness and received two thirds of his kingdom in reward.

Meleager. The son of Oeneus and Althaea. The Fates (q.v.) told his mother he would only die when a certain brand, which was on the fire, was burned. She extinguished and hid it. Meleager was one of the Argonauts (q.v.) and organised the hunt of the Calydonian Boar (q.v.). He fell in love with Atalanta who joined the hunt and having killed the boar himself gave her the hide on the pretext she had touched it first. This set the hunters quarrelling and in the dispute he killed his uncles, brothers of Althaea. She cursed their murderer, not realising the truth, and when she learned the Erinnyes (q.v.) were persecuting him because of the curse burned the brand and committed suicide. Her daughters (save Gorge and Deianeira) were turned into guinea-hens by Artemis. The son of Meleager and Atlanta was Parthenopaeus.

Melpomene. The Muse of Tragedy.

Memnon. The son of Eos (q.v.) and Tithonus, half-brother of Priam (q.v.). The king of Ethiopia who helped the Trojans and killed many Greeks. Achilles (q.v.) met him in single combat while Zeus (q.v.) weighed their fates in the balance. Achilles slew him but Zeus answered his mother's request that he be honoured by having the birds called *Memnonides* rise above his funeral pyre, then fall as a sacrifice. They annually visited his tomb on the Hellespont though one tradition says he survived the war and ruled five generations in Ethiopia before becoming an immortal. The Greeks assumed many monuments, which they called *Memnonia*, were dedicated to him including a huge statue in Egyptian Thebes.

Menelaus. Son of Atreus, younger brother of Agamemnon (q.v.) and husband of Helen (q.v.). When her father chose him from amongst many suitors he made the others swear to help him in any misfortune. He was thus able to summon the Greek forces for the war on Troy (q.v.). At one stage in the war he fought a duel with Paris (q.v.) to decide the war and was winning until Aphrodite (q.v.) carried Paris off. Because he failed to sacrifice to Athene (q.v.) he took eight years to return from Troy to Sparta.

Menoeceus. (1) See **Jocasta.**
(2) See **Seven against Thebes.**

Mentor. Friend and adviser of Odysseus (q.v.) who was too old to go to Troy (q.v.) and remained at Ithaca to watch over Odysseus' interests. Athene (q.v.) took his form to guide Telemachus' (q.v.) search for his father. The name is now synonymous with a trusted counsellor.

Mercury. The Roman equivalent of Hermes (q.v.).

Merope. A Pleiad. Wife of Sisyphus.

Metis. Counsellor of the young Zeus (q.v.) and his first wife. Mother of Athene (q.v.). Herself the daughter of Oceanus (q.v.) and Tethys.

Midas. Son of Gordius. See **Gordian Knot.** His hospitality to Silenus (q.v.) led Dionysus (q.v.) to grant him any wish: he wished that all he touched would turn to gold. When even his food became gold he begged to be relieved of his gift—and was—by bathing in the River Pactolus which was henceforth rich in gold. When he judged Pan (q.v.) a better musician than Apollo (q.v.) the latter gave him asses' ears which he hid under his hat. Only his barber knew, but when his barber told a hole in the ground, reeds grew from it which, via the wind, revealed his secret to the world.

Milanion. Husband of Atalanta (q.v.).

Miletus of Crete. The son of Aria and Apollo (q.v.), a beautiful youth over whom Minos (q.v.) and his brothers Rhadamanthus (q.v.) and Sarpedon quarrelled. Miletus chose Sarpedon and to escape Minos' jealousy they fled to Asia Minor where Miletus founded the city Miletus which bore his name.

Minerva. Etruscan goddess of wisdom, the arts and crafts. The Romans identified her with Athene (q.v.).

Minos. The son of Zeus (q.v.) and Europa (q.v.), brother of Rhadamanthus (q.v.) and Sarpedon (q.v.). Ruler of Crete and supported in this by Poseidon (q.v.) who gave him a magnificent white bull. See **Cretan Bull.** He gave Crete her laws and defended the island with the aid of Talos, a brazen

giant with a bull's head. He pursued the nymph Britomartis for nine months but she leapt into the sea. Artemis (q.v.) deified her and the two shared the epithet Dictynna. While besieging Nisa, the port of Megara, Scylla, the daughter of the king Nisus fell in love with Minos and cropped her hair on which Nisus' life depended. She let Minos into the city but he was repulsed by her parricide and deserted the girl who swam after his ship. According to one tradition her father's spirit in the form of an eagle seized her and she was transformed into the Ciris bird; according to another tradition Minos drowned her and she became a fish. Minos married Pasiphaë (q.v.) who bore him Ariadne (q.v.), Androgeos and Phaedra. When Androgeos won all the events at the Panathenaic games Aegeus (q.v.) had him murdered and in revenge Minos extracted a tribute of seven Athenian youths and maidens who were devoured by the Minotaur (q.v.). He was killed by the daughters of Cocalus of Sicily while pursuing Daedalus (q.v.) and became one of the three judges of the Underworld.

Minotaur. Offspring of Pasiphaë (q.v.) and the Cretan Bull (q.v.) which had the head of a bull and body of a man. It lived in a labyrinth devised by Daedalus (q.v.) where it devoured the maidens and youths of Athens delivered in tribute to Minos (q.v.). It was slain by Theseus (q.v.).

Minyans or **Minyae.** Prehistoric inhabitants of Boeotia (q.v.) and Thessaly whose reputed ancestor was Minyas.

Misenus. Trumpeter of Aeneas (q.v.) who was drowned by a Triton (q.v.) and buried in the Bay of Naples at the port which then bore the name Misenum (the modern Capo Miseno). From the time of Agrippa Misenum was a major Roman naval station.

Mithras. An Iranian deity whose worship was developed in Persia and spread throughout the Middle East. Known to the Greeks from the time of Herodotus his worship spread to Rome under the Republic and from the 2nd century A.D. spread throughout the empire. Mithras was linked with astrology and appears to have been linked with the sun following a fight with the sun-god. But the core of his cult was that man or the soul had fallen from grace and that Mithras could bring redemption and thus eternal life. Very popular with the Roman legions. Mithras was the one serious contender with Christianity for religious supremacy. His ritual involved seven stages of initiation and secret ceremonies conducted in underground caves or artificial subterranean chambers such as that found in London. These temples were called mithraea. *See also* **J35.**

Mnemosyne. "Memory", the daughter of Uranus (q.v.) and by Zeus (q.v.) the mother of the Muses (q.v.).

Moirae or **Moerae.** See **Fates.**

Monoecus. "The lone dweller", Latin name for Heracles (q.v.) who was said to have dwelt alone for a time in the region of modern Monte Carlo.

Mopsus. The son of Apollo (q.v.) and Manto, daughter of Teiresias. When he beat Calchas (q.v.) in prophecy Calchas died of grief.

Morpheus. The Greek *Hypnos.* The son of the god of "Sleep". A god who sends dreams and visions of human form. In Ovid's *Metamorphoses,* Sleep sends him to Alcyone (q.v.) in the form of her dead husband.

Musaeus. A mythical poet who succeeded Orpheus (q.v.), the first poet.

Muses or **Musae.** The daughters of Zeus (q.v.) and Mnemosyne (q.v.) who presided over the arts and sciences. Originally three in number, Hesiod later names nine. Clio was muse of history, Euterpe of lyric poetry and music, Thalia of comedy, Melpomene of tragedy, Terpsichore of song and dance, Erato of mime, Polyhymnia or Polymnia of the hymn, Calliope of epic poetry and Urania of astronomy, though the attributions vary.

Myrmidons or **Myrmidones.** Tribe of southern Thessaly which provided Achilles' (q.v.) contingent at Troy.

Myrtilus. The son of Hermes (q.v.). The charioteer of Oenomaus whose death he caused by removing the lynch pin of his chariot and substituting a wax replica. He did this because Pelops (q.v.) had bribed him with the promise of half his kingdom, but instead Pelops flung him into the sea. He cursed the House of Pelops as he died and his father placed him amongst the stars.

N

Naiads or **Naiades**. Fresh-water nymphs in Greek mythology. They carried off Hylas (q.v.).

Narcissus. See Echo.

Nauplius. A king of Euboea who lured ships returning from Troy (q.v.) to their doom on the promontory of Caphareus by lighting misleading fires.

Nausicaa. Daughter of Alcinous, king of the Phaeacians who found Odysseus (q.v.) after a shipwreck while playing ball with her friends on the beach. She looked after him and her father gave him a ship.

Nectar. The drink of the Greek gods which conferred immortality.

Neleus. Twin of Pelias (q.v.), sons of Poseidon (q.v.) and the nymph Tyro. The twins were exposed by their mother but reared by a horse breeder. When Tyro married Cretheus, king of Iolcus, he adopted the boys who were thus half-brothers of Aeson. Pelias then later seized the kingdom, imprisoned Aeson and expelled Neleus who went to Pylus with Bias and Melampus and became its king. He and all twelve of his sons bar Nestor (q.v.) were killed by Heracles (q.v.) for aiding Augias (q.v.) in his war against Heracles.

Nemesis. Greek goddess, daughter of Oceanus. Originally she was envisaged as allotting to men their share of happiness and unhappiness, thereby chastening the over-fortunate. Later she was portrayed as the punisher of crime, the goddess of retribution. Some say she laid the egg from which Helen (q.v.), Clytemnestra (q.v.) and the Dioscuri (q.v.) were born. She had a sanctuary at Rhamnus from around 430 B.C.

Nemi. A lake in the Alban mountains, site of a sanctuary and sacred wood of Diana (q.v.).

Neoptolemus. Also called Pyrrhus, a son of Achilles (q.v.) and Deidamia. Odysseus (q.v.) and Diomedes (q.v.) persuaded his grandfather Lycomedes to let him go to Troy (q.v.) after his father's death. He was one of the Greeks inside the Wooden Horse. He slew Polites, the son of Priam (q.v.) and Hecuba (q.v.) before their eyes. He killed Priam at the altar of Zeus, smashed the skull of Astyanax (q.v.), Hector's (q.v.) child, and sacrificed Polyxena, Priam's daughter, on his father's tomb. He was given Andromache (q.v.) but back in Greece married Hermione (q.v.) with the blessing of Menelaus (q.v.) despite her prior betrothal to Orestes (q.v.). When their marriage proved barren he went to Delphi (q.v.) to consult the oracle and was slain either by Orestes or the priests of Apollo (q.v.).

Nephele. A phantom conjured up by Zeus (q.v.) to deceive Ixion. She later married Athamas.

Neptune. Italian sea-god whom the Romans identified with Poseidon (q.v.).

Nereids or **Nereides.** Fifty beautiful sea nymphs, the daughters of Nereus (q.v.) and Doris, of whom the most famous were Amphitrite (q.v.) and Thetis (q.v.).

Nereus. An ancient and benevolent sea god, the son of Pontus (the sea) and Ge (q.v.). Husband of Doris, the daughter of Oceanus (q.v.) by whom he was father of the Nereids (q.v.).

Nero. See B44.

Nessus. See Deianeira.

Nestor. King of Pylos, only one of Neleus' (q.v.) twelve sons spared by Heracles. He participated in the Calydonian Boar (q.v.) hunt and the battle of Lapithae (q.v.) and Centaurs (q.v.). The oldest of the Greeks at Troy (q.v.) he was famous for his eloquence and wisdom. The father of Antilochus, a friend of Achilles (q.v.) and one of the bravest Greeks at Troy. Nestor was the only Greek to return home without mishap.

Nike. Goddess of Victory, not only in war but in musical and athletic competitions in Hesiod's Theogony, the daughter of the Titan Pallas and Styx. A minor deity, later envisaged not as one goddess but as several spirits, represented as young girls with wings who flew across the heavens to carry the crown to the victor. Zeus honoured Nike for helping the Olympian gods in the Titanomachia (q.v.). She was sometimes identified with Athene (q.v.).

Niobe. Daughter of Tantalus, sister of Pelops (q.v.) and wife of Amphion (q.v.) by whom she had seven sons and seven daughters (according to Ovid, Homer makes it six of each). She boasted of being

superior to Leto (q.v.) who only had two children and in revenge Apollo (q.v.) slew her sons and Artemis (q.v.) her daughters. She wept for nine days and nights and Zeus (q.v.) then turned her into a stone on Mt. Sipylus.

Nisus. See Minos.

Nomius. "The pasturer", a name given to Pan (q.v.), Apollo (q.v.) and Hermes (q.v.) in their roles as protectors of flocks and pastures.

Notus. The south-west wind, known to the Romans as Auster. The son of Astraeus (q.v.) and Eos (q.v.).

Numa. The name of two Italian warriors in the Aeneid.

Numa Pompilius. Legendary king of Rome. The second king, successor of Romulus (q.v.) he was said to have ruled between 717 and 673 B.C. Said to be of Sabine (q.v.) origin he reorganised Roman religion under the guidance of Egeria (q.v.). He was said to have been initiated into the mysteries of Pythagoras, an obvious anachronism as he predates Pythagoras' 6th century visit to Italy, but his reputed religious reforms signify a new strand in Roman religion, a disinterested search for knowledge as opposed to inspired action. He founded the cult of Janus (q.v.), organised the priests in collegia and established the flamens, and reorganised the Salii whose war dances in honour of Mars (q.v.) reflected a very ancient Italic rite. He also appointed the Pontifex Maximus, a high priest with responsibility for ensuring religious rites were properly performed and for preventing the growth of undesirable foreign cults. He also reformed the Roman calendar to achieve the maximum coincidence of lunar and solar cycles.

Numicius. A sacred river in Latium between Ardea and Lavinium.

Numitor. The grandfather of Romulus (q.v.) and Remus (q.v.).

Nymphae or **Nymphs.** Minor deities, the spirits of nature. These daughters of Zeus (q.v.) were semi-mortal and were generally benevolent, though they could be malevolent particularly to unresponsive lovers. Each was the tutelary deity of a rock, tree, cave or fountain and was better known to the local peasants than the great gods of Olympus (q.v.). Lavishly decorated monumental fountains (a "nymphaeum") were dedicated to the nymphs by both Greeks and Romans.

Nysa, Mt. Mountain in Libya where, according to tradition, Dionysus (q.v.) was raised.

O

Oceanides. Sea nymphs (q.v.) of the ocean, daughters of Oceanus (q.v.). Hesiod says they were 40 in number.

Oceanus. One of the Titans (q.v.), the son of Ge (q.v.) and Uranus (q.v.). The only Titan not to revolt against Uranus (q.v.). In Aeschylus' Prometheus Bound he preaches submission to the authority of Zeus (q.v.). He was seen originally as the river encircling the world from which all rivers and seas sprang. He is thus depicted as the rim on Achilles' (q.v.) shield. The husband of Tethys and by her father of, among others, Metis.

Odysseus. The hero of Homer's Odyssey, itself the model for James Joyce's Ulysses, Ulysses being the Roman name for him. The son of Laertes, king of Ithaca, and Anticleia, daughter of the wily thief Autolycus. However, one tradition makes him the son of Sisyphus (q.v.). He married Penelope (q.v.). Warned by an oracle not to go to Troy (q.v.) he feigned madness when the heralds arrived by sowing salt, but when Palamedes placed his son Telemachus (q.v.) before the plough he was forced to disclose his sanity and join the expedition. Later, at Troy, he avenged himself by having a letter signed in Priam's (q.v.) hand placed in Palamedes' tent. The letter was found and Palamedes was stoned to death. But Odysseus himself tricked Achilles (q.v.) into revealing his true identity and joining the expedition. At Troy Odysseus and Diomedes (q.v.) entered the city at night to kill Rhesus the Thracian and steal his white horses, because it was prophesied that if they drank of the Scamander (q.v.) Troy would not fall. He quarrelled with Ajax (q.v.) over the armour of Achilles and some say he killed him. He captured Helenus and from him learned the secret oracles which told how Troy would fall. In accordance with these he stole the Palladium of Athene (q.v.). It was also Odysseus who devised the stratagem of the Wooden Horse. When Troy fell he took Hecuba (q.v.) as a slave. His journey home lasted ten years and involved many adventures. He first went to Cicones to procure jars of sweet wine and then visited the Lotophagi (q.v.). After leaving them he landed in Sicily where he blinded Polyphemus the Cyclops (q.v.). Next he visited Aeolus (q.v.) and as a result was blown off course and lost all his ships save one at Telepylos. In this he reached Aeaea, land of Circe (q.v.) and on her advice sought the aid of Teiresias, a dead seer in the Underworld. In the land of the Cimmerians he summoned Teiresias' shade, and also those of his mother and former comrades, though Ajax (q.v.) held aloof. Then, with Circe's counsel he navigated the Scylla and Charybdis (q.v.) and neutralised the spell of the Sirens (q.v.) by blocking his crew's ears with wax but having himself tied to the mast that he might hear their song. At Thrinacia his men slaughtered the cattle of Helios (q.v.) and were punished by Zeus (q.v.), all but Odysseus dying in a subsequent shipwreck. He drifted to Ogygia on flotsam, where he spent eight years with the nymph Calypso (q.v.). On a raft he made land at Scheria, was found by Nausicaa (q.v.) and given a ship to Ithaca (q.v.). Here he was recognised by Eumaeus (q.v.) despite his disguise as a beggar. He found Laertes (q.v.) in the country and Penelope (q.v.) besieged by suitors. This drunken and unruly crew were headed by one Alcinous, their most persistent member. Penelope had kept them at bay by promising to marry one of them when she had finished weaving a robe for Laertes: a robe she unpicked each night. But betrayed by her servants she was now being forced to choose a husband. Meanwhile Telemachus (q.v.) who had sailed away to find Odysseus returned to find him with Laertes and they plotted revenge. Still dressed as a beggar Odysseus entered the palace and was recognised only by his nurse Eurycleia and his faithful hound Argus which died on seeing his long lost master. Penelope now announced she would marry the suitor who could fire Odysseus' bow. Only he was able to bend and string it. The suitors having failed Odysseus strung the bow and with Telemachus slew the suitors. The *Odyssey* ends when Athene (q.v.) reconciles the hero and the kinsmen of the suitors who were seeking revenge. Teiresias had prophesied that Odysseus had to set out on another journey to appease Poseidon (q.v.) for the blinding of his son Polyphemus and would then live to an old age until death came from the sea. One tradition tells how Telegonus, Odysseus' son by Circe came looking for his father, landed and began plundering for supplies. Odysseus and Telemachus gave battle and Telegonus killed Odysseus, not recognising his father. He also took Telemachus and Penelope to Aeaca where Circe married Telemachus and he himself married Penelope.

Odyssey. *See under* **Odysseus.**

Oedipus ("Swollen-foot"). The son of Laius, king of Thebes, and Jocasta (q.v.). The Delphic oracle said Laius would be killed by his son so he had the baby exposed on Mt. Cithaeron with a nail driven through its feet—hence "Oedipus". But he was found by a shepherd and raised by Polybus, king of Corinth, as his own son. As an adult Oedipus learned from the oracle that he would kill his own father and marry his own mother and believing himself the son of Polybus, left Corinth. He met Laius on the road and killed him in a quarrel. Laius had been on his way to Delphi to seek advice on ridding Thebes of the Sphinx (q.v.). This Oedipus did and was made king by the Thebans. He married Jocasta and they had four children, Eteocles (q.v.), Polynices (q.v.), Antigone (q.v.) and Ismene (q.v.). When Thebes suffered a plague because of their incest Oedipus contacted the seer Teiresias and learned whose son he was. When she heard the truth Jocasta hanged herself and Oedipus blinded himself with the pins from her dress. With Antigone and later Ismene he went into exile at the grove of the Eumenides (*see* **Erinnyes**) at Colonos in Attica. Here he was received by the gods, having first cursed the sons who had neglected him, saying they would divide their kingdom by the sword.

Oeneus. King of Pleuron and Calydon, husband of

Althaea and father of Tydeus (q.v.), Meleager (q.v.), Gorge and Deineira (q.v.). His realm was seized by his nephews but his grandson Diomedes (q.v.) avenged him and put Andraemon, husband of Gorge, on the throne. He accompanied Diomedes to the Peleponnesus where he was killed by two nephews who had escaped Diomedes. Deineira (q.v.) married Heracles (q.v.).

Oenomaus. A son of Ares (q.v.), king of Elis. An oracle said he would be killed by his son-in-law. Therefore he challenged all his daughter's suitors to a chariot race and if they won they would marry his daughter Hippodameia: if they lost they were put to death. His own chariot was drawn by wind-born horses, a gift from Ares. But he was murdered by Myrtilus at the instigation of Pelops (q.v.).

Oenone. A nymph who loved Paris (q.v.). He deserted her for Helen (q.v.) and when he was wounded by Philoctetes (q.v.) she refused to help him. Then, in remorse at his death, she committed suicide.

Oileus. One of the Argonauts (q.v.), and father of Ajax (q.v.).

Olympia. A small province in the western Peloponnesus, isolated from the centre and east of the Peloponnesus by high mountains. The site of a major sanctuary of Zeus (q.v.) whose worship replaced that of an early female divinity in the 9th century B.C. However, it was not till about 470 B.C. that a magnificent temple was built to Zeus. From 776 B.C. though, the Olympic games had been celebrated at Olympia in honour of Zeus. These quadrennial contests were international in character and an international truce accompanied their celebration. The prestige of the games was great and from 776 Greek chronology was based on the games, an "Olympiad" being a four-year cycle. Hence Olympiad 12, 1 denoted the 1st year in a four-year period after 11 previous Olympiads. If the number of Olympiads is multiplied by 4 and deducted from 776 we have our date *e.g.* 11 × 4 = 44, subtracted from 776 is 732 B.C.

Olympius. A term for any deity or muse inhabiting Olympus and not the Underworld.

Olympus Mt. The highest peak in Greece on the borders of Thessaly and Macedonia. Its 2975 m are almost inaccessible and it was not climbed until 1913. It was believed to be the home of the twelve Olympian gods.

Omphale. Queen of Lydia and widow of Tmolus who purchased Heracles (q.v.) as a slave. He served her for three years and one tradition says he dressed as a woman and swapped clothes with Omphale during this period.

Ops. Roman goddess of plenty, a consort of Saturn (q.v.) and the personification of abundance.

Orcus. The Roman name for Hades (q.v.) and for his realm.

Orestes. The son of Clytemnestra (q.v.) and Agamemnon (q.v.). As a child he was smuggled out of Mycenae by his sister Electra (q.v.) when Clytemnestra and Aegisthus (q.v.) seized power. He took refuge at the court of king Strophius in Phocis, becoming a close friend of Pylades (q.v.), the king's son. When of age he, Pylades and Electra killed Aegisthus and Clytemnestra, and Orestes was punished for his matricide by the Erinnyes (q.v.). He fled to the Acropolis of Athens and embraced the image of the goddess. Athene (q.v.) then summoned the Areopagus to judge his case. Apollo (q.v.), whose oracle had encouraged his crime, defended him on the grounds that fatherhood was more important than motherhood. Athene's casting vote found him innocent. Another tradition says Apollo told him he could be free of the Erinnyes by fetching the statue of Artemis (q.v.) from the Tauric Chersonese. Orestes and Pylades went to Tauris and were seized by the natives for sacrifice to Artemis. But it transpired that his sister Iphigenia (q.v.) was the priestess and she helped them steal the statue and return to Greece. They met Electra and went on to Mycenae where Orestes killed Aegisthus' son and became king. Later he slew his rival Neoptolemus (q.v.) and married his cousin Hermione.

Oreithyia. *See* **Boreas.** He turned her into a wind.

Orion. A giant, son of Poseidon (q.v.) who was a renowned hunter and very handsome. He loved Merope, daughter of Oenopion of Chios and was promised her hand in return for ridding Chios of wild animals. This he did but Oenopion would not give up Merope which led Orion to seduce her. Oenopion, with the help of his father Dionysus, blinded Orion who was told by the oracle he could only recover his sight by going to the east and gazing on the sun as it rose. This he did with the help of Hephaestus (*q.v.*) and once there Eos (*q.v.*) fell in love with him and Helios (*q.v.*) restored his sight. Later he joined Artemis (*q.v.*) in a hunt. Apollo (*q.v.*) angry at his boasting that he would kill all the wild beasts and afraid he would seduce Artemis contrived his death at the unwitting hands of Artemis. She placed his image in the stars, his constellation rising with the sun at the autumnal equinox.

Orpheus. The son of king Oeagrus of Thrace and Calliope (*q.v.*). The Greeks regarded him as the first great poet. He could enchant the beasts and trees with his lyre, a gift from Apollo (*q.v.*). After returning from the voyage of the Argonauts (*q.v.*) he married Eurydice (*q.v.*). His grief at losing her after redeeming her from Hades (*q.v.*) led to a failure to honour Dionysus (*q.v.*) at a Bacchanalia and he was torn to pieces by Bacchae (*q.v.*). The muses buried the pieces at the foot of Mt. Olympus (*q.v.*) save his head which was thrown into the River Hebrus still singing. The head and his lyre eventually floated to Lesbos (*q.v.*) and were finally placed amongst the stars at the request of Apollo and the Muses. *See also* **Orphism J38.**

Orthrus. A giant two-headed dog, the offspring of Typhon (*q.v.*) and Echidne (*q.v.*) and, some say, the father of the Sphinx (*q.v.*) and Chimaera (*q.v.*). It was set to watch the oxen of Geryon (*q.v.*) and was slain by Heracles (*q.v.*).

Ortygia (1) Port of Syracuse in Sicily.

(2) Port of Delos (*q.v.*), birthplace of Artemis (*q.v.*).

Otus and **Ephialtes.** Twin sons of Iphimedeia and Poseidon (*q.v.*), named Aloeidae after their mother's later husband Aloeus. At an early age they imprisoned Ares (*q.v.*) and later swore to rape Hera (*q.v.*) and Artemis (*q.v.*). In a vain effort to achieve this they placed Mt. Pelion on top of Mt. Ossa and attacked Heaven. But Artemis induced them to seek her at Naxos. Here she leapt between them in the form of a doe and they accidentally slew each other. In Tartarus (*q.v.*) their shades were tied back to back by bonds of vipers.

Ovid. *See* **B46.**

P

Palaemon. A sea god, the son of Athamas and Ino who was originally named Melicertes.

Palamedes. *See* **Odysseus.**

Pales. Italic deity of flocks and herds, worshipped on the Palatine.

Palicus. An obscure god or hero worshipped in Sicily and mentioned in the *Aeneid* (*q.v.*).

Palinurus. "Wind Astern", the helmsman of Aeneas. He managed the ship between the Scylla and Charybdis (*q.v.*) and in the storm off the coast of Carthage but later fell asleep and into the sea. He was cast ashore but murdered by local tribesmen. His shade begged Aeneas for carriage across the Styx (*q.v.*) so it could be at rest, but the Sibyl refused as he had not been properly buried. However she promised him a shrine, Capo Pulinuro in Lucania near modern Salerno.

Palladium. A mythical statue of Athene given to Dardanus (*q.v.*) by Zeus (*q.v.*) to ensure the protection of Troy. By one tradition it was stolen by Odysseus (*q.v.*) and Diomedes (*q.v.*). By another Aeneas (*q.v.*) saved it and brought it to Rome where it saved the city several times in its early years.

Pallas. (1) A title of Athene (*q.v.*) given to her by the Achaens. Pallas, Kore and Parthenos signify a virgin, maiden or girl.

(2) One of the 24 Giants (*q.v.*) who rebelled against Zeus (*q.v.*).

(3) A brother of Aegeus (*q.v.*). *See also* **Theseus.**

(4) An ancestor of Evander (*q.v.*).

(5) Evander's son who went to follow Aeneas (*q.v.*).

Pan. A god, half-man, half-goat, said by some to be a son of Zeus (*q.v.*) by others to be the son of Hermes (*q.v.*) and Penelope with whom he inhabited Arcadia. He was a patron of shepherds and herdsmen and a lover of mischief. When not frolicking with the nymphs he liked to startle peasants and flocks inspiring "panic". He loved and

pursued Syrinx whose flight from him resulted in her being transformed into a reed from which he made a seven-piped flute, the syrinx. He also seduced Selene (*q.v.*). Sometimes identified with the Roman Faunus (*q.v.*).

Pandarus. A Trojan archer who broke a truce by shooting at the Greeks. In Chaucer's *Troilus and Criseyde* and Shakespeare's *Troilus and Cressida* he is Cressida's uncle and the lovers' go-between. The word "pandar" is derived from his name for this reason.

Pandora. "All gifts", the first woman fashioned and given life by Hephaestus (*q.v.*) and Athene (*q.v.*). Zeus (*q.v.*) sent her to punish man after Prometheus (*q.v.*) had given him fire. She married the brother of Prometheus, Epimetheus. Her curiosity led her to open a box which it was forbidden to touch, and from it sprang all the evils and diseases which beset mankind. Only hope was left at the bottom of the box.

Parcae. The Roman equivalent of the "Fates" or Horae.

Paris. Son of Priam (*q.v.*) and Hecuba (*q.v.*) who dreamed during her pregnancy that she would bring forth a blazing firebrand. As a child he was exposed on Mt. Ida. Raised by shepherds he was named Paris or sometimes Alexander ("defender of men") because of his courage. He loved and deserted Oenone (*q.v.*) which eventually caused his death. Promised the fairest of women by Aphrodite (*q.v.*) if he gave her the apple of discord, he did as she bade. Reunited with his parents he then left for Sparta whence he seduced Helen (*q.v.*) thus starting the Trojan War. At one point in the war Aphrodite saved him from death in a duel with Menelaus. He shot the arrow which slew Achilles (*q.v.*) at the Scaean Gate but was himself mortally wounded by Philoctetes (*q.v.*).

Parnassus, Mt. 2461 m peak in the Pindus range, north-east of Delphi (*q.v.*). Home of Apollo (*q.v.*) and the Muses (*q.v.*) hence the name "Montparnasse" for the hill in Paris on which centred the university and cultural life of that city. On the original's slopes was also the Corycian Cave, a centre of the Bacchae (*q.v.*).

Parthenon. *See* **L94.**

Parthenope. A nymph whose body was said to have washed up at Neapolis (Naples) around 600 B.C. She gave her name to the short-lived Parthenopean Republic of Naples established by Napoleon in 1799.

Parthenopeus. *See* **Seven Against Thebes.**

Parthenos. *See* **Pallas.**

Pasiphaë. Daughter of Helios (*q.v.*) and Persë, and wife of Minos (*q.v.*). Mother of the Minotaur (*q.v.*) by the Cretan Bull (*q.v.*) and of many children, including Ariadne (*q.v.*), Glaucus and Phaedra, by Minos.

Patroclus. Cousin and bosom companion of Achilles (*q.v.*) whom he met at the court of Peleus (*q.v.*) while in exile for an accidental murder. Slain by Hector (*q.v.*) while wearing Achilles' armour, his death persuaded Achilles to re-enter the Trojan War.

Pausanias. Spartan king who intervened to moderate Lysander's arrogant attitude towards Athens and other Greek cities after the Peloponnesian War.

Pegasus. Winged horse, offspring of Poseidon (*q.v.*) and Medusa (*q.v.*). It was captured by Bellerophon (*q.v.*) at the fountain of Pirene and helped him slay the Chimaera (*q.v.*). It struck Mt. Helicon with its hoof and brought forth the spring of Hippocrene, sacred to the Muses.

Peleus. The son of Aeacus, king of Aegina. With his brother Telamon he killed their half-brother Phocus and the two were expelled to Phthia in Thessaly by Aeacus. Here Eurytion purified them of murder. They took part in the Calydonian Hunt when they accidentally killed Eurytion. They then fled to the court of Acastus (*q.v.*) of Iolcis. Zeus (*q.v.*) married him to Thetis (*q.v.*) though he himself loved Thetis. This was because the oracle foretold that her son would be greater than his father. Their son was Achilles (*q.v.*). All the gods save Eris (*q.v.*) were invited to the wedding and in revenge she cast the Apple of Discord. Peleus later ruled the Myrmidones at Phthia.

Pelias. *See* **Jason.**

Pelicles. Son of Peleus *i.e.* Achilles (*q.v.*).

Peloponnesus. The "island of Pelops" (*q.v.*), the large southern peninsular of mainland Greece, attached to northern Greece by the Corinthian isthmus.

Pelops. Son of Tantalus (*q.v.*) king of Lydia. Tantalus cut him in pieces and served him to the gods at a meal. Only Demeter (*q.v.*) grieving for Persephone (*q.v.*) did not realise and she ate Pelops' shoulder. Zeus (*q.v.*) restored him to life by having Hermes (*q.v.*) boil him in a pot. Demeter gave him an ivory shoulder, said to be the birthmark of his descendants. His shoulder blade was later taken to Troy (*q.v.*) by the Greeks as the oracle said this was necessary if the city were to fall. He married Hippodamia.

Pelorus. One of the Sparti (*q.v.*).

Penates. Roman deities of the home, confused from early times with the *genius* and the Lares. Eventually a wide variety of deities, *e.g.* Mars, Mercury, Venus, were regarded as "*di Penates*" that is, "guardians of the hearth".

Penelope. The wife of Odysseus (*q.v.*), usually seen as a symbol of fidelity. One tradition in the Peloponnesus made her adulterous and the mother of Pan (*q.v.*) by Hermes (*q.v.*) or by all of her many suitors.

Peneus. The son of Oceanus (*q.v.*) and Tethys. A river god and father of Daphne (*q.v.*) and Cyrene (*q.v.*). Identified with the River Peneus in Thessaly.

Penthesilea. Daughter of Otrere and Ares (*q.v.*), queen of the Amazons (*q.v.*) who helped the Trojans. Slain by Achilles (*q.v.*) they fell in love as she died and he later mourned her. When the wretched Thersites mocked his grief Achilles slew him which caused his kinsman Diomedes (*q.v.*) to throw her corpse into the Scamander. It was retrieved and honourably buried.

Pentheus. Grandson of Cadmus (*q.v.*) and king of Thebes. The subject of Euripedes' *Bacchae*. He refused to allow Dionysus (*q.v.*) into the city but the god, in disguise, persuaded him to dress as one of the Bacchae (*q.v.*) and watch their orgies. He was then torn to pieces by the Bacchae, led by his own mother who was in a trance.

Perdix (or **Talos**). See **Daedalus**.

Periclymenus. The son of Neleus (*q.v.*) and brother of Nestor (*q.v.*). An Argonaut (*q.v.*) he could assume any form he chose. Slain by Heracles (*q.v.*).

Periphetes. A giant residing at Epidaurus who murdered travellers with an iron club. Slain by Theseus (*q.v.*) who henceforth carried his club.

Perse. The daughter of Oceanus (*q.v.*). Wife of Helios (*q.v.*) to whom she bore Circe (*q.v.*), Pasiphaë (*q.v.*), Aeetes and Perses (*q.v.*).

Persephone. Daughter of Zeus (*q.v.*) and Demeter (*q.v.*). She spent the winter months with Hades (*q.v.*) when nothing grew and with Demeter she spent the fertile months. Thus she was a goddess of vegetation. She was also queen of the Underworld and was a symbol of death. Known to the Romans as Proserpina. Her companion in the Underworld was Hecate (*q.v.*).

Perses. The son of Helios (*q.v.*) and Perse (*q.v.*) father of Hecate (*q.v.*).

Perseus. Grandson of Acrisius (*q.v.*) king of Argos and the son of Zeus (*q.v.*) and Danae (*q.v.*). Raised at the court of Polydectes who sent him to fetch the head of Medusa (*q.v.*). Hermes (*q.v.*) gave him a sickle with which to do this and told him how, via the Graeae (*q.v.*) he could procure Hades' (*q.v.*) helmet of invisibility, winged sandals and a magic wallet to help him in the task. Once he had the head he petrified the Titan Atlas (*q.v.*) with it. He then flew to Aethiopia where he found Andromeda (*see* **Cassiopeia**). Returning to Seriphos he slew Polydectes, made Dictys (*q.v.*) king and returned to Argos. He later exchanged the kingdom of Argos for that of his cousin Megaperthes of Tiryns.

Phaebus ("Shining"). A name used for Apollo (*q.v.*) at Delos (*q.v.*) where he was associated with Artemis (*q.v.*).

Phaedra. The daughter of Minos (*q.v.*) and wife of Theseus (*q.v.*) to whom she bore Acamas and Demephon. *See also* **Hippolytus**.

Phaeton. The son of Helios (*q.v.*) and Clymene. Helios let him drive the chariot of the sun across the sky but he lost control of it and was killed by a thunderbolt from Zeus (*q.v.*) for almost setting the world on fire. He fell into the River Po and his sisters who mourned him were turned into poplar or alder trees and their tears into amber.

Phalanthus. Mythical founder of Tarentum in Italy.

Phaon. See **Sappho**.

Philemon. The husband of Baucis. This old Phrygian couple once received Zeus (*q.v.*) and Hermes (*q.v.*) with great hospitality.

Philoctetes. The son of Poecas, nephew of Protesilaus, and companion of Heracles (*q.v.*). He lit Heracles funeral pyre and received his bow and arrows. On the way to Troy (*q.v.*) one of the poisoned arrows wounded him, or he was bitten

by a snake on the island of Tenedos. The smell of the wound became so offensive that on the advice of Odysseus (*q.v.*) he was left on Lemnos. Later an oracle revealed that Troy would not fall till the bow and arrows of Heracles were brought to the Greeks and Odysseus and Diomedes (*q.v.*) fetched him to Troy. Here either Machaon or Podalirius, the sons of Asclepius (*q.v.*) cured him of his wound. He slew Paris (*q.v.*) and later settled in Italy.

Philomela. See **Procne**.

Phineus. King of Salmydessus in Thrace and the son of Agenor. He first married Cleopatra, then Idaca who falsely accused her stepsons of improper advances. Phineus imprisoned them and was made blind and pursued by the Harpies (*q.v.*). Eventually the Argonauts (*q.v.*) whose ranks included Zetes and Calais, Cleopatra's brothers, slew the Harpies. Phineus freed the stepsons and told Jason (*q.v.*) what course to set.

Phlegethon ("Blazing"). A river of the Underworld called the "river of flames" by Plato. The shades of those who had committed crimes of violence against their kin were roasted in it until they received forgiveness.

Phlegyas. A king of the Lapithae (*q.v.*) who burnt Apollo's (*q.v.*) shrine at Delphi and was punished for it in the Underworld by having to sit beneath a huge rock which was liable to fall at any time.

Phocis. Small mountainous province of northern Greece which held the oracle of Delphi.

Phocus. See **Peleus**.

Phoebe ("Bright"). In early myth the daughter of Heaven and Earth and mother of Leto (*q.v.*). Later identified with Artemis(*q.v.*) the moon-goddess.

Phoenix ("Red"). (1) Companion and tutor of Achilles (*q.v.*) who tried to reconcile him with Agamemnon (*q.v.*).
(2) The brother of Cadmus (*q.v.*) and Europa (*q.v.*), eponymous ancestor of the Phoenicians.
(3) A mythological Egyptian bird which died on a funeral pyre every 500 years before rising again from the ashes.

Phorcys. A sea-god, the father of Echidne (*q.v.*), Ladon, the Gorgons (*q.v.*) and the Graeae (*q.v.*).

Phrixus and Helle. Brother and sister, the children of Athamas king of Aeolia. Their stepmother, Ino (*q.v.*), had engineered their sacrifice by Athamas out of jealousy but they escaped on a flying ram with a golden fleece sent by Zeus (*q.v.*). Helle fell off into what was henceforth the Hellespont, but Phrixus reached Colchis and sacrificed the ram to Zeus (*see* **Jason**). The ram's image was placed amongst the stars as Aries.

Phyllis. See **Demophon**.

Picus. An ancient Italian god represented as a woodpecker *i.e.* '*picus*'.

Pierides. A name applied to the Muses (*q.v.*). It was derived from the inhabitants of Pieria, on the south coast of Macedonia, who were noted for their worship of the Muses.
Also a name for nine daughters of Pierus king of Macedonia who were defeated in a contest by the Muses and turned into birds.

Pillars of Hercules. Two pillars, Calpe and Abyla, erected on either side of the straits of Gibraltar by Heracles (*q.v.*).

Pilumnus. An ancient minor Italian god, "the spearman".

Pindar. See **B48**.

Pirithous. Son of Ixion (*q.v.*) and Dia, companion of Theseus (*q.v.*) and king of the Lapithae (*q.v.*). He led the fight on the Centaurs (*q.v.*). On the death of his wife Hippodamia he and Theseus abducted the young Helen (*q.v.*) of Troy. She fell by lot to Theseus who, in return and despite misgivings, promised to help Pirithous abduct a daughter of Zeus (*q.v.*) for himself. They attempted to abduct Persephone (*q.v.*) from the Underworld but Hades (*q.v.*) chained them to a rock. Heracles (*q.v.*) later freed Theseus but Pirithous was left to suffer torment for his sins.

Pleiades. The seven daughters of Atlas (*q.v.*) and Pleione and companions of Artemis (*q.v.*). Zeus (*q.v.*) turned them into doves and placed their image in the stars to save them from the attentions of Orion (*q.v.*) who pursued them for five years. A group of seven poets in 3rd century B.C. Alexandria also called themselves the Pleiad.

Plutarch. See **B48**.

Pluto. (1) A Roman name for Hades (*q.v.*), "the rich one" who owns the riches of the earth itself.

(2) A nymph who was mother of Tantalus (*q.v.*) by Zeus (*q.v.*).

Podarces. (1) *See* **Priam.**

(2) Son of Iphiclus, leader of the Thessalians who fought at Troy (*q.v.*).

Polites. A son of Priam (*q.v.*) and Hecabe (*q.v.*), slain before their eyes by Neoptolemus (*q.v.*).

Pollux. The Roman name for Polydeuces. *See* **Castor.**

Polydeuces. *See* **Castor.**

Polydorus. (1) The son of Cadmus (*q.v.*) and Harmonia and ancestor of Oedipus (*q.v.*) and other great Theban kings.

(2) The youngest son of Priam (*q.v.*) and Hecabe (*q.v.*).

Polymnia. *See* **Muses.**

Polynices. The son of Jocasta and Oedipus (*q.v.*), brother of Eteocles (*q.v.*), Antigone (*q.v.*) and Ismene (*q.v.*). *See also* **Seven Against Thebes.** When Creon refused to allow his burial Antigone (*q.v.*) disregarded the order and buried the corpse.

Polypemon. Also known as Procrustes, 'the stretcher'. A robber who tied travellers to a bed and if they were too tall he cut off their legs; if too short he put them on a rack. Theseus (*q.v.*) did the same to him.

Polyphemus. *See* **Cyclopes and Galatea.**

Polyxena. The daughter of Priam (*q.v.*) and Hecuba (*q.v.*) beloved by Achilles (*q.v.*) whose shade requested her sacrifice by Neoptolemus (*q.v.*) after Troy's (*q.v.*) fall. This is the theme of Euripides' *Hecabe*.

Pomona. An Italian goddess of tree-fruits (*poma*) *e.g.* apples. She was a minor deity but had her own priest and sanctuary near Rome. Ovid links her with Vertumnus, an Etruscan god with the power to change his shape. He was god of the changing seasons and the ripening fruits of autumn, and also of money changing. *Vertere* means "change" in Latin. He loved Pomona and pursued her disguised as a harvester, vine-dresser, herdsman and old woman, but only won her when he appeared as himself. His statue stood in the Vicus Tuscus, a busy street of brothels and shops named after him as an Etruscan.

Pontus. The sea, offspring of Ge (*q.v.*) the earth.

Pontus Euxinus. The "Hospitable Sea", the Greek name for the Black Sea. The name was an attempt to flatter and placate a hostile sea which was much feared by sailors.

Porphyrion. *See* **Giants.**

Porsenna. *See* **Lars Porsenna.**

Portunus. A Roman sea-deity associated with harbours.

Poseidon. The Roman N Ntune, a god of earthquakes, and later of the sea. The eldest son of Cronus (*q.v.*) and Rhea. When he and Zeus (*q.v.*) and Hades (*q.v.*) cast lots for their realms he won the sea and had an underwater palace near Aegae in Euboea. Here he kept horses with brazen hoofs and gold manes who drew his chariot across the sea. Its passage calmed the sea. Poseidon created the horse and invented the bridle. As a horse he raped Demeter (*q.v.*) who was disguised as a mare. Their offspring was the horse Arion and the nymph Despoena and, some say, Persephone (*q.v.*). He resented Zeus (*q.v.*) and helped Hera (*q.v.*) and Apollo (*q.v.*) enchain him. In punishment Zeus made him a servant of Laomedon (*q.v.*) and he built the Neptunilia Pergama, the walls of Troy. He helped the Greeks at Troy but baited Odysseus (*q.v.*) who blinded Polyphemus (*q.v.*). He disputed the possession of Athens with Athene (*q.v.*) and lost, but Zeus gave him the Isthmus of Corinth instead. Here the Isthmian games were held in his honour. He married Amphitrite (*q.v.*). By mortal women he had many children including Pegasus (*q.v.*) and the Aloeidae (*q.v.*). He is usually portrayed with a trident which he used to shake the earth.

Priam. The son of Laomedon (*q.v.*) and husband of Hecuba (*q.v.*). Originally called Podarces his name was changed to Priam *i.e.* "ransomed" because Heracles (*q.v.*) spared him and sold him to Hesione (*q.v.*) his sister. He had fifty sons and fifty daughters, nineteen of whom were by Hecuba and included Hector (*q.v.*), Paris (*q.v.*), Helenus (*q.v.*) and Cassandra (*q.v.*). He begged Achilles (*q.v.*) to return Hector's body. Eventually slain at the altar of Zeus (*q.v.*) by Neoptolemus (*q.v.*).

Priapus. The son of Dionysus (*q.v.*) and Aphrodite (*q.v.*). A fertility god whose worship spread from the Hellespont to Greece and later Rome, though he was never taken seriously. He was often portrayed in the form of a red-faced scarecrow with a large detachable phallus and in this role was used to scare birds. The phallus became a truncheon to ward off other intruders. He was also a protector of cultivated gardens and a god of sailors. In Petronius' *Satyricon* he pursues the hero Encolpius and makes him impotent. Horace and Martial write of him lightheartedly and 85 obscene poems about him – '*priapeia*' – exist of unknown authorship. His sacrificial animal was the donkey, a symbol of lust.

Procne. The daughter of Pandion, king of Athens. Pandion gave her to Tereus in return for his assistance and they had a son Itys. But Tereus wanted her sister Philomela. He made Procne a slave and tore out her tongue, then seduced Philomela saying Procne was dead. Procne could only alert her sister and be free by stitching a message to her robe. Once free she slew Itys, cooked pieces of the corpse and fed it to Tereus. When Tereus learnt what had happened he chased the sisters with an axe but the gods turned him into a hawk, Procne into a swallow and Philomela a nightingale though some traditions say it was Philomela who lost her tongue and became a swallow.

Procris. Daughter of Erectheus of Athens and the wife of Cephalus. Eos (*q.v.*) who also loved Cephalus showed him that Procris was easily seduced in return for gold. Procris then fled to Crete and lived for a time with Minos (*q.v.*). On returning to Athens disguised as a youth she brought with her a hound and spear, gifts from Artemis (*q.v.*), which never missed their quarry. Cephalus so wanted the gifts that the couple were reconciled. But Procris suspected Cephalus of having an affair with Eos and followed him on a hunt where he accidentally killed her with the spear.

Procrustes. *See* **Polypemon.**

Proetus. The son of Abas (*q.v.*) king of Argolis. His twin brother Acrisius (*q.v.*) expelled him and he fled to Lydia where he married Anteia (also called Stheneboea) daughter of king Iobates (*see* **Bellerophon**). He later returned to Argolis and forced Acrisius to give him half the kingdom. He ruled from Tiryns whose huge walls he built with the aid of the Cyclopes (*q.v.*). Eventually gave two thirds of his kingdom to Melampus (*q.v.*) and Bias.

Prometheus. A Titan (*q.v.*) and the brother of Epimetheus (*q.v.*) or "afterthought" and Atlas (*q.v.*). Sometimes said to be the maker of mankind. He supported Zeus (*q.v.*) against his brother Titans but stole fire from Olympus and gave it to men. This angered Zeus who took revenge on man through Pandora (*q.v.*) and punished Prometheus by chaining him to a rock in the Caucasus. Here an eagle tore at his liver each day. The liver was renewed daily and Prometheus suffered this torment until Heracles (*q.v.*) rescued him.

Proserpina. Roman counterpart of Persephone (*q.v.*).

Proteus. A sea god and a subject of Poseidon (*q.v.*). He had the power of prophecy and could change his form. He would avoid prophecy by changing form until tightly gripped; then he appeared in his true shape and spoke the truth. Said to live on the isle of Pharos in the Nile Delta. Menelaus (*q.v.*) mastered him while returning from Troy (*q.v.*) and forced him to reveal the way to Sparta.

Psyche. In Greek literature, the "soul" personified, often portrayed as a butterfly. As the centre of emotion she was tormented by "*eros*". Her beauty made Aphrodite (*q.v.*) jealous and she sent Eros (*q.v.*) to torment her. Instead he fell in love with her though he would not let her see him or disclose his identity. But at the bidding of her two sisters she sought to discover who he was. For the first time she saw him, holding a candle above him as he slept, but hot wax fell on him. He woke and left her to seek him. After many trials she found him, became immortal and was united with Eros for ever.

Pygmalion. (1) The king of Tyre and brother of Dido (*q.v.*).

(2) The king of Cyprus who made and fell in love with a maiden's statue. Aphrodite (*q.v.*) answered his prayers and gave the statue life as the girl Galatea. They married and had two sons, Paphus and Metharme. In some versions of the tale he is a sculptor. The basis of Shaw's *Pygmalion* and the musical *My Fair Lady*.

Pylades. Husband of Electra (*q.v.*). *See also* **Orestes.**

Pyramus and Thisbe. The lovers in a tale by Ovid which he heard in the East. Living in Babylon they are forbidden to meet but converse through a chink in a wall. They arrange a meeting at the tomb of Ninus but Thisbe, arriving first, was chased away by a lion and dropped her veil. Finding this, Pyramus thought her dead and committed suicide. She returned and slew herself on his sword. Since that time the nearby mulberry has borne fruit the colour of blood. This is the basis of Bottom's tale in Shakespeare's *A Midsummer Night's Dream*.

Pyrrhus. Another name for Neoptolemus.

Pythia. The priestess of Apollo (*q.v.*) at Delphi (*q.v.*).

Python. A she-dragon of Mt. Parnassus who controlled the oracle at Delphi (*q.v.*). The boy Apollo (*q.v.*) slew her and the Pythia (*q.v.*) took over her task of giving voice to oracles.

Q

Quirinus. A very ancient Roman deity whose cult was centred on the Quirinal. The Romans eventually forgot his original character and he was identified with Mars (*q.v.*) in classical times, though Romulus (*q.v.*) was also supposed to have adopted the name after his deification.

R

Rape of the Sabine Women. An episode recounted by Livy and Ovid to explain the intermarriage of the Roman settlers and natives. Romulus (*q.v.*) and his followers invited the surrounding tribes to celebrate a festival in the Circus Maximus then carried off the native girls. War broke out but the Sabine women, who had been well treated, intervened to restore peace. The event has been the subject of paintings by Poussin and Rubens and of a group of statues by Giovanni da Bologna.

Remus. *See* **Romulus.**

Rhadamanthus. The son of Zeus (*q.v.*) and Europa (*q.v.*), brother of Minos (*q.v.*) and Sarpedon (*q.v.*). Once the ruler of part of Crete but Minos forced him to flee to Boeotia (*q.v.*). Famed for his wisdom and justice he was made one of the judges of the Underworld after his death. He married Alcmene (*q.v.*) on the death of Amphitrion (*q.v.*).

Rhea. (1) A Titaness, daughter of Ge (*q.v.*) and Uranus (*q.v.*). *See* **Cronus.**

(2) *See* **Romulus.**

Rhesus. A Thracian king who helped the Trojans. An oracle said that if his magnificent snow-white horses ate the grass of the Trojan plain and drank of the River Scamander Troy would not fall. Diomedes (*q.v.*) and Odysseus (*q.v.*) raided his camp, slew him, and stole the horses.

Rhodos/Rhode. The daughter of Poseidon (*q.v.*), wife of Helios (*q.v.*).

Rome. The "eternal city" sited on the banks of the Tiber. Traditionally founded in 753 B.C. (year 1 of the Roman calendar) by Romulus (*q.v.*). It only really became a city in the 6th century under the Tarquins. Under the Republic it had a population of two or three hundred thousand, of 450,000 by the time of Augustus and 1,000,000 under the Antonines, though the population was occasionally reduced by wars, fires and plagues.

Romulus. The legendary founder of Rome (*q.v.*), twin brother of Remus and together the sons of Rhea or Rhea Silvia. She was the daughter of Numitor, king of Alba Longa (*q.v.*) who was deposed by his brother. Her uncle compelled her to become a Vestal Virgin (*q.v.*) but she bore Romulus and Remus, according to her, by Mars (*q.v.*). Her uncle then imprisoned her and threw the babies into the Tiber. The shepherd Faustulus (*q.v.*) found a wolf suckling them and reared them. When they reached manhood they returned to Alba Longa, restored Numitor to the throne and set off to found a city of their own. They went to the site of Rome and decided to consult the gods. Romulus chose the Palatine Hill, his childhood home, as the centre of the city, Remus the Aventine (*q.v.*). The gods favoured Romulus, sending him an extraordinary omen of twelve vultures, Remus only six. Thus Romulus was given the honour of founding Rome which he did by ploughing a furrow around the Palatine. As he commenced building the city wall Remus derisively jumped over it, a quarrel ensued and Romulus slew him. Romulus took in fugitives in order to populate the city, found them wives by the "Rape of the Sabine women" (*q.v.*) and reigned for forty years before disappearing in a whirlwind on the Campus Martius. He was deified and identified with the Sabine god Quirinus (*q.v.*).

Rubicon. *See* **L107.**

S

Sabines. A branch of the Samnite race and one of the Sabellian peoples who occupied the Etruscanised area on the middle valley of the Tiber around Falerii. To the south of Rome they held the mountainous land between Rome and Campania. They were a constant threat to early Rome and the tradition that one Titus Tatius, a Sabine prince, was offered joint rule by Romulus (*q.v.*) may indicate a period of Sabine occupation or domination of Rome.

Sabinus. A mythical Sabine king.

Salmoneus. The son of Aeolus (*q.v.*) and brother of Sisyphus (*q.v.*). The founder of Salmone. His pride led him to emulate the thunder and lightning of Zeus (*q.v.*) who slew him and crushed his city with a thunderbolt.

Sarpedon. The son of Zeus (*q.v.*) and Europa (*q.v.*), brother of Minos (*q.v.*) and Rhadamanthus (*q.v.*). The three brothers quarrelled over the love of the youth Miletus (*q.v.*). Sarpedon went to Asia Minor and became king of the Lycians after helping king Cilix of Cilicia defeat them. Zeus allowed him to live three generations and he helped Troy (*q.v.*) in the Trojan war. Patroclus (*q.v.*) slew him.

Saturn. From *Satus i.e.* "sown". Ancient Mediterranean god of agriculture, possibly of Ligurian origin and particularly revered in Sardinia (*q.v.*) and Africa (*q.v.*). Later identified with Cronus (*q.v.*) who supposedly emigrated to Italy after being deposed by Zeus (*q.v.*). Here he presided over a mythical "Golden Age". His temple in Rome was consecrated in 497 B.C. and housed the state treasury. His festival, the Saturnalia, was celebrated near the winter solstice, originally on 17 December but from the 4th century A.D. on New Year's Day. During the celebrations complete licence was given, slaves took the place of their masters, presents were given, a "Lord of Misrule" appointed and merrymaking and disorder of every kind was rife. It may be that in primitive times his worship involved the sacrifice of humans because in classical times rush dummies in human shape (*argei*) were flung into the Tiber each year on 15 May in his honour.

Satyrs. Young spirits of wildlife, the woods and hillsides. Sons of Hermes (*q.v.*) closely associated with Dionysus (*q.v.*). They were possessed by lechery and a love of wine and embodied the fertile force of nature. Usually they were personified with pointed ears, horns and a tail like Pan's (*q.v.*).

Scaean Gate. The "left hand", the gate in the walls of Troy (*q.v.*) where Achilles (*q.v.*) fell.

Scamander, River. River in Asia Minor near Troy (*q.v.*), originally called the Xanthus. Its name was changed when the mythical Scamander (*q.v.*) of Crete founded a colony in Phrygia and jumped into the river.

Scamander. One-time king of Crete, father of Teucer (*q.v.*) by the nymph Idaea and therefore an ancestor of the Trojans.

Sciron. A robber who dwelt on the border of Attica and Megara. He preyed on travellers and forced them to wash his feet on the Scironian rock. He then kicked them off the rock into the sea to be eaten by a giant turtle. Theseus (*q.v.*) slew him.

Scylla. (1) *See* **Minos.**

(2) *See* **Charybdis.**

Scyrus. Aegean isle, half-way between Lesbos and Euboea and off the major trade routes. It was of no importance save in legend: here Achilles (*q.v.*) was hidden by Lycomedes. It was also here that Lycomedes threw Theseus (*q.v.*) from a rock while the hero was in voluntary exile from Athens after giving the city its first constitution. In 470 B.C. Cimon expelled the local populace in order to install Athenian colonists. At the same time he found the reputed body of Theseus and took it back to Athens amidst great pomp.

Selene. Eastern goddess whom the Greeks identified with Artemis (q.v.) and the Romans with Diana (q.v.) or the older moon goddess Luna. Both also identified her with Hecate (q.v.) and thus the moon became associated with sorcery.

Semele. See **Dionysus**.

Semiramis. The wife of Ninus. These two were the mythical founders of Ninus or Nineveh.

Seven Against Thebes. Oedipus (q.v.) cursed his sons for neglecting him, saying they would divide their kingdom by the sword. To avoid this Eteocles and Polynices agreed to rule in turn but Eteocles then refused to give up the throne when his term expired. Polynices sought the help of Adrastus (q.v.) king of Argos and married his daughter Argia while her sister married Tydeus son of Oeneus of Calydon who was in exile because of a murder he had committed. Amphiaraus the seer (brother-in-law of Adrastus) prophesied death for all who marched on Thebes save Adrastus. But on the advice of Tydeus, Polynices bribed Eriphyle into persuading Amphiaraus to join them. These four were joined by Capaneus, Hippomedon and Parthenopaeus. The seven were initially successful but Teiresias (q.v.) prophesied that a Theban royal prince must sacrifice himself to save the city and Menoeceus did so. The fortunes of the seven now waned. Zeus (q.v.) killed Capaneus with a thunderbolt as he stormed the city walls. Tydeus was wounded by Melanippus but Athene (q.v.) intended to save him with an elixir from Zeus. But Amphiaraus, who had a grudge against him, persuaded him to drink the brains of Melanippus which so disgusted Athene she let him die. Hippomedon and Parthenopaeus were also slain. Polynices now fought a duel with Eteocles to settle the matter and both were mortally wounded. Amphiaraus was swallowed up by the earth and only Adrastus survived. See also **Antigone** and **Epigoni**.

Seven Hills of Rome. The Quirinal, Viminal, Esquiline, Caelian, Capitoline, Palatine and Aventine.

Seven Kings of Rome. Traditionally said to be Romulus, Numa Pompilius, Tullus Hostilius, Ancus Martius, Tarquinius Priscus, Servius Tullius and Tarquinius Superbus.

Seven Sages of Greece. Usually held to be Thales of Miletus, Bias of Priene, Solon, Chilo of Sparta who brought the bones of Orestes (q.v.) to Sparta, Periander of Corinth, Pittacus of Mytilene, a democrat, contemporary of Solon and opponent of Alcaeus, and Cleobulus of Rhodes.

Sibyl (Sibylla). A priestess and prophetess who uttered oracles. Localised in several places the term came to be used generically of many sibyls and Varro lists ten. The most famous was at Cumae in Campania and she told Aeneas (q.v.) how to enter the Underworld. Ovid says she was seven generations old when Aeneas met her and that Apollo (q.v.) had granted her request to live as many years as there were grains in a handful of sand. But she had forgotten to seek eternal youth and was now withered with age. In Petronius' *Satyricon* she hangs in a bottle and when asked what she wants replies "I want to die".

Sibylline Books. A Roman tradition tells how a sibyl (q.v.) offered Tarquinius Priscus nine prophetic books which he refused to buy at the price. She destroyed three and he still refused them; she burnt three more and he took the remaining three at the price demanded for the nine. Special priests kept them and they were consulted only when the Senate authorised it in time of need. In 83 B.C. the originals were destroyed by fire but replaced by new ones. Many later additions were made including Jewish and Christian forgeries and fourteen still exist. They were last consulted in the 4th century A.D. and shortly afterwards Stilicho had them burnt. The original books instructed the Romans to convey the sacred stone of Cybele to Rome.

Sigeum. Part of Troy (q.v.). Hence the Dardanelles were known as the "straits of Sigeum".

Sileni, Silenus. Scholars distinguish between *sileni* and satyrs (q.v.) but the two are very similar and the Greeks themselves seem to have made no distinction. They are regarded as companions of Dionysus (q.v.) and have pointed ears, flat noses and the tail of a horse or goat. By the 6th century B.C. one of their number, Silenus, stands out from his fellows for his wisdom and is sometimes said to have been the tutor of Dionysus. His special

knowledge comes from wine drinking and like his fellows he is usually drunk. An old man with horse-ears and tail he proves a good raconteur when captured, though something of a comic drunkard.

Silvanus. Ancient Italian god, a protector of uncultivated land.

Sinis or **Sinnis.** A robber of the Corinthian Isthmus who killed travellers by tying them to the tops of fir trees tied to the ground and then releasing the trees. Theseus (q.v.) slew him in the same fashion.

Sinon. A cousin of Odysseus (q.v.) and grandson of Autolycus the thief. When the Greeks pretended to leave Troy (q.v.) he remained in camp and persuaded the Trojans that the wooden horse was a gift in atonement for the theft of Athene's Palladium (q.v.). Once the horse was inside Troy he signalled the Greek fleet to return.

Sirens. In Homer two sisters who lure sailors to their death by their singing. Odysseus (q.v.) and the Argonauts (q.v.) withstood their fatal charms, the latter because Orpheus (q.v.) outsang them. They have been associated with the modern Galli islands. In non-Homeric tradition their number varies and they are portrayed as having the bodies of birds and heads of either sex. Some say they were daughters of Ge (q.v.) and companions of Persephone (q.v.) who escorted the dead to the Underworld. They were said to feed on the dead. Later they are given the heads of beautiful women and sing to console the dead they escort. Finally they lose their funerary and evil nature and develop fishes' tails like mermaids.

Sisyphus. The son of Aeolus and husband of the Pleiad Merope who bore him Glaucus. He was an ancestor of Bellerophon (q.v.) and also seduced Anticleia, mother of Odysseus (q.v.) and may have been his father. The founder of Ephyra (later Corinth) and an infamous rogue and knave he was condemned in the Underworld perpetually to push a large stone, uphill, only to see it always roll down, hence the term 'labour of Sisyphus' to denote a futile task.

Sophocles. See **B56**.

Spartii. "The sown men" who sprang up when Cadmus (q.v.) sowed the dragon's teeth. They were fully armed and fought amongst themselves until only five remained, Echion, Udaeus, Chthonius, Hyperenor and Pelorus. These helped Cadmus build the Cadmea, citadel of Thebes, and were ancestors of the Thebans. The title was also given to their descendants. Cadmus saved some of the teeth and Jason (q.v.) had to sow these to get the Golden Fleece.

Sphinx. A fabulous monster with a human head and the body of a lion. In Egyptian mythology where it originates it could be of either sex but in Greek myth is a female and lives north of Thebes. It was the offspring of Echidne (q.v.) and Typhon (q.v.) or possibly Orthrus (q.v.) and the Chimaera (q.v.) and plagued Thebes by strangling and devouring all who could not answer her riddle: what walks on four legs at dawn, two at noon and three in the evening? Oedipus (q.v.) answered correctly that it was man who first crawls, then walks upright and finally uses a stick in old age. The sphinx then leapt from her rock and was dashed to pieces.

Stentor. Greek herald in the Trojan war who supposedly had a voice equal to that of fifty men. He died after Hermes (q.v.) beat him in a shouting match. His name gives us the word 'stentorian' meaning extremely loud.

Steropes. One of the Cyclopes (q.v.).

Stheneboea. Another name for Anteia. See **Bellerophon**.

Sthenelus. (1) A king of Mycenae, the son of Perseus (q.v.) and Andromeda (q.v.). The husband of Nicippe by whom he was the father of Alcinoe, Medusa (q.v.) and Eurystheus (q.v.).
(2) The son of Capaneus and Evadne, a companion of Diomedes (q.v.) and one of the Epigoni (q.v.). One of the Greeks in the Wooden Horse (q.v.).
(3) A Trojan and companion of Aeneas (q.v.).

Stheno. One of the Gorgones (q.v.).

Strymon. River in Thrace, believed by the Greeks to be the home of the crane.

Stymphalian Birds. Monsters inhabiting Lake Stymphalus, a marshy area in northern Arcadia. They were huge birds with bronze beaks and claws that ate human flesh. They used their feathers as arrows. The birds were sacred to Ares (q.v.) but Heracles (q.v.) startled them with bronze castanets provided by Athene (*q.v.*) and shot them. Some say they flew to the Black Sea and were found there by the Argonauts (*q.v.*).

Styx. The river of "hate" in the Underworld and flowing several times around its perimeter. When dipped in it Achilles (*q.v.*) was made invulnerable. Ghosts could only cross it if they paid Charon (*q.v.*) to ferry them across and for this purpose a coin was placed beneath the tongue of corpses. On its far bank was Cerberus (*q.v.*). Aristophanes (*q.v.*) and others describe it as a marsh rather than a river though Herodotus (*q.v.*) identifies it with a trickle from the rock near Pheneus. Generally it was associated with the cascade on Mt. Chelmos further west whose cold waters stain the rock black. Plutarch and Arrian say Alexander the Great was poisoned by water from here brought to him in a mule's hoof.

Sul or **Sulis.** A Celtic deity identified with Minerva (*q.v.*) by the Romans. The patron of Aquae Sulis.

Symplegades. Floating islands, like icebergs, at the entrance to the Bosphorus. They clashed together and crushed ships. Jason (*q.v.*), on the advice of Phineus, let loose a dove which made them recoil and as they did so the Argo (*q.v.*) slipped between them. Henceforth they remained stationary.

Syrinx. An Arcadian nymph. *See* **Pan.**

T

Talaus. The father of Adrastus (*q.v.*).

Talos. (1) A mythical brazen giant with a bull's head said to have protected Crete.
(2) *See* **Daedalus.** Another name for Perdix.

Tantalus. A wealthy king, the son of Zeus (*q.v.*) and the nymph Pluto. The father of Pelops, Broteas and Niobe. He was favoured by Zeus and was invited to Olympian banquets but stole nectar (*q.v.*) and ambrosia (*q.v.*) and revealed Zeus' secrets. He received the golden dog made by Hephaestus (*q.v.*) for Rhea (*q.v.*) (which had watched Zeus' cradle) from Pandareus. This incensed the gods but Tantalus denied having seen it. Pandareus was then put to a miserable death and his daughters were abducted by the Harpies (*q.v.*). His numerous other crimes included serving Pelops (*q.v.*) as a meal to the gods. For this he was punished in the Underworld, either by being placed beneath a huge rock which constantly threatened to fall and crush him or by being placed in a lake the waters of which receded whenever he tried to drink, while above his head were boughs of fruit "tantalisingly" behind his reach.

Tarchon. Legendary ancestor of the Etruscan "Tarquins" who lead a group of emigrants from Lydia to Italy and there founded Tarquinii and other Etruscan cities. He became an ally of Aeneas (*q.v.*).

Tarpeia. The daughter of Tarpeius, commander of the Roman garrison on the Capitol during the Sabine (*q.v.*) wars shortly after Rome's foundation. Her story is told by Livy. She treacherously offered to show the way into the citadel if the Sabine chief Tatius would give her that which his men "wore on their shield arms". By this she meant gold torques but instead the Sabines crushed her to death with their shields. The tale is an attempt to account for the name of the Tarpeian Rock (*q.v.*).

Tarpeian Rock. A precipice on the south-west corner of the Capitol from which traitors and other condemned criminals were thrown to their death. The last victim was an equestrian implicated in a conspiracy against Claudius in 43 A.D.

Tartarus. (1) Another name for Hades (*q.v.*) though in Homer it refers to the deepest reaches of the Underworld, a place of punishment to which the Titans (*q.v.*) and Centimani (*q.v.*) were consigned by Cronus (*q.v.*).
(2) Also the name of a son of Ge (*q.v.*) who was father, by his mother, of the monster Typhon (*q.v.*).

Teiresias or **Tiresias.** A blind Theban prophet, who, while young, had come upon Athene (*q.v.*) bathing in the nude. She had therefore blinded him but in compensation gave him the gift of prophecy. He revealed to Oedipus (*q.v.*) the truth of his incest. He helped Thebes against the Seven (*q.v.*) then died after drinking from the well of Tilphussa.

Odysseus (*q.v.*) consulted his shade in the land of the Cimmerians.

Telamon. The son of Aeacus and brother of Peleus (*q.v.*). After the two murdered their half-brother Phocus, his father expelled him to Salamis where he married Glauce and later succeeded her father as king. Next he married Periboea of Athens and she bore him Ajax (*q.v.*). A friend of Heracles (*q.v.*) and with him sacked Troy (*q.v.*). He carried off Hesione who bore him Teucer and his refusal to return her to her brother Priam (*q.v.*) was one cause of the Trojan war.

Telchines. Mythical beings, artists in metal work who made a sickle for Cronus (*q.v.*) and the trident for Poseidon (*q.v.*). They raised the infant Poseidon. At times they were destructive and interfered with the weather. They annoyed Zeus (*q.v.*) who drowned a number of them in a flood, and Apollo (*q.v.*) who took the form of a wolf to savage them.

Telemachus. *See* **Odysseus.**

Telephassa. The mother of Europa (*q.v.*) and Cadmus (*q.v.*) by Agenor.

Telephus. The son of Heracles (*q.v.*) and Auge (a priestess and daughter of Aleus, king of Tegea). Abandoned as a child, the Delphic oracle later directed him to the court of king Teuthras in Mysia where he found his mother married to Teuthras. He later succeeded Teuthras and married Laodice, daughter of Priam (*q.v.*). When the Greeks on their way to Troy (*q.v.*) landed in Mysia he repulsed them, but Dionysus (*q.v.*) caused him to trip on a vine and Achilles (*q.v.*) wounded him. An oracle told him he could only be cured by the one who wounded him while the Greeks were told they could not take Troy without his help. He therefore went to Achilles who cured the wound with rust from his spear and in return Telephus showed the Greeks the route to Troy.

Tempe. A vale in Thessaly where Apollo (*q.v.*) pursued Daphne (*q.v.*) and was purified of the killing of Python.

Tenedos. Small island off the coast of Asia Minor, south west of Troy (*q.v.*). Here Achilles (*q.v.*) slew king Tenes (*q.v.*) and his father Cyncus and here Philoctetes (*q.v.*) was wounded.

Tenes. The son of Apollo (*q.v.*) though reputed to be son of Cycnus, king of Colonae in Troas. His stepmother attempted to seduce him and, when he refused her, made false accusations against him. Cycnus then put Tenes and his sister Hemithea into a chest and cast it adrift at sea. It washed up on the isle of Leucophrys where Tenes became king and gave his name to the island, Tenedos (*q.v.*).

Tereus. *See* **Procne.**

Terpsichore. The muse of song and choral dance, portrayed with a lyre and plectrum.

Teucer. (1) The son of Scamander (*q.v.*) and the nymph Idaca. He gave the land to Dardanus (*q.v.*) on which Dardanus built Dardania. An ancestor of the Trojans.
(2) The son of Hesione and Telamon, half brother of Ajax (*q.v.*) behind whose shield he fought at Troy (*q.v.*).

Teucri. Name for the Trojans derived from that of their ancestor Teucer (*q.v.*).

Teuthras. *See* **Telephus.** The father of the girl Tecmessa. Ajax (*q.v.*) raided the Thracian Chersonese, slew him and abducted Tecmessa.

Tethys. A Titaness, mother of Oceanus (*q.v.*) of Metis.

Thalia. (1) Muse of comedy.
(2) One of the Charities (*q.v.*).

Thebe. The wife of Zethus, who gave her name to Thebes.

Themis. A Titaness, the daughter of Ge (*q.v.*) and Uranus (*q.v.*) and sister of Cronus (*q.v.*). The wife of Zeus (*q.v.*) before Hera (*q.v.*), she bore him the Horae (*q.v.*) and Moerae (*q.v.*). She determined religious rites, instituted laws and was the first to distinguish between that which was permitted and that which offended the divine order. Hence she became the personification of justice and represented the incarnation of divine law.

Therseander. *See* **Epigoni.**

Theocritus. *See* **B59.**

Thersites. A low-minded, ugly and mean spirited wretch amongst the Greek forces at Troy (*q.v.*). He accused Agamemnon (*q.v.*) of prolonging the war to serve his own interest until Odysseus (*q.v.*) beat him into silence.

Theseus. The son of Aethra, a princess of Troezen, by Aegeus (*q.v.*) though one tradition says Poseidon (*q.v.*) fathered him in the form of a bull.

Aegeus left her after seducing her but showed her a rock under which he had hidden his sword and sandals. Theseus was raised secretly by his mother at her father's court, and when he reached adolescence lifted the rock to claim Aegeus' sword and sandals. With these he set off for Athens and on the way had many adventures, slaying the wild sow of Crommyum, Sciron (q.v.), Periphetes (q.v.), Cercyon and Procrustes (q.v.). Arriving at Athens Aegeus recognised the sword and sandals and accepted him as his son despite the plots of Medea (q.v.). Theseus then scattered the Pallantides, fifty nephews of Aegeus and the sons of Pallas who hoped to claim the throne themselves. Next he captured the Cretan Bull (q.v.). But his greatest task was to go voluntarily to Crete to slay the Minotaur (q.v.). As one of the tribute demanded by Minos (q.v.) he was to be sacrificed to the monster but Minos' daughter Ariadne fell in love with him and gave him a sword with which to slay the beast and a thread by which he could retrace his steps through the massive labyrinth in which it lived. The couple then fled to Naxos where he left Ariadne and where she was loved by Dionysus (q.v.) whose sacred island it was. Aegeus tragically killed himself on Theseus' return and the hero then became king of Athens. Either alone or with Heracles (q.v.) he invaded the land of the Amazons and carried off either Antiope or Hippolyte. The Amazons attacked Athens but Theseus defeated them in the middle of Athens. By the Amazon queen he became father of Hippolytus (q.v.). Later he married Phaedra and was father by her of Acamas and Demophon (q.v.). A close friend of Pirithous (q.v.), the two shared many adventures. Eventually he returned again to Athens but was ousted by Menestheus and retired to Scyros where, for some reason he was murdered by Lycomedes. Unlike Heracles, Theseus was not worshipped throughout the Hellenistic world but was very much an Athenian hero and his reputed bones were brought to the city from Scyros in historical times. He is said to have gathered the villages of Attica into one state by the process of *synoecismus*.

Thetis. A Nereid (q.v.) who was raised by Hera (q.v.) and remained attached to her. Zeus (q.v.) and Poseidon (q.v.) desired her but it was foretold that her son would be greater than his father. She was thus forced to marry a mortal, Peleus (q.v.), but only after she had tried to avoid him by changing her shape, becoming various animals including a lion. Their wedding on Mt. Pelion was attended by all the gods save Eris (q.v.). They had a number of children who were killed when Thetis tried to make them immortal by throwing them into the fire. Peleus snatched their seventh child, Achilles (q.v.), from her as she tried yet again. Instead she dipped him in the Styx (q.v.). Angry at not giving birth to an immortal she left Peleus to live with her sister Neireids. She cared for Hephaestus (q.v.) when Zeus threw him into the sea, and for Dionysus (q.v.) though she and Briareus (q.v.) freed Zeus when the other gods enchained him.

Thoas. The son of Andraemon king of Calydon who took forty ships to Troy (q.v.) and was one of the Greeks in the Wooden Horse (q.v.).

Thyades. See **Thyia.**

Thyestes. The son of Pelops (q.v.) and Hippodamia and brother of Atreus, ancestor of the illustrious Atridae family. He and Atreus murdered their half-brother Chrysippus and fled to Mycenae. Here Atreus seized the kingdom and banished Thyestes. Thyestes had seduced Atreus' second wife Aerope and he now tricked Atreus into killing Pleisthenes, his son by his first wife. In revenge Atreus lured Thyestes to Mycenae, slew his three sons and served them to him. Thyestes unknowingly ate them. Not surprisingly he cursed the house of Atreus on learning the truth. The Delphic oracle told Thyestes he could get revenge by fathering a son on his own daughter Pelopia, a priestess at the court of Thres;potus of Sicyon. He raped her and Atreus later married her, believing her to be the daughter of Thresjpotus. He raised Thyestes' son Aegisthus (q.v.) as his own.

Thyia. The first woman to worship and sacrifice to Dionysus (q.v.). She gave her name to the Attic women who participated in the orgies of Dionysus at Parnassus, the Thyiades. These women were also called Thyades, "raging women", a similar name but of different origin.

Thyone. See **Semele.**

Thyrsus. A wand carried by the Maenads, covered with ivy wreaths and surmounted by a fir cone.

Tiryns. City reputedly founded by Proetus (q.v.) and built with the help of the Cyclopes (q.v.). The actual site is a mound 300 yd long on the Gulf of Argolis. It was first inhabited in the 3rd millennium B.C. and held a chief's residence and town. Around 1600 B.C. a larger palace was built and ramparts constructed. In the 14th and 13th centuries the rampart was rebuilt and enlarged. Its impressive ruins remain.

Tisiphone. One of the Eumenides (q.v.).

Titanesses. Sisters of the Titans (q.v.), daughters of Ge (q.v.) and Uranus (q.v.). Their numbers included Rhea (q.v.), Themis (q.v.), Tethys and Mnemosyne.

Titanomachia. The ten-year war, waged in Thessaly by Zeus (q.v.) and the Olympian gods against Cronos (q.v.) and the Titans (q.v.) led by Atlas (q.v.). Ge (q.v.) promised Zeus (who had usurped his Titan father Cronos) victory if he would free the Cyclopes (q.v.) and Hecatoncheires (q.v.) from Tartarus (q.v.). He did and the Cyclopes gave him the thunderbolt, Hades (q.v.) a helmet which conferred invisibility and Poseidon a trident. The three overcame Cronos and the Hecatoncheires stoned the other Titans who were defeated and consigned either to Tartarus or an island far to the west. Here the Hecatoncheires guarded them. Atlas was made to carry the sky as punishment but the Titanesses (q.v.) were spared. The war is the basis of Keats' *Hyperion*.

Titans. The sons of Ge (q.v.) and Uranus (q.v.). There were twelve of them though the lists given of their names are inconsistent. The most often named are Cronus (q.v.), Oceanus (q.v.), Hyperion, Iapetus and Atlas (q.v.). Brothers of the Titanesses (q.v.). When Uranus consigned the Cyclopes (q.v.) to Tartarus (q.v.) Ge persuaded Cronos and his brother Titans to depose Uranus. The Titans were in turn deposed in the Titanomachia (q.v.).

Tithonus. The son of Laomedon and Strymor and a half-brother of Priam (q.v.). By Eos (q.v.) the father of Memnon (q.v.). Eos begged Zeus (q.v.) to make him immortal, which he did, but forgot to ask for perpetual youth. Tithonus grew older and older until Eos tired of looking on him, turned him into a cicada and locked him in a cage.

Tities. One of the three primitive tribes of Rome.

Tityus. A giant son of Ge (q.v.) sent by Hera (q.v.) to violate Leto (q.v.) but Artemis (q.v.) and Apollo (q.v.) slew him with their arrows. In Hades (q.v.) he was pegged to the ground (he covered nine acres) while two vultures picked at his liver.

Tleopolemus. A son of Heracles (q.v.) who settled in Argos and later Rhodes.

Triptolemus. See **Demeter.**

Triton. The son of Poseidon (q.v.) and Amphitrite (q.v.) though sometimes several tritons are spoken of. He was a merman, his upper body being human, the lower fish. He blew a shell-trumpet, the concha, to calm the waves and Ovid tells us that he blew the concha to order the waters to recede after the Flood. (See **Deucalion**).

Troilus. A young son of Priam (q.v.) slain by Achilles (q.v.). His romance with Cressida is a medieval invention.

Trojan War. The ten-year siege of Troy (q.v.) and its eventual sack by Greek forces under Agamemnon (q.v.). The combined forces sought to restore Helen (q.v.) to Menelaus (q.v.). The story of the war is told in Homer's *Iliad* where Achilles (q.v.) is the major hero of the Greeks and Hector (q.v.) of the Trojans. According to Homer the war was ended by the Wooden Horse (q.v.) concocted by Odysseus (q.v.). The war is usually placed by tradition as occurring in the 12th century B.C. The war is not a purely mythical episode. Archaeological evidence from the site of Troy shows that the city occupying the seventh stratigraphical layer was destroyed by fire, though probably in the 14th century B.C. Archaeology also confirms the *Iliad's* description of the main towns in Trojan civilisation together with its picture of the Greek people and army.

Trophonius and Agamedes. Sons of Erginus who built a temple for Apollo (q.v.) at Delphi. They were rewarded by living merrily for six days and dying in their sleep on the seventh. Trophonius later had an oracle of his own at Lebadeia in Boeotia. Here, according to Pausanias, the questioner underwent a complex initiation, was dressed as a sacrificial victim and (carrying a honey-cake to placate the Underworld divinities) descended into a pot-hole. An underground stream swept him along some distance before he was returned to the light having heard invisible speakers in the cavern. Not surprisingly the questioner would look dazed and dejected and it became common to speak of a gloomy person as one who had been consulting Trophonius.

Tros. (1) The grandson of Dardanus (q.v.) and father of Ilus (q.v.) and Ganymede (q.v.). An ancestor of the Trojans, he gave his name to Troy (q.v.).
(2) A small town absorbed by the city of Troy (q.v.).

Troy. Also called Ilium, a city of Asia Minor near the sea not far from the straits of the Dardanelles. From its position the inhabitants could watch the sea traffic between the Aegean and Sea of Marmara. Many traders off-loaded cargo and used the land route to bypass the dangerous straits. Hence in the late 3rd millennium B.C. Troy became very prosperous from trade, a prosperity which returned at various periods in the 2nd millennium. In 1870 the German Heinrich Schliemann, an amateur archaeologist, sought the site near modern Hissarlik in Turkey. He found it and later excavations have distinguished nine strata of occupations, the richest dating from 2200 B.C. and the 7th showing signs of destruction by fire (See **Trojan War**). From the 14th century B.C. the site was of little importance until the Roman occupation when, as Ilium Nevum, it played a large part in provincial life. Homer's Troy had probably absorbed three neighbouring towns, Tros (q.v.), Dardania and Ilium and the names of three tribes, Ilians, Trojans and Dardanians are represented in the myths of its foundation.

Tyche or Tuche. The Roman "Fortuna", and always more popular in Rome. A daughter of Zeus (q.v.) and the goddess of luck who bestowed or denied gifts to men according to her whims. She often accompanied Pluto (q.v.). She is portrayed juggling a ball, symbolising the instability of fate, or with a rudder to guide men's affairs.

Tydeus. Son of Oeneus and Calydon, husband of Deipyle. After committing a murder in his youth he fled to the court of Adrastus (q.v.). See **Seven Against Thebes.**

Tyndareus. The brother of Hippocoon who deposed him as king of Sparta, but Heracles (q.v.) reinstated him. Helen (q.v.) was brought up at his court (she was his wife Leda's (q.v.) child by Zeus (q.v.)). Helen married Menelaus (q.v.) who succeeded Tyndareus. Tyndareus had had all the Greek nobles who sought Helen's hand swear an oath to defend her chosen husband. This was the reason why the Greeks allied in support of Menelaus in the Trojan War (q.v.). Tyndareus also helped Agamemnon (q.v.) expel Thyestes (q.v.) and regain his throne.

Typhon. The monstrous offspring of Ge (q.v.) and Tartarus (q.v.), whose eyes could expel fire and whose limbs ended in snakes' heads. He attacked Olympus and the gods fled to Egypt disguised as animals, Zeus (q.v.) as a ram, Apollo (q.v.) as a cow, Dionysus (q.v.) as a goat, Hera (q.v.) as a white cow, Artemis (q.v.) as a cat, Aphrodite (q.v.) as a fish, Ares (q.v.) as a boar and Hermes (q.v.) as an ibis. Athene (q.v.) did not flee and persuaded Zeus to fight. In a great struggle Zeus was saved by Hermes and Pan (q.v.) and then defeated Typhon with his thunderbolts. He was then buried under Mt. Etna. By Echidne (q.v.) Typhon was father of a variety of monsters.

Tyro. A nymph, the mother of Pelias (q.v.) and Neleus (q.v.) by Zeus (q.v.) and of Aeson by Cretheus. The grandmother of Jason (q.v.).

U

Udaeus. One of the Spartii (q.v.).
Ulysses. The Roman name for Odysseus (q.v.).
Urania. The Muse of Astronomy.
Uranus. The Sky, offspring of Ge (q.v.) the earth and brother of Pontus, the sea. The father by Ge of the Hecatoncheires (q.v.), the Cyclopes (q.v.) and the Titans (q.v.). He threw the rebellious Cyclopes into Tartarus (q.v.). Ge then persuaded the Titans to rise against their father and avenge their brothers. She gave Cronos (q.v.) a flint sickle with

which he castrated Uranus. The blood of Uranus which fell to earth produced the Erinyes and the blood which fell into the sea produced Aphrodite (q.v.). Uranus was deposed but cursed Cronos that his own children depose him.

V

Venus. Originally an Italian deity whose name meant "beauty" or "charm", she was a goddess of vegetable rather than animal fertility. She became identified with Aphrodite (q.v.) by way of Aphrodite's cult at Mt. Eryx in Sicily, said to have been founded by Aeneas (q.v.) on the death of Anchises (q.v.). In 217 B.C. Venus Erycina was given a temple at Rome and became completely associated with Aphrodite taking on her functions and attributes. She was patron goddess of Sulla and Pompey. In the imperial cult she played a very important role as the Julian family claimed descent from Aeneas and therefore Aphrodite. In this context she was Venus Genetrix, creator of all things, the universal mother and life giver.

Vesta. A primitive Roman goddess of the hearth, the counterpart of Hestia (q.v.). She was worshipped in each Roman house and officially in a circular temple in the Forum. The temple held a fire, said to have come from Troy (q.v.) which could never be allowed to go out. It was tended by the Vestal Virgins (q.v.). Her cult was purely Italian and never spread to the provinces.

Vestal Virgins. A college of priestesses of the cult of Vesta (q.v.). There were originally four of them, later six and finally seven. Candidates for the college were chosen at between six and ten years of age; both their parents had to be alive and they underwent a prolonged special training. They served for thirty years under the control of the Pontifex Maximus and during all this period had to remain virgins. The punishment for unchastity was burial alive. However they were highly honoured and had great privileges. For instance they could save from execution any criminal they met on the way to his death. They lived in a large residence near the temple of Vesta. The sacred fire of Vesta was tended by Vestal Virgins up to the 4th century A.D.

Virgil. See **B62.**
Victoria. The Roman goddess of victory, corresponding to the Greek Nike (q.v.).
Vulcan. The Roman god of fire, identified with Hephaestus (q.v.) and sometimes called Mulciber, "the smelter". His name gives us the word "volcano".

W

Wooden Horse of Troy. The "Trojan Horse", a stratagem devised by Odysseus (q.v.) which ended the Trojan War (q.v.). The Greeks had Epeius, son of Panopeus, build a large wooden horse. Athene (q.v.) helped him and it bore an inscription dedicated to her. Then twenty-three or more Greeks including Odysseus, Neoptolemus (q.v.), Sthenelus and Thoas hid inside it. The rest of the Greek force then burnt their camp and put to sea leaving only the wily Sinon (q.v.) to trick the Trojans into dragging the horse into Troy. (See also **Laocöon**). Inside the city Helen (q.v.) patted the horse and called out the names of those she suspected were inside it, but she was accompanied by the Trojan prince Deiphobus and Odysseus stopped the Greeks answering. At night the Greek fleet returned, Sinon let the men out of the horse, the gates of Troy were opened and the city was sacked.

X

Xenophon. See **B66.**
Xuthus. The son of Hellen and husband of Creusa, the daughter of Erectheus, king of Athens. By her the father of Achaeus and Ion. On the death of

Erectheus Xuthus was asked to determine which of the king's sons should succeed him. He chose Cecrops and was expelled to Achaia by the other heirs. Euripedes (*q.v.*) makes Ion the son of Apollo (*q.v.*) and Creusa.

Z

Zagreus. A son of Zeus (*q.v.*). He was torn apart and eaten by Titans (*q.v.*) except for his heart which Athene (*q.v.*) saved. He is sometimes identified with Dionysus (*q.v.*).

Zephyrus. The son of Astraeus and Eus. He was the west wind, originally imagined, like all winds, in the form of a horse. The father of Xanthus and Balius, the talking horses of Achilles (*q.v.*) which Poseidon (*q.v.*) had given to Peleus (*q.v.*) as a wedding gift. The husband of Iris (*q.v.*). He deflected the discus which killed Hyacinthus (*q.v.*). His Roman counterpart was Favonius.

Zetes. *See* **Calais.**

Zethus. *See* **Amphion.**

Zeus. The son of Cronos (*q.v.*) and Rhea (*q.v.*). He deposed his father and defeated the Titans (*q.v.*). Then he and his brothers Hades (*q.v.*) and Poseidon (*q.v.*) cast lots for their kingdoms and Zeus won the sky. The earth was common to all. Zeus was the king of the gods and was identified with Jupiter by the Romans. He was the father of men. In early legend his consort is Dione, but his consort on Mt. Olympus (*q.v.*) is the jealous Hera (*q.v.*). He first married Hetis who bore him Athene (*q.v.*) and his second wife was Themis (*q.v.*) who bore him the Horae and Maerae. Hera bore him Ares (*q.v.*), Hebe (*q.v.*) and Hephaestus (*q.v.*). His sister Demeter (*q.v.*) bore him Persephone (*q.v.*) and Eurynome bore him the Charities (*q.v.*) while by Mnemosyne he was father of the Muses (*q.v.*). By mortal women he was father of Hermes (*q.v.*), Apollo (*q.v.*) and Artemis (*q.v.*) and Dionysus (*q.v.*). Given the thunderbolt by the Cyclopes (*q.v.*) he was known as the thunderer.

IDEAS &
BELIEFS

This section explains many of the ideas and beliefs that have dominated our history during the centuries. The arrangement is alphabetical and the subjects fall broadly into four groups: religious, philosophical, political, and the less mainstream cults and ideas.

IDEAS AND BELIEFS

THIS section explains many of the ideas and beliefs which people have held at different periods in history. Beliefs may be true or false, meaningful or totally meaningless, regardless of the degree of conviction with which they are held. Since man has been moved to action so often by his beliefs they are worth serious study. The section throws a vivid light on human history.

Man has always felt a deep need for emotional security, a sense of "belonging". This need has found expression in the framing of innumerable religious systems, nearly all of which have been concerned with man's relation to a divine ruling power. In the past, people have been accustomed to think of their own religion as true and of all others as false. Latterly we have come to realise that in man's religious strivings there is common ground, for our need in the world today is a morality whereby human beings may live together in harmony.

There is also to be found in man an irresistible curiosity which demands an explanation of the world in which he finds himself. This urge to make the world intelligible takes him into the realm of science where the unknown is the constant challenge. Science is a creative process, always in the making, since the scientist's conjectures are constantly being submitted to severe critical tests. Basic scientific ideas are discussed in **Section F**.

A

Activists, those in a political movement who insist on taking active steps towards their objectives rather than merely putting forward a programme. Lately activism has become an increasingly common facet of political life. This is probably because the undeniably rapid social changes which are taking place across the world at the moment are not generally being followed by appropriate shifts in political structures and ideals.

Acupuncture, a unique medical system originating in China and based on the established therapeutic effects of implanting fine gold needles in specific parts of the body. The site of needle implantation is decided according to traditional texts. The apparent lack of any logical relationship between the implantation sites and any known physiological or anatomical systems within the body once caused acupuncture to be held in low regard by Western medicine. Indeed it was certainly true that acupuncture and other similar practices tended to flourish in parts of the world where orthodox medicine has made little progress or where doctors and trained staff are scarce.

Recent years however have seen a curious and unexpected revival of interest in acupuncture in Europe and America, prompted in large part by the considerable press publicity which has surrounded a number of major surgical operations performed without anaesthesia upon human patients and which have been witnessed by sceptical Western specialists. Considerable controversy still surrounds acupuncture and is likely to continue for many years—possibly because it is hard to envisage a theory to explain its effects which is consistent with orthodox medicine. No doubt the immensely powerful effects of suggestion and hypnosis need to be taken into account. Some recent discoveries on the psychology and physiology of pain which show that severe wound pain may be alleviated by electrical stimulation of the nerve endings in the site of the wound may also have some relevance. It is tempting to take the line that acupuncture is based on some "forgotten" or "hidden" medical system and to assume that it is only because Western scientists are blinkered and hide-bound that it is not being incorporated in a big way into European and American hospitals. But there are always two sides to an argument; whereas the first reports from Western specialists visiting China were filled with grudging acceptance and genuine puzzlement, some recent visitors have brought back less enthusiastic reports. It is clear that the full story about acupuncture, its nature and its practical value has not yet been told. Certainly, in America, where it has been licensed in 15 states, it is the fastest-growing form of medicine.

Adlerian Psychology. In 1911 the Viennese psychoanalyst Alfred Adler (1870–1937) together with his colleague Carl Gustav Jung broke with their friend Sigmund Freud over disputes concerning the latter's theoretic approach to psychoanalysis. Jung and Adler were themselves shortly also to part company, each to set up and develop his own "school" of psychoanalysis. Adler's system of psychotherapy is based on the idea, not of sex as a driving force as in the case of Freud, but on the concept of "compensation" or a drive for power in an attempt to overcome the "inferiority complex" which he held to be universal in human beings. The child naturally feels inferior to adults, but bullying, making him feel insignificant or guilty or contemptible, even spoiling, which makes him feel important within the family but relatively unimportant outside, increases this feeling. Or the child may have physical defects: he may be small or underweight, have to wear glasses, become lame, be constantly ill, or stupid at school. In these ways he develops a sense of inferiority which for the rest of his life he develops a technique to overcome.

This may be done in several ways: he may try to become capable in the very respects in which he feels incompetent—hence many great orators have originally had speech defects; many painters poor eyesight; many musicians have been partially deaf; like Nietzsche, the weakling, he may write about the superman, or like Sandow, the strong man, be born with poor health.

On the other hand he may overdo his attempt and overcompensate. Hence we have the bully who is really a coward, the small man who is self-assertive to an objectionable degree (Hitler, Napoleon, Stalin, and Mussolini were all small men) or the foreigner who like three of these men wanted to be the hero of his adopted country—Hitler the Austrian, Napoleon the Italian, Stalin the Georgian.

But what about the man who can do none of these things, who continues to fail to compensate? He, says Adler, becomes a neurotic because neurosis is an excuse which means "I could have done so-and-so but ..." It is the unconscious flight into illness—the desire to be ill. Adler's treatment involves disclosing these subterfuges we play on ourselves so that we can deal with the real situation in a more realistic way. Adlerian psychoanalysis still attracts supporters, but its golden days were when the founder was at the head of the movement in the U.S.A., when his views were considered to provide a more "acceptable" theory of the mind than the enormously controversial theories of Freud with their strong sexual orientation.

Adventists, a group of American religious sects, the most familiar being the Seventh-Day Adventist Church, which observes Saturday as the true Sabbath. With (1987) more than 5 million members throughout the world, it shares with other Adventists a belief in the imminent second coming of Christ (a doctrine fairly widespread in the U.S.A. during the early decades of the 19th cent. when the end of the world was predicted by William Miller for 1843, then for 1844). Modern Adventists content themselves with the conviction that the "signs" of the Advent are multiplying, the "blessed event" which will solve the world's ills. Believers will be saved, but the sects differ as to whether the unjust will be tortured in hell, annihilated, or merely remain asleep eternally.

Agnosticism. *See* **God and Man.**

Albigenses, also known as Cathari. French heretical sect (named after the town of Albi in Provence) which appeared in the 11th cent. to challenge the Catholic Church on the way true Christians should lead their lives. They followed a life of extreme asceticism in contrast to the local clergy and their faith was adopted by the mass of the population, especially in Toulouse. Condemned as heretics by Pope Innocent III, the sect was exterminated in the savage Albigensian Crusade (1208–29), initially led by Simon de Montfort. (In his thoroughness, de Montfort also succeeded in destroying the high culture of the Troubadours.)

Alchemy, ancient art associated with magic and astrology in which modern chemistry has its roots. The earliest mention of alchemy comes from ancient Egypt but its later practitioners attributed its origins to such varied sources as the fallen angels of the Bible, to Moses and Aaron, but most commonly to Hermes Trismegistus, often identified with the Egyptian god Thoth, whose knowledge of the divine art was handed down only to the sons of kings (cf. the phrase "hermetically sealed"). Its main object was the transmutation of metals. Egyptian speculation concerning this reached its height during the 6th cent. in the Alexandrian period. Brought to Western Europe by the Moslems, one of its most famous Arab exponents was Jabir (*c.* 760–*c.* 815), known to the Latins as Geber, who had a laboratory at Kufa on the Tigris. One school of early Greek philosophy held that there was ultimately only one elemental matter of which everything was composed. Such men as Albertus Magnus (1206–80) and Roger Bacon (1214–94) assumed that, by removing impurities, this *materia prima* could be obtained. Although Bacon's ideas were in many ways ahead of his time, he firmly believed in the philosopher's stone, which could turn base metals into gold, and in an elixir of life which would give eternal youth. Modern science has, of course, shown in its researches into radioactivity, the possibility of transmutation of certain elements, but this phenomenon has little bearing on either the methods of the alchemist or the mysteries with which he surrounded them. In line with the current considerable revival of interest in the occult, alchemy appears to be staging a comeback, at least as a literary if not an experimental topic.

Anabaptists. *See* **Baptists.**

Analytical Psychology, the name given by Carl Gustav Jung (1875–1961) of Zürich to his system of psychology, which, like Adler's (*see* **Adlerian Psychology**), took its origin from Freud's psychoanalysis from which both diverged in 1911. Briefly, Jung differed from Freud: (1) in believing that the latter had laid too much emphasis on the sexual drive as the basic one in man and replacing it with the concept of *libido* or life energy of which sex forms a part; (2) in his theory of types: men are either extrovert or introvert (*i.e.* their interest is turned primarily outwards to the world or inwards to the self), and they apprehend experience in four main ways, one or other of which is predominant in any given individual—sensing, feeling, thinking, or intuiting; (3) in his belief that the individual's unconscious mind contains not only repressed materials which, as Freud maintained, were too unpleasant to be allowed into awareness, but also faculties which had not been allowed to develop—*e.g.*, the emotional side of the too rational man, the feminine side of the too masculine one; (4) in the importance he attaches to the existence of a

collective unconscious at a still deeper level which contains traces of ancient ways of thought which mankind has inherited over the centuries. These are the *archetypes* and include primitive notions of magic, spirits and witches, birth and death, gods, virgin mothers, resurrection, etc. In the treatment of the neuroses Jung believed in the importance of (*a*) the present situation which the patient refuses to face; (*b*) the bringing together of conscious and unconscious and integrating them.

In the 1940s and 50s interest in Jung's ideas waned, at least in academic circles, as the emphasis among experimental psychologists shifted closer and closer to the "hard" scientific line. This was also true in the field of psychoanalysis where the Jungian as opposed to the Freudian point of view became progressively less popular. At the present time this trend is beginning to reverse, and while Jung's offbeat views on astrology, telepathy, etc., are still unfashionable, a reappraisal of the significance of his views on the nature of the unconscious is taking place and many psychologists feel that his contribution to our understanding of the nature of human mental processes has been greatly underrated. *See also* **Psychoanalysis** and **Section Q**.

Anarchism, a political philosophy which holds, in the words of the American anarchist Josiah Warren (1798–1874), an early follower of Robert Owen, that "every man should be his own government, his own law, his own church." The idea that governmental interference or even the mere existence of authority is inherently bad is as old as Zeno, the Greek Stoic philosopher, who believed that compulsion perverts the normal nature of man. William Godwin's *Enquiry Concerning Political Justice* (1793) was the first systematic exposition of the doctrine. Godwin (father-in-law of Shelley) claimed that man is by nature sociable, co-operative, rational, and good when given the choice to act freely; that under such conditions men will form voluntary groups to work in complete social harmony. Such groups or communities would be based on equality of income, no state control, and no property: this state of affairs would be brought about by rational discussion and persuasion rather than by revolution.

The French economist Proudhon (1809–65) was the first to bring anarchism to the status of a mass movement. In his book *What is Property?* he stated bluntly that "property is theft" and "governments are the scourge of God". He urged the formation of co-operative credit banks where money could be had without interest and goods would be exchanged at cost value at a rate representing the hours of work needed to produce each commodity. Like Godwin, he disapproved of violence but, unlike Marx, disapproved of trade unions as representing organised groups.

In communistic anarchism these ideas were combined with a revolutionary philosophy, primarily by the Russians Michael Bakunin (1814–76) and Peter Kropotkin (1842–1921) who favoured training workers in the technique of "direct action" to overthrow the state by all possible means, including political assassination. In 1868 anarchists joined the First International which broke up a few years later after a bitter struggle between Bakuninists and Marxists. Subsequently small anarchist groups murdered such political figures as Tsar Alexander II of Russia, King Humbert of Italy, Presidents Carnot of France and MacKinley of America, and the Empress Elizabeth of Austria.

Anarchism and communism differ in three main ways: (1) anarchism forms no political party, rejects all relationship with established authority, and regards democratic reform as a setback; (2) communism is against capitalism, anarchism against the state as such; (3) both have the final goal of a classless society, but anarchism rejects the idea of an intermediate period of socialist state control accepted by communism. Philosophical anarchists, such as the American writer Henry David Thoreau (1817–62), were primarily individualists who believed in a return to nature, the non-payment of taxes, and passive resistance to state control;

in these respects Thoreau strongly influenced Gandhi as did the Christian anarchist Tolstoy.

Anarchism has traditionally been criticised as being impractical—*e.g.*, in a non-authoritarian society, who is going to look after the sewers or clean the streets?—and there is a good deal of force to this argument. In fact anarchistic ideas became progressively less fashionable in the first half of this century. A curious and probably significant revival of interest has taken place in the past decade, however, probably because of a growing sense of disillusion, particularly on the part of young people, with the progress of orthodox political systems. *See also* **Syndicalism**.

Anglicanism, adherence to the doctrine and discipline of the Anglican Church, as the genuine representative of the Catholic Church. *See* **Church of England**.

Anglo-Catholicism. To Queen Elizabeth I the Church of England was that of the "middle way" in which human reason and commonsense took their place beside Scripture and Church authority. The extent to which these various factors are stressed creates the distinctions between "high" and "low" church. Anglo-Catholics tend to reject the term "Protestant" and stress the term "Catholic" and, although few accept the infallibility of the Pope some Anglo-Catholic churches have introduced much or all of the Roman ritual and teach Roman dogmas. *See* **Catholicism, Tractarianism**.

Animism. To early man and in primitive societies the distinction between animate and inanimate objects was not always obvious—it is not enough to say that living things move and nonliving things do not, for leaves blow about in the wind and streams flow down a hillside. In the religions of early societies, therefore, we find a tendency to believe that life exists in all objects from rocks and pools to seas and mountains. This belief is technically known as *animatism*, which differs from *animism*, a somewhat more sophisticated view which holds that natural objects have no life in themselves but may be the abode of dead people, spirits, or gods who occasionally give them the appearance of life. The classic example of this, of course, is the assumption that an erupting volcano is an expression of anger on the part of the god who resides in it. Such beliefs may seem absurd today. but it is worth realising that we are not entirely free of them ourselves when we ascribe "personalities" of a limited kind to motor cars, boats, dolls, or models which incur our pleasure or anger depending upon how well they "behave".

Anthropomorphism, the attribution of human form, thoughts or motives to non-human entities or life forms from gods to animals. At one end this can be summed up in the once widespread image of God as a "white-bearded old gentleman sitting on a cloud." At the other end is the very common tendency to invest domestic animals and pets with man-like wishes and personalities. At both extremes the belief could be seriously misleading. Firstly, it could be very unwise to assume that God, if he exists, necessarily thinks as humans do and has human interests at heart. Secondly, we shall learn very little about animal behaviour if we look upon them as mere extensions of our own personality, and we do them less than justice if we see them simply as human beings of diminutive intelligence.

Anthroposophy, a school of religious and philosophical thought based on the work of the German educationist and mystic Rudolf Steiner (1861–1925). Steiner was originally an adherent of Madame Blavatsky's theosophical movement (*cf* Theosophy) but in 1913 broke away to form his own splinter group, the Anthroposophical Society, following ideological disputes over the alleged "divinity" of the Indian boy Krishnamurti. Steiner was much influenced by the German poet and scientist, Goethe, and believed that an appreciation and love for art was one of the keys to spiritual development. One of the first tasks of his new movement was the construction of a vast temple of arts and sciences, known as the Goetheanum, to act as the headquarters of the society. This structure, which

was of striking and revolutionary architectural style, was unfortunately burnt down in 1922 to be replaced by an even more imaginative one which today is one of the most interesting buildings of its kind in the world. Anthroposophy, which ceased to expand greatly following its founder's death, is nevertheless well-established in various parts of the world with specialised, and often very well equipped, schools and clinics which propagate the educational and therapeutic theories of the movement. These, which include the allegedly beneficial powers of music, coloured lights, etc., have made an increasing impact on modern educational ideas, but the schools have acquired a reputation for success in the training of mentally handicapped children. Today (1990) there are over 400 Steiner schools worldwide, many clinics and homes for the handicapped, adult education centres, an international management consultancy, and several hundred thousand acres under biodynamic cultivation without the use of chemical pesticides, herbicides, or fertilizers. Interesting work continues to be done, in pharmacology, botany, mathematics and physics, and architecture.

Anticlericalism, resentment of priestly powers and privileges, traceable in England to Wyclif's insistence in the 14th cent. on the right of all men to have access to the Scriptures. The translation of the Bible into the common tongue was a great landmark in the history of the Bible and the English language. Wyclif's principles were condemned by the Roman Church of his time but were readily accepted during the Reformation. Tudor anticlericalism arose from motives ranging from a greedy desire to plunder the riches of the Church to a genuine dislike of the powers of the priesthood whose spiritual courts still had the right to decide on points of doctrine or morals in an age when the layman felt he was well able to decide for himself. In innumerable ways the Church was permitted to extort money from the laity. It is generally agreed, says Trevelyan, that the final submission of church to state in England was motivated quite as much by anticlericalism as by Protestantism. The rise of the Reformed churches in England satisfied the people generally and anticlericalism never became the fixed principle of permanent parties as happened in France and Italy from the time of Voltaire onwards.

Antisemitism, a term first applied about the middle of the last century to those who were anti-Jewish in their outlook. Although this attitude was prevalent for religious reasons throughout the Middle Ages, modern antisemitism differed (*a*) in being largely motivated by economic or political conditions, and (*b*) in being doctrinaire with a pseudo-scientific rationale presented by such men as Gobineau (1816–82) and Houston Stewart Chamberlain (1855–1927), and later by the Nazi and Fascist "philosophers". Beginning in Russia and Hungary with the pogroms of 1882 it gradually spread south and westwards where, in France, the Dreyfus case provided an unsavoury example in 1894. Thousands of Jews from Eastern Europe fled to Britain and America during this period; for in these countries anti-semitism has rarely been more than a personal eccentricity. During the last war the murder of six million Jews by the Nazis and their accomplices led to a further exodus to various parts of the world and finally to the creation of the state of Israel.

The individual Jew-hater makes unconscious use of the psychological processes of projection and displacement: his greed or sexual guilt is projected on to the Jew (or Negro or Catholic) because he cannot bear to accept them as his own emotions, and his sense of failure in life is blamed on his chosen scapegoat rather than on his own inadequacy.

But there are social causes too and politicians in some lands are well versed in the technique of blaming unsatisfactory conditions (which they themselves may have in part produced) upon minority groups and persuading others to do the same. Historically, the Jew is ideally suited for this role of scapegoat; (1) in the Middle Ages when usury was forbidden to

Christians but not to Jews, the latter often became moneylenders incurring the opprobrium generally associated with this trade (e.g., to the simple-minded Russian peasant the Jew often represented, not only the "Christ-killer", but also the moneylender or small shopkeeper to whom he owed money); (2) many trades being closed to Jews, it was natural that they concentrated in others, thus arousing suspicions of "influence" (i.e. Jews are felt to occupy a place in certain trades and professions which far exceeds their numerical proportion to the population as a whole); (3) even with the ending of ghetto life, Jews often occupy en masse some parts of cities rather than others and this may lead to resentment on the part of the original inhabitants who begin to feel themselves dispossessed; (4) Jews tend to form a closed society and incur the suspicions attached to all closed societies within which social contacts are largely limited to members; marriage outside the group is forbidden or strongly disapproved of, and the preservation, among the orthodox, of cultural and religious barriers tends to isolate them from their fellow citizens. In 1990, with the political changes in Russia and Eastern Europe, some observers saw the beginning of a resurgence of anti-semitism See **Racism, Zionism, Judaism.**

Anti-vivisection, opposition to scientific experimentation upon live animals based, according to its supporters, both on the moral grounds of the suffering imposed, and also on the grounds that many doctors and scientists of repute have rejected the value of information gained in this way. It is true that the protagonists of the movement during its early days in the mid-19th cent. included a number of eminent physicians and surgeons. Many people today remain deeply concerned about the moral problems of vivisection, even though without animal experiments we would be unable to test out new drugs for safety before using them on human beings. There are in Britain two or three large national anti-vivisection societies and several smaller ones. Much of their work is co-ordinated through the British Council of Anti-Vivisection Societies. Animal experimentation is controlled by Act of Parliament which makes obligatory the possession of licences by experimenters, inspection of laboratories by the Home Office, and the issue of annual returns of experiments. Many people would like the number of experiments on animals reduced and the law changed to prohibit any experiments in which there is any risk of inflicting suffering. A recent opinion survey showed that while the public approves of medical experiment it strongly disapproves of animals being used for the testing of cosmetics and other chemicals which have nothing to do with medical research. Reform of the Cruelty to Animals Act 1876 has been called for in view of the enormous increase in the number and variety of live animal experiments.

Apartheid, an Afrikaans word meaning "apartness," referred to by South African Government spokesmen as "separate development" or "self-development." To others it means the system of total racial discrimination between black and white South Africans—the permanent inhabitants of the country—as enforced by the National Party since it came to power in 1948. Some degree of racial segregation has existed in South Africa since the earliest days of colonialism in the mid-17th cent. and the policy was continued by the United Party under Smuts and Hertzog from 1934 onwards though it was never a political issue. This changed when the National Party gained power and oppressive measures against the non-white segment of the population have grown steadily under Malan, Strydom, Verwoerd, and Vorster. Apartheid involves the beliefs in racial purity and baaskap, or white supremacy. It means keeping vast African populations in a condition of helotry. Thousands of families are broken up by the pass laws. The official policy of the South African Government is to create separate self-governing black states in which the Africans would be guided to self-government and, it is claimed, eventually to independence. The first so-called Bantu reserve was set up in the Transkei in 1962. But Africans with 70 per cent of the population would have only about 13 percent of the land, and the poorest land at that: cities and mineral areas would remain the reserve of the whites. Total apartheid or complete separation of the black and white races in South Africa remains unlikely to be realised since mining, the main industry of the country, is based on low-paid African labour.

The sports boycott, the conflict between the churches and the government, and the economic need to make more use of African labour, could bring an impetus for change. The increasing economic power of some of the black African states—Nigeria for example, is rich in oil resources—and the elimination of "Europeanism" from the Arab cultures of the North, have led to a steady erosion of the power-base of the white dominant countries such as South Africa. Inevitably, apartheid has shown signs of reaction in response to these external pressures. In 1985, the laws prohibiting inter-racial sex and marriage were abolished. In 1990, under the reforms of President de Klerk, Nelson Mandela (see **B40**) was released from prison, the African National Congress (ANC) was legalised and it seemed that a new political era (and the end of apartheid) might at last be approaching. However, violence and discrimination still remains. See also **Africa, Section C, Part II.**

Aquarius, one of the twelve "signs of the Zodiac". This has recently achieved special significance in the mythology of our time because of the pronouncements of astrologers that the world is shifting out of the 2000-years-old cycle of the Age of Pisces, the fish, into that of Aquarius the water-carrier. The exact date of the transition is a matter of astrological controversy, but the consensus is that it began in 1960 and will be completed sometime in the 24th century. The Aquarian Age is predicted to be one of peace and harmony, replacing the era of strife which, ironically, has marked the dominance of the Christian symbol of the fish. One of the first spaceships to carry man to the moon, for example, was named Aquarius by its crew. See also **Astrology.**

Arianism, formed the subject of the first great controversy within the Christian Church over the doctrine of Arius of Alexandria (d. 336) who denied the divinity of Christ. The doctrine, although at first influential, was condemned at the Council of Nicaea (325), called by the Emperor Constantine, at which Arius was opposed by Athanasius, also of Alexandria, who maintained the now orthodox view that the Son is of one substance with the Father. Arius was banished but the heresy persisted until the 7th cent., especially among the barbarians, the Goths, Vandals and Lombards. Disbelief in the divinity of Christ has formed part of the doctrine of many minor sects since, notably in **Unitarianism** (q.v.).

Assassins, a sect of Moslem Shi'ites, founded by the Persian Hasan i Sabbah (c. 1090), which for more than two centuries established a rule of terror all over Persia and Syria. The coming of the Mongols in 1256 destroyed them in Persia and the Syrian branch suffered a similar fate at the hands of the then Mamluk sultan of Egypt, c. 1270. It was a secret order, ruled over by, a grand master, under whom the members were strictly organised into classes, according to the degree of initiation into the secrets of the order. The devotees, belonging to one of the lower groups, carried out the actual assassinations under strict laws of obedience, and total ignorance of the objects and ritual of the society. It is believed that the latter were given ecstatic visions under the influence of hashish, whence the term hashshashin, which became corrupted to "assassin".

Associationism. In psychology, the Associationist school of the 19th cent. accepted the association of ideas as the fundamental principle in mental life. It was represented in Britain by the two Mills and Herbert Spencer, in Germany by J. F. Herbart (1776–1841). To these, mental activity was nothing but the association of "ideas" conceived of as units of both thought and feeling—the emotion of anger or the perception of a chair were both "ideas"—and apart from them the self did not exist. Personality was simply a series of these units coming and going, adding to or cancelling each other out, in accordance with rigid and mechanistic scientific laws.

Astrology was once the best available theory for explaining the course of human life and bears much the same historical relationship to astronomy as alchemy does to chemistry. Originally it was divided into the two branches of Natural Astrology which dealt with the movements of the heavenly bodies and their calculations, and Judicial Astrology which studied the alleged influence of the stars and the planets on human life and fate. It was the former that developed into modern astronomy; the latter was, and remains, a primitive myth.

Astrology owes most to the early Babylonians (or Chaldeans) who, being largely nomadic in an environment which permitted an unobstructed view of the sky, readily accepted the idea that divine energy is manifested in the movements of the sun and planets. Gradually this concept became enlarged and the relative positions of the planets both in relation to each other and to the fixed stars became important together with the idea of omens—that, if a particular event occurred whilst the planets were in a particular position, the recurrence of that position heralded a recurrence of the same sort of event. Soon the planets became associated with almost every aspect of human life. They were bound up with the emotions, with parts of the body, so that astrology played quite a large part in medicine up to late mediaeval times. Not only was the position of the planet to be considered but also the particular sign of the zodiac (or house of heaven) it was occupying, and it was believed possible to foretell the destiny of an individual by calculating which star was in the ascendant (*i.e.* the sign of the zodiac nearest the eastern horizon and the star which arose at that precise moment) at the time of his birth. Astrology was popular among the Egyptians, the Romans (whose authorities found the Chaldean astrologers a nuisance and expelled them from time to time), and during the Middle Ages when astrologers were often highly respected.

Despite the apparent absurdity of astrological beliefs—for example, how could the pattern of light from stars billions of miles away possibly influence the temperament of single individuals on earth—a substantial number of intelligent and well-educated people take its study in all seriousness. The most interesting "convert" was the psychologist and philosopher, Carl Jung, who conducted a complex experiment in which he compared the "birth signs" of happily married and divorced couples and claimed to find that those most favourably matched in astrological terms were also those more likely to have permanent wedded bliss. Jung's findings were subsequently shown to have been based on a simple statistical fallacy, which did not prevent the brilliant but eccentric psychologist from offering them up as evidence in support of his own theory of "synchronicity" (**J51**), an involved and vaguely metaphysical notion which suggests that events in the universe may be significantly related in a "non-causal" fashion. To add fuel to the controversy however, the French mathematician, Michel Gauquelin, has recently offered up fresh data which apparently supports the general astrological view. In a carefully controlled study he noticed statistically significant correspondences between certain astrological signs and the professions of a large number of Frenchmen whose birth time and date were accurately recorded. Gauquelin claims to have repeated his study on a second large sample of his fellow countrymen, though he has been unable to use English people as the exact times of birth are not recorded on their birth certificates! This apparent shot in the arm for astrology is still a matter of great scientific controversy. though Gauquelin's work has been given support from the distinguished British psychologist. H. J. Eysenck, who has pronounced his statistical data to to be incontrovertible. Both scientists, however, carefully refrain from discussing the implications of these curious findings, and the controversy will no doubt increase rather than decrease in the near future.

Atheism. *See* **God and Man.**

Atlantis, a mythical continent supposed to have lain somewhere between Europe and America and a centre of advanced civilisation before it was inundated by some great natural catastrophe in pre-Christian times. There is little, if any, serious historical or archaeological evidence for its existence, but the legend of the Golden Land destroyed when the waters of the Atlantic closed over it has remarkable staying power and is believed by large numbers of people. Plato wrote convincingly about the wonders of Atlantis in his dialogues *Timaeus* and *Critias*, while other writers have suggested that the biblical story of the Flood is based on fragmentary accounts of the Atlantean deluge. The lost continent is also of occult significance, largely as the result of the writings of W. Scott-Elliott whose book, *The Story of Atlantis* (recently re-published by the Theosophical Society), alleged that by clairvoyance he had been able to contact the spirits of Atlanteans who had been destroyed because of their addiction to black magic. There even exists in Britain today a minor but ardent religious group, the "Atlanteans", who hold that Atlantis still exists today, but on a different metaphysical plane, and that it is possible to communicate with it via individuals with supposedly mediumistic powers (*see* **Spiritualism**). Members of the Atlanteans meet regularly to hear "trance addresses" by one of the high priests of Atlantis, Helio-Arconaphus. Such beliefs are essentially harmless and merely reflect the great variety of religious attitudes which human beings enjoy.

Atomism. In philosophy, the atomists were a group of early Greek thinkers, the most important of whom were Leucippus (fl. *c.* 440 B.C.) and his younger contemporary Democritus (*c.* 460–370 B.C.). Prior to these men, although it had been agreed that matter must be composed of tiny ultimate particles and that change must be due to the manner in which these mingled or separated from each other, it was supposed that there existed different types of particle for each material—*e.g.* for flesh, wood, hair, bone. The atomists taught that atoms were all made of a single substance and differed only in the connections (pictured as hooks, grooves, points, etc.) which enabled them to join each other in characteristic ways. Theirs was the first move towards modern atomic theory and a predecessor of the modern concept of chemical linkages.

Authoritarianism, a dictatorial form of government as contrasted with a democratic one based on popular sovereignty. Its alleged advantages are the avoidance of the delays and inefficiency said to be characteristic of the latter.

Automatism, the production of material, written or spoken in "automatic" fashion—*i.e.*, apparently not under the conscious or volitional control of the individual. This psychologically perplexing phenomenon has occurred from time to time throughout the history of literature and art, and while it has occasionally produced work of great merit (much of William Blake's poetry, Coleridge's "Kubla Khan", etc.) the bulk of it is indifferent and often simply rubbish. Spiritualists claim that the work is produced under the direct guidances of the spirit world, and their argument has attracted considerable attention through the compositions of the pianist Rosemary Brown who, with little or no academic background in musical theory, has produced a number of "original" piano pieces allegedly composed by Beethoven, Mozart, etc., from the astral plane. While few music critics doubt Mrs. Brown's honesty and integrity, most consider her work to be clever pastiche and barely comparable in quality to the masterworks of the dead composers. Nevertheless automatism wants some explaining, and most psychologists today defer judgement, taking the view that it serves to remind us of the fund of material which lies in the unconscious mind, and which is prone to pop up from time to time without warning. Rather similar is the case of Matthew Manning, a young English student who produced clever and artistically intriguing drawings and sketches, allegedly guided by the hands of famous dead artists.

B

Baconian Method, the use of the inductive (as opposed to the deductive or Aristotelian) method of reasoning as proposed by Francis Bacon in the 17th cent. and J. S. Mill in the 19th cent. Deduction argues from supposedly certain first principles (such as the existence of God or Descartes's "I think, therefore I am") what the nature of the universe and its laws *must* be, whereas the only means of obtaining true knowledge of the universe, in Bacon's view, was by the amassing of facts and observations so that when enough were obtained the certain truth would be known in the same way that a child's numbered dots in a playbook joined together by a pencilled line create a picture. However, this is not the way science progresses in practice (*see* **F3(1)**). Bacon underrated the importance of hypothesis and theory and overrated the reliability of the senses. In discussing the scientific tradition, Sir Karl Popper in his book, *Conjecture and Refutations*, says: "The most important function of observation and reasoning, and even of intuition and imagination, is to help us in the critical examination of those bold conjectures which are the means by which we probe into the unknown." Two of the greatest men who clearly saw that there was no such thing as an inductive procedure were Galileo and Einstein.

Bahá'í Faith, a faith which teaches the unity of all religions and the unity of mankind. It arose in Iran from the teachings of the Bab (Mirza Ali Mohammed, 1820–50) and the Bahá'u'lláh (Mirza Husain Ali, 1817–92), thought to be manifestations of God, who in his essence is unknowable. Emphasis is laid on service to others. It has communities in many states and is surprisingly strong in England with a substantial following among university students. Its aims—universal peace, love, fellowship, sexual equality, etc.—are so laudable that it is hard to disagree with anything in the movement. Since the ruling fundamentalist Islamic regime of the Ayatollahs came to power in Iran in 1979 members of the faith have been persecuted. The movement is now guided and administered by an elected order, "The Universal House of Justice". Today (1990) the movement has some 4–5 million followers.

Baptists, a Christian denomination whose distinctive doctrines are that members can only be received by baptism "upon the confession of their faith and sins" and that "baptism is no wise appertaineth to infants." Baptism is therefore by total immersion of adults. Modern Baptists base their doctrines upon the teaching of the Apostles and some hold that the Albigenses (*q.v.*) maintained the true belief through what they regarded as the corruption of the Roman Church in mediaeval times. On the other hand any connection with the Anabaptist movement during the Reformation is rejected and the beginning of the modern Church is traced to John Smyth, a minister of the Church of England who in Amsterdam came under the influence of the Arminians (*q.v.*) and Mennonites. Smyth died in 1612 when the first Baptist church in England was built at Newgate. This, the "General" Baptist Church, rejected Calvinistic beliefs and held the Arminian doctrine of redemption open to all, but some years later a split occurred with the formation of the "Particular" Baptist Church which was Calvinist in doctrine. In 1891 the two bodies were united in the Baptist Union and today the sect is spread throughout the world, notably in the United States.

The Anabaptist movements of Germany, Switzerland, and Holland also practised adult baptism in addition to a primitive communism and demanded social reforms. Persecuted by both Catholics and Protestants, their leader, Thomas Münzer, and many others were burned at the stake (1525). However, this sect was noted for its violence under a religious guise, and its taking over of the state of Münster in 1533 was characterised by wild licentiousness, since, as Antinomians, they believed that the "elect" could do no wrong. A revival begun by Menno Simons (d. 1561), a Dutch religious reformer, led to the formation of the Mennonite sect which, whilst rejecting infant baptism, gave up the objectionable features of the Anabaptists. This reformed sect still exists as small agricultural groups in the original strongholds of the movement and in the United States. There are (1990) 240,000 Baptists in Great Britain.

Beat Generation, a term first used by the American writer Jack Kerouac (d. 1969), author of *The Town and the City* and *On the Road*, to define various groups spread across the face of the country, but notably in New York and San Francisco, who, belonging to the post-war generation, represented a complex of attitudes. Briefly, these were: rejection of the values of the past and lack of conviction in the possibility of a future for humanity—hence an acceptance of nothing but the immediate present in terms of experience and sensations; rebellion against organised authority, not out of any political conviction (as in the case of anarchism), but rather from lack of any interest or desire to control events, nature, or people; contempt for the "Square"—the orthodox individual who, stuck in his rut, "plays it safe" and remains confident of the rightness and decency of his moral values.

The Beat Generation of the 1940s and 50s gave way to the Love generation or Flower people, with their flowers, beads, and cowbells. Their social philosophy was the same—living in the present, unconventionally, seeking personal freedom, believing drugs to be essential, claiming to be acting against the rat race, dissociating themselves from politics, taking a superficial interest in the religions of the East, borrowing much of their language, music, and ideas on dress from the American "*hippy*"; yet believing in the creation of a new and gentler society based on different forms and values.

Both the Beat and Love generations were forerunners in America of an increasing and certainly welcome social awareness on the part of American students. This led in turn to the "campus revolutions" which were disruptive in their early stages but were also influential as part of the wave of public protest against the American involvement in Vietnam.

Behaviourism, a school of psychology founded in 1914 by J. B. Watson (1878–1958), an animal psychologist at Johns Hopkins University, Baltimore. Its main tenet was that the method of introspection and the study of mental states were unscientific and should be replaced by the study of behaviour. When animals or human beings were exposed to specific stimuli and their responses objectively recorded, or when the development of a child, as seen in its changing behaviour, was noted, these alone were methods which were truly scientific. Watson contributed an important idea to psychology and did a great deal towards ridding it of the largely philosophical speculations of the past. But he also went to absurd extremes, as in his view that thought is nothing but subvocal speech, consisting of almost imperceptible movements of the tongue, throat, and larynx (*i.e.*, when we think, we are really talking to ourselves), and his further opinion that heredity is, except in grossly abnormal cases, of no importance. He claimed that by "conditioning", the ordinary individual could be made into any desired type, regardless of his or her inheritance.

The work of Ivan Pavlov had begun about 1901, but was unknown in America until about ten years later, and it was through another Russian, Vladimir Bekhterev, that the concept of "conditioning" was introduced into the country. Bekhterev's book *Objective Psychology*, describing his new science of "reflexology", was translated in 1913 and played a great part in the development of Behaviourist ideas. The conditioned reflex became central to Watson's theory of learning and habit, formation (*e.g.*, he showed that a year-old child, at first unafraid of white rats, became afraid of them when they came to be associated with a loud noise behind the head). Finally all behaviour, including abnormal behaviour, came to be explained in terms of conditioned responses; these were built up by association on the infant's three innate emotions of fear, rage, and love, of which the original stimuli were, for the first, loud noises and the fear of falling; for the second, interference with freedom of movement; and for the third, patting and stroking.

Because of its considerable theoretical simplicity and its implicit suggestion that human behaviour could be easily described (and even modified or controlled), Pavlovian psychology appeared very attractive to the Communist regime in Russia, and before long it became the "official" dogma in universities and research laboratories. Whereas in America and Western Europe its severe limitations became gradually apparent, in Russia these were ignored or disguised for ideological reasons with the inevitable outcome that Soviet psychology failed to evolve and, at one stage, seemed to be no more than a pallid offshoot of physiology. The recent liberalisation which has been taking place throughout Soviet society has led to a considerable broadening of scientific horizons and Pavlovian ideas are no longer looked upon with such unquestioning reverence. In non-Communist countries simple Watsonian behaviourism has evolved into more sophisticated studies of animal learning, largely pioneered by the Harvard psychologist, Skinner. These techniques, which have shown that animals, from monkeys to rats, may be taught to solve a remarkable range of physical problems (such as pressing complex sequences of buttons or levers to escape from a cage) have themselves turned out to be rather disappointing in terms of advancing our general understanding of the workings of the human and animal brain. There is a growing feeling among psychologists that the real keys to the understanding of mankind will only be found through the study of man himself, and not his simpler animal cousins. *See also under entry* **Gestalt Psychology**.

Benthamism. *See* **Utilitarianism**.

Black Power. The division of the world's population into races is now generally agreed by scientists to have arisen as the result of climatic and environmental pressures—the darker, more highly pigmented peoples tending to be better equipped to withstand higher solar output than the fairer, more northerly based types. For various reasons, again largely climatic and environmental, the first great advances in civilisation came from the temporary ascendancy over the black or near-black. Until quite recently—not much more than century ago—the technological gulf between white and black was so vast that the negroid races were often held in slavery by the Europeans and while such a thought might be repugnant to most today, attitudes to coloured people still reflect a notion of inherent white "superiority" which it is easy to deny intellectually but difficult to shake off emotionally. In the U.S.A., the most advanced and at the same time the most tormented multi-racial society in the world, the role of the substantial negroid population has changed dramatically in the last hundred years, shifting from that of slave to friendly servant, and then to near, or theoretical, equal. With this shift has come a corresponding change in the black community's view of itself, from relief at being no longer slaves, to gratitude at being allowed to do the menial jobs in the American society. More recently, with advances in educational opportunity and increasing political liberalisation, the attitude of the Negro in the U.S.A. has shifted yet again—from subservience to intellectual and physical equality, and even, perhaps, to inherent superiority. This new stand, rare at first, but spreading rapidly across America and other parts of the world throughout the 1960s, has crystallised in the concept and ideology of "Black Power". a movement of growing significance and importance in modern society. It is hard to trace the moment at which this formally emerged but one of its first expressions was the use by Negroes of the phrase "Black is beautiful", an apparent wakening of the belief that their colour, physique, features, hair, etc., were in no way aesthetically inferior to those of Europeans. Suddenly, in Negro communities it became no longer fashionable to straighten hair artificially, to bleach the skin or even to copy white American clothing, social habits, speech, and mannerisms. Alongside this highly important

psychological jump—a rejection of the white man's social patterns—came an increasing rejection of his political machinery as well, a belief that the black races should have political autonomy and power of their own and not as part of an integrationist evolution of Caucasian societies.

In the late 60s when the Black Power movement was in its most aggressive phase of expansion, there were real fears that open conflict, almost of civil war dimensions, might break out in American cities, but increasing liberalisation and better opportunities for social advancement and education for Negroes has slightly dulled its sense of purpose. The 70s in fact saw a dramatic change in the state of the American Negro, with blacks penetrating middle-class and professional strata of society—medicine, law, politics, business, science, etc.—at a rate which would have seemed incredible 20 years ago. Urban ghettoes, however, still exist and provide numerous flashpoints for black-white conflict—the city of Boston is a particularly good example—but most observers (black and white) now view the future with more optimism than pessimism. However, the fact that America is fast becoming the best integrated country in the world is at least partly due to the conflicts and injustices which launched Black Power into being. With the death of its leaders, George Jackson, Michael X, Malcolm X, Black Power in Britain has since the 1970s given way to Rastafarianism (*q.v.*).

Bolshevism, an alternative name for **Communism** (*q.v.*), usually used in the West in a derogatory sense. When the Russian Social Democratic Party at a conference held in London in 1903 split over the issue of radicalism or moderation, it was the radical faction headed by Lenin (who subsequently led the 1917 Revolution and became first Head of State of the Soviet Union) which polled the majority of votes. The Russian for majority is *bolshinstvo* and for minority *menshinstvo*; hence the radicals became known as Bolsheviki and the moderates as Mensheviki, anglicised as Bolsheviks and Mensheviks. *See* **Communism**, **Marxism**.

British Israelites, a religious group who hold the race-theory that the English-speaking peoples (of the White Race) are the lineal descendants of the "lost Ten Tribes" of Israel (deported by Sargon of Assyria on the fall of Samaria in 721 B.C.). They believe the Anglo-Saxons to be God's "Chosen People" in the literal sense of the term as it is used in the Old Testament by whom the world will be brought in readiness for the Millennium. The official organisation is the British-Israel World Federation of which the official journal is the *National Message*. Some British Israelites have the notion that the future can be foretold by the measurements of the Great Pyramid.

Buchmanism. *See* **Moral Re-Armament**.

Buddhism, one of the great Oriental religions. It arose against the background of Hinduism in north India in the 6th cent. B.C., its founder (real or legendary) being the Hindu prince Siddhartha Gautama, known as the Buddha or "Enlightened One". Distressed by the problem of human suffering from which even death allowed no escape—since Buddha accepted the Hindu doctrine of a cycle of lives—he left his palace and his beloved family to become a religious mendicant and ascetic, studying with limited success for six years the beliefs of Brahmin hermits and self-torturing recluses. After this long search he sat down under a tree (the Bo-tree) and finally came to understand the cause and release from suffering. The result of his meditations are enshrined in the "four noble truths" which are: (1) that all that lives experiences suffering; (2) suffering is caused by desire; (3) suffering ceases when desire is eradicated; (4) that it can be destroyed by following the "noble eightfold path" whose steps are: right views; right thought; right speech, plain and truthful; right conduct, including abstinence not only from immorality but also from taking life, whether human or animal; right livelihood, harming no one; right effort, always pressing on; right awareness of the past, the present, and the future; and lastly, right contemplation or meditation. The more

J9

man acquires merit by following these rules in his chain of lives, the sooner is *Nirvana* attained; he loses his individuality, not by annihilation, but "as the dewdrop slips into the shining sea," by merging with the universal life.

Buddhism teaches a way of liberation through ethics and meditation; A universal God plays no part in this religion, and in many Buddhist nations no word exists for the concept which was neither affirmed nor denied by Buddha himself but simply ignored. Nor did Buddha claim to be other than a man, although much superstition entered the religion at a later date; prayers were made to Buddha, ritual developed, sacred relics preserved under stupas, and the belief in a succession of Buddhas introduced; the sacred writings (*Tripitaka*) are divided into three parts; for the layman, the monks, the philosophers. They were produced by devotees at three councils—the first held immediately after the death of Buddha at the age of 80, the last at the order of King Asoka in 244 B.C. The founder himself wrote nothing.

Buddhism spread to Sri Lanka, Nepal, Tibet, Mongolia, Indo-China, Myanmar (Burma), Thailand, China, and Japan, although on the whole losing influence in India. In Tibet, Buddhism developed into Lamaism (*q.v.*). In Sri Lanka and Burma it persisted in its pure form (the Theravada), while in China and Japan it developed into the Mahayana with its bodhisattvas and avatars.

Bushido, the traditional code of honour of the Samurai or Japanese military caste corresponding to the European concept of knighthood and chivalry from which it took its separate origin in the 12th cent. Even today it is a potent influence among the upper classes, being based on the principles of simplicity, honesty, courage, and justice which together form a man's idea of personal honour.

C

Cabala, originally a collection of Jewish doctrines about the nature of the Universe, supposedly handed down by Moses to the Rabbis, which evolved into a kind of mystical interpretation of the Old Testament. Students of the history of religious belief have found its origins to be in fact extremely obscure, and some aspects appear to have been lifted from ancient Egyptian sources. Skilled Cabalists hold that the system contains a key to biblical interpretation based on the numerical values of the words and letters of the Scriptures which reveal hidden depths of meaning behind the allegorical Old Testament stories.

Calvinism, the branch of Protestantism founded basically (although preceded by Zwingli and others) by Jean Chauvin (1509–64), who was born in Noyon in Picardy. John Calvin, as he is usually called, from the Latin form of his name, Calvinius, provided in his *Institutions of the Christian Religion* the first logical definition and justification of Protestantism, thus becoming the intellectual leader of the Reformation as the older Martin Luther was its emotional instigator. The distinctive doctrine of Calvinism is its dogma of predestination which states that God has unalterably destined some souls to salvation to whom "efficacious grace" and the gift of perseverance" is granted and others to eternal damnation. Calvinism, as defined in the Westminster Confession, is established in the Reformed or Presbyterian churches of France, Holland, Scotland, etc., as contrasted with the Lutheran churches, and its harsh but logical beliefs inspired the French Huguenots, the Dutch in their fight against Spanish Catholic domination, and the English Puritans. The rule set up under Calvin's influence in Geneva was marred by the burning at the stake of the anatomist Servetus for the heresy of "pantheism", or, as we should say, Unitarianism.

Perhaps its greatest single influence outside the Church was the result of Calvinist belief that

to labour industriously was one of God's commands. This changed the mediaeval notions of the blessedness of poverty and the wickednesss of usury, proclaimed that men should shun luxury and be thrifty, yet implied that financial success was a mark of God's favour. In this way it was related to the rise of capitalism either as cause or effect. Max Weber, the German sociologist, believed that Calvinism was a powerful incentive to, or even cause of, the rise of **capitalism** (*q.v.*): Marx, Sombart, and in England, Tawney, have asserted the reverse view—that Calvinism was a result of developing capitalism, being its ideological justification.

Capitalism is an economic system under which the means of production and distribution are owned by a relatively small section of society which runs them at its own discretion for private profit. There exists, on the other hand, a propertyless class of those who exist by the sale of their labour power. Capitalism arose towards the end of the 18th cent. in England where the early factory owners working with small-scale units naturally approved of free enterprise and free trade. But free enterprise has no necessary connection with capitalism; by the beginning of this century monopolies were developing and state protection against foreign competition was demanded. Capitalism is opposed by those who believe in socialism (*q.v.*), first, for the moral reasons that it leads to economic inequality and the exploitation of labour and the consuming public, and that public welfare rather than private profit should motivate the economic system; secondly, for the practical reason that capitalism leads to recurrent economic crises. The recent world economic crisis has led to great hopes on the part of Marxists and Communists that capitalism is now involved in its final death throes. It is worth commenting however, that the European war of the 1940s, the great depression of the 30s, the first world war and the Russian Revolution were also, in their turn, confidently held up by Communists as heralding capitalism's imminent collapse.

Cartomancy, the art of fortunes or predicting the future by playing cards or by the Tarot pack. The elegant Tarot cards number 78 in all and are probably mediaeval in origin. They are rich in symbolism and include trump cards depicting the devil, the pope, death, the moon, the wheel of fortune, etc., and are an interesting part of our cultural mythology. There is no evidence whatsoever that they can be used in any objective way to divine the future, and professional fortune tellers and clairvoyants who use them almost certainly rely on a little native, basic psychology to achieve their results.

Catholicism. For those who are not Roman Catholics the term "Catholic" has two separate meanings. The more general refers to the whole body of Christians throughout the world, the more specific refers to a particular view of Christianity. In this latter sense the Church of England, the Orthodox Eastern Churches, and others consider themselves "Catholic" meaning that (a) they belong to Christ's Church as organised on an accepted basis of faith and order; (b) they insist on the necessity of "liturgical" worship through established forms (e.g., baptism, holy communion); (c) they emphasise the continuity of Christian tradition by the use of ancient creeds (e.g., the Apostles' Creed, the Nicene Creed) and regard the ministry as a succession (Apostolic succession) deriving from early practice. In this sense there is thought to be no necessary contradiction between Catholicism and Protestantism regarded as a renewal of the Church in the 16th cent. by an appeal to the Scriptures as interpreted by the early Fathers of the Church. This definition obviously excludes Quakers, Christian Scientists, and many Nonconformist sects.

The Roman Catholic Church is the religious organisation of all those who acknowledge the bishop of Rome as head of the Christian Church, recognising him as the lawful successor of St. Peter, who was the apostle appointed by Christ to be the head of the Church.

Whereas in the Protestant Churches prayer and preaching play a central part (each individual soul seeking direct communication with God), in Roman Catholic worship the central service is the Mass, or Holy Eucharist, the seven sacraments (baptism, confirmation, eucharist, penance, extreme unction, orders, and marriage) being administered by a special priesthood. Church discipline and organisation are strong and authoritarian. There are now 7 Catholic provinces in Britain, 30 episcopal dioceses and over 3,000 parishes. In 1982, Pope John Paul II paid the first pastoral visit by a reigning pontiff. In 1990, there were over 900 m. Roman Catholics worldwide. *See* **Papal Infallibility.**

Characterology, the attempt made over many centuries to classify people into personality types on the basis of physical or psychological characteristics. The first attempt was made by Hippocrates in the 5th cent. B.C. who classified temperaments into the *sanguine* (or optimistic), the *melancholic,* the *choleric* (or aggressive), and the *phlegmatic* (or placid); these were supposed to result from the predominance of the following "humours" in the body: red blood, black bile, yellow bile, or phlegm respectively. Theophrastus, a pupil of Aristotle, described, with examples, thirty extreme types of personality (*e.g.* the talkative, the boorish, the miserly, etc.); these were basically literary and imaginative but about the same time "physiognomy" arose which attempted to interpret character from the face. Physiognomy became of importance again during the Renaissance and there are still those today who believe in it in spite of the fact that, broadly speaking, there is no connection whatever between facial features and personality (i.e. although it may be possible to tell from the features that a man is an idiot or some extreme abnormal type and some idea of character may be obtained from an individual's characteristic facial expressions, it is not possible to tell (as Johann Lavater, the best-known physiognomist of the late 18th cent. believed) from the shape of the nose, height of the brow, or dominance of the lower jaw, whether anyone is weak, intellectual or determined). The contention of the 19th cent. Italian criminologist Cesare Lombroso that criminals show typical facial characteristics—prominent cheekbones and jaw, slanting eyes, receding brow, large ears of a particular shape—was disproved by Karl Pearson early this century when he found that 3,000 criminals showed no major differences of features, carefully measured from a similar number of students at Oxford and Cambridge.

It has, however, been noted that people in general tend to be intellectual or emotional, inward- or outward-looking, and this observation is reflected in the classification of the Scottish psychologist, Alexander Bain (d. 1903), into intellectual, artistic, and practical; Nietzsche's Apollonian and Dionysian types; William James's "tender" and "toughminded"; and C. G. Jung's introvert and extrovert.

Some connection has been found between temperament and body-build. The German psychiatrist Ernst Kretschmer (1888–1964) showed that manic-depressive patients and normal people who are extroverted and tend to alternate in mood (as do manic-depressives to an exaggerated degree) were usually short and stout or thick-set in build; schizophrenics and normal people, who both show shyness, serious or introverted reactions, were usually tall and slender. The former of "pyknic" body-build are "cyclothyme" in temperament, the latter with "schizothyme" temperament are of two bodily types—the tall and thin or "asthenic" and the muscularly well-proportioned or "athletic". The American Sheldon has confirmed these observations on the whole and gone into further details. According to him the basic body types are: (1) *endomorphic* (rounded build), corresponding to Kretschmer's pyknic, normally associated with the *viscerotonic* temperament (relaxed, sociable); (2) *mesomorphic* (squarish, athletic build), normally associated with the *somatotonic* temperament (energetic, assertive); and (3) *ectomorphic* (linear build) normally associated with the *cerebrotonic* temperament (anxious, submissive, restless).

Glandular and metabolic factors have considerable effect on human personality and also, to some extent, on physique. It is not too surprising, therefore, to find an association between body build (or "somatotype" as Sheldon termed it) and general mood. However, Sheldon's original clear-cut categories of body-type are no longer looked upon as reliable indicators of personality.

Chartism, a socialistic movement in England (1837–55) which attempted to better the conditions of the working classes. Named after "The People's Charter" of Francis Place (1838), its programme demanded: (1) universal manhood suffrage; (2) vote by ballot; (3) equal electoral districts; (4) annual parliament; (5) payment of members; (6) abolition of their property qualifications. Chartism was supported by the Christian socialists (*q.v.*), J. F. D. Maurice (1805–72), and Charles Kingsley (1819–75) with certain qualifications. The movement, the first mass organisation of the industrial working class, had considerable influence on the evolution of socialist ideas in England. It is worth noting that its demands—with the exception of the unworkable "annual parliament"—have largely been met today, though at the time they were thought by many to be both outrageous and impossible. The movement failed at the time from internal divisions.

Chauvinism, a term applied to any excessive devotion to cause, particularly a patriotic or military one. The word is derived from Nicholas Chauvin whose excessive devotion to Napoleon made him a laughing-stock.

Chirognomy, the attempt to read character from the lines in the hand (as contrasted with chiromancy or palmistry, in which an attempt is made to tell the future in the same way) is an ancient practice which, like astrology (*q.v.*) has no discernible scientific basis but a very considerable popular following. As with astrology, where it is hard to see what kind of link could exist between the constellations and human behaviour, so it is equally hard to see how the configuration of lines on the hand could be paralleled by psychological attributes. This argument might be thought of as irrelevant if palmistry, etc. actually had predictive power, but the plain fact is that when put to a scientific test, practitioners of these arts turn out to show no abilities beyond those with which a normally perceptive individual is equipped.

Chiropractice, the art of manipulation of the joints, in particular the spine, as a means of curing disease, is a slightly fashionable quasi-medical practice. Few qualified doctors employ its questionable principles though, as with its near-neighbour osteopathy, it seems on occasions to be a useful complement to medical treatment. Much controversy surrounds the status of practitioners of fringe medicine of this kind. In America osteopathy (bone manipulation), which seems to be beneficial in many cases for the condition known as prolapsed or "slipped" disc, is becoming gradually merged into orthodox medical practice.

Christadelphians, a religious denomination formed in the U.S.A. in the late 1840s by John Thomas, an Englishman. They strive to represent the simple apostolic faith of the 1st century and hold that the Scriptures are the wholly inspired, infallible Word of God. They believe in the mortality of mankind—the teaching of the immortality of the soul is not of Bible origin and that salvation is dependent of belief followed by a baptism of total immersion in water. They believe in the imminent, personal return of Jesus Christ to the earth to judge the living and dead and reward the righteous with Eternal life.

Christianity, the religion founded by Jesus Christ whose teaching is found in the New Testament's four Gospels. Simple as His creed may seem it soon became complicated by the various ways in which Christians interpreted it, and the differences within the early Church are reflected in the numerous Councils held to define truth from heresy. The Eastern Church of the Byzantine Empire from the 5th cent. onwards had differed in various ways from the See of Rome and by 1054 the breach became permanent. The 16th cent. Reformation was the other great break in the unity of the Church and once Protestantism had given in effect the right to each man to interpret the Scriptures in his own way, the tendency to fragmentation increased so that, by 1650, there were no fewer than 180 sects, mostly dogmatic and intolerant towards each other. Today there are many more, some of which are mentioned in this section under the appropriate headings. Nevertheless there are signs today that the trend of disunity is being reversed. The modern ecumenical movement, which has its roots in the great missionary movement of the 19th cent., aims to bring about a reunion of Christendom by uniting Christians throughout the world on the simple basis of the acceptance of Jesus Christ as God and Saviour, *i.e.*, on the basis of Christian fellowship. The movement finds expression in the World Council of Churches (*q.v.*). The Christian life is expressed in the words of Christ: "Thou shalt love the Lord thy God with all thy heart and thy neighbour as thyself." For many it is the humanitarian side of Christianity that has meaning today; to accept responsibility for others, as well as for oneself. *See* chart, below.

Christian Science claims that it is a religion based on the words and works of Christ Jesus. It draws its authority from the Bible, and its teachings are set forth in *Science and Health with Key to the Scriptures* by Mary Baker Eddy (1821–1910) the discoverer and founder of Christian Science. A distinctive part of Christian Science is its healing of physical disease as well as sin by spiritual means alone.

The Church of Christ, Scientist, was founded in 1879 when 15 students of Mrs Eddy met with their teacher and voted to organize a church designed to commemorate the words and works of the Master, which should reinstate primitive Christianity and its lost element of healing.

A few years later the church took its present and permanent form as The Mother Church, The First Church of Christ, Scientist, in Boston, Massachusetts, which together with its branch churches and societies throughout the world, constitutes the Christian Science denomination. Now (1990) more than 100 years after its founding there are over 2,700 branches in 60 countries, as well as numerous informal groups not yet organized and about 300 organizations at universities and colleges.

Christian Socialism, a movement launched in 1848, a year of revolutions throughout the continent, by a group in England designed to commit the church to a programme of social reform. The leaders, notably J. F. D. Maurice, Charles Kingsley (both Anglican clergymen), and John Ludlow were deeply moved by the wretched conditions of the British working class and the two priests had, indeed, given active support to the Chartist movement (*q.v.*). However, all insisted that socialism in its existing forms ignored the spiritual needs of mankind and must be tempered with Christianity. Tracts were written to expose the sweated industries, the consequences of unrestrained competition and the evils following the enclosure system; but, more concretely, Christian socialism fostered co-operative workshops and distributive societies based on those of the Rochdale pioneers, organised a working-man's college, and set up elementary classes for education. It also supported the emerging trade-union movement.

The traditions of Christian socialism have

Early Christian Church
|
(Church of the Roman Empire)
4th cent.
|
3rd–7th cent. Schisms in the East.
Controversies concerned with the relation of Jesus
Christ to God and to man: Arianism, Nestorianism
Monophysitism, Monotheletism

| Nestorian Church | Armenian Church | Jacobite Church | Coptic Church |

Schism of Eastern and Western Christendoms 1054 A.D.

Western Christendom *Latin* Rome

Eastern Christendom *Greek* Constantinople

Mediaeval Inquisition began c. 1231

Orthodox Eastern Church

Spanish Inquisition began 1481

Counter Reformation and Inquisition at Rome, 16th cent.   *Reformation, 16th–17th cent.*   *Renaissance 15th cent.*

Roman Catholic Church   Protestantism   Humanism

Moravians Lutherans Calvinists Church of England   (*Henry VIII's break with Rome 1534. Excommunication of Elizabeth 1570*)

Presbyterians

Nonconformism

Baptists Congregationalists Methodists Evangelicals Modernists Anglo-Catholics been carried on by the Fabian Society, by adherents of Guild Socialism, and by individuals who reject Marx's teaching of revolutionary change, and seek to bring it about by the methods of action through political parties, education, and encouragement of the unions. They believe that Christ's teachings can only be fully realised in a new society since Christianity implies social responsibility, and material factors are admitted to have an important bearing on the ability to lead a truly religious life. *See also* **Fabian Society, Guild Socialism**.

Church of England. There is some evidence of possible continuity with the Christianity of Roman Britain, but in the main the Church derives from the fusion of the ancient Celtic church with the missionary church of St. Augustine, who founded the See of Canterbury in A.D. 597. To archbishop Theodore in 673 is ascribed its organisation in dioceses with settled boundaries, and in parishes. St. Augustine's church was in communion with Rome from the first, but the Church of England was not brought within papal jurisdiction until after the Norman conquest, and was at no time under the complete domination of Rome. It remains the Catholic Church of England without break of continuity, but during the Reformation the royal supremacy was accepted and that of the pope repudiated. It is the Established Church (*i.e.*, the official church of the realm), crowns the sovereign, and its archbishops and bishops in the House of Lords can act as a kind of "conscience of the state" at every stage of legislation. The Church is organised in two ecclesiastical provinces (Canterbury and York) and 43 dioceses. Its traditional forms of worship are embodied in the Book of Common Prayer, but the Alternative Service Book of 1980 is now widely used. In 1989, Easter communicants were estimated at *c* 1,600,000. In November 1989, the General Synod accepted in principle the ordination of women priests, despite bitter opposition from traditionalists.

The Anglican Communion comprises the churches in all parts of the world which are in communion with the Church of England. All the bishops of the Anglican Communion meet every ten years in the Lambeth Conference (first held in 1867), over which the Archbishop of Canterbury by custom presides as *primus inter pares*. At the 1968 Conference observers and laymen were admitted for the first time. The 1988 Conference paved the way for the eventual consecration of women bishops. The next Conference meets in 1998.

Church of Scotland, the established national church of Scotland, presbyterian in constitution, and governed by a hierarchy of courts—the kirk-sessions, the presbyteries, the synods, and the General Assembly. *See* **Presbyterianism**.

Clairvoyance. *See* **Telepathy**.

Communism, ideally refers to the type of society in which all property belongs to the community and social life is based on the principle "from each according to his ability, to each according to his needs." There would be public ownership of all enterprises and all goods would be free. Since no such society as yet exists, the word in practice refers to the attempt to achieve such a society by initially overthrowing the capitalist system and establishing a dictatorship of the proletariat (Marx identified the dictatorship with a democratic constitution). Communists believe that their first task is the establishment of socialism under which there remain class distinctions, private property to some extent, and differences between manual and brain workers. The state is regulated on the basis "from each according to his ability, to each according to his work". Lenin applied Marx's analysis to the new conditions which had arisen in 20th-cent. capitalist society. Marxism–Leninism develops continuously with practice since failure to apply its basic principles to changed circumstances and times would result in errors of dogmatism. Mao Tse-tung worked out the techniques of revolutionary action appropriate to China; Che Guevara the guerrilla tactics appropriate to the peasants of Latin America. His counsel "It is not necessary to wait until conditions for making revolution exist; the insurrection can create them", was the opposite of Mao Tse-tung's "Engage in no battle you are not sure of winning", and Lenin's

"Never play with insurrection". Two fundamental principles of communism are (1) peaceful co-existence between countries of different social systems, and (2) the class struggle between oppressed and oppressing classes and between oppressed and oppressor nations. Maoism, for example, holds that it is a mistake to lay one-sided stress on peaceful transition towards socialism otherwise the revolutionary will of the proletariat becomes passive and unprepared politically and organisationally for the tasks ahead.

In Russia the civil war developed *after* the revolution; in China the communists fought their civil war *before* they seized power: the Yugoslav partisans won their own guerrilla war *during* their stand against the fascist powers—differences which had important political consequences. Russia suffered three decades of isolationism and totalitarian suppression ("an isolated and besieged fortress") before the advent of Gorbachev has heralded a new openness (*glasnost*) in Soviet politics. Mao Tse-tung held to the orthodox Leninist view about capitalism and communism, regarded détente as a dangerous illusion, and compromise and "revisionism" as a fatal error. The ideological dispute between these two great communist powers which lasted from the '60s to the '80s is ending with the improvement in inter-party relations and today a movement towards détente is taking place. The dramatic collapse of Communism in Eastern Europe during 1989, and the dramatic political developments in Russia in 1990, have thrown into question all the most basic tenets of communism. *See also* **Maoism, Marxism, Trotskyism, and Section C, Part II**.

Confucianism. Confucius (Latinised form of K'ung-Fo-tzu) was born in 551 B.C. in the feudal state of Lu in modern Shantung province. He was thus a contemporary of Buddha, although nobody could have been more dissimilar. Where Buddha was metaphysical in his thought, Confucius was practical; Buddha was original, Confucius had hardly an original idea in his head; Buddha wanted to convert individuals to an other-worldly philosophy. Confucius wanted to reform the feudal governments of his time, believing that in this way their subjects would be made happier. Other religions have in their time, been revolutionary; Confucius was a conservative who wanted to bring back a golden age from the past. The only respect in which Confucius agreed with the Buddha was that neither was particularly interested in the supernatural.

Much of his time was spent in going from the court of one feudal lord to another trying to impress them by his example. For he suffered from the curious belief that the example set by the ruler influences his subjects. He made much of etiquette, trembling and speaking in low tones and behaving with "lofty courtesy" to his inferiors. Promoting the idea of "the golden mean", he was not impressed by heroic deeds or unusual people, and was greatly displeased when he heard that a truthful son had reported that his father had stolen a sheep: "Those who are upright", he said, "are different from this; the father conceals the misconduct of the son, and the son conceals the misconduct of the father." One feels that Confucius would have felt not at all out of place in an English public school. Virtue brings its own reward in this world, ceremonial is important, politeness when universal would reduce jealousy and quarrels; "reverence the spirits but keep them far off." Destiny decides to what class a man shall belong, and as destiny is but another name for Nature prayer is unnecessary, for once having received his destiny, a man can demand and obtain from Nature what he chooses—his own will determines all things.

Congregationalists, the oldest sect of Nonconformists who hold that each church should be independent of external ecclesiastical authority. They took their origin from the Brownists of Elizabeth's days. Robert Browne (*c.* 1550–*c.* 1633), an Anglican clergyman, who had come to reject bishops, was forced with his followers to seek refuge, first in Holland and then in Scotland where he was imprisoned by the Kirk. In later life he changed his views and is disowned by Congregationalists because of his reversion to Anglicanism. His former views were spread by Henry Barrow and John Greenwood who, under an Act passed in 1592 "for the punishment of persons obstinately refusing to come to church" (and largely designed for the suppression of this sect), were hanged at Tyburn. They had preached (a) that the only head of the church is Jesus Christ; (b) that, contrary to Elizabethan doctrine, the church had no relationship to the state; (c) that the only statute-book was the Bible whereas the Articles of Religion and Book of Common Prayer were mere Acts of Parliament; (d) that each congregation of believers was independent and had the power of choosing its own ministers. The body fled once more to Holland and were among the Pilgrims who set sail in the *Mayflower* for America in 1620 whilst those who remained were joined by Puritans fleeing from Charles I. They became free once more to live in England under the Commonwealth only to be repressed again under Charles II. Finally full liberty of worship was granted under William III. In 1833 the Congregational Union of England and Wales was formed which had no legislative power. It had issued a Declaration of Faith by which no minister was bound; he was responsible to his own church and to nobody else. The sect is widespread both in Britain and the U.S.A. where it is held in special honour because of its connection with the Pilgrim Fathers. In 1972 the Congregational Church in England and Wales and the Presbyterian Church of England decided to unite to form the United Reformed Church. The majority of members who did not join comprise the Congregational Federation.

Conservatism. The term "Conservative" came into general use after 1834 in place of the older name of "Tory". The modern Conservative Party has its origins in the period of "Tory Democracy" introduced by Disraeli between 1874 and 1880. Originally the party of church, aristocracy and landed gentry, Conservatism has been increasingly supported since the turn of the century by large business interests. Under Baldwin, Conservative-dominated administration held office for much of the inter-war period. The 1945 Labour victory caused the Conservative Party to undertake a basic review of its philosophy. From 1951 to 1964, Conservatives held office continuously, reaching a peak in Harold Macmillan's 1959 election victory. Though defeated by Labour in 1964 and 1966, the party regained power in 1970 under Edward Heath. The subsequent troubled administration, plagued with problems on the industrial front, ended with the February 1974 election. The subsequent defeat in October 1974, followed by the battle for the Conservative leadership, again caused the party to seek to review its philosophy as it had developed in recent years. Since the three victories of the party in 1979, 1983 and 1987, the Conservatives have rejected government intervention in industry and relied on market forces and a rigid monetarist policy. Privatisation is a fundamental but increasingly controversial part of their programme. On the continent, Conservatism has generally adopted a more right-wing stance. *See also* **Section C, Part I.**

Coptic Church, the sect of Egyptian Christians who, holding "Monophysite" opinions (*i.e.*, refusing to grant the two natures, God and Man, of Christ), were declared heretical by the Council of Chalcedon in 451. They practise circumcision and have dietary laws. Their language is a direct descendant of ancient Egyptian. Like the Armenians, they are regarded as an heretical branch of Eastern Christianity. Their religious head is the patriarch of Alexandria.

Cynics, a school of philosophy founded in the time of Alexander the Great by Diogenes. Choosing to live like a dog by rejecting all conventions of religion, manners, or decency, and allegedly living in a tub. Diogenes unwittingly brought on his school the title "Cynic", meaning not "cynical", as the word is understood today, but "canine". His teacher, Antisthenes, who had been a disciple of Socrates, decided, after the latter's death, that all philosophy was useless quibbling and man's sole aim should be simple goodness. He believed in a return to nature, despised luxury, wanted no government,

no private property, and associated with working men and slaves. Far from being cynics in the modern sense, Diogenes and Antisthenes were virtuous anarchists rather like old Tolstoy (except rather more consistent).

D

Deism. *See* **God and Man.**

Demonism, Demons, and the Devil. Demons are ethereal beings of various degrees of significance and power which are believed to be implicated in men's good, but especially evil, fortune, They are common to most cultures. From the anthropological point of view the demon arose as a widespread concept in the following ways: (1) as a psychological projection into the outer world of man's own good or evil emotions and thoughts; (2) as a survival of primitive animism (*q.v.*), thus spirits are believed to haunt places, trees, stones, and other natural objects; (3) when by warlike invasion the gods of the vanquished become the devils of the conquerors (as when the Jews occupied Canaan); (4) as a primitive belief that spirits of the dead continue after death to hover near their former habitation, and not always entirely welcome to the living; (5) the conception of a supreme source of evil (the Devil or Satan) which took shape among the Jews during their sojourn in Babylon under the influence of Zoroastrianism (*q.v.*), a religion in which the struggle between the two spirits, Good and Evil, reached its height in the imagination of the ancient world. The Satan of the Old Testament was first regarded as one of God's servants (in the Book of Job he goes up and down the earth to see whether God's commands are obeyed), but when the Jews returned from their captivity he had become identified with Ahriman, the spirit of evil, who was in continual conflict with Ahursa Mazda, the spirit of good. As Dr. Margaret Murray has pointed out, the primitive mind ascribed both good and evil to one power alone; the division into God and the Devil, priest and witch, belongs to a higher stage of civilisation. The worship of evil itself, or of its personification in Satan, is a curious practice which seems to have developed hand-in-hand with Christianity and to have received steady support from a small but measurable minority. Many of the ceremonies involved in Satanism or in the so-called Black Mass appear to have been no more than opportunities for sexual excesses of one kind or another—such indulgences being traditionally barred to devout Christians. The alleged power of sex as a form of magic was propagated by the talented but rather mad poet, Aleister Crowley (1875–1947), who scandalised pre-war Europe with his very well-publicised dabblings into Satanism. The self-styled "wickedest man in the world", Crowley was a pathetic rather than shocking figure and died a drug addict. He can hardly be said to have significantly advanced the cause of Demonology, though it has to be admitted that he tried very hard.

Determinism and Free-will. The question of whether man is, or is not, free to mould his own destiny is one which has exercised the minds of philosophers since Greek mythology conceived of the Fates as weaving a web of destiny from which no man can free himself. Socrates emphasised that man could through knowledge influence his destiny whilst ignorance made him the plaything of fate; Plato went further in pointing out that man can, and does, defeat the purposes of the universe and its divine Creator. It is our duty to live a good life, but we can live a foolish and wicked one if we chose. Aristotle wrote "Virtue is a disposition or habit involving deliberate purpose or choice". If this were not so morality would be a sham.

The Problem for Theology. The last of the great philosophers of Antiquity and one of the great influences in moulding Catholic theology was Plotinus (*c.* 204–70). Soul, he taught, is free, but once enmeshed in the body loses its freedom in the life of sense. Nevertheless, man is free to turn away from sensuality and towards God who is perfect freedom; for even when incarnated in matter the soul does not entirely lose the ability to rescue itself. This conception was carried over into the beliefs of the early Christian Apologists because it appeared to be in line with the teaching of Jesus that He had come to save man from sin. Sin implies guilt, and guilt implies the freedom to act otherwise; furthermore an all-good God cannot be responsible for the sin in the world which must be man's responsibility and this again implies freedom. Pelagius (c. 355–c. 425), a Welsh priest, not only believed in free-will but questioning the doctrine of original sin, said that when men act righteously it is through their own moral effort, and God rewards them for their virtues in heaven. This belief became fairly widespread and was declared a heresy by the Church, being attacked notably by St. Augustine (354–430), a contemporary of Pelagius, who believed in predestination—that, since the sin of Adam, God had chosen who in all future history would be saved and who damned. This represents one tradition in Christianity: the determinism which leads to Calvinism (q.v.). St. Thomas Aquinas (1227–74), the greatest figure of scholasticism and one of the principal saints in the Roman Catholic Church, compromised between the two positions in the sense that, believing man to be free, he yet held that Adam's sin was transmitted to all mankind and only divine grace can bring salvation. But even when God wishes to bestow this salvation, the human will must co-operate. God foresees that some will not accept the offer of grace and predestines them to eternal punishment.

The Problem for Philosophy. With the Renaissance, thinkers began to free themselves from the domination of the Church and so study the world objectively and freely without preconceptions. But the more man turned to science, the more he discovered that the world was ruled by apparently inexorable laws and, since the scientist must believe that every event has a cause, he was led back to determinism. Man as part of the universe was subject to law too and all that existed was a vast machine. Francis Bacon (1561–1626) separated the fields of religion and science but left man subject completely to the will of God. Thomas Hobbes (1588–1679) was a rigid determinist and materialist although, having had trouble with the church in France whence, as a royalist, he had fled, he took care to announce that the Christian God is the Prime Mover.

Modern philosophy begins with René Descartes (1596–1650), a Frenchman who tried to reconcile the mechanical scientific universe of his time with the spiritual need for freedom. He did this by separating completely mind and body; the former, he said, is free, the latter completely determined. But, by admitting that the will can produce states of body, he was left with the problem of how this could happen—a problem which the so-called Occasionists solved to their own satisfaction by stating that the will is free and God so arranges the universe that what a person wills happens. Baruch Spinoza (1632–77), a Dutch Jew whose independence of thought led to his excommunication from the Amsterdam Synagogue in 1656, was a complete determinist. He asserted that God and Nature are one, everything that happens is a manifestation of God's inscrutable nature, and it is logically impossible that things could be other than they are. Thus both Hobbes and Spinoza were determinists for entirely opposed reasons. The former as a materialist, the latter because he believed in the absolute perfection and universality of God. Yet the great religious mystic and mathematician Blaise Pascal (1623–62) held that, no matter what reason and cold logic may indicate we *know* from direct religious experience that we are free. John Calvin (1509–64) and Martin Luther (1483–1546) were both determinists. See **Calvinism, Lutheranism**.

To the more practical British philosophers, John Locke (1632–1704) and David Hume (1711–76), free-will was related to personality. Locke believed that God had implanted in each individual certain desires and these determine the will; the desires are already there, but we use our will to satisfy them. Hume argued that a man's behaviour is the necessary result of his character and if he had a different character he would act otherwise. Accordingly, when a man's actions arise from his own nature and desires he is free. He is not free when external events compel him to act otherwise (e.g., if he strikes another because his own nature is such he is free as he is not if he is compelled to do so against his desire). Leibnitz (1646–1716), although as a German metaphysical philosopher holding very different general views, said much the same thing—that choice is simply selecting the desire that is strongest. But most of the 18th cent. thinkers after Voltaire, with the great exceptions of Rousseau and the later German philosophers Kant, Fichte, Schopenhauer, and Hegel, who were initially influenced by him, accepted determinism. Rousseau (1712–78) began to stem the tide by his declaration that man is a free soul striving to remain free and only prevented from being so by society and the cold science which stifles his feeling heart. Once again the will became important as Kant (1724–1804) asserted that belief in freedom is a moral necessity although it cannot be proved by reason; the moral nature of man shows that there is a "transcendental" world beyond the senses where freedom applies. Fichte and Schelling found freedom in the Absolute ego or God, of whom each individual was part and thus also free. Hegel (1770–1831) saw the whole universe as evolving towards self-awareness and freedom in man although this could only be fully realised in a society that makes for freedom. Even God himself only attains full consciousness and self-realisation through the minds of such individuals as are free. This is the goal of the dialectical process. (See **Dialectical Materialism**.)

The Scientist's View. For the scientist the law of cause and effect is a useful hypothesis since, by and large, it is necessary for him to assume that all events are caused. Nevertheless the modern tendency is to think in terms of statistical probability rather than relentless mechanistic causality, and, although the free-will problem does not concern the scientist as such, it is clear that freedom and determinism (assuming the terms to have any meaning at all) are not necessarily opposed. In sociology, for example, we *know* that certain actions will produce certain results upon the behaviour of people in general, e.g., that raising the bank rate will discourage business expansion. But this does not mean that Mr. Brown who decides in the circumstances not to add a new wing to his factory is not using his free-will. Even in the case of atoms, as Dr. Bronowski has pointed out, the observed results of allowing gas under pressure in a cylinder to rush out occur because most of the atoms are "obeying" the scientific "law" relating to such situations. But this does not mean that some atoms are not busy rushing across the stream or even against it—they are, but the general tendency is outwards and that is what we note. Lastly, the modern philosophical school of Logical Analysis would probably ask, not whether Free-will or Determinism is the true belief, but whether the question has any meaning. For what scientific experiment could we set up to prove one or the other true? The reader will note that some of the philosophers mentioned above are using the words to mean quite different concepts.

Dialectical Materialism, the combination of Hegel's dialectic method with a materialist philosophy produced by Karl Marx (1818–83) and his friend Friedrich Engels (1820–95). It is the philosophical basis of **Marxism** (q.v.) and **Communism** (q.v.). "Dialectic" to the ancient Greek philosophers meant a kind of dialogue or conversation, as used particularly by Socrates, in which philosophical disputes were resolved by a series of successive contradictions: a thesis is put forward and the opposing side holds its contradiction or antithesis until in the course of argument a synthesis is reached in which the conflicting ideas are resolved.

From Thesis through Antithesis to Synthesis. Hegel in the 19th cent. put forward the view that this process applies to the course of nature and history as they strive towards the perfect state. But to him, as to the Greeks, the conflict was in the field of ideas. The "universal reason" behind events works through the ideas held by a particular society until they are challenged by those of another which supersedes them and in turn, usually by war, becomes the agent of universal reason until the arrival of a new challenger. Hegel therefore regarded war as an instrument of progress and his Prussian compatriots found no difficulty in identifying their own state as the new agent of progress by universal conquest. Feuerbach, Lassalle, and other early socialists were impressed by some of Hegel's ideas: *e.g.*, that societies evolved (with the assumption that finally their own ideal society would be achieved) and that truth, morals, and concepts were relative so that a type of society that was "good" at one time was not necessarily so at another. But Marx and Engels in effect turned Hegel upside-down, accepted his dialectic but rejected his belief that ideas were the motive force. On the contrary, they said, ideas are determined by social and economic change as a result of materialistic forces. (*See* **Calvinism**, where it is pointed out that the Marxist view is not that Calvin changed men's economic ideas but rather that a developing capitalism unconsciously changed his.) The historical materialism of Marxism purports to show that the inexorable dialectic determines that feudalism is displaced by capitalism and capitalism by creating a proletariat (its antithesis) inevitably leads to socialism and a classless society. The state, as a tool of the dominant class, withers away. Dialectical materialism is applied in all spheres. As a philosophy there is little to be said for it save that it has shown us the close dependence of man's thoughts upon current material and social conditions. But as a battle-cry or a rationalisation of Marxism it wields immense power over the minds of men. *See* **Marxism**.

Dianetics. *See* **Scientology**.

Diggers, one of the many sects which flourished under the Commonwealth (others were the Muggletonians, the Levellers, the Millennarians, and the Fifth Monarchy Men), so-called because they attempted to dig (*i.e.* cultivate) untilled land. Gerrard Winstanley, a profoundly religious man, and leader of the Diggers, believed in the economic and social equality of man and castigated the clergy for upholding the class structure of society. In his book *The True Leveller's Standard Advanced* (1649) he wrote: "Every day poor people are forced to work for fourpence a day, though corn is dear. And yet the tithing priest stops their mouth and tells them that 'inward satisfaction of mind' was meant by the declaration 'the poor shall inherit the earth'. I tell you, the Scripture is to be really and materially fulfilled. You jeer at the name 'Leveller'; I tell you Jesus Christ is the Head Leveller".

Doukhobors, a religious sect of Russian origin, founded by a Prussian sergeant at Kharkov in the middle of the 18th cent., and now mainly settled in Canada. Like many other sects they belong to that type of Christianity which seeks direct communication with God and such bodies tend to have certain traits in common, such as belief in the "inner light", opposition to war and authority in general, and often ecstasies which show themselves in physical ways such as shaking, speaking in strange tongues (glossolalia), and other forms of what to the unbeliever seem mass hysteria. Liturgy, ritual, or ceremony is non-existent. The Doukhobors were persecuted in Tsarist Russia, but in 1898 Tolstoy used his influence to have them removed to Canada where the government granted them uninhabited land in what is now Saskatchewan and seven or eight thousand settled down in peace which they enjoyed for many years. Recently, however, their practices have caused difficulties once more; for even the most tolerant government which is prepared to accept pacifism, total dependence on communally-owned agriculture, refusal to engage in commerce, non-payment of taxes, rejection of the marriage ceremony and separation "when love ceases", finds it difficult to tolerate, as civilisation advances ever closer to Doukhobor communities, their proneness to "put off these troublesome disguises which we wear"—*i.e.*, to walk about naked in the communities of their more orthodox

neighbours. What the future of the Doukhobors in their various sects (for even they have their differences) will be it is impossible to say, but it is difficult to believe that these simple people can long resist the pressure of modern civilisation.

Dowsing. *See* **Radiesthesia**.

Druidism, the religion of Celtic Britain and Gaul of which Druids were the priesthood. They were finally wiped out by the Roman general Suetonius Paulinus about A.D. 58 in their last stronghold, the island of Anglesey. There are two sources of our present beliefs in Druidism: (1) the brief and factual records of the Romans, notably Pliny and Julius Caesar, which tell us that they worshipped in sacred oak groves and presumably practised a religion doing reverence to the powers of nature which must have had its roots in early stone age times and had many cruel rites, *e.g.*, human sacrifice; (2) the beliefs put forward by William Stukeley, an amateur antiquarian who from 1718 did valuable work by his studies of the stone circles at Stonehenge and Avebury. However, influenced by the Romantic movement, he later put forward the most extravagant theories which unfortunately are those popularly accepted by those without archaeological knowledge today. Stonehenge and Avebury were depicted as the temples of the "white-haired Druid bard sublime" and an attempt was made to tie up Druidism with early Christianity, above all with the concept of the Trinity. In fact, these circles have no connection with the Druids. They may have made ceremonial use of them but recent evidence suggests that the megalithic stones at Stonehenge belong to a Bronze Age culture (2100–1600 B.C.). Nor have Druidism and Christianity any relationship. Almost nothing is known of the religion. Yet such were its romantic associations that, even today, one hears of "Druidic" ceremonies practised at the appropriate time of year on Primrose Hill in the heart of London (though whether seriously or with tongue in cheek, one does not know). In Wales the name Druid survives as the title for the semi-religious leaders of the annual festivals of Celtic poetry, drama, and music known as Eisteddfods. Lingering, but now tenuous, druidic connections are to be found in all Celtic parts including Cornwall and Brittany where Eisteddfods are also held.

Dualism, any philosophical or theological theory which implies that the universe has a double nature, notably Plato's distinction between appearance and reality, soul and body, ideas and material objects, reason and the evidence of the senses, which infers that behind the world as we perceive it there lies an "ideal" world which is more "real" than that of mere appearance. In religions such as Zoroastrianism or the Gnostic and Manichaeism heresies, it was believed that the universe was ruled by good and evil "principles"—in effect that there was a good God and a bad one. In psychology, dualism refers to the philosophical theories which believe mind and body to be separate entities. The opposite of dualism is monism which asserts the essential unity of the substance of the universe.

An essential problem in the dualistic view lies in the question as to how and where the two separate and distinct properties of the universe interact. Where, for example, does the "mind" actually mesh with the physical mechanics of the brain and body—where does the ghost sit in his machine? Descartes decided that mind and body must interact somewhere and he selected the pineal gland (an apparently functionless part of the brain) as the spot. But this did nothing to explain how two *totally different* aspects of nature can possibly influence each other, and today most philosophers and psychologists reject dualistic views of life and personality as posing more problems than they solve. *See also* **Psychology, Occam's Razor**.

E

Ecomovement. In the early 1970s widespread publicity was for the first time given to the urgent warnings of ecologists that the current exponential increase in (a) world population, (b) depletion of natural resources, and (c) pollution of the environment could not continue without global catastrophe. The most significant single event in the evolution of what is now being known as the "ecomovement" was probably the publication of the Club of Rome's paper on *The Limits to Growth*. From this sprang a movement, unfortunately initially drawn only from the middle class and better educated, which aimed to reduce environmental pollution, the extravagances of advertising and needless waste of natural resources. Its first campaigns were directed against such obvious targets as disposable glass bottles and unnecessary packaging and wrapping in shops and supermarkets. The ecomovement also protests against industrial firms which pollute rivers and seas against aircraft noise and waste in general. Its early campaigns were greeted with some derision but have achieved dramatic point with the world energy and economic crisis which developed towards the end of 1973. *See* **Section Y.**

Ecumenism, a world movement which springs from the Christian belief that all men are brothers and that the Christian Church should be re-structured to give reality to the belief. Christ's church exists not to serve its own members, but for the service of the whole world. Some see the answer in a united church of a federal type (unity in diversity), others in an organic structure with one set of rules. The period since the convening of the Second Vatican Council by Pope John has been one of fervent discussion among Christian theologians with the aim of promoting Christian unity. *See* **World Council of Churches.**

Education. Education was no great problem to primitive man, but as societies became more complex people began to ask themselves such questions as: *What* should young people be taught? *How* should they be taught? Should the aim of their education be to bring out their individual qualities or rather to make them good servants of the state?

The first teachers were priests who knew most about the traditions, customs, and lore of their societies and thus the first schools were in religious meeting places. This was notably true of the Jews who learned from the rabbis in the synagogue.

The Greeks. We begin, as always, with the Greeks whose city-states, based on slavery, educated men (not women) for the sort of life described in Plato's *Dialogues*—the leisured life of gentlemen arguing the problems of the universe at their banquets or in the market-place. This made it necessary to learn debate and oratory (or rhetoric) especially for those who proposed to take up politics. The Sophist philosophy taught the need to build up convincing arguments in a persuasive manner, to learn the rules of logic and master the laws and customs of the Athenians, and to know the literature of the past so that illustrations might be drawn from it. These strolling philosophers who taught for a fee were individualists showing the student how to advance himself at all costs within his community.

Socrates had a more ethical approach, believing that education was good in itself, made a man happier and a better citizen, and emphasised his position as a member of a group. His method of teaching, the dialectic or "Socratic" method, involved argument and discussion rather than overwhelming others by rhetoric and is briefly mentioned under **Dialectical Materialism** (*q.v.*). Today this method is increasingly used in adult education where a lecture is followed by a period of discussion in which both lecturer and audience participate; for psychologists have shown that people accept ideas more readily when conviction arises through their own arguments than when they are passively thrust down their throats.

Socrates' pupil Plato produced in his book *The Republic* one of the first comprehensive systems of education and vocational selection. Believing that essentially men have very different and unequal abilities he considered that in an idealistic or utopian society they should be put into social classes corresponding to these differences, and suggested the following method: (1) For the first 18 years of a boy's life he should be taught gymnastics and sports, playing and singing music, reading and writing, a knowledge of literature, and if he passed this course sent on to the next stage; those who failed were to become tradesmen and merchants. (2) From 18–20 those successful in the first course were to be given two years of cadet training, the ones thought incapable of further education being placed in the military class as soldiers. (3) The remainder, who were to become the leaders of society, proceeded with advanced studies in philosophy, mathematics, science, and art. Such education was to be a state concern, state supported and controlled, selecting men and training them for service in the state according to their abilities.

Plato's pupil Aristotle even suggested that the state should determine shortly after birth which children should be allowed to live and destroy the physically or mentally handicapped; that marriage should be state-controlled to ensure desirable offspring. However, in their time the leisured and individualistic Sophists held the field and few accepted the educational views of Plato or his pupil.

Rome. The Romans were not philosophers and most of their culture came from Greece. Administration was their chief aptitude and Quintilian (A.D. *c.* 35–*c.* 95) based his higher education on the earlier classical tuition in public speaking, but he is important for emphasising the training of character and for his humanistic approach to the method of teaching that caused his *Institutio oratoria* to be influential for centuries later—indeed one might almost say up to the time of the great Dr. Arnold of Rugby. Education, he believed, should begin early but one must "take care that the child not old enough to love his studies does not come to hate them" by premature forcing; studies must be made pleasant and interesting and students encouraged by praise rather than discouraged when they sometimes fail; play is to be approved of as a sign of a lively disposition and because gloomy, depressed children are not likely to be good students; corporal punishment should never be used because "it is an insult as you will realise if you imagine it yourself". The world became interested not in *what* he taught but *how* he taught it; he was the pioneer of humanistic education and character-training from Vittorino d. Feltre (1378–1446) of Mantua, through Milton and Pope who commended his works to the modern educationists who have studied their pupils as well as their books.

The Middle Ages: The Religious View. With the development of Christianity education once more became a religious problem. The earliest converts had to be taught Christian doctrine and were given instruction in "catechumenal" schools before admission to the group, but as the religion came increasingly into contact with other religions or heresies a more serious training was necessary, and from these newer "catechetical" schools, where the method used was the catechism (*i.e.*, question and answer as known to all Presbyterian children today), the Apologists arose among whom were Clement of Alexandria and the great Origen. From this time education became an instrument of the church and in 529 the Emperor Justinian ordered all pagan schools to be closed.

As typical of the best in mediaeval education whilst the lamp of civilisation burned low during the Dark Ages, after the fall of Roman power, and survived only in the monasteries, we may mention St. Benedict (*c.* 480–*c.* 547) of Monte Cassino. There, in southern Italy, a rule was established which became a part of monastic life in general. Monastic schools were originally intended for the training of would-be monks, but later others were admitted who simply wanted some education; thus two types of school developed one for the *interni* and the other for *externi* or external pupils. Originally studies were merely reading in order to study the Bible, writing to copy the sacred books, and sufficient calculation to be able to work out the advent of holy days or festivals. But by the end of the 6th cent. the "seven liberal arts" (grammar, rhetoric, dialectic, arithmetic, geometry, music, and astronomy) were added.

The Renaissance. The close of the Middle Ages saw the development of two types of secular school. One came with the rise of the new merchant class and the skilled trader whose "guilds" or early trade unions established schools to train young men for their trades but ultimately gave rise to burgher or town schools; the other was the court school founded and supported by the wealthy rulers of the Italian cities—Vittorio da Feltre (mentioned above) presided over the most famous at Mantua.

These Renaissance developments are parallelled in northern Europe by the Protestant reformers who, having with Martin Luther held that everyone should know how to read his Bible in order to interpret it in his own way, were logically committed to popular education, compulsory and universal. In theory this was intended for biblical study, but writing, arithmetic, and other elementary subjects were taught and Luther said that, even if heaven and hell did not exist, education was important. Universal education is a Protestant conception.

Views of Philosophers. From this period onwards people were free to put forward any ideas about education, foolish or otherwise, and to create their own types of school. Of English philosophers who theorised about, but did not practise, education we may mention the rationalist Francis Bacon (1561–1626) who saw learning as the dissipation of all prejudices and the collection of concrete facts; the materialist and totalitarian Hobbes (1588–1679) who, as a royalist, believed that the right to determine the kind of education fit for his subjects is one of the absolute rights of the sovereign power or ruler; the gentlemanly Locke (1632–1704) whose ideal was a sound mind in a sound body to be attained by hard physical exercise, wide experience of the world, and enough knowledge to meet the requirements of the pupil's environment. The end result would be one able to get on with his fellows, pious but wise in the ways of the world, independent and able to look after himself, informed but reticent about his knowledge. Classics and religious study were not to be carried to excess, since Locke held that these subjects had been overrated in the past. Locke's pupil was the well-to-do, civilised young man of the 17th cent. who knew how to behave in society.

Jean-Jacques Rousseau (1712–78), a forerunner of the Romantic movement (*q.v.*), which despised society and its institutions, put emotion at a higher level than reason. His book *Emile* describes the education of a boy which is natural and spontaneous. Society, he holds, warps the growing mind and therefore the child should be protected from its influences until his development in accordance with his own nature is so complete that he cannot be harmed by it. During the first 4 years the body should be developed by physical training; from 5 to 12 the child would live in a state of nature such that he could develop his powers of observation and his senses; from 13 books would be used and intellectual training introduced, although only in line with the child's own interests, and he would be given instruction only as he came to ask for it. Moral training and contact with his fellows to learn the principles of sympathy, kindness, and helpfulness to mankind would be given between 15 and 20. Girls, however, should be educated to serve men in a spirit of modesty and restraint. His own five children he deposited in a foundling hospital.

Summary. Broadly speaking, then, there have been four main attitudes to education: (1) religious, with a view to a life beyond death; (2) state-controlled education, with a view to uniform subservience to authority; (3) "gentle-manly" education, with a view to social graces and easy congress in company; (4) the "child-centred" education, which attempts to follow the pupil's inner nature. It is unnecessary to mention the ordinary method of attempting to instil facts without any considerable degree of co-operation between pupil and teacher in order that the former may, with or without interest, follow some occupation in adult life; for this the philosophers did not consider. Today there

remain the two fundamental principles: education for the advantage of the state and its ideology or education for individual development and freedom.

Four educationists of the modern period who have influenced us in the direction of freedom were Johann Pestalozzi of Switzerland (1746–1827) who, by trying to understand children, taught the "natural, progressive, and harmonious development of all the powers and capacities of the human being"; Friedrich Froebel (1782–1852) of Germany, the founder of the Kindergarten who, like Pestalozzi, was influenced by Rousseau but realised the need to combine complete personal development with social adjustment; Maria Montessori (1869–1952) whose free methods have revolutionised infant teaching; John Dewey (1859–1952) who held that the best interests of the group are served when the individual develops his own particular talents and nature.

Eleatics, the philosophers of Elea in ancient Greece who, at the time when Heraclitus (c. 535–475 B.C.) was teaching that change is all that exists and nothing is permanent, were asserting that change is an illusion. Of the three leaders of this school, Xenophanes asserted that the universe was a solid immovable mass forever the same; Parmenides explained away change as an inconceivable process, its appearance being due to the fact that what we see is unreal; and Zeno (the best-known today) illustrated the same thesis with his famous argument of the arrow which, at any given moment of its flight, must be where it is since it cannot be where it is not. But if it is where it is, it cannot move, this is based, of course, on the delusion that motion is discontinuous. The Eleatics were contemporaries of Socrates.

Empiricism. While not a single school of philosophy, empiricism is an approach to knowledge which holds that if a man wants to know what the universe is like the only correct way to do so is to go and look for himself, to collect facts which come to him through his senses. It is, in essence, the method of science as contrasted with rationalism (*q.v.*) which in philosophy implies that thinking or reasoning without necessarily referring to external observations can arrive at truth. Empiricism is typically an English attitude, for among the greatest empirical philosophers were John Locke, George Berkeley, and David Hume. *See* Rationalism.

Epicureanism. The two great schools of the Hellenistic period (*i.e.* the late Greek period beginning with the empire of Alexander the Great) were the Stoics and Epicureans, the former founded by Zeno of Citium (not to be confused with Zeno the Eleatic) (*q.v.*), the latter by Epicurus, born in Samos in 342 B.C. Both schools settled in Athens, where Epicurus taught that "pleasure is the beginning and end of a happy life." However, he was no sensualist and emphasised the importance of moderation in all things because excesses would lead to pain instead of pleasure and the best of all pleasures were mental ones. Pleasures could be active or passive but the former contain an element of pain since they are the process of satisfying desire not yet satiated. The latter involving the absence of desire are the more pleasant. In fact, Epicurus in his personal life was more stoical than many Stoics and wrote "when I live on bread and water I spit on luxurious pleasures." He disapproved of sexual enjoyment and thought friendship one of the highest of all joys. A materialist who accepted the atomic theory of Democritus, he was not a determinist, and if he did not disbelieve in the gods he regarded religion and the fear of death as the two primary sources of unhappiness.

Epiphenomenalism. *See* **Mind and Body.**

Erastianism, the theory that the state has the right to decide the religion of its members, wrongly attributed to Erastus of Switzerland (1524–83) who was believed to have held this doctrine. The term has usually been made use of in a derogatory sense—*e.g.*, by the Scottish churches which held that the "call" of the congregation was the only way to elect ministers at a time when, about the turn of the 17th and 18th cent., they felt that Episcopalianism was being foisted on them. "Episcopalianism" (*i.e.* Anglicanism) with its state church, ecclesiastical hierarchy, and system of livings presented by patrons was to them "Erastian" in addition to its other "unscriptural practices."

Essenes, a Jewish sect which, during the oppressive rule of Herod (d. 4 B.C.), set up monastic communities in the region of the Dead Sea. They refused to be bound by the scriptural interpretations of the Pharisees and adhered rigorously to the letter of Holy Writ, although with additions of their own which cause them by orthodox Jews today to be regarded as a break-away from Judaism. Among their practices and beliefs were purification through baptism, renunciation of sexual pleasures, scrupulous cleanliness, strict observance of the Mosaic law, communal possession, asceticism. Akin in spirit, although not necessarily identical with them, were the writers of Apocalyptic literature preaching that the evils of the present would shortly be terminated by a new supernatural order heralded by a Messiah who would reign over a restored Israel. The casting out of demons and spiritual healing formed part of these general beliefs which were in the air at that time. The sect has an importance far beyond its size or what has been known about it in the past since the discovery from 1947 onwards of the Dead Sea Scrolls (*see* **Section L**) of the Qumran community occupying a monastery in the same area as the Essenes and holding the same type of belief. These scrolls with their references to a "Teacher of Righteousness" preceding the Messiah have obvious relevance to the sources of early Christianity and have given rise to speculations as to whether Jesus might have been influenced by views which, like His own, were unacceptable to orthodox Jews but in line with those of the Dead Sea communities. They seem to show that early Christianity was not a sudden development but a gradual one which had its predecessors.

Ethical Church, a movement typical of 19th cent. rationalism which attempted to combine atheism (or at any rate the absence of any belief in a God which was inconsistent with reason or based on revelation) with the inculcation of moral principles. Prayers were not used and ordinarily the service consisted in the singing of edifying compositions interspersed with readings from poems or prose of a similar nature by great writers holding appropriate views. It terminated in a talk on an ethical or scientific theme. Conway Hall (built 1929) in Red Lion Square, London, belongs to the South Place Ethical Society, founded by Moncure Conway who preached at their Unitarian chapel in South Place, Finsbury, 1864–97.

Ethnocentrism, the exaggerated tendency to think the characteristics of one's own group or race superior to those of any others.

Eugenics, a 19th-cent. movement largely instigated by the British scientist and mathematician, Sir Francis Galton. Galton argued that many of the most satisfactory attributes of mankind—intelligence, physical strength, resistance to disease, etc.—were genetically determined and thus handed down in the normal process of inheritance. From this he reasoned that selective mating of physical "superior" individuals, and its converse, the controlled limitation on the breeding of criminals or the insane, would lead inevitably to a progressive improvement in the overall standards of the human race. In their simplest form these proposals are incontestable, though they do of course introduce marked restrictions on the choice of the individual for marriage and procreation. Worse yet is the way in which the argument can be misapplied or elaborated—as it was in Nazi Germany—to include the sterilisation of alcoholics, confirmed criminals and even epileptics. Nevertheless there remains the feeling that there are some aspects of eugenics which intuitively at any rate make good sense and of course the widespread application of birth control is itself an enactment of eugenic principles.

Evangelicalism, the belief of those Protestant sects which hold that the essence of the Gospel consists in the doctrine of salvation by faith in the atoning death of Christ and not by good works or the sacraments; that worship should be "free" rather than liturgical through established forms; that ritual is unacceptable and superstitious. Evangelicals are Low Churchmen.

Evangelism, the preaching of the Gospel, emphasising the necessity for a new birth or conversion. The evangelistic fervour of John Wesley and George Whitefield (*see* Methodism) aroused the great missionary spirit of the late 18th and 19th cent. George Fox, founder of the Society of Friends (*q.v.*), was also an evangelist. Evangelists can be Low, High, or Middle Churchmen.

Existentialism, a highly subjective philosophy which many people connect with such names as Jean-Paul Sartre (1905–80) or Albert Camus (1913–60) and assume to be a post-war movement associated with disillusion and a sordid view of life. However, existentialism stems from Sören Kierkegaard (1813–55), the Danish "religious writer"—his own description of himself—in such works as *Either/Or, Fear and Trembling,* and *Concluding Unscientific Postscript.* Between the two wars translations of Kierkegaard into German influenced Martin Heidegger's great work *Being and Time* and the other great existentialist Karl Jaspers; it has strongly influenced modern Protestant theology notably in Karl Barth, Reinhold Niebuhr, and Paul Tillich and beyond that field the French philosopher Gabriel Marcel, the Spanish writer Unamuno in his well-known *The Tragic Sense of Life,* and Martin Buber of Israel in his *I and Thou.* We have it on Heidegger's authority that "Sartre is no philosopher" even if it is to his works that modern existentialists often turn.

Existentialism is extremely difficult for the non-metaphysically-minded to understand, it deals, not with the nature of the universe or what are ordinarily thought of as philosophical problems but describes an attitude to life or God held by the individual. Briefly, its main essentials are: (1) it distinguishes between *essence, i.e.,* that aspect of an entity which can be observed and known—and its *existence*—the fact of its having a place in a changing and dangerous world which is what really matters; (2) existence being basic, each self-aware individual can grasp his own existence on reflection in his own immediate experience of himself and his situation as a free being in the world; what he finds is not merely a knowing self but a self that fears, hopes, believes, wills, and is aware of its need to find a purpose, plan, and destiny in life; (3) but we cannot grasp our existence by thought alone; thus the fact "all men must die" relates to the essence of man but it is necessary to be involved, to draw the conclusion as a person that "I too must die" and experience its impact on our own individual existence; (4) because of the preceding, it is necessary to abandon our attitude of objectivity and theoretical detachment when faced by the problems relating to the ultimate purpose of our own life and the basis of our own conduct; life remains closed to those who take no part in it because it can have no significance; (5) it follows that the existentialist cannot be rationalist in his outlook for this is merely an escape into thought from the serious problems of existence; none of the important aspects of life—failure, evil, sin, folly—nor (in the view of Kierkegaard) even the existence of God or the truth of Christianity—can be proved by reason. "God does not exist; He is eternal," was how he expressed it; (6) life is short and limited in space and time, therefore it is foolish to discuss in a leisurely fashion matters of life and death as if there were all eternity to argue them in. It is necessary to make a leap into the unknown, *e.g.,* accepting Christ (in the case of the Christian existentialist) by faith in the sense of giving and risking the self utterly. This means complete commitment, not a dependence on arguments as to whether certain historical events did, or did not, happen.

To summarise: existentialism of whatever type seems to the outsider to be an attitude to life concerning itself with the individual's ultimate problems (mine, not yours); to be anti-rationalist and anti-idealist (in the sense of being, as it seems to the believer, practical)—in effect it seems to say "life is too short to fool about with argument, you must dive in and become committed" to something. Sartre who called himself an "atheist existentialist" was apparently committed to the belief that "hell is other people," but for most critics the main argument against existentialist philosophy is that it often rests on a highly specialised personal experience and, as such, is incommunicable.

Existential Psychology, a new if rather diffuse movement in modern psychology with no specific founder but with a number of figures who have, perhaps against their will, acquired leader status. One of the key figures is the British psychiatrist, R. D. Laing, whose radical views on psychotherapy are counted as being heretical by the vast majority of his medical colleagues. Laing holds that many so-called neurotic and psychotic conditions are essentially not "abnormal" and merely represent extreme strategies by which an individual may adjust to environmental and personal stress. Instead of attempting to suppress or eliminate the psychosis in the traditional manner, one should lead the patient through it thus allowing the individual's "unconscious plan" for his own adjustment to be fulfilled.

Exorcism, the removal or ejection of an evil spirit by a ritual or prayer. It is easy to forget that the concept of insanity as representing a disorder of the brain, analogous to physical sickness of the body, is fairly recent in origin. Barely two centuries ago it was considered to be appropriate treatment to put lunatics into chains and beat them daily in the hope that the malevolent beings inhabiting them might be persuaded to depart. Tragically, many of the symptoms of severe forms of mental disorder induce such an apparent change in the personality of the individual as to suggest that an alien individual has indeed taken over their body, and this belief is still common in many parts of the world. Most religious systems have developed some ritual or set of rituals for expelling these demons, and while, not surprisingly, the practice of exorcism by the clergy has declined dramatically in the past century, it is still brought into play now and again in such circumstances as alleged hauntings, poltergeist phenomena, etc. From a scientific point of view, exorcism must be counted as a superstitious rite, but its suggestive power in cases of hysteria, and perhaps even more serious mental illnesses, cannot be completely ruled out. General interest in the topic has been stimulated in part by the resurgence of the practice of Black Magic and witchcraft, largely in the form of experimental dabbling by young people, who no doubt become disillusioned when it fails to live up to its promise. Testimony to the pulling-power of this remnant of our superstitious past is the fact that a sensational and terrifying novel, *The Exorcist,* which its author claimed was based on fact, topped the best-seller lists in 1972, and the even more horrific movie-version became one of the most successful (in box office terms) films of all time. The Church of England, incidentally, takes anything but a dismissive line on the matter, and in fact employs a number of ordained priests as "licensed exorcists". These services are apparently much in demand.

F

Fabian Society. In 1848 (the year of *The Communist Manifesto* by Marx and Engels) Europe was in revolt. In most countries the workers and intellectuals started bloody revolutions against the feudal ruling classes which were no less violently suppressed; hence on the continent socialism took on a Marxist tinge which to some extent it still retains. But at the same time England was undergoing a slow but non-violent transition in her political and industrial life which led the workers in general to look forward to progress through evolution. Marxism never became an important movement in England even though it took its origin here.

There were many reasons for this: the agitation of the Chartists (*q.v.*); the writings of Mill, Ruskin, and Carlyle; the reforms of Robert Owen; the religious movement led by the Wesleys; the Co-operative societies; the Christian socialists. Furthermore legislation stimulated by these bodies had led to an extension of the franchise to include a considerable number of wage-earners, remedial measures to correct some of the worst abuses of the factory system, recognition of the trade unions, etc.

This was the background against which the Fabian Society was founded in 1884 with the conviction that social change could be brought about by gradual parliamentary means. (The name is derived from Quintus Fabius Maximus, the Roman general nicknamed "Cunctator," the delayer, who achieved his successes in defending Rome against Hannibal by refusing to give direct battle.) It was a movement of brilliant intellectuals, chief among whom were Sidney and Beatrice Webb, H. G. Wells, G. B. Shaw, Graham Wallas, Sidney Olivier, and Edward Pease. The Society itself was basically a research institution which furnished the intellectual information for social reform and supported all contributing to the gradual attainment by parliamentary means of socialism.

The Webbs's analysis of society emphasised that individualist enterprise in capitalism was a hang-over from early days and was bound to defeat itself since socialism is the inevitable accompaniment of modern industrialism; the necessary result of popular government is control of their economic system by the people themselves. Utopian schemes had been doomed to failure because they were based on the fallacy that society is static and that islands of utopias could be formed in the midst of an unchanging and antagonistic environment. On the contrary, it was pointed out, society develops: "The new becomes old, often before it is consciously regarded as new." Social reorganisation cannot usefully be hastened by violent means but only through methods consonant with this natural historical progression—gradual, peaceful, and democratic. The Fabians were convinced that men are rational enough to accept in their common interest developments which can be demonstrated as necessary; thus public opinion will come to see that socialisation of the land and industries is essential in the same way that they came to accept the already-existing acts in respect of housing, insurance, medical care, and conditions of work.

The Society collaborated first in the formation of the Independent Labour Party and then with the more moderate Labour Party and the trade unions and Co-operative movement. But in general it disapproved of independent trade union action since change should come from the government and take political form. The class-war of Marx was rejected and so too was the idea of the exclusive role of the working class —reform must come from the enlightened co-operation of all classes—not from their opposition.

Faith Healing, the belief and practice of curing physical and mental ills by faith in some supernatural power, either allegedly latent in the individual (as with Christian Science) or drawn in some way from God. It is a characteristic of faith healing that it is supposed to be publicly demonstrable—*i.e.*, a "healer" will hold public meetings and invite sick people to come up to be cured on the platform. In the emotionally charged atmosphere which the healer generates, it is not unusual for people to show immediate and striking improvement in their illness, but the almost invariable rule is for relapses to occur within days or hours after the event. When remission is more permanent, the illness is generally hysterical in origin and will often return to the individual in some other form. Spiritualists claim that the healing in such cases is done not by "faith" but by direct intervention of the spirits of doctors, etc., who have died and passed on to another world. Perhaps the world's most famous faith healer in recent years was Harry Edwards (d. 1976), who had literally millions of letters from all parts of the world asking for the healing attention of his spirit guides. Many doctors, while remaining immensely sceptical about the origins and extent of this kind of therapy, are inclined to admit that it might have benefits when the sickness is mildly hysterical in origin. The real danger, of course, comes when patients seek unorthodox therapy before consulting their doctor.

Falangists. The Fascist Party of Spain founded in 1933 by José Antonio Primo de Rivera, son of the man who was dictator of the country from 1923 to 1930; he was shot by the Republicans. In 1937 the falangists who had shown unwelcome signs of social radicalism were merged with the other right-wing political groups to form the *Falange Española Tradicionalista y de las Juntas de Ofensive Nacional Sindicalistas* which replaced the Cortes (*i.e.* the Government) between 1939 and 1942 when the Cortes was reinstituted. The Falange was the only political party allowed in Spain during the Franco era. *See* **Fascism**.

Fascism. From the end of mediaeval times with the opening up of the world, the liberation of the mind and the release of business enterprise, a new spirit arose in Europe exemplified in such movements as the Renaissance, the Reformation, the struggle for democracy, the rise of capitalism, and the Industrial Revolution. With these movements there developed a certain tradition, which, in spite of hindrances and disagreement or failures, was universally held by both right- and left-wing parties however strongly they might fail to agree on the best means of attaining what was felt to be a universal ideal. The hard core of this tradition involved: belief in reason and the possibility of human progress; the essential sanctity and dignity of human life; tolerance of widely different religious and political views; reliance on popular government and the responsibility of the rulers to the ruled; freedom of thought and criticism; the necessity of universal education; impartial justice and the rule of law; the desirability of universal peace. Fascism was the negation of every aspect of this tradition and took pride in being so. Emotion took the place of reason, the "immutable, beneficial, and fruitful inequality of classes" and the right of a self-constituted élite to rule them replaced universal suffrage because absolute authority "quick, sure, unanimous" led to action rather than talk. Contrary opinions are not allowed and justice is in the service of the state; war is desirable to advance the power of the state; and racial inequality made a dogma. Those who belong to the "wrong" religion, political party, or race are outside the law.

The attacks on liberalism and exaltation of the state derive largely from Hegel and his German followers; the mystical irrationalism from such 19th cent. philosophers as Schopenhauer Nietzsche, and Bergson; from Sorel (*see* **Syndicalism**) came the idea of the "myth", and an image which would have the power to arouse the emotions of the masses and from Sorel also the rationale of violence and justification of force. But these philosophical justifications of fascism do not explain why it arose at all and why it arose where it did—in Italy, Germany, and Spain. These countries had one thing in common—disillusionment. Germany had lost the 1914–18 war, Italy had been on the winning side but was resentful about her small gains. Spain had sunk to the level of a third-rate power, and people were becoming increasingly restive under the reactionary powers of the Catholic Church, the landed aristocracy, and the army. In Marxist theory, fascism is the last fling of the ruling class and the bourgeoisie in their attempt to hold down the workers.

Italian Fascism. The corporate state set up by Benito Mussolini in Italy claimed to be neither capitalist nor socialist, and after its inception in 1922 the Fascist Party became the only recognised one. Its members wore black shirts, were organised in military formations, used the Roman greeting of the outstretched arm, and adopted as their slogan "Mussolini is always right". Membership of the Party was not allowed to exceed a number thought to be suited to the optimum size of a governing class and new candidates were drawn, after strict examinations, from the youth organisations.

The Blackshirts, a fascist militia, existed separately from the army and were ruled by Fascist Headquarters.

At the head of government was Mussolini, "Il Duce" himself, a cabinet of fourteen ministers selected by him and approved by the King to supervise the various functions of government, and the Grand Council or directorate of the Fascist Party, all the members of which were chosen by the Duce. Parliament, which was not allowed to initiate legislation but only to approve decrees from above, consisted of a Senate with life-membership and a Chamber of Fasci and Corporations composed of nominated members of the Party, the National Council of Corporations, and selected representatives of the employers' and employees' confederations. Private enterprise was encouraged and protected but rigidly controlled; strikes were forbidden, but a Charter of Labour enforced the collaboration of workers and employers whose disputes were settled in labour courts presided over by the Party. All decisions relating to industry were government-controlled (*e.g.*, wages, prices, conditions of employment and dismissal, the expansion or limitation of production), and some industries such as mining, shipping, and armaments were largely stateowned.

Italian fascism served as a model in other countries, notably for the German National Socialist Party, in Spain and Japan, and most European nations between the wars had their small Fascist parties, the British version led by Sir Oswald Mosley being known as the British Union which relied on "strong-arm tactics", marches and violence. The Public Order Act of 1936 was passed to deal with it. Although fascism in all countries has certain recognisable characteristics, it would be wrong to think of it as an international movement taking fixed forms and with a clearly thought-out rationale as in the case of communism. There have been minor revivals of interest in Fascism in Italy—presumably as a counter-move against the considerable inroads being made by the Communist party in that country and more recently in France with the emergence of the National Front led by M. Le Pen. During 1989, elections in both West Germany and Austria showed increasing support for extreme right-wing or antiimmigrant parties. During 1990, there was evidence of neo-Fascism in Eastern Germany. *See* **Falange, Nazism**.

Fatalism. *See* **Determinism**.

Feedback Cult is the name given to a curious fad which began in America in 1970 and which is interesting because it incorporates complicated scientific equipment and experimental psychological methods into its practice. The basis of the cult is as follows: for nearly fifty years it has been known that the brain is the source of varied electrical signals of very low power which can be detected by attaching electrodes to the scalp and amplifying the pulses emitted. Much scientific controversy has surrounded these pulses, and their interpretation by skilled clinicians can lead to the detection of hidden cerebral disorders such as tumours, epileptic foci, etc. The presence of one particular rhythm, the so-called alpha wave, which beats at 14 cycles per second—is believed to be dependent upon whether or not the individual is "attending" to something, particularly in the visual field. It is this alpha rhythm, or rather its control, that is the basis of the feedback cult.

During the decade after 1970 it was discovered that when some people are connected to an electroencephalograph (the device which records brain rhythms) and are shown the recorded tracings of their own brain waves as they actually occur, they find it possible to modify and control the nature of the waves—the alpha in particular. This, a scientific curiosity rather than a major discovery, soon caught the attention of followers of yoga and other systems seeking enhanced relaxation, "mental discipline," etc. The argument was advanced that for centuries man had been seeking to exercise control over his own mental activities, without however having much opportunity to assess his success—or lack of it. The use of the EEG with the individual's brain waves "fed back" to him for inspection would remedy this. The result has been a sudden surge of lay interest in electroencephalography and a boom in the sale of small, portable EEG machines. Followers of the cult, who may sit for hours inspecting the output from their own brains and attempting to modify it, at will, claim that the activity promotes mental "relaxation" and a greater and deeper understanding of their own personal problems. Psychologists are understandably extremely dubious about the reality of this as mental therapy.

Fetichism, originally a practice of the natives of West Africa and elsewhere of attributing magical properties to an object which was used as an amulet, for putting spells on others, or regarded as possessing dangerous powers. In psychology the term refers to a sexual perversion in which objects such as shoes, brassières, hair, etc., arouse sexual excitement.

Feudalism. The feudal system took its origins from Saxon times and broadly speaking lasted until the end of the 13th cent. It was a military and political organisation based on land tenure, for, of course, society throughout this period was based almost entirely on agriculture. The activities of men divided them into three classes or estates. The First Estate was the clergy, responsible for man's spiritual needs; the Second was the nobility, including kings and emperor as well as the lesser nobles; the Third was composed of all those who had to do with the economic and mainly agricultural life of Europe. The praying men, the fighting men and administrators, and the toilers were all held to be dependent on each other in a web of mutual responsibilities.

The theory of feudalism, although it by no means always worked out in practice, was as follows: the earth was God's and therefore no man owned land in the modern sense of the word. God had given the pope spiritual charge of men, and secular power over them to the emperor from whom kings held their kingdoms, and in turn the dukes and counts received the land over which they held sway from the king. Members of the Second Estate held their lands on the condition of fulfilling certain obligations to their overlord and to the people living under them, so when a noble received a fief or piece of land he became the vassal of the man who bestowed it. To him he owed military service for a specified period of the year, attendance at court, and giving his lord counsel. He undertook to ransom his lord when he fell into enemy hands and to contribute to his daughter's dowry and at the knighting of his son. In return the lord offered his vassal protection and justice, received the vassal's sons into his household and educated them for knighthood.

The system was complicated by the fact that large fiefs might be subdivided and abbots often governed church lands held in fief from nobles. The serf or toiling man dwelt on the land of a feudal noble or churchman where he rendered service by tilling the soil or carrying out his craft for his manorial lord in return for protection, justice, and the security of his life and land. He was given a share in the common lands or pastures from which he provided for his own needs. In the modern sense he was not free (although at a later stage he could buy his freedom) since he was attached to the soil and could not leave without the lord's permission. On the other hand he could neither be deprived of his land nor lose his livelihood. Feudal tenures were abolished in England by statute in 1660, although they had for long been inoperative. In Japan a feudal system existed up to 1871, in Russia until 1917, and many relics of it still linger on (*e.g.* the *mezzadria* system of land tenure in parts of Italy).

Flying Saucers. In June 1947 an American private pilot, Kenneth Arnold, saw a series of wingless objects flying through the air at a speed which he estimated at thousands of miles an hour. He later told the press that the objects "flew as a saucer would if you skipped it across the water," and the phrase "flying saucers" was erroneously born. What Arnold actually saw has never been satisfactorily explained—it was probably a flight of jet fighters reflecting the sun's rays in a way that made them appear

as discs—but since that date literally hundreds of thousands of people all over the world have reported the sighting of strange objects in the sky, coming in a bewildering range of shapes and sizes. Initially the American Air Force launched an official enquiry—Project Bluebook —to attempt to solve the mystery of these "unidentified flying objects" or "U.F.O.s," which finally folded in 1969 after concluding that the bulk of the sightings were probably misinterpretations of natural phenomena and that there was no evidence for the commonly held view that earth was being visited by spacecraft from some other planetary system. A rather similar conclusion was arrived at by the famous University of Colorado project—the Condon Committee—which published its findings in 1968. Despite this clear-cut official attitude, belief in the existence of flying saucers and their origin as alien space vehicles is exceedingly widespread and is held very strongly by people in all walks of life. In 1959 this striking social phenomenon attracted the attention of the psychologist C. G. Jung. He noticed that the press were inclined to report statements that saucers existed when made by prominent people and not publish contrary statements made by equally prominent people. He concluded that flying saucers were in some way welcome phenomena and in his brilliant little book. *Flying Saucers—a modern myth,* he hypothesised that the U.F.O.s were the modern equivalent of "signs in the skies." It was Jung's contention that the saucers were looked upon as the harbingers of advanced alien civilisations who had come to save the world from its descent into nuclear catastrophe—archangels in modern dress in fact.

Whatever the validity of this imaginative view of U.F.O.s, it is undeniably true that they exercise a great fascination for millions of people, some of whom invest them with definite religious significance. The best example of the open incorporation of flying saucers into a religious belief system is to be found in the Aetherius Society, an international organisation with headquarters in Los Angeles but founded by a former London clerk, George King. Mr. King, who claims to be the mediumistic link between earth and the largely benevolent beings from outer space, regularly relays messages—notably from a Venusian known as Aetherius—to enthusiastic congregations at religious meetings. The sect, which is entirely sincere and dedicated in its beliefs, also makes pilgrimages to the tops of various mountains which have been "spiritually charged" with the aid of the spacebeings in their flying saucers.

Odd though such ideas may seem to most people, they can be readily understood within the context of the very marked decline in orthodox religious belief which we have seen in the past two decades. To an increasing number of people, many of whom feel a desperate need for spiritual guidance and enlightenment, the concepts of the traditionally Western religions seem somehow unsatisfactory. Many therefore turn to cults and splinter groups which use ideas and terminology which to them seem more at home in the twentieth century than those that sprung to life thousands of years ago. To members of the Aetherius Society, for example, the idea that Jesus Christ lives on Venus and rides around in a flying saucer is neither blasphemous nor ludicrous. As long as empty churches testify to the growing, if perhaps only temporary loss of contact between orthodox religions and the man-in-the-street, then one can expect such offbeat ideas as the cults surrounding flying saucers, to expand and flourish.

Fourierism *See* **Utopianism.**

Freemasonry, a widespread, influential secret organisation of English origin. Although it can be traced back to the Middle Ages when itinerant working masons in England and Scotland were organised in lodges with secret signs for the recognition of fellow-members, modern freemasonry first arose in England in the early decades of the 18th cent. The first Grand Lodge was founded in London in 1716 and Freemasons' Hall was opened in 1776. With its clubs for discussion and social enjoyment (women were excluded) it met a need and became a well-known feature of English life. The movement quickly spread abroad to places which had direct trade links with England. The graded lodge structure, the social prestige conferred by membership, the symbolism, ritual and ceremony, and the emphasis on mutual help have had a lasting appeal. Interest in the occult had more appeal on the Continent than in England. Until a decade or so ago, membership conferred definite business and social advantages, particularly in small communities where the leading middle-class figures were generally members. Recently this advantage has markedly declined and freemason lodges nowadays tend to be little more than worthy charitable organisations. Fear of secret societies has given freemasonry many opponents; it was condemned by the Roman Catholic Church, banned by Fascist dictators, and denounced by the Comintern. A statement from the congregation for the doctrine of the faith in 1981 reminded Catholics that under Article 2335 of the Code of Canon Law they are forbidden under pain of excommunication from joining masonic or similar associations.

Freudian theory. *See* **Psychoanalysis.**

Friends, The Society of. *See* **Quakers.**

Fundamentalism is a term covering a number of religious movements which adhere with the utmost rigidity to orthodox tenets; for example the Old Testament statement that the earth was created by God in six days and six nights would be held to be factual rather than allegorical or symbolic. Although the holding of rigid beliefs in the literal truth of the Bible might seem to be frequently contrary to modern scientific findings, the fundamentalists at least do not have the problems of compromise and interpretation to face, and to some people this is no doubt a great attraction.

G

Game Theory, an approach to understanding human and animal behaviour which takes the view that psychological insight is best gained by studying the decisions which all living things make constantly and which govern the course of their lives. It proposes that life is basically a strategic game following complex rules which can probably only be understood by a study of the "decision units" as and when they occur. Because one is dealing with highly variable animals controlled by highly complex brains, and not with simple clockwork or electro-mechanical systems, the study of the rules which operate in the game of life is enormously complicated and thus game theory has quickly taken off into advanced mathematics. Game theory, incidentally, can be used to apply to individual action or to the behaviour of groups. Little of any predictive value has been put forward by the protagonists of this approach, but the use of computers to tackle the complex mathematics involved may well lead to some interesting advances.

Gestalt Psychology. In the latter half of the 19th cent. it became evident to psychologists that in principle there was no good reason why "mental" events should not be just as measurable and manageable as "physical" ones. Intensive studies of learning, memory, perception, and so on were therefore undertaken and the beginnings of an empirical science of psychology were underway. In the early part of the 20th cent. the experiments of Pavlov (*see* **Behaviourism**) and his co-workers suggested that the behaviour of an animal, or even men, might ultimately be reduced to a descriptive account of the activities of nervous reflex loops—the so-called conditioned reflexes. With the publication of Watson's important book on Behaviourism in 1914 it looked as though the transfer of psychological studies from the field of philosophy to that of science could now take place. Actually the over-simplified picture of cerebral and mental pictures which Behaviourism offered

was rather comparable to the billiard ball view of the universe so fashionable in Victorian science. Just as Behaviourism implied that there was a fundamental building block (the conditioned reflex) from which all mental events could be constructed, so Victorian physics assumed that the entire universe could be described in terms of a vast collection of atoms pushing each other around like billiard balls. The development of nuclear physics was to shatter the latter dream and at the same time a challenge to the naïve "reflex psychology" came from the Gestalt experimental school.

The founders of this school were Max Wertheimer, Kurt Koffka and Wolfgang Köhler, three young psychologists who in 1912 were conducting experiments—notably in vision—which seemed to expose the inadequacies of the behaviourist position. The Pavlov-Watson view, as we have said, implied that complex sensory events were no more than a numerical sum of individual nervous impulses. Wertheimer's group proposed that certain facts of perceptual experiences (ruled out of court as subjective and therefore unreliable by Watson) implied that the whole (*Gestalt*) was something more than simply the sum of its parts. For example, the presentation of a number of photographs, each slightly different, in rapid series gives rise to cinematographic motion. In basic terms, the eye has received a number of discrete, "still" photographs, and yet "motion" is perceived. What, they asked, was the sensory input corresponding to this motion? Some processes within the brain clearly *added* something to the total input as defined in behaviourist terms. An obvious alternative—in a different sense modality—is that of the arrangement of musical notes. A cluster of notes played one way might be called a tune; played backwards they may form another tune, or may be meaningless. Yet in all cases the constituent parts are the same, and yet their relationship to one another is evidently vital. Once again the whole is something more than the simple sum of the parts.

The implications of all this appeared to be that the brain was equipped with the capacity to organise sensory input in certain well-defined ways, and that far from being misleading and scientifically unjustifiable, human subjective studies of visual experience might reveal the very principles of organisation which the brain employs. Take a field of dots, more or less randomly distributed; inspection of the field will soon reveal certain patterns or clusters standing out—the constellations in the night sky are a good illustration. There are many other examples, and Wertheimer and his colleagues in a famous series of experiments made some effort to catalogue them and reduce them to a finite number of "Laws of Perceptual Organisation" which are still much quoted today.

Ghosts, belief in ghosts is one of the most common features of supernatural and mystical philosophy. At its roots it is based on the assumption that Man is essentially an individual created of two separate and distinct substances, mind and body. Most religious systems hold to this dualistic view (*see* **Dualism**), arguing that whereas the body is transient and destructible, the mind or spirit is permanent and survives the death of its physical host. The discarnate spirit is normally assumed to progress to some other realm ("Heaven," "Nirvana," "The Spirit World," etc.) whereupon it loses contact with the mortal world. Occasionally, however, for one reason or another, the spirits may not progress and may become trapped and unable to escape the material world. Traditionally this is supposed to occur when the death of the individual is precipitated by some great tragedy —murder, suicide, etc.—when the site of the tragedy is supposed to be haunted by the earthbound spirit. Although the library of the Society for Psychical Research is crammed with supposedly authentic accounts of hauntings of this kind, scientific interest in ghosts has been waning rapidly in recent years. At one time, in particular in the latter part of the 19th cent., with the upsurge of scientific interest in Spiritualism (*q.v.*), there were even attempts to call up ghosts in the laboratory. These led to spectacular opportunities for fraud on the part of Spiritualist mediums and the like, but in the long run added little to the cause of science. As we have said, belief in ghosts is largely dependent upon a parallel belief that the mind or soul of man is something essentially separate from the body. With the decline in belief of this notion (it is now almost totally dismissed by most scientists and philosophers) has come an inevitable decline in belief in ghosts.

Gnosticism. Among the many heresies of early Christianity, especially during its first two centuries, was a group which came under the heading of Gnosticism. This was a system or set of systems which attempted to combine Christian beliefs with others derived from Oriental and Greek sources, especially those which were of a mystical and metaphysical nature, such as the doctrines of Plato and Pythagoras. There were many Gnostic sects, the most celebrated being the Alexandrian school of Valentius (fl. *c.* 136–*c.* 160). "Gnosis" was understood not as meaning "knowledge" or "understanding" as we understand these words, but "revelation." As in other mystical religions, the ultimate object was individual salvation; sacraments took the most varied forms. Many who professed themselves Christians accepted Gnostic doctrines and even orthodox Christianity contains some elements of Gnostic mysticism. It was left to the bishops and theologians to decide at what point Gnosticism ceased to be orthodox and a difficult task this proved to be. Two of the greatest, Clement of Alexandria and his pupil Origen, unwittingly slipped into heresy when they tried to show that such men as Socrates and Plato, who were in quest of truth, were Christian in intention, and by their lives and works had prepared the way for Christ. Thus they contradicted Church doctrine which specifically said *Extra ecclesiam nulla salus*—outside the Church there is no salvation.

God and Man. The idea of gods came before the idea of God and even earlier in the evolution of religious thought there existed belief in spirits (*see* **Animism**). It was only as a result of a long period of development that the notion of a universal "God" arose, a development particularly well documented in the Old Testament. Here we are concerned only with the views of philosophers, the views of specific religious bodies being given under the appropriate headings. First, however, some definitions.

Atheism is the positive disbelief in the existence of a God. **Agnosticism** (a term coined by T. H. Huxley, the 19th cent. biologist and contemporary of Darwin) signifies that one cannot know whether God exists or not. **Deism** is the acceptance of the existence of God, not through revelation, but as a hypothesis required by reason. **Theism** also accepts the existence of God, but, unlike Deism, does not reject the evidence of revelation (*e.g.*, in the Bible or in the lives of the saints). **Pantheism** is the identification of God with all that exists (*i.e.*, with the whole universe). **Monotheism** is the belief in one God, **Polytheism** the belief in many (*see also* **Dualism**).

Early Greek Views. Among the early Greek philosophers, Thales (*c.* 624–565 B.C.) of Miletus, in Asia Minor, Anaximander (611–547 B.C.), his pupil, and Anaximenes (b. *c.* 570 B.C.), another Miletan, were men of scientific curiosity and their speculations about the origin of the universe were untouched by religious thought. They founded the scientific tradition of critical discussion. Heraclitus of Ephesus (*c.* 540–475 B.C.), was concerned with the problem of change. How does a thing change and yet remain itself? For him all things are flames—processes. "Everything is in flux, and nothing is at rest." Empedocles of Agrigentum in Sicily (*c.* 500–*c.* 430 B.C.) introduced the idea of opposition and affinity. All matter is composed of the so-called four elements—*earth, water, air,* and *fire*—which are in opposition or alliance with each other. All these were materialist philosophers who sought to explain the working of the universe without recourse to the gods.

Socrates, Plato, and Aristotle. Socrates (470–399 B.C.) was primarily concerned with ethical matters and conduct rather than the nature of the universe. For him goodness and virtue come from knowledge. He obeyed an "inner voice" and suffered death rather than give up his philosophy. He believed in the persistence of life after death and was essentially a monotheist. Plato (427–347 B.C.) was chiefly concerned with the nature of reality and thought in terms of absolute truths which were unchanging, logical, and mathematical. (*See* **Mind and Matter**.) Aristotle (384–322 B.C.) took his views of matter not from Democritus (atomic view) but from Empedocles (doctrine of four elements), a view which came to fit in well with orthodox mediaeval theology. Matter is conceived of as potentially alive and striving to attain its particular form, being moved by divine spirit or mind (*nous*). (An acorn, for example, is matter which contains the form "oak-tree" towards which it strives.) Thus there is a whole series from the simplest level of matter to the perfect living individual. But there must be a supreme source of all movement upon which the whole of Nature depends, a Being that Aristotle describes as the "Unmoved Mover", the ultimate cause of all becoming in the universe. This Being is pure intelligence, a philosopher's God, not a personal one. Unlike Plato, Aristotle did not believe in survival after death, holding that the divine, that is the immortal element in man, is mind.

Among the later Greek thinkers the Epicureans were polytheists whose gods, however, were denied supernatural powers. The Stoics built up a materialist theory of the universe, based on the Aristotelian model. To them God was an all-pervading force, related to the world as the soul is related to the body, but they conceived of it as material. They developed the mystical side of Plato's idealism and were much attracted by the astrology coming from Babylonia. They were pantheists. The Sceptics were agnostics.

From Pagan to Christian Thought. Philo, "the Jew of Alexandria," who was about 20 years older than Jesus, tried to show that the Jewish scriptures were in line with the best in Greek thought. He introduced the *Logos* as a bridge between the two systems. Philo's God is remote from the world, above and beyond all thought and being, and as His perfection does not permit direct contact with matter the divine *Logos* acts as intermediary between God and man. Plotinus (204–70), a Roman, and the founder of Neoplatonism, was the last of the great pagan philosophers. Like Philo, he believed that God had created the world indirectly through emanations—beings coming from Him but not of Him. The world needs God but God does not need the world. Creation is a fall from God, especially the human soul when enmeshed in the body and the world of the senses, yet (*see* **Determinism**) man has the ability to free himself from sense domination and turn towards God. Neoplatonism was the final stage of Greek thought drawing inspiration from the mystical side of Plato's idealism and its ethics from Stoicism.

Christianity: The Fathers and the Schoolmen. It was mainly through St. Augustine (354–430), Bishop of Hippo in North Africa, that certain of the doctrines of Neoplatonism found their way into Christianity. Augustine also emphasised the concept of God as all good, all wise, all knowing, transcendent, the Creator of the universe out of nothing. But, he added, since God knows everything, everything is determined by Him forever. This is the doctrine of predestination and its subsequent history is discussed under **Determinism**.

In the early centuries of Christianity, as we have seen, some found it difficult to reconcile God's perfection with His creation of the universe and introduced the concept of the *Logos* which many identified with Christ. Further, it came to be held that a power of divine origin permeated the universe, namely the Holy Spirit or Holy Ghost. Some theory had to be worked out to explain the relationships of these three entities whence arose the conception of the Trinity. God is One; but He is also Three: Father, Son (the *Logos* or Christ), and Holy Ghost.

This doctrine was argued by the Apologists and the Modalists. The former maintained that the *Logos* and the Holy Spirit were emanations from God and that Jesus was the *Logos* in the form of a man. The Modalists held that all three Persons of the Trinity were God in three forms or modes: the *Logos* is God creating, the Holy Spirit God reasoning, and God is God being. This led to a long discussion as to whether the *Logos* was an emanation from God or God in another form; was the *Logos* of like *nature* with God or of the same *substance*? This was resolved at the Council of Nicaea (325) when Athanasius formulated the orthodox doctrine against Arius (*q.v.*): that the one God is a Trinity of the same substance, three Persons of the same nature—Father, Son, and Holy Ghost.

St. Thomas Aquinas (1227–74), influenced greatly by Aristotle's doctrines, set the pattern for all subsequent Catholic belief even to the present time. He produced rational arguments for God's existence: *e.g.*, Aristotle's argument that, since movement exists, there must be a prime mover, the Unmoved Mover or God; further, we can see that things in the universe are related in a scale from the less to the more complex, from the less to the more perfect, and this leads us to suppose that at the peak there must be a Being with absolute perfection. God is the first and final cause of the universe, absolutely perfect, the Creator of everything out of nothing. He reveals Himself in his Creation and rules the universe through His perfect will. How Aquinas dealt with the problem of predestination is told under **Determinism**.

Break with Mediaeval Thought. Renaissance thinkers, free to think for themselves, doubted the validity of the arguments of the Schoolmen but most were unwilling to give up the idea of God (nor would it have been safe to do so). Mystics (*see* **Mysticism**) or near-mystics such as Nicholas of Cusa (*c.* 1401–64) and Jacob Boehme (1575–1624) taught that God was not to be found by reason but was a fact of the immediate intuition of the mystical experience. Giordano Bruno held that God was immanent in the infinite universe. He is the unity of all opposites, a unity without opposites, which the human mind cannot grasp. Bruno was burned at the stake in 1600 at the instigation of the Inquisition (a body which, so we are told, never caused pain to anyone since it was the civil power, not the Inquisition, that carried out the unpleasant sentences) for his heresy.

Francis Bacon, who died in 1626, separated, as was the tendency of that time, science from religion. The latter he divided into the two categories of natural and revealed theology. The former, through the study of nature, may give convincing proof of the existence of a God but nothing more. Of revealed theology he said: "we must quit the small vessel of human reason ... as we are obliged to obey the divine law, though our will murmurs against it, so we are obliged to believe in the word of God, though our reason is shocked at it." Hobbes (d. 1679) was a complete materialist and one feels that his obeisance to the notion was politic rather than from conviction. However, he does mention God as starting the universe in motion; infers that God is corporeal but denies that His nature can be known.

From Descartes Onwards. Descartes (1596–1650) separated mind and body as different entities but believed that the existence of God could be deduced by the fact that the idea of him existed in the mind. Whatever God puts into man, including his ideas, must be real. God is self-caused, omniscient, omnipotent, eternal, all goodness and truth. But Descartes neglected to explain how mind separate from body can influence body, or God separate from the world can influence matter.

Spinoza (1632–77) declared that all existence is embraced in one substance—God, the all-in-all. He was a pantheist and as such was rejected by his Jewish brethren. But Spinoza's God has neither personality nor consciousness, intelligence nor purpose, although all things follow in strict law from His nature. All the thoughts of everyone in the world, make up God's thoughts.

Bishop Berkeley (1685–1753) took the view that things exist only when they are perceived, and this naturally implies that a tree, for example, ceases to exist when nobody is looking at it. This problem was solved to his own satisfaction by assuming that God, seeing everything, prevented objects from disappearing when we were not present. The world is a creation of God but it is a spiritual or mental world, not a material one.

Hume (1711–76), who was a sceptic, held that human reason cannot demonstrate the existence of God and all past arguments to show that it could were fallacious. Yet we must believe in God since the basis of all hope, morality, and society is based upon the belief. Kant (1724–1804) held a theory similar to that of Hume. We cannot know by reason that God exists, nor can we prove on the basis of argument anything about God. But we can form an idea of the whole of the universe, the one Absolute Whole, and personify it. We need the idea of God on which to base our moral life, although this idea of God is transcendent, *i.e.*, goes beyond experience.

William James (1842–1910), the American philosopher (*see* **Pragmatism**), held much the same view: God cannot be proved to exist, but we have a will to believe which must be satisfied, and the idea works in practice. Hegel (1770–1831) thought of God as a developing process, beginning with "the Absolute" or First Cause and finding its highest expression in man's mind, or reason. It is in man that God most clearly becomes aware of Himself. Finally Comte (1798–1857), the positivist, held that religion belongs to a more primitive state of society and, like many modern philosophers, turned the problem over to believers as being none of the business of science.

Golden Dawn, Order of, a strange but intellectually influential secret society founded in 1887 by three former Rosicrucians (*q.v.*). The Society, which was but one of the large number of occult organisations which flourished in the latter half of the 19th cent., was particularly interesting because it attracted so many scholarly eccentrics to its ranks. These included the poet W. B. Yeats, the actress Florence Farr, the writers Arthur Machen and Algernon Blackwood and the poetess Dion Fortune. A member with a less savoury reputation was the notorious Aleister Crowley who was ultimately expelled from the order for practising Black Magic. Essentially the movement, like others of its kind, professed to offer important secrets of occult knowledge, and taught its followers the basic principles of White, as opposed to Black Magic. Mainly harmless in their aims and activities, societies such as this served largely as pastimes for individuals of intellectual and academic standing who found the concepts and rituals of the Established Church too dull for their inquisitive minds. Most members of the Order of the Golden Dawn, either became disillusioned when the white magic, which they had so arduously studied, failed to provide any genuine supernatural results and gave up in disgust, or broke away to form their own rival groups. Though these often had equally glamorous names and rituals, they tended to be no more successful and themselves vanished into the mists of obscurity. Today so-called White Magic has become fashionable with many young people, no doubt as the result of the almost total collapse of the authority of orthodox religion, but it is noticeable that such interest is generally to be found among the less well-educated and intelligent. White Magic had its intellectual heyday in the 19th cent. and it is unlikely ever to attract such sustained academic interest again.

Good and Evil.

Early Philosophers' Views. The early Greek philosophers were chiefly concerned with the laws of the universe, consequently it was common belief that knowledge of these laws, and living according to them, constituted the supreme good. Heraclitus, for example, who taught that all things carried with them their opposites, held that good and evil were like two notes in a harmony, necessary to each other. "It is the opposite which is good for us". Democritus, like Epicurus (q.v.), held that the main goal of life is happiness, but happiness in moderation. The good man is not merely the one who *does* good but who always *wants* to do so: "You can tell the good man not by his deeds alone but by his desires." Such goodness brings happiness, the ultimate goal. On the other hand, many of the wandering Sophist teachers taught that good was merely social convention, that there are no absolute principles of right and wrong, that each man should live according to his desires and make his own moral code. To Socrates knowledge was the highest good because doing wrong is the result of ignorance: "no man is voluntarily bad." Plato and Aristotle, differing in many other respects, drew attention to the fact that man is composed of three parts: his desires and appetites, his will, and his reason. A man whose reason rules his will and appetites is not only a good but a happy man; for happiness is not an aim in itself but a by-product of the good life. Aristotle, however, emphasised the goal of self-realisation, and thought that if the goal of life is (as Plato had said) a rational attitude towards the feelings and desires, it needs to be further defined. Aristotle defined it as the "Golden Mean"—the good man is one who does not go to extremes but balances one extreme against another. Thus courage is a mean between cowardice and foolhardiness. The later philosophers Philo and Plotinus held that evil was in the very nature of the body and its senses. Goodness could only be achieved by giving up the life of the senses and, freed from the domination of the body, turning to God, the source of goodness.

Christian Views. St. Augustine taught that everything in the universe is good. Even those things which appear evil are good in that they fit with the harmony of the universe like shadows in a painting. Man should turn his back on the pleasures of the world and turn to the love of God. Peter Abelard (1079–1142) made the more sophisticated distinction when he suggested that the wrongness of an act lies not in the act itself, but in the intention of the doer: "God considers not what is done but in what spirit it is done; and the merit or praise of the agent lies not in the deed but in the intention." If we do what we believe to be right, we may err, but we do not sin. The only sinful man is he who deliberately sets out to do what he knows to be wrong. St. Thomas Aquinas agreed with Aristotle in that he believed the highest good to be realisation of self as God has ordained, and he also agreed with Abelard that intention is important. Even a good act is not good unless the doer intended it to have good consequences. Intention will not make a bad act good, but it is the only thing that will make a good act genuinely good.

In general, Christianity has had difficulties in solving the problem of the existence of evil; for even when one accepts that the evil men do is somehow tied up with the body, it is still difficult to answer the question: how could an all-good God create evil? This is answered in one of two ways: (a) that Adam was given free-will and chose to sin (an answer which still does not explain how sin could exist anywhere in the universe of a God who created everything); (b) by denying the reality of evil as some Christians have chosen to do (e.g., Christian Science q.v.). The Eastern religions, on the other hand (see **Zoroastrianism**), solved the problem in a more realistic way by a dualism which denied that their gods were the creators of the whole universe and allowed the existence of at least two gods, one good and one evil. In Christianity there is, of course, a Devil, but it is not explained whence his evil nature came.

Later Philosophic Views. Hobbes equated good with pleasure, evil with pain. They are relative to the individual man in the sense that "one man's meat is another man's poison." Descartes believed that the power to distinguish between good and evil given by God to man is not complete, so that man does evil through ignorance. We act with insufficient knowledge and on inadequate evidence. Locke, believing that at birth the mind is a blank slate, held

that men get their opinions of right and wrong from their parents. By and large, happiness is good and pain is evil. But men do not always agree over what is pleasurable and what not. Hence laws exist and these fall into three categories: (1) the divine law; (2) civil laws; (3) matters of opinion or reputation which are enforced by the fact that men do not like to incur the disapproval of their friends. We learn by experience that evil brings pain and good acts bring pleasure and, basically, one is good because not to be so would bring discomfort.

Kant (see **God and Man**) found moral beliefs to be inherent in man whether or not they can be proved by reason. There is a categorical imperative which makes us realise the validity of two universal laws: (1) "always act in such a way that the maxim determining your conduct might well become a universal law; act so that you can will that everybody shall follow the principle of your action; (2) "always act so as to treat humanity, whether in thine own person or in that of another, in every case as an end and never as a means."

Schopenhauer (1788–1860) was influenced by Buddhism and saw the will as a blind impelling striving, and desire as the cause of all suffering. The remedy is to regard sympathy and pity as the basis of all morality and to deny one's individual will. This is made easier if we realise that everyone is part of the Universal Will and therefore the one against whom we are struggling is part of the same whole as ourselves.

John Stuart Mill and Jeremy Bentham were both representatives of the Utilitarian school, believing that good is the greatest good (happiness) of the greatest number (see **Utilitarianism**). Lastly, there is the view held mostly by political thinkers that good is what is good for the state or society in general (see **State and Man**).

Graphology, the study of the analysis of human handwriting. There are two approaches to this topic and it is important to separate them clearly. The first involves the attempt on the part of an expert to decide from looking at a signature (a) to whom it belongs, and (b) whether or not it is forgery. This art is a legitimate, though tricky area of study, and graphologists have been called in as expert witnesses in courts of law. The second approach involves attempts to detect such tenuous variables as character from a study of an individual's handwriting, and the facts here are altogether less clear. Psychologists find it difficult enough to assess character or personality in a face-to-face interview and even when they are equipped with a range of special tests. The general opinion here would seem to be that some slight information might be revealed by a careful study of handwriting, but that the overall effect would be too unreliable for this kind of graphology to be of practical value.

Greater World Spiritualists. Spiritualism, as an organised religion, holds the view that the human personality survives death, and that it is possible to communicate with the spirits of those who have died in the physical sense. Greater World Spiritualists make the following declaration of beliefs: 1. I believe in One God Who is Love. 2. I accept the Leadership of Jesus Christ. 3. I believe that God manifests through the Illimitable Power of the Holy Spirit. 4. I believe in the survival of the Human Soul and its individuality after physical death. 5. I believe in the Communion with God, with His angelic ministers, and with the souls functioning in conditions other than the earth life. 6. I believe that all forms of life created by God intermingle, are interdependent and evolve until perfection is attained. 7. I believe in the perfect justice of the Divine Laws governing all life. 8. I believe that sins committed can only be rectified by the sinner himself or herself, through the redemptive power of Jesus Christ, by repentance and service to others; and also the following pledge: 9. I will at all times endeavour to be guided in my thoughts, words and deeds by the teaching and example of Jesus Christ.

Guild Socialism, a British form of syndicalism (q.v.) created in 1906 by an architect, A. J. Penty, who was soon joined by A. R. Orage, S. G. Hobson, and G. D. H. Cole. The background to the movement was the situation that, although at the time the Labour Party had 29 members in the House of Commons, a period of severe economic crisis had shown the government unwilling and the Labourites unable to do anything about it; the workers were resorting again to direct action to secure their demands and the democratic and constitutional methods to which the Fabians had partly persuaded them seemed to have failed. The guild socialists advocated a restoration of the mediaeval guild system as was being recommended by the French syndicalists whose programme involved a return to direct economic action, a functional industrial structure, return of craftsmanship, and distrust of the state. Guild socialists believed that value was created by society as a whole rather than by individuals singly, and that capitalist economists had recommended the acquisition of wealth without emphasising the social responsibilities which wealth should bring. The trade unions were to be organised to take over and run their own industries after nationalisation. Thus guild socialists were not only against capitalism but also against state socialism in which the state took over the control of industry. Political authority was held to be uncongenial to human freedom and therefore nothing was to be gained by the substitution of state bureaucracy for capitalist control. The National Guilds League, formed in 1915, advocated abolition of the wages system, self-government in industry and control by a system of national guilds acting in conjunction with other functional democratic organisations in the community. This body was dissolved in 1925, but the theories of guild socialism have undoubtedly influenced British socialism.

Gurdjieff, Russian–Greek mystic who set up an occult commune at La Prieure in France, to which were attracted a host of the intellectual and literary avant-garde of the 1920s. His teachings, which are immensely obscure, are presented in allegorical form in a lengthy philosophical novel, *All and Everything,* which has the peculiar sub-title "Beelzebub's Tales to his Grandson."

H

Heresy, originally meant a sect or school of thought holding views different from others (*e.g.,* Pharisees and Sadducees within Judaism). Later it came to mean beliefs contrary to orthodox teaching (*e.g.,* Arianism, Apollinarianism, Nestorianism).

Hinduism, the religion and social institutions of the great majority of the people of India. Hinduism has no fixed scriptural canon but its doctrines are to be found in certain ancient works, notably the *Veda,* the *Brahmanas,* the *Upanishads,* and the *Bhagavad-gita.* The dark-skinned Dravidians invaded India between about 3250 and 2750 B.C. and established a civilisation in the Indus valley. They were polytheists who worshipped a number of nature-gods; some elements of their beliefs persisted into Hinduism. They were subdued by a light-skinned Nordic people who invaded from Asia Minor and Iran about 1500 B.C. The language of these Aryan people was Vedic, parent of Sanskrit in which their religious literature (the Vedas) came to be written after many centuries of oral transmission.

The *Veda* or Sacred Lore has come down to us in the form of mantras or hymns of which there are four great collections, the best-known being the *Rig-Veda.* These Vedic Aryans worshipped nature-deities, their favourites being Indra (rain), Agni (fire), and Surya (the sun). Their religion contained no idolatry but became contaminated by the more primitive beliefs of the conquered Dravidians. Sacrifice and ritual became predominant in a ceremonial religion.

As a reaction a more philosophic form arose (c. 500 B.C.) with its scriptures in the *Upani-*

shads. At its highest level known as Brahmanism belief is in a subtle and sophisticated form of monotheism (Brahman is an impersonal, all-embracing spirit), but there is a tolerant acceptance of more primitive beliefs. Thus Vishnu (a conservative principle) and Siva (a destructive principle) grew out of Vedic conceptions. The two great doctrines of Hinduism are *karma* and transmigration. The universal desire to be reunited with the absolute (*atman* or Brahman) can be satisfied by following the path of knowledge. Life is a cycle of lives (*samsara*) in which man's destiny is determined by his deeds (*karma*) from which he may seek release (*moksa*) through ascetic practices or the discipline of Yoga (*q.v.*). Failure to achieve release means reincarnation—migration to a higher or lower form of life after death—until the ultimate goal of absorption in the absolute is reached.

In the great Sanskrit epic poems *Ramayana* and *Mahabharata* the deity takes three forms, represented by the divine personalities of Brahma, Vishnu, and Siva. There are also lower gods, demi-gods, supernatural beings, and members of the trinity may even become incarnate, as Vishnu became identified with Krishna, one of the heroes of the *Mahabharata* and the well-known *Bhagavad-gita.*

The ritual and legalistic side of Brahmanism is the caste system based on the elaborate codes of the *Law of Manu,* according to which God created distinct orders of men as He created distinct species of animals and plants. Men are born to be Brahmans, soldiers, agriculturists, or servants, but since a Brahman may marry a woman from any of these castes, an endless number of sub-castes arise.

Hinduism has always shown great tolerance for varieties of belief and practice. Ideas pleasant and unpleasant have been assimilated: fetichism, demon-cults, animal-worship, sexual-cults (such as the rites of *Kali* in Calcutta). Today, as would be expected in a country which is in the throes of vast social change, Hinduism itself is changing. Under the impact of modern conditions new ideas are destroying old beliefs and customs. *See also* **Jainism, Sikhism.**

Holy Rollers. Contrary to general belief there is no single individual religious group calling themselves Holy Rollers; rather this is a generic term referring to a number of minor revivalist groups whose members work themselves into an ecstatic frenzy in the course of religious worship. Swooning and fainting are probably the most popular methods of expressing this kind of religious ecstasy, but "speaking with tongues" (*i.e.,* babbling nonsense), snake handling (many believers die from snake venom as a consequence) and uncontrolled dancing are also featured. Athletic religious worship of this kind is of course of great interest to psychologists. Anthropologists are equally interested, for they see in such behaviour patterns vivid reminders—if such are needed—that mankind has a history that predates our present culture by millions and not just by thousands of years.

Homoeopathy, a branch of fringe medicine whose motto *Similia Similibus Curantur* (like cures like) sums up its controversial approach to therapy. In essence the homoeopathists claim that a disease can be treated by administering quite minute doses of a substance which produce symptoms (in the healthy person) similar to those induced by the disease itself. The founder and populariser of this unusual approach to medicine was the German Samuel Hahnemann who was born in 1775, a friend of the physician Mesmer who propagated hypnotherapy. Hahnemann lived to see his ideas spread across the civilised world and despite the grave theoretical difficulties implicit in the question of how the very minute dosages actually achieve any result at all, it remained a respectable approach of medicine until the latter half of the last century. Even today a number of qualified doctors still employ homoeopathic ideas within the framework of the national health service, and the late King George V was treated by the eminent homoeopathist, Sir John Weir, but it seems nevertheless to be in slow but steady decline. This is probably due not to any revealed deficiences in homoeopathy itself, but rather to the extraordinary advances which have been made in orthodox medicine in the last few decades.

House Church Movement, a recent development in Christian worship which began in the 1970s. Each house church has an average of 100 members. Groups of members hold services and prayer meetings in private houses. The post of chairman is taken in rotation. The movement has an estimated 95,000 membership, but with a much larger number of participants.

Humanism, the term applied to (1) a system of education based on the Greek and Latin classics; and (2) the vigorous attitudes that accompanied the end of the Middle Ages and were represented at different periods by the Renaissance, the Reformation, the Industrial Revolution, and the struggle for democracy. These include: release from ecclesiastical authority, the liberation of the intellect, faith in progress, the belief that man himself can improve his own conditions without supernatural help and, indeed has a duty to do so. "Man is the measure of all things" is the keynote of humanism. The humanist has faith in man's intellectual and spiritual resources not only to bring knowledge and understanding of the world but to solve the moral problems of how to use that knowledge. That man should show respect to man irrespective of class, race or creed is fundamental to the humanist attitude to life. Among the fundamental moral principles he would count those of freedom, justice, tolerance and happiness.

Today the idea that people can live an honest, meaningful life without following a formal religious creed of some kind does not seem particularly shocking. Persons seeking to find out more about humanism can apply for information to the British Humanist Association, 13 Prince of Wales Terrace, London W8.

Hussites, the followers of John Hus, the most famous pupil of John Wyclif. He was the rector of Prague University and, although it is now by no means certain that his beliefs were heretical, he was condemned to death for heresy and burnt at the stake in 1415 at Constance whence he had come with a safe conduct issued by the Emperor Sigismund of Hungary. The latter based his action on the doctrine that no faith need be kept with heretics, but it is obvious that the main objection to Hus was his contempt for authority of any kind. After their leader's death, the Hussites became a formidable body in Bohemia and Moravia. They took up arms on behalf of their faith, their religion being strongly imbued with political feeling (hostility to Germanism and to the supremacy of the Roman Church). Their religious struggles for reform led to the Hussite Wars during which the movement splintered into several groups.

I

I Ching, the Chinese "Book of Changes" which is supposed to provide a practical demonstration of the truths of ancient Chinese philosophy. The method consists of casting forty-nine sticks into two random heaps, or more simply, of tossing three coins to see if there is a preponderance of heads or tails. The coins are cast six times whereupon the head-tail sequence achieved is referred to a coded series of phrases in the book, which are supposed to relate in some way to the question held in the mind when the sticks or coins are being cast. The phrases are without exception vague, and platitudinous remarks such as "Evil people do not further the perseverance of the superior man," etc., abound. Consequently it is not difficult to read into such amorphous stuff a suitable "interpretation" or answer to one's unspoken question. The I Ching might well be looked upon as an entertaining parlour game, but it is currently a great fad in Europe and America and is taken with great seriousness by an astonishing number of people.

Idealism, in a philosophical sense, the belief that there is no matter in the universe, that all that exists is mind or spirit. *See* **Mind and Matter** and **Realism.**

Illuminati, a secret society founded in 1776 by Adam Weishaupt, a Bavarian professor of canon law at Ingolstadt, in an attempt to combat superstition and ignorance by founding an association for rational enlightenment and the regeneration of the world. "He tried to give the social ideals of the Enlightenment realisation by conspiratorial means" (J. M. Roberts, *The Mythology of the Secret Societies,* 1972). Under conditions of secrecy it sought to penetrate and control the masonic lodges for subversive purposes. Among its members were Goethe and Schiller. The Order spread to Austria, Italy and Hungary but was condemned by the Roman Catholic Church and dissolved in 1785 by the Bavarian government.

Immortality. The belief in a life after death has been widely held since the earliest times. It has certainly not been universal, nor has it always taken a form which everyone would find satisfying. In the early stages of human history or prehistory everything contained a spirit (*see* **Animism**) and it is obvious from the objects left in early graves that the dead were expected to exist in some form after death. The experience of dreams, too, seemed to suggest to the unsophisticated that there was a part of man which could leave his body and wander elsewhere during sleep. In order to save space, it will be helpful to classify the various types of belief which have existed in philosophical thought regarding this problem: (1) There is the idea that, although *something* survives bodily death, it is not necessarily eternal. Thus most primitive peoples were prepared to believe that man's spirit haunted the place around his grave and that food and drink should be set out for it, but that this spirit did not go on forever and gradually faded away. (2) The ancient Greeks and Hebrews believed for the most part that the souls of the dead went to a place of shades there to pine for the world of men. Their whining ghosts spent eternity in a dark, uninviting region in misery and remorse. (3) Other people, and there were many more of these, believed in the transmigration of souls with the former life of the individual determining whether his next life would be at a higher or lower level. Sometimes this process seems to have been thought of as simply going on and on, by others (*e.g.*, in Hinduism and Buddhism) as terminating in either non-sentience or union with God but in any case in annihilation of the self as self. Believers in this theory were the Greek philosophers Pythagoras, Empedocles, Plato (who believed that soul comes from God and strives to return to God, according to his own rather confused notions of the deity. If it fails to free itself completely from the body it will sink lower and lower from one body to another.) Plotinus held similar views to Plato, and many other religious sects in addition to those mentioned have believed in transmigration. (4) The belief of Plato and Aristotle that if souls continue to exist after death there is no reason why they should not have existed before birth (this in part is covered by (3)), but some have pointed out that eternity does not mean "from now on," but the whole of the time before and after "now"—nobody, however, so far as one knows, held that *individual* souls so exist. (5) The theory that the soul does not exist at all and therefore immortality is meaningless: this was held by Anaximenes in early Greek times; by Leucippus, Democritus, and the other Greek atomists; by the Epicureans from the Greek Epicurus to the Roman Lucretius; by the British Hobbes and Hume; by Comte of France; and William James and John Dewey of America. (6) The thesis, held notably by Locke and Kant, that although we cannot prove the reality of soul and immortality by pure reason, belief in them should be held for moral ends. (For the orthodox Christian view *see* **God and Man, Determinism and Free-will.**) From this summary we can see that many philosophies and religions (with the important exceptions of Islam and Christianity) without denying a future life do deny the permanence of the individual soul in anything resembling its earthly form (*see* **Spiritualism, Psychic Research**).

Imperialism, the practice by a country, which has become a nation and embarked upon commercial and industrial expansion, of acquiring and administering territories, inhabited by peoples usually at a lower stage of development, as colonies or dependencies. Thus the "typical" imperialist powers of the 19th cent. and earlier were Britain, Belgium, Holland, Spain, and Portugal, whilst Germany, Italy, and Japan, which either did not have unity during this period or adequate industrial expansion, tried to make good their lacks in this direction by war in the 20th cent. The term "imperialism" is not easy to define today (although often enough used as a term of abuse). There is economic imperialism exerted, not through armies, but through economic penetration. There is what may be described as ideological imperialism, *e.g.*, the anti-communist crusade that led America (in the name of freedom) into a disastrous and widely-condemned war in Vietnam; the dogmatism that led the Soviet Union into the invasion of Czechoslovakia and Israel into occupying neighbouring territories.

Irrationalism. An attitude that puts emotion and passion before reason, and which can be exploited for dubious ends.

Islam, the religion of the Arabic and Iranian world of which Mohammed (570–632) was the prophet, the word signifying submission to the will of God. It is one of the most widespread of religions. Its adherents are called Moslems or Muslims. Islam came later than the other great monotheistic religions (Judaism and Christianity) and drew its inspiration mainly from Judaism and Nestorianism. Mohammed accepted the inspiration of the Old Testament and claimed to be a successor to Moses, but recognised Jesus only as a prophet.

The sacred book of Islam is the Koran. Its revelations are contained in 114 *suras* or chapters; all but one begin with the words: "In the name of Allah, the Merciful, the Compassionate." It is written in classical Arabic, and Moslems memorise much or all of it. Its ethical teachings are high. Like orthodox Judaism Islam is a literal-minded religion lived in everyday life. No Moslem is in any doubt as to exactly how he should carry on in the events of his day. He has five duties: (1) Once in his life he must say with absolute conviction: "There is no God but Allah, and Mohammed is His Prophet". (2) Prayer preceded by ablution must be five times daily—on rising, at noon, in mid-afternoon, after sunset, and before retiring. The face of the worshipper is turned in the direction of Mecca. (3) The giving of alms generously, including provisions for the poor. (4) The keeping of the fast of Ramadan, the holy month, during which believers in good health may neither eat nor drink nor indulge in wordly pleasures between sunrise and sunset. (5) Once in his life a Moslem, if he can, must make the pilgrimage to Mecca. In addition, drinking, gambling, and the eating of pork are forbidden and circumcision is practised. Polygamy is permitted, although decreasing; sexual relations outside marriage are disapproved of; marriage is only with the wife's consent; and divorce may be initiated by either husband or wife. A great advantage in the spread of Islam has been its lack of race prejudice.

Mohammed's main achievements were the destruction of idolatry, the welding of warring tribes into one community, the progress of a conquest which led after his death to the great and cultured empire which spread throughout the Middle East into north Africa, north India, and ultimately to Spain. That it did not spread all over Europe was due to the Muslim defeat by Charles Martel at Poitiers in 732.

During the 1980s, militant Islam became a major political force in Iran (under Ayatollah Khomeini). There were (1990) over 860 m. Moslems in the world.

Britain's Moslem population (1990) numbers c 1.5 million. There are some 385 mosques and numerous prayer centres throughout Britain. The first was established at Woking in Surrey in 1890. The Central Mosque in London has the largest congregation in Britain while other important centres include Liverpool, Manchester, Leicester and Glasgow.

J

Jainism. The Jains are a small Indian sect, largely in commerce and finance, numbering about 2 million. Their movement founded by Vardhamana, called Mahavira (the great hero), in the 6th cent. B.C. arose rather earlier than Buddhism in revolt against the ritualism and impersonality of **Hinduism** (*q.v.*). It rejects the authority of the early Hindu Vedas and does away with many of the Hindu deities whose place is largely taken by Jainism's twenty-four immortal saints; it despises caste distinctions and modifies the two great Hindu doctrines of *karma* and transmigration. Jain philosophy is based on *ahimsa*, the sacredness of all life, regarding even plants as the brethren of mankind, and refusing to kill even the smallest insect.

Jansenism, the name given by the Roman Catholic Church to the heresy of Cornelius Jansen (1585– 1638), a Dutch-born professor of theology at Louvain, derived from his work *Augustinus*, published after his death.

Jehovah's Witnesses, a religious body who consider themselves to be the present-day representatives of a religious movement which has existed since Abel "offered unto God a more excellent sacrifice than Cain, by which he obtained witness that he was righteous." Abel was the first "witness," and amongst others were Enoch, Noah, Abraham, Moses, Jeremiah, and John the Baptist. Pre-eminent among witnesses, of course, was Jesus Christ who is described in the Book of Revelation as "the faithful and true witness." Thus they see themselves as "the Lord's organisation," in the long line of those who through the ages have preserved on earth the true and pure worship of God or, as the Witnesses prefer to call Him, "Jehovah-God."

So far as other people are aware, the movement was founded by Charles Taze Russell (Pastor Russell) of Allegany, Pittsburgh, Pennsylvania, U.S.A. in 1881 under the name, adopted in 1896, of the Watch Tower Bible and Tract Society, which has continued as the controlling organisation of Jehovah's Witnesses. Its magazine, *The Watch Tower Announcing Jehovah's Kingdom*, first published in 1879, and other publications are distributed by the eager members who carry out house-to-house canvassing. The movement has a strong leadership.

Their teaching centres upon the early establishment of God's new world on earth, preceded by the second coming of Christ. Witnesses believe this has already happened and that Armageddon "will come as soon as the Witness is completed." The millenial period will give sinners a second chance of salvation and "millions now living will never die" (the title of one of their pamphlets). The dead will progressively be raised to the new earth until all the vacant places left after Armageddon are filled.

Every belief held by the movement, it is asserted, can be upheld, chapter and verse, by reference to the Scriptures. Witnesses regard the doctrine of the Trinity as devised by Satan. In both wars Witnesses have been in trouble for their refusal to take part in war and it is only fair to add that six thousand suffered for the same reason in German concentration camps.

Jensenism, name given to the minority group of psychologists and educationalists who, in general, support the view of the American professor, Arthur Jensen. The latter's studies of individual variation in learning and of the genetic factor in mental ability has led him to argue that heredity is more crucial in determining intellectual ability than environment. By implication this has put him and his colleagues at the centre of a divisive "race and intelligence" controversy which has acquired some political overtones. In 1978 Professor H. J. Eysenck was physically assaulted by students at a university lecture because he was reputed to be supporting the Jensenist position.

Jesus People, naïve and exhibitionist revival of interest in the teaching and personality of Jesus Christ which featured from the 1960s as part of the American "Hippy" scene. The Jesus people or Jesus Freaks, as they are sometimes called, are generally white but not necessarily of an orthodox Christian background. The cult, like so many others of its kind seems to have developed in California and its adherents adopt the regimental attire (colourful costumes, long hair, beards, etc.) of the modern American Hippy, who is himself a descendant of the Beatnik (*see* **Beat Generation**). Apart from the fact that the long hair and beards are vaguely reminiscent of the Victorian pictorial representation of Jesus, the followers of the present-day cult would seem to have little genuinely in common with the ethos of Christianity, and the movement and its ideals appear to be superficial and probably transitory. A highly successful rock musical, "Jesus Christ, Superstar," blatantly cashes in on the Jesus Freak vogue.

Judaism, the religion of the Jews, the oldest of the great monotheist religions, parent of Christianity and Islam, the development of which is presented in the Old Testament. The creed of Judaism is based on the concept of a transcendent and omnipotent One True God, the revelation of His will in the *Torah*, and the special relation between God and His "Chosen People." The idea of Incarnation is rejected, Jesus is not recognised as the Messiah. The *Torah* is the Hebrew name for the Law of Moses (the Pentateuch) which, Judaism holds, was divinely revealed to Moses on Mount Sinai soon after the exodus of the Israelites from Egypt (1230 B.C.). Many critics deny the Mosaic authorship of the first five books of the Bible and believe them to be a compilation from four main sources known as J(Jahvist), E (Elohist), D (Deuteronomist) and P (Priestly Code), distinguished from each other by the name used for God, language, style, and internal evidence. From the historical point of view an important influence on Judaism may have been the monotheism of Akhenaten, the "heretic" Pharaoh (note, for example, the striking resemblance between Psalm 104 and Akhenaten's "Hymn to the Sun").

The Talmud is a book containing the civil and canonical laws of the Jews and includes the Mishna, a compilation from oral tradition written in Hebrew, and the Gemara, a collection of comments and criticisms by the Jewish rabbis, written in Aramaic. There are in fact two Talmuds: the one made in Palestine (the Jerusalem Talmud), finished at the beginning of the 5th cent., and the other made in Babylon, completed at the end of the 6th cent.

Judaism at the beginning of the Christian era had a number of sects: (1) the Pharisees (whose views include the first clear statement of the resurrection of the just to eternal life and the future punishment of the wicked) who held to the *Torah* and the universality of God; (2) the Sadducees, the upper class of priests and wealthy landowners, to whom God was essentially a national God and who placed the interests of the state before the *Torah*; they rejected ideas of resurrection and eternal life; (3) the Essenes (*q.v.*) who were regarded as a puritanical break-away movement by both parties. The views of the Pharisees prevailed.

Jewish writing continued through the years and some books were added to the *Torah*, among them the Three Major Prophets and certain books of the Twelve Minor Prophets. There were also the Apocalyptic writers who were unorthodox in their preaching of a divinely planned catastrophic end to the world with a "new Heaven and a new earth," preceded by a divine Messiah, and a future life—all of which beliefs influenced early Christianity. Judah Halevi of Toledo (*c*. 1085–*c*. 1140) and Moses Maimonides of Cordova (1135–1204) were the great Jewish philosophers.

Modern movements in Judaism stem from the Enlightenment, notably with Moses Mendels-

sohn in the 18th cent. who accepted, as was the tendency of the period, only that which could be proved by reason. He translated the Pentateuch into German thus encouraging German Jews to give up Yiddish and Hebrew for the language of the land and thereby preparing them for their vast contribution to Western civilisation. One of his disciples, David Friedländer (d. 1834) instituted "reform" Judaism. He wanted to eliminate anything that would hamper the relationships of Jews with their neighbours or tend to call in doubt their loyalty to their adopted state. A similar movement in America (1885) called for the rejection of dietary laws, the inauguration of Sunday services, and the repudiation of Jewish nationalism. Between "reform" and orthodoxy there arose the conservative movement which, in England, includes prayers in English in the service, does not segregate men and woman in the synagogue, and translates the Law in a more liberal way.

Judaism is essentially a social and family religion which, more than almost any other concerns itself with the observances of every aspect of daily life. As in Islam (*q.v.*) details are laid down in the most minute way for the behaviour of the orthodox.

The home is the main Jewish institution and Jews, like Catholics, cannot surrender their religion. Circumcision takes place eight days after birth, and a boy becomes a man for religious purposes at his Bar Mitzvah at the age of thirteen. Women are spared most of this because their place in the home is considered sufficiently sacred. Among festivals are Passover, recalling the Exodus; Rosh Hashanah (the Jewish New Year), the anniversary of the Creation and the beginning of ten days of penitence ending with Yom Kippur (the Day of Atonement), a day of fasting spent in the synagogue; Purim, celebrating the deliverance of the Jews from Haman; and Chanukah, celebrating their victory against the Syrians under their leader Judas Maccabeus. A new and semi-religious festival is the Yom Haatzmaut, the anniversary of the birth of the new Jewish state of Israel. The total numbers of world Jewry are estimated to be over 16 million (1990).

K

Kabbala. *See* **Cabala.**

Ku Klux Klan. After the American Civil War (1861–65) southern conservatives and ex-Confederate leaders began to fear (as they had every reason to do) both Negro and poor White rule. Taxes were rising owing to radical legislation and the tax-burdened and disenfranchised planters finally took to illegal means to achieve their ends by trying to effect an alliance with the poor White and small farmer through appealing to his anti-Negro prejudice.

Hence the Ku Klux Klan was formed in 1866 as a secret society by a small group of Confederate veterans in Tennessee with the intention of frightening Negroes by dressing in ghostly white robes in the guise of the spirits of dead soldiers. But the movement spread like wild-fire throughout the South encouraged by small farmers and planters alike. General Nathan Bedford Forrest was appointed "Grand Wizard" of the Klan "empire" and in every community armed Klansmen riding at night horsewhipped "uppity" Negroes, beat Union soldiers, and threatened carpet-bag politicians (*i.e.*, fortune-hunters from the North). Soon several similar organisations arose, many of which did not stop at torture, burning property, and murder. In fact, although claiming to be a "holy crusade" the Klan was a vicious and contemptible organisation in which former Southern leaders trying to regain control deliberately set poor and middle-class Whites against the Negroes by appeal to race prejudice. Congress struck back with laws and intervention of Federal troops, and after a large number of convictions in South Carolina much of the violence stopped.

After the 1914–18 war the movement, dormant since 1900, revived as a sadistic anti-Negro, anti-Jewish, anti-Catholic society, spreading to the north as well as the south. By 1926, with its white-gowned hooligans and fiery crosses, the Klan began to subside once more. While it revived again in the mid-60s, the Klan has recently suffered a loss of support. Membership in 1990 was estimated at a mere 15,000.

Kuomintang, a Chinese Nationalist party founded in 1891 by Sun Yat Sen. It took part in the first Chinese revolution of 1911 and led the second the following year, dominating south China by 1930 and, under Chiang Kai-shek, who succeeded Sun Yat Sen on his death in 1925, conducted China's defence against Japanese invasion from 1937–45. Sun Yat Sen had attempted to found a democratic republic based on Western parliamentary democracy and in his famous *Testament* laid down the principles upon which the constitution of China should be based. In 1946, Sun Fo, the son of Sun Yat Sen, deplored the party's departure from the principles of social democracy and the welfare of the people in which his father had believed. Beginning as a movement largely inspired by Russia, the Kuomintang under Chiang Kai-shek degenerated into a reactionary and corrupt military oligarchy which, collapsing in 1949, was replaced by the Communist Party, leaving Chiang and his followers to rule Taiwan.

L

Lamaism, the religion of Tibet. Its beliefs and worship derive from the Mahayana form of Buddhism which was introduced into Tibet in 749. The emphasis laid by its founder on the necessity for self-discipline and conversion through meditation and the study of philosophy deteriorated into formal monasticism and ritualism. The Dalai Lama, as the reincarnated Buddha, was both king and high priest, a sort of pope and emperor rolled into one. Under him was a hierarchy of officials in which the lowest order was that of the monks who became as numerous as one man in every six or seven of the population. The main work carried out by this vast church-state was the collection of taxes to maintain the monasteries and other religious offices. Second in power to the Dalai Lama was the Panchen or Tashi Lama believed to be a reincarnation of Amitabha, another Buddha. The last Dalai Lama fled to India in 1959 when the Chinese entered his country. For a brief period following his departure, the Panchen Lama surprised the Western world by publicly welcoming the Communist invasion, but he later renounced the regime and the suppression of Lamaism in Tibet continued unchecked.

Levellers, an English military-politico-religious party prominent in the Parliamentary Army about 1647 which stood for the rights of the people. See **Diggers**.

Liberalism. The Liberal Party is the successor to the Whigs (a nickname derived from *Whiggamore,* used in the 17th cent. for Scottish dissenters) of the 18th and 19th cents. Under Gladstone's two great ministries (1868–74; and 1880–85), and again under Campbell-Bannerman and Asquith (1906–14) much reforming legislation was enacted. The Asquith–Lloyd George split of 1916, and the advent of Labour as a major party after 1918, have caused the Liberals to be relegated as a smaller, third party. In the decade after 1945, there were times when the Liberal Party barely survived. But revivals have since occurred (*see* **D3**) under the leadership of Grimond (1962), Thorpe (1974) and David Steel (1979).

Liberal philosophy is moderately radical and progressive in terms of social reform. But the party strongly disapproves of state control or any form of monopoly, private or public. The main proposals favoured by the party are co-ownership in industry, proportional representation, greater protection of individual liberties, and separate Parliaments for Wales and Scotland. Many younger members of the party hold views to the Left of official party policy. The phenomenon of "community politics" has owed much to these younger, radical Liberals. The

1987 election setback heralded a merger ("democratic fusion") between the Liberals and their SDP Alliance partners. The new Social and Liberal Democratic Party (SLD) was formed in 1988. The first leader of the new party is Paddy Ashdown, MP for Yeovil. The new party (known as the Liberal Democrats) has been faced with the twin problems of putting forward a clear political ideology and also dealing with the continuing Owenite SDP.

Libertarianism, a political belief in free trade, individual liberty and respect for the lives and property of others. Essentially it is the modern day form of classical liberalism. Today the tradition is carried on by, among others: Frederick Hayek, Murray Rothbard, Ayn Rand and Robert Nozick.

Logical Positivism, a school of philosophy founded in Vienna in the 1920s by a group known as "the Vienna circle": their work was based on that of Ernst Mach, but dates in essentials as far back as Hume. Of the leaders of the group, Schlick was murdered by a student, Wittgenstein came to Britain, and Carnap went to America following the entry of the Nazis. Briefly the philosophy differs from all others in that, while most people have believed that a statement might be (*a*) true, or (*b*) false, logical positivists consider there to be a third category; a statement may be meaningless. There are only two types of statement which can be said to have meaning: (1) those which are tautological, *i.e.*, those in which the statement is merely a definition of the subject, such as "a triangle is a three-sided plane figure" ("triangle" and "three-sided plane figure" are the same thing); and (2) those which can be tested by sense experience. This definition of meaningfulness excludes a great deal of what has previously been thought to be the field of philosophy; in particular it excludes the possibility of metaphysics. Thus the question as to whether there is a God or whether free-will exists is strictly meaningless for it is neither a tautological statement nor can it be tested by sense experience.

Lollards, a body of religious reformers and followers of Wyclif who were reviled and persecuted in the reign of Richard II. The name "Lollard" comes from a Flemish word meaning "mutterer"— a term of contempt used to describe the sect. Under Henry V, determined efforts were made to crush the Lollards. Their leader, Sir John Oldcastle, was burnt at the stake (December 1417).

Luddites, a group of peasants and working men who deliberately destroyed spinning and farm machinery in England in the early part of the 19th cent., fearing that such devices would destroy their livelihood. Their name was taken from the eccentric Ned Lud who had done the same in a less organised way two or three decades earlier. The Luddites' worst fears were of course not realised, for far from putting human beings out of work the industrial revolution created jobs for a vastly increased population. Luddism, dormant for over a century, is beginning to appear again, if in muted form. Public anxiety about the rapid growth in computer technology is manifesting itself in the form of such groups as the Society for the Abolition of Data Processing Machines, which while not of course dedicated to the physical destruction of computers, urge for social and even governmental checks on the development of such things as "data banks." These are vast computer memory stores listing comprehensive records concerning all the people living in a city or country and able to cross-reference them in a way that has never previously been possible. Luddism is of considerable historical and social significance.

Lutheranism. The Reformation had a long history before it became, under Luther and Calvin, an accepted fact. The mediaeval Church had held (as the Catholic Church holds today) that the sacraments were the indispensable means of salvation. Since these were exclusively administered by the clergy, any movement which attacked clerical abuses was forced by sheer necessity to deny the Church's exclusive control of the means of salvation, before it could become free from dependence on a corrupt priesthood. Hence the Albigenses and the Waldenses (*qq.v.*), the followers of John Hus and Wycliff (*see* **Anticlericalism**), were bound to deny the authority of the Church and emphasise that of the Bible. Luther began his movement primarily in order to reform the Church from its gross abuses and the famous ninety-five theses nailed to the door of the Church at Wittenberg in 1517 were not primarily theological but moral complaints dealing with the actual behaviour of the clergy rather than Church beliefs. But, unlike the earlier reformers, Luther had arrived at the right moment in history when economic individualism and the force of nationalism were bound, sooner or later, to cause the authorities in Germany to line up on his side. Thus he began with the support of the peasants who were genuinely shocked at the abuse of indulgences and other matters, but ended up by being supported by the noblemen who wanted to destroy the power of the pope over the German states and looked forward to confiscating the lands and property of the Church. When the peasants wanted the reform of actual economic abuses relating to the feudal system, Luther took the side of the nobles against them. The contemporary movement in Switzerland led by Ulrich Zwingli had no such secular support, and Zwingli was killed in 1531.

Martin Luther (1483–1546) was the son of a miner in Eisleben in Saxony, entered the order of Austin Friars in 1505, and later taught at the newly founded university of Wittenberg. After the publication of the theses the real issue so far as the Church was concerned was whether he was willing or not to submit to the authority of his superiors; Luther refused to compromise with his conscience in the famous words: "Here I stand; I can do no other." In a further statement Luther recommended the formation of a German national church, the abolition of indulgences and other means whereby Rome obtained money from Germany, and an end to the celibacy of the clergy. For this he was naturally excommunicated. His teaching was based on the German translation of the Bible, but he was by no means a fundamentalist: *e.g.*, he denied that the Book of Hebrews was written by Paul, would have nothing to do with the Apocrypha, and regarded the letter of James as "an epistle of straw." The Scriptures were open to all and could be interpreted by private judgment enlightened by the Spirit of God. Like Calvin, Luther was a predestinarian and determinist, but he was also a conservative and soon became alarmed about the position taken by many extremists once the Reformation was under way. He had really wanted the Church to reform itself, but when he alienated Rome he had perforce to rely more and more on the secular powers which finally resulted in the state-church form which became pronounced in Prussia and later elsewhere. Whereas Calvin wished the Church to be at least the equal of the State and in some respects its superior, Luther's rebellion resulted in the reverse, a state-controlled episcopalianism. *See* **Calvinism, Presbyterianism**.

Lycanthropy, the belief that men may, by the exercise of magical powers or because of some inherited affliction, occasionally transform into wolves. The so-called werewolf is an important feature of mid-European folklore and much the same can be said of the were-tigers and were-bears of Africa and the Far East. There is, needless to say, no such thing as a genuine werewolf known to biology, but it is not hard to see how legends of their existence could arise. There are a number of mental illnesses in which men may deliberately or unconsciously mimic the actions of animals and there are a number of endocrinological disorders which may cause gross changes in the features of the individuals, including the excessive growth of hair. In times when the physiological bases of such afflictions were not properly understood, sufferers from such complaints could easily be persuaded, either by themselves or others, that they were in fact wolfmen. Once the mythology of lycanthropy is established in a society, then of course it will be used by unscrupulous individuals for their own ends —for example revenge killings by people dressed as animals—thus helping to perpetuate the legend.

M

McLuhanism. According to Marshall McLuhan (1911–80), a Canadian, and former professor of English at Toronto, the *way* people communicate is more important than *what* they communicate: hence his famous slogan, "the medium is the message." There have been two great landmarks in human understanding since we learnt to speak and write: the invention of the printed book and the present electronic revolution. The printed word took us step by step along the linear, logical path to understanding; television comes at us from all directions at once. "Electronic circuitry has overthrown the regime of 'time' and 'space' . . . Its message is Total Change." Thus the spectacle of the Chicago police force clubbing people outside the Democratic Convention in August 1968 was described by Alistair Cooke in a despatch to *The Guardian*, as "a terrifying demonstration of McLuhanism: the millions frozen with terror in front of their television screens." In his essay, "On Reading Marshall McLuhan," Dr. George Steiner (one of the first critics in England to understand him) writes: "Marshall McLuhan posits that Western civilisation has entered, or is about to enter an era of electromagnetic technology. This technology will radically alter the milieu of human perception, the reality co-ordinates within which we apprehend and order sense data. Experience will not present itself serially, in atomized or linear patterns of causal sequence, but in 'fields' of simultaneous interaction." McLuhan's importance lies in alerting us to the present clash between two great technologies, the literate and the electromagnetic, and in his vision, beyond the present chaos, of a world drawn tighter together in a "global village" where identity will merge in collectivity and we shall all be able to co-operate for the common good instead of being split up into warring nations.

Magic, a form of belief originating in very early days and based on the primitive's inability to distinguish between similarity and identity. The simplest example would perhaps be the fertility rites in which it is believed that a ceremony involving sexual relations between men and women will bring about fertility in the harvest. Or the idea that sticking pins in an image of an individual will bring about harm or even death to the real person. Magic is regarded by some as a form of early science in that man in his efforts to control Nature had recourse to magical practices when the only methods he knew had failed to bring the desired results. It filled a gap. By others magic is regarded as an elementary stage in the evolution of religion. It can be said to have served a purpose there too. Yet magic differs from religion, however closely at times it may come to be related with it in this important respect: religion depends upon a power *outside and beyond* human beings, whereas magic depends upon nothing but the casting of a spell or the performance of a ceremony—the result follows automatically.

The idea that "like produces like" is at the roots of imitative magic. It follows that an event can be compelled by imitating it. One engages in swinging, not for pleasure, but to produce a wind as the swing does; ball games are played to get rainy weather because the black ball represents dark rainclouds; other ball games, in which one attempts to catch the ball in a cup or hit it with a stick, represent the sexual act (as some gentlemen at Lords may be distressed to hear) and bring about fertility; in medicine until a few centuries ago herbs were chosen to cure a disease because in some respects their leaves or other parts looked like the part of the body affected (*e.g.*, the common wildflower still known as "eye-bright" was used in bathing the eyes because the flower looks like a tiny eye).

See **Witchcraft, Demonism**.

Malthusianism, the theory about population growth put forward by the Rev. Thomas Malthus (1766–1834) in *An Essay on Population* (1798). His three main propositions were

(1) "Population is necessarily limited by means of subsistence." (2) "Population invariably increases where means of subsistence increase unless prevented by some very powerful and obvious checks." (3) "These checks, and the checks which repress the superior power of population, and keep its effects on a level with the means of subsistence, are all resolvable into moral restraint, vice and misery." In other words, no matter how great the food supply may become, human reproductive power will always adjust itself so that food will always be scarce in relation to population; the only means to deal with this is by "moral restraint" (*i.e.*, chastity or not marrying), "vice" (*i.e.*, birth-control methods), or misery (*i.e.*, starvation). More specifically, Malthus claimed that while food increases by arithmetical progression, population increases by geometrical progression. It is true that these gloomy predictions did not take place in Malthus's time largely owing to the opening up of new areas of land outside Europe, the development of new techniques in agriculture, the growth of international trade to poorer areas, the increased knowledge of birth-control, and developments in medical science which reduced the misery he had predicted. Furthermore, we now know that as a society becomes industrialised its birth-rate tends to fall. Growth in the world's population has increased from about 465 million in 1650 to over 5,000 million in 1990.

Manichaeism, an Asiatic religion which developed from Zoroastrianism (*q.v.*) and shows the influence of Buddhism (*q.v.*) and Gnosticism (*q.v.*), being founded by Mani, a Persian who was born in Babylonia, *c.* 216 A.D. Mani presented himself to Shapur I as the founder of a new religion which was to be to Babylonia what Buddhism was to India or Christianity to the West. His aspiration was to convert the East and he himself made no attempt to interfere directly with Christianity although he represented himself as the Paraclete (the Holy Ghost or "Comforter") and, like Jesus, had twelve disciples. His success in Persia aroused the fury of the Zoroastrian priests who objected to his reforming zeal towards their religion and in 276 Mani was taken prisoner and crucified.

Of Mani's complicated system little can be said here, save that it is based on the struggle of two eternal conflicting principles, God and matter, or light and darkness. Although its founder had no intention of interfering with the West, after his death his followers soon spread the religion from Persia and Mesopotamia to India and China. It reached as far as Spain and Gaul and influenced many of the bishops in Alexandria and in Carthage where for a time St. Augustine accepted Manichaeism. Soon the toleration accorded it under Constantine ended and it was treated as a heresy and violently suppressed. Yet it later influenced many heresies, and even had some influence on orthodox Catholicism which had a genius for picking up elements in other religions which had been shown to appeal to worshippers provided they did not conflict unduly with fundamental beliefs.

Maoism is the branch of communism in China that was shaped by one of the most remarkable statesmen of modern times, Mao Tse-tung (1893–1976). He set the pattern of revolution for poor peasant societies and restored pride and confidence to his fellow countrymen after years of turmoil and brutality. Although Marxist theory guided the Chinese communists in their struggle for liberation from the old, bourgeois and feudal China, it was interpreted in a manner peculiar to China and developed to fit into the Chinese way of life and the "thoughts" of Chairman Mao. As early as 1926 Mao had pointed out that the Chinese proletariat had in the peasantry its staunchest and most numerous ally. "A rural revolution," he said, "is a revolution by which the peasantry overthrows the authority of the feudal landlord class." The struggles of 1925–49 (the Long March of the Red Army, the Anti-Japanese War, the Civil War against Chiang Kai-shek) were the foundations on which present-day China has been built. Maoism is against authoritarianism and for self-reliance; against bureaucracy and for revolutionary momentum; against rivalry

between individuals and for common effort. Great efforts have been made to remove poverty, ignorance, corruption and disease from China. Mao taught that struggle is necessary for the revolution to endure. "Running water does not go stale and door-hinges do not become worm-eaten," Mao reminded his comrades. "We must," he said, "make every comrade understand that the highest criterion for judging the words and deeds of the communists is whether they conform with the best interests and win the support of the broadest masses of the people." The effect of the death of Mao Tse-tung on Chinese communism has been a political direction towards the modernisation of China and away from Marxism and "continuous revolution". *See also* **China, Section C, Part II.**

Marxism. The sociological theories founded by Karl Marx and Friedrich Engels on which modern communist thought is based. Marx and Engels lived in a period of unrestrained capitalism when exploitation and misery were the lot of the industrial working classes, and it was their humanitarianism and concern for social justice which inspired their work. Marx wrote his *Communist Manifesto* in Brussels in 1848 and in his great work, *Das Kapital* (1867), he worked out a new theory of society. Marx showed that all social systems are economically motivated and change as a result of technical and economic changes in methods of production. The driving force of social change Marx found to be in the struggle which the oppressed classes wage to secure a better future. Thus in his celebrated theory of historical materialism he interpreted history in terms of economics and explained the evolution of society in terms of class struggle. (*See* **Dialectical Materialism.**) "In the social production of their means of existence," he wrote, "men enter into definite and unavoidable relations which are independent of their will. These productive relationships correspond to the particular stage in the development of their material productive forces." Marx's theory of historical materialism implies that history is propelled by class struggle with communism and the classless society as the final stage when man will have emancipated himself from the productive process. Marx was the first to put socialism on a rational and scientific basis, and he foretold that socialism would inevitably replace capitalism. His prophecy, however, came to realisation not in the advanced countries as he had envisaged but in backward Russia and China. The collapse of communism (*see* **J12**) in Eastern Europe in 1989 has questioned many of the basic assumptions of Marxism.

Mesmerism, a rapidly vanishing name to denote the practice of hypnosis, which owes its popularity, though not its discovery, to the Austrian physician, Anton Mesmer (1733–1815). Mesmer's contribution was the realisation that a large number of what we would today call psychosomatic or hysterical conditions could be cured (or at least temporarily alleviated) by one or another form of suggestion. Mesmer himself relied on the idea of what he called "animal magnetism," a supposedly potent therapeutic force emanating from the living body which could be controlled by the trained individual. Mesmer used wands and impressive gadgetry to dispense the marvellous force and he effected a remarkable number of cures of complaints, hitherto looked upon as incurable or totally mysterious in origin—the most typical of these being hysterical blindness, paralysis or deafness, nervous skin conditions, and so on. Hypnosis, which is a valid if very poorly understood psychological phenomenon even today, would probably have been developed much further had not efficient general anaesthetics such as ether, nitrous oxide, etc., been discovered, thus greatly diminishing its role as a pain reliever in surgery. Mesmer, who was three parts charlatan, never really troubled to think deeply about the cause of his undoubted success. The first man to treat hysteria as a formal class of illness and who made a scientific attempt to treat it with hypnosis was Ambrose Liébeault (1823–1904). He and his colleagues Hippolyte Bernheim (1840–1919) believed: (*a*) that hysteria was produced by suggestion, and particularly by autosuggestion on the part of the patient, and (b) that suggestion was a normal trait found in varying degrees in everyone. These conclusions are true, but as Freud showed later are far from being the whole truth.

Messianism. Most varieties of religious belief rely on the assumption that the deity is a supernatural being either permeating the universe or dwelling in some other sphere, and normally inaccessible to man. Where divine intervention is necessary, the deity is traditionally believed to nominate a human being—in the case of Christianity, for example, Jesus is believed to be the actual son of God. Messianic cults introduce a novel variant on the traditional theme. In these a human being is held to be God himself. He may either nominate himself for this role, relying on his own personality or native talent to acquire the necessary following, or for one reason or another large numbers of people may alight on one individual and declare him the Messiah. While it might seem that beliefs of this kind would be confined to earlier epochs in man's recorded history, this is in fact not the case. In the past century, and even within recent decades, a number of individuals have been held by groups to be actually divine. Among these were the Dutchman Lourens van Voorthuizen, a former fisherman who declared himself to be God in 1950 and got large numbers to accept his claim; the Anglican priest Henry James Prince, who did much the same thing in 1850; and of course the famous Negro George Baker, who convinced hundreds of thousands of other Negroes that he was "Father Divine." To simple people the idea that God is to be found on earth and that one may even be personally introduced to him, is an obviously attractive one. The trouble is that all self-styled gods to this present date have sooner or later seriously disappointed their supporters by performing that most human of acts—dying.

Metapsychology. Not to be confused with parapsychology (q.v.). The branch or off-shoot of psychology which goes beyond empirical and experimental studies to consider such philosophical matters as the nature of mind, the reality of free-will and the mind/body problem. It was originally used by Freud as a blanket descriptive term denoting all mental processes, but this usage is now obsolete.

Methodism, the religious movement founded by John Wesley in 1738, at a time when the Anglican Church was in one of its periodic phases of spiritual torpor, with the simple aim of spreading "scriptural holiness" throughout the land. Up to that time Wesley had been a High Churchman but on a visit to Georgia in the United States he was much impressed by the group known as Moravians (q.v.), and on his return to this country was introduced by his brother Charles, who had already become an adherent, to Peter Böhler, a Moravian minister in England. Passing through a period of spiritual commotion following the meeting, he first saw the light at a small service in Aldersgate in May 1738 "where one was reading Luther's preface to the Epistle to the Romans" and from this time forth all Wesley's energies were devoted to the single object of saving souls. He did this for fifty years and at the end of his life confessed that he had wasted fifteen minutes at that time by reading a worthless book. Even when he was over eighty he still rose at 4 a.m. and toiled all day long.

Soon Whitefield, a follower with Calvinist views, was preaching throughout the country and Charles Wesley was composing his well-known hymns; John's abilities at this time were taken up in organising the movement described as "People called Methodists." They were to be arranged in "societies" which were united into "circuits" under a minister, the circuits into "districts" and all knit together into a single body under a conference of ministers which has met annually since 1744. Local lay preachers were also employed and to maintain interest the ministers were moved from circuit to circuit each year. These chapel services were not originally meant to conflict with the Church of England of which Wesley still considered himself a member. They were purely supplement-

ary, and it used to be the custom (before the Methodists began to count themselves as Nonconformists) for Methodists to attend Church in the morning and Chapel in the evening.

The class-meeting was the unit of the organisation where members met regularly under a chosen leader to tell their "experiences" upon which they were often subjected to severe cross-examination. At the end of every quarter, provided their attendances were regular, they received a ticket of membership which entitled them to come to monthly sacramental services. If attendance was inadequate the name was removed from the list, without appearance on which nobody was deemed a member. The price of the ticket was "a penny a week and a shilling a quarter" but Wesley was not interested in receiving money from anyone who was not utterly devoted to the cause.

John Wesley introduced four other innovations, some of which were regarded by Churchmen who had previously been willing to commend his efforts in bringing religion to the poorer classes as dangerous: (1) He started the Sunday-school scheme and afterwards enthusiastically supported that of John Raikes, often regarded as the founder of the idea; this was of immense importance in the days before the Education Acts. (2) He reintroduced the Agapae or "love feasts" of the early Church which were fellowship meetings deepening the sense of brotherhood of the society. (3) He began to copy the open-air meetings of the eloquent Whitefield and soon unwittingly produced the most extraordinary results, finding that his sermons led to groans, tears, fainting-fits, and all sorts of emotional expression. Even his open-air lay speakers produced like results and these came to be associated with Methodism and gave significance to the proud Anglican claim that *their* services would be "without enthusiasm." (4) After some hesitation he ventured to consecrate Dr. Thomas Coke, who was being sent as a missionary to America, as a bishop of his church. In addition to Wesley's religious work he was a great educator of the common man. Thus he introduced the cheap book and the church magazine, publishing books of any sort which he thought would edify and not harm even when the views expressed were different from his own—e.g., Thomas à Kempis's *Imitation of Christ* and works of history, biography, science, and medicine in some cases written by himself. In this way the movement with its cheap books and reading rooms had an influence far beyond its actual membership. Both the Anglican Church and the Evangelical movement of Wilberforce and others profited from Wesley's work.

Methodism, especially after Wesley's death in 1791, began, like other movements, to develop schisms. These were the long-standing differences which the Baptist movement (q.v.) had shown too between Arminian and Calvinist sections—i.e., between those who did and those who did not accept the doctrine of predestination. In the case of the Methodists, this led to a complete break in 1811. Then there were differences associated with the status of the laity, or the relationship of the movement with the Anglican Church. The "Methodist New Connection" of 1797 differed only in giving the laity equal representation with the ministers but the more important break of the Primitive Methodists in 1810 gave still more power to the laity and reintroduced the "camp-meeting" type of service. In 1815 the Bryanites or "Bible Christians" were formed, and a further schism which was even brought before the law courts was ostensibly over the foundation of a theological college. The real reason, of course, was that the ministers were becoming more Tory, whilst the laity were becoming more Radical. Finally in 1932, at a conference in the Albert Hall in London, the Wesleyan Methodists, the Primitive Methodists, and the United Methodists became one Church, the Methodist Church.

During 1988, Methodists celebrated the 250th anniversary of the conversion of John Wesley. Adult Methodist membership has fallen recently, from 841,000 in 1930, to 729,000 in 1960 and now to c. 520,000 (1990).

Mind and Matter.

Early Greek Views: Idealism and Dualism. Primitive peoples could see that there is a distinction between those things which move and do things by themselves and others, such as stones, which do not. Following the early state of **Animism** (q.v.), in which spirits were believed to have their abode in everything, they began to differentiate between matter or substance and a force which seems to move it and shape it into objects and things. Thus to the Greek Parmenides (fl. c. 475 B.C.), who was a philosopher of pure reason, thought or mind was the creator of what we observe and in some way not quite clear to himself it seemed that mind was the cause of everything. This is perhaps the first expression of the movement known as Idealism which says, in effect, that the whole universe is mental—a creation either of our own minds or the mind of God. But from Anaxagorus (488–428 B.C.) we have the clearer statement that mind or *nous* causes all movement but is distinct from the substance it moves. He does not, however, think in terms of individual minds but rather of a kind of generalised mind throughout the universe which can be used as an explanation of anything which cannot be explained otherwise. This is the position known as Dualism (q.v.) which holds that both mind and matter exist and interact but are separate entities.

Most people in practice are dualists since, rightly or wrongly, mind and body are thought of as two different things: it is the "commonsense" (although not necessarily the true) point of view. Plato in a much more complex way was also a dualist although he held that the world of matter we observe is in some sense not the genuine world. The real world is the world of ideas and the tree we see is not real but simply matter upon which mind or soul has imprinted the idea of a tree. Everything that exists has its corresponding form in the world of ideas and imprints its pattern upon matter. Mind has always existed and, having become entangled with matter, is constantly seeking to free itself and return to God.

Plato's pupil Aristotle had a much more scientific outlook and held that, although it was mind which gave matter its form, mind is not *outside* matter, as Plato had thought, but *inside* it as its formative principle. Therefore there could be no mind without matter and no matter without mind; for even the lowest forms of matter have some degree of mind which increases in quantity and quality as we move up the scale to more complex things.

So far, nobody had explained how two such different substances as matter and mind could influence each other in any way, and this remains, in spite of attempts to be mentioned later, a basic problem in philosophy.

Two later ideas, one of them rather foolish and the other simply refusing to answer the question, are typified by the Stoics and some members of the Sceptic school. The first is that only matter exists and what we call mind is merely matter of a finer texture, a view which as an explanation is unlikely to satisfy anyone; the other, that of some Sceptics, is that we can know nothing except the fleeting images or thoughts that flicker through our consciousness. Of either mind or matter we know nothing.

Renaissance Attitude. Christian doctrines have already been dealt with (*see* **God and Man, Determinism and Free-will**), and the past and future of the soul is dealt with under **Immortality**. Nor need we mention the Renaissance philosophers who were really much more concerned about how to use mind than about its nature. When they did consider the subject they usually dealt with it, as did Francis Bacon, by separating the sphere of science from that of religion and giving the orthodox view of the latter because there were still good reasons for not wishing to annoy the Church.

17th-cent. Views: Hobbes, Descartes, Guelincx, Spinoza, Locke, Berkeley. Thomas Hobbes in the 17th cent. was really one of the first to attempt a modern explanation of mind and matter even if his attempt was crude. As a materialist he held that all that exists is matter and hence our thoughts, ideas, images, and actions are really a form of motion taking place within the brain and nerves. This is the materialist theory which states that mind does not exist.

Thus there are three basic theories of the nature of mind and body: idealism, dualism, and materialism, and we may accept any one of the three. But, if we accept dualism, we shall have to explain precisely the relationship between body and mind. In some of his later writings Hobbes seems to suggest that mental processes are the effects of motion rather than motion itself; *i.e.*, they exist, but only as a result of physical processes just as a flame does on a candle. This theory of the relationship is known as *epiphenomenalism.*

Descartes, the great French contemporary of Hobbes, was a dualist who believed that mind and matter both exist and are entirely different entities; therefore he had to ask himself how, for example, the desire to walk leads to the physical motion of walking. His unsatisfactory answer was that, although animals are pure automatons, man is different in that he has a soul which resides in the pineal gland (a tiny structure in the brain which today we know to be a relic of evolution with no present function whatever). In this gland the mind comes in contact with the "vital spirits" of the body and thus there is interaction between the two. This theory is known as *interactionism,* and since we do not accept its basis in the function of the pineal gland, we are simply left with the notion of interaction but without the explanation of how it takes place.

One of Descartes's successors, Arnold Guelincx, produced the even more improbable theory of *psychophysical parallelism* sometimes known as the theory of the "two clocks". Imagine you have two clocks, each keeping perfect time, then supposing you saw one and heard the other, every time one points to the hour the other will strike, giving the impression that the first event causes the second, although in fact they are quite unrelated. So it is with the body and mind in Guelincx's view, each is "wound up" by God in the beginning in such a way as to keep time with the other so that when I have the desire to walk, purely unrelated physical events in my legs cause them to move at the same time. A variety of this theory is *occasionism,* which says that whenever something happens in the physical world, God affects us so that we *think* we are being affected by the happening.

The trouble about all these theories is (*a*) that they really explain nothing, and (*b*) that they give us a very peculiar view of God as a celestial showman treating us as puppets when it would surely have been easier to create a world in which mind and matter simply interacted by their very nature. Spinoza, too, believed in a sort of psychophysical parallelism in that he did not think that mind and body interacted. But since in his theory everything is God, mind and matter are simply two sides of the same penny.

John Locke, another contemporary, thought of the mind as a blank slate upon which the world writes in the form of sensations, for we have no innate or inborn ideas and mind and matter do interact although he does not tell us how. All we know are sensations—*i.e.*, sense impressions. Bishop Berkeley carried this idea to its logical conclusion: if we know nothing but sensations, we have no reason to suppose that matter exists at all. He was, therefore, an idealist.

18th cent. Views: Hume, Kant. David Hume went further still and pointed out that, if all we know are sensations, we cannot prove the existence of matter but we cannot prove the existence of mind either. All we can ever know is that ideas, impressions, thoughts, follow each other. We do not even experience a self or personality because every time we look into our "minds" all we really experience are thoughts and impressions. Hume was quick to point out that this was not the same as saying that the self did not exist; it only proved that we cannot know that it does.

Kant made it clear that, although there is a world outside ourselves, we can never know what it is really like. The mind receives impressions and forms them into patterns which conform not to the thing-in-itself but to the nature of mind. Space and time, for example, are not realities but only the form into which our mind fits its sensations. In other words our mind shapes impressions which are no more like the thing in itself than the map of a battlefield with pins showing the position of various army groups at any given moment is like the battlefield. This, of course, is true. From physics and physiology we know that the sounds we hear are "really" waves in the air, the sights we see "really" electromagnetic waves. What guarantee do we have that the source is "really" like the impression received in our brain? Kant was the leader of the great German Idealist movement of the 18th cent. which in effect said: "why bother about matter when all we can ever know is mental?"

19th and 20th cent. Views. The Englishman Bradley, and the Frenchman Henri Bergson in the 19th and early 20th cent. both held in one form or another the belief that mind in some way creates matter and were, therefore, idealists, whereas Comte, the positivist (*q.v.*), and the Americans William James and John Dewey, held that mind is a form of behaviour. Certain acts (*e.g.*, reflexes) are "mindless" because they are deliberate; others which are intended may be described for the sake of convenience as "minded" (*i.e.*, purposeful). But like the majority of modern psychologists—insofar as they take any interest in the subject—they regarded mind as a process going on in the living body. Is there any reason, many now ask, why we should think of mind as being any different in nature from digestion? Both are processes going on in the body, the one in the brain the other in the stomach and intestines. Why should we regard them as "things"? *See also* J43–4.

Mithraism, a sun-religion which originated in Persia with the worship of the mythical Mithra, the god of light and of truth. It was for two centuries one of early Christianity's most formidable rivals, particularly in the West since the more philosophical Hellenic Christianity of the East had little to fear from it. (Arnold Toynbee has described Mithraism as "a pre-Zoroastrian Iranian paganism—in a Hellenic dress"; Manichaeism as "Zoroastrianism—in a Christian dress".) Mithraism was a mystery-faith with secret rites known only to devotees. It appealed to the soldiers of the Roman Army which explains its spread to the farthest limits of the Roman empire and its decline as the Romans retreated. The religion resembled Zoroastrianism (*q.v.*) in that it laid stress on the constant struggle between good and evil and there are a number of parallels with Christianity. *e.g.*, a miraculous birth, death, and a glorious resurrection, a belief in heaven and hell and the immortality of the soul, a last judgment. Both religions held Sunday as the holy day of the week, celebrated 25 December (date of the pagan winter solstice festival) as the birthday of the founder; both celebrated Easter, and in their ceremonies made use of bell, holy water, and the candle. Mithraism reached its height about 275 A.D. and afterwards declined both for the reason given above and, perhaps, because it excluded women, was emotional rather than philosophical, and had no general organisation to direct its course. Yet even today, from the Euphrates to the Tyne, traces of the religion remain and antiquarians are familiar with the image of the sun-god and the inscription *Deo Soli Mithrae, Invicto, Seculari* (dedicated to the sun-god of Mithra, the unconquered). Mithraism enjoyed a brief revival of popular interest in the mid-1950s when workers excavating the foundations of the skyscraper, Bucklersbury House in the City of London, found the well-preserved remains of a Roman Mithraic temple. A campaign to save the temple as a national monument resulted in its now being on open display on a site in front of the skyscraper.

Mohammedanism. *See* Islam.

Monasticism. When in the 4th cent. A.D. Constantine in effect united state and church there were naturally many who hastened to become Christians for the worldly benefits they expected it

to bring in view of the new situation. But there were others who, in their efforts to escape from wordly involvement, went into the deserts of North Africa and Syria to live as hermits and so in these regions there grew up large communities of monks whose lives of renunciation made a considerable impression on the Christian world. They were men of all types but the two main groups were those who preferred to live alone and those who preferred a community life. Among the first must be included St. Anthony, the earliest of the hermits, who was born in Egypt *c.* 250 and who lived alone in a hut near his home for fifteen years and then in the desert for a further twenty. As his fame spread Anthony came forth to teach and advocate a life of extreme austerity, until by the end of his life the Thebaid (the desert around Thebes) was full of hermits following his example. (Not unnaturally, he was constantly assailed by lustful visions which he thoughtfully attributed to Satan.) In the Syrian desert St. Simeon Stylites and others were stimulated to even greater austerities and Simeon himself spent many years on the top of a pillar in a space so small that it was only possible to sit or stand. With some of these men it is obvious that ascetic discipline had become perverted into an unpleasant form of exhibitionism.

The first monastery was founded by Pachomius of Egypt *c.* 315 and here the monks had a common life with communal meals, worship, and work mainly of agricultural type. In the Eastern part of the Empire St. Basil (*c.* 360) tried to check the growth of the extreme and spectacular practices of the hermits by organising monasteries in which the ascetic disciplines of fasting, meditation, and prayer, would be balanced by useful and healthy activities. His monasteries had orphanages and schools for boys—not only those who were intended for a monkish life. But the Eastern Church in general continued to favour the hermit life and ascetic extremes. Originally a spontaneous movement, the monastic life was introduced to the West by St. Athanasius in 339 who obtained its recognition from the Church of Rome and St. Augustine introduced it into North Africa beyond Egypt. The movement was promoted also by St. Jerome, St. Martin of Tours, who introduced it into France, and St. Patrick into Ireland. The monastery of Iona was founded by St. Colomba in 566. But it must be remembered that the Celtic Church had a life of its own which owed more to the Egyptian tradition than to Rome. Unlike the more elaborate monasteries of the Continent those of the early Celtic Church were often little more than a cluster of stone bee-hive huts, an oratory, and a stone cross. It had its own religious ceremonies and its own art (notably its beautifully carved crosses and the illuminated manuscripts such as the Lindisfarne Gospel (*c.* 700) and the Irish Book of Kells dating from about the same time). The Scottish St. Ninian played a major part in introducing Egyptian texts and art to Britain where, mixed with Byzantine influences and the art of the Vikings, it produced a typical culture of its own. Strangely enough, it was the relatively primitive Celts who played almost as large a part in preserving civilisation in Europe during the Dark Ages as the Italians have since. It was St. Columbanus (*c.* 540–615) who founded the great monasteries of Annegray, Luxeuil, and Fontaine in the Vosges country, St. Gall in Switzerland, and Bobbio in the Apennines. So, too, it was the Anglo-Saxon Alcuin (*c.* 735–804) who was called from York by Charlemagne to set up a system of education throughout his empire; the most famous of the monastic schools he founded was at Tours. Among those influenced by him was the philosopher John Scotus Erigena.

Meanwhile from the south, as the disintegrating Roman empire became increasingly corrupt, St. Benedict of Nursia (*c.* 480–*c.* 543) fled the pleasures of Rome to lead a hermit's life near Subiaco. Here he founded some small monasteries, but *c.* 520 made a new settlement, the great monastery of Monte Cassino in southern Italy, where he established a "Rule" for the government of monks. This included both study and work and emphasised that education was necessary for the continuance of Christianity. As his influence spread his Rule was adopted by other monasteries, and schools became part of monastic life. It is not possible to describe the many different orders of monks and nuns formed since, nor the mendicant orders of friars (*e.g.*, Franciscans, Dominicans, Carmelites, Augustinians). Outside the Roman Catholic Church, both Eastern Orthodox and Anglican Christians owe much to the monastic movement. Monasticism, of course, is not peculiar to Christianity and forms a major aspect of Buddhism, especially in the form of Lamaism in Tibet (*q.v.*).

Monophysitism, a heresy of the 5th cent. which grew out of a reaction against Nestorianism (*q.v.*). The majority of Egyptian Christians were Monophysites (Mono-physite = one nature)—*i.e.* they declared Christ's human and divine nature to be one and the same. This view was condemned at the Council of Chalcedon (A.D. 451) which pronounced that Jesus Christ, true God and true man, has two natures, at once perfectly distinct and inseparably joined in one person and partaking of the one divine substance. However, many continued to hold Monophysite opinions, including the Coptic Church (*q.v.*), declaring the Council to be unoecumenical (*i.e.* not holding the views of the true and universal Christian Church).

Montanism, a Phrygian form of primitive Puritanism with many peculiar tenets into which the early Christian theologian Tertullian (*c.* 150–*c.* 230) was driven by his extremist views that the Christian should keep himself aloof from the world and hold no social intercourse whatever with pagans. The sect had immediate expectation of Christ's second coming and indulged in prophetic utterance which they held to be inspired by the Holy Ghost but which their enemies put down to the work of the Devil.

Moral Re-Armament, a campaign launched in 1938 by an American evangelist of Lutheran background, Frank N. D. Buchman (1878–1961), founder of the Oxford Group Movement, and at first associated with the First Century Church Fellowship, a fundamentalist Protestant revivalist movement. On a visit to England in 1920 Buchman preached "world-changing through life-changing" to undergraduates at Oxford, hence the name Oxford Group. This revivalist movement was based on Buchman's conviction that world civilisation was breaking down and a change had to be effected in the minds of men.

Two of the Group's most typical practices were group confession of sins openly and the "quiet time" set aside during the day to receive messages from the Almighty as to behaviour and current problems. In the eyes of non-Groupers the confession (often of trivial sins) appeared to be exhibitionist and there was felt to be a certain snobbery about the movement which made it strongly conscious of the social status of its converts.

The Oxford Group gave way to Moral Re-Armament, the third phase of Buchmanism. M.R.A. men and women lay stress on the four moral absolutes of honesty, purity, love, and unselfishness. They believe they have the ideas to set the pattern for the changing world and, indeed, claim to have aided in solving many international disputes—political, industrial, and racial. Theologians complained of the Groups that their movement lacked doctrine and intellectual content; M.R.A. is no different in this respect.

The peak of public interest in M.R.A. was probably reached in the 1950s. Like so many movements of its kind it relied heavily for its motive force on the dynamism of its founder and leader. With the death of Dr. Buchman and the unexpected demise at an early age of his most promising protégé and successor-designate, the journalist Peter Howard, the movement began to lose its public impact. The phrase "moral rearmament" was coined by the English scientist W. H. Bragg and appropriated by Buchman.

Moravian Church, a revival of the Church of the "Bohemian Brethren" which originated (1457) among some of the followers of John Hus. It developed a kind of Quakerism that rejected the use of force, refused to take oaths, and had no hierarchy. It appears to have been sym-

pathetic towards Calvinism but made unsuccessful approaches to Luther. As a Protestant sect it was ruthlessly persecuted by Ferdinand II and barely managed to survive. However, in the 18th cent. the body was re-established by Count Zinzendorf who offered it a place of safety in Saxony where a town called Herrnhut (God's protection) was built and this became the centre from which Moravian doctrine was spread by missionaries all over the world. Their chief belief (which had a fundamental influence on John Wesley—*see* **Methodism**) was that faith is a direct illumination from God which assures us beyond all possibility of doubt that we are saved, and that no goodness of behaviour, piety, or orthodoxy is of any use without this "sufficient sovereign, saving grace".

Mormons, or **Latter-day Saints**, one of the very numerous American religious sects; founded in 1830 by Joseph Smith, the son of a Vermont farmer, who, as a youth, had been influenced by a local religious revival though confused by the conflicting beliefs of the various denominations. He said that while praying for guidance he had been confronted by two heavenly messengers who forbade him to join any existing church but prepare to become the prophet of a new one. Soon, in a series of visions, he was told of a revelation written on golden plates concealed in a nearby hillside. These he unearthed in 1827 and with the help of "Urim and Thummin" translated the "reformed Egyptian" characters into English. Described as the *Book of Mormon*, this was published in 1830 and at the same time a little church of those few who accepted his testimony was founded in Fayette, N.Y. In addition the first of Joseph Smith's "miracles"—the casting out of a devil—was performed. The *Book of Mormon* purports to be a record of early American history and religion, the American Indians being identified as part of the ten Lost Tribes of Israel. Jesus Christ is believed to have appeared in America after His resurrection and prior to His ascension. Smith's eloquence was able to influence quite educated people, including Sidney Rigdon with whom he went into business for a time. *Doctrine and Covenants* is the title of another book dealing with the revelations Smith claimed to have received. Soon the sect was in trouble with the community both because its members insisted on describing themselves as the Chosen People and others as Gentiles and because they took part in politics, voting as Smith ordered them to. Smith was constantly in trouble with the police. Therefore they were turned out from one city after another until they found themselves a dwelling-place at Nauvoo, Illinois, on the Mississippi.

In 1844 Smith was murdered by a mob, and confusion reigned for a while. Brigham Young, Smith's successor, was quite an extraordinary leader, however, and soon stamped out the warring factions and drove out the recalcitrants, though persecutions from the outside continued. There followed the famous trek of more than a thousand miles across desert country in which he led the way, reaching his journey's end in the forbidding valley of the Great Salt Lake (then outside the area of the United States) on 24 July 1847. By 1851 30,000 Mormons had reached the Promised Land. Here they held their own in a hostile environment and under the practical genius of their leader carried through a vast irrigation scheme and built Salt Lake City which still serves as the headquarters of their sect. In 1850 their pioneer settlement was made Utah Territory, and in 1896 incorporated in the Union. The church was strictly ruled by its leader who also looked after affairs of state for thirty years until his death in 1877.

"Plural marriage" (or polygamy) is one of the things for which the church is best known. Though practised in the early years—as a restoration of the Old Testament practice, as Mormons believe—it was discontinued in 1890, by a formal declaration from Wilford Woodruff, then the President of the Church.

Membership of The Church of Jesus Christ of Latter-day Saints had reached the 7·3 million mark by the end of the 1980s, with members in over 130 nations.

The Reorganised Church of Jesus Christ of

Latter-day Saints with its headquarters at Independence, Missouri, has been separate and distinct since 1852.

Muggletonians, one of the many sects which arose during the Commonwealth but, unlike most of the others (**Levellers** (q.v.), **Diggers** (q.v., Fifth Monarchy Men, and the Millenarians) which tended to have a strongly political aspect, this was purely religious. Founded by two journeymen tailors, Lodowick Muggleton and John Reeve, who interpreted the Book of Revelation in their own peculiar way, it was decided that Reeve represented Moses, and Muggleton, Aaron. They also believed that the Father, not the Son, had died on the cross (an ancient heresy) but added the strange statement that He left Elijah in control during His period on earth. Rejecting the doctrine of the Trinity, they also asserted that God has a human body. Nevertheless, for a time, they had many followers.

Mysticism, a religious attitude which concerns itself with direct relationship with God, "reality" as contrasted with appearance or the "ultimate" in one form or another. All the higher religions have had their mystics who have not always been regarded without suspicion by their more orthodox members, and, as Bertrand Russell points out, there has been a remarkable unity of opinion among mystics which almost transcends their religious differences. Thus, characteristic of the mystical experience in general, have been the following features; (1) a belief in insight as opposed to analytical knowledge which is accompanied in the actual experience by the sense of a mystery unveiled, a hidden wisdom become certain beyond the possibility of doubt; this is often preceded by a period of utter hopelessness and isolation described as "the dark night of the soul"; (2) a belief in unity and a refusal to admit opposition or division anywhere; this sometimes appears in the form of what seem to be contradictory statements: "the way up and the way down is one and the same" (Heraclitus). There is no distinction between subject and object, the act of perception and the thing perceived; (3) a denial of the reality of time, since if all is one the distinction of past and future must be illusory; (4) a denial of the reality of evil (which does not maintain, e.g., that cruelty is good but that it does not exist in the world of reality as opposed to the world of phantoms from which we are liberated by the insight of the vision). Among the great mystics have been Meister Eckhart and Jakob Boehme, the German religious mystics of the 13th and 16th cent. respectively, Acharya Sankara of India, and St. Theresa and St. John of the Cross of Spain. Mystical movements within the great religions have been: the Zen (q.v.) movement within Buddhism; Taoism in China; the Cabalists and Hasidim in Judaism; the Sufis within Islam; some of the Quakers within Christianity.

Mystery Religions. See **Orphism.**

N

Natural Law, the specifically Roman Catholic doctrine that there is a natural moral law, irrespective of time and place, which man can know through his own reason. Originally a product of early rational philosophy, the Christian form of the doctrine is basically due to St. Thomas Aquinas who defined natural law in relation to eternal law, holding that the eternal law is God's reason which governs the relations of all things in the universe to each other. The natural law is that part of the eternal law which relates to man's behaviour. Catholic natural law assumes that the human reason is capable of deriving ultimate rules for right behaviour, since there are in man and his institutions certain stable structures produced by God's reason which man's reason can know to be correct and true. Thus, the basis of marriage, property, the state, and the contents of justice are held to be available to man's natural reason. The rules of positive morality and civil law are held to be valid only insofar

as they conform to the natural law, which man is not only capable of knowing but also of obeying.

Protestant theologians criticise this notion. Thus Karl Barth and many others hold that sinful and fallen man cannot have any direct knowledge of God or His reason or will without the aid of revelation. Another theologian Niebuhr points out that the principles of the doctrines are too inflexible and that although they are the product of a particular time and circumstance, they are regarded as if they were absolute and eternal. In fact, as most social scientists would also agree, there is no law which can be regarded as "natural" for all men at all times. Nor does it seem sensible to suppose that all or even many men possess either the reason to discern natural law or the ability to obey it; whether or not we accept man's free-will (and all Protestant sects do not), we know as a fact of science that people are not always fully responsible for their actions and some not at all.

Nazism, the term commonly used for the political and social ideology of the German National Socialist Party inspired and led by Hitler. The term *Nazi* was an abbreviation of Nazional-socialistische Deutsche Arbeiterpartei. Since 1945, neo-Nazi organizations have emerged in such countries as South Africa. In 1989, extreme right-wing parties polled well in elections in West Germany and Austria and in 1990 neo-Nazis were increasingly evident in East Germany.

Neoplatonism. See **Determinism and Free-will** and **God and Man.**

Nestorian heresy. The 5th cent. of the Christian Church saw a battle of personalities and opinions waged with fanatical fury between St. Cyril, the patriarch of Alexandria, and Nestorius, patriarch of Constantinople. Nestorius maintained that Mary should not be called the mother of God, as she was only the mother of the human and not of the divine nature of Jesus. This view was contradicted by Cyril (one of the most unpleasant saints who ever lived) who held the orthodox view. In addition to his utter destruction of Nestorius by stealthy and unremitting animosity Cyril was also responsible for the lynching of Hypatia, a distinguished mathematician and saintly woman, head of the Neoplatonist school at Alexandria. She was dragged from her chariot, stripped naked, butchered and torn to pieces in the church, and her remains burned. As if this were not enough Cyril took pains to stir up pogroms against the very large Jewish colony of Alexandria. At the Council of Ephesus (A.D. 431) the Western Bishops quickly decided for Cyril. This Council (reinforced by the Council of Chalcedon in 451) clarified orthodox Catholic doctrine (see **Monophysitism**). Nestorius became a heretic, was banished to Antioch where he had a short respite of peace, but later, and in spite of his weakness and age, was dragged about from one place to another on the borders of Egypt. Later the Nestorian church flourished in Syria and Persia and missions were sent to India and China.

New Age, a quasi-religious movement, based on a millenarian mysticism, astrology and ecology. Condemned by many Christians as pagan and heretical. It gained support in the 1980s.

Nihilism, the name commonly given to the earliest Russian form of revolutionary anarchism. It originated in the early years of Tsar Alexander II (1818–81), the liberator of the serfs, who, during his attempts to bring about a constitutional monarchy, was killed by a bomb. The term "nihilist", however, was first used in 1862 by Turgenev in his novel *Fathers and Children.* See **Anarchism.**

Nominalism. Early mediaeval thinkers were divided into two schools, those who regarded "universals" or abstract concepts as mere names without any corresponding realities (Nominalists), and those who held the opposite doctrine (**Realism**) that general concepts have an existence independent of individual things. The relation between universals and particulars was a subject of philosophical dispute all through the Middle Ages.

The first person to hold the nominalist doctrine was probably Roscelin or Roscellinus in the late 11th cent., but very little is known of him and none of his works remains except for a single letter to Peter Abelard who was his pupil. Roscelin was born in France, accused twice of heresy but recanted and fled to England where he attacked the views of Anselm, according to whom Roscelin used the phrase that universals were a *flatus voci* or breath of the voice. The most important nominalist was the Englishman William of Occam in the 13th cent. who, once and for all, separated the two schools by saying in effect that science is about things (the nominalist view) whereas logic, philosophy, and religion are about terms or concepts (the Platonic tradition). Both are justified, but we must distinguish between them. The proposition "man is a species" is not a proposition of logic or philosophy but a scientific statement since we cannot say whether it is true or false without knowing about man. If we fail to realise that words are conventional signs and that it is important to decide whether or not they have a meaning and refer to something, then we shall fall into logical fallacies of the type: "Man is a species, Socrates is a man, therefore Socrates is a species." This, in effect, is the beginning of the modern philosophy of logical analysis which, to oversimplify, tells us that a statement is not just true or untrue, it may also be meaningless. Therefore, in all the philosophical problems we have discussed elsewhere there is the third possibility that the problem we are discussing has no meaning because the words refer to nothing and we must ask ourselves before going any further "what do we mean by God", and has the word "freewill" any definite meaning?

Nonconformism, the attitude of all those Christian bodies, which do not conform to the doctrines of the Church of England. Up to the passing of the Act of Uniformity in 1662 they were called "puritans" or "dissenters" and were often persecuted. The oldest bodies of nonconformists are the Baptists, Independents, and (in England) the Presbyterians; the Methodists, although dating from 1738, did not consider themselves nonconformists until some time later. The Presbyterians are, of course, the official Church of Scotland where it is the Anglicans (known as "Episcopalians") who are technically the nonconformists.

O

Occam's Razor, the philosophical maxim by which William of Occam, the 14th cent. Franciscan has become best-known. This states in the form which is most familiar: "Entities are not to be multiplied without necessity" and as such does not appear in his works. He did, however, say something much to the same effect: "It is vain to do with more what can be done with fewer." In other words, if everything in some science can be interpreted without assuming this or that hypothetical entity, there is no ground for assuming it. This is Bertrand Russell's version and he adds: "I have myself found this a most fruitful principle in logical analysis."

Occultism. See **Magic, Alchemy, Astrology,** and **Theosophy.**

Opus Dei, a Roman Catholic organisation founded in 1928 by the Spanish priest Josemaría Escrivá de Balaguer (1902–75). Its aim is to spread, in all spheres of society, a deep awareness of the universal call to holiness and apostolate, in the fulfilment—with freedom and responsibility—of one's professional work.

Orangemen, members of an Irish society formed in Ulster in 1795 to uphold Protestantism. Their name is taken from King William III, Prince of Orange, who defeated James II at the Battle of the Boyne (1690), hence the enormous banners depicting "King Billy on the Boyne" carried in procession on 12 July each year. The Unionist Party of Northern Ireland (the ruling political party from 1921 to 1972) is largely maintained by the Orange Order. The Order has branches in many English-speaking countries but flourishes chiefly in Ulster.

Orgonomy, a pseudo-psychological theory advanced by the German psychiatrist Wilhelm Reich (1897–1957), a pupil of Freud, who was expelled from Germany for attacking the Nazis and who started life afresh in the U.S.A. like so many of his colleagues. Moving quickly away from orthodox psychoanalytic theories, Reich became increasingly obsessed with the view that all living things were permeated with a unique force or energy which he termed "orgone" and which he believed could be photographed and measured with a geiger counter. The key to the successful flow of orgone throughout the body was sexual intercourse and the resulting orgasm (hence "orgone"). Reich achieved a substantial following for his increasingly bizarre views and when he was sentenced to two-years' imprisonment in 1956 for alleged medical malpractice a "civil rights" controversy developed which has not died down to this date. His unfortunate and rather tragic death in prison has fanned the emotional issues and granted him the important role of martyr to his cause.

Orphism. The Greeks in general thought very little of their gods, regarding them as similar human beings with human failings and virtues although on a larger scale. But there was another aspect of Greek religion which was passsionate, ecstatic, and secret, dealing with the worship of various figures among whom were Bacchus or Dionysus, Orpheus, and Demeter and Persephone of the Eleusinian Mysteries. Dionysus (or Bacchus) was originally a god from Thrace where the people were primitive farmers naturally interested in fertility cults. Dionysus was the god of fertility who only later came to be associated with wine and the divine madness it produces. He assumed the form of a man or a bull and his worship by the time it arrived in Greece became associated with women (as was the case in most of the Mystery Religions) who spent nights on the hills dancing and possibly drinking wine in order to stimulate ecstasy; an unpleasant aspect of the cult was the tearing to pieces of wild animals whose flesh was eaten raw. Although the cult was disapproved of by the orthodox and, needless to say, by husbands, it existed for a long time.

This primitive and savage religion in time was modified by that attributed to Orpheus whose cult was more spiritualised, ascetic, and substituted mental for physical intoxication. Orpheus may have been a real person or a legendary hero and he, too, is supposed to have come from Thrace, but his name indicates that he, or the movement associated with him, came from Crete and originally from Egypt, which seems to have been the source of many of its doctrines. Crete, it must be remembered, was the island through which Egypt influenced Greece in other respects. Orpheus is said to have been a reformer who was torn to pieces by the Maenad worshippers of Dionysus. The Orphics believed in the transmigration of souls and that the soul after death might obtain either eternal bliss or temporary or permanent torment according to its way of life upon earth. They held ceremonies of purification and the more orthodox abstained from animal food except on special occasions when it was eaten ritually. Man is partly earthly, partly heavenly, and a good life increases the heavenly part so that, in the end, he may become one with Bacchus and be called a "Bacchus".

The religion had an elaborate theology. As the Bacchic rites were reformed by Orpheus, so the Orphic rites were reformed by Pythagoras (c. 582–c. 507 B.C.) who introduced the mystical element into Greek philosophy, which reached its heights in Plato. Other elements entered Greek life from Orphism. One of these was feminism which was notably lacking in Greek civilisation outside the Mystery Religions. The other was the drama which arose from the rites of Dionysus. The mysteries of Eleusis formed the most sacred part of the Athenian state religion, and it is clear that they had to do with fertility rites also, for they were in honour of Demeter and Persephone and all the myths speak of them as being associated with the supply of corn to the country. Without being provocative, it is accepted by most anthropologists and many theologians that Christianity, just as it accepted elements of Gnosticism and Mithraism, accepted elements from the Mystery Religions as they in turn must have done from earlier cults. The miraculous birth, the death and resurrection the sacramental feast of bread and wine, symbolising the eating of the flesh and drinking of the blood of the god, all these are common elements in early religions and not just in one. None of this means that what we are told about Jesus is not true, but it surely does mean: (*a*) that Christianity was not a sudden development; (*b*) that the early Church absorbed many of the elements of other religions; (*c*) that perhaps Jesus Himself made use of certain symbols which He knew had a timeless significance for man and invested them with new meaning.

Orthodox Eastern Church. There are two groups of Eastern churches: (1) those forming the Orthodox Church dealt with here which include the ancient Byzantine patriarchates of Constantinople, Alexandria, Antioch, and Jerusalem, and the national churches of Russia, Greece, Yugoslavia, Bulgaria, Rumania, etc. (although Orthodox communities exist all over the world and are no longer confined to geographical areas); (2) the churches which rejected Byzantine orthodoxy during various controversies from the 5th to the 7th cent., notably the Coptic church (*q.v.*) and the Armenian church. Although all Orthodox churches share the same doctrine and traditions they are arranged as national independent bodies each with its own hierarchy. They do not recognise the pope, and the primacy of the patriarch of Constantinople is largely an honorary one. Although claiming to be the One Holy, Catholic, and Apostolic Church its alleged infallibility rests on universal agreement rather than on any one individual, and agreement over the faith comes from the Scriptures interpreted in the light of the Tradition. The latter includes dogmas relating to the Trinity, Christology, Mariology, and Holy Icons; the testimony of the Fathers (St. Athanasius, St. Basil, St. John Chrysostom, St. Cyril of Alexandria, etc.); the canons or rules as formulated by the Councils and the Fathers. The Orthodox Church did not take part in the great Western controversies about the Bible, nor, of course, in the Reformation. Attempts have recently been made to improve relations bebetween Rome and Constantinople: the two Churches agreed in 1935 to retract the excommunications cast on each other in A.D. 1054, which formalised the Great Schism.

Ouspensky, a contemporary of Gurdjieff (*q.v.*), Peter Ouspensky was another obscure mystic of Eastern European origin who believed he had an occult philosophical message to bring to the West. This he embodied in a series of lengthy books which are both humourless and self-indulgent.

Oxford Group. *See* **Moral Re-Armament.**
Oxford Movement. *See* **Tractarianism.**

P

Pantheism. *See* **God and Man.**
Papal Infallibility. The basis of papal infallibility is (*a*) that every question of morals and faith is not dealt with in the Bible so it is necessary that there should be a sure court of appeal in case of doubt, and this was provided by Christ when he established the Church as His Teaching Authority upon earth; (*b*) ultimately this idea of the teaching function of the Church shapes the idea of papal infallibility which asserts that the Pope, when speaking officially on matters of faith or morals, is protected by God against the possibility of error. The doctrine was proclaimed in July 1870.

Infallibility is a strictly limited gift which does not mean that the Pope has extraordinary intelligence, that God helps him to find the answer to every conceivable question, or that Catholics have to accept the Pope's views on politics. He can make mistakes or fall into sin, his scientific or historical opinions may be quite wrong, he may write books that are full of errors. Only in two limited spheres is he infallible and in these only when he speaks officially as the supreme teacher and lawgiver of the Church, defining a doctrine that must be accepted by all its members. When, after studying a problem of faith or morals as carefully as possible, and with all available help from expert consultants, he emerges with the Church's answer—on these occasions it is not strictly an answer, it is *the* answer.

Historically speaking, the Roman Catholic Church of the early 19th cent. was at its lowest ebb of power. Pope Pius IX, in fear of Italian nationalism, revealed his reactionary attitude by the feverish declaration of new dogmas, the canonisation of new saints, the denunciation of all modern ideals in the Syllabus of Errors, and the unqualified defence of his temporal power against the threat of Garibaldi. It is not too much to say that everything regarded as important by freedom-loving and democratic people was opposed by the papacy at that time. In 1870, after a long and sordid struggle, the Vatican Council, convened by Pius IX, pronounced the definition of his infallibility. Döllinger, a German priest and famous historian of the Church, was excommunicated because, like many others, he refused to accept the new dogma. It is difficult not to doubt that there was some connection between the pronouncement of the Pope's infallibility and his simultaneous loss of temporal power.

After the humanism of the Second Vatican Council (1962–5) Pope Paul's encyclical *Humanae Vitae* (1968), condemning birth control, came as a great disappointment to the many people (including theologians, priests, and laymen) who had expected there would be a change in the Church's teaching. The Church's moral guidance on this controversial issue, however, does not involve the doctrine of infallibility. (The Roman Catholic Church teaches that papal pronouncements are infallible only when they are specifically defined as such.) That there is unlikely to be any immediate softening of the Church's line on infallibility was made clear in July 1973 when the Vatican's Sacred Congregation for the Doctrine of the Faith published a document strongly reaffirming papal infallibility. The document also reminded Catholics of their obligation to accept the Catholic Church's unique claims to authenticity.

Parapsychology, the name given to the study of psychical research (*q.v.*) as an academic discipline, and chosen to denote the topic's supposed status as a branch of psychology. The impetus behind parapsychology came from the psychologist William MacDougall who persuaded Duke University in North Carolina, U.S.A., to found a department of parapsychology under J. B. Rhine. Throughout the 1930s and 40s the work of Rhine and his colleagues, who claimed to have produced scientific evidence for the existence of E.S.P., attracted world-wide attention. Increasing reservations about the interpretation of Rhine's results and an apparent lack of any readily repeatable experiments, however, gradually eroded scientific confidence in the topic. The academic status of parapsychology is at the present time exceedingly uncertain. Rhine retired from university life in 1965 and the world-famous parapsychology laboratory at Duke University was closed. On the other hand the American Association for the Advancement of Science recently admitted the Parapsychological Association (the leading organisation for professional parapsychologists) as an affiliated member society. An American government body, the National Institute of Mental Health, has also officially supported some medical research into alleged telepathic dreams, the first "official" grant support of this kind. In Britain a poll of readers in the weekly journal, *New Scientist,* revealed a very high interest in the subject matter of parapsychology, and active research is currently going on at the Dept. of Psychology at Cambridge. Stories of intensive parapsychological research in Soviet Russia are however without foundation and are not supported by Western parapsychologists who have visited Russia.

Parsees. *See* **Zoroastrianism.**
Pavlovian theory. *See* **Behaviourism.**
Pentecostalism, a religious movement within the Protestant churches, holding the belief that an essential feature of true Christianity is a vigorous and profound spiritual or mystical ex-

perience which occurs after, and seemingly reinforces the initial conversion. The origins of modern Pentecostalism appear to lie in the occasion on 1 January 1901 when a member of a Bible College in Topeka, Kansas, one Agnes N. Ozman, spontaneously began to speak in an apparently unknown language at one of the College's religious meetings. This "speaking in tongues" was assumed to be evidence of her conversion and "spirit baptism", and became a feature of most Pentecostal meetings in due course. The movement spread rapidly across America, particularly in rural communities, and also was a strong feature of Welsh religious life in the early part of the century. Pentecostal services are enthusiastic and rousing with a strong emphasis on music and participation on the part of the congregation. Pentecostalism is evangelistic in nature and seems to be gaining in strength at the present time, at the expense of more orthodox and staid versions of Christianity. The fiery character Aimee Semple McPherson was one of its most prominent evangelists.

Phrenology, a psychological "school" founded in 1800 by two Germans, Franz Josef Gall and Johann Gaspar Spurzheim. Gall was an anatomist who believed there to be some correspondence between mental faculties and the shape of the head. He tested these ideas in prisons and mental hospitals and began to lecture on his findings, arousing a great deal of interest throughout both Europe and America, where his doctrines were widely accepted. Phrenology became fashionable, and people would go to "have their bumps read" as later men and women of fashion have gone to be psychoanalysed. Roughly speaking, Gall divided the mind into thirty-seven faculties such as destructiveness, suavity, self-esteem, conscientiousness, and so on, and claimed that each of these was located in a definite area of the brain. He further claimed that the areas in the brain corresponded to "bumps" on the skull which could be read by the expert, thus giving a complete account of the character of the subject. In fact, (a) no such faculties are located in the brain anywhere, for this is simply not the way the brain works; (b) the faculties described by Gall are not pure traits which cannot be further analysed and are based on a long outdated psychology; (c) the shape of the brain bears no specific relationship to the shape of the skull. Phrenology is a pseudo-science; there is no truth in it whatever. But, even so, like astrology, it still has its practitioners.

Physiocrats. A French school of economic thought during the 18th cent., known at the time as *Les Economistes* but in later years named physiocrats by Du Pont de Nemours, a member of the School. Other members were Quesnay, Mirabeau, and the great financier Turgot. The physiocrats held the view, common to the 18th cent., and deriving ultimately from Rousseau, of the goodness and bounty of nature and the goodness of man "as he came from the bosom of nature". The aim of governments, therefore, should be to conform to nature; and so long as men do not interfere with each other's liberty and do not combine among themselves, governments should leave them free to find their own salvation. Criminals, madmen, and monopolists should be eliminated. Otherwise the duty of government is *laissez-faire, laissez passer*. From this follows the doctrine of free trade between nations on grounds of both justice and economy; for the greater the competition the more will each one strive to economise the cost of his labour to the general advantage. Adam Smith, although not sharing their confidence in human nature, learned much from the physiocrats, eliminated their errors, and greatly developed their teaching.

Physiognomy. *See* **Characterology.**

Pietism, a movement in the Lutheran Church at the end of the 17th cent.—the reaction, after the sufferings of the thirty years' war, of a pious and humiliated people against learning, pomp and ceremony, and stressing the importance of man's personal relationship with God. The writings of Johann Georg Hamann (1730-88) who came from a Pietist family of Königsberg influenced Kierkegaard. The Pietist move-

ment was the root of the great Romantic movement of the 18th cent.

Plymouth Brethren, a religious sect founded by John Nelson Darby, a minister of the Protestant Church of Ireland, and Edward Cronin a former Roman Catholic, in 1827. Both were dissatisfied with the lack of spirituality in their own and other churches and joined together in small meetings in Dublin every Sunday for "the breaking of bread". Soon the movement began to spread through Darby's travels and writings and he finally settled in Plymouth, giving the popular name to the "Brethren". Beginning as a movement open to all who felt the need to "keep the unity of the Spirit", it soon exercised the right to exclude all who had unorthodox views and split up into smaller groups. Among these the main ones were the "Exclusives", the Kellyites, the Newtonites, and "Bethesda" whose main differences were over problems of church government or prophetical powers. Some of these are further split among themselves. Readers of *Father and Son* by Sir Edmund Gosse, which describes life with his father, the eminent naturalist Philip Gosse, who belonged to the Brethren, will recall how this basically kind, honest, and learned man was led through their teachings to acts of unkindness (*e.g.*, in refusing to allow his son and other members of his household to celebrate Christmas and throwing out the small tokens they had secretly bought), and lack of scientific rigour (*e.g.*, in refusing for religious reasons alone to accept Darwinism when all his evidence pointed towards it).

Today, the majority of Brethren belong to the "Open Brethren" assemblies and, unlike the "Exclusives" hold that the Lord's Supper (a commemorative act of "breaking the bread" observed once a week) is for all Christians who care to join them. Baptism is required and Brethren believe in the personal premillennial second coming of Christ.

Poltergeist, allegedly a noisy type of spirit which specialises in throwing things about, making loud thumpings and bangings, and occasionally bringing in "apports", *i.e.*, objects from elsewhere. Most so-called poltergeist activities are plain frauds, but the others are almost invariably associated with the presence in the house of someone (often, but not always a child) who is suffering from an adolescent malaise or an epileptic condition. The inference is that those activities which are not simply fraudulent are either due to some unknown influence exuded by such mentally disturbed people, or that they are actually carried out by ordinary physical means by such people when in an hysterical state—*i.e.*, unconsciously. The second hypothesis is much the more probable. *See* **Psychic Research.**

Polytheism. *See* **God and Man.**

Positivism, also known as the **Religion of Humanity,** was founded by Auguste Comte (1798–1857), a famous mathematician and philosopher born in Montpellier, France. His views up to the end of the century attracted many and it would have been impossible throughout that time to read a book on philosophy or sociology that did not mention them, but today his significance is purely of historical interest. In his *Cours de Philosophie Positive* (1830) he put forward the thesis that mankind had seen three great stages in human thought: (1) the theological, during which man seeks for supernatural causes to explain nature and invents gods and devils; (2) the metaphysical, through which he thinks in terms of philosophical and metaphysical abstractions; (3) the last positive or scientific stage when he will proceed by experimental and objective observation to reach in time "positive truth".

Broadly speaking, there is little to complain of in this analysis; for there does seem to have been some sort of general direction along these lines. However, Comte was not satisfied with having reached this point and felt that his system demanded a religion and, of course, one that was "scientific". This religion was to be the worship of Humanity in place of the personal Deity of earlier times, and for it he supplied not only a Positive Catechism but a treatise on Sociology in which he declared himself the High Priest of the cult. Since, as it stood, the religion was likely to appear somewhat abstract to many, Comte drew up a list of historical characters whom he regarded as worthy of the same sort of adoration as Catholics accord to their saints. The new Church attracted few members, even among those who had a high regard for Comte's scientific work, and its only significant adherents were a small group of Oxford scholars and some in his own country. Frederic Harrison was the best-known English adherent and throughout his life continued to preach Comtist doctrines in London to diminishing audiences.

Pragmatism, a typically American school of philosophy which comes under the heading of what Bertrand Russell describes as a "practical" as opposed to a "theoretical" philosophy. Whereas the latter, to which most of the great philosophical systems belong, seeks disinterested knowledge for its own sake, the former (a) regards action as the supreme good, (b) considers happiness an effect and knowledge a mere instrument of successful activity.

The originator of pragmatism is usually considered to have been the psychologist William James (1842–1910) although he himself attributed its basic principles to his life-long friend, the American philosopher, Charles Sanders Peirce (1839–1914). The other famous pragmatist is John Dewey, best-known in Europe for his works on education (for although American text-books on philosophy express opinions to the contrary, few educated people in Europe have taken the slightest interest in pragmatism and generally regard it as an eccentricity peculiar to Americans). James in his book *The Will to Believe* (1896) points out that we are often compelled to take a decision where no adequate theoretical grounds for a decision exist; for even to do nothing is to decide. Thus in religion we have a right to adopt a believing attitude although not intellectually fully convinced. We should believe truth and shun error, but the failing of the sceptical philosopher is that he adheres only to the latter rule and thus fails to believe various truths which a less cautious man will accept. If believing truth and avoiding error are equally important, then it is a good idea when we are presented with an alternative to believe one of the possibilities at will, since we then have an even chance of being right, whereas we have none if we suspend judgment. The function of philosophy, according to James, is to find out what difference it makes to the individual if a particular philosophy or world-system is true: "An idea is 'true' so long as to believe it is profitable to our lives" and, he adds, the truth is only the expedient in our way of thinking ... in the long run and on the whole of course". Thus "if the hypothesis of God works satisfactorily in the widest sense of the word, it is true". Bertrand Russell's reply to this assertion is: "I have always found that the hypothesis of Santa Claus 'works satisfactorily in the widest sense of the word'; therefore 'Santa Claus exists' is true, although Santa Claus does not exist." Russell adds that James's concept of truth simply omits as unimportant the question whether God really *is* in His heaven; if He is a useful hypothesis that is enough. "God the Architect of the Cosmos is forgotten; all that is remembered is belief in God, and its effects upon the creatures inhabiting our petty planet. No wonder the Pope condemned the pragmatic defence of religion."

Predestination. *See* **Calvinism.**

Presbyterianism, a system of ecclesiastical government of the Protestant churches which look back to John Calvin as their Reformation leader. The ministry consists of presbyters who are all of equal rank. Its doctrinal standards are contained in the *Westminster Confession of Faith* (1647) which is, in general, accepted by English, Scottish, and American Presbyterians as the most thorough and logical statement in existence of the Calvinist creed. The Church of Scotland is the leading Presbyterian church in the British Isles.

The Reformation in Scotland was preceded by the same sort of awareness of the moral corruption of the Roman Church as had happened elsewhere, but for various political and emotional reasons, which need not be dis-

cussed here, the majority of the Scottish people (unlike the English who had been satisfied with the mere exchange of Crown for Pope) were determined on a fundamental change of doctrine, discipline, and worship, rather than a reform of manners. The church preachers had learned their Protestantism not from Luther but from Calvin and their leader John Knox had worked in Geneva with Calvin himself and was resolved to introduce the system into Scotland. In 1557 the "Lords of the Congregation" signed the Common Band (*i.e.*, a bond or covenant) to maintain "the blessed Word of God and his congregation" against their enemies, and demanded the right to worship as they had chosen. However, the real-date of the Scottish Reformation is August 1500 when Mary of Guise (the regent for Mary Queen of Scots who was not yet of age) died and the Estates met to settle their affairs without foreign pressure; the *Scots Confession* was drawn up and signed by Knox and adopted by the Estates.

The ideas on which the Reformed Kirk was based are found in the *Scots Confession*, the *Book of Discipline*, and the *Book of Common Order*, the so-called Knox's liturgy. Knox's liturgy, the same as that used in Geneva but translated into English, was used until Laud's attempt to force an Anglican liturgy on the Kirk led to an abandonment of both in favour of "free prayers."

The Presbyterian tradition includes uncompromising stress upon the Word of God contained in the Scriptures of the Old and New Testaments as the supreme rule of faith and life, and upon the value of a highly trained ministry, which has given the Church of Scotland, a high reputation for scholarship and has in turn influenced the standard of education in Scotland. The unity of the Church is guaranteed by providing for democratic representation in a hierarchy of courts (unlike the Anglican Church, which is a hierarchy of persons). The local kirk-session consists of the minister and popularly elected elders (laymen). Ministers, elected by their flocks, are ordained by presbyters (ministers already ordained). Above the kirk-session is the court of the presbytery which has jurisdiction over a specified area; above that the court of synod which rules over many presbyteries; and finally the General Assembly which is the Supreme Court of the Church with both judicial and legislative powers, and over which the Moderator of the General Assembly presides. The function of the elders is to help the minister in the work and government of the kirk. The episcopacy set up by James VI and I, and maintained by Charles I was brought to an end by the Glasgow Assembly (1638), but General Assemblies were abolished by Oliver Cromwell and at the Restoration Charles II re-established episcopacy. The Covenanters who resisted were hunted down, imprisoned, transported, or executed over a period of nearly thirty years before William of Orange came to the throne and Presbyterianism was re-established (1690). Today Presbyterians no less than other Christian communities are looking at Christianity as a common world religion in the sense that the principles which unite them are greater than those which divide them. A small but significant step in the direction of international Christian unity was made in 1972 when the Presbyterian and Congregationalist Churches in England were merged to form the United Reformed Church. *See* **Church of Scotland, Calvinism.**

Protestant, the name first applied to those who favoured the cause of Martin Luther and who protested against the intolerant decisions of the Catholic majority at the second Diet of Speyer (1529), revoking earlier decisions of the first Diet of Speyer tolerating the Reformers in certain cases (1526). In general the name "Protestant" is applied to those Churches which severed connection with Rome at the time of the Reformation. The essence of Protestantism is the acceptance by the individual Christian of his direct responsibility to God rather than to the Church. *See* **Lutheranism, Presbyterianism, Calvinism.**

Psychedelism. For all his recorded history man

has relied upon drugs of one kind or another to make his life more tolerable. These have generally been central nervous system depressants—*i.e.*, alcohol, hashish, etc.—and their use in most societies have been brought under careful government control. Most societies have also at some stage experimented with the use of certain drugs of another class—the hallucinogens. These, far from having the mentally tranquilising characteristics of small doses of alcohol, provoke striking changes in mental alertness, frequently coupled with visionary or hallucinatory experiences. The confusion and disorientation which accompany such states has led to social disapproval of their use in Western countries, and the favoured "legal" drug for centuries has been alcohol. In the 1950s the novelist Aldous Huxley in his essay *The Doors of Perception* wrote of his experiences with the drug mescalin, a derivative of the South American peyotl and a powerful hallucinogen. Huxley put forward the hypothesis that mescalin had given him not only an entirely original psychological experience but had also significantly "heightened" his perceptual ability—a development of the greatest possible interest to artists, writers, and poets. Huxley's book had considerable impact, stimulating other creative individuals into similar experiments, not always with such euphoric results. In England the author Richard Ward reported some frightening moments under the drug LSD in his *A Drug-taker's Notebook* and Huxley amplified the unpredictable nature of the drug-experience in *Heaven and Hell*, published in 1956. Although such experiments were technically illegal, public interest had been considerably aroused and in the 1960s, when it became easy to synthesise the most effective of the hallucinogens, LSD, its use began to be common among certain sections of society. In 1964 a sensational scandal rocked the great American university of Harvard when senior members of the teaching staff, including the psychologist Timothy Leary, were dismissed for using LSD and encouraging students in its use. Unrepentant, Dr. Leary set up a community near New York from whence the cult of psychedelism was propagated.

Psychedelism—which is not really an organised system of belief, but rather an attitude of mind —preaches that through the controlled use of drugs, particularly of the hallucinogenic variety, an individual may be made aware for the first time of the rich fields of experience which lie latent in the unconscious mind. The exploration of these territories will have both a liberating and an enriching effect, the outcome being to "turn on" the individual to the total reality of mind. So convinced do many of the proponents of psychedelia become of the significance of the experience of the so-called LSD "trip," that they are inclined to urge non-trippers to experiment with the drug. Herein, of course, lies one obvious danger, for the drug LSD is potentially a toxic substance which needs to be administered in minute doses if it is not to cause madness or even death. There is also much uncertainty about the possible long-term effects of "tripping," many psychologists and scientists believing that it leads to a progressive disorientation and destruction of the personality, a disintegration of which the individual drug-taker is seldom aware. If there is a credit side to psychedelism it may lie in the clear, if limited, evolution in popular music, art, and design and to a lesser extent, literature which has been inspired by these excursions. The wave of interest in LSD and similar drugs is beginning to slacken off, possibly because of an increasing awareness of the possible grievous side-effects and of the largely illusory nature of the "insights" which the "trip" is supposed to provide. The controversial Dr. Leary, the movement's most literate and influential figure, later disavowed many of his original statements, and warned young people against the indiscriminate use of drugs as an aid to insight or self-awareness.

Psychic Research is a general term for the various approaches to the scientific investigation of the paranormal, in particular supposed extra-sensory powers of the mind, but also mani-festations such as ghosts, poltergeists, spiritualistic phenomena, etc. In recent years the word parapsychology has also come into use, particularly for the investigation of ESP in a laboratory setting, but it is really part of psychic research as the subject's fascinating history reveals.

For all recorded history, and no doubt very much earlier, man has been puzzled at his apparent ability to perceive features of the universe without the use of the normal senses—mind-to-mind contact, dreams about the future which come true, etc. He has also been intrigued by the notion that in addition to the natural world of people and things, there exists in parallel, a *supernatural* world of ghosts, spirits and other similar strange manifestations. Belief in such oddities has been tremendously widespread and still forms one of the major casual conversational topics raised when people see each other socially today. Of course, until the 19th cent. or thereabouts such phenomena, while bizarre, unpredictable and possibly frightening, were not at odds with man's view of himself and his world as revealed through basic religious beliefs. Man was supposed to be in essence a supernatural being with eternal life, and the world was seen as the happy hunting ground of dynamic evil forces which could intervene directly in the lives of humans. The rise of material science in the 19th cent. however began to shake the orthodox religious framework, and as a result in due course scientists began to question the basis of all supernatural powers and manifestations, putting forward the reasonable argument: "if such things *are* real then they should be demonstrable in scientific terms—just as all other aspects of the universe are."

Once having advanced this argument, the next step was to carry it to its conclusion and set about the systematic investigation of the phenomena to see whether they *did* conform in any way to the immensely successful framework of 19th cent. science, and from this step psychic research was born. In fact one can date its origins rather precisely—to 1882 when a group of scholars formed the Society for Psychical Research in London—an organisation which still exists today. The first experiments in this slightly eccentric field of science were haphazard and tended to be confined to spiritualistic phenomena such as table tapping, mediumistic messages, ectoplasmic manifestations, etc., which were having a great wave of popularity among the general public at the time. In fact what one might term as the first phase of psychic research—it has gone through three phases in its history—was really heavily tied up with Spiritualism. Before ridiculing it for this, it is only fair to point out that many of the most eminent figures of the time—the great physicists Sir Oliver Lodge and Sir William Crookes, Alfred Russell Wallace, co-discoverer with Darwin of the theory of evolution by natural selection, the brilliant author and creator of Sherlock Holmes, Sir Arthur Conan Doyle, and many others—became convinced Spiritualists as the result of their early experiments. Nevertheless, despite the ardent support of such intellectual giants, medium after medium was in due course detected in fraud—sometimes of the most blatant kind—and the majority of scientists gradually became more critical and less likely to be taken in by even the subtlest of trickery. As a result, interest slowly shifted from the séance room to a different realm, and as it did so the first phase of psychic research drew to a close.

The second phase was, broadly speaking, the era of the ghost hunter. With the idea of spirits materialising in laboratories seeming intrinsically less and less credible, scientists began to study what struck them at the time to be basically more "plausible" matters—haunted houses, poltergeist phenomena and so on. For some reason the idea of a house dominated by a psychic presence as the result of some tragic history seemed (at the turn of the century) *somehow* scientifically and philosophically more acceptable than did the old spiritualist notions about direct communication with the spirit world. The key figure in the

Atlas of the World

Contents

Symbols

————	Principal Railways	- - - - - -	Internal Boundaries
════	Motorways		
————	Principal Roads	4125	Heights in Metres
▬▬▬▬	International Boundaries	☼	Principal Airports

Height of Land

FT	600	Below Sea Level	0	300	600	1,200	3,000	FT
M	200		0	100	200	400	1,000	M

For Pages 6, 7, 8, 9

FT	600	Below Sea Level	0	600	1,200	3,000	6,000	12,000	18,000	FT
M	200		0	200	400	1,000	2,000	4,000	6,000	M

For Pages 4, 5, 12, 13, 16, 17, 18, 20, 21, 22, 26, 31, 32, 33

FT	600	Below Sea Level	0	600	1,200	3,000	6,000	9,000	12,000	18,000	FT
M	200		0	200	400	1,000	2,000	3,000	4,000	9,000	M

For Pages 10, 11, 27, 28, 29, 30, 36

FT	600	Below Sea Level	0	600	1,200	3,000	4,500	6,000	9,000	12,000	18,000	FT
M	200		0	200	400	1,000	1,500	2,000	3,000	4,000	6,000	M

For Pages 14, 15, 19, 23, 24, 25, 34, 35

© 1990 and Printed in Great Britain by George Philip Ltd., London.

WORLD : Political

Scale 1:135,000,000

4

ICELAND

Reykjavik
Akureyri
Þrúðvölur

Arctic Circle

Faroe Is.
(Den.)

ATLANTIC OCEAN

Shetland Is.

Kristiansund
Trondheim
Østersund

Bergen

N O R W A Y

Narvik
Tromsø

Sogne Fd.
Lillehammer

Hardanger Fd.
Oslo
Drammen
Stavanger

Skagerrak
Göteborg

S W E D E N

Vänern
Örebro
Uppsala
Eskilstuna
Gävle

Vättern
Jönköping
Kalmar
Karlskrona

60

55

50

45

40

35

UNITED KINGDOM

Hebrides

Orkney Is.

N O R T H

S E A

B A L T I C

Glasgow
SCOTLAND
Dundee
Edinburgh
Inverness
Aberdeen
Londonderry
N.I.
Belfast
Isle of Man
Carlisle
Newcastle
REP.
OF IRELAND
Galway
Limerick
Dublin
Liverpool
Manchester
Leeds
York
Hull
Sheffield
ENGLAND
Birmingham
Norwich
Leeds

DENMARK
Aalborg
Kattegat
Aarhus
COPENHAGEN
Esbjerg
Flensburg
Kiel
Malmö

Gdynia
Gdańsk
Szczecin
Bydgoszcz

Hamburg
Rostock
Elbe
East
BERLIN
Magdeburg
GERMANY
Hanover
Bremen
Groningen
Amsterdam NETHER-
The Hague LANDS
Rotterdam

Poznań
Łódź
P O L
Wrocław
Katowice

Cork
C. Clear

Swansea
Cardiff
Bristol
LONDON
Southampton
Portsmouth
Plymouth
Brighton

Dover
Ostend
Calais
Antwerp
BELGIUM
BRUSSELS
LUX.
West
Dortmund
Essen
Cologne
Bonn
Halle
Leipzig
Dresden
Karl-Marx-
Stadt
CZECHOSLOV
Plzeň
PRAGUE
Brno

Scilly Is.
English Channel
Ushant

Cherbourg
Le Havre
Rouen
Caen
Reims

Frankfurt
Wiesbaden
Mainz
Würzburg
Nuremberg

Ostrava
Karvina

Brest
Rennes
Le Mans
PARIS
Metz
Strasbourg
Stuttgart

VIENNA
Bratislava
Linz

Nantes
F R A N C E
Orléans
Tours
Dijon
Mulhouse
Basel
Freiburg
Munich
Salzburg
A U S T R I A
Graz
BUDAPEST
HUNG

BAY OF BISCAY

La Coruña
Finisterre
Vigo
Oporto
Coimbra

Santander
Bilbao
San Sebastian
Bayonne
Bordeaux
Garonne
Toulouse
Perpignan

Limoges
Clermont
Ferrand
Périgueux
St. Etienne
Lyons
Grenoble
SWITZERLAND
Bern
Zürich
Geneva

Milan
Brescia
Trento
Turin
Genoa
La Spezia
Nice
Monaco
Toulon
Marseilles

Venice
Trieste
Ljubljana
Zagreb
Rijeka
Pécs
YUGOS

Bologna
Ravenna
San
Marino
Florence
Leghorn
Ancona

Split
Sarajevo
Dubrovnik

Oviedo
Valladolid
Duero
Zaragoza
Ebro
Barcelona
Andorra

Balearic Is.
Palma
Majorca
Minorca

Corsica
Ajaccio

Tiber
ROME
A D R I A T I C
S E A

LISBON
PORTUGAL
Tagus
Badajoz
Guadiana
MADRID
Toledo
S P A I N

Valencia
Alicante
Murcia
Cartagena

Sardinia
Sassari

Naples
Bari
Taranto
Brindisi

Lagos
Sevilla
Córdoba
Guadalquivir
Granada
Málaga
Gibraltar (Br.)
Str. of
Gibraltar
Tangier
Ceuta (Sp.)
Almería

M E D I T E R R A N E A N

Cagliari

Palermo
Messina
Reggio
Sicily
Catania
Ionian Se

Rabat
Fès
Meknès
Ouahran
(Oran)
Melilla (Sp.)
MOROCCO
Tlemcen

El Djezaïr
(Algiers)
Blida
A L G E R I A
Skikda
Annaba
Constantine
TUNISIA
Tunis
Bizerta
Sousse

Pantelleria
(Ital.)
MALTA

Tyrrhenian Sea

S E A

EUROPE

0   100   200   300   400 miles
0   200   400   600 km

E.E.C. members

E.F.T.A. members

Hammerfest
Pechenga
Murmansk

White Sea
Mezen
Arkhangelsk

N. Dvina

Kotlas

FINLAND

L. Onega

Perm
Sverdlovsk

Kirov
Izhevsk
Zlatoust

Luleå

Kuopio
L. Ladoga
Vyborg

Vologda

UNION OF SOVIET

Ufa

Helsinki
Kronshtadt
Leningrad
Tallinn
ESTONIA
L. Chudskoye
Novgorod
Rybinsk Res.

R. S. F. S. R.

Kostroma
Yaroslavl
Ivanovo
Gorki
Volga
Kazan

SOCIALIST

Ulyanovsk
Kuybyshev
Syzran
Orenburg

REPUBLIC

ampere

Pskov

Riga
LATVIA
epaja
Klaipeda
LITHUANIA
Kaunas
liningrad
Vilnius

Daugavpils
W. Dvina
Vitebsk
Smolensk
Mogilev

MOSCOW

Tula
Orel
Tambov
Penza
Volga
Uralsk
Ural

KAZAKHSTAN

BELORUSSIYA
Minsk
Gomel
Chernigov
Kursk
Voronezh
Don
Saratov
Volgograd

SAW
ND
Białystok
Brest
Bug
Pripet
Zhitomir
Kiev
Lublin
Lvov
Berdichev
U K R A I N E

Dnieper
Kharkov
Voroshilovgrad
Volga
Astrakhan

CASPIAN SEA

ów
owa
Košice
Debrecen
Chernovtsy
Dniester
MOLDAVIA
Kirovograd
Dnepropetrovsk
Krivoy Rog
Nikolayev
Zaporozhye
Taganrog
Donetsk
Rostov
Don
Stavropol
Makhachkala
Derbent

Cluj
ROMANIA
Timişoara
Braşov
sad
Galaţi
Kishinev
Odessa
Kherson
S. of Azov
Kerch
Krasnodar

GEORGIA

Tbilisi

BUCHAREST
Danube
Ploesti
Constanţa
Sevastopol
Novorossiysk
Batumi
AZERBAIJAN
Nagorno-Karabakh
AZ.

Niš
SAW
Sofia
BULGARIA
Sliven
Burgas
Varna
B L A C K   S E A
Sinop
Samsun
Trabzon
Erzurum
ARMENIA
Yerevan
Tabriz

Skopje
Plovdiv
Edirne
Istanbul
Üsküdar
Kastamonu
Ankara
Kayseri
Malatya
Diyarbakir
Mosul
IRAN

Thessaloniki
Bursa
Balıkesir
T U R K E Y
A N A T O L I A
Erzurum

GREECE
İzmir
Aydın
Konya
Adana
İskenderun
Antalya
Aleppo
SYRIA
Euphrates
Tigris
IRAQ
Baghdad

atras
Piraeus
ATHENS
Antalya
CYPRUS
Nicosia
Limassol
Homs

Iraklion
Crete

ENGLAND AND WALES

Map scale: 0 20 40 60 miles / 0 20 40 60 80 100 km

East from Greenwich   COPYRIGHT: GEORGE PHILIP & SON, LTD.

West from Greenwich

8

SCOTLAND

0   20   40   60 miles
0 20 40 60 80 100 km

SHETLAND

Unst
Fetlar
Yell
Whalsay

Shetland Is.

Rona

Mainland

Bressay
Foula   Lerwick

On same scale   Sumburgh Hd.

ATLANTIC

OCEAN

Mainland

Sumburgh Hd.

Fair Isle

N. Ronaldsay

Westray   Eday
Rousay   Sanday
ORKNEY   Stronsay
              Shapinsay
Mainland   Orkney Is.
Kirkwall
Hoy   South
              Ronaldsay

Pentland Firth

NORTH

SEA

C. Wrath   Strathy Pt.   Dunnet Hd. John
                                 Thurso   O'Groats
L. Laxford   Ben Hope   Dounreay
Eddrachillis Bay   Noss Hd.
L. Assynt   Wick
Enard Bay   B. More   Loch Shin
            Assynt 958
                    1081   Lairg
L. Broom   B. Dearg   Golspie
            1084   Dornoch
Ullapool   Dornoch Firth
                            Tain   Tarbat Ness
HIGHLAND
            Ben Wyvis
            1044   Cromarty
Fannich   Dingwall
Conon Beauly   Elgin   Buckie
        Inverness Nairn Forres Keith   Banff
Strome ferry   Fraserburgh
Kyle   Grantown-   Buchan
Lochalsh   Glen Affric on-Spey   Turriff Peterhead
Cuillin   Glen Moriston   Huntly
Hills   Cairn Gorm GRAMPIAN
          L. Arkaig   Gairngorm Mts. Aberdeen
S. Uist   1245   Girdle Ness
          Kingussie Ben Macdhui Ballater
Mallaig   Strath Spey 1311 Braemar Banchory
                    Balmoral Castle Stonehaven
Ben Nevis SCOTLAND Lochnagar
1343   Braes of Angus S. Esk
Fort   Rannoch   Brechin
William   Tummel Pitlochry   Montrose
          Aberfeldy TAYSIDE Forfar
Ben Lawers L. Tay Blairgowrie Arbroath
1214   Sidlaw Hills
B. More Breadalbane   Scone Dundee
996   Firth of Tay
          1174 Tay Crieff Perth
          Ben Chonzie 741   Tayport St. Andrews
          Ben More 983   Fife Ness
          Ben Vorlich   Cupar
          Trossachs   Glenrothes FIFE Leven Anstruther
          L. Katrine Kinross   Bass Rock
          974 Lomond
          Callander Stirling Dunfermline Kirkcaldy
          L. Lomond Bannockburn Buckhaven
CENTRAL   Leith
Helensburgh Grangemouth
Dumbarton Falkirk Edinburgh Haddington
Clydebank   LOTHIAN Musselburgh
Greenock Glasgow Coatbridge   Dunbar
Port Glasgow Paisley Motherwell St. Abb's Hd.
STRATHCLYDE Hamilton Wishaw   Lammermuir Hills
Kilmarnock Carstairs Peebles Berwick-upon-
                    Moorfoot   Tweed
                    Hills Galashiels
Prestwick Lanark   BORDERS Kelso Holy I.
Ayr   Broad   Selkirk Jedburgh Farne Is.
              Law Hawick The Cheviot Alnwick
Girvan   840   816
          Southern Coquet
DUMFRIES Uplands Cheviot Hills
Merrick AND   Hills NORTHUMBERLAND
843 GALLOWAY   Tyne Newcastle
Dumfries   Gretna Green Hexham Blaydon
Castle   Annan   Gateshead
Douglas   Solway Firth Carlisle ENGLAND
Kirkcudbright   CUMBRIA Durham
Wigtown Wigtown Bay Maryport Cross Fell Bishop
Stranraer   Skiddaw 893 Auckland
Portpatrick Luce Workington Penrith
          Bay   Keswick

West from Greenwich   COPYRIGHT. GEORGE PHILIP & SON, LTD.

9

IRELAND

0	20	40	60 miles		
0	20	40	60	80	100 km

A T L A N T I C

O C E A N

Tiree
Staffa
B. More
996
Mull
Iona
Firth of Lorn
STRATHCLYDE
Colonsay
SCOTLAND
Lochgilphead
Rudh a' Mhail
Islay
Bowmore
Gigha
Campbeltown
Mull of Kintyre
North Channel
Arran

Tory I.
Sheep Haven
Lough Swilly
Malin Hd.
Giant's Causeway
Ballycastle
Portrush
Rathlin I.
Fair Hd.
Horn Hd.
Inishowen Pen.
Moville
Buncrana
Foyle
Coleraine
Ballymoney
584
Trostan
Larne
Bloody Foreland
Errigal
752
Derryveagh Mts.
Londonderry
Spern Mts.
Strabane
Sawel
683
Ballymena
Aran I.
Letterkenny
DONEGAL
Gweebarra B.
Glenties
Finn
Lifford
Omagh
Dungannon
Lurgan
(Craigavon)
Banbridge
Downpatrick
Slieve
Donard 852 Newcastle
Mourne Mts.
Carlingford L.
Loughros More B.
Rossan Pt.
Bluestack
Killybegs
Derg
Lower
L. Erne
Enniskillen
Erne
Upper
NORTHERN
IRELAND
Lough
Neagh
Belfast
Newtownards
Ards Pen.
Bangor
Strangford L.
Carrickfergus
Antrim
Larne
Rathlin O'Birne I.
Donegal
ULSTER
Ballyshannon
Donegal Bay
Broad Haven
Erris Hd.
Mullet
Peninsula
Killala Bay
Sligo B.
Sligo
L. Allen
LEITRIM
Finn
Omagh
Dungannon
Portadown
(Craigavon)
Armagh
ARMAGH
Slieve
Gullion
Monaghan
MONAGHAN
Castleblayney
Newry
Warrenpoint
Dundrum
Bay
Dundalk
Dundalk
Bay
Ballina
Ox Mts.
SLIGO
Leitrim
CAVAN
Cootehill
Louth
LOUTH
Ardee
Carlingford L.
Achill Hd.
Achill I.
Nephin
806
L. Conn
Castlebar
Gowna
L. Sheelin
Blackwater
Ceannanus Mor
(Kells)
Drogheda
Balbriggan
Clare I.
Clew Bay
765
Croagh Patrick
Mweelrea
819
Westport
MAYO
Boyle
ROSCOMMON
Carrick-on-Shannon
Longford
LONGFORD
L. Ree
An Uaimh
(Navan)
MEATH
Boyne
Inishturk
Twelve Pins
Mask
Tuam
Roscommon
Inny
Mullingar
WESTMEATH
Athlone
Howth Hd.
Inishbofin
Slyne Hd.
Connemara
L. Corrib
CONNACHT
GALWAY
REPUBLIC
Clara
Maynooth
DUBLIN
Dublin (Baile Átha
Cliath)
Dun
Laoghaire
Kilkieran B.
Galway
Athenry
Ballinasloe
Brosna
Tullamore
OFFALY
Allen
Naas
Celbridge
Liffey
Galway Bay
Gort
Loughrea
Slieve
Aughty
Barrow
L. Derg
Birr
St. Bloom
Mountmellick
Portlaoise
KILDARE
Kildare
Pollaphouca
Res.
754
Bray
Inishmore
Aran Is.
Liscannor Bay
Mal Bay
CLARE
Ennis
OF
LAOIS
Athy
LEINSTER
Lugnaquilla
923
WICKLOW
Wicklow
Mizen Hd.
IRELAND
Roscrea
Carlow
Arklow
Kilkee
Nenagh
Keeper
694
Thurles
Nore
CARLOW
Muine Bheag
Mt. Leinster
796
Gorey
Loop Hd.
Shannon
Foynes
Rathkeale
Limerick
TIPPERARY
Kilkenny
KILKENNY
Enniscorthy
Brandon Bay
Tralee
Fenit
Listowel
LIMERICK
Galtymore
920
Tipperary
St. Naman
722
Cahir
Carrick-on-Suir
Clonmel
WEXFORD
New Ross
Wexford
Wexford Harbour
Rosslare
Great
Blasket
Dingle
St. Mish
Brandon Hill
953
Mitchelstown
Charleville
Rath Luirc
Knockmealdown
Comeragh Mts.
Waterford
Greenore Pt.
Tuscar Rock
Carnsore Pt.
Dingle Bay
KERRY
Mallow
Fermoy
Blackwater
WATERFORD
Tramore
Saltee Is.
Killarney
Dungarvan
Dungarvan Bay
Hook Hd.
Waterford
Harbour
Valentia
Harbour
Macgillycuddy's
Reeks
Carrantuohill
1040
Lakes of
Killarney
Boggeragh Mts.
Youghal
Youghal Harbour
Valentia I.
Cahirciveen
Macroom
Lee
CORK
Midleton
Kenmare River
Caha Mts.
Bandon
Cobh
Ball inskellig B.
Castletown Berehaven
Bantry
Clonakilty
Cork Harbour
Crow Head
Bantry Bay
Galley Hd.
Dunmanus Bay
Mizen Hd.
Baltimore
Clonakilty Bay
Old Head of Kinsale
Fastnet Rock
Clear I.
Clear

FRANCE

0 20 40 60 80 100 miles
0   40   80   120   160 km

Swansea · Newport · LONDON · Southend
Cardiff · Bristol · Bath · Swindon · Mar

E N G L A N D

Taunton · Southampton · Folkestone · Dov
Hastings · C. Gris
Exeter · Exmouth · Chichester · Brighton · Nez
Torquay · Weymouth · Portsmouth · Newhaven · Boulogn
St. Ives · Truro · Plymouth · Ryde · Bournemouth · Montre
Land's · Falmouth · Dartmouth · Portland · Somm
End · Penzance · Eddystone · Le Tréport
Dieppe

E N G L I S H   C H A N N E L   St. Valery
Fécamp · Caux · Yvetot
C. de la Hague · Cherbourg · S.Me
Alderney · Pte. de Barfleur · Barfbec · Roue
Guernsey · St. Peter · Valognes · Le Havre · Trouville · Honfleur · Elbeuf
Channel Is. · Port · Sark · Bessin · Bayeux · Lisieux · Ve
(Br.) · Jersey · St. Helier · St. Lô · Caen · C. · Evreu
Granville · Bocage · Falaise · M · Mante
Ushant · Brest · Morlaix · Mt. St. · Or. · Perche · Dreux · Ve
Pte. de · Mts. · Guingamp · Michel · Avranches · Or · E.L.
St. Mathieu · B⁴ Arrée · St. Brieuc · Dinard · Fougères · Alençon · Chartres
F · R · Dinan · Mayenne · E · Bea
Pte. du Raz · Mts. Noire · C.N. · Rennes · M A I N E
Quimper · I.V. · Laval · May. · Or
Pte. de Penmarch · Quimperlé · Lorient · Mo. · Vilaine · Châteaubriant · Sarthe · Le Mans · Orl
Vannes · I · R
Carnac · Angers · M.L. · Tours · TOURAINE · Amboise · Blois
Quiberon · LA · F · R · I.L. · Loches
Belle I. · St. Nazaire · Nantes · N · Saumur · Chinon
Loire · Cholet · Châtellerault · Châteauroul
Ile de Noirmoutier · Vende · Bocage · Creuse
B A Y · Ile de Yeu · Ve. · P O I T O U · D.S. · Poitiers · Vi.
La Roche · Fontenay · Catine · Vienne
O F · Les Sables d'Olonne · Niort · M A
Ile de Ré · La Rochelle · H.V.
A U N I S · Limoges
B I S C A Y · Ile d' Oléron · Rochefort
Saintes · ANGOUMOIS · LIM
Royan · C · Cognac · Angoulême · Uzerche
Le Verdon · M · Ch. · Périgueux
Médoc · D · Perigord
Pauillac · Libourne · Dordogne · Sarlac
Bordeaux · Gi. · Bergerac
Arcachon · Garonne · G U Y E N · Lo
L.G. · Cahors
L. · Agen · T.G.
Mont-de-Marsan · Mi
Gijón · S. Vicente de · Santander · Gulf of · G A · S C O N Y
Llanes · la Barquera · Torrelavega · Gascony · Armagnac · Auch
Oviedo · Sontona · Biarritz · Orthez · Ge. · Toulouse
Picos de · Reinosa · Guecho · Fuenterrabia · Bayonne · Pau · G.H.
Europa 2648 · Sestao · Guernica · San · B E A R N · Tarbes · Ari.
Sa. de Alba · Durango · Bilbao · Sebastian · Lourdes · Bigorre · H.P.
Léon · Talsa · Roncesvalles · Pic du Midi · Pyrenee
Vitoria · Canfranc P. · Mt. Perdu · Andorra
Astorga · Saldaña · Pancorbo P. · Miranda · Pamplona · 2884 · 335 · La Pa
Sahagún · Burgos · Logroño · Tafalla · 1631 · Jaca
S · P · A · I · N

FRENCH DEPARTMENTS

Code		Department
A.	01	Ain
Ai.	02	Aisne
Al.	03	Allier
A.H.P.	04	Alpes-de-Haute-Provence
H.A.	05	Hautes-Alpes
A.M.	06	Alpes-Maritimes
Ar.	07	Ardèche
Ard.	08	Ardennes
Ar.	09	Ariège
Aub.	10	Aube
Aud.	11	Aude
Av.	12	Aveyron
B.R.	13	Bouches-du-Rhône
Ca.	14	Calvados
Ca.	15	Cantal
Ch.	16	Charente
Ch.M.	17	Charente-Maritime
Che.	18	Cher
Co.	19	Corrèze
	20	Corse a) Haute-Corse
C.O.	21	Côte-d'Or b) Corse du Sud
C.N.	22	Côtes-du-Nord
C.	23	Creuse
D.	24	Dordogne
Dn.	25	Doubs
Dr.	26	Drôme
E.	27	Eure
E.L.	28	Eure-et-Loir
F.	29	Finistère Nord et Sud
G.G.	30	Gard
H.G.	31	Haute-Garonne
Ge.	32	Gers
Gi.	33	Gironde
H.	34	Hérault
I.V.	35	Ille-et-Vilaine
In.	36	Indre
I.L.	37	Indre-et-Loire
Is.	38	Isère
J.	39	Jura
L.	40	Landes
L.C.	41	Loir-et-Cher
Lo.	42	Loire
H.L.	43	Haute-Loire
L.A.	44	Loire-Atlantique
Loi.	45	Loiret
Lot	46	Lot
L.G.	47	Lot-et-Garonne
Loz.	48	Lozère
M.L.	49	Maine-et-Loire
M.	50	Manche
Ma.	51	Marne
H.M.	52	Haute-Marne
May.	53	Mayenne
M.M.	54	Meurthe-et-Moselle
Me.	55	Meuse
Mo.	56	Morbihan
Mos.	57	Moselle
N.	58	Nièvre
No.	59	Nord
O.	60	Oise
Or.	61	Orne
P.C.	62	Pas-de-Calais
P.D.	63	Puy-de-Dôme
P.A.	64	Pyrénées Atlantiques
H.P.	65	Hautes Pyrénées
P.O.	66	Pyrénées (Orientales)
B.R.	67	Bas Rhin
H.R.	68	Haut Rhin
Rh.	69	Rhône
H.S.	70	Haute Saône
S.L.	71	Saône-et-Loire
Sa.	72	Sarthe
Sa.	73	Savoie
H.Sa.	74	Haute-Savoie
	75	Paris
S.Me.	76	Seine-Maritime
S.M.	77	Seine-et-Marne
Yv.	78	Yvelines
D.S.	79	Deux-Sèvres
So.	80	Somme
T.	81	Tarn
T.G.	82	Tarn-et-Garonne
Va.	83	Var
Va.	84	Vaucluse
Ve.	85	Vendée
Vi.	86	Vienne
H.V.	87	Haute Vienne
Vo.	88	Vosges
Y.	89	Yonne
Es.	90	Belfort
	91	Essonne
	92	Hauts-de-Seine
	93	Seine-St. Denis
	94	Val-de-Marne
	95	Val-d'Oise

CORSICA
On same scale

COPYRIGHT. GEORGE PHILIP & SON. LTD.

West from Greenwich
25 20 15 15 20 25 30

ICELAND
On same scale
as general map

ATLANTIC

OCEAN

Arctic Circle

SCANDINAVIA

0		100		200 miles
0	100	200	300	

East from Greenwich
10 15

CZECHOSLOVAKIA

Böhmerwald

LOWER

UPPER

AUSTRIA

BAVARIA

WÜRTTEMBERG

BADEN

FRANCE

LORRAINE

SAAR

SWITZERLAND

TYROL

SALZBURG

STYRIA

CARINTHIA

BURGENLAND

Carnic Alps

FRIULI-VENEZIA GIULIA

VENETO

LOMBARDY

ITALY

Gulf of Venice

JURA

FRANCHE COMTE

SCHWARZWALD

Vienna
Znojmo
Stockerau
Baden
Wiener Neustadt
Semmering 985
Kapfenberg
Leoben
Mur
Graz
Maribor
Zagreb
Karlovac
Kupa
Senj
Krk
Rijeka
Istria
Rovinj
Trieste
Koper
Ljubljana
Celje
Klagenfurt
Villach
Udine
Gorizia
Belluno
Treviso
Venice
Chioggia
Padua
Rovigo
Po
Vicenza
Verona
Adige
Mantua
Cremona
Brescia
Bergamo
Milan
Pavia
Novara
Vercelli
Turin

St. Pölten
Melk
Amstetten
Steyr
Linz
Gmunden
Bad Ischl
Salzburg
Kufstein
Innsbruck
Brenner P.
Bolzano
Merano
Trento
Rovereto

Zwettl
Horn
Krems
Freistadt
Passau
Ried
Gmünd
Budějovice
Klatovy
Písek
Vltava
Třeboň
Tábor
Jihlava
Třebíč
Havlíčkův Brod

Regensburg
Munich
Ingolstadt
Augsburg
Nürnberg
Fürth
Erlangen
Würzburg

Ulm
Stuttgart
Augsburg
Memmingen
Kempten

Zürich
Winterthur
St. Gallen
Feldkirch
LIECHTENSTEIN
Chur
Lecco
Como
Lugano

Basel
Berne
Lucerne
Lausanne
Geneva
Interlaken
Bernese Oberland

Grenoble
Chambéry
Annecy
Grand St. Bernard P.
Mont Blanc 4807
Matterhorn 4477
Mte. Rosa

Dijon
Besançon
Chaumont
Nancy
Metz
Luxembourg

East from Greenwich

ITALY AND
S.E. EUROPE

0   50   100   150   200 miles
0   100   200   300 km

GERMANY

Nuremberg   Plzeň   CZECHO   Ostrava   Jablun

Jihlava   Slavkov

Brno   Slavkov

Augsburg   Ulm   Regensburg   Linz   Salzburg   Bratis

Munich   Isar   Danube   Bruck

Salzburg   Vienna

Belfort   Besançon   Basel   L. of Constance   Inn   Salzburg   Vienna

Dijon   Jura   Basel   Zürich   Innsbruck   T   R   I   A   Brück   Graz   H

Mâcon   Chalon   Berne   SWITZERLAND   Brenner P.   Klagenfurt   Raab   Bulo

Lausanne   Geneva   1371   TYROL   Drava   Klagenfurt   Mur

Geneva   Simplon   Ortler   Trento   Piave   Udine   Ljubljana   Péc

Lyons   Mt. Blanc   3899   Trieste   Zagreb

Grenoble   4807   Como   Bergamo   Brescia   Garda   Vicenza   Gorizia   Rijeka   YUGO

Turin   Novara   Milan   Verona   Padua   Venice   Isonzo   Trieste

Isère   Po   Verona   G. of   Pula   Bons

Durance   Alessandria   Reggio   Ferrara   Venice   BOSNI

Avignon   Riviera   Genoa   Modena   Ravenna   ADRIATIC

Marseilles   Monaco   La   Bologna   Forlì   Bonja Luka

Cannes   Nice   Spezia   Florence   Rimini   San Marino   Zadar   Dinaric Alps

Menton   Gulf of Genoa   Florence   Arno   Dalmati

Toulon   Ligurian Sea   Leghorn   Arezzo   Ancona   Šibenik   Split

C. Corse   Elba   Siena   Perugia   Vis   Lastovo   Dubrovnik

2710   Bastia   Gran Sasso   Sabine Mts.   2914

Mte. Cinto   Civitavecchia   Tiber   ROME   Mt. Gargano

Ajaccio   CORSICA   Caprera   Gaeta   Foggia   Barletta   Bari

Str. of Bonifacio   Volturno   Naples   Vesuvius   1277   Ofanto

Sassari   Olbia   Capri   Salerno   Taran

Mte. del Gennargentu   ▼3719   G. of   Taranto

1834   Cosenza   La Sila   C   M   di L

Cagliari   Tyrrhenian Sea   1929   Catanzaro

Stromboli   Lipari Is.

MEDITERRANEAN   Palermo   Messina   Reggio   Ion

Skikda   Trapani   Sicily   Mt. Etna   C. Spartivento   S

Annaba   Egadi Is.   3340   Catania   Str. of Messina

Bizerta   Marsala   Agrigento   Caltanissetta

Constantine   C. Bon   Siracusa

Tunis   Pantelleria (It.)   C. Passero

ALGERIA   G. of Hammamet   Sousse

Tébessa   Kairouan   Gozo   Valletta

TUNISIA   Lampedusa   MALTA

Sfax   (It.)   4135   ▼

Tozeur   Chott Djerid   Gabès   Kerkennah

Djerba

East from Greenwich

45

40

35

10   15

17

SPAIN
AND PORTUGAL

El Djezair (Algiers)

| 0 | 50 | 100 | 150 miles |
| 0 | 50 | 100 | 200 | 250 km |

MIDDLE EAST

0   100   200 miles

0   100   200   300   km

Division between Greeks and Turks in Cyprus; Turks to the north.

East from Greenwich

ICELAND

ATLANTIC

OCEAN

Jan Mayen

A R C T I C

Spitsbergen

Franz Josef Land

BRITISH
ISLES

North
Sea

Bergen

Trondheim

Hammerfest

North Cape

S

NORWAY

Barents
Sea

Novaya Zemlya

Kara
Sea

DENMARK

Hamburg

Esbjerg

Oslo

S
W
E
D
E
N

Narvik

Murmansk

Kola Pen.

Kolguyev I.

Pechora
Gulf

Putih I.

Dickson

Vaigach I.

Khabarovo

Gulf of Ob

Urengoy

Berlin

Copenhagen

Malmö

Gothenburg

Uppsala

Stockholm

Gävle

Gulf of Bothnia

Tampere

Helsinki

F
I
N
L
A
N
D

G. of Finland

Oulu

Kem

Tornio

Kandalaksha

White
Sea

Onega

Murmansk

N.Dvina

Arkhangelsk

Naryan Mar

Novy
Port

Vorkuta

Taz

West

POLAND

Kaliningrad

Gdańsk

Szczecin

Łódź

Wrocław

Warsaw

Bydgoszcz

Poznań

Riga

LATVIA

ESTONIA

Tallinn

Leningrad

L.Ladoga

Andropov

Vologda

Kotlas

Pechora

Telpos Iz
1617

1894

Vorkuta

S O V I E T

S i b e r i a n

Tomsk

Vilnius

LITHUANIA

Minsk

Kaunas

W.Dvina

Moscow

Kalinin

Yaroslavl

Ivanovo

Kostroma

L.Onega

Kirov

Izhevsk

Berezniki

Perm

Serov

Nizhniy Tagil

Tyumen

Tobolsk

P l a i n

F E D

Ob

Gomel

Vitebsk

Smolensk

Orel

Tula

Penza

Ryazan

Gorki

Uglich

Nizhniy Novgorod

Ulyanovsk

Kazan

Ufa

Zlatoust

Sverdlovsk

Kurgan

Petropavlovsk

Irtysh

Omsk

Novosibirsk

Barnaul

UKRAINE

Lvov

Zhitomir

Dnepropetrovsk

Kirovograd

Kiev

Dnieper

Kharkov

Voronezh

Tambov

Saratov

Chapayevsk

Kuybyshev

Volga

Ural

Orenburg

Orsk

Aktyubinsk

Chelyabinsk

Magnitogorsk

Kokchetav

Pavlodar

Tatarsk

Slavgorod

B

Odessa

Nikolayev

Kishinev

Crimea

Simferopol

Sevastopol

Kerch

Sea of Azov

Novorossiysk

Rostov

Donetsk

Makeyevka

Taganrog

Zaporozhye

Volgograd

Engels

Uralsk

Guryev

K I R G I Z

S T E P P E

Tselinograd

Karaganda

Semipalatinsk

Lenin

Be

Ayaguz

Dz

Black Sea

Samsun

Krasnodar

Maikop

Elbrus 5633

Astrakhan

Ust Urt Plateau

Aral
Sea

Karsakpai

K A Z A K H S T A N

Balkhash

L. Balkhash

Tache

Novorossiysk

TURKEY

Trabzon

Batumi

GEORGIA

Leninakan

Grozniy

Tbilisi

Baku

Krasnovodsk

Anzali

Syr Darya

Aralsk

Kzyl Orda

Dzhambul

Frunze

KIRGHIZIA

Alma-Ata

Kuldja

Przhevalsk

Pk.Pobedy
7439

XIN

U

Erzurum

Diyarbakir

Kars

Van

Yerevan

AZERBAIJAN

ARMENIA

Tabriz

Rasht

Denau

Khiva

Kara Kum

UZBEKISTAN

Bukhara

TURKMENISTAN

Chardzhou

Kzyl Kum

Tashkent

Leninabad

Chimkent

Kokand

Namangan

Andizhan

Kashir

Shache

Tarim Pen

Mosul

IRAQ

Kirkuk

Hamadan

Tehran

Ashkhabad

Bandar-e Torkeman

Mary

Samarkand

Dushanbe

TADZHIKISTAN

Communism Pk.
7495

Pamirs

Termez

Hotan

XIZAN

(TIBET

Baghdad

Basra

Abadan

Kuwait

The
Gulf

Bushire

Shiraz

Esfahan

Yazd

Kerman

(P E R S I A)

I R A N

Mashhad

Herat

AFGHANISTAN

Mazar-i-Sharif

Kabul

Shghr-i-
Zabul

PAKISTAN

Kashmir

Euphrates

ALASKA

Bering Strait

St. Lawrence I. (U.S.A.)

Chukot Sea

Wrangel I.

Beringa I.
Amabarchik

Chukot Range

Gulf of Anadyr

Anadyr

B e r i n g   S e a

O C E A N

Komsomolets I.
October Revolution I.
Bolshevik I.

De Long Is.

East Siberian Sea

New Siberian Is.

Lyakhov Is.

Nizhne Kolymsk

Sredne Kolymsk

Kolyma

Gizhiga

Kamchatka

Komandorskiye Is.

rang Mts.

Taimyr Pen.

L. Taimyr

Laptev Sea

Nordvik

Tiksi

Buluno

Yana

Verkhoyansk

Kolyma Ra.

Shelikhov Gulf

Magadan

Ust Kamchatsk

Klyuchevsk
Vol.

Khatanga

Kotuy R.

Verkhoyansk Range

Lena

Okhotsk

Sea of Okhotsk

Petropavlovsk-Kamchatskiy

ka

ka

lsk

C e n t r a l

Zhigansk

Vilyuisk

Yakutsk

Aldan

Dzhugdzhur Ra.

Shantar Is.

Okha

Sakhalin

S o v i e t   S o c i a l i s t   R e p u b l i c

Circle

S i b e r i a n

Lower Tunguska

loginsk

Lena

Olekminsk

Nikolayevsk

Aleksandrovsk

S.

P l a t e a u

Stony Tunguska

Aldan

Stanovoi Ra.

Sovetskaya Gavan

Gulf of Tartary

Yuzhno-Sakhalinsk

Korsakov

Kuril Is.

Angara

Lena

Bodaibo

Skovorodino

Belogorsk

Amur

Komsomolsk

Birobidzhan

Sikhote Alin Range

nsk

Achinsk

Bratsk

Kirensk

Yablonovy Ra.

Sretensk

Nerchinsk

Blagoveshchensk

Khabarovsk

ovo

Krasnoyarsk

Taishet

Nizhneudinsk

L. Baikal

Chita

Oloyyannaya

Amur

Sapporo

Otaru

Kansk

Tulun

Angarsk

Ulan-Ude

Khilok

Songhua I.

Vladivostok

Hakodate

JAPAN

Kuznetsky

Cheremkhovo

Petrovsk

Hailar

Ussuriysk

znetsk

Minusinsk

Munku-Sardyk
3491

Irkutsk

Kyakhta

Selenga

Harbin

Sea of Japan

Yenisei

Dzhibkhalantu

Ulan Bator

Changchun

Shenyang

Wonsan

vsk

Yingkou

Dandong

Seoul

KOREA

Pusan

Hiroshima

M O N G O L I A

Gobi

N E I   M O N G G O L

Beijing (Peking)

Pyongyang

Inchon

Mokpo

Mason

Nagasaki

JAPAN

mqi

Turpan

C H I N E S E   R E P U B L I C

Baotou

Datong

Tianjin

Dalian

Jinan

Qingdao

Kunsan

S.

Kunsan

op Nur

G

GREAT WALL

Hwang

Lianyungang

Lanzhou

Xi'an

Zhengzhou

U.S.S.R.

| 0 | 200 | 400 | 600 | 800 miles |

| 0 | 200 | 400 | 600 | 800 | 1000 | 1200 | km |

COPYRIGHT GEORGE PHILIP & SON LTD

| 0 | 100 | 200 | 300 | 400 | 500 miles |

| 0 | 200 | 400 | 600 | 800 km |

East from Greenwich

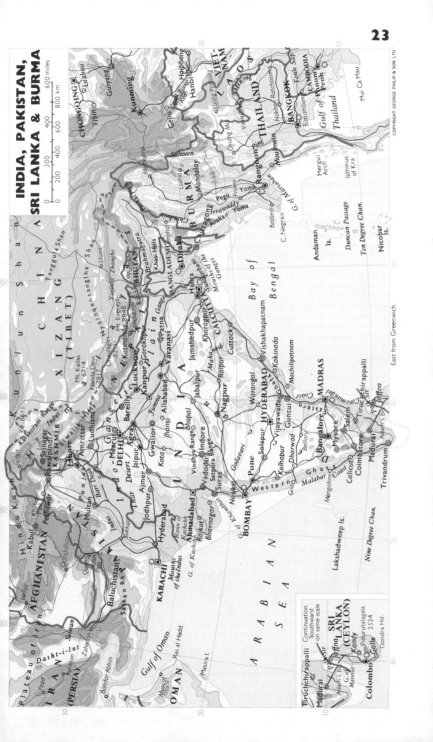

23

INDIA, PAKISTAN, SRI LANKA & BURMA

COPYRIGHT GEORGE PHILIP & SON LTD.

24

CHINA

0 100 200 300 400 500 miles
0 200 400 600 800 km

East from Greenwich

HAINAN
(Same scale as main map)

Haiphong Leizhou Bandao Zhanjiang
Hai Haikou Guangzhou
Tongking WADE 1879

KAZAKHSTAN
KIRGHIZIA
M O N G O L I A
Ulan Bator
Hentei Nuru
Khangai
G o b i
Alxa Zuoqi
NINGXIA (Aut. Reg.)
Yinchuan
XINJIANG UYGUR (Aut. Reg.)
Tarim Pendi
Tien Shan
Qaidam Pendi
Kunlun Shan
Altun Shan
QINGHAI
Qilian Shan
Tanggula Shan
Bayan Har Shan
X I Z A N G (TIBET) (Aut. Reg.)
Lhasa
NEPAL
BHUTAN
BANGLADESH
BURMA
INDIA
KASHMIR
DELHI
New Delhi
HEILONG
Harbin
N E I   M O N G G O L (Aut. Reg.)
Baotou
Hohhot
Datong
Beijing (Peking)
TIANJIN
Taiyuan
SHANXI
GANSU
Lanzhou
Xining
Chengdu
SICHUAN
CHONGQING
GUIZHOU
Guiyang
YUNNAN
Kunming
VIETNAM
Hanoi
GUANGXI ZHUANG (Aut. Reg.)
Nanning
GUANGDONG
GUANGZHOU
HONG KONG (Br.)
Macao
HUNAN
Changsha
JIANGXI
Nanchang
FUJIAN
Fuzhou
TAIWAN (Formosa)
Taipei
Kaohsiung
ZHEJIANG
Hangzhou
SHANGHAI
JIANGSU
Nanjing
ANHUI
Hefei
HUBEI
WUHAN
HENAN
Zhengzhou
SHAANXI
Xi'an
SHANDONG
Jinan
Qingdao
HEBEI
Shijiazhuang
EAST CHINA SEA
YELLOW SEA
SOUTH KOREA
SEOUL
PUSAN
NORTH KOREA
PYONGYANG
SHENYANG
LIAONING
DALIAN
JILIN
Changchun
Khabarovsk
Vladivostok

C H I N A

U.S.S.R.

SAKHALIN

La Pérouse Strait

Cape Soya

Sea of Okhotsk

Svetlaya

Iman

Lesozavodsk

Spassk-Dalni

Tetyukhe
Pristan

Mudanjiang

Jixi

Ussuriysk

Artem

Suchan

Vladivostok

Nakhodka

Yanji

Yaku I.

Rebun

Wakkanai

Rishiri

HOKKAIDO

Rumoi

Mashike

Mt. Asahi
2290

Cape Shiretoko

Abashiri
Bay

L. Kutcharo

Cape Kamui

Otaru

Asahigawa

HOKKAIDO

Obihiro

Kushiro

Nemuro

Sapporo

L. Shikotsu

Mt. Horoshiri
2052

Okushiri

Muroran

Cape Erimo

Hakodate

Cape Esan

Tsugaru Strait

Cape Shiriya

NORTH
KOREA

S E A   O F

J A P A N

Cape Shiragami

Aomori

Cape Henashi

Hirosaki

Noshiro

Hachinohe

L. Towada

Mt. Iwate
2041

Cape Nyudo

Akita

Morioka

Miyako

Kamaishi

TOHOKU

Sakata

Ishinomaki

SOUTH
KOREA

Sado

Yamagata

Sendai

Pohang

Niigata

Mt. Azuma
2024

Fukushima

Cape Suzu
Wajima

Agano

Koriyama

Lake
Inawashiro

Nagaoka

Iwaki

Noto

Toyama

Maebashi

Utsunomiya

Kanazawa

Mt. Hotaka
3190

Tone

Mito

L. Kasumiga

CHUBU

Oki Is.

Cape Kyo

Hida

Choshi

Cape Inubo

TOKYO

KANTO

Matsue

Tottori

Fujiyama
3776

YOKOHAMA

PUSAN

Chugoku Mts.

KYOTO

NAGOYA

Yokosuka

Boso

CHUGOKU

Akaishi Ra.

Cape Hino

Korea Strait

Tsushima

Hiroshima

Okayama

OSAKA

Shizuoka

O I.

Cape Nojima

Shimonoseki

Kure

KOBE

Sakai

Toyohashi

Hamamatsu

KITAKYŪSHŪ

Matsuyama

Takamatsu

Wakayama

Cape Iro

Fukuoka

SHIKOKU

Tokushima

KINKI

Nii Is.

Sasebo

Omuta

Kochi

Miyake Is.

Kumamoto

SHIKOKU

Tosa
Bay

Cape Muroto

Cape Shiono

Nagasaki

Cape Nomo

Miyazaki

Kyushu Mts.

Bungo Channel

Cape Ashizuri

Hachijo I.

KYUSHU

Kagoshima

KYUSHU

O C E A N

Kagoshima Bay

Osumi Bay

Osumi Strait

Osumi
Group

Tanega I.

1935 Yaku I.

Tokara Group

Amami
I.

P A C I F I C

REFERENCE TO PREFECTURES

HOKKAIDO DISTRICT	KANTO DISTRICT	CHUGOKU DISTRICT
1 Hokkaido	17 Gumma	31 Tottori
TOHOKU DISTRICT	18 Tochigi	32 Okayama
2 Aomori	19 Saitama	33 Shimane
3 Akita	20 Ibaraki	34 Hiroshima
4 Iwate	21 Tokyo	35 Yamaguchi
5 Yamagata	22 Chiba	SHIKOKU DISTRICT
6 Miyagi	23 Kanagawa	36 Kagawa
7 Fukushima	KINKI DISTRICT	37 Tokushima
CHUBU DISTRICT	24 Hyogo	38 Ehime
8 Niigata	25 Kyōto	39 Kochi
9 Ishikawa	26 Shiga	KYUSHU DISTRICT
10 Toyama	27 Osaka	40 Fukuoka
11 Fukui	28 Nara	41 Saga
12 Gifu	29 Mie	42 Nagasaki
13 Nagano	30 Wakayama	43 Kumamoto
14 Yamanashi		44 Oita
15 Aichi		45 Miyazaki
16 Shizuoka		46 Kagoshima

JAPAN

0   50   100   150   200 miles

0 50 100 150 200 250 300 km

East from Greenwich

SOUTH-EAST ASIA

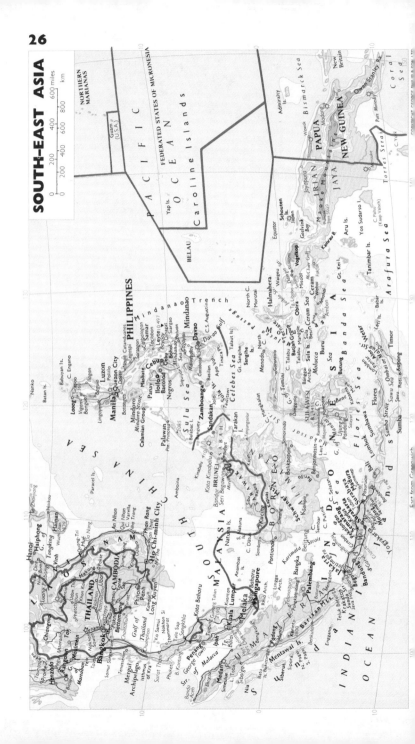

NORTHERN MARIANAS

FEDERATED STATES OF MICRONESIA

Guam (U.S.A.)

PACIFIC OCEAN

Caroline Islands

Yap Is.

BELAU

New Britain

Bismarck Sea

Admiralty Is.

PAPUA NEW GUINEA

IRIAN JAYA

Coral Sea

Torres Strait

Maoke Mts.

Arafura Sea

Tanimbar Is.

Aru Is.

Kei Is.

Banda Sea

MOLUCCAS

Halmahera

Ceram Sea

Ceram

Buru

SULAWESI

CELEBES

Celebes Sea

PHILIPPINES

Mindanao

Mindanao Trench

Leyte

Samar

Cebu

Panay

Negros

Palawan

Sulu Sea

Zamboanga

Sandakan

BRUNEI

SARAWAK

B O R N E O

KALIMANTAN

SOUTH CHINA SEA

Paracel Is.

V I E T N A M

L A O S

THAILAND

Hanoi

Haiphong

Vinh

Ho-Chi-minh City

Phnom Penh

CAMBODIA

Bangkok

Gulf of Thailand

Chiengmai

Moulmein

Mergui Archipelago

M A L A Y S I A

Kuala Lumpur

Singapore

Penang

George Town

Str. of Malacca

Medan

Palembang

Jakarta

I N D O N E S I A

J a v a

Bali

Sumba

Flores

Flores Sea

Java Sea

Timor

Sumbawa

Lombok

Banjarmasin

Pontianak

S u m a t r a

INDIAN OCEAN

Mentawai Is.

Manila

Quezon City

Luzon

Batan Is.

Babuyan Is.

C. Engaño

Baguio

Mindoro

Davao

Menado

Equator

East from Greenwich

miles 0 200 400 600

km 0 200 400 600 800

CANADA

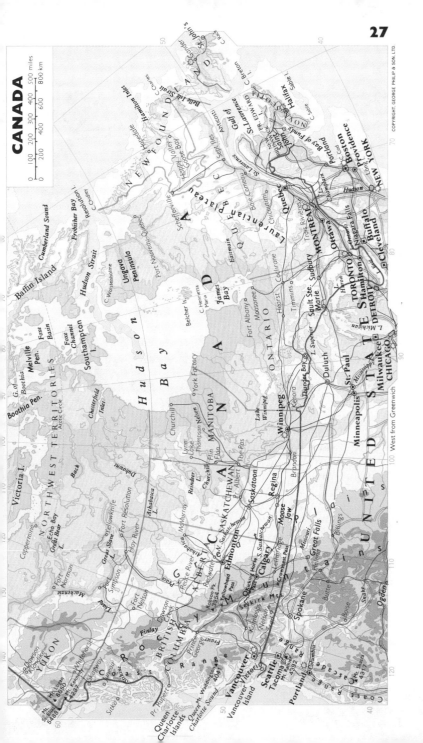

0   100 200 300 400 500 miles
0 200   400   600   800 km

West from Greenwich

50

120

Kamloops

Red Deer

N. Battleford

Prince Albert

Saskatoon

Victoria

Vancouver

Calgary

Drumheller

Rosetown

C A

N

Portage
la Prairie

Rosetown

Regina

C. Flattery

Everett

Sandpoint

Medicine Hat

Lethbridge

Moose Jaw

Brandon

Minot

Tacoma

Seattle

Spokane

W A S H I N G T O N

Gt. Falls

Missouri

M O N T A N A

Glendive

N. DAKOTA

Grand Fork

Portland

Mt.
Rainier 4392

Columbia

Walla Walla

Missoula

Helena

Butte

Yellowstone

Bismarck

Far

Corvallis

Salem

La Grande

Snake

Billings

Aberde

Eugene

O R E G O N

Payette

Boise

I D A H O

S.

DAKOTA

Medford

Klamath Falls

Twin Falls

Snake

Idaho Falls

W Y O M I N G

B l a c k

Rapid City

Gannett Pk.
4202

Hills

Sioux F

Mt. Shasta
4317

Elko

Gt. Salt Lake

Ogden

Casper

Reno

G r e a t

Salt Lake City

Laramie

Cheyenne

N E B R A S K A

Sacramento

N E V A D A

Provo

Long's Pk.
4345

Grand Island

Stockton

Oakland

B a s i n

U T A H

Platte

**San
Francisco**

Mt. Whitney
4418

W
a
s
a
t
c
h

Denver

Ka

Fresno

Grand
Junction

C O L O R A D O

Pikes Pk.
4301

Colorado Springs

K A N S A S

Pueblo

Hutchinson

Bakersfield

Las
Vegas

Death Valley

Colorado

Arkansas

Wichita

Santa Barbara

Grand

Blanca Pk.
4364

Trinidad

U N I T E

D

S

**LOS
ANGELES**

Pasadena

Colorado
Plateau

Canadian

Winslow

Albuquerque

Santa Fé

Amarillo

Pampa

O K L A

Long Beach

A R I Z O N A

**Oklahoma
City**

San Diego

Phoenix

N E W   M E X I C O

Clovis

Lubbock

Wicl
Fall

Mexicali

Gila

Llano
Estacado

Tucson

Las Cruces

Fort Worth

Ciudad
Juarez

El Paso

Pecos

Odessa

Abilene

T   E   X   A

San Angelo

Alpine

Austin

L o w e r   C a l i f o r n i a

Hermosillo

M
E
X
I
C
O

Chihuahua

Rio Grande

**San
Antonio**

Guaymas

Ciudad Obregon

S
i
e
r
r
a

Los Mochis

Nuevo Laredo

Culiacan

Torreón

Monterrey

P A C I F I C

Tropic of Cancer

M
a
d
r
e

Mazatlan

C. San Lucas

San Luis
Potosí

Tamp

O C E A N

G
u
l
f
o
f
C
a
l
i
f
o
r
n
i
a

S
a
c
r
a
m
e
n
t
o

C
a
s
c
a
d
e

S
i
e
r
r
a
N
e
v
a
d
a

C
A
L
I
F
O
R
N
I
A

R
O
C
K
Y

M
O
U
N
T
A
I
N
S

Rio Grande

30

120

100

110

110

100

Projection: Bonne

U.S.A.

0   100   200   300   400 miles

0   200   400   600 km

C A N A D A

MINNE-

SOTA

St. Paul

Minneapolis

IOWA

Des Moines

Council Bluffs

Omaha

St. Joseph

Kansas City

Jefferson City

MISSOURI

Springfield

Tulsa

Fort Smith

ARKANSAS

Little Rock

Dallas

Red

Beaumont

Houston

Galveston

Corpus Christi

Matamoros

WISCONSIN

Green Bay

Madison

Milwaukee

CHICAGO

Peoria

ILLINOIS

Evansville

KENTUCKY

TENNESSEE

MISSISSIPPI

Jackson

ALABAMA

Montgomery

Duluth

Lake Superior

Thunder Bay

Winnipeg

Sault Ste. Marie

Sudbury

Cochrane

Laurentian Plateau

Arvida

Quebec

Frois Rivières

Montreal

Sherbrooke

Saint John

Fredericton

MAINE

Portland

Manchester

N.H.

MASS.

Boston

C. Cod

R.I. Providence

New Haven

Ottawa

Kingston

Lake Huron

Georgian Bay

Toronto

Lake Ontario

Rochester

Hamilton

Buffalo

Albany

Troy

VERMONT

NEW YORK

Newark

N.J.

NEW YORK

Scranton

PENNSYLVANIA

Pittsburgh

Philadelphia

M.D.

Delaware B.

Washington

Richmond

Chesapeake B.

Norfolk

C. Hatteras

Wilmington

Charleston

Savannah

Jacksonville

ATLANTIC

OCEAN

MICHIGAN

Gl. Michigan

Saginaw

London

Windsor

Lake Erie

Detroit

Cleveland

Akron

Grand Rapids

Toledo

Fort Wayne

INDIANA

Columbus

OHIO

Dayton

WEST VIRGINIA

Huntington

Indianapolis

Cincinnati

Louisville

Lexington

Ohio

VIRGINIA

Roanoke

Greensboro

Raleigh

NORTH CAROLINA

Charlotte

Greenville

SOUTH CAROLINA

St. Louis

Nash-ville

Knoxville

Chattanooga

Oak Ridge

A P P A L A C H I A N

Memphis

Birmingham

Gadsden

Atlanta

GEORGIA

Columbus

Dothan

Albany

Monroe

Shreveport

LOUISIANA

Baton Rouge

Mobile

New Orleans

Mississippi Delta

Tampa

St. Petersburg

FLORIDA

West Palm Beach

Freeport

BAHAMAS

Nassau

Miami

Everglades

C. Sable

Key West

Florida Strait

Gulf of Mexico

Havana

Matanzas

C U B A

Camagüey

Yucatan Strait

Sioux City

Cedar Rapids

Austin

Mississippi

Fort Arkansas

Tennessee

Savannah

STATES

C.   Connecticut
D.   Delaware
M.   Maryland
Mass.   Massachusetts
N.H.   New Hampshire
N.J.   New Jersey
R.I.   Rhode Island

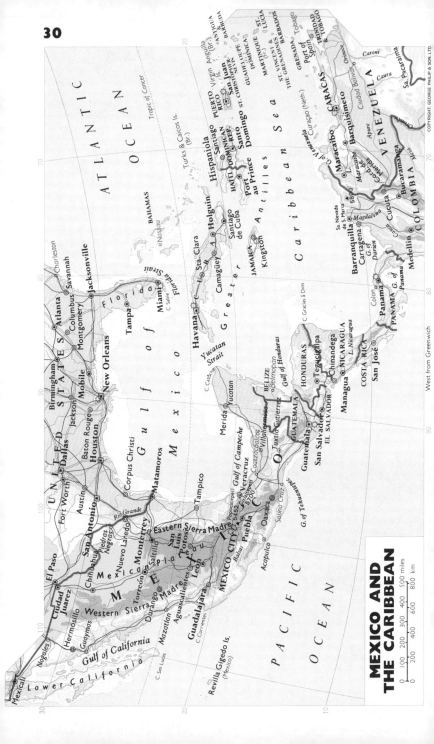

MEXICO AND
THE CARIBBEAN

West from Greenwich

ATLANTIC OCEAN

Tropic of Cancer

Turks & Caicos Is. (Br.)

BAHAMAS

Nassau

Florida Strait

C. Sable

Miami

Tampa

Jacksonville

Savannah

Charleston

Columbus

Atlanta

Montgomery

Birmingham

Jackson

Mobile

New Orleans

Baton Rouge

UNITED STATES

Houston

Dallas

Fort Worth

Austin

San Antonio

Corpus Christi

El Paso

Ciudad Juárez

Chihuahua

Nogales

Hermosillo

Guaymas

Mexicali

Lower California

Gulf of California

C. San Lucas

Mazatlán

Revilla Gigedo Is. (Mexico)

C. Corrientes

Durango

Aguascalientes

Guadalajara

León

MEXICO CITY

Puebla

Orizaba 5750

Popocatepetl 5452

Acapulco

Oaxaca

Salina Cruz

G. of Tehuantepec

PACIFIC OCEAN

Coatzacoalcos

Tuxtla Gutiérrez

Villahermosa

Mérida

Yucatan

Yucatan Strait

C. Catoche

Gulf of Campeche

Veracruz

Tampico

Torreón

Saltillo

Monterrey

Piedras Negras

Nuevo Laredo

Matamoros

Rio Grande

MEXICO

M E X I C O

Western Sierra Madre

Eastern Sierra Madre

Southern Sierra Madre

San Luis Potosí

Gulf of Mexico

Havana

Sta. Clara

Camagüey

Holguín

Santiago de Cuba

C U B A

Greater Antilles

JAMAICA

Kingston

Caribbean Sea

Belmopan

BELIZE

GUATEMALA

Guatemala

San Salvador

EL SALVADOR

HONDURAS

Tegucigalpa

Gulf of Honduras

C. Gracias á Dios

NICARAGUA

Chinandega

Managua

L. Nicaragua

COSTA RICA

San José

PANAMA

Panamá

Colón

G. of Panama

G. of Darién

HAITI

Port au Prince

DOMINICAN REP.

Santo Domingo

Santiago

Hispaniola

PUERTO RICO

San Juan

Virgin Is.

Anguilla

ANTIGUA & BARBUDA

ST. CHRISTOPHER

GUADELOUPE

DOMINICA

MARTINIQUE

ST. LUCIA

ST. VINCENT & THE GRENADINES

BARBADOS

GRENADA

Tobago

TRINIDAD & TOBAGO

Port of Spain

Curaçao (Neth.)

G. of Venezuela

Maracaibo

L. Maracaibo

Barquisimeto

CARACAS

VENEZUELA

Orinoco

Caura

Sa. Pacaraima

Caroni

Ciudad Bolívar

Apure

Mérida

Bucaramanga

Cúcuta

Magdalena

Cauca

Medellín

COLOMBIA

Barranquilla

Cartagena

G. of Darién

Sa. Nevada de Sta. Marta

| 0 | 100 | 200 | 300 | 400 | 500 miles |
| 0 | 200 | 400 | 600 | 800 km |

SOUTH AMERICA

0   200   400   600   800 miles
0 200 400   800   1200 km

CARIBBEAN   SEA

Windward Is.

Sierra Maestra Hispaniola
Santiago de Cuba HAITI DOM.
JAMAICA   Port au REP. S.Juan
Kingston   Prince   PUERTO RICO
(U.S.)
Leeward Is.
BARBADOS
NICARAGUA
COSTA
RICA
Barranquilla Maracaibo G. of Venezuela Curaçao (Neth.)
G. of Cabimas Port of Spain
Darién La Guaira TRINIDAD AND TOBAGO
Cartagena Caracas Puerto Santa Tomé
Barquisimeto Cabello Ciudad Bolívar
Pereira Medellín VENEZUELA Orinoco GUYANA Demerara Georgetown
Manizales Roraima SURINAM Paramaribo
Cali Bogotá Sa.Pacaraima 2810 FR. GUIANA Cayenne
COLOMBIA Orinoco Sa. de
Pasto Casiquiare Tumucumaque
Macapá Amazon I. Equator
ECUADOR Quito Belém
Chimborazo Cotopaxi Putumayo São Luís
6267 5897 Japurá Negro Manaus p.Santarém
Guayaquil Solimões Amazon Teresina Fortaleza
Cuenca Marañón Benjamin Constant Imperatriz C. de São
Iquitos Purus Tapajós Picos Natal Roque
Chiclayo Madeira Paulistano João Pessoa C. Branco
Trujillo S. Antonio Roosevelt Xingu Recife
Pucallpa Falls BRAZIL Barreiros Maceió
PERU Branco Guaporé Araguaia Salvador Aracaju
Callão Lima Huascarán São Francisco Alagoinhas
Pisco Cuzco Plateau of Ilhéus
Lomas Juliaca Mato Grosso Vitória de
Arequipa BOLIVIA Cuyabá Brasília Conquista
Mollendo La Paz Goiânia Montes Pirapora
Tacna Cochabamba Claros
Arica Oruro Santa Cruz Uberlândia Belo
Iquique Sucre Corumbá Horizonte
Potosí Ribeirão Vitória
Tropic of Capricorn Tarija PARAGUAY Preto Campos
Antofagasta Pilcomayo Campinas Niterói
Taltal Ojos del Salado Asunción São Paulo Rio de
6862 Tucumán Corrientes Curitiba Janeiro
Santiago Santos
del Estero Iguaçu
La Serena Falls Blumenau
PACIFIC Aconcagua ARGENTINA Pôrto Alegre
Córdoba Santa Fé Uruguaiana Lagoa dos Patos
Viña del Mar Mendoza Rosario Paraná Bagé Rio Grande do Sul
Valparaíso Santiago URUGUAY Rocha
Juan Buenos Montevideo
Fernández Mercedes Aires Río de la Plata
(Chile) Santa Azul
Concepción Rosa Mar del Plata
OCEAN Colorado Pta. Mogotes ATLANTIC
Valdivia Negro Bahía Blanca
Osorno
Puerto Montt G. of San Matías
Chiloé Chubut Rawson
Chonos Comodoro OCEAN
Arch. Rivadavia
G. of San Jorge

Falkland Is.
Río Gallegos (Br.)
Punta Stanley
Arenas
Magellan's Str. South Georgia
C. Froward Tierra del Fuego (Br.)
Staten I.
C. Horn
Drake Passage

80 60 Tropic of Capricorn
West from Greenwich 50

33

AFRICA

0   200   400   600   800 miles
0   200 400 600 800 1000 1200 km

West from Greenwich 0 East from Greenwich

SÃO TOMÉ & PRINCIPE

Equator

Ascension I.

St. Helena

SOUTH ATLANTIC OCEAN

INDIAN OCEAN

KENYA
Kismayu
Brava
Birico
Lamu
Malindi
Mombasa
Zanzibar
Dar-es-Salaam
Tanga
Pangani
Bagamoyo
TANZANIA
Tabora
Manyoni
Dodoma
Iringa
Kilwa
Lindi
Mtwara
C. Amber
Antsiranana
Andoany
Mahajanga
COMOROS
Mozambique
Pemba
Ibo
MOZAMBIQUE
Quelimane
Chinde
Beira
Sofala
Inhambane
Maputo
Antananarivo
Toamasina
Mananjary
Farafangana
Fianarantsoa
Manakara
Tôlanaro
C. Ste. Marie
Morondava
Toliara
Androka

ZAIRE
Kinshasa
Brazzaville
CONGO
GABON
Libreville
Pointe Noire
Cabinda
Boma
Matadi
Ambriz
Luanda
ANGOLA
Benguela
Lobito
Lubango
Namibe
C. Sta. Maria

NAMIBIA
(SOUTH WEST AFRICA)
Walvis Bay
Swakopmund
Windhoek
Lüderitz
BOTSWANA
Gaborone
Kalahari
ZIMBABWE
Bulawayo
MALAWI
Blantyre
ZAMBIA
Lusaka

SOUTH AFRICA
CAPE PROVINCE
Cape Town
C. of Good Hope
Port Elizabeth
East London
Durban
Johannesburg
Pretoria
Kimberley
Bloemfontein
ORANGE FREE STATE
TRANSVAAL
NATAL
SWAZILAND
TRANSKEI
Pietermaritzburg
Port Nolloth
Tropic of Capricorn

34

AUSTRALIA

| 0 | 100 | 200 | 300 | 400 | 500 miles |
| 0 | 200 | 400 | 600 | 800 km |

PAPUA NEW GUINEA
Lae
Wau
G. of Papua
Mt. Victoria
4073
Port Moresby
Rigo
Torres Strait
Cape York
nce of Wales
I.

Bougainville
Choiseul
SOLOMON
Santa Isabel
D'Entrecasteaux Is.
ISLANDS
Malaita
Louisiade Arch.
S. Cristóbal
Indispensable Str.

of
ria
ellesley
Is.

Cape York Peninsula
Weipa
Coleman
Cooktown

Coral
Sea
PACIFIC

Chillagoe
Mt. Bartle Frere 1611
Normanton
Innisfail
Cairns
Croydon
Norman
arketown
Cloncurry
Selwyn
ajarra
Winton

Townsville
Bowen
Charters Towers
Hughenden
Mackay

OCEAN

QUEENSLAND
Diamantina
Langreach
Emerald
Mt. Morgan
Rockhampton
Windorah
Gladstone
irdsville
Great
Bundaberg
Charleville
Maryborough
Fraser I.
Darling
Gympie
Toowoomba
Brisbane
Cunnamulla
Ipswich
Dirranbandi
Tibooburra
L. Callabonna
Moree
Bourke
Walgett
Grafton
Coffs Harbour
NEW SOUTH
Cobar
Wilcannia
Dubbo
Broken Hill
Menindee
Roto
Newcastle
erborough
Murray
River
WALES
Bathurst
SYDNEY
Mildura
Cootamundra
Wollongong
elaide
Basin
Canberra
Goulburn
Jervis B.
Queanbeyan
Bateman's B.
TERR
Snowy Mts.
Mt. Kosciusko 2230
Wangaratta
Bombala
VICTORIA
Ballarat
MELBOURNE
Colac
Geelong
King I.
Bass Strait
Furneaux Group
Scottsdale
Burnie
Devonport
Launceston
Strahan
Queenstown
TASMANIA
Hobart
Tasman Penin.
P. Davey
P. Arthur
Storm B.
S.E. Cape

Great
Barrier
Reef
Chesterfield Is.
Bird I.
Cato I.
Great Dividing
Grey Range
Warrego
Darling
New England Range
Gwydir Mts.

North C.
Doubtless B.
Kaipara Harb.
Great Barrier I.
Auckland
Devonport
North Island
Thames
Hamilton
Tauranga
B. of Plenty
East C.
North Taranaki Bight
Rotorua
New Plymouth
Gisborne
NEW ZEALAND
Patea
Wanganui
Hawke Bay
Karamea B.
Nelson
Wellington
South Island
Westport
Blenheim
Cook Strait
Ross
Campbell
Waiau
Mt. Cook 3764
Southern Alps
Christchurch
Mt. Aspiring 3035
Lyttelton
Milford Sd.
Canterbury Plains
Chatham Is. (N.Z.)
Kingston
Oamaru
Port Chalmers
Otago Harb.
Dunedin
Bluff
Bluff Harb.
Invercargill
Stewart I.
Southwest C.

NEW ZEALAND
on same scale

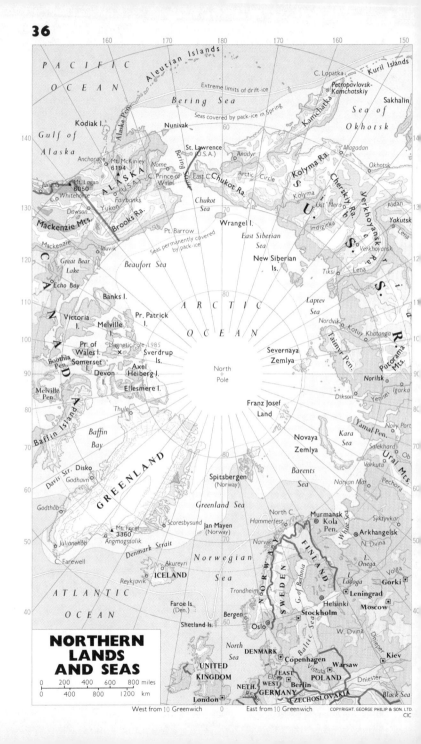

36

PACIFIC OCEAN

Aleutian Islands

Extreme limits of drift-ice

Bering Sea

Seas covered by pack-ice in Spring

C. Lopatka

Kuril Islands

Petropavlovsk-Kamchatskiy

Sakhalin

Sea of Okhotsk

Kodiak I.

Gulf of Alaska

Nunivak

St. Lawrence (U.S.A.)

Anadyr

Kamchatka

Magadan

Okhotsk

Anchorage

Mt. McKinley 6194

Nome

C. Prince of Wales

East C.

Bering Str.

Chukot Ra.

Arctic Circle

Kolyma Ra.

Chersky Ra.

Verkhoyansk Ra.

Aldan

ALASKA (U.S.A.)

Unga

Mt. Logan 6050

Whitehorse

Fairbanks

Dawson

Yukon

Brooks Ra.

Chukot Sea

Kolyma

U. S.

Ust 'Nera

Ob

Verkhoyansk

Yakutsk

Mackenzie Mts.

Mackenzie

Inuvik

Pt. Barrow

Seas permanently covered by pack-ice

Wrangel I.

East Siberian Sea

New Siberian Is.

Indigirka

S.

Lena

Verkhoyansk

Siberia

S.

CANADA

Great Bear Lake

Echo Bay

Beaufort Sea

ARCTIC

Laptev Sea

Tiksi

Lena

Nordvik

Kotuy

Khatanga

R.

Banks I.

OCEAN

Putorana Mts.

Victoria I.

Melville I.

Pr. Patrick I.

80

Taimyr Pen.

Severnaya Zemlya

Norilsk

Igarka

Pr. of Wales I.

Magnetic Pole 1985

Sverdrup Is.

Boothia Pen.

Somerset I.

Axel Heiberg I.

Devon I.

North Pole

Dikson

Yenisey

Ob

Melville Pen.

Ellesmere I.

Franz Josef Land

Novy Port

Yamal Pen.

Thule

80

Kara Sea

Salekhard

Ural Mts.

Baffin Island

Baffin Bay

Novaya Zemlya

Vorkuta

Davis Str.

Disko

Godhavn

GREENLAND

80

Barents Sea

Pechora

Naryan Mar

Godthåb

Spitsbergen (Norway)

North C.

Murmansk

Kola Pen.

Syktyvkar

White Sea

Arkhangelsk

N. Dvina

Julianehåb

Mt. Forel 3360

Scoresbysund

Greenland Sea

Hammerfest

Narvik

Angmagssalik

Denmark Strait

Jan Mayen (Norway)

Norwegian

L. Onega

L. Ladoga

Volga

Gorki

Akureyri

ICELAND

Reykjavik

Sea

Trondheim

NORWAY

SWEDEN

FINLAND

Helsinki

Leningrad

Moscow

ATLANTIC

OCEAN

Faroe Is. (Den.)

Shetland Is.

Bergen

Oslo

G. of Bothnia

Stockholm

W. Dvina

Dnieper

Kiev

NORTHERN LANDS AND SEAS

0   200   400   600   800 miles

0   400   800   1200 km

North Sea

UNITED KINGDOM

DENMARK

NETH.

London

Copenhagen

EAST WEST GERMANY

Berlin

Elbe

Rhine

Baltic Sea

Vistula

POLAND

CZECHOSLOVAKIA

Warsaw

Dniester

Black Sea

West from 10 Greenwich   0   East from 10 Greenwich

COPYRIGHT. GEORGE PHILIP & SON. LTD

CIC

"ghost hunting" era was Mr. Harry Price, an amateur magician who became the scourge of fraudulent mediums, but who staked his name and credibility on the authenticity of the alleged poltergeist phenomena at Borley Rectory in Suffolk, which became world famous through his book, *The Most Haunted House in England*. The ancient rectory's catalogue of ghosts and marvels allegedly witnessed by numerous "reliable witnesses" seemed irrefutable. Unfortunately investigations by the Society for Psychical Research some years after Price's death now make it seem certain that Price was responsible for faking some of the Borley phenomena himself, and with these disclosures scientifically "respectable" ghost hunting took a nasty tumble. Thus, with an increasingly critical attitude developing among scientists, haunted houses and poltergeists gradually began to shift out of favour to usher in the third phase of psychic research.

The date of the commencement of this phase can be identified as 1927 when the Parapsychology Laboratory at Duke University in North Carolina was formed by Dr. J. B. Rhine. Here the emphasis was on laboratory studies along the traditional lines of experimental psychology; spirit forms and poltergeists were ignored in favour of the routine testing of literally thousands of people for telepathy, precognition (the ability to see into the future), etc., almost always involving card tests which could be rigidly controlled and the results statistically analysed. By the 1940s Rhine was claiming irrefutable evidence of telepathy achieved by these means, but once again critical forces began to gather and it was pointed out that results obtained in Rhine's laboratory rarely seemed to be replicable in other scientists' laboratories in different parts of the world. In fact the failure of ESP experiments of this kind to be easily repeatable has turned out to be crucial and has led to a growing scepticism on the part of uncommitted scientists who now question whether psychic research and parapsychology have really advanced our understanding of the world of the paranormal in any way. At the present time the topic is in a highly controversial phase.

Although Rhine's university parapsychology laboratory closed with his retirement in 1965 research in the field has continued ever since, especially with the work of Dr. Helmut Schmidt who has made important contributions. In recent years a new Chair and research laboratory has been introduced at the University of Utrecht in the Netherlands.

To sum up the topic one could say that in a curious way, while the third phase of psychic research is now drawing to a close, the evidence suggests that a fourth phase is appearing, and that this may well feature a return to the study of the more sensational and dramatic phenomena reminiscent of the Victorian séance room. If this is so, a century after its foundation the wheel will have turned full circle and psychic research will be back where it started, without in the opinion of most scientists, having solved any of the basic questions which it had set out to answer. *See* **Parapsychology, Poltergeist, Telepathy, Spiritualism.**

Psychoanalysis, an approach to the study of human personality involving the rigorous probing, with the assistance of a specially trained practitioner, of an individual's personal problems, motives, goals and attitudes to life in general. Often, and quite understandably, confused with psychology (of which it is merely a part), psychoanalysis has an interesting historical background and has attracted the interest of philosophers, scientists and medical experts since it emerged as a radical and controversial form of mental therapy at the turn of the century. The traditionally accepted founder is the great Austrian Sigmund Freud, but he never failed to acknowledge the impetus that had been given to his own ideas by his talented friend, the physiologist Joseph Breuer, who for most of his working life had been interested in the curious phenomena associated with hypnosis. Breuer had successfully cured the hysterical paralysis of a young woman patient and had noticed that under hypnosis the girl seemed to be recalling emotional experiences, hitherto forgotten, which bore some relationship with the symptoms of her illness. Developing this with other patients Breuer then found that the mere recalling and discussing of the emotional events under hypnosis seemed to produce a dramatic alleviation of the symptoms—a phenomenon which came to be known as *catharsis*. Breuer also noticed another curious side-effect, that his women patients fell embarrassingly and violently in love with him, and he gradually dropped the practice of "mental catharsis", possibly feeling that it was a bit too dangerous to handle. This left the field clear for Freud, whose brilliant mind began to search beyond the therapeutic aspects of the topic to see what light might be thrown on the nature of human personality and psychological mechanisms in general. The most important question concerned the "forgotten" emotional material which turned up, apparently out of the blue, during the hypnotic session. Freud rightly saw that this posed problems for the current theories of memory, for how could something once forgotten (a) continue to have an effect on the individual without his being aware of it, and (b) ultimately be brought back to conscious memory again. It must be remembered that at this time memory was considered to be a fairly simple process—information was stored in the brain and was gradually eroded or destroyed with the passage of time and the decay of brain cells. Once lost, it was believed, memories were gone for ever, or at best only partially and inaccurately reproducible. Furthermore, human beings were supposed to be rational (if frequently wilful) creatures who never did anything without thinking about it (if only briefly) beforehand and without being well aware of their reasons for so doing. It was within this framework that Freud had his great insight, one which many people believe to be one of the most important ideas given to mankind. This was simply the realisation that the human mind was not a simple entity controlling the brain and body more or less at will, but a complex system made up of a number of integrated parts with at least two major subdivisions—the conscious and the unconscious. The former concerned itself with the normal round of human behaviour, including the larger part of rational thought, conversation, etc., and large areas of memory. The latter was principally devoted to the automatic control of bodily functions, such as respiration, cardiac activity, various types of emotional behaviour not subject to much conscious modification and a large storehouse of relevant "memories" again not normally accessible to the conscious mind. Occasionally, Freud proposed, an exceedingly unpleasant emotional or otherwise painful event might be so troublesome if held in the conscious mind's store, that it would get shoved down into the unconscious or "repressed" where it would cease to trouble the individual in his normal life. The advantages of this mechanism are obvious, but they also brought with them hazards. With certain kinds of memory, particularly those involving psychological rather than physical pain—as for example a severe sexual conflict or marital problem—repression might be used as a device to save the individual from facing his problem in the "real" world, where he might be able ultimately to solve it, by merely hiding it away in the unconscious and thus pretending it did not exist. Unfortunately, Freud believed, conflicts of this kind were not snuffed out when consigned to the basements of the mind, but rather tended to smoulder on, affecting the individual in various ways which he could not understand. Repressed marital conflicts might give rise to impotence, for example, or even to homosexual behaviour. Guilt at improper social actions similarly repressed might provoke nervous tics, local paralysis, etc, etc. Following this line of reasoning, Freud argued that if the unwisely repressed material could be dredged up and the individual forced to face the crisis instead of denying it, then dramatic alleviations of symptoms and full recovery should follow.

To the great psychologist and his growing band of followers the stage seemed to be set for a dramatic breakthrough not only in mental therapy but also in a general understanding of the nature of human personality. To his pleasure—for various reasons he was never too happy about hypnosis—Freud discovered that with due patience, skill and guidance an individual could be led to resurrect the material repressed in his unconscious mind in the normal, as opposed to the hypnotic, state. This technique, involving long sessions consisting of intimate discussions between patient and therapist became known as psychoanalysis, and it has steadily evolved from its experimental beginnings in the medical schools and universities of Vienna to being a major system of psychotherapy with a world-wide following and important theoretical connotations. Psychoanalysis, as practised today, consists of a number of meetings between doctor and patient in which the latter is slowly taught to approach and enter the *territory* of his subconscious mind, and examine the strange and "forgotten" material within. A successful analysis, it is claimed, gives the individual greater insight into his own personality and a fuller understanding of the potent unconscious forces which are at work within him and in part dictating his goals.

Freud's initial ideas were of course tentative, and meant to be so. He was however a didactic and forceful personality himself, unwilling to compromise on many points which became controversial as the technique and practice of psychoanalysis developed. The outcome was that some of his early followers, notably the equally brilliant Carl Jung and Alfred Adler, broke away to found their own "schools" or versions of psychoanalysis, with varying degrees of success. Today, psychoanalysis is coming under increasingly critical scrutiny, and its claims are being treated with a good deal of reservation. Notable antagonists include the English psychologist Professor H. J. Eysenck who points out that there is little if any solid experimental data indicating that psychoanalysis is a valid method of treating or curing mental illness. Analysists respond by saying that their system is closer to an art than a craft and not amenable to routine scientific experiment. The controversy will no doubt continue for some time to come, but whatever its validity as therapy, the basic ideas behind psychoanalysis—notably the reality and power of the unconscious mind—are beyond question and have given human beings definite and major insights into the greatest enigma of all—the workings of the human mind.

Psychometry, the supposed talent or faculty of divining something about the history and previous owners of an object by holding it in the hand. A common feature of modern Spiritualistic practice, and to a certain extent synonymous with clairvoyance, psychometry is based on an ancient magical assumption that objects somehow take on traces or "memories" of their surroundings which are detectable by specially sensitive individuals. Controlled scientific tests on people claiming to have this power have however proved totally negative. *See also* **Psychic Research**.

Puritans were a separate sect before the accession of Edward VI, but did not become prominent till the reign of Elizabeth. Afterwards they split up into Independents and Presbyterians, and the influence of Oliver Cromwell made the former supreme. Since the Revolution the word has been replaced by 'Nonconformist' or 'Dissenter', but, of course, Romanists in England and Protestant Episcopalians in Scotland are just as much Nonconformists or Dissenters as Baptists or Methodists are.

Pyramidology, a curious belief that the dimensions of the Great Pyramid at Giza, if studied carefully, reveal principles of fundamental historical and religious significance. The perpetrator of this was a Victorian publisher, John Taylor, who discovered that if you divide the height of the pyramid into twice the side of its base you get a number very similar to *pi*—a number of considerable mathematical importance. Later discoveries in the same vein include the finding that the base of the pyramid (when divided by the width of a single casing stone) equals exactly 365—number of days in the year. Many books have been written on the interpretation of the dimensions of the pyramid, none of which has any scientific or archaeological validity. Pyramidology is simply a classic example of the well-known fact that hunting through even a random array of numbers will turn up sequences which appear to be "significant"—always provided that one carefully selects the numbers one wants and turns a blind eye to those that one doesn't! A peculiar variant of pyramidology has recently arisen through the publication of a claim that razor blades kept beneath a cardboard model of a pyramid never lose their cutting edge! Scientific tests have shown that this is not so, but the belief persists—implicit testimony to the mystical power of certain common emblems and symbols.

Pyrrhonism, a sceptical philosophy which doubts everything.

Q

Quakers, a religious body founded in England in the 17th cent. by George Fox (1624–91). The essence of their faith is that every individual who believes has the power of direct communication with God who will guide him into the ways of truth. This power comes from the "inner light" of his own heart, the light of Christ, Quakers meet for worship avoiding all ritual, without ordained ministers or prepared sermons; there is complete silence until someone is moved by the Holy Spirit to utter his message.

In the early days Quakers gave vent to violent outbursts and disturbed church services. Friends had the habit of preaching at anyone who happened to be nearby, their denunciation of "steeple-houses" and references to the "inner light," their addressing everyone as "thee" and "thou," their refusal to go beyond "yea" and "nay" in making an assertion and refusing to go further in taking an oath, must have played some part in bringing about the savage persecutions they were forced to endure. Many emigrated to Pennsylvania, founded by William Penn in 1682, and missionaries were sent to many parts of the world. The former violence gave way to gentleness. Friends not only refused to take part in war but even refused to resist personal violence. They took the lead in abolishing slavery, worked for prison reform and better education. As we know them today Quakers are quiet, sincere, undemonstrative people, given to a somewhat serious turn of mind. The former peculiarities of custom and dress have been dropped and interpretation of the Scriptures is more liberal. Although Quakers refuse to take part in warfare, they are always ready to help the victims of war, by organising relief, helping refugees in distress, or sending their ambulance units into the heat of battle. In Britain the Quakers have (1990) some 18,000 adult members.

Quietism, a doctrine of extreme asceticism and contemplative devotion, embodied in the works of Michael Molinos, a 17th cent. Spanish priest, and condemned by Rome. It taught that the chief duty of man is to be occupied in the continual contemplation of God, so as to become totally independent of outward circumstances and the influence of the senses. Quietists taught that when this stage of perfection is reached the soul has no further need for prayer and other external devotional practices. Similar doctrines have been taught in the Moslem and Hindu religions. *See* **Yoga**.

R

Racism, the doctrine that one race is inherently superior or inferior to others, one of the bases of racial prejudice. It has no connection what ever with the study of race as a concept, nor with the investigation of racial differences, which is a science practised by the physical anthropologist (who studies physical differences), or the social anthropologist (who studies cultural differences). *See also* **Race, Section L**.

Radiesthesia, the detection, either by some "psychic" faculty or with special equipment, of radiations alleged to be given off by all living things and natural substances such as water, oil, metal, etc. The word radiesthesia is in fact a fancy modern name for the ancient practice of "dowsing," whereby an individual is supposed to be able to detect the presence of hidden underground water by following the movements of a hazel twig held in his hands. Dowsers, or water diviners, as they are sometimes called, claim also to be able to detect the presence of minerals and, hard though it may seem to believe, have actually been hired by major oil companies to prospect for desert wells—though without any notable success. The theory of dowsing is that all things give off a unique radiation signal which the trained individual (via his twig, pendulum, or whatever) can "tune in" to, a theory which, while not backed up by any data known to orthodox sciences, is at least not too fantastically far-fetched. It is when radiesthesists claim to be able to detect the presence of oil, water, or precious metals by holding their pendulum *over a map* of the territory and declare that it is not necessary for them to visit the area in person to find the required spot that the topic moves from the remotely possible to the absurdly improbable. Some practitioners of this art state that they are able to perform even more marvellous feats such as determining the sex of chickens while still in the egg, or diagnosing illness by studying the movements of a pendulum held over a blood sample from the sick individual. Such claims when put to simple scientific test have almost invariably turned out as fiascos. Yet belief in dowsing, water-divining, and the like is still very widespread.

There is an important link between radiesthesia and the pseudo-science of *radionics*, which holds that the twig or pendulum can be superseded by complicated equipment built vaguely according to electronic principles. A typical radionic device consists of a box covered with knobs, dials, etc., by which the practitioner "tunes in" to the "vibration" given off by an object, such as a blood spot, a piece of hair, or even a signature. By the proper interpretation of the readings from the equipment the illness, or even the mental state, of the individual whose blood, hair, or signature is being tested, may be ascertained. The originator of radionics seems to have been a Dr. Albert Abrams who engaged in medical practice using radionic devices in America in the 1920s and 30s. The principal exponent in this country was the late George de la Warr who manufactured radionic boxes for diagnosis and treatment of illnesses, and even a "camera" which he believed to be capable of photographing thought. In a sensational court case in 1960 a woman who had purchased one of the diagnostic devices sued de la Warr for fraud. After a long trial the case was dismissed, the Judge commenting that while he had no good evidence that the device worked as claimed, he felt that de la Warr seriously believed in its validity and thus was not guilty of fraud or misrepresentation.

Ranters, a fanatical antinomian (the doctrine that Christians are not bound to keep the law of God) and pantheistic sect in Commonwealth England. The name was also applied to the Primitive Methodists because of their noisy preaching.

Rastafarianism, a Caribbean religious cult which took root among West Indians after the waning of Black Power (*q.v.*) in the mid-1970s. Rastafarians look to Ethiopia as their spiritual and racial home since that country was the one part of Africa not to be colonised. Reggae is their music, prominent in the West Indian Notting Hill Festival held in London during the August Bank Holiday weekend.

Rationalism is defined as "the treating of reason as the ultimate authority in religion and the rejection of doctrines not consonant with reason." In practice, rationalism had a double significance: (1) the doctrine as defined above, and (2) a 19th cent. movement which was given to what was then known as "free-thought," "secularism," or agnosticism—*i.e.*, it was in the positive sense anti-religious and was represented by various bodies such as the Secular Society, the National Secular Society, and the Rationalist Press Association (founded in 1899).

In the first sense, which implies a particular philosophical attitude to the universe and life, rationalism is not easy to pin down although, at first sight, it would appear that nothing could be simpler. Does it mean the use of pure reason and logic or does it mean, on the other hand, the use of what is generally called the "scientific method" based on a critical attitude to existing beliefs? If we are thinking in terms of the use of pure reason and logic then the Roman Catholic Church throughout most of its history has maintained, not that the whole truth about religion can be discovered by reason, but as St. Thomas Aquinas held, the basis of religion—*e.g.* the existence of God—can be rationally demonstrated. Nobody could have made more use of logic than the schoolmen of the Middle Ages, yet not many people today would accept their conclusions, nor would many non-Catholics accept St. Thomas's proofs of the existence of God even when they themselves are religious. The arguments of a First Cause or Prime Mover or the argument from Design on the whole leave us unmoved, partly because they do not lead up to the idea of a *personal God*, partly because we rightly distrust logic and pure reason divorced from facts and know that, if we begin from the wrong assumptions or premises, we can arrive at some very strange answers. If the existence of a Deity can be proved by reason, then one can also by the use of reason come to the conclusions, or rather paradoxes, such as the following: God is by definition all good, all knowing, all powerful—yet evil exists (because it if does not exist then it cannot be wrong to say "there is no God"). But if evil exists, then it must do so either because of God (in which case He is not all good) or in spite of God (in which case He is not all powerful).

Arguments of this sort do not appeal to the modern mind for two historical reasons: (1) many of us have been brought up in the Protestant tradition which—at least in one of its aspects—insists that we must believe in God by faith rather than by logic and in its extreme form insists on God as revealed by the "inner light"; (2) our increasing trust in the scientific method of observation, experiment and argument. Thus, no matter what Aristotle or St. Thomas may say about a Prime Mover or a First Cause, we remain unconvinced since at least one scientific theory suggests that the universe did not have a beginning and if scientific investigation proved this to be so, then we should be entirely indifferent to what formal logic had to say.

The secularist and rationalist movements of the 19th cent. were anti-religious—and quite rightly so—because at that time there were serious disabilities imposed even in Britain by the Established Church on atheism or agnosticism and freedom of thought. They are of little significance now because very little is left, largely thanks to their efforts, of these disabilities.

Finally, although most people are likely to accept the scientific method as the main means of discovering truth, there are other factors which equally make us doubt the value of "pure" logic and reason unaided by observation. The first of these is the influence of Freud which shows that much of our reasoning is mere rationalising—*e.g.*, we are more likely to become atheists because we hated our father than because we can prove that there is no God. The second is the influence of a movement in philosophy which, in the form of logical positivism or logical analysis, makes us doubt whether metaphysical systems have any meaning at all. Today, instead of asking ourselves whether Plato was right or wrong, we are much more likely to ask whether he did anything but make for the most part meaningless noises. Religion is in a sense much safer today than it ever was in the 19th cent. when it made foolish statements over matters of science that could be *proved* wrong; now we tend to see it as an emotional attitude to the universe or God (a "feeling of being at home in the universe," as William James put it) which can no more be proved or disproved than being in love.

Realism is a word which has so many meanings, and such contradictory ones, in various spheres, that it is difficult to define. We shall limit ourselves to its significance in philosophy. In philosophy, "realism" has two different meanings, diametrically opposed. (1) The most usual meaning is the one we should least expect from the everyday sense of the word—*i.e.*, it refers to all those philosophies from Plato onwards which maintained that the world of appearance is illusory and that ideas, forms, or universals are the only true realities, belonging to the world beyond matter and appearance—the world of God or mind. In early mediaeval times St. Thomas Aquinas was the chief exponent of this doctrine which was held by the scholastics as opposed to the Nominalists (*q.v.*). (2) In its modern everyday meaning "realism" is the belief that the universe is real and not a creation of mind, that there is a reality that causes the appearance, the "thing-in-itself" as Kant described it. Material things may not really be what they appear to be (*e.g.* a noise is not the "bang" we experience but a series of shock-waves passing through the atmosphere), yet, for all that, we can be sure that matter exists and it is very possible (some might add) that mind does not.

Reformation, the great religious movement of the 16th cent., which resulted in the establishment of Protestantism. John Wyclif (d. 1384), John Hus (d. 1415) and others had sounded the warning note, and when later on Luther took up the cause in Germany, and Zwingli in Switzerland, adherents soon became numerous. The wholesale vending of indulgences by the papal agents had incensed the people, and when Luther denounced these things he spoke to willing ears. After much controversy, the reformers boldly propounded the principles of the new doctrine, and the struggle for religious supremacy grew bitter. They claimed justification (salvation) by faith, and the use as well as the authority of the Scriptures, rejecting the doctrine of transubstantiation, the adoration of the Virgin and Saints, and the headship of the Pope. Luther was excommunicated. But the Reformation principles spread and ultimately a great part of Germany, as well as Switzerland, the Low Countries, Scandinavia, England, and Scotland were won over to the new faith. In England Henry VIII readily espoused the cause of the Reformation, his own personal quarrel with the Pope acting as an incentive. Under Mary there was a brief and sanguinary reaction, but Elizabeth gave completeness to the work which her father had initiated. *See* **Lutheranism, Calvinism, Presbyterianism, Baptists, Methodism.**

Renaissance is defined in the *Oxford English Dictionary* as: "The revival of art and letters, under the influence of classical models, which began in Italy in the 14th century." It is a term which must be used with care for the following reasons: (1) Although it was first used in the form *rinascita* (re-birth) by Vasari in 1550 and people living at that time certainly were aware that something new was happening, the word had no wide currency until used by the Swiss historian Jacob Burchardt in his classic *The Civilization of the Renaissance in Italy* (1860). (2) The term as used today refers not only to art in its widest sense but to a total change in man's outlook on life which extended into philosophical, scientific, economic, and technical fields. (3) Spreading from Italy there were renaissance movements in France, Spain, Germany, and northern Europe, all widely different with varying delays in time. As the historian Edith Sichel says: "Out of the Italian Renaissance there issued a new-born art; out of the Northern Renaissance there came forth a new-born religion. There came forth also a great school of poetry, and a drama the greatest that the world had seen since the days of Greece. The religion was the offspring of Germany and the poetry that of England."

The real cause of the Renaissance was not the fall of Constantinople, the invention of printing, or the discovery of America, though these were phases in the process; it was, quite simply, money. The birth of a new merchant class gave rise to individualist attitudes in economic affairs which prepared the way for individualism and humanism. The new wealthy class in time became patrons of the arts whereas previously the Church had been the sole patron and controller. Thus the artist became more free to express himself, more respected, and being more well-to-do could afford to ignore the Church and even, in time, the views of his patrons.

It is true that art continued to serve to a considerable extent the purposes of faith, but it was judged from the standpoint of art. Mediaeval art was meant to elevate and teach man: Renaissance art to delight his senses and enrich his life. From this free and questing spirit acquired from economic individualism came the rise of modern science and technology; here Italy learned much from the Arab scholars who had translated and commented upon the philosophical, medical, and mathematical texts of antiquity, while denying themselves any interest in Greek art and literature. Arabic-Latin versions of Aristotle were in use well into the 16th cent. The Byzantine culture, though it had preserved the Greek tradition and gave supremacy to Plato, had made no move forward. But the Greek scholars who fled to Italy after the fall of Constantinople brought with them an immense cargo of classical manuscripts. The recovery of these Greek masterpieces, their translation into the vernaculars, and the invention of printing, made possible a completer understanding of the Greek spirit. It was the bringing together of the two heritages, Greek science, and Greek literature, that gave birth to a new vision. But it was not only Aristotle and Plato who were being studied but Ovid, Catullus, Horace, Pliny and Lucretius. What interested Renaissance man was the humanism of the Latin writers, their attitude to science, their scepticism.

The period *c.* 1400–1500 is known as the **Early Renaissance.** During this time such painters as Masaccio, Uccello, Piero della Francesca, Botticelli, and Giovanni Bellini were laying the foundations of drawing and painting for all subsequent periods including our own. They concerned themselves with such problems as anatomy, composition, perspective, and representation of space, creating in effect a grammar or textbook of visual expression. The term **High Renaissance** is reserved for a very brief period when a pure, balanced, classical harmony was achieved and artists were in complete control of the techniques learned earlier. The High Renaissance lasted only from *c.* 1500 to 1527 (the date of the sack of Rome), yet that interval included the earlier works of Michelangelo, most of Leonardo's, and all the Roman works of Raphael.

Ritualism, a tendency which, during the 19th cent., developed in the High Church section of the Church of England to make use of those vestments, candles, incense, etc. which are usually regarded as features of the Church of Rome. Since some opposition was aroused, a Ritual Commission was appointed in 1904 to take evidence and try to find some common basis on which High and Low Church could agree with respect to ceremonial. The report of 1906 in effect recommended the giving of greater powers to bishops to suppress objectionable practices. Although they are often associated together, it is worth while pointing out that there was no special connection between the Oxford Movement or Tractarians (*q.v.*) and Ritualism because Pusey disliked ritual and even Newman, who eventually went over to Rome, held extremely simple services at his church of St. Mary's.

Roman Catholic Church, the Christian organisation which acknowledges the Pope as the lawful successor of St. Peter, the apostle appointed by Christ to be the head of His Church. The reforming impulse at the Second Vatican Council (1962–5), summoned by Pope John, set in train movements towards religious unity and the reform and modernisation of the Church. Pope Paul made changes in the government and liturgy of the Church but refused to allow birth control, the marriage of priests and a greater role for women in the Roman Catholic Church.

Recent years have seen rapid changes in the Roman Catholic Church and the papacy has found a strong and charismatic leader in Pope John Paul II whose first encyclical *Redemptor Hominus* (1979) declared that the Christian missionary must always begin with "a deep esteem for man, for his intellect, his will, his conscience and his freedom". A historic meeting took place in 1982 between Rome and Canterbury when Pope John Paul II, making the first papal visit to Britain, joined Dr. Runcie in Canterbury Cathedral in the cause of Christian unity. *See* **Cardinals (L22)**.

Romantic Movement or Romanticism is the name given not so much to an individual way of thinking but to the gradual but radical transformation of basic human values that occurred in the Western world round about the latter part of the 18th cent. It was a great breakthrough in European consciousness and arose through the writings of certain men living during the half-century or more following, say, 1760. It arose then because both time and place were propitious for the birth of these new ideas. There was a revolution in basic values—in art, morals, politics, religion, etc. The new view was of a world transcending the old one, infinitely larger and more varied.

To understand the Romantic movement it is necessary first to take note of the climate of thought preceding the great change; then to account for its beginning in Germany where it did (*see* **Pietism**) during the latter part of the 18th cent., and finally to appraise the writings of those men whose ideas fermented the new awakening. Briefly, the shift was away from French classicism and from belief in the all-pervasive power of human reason (the Enlightenment) towards the unfettered freedom that the new consciousness was able to engender. What mattered was to live a passionate and vigorous life, to dedicate oneself to an ideal, no matter what the cost (*e.g.*, Byron).

The ideas of the Englightenment (*e.g.*, Fontenelle, Voltaire, Montesquieu) had been attacked by the Germans Hamann and Herder and by the ideas of the English philosopher Hume, but Kant, Schiller, and Fichte, Goethe's novel *Wilhelm Meister*, and the French Revolution all had profound effects on the aesthetic, moral, social, and political thought of the time. Friedrich Schlegel (1772–1829) said: "There is in man a terrible unsatisfied desire to soar into infinity; a feverish longing to break through the narrow bonds of individuality." Romanticism undermined the notion that in matters of value there are objective criteria which operate between men. Henceforth there was to be a resurgence of the human spirit, deep and profound, that is still going on.

Rosicrucians, an ancient mystical society founded in the 16th cent. by Christian Rosenkreuz which attempted to forge a theoretical link between the great Egyptian religions and the Church of Rome, drawing rituals and philosophy from both camps. The Society did not long survive the death of its founder (he managed to reach the age of 106 incidentally) but has been revived in succeeding centuries by a series of rivalling factions. Perhaps the most famous of these is the Rosicrucian Order (A.M.O.R.C) which has become well-known in the Western world as a result of its heavy advertising in the popular press. Founded by the American H. Spencer Lewis, this offers a simple and good-natured doctrine preaching the Brotherhood of Man, the reincarnation of the soul and the immense latent potential of the human mind. As with many American-based organisations of this kind, the boundary between business and religion is hard to define. It is probably best summed up as a modern secret society which serves an important function in the lives of many people of mystical inclinations.

S

Salvation Army. The religious movement which in 1878 became known by this name arose from the Christian Mission meetings which the Rev. William Booth and his devoted wife had held in the East End of London for the previous thirteen years. Its primary aim was, and still is, to preach the gospel of Jesus Christ to men and women untouched by ordinary religious efforts. The founder devoted his life to the salvation of the submerged classes whose conditions at that time were unspeakably dreadful. Originally his aim had been to convert people and then send them on to the churches, but he soon found that few religious bodies would accept these "low-class" men and women. So it was that social work became part of their effort. Practical help like the provision of soup-kitchens, accompanied spiritual ministration. Soon, in the interests of more effective "warfare" against social evils, a military form of organisation, with uniforms, brass bands, and religious songs, was introduced. Its magazine *The War Cry* gave as its aim "to carry the Blood of Christ and the Fire of the Holy Ghost into every part of the world.'

General Booth saw with blinding clarity that conversion must be accompanied by an improvement of external conditions. Various books had earlier described the terrible conditions of the slums, but in 1890 he produced a monumental survey entitled *In Darkest England and the Way Out.* From that time forward the Army was accepted and its facilities made use of by the authorities. Today (1990) the Army's spiritual and social activities have spread to 89 countries all over the world; every one, no matter what class, colour, or creed he belongs to is a "brother for whom Christ died." Within Britain there are 60,000 active members.

Sandemanians or Glassites, an obscure religious sect whose sole claim to fame is that one of its members was the great Michael Faraday, founder of the science of electromagnetism, who never failed to attend its Sunday services.

Sceptics. From Thales of Miletus (*c.* 624–565 B.C.) to the Stoics in the 4th cent. B.C. philosophers had been trying to explain the nature of the universe; each one produced a different theory and each could, apparently, prove that he was right. This diversity of views convinced the Sceptic school founded by Pyrrho (*c.* 360–270 B.C.) that man is unable to know the real nature of the world or how it came into being. In place of a futile search for what must be for ever unknowable, the Sceptics recommended that men should be practical, follow custom, and accept the evidence of their senses.

Schoolmen. From the time of Augustine to the middle of the 9th cent. philosophy, like science, was dead or merely a repetition of what had gone before. But about that time there arose a new interest in the subject, although (since by then Western Europe was entirely under the authority of the Catholic Church) the main form it took was an attempt to justify Church teaching in the light of Greek philosophy. Those who made this attempt to reconcile Christian beliefs with the best in Plato and Aristotle were known as "schoolmen" and the philosophies which they developed were known as "scholasticism." Among the most famous schoolmen must be counted John Scotus Erigena (*c.* 800–*c.* 877), born in Ireland and probably the earliest; St. Anselm, archbishop of Canterbury (1033–1109); the great Peter Abelard whose school was in Paris (1079–1142); Bernard of Chartres, his contemporary; and the best-known of all, St. Thomas Aquinas of Naples (1225–74), who was given the name of the "Angelic Doctor."

The philosophies of these men are discussed under various headings (**God and Man, Determinism and Free-will**), but being severely limited by the Church their doctrines differed from each other much less than those of later philosophical schools. However, one of the great arguments was between the orthodox Realists (*q.v.*) and the Nominalists (*q.v.*) and a second was between the Thomists (or followers of St. Thomas Aquinas) and the Scotists (followers of John Duns Scotus—not to be confused with John Scotus Erigena). The two latter schools were known as the Ancients, whilst the followers of William of Occam, the Nominalist, were known as the Terminalists. All became reconciled in 1482 in face of the threat from humanism of which the great exponent was Erasmus of Rotterdam (1466–1536).

Scientology, an applied religious philosophy dealing with the study of knowledge, which through the application of its technology, can bring about desirable changes in the conditions of life. The word Scientology comes from the Latin word *Scio* (knowing in the fullest meaning of the word) and the Greek word *Logos* (study of). Developed and founded by author, philosopher and humanitarian L. Ron Hubbard (1911–86). A world-wide organisation with approximately 600 established Churches and affiliated groups in 50 countries. Membership estimated at 7 million (1989). In Scientology the individual is considered to be a soul or spirit of an immortal nature which goes from life to life. Although he has a mind and a body, he is himself a spiritual being called a "Thetan" (taken from the Greek letter theta, meaning thought or spirit). Scientology is traditional in its philosophical approach and although many new phenomena have been discovered, it follows the basic trend of the formal philosophies of the Egyptians, Greeks and great thinkers of the Renaissance, which consider the individual a spiritual rather than an animal being. The ultimate goal of Scientology is "a civilisation without insanity, without criminals and without war, where the able can prosper and honest beings can have rights, and where Man is free to rise to greater heights." Scientologists believe that, by helping persons achieve the State of Clear (a level of spiritual awareness and ability) they can salvage a civilisation that is otherwise doomed. Scientology technology is also used to help people improve conditions in society by dealing with community problems such as drug and alcohol abuse, problems in education, juvenile delinquency, crime and violence. From 1959 until the late 1960s the worldwide headquarters was based in East Grinstead, Sussex and this is now the base for the UK headquarters of the Church.

Shakers, members of a revivalist group, styled by themselves "The United Society of Believers in Christ's Second Appearing," who seceded from Quakerism in 1747 though adhering to many of the Quaker tenets. The community was joined in 1758 by Ann Lee, a young convert from Manchester, who had "revelations" that she was the female Christ; "Mother Ann" was accepted as their leader. Under the influence of her prophetic visions she set out with nine followers for "Immanuel's land" in America and the community settled near Albany, capital of New York state. They were known as the "Shakers" in ridicule because they were given to involuntary movements in moments of religious ecstasy. Central to their faith was the belief in the dual role of God through the male and female Christ: the male principle came to earth in Jesus; the female principle, in "Mother Ann." The sexes were equal and women preached as often as men at their meetings which sometimes included sacred dances—nevertheless the two sexes, even in dancing, kept apart. Their communistic way of living brought them economic prosperity, the Shakers becoming known as good agriculturists and craftsmen, noted for their furniture and textiles. After 1860, however, the movement began to decline and few, if any, are active today.

Shamans, the medicine men found in all primitive societies who used their magical arts to work cures, and protect the group from evil influences. The *shaman* was a man apart and wore special garments to show his authority. Shamanism with its magical practices, incantations, trances, exhausting dances, and self-torture is practised even today by primitive tribes.

Shiites or Shia, a heretical Moslem sect in Persia, opposed by the orthodox Sunnites. The dispute, which came almost immediately after the death of the Prophet and led to bitter feuding, had little to do with matters of doctrine as such but with the succession. After Mohammed's death, there were three possible claimants: Ali, the husband of his daughter Fatima, and two others, one of whom gave up his claim in favour of the other, Omar. The orthodox selected Omar, who was shortly assassinated, and the same happened to his successor as Ali was passed over again. The Shiites are those who maintain that Ali was the true vicar of the Prophet, and that

the three orthodox predecessors were usurpers.

Shintoism, literally means "teaching of the Gods". It is a native Japanese religion, with a strong bias towards ancestor worship and the divine powers of natural forces. Unusual in that it had no recognised founder nor written dogma, Shintoism permeated Japanese life in a most vigorous way until the defeat of the country at the hands of the Allied Powers in 1945. In the 1500 years of its existence the Shinto religion produced tens of thousands of unique and beautiful shrines throughout Japan. Vast numbers of these were destroyed by bombing in the war, but a tolerant decision by the American airforce spared one Shinto centre, Kyoto, from air-attack. Shintoism was disestablished by the American occupying forces in 1945 and the Emperor Hirohito "abdicated" his divine powers. Dissatisfaction among many Japanese with the worldly extravagance of their society has led to a recent revival of interest in Shintoism. Nationalism in Japan has often made use of Shintoism.

Sikhism. The Sikh community of the Punjab, which has played a significant part in the history of modern India, came into being during a period of religious revival in India in the 15th and 16th cent. It was originally founded as a religious sect by Guru (teacher) Nanak (1469–1538) who emphasised the fundamental truth of all religions, and whose mission was to put an end to religious conflict. He condemned the formalism both of Hinduism and Islam, preaching the gospel of universal toleration, and the unity of the Godhead, whether He be called Allah, Vishnu, or God. His ideas were welcomed by the great Mogul Emperor Akbar (1542–1605). Thus a succession of Gurus were able to live in peace after Nanak's death; they established the great Sikh centre at Amritsar, compiled the sacred writings known as the *Adi Granth*, and improved their organisation as a sect. But the peace did not last long, for an emperor arose who was a fanatical Moslem, in face of whom the last Guru, Govind Singh (1666–1708), whose father was put to death for refusal to embrace Islam, had to make himself a warrior and instil into the Sikhs a more aggressive spirit. A number of ceremonies were instituted by Govind Singh; admission to the fraternity was by special rite; caste distinctions were abolished; hair was worn long; and the word singh, meaning lion, was added to the original name. They were able to organise themselves into 12 *misls* or confederacies but divisions appeared with the disappearance of a common enemy and it was not until the rise of Ranjit Singh (1780–1839) that a single powerful Sikh kingdom was established, its influence only being checked by the English, with whom a treaty of friendship was made. After the death of Ranjit Singh two Anglo-Sikh wars followed, in 1845–46, and 1848–49, which resulted in British annexation of the Punjab and the end of Sikh independence. In the two world wars the Sikhs proved among the most loyal of Britain's Indian subjects. The partitioning of the continent of India in 1947 into two states, one predominantly Hindu and the other predominantly Moslem, presented a considerable problem in the Punjab, which was divided in such a way as to leave 2 million Sikhs in Pakistan, and a considerable number of Moslems in the Indian Punjab. Although numbering less than 2 per cent. of the population (*c.* 8 million) the Sikhs are a continuing factor in Indian political life. Demands for Sikh independence led to the storming by Indian troops of the Golden Temple at Amritsar on 6 June 1984. In October 1984, Mrs. Gandhi was assassinated by Sikh extremists. There were at the end of the 1980s *c* 500,000 Sikhs in Britain.

Socialism, is a form of society in which men and women are not divided into opposing economic classes but live together under conditions of approximate social and economic equality, using in common the means that lie to their hands of promoting social welfare. The brotherhood of man inspires the aims of socialism in foreign, colonial, social, and economic policies alike. The word "socialism" first came into general use in England about 1834 in connection with Robert Owen's "village of co-operation" at New Lanark. About the middle of the 19th cent., Charles Kingsley and others established a form of Christian socialism, and William Morris, John Burns, and others founded a Socialist League in 1886. With the development of trade unions the socialist movement took a more practical trend. Fabianism (q.v.) associated in its early days with the names of Beatrice and Sidney Webb and George Bernard Shaw, aims at the gradual reorganisation of society by creating intelligent public opinion by education and legislation. The British Labour Party believes in peaceful and constitutional change to socialism by democratic methods based upon popular consent. The Labour Government of 1945–51 initiated a major period of social reform and public ownership. Though beset by economic difficulties, the 1964–70 Labour Government continued a policy of radical reform. The minority Labour Government (of February–October 1974) and the subsequent administration continued this process, particularly in the area of state intervention in industry. The election defeats of 1979, 1983 and 1987 have inevitably led to a questioning of the future direction the party should take particularly set against the background of the seeming inability of Labour to win seats outside its strongholds of Scotland, Wales and the North. See also Section C, Part I.

Southcottians, followers of Joanna Southcott, who died in 1814 shortly after announcing that (although over 50) she was about to give birth to a divine human being named Siloh. Miss Southcott certainly produced all the symptoms of pregnancy, and was even examined by the Royal physician who pronounced her unquestionably "with child." Although she even went "into labour," no child, divine or otherwise, appeared and she seems to have died of something rather close to a broken heart. Her interesting symptoms would today be classed as "hysterical pregnancy"—a not uncommon condition which may mimic real pregnancy in a remarkable way. Joanna's followers remained loyal to her memory, however, and a tiny sect still survives to this day. Shortly before her death, incidentally, she handed to followers a number of locked and sealed boxes which she indicated contained, among other things, the secret of the universe. These were only to be opened 100 years after her death and then in the presence of 12 bishops. In 1927 one of these boxes unexpectedly turned up and it was ceremoniously opened at the Caxton Hall before a public audience. The organisers had to make do with only one bishop as most of the country's senior clerics pronounced themselves to be too busy to attend. Perhaps it was just as well for Miss Southcott's marvellous box was found to contain only a few rare coins, a horse pistol, a woman's embroidered nightcap, and a slightly improper novel, The Surprises of Love. One of the most endearing qualities of Joanna Southcott must have been her sense of humour.

Spiritualism is a religion which requires to be distinguished from psychical research (q.v.) which is a scientific attempt carried on by both believers and non-believers to investigate psychic phenomena including those not necessarily connected with "spirits"—e.g., telepathy or clairvoyance and precognition. As a religion (although for that matter the whole of history is filled with attempts to get in touch with the "spirit world") Spiritualism begins with the American Andrew Jackson Davis who in 1847 published Nature's Divine Revelations, a book which is still widely read. In this Davis states that on the death of the physical body, the human spirit remains alive and moves on to one or another of a considerable range of worlds or "spheres" where it commences yet another stage of existence. Since the spirit has not died, but exists with full (and possibly even expanded) consciousness, there should be no reason, Davis argues, why it should not make its presence known to the beings it has temporarily left behind on earth. In 1847, the year of the publication of Davis's book, two young girls, Margaret and Kate Fox, living in a farmhouse at Hydesville, New York, began apparently to act as unwitting mediums for attempts at such between-worlds communication. The girls

were the focus for strange rappings and bangs which it was alleged defied normal explanation and which spelt out, in the form of a simple alphabetical code, messages from the spirits of "the dead." The Fox sisters were later to confess that they had produced the raps by trickery, but by that time the fashion had spread across the world and before long "mediums" in all lands were issuing spirit communications (often in much more spectacular form). In the late 19th cent. Spiritualism went into a phase of great expansion and for various reasons attracted the attention of many scientists. Among these were Sir William Crookes, Sir Oliver Lodge, Professor Charles Richet, Alfred Russell Wallace, to say nothing of the brilliant and shrewd creator of Sherlock Holmes, Sir Arthur Conan Doyle. Today many people find it astonishing that people of such brilliance should find the phenomena of the seance room of more than passing interest, but the commitment of the Victorian scientists is understandable if we realise that Spiritualists, after all, claim to do no more than demonstrate as fact what all Christians are called on to believe—that the human personality survives bodily death. Furthermore, at the time of the late 19th cent. peak of Spiritualism, much less was known about human psychology and about the great limitations of sensory perception in typical seance conditions, when lights are dimmed or extinguished and an emotionally charged atmosphere generated. Today the most striking phenomena of the seance room—the alleged materialisation of spirit people and the production of such half-spiritual, half-physical substances as ectoplasm—are rarely if ever produced at Spiritualist meetings. Some say that the most probable explanation for this is that too many fraudulent mediums have been caught out and publicly exposed for the profession to be worth the risks. The movement today, which still has a large and often articulate following, now concentrates on the less controversial areas of "mental mediumship," clairvoyance and the like, or on the very widespread practice of "spirit healing." Where people are not deliberately deluded by bogus mediums acting for monetary reward (a practice which largely died out with the "death" of ectoplasm) Spiritualism probably has an important role to play in the life of many people whose happiness has been removed by the death of a much loved relative or spouse. It does not deserve the violent attacks that are often made on it by orthodox clergy who allege that Spiritualists are communicating not with the souls of the departed but with the devil or his emissaries. See also **Greater World Spiritualists.**

State and Man. Most of the early civilisations such as those of Egypt and Babylonia were theocratic, that is to say, they were arranged in a hierarchy with, at the peak, a king who was also an incarnation of the god. Needless to say, in such circumstances there was no room for philosophising about the nature of the state and the relationship which ought to exist between state and citizens. As usual, we have to turn to ancient Greece for the beginnings of thought about this problem. We do so as briefly as possible since in general it is only the later philosophers whose work has much contemporary interest and, in any case, most people today realise that the political philosophy of a particular time is bound to reflect the actual conditions prevailing then and as such is of mainly theoretical interest today.

The Greek Approach. The early pre-Socratic philosophers Democritus and the Pythagorean school for example, held that the individual should subordinate himself to the whole; they had no doubt that the citizen's first duty was to the state. The Greeks until the time of Plato were not really thinking in terms of individual rights, nor had they given much thought to what form the state should take—they simply accepted it. The first great attempt to describe the ideal state is to be found in Plato's The Republic which is referred to elsewhere (see **Education**). His pupil Aristotle did not try to form a utopia but made many comments on the nature of government. Thus, while agreeing that the state was more important than any individual person, he distinguished between good and bad states, and pointed out that to the extent that the state does not enable its citizens to lead virtuous and useful lives it is evil. A good constitution must recognise the inequalities between human beings and confer on them rights according to their abilities: among these inequalities are those of personal ability, property, birth, and status, as freeman or slave. The best forms of rule were monarchy, aristocracy, and democracy; the worst forms—tyranny, oligarchy (or rule of a powerful few), and ochlocracy (or mob-rule). The later Greek thinkers of Hellenistic times held two opposed points of view. The Epicureans (*q.v.*) taught that all social life is based upon self-interest and we become members of a group for our own convenience; therefore there are no absolute rights and laws—what is good is what members decide at that time to be good, and when they change their minds the law must change too. Injustice is not an evil in any god-given sense; we behave justly simply because if injustice became the general rule, we ourselves should suffer. The Stoics (*q.v.*), on the other hand, held that the state must dominate the individual completely and everyone must carry out, first and foremost, his social duties and be willing to sacrifice everything for it; but the state of the Stoics was no narrowly national one, but one that strove to become a universal brotherhood.

The Christian Approach. The orthodox Christian view is expressed in St. Augustine's book *The City of God.* Here it is held that the church, as the worldly incarnation of the City of God, is to be supreme over the state, and the head of the church is to be supreme over secular rulers. In addition it must be recognised that, whilst the secular ruler can make mistakes, the church does not, since it is the representative of God's kingdom on earth.

The Secular State. During the Renaissance (*q.v.*) people began to think for themselves and the results of their cogitations were not always pleasant; for it was during this time that many rulers, petty and otherwise, were seeking absolute authority. Two notable thinkers at this stage were Niccolo Machiavelli (1469–1527) in Italy and Thomas Hobbes (1588–1679) in England, where, of course, the Renaissance arrived later in history. Both supported absolute monarchy against the former domination of the church. The name of Machiavelli has become a by-word for any behaviour that is cunning and unscrupulous, but he was not really as bad as he is usually painted. It is, indeed, true that in his book *The Prince* he showed in the greatest detail the methods by which a ruler could gain absolute control and destroy civic freedom, but this despotism was intended as merely a necessary intermediate stage towards his real idea which was a free, united Italian nation wholly independent of the church. Hobbes was a materialist whose thesis was that man is naturally a ferocious animal whose basic impulse is war and pillage and the destruction of whatever stands in his way to gain his desires. But if he allowed himself to behave in this way his life would be "nasty, brutish, and short" so he creates a society in which he voluntarily gives up many of his rights and hands them over to a powerful ruler in his own interest. But having done this he must obey; even when the ruler is unjust, as he has no right to complain because anything is better than a return to his natural state. The religion of the king must be the religion of the people and the only things no ruler has the right to do is to cause a man to commit suicide or murder or to make him confess to a crime.

Views of Locke: Live and Let Live. John Locke (1632–1704) disagreed with these views. Man is naturally peaceful and co-operative and therefore social life comes readily to him. He sets up an authority in order to preserve the group and that is why laws are made; but the function of the state is strictly limited to maintaining the public good and beyond this men are to be left free. Therefore absolute power and the doctrine of the Divine Right of Kings were wrong because power ultimately rests with the people who have the right to make and

break governments. It is also wrong that those who make the laws should be able to execute them. This is the important British doctrine of the separation of powers between the legislature and the executive which, in Britain and America, is regarded as one of the bases of democracy.

Rousseau's Social Doctrine. The only other views we need consider here are those of Jean-Jacques Rousseau (1712–78) and Herbert Spencer (1820–1903), since the views of the two important intervening figures, Hegel and Karl Marx, are dealt with elsewhere (*see* **Dialectical Materialism**) and after Spencer we come to a stage where political philosophy begins to merge with sociology and the social sciences. Rousseau is a puzzling figure. On the one hand he has been hailed as the prophet of freedom and on the other as the father of modern totalitarianism. His book *Social Contract* (1762) begins with the words: "Man is born free, and everywhere he is in chains." He says that he is in favour, not merely of democracy, but of direct democracy in which everyone has to give his assent to all measures as in the Greek city-states and in Geneva, of which city he was a citizen. (This method is still in force in respect of some measures in the Swiss cantons.) Natural society is based on a "social contract" or mutual agreement and Rousseau speaks of a "return to nature" which would ensure the sovereignty of the people at all times. Thus far, he seems to agree with Locke but soon we find that he is more akin to Hobbes, since (as we are learning in our own day) nothing is more tyrannical than the absolute rule of all the people. (Public opinion is more Hitlerian than Hitler.) As it turns out, then, the "social contract" consists in "the total alienation of each associate, together with all his rights, to the whole community" and "each of us puts his person and all his power in common under the supreme direction of the general will." Rousseau admired direct democracy in the small city-state, but if his doctrine is applied to large states, then the "general will" becomes absolute. It is in this sense that he is regarded as the forerunner of totalitarianism. Herbert Spencer is quoted only as an example of the inappropriate application of a biological theory to social issues. Influenced by Darwin's thesis of natural selection, he saw in society a struggle in which the fittest survived and the less fit perished. Each individual had the right to preserve himself, but in the case of human beings this depended upon group life in which, to some extent, each individual is limited by the rights of others. But this should not go too far, and he condemned the socialism of J. S. Mill which (*a*) would give over-much protection to the unfit, and (*b*) would give the state powers which it has no right to since the best government is the least government. In accordance with Darwinism free competition was essential.

Stoics, the followers of Zeno, a Greek philosopher in the 4th cent. B.C., who received their name from the fact that they were taught in the Stoa Poikile or Painted Porch of Athens. They believed that since the world is the creation of divine wisdom and is governed by divine law, it is man's duty to accept his fate. Zeno conceived virtue to be the highest good and condemned the passions. (*See* **God and Man, State and Man, Determinism and Free-will** for a more detailed account of their beliefs.)

Subud, a way of worship and living founded by the Javanese mystic Pak Subuh (d. 1987), (known as Bapak), which established its headquarters in England in 1957, and made newspaper headlines because of the presumed miracle cure of the actress Eva Bartok. The basis of Subud (which is a contraction of three Sanskrit words, Susila Budhi Dharma, meaning "right living in obedience to the will of God") is a spiritual exercise, the latihan, in which the individual comes into contact with the Power of God, and which can bring about a purification which will enable the person to realise his or her real self. During the latihan people make an endless variety of spontaneous movements and utter words or chants, comparable perhaps to those of the Christians at the first Pentecost, but at times are completely quiet. Subud has no dogma, and is open to people of any colour, creed or race, and members are encouraged to continue with their own religion. Its ultimate worldly aim is charitable works. Bapak came eventually to stress the importance of business enterprises, both to make Subud secure and to fund its social work. When this happened some members left Subud, feeling that it had become too worldly; others left when some of the enterprises failed. Subud has however spread to about 70 countries, and the number of members remains fairly constant. The most successful enterprise was the conversion of a large country house near Windsor, Anugraha, to serve both as a Conference Centre for business and industrial firms and an International Subud Centre. Subud is of particular interest because it represents an incursion of an Eastern influence, and suggests again that there is a growing dissatisfaction in many quarters with orthodox religion and its contribution to the philosophy of the modern world.

Sunnites, the orthodox sect of Islam as contrasted with the Shiites or Shia (q.v.).

Swedenborgianism. The Church of the New Jerusalem, based on the writings of Emanuel Swedenborg (1688–1772), was founded by his followers eleven years after his death. The New Church is regarded by its members not as a sect but as a new dispensation bearing the same relationship to Christianity as Christianity does to Judaism.

Synchronicity, an attempt by the psychologist, Carl Gustav Jung, to explain the apparently significant relationship between certain events in the physical universe which seem to have no obvious "causal" link. This rather involved concept is easily understood if one realises that almost all scientific and philosophical beliefs are based on the notion that the continuous process of change which is taking place in ourselves and in the universe around us is dependent upon a principle known as causality. We can express this another way by saying that an object moves because it has been pushed or pulled by another. We see because light strikes the retina and signals pass up the nervous system to the brain. A stone falls to the ground because the earth's gravity is pulling it towards its centre, etc., etc. For all practical purposes every event can be looked upon as being "caused" by some other prior event and this is obviously one of the most important principles of the operation of the universe. Jung, however, felt that there is a sufficiently large body of evidence to suggest that events may be linked in a significant (i.e., non-chance) way without there being any true causal relationship between them. The classic example he held to be the supposed predictive power of astrology by which there appears to be a relationship between the stellar configurations and the personality and life-pattern of individuals on earth. Jung was scientist enough to realise that there could be no causal connection between the aspect of the stars and the lives of people billions of miles from them, yet felt the evidence for astrology was strong enough to demand an alternative non-causal explanation. The trouble with synchronicity, which has not made much impact on the world of physics or of psychology, is that it is not really an explanation at all but merely a convenient word to describe some puzzling correspondences. The real question, of course, is whether there really are events occurring which are significantly but not *causally* linked, and most scientists today would hold that there were probably not. Still it was typical of the bold and imaginative mind of Jung to tackle head-on one of the principal mysteries of existence and come up with a hypothesis to attempt to meet it.

Syndicalism, a form of socialist doctrine which aims at the ownership and control of all industries by the workers, contrasted with the more conventional type of socialism which advocates ownership and control by the state. Since syndicalists have preferred to improve the conditions of the workers by direct action, e.g., strikes and working to rule, rather than through the usual parliamentary procedures, they have been closely related to anarchists (q.v.) and are sometimes described as anarcho-syndicalists. Under syndicalism there would be no state; for the state would be replaced by a federation

of units based on functional economic organisation rather than on geographical representation. The movement had bodies in the United Kingdom, where guild socialism (q.v.) was strongly influenced by its doctrines, in France, Germany, Italy, Spain, Argentina, and Mexico, but these gradually declined after the first world war losing many members to the communists. Fascism (q.v.) was also strongly influenced by the revolutionary syndicalism of Georges Sorel.

T

Taoism, a religion which, although in a degenerate state, is still one of the great Eastern creeds. Its alleged founder, Lao-tze, is said to have been born in Honan about 604 B.C.; he is also said to be the author of the bible of Taoism, the *Tao-te-ching,* or in English *The Way of Life,* and to have disapproved of Confucius. This, if true, would hardly be surprising; for Taoism is eminently a mystical religion recommending doing nothing and resisting nothing, whereas **Confucianism** (q.v.) is eminently a practical code of living and its founder insisted on intervening in everything to do with social life. But the truth as revealed by modern scholarship is rather different. We are told that the poems of the *Tao-te-ching* are anonymous and probably originated among recluses in lonely valleys long before the time of Confucius; they were collected and given form at some time late in the 3rd cent. B.C. and their authorship attributed to Lao-tze. It is entirely possible that no such peson ever existed (unlike Confucius, who certainly did), but if there were such a man he appears to have used a pseudonym since "Lao" is not a surname but an adjective meaning "old" and it was customary to attribute important works to old men on account of their supposed wisdom. Lao-tze simply means "the old philosopher", and although the *Tao-te-ching* is one of the most remarkable and instructive books ever written it is as anonymous as the Border Ballads.

It is apparent that the religion learned both from the ancient Chinese mystics and from Brahmanism: *Tao,* the Way, is impalpable, invisible, and incapable of being expressed in words. But it can be attained by virtue, by compassion, humility, and non-violence. Out of weakness comes true strength whereas violence is not only wrong but defeats its own ends. There is no personal God and such gods as men imagine are mere emanations of *Tao* which gives life to all things. *Tao* is Being. Works are worthless and internal renunciation is far better than anything that follows from the use of force because passive resistance convinces the other from within that he is in error, whereas violence only compels the external appearance of conviction whilst inwardly the individual is as before. "It is wealth to be content; it is wilful to force one's way on others."

Later Lao-tze became a divinity and indeed one of a Trinity each worshipped in the form of idols (which the founder had hated). Soon there was worship of the forces of nature: the stars, the tides, the sun and moon, and a thousand other deities among whom Confucius was one. The purest mysticism and wisdom had been utterly corrupted by contact with the world.

Telepathy and Clairvoyance. Telepathy is the alleged communication between one mind and another other than through the ordinary sense channels. Clairvoyance is the supposed faculty of "seeing" objects or events which, by reason of space and time or other causes, are not discernible through the ordinary sense of vision. Such claims have been made from time immemorial but it was not until this century that the phenomena were investigated scientifically. The first studies were undertaken by the Society for Psychical Research, which was founded in 1882 with Professor Henry Sidgwick as its first president. Since then it has carried out a scholarly programme of research without —in accordance with its constitution—coming to any corporate conclusions. In America the centre of this research was the Parapsychology Laboratory at Duke University (*see* **Para-**

psychology) where at one time it was claimed clear scientific evidence for extra-sensory perception (ESP) had been obtained. These claims have been treated with great reservation by the majority of scientists but despite the belief that the study of ESP was going into eclipse, there remains a small but measurable residue of interest in scientific research in this area. It would be odd if some scientists were not interested in ESP because of the enormous weight of anecdotal evidence which has built up over centuries to support it. The weakness of the scientific as opposed to the casual evidence is however exemplified by the failure of ESP researchers to produce a reliable "repeatable" experiment.

Theism. See **God and Man.**

Theosophy (Sanskrit *Brahma Vidya* = divine wisdom), a system of thought that draws on the mystical teachings of those who assert the spiritual nature of the universe, and the divine nature of man. It insists that man is capable of intuitive insight into the nature of God. The way to wisdom, or self-knowledge, is through the practice of **Yoga** (*q.v.*). Theosophy has close connections with Indian thought through Vedic, Buddhist, and Brahmanist literature. The modern Theosophical Society was founded by Mme H. P. Blavatsky and others in 1875, and popularised by Mrs. Annie Besant.

Tractarianism, a Catholic revival movement, also known as the **Oxford Movement** (not to be confused with the so-called Oxford Group), which had its beginnings at Oxford in 1833. The leaders included the Oxford high churchmen E. B. Pusey, J. Keble and J. H. Newman. Through the *Tracts for the Times* (1833–41), a series of pamphlets which were sent to every parsonage in England, they sought to expose the dangers which they considered to be threatening the church from secular authority. The immediate cause of the movement was the Reform Act (1832) which meant that the state was no longer in the safe keeping of Tories and Churchmen but that power was falling into the hands of Liberals and Dissenters. They advocated a higher degree of ceremonial in worship nearer the Roman communion. In *Tract 90* (the last) Newman showed how the Thirty-nine Articles themselves, which were regarded as the bulwark of Protestantism, could be made to square with Roman doctrine. It was obvious which direction the movement was taking and the romanizing tendency was widely resented. In 1845 Newman went over to Rome. Pusey and Keble persisted in their efforts to secure recognition of Catholic liturgy and doctrine in the Anglican Church. Catholicism of the Anglican type (*i.e.*, Catholic in ritual, ceremony, and everything save submission to the Pope) is termed Anglo-Catholicism (*q.v.*).

Transcendental Meditation, popularised in the West by the Maharishi Mahesh Yogi, who achieved sensational worldwide publicity by his "conversion" of the Beatles a few years ago. This is a simple meditational system which it is claimed is an aid to relaxation and the reduction of psychological and physical stress. It is a technique which can be taught in a relatively short, concentrated period of time, provided that someone trained by the Maharishi is the teacher. The pupil or would-be meditator is given a mantra—a meaningless word which acts as a focal point for the imagination—letting his thoughts flow freely while sitting in a comfortable position. Extraordinary claims are made on behalf of the system. As with most cults, religious and occult systems, there is an initial psychological benefit to anyone who becomes deeply involved. Nevertheless, apart from this simple "participation-effect", there is some evidence that the body's autonomic functions (heart rate, respiratory cycle, brain waves, etc.) can be modified by certain individuals including yogis. Whether it is ultimately beneficial to be able to modify these autonomic functions or not is another matter. The TM movement in Britain is based at Mentmore Towers in Buckinghamshire. See also **Feedback Cult.**

Transmigration of Souls. See **Immortality, Buddhism, Hinduism.**

Transubstantiation, the conversion in the Eucharist of the bread and wine into the body and blood of Christ—a doctrine of the Roman Catholic Church.

Trotskyism, a form of communism supporting the views of Leon Trotsky, the assumed name of Lev Bronstein (1879–1940) who, in 1924, was ousted from power by Stalin and later exiled and assassinated in Mexico. Trotsky held that excessive Russian nationalism was incompatible with genuine international communism and that Stalin was concentrating on the economic development of the Soviet Union to an extent which could only lead to a bureaucratic state with a purely nationalist outlook. After the Hungarian uprising in 1956, which was ruthlessly suppressed by the Soviet Armed Forces, a wave of resignations from Western Communist parties took place, many of the dissidents joining the Trotskyist movement.

U

Ufology, cultish interest in the study of strange and unexplained aerial phenomena (unidentified flying objects, hence UFOs). See **Flying Saucers.**

Underground, the name given to an increasingly well-organised group, mainly composed of young people, university students, etc., which propagates anti-establishment and often highly controversial views. Its history, and to some extent its aims, are obscure, but it is a force of increasing power in Western society and its evolution is worth watching with care. The 1960s were years of great metamorphosis in Europe and America with rapid changes taking place in our attitudes to war and peace, to sex and morals, to marriage and family, to church and state. For large sections of the population these changes have been too rapid and too radical by far, but for others they have been too slow. In particular, the liberalisation of the law on the so-called "soft drugs," notably marijuana, is advocated by a vocal and increasing minority of young people. The expression of their views has been finding outlet in magazines and newspapers, privately published and printed, which reach a wide circulation despite the disinclination of many newsagents to stock them. These publications, while frequently containing material of an obscene and, to many people, highly offensive nature, also contain articles, features, and poems by writers of repute, many of whom contribute regularly to more orthodox publications and yet are sympathetic to the "underground cause." The word underground here, incidentally, refers back to the "underground press" that published revolutionary material at great risk in Nazi-occupied territories during the last war. With the exception of the risqué magazine *Private Eye*, which is largely concerned with acid political satire, the first of the genuine underground newsheets was the *International Times* (IT) which was followed in due course by *Oz* and *Rolling Stone*. All three papers were strongly anarchistic in flavour, uneven in literary merit, openly in favour of legalising marijuana ("pot"), and generally quite scandalous to the middle-class and middle-aged. This is not the place to argue the pros and cons of the underground arguments, nor to decide whether our "permissive society" has gone too far or not yet far enough. The important message that the appearance of the whole underground movement implies is that young people, because of greater financial independence, wider opportunities for travel, better education, and easier access to communication channels, such as printing presses, radio transmitters, etc., are beginning to make their admittedly controversial views more widely publicised. Furthermore, this is a trend which will inevitably develop rather than diminish and in the absence of authoritarian repression, these forces will have an increasing impact on our lives. By the early 1970s however signs of the decline in the power of the underground were appearing. One of its leading publications *Oz* had folded and its "drop-out" arguments seemed to be appealing less and less to students and young people. The most likely reason for this is that the movement in its decade of vigorous life was successful in inducing a number of reforms ranging from the propagation of a more liberal attitude to what may be printed, spoken about or shown on stage and screen, and an acceptance by school and university authorities that students should have a greater voice in academic affairs. These reforms, whether welcome or not to the middle-aged and the middle-class, have nevertheless reached fruition in the "permissive" society which in turn appears to have taken much of the steam out of the underground itself. *See also* **Weathermen.**

Unitarianism has no special doctrines, although clearly, as the name indicates, belief is in the single personality of God, *i.e.*, anti-trinitarian. This general statement, however, can be interpreted with varying degrees of subtlety. Thus unitarian belief may range from a sort of Arianism which accepts that, although Christ was not of divine nature, divine powers had been delegated to him by the Father, to the simple belief that Christ was a man like anyone else, and his goodness was of the same nature as that of many other great and good men. Indeed, today many Unitarians deny belief in a personal God and interpret their religion in purely moral terms, putting their faith in the value of love and the brotherhood of man. The Toleration Act (1689) excluded Unitarians but from 1813 they were legally tolerated in England. Nevertheless attempts were made to turn them out of their chapels on the ground that the preachers did not hold the views of the original founders of the endowments. But this ended with the Dissenting Chapels Act of 1845. In America no such difficulties existed, and in the Boston of the 19th cent. many of the great literary figures were openly unitarian in both belief and name: *e.g.*, Emerson, Longfellow, Lowell, and Oliver Wendell Holmes.

Utilitarianism, a school of moral philosophy of which the main proponents were J. S. Mill (1806–73) and Jeremy Bentham (1748–1832). Bentham based his ethical theory upon the utilitarian principle that the greatest happiness of the greatest number is the criterion of morality. What is good is pleasure or happiness; what is bad is pain. If we act on this basis of self-interest (pursuing what we believe to be our own happiness), then what we do will automatically be for the general good. The serious failing of this thesis is (1) that it makes no distinction between the quality of one pleasure and another, and (2) that Bentham failed to see that the law might not be framed and administered by men as benevolent as himself. J. S. Mill accepted Bentham's position in general but seeing its failings emphasised (1) that self-interest was an inadequate basis for utilitarianism and suggested that we should take as the real criterion of good the social consequences of the act; (2) that some pleasures rank higher than others and held that those of the intellect are superior to those of the senses. Not only is the social factor emphasised, but emphasis is also placed on the nature of the act.

Utopias. The name "utopia" is taken from a Greek word meaning "nowhere" and was first used in 1516 by Sir Thomas More (1478–1535) as the title of his book referring to a mythical island in the south Pacific where he sited his ideal society. Since then it has been used of any ideal or fanciful society, and here a few will be mentioned. (The reader may recall that Samuel Butler's 19th cent. novel, describing an imaginary society in New Zealand where criminals were treated and the sick punished, was entitled *Erewhon* which is the word "nowhere" in reverse.) It should be noted that not all utopias were entirely fanciful—*e.g.*, Robert Owen's and François Fourier's beliefs, although found to be impractical, were, in fact, tried out.

Sir Thomas More. More wrote at a time when the rise of the wool-growing trade had resulted in farming land being turned over to pasture and there was a great wave of unemployment and a rise in crime among the dispossessed. More began to think in terms of the mediaeval ideal of small co-operative communities in which class interests and personal gain played

a decreasing part, a society which would have the welfare of the people at heart both from the physical and intellectual points of view. His utopia was one in which there was no private property, because the desire for acquisition and private possessions lay at the root of human misery. There was, therefore, only common ownership of land and resources. Each class of worker was equipped to carry out its proper function in the economic scheme and each was fairly rewarded for its share in production so that there was neither wealth nor poverty to inspire conflict. Nobody was allowed to idle, until the time came for him to retire when he became free to enjoy whatever cultural pleasures he wished, but since the system was devoid of the waste associated with competition, the working day would be only six hours. There was to be compulsory schooling and free medical care for everybody, full religious toleration, complete equality of the sexes, and a modern system of dealing with crime which was free from vindictiveness and cruelty. Government was to be simple and direct by democratically-elected officials whose powers would be strictly limited and the public expenditure kept under close scrutiny. It will be seen that More was far in advance of his age, and to most democratically-minded people in advance of an earlier utopia, Plato's *Republic*, which is described under the heading of Education.

James Harrington. James Harrington published his book *The Commonwealth of Oceana* in 1656 and offered it to Oliver Cromwell for his consideration but without tangible results. Better than any other man of his time Harrington understood the nature of the economic revolution which was then taking place, and, like More, saw the private ownership of land as the main cause of conflict. He put forward the theory that the control of property, particularly in the shape of land, determines the character of the political structure of the state; if property were universally distributed among the people the sentiment for its protection would naturally result in a republican form of government. The Commonwealth of Oceana was a society "of laws and not of men"—*i.e.*, it was to be legally based and structured so as to be independent of the good or ill-will of any individuals controlling it. Thus there must be a written constitution, a two-house legislature, frequent elections with a secret ballot, and separation of powers between legislature and executive—all today familiar features of parliamentary democracy, but unique in his time.

Saint-Simon. The utopias of the late 18th and 19th cent. come, of course, into the period of the industrial revolution and of laissez-faire capitalism. Individual enterprise and complete freedom of competition formed the outlook of the ruling class. Naturally the utopias of this period tended to have a strongly socialist tinge since such theories are obviously produced by those who are not satisfied with existing conditions. Saint-Simon's *New Christianity* (1825) is one such, and by many, Claude Henri, Comte de Saint-Simon (1760–1825) is regarded as the founder of French socialism. His book urged a dedication of society to the principle of human brotherhood and a community which would be led by men of science motivated by wholly spiritual aims. Production property was to be nationalised (or "socialised" as he describes the process) and employed to serve the public good rather than private gain; the worker was to produce according to his capacity and to be rewarded on the basis of individual merit; the principle of inheritance was to be abolished since it denied the principle of reward for accomplishment on which the society was to be founded. Saint-Simon's proposals were not directed towards the poorer classes alone, but to the conscience and intellect of all. He was deeply impressed with the productive power of the new machines and his scheme was, first and foremost, intended as a method of directing that power to the betterment of humanity as a whole.

Fourier. François Marie Charles Fourier (1772–1837), although by conviction a philosophical anarchist who held that human beings are naturally good if allowed to follow their natural desires, was the originator of what, on the face of it, one would suppose to be the most regimented of the utopias. It consisted of a system of "phalanxes" or co-operative communities each composed of a group of workers and technicians assured of a minimum income and sharing the surplus on an equitable basis. Agriculture was to be the chief occupation of each phalanx and industrial employment planned and so carefully assigned that work would become pleasant and creative rather than burdensome. One of his ideas was that necessary work should receive the highest pay, useful work the next, and pleasant work the least pay. The land was to be scientifically cultivated and natural resources carefully conserved. Most of the members' property was to be privately owned, but the ownership of each phalanx was to be widely diffused among members by the sale of shares. Such "parasitic and unproductive" occupations as stockbroker, soldier, economist, middle-man and philosopher would be eliminated and the education of children carried out along vocational lines to train them for their future employment.

The strange thing was that Fourier's suggestions appealed to many in both Europe and the U.S.A. and such men (admittedly no economic or technical experts) as Emerson, Thoreau, James Russell Lowell, and Nathaniel Hawthorne strongly supported them. An American Fourier colony known as Brook Farm was established and carried on for eight years when it was dissolved after a serious fire had destroyed most of its property.

Robert Owen. Robert Owen (1771–1858), a wealthy textile manufacturer and philanthropist, established communities founded on a kind of utopian socialism in Lanarkshire, Hampshire, and in America. Of his New Lanark community an American observer wrote: "There is not, I apprehend, to be found in any part of the world, a manufacturing community in which so much order, good government, tranquillity, and rational happiness prevail." The workers in Lanark were given better housing and education for their children, and it was administered as a co-operative self-supporting community in Scotland. Later in life Owen returned to sponsoring legislation that would remove some of the worst evils of industrial life in those days: reduction of the working day to twelve hours, prohibition of labour for children under the age of ten, public schools for elementary education, and so on. But he lived to see few of his reforms adopted. He also promoted the creation of co-operative societies, the formation of trades unions, labour banks and exchanges, the workers' educational movement, and even an Anglo-American federation.

V

Vegetarianism, a way of life practised by those who abstain from meat. Strict vegetarians (Vegans) also excude all animal products (*e.g.* butter, eggs milk) from their diet.

Vitalism, the philosophical doctrine that the behaviour of the living organism is, at least in part, due to a vital principle which cannot possibly be explained wholly in terms of physics and chemistry. This belief was held by the rationalist thinker C. E. M. Joad (1891–1953) and is implicit in Henri Bergson's (1859–1941) theory of creative evolution. It was maintained by Bergson that evolution, like the work of an artist, is creative and therefore unpredictable; that a vague need exists beforehand within the animal or plant before the means of satisfying the need develops. Thus we might assume that sightless animals developed the need to become aware of objects before they were in physical contact with them and that this ultimately led to the origins of organs of sight. Earlier this century a form of vitalism described as "emergent evolution" was put forward. This theory maintains that when two or more simple entities come together there may arise a new property which none of them previously possessed. Today biologists would say that it is the *arrangement* of atoms that counts, different arrangements exhibiting different properties, and that biological organisation is an essentially dynamic affair.

W

Wahabis, members of an Arabian sect of Islam which originated in the teaching of Muhammad Ibn 'Abd-al-Wahab, born at the end of the 17th cent. He was deeply resentful of the Turkish rule which, in addition to its tyranny, had brought about innovations in the religion which Muhammad regarded as a perversion of its original form. He proceeded to reform Islam to its primitive conditions and impressed his beliefs on Mohammed Ibn Saud, a sheikh who spread them with the aid of his sword. Under the successors of Ibn Saud the power of the Wahabis spread over much of Arabia where it is dominant today in Saudi Arabia. Its particular characteristic is that it refuses to accept symbolic or mystical interpretations of the words of the Prophet and accepts quite literally the teaching of Islam. It is, in fact, a sort of Moslem fundamentalism. Although crushed by the Turks in 1811–15, the movement remains an important element in Mohammedanism.

Waldenses, a movement also known as "The Poor Men of Lyons," founded by Peter Waldo of that city about the same time, and in the same part of southern France, as the Albigenses (*q.v.*) with whom, however, they had nothing in common. Their main belief was a return to Apostolic simplicity, based on reading the Bible in their own language; their doctrines were somewhat similar to those of the Mennonites and the Quakers. However, they did not wish to separate themselves from the Church and were originally protected by several Popes until the Lateran Council of 1215 excluded them mainly for the crime of preaching without ecclesiastical permission. From this time they were subjected to persecution, yet maintained some contact with the Church until the Reformation when they chose to take the side of the Protestants. Situated mainly on the sides of the Alps, half in Piedmont and half in France, they were persecuted or not according to the contemporary political convenience of the Dukes of Savoy, and the major attempt to destroy them called forth Oliver Cromwell's intervention and the famous sonnet of Milton. In spite of torture, murder, deportation, and even the kidnapping of their children, to have them brought up in the Roman Catholic faith, the sect survived, and still exists, having been granted full equality of rights with his Roman Catholic subjects by Charles Edward of Piedmont in 1848.

Weathermen, a radical offshoot of the Students for a Democratic Society formed in 1969, making up the so-called "underground" in the United States of America. It derives its name from a line in Dylan's song "You don't need a weatherman to know which way the wind blows." Unlike most of the loosely-structured organisations involved in the growing anti-establishment front, the Weathermen appear to have direct rather than anarchistic political goals, taking a stand far to the left of traditional politics. Their avowed aim is the total overthrow of the current American political structure, with specific and carefully planned acts of violence as the tools of their trade and the civil police force as one of their prime targets. This has led to a series of bomb explosions, often cunningly planned, and brutal murders of police patrolmen which have deeply shocked the average American citizen. A particularly sinister and ominous feature, to most people's eyes, is the fact that the Weathermen appear to be largely drawn from the highly intelligent and well-educated strata, many of them with well-to-do and/or academic backgrounds. Members of this group make no secret of their contempt for the intellect and political attitudes of the American middle-class, and claim to demonstrate the impotence of Society by their ability to commit flagrant acts of violence with such ease and the equal ease with which they subsequently escape detection and arrest. The elusive nature of the organisation and its uncertain background have led to a number of fantastic speculations about its true origins. One of the oddest of these is the notion, widely held in America, that the Weathermen are in reality financed and backed by the country's extreme *right*—as a means of discrediting in the public eye the slow but steady move towards socialism that seemed to be developing there. The Weathermen appear to have ceased activity in the early 1970s, but bomb outrages in early 1975 were once more perpetrated in their name.

Witchcraft. There are various interpretations and definitions of witchcraft from that of Pennethorne Hughes who states that "witchcraft, as it emerges into European history and literature, represents the old paleolithic fertility cult, plus the magical idea, plus various parodies of contemporary religions" to that of the fanatical Father Montague Summers who says that Spiritualism and witchcraft are the same thing. A leading authority on witchcraft, however, the late Dr. Margaret Murray, distinguishes between Operative Witchcraft (which is really Magic (*q.v.*)) and Ritual Witchcraft which, she says, "embraces the religious beliefs and ritual of the people known in late mediaeval times as 'witches.'" That there were such people we know from history and we know, too, that many of them—the great majority of them women—were tortured or executed or both. Many innocent people perished, especially after the promulgation of the bull *Summis desiderantes* by Pope Innocent VIII in 1484. Himself "a man of scandalous life," according to a Catholic historian, he wrote to "his dear sons," the German professors of theology, Johann Sprenger and Heinrich Kraemer, "witches are hindering men from performing the sexual act and women from conceiving . . ." and delegated them as Inquisitors "of these heretical pravities." In 1494 they codified in the *Malleus Maleficarum* (Hammer of Witches) the ecclesiastical rules for detecting acts of witchcraft. Dr. Murray points out that there have ordinarily been two theories about witchcraft: (1) that there were such things as witches, that they possessed supernatural powers and that the evidence given at their trials was substantially correct; (2) that the witches were simply poor silly creatures who either deluded themselves into believing that they had certain powers or, more frequently, were tortured into admitting things that they did not do. She herself accepts a third theory: that there were such beings as witches, that they really did what they admitted to doing, but that they did not possess supernatural powers. They were in fact believers in the old religion of pre-Christian times and the Church took centuries to root them out. That there existed "covens" of witches who carried out peculiar rites Dr. Murray has no doubt whatever. The first to show that witchcraft was a superstition and that the majority of so-called witches were people suffering from mental illness was the physician Johann Weyer of Cleves (1515–88). His views were denounced by the Catholic Church. Few people realise how deeply the notion of witchcraft is implanted in our minds and how seriously its power is still taken. For example, the Witchcraft Act was not repealed in this country until the 1950s. Furthermore, as late as 1944, when the allied armies were invading Europe, the Spiritualist medium Mrs. Helen Duncan was charged with witchcraft and actually sent to prison—a prosecution which brought forth caustic comments from the then prime minister, Winston Churchill. *See also* **Demonism.**

Women's Liberation Movement, the name given to a loosely organised collection of women drawn from all ages and walks of life which appears to be emerging as a latter-day "supersuffragette" movement. Unlike the original suffragette movement, however, which advocated "Votes for Women," the current version seems to have less definite aims. The principal argument hinges on the fact that with the development of highly efficient methods of contraception (the "pill") women need no longer be "slaves" to their family commitments and the traditional dominant and decision-making role of the male in our society must go. At the same time there should be no more wage or job discrimination against women. The movement has been going from strength to strength in America and is acquiring definite power in local and state politics. In Europe it has made somewhat less dramatic inroads. To many spectators, the movement's bible is the witty if polemical book *The Female Eunuch* by the Australian author Germaine Greer. An equally amusing, if perhaps somewhat less serious counterblast *The Manipulated Man* by the German woman doctor, Esther Vilar, traitorously takes an anti-feminist line. A small victory for the feminist cause has been the slow advance of the unpronounceable abbreviation "Ms" as an acceptable alternative for Mrs or Miss. 1975 saw the passage, in the United Kingdom, of the "Equal Opportunities Act"—a development which would have delighted the suffragettes of seventy years ago.

World Congress of Faiths, an inter-religious movement which aims to break down barriers between faiths. The first step was taken by the world's parliament of religions held in Chicago in 1893; similar gatherings were held subsequently at intervals in Europe; but the actual organisation was formed in 1936 by Sir Francis Younghusband; and now an annual conference is held and educational activity carried on.

World Council of Churches, a union of Christian Churches from all over the world (including the Churches of the Protestant, Anglican, and Orthodox traditions, but excluding the Roman Catholic Church), engaged in extending Christian mission and unity throughout the world. This modern ecumenical movement stems from the great World Missionary Conference held at Edinburgh in 1910. The World Council was founded in 1948 and meets for consultation from time to time. In the light of the 1975 assembly in Nairobi, the Churches have monitored the suppression of human rights throughout the world. The Salvation Army resigned in 1981 in protest at the movement's involvement in African liberation. The next assembly (1991) will be held in Canberra.

Y

Yoga, a Hindu discipline which teaches a technique for freeing the mind from attachment to the senses, so that once freed the soul may become fused with the universal spirit (*atman* or Brahman), which is its natural goal. This is the sole function of the psychological and physical exercises which the Yogi undertakes, although few ever reach the final stage of *Samadhi* or union with Brahman which is said to take place in eight levels of attainment. These are: (1) *Yama*, which involves the extinction of desire and egotism and their replacement by charity and unselfishness; (2) *Niyama*, during which certain rules of conduct must be adopted, such as cleanliness, the pursuit of devotional studies, and the carrying out of rituals of purification; (3) *Asana*, or the attainment of correct posture and the reduction to a minimum of all bodily movement (the usual posture of the concentrating Yogi is the "lotus position" familiar from pictures); (4) *Pranayama*, the right control of the life-force or breath in which there are two stages at which the practitioner hopes to arrive, the first being complete absorption in the act of breathing which empties the mind of any other thought, the second being the ability almost to cease to breathe which allegedly enables him to achieve marvellous feats of endurance; (5) *Pratyahara* or abstraction which means the mind's complete withdrawal from the world of sense; (6) *Dharana* in which an attempt is made to think of one thing only which finally becomes a repetition of the sacred syllable OM; (7) *dhyana*, meditation, which finally leads to (8) *Samadhi* the trance state which is a sign of the complete unity of soul with reality.

Yoga is very old, and when the sage Patanjali (*c.* 300 B.C.) composed the book containing these instructions, the *Yoga Sutras*, he was probably collecting from many ancient traditions. Some of the claims made by Yogis seem, to the Western mind, frankly incredible; but in the West and especially in recent years Yoga methods have been used at the lower levels in order to gain improved self-control, better posture, and improved health. Whether it achieves these ends is another matter, but the genuine Yogi regards this as a perversion of the nature and purpose of the discipline.

Z

Zen Buddhism, a Buddhist sect which is believed to have arisen in 6th cent. China but has flourished chiefly in Japan; for some reason it has of recent years begun to attract attention in the West thanks to the voluminous writings of Dr. D. T. Suzuki and the less numerous but doubtless much-read books of Mr. Christmas Humphreys. But the fact that these writings exist does not explain their being read, nor why of all possible Eastern sects this particular one should be chosen in our times. What is Zen's attraction and why should anyone take the trouble to read about something (the word "something" is used for reasons that will become evident) that is not a religion, has no doctrine, knows no God and no after-life, no good and no evil, and possesses no scriptures but has to be taught by parables which seem to be purposely meaningless? One of the heroes of Zen is the fierce-looking Indian monk Boddhidharma (fl. *c.* 516–34) who brought Buddhism to China, of whom it is recounted that when the Emperor asked him how much merit he had acquired by supporting the new creed, the monk shouted at him: "None whatever!" The emperor then wished to know what was the sacred doctrine of the creed and again the monk shouted: "It is empty—there is nothing sacred!" Dr. Suzuki, having affirmed that there is no God in Zen, goes on to state that this does not mean that Zen denies the existence of God because "neither denial nor affirmation concerns Zen." The most concrete statement he is prepared to make is that the basic idea of Zen is to come in touch with the inner workings of our being, and to do this in the most direct way possible without resorting to anything external or superadded. Therefore anything that has the semblance of an external authority is rejected by Zen. Absolute faith is placed in a man's own inner being. Apparently the intention is that, so far from indulging in inward meditations or such practices as the Yogi uses, the student must learn to act spontaneously, without thinking, and without self-consciousness or hesitation. This is the main purpose of the *koan*, the logically insoluble riddle which the pupil must try to solve. One such is the question put by master to pupil: "A girl is walking down the street, is she the younger or the older sister?" The correct answer, it seems, is to say nothing but put on a mincing gait, to *become* the girl, thus showing that what matters is the experience of being and not its verbal description. Another *koan*: "What is the Buddha?" "Three pounds of flax" is attributed to T'ungshan in the 9th cent. and a later authority's comment is that "none can excel it as regards its irrationality which cuts off all passages to speculation." Zen, in effect, teaches the uselessness of trying to use words to discuss the Absolute.

Zen came to Japan in the 13th cent., more than five centuries after Confucianism or the orthodox forms of Buddhism, and immediately gained acceptance whilst becoming typically Japanese in the process. One of the reasons why it appealed must have been that its spontaneity and insistence on action without thought, its emphasis on the uselessness of mere words, and such categories as logical opposites, had an inevitable attraction for a people given to seriousness, formality, and logic to a degree which was almost stifling. Zen must have been to the Japanese what nonsense rhymes and nonsense books, like those of Edward Lear and Lewis Carroll, were to the English intellectuals. Lear's limericks, like some of the *koans*, end up with a line which, just at the time when one expects a point to be made, has no particular point at all, and *Alice in Wonderland* is the perfect example of a world, not without logic, but with a crazy logic of its own which has no relationship with that of everyday life. Therefore Zen began to impregnate every aspect of life in Japan, and one of the results of its emphasis on spontaneous action rather than reason was its acceptance by the Samurai, the ferocious warrior class, in such activities as swordsmanship, archery,

Japanese wrestling, and later Judo and the Kamikaze dive-bombers. But much of Japanese art, especially landscape gardening and flower-arrangement, was influenced similarly, and Zen is even used in Japanese psychiatry. The very strict life of the Zen monks is based largely on doing things, learning through experience; the periods of meditation in the Zendo hall are punctuated by sharp slaps on the face administered by the abbot to those who are unsatisfactory pupils. Dr. Suzuki denies that Zen is nihilistic, but it is probably its appearance of nihilism and its appeal to the irrational and spontaneous which attracts the Western world at a time when to many the world seems without meaning and life over-regimented. However, it has influenced such various aspects of Western life as philosophy (Heidegger), psychiatry (Erich Fromm and Hubert Benoit), writing (Aldous Huxley), and painting (Die Zen Gruppe in Germany).

Zionism, a belief in the need to establish an autonomous Jewish home in Palestine which, in its modern form, began with Theodor Herzl (1860–1904), a Hungarian journalist working in Vienna. Although Herzl was a more or less assimilated Jew, he was forced by the Dreyfus case and the pogroms in Eastern Europe to conclude that there was no real safety for the Jewish people until they had a state of their own. The Jews, of course, had always in a religious sense thought of Palestine as a spiritual homeland and prayed "next year in Jerusalem," but the religious had thought of this in a philosophical way as affirming old loyalties, not as recommending the formation of an actual state. Therefore Herzl was opposed both by many of the religious Jews and, at the other extreme, by those who felt themselves to be assimilated and in many cases without religious faith. Even after the Balfour Declaration of 1917, there was not a considerable flow of Jews to Palestine, which at that time was populated mainly by Arabs. But the persecutions of Hitler changed all this and, after bitter struggles, the Jewish state was proclaimed in 1948. Today Zionism is supported by the vast majority of the Jewish communities everywhere. In 1990, a major exodus of Jews from Russia to Israel (made possible by the new *glasnost* in Soviet society) seemed likely to mark a new phase in the history of Zionism.

Zoroastrianism, at one time one of the great world religions, competing in the 2nd cent. A.D. on almost equal terms from its Persian home with Hellenism and the Roman Imperial Government. Under the Achaemenidae (*c.* 550–330 B.C.) Zoroastrianism was the state religion of Persia. Alexander's conquest in 331 B.C. brought disruption but the religion flourished again under the Sassanian dynasty (A.D. *c.* 226–640). With the advance of the Mohammedan Arabs in the 7th cent. Zoroastrianism finally gave way to Islam. A number of devotees fled to India there to become the Parsees. In Persia itself a few scattered societies remain.

The name Zoroaster is the Greek rendering of Zarathustra, the prophet who came to purify the ancient religion of Persia. It is thought that he lived at the beginning of the 6th cent. B.C. He never claimed for himself divine powers but was given them by his followers. The basis of Zoroastrianism is the age-long war between good and evil, Ahura Mazda heading the good spirits and Ahriman the evil ones. Morality is very important since by doing right the worshipper is supporting Ahura Mazda against Ahriman, and the evil-doers will be punished in the last days when Ahura Mazda wins his inevitable victory.

The sacred book of this religion is the *Avesta.* If Zoroastrianism has little authority today, it had a very considerable influence in the past. Its doctrines penetrated into Judaism (*q.v.*) and, through Gnosticism, Christianity. The worship of Mithra by the Romans was an impure version of Zoroastrianism. Manichaeism (*q.v.*) was a Zoroastrian heresy and the Albigensianism of mediaeval times was the last relic of a belief which had impressed itself deeply in the minds of men.

GAZETTEER OF THE WORLD

An index and guide to the maps with up-to-date descriptive matter. Each year the Gazetteer is amended to include the latest available population figures.

GAZETTEER OF THE WORLD

Measurement of Geographical Phenomena.

(1) Physical Features.

In using the gazetteer the reader should note that it is impossible to make absolutely correct measurements of geographical phenomena. For example, measurement of height of land above sea-level depends, in the first instance, upon the definition of the elusive concept of sea-level itself. This is constantly changing and so an arbitrary value of *mean sea-level* is normally used, but the value adopted varies from country to country. As a result, height above sea-level has inbuilt inconsistencies and inaccuracies. Similarly, the length of a river will depend upon the scale of the survey from which measurements are made. Large-scale maps and aerial photographs can show in great detail the sinuous course of rivers, whereas a map on a smaller scale must reduce the amount of information shown and thereby the apparent length. We hope to include in a later edition the results of a yet unpublished work by a commission of the United Nations which is attempting to define in precise terms the area of the world's seas and oceans.

The gazetteer now records the heights of mountains, lengths of rivers, and land and sea areas in metric units. English equivalents will be found on p. 1 of the **Atlas**.

(2) Definition of Urban Area.

An even more difficult problem of measurement relates to the definition of the urban area of a town or city. It is possible to define the extent of urban areas in three major ways, by using (1) the administrative area, (2) the physically built-up area, and (3) the socio-geographic, metropolitan area. This latter concept is in many ways the most meaningful for it relates to the notion that a city exerts a strong influence over the population resident beyond its administrative or built-up boundary. For example, the city may provide employment opportunities or shopping and entertainment facilities for a population resident some distance away from it. In order to define "city" in these terms some means of measuring the degree of connection between it and its surrounding hinterland (the city-region) must be found and, needless to say, there is considerable disagreement among workers in this field as to what are the most suitable criteria to use. Different criteria produce different definitions and even

the most recent measurements are obsolete within a short space of time. However, the real significance of this less tangible concept of "city" may be illustrated by the fact that the reform of local government in England rests in part upon the concept of the city-region.

The population figures given in the gazetteer normally relate to the city's administrative area. In the case of some large cities two figures are given—(1) for the administrative city, and (2) for the more extensive metropolitan area which surrounds and includes the administrative city.

The census of the United Kingdom is now based on the reorganised local government areas. Up-to-date population figures perforce refer to these areas which are both fewer in number and larger in size than their predecessors. As a result much local detail is lost in the most recent (post-1971) figures.

Place Names.

Where there have been recent changes in place names, the old name is given in brackets and a cross reference directs the reader to the new name.

Chinese place names.

The romanisation of Chinese characters has long posed problems. The characters which represent sounds cannot easily be "translated" into letters. The first system adopted in Western countries was **Wade-Giles** but this is very European in its approach. In 1975 the Chinese government issued a directive to adopt an alternative system called **Pinyin** which is more Chinese in its approach. This system, which since 1977 has been more widely accepted, is the script used within the Gazetteer and its maps. Cross-references are made from the Wade-Giles to the now official Pinyin version of each place name.

Editor's Note to Readers.

As a result of the indeterminate and dynamic nature of geographical phenomena inconsistencies and inaccuracies are bound to occur in a gazetteer of this size. The editor welcomes comments and criticisms of the entries based upon local knowledge and will try to make the fullest possible use of information received from readers.

ABBREVIATIONS USED IN THE GAZETTEER

GEOGRAPHICAL NAMES

Ala. = Alabama
Ark. = Arkansas
ASSR = Autonomous Soviet Socialist Republic
Atl. Oc. = Atlantic Ocean
B.C. = British Columbia
Brit. = British
BEF = British Expeditionary Forces
Cal. = California
CERN = European Centre for Nuclear Research
Col. = Colorado
Conn. = Connecticut
ČSSR = Czechoslovak Socialist Republic
Del. = Delaware
Eng. = England
E.C. = European Economic Community
Fla. = Florida
Fr. = French
Ga. = Georgia
ICI = Imperial Chemical Industries
Ill. = Illinois
Ind. = Indiana
Kan. = Kansas
Ky. = Kentucky
La. = Louisiana

Land = prov. (W. Germany)
Mass. = Massachusetts
Md. = Maryland
Me. = Maine
Mich. = Michigan
Minn. = Minnesota
Miss. = Mississippi
Mo. = Missouri
Mont. = Montana
NATO = North Atlantic Treaty Organisation
N.C. = North Carolina
N.D. = North Dakota
Neth. = Netherlands
N.H. = New Hampshire
N.J. = New Jersey
N.M. = New Mexico
N.S.W. = New South Wales
N.T. = Northern Territory (Australia)
N.Y. = New York
N.Z. = New Zealand
Oblast = aut. prov. (USSR)
O.F.S. = Orange Free State
Okla. = Oklahoma
Okrug = aut. dist. (RSFSR)
OPEC = Organization of Petroleum Exporting Countries

Ore. = Oregon
Pac. Oc. = Pacific Ocean
Penns. = Pennsylvania
R.I. = Rhode Island
R.o.I. = Republic of Ireland
RSFSR = Russian Soviet Federal Socialist Republic
S.C. = South Carolina
Scot. = Scotland
SHAPE = Supreme Headquarters, Allied Powers, Europe
S.D. = South Dakota
SSR = Soviet Socialist Republic
Tenn. = Tennessee
U.K. = United Kingdom
U.N. = United Nations
USA = United States of America
USSR = Union of Soviet Socialist Republics
Va. = Virginia
Vt. = Vermont
Wash. = Washington
W.I. = West Indies
Wis. = Wisconsin
Wyo. = Wyoming

OTHER ABBREVIATIONS

a. = area
admin. = administrative
agr. = agriculture
alt. = altitude
anc. = ancient
arch. = archaeological
a.s.l. = above sea-level
ass. = associated
aut. rep. = autonomous republic
bdy. = boundary
bldg. = building
bor. = borough
bdr. = border
C. = cape
c. = city; circa, *c.* = about
can. = canton
cap. = capital
cas. = castle
cath. = cathedral
ch. = chief
cm = centimetres
co. = county
C.B. = county borough
col. = colony
colly. = colliery
comm. = commercial
conurb. = conurbation
cst. = coast
ctr. = centre
cty. = country
dep. = department
dist. = district
div. = division
E. = east or easterly
elec. = electrical
engin. = engineering
esp. = especially
est. = estimate
exp. = exports
F. = firth

fed. = federal
fish. pt. = fishing port
fortfd. = fortified
G. = Gulf
gen. = general
G.N.P. = gross national product
gr. = great, group
ha = hectares
gtr. = greater
hgst. = highest
I. = island
impt. = important
inc. = including
indep. = independent
inds. = industries
industl. = industrial
Is. = Islands
km = kilometres
km² = square kilometres
L. = lake
l. = length
lge. = large
l. gov. dist. = local government district
lgst. = largest
lt. = light
m = metres
machin. = machinery
met. a. = metropolitan area
met. co. = metropolitan county
mftg. = manufacturing
mkg. = making
mkt. = market
mm = millimetres
mnfs. = manufactures
mng. = mining
mtn. = mountain
mun. = municipality
N. = north or northerly

nat. = national
non-met. co = non-metropolitan county
nr. = near
p. = population
par. = parish
penin. = peninsula
pref. = prefecture
prin. = principal
prod. = products
prot. = protectorate
prov. = province
pt. = port
R. = river
rep. = republic
residtl. = residential
rly. = railway
S. = south or southerly
shipbldg. = shipbuilding
sm. = small
spt. = seaport
st. = state
sta. = station
sub. = suburb
t. = town
Tan-Zam = Tanzania-Zambia rly.
terr. = territory
tr. = trade
trib. = tributary
Turk-Sib = Turkestan-Siberia rly.
univ. = university
U.D. = urban district
v. = village
W. = west or westerly
wat. pl. = watering place
wks. = works
wkshps. = workshops

A

Aachen (**Aix-la-Chapelle**), t., N. Rhine-Westphalia, **W. Germany**; anc. spa t. in coal-field dist.; industl., route ctr.; contains tomb of Charlemagne; p. (est. 1986) 243,700.

Aalen, t., Baden-Württemberg, **W. Germany**; on R. Kocher; iron, textiles, lens mkg.; p. (est. 1986) 62,800.

Aalst (**Alost**), t., E. Flanders, **Belgium**, 24 km N.W. Brussels; industl., comm. ctr. at rly. junc.; agr. tr.; p. (1982) 78,707.

Aarau, t., cap. of Aargau can., **Switzerland**; precision tools and instruments, shoes, textiles; hydroelectric power; p. (1980) 15,788.

Aare, R., **Switzerland**; flows through Brienz and Thun Ls., thence into Rhine; Aare gorges above Meiringen; lgst R. wholly in Switzerland, 290 km long.

Aargau, can., N. **Switzerland**; occupies lower Aare R. valley; agr. in valleys, wooded uplands; cap. Aarau; a. 1,404 km²; p. (est. 1986) 473,000.

Aba, t., **Nigeria**; N.E. of Pt. Harcourt; mkt., palm oil processing; p. (est. 1983) 216,000.

Abaco, Gt., I., Bahamas, **W.I.**; sheltered harbours, yachting; exp. crayfish; p. (1980) 7,271.

Ābādān, c., **Iran**; spt., major oil terminal and refining ctr. on A.I. in Persian G.; permanently damaged by Iraqi air attack; now closed (1980); p. (est. 1985) 294,000.

Abakan, t., **RSFSR**, on R. A.; recent rly.; sawmilling, food inds.; p. (est. 1985) 147,000.

Abashiri, t., N. cst. Hokkaido, **Japan**; impt. fishing base; p. (1985) 44,285.

Abbeville, t., N. **France**; on R. Somme; connected with Paris and England by canals; sugarmilling, carpets, biscuits, beer; p. (1982) 25,988.

Abbots-Langley, v., Herts., **Eng.**; birthplace of Nicholas Breakspeare (Pope Adrian IV).

Abenrå, spt., S.E. Jutland, **Denmark**; at head of A. fjord and admin. ctr. of S. Jutland prov.; vehicles, clothing, food processing; p. (1981) 15,341.

Abeokuta, t., **Nigeria**; cap. Ogun st.; N. of Lagos; palm oil, textiles; p. (est. 1983) 309,000.

Aberaeron, t., Ceredigion, Dyfed, S. **Wales**; p. (1981) 1,446.

Abercarn, t., Islwyn, Gwent, **Wales**; tinplate, knitting pins; former colliery t.; p. (1981) 17,604.

Aberconwy, l. gov. dist., Gwynedd, **Wales**; lower Conwy valley inc. ts. Conwy, Betws-y-Coed, Llanwrst and Llandudno; p. (est. 1988) 54,100.

Aberdare, t., Cynon Valley, Mid Glamorgan, **Wales**; on R. Cynon: wire cables; former coalmng; p. (1981) 36,621.

Aberdare Range, mtns., Nat. Park, **Kenya**; rise to 4,000 m; form a section of E. rim of Gr. Rift Valley; equable climate attractive to white settlers; camphor forests, fruit and pastoral agr. at higher alts.

Aberdeen, royal burgh, l. gov. dist., Grampian Reg., **Scot.**; between mouths of Rs. Dee and Don; impt. fishing pt. under competition from claims of rapidly growing N. Sea oil ind.; "granite-city"—much granite used in central bldgs.; univ., cath.; p. (est. 1986) 216,273.

Aberdeen, t., S.D., **USA**; ctr. for wheat and livestock region; p. (1980) 25,956.

Aberdeenshire, former co., E. **Scot.** See **Grampian Region**.

Aberfeldy, burgh, Perth and Kinross, **Scot.**; in Strath Tay, 6 km below Loch Tay; mkt.; salmon and trout fishing resort; p. (1981) 1,627.

Abergavenny, t., Gwent, **Wales**; on R. Usk; scene of massacre of Welsh chiefs; light engin., concrete prods.; cattle mkt.; cas.; p. (1981) 9,390.

Aberlour, Charlestown of, burgh, Moray, **Scot.**; on R. Spey, 19 km S. of Elgin; p. (1981) 879.

Abernethy, burgh, Perth and Kinross, **Scot.**; on R. Tay, once cap. of Pictish Kings; p. (1981) 881.

Abersoch, t., Gwynedd, **Wales**; yachting resort.

Abertillery, t., Blaenau Gwent, Gwent, **Wales**; collieries, tinplate; p. (1981) 19,319.

Aberystwyth, t., Ceredigion, Dyfed, **Wales**; on Cardigan Bay at mouth of R. Ystwyth, resort; cas., univ. college; Nat. Library of Wales; p. (1981) 8,666.

Abidjan, c., former cap. of Côte d'Ivoire; pt.; exp. palm oil, cocoa, copra, hardwood, rubber; oil refining at Vridi nearby; p. (est. 1982) 1,800,000 (met. a.). See **Yamoussoukro**.

Abilene, t., Texas, **USA**; univ.; agr. processing, oil refining; p. (1985) 107,600 (c.), 123,100 (met. a.).

Abilene, t., on Smoky Hill R., Kansas. **USA**; childhood home of Eisenhower; p. (1980) 6,572.

Abingdon, Vale of White Horse, Oxon., **Eng.**; mkt. t. on R. Thames; cars, leather gds.; mediaeval and Georgian bldgs.; p. (1981) 22,686.

Abingdon, t., Va., **USA**; timber inds., agr. processing and tr., tobacco; tourist ctr.; p. (1970) 4,376.

Abinger Hammer, v., Surrey, **Eng.**; former centre of Weald iron industry.

Abkhazskaya, aut. rep., Georgian SSR, **USSR**; borders Black Sea; sub-tropical crops, tourism; cap. Sukhumi; a. 8,599 km²; p. (1986) 530,000.

Abo. See **Turku**.

Abomey, anc. cap., former Kingdom of Dahomey. now **Benin**; former slave mkt.; cotton; p. (est. 1975) 41,000.

Abovyan, t., Armenian SSR, **USSR**; 16 km from Yerevan; new model t. founded 1963; planned p. 50,000.

Aboyne and Glentanner, par., Kincardine and Deeside, **Scot.**; on R. Dee nr. Ballater; Highland games; resort; p. (1981) 1,515.

Abraham, Plains of, nr. Quebec, **Canada**; Wolfe's victory over French under Montcalm, 1759.

Abram, t., Gtr. Manchester, **Eng.**; engin.; p. (1981) 7,083.

Abrantes, t., **Portugal**, on Tagus R.; French won battle here in Napoleonic Wars, 1807, dist. of Santarém; p. (1981) 48,653.

Abruzzo, region, central **Italy**; high limestone plateaux, narrow cstl. plain bordering Adriatic; poor agr., livestock; methane; forms part of Mezzogiorno; a. 8,513 km²; p. (est. 1986) 1·3m.

Abu Dhabi, I., emirate, lgst. of **United Arab Emirates**; S.E. Arabian pen.; rich oil reserves; a. 207,200 km²; p. (1985) 670,125.

Abuja, new t., **Nigeria**; planned new cap. for Nigeria built from oil revenue; building slowing down with fall in oil prices.

Abu Qir, v. on A. Bay, **Egypt**; site of anc. Canopus; Battle of the Nile fought in the Bay 1798; offshore gasfield linked by pipeline to fertiliser plants near Alexandria.

Abu Simbel, Nile Valley, **Egypt**; anc. temples carved out of solid sandstone, one to Rameses II and the other to his Queen; saved from waters of Lake Nasser.

Abydos, anc. t. of Phrygia, Asia Minor, in present **Turkey**; resisted Philip of Macedon; famed for story of Leander and Hero.

Abydos, ruined c., Upper **Egypt**; celebrated for its temple of Osiris.

Acajutla, spt., El Salvador; exp. coffee; cement, oil refining, fertilisers; p. (1961) 3,662.

Acapulco de Juárez, spt., Pac. cst., **Mexico**; major modern resort in bay surrounded by steep mtns.; exp. agr. prods.; p. (est. 1986) 300,000.

Accra, c., cap. of **Ghana**; spt.; univ.; airpt.; consumer gds.; p. (1984) 636,067 (c.) 738,498 (met. a. inc. Tema).

Accrington, t., Hyndburn, Lancs., **Eng.**; 32 km N. of Manchester; former cotton ctr.; textile machin., more diversified new inds.; p. (1981) 35,891.

Achill I., Mayo, **R.o.I.**; mtnous.; agr., fishing, tourism at Dugort and Keal; a. 148 km²; p. (est. 1980) 3,200.

Acireale, spt., Sicily, **Italy**; cath.; sulphur springs, bldgs.; p. (1981) 47,888.

Aconcagua, mtn., Andes, **Argentina**; highest peak of Western Hemisphere, alt. 6,956 m.

Aconquija, Nevada de, mtn. range, in E. Andes, N. **Argentina**; rises steeply from Chaco lowland to 5,500 m.

Acre. See '**Akko**.

Acre, st. **W. Brazil**; isolated within Amazon basin; rubber estates; major producer of coagulated rubber; cap. Rio Branco; a. 153,170 km²; p. (est. 1985) 366,100.

Acton. See **Ealing**.

Adamawa Highlands, Nigeria; rise to over 5,490 m; stock rearing.

Adam's Bridge, chain of sandbanks, 35 km long, in Palk Strait, between **India** and **Sri Lanka**; construction of rail causeway mooted.

Adana, t., **Turkey**; on Seijhan R.; ctr. for fruit and cotton, impt. exp, from Turkey; cas.: cap. of A. prov.; 4th. t. of Turkey; Yumurtalik Free Trade Zone (1987); p. (1985) 777,554.

Adapazari, t., **Turkey**; rly. junction; agr. and tr. ctr., silk, linen; high-grade concentrate from low-grade iron ore deposits in Camdagi a.; p. (1985) 152,291.

Adda, R., N. **Italy**; flows through L. Como to R. Po.; agr. in wide valley above L. Como; 240 km long.

Addis Ababa, c., cap. of **Ethiopia**; at 2,440 m in central highlands; terminus of Djibouti rly., ctr. of coffee tr., main concentration of inds. in Ethiopa; consumer gds., food processing; new cotton mill (1981); admin. ctr.; univ., palaces; p. (est. 1985) 1,464,901.

Adelaide, c., spt., cap. of S. **Australia**; on alluvial plain of R. Torrens with Mount Lofty Range to E. and Gulf St. Vincent to W.; growth based on wheat, wool and fruit but heavy inds. since war (nearby coal and iron); cars, electrical goods, textiles, chems., oil refining; p. (est. 1985) 987,100.

Adélie Land (Terre Adélie), **Antarctica**; French terr. and dependency of Réunion.

Adelsberg, t., Yugoslavia. *See* **Postojna.**

Aden, spt., cap. of **Democratic Rep.** of **Yemen**; former Brit. col.; bay behind headlands of Aden t. and Little Aden, excellent anchorage; p. (est. 1984) 318,000.

Aden, G. of W. Arabian Sea; one of most impt. shipping lanes in world; pts. of Aden, Berbera, Djibouti; length 880 km, width 480 km at mouth.

Adige, R., N. Italy; upper course forms impt. routeway through Alps between Italy and N.; flows via Verona to Adriatic; 360 km long.

Adirondack, mtns., **USA**; hgst. peak Mt. Marcy (1,630 m), average height 1,200 m; scenically attractive, ski resorts, sanatoria, iron-ore deposits.

Adlington, t., Lancs., Eng.; nr. Chorley; former cotton spinning t.; p. (1981) 5,626.

Admiralty Is., 27 km of sm. coral Is., one lge. I., S.W. **Pac. Oc.**; part of Papua New Guinea; forms part of Bismarck Archipelago; anc. civilisation; pearl fishing, coconuts; ch. t. Lorengau.; a. 2,072 km²; p. (est. 1977) 30,500.

Adour, R., S.W. France; rises in Pyrenees, enters Bay of Biscay below Bayonne; 331 km long.

Adria, mkt. t., Rovigo, **Italy**; formerly on cst., now 22 km inland, old Etruscan c.; p. (1981) 21,785.

Adrianople. *See* **Edirne.**

Adriatic Sea, branch of the Mediterranean, between Italy and Balkan Peninsula; forms G. of Venice on the N.; chief trading pts., Venice, Trieste, and Ancona on the N., Brindisi and Dürres on the S.; a. 134,680 km², 720 km long.

Adriatic Highway, Yugoslavia; cst. road (in need of repair) across Dinaric Alps motivated by tourist boom.

Adullam or Aidelma, Judean c. of Canaanite origin, S.W. Jerusalem, **Israel**, where David hid in cave from Saul.

Adur, l. gov. dist., West Sussex, **Eng.**; lower A. valley and ts. of Shoreham-by-Sea and Southwick; p. (est. 1988) 56,800.

Adwick le Street, t., South Yorks, **Eng.**; coal; home of George Washington's family; p. (1981) 19,162.

Adygeyskaya (Adygei), aut. region, **RSFSR**; in foothills of Caucasus; mainly agr. and lumbering; cap. Maykop; a. 7,599 km²; p. (est. 1986) 423,000.

Adzharskaya, aut. rep., Georgian SSR, **USSR**; borders Turkey; mtnous.; sub-tropical crops; cap. Batumi; a. 2,849 km²; p. (est. 1986) 382,000.

Aegades, gr. of rocky Is. off W. cst. of Sicily, **Italy**; ch. t. Favignana on I. of that name.

Aegean Is., between **Greece** and **Turkey**; called the Grecian Archipelago, inc. Crete, Cyclades, Sporades, and Dodecanese; a. 3,901 km²; p. (1981) 428,533.

Aegean Sea, branch of the Mediterranean; studded with Is., between **Greece** and **Turkey**; connected through the Dardanelles with Sea of Marmara and thence through the Bosporus Strait with the Black Sea; rich cultural history; coral sponge fishing; recent oil finds contested between Greece and Turkey; length 640 km, width 320 km.

Afan. *See* **Por Talbot.**

Afars and Issas. *See* **Djibouti.**

Affric, Glen, Inverness, **Scot.**; 48 km S.W. of Inverness; hydroelectric power.

Afghanistan, rep. (1973), former kingdom, **Asia**; land locked, lies N. and W. of Pakistan; cap. Kabul; comm. ctrs. Kabul, Kandahar; mtnous.; ch. Rs., Kabul and Helm; intense summer heat, severe winter cold, scanty rainfall; ethnic variety, Pashtuns, Ghilzays, Uzbeks and Tadzhiks; many hill tribes; languages Pashtu and Farsi; religion Islam; geography causes fragmented settlement and slow economic progress; severe drought 1968-

72; 75 percent depend on agric.; heavily dependent on irrigation; wheat staple crop, also cotton, rice, maize; sheep, goats, horses; handicraft inds. (carpets and weaving) more impt. than modern inds.; mineral resources but poor transport hinders development; no rly.; refugees totalled 5,000,000 by 1985; hydroelectr. at Asadabad; a. 647,500 km²; p. (est. 18,136,000 (inc. 2,600,000 nomadic p.);. Invaded by Russian troops, Dec. 1979. Withdrawal completed Feb. 1989.

Africa, second lgst. continent contains 22 per cent of world's land a. but only 11 per cent of p.; diverse physical and cultural conditions; plateaux interrupted in N. and S. by steeply folded, sharply eroded mtn. ranges and by mtn. massifs of Sahara and E. Africa; climate and vegetation vary from hot desert to equatorial rain forest and from Mediterranean woodland to tropical savannah; sparse but ethnically varied p., concentrated mainly along N.W. Mediterranean cst., Nile valley, cst. of W. Africa and N.E. of L. Victoria; little urbanisation; economic development hindered by colonial legacy and neo-colonial international companies, poorly developed transport network, poor soils, inadequate rainfall and fluctuating prices of primary prods. on world mkt.; petroleum deposits providing revenue for devel. in few ctys.; those ctys. without oil severely handicapped by high cost of imports; schemes like Volta R. multipurpose development and the Cabora Bassa dam designed to alleviate this poverty; continent contains 40 per cent of world hydroelectric potential and is storehouse of non-energy producing minerals, but many are exported in unprocessed form; agr. predominant economic activity, except in industl. enclaves of Egypt, Zimbabwe and S. Africa; 60 per cent land devoted to subsistence crops; 50 ctys. had achieved independence by 1977 compared with 4 in 1945; a c. 30,259,000 km²; p. (est. 1984) 536,685,000.

Agadir, spt., S. cst. **Morocco**; wrecked by earthquake, 1960; new t. built S. of former c. in a. of greater geological stability; p. (est. 1981) 246,000.

Agana, cap. of **Guam**; reconstructed after second world war; p. (est. 1980) 3,000 (exc. armed forces).

Agen, t., cap. of Lot-et-Garonne, **France**; mkt. t.; aqueduct and bridge over Garonne R.; fruit tr. and processing; p. (1982) 58,288 (met. a.).

Agincourt (Azincourt), v., Pas-de-Calais, **France**; famed for battle in 1415 between English, led by Henry V and French under d'Albert.

Agra, c., Uttar Pradesh, **India**; on Jumna R., 184 km S.S.E. of Delhi; formerly cap. of Mogul Empire; famous Taj Mahal mausoleum; univ.; p. (1981) 694,191 (c.), 747,318 (met. a.).

Agrigento, t., S. Sicily, **Italy**; spt., exp. sulphur, salt. Formerly Girgenti, founded Akragas, c. 580 B.C., famous for its temples; birthplace of Empedocles; p. (1981) 51,325.

Aguadilla, spt., **Puerto Rico**; exp. coffee and sugar; p. (1970) 21,087.

Aguascalientes, st., Mexico; on central plateau at 1,800 m; agr.; mineral springs; cap. A.; a. 6,472 km²; p. (est. 1983) 593,623.

Aguascalientes, t., cap. of A. st. **Mexico**; alt. over 1,800 m; 416 km N.W. of Mexico City; wide range of local inds.; hot springs; p. (1980) 359,574.

Agulhas, C., rocky projection, 160 km E. of C. of Good Hope, most southerly point of **Africa.**

Ahlen, t., N. Rhine–Westphalia, **W. Germany**; on R. Werse; coal mng., metal and engin. wks.; p. (est. 1986) 51,900.

Ahmadabad, temporary cap. of Gujarat, **India**; Jain temple, mosques; univ.; impt. textile ctr.; oilfield at Nawagam nearby; p. (1981) 2,059,725 (c.), 2,548,037 (met. a.).

Ahmadnagar, c., Maharashtra, **India**; admin. ctr.; old Bahmani cap.; lge. tr. in cotton and silk gds.; p. (1981) 143,937 (c.), 181,210 (met. a.).

Ahrewady. *See* **Irrawaddy.**

Ahvāz (Ahwāz), c., cap. of Khuzestan prov., **Iran**; airpt.; oil, aluminium, steel pipes; new steel plant; p. (1986) 589,529.

Aigues-Mortes, t., Gard dep., **France**; on Rhône delta; canal ctr., once spt., now 5 km from Mediterranean; salt works; much of mediaeval t. preserved; tourism; p. (1982) 4,475.

Aiguille d'Arves, mtn., Dauphiné Alps, S.E. **France**; 3 rock needles; hgst. alt. 3,511 m.

Aiguille du Midi, mtn., Mt. Blanc massif, S.E. **France**; rock needle, funicular rly.; alt. 3,845 m.

Aiguille Verte, mtn., Mt. Blanc massif, S.E. **France**, rock needle overlooking Chamonix; alt. 4,130 m.

Ailefroid, mtn., Dauphiné Alps, S.E. **France**; double summit; alt. 3,962 m.

Ailsa Craig, rocky I., Kyle and Carrick, **Scot.**; alt. 340 m; gannetry.

Ain, dep., **France**; in Jura; mainly agr., famous for pigs and poultry; a. 5,822 km²; p. (1982) 418,300.

Ain, R., **France**; trib. of R. Rhône, flows S.S.W. from Jura; hydroelectric power; 194 km long.

Airdrie, burgh, Strathclyde Reg., **Scot.**; 19 km E. of Glasgow; iron inds., brick and concrete wks., steel tubes, pharmaceutics; p. (1981) 45,643.

Aire, R., West Yorks., **Eng.**; trib. of Ouse; major valley for power production; produces 20 per cent of U.K. power; length 112 km.

Aireborough, t., West Yorks., **Eng.**; woollens; p. (1981) 31,414.

Aisne, dep., **France**; borders Ardennes; forested; mainly agr., sugar-beet; sm. textile ts.; cap. Laon; a. 7.423 km²; p. (1982) 534,200.

Aisne, R., N.E. **France**; navigation improved by regularisation; 240 km long.

Aitolia and Akarnania, Greece; mtnous. prov. on N. side G. of Patras; arable cultivation on cstl. plain; cap. Missolonghi; a. 5,390 km²; p. (1981) 219,764.

Aix-en-Provence, t., Bouches-du-Rhône, **France**; 29 km N. of Marseilles; old cap. of Provence; thermal springs; cultural and comm. ctr., agr., inds.; p. (1982) 124,550.

Aix-la-Chapelle. *See* Aachen.

Aix-les-Bains, health resort, Savoy, **France**; p. (1982) 23,534.

Aizuwakamatsu, t. N. Honshu, **Japan**; lacquer ware, candles; p. (1985) 118,144.

Ajaccio, spt., cap. Corse du Sud, Corcisa, **France**; timber, flour, olive oil, tobacco; tourism; birthplace of Napoleon; p. (1982) 55,279.

Ajman, emirate, one of **United Arab Emirates**; p. (1985) 64,318.

Ajmer, t., Rajasthan, **India**; salt extraction, vegetable oils; p. (1981) 375,593 (met. a.).

Akhaia, prov., **Greece**; impt. currant producing a.; livestock; inc. pt. of Patras; a. 3,134 km²; p. (1981) 275,193.

Akhisar, t., **Turkey**; anc. Thyatira; in fertile agr. basin, p. (1985) 68,553

Akita, pref., **Japan**; a. 11,663 km²; contains Japan's lgst. oilfield and copper mine; mtns. and fertile lowlands; p. (1985) 1,253,000.

Akita, c., **Japan**; cap. Akita pref.; old cas. t., pt; oil refining ctr., fertilisers, wood pulp; p. (1985) 296,381.

'Akko (Acre), c., spt., **Israel**; famous for sieges during Crusades; withstood Napoleon for 61 days in 1799; pt. functions now assumed by Haifa; p. (est. 1982) 39,100.

Akmolinsk. *See* Tselinograd.

Akola, t., Maharashtra, **India**; cotton; p. (1981) 225,412.

Akosombo, pt. **Ghana**; pt. and new t. S. of L. Volta; textile factory being built; planned p. 50,000.

Akranes, t., **Iceland**; N. of Reykjavik; lge. cement wks.; p. (1983) 5,351.

Akron, c., Ohio, **USA**; lge. rubber mftg. ctr.; maize, mills, woollens, machin., chemicals; univ.; p. (1984) 226,900.

Aktyubinsk, t., N.W. Kazakh SSR, **USSR**; at S. end of Ural mtns.; ferro-alloys, engin., lignite, elec. power, chemicals, copper; p. (est. 1985) 231,000.

Akureyri, t., N. **Iceland**; herring fishery, textiles, food processing; 2nd. t. of Iceland; p. (1983) 13,742.

Akyab, *See* Sittwe.

Alabama, st., **USA**; cap. Montgomery, ch. pt. Mobile; "cotton st.", cattle-rearing; fertilisers, chemicals, mng.; lgst. c. Birmingham; settled 1702; admitted to union 1819; st. flower camelia, st. bird yellow-hammer; a. 133,667 km²; p. (1985) 4,021,000.

Alagôas, st., N.E. **Brazil**; hot, dry cattle rearing a., poor st. with low literacy rate; cap. Maceió; a. 28,648 km²; p. (est. 1985) 2,224,200.

Alameda, spt. Cal., **USA**; on I. in San Francisco Bay; impt. naval and air base; pt. inds.; p. (1980) 63,852.

Aland Is. (Ahvenanmaa), group belonging to **Finland** at entrance of G. of Bothnia; a. 1,481 km²; p. (1986) 23,640.

Alaska, Arctic st., **USA**; separated from other sts.; bought from Russia (1868); mtnous.; furs, timber, salmon; major oil and natural gas discoveries on N. slope present difficult ecological problems for exploitation; pipeline from Prudhoe Bay to Valdez; lgst. c. Anchorage; admitted to union 1959; st. flower forget-me-not, st. bird Willow Ptarmigan; cap. Juneau (planned cap. at Willow South never built); a. 1,518,776 km²; p. (1985) 521,000.

Alaska G. of, S. cst. A., **USA.**; semi-circular G. with precipitous csts.; oil in Cook Inlet and Controller B.; a. 5,000 km².

Alaska Highway, from Dawson Creek, B.C., **Canada**, to Fairbanks, Alaska, **USA**; 2,443 km long; built for second world war programme; main supply base and H.Q., Edmonton, Alberta.

Alaska Range, mtn. massif, S.A., **USA**; extends in arc of 640 km; separates S. cst. and N. tundra; S.E. flowing glaciers; many peaks over 3,000 m; Mt. McKinley, 6,182 m.

Alatau, mtns., bdy. of Kazakhstan, **USSR**; and Sinkiang, **China**; group of 5 ranges, outliers of Tien-Shan; alt. up to 4,600 m; highest peak Khan Tengri, 6,954 m.

Alava, Basque prov., N. **Spain**; ch. t. Vitoria; viticulture; a. 3,043 km²; p. (1987) 268,863.

Albacete, prov., S.E. **Spain**; stock-raising; a. 14,864 km². p. (1981) 339,370.

Albacete, t., cap. of A. prov., **Spain**; agr. mkt., fruit, saffron; p. (1987) 125,764.

Alba-Iulia, t., **Romania**; on R. Mures, formerly Carlsburgh; union of Transylvania with Romania proclaimed here 1918; p. (est. 1985) 64,369.

Albania, rep., **S.E. Europe**; lying along Adriatic, adjacent to Yugoslavia and Greece; Chinese economic aid and co-operation ended in 1978; food ch. ind.; petroleum reserves and refining, hydro-electric power, coal, chrome ore, copper, iron ore; first external rail link opened (1986) for ore exports; fastest growing p. in Europe; cap. Tirana; a. 27,529 km²; p. (est. 1987) 3,080,000 of whom 1,000,000 were under 15 years old.

Albano, crater L., **Italy**; tourist attraction 24 km S.E. of Rome; steep sides; a. 8 km².

Albany, mkt. t., Ga., **USA**; on Flint R.; agr. ctr.; cotton, food; p. (1980) 74,471.

Albany, c., cap. of N.Y. st., **USA**; R. pt. on Hudson R.; admin. and industl. ctr.; p. (1984) 99,500 (c.), 842,900 (met. a. with Schenectady-Troy).

Albany, t., **W. Australia**; pt. on King George Sound; founded (1826) as penal col.; first white settlement in W. Australia, established to counter Fr. settlement of W.; p. (1981) 15,222.

Albert, L. *See* Mobutu Seso, L.

Alberta, prov., W. **Canada**; part of prairies; Rockies in W.; wheat, livestock, feed crops; coal less impt. with development of rich oil and gas resources; chemicals, timber; cap. Edmonton; a. 661,188 km²; p. (1986) 2,375,000.

Albertville. *See* Kalemi.

Albi, t., cap. of Tarn dep., **France**; cath., industl. and comm. ctr.; p. (1982) 60,181 (met. a.).

Ålborg, c., cap. of N. Jutland prov., **Denmark**; spt. on S. side of Lim fjord; shipping., cement, textiles; airpt.; p. (est. 1987) 155,000.

Albula Alps, mtn. range, Rhaetian Alps, E. **Switzerland**; summits intersected by low passes; inc. several impt. Dolomitic peaks.

Albuquerque, t., N.M., **USA**; on Rio Grande; alt. 1,525 m.; univ.; food prod., engin.; resort; p. (1984) 350,500 (c.), 449,400 (met. a.).

Albury-Wodonga, t., N.S.W., Vic., **Australia**; regional urban growth ctr. (1974) on Murray R.; p. (est. 1983) 77,970.

Alcalá de Henares, t., **Spain**; nr. Madrid; univ.; birthplace of Cervantes; p. (1981) 142,862.

Alcamo, t., Sicily, **Italy**; nr. ruins of anc. Segesra; p. (1981) 42,059.

Alcatraz, I., Cal., **USA**; San Francisco Bay; former prison.

Alcoy, t., **Spain**; textiles, paper; p. (1981) 65,908.

Aldabra Is., Seychelles Rep.; 400 km N.W. of Madagascar; leased (1971–1985) to Royal Society for wildlife research (unique animal and plant species).

Aldan, R., E. Siberia, **USSR**; flows from Stanovoy Range to Lena R. via Tommot gold-mng. dist.; coal in lower course; 2,682 km long.

Aldeburgh, spt., Suffolk Coastal, Suffolk, **Eng.**; 48 km from Ipswich; famous for annual music festival; p. (1981) 2,911.

Aldermaston, Berkshire, **Eng.**; atomic weapons research ctr.

Alderney, I., Channel Is., **Brit.**; horticulture tourism; a. 794 ha; p. (1986) 2,130.

Aldershot, t., Rushmoor, Hants., **Eng.**; bricks; lge. military camp; p. (1981) 32,654.

Aldridge, t., West Midlands, **Eng.**; plastics,

packing cases; expanded t.; p. with Brown-hills (1981) 87,219.

Alençon, t. cap of Orne dep., **France;** textiles; p. (1982) 32,526.

Aleppo, c., **Syria;** 2nd. c. of Syria; in limestone hills; univ.; mkt and textile ctr.; p. (est. 1985) 1,145,117.

Alès, t., Gard dep., **France;** sm. coalfield; chemicals; p. (1982) 70,180 (met. a.).

Alessandria, t., N. **Italy;** rly. ctr. on Tanaro R.; engin.; p. (1981) 100,523.

Alesund, spt. on Giske I., W. **Norway,** fishing, fish processing; airpt. on I. to N.; p. (est. 1987) 35,000.

Aletsch, glacier, **Switzerland;** in Bernese Alps; lgst. in Europe; length 24 km.

Aletschhorn, mtn., Bernese Alps, **Switzerland;** alt. 4,198 m.

Aleutian Is.; Bering Sea, Alaska, **USA;** chain of over 150 Is. formed from partially submerged peaks of volcanic A. mtn. range; on earthquake belt; U.S. air base.

Alexander Archipelago, S.E. Alaska, **USA;** dense I. system; fjord scenery; well populated; furs, lumbering, fishing; a. 33,670 km².

Alexandria, (El Iskandariyah) ch. pt., **Egypt;** founded by Alexander the Great, 332 B.C.; floating dock; exp. cotton, wheat, rice, gum; second lgst. c. in Africa; new steel plant at El Dikhelia; pt. being expanded and new pt. at Dikhelia; linked to offshore gas field; rapid growth, second lgst. c. in Africa; p. (1985) 2·821m, projected p. (2005) 4,750,000.

Alexandria, c., spt., Va., **USA;** on Chesapeake Bay; indust. t.; p. (1980) 103,000.

Alford, t., East Lindsey, Lincs., **Eng.;** mkt.; brewing, food processing; p. (1981) 2,596.

Alfreton, t., Amber Valley, Derbys., **Eng.;** mkt. t.; formerly coal mng.; hosiery, knitwear; p. (1981) 23,124.

Algarve, prov., anc. kingdom, **Portugal;** in extreme S. of cty; tourism, fishing, fruit; p. (est. 1970) 316,200.

Algeciras, spt., **Spain;** W. of Gibraltar on A. Bay; nearby Campo de Gibraltar scheme for social and economic development to break down Gibraltar's economic isolation; p. (1981) 86,042.

Algeria, indep. st. (1962), N. **Africa;** former French colony; fertile cstl. plain borders Mediterranean Sea where cereal, wine, fruit and olive production and incr. mkt. garden prods. for exp.; Land reform (1980) encouraging livestock; afforestation to prevent N. spread of Sahara; exp. of high grade iron ore, phosphates, petroleum and natural gas are financing ambitious industrialisation plans; incr. tourism; new roads link Saharan oilfields to cst.; cap. El Djezair; 60 per cent of p. under 19; a. 2,373,994 km²; p. (est. 1986) 22,600,000.

Algiers. See **El Djezair**

Alicante, spt., cap of A. prov., **Spain;** wine, fruits; oil refinery; p. (est. 1987) 258,004.

Alice Springs, t., N.T., **Australia;** ch. t., of desert a.; major cattle raising ctr.; natural gas nearby; growth of winter tourism; p. (est. 1986) 22,759.

Aligarh, t., Uttar Pradesh, **India;** 128 km S.E. of Delhi; univ.; p. (1981) 320,861.

Alkmaar, t., **Netherlands;** impt. cheese mkt. on N. Holland canal; p. (est. 1987) 87,000.

Allahabad, t., Uttar Pradesh, **India;** at confluence of Jumna and Ganges Rs.; univ.; Hindu pilgrimage ctr.; p. (1981) 616,051 (c.), 650,070 (met. a.).

Allegheny Mtns., USA; part of Appalachian system, inc. several parallel ranges; water-shed between Atlantic and Mississippi R. drainage; forested, tourism; average alt. 1,500 m.

Allegheny R., Penns., N.Y., **USA;** rises in A. mtns., flows to Ohio R.; Pittsburg met. a. on lower reaches where R. entrenched 120 m below plateau making urban development difficult; used for coal and oil transport; 520 km long.

Allen, Bog of, R.o.I.; peat bogs, peat cutting, cultivation; a. 958 km².

Allentown, t., Penns., **USA;** coal, textiles, cement; p. (1984) 103,900 (c.), 646,700 (met. a.).

Alleppey, spt., Kerala, S. **India;** on sand spit coconut prods, p. (1981) 169,940.

Allerdale, l. gov. dist., Cumbria, **Eng.;** cstl. dist inc. Workington, Maryport, Cockermouth and Keswick; p. (est. 1988) 96,600.

Alliance, t., Ohio, **USA;** iron, steel, engin.; p. (1980) 24,315.

Allier, dep., **France;** N. of Massif Central; coal and iron mng.; mineral springs, wine, wheat; a. 4,786 km²; p. (1982) 369,000.

Alloa, sm. burgh, Clackmannan, **Scot.;** on N. bank of R. Forth; bricks, tiles, glass, distilling p. (1981) 26,390.

Alma-Ata, c., cap. of Kazakh SSR, **USSR;** in foothills of Tien-Shan mtns.; univ.; comm. agr., and ind. ctr.; food processing, machin., printing; p. (1986) 1,088,000.

Almada, t., **Portugal;** on R. Tagus estuary opposite Lisbon; Salazar bridge (opened 1966) links it with Lisbon; p. (1981) 147,690.

Almelo, t., Overijssel, **Neth.;** 40 km S.E. of Zwolle; cotton textile mnfs.; p. (est. 1987) 62,000.

Almeria, spt. on G. of A., S.E. **Spain;** cath.; exp. grapes, oranges; p. (1987) 154,911.

Alnwick, t., l. gov. dist., Northumberland, **Eng.;** cas.; mkt. t.; p. (est. 1988) 30,400 (dist.).

Alor Setar, t., cap. of Kedah, W. **Malaysia;** on main W. cst. road and rly.; p. (1980) 71,682.

Alost. See **Aalst.**

Alpes-de-Haute-Provence (Basses-Alpes), dep., S.E. **France;** mtnous., infertile a. bordering Italy; olives, wines; cap. Digne; a. 6,988 km²; p. (1982) 118,200.

Alpes-Maritimes, dep., S.E. **France;** ceded by Italy in 1860; ch. t. Nice; olives, wines, fruit; a. 3,737 km²; p. (1982) 878,600.

Alphen, t., S. Holland, **Neth.;** on Old Rhine, 16 km S.E. of Leiden; mkt. for dairy produce; p. (est. 1987) 57,000.

Alps, hgst. mtns. in **Europe;** 960 km long, inc. 1,200 glaciers; separates S. and central Europe, forming a climatic divide; major tourist a., winter sports; hydroelec. power; main peaks Mont Blanc (4,814 m), Mont Rosa (4,641 m), Matterhorn (4,509 m).

Als, I., S. **Denmark;** in the Little Belt, a. 337 km²; linked to Jutland by bridge; p. (est. 1970) 53,000.

Alsace-Lorraine, region, E. **France;** bordered to E. by W. Germany and Rhine R; incorporated into Germany at time of unification (1871), returned to France by Treaty of Versailles (1919); impt. iron-ore and iron and steel inds. in Lorraine; regional aid for economic development; well wooded; p. (1982) 1,558,400 (Alsace) See **Lorraine.**

Alsdorf, t., N. Rhine-Westphalia, **W. Germany;** 16 km N. of Aachen; tar-distillation plant; p. (est. 1986) 45,900.

Alston, t., Eden, Cumbria, **Eng.;** in upper reaches of south Tyne in N. Pennines; limestone quarrying.

Altai Mtns., Mongolia, **USSR;** border China; steppes and glaciers; silver and mercury; multi-purpose R. development at Kamenna-Obi; ctr. of USSR atomic ind. at Ust Kamenogorsk; stock-rearing; average alt. 3,000 m, highst. alt. 4,656 m at Tabun Bogdo.

Alta, R., N. Norway; scene of major new h.e.p. sta. fiercely opposed by Lapp residents.

Altamira, caves, N. **Spain;** prehistoric shelters, paintings of animals (Magdalenian).

Altamura, t., Apulia, **Italy;** at foot of Apennines; wines, wool; cath.; p. (1981) 51,328.

Altdorf, t., cap. of Uri can., **Switzerland;** rubber gds., wood workings; statue of William Tell and Tell Theatre; p. (1980) 8,200.

Altenahr, t., N. Rhine-Westphalia, **W. Germany;** site of anc. cas. of Counts von der Marck; metals, wine; p. (est. 1983) 23,400.

Altenburg, t., Leipzig, **E. Germany;** lignite mng., engin., metallurgy, mnfs. playing cards, textiles; p. (1981) 55,827.

Alton, t., East Hants., **Eng.;** breweries, lt. engin.; p. (1981) 14,646.

Alton, t., Ill., **USA;** on Mississippi R.; oil refining; p. (1980) 34,171.

Altona, R. pt. of Hamburg, **W. Germany;** on the Elbe; chemical and fishing inds.; trawler pt.

Altoona, c., Penns., **USA;** rly. t.; p. (1984) 54,600 (c.), 134,400 (met. a.).

Altrincham, mkt. t., Trafford, Gtr. Manchester, **Eng.;** engin.; residtl.; p. (1981) 39,641.

Alva, burgh, Clackmannan, **Scot.;** at S. foot of Ochil Hills, 5 km N. of Alloa; woollens, printing, fruit and fish canning; p. (1981) 4,876.

Alwar, c., Rajasthan, **India;** in hilly agr. region; former cap. of A. princely st.; fort, palace; p. (1981) 145,795.

Alyn and Deeside, l. gov. dist., Clwyd, **Wales;** inc. Connah's Quay, Buckley and Hawarden; p. (est. 1988) 72,600.

Amagasaki, c., **Japan;** nr. Osaka; chemicals polyethylene; iron and steel; oil refining; p. (1985) 509,115.

Amalfi, spt., **Italy**; on G. of Salerno; tourist resort; fisheries; p. (1981) 6,052.

Amapá, fed. terr., N. **Brazil**; on equator; tropical rain forest, sparse p.; a. 137,423 km²; p. (est. 1985) 217,000.

Amārah, Al, pt., **Iraq**; on left bank of R. Tigris 400 km below Baghdad; Arab t. and agr. mkt. at R. crossing; p. (1970) 80,078.

Amārapura, t., **Burma**; on R. Irrawaddy 10 km. S.W. of Mandalay; former cap.; craft inds.

Amarillo, t., Texas, **USA**; oil refining, creameries, meat packing; p. (1984) 162,900 (c.), 190,300 (met. a.).

Amasya, t., **Turkey**; on Yesil-Cekerek R.; tr. ctr.; p. (1985) 53,431.

Amazon, gr. R., **S. America**; drains lgst. a. and carries more water than any other R. in world; main Andean headstreams Huarco Ucayali and Marañón from Peru unite to flow across Brazil to Atl. Oc., receiving waters of many Rs. inc. the Madeira; lgst. rain forest in world; ocean steamers penetrate to Iquitos, Peru, c. 3,680 km from mouth; a. drained c. 6 million km² of sparsely populated cty., mostly in Brazil; length 6,448 km; basin inc. 40% of S. America; ocean pt. Belém.

Amazonas, lgst. st. of Brazil; isolated; tropical rain forest; tree prods.; vast mineral reserves: cap. Manáus; a. 1,595,823 km²; p. (est. 1985) 1,739,600 (mainly Indian).

Amazonas, fed. terr., **Venezuela**; cap. Puerto Ayacucho on Orinoco R., isolated, tropical rain forest; a. 181,300 km²; p. (1981) 45,667.

Amazonia, Peru, Colombia, Brazil; a. covered by Amazon R. and its tribs. and the surrounding lowland; thickly forested; underdeveloped.

Ambala, c., Haryana, **India**; cotton, flour; p. (1981) 121,203.

Ambato, c., **Ecuador**; S. of Quito, on slope of Mt. Chimborazo; alt. 2,702 m; textiles, canned fruits, leather gds.; p. (est. 1984) 114,500.

Amberg, t., Bavaria, **W. Germany**; mediaeval walled t. on R. Vils; specialist steels, textiles; p. (est. 1986) 43,300.

Amber Valley, l. gov. dist., Derbys., **Eng.**; S. of co., nr. Notts.; inc. Alfreton, Ripley, Heanor and Belper; p. (est. 1988) 111,900.

Ambès, t., Gironde, **France**; nr. Bordeaux; oil refining; p. (1982) 2,715.

Ambleside, tourist ctr., Cumbria, **Eng.**; N. of L. Windermere.

Amboise, t., Indre-et-Loire dep., **France**; 24 km E. of Tours; famous cas, and prison; p. (1982) 11,415.

Ambon, I., Moluccas, **Indonesia**; spices, coconuts; a. 818 km²; p. 73,000.

America, the lands of the Western hemisphere, comprising the continents of North and South America, separated by narrow Isthmus of Panama; most N. point over 14,400 km from C. Horn, the extreme S. point; (est. 1984) 750,000,000. *See also* **North, South,** and **Central America**.

Amersfoort, c., Utrecht, **Neth.**; walled c. on R. Eem; rapid growth of light inds.; p. (est. 1987) 92,000.

Amersham, t., Bucks., **Eng.**; Radio chemical Ctr., renamed Amersham International after privatisation (1982); lt. inds., 17th cent. mkt. hall.

Ames, t., Iowa, **USA**; Iowa State Univ. of Science and Technology and many fed. and st. institutes; p. (1980) 45,775.

Amiens, c., cap. of Somme dep; major textile ctr. of **France**, on R. Somme; cath.; p. (1982) 136,358.

Amirante Is., British group, **Indian Ocean**; S.W. of Seychelles.

Amlwch, t., Gwynedd, **Wales**; N. cst of Anglesey; resort; pt.; oil terminal; p. (1981) 3,690.

Amman, c., cap. of **Jordan**; N.E. of Dead Sea; site of biblical Raboth Ammon; textiles, cement, tobacco; airpt.; univ.; p. (est. 1985) 812,500.

Ammanford, t., Dinefwr, Dyfed, **Wales**; anthracite, brick mkg.; p. (1981) 5,711.

Amoy. *See* **Xiamen.**

Ampthill, Mid Beds., **Eng.**; mkt. t.; p. (1981) 5,766.

Amravati, c., Maharashtra, **India**; cotton ctr., univ.; p. (1981) 261,404.

Amritsar, c., Punjab, N.W. **India**; Golden Temple sacred to Sikhs; trade ctr. for shawls and carpets; soaps, paints, engin.; Massacre of Indian nationalists by troops under British control, 1919; p. (1981) 594,844 (met. a.).

Amroha, t., Uttar Pradesh, **India**; pilgrimage ctr.; p. (1981) 112,682.

Amsterdam, spt., cap. of **Netherlands**; at junction of R. Amstel and the IJ; built on 96 Is. joined by 300 bridges, harbour at terminus of N. Sea canal can hold 1,000 ships; two univs., Royal Palace, Bourse; extensive tr.; exp. dairy prod., sugar, tobacco; shipbldg., diamond polishing, aeronautical, marine, elec. machin., oil refining; p. (est. 1987) 682,702 (c.), 1,015,916 (met. a.).

Amu-Dar'ya (Oxus), R., marks boundary between **USSR** and **Afghanistan**; flows from Pamir mtns. to Aral Sea; Kara- and Ksyl-Kum deserts on either bank; rich in fish; 1,395 km long.

Amur (Heilong Jiang), major R. of E. **Asia**; flows from Mongolia between N.E. China and E. Siberia into Pac. Oc. opposite Sakhalin I.; with tribs. Argun and Ussuri forms lgst. R. frontier in world; crossed by Trans-Siberian rly. at Khabarovsk; 2,827 km long.

Anaconda, t., Mont., **USA**; one of lgst. copper mines in world; p. (1980) 12,518 (co.).

Anaheim, t., Cal., **USA**; tourism; Disneyland; p. (1984) 233.500.

Ahahuac, plateau, **Mexico**; average alt. 2,000 m; surrounded by higher cty. inc. volcano Popocatapetl (5,456 m); contains Mexico City heartland of Aztec Mexico; a. c. 3,900 km².

Anambas Is., Indonesia; 240 km W. of W. Malaysia; little development; p. c. 12,000.

Anatolia (Asia Minor), penin. approx. coextensive with Turkey bounded by Black Sea (N.), Mediterranean (S.), Aegean (W.).

Anching. *See* **Anqing.**

Anchorage, t., Alaska, **USA**; timber, salmon fishing and canning; earthquake 28 Mar. 1964; spt.; airpt.; p. (1984) 226,700; 3rd fastest growing t. in USA.

Ancona, spt., central **Italy**; on the Adriatic Sea; founded by Dorians, 1500 B.C.; sugar refineries, shipbldg., petrochemicals; p. (1984) 105,657.

Andalucia, region, covering southern **Spain**; Córdoba, Seville, Jaén and Granada, celebrated ctrs. in Moorish times; irrigation for wines, olives, fruits.

Andaman and Nicobar Is., Bay of Bengal; constituted a union terr., **India**, 1956; hilly remnants of drowned mtn. chain; primitive pygmy tribes; a. 8,327 km²; p. (1981) 188,741.

Anderlecht, t., residtl. and industl. sub. of Brussels, **Belgium**; p. (est. 1983) 94,715.

Andermatt, v., Uri, **Switzerland**; at foot of Mt. St. Gotthard; tourist ctr., winter health resort; p. (1970) 1,589.

Anderson, t., Ind., **USA**; car components; p. (1984) 61,800 (c.), 134,100 (met. a.).

Andes, gr. volcanic mtn. system, **S. America**; extends over 6,400 km from N.-S.; physical and climatic divide rising to over 6,000 m; densely populated; high tropical plateaus; rich in minerals; hgst. peak, Aconcagua (6,965 m).

Andhra Pradesh, st. S.E. **India**; cap. Hyderabad; inc. valleys of lower Godavari and Krishna Rs.; sugar, rice; a. 275,278 km²; p. (est. 1981) 53,549,673.

Andizhan, c. Uzbek SSR, **USSR**; once residence of Khans of Khokan; industl. ctr.; in irrigation a.; cotton, silk; oilfields; p. (est. 1985) 275,000.

Andorra, sm. mtn. st., E. Pyrenees; under joint suzerainty of French President and Bishop of Urgel (Spain); virtually indep.; livestock, wines, tobacco; tourism having fundamental social and economic consequences; alt. 900–3,000 m; a. 495 km²; p. (est. 1985) 35,000.

Andover, mkt. t., Test Valley, Hants., **Eng.**; prehistoric earthwks.; expanded t.; p. (1981) 31,006.

Andria, t., S. **Italy**; Roman remains, cath., palaces; p. (1981) 83,319.

Andropov (Rybinsk), c., cap. of R. oblast, **RSFSR**; on Upper Volga; tr. and shipping ctr. since 16th cent.; site of hydroelectric power sta.; shipbldg., engin.; renamed 1984 to honour dead General Secretary; p. (est. 1985) 251,000.

Andros, lgst. I., **Bahamas**; sponges, sisal, hemp; p. (1980) 8,307.

Andújar, t., **Spain**; on Guadalquivir R.; mineral springs, pottery, soap, textiles, uranium plant; p. (1981) 30,875.

Angara, R., Siberia, **USSR**; trib. of Yenisey; navigable almost its entire length., rises nr. and flows through L. Baykal; length 2,080 km; hydro-electric power.

Angarsk, t., E. Siberia, **USSR**; on R. Angaar 32 km N.W. Irkutsk; engin., saw milling; p. (est. 1985) 256,000.

Angel Falls (Salto del Angel), waterfall, **Venezuela**; nr. Ciudad Bolivar; 980 m drop.

Angerman, R., N. **Sweden** rises nr. Norwegian border, falls to G. of Bothnia; timber transport; 448 km long.

Angers, t., cap, of Maine-et-Loire dep., **France;** on R. Maine; mkt. t. for local produce, fruit, vegetables, Anjou wines, Cointreau; textiles; cath., cas.; p. (1982) 141,143.

Angkor, c., **Cambodia;** jungle-covered ruins of c. from Khmer civilisation; discovered 1860.

Anglesey (Ynys Môn), former co., l. gov. dist., Gwynedd, **Wales;** separated from mainland by Menai Straits; former stronghold of Druids, attacked by Romans A.D. 61; mainly agr. and tourism; p. (est. 1988) 71,000.

Angola, People's Rep. of (Port. W. Africa), W. Africa; interior forms part of central African plateaux, bounded by transitional escarpments in W. which face on to narrow coastal plain; rainfall diminishes from N.–S. with consequent crop zoning; coffee, cotton, oil palm in N., corn, peanuts, sisal in drier interior, cattle in S., semi-desert in S.E.; economy dependent upon primary inds., especially agr.; coffee major exp., produced on plantations; newly discovered oil-fields; diamonds in remote N.E. Luanda dis.; iron-ore mng. impt. at Cassinga; little mftg.; hydroelectric scheme on Cuarza R.; pts. on natural harbours impt. transhipment points for land-locked central African ctys.; indep. 1975, followed by civil war between rival guerrilla groups; cap. Luanda; a. 1,246,375 km²; p. (est. 1987) 9·24m (inc. Cabinda).

Angoulême, mftg. t., Charente, **France;** on R. Charente; cognac, paper; cath.; suffered during Huguenot wars; p. (1982) 50,151.

Angra do Heroismo, t., cap. admin. dist. **Azores;** pt. on Terceira I.; p. (1981) 75,010.

Angren, t., Uzbek SSR, **USSR;** E. of Tashkent; lgst. ctr. of lignite mng. in central Asia; p. (est. 1985) 122,000.

Anguilla I., Leeward Is., **W.I.;** dry climate, thin limestone soil; exp. cotton, salt; a. 91 km²; reverted to Brit. Crown after secession from St. Kitts–Nevis ass. st. 1967; status of separate Brit. dependency and withdrawal from St. Kitts–Nevis ass. statehood 1980; p. (est. 1985) 7,000.

Angus, l. gov. dist., former co., **Scot.;** part of Tayside Reg.; a. 1,937 km²; p. (est. 1986) 93,150.

Anhui (Anhwei), prov., E. central **China;** in delta region of Chang Jiang; a. 140,686 km²; cap. Hefei; soya-beans, rice, tea, coal and iron; p. (est. 1985) 51,030,000.

Aniakchak, volcano, S.W. Alaska, **USA;** rich variety of flora and fauna on crater floor; alt. 1,384 m.

Anjou, former prov. of **France;** mainly S. of lower R. Loire; ch. t. Angers.

Ankara, c., cap. of **Turkey** since 1923; alt. 1,037 m; univ., cultural and admin. ctr.; p. (1985) 2,235,035.

Anklesvar, t., Gujarat, **India;** natural gas, oil; gas pipelines to Ultaran and Barodi; p. (1961) 20,287.

'Annaba, spt., **Algeria;** on fertile plain; fertiliser factory supplied by phosphates from Djebel-Onk; iron and steel complex; p. (est. 1983) 348,322.

Annaberg–Bucholz, t., Karl-Marx-Stadt, **E. Germany;** in Erz Mtns.; cobalt, tin, uranium mng.: p. (est. 1970) 27,892.

Annam, region, **Vietnam;** formerly within French Union; divided by 17th parallel bdy. (1957); a. 147,560 km²; ch. t. Hué.

Annamese Cordillera, cstl. mtn. range, **Laos, Vietnam;** N.–S. watershed between Mekong and S. China Sea; rising to 2,000 m in Ngoc Linh; forested; inhabited by hill tribes.

Annan, royal burgh, Annandale and Eskdale, **Scot.;** on R. Annan, 3 km from its mouth in Solway F.; Chapelcross reactor sta.; p. (1981) 8,285.

Annandale and Eskdale, l. gov. dist., Dumfries and Galloway, **Scot.;** close to Borders Reg. and Eng.; p. (est. 1986) 35,911.

Annapolis, c., cap. of Maryland, **USA;** naval academy; p. (est. 1984) 32,000.

Annapolis Valley, Nova Scotia, **Canada;** famous fruit growing a., especially for apples.

Annapurna, massif, **Nepal;** part of Himalayas; many glaciers in W. and N.W.; alt. 8,080 m.

Ann Arbor, c., Mich., **USA;** on the Huron; univ. of Michigan.; motor lorries, farm implements, scientific instruments; p. (1984) 107,700.

Annecy, t., **France;** dep. of Haute-Savoie; at lower end of beautiful L. Annecy; textiles, paper, watches; resort; p. (1982) 51,953.

Anqing (Anching), c., Anhui prov., **China;** R. pt.

on Chang Jiang; tr. in agr. prods.; p. (est. 1970) 160,000.

Ansbach, t., Bavaria, **W. Germany;** machin., metallurgy, furniture indus.; rly. ctr.; p. (est. 1986) 37,500.

An-shan, c., Liaoning, N. **China;** at foot of Qian Shan, 96 km S.W. of Shenyang; lgst. iron and steel complex in China (fully automated steel plant), elec., chemical and locomotive ind.; p. (est. 1985) 1,258,600.

Antakya (Antioch), anc. c., S. **Turkey;** on R. Orontes; cap. of Hatay prov., major Roman cap. and early ctr. of Christian culture; p. (1985) 107,821.

Antalya, c., S.W. **Turkey;** freeport (1986) with shallow harbour from which Paul and Barnabas sailed to Antakya; tourism; p. (1985) 261,114.

Antananarivo (Tananarive), cap. of **Madagascar;** ctr. of commerce and communications; airpt.; lge meat preserving factories, plastics, radios, car assembly, shoes, knitted gds.; rice mills; univ.; p. (est. 1985) 662,585.

Antarctica, plateau continent within A. circle; snow-covered, extensive ice sheets and glaciers; volcanoes and Is.; alt. 2,000–3,000 m; dependencies of U.K., Australia, N.Z., France, Norway but a. S. of 60° S reserved for peaceful international scientific research; a. 16 million km².

Antarctic Ocean, parts of Pac., Atl. and Indian Oceans, S. of 60° S.; cold and dangerous; no mammalian life other than whales.

Antibes, t., Alpes-Maritimes, N. of Cap d. A., S.E. **France;** spt. on Fr. Riviera; exp. oranges; flowers for perfume mnfs.; resort; Roman remains; p. (1982) 63,248.

Anticosti, barren I. in G. of St. Lawrence, Quebec, **Canada;** well wooded game reserve, lumbering; 224 km by 45 km.

Antigua, anc. c., **Guatemala;** 32 km W. of Guatemala c.; former cap., destroyed by earthquake 1773; comm. ctr. in coffee dist.; notable colonial ruins; tourism; p. (est. 1983) 27,000.

Antigua and Barbuda, Leeward Is., **W.I.;** aut. st. in ass. with Gt. Britain; indep. 1981; semi-arid limestone; 75 per cent p. in N.E.; sugar, cotton, tourism; cap. St. Johns; a. (inc. Barbuda and Redonda) 440 km²; p. (est. 1986) 81,500.

Antilles, Greater and **Lesser,** archipelago enclosing Caribbean Sea and G. of Mexico, **W.I.;** complex political structure, tropical climate and crops; a. c. 259,000 km².

Antioquia, mtnous. dep. **Colombia;** colonial mng.; agr. now more impt.; one of major p. clusters in Colombia inc. dep. cap. Medellin; a 65,791 km²; p. (1985) 4,055,064.

Antisana, volcano, central **Ecuador;** alt. 5,708 m.

Antofagasta, spt., **Chile;** cap., comm. and industl. ctr. of A. prov.; exps. copper from Chuquicamata; situated in desert, water supply 240 km by aqueduct from Andes; p. (est. 1985) 200,300.

Antony, t., Hauts-de-Seine, **France;** brick wks., toys; sub. of Paris; p. (1982) 54,668.

Antrim, former co.; l. gov. dist., N. **Ireland;** fertile lowland a., arable agr.; borders L. Neagh in S.W. and A. mtns. in N.E.; p. (1981) 44,804.

Antrim, mkt. t., N. **Ireland;** on Lough Neagh; linen, nylon; p. (1981) 22,342.

Antsiranana, (Diego Suarez), t., extreme N. of **Madagascar;** oxygen plant; Fr. naval base; p. (est. 1982) 49,000.

An-tung. See Dandong.

Antwerp, (Anvers), low-lying prov., N. **Belgium:** grain, flax; a. 2,859 km²; p. (est. 1983) 799,909.

Antwerp, (Anvers), spt., **Belgium;** on Scheldt R., 88 km from sea; major transit pt. for EC, competes with Rotterdam; oil pt., refineries; diamonds; Gothic cath.; of artistic and historic interest; p. (est. 1984) 488,425.

Anuradhapura, anc. cap., **Sri Lanka;** ctr. of Buddhism; comm. ctr of irrigated rice-growing a. in dry zone; p. (1981) 36,248.

An-yang, c., Henan prov., **China;** coal, cotton ind.; former cap. of Shang dynasty; p. (1984) 534,400.

Anzhero-Sudzhensk, t., S.W. Siberia, **USSR;** nr. Tomsk; coal mng., mng. equipment pharmaceutics; p. (est. 1985) 110,000.

Aomori, spt., N. Honshu, **Japan;** on A. Bay; cstl. tr. of timber, fish with Hokkaido; S. outlet of Seiken Tunnel between Honshu and Hokkaido; cap. of apple-growing A. prov.; p. (1985) 294,050.

Aosta, t., cap. of Val d'Aosta, N. **Italy;** in valley of Dora Baltea at node of trans-Alpine routes; iron inds.; Mont Blanc road tunnel links to Chamonix, Switzerland, opened 1964; cath., p. (1981) 37,682.

Apapa, spt., sub. of Lagos, **Nigeria;** on mainland opposite I. on which Lagos is situated; modern pt. terminus of W. Nigerian rly. system; exp. agr. prods.; imports industl. prods.

Apeldoorn, c., Gelderland, **Netherlands;** holiday resort; royal summer palace of Het Loo; p. (est. 1987) 146,000.

Apennines, mtn. "backbone" of **Italy;** rich in minerals inc. Carrara marble; cultivation on lower slopes; earthquakes, in S.; barrier to E.–W. communications; hgst. alt. 2,916 m, (Grand Sasso d'Italia); length N.–S. 1,280 km; width 120 km.

Apia, spt., N. Upolu, cap. of **W. Samoa;** exp. agr. prods.; p. (1981) 33,170.

Apolda, t., Erfurt, **E. Germany;** ball-casting and museum; p. (est. 1970) 29,087.

Appalachian Mtns., parallel ranges between Atl. Oc. and Mississippi basin, stretching for 2,560 km from Me. to Ala., **USA;** afforestation, hydro-elec. power, coal in N., iron ore in S.; region of human poverty; average alt. 900 m; Mt. Mitchell 2,039 m.

Appenzell, can., N.E. **Switzerland;** divided into the half-cans. Appenzell Inner-Rhoden, a. 174 km², cap. Appenzell; and Appenzell Ausser-Rhoden; textiles, agr.; a. 243 km², cap. Herisau; p. (est. 1986) 62,000.

Appenzell, picturesque t., cap. of A. can., **Switzerland;** on R. Sitter; lace, embroidery; p. (1970) 5,217.

Appian Way, anc. highway; runs from Rome to Campania and S. **Italy.**

Appleby, t., Eden, Cumbria, **Eng.;** mkt. t. on R. Eden; cas.; p. (1981) 2,384.

Appleton, c., Wis., **USA;** industl. c. in rich dairy dist.; p. (1984) 213,800.

Apsheron, peninsula, E. Azerbaydzhan SSR, **USSR;** on W. side of the Caspian; petroleum wells (nr. Baku) and mud volcanoes.

Apulia, region, S.E. **Italy;** hilly, cstl., pastoral plain; grain, fruits, livestock; wine, olive oil; a, 19,347 km²; p. (est. 1986) 4m.

Aqaba, t., **Jordan's** only spt. at head of G. of A., 88 km from Israeli Elat.; exp. phosphates, imports petroleum; p. (est. 1983) 40,000.

Aqaba G., Red Sea, between **Sinai Peninsula** and **Saudi Arabia;** impt. Biblical waterway; few natural harbours, Dahab, Elat, Aqaba main pts; Elat ctr. of mng. a., and airpt.; length 160 km, width 24 km.

Aquila (L'Aquila), t., cap. of Abruzzi prov., **Italy;** on R. terrace of R. Aterno; mkt. and sm. inds. ass. with local farming; holiday resort; cath.; p. (1981) 63,678.

Aquitaine, Basin of, geographical region, S.W. **France;** to W. and S.W. of Central Massif, to N. of Pyrenees, bordered on W. by Atl. Oc.; warm, wet, oceanic climate; rich agr. lowland; inc. Landes, reclaimed sandy area; ch. ts. Bordeaux, Toulouse; p. (1982) 2,646,800.

Arabia, peninsula, **S.W. Asia;** mainly desert plateau, lying between Red Sea and Persian Gulf; inc. Saudi Arabia, South Yemen, North Yemen, Oman, United Arab Emirates, Kuwait, Bahrain, Qatar; coffee, dates, gums, horses, camels; E. Arabia rich in oil reserves; a. 2,590,000 km²; p. 8,000,000.

Arabian Desert, E. **Egypt;** between R. Nile and Red Sea; alt. approx. 350–2,000 m; a. 207,200 km².

Arabian Mtns., ridge along W. and S.W. csts. of **Arabia;** volcanic, hgst. peaks in Yemen Arab Rep.; average alt. 1,500 m, rising to over 3,500 km.

Arabian Sea, N.W. part of Indian Oc., tr. in Arab dhows; width 2,880 km.

Aracaju, spt., cap. of Sergipe st., **Brazil;** sugar, soap, textiles, tanneries; p. (est. 1985) 361,500.

Arad, new t. (1962) **Israel;** in Negev desert, nr. Beersheba; inds. to be based on gasfields at Zohar and Kanaim; chemicals.

Arad, t., **Romania;** industl., route ctr. on R. Mures; p. (est. 1985) 186,000.

Arafura Sea, N. of Australia, S.W. of Papua-New Guinea, and E. of Timor.

Aragua, sm. upland cstl. st., **Venezuela;** lies in densely populated industl., agr., urban and political region of cty.; tropical climate; good road network; cap. Maracay in fertile Aragua valley; a. 7,014 km²; p. (1981) 891,623.

Araguaia, R., Brazil; trib. of Tocatins R.; splits into 2 parts in middle course to form Banaral I.; rapids; length 1,800 km.

Arak, t., **Iran;** mkt. and agr. processing ctr. for

surrounding region on Trans-Iranian rly.; carpets; p. (1986) 268,405.

Aral Sea (Aral'skoye More), inland sea with no outlet, **USSR;** fed by Amu-Dar'ya and Syr Dar'ya Rs.; sparse p. on shore but attempts to develop agr.; a. 63,805 km².

Aran Is.; Galway, **R.o.I.;** inc. anc. religious ctr. and I. of Inishmore; fishing; agr.; a. 47 km²; p. (1971) 2,269.

Arandelovac, t., Yugoslavia; industl. a. based on local sources of refractory clays; tourist resort.

Aranjuez, t., Spain; 18th cent. planned t. on R. Tagus; mkt. gardens; strawberries, asparagus; p. (1981) 35,484.

Ararat, volcanic mtn., **Turkey;** supposed resting-place of Noah's Ark.; 5.168 m.

Ararat, t., Victoria, Australia; former gold rush t. on W. Highway and ctr. for Grampians; p. (1986) 8,015.

Aras (Araxes) R., flows from Bingöl Dağlari mtns. **(Turkey)** to Caspian Sea forming long sections of **USSR–Iran** frontier; valley in rich fruit growing a.; home of anc. civilisation; length 880 km.

Araucania, terr., **Chile;** concentration of A. Indians, especially in Rio Tolten valley; a. 31,761 km²; p. (est. 1984) 675,741.

Arbroath, royal burgh, Angus cst., **Scot.;** engin., textiles, fishing pt.; holiday resort; p. (1981) 24,093.

Arcachon, t., Gironde, S.W. **France;** on S. side of Bassin d'Arcachon, Bay of Biscay; fish. pt., oysters; resort; p. (1982) 13,664.

Arcadia, region of anc. **Greece** in Peloponnesus; tradition of pastoral agr. in dry a.; ch. c. was Megalopolis.

Arctic Ocean, almost landlocked sea extending from N. Pole to Atl. Oc.; flora and fauna of scientific interest; a. 14,089,600 km².

Ardabil, anc. c. in fertile agr. a., Azerbaijan, **Iran;** tr. and route ctr.; carpets; p. (1986) 283,710.

Ardal, t., Norway; on Sogne fiord; site of aluminium wks.

Ardèche, dep., S. **France;** Cevennes Mtns.; olives, wine, silk, minerals; cap. Privas; a. 55,530 km²; p. (1982) 268,400.

Ardennes, hilly wooded region, **Belgium,** N. **France, Luxembourg,** rising to over 600 m; infertile; heavy fighting in both world wars.

Ardennes, dep., N.E. **France;** farming, woollens, iron; cap. Mézières; a. 5,250 km²; p. (1982) 301,900.

Ardglass, sm. t., Down, **N. Ireland;** one of N.I.'s impt. fishing pts.

Ardnacrusha, Clare, **R.o.I.;** power sta. on R. Shannon, 5 km N. of Limerick.

Ardrishaig, sm. spt., Argyll and Bute, **Scot.;** on Loch Gilp, at entrance to Crinan canal; p. (1981) 1,322.

Ardrossan, burgh, Cunninghame, S.W. **Scot.;** re-sort and spt. on Firth of Clyde; oil storage, ship-bldg., road bitumen, engin.; p. (1981) 11,337.

Ards, l. gov. dist., N. Ireland; formerly part of Down; N. of Strangford L.; main t. New-townards; p. (1981) 57,502.

Arecibo, spt., N. cst. **Puerto Rico;** sited in rich agr. a.; local hydroelec. power; p. (1980) 86,766.

Arendal, spt. **Norway;** on Skagerrak; wood pulp, aluminium, shipping; p. (1980) 11,501.

Arequipa, c., **Peru;** cap. of A. prov. and former Inca c.; impt. wool mkt.; alpaca wool inds.; growth point for prov. industl. development; copper mng. nearby; earthquakes frequent; p. (est. 1985) 545,000.

Arezzo, c., cap. of Arezzo prov., Tuscany, **Italy;** hill site in basin within Apennines at junc. of valley routes; in mediaeval times ctr. of learning and the arts; birthplace of Petrarch and Vasari; Gothic cath.; mkt. for silk, wine, olives; p. (1981) 92,105.

Arfon, l. gov. dist., Gwynedd, **Wales;** borders Menai Straits and inc. Bangor and Caernarvon; p. (est. 1988) 55,200.

Argenteuil, t., Val-d'Oise, **France;** N.W. sub. of Paris; industl., mkt. gardens; p. (1982) 96,045.

Argentina, fed. rep., **S. America;** 2nd. in a., 3rd. in p. of S. American sts.; p. predominantly of European origin and highly urbanised; varied relief and climate, inc. Andes, tropical N., Chaco, Pampas, Patagonia in S.; agr. less impt. internally than other S. American sts., yet provides most of exp., inc. meat, wool, wheat, maize, cotton; petroleum, natural gas; cap. Buenos Aires; new cap. to be built on fringe of Patagonia to decentralize power from Buenos Aires by 1989; a. 2,797,109 km² p. (est. 1987) 31·5m.

Argonne, hill ridge, S.E. Paris basin, **France**; composed of greensand; wooded; fighting in 2nd world war; alt. 300 m; a. c. 650 km².

Argos, c. of anc. **Greece**; N.E. Peloponnesus; leading c. in 7th cent. B.C. under King Pheidon; p. (1981) 20,955.

Argostólion, cap. of Cephalonia I., **Greece**; shipbldg.; earthquake 1953; p. (1981) 6,788.

Argyll, former co., N.W. **Scot.**; now divided between Highland and Strathclyde Regs.

Argyll and Bute, l. gov. dist., Strathclyde Reg., **Scot.**; rural a. N.W. of Glasgow conurb.; a. 6,754 km²; p. (est. 1986) 65,586.

Århus, c., **Denmark**; prin. spt. on E. cst. Jutland; admin. ctr. of A. prov.; Gothic cath.; univ.; comm. and industl. ctr.; pt. processing inds., oil refining; p. (est. 1987) 256,000.

Arica, spt., N. **Chile**, free zone; exp. tin, copper, sulphur mainly from Bolivia; rly. to La Paz and oil pipeline connects to Sica-Sica in Bolivia; p. (est. 1985) 155,500.

Ariège, dep., S. **France**; Pyrenees in S., fertile lowland in N.; livestock, fruit, iron, copper; cap. Foix; a. 4,900 km²; p. (1982) 135,200.

Arizona, st., **USA**; home of Apache Indians; much desert, rainfall increasing to E.; many lge. irrigation schemes for cotton, grain, fruit, vegetables; inc. Col. Plateau and Grand Canyon to N.; copper, lead mng. and refining; prin. ts. Phoenix (cap.), Tucson; huge meteorite crater nr. Winslow; admitted to union 1912; st. flower Saguaro Cactus blossom; st. bird cactus wren; a. 295,024 km²; p. (1980) 2,718,000.

Arkansas, st., **USA**; highland in N.W., inc. Ozark, Ouachita mtns., lowland in S.E. where Arkansas R. and Mississippi alluvium; humid climate; cotton cultivation; bauxite, coal, petroleum; admitted to union 1836; st. flower Apple Blossom, st. bird Mockingbird; cap. Little Rock; a. 137,534 km²; p. (1985) 2,359,000.

Arkansas, R., **USA**; rises in Rockies, trib. of Mississippi; completion (1971) of 704 km waterway (17 dams and locks), opening Okla. and Ark. to sea; flows through impt. agr. as.; several major cs. on banks; length 2,334 km.

Arkhangel'sk, c., major spt., **USSR**; on E. side Dvina estuary, White Sea; lge. harbour kept open in winter by ice breakers; fishery headquarters; inds. from local softwood resources; engin.; hydroelec. power; p. (est. 1985) 408,000.

Arklow, U.D., spt., Wicklow, **R.o.I.**; fisheries, pottery; fertiliser plant under construction; resort; p. (1981) 8,646.

Arlberg, Alpine pass, 1,803 m; main western entry to Austria; rly. tunnel 10 km long; road tunnel (1979) 14 km long.

Arles, t., Provence, S. **France**; on Rhône delta; anc. Roman t.; historic bldgs and monuments; van Gogh and Gauguin painted here; p. (1982) 50,772.

Arlington, t., Texas, **USA**; aircraft, missiles; rapid expansion; p. (1984) 213,800; 2nd fastest growing t. in USA.

Arlington, t., Va., **USA**; Arlington National Cemetery contains tombs of the Unknown Soldier and President Kennedy.

Arlon, t., cap. of Luxembourg prov., **Belgium**; p. (1982) 22,364.

Armadale, burgh, West Lothian, **Scot.**; 16 km S.W. Linlithgow; p. (1981) 9,530.

Armagh, former co.; l. gov. dist., **N. Ireland**; lowland in N. rising to over 450 m adjoins R.o.I. border; mainly rural; p. (1981) 48,105.

Armagh, t., A., **N. Ireland**; caths.; linen, whiskey; p. (1981) 12,700.

Armavir, c., Krasnodar Terr., **RSFSR** on Kuban R.; rly. junc.; engin.; food processing; p. (est. 1985) 168,000.

Armenia, constituent rep., **USSR**; former a. divided between Turkey, Russia, Iran; mineral inds.; sub-tropical agr.; hydroelec. stas. under constr.; earthquake 1988; disturbances 1989; cap. Yerevan; a. 30.821 km²; p. (1986) 3,369,000.

Armenia, t., **Colombia**; coffee; p. (est.) 199,459.

Armentières, mftg. t., Nord, **France**; base of British operations against Lille in first world war; textiles; p. (1982) 55,913 (French met. a.).

Armidale, t., N.S.W., **Australia**; univ.; ctr. of New England wool producing dist.; p. (1981) 18,922.

Arnhem, c., cap. of Gelderland prov., **Neth.**; on R. Neder-Rhine; lge. tin smelter; lt. inds. using rubber and rayon; p. (est. 1987) 128,000.

Arnhem Land, N. part of N.T., **Australia**; an aboriginal reserve; bauxite worked, uranium finds.

Arno, R., central **Italy**; flows past Florence and Pisa into Mediterranean; Val d'Arno is the fruitful valley of the R.; length 120 km.

Arnold, t., Gedling, Notts., **Eng.**; almost continuous with Nottingham; hosiery, brick mkg.; p. (1981) 37,242.

Arnstadt, t., Erfurt, **E. Germany**; on R. Gera, 16 km S. of Erfurt; artificial silk, leather gds., engin.; p. (est. 1970) 28,762.

Aroostook, dist., New England, **USA**; produces 12 per cent of USA potatoes.

Arran, I., Cunninghame, **Scot.**; in Firth of Clyde; contains many summer resorts; a. 427 km²; p. (1981) 4,726.

Arras, t., cap. of Pas-de-Calais dep., **France**; historic cap. of Artois; renowned for tapestry; agr. mkt.; brewing, textiles, metal inds.; almost destroyed in first world war; p. (1982) 80,477 (met. a.).

Árta, t., cap. of Árta prov., Epirus, **Greece**; agr. tr. ctr.; Ambracia was its name in anc. Greece; p. (1981) 20,004.

Artemovsk, t., Ukrainian SSR, **USSR**; industl. ctr. in Donets Basin; salt, coal, iron, mercury; p. (est. 1969) 81,000.

Arthur's Seat, famous hill, Edinburgh, **Scot.**; 251 m.

Artois, former prov. of N. **France**; now mainly with dep. of Pas-de-Calais.

Arun, l. gov. dist., West Sussex, **Eng.**; W. section of S. Downs and ts. of Arundel, Littlehampton and Bognor Regis; p. (est. 1988) 130,200.

Arunachal Pradesh, new union terr. (1972), N.E. Assam, **India**; formerly N.E. Frontier Agency; in Himalayas bordering Tibet and Burma; tribal p.; cap. Itanagar; a. 81,424 km²; p. (1981) 631,839.

Arundel, t., Arun, West Sussex, **Eng.**; mkt. t. on Arun R.; Arundel Castle, seat of Duke of Norfolk; p. (1981) 2,235.

Arusha, t., **Tanzania**; S.W. of Mt. Meru; mkt. for coffee; H.Q. of E. African Common Market; airpt. at 1,388 m (W. of t.); p. (1978) 55,281.

Aruwimi, R., **Zaïre**; trib. of R. Zaïre; route of Stanley's famous forest march in 1887; 992 km long.

Arvida, t., S. Quebec, **Canada**; aluminium plant; nearby Saguenay power development.

Arvika, t., N. of L. Vänern, **Sweden**; agr. machin. and implements, pianos, organs; p. (est. 1970) 15,998.

Asahikawa, c., Hokkaido, **Japan**; on Ishikari R.; industl., comm. and rly. ctr. for gr. agr. region; p. (1985) 363,631.

Asansol, t., W. Bengal, **India**; in Damodar valley; rly. junc.; coal mng., iron, steel; p. (1981) 187,039 (c.), 366,424 (met. a.).

Ascension I., part of Brit. col. **St. Helena**, 1,216 km to S.E.; volcanic; ch. settlement Georgetown; nesting place of sooty tern; Brit. earth satellite sta. (1966); airstrip known as Miracle Mile; some arable and pastoral agr.; a. 88 km²; p. (est. 1985) 1,700.

Aschaffenburg, t., Bavaria, **W. Germany**; pt. on R. Main and Trans-European waterway; cas.; synthetic fibres, scientific-based inds.; p. (est. 1986) 59,600.

Aschersleben, t., Halle, **E. Germany**; potash and lignite mng., chemicals, textiles, engin., horticulture; p. (est. 1973) 37,150.

Ascoli Piceno, cath. c., central **Italy**; cap. of A.P. prov.; lies in wooded hills; agr. inds.; (1981) 54,298.

Ascot, v., Berks., **Eng.**; famous racecourse at Ascot Heath.

Ashanti, admin. region, central **Ghana**; formerly powerful native st.; timber, cocoa; growing importance of gold mines (15% Ghana's exp.); new mines opened 1984; cap. Kumasi; a. 24,390 km²; p. (1984) 2,089,683.

Ashbourne, t., Derbys. Dales, **Eng.**; nr. Dovedale; mkt. t.; quarrying, milk processing; p. (1981) 5,960.

Ashburton, t., Teignbridge, Devon, **Eng.**; old

mkt. t., S. gateway to Dartmoor; anc. stannary t.; p. (1981) 3,564.

Ashburton, t., S. Island, **N.Z.;** ctr. of gr. wheat growing dist.; p. (est. 1987) 14,000.

Ashby-de-la-Zouch, t., North West Leics., **Eng.;** local coal-mng., hosiery; p. (1981) 11,518.

Ashby Woulds, t., North West Leics., **Eng.;** clay mng., pottery; p. (1981) 3,015.

Ashdod, pt., Israel; new modern deepwater pt. on Med. cst., 32 km S. of Jaffa.

Ashdown Forest, East Sussex, **Eng.;** heath and woodland; site of former iron industry.

Asheville, c., N.C., **USA;** economic and cultural ctr. of mtnous. region; winter resort; glass; p. (1984) 58,600 (c.), 165,600 (met. a.).

Ashfield, l. gov. dist., Notts., **Eng.;** comprises Sutton-in-Ashfield, Hucknall and Kirkby A.; p. (est. 1988) 107,700.

Ashford, t., l. gov. dist., Kent, **Eng.;** mkt. t., rly. works closing down but may be kept open if channel tunnel started; p. (est. 1988) 95,100 (dist.).

Ashikaga, c., Honshu, **Japan;** cultural ctr.; old silk-weaving ctr.; anc. school with library of Chinese classics; p. (1985) 167,656.

Ashington, t., Wansbeck, Northumberland, **Eng.;** coal mng., p. (1981) 23,658.

Ashkhabad, c., cap. of Turkmen SSR, **USSR;** in foothills of Kopet-Dag mtns.; textiles, clothing, food processing; univ.; p. (1986) 366,000.

Ashland, t., Ky., **USA;** on R. Ohio; iron, steel, lumber, leather; p. (1980) 27,064.

Ashtabula, t., Ohio, **USA;** pt. on L. Erie handling iron ore, coal; many diversified inds.; p. (1980) 23,449.

Ashton-in-Makerfield, t. Gtr. Manchester, **Eng.;** nr. Wigan; former coal mng.; p. (1981) 29,341.

Ashton-under-Lyne, t., Tameside, Gtr. Manchester, **Eng.;** textiles, lt. engin., rubber, tobacco; p. (1981) 44,671.

Asia, largest continent, extends over nearly one-third of the land surface of the earth; chief mtn. ranges, Himalayas, Kunlun, Tien Shan, Altai, Tibetan plateau; ch. Rs., Ob, Yangtze, Yenisey, Lena, Amur, Hwang-ho, Mekong; deserts, Arabia, Thar, Takla Makan, Gobi; some very fertile valleys and plains; climate very varied, extreme in N., monsoonal in S. and E.; gold, coal, oil, iron, manganese, antimony, tin; principal countries in Asia: Turkey in Asia, Israel, Jordan, Iran, Iraq, Afghanistan, India, Pakistan, Sri Lanka, Burma, China, Vietnam, Indonesia, Thailand, Malaysia, Korea, Japan, Bangladesh, Kampuchea, Laos, Philippines, Korea, Syria, Lebanon, Taiwan, and Soviet Asia; industrialisation greatest in Japan, China, Korea, India, and Soviet Asia; a. c. 43,250,000 km²; p. (est. 1984) 2,777,385,000 (58 per cent of world total).

Asia Minor. *See* Anatolia.

Asir, dist., S.W. **Saudi Arabia;** desert cstl. plain with parallel A. mtns.

Askja, volcanic crater, L. and lava plain, E. **Iceland;** surrounded by Dyngju-fjöll Hills; alt. 1,450 m.

Asmara, c., **Ethiopia;** alt. 2,226 m; on rly.; textiles, matches, soap, brewing; p. (est. 1985) 284,748.

Asnières, t., sub. N.W. Paris, Hauts-de-Seine, **France;** regattas; p. (1982) 71,220.

Aspra Spitia, t. central **Greece;** new industl. t. close to Andikira Bay; aluminium wks.

Aspull, t., Gtr. Manchester, **Eng.;** nr. Wigan; former coal mng.; p. (1981) 6,816.

Assab, pt. on Red Sea, **Ethiopia;** oil refinery; p. (est. 1970) 14,900.

Assam, st., **India;** on Brahmaputra R.; valley enclosed by mtns.; forested; extensive tea plantations; rice, cotton, coal; oil development at Rudrasagar; former cap. Shillong; since 1956 4 new sts. carved out – Nagaland (1963), Meghalaya, Manipur, Tripura (1972), and union terrs. of Arunachal Pradesh and Mizoram (1972); a. (1972) 121,973 km²; p. (est. 1981) 19,896,843.

Assen, t., prov. cap. Drenthe, **Neth.;** route ctr.; food processing; p. (est. 1987) 48,000.

Assiniboine, R., Manitoba, **Canada;** joins Red R. at Winnipeg; 720 km long.

Assisi, t., Umbria, central **Italy;** 24 km S.E. of Perugia; birthplace of St. Francis; cath. and old cas.; p. (1981) 24,440.

Assyria, gr. anc. empire, northern plain Mesopotamia (Iraq), cap. Nineveh; drained by R. Tigris; now mainly pastoral farming a.

Astara, pt., Azerbaydzhan, **USSR;** on Caspian Sea, at frontier with Iran; natural gas pipeline.

Asti, t., Italy; route, industl., comm. ctr.; cath.; sparkling wines; p. (1981) 77,681.

Astin Tagh, (Aerchin Shan), mtn. range, S., Sinkiang, **China;** N. branch of Kunlun mtn. system which separates Tibet from Turkestan; rises to 5,000 m.

Astrakhan', c., **RSFSR;** major air and sea pt. on delta of R. Volga, 80 km from Caspian Sea; handles petroleum, timber; lge. fishing fleet; caviar; food and pt. processing inds.; astrakhan fur; cap. A. oblast; univ.; p. (1986) 503,000.

Asturias, region and former kingdom, N.W. **Spain;** S. of Bay of Biscay; now Oviedo prov.; isolated from rest of Spain by Cantabrian mtns.; coal mng; p. (1987) 1,115,016.

Asunción, c., cap. of **Paraguay;** at confluence of Rs. Paraguay and Pilcomayo; 25 per cent of p. of Paraguay in and around A.; admin., industl., comm. ctr.; cath.; p. (1984) 729,307 (met. a.).

Aswan, t., Upper **Egypt;** on Nile at first cataract; anc. name Syene. Aswan dam built 1902, 5 km S. of t., to control Nile flood; lge. cement plant; univ. proposed; p. (1985) 182,700.

Aswan High Dam (107 m high) opened 1971, on R. Nile, **Egypt,** 6 km S. of old Aswan dam, has harnessed R. to bring electricity and irrigation to hundreds of vs. and prevent Nile's flood from being lost into Mediterranean. *See also* Nile.

Asyût, major c. of Upper **Egypt;** nr. A. dam on Nile R.; anc. Lycopolis; noted pottery, wood, ivory carving; caravan tr. ctr.; cap. of A. prov.; p. (1985) 274,400.

Atacama Desert, N. **Chile;** arid coastal tract rich in nitrates; one of world's driest deserts.

Ataléia, t., Minas Gerais, **Brazil;** W. of Sierra des Aimorés; p. (est. 1967) 118,112.

Atami, c., Honshu, **Japan;** on Sagami Bay; seaside hot-spring resort; p. (1985) 49,374.

Atbara, t., Sudan; at confluence of Atbara R. with Nile; heavy inds.; international airpt.; p. (1983) 73,000.

Atbara R., or **Black Nile, Ethiopia** and **Sudan;** trib. of Nile; provides irrigation water for Sudan; length 1,264 km.

Athelney, hill, formerly encircled by marsh nr. Taunton, Somerset, **Eng.;** between the Rs. Tone and Parret; King Alfred's hiding-place.

Athens (Athínai), c., cap of **Greece;** on plain of Attica; admin., economic and cultural ctr.; varied mnfs., notably textiles; anc. c. of Greek art and learning; Acropolis and many splendid temples; univ.; airpt; p. (1981) 885,737 (c.) 3,027,331 (met. a.).

Athens, t., Ga., **USA;** univ.; cotton gds., lumber; p. (1984) 42,500 (c.), 136,600 (met. a.).

Athens, t., Ohio, **USA;** univ.; coal, lt. inds.; p. (1980) 19,743.

Atherstone, t., North Warwicks., **Eng.;** N. of Coventry; mkt. t., coal mng, footwear, granite quarrying.

Athlone, U.D., Westmeath, **R.o.I.;** on R. Shannon; radio sta.; textiles; p. (1981) 9,444.

Atholl, dist., N. Perth and Kinross, **Scot.;** extensive deer forests and grouse moors; a. 1,166 km².

Athos, peninsula, Khalkidhiki, N.E. **Greece;** Mt. Athos (2,034 m) at S. tip, known as Holy Mountain, home of monastic community; ch. t. Karves.

Athy, U.D., Kildare, **R.o.I.;** on Grand Canal; agr. machin.; p. (1981) 5,565.

Atitlán L., S.W. **Guatemala;** volcanic; famed for beauty; dense p. on shore; maize, fishing; a. 137 km².

Atlanta, c., st. cap. Ga., **USA;** univ.; cotton, paper, farm implements, printing, clothing; p. (1984) 426,100 (c.), 2,380,000 (met. a.).

Atlantic City, c., N.J., **USA;** summer resort, convention c.; p. (1984) 36,800 (c.), 290,400 (met. a.).

Atlantic Ocean, 2nd lgst ocean; a. est. 82,440,000 km²; connected to Pac. Oc. by Panama Canal; central ridge of volcanic activity runs S. from Iceland to Antarctic, some peaks emerging as Is. mainly in N. (*e.g.* Azores, Ascension, Tristan da Cunha); S, mainly a barren waste of water; chief deeps: Milwaukee Deep (9,225 m) nr. Bahamas and Nares Deep (8,531 m) nr. Puerto Rico.

Atlas, mtn. range, N.W. **Africa;** extends 2,400 km through Morocco, Algeria, to Tunisia; formed of several chains; mineralised, roads across passes; long been home of Berber tribes; average height 2,500–3,000 m; hgst. peak Jebel Toubkal, 4,141 m.

Atlixco Valley, t., **Mexico;** 16 km S.W. of Puebla; fertile volcanic soils; wheat, fruit, vegetables.

Attica, (Attiki), dep., **Greece;** agr., serving cap. Athens; a. 3,761 km²; p. (1981) 342,093.

Attleboro, c., Mass., **USA;** founded (1669) by immigrants from English Attleborough (Norfolk); jewellery, silverware; p. (1980) 34,196.

Attock, t., **Pakistan;** on Indus R. between Peshawar and Islamabad; oil wells, oil refining; impt. crossing of R. Indus.

Aubagne, t., Bouches-du-Rhône, **France;** bricks, tiles, corks, meat processing; p. (1981) 38,571.

Aube, dep., N.E. **France;** arid, infertile chalk in ctr. and N.W.; wooded and fertile S.E.; drained by Seine and A. Rs.; cap. Troyes; a. 6,024 km²; p. (1982) 289,800.

Aubervilliers, t., Seine-St. Denis, **France;** sub. of Paris; industl.; p. (1982) 67,775.

Auburn, t., N.Y., **USA;** shoes, woollens, farm implements; st. prison; p. (1980) 32,548.

Aubusson, t., Creuse dep., **France;** sited on Creuse R.; fine tapestries and carpets; p. (1982) 6,153.

Auch, t., cap. of Gers dep., **France;** agr., mkt., tr. in Armagnac brandy; agr. processing; p. (1982) 25,543.

Auchterarder, burgh, Perth and Kinross, **Scot.;** 24 km S.W. of Perth; health resort on S. slopes of vale of Strathearn; woollen inds.; p. (1981) 2,895.

Auchtermuchty, burgh, North East Fife, **Scot.;** at S. foot of Lomond Hills, 40 km N.E. of Alloa; distilling; p. (1981) 1,643.

Auckland, spt., c., N.I., **N.Z.;** lgst. c. in N.Z.; seat of government 1845–64; univ.; extensive tr. and shipping; sawmills, sugar refinery, shipbldg., glass; steelwks. projected 40 km S. of A., in Waikato iron sand a.; p. (est. 1987) 148,400.

Auckland Is., uninhabited gr. of S. Pac. Oc.; 320 km off N.Z.; discovered by British (1806); fur seals; a. 606 km².

Aude, dep., S. **France;** mtnous.; fertile N., salt from S. cstl. lagoons; drained by A. R. to Mediterranean; cap. Carcassonne; a. 6,340 km² p. (1982) 281,100.

Audenshaw, t., Gtr. Manchester, **Eng.;** metals, leather, pharmaceuticals; p. (1981) 10,744.

Aue, t., Karl-Marx-Stadt, **E. Germany;** 32 km S.E. of Zwickau; uranium mng., metallurgy, textiles; p. (est. 1973) 32,989.

Aughrim, v., Galway, **R.o.I.;** battle (1691) between William III and James II.

Augsburg, c., Bavaria, **W. Germany;** at confluence of Rs. Lech and Wertach; cath.; theological institute; major industl. ctr., textiles, engin.; route ctr.; p. (est. 1986) 246,000.

Augusta, t., Sicily, **Italy;** on E. cst. peninsula; gd. harbour used as naval base; fishing; lubricants; p. (1981) 38,900.

Augusta, c., Georgia, **USA;** pt.; on Savannah R. and boundary with S.C.; cotton, cotton-seed oil, chemicals, foundries; p. (1984) 46,000 (c.), 368,300 (met. a.).

Aulnay-sous-Bois, t., Seine-St. Denis, **France;** residtl. sub. of Paris; p. (1982) 76,032.

Aurangabad, t., admin. ctr., Maharashtra, **India;** textiles, grain tr.; p. (1981) 316,000

Aurès, mtn. massif, **Algeria;** Berber stronghold.

Aurignac, v., Haute-Garonne, S. **France;** at foot of Pyrenees; caves, paleolithic remains.

Aurillac, t., cap., mkt. t. for dep. of Cantal, **France;** cheeses, umbrellas, leather goods; p. (1982) 33,197.

Aurora, t., Ill., **USA;** rly. wks., foundries, office equipment; p. (1984) 194,800.

Aussig. *See* Usti Nad Labem.

Austin, st. cap., Texas, **USA;** educational and artistic ctr., st. univ.; food processing; international airpt.; p. (1984) 397,000 (c.), 645,400 (met. a.).

Australasia, div. of **Oceania;** inc. Australia, Tasmania, N.Z., New Guinea and neighbouring archipelagos.

Australia, Commonwealth of, lgst. I., smallest continent in world; forms part of **Australasia;** Cook took possession for Britain 1770; Commonwealth proclaimed 1901; fed. of N.S.W.,

Victoria, Queensland, S.A., W. Australia, Tasmania; inc. also Cap. Terr. (Canberra) and N.T.; p. and inds. concentrated around cst. and in st. caps.; 41 per cent live in Gtr. Sydney and Melbourne; agr. economy (sheep, wheat, dairying) giving way to mineral inds. esp. in W.A. where lge. and diverse deposits abound; offshore petroleum deposits; N. cst. tropical, interior dry, S.E. cst. more moderate, Mediterranean climate in S.W.; mtns. in E. form Gr. Dividing Range separating E. cst. from interior, where plains drained by Murray-Darling and L. Eyre R. systems (used for hydroelec. power and irrigation); cap. Canberra; a. 7,682,300 km²; p. (1986) 16,018,350.

Australian Alps, form S. part of Gr. Dividing Range, between E. cst. and interior, **Australia;** extend for 320 km.; contain hgst. mtns. in Australia; Mount Kosciusko (2,228 m.); snow melt vital for irrigation of S.E.; popular tourist and naturalist a.

Australian Antarctic Terr., part of **Antarctica;** between 145° E. and 160° E. and S. of 60° S. excluding Adélie Land; research stas. of Mawson, Davis and Casey.

Australian Bight, Gr.; gr. cstl. indentation S. of Nullarbor Plain, **Australia.**

Australian Capital Territory, fed. terr. surrounding Canberra, seat of Fed. Govt. of **Australia;** also inc. a. around Jervis Bay, originally planned to serve as pt. p. (1986) 258,910.

Austria, rep., **Europe;** after long and glamorous history under the Hapsburg **(L53),** instability between A. and Hungary a cause of first world war; forcibly incorporated in German Reich, 1938, liberated 1945, recovered indep. 1955; almost entirely within Alps; drained mainly by Danube; continental climate; magnificent scenery generates a major tourist ind. but much food must be imported; forests and timber inds.; mineralised, iron-ore of Styria; hydroelec.; inds. located in ts.; cap. Vienna; a. 83,898 km²; p. (est. 1986) 7,565,603, mainly Roman Catholic.

Austria, Lower, st., **Austria;** impt. agr. a.; cap. Vienna; a. (excluding Vienna) 18,384 km²; p. (excluding Vienna) (est. 1986) 1·425m.

Auvergne, old French prov. forming the present deps. of Puy-de-Dôme, Cantal and a small part of Haute-Loire; part of Massif Central; volcanic scenery; ch. t. Clermont-Ferrand; p. (1982) 1,332,200.

Auvergne Mtns., mtns., central **France;** in N.W. of Central Massif; highest peak Puy de Sancy in Mt. Dore, 1,887 m; volcanic landscape.

Auxerre, t., cap. of Yonne dep., **France;** comm. and industl. ctr.; wine; tr.; Gothic cath.; p. (1982) 41,164.

Ava, c., **Burma;** on the Irrawaddy R.; former cap.; many pagodas, now ruins; bridge over R.

Avebury, v., Wilts,. **Eng.;** mediaeval v. outside Neolithic circle and avenues, nr. Silbury Hill; lgst. prehistoric structure in England.

Aveiro, t., **Portugal;** on Vouga estuary, connected to sea by canal; fish. pt. salt from lagoons; p. (1981) 28,625.

Avellaneda, industl. sub. of Buenos Aires, **Argentina;** hides, wool; p. (1980) 330,654.

Avellino, t., cap. of A. prov., **Italy;** on motorway from Naples to W.; monastery; sulphur mng. and refining; hats; p. (1981) 56,892.

Aversa, t. **Italy;** in fertile plain of Campania; agr. and route ctr.; p. (1981) 50,525.

Avesta, t., Kopparberg, **Sweden;** on Dal R.; iron, aluminium and charcoal wks.; p. (est. 1970) 28,545.

Aveyron, dep., **France;** on S.W. rim of Central Massif, inc. Causses limestones; extensive forests; grain, dairying, sheep; coal; cap. Rodez; a. 8,767 km²; p. (1982) 277,800.

Aviemore, t., Badenoch and Strathspey, **Scot.;** on R. Spey, 19 km S.W. of Grantown; winter sports; p. (1981) 2,426.

Avignon, t., cap. of Vaucluse, dep., **France;** anc. Roman t. at crossing of R. Rhône; Provençal tourist ctr.; diversified inds. inc. wine tr.; p. (1982) 91,474.

Avila, t., cap. of A. prov., **Spain;** in Old Castile; univ., cath.; mediaeval architecture; birthplace of St. Teresa; p. (1987) 44,221.

Avon, non-met. co., S. **Eng.;** based on Lower Avon valley and Severnside; major ctrs. of p. at

Bristol and Bath; pt. at Avonmouth; cstl. resort of Weston-super-Mare; bordered by Mendips in S.; a. 1,336 km²; p. (est. 1988) 954,300.

Avon, R., Avon/Wiltshire, **Eng.**; flows from Cotswolds to enter Bristol Channel at Avonmouth; spectacular limestone gorge between Bristol and the sea; length 128 km.

Avon, R., Warwicks, **Eng.**; flows past Stratford-on-A., to reach Severn R. at Tewkesbury; fertile agr. valley; string of ts. along course; length 152 km.

Avon, R., Wilts./Hants./Dorset, **Eng.**; flows past Salisbury into English Channel at Christchurch; length 112 km.

Avonmouth, outport of Bristol, at mouth of R. Avon, **Eng.**; docks; seed crushing, petrol refinery, non-ferrous metal and chemical plants.

Avranches, t., Manche, **France**; Normandy mkt. t.; cider and dairy produce; p. (1982) 10,419.

Awe, Loch, Argyll and Bute, **Scot.**; 13 km W. of Inveraray, bordered by Ben Cruachan; a. 41 km², length 40 km; salmon and trout fishing; hydroelec. sta. at Cruachan.

Axholme, Isle of, flat lowland a., Boothferry, N.W. Lincs., **Eng.**; W. of Trent R.; drained by Vermuyden in 17th cent.

Axminster, t., East Devon, **Eng.**; brushes; flour and sawmills; carpet and press tool mftg.

Ayacucho *See* **Huamanga.**

Aydin, t., **Turkey**; anc. Tralles; rly. and agr. tr. ctr. for surrounding a.; p. (1985) 90,449.

Ayers Rock, N.T., **Australia**; giant terra-cotta monolith rising abruptly to 335 m; sacred to Aborigines; major tourist attraction.

Aylesbury, co. t., Aylesbury Vale, Bucks., **Eng.**; mkt. t.; expanded t.; p. (1981) 48,159.

Aylesbury Vale, l. gov. dist., Bucks., **Eng.**; a. in N.W. of co. inc. Aylesbury and Buckingham; p. (est. 1988) 145,400.

Aylesford, mkt. t., Kent, **Eng.**; N.W. Maidstone.

Ayr, royal burgh, Kyle and Carrick, **Scot.**; pt. on F. of Clyde, 48 km S.W. of Glasgow; Burns born nearby; p. (1981) 49,481.

Ayrshire, former co. **Scot.**; now part of Strathclyde Region.

Aysgarth, v. Richmondshire, North Yorks., **Eng.**; on R. Ure in Wensleydale; famous waterfalls.

Ayutthaya, t., **Thailand**; former cap., on Menam Chao Phraya R. delta; p. (1980) 47,189.

Azarbaijan, E. and **W.,** provs., N. **Iran**; border USSR (Azerbaydzhan SSR) and Turkey; cap. (E.A.) Tabriz; cap. (W.A.) Rezayeh; p. (1986) 4,180,376 (E) and 1,989,935 (W).

Azerbaydzhan, Transcaucasia, constituent rep. **USSR**; Caucasus and Lesser Caucasus separated by hot dry irrigated steppe; impt. oil ind.; disturbances 1989; 86,661 km²; p. (1986) 6,718,000

Azores, Portuguese gr. of physically and climatically attractive Is. in mid-Atlantic about 1,440 km W. of Lisbon; partial indep. by regional gov. (1977); volcanic; fruit, wine; ch. spts: Ponta Delgada, Horta (a major whaling ctr.), Angra do Heroismo; U.S. air bases on Terceira I.; a. 2,569 km²; p. (est. 1986) 253,500.

Azov Sea (Azouskoye More), USSR; joins Black Sea by Kerch strait; receives Don R.; fisheries; a. 36,000 km².

Azpeitia, t., N. **Spain;** mineral springs; local quarrying; timber inds., agr. processing; p. (1981) 12,509.

Azraq Desert Nat. Park, Jordan; first Jordanian nat. park around oasis of Azraq, 96 km E. of Amman; a. 3,900 km².

B

Baalbek, c., **Lebanon,** S.W. Asia; old Heliopolis; ruins; tourism.

Bab-el-Mandeb, strait connecting Red Sea and Indian Oc.; dangerous but impt. shipping lane; length 32 km, width 27 km.

Babergh, l. gov. dist., S. Suffolk, **Eng.**; inc. Sudbury and Hadleigh; p. (est. 1988) 78,500.

Babol, t., **Iran,** Mazandaran prov.; airport; p. (1966) 49,973.

Babylon, anc. cap. of Babylonian Empire, in Euphrates valley about 96 km S. of Baghdad, **Iraq.**

Bacau, t., E. **Romania;** on R. Bistrita; oil, sawmilling, textiles; p. (est. 1984) 169,503.

Bacolod City, t., Negros, **Philippines;** sm. pt.; exp. sugar; p. (est. 1984) 287,830.

Bacton, v., Norfolk, **Eng.**; terminal for S. gasfields in N. Sea.

Bacup, t., Rossendale, S.E. Lancs., **Eng.**; 32 km N. of Manchester; textiles, felts, footwear; p. (1981) 15,259.

Badagri, t., W. of Lagos, **Nigeria;** on the Bight of Benin: formerly a gr. slave pt.; coir sacks.

Badajoz, lgst. prov., **Spain;** gr. reclamation scheme in progress; a. 21,624 km²; p. (1981) 643,512.

Badajoz, c., cap. of B. prov., W. **Spain,** in Estremadura; anc. fortress c.; transit tr.; p. (1987) 120,240.

Baden, t., **Switzerland;** health resort, mineral springs; p. (est. 1974) 67,300.

Baden-Baden, t., Baden-Württemberg. **W. Germany;** fashionable spa; p. (est. 1986) 49,300.

Baden-bei-Wien, wat. pl., **Austria;** 22 km S.W. of Vienna; p. (1981) 23,140.

Badenoch and Strathspey, l. gov. dist., Highland Reg., **Scot.**; mtn. a. S. of Inverness inc. Aviemore and Kingussie; p. (est. 1986) 10,605.

Baden-Württemberg, *Land*, S. **W. Germany;** created 1952; bounded by Rhine in W., drained by Neckar and Donau R. systems; mtnous., inc. Black Forest and Swabian Jura; received much immigrant ind. from E. Europe, so encouraging prosperous and diversified industl. structure; several impt. industl. regions centred on Mannheim, Karlsruhe, and cap. Stuttgart; a. 35,750 km²; p. (est. 1986) 9,326,800.

Bad Lands, S.D., **USA;** stretches of infertile badly eroded soil.

Badrinath, mtn. and t., Uttar Pradesh, **India;** pilgrim shrine of Vishnu.

Badulla, t., **Sri Lanka;** tea; anc. t.; rly. terminus; ctr. of tea estates; p. (1981) 32,954.

Badwater, salt pool, Cal., **USA;** 85 m below sea-level, lowest point in N. America.

Baeza, t., S. **Spain;** anc. Moorish c.; olives, wine; p. (1981) 12,841.

Baffin B., between **Greenland** and **Canada;** joined to Atl. Oc. by Davis Strait, to Arctic Oc. by Nares Strait; open 4 months per year; B.I., in W., ctr. of Arctic research and communications; length 1,120 km, width 100–650 km.

Bagé, t., S. **Brazil;** ctr. of cattle tr.; p. (est. 1985) 106,300.

Baghdad, c., cap. of **Iraq;** anc. c. on R. Tigris; terminus Baghdad rly.; airport; univ.; textiles, gum, bricks, tiles, metal inds.; p. (1977) 3,236,000.

Baghdad, prov. or liwa, **Iraq;** between Iran and Syrian Desert; inc. some of the most fertile lands in the Tigris and Euphrates valleys; p. (est. 1982) 4,038,000.

Baghlan, t., **Afghanistan;** new industl. t. in ctr. of sugar producing a.; alt. 518 m; p. (est. 1982) 41,240.

Bagnolet, t., Seine-St. Denis, **France;** sub. of Paris; famous for "plaster of Paris" from local gypsum; textiles; p. (1982) 32,557.

Bagshot, t., Surrey Heath, Surrey, **Eng.**; heath of same name; historically old postal town, 42 km S.W. of London; residtl.

Baguio, Luzon, N.W. of Manila, summer cap. of **Philippines,** alt. 1,500 m; gold mines; p. (est. 1984) 133,726.

Bahamas, indep. st. (1973) within Brit. Commonwealth, **W.I.;** more than 700 coral atolls; subtropical climate; infertile but valuable tourist tr.; exp. crayfish; cap. Nassau; a. 11,406 km²; p. (est. 1986) 235,000.

Bahawalpur, t., **Pakistan;** former cap. of B. princely st.; impt. bridging point over Sutlej R.; p. (1981) 133,956.

Bahia, st., **Brazil;** cap. Salvador; cattle, cacao, sugar, coffee, tobacco; oil, extensive mineral deposits; a. 560,139 km²; p. (est. 1985) 10,654,500.

Bahía Blanca, spt., **Argentina;** industl. ctr., oil refining; prin. shipping point of S.; exp. oil, grain, wool, hides; p. (1980) 214,000 (c.) 224,000 (met. a.).

Bahrain Is., indep. st. (1971) in Persian G.; low sandy Is. linked by road causeway to Saudi Arabia (1985); springs allow cultivation of dates; oil wells, oil and aluminium refining; trading ctr., declining importance of agr. as incr. salinity of traditional water supplies; cap. Manamah; airpt. at Muharraq; a. 678 km²; p. (est. 1987) 416,275.

Baia, historic v., Campania, **Italy**; beautifully situated on Bay of Naples; celebrated Roman pleasure resort; p. (1981) 2,087.

Baia-Mare, t., N.W. **Romania**; on Somesul R., in region mining copper, lead, zinc, gold, silver; mtn. resort; p. (est. 1984) 131,268.

Baikal L. *See* **Baykal L.**

Baildon, t., West Yorks., **Eng.**; nr. Bradford; moorland resort; p. (1981) 15,904.

Baja, t., **Hungary**; impt. bridging point of R. Danube in Gr. Plain; p. (est. 1984) 40,000.

Baja California. *See* **Lower California.**

Bakar, pt., **Yugoslavia**; S. of Rijeka; new pt. and oil harbour.

Bakersfield, c., Cal., **USA**; ctr. of oil prod. and refining; aircraft assembly; p. (1984) 130,200 (c.), 462,400 (met. a.).

Bakewell, t., Derbys Dales. **Eng.**; tourist ctr. Peak District; agr., mng.; p. (1981) 3,946.

Bakhchisaray, t., Crimea, Ukrainian SSR, **USSR**; old cap. of Tartar Khans; copper, leather; p. 16,000.

Bakhuis Gebergte mtns., W. **Surinam**; major aluminium complex based on local power and bauxite.

Bakony Wald, mtns., **Hungary**; forested; vineyards; bauxite, manganese.

Baku, cap. of Azerbaydzhan SSR, **USSR**; pt. on Caspian Sea; univ.; oil-wells; oil pipeline connects with Batumi; shipbldg.; p. (1986) 1,118,000 (c.), 1,722,000 (met. a.).

Bala, t., Meirionnydd, Gwynedd, N. **Wales**; nr. Denbigh, lt. engin., resort; p. (1981) 1,848.

Bala, L., Meirionnydd, Gwynedd, N. **Wales**; drained by the Dee.

Balaklava, pt., S. Crimea, **USSR**; scene of the charge of the Light Brigade (1854); p. 2,000.

Balashov, t., Saratov area, **RSFSR**; on Khoper R.; engin., aircraft plant; p. (est. 1969) 76,000.

Balaton, L., lgst. in **Hungary**; a. 596 km²; long history of settlement in a.; shores forested; vineyards; tourism.

Balboa, t., **Panama Canal Zone**; pt. on Pac.; p. (est. 1980) 3,000.

Balbriggan, spt., Dublin, **R.o.I.**; hosiery; p. (1981) 6,708.

Baldock, t., North Herts., **Eng.**; on N. edge of Chiltern Hills and Gr. N. Road; hosiery, malting, lt. engin.; p. (1981) 6,679.

Baldwin, t., N.Y., **USA**; on S. Long I.; fisheries; p. (1980) 31,630.

Balearic Is., in Mediterranean Sea, **Spain**; inc. Majorca, Minorca, Ibiza, Formentera; limestone scenery and mild climate encourage tourism which has swamped Moorish influence; agr.; ch. t. Palma; a. 5,014 km²; p. (1987) 700,307.

Bali, I. off Java, **Indonesia**, in Lesser Sundas; equable climate, fertile soil, luxurious vegetation; p. mainly engaged in agr.; noted native dancers; a. (inc. Lombok) 10,196 km²; p. (est. 1983) 2,593,900.

Balikesir, t., **Turkey**; rly. junc.; ctr. of fertile agr. region; p. (1985) 149,989.

Balikpapan, t., Kalimantan, **Indonesia**; new oil refinery; p. (1980) 280,875.

Baliuag, t., Luzon, **Philippines**; rice, bamboo hats, mkt.; p. (est. 1969) 51,400.

Balkan Mtns., Bulgaria; fine alpine meadows, forested; tourism based on Sofia; average alt. 900–1,200 m, hgst. point Botev Peak, 2,377 m.

Balkan Peninsula, the easternmost of the three gr. southern peninsulas of Europe, between the Adriatic and Ionian seas on the W., and the Black Sea, Sea of Marmara and the Aegean Sea on the E., with an area of, roughly, 500,000 km²; includes Turkey, Yugoslavia, Bulgaria, Albania, Greece; ch. mtns.: Rodopi, Pindhus, Balkan; ch. Rs.: Danube, Maritsa, Vardar; ch. Ls.: Scutari, Okhrida.

Balkh. *See* **Wazirabad.**

Balkhash, t., Kazakh SSR, **USSR**; on N. shore of L.B.; smelting, esp. local copper; vermiculite deposits nearby, salt; p. (est. 1969) 77,000.

Balkhash, L., Kazakh SSR, **USSR**; receives Ili R., but has no outlet; salt water; fishing, salt-panning; a. 17,301 km².

Ballachulish, v., Argyll and Bute, **Scot.**; on S. shore of Loch Leven, N.E. of Oban; tourism; ferry across Loch Linnhe, new road bridge.

Ballarat, t., Victoria, **Australia**; 117 km N.W. of Melbourne, former gold-field dist.; mkt. ctr.;

fine examples of 19th century architecture; 2 caths.; p. (est. 1983) 74,990.

Ballater, burgh, Kincardine and Deeside, **Scot.**; on R. Dee, 59 km S.W. of Aberdeen; tourist resort, mineral wells; nr. the royal Highland residence of Balmoral; p. (1981) 1,238.

Ballina, U.D., spt., Mayo, **R.o.I.**; agr. machin. salmon fishing; p. (1981) 6,856.

Ballina, t., N.S.W., **Australia**; at mouth of Richmond R.; resort, fishing; p. (1981) 9,738.

Ballinasloe, U.D., Galway and Roscommon, **R.o.I.**; agr. ctr.; cattle mkt.; terminus of Grand Canal; p. (1981) 6,374.

Ballinrobe, R.D., Mayo, **R.o.I.**; E. of Lough Mask; trout fishing; p. (est. 1985) 1,600.

Ballybunion, resort, Kerry, **R.o.I.**; at mouth of R. Shannon; p. (1981) 1,364.

Ballycastle, spt., mkt. t., Moyle, **N. Ireland**; abbey and cas. ruins; seaside resort; p. (1981) 3,650.

Ballyclare, t., Newtownabbey, **N. Ireland**; paper, linen, dyeing, asbestos-cement prod.; p. (1981) 6,159.

Ballymena, mkt. t., l. gov. dist., **N. Ireland**; on R. Braid; linen and dyeing; p. (1981) 28,166 (t.), 54,459 (l. gov. dist.).

Ballymoney, mkt. t., l. gov. dist., **N. Ireland**; 64 km N.W. of Belfast; linen; p. (1981) 22,742 (dist.).

Ballynahinch, t., Down, **N. Ireland**; 19 km from Downpatrick.

Ballyshannon, spt., Donegal, **R.o.I.**; at mouth of R. Erne; salmon fishery; resort; hydro-electric power plant; p. (est. 1980) 2,500.

Balmoral Cas., Kincardine and Deeside, **Scot.**; royal residence, on R. Dee, 13 km W of Ballater.

Balsas, R., and lowland, **Mexico**; R. flows E. to Pacific through rich agr. valley of Morelos; length 800 km.

Baltic Sea, an arm of Atl. Oc., opens into N. Sea by narrow channels between Denmark and Sweden; joined to Arctic by White Sea Canal; low, dune-backed cst.; shallowness, tendency to freeze reduce its importance for shipping; a. 414,000 km².

Baltic White Canal. *See* **Volga Baltic Waterway.**

Baltimore, industl. c., spt., Md., **USA**; fine harbour nr. head of Chesapeake B.; pt. processing and diversified inds.; steel wks. at Sparrow's Point; educational, cultural ctr., seat of Johns Hopkins univ.; many fine public bldgs. despite disastrous fire of 1904; p. (1984) 763,600 (c.), 2,244,700 (met. a.).

Baltoro Glacier, Karakoram Mtns., **Pakistan**; drains into tribs. of Indus; alt. 3,532 m.

Baluchistan, prov. (revived 1970), **Pakistan**; S. of Afghanistan; largely desert and rugged barren mtns.; cap. Quetta; cereals, potatoes, fruits, dates; new oil and natural gas discoveries; a. 137,011 km²; p. (1981) 4,332,349.

Bamako, cap. c. of **Mali**; impressive site at foot of escarpment on R. Niger; admin. and agr. tr. ctr.; R. pt.; univ.; main industl. ctr. of Mali; p. (1976) 404,022.

Bamberg, c., Bavaria, W. **Germany**; cath.; textiles, elec., leather and engin. inds.; impt. R. pt. on Trans-European waterway; p. (est. 1986) 69,600.

Bamburgh, t., Northumberland, **Eng.**; former cap. of Bernicia and Northumbria; cas.; birthplace of Grace Darling.

Banaba I. *See* **Ocean I.**

Banagher, v., Offaly, **R.o.I.**; impt. crossing of R. Shannon.

Banam, t., **Cambodia**; on Mekong R.; boat-bldg., rice milling; p. 28,000.

Banant, terr., Vojvodina, **Yugoslavia**; major source of petroleum, natural gas, vineyards, but economically backward.

Banbridge, t., l. gov. dist., **N. Ireland**; on Bann R.; linen; p. (1981) 29,768.

Banbury, mkt. t., Cherwell, Oxford, **Eng.**; 128 km from London; aluminium ind., furniture, printing, ladies' wear; expanded t.; p. (1981) 35,796.

Banchory, burgh, Kincardine and Deeside, **Scot.**; on R. Dee, 27 km S.W. of Aberdeen; p. (1981) 4,779.

Banda Is., volcanic gr. in Moluccas, in Banda Sea **Indonesia**; nutmegs and mace; a. 103 km².

Bandama, R., **Ivory Coast**; major power and irrigation scheme at Kossou Dam; length c. 320 km.

Bandar. *See* **Masulipatnam.**

Bandar 'Abbās, spt., S. **Iran**; airport; oil exploration; new deepwater harbour; p. (est. 1982) 175,000.

Bandar Anzali, spt., N. Iran; on Caspian Sea; p. (1967) 59,737.

Bandar-e-Būshehūr (Bushire), spt., S.W. Iran; on Persian G., Iran's major pt.; petrochem. complex project; p. (est. 1982) 120,000.

Bandar-e-Torkeman, spt., N. Iran; on Caspian Sea, on rly. from Tehran; p. (1966) 13,081.

Bandar Khomeynī, spt., Iran, on Persian G., terminus of rly. from Tehran; petrochemical plant; p. (1966) 6.013.

Bandjarmasin, c., cap. of Kalimantan, Indonesia; pt. on Martapura R., nr. confluence with Barito R.; tr. ctr.; oil, timber, rubber, printing plant; p. (1980) 381,286.

Bandon, t., Cork, R.o.I.; on B.R.; agr. processing; p. (1971) 2,257.

Bandung, c., W. Java, Indonesia; industl. and tourist ctr.; tech. institute; radio sta. at nearby Malabar; p. (est. 1983) 1,602,000.

Banff Nat. Park, Canada; first Canadian Nat. Park; in Rocky Mtns.; variegated scenery, many tourist facilities; a. 6,695 km².

Banff, royal burgh, Banff and Buchan, Scot.; on Moray Firth at mouth of R. Deveron; fisheries; tourism; p. (1981) 3,929.

Banffshire, former co., Scot.; lge. part now forms Banff and Buchan l. gov. dist., Grampian Reg.; a. of dist. 1,525 km²; p. of dist. (est. 1986) 83,174.

Bangalore, c., Karnataka, India; well-planned c., former Brit. military sta. and admin. H.Q.; route ctr.; textiles, engin.; p. (1981) 2,914,000.

Bangka (Banka), I., between Sumatra and Kalimantan, Indonesia; tin; a. 11,942 km²; p. 280,000.

Bangkok (Krung Thep), cap. c., Thailand; pt. on Menam Chao Phraya R., 32 km from sea; built originally round canals; major industl. ctr.; royal palace, univ.; p. (1985) 5,363,378.

Bangladesh (East Pakistan), indep. sov. st., S. Asia; within Commonwealth (1972); occupies former Indian prov. of E. Bengal and E. part of Ganges delta; dense rural p. engaged in intensive farming of rice and jute; illiteracy 80 per cent; poor internal communications hinder devel.; exp. textiles; susceptible to flooding and cyclones, cstl. embankment project; open warfare between India and Pakistan (Dec. 1971) resulted in creation of indep. st.; cap. Dacca; a. 142,776 km²; p. (est. 1987) 104,100,000 (+2.6 per cent a year).

Bangor, t., North Down, N. Ireland; spt. on S. shore of Belfast Lough, 16 km N.E. of Belfast; lt. inds.; carpets, hosiery; seaside resort; p. (1981) 46,585.

Bangor, t., S. Me., USA; pt. of entry on Penobscot R.; timber inds., shoes; p. (1980) 31,643.

Bangor, t., Arfon, Gwynedd, Wales; pt. on S. shore of Menai Strait; cath., univ. college; lt. engin.; tourist ctr.; p. (1981) 12,174.

Bangui, c., cap. of Central African Rep.; pt. on R. Ubangi; airpt.; p. (est. 1984) 473,817.

Bangweulu, L., Zambia; 240 km long, 128 km wide, contains 3 islands. Dr. Livingstone died at Illala, on S. shore of this L., in 1873.

Baniyas, spt., Syria; terminus of oil pipeline from Kirkuk, opened 1952.

Banja Luka, t., N. Bosnia, Yugoslavia; caths., mosques; recent industl. development; cellulose; rly. junc.; p. (1981) 183,618.

Banjul (Bathurst), t., cap. of Gambia, Senegambia; pt. at mouth of Gambia R., exp. groundnuts; airport; p. (1983) 44,188.

Banks I., Canada, Arctic Oc.; separated by McClure Strait from Melville I.

Banks Is., gr. of sm. Is. in S. Pacific; N.E. of New Hebrides.

Banks Peninsula, on E. cst. of S.I., N.Z.; prominent feature of Canterbury cst.

Banks Strait, separating Furneaux Is. from Tasmania, Australia.

Bankura, t., W. Bengal, India; on Hooghly R.; shellac, silk; p. (1961) 62,833.

Bann, Upper and Lower R., N. Ireland; rises in Mtns. of Mourne, and flows through Lough Neagh to Atlantic nr. Coleraine; length 144 km.

Bannockburn, moor, nr. Stirling, Scot.; Bruce's victory over Edward II on June 23–24, 1314, established Scotland's independence.

Banovici, basin, Yugoslavia; in Bosnia; brown coal.

Banská Bystrica, region, Slovakia, ČSSR; copper and silver mng., metal wks.; a. 9,230 km²; p. (est. 1986) 78,000 (commune).

Banstead, Surrey, Eng.; dormitory t.; p. (1981) 43,163. See Reigate.

Bantam, t. and dist., W. Java, Indonesia; suffered severely from fever and volcanic eruption; former pt. and sultanate; cattle rearing.

Bantry, t., Cork, R.o.I.; tweed; p. (est. 1980) 3,000.

Bantry Bay, Cork, R.o.I.; Atlantic inlet; natural harbour utilised mainly by oil-storage depot.

Baoding (Paoting), c., Hebei prov., China; on main rly. to Beijing; p. (est. 1984) 522,800.

Baoji (Paoki), c., Shaanxi prov., China; ctr. of arable agr. a.; cotton weaving; nearby gorge on Huang-He used for multi-purpose dams; p. (1984) 352,100.

Baotou (Paotow), c., Mongol Zizhiqu (Inner Mongolia), China; on left bank of Huang-He, on road and rly. routes to E. China; terminus of caravan routes through Gobi Desert and Tarim basin to Turkestan; tr. in non-perishable livestock prods., cereals; modern steel ind.; p. (est. 1983) 1,051,000.

Bar, spt., Dalmatian cst., Yugoslavia; terminal of new Belgrade-Bar rly.; p. (1981) 32,535.

Baracaldo, pt., N.E. Spain; rapidly growing industl. t. on Bilbāo estuary; p. (1981) 117,422.

Baracoa, spt., Cuba; exp. bananas, coconuts; p. (est. 1967) 105,090.

Baranovichi, c., Belorussiya, USSR; admin. ctr. of agr. dist.; impt. rly. ctr.; p. (est. 1980) 135,000.

Barataria Bay, S.E. Louisiana, USA; 56 km S. of New Orleans; ctr. of shrimp ind., petroleum extraction; picturesque stilt vs.; a. 466 km².

Barauni, t., N. Central Bihar, India; oil refining; oil pipelines to Gauhati, and Kanpur and from Haldia; p. (1961) 40,321.

Barbados, I., indep. sovereign st., within Brit. Commonwealth, W.I.; fertile soils; economy based on intensive agr. supporting dense p.; sugar, molasses, rum; fishing; tourism; cap. and spt. Bridgetown; a. 429 km²; p. (est. 1985) 253,000.

Barbary Coast, gen. name applied to Mediterranean cst. of N. Africa between Strait of Gibraltar and C. Bon.

Barberton, t., Ohio, USA; S.W. of Akron; tyre mftg.; p. (1980) 29,751.

Barberton, t., Transvaal, S. Africa; developed from 19th cent. gold rush; ctr. of rich agr. dist.; p. (est. 1967) 13,200.

Barbican, dist., City of London, Eng.; inc. major housing scheme to attract p. back into c.; cultural amenities.

Barbizon, v., nr. forest of Fontainebleau, France; haunt of painters, especially those ass. with the Barbizon school.

Barbuda and Redonda, Is., Leeward Is., W.I.; dependencies of Antigua and Barbuda; sea-island cotton; a. 163 km²; p. (1986) 1,500.

Barcellona, t., N.E. cst., Sicily, Italy; mkt. t.; p. (1981) 36,869.

Barcelona, c., cap. of B. prov., major spt. of Spain; industl. and comm. ctr., "Manchester of Spain", textiles and varied inds.; exp. agr. prod. inc. cork; cath., univ.; p. (1987) 1,703,744.

Barcelona, t., N. Venezuela; cap. of Anzoátegui st.; agr. tr.; brewing; adjoins Puerto la Cruz on Caribbean cst.; joint p. (1981) 156,500.

Barcoo Creak. See Cooper's Creek.

Bardsey, I., Irish Sea; off cst. of Wales, nr. N. point of Cardigan Bay; lighthouse.

Bareilly, c., Uttar Pradesh, India; mkt., sugar refining, cotton mills, bamboo furniture; p. (1981) 386,734.

Barents Sea, part of Arctic Oc., E. of Spitzbergen to N. Cape; impt. cod fisheries; oil potential; short Rs. to be diverted from Sea to Volga to carry water to Karakum Desert.

Bari, c., cap. of B. prov., Apulia, Italy; spt. on Adriatic handling agr. prods.; agr. processing inds., oil refinery; p. (1984) 369,576.

Barinas, t., cap. of B. st., Venezuela; cattle, oil in surrounding Llanos; p. (1981) 109,900.

Barisal, t., Bangladesh; nr. Tetulia at mouth of Ganges; river pt.; gr. damage and loss of life from cyclone 1965; p. (1981) 142,098.

Barito R., Borneo, Indonesia; a. of swampland in lower valley; proposals to develop valley for rice cultivation; length c. 400 km.

Barking and Dagenham, outer bor., E. London, Eng.; on Rs. Roding and Thames; diversified inds. inc. huge R.side Ford motor wks.; high proportion of council housing; p. (est. 1988) 147,600.

Barlad, t., Moldavia, Romania; soap, textiles; p. (1966) 41,060.

Bar-le-Duc, t, cap. of Meuse dep., France; in picturesque Ornain valley; many fine old houses; varied inds.; p. (1982) 20,029.

Barletta, t., spt., **Italy;** diversified pt. processing inds.; wine tr.; p. (1981) 83,719.

Barmouth, t., Meirionnydd, Gwynedd, **Wales;** pt. on Cardigan Bay; chemicals; resort; p. (1981) 2,136.

Barnard Castle, Teesdale, Durham, **Eng.**; mkt. t., resort; woollens, penicillin; cas.; p. (1981) 5,016.

Barnaul, t., W. Siberia, **RSFSR;** route ctr. in cotton-growing dist. nr. industl. Kuznetsk Basin; varied inds.; p. (est. 1980) 542,000.

Barnet, former U.D., Herts., **Eng.**; now outer bor., Greater London; comprising Finchley, Hendon, Barnet, East Barnet and Friern Barnet; p. (est. 1988) 301,400.

Barnsley, t., met. dist., South Yorks., **Eng.**; machin., plastics; carpets; coal-mng. ctr.; p. (est. 1988) 220,900.

Barnstaple, North Devon, **Eng.**; mkt. t., pt. on R. Taw; seaside resort; p. (1981) 19,025.

Baroda, t., Gujarat, **India;** univ.; palaces, Hindu temples; natural gas pipeline from Ankleshwar; oil refining nearby at Jawaharnagar; heavy water plant; p. (1987) 734,473.

Barquisimeto, t., **Venezuela;** well built c.; comm. ctr. for fertile agr. a.; p. (1981) 496,700.

Barra Is., Outer Hebrides, **Scot.**; a. 901 km²; lighthouse on Barra Head; p. (est. 1984) 1,200.

Barrancabermeja, R. pt., **Colombia;** oilfield, oil refining, paper mkg., petrochemicals; p. (est. 1983) 123,000.

Barranquilla, t., **Colombia;** major spt. nr. mouth of Magdalena R.; impt. industl. ctr.; international airpt.; p. (1985) 920,695.

Barreiro, t., Setúbal, **Portugal;** on S. bank of Tagus estuary; agr. processing; p. (1981) 50,863.

Barrow-in-Furness, spt., l. gov. dist., Cumbria, **Eng.**; iron and steel ind. once based on local haematite ores; shipbldg., submarines; p. (est. 1988) 72,400.

Barrow I., W. Australia; since 1967 one of Australia's richest oilfields.

Barrow Point, most N. headland in Alaska, **USA.**

Barry, pt., Vale of Glamorgan, South Glamorgan, **Wales;** rapid growth in 19th cent. as outport of Cardiff; modern light inds., replacing coal and tinplate inds.; p. (1981) 41,681.

Barth, spt., Rostock, **E. Germany;** shipyard engin., furniture, sugar; p. (1963) 12,406.

Bartlesville, t., Okla., **USA;** oil refining, metal inds.; p. (1980) 34,568.

Barton-on-Humber, mkt. t., Glanford, Humberside, **Eng.**; anc. Eng. bor.; S. site of new Humber Bridge; p. (1981) 8,498.

Basel, c., cap. of B. can., 2nd. t. of **Switzerland;** cath., univ.; burial place of Erasmus; comm., industl. rly. ctr. at head of barge navigation on R. Rhine; p. (est. 1985) 175,000 (c.) 364,000 (met. a.).

Basel, can., **Switzerland;** divided into 2 half cantons; (1) B.—Stadt; in immediate vicinity of B.c.; cap. B.; a. 36 km²; p. (est. 1986) 194,000; (2) B.—Land; on N. Jura slopes; watchmaking; cap. Liestal; a. 427 km²; p. (est. 1986) 226,000.

Basford, t., Gedling, Notts., **Eng.**; outskirts of Nottingham; hosiery.

Bashkir (Bashirskaya) ASSR, occupies Belaya R. basin in S.W. Urals, **RSFSR;** impt. mng. and metal inds., inc. major oilfield; arable agr.; cap. Ufa; a. 143,486 km²; p. (1986) 3,864,000.

Basildon, t., l. gov. dist., Essex, **Eng.**; in lower Thames valley; new t. 1949; light inds.; p. (est. 1988) 157,500 (dist.).

Basilicata, region, S. **Italy;** comprising provs. of Potenza and Matera, mtnous. in W., drains to G. of Taranto; arable agr.; a. 9,984 km²; p. (est. 1986) 620,000.

Basingstoke and Deane, l. gov. dist., N. Hants., **Eng.**; 80 km W. of London; expanded t.; engin., light inds.; p. (est. 1988) 139,700.

Basle. See Basel.

Basotho ba Borwa (S. Sotho), Bantu Terr. Authority, O.F.S., **S. Africa;** cap. Witziesnoek; a. 52,000 hectares; p. (est. 1969) 144,000.

Basque Provs., N. **Spain;** comprise 3 provs.: Alava, Guipuzcoa and Vizcaya where Basque language spoken; recent claims that French dep. of Pyrénées-Atlantiques should be inc. within an indep. Basque prov.; regional parliaments for provs. in Spain to help offset separatist moves (1980); lgst. c. Bilbao; p. (1981) 2,141,809.

Basra, t., **Iraq;** cap. of B. prov.; R. pt., 64 km from mouth of Tigris R., on main rly. from Baghdad; exp. agr. prods.; p. (1977) 1,540,000.

Bas-Rhin, dep., E. **France;** N. part of Alsace; extends to Rhine rift valley, inc. Vosges Mtns.; impt. agr. dist.; many industl. ts.; cap. Strasbourg;

a. 4,791 km²; p. (1982) 912,000.

Bass Rock, lighthouse in Firth of Forth, opposite Tantallon Cas., E. Lothian, **Scot.**; gannetry.

Bass Strait, Australia; between Victoria and Tasmania; length 320 km; width 224 km.

Bassano del Grappa; cap. of Vicenza prov., on R. Brenta, **Italy;** light and craft inds.; cath.; p. (1981) 64,676.

Bassein, t., **Burma;** on mouth of Irrawaddy R., univ.; airfield; rice tr. and milling; p. (1983) 335,000.

Bassenthwaite, L., L. Dist., Cumbria, **Eng.**; most N. of lge. Ls.; drained to Solway Firth by R. Derwent; length 6 km, width 1·6 km.

Basses-Alpes. See Alpes-de-Haute-Provence.

Basses-Pyrénées. See Pyrénées-Atlantique.

Basse-Terre, I., cap. of Guadeloupe, **Fr. W.I.**; pt.; p. (1982) 13,656.

Basseterre, t., St. Kitts I., **W.I.**; cap. St. Kitts-Nevis-Anguilla ass. st.; pt.; sugar refining; p. (1980) 14,283.

Bassetlaw, l. gov. dist., N. Notts., **Eng.**; lge. a. based on Worksop and East Retford; p. (est. 1988) 104,800.

Bastia, c. spt., cap. Haute Corse, N.E. Corsica, **France;** lgst. t. of Corsica; agr. exp. and inds.; tourism; p. (1982) 50,596 (met. a.).

Basutoland. See Lesotho.

Bata, t., ch. spt., **Equatorial Guinea;** cap. of Rio Muni prov.; airpt.; p. (est. 1986) 17,000.

Bataan, peninsula and prov., W. Luzon, **Philippines;** mtnous.; inc. t. of Balanga; timber inds., oil refining; proposed nuclear power sta.

Batangas, prov. and spt., S.W. Luzon, **Philippines;** oil refining; agr. tr.; p. (est. 1983) 155,064 (spt.).

Batavia. See Djakarta.

Bath, c., l. gov. dist., Avon, **Eng.**; Roman baths, hot springs, medicinal waters; fine Regency architecture; univ.; elec. engin., metal inds.; p. (est. 1988) 84,800.

Bathgate, burgh, W. Lothian, **Scot.**; coal mng. automobile ind.; p. (1981) 14,388.

Bathurst, t., N.S.W., **Australia;** former gold t., reliant on wool and wheat; diversifying with secondary inds.; with Orange to form site of major inland c. of 200,000; p. (1981) 19,640.

Bathurst, I., off cst. of N.T., **Australia;** separated from Melville I. by Apsley Str.; aboriginal reserve; cypress pine milling; (1981) 1,586.

Bathurst, t., N.B., **Canada;** pt. on Nipisiguit Bay; paper mill; salmon fishing; local mng.; p. (1981) 15,705.

Bathurst. See Banjul.

Bātinah, Al, fertile coastal plain, **Oman,** Arabia; produces early-ripening dates famous for flavour.

Batley, t. West Yorks., **Eng.**; heavy woollens, shoddy; p. (1981) 42,572.

Baton Rouge, st. cap., La., **USA;** on Mississippi; major tr. ctr.; univ.; oil refining, chemical plants; p. (1984) 238,900 (c.), 538,000 (met. a.).

Battambang, prov., **Kampuchea;** N.W. of Phnom-Penh; rice growing, cotton mill; p. (1981) 551,860.

Battersea, dist., London, **Eng.**; S. of R. Thames; famous park; lge. power sta. now disused; part of Wandsworth.

Batticaloa, t., cap. of E. Prov., **Sri Lanka;** on E. cst.; comm. ctr.; p. (1981) 42,963.

Battle, t., Rother, East Sussex, **Eng.**; battle of Hastings 1066; abbey.

Battle Creek, t., Mich., **USA;** on Kalamazoo R.; engin., local cereal prod.; p. (1984) 54,300, (t.), 137,800 (met. a.).

Batu Arang, t., **Malaya;** ctr. of only worked coalfield in Malaya; 45 km from Kuala Lumpur.

Batumi, t., spt. on E. shore of Black Sea; Georgian SSR, **USSR;** oil, engin., citrus fruits, tea; oil pipeline connects with Baku; resort; airpt; p. (est. 1985) 132,000.

Bauchi, t., **Nigeria;** cap. Bauchi st.; ctr. of Jos plateau; tin-mng. ctr.

Bauld, C., northernmost part of Newfoundland, **Canada.**

Bauru, t., São Paulo st., **Brazil;** comm. ctr.; food inds.; p. (1985) 220,900.

Bautzen, t., Dresden, **E. Germany;** on R. Spree; textiles, engin., iron inds.; cath.; p. (est. 1970) 43,670.

Bavaria (Bayern), Land, **W. Germany;** mtnous., bounded in S. by Alps, inc. Böhmerwald, Fichtelgebirge, Franconian Forest; main Rs. Danube and Main; fertile agr. valleys; forestry and agr.; economic life concentrated in ts., esp. cap. Munich, now a focus of p. immigration; rural beauty attracts tourist tr.; celebrated beer; a. 70,220 km²; p. (est. 1986) 11,026,500.

Bavarian Alps, mtn. range, **W. Germany,** along Austrian border; Zugspitze (2,969 m) highest mtn. in W. Germany.

Bavarian Forest. See **Böhmerwald.**

Bawdwin, t., **Burma;** in Shan plateau; impt. mng. ctr.; wolfram, lead, zinc, silver, rubies.

Bayamón, t., **Puerto Rico;** in fertile valley; oil refining; p. (1980) 196,207.

Baybay, t., Leyte, **Philippines;** impt. comm. pt.; p. (est. 1969) 70,200.

Bay City, t., Mich., **USA;** comm. pt. nr. head of Saginaw B.; fishing; pt. processing inds.; p. (1980) 41,593 (c.), 119,881 (met. a.).

Bayeux, t., Calvados, **France;** mkt. t.; cath., museum, Bayeux tapestry; p. (1982) 15,237.

Baykal, L. (**Ozero Baykal**), Siberia, **RSFSR;** sixth largest fresh-water L. in world; basin forms deepest depression in world (1,616 m); many pts. around shores but frozen Nov.–May; skirted by Trans-Siberian rly.; sturgeon, salmon; tourism; a. 35,483 km².

Bayonne, spt., Pyrénées-Atlantique, S.W. **France;** cath.; noted for invention of bayonet; Basque Museum; p. (1982) 127,477 (met. a.).

Bayonne, t., N.J., **USA;** 10 km from New York; chemicals, oil refining; dry docks; p. (1980) 65,047.

Bayreuth, t., Bavaria, **W. Germany;** home of Wagner; famous for musical festivals in national theatre; p. (est. 1986) 72,300.

Baytown, pt., S.E. Texas, **USA;** industl. t., oil refining and exp.; p. (1980) 56,923.

Beachy Head, chalk headland, S.W. of Eastbourne, East Sussex, **Eng.;** 175 m high.

Beaconsfield, t., South Bucks., **Eng.;** residtl; home of Edmund Burke; p. (1981) 10,909.

Beardmore Glacier, Antarctica; one of world's lgst. valley glaciers; over 176 km in length.

Bear I. (**Björnöya I.**), **Norway;** in Arctic Oc., 208 km S. of Spitzbergen; cod fisheries.

Bearsden, burgh, l. gov. dist. with Milngavie, **Scot.;** residtl.; p. (est. 1986) 40,171 (dist.)., (1981), 27,151 (burgh).

Beas (**Bias**), R., Punjab, **India;** trib. of Sutlej R.; part of irrigation scheme.; marked limit of Alexander's advance into India, 327 B.C.

Beattock, pass, S. Uplands, **Scot.;** gives access from valley of R. Clyde to R. Annan; used by main W. cst. rly. route from Carlisle to Glasgow and Edinburgh; alt. 309 m.

Beauce, region, central **France;** flat limestone plateau; arid, few surface streams; thin layer of loam (limon) permits agr.; impt. wheat growing a. ("the granary of France"); p. mainly grouped in vs.

Beaufort Sea, off N. Alaska, **USA;** part of Arctic Oc.

Beaujolais, France; in upper Rhône valley, N.E. Massif Central; wine-growing dist.

Beaulieu, v., Hants, **Eng.;** on Beaulieu R.; Cistercian abbey; car museum.

Beauly, t., Inverness, **Scot.;** on B. R.; ruined priory; p. (1981) 1,145.

Beaumaris, t., Anglesey, Gwynedd, N. **Wales;** pt. on Menai Strait; lt. engin.; resort; p. (1981) 2,088.

Beaumont, t.; 2nd. pt. of Texas, **USA;** ctr. of petrochemical inds.; p. (1984) 123,400 (t.), 391,900 (met. a. with Orange-Port Arthur).

Beaune, t., Cote d'Or, **France;** mediaeval walled t.; ctr. of wine tr.; p. (1982) 21,127.

Beauvais, agr. mkt. t., cap. of Oise dep., N. **France;** cath.; Gobelin tapestry removed to Paris; p. (1982) 54,147.

Bebington, Wirral, Merseyside, **Eng.;** part of pt. of Liverpool; soap, chemicals, engin.; p. (1981) 64,174.

Becancourt, t., Quebec, **Canada;** on S. bank of St. Lawrence; integrated steel mill projected.

Beccles, Waveney, Suffolk, **Eng.;** mkt. t. on R. Waveney S. of Broads; resort, agr. inds.; p. (1981) 8,903.

Béchar (**Colom-Béchart**) t., N.W. Algeria; airpt.; coal; p. (est. 1984) 184,000 (region).

Bechuanaland. See **Botswana.**

Beckum, t., N. Rhine–Westphalia, **W. Germany;** cement, chalk, engin. wks.; p. (est. 1986) 36,500.

Beddington and Wallington. See **Sutton.**

Bedford, co. t., North Beds., **Eng.;** on R. Ouse, 80 km N. of London; gen. engin., inc. marine and elec., bricks, aero research; Bunyan imprisoned here; p. (1981) 74,245.

Bedfordshire, non-met. co., **Eng.;** co. t., Bedford; crossed by Chilterns; agr., mkt. gardening, brickmkg., cement, vehicles, engin.; a. 1,232 km²; p. (est. 1988) 530,700.

Bedfordshire, North, l. gov. dist., Beds., **Eng.;** a. inc. Bedford and surrounding rural a.; p. (est. 1988) 136,800.

Bedfordshire, South, l. gov. dist., Beds., **Eng.;** close to Luton and inc. Dunstable and Leighton-Linslade; p. (est. 1988) 111,500.

Bedford Level, once over 162,000 ha. of peat marsh in S. Fenland, **Eng.;** first successful draining initiated by Earl of Bedford 1634.

Bedlington, t., Wansbeck, Northumberland, **Eng.;** nr. Blyth; coal mng.; electronics; p. (1981) 26,707.

Bedloe's I., or **Liberty I.,** N.Y. harbour, **USA;** on which the statue of Liberty stands.

Bedwas and Machen, t., Rhymney Valley, Mid Glamorgan, **Wales;** gas, coal and coke by-prods.; p. (1981) 13,152.

Bedwellty, t., Islwyn, Gwent, **Wales;** elec. gds., car upholstery; p. (1981) 24,670.

Bedworth, t., Warwicks., **Eng.;** nr. Coventry; coal mng., limestone quarrying, engin., textiles; p. (1981) 41,991. See **Nuneaton.**

Bedzin, t., S. Poland; coalmng. t. in Upper Silesia; p. (1983) 77,000.

Beerenberg, mtn., Jan Mayen I., **Norway,** Arctic Oc.; one of lgst. volcanic cones in world; glaciated; alt. 2,546 m.

Beersheba, t., **Israel;** ctr. for development of the Negev; p. (est. 1982) 112,600.

Beeston and Stapleford, Broxtowe, Notts., **Eng.;** sub. of Nottingham; engin., drugs, telephones; p. (1981) 64,599.

Bègles, t., Gironde, **France;** mftg.; p. (1982) 23,426.

Begovat, t., E. Uzbek SSR, **USSR;** on Syr Dar'ya R.; iron and steel wks.; hydroelectric power; p. (1967) 59,000.

Beihai, spt., Guangxi prov., **China;** seafood cultivation, fishing; food processing and machin. inds.; offshore oil development; port being rebuilt to attract foreign investment as part of new open door policy; growth centre; p. (1984) 172,000.

Beijing (**Peking**), c. and mun., cap. of **China;** cultural ctr. and c. of gr. architectural beauty; for hundreds of years seat of Chinese emperors (Mongol, Ming, Manchu); formerly surrounded by walls; Imperial and Summer palaces; seat of govt.; univ.; Catholic cath. reopened (1985); many sm. factories producing a very wide range of goods, esp. chemicals, computers, textiles, synthetic fibres, machin., precision instruments, printing, publishing; route ctr., rly. junc., airpt.; a. 8,770 km²; p. (1986) 5,860,000.

Beira, spt., **Moçambique;** airpt; rly. runs inland to Harare (Zimbabwe) and Blantyre (Malawi); exp. sugar, maize, cotton; oil pipeline to Umtali; p. (est. 1986) 269,700.

Beirut, c., cap. of **Lebanon;** pt. on Mediterranean; anc. Phoenician c., now busy shipping and mercantile ctr.; silk, wool, fruits; 4 univs.; p. (est. 1980) 702,000.

Beisan (**Bet She'an**), t., **Israel;** in Jordan valley, c. 90 m below sea-level; archaeological finds date from 1500 B.C.; rebuilt since 1948 by Israelis; p. (est. 1970) 11,900.

Bejaia (**Bougie**), spt., Algeria; impt. tr. ctr.; exp. wood, hides; oil pipeline connection to Hassi-Messoud; p. (est. 1983) 124,122.

Belaya Tserkov, t., N. Ukrainian SSR, **USSR;** agr. and comm. ctr.; p. (est. 1985) 181,000.

Békéscsaba, t., **Hungary;** milling; rly. junc.; poultry processing plant; p. (est. 1985) 71,000.

Belau, Rep. of, formerly Western Carolines; group of Is. 300 km. E. of Philippines; renamed 1981; part of U.S. Trust Terr. of Pacific Is.; also known as Palau Is.; p. (1980) 12,116.

Belém, spt., cap. of Pará st., **Brazil;** comm. ctr., ch. pt. of Amazon basin, entrepôt for riverside settlements, exp. forest prod. inc. jute, cocoa and cotton; inds. dominated by food processing and textiles; new steel works; univ.; p. (est. 1985) 1,120,800.

Belfast, l. gov. dist., cap. of **N. Ireland;** on Belfast Lough; Britain's lgst. single shipyard; free-port (1984) for air freight; linen mnf., rope, tobacco, distilling, aircraft, fertilisers, computers; oil refinery on E. side of harbour; univ.; Stormont Castle; p. (1981) 297,983.

Belfort, t., cap. of Belfort dep., E. **France,** in Alsace; fortress t. between Jura and Vosges; heavy inds., rly. wks., cotton ind.; elec. engin.; p. (1982) 52,739.

Belfort (**Territoire de**), dep., **France;** ch. t. Belfort; a. 608 km²; p. (1982) 131,900.

Belgaum, t., Karnataka, **India;** cotton; alt. 760 m; Jain temples; p. (1981) 274,430 (c.), 300,372 (met. a.).

Belgium, kingdom, **W. Europe,** comprises 9 admin. provs.; low-lying except in Ardennes in S.E.; very high density of p., intensive agr.

and highly industl.; severe social and economic problems have resulted from decline of Sambre-Meuse coalfield and associated heavy engin. inds., similar difficulties in textile inds. in N.W.; industl. expansion on Kempenland coalfield in N.E. and around Brussels, Antwerp, and Ghent; heavily dependent upon foreign tr. for economic survival; member of EEC; major spt. of Antwerp competing with Rotterdam for hinterland of N. EC; 2 language groups: Flemish (Dutch dialect) in N., French dialect in S. (Walloon a.); univs. at Brussels, Ghent, Liège, Louvain; cap. Brussels; a. 30,445 km²; p. (est. 1986) 9,860,000.

Belgorod, t., **RSFSR**; N.W. of Kharkov, on N. Donets R.; rly. junc. in agr. region; p. (est. 1985) 280,000.

Belgrade (Beograd), c., cap of **Yugoslavia**; inland pt. on Danube at mouth of Sava R.; industl., admin. and cultural ctr.; univ.; airport; p. (1981) 1,470,073.

Belitung or **Billiton**, I., between Sumatra and Kalimantan, **Indonesia**; tin; a. 4.832 km²; p. 102,375.

Belize, indep. rep. (1981), **Central America**; formerly Brit. Honduras; almost totally underdeveloped; heavy rainfall, hurricanes; tropical forest; only 15 percent of land is cultivated; economy hit by fall in world sugar prices; recent sale of 13 percent of land a. to clear tropical forest for citrus production; 20 per cent unemployed; lowest p. density in Central America; S. dist. of Toledo claimed by Guatamala; new cap. Belmopen; a. 22,962 km²; p. (est. 1986) 171,000.

Belize, c., former cap. of **Belize**; mahogany, dyewoods, bananas; almost devastated by hurricane 31 Oct. 1961; cap. moved to Belmopen 80 km further inland; spt.; p. (est. 1986) 47,000.

Bellery, c., Karnataka, **India**; fort; cotton processing and tr.; p. (1981) 201,579.

Bell Bay, t., Tasmania, **Australia**; on bank of Tamar R.; modern pt. and aluminium refinery (1950s) for processing Queensland bauxite; ferry terminal; now part of Launceston.

Bell I., Newfoundland, E. **Canada**; in Conception Bay, 32 km N.W. of St. Johns; impt. Wabana iron-ore deposits outcrop on N.W. cst., smelted on Pictou coalfield, Nova Scotia; a. 31 km².

Belle Isle Strait, Canada; between Newfoundland and Labrador, on N. shipping route to Canada from Europe.

Belleville, pt., L. Ontario, **Canada**; agr. processing; white marble nearby, cement; light inds.; p. (1981) 34,881.

Belleville, t., Ill., **USA**; industl. ctr., domestic prod., coal; air force training school; p. (1980) 41,580.

Belleville, t., N.J., **USA**; machin., chemicals; p. (1980) 35,367.

Bellingham, t., spt., Wash., **USA**; agr. distribution ctr.; timber inds.; salmon canning; p. (1984) 45,100 (c.), 111,800 (met. a.).

Bellingshausen Sea, borders Antarctica; part of **S. Pac.**; ice floes obstruct passage.

Bellinzona, t., **Switzerland**; on R. Ticino; 22 km N. of Lugano; three castles built on hills dominating t.; rly. engin.; tourism; p. (1980) 16,743.

Bell Rock (Inchcape I.), rock and lighthouse 19 km S.E. of Arbroath, **Scot.**

Belluno, t., cap. of B. prov., Venezia, N. **Italy**; route ctr. at S. foot of Dolomites; cath.; engin.; p. (1981) 36,634.

Belmopen, new cap., **Belize**; at geographic ctr. of cty.; (est. 1986) 3,500.

Belo Horizonte, c., cap. of Minas Gerais st. **Brazil**; impt. inland c.; ctr. rich agr. and mng. region; steel mills, food inds., textiles, diamond cutting; oil pipeline from Guanabara; univ.; one of the fastest growing c. in Brazil, especially since building of Fiat factory; p. (est. 1985) 2,122,100 (+ 72 per cent in 10 years).

Beloretsk, t., Bashkir ASSR, **RSFSR**; in Ural Mtns. on Belaya R.; iron, metal inds.; p. (est. 1969) 66,000.

Belorussiyan SSR, constituent rep., **USSR**; lowlying; timber; agr. on drained marshes; peat; 209,790 km²; p. (1986) 10,002,000.

Belovo, t., W. Siberia, **RSFSR**; in Kuznetsk basin; coal mng., zinc, engin.; p. (est. 1985) 117,000.

Belper, mkt. t., Amber Valley, Derbys., **Eng.**; hosiery, textiles, oil wks., iron foundries; p. (1981) 16,453.

Belsen, v., 24 km N.W. of Celle, **W. Germany**; notorious second world war concentration camp.

Belterra, t., dist., Pará st., N.E. **Brazil**; nr. confluence of Tapajós and Amazon Rs; site of Fordlandia scheme.

Beltsy, t., Moldavian SSR, **USSR**; on trib. of Dniester R.; agr. ctr., food processing; p. (est. 1985) 147,000.

Belvoir (pronounced Beaver), **Vale of**, Melton Leics., **Eng.**; clay vale, cattle, sheep; Stilton cheese; recent discovery of valuable coal deposits (est. 500 m. tonnes).

Bembridge, v., E. cst., I. of Wight, **Eng.**; resort.

Benalla, t., dist., Victoria, **Australia**; pastoral and agr.; p. (1986) 8,490 (t.).

Benares. See **Varanasi.**

Benbecula I., Outer Hebrides, Western Isles, **Scot.**; between Is. of N. and S. Uist; airpt. in N.; fishing; a. 93 km²; p. 900.

Bendigo, c., Victoria, **Australia**; formergoldmng. dist., gold rush 1851; mng. ceased 1955; primary prods.; impt. egg producing ctr.; p. (est. 1983) 62,260.

Benevento, c., Campania, **Italy**; cap. of B. prov. which contains many Roman remains; cath.; agr. processing; p. (1981) 62,636.

Benfleet, t., Castle Point, Essex. **Eng.**; residtl.; p. (1981) 50,240.

Bengal, Bay of, part of **Indian Oc.** washing E. shores of India and W. shores of Burma, receives waters of Rs. Krishna, Ganges; Brahmaputra, Irrawaddy.

Bengbu (Pengpu), c., Anhui, **China**; on Kwo-Ho 168 km. NW of Nanjing; on Tianjin–Nanjing rly; p. (1984) 597,100.

Benghazi, joint cap. (with Tripoli) of **Libya**; spt. and airpt. on G. of Sirte; univ.; former Greek Hesperides; p. (est. 1981) 368,000.

Benguela, t., **Angola**, S.W. Africa; rly. runs inland to Zaïre and Zambia; seaport now lost much tr. to Lobito; p. (est. 1975) 41,000.

Benha, t., **Egypt**; impt. mkt. t., rail and road ctr. in heart of cultivated a. of Nile delta 48 km N. of Cairo; airpt.; p. (est. 1970) 72,500.

Benin City, t., **Nigeria**; cap. of Benin st.; former notorious slave ctr.; p. (est. 1983) 166,000.

Benin, People's Republic of, (Dahomey), indep. st. (1960), **West Africa**; former French Colony; high standard of education reflected in heavy government sector and low level of productive activity in the economy; staple foods of groundnuts, palms, coffee, cocoa; intensive farming in fertile Terre de Barre; land held collectively; full potential of drier N. not yet exploited; concern about desert encroachment; oil found offshore from main pt. Cotonou; inds. process primary prods.; joint Benin-Nigerian rly; much tropical rain forest in S.; dependence on Nigeria; many joint industl. projects; cap. Porto Novo; a. 112,622 km²; p. (est. 1988) 4·45m.

Beni Suef, t., **Egypt**; on Nile, 96 km S. of Cairo; ctr. of fertile agr. a.; carpets, cotton; p. (est. 1983) 146,000.

Ben Lawers, mtn., Perth and Kinross, **Scot.**; by Loch Tay; arctic and alpine flora; alt. 1,215 m.

Ben Macdhui, mtn., Kincardine and Deeside, **Scot.**; Cairngorm gr.; second highest peak in Brit. Is.; alt. 1,310 m.

Ben Nevis, mtn., Lochaber, **Scot.**; volcanic; hgst. peak in Brit. Isles; alt. 1,344 m.

Benoni, t., Transvaal, **S. Africa**; gold mng. ctr.; engin.; p. (1980) 206,810.

Benrath, t., **W. Germany**; on Rhine R. nr. Düsseldorf; R. pt. and industl. t.; chemicals, machin.

Bensberg, t., N. Rhine-Westphalia, **W. Germany**; 16 km from Cologne; leather gds.; mainly residtl.; foundries; cas.; p. (est. 1971) 43,800.

Bensheim, t., Hesse, **W. Germany**; ctr. of fruit and wine dist. on E. edge Rhine valley; textiles, paper, metallurgy; p. (est. 1986) 33,500.

Bentley with **Arksey**, t., South Yorks., **Eng.**; p. (1981) 21,786.

Benton Harbor, t., Mich., **USA**; midway along E. cst. L. Michigan; p. (1984) 14,200 (t), 163,000 (met. a.).

Benue R., Nigeria–Cameroon; rises in Adamawa mtns.; forms ch. trib. of Niger R.; R. pts. and agr. tr.; length 1,392 km.

Ben Vorlich. mtn., Perth and Kinross, **Scot.**; alt. 983 m.

Ben Wyvis, mtn., Ross and Cromarty, **Scot.**; nr. Dingwall; alt. 1,046 m.

Benxi (Penki), c., Liaoning prov., **China**; metallurgical ctr.; p. (1984) 810,500.

Ben-y-Gloe, mtn., Glen Tilt, Perth and Kinross, **Scot.**; alt. 1,120 m.

Beograd. See **Belgrade.**

Beppu, c., Kyushu, **Japan**; hot spring resort; p. (1985) 134,782.

Berbera, pt., **Somalia**, on G. of Aden; exp. livestock from pastoral hinterland; new deep-sea pt. completed 1969; airport; p. (est. 1987) 65,000.

Berchtesgaden, v., W. Germany; mtn. resort 24 km S. of Salzburg; Hitler's mtn. retreat; tourism; potash.

Berck-Plage, resort, Pas-de-Calais, France, on Eng. Channel; p. (1982) 15,671.

Berdichev, t., Ukrainian SSR, USSR; ctr. of sugar a.; engin., lt. inds.; p. (est. 1969) 61,000.

Berdyansk, c., Ukrainian SSR, USSR; pt. on Sea of Azov; agr. ctr.; machin.; health resort; p. (est. 1985) 130,000.

Bere Regis, mkt. t., Dorset, Eng.; Saxon royal residence.

Berezina, R., USSR; trib. of Dnieper; forms part of Baltic-Black Sea waterway; 608 km long.

Berezniki, t., E. European RSFSR; pt. on Kolva R., W. Urals; salt, chemicals, paper; p. (est. 1985) 195,000.

Bergama, t., Turkey; anc. Pergamos, ruins; morocco leather inds.; agr. tr.; p. (1985) 38,849.

Bergamo, c., Lombardy, Italy; 54 km N.E. Milan; cath. and academy; silk industry; p. (1984) 121,033.

Bergen, spt., W. cst. Norway; univ.; most impt. comm. pt. in kingdom; shipping, fishing; mftg. inds.; birthplace of Grieg; p. (est. 1987) 208,809.

Bergen op Zoom, t., N. Brabant, Neth.; sugar refining. engin.; p. (est. 1987) 46,000.

Bergerac, t., Dordogne, S.W. France; impt. bridge over Dordogne R.; mkt. for wines and luxury foods; anc. Huguenot stronghold; p. (1982) 27,704.

Bergisches Land, terr., N. Rhine-Westphalia, W. Germany; specialised iron and steel prod.; chemicals, machin.; inc. ts. of Solingen, Remscheid, Velbert, Wuppertal.

Bergisch-Gladbach, t., N. Rhine-Westphalia, W. Germany; 11 km E. of Cologne, paper, metallurgy, textiles; p. (est. 1986) 101,800.

Berhampur, t., Orissa, India; admin. or educational ctr.; p. (1971) 117,662.

Bering Current (Okhotsk Current, or Oyashio), ocean current, N. Pac. Oc.; flows through Bering Strait from Arctic, along E. cst. of Kamchatka and Japanese Is. Hokkaido, Honshu; relatively cold; moderate summer temperatures along csts. causes fogs.

Bering Sea, part of N. Pac. Oc. between Aleutian Is. and B. Strait; fishing; a. 2,274,020 km².

Bering Strait, narrow sea which separates Asia from N. America, and connects Bering Sea with Arctic Oc.; 58 km wide at narrowest part.

Berkeley, v., Gloucs., Eng.; nr. R. Severn, 24 km N. of Bristol; scene of murder of Edward II; civil nuclear power-sta. closed down 1989.

Berkeley, c., Cal., USA; univ.; chemicals; now inc. in San Francisco; p. (1984) 103,800.

Berkhamsted, Dacorum, Herts., Eng.; mkt. t.; chemicals; cas. ruins, 17th cent. school; birth-place of William Cowper the poet; p. (1981) 15,461.

Berkshire, non-met. co., Eng.; chalk downland inc. Inkpen Beacon, White Horse Hills; drained by Thames and tribs.; residtl.; electronics, biscuits; dairying; Windsor Gr. Park; Ascot racecourse; a. 1,256 km²; p. (est. 1988) 747,100.

Berlin, c., former cap. of Germany, Europe; on Spree R.; divided into 4 occupied zones 1945; Soviet (now E. Berlin), British, American, French (now W. Berlin); W. Berlin forms isolated enclave within E. Germany; focal point of escape attempts from E. to W. led to construction of "Berlin Wall", destroyed 1989; W. Berlin major industl. ctr. aided by American and W. German capital; educational, cultural and tourist ctr.; E. Berlin, cap. of E. Germany, rebuilt as showpiece with high-rise housing, elect. manfs, machin., vehicles, chems. and clothing; p. (est. 1986) 1,879,200, (W. Berlin); (est. 1986) 1,233,309 (E. Berlin).

Bermuda, Brit. gr. coral Is. (360 in no. of which 20 are inhabited) N. Atlantic; about 1,120 km E. of S.C.; Hamilton, on Long I. is the ch. t.; Brit. and US air and naval stas.; favourite winter resort for Americans; inds. attracted by tax incentives; no surface water; total a. 54 km²; p. (est. 1985) 57,145.

Bern, c., cap. of B. can. and fed. cap. Switzerland; on Aare R.; cath., univ.; textiles, musical instruments, chocolate; H.Q. of Postal Union; bear pit; p. (est. 1985) 139,000 (c.) 301,000 (met. a.).

Bern, can., Switzerland; fertile valleys, dairying; watches; hydroelectric power; plans for separate can. in Jura reg.; a. 6,881 km²; p. (est. 1986) 926,000.

Bernard, Great St., one of the Alps in the S. of the Valais, Switzerland; highest point 3,390 m; height of mtn. pass between Italy (Aosta) and Switzerland (Martigny), 2,477 m; famous hospice for travellers in monastery on mtn.; road tunnel completed 1962.

Bernard, Little St., one of Graian Alps, Savoy, S.

of Mt. Blanc, France; pass traversed by Hannibal 218 B.C.

Bernburg, t., Halle, E. Germany; cas.; chemicals, salt mng.; p. (est. 1980) 46,000.

Bernese Oberland (Berner Alpen), alpine region, Switzerland; 35 peaks over 3,000 m inc. Finsteraarhorn and Jungfrau; tourist a. inc. resorts of Interlaken and Grindelwald.

Bernina Alps, Switzerland; alt. 4,050 m.

Berri, t., S. Australia; ctr. of irrigated fruit growing a. on R. Murray; wines; p. (1981) 3,419.

Berri, oilfield, Saudi Arabia; 72 km N.W. of Ras Tannura; the field extends offshore.

Berwick, l. gov. dist., former co., Border Reg., S.E. Scot.; a. of sheep rearing and woollen inds. in S. Uplands; a. 875 km²; p. (est. 1986) 18,748.

Berwick, t., Vic., Australia; satellite of Melbourne; to be expanded to planned p. of 100,000 by 1985; p. (est. 1983) 41,400.

Berwick-upon-Tweed, l. gov. dist., Northumberland, Eng.; spt. on mouth of Tweed; border t., changed between Eng. and Scot. 15 times in history; fishing, lt. engin., tweeds, knitwear; cas. ruins; p. (est. 1988) 26,800 (dist.).

Besançon, t., cap. of Doubs dep., France; cath., observatory, univ.; farm implements, textiles; watch- and clock-making; birthplace of Victor Hugo; p. (1982) 119,687.

Besche, t., Saarland, W. Germany; oil refining.

Beskids, W. and E., (Beskidy Zachodnie), mtn. range, Poland, ČSSR, E. Europe; northern range of Carpathian mtn. system, seldom exceeds alt. 1,200 m, many passes; forested; tourism; length 352 km.

Bessarabia, terr., ceded to USSR by Romania 1940, and now part of Moldavian SSR; agr. region.

Bessemer, t., Ala., USA; iron and steel; p. (1980) 31,729.

Bethany (El Azarieh), v., on Mt. of Olives 6 km W. of Jerusalem, Jordan.

Bethel, anc. c., the modern Beitin, Jordan; 16 km N. Jerusalem.

Bethesda, t., Arfon, Gwynedd, Wales; slate, lt. engin; p. (1981) 4,060.

Bethlehem, t., Jordan; 9 km S.W. Jerusalem; according to Matthew and Luke birthplace of Christ; p. (est. 1980) 14,000.

Bethlehem, t., Penns., USA; 80 km N. of Philadelphia; iron-wks.; univ.; p. (1980) 70,419.

Bethnal Green, dist., London, Eng.; in E. End of London; now in Tower Hamlets.

Béthune, t., Pas-de-Calais, France; rail and canal ctr. for coalfield; mkt. t.; p. (1982) 258,383 (met. a.).

Betteshanger, v., Kent, Eng.; on N. flank of N. Downs, 6 km W. of Deal; coal mng.

Bettws-y-Coed, t., Aberconwy, Gwynedd, Wales; waterfalls; tourism; p. (1981) 658.

Beuel, t., N. Rhine-Westphalia, W. Germany; on E. bank R. Rhine opposite Bonn; chemicals, furniture; p. (est. 1969) 38,668.

Beuthan. See Bytom.

Beverley, l. gov. dist., mkt. t., Humberside, Eng.; famous minster (13th cent.); agr. processing; p. (est. 1988) 114,000.

Beverly, c., Mass., USA; footwear, machin.; p. (1980) 37,655.

Beverly Hills, t., Cal., USA; sub. of Los Angeles; home of many film celebrities; p. (1980) 32,367.

Beverwijk, t., nr. Haarlem, N. Holland, Neth.; agr. prods.; p. (est. 1987) 35,000.

Bewdley, Wyre Forest, Hereford and Worcs., Eng.; mkt. t. on R. Severn; birthplace of Stanley Baldwin; residtl.; p. (1981) 8,742.

Bexhill-on-Sea, t., Rother, East Sussex, Eng.; resort; p. (1981) 35,529.

Bexley, former bor., W. Kent; now outer bor., Greater London, Eng.; inc. Chislehurst and Sidcup (N. of the A.20), Crayford and Erith; p. (est. 1988) 220,400.

Béziers, t., Hérault, France; ctr. of wine, brandy tr. and inds.; chemicals; p. (1982) 78,477.

Bezwada. See Vijayawada.

Bhadravati, t., Karnataka, India; steel; p. (1981) 77,055 (t.), 130,606 (met. a.).

Bhagalpur, t., Bihar, India; agr. tr. ctr. on R. Ganges; p. (1981) 225,062.

Bhamo, t., Upper Burma; on Irrawaddy; inland limit of steam boats; mkt. ctr.; ruby mines; p. 10,000.

Bhandara, cap. of Bhandara dist., Maharashtra, India; 48 km E. of Nagpur; cotton cloth, brass mftg.; p. (1981) 56,025.

Bharuch, t., Gujerat, India; world's lgst. stream urea fertiliser plant; nearby oilfield.

Bhatpara, t., W. Bengal, **India**; on R. Hooghly; industl. t.; jute, engin.; p. (1981) 260,761.

Bhaunager, t., Gujarat, **India**; pt. on G. of Cambay; exp. cotton, oilseeds; p. (1981) 307,121.

Bhilai, t., Madhya Pradesh, **India**; steel plant; rails and rly. sleepers; p. (1961) of industl. t. (1981) 319,450.

Bhim-Gora, sacred pool, place of Hindu pilgrimage, Uttar Pradesh, **India**.

Bhopal, c., cap. of Madhya Pradesh, **India**; impt. tr. ctr.; varied inds.; prehistoric cave paintings nearby; 2,000 killed in world's worst chem. accident (1984); p. (1981) 671,018.

Bhubaneswar, t., cap. of Orissa, **India**; 29 km from Cuttack; admin. ctr.; Hindu temples, pilgrimage ctr.; p. (1981) 219,211.

Bhutan, kingdom, indep. mtn. st., E. Himalayas; heavy monsoon rain, rich tropical vegetation. valuable forests; N.–S. ridges and valleys result in semi-closed communities; first motor link with India opened 1962; cap. Thimphu; a. c. 46,620 km²; alt. 7,558 m (Kula Kangri); p. scattered and nomadic (est. 1985) 1,417,000.

Biafra, Bight of. *See* **Bonny, Bight of.**

Biako, formerly Marcias Nguema (**Fernando Po**).
I., **Equatorial Guinea**; in Bight of Bonny; mtnous.; coffee, cocoa, bananas, timber; p. (est. 1984) 75,000.

Bialystok, t., **Poland**; cap. of B. prov., nr. Grodno; major industl. ctr.; rly. ctr.; p. (est. 1985) 245,000.

Biarritz, t., Pyrénées-Atlantique dep., **France**; on Bay of Biscay; seaside resort; p. (1982) 26,647.

Biberach, t., Baden-Württemberg, **W. Germany**; on R. Kinzig; spa; wood, metal and engin. inds.; p. (est. 1986) 28,000.

Bicester, Cherwell, Oxford, **Eng.**; anc. mkt. t., N.E. of Oxford; p. (1981) 14,436.

Biddulph, t., Staffs. Moorlands, Staffs., **Eng.**; coal mng., machin., textiles, furniture; residtl.; p. (1981) 19,160.

Bideford, Torridge, N. Devon, **Eng.**; pt. on estuary R. Torridge; mkt., boat-bldg.; resort; p. (1981) 12,211.

Biel (Bienne), t., Berne, **Switzerland**; nr. Lake B.; watches; impt. industl. ctr.; p. (est. 1985) 52,000.

Bielawa, t., Wroclaw prov., S.W. **Poland**; textiles; p. (1970) 31,000.

Bielefeld, t., Rhine-Westphalia, **W. Germany**; ch. ctr. of linen industry; machin., bicycles; p. (est. 1986) 299,400.

Biella, t., Vercelli, **Italy**; textiles; p. (1981) 53,572.

Bielsko-Biala, t., Katowice prov., **Poland**; woollens, linen, metal, chemicals; p. (est. 1985) 174,000.

Bien-hoa, t., nr. Ho Chi-minh City, S. **Vietnam**; sugar refining; cotton mills.

Bies-Bosch, reclaimed fenland area between N. Brabant and S.W. **Neth.**; sugar refining, dairying; a. 142 km².

Biggar, sm. burgh, Clydesdale, **Scot.**; 213 m in Southern Uplands; p. (1981) 1,931.

Biggin Hill, Greater London, **Eng.**; nr. Orpington; famous airfield of Battle of Britain.

Biggleswade, t., Mid Beds., **Eng.**; in valley of R. Ivel, 14 km S.E. of Bedford; ctr. of fruit-growing and mkt. gardening dist.; hydraulic machin. tools, hosiery, caravans; p. (1981) 10,928.

Big Horn Mtns., Wyo. and Mont., **USA**; Rockies; favourite film location; attractive agr. valleys; highest alt., 3,600 m.

Bihać, t., **Yugoslavia**; on R. Una; recent industl. development; timber processing.

Bihar, st., N.W. **India**; in Ganges basin; hilly; bulk of p. in agr. N.; irrigation; minerals in S.E.: coal, iron, mica; steelwks. at Jamshedpur, oil refining at Barauni; cap. Patna, admin. ctr. Ranchi; a. 173,882 km²; p. (1981) 69,914,734.

Bihar, t., Bihar, **India**; within middle Ganges valley nr. Patna; p. (1981) 151,343.

Biisk, c., Siberia, **USSR**; ctr. of rich agr. a.; meat packing, textiles; p. (est. 1985) 226,000.

Bijagós, Achipelago dos (Bissagos Is.), off W. cst. **Guinea-Bissau**; c. 14 Is.; coconuts, rice; ch. t. Bolama on Bolama I.; a. 1,554 km².

Bijapur, t., Karnataka, **India**; cotton tr. and inds.; ruins; former cap. of B. kingdom; p. (1981) 147,313.

Bikaner, t., Rajasthan, **India**; in Thar desert; on former caravan route; wool tr., bldg. stone, handicrafts; p. (1981) 253,174 (t.), 287,712 (met. a.).

Bikini, atoll, **Pac. Oc.**; atomic-bomb tests (1946).

Bilaspur, t., Madhya Pradesh, **India**; silks, cottons; p. (1981) 147,218 (t.), 179,791 (met. a.).

Bilbao, spt., N. **Spain**; cap. Basque prov. of Viscaya; formerly famous for rapier making;

iron ore, smelting; pipeline from Ayoluengo oilfield; p. (1987) 382,413.

Billinge and Winstanley, t., Lancs., **Eng.**; former coal-mng. a.; p. (1981) 12,488.

Billingham, t. Cleveland, **Eng.**; on N. of Tees estuary; major petrochemical plant.

Billings, t., Mont., **USA**; agr. tr. ctr. in irrigated a.; sulphur plant; p. (1984) 69,800 (t.), 118,700 (met. a.).

Billingsgate, London, **Eng.**; old river-gate and wharf, formerly ch. fish mkt. of England; now moved to Isle of Dogs.

Bilma (Kawar), oasis t., **Niger**; on caravan route from Tripoli to Agadés and L. Chad; p. c. 1,000.

Billiton I. *See* **Belitung.**

Biloxi, t., Miss., **USA**; fishing, tourist ctr.; US Coast Guard air base; p. (1984) 48,700 (t.) 197,400 (met. a.).

Bilston, t., West Midlands, **Eng.**; part of Wolverhampton; iron and steel.

Bingen, t., Rhineland Palatinate, **W. Germany**; at S. entrance to Rhine gorge; wine; beautiful scenery; tourism; p. (est. 1986) 22,100.

Bingerville, spt., **Ivory Coast**, W. Africa; rubber processing.

Bingham Canyon, t., N. Utah, **USA**; silver, gold, lead; major open pit copper mine; p. (1970) 31.

Binghamton, N.Y., **USA**; on Susquehanna R.; boot factories, aircraft components, cameras; p. (1984) 54,500 (t.), 264,100 (met. a.).

Bingley, West Yorks., **Eng.**; mkt. t. on R. Aire 26 km N.W. of Leeds; textiles, engin., agr.; p. (1981) 28,070.

Bintan I., lgst. island of Riouw archipelago, **Indonesia**; bauxite, tin.

Bintenne, dist., **Sri Lanka**; remote a., sparse p.; lge. Gal Oya reservoir; tea and rubber estates.

Biratnagar, t., S.E. **Nepal**, in the Tarai; jute, sugar, cotton milling, stainless steel; p. (1981) 93,544.

Birbhum, dist., W. Bengal, **India**; cap. Suri; healthy climate; rice, sugar; mnfs. silk, cotton; a. 4,550 km²; p. (1961) 1,446,158.

Birkenhead, Wirral, Merseyside, **Eng.**; spt. on R. Mersey, opposite Liverpool; handles industl. goods; heavy and pt. processing inds.; shipbldg.; p. (1981) 123,907.

Birmingham, c., met. dist., West Midlands, **Eng.**; industl. cap. Midlands, second lgst. c. Gt. Britain; metal inds.; motor vehicles, components and accessories; major growth due to Industl. Revolution; univ. cath.; freeport (1984) for air freight; p. (est. 1988) 993,700.

Birmingham, t., Ala., **USA**; coal, iron, limestone, steel, aircraft, chemicals, textiles; p. (1984) 279,800 (t.), 895,200 (met. a.).

Birnam, v., Perth and Kinross, **Scot.**; location of Birnam Wood in *Macbeth*; former royal forest; p. (1981) 990.

Birobidzhan, or Jewish aut. oblast, **RSFSR**; in Khabarovsk terr.; agr., timber and mng. inds.; a. 35,988 km²; cap. Birobidzhan City; p. (est. 1980) 67,000 (inc. 15,000 Jews).

Birr, U.D. Offaly, **R.o.I.**; mkt. t. on Brosna R.; observatory; p. (est. 1978) 4,000.

Bir Tlacsin, Libya; 192 km S.W. Tripoli; oilfields.

Bisbee, t., Arizona, **USA**; very rich copper deposits, gold, silver, lead; p. (1980) 7,154.

Biscarosse, Landes dep., **France**; 72 km S.W. Bordeaux; rocket and missile testing range projected; p. (1982) 8,979.

Biscay, Bay of, stormy a. of Atl. Oc., W. of France and N. of Spain, from Ushant to C. Ortegal; the Roman Sinus Aquitanicus; heavy seas.

Bisceglie, t., Apulia, **Italy**; spt. on E. cst. 35 km N.W. of Bari; tr. in wine and olives; light inds.; cath.; p. (1981) 45,899.

Bischofswerda, t., Dresden, **E. Germany**; quarrying, glass and iron inds.; rly. ctr.; p. (1963) 11,285.

Bishop Auckland, t., Wear Valley, Durham, **Eng.**; palace of Bishop of Durham; iron, lt. engin.; former coal mng.; p. (1981) 32,572.

Bishopbriggs, sm. burgh, Strathkelvin, **Scot.**; p. (1981) 23,367.

Bishop Rock, isolated rock, lighthouse, Scilly Is., **Eng.**; 58 km S.W. of Land's End, Cornwall; recognised internationally as E. end of trans-Atlantic ocean crossing.

Bishop's Stortford, East Herts., **Eng.**; mkt. t. on Stort R.; light inds.; Hatfield forest nearby; Norman cas.; p. (1981) 22,807.

Biskra, t., **Algeria**; admin. ctr., winter resort; oasis nearby; date mkt.; p. (1966) 59,052.

Bisley, v., Surrey, **Eng.**; ranges of Nat. Rifle Ass. on B. common.

Bismarck, t., st. cap. N.D., **USA**; on Missouri R.; agr. mkt. ctr.; p. (1980) 44,485.

Bismarck Archipelago, volcanic gr., S.W. Pac. Oc., off **New Guinea,** admin. by Australia; p. (est. 1962) 174,115.

Bisotūn, t., **Iran**; in ruins; monuments to Darius I (the Great).

Bissagos Is. *See* **Bijagós, Achipelago dos.**

Bissau, t., cap of **Guinea-Bissau**; former ctr. of slave tr.; airpt.; plans to expand harbour; p. (1979) 109,214.

Bitola, t., Macedonia, **Yugoslavia**; varied mnfs.; recent industl. development; mosques; p. (1981) 137,835.

Bitonto, t., Apulia, on E. cst. 11 km N.W. of Bari; **Italy**; cath.; p. (est. 1968) 41,749.

Bitterfeld, t. Halle, **E. Germany**; lignite mng., engin. chemicals; p. (est. 1970) 28,964.

Bitter Lakes, Isthmus of Suez, **Egypt**, utilised by Suez Canal.

Biwa-ko, lgst. lake in **Japan,** S. Honshu; 101 m a.s.l.; canal to Kyto provides hydroelectric power; superb scenery, historical associations; tourism; a. 675 km².

Biysk or **Bisk,** c., Altai terr., **RSFSR**; pt. on Biya R.; terminus of branch of Turk-Sib. rly.; p. (1983) 221,000.

Bizerte, c., **N. Tunisia**; pt. and naval sta. on Med.; the anc. Hippo Zaritus; fishing, oil refining, steel wks., tyres; p. (1984) 94,509.

Björnborg. *See* **Pori.**

Blaby, l. gov. dist. Leics., **Eng.**; sm. a. S.W. of Leicester; p. (est. 1990) 87,300.

Black Belt, coastlands of Miss. and Ala., **USA**, where black soil prairie land is good for cotton.

Blackburn, t., l. gov. dist., Lancs., **Eng.**; once major cotton weaving ctr.; engin., lt. inds.; p. (est. 1988) 134,400 (dist.).

Black Country, Midlands, **Eng.**; formerly impt. iron-working and coal-mng. dist. mainly in S. West Midlands; now a. of lt. engin.; c. 130 km².

Blackdown Hills, Devon and Somerset, **Eng.**; sandstone hills rising over 305 m.

Black Forest. *See* **Schwarzwald.**

Blackheath, open common, S.E. London, **Eng.**; mustering place of Wat Tyler's (1381) and Jack Cade's (1450) revolutionary peasants; now main attraction of expensive residtl. a.; a. 108 ha.

Black Hills, mtns. between S.D. and Wyo., **USA**; highest., Horney Peak, 2.208 m; form part of Nat. Park.

Black Isle, peninsula, between Cromarty and Beauly Firths, Ross and Cromarty, **Scot.**; agr., fisheries, quarrying; a. 280 km².

Black Mtn., Powys and Dyfed, S. **Wales**; rise to 802 m in Brecknock Van, sandstone plateau; moorland; valleys used for reservoirs; Nat. Park.

Black Mtns., Powys, S. **Wales**; rise to 811 m in Waun Fach.

Blackpool, t., l. gov. dist., Lancs., **Eng.**; on cst. of Fylde dist.; one of major Brit. resorts; p. (est. 1988) 143,800 (dist.).

Black Prairie, region Texas, **USA**; extends 560 km S.W. from Ouachita Mtns. to Austin; contains very fertile Black Waxy and Grande Prairie sub-regions devoted almost entirely to cotton growing; ch. ts., Dallas, Fort Worth, Austin; a. 77,700 km².

Blackrod, t., Gtr. Manchester, **Eng.**; nr. Chorley; former cotton weaving; p. (1981) 5,628.

Black Sea, bordered by 4 sts., **USSR** (N. and E.), **Turkey** (S.), **Bulgaria, Romania** (W.); receives waters of Danube, Dniester, Dnieper, Don. Bug; stagnant and lifeless below 146 m; fisheries in N. and W.; oil exploration by Turkey; a. 424,760 km² (exc. Sea of Azov).

Blacksod Bay, cst. of Mayo, **R.o.I.**

Black Volta, R., rises in **Bourkina Fasso**, flows E. and S. into L. Volta, **Ghana**; length c. 1,200 km.

Blackwater, R., N. Ireland; rising in Dungannon, it forms border with **R.o.I.**; enters L. Neagh; 80 km long.

Blackwater, R., **R.o.I.**; flows from Knockanefune to enter Atl. Oc. at pt. and resort of Youghal; chain of sm. ts. along course; 144 km long.

Blaenau Gwent, l. gov. dist., Gwent. **Wales.**; inland valley a. inc. Ebbw Vale and Abertillery; p. (est. 1988) 77,300.

Blaenavon, t., Torfaen, Gwent, **Wales**; former coal mng.; p. (1981) 6,363.

Blagoveshchensk, t., E. Siberia, **RSFSR**, on Chinese bdr. and R. Amur; wat. pl.; engin., sawmilling, flour milling; on Trans-Siberian rly.; p. (est. 1985) 195,000.

Blair Atholl, v., Perth and Kinross, **Scot.**; tourist resort; cas.; seat of Duke of Atholl.

Blairgowrie and **Rattray,** burgh, Perth and Kinross, **Scot.**; at foot of Scot. Highlands; mkt. t. in Strathmore fruit growing dist.; p. (1981) 7,049.

Blakeney, v., N. Norfolk, **Eng.**; nr. sand spit; yachting; wild fowl.

Blandford or **Blandford Forum,** North Dorset, **Eng.**; on R. Stour; pastoral mkt. t. since 13th cent.; p. (1981) 3,915.

Blantyre, c., **Malawi**; in Shire Highlands; linked by rail to Beira (Moçambique); comm. ctr.; timber processing; p. (est. 1983) 313,600.

Blantyre, v., East Kilbride, **Scot.**; Lower B. birth-place of David Livingstone; p. (1981) 19,816.

Blarney, v., 6 km N.W. Cork, **R.o.I.**; cas. and Blarney stone; p. (1981) 1,500.

Blasket Is., Kerry. **R.o.I.**; rocky Is.; uninhabited since 1953.

Blaydon, t. Tyne and Wear. **Eng.**; former coal mng.; p. (1981) 30,563.

Bled, glacial L., Slovenia, **Yugoslavia**; tourism.

Blenheim, t., S.I., **N.Z.**; fruit; p. (est. 1987) 18,400.

Blenheim, v., **W. Germany**; scene of battle (1704) when English and Austrians under Marlborough defeated the French and Bavarians; **Blenheim Palace,** Woodstock, Oxon. **Eng.**; named in honour of this victory.

Blessington, L., Wicklow, **R.o.I.**; glacial L., now serves as reservoir for Dublin.

Bletchley, Bucks., **Eng.**; expanded t.; p. (1981) 42,450.

Blida. *See* **El Boulaïda.**

Bloemfontein, t. cap. O.F.S., **S. Africa**; on plateau, alt. 1,393 m; route and tr. ctr.; univ.; p. (1985) 232,984 (met. a.).

Blois, t., cap. of Loire-et-Cher dep., **France**; historic t. on Loire R.; Renaissance château; wines; p. (1982) 61,049 (met. a.).

Bloomfield, t., N.J., **USA**; pharmaceuticals, metal and elec. gds.; sub. N.J. c.; p. (1980) 47,792.

Bloomington, t., Ill., **USA**; comm. ctr. and industl. t. in rich agr. and coal-mng. a.; univ.; p. (1984) 46,600 (t.). 122,800 (met. a.).

Bloomington, t., Ind., **USA**; electronic equip-ment, furniture, structural glass; univ.; p. (1984) 52,200 (t.), 100,900 (met. a.).

Bloomsbury, dist., London, **Eng.**; fashionable dist. with many squares; famous for B. gr. of authors in first quarter of 20th cent.; inc. Brit. Museum, Univ. of London.

Bludenz, t., W. **Austria**; cotton, watches; p. (est. 1965) 11,400.

Blue Grass, dist., Ky., **USA**; area where blue grass abundant; horse breeding.

Blue Mountains, t., N.S.W., **Australia**; tourist ctr.; new t. (1947); p. (1981) 55,877.

Blue Mtns., Jamaica; famous for coffee; dense forest; tourism; average alt. 900–1,200 m, ris-ing to 2,294 m in Blue Mtn. peak.

Blue Nile (Bahr-el-Azraq), R., rises in tablelands of Ethiopia, joins the White Nile at Khartoum; its seasonal flooding provides the bulk of water for irrigation in Sudan and Egypt.

Blue Ridge Mtns., S. Penn., Ga., **USA**; inc. Shenandoah valley; superb scenery, resorts; average alt. 600–1,200 m, rising to 1,737 m in Grandfather Mtn.

Bluff, bor., S.I., **N.Z.**; 29 km from Invercargill; spt. for Southland prov., major aluminium tr.; p. (1976) 3,016.

Blumenau, mkt. t., Santa Catarina st., **Brazil**; butter, sugar; p. (est. 1985) 192,900.

Blyth., spt., Northumberland, **Eng.**; on coalfield; now as B. Valley forms l. gov. dist.; p. (est. 1988) 78,500 (dist.).

Bo, t., **Sierra Leone**; gold; admin. H.Q.; p. (1985) 740,510.

Boa Vista, t., R. pt., cap. Roraima st., **Brazil**; p. (est. 1977) 25,000.

Bobbio, t., Emilia-Romagna, **Italy**, in northern Apennines; ctr. European cultural life, 9th-12th cent.; St Columban founded monastery, 612; p. (1981) 4,215.

Bobo Dioulassa, t., **Bourkina Fasso**; agr. tr., gold mng.; p. (1985) 231,162.

Bobigny, N.E. sub of Paris, cap. of Seine-St. Denis dep., **France**; commu indst.; p. (1982) 42,727.

Bobruysk, t., Belorussiyan SSR, **USSR**; pt. on R. Berezina; engin., sawmilling, paper, cellulose, grain; p. (est. 1985) 223,000.

Bocholt, t., N. Rhine-Westphalia, **W. Germany;** machin., textiles, elec. gds.; p. (est. 1986) 66,400.

Bochum, t., N. Rhine-Westphalia, **W. Germany;** heart of Ruhr iron and steel ind.; known since 9th cent.; new (1962) Univ. of Ruhr; p. (est. 1986) 381,200.

Bodensee (L. Constance), S.W. **West Germany** and **Switzerland;** 72 km long, 14 km wide.; R. Rhine flows through; fruit and horticulture on warmer slopes of L.

Bodmin, co. t., North Cornwall, **Eng.;** on S.W. flank of Bodmin moor; china clay, lt. engin.; p. (1981) 12,148.

Bodmin Moor, upland, N.E. Cornwall, **Eng.;** lower slopes cultivated, higher slopes used for sheep pastures; average alt. 300 m, highest point, Brown Willy, alt, 419 m; major ctr. of china clay quarrying.

Bodô, t., **Norway;** nr. Lofoten Is.; spt., fish processing; N. rly, terminus; p. (est. 1987) 35,000.

Bodrum, t., on Aegean cst., **Turkey;** anc. Halicarnassus; 15th cent. Crusader castle; fishing.

Boeotia, region of anc. **Greece;** scene of many battles; Thebes was the ch. c.; home of Hesiod and Pindar; p. (1981) 117,175.

Bogda Ula, massif, Sinkiang, **China;** forms N. perimeter of Turfan depression; 240 km wide, average alt. 4,000 m, rising to 5,479 m in Turpanat Targh.

Bognor Regis, t., Arun, West Sussex. **Eng.;** residtl.; seaside resort; p. (1981) 39,536.

Bogor, t., Java, **Indonesia;** rubber factory, textiles, footwear; p. (est. 1983) 274,000.

Bogota, cap. and lgst. c. of **Colombia;** in E. Cordilleras, 2,745 m a.s.l.; univ., nat. observatory, colonial architecture; political, social and financial ctr. of rep.; p. (1985) 4,185,174.

Bo Hai (Pohai), G. of, N. China; together with G. of Liaotung forms shallow expanse of water almost cut off from Yellow Sea by Liaotung and Shandong peninsulas; receives water and silt from Huang He; a. approx. 38,900 km².

Bohemia, historic region, former kingdom, W. **ČSSR;** plateau drained by R. Elbe; borders W. Germany; agr. dist.; minerals inc. lignite, graphite; textiles, sugar, pottery.

Böhmerwald (Bohemian Forest), forested range of mtns. between **ČSSR** and Bavaria, **W. Germany;** 240 km long; alt. 1,479 m at Aber; region of poor soils; sm. farms; some mng. and quarrying.

Bohol I., Philippines; maize, coconuts, rice; a. 3,864 km²; p. (1970) 674,806.

Boise, t., cap. of Idaho, **USA;** financial ctr.; timber mills; hot springs; p. (1984) 107,200 (c.), 189,300 (met. a.).

Boksburg, t., Transvaal, **S. Africa;** industl.; former coal-mng.; t. p. (1980) 150,287.

Bolan Pass, Baluchistan, **Pakistan;** pass from Pakistan to Afghanistan; summit 1,800 m.

Bolbec, t., Seine-Maritime, **France;** 19 km E. of Le Havre; textiles; elec. engin.; p. (1982) 12,578.

Boldon, t., Tyne and Wear, **Eng.;** coal mng.; p. (1981) 24,171.

Boleslawiec (Bunzlau), t., Lower Silesia, **Poland;** German before 1945; on the Bóbr R., pottery; p. (1970) 30,500.

Boliden, t., N. **Sweden;** impt. deposits of copper and arsenic.

Bolivia, inland rep., S. **America;** land-locked, 9 deps.; cap. nominally Sucre, actual admin. H.Q. La Paz; much US investment but discouraged by nationalism from late 1960s; relief makes transport difficult; moves towards gaining access to cst. via internat. corridor; forests; savannahs; agr. in backward conditions; embryonic industl. devel. suffered from political instability; much social protest against military rule, return to democracy 1982; rubber, quinine, cattle, hides; ch. exp. gas and tin; petroleum; mafia cocaine tr.; exp. illegal narcotics; language Spanish; a. 1,331,661 km²; p. (est. 1985) 6,429,000.

Bollington, t., Cheshire, **Eng.;** nr. Macclesfield; textile finishing; p. (1981) 6,930.

Bologna, c., N. **Italy;** cap. of B. prov. on N. flank of Apennines; impt. route ctr. commanding road and rly. across Apennines to Florence; preserved and restored in Arcadian style by Communist admin.; univ., service t.; p. (1984) 447,971.

Bolsa Island, Cal., **USA;** nuclear power and desalination project in progress.

Bolsena, L., Latium region, **Italy;** occupies lge. extinct volcanic crater in S. of Tuscan Hills

96 km N.W. of Rome; a. (approx.) 129 km²; p. (1981) 3,960.

Bolshoya Volga, t., **RSFSR;** 128 km N. of Moscow, at junct. of Volga and Moscow Volga Canal; Soviet Institute of Nuclear Studies.

Bolsover, t., l. gov. dist., Derbys., **Eng.;** limestone, coal, textiles; cas.; Hardwick Hall 6 km to S., p. (est. 1988) 69,900.

Bolton, t., met. dist., Gtr. Manchester, **Eng.;** cotton, textiles, engin.; p. (est. 1988) 263,600.

Bolton Abbey, North Yorks. **Eng.;** ruined Augustinian Priory.

Bolzano, t., Trentino-Alto Adige **Italy;** on R. Isarco at S. approach to Brenner Pass; resort; p. (1984) 103,009.

Boma, t., **Zaïre;** t., spt.; pt. on estuary of R. Zaïre; exp. timber, cocoa, palm prods., bananas; p. (est. 1970) 61,054.

Bombay, spt., cap. of Maharashtra st., **India;** harbour, docks, rly. ctr.; univ.; greatest cotton ctr. in republic; pt. handles nearly half of India's foreign tr.; oil refinery; film industry; univ., fine public bldgs.; p. (1981) 8,243,405 (met. a.).

Bonaire I., Neth. Antilles; a. 287 km²; p. (1981) 8,753.

Bône. See **Annaba.**

Bo'ness, burgh, Falkirk, **Scot.;** spt. on Firth of Forth, 6 km E. of Grangemouth; foundries, timber yards; p. (1981) 14,669.

Bonifacio, spt., Corse du Sud, Corsica, **France;** opposite Sardinia, on Strait of Bonifacio; p. (1982) 2,736.

Bonin Is., Pac. Oc., **Japan;** 15 Is., volcanic; 960 km S. of Tokyo; a. 103 km²; p. (est. 1970) 300.

Bonn, c., fed. cap. of **W. Germany;** at confluence of Rs. Sieg and Rhine; univ.; seat of W. German parliament; birthplace of Beethoven; founded in Roman times; varied inds. inc. printing, publishing; p. (est. 1986) 291,400.

Bonnet a l'Eveque, mtn., **Haiti;** sheer sides, flat top; site of La Ferrière fortress, alt. 900 m.

Bonneville Dam, Ore., Wash., **USA;** across R. Columbia 64 km above Portland (Ore.), provides irrigation to valleys on Columbia-Snake Plateau; locks permit navigation and provide hydroelectric power.

Bonneville Salt Flats, Utah, **USA;** remains of anc. lake; world automobile speed test, 1937–47.

Bonny, t., S. **Nigeria;** at mouth of R. Bonny. Niger delta; oil terminal.

Bonny, Bight of (Bight of Biafra until 1975), **W. Africa;** bay lying E. of the G. of Guinea between the Niger and C. Lopez.

Bonnyrigg and **Lasswade,** burgh, Midlothian, **Scot.,** 11 km S.E. of Edinburgh, p. (1981) 14,301.

Boothferry, l. gov. dist., Humberside, **Eng.;** lowland a. of I. of Axholme and inc. Goole; p. (est. 1988) 64,100.

Boothia, peninsula on Arctic cst., Franklin dist. **Canada;** separated from Baffin I., by G. of B.

Bootle, t., Sefton, Merseyside, **Eng.;** on E. side of entrance to Mersey estuary; shares line of docks with Liverpool; dockside inds. inc. tanning, ship-repairing; tin plant; p. (1981) 62,463.

Bophuthatswana, indep. Bantu Terr. (1977) not recognised by UN as designed to consolidate apartheid; some mineral wealth (asbestos, platinum) but land produces only 10 per cent of agricultural requirements; heavily dependent on S. Africa; home of Sun City, tourist centre for S. Africa; cap. under construction at Mmabatho; a. 40,330 km²; p. (est. 1985) 1,660,000.

Bor, t., Serbia, **Yugoslavia;** copper mng. and processing; p. (1981) 56,486.

Borås, t., S. **Sweden;** on R. Viske, nr. Göteborg; ctr. of textile and clothing inds.; p. (est. 1986) 100,000.

Bordeaux, spt., cap. of Gironde, **France;** nr. mouth of R. Garonne; cath., univ.; exp. wines, liqueurs, sugar, potatoes, pit props; oil refining nearby; p. (1982) 211,197.

Borders Region, l. gov. reg., **Scot.;** occupies E. half of Southern Uplands; hilly cty. drained by R. Tweed and tribs.; rural a. interspersed by mkt. and mill ts., a 4,670 km²; p. (est. 1986) 101,804.

Bordighera, t., **Italy;** Riviera winter resort; p. (est. 1968) 12,172.

Boreham Wood, t., Herts., **Eng.;** lt. engin., computers, film studios.

Borinage, dist. around Mons, **Belgium;** impt. but declining coalfield.

Borislav, t., Ukrainian SSR, **USSR;** formerly Polish (1919–39); oilfield, natural gas; richest ozocerite deposits in Europe; oil pipeline links to Drogobych and Dashava; p. (est. 1967) 32,000.

Borisoglebsk, t., **RSFSR; USSR;** food processing; p. (est. 1969) 65,000.

Borisov, t., Belorussiyan SSR, **USSR;** defeat of Napoleon, 1812; chemicals, sawmills, hardware; p. (est. 1985) 132,000.

Borkum, I., **W. Germany;** off Ems R. estuary; a. 36 km²; p. (est. 1971) 30,000.

Borlänge, t., **Sweden;** iron, paper, engin. and chemical wks.; p. (est. 1986) 46,000.

Borneo, lgst. I. in Malay archipelago and 3rd lgst. in world; high mtn. range extends from ctr. to N. rising to 4,180 m; low-lying swamp in S.; politically divided into Kalimantan (Indonesian B.), Sabah and Sarawak (E. Malaysia) and Brunei; jungle-covered and underdeveloped; scattered tribes inc. Dyaks; few nodes of development around oilfields (Sarawak and Brunei), as, of forest exploitation (Sabah); new settlement in Barito valley (Kalimantan); a. 738,150 km²; p. (est. 1983) 7,350,000.

Bornholm, I. in Baltic Sea, **Denmark;** mostly granite with poor soils; cattle rearing; kaolin; tourism and fishing impt.; cap. Rønne; a. 543 km²; p. (1983) 47,313.

Bornu, region, **Nigeria;** S.W. of L. Chad; former Moslem st.; a. 132,090 km²; p. (est. 1982) 5,000,000.

Borobudur, Java, **Indonesia;** gr. Buddhist temple; ruins now restored.

Borrowdale, valley, Cumbria, **Eng.;** tourist resort; former graphite mines.

Boscastle, spt., Cornwall, **Eng.;** resort; pilchard fishing; sm. harbour built for slate exp.

Bosnia and Hercegovina, rep., **Yugoslavia;** mtnous., forested, watered by R. Sava and tribs.; one-fourth cultivated; tobacco, cereals, fruit; cattle, sheep, pigs; mineral deposits in Bosnia; cap. Sarajevo; a. 51,199 km²; p. (1981) 4,124,256.

Bosporus or **Strait of Constantinople (Karadeniz Boğazi),** between Black Sea and Sea of Marmara; suspension bridge, first to link Europe and S.W. Asia, opened 1973; badly polluted by sewage from Istanbul and oil spillage from shipping.

Bossier City, t., La., **USA;** oil refineries, rly. wks., chemical and processing plants; p. (1980) 50,817.

Boston, t., l. gov. dist., Lincs., **Eng.;** sm. pt. on Witham R., agr. mkt., fruit and vegetable canning; p. (est. 1988) 52,200 (dist.).

Boston, c., st. cap. Mass., **USA;** fine harbour and leading pt. at head of Boston Bay; cultural, comm. and financial ctr., impt. mkt. for fish and wool; 3 univs.; leading c. in 19th cent.; varied inds. inc. leather, rubber, textiles, shoes and elec. gds.; p. (1984) 507,700 (c.), 4,026,600 (met. a.).

Bosworth or **Market Bosworth,** t., Leics., **Eng.;** battle between Richard III and Henry VII, 1485; see **Hinckley.**

Botany Bay, N.S.W., **Australia;** inlet of Tasman Sea on E. cst., site of landing of James Cook, 1770; 8 km S. of Sydney; resort; first settled by Brit. in 1787; old penal colony; deep-water pt. (1961) for oil tankers supplementary to Pt. Jackson.

Botasani, t., N. Moldavia, **Romania;** in rich pastoral a.; p. (1983) 94,536.

Bothnia, G. of, N. of Baltic; between Finland and Sweden; shallow sea, many Is.

Botswana, Rep. of, indep. sov. st. within Brit. Commonwealth (1966), **Southern Africa;** stretches from Orange R. to Zambesi R., and merges in W. with Kalahari desert; land locked; depends on rly. link to Zimbabwe and S. Africa; coal produced since 1980 to reduce dependence on S. Africa; minerals located but few mined; diamonds since 1971 (50 percent of exp.); copper, nickel; limited livestock agr.; potential arable land of Okavango chobe swamp; few inds. cap. Gaborone; a. 582,000 km²; p. (est. 1986) 1,127,880.

Bottrop, t., N. Rhine-Westphalia, **W. Germany;** once a sm. t., now ctr. of Ruhr coal basin; p. (est. 1986) 112,300.

Bouches-du-Rhône, dep., S. **France;** covers Rhône delta and inc. the Camargue and Crau; lagoon cst.; mainly agr. but inc. industl. complex ass. with cap. of Marseilles; a. 5,270 km²; p. (1982) 1,715,900.

Bougainville, I. seceded from **New Guinea** to form Rep. of N. Solomons; secession ended 1977; major reserve of copper in Panguna valley; new mng. ts. of Anewa Bay and Panguna; forested; a. 10,619 km²; p. (1970) 77,880.

Bougie. See **Bejaia.**

Boulder, t., Col., **USA;** gold- and silver-mng. dist.; univ.; resort; see **Denver.**

Boulder City, t., Nevada, **USA;** nr. Gr. Boulder Dam. gr. engin. project; model t., ctr. for Nat. Park services; p. (1980) 9,590.

Boulogne-Billancourt, S.W. sub. of Paris, **France;** car, aircraft inds.; p. (1982) 102,595.

Boulogne-sur-Mer, t., Pas-de-Calais dep., **France;** on English Channel; comm. and fish. pt.; Channel ferry; pt. inds.; p. (1982) 98,566 (met. a.).

Bounty I., N.Z., S. Pac. Oc.; uninhabited guano covered I.

Bourg-en-Bresse, t., cap. of Ain dep., **France;** route ctr., varied inds.; p. (1982) 43,675.

Bourges, t., cap. of Cher dep., **France;** cath., univ.; industl. and transit ctr.; p. (1982) 79,408.

Bourget, L., Savoie, **France;** tourist a.

Bourkina Fasso, (Upper Volta), W. Africa; landlocked st. under Fr. rule until 1960; savana and low hills, hot and dry desert in N.; p. concentrated in S. and dependent on nomadism and subsistence agr.; many migrate to Ivory Coast and Ghana for work; soil erosion and desert encroachment reduce potential; poorest cty. in Africa; low life expectancies; dependent on aid; much emigration; cap. Ouagadougou; a. 274,123 km²; p. (est. 1987) 8,334,000.

Bourne, t., South Kesteven, Lincs., **Eng.;** home of Hereward the Wake; agr. machin.; p. (1981) 8,142.

Bournemouth, t., l. gov. dist., Dorset, **Eng.;** on S. cst., E of Poole Harbour; seaside resort; conference ctr.; p. (est. 1988) 154,800 (dist.).

Bournville, garden sub. founded by George Cadbury (1897), 6 km S.W. of Birmingham **Eng.;** chocolate and cocoa wks.

Bourton-on-the-Water, v., Gloucs. **Eng.;** tourist ctr.

Bouvet I., uninhabited island in S. Atlantic belonging to **Norway;** a. about 56 km².

Bovey Tracey, v., Devon, **Eng.;** ball clay excavating.

Bow or **Stratford-de-Bow,** Tower Hamlets, E. London, **Eng.;** 5 km from St. Paul's.

Bow, R., Alberta, N.W. **Canada;** head of Saskatchewan R., flows through Banff Nat. Park; irrigation; 504 km long.

Bowdon, t., Gtr. Manchester, **Eng.;** p. (1981) 4,925.

Bow Fell, mtn., Cumbria, **Eng.;** at head of Borrowdale, 6 km N.W. of West Water alt. 903 m.

Bowland, Forest of, W. offshoot of Pennines, Lancs., **Eng.;** between Rs. Lune and Ribble; designated a. of outstanding natural beauty; reservoirs.

Bowling, v., Dunbarton, **Scot.;** on N. bank of R. Clyde, 16 km N.W. of Glasgow; lge. oil refinery; p. (1981) 450.

Bowling Green, t., Ky., **USA;** tr. ctr. for agr. a. producing tobacco, livestock, limestone and dairy prods.; univ.; p. (1980) 40,450.

Bowness, v., Cumbria, **Eng.;** W. end of Hadrian's Wall.

Bowness, t., Cumbria, **End.;** on L. Windermere; tourist ctr.

Box Hill, nr. Dorking, Surrey, **Eng.;** E. of R. Mole gap through N. Downs; chalk; wooded, fine views; alt. 233 m.

Boyle, mkt. t., Roscommon, **R.o.I.;** on R. Boyle; dairying; p. (1971) 1,727.

Boyne, R., **R.o.I.;** flows to Irish Sea; Battle of the Boyne (1690) fought at Oldbridge, 5 km W. of Drogheda; salmon fishing; 128 km long.

Boyoma Falls (Stanley Falls), on Upper Zaïre R., **Zaïre;** nr. equator; originally named after the explorer.

Bozrah, c. of anc. Edom, probably modern Buseira (**Jordan**), S.E. of Dead Sea.

Brabant, prov., **Belgium;** S. section of former Duchy; fertile and wooded; many breweries; mnfs., linen, cloth, paper, lace; cap. Brussels; a. 3,281 km²; p. (1981) 2,221,222.

Brabant, North, prov., **Neth.;** S. of Gelderland; N. half of former Duchy; cattle rearing; grain, hops, beetroot; cap. 's-Hertogenbosch; a. 4,972 km²; p. (1983) 2,093,969.

Brač, I., Adriatic Sea, **Yugoslavia;** lgst. of Dalmatian Is.; tourism, fishing; a. 393 km².

Brackley, t., South Northants., **Eng.;** flour milling, brewing; former prosperous wool tr.; Magdalen College School (1447); p. (1981) 6,527.

Bracknell, t., l. gov. dist., Berks., **Eng.;** on Thames Valley terrace, 16 km S. of Windsor; new t. designated 1949 to meet overspill needs from London; extends N. and W. of old v. of Bracknell; Meteorological Office H.Q., chosen (1983) as one of world's 2 forecasting stas.; engin., sealing compounds, plastics; p. (est. 1988) 98,200.

Brackwede, t. N. Rhine-Westphalia, **W. Germany;** iron and machin.; p. (1969) 26,448.

Bradford, c., met. dist., West Yorks., **Eng.;** 14 km W. of Leeds; comm. ctr. of wool-textile inds.; impt. for worsted; engin. and chem. inds.; univ.; birthplace of Delius and J. B. Priestley; p. (est. 1988) 464,100.

Bradford-on-Avon, t., West Wilts., **Eng.;** on E. flank of Cotswolds from which bldg. stone derived; former ctr. of wool ind.; p. (1981) 8,752.

Bradwell, v., Essex, **Eng.;** at mouth of R. Blackwater; civil nuclear power-sta.

Braemar, dist. in Grampians, Kincardine and Deeside, **Scot.;** containing Balmoral estate.

Braeriach, mtn., **Scot.;** borders Badenoch and Strathspey, alt. 1,296 m.

Braga, t., cap. of B. dist., N.W. **Portugal;** agr. tr. ctr.; religious ctr.; cath.; p. (1981) 63,800.

Bragança, t., cap. of B. dist., N.E. **Portugal;** agr. tr.; p. (1981) 13,900.

Brahmaputra, one of longer Rs. in **Asia;** flows for much of its length through Himalayas and Assam; called **Tsangpo** in Tibet; fertile agr. valley subject to flooding and silting; 2,880 km long.

Braich-y-Pwll, headland, Gwynedd, **Wales.**

Brăila, t., **Romania;** R. pt. on Danube, nr. Galati; grain tr., boatbldg., reed processing; p. (est. 1984) 228,035.

Braintree, t., Mass., **USA;** elec. machin., rubber gds., glassware; p. (1980) 36,337.

Braintree, t., l. gov. dist., Essex, **Eng.;** on Blackwater; rayon mftg., metal windows, engin.; p. (est. 1988) 117,200 (dist.).

Brakpan, t., Transvaal, **S. Africa;** gold mng.; p. (1980) 79,732.

Brampton, t., Ontario, **Canada;** noted for its greenhouses; p. (1986) 188,498.

Brandenburg, t., **E. Germany;** on R. Havel; former cap. of prov. of B.; cath.; tractors, textiles, machin.; p. (1981) 94,680.

Brandenburg. *See* **Neubrandenburg.**

Brandon, t., Manitoba, **Canada;** on Assiniboine R., W. of Winnipeg; comm. ctr. wheat a.; agr. equipment oil refining; p. (1981) 36,242.

Brandon, t., Suffolk, **Eng.;** ctr. of Breckland; expanded t.

Brandon and Byshottles, ts., former U.D., Durham, **Eng.;** former coal-mng. a.; p. (1981) 17,905.

Brandywine Creek, R., Penns., **USA;** Americans defeated by British 1777; length 32 km.

Brantford, t., Ontario, **Canada;** on Grand R., S.W. of Hamilton; leading mnf. t.; farm implements, cycles, bus and truck parts; p. (1986) 76,146.

Brasília, cap. of **Brazil,** Goiás st., 960 km N.W. of Rio de Janeiro; ch. of many cities designed to open up interior of rep.; modern architecture; inaugurated 1960; p. (est. 1985) 1,576,700.

Brasov, t., **Romania;** at foot of Transylvanian Alps; aircraft, engin., lge. German and Hungarian p.; p. (est. 1984) 335,000.

Bratislava, c., cap. of Slovakia, **ČSSR;** pt. on Danube 48 km below Vienna; univ.; industl. and comm. ctr.; textiles, chemicals; engin., oil refining; linked to Mozyr', USSR, by "friendship oil pipeline"; p. (est. 1986) 417,000.

Bratsk, c., central Irkutsk oblast, **RSFSR;** on Angara R., ship-repair yards, lumber, iron-ore, wood processing, chemicals; lge. hydroelectric sta.; p. (est. 1985) 240,000.

Braunschweig. *See* **Brunswick.**

Brava, spt., **Somalia;** leather, shoes; p. (est. 1965) 7,665.

Bray, U.D., Wicklow, **R.o.I.;** on Irish Sea cst.; popular resort; p. (1981) 22,853.

Brazil, Federative Republic of, S. America; a. 8,512,035 km²; 5th lgst. cty. in world, exceeded in size only by USSR, China, Canada and USA; covers variety of land and climate; in S., gr. Brazilian plateau, in N., Amazon R. basin (thickly forested); leading industl. nation of **Latin America;** agr.; coffee, cotton, sugar, cocoa, rubber, fruits, hardwoods; rapid exploitation of rainforests worries conservationists; cattle-raising; vast mineral reserves inc. manganese, iron, gold, diamonds; admin. through 22 sts., 4 terrs., and Fed. Dist.; cap. Brasília; lgst. industl. ctr. São Paulo and Belo Horizonte; many multinational companies, inc. car mftg., chems., construction materials; p. mainly White, Negro, Indian, Mestizo; Portuguese official language; p. concentrated in coastal belt, leaving vast a. of interior relatively underdeveloped; oil shortages led to use of sugar alcohol for cars; incr. finds of oil offshore will lead to oil self-sufficiency by 1999; p. (est. 1987) 141·5m.

Brazos, R., Texas, **USA;** flows through agr. and industl. Young Co. via Waco to industl. Brazosport; length 1,520 km.

Brazzaville, c., cap. of **Congo Rep.;** connected by rly. with the Atlantic at Pointe-Noire; R. pt. under construction; airport; p. (1984) 595,102.

Brechin, royal burgh, Angus, **Scot.;** on S. Esk; cath.; linen, paper, whisky; p. (1981) 7,674.

Breckland, dist., S.W. Norfolk, N.W. Suffolk, **Eng.;** chalk overlain by glacial sands; heathland and coniferous plantations; a. 518 km²; lge. a. within Norfolk forms l. gov. dist., inc. Thetford, Swaffham and East Dereham; p. (est. 1988) 104,300.

Brecknock (Breconshire), former co., **Wales;** now mostly inc. in Powys; sm. parts in Mid-Glamorgan and Gwent; now forms l. gov. dist., within Powys inc. Builth Wells, Hay on Wye and Brecon; p. (est. 1988) 41,100.

Brecon (Brecknock), t., Powys, **Wales;** on R. Usk; agr. ctr.; p. (1981) 7,422.

Brecon Beacons, mtns., S. **Wales;** 8 km S. of Brecon; highest peak 888 m; sandstone moorland; Nat. Park.

Breda, c. N. Brabant prov., **Neth.;** mnf. ctr.; machin., foundries, canneries, refineries; historic t., 13th cent. cath.; p. (est. 1987) 119,000.

Bredbury and Romiley, ts., Gtr. Manchester, **Eng.;** paper, engin., dyeing, textiles; p. (1981) 29,122.

Bregenz, t., cap. of Vorarlberg, **Austria;** on Bodensee; hydroelec. power; textiles; resort nr. Bregenz Forest; p. (1981) 24,561.

Breidha Fjord, lge. inlet, W. cst. **Iceland.**

Bremen, Land, **W. Germany;** a. 404 km²; cap. Bremen; p. (est. 1986) 654,200.

Bremen, c., cap. of Land B., **W. Germany;** old t. on right bank of Weser R., 64 km from N. Sea; new t., founded 17th cent., on left bank; leading pt., industl. and comm. ctr.; but hinterland divided by post-war division of Germany; former member of Hanseatic League; p. (est. 1986) 522,000.

Bremerhaven, c., Bremen, **W. Germany;** outport of Bremen at mouth of R. Weser; docks; impt. passenger and fish. pt.; shipbldg.; united with Wesermünde 1941; p. (est. 1986) 132,200.

Bremerton, t., Wash., **USA;** on Puget Sound; naval dockyard; elec. equipment, machin.; p. (1984) 35,200 (t.), 164,800 (met. a.).

Brendon Hills, Somerset, **Eng.;** extension of Exmoor, rising to over 400 m.

Brenner Pass, lowest Alpine pass from Bolzano (**Italy**) to Innsbruck (**Austria**); used by road and rail; frequent meeting place of Mussolini and Hitler (1940–2).

Brent, outer bor., Greater London, **Eng.;** inc. Wembley and Willesden; p. (est. 1988) 257,200.

Brenta, R., N. **Italy;** rises in picturesque Alpine valley; forestry, silk, tourism; flows to Adriatic Sea; navigable in lower course; length 180 km.

Brentford and Chiswick. *See* **Hounslow.**

Brentwood, t., l. gov. dist., Essex, **Eng.;** residentl.; p. (est. 1988) 70,000 (dist.).

Brescia, c., cap. B. prov., Lombardy, N. **Italy;** industl. ctr.; iron, steel, engin., textiles; many historic bldgs.; p. (1984) 204,278.

Breslau. *See* **Wroclaw.**

Bressay I., Shetland Is., **Scot.;** p. (1971) 251.

Brest, naval pt., Finistère dep., N.W. **France;** base of French Atlantic fleet; used by Germans as fortfd. submarine base 1940–4; exp. agr. prods.; impt. industl. ctr.; p. (1982) 160,355.

Brest (Brest-Litovsk), c., Belorussiyan SSR, **USSR;** nr. Polish border; route ctr. and agr. mkt.; timber, food-processing, textiles. Captured by Germans in 1915. Treaty of Brest-Litovsk signed with Soviet Russia 1918; p. (est. 1985) 222,000.

Bretton Woods, resort, N.H., **USA;** site of US monetary and financial conference, 1944, leading to establishment of the International Monetary Fund and the World Bank.

Briançon, t., Hautes-Alpes, **France;** in upper Durance R. valley; winter sports; p. (1982) 11,851.

Bridgend, t., Ogwr, Mid-Glamorgan, S. **Wales;** industl. trading estate; iron, stone, paper; coal mng.; p. (1981) 15,699.

Bridge of Allen, burgh, Stirling, **Scot.;** 3 km N. of Stirling; p. (1981) 4,668.

Bridgeport, c., Conn., **USA;** on Long Island Sound; impt. industl. c., firearms, hardware, elec. equipment, metal products, plastics; p. (1984) 142,100.

Bridgetown, t., spt., cap. **Barbados;** deepwater

harbour opened 1961; comm. ctr.; exp. sugar, molasses, rum; tourism; p. (est. 1985) 7,466.

Bridgewater Canal, Worsley–Manchester–Runcorn, Gtr. Manchester and Cheshire, **Eng.**; crosses ship canal by means of Barton swing bridge; 61 km long.

Bridgnorth, t., l. gov. dist., Shrops., **Eng.**; cas.; carpets, radio equipment; p. (est. 1988) 51,000.

Bridgwater, t., Sedgemoor, Somerset, **Eng.**; on R. Parrett, 16 km from Bristol Channel; engin., wire rope, fibre fabrics, cellophane; p. (1981) 26,132.

Bridlington, t., East Yorks., Humberside, **Eng.**; on Bridlington Bay, S. of Flamborough Head; fishing; seaside resort; p. (1981) 28,970.

Bridport, West Dorset, **Eng.**; mkt. t.; seaside resort; p. (1981) 6,876.

Brie, region, Marne and Seine-et-Marne deps., **France;** low, level plateau of limestones and clays, S.E. of Paris; loam (limon) cover and plentiful water supply encourage agr.; grains, sugar-beet, fruit, dairy cattle; famous cheese; densely populated.

Brienz, t., **Switzerland;** resort on L. Brienz; wood carving; p. (1970) 2,796.

Brierley Hill, t., West Midlands, **Eng.**; on W. edge of Black Cty.; cut glass, castable metal gds., firebricks, roofing and tiling, iron and steel.

Brigg, mkt. t., Glanford, Humberside, **Eng.**; ctr. of agr. dist. between Lincoln Heights and Wolds; sugar-beet, jam, seed crushing, canning; p. (1981) 5,358.

Brighouse, t., Calderdale, West Yorks., **Eng.**; on R. Calder, 5 km S.E. of Halifax; textiles and engin.; p. (1981) 35,241.

Brightlingsea, t., Tendring, Essex, **Eng.**; on R. Colne; oysters, boatbldg., yachting; p. (1981) 7,245.

Brighton, t., l. gov. dist., East Sussex, **Eng.**; 80 km S. of London on S. cst.; seaside resort and residtl. t.; Royal Pavilion (1817), univ.; lt. inds.; birthplace of Aubrey Beardsley; p. (est. 1988) 149,200, (dist.)

Brindisi, c., Apulia, S. **Italy;** spt. on Adriatic cst., sea and air connections to Middle E.; cath.; cas.; wine, olive oil, silk, petrochemicals; oil refining; p. (1981) 89,786.

Brisbane, t., cap. of Queensland, **Australia;** third c. of A., set on winding B. river, 20 km from attractive sandy cst.; caths., univ.; consumer goods, processing of primary prods.; severe flooding 1974; rapid growth in past 30 years; p. (est. 1985) 1,157,200 (met. a.).

Brisbane Water, t., N.S.W., **Australia;** N. of Broken Bay; rapid growth with electrification of commuting rly. to Sydney; p. (1981) 71,984.

Bristol, c., l. gov. dist., Avon, **Eng.**; pt. on R. Avon 14 km from Bristol Channel; outport at Avonmouth; cath., univ.; docks; aircraft engin., tobacco, paint, printing and lt. inds.; p. (est. 1988) 377,700.

Bristol, t., Conn., **USA;** foundries, ball bearings, clocks, bells; p. (1980) 57,370.

Bristol Channel, arm of Atl. Oc. between S. cst. of Wales and Somerset and Devon, **Eng.**; noted tidal bores.

British Antarctic Territory, Brit. col., created 1962; consists of all land and Is. S. of lat. 60° S. and between 20° and 80° W. longitude; comprising Graham Land peninsula, S. Shetlands, S. Orkneys and smaller Is., excluding S. Georgia and S. Sandwich Is.; a. 1,222,500 km².

British Columbia, W. prov. separated from rest of **Canada** by Rockies, borders Pac. Oc.; little lowland; parallel N.W.–S.E. ranges of Rockies crossed by Rs. Fraser, Columbia, Kootenay and Peace; vast coniferous forest and hydroelec. resources; salmon fishing on cst.; mng.; p. concentrated in S.W. around Vancouver; a. 948,600 km²; p. (1986) 2,889,000.

British Honduras. *See* Belize.

British Indian Ocean Terr., Brit. col., created 1965; consists of the Chagos Archipelago (of which Diego Garcia [Anglo-American naval communications ctr.] is lgst. I.) 1,920 km N.E. of Mauritius, and formerly Is. of Aldabra, Farquhar, and Desroches in the W. Indian Oc. now part of Seychelles Rep.; p. (est. 1982) 3,000.

British Is., archipelago, N.W. **Europe;** comprising 2 lge. Is.; Great Britain, Ireland; and 5,000 sm. Is.; a. 315,029 km².

British Solomon Is. *See* Solomon Is.

British West Africa, formerly comprised Gambia, Sierra Leone, Gold Coast (Ghana), Nigeria, and parts of Togoland and Cameroons. *See* under their separate headings.

Briton Ferry, t., West Glamorgan, S. **Wales;** pt. at mouth of R. Neath; former ctr. for steel wks., engin., ship-breaking.

Brittany, region, N.W. **France;** penin. between Eng. Channel and Bay of Biscay; contrast between productive cst. lands (fishing, early vegetables, tourism) and barren moorland interior; economically depressed; oil refinery projected at St. Livy; p. (1982) 2,703,700.

Brive-la-Gaillarde, t., Corrèze dep., **France;** regional mkt. in fertile basin on edge of Central Massif; p. (1982) 54,032.

Brixham, S. Devon, **Eng.**; incorporated in Torbay; fishing; resort.

Brno (Brünn), c., **ČSSR;** cap. of Moravia; finely situated at confluence of Svratka and Svitava Rs., 109 km N. of Vienna; industl. and communications ctr. with mnfs. of machin., precision tools, textiles; annual tr. fair; p. (est. 1986) 385,000.

Broad Haven, t., new t. planned on St. Brides Bay, **Wales.**

Broadstairs, Thanet, Kent, **Eng.**; seaside resort; 5 km N.E. of Ramsgate; p. (1981) 23,400.

Broads, The, Norfolk, **Eng.**; series of Ls. formed by mediaeval turf cutting in lower alluvial reaches of Rs. Bure, Waveney, and Yare; yachting, fishing, tourism; plans to create a Nat. Park to help relieve pollution; lge. part now forms **Broadland,** l. gov. dist., p. (est. 1988) 104,400.

Brockton, c., Mass., **USA;** S. of Boston; lge. shoe and leather ind., machin.; annual tr. fair; p. (1980) 95,172 (c.), 169,374 (met. a.).

Brockville, t., Ontario, **Canada;** R. pt. on St. Lawrence R. below Thousand Is.; telephone equipment, wire cables, elec, tools; p. (1981) 19,896.

Broken Hill, t., N.S.W., **Australia;** major mng. (silver, lead, zinc) ctr. in arid W. of st.; p. (1981) 26,913.

Bromberg. *See* Bydgoszcz.

Bromley, outer bor. of London, **Eng.**; inc. Beckenham, Orpington, Penge, and part of Sidcup; p. (est. 1988) 298,200.

Bromsgrove, l. gov. dist., Hereford and Worcs., **Eng.**; mkt. t., 21 km S.W. Birmingham; wrought ironwk., lt. engin.; p. (est. 1988) 89,600.

Bromyard, Hereford and Worcs., **Eng.**; sm. mkt. t.

Bronx, The, one of the five bors. of New York City, **USA;** connected by bridges to bor. of Manhattan; residtl. with parks, zoological and botanical gardens, colleges and professional schools; p. (1980) 1,168,972.

Brooklyn, bor., N.Y. City. **USA;** linked with Manhattan bor. by Brooklyn, Manhattan, and Williamsburgh suspension bridges across East R.; and with Staten I. by Verrazano-Narrows bridge (longest in world); mainly residtl. with numerous mftg. and comm. interests; p. (1980) 2,230,936.

Brooks Range, mtns., N. Alaska, **USA;** forms N. section of Rocky Mtns.; Eskimo p.; Arctic climate, flora and fauna; alt. 2,000 m rising to 2,818 m (Mt. Michelson).

Broom, loch on N.W. cst. of Ross and Cromarty, **Scot.**

Brora, t., Sutherland, **Scot.**; on E. cst., 19 km N.E. of Dornoch Firth; ctr. of sm. coalfield; Harris Tweed ind.; tourism; p. (1981) 1,728.

Brownhills, t., West Midlands, **Eng.**; former mng. t.; expanded t.; p. (1981) 18,200.

Brownsville, t., Texas, **USA;** pt. on Rio Grande nr. Mexican border; livestock, sugar-cane, fruit processing, chemicals; p. (1984) 94,700 (t.), 241,100 (met. a. with Harlingen-San Benito).

Broxbourne, t., l. gov. dist., Herts., **Eng.**; on gravel terrace to W. of R. Lea; ctr. of very intensively cultivated dist.; lt. inds.; "dormitory" t. linked with London; p. (est. 1988) 82,500.

Broxtowe, l. gov. dist., Notts., **Eng.**; made up of Beeston and Stapleford and Eastwood; p. (est. 1988) 108,300.

Bruay-en-Artois, t., Pas-de-Calais, **France;** coal mng.; p. (1982) 23,200.

Bruchsal, t., Baden-Württemberg, **W. Germany;** tobacco, paper, machin.; p. (est. 1986) 36,500.

Bruges *See* Brugge.

Brugge (Bruges), c., cap. of W. Flanders prov., N. **Belgium;** once mediaeval t. connected by canal to its outer pt. Zeebrugge; univ.; impt. mkt. for grain, cattle, horses; engin., ship-repairing, elec. gds., glass mkg., textiles, lace; p. (est. 1984) 118,146.

Brühl, t., N. Rhine–Westphalia, **W. Germany;** 13 km S. of Cologne; cas.; lignite; p. (est. 1986) 40,700.

Brunei, indep. st. (1984), **N. Borneo;** enclave of Sarawak; Brit. protectorate since 1888; thriving economy based on Seria and offshore oil and gas fields; oil and gas provide 95 per cent of exp.; need to diversify as reserves dwindle and prices fall; 80 percent of food is imported; agr. therefore being encouraged since only 15 per cent of land is cultivated; cap. Bandar Seri Begawan; a. 5,765 km²; p. (est. 1986) 227,000 of whom 25 per cent are Chinese.

Brünn. *See* Brno.

Brunsbüttelkoog, pt. at mouth of R. Elbe.

Brunswick (Braunschweig), c., Lower Saxony, **W. Germany;** on R. Oker; formerly cap. of st. of Brunswick, now a comm. and industl. ctr.; mnfs. inc. canning, tinplate, optics, pianos, lorries; p. (est. 1983) 257,100.

Brussels (Bruxelles), cap. of **Belgium** and of prov. of Brabant; impt. comm., industl. and cultural ctr.; varied mnfs., inc. pharmaceuticals, electronic equipment, machine tools; lge. oil refinery at Feluy; noted for carpets and lace; occupied by the Germans 1914–18, 1940–4; univ.; mediaeval and Renaissance monuments; H.Q. of EEC; p. (est. 1984) 982,434.

Bryan, t., Texas, **USA;** mkt. ctr., agr. college; p. (1984) 59,000 (t.), 117,400 (met. a.).

Bryansk, c., cap. of B. oblast, **RSFSR,** on Desna R.; rly. junc.; a fortress until 19th cent.; sawmilling, engin., textiles, chemicals, steel; oil pipeline from Kuybyshev; p. inc. Bezhitsa (est. 1985) 430,000.

Brynmawr, t., Gwent, **Wales;** former coal-mng. a.; industl. estate; p. (1981) 5,528.

Brzeg (Brieg), t. Silesia, **Poland;** on R. Oder; German until 1945; textiles, leather, chemicals; p. (1968) 29,000.

Bucaramanga, c., N. central **Colombia,** 900 m a.s.l. in E. highlands of Andes; ctr. of coffee-growing dist.; cigar and cigarette mkg.; p. (1985) 363,900.

Buchan Ness, C., nr. Peterhead, E. Scot.

Bucharest (Buckresti), cap. and lgst. c. of **Romania;** "Little Paris," on the Dambovita, trib. of Danube; cath., univ.; textiles, chemicals, pharmaceuticals, oil refining, engin.; 20 per cent industl. output of rep.; badly damaged by earthquake (1977); p. (est. 1985) 1,975,808.

Buckfastleigh, t., S. Devon, **Eng.;** wool, quarry-ing; nearby Benedictine abbey on site of medi-aeval Cistercian abbey; p. (1981) 2,889.

Buckhaven and Methil, burgh, Kirkcaldy, **Scot.;** on N. Side of Firth of Forth, 13 km N.E. of Kirkcaldy; coal; p. (1981) 18,236.

Buckie, burgh, Moray, **Scot.;** boat- and yacht-bldg.; fisheries; p. (1981) 7,763.

Buckingham, Aylesbury Vale, Bucks., **Eng.;** mkt. t. on R. Ouse, 24 km N.W. of Aylesbury; p. (1981) 6,627.

Buckinghamshire, non-met. co., **Eng.;** crossed by Chilterns and Vale of Aylesbury; rural and wooded, emphasis is on dairy farming; co. t. Aylesbury; mnfs. chiefly in High Wycombe; de-cline in traditional handicrafts (lace mkg. and fur-niture parts); a. 1,882 km²; p. (est. 1988) 627,300.

Buckley, t., Alyn and Deeside, Clwyd, **Wales;** sm. castings; p. (1981) 13,386.

Budapest, cap. and lgst. c. of **Hungary;** stands on both banks of Danube (Buda on right, Pest on left); attractive townscape; univ.; varied mnfs., inc. steel, textiles, chemicals, engin., motorbuses, oil refining; employs 40 per cent industl. workers of Hungary; p. (est. 1987) 2·1m.

Budaun, t., Uttar Pradesh, **India;** agr. process-ing; ruins; p. (1961) 58,770.

Bude. *See* Stratton and Bude.

Budel, t., N. Brabant, S. **Neth.;** 19 km S. of Eind-hoven; major zinc smelter project.

Budge-Budge, t., W. Bengal, **India;** on lower Hooghly R.; hemp, rice; p. (1961) 39,824.

Budleigh Salterton, East Devon, **Eng.;** resort; birthplace of Raleigh nearby; p. (1981) 4,436.

Buena Park, t., Cal., **USA;** agr. processing mkt.; oilfields; p. (1980) 64,165.

Buenaventura, spt., **Colombia;** lumber yards, tan-ning, fish canning; p. (est. 1983) 156,000.

Buenos Aires, c., cap. of **Argentina;** cap. to be rebuilt in Patagonia (by 1989) to decentralise power; B.A. now contains one third of A.'s p.; ch. spt. at head of Rio de la Plata, on E. edge of Pampa; connected to Uruguay, Paraguay, and Brazil by gr. R. system; industl. and tr. ctr. for outlying regions; p. (1980) 2,923,000 (c.) 9,968,000 (met. a.).

Buffalo, c., N.Y., **USA;** pt. on L. Erie; focus of communications on Gr. Ls. has encouraged many heavy inds.; diversified lt. inds.; univ.; p. (1984) 339,000 (c.), 1,204,800 (met. a.).

Bug, R., Ukrainian SSR, **USSR;** known as S. or Ukrainian B.; flows from Volyno–Podolsh up-land to Black Sea; navigable in lower course; 853 km long.

Bug, R., the western Bug rises in the Ukraine, **USSR,** not far from the southern Bug and flows N. to join the Vistula below Warsaw; forms bdy. between Poland and Ukrainian SSR; 774 km long.

Bugul'ma, t., Tatar ASSR, **RSFSR;** oil ctr.; p. (est. 1967) 74,000.

Buganda, prov., **Uganda,** E. Africa; located W. of L. Victoria largely at alt. between 1,300 and 1,800 m; intensive cultivation, cotton (ch. comm. crop), plantains, millets; cap. Kampala.

Builth Wells, t., Brecknock, Powys, **Wales;** on upper course of R. Wye; medicinal springs; p. (1981) 1,287.

Buitenzorg. *See* Bogor.

Bujumbura, t., cap. of **Burundi;** pt. on L. Tan-ganyika; varied inds.; airpt.; p. (1986) 272,600.

Bukavu, t., Zaïre; cement, quinine processing; p. (1982) 209,051.

Bukhara (Bokhara), t., Uzbek SSR, **USSR;** in Amu-Dar'ya valley at W. foot of Tien Shan; agr. mkt. at W. terminus of anc. caravan route from China; modern route ctr.; local natural gas, textiles; p. (est. 1985) 209,000.

Bukittinggi, t., Sumatra, **Indonesia;** in Padang Highlands at 1,068 m; p. 53,700.

Bukoba, t., Tanzania; pt. midway along W. shore of L. Victoria; exp. coffee, rice and other food-stuffs to L. pts. in Kenya and Uganda.

Bukovina, Northern; terr., formerly belonging to Romania, ceded to **USSR** in 1940; now part of Ukrainian SSR; a. 5,542 km²; ch. t. Chernovitsy; Carpathian Mtns., forested; farming, cereals; cattle.

Bulawayo, t., Zimbabwe; impt. rly. ctr.; major ctr. of commerce and heavy engin., airpt.; p. (1982) 413,800.

Bulgaria, People's Rep. of, S.E. Europe; in E. Balkans, bounded by Black Sea in E., and by Danube R. in N. which separates it from Romania; Rodopi range in S.W.; Maritsa R. basin forms central lowland a.; sharp climatic contrasts between winter and summer; fertile lowland areas organised into lge.-scale coopera-tive farms producing grain; impt. exp. tr. in agr. prods., inc. fruit, vegetables, tobacco; rapidly increasing industl. output; mineral and oil resources; popular tourist a. on Black Sea cst.; cap. Sofia; a. 110,911 km²; p. (est. 1987) 8,949,600.

Bunbury, t., spt., **W. Australia;** 3rd. t. of st., exp. hardwoods, coal, mineral sands; growth since 1970 with establishment of alumina refinery and expansion of pt.; p. (1981) 21,749.

Buncrana, U.D., dist. t., Donegal, **R.o.I.;** salmon fishing; seaside resort; p. (1971) 2,955.

Bundaberg, t., Queensland, **Australia;** on Burnett R.; ctr. of sugar refining; p. (est. 1984) 32,880.

Bundoran, v., Donegal, **R.o.I.;** fish, pt. and resort; p. (est. 1978) 1,437.

Bungay, t., Waveney, Suffolk, **Eng.;** mkt. t. on R. Waveney; printing, malting, leather gds.; p. (1981) 4,106.

Bungosuido Channel, Japan; E. entrance into Inland Sea.

Bunzlau. *See* Boleslawiec.

Buraimi, oases lying between **Oman** and **United Arab Emirates;** rich in oil.

Buraydah (Buraida), t. Nejd., **Saudi Arabia;** oasis; tr. ctr.; p. (1974) 69,940.

Burbank, c., Cal., **USA;** airpt.; aeroplanes, film studios; p. (1980) 84,625.

Burdwan, t., W. Bengal, **India;** agr. processing and tr. ctr. in Damodar valley close to Raniganj coalfield; p. (1971) 143,318.

Bure, R., Norfolk, **Eng.;** lower course forms part of Norfolk Broads; joins Yare at Yarmouth; 93 km.

Burg, t., Magdeburg, **E. Germany;** on Ihle Canal; p. (est. 1970) 29,994.

Burgas, c., **Bulgaria;** spt. and comm. ctr. on Black Sea; ch. exp. pt. for rep.; pt. for oil tankers under construction; p. (1985) 182,570.

Burgenland, prov., **Austria;** bordered on E. by Hungary; low-lying in N., agr.; hilly in S.; cap. Eisenstadt; a. 3,962 km²; p. (est. 1986) 267,000.

Burgess Hill, t., Mid Sussex, West Sussex, Eng.; bricks, tiles; p. (1981) 23,542.

Burghausen, t., **W. Germany**; chemicals, oil refining; pipeline to Munich.

Burghead, burgh, Moray, **Scot.**; fish pt., resort; p. (1981) 1,365.

Burgos, c., N. **Spain**; cap. of B. prov.; anc. cap. of Castile and cap. of Franco's regime 1936–9; cath; home of the Cid; tourism, varied inds.; p. (1987) 158,857.

Burgos, prov., Old Castile, **Spain**; cap. B.; a. 14,050 km²; p. (1981) 363,516.

Burgstädt, t., Karl-Marx-Stadt, **E. Germany**; textiles, machin.; p. (1963) 17,167.

Burgundy, former kingdom and prov., N.E. **France**; composed largely of upper valley of R. Saône; famous vineyards; strategic position on route leading between plateau of Vosges and Jura Mtns., from Rhône valley to Rhine valley.

Burhanpur, t., Madhya Pradesh, **India**; anc. walled Mogul c.; textiles, brocades; p. (1971) 105,246.

Burkina Faso. *See* **Bourkina Fasso.**

Burlington, t., S. Ontario, **Canada**; on L. Ontario, sub., N.E. of Hamilton; in fruit-growing a.; industl.; tourism; p. (1986) 116,675.

Burlington, t., Iowa, **USA**; on bluffs of Mississippi R.; machin., furniture; p. (1980) 29,529.

Burlington, t., Vt., **USA**; on L. Champlain; pt. of entry and ch. industl. and comm. t. in st.; mnfs.; p. (1987) 37,500 (t.), 158,857 (met. a.).

Burma, Union of, rep., **S.E. Asia**; Irrawaddy R. basin, developed by British in 19th cent., forms major cluster of p., routeways and source of rice of which B. is one of few exporters; surrounding mtns. relatively underdeveloped, although they are a source of teak and hardwood exps.; almost self-sufficient in petroleum from deposits in N.; natural gas prod. increasingly impt.; monsoon climate; p. mainly Buddhist; secessionist moves in Moslem Arakan st., ch. ts., Mandalay, cap. Rangoon; a. 676,580 km²; p. (est. 1987) 37,850,000. In 1989, Burma was renamed the Union of Myanmar.

Burnham Beeches, Berks./Bucks., **Eng.**; part of anc. forest acquired 1879 for public use; a. 243 ha.

Burnham-on-Crouch, t., Essex, **Eng.**; pt., yachting, boat-bldg.; p. (1981) 6,291.

Burnham-on-Sea, t., Sedgemoor, Somerset, **Eng.**; on Bridgwater Bay; resort; p. (1981) 14,920.

Burnie, spt., Tasmania, **Australia**; pulp and paper mills; impt. mineral pt. (tin); p. (1981) 20,368.

Burnley, t., l. gov. dist., Lancs., **Eng.**; textiles, engin., car accessories; p. (est. 1988) 85,400 (dist.).

Burntisland, royal burgh, Kirkcaldy, **Scot.**; on F. of Forth; p. (1981) 5,875.

Burray, one of the Orkney Is., **Scot.**; p. (est. 1969) 595.

Burrinjuck, t., N.S.W., **Australia**; on Murrumbidgee R., N. of Canberra; site of impt. dam providing irrigation in Riverina dist.

Burry Port, t., Dyfed, **Wales**; p. (1981) 5,951.

Bursa, c., N.W. **Turkey**; noted for its textiles; cap. of anc. Bithynia (3rd cent. B.C.) and later of Ottoman empire; mosques; p. (1985) 612,510.

Burslem. *See* **Stoke-on-Trent.**

Burton-on-Trent, t., East Staffs., **Eng.**; brewing, malting, rubber gds.; p. (1981) 47,930.

Burujird, t., **Iran**; textiles and mkt. ctr. at alt. 1,678 m; p. (1966) 71,486.

Burundi, rep., E. central **Africa**; high plateau on N.E. shore of L. Tanganyika; tropical climate, irregular rainfall; economy based on agr., inc. subsistence crops of manioc, sweet potatoes, and cash crops of cotton, coffee; coffee major exp.; (89 percent of export earnings in 1980); one of poorest states in world; sm. mftg. inds. developing, but no rlys.; home of ruling Tutsi and rebel Hutu; cap. Bujumbura; a. 27,834 km²; p. (est. 1987) 4,927,000.

Bury, t., met. dist., Gtr. Manchester, **Eng.**; on R. Irwell to S. of Rossendale Fells; cotton, textiles; birthplace of Robert Peel; p. (est. 1988) 175,000.

Buryat (Buryatskaya), aut. rep. **RSFSR**; borders L. Baykal; mtnous., forested; lge. mineral deposits; cap. Ulan Ude; a. 350,945 km²; p. (1986) 1,013,000.

Bury St. Edmunds, St. Edmundsbury, Suffolk, **Eng.**; old mkt. t., on R. Lark, abbey ruins; farm implements, sugar-beet processing; expanded t.; p. (1981) 28,914.

Bushey, t., Hertsmere, Herts., **Eng.**; residtl.; p. (1981) 23,240.

Bushir. *See* **Bandar-e-Büshehr.**

Busto Arsizio, t., Varese prov., N. **Italy**; 30 km. N.W. of Milan; cotton milling ctr., iron, steel, rayon, textile machin.; p. (1981) 79,769.

Bute, Kyles of, strait, 10 km between isles of Bute and Argyll, **Scot.**

Buteshire, former co., now part of Strathclyde Region, **Scot.**

Butte, t., Mont., **USA**; mng. t. (copper, zinc. silver, manganese, gold, lead, arsenic); also a farming ctr.; p. (1980) 37,205.

Buttermere, L., Cumberland, **Eng.**

Butt of Lewis, promontory with lighthouse; Lewis, Hebrides, **Scot.**

Buxton, t., High Peak, Derbys., **Eng.**; spa; lime-quarrying nearby; p. (1981) 20,797.

Buzau, t., **Romania**; rly. ctr.; cath.; wheat, timber, petroleum; p. (est. 1984) 129,510.

Bydgoszcz, prov., **Poland**; cap. B.; drained by Rs. Vistula, Brda, and Notec; formerly called Pomorze; salt and lime deposits aid chemical inds.; a. 20,800 km²; p. (est. 1986) 1,090,000.

Bydgoszcz (Bromberg), c., N. central **Poland**; on R. Brda; R. pt., rly. ctr.; elec. equipment, machine tools, timber mnfs.; p. (est. 1985) 361,000.

Byelorussian SSR. *See* **Belorussiyan SSR.**

Byron C., most E. point of **Australia**, Pacific cst. of N.S.W.

Bytom, c., S.W. **Poland**; formerly in Prussian prov. of Upper Silesia; ctr. of Katowice mng. a.; p. (est. 1985) 239,000.

C

Cabinda, enclave, **Angola**; separated by Zaïre R. estuary from Angola; tropical climate encourages thick forest. cover; tropical crops; offshore oil production; uranium; attempts at secession; a. 7,236 km²; p. (1970) 81,265.

Cabot Strait, entrance of G. of St. Lawrence between C. Breton I. and Newfoundland, **Canada.**

Cáceres, c., and cap. of C. prov., W. **Spain**; in Estremadura, above Tagus valley; mkt. t. lies below the old t. topping the hill; p. (1987) 69,770.

Cachar, dist., Assâm, **India**; tea-growing ctr.; a. 6,961 km²; p. (1961) 1,378,476.

Cachoeira, t., Bahia, **Brazil**; historic c.; p. (est. 1985) 138,500.

Cachoeira do Sul, t., Rio Grande do Sul, **Brazil**; p. (est. 1980) 112,500.

Cadarache, t., S. **France**; nr. Aix-en-Provence; nuclear research centre.

Cader Idris, mtn., Gwynedd, **Wales**; alt. 893 m.

Cádiz, maritime prov., S.W. **Spain**; cap. Cádiz; a. 7,321 km²; p. (1981) 988,378.

Cádiz, c., cap. of C. prov., S.W. **Spain**; in Andalusia; pt. on Bay of C.; fortress t., naval base; exp. sherry, cork, fruit, olive oil, tunny fish; univ., cath.; one of the most anc. ts. in Europe, built by Phoenicians, c. 1100 B.C.; p. (1987) 156,113.

Caen, c., cap. of Calvados dep., **France**; church and abbey, tomb of William the Conqueror; univ.; iron-ore mng. and processing; severely damaged in second world war; p. (1982) 117,119.

Caerleon, t., Gwent, **Wales**; on R. Usk, 5 km N.E. of Newport; Roman Isca Silurum; remains still present; agr. machin., tools, bricks; p. (1981) 6,711.

Caernarvon, t., Arfon, Gwynedd, N. **Wales**; pt. on S. shore of Menai strait; cas. where first Prince of Wales (Edward II) was christened; bricks, plastics; p. (1981) 9,506.

Caernarvonshire, former co., N. **Wales**. *See* **Gwynedd.**

Caerphilly, t., Rhymney Valley, Mid-Glamorgan, S. **Wales**; cas.; lt. inds.; former coal-mng. a.; p. (1981) 42,736.

Caesar Mazaca, anc. c., Asia Minor; residence of the Cappadocian Kings; the modern Kayeri, **Turkey.**

Caesarea Palestinae, old c., **Israel**, 32 km S. Mt. Carmel; cap. of Herod the Great.

Caeté, t., Minas Gerais st., **Brazil**; lge. iron and steel wks.; p. (est. 1985) 35,200.

Cagliari, cap. and ch. pt. of Sardinia, **Italy**; univ., cath.; p. (1984) 225,009.

Cahir, t., Tipperary, **R.o.I.**; on R. Suir; anc. cas. and abbey; salmon fishing; p. (1981) 2,082.

Cahors, t., cap. of Lot dep., **France**; comm. ctr.; many historic bldgs., inc. cath., palace; distilleries, shoe factory; p. (1982) 20,774.

Cairngorm, mtns., Moray, Badenoch and Strathspey, **Scot.**; rise to 1,310 m (Ben Macdhui); form part of Highlands; nat. nature reserve of arctic flora and fauna; winter sports.

Cairns, spt., Queensland, **Australia**; on Trinity Bay; bulk sugar terminal; resort for Barrier Reef; p. (est. 1984) 38,700.

Cairntoul, mtn., Kincardine and Deeside, **Scot.**; alt. 1,294 m.

Cairo (El Qâhira), c., cap. of **Egypt**; on E. bank of Nile, at head of delta; lgst. c. in rep.; univ.; mosques, palace; fortress of Babylon in old c.; rapid growth with rural depopulation causing great strain on infrastructure; urban mass-transit rly. (1982) and sewerage renewal scheme (1982) begun but cannot keep pace with growth; p. (1985) 6,205,000; Greater Cairo (est. 1987) 13·3m.

Cairo, Ill., **USA**; at confluence of Mississippi and Ohio; busy traffic ctr.; p. (1970) 6,277.

Caistor, t., West Lyndsey, Lincs., **Eng.**; site of Roman camp in Lincs. Wolds.

Caithness, l. gov. dist., former co., **Scot.**; most N. part of mainland; fish, with much moorland; herring fishery; poor agr.; quarrying; ch. ts. Wick, Thurso; a. 3,152 km²; p. (est. 1986) 27,134.

Cajamarca, t., cap. of C. dep., **Peru**; in mtn. valley, 2,745 m; impt. in Inca times; p. (est. 1985) 185,000.

Calabar, spt., S.E. **Nigeria**; cap. Cross River st.; exp. palm oil, kernels, rubber, ivory, cement; p. (est. 1983) 256,000.

Calabria, region, extreme S.W. **Italy**; mtnous. pen.; highest point Mt. Pollino 2,234 m; ch. R. Crati; socially and economically underdeveloped; cap. Catanzaro; p. (est. 1986) 2·1m.

Calais, spt., Pas-de-Calais, N.E. **France**; cross-channel ferry pt. opposite to and 33·6 km distant from Dover; nearby Sangatte to be exit of proposed Channel Tunnel (1993); p. (1982) 76,935.

Calama, oasis, Antofagasta prov., N. **Chile**; in Atacama desert at foot of Andean Cordillera; water from R. Loa supplies Antofagasta and used for irrigation locally.

Calatafimi, t., Sicily, **Italy**; Garibaldi defeated Neapolitans, May 1860; p. (1981) 8,159.

Calbayog, t., Samar, **Philippines**; hemp tr., fisheries; p. (est. 1984) 113,954.

Calbe, t., Magdeburg, **E. Germany**; on R. Saale; p. (est. 1970) 16,296.

Calcutta, c., cap. of W. Bengal st., **India**; pt. on Hooghly R., lgst. c. in rep. and one of most densely populated areas of world; vast tr. from Ganges plain; univ.; jute-mills, textiles, chems., engin.; exp. jute, cotton, sugar-cane, rice, tea, coal; "black hole" (1756); p. (1981) 3,288,148 (c.), 9,194,018 (met. a. covering 1,036 km²).

Calder, R., West Yorks., **Eng.**, trib of Aire R.

Calderdale, met. dist., West Yorks., **Eng.**; chief t. Halifax; also inc. Todmorden, Brighouse, Hebden Royd, Ripponden and Sowerby Bridge; p. (est. 1988) 195,900.

Calder Hall, Cumbria, **Eng.**; first full-scale nuclear power sta. in world (1956) owned and operated by A E A, produces electricity for nat. grid.

Caldy I., off Dyfed cst., **Wales**; lighthouse; Trappist monastery.

Caledonian Canal, from Moray Firth to Loch Linnhe, **Scot.**, connecting North Sea with Atl. Oc.; 100 km long; opened 1822.

Calf of Man, sm. I., S.W. I. of Man, **Eng.**; a. 250 ha.

Calgary, ch. t., Alberta, **Canada**; ctr. of ranching cty.; lumber mills, tanneries, oil refining, flour milling; p. (1986) 636,104 (c.), 671,326 (met. a.).

Cali, c., cap. of Valle del Cauca dep., W. **Colombia**; 1,068 m on Cauca R.; comm. and transport ctr. for rich agr. a.; p. (1985) 1,397,433.

Calicut (Kozhikade), t., Kerala, **India**; first pt. reached by Vasco da Gama (1498); gave its name to calico cloth; p. (1981) 394,447 (t.), 546,058 (met. a.).

California, st., W. **USA**; admitted to Union 1850; st. flower golden poppy, st. bird California Valley quail; mtnous., forested, fertile valleys; subject to earthquakes from San Andreas fault; rich in minerals, oil, natural gas, gold, silver, copper; fruits; film ind.; attractive climate and scenery;

cap. Sacramento; ch. pt. San Francisco, lgst. c. Los Angeles; most populous st. in USA; a. 411,014 km²; p. (1985) 26,365,000.

California Current, E. **Pac. Oc.**; flows N. to S. along cst. of Ore. and Cal., USA; relatively cold water; reduces summer temp. and causes fog in cst. a. especially nr. San Francisco.

California, G. of, arm of Pac. Oc., N.W. **Mexico**; 1,120 km long; same rift as Imperial and Coachella valleys in S.E. Cal.

Callander, burgh, Stirling, **Scot.**; mkt. t. on R. Teith, 24 km N.W. of Stirling; "the gate of the Highlands," tourism; p. (1981) 2,519.

Callao, c., W. **Peru**; pt. of Lima; sheltered harbour; sacked by Drake in 16th cent.; p. (est. 1985) 515,000.

Calne, North Wilts., **Eng.**; mkt. t. on Marden R.; lge. bacon factory closed (1982); p. (1981) 10,268.

Caltagirone, t., Catania, Sicily, **Italy**; cath.; majolica ware; p. (1981) 35,682.

Caltanissetta, t., cap. of C. prov., Sicily, **Italy**; cath.; agr., sulphur ctr.; p. (1981) 61,146.

Calvados, dep., N.E. **France**; low-lying cty. and damp climate aid dairying; butter and cheese prods.; apple orchards produce Calvados brandy; cap. Caen; a. 5,690 km²; p. (1982) 589,400.

Cam (Granta), R., Cambridge, **Eng.**; trib. of R. Ouse; flows through the "backs" at Cambridge; 64 km long.

Camagüey, c., **Cuba**; comm. ctr. in rich agr. region; cattle, sugar-cane; p. (1985) 279,800.

Camargue, delta dist., Bouches-du Rhône, **France**; at mouth of R. Rhône; famous col. of flamingoes; gypsies; bull-rearing; a. 777 km².

Camberley, t., Surrey, **Eng.**; Royal Military Staff College, Royal Military Academy.

Cambodia. *See* **Kampuchea.**

Camborne, t., Cornwall, **Eng.**; 18 km S.W. Truro; old tin and copper mines; engin., radio-television assembly; textiles, chemicals; p. (1981) 46,482 (inc. Redruth).

Cambrai, t., Nord dep., **France**; on R. Scheldt; textiles (gave its name to cambric), agr. processing; suffered in both world wars; p. (1982) 36,618.

Cambrian Mtns., **Wales**; collective name for mtns. of N. and Central Wales inc. Snowdonia and Cader Idris.

Cambridge, univ. c., co. t., l. gov. dist., Cambridgeshire, **Eng.**; on Cam R.; famous univ. with residtl. colleges; leading ctr. of research-based inds.; p. (est. 1988) 97,800.

Cambridgeshire, non-met. co., **Eng.**; low-lying, sloping from E. Anglian Heights in S.E. to Fens in N.; crossed by Rs. flowing to Wash; rich soils aid intensive agr. and mkt. gardening; inc. former cos. of Huntingdon, Peterborough and Isle of Ely; ch. t. Cambridge; a. 3,408 km²; p. (est. 1988) 651,600.

Cambridgeshire, East, l. gov. dist., Cambs., **Eng.**; a. N.E. of Cambridge inc. Ely; p. (est. 1988) 60,600.

Cambridgeshire, South, l. gov. dist., Cambs., **Eng.**; rural a. surrounding Cambridge; p. (est. 1988) 119,300.

Cambridge, c., Mass., **USA**; 5 km beyond Boston; seat of Harvard Univ. and MIT; mftg.; impt. research ctr.; now inc. in Boston met. a.; p. (1980) 95,322.

Camden, inner bor., N. London, **Eng.**; inc. Hampstead, Holborn, and St. Pancras; p. (est. 1988) 182,600.

Camden, c., N.J., **USA**; pt. of entry on Delaware R., opposite Philadelphia; comm., mftg. and residtl.; iron foundries, chemicals, shipbldg.; p. (1980) 84,910; inc. in Philadelphia met. a.

Camerino, t., central **Italy**; in Apennines; univ. cath.; the anc. Camerium; p. (1981) 7,920.

Cameroon, United Rep. of, unitary st. (1972) W. **Africa**; on G. of Guinea; fed. cap. Yaoundé; dependence on primary exports of coffee and cocoa now reduced by rapid incr. in petroleum production since 1977; growing industrial sector; now graduated to middle income developing country; a. 475,500 km²; p. (est. 1986) 9,880,000.

Cameroon Mtn., volcano, massif, **Cameroon**; cstl. mtn., hgst. in W. Africa; last eruption 1959; alt. 4,072 m.

Campagna di Roma, Latium, **Italy**; malarial coastal plain around Rome; now reclaimed and used for pasture.

Campania, region, S. **Italy**; comprising provs. Avellino, Benevento, Caserta, Naples, Salerno; admin. and comm. ctr. Naples; high p. density; fertile; intensive agr.; p. (est. 1986) 5·7m.

Campbelltown, t., N.S.W., **Australia**; dairy and

poultry ctr. for Sydney; proposed growth ctr. for 340,000; p. (1981) 91,525.

Campbeltown, royal burgh, spt., Kintyre, Argyll and Bute, **Scot.**; distilling, fishing; planned ctr. for construction of off-shore oil platforms; p. (1981) 6,077.

Campeche, spt., S.E. **Mexico**; on G. of Campeche; gives its name to prov. (a. 56,099 km²; p. (1970) 251,556); clothing; exp. timber, sisal hemp; p. (1980) 151,805.

Campina Grande, t., Paraiba, **Brazil**; inland mkt. t. benefitting from industl. devel. from recent SUDENE development plan; p. (est. 1985) 280,700.

Campinas, t., **Brazil**; 88 km N. of São Paulo; coffee; machin.; rubber gds.; p. (est. 1985) 845,000.

Campine or **Kempenland**, region in Limburg and Antwerp provs., **Belgium**; concealed coalfield in heathland a.

Campobasso, t., cap. of C. prov., S. **Italy**; agr. ctr.; famed for cutlery; 15th cent. cas.; p. (1981) 48,291.

Campo Belo, t., Minas Gerais st., **Brazil**; impt. cattle ctr. nr. L. formed by Furnas Dam on Rio Grande; p. (est. 1985) 42,900.

Campo Duran, terr., **Argentina**; oilfield and refining.

Campos, c., Rio de Janeiro st., **Brazil**; ctr. for rich agr. region; sugar refining; p. (est. 1985) 367,100.

Campos do Jordão, t., **Brazil**; alt., 1,699 m; health resort, known as the Switzerland of Brazil; p. (est. 1985) 32,600.

Campsie Fells, range of hills, Stirling, **Scot.**; highest point, 578 m.

Campulung, t., **Romania**, in Walachia, at foot of Transylvanian Alps; summer resort; p. (est. 1970) 26,675.

Canada, indep. st., within Commonwealth; occupies N. part of **N. America**; enclave of Alaska (USA) in N.W.; second lgst. cty. in world, consisting of 10 provs., 2 terrs.; coastal mtns. and Rockies in W., interior plains in ctr., Hudson Bay lowlands in N., plateau a. of Quebec and Newfoundland in E.; many Is. off Arctic cst.; continental climate, severe in interior but moderated on csts.; less than 8 per cent of total land a. classified as cultivated land but agr. prods. (especially wheat) very valuable exp.; enormous forest resources but many economically inaccessible; fur trapping in N., impt. fishing inds. on both Pac. and Atl. csts.; considerable mineral resources; lgst. world producer of asbestos, silver, nickel, zinc.; major oil and gas resources in Alberta; one of most urbanised ctys. in world; p. concentrated along E.–W. axis in S. parts of W. provs. and along Gr. Ls. and St. Lawrence lowland; economy highly integrated with USA; 80 per cent of mftg. inds. based on US investment and 78 per cent of external tr. with USA; major cultural differences between English and French communities; strong separatist movements in Quebec; both nat. languages official (30 per cent p. speak French); cap. Ottawa; a. 9,976,185 km²; p. (1986) 25,354,054.

Canada Dam, Bihar, **India**; on R. Mayurakshi, 256 km from Calcutta.

Canadian Coast Range, mtns., B.C., W. **Canada**; penetrated by deep inlets (fjords) with very little cst. plain; crossed only by R. Skeena in N., R. Fraser in S.

Canadian R., S.W. **USA**; trib. of Arkansas R., not navigable but impt. for irrigation; 1,440 km long.

Canadian Shield (**Laurentian Shield**), **Canada**; vast region of hard anc. rock surrounding Hudson Bay, deeply eroded by ice, and lake covered; mng. and forestry.

Canal du Centre, canal, **France**; links Rhône-Saône valley at Chalon-sur-Saône with R. Loire at Digoin; serves Le Creusot coalfield; length 96 km.

Canal Zone, Panama; strip of land leased to USA since 1903 for Panama Canal; p. (1970) 44,650.

Canaries Current, ocean current, flows S. along N.W. coast of Africa from El Dar-el-Beida to C. Verde; relatively cold and has very marked cooling effect on Saharan coastlands.

Canary Is., or **Canaries**, N. Atl. Oc.; gr. of 7 volcanic Is. belong to Spain, 96 km off cst. ʳrica; desires independence; inc. Tenerife (the

lgst. I.), Gran Canaria, La Palma, Gomera, Hierro, Fuerteventura, Lanzarote; dry sunny climate and impressive volcanic landscape encourage tourism; intensive, irrigated agr. for bananas, tomatoes, oranges and vegetables; cap. Las Palmas, the "Fortunate Isles" of many myths and legends; a. 7,272 km²; p. (1981) 1,444,626.

Canberra, cap. **Australia**; midway between Melbourne and Sydney, lgst. inland c.; rapid growth since cap. established (1912); half work-force employed in government; spacious planned c. centred around L. Burley Griffin, reliant on high car ownership; p. (est. 1985) 251,950.

Candia. See **Iráklion.**

Canea. See **Khaniá.**

Canna, sm. I., Hebrides, **Scot.**; basaltic pillars.

Cannanore, t., Kerala, **India**; exp. timber, coconuts; p. (1981) 60,904 (t.), 157,797 (met. a.).

Cannes, spt., dep. Alpes-Maritimes, **France**; 32 km S.W. Nice; famous resort; perfumes; airpt.; annual spring international film festival; p. (1982) 72,787.

Cannock Chase, upland a., Staffs., **Eng.**; open a. close to Midlands conurb.; now forms l. gov. dist. based on Cannock t.; p. (est. 1988) 87,700.

Canopus, c. of anc. **Egypt**; 19 km E. of Alexandria; here bdy. between Asia and Africa was drawn; Aboukir nr. ruins of temple of Serapis.

Cantabrians (**Sierra de Cantabria**), mtns., N. **Spain**; stretch from Pyrenees to C. Finisterre; form barrier between sea and central plateau; thick vegetation on lower slopes; coal, iron, hydroelec. power; hgst. peak Peña Vieja (2,673 m).

Cantal, dep., S.E. **France**; volcanic a., part of Massif Central; hgst. peak Plomb du Cantal (1,859 m); difficult agr., sparse p.; cap. Aurillac; a. 5,778 km²; p. (1982) 162,000.

Canterbury, c., l. gov. dist., Kent, **Eng**; at foot of N. Downs on R. Stour; univ.; cath. founded A.D. 597 by St. Augustine; shrine of Thomas Becket; for centuries a place of pilgrimage; p. (est. 1988) 131,900 (dist.).

Canterbury, prov., S.I., **N.Z.**; cap. Christchurch; a. 36,104 km²; p. (est. 1985) 422,200.

Canterbury Plains, rich grazing and wheat-growing dist., on merged alluvial fans; S.I., **N.Z.**; ch. t. Christchurch; ch. pt. Lyttelton.

Can-tho, t., **Vietnam**; on Mekong R. delta, tr. ctr.; rice, fish; p. (1973) 182,424.

Canton. See **Guangzhou.**

Canton R. See **Zhujiang.**

Canton, c., Ohio, **USA**; iron and steel, pulleys, hydraulic presses; p. (1984) 89,100 (c.), 404,200 (met. a.).

Canvey I., Castle Point, Essex, **Eng.**; fronting the Thames; expanded t.; resort; radio components, bookbinding, iron and wire wks., oil storage; oil refinery projected; liquid gas terminal; p. (1981) 35,293.

Cap de la Madeleine, t., S. Quebec, **Canada**; varied mnfs.; p. (1981) 32,626.

Cape Breton I., Nova Scotia, **Canada**; coalmng., steelwks.; farming, timber, fishing; ch. t. Sydney; discovered in 1497 by John Cabot; a. 9,324 km²; p. (1981) 127,035.

Cape Canaveral, E. Fla., **USA**; formerly Cape Kennedy; barrier I. separating Banana R. lagoon from Atl. Oc.; military base for testing missiles.

Cape Coast, t., **Ghana**; pt. of G. of Guinea, 96 km S.W. of Accra; cap. of Gold Coast until 1876; exp. cacao; cas.; p. (1984) 51,653.

Cape Cod, low sandy penin., Mass. Bay, **USA**; resort; fishing, boat bldg.; encloses C. C. Bay where Pilgrim Fathers first arrived in America 1620.

Cape Giradeau, t., Mo., **USA**; on Mississippi R.; footwear, clothing; p. (1980) 34,361.

Cape Kennedy. See **Cape Canaveral.**

Cape of Good Hope, S. Africa; famous headland, S. of Cape Town; 305 m high.

Cape Province, prov., **Rep. of S. Africa**; formerly Cape of Good Hope Colony; southernmost tip of Africa; cap. Cape Town; mostly plateau; inc. Transkeian terrs. in E.; sheep raising; wheat, citrus fruits, grapes, tobacco; fisheries; diamond and copper mng. in Namaqualand; automobile assembly, textiles, food canning; a. 721,224 km²; p. (1980) 5,091,360.

Capernaüm, in time of Christ impt. place in Palestine, on N. shore of L. Galilee; the modern Tell Hum (Israel).

Cape Town, c., cap. of Province, and legislative cap. of **Rep. of S. Africa**; spt. on Table Bay, 48 km N. of C. of Good Hope; communication by rail direct with Zimbabwe, Transvaal, O.F.S., and Natal; docks; cath.; univ.; exp. wool, gold, diamonds; oil refinery under construction at Milnerton 10 km N.E., p. (1970) 1,096,257 (met. a.).

Cape Verde Is., archipelago off W. cst. **Africa**; former Portuguese col.; 15 volcanic Is. and islets, divided into two grs.; windward and leeward; a. 4,040 km²; cap. Praia; agr. sugar, fruit-growing; São Vicente fuelling sta. for navigation to S. America; indep. achieved 1975; highest per capita aid levels in world; plans to develop infrastructure; irrigation and reafforestation projects; p. (est. 1987) 350,000.

Cap-Haitien, t., N. **Haiti**; spt., on N. cst.. exp. coffee, cacao, sugar; p. (1982) 64,406.

Capraia, I., 26 km E. of Corsica, belonging to **Italy**; volcanic; part of Genoa prov.

Caprera, I., off N.E. cst. Sardinia, **Italy**; Garibaldi buried here.

Capri, I. and tourist resort in Bay of Naples, **Italy**; famous Blue Grotto; celebrated in times of Augustus and Tiberius; wines; a. 10 km²; p. (1981) 7,489.

Capua, t., Campania, S. **Italy**; on Volturno R.; founded by Etruscans, impt. ctr. under Roman rule, sacked by Gaiseric; modern t. 5 km N. of site of anc. Capua; cath., Roman bridge; p. (1981) 18,053.

Caracas, c., cap. of **Venezuela**; in mtn. valley 921 m a.s.l.; 13 km inland from its pt. La Guaira; modern c.; contains 20 per cent of p. of rep.; cath., univs.; oil, textile mills, sugar refining; p. (1981) 1,816,900 (c.), 2,944,000 (met. a.).

Caradon, l. gov. dist., Cornwall, **Eng.**; a. between Tamar and S. cst.; inc. Looe, Saltash and Liskeard; p. (est. 1988) 74,900.

Carbon County, N. Utah, **USA**; contains immense reserves of gd. coking coal suitable for blast furnaces; not yet developed.

Carbonia, t., Sardinia, **Italy**; built 1937–8 nr. lignite and barytes a.; p. (1981) 32,130.

Carcassonne, c., cap. of Aude dep., S. **France**; historic citadel guarding impt. routeway from Aquitaine to Rhône valley; old c. divided from new by Aude R.; tourism; p. (1982) 42,450.

Cardamom Hills, Kerala, S. **India**; highland formed where W. and E. Ghats meet; rise to over 2,400 m; hgst. land of Indian penin.; rainfall less seasonal than most of India; "China" tea plantations on middle slopes.

Cárdenas, t., W. **Cuba**; pt. on Cárdenas Bay; processes and exp. sugar; p. (est. 1967) 67,400.

Cardiff, c., l. gov. dist., South Glamorgan, cap. of **Wales**; at mouth of R. Taff on Bristol Channel, one of world's gr. coal-shipping pts.; univ. colls., cath., cas.; docks at Barry; iron and steel wks., flour mills; freeport (1984) to help redevelopment of docks; p. (est. 1988) 283,900.

Cardigan, t., Ceredigion, Dyfed, S. **Wales**; at mouth of Teifi R.; former pt., now mkt. ctr.; p. (1981) 4,184.

Cardiganshire, former c., **Wales**. See Dyfed.

Caribbean Sea, part of Atl. Oc., between W.I. and Central and S. America; warm sea, entirely within tropics; a. 19,425 km².

Cariboo Range, mtns., B.C., W. **Canada**; mass of anc. crystalline rocks inside the gr. bend of R. Fraser; widespread occurrence of lode and alluvial gold; mainly above 1,500 m; hgst. point Mt. Sir Wilfred Laurier (3,584 m).

Carinthia (Karnten), prov., **Austria**; cap. Klagenfurt; contains hgst. mtn. in Austria, Grossglockner, alt. 3,801 m; many Ls.; p. (est. 1986) 542,000.

Carlisle, c., l. gov. dist., Cumbria, **Eng.**; on Eden R.; imp. and route ctr.; Norman cas.; cath.; textiles, plasterboard, flour, bacon, biscuits, metal boxes; p. (est. 1988) 102,000 (dist.).

Carlow, co., S.E. Leinster, **R.o.I.**; arable agr. and livestock; co. t. Carlow; a. 896 km²; p. (1981) 39,820.

Carlow, co. t., Carlow co., **R.o.I.**; cath.; mkt., agr. processing; p. (1981) 13,164.

Carlsbad, t., N.M., **USA**; tourist resort; impt. potash deposits; p. (1980) 25,496.

Carlsbad Caverns National Park, N.M., **USA**; in foothills of Guadalupe mtns.; limestone caves; a. 18,600 ha.

Carlton, t., Gedling, Notts., **Eng.**; 3 km N.E. Nottingham; hosiery; p. (1981) 46,456.

Carmarthen, t., l. gov. dist., Dyfed, **Wales**; on Towy R.; impt. agr. ctr.; cas. ruins; p. (est. 1988) 55,800 (dist.).

Carmarthenshire, former co., **Wales**. See Dyfed.

Carmiel, t., N. **Israel**; new t. built built between Acre and Safad, in the Galilean hills.

Carmona, t., **Spain**; Roman walls and necropolis; p. (1970) 24,378.

Carnac, sm. t., Brittany, N.W. **France**; famous for its megalithic monuments; p. (1982) 3,964.

Carnarvon, t., W. **Australia**; on R. Gascoyne; NASA tracking sta.; p. (1976) 5,341.

Carnoustie, burgh, Angus, **Scot.**; on N. Sea; 10 km S.W. of Arbroath; resort; p. (1981) 9,217.

Caroline Is., archipelago in W. Pac. Oc.; internal self-government (1978); 549 in no., lying betweeen the Philippines and the Marshall gr., former Japanese mandate now part of US Pac. Trust Terr.; Western Carolines became **Rep. of Belau** (1981); ch. exp. copra; a. 1,193 km; p. (est. 1967) 66,900.

Caroni, R., Venezuela, hydroelec. complex at confluence Orinoco R.; steelwks.

Carpathian Mtns., range, **E. Europe**; arc of mtns. extending from ČSSR into Ukrainian SSR and Romania; major European range; 1,288 km long; contains oilfields.

Carpentaria, G. of, N. **Australia**; between Arnhem Land and C. York.

Carpentras, t., Vaucluse, **France**; on R. Auzon; antiquities; sweetmeats; p. (1982) 25,886.

Carpi, t., central **Italy**; 16 km N. of Modena; cath.; food processing; p. (1981) 60,507.

Carrantuohill, mtn., Kerry, **R.o.I.**; 1,041 m, loftiest in all Ireland.

Carrara, t., Massa Carrara, central **Italy**; famed for white marble used by Michelangelo; p. (1981) 65,687.

Carrick, l. gov. dist., Cornwall, **Eng.**; stretches across penin. and surrounds Fal estuary; inc. Truro, Penryn and Falmouth; p. (est. 1988) 80,350.

Carrickfergus, t., l. gov. dist., **N. Ireland**; pt. on N. shore of Belfast Lough; textiles, nylon fibres, tobacco inds.; p. (1981) 28,365 (dist.), 17,633 (t.).

Carrickmacross, mkt. t., U.D. Monaghan, **R.o.I.**; p. (1981) 1,768.

Carrick-on-Shannon, co. t., R. D., Leitrim, **R.o.I.**; on flat land in Upper Shannon valley; p. of t. (1981) 1,677.

Carrick-on-Suir, mkt. t., U.D., Tipperary, **R.o.I.**; leather produs.; N.W. of Waterford; p. (1981) 5,511.

Carron, v., Falkirk, **Scot.**; nr. Falkirk; site of first ironwks. in E. Lowlands of Scot.

Carron, Loch, inlet, W. cst., Ross and Cromarty, **Scot.**; followed by rly. from Dingwall to Kyle of Lochalsh.

Carse of Gowrie, Perth and Kinross, **Scot.**; fertile coastal dist. between Perth and Dundee, S. of Sidlaw Hills; soft fruits, especially raspberries.

Carson City, cap. Nevada, **USA**; smallest st. cap. at 1,427 m; tourist ctr.; p. (1980) 32,022.

Carstenz Mtns., Irian Jaya, **Indonesia**; major copper and base metal deposits and mng.; slurry pipeline to pts. on Tipoeka R.

Cartagena, spt., cap. dep. Bolivar. **Colombia**; shares with Barranquilla tr. from Magdalena R. valley; platinum, coffee, chemicals, textiles, fertilisers, oil refinery; drugs summit 1990; p. (1985) 559,581.

Cartagena, t., Murcia prov., S.E. **Spain**; on Mediterranean; spt. and naval base; cath.; shipbldg., metalwkg.: p. (1981) 172,751.

Cartago, t., Colombia; in Cauca valley, ctr. of rich agr. a.; p. (1982) 83,200.

Cartago, c., **Costa Rica**; former cap.; 1,504 m at foot of volcanic Mt. Irazu; coffee, fruits; subject to earthquakes; p. (est. 1983) 27,929.

Cartago Basin, Meseta Central, **Costa Rica**; alt. 5,000 ft.; a. of early Spanish settlement.

Carter Fell, mtn., a summit of the Cheviot hills, on the Eng./Scot. border, 554 m.

Carthage, anc. c., N. **Africa**; on Bay of Tunis; destroyed by Romans 146 B.C.; site is sub. of Tunis.

Casablanca. See El Dar-el-Beida.

Casale Monferrato, t., Piedmont, **Italy**; on R. Po; cath.; cement; p. (est. 1968) 43,896.

Cascade Range, USA and **Canada**; extends N. and S. through B.C., Wash., and Ore. between Rocky Mtns. and Pac. cst.; timber resources, hydroelec. power; hgst. peak Mt. Rainier, 4,395 m.

Cascade Tunnel, longest rly. tunnel in N. America, Wash., **USA**; carries trunk rly. from Spokane to Seattle through Cascade Mtns.; length 12·5 km.

Caserta, t., Italy; on N.E. edge of plain of Campania; impt. route ctr. and agr. mkt.; cath.; palace; p. (1981) 66,318.

Cashel, mkt. t., UD. Tipperary, **R.o.I.**; anc. seat of kings of Munster; ruins of cath. on Rock of Cashel; p. (1981) 2,692.

Casiquiare, R., and canal, **Venezuela**; joins Orinoco to the Rio Negro, a trib. of the Amazon.

Casper, t., Wyo., **USA**; petroleum; airpt.; p. (1980) 51,016.

Caspian Sea, salt lake, **USSR**; largest inland sea in world; a. 422,170 km² but shrinking; 28 m below sea level; maximum depth 975 m; fed by R. Volga; agr. and dense p. on S. shore; pts.; Astrakhan, at mouth of Volga, Baku (oil ctr.).

Casquets, dangerous rocks, 11 km W. of Alderney, Channel Is., **Eng.**; lighthouse.

Cassino, t., Frosinone, **Italy**; in Apennines, on Rapido R.; t. and nearby monastery (Montecassino) destroyed 1944, now rebuilt; p. (1981) 31,139.

Castel Gandolfo, t., central **Italy**; in Alban Hills; papal summer residence; tourist centre; p. (1981) 13,348.

Castellammare del Golfo, spt., N.W. Sicily, **Italy**; wat. pl.; tuna fishing; p. (est. 1968) 15,498.

Castellammare di Stabia, t., Campania, **Italy**; on Bay of Naples, at foot of Vesuvius; historic arsenal and dockyards; mineral springs; cath.; resort; p. (1981) 70,317.

Castellón de la Plana, prov., **Spain**; on Mediterranean, part of anc. Valencia, mainly mtns. a. 6,679 km²; cap. Castellón; p. (1987) 439,266.

Castellón de la Plana, t., **Spain**; on plain inland from Mediterranean cst.; varied agr. inds.; oil refining; p. (1987) 128,664.

Castelnaudary, t., Aude dep., **France**; in strategic gap between Central Massif and Pyrenees; captured by Black Prince 1355; mkt. for cereals; pottery; p. (1982) 11,381.

Castelo Branco, t., **Portugal**, prov. cap. Beira Baixa; agr. mkt. t.; p. (1981) 21,300.

Castelvetrano, agr. t., W. Sicily, **Italy**; wine mkg.; p. (1981) 30,577.

Castile, region in the high plateaux of central **Spain**; former kingdom; divided into Old Castile in N. (Avila, Burgos, Logroño, Santander, Segovia, Soria) and New Castile in S. (Ciudad Real, Cuenca, Guadalajara, Madrid, Toledo). Its dialect became the standard language of Spain.

Castlebar, U.D., cap. Mayo, **R.o.I.**; mkt. t.; pursuit of Brit. by Fr. who captured t. 1798 known as the "Castlebar races"; p. (1981) 6,409.

Castleblayney, U.D., Monaghan, **R.o.I.**; nr. Dundalk; mkt. t.; shoes; p. (1981) 2,425.

Castlecary, v., Central Reg., **Scot.**; sta. on Roman wall; silica, fire clay deposits.

Castle Donington, t., North West Leics., **Eng.**; airpt; power sta.

Castle Douglas, burgh, Stewartry, **Scot.**; nr. R. Dee; nearby cas.; stock mkt.; p. (1981) 3,502.

Castleford, t., West Yorks., **Eng.**; 16 km S.E. of Leeds at confluence of Rs. Aire and Calder; coal mng., chemical, glass, and clothing mnfs.; flour milling, brick mkg.; p. (1981) 36,032.

Castle Morpeth, l. gov. dist., Northumberland, **Eng.**; based on Morpeth; p. (est. 1988) 50,400.

Castle Point, l. gov. dist., Essex, **Eng.**; comprises Canvey I. and Benfleet; p. (est. 1988) 85,500.

Castlereagh, l. gov. dist., **N. Ireland**; inc. S.E. outskirts of Belfast; p. (1981) 61,113.

Castleton, v., Derbys., **Eng.**; on Hope R.; tourist ctr. for the Peak District; nearby fluorspar mines.

Castletown, t., Isle of Man, **Eng.**; former cap.; pt., cas. tower; p. (1986) 3,019.

Castres, t., Tarn, **France**; on R. Agout; former Huguenot stronghold; cath.; textiles, soap, earthenware; p. (1982) 46,877.

Castries, t., cap. St. Lucia, Windward Is., **W.I.**; harbour; p. (1980) 45,763.

Castro-Rauxel or **Kastrop Rauxel,** t., N. Rhine-Westphalia, **W. Germany**; part of Ruhr conurb.; industl.; coal, cement, tar prod., tiles, brandy; p. (est. 1986) 96,100.

Catalonia, region, N.E. **Spain**; ch. industl. a.; comprises 4 provs.; Barcelona, Gerona, Lérida, Tarragona; cap. Barcelona; hilly, drained by Ebro R.; cereals, olive oil, wines; textiles, cars; hydroelec. power stas.; nuclear power sta. projected; a. 32,185 km²; p. (1981) 5,956,598.

Catamarca, t., cap. of Catamarca prov., N.W. **Argentina**; in Andean foothills 128 km S. of San Miguel de Tucumán; ctr. of irrigated oasis producing vines, apricots, cherries, cotton; thermal springs; p. (1980) 88,432.

Catanduanes, I., off S. Luzon, **Philippines**; hilly, fertile; rice, corn, cotton, hemp, coconuts; a. 1,429 km²; p. (1970) 162,679.

Catania, c., Sicily, **Italy**; cap. of C. prov.; pt. on E. cst. at foot of Mt. Etna; rebuilt several times after earthquakes and volcanic eruption; cath., univ., cas.; p. (1984) 380,370.

Catanzaro, t., S. **Italy**; univ.; service ctr., regional cap. of Calabria; p. (1984) 101,622.

Catastrophe, C., S. extremity of Eyre Peninsula, S. **Australia.**

Catawba, R., S. and N.C., **USA**; rises in Blue Ridge Range, flows to Santee R.; extensively dammed; 480 km long.

Caterham and **Warlingham,** ts., former U.D. Tandridge, Surrey, **Eng.**; on N. Downs; residtl.; p. (1981) 33,083.

Cathay, anc. name for China and E. Tartary.

Catoche, C., N.E. point of Yucatan, **Mexico.**

Catskill Mtns., N.Y., **USA**; gr. in Appalachians, W. of Hudson R., well wooded; resort for p. of N.Y. c.; alt. c. 900 m.

Cauca, dep., **Colombia**; cap. Popayán; a. 30,191 km²; p. (1985) 674,824.

Cauca, R., **Colombia**; trib. of Magdalena; 960 km long.

Caucasia, region between Black Sea and Caspian, **USSR**; divided by Caucasus Mtns. into N. or Cis-Caucasia and S. or Trans-Caucasia.

Caucasus (Bol'shoy Kavkaz), mtns., separate RSFSR from Georgian SSR and Azerbaydzhan SSR, **USSR**; run from Black Sea to Caspian Sea; divided into 3 ranges; hgst. summits Mt. Elbruz (5,631 m) and Kasbek (5,047 m); many lofty passes and glaciers; total l. c. 1,520 km.

Caucun, I., off Yucatan penin., **Mexico**; developing tourist ctr.; airpt.

Causses, Les, limestone plateau, Aveyron, Tarn deps., S. **France**; on S.W. flank of Central Massif; caverns, gorges of Rs. Lot and Tarn; sheep provide milk for Roquefort cheese; alt. 900–1,800 m.

Cauvery, R., S. **India**; rises in W. Ghats, flows into Bay of Bengal through Karnataka and Tamil Nadu; length 640 km; lge. irrigation and hydroelec. power project.

Caux, region of Normandy, **France**; fertile loess-covered chalk plateau adjacent to English Channel; arable agr.

Cava de' Tirreni, t., Salerno, **Italy**; summer resort; textiles; p. (1981) 50,558.

Cavaillon, t., Vaucluse, **France**; cath.; ctr. of mkt. gardening dist.; p. (1982) 20,830.

Cavan, inland c., **R.o.I.**; agr. a. with many Ls.; depopulation; borders Ulster; a. 1,932 km²; p. (1981) 6,840.

Cavan, U.D., co. t., Cavan, **R.o.I.**; 115 km S.W. Belfast; mkt.; cath.; p. (1981) 5,035.

Cavite, spt., Luzon, **Philippines**; walled t.; oil refining nearby; p. (est. 1970) 77,100.

Cavour Canal, irrigation canal, Piedmont and Lombardy regions, N. Italy; links R. Po nr. Chivassa with R. Ticino 16 km N.E. of Novara; provides water for 101,000 ha of rice-fields and meadow-land; length 128 km.

Cawnpore. *See* Kanpur.

Caxias, t., Marahão, Brazil; on Itapicuru R. p. (1968) 124,403.

Caxias do Sul, t., Rio Grande do Sul, **Brazil**; wines; p. (1980) 198,683.

Cayambe, volcanic mtn., Andes, **Ecuador**; alt. 5,958 m.

Cayenne, c., cap of French Guiana, at mouth of Cayenne R.; exp. gold; gave its name to Cayenne pepper; p. (1982) 38,135.

Cayman Is., W.I.; consists of Grand Cayman, cap. Georgetown; Little Cayman; and Cayman

Brac.; turtle and shark fishing; a. 259 km²; p. (est. 1987) 22,900.

Ceará, st., N. Brazil; stretches from Brazilian Plateau to Atl. cst.; poor cattle rearing a. with many droughts; cap. Fortaleza; a. 148,078 km²; p. (est. 1985) 5,890,400.

Cebu, one of Visayan Is., Philippines; mtnous.; forested; coal, oil, gold; coconuts, maize; 4,408 km²; p. (1970) 1,632,642 (prov.).

Cebu, t., Cebu I., Philippines; tr. ctr. of Visayan Is.; pt. for abaca and copra; p. (est. 1984) 552,155.

Cedar Falls, t., N. Iowa, USA; on Cedar R.; p. (1980) 36,322.

Cedar Mountain, hill, Va., USA; here Stonewall Jackson defeated Banks in Civil War (second battle of Bull Run, 1862).

Cedar Rapids, c., Iowa, USA; distribution and rly. ctr. for agr. a.; p. (1984) 108,700 (c.), 169,500 (met. a.).

Cegléd, t., Hungary; on edge of Central Plain in fruit growing a.; vehicle repair shops; p. (est. 1984) 40,000.

Celaya, mkt. t., Guanajuato, Mexico; rly. junc.; ctr. of rich farming a.; many inds.; sweetmeats; p. (1980) 219,010.

Celebes. See Sulawesi.

Celje, t., Yugoslavia; industl., agr. ctr., zinc refining, fertilisers; close to Austrian border; p. (1981) 63,877.

Celle, t., Lower Saxony, W. Germany; on R. Aller; cas. was residence of dukes of Brunswick-Lüneburg until 1705; oil refining, machin., textiles; p. (est. 1986) 70,200.

Celtic Sea, a. bounded by S. Ireland, Wales, Cornwall and Brittany; rich natural gas deposits 48 km S.W. of Kinsale.

Central African Republic, indep. st., former empire until 1979; within Fr. Community, Equatorial Africa; formerly Fr. colony of Ubangi-Shari; land-locked upland plateau covered by savannah grassland; S.W. forest zone likely to develop with proposed rail link with Transcameroon rly.; cotton, diamonds; cap. Bangui; a. 622,984 km²; p. (est. 1987) 2,775,000.

Central America, stretch of land between Mexico and S. America, from the Isthmus of Tehuantepec to that of Panama; includes Guatemala, Honduras, Mexico, Nicaragua, Salvador, Costa Rica, Panama, Belize; tropical climate; forests, savannahs; p. (est. 1981) 93,000,000.

Central Asia, usually applied to regions between 30° and 40° N. lat. and 55° and 85° E. long.; Soviet C.A. is the land between China and Afghanistan and the Caspian, consisting of Kazakh SSR, Tadzhik SSR, Turkmen SSR, Uzbek SSR, and Kirghiz SSR.

Central Clydeside Conurbation, conurb., Scot., based on Glasgow and includes other urban areas (Bearsden, Milngavie, Clydebank, Cumbernauld, Kilsyth, East Kilbride, Eastwood, Hamilton, Monklands, Motherwell, Renfrew and Strathkelvin); p. (1981) 1,713,287.

Central Lancashire, new t., Lancs., Eng.; site of 14,186 ha.; t. created from expansion of Chorley and Leyland; biggest new t. in Eng.; p. (1981) 247,224.

Central Region, l. gov. reg., Scot.; stretches from Grampian mtns. to Central Lowlands, the Forth valley; main ts. Falkirk and Stirling; a. 2,631 km²; p. (est. 1986) 271,819.

Central Valley, Cal., USA; valleys of Rs. San Joaquin and Sacramento; main agr. a. of Cal.; vast scheme for irrigation, hydroelec. power, flood control and protection of wildlife.

Cephalonia (Kefalliniá), lgst. of Ionian Is., Greece; mtnous. with fertile valleys; impt. harbours of Argostólion and Lexourion; currant production; a. 751 km²; p. (1981) 31,297.

Ceram. See Seram.

Ceredigion, l. gov. dist., Dyfed, Wales; lge a. inc. Cardigan and Lampeter in S. and Aberystwyth in N.; p. (est. 1988) 67,000.

Cérignola, t., Apulia, Italy; agr. ctr.; Spanish victory over French in Italian wars 1503; p. (1981) 50,682.

Cerigo (Kithira) I., Greece; sm. I. between Crete and Peloponnesus.

Cernauti. See Chernovtsy.

Cerro de Pasco, t., Pasco dep., Peru; mng. ctr. at 4,403 m; univ.; copper, gold, lead, zinc; p. (est. 1970) 29,000.

Cerro Rico, mtn., Bolivia; in Andes, W. of Potosi; alt. 4,782 m; rich silver, tin, tungsten ores.

Cesena, t., Emilia-Romagna, Italy; flourished in Renaissance times; cath., Malatesta library; agr. mkt. t.; p. (1981) 89,640.

České Budějovice (Budweis), t., ČSSR; on R. Vitava, 128 km S. of Prague, major industl. ctr.; pencils, porcelain, brewing, anthracite; p. (est. 1986) 94,000.

Ceský Těšin, t., ČSSR; on Olše R., trib. of Oder; part of former t. of Teschen on Czech side of frontier with Poland; coal mng.

Cessnock-Bellbird, t., N.S.W., Australia; coal mng. declining since 1968; ctr. for Hunter Valley vineyards; p. (1981) 16,916.

Ceuta, spt., Spanish N. Africa, naval base; opposite to and 26 km from Gibraltar; cath.; the anc. Abyia, one of the Pillars of Hercules; p. (1981) 65,263.

Cevennes, mtns., S. France; separating basins of Rhône, Loire, and Tarn; highest point Mt. Mézenc, alt. 1,767 m.

Ceylon. See Sri Lanka.

Chaco, prov., N. Argentina; farming and prairie land; cap. Resistencia; a. 99,632 km²; p. (1980) 692,410.

Chad, indep. st. within Fr. Community, Equatorial Africa; landlocked; focus of trans Sahara and Equatorial tr. routes; N. frontier (Aouzou Strip) rich in minerals and occupied by Libya; valuable uranium and oil reserves but no exploitation; severe droughts (1982–3) reduced cattle and restricted arable crops; cash crops of cotton and ground nuts; cap. Ndjamena; a. 1,282,050 km²; p. (est. 1987) 5,241,000.

Chad, L., lge. sheet of water bordering Nigeria, Niger, Chad and Cameroon; a. 129,500 km² when in flood; varies in extent with season, and is drying up; shallow, many Is., lies between the wooded region of the Sudan and the steppes leading to the Sahara desert; joint project for devel. by neighbouring ctys.

Chadderton, t., Gtr. Manchester, Eng.; engin., chemicals, textiles; p. (1981) 34,013.

Chagos Is., 5 coral Is., Indian Oc.; admin. by Seychelles since 1965; fine harbour in Diego Garcia (Anglo-American naval communications ctr.).

Chainat, t., Thailand; on Menam Chao Phraya; major barrage for hydroelec. power and flood control.

Chalcis, t., Greece; resort for Athens; joined to mainland by swing bridge; p. (1981) 44,867.

Chalfont St. Giles, v., Bucks., Eng.; in London commuter belt; home of Milton.

Châlons-sur-Marne, t., cap. of Marne dep., N.E. France; comm. and industl.; cath., churches; p. (1982) 54,359.

Chālon-sur-Saône, t., Saône-et-Loire dep., E. France; R. pt., comm. ctr. for Burgundy; historic t.; p. (1982) 57,967.

Chambal, R., trib. of R. Jumna, rising in Vindhya hills, Madhya Pradesh, India; major power, irrigation and industl. scheme; agr. in lower valley causing soil erosion, major soil conservation projection; 880 km long.

Chambéry, t., cap. of Savoie dep., S.E. France; leather gds.; tourism; p. (1982) 54,896.

Chambord, v., Loir-et-Cher dep., France; on R. Cosson, trib. of Loire; Renaissance château; p. (1981) 206.

Chamonix, t., Haute-Savoie, France; at foot of Mont Blanc, in valley of R. Arve; winter sports ctr., road tunnel links to Aosta; p. (1982) 9,255.

Champagne, region and former prov., France; covers deps. of Aube, Marne, Haute-Marne, Ardennes, and parts of Yonne Aisne, Seine-etMarne, and Meuse; famous for its champagne wine; wheat, sheep; impt. tr. fairs in Middle Ages., main ctr. Reims. See Champagne Humide and Champagne Pouilleuse.

Champagne Humide, region, France; clay vale, runs 160 km N.E. from Auxerre to Bar-le-Duc; drained by Seine, Aube, Marne, Aisne, and many tribs.; heavily wooded, marshy; where cleared and drained, grain cultivation.

Champagne Pouilleuse, region, France; barren chalk plateau, extends 128 km N.E. from Sens to Reims; drained by Aisne, Vesle, Seine, Aube, Marne; dusty chalk downland pastures; sheep; vine growing on S.-facing valley sides and S.E.-facing escarpment of Falaise de l'Ile de France favours production of Champagne wines; ch. producing ctrs.; Châlons-surMarne, Reims, Epernay.

Champaign, t., Ill., USA; close to Urbana; univ.; foundries; food processing; p. (1984) 60,400 (t.), 170,300 (met. a.).

Champigny-sur-Marne, t., Val-de-Marne dep., France; E. sub. of Paris; varied inds.; p. (1982) 76,260.

Champlain Canal, N.Y., **USA;** follows gap between Adirondack Mtns. and Green Mtns. occupied by Hudson R.; links Albany with L. Champlain and allows through barge traffic between New York and St. Lawrence valley.

Champlain, L., **USA;** N. frontier of N.Y. st.; discharges by Richelieu R. into St. Lawrence; flanked by trunk route from New York to Montreal; forms link between Hudson R. and St. Lawrence waterway; a. 1,126 km².

Chañaral, spt., N. Atacama, **Chile;** lies in gold and copper-mng. a.; p. (1960) 21,098.

Chanda, t., Nagpur, Maharashtra, **India;** anc. temples; p. (1961) 51,484.

Chandausi, t., Uttar Pradesh, **India;** cotton, hemp; rly. ctr.; p. (1961) 48,557.

Chandernagore, t., W. Bengal, **India;** on Hooghly R., N. of Calcutta; founded by French 1686; p. (1961) 67,105.

Chandigarh, union terr. (1966) and former cap. of both Punjab and Haryana sts., **India;** new c. designed by Le Corbusier to replace former cap. Lahore, now in Pakistan; to be sole capital of Punjab on plateau at foot of Himalayas, S.W. of Simla, (now postponed because of Sikh unrest); univ.; a. of terr. 114 km², p. of c. (1981) 451,610.

Changchun, c., Jilin, **China;** rly. ctr.; univ.; China's biggest motor vehicle plant, machine tools; film production centre; p. (1984) 1,809,200.

Changnacheri, t., Kerala, S. **India;** tea, cotton-spinning, silk; p. (1961) 42,376.

Changbai Shan, mtns.; form bdy. between **China** and **N. Korea;** drained by Rs. Yalu and Tumen; hgst. point Pai-t'ou-shan, 2,442 m.

Chang Jiang (Yangtse Kiang), R., **China;** rises in plateau in Xizang Zizhiou (Tibet) and flows E. to E. China Sea nr. Shanghai; one of China's major Rs.; crosses 'Red Basin' of Sichuan, a deep gorge above Yichang and finally a broad level plain; many lge. cs. on its banks inc. Yichang, Nanjing, Wuhan, Zhenjiang, Chongqing; major water control project; navigable by ocean-going vessels for 2,880 km. to Yichang; total length 5,600 km.; longest river in Asia.

Changsha, c., cap. of Hunan prov., **China;** pt. on Xiang Jiang; univ.; tea, rice, antimony; p. (1984) 1,123,900.

Changzhou (Changchow), c., Jiangsu, **China;** in valley of Chang Jiang, on Grand Canal 112 km S.E. of Nanjing; mkt. for intensively cultivated dist.; silk; p. (1984) 512,600.

Channel Is., gr. of self-governing Is. belonging to the Brit. Crown off N.W. cst. France, of which the lgst. are Jersey, Guernsey, Alderney, and Sark; part of the old duchy of Normandy; vegetables, flowers, fruit, granite; two famous breeds of dairy cattle; tourist resort; impt. banking and insurance ctr. encouraged by low taxes; retirement ctr.; a. 194 km²; p. (est. 1985) 130,000.

Chantilly, t., Oise, **France;** famous racecourse; formerly famous for lace and porcelain; p. (1982) 10,208.

Chao Phraya. *See* **Menam Chao Phraya.**

Chaozhou (Chaochow), c., Guandong, S. **China;** on Han R., 32 km N. of Shantou; ctr. of cultivated plain; rice, sugar, tea; linked to Shantou by rly.; p. (1984) 191,400.

Chapala, L., **Mexico;** chiefly in Jalisco st.; attractive site and climate encourage tourism; pastoral agr. on shores; a. 1,080 km².

Chapayevsk, t., Kuybyshev region, **RSFSR;** in Volga valley; chemicals, agr. machin.; p. (est. 1969) 87,000.

Chapelcross, nr. Annan, Annandale and Eskdale, **Scot.;** AEA nuclear power sta., producing electricity for nat. grid.

Chapel-en-le-Frith, mkt. t., High Peak, Derbys., **Eng.;** brake-linings.

Chapra, t., Bihar, **India;** on Ganges R.; ctr. of former saltpetre and indigo tr.; p. (1981) 111,564.

Chard, mkt. t., Somerset **Eng.;** lace, engin., shirt and cotton mftg.; p. (1981) 9,384.

Chardzhou, t., Turkmen SSR, **USSR;** inland pt. on Amu-Dar'ya R.; shipyards, textiles, chemicals; major oil refinery project; p. (est. 1985) 157,000.

Charente, dep., S.W. **France;** cap. Angoulême; ctr. of distilling tr., cognac; a. 5,970 km²; p. (1982) 340,300.

Charente, R., S.W. **France;** rises W. of Limoges and flows into Bay of Biscay below Rochefort; valley slopes beyond Angoulême produce ʼlebrated grapes from which brandy is made ʼognac and Jarnac.

Charente-Maritime, dep., S.W. **France;** cap. La Rochelle; borders Bay of Biscay; wine, wheat; oysters, pilchards; a. 7,229 km²; p. (1982) 512,800.

Charleroi, t., Hainaut, **Belgium;** on R. Sambre; coal mng.; glass; p. (est. 1984) 213,041.

Charleston, c., spt., S.C., **USA;** industl. and comm. ctr. on Atl. cst. founded 1670; scene of onset of Civil War; p. (1984) 67,100 (c.), 472,500 (met. a. with North Charlestown).

Charleston, t., cap. W. Va., **USA;** on Kanawha R.; in bituminous coal dist.; chemicals, glass, tools, oil, natural gas, lumber, coal processing; p. (1984) 59,400 (t.), 267,000 (met. a.).

Charleville-Mézières, twin t., Ardennes dep., N.E. **France;** on Meuse R.; iron, bricks, nails, hardware; p. (1982) 61,588.

Charlotte, c., N.C., **USA;** key rly. junc.; machin., chemicals, textiles; p. (1984) 330,800 (c.), 1,031,400 (met. a. with Gastonia).

Charlotte Amalie, t., cap. of Virgin Is. of **USA;** on St. Thomas I.; excellent natural harbour; former coaling sta.; p. (1980) 11,842.

Charlottenburg, sub. of Berlin, **Germany** (in W. Berlin); on R. Spree.

Charlottesville, t., Va., **USA;** on Rivanna R.; in apple-growing region; univ.; Monticello nearby, home of Jefferson; textiles; p. (1984) 40,600 (t.), 118,300 (met. a.).

Charlottetown, t., ch. pt. Prince Edward I., **Canada;** originally named after Queen Charlotte, consort of George III; univ.; p. (1986) 15,776.

Charlton Kings, t., Cheltenham, Gloucs., **Eng.;** at foot of Cotswolds; p. (1981) 10,785.

Charnwood Forest, upland dist., Leics., **Eng.;** to W. of Soar valley, 19 km N.W. of Leicester; composed of anc. rocks; stone-crushing; largely forests; used for recreation by industl. ts. of E. Midlands; alt. 180–275 m; now forms l. gov. dist. of Charnwood and inc. Loughborough and Shepshed; p. (est. 1990) 151,900.

Charters Towers, t., N. Queensland, **Australia;** fine bldgs. remain from 1872 gold rush; ctr. of agr. dist.; p. (est. 1984) 7,620.

Chartres, t., cap. of Eure-et-Loir dep., **France;** mkt. for cereals from Beauce region; famous Gothic cath.; p. (1982) 77,795 (met. a.).

Châteauroux, t., cap. of Indre dep., **France;** 96 km S.E. of Tours, on R. Indre; agr. ctr., woollens, pottery; p. (1982) 53,967.

Chateau Thierry, t., Aisne, **France;** on R. Marne; mkt. t.; cas.; precision instruments; p. (1982) 14,920.

Châtellerault, t., Vienne, **France;** 64 km S. of Tours on R. Vienne; cutlery, metallurgical and aeronautical engin. Descartes lived here; p. (1982) 36,870.

Chatham, t., Rochester upon Medway, Kent, **Eng.;** on estuary of R. Medway; lt. inds.; famous naval dockyard established by Henry VIII, now closed; p. (1981) 61,909.

Chatham, t., spt., N.B., **Canada;** lumbering, fish exporting; p. (1981) 6,780.

Chatham, c., Ont., **Canada;** on extinct L. plain on R. Thames; agr. prods.; p. (1981) 40,952.

Chatham Is., N.Z. dependency, S. **Pac. Oc.;** volcanic Is.; sheep rearing and fishing; a. 963 km²; lgst. I. Wharekauri; p. (est. 1968) 500.

Chatsworth, par., Derbys., **Eng.;** on R. Derwent; seat of the dukes of Devonshire.

Chattanooga, c. Tenn., **USA;** on Tennessee R.; univ.; rly. ctr.; cottons; iron, steel, chemicals, paper, metals; p. (1984) 164,400 (c.), 422,500 (met. a.).

Chatteris, Fenland, Cambridge, **Eng.;** mkt. t.; p. (1981) 6,180.

Chaudière Falls, on Ottawa R., above Ottawa, **Canada;** hydroelec. sta.

Chauk, t., **Burma;** on R. Irrawaddy; ctr. of oilfield; oil refining; fertilisers.

Chaumont, t., cap. of Haute-Marne dep., **France;** on R. Marne; gloves, leather; p. (1982) 29,552.

Chautauqua, L., N.Y. st., **USA;** summer resort; vineyards.

Chaux-de-Fonds, La, t., can. Neuchâtel, **Switzerland;** ctr. of watchmkg. ind.; p. (1980) 37,234.

Cheadle, t., Staffs. Moorland, Staffs., **Eng.;** metal mnfs.; former coal-mng. a.; p. (1971) 4,070 (dist.).

Cheadle and Gatley, ts., Gtr. Manchester, **Eng.;** textile finishing and bleaching, engin.; residtl.; p. (1981) 58,683.

Cheb, t., **CSSR;** nr. Bavarian frontier; comm. ctr.; machin.; p. (1984) 31,333.

Cheboksary, c., cap. of Chuvash ASSR, **RSFSR;** R. pt. on Volga; agr. ctr.; hydroelec. plant; p. (est. 1985) 389,000.

Checheno-Ingush ASSR, USSR; oilfield, petro-chemicals; p. (1986) 1,222,000.

Cheddar, v., Somerset, **Eng.;** famous limestone caves and gorge in Mendips; cheese, strawberries.

Chefoo. See **Yentai.**

Cheju (Quelpart), I., off **S. Korea,** E. China Sea; extinct volcano Mt. Halla, 1,968 m.

Chekiang. See **Zhijiang.**

Che-ling Pass, on bdy. between Guandong and Hunan, S. **China;** historic route across Nanling mtns., now followed by Wuhan to Guangzhou trunk rly.; alt. 300 m.

Chelm, t., E. **Poland;** nr. Lublin; cath.; flour-milling; p. (1983) 57,900.

Chelmsford, co. t., l. gov. dist., Essex, **Eng.;** 48 km N.E. London; cath.; agr. mkt.; p. (est. 1988) 151,700.

Chelsea, dist., London, **Eng.;** fashionable residtl. dist. See **Kensington.**

Chelsea, t., Mass., **USA;** industl. sub. on Boston harbour; p. (1980) 25,431.

Cheltenham, t., l. gov. dist., Gloucs., **Eng.;** spa; educational ctr.; precision instruments; birthplace of Gustav Holst; p. (est. 1988) 86,400 (dist.).

Chelyabinsk, t., **RSFSR;** major industl. ctr. on Miass R., Siberian lowlands; steel wks.; metallurgy, machin.; on natural gas pipeline from Gazli gasfield; p. (1986) 1,107,000.

Chelyuskin, Cape, most N. point in Asia, in Krasnoyarsk Terr., **RSFSR;** named after Russian navigator who discovered it in 1742.

Chemnitz. See **Karl-Marx-Stadt.**

Chemulpo. See **Inchon.**

Chenab, R., W. Punjab, **Pakistan;** one of "five rivers" of Punjab; rises in Himalayas, flows S.W. into R. Sutlej; dams at Marala and Khanki; c. 1,440 km long.

Chengchow. See **Zhengzhou.**

Chengdu (Chengtu), c., cap. of Sichuan prov., **China;** telecommunications centre, oil refinery; chemicals, electronics, textiles, machin.; p. (1984) 2,539,600.

Chepstow, mkt. t., Gwent, **Wales;** on R. Wye, 3 km above confluence with R. Severn; Severn Bridge links to Aust (Avon); ruined cas.; p. (1981), 9,309.

Chequers, official residence of Brit. prime ministers, 3 km S. of Wendover, Bucks., **Eng.;** gift of Lord Lee of Fareham.

Cher, dep., **France;** cap. Bourges; crossed by Cher R.; chiefly pastoral agr.; a. 7,301 km²; p. (1982) 319,000.

Cher, R., central **France;** rises in Central Massif, joins Loire below Tours; length 320 km.

Cherbourg, spt., Manche, **France;** N. cst. of Contentin peninsula; opposite to and 128 km dist. from Portsmouth; naval arsenal, shipbldg.; metals, ropes, fishing; p. (1982) 85,485 (met. a.).

Cheremkhovo, t., **RSFSR;** N.W. of Irkutsk; coal, engin., chemicals; on Trans-Siberian rly.; p. (est. 1970) 110,000.

Cherepovets, c., **RSFSR;** on Rybinskoye reservoir of R. Volga; steel, engin., sawmills, shipbldg.; p. (est. 1985) 299,000.

Cheribon. See **Tjirebon.**

Cheriton, dist. near Folkestone, Kent, **Eng.;** site for emergence of Channel Tunnel, linked to Sangatte, Calais, France; under construction.

Cherkassy, t., Ukrainian SSR, **USSR;** nr. Kiev, on reservoir formed by Dnieper R.; sugar, engin., sawmilling; p. (est. 1985) 273,000.

Cherkessk, t., **RSFSR;** rly. terminus, industl. ctr.; p. (est. 1985) 102,000.

Chernobyl, Ukraine, **USSR;** site of world's worst nuclear accident (1986).

Chernigov, t., Ukrainian SSR, **USSR;** on Desna R.; caths.; univ.; flour, textiles, chemicals; p. (est. 1985) 278,000.

Chernogorsk, t., **RSFSR;** 16 km N.W. of Abakan; ctr. of Minusinsk coal-mng. basin; p. (est. 1967) 63,000.

Chernovtsy, t., Ukrainian SSR, **USSR;** univ.; Greek cath.; wheat, dairy produce, textiles, engin., chemicals; p. (est. 1985) 244,000.

Cherrapunji, t., Assam, **India;** in Khasi Hills; reputed wettest place in world, average annual rainfall 12,700 mm.

Chertsey, t., Runnymede, Surrey, **Eng.;** on S. bank of R. Thames, 6 km below Staines; residtl.; p. (1981) 43,265.

Cherwell, l. gov. dist., Oxon., **Eng.;** stretches

from Banbury to Bicester; p. (est. 1988) 122,400.

Cherwell, R., trib. of Thames, nr. Oxford, **Eng.;** length 48 km.

Chesapeake Bay, inlet on Atl. cst., **USA;** extending 320 km from mouth of Susquehanna R. to C. Charles; shellfish ind.; bridge-tunnel (opened 1964) spans entrance to Bay; p. of c. (1984) 126,000.

Chesham, t., Bucks., **Eng.;** in heart of Chiltern Hills; printing, textiles, lt. engin.; residtl; p. (1981) 20,655.

Cheshire, non-met. co., N.W. **Eng.;** lowland a. drained by Rs. Dee and Mersey, bounded by Pennines in E.; dairying and mkt. gardening; chemical ind. based on salt deposits around Northwich; heavy inds. in and around Warrington; attracting many high technology inds.; much of co. residtl. for Liverpool and Manchester; cap. Chester; a. 2,323 km²; p. (est. 1988) 955,800.

Cheshunt, t., Herts., **Eng.;** in Lea valley, 11 km S. of Hertford; bricks, mkt. gardening, horticulture; p. (1980) 49,670.

Chesil Bank, Dorset, **Eng.;** shingle ridge enclosing the Fleet lagoon running from I. of Portland to Bridport.

Chester, c., l. gov. dist., Cheshire, **Eng.;** at head of estuary of R. Dee; cath., anc. walls and old timbered houses; Roman c. of Deva site of legionary barracks; engin., metal gds.; p. (est. 1988) 117,100.

Chester, t., Penns., **USA;** on Delaware R. S.W. Philadelphia; called Uppland by Swedish settlers 1643, renamed by William Penn; pt. of entry; shipbldg.; p. (1980) 45,794.

Chesterfield, mkt. t., colly. dist., l. gov. dist., Derbys., **Eng.;** on Rother R.; 13 km S. of Sheffield; variety of heavy inds.; 14th-cent. church with crooked spire; p. (est. 1988) 99,700 (dist.).

Chesterfield Inlet, arm of Hudson Bay, **Canada;** 400 km by 40 km.

Chester-le-Street, t., l. gov. dist., Durham. **Eng.;** clothing, confectionery, sand wkg.; p. (est. 1988) 53,100 (dist.).

Cheviot Hills, range between **Scot.** and **Eng.;** hgst. summit, the Cheviot, 816 m.

Cheyenne, t., cap. of Wyo., **USA;** cattle-ranching dist.; rly. ctr.; p. (1980) 47,283.

Chiana, Val di, valley, central **Italy;** separates Tuscan hills from central Apennines; occupied by upper course of R. Arno, middle course of R. Tiber; followed by main route from Florence to Rome.

Chiang Mai, c., cap of C. prov., and 3rd c. of **Thailand;** rly. terminus on Ping R.; tr. ctr.; teak; p. (1980) 101,594.

Chiapa, R., flows N. from **Guatemala** through **Mexico** to G. of Campeche; impt. routeway in lower course; length 320 km.

Chiapas, Pac. st., **Mexico;** mtnous., forested; bananas, tobacco, sugar and cocoa; cattle; oil reserves; close associations with Guatemala; cap. Tuxtla-Gutierrez; a. 74,408 km²; p. (1980) 2,096,812.

Chiasso, frontier t., S. **Switzerland;** rly. sta. on Italian border; p. (1970) 8,868.

Chiatura, t., Georgian SSR, **USSR;** impt. manganese deposits; p. (est. 1967) 27,000.

Chiba, c., cap. of C. pref. **Japan;** part of Keihin conurb. on Tokyo B.; tr. ctr., giant shipyard, oil refining, aluminium, chemicals, iron and steel; airpt.; p. (1985) 788,920.

Chicago, c., Ill., **USA;** on S. shore of L. Michigan; second lgst. US c.; economic heart of Mid-West; comm. ctr. called "The Loop"; immense tr. by rail and Gr. Ls.; univs.; grain mills, meat packing plants, iron and steel wks.; major iron-ore mkt., electronic equipment, furniture; lgst. airport in world; p. (1984) 2,992,500 (c.), 8,035,000 (met.a.).

Chichester, t., l. gov. dist., West Sussex, **Eng.;** on S. cst. plain, 18 km W. of Arundel; cath.; yachting basin; p. (est. 1988) 105,900 (dist.).

Chickamauga Creek, USA; branch of Tennessee R. above Chattanooga, forming part of Tenn. Valley Authority scheme; Civil War battles; site of Nat. Park.

Chickerell, E. Dorset, **Eng.;** 5 km N.W. of Weymouth; East Fleet, a sea-fed tidal estuary, lies to the west of the village.

Chiclayo, c., Lambayeque dep., **Peru;** mkt. ctr. for irrigated desert a. between Andes and Pac. Oc. producing mainly rice and sugar; p. (1985) 349,000.

Chicopee, t., Mass., **USA**; on Connecticut R. nr. Springfield; p. (1980) 55,112.

Chicoutimi, t., Quebec, **Canada**; pt. on Chicoutimi R.; lumber, pulp, paper; hydroelectric power; p. (1986) 61,083 (t.), 158,468 (met. a. with Jonquière).

Chiemsee, L., lge. lake nr. Munich, **W. Germany**; c. 460 m a.s.l.

Chieti, t., cap. of C. prov., S. **Italy**; cath.; anc. Teate Marrucinorum; Europe's lgst. glass plant, using methane from Abruzzi field; p. (1981) 54,927.

Chigrik, t., Uzbek SSR, **USSR**; new t. (1963) 34 km S. of Tashkent.

Chigwell, t., Epping Forest, Essex, **Eng.**; on borders of Epping Forest; Hainault Estate now incorporated in Redbridge, Greater London; resdtl.; p. (1981) 51,290.

Chihli, Gulf of. See **Pohai**.

Chihuahua, lgst. st. in **Mexico**; dry climate impedes agr.; mng., cotton, cattle, Chihuahua dogs; a. 247,024 km²; p. (1980) 1,933,856.

Chihuahua, c., cap. Chihuahua st., **Mexico**; univ., cath.; ctr. silver-mng. ind.; p. (est. 1986) 390,000.

Chikchi, peninsula, **RSFSR**; world's first Arctic nuclear power sta. being built.

Chikugo, t., N. Kyushu, **Japan**; lgst. coal mines in country; p. (1985) 43,359.

Chilaw, t., Sri Lanka; ctr. of coconut plantations.

Chile, rep., **S. America**; extends between Andes and Pac. for 4,160 km to C. Horn, E. to W. 400 km; Atacama desert; Spanish language; Roman Catholic; similar climate to that of Argentina but lacks space for extensive agr.; dairying, sheep, wool; ch. exp. nitrates, copper, iron-ore, coal, iodine, petroleum, paper; cap. Santiago; ch. pt. Valparaiso; earthquake 1960, hgst. recorded magnitude; domestic and foreign protests against human rights abuses of government; a. 738,494 km²; world's lgst. producer of copper; p. (est. 1987) 12·5 m.

Chillán, t., cap. of Nuble prov., Chile; destroyed 1939 by one of world's worst recorded earthquakes; since rebuilt; agr. and comm. ctr.; p. (est. 1985) 125,400.

Chiloé, I. and S. prov., **Chile**; cap. San Carlos, earthquakes 1939 and 1960; ch. pt. Ancud destroyed 1960; heavy rainfall, tropical forest; a. 23,460 km²; p. (1970) 110,728.

Chilpancingo de los Bravos, t., cap. of Guerrero st., **Mexico**; ctr. of pre-Aztec culture; univ.; p. (1970) 56,904.

Chiltern, l. gov. dist., Bucks., **Eng.**; inc. part of C. Hills and Chesham and Amersham; p. (est. 1988) 87,900.

Chiltern Hills, chalk escarpment, Oxon., Bucks., Beds., and Herts., **Eng.**; cut by no. of impt. gaps used by main communications; sheep and barley; hgst. point 276 m nr. Wendover.

Chimborazo, mtn., **Ecuador**; 6,286 m; Andes; extinct volcano, first explored by von Humboldt (1802), first scaled by Whymper (1880).

Chimbote, spt., **Peru**; steel, iron-ore, coal; tinned fish, fish-meal; p. (est. 1985) 255,000.

Chimkent, t., Kazakh SSR, **USSR**; in W. foothills of Tien Shan; nearby oasis fed by Arys R.; major industl. ctr.; lead smelting; p. (est. 1985) 369,000.

China, People's Republic of, Asia; Third lgst. cty. of world; 22 provs., 3 municipalities and 5 autonomous regions; anc. conservative civilisation overthrown by long civil war and establishment of communist régime (1949); lge. p. crowded on cultivable valleys of Hwang-ho (Yellow R.), Yangtze and Si-kiang in E.; rest of cty. either mtnous. (plateau of Tibet) or desert (Sinkiang); rapid economic growth following onset of communist régime; agr. organised on commune basis, becomes increasingly intensive in S. where climate is less extreme, employs 82 per cent of p.; vast mineral resources; esp. iron ore and coal, many underdeveloped; mineral fuels major export; recent industl. growth; heavy inds. at Wuhan, Baotou and in N.E. (Manchuria); special economic zones to attract foreign investment; poor communications except in E.; increasingly self-sufficient in petroleum; 1984 economic reform liberalised state planning system to allow mkt. forces to restructure all but key sectors; consumer goods and services to be expanded; cap. Beijing; 35 m. only children resulting from one-child family birth control policy; a. 9,595,961 km²; p. (est. 1989) 1,112,000,000, lgst. p. of any country.

'na Sea, part of W. Pacific between Korea and 'lippines; divided by the narrow Formosa

Strait into two areas; E. China Sea, inc. Yellow Sea, and S. China Sea.

Chinandega, mkt. t., cap. of C. dep., **Nicaragua**; sugar refining; p. (est. 1985) 68,000.

Chincho. See **Jinzhou**.

Chindwin, R., **Burma**; ch. trib. of Irrawaddy; rises in Patkai Hills, navigable in rainy season; dense p. on lower reaches; 800 km long.

Chinghai. See **Qinghai**.

Chinkiang. See **Zhenjiang**.

Chingola, t., **Zambia**; copper mng.; metal prod., printing; p. (1980) 145,869.

Chinon, t., Indre-et-Loire, central **France**; on R. Vienne, industl.; ruined cas., once a royal residency; nuclear power sta.; p. (1982) 8,873 (t.), 78,131 (met. a.).

Chinqui, volcano, **Panama**; 3,480 m.

Chinwangtao. See **Qinhuangdao**.

Chioggia, spt., cath. t., N. **Italy**; on I. in G. of Venice; fishing; p. (1981) 53,566.

Chios (Khios) I., in Aegean Sea, **Greece**; mainly agr.; wines, fruits and figs; supposed birthplace of Homer; p. (1981) 49,865.

Chippenham, North Wilts., **Eng.**; mkt. t. on R. Avon; rly. signal and brake equipment, bacon curing, tanning; p. (1981) 19,290.

Chipping Campden, v., Gloucs., **Eng.**; in Cotswold Hills; formerly impt. for woollens; tourism.

Chipping Norton, mkt. t., Oxford, **Eng.**; nr. Banbury; formerly impt. for woollens; p. (1981) 5,035.

Chipping Sodbury, mkt. t., Avon. **Eng.**; 13 km N.E. of Bristol.

Chirchik, c., Uzbek SSR, **USSR**; 32 km N.E. Tashkent; engin., chemicals; hydroelec. power stas.; p. (est. 1985) 153,000.

Chiricahua Mtns., Arizona, **USA**; form part of Coronado Nat. Forest; long inhabited by Apache Indians; spectacular volcanic scenery; alt. 2,987 m.

Chirk, t. Clwyd, **Wales**; on R. Cleriog, S. of Wrexham; slate, formerly coal-mng. a.; cas.

Chislehurst. See **Bromley**.

Chistyakovo. See **Torez**.

Chita, c., rly. ctr., Siberia, **RSFSR**; on upper R. Ingoda, 640 km E. of L. Baykal; coal, engin., chemicals, sawmilling; p. (est. 1985) 336,000.

Chittagong, c., **Bangladesh**; main pt. on Karna-fuli R., nr. Bay of Bengal; exp. jute, tea; oil refining; steel mill; hydroelec. power; p. (1981) 1,391,877.

Chittaranjan, t., West Bengal, **India**; new t. on Barakhar R., in steel ctr. of Damodar valley; rly. locomotive wks.; p. (1961) 28,957.

Chkalov. See **Orenburg**.

Choisy-le-Roi, t., Val-de-Marne dep., **France**, industl. sub. of Paris on R. Seine; p. (1982) 35,531.

Cholet, t., Maine-et-Loire, **France**; textile ctr. on R. Seine; p. (1982) 56,528.

Cholon (Cho Lon), t., S. **Vietnam**; 16 km S.W. of Ho Chi-minh City; ctr. of rice tr.; p. inc. Ho Chi-minh City (1968) 1,682,000.

Cholula, anc. c. of Puebla prov., **Mexico**; Aztec temple, pyramid of Cholula, and other remains.

Chomo Lhari, mtn., Tibet, **China** and **Bhutan**; sacred to Buddhists; part of Himalayas; alt. 7,319 m.

Chomutov, t., N. **ČSSR**; industl. ctr. of lignite mng. a.; coal, steel, glass; p. (1984) 57,398.

Chongqing(Chungking), c., S.E. Sichuan prov., **China**; on Chang Jiang; comm. ctr. of W. China chosen 1983 as centre for experimental economic reforms; ctr. of rich agr. dist. of Red Basin of Sichuan; coal, iron and steel, heavy machin.; lorries, vans, chemical fertilisers; textiles; former treaty pt.; p. (1984) 2,733,700.

Chooz, t., Ardennes, **France**; pressurised water reactor; nuclear power sta. linked with Belgian grid.

Cho Oyu, mtn., between **Nepal** and Tibet, **China**; sixth hgst. in world; alt. 8,225 m.

Chorley, t., l. gov. dist., N. Lancs., **Eng.**; on W. flank of Rossendale Fells, 11 km S.E. of Preston; cotton, engin.; expansion as new t. with Leyland p. (est. 1988) 96,700. See **Central Lancashire**.

Chorleywood, t., Three Rivers, Herts., **Eng.**; nr. Watford; p. (1981) 8,415.

Chorrilos Pass, Argentina; in E. cordillera of Andes at alt. 4,470 m; used by rly. from San Miguel de Tucumán to Antofagasta.

Chorzów(Królewska Huta), t., Upper Silesia, **Poland**; coal, iron and steel, chemicals, engin.; p. (est. 1983) 145,100.

Chota Nagpur, plateau, Madhya Pradesh, **India**; produces lac; impt. mng. ctr.; bauxite, mica.

Chou Kou Tien, site nr. Beijing, **China**; discovery of fossil bones of Beijing (Peking) man (*Sinanthropus pekinensis*).

Christchurch, t., l. gov. dist., Dorset, **Eng.**; on S. cst. 8 km E. of Bournemouth; holiday resort, aircraft. lt. inds.; p. (est. 1988) 40,300 (dist.).

Christchurch, c., Canterbury prov., S.I., **N.Z.**; lgst. c. of S.I.; comm. ctr. for lamb, wool, and grain; cath., univ.; airpt; p. (est. 1987) 167,700.

Christianshab, Danish settlement on Disko Bay, **W. Greenland**; meteorological sta.

Christmas I., in Indian Oc., Australian terr. since 1958; a. 140 km², healthy climate, phosphate deposits; p. (est. 1982) 3,000.

Christmas I., lge. coral atoll in Pac. Oc., one of Line Is.; discovered by Cook 1777; a. 135 km²; nuclear test site, 1957–64.

Chu, R. Kazakh SSR, **USSR**; rises in Tien Shan flows N.W. for 800 km into inland drainage basin; Chumysh Dam provides hydroelectricity and water for intensive cultivation of cotton, sugar-beet, citrus fruits.

Chuanchow. *See* **Quauzhu.**

Chubut, R., **Argentina**; drains from Andes into Atl. Oc.; continual irrigation reducing soil fertility of valley; 640 km long.

Chuchow. *See* **Zhuzhou.**

Chudleigh, mkt. t., Devon, **Eng.**; on R. Teign; stone quarrying.

Chu-kiang. *See* **Zhujiang.**

Chukotskiy, peninsula, **USSR**; extreme N.E.; rich gold deposit; hunting.

Chukyo, industl. area, Honshu, **Japan**; centred on Nagoya; textiles, ceramics, chemicals.

Chula Vista, t., Cal., **USA**; agr., aircraft; p. (1980) 83,927.

Chungking *See* **Chongqing.**

Chuquibamba Mtns. (alt. *c.* 6,400 m), **Peru.**

Chuquicamata, t., N. **Chile**; 3,050 m in Andes; lgst copper mine in world; p. (est. 1970) 29,000.

Chur (**Coire**), t., cap. Graubünden, **Switzerland**; in valley of upper Rhine; historic bldgs.; fruit, wine, tourist ctr.; p. (1980) 32,037.

Church, Hyndburn, sub. of Accrington, Lancs., **Eng.**; engin.; p. (1981) 4,332.

Churchill, R., formerly Hamilton R., flows into Hamilton inlet, cst. of Labrador, **Canada**; magnificent waterfall, Churchill Falls with lge. hydroelec. scheme.

Church Stretton, mkt. t., Shrops., **Eng.**; tourism.

Chusan I. *See* **Zhousan.**

Chusovoy, t., **RSFSR**; in Urals; iron and steel; p. (est. 1969) 62,000.

Chuvash ASSR, aut. rep., **RSFSR**; in middle Volga valley; arable agr., lumbering, food processing; a. 18,407 km²; p. (1986) 1,319,000.

Cibao, lowland a., **Dominican Rep.**, Central America; extends along N. side of Cordillera de Cibao for 180 km; 16–56 km wide; early a. of Spanish settlement; E. part called Vega Real; richest agr. a. of Hispaniola; cacao, tobacco, maize; dense p.; ch. t. Santiago.

Cicero, t., Ill., **USA**; adjoins Chicago; electrical appliances, hardware; p. (1980) 61,232.

Ciechanów, t., **Poland**; 78 km N.W. of Warsaw; agr. inds.; p. (1983) 37,600.

Cienaga, spt., N. **Colombia**; p. (est. 1972) 69,100 (t.), 168,100 (met. a.).

Cienfuegos, t., **Cuba**; sugar, tobacco; picturesque; nuclear power sta. proposed, built with Soviet assistance; p. (1985) 124,600.

Cieszyn, t., Katowice prov., **Poland**; part of former Teschen on Polish side of frontier with ČSSR; p. (1970) 25,200.

Cimpina, t., **Romania**, in Walachia; petroleum ctr.; oil pipeline links to Ploiesti and Constanta on Black Sea.

Cincinnati, c. Ohio, **USA**; route and comm. ctr. on terraces of Ohio R.; food processing and many varied inds.; univs.; p. (1984) 370,500 (c.), 1,673,500, (met. a.).

Cinderford, t., Gloucs., **Eng.**; former ctr. of coalmng. a. of Forest of Dean; new lt. industl. estate.

Cinque Ports, confederation of anc. Eng. pts. on cst. of Kent and Sussex; original 5: Sandwich, Dover, Hythe, Romney, Hastings; Winchelsea, and Rye added later. *See* **L23.**

Cirencester, t., Cotswold, Gloucs., **Eng.**; the Roman Corineum; former woollen t.; p. (1981) 15,622.

Ciskei, Bantu Terr. Authority, **S. Africa**; established 1961 between Fish and Kei Rs. on S.E. cst.; indep. (1981) but only recognised by S. Africa; 40 per cent of males work outside Ciskei;

new cap. Bisho (under construction); cap. Zwelitsha; p. (1980) 677,820.

Citta di Castello, walled t., **Italy**; in upper Tiber valley; impt. in Roman times; Renaissance cath., palaces; p. (1981) 37,242.

Citta Vecchia (**Mdina**), c., central **Malta**; former cap.; Roman remains; cath.

Ciudad Bolivar, c., Bolivar st., **Venezuela**; pt. on Orinoco R.; formerly called Angostura; coffee, cattle; ctr. of new industl. development on lower Orinoco; p. (1981) 181,900.

Ciudad Guayana, c., Bolivar st., **Venezuela**; spt. on R. Orinoco; heavy inds. ctr.; p. (1981) 314,000.

Ciudad Juarez, c., **Mexico**; comm. ctr. on USA border; agr. processing; tourism; p. (est. 1986) 750,000.

Ciudad Madero, t., **Mexico**; styrene and detergent plants, oil refining; p. (1979) 141,571.

Cuidad Obregón, t., Sonora, **Mexico**; on Yaqui R.; ctr. of irrigated agr. a.; p. (1979) 181,733.

Ciudad Presidente Stroessner, t., **Paraguay**; rapidly growing t. close to Itaipú Dam on Parana R.; p. (1982) 60,000.

Ciudad Real, t., cap. of Ciudad Real prov., **Spain**; mkt. t. founded 1255; textiles; p. (1987) 55,072.

Ciudad Real, prov., central **Spain**; mostly at 600 m; covering la Mancha dist.; agr.; cap. C.R.; a. 19,741 km²; p. (1987) 485,639.

Ciudad Rodrigo, old fortress t., Salamanca prov., **Spain**; strategic position nr. Portuguese bdy.; in Peninsular War fell to Fr. (1810) and captured by Wellington (1812); p. (1970) 13,320.

Civitavecchia, t., Latium, **Italy**; pt. for Rome on Tyrrhenian cst., 48 km N. of mouth of R. Tiber; p. (1981) 45,836.

Clackmannan, former co., l. gov. dist., Central Reg., **Scot.**; a. 161 km²; p. (est. 1986) 47,586.

Clacton-on-Sea, t., Tendring, Essex, **Eng.**; on E. cst. 19 km S.E. of Colchester; seaside resort; lt. inds.; residtl.; p. (1981) 43,571.

Clairvaux, v., Aube, **France**; Cistercian abbey.

Clamart, t., Hauts-de-Seine, **France**; sub. of S.W. Paris; p. (1982) 48,678.

Clapham, S. London rly. junction; accident 1988.

Clare, co., Munster, **R.o.I.**; cstl. co. bounded in S. and E. by R. Shannon; mainly agr. and tourism; inc. cliffs of Moher; Shannon airpt. and tax-free industl. development scheme; co. t. Ennis; a. 3,351 km²; p. (1981) 27,701.

Clare I., Clew Bay, Mayo, **R.o.I.**

Clarence Strait, between Melville I. and Darwin, N.T., Australia.

Clarksburg, t., W. Va., **USA**; industl. ctr. for coal mng. a., oil and natural gas fields; machin. glass, pottery; p. (1980) 22,371.

Clarksdale, t., Miss., **USA**; processing ctr. for rich farming a.; p. (1980) 21,137.

Clarksville, t., Tenn., **USA**; on Cumberland R.; tobacco mkt.; p. (1984) 58,000 (t.), 152,600 (met. a.).

Clausthal-Zellerfeld, t., Lower Saxony, **W. Germany**; in Harz mtns.; tourism.

Clay Cross, t., Derbys., **Eng.**; former ctr. coal mng. (first developed by George Stephenson 1838) iron, engin.; p. (1981) 9,725.

Clayton-le-Moors, t., Hyndburn, Lancs., **Eng.**; nr. Blackburn; textile machin., cotton and blanket weaving, bristles, soap; p. (1981) 6,309.

Clear C., southernmost point of Ireland, Clear I., **R.o.I.**; off S.W. cst. of Cork.

Cleare, c., Alaska, **USA**; site of ballistic missile early warning sta.

Clearwater, t., Fla., **USA**; citrus fruit, flowers, fish; resort; p. (1980) 85,528.

Cleator Moor, t. Cumbria, **Eng.**; former colly. t.

Cleckheaton t., West Yorks., **Eng.**; nr. Bradford; woollens, blankets, asbestos.

Clee Hills, Shrops., **Eng.**; between Rs. Severn and Teme; alt. 550 m.

Cleethorpes, t., l. gov. dist., Humberside, **Eng.**; 5 km S. of Grimsby; resort; p. (est. 1988) 68,400 (dist.).

Clent Hills, Hereford and Worcs., **Eng.**; about 16 km S.W. of Birmingham, overlooking valley of R. Stour; recreation; maximum alt. 316 m.

Clerkenwell, industl. dist., London, **Eng.**; immediately N. of the City; noted for jewellry.

Clermont-Ferrand, c., cap. Puy-de-Dôme dep. central **France**; in Auvergne; rubber tyres, chemicals, food inds.; Gothic cath.; Romanesque church; p. (1982) 151,092.

Clevedon, t., Woodspring, Avon, **Eng.**; at mouth of R. Severn; seaside resort; quarrying, bricks, footwear; p. (1981) 17,915.

Cleveland, c., Ohio, **USA**; impt. Gr. Ls. pt. handling iron ore and coal which support a major iron and steel ind.; oil refining, food processing, many varied inds.; univ.; p. (1984) 546,500 (c.), 2,788,400 (met. a.).

Cleveland, non-met. co., N.E. **Eng.**; heavy industl. region centred around ts. of Tees estuary; chems., iron and steel mftg.; inc. part of N. York Moors to S.; a. 583 km²; p. (est. 1988) 553,100.

Cleveland Hills, North Yorks./Cleveland, **Eng.**; part of N. York Moors; once mined for iron ore, impt. potash deposit.

Clichy, t., Hauts-de-Seine, **France**; N.W. sub. of Paris; oil refining, aircraft, automobile components; p. (1982) 47,000.

Clifton, sub., Bristol, Avon, **Eng.**; on R. Avon; mineral springs; famous suspension bridge.

Clifton, t., N.J., **USA**; industl. t., nr. Passaic; p. (1980) 74,388.

Clinton, t., Iowa, **USA**; on Mississippi R.; iron and steel, machin.; p. (1980) 32,828.

Clitheroe, t., Ribble Valley, Lancs., **Eng.**; in Ribble valley; mkt. t. for rural a.; limestone quarrying nearby; p. (1981) 13,552.

Clonakilty, t., Cork, **R.o.I.**; nr. Bandon; sm. harbour; agr. prods.; p. (1966) 2,341.

Cloncurry, t., Queensland, **Australia**; rly junction and air terminal in ctr. of copper field; uranium nearby; p. (est. 1984) 3,040.

Clones, mkt. t. on Ulster border, Monaghan, **R.o.I.**; rly. ctr.; p. (1981) 2,384.

Clonmacnoise, v., Offaly, **R.o.I**; ecclesiastical ruins.

Clonmel, t., Tipperary, **R.o.I.**; on R. Suir; agr. ctr.; fairs; cider, footwear; p. (1981) 12,407.

Clovelly, v., Devon, **Eng.**; seaside resort.

Clowne, t., Derbys., **Eng.**; coal mng.

Cluj, c., **Romania**; in Transylvania on Somesul R.; univs., historic bldgs.; industl. ctr.; p. (est. 1984) 299,786.

Clutha R., R. of S.I., **N.Z.**, hydroelec. power; 320 km long.

Clwyd, co. N. **Wales**; inc. most of Denbigh and Flintshire; mtnous. to S.; N. cstl. resorts inc. Colwyn Bay, Prestatyn and Rhyl; sm. coalfield; lgst. t. Wrexham; a. 2,424 km²; p. (est. 1988) 407,000.

Clwyd, R., Clwyd, N. **Wales**; flows into Irish Sea at Rhyl; length 48 km.

Clydach, t., West Glamorgan, **Wales**; on R. Tawe, 8 km N.E. Swansea; steel wks., nickel refineries.

Clyde, R., Strathclyde Reg., S.W. **Scot.**; flows through industl. belt into Firth of C.; Glasgow, Greenock, Clydebank main pts.; hydroelec. stas.; twin-road tunnel under R. in Glasgow (Whiteinch-Linthouse) completed 1963; 170 km long.

Clydebank, t., l. gov. dist., Strathclyde Reg., **Scot.**; on Clyde adjoining Glasgow; tyres, biscuits; p. (est. 1986) 49,204.

Clyde, Firth of, stretches from Dumbarton to Ailsa Craig, **Scot.**; Bute, Arran, Gr. and Little Cumbrae ch. Is.; 102 km long.

Clydesdale, l. gov. dist., Strathclyde Reg., **Scot.**; small dist. formerly known as Lanark; p. (est. 1986) 58,293.

Coachella Valley, arid region, S.E. Cal., **USA**; part of G. of Cal.; dates and citrus fruits under irrigation from Imperial Valley irrigation system.

Coahuila, st., **Mexico**; 3rd st. of Mexico; lies S. of Texas, bordering Rio Grande valley; main coal deposits; mnfs. impt.; irrigated agr.; cap. Saltillo; a. 142,611 km²; p. (1980) 1,558,401.

Coalbrookdale, v., Salop, **Eng.**; old coal and iron mines; home of iron master Abraham Darby. *See* **Bridges, Section L**.

Coalville, t., North West Leics., **Eng.**; nr. Ashby-de-la-Zouch; coal mng., engin., elastic webbing; p. (1981) 30,832.

Coast Range, mtns., **USA**; along Pac. cst.; wooded ranges causing rain shadow to E. valleys; alt. up to 600 m.

Coatbridge, burgh, Strathclyde Reg., **Scot.**, 16 km E. of Glasgow; coal, iron and steel, prefabricated houses, tubes engin.; p. (1981) 50,866.

Coats I., S. of Southampton I. Hudson Bay, **Canada**.

Coatzacoalcos (Puerto Mexico), spt., **Mexico**; G. of Campeche; oil refinery; chemifertilisers; p. (1980) 186,129.

t., Ont., **Canada**; silver, cobalt, arsenic,

nickel; p. (1971) 2,191.

Cobán, t., **Guatemala**, mkt. t.; coffee and Peruvian bark tr.; p. (est. 1983) 43,538.

Cóbh (**Queenstown**), U.D., Cork, **R.o.I.**; spt. on Great I. in Cork Harbour; lge. docks; H.Q. of Royal Cork Yacht Club; seaside resort; p. (1981) 6,587.

Coburg, t., Bavaria, **W. Germany**; old cas.; wickerwork, furniture, metal, machines, toy inds.; p. (est. 1986) 44,400.

Cochabamba, dep., **Bolivia**; E. of Andes; lgst. p. concentration of Bolivia in C. basin; a. 65,496 km²; p. (est. 1982) 908,674.

Cochabamba, c., cap. of C. dep., **Bolivia**; second lgst. c. in rep.; alt. 2,559 m; univ., cath.; oil refining, shoes, rubber tyres, fruit-canning, modern milk plant; hydroelectric power; p. (est. 1982) 281,962.

Cochin, spt., Kerala, **India**; on Malabar cst.; exp. coconut oil, tea; oil refining; silting pt.; p. (1981) 513,249.

Cochin China, region, formerly part of Indo-China; now roughly coincides with S. Vietnam; comprises the Mekong delta. *See* **Vietnam**.

Cockenzie and Port Seton, small burgh, E. Lothian, **Scot.**; two fishing pts. on F. of Forth; p. (1981) 3,756.

Cockermouth, t., Allerdale, Cumbria, **Eng.**; slate, shoe mftg., plywood, concrete prods.; birthplace of Wordsworth; p. (1981) 7,149.

Cockpit Country, upland a., W. **Jamaica**; classic karst landscape forming rugged upland; some cultivation in hollows; a. 500 km²; alt. 300–800 m.

Coco, R., **Honduras** and **Nicaragua**; flows to Caribbean Sea through economically impt. valley; agr., forestry, mng.; potential as routeway; 480 km long.

Cocos or **Keeling Is.**, 27 coral atolls, **Indian Oc.**; since 1955 terr. of Australia purchased by Australia (1978) to ensure democracy; strategic position S.E. of Sri Lanka, radio and cable sta. German cruiser *Emden* destroyed by Australian cruiser *Sydney* on N. Keeling I. in 1914; uninhabited until 1826; developed by Clunies Ross family for coconut prod.; controlled emigration since 1948 to solve problem of overpopulation; voted to integrate with Northern Territory, Australia (1984); a. 13 km²; p. (est. 1980) 1,000.

Coesfeld, t., N. Rhine–Westphalia, **W. Germany**; textiles, machin.; p. (est. 1986) 31,600.

Cognac, t., Charente, **France**; cognac, bottles; p. (1982) 20,995.

Coiba I., off S. cst. of **Panama**.

Coimbatore, t., Tamil Nadu, **India**; commands Palghat Gap; varied inds. benefit from local hydroelec. power; p. (1981) 704,514 (c.), 920.355 (met. a.).

Coimbra, t., **Portugal**; cath. oldest univ. in Portugal; wine-growing; earthenware mfns.; p. (1981) 74,616 (t.), 138,930 (met. a.).

Colchester, t., l. gov. dist., Essex, **Eng.**; pre-Roman t. of Camulodunum on R. Colne; univ.; lt. inds., engin., oyster fisheries; pt.; p. (est. 1988) 150,200 (dist.).

Cold Fell, mtn., Northumberland, **Eng.**; 622 m.

Cold Harbour, v., Va., **USA**; battles between Grant and Lee 1864.

Coldstream, t., Berwick, **Scot.**; on Eng. border; agr. machin., knitwear; p. (1981) 1,649.

Coleraine, t., l. gov. dist., N. **Ireland**; pt. on R. Bann, 6 km from sea; univ.inen, acrilan mftg., distilling; p. (1981) 46,668 (dist.), 15,967 (t.).

Coleshill, t., l. gov. dist., North Warwickshire, **Eng.**; lurgi gasification plant; new colly. 1965.

Colima, mkt. t., **Mexico**; on Colima R. in fertile valley; univ.; agr. processing; p. (est. 1984) 58,000.

Colima, st., **Mexico**; on Pac. cst.; cap. Colima; pt. Manzanillo; cotton, sugar, rice, coffee; a. 5,203 km²; p. (1980) 339,202.

Colima, volcano (48 km N.E. of c.), **Mexico**; alt. 3,869 m.

Coll, I. off cst. of Mull, Argyll and Bute, **Scot.**; agr. lobster fishing; p. (1981) 951.

Collie, t., W. **Australia**; impt. coal deposits supply power for much of W. Australia; p. (1981) 7,667.

Collingwood, t., Ont., **Canada**; on Georgian Bay, L. Huron; shipbldg., steel; p. (1981) 12,064.

Colmar, t., cap. Haut-Rhin dep., **France**; ctr.

of Alsace textile ind.; attractive mediaeval t.; mkt. for vineyards; p. (1982) 63,764.

Colne, t., Pendle, E. Lancs., **Eng.;** cotton mnfs., felts; p. (1981) 18,203.

Colne, R., Eng.; trib. of Thames rising in Chilterns.

Colne Valley, t., West Yorks., **Eng.;** woollens; p. (1981) 21,659.

Cologne (Köln), c., N. Rhine–Westphalia, **W. Germany;** on Rhine at N. end of Rhine gorge; cath., univ.; impt. R. pt., route and comm. ctr., eau-de-Cologne, electro-technical ind., machin., metallurgy, paper, chemicals, cars, oil refining, textiles; p. (est. 1986) 914,300.

Colombes, t., Hauts-de-Seine dep., **France;** mftg. sub. of Paris on R. Seine; p. (1982) 78,783.

Colombia, rep., N.W. **S. America;** cap. Bogotá; Andes contain most of p.; the savannahs (llanos) to S.E. are almost uninhabited; industl. employment growing; increasingly indep. of USA sphere of influence; agr. impt.; coffee, (50 percent of exports), bananas; major oil reserves discovered (1985), some exp.; eruption of Nevado del Ruiz (1985); a. 1,139,592 km²; p. (est. 1987) 29·7 m.

Colombo, c., cap. of **Sri Lanka;** on W. cst.; univ.; impt. pt. (artificial) built by British; exp. tea, rubber, coconuts; p. (est. 1983) 623,000.

Colón, t., **Panama;** at Atl. end of Panama Canal; free tr. zone; comm. and industl. ctr.; oil refining nearby; p. (1980) 59,840.

Colonsay, I., Inner Hebrides, Argyll and Bute, **Scot.;** 13 km long; ecclesiastical antiquities; p. (inc. Jura 1971) 349.

Colorado, st., **USA;** admitted to Union 1876; st. flower Rocky Mtn. Columbine, st. bird Lark Bunting; hgst. st. in USA; in the Rockies extending up to 4,401 m (Mt. Elbert), no land below 1,000 m; drained by headwaters of Rs. Arkansas and Colorado; major stockrearing a.; many valuable minerals esp. uranium, radium and molybdenum; cap. Denver; a. 270,000 km²; p. (1985) 3,231,000.

Colorado, plateau, Arizona, Utah, Col., N.M., **USA;** arid upland with spectacular scenery, inc. Grand Canyon; alt. 1,500–3,300 m.

Colorado, R., Argentina; flows from Andes to Atl. Oc.; limited irrigation in pastoral valley; length 848 km.

Colorado, major R. of W. **USA;** drains 8% of USA; formed by confluence of Green and Grand Rs.; spectacular canyons inc. Grand Canyon; hydroelec. power from many dams inc. Hoover Dam; irrigation supplies intensive horticultural a. in S. section and consequent rapid decrease in volume to a sm. stream in lower course; length 2,320 km.

Colorado, R., rises N.W. Texas, **USA;** flows to G. of Mexico; irrigation and power; 1,552 km long.

Colorado Desert, Cal., **USA;** inc. Imperial Valley, a fertile irrigated a.

Colorado Springs, t., Col., **USA;** 102 km S. Denver; resort; p. (1984) 247,700 (t.), 349,100 (met. a.).

Colton, t., S.E. Cal., **USA;** fruit- and vegetable-canning; mkt. gardening; p. (1980) 15,201.

Columbia, t., Mo., **USA;** W. of St. Louis; st. univ.; flour, lumber; p. (1984) 63,300 (t.), 106,100 (met. a.).

Columbia, t., st. cap. S.C., **USA;** in ctr. of rich farming a.; textiles, clothing; burned down in Civil War 1865; p. (1984) 98,600 (t.), 433,200 (met. a.).

Columbia, District of (D.C.); area on east bank of Potomac R., coterminus with c. of Washington, cap. of **USA;** a. 179 km²; p. (1985) 626,000.

Columbia, R., major R. of western N. **America;** rises in Rocky Mtns., B.C., flows though Washington, USA; power sources, inc. Grand Coulee Dam, Bonneville Dam; deepwater harbour at mouth; length 2,240 km.

Columbus, c., Ga., **USA;** at head of navigation on Chattahoochee R.; industl. and shipping ctr.; textile mills, food-processing; cotton-ginning machin.; p. (1984) 174,800 (c.), 244,500 (met. a.).

Columbus, t., Ind., **USA;** engin.; leather gds.; p. (1980) 30,614.

Columbus, c., st. cap. Ohio, **USA;** rly. ctr.; st. univ.; machin., paper, aircraft machin., chemicals; p. (1984) 566,100 (c.), 1,279,000 (met. a.).

Colwyn Bay, t., Clwyd, N. **Wales;** on cst. 10 km E. of Llandudno; furniture; seaside resort; p. (1981) 26,278; as **Colwyn** forms basis of l. gov. dist. inc. Abergele; p. (est. 1988) 54,800.

Comayagüela, c., former cap. of **Honduras;** twin c. of Tegucigalpa from which it is separated by Choluteca R.; both cs. administered together as Central Dist.

Combe Martin, v., Devon, **Eng.;** 8 km E. of Ilfracombe; seaside resort.

Comber, t., Ards, **N. Ireland;** linen; p. (1981) 7,600.

Como, c., N. **Italy;** at foot of Alps, on L. Como; oranges, olives; textiles; cath.; tourism; p. (1981) 95,571.

Como, L., N. **Italy;** beautiful mtn. scenery, tourism, villas; a. 145 km².

Comodoro Rivadavia, spt., Chubut prov., **Argentina;** on San Jorge G., 880 km S.W. of Bahia Blanca; military zone; univ.; ch. source of oil in Argentine; oil refining; p. (1980) 96,865.

Comorin, C., most S. point of **India.**

Comoro Is., arch., **Indian Oc.;** in Moçambique channel, midway between African and Madagascar; cap. Moroni; total a. 2,170 km²; turtle fishing; vanilla, copra, sisal, timber, perfume plants; indep. from France declared 1975 but rejected by Mayotte Is. whose future is still undecided; p. (est. 1987) 422,500.

Compiègne, t., Oise, **France;** sugar mills, rope; Armistice signed between Allies and Germany 1918; Fr. surrendered to Hitler 1940; resort; p. (1982) 62,778 (met. a.).

Compton, t., Cal., **USA;** residtl. for Los Angeles; heavy engin., glass, oil refining; p. (1980) 81,286.

Conakry, c., cap. of **Rep. of Guinea;** impt. pt. on offshore islet; exp. iron-ore and alumina; experimental fruit gardens; p. (est. 1983) 705,280.

Concarneau, pt., Finistère, **France;** 19 km S.E. Quimper; fisheries; p. (1982) 18,225.

Concepción, c., prov. cap., **Chile;** shipping ctr. through its pt. Talcahuano; univ.; comm. and cultural t.; severe earthquakes 1939 and 1960; nr. to coalfield; p. (est. 1985) 278,400.

Concepción, prov., **Chile;** cap. C.; Lota-Coronel coalfield lgst. in Chile; a. 5,701 km²; p. (1970) 638,118.

Concepción, t., cap. of C. prov., **Paraguay;** main comm. ctr. for Chaco, pt. on R. Paraguay; p. (1982) 22,866.

Conchos, R., Chihuahua prov., **Mexico;** flows N.E. from Madre Occidental to Rio Grande; cotton under irrigation in upper valley; hydro-elec. power; length 560 km.

Concord, t., Cal., **USA;** residtl. and comm. ctr. in San Francisco met. a.; rapid p. growth; p. (1984) 103,800.

Concord, t., Mass., **USA;** literary ctr.; textiles; p. (1980) 16,293.

Concord, t., st. cap., N.H., **USA;** on Merrimack R.; granite, machin., textiles; p. (1980) 30,400.

Concordia, t., **Argentina;** pt. on Uruguay R.; exp. agr. prod.; p. (1980) 93,618.

Condamine, R., Queensland, **Australia;** trib. of R. Darling; used for irrigation.

Coney I., t., N.Y., **USA;** on Long I., 8 km long, comprises Manhattan Beach, Brighton Beach, W. Brighton, and W. End; seaside resort.

Congleton, t., l. gov. dist., E. Cheshire, **Eng.;** on S.W. margin of Pennines; clothing, textiles; once impt. for silk; p. (est. 1988) 86,600.

Congo, People's Rep. of the, indep. st. within Fr. Community. Equatorial Africa; cap. Brazzaville; agr. and forestry; hardwoods; economy heavily dependent on petroleum; economy hit by fall in world oil prices; a. 342,000 km²; p. (est. 1987) 2,180,000.

Congolese Republic. *See* **Zaïre.**

Congo R. *See* **Zaïre R.**

Conisborough, t., South Yorks., **Eng.;** limestone, bricks, tiles; p. (1981) 16,114.

Coniston, t., Ont., **Canada;** on rly. 13 km E. of Sudbury; nickel smelting; t. built by and for nickel-mng. company.

Coniston Water, L., Cumbria, **Eng.;** focus of tourism in L. Dist.; 8·8 km long.

Conjeeveram. *See* **Kanchipuram.**

Connacht, prov., **R.o.I.;** inc. Galway, Mayo, Sligo, Leitrim, Roscommon; mtnous in W.; farming, fishing; a. 17,775 km²; p. (1981) 106,553.

Connah's Quay, t., Alyn and Deeside, Clwyd, **Wales;** p. (1981) 14,801.

Connaught Tunnel (Can. Pac. Rly.), B.C., **Canada;**

longest in N. America (8 km) 1,500 m under mt. Sir Donald (Selkirk Mtns.).

Connecticut, R., New Eng.; **USA**; middle course forms fine agr. land; investment in navigation, irrigation and flood control; 566 km long.

Connecticut, st., New England, **USA**; one of original 13 sts.; admitted to Union 1788; st. flower mountain Laurel, st. bird robin; humid climate; arable agr.; diversified inds.; many natural harbours on cst.; cap. Hartford; lgst. c. Bridgeport; a. 12,973 km²; p. (1985) 3,174,000.

Connemara, mtns., dist., **R.o.I.**; Co. Galway; many lakes and bogs; tourist resort.

Consett, t., Derwentside, Durham, **Eng.**; on edge of Pennines, 16 km S.W. Newcastle; iron, steel closed (1980), coal mng.; p. (1981) 33,433.

Constance (Konstanz), c., Baden–Württemberg, **W. Germany**; on Bodensee; cath.; textiles, machin., chemicals, elec. inds.; route ctr.; tourism; p. (est. 1983) 69,100.

Constance, L. See **Bodensee**.

Constanţa, ch. spt. S.E. **Romania**; on Black Sea; oil pipeline to Ploiesti and Cimpina; new Danube-Black Sea canal (1984) shortens route of Trans-European waterway to Black Sea; exp. petroleum, wheat; cement, chemicals, machin.; p. (est. 1984) 318,799.

Constantine, c., N.E. **Algeria**; stands 650 m high on gorge of Rhumel R.; planned textile and engin. wks.; p. (est. 1983) 449,000.

Constantinople. See **Istanbul**.

Conwy (Conway), Aberconwy, Gwynedd, spt., N. **Wales**; mediaeval walled t.; at mouth of R. Conway; sm. seaside resort; cas.; quarrying, lt. engin.; p. (1981) 12,969.

Cook, mtn., alt. 3,764 m; hgst. point in S. Alps. and **N.Z.**; 3 peaks.

Cook Inlet, S. cst. Alaska, **USA**; oil pipeline connects oilfields of Granite Point with marine terminal at Dritt R.

Cook Is., Brit. gr. (Rarotonga, lgst.) in **S. Pac.**, annexed to N.Z., 1901; internal self-govt. 1965; bananas, oranges, copra; a. 241 km²; p. (est. 1985) 18,000.

Cookstown, mkt. t., l. gov. dist., **N. Ireland**; cement wks.; p. (1981) 26,402 (dist.), 7,649 (t.).

Cook Strait, channel between N. and S. Is. of **N.Z.**; 24–29 km wide; undersea cable completed 1965.

Cooma, t., N.S.W., **Australia**; mkt. t.; tourist ctr. for Kosciusko Nat. Park; H.Q. of Snowy Mts. Authority; p. (1981) 7,978.

Coonoor, t., Tamil Nadu, **India**; in Nilgiri Hills; sanatorium c. 1,800 m a.s.l.; p. (1981) 44,750.

Cooper Creek (Barcoo), intermittent R., central **Australia**; rises in Warrego Range, Gr. Dividing Range, flows S.W. into marshes of L. Eyre; provides water for livestock in semi-arid region; 1,408 km long.

Copeland, l. gov. dist., Cumbria, **Eng.**; cstl. a. N. of Barrow and inc. Whitehaven and Millom; p. (est. 1988) 71,600.

Copenhagen (København), ch. spt., cap. of **Denmark**; on E. cst. of Sjaelland I.; royal palace, univ., library; naval sta.; freeport; steel, metal, textiles, clothing, breweries; airpt.; p. (est. 1987) 622,275 (c.), 1,346,666 (met. a.).

Copiapó, t., cap. of Atacama prov., **Chile**; copper- and iron-mng. ctr.; p. (1982) 65,001.

Coquet, R., Northumberland, **Eng.**; rises in the Cheviots and flows into North Sea.

Coquimbo, spt., **Chile**; exp. iron. copper, and manganese ores; p. (1983) 73,600.

Coral Sea, Pac Oc., extends from the New Hebrides to Australia.

Coral Sea Islands Territory, Fed. terr., **Australia**; scattered Is., E. of Gr. Barrier Reef, off Queensland cst.; possibility of oil exploration.

Corbeil-Essonnes, t., Essonne, **France**; on R. Seine, 19 km S.E. of Paris; flour mills, printing, paper; p. (1982) 38,081.

Corbridge, t., Northumberland, **Eng.**; on R. Tyne, nr. Hexham; 17th cent. bridge; Roman t. nearby.

Corby, t., l. gov. dist., Northants., **Eng.**; 11 km N. of Kettering; new t.; steel wks., now mostly closed down, shoes, clothing, lamps; p. (est. 1988) 51,000 (dist.).

Córdoba, c., central **Argentina**; univ.; cultural and comm. ctr.; exp. wheat, cattle, lumber; health resort; local hydroelec. power from La Vina; p. (1980) 971,000 (c.), 984,000 (met. a.).

·doba, t., Veracruz, **Mexico**; mkt. t. in ˙ee- growing a.; p. (1980) 126,179.

·, prov., Andalusia, **Spain**; cap. Córdoba;

olives, vines, livestock; a. 13,724 km²; p. (1987) 753,102.

Córdoba, c., Andalusia, **Spain**; cap. of C. prov., on Guadalquivir R.; cath. originally built as a mosque in 8th cent.; tourist ctr.; p. (1987) 298,372.

Corfu (Kérkira), most N. of Ionian Is., **Greece**; traversed by mtns. but largely lowland producing olive oil, figs, wine, oranges; a. 637 km²; p. (1981) 99,477 (prov.).

Corinth (Kórinthos), t., cap. Corinthia prov., **Greece**; at end of Isthmus of C.; occupies site 5 km from anc. classic c. destroyed by earthquake 1858; raisins, wine; p. (1981) 22,658.

Corinth Canal, ship canal, S. **Greece**; traverses Isthmus of Corinth, links G. of Corinth and Ionian Sea with Saronic G. and Aegean Sea; opened 1893; length 5·6 km, depth 8 m.

Corinth, Isthmus of, connects the Peloponnesus with the mainland of **Greece**; cut across by canal.

Corinto, ch. spt., N.W. **Nicaragua**; handles 50 per cent of cty's tr.; exp. hides, sugar, coffee; p. (est. 1985) 24,000.

Cork, c., **R.o.I.**; lgst. and most S.; mtns.; dairying, brewing, agr., fisheries; cap. Cork; a. 7,485 km²; p. (1981) 136,344.

Cork, spt., C.B., Cork, **R.o.I.**; at mouth of R. Lee; cath., univ.; woollens, butter, cattle, brewing, cars, rubber; p. (1981) 91,323.

Corner Brook, c., W. Newfoundland, **Canada**; gd. harbour; iron foundries, cement, gypsum; one of world's lgst. newsprint mills; p. (1981) 24,340.

Cornwall, t., Ont., **Canada**; on St. Lawrence R.; H.Q. of Seaway Authority; textiles, pulp, paper, flour; p. (1981) 46,144.

Cornwall and Isles of Scilly, non-met. co., S.W. **Eng.**; penin. bordering Atl. Oc. and Eng. Channel; granite moorlands supply kaolin; tin mines due to close (1986); mild maritime climate encourages tourism, dairying, and mkt. gardening; many small fishing vs.; co. t. Bodmin; a. 3,515 km²; p. (est. 1988) 460,600.

Cornwall, North, l. gov. dist., **Eng.**; lge. a. on N. cst. stretching from Bodmin to Bude; p. (est. 1988) 71,600.

Coro, c., Falcón, **Venezuela**; on Paraguaná penin.; agr. processing; nearby oil refineries; p. (est. 1980) 71,000.

Corocoro, t., La Paz dep., **Bolivia**; at alt. c. 4,000 m in central Andes, 80 km S. of La Paz; impt. copper-mng. ctr.

Coromandel Coast (Carnatic region), cst. of Tamil Nadu, **India**; where earliest European settlements established; extensive a. of flat land built up by R. Cauvery.

Coronation Gulf, arm of Beaufort Sea; extreme point N. Canadian mainland; discovered by Franklin.

Coronel, spt., **Chile**; coal mng., pt. inds.; p. (1982) 49,257.

Coronel Oviedo, t., **Paraguay**; comm. ctr.; p. (1982) 21,782.

Corpus Christi, c., Texas, **USA**; cotton, oil refining, chemicals; resort; p. (1984) 258,100 (c.), 361,300 (met. a.).

Corréze, dep., S. central **France**; part of Massif Central, mostly over 600 m; sparse p. based on livestock agr. and forestry; cap. Tulle; a. 5,884 km²; p. (1982) 239,000.

Corrib, Lough, Galway and Mayo, **R.o.I.**; drained by Corrib R. into Galway Bay; impt. brown trout fishery; a. 176 km².

Corrientes, t., Argentina; agr. tr. ctr. on Paraná R.; univ.; cattle, sugar, rice, cotton; river navigation reduces isolation; p. (1980) 181,000.

Corryvreckan, strait and whirlpool between Jura and Scarba Is., Inner Hebrides, **Scot.**; whirlpool caused by tidal movement over variable sea bed.

Corse du Sud. See Corsica.

Corsica (Corse), I., **France**; in Mediterranean Sea; violent history in 16th and 17th cent.; high granite peaks (Monte Cinto), mtn. torrents, fertile plains; inland and sea fishing; rapid growth of tourism with little benefit to indigenous Corsicans; split into 2 deps. to help overcome autonomist agitation (1975); Haute Corse, cap. Bastia (1982) 127,200, Corse du Sud, cap. Ajaccio (1982) 102,800; a. 8,721 km²; p. (1982) 230,000.

Corsicana, t., Texas, **USA**; site of first oil drilling in USA; p. (1980) 21,712.

Cortona, t., Tuscany, Italy; nr. Perugia; Roman remains, cath.; p. (1981) 22,281.

Corumbá, pt., Mato Grosso, Brazil; on R. Paraguay; exp. agr. products; mkt. t.; p. (est. 1970) 39,000.

Corunna. See La Coruña.

Corvallis, t., Ore., USA; in fertile farming valley; lumbering; univ.; p. (1980) 40,960.

Coryton, t., Essex, Eng.; on Thames, oil refining; oil pipeline to Stanlow refinery.

Cos (Kos), I., Dodecanese, Greece; in Aegean Sea, second lgst. of gr.; gave name to Cos lettuce; birthplace of Hippocrates; p. (1981) 20,350.

Cosenza, c., S. Italy; ctr. for figs, oranges, olive oil, wine; cath., univ., cas.; p. (1984) 106,376.

Costa Brava, region, Catalonia, Spain; tourism.

Costa del Sol, region, Málaga cst., Spain; tourism.

Costa Rica, rep. Central America; over half p. in equable Meseta Central; cap. San José; forests, volcanic mtns.; agr. 40 per cent G.N.P.; coffee, bananas, cacao; high literacy and living standards; a. 50,909 km²; p. (1985) 2,655,000.

Côte d'Azur, France; Mediterranean littoral E. of Rhône R.; inc. resorts of Nice, Cannes, Monte Carlo, and St. Tropez.

Côte d'Ivoire (Ivory Coast), rep., on G. of Guinea, W. Africa; formerly a Fr. overseas terr.; hot, humid climate; coastal lagoons, interior plateau (300–1,200 m); economy based on subsistence agr. although an impt. coffee and timber producer; world's third lgst. coffee producer; half p. relies on coffee as principle source of income; underdeveloped mineral resources; poorly developed rail network but extensive road system; new pt. at San Pedro; Pt. Bouet outport of former cap. Abidjan; new cap. Yamoussoukro (1983); a. 322,481 km²; p. (est. 1987) 11·1 m.

Côte d'Or, dep., E. France; heart of anc. Burgundy, traversed by R. Saône; cap. Dijon; wines, livestock, iron and steel; a. 8,783 km²; p. (1982) 473,200.

Cotentin, peninsula, N. France; 80 km long; Cherbourg, at its extremity, 128 km from Portsmouth.

Côtes-du-Nord, dep., N. Brittany, France; rugged cst. and Is. and mild climate encourage tourism; mkt. gardens along cst.; many fishing ts.; cap. St. Brieuc; a. 7,218 km²; p. (1982) 539,100.

Cotonou, pt., Benin Rep.; new artificial pt.; fishing; lt. inds.; offshore oilfields (drilling from 1982); p. (est. 1982) 487,020.

Cotopaxi, volcano, (alt. 5,982 m) in the Andes of Ecuador, nr. Quito; loftiest active volcano in the world; recent eruptions have caused great damage to Ecuador.

Cotswold, l. gov. dist., Gloucs., Eng.; lge a. covering C. Hills and inc. Cirencester and Northleach; p. (est. 1988) 75,100.

Cotswold Hills, W. Eng.; limestone escarpment; Gloucs., Oxon.; once famous for woollens; source of Thames and tribs.; highest point Cleeve Cloud, 309 m; tourism.

Cottbus or Kottbus, E. Germany; on R. Spree; rly. ctr.; textile and metal mnfs.; p. (est. 1986) 126,000.

Cottian Alps, mtn. range on border of France and Italy crossed by Hannibal; craggy; max. alt. 2,844 m (Monte Viso).

Coulsdon and Purley. See Croydon.

Council Bluffs, t., Iowa, USA; on Missouri R. nr. Omaha; rly. ctr.; farm implements, paper, machin.; p. (1980) 56,449.

Courantyne, R., Guyana; rises in Serra Acari; passes through bauxite mng. region to Atl. Oc.; navigation in lower course; 720 km long.

Courtrai. See Kortrijk.

Cove and Kilcreggan, burgh, Dumbarton, Scot.; at junc. of Loch Long and R. Clyde; p. (1981) 1,218.

Coventry, c., met. dist., West Midlands, Eng.; 29 km E.S.E. of Birmingham; former ctr. of cycle, motor-cycle, motor-car and aircraft engines, tractors, engin.; tools; chemicals; projectiles, textiles; cath.; univ.; p. (est. 1988) 306,200.

Covilhã, t., Portugal; cloth factories; p. (1981) 21,807 (c.), 60,945 (met. a.).

Covington, t., Ky., USA; on R. Ohio, opp. Cincinnati; machin., leather, furniture; p. (1980) 60,065.

Cowbridge, t., Vale of Glamorgan, South Glamorgan, S. Wales; nr. Cardiff; p. (1981) 1,224.

Cowdenbeath, burgh, Dunfermline, Scot.; 8 km N.E. of Dunfermline; coal; p. (1981) 12,235.

Cowes, resort and pt., Medina, I. of Wight, Eng.;

on estuary of R. Medina; regattas and yacht bldg.; hovercraft; p. (1981) 19,663.

Cowra, t., N.S.W., Australia; famous wheat dist. and site of state experimental farm; p. (1981) 7,900.

Cozumel I., E. of Yucatan peninsula, Mexico.

Cracòw. See Kraków.

Cradle, Mt., mtn., Tasmania, Australia; alt. 1,546 m; Nat. Park.

Cradock, t., Cape Prov., S. Africa; wool tr.; p. (est. 1967) 21,300.

Craigavon, c., l. gov. dist., N. Ireland; new "city in a garden" under construction, 16 km long, merging Portadown and Lurgan, linked by motorway, to provide major base for ind.; p. (1981) 71,416 (dist.), 10,195 (c.).

Crail, royal burgh, North East Fife, Scot.; cstl. resort; p. (1981) 1,158.

Craiova, c., S. Romania, in Wallachia; tr. ctr.; agr. processing, textiles, engin., chemicals; p. (est. 1984) 267,474.

Cramlington, t., Northumberland, Eng.; 13 km N. of Newcastle; new t.; p. (1981) 25,225.

Cranborne Chase, Wilts., Eng.; chalk upland of over 275 m; extension of Salisbury Plain.

Cranbrook, mkt. t., Kent, Eng.; hops and grain; former weaving t.; p. (1971) 16,022 (dist.).

Cranston, t., R.I., USA; machin., chemicals, textiles; p. (1980) 71,992.

Crater L., Ore., USA; in Nat. Park, is a body of water 600 m deep and 10 m across, set in a crater of an extinct volcano, c. 2,400 m high; varied flora and fauna on shore.

Craters of the Moon, dist., Idaho, USA; Nat. Monument of volcanic craters and cones; a. 192 km².

Crato, t., Ceara st., Brazil; ctr. of irrigated area producing cotton, sugar, rice; p. (1960) 27,649.

Crau, La, region, Bouches-du-Rhône dep., S.E. France; dry, pebbly area E. of Rhône delta; winter pasture for sheep.

Craven, dist., central Pennines, Eng.; relatively low limestone plateau, alt. mainly below 240 m; drained by R. Ribble to S.W., R. Aire to S.E.; sheep rearing in valleys, cattle for fattening, root and fodder crops; now forms l. gov. dist. based on Skipton and Settle; p. (est. 1988) 49,500.

Crawley, t., l. gov. dist., West Sussex, Eng.; on N.W. flank of Weald, 14 km S. of Reigate; new t. (1947); engin., pharmaceuticals, metal, leather, wooden gds.; p. (est. 1988) 84,300 (dist.).

Crayford. See Bexley.

Creag Meagaidh, mtn., Lochaber, Scot.; alt. 1,128 m.

Crediton, mkt. t., Devon, Eng.; p. (1981) 6,169.

Cree, R., Wigtown, Scot.; flows into Wigtown Bay.

Crema, industl. and agr. t., N. Italy; S.E. of Milan; cath.; p. (1981) 34,610.

Cremona, t., cap. of C. prov., Lombardy, N. Italy; famed as a ctr. of learning and later for mnf. of violins and violas; revived in last 20 years; birthplace of Stradivari; cath.; pt. on new Milan-Adriatic Waterway; p. (1981) 80,929.

Crete (Kriti), I., E. Mediterranean, lgst. I. of Greece; cradle of Minoan civilisation between 1600 and 1400 B.C.; mild climate; sm. a. of cultivable land; few minerals; part of Greece since Balkan Wars (1913); cap. Iraklion; birthplace of El Greco; a. 8,379 km²; p. (1981) 502,165 (admin. reg.).

Creus, c., juts out into Mediterranean Sea, Spain; nr. Fr. border.

Creuse, dep., in Massif Central, France; soil infertile, harsh climate, limited agr.; a. 5,605 km² p. (1982) 138,500.

Crewe, t., Cheshire, Eng.; 32 km S.E. of Chester; lge. rly. wks.; impt. rly. junc.; aircraft and refrigerator wks.; clothing, engin., motor vehicles; expanded t.; with Nantwich forms l. gov. dist.; p. (est. 1988) 96,800.

Crewkerne, mkt. t., Somerset, Eng.; 13 km S.W. of Yeovil; leather gds.; grammar school (1499); p. (1981) 5,330.

Criccieth, t., Dwyfor, Gwynedd, N. Wales; on N. shore of Cardigan Bay; seaside resort; p. (1981) 1,570.

Cricklade, t., N. Wilts., Eng.; on R. Thames, 13 km N.W. of Swindon; fortified township in Saxon times; p. (1971) 22,368 (dist.).

Crieff, t., Perth and Kinross, Scot.; on R. Earn; summer resort; p. (1981) 5,442.

Crimea (Krym) Peninsula, juts into Black Sea, Ukrainian SSR, USSR; wheat, tobacco, fruit; campaign 1854–55 between Russia and Allied

Forces of Turkey, Britain, France, and Sardinia was chiefly fought out here (Alma, Balaclava, and Sevastopol); tourism.

Crimmitschau, t., Karl-Marx-Stadt, **E. Germany**; nr. Zwickau; impt. textile ctr.; p. (est. 1970) 29,932.

Crinan Canal, across peninsula of Argyll and Bute, S.W. **Scot.**; connects Loch Gilp with Atl. Oc.; 14 km long.

Cristóbal, dist., **Panama Canal Zone**; adjoins Colon at N. entrance to Canal; p. (1970) 11,600.

Croaghpatrick, mtns., May, **R.o.I.**; 766 m.

Croatia, constituent rep., **Yugoslavia**; stretches from Istria on Adriatic cst. to Dinaric Alps; crossed by Drava and Sava Rs.; traditional agr. being replaced by new inds.; impt. aluminium wks. based on local bauxite; chemicals, shipbldg.; new oilfields supply 70 per cent of Yugoslavia's needs; cap. Zagreb; a. 56,524 km²; p. (1981) 4,601,469.

Crocodile R. See Limpopo.

Cromarty, burgh, Ross and Cromarty, **Scot.**; N.E. cst. of Black Isle; offshore oil platforms at Nigg, C.Firth; p. (1981) 685.

Cromer, t., North Norfolk, **Eng.**; on N. cst. of E. Anglia; seaside resort; p. (1981) 6,192.

Cromford, v., Derbys., **Eng.**; Richard Arkwright's first waterpowered mill (1771); cotton.

Crompton, t., Gtr. Manchester, **Eng.**; 3 km S. of Rochdale; cotton, engin., elec. lamps; p. (1981) 19,938.

Crook and Willington, ts., former U.D., Wear Valley, Durham, **Eng.**; varied inds. to replace coal mng.; p. (1981) 21,619.

Crosby, t., Sefton, Merseyside, **Eng.**; on Liverpool Bay 5 km N. of Bootle, Seaforth container pt.; residtl.; seaside resort; p. (1981) 53,660.

Cross, R., S.E. **Nigeria**; rises in Cameroon Highlands, flows W. and S. into G. of Guinea at Calabar; useful inland waterway; 640 km long.

Cross Fell, mtn., Cumbria, **Eng.**; on E. border of co.; alt. 894 m; highest point of the Pennines.

Crotone, t., S. **Italy**; pt. on E. cst. Calabria; electro-chemicals and metallurgical inds.; on site of anc. Crotona founded as Greek col.; home of Pythagoras; p. (1981) 58,281.

Crowland, t., Lincs., **Eng.**; mkt. t. in the Fens, on R. Welland; 8th-cent. abbey ruins.

Crows Nest Pass, B.C., Alberta, **Canada**; southernmost pass across Canadian Rocky Mtns.; used by rly. from Medicine Hat to Syokane (USA); summit 1,360 m.

Croydon, residtl. t., **Eng.**; now outer bor. Greater London; inc. Coulsdon and Purley; lt. inds.; major office ctr.; p. (est. 1988) 317,200.

Crummock Water, L. Dist., Cumbria, **Eng.**; ribbon L.

Csepel, sub., Budapest, **Hungary**; iron and steel, oil refining, leather, paper; p. incorporated with Budapest 1950.

Csongrad, mkt. t., agr. dist., **Hungary**; at junc. of Rs. Tisza and Körös; p. (est. 1984) 22,000.

Cuba, I., indep. rep., **W.I.**; cap. Havana; lies within tropics; highly fertile although half land a. is mtnous.; exp. sugar, nickel, tobacco, rum, citrus fruits; revolution (1959) reoriented economic and political connections away from USA towards USSR; excellent health care and education; 88 per cent of cultivated land in state farms or cooperatives; recent attempts to diversify economy but sugar still 75 per cent of exp; a. 114,494 km²; p. (est. 1986) 10,119,500.

Cubatão, t., **Brazil**; N.E. of Santos; rapidly growing t. from industl. expansion; hydro-electric, oil refinery, petro-chems., new integrated steel wks. to aid vehicle ind. of São Paulo; p. (est. 1980) 66,000.

Cuckfield, mkt. t., Mid Sussex, West Sussex, **Eng.**; p. (1981) 28,254.

Cuckmere, R., Sussex, **Eng.**; passes through S. Downs in beautiful gap; length 37 km.

Cúcuta, t., cap. of Norte de Santander, **Colombia**; close to Venezuelan border; nr. oilfield; destroyed by earthquake, 1875; new planned t.; p. (1985) 407,236.

Cuddalore, spt., Tamil Nadu, **India**; nr. Pondicherry; exp. oilseeds, cottons; p. (1981) 127,625.

Cuddapah, t., Andhra Pradesh, **India**; cotton, cloth factories, millet, rice; p. (1981) 103,125.

Cudworth, South Yorks., **Eng.**; p. (1981) 9,361.

Cuenca, t., cap. of Azuay prov., 3rd. c. of **Ecuador**; in fertile agr. basin of Andes; sugar, tyres, flour mills, Panama hats; p. (est. 1984) 176,900.

┄ca, agr. and mng. prov., central **Spain**; furniture, ┄er, paper; a. 17,063 km²; p. (1987) 213,812.

┄t., cap of C. prov., **Spain**; on gorge above

R. Júcar; mkt. t.; famed in mediaeval times for silver and cloth mnfs.; p. (1987) 41,407.

Cuernavaca, t., cap. of Morelos st., central **Mexico**; anc. Indian t. captured by Cortes; tourist resort; univ.; p. (1980) 232,355.

Cuiabá, t., cap. of Mato Grosso st., **Brazil**; ctr. pastoral a.; gold and diamonds produced; galena deposit nearby; p. (est. 1985) 283,100.

Cuillin Hills, mtns., I. of Skye, **Scot.**; attaining 992 m in Sgurr Alasdair.

Culiacán, c., of Sinaloa, N.W. **Mexico**; anc. c.; Pacific pt. Altata; p. (1980) 560,011.

Culloden Moor, 10 km E. of Inverness, **Scot.**; defeat of Prince Charles Edward Stuart's highlanders by Duke of Cumberland's forces (1746).

Culross, royal burgh, Dunfermline, **Scot.**; belongs to Nat. Trust.; abbey; p. (1971) 523.

Culver City, t., Cal., **USA**; sub. of Los Angeles; lge. motion-picture plant; electronic equipment, machin., chemicals, tools; p. (1980) 38,139.

Cumaná, c., N.E. **Venezuela**; pt. on Caribbean; European settlement since 1510; exp. coffee, cacao; sardine canning; airpt.; p. (1981) 191,900.

Cumaná, G., N. cst., **Venezuela**.

Cumberland, former co., **Eng.**; now part of Cumbria non-met. co.

Cumberland, industl. t., Md., **USA**; on Potomac R.; iron and steel, tyres, glassware; p. (1984) 24,100 (t.), 104,500 (met. a.).

Cumberland Gap, Ky., **USA**; ch. break in high E. wall of Cumberland plateau; gives access from upper Tennessee valley to Cumberland and Ohio valleys; impt. routeway in colonisation of Ky.

Cumberland Is., off cst. of Queensland, **Australia**.

Cumberland Plateau, mtn. region, Ky., Tenn., Ala., **USA**; forms S.W. zone of Appalachian mtn. system terminating abruptly towards Tennessee valley to E., Cumberland valley to W.; drained W. by tribs. of Cumberland and Ohio Rs; composed of horizontal sandstones overlying coal; thinly populated by backward farming communities except where mng. ts. occur in valleys cut down to coal; mainly between 360–900 m.

Cumberland R., Tenn. and Ky., **USA**; trib. of Ohio R., rises in C. plateau; upper course forested; crosses coal-mng. a. and fertile agr. valley; part of Tenn. Valley Authority scheme; hydroelec. power; 1,104 km long.

Cumbernauld, new t. (1955), Strathclyde Reg., **Scot.**; to house 50,000 overspill from Glasgow; mnfs. of adding machines rapidly decl. with use of computers; p. (1981) 48,207; with Kilsyth forms larger l. gov. dist.; p. (est. 1986) 62,503.

Cumbrae, Gt. and Little, Is., in F. of Clyde, off cst. of Cunninghame, **Scot.**

Cumbria, non-met. co., N.W. **Eng.**; centred on L. Dist. where rugged glaciated scenery encourages tourism, sheep-farming, forestry and water storage; Cumberland coalfield on W. cst. where declining heavy inds. being replaced by new lt. inds.; major ts. Carlisle and Barrow; a. 6,809 km²; p. (est. 1988) 489,200.

Cumbrian Mtns., L. Dist., Cumbria, **Eng.**

Cumnock and Doone Valley, l. gov. dist., Strathclyde Reg., **Scot.**, hilly dist. S. of Glasgow; p. (est. 1986) 43,528.

Cundinamarca, dep., **Colombia**; contains many Andean Ls. and the fed. cap Bogotá; a. 23,585 km²; p. (1985) 1,358,978 (excluding Bogota).

Cunene. See Kunene R.

Cuneo, prov., **Italy**; a. 7,433 km²; p. (1981) 548,452.

Cuneo, t., cap. of C. prov., Piedmont, **Italy**; mkt. for prod. of surrounding a.; withstood many sieges under the rule of house of Savoy; p. (1981) 55,875.

Cunninghame, l. gov. dist., Strathclyde Reg., **Scot.**; borders F. of Clyde and inc. I. of Arran; p. (est. 1986) 137,147.

Cupar, royal burgh, North East Fife, **Scot.**; on R. Eden, W. of St. Andrews; linen; sugar-beet; p. (1981) 6,642.

Curaçao, I. (**Neth. Antilles**), off N. cst. **Venezuela**; major ctr. for refining and trans-shipping Venezuelan oil; threatened closure (1985) offset for 5 years to avoid economic collapse (provides 25 percent of C. income); picturesque Dutch archi-tecture in cap. Willemstad; a. 544 km²; p. (1981) 147,388.

Curepipe, t., central **Mauritius**; health resort; p. (1983) 57,613.

Curicó, t., **Chile**; agr. and comm. ctr.; earthquake 1928; p. (1982) 51,743.

Curitiba, c., cap. of Paraná st., **Brazil**; univ.; industl. and comm. ctr. at c. 900 m; coffee, maté, chemicals, pharmaceutical and forest prods., foodstuffs; p. (est. 1985) 1,285,000.

Curragh, plain, Kildare, **R.o.I.**; turf; racecourse.

Curtis I., Queensland, **Australia**; low volcanic I.; wooded; cattle.

Curzola. See **Korčula**.

Cuttack, t., Orissa st., **India**; on Mahanadi R.; long famous for gold and silver filigree work; p. (1981) 269,950 (t.), 327,412 (met. a.).

Cuxhaven, spt., Lower Saxony, **W. Germany**; outport of Hamburg at the mouth of R. Elbe; fine harbour; p. (est. 1986) 56,100.

Cuyahoga Falls, t., Ohio, **USA**; industl. and residtl.; p. (1980) 43,890.

Cuzco, dep., **Peru**; inc. Central Cordilleras, reaching c. 5,800 m; tropical climate; agr. varies with alt.; minerals; cap. C.; a. 144,304 km²; p. (est. 1985) 942,700.

Cuzco, t., cap. of C. dep., S. **Peru**; in Andes at alt. 3,418 m in valley of Urubamba R.; once cap of Incas; sacked by Francisco Pizarro 1533; cath., ruins of Inca fortress; tr. ctr. for agr. prod.; p. (est. 1985) 236,000.

Cwmamman, t., Dinefwr, Dyfed, **Wales**; on R. Loughor; p. (1981) 3,721.

Cwmbran, t., Torfaen, Gwent, **Wales**; in valley of Avon-Lwyd, 8 km N. of Newport; new t. (1949); motor accessories, wire, elec. gds., bricks, tiles, pipes; p. (1981) 44,309.

Cwm Dyli, Gwynedd, **Wales**; hydroelec. sta.

Cyclades (**Kirkádhes**), gr. of about 220 Is., **Greece**; rugged and barren csts, conceal sheltered agr. valleys; ch. t. and pt. Hermoupolis; a. 2,650 km²; p. (1981) 88,458.

Cynon Valley, l. gov. dist., Mid Glamorgan, **Wales**; inland valley inc. Aberdare and Mountain Ash; p. (est. 1988) 64,300.

Cyprus, Rep. of, I., indep. state, E. Mediterranean, 64 km S. of Turkey; N., inc. main pt. of Famagusta, occupied by Turkey from 1974; indep. st. of Turkish Rep. of Cyprus declared (1983) but only recognised by Turkey; varied cst., limestone hills in N., forested mtns. in S., central plains of Messarois in which cap. Nicosia is situated; agr. employs 30 per cent of p.; many irrigation schemes also aid soil and water conservation; land reform programmes to reduce fragmentation of holdings; copper in Troodos mtns. but asbestos of increasing importance; lt. inds. and tourism helping to re-structure economy but agr. provides over 50 per cent of exp., inc. wine, citrus fruit, vegetables; split of cty. by Attila line into 2 separate economics, N. dependent on aid from Turkey but S. developing rapidly since 1974; a. 9,251 km²; p. (est. 1986) 673,100.

Cyrenaica, prov., **Libya**; impt. region in anc. times; Greek col. 7th cent. B.C., Roman prov. 1st cent. B.C., captured by Arabs A.D. 642, part of Ottoman Empire 16th cent.; animal grazing, dates, oil-wells; a. 854,700 km²; p. (est. 1963) 350,024.

Czechoslovak Socialist Republic (**ČSSR**), fed. two-rep. st. (Czech Socialist Rep. and Slovak Socialist Rep.); **Central Europe**; ch. ts. Prague (cap.) Brno, Bratislava, Ostrava, Plzen; Rs. Danube, Elbe, Vltava, Oder of gr. economic importance for landlocked cty.; inds. highly developed; high standard of living; coal, non-ferrous metals, little petroleum; hydro-elec. power; a. 127,897 km²; p. (est. 1986) 15,520,839.

Czeladz, t., S. W. **Poland**; coal; p. (1970) 31,800.

Czernowitz. See **Chernovtsy**.

Czestochowa, c., Katowice prov., S. **Poland**; on Warta R.; rly. and industl. ctr.; iron and steel, textiles; celebrated religious ctr.; monastery; p. (est. 1985) 247,000.

D

Dacca (**Dhaka**), c., cap. of **Bangladesh**; on Buriganga R., old channel of Ganges; jute, muslin, paper mnfs.; medical radioisotope ctr.; univ.; p. (1981) 3,430,312.

Dabrowa Gornicza, t., Katowice, **Poland**; coal, zinc, iron ore; p. (est. 1983) 141,600.

Dachau, t., Bavaria, **W. Germany**; paper, elec. gds., brewing; concentration camp during last war; p. (est. 1986) 32,900.

Dachstein, mtn., Salzkammergut, **Austria**; alt. 2,998 m.

Dacorum, l. gov. dist., Herts., **Eng.**; a. of Chilterns inc. Tring, Berkhamsted and Hemel Hempstead; p. (est. 1988) 133,100.

Dadra and Nagar Haveli, union terr., **India**; admin. ctr. Silvassa; a. 490 km²; p. (1981) 103,677.

Dagenham, dist. former M.B., **Eng.**; now forms part of Greater London bor. of Barking; on N. bank of R. Thames with riverside Ford motor wks.

Dagestan, Caucasian aut rep., **RSFSR**; mtnous.; cap. Makhachkala; cotton, orchards and vineyards; machin., engin. oil; a. 50,246 km²; p. (1986) 1,754,000.

Dagupen, t., Pangasinan, Luzon, **Philippines**; on Lingayen Bay; comm. ctr.; p. (est. 1984) 103,401.

Daharki Mari, t., **Pakistan**; 560 km N.E. of Karachi; fertiliser plant.

Dahlak Archipelago, **Ethiopia**; in Red Sea; only 2 Is. inhabited; noted for pearl fishing.

Dahomey. See **Benin, People's Rep. of**.

Daimiel, mkt. t., Ciudad Real, **Spain**; cheeses, oil, wine; p. (1981) 16,260.

Dakar, spt., cap. of Senegal, **Senegambia**, W. Africa; S.E. of C. Verde behind Gorée I. on Atl. cst.; exp. groundnuts; some industl. development; free tr. zone, international airport; univ. and medical ctr.; p. (est. 1979) 978,553.

Dakhla, oasis, Libyan Desert, **Egypt**; 272 km S.W. of Asyût; dates, olives; stage on caravan route from Cyrenaica to Upper Egypt; site of New Valley Project for irrigation.

Dalälven, R., S. central **Sweden**; length 520 km, used for timber transport.

Da Lat (**Dalat**), t., **Vietnam**; 224 km N.E. Ho Chiminh City; in Annamite hills; nuclear reactor (1963); airport; p. (1973) 105,072.

Dalbeattie, burgh, Stewartry, **Scot.**; granite, dairy prod., gloves; p. (1981) 3,891.

Dalby, t., Queensland, **Australia**; 1961 oil strike of Moonie oilfield; rich volcanic soils aid grain and beef production; p. (est. 1984) 9,590.

Dalgety, t., on Fife cst., **Scot.**; new t. proposed; p. 10,000.

Dalian, spt., Liaoning prov., **China**; seafood cultivation; shipbldg., heavy engin., elec., chemical inds.; fully mechanised pt. and another being built; designated development zone in cty.'s new open door policy; p. (1984) 1,587,800.

Dalkeith, burgh, Midlothian, **Scot.**; 10 km S.E. of Edinburgh; mkt. t.; p. (1981) 11,077.

Dalkey, t., Dublin, **R.o.I.**; on E. cst.; 6 km N. of Wicklow border; resort; residtl.; p. 5,526.

Dallas, c., Texas, **USA**; in cotton- and grain-growing a.; machin., aircraft, petroleum prod.; univ.; scene of assassination of President Kennedy (1963); p. (1984) 974,200 (c.), 3,348,000 (met. a. with Fort Worth).

Dalmatia, region of **Yugoslavia** and prov. of Croatia, N.E. Adriatic cst.; high Karst plateaux; olive oil, wine; tourism; contains many resorts; a. 12,732 km²; p. 622,000.

Daltonganj, t., Bihar, **India**; on R. Koël; coal, cement; p. (1961) 25,270.

Dalton-in Furness, t., Cumbria, **Eng.**; limestone quarrying, textiles; abbey ruins; p. (1981) 10,931.

Daman (**Damão**), spt., **India**; 160 km N. Bombay; fishing, ship-bldg., cotton; former Portuguese settlement; p. (est. 1971), 17,317.

Damanhûr, t., **Egypt**; on W. margin of Nile delta, 40 km S.E. of Alexandria; mkt. for local agr. produce; p. (1986) 221,500.

Damaraland, region, **South-West Africa**; high plateau; admin. by Rep. of S. Africa; pt., Walvis Bay; cattle rearing.

Damascus (Arabic **Esh-Sham**), cap. c., **Syria**; 91 km S.E. of its pt. Beirut; claims to be oldest continuously inhabited c. in world; metal-wk., glass, cement; univ.; p. (est. 1985) 1,196,710.

Dambovitta (**Dimbovita**), R., **Romania**; rises in Mt. Omul (Transylvanian Alps), flows S. through Bucharest to R. Danube, via impt. settlids; 320 km long.

Damietta (**Dumyât**), t., Lower **Egypt**; on main distributary of R. Nile delta; cotton; plans to build new c. for 400,000; p. (1976) 93,488.

Dammam, spt. on Persian G., **Saudi Arabia**; oil pt.; industry, univ.; p. (1974) 127,844.

Damodar, R., Bihar, **India**; flows through India's major coalfields; valley forms ch. industl. a. of India; multipurpose scheme for hydro-electric power, irrigation and flood control.

Dampier, spt., W. **Australia**; on Indian Oc.; new pt. (1965) for shipping iron ore from Mt. Tom Price and Mt. Wittenoom; pelletising plant; p. (est. 1976) 2,727.

Dampier Archipelago, gr. of sm. Is., off N.W. **Australia,** in Indian Oc.

Dampier Strait, Bismarck Archipelago, channel between W. New Britain and Umboi I.

Dampir Strait, channel between Irian Jaya and Waigeo I.

Danakil Land (Dankalia), coastal desert a., mainly in **Ethiopia,** but partly in Djibouti; includes D. depression; potash; sm. pt. and road projected.

Da-nang (Tourane), c., S. **Vietnam**; ch. pt. of Annam on S. China Sea; exp. agr. prod.; p. (1973) 492,194.

Danao, t., Cebu, **Philippines**; rice and sugar dist.; p. (est. 1970) 45,500.

Danapur, t., Bihar, **India**; on Ganges R., nr. Patna; p. (1961) 70,766.

Dandenong, t., Victoria, **Australia**; 30 km E. of Melbourne; growing industl. ctr.; p. (est. 1983) 58,200.

Dandong (Antung), c., Liaoning, **China**; pt. on Yalu R., 24 km from mouth; Chinese frontier sta. on main rly. from China into N. Korea; mkt. for agr. prod.; lumbering; p. (est. 1984) 560,500.

Dannemora, t., **Sweden**; 40 km N.E. of Uppsala; iron ore worked since 1579; p. (est. 1970) 4,147.

Danube (Donau), R., second longest R. in Europe; rises in Black Forest, Germany, and flows E. into Black Sea; forms comm. highway; Iron Gate hydro-electric and navigation project inaugurated by 1978; increased no. of dams causing concern with conservationists; linked by canals with Main, Rhine and Oder; completion of Rhine-Main-Danube canal and Danube-Black Sea canal (1984) now creates Trans-Europe Waterway of 3,500 km.; Vienna, Budapest, Belgrade, and other lge. cs. on its banks; 2,706 km long.

Danube-Tisa Canal, N. **Yugoslavia**; irrigation, flood control, navigable; 261 km long.

Danville, t., Ill., **USA**; coal; mftg. tr.; p. (1980) 38,985.

Danville, t., Va., **USA**; cotton, tobacco; p. (1984) 44,700 (t.), 111,200 (met. a.).

Danzig. *See* Gdańsk.

Dap Cau, t., **Vietnam**; bamboo pulp and paper factories.

Darbhanga, t., Bihar, **India**; rice, oil-seeds, grain, sugar tr.; univ.; p. (1981) 176,301.

Dardanelles, strait between European and Asian Turkey, connecting Aegean Sea with Sea of Marmara; (the anc. Hellespont), 64 km long.

Daresbury, v., Cheshire, **Eng.**; birthplace of C. L. Dodgson (Lewis Carroll).

Dar-es-Salaam, spt., former cap. of **Tanzania**; univ.; textile mill projected; oil refining; pipeline to Ndola, Zambia; naval base and Tanzam rly. built with Chinese aid; p. (est. 1985) 1,096,000.

Darien, region, **Panama**; tortoiseshell, pearls, gold, but agr. is basis of economy; cap. La Palma; a. 15,540 km²; p. (1980) 26,524.

Darien, Gulf of, inlet of Caribbean Sea; separates Colombia and Panama.

Darjeeling, hill t., W. Bengal, **India**; tea, quinine; Himalayan resort; p. (1984) 63,600.

Darkhan, new t., **Mongolia,** on R. Hara; industl.

Darlaston, t., West Midlands, **Eng.**; nuts, bolts, fabricated steel mnfs., drop forgings, car components; pig iron plant closed after 100 years of production.

Darling Downs, plateau, S.E. Queensland, **Australia**; rich agr. region, fertile black soils aid wheat growing; ch. t. Toowoomba.

Darling R., N.S.W., **Australia**; longest trib. of the Murray, forming part of the Murray-Darling Rs. scheme for irrigation and flood control; 2,723 km long.

Darlington, t., l. gov. dist., Durham, **Eng.**; bridge bldg., woollen yarn mnf., engin.; rly. wagons, steel wks.; p. (est. 1988) 99,700 (dist.).

Darmstadt, c., Hesse, **W. Germany**; cas.; comm. ctr.; metallurgical prods., paper, machin., radio, chemicals, plastics; technical univ.; p. (est. 1986) 133,600.

Dart, R., Devon, **Eng.**; rises in Dartmoor, flows S. into English Channel at Dartmouth; picturesque estuary; 74 km long.

Dartford, t., l. gov. dist., Kent, **Eng.**; nr. S. cst. of Thames estuary; Dartford-Purfleet road tunnel (1963); engin., chemicals, quarrying, paper; kt.; p.: est. 1988) 78,400 (dist.).

noor, high granite plateau, S.W. Devon, rough moorland; sheep, cattle, and

wild ponies; granite tors; Nat. Park; tourism; granite quarries, reservoirs; prison at Princetown; china clay (Lee Moor) now extends into Nat. Park; recent discovery of tungsten, lgst. deposit in W. Europe but conflicts with conservation; a. 583 km²; hgst. point High Willays, 622 m.

Dartmouth, spt., S. Devon, **Eng.**; on W. of estuary of R. Dart; Royal Naval College; pottery; yachting, holiday resort; p. (1981) 6,298.

Dartmouth, industl. spt., sub. of Halifax, Nova Scotia, **Canada**; oil refining, shipbldg.; p. (1986) 65,243.

Darvel, burgh, Strathclyde Reg., **Scot.**; on R. Irvine, 13 km E. Kilmarnock; birthplace of Sir Alexander Fleming, discoverer of penicillin; p. (1981) 3,455.

Darwen, t., N.E. Lancs., **Eng.**; on flank of Rossendale Fells, 5 km S. of Blackburn; tile and glaze bricks, paint, wallpaper, plastics; p. (1981) 30,048.

Darwin, c., cap. N.T., **Australia**; pt. and regional ctr., invigorated in the 1950s by nearby uranium mng. (Rum Jungle); devastated by cyclone 1974, rebuilding complete by 1979; international airpt.; p. (est. 1986) 66,000.

Daryal Gorge, Caucasus, Georgian SSR, **USSR**; deep gorge (1,800 m) cut by Terek R.; identified as the classical Caspian or Iberian Gates from which distances were reckoned; forms part of Georgian military road.

Dashava, settlement on Lvov oblast, W. Ukraine, **USSR**; ctr. of rich natural gas field and starting point of gas pipeline to Kiev and Moscow, built after second world war.

Datia, t. Madhya-Pradesh, **India**; stone-walled, palaces; p. (1981) 60,991.

Datong (Tatung), c., Shanxi prov., **China**; impt. coalfield; steam and diesel locomotives; p. (1984) 981,000.

Datteln, t., N. Rhine-Westphalia, **W. Germany**; coal, leather, iron; p. (est. 1983) 37,300.

Daugavpils, t., Latvian SSR, **USSR**; on Dvina R.; textiles, engin., rly. repair wks., food prods.; p. (est. 1985) 124,000.

Dauphiné Alps, mtn. range, S.E. **France**; 24 peaks over 3,050 m.

Daura, t., nr. Baghdad, **Iraq**; oil refining.

Davangere, t., Karnataka, S. **India**; on 600 m plateau in Indian Penin.; p. (1981) 196,621.

Davao, t., Mindanao, **Philippines**; pt. for sugar; p. (est. 1984) 179,521

Davenport, t., Iowa, **USA**; on Mississippi R. where it is spanned by bridges to Rock Island, Molise and East Molise; rly., comm. and industl. ctr.; p. (1984) 102,100 (t.), 380,900 (met. a.).

Daventry, t., l. gov. dist., Northampton, **Eng.**; 14 km S.E. of Rugby; boot-mkg., lt. engin.; wireless-transmission sta.; expanded t.; p. (est. 1988) 63,000 (dist.).

David, t., cap. of Chiriqui prov., **Panama**; timber coffee, cacao, sugar; p. (1980) 49,472.

Davis Strait, channel between Greenland and Baffin I., N.W. Terr., **Canada**; connects Atl. Oc. with Baffin Bay; navigable.

Davos-Platz and **Dörfli,** sts., Grisons, **Switzerland**; Alpine winter resorts; alt. 1,478 m; p. (1980) 10,468.

Dawley, t., The Wrekin, Shrops., **Eng.**; on S.E. flank of the Wrekin: ironwks., pipe, cement, roadstone, asphalt and brick wks., engin.; new t. (1963); p. (1981) 49,137. *See* Telford.

Dawlish, t., Teignbridge, S. Devon, **Eng.**; on S. cst. between estuaries of Rs. Exe and Teign; seaside resort; flower tr.; p. (1981) 10,755.

Dawson, t., Yukon Terr., **Canada**; on Yukon R., nr. Klondike goldfields; asbestos mng. projected 1968; p. (1981) 697.

Dayton, c., Ohio, **USA**; on Great Miami R.; univ.; aircraft, elec. machin., rubber gds.; p. (1984) 181,200 (c.), 930,100 (met. a.).

Daytona Beach, t., Fla., **USA**; resort; shipping, ctr.; motor speed trials; p. (1984) 56,400 (t.), 300,300 (met. a.).

De Aar, t., rly. junc., Cape Prov., **S. Africa**; 500 m. from Cape Town; rlys. from N.W. (Luderitz, Walvis Bay) and S.E. (Pt. Elizabeth, E. London) join Cape Town to Johannesburg trunk rly.; p. (est. 1967) 16,600.

Dead Sea, salt-water L. between Israel and **Jordan**; surface 392 m below level of Mediterranean; a. 881 km², length 76 km, greatest width 15 km, greatest depth 399 m; receives waters of Jordan; high mineral content, very saline; Israeli plans to link to Mediterranean Sea by underground canal to generate hydro-electric power.

Deal, anc. pt., E. Kent, **Eng.**; on S.E. cst., 11 km N.E. Dover; opposite Goodwin Sands; seaside resort; lifeboat service; p. (1981) 25,989.

Dean, Forest of, Gloucs., **Eng.**; between Wye and Severn Rs.; former Royal Forest; Forestry Commission plantations; former coal-mng. a.; tourism; new lt. industl. estates; now forms l. gov. dist.; p. (est. 1988) 77,900.

Dearborn, t., Mich., **USA**; birthplace of Henry Ford; p. (1980) 90,660.

Death Valley, depression, Cal., **USA**; N. of Mojave Desert, 240 km N.E. of Los Angeles; completely arid; floor covered with saline deposits; tourist attraction; depth of valley floor 84 m below sea-level.

Deauville, seaside resort, Calvados dep., N. **France**; on Eng. Channel; racecourse, casino; p. (1968) 5,370.

Debra Markos, t., cap. of Gojam prov., **Ethiopia**; vegetable oil extraction; p. (est. 1980) 40,686.

Debrecen, t., **Hungary**; 183 km E. of Budapest; univ.; ctr. of pastoral dist.; fairs; pharmaceutics, medical instruments, furniture; ctr. of Calvinism: p. (est. 1985) 212,000.

Decatur, t., Ala., **USA**; steel textiles; industl. development after establishment of Tenn. Valley Authority; p. (1980) 42,002.

Decatur, t., Ill., **USA**; on Sangamon R.; industl.; rly. engin., food processing; univ.; p. (1984) 91,900 (t.), 128,600 (met. a.).

Decazeville, t., Aveyron, S. **France**; ctr. of sm. coalfield (no longer worked), metallurgy; p. (1982) 9,204.

Deccan, The, upland of S. **India,** bounded by the Narbada and Kistna Rs.; coincides with Maharashtra st.; area of very fertile lava soils; impt. cotton-growing region.

Dee, R., N. **Wales** and Cheshire, **Eng.**; 144 km long; lge. silted estuary, use for water storage planned.

Dee, R., Kincardine and Deeside, **Scot.**; picturesque, tourism; 139 km long.

Dehiwala-Mt Lavina, t., **Sri Lanka**; on cst. S. of Colombo; p. (est. 1983) 181,000.

Dehra Dun, t., Uttar Pradesh, **India**; scientific research ctr.; sawmills; p. (1981) 211,416 (t.), 293,010 (met. a.).

Deir-ez-Zor, t., **Syria**; on Euphrates R.; on motor route between Damascus and Baghdad; p. (1970) 66,143.

Dej, t., **Romania**; on Somesul R., distillery; p. (1983) 38,229.

Delabole, v., Cornwall, **Eng.**; on N.W. flank of Bodmin Moor; slate quarries.

Delagoa Bay, natural harbour, **Moçambique**; ch. pt. Maputo.

Delaware, st., **USA**; admitted to Union 1787, popular name First State; st. flower Peach Blossom, st. bird Blue Hen Chicken; low-lying a. of Atl. cst. plain; agr., lumber; fertilisers, minerals, leather, chemicals, machin.; cap. Dover; ch. pt. Wilmington; a. 6,138 km²; p. (1985) 622,000.

Delaware Bay, inlet, Atl. cst., **USA**; drowned estuary of R. Delaware, extends 128 km inland from C. May into heart of highly industl. a. of Philadelphia.

Delaware, R., flows between N.Y. st., **USA** along the Penns. border, through N.J. to Delaware Bay; 504 km long.

Delft, c., pt., S. Holland, **Neth.**; on Schie R. (canalised), nr. Rotterdam; technical univ.; ceramics (delft-ware), tool mftg., precision instruments; 13th cent. Old church and 15th cent. New church; p. (est. 1987) 88,000.

Delhi, c., cap. of **India**; on watershed between Rs. Indus and Ganges; made up of Old Delhi with walls, palace, and fort, and New Delhi with admin. ctr.; univ.; p. (1981) 273,036 (New Delhi), 4,884,234 (c.), 5,729,283 (met. a.).

Delhi, union terr., India; hot and arid region between Indus valley and alluvial plain of Ganges; irrigation to support agr.; New Delhi and Old Delhi ch. ctrs.; a. 1,497 km²; p. (1981) 6,220,406.

Delitzsch, t., Leipzig, **E. Germany**; 26 km E. of Halle; sugar, chemicals; p. (est. 1970) 24,270.

Delmarva, peninsula, Del., **USA**; between Chesapeake Bay and Del. Bay; horticulture, poultry, forestry, fishing.

Delmenhorst, t., Lower Saxony, **W. Germany**; nr. Bremen; jute, woollens, linoleum, foodstuffs; p. (est. 1986) 70,500.

Delphi, anc. Phocis, central **Greece**; N. of G. of Corinth; famous for Delphic oracle on Mt. Parnassus.

Del Rio, t., Texas, **USA**; pt. of entry on Rio

Grande; mkt. for agr. a.; grapes; exp. wool; border t., bridge to Mexico; p. (1980) 30,034.

Delyn, l. gov. dist., Clwyd, **Wales**; W. of Dee estuary inc. Holywell, Flint and Mold; p. (est. 1988) 65,100.

Demavend, dormant volcano, **Iran**; hgst. peak in Elburz range, c. 5,673 m.

Demerara, co., **Guyana**; between Essequibo and Demerara Rs.; exp. sugar, molasses, rum.

Demerara, R., **Guyana**; drains N. to Atl. Oc.; bauxite transport.

Denain, t., Nord dep., N. **France**; industl. ctr.; p. (1982) 21,872.

Denbigh, former co., N. **Wales**; now mostly in Clwyd; sm. part in Gwynedd.

Denbigh, t., Glyndŵr, Clwyd, **Wales**; in Vale of Clwyd, 16 km S. of Rhyl; cas.; tourism; dairy prods.; birthplace of Stanley the explorer; p. (1981) 9,040.

Denby Dale, t., West Yorks., **Eng.**; 13 km W. of Barnsley; woollen textiles; earthenware pipes; p. (1981) 13,476.

Den Helder. See Helder.

Denholme, t., West Yorks., **Eng.**; nr. Bradford; dairying, textiles; p. (1981) 2,676.

Denizli, t., **Turkey**; 75 km S.E. of Izmir; gardens —"the Damascus of Anatolia"; nr. site of Laodica; p. (1985) 169,130.

Denmark, kingdom, N.W. **Europe**; part of Scandinavia; member of EC; consists of Jutland peninsula, Is. of Sjaelland, Fyn, Falster, Lolland, and Bornholm, and 400 smaller Is., between N. Sea and Baltic; emphasis on dairy agr., producing butter, eggs, and bacon; increasing industrialisation; industl. prods. now account for 62 per cent of exp.; cap. Copenhagen; a. 42,932 km²; p. (est. 1987) 5,124,794.

Denny and Dunipace, burgh, Falkirk, **Scot.**; 10 km W. of Falkirk; steel castings, precast concrete, p. (1981) 23,172.

Dent du Midi, mtn. gr., Vaud can., S.W. **Switzerland**; rises to 10,694 ft. in Haut Cime.

Denton, t., Gtr. Manchester, **Eng.**; nr. Manchester; felt-hat mkg.; p. (1981) 37,729.

Denton, mkt. t., Texas, **USA**; univs.; food processing; p. (1980) 48,063.

Denver, c., cap. of Col., **USA**; on E. slope of Rockies, on South Platte R.; univs.; oil, electronic equipment, mng. machin., livestock, canning; tourism; p. (1984) 504,600 (c.), 1,791,400 (met. a. with Boulder).

Deogarh, t., Bihar, **India**; temples, place of pilgrimage; p. (1961) 30,813.

Deptford. See Lewisham.

Dera Ghazi Khan, t., **Pakistan**; on W. bank of Indus R.; silk, brass; p. (1981) 103,000.

Dera Ismail Khan, t., **Pakistan**; on Indus R.; admin. ctr., caravan ctr.; p. (1981) 68,000.

Derbent, c., S.E. Dagestan, **RSFSR**; on Caspian Sea; textiles, fish inds., glass; oil and natural gas nearby; p. (est. 1970) 50,000.

Derby, c., l. gov. dist., Derbys., **Eng.**; on R. Derwent; general engin., aero-engines, man-made fibres; p. (est. 1988) 215,400.

Derbyshire, non-met. co., **Eng.**; much of a. occupied by Pennines and Peak Dist. Nat. Park.; coalfield and industl. a. in E.; forms part of Manchester met. a. in N.W.; co. t. Derby; a. 2,631 km²; p. (est. 1988) 924,200.

Derbyshire Dales, l. gov. dist., Derbys., **Eng**; Pennine a. inc. Matlock, Bakewell and Ashbourne; p. (est. 1988) 66,800.

Derbyshire, North East, l. gov. dist., Derbys., **Eng.**; industl. a. of Clay Cross and Dronfield; p. (est. 1988) 96,800.

Derbyshire, South, l. gov. dist., Derbys., **Eng.**; a. S. of Derby and inc. Repton and Swadlincote; p. (est. 1988) 71,600.

Derg, Lough, in basin of R. Shannon, **R.o.I.**; separating Galway and Clare from Tipperary.

Derg, L., Donegal, **R.o.I.**, with cave on I. visited by R.C. pilgrims and known as "St Patrick's Purgatory".

Derwent, lgst R. of Tasmania, **Australia**; flows to Storm Bay via Hobart; hydroelec. power; 190 km long.

Derwent, R., Derbys., **Eng.**; trib. of R. Trent; length 96 km.

Derwent, R., North Yorks, Humberside, **Eng.**; trib. of R. Ouse; length 91 km.

Derwentside, l. gov. dist., Durham, **Eng.**; inc. Consett, Stanley and surrounding a.; p. (est. 1988) 85,900.

Derwentwater, L., Cumbria, **Eng.**; 5 km long.

Desaguadero, R., **Bolivia**; outlet of L. Titicaca; used for irrigation; 320 km long.

Desborough, t., Northants., **Eng.**; boot and shoe mnfs., iron mng.; p. (1981) 6,393.

Des Moines, c., cap. of Iowa st., **USA**; in heart of corn belt; transport and industl. ctr.; univ.; p. (1984) 190,800 (c.), 377,100 (met. a.).

Des Moines, R., Iowa, **USA**; trib. of Mississippi rising in Minn.; 880 km long.

Desna, R., main trib. of Dnieper R., **USSR**; navigable below Bryansk; 1,184 km long.

Des Plaines, t., Ill., **USA**; sub. of Chicago on Des Plaines R.; p. (1980) 53,568.

Dessau, t., Halle, **E. Germany**; at confluence of Mulde and Elbe Rs.; cas.; machin., rly. carriages, paper, sugar, chemicals; route ctr.; p. (est. 1986) 103,000.

Detmold, t., N. Rhine-Westphalia, **W. Germany**; cas.; paints, wood inds.; p. (est. 1986) 66,700.

Detroit, ch. c., pt., Mich., **USA**; busy comm. and industl. ctr.; univ.; gr. grain mart; and ctr. of the "Ford" motor-car wks., aeroplanes, military tanks, synthetic diamonds, pharmaceutics, tools, chemicals, steel; lgst exporting t. on Great Lakes; 850 murders per year; p. (1982) 1,089,100 (c.), 4,577,100 (met. a.).

Detroit, R., channel between L. St. Clair and L. Erie (40 km) separates st. of Mich., **USA**, from Ontario, **Canada**; carries more shipping than any other inland waterway in the world.

Deurne, t., **Belgium**; nr. Antwerp, airport; p. (1982) 76,744.

Deux Sèvres, dept., Poitou-Charentes, **France**; mainly agr.; vineyards; cap. Niort; a. 6,053 km²; p. (1982) 342,500.

Deventer, t., Overijssel, **Neth.**; on IJssel R.; indstl. ctr., Hanse t. in Middle Ages; p. (est. 1987) 65,000.

Devil's Island (I. du Diable), I., Atl. Oc. off **Fr. Guiana**; former penal settlement where Dreyfus was confined in 1894.

Devils Tower, N.E. Wyo., **USA**; tower rock of volcanic origin with fluted columns of igneous rock; alt. 264 m.

Devizes, Kennet, Wilts., **Eng.**; mkt. t., on Kennet and Avon canal at foot of Marlborough Downs; bricks, tiles, bacon-curing; p. (1981) 10,629.

Devonport, spt., N. Tasmania, **Australia**; pt. for fruit dist. of R. Mersey; mnfs. primary prods.; nearby Mersey-Forth power project (1970) attracts growth; p. (1981) 21,424.

Devonport, bor., Auckland, **N.Z.**; naval base and dockyard; sub. of Auckland; p. (est. 1987) 10,550.

Devon, non-met. co., S.W. **Eng.**; between English and Bristol Channels; attractive cstl. scenery; Nat. Parks of Dartmoor and Exmoor encourage tourism; mixed farming; modern lt. inds.; major ctrs. of p. at Plymouth, Torbay, Exeter; a. 6,713 km²; p. (est. 1988) 1,021,100.

Devon, East, l. gov. dist., Devon, **Eng.**; Exmouth, Sidmouth and Seaton on cst. and inland to Honiton and Ottery St. Mary; p. (est. 1988) 118,100.

Devon, North, l. gov. dist., **Eng.**; inc. Exmoor and ts. of Barnstaple, Ilfracombe and Lynton; p. (est. 1988) 84,400.

Dewsbury, t., West Yorks., **Eng.**; on R. Calder, 13 km from Leeds; heavy woollens, shoddy, coalmng.; dyewks.; p. (1981) 48,339.

Dez Dam, over Dez R., Khurzistan prov., **Iran**; opened 1963.

Dezfūl, r., Iran; mkt. ctr.; oil fields nearby; p. (est. 1982) 141,000.

Dhahran, spt., **Saudi-Arabia**; main oil pt. of S.A.; airpt.; College of Petroleum and Minerals; p. 12,001.

Dhanbad, t., Bihar, **India**; lead, zinc, tools, radio assembly, fertilisers; p. (1981) 120,221 (t.), 678,069 (met. a.).

Dhanushkodi, t., Tamil Nadu, **India**; on I. in Palk Strait; ferry pt. for passenger traffic from India to Sri Lanka.

Dhar, t., Madhya Pradesh, **India**; cultural and tr. ctr.; p. (1961) 29,325.

Dharmsala, hill sta., Himachal Pradesh, **India**; 160 km N.E. of Amritsar; sanatorium; c. 1,800 m; imposing mtn. scenery; p. (1981) 14,522.

Dharwar, t., Karnataka, **India**; 112 km E. of Goa; univ.; cotton mnf.; p. (1961) 77,163.

Dhaulagiri, mtn. peak, 8,172 m, **Nepal**, 4 summits in Himalayas.

Dhekélia, Cyprus; Brit. sovereign a. within Rep.; p. (1960) 9,802.

fertile prov., **Oman**, Arabia; sugar-cane, h. t. Salālah; ch. pt. Mirbat.

Dhulia, t., Khandesh dist., Maharashtra, **India**; cotton ind.; rly. ctr.; p. (1981) 210,759.

Diamante, R., Mendoza prov., **Argentina**; rises in Andes, flows E. to R. Salado; irrigates oasis of San Rafael; 320 km long.

Diamantina, t., Minas Gerais, **Brazil**; former diamond mng. ctr.; p. (est. 1985) 37,200.

Dibrugarh, t., Assam, **India**; former terminus of rail communications from Calcutta; since 1965 Indo-Pakistan war river communications disrupted; p. (1961) 58,480.

Didcot, sm. t., Oxon, **Eng.**; 16 km S. of Oxford; ordnance depots closed; Grand Prix engin.; ctr. for steam rly; p. (1981) 15,204.

Diego Garcia, I., Brit. Indian Oc. Terr.; Anglo-American naval communications ctr.; c. 1,000 islanders evacuated to Mauritius 1966–71; major US military staging base projected 1975; part of Brit. Indian Oc. Terr.

Diego Suarez. See **Antsiranana**.

Dieppe, pt., Seine-Maritime, **France**; 56 km N. of Rouen; fisheries, shipbldg., machin.; cross-Channel ferry; p. (1982) 26,000.

Differdange, t., S.W. **Luxembourg**; iron ore; cattle; p. (1981) 16,700.

Digboi, N.E. Assam, **India**; oil fields and refinery; p. (1961) 35,028.

Digne, t., cap. of Alpes-de-Haute-Provence, **France**; nr. Aix; cath.; p. (1982) 16,391.

Dijon, c., cap. Côte-d'Or, E. **France**; the Roman Divonense castrum; route ctr.; Seine-Saône watershed; wine tr.; industl. ctr.; univ., cath.; p. (1982) 145,569.

Dili, t., cap. of **E. Timor**; major spt.; exp. cotton, copra, coffee; p. (1980) 65,451.

Dimitrovgrad, t., **Bulgaria**; founded 1947; fertilisers, chemicals, superphosphate plant, iron, thermo-electric sta.; p. (est. 1968) 44,302.

Dimitrovo. See **Pernik**.

Dinajpur, t., **Bangladesh**; comm. ctr.; univ.; p. (1981) 96,718.

Dinan, t., Brittany, **France**; mediaeval t. above Rance R.; hosiery, brewing; holiday resort; p. (1982) 14,157.

Dinant, t., Namur, **Belgium**; on R. Meuse; mkt. t., tourist resort; exported copperware (*dinanderie*) in Middle Ages; cath.; citadel (1040); p. (1982) 12,008.

Dinard, t., Brittany, **France**; resort, especially for English; p. (1982) 10,016.

Dinaric Alps, mtn. range, **Yugoslavia**, **Albania** and **Italy** (Trieste); extend 640 km along Adriatic; hgst. peak Durmitor, 2,515 m.

Dindigul, t., Tamil Nadu, **India**; 40 km S. of Tiruchirapalli; cigars; p. (1981) 164,103.

Dinefwr, l. gov. dist., Dyfed, **Wales**; inland a. inc. Llandovery, Llandeilo, Ammanford and Cwmamman; p. (est. 1988) 38,900.

Dingle B., Kerry, **R.o.I.**; long inlet of sea on Atl. cst.

Dingwall, royal burgh, Ross and Cromarty, **Scot.**; at head of Cromarty F.; rly. junc.; cattle mkt., admin. ctr.; distilling, handloom weaving; p. (1981) 4,815.

Dinslaken, t. N. Rhine-Westphalia, **W. Germany**, N. of Duisburg; coal, steel, iron, footwear, timber; oil pipeline from Wesseling under construction; p. (est. 1986) 61,300.

Diomede Is., two barren granitic islets in Bering Strait between Alaska and Siberia; accepted bdy. between Soviet and US terr.

Diredawa, t., **Ethiopia**; 40 km N. of Harar; rly. wks.; mkt and comm. ctr.; new cement wks.; p. (est. 1980) 82,024.

Dirk Hartog I., off Shark Bay, W. **Australia**.

Disko U., off W. cst. of **Greenland** in Baffin Bay; contains harbour of Godhavn, cap. N. Greenland; rendezvous for whalers; shrimp beds; a. 8,288 km².

Dismal Swamp, morass, S. Va. and N.C., **USA**; contains L. Drummond and extends 50–65 km S. from nr. Norfolk.

Diss, South Norfolk, **Eng.**; mkt. t. on R. Waveney; 45 km S.W. of Norwich; agr. implements; p. (1981) 5,423.

Distaghil, major peak, Gr. Karakoram, N. Kashmir, **Pakistan**; two summits connected by a ridge, max. alt. 7,890 m.

Distrito Federal, federal dist., **Brazil**; inc. cap. c. of Brasilia; a. 5,815 km²; p. (est. 1985) 1,567,700.

Ditchling Beacon, 10 km N. of Brighton, East Sussex, **Eng.**; hgst point of South Downs, 248 m.

Diu, spt., I., off S. cst. of Bombay, **India**; oil nearby at Kayakov; p. (1960) 14,271.

Dīwānīyah, Ad, t., **Iraq**; cap. D. prov.; on Baghdad–Basra rly.; p. (1965) 181,000 (met. a.).

Diyarbakir, c., cap. of D. prov., central **Turkey**; on Tigris R.; comm. and mnf. ctr.; flour and rice mills; the anc. Amida, old walls, gates, citadel; p. (1985) 305,940.

Djajapura (Sukarnapura), t., cap. of Irian Jaya, **Indonesia**; on Humboldt B., an inlet of Pac. Oc.

Djakarta (Batavia), c., cap. of **Indonesia,** N.W. Java; comm. ctr.; textiles; exps. rubber, tea; printing; airport; p. (est. 1983) 7,636,000.

Djambi, dist., and t., Sumatra, **Indonesia**; on E. cst. plain 160 km N.W. of Palembang; univ.; field; a. (dist.) 44,924 km²; p. (1971) 158,559 (t.).

Djerba, t. and I., **Tunisia,** at S. entrance to G. of Gabès, joined to mainland by causeway; olives, dates, textiles, pottery; a. 510 km²; p. (1975) 70,217.

Djibouti, c. cap. of Djibouti; rly. terminus; main pt. free pt. (1981), container terminal (1985); p. (est. 1987) 250,000.

Djibouti, Rep. of, indep. st. (1981) N.E. **Africa**; former French Somaliland, renamed Fr. Terr. of Afars and Issas 1967; extends inland from straits of Bab-el-Mandeb; economy based on trade through international pt. of D.; plain, mainly below 180 m; hot, dry climate; shark and mother-of-pearl fisheries; little cultivable land; a. 23,051 km²; p. (est. 1987) 470,000 of whom over half live in cap. Djibouti.

Dneprodzerzhinsk, t., Ukrainian SSR, **USSR**; W. of Dnepropetrovsk on Dnieper R.; iron and steel, engin., chemicals; hydroelec. sta. nearby; p. (est. 1985) 271,000.

Dneproges (abbrev. Dnieper hydroelectric sta.), Ukrainian SSR, **USSR**; nr. Zaporoz'ye, on Dnieper: lgst dam and power sta. in Europe; destroyed by Germans, rebuilt 1944–9.

Dnepropetrovsk, c., Ukrainian SSR, **USSR**; on R. Dnieper; univ.; impt. rly. and industl. ctr., using iron ore (from Krivoy Rog), coal (Dombas), manganese (Nikopol) and electric power from Dnieper dam; heavy machin., chemicals; p. (est. 1986) 1,166,000.

Dneprorudnyy, t., Ukrainian SSR, **USSR**; new t. on S. shore of Kakhvota reservoir; p. (1964) 6,000.

Dneprostroy. See **Zaporoz'ye.**

Dnieper (Dnepr), gr. R. of Ukrainian SSR, **USSR**; 3rd longest R. of Europe; rises in Valdai hills, flows into Black Sea, 2,240 km long; connected by canals to Baltic; tribs. inc. Berezina, Pripet, Desna, Orel, Samara; since erection of Dneproges dam navigable for almost entire length.

Dniester (Dnestr), R., Ukraine SSR, **USSR**; rises in Carpathians and flows into the Black Sea; 1,403 km long.

Döbeln, t., Leipzig, **E. Germany**; machin., metallurgy, wood, cigar and sugar inds.; p. (est. 1973) 27,471.

Dobrich. See **Tolbukhin.**

Dobruja, historic region, S.E. **Europe**; along Black Sea cst., S.E. Romania, and N.E. Bulgaria; mainly agr.; ch. pt. Constanta.

Dobšiná, t., **ČSSR**; cave containing ice-field of 0·8 ha; asbestos, iron ore; p. 5,300.

Dodecanese (S. Sporades), gr. of some 20 Greek Is. (originally 12) in S. Aegean Sea; most impt. are Rhodes, Cos, and Leros; Italian 1912–46; p. (1981) 145,071.

Dodoma, cap. of **Tanzania** since 1974; at geographical ctr. of T. in rural a.; p. (est. 1985) 141,000.

Dodworth, t., South Yorks., **Eng.**; nr. Barnsley; coal; p. (1981) 4,922.

Dogger Bank, sandbank in N. Sea, between England and Denmark; depth varies from 6 to 37 m; valuable fishing ground; action between British fleet under Beatty and German fleet under Hipper; *Blücher* sunk Jan. 1915.

Dogs, I. of, riverside dist., formed by bend in the R. Thames off Greenwich, London, **Eng.**; Millwall and India docks, shipbldg. yards.

Doha, t., cap. of **Qatar**; spt. on E. of Qatar peninsula, Persian Gulf; internat. airpt., deep sea pt.; contains 80 per cent of p.; p. (est. 1982) 190,000.

Dokai Bay, inlet, N. Kyushu, **Japan**; landlocked bay on S. side of Shimonoseki Straits; flanked by highly industl. zone inc. Yawata, Wakamatsu, Tobata cs.; requires constant dredging; length 6 km, width 0·8–2·4 km.

Dôle, t., Jura, E. **France**; on R. Doubs, nr. Dijon; industl. ctr.; anc. cap. of Franche-Comté, ceded to France in 1678; birthplace of Pasteur; p. (1982) 27,959.

Dolgarrog, sm. t., Meirionnydd, Gwynedd, **Wales**; site of hydroelectric sta.

Dolgellau, t., Gwynedd, N. **Wales**; agr., quarrying, timber; p. (1981) 2,321.

Dollar, burgh, Clackmannan, **Scot.**; at foot of Ochil hills; p. (1981) 2,480.

Dollar Law, mtn., nr. Peebles, **Scot.**; alt. 817 m.

Dolomites, gr. of limestone mtns., S. Tyrolese Alps, N.E. **Italy**; tourist dist.; peaks assume fantastic forms; principal peak Marmolada 3,355 m.

Dominica, Commonwealth of, W.I.; indep. st. (1978); most N. of Windward Is.; 25 per cent under cultivation; volcanic soils highly suitable for bananas; N.–S. mtn. range has spectacular volcanic scenery; cap. Roseau; a. 751 km²; p. (est. 1987) 94,191.

Dominican Rep., rep., **W.I.**; shares I. of Hispaniola with Haiti; comprises Nat. Dist. (inc. cap. Santo Domingo) and 25 admin. provs.; mtnous. with sub-tropical climate; in path of tropical cyclones; badly devastated by hurricane (1979); comm. economy mainly agr.; transport system geared to exp. of sugar (now declining with U.S. quotas on imports); decline in tobacco sales causing farmers to abandon production; govt. investment in agr. and mng.; oil refining at Nigua; exp. bauxite; tourism growing and leading earner of foreign exchange; official language Spanish; a. 48,430 km²; p. (est. 1985) 6,243,000.

Domodossola, frontier t., Piedmont, N. **Italy**; nr. Alpine tourist resort in Toce valley, nr. Simplon; p. (1981) 20,069.

Don, R., South Yorks., **Eng.**; trib. of R. Ouse, 112 km long.

Don, R., Gordon, **Scot.**; flows into N. Sea nr. Aberdeen; salmon; 131 km long.

Don, major R. of southern **RSFSR**; falls into Sea of Azov below Rostov, its ch. pt.; navigable to Voronezh; ch. trib., Donets; access to Volga by Don-Volga canal; fisheries; 1,955 km long.

Donaghadee, t., Ards, **N. Ireland**; nearest point to Scot.; spt. and seaside resort; p. (1971) 3,687.

Donauwörth, t., W. Bavaria, **W. Germany**; bridge t. on N. bank of Danube at Wörnitz confluence; p. (est. 1968) 11,130.

Donbas, industl. region, Ukrainian SSR, **USSR**; in valleys of Rs. Donets and lower Dnieper; about 23,300 km²; produces 60 per cent of Russia's coal; adjoins Krivoy Rog ironfields; many lge. industl. ts.

Doncaster, t., met. dist., South Yorks., **Eng.**; on Don R., 27 km N.E. of Sheffield; coal mines, tractors, nylon mftg.; racecourse; p. (est. 1988) 291,600.

Donegal, spt., Co. Donegal, **R.o.I.**; on W. cst. on Donegal Bay; homespun tweeds, carpets; p. (1981) 1,725.

Donegal (Tirconnail), co., N.W. **R.o.I.**; fishing poor agr.; cloth, hydroelectric power; co. t. Lifford; a. 4,830 km²; p. (1981) 125,112.

Donets, R., rises in uplands of central **RSFSR**; N.E. of Belgorod, flows S.E. to join R. Don; crosses Donets coalfield; length 1,040 km. See **Donbas.**

Donetsk (Stalino), t., Ukrainian SSR, **USSR**; industl. ctr. of Donets coal basin; iron, steel, engin., chemicals; p. (1986) 1,081,000.

Donges, t., Loire Atlantique, **France**; nr. St. Nazaire; oil refinery; synthetic textiles, plastics; p. (1968) 6,458.

Dongola (Dunqulah), t., **Sudan**; on left bank of Nile above Third Cataract; Old D. was 120 km to S.; p. (est. 1965) 4,970.

Dong Ting (Tung Ting), lge. L., Hunan, **China**; receives water from Xi Jiang and Yuan Rs., drains N. to Chang Jiang; surrounded by flat intensively cultivated land; rice, sugar; size varies with season; max. (in late summer) 6,500 km².

Donner Pass, E. Cal., **USA**; highway pass through Sierra Nevada at 2,176 m.

Donzère-Mondragon, Vaucluse, **France**; site of Rhône barrage supplying hydroelectric power.

Dora Baltea, R., N. **Italy**; rises in Mt. Blanc, flows E. and S. through Val d'Aosta to R. Po at Chivasso; impt. routeway from N. Italy to Switzerland (through Gr. St. Bernard Pass) and France (through Little St. Bernard Pass); 152 km long.

Dorchester, co. t., West Dorset, **Eng.**; mkt. t. on R. Frome; lime, agr., engin.; Roman remains; nearby prehistoric Maiden Castle; linked with the name of Thomas Hardy; p. (1981) 14,049.

Dordogne, dep., S.W. **France**; cap. Périgueux; crossed by Dordogne R.; fertile valleys; p. (1982) 377,500.

Dordogne, R., S.W. **France**; rises in Centra¹

Massif, joins Garonne to form Gironde; vineyards; upper reaches used for hydroelectric power.

Dordrecht, c., nr. Rotterdam, **Neth.**; on R. Merwede; timber, shipbldg., seaplanes; p. (est. 1987) 107,000.

Dorking, t., Mole Valley, Surrey, **Eng.**; on R. Mole to S. of gap through N. Downs; mkt., residtl.; lt. inds.; p. (1981) 21,654.

Dornbirn, t., Vorarlberg, **Austria**; textiles; p. (1981) 38,641.

Dornoch, burgh, Sutherland, **Scot.**; N. of Dornoch F.; resort; p. (1981) 1,006.

Dorset, non-met. co., S. **Eng.**; borders Eng. Channel along attractive cliffed cst. formed by E.–W. limestone ridges; Portland stone quarried; many tourist resorts inc. Bournemouth; mkt. ts. serve agr. interior; a. 2,655 km²; p. (est. 1988) 655,700.

Dorset East, l. gov. dist., Dorset, **Eng.**; rural a. based on W. Minster; p. (est. 1988) 79,600.

Dorset Heights, hills, extend E. to W. across central Dorset, **Eng.**; chalk; pastoral farming, sheep; some cultivation where soil is deep enough; rise to 250–275 m.

Dorset, North, l. gov. dist., Dorset, **Eng.**; mainly rural but inc. ts. of Shaftesbury, Sturminster Newton and Blandford Forum; p. (est. 1988) 54,700.

Dorsten, t., N. Rhine–Westphalia, **W. Germany**; on R. Lippe; coal, iron, elec., chemical inds.; p. (est. 1986) 74,100.

Dortmund, c., N. Rhine–Westphalia, **W. Germany**; on Dortmund–Ems Canal; industl. ctr. and pt. of Ruhr; coal, iron, steel; p. (est. 1986) 568,200.

Dortmund–Ems Canal, N. Rhine–Westphalia, **W. Germany**; links Dortmund on Ruhr coalfield with R. Ems 8 km above Lingen; 144 km long.

Douai, t., Nord, **France**; nr. Lille on Scarpe R.; coal, iron and engin. wks.; bell founding, arsenal; p. (1982) 202,366 (met. a.).

Douala, spt., **Cameroon**; rly. to Yaoundé; exp. hardwoods; p. (est. 1984) 850,000.

Douarnenez, spt., Finistère, N.W. **France**; on D. Bay; sardine fisheries; p. (1982) 17,813.

Doubs, dep., E. **France**; traversed by Jura range and R. Doubs; mainly agr.; watchmkg., motor vehicles; cap. Besançon; a. 5,315 km²; p. (1982) 477,200.

Douglas, t., cap. of I. of Man; 120 km W. of Liverpool, **Eng.**; spt; resort; nearby freeport (1983) gaining from low tax rate; p. (1986) 20,368.

Douglas Point, on shore of L. Huron, Ont., **Canada**; nuclear power sta.

Dounreay, Caithness, **Scot.**; fast-breeder nuclear reactors.

Douro, R., **Portugal** and **Spain**; enters Atl. Oc. below Oporto; known as Duero R. in Spain; l. 776 km; famous port wine a.

Dove, R., Derbs. and Staffs., **Eng.**; trib. of Trent; flows through beautiful dales; 77 km long.

Dovedale, valley, Derbys., **Eng.**; steeply sloping limestone ravine of R. Dove; tourism.

Dover, packet pt., l. gov. dist., Kent, **Eng.**; one of old Cinque pts.; nearest spt. to France the Strait of D. being only 34 km wide; ch. pt. for passenger and mail traffic with Continent; cas.; p. (est. 1988) 106,300.

Dovey, R., **Wales**; flows from Cambrian Mtns. and enters Cardigan Bay by a wide estuary.

Dowlais, dist., Merthyr Tydfil, Mid Glamorgan, S. **Wales**; coal mng., iron founding, engin.

Down, former co.; l. gov. dist., **N. Ireland**; borders Strangford Lough and Dundrum Bay; agr. and fisheries; p. (1981) 52,855 (dist.).

Downham Market, t., West Norfolk, **Eng.**; on R. Ouse; flour-milling, malting, sheet-metal wks.; p. (1981) 4,687.

Downpatrick, t., Down, **N. Ireland**; on R. Quoile; linen; p. (1981) 8,245.

Downs, natural harbour of refuge for shipping between Kent cst. and Goodwin Sands in the English Channel.

Drachenfels, mtn. peak of the Rhine, **W. Germany**; the steepest of the Siebengebirge range, nr. Königswinter; alt. 325 m; ascended by lt. rly.; famous cave of legendary dragon.

Draguignan, t., S.E. **France**; cap. of Var. dep. until 1974; mkt. t., service ctr.; p. (1982) 28,194.

Drakensberg, mtn. chain between Natal and Orange Free State, **S. Africa**, and **Lesotho**; xtending 800 km from Gt. Fish R. to Olifants hgst. peak Mont-aux-Sources 3,283 m; ~osses range by Van Reenen Pass.

~n, spt., **Norway**; nr. Oslo, on the Dram-

men R.; shipyard; exp. timber, wood-pulp, paper; p. (est. 1987) 51,324.

Drancy, t., Seine-St. Denis, **France**; N.E. sub. of Paris; p. (1982) 60,224.

Drava (Drau), R., trib. of Danube, **Austria** and **Yugoslavia**; flows from the Tyrol across Carinthia and Styria, joining Danube nr. Osijek; length 720 km; used for hydroelec. power.

Drax, West Yorks., **Eng.**; thermal elec. power sta. linked to new Selby coalfield.

Drenthe, prov., **Neth.**; on German frontier; cap. Assen; a. 2,663 km²; p. (1983) 424,720.

Dresden, c., **E. Germany**; R. pt. on Elbe, 80 km E. of Leipzig; impt. route ctr.; engin., chemicals, optical and photographic apparatus, porcelain, glass, brewing; fine art collections; scientific research; oil pipeline from Schwedt under construction; p. (est. 1986) 520,000.

Driffield, t., East Yorks, Humberside, **Eng.**; on Yorks. Wolds 21 km N. of Beverley; oil-cake wks.; p. (1981) 9,090.

Drin, R., N. **Albania**; rises in Yugoslavia and flows through deep gorges into Adriatic; hydro-elec. power; 288 km long.

Drina, R., trib. of Sava R., **Yugoslavia**; ch. source of hydroelec. power in rep.; 480 km long.

Dröbak, spt., S.E. **Norway**; winter pt. for Oslo; summer resort.

Drogheda, spt., Louth, **R.o.I.**; considerable tr. in agr. produce, salmon, etc.; stormed by Cromwell in 1649; p. (1981) 22,556.

Drogobych, t., Ukrainian SSR, **USSR**; 64 km S.W. of Lvov; ctr. of lge. oilfields, refineries; mftg.; p. (est. 1968) 56,000.

Droitwich, t., Wychavon, Hereford and Worcs., **Eng.**; brine baths; lt. inds.; expanded t.; p. (1981) 18,073.

Drôme, dep., S.E. **France**; traversed by Alps and watered by Rs. Rhône, Drôme, and Isère; cap. Valence; agr., forestry, sericulture, textile ind.; a. 6,560 km²; p. (1982) 389,200.

Dromore, mkt. t., Banbridge, **N. Ireland**; on Lagan R.; linen; p. (1971) 2,303.

Dronfield, t., North East Derbys., **Eng.**; between Chesterfield and Sheffield; edged tools, engin. and agr. implements; p. (1981) 23,304.

Droylsden, t., Gtr. Manchester, **Eng.**; sub. of Manchester; chemicals; textiles; p. (1981) 22,513.

Drumochter Pass, Grampian Mtns., **Scot.**; carries main Perth to Inverness rly. and main road from Glen Garry into valley of R. Spey; highest alt. reached by any main rly. in Gt. Britain, 453 m.

Dschang, t., **Cameroon**; quinine processing; bauxite mng.

Dubai (Dubay), emirate, one of **United Arab Emirates**, Arabian Gulf; recently developed as free pt. (modelled on Singapore), major comm. ctr. of a.; offshore oil with vast underwater storage tanks; international airpt.; deepwater pt. (Port Rashid) under construction; p. (1985) 419,104.

Dubbo, t., N.S.W., **Australia**; busy road, rail, air junction in rich agr. dist.; p. (1981) 23,986.

Dublin, co., **R.o.I.**; co. t. Dublin; a. (inc. c. of Dublin) 922 km²; p. (1981) 977,700.

Dublin (Irish *Baile Átha Cliath*), C.B., cap. of **R.o.I.**; co. t. Co. Dublin; at mouth of R. Liffey; ctr. of govt., commerce, ind., and culture; cath., univ., Abbey Theatre; brewing, distilling, food processing; Swift was buried here; p. (1981) 525,882 (c.), 915,115 (met. a.).

Dubrovnik (Ital. Ragusa), t., **Yugoslavia**; impt. pt. on Adriatic; retains much of its mediaeval architecture; tourism; airport; p. (1981) 66,131.

Dubuque, t., Iowa, **USA**; pt. on Mississippi R.; varied inds. inc. meat-packing; p. (1980) 62,321.

Dudinka, Arctic spt. on R. Yenisey, **RSFSR**; nickel.

Dudley, t., met. dist., West Midlands, **Eng.**; cas.; engin.; cables, chains; p. (est. 1988) 304,300.

Duisburg, c., N. Rhine–Westphalia, **W. Germany**; R. pt. on E. bank of Rhine at confluence with R. Ruhr, 16 km N. of Düsseldorf; iron and steel inds., machin., textiles, chemicals, pt. inds., route and R. tr. ctr.; p. (est. 1986) 541,600.

Dukeries, dist., Sherwood Forest, Notts., **Eng.**; so called from ducal mansions in dist.; tourism.

Dukinfield, t., Tameside, Gtr. Manchester, **Eng.**; 10 km E. of Manchester; textiles, engin., rope and twine; p. (1981) 18,063.

Dukla Pass, anc. and easy route across Carpathians, joining Poland, Hungary and Slovakia, 497 m a.s.l.

Duluth, pt., Minn., **USA**; at W. end of L. Superior; gr. tr. in grain, timber and iron ore; natural gas pipeline into the Mesabi Iron Range; p. (1984) 86,600 (c.), 253,800 (met. a.).

Dulwich, residtl. sub. in bor. of Southwark, Greater London, **Eng.**; village character with lge. park and public school.

Dumaujváros, t., **Hungary**; new t. built from v. of Dunapentele; iron and steel wks.; paper inds., engin.; p. (1966) 43,400.

Dumbarton, royal burgh, l. gov. dist., Strathclyde Reg., **Scot.**; on N. bank of R. Clyde, 19 km below Glasgow; shipbldg., valve and tube-mkg., iron and brassware; p. (est. 1986) 79,295 (dist.).

Dum-Dum, t., W. Bengal, **India**; ammunition; impt. airpt.; p. (est. 1981) 360,288.

Dumfries, royal burgh, Nithsdale, **Scot.**; on R. Nith, 16 km from Solway F.; p. (1981) 32,084.

Dumfries and Galloway Region, l. gov. reg., **Scot.**; occupies W. half of Southern Uplands; drained by S. flowing rivers to Solway F.; sparse rural p.; a. 6,369 km²; p. (est. 1986) 146,770.

Dumfriesshire, former co., **Scot.**; now part of Dumfries and Galloway Reg.

Dunbar, royal burgh, E. Lothian, **Scot.**; sm. fishing pt.; Cromwell's victory 1650; p. (1981) 6,015.

Dunbartonshire, former co., **Scot.**; now part of Strathclyde Reg.

Dunblane, mkt. burgh, Stirling, **Scot.**; on Allan Water, 8 km from Stirling; Gothic cath. now used as par. church; p. (1981) 6,824.

Dundalk, U.D., cap. of Co. Louth, **R.o.I.**; harbour, rly. ctr.; engin., footwear, tobacco, brewing; p. (1981) 25,663.

Dundee, c., spt., royal burgh, l. gov. dist., Tayside Reg., **Scot.**; on F. of Tay, 80 km N. Edinburgh; jute mnf., engin., computers, refrigerators, clocks, watches, preserves, linoleum; publishing., univ.; p. (est. 1986) 176,208.

Dunedin, c., Otago, S.I., **N.Z.**; univ.; wool and dairy produce; named after the old name of Edinburgh; p. (1987) 76,800.

Dunfermline, royal burgh, l. gov. dist., Fife Reg., **Scot.**; 22 km E. of Alloa; linen, rubber gds., synthetic fibre; birthplace of Charles I and Andrew Carnegie; cap. of Scot. 1057–93; p. (est. 1986) 129,099. (dist.).

Dungannon, mkt. t., l. gov. dist., **N. Ireland**; linen, bricks; p. (1981) 8,295 (t.), 41,039 (dist.).

Dungarvan, U.D., Co. Waterford, **R.o.I.**; spt., mkt. t.; leather processing; p. (1981) 6,631.

Dungeness, headland of shingle, Kent, **Eng.**; 16 km S.E. of Rye; civil nuclear power stas.; linked by power cable to France 1961.

Dunkeld, t., Perth and Kinross, **Scot.**; on R. Tay at entrance to Strathmore; cath.; ecclesiastical ctr. in 9th century; tourist resort.

Dunkirk, spt., Nord dep., **France**; strong fort; gd. harbour and tr.; fisheries, shipbld., oil refining; steel mill; scene of evacuation of B.E.F. 1940; p. (1982) 73,618.

Dun Laoghaire (Kingstown), C.B., Dublin, **R.o.I.**; spt., mail packet sta., fishing; ferry to Eng.; p. (1981) 54,496.

Dunmanway, t., Cork, **R.o.I.**; on R. Brandon; tweeds, blankets.

Dunmow, Great, mkt. t., Uttlesford, Essex, **Eng.**; on R. Chelmer; 16 km N.W. of Chelmsford.

Dunmow, Little, v., 3 km E. of Great Dunmow; Uttlesford, Essex, **Eng.**; historic Dunmow Flitch (ale of bacon); bacon factory closed (1983).

Dunoon, burgh, Argyll and Bute, **Scot.**; on N. side of F. of Clyde, anc. cas.; holiday resort; p. (1981) 9,372.

Duns, burgh, Berwick, **Scot.**; agr. and allied inds.; mkt. t.; cas.; p. (1981) 2,249.

Dunsinane, hill, Sidlaws, **Scot.**; nr. Perth; alt. 309 m; referred to by Shakespeare in *Macbeth*.

Dunstable, t., South Beds., **Eng.**; on N. edge of Chiltern Hills, 6 km W. of Luton; motor vehicles, engin., cement, rubber, and plastic gds.; p. (1981) 30,912.

Duque de Caxias, t., **Brazil**; Brazil's largest oil refinery, petro-chemicals; Alfa-Romeo car plant; p. (est. 1985) 666,100.

Durance, R., S.E. **France**; trib. of Rhône; rapid current, 347 km long; provides irrigation and hydroelec. power.

Durango, c., cap. of D. st., **Mexico**; cath.; silver, gold, copper, iron-ore; p. (1980) 321,148.

Durango, st., N.W. **Mexico**; mng., agr., cotton, wheat; a. 109,484 km²; p. (1980) 1·16 m.

Durant, t., S. Okla, **USA**; cotton gins and compresses, cottonseed oil; p. (1980) 11,972.

Durban, c., **S. Africa**; on Durban Bay; ch. comm. c. of Natal; exp. coal, manganese, wool, hides; oil and sugar refining, chemicals, textiles, engin.; oil pipeline to Johannesburg; univ.; main pt. and seaside resort; p. (1985) 634,301.

Düren, t., N. Rhine–Westphalia, **W. Germany**; on R. Ruhr 37 km S.W. of Cologne; rly. ctr.; iron and steel wks., vehicles; p. (est. 1986) 84,100.

Durgapur, t., W. Bengal, **India**; site of barrage on Damodar R.; p. (1981) 311,798.

Durham, c., co. t., l. gov. dist., Durham, N.E. **Eng.**; sited within a meander of R. Wear; cath., cas., univ.; carpets, organ mftg., confectionery; p. (est. 1988) 85,800.

Durham, non-met. co., N.E. **Eng.**; between Rs. Tyne and Tees; stretches from attractive Pennine moorland in W. to coalfield and industl. a. with many sm. ts. in E.; borders the N. Sea; a. 2,437 km²; p. (est. 1988) 596,800.

Durham, t., N.C., **USA**; tobacco ind., textiles; univ.; p. (1984) 102,000.

Durrës (Durazzo), ch. spt., **Albania**; on Adriatic; pt. for Tirana; tobacco ind., plastics; tourism; p. (1980) 65,900.

Dursley, t., Gloucs., **Eng.**; 21 km S.W. of Gloucester; engin., agr. machin.; 18th cent. mkt. house; p. (1981) 12,626.

Dushanbe, c., cap. of Tadzhik SSR, **USSR**; univ.; industl. and agr. ctr.; rly. junc.; earlier called Stalinabad; 1989 ethnic unrest; p. (1986) 565,000.

Düsseldorf, c., cap. of N. Rhine-Westphalia, **W. Germany**; on R. Rhine, 32 km N. of Cologne; admin. and cultural ctr., art and medical academies; iron, steel, machin., soap, cars, paper, chemical inds.; impt. trans-shipment pt.; p. (est. 1986) 560,600.

Dust Bowl, region, **USA**; name applied to great plains on E. flank of Rocky Mtns.; subject to severe soil erosion by wind, particularly in drought years (1933, 1936) due to destruction of natural vegetation by over-grazing or by excessive ploughing.

Dutch Harbour, t., Unalaska I., Aleutian gr., N. Pac. Oc.; strategic American naval base.

Dvina or Northern Dvina, R., RSFSR; flows to White Sea at Arkhangelsk, formed by the junction of Rs. Sukhona and Vychegda at Kotlas; connected by canal with Neva and Volga; used for timber transport; 744 km long.

Dvina or Western Dvina, R., Latvian SSR, RSFSR, **USSR**; rises in Valdai Hills nr. sources of Volga and Dnieper, flows through Latvia to G. of Riga; connected by canal to Berezina and Dnieper; c. 1,016 km long.

Dwyfor, l. gov. dist., Gwynedd, **Wales**; Lleyn penin. and ts. of Pwhelli, Criccieth and Porthmadog; p. (est. 1988) 27,000.

Dyfed, co., S.W. **Wales**; inc. former cos. of Cardiganshire, Carmarthenshire and Pembroke; upland a. crossed by valleys of Teifi and Towy Rs.; stock rearing and fattening; tourism impt. around cst.; industl. in S.E.; a. 5,765 km²; p. (est. 1988) 348,400.

Dzaudzhikau. See **Ordzhonikidze.**

Dzerzhinsk, c., RSFSR; R. pt. of Oka; chemicals (fertilisers, explosives); p. (est. 1985) 274,000.

Dzhalil, t., RSFSR; new t. 48 km N.E. of Almetyevsk to serve new oilfield there.

Dzhambul, c., Kazakh SSR, **USSR**; on Talas R. and on Turk-Sib rly.; chemicals, food-processing; p. (est. 1985) 303,000.

Dzhezkazgan, t., Kazakh SSR, **USSR**; 560 km W. of L. Balkhash; copper-mines; manganese ore nearby; p. (est. 1985) 102,000.

Dzierzoniow (Reichenbach), t., Wroclaw, S.W. **Poland**; mnf. ctr.; textiles, machin., elec. equipment; formerly in Germany; p. (1970) 32,900.

Dzungaria, inland basin, Xinjiang prov., N.W. **China**; lies between Tien-Shan highlands of Soviet–Chinese frontier and Altai mtns.; former historic kingdom of Zungaria.

E

Ealing, outer bor., Greater London, **Eng.**; comprising former bors. of Acton, Ealing, and Southall; p. (est. 1988) 297,300.

Earl's Court, residtl. a., London, **Eng.**; Bor. of Kensington and Chelsea, contains E.C. exhibition hall.

Earn R., Perth, and Kinross, **Scot.**; issues from Loch Earn (10 km long) and flows into Tay R.; 74 km long.

Easington, l. gov. dist., Durham, **Eng.**; colly. v.; now part of Peterlee new t.; p. (est. 1988) 95,000.

Easington, v., Humberside, **Eng.**; nr. Hull; natural gas terminal.

East Anglia, comprises Norfolk and Suffolk, **Eng.**; former Anglo-Saxon kingdom; one of Britain's most productive agr. regions.

East Anglian Heights, hills, extend S.W. to N.E. across N.E. Hertfordshire, N. Essex, and S.W. Suffolk, **Eng.**; chalk overlain by glacial clays and sands; smooth, rolling surface; region of lge. farms and lge. fields, mixed farms mainly grain; rarely exceed 180 m.

East Bergholt, v., Suffolk, **Eng.**; birthplace of Constable.

Eastbourne, t., l. gov. dist., East Sussex, **Eng.**; on S. cst. to E. of Beachy Head; seaside resort; p. (est. 1988) 80,300.

East Cape, extreme N.E. point of Asia; on Chukchi peninsula, **RSFSR**; Russian name Cape Dezhnova.

East Cape, extreme E. point of **N.Z.**; named by Cook on his first voyage in 1769.

East Chicago, t., Ind., **USA**; L. Michigan; iron and steel wks., oil refining; p. (1980) 39,786.

East Cleveland, t., Ohio, **USA**; residtl.; p. (1980) 36,957.

East Coast Bays, bor., N.I., **N.Z.**; series of settlements on bays N. of Auckland; amalgamated 1954; p. (est. 1987) 31,600.

East Dereham, t., Breckland, Norfolk, **Eng.**; 22 km W. of Norwich; agr. implements; p. (1981) 11,845.

Easter Island, S. Pac. Oc., 3,760 km W. of Chile; various theories to explain origin of gigantic statues; p. (est. 1985) 2,000.

East Grinstead, t., West Sussex, **Eng.**; in ctr. of Weald, 14 km W. of Tunbridge Wells; famous hospital for plastic surgery; p. (1981) 22,263.

East Ham. See **Newham.**

East Hartford, t., Conn., **USA**; industl.; p. (1980) 52,563.

East Indies, name commonly applied to Is. between S.E. Asia and N. Australia, variously known as Malay archipelago, Malaysia, Indonesia.

East Kilbride, t., l. gov. dist., Strathclyde Reg., **Scot.**; 11 km S.S.E. of Glasgow; new t. 1947; lge. agr. machin., aero engines, engin., elec. gds., seawater distillation plant; knitwear, clothing; p. (est. 1986) 81,837.

East Lansing, t., Mich., **USA**; residtl.; univ.; p. (1980) 51,392.

Eastleigh, t., l. gov. dist., Hants., **Eng.**; rly. engin.; many new inds.; p. (est. 1988) 101,000.

East London, spt., C. Prov., **S. Africa**; at mouth of Buffalo R.; holiday resort; trading ctr.; inds. inc. car assembly, textiles, engin.; titanium deposits nearby; p. (1985) 193,819 (met. a.).

East Lothian (Haddington), former co., l. gov. dist., **Scot.**; part of Lothian Reg.; p. (est. 1986) 81,872.

East Main, R., Quebec, **Canada**; flows into James Bay; 432 km long.

Easton, t., Penns., **USA**; on Delaware R.; rly. ctr., coal, steel, machin., p. (1980) 26,027.

East Orange, t., N.J., **USA**; residtl. sub. of New York; p. (1980) 77,690.

East Pakistan. See **Bangladesh.**

East Point, t., Ga., **USA**; textiles, fertilisers; p. (1980) 37,486.

East Providence, t., Rhode I., **USA**; textiles, machin.; p. (1980) 50,980.

East Retford, t., Bassetlaw, Notts., **Eng.**; on R. Idle, 10 km E. of Worksop; rubber, wire ropes, engin.; p. (1981) 19,348.

East Riding, Yorkshire. See **Yorkshire.**

East River, tidal strait about 26 km long and from 180–1,200 m wide; separates the bors. of Manhattan and Bronx from the bors. of Queens and Brooklyn, N.Y., **USA.**

East St. Louis, t., R. pt., Ill., **USA**; on Mississippi R.; lge. stockyards, meat-packing, aluminium, chemicals; p. (1980) 55,200.

Sussex, non-met. co., S.E. **Eng.**; mainly l. urban growth on cst., where resorts, ꞁent and dormitory ts. for London, inc. ꞁ., Hastings and Eastbourne; crossed by S.

Downs in S. terminating at Beachy Head, Ashdown Forest in N.; a. 1,795 km²; p. (est. 1988) 712,800.

East Timor, prov., Indonesia; Port. terr. until 1975; sovereignty claimed by Indonesia and disputed by Portugal; mtnous; underdeveloped; cap. Dili; a. 14,693 km²; p. (est. 1985) 2,294,000.

Eastwood, t., Broxtowe, Notts., **Eng.**; birthplace of D. H. Lawrence; coal; p. (1981) 11,700.

Eastwood, l. gov. dist., Strathclyde Reg.; **Scot.**; part of Central Clydeside conurb.; p. (est. 1986) 56,060.

East Yorkshire (formerly **North Wolds**), l. gov. dist., Humberside, **Eng.**; lge. a. inc. Pocklington, Driffield and Bridlington; p. (est. 1988) 84,800.

Eau Claire, t., Wis., **USA**; on Chippewa R.; agr. mkt.; univ. food processing, varied mnfs.; p. (1984) 53,900 (t.), 136,000 (met. a.).

Ebal, Mt., Israel; opposite Gerizim; alt. 911 m.

Ebbw Vale, t., Blaenau Gwent, Gwent, **Wales**; 27 km N.W. of Newport; coal, iron, tinplate, bricks, pipes, precast concrete; some steel wks. to close; p. (1981) 24,422.

Eberswalde, t., Frankfurt, **E. Germany**; N.E. of Berlin; iron, wood, and cardboard wks., chemicals; p. (1981) 53,183.

Ebro, ch. R. of N.E. **Spain**; flows to Mediterranean from Cantabrian Mtns.; feeds hydroelectric plants, irrigation, esp. around Zaragoza; 928 km long.

Eccles, Gtr. Manchester, **Eng.**; 6 km W. of Manchester; chemicals, oil refining, engin.; p. (1981) 37,166.

Echo L., Tasmania, **Australia**; used to store water for hydroelectric power.

Echuca, t., Victoria, **Australia**; major inland pt. on Murray R. in mid 19th century; in 1970s original pt. and bldgs. restored; p. (1976) 9,075 (inc. Moama).

Écija, t., Seville, **Spain**; olive oil, wine, pottery; the Roman Astigi; p. (1981) 34,619.

Eckernförde, spt., Schleswig-Holstein, **W. Germany**; on Baltic, N.W. of Kiel; p. (est. 1986) 24,500.

Ecrins, mtn. peak, S.E. **France**; hgst. point of massif du Pelvoux and Dauphiné Alps; alt. 4,106 m.

Ecuador, rep., **S. America**; on equatorial Pac. cst., bounded by Colombia to N. and Peru to W. and S.; inc. Galapagos Is. in Pac. Oc.; lowland to E. and W. of central Andes; climate temperate in Andes and hot and humid in lowlands; comm. economy mainly agr. with impt. exp. of bananas, coffee, cocoa; petroleum impt. (68 per cent of exports); pipeline across Andes to pt. of Esmeraldas; communications difficult but vital for economic development; attempts to control illegal narcotics exp.; major pts. Guayaquil and Manta; official language Spanish; cap. Quito; a. inc. Galapagos Is. 454,752 km²; p. (est. 1987) 9·9 m.

Edam, t., N. Holland, **Neth.**; on cst. IJsselmeer; cheese, tool mftg.; p. (est. 1984) 24,019.

Eday, I., Orkney Is., **Scot.**; the Ocelli of Ptolemy; p. (1971) 179.

Eddystone, rock with lighthouse, Eng. Channel; S.W. of Plymouth.

Ede, t., Gelderland, **Neth.**; livestock; pianos; p. (est. 1987) 90,000.

Edea, t., pt., **Cameroon**; aluminium smelting based on nearby hydroelectric power plant.

Eden, Vale of, fertile belt in Cumbria, **Eng.**; between barren hills of Pennines and L. Dist.; occupied by R. Eden; mkt. ts. Appleby and Penrith; now forms l. gov. dist. inc. Penrith, Alston and Appleby; p. (est. 1988) 46,200.

Eder, R., **W. Germany**; joins Fulda R. S. of Kassel; Eder dam lgst. in Germany.

Edessa (Edhessa), t., N.E. **Greece**; agr. tr. ctr.; the anc. Ægae, burial place of Macedonian kings; p. (1981) 16,642.

Edgehill, ridge, 24 km S. of Warwick, **Eng.**; scene of first battle of civil war, 1642.

Edgewater, t., N.J., **USA**; sub., connected by ferry with New York; p. (1980) 4,628.

Edinburgh, c., cap. of **Scot.**, l. gov. dist., Lothian Reg.; royal burgh on F. of Forth; univ., cas.; palace (Holyrood); printing, publishing, brewing, electronics equipment, rubber gds.; Edinburgh Festival in August; Leith, with docks is joined to E.; p. (est. 1986) 438,232.

Edirne, t., **Turkey**; in Thrace, on R. Maritsa; comm. ctr. with tr. in wine, tobacco, silk, perfume; the anc. Adrianople, named after the emperor Hadrian, later cap. of Ottoman sultans 1366–1453; p. (1985) 86,909.

Edmonton, c., cap. of Alberta, **Canada**; fast-growing c. (119 km²) on both sides of N.

Saskatchewan R.; high-level bridge links Strathcona; major military ctr.; univ.; international air ctr.; oilfields and farming; oil and chemical inds.; p. (1986) 573,982 (c.), 785,465 (met. a.).

Edremit, t., Balikesir, **N.W. Turkey;** cereals, opium; silverwk.; p. (1985) 30,159.

Edward, L., on frontier of Uganda and Zaïre, one of the sources of R. Nile; occupies Gr. Rift Valley; alt. *c.* 900 m, 70km long, breadth 51km; salt, fishing, wildlife.

Eger, t., N.E. **Hungary;** mkt. t. in wine producing region; mediaeval fortress t.; p. (est. 1985) 66,000.

Egersund, pt., S. cst. **Norway;** fishing; mentioned in Norwegian sagas; p. (est. 1970) 10,197.

Egham, t., Runnymede, Surrey, **Eng.;** on R. Thames, nr. Staines; contains field of Runnymede; residtl.; p. (1981) 27,817.

Egmont, mtn., N.I., **N.Z.;** extinct volcano; hgt. 2,501 m.

Egremont, mkt. t., Cumbria, **Eng.;** 16 km S. of Whitehaven; limestone; former iron ore mng.

Egypt, Arab Republic of, indep. st., N.E. corner **Africa;** member of Federation of Arab Reps.; 96 per cent a. is desert except Nile valley and delta where 95 per cent of p. live; agr. depends on annual rise of Nile waters and irrigation; cereals, sugarcane, vegetables, fruit; cotton main cash crop; phosphates; oilfield in Sinai and recent finds offshore in G. of Suez and in Western Desert; nat. gas since 1974; 6 oil refineries; major port development on Red Sea to handle mineral exp.; textiles account for ⅓ of manuf. output; cap. Cairo; Aswan High Dam has produced problems; (1) silting up of reservoir (L. Nasser) behind dam; (2) reduction in fertilising silt deposits in lower Nile valley; (3) erosion of Nile delta itself; (4) reduction of fish p. in E. Med.; a. 999,740 km²; p. (est. 1987) 50·7 m (75 per cent illiterate).

Eider, R., **W. Germany;** separates Holstein from Schleswig; flows into N. Sea; 125 m. long.

Eifel, plateau of volcanic rocks, **W. Germany;** lies N. of R. Moselle, forming W. edge of Rhine gorge between Koblenz and Bonn; formerly cultivated, now largely woodland and moorland; farming in valleys; rises to just over 600 m.

Eiger, mtn., one of the hgst. peaks of the Bernese Oberland, **Switzerland;** famous for steep N. wall; alt. 3,978 m.

Eigg, I., Inner Hebrides, **Scot.;** 24 km S.W. of Mallaig; basaltic rocks on cst.; rises to 393 m.

Eilat, new spt., Negev, **Israel;** on G. of Aqaba; growing tourist tr.; copper at Timna; oil pipeline from Ashdod (1970).

Eildon Hills, Roxburgh, **Scot.;** S. of Melrose; hgst. point 422 m.

Eindhoven, c., N. Brabant, **Neth.;** electronic equipment, motor vehicles, tobacco and textile inds.; technical univ.; p. (est. 1987) 191,000.

Eire. *See* **Ireland, Republic of.**

Eisenach, t., Erfurt, **E. Germany;** on R. Hörsel, at foot of Thuringian forest; ctr. of Werra potash field; cars, machin., textiles; birthplace of J. S. Bach; p. (1981) 50,674.

Eisenerz Alps, mtn. range, **Austria;** most N. range of Alps, overlooking Danube valley between Linz and Vienna; impt. iron-ore deposits; alt. from 1,800–2,700 m.

Eisenhüttenstadt, t., Frankfurt, **E. Germany;** iron smelting; terminus of Oder–Spree canal; p. (est. 1970) 45,194.

Eisleben, t., Halle, **E. Germany;** machin., copper- and silver-mng. ctr.; birthplace of Luther; p. (est. 1970) 30,386.

Ekibastuz, t., Kazakh SSR, **USSR;** 120 km S.W. of Pavlodar; ctr. of rapidly developing mng. a. coal, gold, metals; coal-fed generating plant projected to supply power to European Russia; p. (est. 1967) 40,000.

El Aaiun, pt., **Western Sahara;** main pt. for exp. of phosphates; p. (est. 1974) 20,010.

El Alamein, v., **Egypt;** in Libyan Desert 96 km S.W. of Alexandria, scene of Allied victory, second world war; oilfield nearby; terminal nr. Sidi Abd el-Rahman.

Elan, R. Powys, **Wales;** rises on S.E. sides of Plynlimon, flows into R. Wye; lower valley contains series of 4 lge. reservoirs, capacity 45,460 million litres; ch. source of water for Birmingham.

Elâzig, t., E. **Turkey;** dam and hydroelec. project at Keban, 48 km to N.W. at confluence of E. and W. branches of Euphrates; p. (1985) 182,296.

Elba, I., off Tuscan cst., **Italy;** iron ore, wine,

marble, salt; ch. t. Portoferraio; Napoleon's first exile here; a. 363 km²; p. (1981) 10,755.

Elbe (Labe), R., in **CSSR** and **Germany;** rises in Riesengebirge and flows into N. Sea at Cuxhaven; navigable for 840 km of total l. of 1,160 km; connected with Rhine and Weser Rs. by Mittelland canal; forms part of border between E. and W. Germany.

Elbert, mtn., Col., **USA;** hgst. peak of Rocky Mtns. in USA, 4,401 m.

Elblag or **Elbing,** spt., Gdansk, N. **Poland;** shipbldg., machin., vehicles; p. (est. 1983) 115,900.

El Boulaïda (Blida), t., **Algeria;** agr. ctr.; citrus fruits; p. (est. 1983) 191,314.

Elbruz Mt., Caucasus, Georgian SSR, **USSR;** hgst. in Europe (5,636 m), over-topping Mont Blanc by 822 m; twin volcanic peaks.

Elburz, mtn. range, N. **Iran;** bordering on Caspian Sea; hgst. peak, Demavend, 5,642 m.

Elche, t., Alicante, **Spain;** palm groves; oil, soap, footwear; p. (1981) 143,000.

El Dar-el-Beida (Casablanca), c., **Morocco;** pt. on Atl. Oc.; artificial harbour; fish canning, textiles; exp. phosphate; p. (est. 1981) 2·4 m.

Eldorado, radium mine, N.W. Terr., **Canada;** on E. shore of Gr. Bear Lake nr. Arctic Circle; produces 40 per cent of world's radium, sent to Pt. Hope, Ontario, for refining.

El Djezair (Algiers), pt., cap. c. of **Algeria;** old t. surmounted by 16th cent. Casbâh (fortress); univ.; exp. wine, citrus fruit, iron ore; oil refining at Maison Carrée; airpt. at Maison Blanche, 16 km E. of c.; p. (est. 1983), 1,721,607.

Elektrenai, t., Lithuanian SSR, **USSR;** new township nr. Vievis, at site of thermal power sta.

Elektrostal, t., **RSFSR;** 56 km E. of Moscow; steel, engin.; p. (est. 1985) 148,000.

Elephanta I., Bombay Harbour, **India;** Brahmanic caves with monolithic carvings.

Elephant Butte Dam, N.M., **USA;** on Rio Grande; built to control flood water; lake, a. 115 km² supplies irrigation water to 2,020 km² in N.M. and Texas, water also supplied to Mexico.

El Ferrol del Caudillo, spt., **Spain;** on N.W. cst.; fortfd., fishing; p. (1981) 91,764.

Elgin, royal burgh, Moray, **Scot.;** pt. Lossiemouth; woollens, whisky; ruins anc. cath.; p. (1981) 18,905.

Elgin, t., Ill., **USA;** watches, electrical equipment; p. (1980) 63,981.

Elgon Mt., extinct volcano, bdy. of **Kenya** and **Uganda;** 4,300 m; cave dwellings on slopes.

Eli and Earlsferry, burgh, North East Fife, **Scot.;** summer resort; p. (1981) 888.

Elisabethville. *See* **Lubumbashi.**

Elizabeth, t. S. **Australia;** planned t. built 1950s, now merges with Adelaide met. a.; p. (1976) 33,721.

Elizabeth, c., N.J., **USA;** univ.; sewing machines. oil refining, cars, aircraft components; now inc. in Newark; p. (1984) 107,500.

Elk I., Nat. Park, **Canada;** animal reserve, tourism.

El Khârga, oasis, Libyan desert, **Egypt,** 136 km S.W. of Asyût; site of New Valley Project for irrigation.

Elkhart, t., Ind., **USA;** E. of Chicago; paper, machin.; elec. equipment, musical instruments; p. (1984) 43,100 (t.), 142,200 (met. a.).

Elk Mtns., W. Col., **USA;** highest point Castle Peak, 4,305 m.

Elland, t., West Yorks., **Eng.;** on R. Calder, 5 km S.E. of Halifax; textiles; p. (1981) 18,011.

Ellesmere, agr. dist., S.I., **N.Z.;** on Canterbury Plain nr. Christchurch.

Ellesmere, mkt. t., Shrops., **Eng.;** nearby lake; tourism.

Ellesmere I., extreme N. of Arctic **Canada;** barren uninhabited; a. 106,200 km².

Ellesmere Port, t., l. gov. dist., N.W. Cheshire, **Eng.;** on Manchester Ship Canal and 14 km S.S.E. of Liverpool; metal mftg., paper, engin., oil refineries; cars; expanded t.; with Neston forms l. gov. dist.; p. (est. 1988) 79,700.

Elliot Lake, t., N. Ont., **Canada;** ctr. of uranium mines; p. (1981) 16,723.

Ellice Is. *See* **Tuvalu I.**

Ellis I., N.Y. harbour, **USA;** served as ch. immigration ctr., 1892–1943.

Ellon, burgh, Gordon, **Scot.;** on R. Ythan; p. (1981) 6,293.

El Mahalla el Kubra, t., **Egypt;** N. of Cairo on Nile delta; textile ctr.; p. (1986) 362,700.

Elmbridge, l. gov. dist., Surrey, **Eng.;** close to Gtr. London; inc. Esher, Walton and Weybridge; p. (est. 1988) 107,100.

Elmira, t., N.Y., **USA;** rly. gds., farm implements;

famous as burial place of Mark Twain; p. (1980) 35,327.

El Misti, mtn., S. **Peru**; dormant volcano with snow cap; alt. 5,846 m.

Elmshorn, t., **W. Germany**; N.W. of Hamburg; shipbldg.; p. (est. 1986) 41,500.

El Paso, c., Texas, **USA**; on E. bank Rio Grande opposite Ciudad Juárez (Mexico); natural gas distribution, oil refining, metallurgy; tourism; p. (1984) 463,800 (c.), 526,500 (met. a.).

El Salvador. *See* **Salvador.**

El Segundo, t., Cal., **USA**; lge. oil refinery; assembly of aircraft components; p. (1980) 13,752.

Elsinore (Helsingör), t., spt., **Denmark**; shipbldg.; setting of Shakespeare's *Hamlet*; p. (est. 1987) 56,618.

Elstow, v., Beds., **Eng.**; the birthplace of John Bunyan.

Elstree, t., Hertsmere, Herts., **Eng.**; 6 km W. of Barnet; residtl.; films, lt. engin., silk hosiery.

El Teniente, Andean t., central **Chile**; copper mng. and smelting; p. 11,761.

Eluru, t., Andhra Pradesh, **India**; cotton, carpets, hosiery, oil; p. (1981) 168,154.

Elvas, mkt. t., **Portugal**; on Guadiana R.; plums, olives, jams; cath.; once strongly fortfd.; p. (1981) 12,880.

Ely, t., Cambridge, **Eng.**; on S. fringe of Fens; mkt., cath.; agr. ctr.; p. (1981) 10,268.

Ely, I. of. *See* **Cambridgeshire.**

Elyria, t., Ohio, **USA**; mftg.; p. (1980) 57,538.

Emba, R., Kazakh SSR, **USSR**; rises in Urals, flows S.W. to Caspian Sea; crosses productive Ural–Emba oilfield; 608 km long.

Emden, t., Lower Saxony, **W. Germany**; impt. N. Sea pt. nr. mouth of R. Ems and on Dortmund–Ems and Ems–Jade canals; exp. coal and iron from Ruhr; shipyards, fisheries; p. (est. 1986) 49,600.

Emene, t., **Nigeria**; nr. Enugu; steel plant; cement.

Emilia-Romagna, region, N. **Italy**; S. of Po R.; divided into 8 provs.; fertile agr. a.; a. 22,124 km²; p. (est. 1986) 3·9 m.

Emmen, t., Drenthe, **Neth.**; 48 km S.E. of Groningen; elec. machin., ball bearings, tinplate, iron wks.; p. (est. 1987) 92,000.

Emmental, dist., **Switzerland**; dairy produce, especially cheese.

Empoli, t., Tuscany, **Italy**; on R. Arno; textile mnfs., glass; p. (1981) 44,961.

Ems, R., N. **W. Germany**; rises in Teutoburger Wald, flows N. to N. Sea at Emden; 333 km long.

Emscher, R., **W. Germany**; rises in Sauerland, flows W. through heart of Ruhr coalfield to enter R. Rhine at Hamborn; canalised for most of its course; very highly polluted; 88 km long.

Encarnación, pt., cap. of Itapuá dep. S.E. **Paraguay**; on Paraná R.; exp. timber, maté, tobacco, cotton, hides; p. (1982) 27,632.

Enderby Land, Australian terr., S. of C. of Good Hope, **Antarctica.**

Enfield, former M.B., Middlesex, **Eng.**; now outer bor. Greater London; comprising Edmonton, Enfield, and Southgate; p. (est. 1988) 260,900.

Enfield, t., Conn., **USA**; mftg.; p. (1980) 42,695.

Engadine, Switzerland; upper valley of Inn R., health resort; ch. t. St. Moritz; Swiss Nat. Park.

Enggano, I., Sumatra, **Indonesia**; sparse p.; hunting, fishing, shifting cultivation.

Engels, c., **RSFSR**; on Volga; R. pt., mftg. and food-processing ctr.; engin., petroleum refining, textiles; p. (est. 1985) 177,000.

England, southern and lgst political div. of U.K.; bounded by Wales on W., by Scot. on N. and separated from continent of Europe by English Channel and North Sea; highly industl., circa 80 per cent of p. live in urban areas; major trading nation through main pts. London, Liverpool, Southampton; increasing contrast between prosperous S. and depressed N. and W.; very varied geology and topography produce contrasts in landscape, matched by climatic variability; increasingly attractive as tourist area although urban and agr. pressures on rural countryside cause concern in such a ̃nsely populated cty.; excellent road and network improved by construction of ways and rly. electrification between and Glasgow (Scot.); rich and

varied cultural heritage and numerous historic bldgs.; cap. London; a. 130,368 km²; p. (1981) 46,220,955.

Englewood, t., Col., **USA**; sub. of Denver; glasshouses; p. (1980) 30,021.

Englewood, t., N.J., **USA**; elevators, leather gds.; p. (1980) 23,701.

English Channel (La Manche), narrow sea separating England from France; extends from Strait of Dover to Land's End in Cornwall; length 480 km, greatest width 248 km.; to be crossed by Channel Tunnel (1993); *See* **Cheriton.**

Enham-Alamein, Hants., **Eng.**; rehabilitation ctr. for disabled ex-service men; 4 km N. of Andover; lt. inds.

Enid, t., Okla., **USA**; univ.; ironwks., farm implements; wheat mkt.; p. (1980) 50,363.

Enkhuizen, t., R. pt., **Neth.**; on IJsselmeer; p. (1967) 11,231.

Enna (Castrogiovanni), t., Sicily, **Italy**; sulphurmines; famous for its connection with the Proserpine legend; p. (1981) 27,838.

Ennepetal, t., N. Rhine–Westphalia, **W. Germany**; t. created 1949 with merging of Milspe and Voerde; iron, machin.; p. (est. 1986) 33,700.

Ennerdale Water, L., Cumbria, **Eng.**

Enniscorthy, mkt. t., U.D., Wexford, **R.o.I.**; cath.; p. (1981) 7,261.

Enniskillen, t., Fermanagh, **N. Ireland**; brewing, nylon mftg., meat processing; p. (1981) 10,429.

Enschede, c., Overijssel, **Neth.**; textile ctr.; technical univ.; p. (est. 1987) 144,000.

Ensenada, t., **Mexico**; spt., exp. cotton; fishing and fish processing; p. (1980) 175,425.

Entebbe, t., **Uganda**; on L. Victoria; univ.; cotton ginning; airport; p. (est. 1983) 20,472.

Entre Rios, prov., **Argentina**; between Paraná and Uruguay Rs.; wheat, linseed, livestock; cap. Paraná; a. 76,216 km²; p. (1980) 902,241.

Enugu, cap. of E. prov., **Nigeria**; coal; cloth mill; p. (est. 1983) 228,000.

Epernay, t., on S. bank of Marne, **France**; champagne ctr.; p. (1982) 28,876.

Ephesus, anc. Ionian c., in what is now **Turkey**, S. of Izmir; sacked by Goths A.D. 262; excavations.

Epinal, t., cap. of Vosges dep., **France**; on Moselle R.; textiles, printing, liqueur; p. (1982) 51,495 (met. a.).

Epirus, dist., N.W. **Greece**; a. 9,552 km²; p. (1981) 324,541.

Epping Forest, Essex, **Eng.**; forest a. N.E. of London free to public (opened by Queen Victoria 1882); formerly part of royal hunting forest; also l. gov. dist., inc. Chigwell, Waltham Abbey and Ongar; p. (est. 1988) 111,800.

Epsom and Ewell, ts., l. gov. dist., Surrey, **Eng.**; 29 km S.W. of London; residtl., racecourse; p. (est. 1988) 67,500.

Epworth, v., Humberside, **Eng.**; birthplace of John Wesley.

Equatorial Guinea, unitary state, W. **Africa**; former Spanish col.; indep. 1968; comprises 2 provs.; Rio Muni (mainland and Is. of Corisco, Elobey Grande, Elobey Chico) and Biako (Is. of Biako and Pagalu); narrow coastal plain and dissected upland plateau (600 m); economy almost entirely based on agr. and timber; exploration for oil; cap. Malabo on Biako I.; a. 28,051 km²; p. (est. 1987) 384,000.

Erbil, t., Iraq; comm. ctr.; rly. terminus; p. (1965) 134,000 (met. a.).

Erebus, mtn., active volcano, Victoria Land, **Antarctica**; alt. 4,027 m.

Erewash, l. gov. dist., Derbys., **Eng.**; a. close to Nottingham inc. Ilkeston and Long Eaton; p. (est. 1988) 107,900.

Erfurt, admin. dist., **E. Germany**; a. 7,322 km²; p. (1983) 1,238,200.

Erfurt, c., **E. Germany**; on Gera R.; cath., ctr. of mkt. gardening and seed-growing dist.; textiles, machin., foodstuffs, footwear, radios, heavy engin.; p. (est. 1986) 217,000.

Ericht, loch, **Scot.**; in central Grampians; 25 km long; hydroelec. scheme.

Erie, c., N.W. Penns., **USA**; pt. on L. Erie; coal, iron, grain, petroleum; machin., domestic appliances; p. (1984) 117,500 (c.), 282,100 (met. a.).

Erie Canal. *See* **New York State Barge Canal.**

Erie, one of Great Lakes (the shallowest), **N. America**, separating Canada from USA; 386 km long, 48–91 km wide; polluted waters; petroleum resources.

Erith, former M.B., Kent, **Eng.**; on Thames estuary; plastics, paints, varnishes, timber, concrete; now inc. in London bor. of Bexley.

Eritrea, prov., **Ethiopia**; tobacco, cereals, pearl fishing; demands for autonomy; secessionist rebellion crushed (1978); severe drought 1982–3; cap. Asmara, a. 118,503 km²; p. (est. 1980) 2,426,200.

Erivan. *See* **Yerevan.**

Erlangen, t., Bavaria, **W. Germany**; univ.; textiles, elec. and precision engin., gloves; p. (est. 1986) 100,200.

Ermelo,t.,Neth.;ctr.of agr.dist.;p. (est.1987) 26,000.

Ernakuiam, t., Kerala, **India**; cotton, coffee, hides; p. (est. 1970) 213,811 (c.), 493,460 (met. a.).

Erne, R., **N. Ireland/R.o.I.**; links Ls. in Cavan and Fermanagh; 115 km long.

Erode, t., S. Tamil Nadu, **India**; on R. Cauvery; p. (1981) 142,252 (t.), 275,991 (met. a.).

Erzgebirge (Ore Mtns.), mtn. range along border of ČSSR and Germany; reaching highest peak in Mt. Klinovec (1,240 m) in ČSSR; uranium; tourism.

Erzurum, t., **Turkey**; agr. ctr. on fertile plateau *c*. 1,890 m a.s.l.; formerly of gr. strategic importance; univ.; earthquake (1983); p. (1985) 246,053.

Esbjerg, spt., **Denmark**; W. cst. of Jutland; export harbour on N. Sea cst.; exp. agr. prod.; fishing; airport; p. (est. 1987) 80,825.

Esch-sur-Alzette, t., **Luxembourg**; mng. ctr.; steel; p. (1981) 25,100.

Eschwege, t., Hesse, **W. Germany**; cas.; machin.; textiles, leather, cigars, chemicals; p. (est. 1986) 22,900.

Eschweiler, t., N. Rhine-Westphalia, **W. Germany**; N.W. of Aachen; lignite mng., steel, iron metallurgy; p. (est. 1986) 53,100.

Esdraelon, plain, **Israel**; between Carmel and Gilboa Mtns.

Eşfahān (Isfahan, anc. Aspadana), c., central **Iran**; prov. cap.; historic, picturesque c. noted for carpets and metal ware; tourism, airpt.; new steel mill; impt. oil refining ctr.; p. (1986) 1,001,248.

Esher, t., Elmbridge, Surrey, **Eng.**; on R. Mole, residtl.; Sandown Park racecourse; p. (1981) 61,446.

Eshowe, health resort, Natal, **S. Africa**; 64 km from Tugela R.; p. (est. 1967) 4,800.

Esk, R., Annandale and Eskdale, **Scot.**; Cumbria, **Eng.**; attractive agr. valley; flows into Solway F. from confluence of Black and White Esk Rs.; 37 km long.

Eskilstuna, t., **Sweden**; on R. of same name; iron, steel, machin., machin. tools; p. (est. 1986) 88,000.

Eskişehir, t.,**Turkey**; W. of Ankara, anc. Dorylaeum; rly. ctr.; meerschaum; p. (1985) 366,765.

Esmeraldas, prov., **Ecuador**; cap. E. on R. of same name; cacao, tobacco; a. 14,152 km²; p. (1982) 247,870.

Esmeraldas, pt., **Ecuador**; bananas, timber, tobacco, cacao, rubber; gold mines nearby; terminal of petroleum pipeline from Oriente; p. (est. 1984) 105,200.

Esneh. *See* **Isna.**

Espirito Santo, I., **Brazil**; sugar, cotton, coffee, fruits, lumber, thorium; cap. Vitória; a. 40,883 km²; p. (est. 1985) 2,287,900.

Espiritu Santo, I., **New Hebrides**; volcanic I., lgst. of gr.; depopulation.

Essaouira (Mogador), spt., **Morocco**; cereals, almonds, gum-arabic, crude oil; p. (1982) 42,035.

Essen, c., N. Rhine-Westphalia, **W. Germany**; gr. industl. c., ctr. of Ruhr conurbation; coal, steel (Krupp), electric power, engin.; canal links with Dortmund-Ems and Mittelland canals and with Rhine; minster severely damaged in second world war; p. (est. 1986) 615,400.

Essequibo, R.; flows N. from Brazilian border draining half **Guyana**; lower course navigable, rapids; timber in upper valley; 960 km long.

Essex, non-met. co., **Eng.**; bounded on S. by Thames, on E. by N. Sea; co. t. Chelmsford; on London clay and chalk; agr.; wheat, barley, sugar-beet; mkt. gardens; S.W. of co. forms part of Greater London with mftg. subs.; oil refineries at Shell Haven; civil nuclear power sta. at Bradwell; univ. at Colchester; a. 2,637 km²; p. (est. 1988) 1,529,500.

Esslingen, t., Baden-Württemberg, **W. Germany**; on R. Neckar; mach. and rly. shops; textiles,

chemicals, leather gds.; Liebfrauen church (1440); p. (est. 1986) 86,900.

Essonne, dep., **France**; S. of Paris; cap. Ivry; a. 1,810 km²; p. (1982) 988,400.

Estelí, cap., Estelí, **Nicaragua**; on Inter-American Highway; p. (est. 1985) 30,635.

Eston, t., Cleveland, **Eng.**; 5 km E. of Middlesbrough; shipbldg. and repairing.

Estonia (Estoniya), constituent rep. **USSR**; borders on Baltic, G. of Finland, G. of Riga; lowland with many Ls.; farming and dairying, fishing; oil deposits; hydroelec. power; mainly Lutheran; univ.; cap. Tallinn; a. 45;610 km²; p. (1986) 1,541,000.

Estoril, wat. pl. and thermal spa, **Portugal**; N. side of Tagus estuary; holiday resort; p. (1981) 24,312.

Estremadura, maritime prov., **Portugal**; agr., tourism; cap. Lisbon; a. 5,348 km²; p. (1981) 1,064,976.

Estremadura, region, S.W. **Spain**; on the border of Portugal; largely plateau, alt. 450–900 m.; heathy moorland; sheep; less arid conditions than in remainder of central Spain allow olives, vines, cereals; irrigation in valleys of Tagus, Guadiana; govt. project to develop a. in progress.

Esztergom, t., **Hungary**; R. pt. on Danube; iron foundries, machine tools; mineral springs; cath.; p. (est. 1984) 31,000.

Etang de Berre, lagoon, Bouches-du-Rhône, S.E. **France**; E. of Rhône delta; traversed by Rhône-Marseille canal; salt pans; oil refineries . in a.; approx. a. 260 km².

Étaples, t., Pas-de-Calais, **France**; seaside resort; p. (1982) 11,310.

Etawah, t., Uttar Pradesh, **India**; textiles; p. (1981) 112,174.

Ethiopia (Abyssinia), indep. st. N.E. **Africa**; temperate climate as a result of high plateau terrain; coffee most impt. comm. crop, but poor communications inhibit economic development; low per capita income and rapid growth of p.; potential for hydro-electric power is lge., one sta. open on Awash R.; mftg. dominated by textiles; agr. improvements encouraged by Peasant's Association; severe drought began in 1970's and continued in 1980's, affects low-lying and Eastern regions; cap. Addis Ababa; monarchy abolished 1975; a. 1,221,900 km²; p. (est. 1986) 46,000,000.

Ethiopian Highlands, mtns., Ethiopia; rise over 4,500 m; source of headwaters of tribs. of R. Nile.

Etna, volcano, N.E. Sicily, **Italy**; most recent eruptions 1971 and 1979; alt. 3,276 m.

Eton, t., Berks., **Eng.**; on N. bank of R. Thames opposite Windsor; public school, founded by Henry VI; p. (1981) 3,523.

Etruria, anc. dist., **Italy**; now forms Tuscany; home of the Etruscans and part of the Roman empire by 400 B.C.

Etruria, t., Staffs., **Eng.**; part of Stoke-on-Trent; seat of Josiah Wedgwood's potteries (1769).

Ettrick and Lauderdale, l. gov. dist., part of Borders Reg. in Tweed Valley, **Scot.**; p. (est. 1986) 33,223.

Euboea (Evvoia), lgst. of Greek Is., Aegean Sea; mtnous. (Mt. Delphi 1,746 m); vines and olives in lowlands, sheep and goats in highlands; a. 3,864 km²; p. (1981) 188,410.

Euclid, t., Ohio, **USA**; electrical and agr. machin.; p. (1980) 59,999.

Eucumbene Dam and **L.**, N.S.W., **Australia**; major storage of Snowy Mtns. hydroelectric scheme; holds eight times as much water as Sydney harbour.

Eugene, c., Ore., **USA**; univ.; mkt. ctr. for rich agr. and lumbering region; fruit-canning, sawmilling; headquarters of Willamette National Forest; p. (1984) 101,600 (c.), 266,400 (met. a. with Springfield).

Euphrates, lgst. R. in S.W. **Asia**; rises in Armenian uplands and joined by the Tigris enters Persian G. as the Shatt-al Arab; anc. ctr. of civilisation; modern irrigation, navigation, high dam opened 1973 and Ataturk Dam (1981) part of multi-purpose project; 2,848 km long.

Eure, dep., Normandy, **France**; agr., fruit, livestock, textiles; cap. Evreux; a. 6,037 km²; p. (1982) 462,000.

Eure-et-Loire, dep., N. **France**; mainly agr.; cap. Chartres; a. 5,934 km²; p. (1982) 362,000.

Europe, continent; W. peninsula of Eurasian land mass; no well-defined bdy. with Asia but line normally accepted runs along Ural Mtns. to Caspian Sea and Caucasus to Black Sea

Sea of Marmara and Dardanelles; after Australia, Europe is smallest continent in a., but contains 11 per cent of world's p. and even more of world's economic activity; climate varies from Arctic to Mediterranean and from temperate maritime to severe continental; major physical features inc. Alps, Pyrenees in S., Baltic Shield in N.; major political div. between E. and W. Europe along Iron Curtain; W. Europe also divided into economic grs. EEC and EFTA; major concentration of p. and economic activity within Golden Triangle (q.v.), total a. c. 10,360,000 km²; p. (est. 1984) 490,456,000 (excl. USSR).

Euro-port, name of the post-war expansion of the port of Rotterdam, **Neth.**; capable of handling 100,000 tonne oil-tankers; oil refining; European oil supply ctr.

Evanston, t., **USA**; on L. Michigan, sub. of Chicago; univ.; p. (1980) 73,706.

Evansville, c., Ind., **USA**; on Ohio R.; shipping and comm. ctr. for agr. region; coal mng.; p. (1984) 130,300 (c.), 281,300 (met. a.).

Eveneki National Area, Siberia, **RSFSR**; forest and tundra covered; home of Eveneki people; cap. Tura; a. 740,740 km²; p. (1970) 13,000.

Everest, Mt. (Chomolungma = Goddess Mother of the Earth), Himalaya, on frontier of **Nepal** and Tibet, **China**; alt. 8,854 m; hgst. mtn. in the world; Hillary and Tenzing first to reach summit in 1953; within Nepal Nat. Park.

Everett, mftg. t., Mass., **USA**; nr. Boston; iron and steel; p. (1980) 37,195.

Everett, t., Wash., **USA**; on Puget Sound; harbour; comm. ctr.; timber; tourism; p. (1980) 54,413.

Everglades, Fla., **USA**; subtropical a.; extensive marshes; home of Seminole Indians; lge. scale drainage since 1905; early vegetables.

Evesham, mkt. t., Wychavon, Hereford and Worcs., **Eng.**; on R. Avon, in Vale of Evesham, 24 km S.E. of Worcester; fruit ctr.; tourism; p. (1981) 15,271.

Evora, t., cap. of Upper Alentejo prov., S. **Portugal**; mkt. for agr. prod.; cath.; p. (1981) 34,851.

Évreux, t., cap. of Eure dep., **France**; mkt. ctr.; p. (1982) 54,645 (met. a.).

Evros, prov., **Greece**; borders Bulgaria and Turkey; a. 4,191 km²; p. (1981) 148,486.

Exe, R., Somerset and Devon, **Eng.**; rises on Exmoor, flows S. via Exeter to English Channel at Exmouth; 86 km long.

Exeter, l. gov. dist., cath. c., co. t., Devon, **Eng.**; former Roman Isca; E. of Dartmoor on R. Exe; mkt. t.; univ.; aircraft components; airport; p. (est. 1988) 99,600.

Exmoor, Somerset and Devon, **Eng.**; sandstone moorland, deep wooded valleys; Nat. Park.

Exmouth, t., East Devon, **Eng.**; on estuary of R. Exe; holiday resort; p. (1981) 28,787.

Exploits, R., Newfoundland, **Canada**; length 240 km; used for hydroelectric power.

Eye, mkt. t., Mid Suffolk, **Eng.**; 29 km N. of Ipswich; anc. church; p. (1981) 1,786.

Eyemouth, burgh, Berwick, **Scot.**; on E. cst. 14 km N. of Berwick; fishing; p. ((1981) 3,353.

Eyre Lake, shallow salt L., S. **Australia**; 16 m rapid incr. in a. in wet year of 1974 caused lge. incr. in pelican p.; a. 7,800 km².

Eyre Peninsula, S. **Australia**; between Gr. Australian Bight and Spencer G.; iron-ore deposits; a. 51,800 km².

F

Fabriano, t., Marches, **Italy**; in Apennines; cath.; paper mills; p. (1981) 28,708.

Faenza, t., Ravenna, **Italy**; at foot of Apennines; majolica, textiles; p. (1981) 55,003.

Fagersta, t., Västmanland, **Sweden**; iron, steel smelting; p. (est. 1970) 17,054.

Failsworth, t. Gtr. Manchester, **Eng.**; N.E. of Manchester; textiles, elec. gds.; p. (1981) 21,751.

Fairbanks, t., Alaska, **USA**; univ.; sawmilling; mng.; p. (1980) 22,645.

Field, t., Conn., **USA**; chemicals, automobile univ.; p. (1980) 54,849.

midway between Shetland and Orkney; 3rd sanctuary; famous for brightly

patterned, hand-knitted articles.

Fairmont, t., W. Va., **USA**; glass, machin., coal by-products; p. (1980) 23,863.

Faisalabad c. W. Punjab, **Pakistan**; univ. cotton chemicals, fertilizers; p. (1981) 1,092,000.

Faiyum (El Faiyûm), t. and region, N. **Egypt**; oasis nr. L. Karun (anc. L. Moeris), fertilised by Nile water and silt; cereals, sugar-cane, fruits, cotton; archaeological finds; p. of t. (est. 1983) 213,000.

Faisalabad, t., Uttar Pradesh, **India**; rly. junc.; sugar refining; p. (1981) 101,873 (t.), 143,167 (met. a.).

Falaise, t., Calvados, **France**; birthplace of William the Conqueror; p. (1982) 8,820.

Falaise de l'Ile de France, low S.E.-facing escarpment, 80 km S.E. and E. of Paris, **France**; overlooks Champagne Pouilleuse; ch. vine-growing dist. for champagne-wine ind. of Reims, Epernay.

Falcón, st., **Venezuela**; bordering Caribbean Sea; cap. Coro; p. (1980) 507,899.

Falconara Marittima, t., **Italy**; nr. Ancona; spt.; oil refining, shipbldg.; p. (1981) 29,071.

Falkirk, burgh, l. gov. dist., Central Reg., **Scot.**; 16 km S.E. of Stirling; foundries, bricks, chemical, aluminium wks., concrete, timber yards; battles 1298 and 1746; p. (est. 1986) 143,063 (dist.).

Falkland, burgh, North East Fife, **Scot.**; 5 km S. of Auchtermuchty; mkt.; p. (1981) 960.

Falkland Is., Brit. Crown col., **S. Atl.**, comprises E. and W. Falkland and adjacent Is.; known as Malvinas by Argentina; sheep rearing (for wool); cap. Stanley on E. Falkland I.; invasion by Argentina led to Falklands War (1982); airpt. opened (1985) capable of taking long range wide bodied aircraft; a. 12,173 km²; p. (1986) 1,916.

Falkland Is. Dependencies, S. Atl.; inc. Is. of S. Georgia and S. Sandwich; a. 4,092 km²; p. (of S. Georgia) 11 males; now form part of Brit. Antarctic Terr.

Fall River, c., Mass., **USA**; on Mt. Hope Bay; pt. of entry; clothing, rubber gds., food prods., paper; p. (1980) 92,574 (c.), 176,831 (met. a.).

Falmouth, t., Carrick, Cornwall, **Eng.**; on W. side of estuary of R. Fal. 16 km S. of Truro; sheltered harbourage; offshore oil supply base; seaside resort; fisheries, ship repairing, mng., quarrying, lt. engin.; cas.; pt.; p. (1981) 18,525.

False Bay, inlet on E. side of C. of Good Hope peninsula, **S. Africa.**

Falster, I., Baltic, **Denmark**; cap. Nyköbing; p. (1965) 45,906.

Falun, t., Kopparberg, **Sweden**; paper; copper mines now exhausted; p. (est. 1986) 52,000.

Famagusta, t., spt., **Cyprus**; on E. cst.; resort; anc. crusade pt.; p. (est. 1985) 19,400.

Famatina, t., La Rioja prov., **Argentina**; in foothills of Andes, 576 km N.W. of Córdoba; copper-mines.

Fano, t., **Italy**; sm. pt. on Adriatic cst., N. of Ancona; seaside resort; p. (est. 1971) 48,259.

Fareham, t., l. gov. dist., Hants., **Eng.**; at N.W. corner of Portsmouth Harbour; p. (est. 1988) 100,300.

Farewell (Kap Farvel), C., southernmost tip of **Greenland.**

Farewell, C., most N. point S.I., **N.Z.**

Fargo, t., N.D., **USA**; rly. ctr. and R. pt.; grain, farm machin.; p. (1984) 65,700 (t.), 143,400 (met. a.).

Faringdon, mkt. t., Vale of White Horse, Oxon., **Eng.**; Faringdon Folly.

Farnborough, t., Rushmoor, Hants., **Eng.**; 5 km N. of Aldershot military camp; Royal Aircraft Establishment; p. (1981) 45,453.

Farne Is., gr. of islets off Northumberland cst., **Eng.**; bird sanctuary; National Trust.

Farnham, t., Waverley, Surrey, **Eng.**; at N. foot of N. Downs, 16 km W. of Guildford; mkt.; p. (1981) 35,289.

Farnworth, t., Gtr. Manchester, **Eng.**; nr. Bolton, textiles, engin., paper; p. (1981) 24,589.

Faro, spt., cap. of Algarve prov., **Portugal**; cork, figs, oranges; p. (1981) 27,974.

Faroe Is., 320 km N.W. of the Shetlands, Scot.; cap. Thörshavn (Strömö I.); Danish possession but not member of EC; impt. fisheries; a. 1,399 km²; p. (est. 1986) 46,312.

Farrukhabad, t., Uttar Pradesh, **India**; on Ganges R.; gold, lace, brass wk.; p. (1981) 145,793.

Fars, prov., S. **Iran**; agr.; cap. Shîrãz; p. (1982) 2 m.

Fastnet, lighthouse in Atl. Oc., 7·2 km S.W. C. Clear, Irish cst.

Fatima, v., W. **Portugal**, nr. Leiria; R.C. pilgrimage.

Fatshan *See* **Foshan.**

Faversham, pt., Swale, N.E. Kent, **Eng.**; at head of F. creek; mkt.; fruit, hops, bricks, brushes, engin.; p. (1981) 16,098.

Fawley, t., Hants., **Eng.**; on W. shore Southampton Water; lge. oil refinery with pipeline to Staines and Heathrow Airpt.; synthetic rubber.

Fayetteville, t., N.C., **USA**; agr. processing; p. (1984) 66,100 (t.), 251,300 (met. a.).

Feather, R., N. Cal., **USA**; R. project for water supply irrigation, and hydroelectric power.

Featherstone, t., West Yorks., **Eng.**; p. (1981) 14,043.

Fécamp, sm. spt. on cst. of Normandy, **France**; fishing, tourism, 12th cent. abbey; p. (1982) 21,696.

Fedchenko, glacier, lgst. in **USSR**; in Pamir-Altai mtns. of central Asia; 80 km long.

Federal German Republic. *See* **Germany, Fed. Rep. of.**

Feira de Santana, t., Bahia, **Brazil**, inland mkt. t.; recent industl. expansion results from SUDENE development plan; p. (est. 1985) 356,660.

Feldberg, highest peak in Black Forest, **W. Germany**; alt. 1,495 m.

Feldkirch, t., Vorarlberg, **Austria**; on Swiss frontier; p. (1988) 23,745.

Felixstowe, pt., Suffolk Coastal, Suffolk, **Eng.**; now one of country's best container pts.; seaside resort; p. (1981) 20,858.

Felling, Tyne and Wear, **Eng.**; Tyneside mftg. dist.; p. (1981) 36,431.

Feltham. *See* **Hounslow.**

Fenland, l. gov. dist., Cambs., **Eng.**; agr. a. in N. of co. inc. Wisbech, Chatteris, March, Whittlesey and North Witchford; p. (est. 1988) 73,200.

Fens, The, low-lying dist. around the Wash, **Eng.**; artificial drainage begun in 17th cent.; impt. agr. dist.; root crops, wheat, fruit, bulbs; a. 3,367 km².

Feodosiya, t., Ukrainian SSR, **USSR**; in Crimea; major Black Sea pt., tobacco, hosiery; exp. wheat; resort and sanatoria; p. (est. 1968) 59,000.

Ferghana, region, Uzbek SSR, **USSR**; deep basin at W. end of Tien Shan Mtns.; drained W. by R. Syr Dar'ya; semi-arid but extensive irrigation system allows intensive cultivation of cotton, citrus fruits, silk, rice; ch. ts. Kokand, Namangan.

Ferghana, c., Uzbek SSR, **USSR**; hydroelectric power, petroleum refining, textiles; deposits of ozocerite nearby; p. (est. 1985) 195,000.

Fermanagh, former co.; l. gov. dist., **N. Ireland**; bisected by R. Erne and lakes; stock raising, dairying; p. (1981) 51,558 (dist.).

Fermoy, t., Cork, **R.o.I.**; on R. Blackwater; cath.; woollens; p. (1971) 3,237.

Fernando de Noronha, I., fed. terr., N.E. cst. Brazil; penal settlement and mkt. sta.; cap. Vila dos Remédios; a. 26 km²; p. (1980) 1,279.

Fernando Po. *See* **Biako.**

Ferozepore, t., Punjab st., N.W. **India**; rly. t.; admin. ctr.; p. (1961) 97,932.

Ferrara, c., N. **Italy**; nr. head of Po delta; cath., univ., palaces; mkt. for fertile plain; silk, hemp, wine; oil refinery nearby; petro-chemicals; birthplace of Savonarola; p. (1984) 147,328.

Ferro (Hierro), most S. of the **Canary Is.**; a. 275 km²; cap. Valverde; chosen by Ptolemy (A.D. 56) for his prime meridian and used by French scientists in 17th cent.; reckoned as exactly W. 20° of Paris.

Ferryhill, v., Durham, **Eng.**; 8 km S. of Durham, in gap through limestone ridge which separates Wear valley from Tees valley; commands main N. to S. route along lowland E. of Pennines.

Fertile Crescent, an arc of fertile land from the Mediterranean Sea, N. of the Arabian Desert, to Persian G.; home of some very early civilisations and migrations.

Fez (Fès), c., **Morocco**; lies inland 160 km E. of Rabat; one of the sacred cities of Islam; univ. attached to mosque (one of lgst. in Africa); comm. ctr.; p. (est. 1981) 563,000.

Fezzan, prov., S.W. **Libya**; desert plateau with numerous wells and inhabited oases; p. (1964) 78,326.

Ffestiniog (Festiniog), t., Meirionnydd, Gwynedd, N. **Wales**; at head of Vale of Ffestiniog, 14 km E. of Portmadoc; contains Ffestiniog and Blaenau Ffestiniog; slate quarries; pumped-

storage hydroelec. sta. (1963); cement; narrow gauge rly.; p. (1981) 5,437.

Fianarantsoa, t., **Madagascar**; rice mills, meat preserves; p. (est. 1982) 73,000.

Fichtelgebirge, mtn. range, N.E. Bavaria, **W. Germany**; extending into ČSSR, rising to 1,051 m in Schneeberg; forested slopes.

Fiesole, t., Tuscany, **Italy**; on summit of wooded hill overlooking Florence and the Arno; residtl.; 11th cent. cath.; p. (1981) 14,486.

Fife, l. gov. reg., former co., E. **Scot.**; occupies a. between Tay and Forth estuaries; industl. dist. based originally on coalfields; a. 1,305 km²; p. (est. 1986) 343,825.

Fiji, S.W. Pac. Oc., former Brit. col., gained independence in 1970; comprises over 800 Is.; tropical climate; agr. basis of economy, especially sugar and coconut prods.; gold an impt. exp.; forestry and tourism developing; forms ctr. of communications in S.W. Pac. Oc.; international airport at Nadi, ch. pt. and cap. Suva; a. 18,272 km²; cosmopolitan p. (1986) 715,375. Military coup (1987).

Filey, t., North Yorks., **Eng.**; 8 km S.E. of Scarborough; seaside resort; p. (1981) 5,702.

Filton, Bristol, Avon, **Eng.**; aircraft wks.

Finchley. *See* **Barnet.**

Findhorn, t., Moray, **Scot.**; resort; 12th cent. abbey; fishing; p. (1981) 530.

Findlay, t., Ohio, **USA**; on Blanchard R.; agr. machin., tyres, beet sugar refining; p. (1980) 35,594.

Fingal's Cave, Staffa I., Inner Hebrides, W. **Scot.**; basaltic columns.

Finger Lakes, gr. of narrow glacial Ls., N.Y., **USA**; picturesque resorts and state parks.

Finistère (Lat. *finis terrae* = land's end), dep. N.W. **France**, in Brittany; cap. Quimper; fishing, tourism; a. 7,071 km²; p. (1982) 828,700.

Finland, rep., N. **Europe**; part of Scandinavia; low-lying plateau severely eroded by ice to form 60,000 Ls.; economy based on timber (forests cover 72 per cent of a.); world's leading exporter of pulp and paper; increasing importance of metal and engin. inds.; cap. Helsinki; a. 360,318 km²; p. concentrated in S.; p. (1986) 4,925,644.

Finland, G. of, E. arm of Baltic Sea, between Finland and USSR.

Finnart, Dumbarton, **Scot.**; crude oil terminal situated in Loch Long. N.W. Glasgow; pipeline to Grangemouth.

Finnmark, most N. co., **Norway**; inhabited by Lapps; whale fisheries; lge. copper deposits discovered nr. Reppan fjord; a. 48,125 km²; p. (1983) 77,383.

Finsbury. *See* **Islington.**

Finsteraarhorn, highest peak in Bernese Oberland, **Switzerland**; 4,277 m.

Finucane I., pt., W. **Australia**; deepwater pt. to ship ion ore and new t. projected.

Firenze. *See* **Florence.**

Firozabad, t., Uttar Pradesh, **India**; glassware; agr. tr.; p. (1961) 98,611.

Fishguard and Goodwick, spt., Preseli, Dyfed, **Wales**; on S. of Cardigan Bay; steamer connection to Cork and Rosslare (Ireland); p. (1981) 4,908.

Fitchburg, t., Mass., **USA**; paper, machin., textiles; p. (1980), 39,580 (t.), 99,957 (met. a.).

Fitzroy, R., W. **Australia**; flows into King Sound; dry in winter; irrigation; 560 km long.

Fiume. *See* **Rijeka.**

Flamborough Head, promontory of Yorks. cst., **Eng.**; steep chalk cliffs; lighthouse; anc., Brit. earthwork (Danes' dyke).

Flanders, region between R. Scheldt and cst., crossed by Franco–Belgian frontier; Dunkirk, Lille ctrs. of French F.; Belgian F. divided into 2 provs., E. and W., p. (est. 1983) 676,398 and 549,525 respectively; caps. Bruges and Ghent.

Fleet, t., Hart, Hants., **Eng.**; 6 km N.W. of Aldershot; p. (1981) 26,004.

Fleetwood, spt., Wyre, Lancs., **Eng.**; at mouth of Wyre, Morecambe Bay; deep-sea fish. pt.; fish processing; lge. chemical plant nearby; p. (1981) 28,467.

Flensburg, spt., Schleswig-Holstein, **W. Germany**; on Baltic, close to Danish border; shipbld., machin., chemicals, rum distilleries, fishing; p. (est. 1986) 85,700.

Flevosted, t., **Neth.**; admin. ctr. of new S.E. Polder.

Flinders I., Australia; lgst I. in the Furneaux gr., Bass Strait; famous for mutton birds.

Flinders Range, chain of mtns., S. **Australia**; extending 400 km N.E. from head of Spencer G., reaching 1,190 m in St. Mary's Peak; named after Matthew Flinders; uranium ore at Mt. Painter.

Flint, t., Delyn, Clwyd, **Wales**; viscose textile yarn, cas. ruins; p. (1981) 16,454.

Flint, t., Mich., **USA**; motorcars, aircraft engines; p. (1984) 149,000 (t.), 434,100 (met. a.).

Flintshire, former co., N. **Wales**; now part of Clwyd.

Flodden, v. Northumberland, **Eng.**; on R. Till; battle between James IV of Scot. and the English under the Earl of Surrey 1513.

Flora, t., **Norway**; new t. 136 km N. of Bergen; p. (1965) 7,700.

Florence (Firenze), c., Tuscany, **Italy**; on R. Arno; univ.; leather-work; famous for art treasures, cath. and churches; ruled by Medici 1421–1737; birthplace of Dante and Machiavelli; severely affected by heavy floods Nov. 1966; EEC univ.; p. (1984) 440,910.

Florence, t., N.W. Ala., **USA**; on Tennessee R., nr. Wilson dam; textile, steel plants; p. (1984) 36,000 (t.), 135,700 (met. a.).

Flores, I., most northwesterly of Azores gr.; Portuguese; cap. Santa Cruz; French to set up ballistic missiles tracking sta.; a. 142 km²; p. (1970) 5,630.

Flores, I., Indonesia; mtnous.; volcanic, densely forested; a. 22,973 km²; p. (1961) 803,000.

Flores Sea, between Sulawesi and Flores, Indonesia.

Florianópolis, spt., cap. of Santa Catarina st., Brazil; comm. ctr., fishing; p. (est. 1985) 218,900.

Florida, st., **USA**; Sunshine St.; admitted to Union 1845; st. flower Orange Blossom, st. bird Mockingbird; between Atl. Oc. and G. of Mexico; lowlying, swampy, inc. Everglades; sea resorts on Atl. cst.; citrus fruit and subtropical agr.; agr. processing; cap Tallahassee; a. 151,670 km²; p. (1985) 11,366,000; hgst. percentage of p. over 65 in USA (17.6).

Florida Keys, archipelago, **USA**; extends in an arc from S.E. cst. Florida W.S.W. to Key West in G. of Mexico; fishing resorts.

Florida Strait, between Florida and Bahama Is.; course of Gulf Stream from G. of Mexico.

Florina. *See* Phlorina.

Florissant (St. Ferdinand), t., Mo., **USA**; sub. of St. Louis on Missouri R.; p. (1980) 55,372.

Flushing. *See* Vlissingen.

Fly, lgst. R. of Papua New Guinea; flows S.E. from Victor Emmanuel Range to G. of Papua; 1,280 km long.

Fochabers, v., Moray, **Scot.**; nr. mouth of Spey; tourist resort; food canning; p. (1981) 1,496.

Focsani, t., **Romania**; at foot of Transylvanian Alps; wine and grain ctr.; p. (est. 1983) 77,391.

Foggia, cath. c., S. **Italy**; rly. ctr. and mkt. ctr. for plain of Apulia; site of cas. of Frederick II; p. (1984) 157,371.

Foix, t., cap. of Ariège dep., S. **France**; historic t.; p. (1982) 10,064.

Foligno, t., central **Italy**; in Apennines, on Topino R.; cath., textiles, paper; p. (1981) 52,484.

Folkestone, t., Shepway, Kent, **Eng.**; seaside resort; pt. for Folkestone–Boulogne ferry to France 46 km; p. (1981) 43,742. *See* Cheriton.

Fond du Lac, t., Winnebago L., Wis., **USA**; cath.; machine tools, domestic appliances; resort; p. (1980) 35,863.

Fonseca, Gulf of, Honduras; lgst. indentation along Pac. cst. of Central America; sm. pt. of Amapala, US naval base, and new deepwater pt.

Fontainebleau, t., Seine-et-Marne, France; on R. Seine, 56 km S.E. Paris; in former royal forest (a. 17,200 ha); magnificent palace; p. (1982) 18,753.

Fontenoy, v., **Belgium**; nr. Tournai; scene of battle (1745) when the French under Marshal Saxe defeated the English and their allies; p. (est. 1969) 655.

Foochow. *See* Fuzhou.

~landia. *See* Belterra.

~d, N. and **S.,** two headlands on E. cst. Kent, ~etween which are the Goodwin Sands ~well Bay; lighthouses; sea battle be~ ~yter and Monk (1666).

Forest Heath, l. gov. dist., Suffolk, **Eng.**; part of Breckland inc. Mildenhall and Newmarket; p. (est. 1986) 57,600.

Forest Hills, residtl. a., central Queen's bor., N.Y., **USA**; national and international matches played at West Side Tennis Club.

Forest of Dean. *See* Dean, Forest of.

Forfar, royal burgh, Angus, **Scot.**; former cty. t.; jute, linen; p. (1981) 12,742.

Forlì, c., Emilia-Romagna, central **Italy**; route ctr. in Appennine foothills; felt, textiles, footwear; p. (1984) 110,943.

Formby, t., Merseyside, **Eng.**; on W. cst., 10 km S.W. of Southport; residtl.; p. (1981) 25,798.

Formosa, prov., N. **Argentina**; bordering on Paraguay; timber; cap. Formosa; a. 72,067 km²; p. (1980) 292,479.

Formosa. *See* Taiwan.

Forres, royal burgh, Moray, **Scot.**; on Findhorn R. nr. Moray F.; agr., forestry, engin., distilleries; cas.; p. (1981) 8,346.

Forst, t., Cottbus, **E. Germany**; on R. Neisse; E. section of t. Polish since 1945; textiles; p. (est. 1970) 29,284.

Fortaleza, c., cap. of Ceará st., **Brazil**; in the dry Sertão reg. of the N.E.; terminus of cattle droving route; recent growth resulting from planned industl. devel. to revitalise reg.; p. (est. 1985) 1,588,700.

Fort Collins, t., Col., **USA**; ctr. of rich farming a.; grain, sugarbeet, livestock; univ.; p. (1984) 70,700 (t.), 165,700 (met. a.).

Fort de France, cap. of **Martinique,** Fr. W.I.; landlocked harbour; exp. sugar, rum; comm. ctr.; Fr. naval base; p. (1982) 99,844.

Fort George, R., W. Quebec, **Canada**; rises in Labrador and flows into Hudson Bay; 880 km long.

Fort Gouraud, t., **Mauritania**; modern iron-ore mines.

Forth, R., **Scot.**; formed by two headstreams rising to N. of Ben Lomond which meet nr. Aberfoyle; takes meandering course to Alloa, whence it expands into Firth of Forth (q.v.); 165 km long.

Forth, Firth of, lge. inlet, E. cst. of **Scot.**; submerged estuary of R. Forth; navigable by lge. vessels for 64 km inland to Grangemouth; other pts., Leith, Rosyth (naval), Bo'ness; l. (to Alloa) 80 km; the Forth rly. bridge (1890) spans the F. at Queensferry; the road bridge (1964) is the longest suspension bridge in Europe.

Forth and Clyde Canal, Scot.; links F. of Forth at Grangemouth and F. of Clyde at Glasgow; not completely navigable; 61 km long.

Fort Johnston, t., S. **Malawi**; on L. Malombe; new t., 1966; tobacco; airpt.

Fort Knox, Ky., **USA**; nation's gold bullion depository; military air-base.

Fort Lamy. *See* Ndjamene.

Fort Lauderdale, c., Fla., **USA**; on Atl. cst. N. of Miami; lge. marina; citrus fruits, mkt. garden prod.; holiday resort; p. (1984) 149,900 (c.), 2,799,300 (met. a. of Miami inc. Hollywood and military personnel and families).

Fort Myers, t., Fla., **USA**; on G. of Mexico; resort; Edison experimented here; p. (1984) 38,200 (t.), 252,900 (met. a. inc. Cape Coral).

Fortrose, t., royal burgh, Ross and Cromarty, **Scot.**; on S. cst. of Black Isle, on Moray F.; p. (1981) 1,319.

Fort Smith, c., Ark., **USA**; on Arkansas R.; mkt. ctr. for agr. a.; varied mnfs., inc. furniture, glass; coal and zinc mined nearby; p. (1984) 72,600 (c.), 170,100 (met. a.).

Fort Victoria, (Masvingo), t., **Zimbabwe**, agr. and mng. ctr., cattle, historic ruins in Zimbabwe Nat. Park; p. (1982) 30,600.

Fort Wayne, c., Ind., **USA**; at confluence of 2 headstreams of Maumee R.; rly. repair shops; elec. machin. and domestic appliances, originally a Fr. fort; p. (1984) 165,400 (c.), 348,400 (met. a.).

Fort William. *See* Thunder Bay.

Fort William, burgh, Lochaber, **Scot.**; nr. head of Loch Linnhe; at base of Ben Nevis; aluminium factory; pulp- and paper-mill at Corpach; p. (1981) 11,079.

Fort Worth, c., Texas, **USA**; rly. and comm. ctr. on Trinity R.; livestock and grain mkt.; oil refining, meat packing, oilfield equipment; p. (1984) 414,600 (c.), 3,348,000 (met. a.) with Dallas.

Fort Yukon, trading sta. on Yukon R., N.E. Alaska, **USA**.

Foshan (Fatshan), c., Guandong, **China**; S.W. of Guangzhou; iron and steel, textiles; p. (1984) 299,800.

Fos-sur-Mer, t., Bouches-du-Rhône, S. **France**; nr. Marseilles; new deepwater pt. and oil refinery; bauxite terminal; iron and steel plant; p. (1982) 9,446.

Fotheringhay, v., Northampton, **Eng.**; on R. Nene; Mary Queen of Scots beheaded (1587) in F. Castle.

Fougères, t., Ille-et-Vilaine, **France**; cas.; footwear, clothing; p. (1982) 25,131.

Foulness I., S. Essex, **Eng.**; at mouth of R. Crouch; owned by Min. of Defence; site of projected third London airport of Maplin, now abandoned; projected container and oil pt.

Fountains Abbey, ruined 12th cent. Cistercian abbey, North Yorks., **Eng.**; nr. Ripon.

Fowey, sm. spt., Cornwall, **Eng.**; nr. mouth of R. Fowey; exp. kaolin; resort; fishing; p. with St. Austell (1981) 36,639.

Foxe Basin and Channel, to N. of Hudson Bay, between Baffin I. and Southampton I., **Canada**.

Foyers, Falls of, Inverness, **Scot.**; E. of Loch Ness, nr. Fort Augustus; aluminium wks., the first hydroelectric plant erected in Britain (1896).

Foyle, Lough, inlet, **N. Ireland**; between Donegal (R.o.I.) and Londonderry; outlet of R. F.; Londonderry t. at head of inlet.

Foynes Is., **R.o.I.**; oil terminal on N. side, E. of Battery Point.

Foz do Iguacú, t., Paraná, **Brazil**; highway (coffee road) from Paranaguá; rapid growth with opening of Itaipú Dam; p. (est. 1985) 183,400.

Framingham, t., Mass., **USA**; 32 km W. of Boston; lt. inds.; p. (1980) 65,113.

Framlingham, mkt. t., Suffolk, **Eng.**; N.E. of Ipswich; cas. remains.

Francavilla Fontana, t., Apulia, **Italy**; rly. junc.; agr. tr.; p. (1981) 32,588.

France, rep., W. **Europe**; bounded by 3 seas; Eng. Channel, Atl. Oc., Mediterranean; variety of climate and relief; leading agr. cty. of Europe; 75 per cent under cultivation; exps. grain, fruit, vegetables, wine; industl. expansion since second world war; lgst. inds. inc. iron and steel, motor vehicles, aircraft, engin., textiles, chemicals; tourism impt.; EC member; cap. Paris; 96 deps.; excessive social, economic, and political concentration around Paris promotes description of France as "Paris and the French Desert"; recent attempts to break this down using framework of 21 economic planning regions; a. 550,634 km²; p. (est. 1987) 55,622,000.

Franceville, t., **Gabon**, Equatorial Africa; on R. Ogooué; lined to Libreville as part of the Trans-Gabon rly. project; manganese mine opened 1962; founded by De Brazza.

Francistown, t., Botswana, **Southern Africa**; airpt.; butter, coppermng.; p. (est. 1984) 35,960.

Frankenthal, t., Rhineland-Palatinate, **W. Germany**; in industl. dist. of Mannheim-Ludwigshafen, engin., machin.; p. (est. 1986) 44,300.

Frankfurt-on-Main, c., Hesse, **W. Germany**; local point in Rhine-Main urban region; rly. ctr., transit pt.; machin., cars, chemicals, elec. engin., publishing; airport; cath., univ.; birthplace of Goethe; p. (est. 1986) 592,400.

Frankfurt-on-Oder, c., Brandenburg, **E. Germany**; agr. ctr., R. pt., rail junc.; machin., chemicals; E. part of t. (Slubice) Polish since 1945; p. (1981) 81,009.

Frankischer (Franconian) Jura, plateau with steep N.-facing edge, S.E. of W. **Germany**; runs 128 km S.W. from Fichtelgebirge; drained by Regnitz and Altmühl Rs.

Franklin, dist., N.W. Terr., **Canada**; comprising the Is. of Arctic Canada from Banks I. to Baffin I., including Boothia Peninsula and Melville Peninsula; sparsely populated; furs; a. 1,434,943 km².

Františkovy Lázne (Franzensbad), famous spa, W. Bohemia, **CSSR**; 445 m a.s.l., between the Erzgebirge and the Fichtelgebirge.

Franz Josef Land (Zemlya Frantsalosifa), **RSFSR**; archipelago in Arctic Oc. N. of Novaya Zemlya; a. 20,720 km²; mainly ice-covered.

Frascati, t., **Italy**; 19 km S.E. of Rome; summer resort; famous villas and arch. remains; nuclear research ctr.; p. (1981) 18,728.

Fraser I. (Great Sandy I.), Queensland, **Australia**; low sandy I., timber reserve and Nat. Park; concern over ecology caused discontinuation of mineral sand exp. (1977).

Fraser, R., B.C., **Canada**; rises at c. 1,800 m on W. slopes Rocky Mtns.; famous salmon fisheries; routeway; Vancouver nr. delta; 1,360 km long.

Fraserburgh, spt., burgh, Banff and Buchan, **Scot.**; one of the main E. cst. herring pts.; p. (1981) 12,479.

Frauenfeld, t., cap. of Thurgau can., **Switzerland**; 11th cent. cas.; textiles; p. (1980) 18,607.

Fray Bentos, t., cap. of Rio Negro dep., **Uruguay**; pt. on R. Uruguay 80 km from mouth; meatprocessing; p. (est. 1985) 20,091.

Fredericia, t., pt., E. Jutland, **Denmark**; major rly. junc.; textiles, silver and electroplated gds., fertilisers; oil refinery; p. (1981) 29,350.

Fredericton, c., cap. of N.B., **Canada**; on St. John R.; univ., cath.; timber, shoes, plastics; p. (1986) 44,352.

Frederiksberg, sub. of Copenhagen, **Denmark**, with indep. municipal status; p. (1981) 88,167.

Frederikshaab, sm. spt. on W. cst. of **Greenland**; fish processing.

Frederikshavn, fish. pt., N. Jutland, **Denmark**, on Kattegat; p. (1981) 24,938.

Frederikstad, t., **Norway**; at mouth of Glomma R.; ctr. of pulp and paper-producing ind.; electrotechnical inds., shipbldg., fish canning; p. (est. 1987) 27,000.

Frederiksvaerk, t., Sjaelland, **Denmark**; impt. iron and steel wks.

Freetown, c., cap. of **Sierra Leone**; pt. on Atl. Oc.; one of lgst. natural harbours in world; humid, oppressive climate; exp. diamonds, palm oil; engin., food processing, oil refining; fishing; p. (1985) 554,243.

Freiberg, t., **E. Germany**; S.W. of Dresden, at foot of Erzgebirge; mng. academy (silver discovered 12th cent.); metallurgy, textiles, glass, porcelain; p. (1981) 51,377.

Freiburg im Breisgau, c., **Baden-Württemberg, W. Germany**; in Black Forest; cath., univ.; cultural ctr.; tourism; p. (est. 1986) 186,200.

Freising, t., Bavaria, **W. Germany**; N.E. of Munich; cath.; agr. machin., textiles, chemicals; p. (est. 1986) 36,200.

Freital, t., **E. Germany**; S.W. Dresden; glass, uranium ore processing; coalmines nearby; p. (est. 1970) 42,159.

Fréjus, t., Var dep., S.W. **France**; cath., Roman ruins; resort on Fr. Riviera; p. (1982) 32,698.

Fréjus, Col de, Alpine pass, **France** and **Italy**, 2,083 m, under which runs the Mont Cenis tunnel (13·6 km).

Fremantle, spt., W. **Australia**; at mouth of Swan R., 19 km S.W. from Perth, principal pt. in W. Australia and first Australian pt. of call for mail steamers; part of Perth met. a.; giant industl. complex at Kwinana; p. (1981) 22,484.

French Equatorial Africa, formerly included Gabon, Congo (Brazzaville), Ubangi-Shari and Chad, sts. which are now independent.

French Guiana, Fr. Overseas dep., on N. cst. of S. **America**, between Surinam to W. and Brazil to S. and E.; tropical climate; little developed and thinly populated; ch. ctr. of p. and spt. at cap. of Cayenne; economy based on agr., especially sugar and forestry; some gold and bauxite mng.; a. 90,650 km²; p. (est. 1987) 89,000.

French Polynesia, Fr. overseas terr., in **S. Pac. Oc.**; comprising several archipelagos; Society Is., Marquesas Is., Tubuai Is., Tuamotu Is., and Gambier Is.; increased autonomy from 1977; cap. Papeete; a. 4,002 km²; p. (est. 1987) 184,600.

French Somaliland. *See* Djibouti.

French S. and Antarctic Terrs., Fr. overseas terr., comprising several grs. of Is. and Antarctic terr. of Adélie Land; a. 409,220 km²; p. 132 (mainly scientists).

French West Africa, comprised former Fr. cols. of Dahomey (Benin), Ivory Coast, Mauritania, Niger, Fr. Guinea, Upper Volta, Senegal, Fr. Soudan (Mali).

Freshwater, sm. t., I. of Wight, **Eng.**; at W. end of I., 13 km W. of Newport; resort.

Fresnillo de Gonzalez Echeverria, t., Zacatecas, **Mexico**; alt. 2,227 m; mkt. t., silver mng.; p. (1970) 101,316.

Fresno, c., Cal., **USA**; ctr. of vast irrigated fruitgrowing dist.; p. (1984) 267,400 (c.), 564,900 (met. a.).

Fribourg (Freiburg), c., cap. of F. can., **Switzerland**; between Berne and Lausanne; viaduct and bridges; cath., univ.; p. (1980) 37,400.

Fribourg (Freiburg), can., **Switzerland**; mainly dairy farming; cereals, sugarbeet, cheese; a. 1,671 km²; p. (est. 1986) 195,000.

Friedrichshafen, t., **W. Germany**; on Bodensee; machin., boat bldg., motors; resort; p. (est. 1986) 52,100.

Friendly Is. *See* Tonga.

Friern Barnet. *See* Barnet.

Friesland, prov., N. **Neth.**; cap. Leeuwarden; dairying, horses, cattle; natural gas on Ameland I.; a. 3,432 km²; p. (1983) 595,248.

Frimley and Camberley, ts., Surrey Heath, former U.D., Surrey, **Eng.**; 5 km N. of Farnborough; lt. engin., plastics; military training ctr.; p. (1981) 52,017.

Frinton and Walton, Tendring, Essex, **Eng.**; on E. cst., 8 km N.E. of Clacton; seaside resort; p. (1981) 14,651.

Frisches Haff, shallow freshwater lagoon, Baltic cst. of **Poland**; 85 km long, 6–18 km broad.

Frisian Is., chain of Is. stretching from Den Helder to Jutland, along csts. of Neth., Germany, and Denmark; ch. Is. are Texel, Vlieland, Terschelling, Ameland (West F. Is.), Nordeney, Borkum (East F. Is.), Sylt, Föhr, Rømø (North F. Is.); severe erosion; Sylt now half size it was 500 years ago.

Friuli-Venezia Giulia, aut. reg. (created 1963), N.E. **Italy**; comprising 3 provs. Udine, Gorozia, Trieste; p. (est. 1986) 1·2 m.

Frobisher Bay, inlet in S. Baffin I., N. **Canada**, extending 320 km between Cumberland Sound and Hudson Strait.

Frodingham, t., Humberside, **Eng.**; on W. flank of limestone ridge, Lincoln Edge; impt. iron-ore open-cast mines; mnfs. iron and steel.

Frome, mkt. t., Mendip, Somerset, **Eng.**; on R. Frome, 18 km S. of Bath; p. (1981) 14,527.

Frome, R., Dorset, **Eng.**; flows from N. Dorset Downs into Poole Harbour.

Frontignan, t., Hérault, S. **France**; oil refining; pipeline under sea from Sète; produces muscat; p. (1982) 14,961.

Frunze, c., cap. of Kirghiz SSR, **USSR**; univ.; engin., textiles, meat-packing; p. (1986) 618,000.

Fuerteventura, I., **Canary** gr.; a. 1,717 km²; p. (1970) 18,192.

Fujayrah, emirate, one of **United Arab Emirates**, Persian G.; p. (1985) 54,425.

Fujian (Fukien), prov., **China**; cap. Fuzhou; intensive agr., rice and sugar-cane; shellfish raised along cst.; a. 123,103 km²; p. (est. 1985) 26,370,000.

Fujisawa, t., Honshu, **Japan**; bearings, machin.; p. (1985) 328,387.

Fujiyama, extinct volcano, **Japan**; 96 km S.W. of Tokyo; pilgrim resort; hgst. peak of Japan; alt. 3,780 m.

Fukui, c., cap. of F. pref., central Honshu, **Japan**; synthetic fibres, paper; old silk-weaving ctr.; p. (1985) 250,261.

Fukuoka, c., N. Kyushu, **Japan**; pt. on Hakata Bay; univ. ctr., old cas. t.; textiles, dolls, shipbldg.; p. (1987) 1,192,000.

Fukushima, c., N. Honshu, **Japan**; ceramics, foods, steel; publishing; p. (1985) 270,752.

Fukuyama, c., S. Hokkaido, **Japan**; p. (1985) 360,264.

Fulda, t., Hesse, **W. Germany**; nr. Kassel; on R. Fulda; palace, abbey; textiles, metallurgy, rubber; route ctr.; p. (est. 1986) 54,100.

Fulham. *See* Hammersmith.

Fulwood, t., Lancs., **Eng.**; 3 km N.E. of Preston; part of Central Lancashire New Town.

Funchal, cap. of **Madeira Is.**; pt., winter resort; cath.; p. (1981) 119,481.

Fundy, Bay of, inlet between Nova Scotia and New Brunswick, **Canada**; lge. tidal range of 21 m.

Furka Pass, **Switzerland**; between Valais and Uri cans.; 2,433 m.

Furneaux Is., S.E. **Australia**; in Bass Strait, belonging to Tasmania; lgst. is Flinders I.; p. (1966) 1,220.

Furness, dist., Cumbria, **Eng.**; between Morecambe Bay and the Irish Sea.

▸tenwalde, t., Frankfurt, **E. Germany**; on R.   metallurgy, leather, tyres; p. (est. 1970)

³avaria, **W. Germany**; nr. Nürnberg; ~inds.; p. (est. 1986) 98,200.

Fusan. *See* Pusan.

Fuse, t., Honshu, **Japan**; machin., textiles, chemicals; now part of Higashiosaka.

Fushimi, c., Honshu, **Japan**; sub. of Kyoto; p. (1985) 274,932.

Fushun, c., Liaoning, N. **China**; at foot of Changbai Shan, 35 km N.E. of Shenyang; major industl. ctr.; possesses world's thickest bituminous coal seam (127 m) worked by deep and opencast mines; oil refinery based on local oil shales; steelwks., chemicals; electronics; timber inds.; diversification planned; p. (1984) 1,220,000.

Fuskiki, spt., Honshu, **Japan**; serves Toyama c. with metals, coal.

Futa, La, pass, Tusco-Emilian Apennines, N. **Italy**; used by main road from Bologna to Florence; alt. 903 m.

Futa Jalon (Fouta Djalon), upland dist., mostly in **Guinea**, W. Africa with outliers in Liberia and Sierra Leone.

Fuxin (Fuzin), c., Liaoning, N. **China**; ctr. of lge. coalfield; p. (1984) 653,200.

Fuzhou (Foochow), c., cap. of Fujian prov., **China**; at mouth of Min R., major comm. and industl. ctr.; diverse light inds.; became impt. with tea exp.; former treaty pt.; p. (1984) 1,164,800.

Fylde, W. Lancs., **Eng.**; low plain behind coastal sand dunes; pig- and poultry-rearing dist.; ch. t. Blackpool; as l. gov. dist. excluding Blackpool p. (est. 1988) 73,200.

Fylingdales, ballistic missile early warning sta. on N. Yorks. moors, **Eng.**

Fyn, I., **Denmark**; in Baltic Sea; a. 3,419 km²; cap. Odense; dairying, sugarbeet; p. (1971) 433,765.

Fyne, loch on Argyll and Bute cst., W. **Scot.**; an arm of F. of Clyde; offshore oil platform construction: 64 km long.

Fyzabad, t., Uttar Pradesh, **India**; mkt. t.; sugar refineries; p. (1961) 88,296.

G

Gabès, spt., **Tunisia**; on G. of Gabès, 320 km S. of Tunis; dates, henna, wool; p. (1984) 92,259.

Gabon, rep., W. **Africa**; Cameroon to N., Zaïre to S. and E.; tropical climate, hot, humid; much tropical rain forest; forestry main ind. but mng. increasingly impt.; petroleum exp. creating increasing prosperity; manganese at Moanda (S.), iron-ore at Mekambo (N.E.); communications geared mainly to mng. areas; major pts. Libreville (cap.), Port Gentil; Trans-Gabon rly. project to promote exploitation of timber; first part opened 1979; intense forest cover makes internal air services very impt.; airport at Libreville; agr. development limited by small size of p.; a. 266,770 km²; p. (est. 1987) 1,224,000.

Gaborone (Gaberones), cap. **Botswana**; formerly sm. v.; chosen as cap. for new rep., bldg. began 1964; p. (est. 1984) 96,000.

Gadag-Betgeri, t., Karnataka, **India**; cotton and silk weaving; p. (1981) 117,368.

Gaeta, t., naval pt., **Italy**; on promontory on shore of G. of Gaeta; the anc. Caietae Portus; cath.; p. (1981) 22,605.

Gafsa, t., **Tunisia**; phosphate mng. ctr.; p. (1984) 60,870.

Gaillard Cut, excavated channel, **Panama Canal Zone**; carries Panama Canal through Culebra Mtn. from L. Gatun to Pac. Oc.; 11 km long.

Gainesville, t., Fla., **USA**; univ.; mkt. gardening; electronics, wood prod.; p. (1984) 83,100 (t.), 189,900 (met. a.).

Gainsborough, t., West Lindsey, Lincs., **Eng.**; on R. Trent; agr. implements, milling, packing and wrapping machin.; some R. traffic; mkt.; George Eliot's St. Ogg's in *Mill on the Floss*; p. (1981) 18,691.

Gairdner, salt L., S. **Australia**; a. 4,766 km².

Gairloch, sea loch and v., W. Ross and Cromarty, **Scot.**; resort, fishing.

Galapagos, volcanic Is., Pac. Oc.; 960 km W. of **Ecuador** (to whom they belong) on equator; flora and fauna peculiar to each I.; visited by Darwin 1835; now a wildlife sanctuary; a. 7,428 km²; p. (1982) 6,119.

Galashiels, burgh, Ettrick and Lauderdale, **Scot.**; on Gala Water, 3 km above confluence with R. Tweed; tweeds, woollens; p. (1981) 12,294.

Galati or **Galatz**, c., E. **Romania**; major inland pt. on lower Danube; cath.; p. (est. 1984) 286,110.

Galesburg, t., Ill., **USA**; engin., coal mng.; p. (1980) 35,305.

Galicia, historic region, S.E. **Poland** and W. Ukraine, **USSR**.

Galicia, region, N.W. **Spain**; comprising provs. La Coruña, Lugo, Orense, and Pontevedra; p. (1981) 2,811,942.

Galilee, northern div. of Palestine in Roman times, containing the ts. Cana, Capernaum, Tiberias, Nazareth; the ch. scene of Christ's ministry.

Galilee, Sea of (Lake Tiberias), also known as L. Gennesaret; Biblical associations; 207 m below level of Med.; Israel plans to draw water from L. to irrigate Negev; a. 166 km².

Gallarate, t., **Italy**; nr. Milan; textiles; p. (1981) 46,915.

Galle, c., pt. on S.W. cst. of **Sri Lanka**; exp. tea, rubber, coconut oil; suffered from competition with Colombo after construction of modern harbour there; p. (est. 1983) 88,000.

Gallego, R., N.E. **Spain**; rises in Pyrenees, flows S. to R. Ebro at Zaragoza; provides irrigation around Zaragoza; valley used by main rly. across Pyrenees from Pau (France) to Zaragoza; 176 km long.

Gallipoli. See Gelibolu.

Gällivare, dist., N. **Sweden**, in Norrbotton prov.; rich iron-ore deposits; p. (1976) 25,276.

Galloway, anc. dist. S.W. **Scot.**; inc. l. gov. dists. of Stewartry and Wigtown; dairying.

Galloway, Mull of, the extremity of the Rinns of G., the most southern pt. of **Scot.**

Galston, burgh, Kilmarnock and Loudoun, **Scot.**; on R. Irvine, nr. Kilmarnock; p. (1981) 5,295.

Galveston, c., spt., Texas, **USA**; on I. in Bay at entrance to G. of Mexico; gr. cotton and sulphur pt. with lge. exp. of agr. prod.; mills, foundries, food-processing, chemicals; univ., resort; p. (1980) 61,902 (c.), 195,940 (met. a.).

Galway, co., Galway Bay, Connacht, **R.o.I.**; fishery, cattle, marble quarrying; a. 6,351 km²; p. (1981) 57,725.

Galway, co. t., Galway, **R.o.I.**; univ.; spt., fishing; sawmills, textiles, printing; p. (1981) 37,835.

Gambia, The, member st. of **Senegambia**, W. **Africa**, on Atl. Oc.; comprises St. Mary's I. (on which is Banjul, the cap.) and narrow mainland enclave (average width 32 km) extending 320 km inland astride R. Gambia, hot all year, summer rain, but savannah inland; agr. is basis of economy, esp. groundnuts; economic aid from Taiwan; communications developed around Banjul (spt. and airpt.); union with Senegal, 1982; one of Africa's smallest sts.; a. 11,295 km²; p. (est. 1987) 790,000.

Gambia, R., **Senegambia**, rises in Futa Jalon Plateau, flows N. and W. into Atl. Oc. at Banjul; forms main channels of communication through Gambia, 1,120 km long.

Gambier Is., Fr. Polynesia, **S. Pac. Oc.**, 4 coral Is.; a. 31 km².

Gand. See Ghent.

Gandhinagar, new cap. of Gujarat, **India**; on Sabarmati R., 21 km N. of Ahmadabad; under construction; planned initial p. 75,000 rising to 200,000.

Ganges (Ganga), sacred R. of **India**; rises in Himalayas and flows to Bay of Bengal via alluvial cones at foot of Himalayas and by several delta mouths, on one of which stands Calcutta; navigable for lge. ships from Allahabad; delta alone larger than Eng. and Wales; flood plain and delta very fertile and densely populated; removal of irrig. water by India causes friction with Bangladesh; agreement over division of water at Farraka barrage reached (1978); 2,400 km long.

Gangtok, t., cap. of **Sikkim**, E. Himalayas; agr. tr. ctr.; carpets; p. (est. 1971) 15,000.

Gan Jiang (Kan R.), S. **China**; flows N. to L. Poyang; valley provides road route from Guandong to Jianxi prov.; c. 880 km long.

Gansu (Kansu), prov., N.W. **China**; borders Inner Mongolia; cap. Lanzhou; pastoral agr., wheat, cotton, tobacco; coal reserves; rich iron ore deposits; attemps to break down isolation by attracting foreign investment; a. 391,507 km²; p. (est. 1985) 20,160,000.

Gap, t., Hautes Alpes, S.E. **France**; textiles; p. (1982) 32,097.

Gard, dep., S. **France**; in Languedoc, on Mediterranean; cap. Nîmes; vines, olives, sericulture; a. 5,879 km²; p. (1982) 532,000.

Garda, L., between Lombardy and Venezia, **Italy**; variety of scenery, winter resort; a. 370 km²; greatest depth, 346 m.

Gardéz, t., **Afghanistan**; alt. 2,287 m; ctr. of comm. and transport; p. (est. 1984) 10,469.

Garforth, t., West Yorks., **Eng.**; coalmng., lt. inds.; p. (1981) 28,405.

Garigliano, R. and dist., S. central **Italy**; where Liri R. joins Gari R. below Cassino; nuclear power plant.

Garmisch-Partenkirchen, t., Bavaria, W. **Germany**; winter sports; p. (est. 1986) 27,700.

Garo Hills, mtnous. dist., Assam, **India**; a. 8,078 km²; dense forests; p. (1961) 307,228.

Garonne, R., S.W. **France**; rises at foot of Mt. Maladetta (Pyrenees), flows via Toulouse and agr. valley, and enters Gironde estuary 32 km below Bordeaux; 720 km long.

Garrigue, region, Languedoc, S. **France**; low limestone hills, run N.E. to S.W., W. of Rhône delta; semi-arid; Mediterranean vegetation to which region gives name; winter pasture for sheep; olives; Montpellier, Nîmes located on S. flank.

Garut, t., W. Java, **Indonesia**, mtn. resort, lge. spinning mill; p. 24,219.

Gary, c., Ind., **USA**; on S. shore of L. Michigan; leading producer of steel, tinplate, cement; p. (1984) 143,100 (c.), 8,035,000 (met. a. inc. with Chicago).

Gascony, anc. prov., S.W. **France**; now comprises deps. along Atl. cst. and Pyrenees; Landes, Gers, Hautes-Pyrenees, and parts of Lot-et-Garonne, Tarn-et-Garonne, Haute Garonne, Gironde, and Ariège. Battleground in Hundred Years War.

Gastonia, t., N.C., **USA**; impt. textile ctr.; p. (1980) 47,333.

Gateshead, t., met. dist., Tyne and Wear, **Eng.**; on R. Tyne opposite Newcastle; engin., food-processing, pumps, paper; pt.; p. (est. 1988) 206,200.

Gatineau, R., **Canada**; trib. of Ottawa R., which it joins nr. Ottawa; length 480 km; hydroelec. power; forested valley.

Gatwick, West Sussex, **Eng.**; 40 km S. London; first airport in world where trunk road, main rly. line and air facilities combined in one unit.

Gauhati, t., **India**; temporary cap. of Assam being developed in E. suburb of Dispur; univ.; silk, cotton, lace, oil refinery; pipeline from Barauni; p. (1971) 123,783 (t.), 200,377 (met. a.).

Gaul (Lat. _Gallia_), embraced in the lands inhabited by Celtic peoples in Roman times, covering what is now modern France (Gaul proper), Belgium, N. Italy, and parts of Germany, Neth., and Switzerland. South of the Alps was known as Cisalpine Gaul, north of the Alps as Transalpine Gaul.

Gauri-Sankar, mtn. in Himalayas, Nepal and Tibet, **China**; 56 km W. of Mt. Everest; alt. 7,149 m.

Gävle, spt., **Sweden**; timber, textiles, steel, porcelain; p. (est. 1986) 87,000.

Gävleborg, co., **Sweden**; ch. t., Gävle; a. 18,544 km²; p. (est. 1986) 289,000.

Gaya, t., Bihar, **India**; Buddhist pilgrim ctr.; cottons, silks; p. (1981) 247,075.

Gaza, t., N.E. **Egypt**; ch. t. of Gaza Strip (q.v.); anciently the t. where Samson brought down the temple; p. (1985) 1·608 m.

Gazankulu (Machangana), Bantu Terr. Authority (1969), **S. Africa**; home of Shangana and Tsonga p.; cap. Giyana; p. (1980) 514,280.

Gaza Strip, coastal a. under Egyptian admin. since 1949; occupied by Israeli troops, Nov. 1956–March 1957, and since June 1967.

Gaziantep, t., **Turkey**; S.W. of Malatya; mkt. t.; p. (1985) 478,635.

Gazli, Uzbek SSR, **USSR**; 96 km N.W. of Gukhara; natural gas field; pipeline to Chelyabinsk opened 1963; destroyed by earthquake (1976).

Gdańsk (Danzig), c., spt., N. **Poland**; Baltic pt.; on branch of Vistula; annexed to Germany 1939, restored to Poland 1945; shipbldg., machin., chemicals, metals; Gdańsk, Gdynia and Sopot admin. as single c. (Trójmiasto = tricity); p. (est. 1985) 467,000.

Gdynia, spt., Gdańsk, N. **Poland**; competes with spt. of Gdańsk for Polish hinterland; impt. comm., rly. and industl. ctr.; part of the Trójmiasto; p. (est. 1985) 243,000.

Gedling, l. gov. dist., Notts., **Eng.**; Basford, Carlton and Arnold and N.E. outskirts of Nottingham; p. (est. 1988) 110,300.

Geelong, c., Victoria, **Australia**; spt. on Corio Bay (part of Pt. Phillip Bay); expanding comm. and industl. ctr.; improved pt. facilities in 1960s, bulk grain terminal; p. (est. 1983) 143,920.

Gejiu (Kokiu), t., Yunnan prov., **China**; leading tin-mng. ctr. of China; p. (1984) 337,700.

Gela, t., S. Sicily, **Italy**; in cotton-growing a.; petrochemicals; p. (1981) 74,789.

Gelderland, prov., **Neth.**; E. and S. of Utrecht prov., a. 5,022 km²; cap. Arnhem; cereals, tobacco; cattle rearing; p. (est. 1987) 1·8 m.

Gelibolu (Gallipoli), pt. and penin. on the Dardanelles, **Turkey**; scene of unsuccessful landing by British and Anzac troops 1915; 176 km long.

Gelligaer, t., Rhymney Valley, Mid Glamorgan, **Wales**; 6 km N.E. of Pontypridd; coal mng.; p. (1981) 34,118.

Gelsenkirchen, t., N. Rhine–Westphalia, **W. Germany**; in Ruhr conurb. on Rhine–Herne canal; collys., ironwks., glass, chemicals, oil refining; p. (est. 1986) 283,600.

Geneva, c., cap of G. can., **Switzerland**; at exit of Rhône from L. Geneva; cath., univ., former H.Q. of League of Nations; H.Q. of ILO, WHO, and Red Cross; watchmkg., jewellery, elec. gds., optical instruments; tourist resort; birthplace of Rousseau; p. (est. 1986) 160,000 (c), 363,000 (Canton).

Geneva (L. Léman), L., S.W. corner of **Switzerland**; forms a gr. crescent of water, source of poetic inspiration; 371 m a.s.l.; a. 578 km².

Génissiat, France; site of gr. barrage and hydroelec. power sta. on Rhône below Geneva.

Genk, t., Limburg, **Belgium**; stainless steel wks., petrochemicals; p. (1981) 61,502.

Gennevilliers, t., Hauts-de-Seine, **France**; N.W. sub. of Paris; R. pt.; p. (1982) 45,445.

Genoa (Genova), c., ch. pt. **Italy**; cath., univ., palaces; handles one-third of Italy's foreign tr.; pt. and airpt. expansion, shipyards, steelwks., engin., textiles, tanning; p. (1984) 746,785.

George L., N.Y., **USA**; Adirondack mtns.; picturesque resort.

Georgetown, cap., **Cayman Is.**; pt.; p. (est. 1985) 8,900.

Georgetown (Demerara), c., cap. of **Guyana**; on Demerara R.; exp. sugar, cocoa, coffee, timber, gold, diamonds, bauxite; airpt. nearby; botanical gardens; p. (1983) 188,000, 187,056 (met. a.)

Georgetown. *See* **Penang.**

Georgia, st., S.E. **USA**; one of 13 original sts., admitted to Union 1788; st. flower Cherokee Rose, st. bird Brown Thrasher; on Atl. cst.; rising to Appalachians; impt. arable agr.; cotton and lumber inds.; major source of kaolin; ch. ts., Atlanta (cap.), Savannah; a. 152,489 km²; p. (1985) 5,976,000.

Georgia (Gruziya), constituent rep., **USSR**; rich agr., fruit, tobacco, grain; mng. inc. manganese, gold, oil; several hydroelectric power plants; coastal and mtn. resorts; active Jewish community; ethnic unrest 1989; cap. Tbilisi; a. 69,671 km²; p. (1986) 5,239,000.

Georgian Bay, arm of L. Huron, S. Ont., **Canada**; separated from L. by Manitoulin I. and Saugeen peninsula; c. 160 km long, c. 80 km wide; L. pts., Owen Sound, Midland, Parry Sound; Georgian Bay Is., Nat. Park.

Gera, c., cap. of G. admin. dist., **E. Germany**; on White Elster R.; woollens, printing; lignite mined nearby; p. (est. 1986) 132,000.

Geraldton, spt., W. **Australia**; N. outlet for wheat belt; also exps. wool and manganese; early tomatoes; superphosphate; p. (1981) 20,895.

Germany, Democratic Rep. of, and E. Berlin (E. Germany), rep., Central **Europe**; partition from W. Germany complete by 1948; part of N. European Plain; 7th industl. nation of world; lignite field supplies 70 per cent of energy; main inds., optics, electronics and precision machin., chemicals, heavy engin.; member of Comecon; 15 admin. dists. (Bezirke); cap. E. Berlin; a. 108,267 km²; p. (est. 1986) 16,639,877.

Germany, Fed. Rep. of (W. Germany), **W. Europe**; partition complete by 1948; N. half part of N. European Plain; rises in S. to Bavarian 2nd lgst. trading nation of world; mainly with core in Ruhr conurb.; motor chemicals, precision engin.; member urism; 10 admin. dists. (*Länder*);

W. Berlin, former cap. now isolated in E. Germany; cap. Bonn; a. (inc. W. Berlin) 248,459 km²; p. (est. 1986) 61,066,000.

Germiston, t., Transvaal, **S. Africa**; nr. Johannesburg; gold-mng.; rly. wkshps., engin., machin., chemicals; gas pipeline from Sasolburg, p. (1980) 155,435.

Gerona, c., cap. of G. prov., **Spain**; cath.; textiles, chemicals; p. (1987) 67,447.

Gerrards Cross, t., S.E. Bucks., **Eng.**; 14 km E. of High Wycombe; residtl.

Gers, dep. S.W. **France**; cap. Auch; grain, vines, brandy; a. 6,291 km²; p. (1982) 174,154.

Gersoppa Falls, Sharavati R., Karnataka, **India**; hgst. cascade 253 m; hydroelec. power.

Gezira, dist., **Sudan**, N.E. Africa; between Blue and White Niles; c. 12,173 km² capable of irrigation provided by Blue Nile at Sennar Dam; lge-scale growing of high-quality cotton; total a. c. 20,200 km².

Ghadames (Ghudamis), oasis, Sahara Desert, **Libya**; at point where Tunis, Algeria, Libya converge 480 km S.W. of Tripoli.

Ghaghara (Gogra), sacred R., **India**; trib. of Ganges, rises in Tibet, flows through Uttar Pradesh; lge. catchment a. but poorly developed floodplain; 960 km long.

Ghana, rep., W. **Africa**; indep. st., member of Brit. Commonwealth; tropical monsoon climate, but rainfall decreases inland; badly affected by Sahelian drought; S. Ghana more developed than N.; agr. basis of comm. economy and cocoa (of which Ghana is world's lgst producer) 60 per cent of all exp. by value; Volta R. scheme produces power from main dam at Akosombo and an aluminium smelter plant began production in 1967; reservoir decreasing with drought in Sahel and reducing power production; oil refining and production; communications network based on Accra and Takoradi on cst., and inland ctr. of Kumasi; development of road network vital for expansion of comm. agr.; 3 univs.; pts. at Takoradi and Tema closely linked with internal economic growth; cap. Accra; a. 238,539 km²; p. (est. 1987) 13·7 m.

Ghardaia, t., **Algeria**; N. of Sahara; ch. t. of Mzab valley; p. (1966) 30,167.

Ghats, mtn. ranges which border the Deccan plateau in S. **India**. The **Eastern Ghats** are broken by many Rs. and rise only to 1,362 m in Northern Circars. The **Western Ghats** form an almost unbroken range, reaching 2,672 m in Dodabetta in Nilgiri hills; rainfall extremely heavy; forests; hydroelectric power.

Ghaziabad, t., Uttar Pradesh, **India**; on R. Jumna opposite Delhi; p. (1981) 271,730.

Ghazipur, t., Uttar Pradesh, **N. India**; on Ganges, E. of Varanasi; p. (1961) 37,147.

Ghazni, mtn. t., E. **Afghanistan**; once cap. of empire of Mahmud, c. A.D. 1000; now mkt. t.; p. (est. 1982) 31,985.

Ghent, c., cap. of E. Flanders prov., **Belgium**; pt. at confluence of Rs. Scheldt and Lys; cath., univ.; textiles, steel, plastics, chemicals; oil refinery; p. (est. 1984) 235,401.

Ghor, El, depression, **Jordan** and **Israel**, between Sea of Galilee and Dead Sea 3–24 km wide; agr. resettlement scheme.

Giant's Causeway, basaltic columns on promontory of N. cst. of Moyle, N. **Ireland**.

Gibraltar, City of, Brit. terr. at W. entrance to Mediterranean; rocky I., 426 m, joined to Spain by sandy isthmus; few natural resources; economy depends on tourism, Admiralty dockyard, services to shipping, and entrepôt tr., to close 1983; Spanish govt. lays claim to terr.; frontier with Spain opened (1985); a. 6·5 km²; p. (est. 1986) 29,166.

Gibraltar, Strait of, connects Mediterranean with Atl., 13·6 km wide; of strategic importance.

Gidgelpha-Moomba, dist., S. **Australia**; lge. natural gas field; pipeline to Adelaide.

Giessen, t., Hesse, **W. Germany**; on R. Lahn; univ.; various mnfs.; p. (est. 1986) 71,100.

Gifu, t., Central Honshu, **Japan**; cas.; fans, lanterns, textiles; tourism for cormorant fishing; p. (1985) 411,740.

Gigha, I, Argyll and Bute, **Scot.**; off W. cst. of Kintyre; 10 km by 3 km.

Gijón, spt., Oviedo, **Spain**; on Bay of Biscay; gd. harbour; tobacco, petroleum, coal, earthenware; steel wks. nearby; p. (1981) 256,432.

Gila, R., N.M. and Arizona, **USA**; trib. of R. Colorado; used for irrigation in Imperial valley; 1,040 km long.

Gilan, prov., N.W. **Iran**; on Caspian Sea, bounded by USSR; sub-tropical climate; agr., inc. cotton and rice; cap. Rasht; p. (1982) 1,581,872.

Gilbert Is. *See* **Kiribati.**

Gilgit, dist., Kashmir, **India**; mtnous., exceeding 6,000 m on N. and W.; with Ladakh links India with Tibet; p. 77,000.

Gillingham, t., l. gov. dist., Kent, **Eng.**; 3 km E. of Chatham; on R. Medway; naval and military establishments; cement, lt. inds.; p. (est. 1988) 95,300.

Gippsland, dist., S.E. Victoria, **Australia**; between Dividing Range and cst.; main brown coal field supplying local power plants; intensive dairying and mkt. gardens for Melbourne.

Girardot, t., **Colombia**; R. pt. and airport on upper course of Magdalena R.; linked by rly. to Bogotá; coffee, hides, ceramics; p. (est. 1970) 50,000.

Girgenti. *See* **Agrigento.**

Gironde, dep., S.W. **France**; vineyards, grain, fruit, wines; cap. Bordeaux; a. 10,723 km²; p. (1982) 1,122,400.

Gironde, estuary, S.W. **France**; formed by junc. of Rs. Garonne and Dordogne; navigable to Pauillac and Bordeaux.

Girvan, burgh, Kyle and Carrick, **Scot.**; on F. of Clyde, 29 km S.W. of Ayr; summer resort; p. (1981) 7,878.

Gisborne, c., spt., N.I., **N.Z.**; on Poverty Bay, 96 km N.E. of Napier; freezing-wks.; fishing; p. (est. 1987) 29,800.

Giuba, R. *See* **Juba R.**

Giurgiu, t., **Romania**; pt. on Danube; opposite Ruse, Bulgaria; linked by oil pipelines with Ploiesti; p. (1983) 62,740.

Givors, t., Rhône dep., **France**; on Rhône R. 16 km S. of Lyons; mnfs. inc. glass; oil refining near by at Feyzin; p. (1982) 20,554.

Giza, El, t., **Egypt**; on Nile, sub. of Cairo; nr. pyramids of Khufu (Cheops), Khafra (Chephren), and the Sphinx; film ind.; p. (est. 1983) 1,640,000.

Gjövik, t., S. **Norway**; on L. Mjösa; furniture, footwear, lt. inds.; p. (est. 1987) 26,000.

Glace Bay, t., Cape Breton I., Nova Scotia, **Canada**; coal; harbour; p. (1971) 22,276.

Glacier National Park, B.C., **Canada**; mtn. scenery, resorts; a. 1,349 km².

Glacier National Park, Mon., **USA**; Rocky mtns., picturesque; a. 4,040 km².

Gladbeck, t., N. Rhine-Westphalia, **W. Germany**; N. of Essen; coalmng; p. (est. 1986) 76,600.

Gladstone, t., Queensland, **Australia**; pt. exports coal to Japan; alumina plant (1973), oil storage; p. (est. 1984) 25,350.

Glamis, v., Angus, **Scot.**; G. castle childhood home of Queen Elizabeth the Queen Mother, and featured in Shakespeare's *Macbeth.*

Glamorgan, former co., S. **Wales**; now divided into 3 cos., **South, West** and **Mid-Glamorgan.**

Glamorgan, Vale of. *See* **Gwent, Plain of.**

Glanford, l. gov. dist., Humberside, **Eng.**; a. S. of Humber and inc. Brigg and Barton; p. (est. 1988) 72,100.

Glarus, can., **Switzerland**; E. of Schwyz; a. 684 km²; sheep, cheese, cottons; p. (est. 1986) 27,000.

Glarus, t., cap. of can. G., **Switzerland**; on R. Linth; nr. Wessen; p. (1980), 5,800.

Glasgow, c., burgh, l. gov. dist., Strathclyde Reg., **Scot.**; on R. Clyde; leading spt. and 3rd lgst. c. in Gt. Britain; major problems of urban renewal; ctr. of industl. belt; shipbldg., iron and steel, heavy and lt. engin., electronics equipment, printing; univ., cath.; p. (est. 1986) 725,130 (dist.).

Glas Maol, mtn., Angus, Kincardine and Deeside, **Scot.**; part of the Braes of Angus; 1,068 m.

Glastonbury, t., Somerset, **Eng.**; on R. Brue, ruins of 10th century abbey; nearby prehistoric lake villages; p. (1981) 6,773.

Glatz. *See* **Klodzko.**

Glauchau, t., Karl-Marx-Stadt, **E. Germany**; on R. Mulde; woollens, calicoes, dyes, machin.; p. (est. 1970) 32,127.

Gleiwitz. *See* **Gliwice.**

Glen Affric, Inverness, **Scot.**; drained E. to Moray F.; hydroelectric scheme.

Glencoe, Lochaber, **Scot.**; S.E. of Ballachulish; scene of massacre of MacDonalds 1692.

Glendalough, Wicklow, **R.o.I.**; scenic valley with Ls. and monastic ruins; tourism.

Glenelg, t., S. **Australia**; on St. Vincent G.; sub. of Adelaide; first free settlement in Australia; p. (est. 1984) 13,720.

Glen Garry, Perth and Kinross, **Scot.**; used by Perth to Inverness rly. on S. approach to Drumochter Pass.

Glen More, Scottish valley traversed by Caledonian canal, from Fort William to Inverness.

Glenrothes, t., Kirkaldy, **Scot.**; new t. (1948); coal, transistors, mng. machin., photoprecision ind.; p. (1981) 32,700.

Glen Roy, Lochaber, **Scot.**; 24 km N.E. of Fort William; remarkable terraces, remains of series of glacial lakes.

Glen Spean, Lochaber, **Scot.**; used by Glasgow to Fort William rly.

Glittertind, mtn., Opland co., S. **Norway**; highest peak in Scandinavia; alt. 2,483 m.

Gilwice (Gleiwitz), c., S.W. **Poland** (since 1945); coal mng. and steel ctr. of Katowice region; machin., chemicals; p. (est. 1985) 213,000.

Glomma (Glommen), R., S. **Norway**; lgst. R. in Scandinavia; flows to Skaggerak; timber inds.; hydroelec. power; 400 km long.

Glossop, t., High Peak, Derbys., **Eng.**; at foot of Pennines; paper, food-canning, textile finishing; mkt.; p. (1981) 25,339.

Gloucester, cath. c., l. gov. dist., **Eng.**; on R. Severn; the Roman Glevum; cath., on site of Benedictine abbey; aircraft mftg. and repair; engin., nylon; p. (est. 1988) 90,500.

Gloucester, t., Mass., **USA**; pt. at head of G. Harbour; resort, fish-processing; p. (1980) 27,768.

Gloucestershire, non-met. co., W. **Eng.**; situated around lower Severn basin, Cotswolds, Forest of Dean; sheep, dairy and fruit farming; major ctrs. of p. at Gloucester and Cheltenham; a. 2,639 km²; p. (est. 1988) 527,500.

Glyncorrwg, t., Afan, West Glamorgan, **Wales**; 6 km N. of Maesteg; coal-mng. dist.; p. (1981) 8,647.

Glynde, v., Sussex, **Eng.**; nearby Tudor manor and opera house of Glyndebourne.

Glyndŵr, l. gov. dist., Clwyd, **Wales**; lge inland a. inc. Denbigh, Ruthin and Llangollen; p. (est. 1988) 41,500.

Gmünd. *See* **Schwäbish-Gmünd.**

Gniezno (Gnesen), c., W. **Poland**; E. of Poznan; first cap. of Poland (11th cent.); cath.; p. (1983) 66,100.

Goa, Daman and Diu, terr., India; former Portuguese enclaves; iron pyrites, manganese, coconuts, fish, spices, cashew nuts, salt, copra; a. 3,693 km²; p. (1981) 1,086,730.

Goat Fell, mtn., I. of Arran, Cunninghame, **Scot.**; alt. 874 m.

Gobi, steppes and stony or sandy desert, **China** and **Mongolia**; divided into two principal divs.; Shamo in Central Mongolia, and the basins of the Tarim, E. Turkestan; l. about 2,400 km (E. to W.), breadth 800–1,120 km; average elevation 1,200 m; crossed by Kalgan–Ulan Bator highway.

Godalming, t., Waverley, Surrey, **Eng.**; 6 km S.W. of Guildford; first public supply of elec. 1881; Charterhouse School; p. (1981) 18,209.

Godavari, sacred R., **India**; rises in W. Ghats, flows E. across Deccan through gap in E. Ghats to Bay of Bengal; forms lge. delta; used for irrigation and hydroelec. powers; c. 1,440 km long.

Godesberg, Bad, t., N. Rhine-Westphalia, **W. Germany**; nr. Bonn; spa; meeting place of Chamberlain and Hitler 1938; p. (est. 1969) 73,512.

Godhavn, Danish settlement, Disco I., W. of **Greenland**; arctic research sta.; fish processing.

Godthåb, t., admin. ctr., **Greenland**; first Danish col. 1721; sm. pt.; fish processing; p. (est. 1986) 11,209.

Godwin Austen Mt. or **K2,** peak (8,616 m) in Karakoram between Tibet and Sinkiang, **China,** after Everest highest in world; summit reached by Prof. Desio 1954; also named Chobrum.

Gogmagog Hills, Cambs., **Eng.**; low chalk upland, S. of Breckland; traces of Roman entrenchment.

Gora. *See* **Ghaghara R.**

Goiânia, t., cap of Goiás st., **Brazil**; comm. and industl. ctr.; p. (est. 1985) 928,000.

Goiás, st., central **Brazil**; mtnous., forested; stock-raising, tobacco; gold, diamonds; cap. Goiânia, on Vermelho R.; a. 642,061 km²; p. (est. 1985) 4,437,500.

Gökçeada I. (Imbroz I.), off W. Turkey, in Aegean Sea at entrance to Dardanelles; a. 280 km²; p. (est. 1970) 1,856.

Golconda, fort and ruined c., nr. Hyderabad, S. **India**; famous for its legendary diamond troves.

Gold Coast, City of, Queensland, **Australia**; 40 km cstl. a. inc. 18 townships, named 1959; rapid tourist devel. inc. Surfer's Paradise; p. (est. 1984) 116 ′

Golden Gate, strait between San Francisco Bay and Pac. Oc., Cal., **USA;** spanned by Golden Gate Bridge, opened 1937.

Golden Horn, peninsular on the Bosporus, forming the harbour of Istanbul, **Turkey.**

Golden Triangle, a. of Britain and Europe roughly bounded by Birmingham, Frankfurt, and Paris; economic core a. of **W. Europe.**

Golden Vale, dist., Limerick, Tipperary, **R.o.I.;** drained W. to Shannon and E. to Suir; rich farming a., beef and dairy cattle, pigs.

Gold River, t., B.C., **Canada;** on W. cst. of Vancouver I. at junc. of Heber and Gold Rs.; new t. 1967; p. (1981) 2,225.

Golspie, co. t., Sutherland, **Scot.;** p. (1981) 1,491.

Gomal Pass, a pass in Sulaiman ranges, **Pakistan,** leading from Indus valley to Afghanistan.

Gomel′, c., S.E. Belorussiyan SSR, **USSR;** on R. Sozh, trib. of Dnieper; R. pt., agr. ctr.; engin., chemicals, clothing inds.; p. (est. 1985) 465,000.

Gomera, I., Canaries; 21 km S.W. Tenerife; cap. San Sebastian; p. (1970) 19,389.

Gondar, t. N.W. **Ethiopia;** N. of L. Tana; airport; p. (est. 1980) 76,932.

Goodwin Sands, dangerous sandbanks off E. cst. of Kent, **Eng.;** shielding the Down roadstead.

Goodwood, v., West Sussex, **Eng.;** racecourse and motor racing; home of Dukes of Richmond.

Goole, t., Boothferry, Humberside, **Eng.;** second pt. of Hull on Humber; shipbldg., flour milling, fertilisers, alum and dextrine mftg.; p. (1981) 17,127.

Goonhilly Downs, Cornwall, **Eng.;** satellite communications sta. of Post Office.

Goose Bay, t., Labrador, **Canada;** on Churchill R., international airpt.; p. (1981) 7,005

Göppingen, t., Baden-Württemberg, **W. Germany;** between Ulm and Stuttgart; machin., iron, wood, chemicals; p. (est. 1986) 51,400.

Gorakhpur, t., Uttar Pradesh, **India;** on Rapti R., N. of Varanasi; grain, timber; fertilisers; univ.; p. (1981) 290,814 (t.), 307,501 (met. a.).

Gordon, l. gov. dist., Grampian Reg., **Scot.;** formerly part of Aberdeenshire; p. (est. 1986) 70,788.

Gorgān, c. **Iran,** Mazandaran prov.; nr. Caspian Sea; p. (est. 1982) 114,000.

Gori, t., central Georgian SSR, **USSR;** at confluence of Bolshoy, Liakhvi, and Kura Rs.; birthplace of Stalin; p. (1968) 33,100.

Gorinchem, t., S. Holland, **Neth.;** on R. Merwede; p. (est. 1987) 28,000.

Goring Gap, Berks./Oxon., **Eng.;** where R. Thames cuts through Chilterns and Berkshire Downs.

Gorizia (Görz), c., cap. of Gorizia prov., N.E. **Italy;** on Yugoslav border; cas.; agr. mkt., fruit, wine; textile machin.; p. (1981) 41,557.

Gorki or **Gorky** (formerly Nizhni-Novgorod), c., **RSFSR;** cap. of forested G. region, on Rs. Oka and Volga; univ., churches, 13th cent. kremlin; gr. industl. ctr. with heavy engin., steel, textiles, chemicals, oil refining, cars, glass, timber inds.; birthplace of Maxim Gorky; p. (1986) 1,409,000.

Görlitz, t. **E. Germany;** on W. Neisse on Polish border; lignite mines; textile mills; religious mystic Jacob Boehme lived here; p. (1981) 80,831.

Gorlovka, t., Ukrainian SSR, **USSR;** in Donets Basin; coal, chemicals, engin.; oil pipeline connects with Grozny oilfields; p. (est. 1985) 342,000.

Gorno-Altai, aut. region, S.E. Altai terr., **RSFSR;** in Altai mtns. on Mongolian border; cap. Gorno-Altaisk; forested, pastoral agr., mng. (gold, manganese, mercury); a. 92,567 km; p. (1986) 179,000.

Gorno-Altaisk, t., **RSFSR;** cap. of Gorno-Altai aut. region; nr. Chuya highway to Mongolia; food-processing of agr. prod. from region; p. (1986) 39,000.

Gorno Badakhshan, aut. region, S.E. Tadzhik SSR, **USSR;** in Pamirs, bordered by China and Afghanistan; mng. (gold, mica, salt, limestone); livestock; cap. Khorog; a. 63,688 km²; p. (1986) 149,000.

Gornyy Snezhnogorsk, t., **RSFSR;** new t. in Siberia Arctic on R. Hantaiki, 56 km W.N.W. Komsomolsk; tin-mng.

Gorseinon, v., West Glamorgan, S. **Wales;** nr. ?oughour estuary, 6 km N.W. of Swansea; ?r steel-wks., zinc refineries.

Wielkopolski (Landesberg an der c., W. **Poland** (since 1945); industl. ctr.; ?; p. (est. 1983) 113,000.

Gosainthan (Xixabangma Feng), mtn. massif, **Nepal-Tibet (China)** border; part of Himalayas; rises to 8,091 m.

Gosford-Woy Woy, t., N.S.W., **Australia;** electric rly. connecting Sydney (80 km to S.) led to growth of commuting, dairying, mkt. gardening and tourism; p. (1981) 94,369.

Gosforth, t., sub. to Newcastle upon Tyne, Tyne and Wear, **Eng.;** coal mines closed 1948; p. (1981) 23,835.

Goslar, t., Lower Saxony, **W. Germany;** mng. ctr. at foot of Harz mtns.; lt. inds., tourism; p. (est. 1986) 49,000.

Gosport, t., l. gov. dist., Hants., **Eng.;** naval depot W. of Portsmouth to which it is linked by ferry; marine engin.; p. (est. 1988) 76,900.

Göta, R., Sweden; flows from L. Vänern to the Kattegat; also canal connecting L. Vänern with the Baltic; the G. Canal provides a popular tourist trip from.Stockholm to Göteborg.

Götaland, southernmost of 3 old provs. of **Sweden;** a. 87,262 km²; p. (1983) 3,984,336.

Göteborg or **Gothenburg,** c., cap. of Göteborg and Bohus, S.W. **Sweden;** at mouth of R. Göta on Kattegat; second c. in Sweden for commerce and ind.; univ.; shipbldg., oil refining; deepwater tanker terminal; p. (est. 1986) 429,000.

Gotha, t., Erfurt, **E. Germany;** iron, machin., engin., musical instruments, textiles, porcelain, printing, cartography; p. (1981) 57,573.

Gotham, v., Notts., **Eng.;** gypsum mng. and plaster wks.

Gotland, I. in the Baltic, **Sweden;** many historic bldgs.; cap. Visby; tourism; a. 3,173 km²; p. (est. 1988) 56,000.

Göttingen, t., Lower Saxony, **W. Germany;** univ.; scientific instruments, pharmaceutics, film studios; p. (est. 1986) 133,800.

Gottwaldov (Zlin), t., **ČSSR;** 64 km E. of Brno; footwear, leather and domestic woodware inds.; home of Bata footwear; p. (est. 1986) 86,000.

Gouda, t., S. Holland, **Neth.;** on R. IJssel, 18 km from Rotterdam; cheese, candles, ceramics, pipes; p. (est. 1987) 61,000.

Gough I., Atl. Oc. dependency of St. Helena; breeding ground of the great shearwater; guano.

Goulburn, t., N.S.W., **Australia;** commands route across Gr. Dividing Range; in agr. dist. W. of Sydney; cath.; wool, shoes; p. (1981) 21,755.

Goulburn Is., N.T., **Australia;** 2 sm. Is. off N. cst. of Arnhem Land; Methodist Mission sta.

Goulburn, R., Victoria, **Australia;** irrigation.

Gourock, burgh, Inverclyde, **Scot.;** on F. of Clyde, 3 km W. of Greenock; ferry to Dunoon; resort; p. (1981) 11,158.

Gove Peninsula, N.T., **Australia;** N.E. extremiy of Arnhem Land; giant bauxite and alumina production complex (1968); model t. of Nhulunbuy.

Gower, peninsula, W. Glamorgan, **Wales;** tourism.

Gowrie, Carse of, fertile tract N. side F. of Tay, **Scot.;** includes Dundee, Kinnoul, Perth.

Gozo, I. in Mediterranean, belonging to **Malta;** the anc. Gaulos; surrounded by perpendicular cliffs; a. 67 km²; p. (est. 1983) 23,644.

Grado-Aquileia, t., Friuli-Venezia Giulia, N.E. **Italy;** pleasure resort and former Roman spt.; rich in early Christian mosaics and antiquities; Grado joined to mainland by bridge; p. (est. 1968) 10,065.

Graengesberg, dist., Kopparberg co., **Sweden;** on S. fringe of Scandinavian mtns.; iron ore.

Grafham Water, reservoir, Camb., **Eng.**

Grafton, t., N.S.W., **Australia;** on Clarence R.; dairy prod., timber; annual jacaranda festival; p. (1981) 17,005.

Graham Land, Falkland Is. Dependencies, **Antarctica;** mtnous., icebound; discovered 1832.

Grahamstown, t., C. Prov., S. **Africa;** univ. cath.; p. (1970) 41,086.

Graian Alps, mtns. between Savoie, **France,** and Piedmount, **Italy;** hgst. point Gran Paradiso, 4,063 m.

Grain Coast, name formerly applied to cst. of Liberia, **W. Africa;** "grain" refers to spices.

Grammichele, t., E. Sicily, **Italy;** 37 km S.W. of Catania; planned settlement after 1968 earthquake; p. (1981) 13,607.

Grampian Region, l. gov. reg., N.E. **Scot.;** inc. former cos. of Aberdeenshire, Banff, Kincardine and Moray; highland a.; rapid devel. of cst. with N. Sea oil discoveries; a. 8,702 km²; p. (est. 1986) 502,850.

Grampians, mtns. of Scot.; forming natural bdy. between Highlands and Lowlands; inc. Ben Nevis, the hgst. peak (1,344 m), the Cairngorms and Schiehallion.

Granada, t., W. Nicaragua; on L. Nicaragua; in rich agr. region; distilling, soap, furniture; p. (est. 1985) 89,000.

Granada, c., cap. of G. prov., S. **Spain;** in Andalusia, at foot of Sierra Nevada; formerly cap. of Moorish kingdom of G.; univ., cath., famous 14th cent. Alhambra; tourism; p. (1987) 256,800.

Granada, prov., S. **Spain;** traversed by Sierra Nevada; wheat, olives, textiles, liqueurs, paper; a. 12,530 km²; p. (1987) 788,187.

Granby, t., Quebec, **Canada;** on Yamaska R.; sawmills, leather, textiles, rubber, plastics; p. (1981) 38,069.

Gran Chaco, extensive lowland plain, **Argentina, Paraguay,** and **Bolivia,** between Andes and Paraguay–Paraná Rs.; hot, wet, swampy region with forests containing quebracho trees, a source of tannin; potential for petroleum.

Grand Banks, submarine plateau, extending S.E. from Newfoundland, **Canada;** a. 1,295,000 km²; impt. cod fisheries.

Grand Bassam, t., spt., **Ivory Coast;** exp. bananas, palm-kernels; mnf. prefabricated houses; p. (est. 1963) 22,994.

Grand Canal, canal, N. **China;** c. 1,600 km long from Tianjing to Hangzhou; built between A.D. 605–18 and 1282–92; rebuilt for navigation and flood control.

Grand Canary, I., **Canaries;** cap. Las Palmas; tomatoes, bananas, potatoes; tourism; extinct volcanoes; p. (1970) 519,606.

Grand Cayman I., W.I.; a. 220 km²; coconuts; cap. Georgetown; p. (est. 1987) 21,500.

Grand Combin, mtn., **Switzerland;** part of Pennine Alps nr. Italian border; alt. 4,320 m.

Grand Coulee Dam, Wash., **USA;** on Columbia R., 176 km below Spokane; one of lgst. concrete dams in world (1,924,000 kW); reservoir (Franklin D. Roosevelt Lake) recreational a.; supplies irrigation water to 4,900 km² between Rs. Columbia and Snake.

Grande Chartreuse, limestone massif, Isère, **France;** brandy from monastery of La Grande Chartreuse.

Grand Falls, t., Newfoundland, **Canada;** newsprint; falls provide hydroelectric power; p. (1981) 8,765.

Grand Island, t., Nebraska, **USA;** cattle and grain t.; p. (1980) 33,180.

Grand' Mère, t., Quebec, **Canada;** pulp and paper mills; p. (1981) 15,442.

Grand Prairie. See **Black Prairie.**

Grand Rapids, c., Mich., **USA;** on Grand R.; furniture mkg., car and aircraft parts, chemicals, paper; p. (1984) 183,000 (c.), 626,400 (met. a.).

Grand R., Mich., **USA;** enters L. Mich. at Grand Haven, navigable to Grand Rapids; hydroelec. power; 400 km long.

Grand Turk, I., cap. of **Turks and Caicos Is.;** p. (1980) 3,146.

Grange, t., South Lakeland, Cumbria, **Eng.;** on N. cst. of Morecambe Bay; summer resort; p. (1981) 3,646.

Grangemouth, burgh, Falkirk, **Scot.;** on F. of Forth; shipbldg. and repair, marine engin., oil refining, projected oil tanker terminal; petroleum prods., chemicals, pharmaceutics; electronics and elec. ind.; oil pipeline to Finnart; p. (1981) 21,666.

Granite City, Ill., **USA;** iron and steel, tinplate, rly. engin., chemicals; p. (1980) 36,185.

Gran Sasso d'Italia, rugged limestone highlands, Abruzzi e Molise, central **Italy,** in highest part of Apennines, rising to 2,923 m in Monte Corno; Mussolini was rescued from here by German paratroopers 1943; Aquila at foot of Gran Sasso winter sports ctr.

Grantham, t., S. Kesteven, Lincs., **Eng.;** on Witham R.; tanning, agr. machin., engin., brewing, malting, basket mkg.; expanded t.; p. (1981) 30,084.

Grantown-on-Spey, burgh, Badenoch and Strathspey, **Scot.;** on R. Spey; resort; p. (1981) 2,037.

Granville, spt., Manche dep., **France;** on Golfe de St. Malo; fisheries, food-processing; p. (1982) 15,015.

Grasmere, v., Cumbria, **Eng.;** at head of Grasmere L.; home of Wordsworth; p. (1981) 1,100.

Grasse, t., Alpes-Maritimes dep., S.E. **France,** in Provence in hills above Cannes; perfumers; birthplace of Fragonard; p. (1975) 35,330.

Graubünden. See **Grisons.**

Graudenz. See **Grudziadz.**

's-Gravenhage. See **Hague.**

Graves, Pointe de, N. point of Médoc peninsula, **France;** in famous wine dist.

Gravesend, spt., Gravesham, Kent, **Eng.;** S. bank R. Thames facing Tilbury; pilot sta. for Port of London; paper, cement; oil refinery projected; p. (1981) 52,963.

Gravesham, l. gov. dist., Kent, **Eng.;** based on Gravesend and surrounding dist.; p. (est. 1988) 90,200.

Graz, c., cap. of Styria, **Austria;** on R. Mur at foothills of Alps; second lgst. c.; univ., cath.; machin., iron and steel, rly. wks.; p. (1981) 243,166 (c.), 394,981 (met. a.).

Great Altai, range of mtns., lying mainly in **Outer Mongolia** but also in Western Siberia, **USSR;** rising to 4,200 m.

Great Atlas (Haut Atlas), mtn., N.W. **Africa;** alt. c. 2,000 m; part of the Atlas mtns.

Great Artesian Basin, Central **Australia;** underlies plains of Queensland, N.S.W., S. **Australia;** supplies water for cattle and sheep stations; too saline for use in some a. and too hot in others (cooling towers necessary); a. 2 million km.²

Great Australian Bight, wide inlet of **Indian Oc.,** S. cst. of **Australia.**

Great Barrier Reef, coral reef barrier off N.E. cst. of **Australia;** 1,600 km long, 120–160 km from cst.; currently being eaten away by the star fish, *Acanthaster planci;* many reef Is. form Nat. parks.

Great Basin, high plateau region between the Wasatch and Sierra Nevada mtns., **USA;** inc. most of Nevada, parts of Utah, Cal., Idaho, Ore., Wyo.; drainage ctr. Great Salt Lake; a. 543,900 km²; much desert; sparse p.

Great Bear Lake, lge. L., N.W. Terr., **Canada;** c. 280 km long; a. 36,260 km²; outlet through Great Bear R. to Mackenzie R.

Great Belt (Store Bælt), strait Denmark; separates Fyn I. from Sjaelland I.; sinuous shape makes navigation difficult; rly. ferry at narrowest point (18 km) between Nyborg and Korsør; 64 km long; proposed bridge.

Great Britain. See **England, Scotland, Wales, British Isles.**

Great Dividing Range, mtn. system, E. **Australia;** extends, under different local names, from Queensland to Victoria and separates E. cst. plains from interior; reaches max. alt. in Mt. Koskiusko (2,228 m), in Australian Alps, on bdy. between Victoria and N.S.W.

Greater Manchester, former met. co., pt., N.W. **Eng.;** lge. urban a. centred on major comm. ctr. of M., with former cotton spinning ts. to N., inc. Bolton, Bury and Rochdale; dormitory ts. to S.; former concentration on textile mftg. now reduced and inds. diversified; major industl. estate at Trafford Park; p. (est. 1988) 2,577,700.

Great Falls, c., Mont., **USA;** on Missouri R.; lgst. c. in st.; mkt. for irrigated farming a.; ctr. of hydroelectric power, called the "electric city"; copper- and oil-refining, flour mills; p. (1980) 56,725 (c.), 80,696 (met. a.).

Great Fisher Bank, submarine sandbank in N. Sea; 320 km E. of Aberdeen, 160 km S.W. of Stavanger; valuable fishing-ground; depth of water, from 45–75 m.

Great Gable, mtn., Cumbria, **Eng.;** alt. 899 m.

Great Harwood, t., Hyndburn, Lancs., **Eng.;** 8 km N.E. of Blackburn; textiles, aero-engin.; p. (1981) 10,921.

Great Lake, Tasmania, **Australia;** lgst. freshwater L. in Australia.

Great Lakes, N. America; 5 freshwater Ls.; Superior, Michigan, Huron, Erie, Ontario; glacial genesis; frozen 4 to 5 months in winter; traffic in cereals, iron, coal, etc.; major ctr. of heavy inds.; resorts; serious pollution; a. 248,640 km².

Great Plains, lowland a. of central **N. America;** extending E. from Rocky mtns., and S. from Mackenzie to S. Texas.

Great Rift Valley, geological fault system extending from S.W. Asia to E. Africa, 4,800 km in l.; inc. L. Tiberias (Sea of Galilee), Jord-- valley, Dead Sea, G. of Aqaba, Red S--

chain of Ls., notably L. Rudolf and L. Malawi; a branch runs through Ls. Tanganyika, Mobutu and Edward; used increasingly for geothermal power.

Great Salt Lake, shallow salty L., N. Utah, **USA**; in Great Basin plateau of N. America; remnant of L. Bonneville; alt. 1,286 m; varies in size and depth; receives Bear, Jordan and Beaver Rs.; many Is., no outlet.

Great Sandy Desert, W. **Australia**; mostly sand-hills, stony in ctr.; one of A. 3 great deserts.

Great Slave Lake, N.W. Terr., **Canada**; a. 28,490 km²; 496 km long; drained by Mackenzie R.; navigable.

Great Smoky Mtns., Tenn., **USA**; with Blue Ridge mtns. form E. zone of Appalachian mtn. system; hgst peak Clingmans Dome 2,026 m; largely preserved as Nat Park.

Great Torrington, t., Torridge, Devon, **Eng.**; on R. Torridge; mkt.; processing of agr. prod.; p. (1981) 4,107.

Great Wall of China, wall built in N. China along S. edge of Mongolian plateau to keep out invading Mongols; length 2,400 km; begun in Ch'in dynasty by Shih Huang Ti, c. 220 B.C.; present form dates from Ming dynasty (1368–1644).

Great Whale R. (**R. de la Baleine**), Quebec, **Canada**; rises in L. Bienville, flows to Hudson Bay; difficult transport; 400 km long.

Great Yarmouth. See **Yarmouth**.

Greece, rep., S.E. **Europe**; mtnous. peninsula, between Mediterranean and Ægean Sea, inc. many sm. Is. to S., lgst. Crete; inds. increasingly impt. but agr. prods. still ch. exp. (tobacco, olive oil, cotton, citrus fruit, wine); only 25 per cent a. cultivable; economy also helped by lge. merchant fleet and tourism; deposed king in exile; executive power held by military junta 1967–74; 10th member of EC (1981); cap. Athens; a. 132,561 km²; p. (est. 1985) 9,935,000.

Greenland, I., between Arctic Oc. and Baffin Bay; lofty ice-capped plateau; peopled by coastal settlements of Eskimos; fisheries; whale oil, seal skins; lge. uranium deposits, potential for petroleum; first onshore drilling (1984) in Scoresby Land; some coal, lead, zinc; US base at Thule; part of Danish kingdom; internal autonomy (1979) but leaving EC (1985) after results of referendum; cap. Godthåb; a. 2,175,600 km² of which 1,833,720 km² are under a permanent ice-cap; p. (1987) 53,733.

Greenland Sea, Arctic Oc., between Greenland and Spitzbergen; ice-covered.

Green Mtns., Vt., **USA**; part of Appalachians reaching 1,340 m (Mt. Mansfield); Nat. Forest, tourism.

Greenock, spt., burgh, Inverclyde, **Scot.**; on S. shore of F. of Clyde, 40 km W. of Glasgow; container facilities; shipbldg., sugar refining, woollens, chemicals, aluminium casting, tin-plate inds.; birthplace of James Watt; p. (1981) 57,324.

Green River, Wyo., Utah, **USA**; rises in Wind R. Range (major watershed in Rockies); flows via spectacular scenery to Colorado R.; impt. routeway; 1,168 km long.

Greensboro', c., N.C., **USA**; cotton, tobacco, chemicals; regional financial ctr.; educational institutes; p. (1984) 159,300 (c.), 886,100 (met. a. inc. Winston-Salem-High Point).

Greenville, t., Miss., **USA**; on Mississippi R.; deep-water harbour; tr. ctr. for cotton, agr. prod.; chemicals, metal gds.; p. (1980) 40,613.

Greenville, t., S.C., **USA**; univ.; industl. and comm. ctr.; textile mills, farm prod. processing; p. (1984) 57,400 (t.), 592,900 (met. a. with Spartanburg).

Greenwich, outer bor., London, **Eng.**; inc. most of former bor. of Woolwich on S. bank of R. Thames; famous for its hospital, observatory (now moved to Herstmonceux) and R.N. College; longitudes conventionally calculated from Greenwich meridian; p. (est. 1988) 214,500.

Greenwich Village, lower Manhattan, N.Y. city, **USA**; bohemian quarter.

Greifswald, spt., Rostock, **E. Germany**; on Baltic inlet; shipbldg., textiles, wood inds.; p. (1981) 61,388.

⸱eiz, t., Gera, **E. Germany**; paper, textiles, ⸱icals; p. (est. 1970) 39,058.

⸱⸱⸱**W.I.**, most S. of Windward Is.; inc. ⸱⸱o of Grenadines; known as the ⸱⸱nds" as major exp. is nutmeg; ⸱⸱⸱anilla also grown; sugar and sugar

prods.; cotton-ginning; cap. St. George's; former Brit. col., achieved indep. 1974; Pt. Salinas airport opened (1984) to encourage tourism; a. 344 km²; p. (est. 1985) 112,000.

Grenadines, dependency of Grenada I., **St. Vincent and the Grenadines**, **W.I.**; gr. of over 100 sm. Is., between Grenada and St. Vincent, Windward Is.; sea-island cotton.

Grenoble, c., cap. of Isère dep., S.E. **France**; on Isère R. at foot of Alps; univ.; thriving cultural and scientific ctr.; impt. hydroelectric ctr.; science-based inds., joint Franco-German nuclear research reactor; gloves, paper, cement, liqueurs; tourism based on skiing; p. (1982) 159,503.

Gretna Green, v., Annandale and Eskdale, **Scot.**; on Eng. border; famous as place of runaway marriages 1754–1856; p. (1981) 2,809.

Greymouth, spt., S.I., **N.Z.**; on W. cst. at mouth of Grey R.; ch. t. prov. of Westland; grew with gold mng., now replaced by coal and timber; p. (est. 1987) 7,530.

Grimaldi, caves, N.W. **Italy**; remains of prehistoric man, late Paleolithic, found there.

Grimsby, Great, spt., l. gov. dist., Humberside, **Eng.**; on S. bank of R. Humber; major distant waters fish. pt.; food-processing; chemical ind. at nearby Immingham; p. (est. 1988) 89,100.

Grindelwald, v., Bernese Oberland, **Switzerland**; tourist ctr.; p. (1970) 3,511.

Gris-Nez, C., N.E. **France**; nearest point on Fr. cst. to Dover.

Grisons (**Graubünden**), can., E. **Switzerland**; region of glaciers and magnificent peaks; ch. resorts Davos, Arosa, St. Moritz; Swiss Nat. Park; lgst. can.; sparse p.; ctr. Romansch language; a. 7,112 km²; p. (est. 1986) 166,000.

Grodno, c., W. Belorussiyan SSR, **USSR**; pt. on Neman R.; a Polish t. until 1939; machine parts, cloth; historic bldgs.; p. (est. 1985) 247,000.

Groningen, c., cap. of G. prov., **Neth.**; univ.; impt. trading ctr.; p. (est. 1987) 168,000.

Groningen, prov., N.E. **Neth.**; agr. and dairying; major natural gas deposits at Slochteren; a. 2,157 km²; p. (est. 1987) 558,000.

Groote Eylandt, I., G. of Carpentaria; off cst. of N.T., **Australia**; aboriginal reserve; manganese ore-mng.

Grosseto, t., cap. of G. prov., Tuscany, **Italy**; cath.; agr. mkt.; severely affected by floods 1966; p. (1981) 69,523.

Gross Glockner, mtn. (3,801 m) and pass (2,370 m), **Austria**, part of Hohe Tauern range; hgst. peak in Austria.

Groznyy, t., N. Caucasia, **RSFSR**; on R. Terek; naphtha wells, refinery, engin.; starting point of oil pipelines to Makhachkala, Tuapse and Gorlovka; p. (est. 1985) 393,000.

Grudziadz (Graudenz), t., on R. Vistula, Bydgoszcz, **Poland**; mftg.; p. (1983) 92,800.

Grünberg. See **Zielona Góra**.

Gruyères, dist., can. Fribourg, **Switzerland**; cattle; cheese.

Guadalajara, c., cap. of Jalisco st., W. **Mexico**; c. 1,500 m high; impt. industl. and comm. ctr.; textiles, agr. processing, traditional pottery and glassware; cath.; gas pipeline from Salamanca; health resort; p. (est. 1987) 3,000,000.

Guadalajara, c., cap. of G. prov., **Spain**; on Henares R., N. of Madrid; palace of Mendoza family; battle of Spanish Civil War, March 1937, fought nearby; p. (1987) 59,492.

Guadalaviar, R., E. **Spain**; flows into Mediterranean, below Valencia; 208 km long.

Guadalcanal, volcanic I., **Pac. Oc.**; lgst. of Solomon Is.; jungle and mtns.; exp. copra; ch. t. Honiara.

Guadalquivir, R., S. **Spain**; flows through Andalusia via Seville to Atl.; c. 560 km long; hydro-elec. plants; agr.

Guadalupe Hidalgo, place of pilgrimage, N.W. Mexico City, **Mexico**; basilica and shrine; treaty ending Mexican–U.S. war signed here 1848.

Guadarrama, Sierra de, mtn. range, central **Spain**; rugged, forest covered; affects Madrid's climate; reaches 2,431 m.

Guadeloupe, overseas dep. France, **W.I.**; comprises most S. of Leeward gr., Basse-Terre, Grande-Terre, Marie-Galante and other Is.; economy based on sugar exports to France; rapidly rising p. aggravates process of econ. development; attempts to develop tourism and food-processing inds.; ch. comm. ctr. and pt. Pointe à Pitre (Grande Terre); cap. Basse-Terre; a. 1,748 km²; p. (est. 1987) 335,300.

Guadiana, R., forms part of Spanish and Portuguese frontier; flows into G. of Cádiz; Estremadura valley reclamation scheme in progress; 816 km long.

Guam, I., U.S. air and naval base in W. **Pac.**; developing tourist ind.; free-port and tax incentives aid investment; ch. t. Agaña; a. 541 km²; p. (est. 1985) 114,000.

Guanajuato, st., central **Mexico**; average elevation 1,800 m; mng. (silver, gold, tin, copper, iron, lead, opals); a. 30,572 km²; p. (1980) 3,044,402.

Guanajuato, cap. of G. st., **Mexico**; 1,990 m high in gorge; resort; p. (est. 1983) 45,000.

Guangdong (Kwantung), prov., S. China; on S. China Sea; cap. Guangzhou; occupied by delta of Xijiang and its confluents; Hong Kong in estuary; tropical monsoon climate; densely p. on R. plains and valley slopes; intensive farming of rice, sugar, fruits; 2 Special Economic Zones to encourage foreign investment; a. 221, 308 km²; p. (est. 1985) 61,660,000.

Guangzhou (Canton), c., cap. Guangdong prov., S. **China**; industl. and educational ctr.; mnfs. inc. steel, ships, paper, cement; univ.; former treaty pt. and major spt. of S. China but site on Zhujiang R. delta results in silting and expensive harbour wks., hence Chinese interest in Hong Kong; ctr. of revolutionary movement from days of Sun Yat-Sen; p. (1984) 3,221,600.

Guang Zhuang (Kwangsi Chuang), aut. region, S. **China**; borders on Vietnam; cap. Nanning; drained by Xijiang and tribs.; rice most impt. crop; timber from sub-tropical forests; home of the Zhuang people (over 7 million); a. 221,321 km²; p. (est. 1985) 38,060,000.

Guantánamo, c., S.E. **Cuba**; sugar, coffee, bananas, cacao; pt. at Caimanera on G. Bay; p. (1985) 221,500.

Guaporé, R., **Brazil**; rises in Mato Grosso st., forms Brazil–Bolivia bdy. before joining the Mamoré; length 1,440 km.

Guarulhos, c., **Brazil**; N.E. of São Paulo; mechanical and electrical engin.; metals; benefits from rapid industl. growth of São Paulo; p. (est. 1985) 717,700.

Guatemala, rep., **Central America**; straddles Central American isthmus; interior mtnous, with temperate climate; coastal lowlands hot and humid; economy based on agr., coffee accounting for half exp.; timber exploitation, food processing; two oil refineries; trades mainly with USA, ch. pts. Puerto Barrios, San José, Santo Tomas de Castilla; 4 univs.; cap. Guatemala City; a. 108,889 km²; p. (est. 1987) 8,990,000.

Guatemala City, c., cap. of G. rep.; cath., univ.; fruit and vegetable mkts.; coffee tr.; remains Mayan civilisation; partially destroyed by earthquake (1976); p. (est. 1983) 1,300,000.

Guayama, t., **Puerto Rico**; ctr. of agr. region; sugar-milling and food-processing; p. (1970) 36,159.

Guayaquil, ch. pt., **Ecuador**; cap. of Guayas prov. on Guayas R., nr. Bay of G.; recent new pt. nearby and improvement to transport in hinterland; univ., cath.; sawmills, foundries, machin., brewing, oil refinery; p. (est. 1984) 1,387,800.

Guayas, prov., **Ecuador**; cst. lowlands; plantations for coffee, cocoa, bananas, rice; cap. Guayaquil; p. (1982) 2,016,819.

Gubin (Polish **Guben**), border t., **E. Germany/Poland**; on R. Neisse; comm. ctr.; textiles, machin., leather, synthetic fibre.

Gudbrandsdal, valley, S. **Norway**; leads S.E. from Dovrefjell towards Oslo; drained by R. Logan; used by main road Oslo to Trondheim; provides relatively lge. a. of cultivable land; hay, oats, barley, dairy cattle; 368 km long.

Guelph, t., Ont., **Canada**; on Speed R.; univ.; mkt. ctr. in rich farming a.; cloth, elec. equipment; p. (1986) 78,235.

Guernsey, I., Channel Is., between cst. of France and Eng.; tomatoes, grapes (under glass), flowers, cattle, tourist resort, t. and ch. spt. St. Peter Port; banking; a. 6,335 ha; p. (1986) 55,482 (with ass. Is.).

Guerrero, st., S. **Mexico**; on Pac. cst.; mtnous.; cereals, cotton, coffee, tobacco; cap. Chilpancingo; ch. pt. Acapulco; a. 64,452 km; p. (1980) 2,174,162.

Guiana Highlands, plateau, S. **America**; extend c. 1,440 km from E. to W. across S. parts of Venezuela, Guyana, Surinam, Fr. Guiana; steep sides, rounded tops c. 900 m but rise to 2,852 m in Mt. Roraima; chiefly composed of crystalline rocks rich in minerals.

Guienne, former prov., **France**, partly coincides with the Aquitaine basin (q.v.); controlled by England 1154–1451.

Guildford, co. t., l. gov. dist., Surrey, **Eng.**; 48 km S.W. London; on gap cut by R. Wey through N. Downs, cath., univ.; vehicles, agr. implements, lt. inds.; residtl., cas.; p. (est. 1988) 123,200 (dist.).

Guilin (Kweilin), c., Guangxi, **China**; on R. Li; univ.; textiles, sugar refining, timber; noted for its beautiful setting; p. (1984) 446,900.

Guinea, People's Revolutionary Rep. of, rep., **W. Africa**; climate hot and humid on cst. but temperate in higher interior; 95 per cent p. engaged in agr., but bauxite dominates exp. from deposits at Boké, (world's second largest producer); hydroelectric dam and aluminium smelter at Konkouré; all foreigners barred from business in G. (1968); poorly developed transport system, new rly. and pt. at Kamsar for mineral exp.; major spt. at cap. Conakry; socialist economic policies have been adopted since independence from France (1958); a. 245,861 km²; p. (est. 1987) 6·47 m.

Guinea, gen. name for W. African coastlands from Senegal to Angola.

Guinea-Bissau, formerly Portuguese Guinea, W. **Africa**; indep. 1974; cap. Bissau; poor econ. infrastructure; no manf. inds.; depends on agr. of rice, ground-nuts and stock raising; cst. edged by mangroves; offshore oil potential; a. 36,125 km² p. (est. 1987) 920,000.

Guinea, Spanish. See **Equatorial Guinea.**

Guinea Current, ocean current, flows W. to E. along Guinea cst., diverted away from cst. in Bight of Benin by C. Three Points.

Guinea, Gulf of, arm of Atl. Oc. formed by gr. bend of cst. of W. **Africa** between Ivory Coast and Gabon; Bight of Benin and Bight of Bonny are inner bays.

Guisborough, t., Langbaurgh, Cleveland, **Eng.**; at foot of Cleveland hills; former ctr. of iron-mng.; 12 cent. abbey ruins; p. (1981) 19,903.

Guiyang (Kweiyang), c. and cap., Guizhou prov., **China**; univ.; comm. and industl.; coal; iron and steel, textiles, chemicals; p. (1984) 1,352,700.

Guizhou (Kweichow), inland prov., S.W. **China**; upland a. with p. concentrated in valley urban areas; cap. Guiyang; cereals, tung oil; forestry; coal, mercury; a. 176,480 km²; p. (est. 1985) 29,320,000.

Gujarat, st., **India**; formerly part of Bombay st.; cap. temporarily Ahmedabad; new cap. Gandhinager, 21 km N. of A. under construction; oil development in Cambay area; fertiliser plant projected; a. 187,115 km²; p. (1981) 34,085,799.

Gujranwala, c. **Pakistan**; N. of Lahore; power plant, engin.; p. (1981) 597,000.

Gujrat, t., Rawalpindi, **Pakistan**; agr. ctr., handicraft inds.; p. (1981) 154,000.

Gulbarga, t., Karnataka, **India**; cotton, flour, paint; (1981) 221,325.

Gulfport, t., Miss., **USA**; pt. of entry; exp. wood, cottonseed; mnfs., textiles, fertilisers; resort; p. (1980) 39,676.

Gulf Stream, warm current of the Atl. Oc., issuing from G. of Mexico by Fla. Strait. See **L50.**

Guntur, c., Andhra Pradesh, **India**; on E. cst. N. of Madras; cotton mkt.; p. (1981) 367,699.

Gur'yev, c., Kazakh SSR, **USSR**; pt. on R. Ural at entrance to Caspian Sea; oil refining; pipeline to Orsk; p. (est. 1985) 145,000.

Gus-Khrustalnyy, t., **RSFSR**; 64 km S. of Vladimir; impt. ctr. of glass ind.; p. (est. 1969) 65,000.

Güstrow, t., Schwerin, **E. Germany**; S. of Rostock; cas., cath.; mkt. t.; p. (est. 1970) 37,213.

Gütersloh, t., N. Rhine–Westphalia, **W. Germany**; nr. Bielefeld; silk and cotton inds.; famous for its Pumpernickel (Westphalian rye bread); machin., furniture, publishing, metallurgy; p. (est. 1986) 79,400.

Guyana, rep., N. cst. **S. America**; former Brit. col.; largely covered by dense jungle, p. concentrated on narrow coastal belt; economy based on agr., especially sugar and rice; forestry inds. limited by lack of transport; impt. bauxite deposits; high birth-rate creates social and economic problems, especially on overpopulated coastal belt; airport at Timehri; univ. at Turkeyen; cap. Georgetown; a. 214,970 km²; p. (est. 1987) 812,000.

Gwalior, t., Madhya Pradesh, **India**; adjoins Lashkar (q.v.); dominated by rock of Gwalior with Jain sculptures; p. (1981) 539,015 (t.), 555,862 (met. a.).

Gwent, co., S.E. **Wales**; inc. most of Monmouth and

sm. part of Brecon; upland in N. where coalfield and former mng. ts., lowland a. bordering Severn estuary to S. where lge. industl. ts. inc. Newport; a. 1,375 km²; p. (est. 1988) 445,500.

Gwent, Plain of (**Vale of Glamorgan**), lowland dist., South and Mid Glamorgan, S. **Wales**; lies S. of moorland of S. Wales coalfield, extends E. into Monmouth; fertile soils; mixed farming except in industl. areas of Cardiff, Barry.

Gweru, t. **Zimbabwe;** ctr. of farming dist.; shoes, glass, containers; p. (1982) 78,900.

Gwynedd, co., N.W. **Wales;** comprises former cos. of Anglesey, Caernarvon, most of Merioneth and a sm. part of Denbigh; mtnous. a. except cst. and Anglesey; inc. Snowdonia Nat. Park; sparse p. inland where hill farming; cstl. resorts inc. Llandudno; a. 3,867 km²; p. (est. 1988) 239,000.

Gympie, t., Queensland, **Australia;** on Mary R., 106 m. from Brisbane; former goldfield; now dairying and pastoral dist., tropical fruits, especially pineapples; p. (est. 1984) 11,380.

Györ, t., **Hungary;** at confluence of Rs. Raba and Danube; cath.; textile ctr., rolling stock, chemicals, machine tools; p. (est. 1985) 130,000.

H

Haarlem, c., cap. of N. Holland prov., **Neth.;** nr. N. Sea cst.; tulip-growing, textiles, printing; 15th cent. church; p. (est. 1987) 149,000.

Hachinohe, c., Honshu, **Japan;** cas.; fishing, fish-processing, metal-refining; p. (1985) 241,428.

Hackney, inner bor., N.E. London, **Eng.;** incorporates former bors. of Shoreditch and Stoke Newington; furniture, clothing, p. (est. 1988) 188,900.

Haddington, burgh, E. Lothian, **Scot.;** on R. Tyne, 26 km E. of Edinburgh; woollen mnf.; grain mkt., corn mills, lt. engin., hosiery; p. (1981) 8,117.

Hadhramaut, dist., S. **Yemen;** ch. pt. and c. Al Mukallā; fertile coastal valley; frankincense, aloes, tobacco, shawls, carpets; p. (1961) 240,000.

Hadleigh, t., Babergh, Suffolk, **Eng.;** mkt.; flourmilling; p. (1981) 5,876.

Hadrian's Wall, part of frontier barrier, N. **Eng.;** stretching across Tyne-Solway isthmus, 118 km long. See **Roman Walls, Section L.**

Hafnarjördur, t., S. of Reykjavik, **Iceland;** p. (1983) 12,700.

Hagen, t., N. Rhine–Westphalia, **W. Germany;** N.E. of Wuppertal; iron, steel, chemicals, textiles, paper; p. (est. 1986) 206,100.

Hagerstown, t., Md., **USA;** machin., furniture, chemicals, aircraft; p. (1984) 33,000 (t.), 112,000 (met. a.).

Hagersville, t., Ont., **Canada;** gypsum producer.

Hagfors, t., Värmland, **Sweden;** site of lge. iron and steel wks. since 1878.

Hague, The, or **'s-Gravenhage** or **Den Haag,** c., S. Holland, **Neth.;** seat of government; permanent court of international justice; admin. ctr.; urban inds., machin. and metal wares; engin., printing; p. (est. 1987) 445,000.

Haifa, c., ch. spt., **Israel;** on Bay of Acre at foot of Mt. Carmel; terminus of Iraq oil pipeline; oil refining and heavy inds.; p. (est. 1982) 226,100.

Haikou (Hoihow), c., ch. pt. of Hainan I., Guangdong prov., **China;** p. (est. 1970) 500,000.

Hail, t., and oasis, Neid, **Saudi Arabia;** p. (1974) 40,500.

Hailsham, mkt. t., Wealden, East Sussex, **Eng.;** 8 km N. of Eastbourne; mats, rope, and twine; p. (1981) 16,508.

Hainan, I., S. cst. of **China;** densely wooded; monsoon climate; seafood cultivation; sugarcane, rubber, peanuts, sesame main crops; recent industrial development; food processing, cement, electronics; univ.; a. 36,193 km²; p. (1984) 5,893,000.

Hainaut, prov., **Belgium,** adjoining N.E. border of **France;** industl. and agr.; coal- and iron-mines; a. 3,719 km²; p. (1983) 668,618.

Haiphong, c., ch. pt., **Vietnam;** on Red R. delta; comm. and trading ctr.; cotton, thread, soap, glass, enamel ware, fish-canning; former naval base of Fr. Indo-China; p. (1979) 1,279,067.

Haiti, rep., **W.I.,** W. third of I. of Hispaniola; tropical climate modified by alt.; agr. basis of economy; coffee accounts for 45 per cent exp.; irrigation scheme in Artibonite valley; unexploited mineral resources, some bauxite mng. and exp.; sm.-scale inds.; well-developed road network and international shipping services;

cap. Port-au-Prince; corrupt Duvalier dictatorship ousted in 1986. a. 27,713 km²; p. (est. 1986) 5,358,000 (predominantly Black).

Hakodate, c., S. Hokkaido, **Japan;** Seikan tunnel to Honshu (Aomori) under construction; fishing pt.; fish food processing; p. (1985) 319,194.

Halberstadt, t., Magdeburg, **E. Germany;** cath.; metallurgy, rubber inds., engin., sugar refining; rly. junc.; p. (est. 1970) 46,774.

Halden, t., S.E. **Norway;** wood-pulp, paper, footwear, cotton spinning; nuclear research reactor; p. (est. 1987) 26,000.

Haldia, pt., W. Bengal, **India;** nr. mouth of R. Hooghly; satellite pt. for Calcutta to handle coal, ore, grain; oil pipeline to Barauni; refinery.

Hale, t., Trafford, Gtr. Manchester, **Eng.;** residtl.; p. (1981) 16,247.

Halesowen, t., S.W. of Birmingham, West Midlands, **Eng.;** weldless tubes, elec. gds., stainless steel forgings, engin.; p. (1981) 57,453.

Halesworth, t., Suffolk, **Eng.;** on R. Blyth, 14 km S.W. of Beccles; p. (1981) 3,927.

Halifax, spt., cap. of Nova Scotia, **Canada;** univ.; naval sta. and dockyard, open in winter; machin., iron foundries, footwear, oil refining, food-processing; scene of explosion of munitions ship (1917); p. (1986) 113,577 (c.), 295,990 (met. a.).

Halifax, t., Calderdale, West Yorks., **Eng.;** on E. flanks of Pennines; carpets, textiles, machine tools; cast iron wks.; p. (1981) 87,488.

Halle, c., cap. of H. admin. dist., **E. Germany;** on R. Saale; univ.; lignite and potash mined nearby; engin., chemicals, food-processing; p. (est. 1986) 235,009.

Hallstatt, v., Upper **Austria;** in the Salzkammergut; early Iron Age culture type site.

Halmahera, I., **Indonesia;** mtnous., active volcanoes, tropical forests; spices, pearl fisheries, sago, rice; a. 17,218 km².

Halmstad, spt., Kattegat, **Sweden;** iron and steel wks., machin. engin., cycles, textiles, leather, jute, wood-pulp; p. (est. 1986) 78,000.

Hälsingborg. See **Helsingborg.**

Halstead, t., Essex, **Eng.;** on R. Colne, N.W. of Colchester; rayon weaving; p. (1981) 9,276.

Haltemprice, t., Humberside, **Eng.;** p. (1981) 53,633.

Halton, l. gov. dist., **Cheshire, Eng.;** surrounds Mersey R. and inc. Runcorn and Widnes; p. (est. 1988) 124,000.

Haltwhistle, mkt. t., Tynedale, Northumberland, **Eng.;** on R. South Tyne; former coal-mng. dist.

Hama, c., N. **Syria,** on R. Orontes; the anc. Hamath, ctr. of Hittite culture; food tr., rural inds.; p. (1981) 176,640.

Hamadān, t., **W. Iran;** alt. c. 1,800 m; the anc. Ecbatana, cap. of Media; carpets, pottery; airport.; tomb of Avicenna; p. (1986) 274,274.

Hamamatsu, c., S. Honshu, **Japan;** on cst. plain 96 km S.E. of Nagoya; ctr. of impt. cotton-mftg. region; textiles, dyeing, musical instruments, motor cycles; p. (1985) 514,118.

Hamar, t., **Norway;** on L. Mjösa; ctr. of rich agr. dist.; tr. and mftg. inds.; p. (1980) 15,904.

Hamble, Hants, **Eng.;** popular yachting ctr.

Hambleton, l. gov. dist., North Yorks., **Eng.;** inc. Northallerton, Bedale and Thirsk; p. (est. 1988) 77,300.

Hamburg, c., Land H., **W. Germany;** astride R. Elbe, nr. N. Sea; 2nd. lgst. German c. and ch. pt.; freeport since 1189; pt. to be extended by reclaiming Is. of Neuwerk and Scharhörn; diversified tr. inc. liner traffic, barge traffic down Elbe, entrepôt goods; major pt. processing inds., airpt., univ.; cultural and musical ctr.; heavily bombed in second world war; p. (est. 1986) 1,571,300.

Hämeenlinna (Tavastehus), c., cap. of Häme co., S.W. **Finland;** L. pt.; tourist ctr.; birthplace of Sibelius; p. (1986) 42,326.

Hameln (Hamelin), t., Lower Saxony, **W. Germany;** pt. on R. Weser; iron, textiles; scene of legend of the Pied Piper; p. (est. 1986) 55,400.

Hamhung, c., **N. Korea;** industl. and comm. ctr., oil refinery, petrochemicals; coal nearby; p. (1972) 420,000.

Hamilton, spt., cap. of **Bermuda;** tourism. comm. and service ctr.; p. (est. 1985) 3,000.

Hamilton, c., and L. pt., S.E. Ont., **Canada;** at W. end of L. Ont.; univ.; varied metallurgical mnfs., fruit ctr.; p. (1986) 306,728 (c.), 557,029 (met. a.).

Hamilton, ctr. of major pastoral region; N.I., **N.Z.;** on Waikato R.; univ.; p. (est. 1987) 195,300.

Hamilton, burgh, l. gov. dist., Strathclyde Reg.,

Scot.; in Clyde valley, 16 km S.E. of Glasgow; admin. ctr.; elec. gds., carpet mftg., cottons, woollens, knitwear; Rudolf Hess landed near Duke of Hamilton's estate 1941; p. (est. 1986) 106,945.

Hamilton, t., Ohio, **USA**; on Great Miami R.; industl. ctr.; mnfs. metal prods., paper, machin.; p. (1980) 259,000 (inc. Middletown).

Hamm, t., N. Rhine-Westphalia, **W. Germany**; on R. Lippe, in Ruhr conurb.; rly. marshalling yards, iron and steel foundries; p. (est. 1986) 166,000.

Hammerfest, spt., **Norway**; world's most N. t., on Kvalöya I.; fishing; p. (est. 1973) 7,418.

Hammersmith and Fulham, Thames-side inner bor., London, **Eng.**; inc. former bor. of Fulham; industl., residtl.; p. (est. 1988) 149,600.

Hammond, c., N.W. Ind., **USA**; on Grand Calumet R., nr. Chicago; originally slaughtering and meat-pkg. ctr., now ch. mnfs., petroleum and steel prods., soap; p. (1980) 93,714.

Hampshire, non-met. co., S. **Eng.**; inc. Hampshire basin of chalk covered in clay and sand; inc. infertile heath and New Forest; leading pts. Southampton, Portsmouth; lt. inds.; tourism, seaside resorts; co. t. Winchester; a. 3,771 km², p. (est. 1988) 1,542,900.

Hampshire, East, l. gov. dist., Hants., **Eng.**; stretches from Alton to Petersfield; p. (est. 1988) 102,500.

Hampstead, inc. in Greater London, **Eng.**; hilltop v. with nearby heathland. *See* **Camden.**

Hampton, Thames-side t., Richmond upon Thames, London, **Eng.**; Hampton Court Palace; Hampton Wick E. of H. Court.

Hampton, t., S.E. Va., **USA**; oldest English community in US; fishing, oyster and crab packing; p. (1984) 126,000.

Han, R., Hubei, **China**; rises in S.W. Shaanxi prov., flows E. to join Chang Jiang at Wuhan; ch. trib. of Chang Jiang; 1,280 km long.

Han, R., S. **China**; forms rich agr. delta nr. Shantou; c. 400 km long.

Hanau, t., Hesse, **W. Germany**; on Rs. Mein and Kinzig; jewellery ctr., rubber and non ferrous metals inds.; birthplace of Jakob and Wilhelm Grimm, Paul Hindemith; p. (est. 1986) 85,200.

Hanchung. *See* **Hanzhong.**

Hangzhou (Hangchow), c., cap. of Zhejiang prov., E. **China**; picturesque setting at head of H. Bay; former treaty pt., now silted up; silk weaving, chemicals, jute cloth; tourism; p. (1984) 430,000 (c.).

Hankou, c., Hubei, **China**; at junc. of Han and Chang Jiang, 960 km from mouth of Yangtze but accessible to ocean-going ships; ch. comm. and mnf. ctr. of central China; former treaty pt., now part of Wuhan conurb.; machin., chemicals, cigarettes, silk. *See* **Wuhan.**

Hannibal, t., Mo., **USA**; on Mississippi R.; shoes, cement, metal gds.; boyhood home of Mark Twain; p. (1980) 18,811.

Hanoi, c., cap. of **Vietnam**; on Red R.; old Annamese fort, now modern comm. ctr.; univ.; cotton, silks, tobacco, pottery; superphosphate and magnesium phosphate supply bricks, concrete, rubber; p. (est. 1983) 2,674,400.

Hanover (Hannover), c., cap. of Lower Saxony, **W. Germany**; route ctr.; iron, textiles, machin., paper, biscuits, cigarettes, cars, rubberprocessing, chemicals; p. (est. 1986) 505,700.

Hanyang. *See* **Wuhan.**

Hanzhong (Hanchung), c., S.W. Shaanxi, **China**; on Han R.; nr. Sichuan border; agr. and tr. ctr.; former Nancheng; p. (1984) 412,100.

Haparanda, spt., N. **Sweden**; salmon fishing; exp. timber and prod. of the Lapps; p. (1970) 8,963.

Hapur, t., W. Uttar Pradesh, **India**; inc. in sugar, timber, cotton, brassware; p. (1981) 102,837.

Harar, (Harer), t., cap. H. prov., **Ethiopia**; unique African hilltop t. with medieval walls, towers and gates; anc. c. of Islamic learning; overlooks Rift Valley; brewery (1984); p. (est. 1980) 62,921.

Harare (Salisbury), c., cap. of **Zimbabwe**; admin. and industl. ctr. in agr. region with gold and chrome mines nearby; tr. in agr. prods., inc. tobacco; clothing, furniture, fertilisers; univ., airpt.; p. (est. 1982) 656,000 (met. a.).

Harbin (Haerhpin), c., cap. of Heilongjiang prov., **China**; pt. on Sunghua Jiang; tr. and comm. ctr. of N.E. China; exp. soyabeans; food-processing, machin., paper-mills, oil refining, hydro-turbines, textiles; former treaty pt.; p. (1984) 2,592,100.

Harborough, l. gov. dist., S. Leics., **Eng.**; based on Market Harborough and Lutterworth; p. (est. 1990) 69,700.

Harburg-Wilhelmsburg, industl. pt. of Hamburg, **W. Germany**; oil refining.

Hardanger Fjord, W. cst. **Norway**; 120 km long; magnificent scenery; tourism.

Hardt Mtns., W. Germany; northward continuation of Vosges on W. of Rhine rift valley; formerly forested, now largely cleared for pasture; hgst. points reach just over 600 m.

Hardwar, t., Uttar Pradesh, **India**; on R. Ganges; gr. annual fair and pilgrimage; nearby dam; p. (1961) 58,513.

Hargeisa, t., **Somalia**; comm. ctr. of livestockraising region; airport; p. (est. 1987) 400,000.

Haringey, inner bor., Greater London, **Eng.**; comprising former bors. of Hornsey, Tottenham, and Wood Green; p. (est. 1988) 192,300.

Hari-Rud, R., N. **Afghanistan** and **Iran**; the anc. "Arius"; length 1,040 km; (*Rud* = river).

Harlech, t., Gwynedd, **Wales**; on Cardigan Bay 16 km N. of Barmouth; farming; cas.; seaside resort.

Harlem, upper Manhattan, N.Y. city, **USA**; residtl. and business section of c. with lge. Negro p.; depressed economic a. with much poverty.

Harlem, R., N.Y., **USA**; separates Manhattan I. from bor. of Bronx; with Spuyten Duyvi Creek forms waterway 13 km long from East R. to Hudson R.

Harlingen, spt., Friesland, **Neth.**; natural gas; p. (1980) 43,543.

Harlingen, spt., S. Texas, **USA**; ctr. of productive agr. a.; p. (1980) 43,543.

Harlow, t., l. gov. dist., Essex, **Eng.**; in valley of R. Stort, 35 km N.E. of London; new t. (1947); spreads S.W. from nucleus of old mkt. t. of H.; engin., glass, furniture mkg., metallurgy; p. (est. 1988) 72,000.

Harpenden, t., Herts., **Eng.**; in Chiltern Hills, 8 km N. of St. Albans; Rothamsted agr. experimental sta.; residtl.; p. (1981) 27,896.

Harris, S. part of Lewis I., Outer Hebrides, **Scot.**; and several sm. Is.; p. (1971) 2,879.

Harrisburg, c., cap. of Penns., **USA**; on Susquehanna R.; iron and steel ind.; machin., cigarettes, cotton gds.; p. (1984) 52,100 (c.), 570,200 (met. a.).

Harrogate, t., l. gov. dist., North Yorks., **Eng.**; in valley of R. Nidd, 22 km N. of Leeds; spa; favoured a. for retirement; p. (est. 1988) 147,000 (dist.).

Harrow, outer bor., Greater London, **Eng.**; public school; camera mftg.; p. (est. 1988) 197,100.

Harspränget, t., Norrbotten, **Sweden**; lge. hydroelectric plant.

Harstad, ch. t., Lofoten Is., N.W. **Norway**; herring ind., woollen gds.; p. (est. 1987) 22,000.

Hart, l. gov. dist., N.E. Hants, **Eng.**; comprises Fleet and Hartley Wintney; p. (est. 1988) 85,900.

Hartebeestpoort, Dam, Transvaal, **S. Africa**; on R. Crocodile (Limpopo), 40 km W. of Pretoria; supplies water for cultivation, under irrigation, of cotton, maize, tobacco.

Hartford, c., cap. of Conn., **USA**; comm. and insurance ctr.; univ.; sm. arms, typewriters, elec. machin., aircraft engin., ceramics, plastics; Mark Twain lived here; p. (1984) 135,700 (c.), 1,030,400 (met. a.).

Hartland Point, Barnstaple Bay, N. Devon, **Eng.**

Hartlepool, spt., l. gov. dist., Cleveland, **Eng.**; on E. cst., 5 km N. of Tees estuary; shipbldg., lt. inds., timber, iron and steel inds., pipe making; gd. sands for holiday-makers to the S.; p. (est. 1988) 88,400.

Harvey, t., N.E. Ill., **USA**; nr. Chicago; rolling stock, diesel engines, heavy machin.; p. (1980) 35,810.

Harwell, v. Oxon., **Eng.**; 19 km S. of Oxford; AEA nuclear power research establishment.

Harwich, spt., Tendring, Essex, **Eng.**; on S. cst. of estuary of R. Stour; packet sta. for Belgium, Neth., Denmark; docks, container facilities, naval base; p. (1981) 15,076.

Haryana, st. **India**; formed 1966 from Hindispeaking areas of Punjab; former cap. Chandigarh; Hindu speaking a. transferred from Chandigarh (1986); a. 45,584 km²; p. (1981) 12,922,618.

Harz Mtns., range, E. and **W. Germany**; between the Weser and the Elbe; highest peak the Brocken; ch. t. Goslar (W. Germany); forested slopes; rich in minerals; tourism.

Haslemere, t., Waverley, Surrey, **Eng.**; nr. Hindhead; mkt., residtl., lt. inds.; p. (1981) 13,900.

Haslingden, t., Rossendale, Lancs., **Eng.**; on Rossendale Fells, 5 km S. of Accrington; heavy industl. textiles, waste-spinning; textilefinishing; p. (1981) 15,900.

Hasselt, t., prov., Limburg, **Belgium**; mkt. t.; gin distilleries; p. (1982) 65,100.

Hassi Massaoud, t., **Algeria**; lge. oilfield; pipeline to Bejaia; oil refinery.

Hassi R'Mel, t., **Algeria**; lge. natural gasfield.

Hastings, t., l. gov. dist., East Sussex, **Eng.**; on S. cst., midway between Beachy Head and Dungeness; seaside resort; one of the Cinque Ports; cas.; p. (est. 1988) 83,100.

Hastings, c., N.I., **N.Z.**; on Hawke's Bay, nr. Napier; ctr. for fruit growing dist.; fruit-canning; p. (est. 1987) 37,900.

Hatay (Sanjak of Alexandretta), dist., S. **Turkey**; comprising Antioch (now Antakya) and its pt. Alexandretta (now Iskenderun), ceded to Turkey by France 1939; p. (1985) 1,002,252.

Hatfield, t., Welwyn and Hatfield, Herts., **Eng.**; 30 km N. of London; new t. (1948) which grew around old t. of Bishops Hatfield; lt. engin., aircraft; p. (1981) 25,160.

Hathras, t., Aligarh dist., Uttar Pradesh, **India**; sugar, cotton, carved work; p. (1961) 64,045.

Hatteras, Cape, promontory on I. and cays off N.C., **USA**; stormy region, marked by light-house.

Hattiesburg, t., Miss., **USA**; sawmilling, clothing, fertilisers; p. (1980) 40,829.

Haugesund, spt., S. **Norway**; on S.W. cst., 35 m. N. of Stavanger; ch. ctr. of herring fishery; canning inds.; p. (est. 1987) 27,000.

Hauraki Gulf, arm of Pac. Oc.; E. cst. N.I., **N.Z.**; forming entrance to harbour of Auckland; Nat. Park.

Haute Corse. See Corsica.

Haute Garonne, dep., S. **France**; in Languedoc; cap. Toulouse; a. 6,366 km²; p. (1982) 815,000.

Haute-Loire, dep., **France**; mainly in Massif Central; cap. Le Puy; cattle, fruit, vineyards; a. 4,999 km²; p. (1982) 206,500.

Haute-Marne, dep., **France**; mainly in Cham-pagne; metallurgical inds.; a. 6,268 km²; p. (1982) 210,500.

Hautes-Alpes, dep., **France**; mtnous.; on Italian border; sheep; cap. Gap; a. 5,641 km²; p. (1982) 104,500.

Haute-Saône, dep., **France**; inc. part of Vosges mtns.; mainly agr.; cap. Vesoul; a. 5,372 km²; p. (1982) 232,100.

Haute-Savoie, dep., **France**; borders on Italy and Switzerland; reaches highest alt. in Mont Blanc; cap. Annecy; winter sports; a. 4,595 km²; p. (1982) 494,700.

Haute-Pyrénées, dep., S. **France**; rises in S. to steep peaks of Pyrenees, forming bdy. with Spain; Basques live on both sides of border; cap. Tarbes; Lourdes place of pilgrimage; a. 4,533 km²; p. (1982) 228,800.

Haute-Vienne, dep., **France**; entirely in Massif Central; cap. Limoges; cattle-raising; a. 5,488 km²; p. (1982) 355,000.

Haut-Rhin, dep., E. **France**; in lower Alsace; cap. Colmar; ch. industl. t. Mulhouse; a. 3,507 km²; p. (1982) 646,400.

Hauts-de-Seine, new dep., **France**; W. of Paris; cap. Nanterre; a. 176 km²; p. (1982) 1,386,700.

Havana (La Habana), c., cap. of **Cuba**; ch. pt. of W.I., with lge. harbour; cigars, tobacco, sugar, rum, coffee, woollens, straw hats, iron-ore; oil refining on outskirts of c.; p. (est. 1986) 1,993,000 (c.), 2,014,800 (met. a.).

Havant, t., l. gov. dist., **Eng.**; at foot Ports-downs Hill, 10 km N.E. of Portsmouth; p. (est. 1988) 117,500.

Havel, R., **E. Germany**; rises in Neubrandenburg L. region; flows to Elbe R.; partially canalised nr. Berlin; 354 km long.

Haverfordwest, t., Preseli, Dyfed, **Wales**; 10 km N.E. of Milford Haven; agr. mkt.; Norman cas.; p. (1981) 9,936.

Haverhill, t., St. Edmundsbury, Suffolk, **Eng.**; expanded t.; textiles; p. (1981) 17,146.

Haverhill, t., Mass., **USA**; industl.; shipping containers; p. (1980) 46,865.

Havering, outer bor., E. London, **Eng.**; inc. Horn-church and Romford; p. (est. 1988) 235,600.

Hawaii, I., N. central Pac. Oc.; lgst. of Hawaiian gr.; three gr. volcanic mtns., Mauna Kea (4,208 m), Mauna Loa (4,172 m), Hualalai (last erupted, 1801); ch. ctr. Hilo (devastated by tidal wave, 1946); lava deserts, bamboo forests; sugar-cane, cattle, coffee; tourism; deep-sea fishing; admitted to Union 1959; st. flower Hibiscus, st. bird Nene; p. (1980) 92,053.

Hawaiian Is. (Sandwich Is.), st., Pac. Oc., admitted 1959 as 50th st. of **USA**; chain of coral and volcanic Is.; cap. Honolulu on S.E. cst. of Oahu I.; tourism; ctr. of international shipping routes; sugar, pineapples; a. 16,638 km²; p. (1985) 1,054,000.

Hawarden, t., Alyn and Deeside, Clwyd, N. **Wales**; steel plant; home of Gladstone.

Hawes Water, L., Cumbria, **Eng.**; 4 km long.

Hawick, burgh, Roxburgh, **Scot.**; on R. Teviot, 28 km S.W. of Kelso; hosiery, tweed, and woollens; p. (1981) 16,333.

Hawke Bay, prov. dist., N.I., **N.Z.**; on E. cst.; cap. Napier; a. 11,033 km²; p. (est. 1985) 152,800.

Hawkesbury, R., N.S.W., **Australia**; impt. water-way flowing into Broken Bay; spectacular gorges.

Haworth, t., West Yorks., **Eng.**; nr. Keighley; home of the Brontës.

Hawthorne, t., S.W. Cal., **USA**; residtl.; in gas-and oil-producing a.; aircraft and electronics; p. (1980) 56,447.

Hay, t., Brecknock, Powys, **Wales**; on R. Wye; cas.; mkt.; p. (1981) 1,293.

Hay, R., Alberta, **Canada**; flows into G. Slave Lake; 560 km long.

Haydock, t., Merseyside, **Eng.**; coal mng.; inc. H. Park racecourse; p. (1981) 16,584.

Hayes and Harlington. See Hillingdon.

Hayling Island, resort, Hants., **Eng.**; E. of Ports-mouth.

Hayward, t., Cal., **USA**; fruit-canning, poultry; p. (1980) 94,342.

Haywards Heath, residtl. t. West Sussex, **Eng.**

Hazel Grove and Bramhall, sub. of Stockport, Gtr. Manchester, **Eng.**; p. (1981) 41,529.

Hazleton, t., Penns., **USA**; anthracite region; tex-tiles, iron and steel mnfs.; p. (1980) 27,318.

Headingley, sub., Leeds, West Yorks., **Eng.** mainly residtl.; county cricket ground.

Heanor, t., Amber Valley, Derbys., **Eng.**; 11 km N.E. of Derby; hosiery, pottery, prefabricated timber bldgs. mftg.; p. (1981) 24,655.

Heard, I., S. **Indian Oc.**; 448 km S.E. of Ker-guelen I.; Australian possession; volcanic.

Heathrow, site of London airport, **Eng.**; 24 km W. of central London, S. of M4 motorway; on Piccadilly tube line; handles 75 per cent of all U.K. air cargo and 26.7 million passengers in 1982; more imports (by value) than any U.K. port; residtl. a.

Hebburn, t., Tyne and Wear, **Eng.**; on R. Tyne 6 km below Gateshead; shipbldg., engin.; p. (1981) 22,103.

Hebden Royd, t., Calderdale, West Yorks., **Eng.**; cotton factories, dyewks., heavy engin., wool-lens and worsteds; p. (1981) 8,975.

Hebei (Hopeh), prov., N.E. **China**; part of N. China plain; bounded on N. by Great Wall; cap. Shijiaz-huang; wheat, kaoling, cotton, coal mng., a. 194,250 km²; p. (est. 1985) 54,870,000.

Hebrides or **Western Is., Scot.**; grouped as Outer and Inner Hebrides; ch. t. Stornoway, Lewis; a. 7,382 km².

Hebron, t., **Jordan**; 26 km. S.W. of Jerusalem; p. (1967) 43,000.

Heckmondwike, t., West Yorks., **Eng.**; wool textiles; p. (1981) 9,738.

Hedon, t., Humberside, **Eng.**; former spt.; p. (1981) 4,525.

Heerenveen, t., Friesland prov., N. **Neth.**; bicycles; p. (est. 1987) 37,000.

Heerlen, t., Limburg, **Neth.**; 22 km E. of Maas-tricht; coal mng.; p. (est. 1987) 94,000.

Heide, t., Schleswig-Holstein, **W. Germany**; ctr. of Ditmarschen oilfields; p. (est. 1986) 20,700.

Heidelberg, c., Baden–Württemberg, **W. Germany**; on R. Neckar, nr. Mannheim; celebrated univ. cas.; tobacco, wood, leather, rly. carriages; nylon plant projected; p. (est. 1986) 136,200.

Heidenheim, t. Baden–Württemberg, **W. Ger-many**; N.E. of Ulm; textiles, machin., metal-lurgy, furniture; p. (est. 1986) 47,600.

Heilbronn, t., R. pt., Baden–Württemberg, **W. Germany**; engin., vehicles, foodstuffs; p. (est. 1986) 111,700.

Heilongjiang (Heilungkiang), prov., N.E. **China**; separated from USSR by Amur and Ussuri Rs.; mtnous.; crossed by Songhua R. in central plain; maize, soyabeans, millets; opencast coalmines; gold; cap. Harbin; a. 466,200 km²; p. (est. 1985) 32,950,000.

Hejaz, region, **Saudi Arabia**; mainly desert; very poor communications; ch. t. Mecca; a. 388,500 km²; p. (est. 1973) 2,000,000, mainly Bedouin.

Hekla, volcano, **Iceland**; erupted in 1970; alt. 1,554 m.

Helder (Den Helder), t., N. Holland, **Neth.**; on strait between peninsula and I. of Texel; naval base; p. (est. 1987) 63,000.

Helena, st. cap., Mont., **USA**; grew up as gold- and silver-mng. t.; bricks, pottery; resort; p. (1980) 23,938.

Helensburgh, t., Dumbarton, W. **Scot.**; on the Clyde; resort; p. (1981) 16,478.

Helford, R., Cornwall, **Eng.**; oysters, tourism.

Helicon, mtn. gr., **Greece**; abode of classical muses.

Heligoland (**Helgoländ**), sm. I., N. Sea; off mouth of Elbe; ceded by Britain to Germany 1890 in return for Zanzibar.

Hellespont. See **Dardanelles**.

Helmand or **Helmund**, R., **Afghanistan**; flows c. 1,360 km from mtns. of Kabul to Hamun-i-Helmand swamp on Iranian border; cultivation in valley; major irrigation project.

Helmond, t., N. Brabant, **Neth.**; on Zuid-Willemsvaart (canal); textiles; p. (est. 1987) 64,000.

Helmsley, mkt. t., Ryedale, North Yorks., **Eng.**; cas.

Helmstedt, t., Lower Saxony, **W. Germany**; E. of Brunswick; on E. German border; textiles, machin.; p. (est. 1986) 25,500.

Helsingborg (**Hälsingborg**), spt., Malmöhus, **Sweden** industl. ctr.; train ferry to Elsinore, Denmark; p. (est. 1986) 106,000.

Helsingör. See **Elsinore**.

Helsinki or **Helsingfors**, c., cap. of **Finland**; spt. on G. of Finland; harbour ice-bound Jan. to Apr., channel opened by ice-breakers; cultural ctr., univ.; timber, textiles, carpets; exp. mainly timber prods.; p. (1986) 487,581 (c.), 965,233 (met. a.).

Helston, mkt. t., Kerrier, Cornwall, **Eng.**; on R. Cober, 13 km W. of Falmouth; tourist ctr.; famous for festival of floral dance (8 May); fishing, soup-canning; p. (1981) inc. Porthleven, 10,741.

Helvellyn, mtn., L. Dist., Cumbria, **Eng.**; severely eroded by ice; alt. 951 m; sharp ridge of Striding Edge.

Helwan, t., **Egypt**; 24 km S. of Cairo; sulphur springs; iron and steel complex, recently expanded (1982); fertilisers, cement; car assembly.

Hemel Hempstead, t., Dacorum, Herts., **Eng.**; new t. (1947), on S. slopes of Chilterns; scientific glass, elec. engin., cars; p. (1981) 76,257.

Henan (**Honan**), prov., Central **China**; traversed by Huang He; cap. Zhengzhou; densely p. in fertile E.; mainly agr.; wheat, cotton, kaolin, anthracite; a. 167,172 km²; p. (est. 1985) 76,460,000.

Hengelo, t., Overijssel, **Neth.**; industl. ctr.; cattle mkt.; metals, textiles; p. (est. 1987) 77,000.

Hengyang, c., Hunan, **China**; on Xiang Jiang in foothills to S. Chang Jiang plain; on main Guangzhau-Beijing rly.; lead and zinc mines nearby; p. (1984) 551,300.

Hénin-Beaumont, t., Pas-de-Calais, **France**; on coalfield; p. (1982) 26,212.

Henley-on-Thames, t., South Oxfordshire, Oxon., **Eng.**; 8 km N.E. of Reading; mkt. gardening, brewing; annual regatta; p. (1981) 10,976.

Hensbarrow, upland a., Cornwall, **Eng.**; granite; kaolin-mng. dist., kaolin exp. by sea from Fowey; rises to over 300 m; a. 70 km².

Henzada, t., Burma, on Irrawaddy delta; in tobacco and rice-growing dist.; p. (1983) 283,658.

Herakleion. See **Iráklion**.

Herät, c., cap. of H. prov., N.W. **Afghanistan**; on Hari Rud R.; of historic and strategic importance, has been called "the key of India"; crude petroleum and chrome-ore nearby; tr. ctr.; textiles; p. (est. 1982) 150,497.

Hérault, dep. S.W. **France**; in Languedoc; agr.; cap. Montpellier; govt.-sponsored tourist developments along shores of Mediterranean; a. 6,221 km²; p. (1982) 715,500.

Herculaneum, anc. c., S. **Italy**; 6 km E. of Naples; buried along with Pompeii by eruption from Vesuvius A.D. 79; rediscovered 1709; site of modern Resina and Portici.

Hereford and Worcestershire, non-met. co., **Eng.**; crossed by Wye and Severn valleys, separated by Malvern Hills; mainly agr.; beef, dairy and fruit farming; major ts. Hereford and Worcester; a. 3,906 km²; p. (est. 1988) 671,000.

Hereford, c., l. gov. dist., Hereford and Worcs., **Eng.**; on R. Wye; cath.; mkt.; tiles, engin., timber, cider and preserves; furniture, brassware; p. (est. 1988) 49,000.

Herefordshire, South, l. gov. dist., H. and Worcs., **Eng.**; lge rural a. inc. Ross-on-Wye; p. (est. 1988) 51,100.

Herford, t., N. Rhine-Westphalia, **W. Germany**; on R. Werra; cotton, flax, furniture, cigars, confectionery, metallurgy; p. (est. 1986) 59,500.

Herisau, t., cap. of Appenzell Ausser-Rhoden half-can., N.E. **Switzerland**; muslin, embroideries; p. (1980) 14,160.

Herm, sm. I. of **Channel Is.**, English Channel; 6 km N.W. Sark and N.E. of Guernsey; remarkable shell-beach; a. 130 ha; p. (1971) 96.

Hermon, Mount (**Jebel esh Sheikh**), mtn., in Anti-Lebanon range, on **Syria-Lebanon** bdy., nr. Israel; alt. 2,862 m.

Hermosillo, c., cap. of Sonora st., N.W. **Mexico**; on San Miguel R.; oranges; agr. and mng. ctr.; p. (1989) 340,779.

Hermoupolis or **Hermopolis**, t., Syros I., **Greece**; cap. of Cyclades; Aegean pt. and comm. ctr.; p. (1981) 13,876.

Herne, t., N. Rhine-Westphalia, **W. Germany**; pt. on Rhine-Herne canal; industl. t. of Ruhr conurb.; p. (est. 1986) 171,300.

Herne Bay, t., Kent, **Eng.**; on cst., 19 km W. of Margate; p. (1981) 27,528.

Herning, t., Jutland, **Denmark**; knitting ind.; p. (est. 1987) 56,195.

Heröya, S. **Norway**; nuclear power plant; chemicals, fertilisers.

Herstal, t., **Belgium**; nr. Liège; armaments, aero-engines; p. (1982) 38,189.

Herstmonceux, v. nr. Hastings, Sussex, **Eng.**; cas.; frmr. site of Royal Greenwich Observatory.

Hertford, co. t., East Herts., **Eng.**; on R. Lea, 32 km N. of London; pharmaceutics, flour milling, rolling stock, diesels, brewing; p. (1981) 21,412.

Hertfordshire, non-met. co., **Eng.**; borders Greater London on S.; co. t., Hertford, ch. ctr. St. Albans; drained by Rs. Thames and Lea; intensive agr., lt. inds.; new ts. Welwyn, Stevenage, Hatfield, Hemel Hempstead; a. 1,637 km²; p. (est. 1988) 985,900.

Hertfordshire, East, l. gov. dist., Herts., **Eng.**; lge a. inc. Ware, Bishop's Stortford, Hertford and Sawbridgeworth; p. (est. 1988) 118,700.

Hertfordshire, North, l. gov. dist., Herts., **Eng.**; stretches from Baldock, Letchworth and Hitchin to Royston; p. (est. 1988) 112,300.

's-Hertogenbosch, t., **Neth.**; on Rs. Dommel and Aa; cap. of N. Brabant prov.; cath.; cattle mkt.; industl. development; p. (est. 1987) 90,000.

Hertsmere, l. gov. dist., Herts., **Eng.**; a. close to London, inc. Bushey, Elstree and Potters Bar; p. (est. 1988) 88,600.

Hesse, Land, **W. Germany**; part of former Prussian prov. Hesse-Nassau; mainly upland; inds. at Frankfurt, Kassel, Darmstadt; wine produced along Rhine valley; cap. Wiesbaden; tourism; a. 21,103 km²; p. (est. 1986) 5,543,700.

Hetch Hetchy Dam, Cal., **USA**; on R. Toulumne upstream from San Joaquin R.; ch. source of irrigation for middle San Joaquin valley; supplies water and generating power to San Francisco.

Hetton, t., Tyne and Wear, **Eng.**; 8 km N.E. of Durham; coal-mng. dist.; p. (1981) 15,903.

Hexham, mkt. t., Tynedale, Northumberland, **Eng.**; on R. Tyne, 32 km W. of Newcastle; priory; p. (1981) 9,630.

Heywood, t., Gtr. Manchester, **Eng.**; 5 km E. of Bury; chemicals, engin.; p. (1981) 30,672.

Hialeah, t., Fla., **USA**; sub. of Miami; racecourse; p. (1984) 152,200.

Hidalgo, st., central **Mexico**; mtnous. with fertile valleys in S. and W.; cap. Pachuca; mng. (silver, gold, copper, lead, iron, sulphur); maguey (type of lily), tobacco, cotton, coffee; a. 20,868 km²; p. (1980) 1,516,511.

Higashiosaka, c., **Japan**; E. of Osaka; formed from amalgamation of Fuse, Kawachi, Hiraoka and many sm. ts.; p. (1985) 522,798.

Higham Ferrers, mkt. t., East Northants, **Eng.**; 5 km E. of Wellingborough; footwear and leather dressing; p. (1981) 5,189.

Highgate, residtl. dist., N. London, **Eng.**; hilltop v. in bor. of Haringey.

Highland Park, t., Mich., **USA**; sub. of Detroit; grew up with expansion of motor-car ind.; p. (1980) 27,909.

Highland Region, l. gov. reg., N. **Scot.**; rugged mtns. inland; p. concentrated around cst.; offshore oil development; stock raising, forestry, tourism; a. 25,128 km²; p. (est. 1986) 200,764.

High Peak, l. gov. dist., Derbys., **Eng.**; a. of Pennines inc. New Mills, Glossop, Whaley Bridge and Buxton; p. (est. 1988) 84,300.

High Point, t., N.C., **USA**; furniture ctr., hosiery; p. (1980) 63,808.

High Willhays, hgst. summit, Dartmoor, Devon, **Eng.**; 621 m.

High Wycombe, t., Bucks., **Eng.**; 13 km N. of Maidenhead; furniture, paper-mkg., egg processing; in London commuter belt; p. (1981) 60,516.

Hildesheim, t., Lower Saxony, **W. Germany**; at foot of Harz mtns.; cath.; machin., farm implements, textiles, ceramics; p. (est. 1986) 100,600.

Hillah, Al, mkt. t., **Iraq**; on R. Euphrates; nr. anc. Babylon; food tr. rugs, leather; p. (1970) 128,811.

Hilleröd, t., **Denmark**; admin. ctr. of Frederiksborg prov.; p. (1981) 25,411.

Hillingdon, outer bor. Greater London, **Eng.**; comprising former U.D.s of Hayes and Harlington, Ruislip and Northwood Yiewsley, W. Drayton, and former M.B. of Uxbridge; p. (est. 1988) 231,900.

Hilo, t., **Hawaii**; pt. of entry and main tr. and shipping ctr. of I.; tourism; Mauna Loa volcano nearby; p. (1980) 35,269.

Hilversum, t., **Neth.**; nr. Utrecht; radio broadcasting ctr.; noteworthy modern architecture; p. (est. 1987) 85,000.

Himachal Pradesh, st., N.W. **India**; bounded by Tibet on E.; forested mtns., cultivated valleys; cap. Simla; a. 56,019 km²; p. (1981) 4,280,818.

Himalayas, vast chain of mtns. along N. border of India, between the Indus and Brahamaputra Rs., and lying in Pakistan, India, Nepal, Sikkim, Bhutan, and China; made up of several parallel ranges inc. the Siwaliks, the Hindu Kush, and the Karakorams; crossed by passes, mainly in W.; 2,560 km long; hgst. peak Mt. Everest, 8,854 m.

Himeji, c., S. Honshu, **Japan**; mkt. ctr. on shore of Inland Sea, 48 km W. of Kobe; iron and steel ind., heavy engin.; oil refining; p. (1985) 452,916.

Hinckley, mkt. t., Leics., **Eng.**; hosiery, cardboard boxes, dye-wks., engin.; nr. Watling Street; with Market Bosworth forms l. gov. dist. of Hinckley and Bosworth; p. (est. 1990) 98,800 (dist.).

Hindenburg. *See* **Zabrze.**

Hindhead, hill common, Surrey, nr. Haslemere, **Eng.**

Hindiya Barrage, dam, **Iraq**; across R. Euphrates, 48 km above Al Hillah; provides flood control and irrigation in a. between Shatt al Hillah and R. Euphrates.

Hindley, t., Gtr. Manchester, **Eng.**; 3 km S.E. of Wigan; paint, knitwear, rubber, asbestos; p. (1981) 25,537.

Hindu Kush, mtn. range, mainly in N.E. **Afghanistan**; hgst peak Tirich Mir (7,755 m) in Chitral dist., **Pakistan**; Salang tunnel (opened 1964) with 2-lane motor highway cuts H.K. at height of 3,300 m, runs 240 m below mtn. top, 3·2 km.

Hindustan, former name of part of N. **India** between Himalayas and Vindhya ranges.

Hinkley Point, Somerset, **Eng.**; civil nuclear power-sta.; second sta. now being built.

Hirfanli Dam, project on R. Kizilirmak, 144 km S.E. Ankara, **Turkey**, 1961.

Hirosaki, c., Honshu, **Japan**; mkt., lacquer-ware; cas.; p. (1985) 176,082.

Hiroshima, c., S.W. Honshu, **Japan**; on delta of Ota R.; first c. to be destroyed by atomic bomb (6 Aug. 1945); since rebuilt; motor vehicles, shipbldg.; p. (1987) 1,066,000.

Hirschberg. *See* **Jelenia Góra.**

Hispaniola, second lgst. I. of **W.I.**; lies between Cuba and Puerto Rico; divided between Haiti (Fr.-speaking) and Dominican Rep. (Spanish-speaking); complex relief, climate, and vegetation, but strong cultural differences make international bdy. a sharp divide; a. 76,498 km².

Hitchin, t., North Herts., **Eng.**; in gap through Chiltern Hills, 56 km N. of London; lt. engin., tanning, chemicals, distilling; mkt.; p. (1981) 30,317.

Hjälmaren Lake, central **Sweden**; drained into L. Malaren by Esk R.; linked by canal to Arboga; a. 474 km².

Hjörring, c., Jutland, N. **Denmark**; biscuit and clothing wks.; p. (1981) 23,697.

Hobart, cap. and ch. pt. of Tasmania, **Australia**; on R. Derwent; univ.; fruit exp.; mostly light inds.; zinc; cadmium, superphosphates, textiles; p. (est. 1985) 178,100.

Hoboken, t., Antwerp, **Belgium**; shipbldg.; refractory metals; p. (1981) 34,563.

Hoboken, t., N.J., **USA**; on Hudson R. above Jersey City, opp. N.Y. to which it is linked by subway and ferry; pt. for ocean commerce; industl. ctr.; p. (1980) 42,460.

Ho Chi-minh City (Saigon), c., spt., **Vietnam**; former cap. of S. Vietnam; on Saigon R. to E. of Mekong Delta; tree-lined boulevards; cath., univ., modern airport; comm. ctr.; exp. rice, rubber; food processing; p. declining rapidly since reunification of Vietnam; p. (1979) 3,419,978 (inc. Cholon).

Höchst, t., Hesse, **W. Germany**; industl. sub. of Frankfurt-on-Main; site of German chemical ind.

Hochstetter, mtn., S.I., **N.Z.**; in Southern Alps; alt. 3,416 m.

Hoddesdon, t., Herts., **Eng.**; in Lea valley, 6 km S. of Ware; nursery tr., tomatoes, etc.; p. (1981) 29,892.

Hodeida (Al Hudaydah), t., **Yemen Arab Rep.**, on Red Sea; pt. and naval base; exp. dates, hides, coffee; p. (1981) 126,386.

Hódmezővásárhely, t., S.E. **Hungary**; wheat, fruit, tobacco, cattle; natural gas pipeline from Szeged; p. (est. 1984) 54,000.

Hof, t., Bavaria, **W. Germany**; on R. Saale; textiles, iron, machin., porcelain, glass, brewing; p. (est. 1986) 50,600.

Hofei or **Hefei**, c., cap. of Anhui prov., **China**; rice-growing a.; cotton and silk, iron and steel; p. (est. 1983) 830,000.

Hoffman, mtn. peak of the Sierra Nevada, Cal., **USA**; alt. 2,473 m.

Hofuf (Al Hufuf), t., El Hasa, **Saudi Arabia**; dates, wheat, fruit; textiles, brass- and copper-ware; oil-fields nearby; p. (est. 1977) 102,000.

Hog's Back, Surrey, **Eng.**; steep chalk ridge; alt. 154 m.

Hohenlimburg, t., N. Rhine–Westphalia, **W. Germany**; nr. Dortmund; cas.; textiles, iron, steel; p. (est. 1971) 26,500.

Hohenstein-Ernstal, t., Karl-Marx-Stadt, **E. Germany**; textiles, metal gds.; p. (est. 1970) 16,800.

Hohe Tauern, Alpine range, Tyrol, **Austria**; rugged crystalline rocks; highest point Gross Glockner, 3,801 m; traversed by rly. tunnel 8 km long.

Hohhot (Huhehot), c., Nei Mongol (Inner Mongolia), **China**; diesel engines; new woollen mill; p. (1984) 778,000.

Hoihow. *See* **Haikou.**

Hokkaido, lge. I., **Japan**, N. of Honshu; colder than other Is.; less dense p.; temperate agr.; skiing; tunnel link (1983) with Honshu to aid economic development; a. 88,775 km²; p. of pref. (1985) 5,679,000.

Holbaek, t., Sjaelland, **Denmark**; W. of Copenhagen; engin. and motor wks.; p. (1981) 20,634.

Holbeach, mkt. t., S. Lincs., **Eng.**; in Fens, 11 km E. of Spalding; brewing; ctr. of bulb-growing dist.

Holborn. *See* **Camden.**

Holderness, peninsula, l. gov. dist., Humberside, **Eng.**; between R. Humber and N. Sea; agr.; p. (est. 1988) 50,600.

Holguin, t., N.E. **Cuba**; comm. ctr.; sugar, tobacco, coffee, cattle; exps. handled by pt. Gibara; p. (1985) 194,700.

Holland. *See* **Netherlands.**

Holland, N., prov., **Neth.**; inc. Texel Is.; dairying; a. 2,629 km²; p. (1983) 2,308,047.

Holland, Parts of. *See* **Lincolnshire.**

Holland, South, l. gov. dist., Lincs., **Eng.**; fenland a. around Spalding; p. (est. 1988) 66,300.

Holland, S., prov., **Neth.**; crossed by R. Rhine; mkt. gardening; a. 2,927 km²; p. (1983) 3,129,913.

Hollandia, former name of cap. W. Irian, **Indonesia**; renamed Kota Baru by Indonesia, then Sukarnapura, now Djajapura.

Holloman, t., N.M., **USA**; atomic and space research ctr.; site of 1st. man-made atomic explosion.

Hollywood, t., Fla., **USA**; seaside resort on Atl. cst.; cement, furniture; p. (1984) 120,200; part of Fort Lauderdale met. a.

Hollywood, sub. of Los Angeles, Cal., **USA**; ctr. of film industry.

Holmesdale, Vale of, Kent, E. Surrey, **Eng.**; extends along foot of N. Downs escarpment; drained by Rs. Mole, Darent, Medway, Len, Stour; heavy clay soils; ch. ts. Dorking, Reigate, Sevenoaks, Maidstone, Ashford, which have grown up in gaps through hills to N. and S. of Vale; length 96 km, average width 2 km.

Holmfirth, t., West Yorks., **Eng.**; 8 km S. of Huddersfield, textiles, engin.; p. (1981) 21,839.

Holt, mkt. t., N. Norfolk, **Eng.**; 8 km S.W. of Sheringham; 16th-cent. school.

Holt, t., Clwyd, **Wales**; on R. Dee, 11 km S. of Chester; cas. ruins.

Holyhead, spt., Anglesey, Gwynedd, **Wales**; on Holyhead I.; mail packet sta. for Ireland; lt. engin., woodwkg., clocks; site for aluminium smelter; pt. traffic reduced as result of damage to Menai Bridge; p. (1981) 10,467.

Holy I. (**Lindisfarne**), off cst. of Northumberland, **Eng.**

Holy I., Scot., in F. of Clyde, nr. I. of Arran; submarine base.

Holy I., off cst. of Anglesey, Gwynedd, **Wales.**

Holyoke, t., Mass., **USA**; on Connecticut R., above Springfield; paper, machin.; p. (1980) 44,678.

Holywell, mkt. t., Delyn, Clwyd, N. **Wales**; woollen, rayon and paper inds.; p. (1981) 8,905.

Holywood, spt., North Down, **N. Ireland**; on S. shore of Belfast Lough; seaside resort; p. (1981) 9,462.

Homburg (**Bad Homburg**), c., Hesse, **W. Germany**; famous spa; p. (est. 1986) 51,100.

Home Counties, term applied to the geographical counties adjoining London, *i.e.*, Middlesex, Surrey, Essex, and Kent; sometimes Hertfordshire, Buckinghamshire, and Berkshire are included, and occasionally Sussex; (Middlesex and parts of Essex, Surrey, Kent, and Hertfordshire incorporated in Greater London 1965).

Homs, t., **W. Syria**; on R. Orontes in fertile plain; anc. Emesa; steel plants, fertilisers, lt. inds.; pipeline from Kirkūk oil fields; p. (1981) 354,508.

Honan. *See* **Henan.**

Honda, old Spanish t., **Colombia**; on Magdalena R., at rapids; former comm. ctr.; p. (est. 1968) 22,315.

Honduras, rep., straddles Central American isthmus with longest cst. on Caribbean; comprises 18 deps. inc. offshore Bay Is.; coastal lowlands hot and humid, more temperate in interior highlands which rise to over 2,000 m; agr. basis of economy, especially American-owned banana plantations; bananas almost half exp.; some mng.; rlys. oriented to banana-producing areas to facilitate exp.; nationalised forests; land reform; cap. Tegucigalpa; 5 airports.; a. 111,958 km², p. (est. 1985) 4,372,000.

Honduras, British. *See* **Belize.**

Hong Kong, Brit. Crown Col., S.E. cst. **China**, comprises Hong Kong I., Kowloon peninsula and New Territories (on lease from China until 1997); road and rail tunnels link H.K. with Kowloon; deepwater harbour of Victoria has lost much tr. from China; industl. development rapid since second world war yet few natural resources; exp. clothing, toys, electronics, watches; dense p. increased by immigration from China and Vietnam; to return to Chinese sovereignty (1997) with status of special admin. reg.; present capitalist system to remain for 50 years after that; a. 1,068 km², p. (est 1987) 5·6 m.

Honiara, t., cap. of **Solomon Is.**; on Guadalcanal I.; p. (est. 1985) 26,000.

Honiton, t., East Devon, **Eng.**; on R. Otter, 26 km E. of Exeter; mkt.; trout-fishing; once produced lace, an ind. introduced by Flemish refugees; p. (1981) 6,567.

Honolulu, c., cap. of **Hawaii**; on Oahu 1.; social and comm. ctr. and ch. pt. of archipelago; gd. harbour; univ.; airport; fruit-canning, sugar-processing; tourism; p. (1984) 373,200 (c.), 805,300 (met. a.).

Honshu, lgst. I. of **Japan**; contains most of p. along E. cst. in 320 km industl. belt; new Seikan tunnel links I. to Hokkaido; a. 230,300 km²; p. (1980) 93,246,000.

Hoogeveen, t., Drenthe, **Neth.**; fruit- and vegetable-canning; p. (est. 1984) 45,000.

Hooghly, R., arm of Ganges R., **India**; flows into Bay of Bengal; used in jute-milling and navigable as far as Calcutta; 256 km long.

Hooghly Chinsura, t., W. Bengal, **India**; on Hooghly R.; rice-milling; p. (1981) 125,193 (part of Calcutta met. a.).

Hook of Holland (**Hoek van Holland**), spt., **Neth.**; packet sta. with steamer connections to Harwich, Eng.

Hoorn, old fishing t., N. Holland, **Neth.**; on IJsselmeer, 39 km N. of Amsterdam; cattle mkts.; birthplace of Jan P. Coen, founder of Batavia; p. (est. 1987) 54,000.

Hoover Dam, **USA**; on Colorado R.; used for irrigation (parts of Cal., Arizona, and Mexico), flood control and hydroelectric power; Lake Mead, 184 km long, 2–13 km wide, one of world's lgst. man-made Ls.

Hopeh. *See* **Hebei.**

Hor, unlocated biblical mtn. between Dead Sea and G. of Aqaba, the place of Aaron's death.

Horbury, t., West Yorks., **Eng.**; nr. Wakefield; p. (1981) 9,136.

Horeb. *See* **Sinai.**

Hormuz, Strait of, between Persian G. and G. of Oman.

Horn, C., S. **Chile**, most S. point of S. America.

Horncastle, mkt. t., E. Lindsey, Lincs., **Eng.**; at confluence of Rs. Bain and Waring at foot of Lincoln Wolds; mkt.; vegetable-processing; p. (1981) 4,207.

Hornsea, t., Humberside, **Eng.**; on E. cst., N.E. of Hull; seaside resort; p. (1981) 7,204.

Hornsey. *See* **Haringey.**

Horsens, t., Denmark, E. Jutland; on inlet of Kattegat; industl. and comm. ctr.; p. (est. 1987) 54,676.

Horsforth, t., West Yorks., **Eng.**; in Aire valley N.W. of Leeds; cloth, tanning, lt. engin.; p. (1981) 19,290.

Horsham, t., Victoria, **Australia**; on R. Wimmera; pastoral, dairying and agr. dist.; p. (est. 1983) 12,660.

Horsham, t., l. gov. dist., West Sussex, **Eng.**; on R. Arun at W. end of forested dist. of the High Weald; agr., timber, engin., chemicals; Horsham stone once quarried here; Shelley's birthplace; p. (est. 1988) 107,900 (dist.).

Horta, t., cap. of H. dist., **Azores**; on Fayal I.; excellent harbour and base for transatlantic flights; p. (1981) 6,910.

Horten, spt., **Norway**; nr. Oslo; naval base; shipbldg., mftg. inds.; p. (1980) 13,295.

Horton, R., N.W. Terr., **Canada**; flows into Beaufort Sea, Arctic Oc.; reindeer reserve along cst.

Horwich, t., Gtr. Manchester, **Eng.**; on W. edge of Rossendale Fells, N.W. of Bolton; rly. t.; engin.; rly. workshops closed (1983); p. (1981) 17,970.

Hospitalet de Llobregat, t., **Spain**; sub. of Barcelona, in Llobregat valley; p. (1981) 294,033.

Hotan (**Khotan**), c., S.W. Xinjiang, **China**; in fertile H. oasis at base of Kunlun Shan; silk, carpets, jade-ware; on anc. Silk Road; early ctr. of Buddhism; visited by Marco Polo 1274; p. (est. 1970) 50,000.

Hot Springs, c., Ark., **USA**; in Ouachita mtns. S.W. of Little Rock; Nat. Park since 1832; health resort; p. (1980) 35,781.

Houghton-le-Spring, t., Tyne and Wear, **Eng.**; S.W. of Sunderland; former colly. t.; coal-mng. dist.; p. (1981) 31,036.

Hounslow, outer bor., Greater London, **Eng.**; inc. former bors. of Brentford and Chiswick, Heston and Isleworth, Feltham and Hounslow; rubber goods; p. (est. 1988) 190,800.

Housatonic, R., W. Mass., Conn., **USA**; falls attracted early Puritan settlement and industrialisation; dairy farming; 240 km long.

Houston, c., spt., S. Texas, **USA**; on Galveston Bay; gr. pt., lgst. c. of S.; univ.; oil refineries, oilfield machin., steel, chemicals, paper, processing, milling and assembling plants; NASA's manned space flight ctr. and lunar science institute; p. (1984) 1,705,700 (c.), 3,565,700 (met. a.).

Houston Ship Canal, Texas, **USA**; links Houston to head of shallow Galveston Bay and continues through bay to deep water; provides site for heavy inds.; opened 1915; total length 72 km.

Hove, t., l. gov. dist., East Sussex, **Eng.**; on S. cst., contiguous with Brighton; residtl.; holiday resort; p. (est. 1988) 90,700.

Howrah, c., W. Bengal, **India**; on W. bank of Hooghly R., in met. a. of Calcutta; p. (1981) 744,429.

Hoy, I., Orkneys, **Scot.**; lofty cliffs along W. cst., separated from Mainland I. by Sound of Hoy; Old Man of Hoy rock 137 m high; p. (1971) 531 (inc. Walls).

Hoylake, t., Wirral, Merseyside, **Eng.**; on N. cst. of Wirral peninsula; residtl.; golf course; p. (1981) 32,914.

Hradec Králové, t., **ČSSR**; at confluence of Elbe (Labe) and Orlice Rs.; industl. ctr.; mnfs. machin., precision instruments; 14th-cent. cath. and town hall; p. (est. 1986) 100,000.

Huainan (**Hwainan**), c., Anhui prov., central **China**; ctr. of China's ch. coal mng. region; p. (1984) 1,063,000.

Huai He (**Hwai-ho**), R., **China**; flows E. between N. China plain and lower Chang Jiang; subject to disastrous floods and changes of course; since 1950 flood control and irrigation canal to sea; 1,224 km long.

Huamanga (Ayacucho), c., cap. of A. prov., **Peru**; founded by Pizarro in 1539; lies in equable fertile valley; p. (est. 1985) 150,000.

Huambo. *See* **Nova Lisboa.**

Huancayo, t., cap. of Junín dep., **Peru**; in high valley of Andes, c. 3,300 m; textiles; p. (est. 1985) 190,000.

Huang Hai (**Hwang-hai** or **Yellow Sea**), arm of **Pac. Oc.** between Korea and China; branches into Gs. of Bo Hai and Liaotung; shallow sea rapidly infilling; named after yellow silt from Huang He; length 960 km, greatest width 640 km.

Huang He (**Hwang Ho**), R., **China**; the Yellow R., rises in Kunlun Shan; flows c. 4,800 km. into G. of Bo Hai; cuts through Shaanxi in a deep gorge; filled with yellow silt (loess) from this a.; floods frequently and changes course (once entered sea S. of Shandong); in lower part forms fertile plain; now part of multipurpose scheme for hydro-electric power, irrigation and flood control; lgst. dam in China opened at Liuchia in 1975; 4,640 km long.

Huangshi (**Hwangshih**), c., Hubei prov., **China**; main iron and steel ctr. of central China, built since 1950; p. (1984) 435,200.

Hua Shan (**Tsinling Shan**), mtn. range, central **China**; rises to over 1,830 m; watershed between Huang He and Chang Jiang basins; impt. climatic divide between temperate N. China and tropical S. China.

Huarás or **Huaráz**, cap. of Ancash dep., **Peru**; on Santa R., c. 3,000 m; mainly agr., some mng.; avalanche 1941 killed 6,000 inhabitants; p. (1981) 45,116 (predominantly Indian).

Huascarán, extinct volcano, Peruvian Andes, nr. Huarás, 6,773 m high; avalanche 1970 killed 20,000 people.

Hubei (**Hupeh**), prov., central **China**; N. of the Chang Jiang; many Ls. and Rs.; rice, wheat, cotton; iron ores; Wuhan is major industl. ctr. of prov. and central China; cap. Wuhan; a. 186,363 km²; p. (est. 1985) 48,760,000.

Hubli, c., Karnataka, **India**; E. of Goa; textiles, rly. engin.; p. (1981) 527,108.

Hucknall, t., Ashfield, Nottingham, **Eng.**; hosiery, coal; p. (1981) 28,142.

Huddersfield, t., West Yorks., **Eng.**; on edge of Pennines, 16 km S. of Bradford; wool, textiles, chemicals, engin.; p. (1981) 123,888.

Hudson, R., N.Y., **USA**; flows from Adirondacks to N.Y. harbour; with valley of Mohawk R. makes gr. highway of tr. between Great Ls. and N.Y.; scenic beauty; hydroelec. power; 560 km long.

Hudson Bay, gr. inland sea, **Canada**; communicates by Hudson Strait with Davis Strait (Atl. Oc.); ice-free mid-July to Oct.; salmon, cod; a. 1,398,600 km².

Hué, c., **Vietnam**; on Hué R., 16 km from S. China Sea; pt. and tr. ctr.; former cap. of Annam; royal palace; p. (1973) 209,043.

Huelva, coastal prov., S.W. **Spain**; copper mng., vine- and olive-growing, stock-raising, fisheries, brandy distilling; a. 10,117 km²; p. (1987) 436,813.

Huelva, c., cap. of Huelva prov., **Spain**; pt. on G. of Cadiz; oil refining, chemicals, food processing; exp. of minerals from nearby Rio Tinto; p. (1987) 135,938.

Huesca, c., cap. of H. prov., N.E. **Spain**; at foot of Pyrenees on R. Isuela; cath.; agr. ctr.; wine and timber tr. with France; p. (1987) 40,949.

Hugh Town, cap. of the Scilly Isles, **Eng.**; on St. Mary's I.

Huhehot. *See* **Hohhot.**

Hula L. *See* **Waters of Merom.**

Hull, t., S.W. Quebec, **Canada**; within met. a. of Ottawa; sawmills, paper; p. (1986) 58,722.

Hull or **Kingston-upon-Hull**, c., l. gov. dist., Humberside, **Eng.**; major spt. of U.K.; at influx of R. Hull in estuary of Humber; originally laid out by Edward I; lge. docks; premier distant water fishing pt.; inds. inc. oil-extracting, flour milling, sawmilling, chemicals, engin., univ.; p. (est. 1988) 247,000.

Humber, estuary of Rs. Ouse and Trent, **Eng.**; fine waterway; 2–13 km wide, 61 km long; Humber bridge opened (1981), longest single span suspension bridge in world; oil recently found (1981).

Humberside, non-met. co., **Eng.**; inc. most of E. Riding of Yorks., and Humber estuary where growth of pt. processing and chem. inds. and impt. pts. of Hull and Grimsby; iron and steel at Scunthorpe; cstl. resort of Bridlington in N.E.; a. 3,512 km²; p. (est. 1988) 850,500.

Humboldt, R., N. Nevada, **USA**; rises in Ruby Mtns.,

flows for 480 km before disappearing by evaporation and percolation; impt. 19th cent. routeway.

Humboldt Bay, inlet, Cal., **USA**; nuclear experimental breeder reactor.

Humboldt Current. *See* **Peru Current.**

Hume Lake, reservoir, N.S.W., **Australia**; formed by dam where R. Murray leaves Gr. Dividing Range; supplies water for irrigation in upper Riverina dist.; capacity c. 113 million m³.

Hunan, prov., central **China**; S. of the Chang Jiang; hilly in S. and W.; rice, wheat, beans; rich mineral resources, inc. mercury, tin, tungsten; cap. Changsha; Mao Tse-tung came from Hunan peasant stock; a. 205,589 km²; p. (est. 1985) 55,610,000.

Hunedoara, t., H. dist., **Romania**; iron and steel; p. (1983) 87,000.

Hungary, rep., E. **Europe**; bounded by USSR, ČSSR, Romania, Yugoslavia, and Austria; lies in basin of middle Danube (Duna), with plain in E. and Carpathian mtns. in W.; mainly agr.; exp. meat, fruit, vegetables to W. Europe; inds. increasingly impt. and now account for over 50 per cent of income; plans to make H. leading exporter of buses in Europe; 19 cos., cap. Budapest; a. 93,012 km²; p. (est. 1987) 10,622,000.

Hunsrück (= dog's back), forested highlands, Rhineland–Palatinate, **W. Germany**; between Mosel and Nahe Rs.; vineyards on S. slopes; hgst. point 816 m.

Hunstanton, t., West Norfolk, **Eng.**; S.E. shore of Wash; seaside resort; p. (1981) 4,089.

Hunter, R., N.S.W., **Australia**; rises in Liverpool range of Gr. Dividing Range, flows S. and E. into Tasman Sea at Newcastle; world famous grape growing and wine producing reg.; coal exp.; c. 400 km long.

Hunterston, Cunninghame, **Scot.**; civil nuclear power sta.; integrated iron and steel wks., engin. of oil platforms and oil terminal planned.

Huntingdon, t., l. gov. dist., Cambs., **Eng.**; on R. Ouse; expanded t.; canning, engin., processed rubber, confectionery; birthplace of Cromwell and home of the poet Cowper; p. (est. 1988) 147,700.

Huntingdon and Peterborough, former co., **Eng.**; now part of Cambridgeshire non-met. co.

Huntington, c., W. Va., **USA**; on Ohio R.; R. pt. comm. ctr.; rly. wks., steel; p. (1984) 61,100 (c.), 334,000 (met. a. with Ashland).

Huntly, burgh, Gordon, **Scot.**; at confluence of Rs. Bogie and Deveron; agr. mkt.; angling resort; p. (1981) 3,957.

Huntsville, c., Ala., **USA**; textiles; rocket research ctr.; p. (1984) 149,500 (c.), 210,000 (met. a.).

Hupeh. *See* **Hubei.**

Huron, L., between **Canada** and **USA**; one of the Gr. Ls. of the St. Lawrence basin; a. 59,596 km²; 330 km long.

Husum, spt., Schleswig-Holstein, **W. Germany**; on N. Sea cst.; cattle mkt.; p. (est. 1986) 23,800.

Hutchinson, t., Kan., **USA**; salt-mng., meat-packing, flour milling, oil refining; p. (1980) 40,284.

Huyton with Roby, Knowsley, Merseyside, **Eng.**; sub. of Liverpool; p. (1981) 57,671.

Hwai-ho. *See* **Huai He.**

Hwainan. *See* **Huainan.**

Hwang-hai. *See* **Huang Hai.**

Hwang-ho. *See* **Huang He.**

Hwangshih. *See* **Huangshi.**

Hyde, t., Tameside, Gtr. Manchester, **Eng.**; on R. Tame, 11 km S.E. of Manchester; paints, chemicals, food-processing, tobacco, rubber; p. (1981) 35,600.

Hyderabad, ch. c., Andhra Pradesh, **India**; on R. Musi; walled t. and impt. comm. ctr.; univ., nuclear fuel fabrication plant; p. (1981) 2,187,262 (c.).

Hyderabad, c., **Pakistan**; 5 km W. of Indus; 144 km N.E. of Karachi; old cap. of Sind; univ.; noted for silk, gold and silver embroidery; now varied mnfs.; dam at nearby Kotri; p. (1981) 795,000.

Hyndburn, l. gov. dist., Lancs., **Eng.**; inc. Colne Valley ts. of Accrington, Great Harwood, Rishton, Clayton-le-Moors, Church and Oswaldtwistle; p. (est. 1988) 78,900.

Hythe, t., Shepway, Kent, **Eng.**; on S. cst., 5 km W. of Folkestone; one of the Cinque pts.; military canal passing through t., used for boating; p. (1981) 12,723.

I

Iasi (**Jassy**), c., **Romania**; former cap. of Moldavia;

in fertile agr. region; univ., cath.; cultural ctr.; textiles, plastics, chems.; p. (est. 1984) 310,158.

Ibadan, c., cap. Oyo st.; S.W. **Nigeria;** univ.; ctr. of rich agr. a., between the savannah and forest regions; p. mainly Yoruba; crafts, small inds.; p. (est. 1983) 1·1 m.

Ibagué, c., cap. of Tolima dep., **Colombia;** transport ctr.; cotton, tobacco, sugar, leather gds.; p. (1985) 306,078.

Ibarra, t., **Ecuador;** alt. 2,226 m at foot of Imbabura volcano; on Pan-American highway; p. (1982) 53,428.

Iberian Peninsula, S.W. peninsula of **Europe;** containing sts. of Spain and Portugal; lge. a. of high tableland; interior isolation and regionalism; historical and contemporary importance for minerals; a. 593,250 km²; p. (1968) 41,500,000.

Ibiza, I., Balearic gr. in W. **Mediterranean;** Spanish, cath., tourism.

Iceland, rep., N. **Atl. Oc.;** volcanic I. with ice-covered plateaux; glacier fields cover 13,000 km²; only 1 per cent of a. cultivated; cold climate; hot house cultivation using thermal springs; economy dependent on fishing and fish-processing inds.; high standard of living; tourism increasingly impt.; 7 admin. dists.; cap. Reykjavik; a. 102,846 km²; p. (est. 1986) 244,009.

Ichang. See **Yichang.**

Ichinomiya, c., S.E. Honshu, **Japan;** anc. Shinto shrine; textiles, pottery; p. (1985) 257,392.

Ichow. See **Lin-i.**

Icknield Way, prehistoric route running from near Avebury, Wilts., **Eng.;** along the Berkshire Downs, Chilterns and East Anglian Heights into Norfolk, crossing the Thames at Streatley.

Idaho, st., **USA;** Gem State; admitted to Union 1890; St. flower Syringa, St. bird Mountain Bluebird; one of the Rocky Mtn. sts.; rich in minerals; agr. mainly in irrigated Snake R. valley; cap. Boise; a. 216,413 km²; p. (1985) 1,005,000.

Idaho Falls, c., Idaho, **USA;** on Snake R.; food-processing, lumbering; silver, lead, and gold mines nearby; nuclear experimental breeder reactor; p. (1980) 39,590.

Ida Mountains, range, N.W. **Turkey;** volcanic, hot springs; max. alt. Mount Gargarus, 1,768 m.

Idle, t., West Yorks., **Eng.;** in Aire valley, 5 km N. of Bradford; woollens.

Ife, t., **Nigeria;** ctr. of the cacao tr.; univ.; p. (est. 1983) 214,000.

Ifni, enclave, S. **Morocco;** ceded by Spain to Morocco (1969); cap. Sidi Ifni; a. 1,500 km²; p. (est. 1971) 46,000.

Igarka, sm. t., Siberia, **RSFSR;** on R. Yenisey, 640 km from its mouth; graphite plant, nickel-mines, lumber mills; p. (est. 1970) 16,000.

Iglesias, t., Sardinia, **Italy;** N.W. of Cagliari; mng. for lead, pyrites, zinc; p. (1981) 30,117.

Iguaçu, R., trib. of Paraná; mostly in Brazil; famous falls where Argentina, Brazil, and Paraguay meet, excelling Niagara, height 64 m; hydroelec. power potential.

IJmuiden, c., N. Holland, **Neth.;** on cst. at mouth of N. Sea canal; fishing; gasification plant, major iron and steel plant.

IJsselmeer (Lake IJssel), freshwater reservoir, **Neth.;** formerly Zuider Zee; separated from N. Sea by Wieringen–Friesland Barrage; active land reclamation in progress; Wieringermeer drained 1930, N.E. Polder 1942, E. Flevoland 1957, S. Flevoland 1968, Markerwaard to remain undrained; when reclamation complete by end of cent. a. of Neth. will have increased by some 6 per cent.; ch. c. on inlet (IJ) Amsterdam; p. (1982) 101,253.

Ilchester, t., Somerset, **Eng.;** on R. Yeo; N.W. of Yeovil; birthplace of Roger Bacon.

Ilebo, t. Zaire; rlwy. terminus on Kasai R; p. (est. 1976) 142,000

Îles d'Hyères, I. gr., **France;** in Mediterranean off Toulon; tourism.

Ilesha, t., **Nigeria;** tr. ctr., cotton weaving; p. (est. 1983) 273,000.

Ilford. See **Redbridge.**

Ilfracombe, t., North Devon, **Eng.;** sm. pt. on cst. of Bristol Channel; seaside resort; p. (1981) 10,133.

Ilhéus, spt., Bahia, **Brazil;** exp. cacao, timber; losing tr. to lge. pts.; p. (est. 1985) 146,100.

Ili, R., **Central Asia;** rises in Tienshan, China, and flows into L. Balkhash in Soviet terr.; new t. of I. at site of hydroelec. sta.; c. 1,200 km long.

Iligan, t., Mindanao, **Philippines;** integrated steel mill; cement; p. (1984) 181,865.

Ilkeston, t., Erewash, Derbys., **Eng.;** W. of Not-tingham, iron, engin., locknit fabrics, needles, plastics; p. (1981) 33,031.

Ilkley, t., spa, West Yorks., **Eng.;** on R. Wharfe, N.W. of Leeds; local mkt.; p. (1981) 24,082.

Illawara, dist., N.S.W., **Australia;** forming belt of land between S. tableland and cst.; very fertile; dairy farming; coal seams; ch. ts., Kiama, Wollongong, Bulli, Gerringong.

Ille-et-Vilaine, dep., N.W. **France;** on English Channel; a. 6,990 km²; agr.; cap. Rennes; p. (1982) 745,000.

Illimani, one of the high peaks of the Cordillera Real, Andes, **Bolivia,** 6,461 m, E. of La Paz.

Illinois, st., **USA;** Prairie State; admitted to Union 1818; St. flower Native Violet; St. bird Cardinal; in Middle West; named after its principal R., a lge. trib. of Mississippi; many Rs.; cap. Springfield, metropolis Chicago; rich agr.; fuel and mineral resources; major coal-mng. st.; inds. inc. meat-processing, farm implements; a. 146,076 km²; p. (1985) 11,535,000.

Illinois, R., Ill., **USA;** glacial valley; long history of settlement; impt. routeway; 437 km long.

Illyria, region, mainly in **Yugoslavia,** stretching along Adriatic Sea from Trieste in N. to **Albania** in S. and inland as far as Rs. Danube and Morava.

Ilmen, L., **RSFSR,** nr. Novgorod; drained by Volkhov R. into L. Ladoga; a. 932 km²; fisheries.

Ilminster, t., Somerset, **Eng.;** 16 km S.E. of Taunton; cutstone, concrete, collars, radio valves; p. (1981) 3,716.

Iloilo, c., cap. of I. prov., Panay, **Philippines;** ctr. of rly. network; impt. pt. exp. sugar, rice, copra, hemp; p. (est. 1984) 263.422.

Ilorin, t., N. **Nigeria;** on Lagos–Kano rly.; agr. and caravan ctr.; govt. sugar-growing scheme at Bacita; p. (est. 1983) 344,000.

Imabari, t., spt., N.W. Shikoku, **Japan;** on shore of Indian Sea; mnfs. cotton textiles, paper, canned fruits.

Imatra, t., Kymi, **Finland;** hydroelec. power sta. supplies S. Finland; electro-metallurgy; p. (1986) 34,802.

Imbroz. See **Gökçeada I.**

Immingham, pt., Humberside, **Eng.;** on the Humber, N.W. of Grimsby; lge. docks; new deep-sea oil and coal terminals; chemicals engin., refinery nearby at Killingholme.

Imola, t., **Italy;** S.E. of Bologna; cath.; glass, pottery; p. (1981) 60,010.

Imperia, t., **Italy;** on G. of Genoa; sm. pt. olive-growing ctr.; resort; p. (1981) 41,609.

Imperial Valley, S. Cal., **USA;** extends 48 km S.E. from Salton Sea to Mexican bdy.; mainly below sea-level; hot, arid climate; irrigation from Colorado R. chiefly by All-American Canal nr. Yuma; total irrigated a. 405,000 ha; principal crops, fruit, dates, tomatoes, cotton, and dairy prod.

Imphal, cap. of Manipur, **India;** in rice-growing basin in hills of Assam nr. Burma bdy.; p. (1981) 156,622.

Inari L., extensive L., Lappi, **Finland;** outlet into Barents Sea; hydroelec. power; a. 1,774 km².

Ince-in-Makerfield, t., Gtr. Manchester, **Eng.;** nr. Wigan; engin.; p. (1981) 14,498.

Inchon, c., **S. Korea;** on Yellow Sea; pt. for Seoul; exp. soyabeans; rice; textile ctr., steel mill, glass, diesel engines; p. (est. 1986) 1,386,900.

Independence, c., Mo., **USA;** E. of Kansas; oil refining; agr. machin.; p. (1984) 112,100.

India, rep., indep. st. (since 1947), S. **Asia;** second cty. of world by p.; 22 sts. and 9 union terrs.; peninsula bounded by Himalayas in N. extends in wide plateau to Indian Oc. in S.; most of p. concentrated in Indo-Gangetic Plain; unpredictable monsoon climate; heavy dependence on agr.; 70 per cent of p. farmers; few cash crops except cotton (the Deccan), tea (Himalayas) and jute (W. Bengal); 854 languages and dialects impede economic development; strong caste system; 36 per cent literate (compared with 15 per cent in 1961); new inds. expanding rapidly; chems., engin. electronics; cap. New Delhi; main pts. Bombay, Calcutta; a. 3,268,580 km²; p. (est. 1987) 781·4 m. (25 per cent growth in 10 years and 2nd most populated cty. of world).

Indiana, st., **USA;** Hoosier State; admitted to Union 1816; St. flower peony; St. bird Cardinal; in Middle

West, bounded by Mich., Ohio, Ill. and sep. from Ky. by Ohio R.; agr.; coal, limestone, petroleum; steel, metal prods., machin., food prod.; cap. Indianapolis; a. 93,994 km²; p. (1985) 5,499,000.

Indianapolis, c., cap. of Ind., **USA**; on White R.; univ.; rly. ctr.; meat-packing, jet engines, aircraft parts, chemicals, pharmaceutics; p. (1984) 710,300 (c.), 1,194,600 (met. a.).

Indian Ocean extends from S. of Asia and E. of Africa to the C. of Good Hope and C. Leeuwin in Australia, separated from the Pacific by the Malay Archipelago and Australia; a. 75,990,600 km².

Indigirka, R., Yakut ASSR, **RSFSR**; flows into Arctic Oc.; hydroelec. power; 1,760 km long.

Indo-China, S.E. Asia; federation in Fr. Union until end of hostilities July 1954; consisted of the three sts. of Vietnam, Cambodia, and Laos.

Indo-Gangetic Plain, India, Bangladesh and Pakistan; name applied to flat land created by the Indus and Ganges basins; densely populated a.

Indonesia, rep., S.E. Asia; former Neth. E. Indies; made up of many sm. Is. straddling equator for over 4,800 km; many Is. in W. volcanic and E. coral; geothermal energy supply being developed; lgst. Is. inc. Java, Sumatra, Kalimantan (S. Borneo), Sulawesi, and Irian (W. New Guinea); mostly underdeveloped except Java; intensive agr. employs 55 per cent of p.; rapidly developing oil and gas industry but falling oil revenues (70 per cent of exports) hindering economic development; self-sufficient in rice, stored surpluses; 63 per cent p. on Java, Madura and Bali Is.; planned decentralisation to other Is.; cap. Djakarta; a. 1,907,566 km²; p. (est. 1987) 170·2 m.

Indore, c., Madhya Pradesh, **India**; nr. valley of Narbada R.; comm. ctr.; cotton-mills; p. (1981) 829,327.

Indre, dep., central **France**; agr. and industl.; cap. Châteauroux; a. 6,905 km²; p. (1982) 242,000.

Indre-et-Loire, dep., central **France**; drained by Indre and Loire Rs.; vineyards, orchards; cap. Tours; a. 6,156 km²; p. (1982) 506,000.

Indus, R., **Pakistan**, rises in Tibet, flows through Kashmir, Punjab, Sind, to Arabian Sea; 5 tribs. Jhelum, Chenab, Ravi, Beas, Sutlej, form one of world's major R. systems, now used extensively to irrigate the Punjab and the Sind; impt. cotton, wheat, and sugar dist.; hydroelec. power; supported Indus valley civilisation 3000–1500 B.C.; 2,880 km long.

Ingleborough, mtn., near Settle, North Yorks., **Eng.**; underground caves, stalactites; made of limestone and millstone grit; alt. 724 m.

Inglewood, t., S. Cal., **USA**; sub. of Los Angeles; chinchilla farms; furniture, lt. engin., aircraft parts; p. (1980) 94,245.

Ingolstadt, t., Bavaria, **W. Germany**; on Danube, nr. Munich; cas.; machin., cars, tobacco, oil refining; pipeline from Genoa; transalpine oil pipeline from Trieste, through N.E. Italy and Austria to I.; p. (est. 1986) 92,600.

Inhambane, spt., **Moçambique**; sugar, copra, oil-seeds, bricks, soap, tiles; p. (1980) 56,439.

Inishboffin, I., Galway, **R.o.I.**, sm. I. off Connemara; farming, fishing.

Inishmore, lgst. of Aran gr., Galway, **R.o.I.**; fishing.

Inkpen Beacon, hill, Berks., **Eng.**; highest point reached by chalk hills in Eng.; alt. 297 m.

Inland Sea, Japan; between Honshu on N. and Shikoku and Kyushu on S.; sheltered sea with many Is.; ch. spts. Osaka, Amagaski, Kōbe, Okayama, Hiroshima, Kure; Nat. Park; a. c. 9,500 km².

Inn, R., traversing **Switzerland**, the Tyrol, **Austria** and Bavaria; enters R. Danube at Passau; hydroelec. plants; 512 km long.

Innerleithen, burgh, Tweeddale, **Scot.**; on R. Tweed, 8 km S.E. of Peebles; woollen cloth and knitwear; mineral springs; p. (1981) 2,397.

Inner Mongolia (Nei Mongol), Chinese aut. region, N.E. **China**; stretches along S. border of Mongolian People's Rep.; vast steppelands, sparse p.; st. farms for animal husbandry; peat beds; milk-processing; cap Hohhot; a. 1,177,518 km²; p. (est. 1985) 19,850,000.

Innisfail, t., Queensland, **Australia**; ch. sugar-producing ctr. of Australia; p. (1981) 7,933.

Innsbruck, c., cap. of the Tyrol, W. **Austria**; on R. Inn; commands N. approach to Brenner Pass; univ.; tourism; fortfd. 12th cent.; p. (1981) 117,287 (c.), 234,941 (met. a.).

Inowroclaw, t., N. **Poland**; nr. Bydgoszcz; rock-salt. iron pyrites; agr. prod.; p. (1983) 69,300.

Insterburg. See **Chernyakhovsk**.

Inter-American Highway, section of Pan-American Highway system, from Mexico to Panama.

Interlaken, t., Bernese Oberland, Berne, **Switzerland**; on R. Aare between Ls. Thun and Brienz; tourist resort; p. (1970) 4,735.

Intracoastal Waterway, USA; toll-free waterway along Atl. and Gulf of Mexico csts.; completed 1949 using bays, rivers and canals; 4,960 km long.

Inuvik, t., Arctic, **Canada**; above the permafrost; p. (1981) 3,147.

Inveraray, burgh, Argyll and Bute, **Scot.**; nr. head of Loch Fyne; herring fishing.

Inverbervie, burgh, Kincardine and Deeside, **Scot.**; on E. cst., 13 km S. of Stonehaven; linen, rayon inds.; p. (1981) 1,826.

Invercargill, c., S.I., **N.Z.**; on S.E. cst.; sawmills, freezing wks.; aluminium smelter; served by Bluff Harbour; p. (est. 1987) 47,800.

Inverclyde, l. gov. dist., Strathclyde Reg., **Scot.**; inc. F. of Clyde, inc. Gourock and Greenock; p. (est. 1986) 97,227.

Inverell, t., N.S.W., **Australia**; 655 km N. of Sydney; wheat and lamb cty.; tin; p. (1981) 9,734.

Invergordon, burgh, spt., Ross and Cromarty, **Scot.**; on N. side of Cromarty F., 19 km N.E. of Dingwall; former naval pt.; whisky distillery; large aluminium plant was threatened with closure, (1981); p. (1981) 4,050.

Inverkeithing, royal burgh, Dunfermline, **Scot.**; on F. of Forth, nr. Dunfermline; shipbreaking, papermkg., quarrying; p. (1981) 5,751.

Inverkip, par., v., Inverclyde, **Scot.**; 10 km S.W. of Greenock; par. contains Gourock; resort; p. (1981) 896.

Inverness, royal burgh, Inverness, N.E. **Scot.**; on Moray F.; distilling, lt. engin., tweeds; sm. pt. for general cargo; tourism; p. (1981) 39,736.

Inverness-shire, former co., l. gov. dist., N.E. **Scot.**; part of Highland Reg.; a. 11,269 km²; p. (est. 1986) 60,773.

Inverurie, royal burgh, Gordon, **Scot.**; on R. Don, 22 km N.W. of Aberdeen; rly. ctr., mkt. t.; tourism; p. (1981) 7,701.

Inyokern, t., E. Cal., **USA**; naval ordnance research sta.

Ioánnina (Janina), t., Epirus, **Greece**; nr. Albanian frontier; agr. tr.; embroidery; univ.; p. (1981) 44,829.

Iona, I., off cst. of Mull, Argyll, **Scot.**; early Scottish Christian ctr.; restored abbey; St. Columba's burial place; anc. burial place of Scottish kings.

Ionian Is., gr. in Mediterranean, belonging to **Greece**; comprising Corfu, Paxos, Levkas, Cephalonia, Zakinthos, Ithake; severe earthquake 1953; total a. 1,948 km²; p. (1981) 182,651.

Ionian Sea. Mediterranean; between Greece on E.; Italy and Sicily on W.

Iowa, st., **USA**; Hawkeye St.; admitted to Union 1846; St, flower Wild Rose, St. bird Eastern Goldfinch; in Middle West; prairie cty.; watered by Mississippi and Missouri; rich farm land; maize, oats, and other grains; hogs, pigs; processing of farm prod.; flood control, reforestation; diverse inds.; cap. Des Moines; a. 145,791 km²; p. (1985) 2,884,000.

Iowa City, c., S.E. Iowa, **USA**; former st. cap. (1839–56); univ.; p. (1980) 50,508 (c.), 81,717 (met. a.).

Ipin. See **Yibin**.

Ipoh, c., cap. of Perak st., N.W. **Malaya**; tin-mng. ctr.; Chinese rock temples; p. (1980) 300,727.

Ipswich, t., S.E. Queensland, **Australia**; nr. Brisbane; coalmng. ctr.; woollens; p. (est. 1984) 73,680.

Ipswich, co. t., l. gov. dist., Suffolk, **Eng.**; pt. on estuary of R. Orwell; incr. impt. container pt.; exp. timber, grain and malt; birthplace of Cardinal Wolsey; diesel engines, gen. engin.; p. (est. 1988) 114,900.

Iquique, t., N. **Chile**; pt. on Pac. Oc.; exp. nitrates and iodine from Atacama desert; fish-canning; p. (est. 1985) 125,000.

Iquitos, t., N.E. **Peru**; on Amazon, 3,680 km from mouth; comm. ctr.; exp. timber, cotton; sawmills, oil refining; p. (est. 1985) 229,557.

Iráklion (Candia or Herakleion), t., cap. of Crete, **Greece**; impt. spt. on G. of I., arm of Aegean Sea; at foot of terraced hill slopes; wine, olive oil, fruit, fishing; tourism; p. (1981) 102,398.

Iran, former kingdom, Islamic st. (1979), S.W. **Asia;** known as Persia until 1935; interior plateau at c. 900 km, ringed by mtn. ranges of up to c. 5,500 m; much of a. is desert; settled agr. limited to Caspian plain; heavy dependence on oil; oilfields centred on Ābādān; hit by fall in world oil prices and sale losses due to Iraqi air attacks; pipeline to Iskenderun (Turkey) on Mediterranean cst. started (1986) as alternative exp. route; high quality carpets exported, esp. to USA; cap. Tehran; a. 1,626,520 km²; p. (1986) 49,857,384.

Irapuato, c., central **Mexico;** agr. tr. and processing; iron-founding; p. (1980) 246,308.

Iraq, rep., S.W. **Asia;** the anc. Mesopotamia; dominated by 2 Rs., Tigris and Euphrates; much of a. desert and semi-desert but irrigation in S. and centre enables settled agr. for barley, wheat, dates, and tobacco; only outlet to sea at N.W. end of Persian G.; oil principal source of wealth; main oilfield at Kirkūk; main oil pt. at Basra; pipelines to Lebanon and Syria; new inds. based on oil; 14 provs.; cap. Baghdad; a. 435,120 km²; p. (est. 1987) 17,093,000.

Irazu, active volcano, 3,437 m high, **Costa Rica.**

Irbid, t., **Jordan;** comm. and agr. tr. ctr.; p. (est. 1984) 136,000.

Ireland, I., W. of Gt. Britain, separated by Irish Sea; divided politically into R.o.I. (Eire) and N. Ireland (Ulster, part of U.K.); ch. physical features, L. Neagh in N.E., Ls. of Killarney in S.W.; Rs. Shannon, Boyne, Blackwater; mtns. of Mourne, Wicklow, and Kerry; mild moist climate; called "emerald isle" because of grasslands; pastoral agr., especially dairying; tourism; a. 83,937 km²; p. (1981) 4,888,077.

Ireland, Republic of, ind. st., W. **Europe;** comprises 26 of 32 cos. making up I. of Ireland; member of EC since 1973; ring of highlands surround central lowland basin, much of which is peat-covered; economy based on agr., especially dairying; exps. butter, cheese, bacon; new govt.-encouraged inds.; mineral resources; tourism; cap. Dublin; a. 68,894 km²; p. (est. 1986) 3,537,195.

Irian Jaya (formerly Dutch New Guinea, later W. Irian), prov., **Indonesia;** formerly W. New Guinea and Dutch col.; part of Indonesia, 1963; inaugurated as prov., 1969; primitive agr. of rice, poultry, cocoa; few oil deposits; cap. Djajapura; a. (inc. Ternate) 412,784 km²; p. (est. 1983) 1,268,600.

Irish Sea, Brit. Is.; between Gt. Britain and Ireland, connecting N. and S. with Atl. Oc.; 320 km long; 80–224 km wide; greatest depth 840 m; a. 18,130 km².

Irkutsk, c., cap. of I. oblast, **RSFSR;** on Angara R. in E. Siberia; on Trans-Siberian rly., 64 km W. of L. Baykal; univ.; engin., sawmilling, petroleum refining, chemicals, hydroelec. power sta.; p. (1986) 602,000.

Irlam, t., Gtr. Manchester, **Eng.;** engin., tar, soap, glycerine, margarine; steel wks. to close; overspill p.; p. (1981) 19,900.

Ironbridge, t. Shrops., **Eng.;** scene of Darby's iron ind.; derives name from first cast-iron bridge (1779) which here crosses Severn; now inc. in Telford new t.

Iron Country, Utah, **USA;** vast reserves of iron ore; undeveloped due to inaccessibility.

Iron Gate (Portile de Fier), Romania; famous rapids in R. Danube; Romanian–Yugoslavian hydroelectric and navigation project, 1964–71.

Irrawaddy, R., **Burma;** flows S. to Bay of Bengal; navigable for lge. steamers 1,440 km; irrigation wks.; major Asian rice bowl; 2,000 km long.

Irtysh, R., W. Siberia, **USSR;** ch. trib. of R. Ob'; crossed by Turk–Sib rly. at Semipalatinsk and by Trans-Siberian rly. at Omsk; hydroelectric power stas.; ambitious plans to divert R. South now postponed; 2,960 km long.

Irvine, royal burgh, Cunninghame, **Scot.;** nr. mouth of R. Irvine; new t. (1966); cas.; hosiery, lt. engin., bottle wks., chemicals; p. (1981) 32,852.

Irvington, t., N.J., **USA;** industl. sub. of Newark; machin.; p. (1980) 61,493.

Irwell, R., Gtr. Manchester, **Eng.;** flows through Manchester to the Mersey via Manchester Ship Canal; 48 km long.

Isar, R., **Austria** and **W. Germany;** rises in Austrian Tyrol, flows N.E. to Danube; hydroelectric power stas. below Munich; 261 km long.

Isarco, R., N. **Italy;** rises nr. Brenner Pass, flows S. into R. Adige at Bolzano; 80 km long.

Isdud, anc. c. of the Philistines. *See* **Ashdod.**

Ise (Ujiyamada), t., Honshu, **Japan;** sacred c. of Shintoism; p. (1985) 105,455.

Ise Bay, inlet, S. Honshu, **Japan;** flanked by ch. textile mftg. a. of cty, with 5 million people centred on Nagoya; 64 km long, 24–32 km wide.

Iseo, L., N. **Italy;** E. of Bergamo; 124 km².

Isère, dep., S.E. **France;** drained by Rs. Isère and Rhône; cap. Grenoble; mtnous.; cereals; wine, butter, cheese; iron, coal, lead, silver, copper; gloves, silks; a. 8,231 km²; p. (1982) 935,500.

Isère, R., S.E. **France;** rises in Graian Alps, flows W. into R. Rhône nr. Valence; used to generate hydroelec. power; used, with trib. R. Arc, by main rly. from France to N. Italy through Mt. Cenis (Fréjus) tunnel.

Iserlohn, t., N. Rhine–Westphalia, **W. Germany;** S.E. of Dortmund; metal gds.; p. (est. 1986) 89,500.

Isfahan. *See* **Esfahān.**

Ishikari, t., Hokkaido, **Japan;** on cst. of Otaru Bay, 16 km N. of Sapporo; ctr. of second lgst. coalfield in Japan; sm. petroleum production.

Ishimbay, c., Bashkir ASSR, **RSFSR;** on R. Belaya; ctr. of oilfield; oilfields; pipelines to Ufa, Orsk, and Shkaparo; p. (est. 1967) 53,000.

Isiro (Paulis), t., N.E. **Zaïre;** admin. offices; cotton ginneries; rly. repair shops.

Isis, R., headstream of R. Thames, **Eng.;** so named around and above Oxford.

Iskenderun (Alexandretta), spt., S. **Turkey;** recent modernisation for new Iran/Turkey rly.; new steel wks.; p. (1985) 152,096.

Islamabad, new cap. of **Pakistan,** to N. of Rawalpindi below Himalayas; nuclear power sta.; p. (1981) 201,000.

Islay, I. Inner Hebrides, Argyll and Bute, **Scot.;** a. 609 km²; farming, dairying distilleries; p. (1971) 3,827.

Isle of Grain, Kent, **Eng.;** flat promontory at confluence of Thames and Medway, once separated from mainland by a tidal estuary; lge oil refinery; pipelines to Walton-on-Thames and Heathrow Airport.

Isle of Man, Irish Sea; 43 km from **Eng.** (Cumbria) and N. Ireland (Down); high plateau N.E. to S.W.; ch. t. Douglas; old cap. Castletown; admin. according to own laws; tourism; freeport (1983) to take advantage of low tax rate; a. 572 km²; p. (1986) 64,282.

Isle of Wight. *See* **Wight, I. of.**

Islington, inner bor., London, **Eng.;** N. of City; incorporates Finsbury; univ.; residtl.; clocks, precision engin.; p. (est. 1988) 169,200.

Islwyn, l. gov. dist., Gwent, **Wales;** inland ts. of Risca, Abercarn, Bedwellty and Mynyddislwyn; p. (est. 1988) 66,400.

Ismailia (Ismâ'iliya), t., **Egypt;** at mid-point of Suez Canal on L. Timsah; rail connections with Cairo, Suez, Port Said; declined during canal closure; p. (1985) 191,700.

Isna (Esneh), t., Upper **Egypt;** on Nile; agr. ctr.; cottons, pottery; p. (1966) 27,400.

Ispra, t., Varese, **Italy;** nr. L. Maggiore; nuclear research ctr.; p. (1981) 4,629.

Israel, rep., S.W. **Asia;** occupies narrow corridor between Jordan valley and Mediterranean Sea; extends S. into the Negev desert (half a. of rep.); Mediterranean climate enables cultivation of early fruits and vegetables, especially citrus fruits; special feature of agr. is cooperative settlements (Kibbutz); main factor limiting agr. development is availability of water; diamonds hgst. exp. earner; most highly industrialised cty. of S.W. Asia, especially for textiles and clothing; petroleum of increasing impt.; tourism; Jewish rep. since 1948; until then part of the mandate Palestine; surrounded by hostile Arab sts.; difficulties of increasing Jewish immigration; cap. Jerusalem; a. 20,850 km²; nat. a. in dispute, particularly since Arab-Israeli wars of 1967 and 1973; p. (est. 1986) 4,331,300. (75 per cent Jewish).

Issyk Kul, mtn. L., Kirghiz SSR, **USSR;** in Tien-Shan mtns., alt. 1,568 m; a. 6,216 km²; ice-free in winter.

Issy-les-Moulineaux, sub. S.W. Paris, Hauts-de-Seine, **France;** engin.; p. (1975) 48,380.

Istanbul (Constantinople), ch. spt., former cap., **Turkey;** on Golden Horn peninsula on European cst. at entry of Bosporus into Sea of Marmara; divided into old "Stamboul" on S. side, and dists.

of Galata and Beyoglu (Pera) on N.; the anc. Byzantium; magnificent mosque of Sta. Sophia; univ.; industl. and comm. ctr.; tourism; p. (1985) 5,475,982.

Istria, peninsula, N. Adriatic, **Yugoslavia;** ch. c. Pula; agr., olives, vines, oranges, maize; p. Yugoslav and Italian; a. c. 5,200 km².

Itabira, t., Minas Gerais st., **Brazil;** on Brazilian Plateau, 96 km N.E. of Belo Horizonte; lgst. deposits of iron ore in Brazil; p. (est. 1985) 81,800.

Itabuna, t., Bahia, E. **Brazil;** cocoa, livestock; p. (est. 1985) 178,700.

Itajai, spt., Santa Catarina, S. **Brazil;** exp. lumber, cement, agr. prods.; (est. 1985) 104,500.

Italy, rep., S. **Europe;** peninsula extending into Mediterranean; inc. 2 main Is. of Sicily and Sardinia; bounded by Alps to N.; central spine of Apennines; Mediterranean climate; contrast between industrialised N. and less developed agr. S. (Mezzogiorno); member of EC; agr. impt., especially in Po basin; tourism attracted by Roman and Renaissance architecture and by climate; inds. based on hydroelectric power in N., inc. elec. engin., motor vehicles and textiles, centred at Milan and Turin; 19 admin. regions; cap. Rome; a. 301,049 km²; p. (est. 1986) 57,291,000.

Ithaca, t., N.Y., **USA;** on Cayuga L.; seat of Cornell Univ.; elec. clocks; machin.; p. (1980) 28,732.

Ithake, one of the Ionian Is., **Greece;** a. 96 km²; ch. t. Ithake; severe earthquake, 1953.

Itzehoe, t., Schleswig-Holstein, **W. Germany;** founded by Charlemagne; wood, cement, machin.; p. (est. 1986) 31,700.

Ivano-Frankovsk (Stanislav), c., Ukrainian SSR, **USSR;** in Carpathian foothills; industl. ctr.; oilfields nearby; oil refineries, engin.; p. (est. 1985) 210,000.

Ivanovo, t., RSFSR; N.E. of Moscow; textiles, iron and chemical wks.; peat-fed power stas.; p. (est. 1985) 474,000.

Iviza. See Ibiza.

Ivory Coast. See Côte d'Ivoire.

Iwaki, t., Honshu, **Japan;** ctr. of apple producing dist., p. (1985) 350,566.

Iwakuni, t., Honshu, **Japan;** on Inland Sea; p. (1985) 111,831.

Iwo, t., Nigeria; nr. Ibadan; tr. ctr.; p. (est. 1983) 262,000.

Izhevsk. See Ustinov.

Izmail, c., Ukrainian SSR, **USSR;** in Bessarabia, on Danube delta, nr. Romanian border; naval base of Soviet Danube flotilla; former Turkish fortress; p. (est. 1970) 48,000.

Izmir (Smyrna), c., Turkey; at head of G. of I., Anatolia; exp. figs, raisins, tobacco, carpets, rugs; anc. and historic c.; ch. comm. ctr. of the Levant; Nemrut Free Trade Zone (1987); ambitous industl. project, refinery and chem. complex (1972–86); univ.; p. (1985) 1,489,772.

Izmit, c., Turkey; E. end of Sea of Marmara; cereals, tobacco, oil refinery and polythene plant under construction; p. (1985) 233,338.

J

Jabalpur (Jubbulpore), c., Madhya Pradesh, **India;** rly. ctr.; ordnance wks.; p. (1981) 614,162 (c.), 757,303 (met. a.).

Jablonec nad Nisou, t., ČSSR; on R. Neisse; glassware ctr., inc. glass jewellery and imitation stones; p. (1984) 44,742.

Jáchymov, t., ČSSR; spa; uranium mines, pitchblende, lead, silver, nickel, cobalt.

Jackson, t., Mich., **USA;** on Grand R.; locomotives, motorcar accessories, electronic equipment, metal gds.; p. (1984) 37,700 (t.), 145,300 (met. a.).

Jackson, t., cap. of Miss., **USA;** comm. and industl. ctr.; p. (1984) 208,800 (c.), 382,400 (met. a.).

Jacksonville, c., Fla., **USA;** pt. on St. John's R.; impt. ctr. on Atl. cst.; chemicals, shipbldg. and repair, printing, lumber, cigar mftg.; tourism; p. (1984) 578,000 (c.), 795,300 (met. a.).

Jacobabad, t., Sind, **Pakistan;** driest and hottest place in Indian sub-continent; p. (1981) 80,000.

Jacui, R., S. **Brazil;** rises in S. edge of Brazilian Plateau, enters Atl. Oc., through lagoon, Lagoa dos Patos; 560 km long.

Jadotville. See Likasi

Jaduguda, Bihar, **India;** uranium mine and mill to supply India's growing nuclear power production.

Jaén, t., cap. of prov. of Jaén, S. **Spain;** in foothills of Andalusian mtns.; cath.; olive oil, wine, chemicals; p. (1987) 103,698.

Jaffna, spt., N. **Sri Lanka;** on J. peninsula; second t. of rep.; p. (est. 1983) 128,000.

Jaipur, c., cap. of Rajasthan, **India;** univ.; fine fabrics, jewellery; tourism; old cap. Amber is 8 km away; p. (1981) 977,165 (c.), 1,015,160 (met. a.).

Jajce, t., Yugoslavia; in Bosnia, at junc. of Rs. Vrbas and Pliva (hydroelectric power); Fed. People's Rep. of Yugoslavia declared here by Tito (1943).

Jakarta. See Djakarta.

Jalalabad, c., E. **Afghanistan;** on Kābul R., nr. Khyber Pass; univ.; agr. tr. ctr.; p. (est. 1982) 57,824.

Jalapa, c., cap. of Veracruz st., **Mexico;** c. 1,370 m; a.s.l.; luxuriant vegetation; agr. ctr.; tourism; p. (1980) 212,769.

Jalgaon, t., Maharashtra, **India;** in Tapti R. valley nr. Bhusawal; p. (1981) 145,335.

Jalisco, st., Mexico; on Pac. Oc.; traversed by Sierra Madre; well timbered, agr.; minerals; tourism; a. 80,876 km²; p. (1980) 4,293,549.

Jalón, R., Spain; rises in Iberian Mtns., flows N.E. into R. Ebro nr. Zaragoza; valley forms main rly., road route from Madrid to Ebro valley.

Jalpaiguri, t., W. Bengal, **India;** frontier t.; rly. ctr.; p. (1961) 48,738.

Jamaica, rep., **W.I.;** member of Brit. Commonwealth; mtnous.; Blue Mtn. range runs E. to W. and rises to 2,258 m; tropical climate modified by alt.; economy based on agr. and mng.; major exp. crops sugar and bananas; major world producer of bauxite (recent contraction) and alumina; tourist ind. expanding; member of Caribbean Free Trade Association; 25 per cent unemployment; major pts. Kingston, Montego Bay, Pt. Antonio; international airpt.; univ. at cap. Kingston; a. 11,424 km²; p. (est. 1985) 2,337,000, of which 22 per cent are in Kingston.

James, R. Va., **USA;** hydroelec. power in upper reaches, wide estuary in lower course; outlet to Chesapeake Bay; 544 km long.

James Bay, S. arm of Hudson Bay, **Canada;** c. 480 km long, 224 km wide.

Jamestown, spt., cap. of **St. Helena I.;** flax; p. (1976) 1,516.

Jamestown, t., dist., Va., **USA;** nr. mouth of James R., where first English permanent settlement was founded 1607.

Jammu, t., J. and Kashmir, **India;** winter cap. of st.; univ., fort, palace; p. (1981) 206,135.

Jammu and Kashmir, st., N.W. **India;** traversed by ranges of Himalayas; wheat and rice; 1972 agreement divided state between India and Pakistan; disturbances 1989; cap. Indian sector Srinagar, cap. Pakistani sector Muzaffarabad; total a. 222,823 km²; p. (1981) 5,987,389.

Jamnagar, t., Gujarat, **India;** on G. of Kutch; p. (1981) 277,615 (t.), 317,362 (met. a.).

Jamshedpur, c., Bihar, **India;** W. of Calcutta; major industl. ctr. of rep.; Tata iron and steel wks.; engin.; p. (1981) 438,385 (c.), 669,580 (met. a.).

Janina. See Ioánnina.

Jan Mayen I., volcanic I. between Spitzbergen and Iceland, Arctic Oc.; annexed by **Norway** 1929; meteorological sta.; a. 373 km²; p. (1967) 36.

Japan, E. Asia; 4 main Is., Honshu (lgst.), Hokkaido, Shikoku, Kyushu; mtnous.; 18 active volcanoes; subject to earthquakes; only 17 per cent of land cultivable; intensive and mechanised agr.; rice, fruits, vegetables; few animals; inds. highly developed and based on imports of raw material and export of finished prods.; rapid industrialisation since second world war; economic growth has been rapid but appears to be slowing slightly; rapid technological innovation; stable labour management relationships; inds. inc. shipbldg., motor vehicles, textiles, steel, electronics, chemicals, cheap consumer gds.; cap. Tokyo, world financial ctr.; a. 370,370 km²; p. (est. 1987) 122,380,000 (inc. Okinawa and Ryuku Is.).

Japan Current. See Kuroshio.

Japan, Sea of, portion of Pac. Oc. between Korea, USSR, and Japan.

Japurá, R., Colombia, Brazil; rises as Caquetá in Colombian Andes, flows S.E. through Brazil to Amazon; 2,080 km long.

Jari, new t., Amazonia, **Brazil;** ambitious project of timber and pulp plant in the rain forest; not as successful as hoped.

Jaroslaw, t., Rzeszow prov., S.E. **Poland;** on R. San; food-processing; found 11th cent.; impt. tr. ctr. 16th cent.; p. (1970) 29,100.

Jarrow, t., South Tyneside, Tyne and Wear, **Eng.;** on S. bank of Tyne, 11 km below Gateshead; grew up as shipbldg. ctr.; hit by depression of 1930s; hunger march to London 1936; new enterprises introduced; steel and tube wks., oil storage; die-castings, knitting-wool-mkg. at Bede trading estate; the Venerable Bede lived and died here; p. (1981) 27,074.

Jasper National Park, Alberta, **Canada;** Rocky mtns., tourism.

Jaunpur, t., Uttar Pradesh, **India;** mkt. t.; ctr. of Moslem learning and architecture in 15th cent.; p. (1981) 105,140.

Java, I., **Indonesia;** most developed of Indonesian Is.; traversed E. to W. by forested volcanic mtns.; fertile volcanic soils aid intensive rice cultivation; over-populated; contains 70 per cent of cty.'s p. yet only 8 per cent of land a.; exps. inc. coffee, rubber, sugar, copra, teak; noted for silver craft and batik work (anc. craft of fabric decoration); a. 130,510 km²; p. (est. 1983) 96,892,900.

Javari, R., forms bdy. between **Peru** and **Brazil;** trib. of R. Amazon.

Java Sea, part of the **Pac. Oc.** between N. cst. Java, Borneo, and Sumatra.

Jebba, t., **Nigeria;** on R. Niger; dam proposed for 1982.

Jebel Aulia, v., **Sudan;** S. of Khartoum; dam across White Nile R.

Jebel-Hauran, high tableland of **Syria,** alt. c. 1,800 m.

Jedburgh, royal burgh, Roxburgh, **Scot.;** on Jed Water, S.W. of Kelso; tweeds, woollens, rayon; abbey ruins; ctr. of Border warfare in Middle Ages; p. (1981) 4,053.

Jeddah. See Jiddah.

Jefferson City, st. cap. Mo., **USA;** on Missouri R.; univ.; comm. and processing ctr. of agr. a.; shoes, tiles, farm implements; p. (1980) 36,619.

Jelenia Góra (Hirschberg), t., S.W. **Poland** (since 1945), formerly in Lower Silesia; mftg.; spa; p. (1983) 89,300.

Jelgava (Mitau), t., Latvian SSR, **USSR;** on Lielupe R.; textiles, foodstuffs, refractory materials; p. (est. 1972) 58,000.

Jemappes, t., **Belgium;** 5 km W. of Mons; industl.; Fr. victory over Austria 1792; battle of Mons 1914; p. (est. 1969) 12,548.

Jena, c., **E. Germany;** on R. Saale, 72 km S.W. of Leipzig; univ., observatory; optical glass-ware, precision instruments; leading cultural ctr. late 18th and early 19th cent., defeat of Prussians by Fr. 1806; p. (est. 1986) 107,000.

Jensen, t., Utah, **USA;** oil refinery; on R. Green.

Jerez de la Frontera, t., **Spain;** in Andalusia, 22 km N.E. of Cádiz; in fertile agr. a.; sherry; p. (1981) 150,481.

Jericho, v., Jordan Valley, **Jordan;** est. through recent excavations as one of oldest towns in the world (6000 B.C.); p. (1961) 10,284.

Jersey, I., lgst. of **Channel Is.,** 21 km W. of Fr. cst.; potatoes, tomatoes, cauliflowers, flowers, fruit. cattle; tourist resort; banking; ch. t. St. Helier; a. 117 km²; p. (1986) 80,212.

Jersey City, c., N.J., **USA;** E. of Newark, on Hudson R.; comm. and industl. ctr.; diverse inds.; p. (1984) 223,000.

Jerusalem, c., **Israel** and **Jordan;** 811 m a.s.l.; between Dead Sea and Mediterranean; the "Holy City" of the Jews and the sacred c. of the Christians and Moslems; Israeli western sector and Arab eastern sector declared by Israeli parliament (1980) united c. and cap.; modern mftg.; p. (est. 1986) 468,900 inc. E. Jerusalem.

Jervis Bay, inlet of Pac. Oc., Australian Capital Territory, **Australia;** acquired by Fed Govt. as site for establishment of pt. for Canberra 1909; plans to develop pt. and steelworks, a. 73 km².

Jesenice, t., **Yugoslavia;** integrated iron and steel wks.; terminal of Brotherhood and Unity Highway.

Jesselton. See Kota Kinabalu.

Jhang Maghiana, t., **Pakistan;** textiles; mkt.; on R. Chenab; p. (1981) 195,000.

Jhansi, c., Uttar Pradesh, **India;** ctr. rly. ctr., mkt.; formerly of strategic importance; p. (1981) 246,172 (c.), 284,141 (met. a.).

Jharia, t., Bihar, **India;** ctr. of most impt. coal-

field in India; p. (1961) 33,683.

Jhelum, R., W. Punjab, **Pakistan;** most W. of the five Rs. of the Punjab; forms Vale of Kashmir in upper course; Mangla Dam under Indus Waters Treaty, completed 1967.

Jhelum, c., **Pakistan;** on Jhelum R.; p. (1981) 106,000.

Jiamusi (Kiamusze), c., Heilongjiang, **China;** ch. pt. on Songhua R.; p. (1984) 546,500.

Jiangsu (Kiangsu), coastal prov., **China;** on Yellow Sea; low lying a. N. of Chang Jiang delta; rich agr., dense p.; cotton, sericulture, tea, sugar, fish (many Ls.); cap. Nanjing; a. 109,000 km²; p. (est. 1985) 61,710,000.

Jiangxi (Kiangsi), prov., S.E. **China;** in basin of navigable Gan R. which drains through L. Poyang to Chang Jiang; ch. cs. Shanghai, Zhenjiang, Wuxi, Nanchang (cap.); rice, wheat, tea, cotton; tungsten, coking coal, kaolin; a. 172,494 km²; p. (est. 1985) 34,210,000.

Jiddah or **Jeddah,** c., admin. cap., Hejaz, **Saudi Arabia;** on Red Sea, pt. of Mecca; pilgrims; steel mill and oil refinery; new King Faisal Port nearby; univ. (with Mecca); p. (1974) 561,104.

Jihlava, t., Moravia, **ČSSR;** on Jihlava R.; 519 m a.s.l.; timber, grain, textiles; Prague Compactata signed here 1436; p. (1984) 52,828.

Jilin (Kirin), prov., N.E. **China;** N. of Korea and Liaotung peninsula; crossed by Songhua R.; in fertile Manchurian plain; impt. industl. a.; soya beans, grain, lumber, coal, gold, lead; cap. Changchun; a. 186,998 km²; p. (est. 1985) 22,840,000.

Jilin (Kirin), c., Jilin, N.E. **China;** former prov. cap.; on Songhua R., at outlet of Songhua reservoir; impt. position on rly. from Changchun to coastal pts.; chemical fertilisers, steel, oil refinery; p. (1984) 1,114,100.

Jimma, t., **Ethiopia;** ch. prod. Jimma coffee; connected by road with Addis Ababa; Agricultural Technical School; p. (est. 1980) 63,837.

Jinan (Tsinan), c., cap of Shandong prov., **China;** on S. bank of Huang He, 160 km. from G. of Bo Hai; agr. ctr.; textiles, foodstuffs, chemicals, trucks; univ.; p. (1984) 1,394,600.

Jinja, t., **Uganda;** on N. shore of L. Victoria where Nile drains from L. over Ripon Falls; (now inundated by Owen Falls dam 2·4 km upstream); cotton mnfs., copper smelting, flour and maize milling; rly. to Kampala; p. (1980) 45,060.

Jinzhou (Chincho), c., Liaoning prov., **China;** cement, glass, bricks, tiles, paper, wood and pulp, oil; p. (1984) 748,700.

Jiujiang (Kiukiang), c., Jianxi prov., **China;** pt. of Chang Jiang at foot of forested mtn.; entrepôt tr.; former treaty pt.; p. (1984) 378,100.

João Pessoa, t., cap. of Paraíba st., **Brazil;** through its pt. Cabedelo expts. cotton, sugar, minerals; recent industl. expansion results from SUDENE development plan; p. (est. 1985) 397,700.

Joban, dist., N.E. Honshu, **Japan;** third lgst. coalfield in Japan; ch. t. Fukushima.

Jodhpur, t., Rajasthan, **India;** ctr. of Thar desert; old fortress t.; p. (1981) 506,345.

Jogjakarta, c., Java, **Indonesia;** univ., cultural ctr.; handicrafts; citadel with palace; p. (1980) 342,267.

Johannesburg, c., Transvaal, S. **Africa;** univ.; gold-mng. ctr. of Witwatersrand; diamond cutting, engin., textiles, chemicals; oil pipeline from Durban; p. (1985) 1,609,408 (met. a.).

John o' Groat's House, place nr. Duncansby Head, Caithness, **Scot.**

Johnstone, burgh, Renfrew, **Scot.;** on R. Black Cart, nr. Paisley; machine tools, textiles, iron and brass foundry; p. (1981) 42,707.

Johnstown, industl. t., Penns., **USA;** on Conemaugh R.; coal-mng. and steel ctr.; machin.; p. (1984) 33,100 (t.), 259,000 (met. a.).

Johore, st., **Malaysia;** at S. end of Malaya; forested; cap. Johor Baharo; rubber, rice, copra, pineapples; tin, iron, bauxite; a. 18,985 km²; p. (1980) 1,638,229.

Joina Falls, Mali; dam projected for hydroelectric power and irrigation under auspices of Organisation of Riparian States of R. Senegal (Guinea, Mali, Mauritania, Senegal).

Joinville, t., Santa Catarina, **Brazil;** exp. timber, maté tea; textiles, machin., car parts, plastics; p. (est. 1985) 304,400.

Joliet, c., Ill., **USA;** on Des Plaines R., S.W. of Chicago; R. pt.; coal and limestone nearby; rly. engin., oil refining; p. (1980) 77,956.

Joliette, t., Quebec, **Canada;** textile mills, paper, tobacco-processing; p. (1981) 16,987.

Jönköping, t., cap. of J. co., Sweden; safety-matches, textiles, footwear; p. (est. 1986) 108,000.

Jonquière, t., S. Quebec, Canada; paper and pulp mills; p. (1986) 58,467. See Chicoutimi.

Joplin, t., Mo., USA; in dairy and livestock region; lead and zinc mng.; mnfs. metal and leather gds.; p. (1984) 39,700 (t.) 131,900 (met. a.).

Jordan, kingdom, S.W. Asia; bounded by Israel, Syria, Saudi Arabia, and Iraq; consists of high plateau (600 m), Jordan valley, and hill cty. to W. of R. Jordan; only 25 per cent of a. sufficiently humid for agr., much is migratory herding of animals and subsistence agr.; sm. mineral wealth; only outlet to sea Aqaba, pt. on G. of Aqaba; only one single-track rly.; new rail link built to Al-Hara phosphate mines, now major exp.; dependant on oil imports; cap. Amman; W. Bank of R. Jordan occupied by Israeli forces since June 1967; plan mooted (1972) to unify J. and W. Bank to form United Arab Kingdom; a. 101,140 km²; p. (est. 1985) 3,510,000 (80 per cent Moslem and 70 per cent under 24).

Jordan, R., Israel and Jordan; flows S. from Anti-Lebanon along sinuous course, mostly below sea-level to Dead Sea; its rapidly and variant depth render it unnavigable, and no t. of any importance has ever been built on its banks; Jesus was baptised in its waters; contemporary strife over use for irrigation; 368 km long.

Jos, t., central Nigeria; on Bauchi Plateau, 96 km S.W. of Bauchi; impt. tin mines; new steel rolling mill; p. (est. 1983) 149,000.

Jostedalsbre, icefield, W. Norway, lgst. icefield of European mainland; a. 881 km²; rises to 2,043 m.

Jotunheimen, mtn. region, central Norway hgst. in Scandinavia; Galdhopiggen 2,470 m, Glittertind 2,482 m.

Juan Fernández, two rocky volcanic Is., S. Pac. Oc., belonging to Chile; a. 98 km²; the buccaneer Alexander Selkirk marooned here 1704–9 gave idea for Defoe's Robinson Crusoe.

Juan les Pins, resort, Alpes-Maritimes dep., S.E. France.

Juba (Giuba), R., Somalia; narrow fertile valley, imp. agr. a.; 872 km long.

Jubbulpore. See Jabalpur.

Jucar, R., E. Spain; rises in Montes Universales, and flows to Mediterranean; irrigation and hydroelec. power; 400 km long.

Judaea, div. of Palestine in the Roman period.

Juggernaut. See Puri.

Juiz de Fora, t., Minas Gerais, Brazil; textile ctr.; p. (est. 1985) 350,700.

Julfa (Jolfa), c., N. Iran; on frontier with USSR, customs and transit ctr. on overland route from Europe.

Julian Alps, mtn. range, Yugoslavia and Italy; hgst. peak 2,865 m.

Julianehåb, t., S.W. Greenland; N.W. of C. Farewell; tr. ctr., fish. pt.

Jülich, t., N. Rhine–Westphalia, W. Germany; nuclear reactor; p. (est. 1986) 30,200.

Jullundur, c., Punjab, India; rly. ctr.; st. cap. until Chandigarh was built; p. (1981) 408,196.

Jumna, R., N. India; ch. trib. of R. Ganges; rises in the Himalayas and flows past Delhi and Agra to Allahabad; 1,376 km long.

Junagadh, t., Gujarat, India; agr. tr. and food-processing; industl. ctr.; formerly cap. of principality of J.; p. (1981) 118,646.

Jundiaí, t., São Paulo st., Brazil; industl. ctr.; nr. São Paulo; p. (est. 1985) 314,900.

Juneau, c., cap. of Alaska, USA; at foot of Chilkoot mtns., lumbering; fisheries; gold settlement (1881); p. (1980) 19,528. See Willow South.

Jungfrau, peak, Bernese Oberland, Switzerland; height 4,161 m; electric rly. from Kleine Scheidegg to Jungfraujoch.

Junin, t., Argentina; agr. tr., rly. engin., pottery, furniture; p. (1980) 62,080.

Jura, dep., E. France; named from mtn. range on Franco-Swiss border; agr. and pastoral; cap. Lons-le-Saunier; a. 5,053 km²; p. (1982) 243,000.

Jura, I., Argyll and Bute, Scot.; off W. cst.; a. 378 km²; p. (1971) 349 inc. Colonsay.

Jura, mtn. range, Switzerland and France; folded parallel ranges separated by deep R. valleys; hgst. peak Crêt de la Neige, 1,724 m; 240 km long, breadth 48–64 km.

Jura, new canton (1979), Switzerland; between Berne and Basle in a strong French speaking dist. in Jura Mtns; p. (est. 1986) 65,000.

Juruá R., lge. trib. of Amazon; rises in E. Peru and flows through Acre and Amazonas sts., Brazil; over 3,200 km long.

Jutland (Jylland), peninsula, Denmark; intensive agr. and poultry farming; sandy heath in W.; more fertile clay in E. used for dairying; a. 29,554 km²; p. (1971) 2,193,070.

Jyväskylä, t., central Finland; pt. on L. Päijänne; pulp. paper, plywood; univ.; p. (1986) 65,442.

K

K2. See Godwin-Austin, Mt.

Kabardin-Balkar ASSR, aut. rep., Transcaucasia, RSFSR; cap. Nalchik; livestock, lumber, wheat, fruit; non-ferrous metals; hydro-metallurgy plant; a. 12,432 km²; p. (1986) 722,000.

Kabelega Falls (Murchison Falls), on Victoria Nile, Uganda; falls between L. Kioga and L. Mobutu Seso.

Kabinda. See Cabinda.

Kābul, c., cap. of Afghanistan; on Kābul R. S. of Hindu Kush; 2,104 m a.s.l.; excellent climate; univ.; comm. and cultural ctr.; textiles, leather, timber inds.; p. (est. 1982) 1,127,417, rapid inc. from migration.

Kābul, R., flows from Hindu Kush through gorges in Khyber Pass to Indus; site of dam for hydro-elec. power and irrigation; length c. 480 km.

Kabwe (Broken Hill), Zambia; comm. and mng. ctr.; lead, zinc, cadmium, silver; p. (1980) 143,635.

Kachin State, semi-aut. st., Burma; comprising former Myitkyina and Bhamo dists.; home of Kachins; a. 89,042 km².

Kadiyevka, t., Ukrainian SSR, USSR; coal, iron and steel, synthetic rubber; p. (est. 1977) 141,000.

Kaduna, t., N. Nigeria; cap of Kaduna st.; rly. junc.; aluminium wks.; spinning and weaving; new oil refinery; p. (est. 1983) 247,100.

Kaffa, region, Ethiopia; mtnous., forested; natural habitat of coffee plant; p. (est. 1980) 1,615,400.

Kagoshima, c., at S. end of Kyushu I., Japan; pt. on K. Bay; univs., cas.; porcelain, silk and cotton clothing, food-processing, publishing; rocket launching site nearby at Uchinoura; p. (1985) 530,496.

Kahoolawe, I., Hawaiian Is.; a. 117 km²; uninhabited.

Kaieteur Falls, waterfall, Guyana; where R. Potaro leaves Guiana Highlands; among world's hgst. falls (226 m).

K'ai-feng, c., Henan, China; nr. S. bank of Huang He; one of the most anc. cities in China; cottons, chemicals; p. (1984) 619,200.

Kai Islands, Is., Indonesia; between New Guinea and Timor; timber; a. 1,761 km²; p. 51,000.

Kaikoura, t., S.I., N.Z.; on E. cst., 128 km N.E. of Christchurch; in this region are the Kaikoura ranges, in which the hgst. peaks are Tapuaenuku (2,887 m) and Alarm (2,867 m); p. (1971) 1,607.

Kailas (Kang-ti-ssu Shan), range and peak, S.W. Tibet, China; unclimbed sacred mtn.; source of Indus, Ganges, Sutlej and Zangbo (head-stream of Brahmaputra).

Kainji Dam, Nigeria; power sta. transmission system and river transportation on R. Niger.

K'ai-ping, t., Hebei, N. China; second lgst. coal-mng. a. (Kailan mines) in China; coal exported through Qinhuangdao.

Kairouan, holy c. of Moslems, Tunisia; 128 km S.S.E. of Tunis; founded A.D. 670; mosque; p. (1984) 72,254.

Kaiserslautern, c., Rhineland–Palatinate, W. Germany; nr. Mannheim; iron, textiles, machin., tobacco, wood; p. (est. 1986) 96,800.

Kaiser Wilhelm's Land, Australian dependency, Antarctica.

Kakamega, t., Kenya; E. Africa; 48 km N. of Kisumu; ctr. of gold-mng. dist.

Kakinada, t., spt., Adhra Pradesh, India; cotton, oilseeds; p. (1981) 226,409.

Kalahari Desert, region of semi-desert, southern Africa; between Orange and Zambesi Rs.; mainly in Botswana; alt. 1,128 m; a. 51,800 km²; inhabited chiefly by Bushmen.

Kalamata, t., Peloponnesus, Greece; nr. Sparta; figs, currants, flour-milling, cigarette mftg.; p. (1981) 43,235.

Kalamazoo, c., Mich., USA; industl. and comm. ctr. in farming a.; paper, pharmaceuticals; fish hatchery nearby; p. (1984) 77,200 (c.), 215,200 (met. a.).

Kalemie (Albertville), t., **Zaïre**; on L. Tanganyika; rail-steamer transfer point; p. (est. 1967) 86,687.

Kalewa, t., **Burma**; at confluence of Irrawaddy and Chindwin Rs.; coal deposits.

Kalgan *See* **Zhangjiakou.**

Kalgoorlie, t., W. **Australia**; gold mng. ctr. in arid region adjacent to "Golden Mile" auriferous reef; nickel mng. more impt.; nickel smelter (1971); p. (1981) 19,848 (inc. Boulder).

Kalimantan (Indonesian Borneo); straddles equator; sparse p.; poor soils; lge. areas of swamp; plans for reclamation; coal, oil, diamonds, gold in sm. quantities; rice, pepper, copra; a. 539,461 km²; p. est. (1970) 626,000.

Kalinin (Tver), c., **RSFSR**; on upper Volga; diversified inds.; 17th cent. cath. and cas.; p. (est. 1985) 438,000.

Kaliningrad (Königsberg), c., **RSFSR**, former cap. of E. Prussia; on R. Pregel, linked by canal to outer pt. Pillau; univ., cath.; shipbldg., machin., wood-pulp, chemicals, exp. agr. prods.; Kant lived here all his life; p. (est. 1985) 385,000.

Kalisz, t., Poznan, **Poland**; on R. Prosna; industl. ctr., textiles; oldest Polish t. mentioned in 2nd cent. A.D. by Ptolemy; p. (est. 1983) 102,900.

Kalmar, t., spt., S. **Sweden**; on I. in Kalmar Sound; cath., cas.; matches, food inds., shipbldg.; p. (est. 1986) 54,000.

Kalmuk (Kalmytskaya) ASSR, aut. rep., **RSFSR**; on Caspian Sea; harsh and infertile steppe; pastoral agr.; cap. Elista; a. 75,887 km²; p. (1986) 324,000.

Kalna, v., on Mt. Stara Planina, **Yugoslavia**; uranium mine and plant; nuclear power sta.

Kaluga, c., **RSFSR**; pt. on Oka R.; chemicals, engin., hydroelec. power plant; p. (est. 1985) 297,000.

Kalyan, spt., Maharashtra, **India**; nr. Bombay; bricks, tiles; p. (1981) 136,052.

Kalymnos, I., Dodecanese, **Greece**; mtnous.; a. 106 km²; p. 13,600.

Kama, R., **RSFSR**; ch. trib. of Volga which it enters below Kazan; rises in foothills of Urals; lge. hydro-electric sta. at Perm; navigable; 2,016 km long.

Kamaishi, t., spt., N.E. Honshu, **Japan**; serves Kamaishi–Sennin iron-ore field, lgst. worked deposits and reserves in Japan; impt. iron and steel ind.; p. (1970) 72,923.

Kamakura, t., Honshu, **Japan**; on shore of Sagami Bay; tourism; p. (1985) 175,490.

Kamaran I., Red Sea, **Democratic Rep. of Yemen**; formerly under Brit. occupation, 1915–67; a. 57 km²; p. 2,200.

Kamchatka, peninsula, E. Siberia, **USSR**; volcanic ranges; geothermal power sta.; mineral wealth, fisheries on cst., climate cold, wet and foggy; contains part of Koryak nat. okrug; cap. Petropavlovsk.

Kamenets-Podolskiy, t., Ukrainian SSR. **USSR**; on Smotrich R.; lt. inds.; mediaeval fortress t.; p. (est. 1970) 113,000.

Kamensk-Shakhtinskiy, c., **RSFSR**; on Donets R.; coal-mng. ctr., engin., food processing, artificial fibres; p. (est. 1967) 71,000.

Kamensk-Uralsk, c., **RSFSR**; aluminium, iron, steel, engin.; p. (est. 1985) 200,000.

Kamet, Himalayan peak, on border of **India** and Tibet, **China**; 7,761 m; highest mtn. climbed (Smythe, 1931) until 1953 (Everest).

Kamloops, t., B.C., **Canada**; on Thompson R.; formerly Fort Thompson; on transcontinental rlys.; suppl ctr. for mng. and grazing dist.; fruit and livestock mkts.; p. (1986) 61,773.

Kampala, c., cap. of **Uganda**; univ., ch. comm. ctr.; lt. inds., coffee-processing; p. (1980) 458,423.

Kampen, t., Overijssel, **Neth.**; on R. IJssel; cigar-mkg.; p. (est. 1987) 32,500.

Kampot, prov., **Cambodia**; on G. of Siam; ctr. of pepper ind.; p. (1981) 337,879.

Kampuchea, Democratic (Cambodia), S.E. **Asia**; between Thailand and Vietnam; former ass. st. of Fr. Union; cap. Phnom-Penh on Mekong R.; mainly agr., rice, rubber, maize, pepper, kapok, livestock; Tonle Sap impt. for fishing; car assembly, cigarette mkg., textiles, plywood, paper, tyres, cement; oil refinery nr. Kompong Som; new constitution established after civil war 1970–5; invaded by Vietnam (1979) and Khmer Rouge overthrown; a. 181,300 km²; p. (est. 1985) 7,284,000 (lge decrease since 1975 from war, famine and migration).

Kamyshin, t., **RSFSR**; pt. on Volga; textiles, mkt. gardening, grain; p. (est. 1985) 116,000.

Kan, R. *See* **Gan Jiang.**

Kananga (Luluabourg), c., cap. of Kasai Occidental prov., **Zaïre**; on Lulua R.; comm. and communications ctr. in cotton-growing a.; p. (1982) 704,211 (met. a.).

Kanawha, R., W. Va., **USA**; rises in Allegheny mtns., flows into R. Ohio; runs through ch. mng. a. of W. Va. coalfield nr. Charleston.

Kanazawa, c., Honshu, **Japan**; in Kana plain, on Sea of Japan; machin., silk and cotton textiles; landscape gardens. *No* theatre; p. (1985) 176,058.

Kanchenjunga, mtn., on Nepal–Sikkim bdy., N.E. **India**; third hgst. mtn. in world, 8,585 m.

Kanchipuram (Conjeeveram), t., Tamil Nadu, S. **India**; on plain S.W. of Madras; pilgrimage ctr.; textiles; p. (1971) 110,657 (t.). 119,693 (met. a.).

Kandahar. See **Qandahar.**

Kandy, c., **Sri Lanka**; in mtns. in ctr. of I.; 120 km from Colombo; univ. at sub. of Peradeniya; resort in hot season; tea, cocoa; p. (1981) 97,872.

Kangaroo I., lgst. I. off S. **Australia** cst.; tourists attracted by spectacular granite scenery and varied flora and fauna; p. (1976) 3,262.

Kano, c., N. **Nigeria**; emporium for whole of Sudan region; impt. airport and rly. terminus; groundnut ctr.; p. (est. 1983) 487,000.

Kanpur (Cawnpore), c., Uttar Pradesh, N. **India**; on R. Ganges; impt. mftg. ctr.; textiles, chemicals, leather goods, foodstuffs; p. (1981) 1,481,789 (c.), 1,639,064 (met. a.).

Kansas, st., **USA**; called the "sunflower state"; prairie; farming, maize, wheat; cattle, dairying, pigs; coal, petroleum, natural gas, lead, meat packing, flour milling, aircraft, chemicals, machin.; admitted to Union 1861; st. flower sunflower, st. bird Western Meadowlark; cap. Topeka; a. 213,095 km²; p. (1985) 2,450,000.

Kansas, R., Kan., **USA**; trib. of Missouri R., confluence at Kansas City; vegetable growing in valley; periodic flooding; 272 km long.

Kansas City, Kansas and Mo., **USA**; at confluence of Kansas and Missouri Rs.; univ.; gr. livestock mart, car and aircraft assembly, steel prods., meat-packing, food processing; p. (1984) 160,500 (Kansas) 443,100 (Mo.); 1,476,700 (joint met. a.).

Kansu. See **Gansu.**

Kant, t., Kirghiz SSR, **USSR**; 19 km E. of Frunze; to be expanded to industl. c.; proposed p. 100,000.

Kanye, t., **Botswana**, S. Africa; lgst. t. in rep.; p. (1980) 22,000.

Kaohsiung, spt., **Taiwan**; on S.W. cst.; industl. ctr., road and rly. terminus; oil refining, aluminium wks.; p. (est. 1984) 1,285,132.

Kaolack, inland pt., **Senegambia**; 112 km up Saloum R.; groundnut ctr., integrated textile complex; p. (est. 1979) 115,679.

Kaposvár, t., S.W. **Hungary**; on Kapos R.; comm. ctr.; textiles, foodstuffs; p. (est. 1985) 74,000.

Kara-Bogaz-Gol, lge. shallow bay, Turkmen SSR, **USSR**; an arm of Caspian Sea; rapid evaporation allows huge quantities of salt from Caspian to be deposited along its shores (world's lgst. source of Glauber's salt); a. 18,130 km².

Karabuk, t., **Turkey**; N. of Ankara; steel wks.; p. (1985) 94,818.

Karacheyevo-Cherkesskaya, aut. region, **RSFSR**; in Greater Caucasus; cap. Cherkessk; livestock, grain; coal, lead, zinc; a. 14,095 km²; p. (1970) 345,000.

Karachi, c., **Pakistan**; on Arabian Sea, nr. Indus delta; former cap. of Pakistan; univ.; spt., air ctr.; oil refining, industl. gases, steel mill, natural gas from Sui; nuclear power sta.; p. (1981) 5,103,000.

Karaganda, c., Kazakh SSR, **USSR**; on impt. coalfield developed since 1926; supplies industl. ctrs. of Urals; iron and steel wks., power sta.; p. (1986) 624,000.

Kara-Kalpak ASSR, aut. rep., N.W. Uzbek SSR, **USSR**; inc. Ust-Urt plateau, Kyzyl-Kum desert; irrigated agr.; cap. Nukus; a. 165,553 km²; p. (1986) 1,106,000.

Karakorum Range, part of Himalayas between Kashmir and China; many lofty peaks, inc. Mt. Godwin-Austen; Karakorum highway linking Pakistan with Xinjiang prov. of China, opened 1971.

Kara-Kum, sand desert, Turkmen SSR, **USSR**; E. of S.E. shore of Caspian Sea; to be irrigated with water diverted from Rs. which flow to Barents Sea. a. 349,650 km²; canal 1,440 km long across desert.

Karamay (K'o-la-ma-i), t. Xianjiang, **China**; ctr. of lge. oilfield; pipeline to Fushantzu refinery; p. (1984) 180,100.

Kara Sea, Arctic Oc.; E. of Novaya Zemlya; navigation to and from Siberian pts. July–Sept.

Karbala, c., **Iraq**; N.W. of Al Hillah; ctr. of pilgrimage; sacred c. of Moslem Shiite sect; p. (1970) 107,496.

Karelian ASSR, aut. rep., **RSFSR**; between Kola peninsula and Finland; lake-covered, coniferous forests; cap. Petrozavodsk; rich in timber, minerals, precious metals; granite and mica quarried; paper and pulp milling; a. 179,408 km²; p. (1986) 787,000.

Karelian Isthmus, RSFSR; strategic route between Finland and USSR impt. for defence of Leningrad.

Kariba Dam, in Kariba gorge of Zambesi R., on **Zimbabwe–Zambia** border; operated jointly by the two govts.; one of lgst. dams in world with vast artificial lake supplying hydroelectric power to Zimbabwe and the copperbelt of Zambia; badly polluted with use of D.D.T. in tsetse and malaria control; involved resettlement of Batonka peoples; completed 1960; following Rhodesian U.D.I., construction began on a second generating sta. on the Zambian side.

Karikal, former Fr. settlement on E. cst. of **India**.

Karkonosze. See Riesengebirge.

Karl-Marx-Stadt (Chemnitz), c., Karl-Marx-Stadt dist., **E. Germany**; leading industl. ctr.; cotton, woollens, machin., cars, furniture, chemicals, engin.; nr. lignite mines; p. (est. 1986) 314,000.

Karlovac, t., Croatia, **Yugoslavia**; S.W. of Zagreb; chemicals, textiles, food processing; p. (1981) 78,363.

Karlový Vary (Carlsbad), t., Bohemia, **ČSSR**; on R. Ohře; hot mineral springs; health resort; porcelain; p. (1984) 59,183.

Karlskoga, t., **Sweden**; E. of L. Vänern; seat of Bofors armament wks.; iron and steel, explosives, chemicals; p. (1983) 35,539.

Karlskrona, spt., S. **Sweden**; on Baltic Sea; main naval sta.; lighting fixtures, china; p. (1983) 59,696.

Karlsruhe, c., Baden–Württemberg, **W. Germany**; road and rly. ctr.; outport on Rhine; chemicals, engin., elec., tobacco inds., oil refining; nuclear reactor; oil pipeline to Lavera, nr. Marseilles; p. (est. 1986) 268,300.

Karlstad, t., **Sweden**; on N. shore L. Väner; ironwks., engin., machin.; p. (est. 1986) 75,000.

Karnak, t., **Egypt**; on Nile, N. of Luxor; site of the anc. Thebes; ruined temples; p. c. 11,000.

Karnal, t., Haryana, **India**; clothing inds.; p. (1981) 132,107.

Karnataka (Mysore), st., S.W. **India**; borders Arabian Oc.; inc. W. Ghats where high rainfall and hydroelec. power; rainfall decreases to E.; cap. Bangalore; a. 192,203 km²; p. (1981) 37,135,174.

Karpathos, I., Dodecanese, **Greece**; Aegean Sea; between Rhodes and Crete; p. (1981) 4,645.

Karroo, W. Cape Prov., **S. Africa**; high plateau, scrub-covered; irrigated by Verwoerd dam on Orange R.

Kars, t., N.E. **Turkey**; in Armenia, alt. c. 1,800 m, in strategic position nr. Soviet border; p. (1985) 69,293.

Karst, dist., **Yugoslavia**; in Dinaric Alps; gives name to limestone landforms which are well developed here.

Karun, R., S.W. **Iran**; mainly mtn. torrent; difficult access, sparse p.; 752 km long.

Karvina, t., **ČSSR**; on Polish border; ctr. of Ostrava-Karvina coalfield; p. (est. 1986) 75,000.

Kasai, R., Angola and **Zaïre**, Central Africa; rises in Bihé Plateau (Angola) and flows over 1,920 km into R. Zaïre 192 km above Kinshasa; alluvial diamond mng. at Chicopa.

Kasai, former prov., **Zaïre**; agr.; impt. source of industl. diamonds; attempted secession 1960; now divided into E. Kasai (cap. Mbuji-Mayi), and W. Kasai (cap. Luluabourg).

Kāshān, c., central **Iran**; in agr. oasis; carpets, velvet; p. (est. 1982) 110,000.

Kashi (Kashgar) c., Xinjiang, prov., **China**; on anc. imperial silk route through central Asia; growth rapid with irrigation; visited by Marco Polo 1275; p. (1984) 187,100.

Kashmir. See Jammu and Kashmir.

Kassala, t., N.E. **Sudan**; ctr. of cotton-growing dist.; p. (est. 1972) 106,000.

Kassel, c., Hesse, **W. Germany**; on R. Fulda; cas.; machin., vehicles, science-based inds.; route ctr.; p. (est. 1986) 185,400.

Kastamonu, t., N. **Turkey**; cap. of K. prov.; ctr. of dist. rich in minerals; textiles, copper gds.; p. (1985) 46,986.

Katanga. See Shaba.

Kathiawar, peninsula, Gujarat, **India**; between G. of Kutch and G. of Cambay; ch. pt. Bhaunagar; very dry a.

Katmai, Mount, S. Alaska, **USA**; active volcano with crater L.; alt. 2,135 m.

Katmandu (Kathmandu), cap. of **Nepal**; on Vishnumati R., 120 km from Indian frontier; highway to Kodari; hydroelec. sta.; brick and tile wks.; many palaces and temples; p. (1981) 393,494.

Katoomba, t., N.S.W., **Australia**; holiday resort at 1,017 m in the Blue Mountains; since 1947 part of City of Blue Mtns.; p. (1981) 13,942 (inc. Wentworth Falls).

Katowice, prov., S. **Poland**; in Upper Silesia; cap. K.; mng. and industl. a. drained by Warta R.; a. 9,516 km²; p. (1986) 3,946,000.

Katowice, c., S. **Poland**; cap. of K. prov.; impt. iron-mng. and industl. ctr.; heavy machin. chemicals; p. (est. 1985) 363,000.

Katrine, Loch, S.W. Stirling, **Scot.**; beautiful woodland and moorland scenery; source of Glasgow water supply; scene of Scott's *Lady of the Lake*; 13 km long, c. 1·6 km wide.

Katsina, t., **Nigeria**; nr. Niger border; agr. tr. ctr., groundnuts, cotton; rural craft inds.; steel rolling mill; Hausa cultural ctr.; p. (est. 1983) 149,000.

Kattegat, arm of N. Sea linked with Baltic; separates **Denmark** (Jutland) from **Sweden**; 64–112 km wide.

Katwijk, t., S. Holland, **Neth.**; on N. Sea 24 km from the Hague; resort; synthetic resins; p. (est. 1987) 39,000.

Kaufbeuren, t., Bavaria, **W. Germany**; on R. Wertach; textile mnfs.; p. (est. 1986) 41,500.

Kaunas (Kovno), c., Lithuanian SSR, **USSR**; on R. Nemen; R. pt. and comm. ctr.; univ.; 11th cent. c.; metal gds., chemicals, textiles, hydroelec. power; Jewish p. (circa 30 per cent) exterminated during German occupation 1941–4; p. (est. 1985) 405,000.

Kavalla, c., E. Macedonia, **Greece**; on Bay of Kavalla; processes and exp. tobacco; the anc. Neapolis; p. (1981) 56,705.

Kawagoe, c., Honshu, **Japan**; in Kanto plain; silk textiles; p. (1985) 285,435.

Kawasaki, S. sub. Tokyo, Honshu, **Japan**; pt. for import of industl. raw materials; heavy inds.; p. (1987) 1,128,000.

Kawthoolei State, st., **Burma**; former Karen st., extended to inc. areas in Tenasserim and Irrawaddy; a. 30,383 km².

Kayah State, semi-aut. st., **Burma**; on Thai border; forested plateau; tungsten mines; teak; a. 11,730 km².

Kayseri, c., **Turkey**; S.E. of Ankara; textiles, carpets, food tr.; anc. Hittite c.; p. (1985) 373,937.

Kazakh SSR (Kazakhstan), constituent rep., **USSR**; in central Asia; cap. Alma-Ata; steppe with stock-raising; lge. desert areas being made fertile by irrigation; plans to divert Ob R.; grain in N.; coal at Karaganda; asbestos at Dzhetygara; minerals inc. metaborite (richest boron mineral); oil; atomic power sta. to W. of Caspian Sea; cosmodrome at Leninsk, E. of Aral Sea; a. 2,778,544 km²; p. (1986) 16,036,000.

Kazan', c., **RSFSR**; cap. of Tatar ASSR; pt. on Volga; impt. tr. ctr. for E. USSR, Turkestan Bokhara and Iran; cath., univ. (where Tolstoy and Lenin were educated); engin., chemicals, synthetic rubber, textiles, paper, oil refining; natural gas pipeline to Minnibayevo; p. (1986) 1,057,000.

Kazanluk, t., central **Bulgaria**; in region famous for attar of roses; p. (est. 1968) 48,816.

Kazan-retto or **Volcanic Is.**; gr. of Is., W. Pac. Oc. S. of Tokyo; sugar plantations, sulphur; returned to **Japan** by USA 1968.

Kazbek, extinct volcano, N. Georgian SSR, **USSR**; second hgst. peak of Caucasus; alt. 5,045 m.

Kāzerūn, t., S.W. **Iran**; ctr. of agr. dist. where fruit, tobacco, opium, cotton grown; p. (1966) 39,758.

Kazvin or **Qazvin,** c., N.W. **Iran**; transit tr.; carpets, textiles; p. (1983) 244,265.

Kearsley, t., Gtr. Manchester, **Eng.**; chemicals, paper; p. (1981) 11,352.

Keban Dam, S.E. **Turkey**; at confluence of the E. and W. branches of Euphrates.

Kecskemet, c., central **Hungary**; fruit-canning and wine-distilling from locally grown prods.; 4th cent. c.; p. (est. 1985) 104,000.

Kedah, st., **Malaysia**; on Strait of Malacca, N.W. Malaya; rice, rubber, coconuts, tungsten; cap. Alor Star; a. 9,479 km²; p. (1980) 1,116,140.

Kediri, t., E. Java, **Indonesia**; food processing; p. (1980) 221,830.

Keeling Is. See **Cocos Is.**

Keelung (Chi-lung), c., N. **Taiwan**; on E. China Sea; naval base and ch. pt.; exp. agr. prods.; chemicals; gold, sulphur, copper mined nearby; p. (est. 1984) 352,666.

Keewatin, dist., N.W. Terr., **Canada**; barren grounds; fur a. 590,934 km².

Kegworth, v. Leics., **Eng**; scene of recent M1 air crash.

Keighley, t., West Yorks., **Eng.**; in Aire valley, 24 km N.W. of Leeds; engin., woollen and worsteds; p. (1981) 57,451.

Keihin, vast conurb. of Tokyo, Yokohama and Kawasaki, **Japan**; p. (1971) 14,650,000.

Keith, burgh, Moray, **Scot.**; mkt. t. in agr. dist.; p. (1981) 4,315.

Kelantan, st., **Malaysia**; one of most fertile areas on E. cst. Malaya; cap. Kota Bharu; rice, coconuts, rubber; a. 14,815 km²; p. (1980) 893,753.

Kells or **Ceannanus Mor**, mkt. t., Co. Meath, **R.o.I.**; notable for monastic remains and illuminated Book of Kells, now in library of Trinity College, Dublin; p. (1981) 2,623.

Kelso, burgh, Roxburgh, **Scot.**; at confluence of Rs. Teviot and Tweed; p. (1981) 5,609.

Kemerovo, c., **RSFSR**; S.E. of Tomsk; coalmng. ctr.; chemicals, textiles, plastics; p. (est. 1985) 507,000.

Kemi, t., N.E. **Finland**; spt. on G. of Bothnia; sawmills; p. (1986) 26,218.

Kemi, R., N.E. **Finland**; used for hydroelectric power and timber transport; 480 km long.

Kempten, t., Bavaria, **W. Germany**; nr. Bodensee; Benedictine abbey; p. (est. 1986) 57,000.

Kendal, l. gov. dist., Cumbria, **Eng.**; mkt. ctr.; tourism; p. (1981) 23,411.

Kenilworth, t., Warwicks., **Eng.**; 6 km S.W. of Coventry; mkt.; ruined cas.; p. (1981) 19,315.

Kenitra. See **Mina Hassan Tani**.

Kennet, l. gov. dist., Wiltshire, **Eng.**; stretches from Marlborough to Devizes; p. (est. 1988) 67,700.

Kennet, R., Wilts. and Berks., **Eng.**; trib. of R. Thames; followed by main rly. London to W. of Eng.; 70 km long.

Kennington, dist., in London bor. of Lambeth, **Eng.**; inc. the Oval cricket ground, home of Surrey C.C.

Kenosha, t., Wis., **USA**; on W. shore of L. Mich.; p. (1980) 77,685 (t.), 123,137 (met. a.).

Kensington and Chelsea, Royal Borough of, inner bor., W. London, **Eng.**; mainly residtl.; contains Kensington Palace and Gardens; p. (est. 1988) 125,600.

Kent, non-met. co., **Eng.**; intensive agr. mkt. gardening, orchards, hops; "Garden of England"; crossed by N. Downs and Weald; industl. zone bordering Thames and Medway estuaries; tourist resorts and cross-channel ferry pts. on cst. proposed Channel Tunnel link (1993) liable to make lge impact on co.; London commuter hinterland; co. t. Maidstone; a. 3,730 km²; p. (est. 1988) 1,520,400.

Kentucky, E. central st., **USA**; in W. foothills of Appalachians and crossed by tribs. of Mississippi; "Bluegrass" st.; mainly agr.; some coal; cap. Frankfort; lgst. c. Louisville, at falls of Ohio R.; hydroelec. power; tourism; admitted to Union 1792; st. flower Goldenrod, st. bird Cardinal; a. 104,623 km²; p. (1985) 3,726,000.

Kentucky, R., Ky., **USA**; flows from Cumberland plateau to Ohio R.; length 400 km.

Kenya, rep., E. **Africa**; member of Brit. Commonwealth; comprises 7 provs.; straddles equator but climate modified by alt.; marked contrast between sparsely populated and arid N. and well-developed S. where upland climate has attracted the European p.; economy based on prod. and processing of arable and pastoral prods., inc. dairy prod.; relatively well developed cooperative African farming; 80 per cent of p. earn living on the land; most industl. of E. African cty., mostly exp. orientated; growth in exp. of cement and fluorspar; tourism incr. impt; ch. spt. Mombasa, airports at Nairobi and Mombasa; famous for big game; univ.; cap. Nairobi; a. 582,646 km²; p. (est. 1987) 22·1 m.

Kenya, Mt., volcano, **Kenya**; just S. of equator; snow-covered; alt. 5,197 m; 2nd hgst. peak in Africa; Nat. Park.

Kephallenia. See **Cephalonia**.

Kerala, st., **India**; cap. Trivandrum; plantations

producing rubber, tea, pepper; higher proportion of literacy than in any other st.; a. 38,855 km²; p. (1981) 25,453,680.

Kerch, c., Ukrainian SSR, **USSR**; in Crimea, commanding K. strait connecting Black Sea and Azov Sea; spt. and industl. ctr.; metallurgical plant, iron and steel mills, shipbldg., fisheries; iron-ore, vanadium, natural gas nearby; p. (est. 1985) 168,000.

Kerguelen, archipelago, S. **Indian Oc.**; part of Fr. Antarctic terr.; whaling, fishing; famous for K. cabbage (*Pringlea antiscorbutica*).

Kerkrade, t., Limburg prov., **Neth.**; coal mng.; anc. abbey; p. (est. 1987) 53,000.

Kérkira. See **Corfu**.

Kermadec Is., volcanic gr. **Pac. Oc.**; 960 km N.E. of N.Z.; a. 34 km²; met. sta. on Sunday I. (lgst. of gr.); annexed to N.Z. 1887; p. (1986) 5.

Kerman, region, S.E. **Iran**; mtnous., much desert land; agr.; carpet-weaving; coal and iron-ore mng. being developed; recent copper find; irrigation scheme projected; p. (1982) 1,078,875.

Kermän, c., S.E. **Iran**; prov. cap.; carpet-weaving ctr.; textile mftg.; airpt.; mediaeval mosques; multi-million dollar complex for mining and refining copper; p. (1986) 254,786.

Kermānshāh, (Qahremānshahr) t., N.W. **Iran**; cap. of Kermānshāhān prov.; agr., comm. and route ctr.; airpt.; oil refinery; p. (1986) 565,544.

Kern, R., E. Cal., **USA**; one of most impt. power-generating Rs. in st.

Kerrier, l. gov. dist., Cornwall, **Eng.**; a. inc. Lizard penin. and Helston; p. (est. 1988) 86,800.

Kerry, coastal co., Munster, **R.o.I.**; deeply indented cst.; cap. Tralee; tourism; a. 4,703 ·km²; p. (1981) 31,993.

Kerulen, R., N.E. **Mongolia** and **China**; flows parallel to edge of Gobi Desert; a. designated for economic development; 1,256 km long.

Kesteven, North, l. gov. dist., Lincs., **Eng.**; rural a. based on Sleaford; p. (est. 1988) 84,000.

Kesteven, South, l. gov. dist., Lincs., **Eng.**; rural a. and ts. of Grantham and Bourne; p. (est. 1988) 105,200.

Keswick, Allerdale, Cumbria, **Eng.**; on Greta R.; at N. end of L. Derwentwater; tourist ctr.; mkt.; pencils; p. (1981) 5,645.

Kettering, l. gov. dist., mkt. t., Northants., **Eng.**; nr. Wellingborough; footwear; iron mng.; p. (est. 1988) 74,600 (dist.).

Kew, dist., London bor. of Richmond-upon-Thames, **Eng.**; contains Kew botanical gardens.

Keweenaw, peninsula, L. Superior, **USA**; former impt. copper deposits.

Keynsham, t., Wansdyke, Avon, **Eng.**; expanded t.; p. (1981) 20,443.

Key West, c., Fla., **USA**; on I. c. 240 km from mainland; naval sta., coastguard base; cigar-mftg.; tourism; p. (1980) 24,382.

Khabarovsk, c., **RSFSR**; cap. of K. terr., E. Siberia, on Amur R.; cath.; oil refining, aircraft engin., wood and paper inds.; pipeline links with oilfields in N. Sakhalin; transport ctr. of Far East; p. (1986) 584,000.

Khairpur, t., **Pakistan**; nr. Sukkur barrage; textiles; p. (est. 1975) 56,500.

Khakass Autonomous Oblast, admin. div. of Krasnoyarsk region, **RSFSR**; pastoral agr., timber and mng. inds.; a. 61,784 km²; p. (1986) 547,000.

Khandwa, t., Madhya Pradesh, **India**; S. of Indore; cotton, oil-pressing; p. (1981) 114,725.

Khaniá, or **Canea**, c., Crete, **Greece**; in sheltered bay on W. cst.; historic sites; p. (1981) 47,451.

Khanka, L., **China–USSR** border; dairy farming, fishing; branch of Trans-Siberian rly. to W. shore; a. 4,403 km².

Khanty-Mansi, admin. div., **RSFSR**; in W. Siberian lowland; sparse p.; cap. KhantyMansiisk (at confluence of Ob' and Irtysh Rs.); natural gas; a. 556,850 km²; p. (1986) 1,047,000.

Kharagpur, c., W. Bengal, **India**; instal., scientific research ctr.; rly. junc.; p. (1981) 150,475 (c.) 232,575 (met. a.).

Khärg, I., Persian Gulf, **Iran**; oil terminal for supertankers, 48 km from mainland; repeated Iraqi air attacks resulted in floating terminal at Sirri island and plans for replacement terminal.

Khar'kov, c., Ukrainian SSR, **USSR**; impt. industl. ctr. in Donets coal region; cap. of K. region; univ.; cath.; rly. ctr.; extensively rebuilt after second world war; p. (1986) 1,567,000.

Khartoum, c., cap. of the **Sudan**; at confluence of

Blue and White Niles; univ.; famous siege under Gordon 1884–5; p. (1983) 476,218.

Khashm el Girba, t., **Sudan;** new t. on Atbara R., between Khartoum and Ethiopian border; for p. of Wadi Halfa inundated by Aswan L.; sugar refinery.

Khasi Hills, Meghalaya, N.E. **India;** form abrupt S. edge to middle Brahmaputra valley; very heavy monsoon rains on S.-facing slopes; lower slopes forested; middle slopes impt. tea-growing region; rise to over 1,800 m.

Khaskovo, t., **Bulgaria;** woollens, carpets, tobacco; p. (1985) 87,788.

Kherson, c., Ukrainian SSR, **USSR;** 24 km up R. Dnieper from Black Sea; sea and R. pt., rly. junc.; grain, oil refining, engin., textiles, shipbldg; founded by Catherine the Great as fortress t.; p. (est. 1985) 346,000.

Khingan, Gr. and **Little,** mtn. ranges, Inner Mongolia and Heilongjiang prov., N.E. **China;** rich timber resources; rise to over 1,800 m.

Khios or **Chios,** I., **Greece;** in Aegean Sea; wines, figs, fruits; marble; cap. Khios; supposed birthplace of Homer; p. (1981) 48,700.

Khiva, former vassal st. of Russia; now part of Uzbek SSR and Turkmen SSR, **USSR.**

Khiva, c., N.W. Uzbek SSR, **USSR;** in oasis nr. Kara-Kum desert; cottons, carpets; anc. c.; p. (est. 1970) 25,000.

Khmel'nitskiy (Proskurov), c., Ukrainian SSR, **USSR;** on R. Bug; machin. tools, textiles, food inds.; p. (est. 1985) 217,000.

Khmer Republic. See **Kampuchea, Democratic.**

Khor Abdulla, Iraq; in Persian G. nr. Basra; deepwater oil-loading island terminal.

Khorāsan or **Khurasan,** prov., N.E. **Iran;** bounded by USSR and Afghanistan; sparsely p.; agr.; wool; turquoises; cap. Mashhad; p. (1982) 3,264,398.

Khorramshahr, spt., S.W. **Iran,** leading pt. on Persian G.; increased in importance in second world war when harbour facilities expanded; handles major part of foreign trade; main exp. dates; linked by pipeline to oilfields and by road and rail to Ahvāz and Tehran; p. (1976) 146,709.

Khotan. See **Hotan.**

Khovu-Aksy, t., Tuva ASSR, **RSFSR;** on R. Elegest, 80 km S.W. of Kyzyl; new t. 1956; cobalt deposit being developed.

Khulna, c., **Bangladesh;** in low-lying a. in W. Ganges delta; p. (1981) 646,359.

Khunjerab Pass, Kashmir, **India;** 5,000 m. pass in Karakoram Range; links Sinkiang (China) with Pakistan and Middle East; new metal route opened (1982) making shorter route to W. for China and took 20 years to build.

Khuzestan, prov., W. **Iran;** frontier Iraq; leading petroleum ctr.; lge. dams; cap. Ahvāz; p. (1982) 2,196,920.

Khyber Pass, pass in Hindu Kush mtns., between **Pakistan** and **Afghanistan;** followed by route from Peshawar to Kabul; historically most famous route into India, used by many invaders, inc. Alexander the Great.

Kiamusze. See **Jiamusi.**

Kianga-Moura, dist., Queensland, **Australia;** lge. coal-field; coking coal exp. to Japan via Gladstone.

Kiangsi. See **Jiangxi.**

Kiangsu. See **Jiangsu.**

Kicking Horse Pass, mtn. pass (1,628 m), over Rocky Mtns., B.C., **Canada;** used by Canadian Pac. rly.

Kidderminster, t., Wyre Forest, Hereford and Worcs., **Eng.;** on R. Stour 6 km above its confluence with R. Severn; carpets, engin., sugar-beet refining, textile machin., elec. vehicles, drop forgings; p. (1981) 51,261.

Kidsgrove, t., "Potteries," Staff., **Eng.;** 5 km N.W. of Stoke-on-Trent; chemicals, metal wks., rayon, silk and nylon spinning, precast concrete, ceramics; p. (1981) 24,227.

Kidwelly, Dyfed, **Wales;** mkt. t.; sm. harbour; cas.; p. (1981) 3,152.

Kiel, spt., cap. of Schleswig-Holstein, **W. Germany;** univ.; Baltic naval pt.; shipbldg. and allied inds.; elec. gds., textiles, fishing; p. (est. 1986) 243,600.

Kiel Canal (North Sea-Baltic Canal or **Kaiser-Wilhelm-Kanal) W. Germany;** connects Elbe estuary on North Sea with Baltic; 98 km long; opened 1895, reconstructed 1914; internationalised 1919 by Treaty of Versailles, but repudiated by Hitler 1936.

Kielce, c., central **Poland;** cap. of K. prov.; in Swietokrzyskie mtns.; cath., route ctr.; agr. machin., chemicals; minerals quarried in prov.; founded 12th cent.; p. (est. 1985) 201,000.

Kielder, reservoir, Northumberland, **Eng.;** one of lgst. man-made lakes in Europe.

Kiev (Kiyev), c., cap. of Ukrainian SSR, **USSR;** on R. Dnieper; leading cultural, industl. and comm. ctr.; cath., univ.; machin., textiles; in a. of rich mineral deposits; natural gas pipeline runs from Dashava; historic c., once cap. of Muscovite empire; p. (1986) 2,495,000.

Kigali, cap. of **Rwanda;** comm. ctr.; airport; new tungsten and iron foundries; p. (est. 1981) 156,650.

Kigoma, t., W. **Tanzania;** pt. on E. shore of L. Tanganyika; W. terminus of Central rly. to Dar-es-Salaam; p. (est. 1978) 50,044.

Kii, peninsula, **Japan;** highland area and inlet of same name, S. Honshu.

Kikinda, t., Vojvodina, **Yugoslavia;** agr. tr.; rly. junc.; p. (1981) 69,854.

Kilauea, crater, 1,112 m high, on S.E. slope of Mauna Loa, **Hawaii,** one of lgst. active craters in world; over 3 km in diameter.

Kildare, inland co., Leinster, **R.o.I.;** dairying, cereals; co. t. Naas; a. 1,694 km²; p. (est. 1986) 116,015.

Kildare, mkt. t., cap. of Kildare, **R.o.I.;** cath.; close by is the famous racecourse, the Curragh of Kildare; p. (1971) 3,137.

Kilimanjaro, volcanic mtn., N. **Tanzania;** hgst. peak in Africa, 5,895 m; international airpt. at 894 m on Sanya Plain; Nat. Park.

Kilindini, spt., **Kenya;** adjoins Mombasa; the finest harbour on E. cst. of Africa.

Kilkenny, inland co., Leinster, **R.o.I.;** cap. Kilkenny; pastoral farming, black marble; a. 2,062 km²; p. (est. 1986) 73,094.

Kilkenny, t., cap. of Kilkenny, **R.o.I.;** on R. Nore; local mkt., caths., cas.; p. (1981) 16,886.

Killala Bay, Mayo and Sligo, **R.o.I.,** wide bay fed by R. Hoy.

Killaloe, v., Co. Clare, **R.o.I.;** crossing point for R. Shannon; cath.; p. 500.

Killarney, t., U.D., Kerry, **R.o.I.;** local mkt.; tourist ctr. for the Ls. of K.; p. (1981) 7,693.

Killarney, Lakes of, Kerry, **R.o.I.;** Lower, Middle, and Upper, celebrated for their beauty; tourist resorts; Muckross on Middle L. site of anc. abbey.

Killiecrankie, Pass of, Scot.; on R. Garry; at S. approach to Drumochter Pass; used by main rly. Perth to Inverness; scene of battle 1691.

Killingworth, t., Tyne and Wear, **Eng.;** 6 km N.E. of Newcastle; new t.; proposed p. 20,000.

Kilmarnock, burgh, Strathclyde Reg., Scot., forms l. gov. dist., with Loudoun; on R. Irvine, 17 km N.E. of Ayr.; carpet factory closed increasing unemployment to 27 per cent; p. (est. 1986) 81,058 (dist.).

Kilo-Moto, goldfield, Zaïre; in N.E. of st., 80 km W. of L. Mobutu Seso; linked by motor road to R. Zaïre (Kisangani) and L. Mobutu Seso (Kasenyi).

Kilrenny and Anstruther, t., North East Fife, **Scot.,** at entrance to F. of Forth; fishing, hosiery, oilskin mnfs.; p. (1971) 3,037.

Kilrush, sm. spt., U.D., Co. Clare, **R.o.I.;** on R. Shannon; p. (1971) 2,671.

Kilsyth, burgh, Stirling, **Scot.;** at S. foot of Campsie Fells, 16 km W. of Falkirk; See **Cumbernauld.**

Kilwinning, burgh, Cunninghame, Scot.; 8 km E. of Ardrossan; to be incorporated in new t. Irvine; p. (1981) 16,193.

Kimberley, former goldfield dist., W. **Australia;** sparsely populated beef producing a., bauxite and iron mng.

Kimberley, t., B.C., **Canada;** on R. Kootenay; site of Sullivan mine, silver, lead, zinc; ores smelted at Trail; p. (1981) 7,375.

Kimberley, t., C. Prov., **S. Africa;** diamond-mng. dist.; asbestos, manganese, iron, cement, engin.; founded 1871; p. (1985) 149,667 (met. a.).

Kinabalu, Mount, Sabah, **Malaysia;** in Crocker mtns.; hgst. peak in Borneo, alt. 4,104 m.

Kincardine, former co., Scot.; with Deeside forms l. gov. dist. in Grampian Reg.; a. 2,546 km²; p. (est. 1986) 47,822.

Kinder Scout, mtn., N. Derbys., **Eng.;** hgst. point of the Peak dist.; alt. 637 m.

Kindia, t., **Guinea;** rich bauxite deposits worked since 1974 but output restricted by poor rail links.

Kineshma, c., **RSFSR;** on Volga, N.W. of Gorki; pt. for Ivanovo industl. a.; textiles; dates from early 15th cent.; p. (est. 1985) 104,000.

King George's Sound, W. **Australia;** nr. Albany; fine harbour and bay.

Kinghorn, t., Kircaldy, **Scot.;** on F. of Forth, 5 km S. of Kirkcaldy; p. (1981) 2,681.

Kingsbridge, t., South Hams, S. Devon, **Eng.;** at head of Kingsbridge estuary, 16 km S.W. of Dartmouth; mkt.; p. (1981) 4,142.

King's Lynn, spt., West Norfolk, **Eng.;** at mouth of Gr. Ouse; docks; fishing base; agr. machin., canning, chemical fertilisers, shoes; expanded t.; p. (1981) 33,340.

Kingston, t., Ont., **Canada;** E. end of L. Ontario; univ., military college; p. (1986) 55,050.

Kingston, spt., cap. of **Jamaica;** ch. comm. ctr. for J.; landlocked harbour; agr.-processing; univ.; p. (est. 1982) 696,300.

Kingston-upon-Hull. *See* **Hull.**

Kingston-upon-Thames, former M.B., Surrey, **Eng.;** now **The Royal Borough of Kingston-upon-Thames,** outer bor. of Greater London; inc. bors. of Malden and Coombe and Surbiton; residtl. with Richmond Park, Hampton Court, Bushey Park nearby; aircraft parts; p. (est. 1988) 134,500.

Kingstown, spt., cap. of St. Vincent, **W.I.;** cath., botanic gardens; p. (est. 1982) 33,694.

Kingswood, t., l. gov. dist., Avon, **Eng.;** nr. Bristol; elec. vehicles, motor cycles, boots, brushes, tools; school founded by John Wesley; p. (est. 1988) 89,700.

Kington, mkt. t., Hereford and Worcs., **Eng.;** 19 km W. of Leominster; p. (1981) 1,951.

Kinki, dist., S.W. Honshu, **Japan;** agr., industl. and comm. complex centred on Osaka, Kyoto, and Kōbe.

Kinlochleven, v., Lochaber, **Scot.;** at head of Loch Leven; hydroelec. power sta.; aluminium smelting; p. (1981) 1,041.

Kinnairds Head, promontory, nr. Fraserburgh, on N.E. cst., **Scot.**

Kinross, burgh, Perth and Kinross, **Scot.;** on Loch Leven, 26 km N.E. of Alloa; textiles; resort; p. (1981) 3,495.

Kinross-shire, former co., **Scot.;** now part of Perth and Kinross l. gov. dist., Tayside Reg.

Kinsale, U.D., Cork, **R.o.I.;** sm. fish pt. on K. harbour; tourism; natural gas field, gas to be piped to N. Ireland; p. (1971) 1,628.

Kinshasa (Leopoldville), c., cap. of **Zaïre;** above the cataracts on R. Zaïre; univ.; textiles, shoes; founded by Stanley 1887; p. (1984) 2,653,558.

Kinta Valley, S.E. Perak, **W. Malaysia;** tin mng., rubber plantations.

Kintyre, peninsula, Argyll and Bute, **Scot.;** terminates in Mull of Kintyre; 67 km long, 16 km wide.

Kioga (Kyoga), L., **Uganda;** on R. Nile midway between L. Victoria and L. Mobuto Seso.

Kiölen or **Kjölen,** mtn. range, **Norway** and **Sweden;** hgst. point Mt. Sulitjelma, 1,876 m.

Kirghiz SSR (Khirghizia), constituent rep., **USSR;** S.W. of Siberia; mtnous. cty., in Tienshan and Pamir systems; livestock breeding; mineral resources, food processing; cap. Frunze; a 196,581 km²; p. (1986) 4,055,000.

Kiribati (Gilbert Is), indep. st. (1979), former Brit. col., central Pac. Oc.; chain of coral Is. across equator; economy based on phosphate mng. and copra; cap. Tarawa; Ellice Is. separated 1976 and renamed Tuvalu; a. 956 km²; p. (est. 1987) 66,250.

Kirin. *See* **Jilin.**

Kirkburton, t., West Yorks., **Eng.;** S.E. of Huddersfield; woollens; p. (1981) 21,387.

Kirkby, t., Knowsley, Merseyside, **Eng.;** p. (1981) 50,898.

Kirkby in Ashfield, t., Ashfield, Notts., **Eng.;** 16 km N.W. of Nottingham; coal mng.; p. (1981) 24,467.

Kirkby Moorside, t., Ryedale, North Yorks., **Eng.;** nr. Vale of Pickering; mkt.-place; sailplanes, gliders.

Kirkcaldy, royal burgh, l. gov. dist., Fife Reg., **Scot.;** spt. on N. side of F. of Forth; submarine coal mng.; linoleum, potteries, engin.; birthplace of Adam Smith; p. (est. 1986) 148,193.

Kirkcudbright, royal burgh, Stewartry, **Scot.;** on R. Dee at influx into K. Bay, S.W. of Dumfries; agr. ctr., hosiery; cas.; abbey; p. (1981) 3,406.

Kircudbrightshire, former co., **Scot.;** now part of

Stewartry l. gov. dist., Dumfries and Galloway Reg.

Kirkenes, t., Finnmark prov., N.E. **Norway;** on S. arm of Varanger fjord, nr. Soviet border; pt. for iron-mng. dist.

Kirkham, t., Kirklees, Lancs., **Eng.;** textiles; p. (1981) 6,289.

Kirkintilloch, burgh, Strathkelvin, **Scot.;** on Forth and Clyde canal; engin.; p. (1981) 32,992.

Kirklees, met. dist., West Yorks., **Eng.;** comprises Huddersfield, Dewsbury, Batley, Spenborough, Colne Valley, Meltham, Holmfirth, Denby Dale, Kirkburton, Heckmondwike, and Mirfield; p. (est. 1988) 375,300.

Kirkstone Pass, mtn. pass, Cumbria, **Eng.;** used by main road between Ullswater and Windermere Ls.

Kirkūk, t., **Iraq;** most imp. centre of Iraqi oil industry; p. (est. 1972) 559,000.

Kirkwall, royal burgh, Mainland I., Orkneys, **Scot.;** cath.; p. (1981) 5,947.

Kirov, c., **RSFSR;** pt. on Vyatka R.; rly. junc.; engin., saw milling, chemicals, leather inds.; cath.; p. (est. 1985) 411,000.

Kirovabad, c., W. Azerbaydzhan SSR, **USSR;** on Gandzha R.; industl. ctr.; textiles, agr. implements, wine; copper and manganese mines; aluminium plant; p. (est. 1985) 261,000.

Kirovograd, c., Ukrainian SSR, **USSR;** on Ingul R.; cap. of K. oblast; agr. ctr.; engin.; p. (est. 1985) 263,000.

Kirovsk, c., **RSFSR;** on Kola peninsula; apatite and nephelite mng.; chemicals; p. (est. 1967) 50,000.

Kirriemuir, burgh, Angus, **Scot.;** on N. margin of Strathmore, 8 km W. of **Forfar;** jute-weaving; birthplace of J. M. Barrie; p. (1981) 5,308.

Kirtland, t., N.M., **USA;** atomic and space research sta.

Kiruna, t., N. **Sweden;** inside Arctic Circle, N.W. of Luleå; linked by rly. to Narvik (Norway); impt. deposits of iron ore; p. (1983) 28,638.

Kiryu, c., Honshu, **Japan;** major textile ctr.; p. (1985) 131,268.

Kisangani (Stanleyville), t., **Zaïre;** on R. Zaïre nr. Boyoma Falls; airpt.; univ.; p. (1982) 339,210.

Kiselevsk, c., S.W. Siberia, **RSFSR;** coal-mng. ctr. in Kuznetsk basin; p. (est. 1985) 126,000.

Kishinev, c., cap. of Moldavian SSR, **USSR;** on Byk R., trib. of Dniester; cath., univ.; industl., comm. ctr. in rich farming a.; tourism; p. (1986) 643,000.

Kislovodsk, c., **RSFSR;** in N. Caucasus; famous spa; p. (est. 1985) 108,000.

Kismayu, pt., **Somalia;** new deep-water harbour; airpt.; p. (est. 1987) 70,000

Kisumu, spt., cap. of Nyanza prov., **Kenya;** at head of Kavirondo G. on L. Victoria; handles bulk of cotton from Buganda and coffee from N. Tanzania for transhipment E. by rail; lge. brewery; p. (est. 1984) 215,000.

Kitakyūshū, c., N. Kyushu, **Japan;** one of Japan's lgst. muns. on merging (1963) of ts. Moji, Kokura, Tobata, Yawata, and Wakamatsu; sixth c. to enjoy special aut. rights; p. (1987) 1,045,000.

Kitami, c., Hokkaido, **Japan;** mkt.; food-processing; p. (1985) 107,280.

Kitchener, c., Ont., **Canada;** agr. machin., tyres, hardware, agr. processing; p. (1986) 150,604 (c.), 311,194 (met. a.).

Kithira. *See* **Cerigo.**

Kitimat, t., B.C., **Canada;** lge. aluminium smelter powered by hydroelectricity from diversion of R. Fraser trib. through the Rockies; p. (1981) 4,281.

Kitwe, t., **Zambia;** contiguous to mng. township of Nkana, ctr. of copperbelt; p. (1980) 314,794.

Kiukiang. *See* **Jiujiang.**

Kivu, L., on border of **Zaïre** and **Rwanda;** in highlands of Gr. Rift Valley; natural gas discoveries; 1,473 m high, 96 km long.

Kizel, c., **RSFSR;** on Kizel R., on W. slopes of Urals; coal-mng. ctr.; mng. equipment; p. (est. 1967) 55,000.

Kizil, lgst. R. of **Turkey;** rises in Kisil Dagh, flows to Black Sea via Sivas; 1,120 km long.

Kladno, t., ČSSR; 16 km N.W. of Prague; coal-mng. ctr.; iron and steel wks., machin.; p. (est. 1986) 73,000.

Klagenfurt, t., cap. of Carinthia, **Austria**; winter sports ctr.; varied mnfs.; p. (1981) 87,321 (c.), 138,558 (met. a.).

Klaipeda (Memel), c. Lithuanian SSR, **USSR**; ice-free spt. on Baltic Sea; exp. timber, textiles, chemicals, paper; p. (est. 1985) 195,000.

Klamath, mtns., N. Cal., S.W. Ore., **USA**; beautiful ranges containing Nat. Park and Indian reserve; hgst. alt. Mt. Eddy, 2,757 m.

Klamono, t., W. Irian, **Indonesia**; ctr. of oilfield; pipeline to Sorong harbour.

Klerksdorp, t., S. Transvaal, **S. Africa**; gold, diamonds; p. (1980) 238,865.

Klodzko (Glatz), t., S.W. **Poland**; formerly in Prussian Silesia; rly. junc.; on R. Neisse; comm. and mftg.; p. (1970) 26,100.

Klondike, R., Yukon, **Canada**; sm. trib. of Yukon in gold-mng. region; gold rush 1896; 160 km long.

Klyuchevskaya Sopka, one of 18 active volcanoes, **RSFSR**; in N.E. Siberia, on Kamchatka peninsula; alt. 4,748 m.

Knaresborough, t., North Yorks., **Eng.**; 5 km N.E. of Harrogate; mkt.; cas. ruins; p. (1981) 13,375.

Knighton, t., Radnor, Powys, **Wales**; on R. Teme; mkt.; p. (1981) 2,682.

Knockmealdown Mtns., Waterford and Tipperary, **R.o.I.**; highest point 796 m; tourism.

Knob Lake. See **Schefferville**.

Knossos, ruined c., cap. of anc. Crete, **Greece**; S.E. of Iráklion; ctr. of Cretan bronze age culture, 1800 B.C.; archaeological source of knowledge about the Minoans.

Knottingley, t., West Yorks., **Eng.**; on R. Aire, 19 km S.E. of Leeds; engin., glass, tar distilling, chemicals; coal mng; p. (1981) 15,953.

Knowsley, met. dist., Merseyside, **Eng.**; comprises Kirkby, Prescot and Huyton with Roby; p. (est. 1988) 158,400.

Knoxville, c., Tenn., **USA**; univ.; livestock and tobacco mkt.; textiles, marble, plastics, chemicals, aluminium; p. (1984) 174,000 (c.), 589,400 (met. a.).

Knutsford, t., N.E. Cheshire, **Eng.**; mkt.; home of Mrs. Gaskell, author of *Cranford*; p. (1981) 13,675.

Kōbe, c., spt., Honshu, **Japan**; at E. end of Inland Sea; 5th c. of Japan; developed as pt. for Osaka and Kinki plain; iron and steel, shipbldg., rubber; p. (1987) 1,433,000.

Koblenz (Coblenz), t. Rhineland-Palatinate, **W. Germany**; at confluence of Rs. Rhine and Moselle; fine buildings; wine, paper, machin., leather, ceramics; p. (est. 1986) 110,300.

Kōchi, plain and c., Shikoku, **Japan**; early vegetables, double rice cropping; p. (1985) 312,253.

Kodiak I., lgst. of Is. of Alaska, **USA**; 144 km long; forested mtns.; fur-trading, salmon-fishing, canning; earthquake 1964; p. (1980) 4,756.

Kōfu, basin and c., Honshu, **Japan**; rice, vineyards, orchards, silk, wine; p. (1985) 202,405.

Kohat, t., **Pakistan**; on trib. of Indus; military t.; cement wks.; p. (1981) 78,000.

Koh-I-Baba Mtns., **Afghanistan**; spur of the Hindu Kush; highest point 5,380 m.

Kokand, c., Uzbek SSR, **USSR**; in the Ferghana Valley; mftg. ctr., textiles, chemicals, engin.; p. (est. 1985) 166,000.

Kokiu. See **Gejiu**.

Kokkoka (Gamla Karleby), t. **Finland**; on cst. of G. of Bothnia; sulphur plant; p. (1986) 34,615.

Kokomo, c., Ind., **USA**; on Wild Cat R.; ctr. of agr. region; car components; p. (1984) 45,400, (c.), 101,000 (met. a.).

Koko-Nor. See **Qinghai Hu.**

Kokura. See **Kitakyūshū.**

Kola Peninsula, peninsula, **RSFSR**; extension of Lapland; rich mineral deposits; hydroelectric plants and missile base.

Kolar, c., Karnataka, **India**; p. (1981) 144,385 (met. a.).

Kolarovgrad (Shumen), c., cap. of K. prov., N.E. **Bulgaria**; agr. tr., leather, cloth, metal gds.; Moslem architecture; p. (1985) 100,122.

Kolding, c., at head of Kolding fjord, Jutland, **Denmark**; spt. and fishing base; lt. inds.; p. (est. 1987) 57,148.

Kolhapur, c., Maharashtra, S.W. **India**; cap. of former princely st. of K.; bauxite; anc. Buddhist ctr.; p. (1981) 351,000.

Köln. See **Cologne.**

Kolobrzeg (Kolberg), t., N.W. **Poland**; spt. on Baltic cst.; comm. and fishing harbour; resort and spa; p. (1970) 25,400.

Kolomna, c., **RSFSR**; on Moskva R., nr. confluence with Oka R.; industl. ctr.; engin., locomotives, machin., synthetic rubber; p. (est. 1985) 156,000.

Kolomyya, c., Ukrainian SSR, **USSR**; on Pruth R.; in Carpathian foothills; agr. tr., metal gds., oil refining, textiles; p. (est. 1974) 141,000.

Kolwezi, c., S. Shaba, **Zaïre**; comm. ctr. for mng. dist. (cobalt and copper); p. (est. 1976) 77,277.

Kolyma, R., N.E. Siberia, **RSFSR**; flows into Arctic Oc., via Kolyma goldfields; navigable in summer; basin largely covered with tundra, sparsely p.; 2,560 km long.

Komárno, c., **ČSSR**; on left bank, of Danube, opposite Hungarian Komárom, on right bank; R. pt., shipbldg., oil refining; p. (1984) 35,396.

Komi ASSR, aut. rep., **RSFSR**; wooded lowland, pastoral agr.; coal from Pechora basin, oil at Ukhta and Troitsko-Pechorsk; mng. now ch. economic activity; cap. Syktyvkar, lumber ctr.; a. 415,799 km²; p. (1986) 1,227,000.

Komi-Permyak, admin. div., **RSFSR**; forestry, cellulose, paper; cap. Kudymbar; a. 31,080 km²; p. (1970) 212,000.

Komló, t., **Hungary**; new mng. t.; coking coal; p. (est. 1984) 32,000.

Kompong Som (Sihanoukville) c., **Kampuchea**; deepwater pt. on G. of Thailand; linked to Phnom Penh by modern highway; textile mills, tractors, oil refining; p. (1962) 6,578.

Kommunarsk (Voroshilovsk), t., Ukrainian SSR, **USSR**; 40 km S.W. of Lugansk; ctr. of iron, steel and coking inds.; p. (est. 1985) 124,000.

Komsomolsk, c., **RSFSR**; built by volunteer youth labour, after 1932; heavy industl. development; oil refining; pipeline connects with oilfield in N. Sakhalin; p. (est. 1985) 300,000.

Konstantinovka, industl. t., Ukrainian SSR, **USSR**; in heart of Donbas industl. region, 61 km N. of Donetsk; heavy engin., iron and steel, zinc smelting; p. (est. 1985) 114,000.

Konya, c., **Turkey**; cap. of K. prov.; agr. tr. ctr.; mnfs. textiles, carpets, leather gds.; the anc. Iconium, fortress of the Hittite empire; p. (1985) 439,181.

Kooland I., W. **Australia**; rugged I. with iron-ore deposits worked since 1960 and exp. to **Japan**.

Koolyanobbing, mng. t., W. **Australia**; high-grade haematite and limonite ores mined since 1961 and t. constructed as residential and service ctr.; p. (1976) 296.

Kootenay or **Kootenai**, R., flows from B.C., **Canada**; through Montana and Idaho, **USA**, into K. L., draining it by narrow channel into Colombia R.; beautiful scenery; 720 km long.

Kopeysk, t., **RSFSR**; in Urals; lignite mng., agr. and mng. machin.; p. (est. 1985) 100,000.

Korat Plateau, E. **Thailand**; headwaters of Mekong tribs.; cattle-rearing; tr. ctr. Korat.

Korçë (Koritsa), t., S.E. **Albania**; in infertile basin at 854 m nr. Greek border; mkt.; cultural ctr.; p. (1980) 54,300.

Korcula (Curzola), I., **Yugoslavia**; sm. I. in Adriatic Sea; ch. pt. K. a. 277 km²; p. (1961) 10,223.

Korea, Democratic People's Republic of, (N. Korea); occupies N. part of Korean peninsula (N. of 38th parallel), E. **Asia**; bounded on N. by China and USSR; continental climate; cold dry winters, hot humid summers; predominantly mtnous. with many uninhabited offshire Is.; all inds. nationalised and collective agr.; rapid mechanisation, agr. employs 43 per cent working p.; development emphasis on mng. resources of coal, iron-ore and on growth of heavy inds.; most industl. resources located in N. Korea; rapid incr. in industrialisation; transport network under reconstruction after devastation of Korean war; some R. transport, international airport at cap. of Pyongyang; longest surviving hard-line Communist ruling dynasty in Asia (Kim Il-Sung); a. 121,248 km²; p. (est. 1986) 20,550,000.

Korea, Rep. of (S. Korea), occupies S. part of Korean peninsula (S. of 38th parallel); climate resembles N. Korea's, topography less rugged; massive US aid revitalised economy after Korean war and Korea now has one of world's largest foreign debts; 20 per cent work-force engaged in agr.; undergoing rapid industrialisation; textiles, electronics, shipbldg., vehicles; iron and steel ind. at Pusan; fishing is both source of subsistence and exp.; irrigation and power project (1971–81) for 4 Rs.—Hangang, Naktangang, Kum-Gang, and Yongsan-Gang; cap. Seoul; a. 98,992 km²; p. (est. 1987) 41,826,706, (24 per cent in cap.).

Korea Bay, Yellow Sea; between N. Korea and North-East China (Manchuria).

Koriyama, Honshu, **Japan**; textiles, chemicals; p. (1985) 301,672.

Korsör, spt., Sjaelland I., **Denmark**; fine harbour; glass wks.; p. (1981) 15,281.

Kortrijk (Courtrai), t., W. Flanders prov., N.W. **Belgium**; textiles; 13th cent. Notre Dame church; battle of the Spurs 1302; p. (1982) 75,731.

Koryak, admin. div., N.E. Siberia, **RSFSR**; sparse p.; a. 393,680 km²; p. (1970) 31,000.

Kos, I. See Cos, I.

Kosciusko, Mount, N.S.W., in Australian Alps; highest peak in **Australia**; 2,228 m; Nat. Park popular for skiing.

Kosi, R., India; flows from Himalayas to Ganges; site of barrage for hydroelectric power and irrigation.

Košice, c., S.E. Slovakia, ČSSR; lies in fertile basin; major industl. ctr.; heavy inds., iron and steel plant; agr.-processing; univ., Gothic cath.; mediaeval fortress t.; p. (est. 1986) 222,000.

Kosovo-Metohija, aut. region, S.W. Serbia, **Yugoslavia**; mtnous., fertile valleys; stock raising, forestry; dominant Albanian p. causing emigration of Serbs and Montenegrins; ch. t. Priština; a. 10,352 km²; p. (1981) 1,584,441.

Kostroma, c., cap. of K. oblast, **RSFSR**; at confluence of Volga and Kostroma; in flax growing a.; textiles, engin.; cath.; p. (est. 1985) 269,000.

Koszalin (Köslin), c., cap. of K. prov., N.W. **Poland**; nr. Baltic cst.; paper mills, textiles, building materials; p. (1983) 97,800.

Kota, t., Rajasthan, **India**; on R. Chambal; textiles; two nuclear reactors and heavy water plant; p. (1981) 358,241.

Kota Kinabalu (Jesselton), t., cap of Sabah, **Malaysia**; on W. cst.; main rubber st.; rly. terminal; p. (1980) 59,500.

Köthen, t., Halle, **E. Germany**; in former st. of Saxony-Anhalt; lignite mines, sugar-refining, machin., chemicals; p. (est. 1973) 35,798.

Kotka, spt., S.E. **Finland**; on G. of Finland, at mouth of Kymi R.; major exp. pt. for timber, paper, pulp; p. (1986) 58,367.

Kotor, spt., S. Montenegro, **Yugoslavia**; on Bay of K., inlet of Adriatic; cath.; tourism.

Kotri, t., **Pakistan**; on R. Indus, opposite Hyderabad; barrage N. of the t., to help irrigate Sind; p. (1961) 52,685.

Kottbus. See Cottbus.

Koulikoro, t., **Mali**, W. Africa; on upper course of R. Niger; mkt. for groundnuts, gum-arabic, sisal; linked by R. to Timbuktu and Gao; rly. terminus, 1,216 km from Dakar.

Kovrov, c., **RSFSR**; on Gorki rly. line and R. Klyazma; impt. agr. exp. ctr.; engin., textiles; p. (est. 1985) 153,000.

Kowloon, peninsula, S.E. **China**; on mainland opposite Hong Kong I.; pt. installations; major industl. and tr. ctr.; held by Britain on lease expiring 1998; p. (1986) 424,000.

Kozáni, dep., Macedonia, **Greece**; cap. K.; mainly agr.; a. 6,143 km²; p. (1981) 147,051.

Kozhikode. See Calicut.

Kra Isthmus, neck of land between B. of Bengal and G. of Thailand, linking Malay peninsula with continent of Asia.

Kragujevac, t., central Serbia, **Yugoslavia**; on both banks of Lepenica R.; cath.; arsenal and garrison; route ctr., developing agr. and industl. ctr.; p. (1981) 164,823.

Krakatoa (Rakata), volcanic I., Sunda strait, **Indonesia**; between Java and Sumatra; greater part disappeared in violent eruption 1883.

Kraków (Cracow), c., cap. of K. prov., S. **Poland**; pt. on Vistula; cultural ctr., univ. (Copernicus

matriculated here); many historic monuments; inc. c. of Nowa Huta lgst. iron and steel ctr. of rep.; machin., chemicals, farm implements; p. (est. 1985) 716,000.

Kramatorsk, c., Ukrainian SSR, **USSR**; in Donets basin; heavy engin., metallurgy; p. (est. 1985) 192,000.

Kramfors, t., **Sweden**; on G. of Bothnia; paper-mill and sulphite pulp wks.

Krasnodar Territory, region, **RSFSR**; extends from Sea of Azov and Black Sea to N.W. end of Caucasus; contains Kuban steppe and Maikop oilfields; fertile black soil; main pt. Tuapse; many health resorts.

Krasnodar, c., cap. of K. region, **RSFSR**; R. pt. Kuban R.; ctr. of industl. and agr. region; p. (est. 1986) 616,000.

Krasnoturinsk, t., **RSFSR**; in Urals, 9 km N.W. of Serov; aluminium, coal; p. (est. 1969) 61,000.

Krasnovodsk, c., Turkmen SSR, **USSR**; pt. on Caspian Sea; oil-refining ctr.; handles agr. and oil prods.; p. (est. 1986) 58,000.

Krasnoyarsk Territory, extensive region, **RSFSR**; extends across Siberia to Arctic Oc.; traversed by Yenisey and tribs.; minerals, grain from Minusinska basin and timber from coniferous forests; cap. K.; a. of labour camps in Stalin era.

Krasnoyarsk, c., cap. of K. terr., E. Siberia, **RSFSR**; on Trans-Siberian rly. at crossing of Yenesey R.; hydroelectric sta.; industl. ctr.; local copper and iron-ore deposits; ctr. for grain and timber; p. (1986) 885,000.

Krefeld, t., N. Rhine–Westphalia, **W. Germany**; chemicals, steel, machin., textiles, soap; former ctr. of silk inds.; p. (est. 1986) 216,600.

Kremenchug, c., Ukrainian SSR, **USSR**; on R. Dnieper; timber, engin., textiles; hydroelectric sta.; oil refining; p. (est. 1985) 224,000.

Krems, mkt. t., **Austria**; on R. Danube; fruit processing; founded in 10th cent. as imperial fortress; p. (1981) 23,056.

Kreuznach, Bad, t., Rhineland Palatinate, **W. Germany**; on R. Nahe; metallurgy, leather, optical and chemical inds.; viticulture, mineral baths; p. (est. 1986) 39,700.

Krishna (Kistna), R., S. **India**; rises in W. Ghats, flows E. across Deccan plateau into Bay of Bengal; lower valley and delta under intensive rice cultivation; densely populated; 1,360 km long.

Kristiansand, spt., S. **Norway**; on Skagerrak; shipbldg., ships, timber, paper, pulp, fish; electro-metallurgy; p. (est. 1987) 63,290.

Kristianstad, c., cap. of K. prov., **Sweden**; on Helge R.; its pt. Ahus is on Baltic; food-processing, clothing, machin.; founded 1614 as fortress; p. (est. 1986) 70,000.

Kristiansund, spt., W. cst. **Norway**; built on 3 Is.; trawler fleet base; exp. dried fish; heavily damaged in second world war; since rebuilt; p. (est. 1987) 63,293.

Kristinehamn, L. pt. on L. Vänern, central **Sweden**; p. (1983) 26,623.

Krivoy Rog., c., Ukrainian SSR, **USSR**; on R. Ingulets; ctr. of ch. iron-mng. a. of USSR; p. (1986) 691,000.

Krk, I., N. Adriatic Sea, **Yugoslavia**; S. of Rijeke; agr.; tourism; ch. t., K.; p. 14,500.

Krkonose. See Riesengebirge.

Kronshlot (Kronstadt), spt., on I. of Kotlin, **RSFSR**; at head of G. of Finland, nr. Leningrad; Baltic pt. and naval base; scene of naval mutiny which precipitated the Russian revolution; founded by Peter the Great 1710; p. (est. 1970) 50,000.

Kroonstad, t., O.F.S., **S. Africa**; on R. Vals; rly. junc.; agr. mkt.; engin., milling; p. (1970) 50,898.

Kropotkin, c., E. Krasnodar Terr., **RSFSR**; food-processing, engin.; p. (est. 1970) 55,000.

Kruger Nat. Park, N.E. Transvaal, **S. Africa**; game reserve; a. 20,720 km².

Krugersdorp, t. Transvaal, **S. Africa**; gold mng., uranium, manganese; p. (1980) 102,940.

Kuala Lumpur, c., fed. terr., **W. Malaysia**; cap. of Fed. of Malaysia and of Selangor st.; univ.; ctr. of rubber and tin dist.; outport Port Kelang; p. (est. 1986) 1,000,000.

Kuanchow. See Guangzhou.

Kuantan, main t. on E. cst. **W. Malaysia;** linked to Kuala Lumpur; tin mng; p. (1980) 136,625.

Kuching, c., cap. of Sarawak, **Malaysia;** pt. on Sarawak R.; gold discovered nearby at Bau; p. (1980) 74,229.

Kucovë (Qyteti Stalin), Albania; nr. Berat; oil prod. and refining; pipeline connects to Vlore.

Kufra, oasis, **Libya;** dates, barley; on caravan route.

Kuldja. See Yining.

Kumamoto, c., W. Kyushu, **Japan;** 3rd c. of K.; cas., univs.; food inds.; business ctr.; p. (1985) 555,722.

Kumasi, c., cap. of Ashanti region, **Ghana;** univ., aerodrome; road and rly. junc.; ctr. of cocoa-producing a.; bauxite nearby; jute bags; p. (1984) 260,286 (c.), 345,117 (met. a.).

Kumba Konam, t., Tamil Nadu, **India;** on Cauvery delta; silks, cotton; sacred Hindu c.; p. (1971) 113,130.

Kunene (Cunene), R., **Angola;** scheme to channel water from Angola to S.W. Africa; 1,200 km long.

Kungur, t., **RSFSR;** S.E. of Perm; oil ind. equipment; p. (est. 1970) 65,000.

Kun Lun (Kwen Lun), mtn. ranges, Xizang Zizhiou (Tibet), **China;** extend 2,900 km E. from Pamirs along N. edge of high plateau of Xizang Zizhiou; drained N. into inland drainage basin of Lop Nor; alt. frequently exceeds 5,400 m; rising to 7,729 m.

Kunming, c., cap. of Yunnan prov., S.W. **China;** univ.; comm. and cultural ctr., noted for its scenic beauty; iron and steel, milling and boring machin., textiles, chemicals; p. (1984) 1,353,300.

Kunsan, spt., S.W. **S. Korea;** on Yellow Sea, on estuary of R. Kum; p. (1966) 102,800.

Kununurra Dam, Ord R., **W. Australia;** opened 1963; to irrigate 81,000 ha of semi-arid land for cotton, rice, and cattle.

Kuopio, t., **Finland;** on L. Kalki; timber inds.; tourism; p. (1980) 78,529.

Kura, R., rises in **Turkey,** chief R. of Trans-caucasia, **USSR;** flows into Caspian Sea; agr., fishing, hydroelec. power; 1,504 km long.

Kurdistan (Country of the Kurds), includes parts of E. Turkey, Soviet Armenia, N.E. Iraq, and N.W. Iran; attempts at autonomy.

Kure, c., S.W. Honshu, **Japan;** spt. and naval base; engin.; shipbldg.; p. (1985) 226,489.

Kurgan, c., **RSFSR;** on Tobol R.; impt. junc. on Trans-Siberian rly.; tr. in cattle and foodstuffs; agr. engin.; p. (est. 1985) 343,000.

Kuria Muria Is., 5 barren Is. in Arabian Sea off cst. of Oman; admin. by U.K. until 1967.

Kurile Is., chain of volcanic Is., N. Pac., **RSFSR;** extend from Kamchatka to Hokkaido; mainly mtnous.; sulphur, hunting, fishing; Japan claims sovereignty over 4 Is. (Kunashiri, Etor-ofu, Shikotan, Habomai); a. 15,592 km²; p. 18,000.

Kurisches Haff (Kurštu Martos), shallow lagoon, Baltic cst. of Lithuanian SSR, **USSR;** receives water of R. Niemen; narrow entrance to Baltic Sea at N. end of lagoon commanded by pt. of Klaipeda (Memel); length 92 km, maxi-mum width 32 km.

Kurische Nehrung, sandspit, Baltic Sea; almost cuts off Kurisches Haff from Baltic Sea; 88 km long.

Kurnool, t., Andhra Pradesh, **India;** agr. comm. ctr.; p. (1981) 206,700.

Kuroshio (Japan Current), ocean current, flows N.E. along Pac. cst. of Kyushu, Shikoku and S. Honshu, relatively warm water, exerts slight warming influence on this cst. in winter.

Kursk, c., cap. of K. oblast, **RSFSR;** on Tuskor R.; rly. junc.; in fertile fruit-growing a.; engin., textiles, synthetic rubber; p. (est. 1985) 420,000.

Kurume, t., W. Kyushu, **Japan;** on Chikugo plain; comm. ctr.; p. (1985) 222,848.

Kushiro, spt., S.E. Hokkaido, **Japan;** exp. lumber; local coal; fishing; p. (1985) 214,545.

Kustanay, c., Kazakh SSR, **USSR;** on Tobol R.; agr.-processing, lt. inds.; p. (est. 1985) 199,000.

Kütahya, t., cap. of K. prov., central **Turkey;** agr. mkt. ctr.; ceramics; chemical complex; p. (1985) 118,773.

Kutaisi, c., Georgian SSR, **USSR;** on R. Rion (hydroelectric plant); chemicals, textiles, mng. equipment; big coal deposits being mined; mkt. gardening a.; p. (est. 1985) 214,000.

Kut-al-Amara, t., cap. of K. prov., **Iraq;** on R. Tigris; agr. tr. ctr.; p. (1970) 58,647.

Kutch, peninsula, Gujarat st., N.W. **India;** bounded on N. by Pakistan; largely barren except for fertile strip along Arabian Sea; p. (1961) 696,440.

Kutch, Rann of, desert region covered with salt, but flooded during monsoons; nine-tenths belongs to India; one-tenth to Pakistan.

Kutchan, t., S.W. Hokkaido, **Japan;** ctr. of lge. iron-ore field; ore smelted at Muroran.

Kutno, t. Lodz, **Poland;** route ctr.; sm. textile ind.; p. (1970) 30,300.

Kuwait, indep. Arab st., **S.W. Asia;** under Brit. protection until 1961; lies at head of Persian G.; inc. mainland and 9 sm Is.; mainly desert with a few oases; imports most of food re-quirements; possesses 13 per cent of the proved world reserves of oil; heavily dependent on oil and natural gas exports; industl. complex of petrochemical inds. at Shuaiba projected; 48 km S. of Kuwait (cap.) which contains nearly half of p.; freshwater scarce; one of hgst. incomes per capita in world, but most of p. remains poor; a. 24,235 km²; p. (est. 1986) 1,770,000.

Kuwait, c., cap. of **Kuwait;** pt. with natural harbour on Persian G.; univ.; p. (1980) 60,525.

Kuybyshev, c., cap. of K. oblast, **RSFSR;** on R. Volga; major R. pt., rly. junc. on Moscow-Siberian line, airport; hydroelectric power sta.; comm. ctr. with varied mnfs., inc. cars, aircraft, textiles, synthetic rubber; oil refining; grain and livestock exp.; p. (est. 1980) 1,226,000.

Kuzbas (Kuznetsk Basin), industl. region, Siberia, **USSR;** lies S. of Trans-Siberian rly. in upper valleys of Rs. Ob and Tom; second lgst. coal output in USSR, iron and steel mftg., heavy metallurgical ind.; ch. ts., Novo-sibirsk, Novokuznetsk, Kemerovo, Leninsk-Kuznetsky.

Kwangsi Chuang. See Guang Zhuang.

Kwantung. See Guangdong.

Kwanto Plain, S.E. Honshu, **Japan;** lgst. a. of continuous lowland in Japan, extends 128 km inland from Tokyo; plain devoted to inten-sive rice cultivation; higher, drier terraces under mulberry, vegetables, tea, tobacco; very dense rural p.; lge. number of urban ctrs., inc. Tokyo, Yokohama; a. 13,000 km²; p. (1960) 27,000,000.

Kwazulu, Bantu Terr. Authority (1970), E. S. **Africa;** runs 480 km from Moçambique to Cape Prov. but in 29 separate as. interspersed by white as.; cap. Nongoma in N. highland; p. (1980) 3,442,140.

Kweichow. See Guizhou.

Kweilin. See Guilin.

Kweiyang. See Guiyang.

Kwidzyn (Marienwerder), c., Gdansk, N. **Poland** (since 1945); cath., cas.; industl. ctr. nr. Vistula R.; p. (1970) 23,100.

Kwinana, new t. (1952), pt., W. **Australia;** oil refinery and steel plant, alumina reduction, integrated steelwks.; p. (1981) 12,355.

Kyle and Carrick, l. gov. dist., Strathclyde Reg., **Scot.;** lge. dist. inc. t. of Ayr; p. (est. 1986) 113,081.

Kyle of Lochalsh, v., Skye and Lochalsh, **Scot.;** at entrance to Loch Alsh, facing S. end of I. of Skye; terminus of rly. across Highlands from Dingwall; ch. pt. for steamers to N.W. cst.; I. of Skye, Outer Hebrides; p. (1981) 803.

Kymi, R., **Finland;** rises in L. Päijänne, flows to G. of Finland; many Ls., timber transport, hydroelec. power; 144 km long.

Kyoto, c., Honshu, **Japan;** cultural and religious ctr., without lge.-scale inds.; former cap. 794-1868; univ.; shrines, old Imperial palace; p. (1987) 1,479,000.

Kyushu, most S. of 4 major Is. of **Japan;** mtnous.; coal mng. in Chikugo basin; heavy inds.;

agr. on coastal lowlands; joined to Honshu by bridge and rly.; a. 42,007 km²; p. (1960) 12,903,515.

Kyustendil, t., **Bulgaria**; in foothills of Osogovo mtns.; lge. lead and zinc deposits; combined plant for mng. and ore dressing projected.

Kzyl Orda, R. and t., Kazakh SSR, **USSR**; lge. dam to irrigate rice plantations; p. of t. (est. 1985) 183,000.

L

Laaland I. *See* **Lolland I.**

Labrador, mainland a. of prov. Newfoundland, **Canada**; separated from I. by Strait of Belle I.; barren, severe climate; impt. cod fisheries; rich iron ore reserves nr. Quebec bdy.; Churchill R. power project; cap. Battle Harbour; a. 292,219 km²; p. (1981) 31,320.

Labrador City, t., Newfoundland, **Canada**; new t. built 1965, nr. Wabush L. to house workers of iron-ore mines; p. (1981) 11,540.

Labuan, I., Sabah, **Malaysia**; rubber, rice, coconuts; cap. Victoria; a. 81 km²; p. (est. 1970) 7,250.

Laccadive, coral Is., Arabian Sea; about 320 km off Malabar cst. joined with Minicoy and Amindivi Is. to form union terr., **India**; renamed Lakshadweep Is. (1974); coir, coconuts; cap. Kavaratti; a. 28 km²; p. of terr. (1971) 31,798.

Lachine, c., Quebec, **Canada**; on Montreal I. where St. Lawrence R. leaves St. Louis L.; iron and steel, wire, rope; Lachine canal by-passes rapids; summer resort; p. (1981) 37,521.

Lachlan, R. N.S.W., **Australia**; main trib. of R. Murrumbidgee; irrigation; 1,472 km long.

La Coruña, spt., cap. of La Coruña prov., N.W. **Spain**; fishing; p. (1987) 242,437.

Ladakh, dist., of the Upper Indus, **India**, bordering Tibet; ch. t. Leh; isolated and remote; alt. 3,600 m; p. (1981) 68,380.

Ladoga (**Ladozhskoye**), L., Leningrad, **USSR**; a. 18,389 km²; (lgst. in Europe); drained to G. of Finland by R. Neva; fishing; link in new deepwater canal between White and Baltic Seas.

Ladybank, burgh, North East Fife, **Scot.**; 8 km S.W. of Cupar; p. (1981) 1,353.

Ladysmith, t. Natal, **S. Africa**; cotton mills; besieged by Boers 1899–1900; p. (est. 1970) 28,500.

Lae, t., **Papua New Guinea**; pt. on Huon Gulf serving goldmng. dist.; outlet for Morobe; plywood; air ctr.; p. (1980) 61,617.

Lagan (**Laggan**), R., **N. Ireland**; flows into Belfast Lough; canal link to Lough Neagh; 56 km long.

Lagôa dos Patos, L., **Brazil**; drained by Rio Grande do Sul; 224 km long.

Lagôa Mirim, L., on bdy. between **Brazil** and **Uruguay**; drains N.; 176 km long.

Lagos, spt., cap. of **Nigeria**; unhealthy and congested; cap. to be moved to Abuja by 1990; on G. of Guinea; gd. natural harbour; exp. cocoa, groundnuts, palm oil and kernels, timber, hides and skins, cotton, rubber, crude oil; mnfs. textiles, confectionery, chemicals, car assembly; univ.; p. (est. 1983) 1,097,000.

La Grande Chartreuse, limestone region between Chambéry and Grenoble, **France**; famous monastery and liqueur.

La Grande Rivière, N. Quebec, **Canada**; major hydroelec. scheme; mineral and timber inds.

Laguna, dist., Durango st., **Mexico**; former L. bed irrigated by Rs. Nazas and Aguanaval; ch. cotton-growing region in Mexico; ch. t., Torréon; a. 259,000 km².

Lahore, ch. c., **Pakistan**; univ., cath., temples, mosques; textiles, pottery, carpets, industl. gases; atomic research ctr.; second c. of Pakistan; p. (1981) 2,922,000.

Lahti, t., S. **Finland**; wood, plywood, brewing, textiles; p. (1986) 94,205.

Lake Champlain, N.Y., **USA**; forms lowland a. for main routes between Montreal and N.Y.

Lake Charles, t., La., **USA**; spt. at mouth of Calcasieu R.; connected to G. of Mexico by channel; exp. oil, chemicals, rice, cotton; p. (1984) 75,100 (c.), 175,000 (met. a.).

Lake District, almost circular mtnous. a., Cumbria,

Eng.; 17 major and many smaller Ls. formed by glacial erosion and deposition; increasing tourist pressure on Nat. Park as motorways improve accessibility.

Lakeland, c., Fla., **USA**; citrus fruit ctr.; holiday resort; p. (1984) 54,400 (c.), 354,600 (met. a. inc. Winter Haven).

Lakeland, South, l. gov. dist., Cumbria, **Eng.**; lge. a. surrounding Morecambe Bay and inc. Ulverston, Grange, Kendal and Sedbergh; p. (est. 1988) 100,200.

Lake of the Woods, L., Ont., S.E. of Winnipeg, on bdy. between **Canada** and **USA**; in pine forest; tourism.

Lakeview, t., Ont., **Canada**; thermal elec. power plant projected; to be lgst. in world.

Lakshadweep, union terr., **India**; made up of Laccadive, Minicoy and Aminidivi Is; a. 32 km.²; p. (1981) 40,249.

La Linea, t., **Spain**; on isthmus connecting Gibraltar with mainland; p. (1981) 55,590.

La Mancha, plain, Cuidad-Real prov., S. **Spain**; in shallow depression on central plateau, alt. between 450–900 m, drained by headstreams of R. Guadiana; semi-arid climate with hot summers, cold winters; widespread salt deposits; Merino sheep, esparto grass; Spain's lgst. grape-growing region.

Lambaréné, t., **Gabon**; site of Schweitzer's hospital on Ogooué R.; p. (1978) 26,257

Lambayeque, prov., N.W. **Peru**; ctr. of irrigated dists.; sugar, cotton, tobacco; cap. Chiclayo, ch. pt. Pimental; a. 11,948 km²; p. (1982) 674,442.

Lambeth, inner bor., London, **Eng.**; L. palace, residence of Archbishop of Canterbury; p. (est. 1988) 239,500.

Lammermuir Hills, E. Lothian, **Scot.**; highest peak Lammer Law, 529 m.

Lampang, t., **Thailand**; modern sugar plant; p. (1980) 42,301.

Lampedusa, lgst. of Pelagi Is., between Malta and Tunisian cst., belonging to **Italy**; barren limestone; a. 21 km²; p. (1981) 4,792.

Lampeter, t., Ceredigion, Dyfed, S. **Wales**; on R. Teifi; mkt.; univ. college of Wales; p. (1981) 1,972.

Lamu, t., **Kenya**; impt. historical and tourist ctr. on Indian Ocean.

Lanark, former co., central **Scot.**; now forms several sm. l. gov. dists. known as Clydesdale within Strathclyde Reg.

Lanark, royal burgh, Clydesdale, **Scot.**; in Clyde valley 35 km S.E. of Glasgow; hosiery; ctr. of mkt. gardening a.; nr. New Lanark model t. built by Robert Owen; p. (1981) 9,778.

Lancashire, non-met. co., N.W. **Eng.**; major growth of p. in 19th cent. based on prod. of cotton and coal; main industl. ctrs. now outside co. in Merseyside and Gtr. Manchester met. cos.; Pennines in E.; extensive lowland in W.; admin. ctr. Preston, co. t. Lancaster; a. 2,738 km²; p. (est. 1988) 1,381,900.

Lancaster, c., co. t., l. gov. dist., Lancs., **Eng.**; 10 km up R. Lune; mediaeval cas., univ.; linoleum, vinyl, clothing; p. (est. 1988) 131,100.

Lancaster, c., Penns., **USA**; agr. ctr., tobacco mkt.; stockyards; mnfs. linoleum, watches; birthplace of Robert Fulton; p. (1984) 56,300 (c.), 381,300 (met. a.).

Lanchow. *See* **Lanzhou.**

Lancing, v., West Sussex, **Eng.**; on S. cst., 3 km E. of Worthing; seaside resort; lt. inds.; public school.

Landau, t., Rhineland-Palatinate, **W. Germany**; on R. Queich; cigar mftg., wine, iron ind.; here the carriages called Landaus were first made; p. (est. 1986) 35,300.

Landes, dep., S.W. **France**; on Atl. cst.; agr., vineyards, resin; cap. Mont-de-Marsan; a. 9,334 km²; p. (1982) 297,100.

Landes, Les, region, Aquitaine, S.W. **France**; fringes Bay of Biscay from Pointe de Grave to Biarritz; coastal sand dunes and lagoons backed by low, flat plain of alternate sandy tracts and marsh; reclaimed by drainage and afforestation, now over half a. covered by pine forests; turpentine, timber; oilfield.

Land's End, extreme S.W. point of **Eng.** on Cornish cst.

Landshut, t., Bavaria, **W. Germany**; on R. Isar; cas.; elec. inds., glass, metallurgy, textiles, coal; rly. junc.; p. (est. 1986) 57,100.

Landskrona, spt., **Sweden**; on the Sound; shipping and tr. ctr.; agr.-processing; on nearby I. of Ven; Tycho Brahe built his observatory; p. (1983) 35,656.

Langbaurgh, l. gov. dist. Cleveland, **Eng.**; a. of N. York Moors inc. Loftus, Skelton, Gainsborough and Saltburn; p. (est. 1988) 144,800.

Langdale Pikes, L. Dist., **Eng.**; 2 peaks Harrison Stickle (733 m), Pike o'-Stickel (709 m); popular rambling and climbing a.; 5 km W. of Grasmere.

Langebergen, mtns., Cape Prov., **S. Africa;** 240 km E. to W. parallel to S. cst. of Africa; form barrier to access from cst. plain to Little Karroo, broken across by valley of R. Gouritz; max. alt. exceeds 1,370 m.

Langreo, t., N. **Spain;** in Asturias, 19 km S.E. of Oviedo; coal and iron mines; p. (1981) 55,758.

Langres, t., Haute-Marne, **France;** cath., mediaeval fortifications; famous for its cutlery; birthplace of Diderot; p. (1982) 11,359.

Languedoc, region, former prov., S. **France;** inc. deps. Gard, Aude, Hérault, Lozère, Ardèche, Tarn, and parts of Haute Garonne, Tarn-et-Garonne, and Haute Loire; major govt. sponsored investment in tourist inds., along Mediterranean cst.; mono-cultural vine prod., irrigation scheme to aid agr. diversification.

Lannemezan, region, Aquitaine, S.W. **France;** belt 80 km wide stretches over 160 km along foot of Pyrenees W. of Toulouse; consists of immense deltas of glacial gravel deeply cut by tribs. of Rs. Garonne and Adour; valleys liable to severe floods in summer, intervening plateau dry, bare; scantily populated.

Lansing, c., cap of Mich., **USA;** on Grand R. at confluence with Cedar R.; automobiles, chemicals; p. (1984) 128,000 (c.), 416,200 (met. a.).

Lanzarote, I., **Canary Is.;** volcanic mtns.; developing tourist ind.; cochineal; cap. Arrecife; p. (1970) 41,912.

Lanzhou (Lanchou), c., cap. of Gansu prov., **China;** on Huang He; tr. ctr.; oil refining, gaseous diffusion plant, woollen mills, coal mng. nearby; p. (1984) 1,455,100.

Laoag, t., N. Luzon I., **Philippines;** agr.-processing; p. (1970) 69,300.

Laoighis or **Leix Co.,** Leinster, **R.o.I.;** mtns. and bog; inland pasture and tillage; cap. Port Laoighise (Maryborough); a. 1,720 km²; p. (1981) 13,837.

Laon, t., cap. of Aisne dep., **France;** on rocky height above plain; historic fortress t.; cath.; p. (1982) 29,074.

Laois. *See* Laoighis.

Laos, People's Dem. Rep. of, S.E. **Asia;** kingdom until 1975; bordered by China, Vietnam, Kampuchea, Thailand and Burma; formerly part of Fr. Indo-China; under-developed and isolated cty.; considerable mineral resources but only tin exploited; disrupted by civil war, drought, crop pests; economic ctr. is Mekong valley, scene of recent Mekong R. Development Project; elsewhere thickly forested mtns.; 70 per cent of p. engaged in subsistence agr. for dry rice; now produces rice surplus; main exp., hardwoods; no rlys.; royal cap. Luang Prabang, admin. cap. Vientiane; a. 231,399 km²; p. (est. 1986) 3,670,000.

La Paz, dep., **Bolivia;** traversed by Andes; de facto cap. La Paz, legal cap. Sucre; cocoa, coffee, rubber, tin-mng. at Catari; a. 105,377 km²; p. (est. 1982) 1,913,184.

La Paz, c., **Bolivia;** seat of govt.; comm. ctr.; copper, alpaca wool, cinchona, textiles; highest cap. c. in world; p. (est. 1982) 881,404.

Lapland, terr., N. **Europe,** in Norway, Sweden, Finland, and USSR, extending from Norwegian cst. to White Sea; mainly mtn. and moorland, with many lakes; Lapps are nomadic pastoralists with reindeer herds; iron-ore at Kiruna and Gällivare; a. 336,700 km²; p. of Swedish Co. of L. (1983) 118,819.

La Plata, c., spt., **Argentina;** cap. of Buenos Aires prov., univ.; mftg. ctr.; iron and steel, oil refining, refrigerated meat prods.; p. (1980) 459,000 (c.), 565,000 (met. a.).

La Plata, Rio de. *See* Plata, Rio de la.

Laptev Sea (Nordenskjöld Sea), inlet of Arctic Oc.; between Severnaya Zemlya and New Siberian Is., **RSFSR.**

Larache, spt., **Morocco;** on Atl. cst. 64 km S. of Tangier; exp. cork, wool; p. (1982) 63,893.

Laramie, t., W., **USA;** univ.; industl. ctr. for cattle and timber region; rly. engin.; p. (1980) 24,410.

Laredo, t., Texas, **USA;** frontier t. on Rio Grande; smuggling; ctr. of Chicanos; p. (1984) 108,700 (t.), 118,200 (met. a.).

Largo, v., North East Fife, **Scot.;** fishing, holiday resort; birthplace of Alexander Selkirk.

Largs, burgh, Cunninghame, **Scot.;** on F. of Clyde opposite Is. of Bute and Cumbrae; seaside resort, fishing; battle 1263 defeating last attempt by Norsemen to conquer Scot.; p. (1981) 9,763.

Larissa, dep., Thessaly, **Greece;** inc. infertile basin of R. Piniós; cap. Larissa; ch. pt. Volos; p. (1981) 102,426.

Larnaca, spt., **Cyprus;** the anc. Citium; grain, cotton, fruit; oil refinery; growing tourist ctr.; p. (est. 1986) 53,000.

Larne, spt., l. gov. dist., N. **Ireland;** at entrance to Larne Lough; cross channel service to Stranraer; tourism; p. (1981) 29,351 (dist.), 18,224 (t.).

La Rochelle, spt., cap. of Charente-Maritime dep., **France;** on Atl. cst.; its deepwater pt. is La Pallice; cath.; fishing pt.; chemicals, food-processing; tourism; p. (1982) 78,231.

Larut Hills, W. Malaysia; rise to over 1,500 m; lge. tin-field.

Larvik, spt., **Norway;** S.W. of Oslo; seaside resort; engin., pulp, stone; former whaling pt.; p. (est. 1970) 10,376.

Las Cruces, t., N.M., **USA;** on Rio Grande R.; irrigated agr.; univ.; p. (1984) 50,300 (t.), 112,200 (met. a.).

La Serena, c., cap. of Coquimbo prov., **Chile;** 14 km inland from its pt. Coquimbo; cath.; resort; p. (1982) 87,456.

Lashio, t., **Burma;** on R. Salween; rly. terminus; Burma road links with China; ctr. of silver-lead mines; p. 4,638.

Lashkar, c., Madhya Pradesh, central **India;** modern industl. t., adjoining Gwalior.

La Skhirra, pt. on G. of Gabès, **Tunisia;** oil; pipeline to Edjelé.

Las Palmas, prov., Canary Is., **Spain;** inc. Gran Canaria, Lanzarote, Fuerteventura and smaller Is.; intensive irrigated agr. of bananas, tomatoes, potatoes; tourism encouraged by climate and volcanic landscape; a. 4,053 km²; p. (1987) 761,793.

Las Palmas, c., N.E. Gran Canaria, ch. pt. of **Canary Is.;** exp. agr. prods.; cath.; p. (1987) 358,272.

La Spezia, spt., Liguria, N.W. **Italy;** on Bay of Spezia; ch. Italian naval sta., arsenal and docks; maritime inds., elec. machin., olive oil, oil refining; p. (1984) 112,606.

Lassen Peak, Nat. Park, Cascade Range, Cal.; only active volcano in **USA.**

Lasswade. *See* Bonnyrigg and Lasswade.

Las Vegas, c., Nevada, **USA;** noted for its gambling casinos; ranching and mng. a.; p. (1984) 183,200 (c.), 536,500 (met. a.).

Latacunga, t., **Ecuador;** at c. 2,740 m in Andean basin, not far from Cotopaxi volcano; anc. Inca t.; ctr.; p. (1982) 28,764.

Latakia, spt., **Syria;** exp. tobacco, olive oil, sponges; p. (1970) 126,000.

Latina (Littoria), c., cap. of Latina prov., in Latium central **Italy;** in ctr. of reclaimed a. of Pontine marshes; mkt. ctr., on which planned road system converges; built since 1932; nuclear power sta. nearby; p. (1981) 93,738.

Latin America, the Spanish-, Portuguese- and Fr.-speaking countries of N. America, S. America, Central America, and the W.I., inc. the reps. of Argentina, Bolivia, Brazil, Chile, Colombia, Costa Rica, Cuba, Dominican Republic, Ecuador, Salvador, Guatemala, Haiti, Honduras, Mexico, Nicaragua, Panama, Paraguay, Peru, Uruguay, and Venezuela; sometimes Puerto Rico, Fr. W.I., and other Is. of the W.I. are included, and occasionally Belize, Guyana, Fr. Guiana, and Surinam; p. (est. 1984) 397,138,000.

Latium (Lazio), region, central **Italy;** between Apennines and Tyrrhenian Sea, comprising provs. of Rome, Frosinone, Latina, Rieti, Viterbo; a. 17,182 km²; p. (est. 1986) 5·1 m.

Latrobe Valley, one of most impt. economic a. in Victoria, **Australia;** major brown coal and electric power production; secondary inds. attracted by cheap power.

Latvia, constituent rep., **USSR;** declared indep., 1990; on dairying, stock-raising, forestry; cap. Riga; spts. Ventspils, Liepaya; a. 66,278 km²; p. (1986) 2,621,000.

Launceston, t., Tasmania, **Australia;** at head of Tamar estuary, inc. Bell Bay where many heavy inds.; p. (1981) 64,555.

Launceston, t., North Cornwall, **Eng.;** agr. mkt.; quarrying, lt. engin.; p. (1981) 6,199.

Laurencekirk, burgh, Kincardine and Deeside, **Scot.**; agr. ctr. in the Howe of Mearns; p. (1981) 1,296.

Laurion or **Laurium**, pt. on Attic peninsula, **Greece**; lead, manganese, zinc, and silver mines; silver mined 5th cent. B.C.

Lausanne, c., cap. of Vaud can., **Switzerland**; nr. L. Geneva; cath., univ.; impt. rly. junc.; seat of Swiss high courts of justice; tourism; p. (est. 1985) 125,000 (c.), 260,000 (met. a.).

Lauterbrunnen, Alpine valley, Bern can., **Switzerland**; famous for its waterfalls, the highest of which is Staubbach 299 m; tourist and winter sports ctr.

Laval, t., cap. of Mayenne dep., **France**; Mayenne R. divides old and modern parts; cotton, paper, machin., marble; cas., church; p. (1982) 53,766.

Lavenham, t., Suffolk, **Eng.**; a ctr. of the wool tr. in 15th cent., still preserves its mediaeval character.

Lavera, pt., nr. Marseilles, S.E. **France** commencement of 752 km oil pipeline to Karlsruhe, W. Germany; oil refining.

Lawrence, t., Mass., **USA**; on Merrimac R., N.W. of Boston; textiles, paper, footwear, engin.; p. (1980) 282,000 (met. a. inc. Haverhill).

Lawton, t., Okla., **USA**; mnfs. cottonseed oil; p. (1984) 85,600 (t.), 119,400 (met. a.).

Laxey, v., I. of Man, **Eng.**; flour milling, woollen mills, meerschaum pipes.

Lazio. *See* **Latium.**

Lea or **Lee**, R., **Eng.**; rises in Chiltern Hills nr. Luton, flows S. and E. into R. Thames through industl. zone of N.E. London; valley to become a regional park; mkt. gardening a.; 74 km long.

Leamington (Royal Leamington Spa), t., Warwicks., **Eng.**; on R. Leam, trib. of Avon, 3 km N.E. of Warwick; fashionable spa; engin. inds.; p. (1981) 42,953.

Leatherhead, t., Mole Valley, Surrey, **Eng.**; on R. Mole to N. of gap through N. Downs; residtl.; p. (1981) 40,473.

Lebanon, mtn. range, **Lebanon**, extending to cst. of Syria; snow-capped most of year; highest peak Timarum, 3,214 m; famous in anc. times for cedar forests.

Lebanon, rep., S.W. **Asia**; at E. end of Mediterranean Sea; bordered by Syria to N. and Israel to S.; narrow coastal strip backed by mtnous. interior; free mkt. a., with economy based on transit tr.; most of p. involved in tourism, finance and commerce; oil refining based on imports; cap. Beirut; strife-torn by civil war and Israeli invasions; a. 8,806 km²; p. (est. 1987) 2,668,000.

Le Bourget, t., N.E. of Paris, **France**; airpt.; p. (1982) 11,021.

Lebórk (Lauenburg), t. Gdansk, **Poland** (since 1945); in agr. dist.; timber and food inds.; p. (1970) 25,000.

Lebowa Territory, Bantu Terr., **S. Africa**; home of N. Sotho and Ndebele peoples; self-gov. Oct. 1972; cap. Seshego; p. (1980) 1,746,500.

Lecce, c., Apulia, S. **Italy**; agr. and route ctr. with ceramic and glass inds.; anc. Greek col.; baroque churches and palaces; p. (1981) 91,289.

Lecco, t., **Italy**; in Lombardy, on L. Como; iron and copper wks., agr.-processing, cheese; one of first ts. in Europe to be run by elec.; p. (est. 1970) 53,600.

Lech, R., rises in Austria and flows past Augsburg in Bavaria, **W. Germany**, to join Danube; 283 km long.

Le Creusot, t., Saône-et-Loire, **France**; ctr. of one of sm. coalfields bordering the Massif Central; steel, engin.; p. (1982) 32,309.

Ledbury, t., Hereford and Worcs., **Eng.**; at W. foot of Malvern hills; fruit preserving, tanning; 17th cent. mkt. hall; birthplace of John Masefield.

Leeds, c., met. dist., West Yorks., **Eng.**; on R. Aire; at E. margin of Pennines; univ.; lge. clothing ind., varied engin. mnfs., paper and printing; with Bradford forms conurb. of W. Yorks., p. (est. 1986) 709,600.

Leek, mkt. t., Moorland, Staffs., **Eng.**; 18 km N.E. of Stoke-on-Trent; silk mnfs., butter; expanded t.; p. (1981) 19,739.

Lee-on-Solent, t., Hants., **Eng.**; on Southampton Water.

Lees, t., Gtr. Manchester, **Eng.**; textiles; p. (1981) 4,838.

Leeuwarden, c., cap. of Friesland prov., **Neth.**; noted cattle mkt.; rly. junc.; p. (est. 1987) 85,000.

Leeuwin, C., S.W. point of **Australia**; notorious storms; Nat. Park (1971).

Leeward Is., W.I., northern gr. of Lesser Antilles archipelago; so-called because winds in this a. generally blow from E.; inc. Virgin Is. of US; Fr. I. of Guadaloupe, Dutch Is. of St. Eustatius and Saba, and Brit. Leeward Is. (Montserrat, Virgin Is., and former cols. of Antigua, St. Kitt-Nevis, Anguilla).

Legaspi, t., cap. of Albay prov., **Philippines**; spt. in S.E. Luzon; linked by rly. with Manila; p. (est. 1984) 108,864.

Leghorn. *See* **Livorno.**

Legionowa, t., **Poland**; new t. (1951) on outskirts of Warsaw; nr. artificial L. in R. Bug valley; p. (1970) 20,800.

Legnano, t., Lombardy, **Italy**; N.W. of Milan; textiles, machin.; p. (1981) 49,308.

Legnica (Liegnitz), c., Wroclaw, S.W. **Poland** (since 1945); on Katzbach R., in rich agr. region; p. (1983) 96,500.

Leh, cap. of Ladakh, Kashmir, **India**; isolated t. in Himalayas on caravan route to Tibet; p. (1981) 8,000.

Le Havre, spt., Seine-Maritime dep., N. **France**; at mouth of Seine on English Channel; shipbldg., engin., chemicals, ropes, cottons, oil refining; pipeline to Grandpuits; p. (1982) 200,411.

Leicester, c., co. t., l. gov. dist., Leics., **Eng.**; on R. Soar; univ.; footwear, hosiery, knitwear, textile machin.; Roman remains; p. (est. 1990) 275,200.

Leicestershire, non-met. co., **Eng.**; mainly rural, low-lying Midland co., but inc. Charnwood Forest; mixed agr., sm. coalfield; hosiery and footwear inds.; now inc. Rutland; ch. t. Leicester; a. 2,554 km²; p. (est. 1988) 885,500.

Leicestershire, North West, l. gov. dist., Leics., **Eng.**; inc. Ashby de la Zouch, Ashby Woulds, Coalville and Castle Donington; p. (est. 1990) 80,300.

Leiden or **Leyden**, c., S. Holland prov., **Neth.**; on Oude Rijn; famous univ.; printing, textiles, medical equipment; gr. weaving ctr. in Middle Ages; revolt against Spanish rule 1573–4; birthplace of Rembrandt; p. (est. 1987) 107,000.

Leigh, t., Gtr. Manchester, **Eng.**; 8 km S.E. of Wigan; mkt.; coal mng.; textiles; p. (1981) 45,341.

Leigh-on-Sea, t., Essex, **Eng.**; on N. cst. of Thames estuary, 3 km W. of Southend; holiday resort, fishing.

Leighton Buzzard, t., South Beds., **Eng.**; at N.E. end of Vale of Aylesbury; tiles, engin., sand quarrying; p. (1981) 29,772 (inc. Linslade).

Leinster, S.E. prov., **R.o.I.**; bulk of recent Irish p. increase; a. 19,637 km²; p. (1981) 1,294,039.

Leipzig, c., **E. Germany**; comm., industl., and cultural ctr. at junc. of Rs. Pleisse, Elster, and Parthe; famous univ.; inds. inc. publishing, steel, textiles, chemicals, machin., cars; tr. fairs; Bach was organist at Thomaskirche; birthplace of Leibnitz and Wagner; p. (est. 1986) 552,133.

Leiston-cum-Sizewell, t., Suffolk Coastal, Suffolk, **Eng.**; on cst. 6 km E. of Saxmundham; agr. implements; nuclear power sta.; p. (1981) 5,133.

Leith, t., Edinburgh City, **Scot.**; shipbldg., timber, whisky; outport for Edinburgh.

Leith Hill, Surrey, **Eng.**; nr. Dorking; alt. 294 m; Lower Greensand crest.

Leitmeritz. *See* **Litoměřice.**

Leitrim, co., Connacht, **R.o.I.**; agr.; cap. Carrick-on-Shannon; a. 1,588 km²; p. (1981) 1,677.

Leix. *See* **Laoighis.**

Leixões, the modern harbour of Oporto, **Portugal**; oil refinery.

Lek, R., **Neth.**; one of the branches of the Neder Rijn; from Wijk-bij-Duurstede to Krimpen nr. Rotterdam; 64 km long.

Le Locle, t., Neuchâtel, **Switzerland**; ctr. of watch-mkg. ind.; p. (1969) 15,200.

Léman L. *See* **Geneva, L.**

Le Mans, t., cap. of Sarthe dep., N.W. **France**; cath.; linen, ironmongery, chemicals, motor cars, aeroplanes; motor-racing; p. (1982) 150,331.

Lemnos, Greek I., Aegean Sea, **Greece**; 64 km S.W. of Dardanelles; ch. t. Kastro (the anc. Myrina); tobacco, wine; a. 466 km²; part of Lesvos dep.

Lena, one of gr. Siberian Rs., **RSFSR**; rises in Oc.; navigable; 4,480 km long.

Leninabad, c., Tadzhik SSR, **USSR**; on Syr Dar'ya R., S. of Tashkent; silks, cottons, fruit-preserving; hydroelectric power sta.; p. (est. 1985) 150,000.

Leninakan, c., Armenian SSR, **RSFSR**; nr. Turkish border; textiles, engin., rug-mkg.; earthquake 1988; p. (est. 1985) 223,000.

Lenin Dam (Dnieper Dam). *See* **Zaporozh'ye.**

Leningrad, c., cap. of Leningrad oblast, **RSFSR**; at mouth of Neva R.; cultural ctr. with many fine bldgs., inc. winter palace, Hermitage museum, cath., admiralty bldg.; former cap. of Russia; major pt. and industl. ctr.; exp. timber, furs, and raw materials; ice-bound December–March; founded (1703) by Peter the Great as St. Petersburg; p. (1986) 4,359,000 (c.), 4,901,000 (met. a.).

Leninogorsk, c., Kazakh SSR, **USSR**; in Altai mtns.; lead, zinc, and silver mines; metallurgical plants; p. (est. 1967) 70,000.

Lenin Peak (Mt. Kaufmann), Trans-Altai Range, Kirghiz-Tadzhik SSR border, 2nd. hgst. mtn. of **USSR**; adjoining glacier; alt. 7,132 m.

Leninsk-Kuznetski, t., **RSFSR**; in W. Siberia on Inya R.; coalfield in Kuznetsk basin; heavy engin., power sta.; p. (est. 1980) 133,000.

Lenkoran, c., pt. Azerbaydzhan SSR, **USSR**; on Caspian Sea, nr. Iranian border; rice, citrus fruits, tea, fisheries, food-processing; p. (est. 1967) 31,000.

Lennoxtown, t., Stirling, **Scot.**; alum. wks.; p. (1981) 4,825.

Lens, t., Pas-de-Calais dep., N. **France**; industl. ctr. in coal a.; p. (1982) 327,383 (met. a.).

Leoben, t., Styria, **Austria**; lignite mng. ctr.; p. (1981) 31,989.

Leominster, mkt. t., l. gov. dist., Hereford and Worcs., **Eng.**; 19 km N. of Hereford; once famed for woollen ind.; p. (est. 1988) 39,300.

León, c., central **Mexico**; at c. 1,700 m; comm., agr. and mng. ctr. (gold, copper, silver, lead, tin); textiles, leather; p. (est. 1986) 800,000.

León, c., cap. of León dep., N.W. **Nicaragua**; cath., univ.; ctr. for agr. and industl. prods.; footwear, textiles; p. (eest. 1985) 101,000.

León, cap. of L. prov., N.W. **Spain**; gothic cath.; craft inds.; p. (1980) 135,521.

Léopoldville. *See* **Kinshasa.**

Lepontine Alps, major gr., **Switzerland–Italy**; alt. over 3,300 m.

Le Puy, t., cap. of Haute Loire dep., **France**; lace, liqueurs; cath. sited on old volcanic plug; tourism; p. (1982) 25,968.

Lérida, t., cap. of L. prov., **Spain**; on R. Segre; 2 caths.; textiles, leather, glass; p. (1987) 108,207.

Lerwick, t., Shetland Is., **Scot.**; on Mainland; fishing; p. (1981) 7,223.

Lesbos. *See* **Lesvos.**

Les Causses. *See* **Causses, Les.**

Leskovac, t., Serbia, **Yugoslavia**; on Morava R.; in economically backward a.; textiles, soap, furniture, tobacco-processing; p. (1981) 159,001.

Les Landes. *See* **Landes, Les.**

Leslie, burgh, Kirkcaldy, **Scot.**; 11 km N. of Kirkcaldy; paper, bleaching; p. (1981) 3,472.

Lesotho (Basutoland), kingdom, southern **Africa**; surrounded by Rep. of S. Africa; at head of Orange R. and enclosed by Drakensberg mtns.; economy mainly agr., especially pastoral farming; exp. livestock, wool, mohair, diamonds; 50 per cent revenue from U.K. grants; poor communications; many workers migrate to S. Africa (23 per cent in 1981); inds. encouraged by tax concessions becoming increasingly impt.; Highlands Water Project started (1986) to export water from Orange R. to S. Africa and generate hydro-electr. from 6 dams; cap. Maseru; a. 30,344 km²; p. (est. 1987) 1·63 m.

Lesser Antilles. *See* **Antilles.**

Lesvos (Lesbos, Mytilene), I., off Turkey, Aegean Sea, belonging to **Greece**; highest point 939 m; agr., antimony, marbles; cap. Mytilene; a. 1,601 km²; p. (1981) 104,620 (dep.).

Leszno, t., Poznan, W. **Poland**; engin., distilling, tobacco; p. (1983) 59,900.

Letchworth (Garden City), t., North Herts., **Eng.**; at foot of Chiltern Hills, 3 km N.E. of Hitchin; first garden c., founded by Sir Ebenezer Howard 1903; engin., office equipment; expanded t.; p. (1981) 31,835.

Lethbridge, c., Alberta, **Canada**; in foothills of Rockies; ctr. of lge. coal-mng. dist. and of irrigated wheat-growing a.; p. (1986) 58,841.

Le Touquet-Paris Plage, fashionable resort, W. cst. **France**; S. of Canche estuary.

Letterkenny, t., Co. Donegal, **R.o.I.**; on Lough Swilly; tourist ctr.; p. (1981) 6,444.

Leuna, t., Halle, **E. Germany**; 5 km S. of Merseburg; synthetic chemical ind.; oil pipeline from Schwedt; p. (est. 1971) 11,000.

Levant, French and Italian name for E. cst. of Mediterranean.

Leven, burgh, Kirkcaldy, **Scot.**; on N. side of F. of Forth; resort; p. (1981) 8,624.

Leven, L., Perth and Kinross, **Scot.**; ass. with escape of Mary Queen of Scots from Castle I. 1568.

Leverkusen, t., N. Rhine–Westphalia, **W. Germany**; on R. Rhine, N. of Cologne; iron, machin., textiles, chemicals; p. (est. 1986) 154,700.

Levkás or **Santa Maura,** one of Ionian Is., off W. **Greece**; wine, olive oil, currants; p. (1981) 21,863.

Lewes, t., l. gov. dist., East Sussex, **Eng.**; on R. Ouse at N. entrance to gap through S. Downs; mkt., cas., printing, light inds.; p. (est. 1988) 90,800 (dist.).

Lewis, I., Outer Hebrides, **Scot.**; fishing, tweeds; ch. t. Stornoway; a. 1,994 km²; p. (1971) 15,174.

Lewisham, inner bor., London, **Eng.**; inc. Deptford; residtl.; industl.; p. (est. 1988) 228,900.

Lewiston, t., Maine, **USA**; power for textile mill supplied by waterfall since early 19th cent.; p. (1980) 40,481.

Lexington, c., Ky., **USA**; in heart of Blue Grass region; univ.; ch. tobacco mkt. and horse-breeding ctr. of USA; p. (1984) 210,200 (c.), 327,200 (met. a.) inc. Fayette.

Lexington, t., Mass., **USA**; nr. Boston; residtl.; first battle in war of independence 19 Apr. 1775; p. (1980) 29,479.

Leyburn, t., Richmondshire, North Yorks., **Eng.**; in lower Wensleydale; mkt.

Leyden. *See* **Leiden.**

Leyland, t., Lancs., **Eng.**; 8 km S. of Preston; motor vehicles, rubber; p. (1981) 26,567. *See* **Central Lancashire.**

Leyte, one of Visayan Is., central **Philippines**; maize, abaca, rice; Japanese fleet defeated by US in battle of Leyte Gulf 1944; a. 7,213 km²; p. (1970) 1,340,015.

Leyton. *See* **Waltham Forest.**

Lhasa (Lasa), c., cap. of Tibet, **China**; "forbidden" c.; Buddhist ctr., temple, monasteries, shrines; caravan tr. in carpets, silk, lace, gold, tea; pharmaceutical factory, turbine pumps, fertilisers; much hotel bldg. and restoration of Buddhist sites to encourage tourism and break down isolation; p. (1982) 343,200.

Lhotse, mtn., Tibet, **China–Nepal**; 4th hgst. mtn. in world; alt. 8,506 m.

Lianyungang, spt., Jiangsu, **China**; impt. fishing and tea centre; rapid industrial development, esp. mineral processing, chemicals and motors; univ.; attracting foreign investment as 'open' c. under China's new economic policy; p. (1984) 450,000.

Liao-ho, R., Liaoning, N.E. **China**; flows into G. of Liaotung, Yellow Sea; navigable for last 640 km of course; c. 1,600 km long.

Liaoning, prov., N.E. **China**; inc. lower course and delta of Liao-ho; part of N.E. China (formerly called Manchuria); maize, millets, soyabeans; lge. mineral reserves of coal and iron ore; cap. Shenyang; a. 150,220 km²; p. (est. 1985) 36,550,000.

Liaotung, peninsula, N.E. **China**; nr. G. of same name.

Liaoyang, c., E. Liaoning prov., N.E. **China**; in fertile valley of Liao-ho; cotton-growing; textile mills; p. (1984) 565,300.

Liao-yuan, c., S.W. Jilin, **China**; lge. coal-mng. ctr.; p. (1984) 375,600.

Liberec, t., **CSSR**; on R. Neisse; univ.; textiles, chemicals, tr. ctr.; p. (est. 1986) 101,000.

Liberia, rep., W. **Africa**; founded (1847) by free slaves from USA; tropical climate; 72 per cent of p. involved in agr.; few cash crops, inc. rubber and cocoa; rich iron deposits provide main exp.; world's lgst. merchant fleet as result of "flag of convenience"; cap. and ch. pt. Monrovia; a. 99,068 km²; p. (est. 1988) 2·51 m.

Libourne, t., Gironde, **France**; on R. Dordogne, 35 km N.E. of Bordeaux; wine tr.; p. (1982) 23,312.

Libreville, c., cap. of **Gabon**; pt. on G. of Guinea; exp. tropical hardwoods, rubber, cacao; Trans-Gabon rly. project to link L. to Booué to promote timber exploitation; p. (est. 1983) 350,000.

Libya, or **Popular Socialist Libyan Arab Jamahiriyah** (since 1977), rep., N. **Africa**; on Mediterranean cst.; desert conditions prevail; radical attitude towards oil companies as oil accounts for 99 per cent of exp. earnings and forms basis of new-found wealth; petro-chemical inds.; over half working p. are foreigners; most of p. engaged in subsistence agr. (nomadic pastoralism); most food and mnfs. imported; plans for unity with Chad; joint caps. Tripoli (site of government deps.), Benghazi; a. 1,759,537 km²; p. (est. 1986) 3,955,000.

Libyan Desert, part of the Sahara, Africa.

Licata, t., Sicily, **Italy;** spt.; sulphur-processing; p. (1981) 40,050.

Lichfield, c., l. gov. dist., Staffs., **Eng.;** cath.; agr. and lt. inds.; expanded t.; birthplace of Dr. Samuel Johnson; p. (est. 1988) 93,800 (dist.).

Lickey Hills, gr. of hills, Hereford and Worcs., **Eng.;** 6 km S.W. of Birmingham; reveal anc. rocks underlying younger sediments; rise to 292 m, largely wooded.

Liechtenstein, principality, between Austria and Switzerland; official language German; economy based on sm.-scale inds. and tourism in picturesque Alpine scenery aided by mild climate; wine; cap. Vaduz; a. 161 km²; p. (est. 1986) 27,400, one-third foreign born.

Liège (Luik), industl. c., E. **Belgium;** on R. Meuse nr. confluence of Ourthe; cath., univ.; conurb. inc. Herstal, Bressoux, Ougrée, Angleur, Grivegnée; metallurgy, armaments, vehicles, chemicals, textiles, glassware, tyres; p. (est. 1984) 203,065.

Liepaja (Libau), c., Latvian SSR, **USSR;** harbour pt. on Baltic Sea, second to Riga; shipyards, steel-wks., paper mills, chemicals; exp. timber, grain; p. (est. 1980) 108,000.

Liestal, t., cap. of the half-can. Baselland, **Switzerland;** p. (1980) 12,158.

Liffey, R., **R.o.I.;** rises in Wicklow Mtns. and enters Irish Sea at Dublin; water supply for Dublin; inds. along estuary.

Liguria, region, N.W. **Italy;** inc. provs. of Genoa and Porto Maurizio; a. 5,411 km²; p. (est. 1986) 1·8 m.

Ligurian Sea, Mediterranean; N. of Corsica.

Likasi (Jadotville), t., **Zaïre;** ctr. for copper mng. and refining; p. (1982) 146,394.

Lille, c., cap. of Nord dep., N. **France;** on R. Deûle; mftg., comm. and cultural ctr.; former cap. of Fr. Flanders (1668); textiles (the term lisle derived from earlier spelling of city's name), metallurgy, engin.; univ., art museums; p. (1982) 174,039.

Lilongwe, c., main ctr. of Central Region, **Malawi;** replaced Zomba as cap. 1975; p. (est. 1985) 186,800.

Lima, c., cap. of **Peru;** 13 km from its pt. Callao; dominates comm., industl. and social life of cty.; cath., univ.; imposing architecture; seaside subs. Miraflores, Barranco, Chorillos; shanty ts. on outskirts; p. (est. 1985) 5,008,400 (10 times bigger than next c., Arequipa).

Lima, t., Ohio, **USA;** on Ottawa R.; rly. wks., oil, car bodies, refrigerators; p. (1984) 46,000 (t.), 152,200 (met. a.).

Limassol, t., S. **Cyprus;** spt. on Akrotiri Bay; new artificial harbour; ctr. of admin. dist.; wine, agr.-processing; exp. foodstuffs; tourism; p. (est. 1986) 114,000.

Limavady, t., l. gov. dist., **N. Ireland;** mkt.; linen; p. (1981) 26,353 (dist.), 8,015 (t.).

Limbach, t., Karl-Marx-Stadt, **E. Germany;** hosiery, textiles, machines; p. (est. 1970) 25,460.

Limbe. See **Blantyre-Limbe.**

Limburg, prov., N.E. **Belgium;** bordering Neth.; mainly agr.; coal-mng. in Campine region; cap. Hasselt; a. 2,409 km²; p. (1983) 359,005.

Limburg, prov., S.E. **Neth.;** bordering on Belgium and W. Germany; drained by R. Maas; former coalmng.; new inds. to relieve unemployment; a. 2,191 km²; p. (1983) 1,080,516.

Limeira, t., São Paulo, **Brazil;** ctr. of orange cultivation; hats, matches; p. (est. 1985) 187,800.

Limerick, co., Munster, **R.o.I.;** agr., livestock, fishing; a. 3,385 km²; p. (1981) 60,736.

Limerick, C.B., cap. of Limerick, **R.o.I.;** spt. at head of Shannon estuary; bacon, tanning, shipbldg.; p. (1981) 18,002 (c.).

Limmat, R., **Switzerland;** trib. of R. Aare; flows through c. of Zürich; 128 km long.

Lim Fjord, shallow strait, Jutland, **Denmark;** connects N. Sea with Kattegat; contains I. of Mors.

Limoges, c., cap. of Haute-Vienne dep., **France;** to N.W. of Central Massif; anc. t., celebrated in middle ages for goldsmith's work, later for enamel ware and porcelain; cath.; p. (1982) 144,082.

Limón, spt., **Costa Rica;** on Caribbean; oil refining nearby; p. (est. 1983) 38,900.

Limousin, region and former prov., central **France;** to W. of Auvergne; now divided into deps. Haute-Vienne, Corrèze, Dordogne; plateau, average alt. 300 m, composed of old crystalline rocks; exposed damp climate; infertile, some pastoral agr.; kaolin; ch. t. Limoges; p. (1982) 732,500.

Limpopo or **Crocodile R., S. Africa, Moçambique,** and **Zimbabwe;** lower R. forms a fertile valley 1,600 km long.

Linares, prov., central **Chile;** thermal springs in Andes; cereals and vineyards in valleys; cap. Linares; a. 9,816 km²; p. (1970) 189,010.

Linares, t., Jaén prov., **Spain;** silver-lead mines; metallurgical inds.; p. (1981) 51,278.

Lincoln, c., co. t., l. gov. dist., Lincs., **Eng.;** on R. Witham in gap through Lincoln Edge; impt. Roman t.; cath., cas.; heavy engin., iron foundries, bricks, lime, seed milling, malting; p. (est. 1988) 80,400.

Lincoln, c., cap. of Nebraska, **USA;** univ.; educational ctr.; grain and cattle mkt.; flour mills, agr. machin., cars, chemicals, rubber gds.; p. (1984) 180,400 (c.), 203,000 (met. a.).

Lincoln Edge, limestone ridge, Lincs. and Humberside, **Eng.;** runs N. from Ancaster through Lincoln to Humber; narrow ridge with steep scarp slope to W., broken by R. Witham at Lincoln; iron-ore deposits worked in N. nr. Scunthorpe; sheep, barley; rarely exceeds 90 m alt.

Lincolnshire, non-met. co., **Eng.;** between Humberside non-met. co. and the Wash; fertile soil on low-lying fenland; intensive agr., arable crops, bulbs, market gardening; food-processing; formerly divided into 3 admin. parts: Holland, Kesteven, and Lindsey; a. 5,884 km²; p. (est. 1988) 582,600.

Lincoln Wolds, low plateau, Lincs. and Humberside, **Eng.;** runs N. 72 km from Wash to Humber; chalk covered with glacial deposits; mixed farming, grains, roots, sheep; lge. farm units; scantily populated; rises to approx. 135 m.

Lindau, t. Baden–Württemberg, **W. Germany;** on I. in Bodensee; tourist resort; p. (est. 1986) 23,100.

Lindisfarne or **Holy I.,** off cst. of Northumberland, **Eng.;** connected to mainland by stretch of sand and causeway at low tide; abbey founded 635 A.D. as first establishment of Celtic Christianity in Eng.

Lindsey. See **Lincolnshire.**

Lindsey, East, l. gov. dist., Lincs., **Eng.;** lge. a. on E. cst. inc. Louth, Mablethorpe, Horncastle, Woodhall Spa, Skegness and Alford; p. (est. 1988) 117,700.

Line Is., Pac. Oc., coral gr. admin. by U.K., except Palmyra, Kingman and Jarvis, which belong to USA; coconuts; airfields, meteorological slas.

Lin-i (formerly **Ichow**), t., Shandong, **China;** at foot of Shandong Highlands.

Linköping, t., S.E. **Sweden;** aero-engin., pianos, furniture; cath.; p. (est. 1986) 118,000.

Linlithgow, burgh, W. Lothian, **Scot.;** distilling, brewing, paper, shoes; birthplace of Mary Queen of Scots; p. (1981) 9,524.

Linnhe, Loch, Lochaber, Argyll and Bute, Scot.; 21 m. long; entrance to Caledonian canal.

Linslade. See **Leighton Buzzard.**

Linz, c., cap. of Upper **Austria;** pt. on Danube; comm. and industl. ctr. with iron and steel wks.; cath.; p. (1981) 119,910 (c.), 434,634 (met. a.).

Lipa, t., Luzon, **Philippines;** sugar, tobacco, cocoa, maize; processing; p. (est. 1984) 133,540.

Lipari Is. or **Aeolian Is.,** volcanic gr. between Sicily and toe of **Italy;** inc. Stromboli (927 m), Lipari, Vulcano, Salina; olives, grapes, currants, pumice; p. (1981) 10,208.

Lipetsk, c., **RSFSR;** on Voronezh R.; ctr. of iron-ore mng. a.; engin., steel, ferro-alloys; health resort; p. (est. 1980) 405,000.

Lippe, R., **W. Germany;** trib. of Rhine; paralleled by L. canal; forms N. bdy. of Ruhr industl. dist.; 176 km long.

Lippstadt, t., N. Rhine–Westphalia, **W. Germany;** on R. Lippe; metallurgy, textiles rly. ctr.; p. (est. 1986) 60,100.

Liri, R., central **Italy;** rises in Alban Hills, flows S.E. to Cassino and then S.W. to G. of Gaeta; valley followed by main road from Rome to Naples; length 168 km.

Lisbon (Lisboa), c., cap of **Portugal;** on R. Tagus, 14 km from mouth; spt. with fine natural har-

bour; cas., cath., univ.; admin., comm., and industl. ctr.; expanding inds., airpt.; attracts p. from rural areas; p. (est. 1984) 807,937.

Lisburn, t., l. gov. dist., **N. Ireland;** on R. Lagan, 10 km S.W. of Belfast; p. (1981) 82,973 (dist.), 40,391 (t.).

Lisieux, t., Calvados dep., N. **France;** historic t., severely damaged in second world war; cath.; Camembert cheese; p. (1982) 25,823.

Liskeard, mkt. t., Caradon, Cornwall, **Eng.;** on R. Looe at S. edge of Bodmin Moor; p. (1981) 6,316.

Lismore, t., N.S.W., **Australia;** pt. on Richmond R.; dairying, sugar refining, maize, potatoes, textiles, engin., bacon; p. (1981) 24,033.

Lismore, mkt. t., R.D., Waterford, **R.o.I.;** on Blackwater R.; cas.; p. (1975) 900.

Listowel, U.D., Kerry, **R.o.I.;** on R. Feale; cas. ruins; p. (1981) 3,542.

Litherland, t., Sefton, Merseyside, **Eng.;** N. sub. of Liverpool; p. (1981) 21,946.

Lithuania, former constituent rep., **USSR;** borders Baltic Sea; agr. development on reclaimed marshland; dairy farming, stockraising, fishing, timber inds., food-processing, ship bldg., textiles, machin.; cap. Vilna; a. 65,201 km²; p. (1990) 3,700,000. Independence proclaimed, 11 Mar 1990.

Litoměřice, t., **ČSSR;** in Bohemia on R. Elbe (Labe); cath.; brewing, agr. ctr.; p. (1984) 28,844.

Little Belt (Lille Bælt), strait, **Denmark;** separates Fyn I. from Jutland; too shallow for lge. ships; road/rly., motorway bridges cross narrow N. section nr. Frederidicia; 48 km long.

Little Bighorn, R., Wyo., Mont., **USA;** Custer's last battle on ridge overlooking R. (1876); 144 km long.

Littleborough, t., Gtr. Manchester, **Eng.;** textiles and textile finishing; p. (1981) 13,861.

Littlehampton, t., Arun, West Sussex, **Eng.;** on S. cst. at mouth of R. Arun; holiday resort, sm. spt.; p. (1981) 22,181.

Little Lever, t., Gtr. Manchester, **Eng.;** 5 km S.E. of Bolton; residtl. and industl.; p. (1981) 11,439.

Little Rock, c., cap. of Ark., **USA;** N.E. of Hot Springs, on Ark. R. opposite N. Little Rock; comm. and mnf. ctr. in rich cotton and dairy farming a.; bauxite nearby; p. (1984) 170,100 (c.), 492,700 (met. a.).

Littoria. *See* **Latina.**

Liuchow. *See* **Liuzhou.**

Liuzhou (Liuchow), c., Guangxi, S. **China;** on trib. of Xijiang; route ctr. and R. pt.; p. (1984) 446,900.

Liverpool, c., spt., met. dist., Merseyside, **Eng.;** second pt. in Gr. Britain; on N. bank at entrance to Mersey estuary; deep-sea container berths at Seaforth; shipping and ship-repairing; elec. mnfs. and engin., flour milling, sugar refining, seed and rubber processing, cars; cath., univ.; second Mersey tunnel opened 1971; freeport (1984) to help revive docks; p. (est. 1988) 469,600.

Liverpool, t., N.S.W., **Australia;** within met. a. of Sydney; major source of poultry, vegetables and dairy prods. for Sydney; p. (1976) 89,656.

Livingston, new t. (1962), W. Lothian, **Scot.;** p. (1981) 38,594.

Livingstone, t., **Zambia;** on Zambesi R. where rly. bridges R.; stands at c. 900 m; former cap.; sawmilling ctr.; p. (1980) 71,987.

Livorno (Leghorn), spt., cap. of L. prov., **Italy;** on Ligurian Sea; shipbldg., machin., chemicals, iron and steel wks., oil refining; exp. wine, olive oil, textiles, marble; p. (1984) 176,298.

Lizard, The, C., Cornwall, **Eng.;** S. point of Eng.

Ljubljana, c., cap. of Slovenia, N.W. **Yugoslavia;** on trib. of Sava R.; industl. ctr., local coal, hydroelectric power; route ctr.; airport; univ.; mediaeval fortress; ctr. of Slovene nat. movement in 19th cent.; p. (1981) 305,211.

Llanberis, pass, Gwynedd, N. **Wales;** between Snowdon and Clyder Fawr; road carries heavy tourist traffic; summit 356 m; nearby tourist resort of Llanberis.

Llandarcy, v., West Glamorgan, S. **Wales;** on cst. Swansea Bay, Bristol Channel; lge. oil refinery; pipeline to Angle Bay, Pembroke.

Llandeilo, mkt. t., Dinefwr, Dyfed, **Wales;** in vale of Towy, E. of Carmarthen; cas.; p. (1981) 1,614.

Llandovery, t., Dinefwr, Dyfed, **Wales;** on R. Bran, nr. confluence with Towy; mkt. ctr. for rural a.; p. (1981) 1,691.

Llandrindod Wells, t., Radnor, Powys, **Wales;** medicinal waters; p. (1981) 4,186.

Llandudno, t., Aberconwy, Gwynedd, **Wales;** between Gr. Ormes and Little Ormes headlands; resort; p. (1981) 18,991.

Llanelli, l. gov. dist., Dyfed, **Wales;** pt. on Burry inlet, 18 km N.W. of Swansea; industl. and comm. ctr.; coal mng., steel, and tin-plate wks., mng. machin.; cas.; p. (est. 1988) 74,100 (dist.).

Llanfairfechan, t., Aberconwy, Gwynedd, **Wales;** at foot of Penmaenmawr mtn.; seaside resort; granite quarrying; p. (1981) 3,780.

Llanfyllin, t., Powys, **Wales;** anc. mkt. t.; p. (1981) 1,207.

Llangefni, t., Anglesey, Gwynedd, **Wales;** in ctr. of the I.; mkt. and agr. t.; p. (1981) 4,265.

Llangollen, t., Glyndwr, Clwyd, **Wales;** on R. Dee; vale of L., tourist ctr.; annual Eisteddfod; p. (1981) 3,058.

Llanidloes, t., Powys, **Wales;** on R. Severn; surrounded by hills; anc. mkt. house; p. (1981) 2,416.

Llanos, lowland region, **Venezuela** and **Colombia,** S. America; drained by R. Orinoco and tribs.; high temperatures throughout year, but rain chiefly in summer; ch. vegetation, coarse grass which withers during dry season (Dec. to May).

Llanos de Urgel, upland region, Lérida, N.E. **Spain;** semi-arid; formerly steppe-land, now irrigated by R. Segre; vine, olive, maize, tobacco.

Llanrwst, mkt. t., Aberconwy, Gwynedd, **Wales;** on R. Conway; tourist ctr.; p. (1981) 2,931.

Llanstephan, v., Dyfed, **Wales;** at mouth of R. Towy; ruins of Norman cas.

Llantrisant, new t., Taff-Ely, Mid Glamorgan, S. **Wales;** iron-ore quarrying; Royal Mint.

Llanwrtyd Wells, t., Brecknock, Powys, **Wales;** once a spa; resort; p. (1981) 488.

Lleyn, peninsula, Gwynedd, N. **Wales;** from Snowdonia to Bardsey I.; crystalline rocks form hills in E., otherwise low, undulating; pastoral farming, sheep, cattle; sm. seaside resorts; ch. t. Pwllheli; a. 466 km².

Lliw Valley, l. gov. dist., West Glamorgan, **Wales;** comprises Pontardawe and Llwchwr; p. (est. 1988) 61,800.

Llwchwr, t., Lliw Valley, West Glamorgan, S. **Wales;** p. (1981) 26,864.

Llwchwr or **Loughor,** R., S. **Wales;** in lower course forms bdy. between Dyfed and West Glamorgan, empties into Burry inlet.

Loanhead, burgh, Midlothian, **Scot.;** 8 km S.E. of Edinburgh; coal, engin.; p. (1981) 6,135.

Lobito, spt., **Angola;** on Atl. Oc.; 29 km N. of Benguela; fine natural deepwater harbour; rly. terminus; varied exps.; oil-refinery under construction; p. (est. 1976) 70,000.

Locarno, t., **Switzerland;** on L. Maggiore; tourist ctr.; L. treaty 1925; p. (est. 1978) 15,300.

Lochaber, mtnous. l. gov. dist., Highland Reg., **Scot.;** bounded by Loch Linnhe and Loch Leven; inc. Ben Nevis; hydroelec. power; a. 4,465 km²; p. (est. 1986) 19,369.

Lochalsh. *See* **Kyle of Lochalsh.**

Lochgelly, burgh, Dunfermline, l. gov. dist., **Scot.;** nr. Dunfermline; p. (1981), 7,308.

Lochgilphead, co. t., Argyll and Bute, **Scot.;** at head of Loch Gilp, 3 km N. of Ardrishaig; tourist ctr.; p. (1981) 2,459.

Lochmaben, burgh, Annandale and Eskdale, **Scot.;** in Annandale, 11 km N.E. of Dumfries; p. (1981) 1,710.

Lockerbie, burgh, Annandale and Eskdale, **Scot.;** in Annandale, 16 km E. of Dumfries; sheep mkt.; air disaster 1988, caused by terrorist bomb; p. (1981) 3,530.

Lockport, t., N.Y., **USA;** on N.Y. st. barge canal, 38 km N.E. of Buffalo; power from Niagara falls supplies paper, metal, and other inds.; p. (1980) 24,844.

Lodi, t., **Italy;** on R. Adda, S.E. of Milan; cath.; scene of Napoleon's victory over Austrians 1796; p. (1981) 42,873.

Lodore Falls, waterfalls, Cumbria, **Eng.;** in Watendlath beck at foot of Derwentwater.

Łódź, c., cap. of L. prov., central **Poland;** second c. of rep. and ctr. of textile ind.; machin., elec. equipment, chemicals, metals; univ.; cultural ctr.; problems of water-supply; p. (est. 1985) 849,000.

Lofoten Is., storm-swept chain of Is. off N.W. cst.

Norway within Arctic Oc., stretching 240 km; cod and herring fisheries among richest in world.

Loftus, t. Langbaurgh, Cleveland, **Eng.**; on N.E. flank of Cleveland Hills; p. (1981) 8,477.

Logan, Mount, S.E. Yukon, **Canada**, E. of Alaska; alt. 6,054 m; highest mtn. in Canada and second highest in N. America.

Logroño, t., N. **Spain**; on Ebro R.; in wine growing a.; industl. and agr. ctr.; p. (1987) 116,273.

Loire, R., **France**; longest in cty., flows from Cevennes mtns. to Atl. Oc. at St. Nazaire; vineyards and many castles in attractive valley; 1,000 km long.

Loire, dep., E. central **France**; in part of the former provs. of Beaujolais and Lyonnais; agr.; coal mng., cattle raising; cap. St. Etienne; a. 4,799 km²; p. (1982) 737,400.

Loire-Atlantique, dep., W. **France**; mainly agr., salt-marsh on cst.; inds. at cap. Nantes; a. 6,980 km²; p. (1982) 994,700.

Loiret, dep., N. central **France**; agr., vineyards, distilling, mftg.; cap. Orléans; a. 6,812 km²; p. (1982) 537,000.

Loir-et-Cher, dep., central **France**; contains fertile a. of Beauce; cap. Blois; a. 6,421 km²; p. (1982) 296,000.

Lokoren, industl. t., **Belgium**; between Ghent and Antwerp; textiles, chemicals, tobacco; p. (1981) 33,369.

Lokoja, t. **Nigeria**; at confluence of Rs. Niger and Benue; R. pt.; iron-ore nearby.

Lolland or **Laaland**, Danish I. in Baltic Sea; a. 1,241 km²; agr. forests; ch. ts. Maribo, Nakshov; p. (1965) 81,760.

Lomami, R., central **Zaire**; trib. of Zaïre R., rich coal-bearing strata at confluence; 1,812 km long.

Lombardy, Plain of, N. **Italy**; extensive lowland flanked by Alps, Apennines, Adriatic Sea; built up by alluvium from R. Po, its tribs. and R. Adige; intensively cultivated; rice, maize, flax, clover, lucerne, wheat, apples, dairy cattle; densely populated; many industl. ts., Milan, Novara, Pavia, etc.; p. of region (est. 1986) 8·9 m.

Lombok, one of the lesser Sunda Is., **Indonesia**; mtnous. volcanic terrain; Wallace's Line passes between Lombok and Bali; ch. t. Mataram; p. 1,300,000.

Lomé, spt., cap. of **Togo**, W. Africa; on G. of Guinea; deepwater pt.; exp. cacao, cotton, palm prods.; phosphates; p. (est. 1983) 366,476.

Lomond, Loch, Stirling, lgst. loch in **Scot.**, studded with Is., surrounded by hills with Ben Lomond on E. side; a. 70 km².

Lomża, t. Bialystok, **Poland**; on Narew R., metal inds., foodstuffs; p. (1970) 25,500.

London, cap. of UK, **Eng.**; at head of Thames estuary; seat of govt., world ctr. of finance and communication; cultural and artistic ctr.; comprises the City, 12 inner and 20 outer bors.; Port of London; upstream docks now closed; main pt. downstream at Tilbury; currently losing p. and inds. to outer met. a.; univs. (London, Brunel, City), caths., many historic bldgs., theatres, museums, galleries, libraries, and parks; p. (est. 1988) 4,400 (City of London), 2,493,600 (Inner London), 6,735,400 (Greater London).

London, t., Ont., **Canada**; on R. Thames, 104 km W. of Hamilton; industl. ctr.; univ.; p. (1986) 269,140 (c.), 342,302 (met a.).

Londonderry, formerly co.; l. gov. dist., **N. Ireland**; borders R.o.I. and L. Foyle; Sperrin Mtns. in S.; p. (1981) 83,494 (dist.).

Londonderry (or **Derry**), c., l. gov. dist., **N. Ireland**; on left bank of R. Foyle, 6 km upstream from Lough Foyle; shirt mftg.; textiles; acetylene from naphtha; training ctr. for ind.; p. (1981) 62,697 (t.).

Londrina, c., Paraná, **Brazil**; industl. and agr. ctr., coffee, maize, cotton, livestock; p. (est. 1985) 347,700.

Long Beach, c., Cal., **USA**; Pac. cst. resort and industl. suburb of Los Angeles met. a.; p. (1984) 378,800 (c.). *See* Los Angeles.

Longbenton, t., Tyne and Wear, **Eng.**; 5 km N.E. of Newcastle; former coal mng.; expanded t.; p. (1981) 50,646.

Long Eaton, t. Erewash, Derbys., **Eng.**; on R. Trent, 8 km S.W. of Nottingham; former ctr. for lace mftg., elec. cables, flexible tubing, hosiery; p. (1981) 32,895.

Longford, co., Leinster, **R.o.I.**; peat bogs; dairy

farming; co. t. Longford; a. 1,090 km²; p. (1981) 31,140.

Longford, co. t., Longford, **R.o.I.**; cas., cath.; mkt. t.; p. (1981) 6,548.

Long Forties Bank, submarine sandbank, N. Sea; 128 km E. of Aberdeen; valuable fishing-grounds; depth of water, from 45–75 m.

Long I., part of N.Y., **USA**; separated from mainland by East R.; contains Queens and Brooklyn bors. of N.Y. City; mkt. gardening, fisheries, oysters, holiday resorts; a. 4,356 km².

Longreach, t. Queensland, **Australia**; in ctr. of Gr. Australian (artesian) basin; collecting ctr. for cattle and wool; p. (1976) 3,354.

Longridge, t., Ribble Valley, Lancs., **Eng.**; 10 km N.E. of Preston; p. (1981) 7,161.

Longview, t. Texas, **USA**; oil, chemicals, plastics; p. (1984) 73,300 (t.), 168,400 (met. a.).

Longwy, t., Meurthe-et-Moselle dep., N.E. **France**; on Belgian–Luxembourg frontier; upper part fortfd.; lower part industl. with iron and steel ind.; p. (1968) 21,087.

Lons-le-Saunier, cap. of Jura dep., E. **France**; saline springs; agr. ctr.; p. (1982) 21,886.

Looe, t. Caradon, Cornwall, **Eng.**; on Looe estuary; holiday resort; p. (1981) 4,499.

Lopburi, t., **Thailand**; ctr. of haematite iron deposits; former cap.

Lop Nor, marsh, Xinjiang, W. **China**; in Tarim Basin at foot of Altun Shan; ctr. of inland drainage, receives water from R. Tarim; atomic testing grounds.

Lorain, t., Ohio, **USA**; on L. Erie; shipbldg., steelwks., fisheries; p. (1980) 275,000 (met. a.).

Lorca, t., Murcia, **Spain**; agr. prod., woollens, chemicals; bishop's palace; p. (1981) 60,627.

Lord Howe I., forested volcanic I., S. **Pac. Oc.**, 698 km N.E. of Sydney; palm seed ind.; admin. by N.S.W.; p. (1981) 287.

Lorient, spt., Morbihan dep., N.W. **France**; on Atl.; naval shipyard, fishing harbour; p. (1982) 64,675.

Lorraine, region and former prov., N.E. **France**; inc. deps. Moselle, Meurthe-et-Moselle, Meuse, and Vosges; ch. t. Nancy; rich iron-ore deposits; impt. but declining industl. a.; mkt. gardening, vineyards; with Alsace long disputed between Germany and France; p. (1982) 2,318,000.

Los Alamos, t., N.M., **USA**; site of research for first atomic bomb; p. (1980) 11,039.

Los Angeles, c., S. Cal., **USA**; booming modern c. ("the city of angels"), busiest pt. in Cal.; fine harbour; one of world's lgst. urban areas; miles of freeway (2,400 km planned by 1980); many prosperous inds., inc. aircraft, missiles, chemicals, machin., electronic equipment, food-processing, oil refining; film ctr.; p. (1984) 3,096,700 (c.), 12,372,600 (met. a.) with Long Beach.

Lossiemouth, burgh, Moray, **Scot.**; on Moray F., 8 km N. of Elgin; birthplace of Ramsay Macdonald; fishing; p. (1981) 6,801.

Lostwithiel, mkt. t. Cornwall, **Eng.**; on R. Fowey S.E. of Bodmin; anc. Stannary t.

Lot, dep., S.W. **France**; livestock, wine, cereals, coals, iron; a. 5,227 km²; cap. Cahors; p. (1982) 154,500.

Lot, R., S. **France**; trib. of Garonne R., 435 km long.

Lota, pt., Chile; coal-mng. ctr.; ceramics, copper smelting; p. (1982) 62,662.

Lot-et-Garonne, dep., S.W. **France**; agr. (cereals, vines, fruit); cap. Agen; a. 5,385 km²; p. (1982) 298,700.

Lothian Region, l. gov. reg., central **Scot.**; borders F. of Forth, and inc. a. around Edinburgh; mainly industl.; a. 1,753 km²; p. (est. 1986) 741,910.

Lötschental, picturesque valley, Valais, **Switzerland**; ch. v. Kippel.

Loughborough, t., Charnwood, Leics., **Eng.**; on R. Soar 16 km N. of Leicester; engin., elec. gds., chemicals, textiles; univ.; former hosiery t.; bell foundry; p. (1981) 47,647.

Loughrea, mkt. t., Galway, **R.o.I.**; cotton mill; p. (1981) 3,377.

Louisiana, southern st., **USA**; Pelican St.; admitted to Union 1812; st. flower Magnolia, st. bird Eastern Brown Pelican; leading producer of rice, sugarcane, sweet potatoes, also cotton, maize, tobacco, oil, natural gas, lumber; cap. Baton Rouge; New Orleans major pt.; a. 125,675 km²; p. (1985) 4,481,000.

Louisville, c., Ky., **USA**; on Ohio R.; univ.; lgst. tobacco mkt. in world; chemicals, paints, cars, machin., elec. gds., synthetic rubber; p. (1984) 289,900 (c.), 962,600 (met. a.).

Lourdes, t., **France**; on R. Pau; Catholic pilgrim centre.; slate, marble; p. (1982) 17,619.

Lourenço Marques. *See* **Maputo.**

Louth, t., East Lindsey, Lincs., **Eng.**; on E. edge of Lincoln Wolds; abbey ruins; cattle mkt., farm implements, rope mkg., lime, malting, canning; p. (1981) 13,296.

Louth, maritime co., Leinster, **R.o.I.**; mtns., bog and barren land; salmon fishing; cap. Dundalk; a. 818 km²; p. (1981) 55,734.

Louvain (Leuven), c., Brabant prov., **Belgium**; on R. Dyle; univ. (Erasmus taught here); brewing ctr., bell foundries; p. (1982) 84,914.

Low Archipelago. *See* **Tuamotu Is.**

Low Countries, name applied to Belgium and the Neth.

Lowell, c., Mass., **USA**; at junc. of Merrimac and Concord Rs.; 48 km N. of Boston; textiles, machin., chemicals, carpets; birthplace of Whistler; p. (1980) 233,000 (met. a.).

Lower California (Baja California), peninsula, N.W. **Mexico**; separating G. of Cal. and Pac. Oc.; isolated, arid; divided into 2 sts., Baja California (cap. Tijuana), and Baja California, Territorio Sur (cap. La Paz); a. 143,963 km²; p. (1969) 1,150,000.

Lower Hutt, c., N.I., **N.Z.**; rapid industl. devel. in last 45 years; engin., plastics, textiles, vehicle assembly; p. (est. 1987) 63,700.

Lower Saxony (Nieder Sachsen), Land, **W. Germany**; inc. Lüneburg heath and Harz mtns.; cap. Hanover; a. 47,205 km²; p. (est. 1986) 7,196,100.

Lowestoft, fish pt., Waveney, Suffolk, **Eng.**; on E. Anglian cst. 14 km S. of Gr. Yarmouth; holiday resort, nr. Broads; food and fish processing plants; base for N. Sea gas; p. (1981) 55,231.

Lowther Hills, mtns., between Strathclyde and Dumfries and Galloway Regs., **Scot.**; hgst. point 733 m.

Loyalty Is., S. Pac. Oc.; included in Fr. administration of New Caledonia; copra; lgst. Is. Maré, Lifou, Uvéa; a. *c.* 2,100 km².

Lozère, dep., S.E. **France**; traversed by Cevennes mtns.; cap. Mende; a. 5,170 km²; p. (1982) 74,200.

Lualaba, R., **Zaïre**, central Africa; rises nr. Lubumbashi in Shaba prov., flows N. circa 800 km to Kikondja, where joined by R. Lufira to form R. Zaïre; name also applied to main stream of R. Zaïre as far downstream as Ponthierville.

Luanda, c. cap. of **Angola**; pt. on Atl. Oc.; exp. coffee, cotton, palm prod.; industl. ctr.; foodstuffs, tobacco, clothing, plastics; oil refining; hydroelectric power; p. (est. 1982) 1,200,000.

Luang Prabang, c., N.W. **Laos**; at confluence of Mekong and Kahn Rs.; rubber, rice, teak; former royal cap.; p. (est. 1973) 44,200.

Lubbock, c., N.W. Texas, **USA**; on Double Mountain fork of Brazos R.; ctr. of cotton-growing a.; p. (1984) 178,500 (c.), 218,900 (met. a.).

Lübeck, c., pt. of Schleswig-Holstein, **W. Germany**; on Baltic Sea at mouth of Trave R.; cath.; shipbldg., machin., chemicals, textiles, iron, foodstuffs; birthplace of Thomas Mann; p. (est. 1986) 209,200.

Lublin, c., cap. of L. prov., E. **Poland**; motor vehicle and elec. engin.; agr. tr. and processing; cultural ctr., univ.; cas.; p. (est. 1985) 324,000.

Lubumbashi (Elizabethville), t., Shaba, **Zaïre**; copper-mng. ctr.; p. (1982) 451,332.

Lucca, c., cap. of L. prov., Tuscany, **Italy**; cath., churches, palaces; noted for olive oil, pasta, wine; silk, cotton, jute, tobacco inds.; p. (1981) 91,246.

Lucena, t., Córdoba, **Spain**; olive oil, ceramics, gilt metals, wine; p. (1981) 29,717.

Lucenec, t., **CSSR**; on Hungarian border; magnesite, textiles, sawmilling; p. (1984) 27,477.

Lucerne (Luzern), can., **Switzerland**; agr., pastoral, vineyards; oil refinery projected at Schötz/Ettiswil; cap. Lucerne; a. 1,492 km²; p. (est. 1986) 306,000.

Lucerne (Luzern), c., cap. of L. can., **Switzerland**; at N.W. end of L. Lucerne; aluminium gds., sewing machin.; tourist ctr.; p. (est. 1985), 60,606 (c.), 160,000 (met. a.)'

Lucerne, L., **Switzerland**; also known as L. of the Four Cantons; length 37 km; a. 70 km².

Luchon or **Bagnères-de-Luchon,** resort in Fr. Pyrenees, Haute-Garonne dep., S. **France**; warm sulphur springs; winter sports ctr.

Luchow. *See* **Zuzhou.**

Luckenwalde, t., E. **Germany**; on R. Nuthe; textiles, footwear, machin., wood and metals, chemicals; p. (est. 1970) 28,984.

Lucknow, c., cap. of Uttar Pradesh st., N. **India**; on R. Gumti (trib. of Ganges); educational and cultural ctr. with textile inds.; rly. ctr.; scene of 1857 mutiny; p. (1981) 895,721 (c.), 1,007,604 (met. a.).

Lüda, special min., S. Liaoning prov., **China**; comprising Port Arthur Naval Base District and the pts. of Port Arthur and Talien (Dairen); chemicals, machin., shipbldg., textiles; p. (est. 1984) 1·59 m.

Lüdenscheid, t., N. Rhine–Westphalia, **W. Germany**; metal mngs., domestic hardware; supplied structures for first Zeppelins; p. (est. 1986) 73,400.

Lüderitz, t., **Namibia**; rly. pt. on desert cst.; diamonds, fishing; p. (est. 1970) 6,642.

Ludhiana, t., Punjab st., N.W. **India**; S. of Sutlej R.; industl. ctr.; hosiery, knitwear; p. (1981) 607,052.

Ludlow, t., South Shrops., **Eng.**; agr. mkt.; agr. engin.; cas.

Ludwigsburg, t. Baden-Württemberg, **W. Germany**; N. of Stuttgart; cas.; textiles, food-stuffs, machin., toys; p. (est. 1986) 76,000.

Ludwigshafen, t., Rhine-Palatinate, **W. Germany**; on R. Rhine, opposite Mannheim; chemicals, marine diesel engines, metallurgy, glass; R. pt. and rly. junc.; oil pipeline from Rotterdam under construction; p. (est. 1986) 152,200.

Lugano, t., Ticino can., **Switzerland**; on L. Lugano; tourist resort; p. (1980) 27,815.

Lugano, L., lies at S. foot of Alps between **Switzerland** and **Italy**; attractive scenery, tourism; a. 49 km².

Lugansk. *See* **Voroshilovgrad.**

Lugnaquilla, mtn., loftiest summit in Wicklow, **R.o.I.**; 927 m.

Lugo, c., cap. of L. prov., N.W. **Spain**; in Galicia, on Miño R.; in fertile agr. a.; cath.; p. (1987) 77,043.

Lukuga, intermittent outlet of L. Tanganyika, **Zaïre**, linking with R. Zaïre.

Luleå, spt., N. **Sweden**, cap. of Norrbotten co.; on Lule R. at head of G. of Bothnia; iron ore; smelting plant, engin.; p. (est. 1986) 66,000.

Luluabourg. *See* **Kananga.**

Lulworth Cove, sm. inlet, Dorset, **Eng.**; formed by sea breaching limestone cliffs and eroding clay behind; tourism.

Lund, t., S. **Sweden**; 16 km N.E. of Malmö; 11th cent. Romanesque cath.; univ.; publishing ctr.; p. (est. 1986) 83,000.

Lundy I., Bristol Channel, N. Devon, **Eng.**; 19 km N.W. of Hartland Point; wildlife sanctuary; about 5 km long and 1 km wide.

Lune, R., Cumbria, **Eng.**; flows 72 km to Irish Sea; attractive valley.

Lüneburg, t., Lower Saxony, **W. Germany**; on Ilmenau R., S.E. of Hamburg; rly. junc., R. pt.; iron wks., chemicals; dates from 8th cent.; p. (est. 1986) 59,500.

Lüneburg Heath, Lower Saxony, **W. Germany**; lies to S. of Lüneburg; glacial outwash plain of sands and gravels; heather, scrub; some agr. but infertile acid soils.

Lünen, t., N. Rhine–Westphalia, **W. Germany**; in Ruhr conurb.; coal, metallurgy, glass, wood; R. pt. and rly. ctr.; p. (est. 1986) 84,400.

Lunéville, t., Meurthe-et-Moselle .dep., N.E. **France**; in Lorraine, on R. Meurthe; 18th cent. château; p. (1975) 24,700.

Lungi, t., Sierra Leone, W. **Africa**; nr. Freetown; only civil airport in st.

Luoyang (Loyang), c., Henan prov., **China**; industl.; ball bearing and mng. machin.; lge. car and tractor plant, oil refinery, textiles; p. (1984) 1,023,900.

Lupata Gorge, Moçambique, E. Africa; narrow pass occupied by R. Zambezi.

Lurgan, t., Craigavon, N. **Ireland**; textiles, tobacco mftg.; merging with Portadown to form new c. of Craigavon; p. (1981) 20,991.

Lusaka, c., cap. of **Zambia;** comm. and admin. ctr.; at junc. of routes to Tanzania and Malawi; motor assembly, footwear, metal prods., clothing; p. (1980) 538,469.

Lushun. *See* **Lüda.**

Luton, t., l. gov. dist., Beds., **Eng.;** in Chiltern Hills nr. source of R. Lea; motor vehicles, engin., hat mkg., aircraft, gear instruments, chemicals; expanded t.; p. (est. 1988) 167,600.

Lutong, main oil pt. of Sarawak, E. **Malaysia;** oil refining.

Lutsk, c., Ukrainian SSR, **USSR;** pt. on Styr R.; one of oldest ts. in Volhynia; coal mng., machin.; architectural monuments; p. (est. 1980) 146,000.

Lutterworth, t., Leics., **Eng.;** church with relics of John Wyclif, religious reformer; engin.

Luxembourg, prov., S.E. **Belgium;** on Fr. border; wooded and hilly; a. 2,784 km²; cap. Arlon; p. (1981) 221,926.

Luxembourg, grand duchy, W. **Europe;** lies between Belgium, W. Germany, and France; divided into 12 admin. cans.; official language French though German frequently used; well wooded, most of a. over 300 m; economic prosperity based upon iron and steel inds. and lge. deposits of iron-ore; agr. and cattle raising impt.; sm. size of home market makes L. keen member of EC and cap. of L. contains many European organisations; tourist ind. based upon scenery and cas. ts.; a. 2,587 km²; p. (est. 1987) 369,500.

Luxembourg, c., cap. of grand duchy of **Luxembourg;** historic t., perched above valleys of Alzette and Petrusse Rs.; cath.; seat of European Court of Justice; p. (est. 1987) 76,640.

Luxor, v., Upper **Egypt;** on E. bank of Nile; site of Thebes; tomb of Tutankhamun; p. (1985) 137,300.

Luxulyan, St. Austell, Cornwall, **Eng.;** proposed site for nuclear power sta., fiercely opposed.

Luzon, I., lgst. and most N. of **Philippines;** mtn. ranges; fertile Cagayan valley; rice, sugar cane, cotton, coffee, hemp, tobacco; mineral deposits; cap. Manila; a. 104,688 km²; p. (1970) 16,669,724.

L'vov, c., Ukrainian SSR, **USSR;** founded 13th cent.; univ., caths.; major industl. ctr.; petroleum refining; natural gas nearby; p. (1986) 753,000.

Lyalpur, *See* **Faisalabad.**

Lydd, Shepway, Kent, **Eng.;** anc. t. on Romney marsh, at edge of Dungeness shingle; name given to explosive lyddite mnf. here; airport; p. (1981) 4,721.

Lydda, c., **Israel,** S.E. of Tel-Aviv; major airport; mentioned in the Bible and reputed birthplace of St. George; p. (est. 1971) 31,200.

Lydney, t., Gloucs., **Eng.;** in Forest of Dean; spt. on Severn estuary; timber imports; new lt. inds.

Lyme Regis, spt., West Dorset, **Eng.;** on bdy, between Devon and Dorset; holiday resort; p. (1981) 3,447.

Lymington, t., Hants., **Eng.;** on the Solent; ferry to I. of Wight; abbey; p. (1981) 38,698.

Lymm, t., Cheshire, **Eng.;** 8 km W. of Altrincham; mainly residtl.; p. (1981) 10,364.

Lynchburg, c., Va., **USA;** on James R. in foothills of Appalachians; tobacco ctr.; p. (1984) 67,300 (c.), 142,600 (met. a.).

Lyndhurst, v., Hants, **Eng.;** recognised as cap. of New Forest; tourism.

Lynemouth, nr. Blyth, Northumberland, **Eng.;** aluminium smelter.

Lynn, industl. c., Mass., **USA;** on Mass. Bay; footwear, elec. appliances; Mary Baker Eddy lived here; p. (1980) 78,471.

Lynton, t., North Devon, **Eng.;** 27 km W. of Minehead on Bristol Channel; tourist ctr. for Exmoor; sm. harbour of Lynmouth 130 m below; devastating flood of R. Lyn 1952; p. (1981) 2,037.

Lyons, c., cap. of Rhône dep., **France;** at confluence of Rs. Saône and Rhône; silk, rayon, chemicals, engin., heavy lorries; oil refinery nearby; univ.; world ctr. for cancer research; p. (1982) 418,476 (c.), 1,220,844 (met. a.).

Lytham St. Annes, t., N. Lancs., **Eng.;** on N. cst. of Ribble estuary, 6 km S. of Blackpool holiday ctr.; p. (1981) 39,707.

Lyttleton, spt., S.I., **N.Z.,** on N. cst. of Banks peninsula; imp. pt.; p. (1976) 3,327.

M

Ma'an, t., S. **Jordan,** terminus of rly. through Amman to Beirut; Hijaz rail line to Medina; p. (est. 1971) 12,000.

Maas, R., Dutch name for the R. Meuse after it has entered the Neth.

Maastricht, t., cap. of Limburg prov., **Neth.;** on R. Maas; pottery, glass, textiles, brewing; p. (est. 1987) 115,000.

Mablethorpe, t., East Lindsey, Lincs., **Eng.;** holiday resort; p. (1981) 7,456.

Macao, Portuguese col., S.E. **China;** increased indep. since 1975; to be returned to China in 1999; gambling, tourism, recreation for Hong Kong; new deep water port; rapid recent industl. growth (toys, textiles and transistors) with influx of capital resulting from uncertainty over the future of Hong Kong; oldest European col. in Far East (1557); a. 17 km²; p. (est. 1986) 426,4000

Macapá, c., cap. of Amapá st., **Brazil;** at mouth of R. Amazon; rubber, cattle tr.; p. (est. 1985) 169,600.

MacArthur (Ormoc), t., W. Leyte, **Philippines;** pt. and agr. ctr., exp. hemp, rice; p. (est. 1984) 116,474.

Macclesfield, t., l. gov. dist., Cheshire, **Eng.;** at foot of Pennines, 16 km S. of Stockport; on R. Bollin; mkt., textiles, clothing, paper prods., engin.; expanded t.; p. (est. 1988) 152,300.

Macdonald Is., terr. of Australia, **Antarctica.**

Macdonnell Range, mtns., N.T., **Australia;** highest part of desert tableland, centrally situated within the continent; some gold and mica mines, but development hampered by aridity and isolation; highest alt. 1,500 m.

Macduff, spt., burgh, Banff and Buchan, **Scot.;** 3 km E. of Banff; fishing; p. (1981) 3,894.

Macedonia, region of Balkan peninsula, covering parts of Greece, Yugoslavia, and Bulgaria.

Macedonia, dist., **Greece;** mtnous.; cereals, tobacco; chromium; cap. and pt. Salonika; a. 33,945 km²; p. (1981) 2,121,953.

Macedonia, constituent rep., **Yugoslavia;** agr., chromium; cap. Skopje; a. 27,436 km²; p. (1981) 1,909,136.

Maceio, spt. cap. of Alagôas st., **Brazil;** cotton, sugar, tobacco, soap, sawmills, distilleries; p. (est. 1985) 484,100.

Macerata, t., cap. of M. prov., **Italy;** cath., univ.; terracotta, glass, chemicals; p. (1981) 43,782.

Macgillicuddy's Reeks, mtns., Kerry, **R.o.I.;** highest peak, Carantuohil, 1,041 m.

Machala, t., Tibet, **China;** hgst. coalmine in world.

Machilipatnam (Bandar, Masulipatnam), spt., Andhra Pradesh, **India;** on Coromandel cst.; cotton mftg., rice; p. (1981) 138,530.

Machynlleth, t., Powys, **Wales;** on R. Dovey; clothing; tourism; p. (1981) 1,768.

Macintyre, R., N.S.W., **Australia;** forms border between Queensland and N.S.W.; trib. of R. Darling; 645 km. long.

Mackay, spt., Queensland, **Australia;** "Sugar Cap. of Australia"; artificial deep-water pt. for sugar exp.; p. (est. 1984) 22,550.

Mackenzie, R., N.W. Terr., **Canada;** lgst. in N. America; rises in Rocky mtns. as Athabaska, flows into Athabaska L., leaves as Slave R., thence into Gr. Slave L., below which it is known as Mackenzie R., across arctic plains to Beaufort Sea; 4,000 km. long.

Mackenzie Mtns., N.W. Terr., **Canada;** range of Rockies, still much unexplored; game preserve; max. alt. 2,760 m.

Mâcon, t., cap. of Saône-et-Loire dep., **France;** on R. Saône; Burgundy wines; p. (1982) 39,866.

Macon, c., Ga., **USA;** on Ocmulgee R.; industl. and shipping ctr. for agr. a., cotton, livestock; cotton mftg.; p. (1984) 120,200 (c.), 277,900 (met. a.).

Macquarie, I., Australian I., **S. Pac.;** 1,440 km S.E. of Tasmania; rich in wildlife, Tasmanian st. reserve (1972).

Macquarie, R., N.S.W., **Australia;** trib. of R. Darling; 960 km long.

Macroom, t., Cork, **R.o.I.;** on R. Sullane; agr., fishing; p. (1971) 2,256.

Madagascar (formerly **Malagasy Rep.**), I. off Moçabique; former Fr. col.; distinctive evolution of flora and fauna; p. engaged in agr.; rice staple food, coffee and cloves main exp.; inds. based on processing; offshore petroleum deposits; new refinery at ch. pt. of Toamasina; cap. Antananarivo; a. 587,041 km.²; p. (est. 1987) 10,568,000.

Madang, t., **Papua New Guinea;** entrepôt pt. on N. cst.; international airpt.; p. (1971) 16,865.

Madeira, R., **Brazil;** trib. of Amazon; with Mamoré R., c. 3,200 km long.

Madeira Is., volcanic archipelago, Atl. Oc., part of met. **Portugal;** partial autonomy by regional gov. (1977); wine, sugar, fruits; tourism; cap. Funchal on Madeira I., lgst. of gr.; a. 790 km²; p. (est. 1986) 269,500.

Madhya Pradesh, st., **India;** absorbed sts. Bhopal, Vindhya Pradesh, Madhya Bharat, 1956; rice, jute, pulses, oilseeds, cotton; forests; manganese, coal, marble, limestone; cotton textile mftg.; cap. Bhopal; a. 443,452 km²; p. (1981) 52,178,844.

Madinat ash Sha'b (Al Ittihad), cap. of **Democratic Rep. of Yemen;** N.W. of Aden.

Madison, c., cap. of Wis., **USA;** educational and admin. ctr.; univ.; mnfs. agr. tools, footwear; p. (1984) 170,700 (c.), 333,000 (met. a.).

Madiun, t., Java, **Indonesia;** agr. and comm. ctr.; engin.; p. (1980) 150,502.

Madras, c., cap. of Tamil Nadu st., **India;** spt. on Bay of Bengal, on Coromandel cst.; cath.; univ.; comm. and mftg. ctr.; textile mills, tanneries, potteries, chemical plants; oil refinery projected; p. (1981) 3,276,622.

Madras. See **Tamil Nadu.**

Madre de Dios, R., **Bolivia;** trib. of R. Madeira; rises in Peru; 960 km long.

Madrid, c., cap. of **Spain;** and of M. prov. on Manzanares R.; stands at 665 m (highest cap. in Europe) in vast open plains; although remote with relatively few inds. is ctr. of Spanish admin. and communications; univ., cath., Prado gallery; printing, publishing; p. (1987) 3,100,507.

Madura, I., **Indonesia;** off N.E. Java; dry climate, limestone soils; arable and pastoral agr.; salt; a. 4,584 km²; p. c. 2,000,000.

Madurai, t., Tamil Nadu, **India;** univ., impt. textile ctr.; p. (1981) 820,891 (c.), 907,732 (met. a.).

Maebashi, c., central Honshu, **Japan;** N.W. Kanto plain; silk textile ctr.; p. (1985) 277,319.

Maelstrom, tidewater whirlpool, in Lofoten Is., **Norway.**

Maentwrog, v., Gwynedd, N. **Wales;** in Vale of Ffestiniog, 3 km E. of Ffestiniog; ch. hydroelectric power sta. in N. Wales.

Maesteg, t., Ogwr, Mid Glamorgan, **Wales;** dormitory t. for steel wks. at Pt. Talbot; coal mng., cosmetics; p. (1981) 20,888.

Mafeking (Mafikeng) t., N.E. Cape Prov., **Bophuthaswana S. Africa;** famous siege at outbreak of Boer War 1899–1900; p. (est. 1971) 6,493.

Magadan, spt., **RSFSR;** on N. side of Sea of Okhotsk; marine engin.; fishing; p. (est. 1980) 124,000.

Magadi, L., Kenya; in Gr. Rift valley; carbonate of soda extracted.

Magdalena, R., **Colombia;** forms basis of inland navigation system, opening up interior; 1,600 km long.

Magdeburg, c., Magdeburg, **E. Germany;** on R. Elbe; cath.; beet-sugar ctr., sugar-refineries; chemicals, steel, mng. machin., heavy engin.; route ctr. and lge. inland pt.; p. (est. 1986) 289,000.

Magelang, t., Java, **Indonesia;** tr. ctr.; tannery; p. (1980) 123,484.

Magellan, strait, between Tierra del Fuego and Chile, separates Atl. and Pac. Ocs.

Maggiore, L., N. **Italy–Switzerland;** a. 212 km²; contains Borromean Is.; tourist resort.

Magherafelt, l. gov. dist., centred on t. of M., **N. Ireland;** agr. a. bordering L. Neagh; (1981) 30,656 (dist.), 5,044 (t.).

Maghreb, collective name given to Arabic-speaking countries bordering Mediterranean in N. Africa, inc. Algeria, Morocco and Tunisia.

Magnet Mtn., S. Urals, **RSFSR;** very rich deposit of magnetite iron ore; smelted at Magnitogorsk, and in Kuzbas region.

Magnitogorsk, c., **RSFSR;** in S. Urals, on R. Ural; sited on magnetite deposits; metallurgical ctr.; oil pipeline from Shkapovo in Bashkira; p. (est. 1980) 410,000.

Mahajanga (Majunga), t., **Madagascar;** second t. and pt.; meat conserves, sacks, cement; p. (est. 1982) 81,000.

Mahalla El Kubra. See **El Mahalla el Kubra.**

Mahanadi, R., **India;** flows from Orissa to Bay of Bengal; forms extensive delta; sugar and rice growing; 832 km long.

Maharashtra, st., W. **India;** on Arabian Sea; ch. ts. Bombay (cap.), Poona, Nagpur; fertile lava soils; impt. cotton-growing dist. of Deccan; a. 307,477 km²; p. (1981) 62,784,171.

Mahé, former Fr. prov., S. **India;** united with India 1954; cap. Mahé.

Mahon, spt., cap. of Minorca, Balearic Is., **Spain;** p. (1981) 21,624.

Maidenhead, t., Windsor and Maidenhead, Berks., **Eng.;** on R. Thames, 14 km above Windsor; residtl.; p. (1981) 49,038; See **Windsor.**

Maidens, The, gr. of dangerous rocks off Larne cst., **N. Ireland.**

Maidstone, co. t., l. gov. dist., Kent, **Eng.;** on R. Medway; regional ctr.; brewing, paper, agr. tools, confectionery, timber inds.; p. (est. 1988) 136,000 (dist.).

Maiduguri, t., **Nigeria;** cap. Bornu st.; on rly. from Bornu; mkt.; p. (est. 1983) 231,000.

Maikop, c. cap. of Adygei aut. oblast, Krasnodar terr., **RSFSR;** oilfields nearby; oil-refineries, woodwkg., food-processing; p. (est. 1980) 130,000.

Main, R., **W. Germany;** joins Rhine opposite Mainz; linked with Danube via Ludwig canal; and newer Rhine-Main-Danube canal creating waterway from N. Sea to Black Sea of 3,500 km; 448 km long.

Main Range, central mtns. of **W. Malaysia;** rise to over 2,100 m.

Maine, st., New England, **USA;** Pine tree St.; admitted to Union 1820; st. flower White Pine Tassel, st. bird Chickadee; mtnous., with much forest; potatoes, paper, pulp, metals, woollens, shoes, processed foods; cap. Augusta; ch. spt. Portland; a. 86,027 km²; p. (1985) 1,164,000.

Maine-et-Loire, dep., **France;** agr. vineyards; cap. Angers; a. 7,280 km²; p. (1982) 676,100.

Mainland I., lgst. of Shetlands, **Scot. Mainland,** I., lgst. of Orkneys, see **Pomona.**

Mainz, c., cap of Rhineland-Palatinate, **W. Germany;** at confluence of Rs. Rhine and Main; R. pt.; cath., univ., cas.; cement, engin., optical glass, food-processing; p. (est. 1986) 189,000.

Maisons-Alfort, t., **France;** S.E. sub. of Paris; p. (1982) 51,591.

Maitland, t., N.S.W., **Australia;** on R. Hunter, nr. Newcastle; ctr. for fertile Hunter Valley; coal mng. decreasing; p. (1981) 38,865.

Majes, R., S. **Peru;** valley a. site of projected irrigation scheme; 240 km long.

Majorca (Mallorca), lgst of Balearic Is., **Spain;** major tourist ctr.; ch. t. and pt. Palma; a. 3,639 km²; p. (1981) 561,215.

Majunga. See **Mahajanga.**

Makalu, mtn., Nepal and Tibet, **China;** fifth hgst. mtn. in world; part of Himalayas; alt. 8,486 m.

Makasar. See **Ujung Pandang.**

Makassar, strait, **Indonesia;** separates Kalimantan from Sulawesi; 384 km wide.

Makeyevka, c., Ukrainian SSR, **USSR;** in Donets basin; metallurgical and coal-mng. ctr.; p. (est. 1980) 439,000.

Makhachkala, c., cap. of Dagestan ASSR, **RSFSR;** pt. on Caspian Sea; comm. and industl. ctr.; oil refineries linked by pipeline to Grozny fields; p. (est. 1980) 261,000.

Makó, t., **Hungary;** on Maros R., nr. Romanian bdy.; comm. and agr. ctr.; p. (est. 1984) 30,000.

Makran, dist., **Pakistan** and **Iran;** coastal dist.; lowland route between India and Middle E.

Makurdi, t. **Nigeria,** W. Africa; on R. Benue; mkt. for palm prod., groundnuts; rly. bridge across R. Benue.

Makwar, v., **Sudan,** N.E. Africa; on Blue Nile; site of Sennar Dam.

Malabar Coast, India; name applied to W. cst. of India from Goa to southern tip of peninsula at C. Comorin; sand dunes backed by lagoons; coastlands intensively cultivated, rice, spices, rubber, coconuts; ch. pt. Cochin.

Malabo (Santa Isabel), cap of **Equatorial Guinea;** on Marcias Nguema I.; ch. pt. for I., exp. cacao; comm. and financial ctr.; p. (est. 1986) 10,000.

Malacca, st., S.W. **W. Malaysia;** originally part of Brit. Straits Settlements (q.v.); cap. M.; a. 1,658 km²; p. (1980) 464,754.

Malacca, strait, separates Sumatra, **Indonesia,** from **W. Malaysia;** 38 km wide at narrowest point; international routeway but attempts by Malaysia and Indonesia to claim it as territorial water.

Maladetta, with **Pic d'Anéto,** hgst. point in Pyrenees, **Spain;** alt. 3,408 m.

Malaga, c. cap. of Malaga prov., **Spain;** in Andalusia on Bay of M.; impt. spt.; olive oil, wine, fruit; oil pipeline from Puertollano; winter resort; cath., citadel; birthplace of Picasso; p. (1987) 566,330.

Malagassy Rep. See **Madagascar.**

Malakoff, t. S.W. sub. of Paris, Hauts-de-Seine, **France;** residtl. and also industl.; p. (1975) 34,215.

Malang, t., Java, **Indonesia;** ctr. of fertile agr. basin; p. (est. 1983) 560,000.

Mälar, L., S.E. **Sweden;** connected with Baltic by Södertelge canal; 1,260 Is.; length 128 km; a. 1,235 km².

Malatya, c., cap. of M. prov., central **Turkey;** at foot of Taurus mtns.; ctr. of rich agr. a.; fruit, opium; p. (1985) 243,138.

Malawi, land locked rep., Central **Africa;** L. Malawi to S. and E.; tropical climate modified by alt.; few natural resources; economy based on agr.; one of most fertile soils in Africa but only 50 per cent cultivated; exp. tobacco and tea; new cap at Lilongwe (old cap. Zomba); a. 117,614 km²; p. (est. 1987) 7·9 m.

Malawi, L., central **Africa;** southward extension of the Gr. Rift valley; c. 450 m a.s.l.; 560 km by 64 km; drains by R. Shire into R. Zambezi; petroleum under L. bed.

Malaya. See **Malaysia, West.**

Malay Archipelago, lge. gr. of Is. extending 7,680 km from Nicobar Is. in Bay of Bengal to Solomon Is. in Pac.; inc. Sumatra, Java, Kalimantan, Sulawesi, Philippines, New Guinea, Bismarck archipelago.

Malaysia, East, part of **Fed. of Malaysia;** inc. Sarawak and Sabah (formerly Brit. N. Borneo); less developed than W. Malaysia; p. concentrated on cst; hill tribes engaged in hunting in interior; diversification of Malaysian agr. has introduced cocoa as a major crop; oil major exp., exploration off cst.; separated from W. Malaysia by S. China Sea; a. 200,971 km²; p. (est. 1980) 2,318,628.

Malaysia, Federation of, indep. federation (1963), S.E. **Asia;** member of Brit. Commonwealth; inc. W. Malaysia (Malaya) and E. Malaysia (Borneo sts. of Sarawak and Sabah); cap. Kuala Lumpur; a. 329,293 km²; p. (est. 1987) 16·6 m.

Malaysia, West (Malaya), part of **Federation of Malaysia;** consists of wide peninsula S. of Thailand; most developed in W.; world's leading producer of natural rubber; worlds leading exporter of tin; but decline in world prices of both these prod. has encouraged economic diversification; timber exports also declining due to efforts to conserve rainforest; palm oil, petrol, electrical and electronic machin. now impt. export; new gas discoveries, attempts to convert palm oil into diesel fuel; free port at Pasir Gudang to divert exports from Singapore; 35 per cent of p. Chinese; a. 131,588 km²; p. (est. 1985) 15,557,000.

Malbork (Marienburg), t., Gdansk, **Poland;** R. pt. on Nogat R.; cas.; p. (1970) 30,900.

Malden, t., Mass., **USA;** mftg. sub. of Boston; rubber gds., hosiery, furniture; p. (1980) 53,386.

Maldive Is., indep. rep. (1968) former Brit., prot., **Indian Oc.;** chain of coral atolls c. 640 km S.W. of Sri Lanka; 1,067 Is., 193 inhabited; economy based on fishing (bonito and tuna); dried fish main exp.; modernisation of fishing with Japanese aid; coconuts, copra, coconut oil, coir, cowrie shells; cap. Male; former Brit. air base on Gan. I. (until 1976); a. 298 km²; p. (est. 1986) 189,000.

Maldon, t., l. gov. dist., Essex, **Eng.;** sm. pt. at head of Blackwater estuary; agr. machin., steel windowframes, flour-milling; p. (est. 1988) 53,600 (dist.).

Malegaon, t., Maharashtra, **India;** in Satmala Hills N.E. of Bombay; p. (1981) 245,883.

Malham Cove, North Yorks., **Eng.;** in Craven dist. of N. Pennines, 16 km N.W. of Skipton; semicircular amphitheatre limestone cliffs from base of which emerges R. Aire.

Mali, Rep. of, W. Africa; landlocked st.; former Fr. col. of Soudan; dry semi-desert climate in S.; extends into Sahara desert in N.; badly affected by Sahelian drought since 1971; few natural resources; nomadic pastoralist p. in N.; only 20 per cent of a. cultivable; livestock basis of inds. (hides, wool, etc.) and exps.; many minerals but not exploited; cap. Bamako; a. 1,204,350 km²; p. (est. 1987) 8,730,000.

Malinda, t., **Kenya;** growing tourist resort on Indian Ocean cst.

Malin Head, Donegal, **R.o.I.;** most N. point.

Malines (Mechelen), t., **Belgium;** on R. Dyle;

cath.; rly. ctr., textiles, furniture; once famous for lace; p. (1981) 77,269.

Malling, t., Kent, **Eng.;** 5 km W. of Maidstone; fruit, chemicals. See **Tonbridge.**

Mallow, mkt. t., Cork, **R.o.I.;** on R. Blackwater; agr. fishing, flour mills, tanneries, condensed milk, dehydrated foods; p. (1981) 6,572.

Malmesbury, t., North Wilts., **Eng.;** anc. hilltop t. in Cotswolds; mkt.; abbey; elec. engin.; birthplace of Thomas Hobbes; p. (1981) 2,552.

Malmö, c., spt., S. **Sweden;** on the Sound opposite Copenhagen; third lgst. c. in cty.; naval and comm. pt.; former ctr. for shipbldg., textiles, machin.; founded in 12th cent.; car and aerospace engin. plant to relieve unemployment; proposed bridge across Öresund Str. to Denmark; p. (est. 1986) 230,000 (c.), 455,000 (met. a.).

Malta, indep. st. within Br. C. (1964), rep. (1974); I. in Mediterranean, 93 km S. of Sicily; strategic location; former British naval and military base; agr. ch. occupation with ship-repairing at dry-docks of Valletta; sm.-scale inds. growing; tourism exploits Mediterranean climate; major airport at Luqa; awarded George Cross for bravery in second world war; cap. Valletta; a. 316 km²; p. (est. 1986) 343,334. (inc. Gozo and Comino).

Maltby, t., Ryedale, South Yorks., **Eng.;** p. (1981) 16,749.

Malton, mkt. t., North Yorks., **Eng.;** on R. Derwent, in S.W. of Vale of Pickering; brewing; p. (1981) 4,143.

Malvern, t., Hereford and Worcs., **Eng.;** at E. foot of Malvern hills; spa; annual dramatic festival; Elgar lived here; p. (1981) 30,187.

Malvern Hills, narrow ridge forming bdy. between Worcs. and Hereford, **Eng.;** rises very abruptly from Severn valley to over 300 m between Malvern and Bromsberrow; moorland, woodland on lower slopes; now forms l. gov. dist.; p. (est. 1988) 87,900.

Mammoth Cave, Ky., **USA;** to S. of Green R. in hilly forested parkland; spectacular limestone formations (stalactites, stalagmites), lakes and rivers (e.g. Echo R., 110 m below surface) in avenues aggregating 240 km long; included in Nat. Park.

Mamoré, R., N. **Bolivia** and **Brazil;** rises in Andes; 1,920 km long.

Mam Soul, mtn., Kyle of Lochalsh and Inverness, **Scot.;** alt. 1,178 m.

Manacle Rocks, dangerous reef off cst. of Cornwall, **Eng.;** 12 km S. of Falmouth.

Manacor, t., Majorca, **Spain;** artificial pearls, wine, stalactite caves of Drach and Hams; p. (1981) 24,153.

Managua, c., cap. of **Nicaragua;** on S. shore of L. Managua; industl. and comm. ctr.; oil refining, agr. processing, textiles, steel; univ.; 48 km from pt. Puerto Somoza; violent earthquake Dec. 1972; p. (est. 1985) 682,111.

Managua, L., **Nicaragua;** second lgst. L. in Central America.

Manāmah, Al, cap. and ch. pt. **Bahrain,** Persian G.; free pt., comm. ctr.; declining pearl-fishing ind.; linked by causeway to internat. airpt.; p. (est. 1987) 121,986.

Manáus (Manaos), c., cap. of Amazonas st., N.W. **Brazil;** on Rio Negro nr. confluence with Amazon; impt. R. pt., airport.; oil refinery; former rubber ctr.; in free zone (10,360 km²) recently set up to encourage development in Amazonas; new inds. include steel wks., oil refinery; boom now far exceeds 19th century rubber boom; tourism; internat. airpt.; p. (est. 1985) 834,500.

Manche, dep., N.W. **France;** on English Channel; agr. and dairying; cap. Saint Lô; ch. pt. Cherbourg; a. 6,410 km²; p. (1982) 482,600.

Manchester, c., Gtr. Manchester, **Eng.;** on R. Irwell; terminus of Manchester Ship Canal; but only 1 dock out of 8 left open; ctr. of cotton and manmade fibre textile inds.; heavy, lt. and elec. engin., machine tools, petro-chemicals, dyestuffs, pharmaceutical gds.; univ.; comm., cultural and recreational cap. of N.W. Eng.; p. (est. 1988) 445,900 (met. dist.), 2,577,700 (Greater Manchester).

Manchester, t., Conn., **USA;** textiles (silk); p. (1980) 49,761.

Manchester, t., N.H., **USA;** at Amoskeag falls, on the Merrimac R.; textiles, footwear, machin.; p. (1984) 94,900 (c.), 136,400 (met. a.).

Manchester Ship Canal, ship canal, Cheshire/ Merseyside/Gtr. Manchester, **Eng.;** joins Manchester to Mersey estuary at Eastham; can be used by ocean steamers; 57 km long.

Manchuria. *See* **North-East China.**

Mandalay, c., **Burma;** on R. Irrawaddy, 640 km N. of Rangoon; former cap.; lost importance with rise of Irrawaddy delta; many temples, palaces; p. (1983) 532,895.

Manfredonia, mkt. t., Foggia, **Italy;** fish. pt.; cath.; p. (1981) 52,674.

Mangalore, spt., Karnataka, **India;** exp. coffee, coconuts, rice, spices, fertiliser; p. (1981) 172,252 (c), 306,078 (met. a.).

Mangere, N.I., **N.Z.;** 21 km S. of Auckland; international airport (opened 1965).

Mangla Dam, Pakistan; world's lgst. earth-filled dam, on Jhelum R., part of Indus Basin irrigation scheme.

Manhattan, I., N.Y., **U.S.A.;** at mouth of Hudson R.; a. 57 km²; forms major part of bor. of Manhattan of N.Y. City.

Manila, c., S.W. Luzon, **Philippines;** leading c. and ch. pt. of Is.; entrepôt tr.; modern skyscrapers; univ., cath.: major airpt.; p. (est. 1984) 6,720,050 (met. a.).

Manipur, new st. (1972), E. **India;** borders Burma; former princely st.; cap. Imphal; a. 22,274 km²; p. (1981) 1,420,953.

Manisa, c., cap. of M. prov., W. **Turkey;** agr. ctr.; mineral deposits nearby; p. (1985) 127,012.

Manitoba, prov., **Canada;** wheat, rich mineral deposits, fisheries; diverse inds.; cap. Winnipeg; a. 650,090 km²; p. (1986) 1,071,000.

Manitowoc, c., Wis., **USA;** on L. Mich.; shipbldg., aluminium wks., flour mills; p. (1980) 32,547.

Manizales, c., cap. of Caldas, **Colombia;** 2,155 m in the Central Cordillera; in rich coffee a.; route ctr.; p. (1985) 309,821.

Mannar, G., with Palk Strait separates **India** from **Sri Lanka.**

Mannheim, c., Baden-Württemberg, **W. Germany;** major R. pt. at confluence of Rs. Neckar and Rhine, opposite Ludwigshafen; heavy and lt. inds., notably precision instruments, machin., vehicles; p. (est. 1986) 294,600.

Manono, t. **Zaïre;** ctr. for tin-mng.; foundries.

Manresa, industl. t., N.E. **Spain;** in Catalonia; textiles; associated with Ignatius of Loyola; place of pilgrimage; p. (1981) 64,745.

Mansfield, t., l. gov. dist., Notts., **Eng.;** on E. flank of Pennines, 19 km N. of Nottingham; coal mng., sand-quarrying, textiles, footwear, metal boxes, machin.; p. (est. 1988) 100,000 (dist.).

Mansfield, t., Ohio, **USA;** machin. farm tools, paper, rubber gds.; p. (1984) 51,900 (t.), 129,100 (met. a.).

Mansfield Woodhouse, t., Notts., **Eng.;** 3 km N. of Mansfield; stone quarries; Roman remains; p. (1981) 26,725.

Mansûra, c., Lower **Egypt;** pt. on Nile; cotton mftg.; univ. (1972); p. (1985) 328,700.

Mantua, c., cap. of M. prov., N. **Italy;** on R. Mincio; comm. and agr. ctr.; old fortfd. c.; p. (1981) 60,866.

Manukau, c., N.I., **N.Z.;** new c. (1965) formed from amalgamation of suburban communities around Auckland; p. (est. 1987) 181,000, now lgst. c. of N.Z.

Manukau Harbour, N.I., **N.Z.;** lge. shallow inlet on W. cst. of Auckland peninsula; provides additional harbour facilities for spt. of Auckland; recreational sailing; fishing.

Manych, R., **RSFSR;** trib. of R. Don; 480 km long; canal being built through R. to Caspian to provide through connection with Black Sea.

Manzala (Menzala), lagoon, Mediterranean cst., **Egypt;** extends E. from Damietta mouth of Nile to Pt. Said; fringed by salt marsh; a. 2,072 km².

Manzanillo, spt., S.E. **Cuba;** exp. sugar, rice, tobacco; p. (1966) 87,000.

Manzanillo, c. Colima, W. **Mexico;** ch. pt. on Pac. Oc.; exp. coffee, timber, minerals; p. (est. 1970) 21,000.

Maputo (Lourenço Marques), spt., cap. of **Moçambique;** at head of Delagoa Bay; rly. terminus; oil refining, deposits of bentonite worked nearby; ore terminal, much transit tr.; second lgst. pt. in Africa; p. (est. 1986) 882,800.

Maracaibo, spt. cap. of Zulia st., **Venezuela;** deepwater harbour; on W. of narrow entrance on L. Maracaibo; univ.; oilfields and refineries; exp. coffee, cocoa, hardwoods; p. (1981) 888,800.

Maracaibo, G., and L., Zulia st., **Venezuela;** brackish lake, 192 km long, 96 km wide; oilwells on fringes and drilled into lake floor.

Maracay, c., N. **Venezuela;** on L. Valencia, 112 km from Carácas; p. (1981) 440,000.

Maragheh, t., **Iran;** on N. end of L. Urmia; comm. and fruit ctr.; p. (est. 1970) 60,000.

Marajó, I., at mouth of the Rs. Amazon and Pará, **Brazil;** a. 38,850 km².

Maralinga, S. **Australia;** 320 km N.E. Eucla; joint U.K.–Australian atomic testing ground, first weapon exploded here 27 Sept. 1956.

Maranhão, st., N.E. **Brazil;** rice, cotton, sugar, tobacco, coffee, cattle, gold, copper; oil in the Barrierinhas a.; cap. São Luiz; a. 334,812 km²; p. (est. 1985) 4,655,100.

Marañon, R. *See* **Amazon, R.**

Maras, t., S. central **Turkey;** tr. in Kurdish carpets; p. (1985) 210,371.

Marathon, v. and plain, **Greece;** 32 km N.E. of Athens; here the Athenians defeated the Persians 490 B.C.

Marazion, mkt. t., Cornwall, **Eng.;** on Mount's Bay, nr. St. Michael's Mount; pilchard fisheries.

Marble Bar, t., W. **Australia;** 136 km inland by rail from Pt. Hedland; ctr. of Pilbara goldfields; p. (1976) 262.

Marburg on Lahn, t., Hesse, **W. Germany;** univ., cas.; noted for optical instruments; p. (est. 1986) 77,100.

March, mkt. t., Fenland, Cambs., **Eng.;** on R. Nene in Fens; rly. junc.; farm tools; p. (1981) 14,475.

Marches, The, region, central **Italy;** extending from eastern slopes of Apennines to Adriatic cst.; embracing provs. of Macerata, Ascoli-Piceno, Ancona, and Pesaro e Urbino; a. 9,697 km²; p. (est. 1986) 1·4 m.

Marchfeld, plain, Lower **Austria;** between Rs. Danube and Morava which here forms bdy. between Austria and ČSSR.

Marcias Nguema. *See* **Biako.**

Mar del Plata, c., **Argentina;** on C. Corrientes; Atl. cst. resort; p. (1980) 415,000.

Maree, L., Ross and Cromarty, **Scot.;** 21 km long, c. 3 km wide; rocky shores; studded with wooded islets.

Maremma, coastal region along Tyrrhenean Sea, S. Tuscany, **Italy;** once malarial, now drained with wide fertile areas.

Mareotis or **Birket-et-Mariut,** L., Lower **Egypt;** separated from Mediterranean by ridge of sand on which stands Alexandria; 80 km long, 32 km wide.

Margam, t., in Pt. Talbot, West Glamorgan, S. **Wales;** on cst. of Swansea Bay; lge. new steel-wks., lgst. steel-rolling mill in Europe.

Margarita, I., in Caribbean off N. **Venezuela;** tourism; formerly pearl-fishing ctr.; cap. Asunción; a. 1,166 km²; p. (est. 1970) 26,000.

Margate, t., Kent, **Eng.;** W. of N. Foreland, in the Isle of Thanet; seaside resort; p. (1981) 53,280.

Margolan, t., E. Uzbek SSR, **USSR;** in Ferghana Valley; noted for silk ind.; p. (est. 1980) 112,000.

Mari, aut. rep., **RSFSR;** timber, paper inds.; p. (1986) 729,000.

Mariana Is. (Marianas), chain of Is., **W. Pac.;** US Trust Terr.; most impt. are Guam, Saipan, and Tinian; US Commonwealth status planned for N. Mariana Is.; a. 479 km²; p. (est. 1984) 20,000.

Maribor, t., Slovenia, **Yugoslavia;** on Drava R. nr. Austrian border; metallurgical inds.; ctr. of agr. a.; p. (1981) 185,699.

Marília, t., São Paulo st., **Brazil;** coffee, cotton, oil peanuts; p. (est. 1985) 136,500.

Mariinsk Canal. *See* **Volga Baltic Waterway.**

Marion, c., Ind., **USA;** mkt. ctr. within corn belt; varied inds.; p. (1980) 35,874.

Marion, t., Ohio, **USA;** agr. ctr., with varied agr. mnfs.; p. (1980) 37,040.

Maritime Provinces, include Canadian provs. of Nova Scotia, New Brunswick, Prince Edward I.

Maritsa, R., Bulgaria and **Greece;** used for irrigation and hydroelectric power; 416 km long.

Market Drayton, t., North Shrops., **Eng.;** on R. Tern, 21 km S.W. of Newcastle-under-Lyme; agr. implements, nylon mftg.

Market Harborough, t., Harborough, Leics., **Eng.;** on R. Welland, 13 km N.W. of Kettering; elec. engin., foodstuffs, corsetry; p. (1981) 15,934.

Market Rasen, t., West Lindsey, Lincs., **Eng.;** agr. ctr.; racecourse; p. (1981) 2,689.

Markinch, burgh, Kirkcaldy, **Scot.;** 13 km N. of Kirkcaldy; paper mftg., whisky blending and bottling factory closed 1983; p. (1981) 2,044.

Marl, t., N. Rhine–Westphalia, **W. Germany**; in Ruhr; coal mng.; chemicals; p. (est. 1986) 87,800.

Marlborough, t., Wycombe, Wilts., **Eng.**; on R. Kennet in heart of Marlborough Downs; public school; p. (1981) 5,771.

Marlborough, prov., S.I., **N.Z.**; pastoral; a. 10,930 km²; cap. Blenheim; p. (est. 1985) 37,200.

Marlborough Downs, hills, Wilts., **Eng.**; chalk; highest point, Milk Hill, 298 m.

Marlow, t., Bucks., **Eng.**; on R. Thames; mkt., tourist ctr.; home of Shelley; p. (1981) 14,132.

Marmara, Sea of, separates Europe from Asia; connected with Black Sea through the Bosporus, with Aegean Sea through Dardanelles; shores belong to Turkey.

Marne, dep., N.E. **France**; in Champagne; ctr. of champagne ind.; cap. Châlons-sur-Marne; a. 8,205 km²; p. (1982) 544,800.

Marne, R., central **France**; rises in Plateau de Langres, flows across Champagne Humide, Champagne Pouilleuse, and Beauce, joins R. Seine just above Paris; with Marne–Rhine and Marne–Saône canals forms impt. inland waterway linking Seine with Rhine and Rhône valleys; c. 520 km. long.

Marple, t., Gtr. Manchester, **Eng.**; 5 km. E. of Stockport; engin., residtl.; p. (1981) 23,899.

Marquesas Is., volcanic gr. in central **Pac. Oc.**, part of Fr. Polynesia; lgst. Nukuhiva and Hivaoa; mtnous., fertile; exp. copra, vanilla, tobacco, cotton; a. 1,274 km²; p. (1983) 6,548.

Marrakesh, c., **Morocco**; tourist ctr.; leather gds., carpets; p. (est. 1981) 549,000.

Marsa el-Brega, new pt., G. of Sirte, **Libya**; oil pipeline from Zelten; gas liquefaction plant opened 1970; airport.

Marsala, pt., Sicily, **Italy**; on site of anc. Carthaginian settlement; wine ctr.; p. (1981) 79,093.

Marseilles, c., spt., cap. of Bouche-du-Rhône dep., S. **France**; on Provence cst.; passenger and gds. traffic; pt. inds., marine engin., oil refining; oil pipeline to Karlsruhe; industl. expansion at G. of Fos; cath., univ., palace; founded as Massilia by Phocaean Greeks of Asia Minor 600 B.C.; p. (1982) 878,689 (c.), 1,110,511 (met. a.).

Marshall Is., gr. of coral Is., central **Pac. Oc.**; internal self-government (1978), comprising 34 atolls; exp. copra, sugar, coffee; admin. ctr. Jaluit I.; US Pac. Trust Terr.; a. 181 km²; nuclear bomb tests; p. (est. 1984) 35,000.

Martha's Vineyard, I., S.E. Mass., **USA**; state forest; summer resort; ch. ts., Vineyard Haven, Oak Bluffs, Edgartown; summer resort.

Martigny, t., Valais, **Switzerland**; linked by road tunnel to Aosta, Italy; p. 6,572.

Martina Franca, t., S. **Italy**; in Apulia; wine, olive oil; summer resort; p. (est. 1968) 38,771.

Martinique, I., Fr. overseas dep., Windward Is., **W.I.**; dominated by volcanic peak Mt. Pelée which erupted 1902 destroying t. of St. Pierre; hurricanes, earthquakes; economy based on sugar-cane and fruit prod.; much emigration to France; cap. Fort de France; a. 1,088 km²; p. (est. 1987) 328,500.

Martos, t., Jaen prov., Andalusia, **Spain**; castled hilltop t.; wines, sulphur springs; mftg.; p. (1981) 21,672.

Mary (Merv), c., Turkmen SSR, **USSR**; in oasis in Kara-Kum desert; anc. c. founded 3rd cent. B.C.; textile ctr.; p. (est. 1986) 87,000.

Maryborough, t., Queensland, **Australia**; pt. on Mary R.; exp. fruit, sugar, timber, coal; p. (est. 1984) 22,400.

Maryborough. See **Port Laoighise, Ireland.**

Mary Kathleen, t., Queensland, **Australia**; new t., nr. uranium field in Cloncurry a.

Maryland, one of original 13 sts. of **USA**; Old Line St.; admitted to Union 1788; st. flower Black eyed Susan, st. bird Baltimore Oriel; on shores of Chesapeake Bay; humid continental climate; arable agr. and mkt. gardening; sea-fishing; cap. Annapolis; lgst. c. Baltimore; a. 27,394 km²; p. (1985) 4,392,000.

Maryport, t., Allerdale, Cumbria, **Eng.**; former pt.; modern lt. inds. in industl. estate to S. of t.; p. (1981) 11,598.

Masaya, t., W. **Nicaragua**; comm. ctr. in rich agr. a.; p. (est. 1985) 75,000.

Masbate, I., **Philippines**; gold mng.; a. 3,269 km²; p. (1970) 492,868.

Mascarene Is., collective name of **Mauritius, Rodriguez and Réunion, in Indian Oc.**

Maseru, t., cap. **Lesotho**; nr. border with S. Africa on Caledon R.; two new industl. estates to encourage light inds.; tourists from S. Africa; p. (est. 1986) 109,382.

Mashad (Meshed), c., N.E. **Iran**; cap. of Khorassan prov.; linked by oil pipeline to Esfahan; linked by new rly. to USSR border; p. (1982) 1,119,748.

Masham, t., North Yorks., **Eng.**: on R. Ure; 14 km N.W. of Ripon; mkt.

Mashhad, c., N.E. **Iran**; cap. of Khorassan prov.; p. (1986) 1,466,018.

Mashonaland, dist., **Zimbabwe**; a. inhabited by the Mashona tribe; ch. t. Salisbury.

Masjid-i-Sulamain, t., **Iran**; impt. oilfield and refinery; p. (est. 1982) 117,000..

Mask, L., Mayo and Galway, **R.o.I.**; 19 km long 3–6 km wide.

Mason City, t., Iowa, **USA**; on Sheel Rock R.; tr. ctr. of lge. agr. a.; p. (1980) 30,144.

Mason–Dixon Line. See **Section L.**

Massachusetts, st., New England, **USA**; Bay St.; admitted to Union 1788; st. flower Mayflower, st. bird Chickadee; on Atl. cst.; humid continental climate; hilly interior severed by N.–S. Connecticut valley; major fishing ind.; replacement of traditional textile inds. by modern science-based inds., especially around M. Institute of Technology; impt. arable agr. a.; cap. Boston; a. 21,386 km²; p. (1985) 5,822,000.

Massa di Carrara. See **Carrara.**

Massawa, spt., **Ethiopia**, on Red Sea; fine harbour; fishing; fish meal; p. (est. 1980) 32,977.

Massif Central, upland a., **France**; variable geology and scenery inc. volcanic Auvergne and limestone Causses; much rural depopulation, pastoral agr.; industl. ts. inc. St. Etienne based on sm. coalfields in N.E.; others ts. inc. Limoges and Clermont-Ferrand.

Masterton, bor., N.I., **N.Z.**; meat-packing; dairy prods., woollen mills; p. (est. 1987) 18,450.

Masulipatnam. See **Machilipatnam.**

Masvingo. See **Fort Victoria.**

Matabeleland, dist., **Zimbabwe**; a. inhabited by Matabele tribe; ch. t. Bulawayo.

Matadi, spt., **Zaïre**; on R. Zaïre; main pt.; exp. forest prod.; proposed Inga power project nearby; p. (1982) 162,396.

Matagalpa, t., **Nicaragua**; ctr. of agr. a., food processing; second lgst. t. of Nicaragua; p. (est. 1985) 37,000.

Matamoros, irrigated region, **Mexico**; around t. of M. on Rio Grande delta; Mexico's leading producer of cotton.

Matamoros, t., **Mexico**; on Rio Grande; livestock tr. ctr.; p. (1980) 238,840.

Matanzas, spt., cap. of M. prov., **Cuba**; exp. sugar, cigars; rayon plant; p. (1985) 105,400.

Matarani, new spt., S. **Peru**; oil refinery.

Mataró, spt., **Spain**; nr. Barcelona; fisheries, textiles, chemicals, paper; p. (1981) 96,467.

Matera, t., cap. of M. prov., S. **Italy**; stands on limestone ridge cleft by canyon; agr. ctr.; 13th cent. cath. and cas.; p. (1981) 50,712.

Mathura (Muttra), t., Uttar Pradesh, **India**; sacred t. on R. Jumna; Hindu pilgrimage ctr.; textiles; p. (1971) 132,028 (t.), 140,150 (met. a.).

Matlock, t., Derbys. Dales, **Eng.**; on R. Derwent; 24 km N. of Derby; tourist ctr., limestone quarrying, lt. inds.; p. (1981) 20,610.

Mato Grosso, st., **Brazil**; cap. Cuiabá; a. 1,232,081 km²; p. (est. 1985) 1,486,100.

Mato Grosso, plateau, Mato Grosso st., **Brazil**; average alt. 900 m, acts as divide between Amazon and Paraná–Paraguay R. systems; reserves of gold, diamonds, manganese but largely undeveloped; lge. areas of tropical rain forest.

Matosinhos, t., **Portugal**; fish. pt. at mouth of Leca R.; seaside resort; p. (1981) 43,488.

Matrah, t., **Oman**; ch. comm. ctr.; agr. tr.; site of Port Qaboos, deep water pt.; p. (est. 1980) 15,000.

Matsue, c., S.W. Honshu, **Japan**; on L. Shinji; old cas.; p. (1985) 140,000.

Matsumoto, c., central Honshu, **Japan**; machin., food-processing, paper; once impt. for silk; remains of 16th cent. cas.; p. (1985) 197,348.

Matsuyama, c., **Japan**; pt. based inds. of oil refining and petrochemicals; univ., feudal cas.; p. (1985) 426,646.

Matterhorn (Fr. **Mt. Corvin**. It. **Monte Cervino**); alt. 4,477 m; Pennine Alps, **Switzerland**.

Mauchline, mkt. t., Strathclyde Reg., **Scot.**; associated with Robert Burns; p. (1981) 3,776.

Mauna Kea, volcano, **Hawaii**; alt. 4,208 m; now dormant.

Mauna Loa, volcano, **Hawaii**; alt. 4,172 m; one of the world's lgst. volcanoes.

Mauritania, Islamic Rep. of, W. Africa; desert in N., S. more fertile; Senegal R. forms main artery of transport; mainly pastoral agr. (nomadic); severe effects of Sahelian drought since 1971 caused p. to become settled and move to ts.; urban p. 35% (1984); deposits of iron ore (Fort Gouraud) and copper (Bakel Akjoujt); fishing being developed; new pt. development at Nouadhibou; cap. Nouakchott; a. 1,085,210 km²; p. (est. 1987) 2,015,000.

Mauritius, I., indep. st. within Brit. Commonwealth; **Indian Oc.**; volcanic I., surrounded by coral reefs, 800 km E. of Madagascar; subtropical climate, prone to cyclone; racially mixed; dependent on sugar for 95 per cent of exps.; attempts to decr. this dependence by Export Processing Zone (tax-free industrial zone), and incr. tea output; dense p. and unemployment cause social tension; former residents of Chagos Arch. resettled on 2 of Agalega Is.; tourism incr. impt.; cap. Port Louis; a. (inc. Rodriguez and Agalega) 2,038 km²; p. (est. 1987) 1,041,000.

Mawson, Australian national research base, **Antarctica.**

Mayagüez, c., spt., **Puerto Rico**; ctr. of fertile region producing sugar, coffee, tobacco; cultural and educational ctr.; p. (1980) 96,193.

Maybole, burgh, Kyle and Carrick, **Scot.**; 13 km S. of Ayr; commuter centre for Ayr etc; cas.; p. (1981) 4,769.

Mayenne, dep., N.W. **France**; pastoral and agr.; cap. Laval; a. 5,146 km²; p. (1982) 271,500.

Mayfair, dist., City of Westminster, London, **Eng.**; fashionable residtl. and comm. a., to E. of Hyde Park; clubs and hotels.

Mayo, maritime co., Connacht, **R.o.I.**; broken cst., much barren mtn. land, many lge. lakes; agr., fishery; co. t. Castlebar, a. 5,506 km²; p. (1981) 20,695.

Mayotte, ch. I., **Fr.** terr., Comoro Archipelago, Moçambique Channel; rejected indep. to remain Fr. dep. (1975); sugar-cane, vanilla, cacao; a. 363 km²; p. (est. 1987) 73,900.

Mazandaran, prov., N.E. **Iran**; Caspian Sea, borders USSR; subtropical climate; agr.; cap. Sari; p. (1982) 2,375,994.

Mazar-i-Sharif, c., **Afghanistan**; chemical fertilisers from natural gas; textiles, bricks, flourmilling; noted mosque; p. (est. 1982) 110,367.

Mazatlán, c., N.W. **Mexico**; major spt. on Pac. cst.; comm. and industl. ctr.; exp. metals, hides, fish prods., woods; oil refinery; fishing, tourism; p. (1980) 249,988.

Mbabane, cap. of **Swaziland**; stands at c. 1,160 m; admin. ctr.; tin mng.; p. (1982) 38,636.

M'Bao, Senegal, W. Africa; oil refinery.

McMurdo Sound, ice-locked channel, Antarctica; base for many expeditions.

Mead, L., Cal., **USA**; on R. Colorado behind Boulder (Hoover) Dam; world's lgst. reservoir; stores water for irrigation in Imperial Valley and Yuma dist.; tourist attraction; 184 km long.

Meath, maritime co., Leinster, **R.o.I.**; pastoral; co. t., Trim; a. 2,347 km²; p. (1981) 24,015.

Meaux, t., Seine-et-Marne dep., **France**; on R. Marne; cath.; comm. and industl. ctr.; p. (1982) 55,797 (met. a.).

Mecca, holy c. of Islam, cap. of **Saudi Arabia**; birthplace of Mohammed; pilgrimage ctr.; Gr. Mosque enclosing the Kaaba; univ. (with Jidda); p. (1974) 366,801.

Mechelen. See **Malines.**

Mecklenburg, region, **E. Germany**; part of N. European plain, bordering Baltic Sea; Schwerin was cap. of former st.; a. 22,947 km².

Medan, c., cap. of N. Sumatra prov., **Indonesia**; ctr. for rubber, tobacco, tea; printing; univ.; pt. is Belawan; p. (est. 1983) 1,966,000.

Médéa, t., 80 km S. of El Djezair, **Algeria**; projected industl. complex; p. (est. 1983) 84,292.

Medellín, c., cap. of Antiquia prov., **Colombia**; at 1,533 m in Central Cordillera; second c. of rep.; univ.; ctr. of drug trade; coffee; textiles, steel, sugar refining, glass; coal, gold, silver mined nearby; hydroelec. power; p. (1985) 1,506,050.

Medicine Hat, t., Alberta, **Canada**; on S. Saskatchewan R.; rly. junc.; coal, natural gas, flour mills; p. (1981) 40,380.

Medina, c., Hejaz, **Saudi Arabia**; 352 km N. of

Mecca; tomb of Mohammed; place of Moslem pilgrimage; univ.; harbour at Yanbu' on Red Sea; p. (1974) 198,186.

Medina, l. gov. dist., I. of Wight, **Eng.**; N.E. part of I. inc. Ryde, Newport and Cowes; p. (est. 1988) 72,900.

Mediterranean, gr. inland sea, almost tideless, dividing Europe from Africa; communicating with Atl. by Strait of Gibraltar and Black Sea by Dardanelles, Sea of Marmara and Bosporus, E. part touches Asia in the Levant; total length W. to E. 3,520 km; greatest width of sea proper c. 1,120 km; water a. 2,331,000 km²; greatest depth 4,482 m; ch. Is.; Corsica, Sardinia, Sicily, Crete, Cyprus, and the Balearic, Lipari, Maltese, Ionian grs., also Greek arch.

Médoc, region, Gironde, **France**; extending for about 77 km along Garonne R.; noted for wines.

Medway, R., Kent, **Eng.**; flows N.E. past Tonbridge, Maidstone and Rochester (where it becomes estuarial) to mouth of Thames; 112 km long; Medway Bridge completed 1962.

Medway, former l. gov. dist., Kent, **Eng.**; now Rochester upon Medway.

Meekatharra, t., W. **Australia**; Flying Doctor and School of the Air ctr.; p. (1976) 829.

Meerut, c., Uttar Pradesh, **India**; scene of outbreak of Indian mutiny 1857; p. (1981) 417,395 (c.), 536,615 (met. a.).

Meghalaya ("Home of the Clouds"), new st. (1972), **India**; former Khasi-Jaintia Hills and Garo Hills dists. of Assam; cap. Shillong; a. 22,549 km²; p. (1981) 1,335,819.

Meiling Pass, on bdy. between Guandong, Jianxi, S. **China**; provides historic routeway across Nanling mtns., followed by old imperial highway from Nanjing to Guangzhou; alt. c. 300 m.

Meiningen, t., **E. Germany**; on R. Werra; cas.; machin., chemicals, timber inds.; drama ctr. in second half 19th cent.; p. (est. 1970) 25,357.

Meironnydd, l. gov. dist., Gwynedd, **Wales**; based on former co. of Merioneth; stretches from Ffestiniog and Bala to Tywyn and Dolgellau; p. (est. 1988) 31,600.

Meissen, t., Dresden, **E. Germany**; on R. Elbe; cath.; famous porcelain popularly known as Dresden china; p. (1981) 39,276.

Meknès, t., **Morocco**; one of the caps. of M.; agr. ctr., olives; p. (est. 1981) 487,000.

Mekong, R., S.E. **Asia**; rises in Tibet, flows through China, Laos, Kampuchea, and S. Vietnam, entering China Sea in extensive swampy delta; used for sm. boats but many rapids; 4,000 km long; new R. project for flood control, irrigation and hydroelectric power.

Melanesia, archipelago, S.W. **Pac. Oc.**; inc. Admiralty, Solomon, Santa Cruz, New Hebrides, Loyalty, New Caledonian, and Fiji Is.; New Guinea is sometimes included; ethnic region; arable subsistence agr.

Melbourne, c., cap. of Victoria, **Australia**; at mouth of Yarra R. and N. head of Port Phillip Bay; focal point of trade, transport and inds.; produces 30 per cent of total factory output in Australia; varied inds. inc. car and aircraft assembly, petrochemicals, foodstuffs; internat. airport; 2 univs., 2 caths.; p. (est. 1985) 2,916,600 (met. a.), 71 per cent of st. p.

Melilla, spt. and enclave in **Morocco**, on Mediterranean cst., belonging to Spain; exp. iron ore; p. (1981) 53,593.

Melitopol, c., Ukrainian SSR, **USSR**; on Molochnoy R.; ctr. of rich fruit-growing a.; heavy machin., food-processing; p. (est. 1980) 163,000.

Melksham, t., West Wilts., **Eng.**; on R. Avon, 8 km N.E. of Bradford-on-Avon; rubber wks., engin., flour mills, creameries, rope and matting; p. (1981) 9,621.

Melrose, burgh, Ettrick and Lauderdale, **Scot.**; on R. Tweed; 6 km E. of Galashiels; ruined abbey; p. (1981) 2,221.

Melton Mowbray, t., Leics., **Eng.**; on Lincoln Heights, 24 km N.E. of Leicester; mkt., hunting dist.; famous pork pies; footwear, pet foods, Stilton cheese; with surrounding a. forms l. gov. dist. of **Melton**; p. (est. 1990) 43,900 (dist.).

Melun, t., cap. of Seine-et-Marne dep., N. **France**; on R. Seine; agr. tools and prod.; Romanesque church; p. (1982) 82,479 (met. a.).

Melville I., off N. cst., Arnhem Land, **Australia**; Aboriginal settlement; a. 4,350 km²; p. (1976) 542.

Melville I., N.W. Terr., Arctic **Canada**; natural gas; a. 41,958 km².

Memaliaj, t., **Albania**; new mng. t. on banks of R. Vjosa.

Memel. *See* **Klaipeda.**

Memmingen, t., Bavaria, **W. Germany**; rly. junc.; machin., textiles; p. (est. 1986) 37,300.

Memphis, anc. c., **Egypt**; on R. Nile; 19 km S. of Cairo; nearby are Sakkara ruins.

Memphis, c., Tenn., **USA**; on R. Mississippi; rly. ctr., pt. of entry, lgst. c. in st., mkt. ctr. for cotton and hardwoods; cottonseed oil, textiles, farm machin.; natural gas and hydroelectric power; univ.; Martin Luther King assassinated here (1968); p. (1984) 648,400 (c.), 934,600 (met. a.).

Menado, t., Sulawesi, **Indonesia**; second t. of I.; pt. for transit tr.; p. (1980) 217,159.

Menai Strait, separates Isle of Anglesey from mainland, **Wales**; crossed by Telford's suspension bridge (1825) and Britannia rly. bridge (1850).

Menam Chao Phraya, R., **Thailand**; main R. of cty.; dense p. in valley; lge. multi-purpose scheme for hydroelectric power and irrigation; 1,120 km long.

Mendip Hills, Avon/Somerset, **Eng.**; limestone range containing many karst features inc. Cheddar gorge and Wookey Hole; a. of outstanding natural beauty; quarrying; motorway; hgst. point. 325 m; now forms l. gov. dist. within Somerset, inc. Frome, Wells, Shepton Mallet, Glastonbury and Street; p. (est. 1988) 94,000.

Mendoza, prov., W. **Argentina**, on Chilean border; Andean peaks Aconcagua and Tupungato; oilfields; alfalfa, vines, olives, fruit, peppermint; cap. M.; a. 148,783 km²; p. (1980) 1,187,305.

Mendoza, c., cap. of M. prov., W. **Argentina**; stands at c. 730 m in oasis known as "garden of the Andes"; starting point of Transandine rly.; univ.; wine, fruit; petroleum, agr. processing; p. (1980) 119,000 (c.), 606,000 (met. a.).

Mendoza, R., **Argentina**; enters L. Guanacache; used for hydroelectric power; 320 km long.

Menin (**Meenen**), t., **Belgium**; on R. Lys on Fr. border; mediaeval cloth ctr.; tobacco tr., textiles, rubber gds., soap; scene of fierce fighting in first world war; p. (1981) 33,542.

Mentawei Is., S.W. Sumatra, **Indonesia**; hilly and forested; fishing, shifting cultivation.

Menteith, Lake of, Stirling, **Scot.**; contains 3 Is.; 2·4 km by 1·6 km.

Menton, t., Alpes-Maritimes dep. S. **France**; Riviera resort; p. (1982) 25,449.

Meppel, t., Drenthe, **Neth.**; 21 km N. of Zwolle; shipbldg.; p. (1987) 23,106.

Merauke, t. W. Irian, **Indonesia**; pt. on S. cst.; ctr. of livestock raising region.

Mercedes, t., S.W. **Uruguay**; livestock ctr., E. of its pt. Fray Bentos; p. (1985) 37,110.

Mergui, archipelago, Tenasserim cst., S. **Burma**; teak, rice, pearl fishing.

Mérida, c., cap. of Yucatan st., S.E. **Mexico**; sisal-hemp; Spanish colonial architecture; tourism; Mayan ruins; p. (1980) 424,529.

Mérida, c. Badajoz prov., S.W. **Spain**; on Guadiana R.; comm. ctr. of Estremadura; impt. Roman remains; p. (1981) 41,783.

Mérida, t. cap. of M. st., **Venezuela**; in Andes; univ., cath.; tourist ctr.; world's highest cable rly. to Espejo peak (4,690 m); p. (1981) 142,800.

Meriden, t., Conn., **USA**; hardware mftg.; p. (1980) 57,118.

Meridian, t., Miss., **USA**; mkt. ctr. in cotton, livestock, lumber a.; rly. and route ctr.; textiles, clothing; p. (1980) 46,577.

Merioneth, former co., **Wales.** *See* **Meirionnydd.**

Merksem, industl. t., Antwerp, **Belgium**; p. (1982) 41,782.

Merrick, mtn., Wigtown, **Scot.**; hgst. peak in S. Uplands of Scot.; alt. 843 m.

Mersea, I., at mouth of R. Colne, Essex, **Eng.**; oysters; holiday resort; 8 km long, 3 km wide.

Merseburg, c., Halle, **E. Germany**; on R. Saale; ctr. of gr. lignite field; paper mills, chemical wks.; historic c.; p. (1981) 50,932.

Merse of Berwick, region, S.E. **Scot.**; lower valleys of Rs. Tweed and Teviot; glacial clays; arable agr. for barley, wheat; dairy cattle; ch. t. Berwick-on-Tweed; a. 570 km².

Mersey, R., Cheshire/Gtr. Manchester/Merseyside,

Eng.; enters Irish Sea by fine estuary at Liverpool; 109 km long.

Merseyside, former met. co., N.W. **Eng.**; a. around lower Mersey estuary inc. N. Wirral penin., pts. of Liverpool, Birkenhead and Bootle; many chem. and pt. processing inds.; p. (est. 1988) 1,448,100.

Mersin, c., S. **Turkey**; freeport (1986), on Mediterranean cst.; oil refinery; dates from c. 3,600 B.C.; p. (1980) 216,308.

Merthyr Tydfil, t., l. gov. dist., Mid Glamorgan, S. **Wales**; in narrow valley of R. Taff, 35 km N.W. of Cardiff; coal-mng. ctr.; hosiery, aircraft, bricks, elec. domestic gds.; p. (est. 1988) 58,100 (dist.).

Merton, outer bor., Greater London, **Eng.**; inc. former bors. of Mitcham, Wimbledon, and Merton and Morden; p. (est. 1988) 164,100.

Meru, mtn., **Tanzania**, E. Africa; extinct volcano overlooking E. arm of Gt. Rift valley; coffee plantations at alt. 1,500–1,800 m, some rubber below 1,200 m; alt. summit 4,560 m.

Merv. *See* **Mary.**

Mesa, t., Arizona, **USA**; in Salt River Valley, founded by Mormons 1878; agr. ctr., helicopter mftg.; p. (1984) 193,900.

Mesa Central, plateau, **Mexico**; part of Mexican plateau, major a. of comm. agr. (maize, wheat, agave); contains cap. Mexico City; dense p. and industl. comm. ctrs.

Mesa del Norte, plateau, **Mexico**; northern part of Mexican plateau.

Mesabi Range, hills, N.E. Minn., **USA**; vast iron ore deposits, now running out.

Mesa Verde National Park, S.W. Col., **USA**; Indian cliff dwellings.

Mesopotamia, anc. region, S.W. **Asia**; between Tigris and Euphrates Rs.; a. of early civilisation.

Messenia, anc. region, Peloponnesus, **Greece**; corresponding to present Messinia, densely p. agr. dep., cap. Kalamata; a. 3,406 km²; p. (1981) 159,818.

Messina, c., spt., Sicily, **Italy**; opposite Reggio; univ.; exp. fruit, wine, oil; p. (1984) 263,924.

Messina, strait, between Sicily and Italian mainland; length 35 km, minimum width 5 km.

Mesta, R., **Bulgaria**, **Greece**; rises in Rodopi mtns., flows S.E. into Aegean Sea 24 km E of Kavalla; valley famous for tobacco; known in Greece as Nestos; c. 280 km long.

Mestre, t., **Italy**; on lagoon at landward end of causeway linking Venice to mainland.

Meta, R., **Colombia** and **Venezuela**; navigable for 640 km; trib. of R. Orinoco; 1,200 km long.

Metz, c., cap of Moselle dep., N.E. **France**; on R. Moselle 40 km N of Nancy; cultural and comm. ctr. of Lorraine; impt. iron mines; wines, preserved fruits; mediaeval bldgs.; birthplace of Verlaine; p. (1982) 118,502.

Meudon, t., Hauts-de-Seine, **France**; S.W. sub. of Paris; observatory; glass, linen, ammunition; p. (1982) 49,004.

Meurthe, R., N.E. **France**; rises in Vosges and joins Moselle N. of Nancy.

Meurthe-et-Moselle, dep., N.E. **France**; borders on Belgium and Luxembourg; cap. Nancy; a. 5,276 km²; p. (1982) 715,800.

Meuse, dep., N.E. **France**; borders on Belgium; cap. Bar-le-Duc; a. 6,237 km²; p. (1982) 200,200.

Meuse (**Maas**), R., **France**; rises in Haute-Marne, flows past Verdun into Belgium past Namur, and Liège into the Neth. and joins the Waal, left arm of the Rhine; impt. routeway; 912 km long.

Mexborough, t., South Yorks., **Eng.**; on R. Don, 16 km above Doncaster; potteries; p. (1981) 15,683.

Mexicali, c., Baja Cal., **Mexico**; border resort; p. (est. 1986) 460,000.

Mexican Plateau, central plateau, **Mexico**; between the branches of the Sierra Madre; highest point over 2,400 m; impt. landform and a. of human settlement.

Mexico, fed. rep., Central America; inc. 31 sts., and fed. dist. of Mexico City; mtnous.; Sierra Madre covers most of rep.; variety of climate according to alt.; W. mostly desert; one of world's fastest-growing p.; agr. requires irrigation; major world exporter of cotton, fruit, sulphur, silver, oil; 14 oil refineries, new petrochemical complex at Cosoleacaque; rapid industl. expansion for consumer gds.; attempts to decentralise inds. from Mexico City not very successful;

tourism for Americans; cap. Mexico City; a. 1,972,360 km²; p. (est. 1987) 81·2 m.

Mexico, st., Mexico; encircles fed. dist. of Mexico City; cap. Toluca; a. 21,412 km²; p. (1980) 7,545,692.

Mexico City, c., cap. of **Mexico**; lgst. c. in Latin America; on plain at 2,275 m; altitude and basin site trap pollutants; many note-worthy bldgs., cath., univ.; admin., comm. and industl. ctr.; nuclear reactor nearby; lge. earthquake (1985) destroyed many parts of c.; surrounded by shanty ts., growing by 1,000 people per day; p. (est. 1987) 16,000,000 (met. a.); p. (est. 2000) 32,000,000 (lgst. met. a. in world).

Mexico, Gulf of, lge. inlet of Atl. Oc. (1,600 km E. to W. by 1,280 km N. to S.) lying S. of USA and E. of Mexico; communicates by Florida strait with Atl. and by Yucatan strait with Caribbean Sea; submarine oil drilling.

Mexico, Valley of, Meseta Central, **Mexico**; major industl. zone; over 60 per cent by value of Mexican mngs. produced; wide range of inds.; major ctr. Mexico City; attempts to decentralise p. and economic activity throughout Mexico; once ctr. of Aztec p.

Meyrin, t., **Switzerland**; H.Q. of CERN, nr. Geneva.

Mezhdurechensk, t., **RSFSR**; W. Siberia, on R. Rom'; new coal-mng. ctr.; p. (est. 1969) 81,000.

Mezzogiorno, lge. underdeveloped region, southern **Italy**; comprising Abruzzo and Molise, Campania, Basilicata, Apulia, Calabria and the Is. of Sicily and Sardinia; major govt. attempts to develop a.; agr. reforms and industl. growth, oil refining, iron and steel, petrochemicals; contains 35 per cent of p. of Italy, much emigration; much devastated by earthquake (1980); p. (1981) 20,053,334.

Miami, c., Fla., **USA**; on Biscayne Bay, at mouth of Miami R.; famous resort and recreational ctr.; varied inds.; international airport; world's fifth lgst. cargo airpt.; 3rd container pt. on U.S. East cst.; lge. freeport; M. beach across Biscayne Bay; p. (1984) 372,600 (c.), 2,799,300 (met. a.).

Miass, c., **RSFSR**; in Urals, 90 km S.W. of Chelyabinsk; gold-mng. ctr.; cars; p. (est. 1980) 152,000.

Michigan, st., **USA**; Wolverine St.; admitted to Union 1837; st. flower Apple Blossom, st. bird Robin; in valley of Gr. Ls.; industl.; cars, iron and steel gds., petroleum, minerals; some agr.; cap. Lansing; a. 150,779 km²; p. (1984) 9,088,000.

Michigan Lake, 3rd lgst of Gr. Ls. and the only one wholly in **USA**; in basin of St. Lawrence R., enclosed by two peninsulas of the st. of Mich. and by Wis., Ill., and Ind.; a. 61,901 km²; discharges by Straits of Mackinac to L. Huron.

Michipicoten, R., Ont., **Canada**; flows 200 km to L. Superior; iron ore deposits in valley.

Michoacan, st., **Mexico**; on Pac. Oc.; mtnous., rich in minerals; cap. Morelia; a. 60,088 km²; p. (1980) 3,048,704.

Michurinsk, t., **RSFSR**; N.W. of Tambov; engin., textiles, food inds.; agr. exp. ctr.; p. (est. 1980) 102,000.

Micronesia, Federated States of, Is., **S. Pac.**; Internal self-government (1978); Carolines, Marshalls; most are coral atolls; p. (est. 1984) 348,000.

Mid Bedfordshire, l. gov. dist., Beds., **Eng.**; a. N. of Luton and inc. Biggleswade, Sandy and Ampthill; p. (est. 1988) 114,900.

Mid Devon, l. gov. dist., Devon, **Eng.**; based on Tiverton; p. (est. 1988) 63,200.

Middleburg, t. cap. of Zeeland prov., **Neth.**; on Walcheren I. nr. Flushing; margarine, timber, optical instruments; cloth ctr. in mediaeval times; p. (1982) 38,655.

Middlesbrough, t., l. gov. dist., Cleveland, **Eng.**; expanded t.; pt. on S. side of Tees estuary; impt. iron and steel ind., heavy engin., chemicals; p. (est. 1988) 143,200.

Middlesex, former co., S.E. **Eng.**; N. of R. Thames; largely absorbed in Greater London 1964.

Middleton, t., Gtr. Manchester, **Eng.**; in valley of R. Irk; textiles, engin., chemicals, foam rubber; p. (1981) 51,696.

Middleton, t., Ohio, **USA**; on Miami R. and canal; steel, paper; p. (1980) 43,719.

Middlewich, t., Cheshire, **Eng.**; on Rs. Dane, Wheelock and Croco, 8 km N. of Crewe; salt, chemicals, clothing; p. (1981) 8,170.

Mid Glamorgan, co., S. **Wales**; upland in N. dissected by deep R. valleys containing former coal-mng. settlements; lowland to S. borders Bristol Channel; a. 1,018 km²; p. (est. 1988) 535,900.

Midhurst, t., West Sussex, **Eng.**; on R. Rother; famous polo grounds; birthplace of Richard Cobden; p. (1971) 18,983 (dist.).

Midland, t., Texas, **USA**; oilfield ctr., cotton ginning, natural gas; p. (1984) 97,100 (t.), 113,600 (met. a.).

Midlands, region, **Eng.**; comprises non-met. cos. of Staffs, Derbys., Notts., Leics., Warwicks., Northants., and met. co. of West Midlands; impt. a. for lt. engin.

Midlothian, former co., l. gov. dist., Lothian Reg., **Scot.**; adjoins Edinburgh; a. 357 km²; p. (est. 1986) 81,261.

Midnapore, t., W. Bengal, **India**; mkt. for agr. prods.; p. (est. 1971) 71,000.

Mid Suffolk, l. gov. dist., Suffolk, **Eng.**; rural a. inc. Eye and Stowmarket; p. (est. 1988) 77,600.

Mid Sussex, l. gov. dist., West Sussex, **Eng.**; a. inc. Cuckfield and Burgess Hill; p. (est. 1988) 120,000.

Midway Island, I., **Pac. Oc.**; calling-place on airroutes betweeen San Francisco and Asia, midway between Asia and USA (to which it belongs); p. (1981) 2,300.

Mieres, t., Oviedo prov., N. **Spain**; in Asturias; coal-mng. ctr., iron and steel inds.; p. (1981) 58,098.

Mihoro, Gifu, **Japan**; power plant under construction.

Mikkeli, c., cap. of M. prov., **Finland**; L. pt. in Saimaa L. region; p. (1986) 31,763.

Milan, c., cap. of M. prov., N. **Italy**; route ctr. in Lombard plain; second lgst. c. in rep.; ctr. of commerce and ind.; textiles, chemicals, printing, publishing, machin., cars, aircraft, porcelain; cath., univ.; p. (1984) 1,561,438.

Mildenhall, t., Forest Heath, Suffolk, **Eng.**; on R. Lark; 13th cent. church; R.A.F. sta. nearby; expanded t.

Mildura, t., Victoria, **Australia**; on R. Murray; irrigation ctr.; wine, citrus fruits, tomatoes; ctr. for dried fruit; p. (est. 1983) 16,920.

Milford Haven, spt., Preseli, Dyfed, **Wales**; magnificent deepwater harbour recently developed; major tanker terminal (250,000 tonnes); 2 refineries; pipeline from Angle Bay to Llandarcy (nr. Swansea); major white fish pt.; trawlers built and repaired; net mkg.; p. (1981) 13,934.

Milford Sound, inlet, at S. of S.I., **N.Z.**; tourist resort; noted for scenery and rare birds.

Millau, t., Aveyron, **France**; on R. Tarn; glove mnfs.; p. (1982) 22,256.

Millom, t., Copeland, Cumbria, **Eng.**; on N.W. cst. of Duddon estuary; ironwks. (closed 1968 after 100 years); hosiery; declining p.

Millport, burgh, Cunninghame, **Scot.**; on Gr. Cumbrae I., in F. of Clyde; resort; cath.; quarries; p. (1981) 1,489.

Milngavie, burgh, Bearsden and M., Strathclyde Reg., **Scot.**; 8 km N.W. of Glasgow, textiles; p. (1981) 8,654.

Milnrow, t., Gtr. Manchester, **Eng.**; sub. of Rochdale; cotton and waste spinning engin., brick mkg., paper and tub mftg.; p. (1981) 11,759.

Milo or **Melos**, I., Cyclades, **Greece**; cap. Plaka, nr. site of anc. c.; famous statue of Venus of Milo (now in Louvre) found here in 1820.

Milton Keynes, t., l. gov. dist., Bucks., **Eng.**; a. 9,000 ha; site and name of new c. for London overspill to comprise Bletchley, Wolverton and Stony Stratford; Open University; p. (est. 1988) 177,600 (fastest growing t. in Eng.).

Milwaukee, c., Wis., **USA**; lgst. c. and ch. pt. of st.; on L. Mich.; 112 km N. of Chicago; univ.; major mftg. ctr. with numerous inds., notably machin. and transport equipment, meatcanning, beer; p. (1984) 620,800 (c.), 1,567,600 (met. a.).

Min, R., Fujian, S. **China**; descends steeply on S.E. course to enter S. China Sea nr. Fuzhou, length 480 km, navigable.

Min, R., Sichuan, W. **China**; flows S., diverted into irrigation channels; joins Chang Jiang at Yibin; length 800 km, navigable.

Mina Hassan Tani (Kenitra), spt., **Morocco**; exp. grain; p. (est. 1981) 450,000.

Minas Gerais, st., **Brazil**; vast iron ore reserves; gold, diamonds, manganese, uranium, aluminium; cotton, coffee; hydroelec. power sta.; cap. Belo Horizonte; plans for development of heavy inds.; a. 585,472 km²; p. (est. 1985) 14,609,000.

Minas Novas, t., Minas Gerais, **Brazil**; p. (est. 1985) 28,400.

Mina Sulman, free transit pt., **Bahrain**; deepwater pt., dry dock for OPEC super-tankers, entrepôt.

Minatitlán, t., E. **Mexico**; petroleum refineries; petrochemicals; p. (1980) 145,268.

Minch, The, channel between the mainland of **Scot.** and the N. portion of Outer Hebrides, 38–64 km wide; very rapid current.

Minch, The Little, channel between I. of Skye, **Scot.**, and the middle portion of Outer Hebrides, 22–32 km wide.

Minchinhampton, t., Gloucs., **Eng.**; in Cotswolds, 6 km S.E. of Stroud.

Mindanao, second lgst. I. of **Philippines**; forested mtns., volcano Mt. Apo; exp. pineapples, hemp, coconuts, coffee; iron, gold, copper mined; plywoods and veneer, paper, pulp; ch. ts. Zamboanga, Davao; a. of sponsored immigration; lge. Moslem p. seeking indep. for I.; greatest ocean depth Mindanao Deep, off Philippines, 11,524 m; a. 94,628 km²; p. (1970) 7,292,691.

Minden, c., N. Rhine–Westphalia, **W. Germany**; on R. Weser at crossing of Mittelland canal; pt., rly. junc.; cath. (12th–14th cent.) destroyed in second world war; p. (est. 1986) 75,400.

Mindoro, I., **Philippines**, S. of Luzon; mtnous., thickly forested; rice, coconuts grown on cst., a. 9,376 km²; p. (1970) 473,940.

Minehead, t., West Somerset, **Eng.**; at N. foot of Exmoor, on Bristol Channel cst.; mkt., holiday resort; shoe factory closed 1981; p. (1981) 11,176.

Minho, R., separates Portugal from Spain in N.W.; length 272 km.

Minicoy Is., Arabian Sea; joined with Laccadive and Amindivi Is. to form union terr. of India.

Minneapolis, c., Minn., **USA**; on Mississippi R., at falls of St. Anthony; lgst. c. of st., pt. of entry, rly. terminus; wheat mkt., comm. and industl. ctr.; wide range of inds.; univ.; p. (1984) 358,300 (c.), 2,230,900 (met. a.) inc. St. Paul which it faces.

Minnesota, st., **USA**; North Star St.; admitted to Union 1858; st. flower Lady's Slipper, st. bird Common Loon; W. of L. Superior; studded with Ls., many Rs.; iron ore; maize, wheat, livestock, dairying; cap. St. Paul; a. 217,736 km²; p. (1985) 4,193,000.

Minorca (Menorca), I. off **Spain**; 2nd lgst. of Balearic Is.; Mediterranean agr.; developing tourism; cap. Mahón; a. 733 km²; p. (1981) 58,727.

Minsk, c., cap. of Belorussian SSR, **USSR**; lge. rly. junc.; cultural and industl. ctr.; univ.; engin., computers; rebuilt since second world war; p. (1986) 1,510,000.

Minya, c., central **Egypt**; on Nile; cotton tr. ctr.; plans for new c. (1988); p. (1985) 191,800.

Minya Konka, mtn., S.W. Sichuan prov., **China**; in Himalayas; highest peak in China; 7,570 m.

Mirfield, t., West Yorks., **Eng.**; on R. Calder, 5 km S.W. of Dewsbury; woollens; p. (1981) 18,686.

Miri, t., Sarawak, E. **Malaysia**; impt. oil ctr.; p. (1980) 52,125.

Mirzapur, t. Uttar Pradesh, **India**; on R. Ganges; carpets, brassware; p. (1981) 127,787.

Miskolc, c., N.E. **Hungary**; impt. industl. ctr.; iron ore, lignite nearby; varied inds., inc. textiles, porcelain, engin., bricks, refrigeration plants; p. (est. 1985) 211,000.

Mississippi, st., S. **USA**; Magnolia St.; admitted to Union 1817; st. flower Magnolia, st. bird Mockingbird; in lower M. valley; bounded on S. by G. of Mexico; cotton, sweet potatoes, pecan nuts, rice, sugar-cane, sorghum-cane, fruit, livestock raising; petroleum, natural gas; cotton textiles, chemicals, fish-processing; cap. Jackson; a. 123,584 km²; p. (1985) 2,613,000.

Mississauga, c., Ontario, **Canada**; lies to W. of Toronto; part of T. met. a.; p. (1986) 374,005.

Mississippi, principal R. of **USA**; rises in N. Minn. nr. L. Itasca; drains c. 3,170,000 km²; enters G. of Mexico in lge. delta nr. New Orleans; navigable, flood control problems; length 3,760 km (Mississippi–Missouri–Red Rock 6,176 km).

Missolonghi, t., **Greece**; pt. on inlet of G. of Patras; fish. tobacco; Byron died here 1824; p. (1981) 11,375.

Missoula, t., Mont., **USA**; on Klark R.; univ.; rly. wks., agr., fruit, oil refinery; tourism; p. (1980) 33,388.

Missouri, st., central **USA**; Show-me St.; admitted to Union 1821; st. flower Hawthorn, st. bird Bluebird; dominated by Mississippi and Missouri Rs.; predominantly agr.; livestock, maize; coal, iron;

transport equipment; cap. Jefferson City; ch. t. St. Louis; a. 180,456 km²; p. (1984) 5,029,000.

Missouri, longest R. of **USA**; 3,942 km; trib. of Mississippi R.; main headstream Jackson R.; flood, power and irrigation schemes.

Missouri Coteau, hill ridge, N. **America**; runs N.W. to S.E. across prairies of Saskatchewan (Canada), N. and S. Dakota (USA); rises abruptly from 480–600 m.

Mistassini, L., Quebec, **Canada**; 160 km long.

Misurata, t., Tripolitania, **Libya**; on cst. of Mediterranean, 176 km E. of Tripoli; mkt. for local agr. produce; p. (1984) 117,000.

Mitau. See Jelgava.

Mitchelstown, t., Cork, **R.o.I.**; nr. Fermoy; dairy prods.; p. (1966) 2,617.

Mitidja, plain, **Algeria**, N. Africa; borders Mediterranean; intensive cultivation of vine; ch. ts. Algiers, Blida.

Mito, c. Honshu, **Japan**; cas., comm. ctr.; famous for lime trees; site of two nuclear power plants nearby; p. (1985) 288,987.

Mittelland Canal, inland waterway system, **W. Germany**; system of canals and canalised Rs.; links Dortmund–Ems canal nr. Rheine through Minden, Hanover, Magdeburg, Berlin to R. Oder at Frankfurt-on-Oder; makes use of natural E.–W. troughs across the N. German plain.

Mittweida, t., Karl-Marx-Stadt, **E. Germany**; metallurgy, textiles; p. (est. 1970) 19,600.

Miyazaki, c., Kyushu, **Japan**; famous shrine; ctr. of sandy plain with lagoons; p. (1985) 279,118.

Mizoram ("Land of Highlanders"), union terr. (1972); new st. (1986); Assam, N.E. **India**; former Mizo Hills dist. of Assam; 80 per cent p. Christian; 44 per cent literate, higher proportion than any other a. except Kerala; new cap. Aizawl; a. 21,238 km²; p. (1981) 493,757.

Mjosa, lgst. L., **Norway**; 88 km long.

Mladá Boleslav (Jungbunziau), t., Bohemia, **ČSSR**; vehicles, agr. machin., textiles; once ctr. of Bohemian Brethren (followers of John Hus); p. (1984) 47,686.

Moanda, spt. at mouth of Zaïre R., **Zaïre**; oil refinery, aluminium smelter.

Mobutu Sese Seko, L., (**L. Albert**), Zaïre, Uganda; on floor of Gt. Rift Valley; crocodile farming; tourism; main pt. Kasenyi; 160 km long, 32 km wide; alt. 640 m; a. 5,346 km².

Mobile, c., spt., Ala., **USA**; on R. M.; shipbldg. pt. inds.; exp. cotton; p. (1984) 204,900 (c.), 465,700 (met. a.).

Moçambique, former Portuguese prov., indep. st. (1975), **E. Africa**; wide cstl. plain rising inland to 2,100 m; crossed by Zambesi R.; few exp. inc. cashew nuts, cotton, sugar, tea; deposits of coal and bauxite; Beira and Maputo (cap.) serve as import pts. for transit tr.; 40% GNP from tourism and transport; Cabora Bassa Dam in Tete dist.; border with Zimbabwe closed March 1976 now reopened; severely hit by drought since 1984; civil war against Renamo rebels; a. 771,820 km²; p. (est. 1987) 14·59 m.

Moçambique Channel, strait, Indian Oc.; separates Madagascar from mainland of Africa; 1,600 km long, 400–960 km wide.

Moçambique Current, ocean current, flows N. to S. along E. cst. of Moçambique and Natal, E. Africa; relatively warm water.

Moçâmedes. See Namibe.

Mocha or Al-Mukha, t., N. **Yemen**; S.W. Arabia; on Red Sea; formerly noted for exp. of coffee; p. 5,000.

Modane, t., S.E. Savoie, **France**; commands routes via Mont Cenis Pass and tunnel; electrometallurgy; p. (1982) 4,877.

Modena, t., cap. of M. prov. **Italy**; cath.; univ.; textiles, leather, engin.; p. (1984) 178.985.

Modesto, t., Cal., **USA**; fruit (especially peaches), vegetable-processing; p. (1984) 122,200 (t.), 295,700 (met. a.).

Modica, t., S.E. Sicily, **Italy**; agr. ctr.; limestone grottoes, cave dwellings; Cava d'Ispica; p. (1981) 45,769.

Moe. See Yallourn.

Moffat, burgh, Annandale and Eskdale, **Scot.**; 24 km N.W. of Lockerbie; resort; p. (1981) 2,034.

Moffat Tunnel, Col., **USA**; carries trunk rly. from Chicago to San Francisco under Rocky mtns. between Denver and Salt Lake City; 10 km long; alt. 2,774 m.

Mogadishu, c., cap. of **Rep. of Somalia**; on

Indian Oc.; modernised deep-sea pt., airpt.; p. (est. 1985) 1,000,000.

Mogador. See **Essaouira.**

Mogi das Cruzes, t., São Paulo, **Brazil;** agr.; bauxite mng.; p. (est. 1985) 234,900.

Mogilev, c., Belorussiyan SSR, **USSR;** on R. Dnieper; industl.; rly. and route junc.; p. (est. 1985) 343,000.

Mohács, t., S. **Hungary;** on Danube; impt. R. pt.; strategic site; battle 1526; p. (est. 1984) 22,000.

Mohammedia, t., **Morocco,** N. Africa; oil refining; p. (1982) 105,120.

Mohawk, R., N.Y., **USA;** trib. of Hudson R.; followed by impt. road, rly. and canal routes across Appalachian mtns.; 280 km long.

Mojave or **Mohave,** S. Cal., **USA;** desert region of mtns. and valleys; a. 38,850 km².

Moji, spt., Kyushu, **Japan;** exp. coal, cement, timber; linked by bridge to Honshu. See **Kitakyushu.**

Mokpo, spt., W. cst. **S. Korea;** ctr. of food-processing and cotton-ginning; p. (est. 1983) 228,000.

Mol, t., N.E. **Belgium;** nuclear energy research ctr.; p. (est. 1983) 29,970.

Mold, t., Delyn, Clwyd, N. **Wales;** on R. Alyn; chemicals, roadstone; p. (1981) 8,589.

Moldau. See **Vltava.**

Moldavian SSR, constituent rep., **USSR;** fertile fruit growing a. especially for vines; rails. based on fruit; cap. Kishinev; a. 34,188 km²; p. (1986) 4,142,000.

Mole Valley, l. gov. dist., Surrey, **Eng.;** based on Mole R. ts. of Leatherhead and Dorking; p. (est. 1988) 76,200.

Mole R., Surrey, **Eng.;** rises in central Weald, flows N. into R. Thames nr. Molesey; cuts impt. gap through N. Downs between Dorking and Leatherhead; 80 km long.

Molenbeek-Saint-Joan, t., **Belgium;** nr. Brussels; lge mftg. ctr.; p. (est. 1983) 71,181.

Molfetta, spt., Apulia, **Italy;** olive oil, macaroni, wine, caths.; p. (1981) 65,951.

Moline, t., Ill., **USA;** on Mississippi R.; agr. implements, ironwks., flour; p. (1980) 46,278.

Molise, region, central **Italy;** subsistence arable and pastoral farming; a. 4,437 km²; p. (est. 1986) 334,000.

Mollendo, t., S.W. **Peru;** on Pac. Oc.; former outlet for Arequipa; replaced by Matarani; wool textiles, fishing; p. (est. 1970) 14,251.

Mölndal, t., S.W. **Sweden;** paper, textiles; margarine; p. (est. 1986) 50,000.

Moluccas or **Spice Is.,** prov. **Indonesia;** gr. of Is. between Sulawesi and W. Irian; mtnous., fertile; spices, sago, timber, pearls, rice, copra, ch. t. Ternate; attempts at secession by S. Moluccans; a. 496,454 km²; p. (est. 1983) 1,534,300.

Mombasa, spt., **Kenya;** ch. harbour, Kilindini; rly. terminus; oil refinery; exp. tropical produce (ivory, hides, rubber, etc.); fertiliser plant, sheet glass, steel rolling mill; p. (est. 1983) 409, 616.

Mon, I., off cst. of Sjaelland, **Denmark;** a. 233 km²; cap. Stege; p. (1965) 12,318.

Monaco, principality on Mediterranean cst. between France and Italy, W. **Europe;** economy based on tourism; benefits from climate and amenities, inc. famous casino; tax laws attract p. and shortage of land causes M. to build out into sea; much revenue derived from transactional laws, sales of tobacco and postage stamps; cap. Monte Carlo; a. 146 ha; p. (est. 1985) 27,000.

Monadhliath Mtns., Badenoch and Strathspey, **Scot.;** between Spey R. and Loch Ness; hgst. peak Carn Mairg 1,216 m.

Monadnock Mt., peak, 965 m high, N.H., **USA;** name used as a term for the geomorphological feature of an isolated hill which has successfully resisted erosion.

Monaghan, co., **R.o.I.;** mainly pastoral and agr.; a. 1,295 km²; p. (1981) 15,196.

Monaghan, co. t., Monaghan, **R.o.I.;** on the Ulster canal; cath.; p. (1981) 6,172.

Mona Passage, strait, Caribbean Sea; separates Hispaniola from Puerto Rico.

Monastir. See **Bitola.**

Mönch, peak, Bernese Alps, **Switzerland;** 4,101 m.

Monchegorsk, t., **RSFSR;** on L. Imandra; copper and nickel smelting; p. (est. 1969) 53,000.

Mönchengladbach, t., N. Rhine-Westphalia, **W. Germany;** 26 km W. of Düsseldorf; rly. ctr. textiles; p. (est. 1986) 255,100.

Monchique, t., Algarve, **Portugal;** spa; wine, oil,

chestnuts; p. (1981) 9,609.

Moncton, t., N.B., **Canada;** rly. ctr., textiles; oil nearby; p. (1981) 54,743.

Mondego, R., **Portugal;** 208 km long.

Monfalcone, t., N.E. **Italy;** on Adriatic; modern industl. t.; shipbldg., oil refining; p. (1981) 30,277.

Monferrato, low hills, Piedmont, N. **Italy;** S. and S.E. of Turin between valleys of Po and Tanaro; celebrated vineyards, produce Asti Spumante wines; alt. never exceeds 460 m.

Monghyr, t., Bihar, **India;** on R. Ganges; mkt. ctr.; p. (1971) 102,474.

Mongla, pt., **Bangladesh;** on Pussur R.; shipping pt. under construction.

Mongolia, vast elevated plateau in heart of Asia between China and USSR. See **Mongolian People's Rep.** and **Inner Mongolia.**

Mongolia, Inner. See **Inner Mongolia.**

Mongolia, People's Rep. of (Outer Mongolia), central Asia; land-locked, extensive plateau at 1,200 m bordering Gobi desert in S.; dry continental climate with extremely cold winters; pastoral agr. collectively organised for horses, sheep, camels, oxen, and goats; extensive state farms for cereals; cap. Ulan Bator; 80 per cent of tr. with U.S.S.R.; incr. mechanisation; food processing, livestock prods.; a. 1,564,360 km²; p. (est. 1987) 1,965,300.

Monklands, l. gov. dist., Strathclyde Reg., **Scot.;** part of Central Clydeside conurb. inc. Airdrie and Coatbridge; p. (est. 1986) 107,010.

Monmouth, t., l. gov. dist., Gwent, **Wales;** at confluence of Rs. Wye and Monnow; mkt. ctr.; timber, crushed limestone, wrought ironwk.; p. (est. 1988) 81,300 (dist.).

Monmouthshire, former co., S. **Wales;** mostly inc. in Gwent; parts in South and Mid Glamorgan.

Monongahela, R., W. Va., **USA;** joins Allegheny R. at Pittsburgh to form Ohio R.; impt. waterway.

Monopoli, spt., Apulia, **Italy;** oil, wine, fruit, flour tr.; p. (1981) 43,424.

Monroe, t., La., **USA;** cotton ctr., natural gas, paper, printing ink; p. (1984) 56,000 (t.), 142,700 (met. a.).

Monrovia, c., cap. of **Liberia,** W. Africa; free port and industl. free zone on Atl. at mouth of St. Paul R.; exp. rubber, palm oil; ship registration; p. (1984) 425,000.

Mons, c., cap. of Hainaut prov., W. **Belgium,** nr. Fr. border; cath.; inds. linked with Borinage coal-mng. dist.; varied mnfs.; scene of many battles; NATO (SHAPE) H.Q. nearby at Casteau; p. (1982) 93,377.

Montana, st., N.W. **USA;** Treasure St.; admitted to Union 1889; st. flower Bitterroot, st. bird Western Meadowlark; in Rocky mtns. region; cap. Helena; lgst. c. Great Falls; copper, silver, gold, zinc, lead, manganese; coal, petroleum, natural gas; pastoral agr.; Glacier Nat. Park, tourism; a. 377,456 km²; (1985) 826,000.

Montauban, t., Tarn-et-Garonne dep., **France;** on R. Tarn; cath., agr. prod., wines; p. (1982) 53,147.

Montbéliard, t., Doubs dep., **France;** S. of Belfort; textiles, watches, typewriters, vehicles; p. (1982) 128,194 (met. a.).

Mont Blanc, mtn., Alps; on confines of **Italy** and **France;** alt. 4,814 m; longest road tunnel in world (opened to traffic 1965) linking Courmayeur (Italy) and Chamonix (France), length 12 km.

Montceau-les-Mines, t., Saône-et-Loire dep., **France;** coal, textiles, metal-working; p. (1982) 51,290 (met. a.).

Mont Cenis Pass, W. Alps; on bdy. between **France** and **Italy;** approached from W. by Isère–Arc valleys, from E. by Dora Riparia; alt. 2,097 m.

Mont Cenis Tunnel, W. Alps; on bdy. between **France** and **Italy;** carries main rly. from Lyons to Turin under Col de Fréjus; approached from W. by Isère–Arc valleys, from E. by Dora Riparia; opened 1871; 12 km long.

Montclair, t., N.J., **USA;** residtl. sub. of N.Y.; paper gds. manfs.; p. (1980) 38,321.

Mont-de-Marsan, t., Landes dep., **France;** mkt. ctr.; p. (1982) 30,894.

Mont-Dore, spa, Puy-de-Dôme dep., **France;** 48 km S.W. of Clermont-Ferrand; Puy de Sancy (1,887 m) hgst. peak of Mont-Dore mtn. gr.; p. (1982) 2,394.

Monte Bello Is., gr. off N.W. cst., **Australia;** about 136 km N. of pt. of Onslow; first Brit. atomic weapon exploded here 3 Oct. 1952.

Monte Carlo, t., **Monaco;** tourist resort, casino;

p. (est. 1975) 10,000.

Monte Corno, mtn., **Italy**; in Central Apennines; alt. 2,923 m.

Monte Cristo, Italian I., 42 km S. of Elba, in Tyrrhenian Sea; famed by novel by Dumas.

Monte Gargano, peninsula, S. **Italy**; projects into Adriatic Sea nr. plain of Foggia; formed by limestone plateau, alt. over 900 m; pasture on upper slopes, woodland on lower slopes; a. 1,030 km².

Montego Bay, spt., **Jamaica**; main ctr. for tourism; p. (est. 1982) 70,265.

Montélimar, t., Drôme dep., **France**; bricks, tiles, nougat; hydroelectric barrage on R. Rhône; p. (1982) 30,213.

Montenegro, constituent rep., S.W. **Yugoslavia**; agr., pastoral; cap. Titograd; a. 13,812 km²; p. (1981) 584,310.

Monterey, t., Cal., **USA**; S. of San Francisco; resort of artists and writers; sardine ind., fruit and vegetable canneries; p. (1980) 27,558.

Montería, c., cap. of Cordoba prov., **Colombia**; tobacco, cacao, cotton, sugar; p. (1985) 238,081.

Monte Rosa, hgst. peak, 4,637 m, Pennine Alps, on border of **Italy** and **Switzerland**.

Monte Rotondo, hgst. mtn., Corsica, **France**; 2,767 m.

Monterrey, t., cap. of Nuevo León prov., **Mexico**; third lgst. c.; cath.; textiles, brewing, ironwks., minerals; thermoelec. plant; sheet metal; p. (est. 1987) 2,400,000 (met. a.).

Monte Sant'Angelo, hilltop t., **Italy**; on Gargano promontory; notable ctr. of pilgrimage; p. (est. 1981) 16,500.

Montevideo, c., cap. **Uruguay**; major pt. on Rio de la Plata; dominates life of rep. as financial, comm. and industl. ctr.; fisheries, oil-refining, food-processing, tourism; cath., univ.; p. (est. 1980) 1,362,000.

Montgomery, t., gov. dist., Powys, central **Wales**; in upper Severn valley, 13 km N.E. of Newtown; agr. mkt.; cas.; p. (est. 1988) 51,200 (dist.).

Montgomery, t., W. Punjab, **Pakistan**; livestock; leather, cotton; p. (1961) 25,100.

Montgomery, c., cap. of Ala., **USA**; at head of Alabama R.; cotton, livestock, timber, dairying, fertilisers; hydroelec. power; p. (1984) 185,000 (c.), 284,800 (met. a.).

Montgomeryshire. See **Powys.**

Montluçon, t., Allier dep., **France**; on R. Cher; terminus of Berry canal, linking Commentry coalfields with Loire; iron foundries, glassmaking; cas.; p. (1982) 51,765.

Montmartre, dist., N. Paris, **France**; on Butte de M. (101 m), commands superb view S. over Paris; picturesque square, frequented by artists; basilica of Sacré Coeur.

Montparnasse, dist., Paris, **France**; on left bank of Seine R.; haunt of artists and writers.

Montpelier, st. cap., Vermont, **U.S.A.**; sm. t. in Green Mtns. and on Winooski R.

Montpellier, t., cap. of Hérault dep., **France**; 8 km N. of Mediterranean cst. on coastal lowland route to S.W. France; comm. and cultural ctr.; univ.; wines, fruit tr.; silk, chemicals; many anc. bldgs. inc. cath.; p. (1982), 201,067.

Montreal, c., spt., Quebec, **Canada**; at confluence of Ottawa and St. Lawrence Rs.; caths., univs.; major industl., comm. and financial ctr.; extensive harbour installations, lge. grain exp.; diverse mnfs.; lgst. c. and spt. in Canada; p. mainly French-speaking; p. (1986) 1,015,420 (c.), 2,921,357 (met. a.).

Montreuil-sous-Bois, E. sub. Paris, **France**; hothouse flowers and fruit for Paris mkt.; peach growing; mnfs.; p. (1982) 93,394.

Montreux, t., **Switzerland**; on L. Geneva; tourist ctr.; Chillon cas.; p. (1980) 19,685.

Montrose, spt., burgh, Angus, **Scot.**; on E. cst. at mouth of S. Esk R.; chemicals, rope wks., vegetable-canning, boat-bldg., fishing; supply base for N. Sea oil; p. (1981) 12,286.

Mont-Saint-Michel, rocky granite I., in English Channel, off Normandy cst., **France**; tourist ctr. with Benedictine abbey; connected to mainland by causeway; surrounding marshland reclaimed for agr.; alt. 79 m.; p. (1982) 80.

Montserrat, volcanic I., Leeward Is., **W.I.**; chiefly agr.; exp. sea-island cotton, limes, sugar-cane and tomatoes; cap. Plymouth; a. 101 km²; p. (est. 1985) 12,000.

Montserrat, mtn., Catalonia, **Spain**; Benedictine

monastery, alt. 1,236 m.

Monument Valley, Utah and Arizona, **USA**; home of Navajo Indians.

Monza, c., Lombardy, N. **Italy**; 14 km from Milan; cath.; textiles, leather, hats; former royal residence; motor-racing circuit; p. (1984) 122,476.

Moonie, t., Queensland, **Australia**; 320 km W. of Brisbane; oilfields; pipeline to Lytton, at mouth of Brisbane R.

Moose Jaw, c., Saskatchewan, **Canada**; rly. junc.; agr. ctr.; agr. implements, oil refining, p. (1981) 39,941.

Moradabad, c., Uttar Pradesh, N. **India**; rly. junc.; cotton mills, brassware; mosque; p. (1981) 330,051.

Morava, R., ČSSR and **Austria**; trib. of R. Danube; navigable in lower course; 339 km long.

Morava, R., **Yugoslavia**; formed from W. Morava and S. Morava, flows N. into Danube 80 km below Belgrade to Istanbul; 560 km long.

Moravia, region, **ČSSR**; part of Bohemian plateau, drained by Morava R.; inc. fertile agr. a.; mineral resources and industl. ts.

Moray, former co., l. gov. dist., Grampian Reg., **Scot.**; borders M. Firth; arable agr. benefiting from glacial soils; a. 2,230 km²; p. (est. 1986) 84,793.

Moray Firth, arm of N. Sea; on Scottish E. cst., between Highland and Grampian Regs.; plans for lge.-scale industl. expansion; offshore oil platforms at Arderseir; valuable inshore oilfield.

Morbihan, dep., N.W. **France**; on Bay of Biscay; agr., fishing; cap. Vannes; a. 7,094 km²; p. (1982) 590,900.

Mordovian ASSR, **RSFSR**; forested steppe between Rs. Oka and Volga; pastoral agr., lumbering; food processing; a. 25,493 km²; p. (1986) 963,000.

Morea. See **Peloponnesus.**

Morecambe and Heysham, t., N. Lancs., **Eng.**; on S. shore of M. Bay; M. holiday resort; H., pt. for N. Ireland and oil refinery; nuclear power sta. being built on cst. S. of M.; p. (1981) 41,187.

Morecambe Bay, between Lancs. and Cumbria, **Eng.**; isolates Furness dist. of Lancs.; many proposed barrages across Bay, now project increasingly probable as water shortage in N.W. Eng. grows; discoveries of nat. gas.

Morelia, c., cap. of Michoacán st., W. **Mexico**; on rocky hill, 1,891 m in fertile valley; cath.; textiles, pottery; p. (1980) 353,055.

Morelos, inland st., **Mexico**; mtns., forested; arable agr.; cap. Cuernavaca; a. 4,962 km²; p. (1980) 931,675.

Morez, t., Jura dep., **France**; precision instruments, optical equipment; winter sports.

Morgan, t., R. pt., S. **Australia**; transhipment ctr.; from here water pumped from R. Murray and sent by pipeline to Whyalla; p. (1976) 340.

Morgantown, c., W. Va., **USA**; univ.; coal, oil, gas fields; chemicals, heavy ind.; p. (1980) 27,605.

Morioka, c., N. Honshu, **Japan**; textiles, ironwks.; p. (1985) 235,469.

Morlaix, spt., Finistère, **France**; tobacco, paper, brewing, agr.; p. (1982) 19,541.

Morley, t., West Yorks., **Eng.**; 5 km S.W. of Leeds; woollens, stone quarrying; p. (1981) 44,134.

Morocco, kingdom, N.W. **Africa**; csts. on Atl. Oc. and Mediterranean Sea; rises to Atlas mtns. inland; leading world producer of phosphates; other minerals inc. iron-ore, lead and manganese; agr. main occupation, provides 30 per cent of exp.; fishing and tourism well developed; cap. Rabat; a. 466,200 km²; p. (est. 1987) 23·3 m.

Morogoro, t., **Tanzania**, E. Africa; on E. edge of Central African plateau, alt. c. 900 m, 176 km by rail W. of Dar-es-Salaam; ctr. of sisal- and cotton-growing a.

Morón, c., **Venezuela**; on cst. nr. Puerto Cabello; industl.; natural gas, oil refining.

Morón de la Frontera, t., S.W. **Spain**; agr. tr. ctr.; ruined Moorish cas.; p. (1981) 27,311.

Morpeth, t., Castle Morpeth, Northumberland, **Eng.**; finely situated in valley of Wansbeck; coal mng., iron-founding; mkt.; Norman cas. remains; p. (1981) 14,545.

Morro Velho, gold mng. dist., Minas Gerais, **Brazil**; in Serra do Espinhaco; ch. t. Nova Lima.

Mors, I., N. Jutland, **Denmark**; in Lim fjord; a. 357 km²; p. (1965) 25,739.

Morwell, t., Victoria, **Australia**; ctr., for brown coal extraction and briquettes; inds. attracted by cheap power; p. (est. 1983) 18,030.

Moscow, c., cap. of **USSR**, and of **RSFSR**; leading cultural, political, comm., industl. and route ctr. of USSR; on Moskva R.; served by several airpts., R. and canal pts.; contains Kremlin in c. ctr. with Red Square; caths., univs., palaces, many famous theatres and art galleries; p. (1986) 8,533,000 (c.), 8,703,000 (met. a.).

Moscow Sea (**Ucha Reservoir**), artificial L., **RSFSR**; created behind dam on R. Volga at Ivankovo; supplies water to Moscow, maintains level on Moscow–Volga canal, and supplies water to 8 hydroelec. power-stas.; a. 329 km².

Moscow–Volga Canal, **RSFSR**; links R. Volga at Ivankovo with Khimki sub. of Moscow; forms part of Leningrad–Moscow inland waterway; opened 1937; 128 km long.

Moselle, dep., N.E. **France**; iron-ore, coal mng.; metal inds.; cap. Metz; a. 6,224 km²; p. (1982) 1,006,600.

Moselle, R., **France** and **Germany**; trib. of R. Rhine; canalised between Thionville and Koblenz (269 km); lower valley forms famous wine dist.; 525 km long.

Moshi, t., N. **Tanzania**; on southern slope of Mt. Kilimanjaro; ctr. of coffee-growing dist., airpt. at 854 m (S.W. of t.); p. (est. 1976) 52,223.

Mosi-oa-Toenja. See **Victoria Falls**. The local name means "Smoke of the Thunders."

Mosjoen, t., N. **Norway**; recent aluminium wks.

Moskva, R., central **RSFSR**; trib. of R. Oka; Moscow stands on its banks; linked with upper Volga by Moscow–Volga canal (128 km long); 400 km long.

Mosonmagyaróvár, t., **Hungary**; aluminium wks.; agr. machin.; p. (est. 1984) 30,000.

Mosquito Cst., lowland, E. cst. **Nicaragua**; 400 km N.–S., 192 km E.–W.; lumbering, bananas; ch. t. Bluefields; sparse p.

Moss, spt., **Norway**; pulp, paper, machin., textile inds.; p. (est. 1987) 25,000.

Mossamedes. See **Moçâmedes**.

Mossel Bay, pt. and seaside resort, Cape Prov., **S. Africa**; between Cape Town and Port Elizabeth; p. (est. 1967) 15,600.

Mossley, t., Tameside, Gtr. Manchester, **Eng.** 5 km E. of Oldham; mkt. t., textiles; p. (1981) 10,224.

Most, t., **ČSSR**; lignite, chemicals; Druzhba crude oil pipeline extended to chemical wks.; p. (est. 1986) 65,000.

Mostaganem, t., **Algeria**; spt. on Mediterranean cst., E. of Oran; exp. wine and fruits; gas pipeline from Hassi Messoud; p. (1982) 169,526.

Mostar, t., Herzegovina, **Yugoslavia**; on R. Naretva; bauxite, lignite; developing inds., wine, food processing, aluminium plant; p. (1981) 110,377.

Mosul, t., N. **Iraq**; on R. Tigris; in region producing cereals, citrus fruit, cattle; impt. oilfields nearby; metal works; impt. during crusades; p. (1977) 1,220,000.

Motala, t., on L. Vättern, **Sweden**; radio sta.; engin., woollen gds.; p. (est. 1986) 41,000.

Motherwell, burgh, l. gov. dist., Strathclyde Reg., **Scot.**; in Clyde valley, 24 km S.E. of Glasgow; iron, steel, machin., engin., textiles; p. (est. 1986) 148,116.

Moulins, c., cap. of Allier dep., **France**; on Allier R.; leather gds., clothing; cath., ruined château, art treasures; p. (1982) 25,548.

Moulmein, spt., **Burma**, on R. Salween; exp. teak, rice; p. (1983) 219,991.

Mountain Ash, t., Cynon Valley, Mid Glamorgan, **Wales**; in narrow valley 5 km S.E. of Aberdare; coal-mng. a.; p. (1981) 26,231.

Mount Adams, mtn., S. Wash. **USA**; beautiful volcanic scenery in Cascade Range; pine forests; alt. 3,803 m.

Mount Alberta, mtn., W. Alberta, **Canada**; in Canadian Rockies and Jasper Nat. Park; alt. 3,622 m.

Mount Assiniboine, mtn., Alberta, B.C., **Canada**; "Matterhorn" of Canadian Rockies; alt. 3,620 m.

Mount Carmel, mtn., N.W. **Israel**; rises to 554 m and extends 10 km as penin. into Mediterranean Sea, forming S. limit to Bay of Acre; ass. with prophets Elijah and Elisha.

Mount Gambier, t., S. **Australia**; at foot of extinct volcano; forestry, sawmilling of radiata pine; p.

(1981) 19,880.

Mount Goldsworthy, t., W. **Australia**; new t. being developed in iron ore mng. a.

Mount Isa, t., W. Queensland, **Australia**; in Selwyn Range 128 km W. of Cloncurry; copper, silver, lead mng.; p. (est. 1984) 25,020.

Mount Lofty Range, mtn. range, S. **Australia**; forms barrier to routes leaving Adelaide; lower slopes support vineyards and outer suburbs of Adelaide; rises to over 700 m.

Mount Lyell, Tasmania, **Australia**; impt. copper mines, and refinery.

Mount McKinley, Alaska, **USA**; in Alaska Range and Nat. Park; highest point in N. America, c. 6,191 m.

Mountmellick, t., R.D., Laoighis, **R.o.I.**; p. (1961) 22,596 (R.D.).

Mount Newman, W. **Australia**; new t. built 1967 to exploit nearby iron ore.

Mount of Olives, Jordan; ridge (817 m), E. of Jerusalem; Garden of Gethsemane on lower slopes.

Mount's Bay, inlet, S. cst., Cornwall, **Eng.**; 32 km wide; fishery grounds.

Mount Tom Price, t., W. **Australia**; new t., being developed in iron ore mng. a.

Mount Vernon, c., N.Y., **USA**; on Bronx R.; sub. of N.Y.; residtl.; takes name from George Washington's house on Potomac, Va., 24 km S. of Washington D.C.; varied inds., notably electronic equipment; p. (1980) 66,713.

Mourenx, t., Pyrénées-Atlantique, **France**; nr. Lacq; new t., in oil dist.; p. (1982) 9,036.

Mourne Mtns., Newry and Mourne, **N. Ireland**; hgst. peak, 853 m.

Mouscron, t., **Belgium**; textile ctr. nr. Fr. border; p. (1982) 54,562.

Moyle, l. gov. dist., **N. Ireland**; borders N.E. cst.; inc. Rathlin I., Giants Causeway; main t. Ballycastle; p. (1981) 14,251.

Mozambique. See **Moçambique**.

Mudanjiang (**Mutankiang**), c., Heilongjiang prov., **China**; pulp, paper, machin., flour milling; site of dam on Mudan R.; oil shale found locally; p. (1984) 603,300.

Mühlhausen, t., Erfurt, **E. Germany**; on R. Unstrut; textiles, machin., tobacco; p. (1981) 43,348.

Mukden. See **Shenyang**.

Mulhaćen, mtn., Sierra Nevada range, **Spain**; 3,483 m (hgst. peak Europe, outside Alps).

Mülheim-an-der-Ruhr, t., N. Rhine–Westphalia, **W. Germany**; on R. Ruhr; cas.; coal mng., iron, steel., tobacco, engin., elec., oil refining; airpt.; p. (est. 1986) 170,400.

Mulhouse, t., Haut-Rhin dep., **France**; impt. textile ctr.; potash deposits to N. supply chemical inds.; p. (1982) 113,794.

Mull, I., Argyll and Bute, **Scot.**; included in Hebrides; a. 925 km²; pastoral farming, fishing, tourism; ch. t. Tobermory; p. (1971) 1569.

Mullet, The, peninsula, W. cst. Mayo, **R.o.I.**

Mullingar, c. t., Westmeath, **R.o.I.**; on Brosna R.; mkt., agr. ctr.; cath.; p. (1981) 7,854.

Mull of Galloway, S. point of Wigtown, **Scot.**

Multan, t., W. Punjab, **Pakistan**; on R. Chenab; carpets, silks, pottery, steel, thermal sta.; import gas pipeline to Lyallpur; nuclear fuel enrichment plant based on Pakistan's main uranium deposits nearby; p. (1981) 730,000.

Muncie, t., Ind. **USA**; on White R.; iron, steel, glass and paper; p. (1984) 74,200 (t.), 123,600 (met. a.).

Munich or **München**, c., cap. Bavaria, **W. Germany**; on R. Isar; cultural ctr. with univ., cath., many old bldgs.; inds. varied, notably scientific instruments, brewing, elec. engin., chemicals; famous film studios; annual beer festival; p. (est. 1986) 1,274,700.

Münster, c., N. Rhine–Westphalia, **W. Germany**; pt. on Dortmund–Ems canal; heavy machin. with varied mnfs.; cath., univ. and mediæval bldgs. damaged or destroyed in second world war; p. (est. 1986) 267,600.

Munster, prov., S.W. **R.o.I.**; includes cos. Waterford, Kerry, Cork, Limerick, Clare, Tipperary; a. 24,540 km²; p. (1981) 467,531.

Muonio, R., part of bdy. between **Finland** and **Sweden**; flows into G. of Bothnia.

Murano, t., Venice, **Italy**; famous since Middle Ages for glass ind.

Murchison Falls. See **Kabelega Falls**.

Murchison, R., W. **Australia;** flows to Indian Oc., spectacular gorge, Nat. Park; length 1,280 km.

Murcia, prov. and former Moorish kingdom, S.E. **Spain,** on Mediterranean ("Almonds and Raisins Coast"); irrigated agr., cereals and fruit; cap. Murcia; a. 8.467 km²; p. (1987) 1,013,806.

Murcia, c., cap. of Murcia prov., S.E. **Spain;** on R. Segura; cath., univ.; textiles and food inds.; p. (1987) 305,278.

Murgab or **Murghab,** R., **Afghanistan;** flows 400 km to desert swamps.

Murmansk, spt., **RSFSR;** on Kola peninsula; ice-free throughout year; engin., elec. power; fishing, shipbldg.; submarine base; marine power sta. utilising tidal energy projected; p. (est. 1985) 419,000.

Murom, t., **RSFSR;** pt. on Oka R.; anc. t.; textiles, engin.; p. (est. 1985) 121,000.

Muroran, spt., Hokkaido, **Japan;** on W. cst.; impt. iron and steel ctr.; p. (1985) 136,209.

Murray, R., separates N.S.W. and Victoria, **Australia;** major irrigation schemes support intensive agr.; hydro-electric power; 2,560 km long; length Murray-Darling system 3,696 km.

Murrumbidgee, R., N.S.W., **Australia;** trib. of R. Murray; used extensively for irrigation; 2,160 km long.

Mururoa, coral Is., S. **Pac. Oc.;** Fr. nuclear testing site; See **Tuamotu.**

Musa Jebel, mtn., **Egypt;** 2,249 m; identified with the biblical Sinai.

Muscat, t., cap. of **Oman,** Arabia; on S. cst. of G. of Oman; gd. harbour; dates, mother-of-pearl; terminal of oil pipeline; p. (est. 1985) 250,000 (met. a.).

Muscat and Oman. See **Oman.**

Musgrave Range, mtns., on bdy. between S. Australia and N.T., **Australia;** isolated highland in ctr. of continent; arid; rise to 1,520 m.

Muskingum, R., Ohio, **USA;** trib. of Ohio R.; canalised for navigation; 384 km long.

Musselburgh, burgh, East Lothian, **Scot.;** on F. of Forth at mouth of R. Esk; wire, cables, nets, twine; paper mkg.; golf course; p. (1981) 18,805.

Mutankiang. See **Mudanjiang.**

Mutari. See **Umtali.**

Muttra. See **Mathura.**

Muzaffarnagar, t., Uttar Pradesh, **India;** N.E. of Delhi; p. (1981) 171,816.

Muzaffarpur, t., Bihar, **India;** in middle Ganges valley N. of Patna; p. (1981) 190,416.

Mwanza, t., N. **Tanzania;** pt. on L. Victoria; rly. term.; gold and diamonds mined; p. (est. 1985) 134,000.

Mweelrea, mtn., Mayo, **R.o.I.;** 820 m.

Mweru, L., between Zaïre and Zambia; a. 6,993 km² at c. 900 m.

Myanmar. See **Burma.**

Mycenae, anc. c., N.E. Peloponnesus, **Greece;** excavations by Schliemann.

Myingyan, t., **Burma;** on R. Irrawaddy, S.W. of Mandalay; cotton spinning mill, zinc smelting, chemicals, fertilisers.

Myitkyina, t., **Burma;** on R. Irrawaddy; terminus of caravan route to China.

Mymensingh, t., **Bangladesh;** rice, jute; p. (1981) 190,911.

Mynyddislwyn, t., Islwyn, Gwent, **Wales;** in narrow valley of W. Ebbw R., 11 km N.W. of port; elec. gds., kerb- and flagstones; p. (1981) 15,547.

Mysłowice, t., Katowice, **Poland;** ctr. of coalmng. dist.; technical porcelain; p. (1983) 84,800.

Mysore. See **Karnataka.**

Mysore, t., Karnataka, **India;** univ.; new inds. based on hydroelec. power; p. (1981) 476,000.

Mytilene, pt. Aegean Sea, **Greece;** ch. c. of I. of Lesvos (sometimes called Mytilene); p. (1981) 24,991.

N

Naantali, t., S.W. **Finland;** pt. for Turku, on Baltic Sea; oil-refining, chemicals; founded 15th cent.; p. (est.) 2,174.

Naas, co. t., Co. Kildare, **R.o.I.;** former cap. of Leinster prov.; p. (1981) 8,345.

Nabeul, governorate, **Tunisia,** N. Africa; p. (1984) 461,405.

Nablus, t., **Jordan,** N. of Jerusalem; nr. site of anc. Schechem and Jacob's Well; p. (est. 1971) 44,200.

Nadiad, t., Gujarat, **India;** S. of Ahmadabad; p. (1981) 142,689.

Nagaland, st., **India** formerly part of Assam; separate st. since 1963; many border disputes; incorporates Naga Hills and Tuengsang; tribal a., cap. Kohima; a. 16,488 km²; p. (1981) 774,930.

Nagano, c., central Honshu, **Japan;** on R. Sinanogawa, 160 km S.W. of Nigata; cultural ctr.; publishing, machin., food-processing; textiles; p. (1985) 336,967.

Nagaoka, t., N.W. Honshu, **Japan;** lge. oil production ctr.; p. (1979) 177,253.

Nagapattinam, t., Tamil Nadu, **India;** spt. at mouth of R. Vettar; exp. cotton, tobacco, groundnuts; rly. terminus; p. (est. 1971) 68,015.

Nagasaki, c., spt., Kyushu, **Japan;** on narrow peninsula; second c. destroyed by atomic bomb in second world war; impt. shipbldg. ctr. and associated engin.; p. (1985) 449,382.

Nagercoil, t., Tamil Nadu, **India;** extreme S. of Indian peninsula; coconut-processing; p. (1981) 171,684.

Nagh Hamadi (Nag' Hammâdi), t., Upper **Egypt;** on R. Nile 256 km above Asyût; site of barrage (opened 1930) to regulate Nile flood and ensure irrigation of Girga prov.; barrage carries Cairo–Shellal rly. across Nile.

Nagorno-Karabakh, aut. oblast, S.W. Azerbaydzhan SSR, **USSR;** on E. of Lesser Caucasus; forested mtns.; unrest 1990; cap. Stepanakert; a. 4,403 km²; p. (1970) 149,000.

Nagoya, third c. of **Japan;** on Ise Bay, central Honshu; major pt. and industl. ctr.; univ.; textile mills, ceramic ctr., oil-refining; 16th cent. fortress t.; p. (1987) 2,143,000.

Nagpur, c., Maharashtra st., **India;** univ.; admin. ctr.; textiles; Hindu temples; p. (1981) 1,219,461(c.), 1,302,066 (met. a.).

Nagy Banya. See **Baia-Mare.**

Nagykanizsa, t., S.W. **Hungary;** industl. ctr.; heavy equipment, glasswks., beer; p. (est. 1984) 56,000.

Nagykörös, mkt. t., N. **Hungary;** in fruit-growing region; wine, food-processing; p. (est. 1984) 27,000.

Nagymáros, t., **Hungary;** on Danube R. between Budapest and Austrian border; site of hydro-electr. dam built jointly with Austria.

Naha, spt., cap. of Okinawa I., **Ryuku Is.;** p. (1985) 304,000.

Nailsworth, t., Gloucs., **Eng.;** in Cotswold Hills 6 km S. of Stroud; p. (1981) 5,086.

Nain, t., **Iran;** noted for very fine carpets; p. (1967) 40,289.

Nairn, former co., l. gov. dist., Highland Reg. **Scot.;** on Moray F., agr. a.; a. 420 km²; p. (est. 1986) 10,239.

Nairn, royal burgh, Nairn, N.E. **Scot.;** fishing ctr.; cas.; p. (1981) 7,721.

Nairobi, c., cap. of **Kenya;** stands at c. 1,500 m on edge of Kenya highlands; modern c., 528 km from Mombasa; univ.; tourist ctr.; lt. inds.; steel rolling mill; inland ctr. for containers; wildlife game reserve; p. (est. 1983) 1,047,951.

Naivasha, L., **Kenya;** on floor of Gt. African Rift Valley; alt. 1,800 m.

Najaf or **Nejef,** c., **Iraq;** in Euphrates valley; Shiite Moslem pilgrimage ctr.; p. (1970) 179,160.

Nakhichevan, c. Azerbaydzhan SSR, **USSR;** food and wine inds.; ctr. of Nakhichevan aut. region; p. (1970) 33,000.

Nakhichevan ASSR, aut. rep. Azerbaydzhan SSR, **USSR;** borders Iran and Turkey; cotton, tobacco, rice, wheat in irrigated lowlands; salt and mineral deposits; a. 5,439 km²; p. (1986) 272,000.

Nakhodka, t., **RSFSR;** outpt. for Vladivostok on Sea of Japan; new t. 1950; p. (est. 1985) 150,000.

Nakhon Pathom, t., **Thailand;** in central plain, S.W. of Bangkok; mkt. t.; p. (1980) 45,242.

Nakhon Ratchasima, t., **Thailand;** on Mun R., in Korat plateau; rly. junc.; copper deposits nearby; p. (1982) 87,371.

Nakhon si Thammarat, t., **Thailand;** in S. of Isthmus of Kra, on G. of Siam; anc. t.; mkt.; p. (1980) 102,123.

Nakshov, spt., Lolland I., **Denmark;** sugar-refining; p. (1981) 16,216.

Nakuru, t., **Kenya** rift valley (1,837 m), E. Africa; protected bird sanctuary (flamingoes) on L. Nakuru; wool-processing, fertilisers; p. (est. 1972) 47,800.

Nalchik, c., cap. of Kabardino-Balkar ASSR,

RSFSR; in foothills of N. Caucasus; food-processing; tourist resort; p. (est. 1985) 227,000.

Namangan, c., Uzbek SSR, **USSR**; on Syr Dar'ya R., in Ferghana Valley; textiles, leather; p. (est. 1985) 275,000.

Namaqualand, region, S.W. cst. of **Africa**; divided by Orange R. into Gr. N. in S.W. Africa, and Little N. in Cape Prov., Rep. of S. Africa; semi-arid; a. 259,000 km²; copper, diamonds.

Nam Co (Nam Tso), L., Tibet, **China**.

Nam Dinh, t., **Vietnam**, p. 25,000.

Namhol. See **Foshan.**

Namib Desert, desert a. along coastal strip of S.W. Africa for 1,200 km; very dry a., and almost unused.

Namibe (Moçâmedes) pt. **Angola**, S.W. Africa; rail link to Cassinga mines; p. (est. 1981) 100,000.

Namibia, indep. st. (1990); formerly mandated territory under S.Af. rule; became (1990) 50th member of Commonwealth; scanty rainfall; stock rearing; alluvial diamonds from Lüderitz on Orange R.; copper, lead, zinc mng. in Grootfontein dist.; coal and offshore natural gas discovered; minerals provide 60 per cent exp. earnings; ch. pt. Walvis Bay; cap. Windhoek; summer cap. Swakopmund; a. 824,296 km²; p. (est. 1990) 1·3 m.

Namsos, spt., central **Norway**; on Folda fjord; lumber, fish canning; textiles; copper; p. (1980) 11,816.

Namur, c., cap. of N. prov., **Belgium**; at confluence of Meuse and Sambre Rs.; agr. processing, cutlery, glass; p. (est. 1984) 101,861.

Nanaimo, t., B.C., **Canada**; pt. on Vancouver I.; timber and allied inds.; fisheries; boating and yachting; tourism; p. (1981) 21,715.

Nanchong, c., Sichuan, **China**; on Kan R.; major transportation and industl. ctr.; textiles, machin., chemicals, paper; tractor wks.; dates from Sung dynasty (12th cent.); p. (1984) 231,700.

Nancheng. See **Hanzhong.**

Nancy, c., Meurthe-et-Moselle dep., **France**; industl. and admin. ctr.; univ., cath.; chemical ind. (based on local salt); anc. cap. of duchy of Lorraine; p. (1982) 99,307.

Nanda Devi, mtn., Uttar Pradesh, **India**; in Himalayas, 7,822 m; first scaled, 1936.

Nanded, t., Maharashtra, **India**; p. (1981) 191,269.

Nanga Parbat, mtn., N.W. Kashmir, **India**, in W. Himalayas; alt. 8,131 m.

Nanjing (Nanking), c., Jiangsu, **China**; on Chang Jiang; cap. of China during Kuomintang régime 1928–49; famous seat of learning; tombs of founders of Ming dynasty; lge. motor vehicle plant, electronics, precision instruments, insecticides, cotton cloth, oil-refining; road-rail bridge over lowest reaches of Chang Jiang opened 1969; p. (1984) 2,207,500.

Nanling, mtns., S. **China**; form divide between Rs. flowing N. to Chang Jiang and S. to Xi R.; crossed by historic Cheling and Meiling Passes; alt. mainly below 1,800 m.

Nanning, c., cap. of Guangxi prov., **China**; on Yu R.; ch. mkt. on S. frontier; rice transplanter factory; p. (1984) 617,900.

Nan Shan, mtns., central **China**; branch range of Kunlun; rise to over 3,600 m.

Nanterre, N.W. sub. of Paris, **France**; cap. of Hauts-de-Seine dep.; aluminium mftg.; p. (1982) 90,371.

Nantes, spt., cap. of Loire-Atlantique dep., W. **France**; on R. Loire; ocean pt. St. Nazaire; impt. industl. and shipping ctr.; univ., cath., cas.; p. (1982) 247,227.

Nantong (Nantung) c., Jiangsu, **China**; on N. bank of Chang Jiang estuary; cotton; p. (1984) 402,700.

Nantucket, I., Mass., **USA**; official W. of trans-Atlantic sea-crossing; summer resort; fishing; p. (1980) 3,229.

Nantung. See **Nantong.**

Nantwich, mkt. t., Crewe and N. Cheshire, **Eng.**; on R. Weaver, 5 km S.W. of Crewe; brine baths; clothing, food prods.; p. (1981) 11,958; see **Crewe.**

Natyglo and Blaina, t., Blaenau Gwent, Gwent, **Wales**; in narrow valley 3 km N. of Abertillery; footwear, rubber prods.; p. (1981) 9,862.

Napier, c., N.I., **N.Z.**; pt. and ch. c. of Hawke Bay prov. dist.; exp. frozen meat; timber processing, fishing; p. (est. 1987) 49,400.

Naples (Napoli), c., Campania, S. **Italy**; spt. on Bay of N., at foot of Vesuvius, opposite anc. Pompeii; exp. food prods.; impt. industl. ctr.; shipbldg., oil refining, food-processing; cultural and artistic ctr.; univ., cath.; tourism; earthquake, 1980; p. (1984) 1,208,545.

Napo, R., rises in Ecuador; 880 km long.

Nara, c., S. Honshu, **Japan**; anc. religious ctr. and place of pilgrimage; colossal image of Buddha (16·3 m high); cap. of Japan A.D. 710–84; tourism; p. (1985) 327,702.

Nara Basin, Honshu, **Japan**; agr. dist. serving the Kinki plain; intensive rice and vegetable cultivation.

Narayanganj, c., **Bangladesh**; S. of Dacca in middle Ganges delta; p. (1981) 405,562.

Narbeth, mkt. t., South Pembrokeshire, Dyfed, **Wales**; nr. head of Milford Haven; p. (1981) 1,072.

Narbonne, t., Aude dep., S. **France**; in Languedoc; nr. Mediterranean cst.; in wine-growing a.; impt. in Roman times; cath., palace (now town hall); p. (1982) 42,657.

Narew, R., Poland and **USSR**; flows to R. Vistula nr. Warsaw, c. 432 km long; ch. trib. W. Bug.

Narmada, R., central **India**; flows W. through Madhya Pradesh and Gujarat to G. of Cambay; 1,280 km long.

Narrabri, t., N.S.W., **Australia**; 570 km N.W. Sydney; observatory with stellar interferometer (1964); p. (1976) 6,951.

Narrandera, t., N.S.W., **Australia**; on R. Murrumbidgee; collecting ctr. for wool, mutton, wheat, fruits produced in irrigated a.; p. (1976) 4,984.

Narrogin, t., W. **Australia**; major ctr. of wheat belt; p. (1981) 4,969.

Narva, t., N.E. Estonia, **USSR**; textiles, machin., sawmills; hydroelectric power; founded by Danes 1223; p. (est. 1973) 66,000.

Narvik, pt., N.W. **Norway**; sheltered by Lofoten Is.; ice-free; linked by rly. to iron-ore fields in N. Sweden; scene of fierce sea-battles between British and Germans 1940; p. (1980) 19,339.

Naseby, v., Northants., **Eng.**; battle where parliamentarians under Fairfax and Cromwell beat royalists under Charles I and Prince Rupert 1645.

Nashville, c., st. cap. Tenn., **USA**; pt. on Cumberland R.; rly. ctr.; impt. shipping, industl. and educational ctr.; food and tobacco prods., cellophane, rayon; univs. and colleges; p. (1984) 462,500 (c.), 890,300 (met. a.).

Nasik, t., Maharashtra, **India**; on R. Godavari; Hindu pilgrimage ctr.; metal work; p. (1981) 262,428 (t.), 429,034 (met. a.).

Nassau, spt., cap. Bahamas, **W.I.**; exp. forest, sea and agr. prods.; resort; p. (1980) 3,233 (t.), 135,437 (met. a.).

Nassau, t., Cook Is., S. **Pac. Oc.**; **N.Z.** terr.; uninhabited; radio telegraph sta.

Nasser City, t., **Egypt**; rural development at Kom Ombo, N. of Aswan, for resettlement of 50,000 Nubians before formation of Lake Nasser behind the High Dam.

Natal, spt., cap. of Rio Grande do Norte st., **Brazil**; above mouth of Potengi R.; exp. sugar, cotton, salt, carnauba wax, hides; recent industl. expansion results from SUDENE development plan; new textile mills; airport on main routes from Africa to S. America; p. (est. 1985) 512,200.

Natal, prov., S. **Africa**; subtropical coastal climate; sugar-cane, tea, cereals; coal; cap. Pietermaritzburg; a. 91,385 km²; p. (1980) 2,676,340.

Natanya or **Nathania**, t., **Israel**; resort on Mediterranean cst.; food-processing; p. (est. 1971) 62,500.

Natuna Is., Indonesia; I. gr. in S. China Sea, N.W. of Borneo; little developed; a. 2,113 km²; p. 27,000.

Naucratis, anc. c., **Egypt**; between Cairo and Alexandria; excavated by Flinders Petrie and Gardiner.

Naumburg, t., Halle, E. **Germany**; on R. Saale; cath.; textiles, leather, toys, chemicals; p. (est. 1973) 37,106.

Nauplia (Gr. **Nauplion**), pt. and comm. ctr., on E. cst. Peloponnesus, Greece; the anc. Argos; first cap. of indep. Greece 1830–4, when it was superseded by Athens; p. (1981) 10,611.

Nauru, I., indep. rep. (1968), central **Pac. Oc.**; formerly admin. by Australia; coral I., heavily dependent on phosphate-mng.; deposits will be exhausted by 1993 and plans to ship out new soil by UN; a. 21 km²; p. (est. 1985) 8,000.

Navan (An Uamh), U.D., Meath, **R.o.I.**; carpets; lead and zinc ores; p. (1981) 11,136.

Navarre, prov., N. **Spain**; bounded by Pyrenees; thickly wooded; cap. Pamplona; sugar-beet, cereals, cattle, hardwoods, vineyards; former kingdom; p. Basque; p. (1981) 508,722.

Naver, R., Sutherland, **Scot.**; flows N. to Pentland Firth; valley once densely p., cleared early 19th cent. to make room for sheep.

Naxos, I., **Greece**; in Aegean Sea, lgst. of the Cyclades; famous for wine and fruit; a. 425 km²; p. 19,000.

Nazareth, t., **Israel**; 34 km S.E. Acre; home of Jesus Christ; p. (est. 1970) 34,000.

Naze, The, C., S. point of **Norway**.

Nazilli, t., S.W. **Turkey**; on R. Menderes; agr., especially olives; p. (1985) 77,627.

Ndjamena (Fort Lamy), c., cap. of **Chad Rep.**; at confluence of Shari and Logone Rs.; isolated but ctr. of caravan tr.; airpt.; p. (est. 1985) 511,700.

Ndola, t., **Zambia**; nr. bdy. with Zaïre, 176 km by rail N. of Kabwe; ctr. of rich copper-mng. a., less impt. lead- and zinc-mng.; minerals despatched by rail E. to Beira and W. to Lobito Bay; oil refining nearby; international airpt. being built; p. (1980) 282,439.

Neagh, Lough, L., **N. Ireland**; lgst. freshwater L. in Brit. Is.; a. 396 km²; drained by R. Bann.

Neath, t., l. gov. dist., West Glamorgan, **Wales**; 10 km up R. Neath from Swansea Bay; coal, aluminium inds., oil refining; cas., abbey; p. (est. 1988) 65,200 (dist.).

Nebraska, st., **USA**; Cornhusker St.; admitted to Union 1867; st. flower Golden rod, st. bird Western Meadowlark; mainly prairie; cap. Lincoln; farming, meat-packing, wheat, maize, hay, potatoes, sugar-beet, apples, wool, livestock, petroleum, cement; a. 200,147 km²; p. (1985) 1,606,000.

Neckar, R., **W. Germany**; rises between Swabian Jura and Black Forest; flows through Baden-Württemberg to Rhine at Mannheim; 384 km long.

Needles, chalk stacks in English Channel, off W. cst. of I. of Wight, **Eng.**

Neftyne Kamni, t., **USSR**; built on piles over Caspian Sea for Russian oil workers.

Negev, desert, region, S. **Israel**; new a. of irrigated agr.; oil and natural gas; p. (1962) c. 33,000.

Negombo, t., S.W. **Sri Lanka**; at mouth of Negombo lagoon; ctr. of coconut belt; metalware, ceramics; p. (1981) 61,376.

Negril Beach, Jamaica; 40 km W. of Montego Bay; new resort to further Jamaica's tourist tr.

Negri Sembilan, st., W. **Malaysia**; on Strait of Malacca; tin and rubber; cap. Seremban; a. 6,682 km²; p. (1980) 573,578.

Negro Rio, R., **Argentina**; flows into G. of St. Mathias, Atl. Oc.; used for irrigation, partly navigable.

Negro Rio, R., **Brazil**; one of ch. tribs. of R. Amazon; rises in Colombia, joins Amazon nr. Manaus; c. 1,520 km long.

Negro Rio, R., **Uruguay**; flows from Brazil border to Uruguay R.; major multi-purpose project at Rincon del Bonete; 800 km long.

Negros, I., **Philippines**; S. of Mindanao; impt. sugar producing I.; copper deposits; a. 12,704 km²; p. (1970) 2,307,493.

Neheim-Hüsten, t., N. Rhine–Westphalia, **W. Germany**; at confluence of Rs. Möhne and Ruhr; chemicals; p. (est. 1971) 36,300.

Neijiang (Neikiang), c., Sichuan prov., **China**; on To R.; agr. ctr.; p. (1984) 289,100.

Neisse or Nisa, two tribs. of R. Oder, (1) Western or Glatzer Neisse, frontier between Poland and E. Germany, 224 km long; (2) Eastern or Lausitzer Neisse, E. Silesia, Poland, 192 km long.

Neiva, t., **Colombia**; at head of navigation of R. Magdalena; tr. in cattle and coffee; panama hats; p. (1985) 197,445.

Nejd, dist., central **Arabia**; with Hejaz, forms kingdom of Saudi Arabia; mainly desert; impt. oil wells, horses, camels, dates, various fruits; cap. Riyadh; a. 1,087,800 km²; p. (est.) 4,000,000.

Nellore, t., Andhra Pradesh, **India**; admin. ctr.; p. (1981) 237,065.

Nelson, R., **Canada**; drains L. Winnipeg to Hudson Bay; length (with its gr. trib. the Saskatchewan) 2,320 km.

Nelson, t., Pendle, Lancs., **Eng.**; on N. flank of Rossendale 5 km N.E. of Burnley; cotton, iron and brick wks., lt. engin., paper; p. (1981) 30,435.

Nelson, c., S.I., **N.Z.**; pt. nr. head of Tasman Bay; fishing, fruit-packing, timber; coalfield; cath.; p. (est. 1987) 34,500.

Neman (Pol. **Nieman**, Ger. **Memel**), R., Lithua-

nian SSR and Belorussiyan SSR, **USSR**; rises S.W. of Minsk and flows c. 920 km into Kurisches Haff (Courland Lagoon), Baltic Sea, forming sm. delta.

Nene, R., Northants., **Eng.**; rises nr. Naseby and flows 144 km to the Wash.

Nepal, indep. kingdom, S.E. **Asia**; on S. slopes of Himalayas and inc. Mt. Everest; isolated from India by malarial forested zone of Terai; N. mostly tropical forest and jungle; home of Gurkhas; poor infrastructure hinders development; only 5,000 km of road; agr. in fertile valleys, rice, wheat, maize; forestry impt. but deforestation a problem; plans to incr. cottage inds.; cap. Katmandu; a. 141,414 km²; p. (est. 1985) 16,625,000.

Nerbudda. See **Narmada**.

Ness, Loch, L., Inverness, **Scot.**; occupies N.E. end of Glenmore; forms link in Caledonian Canal; very deep; 36·4 km long.

Neston, t., Cheshire, **Eng.**; on N. side of Dee estuary; residtl.; sea bed engin.; p. (1981) 18,415; See **Ellesmere Port.**

Nestos, R. See **Mesta.**

Netherlands, kingdom, N.W. **Europe**; bounded by N. Sea, Belgium and W. Germany; comprises 11 provs.; since second world war has taken advantage of location at mouth of Rhine, opposite Thames estuary, to develop lge.-scale coastal inds., inc. iron and steel at IJmuiden, oil refining, petrochemicals at major European pt. complex of Rotterdam–Europort; similarly major industl. growth in conurbation of Randstad Holland in steering economy far away from formerly predominant agr. basis; agr. still impt. and major sea-flood control schemes around IJsselmeer and Rhine estuary are creating valuable land for intensive agr. in a densely populated cty.; recent discoveries of natural gas in Groningen have also turned cty. into major supplier of energy for European mkts.; practises advanced policy of social welfare; EC member; cap. Amsterdam; seat of govt. at The Hague; a. 36,175 km²; p. (est. 1987) 14,615,125.

Netherlands Antilles (Curaçao), 2 gr. of Is. in Caribbean Sea, part of Lesser Antilles; main gr. off Venezuela inc. Curaçao, Bonaire and formerly Aruba; 2nd gr. inc. volcanic Is. of St. Eustatius, Saba, and St. Maarten (S. part only); agr. of sm. importance as a result of low rainfall; benefits from Venezuelan oil ind.; oil refineries in Curaçao; petrochemical inds.; indep. planned; Aruba separated (1986) with full internal self-government; cap. Willemstad; a. 1,020 km²; p. (1981) 171,620.

Netze. See **Notec.**

Neubrandenburg, c., cap. of N. admin. dist., **E. Germany**; fibreglass, machin., chemicals; p. (est. 1982) 620,600 (dist.).

Neuchâtel, can., **Switzerland**; in Jura mtns.; forested with some pastures; cattle, cheese, wine; watches, cutlery, cottons, hosiery; asphalt from Val de Travers; a. 800 km²; p. (est. 1986) 156,000.

Neuchâtel, cap. of Neuchâtel can., **Switzerland**; on N. slope of Lake Neuchâtel; cas.; univ.; watches, jewellery, condensed milk; p. (1980) 34,428.

Neuchâtel, L., **Switzerland**; at S.E. foot of Jura mtns.; drains N.E. to R. Aare; vineyards on S. facing slopes; remains of lake dwellings, anc. Celtic site of La Tène culture.

Neuilly-sur-Seine, sub., W. of Paris, Hauts-de-Seine, **France**; fine bridge and cas.; engin.; p. (1982) 64,450.

Neumünster, t., Schleswig-Holstein, **W. Germany**; rly. ctr.; leather, paper and textile inds.; p. (est. 1986) 77,900.

Neunkirchen, t., Saarland, **W. Germany**; iron and steel mngs.; coal mng.; p. (est. 1986) 49,500.

Neuquén, prov., S. **Argentina**; natural gas reserves; pipeline planned to feed urban ctrs. of Pampas; p. (1980) 241,904.

Neuquén, t., cap. of N. prov., **Argentina**; at confluence of Rs. Limay and Neuquén, in ctr. of fruit-farming dist.; p. (1980) 90,037.

Neusalz. See **Nowa Sól.**

Neusandetz. See **Nowy Sacz.**

Neuss, c., N. Rhine–Westphalia, **W. Germany**; rly. junc., canal pt.; nr. Rhine, opposite Düsseldorf; metal gds., food-processing; p. (est. 1986) 143,800.

Neustadt, t., Rhineland-Palatinate, **W. Germany**; on R. Haardt; agr. machinery; impt. wine tr.; p. (est. 1986) 48,400.

Neustadt. See **Wiener-Neustadt.**

Neutitschein. See **Nový Jičin.**

Neva, R., **RSFSR**, on which Leningrad stands; drains L. Ladoga to G. of Finland; navigable but liable to flooding; 74 km long.

Nevada, st., **USA**; Silver St.; admitted to Union 1864; st. flower Sagebrush, st. bird Mountain Bluebird; in Rocky mtns., continental climate; mng. basis of economy gold, silver, copper, tungsten, gypsum, iron, lead; livestock agr., timber; tourism; ts. inc. Las Vegas and cap. Carson City; a. 286,299 km²; p. (1985) 930,000.

Nevers, c., cap. of Nièvre dep., **France**; on R. Loire; anc. iron and steel ind.; porcelain and faience; cath., historic bldgs.; p. (1982) 59,274 (met. a.).

Neves, t., Rio de Janeiro st., S.E. **Brazil**; sugar, coffee; p. (1960) 85,741.

Nevis, I., Leeward Is., **W.I.**; cotton, sugar; ch. t. Charlestown; desire for indep. from St. Kitts; a. 130 km²; p. (1980) 9,428.

New Albany, c., Ind., **USA**; on R. Ohio; domestic glassware, furniture, leather, iron and steel, car bodies; p. (est. 1980) 37,103.

New Amsterdam, spt., **Guyana**; on Berbice R.; processes agr. prods. from surrounding lowland; p. (est. 1979) 25,000.

New Amsterdam, Dutch settlement, Manhattan I., **USA**; taken by English 1664, and renamed New York.

Newark, mkt. t., l. gov. dist., Notts., **Eng.**; on R. Trent 27 km N.E. of Nottingham; ball bearings, brewing and malting; cas.; p. (est. 1988) 103,800 (dist.).

Newark, c., N.J., **USA**; meat-packing, printing, elec. gds., paints, chemicals, cars, aircraft, leather; route ctr.; p. (1984) 314,400 (c.; in New York conurbanation).

New Bedford, c., spt., Mass., **USA**; on estuary of R. Acushnet; whale-fishery ctr.; mnfs. cottons, cordage, glass, shoes; resort; p. (1984) 97,700 (c.), 167,700 (met. a.).

Newbiggin-by-the-Sea, t., Wansbeck, Northumberland, **Eng.**; sm. seaside resort; coal mng.; p. (1981) 12,132.

New Brighton, t., Merseyside, **Eng.**; at entrance to Mersey estuary; residtl. dist. of Wallasey, resort.

New Britain, lgst. I., Bismarck Archipelago, **Papua New Guinea**; volcanic mtns.; exp. copra, cacao; a. (with adjacent Is.) 37,814 km²; p. (est. 1970) 154,000.

New Britain, t., Conn., **USA**; iron and brass mnfs.; p. (1980) 73,840 (t.), 142,241 (met. a.).

New Brunswick, maritime prov., **Canada**; forest-clad mtns.; impt. timber inds.; fishing and fish-processing; many minerals; road and rail link with Prince Edward I.; cap. Fredericton; a. 72,481 km²; p. (1986) 710,000.

New Brunswick, t., N.J., **USA**; on Raritan R.; chemicals, motor lorries, leather, hosiery and hardware; univ.; p. (1980) 596,000 (met. a.).

Newburgh, burgh, North East Fife, **Scot.**; on S. side of F. of Tay, 13 km E. of Perth; fish. pt.; linoleum; p. (1981) 2,008.

Newburn, t., Tyne and Wear, **Eng.**; on R. Tyne 5 km W. of Newcastle; pure graphite for nuclear reactors; p. (1981) 43,700.

Newbury, t., l. gov. dist., Berks., **Eng.**; on R. Kennet, 27 km S.W. of Reading; engin., furniture, paper, cardboard boxmaking; mkt.; racecourse; p. (est. 1988) 138,700.

New Caledonia, overseas terr. of **France**; volcanic I. in S. **Pac. Oc.**; nickel and chrome deposits; nickel processing; cap. Nouméa; independence movements to establish separate Melanesian reg. in S. Pacific and much unrest since 1984; referendum on full independence to be held in 1998; a. 22,139 km² p. (est. 1985) 153,000.

Newcastle, c., N.S.W., **Australia**; spt. at mouth of R. Hunter; second c. of st.; lgst. exporter of coal in Australia; iron and steel based on coal resources; new inds. on reclaimed land; mineral sand mng. (rutile, zircon); p. (1981) 258,972.

Newcastle, spt., on Dundrum Bay; Down, **N. Ireland**; resort; p. (1981) 6,246.

New Castle, t., Penns., **USA**; tinplate, glass, steel wire, iron, coal, limestone; p. (1980) 33,621.

Newcastle Emlyn, t., Dyfed, **Wales**; on R. Teifi; p. (1981) 664.

Newcastle-under-Lyme, t., l. gov. dist., Staffs., **Eng.**; 3 km W. of Stoke-on-Trent, on Lyme Brook; coal mng.; brick and tile mnfs.; p. (est. 1988) 117,500.

Newcastle upon Tyne, c., met. dist., Tyne and Wear, **Eng.**; spt. on N. bank of Tyne R., 16 km from N. Sea; shipbldg., heavy engin., chemicals; connected by bridges across Tyne to Gateshead; univ., cath., many fine public bldgs., partially preserved in redevelopment of c. ctr.; airport; new metro system; p. (est. 1988) 279,600.

New Delhi. *See* **Delhi**.

New England, N.S.W., **Australia**; dist. of N. Tablelands; pastoral cty. for sheep and beef; ch. ts. Armidale, Glen Innes, and Tenterfield.

New England, the six N.E. Atl. sts. of **USA**; Me., N.H., Vt., Mass., R.I., Conn.; humid-continental climate, infertile soils, poor agr. conditions; fishing; recent industl. metamorphosis as traditional inds. are replaced by modern science-based, high-value inds.; tourism; ch. t. Boston; p. (1980) 12,349,000.

Newent, mkt. t., Gloucs., **Eng.**; 13 km S. of Ledbury.

New Forest, forest and heathland, Hants., **Eng.**; relic of Royal Forest; now partly owned by Forestry Commission; pasture, ponies, tourism; residtl.; oil reserves but no drilling yet as conflicts with conservation; ch. t. Lyndhurst; rapid growth of p. since 1951; now forms l. gov. dist.; p. (est. 1988) 163,300.

Newfoundland, I., with Labrador, prov., of **Canada**; E. of the G. of St. Lawrence; in E. low; in W. rugged mtns., many Ls.; coniferous forest; fishing, cod, salmon, halibut, lobster, seal; lumber, wood-pulp, paper; iron ore, lead, zinc, copper, asbestos; hydroelec. power; climate is severe; cap. St. John's; a. prov. 404,519 km² (I. 112,300 km², Labrador 292,219 km²); p. (1986) 568,000.

New Galloway, burgh, Stewartry, **Scot.**; on R. Dee; nearby Clatteringshaws hydroelec. sta..

New Guinea, I., S.W. **Pac. Oc.**; N. of Australia; equatorial climate; dense forest; central mtn. chain; lge. a. of lowland in S.; divided politically between Irian Jaya in W. (Indonesia) and Papua New Guinea in E.; economically under-developed; a. 831,390 km². *See* **Papua New Guinea, Irian Jaya.**

Newham, inner bor. Greater London, **Eng.**; W. of R. Lea; contained Royal group of London docks (now all closed); p. and industl. decentralisation from a.; p. (est. 1988) 207,000.

New Hampshire, st., New England, **USA**; borders on **Canada**; Granite St.; admitted to Union 1788; st. flower Purple Lilac, st. bird Purple Finch; forested mtns.; agr., fruit-growing; paper and forest prods.; textiles, shoes; granite; cap. Concord; ch. spt. Portsmouth; ch. mftg. ctr. Manchester; a. 24,097 km²; p. (1985) 998,000.

Newhaven, t., East Sussex, **Eng.**; on S. cst. at mouth of R. Ouse, 14 km E. of Brighton; passenger pt. for Dieppe; boat-bldg. and lt. indus.; p. (1981) 9,857.

New Haven, c., pt., Conn., **USA**; on inlet of Long I. Sound; Yale Univ.; firearms, clocks, hardware, radiators, rubber gds.; p. (1984) 124,200 (c.), 506,000. (met. a.).

New Hebrides. *See* **Vanuatu.**

New Holland, v., rly. terminus, ferry pt. for crossing to Hull, Humberside, **Eng.**

New Ireland, volcanic I., **Papua–New Guinea**, in Bismarck archipelago; mtnous.; ch. pt. Kavieng; exp. copra; a. (with adjacent Is.) 9,842 km²; p. (est. 1987) 78,900.

New Jersey, st., **USA**; Garden St.; admitted to Union 1787; st. flower Purple Violet. st. bird Eastern Gold Finch; on Atl. cst. plain, adjacent to N.Y. c.; intensive agr., mkt. gardening; heavily industrialised; oil refining, glass sand, zinc, iron ore, clay, chemicals, motor vehicles; cap. Trenton; ch. cs. Newark, Jersey City; a. 20,295 km²; p. (1985) 7,562,000.

Newmarket, t., Forest Heath, Suffolk, **Eng.**; at foot of E. Anglian Heights; the "racing capital of England"; p. (1981) 16,235.

New Mexico, st., **USA**; popular name 'Land of Enchantment'; admitted to Union 1912; st. flower Yucca, st. bird Road Runner; N. of Mexico, S. of Col. st.; traversed by Rocky mtns.; dry climate; agr. dependent upon irrigation; dry farming, arable crops, livestock; uranium, potash salts, pumice, beryllium, copper, petroleum; ch. ts., Albuquerque and cap. Santa Fé; a. 315,115 km²; p. (1985) 1,450,000.

New Mills, industl. t., High Peak, Derbys., **Eng.**; at W. foot of Pennines; textile printing, bleaching and dyeing; rayon, paper; confectionery; p. (1981) 9,084.

Newmilns and Greenholm, burgh, Kilmarnock and Loudoun, **Scot.**; on R. Irvine, 19 km E. of Kilmarnock; muslin and lace curtain mnf.; p. (1981) 3,230.

New Mirpir, t., **Pakistan;** new t. 3 km. from old Mirpur submerged by Mangla L. 1967; planned p. 40,000.

New Orleans, c., spt., La., **USA;** on delta of Mississippi R.; the gr. cotton mart of America, busy comm., mftg. and cultural ctr., home of jazz; sugar refining, oil refining; p. (1984) 559,100 (c.), 1,318,800 (met. a.).

New Plymouth, c., spt., N.I., **N.Z.;** on W. cst. at N. foot of Mt. Egmont; oil and natural gas deposits; ctr. of dairy-farming dist.; p. (est. 1987) 44,500.

Newport-on-Tay, burgh, North East Fife, **Scot.;** on S. side of F. of Tay, opposite Dundee; p. (1981) 3,681.

Newport, Medina, cap. I. of Wight, **Eng.;** on R. Medina, in gap through central chalk ridge; mkt.; brewing, joinery, bait mnfs.; prison; p. (1981) 23,570.

Newport, mkt. t., The Wrekin, Shrops., **Eng.;** 13 km N.E. of Wellington; p. (1981) 8,983.

Newport, spt., **Vietnam;** on N. outskirts of Ho Chi-minh City; lge. pt. inaugurated 1967.

Newport, t., R.I., **USA;** on Narragansett Bay; fashionable seaside resort; precision instruments; p. (1980) 29,259.

Newport, t., l. gov. dist., Gwent, **Wales;** on R. Usk, 8 km from its mouth; timber terminal and deep-water berth; engin., iron and steel, aluminium, paperboard, confectionery, chemicals, plastics; p. (est. 1988) 128,100 (dist.).

Newport News, c., spt., Va., **USA;** on N. shore of estuary of James R. on Hampton Roads; lge. harbour; shipbldg.; outlet for Virginian tobacco and Appalachian coal; p. (1984) 154,600 (c.), 1,261,200 (met. a. inc. Norfolk).

Newport Pagnell, mkt. t., Bucks., **Eng.;** on R. Ouse; mnfs. Aston Martin cars; p. (1981) 10,810.

Newquay, t., Restormel, Cornwall, **Eng.;** on N. Cornish cst.; seaside resort; p. (1981) 16,050.

New Quay, t., Ceredigion, Dyfed, **Wales;** on cst. of Cardigan Bay; fishing; resort; p. (1981) 766.

New Radnor, t., Powys, **Wales;** on slope of Radnor Forest, 10 km S.W. of Presteign.

New Rochelle, t., N.Y., **USA;** on Long I. Sound; residtl.; p. (1980) 70,794.

New Romney, t., Shepway, Kent, **Eng.;** nr. S. cst. to E. of Dungeness; in rich agr. dist. of Romney Marsh; Cinque pt.; old harbour silted up by shingle, now a mile from sea; p. (1981) 4,563.

New Ross, mkt. t. U.D., Wexford, **R.o.I.;** brewing and malting; p. (1981) 6,141.

Newry, t., Newry and Mourne, **N. Ireland;** pt. at head of Carlingford Lough; machin., rope, brewing, granite; p. (1981) 19,426.

Newry and Mourne, l. gov. dist., **N. Ireland;** surrounds t. of N., borders R.o.I., Irish Sea; inc. Mtns. of Mourne; p. (1981) 72,748.

New South Wales, st., S.E. **Australia;** first col. established by Brit. in A.; much mineral wealth in tablelands and mtns.; climate equable and well suited to both arable and pastoral agr.; leading agr. st. in Australia; major irrigation schemes in drier E. plains of Murray, Murrumbidgee, and Lachlan Rs.; coal mng. and heavy inds. at Newcastle, Port Kembla, Wollongong; hydroelectric power from Snowy mtns. scheme; lge. concentration of p. in cap. c. of Sydney; a. 801,431 km² (excluding Cap. Terr. of Canberra); p. (1986) 5,531,526.

Newton, t., Mass., **USA;** on R. Charles; in met. a. of Boston; lt. inds.; p. (1980) 83,622.

Newtownabbey, t., l. gov. dist., **N. Ireland;** sub. of Belfast, textiles, lt. inds.; p. (1981) 71,825 (dist.), 56,149 (t.).

Newton Abbot, mk. t., Teignbridge, Devon, **Eng.;** at head of Teign estuary; rly. junc.; pottery, lt. engin.; agr. processing; p. (1981) 20,927.

Newton Aycliffe, t., Durham, **Eng.;** 10 km N.W. of Darlington; new t. (1947); engin., textiles, plastics, paint; p. (1981) 24,720.

Newton-le-Willows, t., Merseyside, **Eng.;** engin., printing, sugar-refining; p. (1981) 19,723.

Newton-Stewart, burgh, Wigtown, **Scot.;** on R. Cree, 8 km N. of Wigtown; mkt.; wool, creameries and agr. inds.; p. (1981) 3,220.

Newtown and **Llanllwchaiarn,** mkt. t., Powys, **Wales;** on R. Severn 13 km S.W. of Montgomery; precision instruments, machine tools; plan for expansion as growth-pole for central Wales; p. (1981) 8,660.

Newtownards, spt., mkt., Ards, **N. Ireland;** 11 km

E. of Belfast; textile and engin. inds.; p. (1981) 20,531.

New Waterway. See **Nieuwe Waterweg.**

New Westminster, t., B.C., **Canada;** spt. on estuary of R. Fraser; exp. timber; agr. ctr., food-processing and canning; fishing; oil refining; forms part of Vancouver met. a.; p. (1981) 38,550.

New York, st., N.E. **USA;** popular name 'Empire St.'; admitted to Union 1788; st. flower Rose, st. bird Bluebird; one of 13 original sts., borders Canada on N., faces Atl. Oc. in S.; Adirondack mtns. in N., with lowland in E. alongside L. Ontario; Hudson valley impt. routeway; humid-continental climate; second lgst. st. in p. size and despite p. movement to W., remains major a. of urbanisation (megalopolis) with comm. and industl. activity; ch. ts. inc. Buffalo, Rochester, Syracuse; st. cap. Albany, metropolis New York city; decline of N. ts. offset by inds. from Quebec, leaving because of separatist moves; dairy farming and intensive agr. serve urban mkts.; a. 128,402 km²; p. (1985) 17,783,000.

New York, c., spt., N.Y., **USA;** on N.Y. Bay at mouth of Hudson R.; lgst. c. in USA and one of lgst. in world; comprises 5 bors., Manhattan, Bronx, Queens, Brooklyn, Richmond; originally founded by Dutch settlers as New Amsterdam on Manhattan I.; gr. comm. ctr. and cultural cap.; univ.; fine parks, bridges, skyscrapers, and deepwater harbour; varied inds., inc. clothing, food-processing, printing and publishing, shipbldg.; despite p. and industl. decentralisation concentration of socially needy in c. causing financial difficulties to c. govt.; 2 intern. airports; p. (1984) 7,164,700 (c.) 17,807,100 (met. a.).

New York State Barge Canal (Erie Canal), N.Y. st., **USA;** links Tonawanda on Niagara R. with Hudson R. via the Mohawk gap through Appalachian mtns.; provides through water route from N.Y. to Gr. Ls.; opened as Erie Canal 1825, improved 1918; length 542 km (with branches 840 km), depth 4 m.

New Zealand, indep. sov. st. within Brit. Commonwealth, S. Pac. Oc.; 1,920 km E. of Sydney, Australia; consists of two major Is., N.I. and S.I., separated by Cook Strait, and several smaller Is., inc. Stewart I. to S.; mtnous., glaciated, volcanic; landscapes with superb scenery; dependent upon pastoral prods., taking advantage of equable climate and excellent grass growing conditions, but mainly reliant on Brit. mkts.; economic diversification; expansion of lt. indus., inc. car assembly, pulp and paper, textiles; hydroelec. potential being developed; oil and natural gas recently discovered; advanced social services; cap. Wellington; ch. pt. Auckland; a. 268,676 km²; p. (1986) 3,261,783.

Neyland, t., Preseli, Dyfed, **Wales;** on Milford Haven; rly. terminus and sm. pt.; p. (1981) 3,097.

Ngami, L., **Botswana,** S.W. Africa; swamp, the remnant of a much larger L.

Ngauruhoe, mtn., N.I., **N.Z.;** an active volcano; 2,292 m.

Niagara, R., forms part of boundary between **Canada** and **USA;** flows from L. Erie to L. Ontario; rapids and famous falls utilised by gr. hydroelec. power sta. heavily polluted with toxic waste; 56 km long.

Niagara Falls, waterfall, Niagara R., on bdy. of **USA** and **Canada;** in two sections, American (51 m high) and Canadian (48 m high), separated by Goat I.; major tourist attraction and hydroelec. power sta.

Niagara Falls, t., Ontario, **Canada;** opposite the falls; hydroelectric power sta.; timber and agr., inds., tourism; p. (1986) 72,107.

Niagara Falls, c., N.Y., **USA;** extends along summit of cliff for 5 km; paper, flour, aluminium, chemicals, hydroelectric power stas.; univ.; p. (1980) 71,384; inc. in Buffalo met. a.

Niamey, t., cap of **Rep. of Niger,** W. Africa; one of the termini (the other is Zinder) of the trans-Sahara motor routes; agr. tr. ctr.; p. (est. 1983) 399,100.

Nicaragua, rep., Central America; civil war (1970), lies across isthmus with Pac. Oc. to W., Caribbean Sea to E.; sparsely populated; central mtn. range, marshy E. cst.; tropical rain forest and climate; limited a. of fertile soils but 70 per cent. p. farmers; main exps. coffee, cotton;

industl. growth was based on US investment, gold and silver mng.; food shortages caused by war and U.S. trade embargo; declining coffee exports, cotton hit by disease; cap. Managua; a. 148,006 km²; p. (est. 1987) 3,500,000.

Nicaragua, Lake, S.W. **Nicaragua;** lgst. L. in Central America; 24 km from Pac. Oc., but discharges into Caribbean via San Juan R.; fisheries; 160 km N.W. to S.E., 67 km S.W. to N.E.

Nicaraguan Depression, lowland, **Nicaragua;** contains Ls. Maragua and Nicaragua.

Nice, c., spt., cap. of Alpes Maritimes dep., **France;** on Mediterranean cst., at foot of Alps; pleasant climate and surroundings; adjoins anc. t. of Cimiez; ceded to France 1860 by Sardinia; resort; fruit and flower exp., perfume mftg.; attracting science-based inds.; major airport; p. (1982) 338,486.

Nicobar Is. See **Andaman and Nicobar Is.**

Nicosia, c., cap. of **Cyprus;** agr. tr. ctr.; textiles, cigarettes, leather, pottery mnfs.; remains of Venetian fortifications; mosques; new airport; cap. of admin. dist. of Nicosia; tourism; p. (est. 1986) 163,700.

Nidd, R., trib. of R. Ouse, North Yorks., **Eng.;** 80 km long.

Nidwalden. See **Unterwalden.**

Nieder Sachsen. See **Lower Saxony.**

Nieuwe Waterweg, ship canal, S. Holland, **Neth.;** connects R. Lek 11 km below Rotterdam with N. Sea cst. at Hook of Holland.

Nieuwveld Range, mtns., Cap Prov., **S. Africa;** part of S. terminal escarpment of African tableland; overlooks Gr. Karroo to its S.; forms impenetrable barrier to routes; mainly over 1,500 m. max. alt. 1,914 m.

Nièvre, dep., central **France;** traversed by Morvan mtns., forests, arable agr.; cap. Nevers; a. 6,887 km²; p. (1982) 239,500.

Nigel, t., Transvaal, **S. Africa;** gold mng.; industl.; p. (est. 1967) 38,400.

Niger, landlocked rep., W. **Africa;** 90 per cent p. dependent upon agr. but only 3 per cent of land cultivated; livestock (cattle, sheep, goats), cotton; exp. of groundnuts main source of wealth; rainfall diminishes to N. giving way to Sahara Desert; discovery and exploitation of uranium (1967), 75 per cent of exp. earnings in 1980 but now declining; fishing in L. Chad; game hunting; close economic ties with France; cap. Niamey; a. 1,253,560 km²; p. (est. 1987) 6,608,000.

Niger, R., W. **Africa;** rises nr. sea in outer mtn. zone of W. Africa as R. Tembi, sweeps round by Timbuktu to delta in G. of Guinea, on circuitous course of 4,160 km, receiving its gr. trib., the R. Benue, about 400 km from the mouth; navigable for 1,600 km; Kainji (Nigeria) hydroelec. plant and dam opened 1969; now organised by international Niger Basin Authority.

Nigeria, fed rep., W. **Africa;** within Brit. Commonwealth; federation of 19 sts.; climate, wet, tropical in S., increasingly dry to N.; main economic development in S.; exp. agr. prods., especially cocoa; exp. hardwoods; economic growth based on cstal. oil deposits (sulphur free); fall in oil prices causing decline in production and exp.; 2nd oil producer in Africa; 6th in world; cap. Lagos, lgst. c. Ibadan; cap. Abuja (1990); a. 923,773 km²; p. (est. 1988) 105,000,000.

Niigata, c., Honshu, **Japan;** pt. on W. cst. exp. locally produced petroleum; chemical inds.; p. (1985) 475,633.

Niihama, c., N. Shikoku, **Japan;** on cst. of Inland Sea, 32 km S.E. of Imabari; refines copper obtained from Besshi mines 19 km to the S.; petrochemicals; p. (1985) 132,192.

Nijmegen, c., E. **Neth.;** on R. Waal, nr. German bdr., 18 km S. of Arnhem; Hanse t. in Middle Ages; historic bldgs., univ.; p. (est. 1987) 147,000.

Nijni-Novgorod. See **Gorki.**

Nikko, t., Honshu, **Japan;** famous temples and shrines; tourist resort; p. (1966) 32,031.

Nikolayev, c., cap. of N. oblast, Ukrainian SSR, **USSR;** major spt. at head of Dnieper–Bug estuary on Black Sea; shipbldg., ctr.; exp. minerals, grains; founded 1784 as fortress; p. (est. 1985) 486,000.

Nikolayevsk, lge. R. pt., Khabarovsk terr., **RSFSR;** on R. Amur; shipyards; fishing, canning, lumbering, oil refining; p. (est. 1967) 32,000.

Nikopol, c., Ukrainian SSR, **USSR;** on Dnieper; manganese mng. ctr.; steel, machin.; p. (est. 1985) 155,000.

Nikšić, t., Montenegro, **Yugoslavia;** N. of Cetinje; bauxite mng., growing industl. ctr.; p. (1981) 72,299.

Nile, longest R. in Africa (see **White Nile** (Bahr-el-Abiad) and **Blue Nile** (Bahr-el-Azrek);); flows through a longer stretch of basin (over 3,920 km in a direct line) than any other R., and along all its windings measures 6,670 km; on Upper Nile navigation is hindered by sudd (floating vegetation); R. rises April, overflows Sept.; formerly cultivation entirely dependent on annual floods, but now assisted by dams, at Asyût, Aswan, Sennar, for regulating flow and navigation; Aswan High Dam completed 1970, but complex problems of delta erosion and dam-lake silting. See also **Egypt.**

Nilgiri Hills, Tamil Nadu, S. **India;** tea-growing dist.; resort a.

Nîmes, c., cap. of Gard dep., S. **France;** in Cevennes; Roman antiquities, notably Maison Carrée; silk, cotton, carpets, wines; tourism; p. (1982) 129,924.

Nineveh, celebrated anc. c., **Iraq,** stood on E. bank of upper R. Tigris, opposite modern Mosul.

Ningbo (Ningpo), c., spt., Zhejiang, **China;** 160 km from Shanghai; leading fish. pt., comm. and mnf. ctr.; exp. agr. and fish prods.; c. opened to foreign investment under new economic reforms; p. (1984) 615,600.

Ningxia Hui, aut. region, N.W. **China;** bounded on N. by Inner Mongolia; dry a. but modern irrigation projects allow growth of spring wheat and rice; coal reserves, salt; cap. Yingchuan; a. 66,408 km²; p. (est. 1985) 4,060,000.

Niobrara, R., **USA;** trib. of Missouri R.; flows from Wyoming to Nebraska; 960 km long.

Niort, c., cap. of Deux-Sèvres dep., W. **France;** noted for mkt. gardens and leather gds. (gloves); birthplace of Mme de Maintenon; p. (1982) 60,230.

Nipigon, Lake, in Thunder Bay dist., Ont., **Canada;** 106 km long, 74 km wide; studded with Is.; discharges by Nipigon R. to L. Superior.

Nipissing, Lake, S. Ont., **Canada;** 855 km²; drained by French R. to Georgian Bay.

Niš, t., **Yugoslavia;** on R. Nishava; route ctr.; rly. engin., developing mftg.; univ.; p. (1981) 643,470.

Nišava, R., **Yugoslavia;** flows N.W. into R. Morava nr. Niš; valley used by trunk rly. from Belgrade to Istanbul; length over 160 km.

Nishapur, mkt. t., N.E. **Iran;** S.W. of Mashhad; in fertile a.; cotton, fruits; famous turquoise mines nearby; birthplace of Omar Khayyám; impt. archaeological finds dating 9th and 10th cent.; p. (1966) 33,482.

Nishinomiya, c., S. Honshu, **Japan;** produces famous liquor called saké; machin., chemicals; p. (1985) 421,267.

Niterói, t., cap. of Rio de Janeiro st., **Brazil;** shipbldg.; residtl. sub. of Rio de Janeiro c. to which it is linked by bridge; p. (est. 1985) 442,700.

Nith, R., S.W. **Scot.;** flows to Solway F., S. of Dumfries; followed by main rly. from Carlisle to Kilmarnock and Glasgow; 114 km long.

Nithsdale, l. gov. dist., Dumfries and Galloway, **Scot.;** a. based on Dumfries; p. (est. 1986) 57,339.

Niue or **Savage I., Pac. Oc.;** one of Cook Is., formerly part of N.Z., self government 1974; ch. pt. Alofi; copra, plaited basketware, sweet potatoes; a. 259 km²; p. (est. 1987) 2,442.

Nivernais, former prov. of **France,** now forming Nièvre prov. and part of Cher.

Nizamabad, t., Andhra Pradesh, **India;** road and rly. ctr. N. of Hyderabad; p. (1981) 183,061.

Nizhneudinsk, t., W. Irkutsk, **RSFSR;** new mftg. t.; p. (est. 1967) 38,000.

Nizhni Novgorod. See **Gorki.**

Nizhniy Tagil, t., **RSFSR;** in Ural mtns.; metallurgical ctr. using ore from Mt. Visokaya; rly. cars, iron, and steel plants, chemicals; p. (est. 1985) 419,000.

No, Lake, Bahr-el-Ghazal prov., **Sudan;** N.E. Africa; vast swamp a., 906 km S.W. of Khartoum; flow of water blocked by papyrus reed and floating weed (sudd).

Nobeoka, t., Kyushu, **Japan;** on E. cst.; p. (1985) 136,381.

Nobi Plain, S. Honshu, **Japan;** at head of Ise Bay; consists of low, badly drained alluvial plain on W. under intensive rice cultivation, with higher, drier, terraces on E. under mulberry, vegetables, pine-woods; very dense urban and rural p.; ch.

textile and pottery mftg. a. in Japan; inc. cs. Nagoya, Gifu, Yokkaichi; a. 1,865 km²; p. (1960) 5,400,000.

Nocera Inferiore, t., **Italy**; nr. Naples; vegetable-canning, textile mnfs.; p. (1981) 47,698.

Nogales, twin ts., Sonora, **Mexico** and Arizona, **USA**; mng. and agr. ctr.; p. (1980) 15,683.

Noginsk, t., **RSFSR**; nr. Moscow; textiles, metals; natural gas pipeline from Central Asia projected; p. (est. 1985) 121,000.

Nola, c., **Italy**; at foot of Vesuvius, 19 km N.E. of Naples; ctr. of fertile arable agr. a. in Campania plain; anc. c., home of Giordano Bruno; p. (1981) 30,979.

Nome, c., W. Alaska, **USA**; on Seward peninsula; gold rush (1900); now admin. and route ctr.; airport; tourism; p. (1980) 2,301.

Noord Brabant, prov., **Neth.**; cap. 's-Hertogenbosch; a. 4,973 km²; p. (est. 1984) 2,103,000.

Noord Holland, prov., **Neth.**; a. 2,722 km²; cap. Haarlem; natural gas in Schermer Polder nr. Alkmaar; p. (est. 1984) 2,307,400.

Noordoostpolder, Overijssel, **Neth.**; land reclaimed from Zuider Zee, 1942; now used for intensive agr.; a. 479 km²; p. (est. 1987) 38,000.

Nord, dep., N. **France**; borders on Belgium and N. Sea; flourishing agr., mng. iron and coal, textile and chemical mnfs.; cap. Lille; a. 5,773 km²; p. (1982) 2,526,300.

Nordenham, pt. on Lower Weser R., Lower Saxony, **W. Germany**; lead and zinc smelting; fishing; p. (est. 1986) 28,800.

Norderney, one of the E. Frisian Is., **W. Germany**; low-lying sand-dunes; resort at Nordseebad.

Nordhorn, t., Lower Saxony, **W. Germany**; nr. Neth. frontier; textiles; p. (est. 1986) 48,000.

Nordkyn, Cape, northernmost pt. of European mainland, Finnmark prov., N. **Norway**.

Nordland, co., N. **Norway**; fjord cst.; p. on cst. lowlands; fishing, livestock; iron-ore, electro-chemical and metallurgical inds. based on local hydroelec. power; spt. Narvik; a. 38,146 km²; p. (1983) 244,974.

Norfolk, non-met. co., E. **Eng.**; low-lying fens in W.; low sandy cst. suffers from erosion; intensive arable agr. on lge. farms; wheat, barley, root crops; inds. based on agr. processing and provision of agr. requisites; tourism intensively developed on Norfolk Broads; cap. Norwich; a. 5,354 km²; p. (est. 1988) 744,300.

Norfolk, c., Va., **USA**; naval base on Hampton Roads; fine deepwater harbour; exp. coal, industl. prods.; shipbldg., car assembly, food-processing, timber inds., fertilisers; p. (1984) 279,700 (c.), 1,261,200 (met. a.).

Norfolk I., remote dependency of Australia; **Pac. Oc.**; volcanic I., 1,676 km N.E. of Sydney; unique ecology; fertile agr.; discovered by Cook 1774; penal settlement 1788–1853; tourism; a. 34 km²; p. (est. 1981) 2,000.

Norfolk, North, l. gov. dist., Norfolk, **Eng.**; cstl. a. inc. Wells-next-the-Sea, Cromer, Sheringham, Walsingham and North Walsham; p. (est. 1988) 94,700.

Norfolk, South, l. gov. dist., Norfolk, **Eng.**; lge. a. inc. Diss and Wymondham; p. (est. 1988) 100,700.

Norilsk, t., Krasnoyarsk terr., **RSFSR**; in N. Siberia; northernmost t. in Russia; mng. of coal, uranium, nickel, copper; natural gas pipeline from W. Siberia; p. (est. 1985) 180,000.

Normandy, historic prov. of **France**; on English Channel; now divided into deps. Manche, Calvados, Eure, Seine-Maritime and part of Orne; Rouen was cap.; Channel Is. were part of the old duchy; conquered England 1066; allied invasion of Europe 1944.

Normanton, t., West Yorks., **Eng.**; 5 km N.E. of Wakefield; coal mng.; p. (1981) 17,256.

Norman Wells, t., N.W. Terr., **Canada**; at confluence of R. Mackenzie and Gr. Bear R., 112 km W. of Gr. Bear L.; ctr. of rich oil-field; p. (1981) 420.

Norrbotten, prov., N. **Sweden**; rich iron deposits at Kiruna; ore exp. via ice-free Narvik on Norwegian cst.; many Ls. and Rs.; highest peak in Sweden, Kebnekaise; cap. Piteå; a. 105,153 km²; p. (est. 1986) 261,000.

Norris Dam, Tenn., **USA**; across R. Clinch at confluence with R. Tennessee, N.W. of Knoxville; lgst. dam Tenn. Valley Authority (TVA); built for flood control and hydroelectric power.

Norrköping, c., S.E. **Sweden**; nr. inlet of Baltic Sea; industl. and shipping ctr.; ocean-going

shipping through Lindö canal; p. (est. 1986) 119,000.

Northallerton, mkt. t., Hambleton, North Yorks.; admin. ctr., **Eng.**; in broad gap between Cleveland hills and Pennines; in dairy farming and agr. dist.; p. (1981) 9,622.

North America, northern continent of W. hemisphere; comprises Greenland (on N. American continental shelf), Canada, USA, Mexico; high W. Cordilleras, inc. Rocky mtns., run N. to S. from Alaska to Mexico; lower range of Appalachian mtns. in E. with vast interior basin, inc. Gr. Ls., Saskatchewan, St. Lawrence, and Miss.–Mo. R. systems; gr. variation in climate and vegetation from subtropical in S. and Mediterranean in W. to Arctic in N. and continental in interior; enormous endowment of natural resources provide basis for vast economies of USA and Canada, but contemporary public concern for natural environment of continent; formerly inhabited by Indians, now mainly occupied by a white p. with lge. European minorities, and an African-based, black p.; p. (est. 1984) 261,120,000 (inc. Hawaii).

Northampton, t., l. gov. dist., Northampton, **Eng.**; on R. Nene; footwear, engin., leather gds.; new t. designation; p. (est. 1988) 182,100.

Northamptonshire, non-met. co., **Eng.**; E. Midlands; chiefly agr.; iron mng. and mftg.; footwear, engin., leather; co. t. Northampton; a. 2,367 km²; p. (est. 1988) 570,300.

Northamptonshire, East, l. gov. dist., Northants., **Eng.**; stretches from Oundle to Irthlingborough, Rushden, Raunds and Higham Ferrers; p. (est. 1988) 66,500.

Northamptonshire, South, l. gov. dist., Northants., **Eng.**; inc. Brackley and Towcester; p. (est. 1988) 66,900.

North Atlantic Drift, drift of surface waters of Atl. Oc. N.E. from Gulf Stream towards Europe; relatively warm; supplies prevailing S.W. winds with warmth and moisture to modify climate of Brit. Is. and N.W. Europe.

Northavon, l. gov. dist., Avon, **Eng.**; a. N. of Bristol, inc. Sodbury; p. (est. 1988) 130,800.

North Bay, t., Ont., **Canada**; on L. Nipissing; air base; tourism, route ctr.; p. (1986) 50,623.

North Berwick, royal burgh, E. Lothian, **Scot.**; on S. of F. of Forth, 32 km E. of Edinburgh; seaside resort; golf course; fishing pt.; p. (1981) 5,388.

North Beveland, I., **Neth.**; in Scheldt estuary; arable agr.; a. 91 km².

North Carolina, st., S.E. **USA**; Tarheel St.; admitted to Union 1789; st. flower Flowering Dogwood., st. bird Cardinal; bounded on E. by Atl. Oc.; one of 13 original sts.; sandy, indented cst., rising in W. to Appalachian mtns.; humid subtropical climate, modified by alt.; agr. impt.; maize, cotton, tobacco; mica; textiles; ch. pt. Wilmington; cap. Raleigh; a. 136,524 km²; p. (1985) 6,255,000.

North Channel, Brit. Is.; gives access from Atl. Oc. to Irish Sea between S.W. Scotland (Galloway) and N.E. Ireland (Larne); length 96 km; narrowest width 24 km.

North China Plain, China; alluvial lowland of Huang-He basin; notorious floods but R. now controlled; wheat and millets; very dense p.

North Crimean Canal, USSR; links R. Dnieper with Black Sea and Sea of Azov, crossing steppes of S. Ukraine and Crimea, terminating at Kerch; first section (123 km long) opened 1963; when completed will be 352 km long, 200 km of which will be navigable.

North Dakota, st., N.W. **USA**; Flickerhill St.; admitted to Union 1889; st. flower Wild Prairie Rose, st. bird Western Meadowlark; rolling prairie, rising from E.-W.; drained by Missouri R., controlled by multi-purpose Garrison Reservoir; arable agr., mainly grains, but eroded "Badlands" in S.; coal mng., petroleum; a. 183,022 km²; p. (1985) 685,000.

North Down, l. gov. dist., **N. Ireland**; borders Belfast Lough; main ts. Bangor, Holywood; p. (1981) 65,666.

North Downs, Surrey/Kent, **Eng.**; chalk escarpment running E. to W. across S.E. Eng.; form "white cliffs of Dover"; followed in part by Pilgrim's Way; Box Hill 233 m.

North-East China, formerly known as Manchuria, comprising provs.—Liaoning, Jilin, Heilongjiang; mtnous., N.W. and E.; drained by N. by Songhua Jiang and S. by Liao Rs.;

forested; soya-beans, wheat, coal, iron; impt. a. for iron and steel; occupied by Japanese in 1931 and returned to China in 1947; p. (est. 1968) 66,000,000.

North East Fife, l. gov. dist., Fife Reg., **Scot.**; a. be- tween F. of Forth and F. of Tay; impt. ts. St. Andrews and Cupar; p. (est. 1986) 66,533.

North-EastFrontierAgency. *See* ArunachalPradesh.

North East Passage, along N. cst. Europe and Asia between Atl. and Pac. *See* **Section L.**

Northern Ireland, part of **U.K.**; occupies N.E. a. of Ireland, consisting of 26 l. gov. dists.; mild, temperate climate, exploited by dairy farming using excellent grass; arable agr. inc. barley, potatoes; traditional inds. inc. linen, shipbldg., food-processing, tobacco; modern inds. encouraged by extensive government aid inc. artificial fibres, carpets, elec. and aero-engin.; heavily dependent upon Brit. mkt.; serious social disturbance since 1969, based upon longstanding religious differences between Roman Catholic and Protestant as a result of discrimination against minority; Stormont Parliament replaced by Assembly (suspended 29 May 1974 and direct rule resumed); returns 12 members to Westminster; a. 14,121 km²; p. (est. 1984) 1,578,000.

Northern Territory, self governing st. (1978) N. **Australia;** variable rainfall decreasing inland from N. to S.; land rises generally N. to S. and reaches over 1,800 m in Macdonnell ranges; lge. semi-nomadic Aboriginal p.; livestock agr. dependent upon rail, road access to mkt.; mng.; newly opened uranium mines abuse aborigine terr.; ch. ts. Darwin on N. cst., Alice Springs; a. 1,356,176 km²; p. (est. 1986) 154,421.

Northfleet, t., Kent, **Eng.**; on S. bank of R. Thames, adjoining Gravesend; cement, paper, rubber, tyres, cables; p. (1981) 26,250.

North Foreland, E. Kent, **Eng.**; chalk headland.

North Island, I., **N.Z.**; one of the two major Is. of N.Z., separated from S.I. by Cook Strait, volcanic mtns., Waikato R. drains I. Taupo, cap. Wellington, spt. Auckland, oil deposits on E. and W. csts.; a. 114,688 km²; p. (1985) 2,439,100.

Northleach, t., Cotswold, Gloucs., **Eng.**; once impt. woollen tr.

North Little Rock, t., Ark., **USA**; agr. processing, engin.; p. (1980) 64,288.

North Ossetian ASSR, RSFSR; on N. slope of Gr. Caucasus; cap. Ordzhonikidze; agr. in valleys; lead, silver, zinc, and oil deposits with metallurgical and food-processing inds.; a. 8,029 km²; p. (1986) 615,000.

North Platte, t., Nebraska, **USA**; on N. Platte R.; p. (1980) 24,509.

North Platte, R., **USA**; rises N. Col., flows 1,088 km through Wyo., across W. Nebraska to join S. Platte at c. of North Platte; extensive power and irrigation developments.

North Rhine–Westphalia, *Land,* **W. Germany**; highly industrialised, coal mng., iron and steel, textiles; a. 34,066 km²; p. (est. 1986) 16,676,500.

North River (Beijiang), Guandong, S. **China;** rises in Nanling mtns., flows S. into Xi Jiang delta; 480 km long.

North Sea, arm of the Atl., E. of Gr. Brit., W. of Norway, Sweden, and N. Germany, and N. of Holland, Belgium, and France; length 960 km, width 640 km; gd. fisheries; major natural gas, coal and oil deposits.

North Sea Canal, ship canal, N. Holland, **Neth.**; connects Amsterdam to N. Sea at Ijmuiden; depth 14 m, length 26 k.

North Shields, t., Tyne and Wear, **Eng.**; Tyne pt.; major new fishing pt. planned; marine engines, chain cables, anchors, rope; mkt.; p. (1981) 41,608.

North Solomons, Rep. of, formed 1975 when Bougainville I. seceded from Papua New Guinea.

North Tonawanda, t., N.Y., **USA**; on Niagara R.; timber tr., paper mnfs.; p. (1980) 35,760.

Northumberland, non-met. co., N. **Eng.**; on border of Scot. along Cheviots and R. Tweed; drained by Tyne, Blyth, Coquet Rs.; pastoral agr., especially sheep; coal mng., with former impt. exp. to London and S.E. Eng.; industl. a. now inc. in Tyne and Wear met. co.; isolation and wild landscape attractive as tourist resort; a. 5,032 km²; p. (est. 1988) 301,400.

Northumberland Straits, separate Prince Edward I. from Nova Scotia and New Brunswick; 14 km combined road and rail tunnel, bridge and causeway to link provs. projected.

Northumbria, Anglo-Saxon kingdom stretching from the Humber to the Forth; conquered by the Danes 9th cent.

North Walsham, mkt. t., North Norfolk, **Eng.**; 22 km N. of Norwich; former wool-weaving ctr.; p. (1981) 7,944.

North-West Passage, between Atl. and Pac. along Arctic cst. of Canada; potentially of gr. importance as a W. outlet for Alaskan oil; sovereignty claimed by Canada but disputed by U.S.A. who claims it is an internat. strait. *See* **Section L.**

Northwest Territories, N.W. region and terr. of **Canada**; N. of 60° Lat. N., between Yukon (W.) and Hudson Bay (E.); comprises 3 dists., Franklin, Mackenzie, Keewatin; varied physical geography, inc. vast areas of lowland with some of highest peaks in E.N. America; tree-line marks physical bdy. between N. and S.; drained in W. by Mackenzie R.; major inds. gold and silver mng. around cap. Yellowknife; petroleum, fur-trapping fisheries; incr. indep. since 1983; a. 3,379,711 km²; p. (1986) 52,000 (two-thirds Eskimos and Indians).

Northwich, t., Cheshire, **Eng.**; on R. Weaver; impt. chemical inds. based originally upon local salt deposits, now much subsidence in a. due to salt extraction; p. (1981) 17,126.

North Wolds. *See* **East Yorkshire.**

North York Moors, limestone plateau, North Yorks./Cleveland, **Eng.**; lies S. of estuary of R. Tees, heather moorland; some pastoral farming on lower slopes; alt. varies from 300–450 m; formerly impt. iron-ore quarrying along N. edge in Cleveland dist.; now potential for potash mng. threatening N.Y.M. Nat. Park.

North Yorkshire, non-met. co., N. **Eng.**; inc. much of former N. Riding; stretches from Pennines (W.) to Vale of York (central), N. York Moors and Yorks. Wolds (E.); crossed by R. Ouse and tribs.; mainly rural, mixed agr.; major ctrs. of p. at York, cstl. resort of Scarborough and spa of Harrogate; a. 8,316 km²; p. (est. 1988) 713,100.

Norton-Radstock, t., Avon, **Eng.**; footwear, sm. coalfield; p. (1981) 18,338.

Norwalk, t., Cal., **USA**; oil refining; p. (1980) 85,286.

Norwalk, t., Conn., **USA**; gd. harbour on Long I. Sound; lt. inds., clothing; formerly impt. oyster ind. diminished by industl. pollution; p. (1980) 77,767.

Norway, kingdom, W. Scandinavia, N. **Europe**; long fjord cst. stretches from Arctic to N. Sea; mtnous.; cool damp climate, influenced by prevailing W. winds; excellent conditions for hydroelectric power and electro-inds.; sm. p. makes N. heavily dependent upon foreign tr., especially exp. of aluminium, wood-pulp, paper, fish; now possesses lge. deposits of petroleum in N. Sea; arable agr. limited to fjord lowlands and a. around cap. Oslo; pastoral transhumance in mtnous. interior; a. 322,600 km², p. (est. 1987) 4,174,005.

Norwich, c., co. t., l. gov. dist., Norfolk, **Eng.**; on R. Wensum just above confluence with R. Yare; univ.; cath., cas.; cult. and agr. ctr.; food mnfs., footwear, printing; decentralization of office employment from London; p. (est. 1988) 117,300.

Norwich, t., Conn., **USA**; sm. pt. on Thames R.; machin., textiles; p. (1980) 38,074.

Nossi-Bé, lgst. of sm. Is., off W. cst. **Malagasy**; sugar, perfumery oils; ch. t. Hellville, resort and ctr. of cst. tr.; a. 337 km²; p. c. 26,000.

Notec (Netze), R., **Poland**; trib. R. Warta; partially navigable; 224 km long.

Notodden, t., S. **Norway**; nr. Tinnfoss falls which provide hydroelectric power; iron smelting, nitrates; p. (1980) 12,877.

Nottingham, c., co. t., l. gov. dist., Nottinghamshire, **Eng.**; a bridging pt. over Trent R.; lace, hosiery, tobacco, pharmaceutical and cycle inds., all based upon local capital; univ., cas., p. (est. 1988) 273,500.

Nottinghamshire, non-met. co., Midlands, **Eng.**; contains part of productive E. Midlands coalfield serving many power stas. along Trent R.; urban growth concentrated mainly on coalfield; ch. and co. t. Nottingham; engin., hosiery; wheat, barley, cattle, roses; brilliantly characterised in writings of D. H. Lawrence; a. 2,165 km²; p. (est. 1988) 1,007,700.

Nouadhibou, pt., **Mauritania**; new pt. for bulk carriers to exp. iron ore; fish processing plants; pelletizing plant; p. (1976) 21,961.

Nouakchott, t., cap. of **Mauritania**, W. Africa; comm. ctr. on caravan route; tr. in agr. prods.; planned industl. zone; rapid growth with mass migration of nomadic p. to shanty ts. as response to Sahelian drought; p. (est. 1985) 500,000.

Nouméa (Port de France), t., cap. of Fr. **New Caledonia**; ch. pt. of Is.; exp. nickel, chrome; p. (1983) 60,112.

Nouvelle Amsterdam, I., **Indian Oc.**; part of Fr. Southern and Antarctic Terrs.; volcanic; ctr. of meteorological research; a. 65 km².

Nova Friburgo, t., Rio de Janeiro, **Brazil**; health resort; p. (est. 1985) 144,000.

Nova Iguaçú, t., Rio de Janeiro, **Brazil**; steel, tyres, chemicals; p. (est. 1985) 1,324,600.

Nova Lima, t., Minas Gerais st., **Brazil**; in Serra do Espinhaço, 16 km S. of Belo Horizonte; adjacent to impt. gold-mines of Morro Velho; p. (est. 1985) 47,400.

Nova Lisboa (Huambo), central **Angola**, Africa; E. of Benguela; rly. repair shops; agr. comm. ctr.; p. (est. 1970) 61,885.

Novara, c., cap. of N. prov., N. **Italy**; agr. and mnf. ctr., textiles, chemicals, cheese; Romanesque church; p. (1984) 102,279.

Nova Scotia, maritime prov., **Canada**; mainly fertile upland and rich valleys with agr. aided by temperate maritime climate; fruit, livestock, dairying; forested uplands along cst. nr Bay of Fundy give rise to impt. timber inds. with many pts. along indented cst.; fishing and fish-processing; local coal supplies, iron and steel ind.; cap. Halifax; a. 54,556 km²; p. (1986) 873,000.

Novaya Kakhovka, c., Ukrainian SSR, **USSR**; built (1951) on K. Sea nr. hydroelec. power sta. on Dnieper R.; tourism.

Novaya Zemlya, archipelago, Arctic Oc., **USSR**; 2 main Is.; lofty and rugged, severe climate; nuclear testing a.; a. 90,750 km².

Novgorod, c., **RSFSR**; on Volkhov R. nr. exit from L. Ilmen; food and timber inds., engin.; in mediaeval times gr. comm. and cultural ctr., cap. of an indep. rep.; architectural monuments; damaged by Germans in second world war; p. (est. 1985) 220,000.

Novi Sad, c., **Yugoslavia**; R. pt. on Danube R., formerly royal free c.; almost destroyed by Austrians 1849; tr. in fruit, wine, vegetables, corn; p. (1981) 257,685.

Novokuybyshevsk, t., **RSFSR**; S.W. of Kuybyshev; lge. oil processing plant; p. (est. 1985) 110,000.

Novo Kuznetsk (Stalinsk), c. **RSFSR**; grew up as iron and steel ctr. of Kuznetsk Basin; engin., chemicals, aluminium, ferro-alloys; p. (1986) 583,000.

Novomoskovsk (Stalinogorsk), c., **RSFSR**; on R. Don; lignite, fertilisers, p. (est. 1985) 147,000.

Novorossiisk, spt., **RSFSR**; on N.E. cst. of Black Sea; engin., textiles; lgst. cement producer in USSR; exp. industl. prods.; p. (est. 1985) 175,000.

Novoshakhtinsk, c., **RSFSR**; on Rostov–Kharkov highway; coal mng., chemicals; p. (1985) 106,000.

Novosibirsk, c., **RSFSR**; on Ob R. and Trans-Siberian rly.; lgst. industl. ctr. of Siberia, nr. Kuznetsk Basin; hydroelec. power; varied inds., uranium nearby; univ.; p. (1986) 1,405,000.

Novo Troitsk, t., **RSFSR**; in Urals, 18 km S.W. of Orsk; cement, special steels; p. (est. 1985) 103,000.

Novovoronezh, **USSR**; on R. Don, S. of Voronezh; nuclear power sta.

Noý Jičín (Neutitschein), t., Moravia, **ČSSR**; farm machin., and eng.; p. (est. 1968) 19,000.

Nowa Huta, t., **Poland**; 10 km S.E. Kraców on Vistula R.; newly developed Lenin metallurgical combine and modern residtl. a. within c. of Kraców; p. (est. 1983) 200,000.

Nowa Sól (Neusalz), t., Lower Silesia, **Poland**; pt. on R. Oder; metal-working, food and timber inds.; p. (1970) 33,300.

Nowgong, t., Assam, **India**; agr. and comm. ctr.; rice, tea; p. (est. 1971) 52,892.

Nowra-Bomaderry, t., N.S.W., **Australia**; on E. cst. at mouth of Shoalhaven R.; expanded (1979) into c. of Shoalhaven; collecting ctr. for coastal agr. prod.; powdered milk, paper mill; p. (1981) 17,887.

Nowy Sącz, t., Kraków prov., S. **Poland**; on Dunajec R.; lignite nearby; rly. engin., mftg.; ctr. of a. renowned for beauty and tourist attractions; p. (1983) 68,300.

Nubia, anc. region, N.E. **Africa**, extending on both sides of Nile from first cataract at Aswan to Khartoum, Sudan; largely desert, some irrigation alongside Nile.

Nuble, prov., **Chile**; borders on Argentina; comprehensive attempt to develop agr.; most industl. development and agr. mkt. at cap. Chillán; a. 14,204 km²; p. (1970) 314,738.

Nueva Esparta, st., **Venezuela**; consists of over 70 Is.; impt. fisheries; cap. La Asunción; a. 1,150 km²; p. (1981) 197,198.

Nueva San Salvador, t., **El Salvador**; agr. comm. ctr. in coffee-growing and livestock region; p. (1980) 69,126.

Nuevo Laredo, c., N.E. **Mexico**; entry point for American tourists driving to Mexico; tr. ctr. in pastoral and arable agr.; a.; p. (1980) 203,286.

Nuevo Léon, st., N.E. **Mexico**; arable agr. needs irrigation in arid climate; impt. iron and steel inds.; cap. Monterrey; a. 65,097 km²; p. (1980) 2,463,298.

Nuku'alofa, cap. of Polynesian kingdom of **Tonga**; p. (1986) 28,899.

Nukus, c., cap. of Karakalpak ASSR, Uzbek SSR, **USSR**; on Amu Dar'ya R. in Khorezm oasis; clothing inds.; p. (est. 1985) 139,000.

Nullarbor Plain, S. **Australia**; low, level, limestone plateau fringing Gr. Australian Bight; arid; treeless, salt-bush scrub; crossed by Trans-continental rly. between Naretha (W. Australia) and Ooldea; rly. is dead straight, dead level for 477 km.

Numazu, t., Honshu, **Japan**; nr. Tokyo; ctr. of industl. dist. with varied mnfs. inc. machin.; p. (1985) 210,484.

Nuneaton, t., with Bedworth forms l. gov. dist., Warwicks., **Eng.**; on Anker R.; coal mng., textiles, lt. inds.; mkt.; birthplace of George Eliot; p. (est. 1988) 116,000 (dist.).

Nunivak, I., Alaska, **USA**; lge. reindeer herds.

Nunjiang, former prov., N.E. **China**; crossed by Nen Jiang, trib. of Songhua Jiang; now part of Heilung-kiang prov.

Nürnberg (Nuremberg), c., Bavaria, **W. Germany**; historic c. of architectural beauty; industl. ctr. with elec. mnfs., machin., heavy vehicles, precision instruments, chemicals, toys, pencils and crayons; rly. junc.; inland pt. on Rhine–Danube waterway; p. (est. 1986) 467,400.

Nusa Tenggara, Is., **Indonesia**; part of Lesser Sunda Is.; p. (1980) 5,461,830.

Nuwara Eliya, hill t., (c. 1,800 m), **Sri Lanka**; health resort; p. (1981) 20,471.

Nyasa, L. *See* Malawi L.

Nyasaland. *See* Malawi.

Nyíregyháza, t., N.E. **Hungary**; ctr. of reclaimed agr. a.; mkt. for tobacco, wine, fruits; domestic ware; p. (est. 1985) 117,000.

Nyborg, pt., **Denmark**; on Fyn I.; terminal of train-ferry across Gr. Belt; shipyards; textile ind.; p. (1981) 15,466.

Nykøbing, spt., Falster I., **Denmark**; varied inds.; admin. ctr. of Storstrøms prov.; p. (1981) 19,038.

Nyköping, spt., **Sweden**; at head of inlet on Baltic cst.; comm. and industl. ctr.; p. (est. 1986) 64,000.

Nystad. *See* Uusikaupunki.

O

Oadby, t., Leics., **Eng.**; 5 km S.E. of Leicester; footwear; with Wigston forms small l. gov. dist., S. of Leicester; p. (est. 1990) 51,100 (dist.).

Oahu, I., **Hawaiian Is.**, Pac. Oc.; sugar, pineapples; tourist tr.; cap. Honolulu; a. 1,564 km²; p. (1980) 797,367.

Oakengates, t., The Wrekin, Shrops., **Eng.**; 24 km N.W. of Wolverhampton; iron and steel, precast concrete, engin.; now part of new t. of Telford; p. (1981) 17,663.

Oakham, t., Rutland, Leics., **Eng.**; mkt.; hosiery, footwear; p. (1981) 7,996.

Oakland, c., Cal., **USA**; on San Francisco Bay; residtl. sub.; cars, shipbldg., fruit canning, elec. machin., clothing, tanneries, chemicals; p. (1984) 351,000 (c.) *See* San Francisco.

Oak Park Village, t., Ill., **USA**; now included in Chicago; birthplace of Ernest Hemingway; p. (1980) 54,887.

Oak Ridge, t., Tenn., **USA**; Atomic Energy Commission's major research ctr.; p. (1980) 27,662

Oamaru, bor., spt., S.I., **N.Z.**; wool, frozen meat; exp. agr. prods.; p. (est. 1987) 12,550.

Oaxaca, st., Pac. cst., S. **Mexico;** mtnous., subsistence agr. in fertile valleys; comm. prod. of coffee, cotton, tobacco; stock-raising; mng. in mtns.; cap. Oaxaca; a. 94,201 km²; p. (1980) 2,518,157.

Oaxaca, c., cap. of O. st., S. **Mexico;** stands at c. 1,500 m; coffee; gold and silver mines; handicraft mkt.; table linen weaving, wool zarapes; tourist ctr.; p. (1980) 157,284.

Ob', R., W. Siberia, **RSFSR;** one of the world's lgst. Rs., flows from Altai mtns. to G. of Ob'; crossed by Turk-Sib. rly. at Barnaul and by Trans-Siberian rly. at Novosibirsk; ch. trib. Irtysh; hydroelec. power; navigable; oilfields in middle section; outlet of Ob basin Novy-Port (Gdansk); plans to divert waters to irrigate Kazakhstan by 2,500 km canal; 4,160 km long.

Oban, spt., burgh, Argyll and Bute, **Scot.;** on F. of Lorne; resort; ctr. for local shipping; woollens, tartans; p. (1981) 8,134.

Obed, Alberta, **Canada;** 240 km W. of Edmonton; major natural gas a.

Obeid, El, t., Kordofan, **Sudan;** economically dependent upon rly. link to Khartoum; agr. tr. ctr.; p. (1983) 140,024.

Oberammergau, v., Upper Bavaria, **W. Germany;** scene of decennial Passion Play; winter sports; p. (est. 1976) 5,000.

Oberhausen, t., N. Rhine–Westphalia, **W. Germany;** industl. ctr. of Ruhr conurb.; rly. junc., canal pt.; p. (est. 1986) 221,500.

Obidos, t., R. p., **Brazil;** 800 km up R. Amazon; cacao, cotton; p. (est. 1968) 25,021.

Obihiro, t., Hokkaido, **Japan;** mkt; sugar-beet refining, flax, dairy prods.; p. (1985) 162,930.

Obuasi, t. **Ghana,** W. Africa; ctr. of gold mng.; lge. deep-level mine, modernised 1984; p. (1970) 40,001.

Obwalden, demi-canton, **Switzerland;** a. 492 km²; p. (est. 1986) 28,000.

Ocaña, t., Magdalena st., **Colombia;** coffee, hides; isolated by difficult transport conditions; p. (est. 1968) 43,481.

Ocean City, t., N.J., **USA;** seaside resort founded by the Methodists; p. (1980) 13,949.

Ocean I. (**Banaba**), **Kiribati,** Pac. Oc.; high grade phosphate (guano) worked by Brit., need for compensation and restoration of land subject of legal action 1971–76; many Banabans evacuated to Rabi I. (Fiji) 1945; future still unsettled; p. (1985) 189.

Oceania, name given to the Is. of the Pacific; comprising Australasia, Polynesia, Melanesia, Micronesia; p. (est. 1984) 24,460,000.

Ochil Hills, volcanic hill-range, **Scot.;** stretching 40 km N.E. to S.W. from F. of Tay to nr. Stirling; loftiest Ben Cleugh 721 m; beautiful glens and valleys.

Odawara, t., **Japan;** pt. with rail connections to Tokyo, 48 km to N.E.; p. (1985) 185,947.

Odemis, t., Asiatic **Turkey;** N.E. of Aydin; tobacco, cereals, silk, cotton, flax, olives, raisins, figs; minerals; p. (1985) 47,475.

Odense, spt., **Denmark;** admin. ctr. of Fyn prov.; varied inds.; exp. dairy prod.; birthplace of Hans Andersen; p. (est. 1987) 173,331.

Odenwald, forested hills, Hesse and Baden-Württemberg, **W. Germany;** highest point Katzenbuckel 626 m.

Oder (Pol. **Odra**), R., central **Europe;** flows from Moravia to Baltic through Silesia and Pomerania, forming from junc. with Neisse R. frontier between Poland and E. Germany; ch. trib. Warta R.; impt. comm. waterway below Wroclaw; 896 km long.

Odessa, t., Texas, **USA;** impt. oil ctr., chemicals, foundry prod., livestock tr.; p. (1984) 108,700 (t.), 144,500 (met. a.).

Odessa, spt., Ukrainian SSR, **USSR;** on Black Sea; cultural, industl. ctr.; cath., univ.; gr. grain exp.; engin., oil refining, chemicals; ice-bound for a few weeks in winter; p. (1986) 1,132,000.

Offaly, co., Leinster, **R.o.I.;** much marshy land (inc. Bog of Allen), barren uplands (inc. Slieve Bloom); pastoral agr.; wheat; p. mainly rural; sm.-scale domestic prods. and agr.-processing inds. in ts.; co. t. Tullamore; a. 1,999 km²; p. (1981) 20,336.

Offa's Dyke, earthwork constructed by Offa, king of Mercia (757–96) as bdy. between the English and the Welsh; still forms part of

border between the two countries; long-distance footpath along the Welsh marches, 269 km.

Offenbach, t., Hesse, **W. Germany;** on R. Main; cas., leather museum; machin., chemicals, leather gds., metals; p. (est. 1986) 107,100.

Offenburg, t., Baden–Württemberg, **W. Germany;** on R. Kinzig; textiles, glass, rly. junc.; cas.; p. (est. 1986) 50,500.

Ogaden, arid region, S.W. **Ethiopia;** on border of Rep. of Somalia; oil exploration with Soviet assistance.

Ogaki, t., Honshu, **Japan;** route ctr. in lowland embayment, 40 km N.W. of Nagoya; p. (1985) 145,909.

Ogbomosho, t., S.W. **Nigeria;** ctr. of agr. dist.; cotton weaving; p. (est. 1983) 527,000.

Ogden, c., Utah, **USA;** stands at 1,324 m., nr. Gr. Salt L.; rly. ctr.; beet-sugar, meat-packing, flour-milling, clothing, cement; p. (1980) 64,407.

Ogdensburg, c., pt., N.Y., **USA;** on St. Lawrence R., opposite Prescott; impt. R. pt.; p. (1980) 12,375.

Ogmore and **Garw,** t., Ogwr, Mid Glamorgan, **Wales;** in narrow valley, 10 km N. of Bridgend; industl.; cas.; p. (1981) 18,220.

Ogooué, R., **Gabon, Congo;** site of Schweitzer's hospital at Lambaréné; 800 km long.

Ogwr, l. gov. dist., Mid Glamorgan, **Wales;** inc. Ogmore, Maesteg and Bridgend inland and Porthcawl on cst.; p. (est. 1988) 137,500.

Ohau, Lake, S.I., **N.Z.;** in Mt. Cook dist.; fed by glaciers; 19 km by 35 km; hydroelectric power potential.

Ohio, R., trib. of Mississippi R., **USA;** formed in Penns., by junc. of Monongahela and Allegheny Rs. at Pittsburgh, thence navigable for 1,560 km to Cairo in Ky.; an impt. comm. waterway for industl. raw materials; flood protection schemes.

Ohio, st., N. **USA;** Buckeye St.; admitted to Union 1803; st. flower Scarlet Carnation, st. bird Cardinal; gr. agr. and industl. region; maize, wheat, cattle; major deposits of coal form basis of heavy inds., especially in major ts. of Cleveland, Cincinnati, Toledo, Akron, Dayton, Youngstown; petroleum; timber inds.; cap. Columbus; a. 106,508 km²; p. (1985) 10,744,000.

Ohre (**Eger**), R., Bohemia, **ČSSR;** rises in Fichtelgebirge, flows N.E. into Labe (Elbe) and through Karlovy Vary; 224 km long.

Ohrid or **Ochrida,** L., forms part of bdy. between **Albania** and **Yugoslavia;** alt. c. 850 m; deepest L. in Balkans; scenic tourist a.; monasteries on shores.

Ohrid or **Ochrida,** t., Macedonia, **Yugoslavia;** on N.E. shore of L.; airport and tourist ctr.; p. (1981) 64,245.

Oich, Loch, L., Gr. Glen, Inverness, **Scot.;** forms part of Caledonian Canal.

Oise, dep., N. **France;** traversed by R. Oise; fertile, forested; cap. Beauvais; a. 5,884 km²; p. (1982) 662,200.

Oise, R., trib. of R. Seine, **France;** canalised navigable to Chauny; 298 km long.

Oita, c., spt., N.E. Kyushu, **Japan;** on Beppu Bay; wire, carbon, iron, and steel; oil refinery; p. (1985) 390,105.

Ojos del Salado, mtn., N.W. **Argentina;** alt. 6,884 m.

Oka, R., Kursk, **RSFSR;** rises S. of Orel, flows past Kaluga, Serpukhov, Kolomna, Ryazan, Murom, to become trib. of Volga at Gorki; navigable, carrying grain and timber; 1,520 km long.

Oka, R., Irkutsk, Siberia, **USSR;** joins Angara R. below Bratsk; 800 km long.

Okayama, c., Honshu, **Japan;** textiles; lt. inds.; p. (1985) 572,423.

Okazaki, t., Honshu, **Japan;** nr. G. of Ovari; industl. ctr.; textiles, chemicals, machin.; p. (1985) 284,996.

Okeechobee, L., S. Fla., **USA;** drains to Atl. Oc. via Everglades; tourist attraction especially for fishing; also comm. fisheries.

Okefenokee, swamp, Ga./Fla., **USA;** forms O. Nat. Wildlife Refuge.

Okehampton, mt. t., West Devon, **Eng.;** on N. flank of Dartmoor; granite quarries; p. (1981) 4,181.

Okha, spt., E. cst. Sakhalin I., **RSFSR;** exp. petroleum; lge. refinery; p. 50,000.

Okhotsk, Sea of, N.E. **Asia;** 1,600 km by 800 km; enclosed by the Siberian mainland, Kamchatka, the Kurils and Sakhalin I.

Oki Is., off cst. of Honshu, **Japan;** a. 350 km².

Okinawa, I., **Japan,** under U.S. control until

1972; lgst. and most impt. of Ryuku Is.
US air bases at Kadena and cap. Naha; a.
1,500 km²; p. (1985) 1,179,000.

Oklahoma, st., USA; Sooner St.; admitted to Union
1907; st. flower Mistletoe, st. bird Scissor tailed
Fly-catcher; prairie, plains and mtns.; continental
climate; cereals, cotton, stock-raising; petroleum,
gas, zinc, coal, gypsum, lead; ch. ind. petroleum
refining; cap. Oklahoma City; a. 181,090 km²; p.
(1985) 3,301,000.

Oklahoma City, c., cap. of Okla. st., **USA;** univ.;
livestock mkt.; tr. and processing ctr.; oil and
by-prods., field machin., flour mills, meat-packing; p. (1984) 443,200 (c.), 962,600 (met. a.).

Okovango, R.; rises in **Angola,** flows to Ngami
depression, **Botswana,** where it forms swampy
delta; 1,600 km long.

Obtyabrsky, t., Bashkir ASSR, **USSR;** on R. Ik;
in new oil-mng. dist., the "New Baku"; p.
(est. 1985) 102,000.

Öland, I., Baltic Sea; off E. cst. **Sweden;**
connected by Europe's longest bridge to
mainland; agr., limestone quarries; ch. t. Borg-
holm; seaside resorts; a. 1,341 km²; p. (1983)
23,874.

Oldbury. See **Warley.**

Oldbury-on-Severn, Avon, **Eng.;** nuclear power
sta.

Old Castile, historical div., **Spain;** now divided
into Santander, Soria, Segovia, Logrono, Avila,
Valladolid, Palencia, and Burgos provs.

Oldenburg, c., Lower Saxony, **W. Germany;** on
R. Hunte nr. Hunte-Ems canal; rly. junc.;
mkt. for horses and cattle; lt. inds.; natural
gas nr. to cst.; p. (est. 1986) 139,300.

Old Fletton, Cambs., **Eng.;** on R. Nene opposite
Peterborough; bricks, gen. and elec. engin.,
beet sugar, fruit and vegetable canning; p.
(1981) 13,657.

Oldham, c., met. dist., Gtr. Manchester, **Eng.;**
on R. Medlock, 11 km N.E. of Manchester;
manmade fibre and cotton textiles, machin.;
recent industl. diversification inc. electro- and
aero-engin., leather, paints; p. (est. 1988)
219,500.

Oldmeldrum, burgh, Gordon, **Scot.;** 6 km N.E. of
Inverurie; p. (1981) 1,358.

Olenek, R., RSFSR; N. Siberia; flows W. of
Lena R. into Laptev Sea, Arctic Oc.; abounds
in fish; 2,160 km long, 960 km navigable.

Oléron, Ile d', I., Charente-Maritime dep., **France;**
lies off estuary of Charente, Bay of Biscay;
oysters, early vegetables; a. 176 km².

Olifant, R., Transvaal, **S. Africa;** trib. of Limpopo; irrigation scheme for intensive agr. in
valley.

Olinda, t., Pernambuco st., **Brazil;** seaside resort;
phosphates; p. (est. 1985) 335,900.

Oliva, t., Valencia, **Spain;** nr. Alicante; wine
dist., ducal palace; p. (1981) 19,232.

Olivos, sub., Buenos Aires, **Argentina.**

Olmütz. See **Olomouc.**

Olney, t., Bucks., **Eng.;** mkt., dairy produce;
annual Shrove Tuesday pancake race.

Oloibiri, S. Nigeria; oilfields; pipeline to Pt.
Harcourt, 128 km W.

Olomouc (Olmütz), ČSSR; industl. ctr., steel wks.,
elec. equipment, textiles, food prod.; cath., univ.;
formerly one of ch. fortresses of Austria; p. (est.
1986) 106,000.

Oloron-Sainte-Marie, t., Pyrénées-Atlantique,
France; in Pyrenean foothills; caths.; p.
(1982) 12,237.

Olsztyn (Allenstein), t., N.W. **Poland;** cap. of
Olsztyn prov.; on R. Alle, 160 km N. of Warsaw; cas.; machin., wood inds.; p. (est. 1985)
147,000.

Olten, c., N. **Switzerland;** rly. junc., on R. Aare;
p. (1970) 21,209.

Olympia, anc. c., Peloponnesus, S. **Greece;** at
confluence of Alphaeus and Cladeus Rs.; site
of gr. temple of Zeus and scene of Olympic
games; modern v. of O. nearby; museum.

Olympia, cap. of Washington st., **USA;** spt. on
Puget Sound; exp. timber; machin., agr.-
processing inds.; p. (1984) 29,200 (c.), 138,300
(met. a.).

Olympus, Mt., highest mtn. in **Greece;** on border
of Thessaly and Macedonia, nr. Aegean cst.;
alt. 2,975 m; regarded by anc. Greeks as home
of the Olympian gods.

Omagh, t., l. gov. dist., **N. Ireland;** on R.;
Stule agr. mkt.; tourist ctr.; p. (1981) 41,110

(dist.), 14,627 (t.).

Omaha, c., Nebraska, **USA;** on Missouri R.;
one of lgst. livestock and meat-packing ctrs. in
US, gold and silver smelting and refining,
steel fabrication, industl. alcohol prod.; univ.;
p. (1984) 334,000 (c.), 607,400 (met. a.).

Oman (Muscat and Oman until 1970), sultanate,
S.W. **Asia;** fertile coastal plain, interior desert
plateau; irrigated agr., especially impt. for
dates; fishing; oil discovered 1964, now main
exp.; a. 212,380 km²; p. (est. 1985) 1,242,000.

Oman, G. of, Arabian Sea; connected through
strait of Kormuz to Persian G.; length 480 km,
width 208 km.

Omaruru, t., S.W. Africa; creamery; aerodrome;
p. (1960) 2,689.

Omdurman, c., central **Sudan,** on Nile, opposite
Khartoum; site of Mahdi's tomb; here
Kitchener defeated the dervishes 1898; native
mkts.; p. (1983) 526,287.

Ometepe, I., L. Nicaragua, **Nicaragua;** volcanic;
alt. 1,753 m.

Omsk, c., W. Siberia, **RSFSR;** at confluence
of Irtysh and Om Rs.; major R. pt. on Trans-
Siberian rly.; in agr. region; engin., chemicals,
textiles, oil refining, food processing; cath.;
founded as fortress 1716; p. (1986) 1,124,000.

Omuta, t., W. Kyushu, **Japan;** on Amakusa
Sea; local coal at Miike giving rise to chemical
inds.; pt. exp. coal; p. (1985) 159,423.

Onega, Lake, RSFSR; between L. Ladoga and
White Sea; second lgst. L. in Europe (L.
Ladoga is lgst.); a. 9,751 km²; ch. c. Petro-
zavodsk; Onega canal forms part of Volga-
Baltic waterway.

Onega, R., RSFSR; flows to G. of Onega; 640 km
long.

Onitsha, t., Nigeria; on R. Niger; agr. tr. ctr.;
p. (est. 1983) 269,000.

Onstwedde, t., Groningen, **Neth.;** mnfs.; p. (1967)
27,666.

Ontario, prov., **Canada;** bounded on N. by
Hudson Bay, on S. by Gr. Ls.; extreme continental climate in N., milder in S. peninsula;
extensive coniferous forest in N.; temperate
agr. in S.; leading mineral producer, nickel,
uranium, copper, gold; well-developed inds.
using plentiful hydroelectric power; agr.-
processing, machin., engin.; cap. Toronto;
contains fed. cap. of Ottawa; a. 1,068,587 km²;
p. (1986) 9,114,000, concentrated in S.E.

Ontario, L., N. America; smallest of the Gr. Ls.
of the St. Lawrence basin, separating the
Canadian prov. of Ont. from N.Y., USA;
navigable, carries industl. raw materials;
polluted waters; a. 19,425 km²; depth 226 m.

Ontario, t., Cal., **USA;** aircraft components;
fruit comm. ctr.; p. (1984) 106,300.

Onteniente, t., Valencia, **Spain;** on R. Clariano;
woollen gds., paper mills; p. (1981) 28,123.

Oosterhout, t., N. Brabant, **Neth.;** nr. Breda;
footwear, tobacco; p. (est. 1987) 47,000.

Ootacamund, t., Tamil Nadu, **India;** in Nilgiri
hills, c. 2,100 m; summer H.Q. of st. govt.;
sanatorium; p. (1961) 50,140.

Opatija (It. Abbazia), t., Yugoslavia; tourist
resort, known as the Nice of the Adriatic; p.
(1981) 29,274.

Opava (Troppau), t., N. Moravia, **ČSSR;** nr.
Polish border; industl. ctr. in agr. a.; p. (1984)
60,961.

Opladen, t., N. Rhine–Westphalia, **W. Germany;**
on R. Wupper; metals, textiles, chemicals; p. (est.
1967) 44,700.

Opland or **Oppland,** co., central **Norway;** mtnous.
N. inc. alpine region of Jotunheimen; fores-
try prods.; a. 24,885 km²; p. (1983) 182,216.

Opole (Oppeln), c., S. **Poland;** on R. Oder; R. pt.,
rly. junc.; cement, metals, furniture; 3 univ.
schools; cap. Prussian prov. of Upper Silesia
1919–45; p. (est 1983) 121,900.

Oporto (Porto), c., spt., **Portugal;** second c. of rep.,
built high above Douro R.; ctr. of port wine tr.;
cath., univ., historic bldgs.; sardine fisheries, cotton
and wool textiles, sugar refining, distilling,
oil refining; outer harbour at Leixões; p. (1981)
327,368 (c.), 1,562,287 (met. a.).

Oradea (Hung. **Nagy Varad**), t., W. **Romania,** on
Crisul Repede R., nr. Hungarian border; p.;
ctr.; baroque architecture; lge. Hungarian rly.
p. (est. 1984) 206,056.

Öraefa Jokull, hgst mtn., **Iceland;** alt. 1,955 m.

Oran. See **Ouahran.**

Orange, t., N.S.W., Australia; in fertile fruit growing a., agr. processing; tourism; with Bathurst is planned growth ctr.; p. (1981) 27,626.

Orange, historic t., Vaucluse, **France;** title founded by Charlemagne passed to William the Silent of the house of Nassau; Roman amphitheatre; tourism; p. (1982) 27,502.

Orange, R., Cape Prov., **S. Africa;** flows from Lesotho to Atl.; part forms S. bdy. between Cape Prov. and Orange Free State; Verwoerd dam (1972) for power, irrigation, flood control; Highlands Water Project (1986) to export water from Lesotho to S. Africa; 2,080 km long.

Orange Free State, prov., **Rep. of S. Africa;** plateau land, Drakensberg to N.E., Rs. Orange, Vaal and Caledon; sheep, cattle, horses, wheat, maize, fruit, tobacco, coal, diamonds; cap. Bloemfontein; a. 128,586 km²; p. (1980) 1,931,860.

Oranienburg, t., Potsdam, **E. Germany;** on R. Havel; industl.; chemicals, metals, machin.; p. (est. 1970) 20,442.

Ord of Caithness, hill, headland, nr. Helmsdale, **Scot.;** alt. 366 m.

Ordos, desert region, Inner Mongolia, **China;** lies S. of Huang He; mean alt. 1,000 m; dry cropping, especially millets; pastoral farming.

Ord, R., W. Australia; in Kimberley dist.; since 1972 Ord Irrigation Project; hydroelectric power.

Ordu, spt., **Turkey;** on Black Sea; exp. manganese; p. (1985) 80,828.

Ordzhonikidze, c., cap. of N. Ossetian ASSR, **RSFSR;** on R. Terek at foot of Caucasus, ind. ctr., metallurgical inds.; natural gas pipeline to Tbilisi; hydroelec. power sta.; p. (est. 1985) 303,000.

Örebro, c., cap. of Örebro prov., **Sweden;** on R. Svartå at entrance to Hjälmar L.; anc. t., cas.; footwear, biscuits; p. (est. 1986) 118,000.

Oregon, st., N.W. **USA;** Beaver St.; admitted to Union 1859; st. flower Oregon Grape, st. bird Western Meadowlark; borders Pac. Oc.; ch. physical features, Coast ranges, Cascade mtn. region, Blue mtns., Columbia R. and tribs., Willamette valley; rainy cst., drier interior (agr. with irrigation); cereals, sugar-beet, fruit, cattle; gold, silver, copper, coal, uranium; fisheries, canning, meat-packing, timber, milling; cap. Salem; a. 250,948 km²; p. (1985) 2,687,000.

Orekhovo-Zuyevo, t., RSFSR; E. of Moscow, on R. Klyazma; textile inds.; p. (est. 1985) 136,000.

Orel, c., **RSFSR;** on R. Oka; univ.; rly. junc.; engin., textile mills, food prods.; birthplace of Turgenev; p. (est. 1985) 328,000.

Orenburg (Chkalov), c., cap. of Orenburg oblast, **RSFSR;** on Ural R.; rly. junc.; food processing, agr. machin.; oil and natural gas in region; p. (1986) 527,000.

Orense, t., cap. of Orense prov., **Spain;** on R. Miñho; flour, leather, iron; p. (1987) 103,397.

Ore Sound, strait, between Sjaelland, Denmark, and S. Sweden; protected by agreement of adjacent countries; freezes occasionally; proposed bridge (1988).

Orford Ness, coastal sandspit, Suffolk, **Eng.;** cas. keep at Orford.

Oriente, prov., **Cuba;** contains mtns. of Sierra Maestra; sugar cane grown in lowlands; manganese mng.; a. 36,592 km²; p. (est. 1970) 2,998,972.

Oriente, terr., **Peru/Ecuador;** for long in dispute between the two ctys., partially settled by treaty (1942); lies E. of Andes, between Putumayo and Marañon Rs.; mainly dense forest, reputedly rich in minerals.

Orihuela, t., Alicante, **Spain;** on R. Segura; leather, textiles, wine; univ., cath.; p. (1981) 49,851.

Orinoco, R., Venezuela; rises in Parima mtns., flows to Atl., connected to Rio Negro and Amazon; impt. industl. development on lower O., based on hydroelec. power and iron ore; experimental scheme to reclaim delta for agr.; 2,368 km long.

Orissa, st., **India;** agr. with few ts.; Hirakud dam across Mahanadi R.; Paradeep being developed as pt.; rice; cap. Bhuvaneshwar; a. 155,825 km²; p. (1981) 26,370,271.

Orizaba, t., Veracruz, **Mexico;** textiles, paper mills, breweries; resort; p. (1980) 114,848.

Orizaba, mtn., Veracruz, **Mexico;** volcanic; called Citlatepetl in Aztec times; alt. 5,704 m.

Orkney, l. gov. reg., **Scot.;** gr. of 68 Is. in N. Sea,

inc. Pomona, Sanday, Westray; 29 inhabited; antiquarian remains, stone circles; farming, fishing; North Sea oil finds; cap. Kirkwall; total a. c. 932 km²; p. (est. 1986) 19,266.

Orlando, c., Fla., **USA;** winter resort; inds. based on citrus fruit and mkt. garden prods.; p. (1984) 137,100 (c.), 824,100 (met. a.).

Orléannais, region and former prov., **France;** inc. deps. of Loire-et-Cher, Loiret, and parts of Eure-et-Loire and Yonne.

Orléans, c., cap. of Loiret dep., **France;** on R. Loire; cath., univ.; regional tr. ctr.; wine, textiles, chemicals, farm implements; statue of Joan of Arc; p. (1982) 105,589.

Ormoc. *See* MacArthur.

Ormskirk, t., West Lancs., **Eng.;** 22 km N.E. of Liverpool; in mkt. gardening a.; lt. engin., clothing; p. (1981) 27,753.

Orne, dep., N. **France;** agr., dairying, stock-keeping, fruit-growing. Camembert cheese; cap. Alençon; a. 6,143 km²; p. (1982) 295,300.

Orontes, R., rises in **Lebanon,** flows through **Syria** past Hama into **Turkey** past Antioch to Mediterranean; unnavigable but used for irrigation; part of valley followed by rly.; irrigated areas intensively cultivated; c. 400 km long.

Oroya, t., **Peru;** impt. mng. and refining ctr.; p. (est. 1970) 35,000.

Orpington. *See* Bromley.

Orsha, c., Belorussiyan SSR, **USSR;** impt. industl. and transport ctr. on R. Dnieper; textiles, metal wks., food-processing; once a frontier fortress; p. (est. 1985) 119,000.

Orsk, c., Bashkir ASSR, **RSFSR;** in Ural mtns. on Ural R.; inds. based on surrounding mng. a.; oil pipeline terminus; oil refining; hydroelectric power sta. nearby; p. (est. 1985) 266,000.

Orta, L., Italy; W. of Lago Maggiore; a. 18 km².

Orthez, t., Pyrénées-Atlantique, **France;** scene of Wellington's victory over Soult (1814); Bayonne hams; p. (1982) 11,542.

Orumiyeh. *See* Rezaiyeh.

Oruro, t., **Bolivia;** cap. of O. prov. at alt. 3,709 m; once impt. ctr. for silver mng.; now other minerals impt.; tin smelter; p. (est. 1986) 184,101.

Oruwala, t., **Sri Lanka;** steel rolling mill.

Orvieto, t., Umbria, **Italy;** on R. Paglia; cath., Etruscan antiquities; wines, olive oil, cereals; pottery; p. (est. 1971) 25,200.

Osaka, c., Honshu, **Japan;** ctr. of Kinki plain; built on delta in shallow O. Bay; comm. ctr.; banking, heavy industry, metals, machin., clothing; p. (1987) 2,648,000.

Osasco, t., São Paulo st., **Brazil;** industl. satellite of São Paulo with traditional and new inds.; p. (est. 1985) 594,200.

Osh, t., S.W. Kirghiz SSR, **USSR;** textiles, food-processing; one of oldest ts. in central Asia; p. (est. 1985) 199,000.

Oshawa, t., Ont., **Canada;** pt. on L. Ont.; motor vehicles; p. (1986) 123,651 (c.), 203,543 (met. a.).

Oshima, I., Tokyo Bay, **Japan;** lgst. and most N. of Izu-shichito gr.; site of volcanic Mt. Mihara (755 m).

Oshkosh, t., Wis., **USA;** on Fox R.; meat packing, flour, motors. *See* Appleton.

Oshogbo, t., **Nigeria;** comm. and educational ctr.; serves agr. dist.; cotton-ginning; new steel rolling mill; p. (est. 1983) 345,000.

Osijek, t., Croatia, **Yugoslavia;** on Drava R.; growing industl. ctr. for textiles and leather; p. (1981) 867,646.

Osinniki, t., **RSFSR;** W. Siberia; new ctr. of coal mng.; thermal power sta.; p. (est. 1969) 67,000.

Osipenko. *See* Berdyansk.

Oslo (Christiania), c., cap. of **Norway;** at head of Oslo Fjord; ch. spt., comm., industl., and cultural ctr.; ice-free harbour, cath., univ.; exp. timber, fish, matches; wood pulp, paper; occupied by Germans 1940–5; p. (est. 1987) 451,099.

Osnabrück, c., Lower Saxony, **W. Germany;** on R. Hase; stands on a branch of the Mittelland canal; inland pt. and industl. ctr.; iron and steel mills; mach., textile and paper mnfs.; p. (est. 1986) 153,800.

Osorno, t., **Chile;** agr. ctr.; in beautiful forested cty.; Germanic influence; food-processing; tourism; p. (est. 1985) 101,000.

Ossett, t., West Yorks., **Eng.;** 5 km W. of Wakefield; woollens, shoddy-processing, engin.; p. (1981) 20,416.

Ostend, spt., **Belgium**; passenger route between Britain and continent of Europe; popular resort; casino, fisheries, shipbldg., textiles, tobacco; p. (1984) 69,039.

Östergötland, co., **Sweden**; on Baltic cst.; rises to uplands of Småland in S. where p. declining; lowland, a. crossed by Gota canal; cap. Linköping; a. 11,050 km²; p. (est. 1986) 395,000.

Östersund, t., Jämtland, **Sweden**; on Storsjön L.; p. (est. 1986) 57,000.

Östfold, co., S.E. **Norway**; hilly a. crossed by R. Glomma; dairy prods. for Oslo; a. 4,178 km²; p. (est. 1983) 234,726.

Ostia, anc. c., **Italy**; once pt. of Rome, at mouth of R. Tiber, founded 4th cent. B.C.; layout revealed by excavations; modern v. of O. nearby on plain reclaimed from salt marsh.

Ostrava, c., **ČSSR**; at junc. of Oder and Ostravice Rs.; industl. ctr. of Ostrava–Karvinna coalmng. region; iron and steel, machin., chemicals, oil refining; p. (est. 1988) 328,000.

Ostrow Wielkopolski, t., Poznan, **Poland**; agr. machin., clothing; p. (1970) 49,500.

Ostrowiec Swietokrzyski (Ostrovets), t., Kielce, **Poland**; on R. Kamienna; ceramic and metallurgical inds.; p. (1970) 50,000.

Oswaldtwistle, t., Hyndburn, Lancs., **Eng.**; at N. foot of Rossendale Fells; chemicals, textiles; p. (1981) 14,519.

Oswego, t., N.Y., **USA**; pt. on L. Ontario; mnfs. hosiery, matches, textiles, boiler engines, paper; p. (1980) 19,793.

Oswestry, t., l. gov. dist., Shrops., **Eng.**; at foot of Welsh mtns., cas.; engin.; p. (est. 1988) 32,500.

Oświecim (Ger. **Auschwitz**), t., Kraków, **Poland**; at confluence of Rs. Iola and Vistula; lge. chemical wks.; German concentration camp (1940–44); p. (1970) 39,600.

Otago, prov., S.I., **N.Z.**; forested mtns.; gold; farming, sheep, fruit; lge. deposit of jade found at head of L. Wakatipu; coalfields; cap. Dunedin; a. 65,320 km²; p. (est. 1985) 182,100.

Otago Harbour, Otago dist., S.I., **N.Z.**; Dunedin and Port Chalmers are ports on this harbour.

Otanmäki, **Finland**; rich deposit of magnetite-ilmenite ore.

Otaru, spt., Hokkaido, **Japan**; herring fisheries; coal mng., lumbering; p. (1985) 172,490.

Otley, t., West Yorks., **Eng.**; on R. Wharfe; printing, machin., wool, paper mkg., leather, furnishings; birthplace of Thomas Chippendale; p. (1981) 13,806.

Otranto, t. S. **Italy**; on Strait O.; once a flourishing c., fine mosaic pavement, cath., cas.; submarine cable sta.; bauxite exp., fishing; p. (est. 1981) 4,811.

Otsu, t., Honshu, **Japan**; on L. Biwa; p. (1985) 234,547.

Ottawa, c. Ont. cap. of **Canada**; on R. Ottawa; univ., caths., parliament bldgs.; hydroelec. power, lumbering, sawmills, paper, flour, leather, matches, machin., ironware; p. (1986) 300,763 (c.), 819,263 (met. a. with Hull).

Ottawa, R., **Canada**; trib. of St. Lawrence, forming bdy. between Ont. and Quebec; timber transport, hydroelec. power; 1,000 km long.

Ottery St. Mary, mkt. t., East Devon, **Eng.**; 16 km E. of Exeter; birthplace of Coleridge; p. (1981) 7,069.

Ottumwa, t., Iowa, **USA**; on Des Moines R.; in coalfield and agr. dist.; iron and steel, meat-packing; p. (1980) 27,381.

Ötzal, valley, **Austria**; longest side valley of R. Inn; tourist dist.

Ouachita or **Washita**, R., Ark., **USA**; trib. of Red R.; 880 km long.

Ouachita National Forest, Ark., Okla., **USA**; part of forested O. highlands.

Ouagadougou, cap. of **Bourkina Fasso**; and comm. ctr.; p. (1985) 442,223.

Ouahran (Oran), spt., N. **Algeria**; founded by Moors 10th cent.; occupied by French 1831-1962; handles wines, wool, cereals, meat, skins; fine roadstead at Mers-el-Kebir; former French naval and military sta.; p. (est. 1983) 663,504.

Oudenaarde (Audenarde), t., **Belgium**, on R. Scheldt; textile ctr.; scene of Marlborough's victory over French 1708; p. (1981) 27,318.

Ouenza, c., **Algeria**; 75 per cent of Algerian iron-ore produced in dist.

Oujda, t., N.E. **Morocco**; comm. ctr.; phosphate, lead and zinc-mng. dist.; p. (est. 1981) 470,500.

Oulton Broad, L., Suffolk, **Eng.**; nr. Lowestoft. See **Broads**.

Oulu, spt., cap. of Oulu prov., N.W. **Finland**; on G. of Bothnia at mouth of R. Oulu; univ.; p. (1986) 97,869.

Oundle, mkt. t., East Northants., **Eng.**; on R. Nene; public school; p. (1981) 3,290.

Ouro Prêto, old colonial t., **Brazil**; former cap. of Minas Gerais st.; grew as gold mng. ctr.; since p. has declined; now other minerals; school of mines; p. (est. 1968) 38,372.

Ouse or Great Ouse, R., **Eng.**; rises in S. Northamptonshire and flows N.E. via the Fens to the Wash; 250 km long.

Ouse, R., East Sussex, **Eng.**; flows to English Channel at Newhaven; 48 km long.

Ouse, R., North Yorks./Humberside, **Eng.**; formed by Rs. Swale and Ure, flows to Humber estuary; 208 km long.

Ovalle, t., Coquimbo prov., **Chile**; ctr. of fruit and pastoral dist.; p. (est. 1970) 61,605.

Overijssel, prov., **Neth.**; dairying, fishing; ch. ind. textiles; a. 3,364 km²; p. (1982) 1,038,369.

Oviedo, coastal prov., N. **Spain**; agr., fruit, sardine, and other fisheries; cap. O.; a. 10,888 km²; p. (1981) 1,129,545.

Oviedo, c., cap. of O. prov., **Spain**; on R. Nalón; cath., univ.; industl. and comm. ctr. for agr. and mng. dists. of Asturias; p. (1981) 168,951.

Owenus, pt., **Liberia**, deepwater pt. built to serve iron ore mines at Belinga.

Owen Falls, Uganda; dam inaugurated 1954; converts L. Victoria into reservoir for irrigation of Egypt and Sudan; also to supply Uganda with hydroelectric power.

Owensboro', t., Ky., **USA**; petroleum; ctr. for stock raising and tobacco growing a.; p. (1980) 54,450 (t.), 85,949 (met. a.).

Owens, L., S. Cal., **USA**; on E. flank of Sierra Nevada, 32 km S.E. of Mt. Whitney; water taken by 360 km-long aqueduct to Los Angeles; a. 311 km².

Owen Sound, t., L. pt., Ont., **Canada**; on S.W. cst. of Georgian Bay, L. Huron; E. terminus of lgst. wheat-carrying L. steamers; linked by rly. to Toronto (200 km) and Montreal; p. (1981) 19,883.

Oxelösund, spt., E. **Sweden**; on Baltic cst., S. of Stockholm; steelwks., glass; p. (1961) 10,007.

Oxford, c., l. gov. dist., Oxon., **Eng.**; between R. Thames and R. Cherwell; 13th cent. univ. and residtl. colleges; printing, cars, elec. engin.; p. (est. 1988) 115,400.

Oxfordshire, non-met. co., **Eng.**; formed by Chilterns and Cotswolds, drained by R. Thames and tribs.; mainly agr. with lge. arable farms; being prospected for new coalfield; ch. t. Oxford; a. 2,611 km²; p. (est. 1988) 579,000.

Oxfordshire, South, l. gov. dist., Oxon., **Eng.**; Wallingford, Thame and Henley-on-Thames; p. (est. 1988) 131,100.

Oxnard, t., Cal., **USA**; citrus fruits, sugar beet, oil refining; p. (1984) 121,200 (met. a.). See **Los Angeles**.

Oxus, R. See **Amu Dar'ya**.

Oyashio. See **Bering Current**.

Oyo, t., **Nigeria**; cotton weaving; mkt.; p. (est. 1983) 185,000.

Ozark Mtns., Okla. and Ark., **USA**; lead, zinc; ch. t, Joplin; forested.

Ozd, t., **Hungary**; iron and steel; p. (1966) 39,900.

P

Paarl, t., Cape Prov., **S. Africa**; summer resort extending along Gt. Berg R.; wines, fruit, tobacco; flour, saw and textile mills; p. (1970) 48,597.

Pabianice, t., **Poland**; nr. Lodz; textiles, farming implements, paper; cas.; p. (1969) 62,000.

Pabna, t., and dist., Bengal, **Bangladesh**; dist. is a fertile alluvial plain; t. serves as trading, industl. and admin. ctr. for a.; hosiery, carpets; p. (1981) 109,065, (t.) 3·4 m (dist.).

Pacasmayo, spt., **Peru**; exp. rice, sugar, cotton, cacao, hides, copper, lead, zinc, silver; p. (1961) 6,000.

Pachitea, R., Peru; rises in Andes, flows N. to R. Ucayali; sm. German immigrant colonies in upper valley; 512 km long.

Pachmarhi, Madhya Pradesh, India; summer cap., tourist ctr.; p. (1961) 6,142.

Pachuca, cap., Hidalgo st., **Mexico;** silver mnfs. and mng.; woollen and leather gds.; p. (1980) 135,248.

Pacific Islands, Trust Terr. of, external terr. of USA held under U.N. trusteeship; consists of Mariana Is. (except Guam), Caroline and Marshall Is., W. Pac. Oc.; inc. 2,141 Is., grouped into 6 admin. dists.; cap. (provisional) Saipan, **Mariana Is.;** total land a. c. 1,800 km²; p. (est. 1985) 154,000.

Pacific Ocean, a. 176,120,000 km²; lgst. ocean in the world; extends from W. cst of America to E. cst. of Asia and Australia and the S. Ocean in the S.; enters Arctic Oc. via Bering Strait; greatest length N. to S. 1,280 km; breadth, 16,000 km; mean depth 3,830 m, 11,524 m in the Mindanao trench; many coral and volcanic Is. in S.W.

Padang, spt., W. cst. Sumatra, **Indonesia;** exp. agr. prods., coffee, copra, rubber and coal; cement mnfs.; univ.; p. (est. 1983) 726,000.

Paddington. See **Westminster, City of.**

Paderborn, c., N. Rhine–Westphalia, **W. Germany;** cath. and other historic bldgs. severely damaged in second world war; foodstuffs, textiles, metals; p. (est. 1986) 110,300.

Padiham, t., Lancs., **Eng.;** at N. foot of Rossendale Fells, textiles, engin., gas appliances; p. (1981) 9,246.

Padstow, mkt. t., Cornwall, **Eng.;** on W. side of Camel estuary in which silting has caused pt. of P. to decline; lt. inds.; seaside resort.

Padua (Padova), c., cap. of P. prov., N.E. **Italy;** cath., arcades, anc. bridges; univ. founded 1222 (Galileo taught here); flourished as artistic ctr.; birthplace of Livy; machin., chemicals, cloth, distilling; agr. ctr.; p. (1984) 230,744.

Paducah, c., Ky., **USA;** pt. on Ohio R.; saw-mills, tobacco, railway wks.; atomic energy plant; p. (1980) 29,315.

Paestum, anc. c., S. **Italy;** S.E. of Salerno; founded by the Greeks 600 B.C.; ruins of temples, Roman forum and amphitheatre.

Pagan, ruined c., central **Burma;** on Irrawaddy R.; founded circa 849, sacked 1299; in ctr. of a. covered with pagodas, place of Burmese pilgrimage; lacquer work.

Pago Pago, spt., cap. of American **Samoa,** S. Pac.; on Tutuila I., magnificent harbour; US naval and radio sta.; airport; p. (1970) 2,491.

Pahang, st., **Malaysia,** central Malaya; isolated from rest of Malaya, less economically developed; largely covered with forest; some rubber production, gold, tin mng.; cap. Kuala Lipis; a. 34,395 km²; p. (1980) 798,782.

Pahlevi. See **Bandar-e-Pahlevi.**

Paignton, t., S. Devon, **Eng.;** incorporated in Torbay; resort; p. (1981) 40,820.

Painted Desert, Arizona, **USA;** a. of bare multicoloured shale and sandstones; arid; a. c. 19,400 km².

Paisley, burgh, Renfrew, **Scot.;** 8 km W. of Glasgow; anc. abbey; shipbldg., chemicals, engin., preserves, car bodies, cotton thread; p. (1981) 84,789.

Paita, pt., **Peru;** exp. cotton, wool, flax, panama hats; lge. whaling sta. to S.; p. 37,000.

Pakistan, Islamic Rep. of, forms part of Indian subcontinent, **S. Asia;** formerly split into two separate units, E. Pakistan (cap. Dacca) and W. Pakistan, (cap. Lahore), 1,600 km apart; politically separate since 1972; W. part now forms Pakistan; rejoined Commonwealth 1989; E. part indep. st. of Bangladesh; dry semi-desert, irrigated by Indus R. and tribs.; cash crops, sugar, wheat, cotton; natural gas fields; new cap. Islamabad; main spt. Karachi; a. 803,944 km²; p. (est. 1987) 102,200,000 (+ 3.1 per cent. a year).

Paknampoh, t., **Thailand;** on R. Menam, at upper limit of navigation; terminus of private rly.; fish breeding in L. created from swamp.

Pakokku, t., Upper **Burma;** pt. on Irrawaddy R.; shipping ctr. for a. producing sugar, tobacco, peanuts, teak, petroleum; Yenangyaung oilfields nearby; p. (est. 1962) 156,960.

Paktia, prov., Afghanistan; mtnous., forested; difficult to govern, inhabited by sm. and indep.

tribes, but sparse p.; livestock basis of agr.; timber exp; a. c. 12,950 km²; p. (est. 1984) 525,000.

Palau Is.; See **Belau**

Palawan I., Philippines; elongated I., rising to 1,731 m; coffee, resin, timber; sparse p.; a. 11,784 km²; p. (1970) 232,322.

Palembang, cap. of S. Sumatra prov., **Indonesia;** R. pt. of Musi R., 80 km from sea; terminus of S. Sumatran rly. systems; exp. coffee and petroleum prods. from nearby oilfields; inds. based on agr. processing and oil refining; p. (1981) 903,000.

Palencia, t., cap. of P. prov., N.W. **Spain;** industl. ctr.; rly. engin.; cath.; p. (1987) 75,951.

Palermo, spt., Sicily, **Italy;** cath., univ.; shiprepairing; processes agr. prod. from surrounding fertile Conca d'Oro; p. (1984) 712,342.

Palestine or **The Holy Land,** historic region, bounded by Syria and Lebanon on the N., Jordan on the E., the Egyptian prov. of Sinai on the S., and the Mediterranean on the W.; a. when under Brit. mandate 2,701 km²; p. (est. 1948) 782,000. See **Israel.**

Palghat, t., Kerala, **India;** commands Palghat gap through W. Ghats; p. (1981) 117,986.

Palitana, t., Gujarat, **India;** t. of Jain temples inhabited by priests and their servants; p. (1961) 24,581.

Palk Strait, India; separates India from Sri Lanka.

Palma de Mallorca, spt., Mallorca I, **Spain;** cath., palaces, varied inds.; agr. exp.; well-known tourist resort; p. (1987) 306,840.

Palm Beach, t., Fla., **USA;** Atl. coastal resort; permanent p. (1980) 9,729.

Palmerston North, c., N.I., **N.Z.;** rly. junc. at ctr. of Manawatu R. lowlands; sheep and dairy prod.; univ.; p. (est. 1987) 60,600.

Palmira, t., W. **Colombia;** agr. ctr. in Cauca valley; p. (est. 1983) 179,000.

Palm Springs, Cal., **USA;** resort; p. (1980) 32,366.

Palmyra, anc. c. in Syrian desert, 192 km. N.E. of Damascus; Bible name Tadmor = city of palms; extensive ruins.

Palmyra Is. See **Line Is.**

Palo Alto, t., sub. development 48 km S.E. San Francisco, **USA;** attractive wooded site of variable relief; on shore of San Francisco Bay peninsula; Stanford Univ.; science-based inds.; p. (1980) 55,225.

Palomar, Mount, peak, 1,868 m high, S. Cal., **USA;** observatory with 5,080 mm reflecting telescope.

Palos de la Frontera, t., Huelva, S.W. **Spain;** on Rio Tinto; starting point for Columbus in 1492; pt. now silted up; p. (1981) 4,014.

Palua, pt., **Venezuela;** pt. of shipment for iron mines at El Pao; nearby Caroni hydroelec. plant built to serve steel wks. and aluminium plant.

Pamir Mtns., high mtn. plateau ("roof of the world"), Tadzik SSR, **Central Asia;** Mt. Communism (7,400 m) climbed by Russo-British team 1962; name derives from high mtn. valleys known as "Pamirs."

Pampas, Argentina; vast plains stretching from the Rio Negro on the S. to the Gran Chaco in the N., and E. from the Andes to the Atl.; woodless, level country; rich pastures in E., supporting countless numbers of sheep and cattle, a major influence upon the Argentinian economy, source of livestock exps.; W. mostly barren.

Pamplona, t., Norte de Santander, **Colombia;** agr., comm. and tr. ctr.; inds. based on agr. processing; p. (1970) 22,800.

Pamplona, c., cap. of Navarre, N. **Spain;** at foot of Pyrenees, anc. Baxque c.; cath., fortress, univ.; industl. ctr. with varied mnfs.; p. (1987) 178,666.

Panama, rep., Central America; narrow strip of terr. at S. end of isthmus separating N. and S. America; mtnous. and tropical, thickly forested; 9 prov. and 1 autonomous Indian reservation; split by Canal Zone from which rep. earns 25 per cent of revenue; to have control over zone by 2000; shipping registration and other services impt.; subsistence agr.; exp. bananas, shrimps, sugar, coffee; rich copper deposits found 1975; poor communications; US invasion 1989, with objective of overthrowing General Noriega. See **section C, Part II.** Cap. Panama City; a. 74,009 km²; p. (est. 1987) 2,277,000.

Panama Canal Zone, Panama; strip of land 82 km long 16 km wide on either side of Canal, leased to USA for military base; control of shipping to Panama by 2000; a. 1,675 km²; p. (est. 1976) 44,000.

Panama, c. spt., cap. of **Panama;** free pt. at S. entrance to Canal; cath.; oil refining, steel rolling mill, cement plant, lt. inds.; contains 25 per cent p. Panama rep.; p. (est. 1984) 424,200.

Panama City, t., Fla., **USA;** pulp and paper mill; resort; p. (1984) 34,100 (t.), 108,500 (met. a.).

Pan American Highway, international road project, not yet fully complete, from Alaska to Chile, down W. csts. of continents; section between USA and Mexico is called Central American Inter-American Highway.

Panay, I., **Philippines;** between Negros I. and Mindoro I.; coconuts, maize grown in E., fertile lowland; ch. t. Iloilo; a. 11,515 km²; p. (1970) 2,116,545.

Pančevo, t., N.E. Serbia, **Yugoslavia;** agr. ctr. for grain growing a., flour-milling; developing industl. ctr., fertilizers, oil refining; p. (1981) 123,791.

Pangalanes Canal (Canal Des Pangalanes), Malagasy Rep.; follows E. cst from Farafangana to Tamatave, through series of lagoons; 480 km long.

Panipat, t., Haryana, N.W. **India;** on Jumna R.; on route from Afghanistan to central India; scene of battles; p. (1981) 137,927.

Panjim, cap. of Goa, **India;** pt.; old cap. (Velha Goa) in ruins; p. (1981) 43,165.

Panjsher Valley, Afghanistan; silver and mica mines.

Pantelleria, volcanic I., Mediterranean, **Italy;** midway between W. Sicily and Tunisia; figs, raisins, vines, capers, cereals; fishing; a. 150 km²; ch. t. P.; p. (1981) 7,917.

Pantin, N.E. sub., Paris, Seine-St. Denis, **France;** glasswks., sugar refining, tobacco factories, chemicals, leather, tallow; p. (1982) 43,553.

Paoki. See Baoji.

Paoting. See Baoding.

Paotow. See Baotou.

Papakura, c., N.I., **N.Z.;** residtl. a. for Auckland; p. (est. 1987) 23,600.

Papaloa, R., **Mexico;** agr. and industl. development; Papaloan project for flood control and electricity generation.

Papal States, Italy, areas ruled by the Pope until 1870; comprised Latium, Umbria, the Marches, and Emilla-Romagna.

Papatoetoe, c., N.I., **N.Z.;** residtl. ctr. close to Auckland; p. (est. 1987) 21,900.

Papeete, t., pt., **Tahiti I.,** Pac. Oc.; cap. Tahiti and of Fr. Settlements in Oceania; exp. copra, vanilla, phosphates and mother-of-pearl; p. (1983) 78,814.

Paphos, admin. dist., W. cst. **Cyprus;** anc. c.; Old P. dates from 3000 B.C., New P. impt. spt.; rich deposits of copper and iron pyrites, sulphur in Vretsia a.; scene of ambitious project (completed 1983) to grow tropical fruits (mango, avocado, papaya) with irrigation; p. (est. 1986) 23,000 (c.).

Papua New Guinea, E. New Guinea, S.E. Asia; indep. st. (1975); mtnous., thickly forested; under-developed; copra, rubber and timber prods.; many valuable reserves of gold and copper; cap. Pt. Moresby; a. 461,693 km²; p. (est. 1987) 3,480,000.

Pará, st., **Brazil;** densely forested; rubber, fruits, cacao, Brazil nuts; massive iron ore deposits in Serra do Carajás with new road and rail access; cap. Belem; a. 1,228,061 km²; p. (est. 1985) 4,318,400.

Paracel Is., S. China Sea; claimed by China, Taiwan and Vietnam.

Paraguay, landlocked rep., **S. America;** undulating cty.; swamps, forest; hot summers, warm winters, high but seasonal rainfall; sm. densely populated areas, lge. areas with no p.; most economically developed in E.; in and around cap. Asunción 25 per cent p.; economy based on agr., decline of meat and timber but agr. expansion in other prods.; cereals, livestock, fruit, cotton, oil-seeds, but food imported; aid from USA for rural development; few fuel resources (a few oilfields in the Chaco Borea) and low energy consumption; hydroelectric plant on Paraná (Itaipu dam), Paraguay Rs. and at Guaira Falls; electricity exp. to Brazil; new inds. with cheap power; first steel mill (1982); some agr. based inds.; a. 406,630 km²; p. (est. 1986) 3,788,196.

Paraguay, R., **S. America;** rises in plateau of Mato Grosso, flows S. and joins R. Paraná nr. Corrientes; forms bdy. between Brazil and Bolivia, Brazil and Paraguay; impt. navigable waterway to Cáceres (Brazil); 1,920 km long.

Paraíba, st., N.E. **Brazil;** livestock, cotton, sugar cane; tin, scheelite; cap. João Pessoa; a. 56,462 km²; p. (est. 1985) 3,008,500.

Paraíba do Sul, R., S. **Brazil;** rises in São Paulo st., and flows between Rio de Janeiro and Minas Gerais to Atl. N.E. of Rio de Janeiro; forms routeway between São Paulo and Rio de Janeiro; 1,040 km long.

Paramaribo, spt., cap. of **Surinam;** on Surinam R.; exp. bauxite, timber, rubber, rice, fruit; t. built on grid pattern with canals and tree-lined streets; p. (1980) 192,810.

Paraná, c., cap. of Entre Rios prov., N.E. **Argentina;** pt. of P. R. for grain, cattle, sheep; road tunnel to Santa Fé; p. (1980) 162,000.

Paraná, R., S.W. **Brazil;** formed by junc. of Rs. Rio Grande and Paranaíba; flows W. between Paraguay and Argentina; flows into Rio de la Plata; navigable to Brazil frontier nr. Iguaçu Falls; forms part of international inland waterway system; hydroelec. power, Itaipú lgst. sta. in world; joint hydroelec. scheme between Paraguay, Brazil and Argentina; 3,280 km long; rapid rise in p. with indust. expansion from electricity.

Paraná, st., S. **Brazil;** between Paraná R. and Atl. Oc.; extensively forested; maté, timber, coffee; cap. Curitiba; a. 201,287 km²; p. (est. 1985) 8,130,900.

Paranaguá, spt., Paraná st., **Brazil;** ch. pt. for Paraná; in lagoon harbour; modern highway links with Asunción (Paraguay); p. (1986) 94,800.

Paradubice, t., **ČSSR;** univ., cath.; rly. junc., industl. ctr.; distilling, oil refining; p. (est. 1986) 94,000.

Paricutín, Mt. Michoacán, **Mexico;** volcano formed between 1943 and 1952, 2,501 m high; of great interest to scientists.

Paris, c., cap. of **France;** dominates rep. politically, economically, and socially, partly as result of extreme centralisation of political power in cap.; on R. Seine, 176 km from mouth, in ctr. of Paris Basin; forms major ctr. of communications; planning of Haussmann gives spacious appearance, 12 boulevards radiate from Arc de Triomphe; many historic bldgs., especially on and around Ile de la Cité, an I. on R. Seine, site of cath. of Notre Dame; major cultural and tourist ctr.; univs.; comprises 20 admin. arrondissements; major ctr. of inds. with concentration of modern science-based inds. hindering planned attempts at decentralisation; p. (1982) 2,188,918 (c.), 8,706,963 (met. a.).

Paris Basin, concentric limestone escarpments form saucer-shaped depression with Paris at ctr.; impt. agr. dist., wheat, dairy prod. and wines.

Parkersburg, t., W. Va., **USA;** on Ohio R.; iron- and steel-wks., oil and natural gas, coal, glassware, rayon, porcelain; p. (1984) 39,400 (t.), 157,900 (met. a.).

Parkes, t., N.S.W., **Australia;** mkt.; rly. junc.; radio telescope; p. (1981) 9,047.

Parma, c., cap. of P. prov., **Italy;** between Apennines and Po R.; tr. ctr. rly. junc.; food-processing, wine, Parmesan cheese, precision instruments, agr. machin.; Roman remains, many historic bldgs., univ., cath.; p. (1984) 177,062.

Parma, t., Ohio, **USA;** motor vehicle parts; residtl.; p. (1980) 92,548.

Parnaíba, spt., Piaui, **Brazil;** agr. comm. ctr., cotton, cattle; exp. agr. prods.; p. (1986) 116,206.

Parnaíba, R., rises in Brazil; flows into N. Atl. Oc., forms bdy. between Maranhão and Piauí; 1,200 km long.

Parnassus, mtn. ridge, **Greece;** 133 km N.W. of Athens, nr. the anc. Delphi, the modern Liakhura; hgst. peak Licoreia 2,461 m.

Parnu or Pyarnu, spt., S.W. Estonian SSR, **USSR;** of G. of Riga; exp. timber flax; health resort; p. (est. 1970) 46,000.

Páros, I., Grecian Archipelago; W. of Naxos; source of Parian marble; cap. P.; a. 163 km²; p. (1961) 7,800.

Parramatta, c., N.S.W., **Australia;** pt. nr. head of Parramatta R. in met. a. of Sydney; 2nd Brit. settlement in Australia; p. (1978) 131,655.

Parrett, R., Somerset, **Eng.;** flows to Bristol Channel, nr. Bridgwater; 56 km long.

Pasadena, c., Cal., **USA;** N. of Los Angeles; in fruit-growing region, base of San Gabriel mtns.; 5,080 mm telescope on Mt. Palomar; famous for its carnival; p. (1984) 125,000; inc. in met. a. of Los Angeles.

Pasco, t., Wash., **USA**; on Snake R.; atomic energy plant; p. (1980) 18,425.

Pasco. *See* **Cerro de Pasco.**

Pas-de-Calais, dep., N. **France**; impt. heavy industl. a. based upon local extensive coal deposits; heavy inds. inc. iron and steel, but many ts. in decline as importance of coal diminishes; prosperous agr. based on arable farming; N. cst. faces English Channel and inc. pts. of Calais and Boulogne; severe devastation in both world wars; cap. Arras; a. 6,750 km²; p. (1982) 1,412,200.

Pasir Gudang, free port , **Malaysia**; across Jahore Str. from Singapore; opened (1984) to divert M.'s exports from Singapore.

Passage West, U.D., Cork, **R.o.I.**; declining pt., fishing; p. (1961) 2,000.

Passaic, c., N.J., **USA**; rubber gds., springs, steel cabinets, tin cans; p. (1980) 52,463.

Passau, c., **W. Germany**, at confluence of Rs. Danube, Inn and Ilz, nr. Austrian frontier; trans-shipment base, inds. inc. leather, porcelain, tobacco and brewing; cath., picturesque tourist ctr.; p. (est. 1986) 52,700.

Passchendaele, t., **Belgium**; strategic point in first world war; battle 31 July–6 Nov. 1917; p. (est. 1969) 3,112.

Passero I., Mediterranean Sea; off S.E. cst. of Sicily, **Italy.**

Passy, residtl. part of W. Paris, **France**; between Bois de Boulogne and right bank of Seine; residence of Balzac.

Pasto, t., cap. of Narino dep., **Colombia**; on flank of Pasto volcano; univ.; agr. comm. ctr.; gold nearby; p. (1985) 252,115.

Patagonia, extensive region, E. of Andes, **Argentina/Chile**; elevated plateau, arid, sterile; prin. Rs. Colorado, Río Negro, and Chubut; impt. source of oil at Commodoro Rivadavia; lge. tracts of grazing for livestock; much of p. Welsh descendants; plans to decentralise cap. of A. to small Ts. of Viedma and Carmen de Patagones.

Patan, c. **Nepal**; impt. ctr. of Buddhism; gold and silver gds.; p. (1981) 79,875.

Patani or **Pattani,** pt., S. **Thailand**; on E. cst. of Malay peninsula; spices, rubber, coconuts; tin mng.; former Malay sultanate; p. of t. (est. 1964) 19,902.

Paterno, t., Sicily, **Italy**; N.W. of Catania; cath. cas.; mineral springs, wines; p. (1981) 45,144.

Paterson, c., N.J., **USA**; on Passaic R. whose falls provide hydroelectric power for gr. silk mnf. ind.; now inds. diversified; in addition to textiles and textile machin., aeroplane engines, metallurgical inds., electronic equipment; p. (1984) 138,800 inc. in met. a. of New York.

Patiala, t., Punjab, **India**; metal gds., flour; cement; p. (1981) 206,254.

Patino Mines. *See* **Unicia.**

Pátmos, I., one of the Dodecanese, **Greece**; in Aegean Sea; a. 34 km²; p. (est.) 3,000. (According to Rev. 1. 9. the exiled St. John wrote the Revelation here.)

Patna, c., cap. of Bihar, **India**; univ.; rly. junc.; agr. tr., rice, oilseeds, cotton; handicraft inds.; p. (1981) 776,371 (c.), 918,903 (met. a.).

Patras (Pátrai), spt., cap. of Akhaia, **Greece**; citadel and cas., exp. currants, raisins, figs, olive oil; inds. based on agr. processing; p. (1981) 141,529.

Pau, c., cap. of Pyrénées-Atlantique dep., **France**; on Gave-de-Pau; impt. mkt. and regional ctr.; summer and winter resort; linen, chocolate, hams, wine; natural gas nearby; p. (1982) 85,766.

Pauillac, t., Gironde dep., **France**; pt. on Gironde estuary; ships, wines, timber; oil refinery, natural gas; p. (1982) 6,359.

Paulo Affonso, falls, São Francisco R., **Brazil**; 79 m; Tres Marías dam and power sta. opened 1960; in Nat. Park.

Pavia, c., prov. cap., N. **Italy**; on R. Ticino; route ctr. and agr. mkt. in Po valley; olives, wine, Parmesan cheese; oil refining at Spineto; walled c.; battle 1525; birthplace of Lanfranc; p. (1981) 85,029.

Pavlodar, pt., Kazakh SSR, **USSR**; on R. Irtysh; chemicals, sulphates, agr. machin., locomotives, aluminium, oil processing; food prod.; p. (est. 1985) 315,000.

Pawtucket, c., R.I., **USA**; on Pawtucket R. at head of navigation; first water-power cotton spinning factory in USA 1790; textiles remain most impt. ind.; p. (1980) 71,204.

Paysandú, dep., W. **Uruguay**; rich pastoral a.; ranching, cattle, sheep; arable agr., cereals, mkt. gardening around c. of P.; a. 13,406 km²; p. (1985) 103,487.

Paysandú, cap. of P. dep., W. **Uruguay**; pt. on Uruguay R. with meat-packing, soap and footwear inds.; p. (1985) 74,014.

Pazardzhik, t., **Bulgaria**; on main rly. line to Istanbul; industl., hemp spinning and weaving; p. (1985) 77,378.

Paz de Rio, t., Boyacá, **Colombia**; iron and steel wks.; iron ore, coal, limestone nearby; hydro-elec. sta. projected.

Peace, R., **Canada**; one of ch. headstreams of Mackenzie R.; rises in Rocky mtns., and flows generally N. to Gr. Slave R. nr. L. Athabaska; a. of very mild climate in lower course, fertile agr. valley; 1,680 km long.

Peak Dist., Pennine hill dist., mid-**Eng.**; extends from Chesterfield to Buxton, and Ashbourne to Glossop; composed of limestone with typical karst features; within P.D. Nat. Park, tourist and recreation a. for cities to E. (Sheffield) and W. (Manchester); limestone quarrying for cement; Kinder Scout 634 m.

Pearl Harbor, landlocked harbour, Oahu I., **Hawaiian Is.**, one of finest natural harbours in E. Pac.; US naval base; attacked by Japanese without warning 7 Dec. 1941. (7.55 a.m., local time).

Pearl Is., archipelago, G. of Panama; sea fishing, pearls.

Pearl R. *See* **Chu-kiang.**

Pechenga (Petsamo), spt., **RSFSR**; on inlet of Barents Sea; formerly Finnish, ceded to USSR Sept. 1944; ice-free throughout year; exp. nickel, timber, cobalt.

Pechora, dist., **RSFSR**; E. of Urals; one of 4 main coalfields of USSR; coking coal; ch. ts., Vorkuta and Inta.

Pechora, R., **RSFSR**; rises in Urals and flows N. into Arctic Oc.; 1,120 km navigable between June and Sept. for transport of timber from its basin; fishing; 1,792 km long.

Pecos, R., N.M. and Texas, **USA**; trib. of Rio Grande; water control schemes provide irrigation for lge. a.; 1,482 km long.

Pécs, c., S.W. **Hungary**; on Yugoslav border; one of oldest and most pleasantly situated ts. of Hungary; cath., univ., airport; in coal-mng. a.; coke, chemicals, majolica, leather gds., engin., brewing; p. (est. 1985) 179,000.

Peebles, royal burgh, Tweeddale, **Scot.**; on upper course of R. Tweed; woollen cloth, knitwear; mkt., tourist ctr.; p. (1981) 6,705.

Peeblesshire, former co., S. **Scot.**; now part of Borders Reg.

Peel, t., I. of Man, **Eng.**; resort, fishing pt. midway along W. cst.; cas., cath.; p. (1986) 3,660.

Peel Fell, mtn. Northumberland, Eng.; 1,964 ft.

Pegu, c., Pegu prov., S. **Burma**; R. pt., rly. junc.; many temples, notably Shwe May Daw Pagoda; once cap. of Burmese kingdom; came under Brit. rule 1852; p. (1983) 150,447.

Pegu Yoma, mtns., **Burma**; between valleys of Rs. Irrawaddy and Sittang; thickly forested with teak which is comm. exploited and forms impt. exp.

Peine, t., Lower Saxony, **W. Germany**; N.W. of Brunswick; iron, furniture, textiles; p. (est. 1986) 45,600.

Peipus, Lake, Estonian SSR, **RSFSR**; drained by Narva R. into G. of Finland; Pskov lies to S.; scene of Alexander Nevsky's victory over the Germans 1242; a. 3,626 km².

Pekalongan, t., N. cst. Java, **Indonesia**; exp. sugar, rubber; p. (1980) 132,558.

Peking. *See* **Beijing.**

Pelagi, gr. of Italian Is., inc. Lampedusa and Linosa, between Malta and Tunisian cst.

Pelée, mtn., **Martinique**; active volcano, devastated town of St. Pierre 1902; alt. 1,342 m.

Pella, dep. of Macedonia, **Greece**; mtnous.; cotton, wheat, tobacco; cap. Edessa; a. 2,802 km²; p. (1981) 132,386.

Peloponnesus (Peloponnisos), peninsula, S. **Greece**; separated from mainland by G. of Corinth, but joined in N.E. by Isthmus of Corinth; mtnous.; livestock agr., drought-resistant sheep and goats; ch. ts., Kalamata, Tripolis; a. 21,642 km²; p. (1981) 1,012,528.

Pelotas, t., Rio Grande do Sul, **Brazil**; pt. on lagoon S.S.W. Pôrto Alegre; meat-packing and industl. ctr.; p. (est. 1985) 278,400.

Pemba, I., part of **Tanzania**; cloves, copra, coconuts; exp. mangrove bark for tannin; a. 984 km²; p. (est. 1985) 257,000.

Pemba (Port Amelia), spt., **Moçambique**; sisal, coconuts, cotton, maize, groundnuts; p. (1980) 41,166.

Pembroke, mkt. t., South Pembs., Dyfed, **Wales**; on S. side of Milford Haven; sm. pt.; dock facilities; cas., ruins of Monkton priory; birthplace of Henry VII; p. (1981) 15,618.

Pembroke Dock, Dyfed, **Wales**; site of government dockyard (1814) with consequent growth of a new t.

Pembrokeshire, former co., **Wales**. *See* Dyfed.

Pembrokeshire, South, l. gov. dist., Dyfed, **Wales**; from Pembroke and Tenby on cst. to Narbeth inland; p. (est. 1988) 41,900.

Penang, I., st. W. **Malaysia**; cap. Georgetown, pt. for N. Malaya handling rubber and tin; paper mill; the first Brit. Straits Settlement (*q.v.*); linked by bridge (1985) to mainland; longest bridge (13 km.) in Asia; a. 1,036 km²; p. (1980) 954,638.

Penarth, t., Vale of Glamorgan, South Glamorgan, **Wales**; former sm. pt. on Severn estuary, 3 km S. of Cardiff; seaside resort; p. (1981) 24,000.

Pendle, l. gov. dist., Lancs., **Eng.**; ts. of Barrowford, Colne and Nelson; p. (est. 1988) 84,400.

Pengpu. *See* Bengbu.

Penicuik, burgh, Midlothian, **Scot.**; on R. Esk; paper; p. (1981) 17,430.

Penistone, t., South Yorks., **Eng.**; on R. Don; steel; mkt.; p. (1981) 8,990.

Penki. *See* Benxi.

Penmaenmawr, t., Aberconwy, Gwynedd, **Wales**; 6 km. S.W. of Conway; resort; p. (1981) 3,903.

Pennine Alps, Switzerland; div. of Alpine system; ch. peaks; Mont Blanc (4,814 m) Monte Rosa (4,637 m), Matterhorn (4,477 m); winter sports.

Pennine Range, mtn. range, "backbone of England," extends 224 km southwards from Cheviot hills to Derbyshire; limestone, millstone grit; moorland sheep, dairying in valleys, quarrying, tourism; inc. Peak Dist. Nat. Park and Pennine Way long distance route; water supply, forestry; Cross Fell, 895 m.

Pennsylvania, st., **USA**; 'Keystone St.'; admitted to Union 1787; st. flower Mountain Laurel, st. bird Ruffed Grouse; originally proprietary colony of Penn family, later one of the 13 original sts. in the Union; traversed N.E. to S.W. by Appalachians; ch. Rs.: Delaware, Susquehanna, Allegheny, and Monogahela; major industl. st.; iron and steel, coal (bituminous and anthracite), natural gas, petroleum; maize, wheat, oats, rye; textiles, machin., motor cars, tobacco; cap. Harrisburg; ch. ts.; Pittsburgh, Philadelphia; a. 117,412 km²; p. (1985) 11,853,000.

Penrith, t., N.S.W., **Australia**; in Sydney met. a.; ctr. for mkt. gardening; p. (1976) 79,038.

Penrith, mkt. t., Eden, Cumbria, **Eng.**; at N. foot of Shap Fell, 29 km S.E. of Carlisle; agr. mkt.; tourist ctr.; p. (1981) 12,205.

Penryn, t., Carrick, Cornwall, **Eng.**; on R. Fal estuary; sm. pt., boat repairs; once ctr. of granite quarrying; p. (1981) 5,090.

Pensacola, t., Fla., **USA**; on N. shore of P. Bay; originally a Spanish settlement, retaining much Spanish influence in squares, bldgs., street names; fishing, sea food inds.; naval air training school; p. (1984) 62,000 (t.), 318,700 (met. a.).

Penticton, B.C., **Canada**; comm. fruit ctr.; p. (1981) 23,181.

Pentonville, dist., London, **Eng.**; prison; birthplace of John Stuart Mill.

Pentland Firth, strait, between Orkney Is. and Caithness, **Scot.**, connecting N. Sea and Atl. Oc.; dangerous tidal currents.

Pentland Hills, range, **Scot.**; extend from Lanark to Edinburgh; Scald Law, 578 m.

Penwith, l. gov. dist., Cornwall, **Eng.**; S.W. tip of Cornwall inc. Penzance, St. Just and St. Ives; p. (est. 1988) 59,300.

Pen-y-Ghent, peak, Pennines, North Yorks., **Eng.**; alt. 680 m.

Penza, c., cap. of P. oblast, **RSFSR**; on Sura R.;

rly. junc.; agr. ctr., especially for grain tr. to Moscow; food-processing and wide range of mnfs.; oil pipeline from Mozyr'; p. (1986) 532,000.

Penzance, t., Penwith, Cornwall, **Eng.**; on Mount's Bay; tourist ctr.; ferry to Scilly Isles; engin.; birthplace of Sir Humphrey Davy; p. (1981) 19,521.

Peoria, t., Ill., **USA**; machin., domestic gds.; grain tr.; univ.; p. (1984) 117,100 (t.), 355,900 (met. a.).

Perak, st., **W. Malaysia**; ch. tin-dredging a., in basin of Perak R.; rubber; cap. Taiping; a. 20,668 km²; p. (1980) 1,805,198.

Pereira, t., Caldas, **Colombia**; cath.; comm. ctr. for coffee; p. (1985) 301,715.

Perekop, Isthmus of, connects Crimea with Ukraine, **USSR**.

Pergamino, t., Buenos Aires, **Argentina**; road and rail focus in maize-growing dist.

Périgord, dist., S.W. **France**; limestone plateau crossed by Dordogne R.; famous for truffles.

Périgueux, t., cap. Dordogne, **France**; on R. Isle; cath.; famous for pâté de foie gras; engin., china; p. (1982) 59,716 (met. a.).

Perim, I. in strait of Bab-el-Mandeb at S. entrance to Red Sea; part of **Democratic Rep. of Yemen**; former coaling sta.; a. 13 km²; p. 1,700.

Perlis, st., W. **Malaysia**; agr. dist. for rice and coconuts; tin; a. 803 km²; p. (1980) 148,276.

Perm, oblast, **RSFSR**; major mng., timber, and paper dist.; produces oil (Krasnokamsk), coal (Kizel), hydroelectricity, and potash (Solikamsh); cap. Perm.

Perm (Molotov), c., cap. of P. oblast, **RSFSR**; on Kama R.; machin., chemicals, oil refineries; univ.; p. (1986) 1,066,000.

Pernambuco, st., N.E. **Brazil**; mtnous. interior, cst. fertile; cap. Recife; sugar, cotton, manioc, tobacco, fruits; a. 98,322 km²; p. (est. 1985) 6,743,500.

Pernik (Dimitrovo), c., **Bulgaria**; iron and steel inds.; p. (1985) 94,845.

Pernis, t., opposite Rotterdam, **Neth.**; lge. oil refinery; pipeline to Wesserling (nr. Cologne). *See also* Terneuzen.

Perovo, t., **RSFSR**; nr. Moscow; engin., chemicals; agr. research institute; p. inc. in Moscow.

Perpignan, c., cap. of Pyrénées-Orientales dep., **France**; nr. Spanish border and Mediterranean; on Paris–Barcelona rly.; mkt. and comm. ctr. for wines and fruits; cath.; tourism; p. (1982) 113,646.

Persepolis, anc. c., **Iran**; former cap. of Persian empire, now in ruins; tourism.

Pershore, t., Wychavon, Hereford and Worcs., **Eng.**; on R. Avon; ctr. of fruit-growing a.

Persia. *See* Iran.

Persian Gulf, inlet from Indian Oc. through G. of Oman and Strait of Kormuz, between Iran and Arabia; oilfields in surrounding land and now in G. itself; ch. pts. Bandar-e-Busehr, Abadan, Kuwait, Dubai; Bahrain, Iget. I.

Perth, c., cap. of W. **Australia**; on R. Swan; well planned garden c.; univ., cath., airport; many employed in services; inds. moving to Fremantle (pt.) or to Kwinana; p. (est. 1986) 83,000 (c.), 1,030,000 (met. a., a 71 per cent of st. p.).

Perth, c., royal burgh, Perth and Kinross, **Scot.**; on R. Tay; rly. junc.; cap. of Scot. until assassination of James I, 1437; dyeing, textiles, whisky distilling; cath., historical associations; p. (1981) 41,998.

Perthshire, former co., **Scot.**; now part of Perth and Kinross, l. gov. dist., Tayside Reg.; p. (est. 1986) 122,988.

Peru, Andean rep., **S. America**; consists of 3 N.W.–S.E. regions; Costa (cst.) Sierra (Andes, rising to over 6,100 m) and Selva (interior *montaña* and R. basins); 40 per cent p. in Costa, 60 per cent in Sierra, yet Selva covers 70 per cent total a.; ch. Rs. Ucayali, Marañon; L. Titicaca shared with Bolivia; El Misti volcano in S.; cap. Lima on Pac. cst. with 20 per cent p.; agr. diversified and being extended by irrigation schemes; fishing main single ind.; mng. impt. in Andes; major world producer of silver, phosphates, potash, copper, petroleum; social, economic and political problems provoking guerrilla insurgents; inflation 103 per cent; a. 1,249,048 km²; p. (est. 1987) 20·7 m.

Peru Current (Humboldt), ocean current, S. Pac.

Oc.; flows N. along cst. of N. Chile and Peru; causes clouds and fog.

Perugia, t., Umbria, **Italy**; on R. Tiber; univ., observatory; woollens, silks, lace; foodstuffs, furniture, pottery, chemicals, agr. machin.; p. (1984) 144,064.

Pervouralsk, t., **RSFSR**; in Urals; metallurgical ctr.; p. (est. 1985) 136,000.

Pesaro, c., central **Italy**; on Adriatic cst.; agr. ctr., seaside resort; birthplace of Rossini; p. (1981) 90,412 (inc. Urbino).

Pescadores Is. (**P'eng-hu Lieh-tao**), archipelago, between Taiwan and mainland **China**; fishing, fish-processing; a. 132 km²; p. 86,000.

Pescara, c., cap. of P. prov., S. **Italy**; on estuary of R. Aterno; fish. pt., olive oil, soap, pasta, pottery; resort; birthplace of D'Annunzio; p. (1984) 131,974.

Peshawar, c., cap. of North-West Frontier Prov., **Pakistan**; 18 km E. of Khyber pass; commanding route to Afghanistan; military sta.; univ.; handicrafts, textiles, furniture; p. (1981) 555,000.

Petah Tikva, oldest modern Jewish settlement in **Israel** (1878); ctr. for oranges; mnfs. inc. textiles; p. (est. 1982) 124,000.

Petaling Jaya, t., **W. Malaysia**; industl. estate nr. Kuala Lumpur; tyres, aluminium rolling mill.

Peter I., uninhabited I., **Antarctic Oc.**, belonging to Norway; a. c. 243 km².

Peterborough, t., Ont., **Canada**; flour-milling, elec. machin., trailers, agr. equipment, plastics, textiles, paper; p. (1986) 61,049.

Peterborough, c., l. gov. dist., Cambs., **Eng.**; on R. Nene on margin of Fens; cath.; rly ctr.; ctr. of brick ind. (Oxford clay around Fletton); diesel engines, agr. machin., gen. engin.; major planned expansion as new t.; p. (est. 1988) 152,900, (53,471 in 1951).

Peterborough, Soke of. See **Cambridgeshire**.

Peterhead, spt., burgh, Banff and Buchan, **Scot.**; on E. cst., 43 km N.E. of Aberdeen; herring fisheries, leading U.K. fish. pt. by value of fish landed (1982); fish-processing, granite quarrying; supply base for N. Sea oil; p. (1981) 17,015.

Peterlee, new t. (1948), Durham, **Eng.**; coal-mng. dist.; textiles, science-based inds.; p. (1981) 22,756.

Petersfield, t., East Hants., **Eng.**; on R. Rother, N.W. of Chichester; mkt.; p. (1981) 10,001.

Petra, anc. c., **Jordan**; temples, rock tombs and Roman ruins; called Sela in Bible (2 Kings 14. 7); rediscovered by Burckhardt 1812.

Petropavlovsk, t., Kazakh SSR, **USSR**; on Ishim R.; rly. junc.; flour, leather, meat canneries, furs, engin.; p. (est. 1985) 226,000.

Petropavlovsk-Kamchatsky, t., **RSFSR**; spt. on Pac. cst.; shipyard, timber mills, engin.; fishing and whaling fleet; p. (est. 1985) 245,000.

Petrópolis, t., Rio de Janeiro, **Brazil**; health resort, c. 700 m a.s.l.; cath.; p. (est. 1985) 275,100.

Petsamo. See **Pechenga**.

Petten, t., **Neth.**; 48 km N.W. of Amsterdam, on cst.; atomic research ctr.

Petworth, mkt. t., West Sussex, **Eng.**; in Rother valley, 19 km N.E. of Chichester; associated with Turner.

Pevensey Levels, marshy a., East Sussex, **Eng.**; lie behind coastal sand-bars between Eastbourne and Bexhill, extend 8 km inland to Hailsham; now largely drained, cattle pastures; a. 62 km².

Pforzheim, t., Baden-Württemberg, **W. Germany**; S.E. of Karlsruhe; gold, silver, metal wks., jewellery; p. (est. 1986) 104,500.

Phan Thiet, spt., **Vietnam**; exp. dried and salt fish; p. 5,000.

Phetburi, t. and prov., **Thailand**; on Isthmus of Kra crossed by Phetburi R.; p. (1960) 24,654 (t.), 237,835 (prov.).

Philadelphia, c., pt., Penns., **USA**; on Delaware R.; comm., industl. and cultural ctr.; univ., R.C. cath., masonic temple, mint, academy of fine arts; shipbldg., locomotives, machin., surgical instruments, carpets, woollens, cottons, worsteds; sugar, and petroleum refining; ctr. of War of Independence 1775–1783; founded as Quaker col. by William Penn 1682; p. (1984) 1,646,700 (c.), 5,755,300 (met. a.).

Philae, I. in Nile R., **Egypt**; flooded by waters of Aswan Dam; contains anc. ruined temples which have been removed to a safer site.

Philippeville. See **Skikda**.

Philippines, Rep. of, S.E. **Asia**; chain of 7,100 Is. in Pac. Oc., stretching over 1,760 km; ch. Is. Luzon, Mindanao, Negros, Cebu, Mindoro, and Palawar; lie in track of cyclones; tropical climate; mtnous., agr. aided by intricate terracing system; most Is. underdeveloped except Luzon where p. concentrated; subsistence agr. rice and maize; 60 per cent of households live below the poverty line; coconuts major export crop; sugar impt. once but falling world prices have curtailed production; electronics and garments also exported; income generated by Filipinos working abroad sending wages home; geothermal energy used; coconut shells burnt for fuel; cap. Quezon City (admin. functions at Manila); a. 299,681 km²; p. (est. 1987) 57·4 m.

Phlorina (Florina), t., Macedonia, **Greece**; in basin at 900 m, 16 km from Yugoslav border; agr. ctr.; p. (1981) 12,573.

Phnom-Penh, c., cap. of **Kampuchea**, S.E. **Asia**; pt. on Mekong R.; handles ships up to 2,500 tonnes; linked to Kompong Som by modern highway; multi-purpose dam to W.; univ., royal palace; airport; much reduced in size and importance since Communist takeover; p. (est. 1986) 700,000.

Phoenix, c., Arizona, **USA**; on Salt R., ctr. of Salt River Valley irrigated region; electronics research, steel, aircraft, clothing; p. (1984) 853,300 (c.), 1,714,800 (met. a.).

Phoenix Group, Is., **Pac. Oc.**; part of Kiribati; a. 41 km²; US have some rights over Canton and Enderbury; Canton used as international airport; p. (1985) 24.

Phuket I., Thailand; off Kra Isthmus; main alluvial tin-working region of Thailand; ch. t. Phuket where a tin-smelting plant is to be established; a. 534 km².

Piacenza, c., cap. of P. prov., **Italy**; in Emilia-Romagna, on R. Po; agr. and comm. ctr.; cath., palaces, arsenal; cars, chemicals, cement; p. (1984) 107,617.

Piatra-Neamt, t., Moldavia, **Romania**; timber, pharmaceuticals, soap; oil refineries; p. (est. 1984) 105,108.

Piaui, st., **Brazil**; semi-arid, underdeveloped dist.; thorn scrub; livestock rearing; cap. Teresina; a. 249,319 km²; p. (est. 1985) 2,419,500.

Piave, R., N.E. **Italy**; flows to Adriatic, 200 km long.

Picardy, former prov., **France**; included the Somme dep. and parts of Pas-de-Calais, Aisne and Oise; old battle sites, Agincourt and Crécy; rich agr. a.; textiles; p. (1982) 1,740,000.

Pichincha, prov., **Ecuador**; p. concentrated in Andes; many natural resources inc. lime, gypsum, silver; tropical hardwoods; cattle raising; cap. Quito; a. 16,105 km²; p. (1982) 1,369,059.

Pickering, mkt. t., Ryedale, North Yorks., **Eng.**; on N. margin of Vale of P.; church with murals; cas.; gas terminal; p. (1981) 5,942.

Pickering, Vale of, North Yorks., **Eng.**, wide, flat-floored vale, once occupied by glacial lake; bounded to N. by N. York Moors, to S. by York Wolds; drained W. by R. Derwent, alluvial soils, marshy in ctr.; crop farming along margins, cattle grazing in damper meadows in ctr., ch. ts. Pickering, Malton, Helmsley.

Picos de Europa, mtn. massif, N. **Spain**; hgst. massif in Cantabrian mtns., rising to 2,650 m; partially inc. in Nat. Park.

Picton, t., S.I., **N.Z.**; freezing wks.; tourist and fishing ctr.; p. (1976) 3,276.

Pictou, t., Nova Scotia, **Canada**; on Northumberland Strait; founded by Scottish settlers; p. (1981) 4,628.

Pidurutalagala, mtn., **Sri Lanka**; alt. 2,530 m; hgst. peak in rep.

Piedmont, region, N. **Italy**; rice, wheat, vines, fruits; cottons, woollens; a. 25,416 km²; p. (est. 1986) 4·4 m.

Pietermaritzburg, c., cap. of Natal, **S. Africa**; named after Piet Retief and Gerhardus Maritz, two Boer leaders; lt. inds.; tanning; iron-ore mng. in a.; part of univ. of Natal; 2 caths.; p. (1985) 192,417 (met. a.).

Pietersburg, t., Transvaal, **S. Africa**; gold, asbestos, tin; comm. ctr. for cereals, tobacco, cotton, citrus fruits; p. (est. 1975) 27,000.

Pila (Schneidemühl), t., N.W. **Poland** (since 1945); formerly in Prussian prov. of Pomerania; tr. ctr., lignite mines nearby; p. (1983) 64,600.

Pilar, t., **Paraguay**; impt. R. pt.; sawmills; textiles; p. (1984) 26,352.

Pilbara, dist., W. **Australia**; extensive iron mng.; other minerals inc. salt, oil, nat. gas; rapid growth of p.; p. (est. 1975); 35,000 (1960) 2,250.

Pilcomayo, R., northernmost R. of **Argentina**; rises in Bolivian Andes, flows across the Gran Chaco, to enter Paraguay, joining the Paraguay R. nr. Asunción; hydroelec. power; 1,120 km long.

Pilibhit, t., Uttar Pradesh, N. **India**; admin. ctr.; sugar-refining; p. (1961) 57,527.

Pilsen. See **Plzeň.**

Pinar del Rio, c., prov. cap., **Cuba**; tobacco; p. (1985) 100,900.

Pinawa, t., Manitoba, **Canada**; 88 km N.E. of Winnipeg; nuclear research; p. (1982) 2,011.

Pindus, mtn. chain, between Thessaly and Albania, **Greece**; hgst. peak 2,455 m.

Pingxiang, c., Jianxi, **China**; supplies coking coal to Wuhan. p. (1984) 1,270,400.

Pinneberg, t., Schleswig-Holstein, **W. Germany**; N.W. of Hamburg; rose cultivation, metals, leather; p. (est. 1986) 35,600.

Pinsk, c., Belorussiyan SSR, **USSR**; in Pripet Marshes, pt. on Pina R.; paper, wood-working inds., matches; Jewish residents exterminated during German occupation second world war; p. (est. 1985) 109,000.

Piombino, t., **Italy**; mainland pt. for island of Elba; steel wks.; p. (1981) 39,389.

Piotrkow Trybunalski, t., **Poland**; cas.; timber and glass inds.; new textile combine; p. (1983) 77,000.

Piqua, t., Ohio, **USA**; N. of Dayton: ironwks., woollens; nuclear reactor; p. (1980) 20,480.

Piracicaba, t., São Paulo, **Brazil**; ctr. of agr. dist.; sugar-refining, brandy, flour; p. (est. 1985) 252,900.

Piraeus, c., **Greece**; pt. of Athens and prin. pt. of Greece; major industl. and comm. ctr.; p. (1981) 196,389.

Pirmasens, t., Rhineland–Palatinate, **W. Germany**; S.W. of Mannheim; footwear, leather gds.; p. (est. 1986) 46,100.

Pirna, t., Dresden, **E. Germany**; on R. Elbe; textiles, paper, glass; p. (est. 1973) 49,946.

Pirot, t., **Yugoslavia**; nr. Bulgarian border; in economic development a.; p. (1981) 69,653.

Pisa, c., **Italy**; at head of Arno delta, 19 km N.E. of Livorno; famous leaning tower, cath., univ.; textiles, chemicals, engin.; airport; tourism; p. (1984) 103,894.

Pisco, spt., **Peru**; famous for P. brandy; p. (est. 1970) 28,519.

Pistoia, t., Tuscany, **Italy**; on Arno plain, N.W. of Florence; iron and steel gds., macaroni; p. (1981) 92,274.

Pit, R., Cal., **USA**; rises in Goose L.; cuts spectacular gorges in the Cascades; used for hydroelectric power.

Pitcairn I., E. Pac. Oc., Brit. col.; inc. atolls of Ducie and Oeno and I. of Henderson; sweet potatoes, bananas, oranges, coconuts; a. 5 km²; p. mostly descendants of mutineers of the *Bounty*; p. (1986) 57.

Pitch Lake, Trinidad, **W.I.**; S. of I., 16 km S.W. of San Fernando; natural deposit of asphalt; tourism; a. 86 ha.

Pitea, spt., N. **Sweden**; on G. of Bothnia; sawmills; p. (1983) 38,700.

Pitesti, t., **Romania**; on Arges R.; petroleum, fruit, grain; lge. automobile plant; oil refinery under construction; p. (est. 1985) 154,000.

Pitlochry, burgh, Perth and Kinross, **Scot.**; on R. Tummel, 6 km S. of Pass of Killiecrankie; summer resort; distilleries, hydros; p. (1981) 2,610.

Pittenweem, burgh, North East Fife, **Scot.**; at entrance to F. of Forth; fisheries; p. (1981) 1,537.

Pittsburgh, c., Penns., **USA**; univ.; R.C. cath.; pt. on Ohio R.; ctr. of richest American coalfield; natural gas, petroleum, iron and steel, machin., metal gds., meat-packing, glass, aluminium, chemicals, p. (1984) 402,600 (c.), 2,372,000 (met. a.).

Pittsfield, c., Mass., **USA**; textiles, paper, plastics, elec. machin.; resort; p. (1980) 51,974.

Piura, t., N. **Peru**; on Piura R.; oldest Spanish t. in Peru; cotton mkt. and processing, p. (est. 1985) 266,000.

Pladju, t., S. Sumatra, **Indonesia**; oil refining; linked by pipeline with Tempino and Bejubang.

Plata, Rio de la (Plate R.), estuary between **Argentina** and **Uruguay**; receives waters of Rs. Paraná and Uruguay; cst. provides sites for lge. spts., Buenos Aires, La Plata, Montevideo.

Platte, R., Nebraska, **USA**; formed by union of N. Platte and S. Platte Rs.; total length 2,240 km; irrigation, hydroelec. power.

Plauen, t., Karl-Marx-Stadt, **E. Germany**; textiles, machin., cable, leather, paper, radios; rly. junc; p. (1981) 78,800.

Plenty, Bay of, prov. and bay, N.I., **N.Z.**; on E. cst.; 208 km wide; p. (1976) 472,083.

Plettenberg, t., N. Rhine–Westphalia, **W. Germany**; on R. Lenne; iron wks.; p. (est. 1986) 27,600.

Pleven, t., **Bulgaria**; many mosques; famous siege 1877; textiles, wines; p. (1985) 129,782.

Plitvička Jezera, lakes, **Yugoslavia**; beautiful scenery; tourism; fishing.

Ploče, new spt., **Yugoslavia**; on Dalmatian cst.; industl. and rly. ctr.

Plock, t., Poland; on R. Vistula, nr. Warsaw; agr.; oil refinery and petrochemical plant; food processing; agr. machin.; p. (est. 1983) 112,400.

Ploiești, t., Prahova dist., **Romania**; petroleum, engin.; p. (est. 1984) 232,462.

Plovdiv (Philippopolis), c., **Bulgaria**; on R. Maritsa; univ., Greek cath.; second c. of rep.; agr. processing, clothing, metals, engin.; p. (1985) 342,201.

Plymouth, c., spt., l. gov. dist., S. Devon, **Eng.**; on Plymouth Sound; comprises the "three towns" of Plymouth, Devonport, and Stonehouse; Brit. fleet faced Armada 1588; R.C. cath., guildhall, museum; Naval dockyard, planned privatisation (1987); seaside resort; fishing and fish-canning, lt. inds.; recently discovered deposit of tungsten, thought to be lgst. in W. Europe but lies within Dartmoor Nat. Park; p. (est. 1988) 258,100.

Plymouth, ch. t., Montserrat I., **W.I.**; p. (est. 1985) 3,500.

Plymouth, spt., Mass., **USA**; on Plymouth Bay, S.E. of Boston; here Pilgrim Fathers landed 1620 from *Mayflower* to form first English col.; Pilgrim Hall, Pilgrim Rock; textiles, cordage, machin.; tourism; p. (1980) 7,232.

Plynlimmon, mtn., Powys and Dyfed, **Wales**; alt. 753 m; source of R. Severn.

Plzeň (Pilsen), c., W. Bohemia, **ČSSR**; ctr. of coal-mng. region; famous for beer and Lenin (former Škoda) armament wks.; p. (est. 1986) 175,000.

Po, R., **Italy**; flows from Monte Viso, through Piedmont and Lombardy to the Adriatic; valley forms a major component of N. Italian lowland; natural gas deposits in valley; liable to flooding; 648 km long.

Pocklington, mkt. t., East Yorks., Humberside, **Eng.**; foot of York wolds, 19 km E. of York; ctr. of agr. dist.; 16th cent. grammar school.

Podolsk, t., RSFSR; on main rly. from Moscow to S.; engin., tin-smelting, food-processing; p. (est. 1985) 208,000.

Pohai. See **Bo Hai.**

Point-à-Pierre, Trinidad; oil refinery; natural gas pipeline from Forest Reserve field.

Point-à-Pitre, ch. t. and pt. Guadeloupe, **Fr. W.I.**; on Grande Terre I.; exp. agr. prods., bananas, sugar; p. (1982) 25,310.

Pointe-des-Galets or **Le Port,** ch. pt., **La Réunion** (Fr.), Indian Oc.

Pointe-Noire, spt., **Congo Rep.**; airport, rly. to Brazzaville; agr. exp.; potash deposits nearby; linked to deepwater terminal for bulk carriers but mine closed due to flooding; petroleum refinery (1982); gas reserves; p. (est. 1980) 185,110.

Point Fortin, t., **Trinidad**; oilfield and refinery.

Poitiers, c., cap. of Vienne dep., **France**; many attractive bldgs., cath.; agr. tr.; mnfs. chemicals, hosiery; Black Prince defeated Fr. 1356; p. (1982) 82,884.

Poland, People's Republic, **E. Europe**; history dominated by constantly changing sovereignty between E. and W. powers; strong national identity, based esp. on Catholic church; mainly lowland; continental climate; economy retarded by history of political fluctuation; growth of export-based inds. almost halted in 1980s depression; major ctr. of mng. and heavy inds. in conurb. of Upper Silesia, agr. land remains largely in private ownership, but govt. attempts to rationalise farm structure, major pts. at Gdynia, Gdansk, and Szczecin, international airport at cap. Warsaw, 17 historic provs. to be replaced by 49 large dists.; border with Germany fixed along Oder-Neisse line; a. 311,700 km²; p. (est. 1987) 37·7 m.

Polotsk, c., Belorussiyan SSR, **USSR;** cath.; gasoline prod., oil refining; pipeline to Latvian pt. of Ventspils; food processing; p. (est. 1970) 64,000.

Polotskiy, t. Belorussiyan SSR, **USSR;** 13 km W. of Polotsk; new oil workers' t. 1963.

Poltava, c., Ukrainian SSR, **USSR;** industl. and food-processing ctr. in rich agr. dist.; countryside described in Gogol's work; textiles, synthetic diamond plant; battle 1709 between Swedish and Russian armies; p. (est. 1985) 302,000.

Polynesia, ethnic region, **Oceania;** I. grs. in Pac. Oc. within 30° N. and S. of equator; between longitude 135° E. and W.; p. (est. 1984) 498,000.

Pomerania, former prov., N. Germany; in post-war redivision part E. of R. Oder to **Poland;** part W. of R. Oder incorporated in Mecklenburg, **E. Germany;** farming, shipbldg., fishing.

Pomona or **Mainland,** lgst of the Orkney Is., **Scot.;** Kirkwall (cap.) and Stromness on I.; p. (1970) 87,384.

Pomorze. *See* **Bydgoszcz.**

Pompeii, ruined c., **Italy;** stood 21 km S.E. of Naples, at foot of Vesuvius; destroyed A.D. 79 by volcanic eruption, site re-discovered 1748; many interesting excavations; also modern c. nearby; fine church with famous collection of silver and gold plate; p. (1981) 22,896.

Ponape, volcanic I., Caroline Is., **W. Pac. Oc.;** copra, ivory, nuts, starch, bauxite; a. 334 km².

Ponce, c., **Puerto Rico;** recently improved harbour on S. cst.; well connected with other ts. in rep.; ctr. of fertile, irrigated sugar-cane a.; industl. ctr.; p. (1980) 189,046.

Pondicherry, spt., Tamil Nadu st., **India;** on Coromandel cst.; cap. of P. terr.; tr. ctr. for local prod.; p. (1981) 162,639.

Ponta Delgada, ch. t., spt., San Miguel I., **Azores;** attractive scenery, mild climate attract tourists; p. (1981) 21,940.

Ponta Grossa, t., Paraná, **Brazil;** rly. junc.; comm. ctr.; maté, rice, timber, tobacco, bananas, cattle, jerked beef; p. (est. 1985) 224,000.

Pontardawe, t., Lliw Valley, West Glamorgan, S. **Wales;** on R. Tawe, N.E. of Swansea; zinc smelting and refining; p. (1971) 29,431 (dist.).

Pontchartrain, Lake, shallow L., lower Mississippi flood plain, **USA;** connected by canal to New Orleans 10 km to S., and by deltaic channels to G. of Mexico.

Pontefract, mkt. t., West Yorks., **Eng.;** 11 km E. of Wakefield; coal, furniture, confectionery, mkt. gardening; cas. ruins; p. (1981) 31,971.

Pontevedra, prov., **Spain;** on deeply indented Atl. cst.; transatlantic pt. Vigo; scenery and fiesta attractions for tourists; agr., livestock, timber, fisheries; cap. P.; a. 4,390 km²; p. (1987) 902,895.

Pontevedra, c., cap. of P. prov., N.W. **Spain;** fish. pt., handicrafts, agr. tr.; p. (1987) 67,314.

Pontiac, t., Mich., **USA;** on Clinton R.; fishing and shooting, motor cars, rubber gds., machin., varnish; p. (1980) 76,715.

Pontianak, t., cap. of Kalimantan, **Indonesia;** exp. rubber, copra; rubber processing; p. (est. 1983) 355,000.

Pontine Is., off W. cst. of Italy; in Tyrrhenian Sea; a. 11·6 km²; p. 6,000.

Pontine Marshes, region, Latium, S. Italy; coastal zone S.E. of Rome extending from Velletri to Terracina; formerly highly malarial fens, largely drained and colonised 1930–35; 3,200 new farms, 4 new ts.; ch. t. Littoria; a. 647 km².

Pontresina, t., Grisons, **Switzerland;** E. of St. Moritz; tourist resort; p. (est. 1970) 1,250.

Pontypool, t., Torfaen, Gwent, **Wales;** coal, steel, glass, bricks, tin galvanising, nylon at Manhilad;

p. (1981) 36,761.

Pontypridd, t., Taff-Ely, Mid Glamorgan, **Wales;** on R. Taff, 19 km N.W. of Cardiff; coal, iron-founding; p. (1981) 32,992.

Pool Malebo (Stanley Pool), Congo and **Zaïre;** lake formed by expansion of R. Zaïre; length 40 km.; width 26 km.

Poole, t., l. gov. dist., Dorset, **Eng.;** spt. on Poole Harbour, 6 km W. of Bournemouth; imports clay for local pottery inds. petroleum production began 1979; tourism, yachting, marine engin., chemicals; p. (est. 1988) 130,700.

Poona. *See* **Pune.**

Poopó, salt L., Oruro dep., **Bolivia;** fed from L. Titicaca by R. Desaguadero, which flows over saline beds; no outlet; c. 3,600 m a.s.l.; a. 2,600 km².

Popayan, c., S.W. **Columbia;** 1,677 m above Cauca R.; cath., univ.; food processing, coffee, flour; mng. nearby; p. (1985) 166,178.

Poplar. *See* **Tower Hamlets.**

Popocatepetl, volcano, nr. Puebla, **Mexico;** alt. 5,456 m; dormant since 1702.

Porbander, spt., Gujarat, **India;** exp. silk, cotton; imports coal, dates, timber, machin., petroleum; birthplace of Mahatma Gandhi; p. (1971) 96,881.

Pori (Björneborg), spt., S. **Finland;** at mouth of R. Kokemäen; copper refinery, rolling mills, match, paper and pulp wks.; p. (1986) 77,805.

Porirua, c., Wellington, N.I., **N.Z.;** dormitory for Wellington; p. (est. 1987) 43,600.

Porjus, t., Norrbotten, N. **Sweden;** on R. Lulea, hydroelectric plant supplies power to iron-ore mng. dists. of Gallivare and Kiruna, also to Narvik rly.

Porsgrunn, spt., **Norway;** timber, shipping, engin., porcelain, explosives; p. (est. 1987) 31,000.

Port Adelaide, main pt., S. **Australia;** serves Adelaide; exp. agr. prods. from hinterland; imports bulk cargoes (petroleum, phosphate, limestone); p. (1976) 36,020.

Portadown, t., Craigavon, N. **Ireland;** on R. Bann, 40 km S.W. of Belfast; linen, food processing; merged with Lurgan to form new c. of Craigavon; p. (1981) 21,333.

Portaferry, spt., Ards, **N. Ireland;** shipping fisheries; p. (1966) 1,426.

Portage la Prairie, t., Manitoba, **Canada;** sm. pt. on Assiniboine R.; grain and potato tr.; p. (1981) 20,709.

Port Alberni, spt., Vancouver I., B.C., **Canada;** exp. timber; fisheries; timber inds.; p. (1981) 19,892.

Port Alfred, pt., **Canada;** upper St. Lawrence R.; imports bauxite for smelting at Arvida.

Port Amelia. *See* **Pemba.**

Portarlington, mkt. t., Offaly, **R.o.I.;** farming; first place to have elec. power-sta. using local peat fuel; p. (1966) 2,804.

Port Arthur. *See* **Thunder Bay.**

Port Arthur (China). *See* **Lushun.**

Port Arthur, t., Texas, **USA;** pt. on L. Sabine; exp. petroleum, chemicals, grain; p. (1980) 61,251.

Port Arzew, pt., **Algeria;** world's first plant to liquefy natural gas (1964); oil pipeline from Haoud el Hamra; oil refinery.

Port Augusta, t., spt., S. **Australia;** at head of Spencer G.; fine harbour; salt field; exp. wheat, fruit; impt. rly. junction; p. (1981) 15,575.

Port-au-Prince, c., cap. of **Haiti;** spt. on bay in G. of La Gonave; cultural and political ctr.; univ., cath.; food processing and exp.; oil refinery; p. (est. 1984) 462,000 (c.), 738,000 (met. a.).

Port Blair, spt., cap. of Andaman and Nicobar Is. p. (1981) 49,634.

Port Chalmers, t., bor., S.I. **N.Z.;** container pt., timber exp.; p. (1976) 3,123.

Port Colborne, t., Ont., **Canada;** pt. on L. Erie; iron smelting; nickel and copper refining; power from Niagara falls; p. (1981) 19,225.

Port Elizabeth, spt., Cape Prov., S. **Africa;** on Algoa Bay; bilingual univ.; exp. skins, wool, ostrich feathers, mohair; foundries, soap, chemicals, car assembly, food preservation, sawmills; p. (1985) 651,993 (met. a.).

Port Erin, v., I. of Man, **Eng.;** on S.E. cst.; seaside resort, fisheries.

Port Essington, N. point, of Coburg peninsula, N.T., **Australia;** pearl culture experiments.

Port Etienne, *See* **Nouadhibou.**

Port Franequi, *See* **Ilebo.**

Port Fuad, t., **Egypt;** N. entrance to Suez Canal.

Port Gentil, spt., **Gabon.** Eq. Africa; exp. palm-oil, mahogany, ebony; sawmills, fishing, centre of Gabon's main oil reserves, oil refining; p. (1983) 123,300.

Port Glasgow, burgh, spt., Inverclyde, **Scot.;** on S. bank of R. Clyde, 27 km below Glasgow; shipbldg. and repairing, textiles, rope, canvas mftg.; p. (1981) 21,554.

Port Harcourt, spt., **Nigeria;** 48 km from sea on E. branch of Niger delta; terminus of E. Nigerian rly. system; tin, palm oil, groundnuts; bitumen plant, tyres; oil refining; p. (est. 1983) 296,000.

Porthcawl, t., Ogwr, Mid Glamorgan, **Wales;** on cst. 16 km S.E. of Pt. Talbot; resort; p. (1981) 15,566.

Port Hedland, sm. spt., **W. Australia;** new t. being built 8 km inland to absorb impact of Mt. Newman ore project; twin ts. to be linked by industl. belt; exp. iron ore to Japan; p. (1981) 12,948.

Porthmadog (Portmadoc), t. Dwyfor, Gwynedd, **Wales;** pt. on Tremadoc Bay; terminus of Ffestiniog lt. rly.; p. (1981) 3,927.

Port Hope, t., Ont., **Canada;** midway along N. shore of L. Ont., fruit, dairying, radium refining; p. (1981) 9,992.

Port Huron, t., Mich., **USA;** on L. Huron; summer resort, dry docks, grain elevators; motor-car parts; p. (1980) 33,981.

Portici, spt., Campania, **S. Italy;** on Bay of Naples; dockland sub. of Naples; p. (1981) 79,259.

Portile de Fier. *See* **Iron Gate.**

Portishead, pt., Woodspring, Avon, **Eng.;** on Severn estuary 5 km S.W. of Avonmouth; shipping; p. (1981) 11,331.

Port Jackson, N.S.W., **Australia;** deep natural harbour used by Sydney and crossed by Sydney bridge.

Port Kelang (Port Swettenham), major spt. of **Malaysia;** 48 km W. of Kuala Lumpur; exp. primary prods. inc. tin, rubber, fruit; imports mnfs.; p. 11,300.

Port Kembla, spt., N.S.W., **Australia;** part of Wollongong; artificial pt. built to exp. coal; many expansion programmes; integrated steel-works; p. (1976) 197,127 (inc. Wollongong).

Portknockie, burgh, Grampian Reg., **Scot.;** on N. Buchan cst., 8 km E. of Buckie; sm. fish. pt.; p. (1981) 1,237.

Portland, t., Weymouth and P., Dorset, **Eng.;** 6 km S. of Weymouth on sheltered N.E. side of I. of Portland; lge artificial harbour; naval base, prison; p. (1981) 10,915.

Portland, t., spt., Me., **USA;** comm. cap. of Me.; lge fisheries; paper, pulp, lumber, processed food, clothing; p. (1984) 61,800 (t.), 201,200 (met. a.).

Portland, c., Ore., **USA;** gr. wheat and wool tr.; flour milling, shipbldg., fishing and canning, aluminium, lumber; p. (1984) 365,900 (c.), 1,340,900 (met. a.).

Portland Canal, fjord, N.W. cst of America, forming bdy. between Alaska and B.C.

Portland, I. of, Dorset, **Eng.;** limestone mass, linked to mainland by shingle spit, Chesil Bank, terminates S. in Portland Bill; naval base, Borstal institution; limestone quarrying; masonry wks.

Portlaoighise, mkt, t., Laoighis, **R.o.I.;** flour, malting; p. (1981) 7,756.

Port Louis, c., cap., of **Mauritius;** on Indian Oc.; exp. sugar; contains 42% of Mauritius p. in met.a.; port extension and bulk sugar terminal; p. (est. 1986) 138,482.

Port Macquarie, t., N.S.W., **Australia;** former penal settlement on Hastings R.; resort; p. (1981) 19,581.

Port Moresby, t., cap. of **Papua New Guinea,** 2,880 km from Sydney; spt., airpt.; univ.; p. (est. 1986) 141,500.

Port Nelson, spt., Manitoba, **Canada;** on cst. of Hudson Bay at mouth of R. Nelson; linked by rly. to trans-continental systems; exp. wheat, minerals; closed by ice for 7 months each year.

Port Nolloth, spt., Cape Prov., **S. Africa;** serves copper- and diamond-mng. dists.; declining crayfish pt.

Pôrto Alegre, c., cap. of Rio Grande do Sul st., **Brazil;** exp. lard, preserved meats, rice, timber, tobacco; textiles, chemicals, furniture,

brewing, metallurgy; oil refinery under construction; pipeline connects with Rio Grande; 2 univs.; p. (est. 1985) 1,275,500.

Portobello, resort, **Scot.;** on F. of Forth, 5 km E. of Edinburgh; bricks, pottery, paper.

Port of Spain, c., cap. of **Trinidad;** attractive c. with squares; 2 caths., mosque; spt. exp. cocoa, sugar, asphalt, oil; natural gas pipeline from Penal; food processing; p. (est. 1982) 59,649.

Porto Marghera, spt., Venezia, **N. Italy;** the modern pt. of Venice, reached by ship canal dredged through shallow lagoon; oil refineries; chemicals, metal refining.

Porto Novo, t., cap. of **Benin Rep.;** on coastal lagoon; spt.; fishing; many old colonial bldgs.; p. (est. 1982) 208,258.

Pôrto Velho, c., cap of Rondônia st., **Brazil;** in a. producing maize, rice, rubber, tin; p. (est. 1985) 202,000.

Portoviejo, t., **Ecuador;** mkt. and comm. ctr. for agr. dist.; p. (est. 1984) 120,900.

Port Phillip, lge. inlet., Victoria, **Australia,** land-locked bay, Melbourne on N., Geelong on W.

Port Pirie, t., spt., **S. Australia;** major pt. on Spencer Gulf; refines zinc and lead from Broken Hill; exp. wheat; p. (1981) 14,695.

Port Radium, t., N.W. Terr., **Canada;** on Gr. Bear L.; pitchblende deposits; p. (1981) 56.

Portree, spt., v., I. of Skye, **Scot.;** landlocked harbour on P. Bay, Sound of Raasay; fishing; tweed mill; p. (1981) 1,533.

Portrush, spt., Coleraine, **N. Ireland;** 8 km N. of Coleraine; tourism; p. (1981) 5,114.

Port Said, (Bur Sa'id), spt., **Egypt;** at N. end of Suez Canal; free tr. a.; impt. fuelling sta.; entrepôt tr.; p. (1985) 374,000.

Port St. Mary, v., I. of Man, **Eng.;** on S.E. cst.; resort; fisheries, boat-bldg.

Portsdown Hill, chalk ridge, Hants., **Eng.;** extends E. to W. behind Portsmouth from Havant to Fareham.

Portsea I., fortfd. I., between Portsmouth and Langston harbours, Hants., Eng.

Portslade-by-Sea, t. East Sussex, **Eng.;** W. of Hove; p. (1981) 18,128.

Portsmouth, c., naval pt., l. gov. dist., Hants., **Eng.;** opposite I. of Wight; naval establishment; Portsmouth is the garrison t.; Portsea has the naval dockyards, Landport is residtl., and Southsea is a popular resort; naval dock yard closed (1984) fleet maintenance and repair; across the harbour is Gosport; shipbldg.; gen. mnfs.; birthplace of Dickens and I. K. Brunel; p. (est. 1988) 183,800.

Portsmouth, t., N.H., **USA;** summer resort, naval dockyard, cotton; the 1905 Peace Treaty between Japan and Russia was negotiated here; p. (1984) 27,800 (t.), 206,500 (met. a.).

Portsmouth, t., Ohio, **USA;** iron and steel gds., aircraft, boots, shoes, bricks; p. (1980) 25,943.

Portsmouth, spt., Va., **USA;** naval dockyard; farm produce, cotton, rly. wks.; p. (1984) 108,000; inc. in Norfolk met. a.

Portsoy, burgh, Banff and Buchan, **Scot.;** spt. 8 km W. of Banff; fisheries and meal milling; p. (1981) 1,784.

Port Stanvac, S. Australia; 24 km S. of Adelaide; oil refining.

Port Sudan, spt., **Sudan;** 48 km N. of Suakin; linked by rail to Atbara and Khartoum; oil refining; p. (1983) 206,727.

Port Sunlight, Merseyside, **Eng.;** garden v. founded 1888 by Lord Leverhulme for the employees of the Port Sunlight factories.

Port Swettenham. *See* **Port Kelang.**

Port Talbot, t., l. gov. dist. West Glamorgan, **S. Wales;** on E. side of Swansea Bay; impt. iron and steel ind., copper, coal; new deep-water harbour serves as ore terminal; p. (est. 1988) 49,000 (dist.).

Port Taufiq, spt., **Egypt;** S. end of the Suez canal.

Portugal, rep., Iberia, **W. Europe;** member of EC (1986); mild temperate climate on cst., drier and hotter in interior; economy based on an inefficient agr. sector, located in wide fertile valleys, and associated processing inds.; major exp. of cork, but few industl. raw materials; textiles; post-war growth of tourist inds.; cap. and airport Lisbon; a. 91,945 km²; p. (est. 1986) 10,290,000.

Portuguesa, st., **Venezuela;** inc. llanos plains; livestock raising; cap. Guanare; a. 15,200 km²; p. (1981) 424,984.

Portuguese Guinea. *See* **Guinea-Bissau.**

Portuguese Timor. *See* **East Timor.**

Porvoo, spt., S. **Finland**; on G. of Finland; exp. ctr. for forest prods.; p. (1982) 19,195.

Porz, t., N. Rhine-Westphalia, **W. Germany**; on R. Rhine, S.E. of Cologne; glass, metals, paper; p. (est. 1967) 71,800.

Posadas, c., cap. of Misiones prov., N.E. **Argentina**; on upper Paraná R.; on border of Paraguay; yerba-maté, tobacco, cereals; connection for Iguaça falls; p. (1980) 144,000.

Posen. *See* Poznań.

Pössneck, t., Gera, **E. Germany**; S.E. of Weimar; porcelain, textiles, leather; p. (est. 1970) 19,074.

Postillon Is., Lesser Sunda Is., **Indonesia**; coconuts.

Postojna (Adelsberg,) t., **Yugoslavia**; 32 km N.E. of Trieste; extensive grotto and stalactite cavern.

Potchefstroom, t., Transvaal, **S. Africa**; on Mooi R.; univ.; agr.; malt, timber, engin.; p. (1970) 68,207.

Potenza, t., cap. of P. prov., **Italy**; on hill 220 m above Basento R.; agr. and industl. ctr.; univ.; p. (1981) 64,358.

Poti, spt., Georgian SSR, **USSR**; exp. manganese; fish processing, timber-milling, engin.; p. (est. 1987) 54,000.

Potomac, R., **USA**; divides Va. from Md.; flows past Wash., to Chesapeake Bay; 464 km long.

Potosí, dep., **Bolivia**; famous for silver- and tin-mines; zinc ore; cap. Potosí; a. 116,630 km²; p. (est. 1982) 823,485.

Potosí, c., **Bolivia**; on slope of Cerro Gordo de Potosí, 4,072 m a.s.l.; tin, silver, copper, lead mng.; p. (est. 1982) 103,183.

Potsdam, c., cap. of admin. dist., **E. Germany**; on R. Havel, 29 km S.E. of Berlin; beautiful parks and gardens, many palaces; scene of conference between Allies on bdy. questions, 1945; motor and locomotive wks., engin.; precision instruments; p. (est. 1986) 140,000.

Potteries, The, dist., N. Staffs., **Eng.**; ctr. of earthenware ind., comprising ts. Burslem, Hanley, Fenton, Tunstall, Stoke and Longton.

Potters Bar, t., Hertsmere, Herts., **Eng.**; residtl.; in London commuter belt; p. (1981) 23,159.

Poulton-le-Fylde, t., Lancs., **Eng.**; ctr. of mkt. gardening, poultry rearing dist.; p. (1981) 17,608.

Powys, co., central **Wales**; mtnous. a. made up of former cos. of Radnorshire, Montgomery and most of Brecon and bordering Eng.; forestry, stockraising and water catchment for Eng.; crossed by Rs. Wye and Severn; sparse p.; a. 5,076 km²; p. (est. 1988) 114,900.

Powys, Vale of, Powys, **Wales**; drained by R. Severn; cattle-rearing; ch. t. Welshpool.

Poyang Hu, lge. L., Jiangxi, **China**; on S. margin of Chang Jiang plain; surrounded by flat, intensively cultivated land, rice, sugar, mulberry; size varies greatly with season, max. a. (in late summer) 4,662 km².

Poznań, prov., W. **Poland**; drained by Warta and Notec Rs.; mainly agr.; stock-raising; mnfs. inc. locomotives; a. 26,705 km²; p. (est. 1986) 1,308,000.

Poznań, c., cap. of P. prov., **Poland**; on Warta R.; route ctr., industl. and educational ctr.; cath. univ.; engin., iron-founding, chemicals; anc. c., once cap. of Poland; p. (est. 1985) 553,000.

Pozzuoli, t., **Italy**; 3 km W. of Naples; anc. Puteoli; mineral baths, ordnance wks.; Roman ruins; p. (1981) 70,350.

Prague (Praha), c., cap. of **ČSSR**; picturesque, anc. c. on R. Vltava; comm. and cultural ctr.; univ. (founded 1348); outstanding architecture; extensive mnfs.; machin., sugar, leather, milling, chemicals; p. (est. 1986) 1·19 m.

Prahova, R., Walachia, **Romania**; rises in Transylvanian Alps, flows S. into R. Ialomita; c. 176 km long.

Prato, t., **Italy**; 13 km N.W. of Florence; cath., mediaeval cas. and fortifications; cottons, woollens, machin.; p. (1984) 161,705.

Predeal Pass, **Romania**; carries main road and rly. across Transylvanian Alps from Bucharest to Brasov; alt. over 1,200 m.

Pregel, R., **Poland**; flows to Frisches Haff, nr. Kaliningrad; 200 km long.

Prek Ihnot, **Khmer Rep.**; power and irrigation development project on lower Mekong R.

Prerov, t., **ČSSR**; S.E. of Olomouc; hardware, textiles; p. (1984) 50,241.

Presall, t., Wyre-Lancs., **Eng.**; N. of Blackpool; p. (1981) 4,608.

Prescot, mftg. t., Knowsley, Merseyside, **Eng.**; 6 km. S.W. of St. Helens; mkt., elec. cable ind.; p. (1981) 10,992.

Preseli, l. gov. dist., Dyfed, **Wales**; W. penin. with ts. of Fishguard, Haverfordwest and Milford Haven; p. (est. 1988) 70,700.

Prešov, mkt. t., **ČSSR**; linen mnfs.; p. (est. 1986) 83,000.

Prestatyn, t., Rhuddlan, Clwyd, **Wales**; on N. cst., 5 km E. of Rhyl; seaside resort; p. (1981) 16,439.

Presteign, mkt. t., Radnor, Powys, **Wales**; on R. Lugg, 16 km N.W. of Leominster; p. (1981) 1,213.

Preston, t., l. gov. dist., Lancs., **Eng.**; pt. on R. Ribble; textiles, engin., aircraft wks.; p. (est. 1988) 128,100 (dist.).

Prestonpans, burgh, E. Lothian, S.E. **Scot.**; on F. of Forth, 14 km E. of Edinburgh; scene of Jacobite victory 1745; p. (1981) 7,620.

Prestwich, t., Gtr. Manchester, **Eng.**; in valley of R. Irwell, 6 km N.W. of Manchester; cotton bleaching and dyeing, soap, furnishings; p. (1981) 31,198.

Prestwick, burgh, Kyle and Carrick, **Scot.**; on F. of Clyde, 5 km N. of Ayr; golfing ctr. and trans-atlantic airpt. and freeport (1984); resort; p. (1981) 13,532.

Pretoria, c., Transvaal, admin. cap. of **Rep. of S. Africa**; univ., tr. ctr.; inds. inc. engin., chemicals, iron, and steel; p. (1985) 822,925 (met. a.).

Preveza, ch. pt. and t. of P. dep. of Epirus, N.W. **Greece**; guards G. of Arta; p. (1981) 13,624.

Pribilof Is., off S.W. Alaska, **USA**; seal fur; a. 168 km²; p. (est.) 550.

Pribram, t., Bohemia, **ČSSR**; impt. lead and silver mines, zinc, barium and antimony; p. (1984) 38,787.

Prijedor, t., Bosnia and Hercegovina, **Yugoslavia**; on E. flank of Dinaric Alps, 104 km S.E. of Zagreb; rly. junc.; iron-ore mines.

Prilep, t., Macedonia, **Yugoslavia**; mkt., refractory materials, tobacco processing; p. (1981) 99,770.

Primorskiy Kray, terr., **RSFSR**; S.E. Siberia, on Sea of Japan; coal, iron ore, and various metals in vicinity; fisheries; millet and rice; slow economic development results from isolation; wants economic links with China; ch. cs., Vladivostok (cap.), Ussuriysk; a. 168,350 km²; p. (1970) 1,722,000.

Prince Albert, t., Saskatchewan, **Canada**; lumbering, furs; p. (1981) 31,180.

Prince Edward I., prov., **Canada**; sm. I. in G. of St. Lawrence; physically poorly endowed; rocky, with thin soils; pastoral agr., fur-farming, fishing; cap. Charlottetown; a. 5,657 km²; p. (1986) 127,000.

Prince George, t., B.C., **Canada**; oil refining; lumbering, mng., fur tr.; p. (1986) 67,621.

Prince Rupert, t., B.C., **Canada**; Pac. pt. of Canadian National rly.; service ctr., fishing and fish-processing; p. (1981) 18,402.

Princeton, bor., N.J., **USA**; seat of Princeton Univ.; p. (1980) 12,035.

Principe. *See* São Tomé.

Pripet Marshes, Belorussiyan SSR, **USSR**; forested swampy region crossed by Pripet R. and its streams; greater part reclaimed; coal and petroleum; a. 46,620 km².

Pripet (Pripyat), R., Belorussiyan SSR, **USSR**; trib. of R. Dnieper; 560 km long.

Pristina, c., cap. of Kossovo aut. region, S.W. Serbia, **Yugoslavia**; on Sitnic R.; admin. ctr.; many mosques; p. (1981) 210,040.

Prokopyevsk, t., S.W. Siberia, **RSFSR**; in Novosibirsk dist.; one of the main coalfields of Kuznetsk Basin; mng. machin., metallurgy; p. (est. 1985) 274,000.

Prome, c. **Burma**; pt. on R. Irrawaddy; connected by rail and road to Rangoon; tr. in rice, cotton, tobacco; one of oldest cs. in Burma, founded 8th cent.; p. (est. 1973) 148,000.

Proskurov. *See* Khmel'nitskiy.

Prostejov, t., N. Moravia, **ČSSR**; rly. junc.; agr. machin., textiles; historic bldgs.; p. (1984) 51,100.

Provence, region and former prov., S.E. **France**; along Mediterranean; now embraces deps. of Var, Bouches-du-Rhône, Vaucluse and parts of Alpes-de-Haute-Provence and Alpes-Maritimes; tourism; fastest growing p. of France; mkt. gardening; intensive investment along cst.

Providence, c., R.I. **USA**; at head of Narragansett Bay; univ.; jewellery, textiles, silverware, rubber gds., machin., oil, coal; p. (1984) 154,100 (c.), 1,095,000 (met. a.).

Provo, t., Utah, **USA**; at base of Wasatch mtns., nr. shore of Utah L.; univ.; flour, bricks, blast furnaces; p. (1984) 74,100 (t.), 240,600 (met. a.).

Prudhoe, Tynedale, Northumberland, **Eng.**; former coal mng. t.; chemicals, paper; p. (1981) 11,820.

Prudhoe Bay, N.E. Alaska, **USA**; ctr. of recent extensive oil finds; arctic conditions make extraction and transport of oil difficult and ecologically dangerous but despite opposition from environmentalist groups 1,262 km pipeline to ice-free pt. of Valdez.

Prussia, former kingdom (1701–1806); former st. (1806–1945), **Germany**; consisted of 13 provs., cap. Berlin; formally abolished 1947; E. Prussia partitioned between USSR and Poland.

Pruszkow, t., **Poland**; nr. Warsaw; elec. plant; engin.; p. (1983) 52,100.

Prut, R., flows between **Romania** and **USSR**; from the Carpathian mtns. to the Danube R.; 576 km long.

Przemysl, c., S.E. **Poland**; on San R. (trib. of Vistula) nr. bdy. between Poland and Ukrainian SSR; anc. fortress t.; sewing machin.; p. (1983) 64,100.

Pskov, c., **RSFSR**; on R. Velikaya, nr. entry to L. Peipus; rly. junc.; flax tr.; historic bldgs.; scene of abdication of Nicholas II, March 1917; p. (est. 1985) 194,000.

Pudsey, t., West Yorks., **Eng.**; between Leeds and Bradford; woollens; p. (1981) 38,977.

Puebla de Zaragoza, c., cap. of P. st., **Mexico**; one of oldest and most impt. cs. of rep.; fine cath., theatre, univ.; cotton mills, onyx quarries, glazed tiles; p. (est. 1986) 1,050,000.

Puebla, st., **Mexico**; on interior plateau at 2,400 m; fertile valleys for coffee and sugar; mng. impt.; dense p.; a. 33,991 km²; p. (1980) 3,279,960.

Pueblo, c., Col., **USA**; on R. Arkansas, in foothills of Rockies; iron and steel ctr.; coal and various metals nearby; p. (1984) 100,000 (t.), 124,900 (met. a.).

Puente-Genil, t., Córdoba, **Spain**; olive oil, quince pulp; p. (1981) 25,615.

Puerto Barrios, pt., **Guatemala**; rly. terminus; oil refining; p. (est. 1983) 39,000.

Puerto Cabello, spt., N. **Venezuela**; on Caribbean nr. Valencia; excellent harbour; linked by rail and highway to Carácas; asbestos, vegetable oils, soap, candles, meat-packing; p. (est. 1980) 94,000.

Puerto Cortés, spt., N.W. **Honduras**; on Caribbean; exp. bananas, hardwoods; p. (est. 1983) 40,230.

Puerto de Santa Maria, El, spt., S.W. **Spain**; on Bay of Cadiz; exp. mainly sherry; p. (1981) 45,933.

Puerto la Cruz, t., **Venezuela**; 16 km from Barcelona; oil refining; p. with Barcelona (est. 1980) 267,000.

Puerto Limón. *See* Limón.

Puerto Montt, spt., **Chile**; in sheep-farming dist.; S. terminus of rlys.; devastated by earthquake 1960; p. (est. 1982) 87,971.

Puerto Ordaz. *See* Santo Tomé de la Guayana.

Puerto Rico, I., terr. of USA, **W.I.**; since 1952 free commonwealth ass. with USA; democratic economic growth aided recently by falling birth-rate; mtnous., eroded soils, alt. modifies tropical climate; exp. mnfs., but agr. impt. internally; 80 per cent land under cultivation, sugar, tobacco, coffee; tourism; cap. San Juan; a. 8,866 km²; p. (est. 1985) 3,451,000.

Puerto Saurez, R. pt., **Bolivia**; on R. Paraguay; collecting ctr. for rubber, coffee, Brazil nuts.

Puerto Varas, t., **Chile**; tourist ctr. in Chilean "Switzerland"; p. (est. 1970) 33,000.

Puget Sound, Wash., **USA**; inlet of Pac. Oc.

Puket. *See* Phuket.

Pula, spt., Croatia, **Yugoslavia**; on Adriatic; industl. ctr. with shipyards, docks, and various inds.; ch. naval base of Hapsburg empire; tourism; Roman remains; p. (1981) 77,278.

Pulia. *See* Apulia.

Puna, cold, bleak, and barren plateau of Andes in **Peru** and **Bolivia**, 3,600–5,500 m.

Pune (Poona), c., Maharashtra, **India**; in W. Ghats; temperate pleasant climate; cultural, educational (univ.) and political ctr.; military base; agr. tr. ctr.; cotton gds., paper; p. (1981) 1,203,351 (c.), 1,686,109 (met. a.).

Punjab, region N.W. Indus plains, Indian sub- continent; extensive irrigation from the "five

rivers"—Jhelum, Chenab, Ravi, Bias, Sutlej; now divided politically between **India** and **Pakistan**; impt. cotton, wheat, and sugar dist.; coal deposits.

Punjab (East), former st., **India**; partitioned on linguistic basis 1966; Punjab-speaking Punjab st. (a. 50,375 km²; p. (1981) 16,788,915 inc. 55 per cent Sikh); and Hindi-speaking Haryana st. (a. 44,056 km²; p. (1981) 12,922,618; joint cap. Chandigarh until 1986.

Punjab (West), prov., **Pakistan**; old prov. revived 1970; p. (1981) 47,292,441.

Punta Arenas, c., cap. of Magallanes prov., S. **Chile**; most S. c. in world; mutton, wool; coal nearby; natural gas pipeline from Kimiri-Aike; p. (est. 1985) 102,300.

Puntarenas, spt., **Costa Rica**, on G. of Nicoya; fishing; fish-processing; resort; p. (est. 1983) 286,082.

Purbeck, I. of, sm. peninsula, Dorset cst., **Eng.**; anc. v. of Corfe Castle in ctr.; limestone ("Purbeck marble") quarries; site of Britain's lgst. onshore oilfield; once a royal deer forest; now forms l. gov. dist. inc. Wareham and Swanage; p. (est. 1988) 46,200.

Puri, dist., Orissa, **India**; cap. P. famous for its temple and festival of the god Vishnu and his monster car, Juggernaut; p. (1961) 1,865,439.

Purley; rail accident 1989 *See* Croydon.

Purus, R., **Peru** and **Brazil**; rises in Andes, flows to Amazon R. through underdeveloped a.; 3,360 km long.

Pusan, main pt. of **S. Korea**; on Korean Strait at head of Naktong R. basin; textiles; steel mill at Pohang nearby; Korea's first nuclear power sta.; p. (est. 1986) 3,514,800.

Pushkin, c., **RSFSR**; nr. Leningrad; summer palaces of Tsars; Pushkin museum; Pulkovo observatory nearby; p. (est. 1966) 66,000.

Puteaux, sub. Paris, **France**; woollens, dyes, engin., printing; p. (1982) 36,143.

Putney, sub. of London, **Eng.**; residtl.; Thames-side dist.

Putrid Sea. *See* Sivash.

Putumayo, R., trib. of R. Amazon; rises in Colombia, forming bdy. with Ecuador and Peru; here in wild-rubber region, Roger Casement exposed cruel exploitation of native labour; 1,600 km long.

Puy-de-Dôme, extinct volcano, Massif Central, **France**; hgst peak of Auvergne mtns., 1,466 m.

Puy-de-Dôme, dep., **France**; in Auvergne; cap. Clermont-Ferrand, industl. ctr. Thiers; a. 8,003 km², p. (1982) 954,700.

Puymorens Tunnel, Pyrenees, on bdy. between **France** and **Spain**; carries main rly. between Toulouse and Barcelona.

Pwllheli, t., Dwyfor, Gwynedd, N. **Wales**; sm. pt. on S. cst. Lleyn peninsula; seaside resort; inshore fishing, boat-bldg.; p. (1981) 3,989.

Pyatigorsk, c., N. Caucasus, **RSFSR**; ctr. of Caucasian mineral water springs; Lermontov shot here in duel 1841; p. (est. 1985) 118,000.

Pylos, pt., S.W. Peloponnesus, **Greece**; shipbldg. and repair yard, heavy metal wks. projected; sea-battles 1827 (Navarino), 425 B.C.

Pyongyang, c., cap. of **N. Korea**; stands high above Taedong R.; major industl. ctr. with coal and iron ore deposits nearby; univ.; many historic relics; p. (est. 1981) 1,280,000.

Pyrenees, range of mtns., **S.W. Europe**; dividing France from Iberian Peninsula; 432 km long; hgst peak Pic d'Anéto (Maladetta) 3,408 m.

Pyrénées-Atlantique, dep., S.W. **France**; mainly agr.; sheep and cattle raising; ch. ts. Pau (cap.), Bayonne, Biarritz; a. 7,713 km²; p. (1982) 551,000.

Pyrénées-Orientales, dep., S. **France**; on Mediterranean; wine, fruit, olives; cap. Perpignan; a. 4,141 km²; p. (1982) 339,700.

Pyrgos, t., Elis, S.W. **Greece**; has suffered from earthquakes; p. (1981) 21,958.

Q

Qaidam (Tsaidam), depression, Qinghai prov., **China**; a. of salt marsh and Ls.; rich deposits of oil; state farms for intensive animals husbandry.

Qacentina (Constantine), c., N.E. **Algeria**; 650 m. alt. on gorge of R. Rhumel; textile and engin. wks.; lge tractor and diesel engine complex; p. (est. 1983) 448,578.

Qandahar, c., former cap of **Afghanistan**; alt. 1,037 m.; fruit preserving and canning; airpt. built with U.S. aid; textiles; p. (est. 1982) 191,345.

Qarun (**Birker el Qarum**). *See* **Karun.**

Qatar, emirate, indep. st. (1971), **Arabia;** crown prince appointed (1979); peninsula on Persian G.; economy based on oil; inland production declining, but increasing offshore drilling; political stability less certain after withdrawal of Brit. military protection (1971); cap. Doha; a. 10,360 km²; p. (est. 1987) 371,863, of whom 75 per cent are foreign nationals.

Qattara Depression, N. **Egypt;** 134 m below sea level, salt marsh produced by seepage and evaporation of artesian water; marshes; few inhabitants; scheme to flood depression with sea water to generate electricity now under construction.

Qena or **Kene,** t., central **Egypt;** on R. Nile; water jars and bottles; agr. tr., cereals, dates; p. (est. 1970) 77,600.

Qingdao (**Tsingtao**), c., Shandong prov., **China;** spt. with excellent harbour at head of bay; tourism impt.; mnfs. locomotives, cement, textiles, machin., chemicals; special development zone to attract high technology inds.; oil jetty for Shengli oil field; p. (est. 1984) 1,229,500.

Qinghai (**Tsinghai**), prov., W. **China;** between Xinjiang and Xizang Zizhou (Tibet), inc. c. plateau; local coal and iron ore but exploitation hindered by isolation; two new iron and steel plants; new rly.; massive hydro-electricity plant; international airpt. link with Hong Kong; attempts to increase economic development; oil exploration; a. 721,004 km²; p. (est. 1985) 4,020,000.

Qinghai Hu (**Koko Nor**), salt L., Qinghai prov., **China;** at over 3,000 m. in Tibetan highlands; a. 5,957 km²; no outlet.

Qinhuangdao (**Chinwangtao**), c., spt., former treaty pt., Hebei, N. **China;** on Yellow Sea cst. 240 km N.E. of Tianjin; only good natural harbour on N. China cst.; exp. coal from Gailan mines; machin., textiles, chemical inds.; designated a development zone to attract foreign investment; p. (1984) 425,300.

Qiqihar (**Tsitsihar**), c., Heilongjiang prov., N. **China;** on Vladivostok portion of Trans-Siberian rly.; food processing and tr., chemicals; potential oilfield; p. (1984) 1,246,000.

Qisil-Qum, desert region, **Central Asia;** covering dried-up a. of extended Pleistocene Aral Sea.

Qizan, spt., **Saudi Arabia;** cereals, pearl-fishing, salt.

Qom (**Qum**), c., **Iran;** pilgrimage ctr., shrine of Fatima; rly. junction; p. (1986) 550,630.

Qornet es Sauda, mtn., Lebanon range, Levant, **Lebanon;** max. alt. 3,050 m.

Quantock Hills, Somerset, **Eng.;** S. of Bridgwater Bay; hgst. pt. 385 m; a Nat. Park.

Quauzhu. *See* **Zhengzhou.**

Queanbeyan, t., N.S.W., **Australia;** rapid growth as commuter ctr. as only 13 km from Canberra; pastoral, dairying dist.; mkt. and service ctr.; p. (1981) 19,056.

Quebec, c., cap. of Q. prov., **Canada;** spt. with fine harbour on St. Lawrence R. at mouth of St. Charles; cultural cap. of French Canada; inds. based on local raw materials of timber, agr. prods.; oil refining at St. Romauld; historic c. with many fine bldgs., univ., tourism; p. (1986) 164,580 (c.), 603,267 (met. a.).

Quebec, prov., **Canada;** mainly within Canadian Shield; continental climate; forests and timber inds.; agr. in S.; hydroelectric power and abundant minerals; p. mainly French-speaking; ch. cs., Quebec (cap.), Montreal; strong separatist movements causing decline in investment and movement of some inds. to USA; a. 1,540,687 km²; p. (1986) 6,540,000.

Quebec-Labrador Trough, Canada; geological formation extending through central Quebec prov. to Ungava Bay, Hudson Strait; immense reserves of iron-ore (locally "red-gold").

Quedlinburg, t., Halle, **E. Germany;** at foot of Harz mtns.; cas., cath.; aniline dyes, metals, engin., horticultural mkt. t.; p. (est. 1970) 30,829.

Queen Charlotte's Is., archipelago, N. of Vancouver I., off cst. B.C., **Canada;** halibut fishing, lumbering; p. (1981) 2,770.

Queen Charlotte Sound, strait, separating Vancouver I. from B.C. mainland, a continuation of Johnstone Strait.

Queen Elizabeth Is., Canada; I. gr. in Canadian Arctic; most N. land of N. America; a. 349,443 km²; p. (1981) 131.

Queen Maud Land, Norwegian sector of **Antarctica;** ice crystal mtns., 3,050 m high for 160 km along cst.

Queens, bor., N.Y. City, **USA;** residtl. dist.;

lgst. bor. of N.Y. c.; p. (1980) 1,891,325.

Queensbury and Shelf, t., West Yorks., **Eng.;** textiles; p. (1981) 11,658.

Queensferry, royal burgh, Edinburgh City, **Scot.;** at S. end of Forth road and rail bridges; p. (1981) 7,529.

Queensland, st., N.E. **Australia;** sub-tropical a. rising from cst. to Gt. Dividing Range and Western Plains (inc. Gt. Artesian Basin); Barrier Reef off cst.; p. concentrated on cst. where sugar cane and tropical fruits grown, popular all year tourist resorts and retirement ctrs. (no death duties); all year mkt. gardening replaced by extensive cattle and sheep ranching in W.; mng. boom since 1960; coal, copper, uranium, bauxite; oil at Moonie; since 1970 rapid increase in mfg.; cap. Brisbane; a. 1,727,200 km²; p. (1986) 2,624,595.

Queenstown. *See* **Cobh.**

Queenstown, t., Tasmania, **Australia;** copper mng. t.; prosperity depends on continuation of mng. at Mount Lyell; p. (1976) 4,520.

Queenstown, t., Cape Prov., **S. Africa;** in agr. region producing wool and wheat; p. (est. 1970) 40,000.

Quelimane, pt., **Moçambique;** at head of estuary; rly. terminus; exp. copra, sisal, tea; notorious in 18th and 19th cent. as slave mkt.; p. (1980) 60,151.

Quelpart. *See* **Cheju.**

Quemoy, gr. of Is. off Chinese mainland nr. Amoy, held by Nationalist forces; p. (est.) 50,000 (plus garrison of 40,000).

QueQue, t., **Zimbabwe;** major new steel works has attracted many ancillary inds.; p. (1982) 47,600.

Querétaro, t., cap. of Q. st., **Mexico;** state of pre-Aztec settlement at 1,881 m; cath., many colonial bldgs.; old cotton ind.; p. (1979) 185,812.

Querétaro, st., **Mexico;** in Central Plateau; arid with fertile valleys; variety of crops; mng. impt.; famous for opals; cap. Q.; a. 11,479 km²; p. (1980) 726,054.

Quetta, t., cap. of Baluchistan, **Pakistan;** at 5,000 ft., commands routes to Bolan Pass; ctr. of irrigated agr. a.; military ctr.; coal mng. nearby; damaged by severe earthquake (1935); p. (1981) 285,000.

Quezaltenango, t., S.W. **Guatemala;** second c. of rep.; at 2,333 m at foot of Santa Maria volcano; univ.; comm. ctr. for rich agr. region; textiles, handicrafts; p. (est. 1983) 66,000.

Quezon City, cap. **Philippines;** new sub. 16 km N.E. of Manila; cap. since 1948; univ.; p. (est. 1984) 1,326,035.

Quibdó, t., **Colombia;** in forested a. on R. Atrato; platinum, gold mng.; p. (1985) 85,085.

Quillon, t., Kerala, **India;** on Malabar cst., ctr. of coconut tr. and processing; p. (1981) 137,943 (t.), 167,598 (met. a.).

Quimes, t., Buenos Aires, **Argentina;** on Rio de la Plata estuary; English public school; resort; oil refining, textiles, chemicals, glass; p. (1980) 441,780.

Quimper, ch. t., Finistère, **France;** tourist ctr. for S. Brittany; Breton pottery; Gothic cath.; p. (1982) 60,162.

Quincy, t., Ill., **USA;** at bridging point of R. Mississippi; agr. machin., clothing, footwear, food inds.; p. (1980) 42,554.

Quincy, t., Mass., **USA;** in Mass. B., 13 km S.E. of Boston; shipbldg. ctr.; p. (1980) 84,743.

Quindio, pass, **Colombia;** provides impt. routeway through Cordillera Central; 11,099 ft.

Qui Nhon, t., S. **Vietnam;** on E. cst.; tr. in coconut prods.; fishing; p. (1973) 213,757.

Quintana Roo, st., S.E. **Mexico;** on Caribbean; low-lying swamp, underdeveloped; cap. Chetumal; a. 50,344 km²; p. (1980) 209,858.

Quito, c., cap. of **Ecuador;** in Andes at 2,852 m, 24 km S. of equator; anc. Inca c., cath., univ., slower growth than coastal ts.; impt. textile ctr.; p. (est. 1986) 1,093,278.

Quorndon or **Quorn,** sm. t., Leics., **Eng.;** on R. Soar, 5 km S. of Loughborough; ctr. of fox-hunting dist.

R

Raake, t., N. **Finland;** spt.; iron wks.

Raasay, I., E. of Skye, Skye and Lochalsh, **Scot.;** 21 km long, 5·6 km wide.

Rab I., at head of Adriatic, **Yugoslavia;** tourism; a. 192 km²; p. (1961) 8,369.

Rabat, c., cap. of **Morocco;** spt. at mouth of Bu

Regreg R. on Atl. cst.; cath., univ.; textiles, carpets, rugs; p. (1982) 893,402.

Rabaul, spt., New Britain, **Papua New Guinea**; ch. pt., exp. copra; damaged by volcanic eruption (1937) former cap. of New Guinea; p. (1980) 14,973.

Raciborz (**Ratibor**), t., Upper Silesia, **Poland** (since 1945); on R. Oder; textiles, metals, wood engin.; p. (1983) 55,600.

Racine, c., Wis., **USA**; sm. pt. on L. Mich., 16 km S. of Milwaukee; agr. machin., tractors, car parts; p. (1980) 85,725 (c.), 173,132 (met. a.).

Radcliffe, t., Gtr. Manchester, **Eng.**; N.W. of Manchester; paper, rubber, paint, engin.; p. (1981) 30,501.

Radebeul, t., Dresden, **E. Germany**; on R. Elbe; satellite of Dresden; p. (est. 1970) 39,626.

Radium Hill, v., S. **Australia**; ctr. for radium mng. 1920–30 and uranium later; mines now closed (since 1961).

Radnorshire, former co., Central **Wales**. *See* **Powys.** Now as Radnor l. gov. dist. inc. Knighton, Presteigne and Llandrindodd Wells; p. (est. 1988) 22,600.

Radom, t., **Poland**; in Radomska Plain; route ctr.; metal and chemical inds.; lge. tobacco factory; p. (est. 1985) 214,000.

Radomosko, t., **Poland**; on edge of Lodz Upland; metallurgical wks., food inds.; bentwood chairs for exp.; p. (1970) 31,200.

Radzionkow, t., Katowice, **Poland**; new t. (1951); p. (1970) 27,800.

Ragaz, Bad, spa, St. Gall can., **Switzerland**; at mouth of Tamina R.; hot springs from nearby v. of Pfäfers; p. (1960) 2,699.

Ragusa. *See* **Dubrovnik.**

Ragusa, t., Sicily, **Italy**; oil and asphalt production; p. (1981) 64,492.

Rahway, t., N.J., **USA**; on R. Rahway; residtl. for N.Y. business men; p. (1980) 26,723.

Raichur, t., Karnataka, **India**; comm. ctr.; agr. processing; p. (1981) 124,762.

Rainford, t., Merseyside, **Eng.**; nr. St. Helens; former coal-mng. a.; p. (1981) 8,941.

Rainier, mtn., Wash., **USA**; 4,432 m; forms Nat. Park.

Rainy, L., on border of Canada and Minn., **USA**; drained by Rainy R. to L. of the Woods.

Raipur, t., Madhya Pradesh, **India**; ctr. of fertile rice growing a.; p. (1981) 338,245.

Rajahmundry, t., Andhra Pradesh, **India**; on delta of Godivari R.; agr. tr.; p. (1981) 203,358 (t.), 268,370 (met. a.).

Rajasthan, st., **India**; dry a. inc. Thar desert; sparse p. where primitive irrigation; agr., millets, pulses, cotton; impt. gypsum deposits; cap. Jaipur; a. 342,274 km²; p. (1981) 34,261,862.

Rajkot, t., Gujarat, **India**; p. (1981) 445,070.

Rajshahi, t., Rajshahi dist., **Bangladesh**; on R. Ganges; univ.; silk inds.; p. (1981) 253,740.

Raki-Ura I. *See* **Stewart I.**

Raleigh, c., cap. of N.C., **USA**; educational ctr. univ.; printing, cotton tr. and processing; p. (1984) 169,300 (c.), 609,300 (met. a.).

Ralik, W. chain of Is., Marshall gr., **Pac. Oc.**; lgst. atoll Kwajalein; parallel with Ratak chain.

Ramat Gan, t., **Israel**; in plain of Sharon; univ.; lt. inds.; p. (1982) 118,300.

Rambouillet, t., Yvelines, **France**; nr. Versailles; anc. château; p. (1982) 22,487.

Rameswaram, t., S. **India**; on Rameswaram I., Palk Strait; contains Dravidian temple, Hindu holy place of pilgrimage; p. (1961) 6,801.

Ramla, t., **Israel**; S. of Lydda; former cap. of Palestine; ass. with crusaders; p. (est. 1970) 30,800.

Rampur, t., Uttar Pradesh, **India**; N.W. of Bareilly; agr. tr.; sugar refining; chemicals; cap. of former princely st. of R.; p. (1981) 204,610.

Ramree I., **Burma**; in Bay of Bengal, off Arakan cst.; 80 km long.

Ramsbottom, t., Lancs., **Eng.**; on R. Irwell, 6 km N. of Bury; engin., paper, textiles; p. (1981) 17,799.

Ramsey, mkt. t., Cambs., **Eng.**; on edge of Fens, 11 km N. of St. Ives; engin.; abbey ruins; p. (1981) 5,828.

Ramsey, t., spt., I. of Man, **Eng.**; on N.E. cst.; holiday resort; p. (1986) 5,778.

Ramsgate, t., Kent, **Eng.**; on S. cst. of I. of Thanet; seaside resort; p. (1981) 39,642.

Rancagua, t., Colchagua prov., **Chile**; ctr. of fertile valley in Andean foothills; tractors, agr. processing; p. (est. 1985) 155,200.

Rance, R., Brittany, **France**; world's first major tidal hydroelectric power sta. (opened 1966).

Ranchi, t., Bihar, **India**; hot season seat of govt. in Chota Nagpur plateau; univ.; heavy engin.; p. (1981) 489,626 (t.), 502,771 (met. a.).

Rand. *See* **Witwatersrand.**

Randers, pt., **Denmark**; on Randers Fjord, inlet of Kattegat; machin., foundries; exp. dairy prod.; mediaeval monastery; p. (est. 1987) 61,094.

Randfontein, t., Transvaal, **S. Africa**; gold-mng. ctr.; uranium plant; p. (est. 1970) 2,951.

Randstad, conurb., **Neth.**; Dutch "urban ring." inc. Rotterdam, The Hague, Leiden, Amsterdam and Utrecht, contained within radius of 16 km; a. of rapid industrialisation.

Rangitaiki, R., N.I., **N.Z.**; flows into Bay of Plenty; 192 km long.

Rangoon, c., cap. of **Burma**; on E. arm of Irrawaddy delta; 2 caths., many mosques, temples and pagodas; replaced Mandalay as cap.; ctr. of rice tr. and exp.; oil refining; teak collecting ctr.; p. (1983) 2,458,712.

Rangpur, t., **Bangladesh**; on R. Ghaghat; jute; p. (1981) 153,174.

Raniganj, t., W. Bengal, **India**; coalfield in Damodar basin; engin.; p. (1981) 48,702 (t.), 119,101 (met. a.).

Rannoch, Loch, Perth and Kinross, **Scot.**; 14 km long, 1·6 km wide; drained to R. Tay.

Rapallo, t., Liguria, N.W. **Italy**; on G. of Genoa, 35 km E. of Genoa; most celebrated resort on Italian Riviera di Levante; p. (1981) 28,318.

Rapanui. *See* **Easter I.**

Rapid City, t., S.D., **USA**; second t. of st.; comm. ctr. for agr. and mng. a.; p. (1980) 46,492.

Rarotonga, volcanic I., **Pac. Oc.**; lgst. of Cook Is.; fruit canning; ch. t. and pt. Avarua; p. (1981) 9,530.

Ra's al Khaymah. *See* **United Arab Emirates.**

Rasht (**Resht**), c., **Iran**; cap. of Gilan prov., in a. producing rice, cotton, silk; carpets; nearby Pahlevi serves as pt.; p. (1986) 293,881.

Ras Lanuf, oil terminal, on G. of Sidra, **Libya**; pipeline from Hofra oilfield.

Ras Tannura, spt., Nejd, **Saudi Arabia**; lge. oil refinery; oil exp.

Ratak, E., chain of Is., Marshall gr., **Pac. Oc.**; ch. I. Majuro; parallel with Ralik chain.

Rathenow, t., Potsdam, **E. Germany**; on R. Havel; optical and precision instruments; p. (est. 1970) 29,823.

Rathlin, I., off Fair Head, Moyle, **N. Ireland**; 8 km by 1·6 km.

Ratibor. *See* **Racibórz.**

Ratingen, t., N. Rhine–Westphalia, **W. Germany**; N.E. of Düsseldorf; textiles, machin., glass; famous for Blue L.; p. (est. 1986) 89,200.

Ratisbon. *See* **Regensburg.**

Ratlam, t., Madhya Pradesh, **India**; rly. junc. in Malwa Plateau; p. (1981) 142,319.

Ratnapura, t., **Sri Lanka**; former ctr. of gem mng.; p. (1981) 37,354.

Rauma, spt., S.W. **Finland**; on Baltic Sea; p. (1986) 30,909.

Raunds, t., East Northants., **Eng.**; 8 km N.E. of Wellingborough; p. (1981) 7,401.

Raurkela, t., Orissa, **India**; steel, tinplate, iron, fertilisers; p. (1981) 322,610.

Ravenglass, t., Cumbria, **Eng.**; nr. mouth of R. Esk; old pt.; Roman remains.

Ravenna, c., cap. of Ravenna prov., Emilia-Romagna, **Italy**; on reclaimed plain nr. Po delta; connected to Adriatic by canal; ctr. of fertile agr. dist., agr. processing; new inds. aided by discovery of methane N. of c.; oil refineries, chemicals, fertilisers; cath., mausoleum, famous mosaics; p. (1984) 137,453.

Ravenna, prov., Emilia-Romagna, **Italy**; N. Italian plain rising to Apennines; fertile agr. a.; cap. R.; a. 1,852 km²; p. (1981) 358,654.

Ravensburg, t., Baden-Württemberg, **W. Germany**; nr. Konstanz; engin., textiles; p. (est. 1986) 43,200.

Ravenscraig, t., nr. Motherwell, Strathclyde Reg., **Scot.**; hot strip steelmill; cold reduction mill at Gartcosh 13 km away; planned closure of steel wks.

Ravi, R., Punjab, **India**; trib. of Chenab; used for irrigation; 720 km long.

Rawalpindi, c., **Pakistan**; seat of govt. until completion of Islamabad; admin., comm. and rly. ctr.; foundries, oil refining, industl. gases; p. (1981) 928,000.

Rawmarsh, t., South Yorks., **Eng.**; 3 km N.E. of Rotherham; engin.; p. (1981) 18,985.

Rawtenstall, t., Rossendale, Lancs., Eng.; on R. Irwell in ctr. of Rossendale Fells; felts; footwear, textiles; p. (1981) 22,231.

Rayleigh, t., Rochford, Essex, Eng.; 8 km N.W. of Southend; lt. inds.; dormitory for London; p. (1981) 29,146.

Ré, Ile de, I., W. cst. of Charente-Maritime dep. France; off La Rochelle; citadel (built 1681) at St. Martin de Ré is now a prison.

Reading, t., l. gov. dist., Berks., Eng.; at confluence of Rs. Thames and Kennet; univ.; biscuits, engin., electronics, mkt. gardening, tinbox mftg. printing; p. (est. 1988) 132,400.

Reading, c., Penns., USA; on Schuylkill R.; steelwks. using local coal, optical gds.; p. (1984) 78,400 (c.), 317,200 (met. a.).

Recife, spt., cap. of Pernambuco st., N.E. Brazil; fine natural harbour; univ.; processing and exp. of sugar from surrounding a.; "Venice of Brazil" because of I. and peninsula site; lge. petrochemical wks. nearby; recent industl. expansion and diversification; engin., chem., electrical and telecommunications equipment; integrated steel wks.; p. (est. 1985) 1,289,600.

Recklinghausen, t., N. Rhine-Westphalia, W. Germany; nr. Dortmund; collieries, iron, machin., textiles, chemicals; p. (est. 1986) 117,600.

Recôncavo, dist., Bahia st., N.E. Brazil; surrounds bay at mouth of R. Paraguassu; intensive cultivation of sugar-cane, cotton, tobacco, rice, by Negro farmers; oil production; ch. ts. São Salvador, Cachoeira.

Redbridge, outer bor., E. London, Eng.; incorporates Ilford, Wanstead and Woodford, Chigwell (Hainault Estate), Dagenham (N. Chadwell Heath ward); mainly residtl.; p. (est. 1988) 230,800.

Redcar, t., Cleveland, Eng.; lge. iron and steel wks.; p. (1981) 84,931.

Redcliff, t., Zimbabwe; iron-mng.; iron and steel wks.; fertilisers.

Red Deer, t., Alberta, Canada; on Red Deer R.; mkt. t. in farming a.; lge. natural gas processing plant nearby; p. (1986) 54,425.

Redditch, t., l. gov. dist., Hereford and Worcs., Eng.; 19 km S. of Birmingham; needles, fishing tackle, cycles, springs, aluminium alloys; new t. (1964); p. (est. 1988) 77,500 (dist.).

Redlands, t., Cal., USA; univ.; citrus fruit packing and canning; p. (1980) 43,619.

Redonda, I., Leeward gr., Antigua and Barbuda; between Montserrat and Nevis; uninhabited.

Redondo Beach, t., Cal., USA; residtl.; tourism; p. (1980) 57,102.

Red R. (China and Vietnam). See Song-koi.

Red R., USA; southernmost of lge. tribs. of Mississippi R.; derives name and colour from red clay in upper course; dammed for flood control and hydroelec. power; 2,560 km long.

Red R. of the North, USA; rises in Minn., flows N. into Canada to empty into L. Winnipeg; 1,040 km long.

Redruth, t., Cornwall, Eng.; once major ctr. of tin mng.; most mines now closed, although recent revival of some; p. (1981) 46,482 (inc. Camborne).

Red Sea, arm of sea separating Arabia from Africa; connects with Indian Oc. by Straits of Bab-el-Mandeb; extension of Great African Rift Valley which further N. encloses the Dead Sea; 2,240 km long.

Redwood City, t., W. Cal., USA; timber tr.; electronics; p. (1980) 54,951.

Ree, Lough, L., R.o.I.; between Roscommon, Longford and Westmeath, an extension of R. Shannon; 27 km long.

Regensburg (Ratisbon), c., R. pt., Bavaria, W. Germany; N.E. of Munich on R. Danube; timber processing, chemicals; p. (est. 1986) 123,800.

Reggio di Calabria, spt., Calabria, Italy; on Strait of Messina; cath.; fishing, ferry to Sicily; mkt. for citrus fruit; tourism; agr. processing; rebuilt after 1908 earthquake; p. (1984) 175,646.

Reggio nell' Emilia, c., cap. of prov. of same name, in Emilia-Romagna, N. Italy; at foot of Apennines; Renaissance church of the Madonna della Ghiara; locomotives, aircraft, agr. engin.; birthplace of Ariosto; p. (1984) 131,075.

Regina, t., cap. of Saskatchewan, Canada; ctr. of wheat growing dist. of Prairies; connected by pipeline to Alberta oilfields; oil refining, chemicals, agr. machin.; p. (1986) 175,064(c.), 186,521 (met. a.).

Rehovoth, Israel; t., in citrus fruit dist.; Weizmann Institute of Science; p. (est. 1970) 36,600.

Reichenbach, t., Karl-Marx-Stadt, E. Germany; at foot of Erzgebirge; p. (est. 1970) 28,818.

Reichenberg. See Liberec.

Reigate, t., Surrey, Eng.; at foot of N. Downs, 8 km E. of Dorking; dormitory for London; with Banstead forms l. gov. dist.; p. (est. 1988) 113,600 (dist.).

Reims, c., Marne dep., N.E. France; on R. Vesle; famous Gothic cath.; univ.; champagne ctr., textiles; p. (1982) 181,985.

Reindeer L., Saskatchewan, Manitoba, Canada; Indian settlement on shore; a. 6,475 km².

Rejang R., Sarawak; navigable for 72 km by ocean boats; main R. of Sarawak.

Rembang, pt., N. cst. Java, Indonesia; in dry limestone R. plateau; proposed nuclear power plant; p. (est. 1960) 75,000.

Remscheid, t., N. Rhine-Westphalia, W. Germany; nr. Düsseldorf; iron and steel ctr.; machin. tools; p. (est. 1986) 121,000.

Renaix. See Ronse.

Rendsburg, t., Schleswig-Holstein, W. Germany; on Kiel Canal; shipbldg., elec. gds.; p. (est. 1986) 30,600.

Renfrew, royal burgh, Renfrew, Scot.; nr. R. Clyde, 8 km W. of Glasgow; p. (1981) 21,396.

Renfrewshire, former co., central Scot.; now reduced in size and forms l. gov. dist. within Strathclyde Reg.; a. of l. gov. dist. 308 km²; p. (est. 1986) 203,220.

Renkum, t., Gelderland. Neth.; 13 km W. of Arnhem; paper mnfs.; p. (est. 1987) 34,000.

Rennes, c., cap. of Ille-et-Vilaine dep., France; only major inland t. of Brittany, in fertile agr. basin; univ., comm. ctr.; cars, engin.; p. (1982) 200,390.

Reno, lgst. t. of Nevada, USA; univ.; st. agr. college; famous for easy divorce procedure and gambling; p. (1984) 105,600 (t.), 211,500 (met. a.).

Repton, t., South Derbyshire, Eng.; famous public school in priory; former Saxon cap. of Mercia.

Resende, t., Rio de Janeiro st., Brazil; chemicals, rly. junc.; univ.; p. (est. 1985) 102,900.

Resht. See Rasht.

Resina, t., S. Italy; on Bay of Naples at W. foot of Vesuvius; nr. site of anc. Herculaneum; resort; p. (est. 1970) 52,451.

Resistencia, t., cap. of Chaco terr., Argentina; served by R. pt. of Barranqueras on R. Paraná; tr. in cattle, timber, cotton; agr. processing; p. (1980) 174,000 (c.), 220,000 (met. a.).

Resita, t., Banat region, Romania; developing steel inds. based on local iron ore; heavy engin.; p. (est. 1984) 102,564.

Restormel, l. gov. dist., Cornwall, Eng.; inc. N. and S. cst. and ts. of Newquay and St. Austell; p. (est. 1988) 85,700.

Retalhuleu, t., cap. of R. dep., Guatemala; comm. ctr. for coffee, sugar; p. (est. 1970) 42,000.

Réunion (Ile de Bourbon), I., overseas terr. of France; in Indian Oc., between Mauritius and Madagascar; volcanic I.; impt. sugar producer; cap. St. Denis; a. 2,512 km²; p. (est. 1987) 564,600.

Reus, t., Tarragona, prov., Spain; textiles; agr. tr.; p. (1981) 75,987.

Reuss, R., Switzerland; flows N. from the St. Gotthard Pass through L. Lucerne, joining Aare R. nr. Brugg; 157 km long.

Reutlingen, t., Baden-Württemberg, W. Germany; S. of Stuttgart; textiles, metals, machin., leather; p. (est. 1986) 97,900.

Reval. See Tallin.

Revelstoke, t., B.C., Canada; rly. junc.; in timber producing a.; ctr. for R. Nat. Park; p. (1981) 5,544.

Revillagigedo Islands, archipelago, Pac. Oc., off S.W. Mexico; ch. Is., Socorro, San Benedicto (volcano suddenly arose on I. 1952).

Reykjavik, c., cap. of Iceland; on S.W. cst.; impt. fish. pt.; fish exp. and processing; water piped from geysers; airport; univ.; 2 caths.; p. (est. 1984) 130,175.

Rezayeh, (Orūmiyeh) c., Iran; cap. of W. Azerbaijan prov.; comm. ctr. of agr. region; p. (1986) 304,823.

Rheidol, R., Dyfed, Wales; flows from Plynlimmon in deeply incised valley (Devil's Bridge) to Aberystwyth; hydroelec. power; 38 km long.

Rheine, t., N. Rhine-Westphalia, W. Germany; on R. Ems; textiles, machin.; p. (1983) 71,200.

Rheingau, dist., W. Germany; famous wine a. on right bank of Rhine from Biebrich to Assmanshausen.

Rheinhausen, t., Rhine-Westphalia, W. Germany;

on left bank of Rhine opposite Duisburg; coal mng., iron, textiles.

Rheydt, t., N. Rhine-Westphalia, **W. Germany**; twin c. of adjacent Mönchengladbach; textiles, machin.

Rhin (Bas). *See* Bas Rhin.

Rhine, R., rises in Switzerland, can. Grisons, passes through L. Constance, skirts Baden, traverses Hesse, Rhineland, and the Neth., flowing to N. Sea by two arms, Oude Rijn and the Waal (the latter discharging finally by the Maas); famous for its beauty, especially between Bonn and Bingen; ch. falls at Schaffhausen; once a natural barrier between E. and W. Europe spanned by 30 rly. bridges; linked to Rhône by 1985 and Rhine-Main-Danube canal allows navigation from N. Sea to Black Sea for 3,500 km. (Trans European waterway); very polluted; 1,280 km long.

Rhine-Hern, canal, **W. Germany**; impt. Ruhr waterway, part of Mitelland Canal; 38 km long.

Rhineland Palatinate (Rheinland-Pfalz), *Land*, **W. Germany**; borders France, Luxembourg and Belgium; drained by Rhine and Moselle, inc. Hunsrück and Eifel mtns.; arable agr. in Rhine valley; vineyards; cap. Mainz; a. 19,852 km; p. (est. 1986) 3,611,400.

Rhode Island, st., New England, **USA**; 'Little Rhody'; admitted to Union 1790; st. flower violet, st. bird R.I. Red; washed by Atl. Oc.; surrounded by Mass. and Conn.; divided by Narragansett Bay, with many Is. lgst. being that from which the st. takes its name; smallest and most densely populated st.; famous for poultry; major ind. textiles; cap. Providence; a. 3,144 km²; p. (1985) 968,000.

Rhodes (Rhodos), I., Dodecanese Is.; off S.W. cst., Anatolia, belonging to **Greece**; cap. R.; p. (1981) 87,831.

Rhodes, cap. of I. of Rhodes, **Greece**; on N.E. cst.; picturesque; p. (1981) 41,425.

Rhodesia. *See* Zimbabwe.

Rhodope Mtns. *See* Rodopi Mtns.

Rhondda, t., l. gov. dist., Mid Glamorgan, **Wales**; in narrow R. valley; coal-mng. ctr.; lt. inds. introduced since 1930s depression; picturesque a. in upper R. valley; p. (est. 1988) 76,600.

Rhône, dep., S.E. **France**; drained by R. Rhône and its trib. R. Saône, which unite at Lyons; agr. grain, potatoes, wine; vine-growing, many mnfs., silks, textiles; cap. Lyons; a. 2,859 km²; p. (1982) 1,440,900.

Rhône, R., **Switzerland** and **France**; rises in Rhône glacier of St. Gotthard mtn. gr., and flows through L. of Geneva and E. France to G. of Lyons in Mediterranean; power stas. at Sion and Geneva; canals, dams, locks and power stas. form part of Fr. Rhône Valley project (1937–72); linked to Rhine by 1985; 811 km long.

Rhône-Saône Corridor, routeway, **France**; impt. transport artery using Rhône, Saône R. valleys as a means for linking Paris, Lorraine and Rhine rift valley with Mediterranean cst.; rlys., roads, with major pt. of Marseilles serving the S. terminus.

Rhuddlan, l. gov. dist., Clwyd, **Wales**; cstl. a. of Rhyl, Prestatyn and St. Asaph; p. (est. 1988) 56,100.

Rhyl, t., Rhuddlan, Clwyd, N. **Wales**; at entrance Vale of Clwyd; resort developed from sm. fishing v.; serves Lancs. conurbs.; p. (1981) 22,714.

Rhymney, t., Mid Glamorgan, **Wales**; on R. Rhymney, E. of Merthyr Tydfil; former colly. and iron founding ctr.; engin.; p. (1981) 7,360.

Rhymney Valley, l. gov. dist., Mid Glamorgan, **Wales**; based on Rhymney and inc. Caerphilly, Bedwas and Gelligaer; p. (est. 1988) 104,500.

Ribble, R., North Yorks., Lancs., **Eng.**; rises in Pennines, flows W. to Irish Sea nr. pt. of Preston; 120 km long.

Ribble Valley, l. gov. dist., N. Lancs., **Eng.**; inc. Forest of Bowland and ts. of Clitheroe and Longridge; p. (est. 1988) 52,800.

Ribe, mkt. t., Jutland, S. **Denmark**; admin. ctr. of R. prov.; impt. mediaeval c.; Romanesque cath.; many fine bldgs.; p. (est. 1970) 8,224.

Ribeirão Prêto, t., São Paulo st., **Brazil**; mkt. in rich agr. a., coffee, cotton, sugar; p. (est. 1985) 384,600.

Richard's Bay, Natal, **S. Africa**; new pt. to supplement congested Durban; on natural harbour; silting problem but designed for bulk carriers; plans to attract ass. industl. development.

Richborough, pt., Kent, **Eng.**; at mouth of R.

Stour; Caesar's ch. pt., Roman remains; pt. has been privately redeveloped; chemicals.

Richmond, t., North Yorks., **Eng.**; at E. foot of Pennines on R. Swale; mkt. t., agr. tr.; 14th cent. grammar school; Norman cas.; now as Richmondshire forms l. gov. dist. with surrounding a. of Aysgarth and Leyburn; p. (est. 1988) 51,600 (dist.).

Richmond, c., Cal., **USA**; deepwater pt.; oil refining; car assembly, chemicals, electronics; p. (1980) 74,676.

Richmond, c., cap. of Va., **USA**; on falls on R. James; pt. at head of navigation; financial, and tr. ctr.; tobacco inds. and mkt.; chemicals, iron and steel; p. (1984) 219,100 (c.), 796,100 (met. a.).

Richmond-upon-Thames, outer bor., Greater London, **Eng.**; inc. Barnes, Richmond and Twickenham; industl. and residtl.; beautiful park and riverside scenery; p. (est. 1988) 160,800. *See also* Kew.

Rickmansworth, t., Three Rivers, Herts., **Eng.**; residtl. sub of London; p. (1981) 29,408.

Rideau Canal, Ont., **Canada**; from Ottawa R. at Ottawa to Kingston on L. Ontario; 211 km long.

Riesa, t., Dresden, **E. Germany**; R. pt. on Elbe R. nr. Meissen; p. (1981) 51,857.

Riesengebirge, mtn. range, between Silesia **(Poland)** and Bohemia **(CSSR)**; highest peak Schneekoppe (Czech Snežka, Polish Sniezka), 1,604 m.

Rieti, Latium, **Italy**; an anc. Sabine c. with mediaeval townscape, in fertile Apennine basin; route ctr. and cap. of R. prov.; chemicals, sugar refinery, textiles; p. (1981) 43,079.

Riff or **Rif**, mtns., **Morocco**, N.W. Africa; extend along N. African cst. for 320 km from Straits of Gibraltar; inaccessible and economically unattractive, terr. of semi-nomadic tribes; rise to over 2,100 m in many places.

Riga, cap. of Latvian SSR, **USSR**; Baltic pt.; exp. wheat, flax, hemp, dairy produce; industl. ctr., diesel rly. engin., furniture; univ.; local bathing beaches; p. (1986) 890,000.

Rigi, mtn., nr. L. Lucerne, **Switzerland**; viewpoint reached by rack and pinion rly.; 1,801 m.

Rijeka-Susak, c., Croatia, **Yugoslavia**; formerly Fiume, ceded to Yugoslavia by Italy after second world war; rival pt. to Trieste on Adriatic Sea; oil refining, shipbldg., tobacco, chemicals; hydroelectric power; p. (1981) 193,044.

Rimac, R., Lima dep., **Peru**; rises in W. cordillera of Andes and flows W. to Pac. Oc.; provides water for irrigation and for c. of Lima; 120 km long.

Rimini, c., Emilia-Romagna, **Italy**; on Adriatic cst. at junc. of Via Emilia and Via Flaminia; mkt. for fertile agr. a.; sm. inds.; bathing resort; p. (1984) 129,506.

Ringerike, t., Buskerud, **Norway**; new t., 40 km N.W. of Oslo and inc. former t. of Hönefoss; p. (est. 1987) 27,000.

Riobamba, c., Chimborazo, **Ecuador**; on R. St. Juan; woollens, cotton gds., cement, ceramics; Inca palace ruins; p. (1982) 149,757.

Rio Branco, R., flows c. 560 km from Guiana Highlands through Brazil to join Rio Negro.

Rio Branco, t., cap. of Acre st., **Brazil**; p. (est. 1985) 145,900.

Rio Cuarto, t., Cordoba prov., **Argentina**; agr. ctr.; p. (1980) 110,000.

Rio de Janeiro, c., spt., S.E. **Brazil**; cap. of Guanabara st., on G. Bay, Alt. Oc.; former fed. cap.; beautiful natural harbour, many fine bldgs., Sugar Loaf mtn., Copacabana beach; flourishing tr. and inds.; mnfs. inc. textiles, foodstuffs, pharmaceutics, china, sheet glass; oil refining; p. (est. 1985) 5,615,100.

Rio de Janeiro, st., S.E. **Brazil**; on Atl. Oc.; consolidated with Guanabara (1975); consists of cst. plain, central Sero do Mar escarpment, fertile Paraíba R. basin in W.; coffee, sugar, fruit; ctr. of heavy ind.; cement, textiles, sugar refineries at Campos, steel wks. at Volta Redonda; offshore oil finds in Campos basin; cap. Niterói; a. 42,735 km²; p. (est. 1985) 12,695,400.

Rio Grande, headstream of R. Paraná., **Brazil**; Furnas dam, Estreito dam for hydroelec. power; 1,040 km long.

Rio Grande, R., flows from st. of Col. through N.M. to G. of Mexico; forms bdy. between Texas, **USA** and **Mexico**; Elephant Butte,

Caballo, and Falcon multi-purpose dams; known also as Rio Grande do Norte and Rio Bravo; c. 3,016 km long.

Rio Grande do Norte, st., N.E. **Brazil;** cst. plain rising to S. plateau; climate semi-arid; cotton, sugar, salt, scheelite; cap. Natal; a. 53,038 km²; p. (est. 1985) 2,112,000.

Rio Grande do Sul, st., S. **Brazil;** grassy plains, rolling plateaux; cool climate; stock-raising, meat-processing, wheat, wine, wool; lge. coal deposits at São Jeronimo; cap. Pôrto Alegre; a. 267,684 km²; p. (est. 1985) 8,471,900.

Rioja, region and prov., N. **Spain;** upper Ebro valley; famous for wines and orange groves; ch. ctr. Logroño; p. (1987) 260,964.

Riom, t., Puy-de-Dôme dep., **France;** former cap. of Auvergne; old bldgs. built of lava; p. (1982) 18,901.

Rio Muni, terr., **Equatorial Guinea;** former Spanish terr., on cst. between Cameroon and Gabon, inc. offshore Is. of Corisco, Elobey Grande, Elobey Chico; with Biako forms Equatorial Guinea; equatorial forest; exp. tree prods. of cacao, coffee, hardwood; ch. t. Bata; a. 26,003 km²; p. (1968) 183,000.

Rion, R., Georgian SSR, **USSR;** flows from Caucasus to Black Sea; lower half navigable; hydroelec. sta. at Kutaisi. (In Greek mythology the R. Phasis of the Argonauts.)

Rio Negro, prov., **Argentina;** in N. Patagonia; irrigated agr. in R. valley, fruits, grain crops; elsewhere stock-raising; cap. Viedma; a. 201,010 km²; p. (1980) 383,896.

Rio Negro, dep., **Uruguay;** livestock fattening from N. Uruguay; grain crops; ch. t. and cap. Fray Bentos; a. 8,466 km²; p. (1985) 48,241.

Rio Tinto, t., **Spain;** at W. end of Sierra Morena 64 km N.E. of Huelva; major world ctr. of copper production.

Riouw-Lingga Archipelago, I. gr., **Indonesia;** S. of Malaya; Bintan lgst. I. where bauxite mng.; pepper and rubber cultivation; a. 5,905 km²; p. (1961) 278,966.

Ripley, mkt. t., Amber Valley, Derbys., **Eng.;** 11 km N.E. of Derby; coal, iron, heavy engin., bricks, agr. implements; p. (1981) 18,691.

Ripon, c., North Yorks., **Eng.;** on R. Ure; cath.; old mkt. square; old custom of wakeman; tourism; p. (1981) 11,952.

Risca, t., Gwent, **Wales;** on R. Ebbw; former coal-mng. dist.; limestone quarrying; bricks, plastics; p. (1981) 14,860.

Risdon, t., Tasmania, **Australia;** first white settlement in Tasmania, opposite Hobart; electrometallurgy.

Rishton, t., Hyndburn, Lancs., **Eng.;** at N. foot of Rossendale Fells, 6 km N.E. of Blackburn; p. (1981) 6,212.

Rive-de-Gier, t., Loire dep., **France;** on R. Gier, nr. Lyons; coal mng., iron and steel, glass; p. (1982) 15,850.

Rivera, dep., **Uruguay;** on Brazilian border; noted for cattle and sheep ranches; cap. R.; a. 9,824 km²; p. (1985) 88,800.

Rivera, t., cap. of R. dep., **Uruguay;** on Brazilian frontier opposite Santa Ana; agr. mkt.; p. (1985) 56,335.

Riverina, pastoral cty., N.S.W., **Australia;** between Lachlan-Murrumbidgee and Murray Rs.; merino sheep in W., good wheat yields in E.; gtr. crop variety with irrigation; a. 68,894 km²;.

River Rouge, t., Mich., **USA;** ctr. of Ford car mnf.; many heavy inds.; rapidly growing t. p. (1980) 12,912.

Riverside, t., Cal., **USA;** ctr. for citrus fruit packing and tr.; resort; p. (1984) 182,200; inc. in met. a. of Los Angeles.

Riviera, the belt of cst. between the Alps and the Mediterranean from Spezia to Hyères, **France** and **Italy;** picturesque scenery, sheltered, mild climate; fashionable health resorts.

Riyadh, t., royal cap. of **Saudi Arabia;** 368 km inland from Persian G.; palace; univ.; route and tr. ctr., linked by rail with pt. of Zahran; p. (1974) 666,840.

Rizaiyeh (Urmia), c., cap. of Azerbaijan prov., **Iran;** nr. L. Urmia; comm. ctr.; birthplace of Zoroaster; p. (1983) 262,588.

Rizal, prov., central Luzon, **Philippines;** rapidly growing prov. in fertile Central Plain; new inds. developing; cap. Pasig; a. 2,049 km²; p. (1970) 2,781,081.

Rize, t., **Turkey;** nr. Trabzon, on Black Sea; ctr. of Turkish tea inds.; p. (1985) 50,221.

Road Town, spt., Tortola; cap. of the Brit. **Virgin Is.;** tr. in fish, poultry; p. (est. 1983) 3,000.

Roanne, t., Loire dep., **France;** on R. Loire; château ruins; textiles; p. (1982) 81,786 (met. a.).

Roanoke, R., Va., and N.C., **USA;** flows into Albemarle Sound; hydroelec. power; 656 km long.

Roanoke, c., S.W. Va., **USA;** between Blue Ridge and Allegheny mtns.; rly. junc.; engin. p. (1984) 100,700 (c.), 222,700 (met. a.).

Roanoke I., off cst. N.C., **USA;** attempted settlement of colony by Raleigh.

Roaring Creek, Belize, Central America; site of new cap. 80 km inland, at junc. of W. highway with Hummingbird highway.

Robben I., at entrance of Table Bay, Cape Prov., **S. Africa;** penal settlement and former leper colony.

Robin Hood's Bay, v., North Yorks., **Eng.;** picturesque site in inlet; tourism, fishing.

Robson, Mt., Canada; on R.C. and Alberta border; alt. 3,956 m; in Nat. Park.

Rocha, dep., **Uruguay;** borders Atl. Oc.; a. of cattle and sheep rearing; cap. R.; a. 11,850 km²; p. (1985) 66,440.

Rochdale, t., met. dist., Gtr. Manchester, **Eng.;** at S. foot of Rossendale Fells, on R. Roch; textiles, engin., asbestos; co-operative movement started here 1844; p. (est. 1988) 206,800.

Rochefort, t., Charente-Maritime dep., **France;** fishing pt.; former impt. naval base; p. (1982) 27,716.

Rochelle, La, t., cap. of Charente-Maritime dep. **France;** on Bay of Biscay; fishing pt.; shipbldg.; pt. tr. declining; p. (1982) 78,231.

Rochester upon Medway, t., l. gov. dist., Kent, **Eng.;** on R. Medway, adjoining Chatham; cath., cas.; many associations with Dickens; aeronautical, elec. and mechanical engin., paint, varnish, cement; p. (est. 1988) 146,600 (dist.).

Rochester, t., Minn., **USA;** famous for Mayo clinic, and Mayo medical research ctr.; p. (1980) 57,890.

Rochester, c., N.Y., **USA;** on Genesee R.; univ.; cameras, films, optical instruments, thermometers, electronic equipment; hydroelectric power; p. (1984) 242,600 (c.), 989,000 (met. a.).

Roche-sur-Yon, La, t., cap of Vendée dep., **France;** on R. Yon; built by Napoleon I; p. (1982) 48,156.

Rochford, l. gov. dist., Essex, **Eng.;** cstl. a. inc. Rochford and Rayleigh; p. (est. 1988) 74,400.

Rock, R., Wis., Ill., **USA;** formerly home of native Indians; focus of white settlement since 1830; 456 km long.

Rockall, sm. I., **Atl. Oc.;** lies 320 km W. of Outer Hebrides; forms hgst. part of submarine bank which forms gd. fishing-ground; uninhabited; annexed by Britain 1955; formally incorporated into Inverness-shire (1972) to ensure control of suspected oil and natural gas deposits; claimed also by Ireland and Iceland; rock samples aged 1,000 million years place it with some Canadian rocks.

Rockall Deep, submarine trench, N. **Atl. Oc.;** between N.W. Ireland and Rockall I.; suspected oil and natural gas reserves.

Rockford, c., Ill., **USA;** serves agr. dist.; agr. machin., machin. tools; p. (1984) 136,500 (c.), 278,800 (met. a.).

Rockhampton, t., pt., Queensland, **Australia;** on Tropic of Capricorn; outlet for vast pastoral and mng. a.; comm. cap. of central Queensland; meat-preserving; p. (est. 1984) 54,630.

Rockingham, t., W. **Australia;** satellite of Perth; major pt. planned to serve Kwinana; p. (1981) 24,932.

Rock Island, c., Ill., **USA;** on R. Mississippi; former site of US arsenal; agr. machin., timber and agr. processing; p. (1980) 46,928.

Rocky Mtns., vast mtn. chain, N. **America;** extend from Alaska, through Canada, USA to Mexico; made up of several parallel ranges separated by intermontane basins and plateaux; barrier to spread of settlers to W. cst. in 19th cent.; climatic barrier; extensive snow and glacier fields in N.; dry desert landscapes in S.; many Nat. Parks; sparse p.; hydroelectric power; hgst. peak Mt. Logan (6,054 m); length 5,120 km.

Rodez, t., cap. of Aveyron dep., **France;** on R. Aveyron; cath.; woollens; p. (1982) 26,346.

Rodopi (Rhodope) Mtns., range S. **Bulgaria;** rise to 3,100 m.

Rodosto. *See* **Tekirdag.**

Rodriguez, I., Brit. dependency of **Mauritius,** Indian Oc.; 560 km N.E. of Mauritius; mainly agr. and fishing; cap. Port Mathurin; a. 109 km²; p. (1983) 33,082.

Roermond, t., Limburg prov., **Neth.**; on R. Maas; minster; textiles; p. (est. 1987) 38,000.

Roeselare, (**Roulers**) t., W. Flanders, **Belgium**; on R. Lys, nr. Kortrijk, textile ctr.; p. (1981) 51,984.

Rogerstone, t., Gwent, **Wales**; on R. Ebbw; lge. aluminium wks.

Rohtak, t., Haryana, **India**; N.W. of Delhi; p. (1971) 124,755.

Roissy-en-France; 26 km N.E. of Paris, **France;** site of Charles de Gaulle airport; p. (1982) 1,411.

Roman, t., **Romania**; on R. Moldava; cath.; agr. processing; p. (1983) 67,962.

Romania (Rumania), Socialist Rep. of, S.E. Europe; bounded by USSR, Hungary, Yugoslavia, Bulgaria, and Black Sea; Carpathian mtns., Transylvanian Alps, wide Walachian plain, Moldavian plateau; drained by Danube and its tribs.; cold winters and hot summers; since second world war transformation of economy from agr. to industl. basis, although agr. still impt., contributing many exps., especially timber, wine, fruit; major pt. Constanta on Black Sea; oilfields at Ploiesti; cap. Bucharest; ch. tr. partners USSR and E. Europe; Danube used for navigation; Iron Gates power and navigation system being constructed in co-operation with Yugoslavia; tourism from W. Europe and N. America encouraged; measures to stimulate birth rate; revolution 1989, popular uprising against Ceaucescu dictatorship; a. 237,428 km²; p. (est. 1987) 22·9 m.

Rome (Roma), cap. of **Italy**, and of Latium and Rome prov.; on R. Tiber, 24 km from sea; in Roman legend founded by Romulus 753 B.C.; once cap. of anc. Roman empire; inc. Vatican c., ctr. of Roman Catholic Church; situated on original "seven hills," and along the R.; leading cultural ctr.; St. Peter's church, Colosseum, Pantheon; univ.; admin. ctr.; tourism; created cap. of United Italy 1871; p. (est. 1986) 2,815,457.

Romford. *See* **Havering.**

Romney Marsh, coastal marsh, Shepway, Kent, **Eng.**; formed by blocking of R. Rother by shingle spit of Dungeness which extends from Rye to Hythe; largely drained; pastures for special Romney Marsh breed of sheep; a. 129 km².

Romsey, t., Test Valley, Hants., **Eng.**; on R. Test, 14 km N.W. of Southampton; mkt. ctr.; Norman abbey; p. (1981) 12,941.

Ronaldshay, North, most N. of Orkney Is., **Scot.**; p. (1971) 134.

Ronaldshay, South, most S. of Orkney Is. **Scot.**; p. (1971) 991.

Roncesvalles, mtn. pass in Pyrenees, Navarre, **Spain**; 32 km N.E. of Pamplona; defeat and death of Roland 778.

Ronda, t., Málaga, **Spain**; in Andalusia; anc. Moorish t., divided by deep gorge crossed by bridge; p. (1981) 31,383.

Rondônia, st., **Brazil**; on Bolivian border; forest covered; forest prods.; nomadic Indian tribes; cap. Pôrto Velho; a. 243,071 km²; p. (est. 1985) 908,900.

Rønne, t., **Denmark**; cap. of Bornholm I.; fish. pt.; shipyards, ceramics; p. (1981) 14,413.

Ronse (Renaix), t., **Belgium**; nr. Ghent; textile ctr.; p. (1982) 24,287.

Roodepoort-Maraisburg, t., Transvaal, **S. Africa**; ctr. Witwatersrand goldfields; p. (1980) 165,315.

Roosendaal, t., S.W. of N. Brabant, **Neth.**, sugar-refining; p. (est. 1987) 58,000.

Roosevelt Dam (1903–11), Arizona, **USA**; on R. Salt in canyon E. of Phoenix on edge of Col. plateau; used for irrigation and hydroelectric power; part of Salt river project.

Roquefort-sur-Soulzon, t., S.E. Aveyron, **France**; caves in limestone cliffs used for ripening cheese; p. (1982) 880.

Roraima, mtn., at junc. of boundaries of **Brazil, Guyana,** and **Venezuela**; 2,852 m, hgst. point of Guiana Highlands.

Roraima (Rio Branco), fed. terr., **Brazil**; underdeveloped rain forest; cap. Boa Vista; a. 214,320 km²; p. (est. 1985) 102,500.

Rosa Monte, Pennine Alps, Swiss-Italian border; alt. 4,637 m.

Rosario, t., Santa Fé, **Argentina**; second t. of rep.; R. pt. on Paraná R.; agr.-processing,

iron and steel, lt. inds.; univ., cath.; p. (1980) 794,000 (c.), 957,000 (met. a.).

Roscommon, co. t., Roscommon, **R.o.I.**; mkt.; cas., priory; p. (1981) 1,673.

Roscommon, inland co., Connaught, **R.o.I.**; extensive peat bog and Ls.; pastoral agr., cap. R.; a. 2,458 km²; p. (1981) 8,454.

Rosetta (Rashid), t., Lower **Egypt**; nr. Rosetta mouth of Nile; Rosetta stone found nearby gave key to Egyptian hieroglyphics; p. (1966) 36,700.

Roskilde, t., spt., Sjaelland, **Denmark**; former cap.; cath. contains tombs of kings; admin. ctr. of R. prov.; p. (1981) 39,659.

Ross and Cromarty, former co., l. gov. dist., Highland Reg.; **Scot.**; extends from N. Sea to Atl. Oc.; most of a. over 300 m, lake-covered; cattle breeding, fishing, tourism; a. 4,999 km²; p. (est. 1986) 47,906.

Rossendale Fells (or Forest), upland, S.E. Lancs./Gtr. Manchester, **Eng.**; extension of Pennines between Rs. Mersey and Ribble; millstone grit moorland used for reservoirs; alt. mainly above 360 m; now forms l. gov. dist. in Lancs. inc. ts. of Haslingden, Rawtenstall, Bacup and Whitworth; p. (est. 1988) 64,600

Ross Dependency, Antarctica; N.Z. sector; inlet of Ross Sea; a. 414,400 sq. km.

Rosslare, spt., Wexford, **R.o.I.**; on extreme S.E. of Ireland; steamer connections to Fishguard.

Ross-on-Wye, t., South Herefordshire, Hereford and Worcs., **Eng.**; mkt., tourism; p. (1981) 7,182.

Ross Sea, sea extending to 85° S. in **Antarctic**.

Rostock, c., cap. of R. dist., **E. Germany**; pt. nr. Baltic cst., outport of Warnemünde; shipbldg., fish-processing, chemicals; univ.; mediaeval t.; p. (1986) 246,000.

Rostov, c., **RSFSR**; pt. on R. Don, nr. Azov Sea (Black Sea); one of Russia's finest and oldest cs.; ctr. of agr. dist.; grain mkt.; agr.-processing; univ.; p. (1986) 993,000.

Rosyth, t., Dunfermline, **Scot.**; naval dockyard privatisation planned (1987).

Rothamsted, v., Herts., **Eng.**; in Chiltern Hills, S. of Harpenden; famous agr. research sta.

Rother, l. gov. dist., East Sussex, **Eng.**; rural a. inc. Rye, Bexhill and Battle; p. (est. 1988) 84,700.

Rother, R., Derbys. and South Yorks., **Eng.**; flows to R. Don at Rotherham; 34 km long.

Rother, R., East Sussex and Kent, **Eng.**; rises in the Weald, flows S.E. into English Channel at Rye; 50 km long.

Rotherham, t., met. dist., South Yorks., **Eng.**; on R. Don, 6 km N.E. of Sheffield; iron, steel, wire, springs, glass; p. (est. 1988) 251,800.

Rothes, burgh, Moray, **Scot.**; on R. Spey 19 km S.E. of Elgin; p. (1981) 1,429.

Rothesay, royal burgh, Argyll and Bute., **Scot.**; on E. cst. of I. of Bute in F. of Clyde; tourism; p. (1981) 5,408.

Rothwell, t., West Yorks., **Eng.**; on R. Aire, 5 km S.E. of Leeds; coal-mng. ctr., engin.; p. (1981) 29,142.

Rotorua, c., leading spa of **N.Z.**; on volcanic plateau, Auckland, N.I.; hot springs; p. (1981) 48,314.

Rotterdam, c., spt. **Neth.**; Europe's lgst. spt., on Nieuwe Maas, part of Rhine-Maas-Scheldt delta; linked to outport Europoort (*q.v*) by New Waterway; serves hinterland of Rhine valley and central Europe; freeport; processing of imports, especially oil refining and petrochemical inds.; badly damaged in second world war; p. (est. 1987) 572,000.

Roubaix, t., Nord dep., **France**; nr. Lille; on Roubaix canal close to Belgian frontier; major textile ctr., especially for woollens; p. (1982) 101,886.

Rouen, c., Seine-Maritime dep., **France**; gr. R. pt., 125 km up R. Seine; oil refining, textiles, chemicals; cath.; Joan of Arc burned here; birthplace of Corneille and Flaubert; badly damaged in second world war; p. (1982) 105,083.

Rousay, Orkney Is., **Scot.**; p. (1971) 256.

Roussillon, former prov., S. **France**; now dep. of Pyrénées-Orientales; irrigated by many sm. streams; olives, wine, fruit; historical cap. Perpignan.

Rovaniemi, t., **Finland**; on Kemi R.; timber and saw mills; p. (1986) 32,769.

Rovigo, prov., Venetia, **Italy**; part of N. Italian plain extending to Adriatic; impt. agr. dist.;

cap. R.; a. 218 km²; p. (1981) 253,508.

Rovigo, t., cap. of R. prov., **Italy;** on R. Adige, cath., cas. ruins, palace; p. (1981) 52,218.

Rovno, c., cap. of R., oblast, Ukrainian SSR, **USSR;** rly. junct.; industl. ctr.; ruins of mediaeval palace; p. (est. 1985) 221,000.

Roxburgh, former co., S. **Scot.;** sheeprearing hilly cty. with wool-based inds.; new forms l. gov. dist. in Borders Reg.; a. 1,538 km²; p. (est. 1986) 35,225.

Royal Oak, t., Mich., **USA;** residtl.; Detroit zoological park here; p. (1980) 70,893.

Royston, mkt. t., North Herts., **Eng.;** at N. foot of E. Anglian Heights, 11 km N.E. of Baldock; p. (1981) 11,799.

Royton, t., Gtr. Manchester, **Eng.;** 13 km N.E. of Manchester; textiles; p. (1981) 21,233.

Ruanda-Urundi. See **Rwanda** and **Burundi.**

Ruapehu, highest mtn., N.I., **N.Z.;** volcanic peak at S. extremity of central volcanic dist.; crater L. at summit; alt. 2,798 m.

Rubicon, R., central **Italy;** flows to Adriatic; crossed by Julius Caesar and his armies 49 B.C.; has been identified with the Fiumicino or the Uso.

Rubtsovsk, t., W. Siberia, **RSFSR;** agr. engin.; p. (est. 1985) 165,000.

Ruby Mines, dist., Mandalay, Upper **Burma;** hilly region of Shan plateau, once famous for rubies.

Ruda Slaska, t., Katowice, **Poland;** coal-mng. ctr.; iron and steel wks.; p. (est. 1985) 165,000.

Rudnyy, t., Kazakh SSR, **USSR;** new t. 48 km S.W. of Kustanay; iron-ore mng. and dressing plant supplying Magnitogorsk; p. (est. 1985) 116,000.

Rudolf, L., N.W. **Kenya;** in Great Rift Valley; a. 9,065 km²; ctr. of semi-arid region; renamed **Turkana.**

Rudolph I., N. of Franz Josef Land Arctic Oc.; Russian naval base; met. sta.

Rudolstadt, t., E. Germany; on R. Saale, in former seat of Thuringia; seat of counts of Schwarzburg-Rudolstadt (1584–1918); tourism; porcelain; p. (est. 1970) 31,539.

Rueil-Malmaison, sub. of Paris, **France;** château; tomb of the empress Josephine; p. (1982) 64,545.

Rufiji, R., Tanzania; E. Africa; flows to Indian Oc.; 720 km long.

Rufisque, t., Senegambia; sm. spt. nr. Dakar; growing industl. ctr. for consumer gds.; p. (est. 1967) 60,000.

Rugby, mkt. t., l. gov. dist., Warwicks, **Eng.;** on R. Avon, 18 km E. of Coventry; famous public school; elec. and gen. engin., motor and aircraft patterns; p. (est. 1988) 86,300 (dist.).

Rugeley, mkt. t., Staffs, **Eng.;** on R. Trent, 14 km S.E. of Stafford; coal, iron, tanning; expanded t.; p. (1981) 24,340.

Rügen, I., E. Germany; in Baltic Sea, off Stralsund; ch. t. Bergen; pt. Sassnitz, terminus of train ferry; steamer services to Trelleborg, Sweden.

Ruhr, industl. dist., **W. Germany;** lies to E. of R. Rhine, on either side of R. Ruhr; rich coalfield; impt. iron and steel, heavy engin. inds. based on local coal and iron ore from Luxembourg, Spain, Sweden; water communications to N. Sea along R. Rhine and Dortmund–Ems Canal; ch. ts. Essen, Duisburg, Düsseldorf, Dortmund, Bochum.

Ruhr, R., W. Germany; trib. of Rhine; flows S. of Ruhr conurb.; 232 km long.

Rukwa, L., E. **Africa;** between L. Tanganyika and L. Malawi in the rift valley; 48 km by 19 im; a. increasing.

Rum, I., Inner Hebrides, Lochaber, **Scot.;** nature reserve, highland ecology; a. 168 km².

Rumaila, Iraq; oilfield; pipeline links to the Zubair–Fao system.

Rum Jungle, N.T., **Australia;** 64 km S.E. of Darwin; site of Australia's first major uranium project; ceased operation in 1970.

Runcorn, t., Halton, Cheshire, **Eng.;** on S. side of Mersey estuary; new t. (1964); chemicals; pipeline carrying petrochemical feedstock from Teeside; new Runcorn–Widnes bridge over Mersey and Manchester Ship Canal opened 1961 (lgst. span arch in Europe); p. of new t. (1981) 63,813.

Rungis, Paris, **France;** site of major new mkt. to replace Les Halles; nr. Orly airpt., Val de Marne dep.; p. (1982) 2,650.

Runnymede, l. gov. dist., Surrey, **Eng.;** comprises Egham and Chertsey; p. (est. 1988) 71,300.

Ruse, t., Bulgaria; on R. Danube, opposite Giurgiu in Romania; univ.; Roman t.; agr. processing; p. (1985) 183,746.

Rushcliffe, l. gov. dist., Notts., **Eng.;** a. S.E. of Nottingham inc. West Bridgeford; p. (est. 1988) 99,300.

Rushden, t., East Northants., **Eng.;** 5 km E. of Wellingborough; shoes; p. (1981) 22,253.

Rushmoor, l. gov. dist., H nts., **Eng.;** small a. of Farnborough and Aldershot; p. (est. 1988) 77,000.

Rüsselsheim, t., W. Germany; impt. car factory; p. (est. 1986) 57,300.

Russian Soviet Federated Socialist Republic (RSFSR), constituent rep., **USSR;** lgst. rep. by a. and p.; economic development; inds. centred on Leningrad and Moscow with new inds. being developed in Urals and Kuznetz basin; extends from Baltic to Pac. Oc. (8,000 km), from Arctic to Caspian Sea (4,000 km); part of N. European plain in W. and Siberian plain in E., separated by Ural mtns.; major Rs. Volga, Don, Ob, Yenisey, Lena, Amur; gr. variety in climate and p. density; major agr. region for wheat, sugar-beet, livestock; vast mineral deposits have aided economic growth; oil around Volga valley; metallic ores from Ural and Black Sea; hydroelectric power from Volga, Yenesey and Ob Rs.; cap. Moscow; a. 16,838,885 km²; p. (1986) 144,027,000.

Rustavi, t., Georgian SSR, **USSR;** new t., 32 km S.E. Tbilisi; iron and steel; lge. metallurgical plant; p. (est. 1985) 143,000.

Rustenburg, t., Transvaal, **Africa;** on N.W. edge of High Veld, 96 km W. of Pretoria; local mkt. for agr. produce; agr.-processing; p. (1970) 52,657.

Rutbah, t., Iraq; on oil pipeline from Iraq to Haifa; impt. ctr. on trans-desert routes.

Rutherglen, royal burgh, Strathclyde Reg., **Scot.;** on R. Clyde, S.E. of Glasgow; chemicals, tubes, paper, wire ropes, bolts.

Ruthin, t., Glyndwr, Clwyd, **Wales;** Vale of Clwyd, 13 km S.E. of Denbigh; p. (1981) 4,430.

Rutland, former Midland co., **Eng.;** sm. co. of 394 km², now part of Leics. and l. gov. dist. based on Oakham; p. (est. 1990) 36,900.

Rutland Water, reservoir, Leics., **Eng.**

Ruwenzori mtn. range, on **Uganda-Zaïre** border; overlooking W. arm of Gt. Rift Valley, midway between L. Mobutu Seso and L. Edward; hgst. peaks, Mt. Margherita (5,123 m), Mt. Alexandra (5,109 m); lower slopes covered in equatorial rain forest, coffee plantations on middle slopes above 1,500 m.

Rwanda, indep. rep., Central **Africa;** former kingdom of Ruanda, part of UN trust terr. of Ruanda-Urundi under Belgian admin. (until 1962); sm., landlocked st., S. of equator, consisting of upland plateau at 1,200 m; mainly subsistence agr. under gt. strain with rapid p. growth; coffee (ch. exp.), cotton, pyrethrum (3rd lgst. world producer), cattle; tin, tungsten and natural gas discoveries; little ind.; cap. Kigali; a. 26,338 km²; p. (est. 1986) 6,320,000.

Ryazan, c., cap. of R. oblast, **RSFSR;** on Oka R.; food inds., agr. machin., footwear, chemicals; mediaeval architecture; p. (est. 1985) 494,000.

Rybinsk. See **Andropov.**

Rybinsk Sea (Rybinsk Reservoir), RSFSR; artificial L.; created behind dams on R. Volga and R. Sheksna at Rybinsk; part of scheme to regulate flow of R. Volga and to incorporate it in a vast inland waterway system; opened 1945; a. 3,885 km.

Rybnik, t., Katowice prov., S.W. **Poland;** ctr. of coal-mng. dist.; p. (est. 1983) 133,000.

Rydal Water, L., nr. Ambleside, Cumbria, **Eng.;** adjacent v. contains Rydal Mount, home of Wordsworth.

Ryde, t., Medina, I. of Wight, **Eng.;** on N.E. cst.; yachting ctr. and seaside resort; boat and yacht bldg.; steamer connection across Spithead to Portsmouth; p. (1981) 24,346.

Rye, t., Rother, East Sussex, **Eng.;** at mouth of R. Rother to W. of Dungeness; one of the Cinque pts.; Ypres cas.; tourist ctr.; p. (1981) 4,293.

Ryedale, l. gov. dist., North Yorks., **Eng.;** lge. a.

inc. Malton, Pickering, Norton, Kirby Moorside and Helmsley; p. (est. 1988) 90,800.

Ryton, t., Tyne and Wear, **Eng.;** on R. Tyne, W. of Newcastle; p. (1981) 15,023.

Ryukyu Is., archipelago, between Kyushu I., **Japan,** and Taiwan; ch. t. Naha on Okinawa I.; following second world war Is. S. of Lat. 30° N. occupied by USA; Amami and Tokara grs. returned to Japan 1953; American military installations on Okinawa withdrawn 1972; lge. Is. mtnous., volcanic; sweet potatoes, sugarcane, pineapples; 3 lge. oil refineries; a. 2,196 km²; p. (1985) 1,179,000.

Rzeszów, c., cap. of R. prov., S.E. **Poland;** at foot of Carpathian highlands; route ctr.; growing industl. t.; p. (est. 1983) 134,400.

Rzhev, c., **RSFSR;** on Volga R.; rly. ctr. on main line to Moscow; agr. processing; p. (est. 1970) 49,000.

S

Saale, R., **E. Germany;** rises in Fichtelgebirge flows N. through Thuringia to Elbe; attractive, well wooded valley; irrigation; hydroelec. power; 360 km long.

Saalfeld, t., Gera, **E. Germany;** on R. Saale; famous cas., iron-mng.; machin., chocolate; p. (est. 1970) 33,405.

Saarland, Land, **W. Germany;** heavy inds. based on lge. coalfields; drained by R. Saar; cap. Saarbrücken; admin. by League of Nations 1919–35, returned to Germany after plebiscite; economic attachment to France after second world war; reunited politically with W. Germany 1957; a. 2,567 km²; p. (est. 1986) 1,042,100.

Saarbrücken, c., cap. of Saarland, **W. Germany;** on R. Saar, nr. Fr. border; cas.; rich coalfield; iron and steel wks., textiles, leather, paper, oil refining at Klarenthal nearby; p. (est. 1986) 184,400.

Saaremaa (Osel), I., Baltic Sea; at entrance to G. of Riga, Estonian **SSR;** low plateau, bleak and barren; ch. t. Kingisepp (Kuressaare); a. 2,720 km².

Saarlouis (Saarlautern), Saarland, **W. Germany;** on R. Saar; coal mng.; wood and metal inds.; founded by Louis XIV; birthplace of Marshal Ney; p. (est. 1986) 37,400.

Sabadell, t., **Spain;** N.W. of Barcelona; textiles, fertilisers, paper; p. (1981) 176,554.

Sabah, E. Malaysia; attempted secession 1975; formerly N. Borneo; underdeveloped; tropical forest; forest prods., inc. rubber, the major exp.; main pt. Sandakan; cap. Kota Kinabalu; a. 76,112 km²; p. (1980) 1,011,046

Sabahiyah, t., **Kuwait;** new t. being built between Ahmadi and Fahahil.

Sabara, t., Minas Gerais, **Brazil;** historic c.; museum of gold; p. (est. 1968) 26,464.

Sabine, R., Texas and La., **USA;** flows through S. Lake (an expansion of the R. 29 km long) to G. of Mexico; 936 km long.

Sable I., off S.E. cst. Nova Scotia, **Canada;** sandy I., scene of many shipwrecks.

Sacramento, c., st. cap. Cal., **USA;** on R. Sacramento; shipping and industl. ctr.; rly. wk.-shps., smelting, meat and fruit packing, flour, lumber, metal prods., rocket and missiles ind.; p. (1984) 304,100 (c.), 1,219,600 (met. a.).

Sacramento, R., Cal., **USA;** forms N. section of Central Valley projected for irrigation, hydroelectric power and flood control; 624 km long.

Saddleback (Blencathara), mtn., Cumbria, **Eng.;** nr. Keswick; alt. 868 m.

Saddleworth, t., Gtr. Manchester, **Eng.;** in Pennines, 8 km N.E. of Oldham; woollens, paper mkg., engin.; p. (1981) 21,851.

Saffron Walden, mkt. t., Uttlesford, Essex, **Eng.;** on E. Anglian heights; cas., abbey ruins; saffron crocus once cultivated here; p. (1981) 12,515.

Safi, spt., **Morocco;** on Atl. Oc.; linked by rail

to phosphate deposits at Youssoufia; pottery, fish-processing; resort; p. (est. 1981) 256,000.

Saga, c., cap. of S. pref., Kyushu, **Japan;** coal-mng. ctr., textiles, ceramics; p. (1985) 168,254.

Saganoseki, t., N.E. Kyushu, **Japan;** on Bungo strait; impt. gold, copper, and silver mines; smelting.

Sagar, t., Karnataka, **India;** nr. Krishna R. valley; p. (1981) 207,401.

Saginaw, c., Mich., **USA;** on R. Saginaw; former fur and lumbering region; coal; beans, sugarbeet; various mnfs.; p. (1984) 73,700 (c.), 411,900 (met. a.).

Saguenay, R., Quebec, **Canada;** trib. of St. Lawrence R.; outlet of L. St. John; used for hydroelec. power; tourism; length c. 176 km.

Sagunto, t., **Spain;** nr. Valencia; integrated steelwks. projected; anc. t., sieged by Hannibal; p. (1981) 54,759 (met. a.).

Sahara, the gr. N. African desert between the Sudan and the Barbary sts., extending from the Atl. to the Nile, inc. Tripoli and Fezzan; a. 16,835,000 km²; numerous oases with ts. and tr. ctrs.; oil pipelines to Algerian and Tunisian csts.; p. (est. 2,500,000), nomadic Arab and Berber tribes.

Saharan Arab Democratic Rep. See **Western Sahara.**

Saharan Atlas, S. range of Atlas mtns. in Algeria; ch. peaks., Jebel Aurès, 2,331 m. J. Aissa, 2,242 m, J. Ksel, 2,011 m.

Saharanpur, c., Uttar Pradesh, N.W. **India;** wood-carving, furniture, agr.-processing inds.; p. (1981) 295,355.

Sahel, region of **W. Africa,** inc. Chad, Mali, Mauritania, Niger, Senegal and Bourkina Fasso, which suffered severe famine and drought 1972–4 and 1984–5 caused by desertification of an area marginal to Sahara Desert.

Saïda (Sidon), t., **Lebanon;** on Mediterranean, S. of Beirut; terminus of oil pipeline from Saudi Arabia; refinery; p. (est. 1980) 24,740.

Saigon. See Ho Chi-minh City.

Saimaa, L. system, **Finland;** a. of water which forms basin of R. Vuoksi; canal connects with C. of Finland and runs partly through Soviet terr.; a. 1,699 km².

Saingdin Falls, Burma; on Kaladan R.; site of new hydroelec. power sta.

St. Abb's Head, rocky promontory, lighthouse, Berwick, **Scot.**

St. Albans, c., l. gov. dist., Herts., **Eng.;** on N. margin of Vale of St. Albans, 32 km N.W. of London; faces remains of Roman Verulamium across R. Ver; lt. inds., electronics, instrument mkg.; cath.; residtl.; p. (est. 1988) 128,500.

St. Amand, t., Cher dep., **France;** on R. Cher; Roman remains; new recreational park; p. (1982) 12,801.

St. Andrews, royal burgh, North East Fife, **Scot.;** seaside resort; univ.; famous golf course; p. (1981) 11,302.

St. Anthony, waterfalls, on R. Mississippi; **USA;** predominant factor in site of Minneapolis.

St. Asaph, t., Rhuddlan, Clwyd, N. **Wales;** on R. Clwyd; p. (1971) 11,755 (dist.).

St. Austell with Fowey, mkt. ts., Restormel, Cornwall, **Eng.;** on S. flank of Hensbarrow; ctr. of Cornwall's china clay ind.; p. (1981) 36,639.

St. Barthélemy, Fr. I., **W.I.;** dependency of Guadeloupe; cash crops of sugar, bananas, cacao; cap. Gustavia; p. (1982) 3,059.

St. Bees Head, promontory, 4 km N.W. of St. Bees, Cumbria, **Eng.;** freestone quarries, anhydrite.

St. Bernard Pass, Great, on Italian–Swiss bdy., W. Alps; carries main road from W. Switzerland to Plain of Lombardy; 2,477 m a.s.l.; road tunnel (5·6 km) constr. 1958–62 links Cantine de Proz (Valais can., Switzerland) and St. Rhémy (Italy); under tunnel will run projected 416 km pipeline from Genoa to Aigle.

St. Bernard Pass, Little, on French–Italian bdy. W. Alps; links Isère valley with Val d'Aosta; alt. 2,190 m.

St. Boniface, t., Manitoba, **Canada;** sub. of Winnipeg; meat-packing, petroleum prods.

St. Bride's Bay, Dyfed, **Wales.**

St. Brieuc, t., cap. of Côtes-du-Nord dep., N.W. **France;** sm. fish. pt.; iron and steel wks.; cath.; p. (1982) 51,399.

St. Catharines, c., Ont., **Canada;** on Welland Ship Canal; mkt. for Niagara fruit-growing region; agr. implements, textile, paper and flour mills, vehicle components; resort; p. (1986) 123,455 (c.), 343,258 (met. a. with Niagara).

St. Chamond, t., Loire, **France**; nr. St. Etienne; ribbons, rayon; rly. wks.; coal mng.; p. (1982) 82,059 (met. a.).

St. Clair, L., Canada–USA; part of link between L. Huron and L. Erie; a. 1,191 km².

St. Clair, R., N. America; flows from L. Huron through L. of St. Clair into L. Erie; forms bdy. between Mich. (USA) and Ont. (Canada); impt. link in Gr. Ls. waterway; length 136 km, depth dredged to 6 m.

St. Clair Shores, t., Mich., **USA**; residtl. sub. of Detroit; p. (1980) 76,210.

St. Cloud, W. sub. of Paris, **France**; fine park; porcelain; p. (1982) 28,760.

St. Cloud, t., Minn., **USA**; on R. Mississippi; granite quarries; st. college; p. (1984) 42,100 (t.), 171,300 (met. a.).

St.-Cyr-l'Ecole, t., Yvelines, **France**; once famous for military school founded by Napoleon; bldgs. destroyed second world war; p. (1982) 16,380.

St. Davids, t., Dyfed, **Wales**; 24 km S.W. of Fishguard; on site of anc. Minevia; cath., ruins of Bishop Gower's palace (1342); p. (1981) 1,800.

St. David's Head, promontory, Dyfed, **Wales.**

St. Denis, t., N. sub., Paris, **France**; on R. Seine; abbey, burial place of Fr. kings; chemicals., machin.; p. (1982) 91,275.

St. Denis, spt., cap. of Ile de la Réunion (Fr.), Indian Oc.; p. (1982) 109,072.

St. Dié, t., Vosges, **France**; on R. Meurthe; cath.; textile ctr., hosiery; p. (1982) 24,816.

St. Dizier, t., Haute-Marne, dep. **France**; on R. Marne; metallurgy; p. (1982) 37,445.

St. Edmundsbury, l. gov. dist., Suffolk, **Eng.**; based on Bury St. Edmunds and inc. Haverhill; p. (est. 1988) 92,300.

St. Elias, mtns., Alaska, **USA**; and Yukon, **Canada**; inc. Mt. McKinley (5,780 m); source of world's lgst. icefield outside polar regions.

Saintes, t., Charente-Maritime dep., **France**; cath.; Roman antiquities; suffered in Huguenot wars; agr. implements; earthenware; p. (1982) 27,486.

St. Etienne, t., cap. of Loire dep., **France**; nr. Lyons; in sm. coal basin on edge of Central Massif; famous for firearms; modern inds. inc. engin., dyes, chemicals, textiles, glass; p. (1982) 206,688.

St. Gall (St. Gallen), t., cap. of can. St. G., **Switzerland**; founded around Benedictine monastery (7th–8th cent.); embroidered cottons; p. (1985) 73,000.

St. Gall (St. Gallen), can., **Switzerland**; borders L. Constance, rising to S.; mainly industl.; ch. ind. textiles; cap. St. G.; a. 2,012 km²; p. (est. 1986) 404,000.

St. George's Channel, Brit. Isles, part of Irish Sea, separating Wales from Ireland.

St. George's, t., cap. of Grenada, **W.I.**; ch. spt.; built around submerged volcanic crater forming St. G. Bay; p. (est. 1980) 8,000.

St. Germain-en-Laye, t., Yvelines, **France**; on R. Seine; outer sub. of Paris; residtl.; popular resort; birthplace of Debussy; p. (1982) 40,829.

Saint Gotthard, mtn. gr., Alps, S. central **Switzerland**; crossed by St. G. pass (2,115 m); rly. passes through St. G. tunnel (14·8 km, max. alt. 1,155 m); road tunnel (16·3 km) opened 1980, longest in world; motorways linking pass with Zürich, Basle, and Lugano being built.

St. Gowan's Head, promontory, Dyfed, **Wales.**

St. Helena, I., Brit., col., **Atl. Oc.**; 1,920 km from W. cst. Africa; spt. and only t. Jamestown; Napoleon imprisoned 1815–21, and Boer captives 1900; famous for its wirebird, species of plover peculiar to I.; a. 122 km²; p. (est. 1985) 6,000.

St. Helens, t., met. dist., Merseyside, **Eng.**; 19 km E. of Liverpool; connected by canal with R. Mersey; coal, iron, alkali; copper smelting, glass, fibreglass, plastics; p. (est. 1988) 187,600.

St. Helier, spt., Jersey, Channel Is., **Eng.**; resort; cas.; tr. in early vegetables; p. (1976) 26,343.

St. Hyacinthe, t., spt., Quebec, **Canada**; on Yamaska R.; cath.; famous for organs; lt. inds.; p. (1981) 38,246.

St. Ives, t., Penwith, Cornwall, **Eng.**; at entrance to St. Ives Bay; fishing, holiday resort; p. (1981) 10,985.

St. Ives, t., Camb., **Eng.**; on R. Ouse, 6 km E. of Huntingdon; borders the Fens; R. Ouse crossed by 16th cent. bridge containing a chapel; p. (1981) 12,278.

St. Jean, t., Quebec, **Canada**; on Richelieu R.; timber, grain exps.; textiles, sewing machines, p. (1981) 35,640.

Saint John, c., spt., N.B., **Canada**; lgst. c. of N.B.; ice-free pt.; lge. dry docks; rly. terminus; impt. inds. inc. sugar- and oil-refining, paper, textiles; p. (1986) 76,381 (c.), 121,265 (met. a.).

St. John, L., Quebec, **Canada**; on Saguenay R.; tourism; a. 971 km².

St. John, R., Maine, N.B., **Canada, USA**; flows to B. of Fundy forming section of international boundary; 720 km long.

St. John's, t., cap. of Antigua, **W.I.**; pt., airpt.; cath.; ch. comm. ctr. of I.; p. (est. 1982) 30,000.

St. John's, c. spt., cap. of Newfoundland, **Canada**; on E. cst.; first English settlement in America early 16th cent.; gr. tr. in fish with allied inds.; univ., 2 caths.; p. (1986) 96,216 (c.), 161,901 (met a.).

St. Johns, R., **USA**; drains swamps of central Fla., 21 km from Atl. Oc.; 560 km long.

St. John's Wood, residtl. dist., Westminster London, **Eng.**; contains Lord's Cricket Ground.

St. Joseph, t., Mich., **USA**; pt. on L. Mich.; ctr. of fruit-growing a.; resort; p. (1980) 9,622.

St. Joseph, t., Mo., **USA**; declining pt. on R. Mississippi; agr. tr. and processing; p. (1980) 76,691 (t.), 101,868 (met. a.).

St. Just, t., Penwith, Cornwall, **Eng.**; nr. Lands End, 10 km W. of Penzance; former tin-mng. ctr.; p. (1981) 4,047.

St. Kilda, rocky I., most W. of the Hebrides, **Scot.**; 5 km long; bird sanctuary, famous for its wren, a sub-species.

St. Kitts-Nevis, Leeward gr. of Is., **W.I.**; aut. st. in association with Gt. Britain; indep. (1983); sugar, sea island cotton, molasses; a. 262 km²; cap. Basseterre; p. (est. 1987) 47,000.

St. Laurent, t., Quebec, **Canada**; industl. t. on Montreal I., W. of Montreal; p. (1986) 67,002.

St. Lawrence, G. of, Canada; arm of Atl. Oc., partly enclosed by Newfoundland and Nova Scotia; impt. fisheries.

St. Lawrence I., Alaska, **USA**; in Bering Sea; 160 km long.

St. Lawrence, R., Canada; major outlet from Gr. Lakes; forms bdy. between USA and Canada; ch. tribs. Ottawa, Richelieu, St. Maurice, Saguenay Rs.; with St. L. Seaway forms a major waterway facing Europe; grain, timber, oil, iron-ore traffic; used for hydroelectric power; total length from source (St. Louis) 3,360 km.

St. Lawrence Seaway, N. America; joint Canada–USA project links head of the Gr. Lakes with Atl. Oc., providing channel for lge. ocean-going vessels to reach American continent; provides major source of hydroelectric power to industl. a.; opened 1959.

St. Lô, t. cap. of Manche dep., N.W. **France**; built on rocky hill overlooking R. Vire; cath.; p. (1982) 24,792.

St. Louis, t., Ile de la Réunion, **Indian Oc.**; p. (1962) 7,753.

St. Louis, t., Senegambia, W. Africa; at mouth of R. Senegal; cath.; former cap.; comm. ctr.; impt. fish. pt.; p. (est. 1980) 97,000.

St. Louis, c., Mo., **USA**; on R. Mississippi 16 km below confluence of Rs. Mississippi and Missouri; two univs., impt. rly. and river junc.; mkt. for furs, livestock, grain, farm prod.; banking and fin. ctr.; varied mnfs.; machin., cars, aircraft, leather gds., beer, chemicals; p. (1984) 429,300 (c.), 2,398,400 (met. a.).

St. Lucia I., fully indep. st. (1979); Windward Is., **W.I.**; volcanic, forested, fertile valleys; exp. bananas and other tropical agr. prod.; airpt.; cap. Castries; a. 616 km²; hurricane disaster 1980; p. (est. 1987) 143,600.

St. Malo, spt., Ile-et-Vilaine dep., N.W. **France**; on Normandy cst.; cath.; once fortfd.; shipping, fishing, and tourist inds.; p. (1982) 47,324.

St. Martin, I., Leeward Is., **W.I.**; N. part Fr. dependency of Guadeloupe, S. part belongs to Neth. Antilles; divided since 1648; ch. exp. salt; total p. (1981) 13,156.

St. Marylebone. See **Westminster, City of.**

St. Mary's I., Scilly Is., **Brit. Isles.**

St. Maur-des-Fossés, residtl. garden sub. of Paris, Val-de-Marne dep., **France**; p. (1982) 80,954.

St. Maurice, v., Valais, **Switzerland**; nr. Martigny; 6th-cent. abbey; once a leading Burgundian t.; p. c. 10,000.

St. Maurice, R., Quebec, **Canada**; trib. of St. Lawrence R.; used for timber transport and hydroelec. power; 520 km long.

St. Mawes, v., Cornwall, **Eng.**; on E. cst. of estuary of R. Fal; cas.; holiday resort, fishing.

St. Michael's Mt., castled rock, Cornwall, **Eng.**; the anc. Ictis; alt. 70 m.

St. Monance, burgh, North East Fife, **Scot.**; resort; p. (1981) 1,248.

St. Moritz, resort and winter sports ctr., **Switzerland**; in the Upper Engadine; alt. 1,857 m; p. (1970) 5,699.

St. Nazaire, t., Loire-Atlantique dep., **W. France**; spt. at mouth of R. Loire, outport for Nantes; growing pt. and industl. ctr.; shipyds., iron and steel, fertilisers, aircraft, oil refining; p. (1982) 68,947.

St. Neots, mkt. t., Cambs. **Eng.**; on R. Ouse, 16 km N.E. of Bedford; brewing, milling, paper-mkg.; expanded t.; p. (1981) 21,185.

St. Nikilaas, mftg. t., E. Flanders, **Belgium**; nr. Antwerp; textile ctr., carpets; p. (1982) 25,432.

St. Omer, t., Pas-de-Calais dep., N. **France**; ctr. of mkt.-gardening a.; textiles, food inds.; cath., abbey ruins; p. (1982) 53,748 (met. a.).

St. Ouen, N. sub. of Paris, Seine-St. Denis dep., **France**; on R. Seine at base of Butte de Monmartre; metals, chemicals, glues, tanning; p. (1982) 43,743.

St. Pancras. See **Camden.**

St. Paul, spt., Ile de la Réunion, **Indian Oc.**; p. (1968) 43,129.

St. Paul, c., cap. of Minn., **USA**; faces Minneapolis across Mississippi; cath.; univ.; ctr. of agr. dist.; agr. mkt. and processing; car assembly, oil refining, electronics; p. (1984) 265,900 (c.), 2,230,900 (met. a. with Minneapolis.)

St. Paul, I., **Indian Oc.**; bare volcanic islet rising to 493 m; part of Fr. Southern and Antarctic Terr.; uninhabited.

St. Peter Port, spt., cap. of Guernsey, **Channel Is.**; exp. fruit, flowers, vegetables; resort; p. (1971) 16,303.

St. Petersburg, c., Fla., **USA**; resort on Tampa Bay; p. (1984) 241,300 (part of Tampa met. a.).

St. Pierre, t., Martinique t., Fr. **W.I.**; utterly destroyed and all inhabitants save one by eruption of Mt. Pelée 1902; tourism.

St. Pierre, t., Réunion, **Indian Oc.**; sm. artificial harbour; p. (est. 1971) 43,808.

St. Pierre and Miquelon, Fr. dep., consisting of 8 sm. Is. off S. cst. of Newfoundland; a. of St. Pierre gr. 26 km²; a. of Miquelon gr., 215 km²; ch. t. St. Pierre, fisheries; p. of St. P. and M. (est. 1987) 6,300.

St. Pölten, t., Lower **Austria**; nr. Vienna; founded round an abbey; textiles, machin.; p. (1981) 50,419.

St. Quentin, t., Aisne dep., **France**; on R. Somme; impt. textile ctr.; p. (1982) 65,067.

St. Raphaël, t., Var dep., S.E. **France** resort on Fr. Riviera, S.W. of Cannes; marina; p. (1982) 24,310.

St. Rémy, t., Bouches-du-Rhône dep., **France**; Roman antiquities; p. (1982) 8,439.

St. Thomas, t., Ont., **Canada**; ctr. of agr. dist.; rly. ctr.; lt. inds.; p. (1981) 28,165.

St. Thomas, t., Atl. Oc.; main economic ctr. of **USA Virgin Is.**; 80 per cent of p. live in pt. of Charlotte Amalie; tourism; p. (1980) 44,218.

St. Thomas I. See **São Tomé.**

St. Trond, t., Limburg, **Belgium**; impt. fruit mkt.; p. (1982) 36,591.

St. Tropez, t., Var dep., S.E. **France**; on Fr. Riviera; popular, expanding tourist resort; marina; p. (1982) 6,248.

St. Vincent, c., S.W. **Portugal**; Spanish fleet defeated by British 1797.

St. Vincent, Gulf of, lge. inlet, S. **Australia**; penetrates 160 km inland, max. width 65 km; Pt. Adelaide is on E. side.

St. Vincent, I., fully ind. st. (1979); **St. Vincent and the Grenadines**; one of Windward gr., **W.I.**; volcanic; exp. bananas, arrowroot from alluvial soils in S.W. which has majority of p.; subsistence agr. on hill slopes; cap. Kingstown; inc. 5 Is. in Grena-

dines; a. 389 km²; p. (est. 1985) 138,000.

Sakai, sub. of Osaka, Honshu, **Japan**; industl. ctr., engin., chemicals, textiles, electricity generation; p. (1985) 818,368.

Sakhalin, I., off cst. of Siberia; with Kuriles forms Sakhalin oblast of **RSFSR**; herring fisheries, coal, naphtha, alluvial gold, oil, timber, natural gas; oil pipelines connected to Komsomolsk and Khabarovsk refineries; a. c. 63,610 km²; p. (1970) 616,000.

Sakashima Is. See **Ryuku.**

Sakura-jima, peninsula, S. Kyushu, **Japan**; former I. joined to mainland by lava flows; famed for fruit and vegetables.

Sala, t., Västmanland, **Sweden**; silver mine worked for over 400 years, now to limited extent; lime, bricks; p. (1961) 11,015.

Salado, R., N.W. **Argentina**; impt. Andean trib. of Paraná R.; 800 km long.

Salamanca, t., Guanajuato st., **Mexico**; oil refining; ammonia plant; natural gas pipeline to Guadalajara; p. (1980) 160,040.

Salamanca, t., cap. of S. prov., **Spain**; on R. Tormes; old univ., 2 caths., many convents; p. (1987) 155,612.

Salamis, I., **Greece**; opposite harbour of Athens; spt. and ch. t. S.; famous naval battle 480 B.C.; p. (1981) 20,807.

Salar de Uyumi, windswept, dry, salt flat, S.W. **Bolivia.**

Salavat, t., **RSFSR**; in Bashkiria, 144 km S. of Ufa; ctr. of oilfield; glass factory; became t. in 1954; p. (est. 1985) 149,000.

Sala-y-Gomez, barren, uninhabited volcanic I., **Pac. Oc.**; belonging to Chile, 328 km E.N.E. of Easter I.

Salazar, **Mexico**; nr. Mexico City; alt. 2,897 m; nuclear reactor for radioisotopes for medical, industl. and agr. purposes.

Salcombe, t., South Hams, S. Devon, **Eng.**; mkt.; fishing; resort; p. (1981) 2,374.

Saldanha Bay, inlet on W. cst. C. of Good Hope, **S. Africa**; whaling, fishing; fish-canning at t. of S.B.; p. (1960) 2,195 (t.).

Sale, t., Victoria, **Australia**; tr. of lge. irrigated agr. a.; gas processing and crude oil stabilisation plant (1969) ; p. (est. 1983) 13,800.

Sale, t., Trafford, Gtr. Manchester, **Eng.**; residtl. sub. of Manchester; p. (1981) 57,824.

Sale or **Salch**, spt., Fez, **Morocco**; former pirate headquarters; fishing, fish-processing, carpets; p. (1982) 289,391.

Salekhard, t., R. pt., N.W. Siberia, **RSFSR**; on R. Ob; fisheries, collecting ctr. for furs; exp. timber; p. c. 22,000.

Salem, t., Tamil Nadu, **India**; industl. ctr., rly. junc. in picturesque valley; local iron ore, manganese mng.; mineral processing, textiles; p. (1981) 361,394 (t.), 518,615 (met. a.).

Salem, t., Mass., **USA**; 24 km from Boston; one of oldest New England ts.; many fine bldgs.; textiles, leather prods., machin., electronics; p. (1980) 38,220.

Salem, t., st. cap. Ore., **USA**; on Willamette R.; univ.; fruit packing, flour milling and canning; p. (1984) 90,300 (t.), 255,200 (met. a.).

Salemi, t., Sicily, **Italy**; the anc. Halicyæ; famous Norman cas., terracotta vases; p. (1981) 12,289.

Salerno, c., cap. of Salerno prov., in Campania, S. **Italy**; on G. of S.; fishing pt. and comm. ctr.; machin., textiles, food processing; univ.; famous for Allied landing 1943; p. (1984) 156,921.

Salford, c., met. dist., Gtr. Manchester, **Eng.**; on R. Irwell, adjoining Manchester; inc. terminal docks of Manchester Ship Canal; univ.; varied inds.; p. and industl. decentralization; p. (est. 1988) 235,600.

Salgótarján, t., N. **Hungary**; coal mng., agr. machin., tools, glass; p. (est. 1985) 49,000.

Salina, t., Kan., **USA**; on Smoky Hill R.; univ.; flour milling, cattle mkt., farm implements; p. (1980) 41,843.

Salinas, t., Cal., **USA**; comm., tr. and processing ctr. for fertile Salinas valley; birthplace of John Steinbeck; p. (1984) 87,600 (t.), 319,200 (met. a.).

Salinas, R., Cal., **USA**; rises in US Coast Range, flows N.W. into Bay of Monterey, Pac. Oc.; fertile valley floor irrigated to produce hard and stone fruits, mkt. garden produce (especially lettuce), alfalfa; 166 km long.

Salinas-Grandes, Las, gr. salt marsh region, **Argentina**; provs. Santiago del Estero and Cordoba; dry, no Rs.

Salisbury, t., South **Australia;** part of Adelaide; research ctr. for long-range weapons; p. (1976) 77,476.

Salisbury (New Sarum), cath. c., l. gov. dist., Wilts., **Eng.;** on S. edge of Salisbury Plain at confluence of Rs. Avon and Wily; Old Sarum to N. was the Roman Sorbiodunum and present site represents a move (1220) to a more sheltered and better watered a. in valley; cath. pure Early English with tallest spire in Eng. (123 m); ctr. mediaeval woollen ind.; regional ctr. with engin. and food-processing inds.; p. (est. 1988) 101,000 (dist.).

Salisbury. *See* Harare.

Salisbury Plain, Wilts., **Eng.;** chalk upland, N. of Salisbury; Stonehenge; army training a.; a. 777 km².

Salonika. *See* Thessaloniki.

Salmon, R., Idaho, **USA;** canyon c. 1·6 km deep and 16 km wide in places; rapids navigable downstream only, thus its name of River of No Return; l. c. 680 km.

Salop. *See* Shropshire.

Salpau Selka, Finland; most S. gravel ridge.

Salsette, I., India; connected by bridge and causeway with Bombay; popular seaside resort at Juhu; a. 624 km².

Salt, R., Arizona, **USA;** rises in Colorado plateau, flows into Gila R. below Phoenix; rich, irrigated fruit growing valley in lower course; many multipurpose schemes in Salt River Valley project; length 384 km. *See also* **Roosevelt Dam.**

Salta, c., cap. of Salta prov., **Argentina;** on R. Salta; picturesque c. with colonial atmosphere, cath.; comm. ctr. for rich agr. a.; p. (1980) 261,000.

Saltash, mkt. t., Caradon, Cornwall, **Eng.;** on W. side of Tamar estuary; lowest bridging point of Tamar by Brunel's rly. bridge (1859) and toll road bridge; p. (1981) 12,659.

Saltburn and Markse-by-the-Sea, t., Langbaurgh, Cleveland, **Eng.;** seaside resort; 16 km E. of Middlesborough; p. (1981) 19,989.

Saltcoats, burgh, Cunninghame, **Scot.;** on Firth of Clyde 3 km S. of Ardrossan; sm. harbour; hosiery; mainly residtl.; p. (1981) 12,807.

Saltillo, c., cap. of Coahuila st., **Mexico;** comm., industl., and mng. ctr.; p. (1980) 321,758.

Salt Lake City, c., cap. of Utah, **USA;** nr. Gr. Salt L., H.Q. of Mormonism; temple and univ.; agr. comm. ctr. for irrigated a.; meat packing; p. (1984) 164,800 (c.), 1,025,300 (met. a.).

Salto, c., cap. of S. dep., **Uruguay;** on Uruguay R., nr. Concordia (Argentina); rly. and tr. ctr. for agr. a.; citrus fruit, grapes, wine; p. (1985) 80,787.

Salton Sea, L., S. Cal., **USA;** 80 m below sealevel in depression which extends N.W. from head of G. of Cal.; ctr. of inland drainage; a. 699 km². *See also* **Imperial Valley.**

Salvador, spt., cap. of Bahia, **Brazil;** Brazil's first cap.; many years of economic stagnation now replaced by rapid growth; Brazil's first oil strike here in 1939; refining less impt. than petrochemicals at Camaçari complex (started 1972); new pt., naval base; hydro-elect. from Paulo Afonso encouraging many new light inds.; cement, aluminium, laminated timber, special alloys; p. (est. 1985) 1,811,400.

Salvador, El, rep., on Pac. cst. of Central America; bounded by Guatemala to W. and Honduras to N. and E.; comprises 14 administrative departments; temperate volcanic uplands, hot humid coastal lowlands; comm. economy mainly agr., especially coffee, also developing comm. fisheries and iron and steel ind.; electric power from dam across Lempa R.; well-developed transport system, inc. Pan-American Highway; pt. at Acajutla and airport at Ilopango; member of Central American Common Market; protracted guerrilla warfare during much of the 1980s; cap. San Salvador; a. 21,331 km²; p. (est. 1985) 5,480,000.

Salween, R., S.E. **Asia;** rises in E. Tibet, crosses Yunnan, descending from Burma to empty in G. of Martaban; many rapids; navigable to Moulmein; hydroelec. scheme; 2,880 km long.

Salzburg, c., cap. of Salzburg prov., **Austria;** on R. Salzach; cath., cas.; birthplace of Mozart;

tourist resort; annual music festival; p. (1981) 139,426 (c.), 267,277 (met. a.).

Salzburg, prov., **Austria;** adjoins Bavaria and the Tyrol, on N. slope of E. Alps; pastoral agr.; timber and some mineral wealth; hydro-electric power; cap. Salzburg; a. 7,154 km²; p. (est. 1986) 460,000.

Salzgitter, t., Lower Saxony, **W. Germany;** S.W. of Brunswick; steel, engin., wagon bldg., fertilisers; p. (est. 1986) 105,400.

Salzkammergut, lake dist., Upper **Austria;** saline baths at Aussee and Ischl; tourist region; stock-raising forestry.

Samar, I., Philippines; separated from Leyte by narrow strait; mainly forested mtns.; hemp, rice in lowlands; cap. Catbalogan; typhoons; a. 13,080 km²; p. (1970) 997,336.

Samarkand, c., Uzbek SSR, **USSR;** one of oldest cs. in world, sited in productive oasis on Zeravshan R.; many historical associations and anc. bldgs; agr. tr. ctr.; food processing; cotton, silk; univ.; p. (est. 1985) 371,000.

Samarra, t., Iraq; on Tigris R., N. of Baghdad; holy c. of Shiite sect; p. c. 10,000.

Sambalpur, t., Orissa, **India;** on Hirakud reservoir of Mahandi R.; p. (1971) 64,675.

Sambhar, salt lake, Rajasthan, **India;** exploited on lge. scale; a. 233 km².

Sambre, R., trib. of R. Meuse at Namur; crosses Franco-Belgian coal basin; part of N. Fr.–S. Belgian waterway system; 176 km long.

Samnan, t., N. **Iran;** in foothills of Elburz mtns.; iron, sulphur ores, petroleum.

Samoa, archipelago, S. **Pac. Oc.;** volcanic mtns., tropical climate; agr., fishing; comprises (1) American Samoa, a. 197 km²; p. (est. 1985) 35,000; (2) Western Samoa, indep. st., cap. and ch. spt. Apia; a. 2,841 km²; p. (est. 1985) 163,000. *See* **Western Samoa.**

Sámos, I., Aegean Sea, off W. cst. Anatolia, belonging to **Greece;** mtnous., fine climate, fertile soils; wine, tobacco, Med. crops; ch. t. Vathy; a. 466 km²; p. (1981) 40,519.

Samothrace, I., Aegean Sea, **Greece;** barren, mtnous.; sparse p.; goats, grain, olives, sponge fishing; a. 184 km²; p. c. 4,000.

Samsö, I., Kattegat, **Denmark;** a. 109 km²; p. (est. 1965) 5,852.

Samsun, spt., Trabzon, **Turkey;** on Black Sea cst.; exp. tobacco, grain, timber, wax, wool, skins, copper gds., antimony, chemical complex; p. (1985) 240,674.

San, R., S.E. **Poland;** trib. of R. Vistula; bdy. between Poland and Ukraine; navigable in lower course; 442 km long.

Sana'a, c., cap. of **Yemen Arab Rep.;** walled c. at 2,217 m; tr. in silk, cottons, hides, grapes; handicraft inds.; Islamic cultural and educational ctr.; p. (1981) 277,818.

San Andreas Fault, Cal., **USA;** shearing plate bdy. which extends from G. of Cal. to San Francisco; stress liable to cause sudden sharp earthquake as it did in 1906. *See* **F9.**

San Angelo, t., Texas, **USA;** on R. Concho; cattle, wool, mohair mkt.; dairy produce, petroleum, machine-shop prod.; p. (1980) 73,240.

San Antonio, sm. coastal t., Angola, Africa; at mouth of R. Zaïre; serves as occasional pt. of embarkation for travellers from lower regions of Zaïre.

San Antonio, spt., Chile; nearest pt. for Santiago; holiday resort; agr. prods.; exp. copper; p. (1982) 65,174.

San Antonio, C., most W. point of Cuba.

San Antonio, c., cap. of Bexar co., Texas, **USA;** in fertile San Antonio valley; serves farming and livestock a.; oil refining, food processing, meat packing; military installations in a.; warm climate attracts winter tourist tr.; Mexican atmosphere; siege of Alamo (1836); p. (1984) 842,800 (c.), 1,188,500 (met. a.).

San Bernardino, c., Cal., **USA;** founded and planned by Mormons (1852) rly. ctr.; citrus fruit packing and tr.; p. (1984) 130,400; inc. in Los Angeles met. a.

San Bruno, t., Cal., **USA;** 16 km S. of San Francisco; site of international airpt.; printing, mainly residtl.; p. (1980) 35,417.

San Carlos, t., Luzon, **Philippines;** p. (est. 1984) 107,080.

San Cristóbal, c., cap. of Táchira st., **Venezuela;** at 830 m nr. Colombian bdy.; mng. and comm. ctr.; coffee, cacao, sugar; food-processing, cement; cath.; p. (1981) 198,600.

Sancti Spiritus, t., Las Villas, **Cuba;** comm. ctr. in grazing dist.; tr. in sugar tobacco; agr. processing; p. (est. 1983) 74,000.

Sandakan, t., Sabah, **Malaysia;** fine natural harbour on N.E. cst.; exp. agr. prods., timber, rubber; sawmilling, fishing; p. (1980) 74,000.

Sanday, I., Barra Is., Orkney, **Scot.;** flat, many shipwrecks; agr., fishing; p. (1971) 592.

Sandbach, mkt. t., Cheshire, **Eng.;** 8 km N.E. of Crewe; salt, chemicals, comm. vehicles; p. (1981) 14,747.

Sandefjord, t., Vestfold prov., S.E. **Norway;** whaling pt. nr. mouth of Oslo Fjord; shipyds., whale-processing; chemicals; p. (est. 1987) 35,441.

Sandhurst, v., Berkshire, **Eng.;** 16 km S.E. of Reading; Royal Military Academy, National Army Museum.

Sandia, t., N.M., **USA;** atomic research ctr.

San Diego, c., Cal., **USA;** first Spanish settlement in Cal. 1542; on Pac. cst., 16 km N. of Mexican border; fine natural harbour, naval base; fish-canning, aircraft; comm. ctr. for fruit-and vegetable-growing dist.; p. (1984) 960,500 (c.), 2,063,900 (met. a.).

Sandlings, The, S.E. Suffolk, **Eng.;** a. of glacial sands, forming heathland; difficult agr. conditions.

Sandown-Shanklin, t., South Wight, I. of Wight, **Eng.;** on Sandown Bay; resort; p. (1981) 16,852.

Sandringham, v., Norfolk, **Eng.;** Royal residence since 1861.

Sandusky, c., Ohio, **USA;** on S. cst. L. Erie; tr. in coal, fruit, foodstuffs; paper, farm implements, chemicals; summer resort of Cedar Point nearby; p. (1980) 31,360.

Sandviken, t., Gävleborg, **Sweden;** impt. steel inds.; p. (est. 1986) 40,000.

Sandwell, met. dist., West Midlands, **Eng.;** comprises Warley and West Bromwich; p. (est. 1988) 296,300.

Sandwich, t., Kent, **Eng.;** Cinque pt. at mouth of Stour R.; harbour silted up 16th cent.; mkt. lt. inds.; p. (1981) 4,227.

Sandwich Is., dependency of Falkland Is., Brit. Crown col. S. **Atlantic.**

Sandy, t., Mid Beds., **Eng.;** 5 km N.W. of Biggleswade; mkt. gardening; p. (1981) 8,048.

Sandy Hook, peninsula, N.J., **USA;** projects into lower bay of N.Y.; government reservation.

San Felipe, cap. of Aconcagua prov., **Chile;** 72 km N. of Santiago; agr., copper and gold-mng. ctr.; p. (1982) 38,254.

San Felipe, cap. of Yaracuy st., **Venezuela;** ctr. of agr. dist. producing coffee, sugar and other tropical prods.; p. (est. 1980) 42,905.

San Fernando, N.W. sub. of Buenos Aires, **Argentina;** spt. on Rio de la Plata; industl. ctr., footwear, furniture, fish canning.

San Fernando, cap. of Colchagua prov., **Chile;** agr. mkt. ctr.; p. (1982) 38,871.

San Fernando, t., Bay of Cadiz, S. **Spain;** pt. has naval arsenal; salt mftg.; much of surrounding marshland now reclaimed; p. (1981) 78,048.

San Fernando, spt., Trinidad, **W.I.;** on W. cst. 40 km S. of Port of Spain; exp. sugar, asphalt, petrol; p. (1980) 33,400.

San Fernando, t., **Venezuela;** ctr. cattle ranching region of upper Llanos; oil; p. (1980) 54,000.

San Francisco, c., Cal., **USA;** spt. on S. F. Bay; entrance spanned by Golden Gate Bridge; attractive hilly site; cosmopolitan c. with several immigrant quarters; comm. and financial ctr. with many varied inds.; univ.; sudden earthquake (1906) destroyed much of c. (*see* **F9**); p. (1984) 712,800 (c.), 5,684,600 (met. a. with Oakland).

Sangihe Is., Indonesia; volcanic archipelago between Kalimantan and Philippines; sago, nutmeg, copra; ch. t. and spt. Tahuna; a. 813 km²; p. c. 90,000.

San Gimignano, hill t., Tuscany, **Italy;** overlooks Val d'Elsa; 13th cent. mediaeval t., preserved as national monument; tourist ctr.; p. (1981) 7,877.

San Giovanni in Fiore, t., Calabria, **Italy;** agr. ctr. at 1,006 m nr. confluence of Neto and Arvo Rs.; p. (1981) 20,154.

Sangli, t., Maharastra, **India;** nr. Miraj on Karnataka border; p. (1981) 269,000 (met. a.).

Sangre de Cristo Mtns., part of Rocky mtns. **USA;** name (Span.—Blood of Christ) derives from reddish hue seen at sunset; highest summit Blanca Peak 4,367 m.

San Joaquin, R., Cal., **USA;** forms part of Central Valley project for irrigation of farmlands of R. valley; 512 km long.

San José, prov., **Costa Rica;** bauxite mng. nr. San Isidro del General projected with road to Punta Uvita where sm. pt. will be built; cap. San José.

San José, c., cap. of **Costa Rica;** sited at c. 1,160 m in S. J. basin; cath., univ., observatory, theatre, park; ch. industl. and comm. ctr. of rep.; oil refining, agr. processing; major route ctr., international airport; p. (1984) 241,464.

San José, t., cap. of San José prov., **Uruguay;** impt. mkt.; flour-milling; p. (est. 1971) 27,500.

San José, c., Cal, **USA;** in fertile Santa Clara valley; fruit and vegetable canning and processing, chemicals, paper, electronics; p. (1984) 686,200 (c.); inc. in met. a. of San Francisco.

San Juan, prov., **Argentina;** at foot of Andes; gold, copper mng.; cap. S. J.; a. 89,179 km²; p. (1980) 469,973.

San Juan, c., cap. of San Juan prov., **Argentina;** comm. ctr. of agr. a., tr. in wine, fruit, cattle; p. (1980) 118,000 (c.), 292,000 (met. a.).

San Juan, c., cap. of **Puerto Rico;** built in part on I.; major spt. on N.E. cst.; exp. agr. prod. to **USA;** agr. processing; modern inds. inc. oil refining, cement, metallurgy, pharmaceuticals; cath., univ.; p. (1980) 1,086,000 (met. a.).

San Juan, R., **Central America;** divides Nicaragua and Costa Rica; plans made for its canalisation, which would give both countries a clear waterway from Caribbean to Pac.; 144 km long.

San Juan, R., Col., N.M., and Utah., **USA;** flows in goose-neck incised meanders; Navajo Dam part of Colorado River storage project, bringing irrigation to Navajo Indian reservation; 640 km long.

San Juan del Norte (Greytown), pt. on Caribbean cst. of **Nicaragua;** silting; sm. exp. of bananas, hardwoods; p. (1963) 599.

San Juan del Sur, spt., on Pac. cst., **Nicaragua;** exp. ctr. for coffee, sugar, cocoa, balsam; p. (est. 1970) 4,223.

Sankt Ingbert, t., Saarland, **W. Germany;** N.E. of Saarbrücken; coal mng.; iron, glass, machin., textiles, leather; p. (est. 1986) 40,500.

Sankt Pölten, t., Lower **Austria;** rly. and industl. ctr.; hydroelectric power sta.; p. c. 41,000.

San Leandro, t., Cal., **USA;** food processing; Portuguese residents have annual religious festival; p. (1980) 63,952.

San Lorenzo, t., **Argentina;** 22 km N. Rosario; lge. chemical wks., oil refining.

Sanlúcar de Barrameda, pt., Cadiz prov., **Spain;** nr. mouth of R. Guadalquivir; wines and agr. prod.; mediaeval cas.; bathing resort; p. (1981) 48,496.

San Luis, c., cap. of S. L. prov., **Argentina;** ctr. of cattle, grain, wine producing dist.; rich mineral deposits in surrounding a.; hydroelectric power sta. and irrigation dam nearby; p. (1980) 212,837.

San Luis Potosi, st., **Mexico;** leading mng. st.; metals melting, food-processing; cap. San Luis Potosi; a. 63,235 km²; p. (1980) 1,670,637.

San Luis Potosi, t., cap. of San Luis Potosi st., **Mexico;** industl. and comm. ctr.; metallurgy textiles; cath.; palace; p. (1980) 406,630.

San Marino, sm. indep. rep., **Italy;** in Apennines nr. Rimini; has kept its independence since 4th cent. A.D.; exp. wine, textiles, building stone; cap. San Marino; a. 62 km²; p. (est. 1986) 22,638 resident citizens.

San Marino, t., cap. of **San Marino rep.;** on slope of Mt. Titano, 19 km. S.W. of Rimini; tourism; p. (est. 1986) 4,363.

San Miguel, t., **El Salvador,** at foot of San Miguel volcano; sisal-fibre, coffee, cattle, cotton, indigo; cath.; p. (1980) 157,838.

San Miguel de Allende, t., Guanajuato st., **Mexico;** picturesque hilly site; famous art institute.

San Miguel de Tucumán, c., cap. Tucumán prov.,

Argentina; on R. Sali; univ.; breweries, sawmills, flour, sugar; p. (1980) 394,000, (c.), 499,000 (met. a.).

San Millán de la Cogolla, Spain; oldest (6th cent.) monastic foundation in Spain; in Cárdenas valley (Logrono prov.); p. (1981) 298.

San Nicolas, R. pt., **Argentina**; on Paraná R.; cattle, flour, agr. prod., distillery, steel plant; p. (1980) 96,313.

Sanniya Hor, shallow L., **Iraq**; linked to R. Tigris; acts as flood control reservoir.

Sanok, t., Rzeszow prov., S.E. **Poland**; picturesque site on steep banks of San R.; industl. ctr., comm. vehicles, rubber gds.; p. (1970) 21,600.

San-Pedro, spt., **Côte d'Ivoire**; new pt. (1970) linked with development of timber production in hinterland and to Bangolo iron ore deposits; iron pelletizing plant; p. (est. 1980) 50,000.

San Pedro, spt., a. of Los Angeles, Cal., **USA**; shipyds., oil refining, fruit canning.

San Pedro de Macoris, spt., **Dominican Rep.**; on Caribbean; exp. sugar, sugar prods.; clothing, soap; p. (est. 1982) 115,000.

San Pedro Sula, t., **Honduras**; ctr. for banana and sugar inds.; food processing; p. (est. 1983) 345,000.

Sanquhar, burgh, Nithsdale, **Scot.**; coal mng., brick mkg.; p. (1981) 2,169.

San Rafael, t., **W. Argentina**; comm. ctr. for agr. a.; food processing, meat, wine, fruit; p. (1980) 70,477.

San Remo, sm. pt., **Italy**; winter resort on Italian Riviera; flower mkt., olive oil, lemons, wine; 12th cent. church; p. (1981) 60,787.

San Salvador (Watling's I.), Bahama Is., **W.I.**; discovered by Columbus 1492, his first sight of the New World; a. 155 km²; p. (1980) 804.

San Salvador, c., cap. of **El Salvador**; stands c. 600 m a.s.l.; ch. comm. and industl. ctr.; food processing, textile and tobacco inds.; univ., observatory; oil refining; liable to earthquakes; p. (1981) 452,614.

Sansanding, t., **Mali**, W. Africa; lge. barrage across R. Niger.

San Sebastian, c., cap. of Guipúzcoa prov., N. **Spain**; spt. on Bay of Biscay, at foot of Mt. Urgull; seaside resort; fishing, textiles, paper, glass; captured by Wellington 1813; p. (1987) 176,586.

San Severo, mkt. t., S. **Italy**; hilltop site, 24 km N.W. of Foggia, Apulia; cath.; wine ctr., cream of tartar, bricks; p. (1981) 54,273.

Santa Ana, c., W. **El Salvador**; second lgst. c. of rep.; coffee, sugar, cattle; Santa Ana volcano nearby; p. (1980) 204,570.

Santa Ana, c., Cal., **USA**; S.E. of Los Angeles; in fruit farming a.; fruit pkg., walnuts, oranges; p. (1984) 225,400 inc. in Los Angeles met. a.

Santa Barbara, c., Cal., **USA**; resort on Pac. cst.; picturesque setting, mild climate; p. (1984) 76,900 (c.), 322,800 (met. a.).

Santa Barbara Is., **USA**; along S. cst. of Cal.; inc. Santa Catalina I., a favourite resort.

Santa Catarina, st., **Brazil**; between Atl. and Argentina; tobacco, manioc, fruit, hogs; impt. coal producer; cap. Florianópolis; a. 95,830 km²; p. (est. 1985) 4,085,900.

Santa Clara, c., **Cuba**; attractive site at over 360 m; agr. and comm. ctr. for sugar and tobacco; decisive victory for guerrilla army of Fidel Castro 1959; p. (1985) 178,300.

Santa Clara, c., W. Cal., **USA**; citrus fruit pkg.; electronics, plastics, chemicals; univ.; p. (1980) 87,700.

Santa Clara Valley, Cal., **USA**; extends S. from San Francisco Bay; intensive fruit-growing under irrigation, prunes; ch. t. San José.

Santa Cruz, c., cap. of S.C. dep., **Bolivia**; alt. 457 m; agr. mkt. for sugar, coffee, rice, cattle; oil refining; gas pipeline planned; international airport; impt. reserves iron ore; univ.; p. (est. 1982) 376,917.

Santa Cruz de la Sierra, t., **Bolivia**; on R. Piray; sugar, flour; distilling; p. (1982) 376,917.

Santa Cruz de Tenerife, pt. on Tenerife I., **Canary Is.**; cap. of S.C. de T. prov., Spain; gd. harbour, oil refinery; exp. agr. prods.; developing resort in attractive a. with mild climate; p. (1986) 211,209.

Santa Cruz Is., volcanic gr., S. Pac. Oc.; part of Solomon Is.; exp. copra.

Santa Fé, c., cap. of S.F. prov., **Argentina**; impt. R. pt. on I. in Salado R.; comm. ctr. for surrounding grain and livestock a.; food processing; univ., cath.; p. (1980) 292,000.

Santa Fé, t., N.M., **USA**; at base of Sangre de Cristo range; oldest capital in US founded by Spaniards 1610; tourist and comm. ctr.; p. (1984) 52,300 (t.), 100,500 (met. a.).

Santa Isabel. *See* **Malabo.**

Santa Maria, t., Rio Grande do Sul, **Brazil**; rly. junc., rly. engin., agr. tr. and processing; p. (est. 1985) 197,200.

Santa Maria de Garoña, Spain; nr. Burgos; nuclear power plant being built.

Santa Marta, spt., cap of Magdalena dep., **Colombia**; banana pt. on deep bay at mouth of Manzanares R., serving local plantations; p. (1985) 225,936.

Santa Monica, c., Cal., **USA**; W. of Los Angeles; attractive site on Santa Monica Bay; aircraft, plastics, cosmetics; p. (1980) 88,314.

Santander, c., cap. of Santander prov., N. **Spain**; spt. and seaside resort on Bay of Biscay; exp. iron and zinc ore, agr. prods.; heavy inds., shipbldg., oil refining, chemicals; former summer resort of Spanish court; cath.; p. (1987) 187,222.

Santarém, t., Pará, **Brazil**; rubber, cacao, Brazil nuts, sugar; p. (est. 1985) 227,400

Santarém, t., cap. of Ribatejo prov., **Portugal**; on slope of hill overlooking Tagus R.; Moorish cas.; mkt. for agr. prod.; p. (1981) 52,138.

Santa Rosa, t., cap. of La Pampa terr., **Argentina**; p. (1980) 51,689.

Santa Rosa, t., Cal., **USA**; tr. and industl. ctr. for Somona Valley fruit-growing a.; p. (1980) 300,000 (met. a.).

Santiago, c., cap of **Chile** and S. prov.; planned t. ctr. in broad valley of Mapoche R., one of lgst. and most attractive cs. in S. America; cultural, comm., political and financial ctr., focus of routes; univ.; textiles, chemicals, paper, iron and steel; rapidly growing p.; p. (est. 1985) 4,318,305 (met. a.).

Santiago de Compostela, c., La Coruña, **Spain**; on R. Sar, surrounded by hills; univ., palace, cath. (with tomb of St. James); famous place of pilgrimage; agr. tr., food processing, tourism; p. (1981) 72,993.

Santiago de Cuba, c., **Cuba**; spt. on S. cst., exp. minerals, agr. prods., sugar, tobacco; oil refining, cigars, soap; cath., univ.; p. (1985) 358,800.

Santiago del Estero, c., cap. of S. del E. prov., **Argentina**; transportation ctr. of Argentine Chaco; agr. tr. ctr., cattle, food processing; p. (1980) 149,000.

Santiago de los Caballeros, t., **Dominican Rep.**; comm. agr. ctr. in fertile a.; food processing, coffee, rice, tobacco; cigars, cigarettes; p. (est. 1982) 394,000.

Santis, mtn., on border cans. St. Gallen and Appenzell, **Switzerland**; alt. 2,506 m. Europe's hgst. television transmitter on summit.

Santo Andre, c., **Brazil**; part of industl. complex built to S.E. of São Paulo to relieve congestion; specialises in metalware and chems., p. (est. 1985) 637,000.

Santo Domingo, cap. **Dominican Rep.**; pt. on S. cst. exp. agr. prods.; reputed burial place of Columbus; univ.; p. (1981) 1,313,172.

Santo Tomé de la Guayana (Puerto Ordaz) c., S.E. **Venezuela**; new industl. c. nr. confluence of Orinoco and Caroni Rs.; iron mines, steel, hydroelec. power and aluminium plants in a.; vast industl. complex projected.

Santorine. *See* **Thira.**

Santos, c., spt., São Paulo, **Brazil**; world's ch. coffee pt.; also exp. oranges, bananas, cotton, and industl. prod. from modern harbour; p. (est. 1985) 461,096.

San Vicente, t., cap. of S.V. dep., **El Salvador**; ctr. for coffee, sugar, tobacco; mnfs. leather gds., shawls, hats; p. (1980) 62,175.

São Bernardo, c., **Brazil**; part of industl. complex built to relieve congestion in São Paulo which lies to N.W.; p. (est. 1985) 565,600.

São Caetano, c., **Brazil**; ctr. for metalwk. built to S.E. of São Paulo to relieve congestion; p. (est. 1985) 171,200.

São Carlos, t., São Paulo st., **Brazil**; 192 km N.W. of São Paulo; ctr. of coffee-growing a.; textiles, refrigerators, furniture; p. (est. 1985) 140,400.

São Francisco, R., **Brazil**; flows from Minas Gerais prov. to Alt.; navigable for 1,440 km of middle course; used for hydroelectric power at Paulo Afonso falls and Três Marias dam; 2,560 km long.

São Goncalo, t., Rio de Janeiro, **Brazil**; fast-growing t.; p. (est. 1985) 731,000.

São Jeronimo, t., Rio Grande do Sul, **Brazil**; low-grade coal; p. (est. 1985) 30,600.

São João do Meriti, t., Rio de Janeiro, **Brazil**; industl. and comm. ctr.; p. (est. 1985) 459,100.

São José dos Campos, t., São Paulo, **Brazil**; ctr. of Brazil's aircraft ind.; synthetic fibres, telecommunication equipment, chems., motor vehicle components; p. (est. 1985) 374,500.

São Leopoldo, t., Rio Grande do Sul, S. **Brazil**; 32 km N. of Porto Alegre; mkt. t.; p. (est. 1985) 114,100.

São Luis, pt., cap. of Maranhão st., **Brazil**; on São Luis I.; noted cultural ctr. in 19th cent.; new aluminium plant (1984); p. (est. 1985) 564,400.

São Miguel, I., Azores; lgst. and most productive I. of archipelago; ch. t. and spt. Ponta Delgada, exp. agr. prods., pineapples; volcanic landscape a tourist attraction; p. (1981) 131,908.

Saône, R., **France**; rises in Vosges and flows to R. Rhône at Lyons; navigable, canalised; 451 km long.

Saone-et-Loire, dep., **France**; mtnous.; noted vineyards; cap. Mâcon; a. 8,627 km²; p. (1982) 571,500.

São Paulo, st., **Brazil**; on Atl. cst.; major industl. a. of S. America; coffee, cotton, sugar, rice, maize; vehicles, elec. gds., chemicals, textiles, telecomm. equipment, metal-wkg. plants; cap. São Paulo; Santos lgst pt. in Brazil; a. 247,226 km²; p. (est. 1985) 29,541,900.

São Paulo, c., cap. of São Paulo st., **Brazil**; fast-growing c., comm. and industl. ctr. of rep. and leading c. of S. America; vehicles, machin., elec. gds., textiles, pharmaceuticals; aluminium refinery; nearby pt. Santos ships rich agr. prod. from hinterland; 20 per cent reduction in employment in severe recession (1980–3); 2 univs., cath.; p. (est. 1985) 10,099,100.

São Roque, Cape of, Rio Grande do Norte, N.E. **Brazil**; most N.E. point of S. America.

São Tomé, cap. **São Tomé and Principe**; p. (est. 1985) 30,000.

São Tomé and Principe, former Port. col.; **W. Africa**; volcanic Is. in G. of Guinea; cocoa, coffee; cap. São Tomé; a. 963 km²; airpt. extended to encourage tourism; indep. achieved as democratic rep. 1975; p. (est. 1987) 113,000.

São Vicente, c., S.E. São Paulo, **Brazil**; first Portuguese settlement in Brazil (1532), on I. off mainland; sub. of Santos; fashionable beach resort; p. (est. 1985) 240,800.

Sapele, t., Benin st., **Nigeria**; S. of Benin; lge. lumber mill and plywood plant.

Sapporo, c., Hokkaido, **Japan**; main t. of Hokkaido; planned t.; univ.; brewing, dairy processing, sawmills; p. (1987) 1,596,000.

Saqqara, v., **Egypt**; necropolis of anc. Memphis; step pyramids; p. (1966) 12,700.

Sarajevo, c., cap. of Bosnia and Hercegovina, **Yugoslavia**; major route ctr., airport; ctr. of Yugoslav Moslems; mosques, caths.; diversified mnfs., metallurgy, elec. prods., textiles, tobacco, pottery; assassination 28 June 1914 of Archduke Francis Ferdinand precipitated First World War; p. (1981) 448,500.

Saransk, c., Mordovian ASSR, **RSFSR**; 232 km S.E. of Gorki; univ.; elec. equipment, engin., agr. processing; p. (est. 1985) 307,000.

Sarapul, c., **RSFSR**; pt. on R. Kama; radio equipment, machin., footwear, gloves; p. (est. 1985) 110,000.

Sarasota, Fla., **USA**; exp. fruit, veg.; resort; p. (1984) 52,300 (t.), 237,600 (met.a.).

Saratoga Springs, N.Y., **USA**; summer resort at foot of Adirondack mtns., mineral springs; horse-racing; casino; p. (1980) 23,906.

Saratov, c., **RSFSR**; pt. on R. Volga; regional ctr. for agr. prod. of lower Volga valley and oil from Baku; univ.; engin., ball-bearings, textiles, oil refining, sawmilling; p. (1986) 908,000.

Sarawak, st., E. **Malaysia**; mtnous. inland with sparse p.; rubber, sago, pepper grown along coast.; oil; cap. Kuching; a. 121,914 km²; p. (1980) 1,235,553.

Sardinia, I., aut. region, **Italy**; mtnous., dry climate; fertile Campidano plain with fruit, wines, sheep; zinc and lead mng.; tourism; fishing; major petrochemical complex at Ottana; part of former kingdom of Sardinia belonging to house of Savoy; a. 24,002 km²; p. (est. 1986) 1·6 m.

Sargasso Sea, zone S.W. of N. Atl. Oc.; relatively still sea within swirl of warm ocean currents; noted for abundance of gulf-weed on its surface, rich in marine life; named by Columbus.

Sari, c., cap. of Mazandaran prov., **Iran**; p. (1983) 124,663.

Sark, I., **Channel Is.**; 10 km E. of Guernsey; picturesque scenery; tourist ctr.; farming; a. 516 ha; p. (est. 1986) 550.

Sark, R., forms extreme W. bdy. between **Scot.** and **Eng.**

Sarnia, c., and pt., Ont., **Canada**; on St. Clair R.; connected to Port Huron by rly. tunnel; oil refineries, petrochemical inds., agr. tr.; p. (1981) 50,892.

Sarno, t., Campania, **Italy**; spa at foot of mtns. on E. edge of fertile Sarno plain; agr. mkt., textile ctr.; cas.; p. (1981) 30,583.

Šar-Planina, **Yugoslavia**; nr. Skopje; impt. chrome deposits; attractive site, ctr. of mtn. tourism.

Sarpsborg, t., **Norway**; on R. Glommen; lgst. pulp and paper concern in kingdom; hydroelectric power sta.; p. (1980) 12,035.

Sarreguemines, t., Moselle dep., **France**; in Lorraine; potteries based on local clay; coal mng.; p. (1982) 25,178.

Sarthe, dep., N.W. **France**; undulating surface; farming, apples, livestock; coal, linen, potteries; cap. Le Mans; a. 6,247 km²; p. (1982) 500,600.

Sarthe, R., **France**; trib. of R. Loire; 265 km long.

Sasebo, spt., Kyushu, **Japan**; ctr. of coalfield; engin., shipbldg.; p. (1985) 250,635.

Saskatchewan, prov., **Canada**; coniferous forests and plains; Rs. Saskatchewan and Churchill; many lge. Ls.; extreme climate; hydroelec. power; gr. wheat prov.; livestock, dairying; oil, copper, uranium, helium plants, furs, fisheries; cap. Regina; a. 651,903 km²; p. (1986) 1,010,000.

Saskatchewan, R., **Canada**; flows from Rocky mtns. through L. Winnipeg and thence by R. Nelson to Hudson Bay; 2,320 km long.

Saskatoon, c., Saskatchewan, **Canada**; grew rapidly after arrival of rly. (1890); comm. ctr. for grain producing a.; meat packing and tr.; varied inds., cement, oil refining; univ.; p. (1986) 177,641 (c.), 200,665 (met. a.).

Sasolburg, t., O.F.S., **S. Africa**; oil from coal production; gas pipeline to Germiston a. p. (1960) 12,557.

Sassari, t., Sardinia, **Italy**; nr. G. of Asinara; cath., univ.; palaces; tobacco and macaroni wks., cheese; p. (1984) 119,781.

Sattahip, pt., **Thailand**; new pt. inaugurated 1967.

Satu-Mare, t., N.W. **Romania**; agr. machin., handicraft inds. based on local prods., food-processing; cath.; p. (est. 1984) 125,819.

Saudi Arabia, kingdom, Arabian peninsula, S.W. **Asia**; mainly desert, agr. in oases and S.W. upland region of Asir; lgst. producer of oil in Middle East; oil sales account for 85 per cent govt. revenue; steel inds. and oil refinery at Jiddah, petrochemicals developing at Dammam; Moslem holy cs. Mecca and Medina; cap. Riyadh (royal), Mecca (religious), Jiddah (admin.); main pt. King Faisal Port.; a. 2,400,930 km²; p. (est. 1987) 13·6 m. (1,500,000 foreign workers).

Sauerland, dist., N. Rhine–Westphalia, **W. Germany**; plateau, alt. from 150–450 m E. of Rhine; agriculturally poor, largely forested; crossed by R. Wupper, with which are associated industl. ts. Wuppertal (textiles), Solingen and Remscheid (cutlery and special steel); supplies hydroelectric power to Ruhr.

Sault Ste. Marie, t., Ont., **Canada**; pt. on St. Mary's R., opposite Sault Ste. Marie, Mich., to which it is connected by bridge; pulp, paper, iron and steel; tourist ctr. for L. and forest region; p. (1986) 80,905.

Sault Ste. Marie, t., Mich., **USA**; pt. on St. Mary's R.; opposite Sault Ste. Marie, Ont.; calcium carbide; tourist ctr. for fishing, hunting a.; p. (1980) 14,448.

Sault Ste. Marie Canals ("Soo"), **Canada** and **USA**; twin canals on Canadian and American side of shallow channel linking L. Superior and L. Huron; traversed by all wheat and iron-ore traffic from L. Superior pts.; length (Canadian) 2 km; depth 5 m.

Saumur, t., Maine-et-Loire dep., **France**; on R. Loire, 48 km S.W. of Tours; sparkling wines, brandy; flower, vegetable mkt.; cas.; p. (1982) 33,953.

Sauternes, v., Gironde, **France**; name applied to white wines of dist.

Sava, R., Slovenia, **Yugoslavia**; joins Danube at Belgrade; used for hydroelectric power; agr. in valleys; transport axis; 928 km long.

Savage or **Niue,** Cook Is., **Pac. Oc.**; under **N.Z.**; ch. exp. native plaited ware, bananas, copra, and sweet potatoes; ch. pt. Alofi; a. 259 km²; p. (est. 1986) 3,000.

Savaii I., lgst. of Samoan gr., **Pac. Oc.**; volcanic, mtnous., fertile; exp. bananas, copra, cocoa; a. 1,821 km²; p. (1981) 43,150.

Savannah, c., Ga., **USA**; spt. nr. mouth of Savannah R.; rly., fishing and comm. ctr. for Sea Is., Savannah valley and surrounding plantations; mkt. for naval stores; sugar refining, paper, oil refining, diverse mnfs.; tourist ind. stimulated by mild climate; p. (1984) 145,000 (c.), 232,900 (met. a.).

Savannah, R., **USA**; flows between Ga. and S.C., to Atl. Oc.; used for hydroelectric power; 720 km long.

Saverne, Col de, low pass, N.E. **France**; carries trunk rly. from Paris to Strasbourg and the East between Vosges and Hardt mtns.; gradual approach from W., steep descent to E. into Rhine valley.

Savoie (Savoy), dep., **France**; borders Italy in Savoy Alps; part of former duchy; dairying and vineyards; hydroelectricity forms basis of metallurgical inds.; first Fr. National Park (Vanoise Park); cap. Chambéry; a. 6,188 km²; p. (1982) 320,600.

Savona, spt., Genoa, **Italy**; cath.; iron, shipbldg., glass and tinplate wks.; exp. preserved fruits and tomatoes; imports coal, oil, iron-ore; p. (1981) 75,353.

Savonlinna, t., Mikkeli, E. **Finland**; in Saimaa L. region; route ctr.; timber inds.; p. (1986) 28,608.

Sawankalok, t., **Thailand**; impt. teak collecting ctr.

Sawbridgeworth, t., East Herts., **Eng.**; on R. Stort, 6 km S. of Bishops Stortford; malting, fruit preserving; p. (1981) 7,777.

Saxham, t., Suffolk, **Eng.**; agr. machin.

Saxmundham, mkt. t., Suffolk Coastal, Suffolk, **Eng.**; 29 km N.E. of Ipswich; p. (1981) 16,235.

Saxony, region, **E. Germany**; turbulent political and territorial history, now comprises admin. dists. of Leipzig, Dresden, Karl-Marx-Stadt. Halle and Magdeburg; inc. Erzgebirge in S., Vogtland in W. and N. European plain; drained by N. flowing Rs. Elster, Pleisse, Mulde, Elle, Neisse, Spree; kaolin deposits basis for porcelain ind. at Meissen; industrialised in 19th and 20th cent. with notable textile ind.; coal mng. nr. Zwickau; inds. concentrated around Karl-Marx-Stadt; cap. Dresden; comm. ctr. at Leipzig; a. 16,996 km².

Sayan Mtns., range of mtns.; between Rs. Yenisey and Angra, **RSFSR**; form part of Sino-Soviet border; mineral resources.

Scafell Pike, mtn., Cumbria, **Eng.**; in Cumbrian Mtns, Lake Dist.; highest in Eng.; alt. 979 m.

Scalby, t., North Yorks., **Eng.**; 5 km N.W. of Scarborough; p. (1981) 9,228.

Scalloway, Shetlands, **Scot.**; on W. cst. of Mainland; the anc. cap.; ruined cas.; fish. pt.; p. (1981) 1,018.

Scalpay, I., off E. cst. of Skye, **Scot.**

Scalpay, I., Harris, Outer Hebrides, **Scot.**; p. (1981) 466.

Scandinavia, name given to lge. peninsula in N.W. **Europe**; comprises kingdoms of Sweden and Norway; sometimes inc. Denmark, Finland and Iceland; rugged a. of anc. peneplained rocks; climate varies from arctic (N.) to humid maritime (S.W.); rich in timber and mineral ores. esp. iron and copper; W. cst. waters valuable fishing grounds.

Scapa Flow, strait, N. **Scot.**; between Pomona and Hoy, Orkney Is.; surrendered German fleet scuttled 1919; Brit. battleship *Royal Oak* sunk at anchor 1939.

Scarba, I., Argyll and Bute, **Scot.**; off N. end of Jura, red deer in woods and moorlands.

Scarborough, c., Ontario, **Canada**; part of Toronto met. a.; p. (1986) 484,676.

Scarborough, t., l. gov. dist., North Yorks., **Eng.**; on E. cst.; seaside resort; cas.; former spa; p. (est. 1988) 105,400 (dist.).

Scarpanto. See **Karpathos.**

Schaffhausen, most. N. can., **Switzerland**; on R. Rhine; pastoral, forested; cereals, fruit, vegetables, wine; hydroelectric power from S. falls on Rhine; cap. S.; a. 298 km²; p. (est. 1986) 70,000.

Schaffhausen, c., cap. of S. can., **Switzerland**; on

Rhine below L. Constance; falls to S.W. of c.; hydroelectricity supplies power for electrochemical ind. and aluminium wks.; p. (1980) 34,250.

Schaumburg-Lippe, former st., between provs. of Hanover and Westphalia, Germany, now part of Lower Saxony, **W. Germany**; farming, coal mng.

Schefferville, t., **Canada**; 576 km N. of St. Lawrence estuary and connected to it (at Seven Islands) by rly.; ctr. of iron-ore mines in Quebec-Labrador trough; p. (1981) 1,997.

Scheldt (Dutch **Schelde,** French **Escaut**), R., **France, Belgium, Neth.**; rises in Aisne, France, flows to N. Sea forming extensive delta with Rhine (Rijn) and Meuss (Maas) in Netherlands; navigable; 432 km long; network of canals.

Schenectady, c., N.Y., **USA**; on Mohawk R., N.W. of Albany; electrical plants, locomotive wks.; p. (1980) 67,972.

Scheveningen, seaside resort, **Neth.**; 3 km N.W. of The Hague; fish. pt.

Schiedam, t., **Neth.**, on Nieuwe Maas, 4 km downstream from Rotterdam; forms part of Rotterdam–Europort; diverse pt.-based inds.; gin; p. (est. 1987) 69,000.

Schiehallion, mtn., Perth and Kinross, **Scot.**; alt. 1,082 m.

Schio, t., Veneto, **Italy**; at foot of Alps on Leogra R.; woollens, textiles, machin.; p. (1981) 35,596.

Schlei, narrow inlet of Baltic, Schleswig-Holstein, **W. Germany**; 40 km long.

Schleswig, t., Schleswig-Holstein, **W. Germany**; fish. pt. on Schlei inlet; lt. inds.; p. (est. 1986) 23,300.

Schleswig-Holstein, *Land*, **W. Germany**; occupies S. part of Jutland peninsula; a. disputed between Denmark and Prussia in 19th cent.; mainly agr.; many sm. pts.; crossed by Kiel Canal; cap. Kiel; a. 15,664 km²; p. (est. 1986) 2,612,700.

Schneidemüthl. See **Pila.**

Schönebeck, t., Magdeburg, **E. Germany**; pt. on R. Elbe; metals, chemicals, machin.; p. (est. 1970) 46,146.

Schoonebeek, v., Drenthe, **Neth.**; S. of Emmen; lge. oilfield.

Schouten I., W. Irian, **Indonesia**; in Geelvink Bay; p. 25,487.

Schouwen-Duiveland, I., Zeeland prov., **Neth.**; cap. Zierikee; formerly 2 separate Is.,

Schuylkill, R., Penns., **USA**; flows into Delaware R.; navigable; length 208 km.

Schwäbish-Gmünd, t., Baden-Württemberg, **W. Germany**; at foot of Swabian Jura, E. of Stuttgart; clocks, glass, optical, precious metal and jewellery inds.; mediaeval and baroque bldgs.; p. (est. 1986) 56,100.

Schwarzwald (Black Forest), forested mtn. range, Baden-Württemberg, **W. Germany**; highest peak Feldberg 1,496 m; tourism; famous for clock and toy inds.

Schwechat, t., **Austria**; nr. Vienna; oil refining; pipeline to Trieste; p. (1961) 13,403.

Schwedt, t., Frankfurt, **E. Germany**; on R. Oder; lge. oil refinery; pipeline from Mozyr' (USSR); paper, fertilisers; p. (1981) 52,291.

Schweinfurt, t., Bavaria, **W. Germany**; on R. Main, N.E. of Würzburg; metals, machin., ball bearings, dyes, brewing; p. (est. 1986) 50,600.

Schwelm, t., N. Rhine-Westphalia, **W. Germany**; E. of Wuppertal; metals machin., textiles; p. (est. 1986) 29,800.

Schwenningen, t., Baden-Württemberg, **W. Germany**; clocks, precision instruments, optical apparatus; p. with Villingen (est. 1986) 76,200.

Schwerin, c., cap. of Schwerin, **E. Germany**; on Schwerin L., surrounded by smaller Ls.; comm. and industl. ctr. of agr. dist.; food processing, engin., furniture; cath., cas.; p. (est 1986) 128,000.

Schwyz, can., **Switzerland**; mtnous. in S.; forested; dairying impt.; original member of confederation; cap. S.; a. 907 km²; p. (est. 1986) 103,000.

Schwyz, c., of Schwyz can., **Switzerland**; tourist ctr. nr. Lucerne; p. (1980) 12,100.

Sciacca, sm. pt., Sicily, **Italy**; nr. Agrigento; mineral springs; p. (1981) 34,294.

Scilly Is., archipelago, l. gov. dist., 45 km. S.W. of Land's End, Cornwall, **Eng.**; early flowers and vegetables benefit from mild winter climate; tourism; p. (est. 1988) 1,900.

Scioto, R., Ohio, **USA**; joins Ohio at Portsmouth; 400 km long.

Scone, par., Perth and Kinross, **Scot.**; place of residence and coronation of early Scottish kings; from here Edward I removed Stone of Destiny to Westminster Abbey 1297; tourist ctr.; civil aerodrome.

Scoresby Sound, E. **Greenland**; lgst. fjord system in the world; length 304 m; fishing and hunting; onshore oil drilling (1984).

Scotland, Brit. Is., N. part of **Gt. Britain**; 12 Gov. Regs.; home affairs admin. by Dept. of Sec. of State for Scot.; physically divided into 3 parts; (1) the Highlands and Is., an upland a. suffering from depopulation, economically reliant on stock-rearing, tourism, hydroelec. power, whisky and fishing; intrusive impact of N. Sea oil on N.E. cst.; (2) the Central Lowlands, containing most p., based in industl. ts. on sm. coalfields, inc. lgst. c. Glasgow and cap. Edinburgh; (3) the S. Uplands, a stock-rearing a. bordering Eng.; a. 78,772 km²; p. (est. 1984) 5,146,000.

Scrabster, pt. nr. Thurso, **Scotland**; main ferry terminal for Orkneys.

Scranton, c., Penns., **USA**; on Lackawanna R.; anthracite ctr.; chemicals, shoes, textiles; univ.; p. (1984) 83,700 (c.), 726,800 (Scranton N.E. met. a.).

Scunthorpe, t., l. gov. dist., Humberside, **Eng.**; on Lincoln Edge, 10 km S. of Humber; iron, limestone mng. and major iron and steel ind.; p. (est. 1988) 60,500.

Scutari (Albania). *See* Shkodër.

Scutari (Turkey). *See* Usküdar.

Seaford, t., East Sussex, **Eng.**; 5 km E. of Newhaven; seaside resort; declined as a pt. with shift of Ouse R. channel to Newhaven; p. (1981) 17,785.

Seaforth, Loch, Lewis, Outer Hebrides, **Scot.**; 22 km long.

Seaham, spt., Durham, **Eng.**; Seaham Harbour on E. cst. 6 km S. of Sunderland; modern colly. workings extend under sea; p. (1981) 21,130.

Sea Islands, USA; chain of Is. off Atl. cst. of S.C., Ga. and Fla.; formerly impt. for sea-island cotton but since 1919 infested with boll weevil.

Seathwaite, v., Cumbria, **Eng.**; 11 km from Keswick, close to Styhead (436 m); exceptionally heavy annual rainfall (above 3,800 mm).

Seaton, t., East Devon, **Eng.**; on Lyme Bay at mouth of R. Axe, seaside resort; freestone quarries; p. (1981) 4,974.

Seaton Carew, t., Cleveland, **Eng.**; site for nuclear power sta. nr. mouth of R. Tees; seaside resort.

Seaton Valley, t., Blyth Valley, Northumberland, **Eng.**; coal mng.; expanded t.; p. (1981) 46,141.

Seattle, c., Wash., **USA**; spt. between Puget Sound and L. Wash.; S.E. is Mt. Rainier, N.E. Mt. Baker; tr. with Far East and Alaska from wooded, agr. hinterland; fishing and fish exp.; lgst. c. of Wash., a major industl. and comm. ctr.; aircraft (home of Boeing), shipbld., food processing; univs. cath.; p. (1984) 488,500 (c.), 2,207,800 (met. a.).

Secunderabad, t., Andhra Pradesh, **India**; now incorporated within Hyderabad; comm. ctr., rly. junc.; p. (1981) 135,994.

Sedan, t., Ardennes dep., **France**; on R. Meuse; machin., metal ware, woollens, flour; Napoleon III surrendered to Prussians 1870; p. (1982) 24,535.

Sedbergh, mkt. t., South Lakeland, Cumbria, **Eng.**; woollen ind., public school.

Sedgefield, t., l. gov. dist., S.E. Durham, **Eng.**; in fertile agr. a.; cattle mkt.; racecourse; p. (est. 1988) 88,400.

Sedgemoor, l. gov. dist., Somerset, **Eng.**; based on Bridgwater, Burnham and surrounding a.; p. (est. 1988) 96,400.

Sefton, met. dist., Merseyside, **Eng.**; comprises Crosby, Bootle and Litherland; p. (est. 1988) 297,600.

Ségou, t., R. pt., **Mali**; W. Africa; on R. Niger; ctr. of irrigation scheme; cotton, hides, cattle; once cap. of former kingdom; p. (1976) 64,890.

Ségou Canal, Mali, W. Africa; leaves R. Niger 6 km below Bamako, extends 208 km N.E. to Segou; irrigates 7,770 km² on right bank of Niger and assists navigation.

Segovia, c., cap. of S. prov., Old Castile, **Spain**; on rocky hill above Eresma R.; Roman aqueduct, cath.; p. (1987) 53,849.

Segovia, R., rises in N.W. Nicaragua, flows N.E. to Caribbean; forms part of S. limit of Mosquito cst., and bdy. between **Honduras** and **Nicaragua**; 480 km long.

Segre, R., Lérida, N.E. **Spain**; rises in E. Pyrenees flows S.W. into R. Ebro; water irrigates the a. around Lérida, the lgst. block of irrigated land in Spain; c. 272 km long.

Segura, R., **Spain**; flows to Mediterranean at Guardamar; 288 km long.

Seibersdorf, Austria; ENEA experimental food irradiation project.

Seïkan Tunnel, Japan; links Honshu with Hokkaido under Tsugaru strait; 37 km long.

Seine, R., **France**; rises in Côte d'Or dep. and flows past Paris and Rouen to English Channel at Havre; navigable, part of French waterway network; 757 km long.

Seine-et-Marne, dep., N. **France**; agr., stock-raising, dairying; impt. source of food for Paris mkts.; Brie cheese; cap. Melun; a. 5,892 km²; p. (1982) 887,100.

Seine-Maritime, dep., N. **France**; undulating and fertile; grain, dairying; heavy inds. at cap. Rouen; oil refineries; beach resorts; p. (1982) 1,191,000.

Seine-Saint Denis, dep., N.E. Paris, **France**; mkt. gardens; cap. Bobigny; p. (1982) 1,321,000.

Seistan and Baluchistan, twin prov., **Iran**; co. ts. Zabol, Zahedan; rly. terminus Pakistan rly. from Quetta through Mirjaveh.

Sekondi-Takoradi, t., S.W. **Ghana**; spt. on G. of Guinea; developed after construction of rly. (1903) to tap mineral, agr. and forest wealth of hinterland; deepwater harbour at Takoradi constructed 1928; fisheries, saw milling; p. (1984) 91,874 (c.), 160,868 (met. a.).

Selangor, st., central Malaya, **W. Malaysia**; former sultanate; economically well developed; chemicals, rubber, tin, coal, pineapples; ch. pt., Pt. Swettenham; fisheries; new st. cap. designated at Klang to relieve congestion of Kuala Lumpur; p. (1980) 1,515,536.

Selby, mkt. t., l. gov. dist., North Yorks., **Eng.**; on R. Ouse, 20 km. S. of York; anc. abbey church; flour milling, flax, oil-cake; development of major coalfield since 1983 linked to bldg. of power sta. in Aire Valley; p. (est. 1988) 90,900 (dist.).

Sele, R., S. **Italy**; rises in S. Apennines, flows W. into G. of Salerno; headwater carried E. through gr. Apennine tunnel (11 km) to irrigate plateau of Apulia in S.E. Italy.

Selenga, Asiatic R., rises in **Mongolia**, enters **USSR** nr. Kiachta from where it is navigable to its delta in L. Baykal; c. 1,100 km long.

Selkirk, royal burgh, Etterick and Lauderdale, **Scot.**; on Etterick Water; 6 km S. of Galashiels; mkt. t.; tartans, tweeds; p. (1981) 5,417.

Selkirk Mtns., B.C. **Canada**; run N.W. to S.E. parallel with Rocky mtns.; anc. rocks, highly mineralised; rise to over 2,700 m.

Selkirkshire, former co., S. **Scot.**; now part of Borders Reg.

Sellafield, nuclear power plant, Cumbria, **Eng.**; formerly Windscale; reprocesses nuclear waste.

Selma, t., Ala., **USA**; on Alabama R., in cotton, dairying, lumbering region; food processing, fertilisers; p. (1980) 26,684.

Selsey Bill, peninsula between Bognor Regis and Portsmouth, West Sussex, **Eng.**

Selukwe, t., **Rhodesia**; alt. 1,444 m; gold mng., chrome ore, molybdenum; ranching.

Selwyn Range, mtns., Queensland, **Australia**; extend 560 km W. from Gr. Dividing Range.

Semarang, spt., Java, **Indonesia**; exp. sugar, tobacco, tapioca, kapok; shipbldg., rly. repairs, cement, sawmills, tyres, elec. equipment; univ.; p. (est. 1983) 1,269,000.

Semipalatinsk, t., Kazakh SSR, **USSR**; on R. Irtysh; lge. meat-packing plant; textiles, engin.; rich gold deposit found in a. 1965; p. (est. 1985) 317,000.

Semmering Pass, low pass, **Austria**; provides route across E. Alps for rly. from Vienna to Venice; scenic resort; alt. below 915 m.

Semnan, t., Central Prov., **Iran**; comm. ctr. for tobacco growing region; p. (1986) 418,152.

Sena, t., Moçambique; on R. Zambesi; iron-ore mng.

Sendai, t., Honshu, **Japan**; cas.; univ.; metallurgy, food processing, lacquer ware; p. (1985) 700,248.

Senegal, member st., **Senegambia**, W. cst. Africa; flat savannah; tropical climate with long dry season; agr. main occupation, groundnuts accounting for 72 per cent exp.; production hit by severe drought (1982–3); groundnut and agr.

processing provide industl. basis; bauxite, phosphate, titanium, zirconium mng.; oil refinery at cap. Dakar; a. 197,109 km²; p. (est. 1987) 6·79 m. *see* **Senegambia**.

Senegal, R., W. Africa; flows from Kong mtns. W. and N.W. to Atl. at St. Louis, above Cape Verde; lower valley forms fertile agr. land; partially navigable; plans for economic development of valley; joint water scheme with 3 dams to relieve water shortages, improve navigation and provide hydro-electric power for Mali, Senegambia and Mauritania; 1,600 km long.

Senegambia, rep., W. Cst Africa; formed (1982) from unification of Senegal and Gambia following attempted coup (1981); secessionist attempts (1982). *See* **Senegal** and **Gambia**.

Senftenberg, t., Cottbus, **E. Germany;** inds. based on local lignite deposits; glassware, tiles; p. (est. 1970) 24,301.

Senigallia, t., **Italy;** resort and spt. on Adriatic; fishing and agr. ctr., food processing, agr. machin.; p. (1981) 40,108.

Senlis, t., Oise dep., **France;** Gallo-Roman wall; tourist ctr. in forested region, 43 km N.E. of Paris; mkt. t., furniture, rubber gds.; p. (1982) 15,280.

Sennar, t., **Sudan;** on Blue Nile, on rly. route to Khartoum, Suakin, Pt. Sudan; dam for irrigation, flood control and hydroelectric power; p. c. 8,000.

Sens, t., Yonne dep., **France;** on R. Yonne; known to Romans as Agedincum; Gothic cath.; agr. tr., food processing, farm implements, boots, chemicals, cutlery; p. (1982) 27,501.

Sensuntepeque, t., **El Salvador;** pottery, distilling; p. (1980) 50,448.

Senta, t., **Yugoslavia;** pt. on Tisa R.; agr. ctr.; food processing, agr. machin., chemicals; p. (1971) 24,714.

Seoul, c., cap. of **S. Korea;** in Han R. valley; food processing, textiles, rly. engin.; univs., anc. walls; international airport, connected by rly. to outport of Inchon; host of 1988 Olympic games; p. (est. 1986) 9,639,100.

Sepik, R., N. New Guinea; flows E. to Bismarck Sea; drains vast mtn. a.; very fast flow; navigable by shallow craft; 800 km long.

Sept Isles (Seven Islands), pt., on St. Lawrence, Quebec, **Canada;** iron brought by rail from Schefferville; airline service but no highway; p. (1981) 29,262.

Sequoia National Park, Cal., **USA;** sequoia trees.

Seraing, t., Liège, **Belgium;** on R. Meuse; coal mng.; iron and steel heavy inds.; seat of famous Cockerill iron wks. (1817) and glass wks. (1825); p. (1982) 63,749.

Seram (Ceram), I., Moluccas, **Indonesia;** W.-E. mtn. range rising to 3,357 m; tobacco; sago; a. 17,143 km²; p. (1961) 73,453.

Serampore, t., W. Bengal, **India;** former Danish settlement; cotton and silk weaving, pottery, jute and paper mills; p. (1981) 127,304.

Serbia, constituent rep., N.E. **Yugoslavia;** lgst. and most impt. rep., "bread basket" of Yugoslavia; grain, fruit; mng. copper and antimony; cap. Belgrade; a. 87,879 km²; p. (1981) 9,313,676.

Seremban, t., cap. of Negri Sembilan st., **W. Malaysia;** on Linggi R.; linked by rly. to Pt. Dickson; comm. ctr. for rubber and tin a.; p. (1980) 136,625.

Sereth, R., rises in Carpathians, W. Ukrainian SSR, **USSR,** and enters **Romania** to join Danube above Galati; 720 km long.

Sergipe, cst. st., **Brazil;** sandy cst. rising to undulating plateau in interior; well wooded and cropped for sugar, cotton; drier interior devoted mainly to stock-raising; oil deposits; a. 21,054 km²; p. (est. 1985) 1,297,500.

Sergo. *See* **Kadiyevka.**

Seria, t., **Brunei;** coastal t., protected from sea by 8 km dyke; oil ctr., linked by pipeline with Lutong; p. (1981) 23,511.

Serov, t., **RSFSR;** in Urals; iron and steel; natural gas pipeline from Ingrim; p. (est. 1985) 102,000.

Serowe, t., **Botswana,** Southern Africa; seat of Bamanguato tribe; mkt. ctr.; lge coal reserves widening economic base of Botswana and reducing dependence on S. Africa; p. (est. 1984) 28,980.

Serpukhov, t., R. pt., **RSFSR;** on R. Oka, planned canal link to Moscow; p. (est. 1985) 142,000.

Serra da Mantiqueira, mtn. range, hgst. in **Brazil.**

Serra do Espinhaco, mtns., **Brazil;** highest peak, Itambe, 2,045 m; iron-ore deposits.

Serra do Mar, mtns., **Brazil;** form steep E. edge of Brazilian Plateau S. from Rio de Janeiro.

Serrai (Seres), dep., Macedonia, N. **Greece;** N. mtns. form frontier with Bulgaria in gorge of Struma R. valley; lower Struma R. basin fertile agr. a., producing cotton, tobacco; mkt. ctr. at cap. Serrai; a. 4,053 km²; p. (1981) 46,317 (t.).

Sertão, semi-arid hinterland. N.E. **Brazil;** stock-raising, but drought causes migration to Amazon basin; hydroelectric power and irrigation schemes; focus of social unrest documented in Brazilian novels.

Sesto San Giovanni, sub., Milan, **Italy;** machin., glass, chemicals, plastics; p. (1981) 94,738.

Sète, spt., Hérault dep., **France;** on Med. cst.; chemicals, fisheries; exp. oysters, brandy, wine; oil pipeline under sea to Frontignan; importance originally based upon canal network, now supplanted by rlys.; tourism of growing importance; p. (1982) 58,865 (met. a.).

Setesdal (Saetersdal), Aust-Agder, S. **Norway;** remote valley retaining traditional social customs; arable pastoral agr.

Sétif. *See* **Stif.**

Seto, t., central Honshu, **Japan;** porcelain ctr. (since 13th cent.); based on local deposits of kaolin; p. (1985) 124,625.

Setouchi, dist., S.W. Honshu, **Japan;** rice, mandarin oranges, reeds, salt, textiles; part of Japan's industl. belt.

Setté Cama, spt., **Gabon,** Equatorial Africa; open roadstead, landing difficult owing to swell; exp. timber; oil nearby.

Settle, mkt. t., Craven, North Yorks., **Eng.;** on R. Ribble in heart of Craven dist.; tourist ctr. for limestone cty. of N. Pennines; textiles.

Settsu Plain, S. Honshu, **Japan;** at head of Osaka Bay at E. end of Inland Sea; intensively cultivated alluvial lowlands, ch. crops, rice, vegetables, oranges; gr. industl. belt extends along cst. through Kobe, Osaka, Kishiwada; engin., chemicals, textiles; a. 1,295 km².

Setubal, t., Estremadura, S. **Portugal;** impt. pt. on Sado R., estuary; exp. cork, wine, oranges; fishing, fish processing, shipyds.; p. (1981) 78,274.

Sevan (Gokcha), lge. L., Armenian SSR, **USSR;** alt. 1,934 m; never freezes; surrounded by high barren mtns.; drained by Razdan R.; several hydroelectric power stas.

Sevastopol, spt., Ukrainian SSR, **USSR;** built on ruins left after famous siege 1855; Black Sea resort; rebuilt after second world war; one of most beautiful Crimean cs.; p. (est. 1985) 341,000.

Sevenoaks, mkt. t., l. gov. dist., Kent, **Eng.;** in Vale of Holmesdale; residtl.; agr., lt. inds.; Knole Park; public school founded in 1432; p. (est. 1988) 107,300 (dist.).

Severn, R., Ont., **Canada;** flows to Hudson Bay; tr. post at mouth; 560 km long.

Severn, R., W. of **Eng.** and **N. Wales;** rises in Powys and flows to Bristol Channel; suspension bridge at estuary opened 1966; several proposals for major economic development around shores of estuary; 344 km long.

Severn Tunnel, Eng.; under estuary of R. Severn between Pilning (Avon) and Severn Tunnel Junction (Gwent); carries main rly. from London to S. **Wales;** longest main-line rly. tunnel in Brit. Is.; 7 km long.

Severodvinsk, t., **RSFSR;** on Dvina Bay, White Sea; metals, bldg. materials; p. (est. 1985) 230,000.

Seville, c., cap. of Seville prov. and of Andalusia, **Spain;** spt. on Guadalquivir R., canal link with Atl. Oc.; exp. agr. prod., imports industl. raw materials; major industl., comm. and cultural ctr.; diverse mnfs.; beautiful c. with Moorish influence, prominent in narrow streets of ctr. a.; Alcázar palace; Gothic cath.; bullfighting, tourist ctr.; p. (1987) 655,435.

Sèvres, t., Hauts-de-Seine, dep., N. **France;** S.W. sub. of Paris on Seine R.; celebrated porcelain mnfs.; headquarters of International Bureau of Weights and Measures; p. (1982) 20,225.

Seward, t., S. Alaska, **USA;** rly. terminal, airfield and ice-free harbour make it an impt. supply ctr. for interior Alaska; p. (1980) 1,843.

Seychelles Is., indep. rep. (1976), **Indian Oc.;** consists of 86 Is. (37 granitic, 49 coralline), among most beautiful in world; lgst. I. Mahé; cap. Victoria; fishing, heavy dependence on tourism pays for dependence on imported food; petroleum exploration; exp. copra, cinnamon bark; famous for species of nut; total a. 404 km²; p. (est. 1987) 67,000.

Seyne, or **La Seyne-sur-Mer.** t., Var dep., **France;** nr. Toulon; shipbld.; p. (1982) 58,146.

Sfax, spt., **Tunisia;** admin. ctr.; exp. phosphate, olive oil, salt, esparto grass, cereals, dates, hides; imports food, coal, textiles, soap; sponges; fishing; natural gas found in a.; surrounded by irrigated gardens and olive groves; p. (1984) 231,911.

Sgurr Mor, mtn., Ross and Cromarty, **Scot.;** alt. 1,109 m.

Shaanxi (Shensi), prov., N. **China; Great Wall** runs nr. N. border with Inner Mongolia; from N.–S. four main regions: (1) dry, fertile loess plateau, notorious famine region, but increasingly irrigated; (2) fertile Wei R. valley, ctr. of p. and agr.; (3) Hua Shan (4) agr. a. of upper Han R.; grain, livestock; coal, petroleum; developing transportation network aiding economic development; cap. Xi'an; a. 188,860 km²; p. (est. 1985) 29,660,000.

Shaba (Katanga), prov., **Zaïre;** many varied mineral deposits inc. copper, tin, iron-ore, cobalt, radium; cap. Lubumbashi; a. 466,200 km²; (est. 1981) 3·8 m).

Shache (Yarkand), c., Xinjiang prov., **China;** tr. ctr. in S. oasis; tr. in wheat, rice, beans, fruit, carpets, textiles; p. (est.) 60,000

Shache (Yarkand), R., Xinjiang prov., **China;** trib. of Gan R.; 800 km long.

Shaftesbury, mkt. t., North Dorset, **Eng.;** Saxon hilltop t., abbey ruins; ctr. for agr. a.; p. (1981) 4,942.

Shahjahanpur, t., Uttar Pradesh, **India;** on Deoha R.; agr. mkt. t. and rly junc.; grain, sugar tr. and processing; p. (1981) 185,396 (t.), 205,095 (met. a.).

Shakhty (Alexandrovsk Grushevski), t., **RSFSR;** anthracite mng. in Donets Basin; leather, textiles, metal wkg., food inds.; p. (est. 1985) 221,000.

Shamaldy-Say, t., Kirghiz SSR, **USSR;** new t. on site of Uch-Kurgan hydroelectric power sta.

Shandaken Tunnel, N.Y. st., **USA;** carries water under Catskill mtns. to augment water supply of c. of N.Y.; 29 km long.

Shandong (Shantung), coastal prov., N. **China;** S. of fertile plain of Huang He; dense p. but agr. potential limited by dry climate; wheat, millet, maize, soyabeans, cotton, hemp, fruits; E. mtns. contain coal, iron, bauxite, kaolin; iron and steel inds. and cotton mills at main industl. ts. of Jinan and Qingdao; special economic zones to encourage foreign investment; birthplace of Confucius at foot of sacred peak Tai; cap. Jinan; a. 146,198 km²; p. (est. 1985) 76,370,000.

Shanghai, c. and mun., **China;** major spt. on left bank of Huangbu; its strategic location developed, largely by Brit. businessmen, as ctr. for imperialist trading; rich agr. region; handles major share of Chinese shipping but dredging required; machin., chemicals, electronics, cars, steel, shipbldg., are main inds.; major educational and research ctr.; open to foreign investment, esp. for high technology inds.; a. 6,186 km²; 3rd most populous c. in world; p. (1984) 12,047,800 (prov.), 6,881,000 (c.).

Shannon Airport, Clare, **R.O.I.;** N.W. of Limerick; on main transatlantic air route; ctr. of customs-free industl. estate built (1958) to compensate for decline in air traffic with larger planes; p. (1981) 7,998 (t.).

Shannon, R., **Ireland;** separates Connaught from provs. of Leinster and Munster, flows to Atl. at Loop Head; hydroelectric power sta. at Ardnacrusha; 358 km long.

Shan State, div., **Burma;** elevated plateau through which flows Salween R.; impt. mng. dist., lead, zinc, silver at Bawdwin, smelters at Namtu; also tungsten, tin, antimony, manganese; home of Shan people; former Shan and Wa sts.; cap. Taunggyi; a. 155,801 km².

Shantou (Swatow), c., spt., S.E. Guandong, **China;** at mouth of Han R.; mftg. and exp. tr.; univ.; special economic zone to attract foreign inds. and new dock being built; p. (1984) 899,900.

Shanxi (Shansi), prov., N. **China;** bounded W. and S. by Huang He; mainly high plateaux; fertile loess deposits, but drought conditions limit agr. potential; dry crops and livestock; coal, iron-ore, petroleum; cap. Taiyuan; a. 156,420 km²; p. (est. 1985) 26,000,000.

Shaohing. *See* Shaoxing.

Shaoxing (Shaohing), c., N. Zhejiang prov., S.E. **China;** agr. ctr. on Hangzhou Bay; rice, wheat, cotton; p. (1984) 244,100.

Shaoyang, c., Hunan prov., **China;** coal and iron mng.; timber; p. (1984) 416,500.

Shap, mkt. t., Cumbria, **Eng.;** nearby in Shap Fell 279 m, an impt. pass traversed by rly. and by a main road; granite quarries.

Shapinsay, Orkney Is., **Scot.;** p. (1971) 346.

Shari, R., central **Africa;** formed by several head-streams in Central African Rep., flows across Chad Rep. into L. Chad in wide delta; navigable.

Shārjah, emirate, member of the **United Arab Emirates** (1971), Persian Gulf; international airport at cap. Shārjah (p. 25,000); natural harbour at Khawr Fakhan; oil exploration, fishing; p. (1985) 268,722.

Sharon, plain, **Israel;** citrus fruits, vines, poultry.

Shashi, t., S. Hubei prov., **China;** agr. mkt. ctr. and canalised R. pt.; tr. in cotton, grain; flour milling, textiles; p. (1984) 246,800.

Shasta Dam, Cal., **USA;** dams water of Rs. Pit, McCloud, Sacramento for hydroelectric power; irrigation, flood control and reclamation of lower Sacramento valley.

Shatt-al-Arab, R., **Iraq;** formed by union of Tigris and Euphrates, flows thence to head of Persian G.; swampy delta in rich agr. a.; deepest-water line of R.'s estuary defined (1975) as new Iraq/Iran bdy.; 192 km long.

Shawinigan Falls, c., Quebec, **Canada;** pulp and paper, chemicals, aluminium inds., powered by hydroelectric power from falls on St. Maurice R.; p. (1981) 23,011.

Shawnee, c., Okla., **USA;** rly. and tr. ctr. for rich agr. a.; electronics, aircraft components; p. (1980) 26,506.

Sheaf, R., South Yorks., **Eng.;** rises in S.E. Pennines, flows N.E. to join R. Don at Sheffield; 18 km long.

Shebelinka, natural gas fields nr. Kharkov, Ukrainian SSR, **USSR;** pipelines to Kharkov-Bryansk and Dnepropetrovsk–Odessa.

Sheboygan, t., Wis., **USA;** on L. Michigan; ctr. for dairy farming and resort a.; cheese, leather gds., hardware; p. (1984) 47,700 (t.), 102,100 (met. a.).

Sheerness, Kent, **Eng.;** on I. of Sheppey at entrance to estuary of R. Medway; former royal dockyard and garrison; deepwater comm. pt.; electronics, furniture, coach bldg.

Sheffield, c., met. dist., South Yorks., **Eng.;** on cramped site at confluence of Rs. Sheaf and Don; univ.; heavy engin. ctr., famous for high quality steels, cutlery, tools; major post-war redevelopment of c. ctr. with ambitious and imaginative housebldg. programme by a socially conscious local council, taking advantage of hilly site has turned S. into a very attractive modern c.; p. (est. 1988) 528,300.

Sheksna, R., **RSFSR;** rises in L. Beloye and flows S. to Rybinsk Reservoir; forms part of Volga–Baltic waterway; 160 km long.

Shellhaven, oil refineries, Essex, **Eng.;** on N. side of Thames estuary, nr. Standord-le-Hope.

Shenandoah National Park, Va., **USA;** extends along forested Blue Ridge mtns.; views of Shenandoah valley and Allegheny mtns.

Shenandoah, R., Va., **USA;** trib. of Potomac R.; picturesque valley noted for rich apple orchards and pastures; scene of several campaigns in Civil War; 272 km long.

Shensi. *See* Shaanxi.

Shen-yang (Mukden), c., cap. of Liaoning prov., N.E. **China;** on Hun R. in narrowest part of lowland with hilly country on both sides; impt. rly. junc. with main routes N. to Harbin and Trans-Siberian rly., S. to Beijing, Luta and into Korea; comm. and educational ctr.; impt. textile ctr., heavy inds., cement, chemicals, machin.; agr. tr.; univ.; p. (1984) 4,134,800.

Shenzhen, special economic zone, Guandong, **China;** a. selected (1980) to encourage foreign investment; close to Hong Kong; soft drinks, cement, electronic equipment, petrochems. relocated from Hong Kong; spt.; univ.; planned nuclear power plant to supply Hong Kong; p. (1984) 337,000 (146,000 temporary workers).

Shepparton-Mooroopna, t., Victoria, **Australia;** ctr. of vegetable and orchard a. of Goulburn valley irrigation; p. (est. 1983) 37,530.

Sheppey, I. of, Kent, Swale, **Eng.;** in Thames estuary E. of mouth of R. Medway; cereals, sheep-raising; new steel wks.; ch. t., Sheerness; a. 117 km².

Shepshed, t., Charnwood, Leics., **Eng.**; 5 km W. of Loughborough; hosiery; p. (1981) 11,151.

Shepton Mallet, mkt. t., Mendip, Somerset, **Eng.**; at foot of Mendip Hills, 8 km S.E of Wells; old woollen ctr.; bacon curing, brewing; p. (1981) 6,303.

Shepway, l. gov. dist., S.E. Kent, **Eng.**; cstl. a. of Folkestone, Hythe, New Romney and Lydd; p. (est. 1988) 87,600.

Sherborne, mkt. t., West Dorset, **Eng.**; 6 km E. of Yeovil; famous abbey and school; Norman cas. ruins; glass fibre; p. (1981) 7,572.

Sherbrook, t., S.E. Quebec, **Canada**; comm. and mkt. ctr. for surrounding agr. region; inds. based on local sources of hydroelectric power from Magog R.; textiles, paper mills, machin., flour milling; deposits of asbestos nearby; p. (1986) 74,438 (c.), 129,960 (met. a.).

Sheringham, t., North Norfolk, **Eng.**; on cst. 6 km W. of Cromer; resort; fishing; p. (1981) 5,515.

Sherwood Forest, anc. royal woodland, Notts., **Eng.**; now restricted to infertile Bunter Sandstone cty.; inc. several estates and parks, notably the Dukeries.

Shetland Is., **Scot.**; 80 km N.E. of the Orkneys; about 100 in gr., ch. I., Mainland; lge. number of rainy days, but climate mild and tourism attracted by isolation, scenery and wildlife; Fair Isle famous for knitted clothes; fishing, livestock, agr., potatoes; rapid growth with oil drilling in N. Sea; lge oil terminal of Sullum Voe; lge. elderly p. due to attractions as a retirement a.; ch. t. Lerwick; a. 1,427 km²; p. (est. 1986) 23,580 (1971 – 17,080).

Shibin el Kôm, Menûfîya, **Egypt**; rly. and mkt. ctr. in agr. a. of Nile delta; tobacco, textiles; p. (1985) 129,600.

Shigatze. *See* Zigaze.

Shijiazhuang (**Shihkiachwang**) c., Hebei prov., **China**; cotton milling, glass mftg.; grew rapidly with coming of rly.; p. (1984) 1,127,800.

Shikarpur, t., N. Sind, **Pakistan**; tr. ctr. for grain, precious stones; engin., food processing; p. (1981) 88,000.

Shikoku, I., **Japan**; S. of Honshu; smallest of Japan's 4 main Is.; sparsely populated, mtnous. interior, heavily forested; arable agr. in lowlands; ch. cs., Matsuyama, Kochi, Tokushima; a. 18,772 km²; p. (1980) 4,163,000.

Shilka, R., E. Siberia, **RSFSR**; trib. of R. Amur; 552 km long.

Shillelagh, v., R.D., Wicklow, **R.o.I.**; oak forest, gave its name to oak or blackthorn cudgel.

Shillong, c., cap. Meghalaya, former cap. of Assam, **India**; at alt. 1,372 m in Khasi hills; ctr. of impt. tea-growing dist.; admin. technical education; pleasant climate attracts summer tourists; p. (1981) 109,244 (c), 174,703 (met. a.).

Shimizu, spt., **Japan**; exp. tea, oranges; fishing; p. (1985) 242,166.

Shimoda, spt., Honshu, **Japan**; between Nagoya and Yokohama; fishing; p. (1970) 30,318.

Shimoga, t., Karnataka, **India**; on Tunga R.; cotton-ginning, rice-milling; p. (1981) 151,783.

Shimonoseki, spt., Honshu I., **Japan**; at extreme S.W. of I.; tunnel and bridge links island of Kyushu; rly. ctr.; engin., chemicals based on local coal; fishing; p. (1985) 269,167.

Shin, Loch, Sutherland, **Scot.**; 26 km long; drained by R. Shin to R. Oykell.

Shipka Pass, **Bulgaria**; over the Balkan mtns., 75 km N.E. of Plovdiv.

Shipley, t., West Yorks., **Eng.**; on R. Aire, 13 km N.W. of Leeds; worsted mnfs.; inc. model v. of Saltaire, built by Titus Salt (1851) to house his alpaca mill workers; p. (1981) 27,894.

Shiraz, c., cap. of Fars prov., **Iran**; beautifully sited in vine-growing dist.; textiles, rugs, metal wks., lt. elec ind., tourist ctr.; tombs of mediaeval poets Saadi and Hafez; known as "city of roses and nightingales"; pleasant winter climate; univ., airpt.; oil refinery; petrochemical complex; fertilisers; p. (1986) 848,011.

Shire, R., flows out of L. Malawi south through **Malawi** and **Moçambique** to Zambesi; lge. hydro-elect. potential; 592 km long.

Shirwa or **Chilwah**, shallow L., **Malawi**; 64 km long, 22 km wide; has 4 Is.

Shizuoka, c., cap. of S. pref., Honshu, **Japan**; pt. on Suruga Bay; impt. ctr. for tea and oranges; lacquer-ware, textiles; p. (1985) 468,362.

Shkodër (**Scutari**), c., N. **Albania**; stands at foot of L. Scutari, 26 km from Adriatic; mkt. ctr., tobacco, cement, textiles; enjoyed greatest comm. prosperity after Ottoman conquest;

several mosques; new rail link (1986) to Titograd, Albania's first external rail link, used mainly for metal ore export; p. (1980) 66,500.

Shkodër (**Scutari**), L., on borders of Montenegro (**Yugoslavia**) and **Albania**; outlet via R. Boyana into Adriatic, 46 km long.

Sholapur, c., Maharashtra, **India**; between Hyderabad and Poona; rly. junc., impt. textile ctr.; p. (1981) 511,103.

Shoreham-by-Sea, t., Adur, West Sussex, **Eng.**; at mouth of R. Adur, 6 km E. of Worthing; spt. and mkt. t.; oil jetty; boat bldg., chemicals, soap, preserves; p. (1981) 20,827.

Shoshone Falls, on Snake R., Idaho, **USA**; height 61 m, used for irrigation projects.

Shott el Jerid, Algeria and Tunisia; deep depression in the desert.

Shotts, plateau, N. **Africa**; upland region with salt Ls., within Atlas mtns.

Shreveport, c., La., **USA**; industl. ctr. in cotton-growing dist.; petroleum; p. (1984) 220,000 (c.), 360,900 (met. a.).

Shrewsbury, co. t., Shrops., **Eng.**; on R. Severn 19 km above Ironbridge gorge between the Wrekin and Wenlock Edge; agr. and dairy equipment, machin., elec. gds.; cattle and sheep mkt.; public school; with Atcham forms l. gov. dist.; p. (est. 1988) 90,900.

Shropshire (**Salop**), non-met co., **Eng.**; on Welsh border, crossed by R. Severn; fine pastoral cty.; with hills and woodland, agr. and dairying; industl. activity at co. t. Shrewsbury; a. 3,489 km²; p. (est. 1988) 400,800.

Shropshire, North, l. gov. dist., Shrops., **Eng.**; a. N. of Shrewsbury and inc. Market Drayton; p. (est. 1988) 56,200.

Shropshire, South, l. gov. dist., Shrops., **Eng.**; S. of Shrewsbury and inc. Ludlow; p. (est. 1988) 36,000.

Shusha, t., Azerbaydzhan SSR, **USSR**; health resort; silk spinning, rug making; Armenian p. massacred by Tartars 1926; p. *c.* 6,000.

Shustar, t., **Iran**; carpets, woollens, pottery; shallow-draught boats can reach Shallili, nr. S. by R. Karun; p. (1966) 21,999.

Sialkot, t., **Pakistan**; N.E. of Lahore; sports gds., musical and surgical instruments, paper; agr. tr. and processing ctr.; p. (1981) 296,000.

Siam. *See* Thailand.

Siam, G. of, lge. inlet, S. China Sea; sheltered with shallow water; length 616 km N.W. to S.E.

Sian. *See* Xi'an.

Siangtan. *See* Xiangtan.

Siauliai, t., Lithuanian SSR, **USSR**; 184 km N.W. of Vilna; impt. rly. junc.; food and leather inds.; p. (est. 1986) 130,000.

Sibenik, t., Croatia, **Yugoslavia**; Adriatic spt.; exp. timber, bauxite; aluminium, chemical and textile inds.; p. (1981) 80,148.

Siberia, terr., **USSR**; extends from Urals to Sea of Okhotsk and Bering Strait, bounded by Arctic on N. and by Mongolia and Turkestan on S.; climate mostly severe; ch. cs., Novosibirsk (cap. W. S.) and Irkutsk (cap. E. S.); rich in coal, iron, minerals; oil and gas in W. Siberian lowland; liquified coal pipeline under construction to Moscow; p. and economic activity clustered around rlys., esp. Trans-Siberian rly.; a. *c.* 12,950,000 km²; p. (est. 1983) 29,587,000.

Sibiu, t., central **Romania**; picturesque site at foot of Transylvanian Alps; retains mediaeval character despite being an impt. industl. ctr.; lge. German minority p.; caths.; p. (1984) 173,115.

Sibu, t., Sarawak, E. **Malaysia**; 128 km up R. Rejang; comm. ctr. at head of ocean navigation; airport; p. (1980) 86,000.

Sichuan (**Szechwan**), prov., S.W. **China**; mostly occupied by Chang Jiang; known as Red Basin because of colour of its sandstone; fertile a. with mild climate; rice, tea, citrus fruits, tobacco, sugar-cane; lge coal reserves; exp. tung oil; silk producing a.; most populous prov.; cap. Chengdu; a. 568,977 km²; p. (est. 1985) 101,120,000.

Sicily, lgst. I., Mediterranean Sea; former kingdom and now aut. region of **Italy**; pleasant climate, mtnous.; fertile lowlands, especially plain of Catania, but gr. hampered by primitive methods, absentee landlords and need for irrigation; lge. range of Mediterranean crops; fishing; sulphur; petroleum reserves, refining and petrochemical inds.; volcanic Mt. Etna erupted in 1971; a. 25,708 km²; p. (est. 1986) 5·1m.

Sidi-bel-Abbès, t., W. **Algeria**; old fortress t., become

H.Q. of Fr. Foreign Legion; agr. mkt. ctr. for region producing grain, grapes, olives, livestock; p. (est. 1983) 146,653.

Sidlaw Hills, low mtn. range, Tayside Reg., **Scot.;** max. alt. 455 m.

Sidmouth, mkt. t., East Devon, **Eng.;** on S. cst., 24 km S.E. of Exeter; seaside resort; retirement ctr.; p. (1981) 12,446.

Sidon. See **Saïda.**

Siebengebirge, sm. wooded range of seven hills, **W. Germany;** of volcanic origin rising to 457 m on right bank of Rhine; famous for Drachenfels association with the Siegfried saga.

Siedlce, t., **Poland;** 88 km E. of Warsaw; rly. junc.; agr. inds.; p. (1983) 61,300.

Siegburg, t., N. Rhine–Westphalia, **W. Germany;** on R. Sieg; Benedictine abbey; dyes, iron, ceramics; p. (est. 1986) 34,100.

Siegen, t., N. Rhine–Westphalia, **W. Germany;** on R. Sieg; 2 cas.; iron mng. and smelting, machin., leather; p. (est. 1986) 107,300.

Siemianowice Slaskie, t., **Poland;** nr. Kotowice; ctr. of mng., industl. region; iron and steel, machin.; cas.; p. (1983) 79,600.

Siena, hill-town, Tuscany, **Italy;** 51 km S. of Florence; spreads over three hilltops with Piazza del Campo in between where celebrated Palio festival (horse-races) are held; 13th- and 14th-cent. arch., cath.; agr. mkt., tanning, glass, textiles, bricks; *panforte* confectionery; tourist ctr.; p. (1981) 61,989.

Sierra Leone, rep., W. cst. **Africa;** mangrove swamps on cst., high plateau, with peaks over 1,800 m in interior; climate hot, humid; economy based on subsistence agr. with rice, coffee and cocoa for exp.; iron ore mng. restarted (1983) at Marampa; main exp. diamonds, notorious smuggling problem; fishing along cst.; cap. Freetown; a. 72,326 km²; p. (est. 1987) 3·85m.

Sierra Madre Occidental, mtn. range, **Mexico;** volcanic, forms W. edge of Mexican plateau; average alt. 2,100 m.

Sierra Madre Oriental, mtn. range, **Mexico;** limestone, forms E. edge of Mexican plateau; average alt. 2,400 m.

Sierra Maestra, mtn. range, Oriente prov., S.E. **Cuba;** rises abruptly from cst.; rich in minerals.

Sierra Morena, mtn. range, **Spain;** between Guadalquivir and Guadiana basins, highest point 1,677 m; rich in minerals.

Sierra Nevada, mtn. range, Granada, **Spain;** highest summit Mulhacén 3,483 m.

Sierra Nevada, mtn. chain, Cal., **USA;** highest peak Mt. Whitney 4,544 m; nat. parks.

Sierra Nevada de Mérida, mtn. range, W. **Venezuela;** extends N.E. from San Cristóbal to Barquisimeto; extension of E. range of Andes, alt. over 4,880 m; impt. coffee plantations from 900–1,800 m on slopes.

Sierra Pacaraima, mtn. range, Brazil, **Venezuela;** forms part of international bdy. and watershed between Amazon and Orinoco basins.

Sighet, frontier t., N. **Romania;** on R. Tisa, on border with USSR; extreme, continental climate; timber, agr. and livestock tr.; cotton textiles; p. (est. 1970) 33,361.

Siglufjörd, spt., N. **Iceland;** impt. herring fisheries; p. (1970) 2,161.

Sigtuna, t., Stockholm, **Sweden;** on Mälaren L.; first cap. of Sweden; educational ctr., tourist resort; p. (1983) 28,681.

Sihanoukville. See **Kompong Som.**

Sikhote-Alin, mtn. range, S.E. Asiatic **RSFSR;** rises to 1,800 m and extends for 1,200 km parallel to Pac. cst.; hinders access to W. basins; forestry, minerals.

Si-Kiang. See **Xi Jiang.**

Sikkim, st., **India;** on S. slopes of Himalayas; incorporated as 22nd st. 1975; forest covered; economically underdeveloped; scene of rivalry between India and China; cap. Gangtok; a. 7,110 km²; p. (1981) 316,385.

Sila, La, massif, Calabria, S. **Italy;** granite mass occupying full width of peninsula; alt. over 1,060 m, max. 1,930 m.

Silchester, par., Hants., **Eng.;** ruins of Roman t., Calleva Atrebatum; impt. ctr. of Roman communications network.

Silesia (Polish **Slask,** Czech **Slezsko,** German **Schlesien**), geographical region, Central **Europe;** since 1945 divided between Poland, CSSR and E. Germany; extends along both banks of Oder R.; bounded in S. by Sudeten mtns.; forested

mtns., fertile arable agr. in lowlands; major concentration of economic activity based on coalfield of Upper Silesia (ceded to Poland 1922); complex territorial history; now forms highly urbanised industl. conurb. mainly in Poland, admin. by Katowice, Opole, Wroclaw, Wroclaw (c.), and part of Zielona Gora; CSSR portion forms part of N. Moravia; E. Germany retains sm. part of Lower Silesia W. of Neisse R.; total a. 46,600 km².

Silistra, t., **Bulgaria;** on Danube opposite Romanian t. of Calarasi; cereals and timber tr.; mnfs. foodstuffs, ceramics, furniture; mosques; p. (est. 1970) 38,500.

Silkeborg, t., Jutland, **Denmark;** tourist resort in beautiful forest and lake region; p. (1981) 33,304.

Silsden, t., West Yorks., **Eng.;** wool textiles; p. (1981) 6,742.

Silver Spring, t., Md., **USA;** sub. N. of Washington, D.C.; science-based inds. and research laboratories; p. (1980) 72,893.

Simcoe, L., S. Ont., **Canada;** several resorts; boating, fishing; 48 km by 42 km.

Simeulue, I., S.W. of Sumatra, **Indonesia;** primitive islanders; fishing and shifting cultivation.

Simferopol, t., Ukrainian SSR, **USSR;** on R. Salghir nr. Sevastopol; industl. ctr. in rich agr. a., fruit-canning, tobacco, machin.; p. (est. 1980) 307,000.

Simla, t., Himachal Pradesh, **India;** famous hill-station c. 2,158 m high on forested ridge of Himalayas, 280 km N. of Delhi.

Simonstown, W. Cape Prov., **S. Africa;** naval sta, docks; p. (est. 1970) 12,091.

Simplon, mtn., **Switzerland;** alt. 3,567 m; the pass over the Simplon (alt. 2,011 m) from Domodossola, Italy, to Brig in the Rhône valley, Switzerland, was originally made by Napoleon I. The Simplon rly. tunnel leads from Brig on the Swiss side to Iselle in the Val di Vedro on the Italian and is the longest in the world, 19.7 km.

Simpson Desert, Central **Australia;** uninhabited arid a. covered in ridge dunes and spinifex; a. 77,000 km².

Sinai, peninsula, easternmost part of **Egypt;** between Gs. of Aqaba and Suez, at head of Red Sea; mainly desert in N., granitic ridges in S. rising to 2,592 m at Jebel Katrun; Jebel Musa or Mt. Sinai (2,244 m) is one of numerous peaks; mineral resources; coal mine at Maghâra; occupied by Israeli troops, Nov. 1956–March 1957, and since June 1967; phased Israeli withdrawal began 1979 after the Israeli–Egypt settlement; a. 28,632 km².

Sinaia, t., S. **Romania;** health and winter sports resort in Transylvanian Alps; until 1947 summer residence of Romanian kings; palaces; p. (est. 1971) 12,000.

Sinaloa, st., **Mexico;** on G. of Cal.; agr. and mng., rich in gold, silver, copper, iron and lead; cereals on uplands; sugar, cotton on lowlands; cap. Culiacán; a. 48,482 km²; p. (1980) 1,880,098.

Sind, prov. (revived 1970), **Pakistan;** lower Indus valley; dry climate; E. part reaches edge of Thar desert; agr. depends on irrigation; irrigated by Sukkur and Kotri systems; wheat, rice, cotton, oilseeds, sugar-cane, fruits; handicraft inds. in ts.; ch. ts., Karachi, Hyderabad, Sukkur, Shikarpur; a. 129,500 km² p. (1981) 19,028,666.

Singapore, rep., S.E. **Asia;** I. separated from Malaysian mainland by Johore Strait and linked by causeway; equatorial climate; cap. Singapore on S cst. has fine natural harbour; p. (est. 1985) 2,558,000, second largest port in the world; world ctr. of rubber and tin mkts.; tr. in machinery, petrol prods., mnfs., with Japan, Malaysia and USA; increasingly impt. as regional financial centre; oil refining, shipbldg., but industl. development slowing down since 1985; only 20 per cent of land cultivated; fruit, mkt. gardening; second hst. standard of living in Asia; reduction in Brit. military presence from base on N. cst. of I.; a. 620 km²; p. (est. 1987) 2,613,000 (rep.).

Singhbhum, dist., Bihar, **India;** iron and steel wks. based on local iron mng.; a. 13,445 km²; p. (1961) 2,049,911.

Sinhailion. See **Lianyungang.**

Sining. See **Xining.**

Sinkiang-Uighur. See **Xinjiang Uygur.**

Sinop, cap. of S. prov., **Turkey;** sm. pt. with gd. harbour on Black Sea but poor communications with hinterland; p. (1985) 23,148.

Sintra (Cintra), t., **Portugal**; summer resort, 29 km from Lisbon; Moorish castle, royal palace; p. (1981) 126,010 (met. a.).

Sinuiju, c., W. **N. Korea**; spt. at mouth of Yalu R. on Yellow Sea; linked by bridge to Antung (China); industl. ctr.; chemicals, aluminium inds., using power from Supung Dam; p. (1981) 305,000.

Sinyang. See **Xinyang.**

Sion, t., cap. of Valais can., **Switzerland**; on R. Rhône; built on two castled hills; cath.; horticultural mkt. ctr.; hydroelectric power stas. and coal mines nearby; p. (1980) 22,877.

Sioux City, Iowa, **USA**; on R. Missouri; meatpacking, foundries, elec. gds., cement; p. (1984) 81,800 (c.), 118,200 (met. a.).

Sioux Falls, t., S.D., **USA**; on Big Sioux R.; in rich wheat region; machin., cars, farming implements; nuclear reactor; p. (1984) 87,600 (t.), 118,100 (met. a.).

Siping (Szeping), c., Jilin prov., **China**; agr. distributing ctr.; cement; p. (1984) 353,300.

Siret, R., **Romania**, **USSR**; flows E. from Carpathians to Danube; steep forested left bank, fertile terraced right bank; hydroelectric power and irrigation schemes; 448 km long.

Sisak, t., Croatia, **Yugoslavia**; developing indust. ctr. and R. pt.; iron and steel, oil refining.

Sistan and Baluchistan, twin prov., **Iran**; bounded by Afghanistan and Pakistan; cap. Zahedan; much desert land; arid, very hot; p. (1982) 664,292.

Sitapur, t., Uttar Pradesh, **India**; rly. junc.; agr. tr. ctr.; eye hospital; p. (1981) 101,210.

Sitra, I., Persian G.; forms part of st. of **Bahrain**, 5 km long and 1·6 km wide; oil pipeline and causeway carrying road extends out to sea for 5 km to deep-water anchorage; oil refinery; power sta. and desalinisation plant.

Sittang, R., **Burma**; rises in Pegu Yoma, flows S. to. G. of Martaban through delta; valley intensively cultivated, delta forested; irrigation project; 976 km long.

Sittard, mkt. t., Limburg, **Neth.**; tanning; p. (est. 1987) 44,000.

Sittingbourne and Milton, mkt. t., Swale, Kent, **Eng.**; on Milton Creek, 14 km E. of Chatham; paper mills, brick wks.; cement; insecticides; ctr. of fruit-growing dist.; p. (1981) 33,645.

Sittwe (Akyab), spt., **Burma**; at mouth of Kaladan R.; exp. rice; (1983) 143,000.

Sivas, c., cap. of S. prov., **Turkey**; impt. tr. and agr. ctr. in Kizil Irmak valley; cement, rugs; copper mng. nearby; foundations of modern Turkey laid here by Atatürk 1919; p. (1985) 198,553.

Sivash Sea or Putrid Sea, lagoon on N.E. cst. of Crimea, **USSR**; 20 per cent salt; a. 2,590 km².

Siwa, oasis, **Egypt**; in Libyan Desert, c. 480 km S.W. of Alexandria; dates, olives; remains of temple of Zeus Ammon (visited by Alexander the Great); 32 km long, 1·6 km wide; p. (1966) 3,600.

Sizewell, Suffolk, **Eng.**; nuclear power sta.; plans to build Britain's 1st pressurised water nuclear reactor here.

Sjaelland, I., **Denmark**; lgst. I., separated from Fyn I. by the Gr. Belt; fertile glacial clays but rapidly spreading ts.; ch. c. Copenhagen; a. 7,356 km²; p. (1965) 2,055,040.

Skagerrak, arm of N. Sea, giving access to the Kattegat, between Norway and Denmark, 112–144 km wide.

Skagway, sm. spt., Alaska, **USA**; at head of Lynn Canal inlet, 640 km N.W. of Prince Rupert; linked by rly. to Whitehorse on upper R. Yukon; boomed in gold rush (1898), p. 15,000, subsequently declined; p. (1980) 768.

Skåne (Scania), prov. and peninsula, extreme S. of **Sweden**; corresponds approx. to cos. Malmöhus, Kristianstad; most favoured part of Sweden in relief, soil, climate; intensive farming, wheat, barley, sugar-beet, fodder crops, dairy cattle; ch. ts. Malmö, Lund, Hälsingborg; a. 10,939 km², p. (1983) 1,024,152.

Skaraborg, co., **Sweden**; between Ls. Vänern and Vättern; dairy agr.; a. 8,467 km²; p. (est. 1986) 270,000.

Skara Brae, prehistoric v. Mainland, Orkneys, **Scot.**; v. excavated from under sand dunes.

Skarzysko-Kamienna, t., Kielce, **Poland**; ctr. of developing metallurgical ind.; p. (1970) 39,200.

Skaw The (Grenen), C., at extreme N. of **Denmark**.

Skeena, R., B.C., **Canada**; rises in N. Rocky mtns., flows S.W. to Pac. Oc. at Prince Rupert; lower valley used by Canadian National Rly.;

640 km long.

Skegness, t., East Lindsey, Lincs., **Eng.**; on E. cst.; resort; lt. engin.; p. (1981) 14,425.

Skelleftea, t., N. **Sweden**; on Bothnia G.; growing since discovery of Boliden ores nearby; iron and copper ore smelting; p. (est. 1986) 74,000.

Skelmersdale, t., West Lancs., **Eng.**; coal, bricks, drainpipes; new t. (1961); p. (1981) 39,144.

Skelton and Brotton, t., Langbaurgh, Cleveland, **Eng.**; at N. foot of Cleveland hills, 16 km E. of Middlesbrough; steel flooring; p. (1981) 16,208.

Skiddaw, mtn., Cumbria, **Eng.**; E. of Bassenthwaite L.; alt. 931 m.

Skien, spt., Bratsberg, **Norway**; on R. Skien; saw-mills, timber tr.; birthplace of Ibsen; p. (est. 1987) 47,000.

Skikda (Philippeville), t., spt., **Algeria**; exp. prods. from Saharan oases; oil pipeline to Mesdar; vast petrochemical plant; p. (est. 1983) 141,159.

Skipton, t., Craven, North Yorks., **Eng.**; on R. Aire; cotton and rayon inds.; cas.; p. (1981) 13,246.

Skopje, t., cap. of Macedonia, **Yugoslavia**; anc. Scupi, one of oldest ts. in Balkans; oriental appearance; destroyed by massive earthquake (1963); food processing, iron and steel wks.; new oil refinery; airpt., route ctr.; p. (1981) 506,547.

Skövde, t., **Sweden**; between Ls. Vänern and Vättern; garrison t., chemicals, cement; p. (est. 1986) 46,000.

Skye, I., lgst. of Inner Hebrides, Skye and Lochalsh, **Scot.**; mtnous.; sheep-farming and fisheries; tourism; only t. Portree; a. 1,417 km²; p. (est. 1986) 11,526 (dist.).

Skyros, I., Sporades, **Greece**; in Aegean Sea; mainly agr.; a. 199 km²; p. (1961) 2,882.

Slagelse, t., Sjaelland, **Denmark**; food inds.; iron wks.; 11th cent. church; p. (1981) 28,539.

Slave Coast, name given to the Guinea cst. of W. Africa between the Volta and Niger deltas where slaves were shipped from 16th to 19th cent.

Slave, R., N.W. Terr., **Canada**; flows into Gr. Slave L.; length 416 km.

Slavonia, historic region, **Yugoslavia**; between Drava R. (N.) and Sava R. (S.); now part of rep. of Croatia; ch. t. Osijek.

Slavyansk, t., Ukrainian SSR, **USSR**; in Donets basin; chemicals, engin.; p. (est. 1985) 143,000.

Sleaford, mkt. t., North Kesteven, Lincs., **Eng.**; 19 km N.E. of Grantham; agr. and agr. implements; p. (1981) 8,523.

Sleat, Sound of, Lochaber, Skye and Lochalsh, **Scot.**; separates I. of Skye from the mainland; 11 km wide.

Slezsko. See **Silesia.**

Sliema, t., **Malta**; E. of Valletta; resort; p. (est. 1983) 20,123.

Slieve Bloom, hill range, Offaly and Laoghis cos., **R.o.I.**; highest point 529 m.

Slieve Donard, mtn., **N. Ireland**; highest of the Mourne mtns.; alt. 835 m.

Sligo, co., Connacht, **R.o.I.**; borders Atl. Oc.; rises to Ox Mtns. over 600 m; pastoral agr.; fishing; co. t. S.; a. 1,909 km²; p. (1981) 18,002.

Sligo, co. t., Sligo, **R.o.I.**; on S. Bay; pt., exp. agr. prods.; abbey ruins; cath.; p. (1981) 17,232.

Slioch, mtn., Ross and Cromarty, **Scot.**; 981 m.

Sliven, t., **Bulgaria**; in Balkan mtns.; impt. woollen mnf. ctr.; carpets; p. (1985) 102,455.

Slough, t., l. gov. dist., Berks., **Eng.**; on river terrace N. of R. Thames, 37 km W. of London; many lt. inds.; p. (est. 1988) 100,300.

Slovakia (Slovak Socialist Rep.), **ČSSR**; extends from Carpathians to Danube valley; prosperous agr.; cap. Bratislava; with Czech Socialist Rep. forms Fed. Rep. of Czechoslovakia; a. 48,956 km²; p. (est. 1970) 4,563,460.

Slovenia, constituent rep., **Yugoslavia**; mtnous., but many minerals inc. coal; highly developed region; cap. Ljubljana; growing separatist demands; a. 16,229 km²; p. (1981) 1,891,864.

Slupsk (Stolp), t., N.W. **Poland** (since 1945); formerly in Pomerania; on R. Stupia, nr. Baltic Sea; cas.; wood, metal, food processing; p. (1983) 90,600.

Småland, historic prov., S. **Sweden**; barren upland a. S. of L. Vättern; moorland, deciduous forest; contrasts greatly with remainder of S. Sweden; a. 29,322 km²; p. (1983) 701,525.

Smederevo, t., Serbia, **Yugoslavia**; nr. Belgrade; pt. on R. Danube; walled t.; steel wks.; p. (1981) 107,366.

Smethwick. *See* **Warley.**

Smolensk, c., cap. of S. oblast, **RSFSR**; on upper Dnieper; anc. c. damaged in many wars; route ctr.; vehicles, machin., food processing; p. (est. 1985) 331,000.

Smyrna. *See* **Izmir.**

Snaefell, highest mtn., **I. of Man**; alt. 620 m.

Snake R., or **Lewis Fork**, trib. of Columbia R., flows from Wyo. to Wash., **USA**; gorges; hydroelectric power; 1,680 km long.

Sneek, t., Friesland, **Neth.**; butter, cheese mkt.; yachting ctr.; p. (est. 1987) 29,500.

Sneeuwbergen, mtn. range, Cape Prov., **S. Africa.**

Snowdon, mtn., Gwynedd, **Wales**; highest in Eng. and Wales, alt. 1,086 m; forms part of Snowdonia Nat. Park.

Snowy Mtns., N.S.W., **Australia**; part of Australian Alps inc. Australia's hgst. peak (Mount Kosciusko); rise to over 2,000 m; S.M. scheme (1950) diverts water from headstreams in tunnels through mtns. to provide water for irrigation and hydroelectric power; completed 1972.

Snowy, R., N.S.W. and Victoria, **Australia**; rises in Mt. Kosciusko, flows S. into Bass strait 128 km W. of C. Howe; part of Snowy Mtn. scheme; 432 km long.

Soar, R., Leics., Notts., **Eng.**; rises S. of Leics., flows N.W. to join R. Trent; 69 km long.

Sobat, R., **Sudan** and **Ethiopia**; made up of several sm. Rs.; trib. of White Nile; 800 km long.

Soche. *See* **Yarkand.**

Sochi, t., **RSFSR**; on Black Sea at foot of main Caucasian range; health resort with subtropical climate and sulphur springs; developed since 1933; p. (est. 1985) 310,000.

Society Is., Fr. Polynesia, S. Pac. Oc.; comprise Windward Is. (Tahiti, Moorea, Mehetia, etc.) and Leeward Is. (Huahune, Raiatea, etc.); visited by Captain Cook; main prods. phosphate and copper; cap. Papeete; a. 1,647 km²; p. (1983) 142,129.

Socotra, I., G. of Aden, Indian Oc.; since 1967 part of **Democratic Rep. of Yemen**; under Brit. protection 1886–1967; lofty tableland; myrrh, frankincense, aloes; cap. Tamrida; a. 3,626 km²; p. (est.) 12,000.

Sodbury, t., Northavon, Avon. **Eng.**; former coalmng. ctr.; expanded t.

Söderhamn, spt., **Sweden**; on G. of Bothnia, N. of Gavle; timber, wood-pulp; p. (est. 1983) 30,736.

Södermanland, co., **Sweden**; between Baltic cst. and L. Mälar; cattle-rearing; mng.; a. 6,822 km²; p. (est. 1986) 250,000.

Södertälje, t., **Sweden**; on S. canal linking L. Mälar with Baltic cst.; vehicles, chemicals, tobacco; p. (est. 1986) 80,000.

Soest, c., N. Rhine–Westphalia, **W. Germany**; one of oldest ts., member of Hanseatic league; suffered heavily in second world war; soap, textile machin., engin.; p. (est. 1986) 42,000.

Soest, t., Utrecht, **Neth.**; residtl., agr. ctr.; p. (est. 1987) 41,000.

Sofia, c., cap. of **Bulgaria**; Roman Serdica, and Triaditsa of Byzantine Greeks; nr. Yugoslav border; impt. route ctr. and ch. industl. ctr. of rep.; machin., textiles, chemicals, elec. engin.; cath., univ., and many historic bldgs.; p. (1985) 1,114,962.

Sogne Fjord, Norway; longest fjord in Norway; length 176 km; tourism.

Sogn og Fjordane, co., W. **Norway**; borders Atl. Oc., indented by Sogne Fjord; lge. hydroelectric power resources; tourism; a. 18,480 km²; p. (1983) 106,140.

Sohag, t., **Egypt**; on R. Nile; cotton processing; p. (est. 1983) 274,000.

Soho, dist., London, **Eng.**; settled by Fr. Huguenots 16th cent.; high proportion of foreign residents, sometimes known as London's "Latin quarter"; night-clubs, theatres, restaurants, filmcompany offices.

Soissons, t., Aisne dep., **France**; anc. Augusta Suessionum; commands N.E. approaches to Paris; cath.; agr. tr.; p. (1982) 32,236.

Sokoto, t., **Nigeria**, W. Africa; founded 1809 as

cap. of native st. of S., p. mainly Hausa and Fulani; tr. ctr.; p. (est. 1981) 143,000.

Solent, The, strait separating I. of Wight from Hampshire mainland, **Eng.**;

Solihull, t., met dist., West Midlands, **Eng.**; 8 km S.W. of Birmingham; residtl.; motor vehicles chemicals; p. (est. 1988) 205,000.

Solikamsk, t., **RSFSR**; on R. Kama; chemicals from local potash; rapidly growing t.; p. (est. 1985) 106,000.

Solingen, t., N. Rhine–Westphalia, **W. Germany**; 24 km E. of Düsseldorf; cutlery ctr.; p. (est. 1986) 158,400.

Solnechnyy. *See* **Gornyy Snezhnogorsk.**

Solomon Is., S. Pac. Oc.; internal self-gov. (1976); full independence (July 1978); archipelago of volcanic Is.; N. Is. form part of Papua New Guinea; remainder Brit.; dependent on exp. of copra, timber, fish; threatened by insect pests; a. 29,785 km²; p. (est. 1985) 270,000 (mostly Melanesian).

Solothurn (Soleure), can., N.W. **Switzerland**, crossed by Jura mtns., and R. Aare; 97 per cent cultivated; dairying; many industl. ts.; cap. S.; a. 793 km²; p. (est. 1986) 219,000.

Solothurn (Soleure), t., cap. of S. can., **Switzerland**; on R. Aare; anc. t.; cath.; watches, motor mnf.; p. (1980) 15,778.

Solway Firth, arm of **Irish Sea**, Dumfries and Galloway Reg., Scot., and Cumbria, **Eng.**; 6 km long.

Somalia (Somali Democratic Rep.), E. cst. **Africa**; narrow cst. plain in N., widens in S., interior plateau reaching *c.* 2,400 m; dry, hot climate; 75 per cent. p. nomadic; livestock herding; permanent agr. in irrigated R. valleys; sugar, banana plantations in Webi Shebeli and Juba Rs. in S.; potential for mineral exploitation; cap. Mogadishu; recent conflict with Ethiopia; recent influx of immigrants from Ethiopia; a. 637,658 km²; p. (est. 1987) 6,110,000.

Somaliland, French. *See* **Djibouti.**

Sombor, t., Serbia, **Yugoslavia**; cattle, grain tr.; textiles; p. (1981) 99,168.

Somersby, v., Lincs., **Eng.**; the birthplace of Tennyson.

Somerset, non-met. co., S.W. **Eng.**; inc. part of Exmoor, Mendips, Quantocks and Blackdown hills; to N. is drained marshland of Somerset levels; dairying; coastal resorts; co. t. Taunton; a. 3,458 km²; p. (est. 1988) 457,700.

Somme, dep., N. **France**; borders Eng. Channel; crossed by R. Somme; low-lying agr. a.; textile inds.; cap. Amiens; a. 6,327 km²; p. (1982) 543,600.

Somme, R., **France**; flows in deps. Aisne and Somme to English Channel; scene of battles 1916; linked to Rs. Oise and Scheldt by canal 186 km long.

Somport Tunnel, on bdy. **France–Spain**; carries main rly. from Pau to Zaragoza under Pyrénées; 8 km long.

Sönderborg, spt., S. Jutland, **Denmark**; older part of c. on Als I.; palace; textiles; p. (1981) 26,885.

Sondrio, t., cap. of S. prov., **Italy**; commands the Adda valley, impt. routeway through Alps; agr. mkt.; textiles; p. (1981) 22,747.

Songhua R., (**Sungari** R.), N.E. **China**; trib. of R. Amur; length 1,840 km.; hydroelectric power.

Songkhla, t., **Thailand**; most S. t.; ctr. of rubber growing dist.; third t. of cty.; p. (1980) 172,604.

Song-koi (Red R.), R., rises in Yunnan plateau, S.W. **China**, flows S.E. through N. **Vietnam**, enters G. of Tongking; Hanoi is nr. head of delta; Haiphong nr. one of R. mouths; lower valley densely populated and intensively cultivated; *c.* 1,280 km long.

Sonora, st., **Mexico**; on G. of Cal.; crossed by Sierra Madre Occidental; irrigated agr.; ch. producer of wheat, cattle; fish exp.; cap. Hermosillo; a. 182,535 km²; p. (1980) 1,498,931.

Sonoran Desert, Arizona, **USA**; alt. 900 m; enclosed basins and salt marshes.

Sonsonate, t., **El Salvador**; old t. with cath.; comm. ctr. of richest agr. region of rep., famed for coffee and dairy prod.; nr. Isalco volcano; p. (1980) 67,229.

"Soo" Canals. *See* **Sault Ste. Marie Canals.**

Soochow. *See* **Suzhou.**

Sopot, spt., **Poland**; on Gdansk Bay; resort, spa; part of Trójmiasto; p. (1983) 51,500.

Sopron, t., N.W. **Hungary**; on R. Hunte; nr. Austrian border; textiles, chemicals; p. (est. 1983) 55,000.

Sorau. *See* Zary.

Soria, t., cap. of prov. of Soria, **Spain**; on R. Duero at *c.* 900 m; agr.-processing; retains mediaeval appearance; p. (1987) 31,507.

Sorocaba, t., São Paulo st., **Brazil**; linked to São Paulo by 3 major highways yet has not attracted many new inds. unlike rest of reg.; textiles and food processing dominate; p. (est. 1985) 328,800.

Sorrento, cst. t., S. **Italy**; nr. S. extremity G. of Naples; popular resort, celebrated for its wines in anc. times; p. (1981) 17,301.

Sosnowiec, t., Katowice prov., **Poland**; coal-mng. ctr., iron wks.; metal and textile inds.; cas.; p. (est. 1985) 255,000.

Soufrière, volcano, St. Vincent, **W.I.**; alt. 1,235 m.

Sound, The, channel between Kattegat and Baltic, 5 km across at narrowest part; proposed tunnel between Denmark and Sweden.

Sousse (Susa), spt., **Tunisia**; exp. olive oil, phosphates; resort; p. (1984) 83,509.

South Africa, Republic of, lies in most S. part of Africa between Atl. and Indian Ocs.; comprises 4 provs., Cape Prov., Natal, O.F.S., Transvaal; narrow cst. plain, several interior plateaux (600–1,800 m) with upland grasslands (Veld) and fringed by escarpments; climate warm and sunny; most highly developed cty. in Africa, based on mineral resources of gold and diamonds, and more recent successful economic diversification; coal in Witbank and Vryheid dists. serves iron and steel ind. at Pretoria; growing textile, foodprocessing inds. at pts. Cape Town, Durban and rubber at Pt. Elizabeth; agr. dependent upon water supply; rich fruit growing a. around Cape Town, extensive grain growing and pastoral areas extended by irrigation; enforces practice of apartheid; caps. Pretoria (admin.), Cape Town (legislative), Bloemfontein (judicial); a. 1,224,254 km²; p. (est. 1987) 33 m. (including homelands).

South America, S. continent of Western Hemisphere; inc. all ctys. S. of Panama. *See* **Latin America**.

Southampton, c. spt., l. gov. dist., Hants., **Eng.**; at head of Southampton Water on peninsula between estuaries of Rs. Test and Itchen; univ.; decline of passenger liners, now one of Britain's biggest container pts.; ship repairing, oil refining, cable mkg., electronics, synthetic rubber; freeport (1984); p. (est. 1988) 196,700.

Southampton Water, inlet, Hants., **Eng.**; comprises drowned estuaries of Rs. Itchen and Test; gives access from Solent and Spithead to spt. of Southampton; 14 km by 1·6–2·4 km.

South Australia, st. of the **Australian Commonwealth**; the "desert state"; barren undulating interior forms part of central plateau of continent but inc. mtns. in S. and S.E. and L. Eyre basin 12 m below sea level; Nullarbor Plain in S.W.; sheep in S.E., intensive agr. in Murray R. valley; some interior mng. inds. but st. cap. of Adelaide contains most inds. and 69 per cent of p.; a. 984,381 km²; p. (1986) 1,382,550.

South Bend, c., Ind., **USA**; on St. Joseph R.; ctr. of fruit and dairy region; motorcars, aircraft, agr. machin.; p. (1984) 107,100 (c.), 239,800 (met. a.).

South Bucks, l. gov. dist., Bucks., **Eng.**; based on Beaconsfield; p. (est. 1988) 60,000.

South Carolina, st., **USA**; 'Palmetto St.'; admitted to Union 1788; st. flower Carolina Jessamine, st. bird Carolina Wren; level in E., mtns. in W.; subtropical climate; part of cotton belt; pigs and maize also impt.; cotton textiles; cap. Columbia; a. 80,432 km²; p. (1985) 3,347,000.

South Dakota, st., **USA**; 'Cayote St.'; admitted to Union 1889; st. flower Pasque flower, st. bird Ring Necked Pheasant; lies in Gt. Plains; crossed by R. Missouri; irrigated agr.; part of spring wheat belt, but now more diversified crops; agr. processing; cap. Pierre; a. 199,552 km²; p. (1985) 708,000 (inc. 25,000 Indians).

South Downs, chalk escarpment, East and West Sussex and Hants., **Eng.**; stretch from Chichester to Eastbourne; rise to over 240 m.

Southend-on-Sea, t., l. gov. dist., Essex, **Eng.**; on N. side of Thames estuary; varied lt. inds.; air

ferry terminal; resort; dormitory for London; p. (est. 1988) 165,400.

Southern Alps, mtns., S.I., **N.Z.**; alt. 3,000 m.

Southern Ocean, surrounds **Antarctica**; pack ice.

Southern Uplands, region, S. **Scot.**; broad belt of hilly cty., N. part bleak moorland, S. part deeply cut by glens; sheep-rearing; dairying in valleys.

South Georgia, Brit. I., S. Atl. Oc.; dependency of **Falkland Is.**; former whaling ctr.; a. 4,144 km².

South Glamorgan, co., S. **Wales**; mostly lowland borders Bristol Channel; inc. lge. industl. ts. and pts. of Cardiff and Barry; a. 417 km²; p. (est. 1988) 403,400.

South Hams, l. gov. dist., S. Devon, **Eng.**; a. between Torquay and Plymouth inc. Totnes, Kingsbridge and Salcombe; p. (est. 1988) 75,700.

South I., lge. I., **N.Z.**; inc. S. Alps (highest Mt. Cook, 3,764 m), Canterbury Plains, impt. sheep-rearing dist.; cool climate; considerable hydroelectric power resources; tourism; a. 150,461 km²; p. (est. 1985) 852,200 (only 26 per cent of N.Z. p.).

South Kensington, dist., W. London, **Eng.**; contains Victoria and Albert Museum, Geological and Science Museums, British Museum of Natural History, Commonwealth Institute, Albert Hall.

South Orkney Is., Antarctica; S.W. of S. Georgia; part of Brit. **Antarctic Terr.** (1962); meteorological sta.

South Ossetian, aut. oblast, Georgian SSR, **USSR**; in Caucasus mtns.; goat and sheep rearing dist.; a. 3,898 km²; p. (1986) 99,000.

Southport, t., Sefton, Merseyside, **Eng.**; on S. side of Ribble estuary; 29 km N. of Liverpool; leisure centre; residtl.; p. (1981) 89,745.

South Ribble, l. gov. dist., Lancs., **Eng.**; a. S. of Preston and inc. Walton-le-Dale; p. (est. 1988) 100,200.

South Sandwich Is., Antarctica; dependency of **Falkland Is.**; sm. volcanic Is.; a. 337 km².

South Shetland, archipelago, S. Atl. Oc.; 640 km S. of C. Horn; part of **Brit. Antarctic Terr.** (1962).

South Shields, t., Tyne and Wear, **Eng.**; pt. on S. bank at mouth of R. Tyne; holiday resort; marine engin., new lt. inds.; p. (1981) 87,203.

Southwark, inner bor., London, **Eng.**; S. of R. Thames, incorporating former bors. of Bermondsey and Camberwell; cath.; site of former Globe theatre; p. (est. 1988) 217,000.

South West Africa. *See* **Namibia**.

Southwick, t., Adur, West Sussex, **Eng.**; on S. cst. 6 km W. of Brighton; p. (1981) 11,388.

South Wight, l. gov. dist., I. of Wight, **Eng.**; inc.. Ventnor and Sandown-Shanklin; p. (est. 1988) 56,900.

Southwold, spt., Waveney, Suffolk, **Eng.**; on E. cst. 13 km S. of Lowestoft; fishing; resort; p. (1981) 1,795.

South Yorkshire, former met. co., **Eng.**; mainly industl. a. E. of Pennines; inc. productive coalfield nr. Barnsley and Doncaster and steel producing ts. of Sheffield and Rotherham; p. (est. 1988) 1,292,700.

Sovetsk (Tilsit), t., **RSFSR** (since 1945); on R. Niemen, formerly in E. Prussia; timber and paper inds.; famous for Treaty of Tilsit between Napoleon and Russia 1807; p. (est. 1970) 65,000.

Sowerby Bridge, t., Calderdale, West Yorks., **Eng.**; on R. Calder, 5 km W. of Halifax; woollens; p. (1981) 15,546.

Spa, t., Liège, **Belgium**; mineral springs, resort; gave name to "spas"; p. (1981) 9,619.

Spain, indep. sov. st., Iberia, S.W. **Europe**; member of EC (1986); lge. land a. takes up 80 per cent of Iberian peninsula and helps to make climate continental; mtnous. interior and narrow coastal strip encourages regional isolation and development of regional culture; civil war 1936–9 hindered modern economic growth; economy based on agr., but much of land is arid and although industl. raw materials in N. Spain and an oil refinery under construction at Bilbao, economic development has depended largely upon the spectacular growth of tourism; 42 million visitors each year; Europe's biggest car exporter; inds. attracted by cheap labour; monarchy revived 1975; cap. Madrid; a. 504,747 km²; p. (est. 1986) 38,891,313.

Spalding, mkt. t., South Holland, Lincs., **Eng.**; in Fens, 16 km up R. Welland from Wash; agr., bulb mkt., agr. machin., sugar-beet, fruit canning; p. (1981) 18,223.

Spandau, t., Potsdam, **E. Germany;** previously gr. military ctr.; at confluence of Rs. Havel and Spree; now part of Berlin.

Spanish Guinea. See **Equatorial Guinea.**

Spanish Sahara (Spanish West Africa). See **Western Sahara.**

Sparrows Point, t., Md., **USA;** situated on Chesapeake Bay; impt. iron and steel inds.

Sparta (Spárti), famous anc. c., **Greece;** on R. Eurotas, in Peloponnesus; passed under Roman rule 146 B.C.; modern c. dates from 1834; p. (1981) 14,388.

Spelthorne, l. gov. dist., Surrey, **Eng.;** close to Gtr. London; inc. Staines and Sunbury-on-Thames; p. (est. 1988) 85,800.

Spencer Gulf, lge. inlet, S. **Australia;** penetrates 384 km inland, many impt. pts. along cst. (Whyalla, Pt. Pirie, Pt. Augusta).

Spennymoor, t., Durham, **Eng.;** growing industl. t. S. of Durham; p. (1981) 20,630.

Sperrin Mtns., Strabane, **N. Ireland;** peat-covered schists; Sawell, 683 m.

Spey, R., Moray, Badenoch and Strathspey, the most rapid in **Scot.,** flows N.E. to Moray Firth; used for hydroelec. power; 171·2 km long.

Speyer, t., Rhineland–Palatinate, **W. Germany;** Roman origin; Romanesque cath.; famous Diet 1529 condemning Reformation gave rise to term "Protestant"; cas; publishing, engin.; p. (est. 1986) 42,900.

Spitalfields, par., E. London, **Eng.;** formerly noted for silk weaving, introduced by Huguenots 17th cent.; name derives from spital or hospital of St. Mary, founded 12th cent.

Spithead, roadstead, between Portsmouth and I. of Wight, **Eng.;** used by ships of Royal Navy.

Spitsbergen (Svalbard), I. gr. belonging to **Norway;** within Arctic; mtnous.; sealing and whaling; coal mng.; asbestos, copper, gypsum; a. 62,921 km²; p. (1986) 3,942.

Split (Spalato), t., **Yugoslavia;** spt. on Adriatic; second spt. of rep.; airport; food processing; p. (1981) 235,922.

Spokane, c., Wash., **USA;** on R. Spokane at falls used for hydroelec. power; timber tr. impt.; flour and saw mills, elec. gds.; lge. aluminium wks.; p. (1984) 173,300 (c.), 352,900 (met. a.).

Spoleto, c., Umbria, central **Italy;** cath., many Roman remains; textiles; p. (est. 1981) 36,839.

Sporades, scattered Is. belonging to **Greece** in Aegean Sea, inc. Skyros, Skiathos and Skopelos.

Spratley Is., S. **China Sea;** cluster of about 50 reefs and sand bars, thought to contain petroleum; ownership disputed by China, Taiwan, Philippines, and Vietnam.

Spree, R., **E. Germany;** flows W. past Berlin to the Havel at Spandau; 363 km long.

Spremberg, t., Cottbus, **E. Germany;** on R. Spree; cas., older part of t. on I.; glass, textiles; p. (est. 1970) 22,629.

Springfield, c., cap. of Ill., **USA;** in rich agr. and coal mng. a.; farming and elec. machin., food processing; home of Abraham Lincoln; p. (1984) 101,600 (c.), 190,100 (met. a.).

Springfield, c., Mass., **USA;** varied mnfs.; US armoury establ. 1794; p. (1984) 150,500 (c.), 515,900 (met. a.).

Springfield, c., Mo., **USA;** agr. ctr.; flour milling, engin.; p. (1984) 136,900 (c.), 217,200 (met. a.).

Springfield, t., Ohio, **USA;** agr. mach., motor lorries; p. (1980) 72,563 (c.), 183,885 (met. a.).

Springs, t., Transvaal, **S. Africa;** E. of Johannesburg; gold mng., engin., cars, elec. gds.; uranium plant; p. (1980) 153,974 (met. a.).

Spurn Head, Humberside, **Eng.;** sand spit at mouth of Humber estuary.

Sri Lanka (Ceylon), indep. rep. (1972) within Brit. Commonwealth (1948); in **Indian Oc.;** S.E. of India; fertile plains with cash crops of coconuts and rubber (S.W.) but dry in N.; mtnous. interior ameliorates climate where tea cultivation; varied p. composition inc. Sinhalese (70 per cent of p.), Tamils, Burghers (Portuguese and Dutch); agitation for Tamil independence; dependent on exp. of primary produce; inds. growing; cap. and ch. spt. Colombo; a. 65,610 km²; p. (est. 1985) 15,800,000.

Srinagar, t., cap. of Kashmir, **India;** in vale at c. 1,600 m. on Jhelum R. in W. Himalayas;

beautiful surrounding cty.; summer resorts; mnfs. silks, woollens, carpets; tourism; p. (est. 1981) 520,000.

Srirangam, t., Tamil Nadu, **India;** on R. Cauvery; temple dedicated to Vishnu; pilgrimage ctr.; p. (1981) 64,241.

Stade, t., Lower Saxony, **W. Germany;** nr. Hamburg; pt. on R. Schwinge; leather, wood, textiles; p. (est. 1986) 43,000.

Staffa, I. on Inner Hebrides, **W. Scot.;** 10 km N. of Iona, off W. cst. Mull; grand basaltic caverns, inc. Fingal's Cave, 69 m long, 13 m wide, 20 m high.

Stafford, co. t., l. gov. dist., Staffs., **Eng.;** on R. Sow, 24 km N. of Wolverhampton; heavy elec. and other engin.; expanded t.; p. (est. 1988) 117,900 (dist.).

Staffordshire, non-met. co., W. Midlands, **Eng.;** plain drained by R. Trent and tribs.; N. Staffs. coalfield inc. a. of "Potteries"; S. Staffs. coalfield now inc. in W. Midlands met. co.; a. 2,717 km²; p. (est. 1988) 1,032,900.

Staffordshire, East, l. gov. dist., Staffs., **Eng.;** stretches from Uttoxeter to Burton-on-Trent; p. (est. 1988) 95,700.

Staffordshire Moorlands, l. gov. dist., Staffs., **Eng.;** borders S. Pennines and inc. Leek, Biddulph and Cheadle; p. (est. 1988) 97,100.

Staffordshire, South, l. gov. dist., Staffs., **Eng.;** a. bordering W. Midlands conurb.; p. (est. 1988) 108,100.

Staines, mkt. t., Spelthorne, Surrey, **Eng.;** on R. Thames, 6 km S.E. of Windsor; linoleum, machin.; nr. birthplace of Matthew Arnold; p. (1981) 53,823.

Stainmore, pass, North Yorks./Durham, **Eng.;** crosses N. Pennines from Greta valley into upper Eden valley; used by main road; alt. 418 m.

Staithes, v., North Yorks., **Eng.;** potash mng.

Stalin. See Brasov.

Stalinabad. See Dushanbe.

Stalingrad. See Volgograd.

Stalino. See Varna.

Stalino. See Donetsk.

Stalinogorsk. See Novomoskovsk.

Stalinsk. See Novo Kuznetsk.

Stalybridge, t., Gtr. Manchester, **Eng.;** on R. Tame, 13 km E. of Manchester; cotton and wool engin., plastics, rubber, gds., elec. cables; p. (1981) 26,396.

Stamboul. See Istanbul.

Stamford, mkt. t., Lincs., **Eng.;** old bldgs., one of 5 Danelaw ts.; agr. inds., elec. gds., plastics; p. (1981) 16,153.

Stamford, c., Conn., **USA;** on shore of Long I. Sound; chemicals, engin.; p. (1984) 101,900 (c.), inc. in New York met. a.

Stanislav. See Ivano-Frankovsk.

Stanley, t., Derwentside, Durham, **Eng.;** former colly. dist.; p. (1981) 41,210.

Stanley, spt., cap of Falkland Is.; former whaling port., contains over half p. of Falklands; p. (1986) 1,200.

Stanley Falls. See Boyoma Falls.

Stanley Pool. See Pool Malebo.

Stanleyville. See Kisangani.

Stanlow, Ches., **Eng.;** petrol refinery, oil storage, docks, chemicals, linked to Anglesey by pipeline.

Stanovoi Mtns., range of mtns., **USSR;** extending from N. of R. Amur to nr. Sea of Okhotsk.

Stara Zagora, t., central **Bulgaria;** textiles, agr. processing; educational ctr.; p. (1985) 150,906.

Stargard Szczecinski, t., N.W. **Poland** (since 1945); formerly in Pomerania; rly. junc.; metal chemical, and food inds.; devastated in second world war; p. (1983) 63,300.

Start Point, C., nr. Dartmouth, Devon, **Eng.**

Stassfurt, t., Magdeburg, **E. Germany;** in gr. potash mng. region; chemicals, machin., metals; p. (est. 1973) 26,270.

Staten I., the most S. point N.Y. st. **USA;** shipyds.; linked with Brooklyn by Verrazano–Narrows bridge (opened 1964); resdtl.

Staten I., off Tierra del Fuego, **S. America.**

Stavanger, spt., cap. of Rogaland prov., S.W. **Norway;** comm. and industl. ctr.; fish curing and canning; oil refinery at Sola; cath., airport; p. (est. 1987) 95,437.

Staveley, t., Derbys., **Eng.;** 5 km N.E. of Chesterfield; coal, iron, chemicals, concrete and iron pipes; p. (1981) 17,828.

Stellenbosch, t., Cape Prov., **S. Africa;** 40 km. E.

of Cape Town; univ.; wines, saw milling, brick and tile mkg.; p. (est. 1975) 30,000.

Stelvio Pass, between **Italy** and **Switzerland;** road pass, alt. 2,762 m.

Stendal, c., Magdeburg, **E. Germany;** impt. rly. junct.; sugar, metal and food inds.; cath.; Stendhal (Henri Beyle) took his name from the c.; p. (est. 1973) 37,925.

Stepney. *See* **Tower Hamlets.**

Sterlitamak, t., Bashkir ASSR, **RSFSR;** on S.W. flank of Ural mtns.; impt. oil refineries on "second Baku" oilfield; linked by pipeline to Togliatti; p. (est. 1985) 240,000.

Stettin. *See* **Szczecin.**

Stettiner Haff, lagoon, **E. Germany** and **Poland;** separated from Baltic Sea by Is. Usedom and Wollin; receives R. Oder; 56 km long.

Stevenage, t., l. gov. dist., Herts., **Eng.;** 6 km S.E. of Hitchin; first new t. to be designated under the New Towns Act 1946; old t. known in Domesday as Stevenach; agr., lt. engin., school furniture, elec. goods., chemicals, aircraft parts; p. (est. 1988) 73,700.

Stevenston, burgh, Cunninghame, **Scot.;** explosives factory; p. (1981) 11,328.

Steventon, v., Hants., **Eng.;** birthplace of Jane Austen.

Stewart I., S. of S.I., **N.Z.;** a. 1,735 km²; rises to over 900 m; famous for oysters.

Stewarton, burgh, Kilmarnock and Loudoun, **Scot.;** woollens, carpets; p. (1981) 6,383.

Stewartry, l. gov. dist., Dumfries and Galloway, **Scot.;** replaces old co. of Kirkcudbright; p. (est. 1986) 23,136.

Steyning, v., West Sussex, **Eng.;** on R. Adur, 6 km N. of Shoreham at entrance to gap through S. Downs; residtl.

Steyr, t., **Austria;** at confluence of Rs. Enns and Steyr; industl. ctr.; historic bldgs.; p. (1981) 38,942.

Stif (Sétif), t., N.E. **Algeria;** agr. ctr. for surrounding plateaux; grain, livestock; phosphates in a.; p. (est. 1983) 186,978.

Stilton, v., Cambs., **Eng.;** 10 km S.W. of Peterborough; famous for cheese.

Stirling, royal burgh, Stirling, **Scot.;** on R. Forth in gap between Campsie Fells and Ochil hills; cas., univ.; coal mng., engin., concrete, wool, rubber gds.; p. (1981) 38,638.

Stirlingshire, former co., central **Scot.;** on S. edge of Grampians; now forms l. gov. dist. within the Central Reg.; a. of l. gov. dist. 2,168 km²; p. (est. 1986) 81,170.

Stockholm, c., cap. of **Sweden;** freeport; on I. at outlet of L. Malar; called the "Queen of the Baltic" for the beauty of its surroundings; comm. ctr.; machin., textiles, leather, sugar, chemicals; univ. and many academic institutions; p. (est. 1986) 663,000 (c.), 1,420,000 (met. a.).

Stockport, t., met. dist., Gtr. Manchester, **Eng.;** on R. Mersey, S.E. of Manchester; cotton manmade fibres, engin.; p. (est. 1988) 290,900.

Stocksbridge, t., South Yorks., **Eng.;** iron and steel; p. (1981) 14,015.

Stockton, t., Cal., **USA;** R. pt. on San Joaquin R.; agr. processing, farm implements; p. (1984) 171,700 (t.), 398,600 (met. a.).

Stockton-on-Tees, mkt. t., l. gov. dist., Cleveland, **Eng.;** 6 km W. of Middlesbrough; impt. iron and steel inds., plywood; first rly. for passenger traffic opened 1825 between Stockton and Darlington; 18th cent. town hall; racecourse; p. (est. 1988) 176,800.

Stoke Newington. *See* **Hackney.**

Stoke-on-Trent, c., l. gov. dist., Staffs., **Eng.;** at S.W. foot of the Pennines; formed in 1910 by union of the "five towns" of Arnold Bennett's novels, Hanley, Burslem, Tunstall, Longton, and Fenton (with Stoke-upon-Trent); ceramics, coal, iron and steel, engin., brick and tile works, precast concrete, rubber gds.; p. (est. 1988) 246,800.

Stolberg, t., N. Rhine–Westphalia, **W. Germany;** E. of Aachen; metals, glass, wood, chemicals; p. (est. 1986) 56,400.

Stolp. *See* **Slupsk.**

Stone, mkt. t., Staffs., **Eng.;** on R. Trent, 11 km S. of Stoke-on-Trent; footwear, tiles, porcelain, scientific glassware; p. (1981) 12,115.

Stonehaven, t., burgh, Kincardine and Deeside, **Scot.;** fish. pt. on E. cst., 22 km S. of Aberdeen, distilling, net mftg.; p. (1981) 7,885.

Stonehenge, prehistoric gr. of monumental stones, on Salisbury Plain, Wilts., **Eng.;** date of erection est. between 2100–1600 B.C.

Stornoway, spt., burgh, **Scot.;** on E. cst. of I. of Lewis, Outer Hebrides; ctr. Harris Tweed ind.; fishing ctr.; p. (1981) 8,660.

Stour, R., Kent, **Eng.;** flows past Canterbury to Pegwell Bay; 64 km long.

Stour, R., Somerset, Dorset, **Eng.;** trib. of R. Avon; 88 km long.

Stour, R., Suffolk and Essex, **Eng.;** flows E. to sea at Harwich; 67 km long.

Stour, R., Hereford and Worcs./West Midlands, **Eng.;** trib. of R. Severn; 32 km long.

Stourbridge, t., West Midlands, **Eng.;** on R. Stour; 14 km W. of Birmingham; brick and glass wks.; p. (1981) 54,661.

Stourport-on-Severn, mkt. t., Wyre Forest, Hereford and Worcs., **Eng.;** at confluence of Rs. Stour and Severn; carpets, iron and steel gds., porcelain, ceramics; old canal and R. pt.; p. (1981) 19,092.

Stowmarket, t., Mid Suffolk, **Eng.;** on R. Gipping, 18 km N.W. of Ipswich; I.C.I. paint factory; p. (1981) 10,910.

Strabane, t., l. gov. dist., **N. Ireland;** agr. ctr., shirt mkg.; p. (1981) 34,871 (dist.), 10,340 (t.).

Straits Settlements, former Brit. crown col. of Penang, Malacca, and Singapore, established 1867, dissolved 1946. *See* **Malaysia, West.**

Stralsund, spt., Rostock, **E. Germany;** opposite Rügen I.; grain tr., machin., metals, fish smoking, shipbldg.; p. (1981) 74,421.

Strangford Lough, arm of sea, Down and Ards, **N. Ireland;** 29 km long, 10 km wide at entrance.

Stranraer, royal burgh, Wigtown, **Scot.;** at head of Loch Ryan; steamer service to Larne, N. Ireland; creameries, brewing, knitwear; cas.; mkt.; p. (1981) 10,837.

Strasbourg, c., cap. of Bas-Rhin dep., E. **France;** impt. pt. in Rhine valley on Ill R., 16 km S. of confluence with Rhine; terminus of Marne–Rhine and Rhône–Rhine canals; industl., comm. and cultural ctr. of economically impt. Alsace region; food processing and varied mnfs.; historic c., with many fine bldgs., inc. cath., univ., imperial palace; surrendered to Germany 1871, recovered 1919; meeting-place of European Parliament; p. (1982) 252,264.

Stratford. *See* **Newham.**

Stratford-on-Avon, t., l. gov. dist., Warwicks., **Eng.;** on R. Avon; birthplace of Shakespeare; memorial theatre, library; many bldgs. ass. with Shakespeare; tourist ctr. in attractive setting; lt. inds.; p. (est. 1988) 106,800 (dist.).

Strathclyde Region, l. gov. reg., Central **Scot.;** indust. dist. formed around Glasgow, inc. ts. on Ayr and Lanarkshire coalfields; borders the F. of Clyde; a. 13,794 km²; p. (est. 1986) 2,344,585.

Strathkelvin, l. gov. dist., Strathclyde Reg., **Scot.;** part of Central Clydeside conurb.; p. (est. 1986) 89,274.

Strathmore, lowland belt, central **Scot.;** flanked to N. by Grampians, to S. by Sidlaw and Ochil hills; drained by Rs. Earn, Tay, Isla, S. Esk; famous for cereals and small fruits; length 96 km, width 11–16 km.

Strathspey, valley of the Spey, **Scot.;** 112 km long.

Stratton and Bude, North Cornwall, **Eng.;** 19 km S. of Hartland Point; resort; p. (1981) 6,783.

Straubing, t., Lower Bavaria, **W. Germany;** agr. mkt. ctr.; machin.; p. (est. 1986) 41,600.

Strawberry, R., Utah, **USA;** on E. slopes of Wasatch mtns. 128 km S.E. of Salt Lake City; dammed to supply irrigation water led through tunnel under Wasatch mtns. to 259 km² cultivable land round L. Utah.

Street, t., Mendip, Somerset, **Eng.;** at foot of Polden Hills, 11 km S.W. of Wells; footwear, leather; p. (1981) 8,803.

Stretford, t., Gtr. Manchester, **Eng.;** borders Manchester Ship Canal; inc. Trafford Park industl. estate; residtl.; Lancashire co. cricket ground, Manchester United football ground at Old Trafford; p. (1981) 47,600.

Stromboli, I., Lipari Is., Tyrrhenian Sea, N. of Sicily, **Italy;** active volcano, alt. 927 m.

Stromness, burgh, Mainland, Orkney Is., **Scot.;** 21 km W. of Kirkwall; mkt., fish. pt.; p. (1981) 1,816.

Stronsay, Orkney Is., **Scot.;** p. (1971) 439.

Stroud, mkt. t., l. gov. dist., Gloucs., **Eng.;** on R. Frome, in Cotswolds; former ctr. of impt. cloth ind. in W. Eng.; woollens, dyes, plastics, engin.; p. (est. 1988) 110,500.

Sturminster Newton, t., North Dorset, **Eng.;** impt.

cattle mkt. on Stour R.; creameries.

Sturts Stony Desert, a. N.W. of S. **Australia;** named after Charles Sturt, explorer.

Stuttgart, c., cap. of Baden–Württemberg, **W. Germany;** on Neckar R.; cas., cath., rly. junc.; industl. and comm. ctr.; publishing, science-based inds.; oil refinery nearby; p. (est. 1986) 565,500.

Styria, prov., **Austria;** borders Yugoslavia on S.; mtnous. with forests and pastures; lignite and iron mng., inds. around cap. Graz; grain, wine, fruit, stock-rearing; tourism; p. (est. 1986) 1·18 m.

Suakin, former pt., **Sudan,** N.E. Africa; on Red Sea; now used only for pilgrim traffic to Jeddah; replaced by Pt. Sudan; plans for new pt.

Subotica, t., Serbia, **Yugoslavia;** univ.; agr. ctr. with Hungarian culture; agr. processing; expanding industl. ctr.; p. (1981) 154,611.

Suceava, t., S. Bukovina, N.E. **Romania;** mkt. t. on Suceava R.; once the residence of Moldavian princes; p. (1983) 85,250.

Suchow. *See* Zuzhou.

Sucre, c., cap. of Chuquisaca dep. and *de jura* cap. of **Bolivia** (La Paz is *de facto* cap.); in valley of Andes at 2,600 m; agr. ctr., oil refining; p. (est. 1982) 79,941.

Sucre, st., **Venezuela;** on Caribbean cst.; coffee and cacao; fishing impt.; fish canning at cap. Cumaná; a. 11,800 km²; p (1981) 585,698.

Sudan, The, rep., N.E. **Africa;** climatic transition from N. desert to rainy equatorial S.; mainly plateaux, dissected by Nile R. system; sporadic conflict between N. and S.; 3 southern provs. now form an autonomous reg.; long staple cotton, grown in irrigated areas, provides most valuable exp.; gum arabic from lge. forest areas; food processing; dams constructed on Atbara and Blue Nile Rs.; suffering from drought in 1980s; Khartoum; a. 2,530,430 km²; p. (est. 1987) 25,550,000.

Sudbury, t., Ont., **Canada;** nickel, copper mng.; refining; univ.; p. (1986) 88,717 (c.), 148,877 (met. a.).

Sudbury, t., Babergh, Suffolk, **Eng.;** on R. Stour, 19 km N.W. of Colchester; p. (1981) 15,524.

Sudene, terr., N.E. **Brazil;** government sponsored economic development.

Sudetenland, region of ČSSR bordering Germany, until 1945 German-speaking; annexed by Hitler 1938, recovered by ČSSR 1945; named after Sudeten mtns.; contains 20 per cent of p. of ČSSR.

Sudeten Mtns. or **Sudetes,** mtn. range along borders of ČSSR and **Poland;** separating Bohemia and Moravia from Silesia; mineral resources.

Suez (Es-Suweis), spt., **Egypt;** the anc. Arsinoë; at head of G. of Suez (arm of Red Sea) and S. entrance of Suez canal, which crosses the isthmus of Suez to the Mediterranean at Port Said; Port Tewfiq adjoining has quay and docks; declined during closure of canal 1967–75; oil refining, fertilisers; p. (1985) 254,000.

Suez Canal, ship canal, **Egypt;** connects Mediterranean Sea (Pt. Said) with Red Sea (Suez) through Ls. Manzala, Timsah, and Bitter; length 162 km; closed after Arab-Israeli war of June 1967; reopened 1975; tunnel links Egypt and Israel (1980); widening and deepening of canal to accommodate larger oil tankers, complete (1980).

Suez, G., Red Sea; N.W. arm of Red Sea between Arabian desert and Sinai peninsula, **Egypt;** southern approach to Suez canal; length 304 km., width varies from 19–40 km.

Suffolk, non-met. co., E. Anglia, **Eng.;** bounded on E. by N. Sea, drowned coastline; rises to 90 m in E. Anglian Heights in W.; impt. agr. a., lge. farms, mixed farming; inds. based on agr.; many expanded ts. in S.; formerly divided into 2 admin. parts; co. t. Ipswich; a. 3,800 km²; p. (est. 1988) 638,600.

Suffolk Coastal, l. gov. dist., E. Suffolk, **Eng.;** lge. rural a. inc. ts. of Leiston-cum-Sizewell, Saxmundham, Aldeburgh, Woodbridge and Felixstowe; p. (est. 1988) 111,300.

Suhl, admin. dist., **E. Germany;** inc. Thuringian Forest; expanding inds. based on local potash and iron ore; a. 3,877 km²; p. (1982) 549,500.

Suhl, t., Suhl, **E. Germany;** once famous for armaments; motor-cycles; p. (1981) 49,849.

Sui, Baluchistan, **Pakistan;** natural gas; pipeline to Karachi.

Sukhumi, spt., Georgian SSR, **USSR;** agr. processing; resort; p. (est. 1985) 126,000.

Sukkur, t., **Pakistan;** major bridging point of R. Indus; 368 km N.E. of Karachi; dam for irrigation; thermal sta.; p. (1981) 193,000.

Sulaymāniyah, t., **Iraq;** in hill dist. nr. Iran border; p. (1970) 98,063.

Sula Is., I. gr. in Molucca Sea, E. of Sulawesi, **Indonesia;** little developed.

Sulawesi (Celebes), I., **Indonesia;** mtnous., lge. forests; copra, coffee, gold, nickel, copper, asphalt; ch. pts. Menado, Makasar; a. 189,484 km²; p. (est. 1983) 11,112,200.

Sullum Voe, Shetland Is., **Scot.;** oil terminal and receiving ctr. for N. Sea oil.

Sultanabad. *See* Arak.

Sulu Is., Philippines; archipelago between Borneo and the Philippines; inc. over 400 volcanic Is. and coral islets; a. 2,461 km²; under US control 1899–1940.

Sumatra, I., **Indonesia;** relatively underdeveloped; sparse p.; main development in Cultuurgebied, rubber, oil palm, sisal, tobacco; impt. oil deposits and new oil refineries; a. 473,607 km²; p. (1981) 30,928,500.

Sumba or **Sandalwood I.,** S. of Flores, **Indonesia;** horse-breeding; rice, maize, tobacco, timber, cinnamon; cap. Waingapu; a. 11,150 km²; p. (1971) 251,126.

Sumbawa, I., **Indonesia;** between Flores and Lombok; wet climate, sparse p.; a. (inc. nearby Is.) 13,572 km²; p. (1980) 320,000.

Sumgait, t., Azerbaydzhan SSR, **USSR;** on Caspian Sea; 40 km N.W. of Baku; metallurgical ind.; chemicals; p. (est. 1985) 223,000.

Sumy, t., Ukrainian SSR, **USSR;** engin., chemicals, textiles, agr. processing; p. (est. 1985) 256,000.

Sunbury-on-Thames, t., Spelthorne, Surrey, **Eng.;** W. of London; residtl., water wks., gravel pits; petrol research establishment; p. (1981) 39,075.

Sunda Is., Indonesia; between S. China Sea and Indian Oc.; form two grs., Greater Sunda Is., inc. Java, Sumatra, Borneo, Sulawesi, Banka, and the Lesser Sunda Is. (renamed Nusa Tenggara 1954) inc. Bali, Lombok, Sumbawa, Timor.

Sundarbans, The, tract of forest and swamps, fringing the delta of the Ganges, **India/Bangladesh;** 130 km wide; rice grown in N.; tigers and crocodiles found in S.

Sunda Strait, between Java and Sumatra, **Indonesia;** 21 km wide, contains the volcanic I. of Krakatao.

Sunday I., lgst. and only inhabited of Kermadec Is., **N.Z.;** 32 km in circuit; meteorological and radio sta.

Sundyberg, t., **Sweden;** adjoins Stockholm; chemicals, paper; p. (1983) 26,985.

Sunderland, spt., met. dis., Tyne and Wear, **Eng.;** at mouth of R. Wear; precision and aero-engin., clothing, glass, shipbldg.; car plant; p. (est. 1988) 296,100.

Sundsvall, spt., Västernorrland, **Sweden;** on a wide bay of the Baltic nr. Hernösand; timber and wood-pulp inds.; p. (est. 1986) 93,000.

Sungari. *See* Songhua R.

Sunnyvale, t., Cal., **USA;** ctr. of fruit-growing a.; lt. inds.; p. (1984) 110,600 (t.), inc. in San Francisco met. a.

Superior, t., Wis., **USA;** at head of L. Superior; tr. in grain, timber, coal; shipbldg. and flour mills; oil refining; p. (1980) 29,571.

Superior, L., N. America; lgst. sheet of fresh water in the world; lies between **Canada** and **USA;** one of chain of gr. Ls. in St. Lawrence system; outlet to L. Huron by St. Mary's R., receives waters of St. Louis, Pigeon and Nipigon; impt. waterway; a. 82,880 km².

Surabaya, spt., Java, **Indonesia;** ch. naval base; handles nearly half Indonesia's tr.; shipbldg., oil refining, food processing; p. (est. 1983) 2,289,000.

Surakarta (Solo), Java, **Indonesia;** on Solo R.; tr. ctr. for agr. region; former sultan's palace; p. (1980) 469,888.

Surat, c., Gujarat, **India;** on R. Tapti; textile ctr.; notable as first English trading post 1612; p. (1981) 776,583 (c.), 913,806 (met. a.).

Surbiton, Gtr. London, **Eng.;** on R. Thames, inc.

in Royal Borough of Kingston-upon-Thames; residtl.; lt. engin., bricks, tiles, elec. components.

Suresnes, t., Hauts-de-Seine dep., **France**; sub. of Paris; cars, chemicals; p. (1982) 35,744.

Surinam (Dutch Guiana), former self-gov. terr. of Neth.; indep. 1975; **S. America**; sub-tropical climate; p. concentrated on cst. where rice, sugar, and citrus fruits grown; great agr. potential; main exp. bauxite (80 per cent of total exp. though recently declining); iron ore, timber, hydro-electr.; cap. Paramaribo; a. 163,265 sq. km; oil finds (1986); p. (est. 1985) 375,000.

Surinumu Dam, 48 km from Port Moresby, **Papua New Guinea**; part of hydroelectric scheme; opened 1963.

Surrey, non-met. co., S. **Eng.**; S. of R. Thames inc. part of N. Downs; serves as dormitory a. and recreational dist. for London; mkt. gardening, dairying; co. t. Guildford; a. 1,655 km²; p. (est. 1988) 999,800.

Surrey Heath, l. gov. dist., Surrey, **Eng.**; based on Bagshot, Frimley and Camberley; p. (est. 1988) 83,600.

Susa. See **Sousse**.

Susquehanna, R., N.Y., Penns., and Md., **USA**; flows to Chesapeake Bay through highly industl. a.; routeway W. from Philadelphia and Baltimore across Appalachian mtns.; not navigable; hydroelectric power; 675 km long.

Sussex. See **East Sussex**, and **West Sussex**.

Susten Pass, alpine road, alt. 2,225 m between Hasli Tal and Reuss valley, links Bernese Oberland with Gotthard road, Switzerland.

Sutherland, l. gov. dist., former co., Highland Reg., **Scot.**; stretches from Atl. Oc. to Moray F.; sparsely p. reg.; a. 3,152 km²; p. (est. 1986) 13,212.

Sutlej, R., **Pakistan**; rises in the Himalayas and flows to the R. Indus; used for lge. scale irrigation; 1,600 km long.

Sutton, outer bor., Greater London, **Eng.**; inc. former bors. of Beddington and Wallington, Sutton and Cheam, and Carshalton; residtl.; p. (est. 1988) 168,000.

Sutton Coldfield, t., West Midlands, **Eng.**; 10 km N.E. of Birmingham; residtl.; hardware, plastics; p. (1981) 86,494.

Sutton-in-Ashfield, t., Ashfield, Notts., **Eng.**; 5 km S.W. of Mansfield; lt. engin.; hosiery; coal-mng. dist.; p. (1981) 41,270.

Suva, c., cap. of Fiji Is.; on Viti Levu I.; fine harbour; exp. coconut prods., sugar; international airport; p. (1986) 69,481.

Suwalki, t., N.E. **Poland**; nr. Lithuanian bdy.; timber, grain, woollens; p. (1983) 46,600.

Suwannee, R., Fla., and Ga., **USA**; flows to G. of Mexico; known as "Swanee River", 400 km long.

Suzhou (Soochow), c., Jiangsu, **China**; nr. Shanghai; former treaty pt.; textile ctr.; p. (1984) 695,500.

Svendborg, spt., Fyn, **Denmark**; exp. dairy prods.; textiles, machin.; p. (1981) 23,845.

Sverdlovsk (Ekaterinburg), c., cap. of S. oblast, **RSFSR**; on R. Iset in E. foothills of Ural mtns.; on Trans-Siberian rly.; industl. expansion during second world war; heavy machin., metallurgical and chemical plants; univ.; p. (1986) 1,316,000.

Svir, R., **USSR**; flows between L. Onega and L. Ladoga; hydroelectric power; navigable; 200 km long.

Svishtov (Sistova), t., N. **Bulgaria**; R. pt. on Danube in vine-growing dist., nr. Romanian bdr.; cath., univ.; p. (est. 1968) 22,456.

Swabia, historic region, mediaeval duchy, **Germany**; now forms part of Baden-Württemberg and Bavaria; contains Black Forest.

Swabian Alps, mtns., Baden-Württemberg, **W. Germany**; inc. the Swabian Jura range between valleys of Neckar and Danube.

Swadlincote, t., South Derbys., **Eng.**; 5 km E. of Burton-on-Trent; potteries, engin., clothing, coal-mng. ctr.; p. (1981) 23,388.

Swaffham, mkt. t., Breckland, Norfolk, **Eng.**; fruit canning; p. (1981) 4,776.

Swale, R., North Yorks., **Eng.**; joins R. Ure to form R. Ouse, 96 km long.

Swale, l. gov. dist., mid Kent, **Eng.**; nr. Thames estuary inc. Sittingbourne, Faversham and I. of Sheppey; p. (est. 1988) 115,300.

Swanage, mkt. t., Dorset, **Eng.**; on bay, E. cst. I. of Purbeck; seaside resort; p. (1981) 8,647.

Swansea, c., spt., l. gov. dist., West Glamorgan, **Wales**; on Swansea Bay; univ.; grew with exp.

of coal; now imports minerals; copper and zinc refining; steel, aluminium, wire, plastics; p. (est. 1988) 186,900 (dist.).

Swatow. See **Shantou**.

Swaziland, indep. kingdom, S. **Africa**; within Brit. Commonwealth (1968), govt. based on tribal communities; bordered by S. Africa on S., W., and N. and by Moçambique on E.; four north-south regions; high, middle, low veld and Lebombo escarpment; rainfall increases with alt.; agr. basis of economy and sugar impt. exp., but iron-ore major exp.; asbestos mng., food processing inds.; cattle raising main internal activity; cap. Mbabane; a. 17,363 km²; p. (1987) 710,000.

Sweden, kingdom, Scandinavia, N.W. **Europe**; divided into admin. purposes into 24 cos.; cap. c. Stockholm; mtnous. in N. and S. with central lowland belt containing major agr. a. and lge. proportion of p.; sm. home mkt. makes for dependency on exps., especially of mftg. products and minerals; inc. high-grade iron-ore from Kiruna and Malmberget, N. of Arctic circle; development of high-value science-based inds.; furniture, porcelain and glass mnfs. have international reputation; social democratic st. since 1932; remained neutral in second world war; highly advanced system of social security; a. 449,792 km²; p. (1985) 8,360,178.

Świdnica (Schweidnitz), t., **Poland** (since 1945); formerly in Lower Silesia; metals, elec. machin., leather, textiles; p. (1983) 59,400.

Swilly, Lough, N.E. Donegal, **R.o.I.**; arm of Atl. Oc. between Fanad Point and Dunaff Head; extends 40 km inland.

Swindon, t., Thamesdown, Wilts., **Eng.**; in upper Thames Valley (Vale of White Horse), 43 km S.W. of Oxford; impt. rly. junc.; rly. workshops closed (1986); mkt. for local dist.; heavy engin., textiles, tobacco; expanded t.; growing ctr. for micro-electronics inds.; p. (1981) 91,136.

Świnoujście (Swinemünde), spt., N.W. **Poland** (since 1945); formerly in Pomerania; on I. of Usedom (Uznam), Baltic Sea; spt. for Szczecin; spa and summer resort; fishing; p. (1983) 45,000.

Swinton and Pendlebury, ts., Gtr. Manchester, **Eng.**; 8 km W. of Manchester; cotton spinning, coal, engin.; p. (1981) 39,621.

Switzerland, confederation, central **Europe**; landlocked mtnous. st. with major physical features dominated by Alpine mtn. system; divided into 26 cantons and half-cantons for purposes of govt.; 3 official languages; German (72 per cent), French (20 per cent), Italian (6 per cent) in addition to Romansch; like Norway, major natural resource is water power; industl. specialisation on precision engin., especially watch and clock mnfs.; agr. in valleys with impt. output of dairy prod.; transhumance between mtn. pastures and valley bottoms; tourism provides valuable source of income; neutral; voted to remain nonmember of U.N. (1986); cap. Berne; a. 41,310 km²; p. (est. 1986) 6,523,400.

Sydney, c., cap. of N.S.W., **Australia**; pt. and c. built around natural harbour of Pt. Jackson, crossed by S. Harbour Bridge and bordered by many impt. bldgs. and parks (Opera House, Government bldgs.); one of best harbours on E. cst., pt. developed with improved transport; site of first European settlement; contains 61 per cent of state p., 22 per cent of Australia's p.; covers vast a. as suburbs grow rapidly; caths., 3 univs.; airpt. on Botany Bay where heavy inds. developing; services most impt. employment, vast range of inds.; p. (est. 1985) 3,391,600 (met. a.).

Sydney, spt., Cape Breton I., Nova Scotia, **Canada**; coal mng. and exp.; steel, chemicals; p. (1981) 29,444.

Syktyvkar, c., Komi ASSR, **RSFSR**; R. pt. on Vychegda R.; shipyds., sawmilling, engin.; cultural ctr. of Komi people; p. (est. 1985) 213,000.

Sylhet, t., **Bangladesh**; on Surma R. in tea growing dist.; fertilisers; p. (1981) 168,371.

Syracuse, c., S.E. Sicily, **Italy**; old t. on Ortygia I., off E. cst., modern t. on mainland, connected by bridge; founded c. 734 B.C.; ctr. of anc. Greek culture; exp. olive oil, oranges, lemons, wine; chemicals at Priolo; many Greek and Roman remains; p. (1984) 118,690.

Syracuse, c., N.Y., **USA**; on Erie Barge canal; impt. industl. ctr. for chemicals, electronics, machin.; formerly salt-producing ctr.; univ.; p. (1984) 164,200 (c.), 650,500 (met. a.).

Syr Dar'ya, one of main Rs. of central Asia; formed in Ferghana Valley in Uzbek SSR, **USSR**; flows through Tadzhik SSR and Kazakh SSR to Aral Sea; not navigable but used for irrigation and hydroelectric power; 2,400 km long.

Syria (Syrian Arab Rep.), S.W. **Asia**; on E. cst. Mediterranean; much of a. mtnous. and semi-desert; climate hot, but cold winters in highland interior; 32 per cent p. engaged in agr. which provides 20 per cent nat. income; mainly pastoral, but grains, fruit and cotton grown in well watered Euphrates R. valley and along cst.; oil exp. since 1968; phosphate mines in Palmyra a.; textiles, food processing in Aleppo and cap. Damascus; a. 187,086 km²; p. (est. 1986) 10,610,000 (inc. Palestinian refugees).

Syriam, t., **Burma**; nr. Rangoon; main oil refining ctr. of cty.

Syros or **Syra**, I., one of Cyclades, Aegean Sea, S. **Greece**; heath-covered; most populous of Cyclades; ch. t. Hermoupolis; p. (1971) 19,000.

Syzran, c., **RSFSR**; impt. R. pt. on Volga nr. confluence with Syzran R.; rly. ctr.; engin., oil refining; p. (est. 1985) 173,000.

Szazhalombatta, t., **Hungary**; on Danube, 24 km S. of Budapest; lgst. oil refinery in rep.; oil supplied through Druzhba pipeline.

Szczecin (Stettin), c., N.W. **Poland** (since 1945); formerly cap. of Prussian prov. of Pomerania; impt. spt. at mouth of R. Oder; deep-sea fishing base; shipbldg., metallurgy, engin., chemicals, technical univ.; p. (est. 1985) 391,000.

Szczecin, prov., **Poland**; borders Baltic Sea; drained by R. Oder; mainly agr.; a. 31,339 km²; p. (est. 1986) 951,000.

Szechwan. See **Sichuan**.

Szeged, t., **Hungary**; nr. confluence of Rs. Tisza and Maros; anc. R. pt. destroyed by floods 1879, since rebuilt; univ.; tr. in cereals, paprika; textiles; p. (est. 1985) 186,000.

Szekesfehérvár, t., **Hungary**; nr. Budapest; mkt. t., with aluminium and metal inds.; food processing; known since Roman times; once cap. of Hungarian kings; p. (est. 1985) 113,000.

Szeping. See **Siping**.

Szolnok, t., **Hungary**; pt. on R. Tisa, E. of Budapest; route ctr.; machin., paper, cellulose, chemicals; p. (est. 1985) 81,000.

Szombathely, t., W. **Hungary**; rly. ctr.; agr. machin., textiles, shoes; birthplace of St. Martin of Tours (c. A.D. 316); p. (est. 1985) 87,000.

T

Tabasco, coastal st., **Mexico**; on Bay of Campeche; low-lying; rapid development with drainage of swamps; cash crops of cacao, coffee, sugar, tobacco; major petroleum deposits aiding industl. development; cap. Villa Hermosa; a. 25,335 km²; p. (1980) 1,149,756.

Table Bay, inlet of Atl., cst. of C. of Good Hope, **S. Africa**; site of Cape Town.

Table Mountain, Cape Prov., **S. Africa**; nr. Cape Town; alt. 1,082 m.

Tabor, t., **ČSSR**; S. of Prague, on R. Luznice; rly. junc.; textiles, tobacco; p. (1984) 33,757.

Tabora, t., central **Tanzania**, E. Africa; at junc. of rlys. from Dar es Salaam and L. Victoria; p. (est. 1985) 134,000.

Tabriz, c., **Iran**; cap. of Azerbaijan; metal inds., carpets, leather, soap; famous blue mosque; univ.; impt. oil refining ctr.; p. (1986) 994,377.

Tachira, st., **Venezuela**; mtnous. inland st. bordering Colombia; coffee; cap. San Cristobal; a. 11,100 km²; p. (1981) 660,234.

Tacna, t., cap. of Tacna prov., **Peru**; in fertile valley of mtnous. region; agr. t.; p. (est. 1985) 126,000.

Tacna, prov., **Peru**; mtnous. and arid, some irrigated valleys; transferred from Chile by treaty 1929; cap. T.; subject to earthquakes; a. 12,769 km²; p. (est. 1985) 126,000.

Tacoma, spt., Wash., **USA**; on Puget Sound; shipping, fishing; grew with Alaskan and Pac. tr.; port inds. and agr. processing; p. (1984) 159,400, inc. in Seattle met. a.

Tacuarembo, dep., **Uruguay**; N. of Rio Negro R., which provides hydroelectricity; mainly agr.; cap. T.; a. 15,812 km²; p. (1985) 82,809.

Tadoussac, v., Quebec, **Canada**; on R. Saguenay, where it enters St. Lawrence R.; tourist ctr.; oldest settlement in Canada (1599); p. (1981) 900.

Tadzhik (Tadzhikistan) SSR, constituent rep., **USSR**; borders China and Afghanistan; mainly mtnous., inc. Pamirs and Turkestan and part of highly cultivated Ferghana Valley; cattle breeding; cotton main cash crop; impt. oil and hydroelec. power resources; riots, 1989; cap. Dushanbe; a. 144,263 km²; p. (est. 1985) 4,500,000.

Taegu, c., **S. Korea**; textiles, agr. processing; p. (est. 1986) 2,029,900.

Taejon, t., **S. Korea**; S. of Seoul; fish, petroleum; p. (1980) 851,642.

Taff, R., Powys, South and Mid Glamorgan, **Wales**; rises in Brecon Beacons, flows S.E. across coalfield to Bristol Channel at Cardiff; 64 km long.

Taff-Ely, l. gov. dist., Mid Glamorgan, **Wales**; inland ts. of Pontypridd and Llantrisant; p. (est. 1988) 94,900.

Tafilalet, Morocco, N. Africa; oasis of the Sahara, E. of Atlas; dates.

Tagab, c., **Afghanistan**; in Panjshir R. valley N.W. of Kābul; p. (est. 1979) 106,777.

Taganrog, c., **RSFSR**; spt. on Sea of Azov; iron and steel, engin.; site of fortress founded by Peter the Great 1698; birthplace of Chekhov; p. (1985) 289,000.

Tagliamento, R., N.E. **Italy**; rises in Carnic Alps, flows W. into Adriatic; 160 km long.

Tagus, R., **Spain** and **Portugal**; rises in E. Spain and flows across the Meseta to Atl. Oc. at Lisbon where there is a magnificent new bridge; its estuary forms one of the finest harbours in Europe.

Tahiti, ch. I., Society Is., **Fr. Polynesia**; contains Papeete, main admin. ctr. of Fr. Oceania; fertile alluvial belt; exp. copra, phosphates, vanilla; tourism; a. 1,041 km²; p. (1983) 115,820.

Taichow. See **Taizhou**.

Taichung, t., **Taiwan**; agr. mkt.; food processing; p. (est. 1984) 655,196.

Taif, t., Hejaz, **Saudi Arabia**; 80 km E. of Mecca; 1,800 m a.s.l.; summer resort; p. (1974) 204,857.

Tai Hu, L., Jiangsu, **China**; focus of intensive system of small canals and waterways, 96 km N. of Shanghai; a. c. 260 km².

Taimyr Peninsula, N. cst., Siberia, **USSR**; terminates with C. Chelyuskin; occupies most of Taimyr National Area, inhabited by nomadic Samoyeds; p. (1986) 54,000.

Tainan, t., S.W. cst. of **Taiwan**; former cap.; univ.; p. (est. 1985) 622,000.

Taipei, c., cap. of **Taiwan**; on cst. plain in N. Taiwan, nucleus of major industl. a.; major transport ctr.; international airpt.; univ.; p. (est. 1986) 2,560,000.

Taiwan (Formosa), I., off cst. of S.E. **China**; beautiful I. with intensive agr. on W. cst.; most densely populated cty. in the world; part of Japan 1895–1945; returned to China 1945; occupied by Nationalist government since 1949; growing political isolation; USA aid has built growth economy, textiles, plastics, electronics exp. to USA esp.; cap. Taipei; a. 35,975 km²; p. (est. 1987) 19.7 m.

Taiyüan, c., cap. of Shanxi prov., N. **China**; on Fen R.; walled c.; univ.; ctr. of rapid industl. development; integrated iron and steel plant; chemicals, machin., paper, textiles; p. (1984) 1,838,100.

Taiz, t., **Yemen Arab Rep.**; in fertile valley; former cap.; p. (1981) 119,573.

Taizhou (Taichow), c., Jiangsu prov., **China**; rice ctr.; p. (1984) 161,300.

Takamatsu, t., **Japan**; N. cst. Shikiku; ferry terminal; univ.; tourism; p. (1985) 327,001.

Takaoka, t., Honshu, **Japan**; ctr. of rice tr.; lacquer wk.; cars; p. (1985) 175,780.

Takapuna, c., N.I., **N.Z.**; connected by motorway to Auckland; residtl. ctr.; p. (est. 1987) 70,000.

Takasaki, t., Honshu, **Japan**; radiation chemistry research ctr.; textiles; p. (1985) 231,764.

Taklimakan Shamo, desert, W. **China**; basin of inland drainage; home of the Turko people; surrounded by a ring of oases.

Takoradi. *See* **Sekondi-Takoradi.**

Talara, t., N. **Peru**; on C. Pariñas; spt.; ctr. of petroleum refining; p. (est. 1972) 30,000.

Talaud I., Indonesia; N.E. of Sulawesi; copra; underdeveloped; a. 1,279 km².

Talavera de la Reina, t., Toledo prov., central **Spain**; on Tagus R.; ceramics; scene of battle 1809; p. (1981) 69,307.

Talca, prov., **Chile**; predominantly agr.; various irrigated crops; livestock; cap. T.; a. 9,637 km²; p. (1982) 266,150.

Talca, t., cap. of Talca prov., **Chile**; S. of Santiago; lge. mftg. ctr.; matches, footwear, paper, and flour mills, foundries; p. (est. 1985) 136,200.

Talcahuano, spt., **Chile**, nr. Concepción; naval sta.; steel plant at Huachipato; fish processing, oil refining; p. (est. 1985) 215,100.

Talien. *See* **Lushun.**

Tallahassee, t., Fla., **USA**; univ.; timber-based inds.; p. (1984) 112,300 (t.), 207,600 (met. a.); fastest growing t. in USA.

Tallinn, spt., cap. of Estonian SSR, **USSR**; on G. of Finland; diverse inds. inc. radio equipment; mediaeval architecture; p. (1986) 472,000.

Tamale, t., cap. of Kaduna st., **Ghana**, W. Africa; admin. ctr.; cotton milling, peanut processing; p. (1984) 83,653.

Tamar, R., Tasmania, **Australia**; formed at confluence of N. Esk and S. Esk at Launceston, flows into Bass Strait nr. George Town.

Tamar, R., Devon and Cornwall, **Eng.**; flows S. to Plymouth Sound; 72 km long.

Tamatave, *See* **Toamasina.**

Tamaulipas, st., **Mexico**; on G. of Mexico, S. of Texas; petroleum is main resource; fishing along lagoon cst.; cotton, livestock; cap. Ciudad Victoria; a. 79,593 km²; p. (1980) 1,924,934.

Tambao, t., **Bourkina Fasso**; rich deposits of manganese could diversify economy and provide valuable exports; development depends on railway extension.

Tambov, c., cap. of Tambov oblast, **RSFSR**; on Tsna R.; regional ctr. serving agr. dist.; engin.; p. (1985) 296,000.

Tameside, met. dist., Gtr. Manchester, **Eng.**; comprises Dukinfield, Ashton-under-Lyne, Hyde and Mossley; p. (est. 1988) 216,800.

Tamil Nadu (formerly **Madras**), st., **India**; on S.E. cst. of peninsula; home of Tamils; crossed by R. Cauvery; dry crops; acute water shortages relieved by water and sewerage development plan; ch. ts. Madras, Madura; a. 130,357 km²; p. (1981) 48,408,077.

Tampa, c., Fla., **USA**; popular winter resort, cigar factories, phosphates, electronics; fruit growing and canning; p. (1984) 275,500 (c.), 1,810,900 (met. a.).

Tampere (**Tammerfors**), t., S. **Finland**; on rly. between Helsinki and Vaasa; textiles, leather, paper, based on local hydroelec. power; cath.; p. (1986) 169,994.

Tampico, spt., **Mexico**; on R. Panuco, 14 km from G. of Mexico; exp. petroleum; oil refining, fish processing, chemicals; tourism; p. (est. 1986) 350,000.

Tamworth, t., N.S.W., **Australia**; impt. service and shopping ctr. for N. Tablelands; p. (1981) 29,657.

Tamworth, t., l. gov. dist., Staffs., **Eng.**; on R. Tame, 8 km S.E. of Lichfield; anc. cas.; lt. engin.; expanded t.; p. (est. 1988) 68,100 (dist.).

Tana, lge. freshwater l., N.W. **Ethiopia**, nr. Gondar; source of Blue Nile, surrounded by marsh, papyrus swamp.

Tana, R., **Kenya**; rises nr. Mt. Kenya and flows to Indian Oc.; impt. elephant habitat in valley; 4 major hydro-elect. sta., 5th opening 1987; 800 km long.

Tananarive. *See* **Antananarivo.**

Tandridge, l. gov. dist., Surrey, **Eng.**; S. of Gtr. London, inc. Caterham and Godstone; p. (est. 1986) 75,600

Tanga, spt., **Tanzania**, E. Africa; on plateau overlooking Tanga Bay; rly. terminus; new plywood plant; p. (est. 1985) 123,000.

Tanganyika, gr. L., E. **Central Africa**; lies in Gt. Rift Valley; c. 672 km long, 24–32 km

wide; second lgst. L. in Africa and except for L. Baykal deepest L. in world; c. 823 m a.s.l.; discovered by Burton and Speke 1858, explored by Livingstone and Stanley 1871.

Tangier, free pt., **Morocco**, N. Africa; on Strait of Gibraltar; no longer internationalised zone but integral part of kingdom of Morocco; summer cap.; shipyard; cigarettes, fishing; p. (est. 1981) 304,000.

Tangshan, c., Hebei prov., **China**; impt. industl. ctr.; steel, machin.; textiles, cement, oil refining; devastated by a series of earthquakes (1976); p. (1984) 1,366,100.

Tanimbar Is., Indonesia; gr. of Is. in Banda Sea, S. Moluccas; forests, swamps; maize, rice, coconuts, sago; p. (est. 1975) 50,000.

Tanta, t., Lower **Egypt**; 88 km N. of Cairo; impt. rly. junc.; religious fairs; cotton processing; univ. proposed; p. (1985) 364,700.

Tanzania, rep., E. cst. **Africa**; inc. Is. of Zanzibar and Pemba, united since 1964; narrow coastal plain rises to inland plateau (Mt. Kilimanjaro, 5,895 m, hgst. peak in Africa); climate varies with alt., tropical in Zanzibar, temperate inland; predominantly subsistence agr., maize, millet, groundnuts, livestock; comm. crops inc. sisal, sugar, cotton, coffee; cloves on Is., especially Pemba; food processing, textile inds.; 5-year planning system to assist economic development especially in rural a.; old cap. Dar es Salaam; new cap. Dodoma (since 1974); a. 939,706 km²; p. (est. 1987) 23,200,000.

Taormino, resort, E. Sicily, **Italy**; 230 m above sea at foot of Mt. Etna; magnificent scenery and anc. ruins.

Tapachula, c., Chiapas st., S. **Mexico**; on Pac. cst. lowlands; comm. ctr. for agr. dist.; p. (1970) 108,464.

Tapti, R., W. **India**; flows W. to G. of Cambay from Betul dist., Madhya Pradesh; 702 km.

Tarai, marshy, jungle tract at foot of Himalayas, **India**, **Nepal**; barrier to economic development of Nepal, now much modified and reduced in area by human occupation.

Taranaki, prov., N.I., **N.Z.**; impt. stock rearing and dairying a.; offshore oil and gas fields; a. 9,713 km²; p. (est. 1985) 108,200.

Taranto, t., Lecce, **Italy**; on G. of Taranto, inlet of Ionian Sea; maritime arsenal with gr. comm. and industl. interests; strong cas.; steel wks.; cement; oil refinery; famous for its oyster and mussel fisheries; p. (1984) 243,120.

Tarapacá, prov., N. **Chile**; hot, arid desert; nitrate deposits; a. 55,270 km²; p. (1982) 273,427.

Tarascon, t., Bouches-du-Rhône dep., **France**; connected by bridges with Beaucaire on. opposite bank of R. Rhône; old cas., famous festival; p. (1982) 11,024.

Tarawera Mtn., volcanic peak, N.I., **N.Z.**; 305 m; in Hot Springs dist.; eruption 1886 destroyed L. Rotomahana (water later returned to form bigger and deeper L.).

Tarbes, t., cap. of Hautes-Pyrénées dep., **France**; on R. Adour; cath.; p. (1982) 54,055.

Targul-Mures, c., Romania; on R. Mures; ch. t. of Magyar aut. region in Transylvania; old fort, Gothic Calvinist cath.; agr. tr. and processing; p. (est. 1972) 106,159.

Tarifa, t., **Spain**; on Gibraltar Strait; most S. point of mainland of Europe; fish tr., cereals, oranges, wines; p. (1981) 15,220.

Tarija, prov., **Bolivia**; part of Gran Chaco rising to W.; extensive agr. and forests; cap. T.; a. 64,196 km²; p. (est. 1982) 246,691.

Tarija, t., cap. of T. prov., **Bolivia**; alt. 1,906 m; cath., univ.; mkt. t.; p. (est. 1982) 54,001.

Tarim Basin, depression, Xinjiang, **China**; desert with oases; crossed by Silk Road; anc. civilisation; state farms for wheat, millet, maize, cotton.

Tarn, dep., S. **France**; watered by Tarn and its tribs.; between Central Massif and basin of Aquitaine; mainly agr.; cap. Albi; a. 5,781 km²; p. (1982) 340,400.

Tarn, R., **France**; trib. of R. Garonne; rocky gorge 50 km long in its upper course; 376 km long.

Tarn-et-Garonne, dep., W. **France**; alluvial plain formed by Rs. Tarn, Garonne and Aveyron; mainly agr.; cap. Montauban; a. 3,730 km²; p. (1982) 190,300.

Tarnow, t., Poland; E. of Kraków; industl. ctr.; lge. nitrogen factory; synthetic fibres, metallurgy; cath.; p. (1983) 111,000.

Tarpon Springs, t., Fla., **USA**; pt.; main source of sponges in USA.

Tarragona, prov., **Spain**; on Mediterranean; vineyards and agr.; cap. Tarragona; a. 6,283 km²; p. (1987) 526,968.

Tarragona, spt., cap. of T. prov., **Spain**; at mouth of R. Francoli; exp. agr. prod. of Ebro valley; cath.; many Roman remains, inc. aqueduct; liqueur; p. (1987) 107,356.

Tarsus, anc. c., S. **Turkey**; nr. Adana; orange and citrus groves; ruined Roman temple; birthplace of St. Paul; p. (1985) 146,502.

Tartary or **Tatary**, region, **Central Asia**; now divided into Chinese or E. Turkestan, and W. Turkestan, USSR.

Tartu, c., Estonian SSR, **USSR**; pt. on Emayygi R.; rly. junc.; famous univ. founded 1632; agr. machin., tobacco ind.; p. (1985) 111,000.

Tashkent, c., cap. of Uzbek SSR, **USSR**; cultural, industl. and scientific ctr. of central Asia; on Trans-Caspian rly. in fertile Ferghana valley; univ.; diverse inds.; terminus of gas pipeline; p. (1986) 2,073,000.

Tasman Bay, lge inlet, S.I., **N.Z.**; penetrates N. cst., between Separation Point and D'Urville I.; enclosed by mtns., sheltered, fertile, coastal fringe; ch. ts. Nelson, Motueka.

Tasman Glacier, S.I., **N.Z.**; one of the lgst. in the world.

Tasmania (formerly **Van Diemen's Land**), I., st., **Australia**; smallest and least populous st. of Australia, second to be colonised (in 1803); mountainous with rugged cst.; temperate climate aids hydro-electric development and consequent rapid industl. expansion; plans for hydro-electric sta. on Franklin R. to help relieve high unemployment but fiercely opposed because of region's rare and striking natural beauty; 9 Nat. Parks; mng.; pastoral agr.; forestry; cap. Hobart; a. 67,897 km²; p. (1986) 446,473.

Tasman Sea, Australia; part of Pac. Oc. between Australia and New Zealand.

Tatabánya, t., N. **Hungary**; lignite mng. ctr.; aluminium refining, chemicals; p. (est. 1985) 76,000.

Tatar ASSR, USSR; in middle Volga valley; wooded steppeland; extensive oil deposits and natural gas fields; cap. Kazan; a. 67,988 km²; p. (1986) 3,531,000.

Tatra Mtns., highest mtn. gr. of W. Carpathians, on border of **ČSSR** and **Poland**; highest peak Gerlach in Slovakia, 2,664 m; mountaineering and winter sports.

Tatung. See Datong.

Taubaté, t., São Paulo st., **Brazil**; industl. ctr.; p. (est. 1985) 205,900.

Taunton, co. t., Somerset, **Eng.**; on R. Tone at W. end of Vale of Taunton; old cas.; with Wellington forms l. gov. dist. of **Taunton Deane**; p. (est. 1988) 94,100 (dist.).

Taunton, t., Mass., **USA**; cotton, iron foundries, machin., plastics; p. (1980) 45,001.

Taunus, mtn. range, Hesse, **W. Germany**; between Rs. Lahn and Rhine and Main; forests, vineyards and spas.

Taupo, L., N.I., **N.Z.**; lgst. L. in N.Z.; geysers, hot springs in vicinity; 40 km by 27 km.

Tauranga, t., N.I., **N.Z.**; spt. on Bay of Plenty; tourism; fishing; p. (est. 1987) 42,400.

Taurus Mtns., range, S. **Turkey**; rise to over 3,660 m.

Tavastehus. See Hämeenlinna.

Tavistock, mkt. t., West Devon, **Eng.**; on R. Tavy; anc, stannary t.; Drake born nearby.

Taw, R., Devon, **Eng.**; flows from Dartmoor to Barnstaple Bay; 80 km long.

Taxco, t., **Mexico**; alt. 1,700 m; gold- and silver-mng.; tourist ctr.; anc. Aztec t.; p. (1970) 64,368.

Taxila, ruined c., **Pakistan**; nr. Rawalpindi; anc. seat of learning; ruins of Buddhist univ.

Tay, R., **Scot.**; flows S.E. from Loch Tay in Perth and Kinross, to Firth of Tay; longest R. in Scot., 188 km; salmon fisheries.

Tay, Firth of, lge. inlet, E. cst. **Scot.**; extends inland almost to Perth.

Tayeh, t., Hupeh, **China**; lies to S. of Yangtze R., 67 km S.E. of Wuhan; impt. iron-ore deposits; supplies Hwangshih; iron and steel inds., heavy engin.

Tayport, burgh, North East Fife, **Scot.**; at entrance to Firth of Tay; opposite Broughty Ferry; linen, jute; p. (1981) 3,014.

Tayside, l. gov. reg., **Scot.**; inc. former cos. of Perth and Angus bordering the Highlands; a. 7,500 km²; p. (est. 1986) 392,346.

Tbilisi (Tiflis), c., Georgian SSR, **USSR**; route ctr. on Kura R.; major admin., economic and cultural ctr. of Transcaucasia; machin., textiles, tanneries, furniture, food processing; power from hydroelectric power stas.; anc. tr. ctr.; some mediaeval fragments in c. ctr.; p. (1986) 1,174,000.

Tczew (Dirschau), t., Gdansk prov., N. **Poland**; pt. on Vistula; rly. junc.; agr. implements; p. (1983) 56,700.

Team Valley, Tyne and Wear, **Eng.**; impt. trading estate has been developed here.

Tebessa, t., N.E. **Algeria**; in Atlas mtns., at 851 m; mkt.; carpets; phosphate deposits nearby; p. (est. 1986) 41,000.

Tees, R., N. **Eng.**; rises on Cross Fell, Cumbria, flows E. to N. Sea between Hartlepool and Redcar; heavy inds. in lower section; 112 km long.

Teesdale, l. gov. dist., Durham, **Eng.**; Pennine a. inc. Barnard Castle; p. (est. 1988) 24,900.

Teesport, oil refinery, between Redcar and Middlesbrough, Cleveland, **Eng.**

Teesside, former admin. dist., Cleveland, **Eng.**; inc. Middlesbrough, Redcar, Thornaby-on-Tees, Stockton-on-Tees, Billingham, and Eston; p.(1981) 382,689.

Tegal, spt., Java, **Indonesia**; textiles, sugar refining; lge. dam nearby; p. (1980) 131,728.

Tegucigalpa, c., cap. of **Honduras**; on R. Choluteca at 976 m; inter-ocean highway connects with Caribbean and Pac. Oc.; former ctr. of silver mng.; inc. Comayagüela, the modern part of c., where the nat. univ. is situated; p. (est. 1985) 571,400.

Tehran (Teheran), c., cap. of **Iran**, 112 km S. of Caspian Sea; mftg. and comm. ctr.; modern bldgs.; gas pipeline to USSR; international airpt.; univ.; car assembly, textiles, chemicals, glass; new oil refinery; ctr. for more than 90 per cent of all industl. firms in Iran; p. (1986) 6,022,078.

Tehuantepec, Isthmus of, separates G. of Mexico from Pac. Oc. at narrowest point of **Mexico**; width 200 km.

Teifi, R., S. **Wales**; rises in Cambrian mtns., flows S.W. to Cardigan Bay; 150 km long.

Teign, R., Devon, **Eng.**; flows to sea at pt. of Teignmouth from Dartmoor; picturesque estuary; 48 km long.

Teignbridge, l. gov. dist., S. Devon, **Eng.**; lower T. valley and ts. of Dawlish, Teignmouth, Newton Abbot and Ashburton; p. (est. 1988) 108,000.

Teignmouth, t., Teignbridge, Devon, **Eng.**; at mouth of R. Teign, 21 km S. of Exeter; resort; revival of pt. with ball clay exp.; p. (1981) 13,264.

Tekirdag, t., **Turkey**; on Sea of Marmara, W. of Istanbul; former Greek settlement; p. (1985) 63,215.

Tel Aviv-Jaffa, c., **Israel**; on Mediterranean; lgst. c. of cty.; financial and cultural ctr.; univ.; founded by Zionists 1909; p. (est. 1982) 325,700.

Telemark, co., **Norway**; borders Skagerrak; mtnous., lake-covered, much forested; hydro-electric power forms basis for electrochemical inds.; a. 15,118 km²; p. (1983) 161,939.

Telford, new t. (1963), Shropshire, **Eng.**; 32 km W. of Wolverhampton; p. (1981) 103,411.

Tellicherry, t., spt., Kerala, **India**; exp. pepper; lge. college; furniture; p. (1961) 44,763.

Telok Betong, spt., Sumatra, **Indonesia**; exp. pepper, agr. products; p. (1971) 198,986.

Tema, t. (opened 1962), nr. Accra, **Ghana**; deepwater harbour, oil refinery, aluminium smelter; impt. industl. development; p. (1984) 60,767.

Teme, R., on border of Wales and Hereford and Worcs., **Eng.**; trib. of R. Severn; 112 km long.

Temir-Tau, c., Kazakh SSR, **USSR**; on Nura R.; industl. ctr.; iron, steel, synthetic rubber, soda; lge. thermal power sta.; p. (1985) 225,000.

Temuco, c., cap. of Cautin prov., **Chile**; cath.; tr. in cereals, apples, timber; Araucanian Indian mkt.; p. (est. 1985) 166,200.

Tenali, t., Andhra Pradesh, **India**; nr. Guntur in Krishna delta; p. (1981) 119,257.

Tenasserim, div., lower **Burma**; on Thailand border; extends along Isthmus of Kra; tin and rubber; a. 92,945 km². p. (1983) 917,628.

Tenby, mkt. t., S. Pembs., Dyfed, **Wales;** on W. side of Carmarthen Bay, Bristol Channel; seaside resort; walled cas. t.; p. (1981) 4,814.

Tendring, l. gov. dist., E. Essex, **Eng.;** inc. cstl. ts. of Harwich, Frinton, Clacton and Brightlingsea; p. (est. 1988) 129,600.

Tenerife, I., **Canary Is.;** volcanic landscapes and mild climate attracts tourists; cap. Santa Cruz; a. 2,025 km²; p. (1970) 500,381.

Tennessee, R., Tenn., Ky., **USA;** lgst. and most impt. branch of Ohio R.; valley once liable to flooding, now controlled by dams, and improved by the Tenn. Valley Authority; 1,251 km long.

Tennessee, st., **USA;** 'Volunteer St.'; admitted to Union 1796; st. flower Iris, st. bird Mockingbird; rises to Appalachians in E., crossed by Tennessee R. and tribs.; a. of heavy rainfall and severe soil erosion necessitated the public Tenn. Valley Authority scheme of conservation, dam bldg., and afforestation; cheap hydroelectric power and attracting new inds., many reservoirs attract tourists; cap. Nashville; a. 109,412 km²; p. (1985) 4,762,000.

Tenterden, mkt. t., Kent, **Eng.;** 13 km N. of Rye; grew with wool tr., church with famous tower; p. (1981) 6,209.

Teófilo Otoni, t., Minas Gerais, **Brazil;** semiprecious stone polishing; p. (est. 1985) 126,200.

Tepic, c., cap. of Nayarit st., **Mexico,** comm. ctr. for agr. dist.; nr. Sanguaney volcano; p. (1980) 177,007.

Teplice, wat. pl., **ČSSR;** N.W. of Prague; textile and hardware inds.; mineral springs; p. (1984) 53,508.

Teramo, c., cap. of T. prov., **Italy;** 24 km from Adriatic; route and agr. ctr.; cath.; textiles; the anc. Interamnium; p. (1981) 51,092.

Terek, R., N. Caucasia, **RSFSR;** flows to Caspian Sea; used for irrigation and hydroelectric power in lower course; 592 km long.

Teresina, t., cap. of Piaui st., **Brazil;** comm. ctr.; lt. inds.; p. (est. 1985) 476,100.

Terezopólis, t., Rio de Janeiro, **Brazil;** health resort; textiles; p. (est. 1985) 115,900.

Terneuzen, t., Neth.; on W. Schelde R.; pipeline to be constructed to carry ethylene from Pernis; p. (est. 1987) 35,000.

Terni, t., Perugia, **Italy;** among the Apennines; iron and steel wks.; arms factory; cath.; p. (1984) 111,347.

Ternopol (Tarnopol), t., Ukrainian SSR, **USSR;** E. of Lvov; rly. junc.; mkt.; agr. machin., food inds.; p. (1985) 182,000.

Terrassa, t., Barcelona, **Spain;** textile ctr.; p. (1981) 147,780.

Terre Adélie, name given to Fr. terr. and I. in Antarctic; est. a. 424,400 km².

Terre Haute, t., Ind., **USA;** coal, natural gas, flour, paper, glass, foundries; p. (1984) 58,800 (t.), 134,500 (met. a.).

Terreón, t., Coahuila, **Mexico;** ctr. of comm. agr.; oil pipeline connects to Chihuahua; thermo-elec. plant; p. (1969) 243,234.

Teruel, t., cap. of Teruel prov., **Spain;** on R. Turia; walled t., cath.; p. (1987) 27,475.

Test Valley, l. gov. dist., W. Hants., **Eng.;** stretches from Andover to Romsey; p. (est. 1988). 102,300.

Tete, t., central **Moçambique;** on R. Zambesi; ctr. of coalfield; iron-ore, graphite, radioactive materials.

Tetovo, t., Macedonia, **Yugoslavia;** chemicals, electro-metallurgy, textiles.

Tetuan, ch. spt., **Morocco,** N. Africa; walled t. p. (est. 1981) 372,000.

Teviot, R., Roxburgh, **Scot.;** trib. of R. Tweed; 59 km long.

Tewkesbury, mkt. t., l. gov. dist., Gloucs., **Eng.;** on R. Avon, close to confluence with R. Severn; Norman abbey; p. (est. 1988) 87,200.

Texarkana, t., Texas and Ark., **USA;** bdy. passes down middle of main street; timber and cotton region; total p. (1984) 32,900 (t.), 118,500 (met. a.).

Texas, st., S.W. **USA;** 'Lone Star St.'; admitted to Union 1845; st. flower Bluebonnet, st. bird Mocking bird; second lgst. st. by a.; borders Mexico; dry plains in W., humid cst. in E.; problems of soil erosion yet leading agr. st.; leading producer of petroleum and natural gas; cap. Austin; a. 692,408 km²; p. (1985) 16,370,000.

Texel, one of the W. Frisian Is., **Neth.;** scene of several naval battles; p. (1967) 11,003.

Thailand (Siam), kingdom, **S.E. Asia;** 4 main regions; parallel N.–S. hill ranges (2,400 m) and valleys in N. producing teak; rice growing, fertile plain of Chao Phraya R. in ctr.; thinly populated E. plateau, drained by Mekong; S. coastal strip on G. of Siam; monsoon climate; predominantly agr., accounting for 60 per cent of p. and 60 per cent of exports; fifth lgst. exporter of foodstuffs in the world, mainly rice, tapioca, rubber and maize to U.S.A., Japan & Singapore esp.; desire to conserve rainforest now resulting in the intensification of agr.; recent offshore gas discoveries; mnfg. development centres on cap. Bangkok, but has slowed down since 1985; tourism and fishery increasingly impt.; a. 519,083 km²; p. (est. 1987) 53·6 m.

Thal Desert, Pakistan; W. of Punjab; now irrigated for wheat and cotton.

Thame, mkt. t., South Oxford, **Eng.;** on R. Thame, 11 km S.W. of Aylesbury; p. (1981) 8,533.

Thames, R., **Eng.;** rises in Cotswold hills and flows past Oxford, Reading, Windsor, and London to the N. Sea; tribs. inc. Windrush, Cherwell, Thame, Kennet, Colne, Lea, and Roding; estuary impt. industl. a. with many oil refineries; flood barrier at Silvertown in Woolwich (1983), 336 km long.

Thamesdown, l. gov. dist., N.E. Wilts., **Eng.,** based on Swindon; p. (est. 1988) 168,800.

Thameshaven, lge. oil refinery, Essex, **Eng.;** on N. cst. of Thames estuary 13 km below Tilbury.

Thana, t., Maharashtra, **India;** textiles, chemicals; p. (1981) 309,897.

Thanet, I. of, lge. promontory, N.E. extremity of Kent, **Eng.;** formed by bifurcation of R. Stour; now also l. gov. dist. which contains Margate, Ramsgate, and Broadstairs; p. (est. 1988) 129,700.

Thanjavur, t., Tamil Nadu, **India;** silks, carpets, jewellery, inlaid metals; impt. Brahman ctr.; p. (1981) 184,015.

Thar Desert, on bdy. of **India** and **Pakistan;** covers slopes between N.W. Deccan and R. Indus; barren, lack of Rs. or level land prevents irrigation; crossed by caravan routes.

Thebes, c. of Boeotia, in anc. **Greece;** Mycenaean site; destroyed by Alexander the Great 335 B.C.; modern c. of Thivai occupies site; p. (1981) 18,712.

Thebes, c. of anc. **Egypt;** on banks of Nile; site now partly occupied by vs. Karnak and Luxor; archeological discoveries in Valley of the Kings 1922, inc. tomb of Tutankhamun.

The Entrance, t., N.S.W., **Australia;** tourist resort on waterway from L. Tuggerah to Tasman Sea; fishing; p. (1981) 37,891.

Thermopylae, celebrated pass between Mt. Oeta and the sea, N.E. **Greece;** heroic battle between Spartans and Persians 480 B.C.

Thessaloniki, c., **Greece;** spt. at head of G. of T.; with fiscal free zone; second c. of Greece; impt. route and industl. ctr.; univ.; p. (1981) 406,413.

Thessaly, prov., central **Greece;** fertile plain drained by R. Pinios; mainly agr.; a. 13,489 km²; p. (1981) 695,654.

Thetford, t., Breckland, Norfolk, **Eng.;** on Little Ouse; industl. estate for London overspill; fruit and vegetable canning, pulp mftg., engin.; p. (1981) 19,591.

Thetford Mines, t., Quebec, **Canada;** asbestos mng. ctr.; p. (1981) 19,965.

Thienen (Tirlemont), t., Brabant prov., **Belgium;** ctr. of Belgian beet-sugar refining; captured by Marlborough 1705; p. (est. 1981) 32,620.

Thiès, t., **Senegambia;** rly. ctr. and wkshps.; aluminium, phosphate quarrying; p. (1976) 117,333.

Thimphu, t., cap. **Bhutan;** hydroelectric plant; 176 km road link to Phuntsholing (Sikkim) 1968; p. (est. 1987) 15,000.

Thionville, t., Moselle dep., N. **France;** in Lorraine ironfield conurb.; metallurgical and chemical inds.; p. (1982) 138,034 (met. a.).

Thira (Santorine), volcanic I., Cyclades, **Greece;** wine prods.; max. alt. 567 m; a. 75 km²; p. c. 10,000.

Thirlmere, L., Cumbria, **Eng.;** 5 km long; furnishes part of water supply of Manchester.

Thirsk, mkt. t., Hambleton, North Yorks., **Eng.;** in wide gap between Pennines and Cleveland hills, 11 km S.E. of Northallerton; racecourse.

Thompson, R., B.C., **Canada;** trib. of R. Fraser; forms impt. routeway through Rocky mtns.; 448 km long.

Thornburi, c., Thailand; on R. Menam opposite Bangkok; second c. of T.; former cap., "Temple of Dawn"; lt. inds.; p. (1970) 627,989.

Thorez (Chistyakovo), Ukrainian SSR, USSR; coal mng.; p. (est. 1967) 95,000 (c.), 300,000 (met. a.).

Thornaby-on-Tees. See Teesside.

Thornbury, mkt. t., Avon, Eng.; 16 km N. of Bristol; aircraft mftg.; expanded t.

Thornton Cleveleys, t., Wyre, Lancs., Eng.; 6 km N.E. of Blackpool; resort; p. (1981) 26,139.

Thörshavn, c., cap. of Faroe Is.; on Stromo I.; fish. pt.; anc. fortress; lighthouse; p. (est. 1986) 15,287.

Thousand Isles, gr. of over 1,500 Is. in St. Lawrence R. which extend up-river for c. 48 km from Brockville to Gananoque, at junc. of L. Ont. and St. Lawrence R.; partly in N.Y. st. and partly in Canada.

Thrace, anc. name of terr. in S.E. Europe, part of which has been added to Greece; successively under Macedonian, Roman, Byzantine, and Turkish rule, before passing to Greece; tobacco; a. 8,586 km²; p. of dep. (1981) 345,220.

Three Rivers, l. gov. dist., S.W. Herts., Eng.; close to London and inc. Rickmansworth and Chorleywood; p. (est. 1988) 80,000.

Thule, N.W. Greenland; 1,600 km from N. Pole; American air base and site of ballistic missile early warning sta.; spt. open 2–3 months per annum.

Thumba, Kerala, India; space science and technological ctr.

Thun, L., Berne can., Switzerland; occupies valleys of R. Aare where it leaves Alpine region; separated from L. Brienz by deltaic neck of land on which is Interlaken; a. 98 km².

Thun, t., Berne, Switzerland; on N.W. end of L. Thun; cas. on hill above t.; tourism; p. (1980) 36,891.

Thunder Bay, t., Canada; formed from Port Arthur and Port William; pt. on N.W. cst. of L. Superior; grain exp. ctr.; p. (1986) 112,272 (c.), 122,217 (met. a.).

Thurgau, can., N.E. Switzerland; on L. Constance, bordered by R. Rhine; prosperous agr. a.; inds. ass, with textiles; cap. Frauenfeld; a. 1,005 km²; p. (est. 1986) 192,000.

Thuringia, former st., E. Germany; bordered by Bavaria, Saxony-Anhalt, Lower Saxony, and Hesse; drained by Rs. Saale and Werra; crossed by Thüringer Wald and extending to Harz mtns.; fertile arable agr. a.; now comprises dists. of Erfurt Suhl and Bera.

Thuringian Forest or Thüringer Wald, forested range of hills E. Germany; rising to 982 m in Beerberg; famous for romantic scenery and legends; resorts.

Thurles, mkt. t., Tipperary, R.o.I.; on R. Suir; agr. processing; cath., cas.; p. (1981) 7,352.

Thurrock, t., l. gov. dist. Essex, Eng.; on Thames, nr. Tilbury; oil refining, metal refining, cement, paper board; p. (est. 1988) 124,400.

Thurso, burgh, Caithness, Scot.; nr. Dounreay; anc. stronghold of Vikings; p. (1981) 9,038.

Tianjing (Tientsin) c. and mun., China 112 km S.E. of Beijing; impt. pt. using poor harbour on Hai R.; industl. ctr., oil refining, textiles, elec. instruments, steel rolling mills, machine tools, chemicals, tobacco, food processing; univ.; p. (est. 1985) 7,990,000 (met. a.), (1984) 5,312,100 (c).

Tiaret, t., W. Algeria; N. Africa; in strategic pass; walled; agr. mkt.; cereals, wool, cattle; p. (1966) 37,059.

Tiber, R., Italy; flows from Apennines to Mediterranean, passing through Rome; 352 km long.

Tiberias, t., Israel; on Sea of Galilee (L. Tiberias); agr. ctr.; health resort with medicinal springs; p. (est. 1970) 23,900.

Tibesti, mtns., on bdy. between Libya and Chad, Equatorial Africa; barren in spite of slight rainfall; mainly above 1,800 m max. alt. 3,401 m.

Tibet (Xizang Zizhiqu), aut. region, China; lofty plateau called "the roof of the world" its lowest plains being 3,660 m a.s.l.; semi-desert; network of roads inc. one across Himalayas to Katmandu; pastoral agr. sheep; arable agr. in R. valleys, especially Zangbo valley, wheat, barley, fruit, vegetables; tr. of wool, musk, gold, skins, drugs traditionally carried by yaks which can stand intense cold; salt, alluvial gold, radioactive ores; recent liberalisation by China encouraging restoration of Buddhist temples and monastries,

tourism and incr. in economic contact with outside world. cap. Lhasa; a. 1,217,308 km²; p. (est. 1985) 1,970,000.

Ticino, R. Switzerland and Italy; trib. of Po; forms S. approach to St. Gotthard Pass; irrigation in lower course; length 240 km.

Ticino, can., Switzerland; on S. slopes of central Alps, bordering Italy; contains parts of Ls. Maggiore and Lugano; mainly pastoral agr., but wine, corn, tobacco in valleys; industl. a., in S. based on hydroelectric power, chemicals, metallurgy; many tourist resorts inc. Locarno, Lugano; cap. Bellinzona; a. 2,813 km²; p. (est. 1986) 277,000.

Ticonderoga, V., N.E., N.Y., USA; resort between Ls. George and Champlain; L. George falls provide hydroelectric power for paper mill; local graphite used in pencil ind.; p. (1980) 2,938.

Tideswell, t., Derbys., Eng.; tourist ctr.; limestone quarrying in a.; lge. 14th cent. church known as "cath. of the Peak." p. c. 1,500.

Tidore I., Moluccas, Indonesia; volcanic; densely populated; coffee, tobacco, spices, fruit; a. 78 km²; p. (est. 1969) 70,000.

Tien Shan (= Celestial Mtns.) mtn. chain, central Asia, along China–USSR border; highest peak 7,320 m; source of Syr-Dar'ya, Chu, Ili and many other Rs.

Tierra del Fuego, archipelago, southernmost part of S. America; separated from Patagonia by Strait of Magellan; divided politically between Chile and Argentina; timber, pastoral agr. sheep; oilfield at Rio Grande; mng.; a. c. 47,900 km²; p. (1980) 29,451.

Tigre, st., Ethiopia; formerly an independent kingdom; cap. Adua; severe drought 1982–3.

Tigris, R., S.W. Asia; rises in Taurus mtns. S. Turkey, flows through Iraq where it is joined by the Euphrates and proceeds to Persian G.; comm. routeway; dam projected 56 km N. of Mosul; many of the earliest cs. located in valley; 1,840 km long.

Tijuana, t., Baja Cal. st., Mexico; resort catering for Americans; casinos, race-tracks, bull-fights; p. (est. 1986) 420,000.

Tiksi, t., USSR; Arctic spt., at mouth of Lena R.; local coal deposits; linked by air and R; to Yakutsk.

Tilburg, c., N. Brabant, Neth.; nr. Breda; woollens, textiles, tobacco, leather; p. (est. 1987) 154,000.

Tilbury, pt., Essex, Eng.; on N. Bank of R. Thames 32 km E. of London; within Port of London; major container terminal.

Tilimsen (Tlemcen), t., N. W. Algeria; picturesque medieval t.; agr. ctr. in fertile region; textiles, furniture, handicrafts; p. (est. 1983) 146,089.

Tillicoultry, burgh, Clackmannan, Scot.; on Devon R.; woollen and worsted fabrics, paper; p. (1981) 6,154.

Tilsit. See Sovetsk.

Timaru, c., S.I., N.Z.; E. cst. spt., exp. frozen foods; fishing; regional ctr. for S. Canterbury; p. (est. 1987) 27,700.

Timbuktu, Mali, W. Africa; nr. Niger R. on border of Sahara; salt tr., handicraft inds.; flourished as comm. mart and Moslem ctr. 14th–16th cent.; p. (1975) 10,500.

Timisoara, c., W. Romania; comm., industl. and educational ctr.; univ., 2 caths., cas.; once a frontier fortress; p. (est. 1984) 309,258.

Timmins, t., Ont., Canada; gold mng. declining; vast deposits of copper, zinc, silver, discovered 1964; timber inds., brewing; p. (1981) 46,114.

Timok Basin, Serbia, Yugoslavia; industl. region; coal mng., copper smelting, chemicals, glass, food processing; arable agr., vines.

Timor, lgst. of Lesser Sunda Is., E. Indies; divided politically until 1975 into W. Timor part of Indonesia and Port Timor; now both part of Indonesia; a. 33,748 km²; p. (est. 1970) 3,085,541.

Timor Sea, that part of the Indian Oc. N.W. of W. Australia, and S. of Timor I.

Timsah, L., Egypt; sm. L. midway along Suez Canal; formerly used for recreational purposes by Brit. garrison in Canal zone.

Tinogasta, t., Catamarca prov., Argentina; in E. foothills of Andes, 192 km N.W. of Catamarca; impt. copper mines.

Tintagel, v., Cornwall, Eng.; ruined Norman cas.; reputed birthplace of King Arthur; tourism.

Tintern, v., Gwent, **Wales**; Cistercian abbey.

Tinto, R., Huelva prov., S.W. **Spain**; in Andalusia; flows W. to Alt. Oc.; gives its name to Rio Tinto copper mng. region which it crosses; 104 km long.

Tipperary, inland co., Munster, **R.o.I.**; drained by Rs. Suir and Shannon; mtnous., Knockmealdown and Galty mtns.; fertile Golden Vale in S.W.; dairying, sugar-beet; divided into N. and S. Ridings; co. t. Clonmel; p. (1981) 20,276 (N.R.), 30,018 (S.R.).

Tipperary, t., Tipperary, **R.o.I.**; 46 km S.E. Limerick; dairy processing; p. (1981) 4,929.

Tiranë, t., cap. of **Albania**; rapid growth since becoming cap. 1920; many new inds.; agr. processing, engin., clothing, glass; univ.; airport; p. (1981) 210,757.

Tiraspol, c., S.E. Moldavian SSR, **USSR**; on R. Dniester; agr. processing ctr.; heat and power sta. recently constructed; p. (1985) 162,000.

Tiree, I., Inner Hebrides, **Scot.**; off cst. of Mull; 22 km long, up to 10 km wide; sm. freshwater lochs and prehistoric forts; p. (1971) 1,019 (inc. Coll).

Tiruchirapalli (Trichinopoly), c., Tamil Nadu, S.E. **India**; on R. Cauvery; rly. ctr.; textiles, cigars, goldsmithery; p. (1981) 362,045.

Tirunelveli (Tinnevelly), c., Tamil Nadu, S.E. **India**; agr. tr. ctr. with sugar refinery; p. (1981) 324,000.

Tiruppur, t., Tamil Nadu, **India**; nr. Coimbatore; p. (1981) 165,223 (t.), 215,859 (met. a.).

Tisa (Tisza), R., E. **Europe**; rises in E. Carpathians, W. Ukraine, flows across Hungary into Yugoslavia where it joins the Danube 72 km below Novi Sad; ch. tribs. Koros and Mures; length c. 960 km; navigable in part.

Titicaca, L., **S. America**; between two ranges of Andes, on borders of Bolivia and Peru; 3,812 m a.s.l.; highest lge. L. in world; max. depth 300 m; crossed by steamers; fishing; a. c. 8,300 km².

Titograd (Podgorica), t., cap. of Montenegro, S. **Yugoslavia**; nr. Albanian frontier; anc. t. but now mainly modern with growing industl. activity; agr. processing, aluminium smelting; airport; p. (1981) 132,290.

Titov Veles, t., central Macedonia, **Yugoslavia**; on R. Vardar, and main rly. to Belgrade; recent industl. growth; textiles; p. (1981) 64,799.

Tiverton, mkt. t., Mid Devon, **Eng.**; 22 km N. Exeter; once famous for lace; textiles, engin.; p. (1981) 16,539.

Tivoli, the anc. Tibur, nr. Rome, **Italy**; on Aniene R., magnificent situations; hydroelec. power; resort; remains of Hadrian's villa; p. (1981) 50,969.

Tjirebon (Cheribon), spt., Java, **Indonesia**; on N. cst. 192 km E. of Djakarta; rice, tea, coffee tr.; ctr. of irrigation scheme; oil refining; p. (1971) 178,529.

Tlaxcala, smallest st., **Mexico**; on Mesa Central; dense p.; mainly agr.; cap. T.; a. 4,027 km²; p. (est. 1983) 611,650.

Tlemcen. See Tilimsen.

Toamasina (Tamatave), t., **Madagascar**; lge seapt. on Indian Oc., handles 70 per cent of M. tr.; industl. complex, car assembly, oil refinery; p. (est. 1982) 83,000.

Tobago, southernmost I., Windward Is., **W.I.**; volcanic, forested, picturesque, irregular topography; resorts utilising pleasant climate; exp. coconuts, copra, cacao, limes; ch. t. Scarborough; seeks internal self-gov.; a. 300 km²; p. (1980) 40,700. See Trinidad and Tobago.

Tobata. See Kitakyushu.

Tobermory, burgh, Argyll and Bute, **Scot.**; on I. of Mull at N. entrance to Sound of Mull; fish. pt., resort; p. (1981) 843.

Tobol, R., W. Siberia, **RSFSR**; trib. of R. Irtysh; navigable in lower course; 800 km long.

Tobolsk, t., W. Siberia, **RSFSR**; R. pt. on Irtysh R.; shipbldg., sawmilling, fishing; p. (est. 1967) 47,000.

Tobruk, spt., **Libya**, N. Africa; on cst. 352 km E. of Benghazi; exp. oil, served by pipeline from Libyan oilfields; p. (1984) 94,006.

Tocantins, R., central **Brazil**; rises in Goias prov., flows N. across plateau of Brazil through Pará estuary to Atl. Oc.; navigation interrupted by rapids 320 km above Pará; ch. trib. Araguaya R.; 2,560 km long.

Toce, R., N. **Italy**; rises in Lepontine Alps, flows

S. and S.E. into L. Maggiore; valley used by trunk rly. from Milan to Berne as S. approach to Simplon Tunnel; 86 km long.

Tocopilla, spt., **Chile**; exp. nitrate, copper ore, sulphates, iodine; p. (1982) 26,123

Todmorden, mkt. t., Calderdale, West Yorks., **Eng.**; nr. source of R. Calder, 10 km N.E. of Rochdale; cottons, machin.; p. (1981) 14,665.

Togliatti (Tol'yatti), c., **RSFSR**; on R. Volga 56 km W.N.W. of Kuybyshev; engin., motor wks., natural gas pipeline to Moscow; chemicals; p. (1986) 610,000.

Togo, Rep. of, W. Africa; narrow strip between Ghana (W.) and Benin (E.); N. and S. lowlands separated by mtns. (1,000 m); climate hot and humid, but drier savannah conditions in N.; coffee on slopes of central mtns., cacao, copra in S., maize in N.; phosphate mng., major iron ore deposits in N. now form ch. exp.; developing food-processing inds.; cap. Lomé; a. 54,960 km²; p. (est. 1988) 3·25 m.

Tokaido, Japan, one of gr. feudal highways, along S. cst. Honshu, now forms main line of modern communications network.

Tokaimura, v., Ibaraki, **Japan**; nuclear reactor and lge. nuclear power sta.

Tokaj, t., **Hungary**; at confluence of Bodrog and Tisa Rs.; nearby slopes of Hegyalla produce Tokay wine; p. (1960) 5,031.

Tokat, t., cap. of T. prov., **Turkey**; copper refining, leather mnfs.; p. (1985) 73,008.

Tokelau or Union Isles, gr. of 3 coral atolls, S. Pac., N. of W. Samoa, belonging to N.Z.; Fakaofo, Nukunono and Atafu; natives are Polynesians; subsistence economy; copra; a. 10 km²; p. (est. 1986) 1,690.

Tokoroa, co. t., N.I., **N.Z.**; kraft paper, pulp, and sawn timber; p. (est. 1987) 17,400.

Tokushima, t., Shikoku, **Japan**; spt. on E. cst.; mkt. ctr., cotton mnfs.; p. (1985) 257,886.

Tokyo, c., cap. of **Japan**; spt. with deepened harbour handling mainly S. coastal tr.; major industl. ctr. with diverse mnfs. and major problems of pollution; built on marshy site with much expensive reclamation from sea; planned decentralisation of p. and economic activity in progress; with Osaka-Kobe-Kyoto conurbs. (480 km long ribbon development) spoken of as Tokaido (q.v.) megalopolis; major educational ctr. with many univs.; p. (1987) 8,348,000 (c.).

Tolbukhin, t., N.E. **Bulgaria**; comm. and agr. ctr. of Dobruja; food-processing, textiles, furniture, agr. machin.; formerly Dobrich, renamed in honour of Russian soldier who took it from Germans during World War II, 1944; p. (1985) 109,069.

Toledo, prov., **Spain**; mtnous.; agr., vineyards, stock-raising; a. 15,346 km²; p. (1987) 487,867.

Toledo, anc. c., cap. of T. prov., **Spain**; in New Castile; on hill above Tagus R.; Gothic, Moorish, and Castillian architecture; picturesque narrow streets; Alcázar citadel; associated with El Greco; sword mkg. still flourishes; sm. arms; tourism; p. (1987) 58,297.

Toledo, c., Ohio, **USA**; rly. ctr. and L. pt. with natural harbour on Maumee R.; exp. mnfs., oil, coal, agr. prod.; imports iron-ore; glass mkg., shipbldg., car components and many varied mnfs.; p. (1984) 343,900 (c.), 610,800 (met. a.).

Tolentino, t., in the Marches, central **Italy**; on R. Chienti; mediaeval walls and houses; cath.; sm. handicraft inds.; spa and tourist ctr.; p. (est. 1981) 17,984.

Tolosa, t., Guipúzcoa prov., **Spain**; in the Basque cty.; mediaeval bldgs., and armour; paper mills; p. (1981) 18,894.

Tolpuddle, v., Dorset, **Eng.**; 11 km N.E. of Dorchester; famous for "Tolpuddle martyrs," agr. labourers condemned to transportation for trying to form a trade union (1834).

Toluca, c., cap. of Mexico st., central **Mexico**; stands at 2,672 m; brewing, flour, cottons, pottery; especially noted for basket weaving; p. (1980) 357,071.

Tol'yatti. See Togliatti.

Tom, R., Siberia, **RSFSR**; flows through Kuznetsk Basin and joins R. Ob; 704 km long.

Tomaszow Mazowiecki, t., Lodz prov., central **Poland**; industl. t. on Pilica R., surrounded by forests; textile ind., artificial silk; p. (1983) 65,600.

Tombigbee, R., Miss., **USA**; flows S. to join

Alabama R. to form Mobile and Tensaw Rs.; navigable, partially canalised; length 654 km.

Tomsk, c., cap. of marshy T. oblast, **RSFSR**; one of few lge. ts. in N. Siberia; major pt. on R. Tom; rly. junc. on Trans-Siberian rly.; educational ctr.; univ., cath.; engin., chemicals; p. (1985) 475,000.

Tonawanda, t., N.Y. st., **USA**; on Niagara R. at terminus of Erie Barge Canal; steel, plastics, chemicals; power from Niagara Falls, adjacent to N. Tonawanda; p. (1980) 18,693.

Tonbridge, t., Kent, **Eng.**; on R. Medway; food processing; lt. inds., inc. cricket balls; Norman cas. gatehouse; public school; with Malling forms l. gov. dist.; p. (est. 1988) 101,200 (dist.).

Tone, R., Honshu, **Japan**; flows E. across Kanto Plain to Pac. Oc., N. of Tokyo; longest R. in Japan.

Tonga, I. gr., S. Pac. Oc.; Polynesian kingdom, gained independence 1970; 158 coral and volcanic Is.; 50 per cent. p. on Tongatabu I.; exp. copra, bananas; fishing; oil discovered 1969; airport; cap. Nuku'alofa; a. 699 km²; p. (1986) 94,535.

Tongariro, volcanic peak, N.I., **N.Z.**; nat. park in ctr. of volcanic dist.; alt. 1,970 m.

Tongeren (Tongres), t., Limburg prov., N.E. **Belgium**; mkt. ctr. for fertile Hesbaye region; historic bldgs.; p. (1982) 29,765.

Tonghua (Tunghwa), c., S.W. Jilin, **China**; rly junc.; soya bean processing; local iron and coal reserves; p. (1984) 363,400.

Tonkin, region, N. **Vietnam**; mtns. in N. and W., alluvial plain in E. around delta of Red R., containing most p. and lge. cs.; fertile agr.; ch. t. Hanoi; ch. pt. Haiphong; a. 104,973 km².

Tonle Sap, L., **Kampuchea**; major comm. fishing a.; L. acts as natural reservoir to control floods of Mekong R.

Tönsberg, c., Vestfold prov., S.E. **Norway**; one of oldest Norwegian cs., on Skagerrak at entrance to Oslo fjord; ctr. of whaling fleet; oil mills; p. (est. 1970) 11,260.

Toowoomba, t., S.E. Queensland, **Australia**; regional ctr. for Darling Downs, a rich wool and beef a; planned with parks and gardens: agr. based inds., engin.; p. (est. 1984) 74,360.

Topeka, c., cap. of Kansas st., **USA**; on Kansas R.; impt. tr. ctr. in rich agr. region; food processing, rly. ctr. and engin.; p. (1984) 118,900 (c.), 159,000 (met. a.).

Torbay, l. gov. dist., S. Devon, **Eng.**; formed by amalgamation of Torquay, Paignton and Brixham; located around Tor Bay; tourism; p. (est. 1988) 118,900.

Torcello, I., with anc. Byzantine cath., on lagoon nr. Venice, **Italy**.

Torfaen, l. gov. dist., Gwent, **Wales**; based on Pontypool, Cwmbran and Blaenavon; p. (est. 1988) 92,400.

Torgau, t., **E. Germany**; R. pt. on Elbe; industl. ctr.; American and Soviet armies met here 1945; p. (est. 1970) 21,688.

Torne, R., N. **Europe**; rises in Sweden, drains L. Tornetrask and flows S.W. to G. of Bothnia, forming Finno–Swedish bdy.; rich in salmon; 512 km long.

Torness, East Lothian, **Scot.**; site of advanced gas cooled nuclear power sta.

Toronto, c., cap. of Ont. prov., **Canada**; major Gt. Ls. pt., on L. Ont.; spacious harbour; exp. lge. quantities of wheat; comm., financial, industl. and educational ctr.; many varied mnfs., univ.; notable bldgs , parks; a. 622 km²; p. (1986) 612,289 (c.), 3,427,168 (met. a.), lgst. c. of C.

Torpoint, t., Cornwall, **Eng.**; on Plymouth Sound; p. (1981) 8,423.

Torquay, t., S. Devon, **Eng.**; incorporated in Torbay; on N. side of Tor Bay; seaside resort with all-year season.

Torre Annunziata, Campania, **Italy**; at foot of Vesuvius; spt., spa, bathing resort on Bay of Naples; arms factory; pasta mnf.; p. (est. 1981) 57,097.

Torre del Greco, t., Campania, **Italy**; spt. and resort on Bay of Naples at foot of Vesuvius; coral fishing; pasta mnf.; p. (1984) 104,654.

Torremolinos, cst. resort, **Spain**; S. of Malaga; p. (1981) 22,535.

Torrens, L., S. **Australia**; 2nd lgst. salt L. in A.; varies from brackish lake to salt marsh.

Torreon, c., Coahuila, N. **Mexico**; developed rapidly after growth of cotton in surrounding Laguna dist.; cotton mills, rubber, smelting, food processing; rly. connection with ts. in S. Mexico; p. (1980) 363,886.

Torres Strait, between C. York, Queensland, **Australia**, and **New Guinea**; 144 km wide, strong tidal currents endanger navigation; contains volcanic and coral Torres Strait Is., 20 of which are inhabited by Australian Melanesians.

Torridge, R., Devon, **Eng.**; flows from Hartland dist. to a confluence with the Taw at Bideford Bay; 85 km long.

Torridge, l. gov. dist., N.W. Devon, **Eng.**; inc. N. cst. ts. of Northam and Bideford and stretches inland to Great Torrington; p. (est. 1988) 51,200.

Tortona, t., Piedmont, N. **Italy**; on Scrivia R.; textiles, metallurgy, engin., wines; cath.; the Roman Dertona; p. (1981) 28,806.

Tortosa, c., Tarragona prov., N.E. **Spain**; pt. on Ebro R., 35 km from mouth; food processing, soap, pottery; cath.; impt. Moorish t.; p. (1981) 31,445.

Tororo, t., **Uganda**; lge. chemical wks., cement, fertilisers.

Tortuga or **Ile de la Tortue**, I., Caribbean Sea; off N. cst. **Haiti**; provides shelter from N.E. tr. winds for Port-de-Paix; private development to convert I. into free pt. with tax incentives for inds.; scenic attractions being tapped to develop tourist tr.; airport under construction; subsistence agr. fishing; a. c. 65 km².

Torun (Ger. Thorn), c., Bydgoszcz prov., **Poland**; rly. junc., pt. on Vistula; industl. ctr.; chemicals, elec. gds., clothing, metallurgy, engin., food processing; univ. bears name of Copernicus who was born here; p. (est. 1985) 186,000.

Tory I., off N.W. cst., Donegal, **R.o.I.**; lighthouse; fishing; p. c. 200.

Totnes, t., South Hams, Devon, **Eng.**; on R. Dart 10 km N.W. of Dartmouth; mediaeval t.; agr. mkt., food processing; p. (1981) 5,627.

Tottenham. See **Haringey**.

Tottori, t., Honshu, **Japan**; spt. on Sea of Japan, exp. lumber, raw silk, fruit; industl. ctr.; p. (1985) 137,060.

Touggourt or **Tuggurt**, t., S. **Algeria**; on edge of Sahara; rly. terminus; dates; p. (1961) 26,000.

Toulon, c., Var dep., S.W. **France**; reinstated as cap. of Var dep. (1974); on Mediterranean cst.; base of Fr. navy; fine natural harbour; comm. pt. and industl. ctr.; many fine bldgs.; Port-Cros Nat. Park nearby; p. (1982) 181,405.

Toulouse, c., cap. of Haute-Garonne dep., S. **France**; in Languedoc on Garonne R. and Canal du Midi, commanding route through Gate of Carcassonne; industl. and agr. tr. ctr.; food processing, varied mnfs.; many fine bldgs., notably mediaeval univ., basilica, Gothic cath.; p. (1982) 354,289.

Touraine, region and former prov. of **France**, of which Tours was the cap.; now occupied by Indre-et-Loire dep. and part of Vienne dep.; known as the "garden of France."

Tourcoing, c., Nord dep., N. **France**; 16 km N.E. of Lille; with twin t. of Roubaix forms major wool textile ctr.; p. (1982) 97,121.

Tournai, c., Hainaut prov., W. **Belgium**; on R. Scheldt, nr. Mons; historic c.; famous cath.; textiles, carpet mftg., ctr. of cement ind.; p. (1982) 67,576.

Tours, c., cap. of Indre-et-Loire dep., **France**; in Touraine, on R. Loire; tourist ctr. for the châteaux of the Loire; route ctr.; agr. inds.; printing, engin.; Gothic cath.; p. (1982) 136,483.

Towcester, mkt. t., South Northants., **Eng.**; 14 km S.W. of Northampton; "Eatanswill" of *Pickwick Papers*.

Tower Hamlets, inner bor., E. London, **Eng.**; inc. former bors. of Bethnal Green, Stepney and Poplar; undergoing rapid economic and social change as p. and inds. are decentralised; site of lge. a. of London Docks (now all closed) with allied dockland inds.; clothing, brewing; p. (est. 1988) 161,800.

Townsville, spt., Queensland, **Australia**; coastal outlet for rich dairying, pastoral and mng. a. along Great Northern Rly; artificial harbour; univ.; copper refining; p. (est. 1984) 82,140.

Towton, v., North Yorks., **Eng.**; nearby Towton field, scene of bloodiest battle of Wars of the Roses 1461: Lancastrians under Henry VI defeated by Yorkists under Edward IV.

Towy, R., S. **Wales**; flows S.W. of Carmarthen Bay; 104 km long.

Toyama, c., Honshu, **Japan**; on Etchu plain to E. of Noto peninsula; regional admin. and comm. ctr.; patent medicines, aluminium smelting, machin.; p. (1985) 314,111.

Toyohashi, t., Honshu, **Japan**; food processing, textiles; p. (1985) 322,142.

Trabzon or **Trebizond**, spt., **Turkey**; on Black Sea; exp. tobacco, food prods., carpets; once a gr. tr. ctr. on caravan route between Persia and Europe; founded 8th cent. B.C. by Greek colonists; p. (1985) 142,008.

Trafalgar, C., S.W. cst., Cadiz, **Spain**; Nelson's famous victory 1805.

Trafford, met. dist. Gtr. Manchester **Eng.**; comprises Sale, Hale, Altrincham, Urmston and Stretford; p. (est. 1988) 215,800.

Trail, t., B.C., **Canada**; lgst. metallurgical smelter in Commonwealth using local non-ferrous metals; processing; p. (1981) 22,939.

Tralee, mkt. t., spt., Kerry, **R.o.I.**; on R. Lee; exp. grain, butter; p. (1981) 16,495.

Trani, spt., N. Apulia, **Italy**; on Adriatic; mkt. t. for fertile coastal a.; fishing, food processing; cath., cas.; p. (est. 1981) 44,235.

Transbaykal, region, Siberia, **RSFSR**; E. of L. Baykal; mineral wealth; ch. t., Chita.

Transcaucasia, region between the Black Sea and the Caspian Sea, **USSR**; comprising the constituent reps. of Georgia, Armenia, and Azerbaydzhan; ch. t. Tbilisi.

Transkei, indep. Bantu Terr. (1976), **S. Africa**; not recognised by UN as designed to consolidate apartheid; mainly agr., maize and livestock; heavily dependent on S. Africa; p. mainly employed in mines in Transvaal and Orange Free State; cap. Umtata; a. 42,849 km²; p. (est. 1984) 2·9 m.

Transvaal, prov., **Rep. of S. Africa**; high veld plateau (900–1,200 m) with Kruger Nat. Park in N.E.; hot summers, temperate winters; livestock on grasslands, grains, citrus fruits and temperate crops on irrigated land; lge. mineral wealth, especially gold in Witwatersrand; diamonds, uranium, platinum; inds. in ch. cs., Johannesburg and cap. Pretoria; a. 286,066 km²; p. (1980) 8,350,500.

Transylvania, historic region and prov., central **Romania**; high plateau surrounded by Carpathians; forested; mineral wealth not yet fully realised; arable agr. in valleys; ch. ts. Cluj, Brasov.

Transylvanian Alps, range of mtns., **Romania**.

Trapani, t., cap. of T. prov. W. Sicily, **Italy**; spt. on promontory, sheltering natural harbour; exp. wine, pasta, tuna fish caught locally; p. (1981) 71,927.

Traralgon, t., Victoria, **Australia**; industl. growth based on Yallourn brown coal; tourism; p. (1986) 19,233.

Trasimeno, L., Umbria, central **Italy**; occupies lge. extinct volcanic crater; drained S. to R. Tiber; a. c. 155 km².

Tras-os-Montes e Alto-Douro, prov., N. **Portugal**; high, bleak plateau, cultivated valleys; climate cold except in S.; port wine cty. of Douro R.; remote, sparsely populated; a. 11,834 km²; p. (1960) 667,054.

Trawsfynydd, Gwynedd, **Wales**; within N. Wales Nat. Park; nuclear power sta.

Trebizond. See **Trabzon**.

Tredegar, t., Blaenau Gwent, Gwent, **Wales**; in narrow valley 5 km W. of Ebbw Vale; engin.; home of Aneurin Bevan; p. (1981) 16,446.

Treforest, t., Mid Glamorgan, **Wales**; on R. Taff; lge. trading estate established in 1930s to alleviate unemployment in primary inds. of S. Wales; aircraft accessories, electronics, chemical, pharmaceutical, rayon, metal wks.

Trelleborg, spt., S. **Sweden**; on Baltic Sea; most impt. rubber factory in cty.; p. (1983) 34,146.

Trengganu, st., **Malaysia**; N.E. Malaya; rice, rubber, coconuts; tin, iron; cap. Kuala Trengganu; a. 13,080 km²; p. (1980) 540,627.

Trent, R., **Eng.**; rises in N. Staffs, flows round S. Pennines and joins the Ouse to form estuary of the Humber; many power stas. along its banks; polluted waterway, especially between Humber and Nottingham; 240 km long.

Trentino-Alto Adige, aut. region, N.E. **Italy**, between Austrian and Swiss Frontiers and L. Garda; embraces provs. Trento and Bolzano; cap. Trento; formerly called Venetia Tridentina; a. 13,598 km²; p. (est. 1986) 880,000.

Trento, t., cap. of Trento prov. and ch. t. of Trentino-Alto Adige, N. **Italy**; on R. Adige and route to Brenner Pass; chemicals, cement, elec. engin.; picturesque t.; cath.; p. (1981) 99,179.

Trenton, c., cap. N.J. st., **USA**; on Delaware R.; transport and industl. ctr.; noted for its wire-rope and pottery inds., established mid-19th cent.; crockery, machin., metal and rubber gds.; p. (1980) 92,124 (c.), 307,863 (met. a.).

Tres Arroyos, t., E. **Argentina**; agr. and livestock ctr.; p. (1960) 40,000.

Trèves. See **Trier**.

Treviso, c., cap. of T. prov., Venetia, N.E. **Italy**; on R. Sile; agr. ctr. on fertile Venetian plain; silk mills, paper, furniture, fertilisers, pottery; p. (1981) 87,696.

Trichinopoly. See **Tiruchirapalli**.

Trichur, t., Kerala, **India**; comm. and educational ctr.; p. (1981) 77,923 (t.), 170,122 (met. a.).

Trier (**Trèves**), c., Rhineland-Palatinate, **W. Germany**; on R. Moselle; Roman origin. (Augusta Trevorum, the Rome of the North), cath., Porta Nigra; ctr. of Moselle wine reg.; textiles, leather goods; birthplace of Marx; p. (est. 1986) 93,100.

Trieste, spt., cap. of T. prov., Friuli-Venezia Giulia, N.E. **Italy**; shipbldg., fishing, oil refining; pipeline to Schwechat, nr. Vienna; cath., cas., Roman antiquities; univ.; p. (1984) 246,305.

Trieste Free Territory, former free st. on the Adriatic; constituted by Peace Treaty with Italy, 1947, as compromise between conflicting Yugoslav and Italian claims; a. 743 km²; Zone A handed over to Italy, Zone B to Yugoslavia 1954. Yugoslav/Italian agreement 1975 settled border dispute and established free industl. zone on both sides of border in region of Sezana-Fernetti.

Trikkala, t., cap. of T. dep., W. Thessaly, N. **Greece**; mkt. t. for pastoral prods.; damaged by earthquake 1954; p. (1981) 45,160.

Trim, co. t., U.D., Meath, **R.o.I.**; mkt. t. on R. Boyne; anc. seat of Irish Parliament; p. (1966) 1,467.

Trincomalee, t., N.E. cst. **Sri Lanka**; excellent natural harbour; formerly a British naval base; p. (1981) 44,913.

Tring, mkt. t., Dacorum, Herts., **Eng.**; in gap through Chiltern hills, 14 km N.W. of Hemel Hempstead; p. (1981) 10,683.

Trinidad, t., cap. of Beni dep., **Bolivia**; exp. beef by air, but development hampered by isolation; p. (1976) 27,487.

Trinidad, I., **W.I.**; N. of Venezuela; climate warm and humid; oil, natural gas, asphalt, sugar, rum, coconut oil, molasses, citrus fruits; tourism; cap. Port of Spain; a. 4,828 km². See **Trinidad and Tobago**.

Trinidad, t., central **Cuba**; picturesque old t. of colonial period declared a national monument; p. (est. 1967) 57,840.

Trinidad and Tobago, indep. st. within Commonwealth (1962), rep. (1976), **W.I.**; main exps. crude oil and petroleum prods. which with natural asphalt represent over 20 per cent national income; lge. offshore gas reserves; oil refining; tropical crops and food processing; sugar, molasses, rum, fruits, textiles; cap. and major spt. Port of Spain; internal self-gov. sought by Tobago; a. 5,128 km²; p. (est. 1987) 1,220,000.

Trinity, R., Texas, **USA**; flows S.E. to Galveston Bay; used for reservoirs; valley contains lge. p. and much economic activity; 800 km long.

Trino, Piedmont, N. **Italy**; 18 km S.S.W. of Vercelli; nuclear power sta.; p. (1981) 9,067.

Tripoli, c., **Lebanon**; spt. on Mediterranean; admin. ctr. for N. Lebanon; terminus of oil pipeline from Iraq; oil refining; exp. agr. prods.; p. (est. 1980) 175,000.

Tripoli, c., joint cap. of **Libya** (with Benghazi), on Mediterranean; stands on edge of palm-oasis, site of anc. Oea; tourist, comm. and mnf. ctr.; gd. harbour; p. (1981) 858,000.

Tripura, st. **India**; N.E. Ganges delta, bordering Assam and Bangladesh; cap. Agartala; rice, jute, cotton, sugar-cane; a. 10,360 km²; p. (est. 1981) 2,053,058.

Tristan da Cunha, sm. gr. S. Is., S. **Atl. Oc.**; dependency of Brit. col. (t. Helena; ch. I. Tristan; evacuated 1961 volcanic eruption) but resettled 1963; weather sta. (Gough I.); a. 117 km²; p. (1984) 315.

Trivandrum, c., cap. of Kerala st., S.W. **India**; pt. on Arabian Sea; textiles coconut processing; univ.; p. (1981) 483,086 (c.), 520,125 (met. a.).

Trnava, c., W. Slovakia, **ČSSR**; mkt. t. in fertile agr. region on Váh R.; food processing, steel wks.; cath., monasteries, called "little Rome"; p. (est. 1986) 70,000.

Trnovo or **Tirnovo**, c., **Bulgaria**; on Jantra R.; food processing, textiles, leather; anc. cap. of Bulgaria; p. (est. 1970) 42,344.

Trogir, t., S. Croatia, **Yugoslavia**; sm. pt. and seaside resort, partly sited on I. of Čiovo; mediaeval bldgs., inc. cath., palaces; p. c. 20,000.

Trois Rivières, t., Quebec, **Canada**; industl. ctr. on St. Lawrence R.; noted for newsprint; hydroelectric power from St. Maurice R.; p. (1986) 50,122 (c.), 128,888 (met. a.).

Trojmiasto (Tri-City), **Poland**; name given to the three municipalities of Gdansk, Gdynia, and Sopot, a loosely-knit conurb.

Trollhättan, t., S.W. **Sweden**; on Göta R., nr. T. falls which generate power for metallurgical and chemical inds.; car and aircraft com- ponents; p. (est. 1986) 49,000.

Trombay, I., off Bombay, **India**; oil refining; atomic reactor; uranium processing and nuclear waste reprocessing plant; zirconium metal produced; fertilisers.

Troms, co., N. **Norway**; deep fjords, offshore Is.; fishing, livestock, boat-bldg.; cap. Tromsö; a. 25,916 km²; p. (1983) 147,690.

Tromsö, t., cap. of Troms prov., N. **Norway**; spt. on sm. I. of T. in Norwegian Sea; arctic fishing, sealing; fish processing; p. (est. 1987) 49,000.

Trondheim, c., spt., **Norway**; on W. cst. on S. side of T. fjord; shipbldg., engin.; exp. timber and wood-pulp, butter, fish, copper; anc. cath., burial place of early Norwegian kings and place of coronation of recent sovereigns; p. (est.1987) 134,496.

Troon, burgh, Kyle and Carrick, **Scot.**; on F. of Clyde, 10 km N. of Ayr; gd. harbour and grav- ing docks; shipbldg.; hosiery; seawater distil- lation research ctr. project; resort; p. (1981) 14,254.

Troppau. *See* **Opava.**

Trossachs, Stirling, **Scot.**; picturesque wooded glen; tourist resort.

Troste, nr. Llanelly, **Wales**; steel strip mill, tin plate.

Trouville, t., Calvados dep., N. **France**; popular seaside resort and fishing pt. on Normandy cst.; p. (1982) 6,012.

Trowbridge, mkt. t., West Wilts., **Eng.**; cloth wks., bacon curing, dairying, engin.; p. (1981) 22,984.

Troy, c., N.Y., **USA**; at confluence of Rs. Hudson and Mohawk; gr. shirt-mftg. ctr.; p. (1980) 56,638.

Troyes, c., cap. of Aube dep., N.E. **France**; on R. Seine; once cap. of Champagne; hosiery, textile machin., food processing; magnificent cath.; site of mediaeval fairs which standard- ised Troy weight; p. (1982) 64,769.

Trucial States. *See* **United Arab Emirates.**

Trujillo, c., N.W. **Peru**; comm. and mkt. ctr. for irrigated agr. region, on Moche R., in foothills of Andes; sugar, cocaine; univ., cath.; p. (est. 1985) 421,000.

Trujillo, t., cap. of T. st., W. **Venezuela**; on Transandean highway at 805 m; agr. mkt. for region producing coffee, cacao, tobacco, maize; p. (est. 1985) 421,000.

Truro, t., Nova Scotia, **Canada**; on Salmon R.; hosiery, lumber mills, printing, metallurgy, machin.; p. (1981) 39,751.

Truro, c., Carrick, Cornwall, **Eng.**; at confluence of Rs. Kenwyn and Allen; mkt. t. and former sm. pt.; admin. ctr. of Cornwall; cath.; p. (1981) 16,277.

Tsaidam. *See* **Qaidam.**

Tsamkong. *See* **Zhanjiang.**

Tsangpo. *See* **Zangbo.**

Tschenstokov. *See* **Czestochowa.**

Tselinograd, c., Kazakh SSR, **USSR**; cap. Virgin Lands terr.; on Ishim R., nr. Karaganda coalfield; chemicals, agr. machin.; p. (1985) 262,000.

Tsinan. *See* **Jinan.**

Tsinghai. *See* **Qinghai.**

Tsinling Shan. *See* **Hua Shan.**

Tsingtao. *See* **Qingdao.**

Tsitsihar. *see* **Qiqihar.**

Tskhinvali, c., N. Georgian SSR, **USSR**; elec. prods., lumber mills, fruit canning; p. (1970) 30,000.

Tsu, t., Honshu, **Japan**; textiles; p. (1985) 150,692.

Tsugaru Strait, **Japan**; separates Is. Hokkaido and Honshu; links Sea of Japan with Pac. Oc.; 72 km long, 24–32 km wide.

Tsuruga, spt., **Japan**; on W. cst. Honshu; rayon textiles, cotton, atomic power plant; p. (1970) 56,445.

Tuam, mkt. t., R.D., Galway, **R.o.I.**; sugar refining; p. (1981) 4,366 (t.).

Tuamotu, coral archipelago, Fr. Polynesia, S. **Pac. Oc.**; pearl fisheries; p. of gr. (est. 1983) 11,793.

Tuapse, c., S. Krasnodar terr., **RSFSR**; at foot of Caucasus on Black Sea; major petroleum pt. at W. end of pipeline from Baku and Makhachkala; oil refineries; p. (est. 1967) 49,000.

Tubarao, t., Santa Catarina st., S. **Brazil**; on E. cst., 280 km N.W. of Pôrto Alegre; coal mines; p. (est. 1968) 59,210.

Tübingen, t., Baden-Württemberg, **W. Germany**; on R. Neckar; 15th cent. univ., cas.; mediaeval c. ctr.; birthplace of Hölderlin; p. (est. 1986) 76,200.

Tubuai, archipelago, Fr. Polynesia. S. **Pac. Oc.**; a. 163 km²; p. (1977) 5,208.

Tucson, c., S.E. Arizona, **USA**; mkt. and dis- tribution ctr. on Santa Cruz R.; cultural ctr. and winter resort based on Spanish heritage and warm dry climate; food processing, missile components; p. (1984) 365,400 (c.), 594,800 (met. a.).

Tucumán. *See* **San Miguel de Tucumán.**

Tudela, t., Navarre, N. **Spain**; mkt. ctr. for fertile fruit-growing dist. and I. of La Majana in Ebro R.; fine cath., Roman bridge; p. (1981) 24,629.

Tula, c., cap. of T. oblast, **RSFSR**; mnf. ctr. in Moscow industl. region; local iron and lignite mng.; Yasnaya Polyana, home of Tolstoy, nearby; p. (1986) 534,000.

Tulare, L., S. Cal., **USA**; ctr. of inland drainage 64 km S. of Fresno; streams feeding it used for irrigation; in drought years L. dries up com- pletely; a. 233 km².

Tullamore, mkt. t., U.D., Offaly, **R.o.I.**; on Grand Canal; farming, distilling, brewing; p. (1981) 7,901.

Tulle-sur-Mer, t., cap. of Corrèze dep., **France**; firearms, textiles; p. (1982) 20,642.

Tulsa, c., Okla., **USA**; impt. oil ctr., based on lge. local deposits; machin., aeroplanes; well laid out with many parks; p. (1984) 374,500 (c.), 725,600 (met. a.).

Tumaco, t., S.W. **Colombia**; spt. on Pac. Oc., on sm. I. off cst.; exp. agr. prods.; climate hot and humid; p. (est. 1968) 80,279.

Tummel, R., Perth and Kinross, **Scot.**; trib. of R. Tay; used by Perth to Inverness rly. as S. approach to Drumocheter Pass; hydroelec. scheme nr. Pitlochry; 88 km long.

Tunbridge Wells (officially **Royal Tunbridge Wells**), t., l. gov. dist., Kent, **Eng.**; on border of East Sussex; chalybeate waters; attractive 17th cent. promenade known as "The Pan- tiles"; p. (est. 1988) 99,300 (dist.).

Tunghwa. *See* **Tonghua.**

Tung Ting Hu. *See* **Dong Ting.**

Tunguska, Upper, Stony and Lower, Rs., Siberia, **USSR**; all rise in Sayan mtns. nr. L. Baykal and flow N.W. through forested cty. into R. Yenisey.

Tunguska Basin, coalfield between Yenisey and Lena Rs., **RSFSR**; main is., Norilsk, Igarka, Yeni- seysk.

Tunis, c., cap. of **Tunisia**, N. Africa; spt. on inlet of Mediterranean; exp. raw materials; base for fishing fleets; univ., notable mosques; tourist ctr.; ruins of anc. Carthage to N.E.; p. (1984) 596,654.

Tunisia, indep. st., N. **Africa**; bounded by Algeria on W., by Libya on E., indented Mediterranean cst.; Atlas mtns. penetrate into N.; temperate cst. climate, hot and dry in S. desert; agr. and mng. basis of economy; wheat, olive oil, wine, fruits, limited to wetter coastal areas and irrigated valleys; phosphates around Ghafsa; iron ore and land in N.W.; steelwks. at Menzel Bourguiba; chemical and paper inds. based on local phosphates; economy hit by fall in world oil prices and lower remittances from Tunisians working abroad (immigration controls in France); cap. Tunis; a. 164,108 km²; p. (est. 1987) 7·6 m.

Tunja, c., cap. of Boyacá dep., **Colombia**; route and agr. tr. ctr.; p. (1985) 95,503.

Turda, t., Transylvania, **Romania**; local salt

mines and quarrying aid chemical and ceramic inds.; p. (1983) 59,695.

Turfan, depression, E. Xinjiang prov., **China**; on S. slopes of Tien Shan mtns.; desert a. irrigated by wells and canals for animal husbandry, fruit, cotton, grain; 275 m below sea level; ch. t. Turfan; archaeological finds.

Turgutlu (Kassaba), t., Manisa prov., **Turkey**; 48 km E.N.E. of Izmir; lignite, cotton, melons; p. (1985) 65,740.

Turin or **Torino**, c., cap. of T. prov., N. **Italy**; on R. Po at confluence with the Dora Riparia; former cap. of Piedmont and kingdom of Sardinia; univ., cath., many historic monuments; headquarters of Italian motor ind.; clothing, machin., furniture, chemicals; oil refinery nearby; p. (1984) 1,069,013.

Turkana, L. See **Rudolf, L.**

Turkestan E., terr. included in Xinjiang, **China**; separated from W. or former Russian Turkestan by Pamir plateau; mainly desert.

Turkestan W., terr. of **USSR**; inc. Turkmen SSR, Uzbek SSR, Tadzhik SSR, Kirghiz SSR, and part of Kazakh SSR.

Turkey, rep., S.W. **Asia** and E. **Europe**; occupies mtnous. Anatolian penin.; equable climate on coastal margins, continental severity in interior; economy predominantly agr. but hampered by poor land resources; grain grown on Anatolian plateau and a Mediterranean variety of crops around cst.; noted for tobacco; industl. development based on mng. resources and oil in S.E.; lge cities in W. act as magnet for the poorer areas of E.; 30 percent of p. in 5 cities; many migrate to Europe & Middle East as migrant workers; cap. Ankara; a. 814,578 km²; p. (1985) 50,664,000.

Turkmen (Turkmenistan), **SSR**, constituent rep., **USSR**; borders on Afghanistan, Iran, and the Caspian Sea; much of a. in Kara-Kum desert; agr. based on irrigation; fruit, cotton, wool; sulphates, petroleum; p. concentrated in oases and industl. ctrs. of cap. Ashkhabad, Mary-Chadzhou, along Trans-Caspian rly.; a. 491,072 km²; p. (1986) 3,271,000.

Turks and Caicos, Is., Caribbean Sea, **W.I.**; about 30 sm. Is., geographically S.E. continuation of Bahamas; dry climate, poor limestone soil; exp. salt, crawfish; cap. Grand Turk; a. 430 km²; p. (est. 1985) 8,000.

Turku (Abo), spt., S.W. **Finland**; on Baltic Sea; ctr. of fertile agr. a.; exp. agr. prods.; industl. ctr.; shipbldg., steel, machin., textiles; Finnish and Swedish univs.; p. (1986) 161,188.

Turnhout, t., N.E. **Belgium**, nr. Antwerp, on Campine canal; textiles, lace, printing; p. (est. 1983) 37,567.

Turnu Severin, c., S.W. **Romania**; R. pt. on Danube below Iron Gate cataracts; grain, salt, petroleum tr., shipbldg.; p. (1985) 97,862.

Tuscaloosa, c., Ala., **USA**; on Black Warrior R.; rly. and industl. ctr. based on local coal, iron, cotton, timber; univ.; p. (1984) 73,200 (c.), 138,900 (met. a.).

Tuscany, region, central **Italy**; inc. provs. Arezzo, Firenze, Livorno, Siena, Grosseto, Lucca, Pisa, Massa and Carrara, Pistoia; mainly mtnous., drained by Arno R. system; wines, olive oil, cereals; iron ore from Elba, marble from Apuan Alps around Carrara; pt. at Livorno (Leghorn); cap. Firenze (Florence); a. 22,989 km²; p. (est. 1986) 3·6 m.

Tuticorin, t., Tamil Nadu, S.E. **India**; on G. of Manaar; fertiliser plant; declining cotton and tea pt.; heavy water plant; p. (1981) 192,949 (t.), 250,677 (met. a.).

Tuttlingen, t., Baden-Württemberg, **W. Germany**; on R. Danube; surgical instruments; footwear; p. (est. 1986) 30,800.

Tuva ASSR, **RSFSR**; bounded by Siberia and Mongolia; mtn. basin, forested; timber inds., coal mng., asbestos, pastoral agr.; cap. Kyzyl; a. c. 165,800 km²; p. (1986) 282,000.

Tuvalu Is., formerly Ellice Is., until 1975 part of Gilbert and Ellice Is., W. **Pac. Oc.**; indep. (1979); p. mainly Polynesian; cap. Funafuti; coconut cultivation in high temps on poor coral soils; exp. copra; a. 25 km²; p. (1985) 8,229.

Tuxtla Gutiérrez, c., cap. of Chiapas st., **Mexico**; in fertile valley at 450 m; ctr. for sisal, tobacco, coffee, cattle; on Inter-American Highway; Mayan ruins nearby; p. (1980) 166,476.

Tuz, L., **Turkey**; salt L.; a. 1,619 km² in winter much reduced in summer.

Tuzla, t., Bosnia-Hercegovina, **Yugoslavia**; salt, lignite, coal; hydroelectric power in a.; agr. mkt. ctr.; textiles; p. (1981) 121,717.

Tweed, R., S.E. **Scot.**; rises in Tweeddale, and reaches sea at Berwick; salmon fisheries; length 155 km.

Tweeddale, l. gov. dist., Borders reg., **Scot.**; based on upper Tweed valley around Peebles; p. (est. 1986) 14,608.

Twelve Pins, star-shaped mtn. range, Galway, **R.o.I.**; Benbaum, 730 m.

Twickenham. See **Richmond-upon-Thames.**

Tychy, t., Katowice prov., **Poland**; on edge of Upper Silesian industl. a.; surrounded by forest; brewing; p. (est. 1985) 182,000.

Tyler, c., Texas, **USA**; oil ctr. on E. Texan field; agr. ctr. for local mkt. gardening; famous for rose growing; p. (1984) 73,000 (c.), 144,600 (met.a.).

Tyne, R., Tyne and Wear, Durham and Northumberland, **Eng.**; formed by confluence of N. Tyne and S. Tyne at Hexham; flows E. to sea at Tynemouth and S. Shields; valley gives easy route across mtns. from Newcastle to Carlisle; lower course forms harbour (with shipbldg. and other wks.) from Newcastle to Tynemouth; road tunnel between Wallsend and Jarrow; 128 km long.

Tynedale, l. gov. dist., W. Northumberland, **Eng.**; lge. inland a. inc. Haltwistle, Hexham and Prudoe; p. (est. 1988) 56,300.

Tynemouth, t., North Tyneside, Tyne and Wear, **Eng.**; pt. on N. bank of Tyne R.; ruined priory and cas.; residtl., resort; p. (1981) 60,022.

Tyne and Wear,former met. co., N.E. **Eng.**; mainly industl. a. around lower T. and W. Rs.; inc. Newcastle-upon-Tyne, Tynemouth, Gateshead, South Shields and Sunderland; traditionally ass. with shipbldg. and coal mng., but inds. incr. diversified; p. (est. 1988) 1,130,500.

Tyneside, North, met. dist., Tyne and Wear, **Eng.**; comprises Tynemouth, Whitley Bay and Wallsend; p. (est. 1988) 192,900.

Tyneside, South, met. dist., Tyne and Wear, **Eng.**; comprises Jarrow, Hebburn and South Shields; p. (est. 1988) 155,700.

Tyre (Sur), **Lebanon**; anc. Phoenician c. and spt., founded c. 15th cent. B.C.; now sm. comm. t., tr. in cotton, tobacco; p. (est. 1980) 14,000.

Tyrol, Alpine region, **Europe**; falls within Austria and Italy, linked by Brenner Pass; embraces highest peaks of Austrian Alps, culminating in Ortler Spitz; two-fifths forest, timber inds.; mtn. pasture; tourism; Austrian prov. of Tyrol; cap. Innsbruck; a. 12,650 km²; p. (est. 1986) 606,000.

Tyrone, former co., N. **Ireland**; now replaced by Strabane, Omagh, Dungannon and Cookstown l. gov. dists.

Tyrrhenian Sea, part of Mediterranean between Italy and Corsica, Sardinia and Sicily.

Tyumen, c., **RSFSR**; one of oldest Siberian ts., rly. ctr. on Trans-Siberian rly., R. pt. on Tura R.; many heavy inds.; ctr. of oil and natural gas region; p. (1985) 425,000.

Tywyn, mkt. t., Meirionnydd, Gwynedd, **Wales**; on cst. of Cardigan Bay, 5 km N.W. of Aberdovey; major floods 1990; p. (1981) 4,551.

Tzekung. See **Zigong.**

Tzepo. See **Zibo.**

U

Ubangi, major R., **Central Africa**; trib. of R. Zaïre, rises on bdr. of Central Africa Emp. and Zaïre flows W. and S. to join Zaïre R. at Irebu; partially navigable; 2,240 km long.

Ube, spt., S. Honshu, **Japan**; coal mng. and industl. ctr.; machin., synthetic petroleum; p. (1985) 174,854.

Ubeda, t., Jaén prov., **Spain**; on plateau between Guadalquivir and Guadalimar; food processing, olive oil, soap; p. (1981) 27,441.

Uberaba, t., Minas Gerais, **Brazil**; ctr. of cattle rearing and arable agr. region; sugar milling, mnfs. lime; p. (est. 1985) 245,900.

Ucayali, R., **Peru**; headstream of R. Amazon; over 2,240 km long, navigable for 1,600 km.

Uckfield, mkt. t., East Sussex, **Eng.**; 13 km N.E.

of Lewes; a. ctr. of former Sussex iron ind.
Udaipur, c., Rajasthan, N.W. **India;** in picturesque valley at 760 m a.s.l.; cap. of former princely st. of U.; maharajah's palace; p. (1981) 232,588.
Uddevalla, spt., S. **Sweden;** N. Göteborg; former shipyds., prefab. houses, timber, granite quarrying, textiles; p. (est. 1986) 46,000.
Udi, t., S. **Nigeria,** W. Africa; 160 km N. of Pt. Harcourt; impt. mng. ctr. on Enugu coalfield; linked by rail to Kaduna and Pt. Harcourt.
Udine, c., cap. of U. prov., Friuli-Venezia Giulia, N.E. **Italy;** between Alps and G. of Venice; route and industl. ctr. in agr. region; textiles, chemicals, engin., leather, woodwork; cath., many attractive bldgs., piazzas; severe earthquakes (1976); p. (1984) 101,179.
Udmurt ASSR, RSFSR; part of Urals industl. a.; two-fifths forested; timber inds.; arable agr.; flax; steel inds. at cap. Izhevsk, Votkinsk, Sarapul; p. (1986) 1,572,000.
Udokan Khrebet, mtns., **RSFSR;** world's lgst. reserve of copper.
Ufa, c., cap. of Bashkir ASSR, **RSFSR;** in Urals industl. a., at confluence of Rs. Belaya and Ufa; p. (1986) 1,077,000.
Uganda, rep., E. **Africa;** dictatorship overthrown (1979); 4 regs. established for economic devel.; equatorial cty., climate modified by alt.; forms part of E. African plateau (1,200 m); well-developed economy; coffee, tea, tobacco, cotton for exp.; developing pastoral economy, fishing on L. Victoria; copper at Kilembe, tin; hydroelectric power from Owen Falls, second project at Kabelega Falls; electricity exp. to Kenya; savannah areas contain abundant wildlife in Nat. Parks and Game Reserves; cap. Kampala; a. 235,887 km²; p. (est. 1987) 16,789,000.
Uist, N. and S., Is., Outer Hebrides, N.W. **Scot.;** indented csts.; N. Uist boggy in E., hilly in W.; S. Uist smaller but mtnous.; crofting, fishing; p. (1971) 1,726 (N.), 3,872 (S.).
Uitenhage, t., Cape prov., **S. Africa;** fruit, wool, rly. wks., tyres, car assembly, textiles; summer resort; p. (1970) 69,048.
Ujiji, t., in sm. terr. same name (a. 2,383 km²) on E. shore L. Tanganyika, **Tanzania;** where Stanley found Livingstone 1871; p. c. 14,000.
Ujiyamada. *See* Ise.
Ujjain, t., Madhya Pradesh, **India;** sacred c. and formerly cap. of Malwa; univ.; p. (1981) 282,203.
Ujpest, industl. sub., Budapest, **Hungary;** elec. engin., leather, shoes, textiles, furniture, pharmaceuticals; p. 76,000.
Ujung Pandang (Makasar), c., Sulawesi, **Indonesia;** in dist. of rich volcanic soils; major spt. and airpt., entrepot tr.; p. (est. 1983) 888,000.
Ukhta t., **RSFSR;** ctr. of natural gas field in Pechora Basin; p. (est. 1969) 57,000.
Ukrainian SSR, constituent rep., **USSR;** in Eastern Europe; of dominating importance in Soviet economy; drained by Rs. Dnieper Dniester, S. Bug, Donets; Pripet Marshes in N., wooded steppes in ctr., fertile black-earth a. in S.; major wheat-growing a. of Europe; highly mineralised, many industl. raw materials and ctrs. of metallurgical and heavy inds.; cap. Kiev; a. 582,750 km²; p. (1986) 50,973,000.
Ulan Bator, c., cap. of **Mongolian People's Rep.;** in stock-raising region; industl. ctr. of cty.; woollen gds., saddles, knitwear; new indust. ctr. at Darkhan nearby; rly. link to China and USSR; contains one-quarter of p. of rep.; p. (est. 1984) 479,500.
Ulan-Ude (Verkhneudinsk), t., Siberia, **RSFSR;** major route and mnf. ctr.; pt. on R. Ude, junc. on Trans-Siberian rly., linked by rail to Peking; engin., textiles, glass, leather; p. (1985) 335,000.
Ullapool, v., Ross and Cromarty, **Scot.;** fish. pt. (herring landings), on L. Broom, 72 km N.W. of Inverness; landed more fish in 1981 than any other British pt.; attractive mtn. and cst. scenery in a.; p. (1981) 1,142.
Ullswater, L., Cumbria, **Eng.;** 13 km long; supplies water to Manchester; attractive tourist a.
Ulm, c., Baden-Württemberg, **W. Germany;** route ctr. at limit of barge navigation on Danube, although navigable limits being extended by canalisation; food-processing, metal gds., textiles, cement; p. (est. 1986) 100,700.
Ulsan, t., **South Korea;** oil refining, fertilisers;

nuclear power sta. (1983) built to reduce oil imports; p. (1980) 418,415.
Ulster. *See* **Northern Ireland.**
Ulúa-Chamelhcón, R. basin, N. cst. **Honduras;** major banana region of Central American cst.
Ulva, I., Argyll and Bute, **Scot.;** off W. cst. of Mull; 8 km long.
Ulverston, mkt. t., South Lakeland, Cumbria, **Eng.;** nr. Morecambe Bay; antibiotics, elec. gds., tanning; p. (1981) 11,963.
Ul'yanovsk (Simbirsk), c., cap. of U. oblast, **RSFSR;** industl. ctr. of middle Volga region; birthplace of Lenin whose real name was **Ulyanov;** p. (1986) 567,000.
Uman, c., Ukrainian SSR, **USSR;** at confluence of Kamenka and Umanka Rs.; rly. junc.; agr.-processing; p. (est. 1969) 64,000.
Umanak, t., W. **Greenland;** hunting and fishing base on arm of Baffin Sea; marble mng.; p. (est. 1968) 2,348.
Umbria, region, central **Italy;** comprising provs. of Perugia and Terni, crossed by Apennines and upper Tiber; agr. mainstay of economy; inds. based on hydroelectric power at Terni; chemicals; developing tourist tr.; cap. Perugia; a. 8,472 km²; p. (est. 1986) 818,000.
Ume, R., **Sweden;** flows S.E. to the G. of Bothnia; length 400 km.
Umeå, c., cap. of Västerbotten prov., N.E. **Sweden;** on G. of Bothnia at mouth of Ume R.; cultural ctr.; woodpulp; p. (est. 1986) 86,000.
Umm-al-Quaywayn, emirate, member of **United Arab Emirates;** p. (1985) 29,229.
Umm Qasr, t., **Kuwait;** on Iraq border; new deepwater port planned.
Umtali (Mutare), t., **Zimbabwe;** comm. ctr. for rich agr. a.; oil refinery at Feruka; pipeline to Beira; paper milling, food processing, vehicle assembly; p. (1982) 69,600.
Umtata, t., Cape Prov., **S. Africa;** admin. ctr. for Transkei terrs.; cath.; p. (1976) 24,805.
Uncia, t., Oruro dep., **Bolivia;** alt. 3,900 m in E. Cordillera of Andes, 96 km S.E. of Oruro; site of impt. Patino tin mines.
Ungava Bay, arm of Hudson Strait, projecting into Labrador, N.E. **Canada;** minerals abundant, recent exploitation of impt. medium and low-grade iron deposits.
Union of South Africa. *See* **South Africa, Rep. of.**
Union of Soviet Socialist Republics (USSR), E. **Europe,** N. **Asia;** major world economic and political power; ctr. of European communist bloc; extends over 9,600 km W.-E., 4,800 km N.-S.; continental climate with marked regional variations; comprises 1 fed. rep. and 14 constituent reps.; centrally planned economy emphasising development of heavy inds. at major sources of natural resources, and development of new resources in E.; timber inds. and textiles impt. with more recent developments in consumer inds.; recent slowing of economic growth; lge.-scale, mechanised agr. with planned prod. reflecting regional variations in physical conditions; transport emphasis on rlys. to open up remote E. regions, but more recent road bldg. programme; recent reforms aim to liberalise economy and politics a little; 27 major pts. inc. Leningrad, Arkhangelsk, Riga, Murmansk, Odessa, Baku, Vladivostok; cap. Moscow; a. 22,272,290 km²; p. (est. 1988) 284,500,000 (3rd. lgst. p. of any cty.).
United Arab Emirates (Trucial Sts.), indep. sov. st. on Persian G., S.W. **Asia;** formed (1971) from Trucial Sts. (Abū Dhabi, Ajmān, Dubai, Al Fujayrah, Ra's al Khaymah, Shārjah, Umm-al-Quaywayn) after withdrawal of Brit. forces and termination of special defence treaty (1820-1971); p. immigration from Middle and Far East as oil-based economic growth proceeds, esp. in Abu Dhabi; a. 82,880 km²; p. (est. 1986) 1,770,000 (65 per cent non national).
United Kingdom, cty., N.W. **Europe;** separated from continent of Europe by English Channel; consists of Gr. Britain (Eng., Wales, Scot.) and N. Ireland; a. 244,022 km²; p. (est. 1985) 56,125,000.
United States of America, fed. rep., N. **America;** world's major economic power and one of the 2 political "super powers"; variety of climatic and physical conditions (*see* **N. America**); economically self-supporting, but imports petroleum, coffee, machin., textiles; extremely diversified mnfs.; exp. capital goods, industl. supplies, vehicles and food; consists of 50

sts. and Dist. of Columbia, co-extensive with cap. of Washington; outlying dependencies inc. Puerto Rico, U.S. Virgin Is., Panama Canal Zone, Guam, American Samoa, Trust Terr. of the Pac. Is.; assertive foreign policy; a. 9,363,169 km²; p. (1986) 241,489,000.

Unst, I., Shetlands, **Scot.**; most N. of gr.; length 20 km; p. (1971) 1,127.

Unterwalden, can., **Switzerland**; divided into Obwalden and Nidwalden; dairying, fruit and livestock; cap. Stans; a. 767 km²; p. (est. 1986) 58,000.

Upernavik, t., W. **Greenland**; on sm. I. in Baffin Bay; sealing and whaling base; meteorological sta.; p. (est. 1968) 1,930.

Upper Austria, prov., **Austria**; borders on W. Germany and CSSR; hilly and forested; drained by Danube R. system; inc. Salzkammergut resort a.; agr., forestry; inds. centred on Linz (cap.), Steyr and Wels; a. 11,979 km²; p. (est. 1986) 1·29 m.

Upper Hutt, c., N.I., **N.Z.**; shares rapid industl. growth of Hutt Valley; p. (est. 1987) 31,000.

Upper Volta. *See* **Bourkina Fasso.**

Uppingham, mkt. t., Leics., **Eng.**; 16th cent. school.

Uppsala, c., cap. of U. prov., **Sweden**; on R. Sala, 72 km from Stockholm; historic ctr. of anc. Sweden; cultural ctr., famous univ. (Linnaeus taught there); cath.; lt. inds.; p. (est. 1986) 158,000.

Ur, anc. Chaldean c., **Iraq**; 208 km W.N.W. of Basra; ruins; flourished about 3,000 B.C.

Ural, R., **RSFSR**; flows S.W. and S. to Caspian Sea; used for domestic and industl. water supply; navigable; 2,400 km long.

Ural Mts., **USSR**; mtn. system, forms bdy. between Europe and Asia and separates Russian plain from W. Siberian lowlands; extends N.-S. for 2,400 km; highest peaks Narodnaya and Telpos-Iz; rich mineral resources have given rise to huge ctrs. of heavy ind., inc. Sverdlovsk, Chelyabinsk, Magnitogorsk.

Uralsk, N.W., Kasakh SSR; **USSR**; on R. Ural; grain-trading and cattle-mart ctr.; flour, leather, woollens, iron-ware; p. (1985) 192,000.

Uranium City, N. Saskatchewan, **Canada**; nr. N. shore of L. Athabasca, ctr. of Beaverlodge uranium-mng. a.; founded 1951; p. (1981) 2,748.

Urawa, t., Honshu, **Japan**; sub. of Tokyo; p. (1985) 377,233.

Urbino, t., in the Marches, central **Italy**; agr. mkt. and route ctr.; picturesque tourist ctr.; cath., univ., palace; p. with Pesaro (1981) 15,918.

Ure, R., North Yorks., **Eng.**; flows E. and S.E. to the Swale to form the Ouse; upper part of valley known as Wensleydale; 80 km long.

Urengoy, dist., Siberia, **USSR**; lge. natural gas field with 5,400 km. pipeline to W. Europe.

Urfa, t., **Turkey**; nr. Syrian bdr.; handicrafts, local agr. tr.; p. (1980) 147,488.

Urgench, t., cap. of Khorezm oblast, W. Uzbek SSR, **USSR**; pt. on Amu Dar'ya R. in Khiva oasis; cotton, food-processing; p. (1985) 116,000.

Uri, can., **Switzerland**; S. of L. of Lucerne; forest and mtns.; traversed by St. Gotthard rly. and R. Reuss; sparse p., German speaking; cap. Altdorf; a. 1,075 km²; p. (est. 1986) 133,500.

Urmia, L., nr. Tabriz, N.W. **Iran**; 136 km by 48 km; salt and shallow; no outlet.

Urmston, Trafford, Gtr. Manchester, **Eng.**; residtl. sub. of Manchester; inc. part of Trafford Park industl. estate; p. (1981) 44,009.

Uruapan, t., Michoacán, W. **Mexico**; mkt. ctr. for semi-tropical mtnous. a.; famous handicrafts; parks, gardens; p. (1980) 146,998.

Urubamba, R., **Peru**; rises in E. Cordillera of Andes; forms one of headstreams of R. Amazon; length 560 km.

Urubupunga, t., Brazil; new. t. for 10,000, at site of hydroelectric power sta.

Uruguaiana, t., **Brazil**; on R. Uruguay; cattle ctr.; jerked beef, soap, candles; p. (est. 1985) 105,900.

Uruguay, rep., **S. America**; smallest of S. American reps.; situated on N. bank of Rio de la Plata estuary; low hills in N.; temperate climate; 60 per cent land a. devoted to live-stock rearing, especially cattle, sheep, based on extensive natural grasslands; arable land in S., grains; ch. t. Montevideo, cap. and main ctr. of inds.; food processing, leather, metallurgy, textiles, rubber; inflation 83 per cent; a. 186,925 km²; p. (est. 1986) 2,982,000.

Uruguay, R., **S. America**; rises in S. Brazil, flows 1,360 km to Rio de la Plata; forms bdy. between Argentina and Uruguay and part of bdy. between Argentina and Brazil.

Ürümqi (Wulumuchi), c., cap. of Xinjiang Aut. Reg., N.W. **China**; admin., comm. and industl. ctr.; iron and steel, cement, textiles, nitrogenous fertilisers, agr. machin.; local coal, tin, silver mng.; p. (1984) 1,147,300.

Usak, t., **Turkey**; connected by rail with Izmir; noted for pile carpet-weaving; p. (1985) 88,267.

Usambara, mtns., N.E. **Tanzania**; scene of early European settlement (1902); lumber, tea, coffee produced on slopes; max. alt. 2,560 m.

Usedom (Uznam), I., Baltic Sea; off mouth of R. Oder; since 1945 E. part belongs to **Poland**, W. (the larger part) to E. **Germany**; a. 445 km²; p. 45,000.

Ushant, I., off cst. of Finistère, **France**; at entrance to English Channel; it was off Ushant that Lord Howe gained his gr. naval victory on the "glorious first of June" 1794; lighthouse, fishing; p. 2,000.

Ushuaia, t., **Argentina**; most S. t. in world; sheep farming, timber, furs; freezing plant; p. (1980) 11,000.

Usk, mkt. t., Gwent, **Wales**; 13th cent. cas.; p. (1981) 1,907.

Usk, R., Gwent, S. **Wales**; flows S. past Newport to Bristol Channel; picturesque, gd. fishing; 91 km long.

Usküdar (Scutari), t., **Turkey**; on Bosporus, opposite Istanbul; mkt. ctr.; new bridge to European side of Bosporus; Crimean memorial cemetery for Brit. troops; Muslim cemeteries; p. (1965) 133,883.

Uspallata Pass, 3,800 m high over Andes between Mendoza, **Argentina**, and Santiago, **Chile**; monument "Christ of the Andes" marks international bdy. settlement; used by Mendoza–Valparaiso rly.

Ussuri, R., rises in Maritime prov. of **RSFSR**, flows *c.* 800 km to R. Amur; final 480 km forms Sino-Soviet bdy.

Ussuriysk (Voroshilov), t., **RSFSR**; 112 km N. of Vladivostok; rly. junc. of Trans-Siberian and Chinese Eastern rlys.; engin., agr. prod.; p. (1985) 156,000.

Ustica, I., Palermo, **Italy**; basalt; agr., fishing, handicrafts; a. 8 km²; p. (1981) 1,157.

Usti-nad-Labem (Aussig), c., Bohemia, **ČSSR**; R. pt. on Elbe; route and industl. ctr.; chemicals, textiles, machin.; p. (est. 1986) 91,000.

Ustinor (Izhevsk), c., cap. of Udmurt ASSR, **RSFSR**; steel ctr., engin.; p. (1986) 620,000.

Ust Kamenogorsk, c., Kazakh SSR, **USSR**; on Irtysh R.; mng. ctr.; food processing, clothing, furniture; hydroelectric power sta. nearby; p. (1985) 307,000.

Usumbura. *See* **Bujumbura.**

Utah, st., **USA**; 'Beehive St.'; admitted to Union 1896; st. flower Sego Lily, st. bird Sea Gull; Rocky mtns. in E.; forms part of Gr. Basin in W.; Gr. Salt L. in N.W.; dry continental climate; poor agr. conditions, soil erosion; copper, gold; tourism; Nat. Parks; cap. Salt L. City; a. 219,932 km²; p. (1985) 1,645,000.

Utica, c., N.Y., **USA**; on Mohawk R. and Barge Canal; in rich dairying region; textiles, electronics, tools, firearms; p. (1984) 72,900 (c.), 321,400 (met. a. inc. Rome).

Utrecht, prov., **Neth.**; on Old Rhine (Oude Rijn); univ., cath.; chemical and cigar factories; printing, machin., woollens, silks, velvets; major transport and financial ctr.; picturesque; p. (est. 1987) 229,000.

Utrecht, cap., prov., **Neth.**; between Gelderland and N. and S. Holland; fertile agr., cattle rearing, horticulture; a. 1,362 km²; p. (1983) 923,182.

Utsunomiya, t., Honshu, **Japan**; ctr. for Nikko Nat. Park; p. (1985) 405,384.

Uttar Pradesh, st., **India**; Himalayas on N. bdy., drained by Ganges and Jumna; irrigation; wheat, rice, millet, barley, maize, cotton, sugar, oil-seeds; ch. ts. Allahabad, Lucknow (cap.), Varanasi, Kanpur, Agra, Meerut; a. 293,732 km²; p. (1981) 111,000,000; (p. increasing by 2 million a year).

Uttlesford, l. gov. dist., Essex, **Eng.**; inc. Saffron Walden and Dunmow; p. (est. 1988) 66,100.

Uttoxeter, t., East Staffs., **Eng.**; on R. Dove; machin., biscuit mftg.; expanded t.; p. (1981) 10,012.

Uusikaupunki (Swed. **Nystad**), spt., Abo-Bjorneborg, S.W. **Finland**; on G. of Bothnia; p. (1982) 13,768.

Uzbek (**Uzbekistan**) **SSR**, constituent rep., **USSR**; crossed by Rs. Amu Dar'ya and Syr Dar'ya; contains part of fertile Ferghana Valley; intensive farming based on irrigation; rice, cotton, fruits, silk, cattle, sheep; ch. cs. Tashkent (cap.), Samarkand; alluvial gold deposits and bauxite in Kizil-Kum desert; a. 412,250 km²; p. (1986) 18,479,000.

Uzhgorod, c., Ukrainian SSR, **USSR**; economic and cultural ctr.; friendship pipeline from Kuybyshev; univ.; p. (1985) 107,000.

V

Vaal, R., **S. Africa**; rises in Drakensberg mtns., flows between the Transvaal and Orange Free State to join the Orange R. nr. Kimberley. V. dam irrigates lge. a. of Witwatersrand; 896 km long.

Vaasa, c., cap. of Vaasa prov., W. **Finland**; pt. on G. of Bothnia; exp. timber and timber prods.; agr. ctr.; food processing, textiles, timber inds.; p. (1986) 54,253.

Vác, t., **Hungary**; on R. Danube; comm. ctr.; summer resort for Budapest; cath.; p. (est. 1984) 36,000.

Vadso, cap. of Finnmark prov., N.E. **Norway**; ice-free Arctic pt. on N. side of Varangar fjord; whaling and fishing base; p. (est. 1970) 5,625.

Vaduz, mkt. t., cap. of **Liechtenstein**; nr. Rhine; sm. tourist resort; p. (est. 1986) 4,920.

Vaigach, sm. I., between Novaya Zemlya and mainland of **USSR**; geological extension of Urals; low-lying reindeer pasture; seal fishing.

Valais, can., **Switzerland**; in upper valley of R. Rhône; surrounded by mtns., forested on slopes; vines and cereals in valleys; ch. resort Zermatt, cap. Sion; a. 5,234 km²; p. (est. 1986) 233,000.

Valdai Hills, morainic ridges between Leningrad and Moscow, **RSFSR**; rise to c. 348 m and form ch. watershed of E. European Rs., Vlga, Dvina and Dniester.

Val d'Aosta, aut. region, N.W. **Italy**; high Alpine ctr., borders France and Switzerland; cap. Aosta; agr., hydroelectric power; winter resorts; a. 3,263 km²; p. (est. 1986) 114,000.

Val-de-Marne, dep., S.E. of Paris, **France**; cap., Créteil; a. 243 km²; p. (1982) 1,191,500.

Valdez, t., Alaska, **USA**; ice-free pt., fishing; terminal of oil pipeline from North Slope; p. (1980) 3,079.

Valdivia, c., cap. of V. prov., S. **Chile**; on R. Callecalle nr. the sea (pt. Corral); damaged by earthquake and tidal wave 1960; univ.; metal, wood and leather gds.; paper, flour, brewing; p. (est. 1985) 104,500.

Val d'Oise, dep., N.W. of Paris, **France**; cap. Pontoise; a. 1,248 km²; p. (1982) 920,500.

Valdosta, t., Ga., **USA**; rly. and tr. ctr. for region producing tobacco, cotton, timber; p. (1980) 37,596.

Valence, t., cap. of Drôme dep., S.E. **France**; on R. Rhône; silks., hosiery, vineyards; agr. mkt.; p. (1982) 68,157.

Valencia, region, E. **Spain**; on Mediterranean; comprises provs. of Alicante, Castellón de la Plana and Valencia; mtnous., with densely populated, fertile coastal plain; irrigation makes a. a major producer of Mediterranean fruit and crops; a. 23,305 km² p. (1987) 2,088,302.

Valencia, c., cap. of V. prov., E. **Spain**; pt. on Mediterranean at mouth of R. Turia; one of most impt. agr. ts. of cty., and active industl. and comm. ctr.; univ., cath.; resort; p. (1987) 732,491.

Valencia, c., N. **Venezuela**; nr. L. Valencia; ctr. of agr. a., sugar-cane, cotton; leading industl. t.; cattle mart; cotton mills, meat packing; cath.; p. (1981) 616,000.

Valenciennes, c., Nord dep., N. **France**; in Hainaut cty. on R. Escaut (Scheldt); metallurgical and chemical inds.; once famous for hand-made lace; birthplace of Froissart and Watteau; p. (1982) 349,505 (French met. a.).

Valentia, I., S.W. Kerry, **R.o.I.**; in Dingle Bay; agr., fishing; 10 km by 3 km.

Vale of Glamorgan, l. gov. dist., South Glamorgan, **Wales**; inc. cstl. ts. of Penarth, Barry and Cowbridge; p. (est. 1988) 119,500.

Vale of White Horse, l. gov. dist., Oxon., **Eng.**; based on Abingdon, Faringdon and Wantage; p. (est. 1988) 112,300.

Vale Royal, l. gov. dist., Ches., **Eng.**; a. in ctr. of co. and inc. saltfield ts. of Northwich and Winsford; p. (est. 1988) 113,300.

Valladolid, c., cap. of V. prov., **Spain**; on R. Pisuerga (trib. of Douro); grain tr.; route, industl. and comm. ctr.; food processing, textiles; cath., univ.; p. (1987) 329,206.

Valle del General, upland, S.W. **Costa Rica**; pioneer subsistence agr., maize, tropical fruit, cattle; improving transport.

Vallejo, t., Cal., **USA**; at mouth of Napa R. on San Pablo Bay; pt. and processing ctr. for farm prod.; naval shipyard; p. (1980) 334,000 (met. a.).

Vallenar, t., Atacama prov., **Chile**; agr. ctr.; dried fruit, wines; iron ore nearby; p. (1982) 42,309.

Valletta, c., cap. of **Malta**; ch. spt. on rocky penin. of Mt. Scebarras, E. cst.; formerly naval base; cath., univ.; p. (est. 1983) 14,096.

Valli di Comacchio, lagoon a., N.E. **Italy**; ctr. of an impt. eel industry; a. 259 km².

Valparaiso, c., central **Chile**; leading pt. on Pac. cst. of S. America; attractive c. with backdrop of steep hills; mftg., comm. and industl. ctr. of rep. with textile mills, sugar refineries, paint, shoe and chemical factories; univ.; p. (est. 1985) 273,006.

Valtellina, fertile valley, **Italy**; in Lombard Alps above L. Como; impt. for vine cultivation; hydroelectric power resources; tourism.

Van, c., cap. of Van prov., S.E. **Turkey**; stands at 1,726 m on shore of salty L. Van; tr. ctr. of wheat-growing a.; new Turkish–Iranian rail link; p. (1985) 110,653.

Vancouver, c., B.C., **Canada**; Pac. cst. spt. with excellent natural harbour; international airport and terminus of transcontinental rly.; timber inds., shipbldg., fishing, oil and sugar refining; exp. prod. from these inds.; protection by mountains and mild climate make c. a major tourist ctr.; univ.; p. (1986) 431,147 (c.), 1,380,729 (met. a.).

Vancouver, I., B.C., **Canada**; off W. cst.; mtnous., forested; woodpulp, paper; indented cst. provides many natural harbours; fishing; cap. Victoria; a. 33,797 km².

Vancouver, t., Wash., **USA**; spt. on Columbia R. opposite Portland (Ore.); exp. grain, timber; food processing; p. (1980) 42,834.

Vandellos, Tarragona, **Spain**; nuclear power sta.; p. (1981) 3,838.

Vanderbijlpark, t., Transvaal, **S. Africa**; on Vaal R.; ctr. for steel wks.; p. (1980) 294,082.

Vänern, lge. L., **Sweden**; W.N.W. of L. Vättern, with which it is connected by canal (and thence with the Baltic); a. 5,566 km².

Vänersborg, L. pt., **Sweden**; on tongue of land between R. Göta and the Vasobotten (southernmost bay of L. Väner); footwear, wood and sulphite pulp; p. (1983) 34,976.

Vannes, t., cap. of Morbihan dep., N.ᵂ. **France**; sm. pt. on S. cst. Brittany; cath.; dates from Roman times; p. (1982) 45,397.

Vanuatu, (**New Hebrides**), former Anglo-French condominion, S. **Pac. Oc.**; between New Caledonia and Fiji Is.; indep. st. 1980; strong separist moves in Santo I.; mostly subsistence agr.; few cash crops; ch. crop coconuts; no worked minerals; thickly forested; cap. Pt. Vila; a. 14,763 km²; p. (est. 1987) 141,400.

Var, dep., S.E. **France**; in Provence, on Mediterranean; mainly agr. with some inds. at Draguignan and Toulon (cap. since 1974); bauxite at Brignoles; rapid growth of p.; inc. many coastal resorts; a. 6,042 km²; p. (1982) 705,500.

Varanasi (**Benares**), c., Uttar Pradesh, **India**; famous holy c. on Ganges, 640 km N.W. of Calcutta; place of annual pilgrimage; univ.; handicrafts, brasses, brocades, embroideries, now debased; p. (1981) 708,647 (c.), 791,162 (met. a.).

Varanger Fjord, inlet of Arctic Oc. into Finnmark, **Norway**; iron mng. on S. shore.

Vardar, R., flows through Yugoslav and Greek Macedonia into Aegean Sea nr. Salonika; inc. V. agr. region; hydroelectric power; routeway; 448 km long.

Varde, t., W. Jutland, **Denmark**; agr. and route ctr.; food processing; steelwks.

Vardö, t., Finnmark prov., N.E. **Norway**; sm.

ice-free pt. on Vardoy I. with fish and oil interests; p. c. 3,500.

Vares, t., Bosnia, **Yugoslavia**; iron mng.; developing mnfs.

Varese, t., Lombardy, **Italy**; in Alpine foothills; resort and industl. ctr.; engin., furniture, paper, textiles, wines; p. (1981) 90,527.

Värmland, prov., **Sweden**; agr., iron mng. and processing, timber inds.; cap. Karlstad; a. 19,236 km²; p. (est. 1986) 279,000.

Varna, t., **Bulgaria**; spt. on Black Sea; industl. ctr. of heavy inds.; summer resorts on cst. nearby; p. (1985) 302,208.

Varnsdorf, t., **CSSR**; rly. junc. on German bdr.; impt. textile ctr.; p. (est. 1968) 13,912.

Västerås, c., cap. of Västmanland prov., **Sweden**; on L. Mälar; impt. elec. and metallurgical inds.; power sta.; impt. mediaeval c., cath., cas.; p. (est. 1986) 118,000.

Västerbotten, prov., **Sweden**; forested; timber inds.; cap. Umeå; a. 59,153 km²; p. (est. 1986) 245,000.

Västernorrland, prov., **Sweden**; forests and timber inds.; cap. Harnosand; a. 25,706 km²; p. (est. 1986) 261,000.

Vastervik, t., Kalmar prov., **Sweden**; on Baltic cst. engin., chemicals, paper; p. (est. 1986) 40,000.

Västmanland, prov., **Sweden**; N. of L. Mälar; mkt. gardening in S.; iron and silver mng. in N.; iron and steel inds.; cap. Västerås; a. 8,363 km²; p. (est. 1986) 254,000.

Vasto, t., Abruzzi e Molise, **Italy**; agr. ctr. on steep-sided, vine-producing plateau; sm. Adriatic fishing pt.; p. (1981) 30,036.

Vatican City, indep. sov. Papal st., **Italy**; forms an enclave in Rome; inc. Papal residence, St. Peter's cath.; a. 44 ha; p. (est. 1985) 1,000.

Vatna Jökull, mtn., **Iceland**; elevated snowfield; active volcano; alt. 2,120 m.

Vättern, L., **Sweden**; 40 km S.E. L. Vänern; a. 1,898 km².

Vaucluse, dep. S.E. **France**; in Provence; cap. Avignon; a. 3,577 km²; p. (1982) 428,900.

Vaud, can., W. **Switzerland**; N. of L. Geneva; forests and vineyards; cap. Lausanne; a. 3,209 km²; p. (est. 1986) 550,000.

Växjö, t., S. **Sweden**; engin., timber wks., hosiery; p. (est. 1986) 67,000.

Vejle, spt., Jutland, **Denmark**; admin. ctr. V. prov.; industl.; p. (1981) 43,300.

Velbert, t., N. Rhine-Westphalia, **W. Germany**; N.W. of Wuppertal; metal ind., locks and keys; p. (est. 1986) 88,600.

Vélez-Málaga, t., Málaga prov., S. **Spain**; famous for wine, raisins, sugar, olive oil; Moorish cas.; p. (1981) 41,776.

Veliki Ustyug, t., **RSFSR**; R. pt. on Sukhona R.; shipyards, mftg.; p. (est. 1967) 35,000.

Velletri, t., central **Italy**; at foot of Alban hills overlooking Pontine marshes; noted for its wine; Garibaldi routed Neapolitans here 1849; p. (1981) 41,114.

Vellore, t., Tamil Nadu, **India**; agr. mkt. t.; scene of Sepoy mutiny 1806; p. (1981) 174,274 (t.), 247,041 (met. a.).

Velsen, t., N. Holland prov., **Neth.**; nr. entrance to N. Sea Canal, inc. IJmuiden iron and steel wks.; lge. paper mill; p. (est. 1987) 57,000.

Veluwe, dist., Gelderland, **Neth.**; between Arnhem and IJselmeer; low hills of glacial sands and sand-dunes; heathland and pinewoods; relatively low p. density.

Venda, Bantu homeland, Transvaal, **S. Africa**; 3rd homeland granted "independence" (1979); nr. Zimbabwe border; p. (1985) 459,986.

Vendée, dep., W. **France**; on Bay of Biscay; fish. pts., beach resorts, agr. pasturage, vineyards; cap. La Roche-sur-Yon; a. 6,972 km²; p. (1982) 483,400.

Vendôme, t., Loir-et-Cher dep., **France**; on R. Loire; leather gds., cottons; mediaeval cas.; p. (1982) 18,218.

Venetia (Veneto), region, N.E. **Italy**; between the Alps and the Adriatic; embraces provs. Vicenza, Verona, Venice, Udine, Treviso, Padua, Belluno and Rovigo; mtnous. in N., inc. Dolomite Alps; fertile plain of Po R. in S.; intensive arable agr.; ch. c. Venice; a. 18,384 km²; p. (est. 1986) 4·4 m.

Venezia Giulia. See **Friuli-Venezia Giulia**.

Venezuela, fed. rep., N. cst. **S. America**; wealth derived from long-established oil ind. (90 per cent of exp. are oil); tropical climate, with temper-

ate uplands, tropical forests and tall grass savannah lands (llanos); most economically advanced a. around cap. Carácas and oilfield a. of L. Maracaibo; counter pole of development based on hydroelectric power resources and iron ore in Caroní R. region; growing steel inds., government investment in lge. agr. areas, esp. maize and cereals; coffee from highlands main comm. agr. crop and exp.; large foreign debt; a. 912,050 km²; p. (est. 1987) 18·3 m.

Venice (Venezia), c., cap. of V. prov. and ch. c. of Venetia, N.E. **Italy**; built on gr. of islets within lagoon in G. of V., at head of Adriatic; splendid architecture, rich in art treasures and historic associations; extensive canal network, inc. Grand Canal, intensive use leading to erosion of bldgs.; gradually sinking into Adriatic, lge.-scale projects to preserve c.; industl. zone on landward side in subs. of Porto Marghera and Mestre; craft and heavy inds.; p. (1984) 340,873.

Venlo, t., **Neth.**; on R. Maas; agr. mkt. and rly. junc.; chemicals, optical instruments, electric lamps; p. (est. 1987) 64,000.

Ventimiglia, t., Liguria, N.W. **Italy**; on Mediterranean cst. on Fr. border; cath.; flower mkt.; tourism; p. (1981) 26,373.

Ventnor, t., South Wight, I. of Wight, **Eng.**; on S. cst. 18 km S. of Ryde; mild climate, tourist and health resort; p. (1981) 7,941.

Veracruz, st., E. **Mexico**; narrow coastal plain rising to Sierra Madre Oriental; contains volcano Orizaba; recent agr. improvements; growth of petroleum inds.; cap. Jalapa; a. 71,836 km²; p. (1980) 5,264,611.

Veracruz, c., V. st., E. **Mexico**; spt. on G. of Mexico; comm. and industl. ctr. of oil region; nearby Laguna Grande, Mexico's first nuclear power sta. (1984); nr. site where Cortés landed 1519; p. (1980) 305,456.

Vercelli, c., cap. of V. prov., N. **Italy**; in Piedmont, on Sesia R.; rice mkt. for lge. irrigated plain textiles, machin., aircraft parts; p. (1981) 52,488.

Verde, Cape, most W. part of **Africa**; site of Dakar, cap. of Senegal.

Verdun, t., Quebec, **Canada**; sub. of Montreal; p. (1986) 60,246.

Verdun, t., Meuse dep., N.E. **France**; in Lorraine, on R. Meuse; strategic ctr. with varied mnfs.; 12th cent. cath.; scene of famous battle 1916; p. (1982) 24,120.

Vereeniging, c., Transvaal prov., **S. Africa**; on Vaal R.; coal, iron and steel, bricks; Treaty of Vereeniging 1902 ended Boer War; p. (1985) 540,142 (met. a.).

Verkhneudinsk. See **Ulan-Ude**.

Verkhoyansk, t., Yakutsk ASSR, **RSFSR**; in N.E. Siberia; coldest permanently inhabited place in world; mean Jan. temp. of −59° F.; ctr. of fur trapping a.; p. c. 2,000.

Vermont, st., New England, **USA**; 'Green Mtn. St.'; admitted to Union 1791; st. flower Red Clover, st. bird Hermit Thrush; traversed by the Green mtns.; farming, dairying, stock-raising, lumbering, quarrying, machine tool and textile mftg.; traditional inds. revitalised by new inds. coming from neighbouring Quebec; cap. Montpelier; famous for autumn colours; a. 24,887 km²; p. (1985) 535,000.

Verona, c., cap. of V. prov., N.E. **Italy**; on R. Adige; commands route from central Europe to Brenner pass and from Venice to Milan; cath. and notable monuments; active agr. tr. and inds., printing; p. (1984) 261,947.

Versailles, c., cap. of Yvelines dep., N. **France**; S.W. sub. of Paris; famous royal palace; mkt. gardening, distilleries; Treaty of Versailles 1919; p. (1982) 95,240.

Verviers, t., **Belgium**; nr. Liège; ctr. of textile ind. in Ardennes; p. (1982) 54,800.

Vestmannaeyjar or **Westman Is.**, archipelago, S. W. **Iceland**; impt. cod fishing ind. based on Heimaey I; p. (1983) 4,743.

Vesuvius, famous active volcano, S. **Italy**; on shore of Bay of Naples; alt. c. 1,186 m; its eruption in A.D. 79 destroyed Pompeii and Herculaneum, and frequent eruptions have since been recorded; observatory founded 1844; funicular rly. from base of mtn. to rim of crater existed from 1880 to 1944 (destroyed by eruption).

Veszprem, c., **Hungary**; in fruit-growing dist., 96 km S. of Budapest; cath., univ. for chemical ind.; p. (est. 1985) 65,000.

Vevey, t., Vaud can., **Switzerland**; on N. shore of L. Geneva; beautiful situation; chocolate, watches; resort; p. (1970) 17,957.

Viareggio, beach resort, Tuscany, **Italy**; on Tyrrhenian Sea, nr. Pisa; monument to Shelley; p. (1981) 58,136.

Viborg, t., Jutland, **Denmark**; admin. ctr. V. prov.; comm. and route ctr.; anc. cath.; textiles, machin., food processing; p. (1981) 28,659.

Vicenza, c. cap. of V. prov., N.E. **Italy**; in Venetia; mkt. ctr. for surrounding fertile agr. plain; textiles, iron and steel; many examples of Palladian architecture; p. (1984) 112,771.

Vichy, t., Allier dep., **France**; on Allier R.; famous spa; hot mineral springs; lge. exp. of V. water; seat of Pétain govt. during German occupation 1940–3; p. (1982) 63,501 (met. a.).

Vicksburg, t., Miss., **USA**; R. pt., on bluffs of Mississippi at junc. of Yazoo canal; shipping and mftg. ctr. in cotton and timber region; prominent in American Civil War; Confederate surrender 1863; p. (1980) 25,434.

Victoria, st., **Australia**; settled rapidly in 19th century with gold rush; now most densely populated yet smallest mainland st.; Latrobe brown coal, offshore natural gas, hydroelectric power encourage rapid industrialisation; dominated by cap. Melbourne; rural a. of Great Dividing Range produces wheat, sheep and dairy prods.; a. 227,516 km²; p. (1986) 4,160,856.

Victoria, c., cap. of B.C., **Canada**; spt. on Vancouver I.; fishing and fish-processing; sawmills, chemicals, cement; beautiful scenery; tourist ctr.; p. (1986) 66,303 (c.), 255,547 (met. a.).

Victoria, main pt. and harbour between **Hong Kong I.** and Kowloon; built on reclaimed land; admin. ctr. of Hong Kong; p. (1976) 501,680.

Victoria, t., cap. of Labuan I., Sabah, **Malaysia**; fine harbour; p. 3,213.

Victoria, t., cap. of **Seychelles**, Ind. Oc.; harbour on lgst. and most impt. I. of Mahé.

Victoria, t., S. Texas, **USA**; comm. ctr. in prosperous agr. a.; local oilfields; p. (1980) 50,695.

Victoria Falls (Mosi-oa-Toenja), on R. Zambesi, **Zambia**; discovered by Livingstone 1855; falls are 1,674 m wide and broken by islands and rocks.

Victoria, Lake, lgst. L. of **Africa**; bordered by Kenya, Uganda, Tanzania; in depression of Gt. Rift Valley, at alt. 999 m. a. c. 67,340 km²; discharges into Victoria Nile; impt. fisheries; discovered by Speke 1858.

Victoria Land, region, **Antarctica**; discovered by Ross in 1841.

Victoria Nile, R., **Uganda**; E. Africa; name of R. Nile from its source at L. Victoria until it enters L. Mobuto Seso.

Vienna (Wien), c., cap. of **Austria**; R. pt. on branch of Danube; surrounded by Wiener Wald (Vienna forest) and Carpathian foothills; major industl., comm. and transport ctr.; many fine bldgs., inc. univ., cath., Rathaus, parliament bldgs., magnificent Prater park; influential ctr. of music, cultural and scientific ctr.; home of Haydn, Mozart, Beethoven, Schubert, Mahler, Brahms, and Freud; p. (1981) 1,531,346 (c.), 2,044,331 (met. a.).

Vienne, dep., W. **France**; drained by R. Vienne; mainly agr. dist.; cap. Poitiers; a. 7,021 km²; p. (1982) 371,428.

Vienne, t., Isère, **France**; nr. Grenoble, on R. Rhône; textiles, metallurgical inds.; Roman remains; overshadowed by Lyons 27 km to N.; p. (1982) 372,000.

Vienne, R., **France**; trib. of the Loire; rises in Massif Central; 354 km long.

Vientiane, admin. cap., **Laos**; pt. and comm. ctr. on Mekong R.; p. (1985) 377,409.

Viersen, t., N. Rhine–Westphalia, **W. Germany**; S.W. of Krefeld; textiles, machin., furniture, paper ind.; p. (est. 1986) 78,100.

Vierzon, t., Cher dep., **France**; on R. Cher; bricks, tiles, porcelain from local sands, clay; agr. machin.; p. (1982) 34,886.

Vietnam, Socialist Rep. of, S.E. **Asia**; comprises regions of Cochinchina and Tonkin in former French Indo-China; from 1954–1976 two separate countries, N. and S. Vietnam, based on two rivers, Song-koi and Mekong respectively, and separated by the high Annamite

chain of mtns.; long period of civil war resulted in reunification; intensive agr. based on rice cultivation now largely collectivised; monsoon climate and river irrigation aid high yields; coffee, tea, rubber, sugar, main comm. crops but much devastation as result of war; minerals mainly concentrated in the N. with impt. anthracite deposit at Quang-Yen; industl. devel. also mainly in N. around Hanoi and ch. pt. Haiphong; hill tribes practising subsistence agr. inhabit the intervening Annamite mtns.; since reunification ts. declining rapidly; a. 335,724 km²; p. (est. 1986) 61,950,000.

Viet-Tri, t., N. **Vietnam**; 128 km N.W. of Hanoi; chemicals, paper mill, sugar refining.

Vigevano, t., Lombardy, **Italy**; on R. Ticino; impt. agr. and industl. ctr.; footwear, plastics, textiles; cath.; p. (est. 1981) 65,228.

Vigo, spt., **Spain**; transatlantic pt. on V. Bay; processing of imports; oil refining; p. (1981) 261,329.

Vijayanagar, ruined c., S.E. **India**; once cap. c. of Hindu empire in S. Deccan; 96 km in circumference; destroyed by Moslem forces at battle of Talikota 1565.

Vijayavada, t., Andhra Pradesh, **India**; rly. junc., comm. ctr.; irrigation dam, Kistna R.; p. (1981) 454,577 (t.), 543,008 (met. a.).

Vila Real de Santo António, pt., Faro, **Portugal**; on W. bank of Guadiana R.; exp. copper ore, fish, fruit; p. (1981) 7,390.

Villach, t., Carinthia, S. **Austria**; at junc. of Gail and Drava Rs.; impt. route ctr.; tourism; p. (1981) 52,692.

Villahermosa, c., cap. of Tabasco, S.E. **Mexico**; agr. mkt., sugar processing; rich local petroleum deposits; p. (1980) 250,903.

Villa Maria, t., **Argentina**; rly. junc.; ctr. of grain, timber, dairying dist.; p. (1980) 67,490.

Villarrica, t., S.E. **Paraguay**; agr. tr. ctr. for cattle, tobacco, fruit; wines, yerba-maté grown in surrounding a.; p. (1982) 21,203.

Villavicencio, t., E. **Colombia**; in foothills of Andes; comm. ctr. for the *llanos*; cattle tr.; p. (1985) 182,298.

Villaviciosa, t., Oviedo prov., N.W. **Spain**; major fishing pt. on Bay of Biscay; p. (1981) 15,703.

Villeurbanne, t., Rhône dep., **France**; forming part of Lyons agglomeration; metallurgy, chemicals, leather, textiles; p. (1982) 118,330.

Vilnius, (Pol. Wilno), c., cap. of Lithuania on Vilija R. (trib. of Niemen); cultural ctr., cath., univ., historic bldgs.; held by Poland 1920–39; lt. inds., food processing; p. (1987) 566,000.

Vilyui, R., Yakut ASSR, **RSFSR**; flows E. from Siberian uplands into Lena R.; R. basin impt. agr. and mng. a.; fishing; 2,400 km long.

Vimy, t., Pas-de-Calais dep., N. **France**; nearby Vimy Ridge, site of Allied victory led by Canadians 1915; p. (1982) 3,621.

Viña del Mar, t., seaside t., central **Chile**, nr. Valparaiso; fashionable S. American resort; oil and sugar refining, textiles; p. (est. 1985) 258,400.

Vincennes, t., Val-de-Marne dep., **France**; sub. of Paris; famous cas. and Bois; industl. and residtl.; p. (1982) 43,068.

Vindhya Hills, mtn. range, central **India**; separating the Deccan from the Ganges basin; c. 640 km long.

Vinnitsa, t., Ukrainian SSR, **USSR**; on R. Bug 192 km S.W. of Kiev; agr. mkt. t.; engin. chemicals, textiles; p. (1985) 367,000.

Virginia, st., **USA**; one of original 13 sts.; 'Old Dominion' St.; admitted to Union 1788; st. flower Dogwood, st. bird Cardinal; wide Atl. coastal plain rising inland to Blue Ridge; famous for high quality "Virginia Leaf" tobacco; industl. ts. of Norfolk, Richmond, Portsmouth and Newport News; cap. Richmond; a. 105,711 km²; p. (1985) 5,706,000.

Virgin Is. (**Brit.**), **W.I.**; gr. of Is. E. of Greater Antilles; most impt. Tortola, Virgin Gorda, Anegada; water scarcity, semi-subsistence agr. economy; livestock, fish, fruit, vegetables; a. 153 km²; p. (est. 1985) 13,000.

Virgin Is. (**USA**), **W.I.**; external terr. of USA E. of Greater Antilles, 64 km E. of Puerto Rico; 3 main Is., St. Thomas, St. John, St. Croix; bought from Denmark 1917; favourite tourist a. in Caribbean; cap. Charlotte Amalie on St. Thomas; livestock, sugar; rum distilling;

a. 344 km²; p. (est. 1985) 105,000.

Vis (Lissa), I., off Dalmatian cst., Adriatic, **Yugoslavia**; fish-canning ctr.; a. 91 km²; anc. remains; resort; sea battle 1866 between Italian and Austrian ironclads; p. 3,000.

Visby, old spt., **Sweden**; on Gotland I. in Baltic Sea; rich in historic interest; resort; p. (est. 1984) 20,000.

Vishakhapatnam, spt., Andhra Pradesh, **India**; deepwater harbour on Bay of Bengal; exp. manganese and oilseeds from Madhya Pradesh; shipbldg.; p. (1981) 565,321 (t.), 603,630 (met. a.).

Vistula, R., Poland; rises in Beskids range of Carpathians, flows through Poland past Krakow to Baltic Sea nr. Gdansk; forms major link in E. European waterway system; coal and timber transport; 1,056 km long.

Vitebsk, c., Belorussiyan SSR, **USSR**; R. pt. on W. Dvina and impt. rly. junc., in agr. region; textiles, machine tools, food processing; p. (1985) 335,000.

Viterbo, c., cap. of V. prov., **Italy**; N. of Rome; agr. ctr., food-processing; 12th cent. cath. and historic bldgs.; p. (1981) 57,632.

Vitim, R., E. Siberia, RSFSR; flows to R. Lena; navigable for 5 months of year; coal and grain tr.; 1,400 km long.

Vitória, spt., Espírito Santo, **Brazil**; new ocean terminal capturing tr. from Rio de Janeiro; exp. coffee, cocoa, fruit, iron ore; sugar refining, shoes, textiles, cement; p. (est. 1985) 254,400.

Vitoria, c., cap. of Alava prov., **Spain**; in Basque cty.; stands on hill at 534 m; furniture mnf.; defeat of Fr. by Wellington 1813; p. (1981) 192,773.

Vitry-le-François, t., Marne dep., N.E. **France**; on Marne R.; industl., textiles, earthenware; agr. mkt. for Champagne Pouilleuse; p. (1982) 18,829.

Vitry-sur-Seine, S.E. sub., Paris, **France**; flower growing on sand and gravel terraces of Seine R., acreage being reduced by competition from housing and inds.; p. (1982) 85,820.

Vittoria, t., Sicily, **Italy**; mkt. for wine; p. (1981) 50,222.

Vittorio Veneto, t., **Italy**; N. of Venice; resort; textiles; p. (1981) 30,028.

Vizcaya, Basque prov., N. **Spain**; on Bay of Biscay; iron mng.; iron and steel inds.; dense p.; cap. Bilbao; a. 2,165 km²; p. (1987) 1,182,358.

Vlaardingen, t., S. Holland prov., **Neth.**; 8 km W. of Rotterdam, on Nieuwe Maas; leading fish. pt.; p. (est. 1987) 75,000.

Vladimir, c., cap. of V. oblast, **RSFSR**; between Gorki and Moscow, on trib. of Oka R.; founded 12th cent.; caths., historic bldgs.; machine tools, agr. machin., textiles; p. (1985) 331,000.

Vladimir-Volynski, c., N.W. Ukrainian SSR, **USSR**; one of oldest Ukrainian settlements, founded 9th cent.; agr. mkt. ctr.; p. (est. 1967) 23,000.

Vladivostok, c., spt., **RSFSR**; ch. pt. and naval base on Pac.; terminus of Trans-Siberian rly. and airline from Moscow; ch. cultural ctr. of Far East; shipyards, fisheries, oil refining, engin., chemicals; economic development in hinterland hindered by distance from major ctrs. of p. and ind.; p. (1986) 608,000.

Vlieland, Friesian I., at entrance to IJsselmeer, **Neth.**; resort, nature reserve.

Vlissingen or **Flushing**, spt., Zeeland prov., S.W. **Neth.**; on Walcheren I.; shipyards, oil refining, fishing; resort; birthplace of Admiral de Ruyter; p. (est. 1987) 45,000.

Vlonë, spt., S.W. **Albania**; on Strait of Otranto, Adriatic Sea; salt; oil pipeline connects from Kucovë nr. Berat; p. (1980) 58,000.

Vltava or **Moldau**, R., Bohemia, **ČSSR**; rises in Sumava mtns. (Bohemian Forest) and flows to R. Elbe below Prague; used for hydroelectric power; c. 416 km long.

Voghera, t., Lombardy, **Italy**; rly. junc. and agr. mkt.; textiles, machin. engin.; cas., cath.; p. (1981) 42,639.

Voi, t., **Kenya**, E. Africa; 144 km N.W. of Mombasa on rly. to Nairobi; branch connection with Tanzania rly. system allows agr. prod. from Arusha and Moshi dists. to pass through Mombasa as alternative to Tanga; new shoe factory.

Voiron, t., Isère dep., **France**; on Morge R., 24 km N.W. of Grenoble; textiles, paper; p. (1982) 19,658.

Vojvodina, aut. prov., N. Serbia, **Yugoslavia**; impt. and fertile agr. dist. crossed by Danube R.; intensive agr., prosperous and dense p.; fruit, vegetables, livestock, food processing; ch. c. Novi Sad; a. 22,489 km²; p. (1981) 2,034,772.

Volcano Is., Japan; 3 volcanic Is. in Pac. Oc., S. of Japan, admin. by USA until 1968, now Japanese.

Volga, R., USSR; rises in Valdai hills, flows in serpentine course to Caspian at Astrakhan in wide delta; ch. tribs., Oka, Sura, Vetluga, Kama, Samara; major waterway linked to Baltic Sea, Azov, and Black Seas, and to Moscow; hydroelectric developments reducing sturgeon in Caspian Sea and caviar prod. declining; longest R. in Europe, 3,720 km.

Volga Baltic Waterway (Mariinsk Waterway), RSFSR; inland deepwater navigation network linking Black Sea and Caspian Sea in S. with Baltic Sea and White Sea in N.

Volgograd (Stalingrad), c., **RSFSR**; R. pt. on Volga and major rly. ctr.; exp. raw materials, fish; industl. ctr. for steel, engin., chemicals, oil refining; hydroelectric power sta.; fierce siege and successful defence 1942 turning point of second world war; p. (1986) 981,000.

Volhynia, historic region, Ukrainian SSR, **USSR**; on Polish frontier; rich agr. lowland; coal mng. at Novovodinsk; cap. Lutsk.

Volkhov, R., RSFSR; flows from L. Ilmen to L. Ladoga; navigable; hydroelectric power sta. and aluminium smelting plant at Volkhov (Leningrad oblast); 208 km long.

Volkingen, t., Saarland, **W. Germany**; on Saar R., 13 km W. of Saarbrücken; coal mng., iron and steel; p. (est. 1986) 43,100.

Vologda, c., **RSFSR**; R. and rly. junc. on upper Sukhona R.; in dairying a.; engin., textiles, sawmilling, paper, dairy inds.; cath., historic bldgs.; p. (1985) 269,000.

Volos, spt., **Greece**; at head of G. of V.; impt. transport, industl., comm. ctr.; exp. agr. prods.; car mnfs.; p. (1981) 71,378.

Volsk, c., **RSFSR**; R. pt. on Volga R.; cement, tanneries, metallurgy, food processing; p. (est. 1969) 71,000.

Volta (White Volta), major R., **W. Africa**; drains extensive terr. in Niger bend, flows S. through Ghana to delta on Guinea cst., 112 km E. of Accra; main means of communication but rapids make through navigation impossible; Volta R. project for industrialisation of Ghana; dam and power plant at Akosombo, aluminium smelter at Tema; power decr. with decline in reservoir size from drought in Sahel; 1,520 km long. See also Black Volta.

Volta Redonda, t., Rio de Janeiro, **Brazil**; state-owned steel plant; p. (est. 1985) 220,100.

Volterra, hill t., Tuscany, **Italy**; Etruscan and mediaeval walls; alabaster, salt; p. (1981) 14,080.

Volzhsky, t., **RSFSR**; new industl. t. on Volga R.; aluminium smelting, chemicals; p. (1985) 245,000.

Voorburg, t., **Neth.**; industl. ctr. E. of the Hague; p. (est. 1987) 41,000.

Vorarlberg, prov., **Austria**; forestry, dairying, tourism; inds. based on hydroelectric power; textiles; cap. Bregenz; a. 2,600 km²; p. (est. 1986) 312,000.

Vorkuta, ctr. of Pechora coal basin, **RSFSR**; beyond Arctic circle, which supplies entire European N. RSFSR; p. (1985) 108,000.

Voronezh, c., **RSFSR**; R. pt. on Voronezh R. nr. junc. with Don; impt. comm. ctr. in fertile agr. dist.; machin., rubber, oil refining, food processing; nuclear power sta.; univ., cath.; p. (1986) 860,000.

Voroshilovgrad, industl. t., Ukrainian SSR, **USSR**; S. of R. Donets in Donbas Region; impt. rly. engin. factories; textiles; p. (1986) 503,000..

Voroshilovsk. See **Kommunarsk**.

Vosges, dep., E. **France**; on Franco–German frontier; dairying, vineyards, stone quarrying; textiles; cap. Epinal; a. 5,970 km²; p. (1982) 395,400.

Vosges, highlands, E. **France**; structurally similar to Black Forest, from which they are separated by Rhine rift valley; forested slopes, vineyards; source of Meurthe, Moselle, Sarve, Ill, and Saône Rs.; highest summit Ballon de Guebwiller, 1,425 m.

Voskresensk, t., **RSFSR**; S.E. Moscow; lignite, chemicals, fertilisers; p. (est. 1969) 61,000.

Votkinsk, t., **RSFSR**; 61 km N.E. of Izhevsk;

lge. engin. plant; hydroelectric power sta.; birthplace of Tchaikovsky; p. (est. 1969) 73,000.

Vranja, t., **Yugoslavia**; flax and hemp culture and mnf.; developing industl. ctr. based on handicrafts; p. (est. 1965) 19,000.

Vratsa, t., **Bulgaria**; on R. Vratcanska; jewellery, wine, silk, tanning; p. (est. 1968) 45,232.

Vrsac, t., **Yugoslavia**; milling, wine, brandy; p. (1981) 61,005.

Vulcano, I., Lipari gr., **Italy**; off N.E. cst. Sicily; active volcano; gave its name as generic title for this type of mtn.

Vyatka, R., **RSFSR**; rises in foothills of Urals, flows past Kirov into Kama R.; timber transport, fishing; c. 1,360 km long.

Vyborg (Viipuri), c., **RSFSR**; spt. on G. of Finland, occupies strategic site on Karelian Isthmus, N.W. of Leningrad; Finnish until 1945; exp. timber; shipyards, engin., food processing; p. (est. 1969) 65,000.

Vychegda, R., **RSFSR**; rises in Urals, flows W. to N. Dvina R.; timber transport; 1,120 km long.

Vyrnwy, L., reservoir, Powys, **Wales**; with dam 360 m long supplies water for Liverpool; a. 454 ha.

Vyshni-Volochek, t., **RSFSR**; 118 km N.W. of Kalinin; flour milling, textiles, glass inds.; p. (est. 1969) 73,000.

W

Waal, R., **Neth.**; S. arm of R. Rhine.

Waco, c., Texas, **USA**; in Brazos valley; route ctr., airport; regional cultural ctr.; univ.; textiles, leather; p. (1984) 104,100 (c.), 182,100 (met. a.).

Waddenzee, stretch of shallow water between W. Frisian Is. and Neth. mainland.

Wadebridge, spt., Cornwall, **Eng.**; at head of Camel estuary, 10 km N.W. of Bodmin; agr. mkt.

Wadi Halfa, t., **Sudan**; on R. Nile at second cataract; rly. terminus of Sudan rlys.; inundated by Aswan L.; new t. Khashm el Girba for inhabitants.

Wadi Medani, t., cap. of Blue Nile prov., **Sudan**; ctr. of cotton growing dist.; p. (1983) 141,065.

Wagadugu. See **Ouagadougou**.

Wagga Wagga, t., N.S.W., **Australia**; on R. Murrumbidgee; ctr. of agr. and pastoral dist.; p. (1981) 36,837.

Wahiawa, t., Oahu I., **Hawaii**; pineapples; p. (1970) 37,329.

Waikaremoana, L., N.I., **N.Z.**; hydroelectric power.

Waikato, R., N.I., **N.Z.**; rises in L. Taupo and flows N.W. into Tasman Sea; coalfields, hydroelec. power stas.; longest R. of N.Z.; 422 km long.

Wairakei, N.I., **N.Z.**; on L. Taupo; health resort; geothermal power sta.

Waitemata, c., N.I., **N.Z.**; part of Auckland on picturesque inlet; p. (est. 1987) 98,500.

Wakamatsu. See **Kitakyushu**.

Wakatipu, L., Otago, S.I., **N.Z.**; 83 km long, 5 km wide, 360 m deep, 320 m a.s.l.

Wakayama, spt., Honshu, **Japan**; textiles; new iron and steel plant; p. (1985) 401,357.

Wakefield, c., met. dist., West Yorks., **Eng.**; on R. Calder; 13 km S. of Leeds; cath.; ctr. of coal-mng. a.; woollen and worsted gds., chemicals, engin.; p. (est. 1988) 311,600.

Wakefield, t., Va., **USA**; on Potomac R., nr. Fredericksburg; birthplace of George Washington; p. (1980) 1,355.

Wake I., coral atoll, **Pac. Oc.**; between Marianas and Hawaii; comm. and naval base on route to Far East, belonging to USA.

Walachia, region, S. **Romania**; wide plain bounded by Transylvanian Alps and separated from Yugoslavia by Danube; rich agr. a., "the bread-basket of Romania"; Ploiesti oilfields; inds. nr. ch. c. Bucharest; a. 76,563 km²; p. c. 7,500,000.

Walbrzych (Waldenburg), c., S.W. **Poland** (since 1945); formerly in Lower Silesia; industl. and mng. ctr. at 427 m; porcelain, machin., engin.; p. (est. 1983) 137,400.

Walchensee, Lake, Bavaria, **W. Germany**; a. 16 km²; hydroelectric power sta.

Walcheren, I., Zeeland prov., S.W. **Neth.**; in N. Sea at entrance to Scheldt estuary; mainly agr.; ch. ts., Vlissingen, Middelburg; flooded 1944 to stop German advance; tourism.

Waldenburg. See **Walbrzych**.

Wales, principality, **Great Britain**; mostly mtnous.; Cambrian mtns. rise to 1,085 m at Snowdon; contrast between N. and Central Wales (pastoral farming, forestry, water supply, tourism, rural depopulation) and S. Wales (coalfield, metal-based inds., lge. ts.); cap. Cardiff; a. 20,761 km²; p. (est. 1987) 2,836,200 (26 per cent Welsh speaking).

Wallasey, t., Wirral, adjoining Birkenhead, Merseyside, **Eng.**; residtl., seaside resort (New Brighton); p. (1981) 90,057.

Wallensee, L., **Switzerland**; 18 km long.

Wallingford, t., South Oxon., **Eng.**; on R. Thames, to N. of its gap between Chilterns and Lambourn Downs; p. (1981) 6,328.

Wallis and Futuna Is., gr. of coral Is., S. **Pac. Oc.**; overseas terr. of France; copra; a. 275 km²; p. (est. 1987) 14,800 (mostly Polynesians).

Wallsend, t., Tyne and Wear, **Eng.**; on N. bank of Tyne, 6 km below Newcastle; Tyne tunnel links with Jarrow; shipbldg., engin., iron, plywood; at end of Hadrian's Wall; p. (1981) 44,699.

Walmer, t., Kent, **Eng.**; 3 km S. of Deal; holiday resort; cas., residence of Warden of Cinque Ports.

Walney, I., off cst. of Cumbria, **Eng.**; opposite Barrow.

Walsall, t., met. dist., West Midlands, **Eng.**; 8 km E. of Wolverhampton; leather and iron gds., engin., steel tubes; p. (est. 1988) 262,300.

Walsingham, v., North Norfolk, **Eng.**; many old bldgs., priory ruins, abbey; mediaeval pilgrimage ctr.

Walsum, t., N. Rhine–Westphalia, **W. Germany**; at confluence of Rhine and Emscher canal; R. pt. for Oberhausen steelwks.; p. (est. 1969) 48,262.

Waltham, c., Mass., **USA**; nr. Boston; science-based inds.; univ.; p. (1980) 58,200.

Waltham Abbey, t., Epping Forest, Essex, **Eng.**; 21 km N.E. London, on edge of Epping Forest; glasshouses (tomatoes); Norman nave of abbey part of parish church; p. (1981) 19,432.

Waltham Forest, outer bor., E. London, **Eng.**; incorporating former bors. of Chingford, Leyton, Walthamstow; industl. and residtl.; p. (est. 1988) 213,300.

Walthamstow. See **Waltham Forest**.

Walton and Weybridge, ts., Elmbridge, Surrey, **Eng.**; on R. Thames, 27 km S.W. of London; eng., aircraft; p. (1981) 49,237.

Walton-le-Dale, t., South Ribble, N.E. Lancs., **Eng.**; on R. Ribble, 3 km E. of Preston; mkt. gardening, cottons, timber; p. (1981) 29,000.

Walvis Bay, spt., South Africa, enclave in **Namibia**; on Walvis Bay, Atl. Oc.; fishing, fish processing; impt. base for S. Africa who wishes to keep it separate from Namibia; p. (est. 1980) 25,000.

Wandsworth, inner bor., S.W. London, **Eng.**; inc. Battersea; on R. Wandle at influx into Thames; oil mills, metal wks., paper, brewing; p. (est. 1988) 257,100.

Wanganui, c., N.I., **N.Z.**; pt. on R. Wanganui; tr. ctr. for wool, grain, meat, dairy prod.; agr. processing, steel-pipes, fertilisers; iron ore deposits; p. (est. 1987) 38,200.

Wanganui, R., N.I., **N.Z.**; famous for its beauty; 265 km long.

Wangaratta, t., Victoria, **Australia**; 232 km from Melbourne; ctr. of varied agr. dist. supplying prods. (milk, wool) for processing; p. (1981) 16,630.

Wankie, t., **Zimbabwe**; site of coal-mng. ind.; 344 km N.W. of Bulawayo; new coal fired power sta.; p. (1982) 39,200.

Wanne-Eickel, t., N. Rhine–Westphalia, **W. Germany**; pt. on Rhine–Herne canal; coal-mng. ctr. of Ruhr; p. (est. 1969) 100,300.

Wansbeck, R., Northumberland, **Eng.**; flows E. from Pennines into N. Sea 5 km N. of Blyth.

Wansbeck, l. gov. dist., Northumberland, **Eng.**; inc. Newbiggin, Ashington and Bedlington; p. (est. 1988) 59,000.

Wansdyke, l. gov. dist., S. Avon, **Eng.**; inland a. inc. Keynsham, Bathavon and Clutton; p. (est. 1988) 82,200.

Wantage, mkt. t., Oxon., **Eng.**; in Vale of the White Horse; birthplace of King Alfred; p. (1981) 8,765.

Wapping, Thames-side dist., London, **Eng.**

Warangal, t., Andhra Pradesh, **India**; textiles, carpets; p. (1981) 335,150.

Ware, mkt. t., East Herts., **Eng.**; on R. Lea; 3 km N.E. of Hertford; p. (1981) 14,203.

Wareham, mkt. t., Purbeck, Dorset, **Eng.**; on R. Frome, on N. of I. of Purbeck, 13 km S.W. of Poole; agr. machin., pipes; p. (1981) 4,577.

Warley, t., Sandwell, West Midlands, **Eng.**; inc. Smethwick, Oldbury and Rowley Regis; varied inds.; p. of dist. (1981) 163,567.

Warminster, t., West Wilts., **Eng.**; on Wylye watershed at edge of Salisbury Plain; agr. mkt., gloves; p. (1981) 15,065.

Warnemünde, spt., **E. Germany**; ferry pt. for rail traffic between Berlin and Copenhagen; shipbldg.; outport for Rostock; resort.

Warrego, R., Queensland, N.S.W., **Australia**; trib. of R. Darling; 640 km long.

Warren, t., Ohio, **USA**; on Mahoning R.; iron and steel mftg.; p. (1984) 152,000.

Warrenpoint, spt., Newry and Mourne, **N. Ireland**; at head of Carlingford Lough; p. (1981) 4,798.

Warrington, t., l. gov. dist., Cheshire, **Eng.**; on R. Mersey and Manchester Ship Canal; metal inds. (wire-drawing), chemicals, brewing, paper; expanded as new c. (to take people from Manchester) with p. (1991) 205,000; attracting high technology inds.; p. (est. 1988) 186,000 (dist.), (1981) 134,327 (t.).

Warrnambool, t., spt., Victoria, **Australia**; former pt. on Lady Bay; wool processing, rugs, blankets; p. (est. 1983) 27,000.

Warsaw (**Warszawa**), c., cap. of **Poland**; on R. Vistula; devastated in second world war; facsimile rebuilding based on Canaletto's paintings; cath., univ.; rly. ctr.; iron, steel, engin., textiles, chemicals; p. (est. 1985) 1,649,000.

Warsop, t., Notts., **Eng.**; 6 km N.E. of Mansfield; limestone, gravel; p. (1981) 13,675.

Warta, R., **Poland**; trib. of R. Oder; connected to R. Vistula by canal; 720 km long.

Warwick, t., Queensland, **Australia**; sawmilling, agr. processing; p. (est. 1984) 9,540.

Warwick, co. t., l. gov. dist., Warwicks., **Eng.**; on R. Avon, 13 km S.W. of Coventry; cas.; agr. implements, brewing, malting; p. (est. 1988) 116,400 (dist.).

Warwick, c., R.I., **USA**; on Narragansett Bay; textile ctr.; p. (1980) 87,123.

Warwickshire, non-met. co., W. Midlands, **Eng.**; undulating, drained by tribs. of Rs. Severn and Trent, crossed by Cotswolds to S.; sm. coalfield to N.; potential new coalfield in S.; much of industl. N. now inc. in West Midlands met. co.; a. 1,981 km²; p. (est. 1988) 484,600.

Warwickshire, North, l. gov. dist., Warwicks., **Eng.**; close to Midlands conurb., based on Atherstone; p. (est. 1988) 59,100.

Wassatch Mtns., range of Rocky mtns., Utah and Idaho, **USA**; alt. 3,600 m.

Wash, The, bay, N. Sea between Lincs. and Norfolk, **Eng.**; 35 km long, 24 km wide; partly reclaimed to form the Fens; proposed barrage to aid further reclamation and water storage.

Washington, t., Tyne and Wear, **Eng.**; 8 km S.E. of Gateshead; coal, iron and steel, stone quarrying, chemicals; new t. 1964; p. (1981) 47,445.

Washington, co., cap. of **USA**; in Dist. of Columbia on Potomac R.; c. planned as national seat of Government; White House, Capitol, 5 univs.; over half p. Black; p. (1984) 622,800 (c.), 3,369,600 (met. a.).

Washington, st., **USA**; 'Evergreen St.' admitted to Union 1889; st. flower Western Rhododendron, st bird Willow Goldfinch; in extreme N.W., stretching from Pac. Oc. into Rocky mtns.; over half a. forested; Colombia R. and tribs. provide hydroelectric power; timber, fishing, tourism; cap. Olympia; a. 176,617 km²; p. (1985) 4,409,000.

Wast Water, L. Dist., deepest L. in **Eng.**; 5 km long, 79 m deep.

Watchet, t., West Somerset, **Eng.**; sm. pt. on cst. of Bristol Channel; paper mkg., fishing; p. (1981) 3,050.

Watenstedt-Salzgitter. *See* **Salzgitter.**

Waterbury, c., Conn., **USA**; on Naugatuck R.; ctr. of brass ind. and metal gds.; p. (1984) 102,900 (c.), 208,200 (met. a.).

Waterford, co., Munster, **R.o.I.**; mtnous. co. in S.E.; mainly agr., dairying, pigs; fishing; co. t. Waterford; a. 1,867 km²; p. (1981) 38,473.

Waterford, co. t., spt., Waterford, **R.o.I.**; on R. Suir; cath.; brewing, fishing, glass mnfs.; p. (1981) 38,478 (t.).

Waterloo, t., Brabant prov., **Belgium**, nr. Brussels; battle nearby 1815; p. (1982) 24,936.

Waterloo, t., Ont., **Canada**; industl. sub. of Kitchener; p. (1986) 58,718

Waterloo, c., Iowa, **USA**; on Cedar R.; agr. prod. and tools; p. (1984) 75,700 (c.), 161,800 (met. a.).

Waters of Merom (**L. Hula**), Upper Galilee, **Israel**; extensive drainage completed 1957; a. 14 km².

Waterton Glacier International Peace Park, Albert and Mont., **Canada** and **USA**; glacial and lake scenery; a. 596 km².

Watertown, t., Mass., **USA**; on Charles R.; textiles, clothing; p. (1980) 34,384.

Watertown, t., N.Y., **USA**; on Black R.; engin., paper; p. (1980) 27,861.

Watford, t., l. gov. dist., Herts., **Eng.**; on R. Colne, 26 km N.W. of London; mkt.; varied inds., inc. lt. and elec. engin., paper, printing; p. (est. 1988) 75,200.

Wattenscheid, t., N. Rhine–Westphalia, **W. Germany**; E. of Essen; coal, metals, footwear; p. (est. 1980) 67,653.

Waukegan, c., Ill., **USA**; on L. Michigan; summer resort; steel, brass, motors, sugar refining; p. (1980) 67,653.

Wauwatosa, t., Wis., **USA**; sub. of Milwaukee; metals, concrete, chemicals; p. (1980) 51,308.

Waveney, R., Norfolk and Suffolk, **Eng.**; 80 km long.

Waveney, l. gov. dist., Suffolk, **Eng.**; based on Lowestoft, Beccles and Bungay; p. (est. 1988) 106,500.

Waverley, l. gov. dist., Surrey, **Eng.**; inc. Farnham, Godalming and Haslemere; p. (est. 1988) 109,700.

Wayatinah, hydroelectric commission v., Tasmania, **Australia**; dam, lagoon and power sta. at confluence of Rs. Nive and Derwent.

Wazirabad (**Balkh**), t., **Afghanistan**; anc. Bactra, cap. of Bactria, called the "mother of cities", destroyed by Genghiz Khan 1221; textile plant projected; p. c. 13,000.

Weald, The, wooded and pastoral tracts S.E. **Eng.**; extending from Folkestone, Kent, through Surrey, Hants., and Sussex to the sea at Beachy Head; former a. of iron working; name derived from German *Wald* = forest.

Wealden, l. gov. dist., East Sussex, **Eng.**; stretches from Uckfield to S. cst.; p. (est. 1988) 133,900.

Wear, R., Durham/Tyne and Wear, **Eng.**; rises in Pennines, flows through Durham to N. Sea at Sunderland; 96 km long.

Wear Valley, l. gov. dist., Durham, **Eng.**; Pennine a. inc. Bishop Auckland, Crook and Willington; p. (est. 1988) 64,100.

Weaver, R., Cheshire, **Eng.**; industl. trib. of R. Mersey; 72 km long.

Weddell Sea, arm of S. Atl. Oc., **Antarctica**; whaling and sealing.

Wednesbury, t., West Midlands, **Eng.**; former metal wkg. t.

Wednesfield, t., West Midlands, **Eng.**; metal tubes, materials handling equip.; expanded t.

Wei, R., Shaanxi prov., W. **China**; rises in highlands of Kansu, flows E. between highlands of Shaanxi and Hua Shan to join Yellow R; valley contains very fertile loess soils; formed cradle of Chinese civilisation; c. 800 km long.

Weifang, c., Shandong prov., **China**; coal-mng. ctr.; tobacco processing; p. (1984) 1,033,200.

Weihai, spt., Shandong prov., **China**; naval base; fishing; vegetable-oil processing, textiles; p. (1984) 216,400.

Weimar, t., Erfurt, **E. Germany**; on R. Ilm; ctr. of music and culture in 19th cent., associated with Goethe, Schiller, Nietzsche, Liszt, Herder; scene of establishment of German rep. 1919; elec. and metal inds., textiles, musical instruments, glass; p. (1981) 63,725.

Weipa, Queensland, **Australia**; Aboriginal community t. since 1965 taken over by Queensland to overcome opposition to bldg. of new t., pt., and alumina plant; bauxite nearby at Aurukin; p. (1976) 2,876.

Weisshorn, mtn. peak, **Switzerland**; alt. 4,505 m.

Wejherowo, t., Gdansk, **Poland**; on R. Reda; mediaeval stronghold; palace; p. (1970) 33,700.

Welkom, t., O.F.S., **S. Africa**; ctr. of O.F.S. goldfields; p. (1980) 176,608 (met. a.).

Welland, t., Ont., **Canada**; on Welland Canal; industl. t.; p. (1981) 45,448.

Welland, R., Northants. and Lincs., **Eng.**; rises in Northampton heights and flows N.E. into the Wash; 112 km long.

Welland Ship Canal, Ont., **Canada**; connects Ls. Erie and Ont.; 43 km long; 2-lane waterway.

Wellingborough, t., l. gov. dist., Northants., **Eng.**; on R. Nene, 14 km N.E. of Northampton; mkt.; footwear; expanded t.; p. (est. 1988) 66,200 (dist.).

Wellington, mkt. t., The Wrekin, Shrops., **Eng.**; brewing, sugar refining, timber, toys; name derived from "Watling Town" (stood on Watling Street); with Dawley and Oakengates forms new t. of Telford; p. (1981) 15,699.

Wellington, mkt. t., Somerset, **Eng.**; 10 km S.W. Taunton, anc. woollen ind. still survives; dairy prod.; p. (1981) 10,567.

Wellington, c., spt., N.I., cap. of **N.Z.**; univ.; impt. exp. ctr. for dairy prod., wool, meat; new inds. developing in Hutt valley with vehicle assembly, rubber, oil refineries; p. (est. 1987) 136,000.

Wellington, prov., N.I., **N.Z.**; mtnous., pastoral and dairy farming; a. 28,153 km²; p. (est. 1985) 587,700.

Wells, cath. t., Mendip, Somerset, **Eng.**; on S. flank of Mendip hills; cath.; bishop's palace; paper mftg.; tourism; p. (1981) 8,374.

Wels, t., Upper **Austria**; on Traun R.; mkt. for agr. a.; cas.; p. (1981) 51,060.

Welshpool, mkt. t., Powys, **Wales**; on R. Severn; nearby is Powys cas.; p. (1981) 7,030.

Welwyn Garden City, t., Welwyn-Hatfield, Herts., **Eng.**; 34 km N. of London; founded by Sir Ebenezer Howard (1920) as first satellite t. of London; new t. 1948; pharmaceuticals, plastics, radio, and electronics, lt. inds.; p. (1981) 40,496.

Welwyn-Hatfield, l. gov. dist., Herts., **Eng.**; comprises Welwyn Garden City and Hatfield; p. (est. 1988) 93,400.

Wembley, former M.B., Middx., **Eng.**; now inc. in Brent outer bor. Greater London; lt. inds., sports ctr.; British Empire Exhibition 1924-5.

Wenlock Edge, narrow ridge, Shrops., **Eng.**; extends 29 km S.W. from Much Wenlock to Craven Arms; limestone; moorland, mainly above 290 m.

Wensleydale, North Yorks., **Eng.**; valley in N. Pennines drained E. by R. Ure; cattle reared for fattening on lowland farms; some dairying (cheese); length 56 km.

Wenzhou (Wenchow), c., spt., Zhejiang prov., **China**; pt. on estuary of Wu R., E. China Sea; fishing, coastal tr.; exp. wood, tea, agr. prod.; univ.; textile, leather and medicine inds.; designated an economic development zone, communications being improved; p. (1984) 519,100.

Wernigerode, t., Magdeburg, **E. Germany**; on N. slopes of Harz mtns.; mediaeval cas.; tourism; p. (est. 1970) 32,662.

Wesel, t., N. Rhine–Westphalia, **W. Germany**; R. pt. at confluence of Rs. Lippe and Rhine, Ruhr conurb.; p. (est. 1986) 54,600.

Weser, R., **W. Germany**; formed by confluence of Fulda and Werra Rs. at Münden; flows N. to N. Sea at Bremerhaven; linked by Mittelland canal to Rhine, Ems, and Elbe; navigable for entire length of 330 m.

Wesermünde. *See* **Bremerhaven**.

Wessex, anc. kingdom, S. **Eng.**; inc. Berks., Hants., Wilts., Dorset, Somerset and Devon.

West Bengal, st., N.E. **India**; W., mainly Hindu section of former presidency of B. (Muslim E.B. now Bangladesh); on Ganges delta and flood plain; humid sub-tropical climate; very dense p.; rice, jute; ch. c. Calcutta; a. 87,617 km²; p. (1981) 54,580,647.

West Bridgford, t., Rushcliffe, Notts., **Eng.**; at junc. of Grantham canal with R. Trent; residtl. sub. of Nottingham; p. (1981) 28,073.

West Bromwich, t., Sandwell, West Midlands, **Eng.**; on R. Thame, 8 km N.W. of Birmingham; heavy engin. and allied inds., chemicals, springs, oil refining; p. (1981) 154,930.

West Derbyshire. *See* **Derbyshire Dales**.

West Devon, l. gov. dist., Devon, **Eng.**; rural W. of Dartmoor and ts. of Tavistock and Okehampton; p. (est. 1988) 43,900.

West Dorset, l. gov. dist., Dorset, **Eng.**; inc. Lyme Regis, Bridport, Sherborne and Dorchester; p. (est. 1988) 85,200.

Western Australia, st. of the **Australian Commonwealth**; cut off from the rest of A. by desert; lgst. st., nearly a third of continent with only 9 per cent of p. concentrated in S.W. around st. cap. of Perth in fertile Mediterranean-like a.; diversity of relief, Hammersley range in N.W., Kimberley range in N.E., Gibson desert in interior; rich but irregularly distributed mineral deposits; intensive agr. in S.W., wheat and sheep in interior; a. 2,525,500 km²; p. (1986) 1,459,019.

Western Desert, Egypt; part of Libyan Desert; inc. Qattara depression; coastal road from Cairo to Tripoli; fighting in second world war.

Western Isles, l. gov. reg., **Scot.**; remote a. of Outer Hebrides where pastoral farming and fishing have been the traditional livelihood for some time; p. (est. 1986) 31,494.

Western Pacific High Commission Territories, inc. Solomon Is. and Kiribati and Tuvalu Is.

Westernport, inlet, Vic., **Australia**; major heavy industl. a. close to Melbourne, rapidly growing.

Western Sahara (Spanish Sahara), N.W. African cst.; comprising Rio de Oro and Sagui el Hamra; desert; rich phosphate mines at Bou Craa connected to El Aaiun pt. by rly.; upon decolonisation terr. split between Morocco and Mauritania (1976) but declared Saharan Arab Democratic Rep. by Algerians (Polisario) and still disputed; intermittent fighting by Polisario continues; a. 265,993 km², p. largely nomadic (est. 1985) 155,000.

Western Samoa, indep. sov. st., S. **Pac. Oc.**; member of Commonwealth (1970); gained independence from N.Z. 1962; consists of 2 lge Is. (Savai'i, Upolu) and 7 sm. Is.; 70 per cent p. in agr.; c. 30 per cent a. devoted to bananas; exp. bananas, copra, cacao beans; ch. spt. Apia on Upolu I.; a. 2,841 km²; p. (est. 1985) 163,000.

Westerwald, plateau of old volcanic rocks, **W. Germany**; ending in steep slope E. of R. Rhine; fertile soil; pastureland or deciduous woodland; sm. quantities of iron ore in Siegerland.

West Glamorgan, co., S. **Wales**; borders Bristol Channel; inc. Gower Penin. and lge. industl. ts. of Swansea, Neath and Port Talbot; impt. metal refining and engin. inds.; a. 816 km²; p. (est. 1988) 362,900.

West Ham, former C.B., Essex, **Eng.**; sub. to E. of London; bordered by Rs. Thames and Lea; now inc. in Newham bor., Greater London.

West Hartford, t., Conn., **USA**; residtl. sub. of Hartford; metal gds., ctr. for dairying, tobacco-growing dist.; p. (1980) 61,301.

West Indies or **Antilles**, I. grs., **Atl. Oc.**; extend between csts. of Fla. and Venezuela, separating Caribbean Sea and G. of Mexico from Atl.; inc. Cuba, Haiti, Dominican Rep., Bahamas, Barbados, Jamaica, Leeward Is., Trinidad and Tobago, Windward Is., Guadeloupe, Martinique, Curaçao, Puerto Rico, Virgin Is.; mostly volcanic and coral Is.; former colonial terrs. developed for plantation agr. worked by W. African slaves; most of indigenous Indians killed.

West Irian. *See* **Irian Jaya**.

West Lancashire, l. gov. dist., Lancs., **Eng.**; N. of Merseyside, inc. Skelmersdale and Ormskirk; p. (est. 1988) 105,400.

West Lindsey, l. gov. dist., Lincs., **Eng.**; lge. a. N. of Lincoln and inc. Market Rasen and Gainsborough; p. (est. 1988) 76,800.

West Lothian, l. gov. dist., former co., Lothian Reg., **Scot.**; industl. dist. in Central Lowlands close to Edinburgh; a. 417 km²; p. (est. 1986) 140,545.

Westmeath, co., Leinster, **R.o.I.**; low-lying, drained by R. Shannon, many Ls.; dairying; co. to Mullingar; ch. t. Athlone; a. 1,834 km²; p. (1981) 27,609.

West Mersea, t., Essex, **Eng.**; on Mersea I.; p. (1981) 5,514.

West Midlands, former met. co., **Eng.**; mainly industl. a. centred around Birmingham and the S. Staffs. coalfield (Black Country) and Coventry and the Warwicks. coalfield; many forms of engin. and light inds. inc. vehicle mftg.; p. (est. 1988) 2,617,200.

Westminster, City of, inner bor., London, **Eng.**; on N. bank of R. Thames; W. of City of London; incorporates former bors. of Paddington and St. Marylebone; contains Houses of Parliament, Westminster Abbey, Government offices, Royal Palaces (Buckingham Palace and St. James's); p. (est. 1988) 169,700.

Westmorland, former co., **Eng.**; now part of **Cumbria** non-met. co.

West Norfolk, l. gov. dist., Norfolk, **Eng.**; lge. a. inc. Hunstanton, King's Lynn and Downham Market; p. (est. 1988) 134,100.

Weston-super-Mare, t., Woodspring, Avon, **Eng.**; on Bristol Channel, 32 km S.W. of Bristol; holiday resort; expanded t.; p. (1981) 57,980.

West Orange, t., N.J., **USA**; elec. equipment; home of T. A. Edison; p. (1980) 39,510.

West Oxfordshire, l. gov. dist., Oxon., **Eng.**; in Cotswolds and ts. of Chipping Norton, Witney and Woodstock; p. (est. 1988) 97,800.

West Pakistan. See **Pakistan.**

West Palm Beach, Fla., **USA**; domestic hardware; spt.; tourism; p. (1984) 67,600 (t.), 692,200 (met.a.).

Westphalia. See **North Rhine-Westphalia.**

West Point, military sta., N.Y., **USA**; on Hudson R.; military academy.

Westport, spt., U.D., Mayo, **R.o.I.**; on Clew Bay; fishing; mkt.; p. (1981) 3,379.

Westray, I., Orkney Is., **Scot.**; 16 km long; p. (1971) 841.

West Somerset, l. gov. dist., Somerset, **Eng.**; inc. Exmoor and cstl. ts. of Watchet and Minehead; p. (est. 1988) 31,500.

West Sussex, non-met. co., S.E. **Eng.**; crossed by E.–W. chalk ridge of S. Downs and forested Weald; diverse agr.; dormitory, retirement and tourist ts. on cst. inc. Bognor Regis and Worthing; Crawley new t. in N.; a. 2,015 km²; p. (est. 1988) 703,400

West Virginia, st., **USA**; 'Mountain St.' admitted to Union 1863; st. flower Big Rhododendron, st. bird Cardinal; inc. Allegheny plateau; impt. mng. st. for coal; fruit farming; many industl. ts.; cap. Charleston; a. 62,629 km²; p. (1985) 1,936,000.

Westward Ho!, v., N. Devon, **Eng.**; named after Kingsley's novel.

West Wiltshire, l. gov. dist., Wilts., **Eng.**; stretches from Melksham, Bradford-on-Avon and Trowbridge to Warminster; p. (est. 1988) 106,200.

West Yorkshire, former met. co., **Eng.**; industl. and mainly built-up a. E. of Pennines; traditionally ass. with woollen textile mftg.; inc. major ctrs. of Bradford and Leeds; p. (est. 1988) 2,056,600.

Wetar I., Indonesia; N. of Timor I.; mtns.; underdeveloped; sparse p.; a. 31,080 km².

Wetherby, t., West Yorks., **Eng.**; on R. Wharfe; mkt., t.; racecourse.

Wethersfield, t. Conn., **USA**; oldest settlement (1634) in st.; aircraft parts, agr. implements; p. (1970) 26,662.

Wetterhorn, mtn., **Switzerland**; alt. 3,710 m.

Wetzlar, t., Hesse, **W. Germany**; on R. Lahn; metallurgical and optical inds.; p. (est. 1986) 50,300.

Wexford, coastal co., Leinster, S.E. **R.o.I.**; mixed farming, fishing; cap. Wexford; a. 2,334 km²; p. (1981) 32,237.

Wexford, t., cap. of Wexford; Leinster, S.E. **R.o.I.**; on R. Slaney; agr. processing; outport at Rosslare; p. (1981) 11,417.

Wey, R., Hants., Surrey, **Eng.**; rises in W. Weald, flows N. into R. Thames nr. Weybridge; cuts impt. gap through N. Downs at Guildford; length 56 km.

Weybridge. See **Walton and Weybridge.**

Weymouth and Portland, t., l. gov. dist., Dorset, **Eng.**; on Weymouth Bay, 13 km S. of Dorchester; torpedo and boatbldg., bricks, tiles, engin.; holiday resort; p. (est. 1988) 64,000.

Whaley Bridge, t., High Peak, Derbys., **Eng.**; textile bleaching and finishing; p. (1981) 5,501.

Whangarei, c., N.I., **N.Z.**; deep harbour; oil refining; natural gas pipelines from Kapuni; fertilisers, sheet glass; p. (est. 1987) 39,800.

Wharfe, R., West and North Yorks., **Eng.**; trib. of R. Ouse; 96 km long.

Wheeling, c., W. Va., **USA**; pt. on Ohio R.; comm. and mftg. ctr. in coal and natural gas a.; iron, stecl, and metal plants; p. (1984) 42,100 (c.), 183,200 (met. a.).

Whickham, t., Tyne and Wear, **Eng.**; nr. Gateshead; chemicals, paper; p. (1981) 31,543.

Whitburn, burgh, W. Lothian, **Scot.**; 32 km S.W. of Edinburgh; coal, limestone; p. (1981) 12,559.

Whitby, t., North Yorks., **Eng.**; at mouth of R. Esk, 27 km N.W. of Scarborough; anc. spt. and fishing t.; residtl. and coastal resort; abbey; famous for jet ornaments; potash to be mined nearby; p. (1981) 13,763.

Whitchurch, t., Shrops., **Eng.**; 21 km S.W. of Crewe; structural steel, dairy prods.

White, R., Ark. and Mo., **USA**; trib. of Mississippi; hydroelectric power; 1,104 km long.

Whiteadder, R., Berwick, **Scot.**; trib. of R. Tweed; 54 km long.

Whitehaven, spt., Copeland, Cumbria, **Eng.**; on Solway F. 5 km N. of St. Bees Head; coal, methane gas, cement, chemicals; p. (1981) 26,714.

Whitehead, t., Carrickfergus, **N. Ireland**; at entrance to Belfast Lough; seaside resort; p. (1966) 2,740.

Whitehorse, t., cap. of Yukon terr., **Canada**; ctr. coal and copper mng., hunting and fur trapping; once a gold "boom town"; H.Q. Royal Canadian Mounted Police; end of Alaska highway linking Edmonton, Alberta; p. (1986) 15,199.

White Mtns., part. of Appalachian system, N.H., **USA**; highest summit Mt. Washington, 1,918 m.

White Nile (Bahr-el-Abiad), R., **Sudan**; N.E. Africa; strictly, name applied to stretch of R. Nile between L. No and Khartoum; 800 km long.

White Plains, t., N.Y., **USA**; on Bronx R.; residtl.; battle 1776; p. (1980) 46,999.

White Russia. See **Belorussiyan SSR.**

White Sea or G. of Arkangelsk, inlet of Barents Sea, **USSR**; frozen for 6 months of year; connected to Baltic Sea by deep-water canal; impt. fisheries.

Whitley Bay, t., North Tyneside, Northumberland, **Eng.**; 5 km N. of Tynemouth; seaside resort; plastics; p. (1981) 37,079.

Whitstable, spt., Kent, **Eng.**; on Thames estuary 10 km N. of Canterbury; holiday resort, oysters; p. (1981) 27,896.

Whittlesey, t., Fenland, Cambs., **Eng.**; in the Fens, 13 km W. of March; bricks, mkt. gardening; p. (1981) 11,812.

Whyalla, t., spt., S. **Australia**; t. on N.W. shore of Spencer Gulf developed by Broken Hill Co. in 1901 as terminal for Iron Knob iron exp.; major iron and steel wks.; shipbldg. now in difficulties; p. (1981) 29,962.

Wichita, c., Kan., **USA**; in Arkansas valley; rly. wks., oil refineries and equipment, meatpacking ctr. in agr. and stock-raising region; univ.; p. (1984) 283,500 (c.), 428,600 (met. a.).

Wichita Falls, c., Texas, **USA**; oil refining, ctr. in agr. and ranching a.; p. (1984) 98,900 (c.), 126,200 (met. a.).

Wick, spt., sm. burgh, Caithness, **Scot.**; on E. cst., 22 km S. of John O'Groats; airport to Orkneys and Shetlands; herring fishing ctr.; p. (1981) 7,933.

Wicklow, coastal co., Leinster, **R.o.I.**; crossed by Wicklow mtns.; pastoral agr. and tourism; cap. Wicklow; a. 2,033 km²; p. (1981) 45,843.

Wicklow, t., cap. of Wicklow, Leinster, **R.o.I.**; on S.E. cst., 56 km S. of Dublin; mkt.; sm. seaside resort; p. (1981) 5,341.

Wicklow, mtns., Wicklow, **R.o.I.**; highest summit Lugnaquillia, 927 m.

Widecombe, v., Devon, **Eng.**; Dartmoor tourist ctr.; famous through ballad "Widecombe Fair."

Widnes, t., Halton, Cheshire, **Eng.**; on R. Mersey 19 km E. of Liverpool; impt. chemical inds.; expanded t.; p. (1981) 54,411.

Wiener Neustadt, t., Lower **Austria**; rly. and industl. ctr.; heavy machin.; founded 1192; anc. bldgs., cas., cath.; education ctr.; p. (1981) 35,006.

Wieringermeer Polder, reclaimed a., N. Holland, **Neth.**; N.W. of IJsselmeer; a. 202 km².

Wiesbaden, c., cap. of Hesse, **W. Germany**; on Rhine, at S. foot of the Taunus; famous spa.; cas.; ctr. for Rhine wines; chemicals, metal gds.; p. (est. 1986) 266,500.

Wigan, t., met. dist., Gtr. Manchester, **Eng.**; 26 km. N.E. of Liverpool; engin., chemicals, cement, food processing, paper; former coalmng. ctr.; p. (est. 1988) 307,600.

Wight, I. of, non-met. co., **Eng.**; English Channel,

separated from Hampshire by Spithead and the Solent; crossed by chalk hills, terminating in the Needles; popular holiday resort; ch. ts., Newport, Ryde, Cowes; a. 381 km²; p. (est. 1988) 129,800.

Wigston, t., Leics., **Eng.**; 6 km S. of Leicester; engin., hosiery; p. (1981) 31,900. *See* **Oadby**.

Wigtown, l. gov. dist., former co., Dumfries and Galloway Reg., **Scot.**; along N. cst. of Solway F.; impt. dairying reg.; a. 1,712 km²; p. (est. 1986) 30,384.

Wigtown, sm. burgh, Wigtown, **Scot.**; on W. Bay, Solway F.; shares admin. with Newton Stewart; p. (1981) 1,015.

Wilhelmshaven, c., Lower Saxony, **W. Germany**; on inlet of N. Sea, 64 km N.W. of Bremen; ch. German naval base until 1945; industl. ctr. with heavy machin., elec. equipment, textiles, furniture; oil pipeline; p. (est. 1986) 94,900.

Wilkes-Barre, c., Penns., **USA**; on Susquehanna R.; industl. ctr. in rich anthracite mng. a.; p. (1980) 51,551.

Wilkes Land, Antarctica; featureless plateau, alt. 2,900 m; immense glaciers; U.S. base taken over by Australia 1959.

Willamette, R., Ore., **USA**; rises in Cascade mtns., flows N. into Columbia R. below Portland; valley gives rich agr. land, wheat, rootcrops, dairy prod., hard and soft fruits; ch. ts. Eugene, Salem, Oregon City, Portland; used for hydroelectric power; 480 km long.

Willemstad, pt., cap. of Neth. **Antilles**; on Curaçao I.; oil refining; tourism; p. (est. 1983) 50,000.

Willenhall, t., West Midlands, **Eng.**; locks and keys, drop forgings.

Willesden, former M.B., Middx., **Eng.**; now inc. in Brent outer bor., Greater London impt. rly. junc., residtl. and industl.

Williamsburg, c., Va., **USA**; between James and York Rs.; historic t., settled 1632; rebuilt in 1920s to original plan; in Colonial Nat. Historical Park; p. (1980) 9,870.

Williamsport, t., Penns., **USA**; on Susquehanna R.; rly. ctr., timber, machin.; summer resort; p. (1984) 32,300 (t.), 117,100 (met. a.).

Willow South, was to be new cap. (1977), Alaska, **USA**; replacing Juneau; closer to ctr. of p.; lack of finance halted construction.

Wilmington, t., spt., Del., **USA**; on Delaware R.; shipbldg., machin., iron and steel wks.; chemicals; leather, cork, rubber gds.; p. (1980) 523,000 (met. a.).

Wilmington, spt., N.C., **USA**; exp. cotton, tobacco, timber, fertilizers, shipbldg., textiles, chemicals; p. (1984) 44,800 (t.), 110,400 (met. a.).

Wilmslow, t., Cheshire, **Eng.**; on R. Bollen, 10 km S.W. of Stockport; residtl.; pharmaceuticals; p. (1981) 30,207.

Wilton, t., Wilts., **Eng.**; on R. Wylye, 5 km W. of Salisbury; agr. mkt., carpets, felt; anc. cap. of Wessex; many old bldgs.; p. (1981) 4,005.

Wilton, industl. estate, Cleveland, **Eng.**; on S. side of Tees estuary; heavy organic- and petro-chemicals; nylon polymer plant.

Wiltshire, non-met. co., **Eng.**; crossed by chalk downland and Salisbury Plain; barley, wheat, dairying, pigs; co. t. Salisbury; a. 3,484 km²; p. (est. 1988) 557,000.

Wiltshire, North, l. gov. dist., Wilts., **Eng.**; rural a. inc. ts. of Calne, Chippenham and Malmesbury; p. (est. 1988) 113,300.

Wimbledon, dist., London, **Eng.**; lge. open common; site of international tennis tournament; part of London Bor. of Merton.

Wimborne. *See* **Dorset East**.

Wimborne Minster, mkt. t., Dorset, **Eng.**; on R. Stour; Roman site and home of Saxon kings; Badbury Rings earthworks nearby; p. (1981) 5,531.

Winchcomb, t., Gloucs., **Eng.**; nr. Cheltenham; old mills; pottery, paper; nearby cas.

Winchelsea, t., c., East Sussex, **Eng.**; 3 km S.W. of Rye; once impt. walled spt. and Cinque port, now 3 km inland.

Winchester, cath. c., l. gov. dist., Hants., **Eng.**; on R. Itchen, 19 km N. of Southampton; anc. Anglo-Saxon cap.; meeting place of parliaments until time of Henry VII; magnificent cath., famous public school; p. (est. 1988) 96,000.

Windermere, lgst. English L., in Cumbria; outlet to Morecambe Bay; supplies water to Manchester; 16 km long, 1·6 km wide.

Windhoek, t., cap. of Namibia; in hills at 1,700 m; comm. ctr., agr. processing; tr. in karakul (Persian lamb); p. (est. 1983) 104,100.

Windrush, R., Oxford, Gloucs., **Eng.**; trib. of R. Thames.

Windscale. *See* **Sellafield**.

Windsor, c., pt., Ont., **Canada**; on Detroit R., linked to Detroit, USA, by tunnel, bridge and ferry; ctr. for car mftg., salt wks., chemicals, paints; univ.; p. (1986) 193,111 (c.), 253,988 (met. a.).

Windsor, New, t., Berks., **Eng.**; on R. Thames, 32 km W. of London; famous royal cas. (founded by William the Conqueror) and park, St. George's Chapel and the Royal Mausoleum; with Maidenhead forms l. gov. dist.; p. (est. 1988) 127,400.

Windward Is., W.I., extend S. from Leeward Is.; consist of Fr. Martinique and former Brit. cols. of Grenada, St. Vincent, St. Lucia and Dominica with their dependencies (the Grenadines divided between Grenada and St. Vincent) which attained associated statehood 1967; sm. limited resources, economically depressed; volcanic; p. (est. 1984) 419,000.

Windward Passage, channel, 96 km wide, between Cuba and Haiti.

Winnebago, L., Wis., **USA**; 43 km long; lgst. L. in Wis.

Winnipeg, c., cap. of Manitoba, **Canada**; at junc. of Red and Assiniboine Rs.; cath., univ., rly. ctr.; ch. world wheat mkt.; meat packing and food processing; lgst. garment mnf. ctr. in cty.; oil refining; p. (1981) 564,473 (inc. St. James).

Winnipeg, L., Manitoba, **Canada**; 64 km N. of Winnipeg; 416 km long, 49–96 km wide; contains several lge. Is. (Reindeer, 181 km²; Big I., 155 km²); used for hydroelectric power.

Winnipegosis, L., Manitoba and Saskatchewan, **Canada**; a. (exclusive of Is.) 5,180 km²; 80 km W. of L. Winnipeg, into which it drains.

Winsford, t., Cheshire, **Eng.**; on R. Weaver; 6 km S. of Northwich; ctr. of salt inds., chemicals; expanded t.; computer peripherals; p. (1981) 26,915.

Winston-Salem, t., N.C., **USA**; formed 1913 from union of 2 adjacent ts.; tobacco ctr.; p. (1984) 143,400.

Winterthur, t., Zurich, **Switzerland**; on Eulach R.; rly. ctr., locomotives, machines, cottons; p. (1985) 84,000.

Wirksworth, t., West Derbys., **Eng.**; in Pennines, 8 km S. of Matlock; limestone, fluorspar wks.; ctr. of Derbys. former lead mng.; p. (1981) 5,492.

Wirral, penin., met. dist., Merseyside, **Eng.**; between estuaries of Dee and Mersey; residtl.; comprises Wallasey, Birkenhead, Bebington and Hoylake; p. (est. 1988) 334,800.

Wisbech, t., Fenland, Cambs., **Eng.**; on R. Nene, 18 km from its mouth in the Wash; mkt. gardening, fruit growing and canning, agr. implements; p. (1981) 17,332.

Wisconsin, st., **USA**; 'Badger St.'; admitted to Union 1848; st. flower Wood Violet. st. bird Robin; bounded by Gr. Ls.; lowlying; leading dairying st.; industl. ts. around Gt. Ls.; cap. Madison; ch. t. Milwaukee; a. 145,439 km²; p. (1985) 4,775,000.

Wisconsin, R., Wis., **USA**; trib. of R. Mississippi; used for hydroelectric power; 960 km long.

Wismar, spt., Rostock, **E. Germany**; on Baltic Sea, N. of Schwerin; oil pt. and industl. ctr. with shipyards and food processing inds.; p. (1981) 57,718.

Witbank, t., Transvaal, **S. Africa**; leading coalmng. dist. with power sta. and carbide and cyanide factories; p. (1970) 50,581.

Witham, t., Essex, **Eng.**; 14 km N.E. of Chelmsford; ctr. of mkt. gardening a.; expanded t.; p. (1981) 25,373.

Witham, R., Leics. and Lincs., **Eng.**; flows into the Wash; cuts impressive gap through Lincoln.

Witney, t., Oxford, **Eng.**; on R. Windrush, 16 km W. of Oxford; woollens, blankets, gloves; p. (1981) 14,109.

Witten, t., N. Rhine–Westphalia, **W. Germany**; on R. Ruhr; glass, machin., metals, chemicals, optical inds.; p. (est. 1986) 102,200.

Wittenberg, t., Halle, **E. Germany**; on R. Elbe; ctr. of Reformation and burial place of Luther (Schlosskirche); cas.; machin., textiles; p. (1981) 53,874.

Wittenberge, t., Schwerin, **E. Germany**; on R. Elbe; rly. junc., repair wkshps., machin.; p. (est. 1970) 33,028.

Witwatersrand, dist., Transvaal, **S. Africa**; gold-mng. dist. producing over quarter of world's gold.

Wivenhoe, t., Essex, **Eng.**; on R. Colne; boat-bldg., oysters, lt. inds.; p. (1981) 6,470.

Włocławek, t., river pt., N. **Poland**; on R. Vistula; impt. paper mnfs., ceramics; p. (est. 1983) 113,400.

Woburn, t., Beds., **Eng.**; 8 km N.E. of Leighton Buzzard; Woburn Abbey (seat of Dukes of Bedford).

Woking, t., l. gov. dist., Surrey, **Eng.**; 6 km N. of Guildford; residtl.; p. (est. 1988) 86,100.

Wokingham, mkt. t., l. gov. dist., Berks., **Eng.**; 8 km S.E. of Reading; agr. tr. and machin., bricks; p. (est. 1988) 150,000.

Wolds, The, chalk downland, Lincs., Humberside, **Eng.**; extend S. to E. Anglian Heights; traditional pastoral agr. changing to extensive arable farming; 72 km long.

Wolfenbüttel, t., Lower Saxony, **W. Germany**; on R. Oker, 11 km S. of Brunswick; noted for ducal library, founded 17th cent., of which Leibnitz and Lessing were librarians; p. (est. 1986) 48,600.

Wolf Rock, isolated rock with lighthouse, at approach to English Channel from Bay of Biscay; 14 km S.W. of Lands End, Cornwall.

Wolfsburg, t., Lower Saxony, **W. Germany**; on R. Aller, N.E. of Brunswick; Volkswagen wks.; p. (est. 1986) 122,000.

Wolin, I., Baltic Sea; off mouth of R. Oder, **Poland**; Nat. Park; fishing, tourism; a. 344 km²; p. (est. 1966) 2,867.

Wollongong Greater, t., N.S.W., **Australia**; 7th. c. of A.; heavy inds. attracted by local coal especially at Pt. Kembla; iron, steel, chems.; Australia's only tinplate plant; p. (1981) 208,651.

Wolsingham, t., Durham, **Eng.**; on R. Wear; impt. steel wks.

Wolverhampton, t., met. dist., West Midlands, **Eng.**; heavy and lt. engin., boilers, rayon, elec. engin. and apparatus, iron wks., aircraft and motor components, hollow-ware, tools, strong-rooms and safes, paints; p. (est. 1988) 249,400.

Wolverton, t., Bucks., **Eng.**; on R. Ouse, 24 km S.W. of Bedford; rly.-carriage wks.; p. (1981) 22,249.

Wombwell, t., South Yorks., **Eng.**; at E. foot of Pennines, 11 km N. of Sheffield; coal mng., bricks; p. (1981) 16,628.

Wonsan, spt., **N. Korea**; on Sea of Japan; major pt. and rly. ctr.; Japanese naval base in second world war; oil refining; p. (1981) 398,000.

Woodbridge, t., Suffolk Coastal, Suffolk, **Eng.**; on R. Deben; engin., brush mkg.; p. (1981) 7,224.

Wood Green, former M.B., Middx., **Eng.**; now inc. in Haringey outer bor., Greater London.

Woodhall Spa, t., East Lindsey, Lincs., **Eng.**; 6 km S.W. of Horncastle; former spa, bromo-iodine springs; resort; p. (1981) 2,445.

Woodspring, l. gov. dist., Avon, **Eng.**; S. of Bristol and inc. Clevedon, Portishead, and Weston-super-Mare; p. (est. 1988) 189,100.

Woodstock, t., Ont., **Canada**; on R. Thames; ctr. of agr. dist.; lt. mnfs. based on hydro-electric power; p. (1981) 26,603.

Woodstock, t., Oxford, **Eng.**; on Glyme R., 11 km N.W. of Oxford; glove mnfs.; Blenheim Palace; p. (1981) 2,036.

Wookey Hole, cave, Mendip Hills, Somerset, **Eng.**; at foot of limestone hills, 3 km N.W. of Wells; R. Axe emerges from the cave.

Woolwich, dist. former met. bor., London, **Eng.**; on either side of R. Thames; impt. Tudor dockyard, now closed; now part of Greenwich and Newham bors.

Woomera, S. **Australia**; c., 432 km N.W. of Adelaide; base for joint U.K.–Australian guided-weapon testing range extending N.W. across the continent; established 1947; p. (1981) 1,658.

Woonsocket, t., R.I., **USA**; on Blackstone R.; textiles, rubber gds.; p. (1980) 45,914.

Worcester, l. gov. dist., Hereford and Worcs., **Eng.**; on R. Severn, 38 km N. of Gloucester; cath.; machin., porcelain, glove mkg.; birthplace of Elgar; p. (est. 1988) 81,200.

Worcester, t., Cape Prov., **S. Africa**; viticultural and industl. ctr.; Goudini spa nearby; p. (1980) 162,000 (c.), 373,000 (met. a.).

Worcester, c., Mass., **USA**; univ.; cultural ctr.; machine tools, elec. engin.; p. (1984) 159,800 (c.), 404,700 (met. a.).

Worcestershire, former Midland co., **Eng.**; now

part of Hereford and Worcs. non-met. co. and West Midlands met. co.

Workington, t., Allerdale, Cumbria, **Eng.**; sm. spt. on Solway F. at mouth of Derwent R., first Bessemer steel plant, heavily dependent upon iron and steel wks. closed (1981), engin.; industl. diversification on nearby industl. estates, inc. bus wks.; p. (1981) 27,581.

Worksop, t., Bassetlaw, Notts., **Eng.**; 24 km S.E. of Sheffield; coal-mng. dist.; brewing, knit-wear, glass, flour; p. (1981) 36,893.

Worms, t., Rhineland-Palatinate, **W. Germany**; on left bank of Rhine; historic ctr.; famous imperial diet 1521 when Luther refused to retract; scene of *Nibelungenlied*; ctr. for Liebfraumilch wines; chemical, textile, leather and metal inds.; p. (est. 1986) 72,000.

Worms Head, promontory, on West Glamorgan cst., Gower peninsula, **Wales**.

Worsley, t., Gtr. Manchester, **Eng.**; ctr. of coal-mng. dist.; p. (1981) 49,021.

Worthing, t., l. gov. dist., West Sussex, **Eng.**; on S. cst., 16 km W. of Brighton; holiday resort, retirement ctr. in mkt. gardening dist.; p. (est. 1988) 98,200.

Woy Woy, t., N.S.W., **Australia**; resort and commuter t. for Sydney; clothing; p. inc. in Gosford.

Wrangel I., Arctic Oc., off Khabarovsk terr., **RSFSR**; weather sta.

Wrath, C., N.W. Sutherland, **Scot**.

Wrekin, hill, Shrops., **Eng.**; alt. 403 m.

Wrekin, The, l. gov. dist., Shrops., **Eng.**; inc. Newport, Wellington, Oakengates and Dawley; p. (est. 1988) 134,200.

Wrexham, t., Clwyd, **Wales**; 18 km S.W. Chester; tyres, synthetic fibres, clothing; as **Wrexham Maelor** forms l. gov. dist.; p. (est. 1988) 117,000.

Wrocław (Breslau), c., Silesia, **Poland**; on R. Oder; impt. route ctr. and R. pt.; univ., cath.; rapid industl. development; ctr. of electronics inds.; p. (est. 1985) 636,000.

Wrocław (Breslau), prov., Lower Silesia, **Poland**; until 1945 part of Germany; heavy inds. based on local minerals; cap. Wrocław; a. 24,740 km²; p. (est. 1986) 1,119,000.

Wroxeter, v., Shrops., **Eng.**; on R. Severn, 8 km S.E. Shrewsbury; Roman sta. Uriconium.

Wuchow. *See* **Wuzhou**.

Wuhan, c., Hubei prov., **China**; formed by union of Hankan, Hanyang and Zhifang; major metropolis on Chang Jiang; integrated iron and steel wks., machine tools, walking tractors, textiles, shipbldg.; univ.; p. (1984) 3,337,500.

Wuhu, c., Anhui prov., **China**; former treaty pt. on Chang Jiang; textiles; p. (1984) 491,700.

Wupper, R., **W. Germany**; trib. of Rhine; industl. concentration along middle course; 64 km long.

Wuppertal, t., N. Rhine–Westphalia, **W. Germany**; formed by amalgamation of Barmen and Elberfeld; textiles, rubber gds., paper, metals, pharmaceuticals; p. (est. 1986) 374,200.

Württemberg-Hohenzollern, former st., **W. Germany**; since 1952 part of Baden–Württemberg.

Würzburg, c., Bavaria, **W. Germany**; on R. Main; univ., cath.; historic bldgs., engin., chemicals, printing; p. (est. 1986) 127,100.

Wurzen, t., Leipzig, **E. Germany**; on R. Mulde; cath., cas.; machin., furniture, leather, foodstuffs; p. (est. 1970) 24,164.

Wuxi (Wusih), c., Jiangsu prov., **China**; on N. shore of Tai L., 120 km W. of Shanghai; univ.; industl. ctr. with cotton mills, chemical wks.; former treaty pt.; p. (1984) 825,100.

Wuzhou (Wuchow), c., R. pt., Guangxi, **China**; on Xijiang; tr. ctr.; exp. tung oil, hides; p. (1984) 256,500.

Wyandotte, t., Mich., **USA**; on Detroit R.; salt deposits; chemical ind.; p. (1980) 34,006.

Wychavon, l. gov. dist., Hereford and Worcs., **Eng.**; inc. Vale of Evesham and Pershore in S. and Droitwich in N.; p. (est. 1988) 101,000.

Wycombe, l. gov. dist., Bucks., **Eng.**; close to Oxon. and inc. High Wycombe and Marlow; p. (est. 1988) 156,300.

Wye, R., Bucks., **Eng.**; rises in Chiltern hills, flows S.E. to R. Thames at Cookham.

Wye, R., **Eng.** and **Wales**; rises in Plynlimmon, flows S.E. into R. Severn at Chepstow; forms deeply incised valley at Symond's Yat; 208 km long.

Wye, t., Kent, **Eng.**; nr. Ashford; impt. agr.

college (Univ. of London).

Wylfa Head, Anglesey, Gwynedd, N. **Wales**; nuclear power sta.

Wymondham, t., South Norfolk, **Eng.**; 14 km S.W. of Norwich; mkt.; Benedictine abbey founded 1107; p. (1981) 9,811.

Wyoming, st., **USA**; 'Equality St.'; admitted to Union 1890; st. flower Indian Paintbrush, st. bird Meadowlark; inc. areas of Rocky mtns. and great plains; Yellowstone Nat. Park; scant rainfall; irrigation; cattle and sheep ranching; petroleum; sparse p.; cap. Cheyenne; a. 253,597 km²; p. (1985) 509,000.

Wyre, R., Lancs., **Eng.**; rises in Pennines, flows W. into Lancaster Bay at Fleetwood; 45 km.

Wyre, l. gov. dist., Lancs., **Eng.**; inc. Preesall, Fleetwood and Thornton Cleveleys; p. (est. 1988) 103,000.

Wyre Forest, l. gov. dist., Hereford and Worcester, **Eng.**; inc. Bewdley, Kidderminster and Stourport; p. (est. 1987) 94,400.

X

Xanthi, t., Thrace, **Greece**; on R. Mesta; ctr. of tobacco-growing a.; p. (1981) 88,777.

Xanthus, ruined c., **Turkey**; on R. Xanthus; destroyed 43 B.C.; tourism.

Xauen, t., Morocco, N. Africa; holy t. founded 15th cent.; p. (1960) 13,712.

Xiamen (Amoy), c., Fujian, **China**; rail link to Jianxi; tea, fruit, machin., chemicals, textiles, electronics, tourism; univ.; formerly treaty pt.; in special Economic Zone to encourage foreign investment; new pt. (1982); 100 factories planned; p. (1984) 532,600.

Xi'an (Sian), cap. of Shaanxi prov., **China**; impt. route and industl. ctr.; machin.; tourism; research ctr.; iron and steel, textiles, chemicals; p. (1984) 2,276,500.

Xiangtan (Siangtan), c., Hunan prov., **China**; on navigable Xijiang; regional tr. ctr., tea, cotton, electrical goods, machin., textiles; Mao Tse Tung born nearby; p. (1984) 501,700.

Xi Jiang (Si Kiang), ch. R., S. **China**; headstreams rise in Yunnan plateau, R. then flows E. enters S. China Sea through lge delta nr. Hong Kong; lower valley intensively cultivated, rice, sugar cane, tea; tropical climate permits continuous cultivation of most crops through year; valley densely populated; c. 2,000 km. long.

Xingu, R., **Brazil**; trib. of Amazon; navigable in its lower course; Nat. Park and Indian reserve threatened by new cattle ranches; 1,920 km long.

Xinhailion. *See* Lianyungang.

Xining (Sining), cap. of Qinghai prov., **China**; ctr. of spring wheat a.; woollen mills, iron and steel; new rly. completed to help reduce isolation; p. (1984) 576,400.

Xinjiang Uygur (Sinkiang-Uighur), aut. region, N. W. **China**; borders USSR and Kashmir; very dry climate; remote until new roads and rlys. penetrated a.; ethnic minority p. of Turkish background and Islamic faith; many attempts to develop natural resources and industry by Chinese government; pastoral agr.; sheep, goats; new st. arable farms, wheat, maize, millet; lge. oil reserves; cap. Ürümqi; a. 1,646,800 km²; p. (est. 1985) 13,440,000.

Xinyang (Sinyang), t., S. Henan, **China**; regional ctr. for S. Henan and Hubei; p. (1984) 226,600.

Xizang Zizhiqu. *See* Tibet.

Y

Yablonovy, mtn. range, Siberia, **RSFSR**; E. of L. Baykal; highest peak, Sokhondo, 2,510 m; crossed by Trans-Siberian rly.

Yaila Mtns., Ukrainian SSR, **USSR**; form S.E. margin of Crimea penin., extend from Sevastopol to Kerch; form marked climate barrier between Black Sea littoral (Soviet Riviera) N. part.

Yakima, t., Wash., **USA**; agr. ctr. of irrigated valley, noted for fruit; p. (1984) 48,900 (t.), 179,500 (met. a.).

Yakima, R., Wash., **USA**; trib. of Columbia R.; used for irrigation; 333 km long.

Yakut ASSR, aut. rep., **RSFSR**; borders Arctic Oc.; home of Yakuts; tundra and forest region, isolated; fur trapping, diamond and gold mng., state farms; a. 3,963,355 km²; p. (1986) 1,001,000.

Yakutsk, t., cap. of Yakut ASSR, **RSFSR**; pt. on Lena R.; univ.; airport; p. (1985) 180,000.

Yallahs Valley, Jamaica; severe soil erosion; govt. improvement scheme of afforestation and new crops; a. 181 km².

Yallourn, t., Victoria, **Australia**; ctr. of lignite mng. a.; p. (1976) 18,710 (inc. Moe).

Yalta, spt., Ukrainian SSR, **USSR**; sub-tropical resort on Black Sea, sheltered by Yaila mtns.; conference between Churchill, Roosevelt, and Stalin 1945; p. (est. 1969) 57,000.

Yalu, R., forms bdy. between N.E. China, and N. **Korea**; flows into Yellow Sea; used for hydro-electric power.

Yamagata, t., Honshu, **Japan**; ctr. of rice-growing a.; cas.; p. (1985) 245,159.

Yamaguchi, t., cap. of Y. prov., S.W. Honshu, **Japan**; cas.; comm. ctr., chemicals; p. (1985) 124,213.

Yamal-Nenets National Okrug, RSFSR; inc. Yamal penin.; permafrost; hunting, fishing; cap. Salekhard; lge. natural gas finds; a. 670,810 km²; p. (1970) 80,000.

Yambol, t., **Bulgaria**; on R. Tunja; ruined mosque; agr. tr.; recent inds. inc. canning, farm machin., textiles, ceramics; p. (1985) 90,215.

Yamethin, dist., Upper **Burma**; teak forests, rice; ch. t. Yamethin; site of irrigation project; p. 9,291.

Yamoussoukro, t., Côte d'Ivoire; new cap. replaced Abidjan (1983) to relieve congestion; p. (1983) 70,000.

Yana, R., Siberia, **USSR**; flows into Arctic Sea; navigable; 1,600 km long.

Yangchow. *See* Yangzhou.

Yangchuan. *See* Yanqan.

Yangi-yer, t., Uzbek SSR, **USSR**; founded 1957 as ctr. for new irrigated cotton lands of E. Uzbekistan.

Yangon. *See* Rangoon.

Yangtze River. *See* Chang Jiang.

Yangzhou, c., Jiangsu, **China**; in valley of Chang Jiang, N.W. of Shanghai; mkt. for local agr. prods.; p. (1984) 382,200.

Yanqan (Yangchuan), c., Shaanxi prov., **China**; iron working ctr.; p. (1982) 477,600.

Yantai, spt., Shangdong prov., **China**; anc. c.; food processing, light ind., textiles, cement, steel; exp. foodstuffs esp. prawns & wines; pt. being enlarged as c. declared an economic development zone to attract foreign investment, esp. high technology; p. (1984) 699,400.

Yaoundé, t., cap. of Cameroon Rep., W. **Africa**; lt. inds. inc. beer, cigarettes, textiles; p. (est. 1984) 650,000.

Yapura, R., Brazil and Colombia, S. America; trib. of R. Amazon; length 2,400 km.

Yaracuy, st., **Venezuela**; crossed by Y. valley impt. agr. a. for bananas, coffee, sugar, tobacco; crossed by Pan-American Highway; cap. San Felipe; a. 7,099 km²; p. (1981) 300,597.

Yare, R., Norfolk, **Eng.**; flows E. to N. Sea at Gorleston; forms part of Norfolk Broads navigable waterways; 80 km long.

Yarkand. *See* Shache.

Yarmouth, spt., Nova Scotia, **Canada**; fisheries; p. (1981) 7,475.

Yarmouth, Great, pt., l. gov. dist., Norfolk, **Eng.**; at mouth of R. Yare; holiday resort; fish and food processing plants; base for N. Sea gas; p. (est. 1988) 88,000 (dist.).

Yaroslavl, c., cap. of Y. oblast, **RSFSR**; on upper Volga in Moscow industl. region; founded 1010; comm. and industl. ctr.; mnfs. inc. textiles, motor vehicles, synthetic rubber, agr. machin.; Volkov theatre, 12th cent. monastery, churches; p. (1986) 630,000.

Yasan, N., **Bulgaria**; lge. refinery and petro-chemicals complex.

Yatsushiro, t., Kyushu, **Japan**; p. (1985) 108,790.

Yazd, c., Isfahan prov., **Iran**; in desert a. at 1,190 m; fine silks, carpets; p. (1986) 248,874.

Yazoo, dist., Miss., **USA**; flood plain of R. Mississippi and R. Yazoo; very fertile alluvial soil, but subject to disastrous floods; one of ch. cotton-growing dists. in USA.

Yegoryevsk, t., **RSFSR**; 115 km S.E. of Moscow; lge textile ind.; phosphorite deposits; p. (est. 1969) 65,000.

Yeletz, t., **RSFSR**; on R. Sosna; grain and cattle tr.; cultural ctr.; rly. junc.; p. (1970) 101,000.

Yell, I., Shetlands, **Scot.**; 27 km long; covered in peat moorland; p. (1971) 1,143.

Yellowhead Pass, B.C., Alberta, **Canada**; most N. and lowest of main passes across Rocky mtns.; carries Canadian Nat. rly. on route from Edmonton to Vancouver and Prince Rupert; summit alt. 1,130 m.

Yellowknife, t., N.W. Terr., **Canada**; on N. shore of Gr. Slave L.; ctr. of impt. gold-mng. dist.; linked by air to Edmonton, Alberta; p. (1986) 11,753.

Yellow R. *See* **Huang He.**

Yellow Sea. *See* **Huang Hai.**

Yellowstone, L., Wyo., **USA**; 32 km long, 24 km wide; alt. 2,360 m; in Y. Nat. Park.

Yellowstone National Park, N.W. Wyo., **USA**; volcanic scenery, geysers; a. 8,956 km².

Yemen Arab Republic (N. Yemen), S.W. Arabian penin.; climate hot and humid in semi-desert cst. strip; summer rainfall inland on high plateau; land slopes down in E. to desert of Rub'al Khali; agr. basis of economy; irrigated terraced, fertile land in highlands; millet, maize, sorghum, oats, fruits; Mocha coffee main exp.; expanding cotton a. in Tihama cst. a.; first oil fields discovered (1984); severe earthquake (1982); ch. spt. Hodeida; cap. Sana'a; strained relations with S. Yemen; a. 194,250 km²; p. (est. 1987) 6,533,265.

Yemen, People's Democratic Rep. of (S. Yemen), S.W. **Arabia**; comprises strategic pt. of Aden and much desert terr.; independence proclaimed 1967 when Brit. troops withdrawn; hot, dry climate; Brit. withdrawal, decline of tourism and closure of Suez Canal resulted in economic decline; subsistence agr., little comm. exploitation of rich fishing grounds; oil refinery at Aden; cap. Madinat ash Sha'b (N.W. of Aden); strained relations with N. Yemen; a. 290,274 km²; p. (est. 1987) 2,278,000.

Yenangyaung, t., R. pt., **Burma**; on left bank of R. Irrawaddy, 448 km N. of Rangoon; ctr. of Burma oilfields.

Yenisey, R., Siberia, **RSFSR**; rises in Sayan mtns., flows N. into Arctic Oc.; ch. tribs., Angara, Stony Tunguska, Lower Tunguska; hydroelectric power sta. at Krasnoyarsk; linked to Ob R. by canal; middle course navigable; 5,280 km long.

Yentai (Chefoo). *See* **Yantai.**

Yeo or **Ivel,** R., Dorset, Somerset, **Eng.**; trib. of R. Parrett; 38 km long.

Yeovil, mkt. t., l. gov. dist., Somerset, **Eng.**; on R. Yeo; glove mnf., aero-engin., agr. machin., dairy processing; p. (1988) 141,700 (dist.).

Yerevan or **Erivan,** c., cap. of Armenian SSR, **USSR**; on Zanga R. in deep valley of Caucasus mtns.; earthquake 1988; major science-based, industl. ctr.; earthquake 1988; p. (est. 1980) 1,036,000.

Yes Tor, second highest summit, Dartmoor, Devon, **Eng.**; 618 m.

Yevpatoriya or **Eupatoria,** spt., Crimea, on Black Sea, **USSR**; popular resort; children's sanatoria; chemicals, leather, locks, dried fish; new pt. being built; p. (est. 1969) 75,000.

Yezd. *See* **Yazd.**

Yibin (Ipin), c., Sichuan prov., **China**, at junction of Chang Jiang and Min Jiang; p. (est. 1970) 275,000.

Yichang (Ichang), c., S.W. Hubei, **China**; on Chang Jiang; site of famous gorges; terminus of lge. vessels from Shanghai.

Yiewsley and West Drayton, former U.D., Middx., **Eng.**; now inc. in Hillingdon outer bor. Greater London; varied lt. inds.

Yinchuan, t., cap. of Ninxia, aut. region, **China**; on Huang He; ctr. of fertile agr. a.; new lt. inds.; p. (est. 1982) 576,000.

Yingkou (Yingkow), c., Liaoning prov., N.E. **China**; 32 km upstream from mouth of Liao R.; soyabean prods.; p. (est. 1970) 215,000.

Yining (Kuldja), c., Xinjiang prov., **China**; on highway to Turkestan; coalfield; recent industl. development inc. iron and steel; p. (est. 1970) 160,000.

Ynys Môn. *See* **Anglesey.**

Yokkaichi, c., spt., S. Honshu, **Japan**; on Ise Bay, 37 km S. of Nagoya; textiles, petrochemicals, synthetic rubber, porcelain; p. (1985) 263,000.

Yokohama, leading spt., Honshu, **Japan**; on W. shore of Tokyo Bay; steel, chemicals, cars, oil refining, shipyards; univs.; with Tokyo and Kawasaki forms conurb. of Keihin; p. (1987) 3,113,000.

Yokosuka, spt., Honshu, **Japan**; S. of Tokyo; holiday resort; thermal power sta.; p. (1985) 427,087.

Yonkers, c., N.Y., **USA**; on E. bank of Hudson R.; residtl.; lt. inds., textiles; p. (1984) 191,200; part of N.Y. met. a.

Yonne, dep., **France**; in S.E. of Paris basin, inc. Champagne, Burgundy, Orléanais; drained by R. Yonne; cap. Auxerre; agr., Chablis wines; a. 7,495 km²; p. (1982) 309,500.

Yonne, R., **France**; major trib. of R. Seine; 288 km long.

York, c., co. t., l. gov. dist., North Yorks., **Eng.**; on R. Ouse; in central position in Vale of York; anc. part of c. enclosed by walls; minster, cas., univ.; chocolate, confectionery, rly. wkshps.; p. (est. 1988) 100,600 (dist.).

York, c., Penn., **USA**; ctr. of fertile agr. region; varied inds., inc. agr. tools, machin., textiles, metal gds.; p. (1984) 44,400 (c.), 391,400 (met. a.).

York, C., Queensland, **Australia**; most N. point on mainland of Australia.

York, Vale of, broad lowland, North Yorks., **Eng.**; between Pennines and N. Yorks. Moors and Yorks. Wolds; drained to Humber by R. Ouse and tribs.; glacial and alluvial soils have required draining; crop farming, wheat, barley, root-crops, associated with fattening of beef cattle; settlement mainly marginal; cap. t. York; length 96 km, width from 16 km in N. to 48 km in S.

Yorke, penin., S. **Australia**; separates Spencer G. and G. of St. Vincent; 160 km long, 48 km wide.

Yorkshire, former co., **Eng.**; formerly divided into 3 separate admin. parts (Ridings) N., E., and W.; now split into 3 non-met. cos., Cleveland, North Yorks., and Humberside and 2 met. cos. West Yorks. and South Yorks.

Yorkshire Moors, hills, North Yorks. and Cleveland, **Eng.**; inc. N. Yorks. Moors, Cleveland hills and Hambleton hills; bounded to N. by Tees valley, S. by vale of Pickering, W. by Swale valley, E. by sea; composed of oolitic limestone; gd. sheep pastures; impt. iron-ore deposits worked in Cleveland hills; max. alt. 454 m.

Yorkshire Wolds, hills, Humberside, **Eng.**; extend N.E. from Humber and terminate in Flamborough Head; chalk; gd. sheep pasture; average alt. 180 m.

Yorktown, v., Va., **USA**; scene of surrender by Lord Cornwallis to Washington 1781.

Yosemite National Park, Cal., **USA**; in Sierra Nevada; contains Yosmite creek and canyon with three famous cataracts.

Yoshkar-Ola, t., Mari ASSR, **RSFSR**; 128 km N.W. of Kazan; cultural ctr.; wood processing, food inds.; p. (1985) 231,000.

Youghal, spt., U.D., Cork, **R.o.I.**; on estuary of the Blackwater; resort; p. (1981) 5,870.

Youngstown, c., Ohio, **USA**; on Mahoning R.; 91 km N.W. of Pittsburgh; ctr. of one of most impt. iron and steel dists. in USA; heavy engin.; univ.; p. (1984) 108,000 (c.), 518,100 (met. a.).

Yoyang. *See* **Yueyang.**

Ypres (Ieper), t., W. Flanders prov., N.W. **Belgium**; textiles and textile machin.; ctr. of cloth ind. in middle ages; scene of battles 1914–17; p. (1981) 34,426.

Ypsilanti, t., Mich., **USA**; on Huron R.; residtl.. agr. mkt., mnfs.; univ.; p. (1980) 24,031.

Ystwyth, R., Dyfed, **Wales**; flows 40 km to join R. Rheidol at Aberystwyth.

Yuan, R., N.W. Hunan prov., **China**; flows into Dongting Hu and Chang Jiang R.; rapids; 640 km long.

Yucatán, st., S.E. **Mexico**; limestone lowlands poor soils; henequen (sisal hemp), chicle (resin from which chewing gum is made); cap. Mérida; a. 61,968 km²; p. (1980) 1,034,648.

Yueyang (Yoyang), t., Hunan, **China**; at outlet of Dongting Hu and Chang Jiang; p. 4,800.

Yugoslavia, Socialist Fed. Rep., S.E. **Europe**; comprises reps. of Serbia, Croatia, Macedonia, Montenegro, Slovenia, Bosnia, Hercegovina, and aut. regions of Kosovo and Vojvodina; long W. cst. on Adriatic Sea with well-developed limestone karstic topography; hilly interior; climate Mediterranean on cst., continental in interior; distinctive political development after second world war; refused to accept Soviet hegemony; well-developed links with W.; with major attempts to industrialise, based on energy, heavy and consumer inds. less p. engaged in agr.; economic decision-making increasingly freed from central control; developing tourist tr., especially with countries of W. Europe, based on climate and attractive Adriatic littoral, with many sm. Is.; cap.

Belgrade; a. 255,698 km²; p. (est. 1987) 23·4 m.

Yukon, R., Canada and Alaska, **USA**; flows N.W. and W. into Bering Strait; navigable for 1,920 km; 3,200 km long.

Yukon Territory, prov., N.W. **Canada**; mtnous. (Mt. Logan 6,050 m); gold, silver, lead, zinc; Alaska Highway links with B.C. and Alberta; ch. ts. Dawson, and Whitehorse (cap.); incr. indep. since 1983; a. 536,327 km²; p. (1986) 24,000.

Yuma, t., Arizona, **USA**; at confluence of Rs. Gila and Colorado, nr. Mexican bdr.; ctr. of irrigated agr. region; p. (1980) 42,481.

Yumen, c., N.W. Gansu prov., **China**; leading petroleum ctr.; drilling equipment, precision instruments; on Old Silk Road to Xinjiang; p. (1984) 158,100.

Yunnan prov., S. **China**; adjoins Burma; mtnous. a. of minority groups; rice, tobacco, tea, cotton; copper, tin; cap. Kunming; a. 420,466 km²; p. (est. 1985) 33,620,000.

Yuzhno-Sakhalinsk, t., **RSFSR**; at S. end of Sakhalin I.; paper, lt. inds.; p. (1985) 158,000.

Yvelines, new dep., **France**; W. of Paris; cap. Versailles; a. 2,271 km²; p. (1982) 1,192,600.

Yverdon, t., Vaud, **Switzerland**; typewriters; p. (1980) 20,802.

Z

Zaandam, t., **Neth.**; industl. dist.; rly. junc.; timber-based inds.; p. (1982) 129,864.

Zabrze, t., Upper Silesia, Katowice, **Poland**; impt. coal-mng. ctr. with associated heavy inds.; cultural ctr.; p. (est. 1985) 198,000.

Zacapa, t., cap. of Z. prov., **Guatemala**; mkt. t. at rly. junc.; tobacco tr. and processing; sulphur springs; p. (est. 1983) 36,000.

Zacatecas, st., **Mexico**; on central plateau a. 2,100 m; dry, agr. dist.; sm. mng. ctrs.; a. 72,836 km²; p. (1980) 1,145,327.

Zacatecas, t., cap. of Z. st., **Mexico**; cath.; ctr. of silver mng., pottery, clothing; p. (1970) 56,829.

Zacatecoluca, t., **El Salvador**; cigar mkg., hand looms; coffee, cotton, sugar, vanilla in a.; p. (1980) 78,751.

Zadar (Zara), t., **Yugoslavia**; spt. on Croatian cst. of Adriatic Sea; formerly Italian (1920–47); Roman remains; cath.; car ferry to Pesaro (Italy); tourism; p. (1981) 116,174.

Zagan (Sagan), t., Zielona Gora, W. **Poland** (since 1945); on R. Bober; cas.; textiles, paper, lignite mines; p. (1970) 21,500.

Zagazig, t., **Egypt**; on Nile Delta; tr. ctr. of fertile agr. a. producing cotton, grains; cotton mills; p. (est. 1983) 256,000.

Zagorsk, c., **RSFSR**; 70 km N.E. of Moscow; woodcarving, toy mkg.; site of famous Troitse-Sergiyeva Lavra monastery, converted into museum 1920; p. (1985) 112,000.

Zagreb, c., **Yugoslavia**; cap. of Croatia; on Sava R.; cath., univ.; tr. fair; many inds., notably petrochemicals based on local petroleum reserves, elec. engin.; airport; second c. of rep.; p. (1981) 768,700.

Zagros, mtns., **Iran**; inc. Iran's major oilfield; highest peak Zardesh Kuh, 4,551 m.

Zahedan, c., **Iran**; cap. of Sistan and Baluchistan prov.; airport; terminus of rly. from Pakistan; p. (est. 1982) 165,000.

Zahle, t., **Lebanon**, S.W. Asia; on slopes of L. mtn.; p. (est. 1980) 46,800.

Zaïre, Rep. of, Central Africa; comprises eight provs. (caps. in brackets): Bas-Zaïre (Matadi), Bandundu (Bandundu), Equateur (Mbandaka), Haut-Zaïre (Kisangani), Kivu (Bukavu), Shaba (Lubumbashi), Kasai Oriental (Mbuji-Mayi), Kasai Occidental (Kananga); lies in vast basin of Zaïre R., mtns. on E. and S. borders; climate equatorial in N., tropical in S.; agr. exp. inc. palm oil, cotton, coffee, but economy based on mng., diamonds (Kasai), cobalt, non-ferrous metals (Shaba), major world producer of copper; radium deposits nr. Lubumbashi; extensive navigation on Zaïre R.; main pt. Matadi on estuary linked by rail to cap. Kinshasa; a. 2,345,457 km²; p. (est. 1987) 31,780,000.

Zaïre, gr. R. of **Equatorial Africa;** numerous tribs., drains 3,885,000 km²; navigable from sea to Matadi for ocean steamers, from Matadi to Pool Malebo interrupted by rapids and falls, again navigable to Boyoma Falls; proposed power project to be lgst. in Africa; estuary 11–16 km wide; c. 4,800 km long.

Zakinthos (Zante), Ionian I., **Greece**; cap. Zakinthos (Zante); devastated by earthquake 1953; currants, wine, olives; a. 717 km²; p. (1981) 30,014.

Zakinthos (Zante), t., Zakinthos I., **Greece**; spt. on E. cst.; agr. tr. and processing; p. (1981) 9,764.

Zakopane, t., **Poland**; in High Tatra mtns.; base for mountaineering and winter sports; health resort; tourism; p. (1983) 29,700.

Zalaegerszeg, t., **Hungary**; in Göcsej dist.; oil refining; mkt. t. for grain and livestock; p. (est. 1985) 62,000.

Zambesi, R., S.E. **Africa**; flows E. to Moçambique Channel, Indian Oc.; forms frontier between Zambia and Zimbabwe; inc. Victoria Falls and Kariba and Cabora Bassa dams; navigable but impeded by rapids; 3,520 km long.

Zambia, rep., Central Africa; member of Commonwealth; tropical climate, modified by alt.; plateau (1,200 m); subsistence agr.; livestock on uplands free from tsetse fly; mng. basis of economy, especially in copperbelt; world's 4th lgst copper producer; exp. disrupted by Rhodesian U.D.I. (1965); falling copper output as mines near exhaustion; need to develop alternative routes to cst.; pipeline from Ndola to Dar-es-Salaam; construction of Tan-Zam rly. financed by Chinese aid; cap. Lusaka; a. 752,618 km²; p. (est. 1987) 7·6m.

Zamboanga, t., Mindanao, **Philippines**; spt. on Basilian Strait, exp. prod. timber; p. (est. 1984) 379,194.

Zamora, prov., **Spain**; borders Portugal; drained by R. Duero; cereals, wine, merino sheep; cap. Zamora; a. 10,559 km²; p. (1987) 222,240.

Zamora, t., cap. of Zamora prov., **Spain**; on R. Duero; cath.; agr. tr. and processing ctr.; developing mnfs.; p. (1987) 60,708.

Zamosc, t., Lublin, **Poland**; Renaissance planned t. in valley of Lubianka R.; industl., comm. and cultural ctr. for E. part of Lublin prov.; p. (1983) 52,900.

Zanesville, t., Ohio, **USA**; textiles, pottery, machin.; p. (1980) 28,655.

Zangbo (Tsangpo), R., Tibet, **China**; one of headstreams of R. Brahmaputra; 1,350 km. long.

Zanjan, c., **Iran**; cap. of Gilan prov.; cotton, woollen gds.; p. (1986) 215,458.

Zanzibar, terr., E. **Africa**; comprises Is. of Z. and Pemba; joined Tanganyika to form **Tanzania** (1964); major world source of cloves; coconut and coconut prod. major exp. and basis of processing inds.; cap. Zanzibar; a. 2,642 km²; p. (est. 1985) 571,000.

Zanzibar, spt., Zanzibar I., **Tanzania**; on W. cst. 35 km from E. Africa; outlet for clove exp., entrepot tr.; former slave mkt.; p. (est. 1985) 133,000.

Zaporozh'ye, t., Ukrainian SSR, **USSR**; on R. Dnieper, dam and hydroelec. power sta.; metal inds. based on Donets coal and Krivoi Rog iron ore; p. (1985) 852,000.

Zaragoza, prov., **Spain**; largely barren plain suffering from climatic extremes; a. 17,122 km²; cap. Z.; p. (1987) 826,160.

Zaragoza, cap. Z. prov., **Spain**; on R. Ebro; 2 caths., univ.; former cap. of Aragon; rly. junc.; comm. ctr.; p. (1987) 575,317.

Zarate, t., Entre Rios, **Argentina**; paper wks., agr. ctr., meat packing; p. (1980) 65,504.

Zaria, c., N. **Nigeria**; founded 15th cent., old part surrounded by walls; univ., cotton ctr.; rly. ctr., p. (est. 1983) 274,000.

Zary (Sorau), t., Zielona Gora, **Poland** (since 1945); textiles; p. (1970) 28,400.

Zawiercie, t., **Poland**; industl. ctr.; coal, iron, textiles, glass; p. (1983) 55,600.

Zdunska Wola, t., **Poland**; nr. Lodz; textiles, engin.; p. (1970) 29,100.

Zealand. See **Sjaelland.**

Zeebrugge, spt., **Belgium**; 14 km N. of Bruges; exp. coal, chemicals; oil refining; linked by canal to Bruges.

Zeeland, prov., **Neth.**; a. covering part of Scheldt estuary and Is.; low-lying; dairying; cap. Middelburg; a. 1,787 km²; p. (1983) 354,863.

Zeist, t., Utrecht, **Neth.**; chemicals, toys; p. (est. 1987) 60,000.

Zeitz, t., Halle, **E. Germany**; textiles, chemicals; p. (est. 1970) 46,736.

Zelenodolsk, t., **RSFSR**; on R. Volga, 40 km W. of Kazan; rly. junc.; sawmills; p. (est. 1969) 76,000.

Zelten, Libya, N. Africa; oilfield; 320 km S. of Benghazi; pipeline to Mersa al-Brega.

Zenica, t., **Yugoslavia;** lge. iron and steel wks.; ctr. of Z. basin; rly. junc.; p. (1981) 132,733.

Zeravshan, R., Tadzhik SSR and Usbek SSR, **USSR;** flows for 736 km before evaporating in desert region N. of Chardzhou.

Zetland. *See* **Shetland.**

Zgierz, t., Lodz. prov., central **Poland;** nr. source of R. Bzura; textiles, chemicals, textile machin.; p. (1970) 42,800.

Zhangjiakou (Kalgan), c., Hebei, **China;** nr. Great Wall, 160 km N.W. of Beijing; a main route to Mongolia; tea wool, hides; p. (1984) 607,900.

Zhangzhou (Chuangchow), c., Fujian prov., **China;** former pt. now silted up; p. (1984) 210,600.

Zhanjiang (Tsamkong), c., Guandong prov., **China;** spt. on Liuzhou peninsula; machin., chemicals, elec. inds.; designated economic development zone; cotton, milling, leather mnfs.; p. (1984) 899,500.

Zhdanov (Mariupol), spt., S.E. Ukrainian SSR, **USSR;** on Sea of Azov; metallurgical ctr., chemicals; fishing and fish-processing; p. (1985) 522,000.

Zhengzhou, (Quauzhu), c., cap. Henan prov., **China;** 24 km. S of Huang He where it emerges on to N. China Plain; impt. route ctr. and rly. junc.; p. (1984) 1,551,600.

Zhenjiang (Chinkiang), c., Jiangsu, **China;** former treaty pt. on Chang Jiang, 77 km. below Nanjing; tr. ctr.; p. (1984) 397,300.

Zhijiang (Chekiang), coastal prov., S.E. **China;** cap. Hangzhou; impt. rice growing a.; major natural gas field; a. 102,269 km²; p. (est. 1985) 39,930,000.

Zhitomir, t., Ukrainian SSR, **USSR;** engin., clothing; route ctr.; p. (1985) 275,000.

Zhousan (Chusan), I., and archipelago off E. cst. of China and Chang Jiang delta; ch. ctr. Dinghai on Zhousan I.; valuable fishing grounds.

Zhuhai, special economic zone, **China,** N. of Macau; selected (1983) to attract foreign investment; new pt.; p. (1984) 144,400.

Zhujiang (Chukiang or Pearl R.), Guandong, S. **China;** one of most impt. waterways of China; 176 km. long from Guangzhou to Hong Kong; fertile delta known as "land of fish, rice and fruit"; around Guangzhou network of elec., drainage and irrigation stas; built since 1959; estuary now silting.

Zhuzhou (Chuchau), c., Hunan prov., **China;** on Xiang Jiang; rly.; p. (1984) 487,800.

Zibo (Tzepo), c., Shandong, **China;** formed by merging of several coal mng. ts. in the 1950s; p. (1984) 2,280,500.

Zielona Gora (Grünberg), c., W. **Poland** (since 1945); in valley surrounded by wooded hills; admin. and industl. ctr., cap. of Z.G. prov.; textiles, food processing, machin.; viticulture; p. (1983) 107,800.

Zielona Gora, prov., **Poland;** borders E. Germany; glacial sands, wooded; brown coal deposits; cap. Z.G.; a. 14,514 km²; p. (est. 1983) 107,800.

Zigaze (Shigatze), t., Tibet, **China;** on R. Zangbo; tr. ctr. on main caravan routes; p. c. 2,000.

Zigong (Tzekung), c., Sichuan, **China;** petroleum, natural gas, salt wks.; p. (1984) 899,700.

Ziguinchor, t., **Senegambia;** pt. on R. Casamance; exp. groundnuts; p. (1979) 79,464.

Zilina, t., Slovakia, **ČSSR;** on R. Vah; paper, fertilisers; p. (est. 1986) 92,000.

Zimbabwe, Central Africa; former Brit. col. (Rhodesia); indep rep. 1980; landlocked st.; much of land high veld above 900 m covered in savannah; impressive economic growth with removal of sanctions and end of warfare; manuf. limited by lack of skilled labour; still heavy dependence on agr., maize and tobacco; mng. also impt.; Wankie coal mine lgst. in world; also asbestos, chrome and copper; power from Kariba dam encourages lt. inds.; cap. Harare; a. 389,329 km²; p. (est. 1987) 8,640,000.

Zimbabwe National Park; site nr. Victoria,

Mashonaland, of ruined t. built c. 15th cent. A.D. by a Bantu people; discovered 1868.

Zinder, t., **Niger,** W. Africa; terminus of trans-Saharan motor route; tr. ctr.; former cap.; second t. of Niger; p. (est. 1981) 75,000.

Zion National Park, Utah, **USA;** contains Z. canyon; a. 596 km².

Zipaquirá, t., **Colombia;** 48 km N. of Bogotá; salt mng., chemicals; cattle-rearing a.; p. (est. 1968) 28,812.

Zistersdorf, t., Lower **Austria;** recently developed oilfields.

Zittau, t., Dresden, **E. Germany;** on R. Mandau; woollens, linens, machin., cars, chemicals; p. (est. 1970) 43,087.

Zlatoust, t., S.W. **RSFSR;** in Ural mtns.; metallurgical ctr.; steel, chemicals, sawmilling; p. (1985) 204,000.

Zletovo, terr., N.E. Macedonia, **Yugoslavia;** oil shales, lead, zinc deposits.

Zlin. *See* **Gottwaldov.**

Znojmo or **Znaim,** t., **ČSSR;** anc. t., cas.; ctr. of fertile agr. dist.; p. (1984) 38,321.

Zomba, t., former cap. of **Malawi,** 884 m a.s.l. on slopes of Zomba mtn., 67 km N.E. Blantyre; Malawi's univ. t.; p. (est. 1983) 46,000.

Zonguldak, t., **Turkey;** spt. on Black Sea; coalmng. a.; p. (1985) 117,879.

Zorita De Los Canes, Guadalajara, **Spain;** on R. Tagus; nuclear power plant.

Zrenjanin, t., Vojvodina, **Yugoslavia;** pt. on R. Begej; ctr. of agr. dist.; agr. processing; p. (1981) 139,300.

Zuetina, oil pt. (1968), **Libya;** pipeline links shore storage sta. with offshore berths.

Zug, smallest can., **Switzerland;** drained by R. Reuss; contains part of L. Z.; dairying, fruit; cap. Z.; a. 241 km²; p. (est. 1986) 82,000.

Zug, t., cap. of Zug can., **Switzerland;** on L. Z.; elec. engin., printing; p. (1980) 21,609.

Zugspitze, mtn., Bavarian Alps, on Bavarian-Austrian bdr.; highest peak in **Germany,** 2,965 m; connected by rack-and-pinion to Garmisch-Partenkirchen at foot.

Zuider Zee. *See* **IJsselmeer.**

Zulia, st., **Venezuela;** centred on L. Maracaibo, producing 70 per cent of Venezuelan oil; timber reserves; cap. Maracaibo; a. 63,902 km²; p. (1980) 1,674,252.

Zululand, Bantu homeland, Natal, **S. Africa;** sugar on coastal plain, livestock on interior plateau; cap. Eshowe; a. 27,006 km²; p. (1970) 2,106,774.

Zürich, c., cap. of Z. can., **Switzerland;** on L. Z. and R. Limmat; cath., univ.; leading world banking ctr.; inds. inc. textiles, paper; p. (est. 1985), 351,000 (c.), 840,000 (met. a.).

Zürich, can., **Switzerland;** forested and agr. a. stretching N. from L. Z.; inds. at cap. Z. and Winterthur; a. 1,728 km²; p. (est. 1986) 1,132,000.

Zürich, L., **Switzerland;** drained by R. Limmat; length 40 km.

Zutphen, t., Gelderland, **Neth.;** on R. Ijssel; textiles, paper; Sir Philip Sidney died here 1586; p. (1982) 31,919.

Zuzhou (Suchow), c., Jiangsu, **China;** at junct. of N. China plain and Chang Jiang basin; impt. rly. junct.; p. (est. 1970) 1,500,000.

Zuzhou (Luchow), c., Sichuan, **China;** coal, iron, kaolin; synthetic ammonia plant; p. (est. 1970) 225,000.

Zweibrücken, t., Rhineland-Palatinate, **W. Germany;** nr. Saarbrücken; cas.; machin., footwear, textiles; p. (est. 1986) 32,700.

Zwickau, c., Karl-Marx-Stadt, **E. Germany;** on R. Mulde; cas.; coal, motors, machin., textiles; birthplace of Schumann; p. (est. 1986) 121,000.

Zwolle, t., Overijssel, **Neth.;** canal ctr.; cattle mkt.; p. (est. 1987) 89,000.

Zyrardow, t., **Poland;** nr. Warsaw; specialised textile ctr.; p. (1970) 33,200.

Zyryanovsk, t., Kazakh SSR, **USSR;** lead, zinc; p. (est. 1969) 56,090.

GENERAL
INFORMATION

Some three thousand entries, including a number of scientific terms
and explanations. Cross references
direct the reader to fuller information elsewhere in the book.

MEASUREMENTS ARE GIVEN IN METRIC UNITS

Abbreviations

mm = millimetre		m^2 = square metre	
cm = centimetre		km^2 = square kilometre	
m = metre		ha = hectare	
km = kilometre		m^3 = cubic metre	
km/h = kilometres per hour		s = second	
g = gram		min = minute	
kg = kilogram		h = hour	
tonne = metric ton			

Equivalents

Length   *Reciprocal*
1 cm = 0·394 in   2·540
1 m = 1·094 yd   0·914
1 km = 0·621 mile   1·609

Area
1 m^2 = 1·196 yd^2 0·836
1 km^2 = 0·386 $mile^2$ 2·590
1 hectare = 2·471 acres   0·405

Volume
1 m^3 = 1·308 yd^3 0·765
1 litre = 0·220 gallon   4·546

Mass
1 kg = 2·205 lb   0·454
1 tonne = 0·984 ton   1·016

Temperature
$C = (F - 32) \div 1·8$
$F = (1·8 \times C) + 32$

See also **Metric Equivalents, F66–70**

GENERAL INFORMATION

A

Aard-vark (Dutch *aarde* = earth + *vark* = pig), a large nocturnal mammal found only in Africa. It feeds on termites and ants, whose nests it excavates with its enormous claws.

Abacus, a device for making arithmetical calculations, consisting of parallel bars on which are strung movable coloured beads. The earliest form of this instrument was used in Mesopotamia about 3000 B.C., and its use spread westwards throughout the Graeco-Roman world and eastwards to China. An efficient form of the abacus is still used today in parts of Asia.

Abdication. The term usually refers to the renunciation of the royal office by a reigning monarch. Both Edward II (1327) and Richard II (1399) were forced to abdicate, James II left the throne vacant without waiting for a formal deposition, and the abdication of Edward VIII was effected by the Declaration of Abdication Act, 1936. Since 1688 when Parliament declared James II to have abdicated by reason of desertion and subversion of the constitution, no British monarch can abdicate without the consent of Parliament.

Aberration, in astronomy, is the apparent displacement of a star due to the speed of the observer with the earth (*see* **Parallax**). In optics (i) spherical aberration is when there is blurring of the image and fringes of colour at its edges, due to failure of lens to bring light to a single focus; (ii) chromatic aberration is due to the refractive index of glass being different for light of different colours. For instance, violet light is bent more than red.

Abiogenesis, or spontaneous generation; the origination of living from non-living matter. The term is applied to such discredited ideas as that frogs could be generated spontaneously by the action of sunlight on mud, or maggots arise spontaneously in dead meat without any eggs from which the maggots hatch being present. Spallanzani (1729–99) upset the hypothesis of spontaneous generation; Pasteur dealt it a death-blow.

Abominable Snowman. *See* **Yeti.**

Aborigines, a term first applied to an ancient mythical people of central Italy, derives from the Latin *ab origine* = from the beginning. It now signifies the original inhabitants of any country, in particular the aboriginal tribes of Australia. In contrast to their highly complex social and religious customs, the material culture of Australian aboriginals is very low and ill adapted to stand up to contact with European civilisation. Originally estimated at 300,000, their number has dropped in the last 200 years to some 80,000. The 1988 Australian bicentenary focused attention on their lack of legal right to ancient tribal lands and their welfare problems.

Absolute Temperature, Absolute Zero. This is a refined notion requiring some study of thermodynamics for its full understanding. For setting up an absolute temperature scale one must first assign a numerical value to one fixed temperature. For this, the triple point of water has been chosen, *i.e.,* the temperature at which solid, liquid, and gaseous water are all in equilibrium. The triple point is defined to be 273·16 K where K is read for kelvin (after Lord Kelvin). This temperature is 0·01°C on the Celsius scale (*q.v.*) and is thus very close to the melting point of ice. Suppose the pressure and volume of a mass of gas are measured (i) at the triple point of water, giving (pV)tr as the product of the pressure and volume; and (ii) at any unknown temperature T K, giving (pV) as the product. Then the absolute temperature, T K, is defined by

$$T\,\text{K} = 273\cdot16\,\frac{(pV)}{(pV)\text{tr}}$$

It is to be understood that the gas pressure is very low. The nature of the gas is immaterial. More subtly, it can be shown that the temperature so defined is identical with that derived in a rather abstract way in the science of thermodynamics. The absolute scale is therefore also called the thermodynamic scale. Absolute temperatures can be obtained from Celsius temperatures by adding 273·15; thus the absolute temperature of melting ice is 273·15 K. Conversely, absolute zero is a temperature 273·15 K below the temperature of melting ice, *i.e.,* −273·15°C. Theory shows that absolute zero is unattainable, but it has been approached to within about 1 millionth of a degree. Within ten or so degrees of absolute zero, matter develops some remarkable properties. *See* **Kelvin, Cryogenics, Superconductor, Helium.**

Abstract Art, a term applied to 20th cent. plastic arts in which form and colour possess aesthetic value apart from the subject. Usually represented as a modern movement beginning with Cézanne. The idea is ancient, abstract design being found in the Neolithic period, in folk-art, and particularly in Moslem art (which forbids naturalistic representations especially of the human figure). Among those in the tradition are Kandinsky, Braque, Mondrian, Calder.

Acetic Acid, an organic acid produced when ordinary (ethyl) alcohol is fermented by the organism called *Acetobacter aceti.* The same oxidation process yields vinegar: this is a weak and crude solution of acetic acid obtained by trickling dilute alcoholic liquor over beechwood shavings at 35°C. The souring of wine is due to the same process. Acetic acid is used as a food preservative and flavouring material, and in the manufacture of cellulose acetate and white lead.

Acetylene (also called ethyne), a compound of carbon and hydrogen prepared from calcium carbide and water. A very reactive gas, it is used industrially on a large scale to prepare acetaldehyde, chlorohydrocarbon solvents, and many intermediates for plastics manufacture. Burns in air with a highly luminous flame, formerly used for lighting purposes, but is now widely used, with oxygen, in welding. For safe storage and transportation it is dissolved in acetone.

Acid Rain is the name given to rain, snow or sleet contaminated with acid substances so that its acidity is greater than the limit expected by normal concentrations of carbon dioxide dissolving in the rain to give carbonic acid (pH 5·5–5·6). The pH (*see* **L95**) of acid rain therefore is less than about 5·5. The increased acidity is caused by larger concentrations of a number of contaminants, principally the strong acids, nitric and sulphuric, which arise from industrial effluents containing oxides of nitrogen and sulphur. The European emission of sulphur dioxide doubled between 1940 and 1980. In some European and North American areas such contamination can give a rain pH as low as 3 (which is 100 times more acid than pH 5). The acid rain can mark fruit and leaves, and adversely affect soil but its main effect is on the aquatic ecosystems especially in regions which cannot naturally buffer acidic inputs such as those with thin soils and granite rocks. It is likely that the disappearance of fish from many Scandinavian lakes has been the result of pollution by acid rain.

Acids, substances having a tendency to lose a positive ion (a proton). This general definition overcomes difficulties of earlier views which merely described their properties and asserted that they are chemically opposite to bases. As a whole acids contain ionisable hydrogen, replaceable by a metal, to form a salt. Inorganic acids are compounds of non-metals or metalloids, *e.g.,* sulphuric, phosphoric acid. Carboxylic acids contain the group –COOH. *See* **F25.**

Actinides, the fourteen metallic elements from thorium (no. 90) to lawrencium (no. 103). All known isotopes of these elements are radioactive and those with atomic number greater than 92 (uranium) have been produced only in significant quantities artificially. Plutonium (no. 94) is obtained from uranium during the course of nuclear reactor operation and the higher transuranic elements can be made from it by the successive capture of neutrons or nuclei of light atoms. The availability of only minute quantities of short-lived isotopes makes the determination of the physical and chemical properties of the higher actinides very difficult. Claims for the discovery of new elements can therefore be controversial and since the discoverers can name the elements their naming is also controversial. There were three different reports for Nobelium (no. 102). Lawrentium (no. 103) is called Jolistium by Russian authors. Element no. 104 was reported in 1964 by a Russian group and called Kurchatovium but is called Rutherfordium (Rf) in the West. Element no. 105 has been named Hahnium (Hn).

Advent, a period devoted to religious preparation for the coming celebration of the Nativity (Christmas). It includes the four Sundays immediately preceding the festival.

Advocatus Diaboli ("the devil's advocate"), a Roman Catholic functionary who presents opposing evidence in regard to the life of any deceased person it may be proposed to canonise.

Aerodynamics, the science of gases (especially air) in motion, particularly in relation to aircraft (aeronautics). The idea of imitating the birds by the use of wings is of ancient origin. Leonardo da Vinci first carried out experiments in a scientific manner. The invention of the balloon in 1783 and the researches of scientists and engineers in the 19th cent. ultimately led to the development of the aeroplane.

Aerolites, the name given to the class of meteorites composed chiefly of heavy silicates. The other two main classes are *siderolites* (nickel-iron and silicates) and *siderites* (nickel-iron).

Aerosol, a suspension of a liquid in a gas; for example, a fog is very small drops of water suspended in air. Formed by spraying the liquid in air, aerosols are used to disperse liquid over a wide area in crop spraying, air freshening and pest control. *See also* **Fluorocarbons.**

Afrikander, type of cattle bred in South Africa.

Afrikaner, an Afrikaans-speaking South African, usually of Dutch descent.

After-damp occurs in a mine after an explosion, causing suffocation. It is composed mainly of carbon dioxide and nitrogen and contains water vapour and carbon monoxide (produced by the burning, in a restricted supply of air, of fine coal dust).

Agaric, large fungi of the family *Agaricaceae*, which includes the mushroom and what are popularly called "toadstools", though the idea that these two lay terms sharply differentiate between edible and poisonous fungi is an incorrect one. Characteristic of the agarics is the presence of a cap or *pileus* (bearing underneath the spore-shedding gills) and a stalk or *stipe*.

Agave, the American aloe or Century Plant which sometimes does not attain to flowering maturity under sixty or seventy years, and then dies. The flower spray may reach a height of 6 m and in its development the rush of sap is so great that the Mexicans collect for brewing the strong spirit called mescal. 1,000 litres of sap can be obtained from a single plant. Some species of agave yield sisal used for making cord and rope.

Aggression. After many years of consideration a definition of aggression was agreed at the United Nations in 1974. It is the use of armed force by a state against the sovereignty, territorial integrity, or political independence of another state or in any other manner inconsistent with the Charter of the UN.

Air, a mixture of gases in the earth's atmosphere, the main constituents being nitrogen, oxygen and argon. Dry air contains these gases in the following proportions by volume: nitrogen 78·06%, oxygen 21%, argon 0·94%. Other gases are also present in small amounts. Of particular importance are water vapour and carbon dioxide. Water vapour is not only critical for life forms on land but also a major

factor in the behaviour of the atmosphere—weather and climate. Carbon dioxide is utilised by green plants in photosynthesis (**F32**). Air also contains traces of ammonia, nitrogen oxides, hydrogen, sulphur dioxide, ozone, and of the rare gases, helium, krypton, neon and xenon. Near cities and industrial areas there are also large quantities of dust and smoke particles (up to 100,000 particles per cc), and traces of other gases from industrial processes. A litre of air at 0°C and 760 mm pressure weighs 1·2932 g. *See also* **Atmosphere, Pollution.**

Air Glow is the general name given to a large number of relatively weak optical emissions from the earth's upper atmosphere in the height range 70 to 400 km (approx.). It is distinct from the aurora polaris (*q.v.*) which is usually much brighter and normally only observable at high latitudes. Air glow is produced by a combination of photochemical reactions in the upper atmosphere, excitation by photoelectrons, or by solar ultra-violet light. In the latter case it is more correctly called "dayglow." These emissions occur in the ultra-violet and infra-red spectral regions as well as in visible light.

Alabaster, a soft crystalline form of sulphate of lime, or granulated gypsum, easily worked for statuary and other ornamental articles, and capable of being highly polished. Volterra, in Tuscany, yields the finest; that in highest ancient repute came from Alabastron in Egypt, near to the modern Antinoë.

Alb, white vestment reaching to the feet, worn by priests in religious ceremonies.

Albatross, a large sea-bird of almost puru white, black and white, or brown plumage. It nests in colonies on remote islands, but at other times rarely approaches land. Of the thirteen species, nine are found in the southern oceans, one in the tropics, three others in the North Pacific

Albert Memorial, a large Gothic monument designed by Sir George Gilbert Scott, and embellished with sculptures by eminent artists. Erected in memory of Prince Albert in Kensington Gardens at a cost of £120,000.

Alcázar the palace at Seville, famed for the beauty of its halls and gardens, in ancient days the residence of the Moorish kings.

Alchemy. *See* Section J.

Alcohols. A class of organic compounds of general formula R–OH, where R is an aliphatic radical. "Alcohol" is the name used for ethyl alcohol (ethanol); this is produced by distilling fermented liquors, and synthetically from ethylene, a product of petroleum cracking. Industrially ethyl alcohol is used in the manufacture of chloroform, ether, perfumes, etc. Diluted with wood alcohol or other denaturants ethyl alcohol is called "methylated spirits"; the denaturants are varied according to the industrial purposes for which it is required, the methylated spirits then being largely exempt from duty. Wood alcohol (methyl alcohol or methanol) can be obtained by distilling wood or synthetically from water gas.

Alcoholic Strength. In 1980 Great Britain adopted the OIML (International Organisation of Legal Metrology) system of spirit strength measurement in metric units as required by EEC directive. The alcoholic strength of wine is expressed in percentage volume ("% vol") terms, *i.e.*, the number of volumes of pure alcohol in 100 volumes of the product at 20°C. For spirits the quantity for duty is the litre of alcohol at 20°C. For example, a case of 12 bottles of 75 cl each = 9 litres; at 40% volume 9 litres = 9 × 40% = 3.60 litres of alcohol. The alcoholic strength of spirits and liqueurs appearing on bottle labels is increasingly shown in % vol. terms (*e.g.*, "40.5% vol"). The USA continues to use the US proof gallon (1.37 US proof gallons = 1 British proof gallon).

Aldehyde, the generic term for a class of chemical compounds of general formula R–CHO, where R is an organic radical. Except for formaldehyde, which is a gas, aldehydes are volatile liquids. They are produced by oxidation of primary alcohols. Most important aldehyde is formaldehyde (methanal) used in making the plastics described as formaldehyde resins. Formalin (formaldehyde solution in water) is much used for preserving zoological specimens.

Alder, a river-side tree of the genus *Alnus*, including some 30 species and found in north temperate regions and the Andes. The only species native to Britain is *A. glutinosa*, which has been described as "guardian of river-banks" because of the way its roots bind together the sand and stones, and so slow down erosion. The wood is used for furniture and charcoal.

Aldine Editions are the beautiful books printed in Venice by the Renaissance printer Aldo Pio Manuzio and his family between 1490 and 1597. Italics were first introduced in these books.

Algae, flowerless plants living mostly in water. Seaweeds and the green pond scums are the best known algae. The green powder found on trees is a microscopic alga (*Protoccus*). See **F42**(1).

Algebra, a branch of mathematics in which symbols are used in place of numbers. Sir Isaac Newton styled it the "universal arithmetic". The Chinese were able to solve the quadratic equation before the Christian era but it was Al-Khowarizmi, an Arab mathematician in the early 9th cent., who introduced algebra to Europe.

Alhambra, the ancient palace of the Moorish kings at Granada in Spain, built in the 13th and 14th cent. Though part of the castle was turned into a modern palace under Charles V, the most beautiful parts of the interior are still preserved—the graceful halls and dwelling-rooms grouped round the Court of Alberca and the Court of Lions, with their fountains, arcades, and lovely gardens.

Aliphatic describes derivatives of hydrocarbons having chains of carbon atoms, as distinct from rings of carbon atoms as in benzene (*see* **Aromatic**). The gas butane is aliphatic.

Alkali, the general name given to a number of chemicals which are bases (*q.v.*). The term should be limited to the hydroxides of metals in the first and second group of the periodic table and of ammonia, *e.g.*, NaOH, KOH. They are used commercially in the manufacture of paper, glass, soap, and artificial silk. The word comes from the Arabic *al-kali* meaning calcined wood ashes. Alkalis are extremely soluble in water and neutralise acids to form salts and water.

Alkaloids, a large group of natural products which contain nitrogen; they are usually basic. Isolated from plants and animals, they include some hormones, vitamins, and drugs. Examples are nicotine, adrenalin, and cocaine. Many alkaloids are made synthetically for medicinal use, *e.g.*, morphine, quinine. Their function in plants is not well understood. *See* **Belladonna**.

Alligator, the crocodile of America, found in the lower Mississippi and adjacent lakes and marshes. There is also a Chinese species. Alligators have broader snouts than other crocodiles.

Allotropy. Depending on the temperature, pressure or method of preparation, an element may exist in one of several forms, each having different physical properties (crystal structure, electrical conductivity, melting point, etc.). This is known as allotropy and the different forms of the element are called allotropes. Many elements exhibit allotropy, *e.g.*, sulphur, phosphorus, oxygen, tin and carbon, the most well-known allotropes of carbon being diamond and graphite.

Alloys are combinations of metals made for their valuable special properties, *e.g.*, durability, strength, lightness, magnetism, rust-resistance, etc. Some well-known ones are brass (zinc + copper), coinage bronze (copper + zinc + tin), steels (iron + carbon + various other materials), soft solder (tin + lead), dental fillings (mercury + various ingredients).

All Saints' Day (Nov. 1) is common to both the Anglican and Roman Catholic Churches, and is in commemoration of the saints generally, or such as have no special day set apart for them. Instituted by Pope Boniface IV, early in the 7th cent., this ecclesiastical festival was formerly called "All Hallows".

All Souls' Day (Nov. 2) is a festival of the Roman Church, intended for the mitigation by prayer of the sufferings of souls in purgatory. The commemoration was enjoined by Abbot Odilo of Cluny during the 11th cent. upon the monastic order over which he presided, and was afterwards adopted generally throughout the Roman Communion.

Allspice, a flavouring obtained from a West Indian tree of the myrtle family, *Pimenta officinalis*, likened to the flavour of cinnamon, nutmeg and cloves combined. The berries resemble peppercorns and are used as a spice in mincemeat, etc.

Alluvium, river transported deposits of sand, mud and gravel which accumulate to form distinctive features such as levées, flood plains and deltas. The frequent renewal of alluvium by flooding causes riverine lands to be some of the most fertile. In Asia alluvial lands support high densities of population, *e.g.*, The Hwang-ho plains and the Ganges delta.

Almond, the fruit of the *Amygdalus communis*, originally indigenous to Persia, Asia Minor and N. Africa; now cultivated in Italy, Spain, France, the USA and Australia. It yields both bitter and sweet oil. Bitter almond oil is obtained by macerating and distilling the ripe seeds; it is used for flavouring and scenting purposes, its fragrant odour being due to the presence of benzaldehyde and hydrogen cyanide. When the seeds are pressed sweet almond oil results: this is used in perfumery, and also as a lubricant for very delicate machinery.

Almuce, a fur stole worn by certain canons.

Aloe, large plants of the lily family, with about 180 species found mainly in the S. African veldt and karroo. The bitter purgative drug (aloes) is prepared by evaporating the plant's sap. *See* **Agave**.

Alpaca, a South American ruminant related to the llama whose long, fine wool is woven into a soft dress fabric known by the same name. Sir Titus Salt first manufactured alpaca cloth (1836). Saltaire, near Bradford, remains to evidence the success which for many years attended the enterprise.

Alpha Particle, or alpha-ray, fast-moving helium nucleus ejected by some radioactive atoms, *e.g.*, polonium. It is a combination of 2 neutrons and 2 protons. *See* **F12**.

Alphabet (so called from the first two letters of the Greek alphabet—alpha, beta) is the term applied to the collection of letters from which the words of a language are made up. It grew out of the knowledge that all words can be expressed by a limited number of sounds arranged in various combinations. The Phoenicians were the first to make use of an alphabetic script derived from an earlier Semitic alphabet (earliest known inscriptions *c.* 1500–950 B.C.) from which all other alphabets have sprung. The stages in the development of the alphabet were mnemonic (memory aids), pictorial (actual pictures), ideographic (symbols), and lastly phonetic. All the ideographic systems died out, with the exception of that of the Chinese.

Altimeter, an instrument used in aircraft to estimate altitude; its usual essential feature is an aneroid barometer which registers the decrease of pressure with height. Roughly 1 millibar corresponds to 9 m. To read an aircraft altimeter correct for its destination, the zero setting must be adjusted for difference of ground height and difference of surface pressure, especially when pressure is falling or when flying towards low pressure.

Altitude, an astronomical term used to signify the angular elevation of a heavenly body; this is measured with a quadrant or sextant. In aeronautics it is the height (in feet or metres) above sea-level.

Alto-Relievo, a term applied to sculptured designs which are depicted in prominent relief on a flat surface, technically signifying that the projections exceeds one-half the true proportions of the objects represented. Basso-relievo is carving kept lower than one-half such projection.

Alum is a compound salt used in various industrial processes, especially dyeing, its constituents being the sulphate of one univalent metal or radical (*e.g.*, potassium, sodium, ammonium, rubidium, caesium, silver, thallium) and the sulphate of a tervalent metal (*e.g.*, aluminium, iron, chromium, manganese), and water of crystallisation.

Alumina is the oxide of aluminium. Very valuable as a refractory material. The ruby is almost 100 per cent. alumina; so also are the emerald, oriental amethyst, etc. An hydrated aluminium oxide is bauxite, chief ore of aluminium from which the metal is extracted electrolytically.

Aluminium, element no. 13, symbol Al, is a light metal which conducts electricity well. Its specific gravity at 20°C is 2·705. Melting point of aluminium is 660·2°C. It is made commercially by electrolysing bauxite dissolved in cryolite (double fluoride of aluminium and sodium). Aluminium alloys are being increasingly used for construction purposes.

Amadavat, a popular cage bird of the weaver family, mainly crimson with spots, so named because the first specimens came from Ahmadabad in India about 1700.

Amalgam is the term applied to any alloy of which mercury forms a part.

Amber, a brittle resinous substance; in origin, fossilised resin. Obtained mostly from the Baltic coasts, and used for ornaments, pipe mouth-pieces, etc.

Ambergris is a waxy substance produced in the intestines of the sperm whale, and generally found floating on the sea. It is a valuable perfumery material.

Amblyopsis, a species of fish, practically sightless, and with inoperative organs of hearing and feeling, that inhabit the Mammoth Cave of Kentucky. A remarkable illustration of the failure of senses not brought into use.

America's Cup. In 1851 the Royal Yacht Squadron put up for competition a silver cup that has become the most famous trophy in yachting. In that year the New York Y.C. sent the schooner *America* across the Atlantic to compete in a 53-mile (85 km) race round the Isle of Wight; it captured the trophy which now bears its name. Until 1983 none of the many challenges by yachtsmen from Great Britain, Canada, and latterly, Australia, had been successful. In that year, however, in Rhode Island Sound *Australia II*, skippered by John Bertrand, won on the 25th challenge. After 132 years the silver ewer was handed to the Royal Perth Y.C. The triumph was short-lived. In 1987 the Cup returned to America, and the 1988 race was eventually awarded to America, having at one stage been awarded to New Zealand.

Amethyst, the violet variety of quartz, used as a precious stone, containing traces of manganese, titanium and iron. The finest coloured specimens come from Brazil and the Urals.

Amice, a white linen vestment worn by Roman Catholic and many Anglican priests when officiating at Mass or Holy Eucharist.

Amines, organic chemicals composed of carbon, hydrogen and nitrogen. They are derived from ammonia, which they resemble in smell and chemical characteristics. The smell of bad fish is due to the presence of amines. Important industrially as intermediates in a wide variety of products, for example, the synthesis of dye-stuffs and man-made fibres such as nylon.

Amino acids, organic compounds containing an amine group and a carboxylic acid group. They are the "building bricks" of proteins (*q.v.*).

Ammeter, an instrument for measuring the current flowing in an electric circuit. A contraction of ampere-meter. *See* **Ampere.**

Ammonia, a colourless gaseous compound comprising three atoms of hydrogen to one of nitrogen. Formerly it was made by heating the horns and hoofs of deer, acquiring the name of spirits of hartshorn. The ammonia of commerce is now procured by coal decomposition in the course of gas-making and by direct synthesis. In the very important Haber process of ammonia production by fixation of atmospheric nitrogen, the nitrogen is made to combine with hydrogen and the ammonia so prepared is converted into nitric acid, ammonium nitrate or ammonium sulphate. The Haber process made Germany self-sufficient in nitrates in the first world war, and was afterwards exploited all over the world.

Ammonites, extinct animals related to the Nautilus. The chambered shell is coiled, usually in a plane spiral, and they are confined to Mesozoic rocks.

Ammonium, the basic radical of ammonium salts. Composed of one atom of nitrogen and four of hydrogen, it behaves chemically like an ion of a monovalent alkali metal. Ammonium

chloride is known as "sal ammoniac". "Sal volatile" is ammonium carbonate.

Amnesty, an act of grace by which a ruler or governing power pardons political offenders.

Amorphous, a term used to indicate the absence of crystalline form in any body or substance.

Ampere, unit of electric current in the SI system of units; named after André Marie Ampère, who in the 1820s helped to lay the foundations of modern electromagnetism. Defined as that constant current which, if maintained in two parallel rectilinear conductors of infinite length, of negligible circular cross section, and placed at a distance of one metre apart in a vacuum, would produce between these conductors a force which is equal to 2×10^{-7} newton per metre length.

Amphibia. *See* **F36**(2).

Amphioxus *or* **Lancelet,** a primitive chordate (**F36**(2)), occurring in sand-banks around British shores and elsewhere.

Anabolism. *See* **Catabolism.**

Analysis is one of the major branches of modern pure mathematics and includes the theories of differentiation, integration, differential equations and analytic functions.

Anarchism. *See* **Section J.**

Anchor, an instrument used for keeping ships stationary. Great improvements have been introduced in recent years, stockless anchors being now chiefly used, consisting of a shank and a loose fluke. Lloyd's rules prescribe the number and weight of anchors which must be carried by merchant ships.

Anchorite is a religious person who retires into solitude to employ himself with holy thoughts. Among the early Christians, anchorites were numerous, but in the Western Church they have been few. Their reputation for wisdom and prescience was high, and kings and rulers in olden days would visit their cells for counsel. An anchorite or "ankret" was in mediaeval times a source of fame and profit to the monastic house within which he was voluntarily immured.

Anchovy, a fish of the herring family, distinguished by its large mouth and projecting snout, plentiful in the Mediterranean and much esteemed when cured.

Ancient Lights are rights of light enjoyed by a property owner over adjoining land. Such a right is obtained either by uninterrupted enjoyment for twenty years, or by written authority, and once legally established cannot be upset, no building being permissible that would seriously interfere with the privilege.

Anemometer, an instrument for measuring the strength of the wind. In the most widely used pattern the rotation, about a vertical axis, of a group of hemispherical or conical cups gives a measure of the total flow of air past the cups, various registering devices being employed. The Dines anemograph provides a continuous record of the variation in both velocity and direction; changes of pressure produced in a horizontal tube, kept pointing into the wind by a vane, cause a float, to which a pen is attached, to rise and fall in sympathy with the gusts and lulls. The recently devised hot-wire anemometer, depending upon the change of electrical resistance experienced by a heated wire when cooled, enables very gentle air currents to be investigated.

Aneroid is the kind of barometer which does not depend upon atmospheric support of a mercury (or other liquid) column. It consists of a metallic box, partially exhausted of air, with a corrugated lid which moves with atmospheric changes. A lever system magnifies the lid movements about 200 times and atmospheric pressure is read from a dial. The construction of the vacuum chamber provides automatic compensation for temperature changes. An aneroid barometer is the basic component of an altimeter.

Angelica, an aromatic plant of the Umbelliferae order, *Angelica officinalis*, valuable as a flavouring and possessing medical properties. In olden times supposed to protect against poison.

Angelus, a church bell rung in Roman Catholic countries, at morn, noon, and sunset, to remind the faithful to say their Angelic Salutation.

Angevin Dynasty includes the Plantagenet kings from Henry II to Richard II. The name was

L 7

derived from Henry II's father, Geoffrey, Count of Anjou.

Angles, a northern tribe originally settled in Schleswig, who with the Saxons and Jutes invaded Britain in the 5th cent.

Angström, a unit of wavelength, named after the Swedish physicist A. J. Angström (1814–74), equal to one hundred-millionth of a centimetre (10^{-8} cm). It is used to measure wavelengths of light, X-rays, etc.

Aniline, a simple aromatic compound ($C_6H_5NH_2$) related to benzene and ammonia. It is obtained from coal-tar. The name recalls the fact that it was first prepared by distilling indigo (*anil* is Portuguese for indigo). In 1856 W. H. Perkin (1838–1907) discovered the first aniline or coaltar dye, mauve, and thus founded the modern dyestuff industry.

Animal Kingdom. *See* **F36.**

Anise, an umbelliferous plant (*Pimpinella anisum*) found in Egypt and the Levant, and valued for its fruit, aniseed, possessing certain medicinal properties and yielding an aromatic, volatile oil, Also used in cooking. The anise of the Bible is *Anethum graveolens, i.e.,* dill.

Annates were acknowledgments formerly paid to the Popes by way of fee or tax in respect of ecclesiastical preferment and consisted usually of a proportion of the income ("first-fruits") of the office. Introduced into England in the 13th cent.; annexed to the Crown under Henry VIII; transferred to a perpetual fund for the benefit of the poorer clergy in 1704. *See* **Queen Anne's Bounty.**

"Annual Register", a yearly record of political and literary events, founded by Edmund Burke (as editor) in 1759 and Robert Dorsley, the bookseller.

Annunciation, Feast of the (March 25), is a Church festival commemorating the message of the in- carnation of Christ brought by the angel Gabriel to the Virgin Mary, hence the title Lady Day.

Anointing is the pouring of consecrated oil upon the body as a mark of supreme honour. In England it is restricted chiefly to the ceremony of the monarch's coronation, and the spoon with which the oil is applied forms part of the English regalia. In the Roman Catholic Church anointing represents the sacrament of extreme unction.

Ant. There are about 6,000 species of ants, which belong to the same order (Hymenoptera) as the bees, wasps and ichneumon flies. They are social in habit, living in communities of varying size and development. There are three basic castes in ants—the females or *queens,* the *males,* and the *workers* (the last-named being neuter), although specialised forms of workers are sometimes found, *e.g.,* the *soldiers* of the harvesting ants. In the communities of those species of ants which evolved most recently there is a highly complex social life and well-developed division of labour. Some species of these ants make slaves of other species, stealing the cocoons before the adult forms emerge. Many ants "milk" green-flies, which they protect for their honey-like secretion, and most ants' nests contain many "guests", such as beetles and silver fish. Some ants harvest grains of corn, and others, from S. America, live on fungi which they cultivate in underground "mushroom beds".

Antarctic Exploration. In earlier centuries it was thought that a great continent must exist in the southern hemisphere, around the South Pole, to balance the known land masses in the north. Its supposed extent was greatly reduced in the 18th cent., particularly when Capt, Cook sailed for the first time south of the Antarctic Circle and reached the edge of the ice-pack. A portion of the ice-covered continent—the coast of Graham Land—was first sighted by Lieut. Edward Bransfield in 1820. Explorers of several other nations sighted portions of the coast-line in other quarters, but the first extensive exploration was made by Capt. James Clarke Ross, who with the *Erebus* and *Terror* penetrated into the Ross Sea in 1841, and discovered the great Ross Ice Barrier in 78° South lat. Interest in the Antarctic did not revive until after 1890, when an international scheme of research was drawn up. A Norwegian, C. E. Borchgrevink, in 1898–1900, was the first to

winter in the Antartic and to travel on the ice barrier. The British share in this work was carried out by Capt. R. F. Scott's expedition in the *Discovery,* 1901–4. Scott's party sledged across the barrier to 82° 17′ South, then a record "farthest south". A little later, Ernest Shackleton beat this by travelling to within 160 km of the South Pole. The Scottish polar explorer William Spiers Bruce led the Scottish national Antarctic Expedition of 1902 in the *Scotia* and discovered Coats Land and founded a meteorological observatory on the South Orkneys. In 1910 Scott organised his second expedition in *Terra Nova,* and became engaged against his will in a "race for the Pole" when, after his departure, the Norwegian Arctic explorer, Roald Amundsen, suddenly announced that he was sailing for the Antarctic. Amundsen set up his base at the eastern end of the Barrier, and, relying on dog teams for hauling his sledges, reached the Pole on 14 December 1911. Meanwhile Scott and his party, their start delayed by adverse weather, were marching southwards, man-hauling their sledges, for Scott was against the use of dogs. After an arduous journey they reached the Pole one month after Amundsen. The return was a struggle against the weather and increasing weakness, probably due to scurvy, until at last they perished within a few kilometres of their base. After the first world war the development of the whaling industry greatly stimulated further exploration. Outstanding expeditions included that of Admiral R. E. Byrd, 1929, when he flew over the South Pole; the British Graham Land expedition, 1934, which carried out the first extensive mapping of any part of the Antarctic continent; and the US Navy's Antarctic Expedition of 1940, when the whole continent was circumnavigated and great areas photographed from the air. In recent years valuable work has been done by the first International expedition, the Norwegian–British–Swedish Expedition to Queen Maud Land, and by the French in Adélie Land. The Falkland Island Dependencies Survey, set up during the war, has continued the scientific exploration of Graham Land. The Antarctic was the scene of high adventure during the International Geophysical Year (1957–58), when scientists from many countries participated in the explorations. The Commonwealth Trans-Antarctic Expedition set out from opposite sides of the continent and met at the South Pole, the UK party, led by Sir Vivian Fuchs, from the Falklands, and Sir Edmund Hillary and his party from New Zealand. The UK party accomplished the first crossing of the White Continent in 99 days. Their scientific work included the marking of seismic and complementary gravimetric studies at frequent intervals along the 3,540 km traverse. Since the Antarctic is becoming important for many reasons, in weather forecasting, in the whaling industry, and as a possible centre for world air routes, the tempo of exploration and research will become even faster in the future.

Anteaters, a small family (the Myrmecophagidae) of mammals from Central and South America. They feed on ants, termites and other insects which they gather with a long tongue covered with sticky saliva.

Antennae, paired feelers of insects and crustaceans, In radio, the term "antenna" is equivalent to "aerial".

Anthem, a choral composition, with or without instrumental accompaniment, usually sung after the third collect in the Church of England services. The words are from the Scriptures, and the composition may be for solo voices only, for full choir, or for both. Among the chief British composers of anthems are Tallis, Purcell, Croft, Boyce, Goss and Stainer.

Anthracite is a black coal with a brilliant lustre. It contains 92 per cent. and over of carbon and burns slowly, without smoke or flame. *See* **Coal.**

Anthropoid, meaning "resembling man", a suborder of the primate mammals including man and also the gibbon, chimpanzee, orang-utan, and gorilla.

Anthropology. *See* **Section F, Part V.**

Antibiotics, a collective name for any substance

derived from micro-organisms or fungi which is capable of destroying infections, *e.g.*, penicillin. *See* **Section P.**

Anticyclone, a region where barometric pressure is greater than that of its surroundings. Such a system is distinguished on weather charts by a pattern of isobars, usually circular or oval-shaped, enclosing the centre of high pressure where the air is calm. In the remaining areas light or moderately strong winds blow spirally outwards in a clockwise direction in the Northern Hemisphere (and in the reverse direction in the Southern Hemisphere), in accordance with Buys Ballot's law (an observer with back to wind in Northern Hemisphere has lower pressure to left; in Southern to right). Over the British Isles anticyclonic weather is generally quiet and settled, being fair, warm, and sunny in summer and either very cold and often foggy or overcast and gloomy in winter. These systems move slowly and sometimes remain practically stationary for days at a time, that over Siberia being particularly well defined. Extensive belts of almost permanent anticyclones occur in latitudes 30° N and 30° S. Persistent anticyclonic weather with easterly winds during the months December to March, 1962–3, brought the coldest and hardest winter to Britain since 1740.

Antimony. Metal element, no. 51, symbol Sb. In group 5 of the periodic table. Exists in various forms, the stable form being a grey metal with a layer structure. The other forms are non-conductors. On being burned, it gives off dense fumes of oxide of antimony. By itself it is not of special utility; but as an alloy for hardening other metals, it is much used. As an alloy with lead for type-metal, and with tin and copper or zinc for Britannia-metal, it is of great value. Most important antimony ore is stibnite (antimony sulphide).

Anti-Pope, one elected in opposition to one held to be canonically chosen; commonly applied to the popes Clement VII and Benedict XIII, who resided at Avignon during the Great Schism (1378–1417).

Anti-proton, the "negative proton", an atomic particle created in high energy collisions of nuclear particles. Its existence was confirmed in Oct. 1955. *See* **Section F.**

Antisemitism. *See* **Section J.**

Antlers are the branched horns of deer, the branches being called tines. Antlers originate as outgrowths of the frontal bone, and are usually shed once a year. Except in the reindeer and caribou they are restricted to the male.

Apartheid. *See* **Section J.**

Ape, a term applied to the gorilla, chimpanzee, orang-utan and gibbon—the anthropoid apes.

Aphelion, the point in the orbit of a planet farthest from the sun; the opposite of perihelion. At aphelion the earth is $1 \cdot 52 \times 10^8$ km from the sun.

Aphids, green-flies or plant lice, a numerous species of destructive insects living on young shoots and foliage, some on roots. Reproduction is by parthenogenesis (virgin birth).

Apis, the sacred bull worshipped by the ancient Egyptians; also the scientific name for the bee.

Apocalyptic writings are those which deal with revelation and prophecy, more especially the Revelation of St. John.

Apocrypha (hidden writings), the books which were included in the Septuagint (Greek) and Vulgate (Latin) versions of the Old Testament but ex- cluded from the sacred canon at the Reformation by the Protestants on the grounds that they were not originally written in Hebrew nor re- garded as genuine by the Jews. The books include: 1 and 2 Esdras, Tobit, Judith, additions to Esther, Wisdom of Solomon, Ecclesiasticus, Baruch, Song of the Three Holy Children, History of Susannah, Bel and the Dragon, Prayer of Manasses, 1 and 2 Maccabees. The term is usually applied to the additions to the Old Testament, but there are also numerous Christian writings of the same character. *The New English Bible,* which contains the Apocrypha, was published in 1970.

Apogee, that point in the orbit of a heavenly body which is farthest from the earth; used in relation to the sun, moon and artificial satellites. The sun's apogee corresponds to the earth's aphelion. *See* **Perigee.**

Apostasy is a revolt, by an individual or party, from one form of opinions or doctrinate to another. Julian, the Roman Emperor (331–63), brought up as a Christian, became converted to paganism and on coming to the throne (361), proclaimed religious toleration. Hence his name, Julian the Apostate.

Apostles. The twelve apostles who were disciples of Jesus were: Simon Peter and Andrew (his brother), James and John (sons of Zebedee), Philip, Bartholomew, Thomas, Matthew, James, Thaddaeus, Simon, and Judas Iscariot. After the Ascension Matthias was chosen to take the place of Judas. St. Paul was the leading apostle in the mission to the Gentiles, though he was not one of the twelve. St. Barnabas has also been called an apostle.

Apostles' Creed, the name of the most ancient of the Church's statements of its belief: "I believe in God the Father Almighty; and in Jesus Christ his only Son our Lord, who was born of the Holy Ghost and the Virgin Mary...." A later version is used in the Church of England at morning and evening prayer.

Apostolic Fathers were the immediate disciples or followers of the apostles, especially such as left writings behind. They included Barnabas, Clement of Rome, Ignatius of Antioch, Hermas, Papias of Hieropolis and Polycarp.

Appeasement Policy. The name of the policy during 1937 and 1938 of yielding to the demands of Hitler and Mussolini in the hope that a point would be reached when the dictators would co-operate in the maintenance of peace. The policy culminated in the Munich Agreement (which was the subject of much criticism) after a series of concessions including the recognition of the Italian conquest of Abyssinia and the German annexation of Austria. The policy was finally demonstrated as futile when Hitler seized Czechoslovakia in March 1939.

Appian Way, the oldest and finest of the Roman roads originally laid by Appius Claudius (312 B.C.) from Rome to Capua and thence to Brundisium (Brindisi).

Approved Schools were residential schools, subject to Home Office inspection, for the training of young persons under 17 who, because of disturbed behaviour as a result of unfavourable influences such as bad environment or parental neglect, were guilty of offences or in need of care and protection and had been sent to them by magistrates from juvenile or other courts. The approved school order was abolished by the Children and Young Persons Act 1969. Such young people may now be committed to the care of a local authority and accommodated in a system of community homes ranging from children's homes to borstal type institutions.

April, the fourth month of the year, from the Roman *Aprilis* derived from *aperire* "to open" —the period when the buds begin to open.

Apse is a semicircular recess, arched or dome-roofed, at the end of the choir, aisles, or nave of a church.

Aqueducts are conduits in which water flows or is conveyed from its source to the place where it is to be used. Most famous builders were the Romans and the oldest Roman aqueduct was the Aqua Appia, which dates from about 310 B.C. Among modern aqueducts may be mentioned that of Glasgow, which brings water to that city from Loch Katrine; that of Manchester, which taps Thirlmere; that of Liverpool, with Lake Vyrnwy in North Wales as its source, and the Fron Aqueduct, Powys, which carries water from the Elan Valley to Birmingham.

Arabian Nights Entertainment or **Book of a Thousand and One Nights,** a collection of fascinating tales of the Orient, of mixed Indian, Persian, Arabic, and Egyptian origination, and first made known in Europe by Antoine Galland's French translation (1704–17) from Arabian texts. The "master" tale tells how the princess Shahrazad so beguiles the king through the telling of the tales over one thousand and one nights that her life was spared. English translators include E. W. Lane (1840), Sir Richard Burton (1885–8), John Payne (1882–4).

Arabic Numerals. The modern system of numbering, 0, 1, 2, 3, 4, 5, 6, 7, 8, 9, in which the digits depend on their position for their value is called the Arabic numerical notation. The method is, in fact, of Indian origin. By the 9th cent. Hindu science was available in Arabic, and the Persian mathematician Al-Kwarizimi (*c.* 830) in his *Arithmetic* used the so-called "Arabic" system of numbering. Gradually the method spread to Europe, taking the place of the Roman system which was useless for calculation. The West is indebted to the Arabs for the zero symbol, the lack of which had been a serious drawback to Greek mathematics. It made the invention of decimal fractions possible.

Aragonite, the unstable form of calcium carbonate found as a mineral in some young deposits. It crystallises in the orthorhombic system but tends to revert to calcite.

Aramaic Languages, the Semitic dialects current in Mesopotamia and the regions extending southwest from the Euphrates to Palestine from about the 12th cent. B.C. until after the rise of Islam, when Aramaic was superseded by Arabic. Both Aramaic and Greek were spoken in Palestine during the time of Christ.

Archaeopteryx, a fossil bird providing a connecting link between reptiles and birds. It had feathers, jaws with teeth, no bill, reptilian bones and skull, a long tail, and it probably used its fore-limbs for gliding flight. The first specimen, found in 1861, in the Solenhofen limestone of Bavaria, is in London's Natural History Museum.

Archbishop, the chief of the bishops of an ecclesiastical province in the Greek, Roman, and Anglican churches. In the Church of England there are two archbishops, the Archbishop of Canterbury, called the Primate of *all* England, and the Archbishop of York, styled the Primate of England.

Archimedes' Principle. When a body is weighed in air and then in any fluid, the apparent loss in weight is equal to the weight of fluid displaced. This scientific fact was noted by the Syracusan philosopher Archimedes (287–212 B.C.) and is frequently used as a basis for density measurements.

Architecture, the art and science of building. The provision of shelter for mankind by the orderly arrangement of materials in a manner which expresses man's attitude to living. The forms which buildings take are the outcome of the function for which they are to be used, of the architect's aesthetic sensibility and the structural method adopted. Until the last hundred years structural methods were limited to timber frames, and columns, lintels, load-bearing walls, arches, vaults, and domes in brick or stone. From these few basic elements have evolved the great variety of historic styles of building to be found throughout the world. To give but one example, the Greeks created those systems of decorated columns and beams, known as the Orders, which were adapted by the Romans, revived decoratively rather than structurally during the Renaissance and are still used in debased form on the more presumptuous type of modern building. In recent years, however, architecture has taken on a new meaning. Once confined to the rich, in the form of Church, State or Commerce, it is now, with the coming of democracy, recognised as an essential social service for all. This, and the development of new structural techniques and materials (steel, aluminium, sheet glass, reinforced concrete, plastics and plywoods, to name a few), have made the interest in historic styles, the mainstay of the older architect, of secondary importance. Modern architecture is the creation of buildings with the highest possible standards of functional performance in terms of efficient planning and structure, good artificial and natural lighting, adequate heating or cooling, and proper acoustic conditions consistent with the price the client can afford to pay. At the same time the architect's task is to design a structure and the spaces the structure delimits, internally and externally which are aesthetically stimulating and satisfying, and well related to the land and buildings around.

Arctic Exploration. Modern exploration of the Arctic begins in the 16th cent. when men sought to reach the East Indies by sailing through the Arctic to the Pacific Ocean. The North-east Passage, via the shores of northern Asia, was the first attempted. In 1553 and 1554 the English navigators Sir Richard Chancellor and Stephen Burrough sailed into the White Sea, but were prevented by storms and ice from advancing farther eastwards. The project was later revived by the Dutch; Barendts in 1594 discovered Spitsbergen, but also failed to get beyond Novaya Zemlya. It was not, in fact, until 1879 that the Swede, A. E. Nordenskjöld, in the *Vega,* succeeded in reaching the Pacific. The attempts to find a North-west Passage were more numerous and determined. In 1585 John Davis penetrated Davis Strait and coasted along Baffin Island. Hopes ran high when Henry Hudson discovered Hudson Bay in 1610, but a practicable passage continued to elude explorers. The problem was to find a navigable route through the maze of channels in the short summer season, and to avoid being frozen in with supplies exhausted. After the Napoleonic Wars the Admiralty sent out many naval expeditions which culminated in Sir John Franklin's expedition with the *Erebus* and *Terror* in 1845. The ships were beset by ice in Victoria Channel and, after Franklin's death, were abandoned by their crews, who perished from scurvy and starvation on their march southwards. To ascertain their fate, several further expeditions were despatched, and the crew of the *Investigator,* commanded by R. J. M'Clure, sailing eastwards from Bering Strait, were the first to make the Passage, though in doing so they were obliged to abandon their ship. It was thirty years before the Norwegian, Roald Amundsen, succeeded in sailing the *Gjoa* from the east to west. In the meantime, the North Pole had become the goal of explorers. Nansen, in 1893, put the *Fram* into the ice-pack to drift across the Polar basin, and himself made an unsuccessful attempt on the Pole across the pack. This was eventually achieved by the American explorer Robert E. Peary, who after several expeditions in the North Greenland region, sledged to the Pole with Eskimo companions in 1909. The next phase was the employment of airships and aeroplanes in Arctic exploration. In 1926 Admiral Byrd made the first flight over the Pole, and in the same year Amundsen and Lincoln Ellsworth flew the airship *Norge* from Spitsbergern to Point Barrow Alaska. Two years later, the *Italia,* commanded by the Italian, Nobile, was wrecked on a return flight from the Pole, and Amundsen lost his life in an attempt to rescue the survivors. With modern developments in aircraft and navigation, flights over the Polar basin are almost a routine matter. The first voyage under the North Pole was made in August 1958 by the American nuclear-powered submarine *Nautilus.*

Arenaceous Rocks, the rocks composed of grains of sand, chiefly sandstones; quartz is the most abundant mineral in these rocks.

Argillaceous Rocks are a sedimentary group, including the shales and clays.

Argon, chemical element no. 18, symbol A. This was the first of the inert gases (**F14**) to be isolated from air by Rayleigh and Ramsay in 1894. Argon is used for filling gas-filled metal filament electric lamps. In gas discharge tube it gives a blue glow. *See also* **Rare Gases.**

Arithmetic, the branch of mathematics that deals with numerical calculations as in counting, measuring, weighing. The early civilisations used simple arithmetic for commercial purposes, employing symbols and later letters of the alphabet as numerals. When Hindu-Arabic numerals replaced Roman numerals in the Middle Ages it meant a great step forward and led to rapid developments—the invention of logarithms, slide-rule, calculating machines.

Arithmetic Progression, a sequence of numbers in which the successor of each number is obtained by adding or subtracting a fixed number, for example 2, 5, 8, 11, ... or 100, 95, 90, 85. ...

Ark of the Covenant was the sacred chest of the Hebrews and symbolised God's presence. It was overlaid with gold inside and outside. It accompanied the Israelites into battle and was once captured by the Philistines. Eventually it found a resting-place in Solomon's Temple.

Armada, Spanish, the naval expedition fitted out

by Philip II of Spain in 1588 against England, commanded by the Duke of Medina Sidonia. It comprised 129 ships, was manned by 8,000 sailors and carried 19,000 soldiers and more than 2,000 cannon. Against this formidable force Elizabeth had only 80 ships, manned by 9,000 sailors, under Lord Howard of Effingham, under whom served Drake, Hawkins and Frobisher. The British Fleet awaited the Armada off Plymouth, and at Tilbury there was a considerable defensive land force under the command of the Earl of Leicester. On 19 July the ships of the Armada were sighted off the Lizard, disposed in a crescent 11 km long from horn to horn. The excellent manoeuvring of the English, their fire-ships and a gale from the N.W. combined so effectively to cripple the Spanish ships that the Armada was scattered, only 63 of the original fleet of 129 reaching home via the North of Scotland. It was impossible to embark the army of Parma waiting in the Netherlands. Elizabeth had a medal struck bearing in Latin the inscription, "God blew and they were scattered".

Armadillo, a genus of animals related to the sloths and anteaters, belonging to South America, and carrying a hard bony covering over the back, under which one species (*Tolypeutes*) can completely conceal itself when attacked, rolling itself up like a hedgehog.

Armageddon, according to the Revelation of St. John, the great battle in which the last conflict between good and evil is to be fought.

Armillary Sphere, an early form of astronomical apparatus with a number of circles representing equator, meridian, ecliptic, etc. Used by Hipparchus and Ptolemy and up to the time of Tycho Brahe for determining the position of the stars.

Aromatic. A term used by chemists, originally to describe compounds like benzene, having a characteristic smell. It is a term which implies a collection of chemical characteristics, the salient features being a flat ring structure and a general similarity to benzene.

Arsenic, a metalloid element, no. 33, symbol As in group 5 of the periodic table usually met with as a constituent of other minerals, sometimes by itself. Its compounds are very poisonous. Lead arsenate is a powerful insecticide used for spraying fruit trees. The more stable allotropic form (grey) has a layer structure, and conducts electricity.

Art Deco, the name given by modern collectors to the decorative style of the 1920s and 1930s; it is derived from the long official name of the Paris Exhibition of 1925, which was almost exclusively devoted to "les Arts Décoratifs". Art Deco runs parallel in time with Functionalism (*q.v.*) but unlike that austere and philosophical style, Art Deco is gay, elegant and even frivolous, being a creation of fashionable Paris. It is related superficially to Cubism, using squares, circles and triangles in interesting combinations for ornament. Another popular motif is the modern girl with her shingled head dancing the tango or drinking cocktails. The style is brash and worldly, but in its best expressions full of charm and vitality. Famous names within the style are the glassmaker René Lalique (1860–1945), the fashion designers Gabrielle Chanel and Elsa Schiaparelli, and the decorator and illustrator Erté (Roman de Tirtoff, b. 1829). There has been a nostalgic revival of Art Deco, *e.g.*, in films like "Bonny and Clyde" (1967) or "The Great Gatsby" (1974) based on F. Scott Fitzgerald's novel (1925).

Artesian Wells take their name from Artois in France, where the first wells of this kind were constructed in 1126. They are to be found only when a water-bearing bed is sandwiched between two impervious beds. When a boring is made to the lower part of the bed, the pressure of water is sufficient to cause the water to overflow at the surface. Artesian wells were known to ancient Egypt and China, and have existed in the Sahara since the earliest times. The fountains in Trafalgar Square were once fed by artesian wells sunk through the London clay into the chalk about 250 m.

Articles. The *Six Articles* are those contained in an Act of Henry VIII, and were of Roman Catholic origin. The *Thirty-nine Articles* were drawn up for the English church at the Reformation. They are printed at the back of the Prayer Book. Candidates for holy orders in the Church of England are required to subscribe to them, though the form of assent has been modified.

Art Nouveau (German *Jugend Stil*) was prevalent in architecture and decoration in Europe and the USA *c.* 1885–1910. It was rooted in the thoughts of Ruskin and William Morris. In reaction against the impersonal uniformity of industrial products which were flooding the market, artists turned to Nature for their inspiration, choosing organically growing forms, flowers or animals, as motifs for decoration or even for shaping whole objects. Another favourite motif was Romantic Woman with long robes and flowing hair, as interpreted so beautifully by Aubrey Beardsley. The sharply undulating line with a whiplash rhythm is a recurring theme. Famous names are the glass-makers Emile Gallé in France and Louis Comfort Tiffany in New York, the English goldsmith Charles Robert Ashbee (1863–1942), Henry Van de Velde (1867–1942) in Belgium and Charles Rennie Mackintosh (1868–1928) in Scotland, both architects and interior decorators, and in pure architecture Antonio Gaudí in Barcelona (1852–1926) and Victor Horta of Brussels (1861–1946).

Arts and Crafts Movement, the English revival of decorative art which began about 1875 as a revolt against the existing vulgarity of internal decoration and furnishings and the pettiness of academic art. Inspired by William Morris and Burne-Jones together with Rossetti, it was strongly influenced by the former's mediaevalism, his hatred of industrialism, and his own version of socialism which included the regeneration of man by handicrafts. His firm of Morris & Co. produced wallpapers, tapestries, furniture, stained-glass windows, carpets and fabrics in a style totally different from that of contemporary Victorian decoration. Morris's Kelmscott Press did much to raise the standards of book design and printing. *See* **Art Nouveau.**

Arum, a genus of plants of the *Araceae* family of which there is but one British species, the wake-robin or cuckoo-pint, sometimes also styled "Lords and Ladies".

Arundel Marbles, a collection of ancient Greek sculptures formed by Thomas Howard, Earl of Arundel in the 17th cent. and presented to Oxford University by his grandson, Henry Howard, who became Duke of Norfolk.

Aryans, nomadic peoples who made their way in successive waves from the Eurasian steppes to the Indus and the Nile during the first half of the 2nd millennium B.C. They crossed the Hindu Kush into N.W. India and settled in the valleys of the Indus and Ganges, where an earlier Indus civilisation had flourished, *c.* 3240–2750 B.C. Their religious ideas are reflected in the Veda (oldest Hindu scriptures, written down many centuries later in Vedic, parent language of Sanskrit). Those who made their way to Syria and Egypt founded the Hyksos empire (*c.* 1720–1550 B.C.). The Aryans introduced the horse-drawn chariot and spoke a language from which the great Indo-European family of languages is derived, with one group in India and Iran, and another in Europe. Because of the misuse of the term by the Nazis, Aryan is now referred to as proto-Indo-European.

Asafoetida, an acrid, strong-smelling gum resin exuded from the stem of umbelliferous plant, *Ferula foetida*, found in Iran and Afghanistan. Formerly used medicinally to treat hysteria; still used in cooking in India, Iran and France.

Ascension Day, or Holy Thursday, is the 40th day after Easter.

Ascot Races are an annual fashionable function dating from 1711 and taking place on Ascot Heath, only 10 km from Windsor, in June. These races have always had royal patronage. The course is c. 3 km long.

Ash, a familiar deciduous tree of the genus *Fraxinus,* of over 60 species, native to North temperate regions. The ash held an important place in Norse mythology, as it was supposed to support the heavens with its roots in Hell. The species native to Britain, and to Europe, is *F. excelsior,* a tall tree with compound leaves, greenish flowers, winged seeds, and black buds in winter. It is a valuable timber tree, tough and elastic, and largely used for wheels and handles. The rowan, or mountain ash, *Sorbus aucuparia*, with similar leaves and orange berries, belongs to a different family. *F. pendula* or weeping ash is a strain which makes an ideal natural summer house.

Ashes, The, the symbol which distinguishes the winning cricket team in the Australian Test Matches. In 1882 the Australians won at the Oval by 7 runs. After the match the following epitaph appeared in the *Sporting Times*: "In affectionate remembrance of English Cricket which died at the Oval on 29 Aug. 1882, deeply lamented by a large circle of sorrowing friends and acquaintances. R.I.P. NB. The body will be cremated and the ashes taken to Australia." When the English Eleven went to Australia the same winter it was said that they had come to recover the "ashes". England won two out of three matches, and after the third match the ashes of what is now generally believed to have been a stump were presented in an urn to Ivo Bligh, later Lord Darnley. He bequeathed the urn to the M.C.C., and it is now in the Memorial Gallery at Lord's.

Ash Wednesday, first day of Lent, the seventh Wednesday before Easter.

Assassination, treacherous murder for political ends, usually of a ruler or distinguished person. Among the most notable: Julius Caesar, 44 B.C.; Thomas Becket, 1170; David Rizzio, 1566; William the Silent, 1584; Henry IV of France, 1610; Jean Paul Marat, 1793; Abraham Lincoln, 1865; Alexander II of Russia, 1881; Archduke Francis Ferdinand of Austria, 1914; Dr. Dollfuss, 1934; King Alexander of Yugoslavia, 1934; Mahatma Gandhi, 1948; King Abdullah of Jordan, 1951; Liaquat Ali Khan, 1951; King Feisal of Iraq, 1958; Mr. Bandaranaike, 1959; President Kennedy, 1963; Malcolm X, 1965; Dr. Verwoerd, 1966; Dr. Martin Luther King, 1968; Senator Robert Kennedy, 1968; Mr. Tom Mboya, 1969; King Faisal of Saudi Arabia, 1975; Lord Mountbatten, 1979; John Lennon, 1980; President Sadat, 1981; Mrs. Indira Gandhi, 1984; Olof Palme, 1986; Abu Jihad, 1988 and Sheikh Hassan Khaled, Grand Mufti of the Lebanon, 1989.

Asteroids or the minor planets are relatively small objects which move in orbits mainly between those of Mars and Jupiter. The first to be discovered (by Piazzi in 1801) was Ceres. Many thousands more have since been discovered, of which nearly 2,000 now have well-determined orbits and have been named. The largest are Ceres (800 km), Pallas (500 km), Vesta (530 km) and Juno (240 km). Few others have diameters of more than 80 km, while those of the majority are less than 5 or 10 km. Of particular interest are the Trojan group, located at the two stable "Lagrangian" points in Jupiter's orbit round the sun, where their locations make isosceles triangles with the sun and Jupiter. Also, a number of asteroids have orbits like that of Icarus which at perigee (*q.v.*) comes close to the sun.

Astrolabe, a mediaeval scientific instrument for taking altitudes, observing the sun by day and the stars by night, and used for telling the time and finding the latitude. Used by the ancient Greeks, later by the Arabs and Persians, and introduced into Europe by way of Spain in the 14th cent. Chaucer is said to have sent his son Lois, a ten-year-old student at Oxford, an astrolabe with a treatise on its use in 1391.

Astrology. See **Section J.**

Astronomical Unit, the mean distance between the centres of the sun and earth, or the semimajor axis of the earth's orbit, has a value of about $1 \cdot 495979 \times 10^8$ km (149,597,900 km). This value has been constantly improved over the past 300 years, first using observations of the planets, later transits of Venus across the sun's disc, then observations of minor planets such as Eros as they came near the earth, and now by the transit time of a radar beam bounced off the planet Venus. The astronomical unit is a fundamental quantity in astronomy.

Astronomy. The Pythagoreans believed the stars and planets moved with uniform circular velocity in crystalline spheres, centred round the earth (the "harmony of the spheres"). Hipparchus (190–120 B.C.) made the first star catalogue, discovered the precession of the equinoxes and introduced the idea of epicyclic motion. His planetary system, in the form it was presented by Ptolemy 200 years later, held until the Renaissance when Copernicus revived the heretical view first put forward by Aristarchus of Samos (310–230 B.C.) that the sun and not the earth was at the centre. Galileo, accurate observer and experimenter, went beyond Copernicus; helped by the contributions of Tycho Brahe, Giordano Bruno, Kepler and others, he was able to overthrow the Ptolemaic system of the heavenly spheres and Aristotelian philosophy and pave the way for Newton and modern astronomy. To Galileo we owe the conception of acceleration; to Newton the theory of universal gravitation; they showed that the same laws govern both celestial and terrestrial physics. Three landmarks in more recent times were the discovery of Uranus by Herschel in 1781 which extended the solar system as then recognised; the estimation by Hubble in 1924 of the distance of Andromeda, which showed that our Galaxy was just one of many; and Einstein's theory of relativity which improved on Newton's theory of the solar system by bringing gravitation into the domain of space-time. Today radiotelescopes and space probes are advancing astronomical knowledge and making it possible to explore regions beyond the scope of optical telescopes. The following have held the position of Astronomer Royal (period of office in brackets): John Flamsteed (1675–1719), Edmund Halley (1719–42), James Bradley (1742–62), Nathaniel Bliss (1762–65), Nevil Maskelyne (1765–1811), John Pond (1811–35), Sir George Airy (1835–81), Sir William Christie (1881–1910), Sir Frank Dyson (1910–33), Sir Harold Spencer Jones (1933–55), Sir Richard Woolley (1956–72), Sir Martin Ryle (1972–82), Professor Sir Francis Graham Smith (1982–). See **F5–7,** *also* **Radio Astronomy.**

Astrophysics, a branch of astronomy concerned with the physical nature and constitution of the various objects within the universe. Recent developments in radio astronomy and in space research technology, opening up gamma-ray, X-ray, ultra-violet and infra-red parts of the spectrum, have contributed to the major recent advances in this science.

Athanasian Creed, one of the three ancient creeds of the Christian Church, often referred to as the *Quicunque Vult,* is a statement of the doctrine of the Trinity and the Incarnation, and though named after St. Athanasius, it is thought to be the work of St. Ambrose (339–97).

Atmosphere is the gaseous envelope of the earth, and consists of a mixture of gases (*see* **Air**) and water vapour, the variability of the latter being of great importance meteorologically. The ozone layer, which absorbs solar ultra-violet radiation which would be lethal to plant life if it reached the ground lies between 12 to 50 km above the earth. The lower level of the atmosphere up to a height of about 12 km (10 km at the Poles and 16 km at the Equator) is known as the *troposphere,* and it is in this region that nearly all weather phenomena occur. This is the region of most interest to the forecaster studying temperature, humidity, windspeed, and the movement of air masses. Temperature falls with height by about 1°C per 152 m in this layer. The *tropopause* is the boundary between the troposphere and the *stratosphere.* Temperature varies little in the lower levels of this region: it is mainly cloudless, and has no vertical currents. Strangely enough, the lowest temperatures of the atmosphere are to be found not at the Poles, but at about 18 km above the Equator, where a temperature as low as $-80°C$ has been recorded! Temperatures begin to rise about 32 km from the earth's surface at about the same rate as they fall in the troposphere owing to the absorption of solar radiation by the concentration of ozone. The stratospheric air is extremely dry. Near the 100 km level a number of important atmospheric phenomena occur. Above this level the oxygen becomes predominantly monatomic in contrast to the normal diatomic form at lower altitudes. This is the *ionosphere* (*q.v.*). This layer acts as an electrical radio mirror which makes long-distance radio transmission possible. The region of the Van Allen belts (*q.v.*) above the earth is called the magnetosphere (*q.v.*). The auroras are most frequently observed at altitudes between about 100 and 400 km but do extend at times far higher. Many aspects of the upper air can only be studied through space-research techniques. These include the composition and temperature of the charged particles in the ionosphere, the location of the electric currents in the ionosphere which produce the regular variations of the compass needle, as well as those which circulate during magnetic storms, the variation of the intensity of different radiation in the air-glow (*q.v.*) with height, the composition of the air at heights above 32 km, and so on. In addition, the pressures, density, temperatures, and wind distribution of the neutral atmosphere can be studied more directly, in much greater detail, and up to much greater altitudes than is possible if one is confined to the use of equipment on the ground. Instruments outside the atmosphere can make systematic observations on a world-wide basis of the atmospheric circulation, through observation of cloud cover and of the thermal radiation into space from the atmosphere. Such observations are of great importance for meteorology. *See also* **Ionosphere.**

Atmospherics are electrical impulses which are believed to originate in atmospheric electrical discharges such as lightning. They give rise to crashing background noises in the loudspeakers of radio sets, interfering with reception at distances of up to 6,400 km from the centre of the disturbance. The location of atmospherics with the aid of radio direction-finding methods gives warning of the approach of thunder-storms.

Atom. *See* **F10-17, F23.**

Atomic Pile, an apparatus containing a fissionable element and a moderator, such as heavy water or graphite, in which a self-sustaining fission process proceeds at a controllable rate. The first atomic pile, constructed on a squash court at Chicago, was operated for the first time on 2 December 1942, under the direction of Enrico Fermi. The pile contained 12,400 lb (5,580 kg) of uranium. *See* **Nuclear Reactors.**

Augsburg Confession, name given to the doctrine of faith of the Lutheran churches, drawn up by Melanchthon and endorsed by Luther for the Diet of Augsburg (1530).

August, named after the Emperor Augustus, because it was his "lucky" month.

Auks, duck-like sea-birds, black and white, with short, narrow wings, compact bodies and legs set well back. Breed in colonies on rocky coasts of N. Europe (incl. British Isles) and spend most time in coastal waters. Migrate south in winter. The Auk family includes the Razorbill, Little Auk, Guillemot and Puffin. The Great Auk became extinct in the 19th cent. after ruthless hunting for the sake of its feathers.

Aurora polaris. This wonderful phenomenon of the night sky is a common sight at high northern and southern latitudes, where it is called the aurora borealis and the aurora australis respectively. It is visible less often at temperate latitudes, and only rarely in the tropics. The auroral ovals, or zones of maximum frequency of aurora, surround both of the earth's geo-magnetic poles, and the northern auroral oval includes the northern parts of Scandinavia, Canada and Alaska. The aurora is the visible manifestation of complex plasma processes occurring within the earth's magnetosphere (*q.v.*), whereby streams of high-energy electrons and protons (mainly) are accelerated and dumped via the earth's magnetic field lines into the upper atmosphere. This mechanism produces the light emission of the aurora. The brightest aurora, which may also extend to lower latitudes, occurs during geomagnetic storms, which are complex and large-scale plasma instabilities within the magnetosphere triggered by fluctuations in the solar wind (*q.v.*) —usually ascribed to "M" regions on the sun

associated with coronal holes, flares and active sunspot groups. Auroral displays may take several forms—a faint glow, a diffuse ribbon of light crossing the heavens, great folded waving curtains or draperies, or the entire sky may be flooded with a rapidly varying brilliant panoply of light. Specially instrumented spacecraft which can directly explore the magnetosphere and high-latitude ionosphere have provided a great deal of our knowledge about this fascinating and complex phenomenon. The aurora is a kind of light essentially different from that of the rainbow which is a partly subjective phenomenon. Each beholder sees his own rain-bow, whose light is sunlight refracted and reflected by many raindrops. The raindrops that produce his rainbow depend on his position as well as on the direction of the sun. The aurora, on the contrary, is a light as objective as that of a candle, though produced differently. It is a self-luminescence of the air in particular regions of the atmosphere that lie far above the clouds.

Austerlitz, Battle of, was fought near Brünn, in Moravia, on 2 December 1805, when Napoleon defeated the Russians and Austrians under Kutuzov.

Auto-da-Fé, or Act of Faith, was the ceremony connected with the sentencing of heretics under the Inquisition of Spain and Portugal, the persons found guilty being imprisoned or burned alive. The ceremony took place in some public square, sometimes in the presence of the king and court.

Automation is a modern word used to designate the adoption of methods of automatic control either of manufacturing processes or of any business process involving a large mass of routine work. The word is used in broader and narrower senses. In its broadest sense it covers any form of mechanisation which largely replaces human labour by the work of automatic or semi-automatic machines, such as has been in progress continuously since the Industrial Revolution; but it it better kept to a narrower meaning, in which it is confined to the recent development of electronic or similar devices, involving feedback (automatic detection and correction of malfunction). Human labour is eliminated save for that needed for watching and maintaining the elaborate machines used. In this sense, automation has been spreading rapidly in advanced countries.

Autumn, the third season of the year, begins with the autumnal equinox, and ends with the winter solstice, but the term is generally understood as covering the period from mid-August to mid-November.

Auxins, "plant hormones", organic substances produced by plants to regulate growth. Synthetic auxins are now widely used, *e.g.*, for promotion of root formation in cuttings, differential weed control, prevention of premature dropping of fruit, in storage of potatoes and hard fruit, and to overcome frost damage to fruit buds.

Average is a single number designed to give a typical example of a set of numbers, *e.g.*, a cricketer's batting average for a season gives an idea of his typical score. There are several kinds of average and their uses are studied in the science of statistics (*q.v.*). A statement that "so and so is the average value" can be misleading if one does not know which average is meant. Three common averages are: the arithmetic average (or mean), the mode, and the median. The arithmetic average of n numbers is found by adding them together and dividing by n; this is a very common method of averaging. The mode of n numbers is the most frequently occurring number. The median is the middle number, *i.e.*, the number which is smaller than just as many of the other numbers as it exceeds. Of the numbers 1, 2, 2, 2, 2, 3, 4, 5, 6, 8, 9, the arithmetic means is 4, the mode is 2, the median is 3.

Avocet, a graceful wading bird related to the stilts, of black-and-white plumage, bluish legs, and slender upturned bill. There are four species. Avocets nest in colonies. There are now over 200 breeding pairs, mainly in E. Anglia.

Avogadro's Hypothesis. This is a fundamental concept of chemistry. Equal volumes of all gases under the same conditions of temperature and pressure contain the same number of molecules. This law was instrumental in assigning the formulae of molecules. The hypothesis was put forward in 1811, but was not generally accepted until 1860.

Avogadro's Number. *See* **F24.**

Aztecs, the name of a native and powerful race found in Mexico when the Spaniards first discovered that country, and with difficulty subdued.

B

Babiroussa, a ferocious, long-legged wild pig, native of Sulawesi, sometimes called the horned-hog, because of the long upper tusks in the male, which are developments of the canine teeth which grow upwards, piercing the upper lip, and curving backwards, often broken in fighting.

Baboon, monkeys belonging to the African genus *Papio*. They are considered the lowest of the Old World (Catarrhine) monkeys, and walk on all fours. In the main terrestrial, but take to trees after food. The mandrill is closely related.

Babylonian Captivity, the period spent by the Jews in Babylon after Jerusalem was captured by Nebuchadnezzar, the Babylonian emperor, in 586 B.C. Traditionally the captivity lasted 70 years, but when Babylon was in turn taken by Cyrus in 538 B.C., the exiles were permitted to return to Jerusalem. The term is also applied in church history to the period 1309–78 when the papacy moved to Avignon, into the control of the French monarchy.

Bacteria. *See* **F41.**

Bacteriophage (Phage), literally "bacteria eater", *i.e.*, a virus which specifically infects bacteria. In common with viruses which attack animal or plant cells, isolated phages are inert, and can only reproduce by making use of the chemical apparatus of a more sophisticated host cell (in this case a bacterium). However phages may be of two types, virulent or temperate. Virulent phages completely disrupt the normal functioning of the infected bacterium and adapt its reproductive mechanism to produce more phage. This eventually kills the bacterium and the newly assembled phages are released. Temperate phages on the other hand may enter into a remarkable symbiotic relationship with the bacterium, known as lysogeny. The phage genetic material is incorporated into that of the bacterium and is reproduced each time the still functioning bacterium subsequently divides. Furthermore the bacterium is immune from attack by potentially virulent phages of the same type. When such lysogenic bacteria die, phage particles may again be released. Phages carried in lysogenic bacteria are in a state known as prophage and it is often difficult to obtain pure, prophage-free strains of bacteria. Because of their relatively simple structure, phages have been extensively used in research on genetics and molecular biology.

Badger, a carnivorous mammal related to the weasel, of nocturnal and burrowing habits, inoffensive, subsisting chiefly on roots and insects, though sometimes mice, young rabbits and eggs form part of its diet. Badger-baiting was a favourite sport in Britain until it was prohibited in the middle of 19th cent. The badger does little harm and quite a lot of good; badger digging is to be condemned as a cruel sport. In Britain the badger is protected by an Act of Parliament passed in 1973, but the Ministry of Agriculture officials may destroy the animal in areas where bovine tuberculosis has been found.

Bagpipe. Once popular all over Europe, this instrument is still played in Scotland, Ireland, Brittany and elsewhere. The bag acts as a reservoir of air and, when squeezed by the player's arm, forces air through the pipes. One of these, the Chanter pipe, provides the tune and is played by the fingers as in a flageolet. The remainder, the Drone pipes, give a continuous, unvarying note.

Bailey Bridge, invented by Sir Donald Bailey and first used in the N. African campaign 1942–3. Built up of prefabricated girders, it can be

easily transported and erected.

Bailiwick, a feudal term denoting the limits of a bailiff's jurisdiction. The term has survived in the Channel Islands, where Jersey and Guernsey are Bailiwicks.

Balance of Power was the doctrine in British policy whereby European groups should be so balanced as to prevent the emergence of a dominating Power. Thus the balance was maintained between the Triple Alliance (Germany, Austria and Italy) and the Triple Entente (Great Britain, France and Russia) and preserved peace from 1871 to 1914. After the first world war there was tentative support of Germany's re- covery to counterweigh the possible French hegemony; but when Germany's power grew under Hitler culminating in the second world war, Britain, France and Russia again became allies. By the end of the war the old system of a balance of power centred upon Europe collapsed to give way to a thermonuclear balance of power between the super-Powers, the Soviet Union (Warsaw Pact) and the United States (Nato alliance). The dramatic collapse of communism during 1989 in much of Eastern Europe, and the likelihood of German reunification, will all change the balance of power.

Baldachin (It. *Baldachino*), a canopy usually supported by four pillars over throne, altar, or other sacred object. The name is also applied to the silken canopy used in processions by the priest who carries the Host.

Balearic Crane, the crowned crane of the Balearic Islands and the North African mainland, distinguished by its yellowish, black-tipped occipital tuft and by its trumpet note.

Baleen *or* "whalebone" the name given to a series of horny plates growing from the roof of the mouth in those whales classified as Whalebone or Baleen Whales (*Mystacoceti*). There are 300–400 or so plates on each side, and their inner edges are frayed, the whole system constituting a filter for collecting minute organisms used for food. The Baleen Whales include the Right-Whales, the Pacific Grey-Whale and the Rorquals. *See* **Whales.**

Ballet is a combination of four arts; dancing, music, painting, and drama, each of which is ideally of equal importance. The movement of the individual dancers and the "orchestration" of the whole group is in the hands of the choreographer. The dancer's training follows certain basic rules but save in classical ballet there is considerable freedom of movement. Ballet as we know it today developed professionally at the Court of King Louis XIV of France, though it owes its origins to Italy and in the earliest times to Greece and Rome. Its movements were made up from the dances of courtiers, country folk and tumblers. Technique grew more complex as costume became modified, the body gaining complete freedom with the invention of tights. A succession of great dancers—French, Italian and latterly Russian left their imprint on the art. Contemporary ballet reflects the aesthetics of the Russian, Sergei Diaghilev. In England Dame Ninette de Valois has laid the foundation of a national ballet, at Sadler's Wells and Covent Garden, with a personality that reflects the national character. A Royal Charter was granted in 1957 setting up the Royal Ballet to co-ordinate the activities of the Sadler's Wells group.

Ballistics, the science dealing with the motion of projectiles, especially shells, bombs and rockets. Great advances have been made in this science.

Balloon, the modern balloon consists of a bag of plastic material inflated with a gas lighter than air. The first ascent by man in a hot-air balloon was made on 21 November 1783, and in a hydrogen balloon on 1 December 1783. The most famous of the early scientific flights by manned balloons were those of the Englishmen Coxwell and Glaisher, in 1862, when a height of 11 km was reached. The first aerial crossing of the English Channel by Blanchard and Jeffries was made on 7 January 1785. Piccard's ascent to 16 km, in 1931, marked the conquest of the stratosphere. Four years later the American balloon *Explorer II*, inflated with nearly 112,000 m³ of helium, carried a team of scientists with their floating laboratory to an altitude of 23 km. In 1957 a pressurised balloon carrying an American doctor rose 31 km above the Earth. Captive kite-balloons were widely used in the war as defensive measures against air attack. Meteorologists send their instruments up in balloons to collect data about the upper atmosphere, and of recent years physicists have learned much about cosmic radiation from the study of photographic plates sent to the upper regions in balloons. Ballooning as a hobby is carried on by a number of enthusiasts.

Balsam, a big genus (140 species) of flowering plants. Many species are cultivated for their showy flowers, *e.g.*, *Impatiens noli-me-tangere*, the yellow balsam or "touch-me-not", so called because the fruit explodes when touched, slinging out the seeds. Balsam fir is a conifer (*Abies balsamea*) from which Canada balsam gum is obtained.

Bamboo, a genus of strong grasses, some species growing to over 36 m in height; much used by oriental peoples for all kinds of purposes. The young shoots of some species are tender and esculent.

Banana (family *Musaceae*), a large herbaceous plant cultivated in moist regions of the tropics, and one of the most productive plants known. The main areas of commercial cultivation are in tropical America, the Canary Islands and West Africa. World production is estimated at 20 million tonnes, of which only 3 million are for trade.

Bandicoots, Australasian marsupial mammals, of the size of a large rat or rabbit. They are burrowing animals living largely on insects. The rabbit-eared bandicoot, restricted to Australia, has shrew-like snout, long ears like a rabbit, long crested tail, and a silky coat. The long-nosed bandicoot has a spiny coat and comes from E. Australia. The pig-footed bandicoot has two functional toes on the foot, like a pig.

Bank Rate, the rate at which the Bank of England is prepared to lend to the clearing banks. If raised it has the immediate effect of raising the rate of discount on Treasury Bills. Known as the Minimum Lending Rate from Oct. 1972 to Aug. 1981. *See* **Section G.**

Bantu (native word = people), term loosely used for large family of Negro races of Southern Africa.

Baobab, a tropical African tree. The species *Adansonia digitata* is one of the largest trees known, though not the tallest; the trunk can reach 9 m in thickness. The fruit is woody, but its juice provides a cooling beverage. The bark yields a fibre used for making rope and cloth.

Barbary Ape, a large monkey belonging to the genus *Macaca.* It is the only monkey living in relative freedom in Europe, a small colony being found on the Rock of Gibraltar. It has no tail.

Barberry, a genus of berry-producing shrubs containing a hundred species. Several species are cultivated for their flowers and bright berries. Has an interesting pollination mechanism; the base of each stamen is sensitive to touch, and insects probing for nectar cause top of stamen to spring inwards, so dusting visitor's head with pollen which can then be carried to the next flower visited. The common barberry (*Berberis communis*) harbours one stage of the fungus that causes rust of wheat.

Barbican, a fortified entrance to a castle or city, with projecting towers. In the London area called Barbican there was formerly a barbican in front of the city gates.

Barbiturates. A group of drugs derived from a parent compound called barbituric acid: phenobarbitone is the best-known example. They induce sleep and are used in the manufacture of sleeping pills and sometimes as anaesthetics, but they have the disadvantage of being habit forming. *See* **Index to Section P.**

Barbizon School, a school of mid-19th-cent. landscape painters whose main tenet was a return to nature with an exact rendering of peasant life and country scenery painted on the spot. It was named after the village of that name in the Forest of Fontainebleau, where its chief members—Millet, Theodore Rousseau, Daubigny and Diaz—made their home. Their practice of painting direct from nature, which was far from universal at that time, made them the precursors of Impressionism (*q.v.*).

Barcarolle, a Venetian gondolier's song applied to instrumental as well as vocal compositions.

Bard, among the ancient Celts a poet or minstrel whose mission was to sing of heroic deeds. He was supposed to have the gift of prophecy, and was exempt from taxes and military service.

Barilla, soda carbonate or soda ash obtained by burning certain salt-marsh plants (*e.g.*, the saltwort, *Salsola kali*). It used to be in great demand, until the product of the Leblanc and then the Solvay ammonia-soda process was made available by the chemical industry.

Barium, metal element, no. 56, symbol Ba. In group 2 of the periodic table. The metal is soft and easily cut. It occurs as the sulphate and carbonate in nature. It was first prepared by Sir Humphry Davy in 1808, as an amalgam, by electrolysis of barium chloride. The pure metal was not isolated until 1901.

Barium meal. Barium sulphate is opaque to X-rays and before X-ray pictures of the alimentary canal radiologists give a "barium meal" to the patients so that the alimentary canal shows up more clearly.

Barnacles constitute a sub-class (*Cirripedia*) of the Crustacea. The barnacle fouling the bottom of ships is the Goose Barnacle, which has a long muscular stalk and a shell composed of five plates. The Acorn Barnacles, which cover rocks, breakwaters, etc., just below high-water mark are similarly constructed, but have no stalk. The manner of feeding of barnacles was vividly described by T. H. Huxley, who said the barnacle is "a crustacean fixed by its head kicking the food into its mouth with its legs". It was a naval surgeon, J. Vaughan Thompson, who discovered in 1830 that barnacles have a free-swimming larva (or nauplius). In the Middle Ages a curious myth grew up to the effect that the Barnacle changed into a sea-bird called, for that reason, the Barnacle Goose.

Barometer is an instrument for measuring atmospheric pressure, invented at Florence by Torricelli, pupil of Galileo, in 1644. The standard method consists of balancing the air column against a column of mercury, used on account of its high density. The mercury is contained in a long glass tube, closed at one end, and inverted in a cistern also containing mercury. The height of the mercury column, supporting the air column, is taken as the pressure at the time, and can be read off very accurately by means of a vernier scale. Present-day tendency is to express the readings in units of pressure instead of length, the millibar being adopted (1 mb = 1,000 dynes per sq. cm.; 1,000 mb ≡ 75 cm of mercury approx.). The standard instrument is correct for pressures at 0°C in Lat. 45°, so that corrections have to be applied for temperatures and latitudes other than these. Also a correction has to be made for reducing the pressure to mean sea level. *See* **Aneroid.**

Baron, title given in feudal England to a man who held his land directly from the king by military or other honourable service. The first baron created by letters patent was John Beauchamp de Holt, Baron of Kidderminster, in 1387. A baron is a member of the fifth and last grade of the peerage of the United Kingdom and is addressed as "Lord". Life peers and life peeresses rank with hereditary barons and baronesses according to the date of their creation. In Scotland the term baron is used of the possessor of a feudal fief, or the representative by descent of such a fief. The equivalent of the English baron, as a rank of the Scottish peerage, is Lord of Parliament.

Baronet, the lowest hereditary title, instituted by James I to provide funds for the colonisation of Ulster. The first baronet was Sir Nicholas Bacon. Between 1964 and 1983 no recommendations for hereditary honours were made.

Baroque, a term used for the art style of the period *c.* 1600–1720 which was the artistic accompaniment of the Jesuit counter-Reformation. Its most obvious characteristics are: (*a*) its emotional appeal and dramatic intensity both related to its deliberate intention as propaganda ("a good picture makes better religious propaganda than a sermon" said one of its exponents); (*b*) in architecture, a style which is heavily and sometimes almost grotesquely ornate, plentifully covered with voluptuous sculpture on which draperies float rather than hang, with twisted and spiral instead of plain or fluted columns, and unnecessary windows or recesses added for ornament rather than use; (c) its emphasis on the whole at the expense of the parts such that a building's sculpture merges into its architecture and both into its painting (Baroque paintings are as closely knit as a jigsaw puzzle so that one cannot isolate individual figures as would be possible in a Renaissance one). Baroque architecure owing to its origin is found mainly in the Catholic countries; Italy, France, Austria, Bavaria, e.g., the Barberini Palace, Rome, designed by its greatest exponent Bernini and others; the Church of the Invalides, Paris. Baroque artists include Caravaggio, Guido Reni, Murillo and Rubens the greatest Northern Baroque painter. The Baroque style merges gradually into **Rococo** (q.v.).

Barque, a small sailing vessel with three or four masts. A three-masted barque has fore- and mainmasts square-rigged, the mizzenmast fore- and aft-rigged.

Barrow is an ancient artificial mound of earth or stone raised over the site of a burial. In Britain barrows were built from 2500 B.C. until the late Saxon period, but the Egyptian are the earliest barrows known, the great pyramids being a spectacular development of the custom of ceremonial burial. Silbury Hill, south of Avebury, is the biggest artificial mound in Europe, 512 m in circuit at the base, 96 m at top, and 41 m high.

Bartholomew, Massacre of St., occurred in Paris on the night of 24 August 1572, when over two thousand Huguenots were massacred by order of the Catholic French Court.

Baryons, the group of heavier subatomic particles which includes the proton, neutron, lambda and omega-minus particles (and their corresponding anti-particles, called anti-baryons). Baryons interact by means of all the known forces of nature (strong, weak, electromagnetic and gravitational). However, in any closed system the total baryon number (i.e., the number of baryons minus the number of anti-baryons) is constant. This means that the proton, being the lightest known baryon, must be stable against spontaneous decay. Unlike the lighter leptons (q.v.), baryons are now thought to have internal structure reflecting the fact that they are composed of quarks (q.v.). See **F15.**

Basalt Rocks are fine-grained, dark coloured, of igneous origin and occur either as lava flows as in Mull and Staffa, or as intrusive sheets, like the Edinburgh Castle Rock and Salisbury Crags. One of the most noted examples of columnar basalt is that of the Giant's Causeway in Ireland.

Basanite, a smooth black siliceous mineral, or flinty jasper; a crypto-crystalline quartz used as a touchstone for testing the purity of gold, etc., by means of the mark left after rubbing the metal with it. Sometimes styled the Lydian stone.

Base, a substance having a tendency to accept a proton (H⁺). This is a wide definition and covers unconventional types of compounds. In aqueous solution bases dissolve with formation of hydroxyl ions, and will neutralise an acid to form a salt. In non-aqueous solvents, like liquid ammonia or hydrogen fluoride, compounds classically regarded as salts can be bases, e.g., sodium fluoride is a base in hydrogen fluoride solution.

Basilisk, is a lizard of aquatic habits, with an elevated crest (which it can erect or depress at will) down the centre of its back.

Basques, people of N. Spain and S.W. France, oldest surviving racial group in Europe, who have preserved their ancient language which is unrelated to any other tongue.

Bas-Relief ("low relief"), a term used in sculpture to denote a class of sculptures the figures of which are only slightly raised from the surface of the stone or clay upon which the design is wrought.

Bastille, a castle or fortress in Paris, built in the 14th cent., and used as a state prison, especially for political offenders. Its bad repute as an instrument of despotism excited the hatred of the populace, who stormed and demolished it

on 14 July 1789, at the beginning of the Revolution.

Bastinado, an oriental punishment, by beating with a pliable cane on the soles of the feet.

Bats. These mammals fly by means of a membrane stretched between each of the long fingers of the hand and between the fifth finger and the body. Another membrane stretches between the legs and the tail. Most British bats, including the pipistrelle, long-eared bats, noctules, belong to the family Vespertilionidae (with the exception of the horseshoe bats which belong to the family Rhinolophidae). These all feed on insects which they catch on the wing. The problem of how bats can detect their insect prey and avoid obstacles when flying in total darkness has interested zoologists for a very long time. The problem was solved with the advent of sensitive ultrasonic recording devices. Blindness does not affect this ability but deafness leave bats comparatively helpless. One of the most interesting types of bat is the fishing bat (*Noctilio*) found in central America, which can detect fish by being able to receive echoes from the ripples they make on the water surface. *See also* **Ultrasonics.**

Bath, Order of the, Britain's second oldest order of knighthood. Exclusive to men since its institution by Henry IV in 1399, women became eligible for admission to the order in 1971. The order has three grades: Knight Grand Cross (G.C.B.), Knight Commander (K.C.B.), and Companion (C.B.). Women members of the order are known as Dame Grand Cross, Dame Commander and Companion.

Battery, Electric, the common term for an electric cell but really meaning a combination of two or more cells. A cell is a device for converting stored chemical energy into electricity which can then be used for heat, light, traction, or any desired purpose. A *primary* cell will do this until the chemical action is completed and the cell is then useless. In a *secondary* cell, the chemical actions are reversible and the cell can be returned to its initial condition and used again. This is done by passing an electric current through—a process called recharging. A common primary cell is the Leclanché dry cell; used in torches. This works by the action of sal-ammoniac on electrodes made of zinc and carbon. About a century after it came into common use it is still the chief source of power for portable equipment in armed forces. A common secondary cell is the lead and sulphuric acid accumulator used in cars. Many other types of cell are known and some are under development because the demands of space travel, medicine, warfare, etc., call for batteries of lighter weight, greater reliability, or special properties. *See* **Fuel Cell, Energy Conversion.**

Bauhaus, a German institution for the training of architects, artists and industrial designers founded in 1919 at Weimar by Walter Gropius, (d. 1969). It was closed by Hitler in 1933 and re-opened at Chicago. The Bauhaus doctrine held that there should be no separation between architecture and the fine and applied arts; that art, science and technology should co-operate to create "the compositely inseparable work of art, the great building". Thus it was an organisation with a social purpose. The original institution, at the instigation of Gropius, included on its teaching staff not only architects and technicians but also such noted artists as Paul Klee and Wassily Kandinsky.

Bauxite, the chief ore of aluminium. Chemically it is aluminium oxide. Aluminium metal is made industrially by electrolysing purified bauxite dissolved in fused cryolite. Chief producing areas; Jamaica, Australia, Surinam, USSR, Guyana, France, Greece, Guinea, USA, Hungary, Yugoslavia.

Bayeux Tapestry, a famous tapestry representing the conquest of England by William the Conqueror. It is embroidered on a band of linen 70 m long and 51 cm wide in blue, green, red and yellow, divided into 72 scenes ranging over the whole story of the conquest. The accepted view is that the tapestry was commissioned for Bayeux Cathedral, but a new interpretation is that it is an Anglo-Norman secular work of art, much influenced by the contemporary *chansons de geste* (songs of deeds), executed by

English embroiderers for a Norman patron. A representation can be seen in the Victoria and Albert Museum in London.

Beagle, a small hound that tracks by scent, and extensively used for hare hunting.

Bears belong to the Ursidae family of the Carnivora. They are plantigrade mammals, walking (like man) on the soles of their feet. Found in most parts of the world except Australia. The common Brown Bear was once spread over the whole of Europe; it became extinct in England about the 11th cent.; 2–2·5 m in length, and stands 1 m or more at the shoulder. The Grizzly Bear of N. America is larger, and the coat is shorter and greyer. The Polar Bear is remarkable in having a white coat all the year round; it spends much time in water, and unlike other bears is entirely carnivorous. Bearbaiting was made illegal in England in 1835.

Beaufort Scale of wind force is used to specify numerically the strength of the wind. Since the introduction of anemometers to measure the actual velocity, equivalent values of the ranges in miles per hour at a standard height in the open have been assigned to the Beaufort numbers. See **Section Z.**

Beaver, a genus of mammals of the Rodentia order, with short, scaly ears, webbed hind feet, and a long broad scaly tail. They grow up to 1·2 m long, and live in communities, constructing dams and lodges where they breed. A campaign was launched in 1977 to bring back beavers to Britain where they have been extinct for several hundred years after being mercilessly hunted for their valuable pelt.

Bedlam (a corruption of Bethlehem) was a priory in Bishopsgate, afterwards converted into a hospital for lunatics. The asylum was transferred to St. George's Field, Lambeth, in 1815. The term "bedlamite" came to be applied to any person behaving like a madman.

Beech, a deciduous tree belonging to the genus *Fagus* of some eight or nine species found in north temperate regions. The common beech, *F. sylvatica,* is believed to be native to Britain and is one of our finest trees, with massive trunk, long, pointed winter buds, and smooth, grey bark. There is little undergrowth under its dense shade. It is shorter-lived than the oak taking about 200 years to reach full size and then declining. The timber of beech has a variety of uses, e.g., spoons, handles, tools, and chairs.

Bee-eater, name of a family of brilliantly coloured birds closely related to the rollers and kingfishers inhabiting the tropical and sub-tropical parts of Africa, Asia and Europe. The European species successfully nested in Britain for the first time in 1955 and a pair nested in Alderney in 1956. With their long curved beaks they catch insects on the wing, especially bees and butterflies, and lay their eggs in dark tunnels.

Beefeater, See **Yeomen of the Guard.**

Beeswax, the secretion of the bee, used for the formation of the cells or honey-comb of the hive; when melted it is what is commercially known as yellow wax, white wax being made by bleaching. Being impervious to water, it acts as a good resistant and is an article of much utility.

Beetles (Coleoptera) constitute one of the biggest orders of insects, numbering over 200,000 species. There are two pairs of wings; the hind pair are used for flight, while the front pair are hardened to form a pair of protective covers (elytra). Some beetles have lost the power of flight and then the elytra are joined together.

Bel and the Dragon is the title of certain supplementary chapters to the "Book of Daniel" of an apocryphal character. First appeared in the Septuagint, but the Jewish Church did not accept it as inspired. In 1546 the Council of Trent declared it to be canonical.

Bell, a hollow body of metal used for making sounds. Bells are usually made from bellmetal, an alloy of copper and tin. Small bells used for interior functions are often made of silver, gold or brass. Ordinary hand-bells are of brass. From the 7th cent. large bells have been used in England in cathedrals, churches and monasteries. The greatest bell in the world is the "King of Bells" in the Kremlin at Moscow which weighs about 198 tonnes, is 627 cm high and 691 cm in diameter. It was cast in 1733 but cracked in the furnace (the

broken part weighed 11 tonnes) and is now preserved as a national treasure. Other large bells in Russia include the 171 tonne one at Krasnogvardersk, near Leningrad, and the one of 110 tonnes at Moscow. The Great Bell (Great Paul) at St. Paul's, cast in 1881, weighs nearly 17 tonnes and is the largest in the United Kingdom. Other gigantic bells are the Great Bell at Peking (53 tonnes); Nanking (22 tonnes); Cologne Cathedral (25 tonnes); Big Ben, Westminster (over 13 tonnes); Great Peter, York Minster (10 tonnes). The Curfew Bell is rung in some parts of England to this day, notably at Ripon. The number of changes that can be rung on a peal of bells is the *factorial* of the number of bells. Thus four bells allow 24 and eight bells 40,320.

Belladonna or **Deadly Nightshade** (*Atropa belladonna*), a well-known poisonous wild plant found in Southern Europe and Western Asia. The alkaloid atropine it contains is valuable in medicine, although a large dose is poisonous.

Bell, Book and Candle. To curse by "bell book, and candle" was a form of excommunication in the Roman Church ending with the words: "Close the book, quench the candle, ring the bell".

Benedicite, the canticle in the Book of Common Prayer, known also as "The Song of the Three Holy Children".

Benedictines are monks and nuns of the Benedictine Order who live under the rule of St. Benedict—the monastic code whose influence on the religious and cultural life of the West has been so powerful. The rule is marked by an absence of extravagant asceticism. The greatest of the early Benedictines was Pope Gregory I (590–604) who sent St. Augustine of Canterbury to Anglo-Saxon England. Gregorian plainsong is named after him.

Benzene. An aromatic hydrocarbon obtained from coal tar and some petroleum fractions. It is a volatile inflammable liquid with a characteristic smell. The molecule consists of a flat ring of six carbon atoms, each bound to one hydrogen atom. Benzene is the parent member of many aromatic organic compounds and is widely used in industry to synthesise intermediates for fibres, dyestuffs, explosives and pharmaceutical chemicals.

Berlin Wall, construction dividing Berlin. Symbol of the Cold War. Built 13 August 1961. Dismantling began in 1989.

Beryl, a mineral, of which the emerald is a grass-green variety. Composed of beryllium and aluminium silicates. The pure mineral is colourless; the colour of most beryl comes from traces of impurities, notably iron and chromium. Otherwise it is yellowish, greenish-yellow, or blue, and is found in veins which traverse granite or gneiss, or embedded in granite, and sometimes in alluvial soil formed from such rocks.

Beryllium. Metallic element, no. 4, symbol Be. Very similar to aluminium, it is stronger than steel and only one-quarter its weight. It is not very abundant, its main source is the mineral, beryl. Copper containing 2 per cent. beryllium is used for making springs. Because of its special properties the metal is used as a component in spacecraft, missiles and nuclear reactors. This accounts for its recent development on a technical scale. The metal powder is toxic.

Bessemer Process for making steel depends on the forcing of atmospheric air into molten pig iron to burn out the impurities. Ousted by the oxygen converter. See **Steel.**

Betel, the leaf of an Indian climbing plant, of pungent, narcotic properties. It is destructive to the teeth, and reddens the gums and lips.

Bhang, the Indian name for the hemp plant *Cannabis sativa,* the leaves and seed-capsules of which are chewed or smoked. The drug which comes from flowers of the female plant is called hashish in Arabia and marihuana in the U.S.A.

Bible (Greek *biblion* = scroll of paper; pl. *biblia* = writings) includes the Hebrew sacred Scriptures (Old Testament) and those held sacred by the Christians (New Testament). The Old Testament— the prehistoric portion—consists of 39 books, and is divided into three parts: (1) the Law, (2) the Prophets, (3) Miscellaneous Writings, The Old Testament was written in Hebrew except for parts of Ezra and Daniel, which were in Aramaic. It was not until the 9th cent. A.D. that a complete Hebrew text was made, the so-called Massoretic text. Before that the main versions were the Alexandrian Greek translation (Septuagint) made in the 2nd cent. B.C. and St. Jerome's Latin Vulgate of the 4th cent. A.D. (It was Jerome who used the Latin word "testament" (formed from *testis* = a witness).) Portions were translated into the Anglo-Saxon in the 8th cent. and the Venerable Bede put the greater part of St. John's gospel into English, but it was not until 1535 that a complete, printed English version appeared—the Coverdale Translation. The Authorised Version dates from 1611 in the reign of James I, and its beautiful phraseology has given it a lasting appeal. The Revised Version dates from 1885. *The New English Bible*, with the Apocrypha, was published in 1970. It is a new translation in plain English prose of the earliest Hebrew, Aramaic, and Greek manuscripts. The finding of the Dead Sea Scrolls (since 1947) has added to our knowledge of Scripture. By 1990 the complete Bible had been translated into 310 languages, the New Testament alone into 695.

Biedermeier, style in interior decoration and the decorative arts developed from Empire (*q.v.*). It was created in Vienna *c.* 1815 and the name was derived from a fantasy figure in Viennese writing personifying all that which is sedate and bourgeois. Biedermeier furniture is less austere and grandiose than Empire's predecessors, more intimate and homely. A most important creation is the large circular table on a stem-like foot, which became the centre of family life, around which chairs could be grouped freely, not formally against walls as previously. In Vienna itself the style died out *c.* 1830, but in other Continental countries it survived well into the second half of the 19th cent. Its English equivalent is Early Victorian.

Billion, formerly in English usage a million million; now a thousand million or 10^9.

Bill of Rights, or Declaration of Rights, was the document setting forth the conditions upon which the British throne was offered to William and Mary in 1688. This was accepted and ultimately became an Act of Parliament.

Binary Notation, for numbers, is a way of representing numbers using only two digits, 0 and 1. Electronic digital computers handle numbers in this form and many people these days are having to learn it. Many school children find it both easy and fascinating—as did the great philosopher and mathematician Leibniz. The ordinary, or decimal numbers, 0, 1, 2, 3, 4, 5, 6, 7, 8, 9, 10 are written in binary notation as follows: 0, 1, 10, 11, 100, 101, 110, 111, 1000, 1001, 1010. The reader might divine the rules from this. The point is you "carry 1", *i.e.*, move the digit 1 a place to the left, when you reach 2. In decimal notation you move 1 a place left when you reach 10. In other words, instead of columns for units, tens, hundreds, thousands, etc., the columns are for units, twos, fours, eights, etc. In binary notation: "1 + 1 = 0 with 1 to carry". Since every digit in binary notation is either 0 or 1 it requires one bit of information to specify a binary digit.

Biological Clock. All living organisms undergo cyclical changes in activity of some sort. These are linked to the changes in their environment which are produced by the alternation of night and day, the phases of the moon and the tides, and the cycle of the seasons. These cycles of activity frequently persist if the organism is put into a constant environment in which there appear to be no external clues as to what time or what season it is. A squirrel, for example, wakes up at about the same time each evening even when it is put into constant darkness. It is usual to refer to these activity patterns as being driven by a biological clock inside the organism. But very little is known about how these biological clocks work.

Biological Warfare, is the use for warlike purposes of bacteria, viruses, fungi, or other biological agents. These can be used to spread distress, incapacity, disease or death among the enemy's people or livestock. One of the strange uses to which mankind puts its science is to make

naturally infective organisms even more virulent for military use. This sort of research can be done in many countries; it is much cheaper and easier to hide than nuclear weapons development.

Biosensors, micro-electronic or optoelectronic devices used to sense the presence of chemicals. This new technique for diagnosis and analysis could have a host of applications in medicine (*e.g.* blood analysis), industry *etc*.

Biosphere, that part of the earth in which life exists—a very thin layer near the surface bounded by regions too hostile for life processes to occur. The upper limit is at about 9,000 m above sea level and the lower limit at about 10,000 m in the deep oceans. Ample supplies of solar energy, liquid water and places where liquid, solid and gas all meet seem to be requirements for a biosphere to exist and for all the biological cycles of water, oxygen, mineral, nitrogen, etc., to function.

Birch, a genus of deciduous trees including about 40 species and found only in northern regions. Birches native to Britain, and to Europe generally, are of two species—the silver birch, *Betula pendula*, with its graceful, drooping branches and triangular leaves, and the white birch, *Betula pubescens*, which has erect branches and soft oval leaves. Birch timber is an important plywood timber, the bark is used for tanning leather, and wintergreen oil comes from the bark of black birch, *Betula lenta*, a North American species. The birch is not a long-lived tree, few standing for more than a hundred years. The tallest recorded is at Woburn in Bedfordshire, 31 m high.

Birds, or Aves, are, next to mammals, the highest class of animal life. There are two kinds of modern birds—*Carinatae*, possessing keeled breast-bones and having power of flight; *Ratitae*, having raft-like breast-bones, and incapable of flight; and a sub-class of fossil birds, Archaeornithes, including *Archaeopteryx*. Estimates of the total number of birds breeding in the British Isles vary, but there are 229 breeding species. Of these the commonest are wrens, of which there are 10 million breeding pairs, house sparrows, blackbirds and chaffinches with up to 7 million pairs each, robins with 5 million and starlings with 3·5 million pairs.

The wheatear is usually the first of the migratory birds to return, often reaching Britain at the end of February and always before the middle of March; the sand martin is the first of the "early swallows" to return, followed by the house martin. The first cuckoo arrives about the middle of April, and the whinchat, garden warbler, and sedge warbler during the last week in April. The nightjar, spotted flycatcher, and red-backed shrike are not seen until the first week in May. The swift is among the last to return from Africa and the earliest to depart. Bird-nesting is illegal in Britain. With the passing of the Wildlife and Countryside Act in 1980 the trapping and caging of robins, nightingales, larks, kingfishers, cuckoos, owls, martins, fieldfares, flycatchers, ravens and other birds was made illegal in Britain. *See also* **F36(2)**.

Birds of Paradise, over 40 species of tropical birds inhabiting the dense forests of New Guinea and neighbouring islands. The male birds are remarkable for their brilliant plumage, long tail feathers, and ruffs on wings and neck, which are displayed to advantage during courtship. Related to the Bower Birds of Australia.

Biretta, a four-cornered head-covering worn by ecclesiastics of the Roman Church and varying in colour according to the rank of the wearer. A cardinal's biretta is red, a bishop's purple, a priest's black.

Bise, a keen dry north wind prevalent in Switzerland and South France.

Bishop is a Christian ecclesiastic, a person consecrated for the spiritual government of an area, a diocese or province, to the spiritual oversight of which he has been appointed (diocesan bishops), or to aid a bishop so appointed (suffragan bishops). In the Church of England there are forty-three diocesan bishops, all nominated by the Crown. Two, Canterbury and York, are archbishops having primacy in the respective provinces. The archbishops of Canterbury and York and the bishops of London, Durham and Winchester and twenty-one other diocesan bishops in order of seniority are spiritual peers, and sit in the House of Lords. The (Disestablished) Church of Ireland has two archbishops and twelve bishops; the (Disestablished) Church of Wales an archbishop and five bishops and the Episcopal Church in Scotland seven bishops. *See also* **Cardinal.**

Bismuth, metallic element, no. 83, symbol Bi, in group 5 of the periodic table. Like antimony, the stable form is a grey, brittle, layer structure; electrical conductor. It is readily fusible, melting at 264°C and boiling at about 1420°C. Wood's metal, an alloy with one of the lowest melting points (under 65°C, so that a spoon made of it will melt when placed in a cup of hot tea), contains four parts bismuth, two parts lead, one part tin, one part cadmium.

Bison, a genus of wild cattle, distinguished from the ox by its shorter, wider skull, beard under the chin, high forequarters, and, in winter, a great mane of woolly hair covering head and forequarters. There are two species, the European and the American bison, both now protected in game reserves.

Bit, formerly the word often referred to the metal piece in the mouth of a bridled horse, now more likely to be a technical expression in the mouth of a computer expert. A bit is a unit of information; it is the information that can be conveyed by indicating which of two possibilities obtains. Any object that can be either of two states can therefore store one bit of information. In a technical device, the two states could be the presence or the absence of a magnetic field, or of an electric voltage. Since all numbers can be represented in the binary system (*see* **Binary Notation**) by a row of digits which are *either* 0 *or* 1, it takes one bit of information to specify a binary digit. Bit is short for binary digit.

Bittern, a bird of the heron genus, with long, loose plumage on the front and sides of the neck. It is a solitary bird inhabiting marshes, but rare in Britain.

Bivalves, shell-fish whose shell consists of two hinged valves, lying one on each side of the body, such as mussels, oysters and cockles.

Blackbird, or Merle, a member of the Thrush family, a familiar song bird in Britain. Male is all-black with orange bill; female is mottled brown with brown bill; the young are spotted brown.

Blackcock and Greyhen (as the female is called) are closely related to the Capercaillies but smaller. They nest on the ground and prefer wooded country to open moors. Found in northern half of northern hemisphere. Polygamous, they perform excited courtship dances; the male is a handsome blue-black bird with white undertail, the female dark brown mottled.

Black Death, the plague which swept across Europe in the years 1348–50, beginning in the ports of Italy, brought in by merchant ships from Black Sea ports. It was the worst scourge man has ever known; about a quarter of the European population was wiped out in the first epidemic of 1348. It reached England in the winter of that year. The disease was transmitted to man by fleas from black rats, though this was not known at the time, the specific organism being *Bacillus pestis.* The disease continued to ravage Europe in recurrent outbreaks up to the late 17th cent. The epidemic which raged in England in 1665 wiped out whole villages and one-tenth of London's population of 460,000. Samuel Pepys wrote a grim account of it in his *Diary. See also* **Labourers, English Statute of.**

Black Hole of Calcutta, the name given to the place where a captured British garrison was confined in 1756, during the struggle for India between the French and British. Into a noisome space, about 6 m square, 146 persons were driven and only 23 were found alive the next morning. The authenticity of the story has been called into question, but after sifting the evidence Professor H. H. Dodwell, in the *Cambridge History of the British Empire,* believes it to be substantially true.

Black Holes. *See* **Astronomy, Section F, Part I.**

Black-letter, the Old English or Gothic type first used in printing blocks.

Black Power. *See* **Section J.**

Black Woodpecker (*Dryocopus martius*), a black

bird about the size of a rook, with slightly crested scarlet crown, found in parts of Europe.

Blenny, a group of marine fishes with spiny rays part of the fin running along the back. Several species are found around the British coast.

Blood Groups. *See* **Index to Section P.**

Bloody Assizes, the assizes conducted in 1685 by George Jeffreys, Lord Chief Justice, at which participants in the Duke of Monmouth's rebellion against King James II were tried. They were marked by relentless cruelty.

Bluebird, a migratory bird of North America, deriving its name from its deep blue plumage, it has a pleasant warbling song and is a familiar sight in the woods from early spring to November. In India and Malaya there is the Fairy Blue-bird; the male is black with shiny blue upper parts. Used as the symbol of happiness by Maeterlinck in his play *The Blue Bird.*

Blue Peter, a blue flag with a white square in the centre, is hoisted 24 hours before a ship leaves harbour (the letter P in the alphabet of the International Code of Signals).

Blue Ribbon, a term in general use to denote the highest honour or prize attainable in any field or competition. Thus the Derby is the blue ribbon of the turf. The expression is derived from the highest Order of Knighthood in the gift of the British Crown, the insignia of which is a garter of blue velvet.

Blue Stocking, a term used to describe a learned or literary woman, particularly if pedantic and undomesticated. It is said that the term derives from the Bas-Bleu club of Paris, which was attended by the literary savantes of the 17th cent. In England a similar literary club was formed about 1780, whose members were distinguished by their blue stockings.

"Blue" Sun, Moon, etc., a phenomenon caused by the scattering of sunlight by transparent particles suspended in the atmosphere, the effect being that blue light is transmitted, and red light extinguished to direct vision. The dust from the Krakatoa eruption in 1883 and the drifting layer of smoke from the forest fires in Alberta, Canada, in September 1950 gave rise to "blue" moons and suns, phenomena sufficiently rare to be described as occurring "once in a blue moon". In the cold climatic conditions of the Pamirs and the far north, vegetation is said to look "blue" on account of the rays of high calorific value (red, yellow, green) being absorbed, while only the blue and violet are transmitted. It was Tyndall who first explained the blue colour of the sky.

Boa, a term applied to a family of snakes of large size, some attaining a length of 9 m. They are not poisonous, but kill their prey by crushing —constriction—hence the name "boa constrictor". They occur both in the Old World and the New, but are more abundant in the latter. Most Boas retain the eggs within the body until young are fully developed, whereas the Pythons almost all lay leather-shelled eggs.

Boar, or Wild Hog, an animal largely distributed over the forest regions of Europe, Asia, Africa and South America. It has a longer snout and shorter ears than its descendant the domestic hog, and is provided with tusks. Having to forage for itself, it is a more active and intelligent animal than the pig of the sty, and offered good sport to the hunter.

Boat, an open vessel, propelled by oars or sails, or both. The boats of a ship of war are the launch, barge, pinnace, yawl, cutters, jolly boat and gig; of a merchant vessel, the launch, skiff, jolly boat or yawl, stern boat, quarter-boat and captain's gig. Every ship is compelled to carry adequate, fully provisioned and equipped lifeboats.

Bode's Law, a numerical relationship formulated by Bode in 1772 (though pointed out earlier by J. D. Titius of Wittenberg), which states that the relative mean distances of the planets from the sun are found by adding 4 to each of the terms 0, 3, 6, 12, 24, 48, 96, and dividing each number by 10. The gap between Mars and Jupiter caused Bode to predict the existence of a planet there, which was later confirmed by the discovery of Ceres and other minor planets. The law breaks down however, for Neptune and Pluto.

Boer War lasted from 11 October 1899, when the

Boers invaded Natal, to 31 May 1902, when the Treaty of Vereeniging ended hostilities. At first the operations of the British troops in Cape Colony were unsuccessful and disastrous reverses were sustained. Lord Roberts was then sent out as Commander-in-Chief, with Lord Kitchener as Chief-of-Staff, and from February 1900, when Kimberley was relieved and Cronje was compelled to surrender and Ladysmith and Mafeking were relieved, the struggle was practically over.

Boiling-point is the temperature at which a liquid boils. At that point the pressure of the vapour is equal to the pressure of the atmosphere. Under increased pressure the b.p. rises and under less pressure, as on the top of a mountain, it is lower. At standard atmospheric pressure (760 mm of mercury) the b.p. of water is 100°C; alcohol 78·4°C; ether 35·6°C.

Books, Classification of. All libraries are classified to facilitate reference, but the favourite system is the Dewey Decimal System, which divides the whole field of knowledge into ten Main Classes; General Works; Philosophy; Religion; Sociology; Philology; Natural Science; Useful Arts and Applied Science; Fine Arts; Literature; History (including geography and travel and biography). Each of these Main Classes is again subdivided into ten main divisions. As an example: the main class of Sociology receives the number 300. This range 300 to 400 (the next main class) is graduated into tens, and Economics is 330. The range 330 to 340 is again graduated, and the subject of Labour and Capital is 331. This process is carried on by decimals so that 331·2 deals with Remuneration for Work, 331·22 with Wage Scales, and 331·225 with Extra Pay.

Borax (Sodium Pyroborate) is a white, soluble, crystalline salt. It is widely and diversely used, e.g., as a mild antiseptic, in glazing pottery, in soldering, in the making of pyrex glass, as a cleansing agent and sometimes as a food preservative. Borax occurs naturally in the salt lakes of Tibet, where it is called tincal.

Bore. In physical geography, an almost vertical wall of water which passes upstream along certain estuaries. Its formation requires special conditions of river flow, incoming high tide, and shape of river channel. It can be spectacular and dangerous on some rivers. In Britain the best known is the Severn bore which can be over a metre high and move at 16–19 km/h. In some parts of Britain the bore is called an eagre.

Boron. A metalloid element, no. 5, symbol B. There are two forms, one crystalline, the other amorphous. It is not very abundant in nature but occurs in concentrated deposits. It is best known in boric acid, which is used as a mild antiseptic (called boracic acid) and borax (q.v.). Boron compounds are essential to some plants, e.g., beans. Used in the preparation of various special-purpose alloys, such as impact resistant steel. Compounds of boron and hydrogen are used as rocket fuels.

Borstal, an institution where young offenders between 15 and 21 on conviction may be sent for detention and reform. Emphasis is placed on vocational training in skilled trades. The Children and Young Persons Act 1969 makes provision for the minimum age to be raised to 17, if and when the Home Secretary makes an order to that effect. The first was opened in 1902 at the village of Borstal, near Rochester in Kent.

Boston Tea Party, an incident which occurred on 16 December 1773, on board some tea-ships in Boston Harbour. High taxation imposed by the British Parliament under George III had caused bitter feelings, and instigated by popular meetings, a party of citizens, disguised as Indians, boarded the tea-ships and threw the tea overboard. This incident was a prelude to the American War of Independence (1775–83) which resulted in Britain's loss of her American colonies.

Bounds Beating, an old Anglo-Saxon custom. The parish clergyman and officials go round the parish boundaries accompanied by boys who beat the boundary stones with long sticks of willow. The ceremony takes place on the Rogation days preceding Ascension Day.

Bourgeoisie, a term used by Marxists to indicate those who do not, like the proletarian, live by the sale of their labour. They include, on the one hand, industrialists and financiers or members of the liberal professions and, on the other, small artisans and shop-keepers who, although their standard of living may not be appreciably higher (and today is often lower) than that of the proletariat, are described as the "petty bourgeoisie". According to the Marxist view of history, the bourgeoisie arose with modern industrialism after it had overthrown the old feudal aristocracy and replaced it as ruling class.

Bovine Spongiform Encephalopathy (BSE), see **Mad Cow Disease.**

Bow, an instrument for propelling arrows, and, in the days when it was a weapon of war, was usually made of yew or ash, and was about 2 m long, with an arrow c. 1 m long. It was the weapon with which Crécy, Poitiers and Agincourt were won. The cross-bow was Italian and was adopted in France, but did not become popular in Britain.

Bow Bells is the peal of the London church of St. Mary-le-Bow, Cheapside, within sound of which one must be born to be entitled to be called a "cockney". Bow Bells had not been heard since 1939, but they once again rang out over the City of London on 20 December 1961.

Bowdlerise, to expurgate a book. Derived from Thomas Bowdler (1754–1825), the editor of the Family Shakespeare, in which "those words and expressions are omitted which cannot with propriety be read aloud in a family". He treated Gibbon's *History of the Decline and Fall of the Roman Empire* in the same way, omitting "all passages of an irreligious and immoral tendency". Such prudery met with ridicule and hence the words "bowdlerism" "bowdlerist", etc.

Bower Bird, native to Australia and New Guinea and related to the Bird of Paradise, though often less striking in appearance. In the mating season the male builds a "bower" of sticks and grasses for courtship displays and as a playground. The Gardener Bower Bird of Papua makes a lawn in front of his bower and adorns it with bright coloured pebbles and flowers which are replaced as they wither. The female builds her nest away from the bower.

Boycott, a term used in connection with a person that the general body of people, or a party or society, refuse to have dealings with. Originally used when Captain Boycott (1832–97) was made the victim of a conspiracy by the Irish Land League which prevented him making any purchases or holding any social intercourse in his district. He had incurred the League's hostility by a number of evictions.

Brass, an exceedingly useful alloy of copper and zinc. Much brass is about two-thirds copper but different proportions give different properties. It is harder than copper and easily worked. Brass in the Bible (Matt. x, 9) probably refers to bronze.

Breadfruit Tree (*Artocarpus altilis*), a native of the South Sea Islands; the fruits are a brownish green, about the size of a melon, and contain a white pulpy substance which is roasted before being eaten. The tree grows 12 m or more. Captain Bligh's ship *Bounty* was on a voyage to Jamaica carrying a cargo of 1,000 breadfruit trees when the mutiny occurred.

Breeder Reactor, a kind of nuclear reactor (q.v.) which besides producing energy by the fission process also produces ("breeds") more nuclear fuel at the same time. A typical reaction is: a neutron induces fission of a U-235 nucleus which breaks up into two medium-sized nuclei and some neutrons; one of the latter then enters a U-238 nucleus turning it into U-239 which then decays radioactively *via* neptunium into plutonium which is useful fuel. There are technical problems in breeder reactors which have delayed their practical use but the "breeding" principle is so valuable that experiments have gone on for many years in, e.g., Scotland and Idaho, and breeder reactors will no doubt increase in importance the more the supply of natural nuclear fuel appears to become depleted. See also **Nuclear Reactors.**

Breviary (Lat. *breviarium* = abridgment), the short prayer-book of the Roman Catholic Church which gives the Divine Office, *i.e.*, the services to be said daily. The directions for Mass are in the Missal. The current Roman breviary is a simplified version of the one decreed by the Council of Trent, 1568. *See also* **Matins.**

Bridges are structures for continuing a road, railway, or canal across a river, valley, ravine, or a road or railway at a lower level. From early times bridges were made of timber, stone, or brick, and it was not until the 19th cent. that wrought- and cast-iron were used. Today the materials mostly used are steel and reinforced concrete. Among the most famous of ancient bridges is that of S. Angelo at Rome, built by Hadrian as the Pons Aelius, A.D. 134. The Rialto bridge at Venice dates from 1588. The Ponte Santa Trinita at Florence, one of the finest Renaissance bridges and deemed the most beautiful in the world, was destroyed by German mines in 1944 but has now been reconstructed just as it was before. The first stone bridge across the Thames was begun in 1176. It had 19 arches and was lined with houses and stood until 1831 when it was replaced by the granite bridge designed by Sir John Rennie which stood until 1972. This has been replaced by a three-span concrete bridge with a six-lane carriageway and two footways. The first cast-iron bridge (recently repaired) was built by Abraham Darby at Coalbrookdale, Shropshire, in 1779. Telford's Menai suspension bridge (1825) has since been enlarged, the original design maintained. Another example of Britain's supremacy in constructional iron-work was Robert Stephenson's tubular bridge across the Menai Straits (1850), the prototype of all modern plate girder railway bridges. Other famous bridges are the Niagara (suspension), Forth railway bridge (cantilever), London Tower bridge (suspension), Tay railway bridge, Victoria Jubilee bridge across the St. Lawrence at Montreal (an open steel structure), Sydney Harbour bridge, Lower Zambesi bridge, Storstrom bridge in Denmark, Howrah bridge at Calcutta, Volta bridge of Ghana, Auckland Harbour bridge, Verrazano-Narrows bridge spanning New York's harbour from Brooklyn to Staten I., exceeding by 18 m the centre span of San Francisco's Golden Gate bridge, Rio-Niterói bridge in Brazil. Britain has undertaken in recent years the largest bridge building programme for over a century. The bridges include the road suspension bridge across the Firth of Forth, completed 1964, the Severn suspension bridge (from which the design principles for the new bridge across the Bosporus were taken) and the Tay road bridge, both completed 1966, the Tinsley viaduct, near Sheffield, opened 1968 and the new Humber suspension bridge, linking the ports of Hull and Grimsby, opened in 1981. When completed, it was the longest single-span suspension bridge in the world (1,410 m).

Bridleway. In English law (sec. 27(6) of the National Parks and Access to the Countryside Act 1949) a highway over which the public have the following, but no other, rights of way, that is to say, a right of way on foot and a right of way on horseback or leading a horse, with or without a right to drive animals of any description along the highway.

Britannia Metal, an alloy of tin, antimony and copper, harder than pure tin, corrosion-resistant, used for teapots, jugs (often electro-plated).

British Association for the Advancement of Science, The, was founded in 1831 by a group of British scientists under the leadership of Charles Babbage (1792–1871) to stimulate scientific inquiry and promote research in the interest of the nation. Its meetings are held annually in different cities of the United Kingdom.

British Museum, was created by an Act of Parliament in 1753, when the Sir Hans Sloane collection, which the British Government had acquired for £20,000, was added to the Cottonian Library and the Harleian Manuscripts. It was opened to the public in 1759 at Montague House Bloomsbury. The acquisition of the library of George III (known as the King's Library) in 1823 led to the construction of the present building with the new wing (1829), quadrangle (1852), domed reading room (1857), and later additions. The books and the reading room are now part of the British Library (*see* **Libraries**). The Natural History Department was transferred to South Kensington in the 1880s. As a museum it is perhaps the most famous in the world, since it has many priceless collections of sculptures, antiquities, prints and drawings coins and medals. Its treasures include the Elgin Marbles (*q.v.*), the Rosetta Stone (*q.v.*), the Portland Vase (*q.v.*).

British Rail (British Railways). The name under which the railways of Britain were unified on 1 January 1948. Instead of the former four main railway systems six regions were formed: London Midland region (former L.M.S.R.), Western (former G.W.R.), Southern (formerly S.R.), Eastern (southern area of former L.N.E.R.), N.E. region (N.E. of former L.N.E.R.), Scottish region (Scottish system of the former L.M.S.R. and L.N.E.R.). Under the Transport Act 1962 the British Railways Board was set up to manage railway affairs. The most far-reaching change in the modernisation and re-equipment programme since 1955 has been the replacement of steam traction by electric and diesel locomotives. Under the chairmanship of Lord (then Dr.) Richard Beeching the British Railways Board planned a viable railway system by closing uneconomic branch lines, by developing new services on the liner train principle, and by utilising a more limited trunk route system. Under the Transport Act 1968 some railway passenger services are eligible for grants on social grounds, including urban railways and unprofitable rural services. High-speed inter-city passenger services linking the main centres of Gt. Britain came into operation in 1976 and in 1985 it was announced that the Advanced Passenger Train (the Electra) would go into production. The name was changed to British Rail in 1964. In 1988, British Rail were beginning to plan for the challenge of the Channel Tunnel, (*see* **L24**) due to open in 1993.

British Standard Time, The British Standard Time Act of 1968 put Britain an hour ahead of Greenwich Mean Time (GMT) throughout the year for an experimental 3 years. This brought Britain into line with countries in Western Europe where Central European Time is observed. In 1970 Parliament called for the restoration of the previous position—BST in the summer months and GMT in the winter months—as from 31 October 1971. In the late 1980s, the debate has reopened.

Brocken-spectre or Glory. The series of coloured rings which an observer sees around the shadow of his own head (or an aeroplane in which he is travelling) as cast upon a bank of mist or thin cloud. This effect is produced by reflection and refraction of sunlight in minute water-droplets in the air just as in a rainbow.

Bromine. A non-metal element, no. 35, symbol Br, member of the halogen family (*q.v.*). It is a red, evil-smelling liquid (Greek *bromos*, a stink). It is an abundant element. In the USA bromide is extracted from sea-water on a large scale. It unites readily with many other elements, the products being termed bromides. Its derivatives with organic compounds are used in synthetic chemistry. Bromoform is a liquid resembling chloroform. Bromides are used in medicine to calm excitement.

Bronze is primarily an alloy of copper and tin, and was one of the earliest alloys known, the Bronze Age (began c. 4,000 B.C. in Middle East) in the evolution of tool-using man coming before the Iron Age (c. 2,000 B.C.) Some modern bronzes contain zinc or lead also, and a trace of phosphorus is present in "Phosphor-bronze".

BSE, *see* **Mad Cow Disease.**

Bubble Chamber. An instrument used by physicists to reveal the tracks of fast fundamental particles (*e.g.*, those produced in large accelerating machines) in a form suitable for photography; closely related to the Wilson cloud chamber (*q.v.*), but the particles leave trails of small bubbles in a superheated liquid (often liquid hydrogen) instead of droplets of liquid in a supersaturated gas; invented in 1952 by the American physicist, Dr. D. Glaser, Nobel Prizeman, 1960, and developed by Prof. L. W. Alvarez, Univ. of California, Nobel Prizeman, 1968.

Buckingham Palace, London residence of British sovereigns since 1837. Originally built for the Duke of Buckingham (1703); bought by George III in 1762 and remodelled by Nash 1825–36.

Buddhism. *See* Section J.

Buntings, name of a group of finches, seed-eating birds, usually found in open country. The Yellowhammer, Reed Bunting, Corn Bunting and Cirl Bunting are resident in Britain; the Snow Bunting (which breeds in small numbers in Scotland) and Lapland Bunting are regular winter visitors. The Ortolan is a rare visitor.

Butane, a colourless inflammable gas made of carbon and hydrogen; formula C_4H_{10}. Found in natural gas and made as a by-product of oil refining. Butane, like propane (*q.v.*), can easily be liquefied and moved safely in cans and tanks. It is thus used as a "portable gas supply"; also used in internal combustion fuels.

Byzantine Art developed in the eastern part of the Roman empire after Constantine founded the city of Constantinople (A.D. 330). It has many sources—Greek, Syrian, Egyptian and Islamic —and reached its zenith in the reign of Justinian (527–65). The major art form was ecclesiastical architecture, the basic plan of which was Roman—either basilican (symmetrical about an axis) or centralised (symmetrical about a point). Arched construction was developed, and the dome became the most typical feature, although, unlike the Roman dome which was placed on a round apartment, the Byzantine dome was placed on a square one on independent pendentives. Frequently small domes were clustered round a large one as in the case of the great church of Santa Sophia (537), the climax of Byzantine architecture. Usually the churches were small and include those of SS. Sergius and Bacchus, Sta. Irene (in Constantinople), S. Vitale in Ravenna, and the much later and larger St. Mark's in Venice. Byzantine art also took the form of miniatures, enamels, jewels, and textiles, but mosaics, frescos, and icons (*q.v.*) are its greatest treasures.

C

Cacao, Theobroma cacao, is an evergreen tree, from 4–6 m high, growing abundantly in tropical America, West Africa, the West Indies, Sri Lanka, etc., yielding seeds, called cocoa beans from which cocoa and chocolate are manufactured. The fruit is 17–25 cm long, hard and ridged; inside are the beans, covered with a reddish-brown skin, which are first fermented, then dried. The trees mature at five to eight years and produce two crops a year.

Cactus, a family of flowering plants numbering about a thousand species adapted to living in very dry situations. The stem is usually fleshy, being composed of succulent tissue, remarkably retentive of water; commonly equipped with sharp thorns which deter animals from eating them. The roots are generally very long, tapping soil water over a large area; a "prickly pear" cactus may have roots covering a circular area 7 m or more in diameter. The leaves are commonly insignificant or absent, and the stem takes over the photosynthetic leaf function and becomes accordingly flattened to expose greater area to sunlight and air. In some kinds of cactus (*e.g.*, *Echinocactus*) the stem is shaped almost like a sea-urchin.

Cadmium. A metallic element, no. 48, symbol Cd, chemically similar to zinc and mercury. Used in alloys to lower the melting point, as in Wood's metal with bismuth and tin. Alloyed with copper to make electric cables. Like zinc, it is a protective metal and is used in electroplating. The cadmium-vapour lamp gives a characteristic frequency used in measuring wavelength.

Caesium, also spelt **Cesium,** is an alkali metal element, no. 55, symbol Cs, in first group of the periodic table. It resembles rubidium and potassium and was discovered by Bunsen and Kirchoff in 1860. It was the first element whose existence was discovered spectroscopically. The caesium atom consists of a heavy nucleus surrounded by 55 electrons, 54 of which are arranged in stable orbits, and one of

which, known as the valency electron, is in a less stable orbit surrounding them. Used in the construction of photo-electric cells and as an accurate time standard (atomic clock).

Calcium, a silvery-white metallic element, no. 20, symbol Ca. It melts at 810°C and is very reactive. It was discovered by Sir Humphry Davy in 1808, but not until 1898 was it obtained pure, by Moissan. Does not occur as metal in nature, but calcium compounds make up a large part of the earth's crust. Most important calcium sources are marble, limestone, chalk (all three are, chemically, calcium carbonate); dolomite, which is the double carbonate of calcium and magnesium; gypsum, a hydrated calcium sulphate; calcium phosphate and calcium fluoride. Igneous rocks contain much calcium silicate. Calcium compounds are essential to plants and are used in fertilisers. Animals require calcium and phosphorus for bone and teeth formation; deficiency is treated by administration of calcium phosphate. Strontium is chemically similar to calcium, and the radioactive strontium 90 from atomic "fall-out" is therefore easily assimilated by the body.

Calendar, a collection of tables showing the days and months of the year, astronomical recurrences, chronological references, etc. The Julian Calendar, with its leap year, introduced by Julius Caesar, fixed the average length of the year at 365¼ days, which was about 11 minutes too long (the earth completes its orbit in 365 days 5 hours 48 minutes 46 seconds of mean solar time). The cumulative error was rectified by the Gregorian Calendar, introduced in Italy in 1582, whereby century years do not count as leap years unless divisible by 400. This is the the rule we now follow. England did not adopt the reformed calendar until 1752, when she found herself 11 days behind the Continent. The Gregorian Calendar did not come into use in Russia until 1918. Old Style and New Style dates are identified as "O.S." "N.S.".

Calends, the first day of the month in the Roman calendar.

Calorie. Unit of quantity of heat. The "small" or fundamental calorie is the amount of heat required to raise the temperature of 1 gram of water from 14·5° to 15·5°C and is equal to 4·185 joules. This is the gram-calorie used in physics and chemistry. The large Calorie (written with a capital C), commonly used in nutritional connotations, is equal to 1000 small calories and is called the kilogram-calorie.

Calvinism. *See* Section J.

Calypso, West Indian song in the form of a doggerel lampoon composed spontaneously and sung to a guitar.

Cambridge University had a sufficiently good teach- ing reputation to attract Oxford students in 1209, when lectures at their own university were suspended. In 1226 it had a Chancellor who was recognised by King and Pope. The first college to be founded was Peterhouse in 1284. The university was reorganised and granted a Charter of Incorporation by an act of Elizabeth in 1571. The colleges with their dates of foundation are Christ's (1505), Churchill (1960), Clare (1326), Clare Hall (1966), Corpus Christi (1352), Darwin (1964), Downing (1800), Emmanuel (1584), Fitzwilliam (1966), Gonville and Caius (1348), Jesus (1496), King's (1441), Magdalene (1542), Pembroke (1347), Peterhouse (1284), Queens' (1448), St. Catharine's (1473), St. Edmund's House (1896), St. John's (1511), Selwyn (1882), Sidney Sussex (1596), Trinity (1546), Trinity Hall (1350), Wolfson (1965). The women's colleges are: Girton (1869), Newnham (1871), New Hall (1954), Hughes Hall (formerly Cambridge T. C.) (1885), and Lucy Cavendish Collegiate Society (1965) (for women research students and other graduates; took undergraduates in 1970s). Women were admitted to degrees (though not allowed to sit for examination) in 1920, and to full membership of the University in 1948. All colleges now admit both men and women students. The last college to admit women was Magdalene College (1988). The most recent foundation is Robinson College (1977).

Camel, a large ruminant quadruped, inhabiting Asia and Africa, where it is largely used as a beast of burden. There are two species—the

Arabian camel or dromedary, with only one hump; and the Bactrian, or double-humped camel. There are no wild dromedaries, and the only wild bactrians occur in the Gobi Desert. The camel is able to go for long periods without water, not, as was formerly believed, because it stored water in its hump, but because of the unique mechanism of its physiology which enables it to conserve water at the expense of not sweating until 40°C is reached.

Campanile, or bell-tower, is separate from but usually adjoining its parent church. The most famous are in Italy. Giotto's tower at Florence, adjoining the cathedral of Santa Maria del Fiore, is architecturally the finest in the world. Others are at Cremona, the loftiest in Italy (110 m) and Pisa (the leaning tower). The magnificent pointed campanile of St. Mark's, Venice, which collapsed in 1902 and has since been rebuilt in its original form, was begun in 902.

Canal, an artificial watercourse used for navigation which changes its level by means of locks. The completion of the Bridgewater Canal in 1761 to take coal from Worsley to Manchester marked the beginning of canal building in industrial Britain. There are over 4,000 km of navigable inland waterways in Great Britain today, c. 3,200 km of which are under the control of the British Waterways Board set up by the Transport Act 1962. The English network is based on the four great estuaries, Mersey, Humber, Severn and Thames. Under the Transport Act 1968, the Board is enabled to maintain an extensive network of amenity waterways. Some 70m. tonnes of freight are carried each year on Britain's canals. The Board has a turnover of c. £20m. (1988–89).

Candela unit of luminous intensity, symbol cd. An idea of the value which this unit represents may be gained from the fact that light obtained from a 40 W filament-type electric lamp or bulb is approximately the same as would be given by a point source of luminous intensity 30 cd. *See* **S.I. units, F66.**

Candlemas, an English and Roman Church festival in celebration of the Purification of the Virgin Mary. The date is 2 February.

Canon, a term applied to signify a recognised rule for the guide of conduct in matters legal, ecclesiastical and artistic, or an authoritative ordinance: thus we have Canonical Scriptures, Canon Law, etc. A Canon is also a dignitary of the Church, usually a member of a cathedral chapter in the Anglican communion, or in the Roman Church a member of an order standing between regular monks and secular clergy.

Canonical Hours were seven in number in the Western Church; Matins and Lauds, before dawn; Prime, early morning service; Terce, 9 a.m.; Sext, noon; Nones, 3 p.m.; Vespers, 4 p.m.; Compline, bed-time.

Canonisation, the entering of one of the faithful departed on the list of saints of the Roman Catholic Church. The rules governing canonisation were simplified by papal decree in 1969. The forty English martyrs, of whom Edmund Campion was one, executed between 1535 and 1679 and beatified long ago, were canonised in 1970. Beatification, by which a person is called blessed, is usually followed by canonisation, but not necessarily.

Canticles, the name given to the scriptural passages from the Bible sung by the congregation in the various Christian liturgies. They are the *Bene-dicite, Benedictus, Magnificat, Nunc Dimittis.*

Capercaillie, the largest of the grouse family, found in the Scottish highlands and the pine forests and mountainous regions of Northern and Central Europe and Asia.

Capet, the family name of the royal house of France, founded by Hugh Capet in 987, with its collateral branches. The main line of the dynasty came to an end in 1328 with the death of Charles IV when the throne passed to the related house of Valois. The direct Valois line ended in 1498 with the death of Charles VIII. The first of the Bourbon line was Henry IV whose descendants ruled France (except during the French Revolution and the Napoleonic era) until 1848.

Capitalism. *See* **Section J.**

Capuchins are members of a mendicant order of Franciscans, founded in the 16th cent. with the aim of restoring the primitive and stricter observance of the rule of St. Francis, so called from the capuce or pointed cowl worn by them.

Carat, a term used in assessing the value of gold and precious stones. In connection with gold, it represents the proportion of pure gold contained in any gold alloy, and for this purpose the metal is divided into 24 parts. Thus 24-carat indicates pure gold, and any lesser number of carats shows the proportion of gold contained in the alloy. The carat as a measure of weight is now obsolete, having been replaced by the *metric carat* of 0·2 grams.

Caravan, a band of travellers or traders journeying together for safety across the Eastern deserts, sometimes numbering many hundreds. There are several allusions to caravans in the Old Testament. The great caravan routes of this period from Egypt to Babylon and from Palestine to Yemen linked up with the Syrian ports and so with Western sea commerce. Many wars have been fought in the past over their control.

Carbohydrates. *See* **Diet, Section P.**

Carbon, a non-metallic chemical element no. 6, symbol C, which occurs in crystalline form as diamonds and graphite; amorphous forms of carbon include charcoal and soot, while coke consists mainly of elementary carbon. The biochemistry of plants and animals largely hinges upon carbon compounds. The study of carbon compounds is called Organic Chemistry. **Carbon 14.** A radioactive isotope of carbon, with a half-life c. 6,000 years, used in following the path of compounds and their assimilation in the body. Also used in determination of the age of carbon-containing materials such as trees, fossils and very old documents.

Carbonari, members of a secret political society originating in Naples, and at one time very numerous. Their chief aim was to free Italy from foreign rule, and they exerted considerable influence in the various revolutionary movements in the first half of the 19th cent. Their name was adopted from the charcoal-burners (*carbonari*), and their passwords, signs, etc., were all in the phraseology of the fraternity.

Carbon dioxide. Commonest of the oxides of carbon. It is formed when carbon and its compounds are burnt with abundant supply of air, and when carbon compounds are oxidised in the respiration process of animals. The atmosphere contains carbon dioxide to the extent of about 325 ppm and is increasing by about 1 ppm per year, principally because of the burning of fossil fuels and possibly because of deforestation which not only leaves more oxidisible material but lowers the amount of carbon dioxide removed by photosynthesis (**F32**).

Carbon monoxide is a colourless gas with no taste or smell. It is formed when coal and coke are burnt with a restricted supply of air; the blue flame to be seen in a coke brazier, for instance, is the flame of carbon monoxide. This gas is very poisonous, forming with the haemoglobin of the blood a compound which is useless for respiration and cherry red in colour, which gives a visible sympton of poisoning by carbon monoxide. With nickel it forms a volatile compound, called nickel carbonyl, and this reaction is the basis of the Mond process for extracting nickel.

Cardinal, one of the chief dignitaries of the Roman Catholic Church who constitute the Pope's council, or Sacred College, and when the papal chair is vacant elect by secret ballot a Pope from among themselves. There are three orders: cardinal bishops, members of the Roman Curia (the central administration of the Church) and bishops of sees near Rome; cardinal deacons, also members of the Curia, holding titular bishoprics; and cardinal priests who exercise pastoral duties over sees removed from Rome, though some are members of the Curia. Pope John Paul I, who had been elected in Aug. 1978 to succeed Pope Paul VI, died suddenly after only 33 days. He was succeeded by Pope John Paul II (Cardinal Karol Wojtyla, Archbishop of Cracow). Pope John Paul II announced 25 new cardinals in 1988, bringing the total number to 161. Papal insignia were trimmed of embellishment by papal decree in 1969 with the abolition, subsequently revoked, of the famous red hat (the galero) and the shoes with buckles. Cardinals must now retire at 80.

Cardinal Virtues, according to Plato these were justice, prudence, temperance, fortitude—*natural* virtues as distinct from the *theological* virtues of the Roman Catholic Church, faith, hope, charity. The phrase "seven cardinal virtues", combining the two, figures in mediaeval literature. *See* **Sins, Seven Deadly.**

Carmelites, a body of mendicant friars taking their name from Mount Carmel, where the order was first established in the 12th cent. The original rule of the order required absolute poverty, abstinence from meat and a hermit life. The rigidity of the rule of the order was mitigated by Innocent IV. They wear a brown habit with white mantle, hence their name of White Friars. The order of Carmelite nuns was instituted in the 15th cent.

Carolingians, dynasty of Frankish rulers founded in the 7th cent. The family was at its height when represented by Charlemagne. It ruled, with interruptions, until 987 when the Capetian dynasty succeeded.

Carp, a well-known fresh-water fish, found in plenty in most European and Asiatic still waters; reaches a length of about 60 cm and under favourable conditions lives for about 40 years. Familiar British members of the family are the roach, rudd, dace, chub, gudgeon, tench, minnow, barbel, bream and bleak. The goldfish, popular in ornamental ponds, is the domesticated variety of a Far Eastern member of the carp family.

Carthusians, an order of monks founded in 1084 by St. Bruno at the Grande Chartreuse near Grenoble, and introduced into England about a century later. They built the Charterhouse (corruption of Chartreuse) in London in 1371. The chief characteristics of the order are a separate dwelling-house in the precincts of the charterhouse for each monk, and the general assembly in the Church twice in the day and once at night. They wear a white habit, with white scapular and hood. The liqueur *Chartreuse* was invented by the order and is still their secret. For many years they have derived large revenues from its sale. The order of Carthusian nuns was founded in the 12th cent.

Casein, the chief protein in milk and cheese. It is coagulated by the action of rennet or acid. An important class of plastics ("casein plastics") are produced from it, and these plastics are converted into buttons, kitting-needles, etc. 36,000 litres of milk yield about 1 tonne of casein.

Cassowary, a genus of ostrich-like birds which, together with the emu, forms a separate order found only in Australasia. All species are black, with brightly coloured necks, and with a horny crest on the head. Noted for fleetness.

Castor-oil Plant (*Ricinus communis*), an African shrub now cultivated in most tropical countries. It has broad palmate leaves and bears a spiny fruit containing seeds which when pressed yield the well-known oil.

Cat, the general name for all members of the class *Felidae* of the carnivorous order, from the lion down to the domestic cat. The latter is believed to be descended from the European and African wild cats. Egypt is credited with having been the first country in which the cat was domesticated.

Catabolism, Anabolism, are the terms used to describe the two types of metabolic pathway. Catabolic pathways are routes by which large organic molecules are broken up by enzymes into their simpler constituents *e.g.,* starch into glucose. The anabolic pathways are the routes by which complex molecules are synthesised from simple sub-units, *e.g.,* proteins from amino acids.

Catalyst. A substance which alters the rate of reaction without itself being chemically changed. Various aluminium and titanium compounds are catalysts in the formation of polythene from ethylene. Palladium catalyses the reaction of hydrogen with oxygen (hence its use in gas lighters). Enzymes in the body hasten the breakdown of carbohydrates and proteins by catalytic action. *See* **F26.**

Cataracts are gigantic waterfalls. The most famous are those of Niagara in North America, the Orinoco in South America, the Victoria Falls on the Zambesi in Africa, and the Falls of the Rhine at Schaffhausen.

Catechism, an elementary book of principles in any science or art, but more particularly in religion, in the form of questions and answers. There is a great variety of these, including the Lutheran, prepared by Luther in 1529, Calvin's Geneva (in 1536), and the Anglican, in the Book of Common Prayer.

Caterpillar, the larva of a butterfly or moth, worm-like in its segmented body, with 3 pairs of jointed true legs, often curiously marked and coloured, and frequently more or less hairy.

Cathedral, the chief church of a diocese, so called from its containing a Bishop's seat, or episcopal chair. The town in which it is situated is a cathedral city. Some celebrated cathedrals are St. John Lateran of Rome, Notre Dame of Paris, the cathedrals of Cologne and Milan, St. Paul's in London, Canterbury Cathedral, York Minster, and the cathedrals of Durham, Bristol, Gloucester, Peterborough, Exeter, Liverpool, and Coventry (destroyed by bombs, now rebuilt),

Catholicism. *See* **Section J.**

Cat's eye, a kind of quartz, much valued as a gem, opalescent, and of various shades.

Cavalier, a name adopted during the troubles of the Civil War to designate the Royalist party; it is also used generally in reference to a knightly, gallant or imperious personage.

Caves, natural hollow places in the earth, frequently found in Carboniferous limestone areas. The underground caves are formed by the action of rainwater carrying carbon dioxide, a dilute acid which slowly attacks the limestone rocks. The main caves in the British Isles are in the Mendips, Derbyshire, Yorkshire, S. Wales and in County Clare. Many British inland caves are thought to have been formed at the end of the Ice Age when there was a rise in the water table. The floods of September 1968 moved masses of débris in some of the British caves, redistributing it in a major way; new routes were blocked and old passages reopened. The scientific study of caves is known as spelaeology.

Cedar, a dark-leaved, cone-bearing, horizontal-branched evergreen tree that grows to a considerable height and girth, the best known species in Britain being the Cedar of Lebanon, which was introduced in the 17th cent.

Celluloid, one of the first synthetic thermoplastic materials, discovered by Alexander Parkes in 1865 when he was attempting to produce synthetic horn. It is made by treating cellulose nitrate with camphor and alcohol. Photographic film is made of a similar, but less-inflammable material, formed by the use of cellulose acetate instead of the nitrate.

Cellulose, a carbohydrate, and a constituent of nearly all plants. Cellulose occurs in an almost pure state in the fibres of linen (flax), absorbent cotton, jute, and filter-paper (used in laboratories).

Celsius was an 18th cent. Swedish scientist (**B13**) after whom the modern Celsius temperature scale is named. Since 1954, °C stands for "degree Celsius" instead of "degree Centigrade" but this is only a change in name. Both symbols refer to the temperature scale which calls the melting point of ice 0°C and the boiling point of water at one atmosphere pressure 100°C. *See* **Absolute Temperature.**

Celts, an ancient race found late in the third millennium B.C. in S.W. Germany, united by a common language and culture, who spread westward into Spain, northward into Britain, eastward to the Black Sea, reaching Galatia in Asia Minor. The "La Tène" iron-age Celts invaded Britain *c.* 250 B.C. After Britain was conquered by the Romans and invaded by the Angles and Saxons there remained as areas of Celtic speech only Wales (Brythonic speakers), Ireland, Scotland, the Isle of Man (Gaelic speakers), and in Cornwall. The late Celtic period in Britain produced a distinctive Christian art (*e.g.,* the Lindisfarne Gospel *c,* 700, and the Irish Book of Kells, dating from about the same time). Surviving Celtic languages are Welsh, Irish, Breton and Scots Gaelic; Cornish survived until the 18th cent. and Manx Gaelic is on the point of extinction.

Centrifuge, a machine which produces large accelerations by utilising the radial force caused by rotating a body about a fixed centre. Centrifuges have found extensive application in modern science. They can be used for the separation of one size of particle from another in biochemistry or in the training of astronauts where the accelerations occurring during rocket lift off can be simulated in a centrifuge on the ground.

Ceramics, are substances in which a combination of one or more metals with oxygen confers special and valuable properties. These include hardness, and resistance to heat and chemicals. Ceramic comes from the Greeek word for pottery, and pottery materials of mud and clay were probably the first man-made ceramics. Nowadays the range is enormous and growing; apart from all the pottery materials, there are firebricks, gems, glasses, concretes, nuclear reactor fuel elements, special materials for electronic devices, coloured pigments, electrical insulators, abrasives, and many other things. The scientific study of ceramics is part of materials science (*see* **Materials Science**). The need to design ceramic objects has inspired great art, and the production of ceramics has become a major industry.

Cerium, a scarce metallic element, no. 58, symbol Ce, discovered by Berzelius in 1803. A mixture of cerium and thorium nitrates is used in the manufacture of gas mantles, which owe their incandescent property to the deposit of cerium and thorium oxide with which they are coated.

Cern, French acronym for the European Laboratory for Particle Physics in Geneva. In 1989, the Large Electron Positron collider (LEP) was opened there. It recreates the swirl of matter just after the 'Big Bang' which scientists believe created the universe 15 billion years ago.

Chain reaction. *See* **F13(1).**

Chalcedony, a mixture of crystalline silica and amorphous hydrated silica, *i.e.*, of quartz and opal. It has a waxy lustre, and is much used by jewellers for necklaces, bracelets, etc. Commonly it is white or creamy. Its bright orange-red variety is called carnelian; its brown variety, sard. Chrysoprase, plasma, bloodstone are varieties which are respectively pale apple-green, dark leek-green, green with red spots.

Chalk, a white limestone, calcium carbonate, found in the Upper Cretaceous deposits (formed from the shells of minute marine organisms). As chalk is porous, few streams form on its surface and consequently it is eroded slowly, although generally speaking it is a soft rock. Its juxtaposition with soft impervious clay in some areas results in its forming steep ridges known as escarpments, *e.g.*, N. and S. Downs and Chilterns. In contrast to the dry upland surfaces of chalk, lower levels are frequently saturated with water which emerges as springs.

Chamberlain, Lord, the senior officer of The Royal Household who is responsible for all ceremonial within the palace (levées, courts, garden parties, entertainment of foreign royalties and heads of state) but not the coronation or state opening of parliament. He is also in charge of appointments to The Royal Household. His office as censor of plays was abolished in 1968.

Chamberlain, Lord Great, one of the great officers of state whose duties are now mainly ceremonial. He attends the monarch at the state opening of parliament and at the coronation and is custodian of the Palace of Westminster (Houses of Parliament). The office is hereditary, dating from Norman times, and is held for one reign in turn by the descendants of the De Veres, Earls of Oxford. The present Lord Great Chamberlain is the Marquess of Cholmondeley.

Chameleon, a family of lizards with numerous species. Their ability to change colour is well known, but exaggerated, and is due to the movement of pigment cells beneath the skin. They are slow in movement, arboreal, and mainly insectivorous. Found in Africa, India, Sri Lanka, Madagascar and Arabia.

Chamois, a species of antelope, native of Western Europe and Asia. About the size of a goat, it lives in mountainous regions, and possesses wonderful leaping power, so that it is very difficult to capture. Its flesh is much esteemed, and from its skin chamois leather is made, although today sheep and goat skins are usually substituted. The mating season is October–November and the fawns are born in May or June. Live to be 20–25 years old.

Channel Tunnel, a scheme to bore a tunnel through 32–48 km of chalk under the sea between Dover and Calais has been a subject for discussion ever since Albert Mathieu first conceived the idea as a practical possibility in 1802. In the 1830s proposals for a bridge were made. In the 1980s plans for a cross channel fixed link began to surface again although it was stated clearly that the project would have to be entirely financed from private capital. The British and French Governments called for the submission of plans for a fixed link by November 1985, stating that the selection of the winning proposal would be made in January 1986.

The announcement in January 1986 of the intention by Britain and France to construct a 31-mile tunnel under the Channel between Cheriton, Kent and Frethun in northern France has brought the idea of a Channel Tunnel very close to realisation. According to the plans by 15 May 1993 a direct "fixed link" will be ready for travellers to and from the continent. Bitter controversy has surrounded the route of the proposed rail link. In early 1990, the Channel Tunnel faced serious financing problems as well as continued controversy over the proposed high-speed rail link.

Chapel Royal, the church dedicated to the use of the Sovereign and Court. There are, among others, chapels royal at St. James's Palace, Buckingham Palace, Windsor, Hampton Court, the Tower, and Holyrood. *See also* **E4(2).**

Charcoal, a term applied to wood that has been subjected to a process of slow smothered combustion. More generally it refers to the carbonaceous remains of vegetable, animal, or combustible mineral substances submitted to a similar process. Charcoal from special woods (in particular buckthorn) is used in making gunpowder. Bone charcoal finds use in sugar refining, as it removes dark colouring matter present in the crude syrup.

Chasuble, a sleeveless vestment worn by ecclesiastics over the alb during the celebration of Mass. It is supposed to symbolise the seamless coat of Christ.

Cheese, an article of food made from the curd of milk, which is separated from the whey and pressed in moulds and gradually dried. There are about 500 varieties differing with method of preparation and quality of milk. They used to be made in the regions after which they are named but nowadays many of them are mass-produced, *e.g.*, Cheddar is made not only in all parts of Britain but in Canada, New Zealand, Australia, Holland and the USA. Cheeses may be divided into 3 main classes: (1) soft, *e.g.*, Camembert, Cambridge, l'Evêque; (2) blue-veined, *e.g.*, Stilton, Gorgonzola, Roquefort (made from ewe's milk), (3) hard-pressed, *e.g.*, Cheddar, Cheshire, Gruyère, Parmesan, Gouda.

Cheetah or "hunting leopard", the large spotted cat of Africa and Southern Asia, the swiftest four-footed animal alive.

Chemical Warfare. This term is usually restricted to mean the use in war of anti-personnel gases, aerosols and smokes, although explosives, napalm, herbicides and defoliants are also chemical agents that are used in war. Anti-personnel chemical weapons may be classified as (*a*) vesicants (agents which produce skin blisters, *e.g.*, mustard gas); (*b*) lacrimators (*e.g.*, the original tear gas, CN, and its British-developed successor CS now preferred for riot control); (*c*) sternutators (sneeze and vomiting agents, usually arsenic compounds, *e.g.*, Adamsite DM); (*d*) nerve gases (extremely lethal agents which incapacitate the nervous system, *e.g.*, the G-agents developed during the second world war and the more powerful **V**-agents developed subsequently); (*e*) lung irritants *e.g.*, phosgene and chlorine). Most of these chemicals can be lethal at sufficiently high concentrations and for this reason it is doubtful whether there exists the "humane" chemical agent which instantly incapacitates but leaves no long-term side effects.

The first occasion when poison gas was used on a large scale was in the first world war; more than 100,000 fatalities resulted from the use of principally chlorine, phosgene and mustard gas.

Worldwide revulsion at the hideous effects of chemical weapons and their potential as indiscriminate weapons of mass destruction resulted in the Geneva Protocol of 1925 which prohibited the use of both chemical and bacteriological weapons. It has now been ratified by over 90 nations including all the major powers (although Japan and America are only recent signatories). The Protocol has been generally well observed although notable violations have been by the Italians in Abyssinia (1935–6), the Japanese in China during the second world war, the Americans in S.E. Asia in the 1960s and Iraq (against the Kurds in the 1980s). See also **Biological Warfare.**

Chemistry is the science of the elements and their compounds. It is concerned with the laws of their combination and behaviour under various conditions. It had its roots in alchemy and has gradually developed into a science of vast magnitude and importance. Organic chemistry deals with the chemistry of the compounds of carbon; inorganic chemistry is concerned with the chemistry of the elements; physical chemistry is concerned with the study of chemical reactions and with the theories and laws of chemistry. See **F23–8.**

Chernobyl Disaster Site in the Ukraine of 1986 Soviet nuclear disaster, which caused major radioactive fallout across many countries.

Chestnut, the fruit of trees of the genus *Castanea*, members of the family *Fagaceae*. C. *sativa* is the sweet or Spanish chestnut, C. *dentata* the American chestnut and C. *crenata* the Japanese chestnut. The nut is edible. The wood is used in carpentry and fencing. See also **Horse Chestnut.**

Chiaroscuro, a term used in painting to denote the disposition of light and shade. Rembrandt is unrivalled as a painter for his contrasts of light and shadows.

Chiltern Hundreds, three hundreds—Stoke, Burnham and Desborough—the stewardship of which is now a nominal office under the Chancellor of the Exchequer. Since about 1750 the nomination to it has been used as a method of enabling a member of Parliament to resign his seat on the plea that he holds an office of honour and profit under the crown. An alternate symbolic post for an M.P. giving up his seat is the stewardship of the Manor of Northstead in Yorkshire which has been used in the same way since 1841.

Chimpanzee, a large anthropoid ape, a native of tropical Africa, of a dark brown colour, with arms reaching to the knee, and capable of walking upright. Its brain is about a third of the weight of the human brain, but is anatomically similar. The animal has considerable intelligence and powers of learning. A suitable subject for space flight experiments.

Chinchilla, a South American burrowing rodent. Grey in colour, and white underneath. It is greatly esteemed for its beautiful fur.

Chippendale Furniture was introduced in the reign of George I by Thomas Chippendale, a cabinetmaker from Yorkshire who migrated to London and set up for himself in St. Martin's Lane, Charing Cross. He was fonder of inventing designs for furniture than of making it, and in 1752 published a book of patterns; the London furniture-makers of the day soon began to model their work upon it.

Chivalry an international brotherhood of knights formed primarily during the 13th cent. to fight against the infidels in the Crusades. For the French the major battle was against the Moslems in the Holy Land and North Africa, the Spaniards fought the same enemy in their own country, and the Germans were concerned with the heathen of Baltic lands, but Chaucer's "very perfect gentle knight" had fought in all these areas. One did not easily become a knight who had to be of noble birth and then pass through a period of probation, beginning as a boy page in the castle of some great lord, serving his elders and betters humbly while he was taught good manners, singing, playing musical instruments, and the composition of verse. Probably he learned Latin, but he certainly learned French, which was the international language of knights as Latin was of scholars. At fourteen he became a squire and learned to fight with sword, battle-axe and lance, and to endure conditions of hard living while carrying out his duties of waiting on his lord, looking after his horses, and in time accompanying him in battle. Only if he showed himself suitable was he finally knighted by a stroke of the hand or sword on the shoulder from the king or lord. Knighthood was an international order and had its special code of behaviour; to honour one's sworn word, to protect the weak, to respect women, and defend the Faith. To some extent it had a civilising effect on the conduct of war (e.g. knights of opposing sides might slaughter each other in battle but feast together after), but, since war was regarded as the supreme form of sport, it hardly contributed to peace.

Chlorine, a gaseous element, no. 17, symbol Cl, of the halogen family, first isolated in 1774 by Scheele by the action of manganese dioxide in hydrochloric acid. It unites easily with many other elements, the compounds resulting being termed chlorides. The gaseous element is greenish-yellow, with a pungent odour. It is a suffocating gas, injuring the lungs at a concentration as low as 1 part in 50,000, and was used during the first world war as a poison gas. Has a powerful bleaching action, usually being used in form of bleaching powder, made by combining lime and chlorine.

Chloroform, a volatile colourless liquid, compounded of carbon, hydrogen, and chlorine. It is a powerful solvent, not naturally occurring but synthesised on a large scale. When the vapour is inhaled it produces unconsciousness and insensibility to pain. It owes its discovery to Liebig, and its first application for medical purposes to Sir James Young Simpson.

Chlorophyll, the green pigment contained in the leaves of plants, first discovered by P. J. Pelletier (1788–1829) and J. B. Caventou (1795–1877) in 1818. Enables the plant to absorb sunlight and so to build up sugar. The total synthesis of chlorophyll was reported in 1960 by Prof. R. B. Woodward. This was an outstanding achievement in the field of organic chemistry. See **Photosynthesis, F32(1).**

Chouans, the name given to the band of peasants, mainly smugglers and dealers in contraband salt, who rose in revolt in the west of France in 1793 and joined the royalists of La Vendée. Balzac gives a picture of the people and the country in which they operated in his novel *Les Chouans.* They used the hoot of an owl as a signal—hence the name.

Chough, a member of the crow family, of glossy blue-green-black plumage, whose long curved bill and legs are coral red. It used to be abundant on the cliffs of Cornwall, but its haunts are now restricted to the rocky outcrops of the western coasts and in the mountains near by. It nests in cleft rocks and caves. The Alpine chough with yellow bill inhabits the mountainous districts of Europe and Asia and is not found in Britain. It was found at c. 8,200 m on Everest.

Christmas means "mass of Christ" from the old English *Cristes maesse*, which is celebrated by the Western church on 25 December. The actual day on which Christ was born is not known and there is some uncertainty about the year. 25 December as the day of Nativity was not generally observed until the 5th cent. A.D., though, as the winter solstice, it had long been observed as a pagan festival of *sol invictus* (unconquered sun). The first Christmas card dates from about 1843 and the Christmas tree, of pagan origin, was introduced into England from Germany where it had been a tradition since the Middle Ages. Santa Claus is a corruption of Santa Nikolaus (St. Nicholas) patron saint of children, whose feast day properly falls on 6 December.

Chromium, a very hard, bluish-white metal element, no. 24, symbol Cr, melting at very high temperature (above 1,900°C). Its chief ore is chromite or chrome iron-ore (ferrous chromite). "Ferro-chrome" is produced by heating chromite and anthracite in an electric furnace, and chrome steels are prepared by adding the pre-calculated amount of ferro-chrome to melted steel. Best known chrome steel is stainless steel first made by Brearley in 1912 and since then developed greatly at Sheffield. A typical formula is 18 per cent. chromium, 8 per cent. nickel, 74 per cent. iron. Equally important are Stellite alloys, containing chromium, cobalt, tungsten (or molybdenum), which have made possible modern high-speed cutting tools. Dies used in manufacture of plastics are commonly of chrome steel. The elementary metal finds little use alone except in chromium-plating for motor cars, etc.

Chromosomes, the structures contained within the nucleus of every animal and plant cell by which genetic information is transmitted. The chromosome number in somatic (body) cells is constant for each species of plant and animal, e.g., man (46), cat (38), mouse (40) honey bee (16), fruit fly *Drosophila* (8), potato (48). Chromosomes are long molecules composed of deoxyribonucleoproteins (*i.e.*, proteins and DNA). Human chromosomes have been the subject of much recent research since it has been found that certain disorders are associated with chromosomal aberration, e.g., in Mongolism an extra chromosome is present. See also **Genes, Chromosome Theory (F31), Cell Division (F34).**

Church Commissioners. The Church Commissioners were established in 1948 by the amalgamation of Queen Anne's Bounty (established 1704) and the Ecclesiastical Commissioners (established 1836) to administer Church revenues and to manage Church property.

Cid, El, a famous Spanish hero of the 11th cent., Don Rodrigo Diaz de Vivar, also called Cid Campeador, whose exploits, against Christians and Moors alike, are celebrated in poem and play.

Cilia, minute hair-like projections on the surface of some cells, which beat together in wavelike movements like the wind over a corn-field. These movements can be used as a means of locomotion as in the aquatic organism paramecium. Cilia are also found on the outer layers of the human trachea where they waft particles upwards to the throat, thus protecting the lungs. See **F37, Index to Section P** and **Flagella.**

Cinque Ports, a number of seaport towns on the coast of Kent and Sussex, originally five; Hastings, Romney, Hythe, Dover and Sandwich. Winchelsea and Rye were added later. These ports were required to furnish a certain number of ships, ready for service, and in return they were granted many privileges. The official residence of the Lord Warden is Walmer Castle, near Dover. The holder of the office is the Queen Mother, the first-ever woman to be appointed.

Cistercians, an order of monks and nuns taking their names from Citeaux, near Dijon, where their first monastery was established in 1098. The order was noted for the severity of its rule. They were famous agriculturists. The habit is white, with a black cowl or hood.

City Technology Colleges (CTCs), new concept of educational institute introduced by the Conservative Government after 1987. The first three to be opened were at Solihull, Nottingham and Middlesbrough.

Civil List is the annual sum payable to the Sovereign to maintain the Royal Household and to uphold the dignity of the Crown. The amount is granted by Parliament upon the recommendation of a Select Committee and has to be settled afresh in the first six months of a new reign. The Civil List of Queen Victoria was £385,000; Edward VII and George V, £470,000; Edward VIII and George VI, £410,000; Elizabeth II £475,000. Since 1972 the Civil List allowances have been increased each year to keep pace with inflation. The figures for 1990 are as follows: The Queen's Civil List £5,090,000, Her Majesty Queen Elizabeth The Queen Mother £439,500, HRH The Duke of Edinburgh £245,000, HRH The Princess Royal £154,500, HRH The Duke of York £169,000; HRH The Princess Margaret £148,500; and HRH The Prince Edward, £20,000.

The Prince of Wales is entitled to tax-free revenue from the Duchy of Cornwall. Other resources available to the Queen include (1) the sums which Parliament votes to government departments each year, e.g., upkeep of palaces (Dept. of the Environment) royal yacht Britannia and the royal flight (Min. of Defence); (2) privy purse (revenues of the Duchy of Lancaster); (3) personal fortune, the size of which is not disclosed. The Queen pays no direct taxes. 80–100 per cent. of the annuities received by other members of the Royal family are treated as tax-free expenses. The system under which annual payments are made by the Government to the Queen was changed by the Civil List Act 1975; payments are now included in the annual estimates in the same way as the expenditure of a government department, and subject to scrutiny in the House of Commons. The Civil List now provides only for the Sovereign, the consort of a Sovereign, their children, and the widows of those children.

Cleopatra's Needle on the Thames Embankment is of the time of Tuthmosis III (1500–1450 B.C.). The monolith had nothing to do with Cleopatra, as it only came to Alexandria after her death. It was first erected at the Biblical On (Greek Heliopolis), sacred City of the Sun. It was presented to the British Government by Mehemet Ali in 1819, but not brought to this country until 1878. Weight c. 183 tonnes; height, 20·8 m.

Climate has been defined by Professor H. H. Lamb as the total experience of the weather at any place over some specific period of time. Not only averages but extremes of temperature, variation of humidity, duration of sunshine and cloud cover, amount of rainfall and frequency of snow, frost, gales, etc., are amongst the data normally investigated. The interiors of great land masses are characterised by large ranges of temperature and low rainfall (continental climate), while proximity to oceans has an ameliorating effect with increase in rainfall (oceanic climate). Presence of mountain ranges and lakes and configuration generally produce local modifications of climate, also apparent between the centre and the outlying suburbs of a city. Latitude introduces zones of climate, e.g., tropical rain, subtropical steppe and desert, temperate rain and polar. The climate is always changing in greater or less degree. Every year, every decade, every century brings a somewhat different experience. The tendency between 1880 and 1940 was for most parts of the world to become warmer. Now environmentalists are concerned about the "greenhouse effect" (see **Y10–11**).

Clock, a device for measuring the passage of time. The earliest timekeeper was the shadow-clock, a primitive form of sundial, used in Ancient Egypt about 1500 B.C. To find the time at night the water clock or clepsydra was used. The sand-glass dates from the 15th cent. No one knows when the first mechanical clocks were invented, but it is known that a complicated mechanical clock driven by water and controlled by a weighbridge escarpment was built in Peking in 1090. The Dover Clock in the Science Museum is not the earliest surviving clock in England, as was once believed, but early 17th cent. The Salisbury Cathedral clock dates from 1386 and that of Wells Cathedral from 1392. The pendulum clock was invented by the Dutch scientist Christiaan Huygens (1625–95). The first watches were made in Nuremberg shortly after 1500. The marine chronometer is a high-precision timepiece used at sea for giving Greenwich mean time. The quartz-crystal clocks are accurate to one thousandth of a second a day, and the improved atomic clock, developed at the British National Physical Laboratory, which makes use of the natural vibrations of the caesium atom, is an almost absolute measure of time. Its accuracy of 1 sec. in 300 years has been improved to 1 sec. in 1,000 years.

Cloud Chamber, an apparatus invented by C. T. R. Wilson in which the tracks of atomic particles can be made visible. Just as the vapour trails tell of the track of an invisible aircraft high up in the air, so the vapour trails of an unseeable particle can tell of its behaviour. The rays under investigation pass through a chamber containing a gas, e.g., air thoroughly cleansed of dust, supersaturated with water, or alcohol-vapour. As the particle passes through it forms a track of tiny water droplets which can be photographed. After a long and honourable history this wonderful instrument is now virtually obsolete. A later ingenious device for tracking fast fundamental particles is the Bubble chamber (q.v.).

Clouds are formed by the cooling of moist air, the type depending on the way the air cools and the height at which condensation occurs. There are three main classes: (1) high cloud (about 6,100 m)—cirrus (delicate and fibrous), cirrostratus (thin white veil), and cirrocumulus (delicately rippled) consisting of ice crystals; (2) medium cloud (above 2,100 m)—altostratus (dense, greyish veil) and altocumulus (broken flattened cloudlets)—chiefly water particles, often supercooled; (3) low cloud (from near ground to 2,100 m)—cumulus (fair weather, broken, dome-topped), cumulominbus (heavy, towering to great heights), stratocumulus (layer of globular masses or rolls), stratus (like fog but off the ground), nimbostratus (low, rainy cloud). The highest clouds of all, and the rarest, are the noctilucent, seen only on summer nights in high latitudes. They form at about 80 km above the earth and consist of ice-coated dust from meteors.

Clover, plants of the *Trifolium* genus, family *Leguminosae,* with about 250 species. These are "nitrogen fixing" plants and include red clover, white clover, alsike clover and crimson clover. They are of great importance in agriculture because in a good pasture they supply directly or indirectly most of the protein available to the animals. Seed of "wild white" clover has been accepted since about 1939 as the indispensable plant of good United Kingdom grassland, largely through the efforts of pioneers like D. A. Gilchrist (1859–1927).

Coal. Until recently the most important single fuel has been coal. It is a mineral of organic origin, formed from the remains of vegetation which over millions of years has changed to coal by the effects of heat and pressure from overlying rock or water. All coal contains moisture, inflammable volatiles, mineral impurities (some of which remain as coal ash after the coal is burnt), and fixed carbon (the coke that is left after the volatiles have been driven off). The relative proportions vary—from Anthracite, a hard coal containing the highest proportion of fixed carbon, to Lignite or brown coal which is little more than a hard peat. World reserves of bituminous coal have been estimated at $7 \cdot 5 \times 10^{12}$ tonnes. If one adds the reserves of brown coal and lignite, this figure is increased by about 15 per cent. The proportion of the reserves that could be economically recovered varies from country to country and estimates vary from 50 to 100 per cent of the reserves. The reserves are highly localised—over half being located in the Soviet Union. In the United Kingdom coal has formed the basis of past industrial prosperity. Peak output occurred in 1913 when 290 million tonnes were mined one third of which was exported. At the end of the second world war production had fallen to 186 million tonnes and was far below demand. In 1947 the British coal industry was brought under public ownership and all its assets were vested in the National Coal Board. During the next ten years great efforts were made to increase coal output but, quite suddenly in 1956, demand for coal fell as oil became a popular fuel and the problem was to cut back the coal industry without causing undue social problems. The fall in demand was accompanied by increasing productivity, both mines and miners having been cut in their numbers by over half. Then as a result of the high cost of oil in 1973 came expansion of the industry. From 1984 the coal industry faced a bitter strike over plans to make large-scale pit closures. The defeat of the miners weakened the NUM and its leader, Arthur Scargill. In 1988–89 coal production was $103 \cdot 8$ m-tonnes.

Coat of Arms, in heraldry, a device containing a family's armorial bearings. In mediaeval times the coat upon which such device was embroidered; knights wore it over their armour.

Cobalt, element no. 24, symbol Cr, a white metal melting at 1490°C. Two main ores are *cobalt glance* (in which the element is combined with arsenic and sulphur) and *smaltite* (cobalt arsenide). The principal sources are Ontario and Zaire. Various cobalt alloys are important, *e.g.*, stellite, ferrocobalt and carboloy. Its monoxide is an important colouring medium, and is used for colouring glass and porcelain blue.

Cobra, hooded and very venomous snakes. The best known species are the Indian Cobra, the Egyptian Cobra, and the Black-necked Cobra. Their food consists chiefly of small rodents,

The King Cobra is almost exclusively a snake-eater. "Spitting" Cobras (or Ringhals) of S. Africa are a related genus, capable of spitting their venom several yards.

Coca, a S. American shrub, *Erythroxylon coca*, also cultivated in Java. The leaves yield cocaine, classified as a dangerous drug. When the natives chew the leaves they are enabled to withstand hunger and fatigue, as cocaine acts both as a mental stimulant and as an anaesthetic on the mucous lining of the stomach.

Cochineal or **Carmine,** a dyestuff consisting of the dried bodies of the female scale insect (*Dactylopius coccus*) which feeds on cacti. Of ancient origin, the dye was well known to the Aztecs, and was used widely in the Middle Ages. The scarlet tunics worn by the English during the Napoleonic wars owed their colour to carmine.

Cockatoo, a member of the parrot family, bearing a crest of feathers on the head, native to Australia and adjacent regions. Predominant colour is white tinged with yellow or scarlet while some species have dark plumage. The cockatoo of New Guniea is slaty black with pale red cheeks and can crack Kanary nuts which usually require a hammer to break them open.

Cockchafer (*Melolontha*), one of the most destructive of beetles, the larvae feeding on roots. It is about $2 \cdot 5$ cm in length, of a brownish colour, and emits a loud whirring sound when flying.

Cockle, the popular name of the bi-valve shellfish of the genus *Cardium*, found plentifully in sandy bays near low-water line.

Cockroach, inaccurately called the "black beetle"; a pest of bakeries and kitchens. In Britain two species are commonly found; the Common Cockroach (*Blatta orientalis*), resident since the time of Elizabeth I, dark brown, about $2 \cdot 5$ cm long, with the wing covers long in the male and short in the female; and the German Cockroach (*Blatta germanica*), now the most common, half the size, dark yellow, with both sexes fully winged. All species have long antennae and flattened, leathery, shiny bodies. They are nocturnal and omnivorous.

Coconut Palm (*Cocos nucifera*), a tropical tree, growing to a height of 30 m, with a slender trunk surmounted by giant feather-like leaves. One of the most important sources of food and raw material for people living in the tropics. The juice of the fruit, or coconut, is drunk; the kernel is eaten fresh or dried to form copra, which yields animal feeding stuffs and oil, used in the manufacture of soap, margarine, cosmetics, synthetic rubber, etc.; leaves are used for thatching; leaf stalks for canes, fence posts, needles, etc., and the trunk for houses and bridges. Main producing areas: Indonesia, Philippines, Malaysia, Sri Lanka and S. India.

Codes, a term used to designate a system of laws properly classified. The Code of Hammurabi, king of Babylon, *c.* 1751 B.C., had extensive influence over a long period. The Romans formulated several codes of historic importance including the Theodosian Code which summarised the Roman laws from the time of Constantine to 438 A.D. The final codification was made under order of the Emperor Justinian by his chief minister Tribonian and published in 529 with a new edition in 534. The most important of modern codes is the *Code Napoléon*, compiled between 1803 and 1810, and still in force. It has been used as an example for the codification of the laws of a number of countries from America to Japan. Under Frederick the Great the law of Prussia was codified. English law has never been codified, although the law on certain subjects has been gathered up into a single statute. The Law Commission Act, 1965, was passed to consolidate and codify the law.

Codex, a manuscript volume of the Scriptures comprising the Sinaiaticus of the 4th cent., the Vatican codex of the same period, the Alexandrine codex of the 5th cent., and others. The British Museum, in 1933, purchased the *Codex Sinaiticus* from the Soviet Government for £100,000. The Sinaiaticus was written on 347 vellum leaves some fifteen to sixteen hundred years ago and the binding into 2 volumes was completed by Douglas Cockerill and his son in 1936. It was sold to an American in 1981 for $5·2 million.

Coffee, a shrub found originally in Arabia and Ethiopia, but now extensively grown in Brazil, Colombia, Ivory Coast, Uganda, Angola and Central America. It yields a seed or berry which after undergoing the necessary preparation, is ground and used in most countries as a breakfast beverage. The best coffee is the Mocha, an Arabian variety. The stimulating effect of coffee is due to the caffeine, which is also present in tea. The beverage was introduced into Europe in the 16th cent., and the first London coffee shop was opened in 1652.

Coke is the solid residue remaining when coal is carbonised and nearly all the volatile constituents have been driven off. Used as fuel, and as an agent for reducing metallic oxides to metals, *e.g.*, iron ore to iron, in the manufacture of steel.

Colorado Beetle, a serious pest of potato crops. Both adults and larvae feed on the foliage where the orange eggs are laid. The grub is reddish, with two rows of small black spots on each side. The adults are about 1·2 cm long with yellow and black striped wing cases. The beetle is avoided by birds because of its nasty taste, and is controlled by arsenical sprays.

Colosseum, the name of the Flavian amphitheatre at Rome, begun by Vespasian and finished by Titus A.D. 80. In general outline it still remains one of the most magnificent ruins in the world. In the arena of this great building the famous gladiatorial displays and mimic naval battles used to be given, and about 50,000 spectators could be accommodated.

Colossus is the name which the ancients gave to any statue of gigantic size. The Colossus at Rhodes, which was a bronze statue of the sun god, Helios, was the most famous, and reckoned among the seven wonders of the world. It stood over 30 m high at the mouth of the harbour. There is no truth in the legend that ships could pass between its legs. It fell in an earthquake in 224 B.C.

Colugo, also known as "flying lemur", caguan or kubuk, a remarkable mammal which may be regarded as an aberrant insectivore or an aberrant form of the earliest ancestor of the bats. It has nothing to do with lemurs. There are two genera, one inhabiting the Philippines and one inhabiting Malaya. They have a parachute-like membrane which covers them from the neck to the tip of the tail, by means of which they can glide from treetop to ground, a distance of up to 64 m.

Column, in architecture, is an upright solid body serving as a support or decoration to a building. Columns consist of a pedestal, a shaft, and a capital, over which the supported entablature rises. They are named according to the styles of architecture of which they form part, being Doric, Tuscan, Ionic, Corinthian or Composite as the case may be.

Comets are celestial bodies which generally move about the solar system in elongated elliptical or nearly parabolic orbits. Most comets are in the latter category, having extremely long orbital periods, up to millions of years, and have therefore only been seen once in recorded history. They spend most of their lifetimes at extremely large distances from the sun, far outside Pluto's orbit. Those in elliptical orbits appear periodically and a few have been observed regularly. Halley's comet, named after Edmund Halley, who first correctly predicted that this comet would reappear in 1758, was first observed in Roman times and is one of the brightest of the periodic comets. The nucleus of a comet, which appears as a faint star when the comet is very far from the sun, is believed to be a frozen mixture of dust and materials called "ices"— CO_2, H_2O, NH_3 and CH_4, frozen at the low temperatures in the outer solar system. Approaching the sun, the comet is heated by sunlight and the surface "ices" are first vaporised and later photo-dissociated and ionised by sunlight, also freeing the surface dust. The dust, gases and ions produce the fuzzy appearance of the coma of the comet. Under the influence of sunlight acting on dust, and the solar wind and interplanetary field acting on the ions, the cometary tail (often multiple) is produced. This may stretch up to 200 million km, pointing away from the sun. Donati's comet (1858) was possibly the most spectacular of all and was visible even in daylight. Kohoutek's comet (1975) was the first to be observed from space, by the American Skylab and Russian Soyuz, and many exciting new space studies were conducted during the last return of Halley's comet in 1985. *See also* **F4(1)**.

Commons are the remnants of the mediaeval open fields round villages in which the villagers had rights in common, *e.g.*, (i) estover—the right of taking wood for house building or firewood; (ii) pasture—the right of grazing beasts; (iii) turbary—the right of digging turf; (iv) piscary—the right to fish. Many of these common lands were enclosed during the agrarian revolution which went on steadily in England from the 15th cent. onwards, and with their enclosure common rights vanished. A Royal Commission on Common Land described the commons in 1965 as the "last reservoir of uncommitted land" which provide, as far as the public is concerned, by far the largest part of the accessible open spaces of the country. Under the Commons Registration Act, 1965, it was the duty of County Councils and County Borough Councils to make a register of all common land and all town and village greens in their areas.

Commons, House of, the Lower House of the British Parliament. *See* **Section D**.

Commune of Paris has twice played a dramatic part in the history of France. In 1792 it was able, through its control of the administrative organisation of Paris, to override the National Assembly. In 1871, after the withdrawal of the Prussian troops, it tried to assert its authority. Public buildings were destroyed by members of the Commune and civil war raged during April and half May, but Government troops savagely suppressed the rising.

Community Charge, *see* Poll Tax **(H20)**.

Compass *or* **Mariner's Compass.** It has been known since very early times that an iron needle, suspended freely to hang horizontally when not magnetised, comes to rest roughly along the geographical north-south line when magnetised. Further, it generally does not hang horizontally. This is the essential behaviour of the *compass*, a navigational instrument whose invention is obscure but which seems to have been known to the Chinese 4,500 years ago. That the behaviour of the compass shows the existence of a *magnetic field* associated with the Earth was first fully recognised by William Gilbert in 1600. Aircraft and ships now largely employ gyrostatic compasses which are not affected by electrical and magnetic disturbances. Sperry, Brown and Anschütz are three important types of gyroscopic compass.

Composite Materials, or more simply composites, are materials which derive useful properties by combining the virtues of two or more components. Combining clay with straw to make tougher bricks is an ancient example in which fibres (straw) are embedded in a matrix or body (the clay). A modern example is fibreglass in which glass fibres are embedded in a plastic matrix. Nature also uses composites as in bamboo in which a lignin matrix binds together the fibres of cellulose to make a light strong structure. Composites may contain flakes or particles embedded in the matrix instead of fibres—it depends on the application. Although the idea is not new composite technology has made rapid strides in the last few decades guided by scientific insight into the nature of solids and the origin of their strengths and weaknesses. The motivation had been that scientifically designed composites offer materials with exceptional strength/weight ratio, desirable magnetic properties and other technological advantages which meet the extreme demands of a variety of industries. For example, composite aluminium containing boron fibres or resin containing graphite fibres can have strength/weight ratios over twice that of high-strength solid aluminium. Composites of many kinds are now widespread in industrial use and are attracting much research and development.

Computer, a technical device for accepting an input of information, processing this information according to some prescribed programme of operations and supplying an output of processed information. Many types of operation can be performed on many types of information and computers are now indispensable in science, business, warfare, government and other activities. Early thinkers in this field were Pascal (17th cent.), Babbage (19th cent.) and Turing (1930s), but electronic computers as we know them appeared during the second world war and the first commercial machine was on sale in 1950. Computers are millions of times faster than human beings at computing; and the introduction of computers into an organisation does more than just speed up the calculations, it tends to transform the whole nature of the organisation. The possibilities for future developments seem enormous. Analogue computers and digital computers are two different kinds stemming from the difference between *measuring* and *counting.* Analogue types handle data that is repeated by physical quantities of continuously variable size such as voltages or lengths. These quantities can be made to vary like the quantities in a problem which the computer is set to solve; the problem is thus solved by analogy. A slide rule is a rudimentary analogue computer in which numbers are represented by lengths of rule. Digital computers handle actual numbers expressed in digits and the quantitiees in the problem are represented by discrete numbers. These can all be expressed in binary form and thus stored or handled in bits. *See* **Bit, Binary Notation.**

Conclave, an assembly of Roman Catholic cardinals met together to elect a pope. The last Conclave was held in the Vatican in Oct. 1978 when Cardinal Wojtyla, Archbishop of Cracow, was elected Pope John Paul II.

Concordat, an agreement of convention between the Pope and a secular government regarding ecclesiastical matters. The Concordat of Worms in 1122 between Calixtus II and the Emperor Henry V was famous as deciding a long struggle in regard to investiture. In 1801, Napoleon concluded a concordat with Pius VII defining the restored relations between the head of the Church and the French Roman Catholics.

Condor, a large eagle of brilliant black plumage with a circlet of white feathers round its neck. It is a native of the Andes.

Confederation is a free association of sovereign states united for some common purpose. It s to be distinguished from a Federation, which is a union of states with one central government, each state relinquishing its sovereignty, though retaining some independence in internal affairs.

Confucianism. *See* **Section J.**

Coniferae are cone-bearing trees, including firs, pines, cedars, cypresses, junipers, yews, etc., and are widely distributed in temperate regions.

Conservatism. *See* **Section J.**

Constitution, the fundamental organic law or principles of government of a nation, state, society, or other organisation, embodied in written documents, or implied in the institutions and customs of the country or society. The government of the USA, unlike Great Britain, works upon a written Constitution. It was framed when the USA came into existence as a sovereign body, when the Constitution built a republic out of a federation of thirteen states, based on representative government. The constitution was adopted in 1789, and its strength has been tested by the fact that, substantially unchanged, it is the groundwork for a federation which now comprises fifty states. *See also* **Sections C and D.**

Continent, a word used in physical geography to denote the larger continuous land masses in contrast to the great oceans of the earth. They are: Eurasia (conventionally regarded as 2 continents, Europe and Asia), Africa, North America, South America, Australia and Antarctica. (Australasia is Australia, New Zealand and adjacent islands. Oceania is Australasia and the many islands of the S.W. Pacific.)

Continental Drift. The hypothesis of drifting continents is due to F. B. Taylor, an American geologist who published his theory in 1908, and to the Austrian meteorologist Alfred Wegener in 1910. The latter was impressed by the matching coasts of South America and Africa, which seemed to him to fit together like the pieces of a jigsaw puzzle. Since then many other people have taken up and developed the

idea. Acccording to Wegener, at one time there were two primary super-continents. Laurasia and Gondwanaland. The one in the northern hemisphere consisted of North America, Europe, and the northern part of Asia. Its southern counterpart included Antarctica, Australia, India, Africa and South America. These super-continents broke up, and their various bits moved apart. In particular, the southern hemisphere continents drifted radially northwards away from the south pole, and the two Americas shifted westwards from Europe and Africa. What would have been the leading edges of the land masses on this hypothesis, are now heavily buckled up into mountain belts, such as the Cordillera and the Alpine-Himalayan chain. The resistance afforded to drifting by the strong ocean floors may well have been the cause of such structures. Despite the wealth of geological facts which have a bearing on the problem of continental drift, none of these has been able to decide the issue in a conclusive manner. Further studies of rock magnetism (*q.v.*) and of fossil climates should ultimately establish the concept of continental drift on a firm basis. *See also* **Earth, F8.**

Conurbation, a term used in reference to an extensive and continuous area of urban land-use. Conurbations are frequently formed by the physical coalescence of several formerly freestanding towns. They may themselves coalesce to form a higher order of physical urbanisation, known as a megalopolis. The seven conurbations officially recognised in the UK are Greater London, W. Midlands, S.E. Lancashire, W. Yorkshire, Merseyside, Tyneside and Clydeside, of which the first five are said to form the English megalopolis. In common with other old and well-developed cities throughout the capitalist world, conurbations in Britain show a marked decline in population and employment.

Convention is an assembly of delegates, representatives, members of a party met to accomplish some specific civil, social, political, ecclesiastical or other important object.

Convocation, an assembly called together to deliberate ecclesiastical affairs. In the Church of England the provinces of Canterbury and York each have their convocation. The term is also applied to assemblies of the graduates of certain universities.

Coot. A very widely distributed bird of the rail family and a common resident of the British Isles. The adult is black with a conspicuous white bald shield on the forehead and a white bill. The juvenile is brownish grey with whitish breast and throat. The coot flies heavily, but swims well. It dives frequently and can remain submerged for a considerable time. It is pugnacious and in winter gregarious. The food is chiefly vegetable. The large nest is usually built among aquatic vegetation and the young are fed by both parents. Another species, the Crested Coot, occurs in S. Europe.

Copper, one of the most familiar of metals, element no. 29, symbol Cu, used in ancient times as an alloy with tin in producing bronze, and preceding iron as an industrial material. Copper ores are most abundant in the USA, Chile, Canada, Zambia and Zaïre. All copper compounds are poisonous.

Copyright. Under the Copyright Act, 1956, copyright subsists in every original literary, dramatic musical, and artistic work if the author is a British subject or a citizen of the Republic of Ireland or resident in the United Kingdom, or if the work is first published in the United Kingdom. The Act provides that, except in certain special cases, the author of the work shall be the first owner of the copyright, and there are no formalities, such as registration or payment of fees, to be accomplished. Copyright includes the right to reproduce the work in any material form, to perform the work in public, or, if the work is unpublished, to publish the work. The Act also protects sound recordings, films and television and sound broadcasts. Literary, dramatic, musical and artistic works which enjoy the protection of the Act are automatically protected in those countries which are parties to the Berne Copyright Convention or the Universal Copyright Convention. In general, copyright in literary, dramatic, musical and artistic works is vested in the author for the period of his lifetime and 50 years following after which it passes into the public domain and becomes freely available to any who wish to make use of it. The Copyright Libraries, entitled to receive copies of books published in the United Kingdom are given under **Libraries.** The Berne Copyright Convention and the Universal Copyright Convention were revised at a diplomatic conference held in Paris in 1971. The effect of the revisions allows any national of a developing country to obtain, under certain conditions, a compulsory licence to translate and publish a copyright work for the purpose of teaching, scholarship and research, upon payment of compensation to the copyright owner of the original work. The Government Department responsible for matters in connection with copyright is the Industrial Property and Copyright Department, 25 Southampton Buildings, London, WC2A 1AY.

Coral, an order of small marine animals closely related to the sea-anemone, but differing from it in their ability to develop a limy skeleton. They multiply sexually and by budding. The structure of the coral secretions assumes a variety of forms, fan-like, tree-like, mushroom shape, and so forth. Red coral (the skeleton of *Corallium rubrum*) is mainly obtained from the Mediterranean. The coral reefs of the Pacific and Indian Oceans are often many miles in extent. Living corals occur only in warm seas at about 23°C.

Cordite, a smokeless explosive adopted for small arms and heavy artillery by the British Government in the naval and military services in 1889, and composed of 58 parts of nitro-glycerine, 37 of gun-cotton, and 5 of vaseline. It is a jelly or plastic dough, and used in the form of sticks. Invented by Sir Frederick Abel and Sir John Dewar in 1889.

Cork, the bark of a species of oak, *Quercus suber*, grown largely in the South of Europe and North America. The cork tree is said to yield bark every six to ten years for 150 years, and grows to a height of from 6–12 m. Its lightness, impermeability, and elasticity enable it to be used for a variety of commercial purposes, especially for stoppers of bottles.

Cormorant, a large, long-billed water-bird which captures fish by diving. The common cormorant has bronze-black plumage with white cheeks and sides and is found round the sea coasts of most parts of the world, including the British Isles. It nests in colonies on sea cliffs and rocky ledges. The Shag or Green Cormorant is a smaller bird with green-black plumage and a crest.

Corncrake. *See* **Landrail.**

Corn Laws were statutes intended for the benefit of British agriculture, and restricted import and export of grain. From the 14th to the mid-19th cent. such laws were in force, and were often of a stringent nature. They became so oppressive and caused corn to reach so high a price that the poorer classes were plunged into distress. A powerful anti-corn law agitation was organised of which Cobden, Bright and Villiers were the leaders, and Sir Robert Peel, in 1846, at the time of the Irish potato famine, carried through free trade. The repeal of the Corn Laws marked an important phase in the transformation of an agricultural to an industrial Britain.

Corona or **Solar Corona,** the outer atmosphere of the sun. This glows by virtue of light emitted by the sun and scattered by electrons and dust particles at various heights in the sun's atmosphere and also by light emitted from ionised atoms in the corona itself. Corona light is much fainter than the bright disc of the sun and is invisible against the normal blue of the sky. During total solar eclipses, the corona can be seen by the human eye as a faint glow extending irregularly outwards a few solar diameters from the sun. The sun's atmosphere extends much further than this but is invisible to the eye at large distances from the sun. The corona gases are thought to be very hot (millions of degrees) and in complex violent motion; the gross structure of the corona is connected with the sunspot cycle.

Cortes, the name of the Parliamentary assemblies of Spain and Portugal.

Cosmic Rays are a form of radiation coming from outer space, of deep penetrating power and of great scientific interest. The rays consist of extremely energetic atomic particles—protons, electrons and some heavier nucleons—travelling at speeds very close to that of light. A complex series of events result from their collision with the atmosphere, giving rise to showers of secondary high-energy particles containing many of those listed on **F16.** Cosmic rays are now investigated with instruments buried in deep mines, as well as those in satellites, and the great interest is because we now believe their origin to be in, or associated with, some of the most interesting objects in the universe—supernovae, neutron stars, pulsars and perhaps some gigantic galactic nuclei. *See* **F3(2).**

Cosmology is the science which studies the whole universe, its origin, its nature, its size, age and evolution. It is presently a very active science because of many new discoveries of radio astronomy and space astronomy (X-ray, ultraviolet and infra-red) of extremely distant and luminous objects whose radiation has taken many thousands of millions of years to reach us, and whose explanation is taxing many of the world's best theoretical scientists. *See* **F3–8.**

Cotton, the name of a plant of several species bearing large yellow flowers with purple centres. These centres expand into pods, which at maturity burst and yield the white fibrous substances known as cotton. The raw cotton contains a large proportion of seeds which are removed by "ginning". Long before the Christian era, cotton had been grown and used with great skill in India to make fabrics. The industry was not introduced into England until the middle of the 17th cent. when Protestant refugees from Flanders came to settle in the wool textile districts of East Anglia and Lancashire. With improvements in machinery and expansion of overseas trade in the 18th and 19th cent., Lancashire became the centre of the world's cotton industry but since the second world war man-made fibres have taken the place of cotton.

Coulomb, a unit of electric charge, named after the French naval engineer, Charles Augustin de Coulomb (1736–1806), equal to the quantity of electricity transferred in one second by a current of one ampere.

County. Since the recent reorganisation of local government in the United Kingdom the distinction between *administrative* counties and *geographical* counties no longer exists. Certain geographical counties have disappeared (*e.g.*, Rutland and Pembroke), new counties have appeared (*e.g.*, Avon and Gwynedd), while former counties have been modified (*e.g.* Glamorgan and Yorkshire).

Coup d'Etat, a violent change in the government of a state carried out by force or illegally. Examples are the overthrow of the French Republic in 1851 by Louis Napoleon, who then became Emperor, and more recently the military *coups* in the Middle East which brought about the abdication of Farouk of Egypt in 1952 and the assassination of Feisal of Iraq in 1958.

Court Leet, a court of record held annually before the steward of any particular manor or lordship; originally there was only one court for a manor, but in the time of Edward I it branched into two, the court baron and the court leet.

Coypu or **Nutria rat,** a large beaver-like rodent found in S. America; it became wild in E. Anglia, where it caused damage to dykes and crops, having escaped from farms where it is bred for its fur. Eradicated in E. Anglia by 1989.

Crack, highly addictive drug, cheap to produce. Inhaled or smoked. Epidemic fears in U.S.A.

Crane, a large, graceful wading-bird with elegant long legs and neck, greyish plumage, superficially resembling the heron and related to the bustard. They migrate in ' or ' formation and have trumpet-like voices. There are several species, found in all continents except S. America, including the Crowned Crane with golden coronet and the Demoiselle with tuft-like crest of white feathers. The Common Crane nested in East Anglia in mediaeval times.

Credit is an advance of money or of goods or services in consideration of a promise of payment later. Trade credit is such an advance from trader to customer; bank credit is an advance of money by a bank to a client, whether a business firm or a private person, in consideration of an interest payment by the borrower.

Creed (Latin *credo* = I believe), a formal statement of belief. The three orthodox Christian creeds are the Apostles' Creed (a summary of their teaching), the Nicene Creed (drawn up by the Church Council at Nicaea in A.D. 325 to define its theological doctrines), and the Athanasian Creed (concerning the nature and divinity of Christ). *See also* under individual headings.

Cremation, the ancient custom, revived in modern times, of burning the dead. Cremation was first legalised in Great Britain in 1885 and the first crematorium opened at Woking in that year. Application for cremation must be accompanied by two medical certificates.

Cricket, a genus of insects of the grasshopper order which move by leaps. The male produces a chirping noise by rubbing its wing-covers together. Just as the males inherit the nerve machinery for emitting the song of the species, so the females receive and respond to that song and to no other.

Crimean War (1853–56). This war between Russia and the allied powers of Turkey, England, France and Sardinia, was connected with the Eastern Question (*q.v.*) and the desire of Russia for a port on the Mediterranean. Chief engagements were the Alma, Balaclava and Inkerman. Fighting virtually ceased with fall of Sevastopol in September 1855. Treaty of Paris signed 30 March 1856.

Crocodiles and their allies (alligators, caimans and gavials) are the largest of modern reptiles. They are well equipped for a predatory life in shallow waters, having powerful tails and strong jaws. Their eggs are laid on land, in sand or decomposing vegetation.

Crow, a family of birds including many well-known species such as the rook, raven, jackdaw, carrion crow, hooded crow, magpie, nutcracker, jaw and chough.

Crusades were military expeditions undertaken by some of the Christian nations of Europe with the object of ensuring the safety of pilgrims visiting the Holy Sepulchre and to retain in Christian hands the Holy Places. For two centuries nine crusades were undertaken: First, 1095–99, under Godfrey of Bouillon, which succeeded in capturing Jerusalem; Second, 1147–49, led by Louis VII of France, a dismal failure, which ended with the fall of Jerusalem; Third, 1180–92, in which Richard I of England took part, making a truce with Saladin; Fourth, 1202–4, led by French and Flemish nobles, a shameful expedition, resulting in the founding of a Latin empire in Constantinople; Fifth, 1217–21, led by John of Brienne; Sixth, 1228–29, under the Emperor Frederick II; Seventh, 1248–54, under St. Louis of France; Eighth, 1270, under the same leadership, but cut short by his death on an ill-judged expedition to Tunis; Ninth, 1271–72, led by Prince Edward of England, which accomplished nothing. Millions of lives and an enormous amount of treasure were sacrificed in these enterprises and Jerusalem remained in the possession of the "infidels". The chief material beneficiaries were the Italian maritime cities; the chief spiritual beneficiary was the Pope; but in literature and the arts both Europe and the Levant benefited enormously from the bringing together of the different cultures.

Cryogenics (Greek roots: productive of cold) is the science dealing with the production of very low temperatures and the study of their physical and technological consequences. "Very low" is often taken to mean below about $-150°C$. The growth of cryogenics (essentially a 20th-cent. science) is connected with the discovery of how to liquefy all gases including even helium which resisted liquefaction until 1908. Scientifically, cryogenics is important partly because special phenomena (*e.g.*, superconductivity (*q.v.*)) appear at lower temperatures and partly because more can be learned about ordinary properties by studying them in the absence of heat. Technologically, cryogenics is becoming more and more significant, for example, liquefied gases are rocket propellants, superconductors make valuable magnets, tissue-freezing techniques (using very cold liquids) have been

introduced into surgery. *See* **Absolute Temperature.**

Crystal, in everyday usage, a solid chemical substance bounded by plane surfaces which show a regular geometrical arrangement as, *e.g.*, quartz crystals, rock salt, snow flakes. In physics the term means any substances whose atoms are arranged in a regular three-dimensional array. This includes most solids, even those not particularly crystalline in appearance, *e.g.*, a lump of lead. *See also* **Glass** and **Liquid Crystals.**

Cubism, the name of a revolutionary movement in art created in the years 1907–9 by the two painters Picasso and Braque. Rejecting purely visual effects, they approached nature from an intellectual point of view, reducing it to mathematical orderliness. Its respectable grandparent was Cézanne who had once written: "you must see in nature the cylinder, the sphere, and the cone"—a concept which, together with the contemporary interest in Negro sculpture, moved the two founders of the movement to experiment with the reduction of natural forms to their basic geometrical shapes. In practice, this meant combining several views of the object all more or less superimposed in order to express the idea of the object rather than any one view of it. The name Cubism was derisive and the movement aroused the same opposition as Impressionism, Fauvism and the later Futurism. Picasso's *Les Demoiselles d'Avignon* (1907; Museum of Modern Art, New York) was his first Cubist painting. Three phases are recognised: (1) Cubism under the influence of Cézanne; (2) high or analytical Cubism (*c.* 1909–12) concentrating on the breaking-down of form to the exclusion of interest in colour; (3) synthetic Cubism (*c.* 1913) making use of *collage* in which pieces of pasted-on paper (illustrations, wallpaper, newspaper) and other materials were used in addition to paint. Amongst other early cubist painters were Metzinger, Gleizes, Gris and Léger.

Cuckoo, a well-known migratory bird which is found in Great Britain from April to July, hawk-like in shape, with a very characteristic note, uttered during the mating season only by the male. The hen has a soft bubbling call. It lays its eggs in the nests of other birds, *e.g.*, the meadow pipit and hedge sparrow, but only one egg in each nest. Feeds mainly on insects, particularly hairy caterpillars.

Cuneiform, (Latin = *wedge-shaped*), an ancient method of writing by impressing wedge-like strokes into tablets of damp clay which when dried and hardened formed a permanent script, Cuneiform writing developed from its original pictographic form into a phonetic writing and can be traced back to the non-Semitic Sumerians of ancient Mesopotamia, the earliest civilisation known to us. It passed to the Semitic Accadians of Babylonia in the 3rd millennium B.C. who adapted it to their own language. Decipherment by Sir Henry Rawlinson, 1835.

Curfew (Old F. *covre-feu* = cover fire), a regulation common throughout Europe in mediaeval times by which, at a fixed hour in the evening, the church bell was rung as a signal that fires were to be put out and the people were to go to bed. The custom originated in the fear of fire when buildings were built of timber. Nowadays a curfew is imposed by the military in areas where riots or disturbances are expected, compelling the civilian population to remain indoors after nightfall.

Curia, the central government of the Roman Catholic Church. By the reform which came into force on 1 January 1968, its twelve Sacred Congregations or "ministries" were reorganised and reduced to nine. The aim of the reform was to streamline the Curial offices so that the Church's machinery can cope with modern problems, so favouring the desires expressed by the Ecumenical Council convened by Pope John.

Curie, a measure of the rate at which radioactive material emits radiation. One curie is a disintegration rate of $3 \cdot 7 \times 10^{10}$ disintegrations per second.

Curlew, a wading-bird of which there are several species. It frequents marshy places, feeds on worms, insects, molluscs and berries and possesses a very long, down-curved bill.

Currency is the name given to the types of cash money—metal or paper—in use in an area (*e.g.* pound, sterling, dollar, franc). It also designates the actual coins or notes issued. Its amount is usually subject to regulation by the Government, or by a Central Bank acting on the Government's behalf. Britain changed over to a £-based decimal currency in February 1971. On 1 January 1985, ½p coins ceased to be legal tender. The old 'halfpenny' first appeared in 1280. *See also* **National Currencies, Section Z.**

Cybernetics, the science concerned with the automatic control and communication processes in both animals and machines. Thus it is concerned with brain function, information theory, electronic computers, and automation.

Cyclone, a term usually applied to a tropical revolving storm. Cyclones often occur towards the end of the hot seasons and are mainly confined to tracks in the western areas of the oceans, being known as hurricanes (Caribbean and Pacific), cyclones (Indian Ocean) and typhoons (China Seas). The circulation of air in a cyclone is similar to that in the *depression* of temperate latitudes, but the region of low pressure is much more localised and the pressure gradients steeper. Winds of hurricane strength and torrential rain occur generally, although at the centre of the storm there is a small area, known as the "eye", where fair, calm weather prevails.

Cyclotron, a machine for accelerating charged particles such as protons to very high energies. Devised by E. O. Lawrence in California in 1930, it uses a magnetic field to make the particles traverse nearly circular paths and an electric field to give them an additional pulse of energy each time round. The accelerated particles impinge on targets, and the resulting events are a basic source of information for nuclear physicists. The cyclotron is obsolescent and has led to the development of other machines, *e.g.*, betatrons, synchrotrons. Britain has two major national high-energy machines: a 7 GeV proton synchroton (to be closed and replaced by a "spallation neutron source"), and a 5 GeV electron synchrotron. The European Organisation for Nuclear Research (CERN), carries out research at higher energies. *See* **L24.**

D

Dactylopterus, a fish of the gurnard family, with wing-like pectoral fins; sometimes known as the flying fish, though that appellation is more generally given to *Exocaetus exiliens*.

Dadaism (French *Dada* = hobby-horse) was a hysterical and nihilistic precursor of **Surrealism** (*q.v.*) resulting from the shock produced by the first world war. Beginning in Zurich about 1915, it spread to other continental cities, such as Berlin and Paris, dying out in 1922. The movement was deliberately anti-art, destructive, and without meaning: it intended to scandalise by such tricks as "compositions" made out of anything that came to hand—buttons, bus tickets, pieces of wire, bits of tin, etc. Other excesses included incoherent poetry, Dada night-clubs, plays, and short-lived newspapers. Many Dadaist painters became Surrealists at a later stage, but where Surrealism is a deliberate attempt to present subconscious and dream-like images, Dadaism was sheer anarchism. Leading Dadaists were Hans Arp, Marcel Duchamp, André Breton, Kurt Schwitters and Max Ernst.

Daddy Longlegs, or **Crane-fly,** a slender long-legged fly of the family Tipulidae. The larvae which do damage to lawns and plants are called leather-jackets. The Americans call Harvestmen (*q.v.*) daddy longlegs.

Daguerreotype, the first practical photographic process, invented in Paris by M. Daguerre during the years 1824–39. The light-sensitive plate was prepared by bringing iodine in contact with a plate of silver. After exposure a positive image came by development of the plate in mercury vapour. Even for open-air scenes the first daguerreotypes involved exposure of 5–10 minutes. The picture came in one copy and the process was therefore of limited use. The wet collodion process (1851) rendered the technique obsolete.

Dail Eireann, the name of the national parliament of the Irish Republic.

Dalai Lama, the temporal and religious leader of Tibet. The present Dalai Lama, Tenzin Gyabo (b. 1935), the 14th reincarnation, fled to India from Tibet in 1959. He was awarded the 1989 Nobel Peace Prize.

Damaskeening, the art of inlaying one metal upon another, largely practised in the East in medi-aeval times, in the decoration of sword blades.

Dandies, the name given to a class of exquisites prominent in early Victorian days, and who attracted attention by excessive regard for dress.

Danegeld, a tax imposed in England in Anglo-Saxon times to raise funds for resisting the Danes or to buy them off. Edward the Confessor abolished the tax, but it was revived by the Conqueror and subsequently retained, under another name, after the danger from the Danes was past. It is the basis of all taxation in this country. Domesday Book (*q.v.*) was originally drawn up for the purpose of teaching the State how to levy the tax.

Danelaw, the law enforced by the Danes in the kingdoms of Northumbria, East Anglia, and in the districts of the five (Danish) boroughs—lands grouped round Leicester, Nottingham, Derby, Stamford and Lincoln—which they occupied during the Viking invasions of the 9th and 10th cent. The country occupied was also called the Danelaw or Danelagh.

Darter, 1. Snakebirds, a genus of the pelican family, with long, pointed bill and serpent-like neck and resembling cormorants in appearance. There are 5 species. 2. Numerous species of small freshwater fish belonging to the perch family, found in N. America.

Date Palm. *Phoenix dactylifera,* one of the oldest known food plants widely cultivated in N. Africa and W. Asia. It grows to 30 m and continues to bear for 2 or 3 centuries, its fruit being of great value as a food. From the leaves the Africans make roofs for their huts; ropes are made from the fibrous parts of the stalks; and the sap furnishes a stimulating beverage.

Dauphin, the title borne by the eldest sons of the Kings of France from 1349 to 1830.

Day is the most natural unit of time and may be defined as the period of rotation of the earth relative to any selected heavenly body. Relative to the sun it is called the *solar day*. Relative to a fixed star it is called the *sidereal day*. Owing to irregularities in the earth's movements, the time taken for the earth to rotate through 360° relative to the sun is variable, and so the *mean solar day* of 24 hours has been introduced, which is the average throughout the year. The *mean solar day* is our standard, used for purposes of the calendar, and astronomers use *sidereal* clocks to check mean solar time. In practice, for conveniecence, the sidereal day is determined by the earth's rotation relative to the vernal equinox or first point of Aries, and is equal to 23 hours 56 minutes and 4·091 seconds of mean solar time (*i.e.*, about 4 minutes shorter than a solar day). *See* **Time.**

DDT (dichloro-dephenyl-trichloroethane). A very powerful insecticide which has had wide success in the control of diseases, such as malaria and typhus which are carried by insects. Mosquito swamps are sprayed with DDT to kill the carriers. Because this toxic chemical breaks down very slowly it builds up in birds and animals and its use is now banned in Britain. Its detection in Antarctic wild life confirmed that DDT pollution was virtually worldwide.

Deacon, an ecclesiastical official, who assists in some of the smaller ministerial duties in church or chapel; in the Anglican Church he ranks below a priest.

Dead Languages are such as the ancient Greek and Roman tongues, which are no longer spoken but are preserved in literature.

Dead Sea Scrolls, a group of ancient Jewish documents, consisting of scrolls and fragments which have been recovered since 1947 in the vicinity of Qumran near the Dead Sea and which represent one of the most important finds ever made in the field of biblical archaeology and Christian origins. The scrolls written in Hebrew or Aramaic, were found in caves, the first by chance by an Arab shepherd in 1947. These consisted of biblical texts older by a thousand years than the earliest Hebrew manuscript of the Old Testament (A.D. 895). Many fragments have since been discovered, comprising the whole of the Old Testament with the exception of Esther. In addition there are commentaries and other non-biblical writings, including one called "The War of the Sons of Light with the Sons of Darkness". The writing on the scrolls indicates that they were written over a period of two centuries, the greater proportion before the birth of Christ. A nearby ruin is believed to have been the home of a religious sect called the Essenes (**J18**), to whom the scrolls belonged. By the aid of the latest scientific techniques, including radiocarbon tests, the age of the scrolls is being accurately determined. An account of the scrolls and their implications is given in Edmund Wilson's *The Dead Sea Scrolls: 1947–1969*.

Dean, a Church of England dignitary, ranking below a bishop, and the head of the chapter of a cathedral. A rural Dean supervises a *deanery* or group of parishes. There are also Deans of Faculties in some universities, and at Oxford and Cambridge the Dean is in charge of chapel services and disciplinary arrangements.

Death Watch Beetle (*Xextobium rufovillosum*), a wood-boring beetle, larger than the common furniture beetle, found chiefly in the old oak beams of churches and other historic buildings. The grub bores from 4–12 years. The name "death watch" comes from the superstition that the ticking sound, made by the beetle striking its head against the wood, is a sign of approaching death. The death watch beetle found in the roof of Westminster Hall was smoked out by means of an insecticide called gamma benzine hexachloride. *See also* **Furniture Beetle, Woodworm.**

Decalogue, name given to the Ten Commandments of the Old Testament. There are two versions of them, differing in detail: Exodus xx. 2–17 and Deuteronomy v. 6–21. They are of Hebrew origin and are recognised by Jews and Chris- tians as the divine law given by God to Moses on Mt. Sinai. Most of them are prohibitions in contrast to the beatitudes (pronounced by Christ in the Sermon on the Mount) which are positive, *e.g.*, Blessed are the merciful.

December, the last month of the year in our calendar, and the tenth in the old Roman.

Deciduous Trees are such as shed their leaves at certain seasons as distinguished from evergreens or permanent foliaged trees or shrubs.

Declaration of Independence was an Act by which the American Congress, on 4 July 1776, declared the American colonies to be independent of Great Britain. "Independence Day" is a holiday in the United States.

Defender of the Faith (*Defensor Fidei*), a title conferred upon Henry VIII by Pope Leo X in 1521 for entering the lists against Luther with his pamphlet in defence of the Seven Sacraments. After Henry assumed headship of the Church of England the Pope withdrew the title but it was confirmed to him by Parliament in 1544 and has been used ever since by English monarchs.

Deflation is a policy designed to bring down costs by reducing the supply of means of payment. It is usually advocated as a remedy for inflation, and in this connection is nowadays more often referred to as monetarism. It usually results in a fall in employment. *See* **Section G.**

Dehydrate, to eliminate the water from a substance. The process of dehydration is now used in the food industry, as a result of wartime research, in making such things as dried egg and packet soups. Most vegetables contain over 90 per cent of water, and much of this can be removed under vacuum at low temperatures without appreciably impairing the flavour. The lightness of the dehydrated products is an advantage when supplies have to be transported.

Deliquescence, the process of dissolving by the absorption of moisture from the atmosphere. For instance, chromic acid crystals on exposure to the air quickly deliquesce.

Delta, a triangular tract of land between diverging branches of a river at its mouth, and so called from its general resemblance to the Greek letter Δ *delta*. The best-known examples are the deltas of the Nile, the Ganges, the Niger and the Mississippi.

Deluge, a flood, commonly applied to the story of the Deluge in the Bible, in which Noah and the Ark figure. A similar tradition lingers in the mythologies of all ancient peoples.

Democratic Party, one of the two great American political parties, originated about 1787, advocating restrictions on the federal governments and in opposition to the federalists. It was in 1825 that a group who were in favour of high tariffs seceded, later to become the Republican Party. The Democratic Party was split again over slavery before the Civil War (1861–65), and in the main the southern states have been supporters of the Democrats. The economic depression helped the Democrats to power in 1932 (*see* **New Deal**) and they held office until 1953 when Eisenhower became President. In 1960 Kennedy narrowly won the Presidency and in 1964 Lyndon Johnson swept in with a landslide victory over the Republican candidate. In 1968 and 1972 the Democratic candidates were beaten by Nixon. In 1976 Jimmy Carter won an easy victory, but since then the Democrats have lost three successive presidential elections (1980, 1984, 1988). The symbol of the party is a donkey, invented, like the Republican's elephant, by the cartoonist Thomas Nast.

Dendrite, a stone or mineral on or in which treelike tracery appears, the result of the action of the hydrous oxide of manganese.

Density, a measure of the mass per unit volume of a material, usually expressed in grams per cubic centimetre. *Specific gravity* is the ratio of the density of a material at the termperature under consideration to that of water at the temperature of its maximum density (4°C). In grams per cubic centimetre the density of gold is 19·3, silver 10·5, lead 11·3, water 0·99997, air 0·00129.

Depreciation of a currency is a fall in its relative value in terms of gold or of other currencies. The term is most often used to indicate a fall in the value of one country's money in relation to others. *See* **Section G.**

Depression, a region where barometric pressure is lower than that of its surroundings. These areas of low pressure are usually less extensive than anticyclones (*q.v.*) and may vary from hundreds to thousands of kilometres in diameter. The winds, often of gale force where the depression is deep, blow round the system in an anticlockwise direction in the Northern Hemisphere (in the reverse direction in the Southern Hemisphere). Well above the earth's surface the winds blow along rather than down the pressure gradient but near the surface, friction causes the winds to blow slightly (*c.* 15°) across the isobars. The depression exists only as long as more air diverges out of its upper parts than converges into its lower parts. The majority of depressions which cross the British Isles travel from the Atlantic, sometimes in series or families at rates from a few kilometres to a thousand kilometres a day, bringing their generally unsettled weather with them.

Desalination, the process of removing minerals, chiefly salt, from sea or brackish water to provide pure water for drinking or industry. Small-scale desalinisation by distillation has been practised for many years on ships and small islands. By the 1960s, many large-scale distillation plants were in operation, many of them in hot dry countries as in the Middle East. Kuwait, for example, used oil revenues to buy desalination plant and powers the plant with natural gas. As water for large population centres becomes more precious and desalinisation techniques more efficient, the process may be more and more used though it is expensive in capital outlay and in the cost of heating required to distil the water. Methods other than distillation are under investigation but not as yet much used.

Deserts, vast, barren, stone or sandy wastes where there is almost no rainfall and little or no vegetation. These regions are found in the interior of the continents Africa, Asia and America between 20° and 30° north and south of the equator. Europe is the only continent without deserts. The most famous are the Sahara, the largest in the world, the Gobi desert of central Asia, the Kalahari desert of south-west Africa and the great Australian desert. The marginal extension of deserts (desertification) is a topic of considerable debate. The increasing size of deserts is thought to result from either climatic change or the interference by man.

Detention Centres in Britain are for young people (boys and girls) over 14 but under 21 who have been found guilty of an offence for which an adult could be sent to prison. A rigorous regime of "Short Sharp Shock" was introduced by the Home Sec. in 1980 in some detention centres.

Determinism and Free-will. See **Section J.**

Deuterium or "heavy hydrogen". The second isotope of hydrogen; the third is called tritium. Deuterium atoms have in their nuclei a neutron as well as a proton; tritium nuclei have two neutrons and one proton. In ordinary hydrogen gas about one out of every 5,000 atoms is a deuterium atom. Deuterium was discovered in 1932 by Professor Harold Urey. The oxide of deuterium corresponding to water is called "heavy water". The nucleus of the deuterium atom is called a deuteron. An anti-deuteron consisting of anti-proton and anti-neutron was produced at Brookhaven in 1965, the first compound anti-nucleus ever to be produced.

Devaluation is a definite, official downward valuation of a country's currency in terms of its exchange value with other currencies. The £ was devalued in 1949, when an official exchange rate of £1 = \$2.8 was established, and again in 1967, to a rate of £1 = \$2.4. Since 1972 there has been greater flexibility in exchange rates and national currencies have been allowed to "float". See **Section G, Part IV.**

Devonian System in geology refers to the strata between the Silurian and the Carboniferous formations. It includes the Old Red Sandstone formation. The fauna of the Devonian include the group of fishes known as the Rhipidistra (on the evolutionary route towards the amphibians), Actinistia (coelacanth), and the Dipnoi or lung fishes. See **F48.**

Dew, moisture deposited by condensation of water vapour on exposed objects especially during calm, cloudless nights. The loss of heat from the ground after sunset, by radiation, causes the layer of atmosphere close to the surface to be chilled below the temperature, known as the dew-point, at which the air is saturated with vapour. Part of the vapour condensed may be transpired from blades of grass and foliage of plants.

Dew Pond is a shallow artificial pond which is on high ground and rarely dries up, even during prolonged droughts, despite being used by cattle and sheep as a drinking source. The name arose from the belief that dew deposits at night provided the moisture for replenishment. Drainage of rain-water and mist condensed on neighbouring trees and shrubs are probably more important factors.

Dialectical Materialism. See **Section J.**

Diamond, a mineral, one of the two crystalline forms of the element carbon (the other is graphite), the hardest known substance, used as a gem and in industry. India was the first country to mine diamonds (the Koh-i-noor, which means "mountain of light", known since 1304, came from Golconda near Hyderabad and came into British possession when the Punjab was annexed in 1849). The celebrated diamond mines of South Africa were discovered in the 1870s. Other important diamond producing countries are Zaïre, USSR, Congo, Ghana, Sierra Leone, Namibia, Angola, Tanzania. The world's biggest diamond is the 3,106-carat Cullinan, discovered near Pretoria, South Africa, in 1905. Diamonds can be made artificially by subjecting carbon to very high temperatures and pressures; many industrial diamonds are made this way. Antwerp is the main diamond centre of the world, London the main marketing centre, Amsterdam the main diamond cutting centre.

Diatoms. One-celled algae, common in fresh and salt water. Distinctive feature is the siliceous wall which is in two halves, one fitting over the other like the lid of a box. These walls are often very finely and beautifully sculptured. The diatoms constitute a class of the plant kingdom known as the Bacillariophyta. *Diatom ooze* is a deep-sea deposit made up of diatom shells. *Diatomite* or *diatomaceous earth* is the mineral form that such diatom oozes assume (sometimes known as kieselguhr which mixed with nitroglycerine yields dynamite).

Diesel Engine, an engine in which the liquid fuel is introduced into a compressed or partially compressed charge of air, and which does not need an extraneous source of ignition. The modern oil engine has been evolved mainly from the principles enunciated by Herbert Akroyd-Stuart in his patent of 1890 and, like the steam and other inventions, represents the improvements achieved by many men, including those by Rudolf Diesel of Germany, in respect of high compression pressures and greater fuel economy.

Diet, in German history, an assembly of dignitaries or delegates called together to debate upon and decide important political or ecclesiastical questions. The most famous imperial Diets were those held at Worms (1521), Speyer (1529), and Augsburg (1530), all of which dealt with matters of religious conflict arising from the Reformation.

Diffusion is the process of mixing which occurs when two liquids or gases are in contact. It is most rapid between gases, and, as laid down by Graham's law, "the rates of diffusion of different gases are in the inverse proportion to the square roots of their relative densities". Diffusion arises through the continual movement of molecules. Even in solids diffusion can occur. If a block of gold and a block of silver are welded together, after some time particles of gold are found in the silver, and *vice versa.*

Dimensions in common speech are the magnitudes of length, breadth and thickness giving, the size of an object, thus a line has only one dimension: length; a plane surface two: length and breadth; and a solid three: length breadth and thickness. In mathematics, hypothetical objects with any number of dimensions are considered. In physics and mechanics, dimensions are numbers which relate the units in which any quantity is measured to the so-called fundamental units. The latter are usually but not necessarily those of length, mass and time. "Dimensional analysis" is an important technique of scientific reasoning.

Dimorphism, the quality of assuming two distinct forms. For instance, carbon, which is graphite in one form, is the diamond in another.

Dinosaur, the name given to a group of extinct reptiles of the Mesozoic period, some of which were of immense size—much larger than crocodiles. See **Diplodocus.**

Dip Needle. Instrument for measuring the *dip* or inclination of the earth's magnetic field.

Diplodocus, one of the best known of the extinct mammoth dinosaurs. Fossil remains have been discovered in the Jurassic rocks of the United States. Some reached a length of over 24 m.

Dipnoi *or* **Lung Fishes.** These have the air bladder adapted to function as a lung, and they can remain alive when the stream or marsh in which they live dries up. Species of lung fish occur in Australia, Africa and S. America.

Diptera, an order of insects. Their main characteristic is that they are two-winged, and the common house-fly is the best-known example. There are at least 50,000 species of these insects, including gnats, blow-flies, mosquitoes, tsetses.

Diptych was a folding two-leaved tablet of wood, ivory, or metal, with polished inner surfaces, utilised for writing with the style by the ancient Greeks and Romans. The same term was applied to the tablets on which the names of the persons to be commemorated were inscribed in the early Church. In art any pair of pictures hinged together is styled a diptych, a set of three, a triptych.

Discus, a circular piece of metal or stone about 30 cm in diameter, used in athletic contests by the ancient Greeks and Romans. Throwing the discus was a very favourite game, which was deemed worthy of celebration in Myron's famous *Discobolus* (c. 460 B.C.–450 B.C.), the best copy of which is in Rome.

Disk, an astronomical term denoting the seemingly flat surface of celestial bodies as seen by the eye.

Distillation, a process used to separate liquids of different boiling points. This is effected by placing the mixture in a distillation apparatus and heating. The liquid with the lower boiling point distils over first, the vapour being condensed and collected, forming the first *fraction*. With continued heating the second liquid reaches its boiling point, distils over and the mixture is said to be *fractionated*. Mixtures of liquids with close very high boiling points require more elaborate apparatus. Fractional distillation is a common process in the chemical industry, particularly in the refining of petroleum.

Diwali, the festival of light, marking the triumph of good over evil, celebrated by Hindus, Sikhs and Jains. Sweets and gifts are exchanged.

DNA (Deoxyribonucleic acid), a polymer molecule in the form of a double-strand helix containing many thousands of sub-units. Contains the genetic information coded in sequences of sub units called bases. The Nobel Prize for medicine was awarded in 1962 for the discovery of the structure of DNA; that for 1968 for interpreting the genetic code and its function in protein synthesis. *See* **Nucleic Acids.**

Docks are enclosed water spaces where ships rest while being loaded or unloaded, repaired, or waiting for cargo. There are three main types: the wet dock in which water is maintained at the level of high tide so that vessels remain afloat while loading and unloading; the tidal dock, with open entrance to permit free ebb and flow of tide (*e.g.,* Glasgow, Southampton (which has double tides)); and the dry dock, or graving dock, for overhauling and repairing vessels, so constructed that, after a ship has been docked, the water can be drawn off (*e.g.,* Southampton, Tilbury). The floating dock is a type of dry dock. Technological advances in the handling of cargo, *e.g.,* containers (sealed boxes of cargo), have led to modernisation of the docks and labour practices.

Dodo, an extinct bird, giant and flightless, which lived on the island of Mauritius up until 250 years ago. Another species, the white dodo, lived on Réunion. Some reached exceptional sizes. By the end of the 17th cent. Mauritius, Rodriguez, and Réunion had all been colonised, and the dodo along with many other birds vanished forever because of their inability to stand up to man and the animals imported into the islands.

Dog-days, a period of 40 days (3 July–11 August) when Sirius rises and sets with the sun. The ancient superstition, which can be traced back in Greek literature to Hesiod (8th cent. B.C.), was that this star exercised direct influence over the canine race.

Doge, the chief magistrate in the former republics of Venice (697–1797) and Genoa (1339–1797, 1802–5).

Dogfish, a large family of small sharks, seldom more than 1 m in length. The flesh is sold as "rock salmon". The eggs are contained in horny cases called "mermaid's purses". The commonest of the British dogfishes are the spur-dogs.

Doldrums, a nautical term applied to those areas of the Atlantic and Pacific within a few degrees of the Equator towards which the trade winds blow and where the weather is calm, hot and sultry. Pressure is low and the air often rises to produce heavy tropical rainfall and squalls, rendering navigation difficult.

Dolomite, a name applied to a limestone containing appreciable magnesium; also the mineral dolomite, a double carbonate of magnesium and calcium.

Dolphin, a mammal of the whale order, from 2–2·4 m long, with a long, sharp snout, and of an active disposition. They abound in most seas and swim in shoals. A few species live in large rivers (Ganges and Amazon). They can cruise for long periods at around 15 knots and produce bursts of speed in the region of 20 knots, the water apparently flowing smoothly past their bodies. Dolphins are some of the most intelligent of mammals and are currently the subject of scientific experiments in communication. Name also for the fish, dorado.

Domesday Book is the famous register of the lands of England framed by order of William the Conqueror. According to Stowe, the name was derived from *Domus dei*, the name of the place where the book was deposited in Winchester Cathedral; though by others it is connected with doom in the sense of judgment. Its compilation was determined upon in 1085, in order that William might compute what he considered to be due to him in the way of tax from his subjects. William sent into each county commissioners to make survey. They were to inquire the name of each place, the possessor, how many hides of land were in the manor, how many ploughs were in demesne, how many homagers, villeins, cottars, serving men, free tenants, and tenants in soccage; how much wood, meadow, and pasture; the number of mills and fish ponds; what had been added to or taken away from the place; what was the gross value at the time of Edward the Confessor. So minute was the survey that the Saxon chronicler of the time reports "there was not a single hide, nor one virgate of land, nor even, it is shame to tell, though it seemed no shame to do, an ox, nor a cow, nor a swine was left that was not set down". The record, which did not take in Northumberland, Cumberland, Durham and parts of Lancashire and Westmorland, was completed in 1086, and was comprised in two volumes—one a large folio, sometimes called the Little Domesday, which deals with Essex, Norfolk and Suffolk, the other a quarto, sometimes called the Great Domesday. The first is written on 384 double pages of vellum in one and the same hand, and in a small but plain character, each page having a double column. The quarto is written on 450 pages of vellum, but in a single column and in a large, fair character. The original is preserved in the Public Record Office. *See also* **Danegeld.**

Dominicans, an order of mendicant preaching friars founded by St. Dominic in Languedoc in 1215 and confirmed by the Pope in 1216. The rule of the order was rigorous. The dress was a white habit and scapular with a long black mantle. This gave them the name of Black Friars. Their official name is Friars Preachers.

Donjon, the keep, or inner tower of a castle, and the strongest and most secure portion of the structure. This was the last refuge of the garrison, and there was usually a prison on the lower floor, hence the name *dungeon*.

Don Juan, the legendary hero of many famous works, supposedly based on the life and character of the unscrupulous gallant Don Juan Tenorio of 14th-cent. Seville. The first dramatisation of the legend and the most famous is Tirso de Molina's *El Burlador de Sevilla*. Don Juan was also the subject of Molière's *Le Festin de Pierre*, Mozart's *Don Giovanni*, Byron's *Don Juan*, and José Zorilla's *Don Juan Tenorio*. The latter is played on All Saints' Day throughout Spanish-speaking countries.

Don Quixote, the "knight of the doleful countenance", the hero and title of Cervantes' classic novel of 16th-cent. Spain. Don Quijote de la Mancha, a gentle country gentleman of lofty but unpractical ideals, having read many chivalric romances, believes he is called upon to redress the wrongs of the world. Mounted on his nag Rosinante and accompanied by his companion Sancho Panza, a hard-headed and practical peasant, he sets out on his journeys of knight-errantry.

Dormouse, a family of small, squirrel-like rodents widely distributed throughout Europe and Asia, and living mainly on fruit and nuts. It is of nocturnal habits and sleeps through the winter.

Dot, a French term indicating the property which a wife brings to her husband on marriage and is usually settled on the woman, being her separate property, though the income from it may go towards the general household expenses.

Dotterel, a handsome bird of the plover family found in northern Europe and Siberia. Nests in the Cairngorms, the Grampians and E. Ross. Very tame.

Doukhobors. *See* **Section J.**

Drachm (or Drachma), an ancient Greek silver coin and weight. One drachma was equivalent to six obols. The word has survived as the name of a weight: Avoirdupois, one-sixteenth part of an ounce; Apothecaries' Weight, one-eighth part of an ounce.

Drag. Term used in mechanics for resistance offered by a fluid to the passage of a body moving through it. When speed of sound is reached drag increases abruptly. The lift/drag ratio gives the aeroplane designer his measure of aerodynamic efficiency.

Dragon, a fabulous monster common to folk-lore in most countries; generally represented as a winged reptile with fiery eyes and breath of flame. A dragon guarded the garden of the Hesperides; in the New Testament there is mention of the "dragon, that old serpent, which is the devil"; St. George, England's patron saint, is supposed to have overcome the dragon; mediaeval legend abounds in dragons; in heraldry the dragon has also a conspicuous place; and in China it was the imperial emblem.

Dragonet, the name of the fish of the *Callionymus* genus, beautifully coloured, and about 30 cm in length. They are common on the British coast and in the Mediterranean.

Dragon Fly, the common name of a well-known order of insects having two pairs of membraneous wings, and often of very brilliant colours. They are swift of flight and may be seen hovering over sheets of water in the sunshine all through the summer. Their chief food is mosquitoes.

Dragon's Blood, a dark-red resinous substance obtained from the fruit of a Malay palm, and possessing medicinal virtues. In a special technique used for making line blocks in printing, dragon's blood is used.

Drawbridge, a bridge that can be lifted up so that no passage can be made across it. It was a usual feature of a fortified castle in the Middle Ages, and was raised or lowered by chains and levers. It spanned the fosse, and on the approach of an attacking party was raised and formed a special barricade to the gate. Modern drawbridges are such as are raised to allow of the passage of boats up and down a river or estuary. The Tower Bridge is a famous London bridge of this type.

Drongo. The King Crow or Indian Black Drongo is frequently seen in India perched on branches or telegraph wires, darting suddenly to catch insects and to attack crows and hawks. Other members of the family are found in Asia, Africa and Australia. Its plumage is black with steel-blue gloss.

Drosophila or **Fruit Fly.** More has been learnt by geneticists from breeding experiments with this insect than with any other.

Dross, the name generally applied to the refuse of molten metal, composed of slag, scales and cinders.

Drought occurs when there has been an absence of rain for a long period or a marked deficiency of precipitation over a much longer period in a climatic zone where precipitation is ordinarily adequate for vegetation or agriculture, river flow and water supplies. It is different from aridity which refers to the extreme dryness of desert or arid regions where rainless periods characterise the climate. Hitherto in the British Isles "an absolute drought" was defined as "a period of at least 15 consecutive days without measurable rainfall", but arbitrary definitions of this type are not now normally used. In the British Isles droughts occur from time to time but very long rainless spells at a place are rather rare. The longest recorded spell in the British Isles with no measurable daily rainfall lasted 61 days at Liss (Hants) from 16 March to 15 May 1893. Over the country as a whole the 12-month period beginning 1 May 1975 was the driest such period since records began, with less than 60 per cent. of normal precipitation in parts of the Midlands and S.W. England.

Druidism. See **Section J.**

Drupe is the scientific term for stone fruit. The stone forms the inner part (endocarp) of the fruit, and encloses a seed or kernel which is liberated after the flesh part (pericarp) has rotted.

Dry-rot, the term was first used about 1775 to describe the fungal decay of timber in buildings. Creosote distilled from coal tar is the standard material for preservation of timber, and penta-chlorophenol and copper naphthenate are two compounds now extensively used. Dry wood always escapes dry-rot. Chief fungi causing dry-rot are *Merulius* and *Poria.*

Duck, water bird smaller than the related goose and swan, which together form the family Antidae. Duck refers to the female, drake to the male. The duck family falls into two separate groups: the river or freshwater (surface feeding) ducks, such as the mallard, pintail, wigeon, shoveler, mandarin, teal, garganey; and the sea (diving) ducks, such as the goldeneye, pochard, scoter, eider, and the fish-eating mergansers or "sawbills". The ancestor of all domestic breeds, with the exception of the muscovy, is the mallard.

Duckbill, *Ornithorhynchus anatinus,* also duck-billed platypus, a fur-covered, egg-laying, nest-building mammal inhabiting Australia and Tasmania. It has webbed feet and a muzzle like a duck's bill and is about 50 cm long.

Ductility is a property possessed by most metals which renders them capable of being stretched without breaking. Gold is the most, and lead the least ductile of metals, the order being gold, silver, platinum, iron, copper, palladium, aluminium, zinc, tin, lead. In animated nature the spider and the silkworm produce secretions of notable ductility.

Dugong. A marine mammal, belonging to the order Sirenia (sea-cows). Inhabits Red Sea and Indian Ocean; also found as far East as the Philippines and Australia. Lives on sea-weed. Related to the Manatee.

Duke, the highest rank in the British peerage. Edward, the Black Prince, eldest son of Edward III, who died before his father, was the first English duke, being created Duke of Cornwall in 1337. Since then all Princes of Wales have held that title.

Dukeries, a stretch of English woodland and park country, mainly in Nottinghamshire, comprising the adjacent demesnes of several English dukes and nobles. The Dukeries include Sherwood Forest and the estates of Welbeck Abbey, Clumber Park, Worksop Manor and Thoresby Hall.

Dunes. Sand dunes are elliptical or crescent-shaped mounds of loose sand produced by wind action. The dune has a gentle slope on windward side; a steep slope on the leeward side.

Dunlin, very common small wading-bird of the Sandpiper family nesting in Britain. Its range extends to other areas where it also breeds.

Dunmow Flitch, a custom which originated in the parish of Little Dunmow, Essex, in the reign of Henry III, which was that the husband who was prepared to swear before the prior, convent, and townsfolk of Dunmow that he had not repented of marriage or quarrelled with his wife for a year and a day, should be rewarded with the gift of a flitch of bacon. The custom has frequently been revived.

Dunnock (*Prunella modularis*), a small bird of rich brown and dark grey plumage common in gardens and hedgerows. Sings a cheerful song all the year round. Called hedge-sparrow in southern England. Another member of the same family, the larger Alpine Accentor (*Prunella collaris*), is found on rocky mountain slopes of Europe and Asia.

Duodecimo, a sheet of paper folded into twelve leaves, written "12mo".

Durbar, a term used in India from the Persian word *darbár* meaning "court" or "audience". It may be either a council for administering affairs of state, or a purely ceremonial gathering. The word was applied to great ceremonial gatherings like Lord Lytton's durbar for the proclamation of the Queen-Empress in 1877 and the Delhi durbar of 1911.

Dust, solid particles of matter floating in the atmosphere, produced chiefly by volcanic eruptions, sand-storms in desert regions, and industrial and domestic smoke. When the island of Krakatoa erupted in 1883, more than 4 km² of dust was thrown into the air and carried three times round the earth by the explosive wave. The particles in dust-storms are much finer than those in sand-storms and are swept up to far greater heights. The local whirlwinds which form over loose dry soils are termed dust-devils.

Dyke. A wall-like intrusion of igneous rock

which cuts across the bedding or other layered structure of the country rock; the word also signifies in alternative usage, a sea-wall and an open drain.

Dynamite, a powerful explosive whose chief element is nitro-glycerine. It was discovered by Nobel in 1867, who absorbed nitro-glycerine in kieselguhr; has a disruptive force of about eight times that of gunpowder.

Dynamo. Machine for transforming mechanical energy into electrical energy. Depends on principle of electromagnetic induction whereby a current is produced in a conductor (e.g., copper wire) traversing a magnetic field. The two essential parts of a dynamo are the conductors or armature and the field magnets.

Dynasty, a succession of monarchs of the same family, as the Carolingian dynasty, the Bourbon dynasty, the Plantagenet dynasty, etc.

E

Eagle, large bird of prey with huge hooked bill, related to the buzzard, kite, hawk, harrier, falcon and vulture, together forming the family Falconidae. There are many species to be found throughout the world, the Golden, Imperial, Tawny, Spotted and Lesser Spotted being found in Europe. The Golden Eagle, a magnificent-looking bird, nests in the Scottish Highlands, and the White-tailed Sea Eagle, which used to breed in Britain, is now only an occasional visitor. The eagle has been the symbol of royal power since the earliest times, and the American or Bald Eagle is the emblem of the United States.

Earl, a British title of nobility of the third rank, duke and marquis coming first and second. The title dates from Saxon times, and until 1337 ranked highest in our peerage.

Earl-Marshal, in England ranks as the eighth of the great officers of state, is head of the College of Arms, attends the sovereign in opening and closing the session of Parliament, arranges state processions (especially coronations) and assists in introducing newly created peers in the House of Lords. The office is hereditary in the family of the Dukes of Norfolk.

Earth, our habitable globe, is the third of the planets of the solar system in order from the sun and on an average throughout the year takes 24 hours to turn completely round relative to the sun, the whole earth revolving round the sun in a slightly elliptical orbit once in a year of 365·2564 days. The mean distance of the earth from the sun is 149,597,900 km. Recent earth satellite studies have shown that small variations of the surface gravity field (or geoid) occur which are believed to be related more to the structures deep within the earth's mantle than to the location and dimension of crustal features, such as oceans, continents and mountain ranges. The crust consists of a skin, 30 km thick under the continents, but only about 6–8 km thick under the ocean bed, comprised of rocks and sediments or soil. At the base of the crust is a sharp discontinuity (the Mohorovičić Discontinuity) to denser rocks of the mantle. This region, nearly 3,000 km thick, is in a process of slow but inexorable change, one of convection responding to heat sources (due mainly to radioactivity of the materials within the earth). This slow convection is responsible for many changes in the surface of the earth—continental drift (q.v.), earthquakes and volcanic activity. The core is a region of very high density and temperature, comprised of heavy elements such as iron and nickel. The crustal rocks are mainly comprised of oxygen, silicon, aluminium, sodium, potassium, iron, calcium and magnesium, with traces of many other elements. The mass of the earth is about 6,000 million million million tonnes, and it was formed about 4,600 million years ago. The earth has one natural satellite, the moon. See also **F8–10.**

Earthquake, a sudden violent disturbance of the earth's crust; the region of the surface immediately above the "focus", or source where the earthquake originates, is termed the "epi-

centre". On account of their destructive power earthquakes have attracted attention from the earliest times, but accurate study dates only from the last century and the development of a world-wide network of recording stations from the present one. The majority of severe earthquakes result from fractures, usually along existing faults, in underlying rock strata subjected to great strains, the shearing movement sometimes extending to the surface. These dislocations set up vibrations which are propagated as waves throughout the bulk of the earth or round the crust. Frequently the main shock is followed by a series of smaller aftershocks. Minor local earthquakes may be attributed to the effects of volcanic activity, but most of the larger ones originate in non-volcanic regions along well-marked lines of weakness in the earth's crust. Generally the ground is felt to tremble, undergoing oscillations which may gradually or suddenly increase to a maximum and accompanied by sounds. When there is movement of the sea-bed a tsunami (q.v.) may result. One of the greatest of historic times was that which destroyed and flooded Lisbon in 1755. Among the notable shocks of the present century rank those of San Francisco (1906), Messina, Italy (1908), China (1920), Japan (1923), Napier, New Zealand (1931), Ionian Is. (1953), Morocco (1960), Chile (1960), Iran (1962), Yugoslavia (1963), Alaska (1964), E. Turkey (1966), W. Sicily (1968), Peru (1970), China (1976), S. Italy and North Africa (1980), N.E. Turkey (1983), Mexico (1985) Armenia (1988), and Romania, (May 1990). The most devastating earthquake in recorded history hit Shanxi (China) in 1556, killing 830,000 people. See also **Richter Scale** and **F9(2).**

Earthworm, of which there are several species, has a cylindrical body, tapering at both ends and segmented into rings. It moves by contraction of its rings, aided by retractive bristles; is eyeless, but has a mouth, gullet and stomach. Earthworms exist in immense numbers, and perform an important part in the scheme of nature by loosening the soil and rendering it more amenable to tillage. They also form a valuable food for birds and many mammals, and are unequalled as bait for certain kinds of fish.

Earwig, a genus of insects possessing two pairs of wings and anal forceps. It is nocturnal, lives on vegetable matter, and hides by day under stones or in flowers, e.g., dahlias. The old belief that it deliberately creeps into people's ears is altogether unfounded.

Easter, the annual Christian festival in commemoration of the resurrection of Christ, the English name being derived from Eostre, goddess of Spring. The date cannot fall earlier than 22 March nor later than 25 April. Many disputes arose among the early Christians as tt the proper time to celebrate this day which governs all other movable feasts. It was eventually ruled at the Council of Nicaea in 325 that Easter Day should be the first Sunday after the full moon following the vernal equinox. If this happens to be a Sunday, then Easter Day is the Sunday after. See also **Section Z.**

Eastern bloc, Communist states of eastern Europe, including the Warsaw Pact countries as well as Albania and Yugoslavia.

Eastern Front, the battlefront between Russia and Germany in both World Wars.

Eastern Question, a term formerly applied to the problems arising from the instability of the Mohammedan power of Turkey and its relations with the other nations of Europe. Later connected with other problems of the Near East such as the possession of Constantinople and the position of the Balkan states.

East India Company was incorporated by Elizabeth in 1600. In 1613 the Company set up a factory at Surat, India, and in 1662 Bombay came under the Company's influence and developed into an important trading port. Dupleix wanted to establish French power in India and a struggle for supremacy took place. Clive gained the victory for England and thenceforward British dominion in India remained undisputed except by native princes. In 1772 Warren Hastings was appointed the first Governor-General and in 1784 Pitt's India Act established a Board of Control for the India Company. A great

EAU-ELD

L 38

GENERAL INFORMATION

increase of trade resulted, and this rule continued down to 1858, when, as a result of the mutiny, the Crown assumed the sovereignty. With the passing of the Indian Independence Act of 1947, British dominion ended.

Eau-de-Cologne, a popular distilled perfume first manufactured at Cologne in the 18th cent. by Johann Maria Farina, an Italian, and since made in large quantities in Cologne and elsewhere.

Ebony, a name applied to various hard black woods, the best of which are grown in Mauritius and Sri Lanka. There are also Indian and American varieties. Only the inner portions, the heartwood, of the trees are of the necessary hardness and blackness. Ebony is largely used in ornamental cabinet work, for piano keys, canes, etc.

Ecce Homo ("Behold the Man!"), used in reference to the pictures and sculptures representing Christ crowned with thorns.

Ecclesiastical Courts, courts for administering ecclesiastical law and maintaining the discipline of the Church of England. Introduced by the Normans. Originally they had jurisdiction over both clergy and laity.

Eclipse, the partial or complete obscuring of one heavenly body by another. An eclipse of the sun occurs when the moon, which is 1/400th of the diameter of the sun and about 1/390th as far away, obscures some portion of the sun as seen by an observer on the earth. A total eclipse occurs when the whole of the sun's disc is covered by the moon. Astronomers travel many thousands of miles to observe the outer layers of the sun and its corona, which is only possible when the light from the sun is totally obscured by the moon during the few minutes of an eclipse. The total solar eclipse of 7 March 1970, as seen from Mexico, was watched by millions on their television screens. Total solar eclipses have occurred over parts of the British Isles in the years 1424, 1433, 1598, 1652, 1715, 1724, 1927, 1954 (visible from the Shetland Is.), and the next will be seen only from near Land's End on 11 August 1999. *See also* **Z11.**

Ecliptic is the sun's apparent path in the sky: the great circle described by the sun from west to east in the course of a year. The sun is exactly on the equator on approx. 21 March, and 23 September, and the points where the celestial equator and ecliptic intersect on these days are called the *equinoctial points.* On approx. 21 June and 22 December the sun reaches its greatest and least midday elevation and its greatest distance north and south of the equator, and the points on the ecliptic on these days are called the *solstices* (*see* **Seasons, Section Z**). These four points are equidistant from each other by 90°. The angle of the ecliptic to the earth's equator is called the obliquity of the ecliptic. Due to the gravitational perturbations of the other planets, both the equinoctial point and the obliquity of the ecliptic change with time. The present value of the obliquity is about 23·5.

Ecology, a term first described by the German biologist Haeckel in the 19th cent., is the study of the inter-relationships between living organisms and their environment. **Autecology** is the study of the environmental relationships of *individual* plants and species. **Synecology** is the study of plant and animal *communities* living together as groups and the relationship of these to their environment. Since 1935 the ecosystem has been the major unit of study in synecology. *See also* **F44–7** and **Section Y.**

Ecumenical Council, a general council of the Christian Church summoned when important questions of Church doctrine and policy are to be decided. The early councils were predominantly Greek and convoked by the emperor. Those summoned by the pope when they meet at the Lateran Palace in Rome are called Lateran Councils; others have met at Constance, Florence, Trent and the Vatican. Their decisions are not binding on the rest of Christendom. Only 21 Ecumenical Councils have been held in the history of Christendom. The first was held at Nicaea in 325 when the mystery of the Trinity was defined. The 21st (known as the 2nd Vatican Council), convened by Pope John, opened in October 1962 in St. Peter's, Rome, and ended in December 1965. Two of

the principal themes were the reunion of all Christians with the Church of Rome and the Church's place in the modern world. At the last session of the Council the Pope announced his decision to establish for the first time an international synod of bishops in Rome for consultation and collaboration in the government of the Roman Church. This Senate of Bishops provides the balancing factor alongside the Curia, which represents the Papacy and not the episcopacy.

Edda, the name given to two important collections of early Icelandic literature—*the Elder or Poetic Edda,* poems handed down from the 9th and 10th cent., probably Norwegian in origin, and the *Younger* or *Prose Edda* of Snorri Sturluson compiled about 1230. They treat of mythical and religious legends of an early Scandinavian civilisation.

Eddystone Lighthouse, 21 km south of Plymouth, is one of the most isolated in the world. The tower is 51 m high, and its light can be seen for 28 km. The present structure is the fourth that has occupied this dangerous position. The first was of wood, completed by Winstanley in 1698, but it was destroyed by storm in 1703. In 1708 a second and stronger lighthouse was built by Rudyerd. This lasted until 1755, when it was destroyed by fire. Smeaton built the third lighthouse of granite and this withstood storm and tempest for over a hundred years, 1759–1881. The present lighthouse, also of granite, was built 1879–81 on a nearby rock by Sir James Douglass.

Eels, edible fishes of the order Apodes, with snakelike body covered with minute scales embedded in the skin. The common or freshwater eel *Anguilla anguilla* is found in the Atlantic coastal areas of N. America and Europe and in the Mediterranean, and breeds S.E. of Bermuda. The electric eel of S. America is a variety of great interest, being able to cause electric shocks.

Egghead, a term used derogatively to describe the more intelligent and thoughtful people. Frequently applied in USA to the late Adlai Stevenson, who is said to have responded with the appeal: "Eggheads of the world unite. You have nothing to lose but your brains."

Egret, a slender, graceful bird of the heron family, of pure white plumage, famed for its beautiful silky plumes (aigrettes), which appear in the breeding season, and for which it was ruthlessly hunted and would have been exterminated had not international action been taken to protect it. The Little Egret with black bill, black legs, and yellow feet breeds in Mediterranean lands.

Eider, a large diving duck, found along the rocky coasts of northern latitudes, well known for the beautifully warm soft down, called "eider down", which the female bird plucks from her breast to line her nest. In Norway and Iceland the haunts of the eider are preserved and the birds protected by law on account of the much prized "eider down", which is collected from the nests just before the breeding season. "Eider down" is so elastic that a kilogram of it will fill an ordinary bed covering.

Eiffel Tower, built by the French engineer Alexandre Gustave Eiffel (1832–1923) for the Paris Exhibition of 1889. The tower which is made of iron is 300 m high and weighs about 7,000 tonnes.

Eisteddfod (a sitting) was originally a congress of Welsh bards and minstrels, and dates from before the 12th cent. These assemblies, discontinued for a long period, were resumed in 1819, and have been held yearly since, each lasting three or four days. Their object is to foster the Welsh patriotic spirit; they are devoted to orations and competitions in poetry, singing and harp-playing, prizes being awarded to the successful contestants.

Eland, largest species of antelope, native of Africa; large pointed horns, stands 1·5 m high at the withers, and weighs several hundred kg.

Elder, small trees of the *Sambucus* genus, with pinnate leaves, and clusters of white flowers and, later, small purplish-black berries. The black elder, the best known, is common in most parts of Europe, and thrives in Britain. A wine is made from its berries.

El Dorado, a "golden land", was an idea much favoured in the days of the early Spanish explorers. It was believed that somewhere on the South American continent there was a country abounding in gold and precious stones. Many expeditions were fitted out to discover it. Sir Walter Raleigh also went forth on this illusive quest. The term is still used in regard to any place of rich promise.

Eleatics. See **Section J.**

Electret, a piece of solid matter which retains a permanent electric polarisation analogous to the magnetic polarisation of a permanent magnet. There are various recipes for making them; carnauba wax is a common constituent.

Electricity. See **F21,** also **Energy Conversion.**

Electric Telegraph may be said to date from 1836, when Sir Charles Wheatstone and his co-inventor Cooke introduced their Single-Needle instrument, which was soon followed by the Double-Needle apparatus, Morse, in 1837, invented his famous recording instrument. The first electric cable was between Dover and France, and was laid in 1850. The first Atlantic cable was laid in 1858, and the second in 1866. It was in 1899 that the first Marconi wireless telegraph messages were sent between England and France.

Electroencephalograph, an instrument which records the minute voltages produced by the electrical activity of the brain by means of electrodes taped to the scalp. The record of brain waves, known as EEG, shows that there is a general cycle of activity in the brain that underlies both sleep and wakefulness.

Electrolysis is the condition established when an electric current passes through a conducting substance, between electrodes, resulting in decomposition and separation into constituents. Water thus becomes decomposed into hydrogen and oxygen.

Electromagnetic waves. See **F14.**

Electron. See **F11, 16.**

Electronic Music, music composed of electronically generated sound, recorded on tape and played through loudspeakers. Modern technical developments mean that in theory, and to a large extent in practice, a composer can generate and record *any* sequence of sounds he likes, varying at will pitch, intensity, reverberation, rhythm, intervals and all other audible qualities. Such limitless freedom of choice imposes on him severe problems of selection, notation and intellectural and artistic organisation. Though widely composed and performed, *i.e.*, played through loudspeakers or broadcast, electronic m sic as an art form must still be regarded as experimental and controversial, though its use as' incidental or "atmospheric" music in radio and television is well established. Among the well-known composers are Babbitt, Berio, Koenig and Stockhausen.

Electronic News Gathering (ENG), also known in the United States as Electronic Journalism (EJ) or Electronic Camera Coverage (ECC), is a system for obtaining television pictures by means of very lightweight, portable electronic cameras. ENG is highly suited to the coverage of news events. It is usually operated by a crew of two—cameraman and engineer—who are also equipped with a van or field car serving as a mobile base. Pictures from the unit can be used in three ways: they can be transmitted "live", beamed back by radio link to the studio, or recorded on to a videotape cassette on site and taken back to headquarters for editing and transmission. The chief advantage of ENG lies in its speed, as the use of electronic equipment avoids the delay which occurs in the chemical processing of film before it can be transmitted.

Electronics. The science which deals with the behaviour and control of free electrons. It started with the discovery of the electron by Sir J. J. Thomson in 1897. The practical applications, constituting electronic engineering, have given us radio, radar, photo-electric cells, cathode-ray oscillographs, electronic microscopes, television. Nowadays electronics uses devices like transistors such that the electrons move inside solid matter instead of *in vacuo*. This is sometimes referred to as "solid state electronics". See also **Microelectronics.**

Electron Microscope. A microscope in which beams of electrons are focused by magnetic lenses in a manner analogous to the focusing of light beams in the ordinary optical micro-

scope. Modern electron microscopes have very high resolving power and can magnify up to 1,500,000 times, making it possible to explore the cell and the virus. A development of the electron microscope is the scanning electron microscope (stereoscan), developed at Cambridge, which can examine an essentially thick object, giving a very large depth of focus.

Electronvolt, unit of energy used in nuclear physics. It is the amount of energy required to move one electronic charge through a potential difference of one volt. It is very small—$1·6 \times 10^{19}$ joules—and therefore suited to atomic physics. 1 MeV = a million electronvolts; 1 GeV = a thousand million electronvolts; these larger units are used in high energy physics.

Elementary Particle, one of the basic constituents of the material universe. The idea that matter consists of tiny particles goes back to classical times but the modern concept of the atom grew out of the chemistry and physics of the 19th cent. With the discovery of the electron in 1897 and the rise of nuclear physics in the 20th cent., the chemical atom was understood to be a structure built of even more fundamental particles—the electron, the proton and the neutron. In the last few decades, many more particles have been discovered, especially in the study of cosmic rays and by the use of large accelerating machines like those at CERN (Geneva) and Brookhaven National Laboratory (Long Island, New York). Among the later discoveries are the neutrino, the positron, the antiproton, the muon, the pion. These differ in electric charge and mass and other intrinsic properties and many have only a very short lifetime before they change into something else. Whether there is a small number of really elementary particles out of which all the others can be constructed is an unanswered question of contemporary physics. See **F15-17.**

Elements. In chemistry, substances which cannot be separated into two or more simpler chemical substances. 91 elements are found naturally on the earth, some are observed spectroscopically in the stars and planets, and a further fourteen have been made artificially. Between them these elements can appear in some 1,200 different isotopes, of which 317 occur in Nature. (There are 274 stable isotopes among 81 stable elements.) See **F6, F23,** and **F64.**

Elephant, a proboscidian mammal of which only two species survive—the Asiatic, in India, and the African elephant. No other animals possess a trunk. Both males and females have large ivory tusks, of considerable commercial value. The Indian elephant is usually about 2·7 m high and weighs about 3 tonnes; African elephants are larger, weighing about 6 tonnes, and are usually much fiercer. Several fossil elephants are still larger bulk have been discovered, including the mammoth and the mastodon. The Indian elephant is domesticated and used as a beast of burden, and may live 70 years. Concern had mounted by 1990, that, with 70,000 elephants slaughtered annually for their ivory, the elephant would be extinct in the wild within ten years. Demand for ivory is greatest in Hong Kong, Japan and the Middle East.

Eleusinian Mysteries, festivals common throughout ancient Greece, agricultural in their symbolism.

Elgin Marbles, a collection of ancient Greek sculptures and architectural fragments got together by the 7th Earl of Elgin and brought to England between 1802 and 1812. These celebrated treasures had originally formed part of the Parthenon at Athens, and were probably carved by pupils of the sculptor Phidias. Lord Elgin expended over £70,000 upon them, and they were purchased for £35,000 for the British Museum, where they can now be seen displayed.

Elk, the largest animal of the deer family, possessing enormous antlers, and standing, when mature, about 2 m high. The American moose is of the same family.

Elm, a stately, wide-spreading tree having some 20 species spread over north-temperate regions, several of which are native and peculiar to Britain. The grandest of the field elms is the English elm, *Ulmus procera,* which may reach a height of *c.* 42 m and a girth of 8 m. The wych elm, *U. glabra,* or Scots elm, is a valuable hardwood and used in boat-building. The fungus that causes Dutch elm disease is carried from tree to tree by a bark beetle. The fungus came from infected veneer logs from central Europe. Ironically the disease was named after the Dutch workers who discovered its cause!

Elzevir, the name of a celebrated family of Dutch printers, who produced editions of Latin, French and German classics, which were highly valued for their beauty of type and accuracy of printing. They flourished in the 17th cent.

Ember-days are set apart for fasting and prayer in the Western Church, at the periods appointed for ordination, viz., the Wednesday, Friday and Saturday after the first Sunday in Lent, Whit-Sunday, 14 September (Holy Cross Day), and 13 December (St. Lucia's Day); of very ancient origin.

Embossing, the art of stamping in relief, letters or designs upon pliant substances.

Emerald. The rich green variety of beryl (beryllium aluminium silicate). The colour is due to the presence of chromium oxide.

Empire, the style created in France during the reign of Napoleon in architecture and all the arts. It is austerely classical, making much use of columns, pediments and the like in buildings as well as furniture, with eagles and sphinxes, reminiscent of Napoleon's campaigns, as ornaments. The style is heavy, grandiose and with a strong element of the heroic. A typical monument is the *Arc de Triomphe* in Paris (begun 1806), almost a repetition of a Roman model. In painting Jacques Louis David interpreted the style with heroic subjects taken from classical mythology or from Napoleon's career. The style was transmitted to the rest of Europe, remaining magnificent and rich at all the Bonaparte courts. In bourgeois surroundings in Germany and Scandinavia it became simple and domesticated but retained its essence of classical dignity.

Encaenia, a festival commemorating a dedication; at Oxford University the annual commemoration of benefactors, accompanied by the conferring of honorary degrees, is held in June.

Encyclical Letters, a term used in reference to letters addressed by the Pope to his bishops upon matters of doctrine or discipline.

Encyclopaedists, a term first applied to the eminent writers who collaborated in the French *Encyclopédie* (1751-65). They included Diderot, D'Alembert, Voltaire, Helvetius; their writings generally were sceptical as to religion, destructive as to politics and had great influence in popularising the social ideas which afterwards resulted in the French Revolution.

Energy. One of the most fundamental concepts of science. A body in motion possesses *kinetic energy* as a result of the *work* done by the forces creating the motion. But a force which does work to stretch a spring does not create motion. Instead, the work is stored up in the spring and is one example of *potential energy*. A raised body also possesses potential energy which turns into kinetic when the body falls. The *heat energy* contained in a body is the sum of the kinetic and potential energy of the constituent atoms which are vibrating all the time. Heat and motion are obtainable from electrical, magnetic, chemical, atomic, and other sources, and physicists therefore define corresponding forms of energy. The vital point is that all forms of energy are transferable into one another *without loss or gain*. This is the Law of Conservation of Energy. It is one of the most fundamental laws of science, and its general validity is the reason why energy is an important idea. Since Einstein, it has been recognised that mass also is interchangeable with energy. See **F18,** *also* **Nuclear Energy.**

Energy Conversion. For practical purposes it is frequently necessary to change energy from one into another of its many forms; indeed almost every activity does this in one way or another. The primary sources of energy are the sun, uranium and other elements from which nuclear energy can be drawn, and the tides. The sun is not much used *directly* because its heat is intermittent and not very intense, but solar cookers and refrigerators have been invented and solar batteries (*q.v.*) are used in spacecraft. The sun can be used *indirectly* because it has produced, *via* living processes, fossil fuels like coal and oil and still continues to generate winds, rain and rivers and hence

hydroelectric and wind power. Commonly both fossil fuels and the energy of river or tidal waters are converted into electricity. Windmill type electricity generators are also quite common. The bulk of electricity production is a two-stage process: first fossil or nuclear fuel is used to create heat (*see* **Nuclear Reactors**); then the heat is used to raise steam and drive generators. Efforts are being made to convert heat into electricity more directly, *e.g.*, by using thermoelectric or thermionic effects (*q.v.*), but these have not been used for large-scale production. Once electrical energy is available, factories can make chemical batteries in great numbers and these can then be used as portable energy sources, as can petrol and other refined forms of fossil fuel. See **Battery, Fuel Cell, Solar Battery.**

Engraving is the art of cutting or otherwise forming designs of pictures on wood, stone, or metal surfaces for reproduction by some method of printing. Wood-engraving was the earliest in the field, dating from the 15th cent. Later, engraving on steel and copper plates was introduced, and mezzotint, lithography, stipple, aquatint, etc. Most modern methods of reproduction are based on photography.

Entablature, that portion of a building which surmounts the columns and extends to the roof of the tympana of the pediments; it comprises the architrave, the frieze and the cornice.

Enthalpy, another name for the heat content (H) of a system in thermodynamics. If a system generates heat it is presumed that the heat comes from the enthalpy of the system which by the 1st law of thermodynamics (**F20**) thus falls. It can be combined with the entropy (S) in an equation which defines the important thermodynamic quantity called the Gibbs Free Energy: $G = H - TS$ where T is the thermodynamic temperature. G is important in the prediction of chemical change (**F20**).

Entropy, one of the most important quantities in thermodynamics, symbol S. According to Clausius' statement of the Second Law (**F20**) the entropy of an isolated system cannot decrease. Although introduced by Clausius it arose from a consideration of Carnot's studies of the limitation of the convertibility of heat into work. It is most easily viewed as disorder in the statistical approach introduced by Boltzmann. This may be illustrated by considering the separate sets of coloured balls in a box. This is an ordered arrangement (of low entropy). The natural tendency is for the balls to mix and for the colours to become disordered (of higher entropy). We do not expect the opposite process for the balls to spontaneously separate, *i.e.*, we do not expect the entropy to decrease. In the context of energy changes, say in heat engines, the entropy change is equal to the heat change divided by the (thermodynamic) temperature (*see* **L3**).

Enzymes. Organic catalysts which accelerate chemical processes occurring in living organisms. There are a large number present in the cell, and most have a high degree of specificity. Enzyme mechanisms are the key to basic biological processes. See **F32(1).**

Ephemoptera or **May-flies,** an order of insects. In the larval condition they exist from two to three years aquatically, but no sooner do they arrive at maturity than their lives are hurried to a close. They rise up in pyramids on warm summer nights, take no food, propagate and perish. The Latin name expresses the fact that the adults have an ephemeral existence.

Epiphany, a Christian festival celebrated on January 6, originally an old solstice festival, celebrating the birth of light.

Equator, the imaginary great circle of the earth, every point of which is 90 degrees from the earth's poles, and dividing the northern from the southern hemisphere. It is from this circle that the latitude of places north and south is reckoned. The celestial equator is the circle in which the plane of the earth's equator meets the celestial sphere (the imaginary sphere, in which the observer is at the centre, used for representing the apparent positions of the heavenly bodies).

Equinox, the time when the sun crosses the plane of the earth's equator, making day and night of equal length.

Eras are distinctive periods of time associated with some remarkable historical event or personage. *The Christian era* is computed according to a 6th-cent. reckoning to begin with Jesus's birth, A.D. 1. The date is placed some years too late. Scholars now believe that Jesus was born *c.* 4 B.C. The *Jewish era* dates from 3761 B.C.; the *Julian era* from the alteration of the calendar by Julius Caesar 45 B.C.; the *Mohammedan era* from the date of the *Hejira*, or the flight of Mohammed from Mecca to Medina, which is A.D., 622, 16 July, in the Julian Calendar.

Erbium, belongs to the group of rare-earth metals discovered by Mosander in 1842. Element no. 68, symbol Er.

Erg, the unit of work and energy in the centimetre-gram-second system; the energy involved when a force of 1 dyne moves its point of application through a distance of 1 cm.

Ernie, the name given to the "electronic random number indicator equipment", the electronic machine which selected the prizewinning numbers in the first Premium Bond draw, June 1957.

Eros. This asteroid is 24–32 km in diameter. It comes closer to the earth than any other member of the solar system with the exception of the moon and several very small asteroids. Determination of solar parallax based on observations of Eros in 1930–31 yielded until then the most accurate estimate of the distance of the sun from the earth. *See* **Astronomical unit.**

Erse, a term used by Lowland Scottish, and English writers for the Gaelic language spoken in the Highlands of Scotland. Sometimes erroneously applied to Irish, the Gaelic language as spoken in Ireland and revived as an official language in recent times. Dr. Johnson, Sir Walter Scott, and other writers used "Erse" to signify Scottish Gaelic. The language of the Scottish Lowlands (that used by Robert Burns) is related to the English language and not to Gaelic and is variously termed Scots, Braid Scots, the Doric, the Scottish vernacular, and fashionably of late, Lallans.

Escurial or **Escorial**, Spanish monastery built in the mountains near Madrid by Philip II to commemorate the victory over the French at Saint-Quentin (1557). A palace was added later and it also includes a church, library and royal mausoleum. Built in granite in sombre style, it is one of the finest buildings in Europe.

Eskimo. Popular name for the Inuit peoples of the Arctic, living in Canada, Greenland, Alaska and the northern territories of Russia.

Esperanto, an artificial international language created by L. Zamenhof of Warsaw and first published in 1887. It does not seek to replace national languages but to serve as a second language for international communication. It is based on the internationality of many words in the principal modern languages, and is entirely phonetic in spelling and pronunciation. In 1990 there are *c.* 10,000 British speakers of the language. Other artificial languages are Volapuk and Ido.

Estates of the Realm in Great Britain are the Lords Spiritual, the Lords Temporal and the Commons. They are the great classes invested with distinct political powers, and whose concurrence is necessary to legislation.

Esters. Organic chemicals formed by combining an alcohol with an acid. They have a pleasant smell, and occur naturally in plants as the scent of flowers. Manufactured for use in the perfumery industry, and as flavourings in food. Some esters are used as solvents, notably amyl-acetate ("pear drops") in quick-drying paints. The polymeric fibre "Terylene" consists of chains of molecules containing many ester groups, formed by reacting an alcohol having two alcoholic (OH) groups with an acid having two acid (COOH) groups.

Etching, a technical method for producing graphic work and works of art. A plate, traditionally of copper, is covered with wax; the design or picture desired is drawn with a sharp implement which penetrates the wax. When the plate is exposed to the action of an acid this will etch into the copper where the lines have been drawn. The wax is then removed, ink is applied to the plate with its engraving, and the design or picture can be printed on to paper in many copies. Rembrandt, Goya and others made great and original works of art in the technique, but it was also widely used for reproductive purposes before the invention of photography. Hogarth painted his famous pictures in oil and reproduced them graphically.

Ether, in chemistry, is a volatile inflammable liquid composed of carbon, hydrogen and oxygen. It is a valuable anaesthetic obtained by heating alcohol with sulphuric acid. In physics, in the 19th cent., all space was supposed to be filled with a substance called ether, the chief property of which was to carry light waves, *i.e.*, light was supposed to be waves in this all-pervading medium known as the ether. Speculation and experiment concerned with the ether were very fruitful in advancing physics. Ultimately the attempts by Michelson and Morley to detect the motion of the earth through the ether were unsuccessful in this respect but profoundly successful in stimulating the theory of relativity. The ether concept has now been abandoned. *See also* **F17**(2).

Ethylene (also called ethene). A gas compounded of carbon and hydrogen, it is related to acetylene and ethane. Industrially it is obtained as a by-product in petroleum refining. It has wide uses as a starting material in the industrial manufacture of intermediates, especially alcohol. Its most important application is in the production of polythene (poly-ethylene). *See* **Catalyst.**

Etruscans, people believed to have come from Asia Minor who colonised Italy about 900 B.C., settled in what is now Tuscany and part of Umbria, reached the height of their civilisation about 500 B.C., and were ultimately absorbed by the Romans. They were skilled technicians in bronze, silver and goldwork, and excelled in the art of granular decoration.

Eucalyptus. This genus includes 300 species of evergreen, leathery-leaved trees native to Australia. The oils yielded by different species vary a great deal in their scent and other properties and are chiefly used in pharmacy and perfumery; about 30 species produce oils suitable for medicinal use. Other species produce timber.

Euro-dollar Market. An international financial market, located mainly in Britain and Europe, for lending and borrowing dollars, *i.e.*, titles to dollar deposits in United States banks.

Europium, element no. 63, symbol Eu, discovered by Demarcay in 1906. A member of the rare-earth metal group.

Evaporation is the process by which a solid or liquid is resolved into vapour by heat. The opposite process is condensation. Wherever a liquid or solid surface is exposed, evaporation takes place into the space above. If the vapour is continually removed the solid or liquid vanishes into vapour; the higher the temperature the quicker the process. If the vapour is confined, then it collects, getting more concentrated until as many atoms of vapour are condensing as are evaporating. The vapour is then said to be saturated. Evaporation of water from sea, soil, plants, skin, etc., is continuously in progress, so it is a process of fundamental importance to meteorology, botany, physiology, industry, *etc.*

Everest Expeditions. For many years after Mt. Everest had been shown to be the highest mountain in the world, political conditions in Nepal, lying south of the summit, and in Tibet, to the north, prevented mountaineers from attempting an ascent. At last in 1921 the Tibetan authorities gave permission, and the first expedition, organised, as were all subsequent British expeditions, by a joint committee of the Royal Geographical Society and the Alpine Club, and led by Col. C. K. Howard-Bury, was sent out. This was primarily a reconnaissance; besides mapping the northern flanks, it found a practicable route up the mountain. By 1939, six further expeditions had climbed on the northern face. Some were baulked by bad weather, others by problems previously little known, such as the effect of high altitudes on the human body and spirit. Nevertheless, notable climbs were accomplished. In 1924, for example, Col. E. F. Norton reached 8,589 m, and it was on this expedition that G. L. Mallory and Andrew Irvine were seen going well at about the same height. They never returned, however, and what disaster befell them is not known. After the war, political conditions again closed the Tibet route: permission was eventually obtained from the Nepalese Government to make the attempt from the south. In 1951 a reconnaissance expedition under Eric Shipton reached the ice-fall at the exit of the Western Cwm (a high valley lying south-west of the massif), and reported favourably on the prospects for an ascent. The first attempt from this side was made the following year by a Swiss expedition led by Dr. E. Wyss-Dunant, two members of which made an attempt on the summit, but were stopped at approx. 8,601 m by the intense cold and the very strong winds. When the British 1953 Expedition led by Col. John Hunt (now Lord Hunt), was being organised, stress was laid on three main points; proper acclimatisation of the climbers; use of oxygen for the final stages; and the establishment of very high altitude camps, so that the final assault parties would set out fresh and unencumbered. Great attention was also paid to recent developments in diet, clothing and equipment. In all these matters the 1953 expedition was able to draw on the accumulated experience of its predecessors. By the end of April, a base camp had been established below the ice-fall, and with the aid of thirty-four Sherpa porters supplies had been carried up into the Western Cwm. The next critical stage was the ascent of the steep head of the cwm, the Lhotse face, with the threat of avalanches always present. By most strenuous efforts, a camp was established on the South Col (7,869 m) on 21 May. From this camp on 26 May, T. D. Bourdillon and R. C. Evans climbed the South Peak of Everest (8,760 m), then the highest altitude ever attained. On 28 May Edmund Hillary and the Sherpa leader, Tenzing Norgay, spent the night at the highest camp (8,510 m) and on the following day, 29 May, climbed to the South Summit, negotiated the difficult final ridge, and reached the summit of Everest.

Evolution, in the words of Sir Julian Huxley (d. 1975), "a natural process of irreversible change which generates novelty, variety and increase of organisation". The theory, as laid down by Darwin, is that all existing species, genera and classes of animals and plants have developed from a few simple forms by processes of change and selection. Up to the time of Darwin a large part of the civilised world believed that life had been created suddenly at the beginning of the world which God had created, according to Archbishop Usher, on 22 October 4004 B.C. The evidence of the rocks, however, has given a more convincing theory of creation, and by studying the fossils preserved in the various layers of the earth's crust the past history of the earth's life has been pieced together. Darwin has been called the Newton of biology. See also **Section F.**

Exchequer, which derives its name from the checkered tablecloth on which accounts were calculated in early Norman times, is a term connected with the revenues of the Crown. In former times it had jurisdiction in all revenue matters. The term Exchequer is now applied to the Governmental department which deals with the public revenues, the working head of which is the Chancellor of the Exchequer.

Existentialism. See **Section J.**

Exploration. Modern exploration began in the second half of the 15th cent. with the voyages of the great Portuguese and Spanish discoverers. They were followed by sailors of other European nations, who profited from their developments in navigation and from their charts, and in less than one hundred years the coastlines of much of the Americas, Africa and South-west Asia had been revealed and the globe circumnavigated. The motives of these early explorers were mixed: they were seeking adventure, trade, plunder, national power and the conversion of the heathen. Few if any were directly interested in advancing scientific knowledge. But from the reports of their voyages and travels, scholars at home compiled descriptions of the strange new world which stimulated their successors to undertake more systematic enquir-

ies. One of the earliest English expeditions to be despatched for scientific research was that of William Dampier on the *Roebuck,* which was sent out by the Admiralty in 1699 to examine the coasts of North-west Australia. In the 18th cent. British explorers were at work mainly in the Pacific Ocean, with the object of breaking the Spanish monopoly of trade. Capt. James Cook sailed thither in 1769 to observe first the transit of Venus at Tahiti, and then to search for the alleged great southern continent. On this voyage he discovered and charted much of the coasts of New Zealand and the east coast of Australia. On his second voyage he was the first to sail across the Antarctic Circle, and he showed that the southern continent was much smaller than had been supposed. By 1800 the general outlines of the continents, except for Antarctica were known, and explorers in the 19th cent. were largely engaged in opening up the interiors. In Africa British explorers solved two problems which had puzzled men for centuries: Mungo Park and Richard Lander established the true course of the River Niger, and Sir Richard Burton, J. H. Speke, Sir Samuel Baker and others revealed the true sources of the Nile. The greatest African explorer of that age was undoubtedly David Livingstone, the missionary, who in three great journeys explored the Zambesi and the region of the Great Lakes, spreading the Gospel, fighting the slave trade, and opening up the interior to settlement and trade. In North America Alexander Mackenzie was the first to cross the main breadth of the continent from sea to sea. In Asia motives were also mixed; men like Charles Doughty, who explored in Arabia, and Sir Francis Younghusband, who journeyed from China to India across the Gobi and the Himalayas, were impelled by a love of adventure and the quest for knowledge, but political considerations were often involved. In recent years, with the main features of the world's surface known, exploration has become more intensive. Teams of scientists go out to study restricted areas in detail. An Antarctic expedition can contribute to our knowledge of world weather, or by biological research into the life history of whales, can help to improve our food supplies. Similarly, expeditions in Africa can help to check the loss of valuable agricultural land through soil erosion, or to develop areas of settlement by schemes for irrigation and power. And there are still great areas to be adequately mapped. All these problems are inter-related, and in solving them the modern explorer can call on many improved techniques and instruments—the aeroplane, the aerial camera, tracked motor vehicles, radio, in fact all the resources of modern science. But the human element is still vital.

Explosives, substances which burn violently to produce gases in such volume that an explosion is induced. Gunpowder was the first explosive to be used; Roger Bacon's powder, consisting of charcoal, sulphur and saltpetre, was the only effective explosive until the 19th cent., but it was difficult to control. Nitroglycerine (glyceryl trinitrate) was first compounded in 1847 by adding glycerine to a mixture of sulphuric acid and nitric acid. In 1866 Alfred Nobel discovered how to make dynamite by absorbing nitroglycerine in the fine sand kieselguhr. Cordite was the joint invention of Sir Frederick Abel and Sir James Dewar (1889). It came into general use as a propellant. High explosives, providing bursting charge for shells and bombs, include TNT (trinitrotoluene), picric acid, cyclonite (RDX) and many others. Slurry explosives can be pumped on to the site and therefore offer advantages in transportation and safety; they are also waterproof. Chemical explosives have been eclipsed by nuclear explosives which have developed from the first atom bomb (dropped on Hiroshima 6 August 1945) to the 100-megaton hydrogen bomb.

Expressionism, a modern art movement confined primarily to the non-Latin countries of Europe which sought to give expression to intimate and personal emotions by means of distortions of line and colour and simplified style which carried a greater impact in terms of feeling. Broadly speaking, this has been characteristic of northern art in general. (*See* **Gothic.**) The term is usually used of the modern movement which influenced the Post-impressionists and subsequent movements in France. Tired of the naturalism of the Impressionists, such artists as van Gogh, Gauguin, Matisse and Rouault, together with the Fauvists (*q.v.*) made use of simple outlines and strong colours. Apart from Toulouse-Lautrec, the principal Expressionists were Norwegian, like Munch, or German, like the painters of *Die Brücke* and *Der Blaue Reiter* groups. Individual artists were Ensor, Kokoschka, Nolde, Rouault and Soutine.

F

Fabian Society. *See* **Section J.**

Fables are fictitious narratives intended to enforce some moral precept, and may be either in prose or verse, and deal with personified animals and objects or with human beings. Aesop in ancient times and Hans Christian Andersen and the Brothers Grimm (in many of their stories) in later days, have given fables. Mention must also be made of La Fontaine's and Krylov's fables.

Fairs were established in mediaeval times as a means of bringing traders and customers together at stated periods, and formed the chief means of distribution. The great English fairs of early times were those of Winchester and Stourbridge near Cambridge. Traders from the Netherlands and the Baltic gathered there with the great merchants of London, and goods of every kind, wholesale and retail, were sold. One of the biggest trade fairs was at Nijni-Novgorod, founded in the 17th cent.; other big continental fairs were those of Leipzig (founded in the 12th cent.), Lyons and Prague. Expositions of advanced industrial products are today popular, *e.g.*, Expo 67 held in Montreal.

Fairy Rings are the circles caused in grassland by certain fungi. The circles expand outwards as the fungus spreads, the fruiting bodies being at the periphery. Farther inward where the fungi are decaying the grass grows more strongly, fertilised by the nitrogen released from the rotting fungi. In olden times these rings were held to be the scene of fairy dances.

Falcon, name given to diurnal birds of prey which belong to the same family, *Falconidae*, as the hawk, eagle, buzzard, kite and harrier. They are swift of wing and feed on birds and small mammals. These birds have long, pointed wings, strong, hooked and notched bill, long, curved claws and an eye of great power. They are found all over the world. Those that breed in Britain are the Kestrel (the most common), Hobby (one of the swiftest of European birds), Merlin and Peregrine, a swift and magnificent bird with slate-grey back, blackish crown, black "moustache" and whitish breast. Other members of the family are the Gyr Falcon from northern latitudes, Iceland and Greenland, which is a winter visitor to Britain, the Lanner, Saker, Eleonora's falcon, Red-footed falcon and the Lesser Kestrel. The Gyr Falcon and the Peregrine were used in the sport of falconry in olden times. Because of its fearlessness and larger size, the female bird was used. When the quarry was sighted, the bird was unhooded, set free, and after mounting high into the air would dart swiftly down to strike the prey. The heron was the usual victim.

Fall-out. Radioactive material produced by nuclear explosions which may cause bodily and genetic damage. (1) *Local fall-out*, due to the return to earth of larger particles, occurs locally, and within a few hours after the explosion; (2) *Tropospheric fall-out*, due to particles which remain in the troposphere and come down within a month or so, possibly all over the world, but within the altitude in which the explosion occurred; (3) *Stratospheric fall-out*, which comes from fragments taken up into the stratosphere and then deposited, in the course of many years, uniformly all over the globe. The two radioactive materials which have given rise to the greatest concern for the health of the individual are strontium-90 and iodine-131.

Both these materials are liable to become concentrated in certain parts of the human body, strontium-90 in bone and iodine-131 in the thyroid gland. Radiation exposure may produce genetic effects, that is effects which may show up in succeeding generations. An extensive survey was carried out by scientists of the US Atomic Energy Commission on the islands of Bikini atoll, site of some 23 nuclear tests, 1946–58. Their records, published in 1969, revealed that the intensity of radioactivity underneath the point of explosion was still exceedingly high. Most of the radiation remaining was due to the radioactive isotope caesium-137. The variation in intensity from one place to another seemed to be correlated with the variations of vegetation: where there was little vegetation weathering had been rapid. (The nuclear test ban treaty, 1963, applies to all nuclear tests except those held underground.)

Fantail, a variety of the domestic pigeon; also a genus of Australian birds of the *Muscicapidae* family. A small New Zealand bird is called a fantail.

Fan Tracery, a complicated style of roof-vaulting, elaborately moulded, in which the lines of the curves in the masonry or other material employed diverge equally in every direction. It is characteristic of the late Perpendicular period of Gothic architecture, and may be seen in St. George's Chapel at Windsor and the Chapel of Henry VII at Westminster Abbey.

Farmer-General, the name given to the financiers who in the days of the old French monarchy farmed certain taxes, contracting to pay the Government a fixed sum yearly, on condition that the unspecified taxes were collected and appropriated by themselves. The revolution of 1789 swept the Farmer General away.

Fascism. *See* **Section J.**

Fata Morgana, the name given to a curious mirage often observed over the Straits of Messina, attributed to the magic of the fairy Morgana, half-sister of King Arthur, who was fabled to live in Calabria.

Fathers of the Church were early writers who laid the foundations of Christian ritual and doctrine. The earliest were the Apostolic Fathers (*q.v.*). The Four Fathers of the Latin Church were St. Ambrose, St. Jerome, St. Augustine and St. Gregory the Great. The Four Fathers of the Greek Church were St. Basil, St. Gregory Nazianzen, St. John Chrysostom and St. Athanasius.

Fathom, a nautical measure, the six-foot stretch (1·8 m) of a man's arms. Replaced by the metre on British Admiralty charts, but continued on yachtsmen's coastal charts.

Fatigue, a condition leading to breakage when a solid component, *e.g.*, an axle, is subjected to a large number of fluctuating repetitive stresses. Fatigue is the cause of most failures in service of metal engineering components though fatigue is not confined to metallic materials alone. Fatigue failures result from the *repetition*, not simply from the *size* of the stresses; indeed, fatigue breakage can result from stresses much lower than the material could stand if the load were applied steadily. Fatigue causes minute cracks, usually at the surface, which grow and spread. Early detection is difficult and fatigue, discovered by the railway engineers of the 19th cent., remains a severe engineering problem.

Fats are important foodstuffs. In physiology they constitute a valuable form of reserve food. They contain carbon, hydrogen and oxygen; chemically they are described as esters of glycerol (glycerine). Commonest fats are stearin, palmitin and olein, esters formed by the combination of glycerol with stearic, palmitic and oleic acid respectively. Fats are converted into soap by alkali; this process (saponification) also releases glycerol.

Fault, a term designating a breakage coupled with displacement of geological strata. *See* **F9(2).**

Fauvism (French *Fauve* = wild beast), a term used, at first contemptuously, to describe the work of a group of French painters who first exhibited at the Salon d'Automne in Paris in 1905. The most prominent among them was Henri Matisse. Forms are freely distorted and colours are selected and applied for their emotive power with no necessary reference to the "real" colour of the object in question. Other famous *Fauves* were Derain, Vlaminck and Rouault. By 1908 the group had lost its cohesion and its members went their separate ways.

February, the second month of the year, contains in ordinary years 28 days, but in leap years 29 days. When first introduced into the Roman calendar by Numa, *c.* 700 B.C. it was made the last month of the year, preceding January, but in 452 B.C. the position of the two months was changed, February following January.

Federation. *See* **Confederation.**

Félibrige, a movement founded in 1854 to revive the ancient glories of Provence, initiated by the French poet Frédéric Mistral.

Felspar, the name given to a group of minerals, silicates of aluminium with some calcium and sodium, or potassium, which make up probably more than half of the earth's crust. It is formed in granite and other rocks, both igneous and metamorphic.

Fenestella, the niche set apart on the south side of the altar for the piscina in Roman Catholic churches.

Fermentation, the action of chemical ferments or *enzymes* in bringing about chemical changes in the materials of living animals and plants, *e.g.,* the breaking-down of sugar by yeast into alcohol.

Ferret, a domesticated polecat. It is about half the size of a cat and is bred in captivity to hunt rats and rabbits. It has a long sinuous body and short legs which enable it to enter rabbit and rat holes and chase the quarry out to guns or into nets. Such ferreting is a popular country sport.

Ferrites are compounds containing iron, oxygen, and one or two of a certain range of other possible metallic elements. Ferrites have recently become very important technically, because, unlike ordinary magnetic materials, they combine strong magnetism with electrical insulating properties. Ferrite-rod aerials are now common in portable radios, and ferrite devices are used in radar. *See* **F22**(2).

Feudalism. *See* **Section J.**

Fieldfare, the largest member of the thrush family, a regular winter visitor to Britain from Scandinavia. It is brown in colour with a lighter spotted breast and a grey head.

Field-Marshal, the highest ranking title in the British army, and only bestowed on royal personages and generals who have attained great distinction. The first British Field-Marshal was created in 1736, when John, Duke of Argyll, had the title conferred upon him by George II.

Fifth Column. When Franco, the Spanish dictator, revolted against the Spanish Republic in 1936 and attacked Madrid with four armies, his commander, General Mola declared that a group of fascists within the city was assisting the besiegers. The term is used to describe a body of spies within a fighting front.

Fighting-Fish, small pugnacious Siamese fish with long caudal and ventral fins. They are kept in glass globes in Siam, and when brought into contact will fight to the death, these encounters being the occasion of much gambling.

Filibuster, a name first given to pirates and buccaneers in the 17th cent. who took possession of small islands or lonely coast lands, and there maintained themselves apart from any governing authority. In later times the term was used to specify men taking part in expeditions whose object was to appropriate tracts of country, and settle upon them in disregard of international law. The most notable expeditions of this kind in modern times were those of Narciso Lopez against Cuba in 1850–51, and of William Walker against Nicaragua, between 1855 and 1860. Both leaders were captured and executed. The term is also used to express the right of a minority in the United States Senate for unlimited debate, which is used on occasions to delay legislation.

Finches, a large family of small birds belonging to the Passerine or perching order of birds. There are about 200 species, including greenfinch, hawfinch, chaffinch, goldfinch, siskin, bullfinch, crossbill, linnet, twite and bunting.

Fir, a cone-bearing tree with small evergreen leaves and of considerable use as timber. There are two types: the Silver Firs and the Douglas Firs numbering about 25 species. All these firs attain to a considerable height, and all yield turpentine or other resinous material.

Fire-damp. *See* **Methane.**

Fire-Fly, a small winged insect of the *Eleteridae* family, is able to throw out a strong phosphorescent light in the dark. There are some remarkable specimens in tropical countries.

Fire of London, of 1666, extended from East to West, from the Tower to the Temple church, and northward to Holborn Bridge. It broke out in a baker's shop in Pudding Lane, and lasted four days, and destroyed 87 churches, including St. Paul's Cathedral, and many public buildings, among them the Royal Exchange, the Custom House and the Guildhall. In the ruins were 13,200 houses and 400 streets. About 100,000 people were made homeless yet in about 10 years all the houses had been rebuilt. The plague had not disappeared from London when the fire occurred.

Firkin, a former measure of capacity, the fourth part of a barrel, now only used in reference to a small cask or tub for butter, lard, allow, etc.

Fischer-Tropsch Process. A process for making synthetic petrol from carbon monoxide and hydrogen. The synthesis is accelerated by cobalt-thoria and nickel-thoria catalysts.

Fish Louse. Parasitic crustacea found on marine and fresh-water fishes and whales.

Fission, Nuclear. A nuclear reaction in which the nucleus of an atom (*e.g.,* uranium 235, plutonium) captures a neutron, and the unstable nucleus so produced breaks into two nearly equal fragments and throws out several neutrons as well. In biology the term fission is applied to reproduction by fragmentation of a single-cell organism, as in amoeba. *See* **F13**(1).

Flagella, single hair-like projections found on many micro-organisms. Their sole function is, by complicated motion, to move the organism about. They are longer and less versatile than cilia (*q.v.*).

Flag Officer, a British naval officer who enjoys the right of carrying a flag at the mast-head of his ship, and is of the rank of Admiral of the Fleet, Admiral, Vice-Admiral or Rear-Admiral.

Flagship, the ship that flies the Admiral's flag, and from which orders proceed.

Flamingo, a strangely beautiful, extremely slender wading bird of white and rose-pink plumage with long, slender legs and neck and a long, down-curved bill with which it rakes the mud and obtains its food of worms and molluscs. The wings are bright crimson, bordered with black, and a flock in flight is a picture of singular beauty. There is a large and famous colony in the Camargue, S.E. France.

Flash-Point. This is found by heating an oil in a special cup and taking the temperature at which sufficient vapour is produced to ignite when a small flame is applied. It is an index of the inflammability of oils.

Fleas. Fleas are small parasitic insects belonging to the order *Aphaniptera* (so called because these creatures have no wings). They obtain their food by sucking blood from their host. They are laterally compressed, which immediately distinguishes them from lice. The human flea (*Pulex irritans*) is able to jump vertically a distance of over 18 cm.

Fleet Prison, a noted debtors' prison that stood on the east side of Farringdon Street, London. It was notorious for the cruelties inflicted on prisoners, particularly under the wardenship of Thomas Bainbridge who took charge in 1728. It was pulled down in 1846.

Fleet Street, a famous thoroughfare in London, now the centre of journalism and newspaper-dom, though it was long celebrated for its taverns where the literary coteries of the day were wont to meet. It takes its name from the Fleet stream which used to run from Hampstead through Holborn to the Thames at Black-friars.

Flemings, the Dutch-speaking people of Flanders, whose ancestors of mediaeval times excelled in the textile arts: England owes its early eminence as a manufacturing nation to the migration of numbers of Flemings to this country in the 16th and 17th cent. *See also* **Walloons.**

Fleur de Lis, the former national emblem of France, the flower of the lily. It was superseded by the Tricolour in 1789, but is still adhered to by the supporters of the old French royalties.

Flint, consists of granular chalcedony with some opaline silica, and occurs as nodules and bands in the Chalk. It is hard and has a conchoidal fracture, so enabling it to be used in making cutting implements in prehistoric times. Before the invention of lucifer matches, it was used along with steel for striking lights.

Flint implements are objects found in the younger geological strata, and constituting evidence of the condition and life of the period. They include knives, clubs, arrow-heads, scrapers, etc., used as weapons, tools and possibly as surgical instruments and in religious ceremonies. Similar to prehistoric specimens are the flint and obsidian implements of some of the primitive peoples of today. Ritual weapons and sacrificial knives continued to be made of stone long after the introduction of metals for practical purposes.

Flounder, one of the most familiar of the smaller flat fishes common round the British coasts, and seldom attaining a weight of over 1·3 kg.

Fluoridation, the process of adding the element fluorine, in the form of suitable compounds, to something deficient in it. Commonly met with as a proposal to add fluorides (fluorine compounds) to drinking water to combat dental decay, especially in children. Some toothpastes are fluoridated and fluoride can also be taken as tablets and in other ways. In 1976 a working party of the Royal College of Physicians recommended that water supplies should be fluoridated when the natural fluoride level is below 1 mg/litre. This recommendation drew on many investigations throughout the world giving evidence for the effectiveness of fluoride in the prevention of decay without harmful side-effects. There is, however, a body of opinion unconvinced by this and opposed to adding fluoride to drinking water, one argument being that to take or not to take fluoride should be a personal decision.

Fluorine, chemical element, no. 9, member of the halogen family, symbol F, it is found in combination with calcium in fluorspar, and occurs in minute quantities in certain other minerals. Discovered by Scheele in 1771, it was first obtained by Moissan in 1886. A pale yellow gas, it is very reactive and combines with most elements except oxygen. Its acid, hydrogen fluoride, etches glass, the fluorine combining with the silicon to form volatile silicon fluoride. Organic fluorine compounds have found use as very stable polymers which resist a wide variety of chemical actions.

Fluorescent Lamp. *See* **Electric Light and Ultra-Violet Rays.**

Fluorocarbons are hydrocarbons in which some or all of the hydrogen atoms have been replaced by atoms of chlorine or fluorine. They are non-toxic, non-flammable and chemically inert gases or low boiling point liquids. These properties make them very suitable for use as refrigerants, and propellants in fire-extinguishers and aerosols. The most widely used fluorocarbons are the chlorofluoromethanes (CCl_2F_2, CCl_3F and $CHClF_2$). In 1974 it was first suggested that the vast release of fluorocarbons into the atmosphere due to the greatly increased use of aerosols could cause a significant depletion of the protective ozone (*q.v.*) layer in the upper atmosphere. The mechanism for this involves the decomposition of fluorocarbons at high altitudes as a result of intense solar irradiation. The chlorine atoms so released can then catalyse the conversion of ozone into ordinary molecular oxygen. The degree of ozone depletion that will result is a matter of considerable current controversy. Similarly, opinions differ as to the detrimental effect ozone depletion might have on the incidence of skin cancer and on the climate.

Fluorspar, a mineral; chemically calcium fluoride. Can be colourless, green or yellow, but is most commonly purple. Blue fluorspar under the name of Derbyshire "blue John" has been used for ornamental purposes.

Fly, the popular name for a large number of insects with one pair of wings and a proboscis ter-

minating in a sucker through which fluid substances can be drawn up. The best-known species are the common house-fly, the bluebottle and the blow-fly. In the larval form flies are maggots, and feed upon decaying substances, animal flesh, etc. Flies are able to walk upon ceilings or upright surfaces by having suckers at the soles of their feet. *See* **Diptera.**

Flycatcher, name of a large family of small birds, the Muscicapidae. They are insect feeders, catch their food in the air, and are distributed over most countries of the world. The spotted and the pied nest in Britain, which they visit from April to September.

Flying Fish are frequently to be seen in southern waters, and are capable of gliding considerable distances without touching the water. To build up speed for its "take-off" the fish swims rapidly, to break the surface at 24–32 km/h. Maximum air speed is about 64 km/h.

Flying Fox, a member of the bat family, but of much larger size, and confined to the tropical and sub-tropical Old World. Like the bats, it is nocturnal, but it feeds entirely on fruits.

Flying Lemur. *See* **Colugo.**

Flying Lizard, or *Draco,* an Asiatic lizard, possessing wing-like projections from each side which enable it to make flying leaps through the air, though not sufficient for continuous flight.

Flying Saucers, the name given to certain saucer-like shapes which have on occasion been seen travelling through the atmosphere. For some time speculation was rife, especially in America, but it is now believed that when not hallucinations, meteorological or cosmic-ray balloons, they are nothing more than atmospheric phenomena like mirages or mock suns caused by unusual atmospheric conditions. Described by Dr. Menzel, astrophysics professor at Harvard, "as real as rainbows are real, and no more dangerous". It has been suggested that the study of some of the people who report the sighting of unidentified flying objects (UFOs) would be more rewarding than the investigation of what they saw! *See also* **Section J.**

Flying Squirrel, rodents of which there are several species in Europe, Asia and America. It possesses a parachute-like fold of skin by means of which it projects itself through the air. In appearance they are much like ordinary squirrels, to which they are related. The African flying squirrels belong to a different family.

Fog is caused by the presence of particles of condensed water vapour or smoke in the surface layers of the atmosphere, the term being applied meteorologically when the resulting obscurity is such as to render objects invisible at distances of up to 1 km. Fogs are frequently formed when the air near the ground is cooled below its dew-point temperature by radiation on a still, cloudless night; by flowing over a relatively cold land or water mass; or by mixing with a colder air stream. An accumulation of smoke over a large city may cause a high fog cutting off the daylight and producing gloom. *See* **Pollution, Aerosol.**

Foliation, a geological term applied to rocks whose component minerals are arranged in parallel layers as the result of strong metamorphic action.

Folio, a printing term for a sheet of paper folded once, a half sheet constituting a leaf.

Folklore concerns itself with the mental and spiritual life of the people—both civilised and primitive—as expressed in the traditional beliefs, customs, institutions and sayings that have been handed down from generation to generation by word of mouth and with the observation, recording and interpretation of such traditions. (The word *folklore* itself was first suggested and used—as two words *Folk Lore*—by W. J. Thoms in the *Athenaeum* of 22 August 1846, and was at once adsorbed into the English language.) Traditional lore of the kind included in the term folklore takes many forms and ranges from omens of good and bad luck (spilling the salt, breaking a mirror, dropping an umbrella, etc.) and the wearing of amulets or the possession of talismans (such as the horseshoe) as protection against misfortune, to elaborate ceremonial dances such as the Abbots Bromley Horn Dance, the Hobby horses of Padstow and Minehead the Northern sword-dances and the Christmas mummers' plays. Especially important are the beliefs and customs associated with birth, babyhood, marriage and death such being occasions when the individuals concerned require special protection or when unusual happenings can be used for foretelling their future. The child born on a Sunday will be the luckiest; rocking on an empty cradle will ensure the speedy arrival of a new baby; throwing an old shoe after a newly-married couple brings them luck; the bride should be carried over the threshold of the new home; on the sea-coast, death is believed to take place at the ebb-tide; the bees must be told of the death of the master of the house, or they will leave the hive. Another very large section of the subject deals with the traditional sayings and practices associated with particular days and seasons of the year—calendar customs, as they are called. The eating of pancakes on Shrove Tuesday; Mother Sunday customs and the simnel cake; Good Friday as the right day for planting potatoes, but emphatically the wrong day for washing clothes or cutting one's finger-nails; the necessity of wearing something new on Easter Sunday; the children's maypole dances and May garlands; midsummer fires; All Hallowe'en as the most favourable occasion for divining the future—especially in respect of marriage—and for games and sports such as apple-bobbing; the numerous practices accompanying the harvest. All these are examples of calendar customs; their full story would occupy several volumes. Folklorists are interested in all such oral tradition because they think that to a large extent it represents what folk have mentally stored up from the past and transmitted to their descendants throughout the centuries, and because therefore it is able to assist other historic methods—ethnographical, linguistic, archaeological, etc.—in the elucidation of the early story of man. In those countries with a great diversity of peoples in all stages of culture, a knowledge of folklore and what it can teach of the mind of man is of great importance to administrators. The Folk-Lore Society was founded in 1878, and that part of the subject represented by song and dance has now its own organisation in the English Folk Dance and Song Society.

Footpath. In English law a highway over which the public have a right of way on foot only, other than such a highway at the side of a public road. *See also* **Long-Distance Walks.**

Force, as a term in physics, signifies an influence or exertion which, when made to act upon a body, tends to move it if at rest, or to affect or stop its progress if it be already in motion. In the c.g.s. system, the unit of force is the dyne; in the foot-pound-second system, the poundal; in the SI system, the newton.

Formaldehyde. Chemically it lies between methyl alcohol and formic acid; oxidation of methyl alcohol yields formaldehyde, and oxidation of formaldehyde produces formic acid. It is used as a disinfectant, in silvering mirrors, and in the manufacture of phenol-formaldehyde plastics (of which bakelite is the best-known example). Solutions of formaldehyde in water, formalin, are used to preserve biological specimens.

Forme, a body of letterpress type, composed and secured for printing from; or a stereotype or electrotype. The former is used more for newspaper formes and the latter in good book work.

Formic Acid can be obtained from a colourless fluid secreted by ants and other insects and plants. It is a strong irritant. Commercially it is obtained from sodium formate, which is synthesised by the absorption of carbon monoxide in caustic soda. It is used in the electroplating, tanning and textile industries.

Fossils. Remains of animals and plants, or direct evidence of their presence, preserved in rocks. They include petrified skeletons and shells, leaf imprints, footprints, etc.

Four Freedoms, a phrase coined by President Roosevelt in January 1941, embodying what should be the goal of the Allies. They were (1) Freedom of speech and expression; (2) Freedom of every person to worship God in his own way; (3) Freedom from want; (4) Freedom from fear.

Fox, carnivorous animal of the canine family, found in considerable numbers in most parts of the world. The common fox *Vulpes vulpes* of Europe is a burrowing animal of nocturnal habits, living upon birds, rabbits and domestic poultry, in the capture of which it displays much cunning. The fox in Britain is preserved from extinction chiefly for hunting purposes. Among other notable species are the Arctic fox and the red fox of North America, of which the valuable silver fox, coveted for its fur, is a variety.

Fox-Shark *or* **Thresher Shark,** a large species of shark common in the Atlantic and in the Mediterranean. It is very destructive to small fish, but although it attains a length of 4·5 m it is not dangerous to man.

Franciscans. *See* Friars.

Franco-German War (1870–71) was opened by a declaration of war by Napoleon III, but the Germans who were better prepared than the French, won victory after victory. On 12 September Napoleon with 104,000 men were made prisoners at Sedan, a republic was then proclaimed, and Paris sustained a four months' siege. In the end France ceded Alsace and part of Lorraine to Germany, who claimed a war indemnity of £200 million.

Frankincense is of two kinds, one being used as incense in certain religious services and obtained from olibanum, an Eastern shrub, the other is a resinous exudation derived from firs and pines, and largely used in pharmacy.

Franklin, the name given in feudal times to a country landowner who was independent of the territorial lord, and performed many of the minor functions of local government, such as serving as magistrate.

Freeport, a port exempt from customs duties and regulations. The north German towns of the Hanseatic League (**L56**) were among the earliest and most famous freeports.

Freira, small grey and white sea bird. Extremely rare, it nests on the island of Madeira. Likely to become the first European species to face extinction since the Great Auk in 1844.

Fresco, a painting executed upon plaster walls or ceilings, a technique which has remained unchanged since it was practised by the great Renaissance artists.

Friars, members of certain mendicant orders of the Roman Catholic Church. The four chief orders are the Franciscans or Grey Friars, the Dominicans or Black Friars, the Carmelites or White Friars and the Augustinians (Austin Friars).

Friday, the 6th day of the week, named after Frigga, the wife of Odin. It is the Mohammedan Sabbath, a general abstinence day of the Roman Catholic Church, and according to popular superstition, an unlucky day.

Friends, The Society of. *See* Quakers, Section J.

Frigate-Bird, a web-footed bird widely distributed over tropical latitudes, and deriving its name from its great expanse of wing and forked tail, resembling the shape of a swift vessel. It feeds on flying fish mostly, being unable to dive and also steals from other birds. A frigate-bird was found dying on the Hebridean island of Tiree in July 1953; only twice previously had one been recorded in Europe—the first on the German coast in 1792, and the second on the coast of France in 1902.

Frog, a familiar amphibian, breathing through gills in the earlier (tadpole) part of its existence and through lungs later. It remains three months in the tadpole stage. The frog hibernates underwater in the mud during the winter.

Frost occurs when the temperature falls to, or below, 0°C, which is freezing point. Hoar frost is applied to the needles or feather-like crystals of the ice deposited on the ground, in the same manner as dew. Glazed frost is the clear icy coating which may be formed as a result of rain falling on objects whose temperatures are below the freezing point. These layers of ice, often rendering roads impassable for traffic, damaging overhead power and communication systems and endangering aircraft, can also be caused by condensation from warm, damp winds coming into contact with very cold air and freezing surfaces.

Froth-Hopper *or* **Frog-Hopper.** A family of bugs

(belonging to the insect order *Hemiptera*) which in the larval stage surround themselves with a protective mass of froth ("cuckoo spit"). These insects, which suck the sap of plants, bear a faint resemblance to frogs, and the adults possess great leaping powers.

Fuel Cells. A recent development is a type of battery into which the active chemicals are fed from external fuel tanks. This is the *fuel cell*, which is being developed in a number of versions in several countries. One was demonstrated in action when in 1959 Bacon of Cambridge University used his fuel cell to drive a fork-lift truck and a welding machine. The Bacon fuel cell consists of two electrodes of porous nickel dipping into a solution of caustic potash in water. One electrode is supplied with hydrogen gas from an outside cylinder and the other with oxygen. These gases, forming layers on the nickel, are the active chemicals. The oxygen combines with water to make two negatively charged ions, each consisting of an oxygen and a hydrogen atom joined together (a hydroxyl ion). The hydroxyl ions travel through the solution to the hydrogen electrode, where they combine with hydrogen to form neutral water. Their negative charge (one electron per ion involved) has now arrived at the hydrogen electrode and is ready to flow back to the other electrode through any outside circuit that is provided. This flow constitutes the useful electric current, and it has been provided at the expense of creating water out of the original hydrogen and oxygen. The water can be removed in the form of steam. What is the advantage of all this? In the first place the fuel gases are easy to make and to store in cylinders. Supplying a new gas cylinder is easier and quicker than recharging an ordinary accumulator. Furthermore, a fuel cell is lighter for a given power than an accumulator; satellite designers have found them useful. The fuel cell is not damaged by heavy overloading, and this is valuable for application to vehicle driving. Fuel-cell-driven buses could combine the advantage of diesel buses and trolleybuses. Fuel cells are still in the development stage. It is not certain how they will compete with combustion engines or, in the oil-less future, with improved ordinary batteries.

Fulani, a non-Negro people of Hamitic stock widely distributed in N.W. Africa, chiefly in Nigeria. There are two main branches: the dark-skinned Fulani, settled farmers and city dwellers, Moslem in religion; and the light-coloured Bororo'en who are semi-nomadic herdsmen. The Fulani are different from any tribe in W. Africa though they resemble in some ways the Masai of E. Africa. The Fulani conquered the Hausa states at the beginning of the 19th cent. which passed under British suzerainty after 1903. Sokoto, built in 1810, was capital of the Fulani empire.

Fuller's Earth, a special kind of clay or marl possessing highly absorbent qualities, originally used in the "fulling"—that is, cleansing and felting—of cloth. Now used in clarifying oils. Deposits in America and in south of England.

Function. In mathematics, one quantity y is said to be a function of another quantity x, written $y = f(x)$, if a change in x results in some corresponding change in y. Thus $\sin x$ or $\log x$ are functions of x. If y depends not only on x but on several other quantities as well, y is called a function of many variables.

Functionalism, in architecture, a movement originated by Le Corbusier, Swiss-born French architect and town-planner, who applied the austere principles of the Purist movement in painting to his own art. From about 1924 he designed in concrete, steel and glass, buildings in which every part had a significance in terms of function on the theory that objects created to carry out their particular function to perfection cannot help being beautiful. "A house is a machine for living in." The style was in vogue between the two wars, and although its severity became somewhat modified, it is still the basis of most modern architecture.

Fungi, a class of simple plants, which reproduce from spores and lack the green colouring matter *chlorophyll*. It includes moulds, rusts, mildews, smuts, mushrooms, etc. Potato blight is a

fungus disease which caused the failure of the potato crop in Ireland in 1846. 50,000 different fungi are known. *See also* **F42(1), P8(1)**.

Furniture Beetle (*Anobium punctatum*). The common furniture beetle is responsible for 80 per cent of all woodworm damage and is the great pest of the comparatively modern house, causing damage in the main to softwood roofing and flooring timbers. Adults are 3 mm long. The grub tunnels for about 33 months. *See also* **Woodworm, Death Watch Beetle**.

Futurism, an Italian school of art and literature initiated by Marinetti, an Italian writer and mountebank friend of Mussolini at a later period. Its origin took the form of a manifesto published in Paris in 1909 in which Marinetti glorified violence, war and the machine age. In its aggression it favoured the growth of fascism. One of the distinctive features of Futurist art was the use of the principle of "simultaneity" in which the same figure (*e.g.*, a woman descending a flight of stairs) is represented in successive positions like film "stills" superimposed on each other. In spite of two further manifestoes it was not until 1911 that the first examples of Futurist painting and sculpture appeared by the artists Severini, Balla and Boccioni. Apart from the principle of simultaneity, Futurism derived from Cubist and Post-impressionist techniques. The movement faded out early in the first world war.

G

Gabardine, a long, loose, coarse, over-garment, worn by men of the common class in the Middle Ages, and prescribed by law as the distinctive garment of the Jews. The name is now given to a closely woven cloth of wool and cotton used to make raincoats.

Gabbro, a kind of igneous rock, often very coarse-grained, containing a good deal of plagioclase felspar, and monoclinic pyroxene; it may occasionally also include biotite, magnetite, ilmenite and hornblende. A gabbro containing nickel at Sudbury in Canada is one of the richest sources known of that metal.

Gadfly, a widely distributed family of flies with only one pair of wings, including the horse fly. The females are very voracious, being able to bite through the skin and suck the blood of animals. The males are harmless.

Gadolinium. An element, no. 64, symbol Gd, belonging to the rare-earths metals discovered in 1886 by Marignac. It is strongly magnetic.

Gaelic, relating to the Gaels and their language, a term now applied only to the Celtic people inhabiting the Highlands of Scotland, but formerly also to the Celts of Ireland and the Isle of Man.

Galago, "Bush Babies", related to the lemur, native to Africa, large-eyed, in keeping with its nocturnal characteristics.

Galaxy *or* **Milky Way Galaxy** is the huge disk-shaped cloud of gas and stars (some 100,000 million, one of which is the sun) that is turning in space like a great wheel, with a diameter of about 100,000 light years. The Milky Way (that part of the heavens in Milton's words "powdered with stars") is really only a small part of this disk, and every star in the galaxy is moving round the centre under the gravitational control of the whole. The sun and planets lie near the edge of the disk, and it takes them about 250 million years to travel once round. The number of stars that can be seen with the unaided eye is about 3,000, and they all belong to the Milky Way Galaxy, as do most of the stars that can be seen with anything but the greatest telescopes. With the large modern optical and radar telescopes many other systems, similar in size and weight to our galaxy, have been discovered, scattered more or less uniformly through space, and the universe is said to include at least 10,000 million such galaxies. *See also* **F4(2)**.

Gale, a high wind now technically defined as one of at least Beaufort force 8. Between thirty and forty gales a year occur on the north and west coasts of the British Isles and only about half of this number in the south-east. At St.

Ann's Head, Dyfed, the anemometer registered a gust of 113 mile/h (182 km/h) on 18 Jan. 1945, which is a record for these islands. Gusts exceeding 113 km/h are rarely experienced in London. Gale warnings are issued for specified areas by the Meteorological Office, the warnings taking the form of radio broadcasts and the hoisting of storm signals at certain points on the coast. *See* **Beaufort Wind Scale, Section Z.**

Gall, abnormal vegetable growths caused by insects, mites, bacteria, or fungi, found on all parts of the plant. Oak-apples, Robin's pincushion (on wild rose), "witches' brooms" (on trees) are examples. Some are useful commercially, *e.g.*, oak apples yield tannic acid and the black oak gall is used in America as animal food.

Galleon, the name given to the old three-decked Spanish treasure vessels employed in conveying the precious minerals from the American colonies to Spain. The term is often applied to any large, especially stately, sailing vessel.

Galley, an oar-propelled sea-boat used by the ancient Greeks and Romans for transport purposes, manned by slaves. They were also used as warships from classical to relatively modern times, *e.g.*, Lepanto 1571. When so used the sides were raised to protect the rowers.

Gallic Acid, obtained from gall nuts, sumach, tea, coffee, and the seeds of the mango, is used in the manufacture of inks and as an astringent in medicine. It was discovered by C. W. Scheele (1742–86), a Swedish chemist.

Gallium, metallic element, no. 31, symbol Ga, related to aluminium, but which can be cut with a knife. It was discovered spectroscopically by L. de Boisbaudran in 1875. Long before Mendeleyev had predicted that an element with its properties would be found to fill the then existing gap in the Periodic Table; this gap came immediately below aluminium, so he suggested the name "eka aluminium" for it.

Gallup Poll, a system, introduced by Dr. Gallup in the United States, for testing public opinion on topical subjects by taking a test poll on questions framed to elicit opinions.

Galvanised Iron is iron coated with zinc. The name comes from the fact that such a coat protective against rust could be deposited electrolytically. Electrodeposition is sometimes used, but the cheaper and more common process depends on dipping the iron in a bath of molten zinc.

Gamboge, a resinous gum obtained from the sap of *Garcinia morella*, a tree native to Thailand, Cambodia and Sri Lanka, and used as a yellow pigment in paints and also as a purgative.

Game is the term applied to wild animals which are protected from indiscriminate slaughter by Game Laws. In the United Kingdom game comprehends deer, hares, pheasants, partridges, grouse, black game, moor game, woodcocks, bustards and certain other birds and animals of the chase. Game can only be killed (with few exceptions) by persons holding game licences. Occupiers of land and one other person authorised by them in each case are allowed to kill hares and rabbits on their land without licence. Game cannot be sold except by a person holding a proper licence. There is a "close time" prescribed for the different classes of game; for instance, the selling or exposing for sale of any hare or leveret during March, April, May, June or July is prohibited by law. Grouse cannot be shot between 11 December and 11 August; partridges between 2 February and 31 August; pheasants between 2 February and 30 September; and black game between 11 December and 10 August. In regard to foxes and stags, custom prescribes a certain law which sportsmen observe. Game reserves are legally protected areas where natural vegetation and wild life are allowed to remain unmolested by sportsmen or those who might destroy for economic ends.

Gaming, or **Gambling**—*i.e.*, staking money on the chances of a game—differs from betting in that it depends upon the result of a trial of skill or a turn of chance. The Betting and Gaming Act of 1959, passed by the Macmillan administration, replaced all the old laws on gaming, which went back to an Act of 1541 entitled "An Acte for Mayntenance of Artyllarie and debarringe

of unlauful games", under which some games were unlawful if played for money in any circumstances. Roulette and any game of dice were among such games. Under the 1959 Act any game was lawful, subject to certain conditions. Since then the Betting, Gaming and Lotteries Act, 1963, and the Gaming Act, 1968, have been passed, to deal with unlawful gaming and to prevent the exploitation of gaming by commercial interests. The playing of bingo is now restricted to clubs licensed for bingo only. The Gaming Board in its evidence to the Royal Commission on Gambling (1976) recommended a new Gambling Authority or Commission to ensure that any legalised gambling is not penetrated by criminals.

Gammexane, a powerful insecticide, used particularly to kill the tsetse fly and mosquito.

Gangue. Useless minerals associated with metallic ores.

Gannet, a fish-eating bird which dives on its prey from a great height, swallowing it under water, is found in large numbers off the coast of Scotland, and has breeding stations in the Hebrides, St. Kilda, Ailsa Craig, the Bass Rock, Grassholme Island and on Ortac and Les Etacs (rocks off Alderney). It is a bird of white plumage, black tips to long narrow wings and wedgeshaped tail, and weighs about 3 kg. The gannet breeds in colonies on ledges of steep, rocky, island cliffs. Related to the cormorants, pelicans and frigate-birds.

Garden Cities in England were founded by Ebenezer Howard (1850–1928), and his ideas were put forward in his book *Tomorrow—A Peaceful Path to Real Reform* (later re-issued as *Garden Cities of Tomorrow*). New towns should be so placed and planned as to get the best of town and country life, an adaptation of the model villages of certain industrial philanthropists such as Salt, Richardson, Cadbury, Leverhulme and others. The Garden City Association (later the Town and Country Planning Association) was formed in 1899, and the first garden city was begun at Letchworth in 1903 and successfully established. Welwyn Garden City was also Howard's foundation, established in 1919.

Gardener-Bird, a bird possessing many of the characteristics of the bower bird, and found only in Papua–New Guinea. *See also* **Bower Bird.**

Gargantua, the giant hero of Rabelais' satire, of immense eating and drinking capacity, symbolical of an antagonistic ideal of the greed of the Church.

Gargoyle, a projecting spout for carrying off water from the roof gutter of a building. Gargoyles are only found in old structures, modern waterpipe systems having rendered them unnecessary. In Gothic architecture they were turned to architectural account and made to take all kinds of grotesque forms—grinning goblins, hideous monsters, dragons and so forth.

Garlic, a bulbous plant of the same genus as the onion and the leek, and a favourite condiment among the people of Southern Europe. It possesses a very strong odour and pungent taste and its culinary use is agelong.

Garnet, a group of minerals; chemically they are orthosilicates of the metals calcium, magnesium, titanium, iron, aluminium. Garnets can be coloured yellow, brown, black, green or red; the blood-red garnet is an important gemstone.

Garrotte, a method of strangulation used as capital punishment in Spain, and consisting of a collar which is compressed by a screw that causes death by piercing the spinal marrow. Garrotting was also applied to a system of highway robbery common in England in 1862–63, the assailants seizing their victims from behind, and by a sudden compression of the windpipe disabling them until the robbery was completed.

Garter. The Most Noble Order of the Garter was founded (*c.* 1348) by King Edward III, and is the premier order of knighthood in Great Britain. The traditional story associating the garter and the motto with the Countess of Salisbury, who it was said dropped her garter while dancing with the King, who remarked "honi soit qui mal y pense" cannot be accepted. The order was originally limited to the

Sovereign and 25 knights, but the number has been extended, and it may now be bestowed on royal personages and leading representatives of the British peerage. The insignia of the order are the garter of dark-blue velvet with the motto in letters of gold, the mantle of dark-blue velvet lined with white silk, the surcoat and hood, and the gold-and-enamel collar. The garter is worn on the left leg below the knee and by women as a sash over the left shoulder. A famous recent recipient of the Garter has been James Callaghan (1987). See **Knighthood.**

Gas is an elastic fluid substance, the molecules of which are in constant rapid motion, and exerting pressure. The technique whereby gases are liquefied depends on increasing pressure and diminishing temperature. Each gas has a critical point; unless the temperature is brought down to this point no amount of pressure will bring about liquefaction. Last gas to be liquefied was helium (1908) which boils at $-209°C$.

Gas from coal was first used as an illuminating agent by William Murdoch towards the end of the 18th cent. in Birmingham, and about 1807 was introduced in London, one side of Pall Mall being lighted with it. It became widely used as an illuminant, and for space heating and cooking. In the U.K. increasing attention has been paid to the use of a primary fuel—natural gas—instead of producing gas from coal or oil.

Gas, Natural, natural mixture of gases often present with deposits of petroleum, found issuing from the ground in many parts of the world—in the oilfields of Venezuela and the Caucasus, in China, Saudi Arabia, but chiefly in North America. Its chief component is methane. Large industrial centres have made use of this gas since the latter part of the 19th cent., but much of this valuable fuel still goes to waste. Pipelines have been constructed to deliver the gas to where it is wanted. Britain began to ship liquid methane from the Saharan oilfield in 1964. Some of the world's largest natural gas fields have recently been discovered in the North Sea and are being actively exploited. Domestic gas appliances have to be modified if the natural product is substituted for ordinary town gas because the burning characteristics are different. Oil production from the North Sea fields began in 1975 and the main single source of gas in the UK is now natural gas.

Gas Turbine. In this kind of engine mechanical movement is produced by a jet of gas impinging on a turbine wheel; used in aeroplanes, locomotives and ships. These engines are mechanically simple compared with internal combustion engines, and require less maintenance.

Gauge, a standard dimension or measurement, applied in various branches of construction. Thus the standard railway gauge is 4 ft 8½ in (143·5 cm) in the UK, USA and most European countries. The Soviet Union uses the broader gauge of 5 ft (152 cm). Narrow railway gauges of different standards are in use on very steep inclines in various countries. Other standard gauges are fixed in building and gun-boring.

Gauls were inhabitants of ancient Gaul, the country which comprised what is now France, Belgium and parts of the Netherlands, Switzerland and Germany.

Gault, a stratum of blue clay between the Lower Greensand and the Chalk. A typical section of the Gault can be seen at Folkestone.

Gauss, a unit of magnetic induction in the c.g.s. system, named after the great German mathematician and astronomer, K. F. Gauss.

Gavelkind, an old English custom of land tenure in Kent and other places in England, whereby on the death, intestate, of a property owner his property is divided equally among his children and not according to the law of primogeniture.

Gazelles, a group of small, graceful antelopes which live in the drier regions of Africa and Asia. They can run very fast: speeds of over 64 km/h have been recorded.

GCSE, (General Certificate of Secondary Education), the new school-leaving examination, introduced in 1988, which replaced the existing GCE and CSE.

Geiger Counter, an electrical device, invented by Geiger, which can detect individual atomic particles, e.g., electrons, protons, etc. It often consists of a tube of gas at a few cm Hg pres-

sure, fitted with two electrodes—a cylinder and an axial wire. A high voltage is kept across the electrodes, and the passage of a charged particle through the gas releases ions which permit a momentary discharge between the electrodes. Electronic circuits register this discharge as a "count". Geiger counters are used to detect and measure radioactivity and cosmic rays both for technical and research purposes.

Gelatine, a transparent, tasteless, organic substance obtained from animal membranes, bones, tendons, etc., by boiling in water. It is of various kinds, according to the substance used in making it. Isinglass, the purest form of it, is made from air-bladders and other membranes of fish, while the coarser kind—glue—is made from hoofs, skin, hides, etc. Its constituents are carbon, hydrogen, oxygen and nitrogen. Gelatine is applied to an immense variety of purposes, from the making of food jellies to photographic materials.

Gemsbok, a large South African antelope of the open dry plains, sandy coloured with black and white markings on its face, and with long straight horns.

General, a military title next in rank to that of Field-Marshal, the highest officer in the army.

Generation, a time-measure reckoned at about 30 years when children are ready to replace parents; also the body of persons existing at the same time or period. According to a UN report in 1958 "one can no longer think of generations in traditional terms. Interests and activities are today changing so fast that sets of young people not more than seven or eight years apart in age may be as far apart in their thinking and behaviour as two generations once were." The generation gap is now even fewer years apart.

Generation, Spontaneous. See **Abiogenesis.**

Genes, the elementary units of heredity. They exist as highly differentiated regions arranged along the length of the chromosomes which the nuclei of cells carry. A chromosome may carry hundreds or even thousands of genes, each with its own particular structure and specific properties. The position of a particular gene on a chromosome is called its locus. The material of the gene is DNA (q.v.). See **F34.**

Genesis, the first book of the Pentateuch, compiled in the 5th cent. B.C. from earlier documents, which carries the scriptural narrative from the creation to the death of Joseph. Sometimes there is disagreement, as in the story of the creation, Gen. i and ii. Gen. i reflects the views of the ancient Greek scientist Thales (c. 640–546 B.C.) and may be said to be the first scientific account of the creation of the world. The conditions described around the figures of Abraham, Isaac, Jacob and Joseph have a genuine historical basis.

Genetic Code. The elucidation of the structure of DNA (q.v.) for which Crick, Wilkins and Watson were jointly awarded the 1962 Nobel Prize for medicine, revealed the code or chemical dictionary out of which messages serving as blueprints for living structures can be made. See **Protein synthesis, F34.**

Genetic Engineering is the name given to the introduction of human choice and design criteria into the construction and combination of genes. This refers not to breeding by selection, a traditional process, but to the biochemical alteration of the actual DNA in cells (see **Section F, Part IV**) so as to produce novel self-reproducing organisms. Such manipulations became possible when techniques were recently discovered for severing and rejoining DNA molecules and inserting sections into them. Many people regard this development as fraught with enormous significance. Like nuclear power, it can lead to good, to evil, and to accidental hazards, not all of which can be foreseen. Thus when biologists realised they could create new lifeforms, e.g., bacteria, with novel genes, they appreciated that, as well as medically beneficial strains, new virulent forms might by accident be produced and escape into the world. Ultimately, not imminently, men may be able to design the genes of higher animals and even of man himself and thus consciously influence biological evolution. Many scientists have been brought by these possibilities up against an old problem: is science going too far too fast?

Genetics. See **F30**(2).

Geneva Convention, an agreement made by the European Powers at Geneva in 1864, establishing humane regulations regarding the treatment of the sick and wounded in war and the status of those who minister to them. All persons, hospitals, hospital ships are required to display the Geneva cross—a red cross on a white ground. A second conference held at Geneva in 1868 drew up a supplementary agreement. An important result of this Convention was the establishment of the Red Cross Society in 1870.

Genocide is an international crime, defined by the General Assembly of the United Nations in 1948 as "acts committed with intent to destroy, in whole or in part a national, ethnic, racial or religious group as such". The UN Convention came into force in 1951.

Genus, a term applied in biology to designate a group of similar species. A group of similar genera is called a family. See **F35**(2).

Geodesy, the science of calculating the configuration and extent of the earth's surface, and determining exact geographical positions and directions, with variations of gravity etc. Land-surveying is a branch of geodesy.

Geography, science concerned with the spatial organisation of natural features and life and man-made artifacts upon and immediately above the surface of the earth. It is increasingly concerned with the processes by which such patterns are generated and this concern is leading to both a greater degree of specialisation within the subject and the merging of its constituent parts with related disciplines of economics, sociology, political science, geology, biology and meteorology.

Geology, the science which deals with the condition and structure of the earth, and the evidence afforded of ancient forms of life. The geological strata are classified in the following categories: *Primary* or *Palaeozoic* (the oldest fossil-bearing rocks including the Cambrian, Ordovician, Silurian, Devonian, Carboniferous, Permian); *Secondary* or *Mesozoic* (Triassic, Jurassic, Cretaceous); *Tertiary* or *Cainozoic* (Eocene, Oligocene, Miocene, Pliocene, Pleistocene); *Post tertiary* (most recent rocks). See **F48**.

Geometrical Progression is a term used to indicate a succession of numbers which increase or decrease at an equal ratio—as 3, 9, 27; or 64, 16, 4.

Geometry is the branch of mathematics which demonstrates the properties of figures, and the distances of points of space from each other by means of deductions. It is a science of reason from fundamental axioms, and was perfected by Euclid about 300 B.C. The books of Euclid contain a full elucidation of the science, though supplemented in modern times by Descartes, Newton and Carnot. Of recent years non-Euclidean geometry has been developed.

Geophysics, the branches of physics which are concerned with the earth and its atmosphere. Meteorology, geomagnetism, aurora and airglow, ionosphere, solar activity, cosmic rays, glaciology, oceanography, seismology, nuclear radiation in the atmosphere, rockets and satellites—all these are geophysical subjects. The object of the International Geophysical Year, 1957–58, was to investigate the physical phenomena occurring on and around the earth by means of carefully co-ordinated observations made simultaneously all over the globe.

Geothermal Energy. Some of the heavy elements within the earth's crust are radioactive and this gives rise to a temperature rise towards the centre of the earth. The practical exploitation of this geothermal energy comes about when there are hot springs or geysers. It is believed that these are caused by rainwater slowly percolating down to the hot rocks and blowing out as steam. The homes of people living in Reykjavik are heated by geothermal steam and there are a number of small power stations in various parts of the world. Although the costs in the few cases where geothermal power has actually been exploited are remarkably low, the expense of drilling, etc., required when attempting to exploit the heat in the rocks where surface manifestations do not occur, is likely to limit the use of this source of power.

Geothermal Heating. The earth's interior is hot and in certain localities, often adjacent to volcanic or earthquake-prone regions, reservoirs of hot water or steam exist at accessible depths. Natural hot geysers occur in many such places and people, *e.g.*, the ancient Romans and present-day Japanese, use natural hot water for bathing, cooking and laundry. Occasionally the subterranean reserves permit large-scale power generation by drilling for hot steam and passing it into turbines to produce electricity. Pioneering work on this was done at Lardarello in Italy which can produce hundreds of megawatts. Other sites are in New Zealand, California, Japan and Iceland. There are possibilities in S.W. England.

Germanium. A grey, hard, brittle chemical element, no. 32, symbol Ge, chemically related to silicon and tin. Discovered by Winkler in 1886. Its richest ore is germanite containing 6% of the metal. Coal is also a relatively rich source. Since 1948 it has assumed great importance as a semi-conducting material for making transistors (*q.v.*). Because of this it has been so intensively studied that more is known about its physical properties than about those of any other element.

Gesta Romanorum (Latin = deeds of the Romans), a mediaeval collection of Latin stories of unknown authorship which circulated widely in Europe during the Middle Ages. First printed in the 15th cent. The stories were used by Chaucer, Shakespeare and other writers who found many romantic incidents and legends which they were able to turn to good account.

Gestation, the carrying of young in animals during pregnancy, varies considerably in its length. In the case of an elephant, the period is 21 months; a camel, 12 months; a cow, 9 months; a cat, 8 weeks; a horse, 48 weeks; a dog, 9 weeks; and a pig, 16 weeks. Hens "sit" for 21 days; geese, 30; swans, 42; turkeys, 28; pigeons, 18.

Geysers, hot springs of volcanic origination and action, are remarkable for the fact that they throw out huge streams of boiling water instead of lava as in the case of a volcano. The most famous geysers are those of Iceland, which number over a hundred, the principal one having an opening of 21 m in diameter and discharging a column of water to a height of 61 m. There are also geysers in the Yellowstone region of America, and some in New Zealand.

Ghost-Moth or **Ghost Swift,** an interesting nocturnal insect (*Hepialus humuli*) common in England, possessing in the male a white collar and known for its habit of hovering with a pendulum-like action in the twilight over a particular spot where the female is concealed.

Gibbon, the name of a long-armed ape mainly inhabiting S.E. Asia. It is without tail, and possesses the power of very rapid movement among the trees of the forests.

Gin, a well-known spirit distilled from malt or barley and flavoured with the juniper berry. The principal varieties are the English and American, known as "Gin" or "Dry Gin", and the Dutch, referred to as "jenever" or "Hollandse jenever". In Germany and Austria it is called "Schnapps". The word "Gin" is an abbreviation of "Geneva", both being primarily derived from the French genièvre (juniper).

Giraffe, the tallest of existing animals, reaching a height of from 5–6 m when full grown. Its sloping back and elongated neck seem to be the natural evolution of an animal that has to feed on the branches of trees. It is a native of Africa, is of a light fawn colour marked with darker spots and has a prehensile tongue.

Giralda, a beautiful and remarkable example of Arabian art, erected in 1195 at Seville, still in existence.

Glaciers form in the higher Alpine ranges, and are immense consolidated masses of snow, which are gradually impelled by their force down the mountain-sides until they reach a point where the temperature causes them to melt, and they run off in streams. From such glaciers the five great rivers, the Rhine, the Po, the Rhône, the Inn and the Adige, have their source. The longest of the Swiss glaciers is the Gross Aletsch, which sometimes extends over 16 km. Some of the glaciers of the Himalayas are four times as long. The Muir in Alaska is of enormous magnitude, and that of Justeldals Brae in Norway is the largest in Europe.

Gladiators were professional athletes and combatants in ancient Rome, contesting with each other or with wild beasts. At first they were drawn from the slave and prisoner classes exclusively, but so much were the successful gladiators held in esteem that men came to make a profession of athletics, and gladiatorial training schools were established. When a gladiator was vanquished without being killed in combat, it was left with the spectators to decide his fate, death being voted by holding the hands out with the thumb turned inward, and life by putting forth the hands with the thumb extended. Gladiatorial shows were the chief public displays in Rome from the 3rd to the 4th cent. A.D.

Glass is an amorphous, man-made substance, fluid when hot, solid, though fragile, when cooled. It is made of sand mixed with an alkaline flux, usually soda or potash. While hot, glass can be formed into almost any shape by moulding, blowing or, since the early 19th cent., by machine pressing. Unrefined glass normally has a greenish tinge, due to the iron content of most sands, but it is transparent or at least translucent. To make truly colourless glass is a difficult and expensive process, and such glass resembling the natural mineral, rock crystal, is given the name crystal. Glass can be tinted by the addition of various metallic oxides, cobalt producing blue, manganese mauve, etc. Because it is at once solid and transparent, glass is the perfect material for windows for which it has been used since Roman times. And since it can be made cheaply and is easy to clean, it has been used for containers in homes, shops and pharmacies, again since Roman days. Glass can also be made into things of beauty, by the use of coloured glass and by cutting, engraving, painting and gilding. The earliest vessels of glass so far found come from Egypt and date back to c. 1500 B.C. With the invention of glass-blowing in the 1st cent. A.D., the use of glass spread throughout the Roman empire. Many varieties were made, including superb art glass like the Portland vase (q.v.) The Arabs were great glassmakers from the 7th to 15th cent. During the Renaissance the Venetians created luxurious art glass, rich in colour and often manipulated into fantastic forms, Bohemia's 17th-cent. glass is wonderfully engraved with pictures and cut into glittering facets. During the 1670s in England George Ravenscroft invented a new, heavy, water-clear crystal, with an addition of lead as the magic ingredient, and English lead glass is still the basis for all modern crystals.

Glass-Snake, genus, Ophisaurus, of legless lizards with long fragile tails capable of re-generation when broken. Six species are known; in S.E. Europe, S.W. Asia, Indo-China and N. America. Attains a length of about 60 cm; main colouring, green, with black and yellow markings.

Glauconite. A green mineral, chemically a hydrated silicate of potassium and iron. Commonly found in marine sands (hence these rocks are known as "greensands") and sandstones.

Glaucus is a curious genus of sea slugs often called the Sea Lizard belonging to the molluscs. It is without shell and has a soft body, with horny mouth and four tentacles. It is a native of the Atlantic, and is not more than 30 cm in length.

Glee, an unaccompanied piece for three or more voices. Glee-singing was popular in England during the 18th and early 19th cent. and glee-clubs are still in existence.

Globigerina, an oceanic unicellular animalcule with a perforated shell, and occurring in certain parts of the Atlantic in such vast numbers as to form a bed of chalk ooze with their empty shells.

Glockenspiel, an instrument composed of metal bars each of which is tuned to a note. The bars are struck by hand-hammers and give forth chiming sounds.

Glow-worm, a beetle, possessing the power (much stronger in the female than the male) of emitting phosphorescent light from the hind end of the body. The female is wingless.

Glucinium. See **Beryllium**.

Glucose, Dextrose or **Grape Sugar** is a carbohydrate (q.v.). It is produced by hydrolysis from cane sugar, dextrine, starch, cellulose, etc., by the action of reagents. It also occurs in many plants, fruits and honey. For brewing purposes glucose is prepared by the conversion of starch by sulphuric acid. Malt also converts starch into glucose.

Glutton or **Wolverine**, the biggest animal of the weasel family, inhabits the northernmost parts of Europe and America. In build it resembles the bear, and is rather larger than a badger. Its fur is of a brown-black hue, but coarse.

Glycerine or **Glycerol**, occurs in natural fats combined with fatty acids, and is obtained by decomposing those substances with alkalis or by superheated steam. It is colourless and oily and sweet, and is put to a variety of commercial uses, being widely utilised for medicaments, for lubricating purposes, and in the manufacture of nitro-glycerine.

Glycols. Organic compounds containing two alcohol groups. Ethylene glycol is the most widely known example; it is used as an antifreeze in motor-car radiators on account of its property of greatly reducing the freezing point of water. Also used in the manufacture of "Terylene". See **Esters**.

Glyptodon, an extinct species of gigantic armadillo, fossil remains of which have been discovered in S. America. It was some 2·7 m long, carried a huge tortoise-like shell and had fluted teeth.

Gneiss, a metamorphic rock usually containing quartz, felspar and mica. It is banded, the light-coloured minerals being concentrated apart from the dark minerals.

Gnosticism. See **Section J**.

Gnu or **Wildebeest**, a large antelope from Africa south of the Sahara, distinguished by its excessively short thick neck and large head with a pronounced roman nose. There are two species; the white-tailed gnu is almost extinct, the brindled gnu is still common and migrates in large herds.

Goat-Moth (Cossus cossus), a large moth of the Cossidae family, common in Britain, evil-smelling and very destructive in the larval stage to trees of the poplar and willow genus, into the wood of which the caterpillar bores during its three years' period of development.

Goats are horned ruminant quadrupeds, indigenous to the Eastern Hemisphere, but now domesticated in all parts of the world. Though related to the sheep, they are a much hardier and more active animal. The male has a tuft of hair under the chin. Many species, including those of Cashmere and Angora, are valuable for their hair, which is used for fine textile fabrics. The milk of the goat is nutritive, and goat-skins are in good demand for leather for gloves, shoes, etc.

God and **Man**. See **Section J**.

Gog and **Magog**, two legendary City of London giants, supposed to be the offspring of certain wicked daughters of the Emperor Diocletian and a band of demons. They were brought captive to London and made to serve as prisoners at the Palace of Brute, which stood on the site of Guildhall. Effigies of the giants have stood in Guildhall since the time of Henry V. They were destroyed in the Great Fire of 1666, replaced in 1672 and used to be carried through the streets of London in the Lord Mayor's Show. The present figures, carved in lime wood by Mr. David Evans, replaced those carved in 1708 by Richard Saunders, which were destroyed in an air raid during the last war.

Gold. Metallic element, no. 79, symbol Au (Latin Aurum) related to silver and copper, the coinage metals. The greatest amount of gold is obtained by treating gold-bearing quartz by the cyanide process. The gold is dissolved out by cyanide solution, which is then run into long boxes filled with zinc shavings when the gold is precipitated as a black slime. This is melted with an oxidising agent which removes the zinc.

Gold-Beaters' Skin is the outside membrane of the large intestine of the ox, specially prepared and used by gold-beaters for placing between the leaves of gold while they beat them. Thin membrane is of great tenacity, and gets beaten to such extreme thinness that it is used to put on cuts and bruises.

Gold Standard. Under the gold-standard system which was widely prevalent up to 1941, each gold-standard country fixed the value of its currency in terms of a weight of gold of a certain fineness and was, broadly speaking, ready to exchange its currency freely for gold, which could then be exported without restriction. This involved keeping a gold reserve big enough to meet all likely demands and also to serve as a backing for the issue of notes. The gold standard had to be given up during the first world war; and though it was in substance restored in Great Britain in 1925 (when Churchill was Chancellor), the restoration was never complete, as the gold reserve remained too small for complete freedom to export to be practicable. Sterling had to be devalued in the financial crisis of 1931 (which brought about the fall of the Labour Government) and Great Britain was forced off the gold standard. Imbalance in payments between countries is financed by transfers of gold or foreign exchange. Such reserves are known as international liquidity. *See also* **Section G, Parts II and IV.**

Goldeneye, a species of wild duck, widely distributed over Arctic regions. It is a passage-migrant and winter-visitor to the British Isles. Has nested in Cheshire. Distinguished by a large white spot in front of each eye on a dark ground.

Golden Dawn. *See* **Section J.**

Golden Number, the number of any year in the metonic cycle of 19 years, deriving its name from the fact that in the old calendars it was always printed in gold. It is found by adding 1 to the number of the year A.D. and dividing by 19, the remainder being the Golden Number; or, if no remainder, the Golden Number is 19. The only use to which the Golden Number is put now is in making ecclesiastical calculations for determining movable feasts.

Goldsmiths Company, one of the richest London City Companies; the official assayers of gold and silver, invested with the power of "hall-marking" the quality of objects made from these metals. First charter granted in 1327.

Gondola, the old regulation black boats so common on the canals of Venice, propelled by a gondolier with one oar who stands at the stern. The covered part in the centre (*felze*) is rarely seen nowadays as most passengers are tourists who want to see the city.

Gonfalon, the pennon affixed to a lance, spear or standard, consisting usually of two or three streamers and made to turn like a weather-cock.

Gophers. Rodent mammals. The pocket gophers are stout-bodied burrowers common in the USA. The slender burrowing gophers, also called "ground squirrels", occur in central and western USA. The sisel or suslik is a related European species. They are a great pest among grain crops.

Gordon Riots of 1780 were an anti-popery agitation fomented by Lord George Gordon. Called also "No-Popery Riots".

Gorilla, the largest of the anthropoid apes, found in the forests of Equatorial Africa, and at maturity standing from 1·2–1·5 m high.

Goshawk (*Accipter gentilis*), a diurnal bird of prey, fearless and extremely agile; loves wooded country and is very destructive of poultry and game-birds. It resembles the peregrine falcon in appearance, but has shorter, rounded wings. This bird was a great favourite of falconers in mediaeval times.

Gospels are those portions of the New Testament which deal with the life, death, resurrection and teachings of Christ. They are the gospels of Matthew, Mark, Luke and John, all compiled in the later part of the 1st cent. The first three are called the *synoptic gospels* because of their general unity of narrative. Mark was the first to be written and John the last, and it is to Mark that one should turn for the most reliable source of knowledge of the life of Jesus. The word *gospel* comes from two Anglo-Saxon words *gode* (good) and *spell* (tidings), a translation of the Greek *evangelion* = evangel, evangelist.

Gothic, the predominant style of architecture in northern Europe from 12th–15th cent. Its most striking characteristic is the extensive use of the pointed arch, but this is really a mere external reflection of the important structural invention of the 12th cent., that of the rib vault, whereby the whole pressure of the stone vaulting is supported on slim ribs which cross each other at a rising centre. On the outside of the building, the pressure from the vaults is caught up and supported by flying buttresses. A complete Gothic construction gives a marvellous effect of airy lightness, also of something striving upwards, towards the heavens, and this is further accentuated when the churches are crowned by lofty towers and spires. The vital structural elements of Gothic architecture were first put into use in the abbey church of St. Denis in Paris *c.* 1140. The style was further developed in a glorious sequence of cathedrals in northern France: Notre Dame in Paris, Rheims, Amiens, Beauvais and others. When, as in Chartres, the windows are filled with stained glass of glowing colours and the doorways flanked with magnificently carved life-size figures of saints and apostles, the whole effect is one of unsurpassed solemnity and grandeur. From France the style spread to other lands in each of which it developed its own characteristics; thus the English churches tended to have massive towers and delicate spires and, as at Salisbury, were often set in open grounds surrounded by lawns; Flemish and Dutch churches were sometimes built of brick as were those in north Germany and Scandinavia; in Spain the Flamboyant style was followed. The main Gothic cathedral in Italy, that of Milan, although begun in 1386 was not completed until the early 19th cent. Late English Gothic is seen, for example, in King's College Chapel, Cambridge, Henry's Chapel at Westminster and St. George's Chapel at Windsor (all *c.* 1500). Gothic is also found in secular buildings, *e.g.*, Little Wenham Hall in Suffolk, the castle at Ghent, the town halls of Louvain and Middelburg and the streets of Gothic houses in Bruges still in use today. Virtually Gothic as a style (excluding the "Gothic revival" of 19th cent. England) ended at the close of the 15th cent. Gothic art is best seen in the illuminated manuscripts of the 13th and 14th cent. and in the church sculpture. Its characteristic is a complete departure from the cool, perfectionist realism of classical times with distortion to produce emotional effects. The human figures are not ideal forms but recognisable as people we might meet in the street: yet there was also the element of wild imagination, intricate design and a wealth of feeling which might be grotesque, humorous, macabre, or even obscene. Gothic style also found expression in the decorative arts, retaining its architectural character even in small-scale works like caskets, chalices and the like in metalwork and ivory.

Goths. A Teutonic people who originally came from southern Sweden (Gotland) and by the 3rd cent. were settled in the region north of the Black Sea. They began to encroach on the Roman Empire and early in the 4th cent. split into two divisions: the "wise" Goths or Visigoths between the Danube and the Dniester (referred to as the West Goths), and the "bright" Goths or Ostrogoths in southern Russia on the Dnieper (referred to as the East Goths). The Ostrogoths were conquered by the Huns *c.* 370, while the Visigoths under Alaric devastated Greece and sacked Rome in 410. Eventually the Visigoths spread to France and Spain and their last king Roderick fell in battle against the Moors in 711. The Ostrogoths regained their independence on the death of Attila in 453 and under their king Theodoric the Great conquered Italy in 493. They lost their identity after Justinian regained Italy, 525–552.

Gourd Family *or* **Cucurbitaceae.** This family of about 650 species of flowering plants includes the gourds, pumpkins, cantaloupes, cucumber, gherkin, water-melon and squashes. Most abundant in the tropics, the cucurbits are mainly climbing annuals with very rapid growth. The bathroom loofah is the skeleton of one cucurbit fruit, *Luffa cylindrica.* The squirting cucumber is another member of the family.

Governor. A device attached to an engine, turbine, compressor, etc., which automatically controls the engine's speed in accordance with power demand. Most governors depend upon the centrifugal action of two or more balls which are thrown outwards as their speed of rotation increases and actuate a throttle valve or cut-off. The centrifugal governor was invented by Thomas Mead, patented by him in 1787. Watt adapted it to the steam engine.

Grail, Legend of the Holy, a tale of Celtic origin which became part of Arthurian legend and the subject of many mediaeval quest-romances. According to the Christian version the grail was the cup which Christ used at the Last Supper, brought to England by St. Joseph of Arimathea.

Grand Prix, the "French Derby" was established by Napoleon III, in 1863. It is the chief French race and is an international competition of three-year-olds.

Granite is a coarsely crystalline igneous rock consisting of quartz and alkali felspars plus mica or hornblende. It is a much used ornamental and building stone; it forms the high ground of Dartmoor and Bodmin Moor.

Graphite *or* **Plumbago,** commonly called blacklead, is a form of carbon occurring in foliated masses in marble, schist, etc. It is soft, will make black marks on paper or other plain surfaces, and is mainly used for lead pencils. It is also a valuable lubricant. Pure graphite has found a new use with the construction of atomic piles. Important deposits occur in Siberia, Sri Lanka, Malagasy, Canada and USA.

Graptolites, fossil animals confined to Cambrian, Ordovician and Silurian strata. Once classified as hydrazoa but now considered more likely to be hemichordates.

Grasshopper. There are many species of these leaping insects which are related to the locusts and crickets. Most are vegetarians; some eat flies and caterpillars also. The chirping sound they make is made by scraping the hind legs against the wings; in some species a noise is produced by rubbing the wings together.

Gravitation. One of the four, possibly five, types of force known to physics. The others are electromagnetic, nuclear (two types) and colour forces. Gravitational forces are an attraction that one piece of matter has for another; they dominate astronomical phenomena, but inside the atom they are negligible compared with the other types of force. Einstein's General Theory of Relativity is the only theory at present extant which attempts to interpret gravitational forces in terms of more fundamental concepts. *See* **F15(1), 18(2).**

Graylag, the ordinary wild grey goose of Europe, the species from which domestic geese are derived; frequents fens and marshes; breeds in Iceland, Scandinavia and Scotland; distinguished by pinkish legs and feet and lack of black markings on bill.

Grebe, a diving bird of beautiful plumage found over a great part of the world on lakes and oceans. The two species familiar in Great Britain are the Dabchick or Little Grebe and the large and handsome Great Crested Grebe, which has a feathery tuft, lost in the autumn, on each side of the head. Grebes have remarkable courtship displays. The breast feathers are of a downy softness and silver lustre, for which they were formerly much hunted.

Greek Art. *See* **Hellenic Art.**

Greek Fire, a combustible supposed to have been composed of sulphur, nitre, naphtha and asphalt, used with destructive effect by the Greeks of the Eastern Empire in their wars.

Greek Kalends, equivalent to never, as only the Romans, not the Greeks, had kalends.

Green Revolution. The "green revolution" is principally due to the American agricultural expert, Dr. Norman Borlaug, who worked in Mexico on the development of new improved strains of wheat, rice, maize and other cereals. The application of new plant varieties transformed the agricultural prospects of India, Pakistan, Sri Lanka, Mexico, the Philippines and other underdeveloped countries; food importers turned into exporters. However of late the inequity in the distribution of fertilisers has affected the grain production of these countries. For his pioneering work Dr. Borlaug was awarded the 1970 Nobel peace prize. *See* **Section G, Part III.**

Greenwich Mean Time. The first Nautical Almanac, for the use of navigators and astronomers, was published by the Astronomer Royal in 1767. It was based on the meridian at Greenwich, with longitude measured east and west of 0°. A master clock, which still exists, was built at Greenwich Observatory in 1852 to control the railway station clocks and Greenwich Mean Time, or Railway Time as it was sometimes called, prevailed. In 1884 Greenwich was chosen as the prime meridian of the world and GMT became known as Universal Time. The timekeeping role is now to be done by the International Bureau of Weights and Measures. GMT will become CUT (Coordinated Universal Time) *See also* **British Standard Time** and **F68.**

Gregorian Calendar. *See* **Calendar.**

Gresham's Law states that if money, *i.e.*, money with the higher intrinsic value, and bad money are in circulation together, the bad money will tend to drive out the good money from circulation. For instance, the good money is more likely to be melted down or demanded in payment by foreign creditors.

Gretna Green, a celebrated village in Annandale and Eskdale, just over the border from England, where runaway marriages were performed from 1754 to 1856, though only completely stopped during present century.

Griffin, in ancient mythology, a winged creature with an eagle's head and the body of a lion, found in ancient sculptures of Persia and Assyria. Its origin is traced to the Hittites.

Grilse, a young salmon that has only been once to the sea.

Grimm's Law, formulated by Jacob Grimm, an eminent German philologist, lays down a principle of consonantal change in the Germanic languages. For instance, Lat. *pater,* Eng. *father,* Ger. *Vater;* Lat. *frater,* Eng. *brother,* Ger. *Bruder;* Lat. *decem,* Eng. *ten,* Ger. *zehn.*

Grogram (French = *gros grain*), a kind of rough fabric made of wool and some other fibre, such as silk, mohair or cotton, formerly much used for commoner kinds of wearing apparel.

Grotto, a natural or artificial cave. Among the most famous are the blue grotto of Capri and the grotto of Antiparos (Cyclades, Aegean).

Ground Wave, that part of the energy emitted by a radio transmitter which travels along the ground; as opposed to the sky wave which is reflected back to earth by the ionosphere. With the lower radio-frequencies, the ground wave can be picked up over several thousand miles; in the broadcasting band, over a hundred or so miles; it is virtually useless at high frequencies.

Grouse, game bird of the northern latitudes where some 20 species occur. They are stout, compact, ground-dwelling birds, protectively plumaged (the willow grouse turns white in winter), the male usually being larger and more brightly coloured than the female. The red grouse of the British moorlands has been introduced into Belgium and W. Germany. Of the same family are the blackcock, ptarmigan, capercaillie, American prairie-hen and the partridge. Grouse shooting begins in Britain on Aug. 12.

Guanaco, a large species of llama, common to South America, and utilised as a beast of burden.

Guano, the excrement of sea-birds, found in large quantities on the rocky islands of the western coasts of South America and Nauru Is. It forms a useful fertilising agent, being rich in phosphate and ammonia, and first came into use in 1841, since which time Peruvian guano has been a recognised article of commerce. Beds of guano from 15–18 m in thickness are not uncommon. Fish guano and bat guano from caves in South America and the Bahamas are also used as fertilisers.

Gudgeon, a small fresh-water fish of the carp family with 2 small barbels on the upper lip.

Guelph and Ghibelline, italianised forms of the German words "Welf" and "Waiblingen", the names of two rival princely families whose conflicts made much of the history of Germany and Italy during the Middle Ages. The feuds between these two factions continued in Italy during the campaigns of Emperor Frederick I, and later developed into the fierce struggles of the 13th cent. between emperor and pope. In Italy the Ghibellines supported the side of the German emperors and the Guelphs the cause of the Pope. The present Royal Family of England and other Northern monarchies are descended by different routes from the Guelph George I, Duke of Brunswick-Lüneburg of the House of Hanover.

Guildhall, the place of assembly of the members of a guild, and at one time, when guilds were in full strength, was practically the Town Hall. The London Guildhall is today the hall of meeting for the City of London Corporation.

Guilds for the fostering and protection of various trades have existed in England since Anglo-Saxon times, and from the 12th to the 16th cent. exercised great influence and enjoyed many privileges. There were trades' guilds and craftsmen's guilds, and in all large cities and towns there was a guild hall. Their successes in the Middle Ages led to many monopolistic abuses, and in the end it became necessary to free the country from their restrictive power. The City Guilds (Livery Companies of the City of London) derive their name from the distinctive dress assumed by their members in the 14th cent. There are 84 Guilds in existence.

Guild Socialism. See **Section J**.

Guillemot, a genus of sea-birds of the auk family, common in Northern Europe, two species—the Common Guillemot and the Black Guillemot—being natives of our own sea coasts, nesting on the cliffs. Brünnich's Guillemot, an Arctic species, is a rare straggler in the British Isles.

Guinea, an English gold coin of the value of twenty-one shillings, current from 1663-1817, and deriving its name from the first guinea coinage having been struck from gold obtained on the coast of Guinea.

Guinea-Pig, a rodent of the cavy family about 25 cm in length and with a tail so short that it does not project outside the body. It makes an excellent pet, though easily frightened. Its ancestors were species of the wild cavy of S. America said to have been domesticated by the Incas of Peru.

Gules, a heraldic term, denoting a rose of red tincture, indicated by vertical lines drawn or engraved without colour.

Gulf Stream is confined entirely to the western side of the N. Atlantic and is the warm-water current flowing through the Straits of Florida from the Gulf of Mexico parallel to the American coast up as far as Cape Hatteras. From there it continues north-eastwards as a slower, broader, cooler (yet even so, relatively warm) drift of water, merging with the North Atlantic Drift and losing its identity about 40° N. Lat., 60° W. Long. It is a common error to attribute the warmth of the British Isles and Western Europe generally to the Gulf Stream but this has no influence whatever except in so far as it feeds the North Atlantic Drift. Both the Gulf Stream and the North Atlantic Drift owe their movement to the direction of the prevailing winds, and it is the south-westerly airstream coming from warmer regions and passing over the surface waters of the Atlantic Drift that brings the warmth inland to influence the climate of Western Europe.

Gull. An extremely well-known, long-winged sea-bird with rather short legs and webbed feet. In almost all adults the body and tail are white whilst the back and most of the wings are grey or black. In the majority of cases the plumage of juveniles is partly or entirely dusky. Gulls are omnivorous, and are very useful as scavengers. They follow ships and quickly seize upon any refuse which may be thrown overboard. There are 44 species, which vary in size from moderately small to large. With certain exceptions, such as the Kittiwake in the North Atlantic, they are not found very far from land. They are sociable and mostly breed in colonies on cliff-ledges, on islands, beaches and sandhills and among vegetation in swamps, sometimes a long way from the sea. The nest is usually substantial, and the eggs generally number from two to three. Of the 29 species breeding in the northern hemisphere, 14 occur in the British Isles. The pure white Ivory Gull is the most northerly of birds. Sabine's and the Swallow-tailed Gull have forked tails. Ross's Gull has a black ring round the neck and one species, Franklin's Gull, migrates from the North, where it breeds, to pass the winter in the Southern hemisphere.

Gums are glutinous compounds obtained from vegetable sources, soluble in cold or hot water, but not in alcohol. There are innumerable varieties. Gum Arabic is exuded from a species of acacia grown in Senegal, the Sudan, Arabia, India and other countries, and is a valuable commercial product, used in dyeing, ink-making, as a mucilage, and in medicine. India-rubber is an elastic gum. Gums are also made from starch, potatoes, wheat, etc., from seeds, bark, roots and weeds. Many so-called gums are resins.

Gun-Cotton, a powerful explosive manufactured by subjecting a prepared cotton to the prolonged action of a mixture of three parts sulphuric acid and one part of nitric acid. It burns without explosion on ignition, but by percussion explodes with a force five times greater than gunpowder does.

Gunpowder, also called "black powder", the oldest of explosive mixtures, consists of saltpetre, sulphur and charcoal, intimately mixed, the proportions being varied for different intended uses.

Gunpowder Plot was a conspiracy by a desperate band of Roman Catholics in the reign of James I to avenge the harsh treatment to which Catholics were subjected. Barrels of gunpowder were secreted in the vaults underneath the Houses of Parliament, and it was proposed to fire these when the King and his Ministers assembled on 5 November 1605. The plot was betrayed and Guy Fawkes and his co-conspirators were arrested and executed. The date serves to perpetuate the ancient custom of burning the effigy of Fawkes, a custom in which young people are the most enthusiastic participants, with bonfires, fireworks, etc.

Gurnard, a sea-fish, with large, bony head and diminutive body, of which there are some forty species. They are plentiful in British waters.

Gymnasium, originally the name given in ancient Greece to the public places where Greek youth used to exercise and receive instruction. Plato, Aristotle and other great teachers lectured there. The Greek institution was never very popular with the Romans, and it was not until the 18th and 19th cent. that the cult of combining physical with intellectual activity again found a place in educational systems. In Germany the name was applied to the classical grammar school; in this country and America to the halls where gymnastics were practised.

Gypsies, a nomadic race, believed to be of Indian origin; their language, Romany, is related to the languages of N.W. India. The Rom are spread over many parts of the world, but are most common in Europe where they appeared towards the end of the Middle Ages. The English name *gypsy* comes from the Spanish *gitano* = Egyptian; other European names are *Zigeuner* (Ger.), *zingaro* (It.), *fzigany* (Magyar), all resembling the Persian *singar* = a saddler. Their history has been one of persecution. Hitler treated them like the Jews. In Britain since the war they have been kept increasingly on the move, but in 1968 Parliament passed a Bill to make the provision of sites a duty of local authorities. However, it is likely at the present rate of building to be many years before the 4,500 gypsy households have a site. Economic pressure has largely removed their traditional crafts of tinkering, basket-making, peg-making. The majority now deal in scrap-iron.

Gypsum, a whitish mineral consisting of hydrated sulphate of calcium. The finest gypsum is alabaster. When heated gypsum is converted into the powder called Plaster of Paris; the water it loses can be taken up when the plaster is wetted, and the reconversion of Plaster of Paris into gypsum accounts for the way in which the former sets hard. The name "Plaster of Paris" came from the location of important gypsum quarries in the Montmartre district of Paris. It was found after the flood disasters of January 1953 that gypsum could undo the effect of sea-water. By spreading it for the rain to wash into the soil, thousands of acres of farmland in Holland and Britain were made productive again.

Gyroscope is a symmetrical rapidly rotating object, typically wheel-like, which because of its mass and rotation possesses a lot of the dynamical property known as angular momentum. Basic dynamical laws tell us that angular momentum is conserved and a consequence of this is that the axis of rotation tends to stay pointing in the same direction. Disturbing influences make a gyroscope's motion complicated but the general effect of the presence of a gyroscope attached to any body is to help to stabilise the body's motion. This is made use of in reducing the rocking of ships and in compasses and control systems in aircraft, torpedoes and missiles.

H

Habeas Corpus, the name given to a writ ordering the body of a person under restraint or imprisonment to be brought into court for full inquiry into the legality of the restraint to be made. The first Habeas Corpus Act was passed in 1679, though nominally such a right had existed from Magna Carta, but some of the more despotic kings had disregarded it. In times of public peril the privilege of *habeas corpus* is sometimes temporarily suspended, many instances occurring in the history of Ireland and during the first and second world wars.

Haber Process, the important industrial process for synthesising ammonia from atmospheric nitrogen. Nitrogen and hydrogen are combined at high pressure (*c.* 350 atmospheres) and moderately high temperature (500°C) using a catalyst (made largely of iron). A yield of 30% is obtained. The majority of the world's ammonia is produced in this way or from methods derived from it.

Habsburg (Hapsburg), the ruling house of Austria, 1282–1918; held title of Roman Emperor, 1438–1806, except for 1740–5. The aggrandisement of the Hapsburg family was mainly brought about by a series of fortunate marriages. In 1521 when the Hapsburg power was at its zenith, Charles V divided his dominions into two branches—Austrian Hapsburg and Spanish Hapsburg. The Hapsburg Danubian Monarchy dates from 1526 when the Hungarian and Bohemian crowns were united with the Austrian patrimony of the Hapsburg. The triple union lasted 400 years. The murder of the heir to the Hapsburg thrones, Francis Ferdinand, at Sarajevo in 1914, provoked the outbreak of the first world war. Francis Joseph's great-nephew, Charles, went into exile in 1918. (Prof. C. A. Macartney's authoritative work, *The Habsburg Empire, 1790–1918,* was published in 1969.)

Haddock, one of the best-known fishes abounding in northern seas and averaging about 1·8 kg in weight. Related to the cod. Largely used for curing, and sold as "finnan haddies".

Hade of veins, a mining term indicating the particular inclination that any vein, seam or strata may have from the perpendicular; thus, in Weardale the veins mainly "hade" to the north.

Hadrian's Wall. *See* **Roman walls.**

Haematite, ferric oxide, one of the principal iron ores, containing about 70% of the metal. It is usually found in kidney-shaped masses, and is specular, red or brown, in thin fragments but greyish in bulk.

Haemocyanin, the respiratory pigment of crustaceans and molluscs. It functions like haemoglobin, from which it differs in containing copper instead of iron and being blue when oxidised instead of red. *See* **F39(1).**

Haemoglobin, the pigment containing iron which gives red blood corpuscles their colour. It is a respiratory pigment, having the property of picking up oxygen when the blood passes through the lungs to produce the compound known as oxyhaemoglobin. In other parts of the body the oxyhaemoglobin breaks down, liberating oxygen, which is used in the oxidation process (respiration) that the body tissues carry on. *See* **F38(2).**

Hafiz, besides being the pseudonym of a famous

Persian poet, is a title conferred upon any Mohammedan who has committed the whole of the Koran to memory.

Hafnium, a metallic element, no. 72, symbol Hf, discovered by Coster and Hevesy in 1922 and important in the atomic-energy field. It occurs in most zirconium minerals to the extent of about 5%.

Hagiology, a branch of literature that is wholly given up to the history of the saints, and the setting forth of the stories and legends associated with their names.

Hail, hard, roughly spherical balls of ice, consisting of white cores covered by layers of both transparent and opaque ice, frequently falling during thunderstorms. They usually do not exceed 2·5 cm in size, but hailstones as large as tennis balls have been observed. The general theory of a hailstone is that near the top of a cumulonimbus cloud a raindrop becomes frozen, grows in size by condensation and through collisions with snow particles, and eventually becomes so weighty as to overcome the ascending air currents in the cloud. Falling, it first encounters supercooled water drops, immediately freezing on it, increasing the white core, and then at lower levels ordinary water drops, freezing more slowly, producing a layer of clear ice. Before the hailstone arrives at the ground gusts and lulls may transport it several times up and down both regions, adding alternate coatings of soft white and hard clear ice.

Halcyon, a term associated in olden times with the kingfisher and days of soothing calm, "halcyon days" being a frequently used expression. The legend was that the kingfisher laid its eggs on the surface of the sea at the time of the winter solstice when the sea was unruffled. (Halcyon is the Greek for kingfisher.)

Halibut, one of the largest of the flat fishes, averaging when full grown from 1·2–1·8 m in length, and highly esteemed for the table. Specimens of still larger size occasionally occur. It is plentifully distributed. Its two eyes are on the right side of the head.

Hallmark. A mark or group of marks, impressed by an assay office on gold or silver articles (and on platinum since 1974) guaranteeing the standard of fineness of the precious metal used in them. These marks, which have been applied to silver made in London since the beginning of the 14th cent. and perhaps earlier, make it possible to establish the year and place of assay and also the name of the maker. English pieces of silver usually have not less than four marks, viz., (1) town mark; (2) maker's mark; (3) date letter; (4) sterling mark.

The town mark is rarely changed; in London a crowned leopard's head was used from the earliest days until 1820 with only minor modifications, except for the period 1697–1720 when a lion's head erased was substituted; since 1820 the crown has been omitted.

Until the late 17th cent. a symbol was often used as a maker's mark, from 1696–1720 the first two letters of the maker's surname, and subsequently the maker's initials. Owing to the destruction of the earlier mark plates at Goldsmiths' Hall no maker's name prior to the late 17th cent. can be identified with certainty.

The London date letter is changed at the end of May each year, so each letter covers seven months of one year and five months of the following. The London date cycle has usually consisted of twenty letters: the alphabet of each cycle is of different style, and the letters are enclosed in shields of different shape.

The sterling mark, the lion passant, was introduced in 1544 and continued in use until 1697, when the higher Britannia standard was introduced in order to discourage the practice current amongst goldsmiths of melting down coin of the realm to make plate. The leopard's head crowned and the lion passant were then replaced by a figure of Britannia and a lion's head erased. Though the regulation imposing a higher standard was withdrawn in 1720, a small amount of Britannia standard silver continued to be made and still is made.

From 1784 until 1890 a plate tax was levied on all silver assayed in Great Britain and an additional duty mark, the sovereign's head, was used during this period. A Jubilee mark bearing the head of George V and of Queen Mary was used between the years 1933 and 1935, and in 1953 a coronation mark with the head of Queen Elizabeth was introduced.

Under the Hallmarking Act 1973 the hall-marking of platinum is now compulsory; the hallmark symbol is an orb surmounted by a cross and encompassed by a pentagon; assay offices London and Birmingham.

Halloween (31 October), the eve of All Saints' Day, a time associated, especially in Scotland, with certain pleasing superstitions attractively set forth in Burns's famous poem "Hallowe'en". It is the night when young men and maidens are supposed, by observing certain rites, to have their future wives and husbands disclosed to them.

Hallucinogen, a drug which acts upon the brain to create sensory illusions or hallucinations with a variety of emotional effects. One of the most widely studied is LSD (q.v.) which will produce symptoms very similar to those found in some mental disorders.

Halo, a luminous circle usually of 22° radius, surrounding sun or moon, produced by the refraction and reflection of light by ice crystals of high cirrus cloud. It is a very common occurrence, in the British Isles almost one day in three. The inner side is red and the outer a whitish-yellow colour. "Mock suns", i.e., patches of light at the same elevation as the sun are much rarer occurrences, sometimes being of great beauty and brilliance. Halo is the Greek for threshing-floor. See **Corona.**

Halogens, the group name for the five non-metallic elements fluorine, chlorine, bromine, iodine and astatine. The term "halogen" means "salt-producer".

Halteres, the modified hind-wings of the two-winged flies or Diptera (e.g., the house-fly). The equilibrium in flight of these insects depends on the halteres, which are commonly called "balancers".

Hampton Court Conference, presided over at Hampton Court Palace by James I in 1604 and which brought about his authorised translation of the Bible, had an important bearing on the religious differences of the time. James refused to grant tolerations to the Puritans. This sowed the seeds of civil war. Following the conference three hundred English Puritan clergy were ejected from their livings.

Hanaper Office, a former Chancery office, deriving its name from the fact that its writs and papers were kept in a hanaper (hamper). The Chancellor's office thus came to be known as the Hanaper. The Comptrollers of the Hanaper were abolished in England in 1842.

Hand, a measure of 4 in (10 cm), the average size of the palm; used in reckoning height of horses.

Handfasting, an informal marriage custom once prevalent in Scotland, whereby a man and woman bound themselves to cohabit for a year and a day, and at the end of that period either confirmed their contract by a regular marriage or separated.

Hanoverians, Royal dynasty which ruled Great Britain and Ireland, from 1714 to 1901. From the Brünswick-Luneburg branch of the Guelph family, they took their name from the German state of Hanover where they were Electors of the Holy Roman Empire. Their succession to the English, and later British, crown was secured by the 1710 Act of Settlement. In 1837 the crown of Hanover went to the uncle of Queen Victoria, Ernest, Duke of Cumberland and the personal union of the Hanoverian and British crowns ceased.

The British Hanoverian monarchs were George I (ruled 1714–27); his son George II (1727–60); George III, grandson of George II (1760–1820); his eldest son George IV (1820–30 and Prince Regent from 1812); William IV, third son of George III (1830–37) and Queen Victoria, granddaughter of George III (1837–1901).

Hansard, the title given to the official reports of Parliamentary debates, so named after Luke Hansard who in 1774 became partner in a firm of printers to the House of Commons. His son T. C. Hansard was first the printer and then the publisher of an unofficial series of parliamentary debates inaugurated by William Cobbett in 1803. In 1909 production was taken over by

H.M. Stationery Office and today's volumes contain full, substantially verbatim, reports of what is said in both Houses of Parliament.

Hanseatic League was a confederation of North German towns established about 1241 for purposes of mutual protection in carrying on international commerce. The League became so powerful that it was able to dominate the foreign trade of Norway, Sweden, Denmark, and even to some extent of London. A branch was established in London and had its guild hall in Cannon Street for hundreds of years. The League existed down to the middle of the 17th cent. Hamburg, Lübeck and Bremen are the only cities which, as free ports, still by commercial courtesy retain the name of Hanse towns. *Hansa* is Old High German for Association or Merchants' Guild. See also **Freeport.**

Hapsburg, see **Habsburg.**

Hara-kiri, the custom of suicide, as formerly practised in Japan, when in disgrace.

Hardware, the electrical, electronic, magnetic and mechanical parts of a computer or data-processing system. See also **Software** and **Section V.**

Hare, a rabbit-like animal with longer ears and legs. There are many kinds of hare distributed over the northern hemisphere and in Africa south to the Cape. They do not burrow as do rabbits but rely on camouflage, speed and mobility for safety. See **Game.**

Harleian MSS. comprise some thousands of volumes of MSS. and documents, collected by the first Earl of Oxford (1661–1724) and his son Edward. After the death of the latter, his widow handed the MSS. over to the nation for £10,000, and they are deposited in the British Museum.

Harlequin, the buffoon of ancient Italian comedy. As adapted to the British stage, however, harlequin is a pantomime character only, in love with Columbine, appearing in parti-coloured garments and carrying a wand, by which he exercises a magic influence in thwarting the fantastic tricks of the clown and pantaloon.

Harmattan, a dry wind which may blow between January and May across the Sahara to the Gulf of Guinea. Although affording relief from the tropical heat, vegetation withers because of its extreme dryness and much irritation is caused by the clouds of fine dust which it carries.

Harmonic Motion, regular periodic motion of the kind exemplified by a ball bobbing up and down at the end of a spring, and by the piston in a steam engine. It may be simple (simple harmonic motion) or composed of two or more simple harmonic motions. In simple harmonic motion the acceleration is proportional to the distance of the moving body from its original rest position.

Harp-seal, the ordinary Greenland seal, with a dark harp-shaped marking on its back, hence its name. It abounds in Newfoundland waters and further northward towards the Arctic.

Harpy Eagle, a large bird of prey named from the winged monsters of Greek mythology, inhabiting the forest regions of Central and South America. There are eight species, one with handsome grey plumage and large crest which attacks and kills animals much larger than itself, and was called by the Aztecs "winged wolf".

Harrier, a bird of prey of the falcon family; of the various species distributed over the world, three breed in Britain: the moorland Hen harrier, the Marsh harrier and Montagu's harrier. They are large birds with long tails, long legs, long wings and gliding flight. They nest on the ground and eat small mammals, frogs, lizards and small birds.

Hartebeest, common African antelope of a grey-brown colour, with ringed and knotted horns bending backward and tapering to sharp points: gregarious, of large size. There are several species.

Harvest Bug, a very small insect, of a dark red colour, which appears in large numbers in the fields in autumn, and is peculiarly irritating to animals and man by the tenacity with which it attaches itself to the skin and burrows underneath. Probably the larvae of spinning mites (Trombidoids). In the USA they are called "chiggers".

Harvest Moon, the full moon that occurs nearest to the autumn equinox, in September. It rises for several nights running about the same time, and yields an unusually brilliant series of moonlight nights.

Harvestmen are, like spiders, members of the arachnid class but belong to the distinctly different order of Phalangida. They are common in the countryside in autumn and have small oval bodies and eight long slender legs which besides being mere organs of locomotion also act as sense organs. Known as "daddy longlegs" in America and UK.

Hashish, an Arabic word for the narcotic substance prepared from the hemp plant (*Cannabis sativa*). It is known by a variety of names, *e.g.*, bhang in India and marijuana in America.

Hatchment, in heraldry, is a square board, in vertical diagonal position, placed outside a house or on the tomb at the death of a member of a family and so arranged that it indicates the sex and condition of the deceased.

Hawfinch, a well-known European bird of the finch family, having a variegated plumage, a sturdy bill and black-and-white tail. In England it is found in the Midland and Eastern counties, and locally in Scotland.

Hawk. This name is applied to almost any diurnal bird of prey other than eagle, falcon or vulture, but in its strict sense applies only to the *Accipiter* genus—the small Sparrow Hawk and the larger Goshawk, round-winged, long-tailed birds with barred under-parts. They prey upon small birds captured in flight and small mammals.

Hawk-moths, large species of moths, thick of body and strong of wing, which fly with rapid swooping motion, hence the name. There are numerous handsome species in Britain.

Hearth-Money was a tax laid on hearths (in all houses paying the church and poor rates). Charles II introduced it in 1662, and it was repealed in the reign of William and Mary.

Heat, after prolonged controversy over whether or not heat is a "substance" (formerly called "caloric"), it was established in the 19th cent. that heat is a form of energy; it is in fact the combined kinetic and potential energy of the atoms of which a body is composed. Heat can be turned into other forms of energy, *e.g.*, a red hot body loses heat by radiating it in the form of electromagnetic waves ("radiant heat"—chiefly infra-red rays). Heat may also be transferred from one place to another by conduction and, in fluids, by convection. All three processes occur when a glowing fire heats a room. A unit quantity of heat is the calorie, which is the amount of heat sufficient to raise the temperature of 1 g of water by 1°C. In general, adding heat to a body raises its temperature. The number of calories required per gram of material to raise the temperature 1°C is called the *specific heat* of the material. However, adding heat may not raise the temperature-but may instead cause a change of state, *e.g.*, from solid to liquid (melting) or liquid to gas (evaporation). The amount of heat required to melt 1 gram of a solid is called the latent heat of melting. Similarly, there is a latent heat of evaporation. Strictly speaking, the specific and latent heats of a substance depend on how much its pressure and volume are allowed to vary during the measurements. Water has a high specific heat, and this makes the oceans a vast heat reservoir, a factor of great meteorological significance. The science of heat is called thermodynamics, and is of great importance in physics and chemistry. **F20**(1).

Heat Pump, essentially a refrigerator working in reverse, *i.e.*, a device which warms up one place, say, a house by releasing into it heat transferred from another place, say, the air or earth outside the house. The idea is attributed to Lord Kelvin (1852) and later Haldane used a heat pump to heat his house in Scotland. In Summer, a house could be cooled by operating the device in reverse. As in a domestic refrigerator, the heat is transferred by a suitable fluid whose circulation has to be driven by an external supply of energy, *e.g.*, by running a mechanical compressor. With good design and favourable conditions, the energy required to run the heat pump is considerably less than would be required to produce the same warming effect directly. Since the 1930s heat pumps have

been produced commercially for domestic and industrial use but, as always, careful consideration is needed to decide whether in a particular application they are cheaper to run than alternative methods of heating.

Heath, flowering plants of the *Ericaceae* family. Heaths are widely distributed over uncultivated spaces of Europe and Africa. In Britain they are represented by heather (of which there are several species) and ling (*Calluna vulgaris*), which cover thousands of acres of moorland. Some of the African or Cape heaths are very beautiful and much prized by florists. One species of heath (*Erica arborea*) which grows in S. Europe and N. Africa has close-grained woody rootstock used for making briar pipes. In N. Europe acid heathlands, dominated by heather and ling, form one of the most widespread vegetation areas created by man through the destruction of former oak forests, grazing and burning.

Heat Wave is a spell of very hot weather, due chiefly in the British Isles to a warm southerly current of air caused by the presence of an anticyclone over western or central Europe at the same time as a depression is stationary over the Atlantic. High humidity increases the discomfort.

Hegira, an Arab term signifying departure or flight, used in reference to Mohammed's departure from Mecca, A.D. 622, from which date the Mohammedan era is reckoned.

Helicopter, heavier-than-air aircraft which obtains its lift from blades rotating above the fuselage in windmill-fashion. The first successful helicopters were the Focke-Wulf 61, a German machine (1936), and the VS-300, designed by Igor Sikorsky, flown in 1937. Helicopters can hover, and rise and descend vertically, in addition to being capable of horizontal flight.

Heliotrope, a favourite sweet-scented flowering plant, common in tropical and sub-tropical countries; the Peruvian heliotrope is the "cherry pie" of our summer garden borders.

Helium, a gaseous element, no. 2, symbol He, first discovered by means of the spectroscope in the sun's atmosphere. This discovery, made in 1868 by the astronomer Sir Norman Lockyer, was followed in 1895 by Sir William Ramsay's proof that the element existed on earth. He found it in the uranium ore, clevite. Later it was established that helium is formed by the radioactive decay of many elements which emit α-particles (nuclei of helium atoms) and is contained in all radioactive minerals. The largest source of helium is natural gas, the richest in helium being the gas from certain wells in Utah, USA. Next to hydrogen, helium is the lightest gas known, has a lifting power equal to 92% of hydrogen and the advantage that it is inert and non-inflammable. It is used for inflating airships. Ordinary air contains 1 part in 200,000 of helium. It was the last gaseous element to be liquefied, this being achieved by Onnes in 1908 in Leyden. Liquid helium has many remarkable properties only imperfectly understood. As well as being scientifically fascinating it is indispensable in cryogenics (*q.v.*) as a medium for cooling other substances to temperatures near absolute zero. Hydrogen fusion in the "H bomb" produces helium.

Hellebore, a plant of the *Ranunculaceae* (buttercup) family. The best-known British examples are the green and stinking varieties. There is also a garden kind which flowers in December called the Christmas Rose. Hellebore yields a bitter substance which forms a drastic purgative, but is now little used.

Hellenic Art. The art of ancient Greece may be roughly divided into three periods: the prehistoric period (*c.* 1500–1000 B.C.) of the bronze age Mycenaeans; the archaic period (*c.* 600–500 B.C.); and the classical period (*c.* 500–300 B.C.). Of the first period centred on Mycenae on Peloponnesus but extending to the coasts of Asia and the city of Troy we can mention only the massive stone gateways and the shaft graves of Mycenae, where the archaeologist Schliemann discovered painted vases, gold cups, bronze swords and ornaments of what had once been a great, if primitive, civilisation. During the archaic period sculpture was the principal form of art expression. The magnificent male and female figures are reminiscent of Egyptian art, but are distinctive in liveliness of facial expression. The vase-paintings of this period became more elaborate, depicting scenes from mythology or ceremonial events. Typical of classical Greek art is the representation of the beautiful and healthy human body deliberately posed and often carrying out heroic or athletic acts. The vast majority of these statues are known to us only through Roman copies. The *Hermes* of Praxiteles (born *c.* 385 B.C.) is possibly the only existing statue which can be assigned with any degree of certainty to an individual artist. Almost the whole of the Greek genius in architecture was expended on temples which are all basically similar in design—a rectangle with a low-pitched gabled roof resting on side walls. The three orders Doric, Corinthian and Ionic mainly referred to the type of column used, but naturally the whole building was influenced thereby. Some of the main buildings are on the Acropolis, a hill outside Athens, on which stand the Parthenon (from the outer frieze of which the Elgin marbles (*q.v.*), now mostly in the British Museum, were taken), the Erechtheum, famous for its Porch of Maidens, and the gateway known as the Propylaea with its broad flight of marble steps. Apart from that on vases, no Greek painting has come down to us, although Greek painters existed and were noted in their time. All we have are copies in mosaic and fresco made by the Romans, at Naples and Pompeii. Of Greek literature in prose, verse and the drama little can be said here. To the early period (*i.e.*, the archaic age) belong Homer's *Iliad* and *Odyssey*. Hesiod's long poem *Work and Days* and Sappho's love poems, and Pindar's Odes. The period of Pericles in the 5th cent. B.C. produced more great literature than any comparable period in history: the philosophical writings of Plato and Aristotle, the tragedies of Aeschylus, Euripides and Sophocles, the comedies of Aristophanes—all these are still part of the European tradition, and together with Greek architecture played a major part in the Renaissance (*see* **Section J**).

Hellenistic Art, the age of the period of Greek civilisation which began with the conquests of Alexander the Great (356–323 B.C.) and lasted until his former empire (which encompassed most of the Middle East and part of North Africa) was conquered by the Romans in 146 B.C. Culturally it was an important period because it spread Greek culture far beyond its original boundaries—even as far as the north of India, and its centres spread from Athens to the cities of Alexandria in Egypt, Antioch in Syria and Pergamum in Asia Minor. But equally Eastern culture spread to the West: democracy was replaced by absolute monarchy, cosmopolitanism took the place of the Greek tendency to believe that all who were not Greeks were barbarians, and mystical philosophies took the place of Greek rationalism. This was a sensuous, secular, pleasure-loving, rootless society, and these tendencies were reflected in its art. Hellenistic sculpture was sensual, effeminate and violently emotional, depicting individuals and not always noble or beautiful ones. (Classical Greek sculpture was idealistic, showed types rather than individuals and appealed to the intellect rather than the emotions.) Some of the best examples came from the school at Pergamum and later from the island of Rhodes, and the titles themselves speak of their nature: *The Dying Gaul, Gaul Slaying his Wife and Himself* and the famous *Laocoön* (representing Laocoön and his two sons being crushed by two enormous serpents). All these date from about 240 to 50 B.C.—for the culture did not immediately end with the Roman conquest. The enormous frieze of the altar of the temple in Pergamum depicts a battle between gods and giants with tremendous realism and brutal violence far removed from the serene art of classical times. Portrait sculpture is typical of Hellenistic art, where it may almost be said to have been invented, since such ventures in the past had been idealistic rather than realistic. The great Hellenistic cities were geometrically planned and fine public buildings made their appearance in which the slender and graceful

Ionic of the ornate Corinthian columns took the place of the more austere and heavy classical ones. Alexandria was celebrated for its vast libraries and was the centre of a brilliant intellectual life (the Septuagint or Greek translation of the Bible was prepared here). Here too worked the mathematicians Euclid and Archimedes, the physicians Erasistratus and Herophilus, and the geographer Pytheas. But Hellenistic literature was a pale reflection of the glories of the past and we mention only the comedies of Menander and the pastoral verse of Theocritus of Syracuse.

Hemiptera, the order of insects to which belong the true bugs. Their wing structure is in most species incomplete, hence the term hemiptera (half-wing). This order includes the familiar water insects, the water boatman and water skater, also the aphids, cicadas, leaf hoppers, scale insects.

Hemlock, a plant of the *Umbelliferae* family, growing in all parts of Britain, and containing a strong alkaloid poison. Used medicinally, this alkaline substance is of considerable service, being a powerful sedative. According to Pliny, hemlock was the poison used by the Athenians in putting criminals to death.

Hemp (*Cannabis sativa*), name of a plant native to Asia, now cultivated widely for the valuable fibre contained in the stalk or in some species in the leaves. Hemp fibre has been replaced by cotton for textiles and by jute for sacks and is now chiefly used for cordage and twine. It contains a resinous substance from which the narcotic hashish is made. The seed yields a valuable oil. The term hemp is also used for other fibre plants, including manila hemp from the Philippines, sunn hemp from India, sisal from W. and E. Africa and phormium from New Zealand.

Henbane, a plant found in Britain and other parts of Europe and Northern Asia. It belongs to the potato family *Solanaceae*, grows mostly on waste ground and bears yellow-brown flowers veined with purple. The leaves yield a poisonous alkaloid substance which, medicinally prepared and administered, is of great use. Tincture of henbane is often preferred to laudanum.

Heptarchy, a word derived from the Greek *hepta*, seven, and denoting the seven kingdoms (*archai*) into which Anglo-Saxon England was divided before 900. The seven were Kent, Essex, Sussex, Wessex, Mercia, East Anglia and Northumbria.

Heracleum, a plant of the *Umbelliferae* family, common in southern and central Europe, though only one species, the cow parsnip, grows in England. It has a bitter root, and from the juice of the stem an intoxicating liquor is occasionally prepared.

Herald, an officer of state empowered to make formal proclamations and deliver messages from the sovereign or other high personage whom he serves. In the developments which took place in armorial bearings, the herald was the functionary charged with the duty of their proper depiction.

Heraldry, the knowledge of armorial bearings, was mainly the outcome of the love of outward distinction which prevailed in mediaeval times, "Heraldry," says Stubbs, "became a handmaid of chivalry, and the marshalling of badges, crests, coat-armour, pennons, helmets and other devices of distinction grew into an important branch of knowledge." The *shield*, or *escutcheon*, is the ground upon which armorial signs are traced, the colour of the shield being called the *tincture*, the signs recorded the *charges*. There are seven *tinctures—or* (gold), *argent* (silver), *gules* (red), *azure* (blue), *vert* (green), *purpure* (purple) and *sable* (black). The *charges* are classed as "Honourable" and "Subordinate" ordinaries, comprising lines and geometrical forms; and "Common" ordinaries, which latter includes all representations of natural objects. There is also a system of external signs, such as crowns, coronets, mitres, helmets, mantlings, wreaths and crests, each having its distinctive significance. For other distinguishing marks *see* **Hatchment, Quartering, Rampant.**

Heralds' College or College of Arms, was incorporated by Richard III in 1483. Its head is the Earl Marshal (an office hereditary in the family of the Dukes of Norfolk), and there are three Kings of Arms, six Heralds and four Pursuivants. The business transacted is wholly connected with the tracing of genealogies and the granting of armorial bearings. In Scotland the Heraldic functions are performed by the Lord Lyon King of Arms.

Herbarium, a systematically classified collection of preserved plants. One of the largest in the world is at the Royal Botanic Gardens at Kew.

Heredity is the study of the transmission of physical and mental characteristics from one generation to another. Gregor Mendel (1822–84), a great experimenter in the field of inheritance, established the principle embodied in Mendel's law in his work published in 1866. The ideas which he then put forward were forgotten until the early years of this century, but today they form the basis of the modern study of genetics. Genes are the units of heredity; they are contained in the chromosomes of the cell nucleus. In human cells there are 46 chromosomes—22 pairs of characteristic shape, and a 23rd (the sex chromosomes) similar in women and dissimilar in men, which unite in the process of fertilisation. An individual can only develop, even under the most favourable surroundings, as far as his inherited characteristics, i.e., his genes will allow him to do. It is in the development of personality that the interplay between heredity and environment becomes most apparent. *See* **Evolution, Section F, Part IV.**

Hermaphrodite, animals or plants possessing both male and female reproductive organs, e.g., snail, earthworms, most flowering plants.

Hermit Crab, a decapod, with a soft asymmetrical body which it protects by thrusting it into an empty gastropod shell, e.g., whelk, which it carries about, only abandoning it when necessary for a larger one. Found in all seas, many live in commensal relationship with sea anemones etc.

Heron, a large wading bird with long curved neck and pointed bill, is a member of the *Ardeidae* family, of which there are many species. Egrets and bitterns are included as herons. Herons are to be met with in marsh lands and near rivers and lakes, where they feed on fish and frogs. They nest in trees in large numbers, these colonies being called heronries. The common heron is native to England, and other species from the Continent are frequent visitors.

Herring (*Clupes harengus*), an important food-fish inhabiting the North Sea which has been subjected to overfishing. In Britain the herring industry is based on the Shetlands and the coastal ports of E. Scotland and N.E. England. Marine biologists have recently reported on its unique structure for hearing which makes it receptive to sound frequencies over a very wide range and able to determine distance, direction and sound of a source of sound.

Hibernation, the dormant condition in which numerous mammals, reptiles, amphibians, insects, plants, etc., pass the winter. The rate of metabolism slows down, and the body temperature drops to that of the surroundings. Work on these low temperatures and their physiological effect has led to improved surgical techniques. Animals of the torrid regions pass through an analogous period (aestivation) during the hot season, when the sources of food are dried up.

Hickory, several species of American tree of the walnut family, remarkable for its very hard, solid, heavy white wood, and bearing an edible, four-lobed nut.

Hieratic Art, a type of art (typified by the major part of the art of ancient Egypt) which is (a) exclusively religious and (b) conventionally based on earlier forms and traditions.

Hieroglyphics are the earliest form of pictured symbolic expression, and are supposed to have been introduced by the ancient Egyptians. They consist of rude depictions of animals, plants, signs and objects, and in their later examples express, in abridged form, ideas and records from which significant historical information has been gleaned. The deciphering of Egyptian hieroglyphics long formed an ardent study, but gradually the key to the riddle was discovered, and most of the ancient records can now be understood. Besides the Egyptian there are also Hittite, Minoan and Mayan hieroglyphic scripts. *See* **Rosetta Stone.**

Hi-Fi means high fidelity and refers to gramophones, tape recorders and similar apparatus which will *faithfully* reproduce sounds. It is not too difficult these days to amplify electrical signals without distorting them much; it is more difficult to turn electrical impulses into exactly equivalent sound waves (with a loudspeaker, for example) or *vice versa* (with a microphone or gramophone pick-up). Pick-up and loudspeakers are therefore often the weak links in domestic hi-fi and faults in their design, deficiencies in the electronic amplifiers, imperfect gramophone motors can all contribute to audible results ranging from the tolerable to the execrable. Almost perfect sound reproduction is however available to enthusiasts possessing a suitable combination of discrimination, know-how and financial resources. There are periodical magazines which provide guidance.

Hindi, the official language of India.

Hinduism. *See* Section J.

Hindustani, the spoken form of Hindi (written in Devanagari script) and Urdu (written in Arabic characters).

Hippogriff, a fabulous animal like a horse in body, but with the head, wings and front legs and claws of an eagle. The monster frequently appears in the romances of the Middle Ages.

Hippopotamus or "river-horse" the largest living representative of the hippopotamidae family, widely distributed over Africa, where it lives in herds. It is of immense bulk, attaining a length of 3·6 m and a weight of 4 tonnes and stands about 1·5 m high. Its skin is hairless and about 5 cm thick, and it has a pair of tusks often weighing as much as 2·7 kg. It leads an amphibious way of life, and lives entirely on vegetation, both aquatic and terrestrial. The pigmy hippopotamus, which occurs in forests and swamps in W. Africa, is only half the size.

Histology is the study of the structure of plant and animal tissues. These mainly consist of groups of cells with similar functions, e.g., muscle, brain tissue.

Hittites, an ancient race (often mentioned in the Old Testament) who inhabited Cappadocia (region of Eastern Asia Minor) from the third to the first millennium B.C. Excavations have revealed that they attained a high level of civilisation round about 1350 B.C. The Hittites were rivals of Egypt, disputing with the Pharaohs the mastery of the Middle East. They were the first to smelt iron successfully.

Hobby, a bird of the falcon family, 30–35 cm long. Local breeding visitor to England and Wales, April–September; irregular visitor to Scotland and Ireland. They winter in Africa.

Hog, the common name of animals of the Suidae family, including the wild boar, pig and sow. The wild boar, *Sus scrofa,* is the common ancestor. The skin of the hog is covered with bristles, the snout truncated and each foot has four hoofed toes. Hogs are omnivorous feeders and eat almost anything that is given them.

Hogmanay, the Scottish New Year's Eve festival and a national holiday of the country. The custom of demanding Hogmanay bread is still upheld in many parts of Scotland.

Hogshead, a cask of varying capacity, also a specific measure. In the old English measure a hogshead was 63 old gallons of wine (= 52½ imperial gallons = 238·6 litres). Of beer 54 old gallons make a hogshead.

Holly, a hardy evergreen shrub, largely grown in England. Its bright dark green prickly curved leaves and clusters of red berries are familiar in all parts of the country, and used as house decoration between Christmas Eve and Twelfth Night, probably a relic from Roman and Teutonic customs. Its wood is white and hard, valued for carved work, while its bark yields a gummy substance which is converted into bird-lime.

Hologram, a photographic record, taken under special optical conditions, of light reflected from a scene or object. The hologram is typically a piece of film. However it is nothing like a photographic negative of the ordinary kind;

for one thing it will show an unintelligible pattern of light and dark patches. Nevertheless if it is illuminated (again under special optical conditions) the light coming through it will form a *three dimensional* image of the original object. Another radical difference between a hologram and an ordinary film is that if the hologram is cut up, each fragment can be used to construct the entire image. Holography, as a method of recording and reproducing photographic information, was conceived by Gabor in 1947 but was only fully realised in practice after the invention of the laser (*q.v.*), which made available powerful sources of coherent light. The use of laser light is one of the "special conditions" referred to above. Technical applications are being explored in many laboratories. Gabor received the 1971 Nobel prize for his discovery and invention.

Holy Alliance, an alliance ostensibly for conserving religion, justice and peace in Europe, but used for repressing popular tendencies towards constitutional government. Formed by Alexander I of Russia, Francis I of Austria and Frederick William III of Prussia, at Paris on 26 September 1815. Subsequently joined by all the sovereigns of Europe, except the Pope and the King of England. It ended after the 1830 revolution in France.

Holy Coat of Trèves, a garment preserved in the Cathedral of Trèves and said to have been worn by Christ. It was brought from Jerusalem by the Empress Helena in the fourth century.

Holy Roman Empire, the title traditionally given (although the term "Holy" does not appear in a document until 1157) to the revived Empire when the German king Otto I was crowned in Rome by Pope John XII in 962. It endured until Napoleonic times (1806) two years after Francis II had assumed the title of Emperor of Austria.

Holy Rood, an annual Roman Catholic festival held on 14 September to celebrate the Elevation of the Cross in commemoration of its re-erection in Jerusalem by the Emperor Heraclius in 628 after retaking it from the Persians. Also included in the Church of England calendar.

Holyrood, the ancient royal palace at Edinburgh, dating from the 15th cent., and inhabited by many Scottish sovereigns, notably Mary Stuart, the rooms occupied by her (including the one in which Rizzio was murdered) being still shown. It is now known as Holyrood House and is still used as a royal residence.

Holy Water, water blessed by a priest and kept in small fonts at the entrance to Roman Catholic and some Anglican churches, and used by worshippers going in, and out, or by priests in sprinkling.

Holy Week is the week preceding Easter Sunday, and embraces the days of the Sufferings of Christ. It includes Good Friday and Holy Saturday.

Homoeopathy. *See* Section J.

Honey, the sweet syrup formed by bees from the nectar of flower, the sucrose in the nectar being converted into a mixture of the simple sugars, glucose and fructose. Hybla, an ancient town of Sicily, on the southern slope of Mt. Etna, was famous for its honey.

Honey-eater, an Australian bird (of which there are many species) provided with a long curved bill and tufted tongue. It lives by sucking the nectar from the flowers which abound in rural parts of Australia and New Zealand.

Hookah, an Oriental pipe for tobacco smoking, the smoke being drawn through the water of a goblet (commonly a coconut shell) by means of a long flexible tube.

Hoopoe, a remarkably handsome bird with vivid black and white-barred wings and tail and black-tipped crest which opens like a fan. Ranges over Europe, Asia and Africa. It has bred in England and Wales and occurs in the British Isles in small numbers at all seasons. Other species are confined to Africa, Madagascar and India.

Hops, the female "cones" of the hop plant used in brewing; their essential oils give beer an aromatic flavour, and their tannin and resin act as a preservative as well as accounting for the bitter taste desired. The hop is a perennial climber belonging to the mulberry family. The male and female organs are on separate plants; as only the female flower-heads are commercially

useful, female plants predominate in a hop garden, only a very few male plants being grown so that the female flowers can be fertilised.

Horizon, the limit of vision, the apparent line where sea and sky, or land and sky meet. This is termed the visible horizon. An ordinary person at the height of 1·5 m can see for 4·8 km, at 6 m 9·6 km, at 15 m 14·8 km and at 305 m 67·5 km. The figures are approximate.

Hormone, a chemical substance which is released by one part of the body and produces a response in other parts after having been carried there by the bloodstream or some other transport system. Prolactin, for example, is a hormone produced by the pituitary gland of nursing mothers and serves to stimulate and maintain the milk supply.

Horn *or* **French Horn,** a brass instrument of the trumpet family (*i.e.*, played by three valves) whose tube is very thin and long (Horn in F = 12 ft). In consequence the tube is curled in a complicated manner. Owing to the sweet tone it is capable of producing, the Horn sometimes plays as part of the wood-wind.

Hornbill, large bird found in Africa and oriental regions. Some species have a casque or a horny growth above the very powerful beak. It feeds on fruits. When the female has laid her eggs in the hollow of a tree, the male bird stops up the entrance, and keeps her imprisoned until the hatching is completed and the young ones are able to fly. There are about 45 species.

Hornblende, the commonest member of the amphibole group of minerals, a silicate of calcium, magnesium, iron and aluminium, of a dark green colour. It is a constituent of numerous rocks, including diorite, syenite and hornblende schist.

Horned Viper, any of a number of species of African viper which have scales over each eye resembling horns. Their bite is usually very poisonous. The significance of the horns is not known.

Hornet, a general name for many of the bigger wasps. It usually nests in hollow trees, and despite its rather fiercesome appearance does not sting unless unduly provoked.

Horology, the science of time-measurement, including the construction and management of clocks, watches, etc. Instruments of this kind are not known to have existed before the 12th cent. and until the introduction of the pendulum in the 17th cent., clocks were ill-regulated and inaccurate. The time-recording mechanisms of the present day include (*a*) the *clock*, which shows the hours and minutes by hands, and strikes the hours, and sometimes quarters; (*b*) the *timepiece*, which is not generally a fixture and shows the time, but does not strike; (*c*) the *watch*, which is a pocket time-keeper; (*d*) the *chronometer*, which indicates the minutest portions of times; (*e*) electric timepieces, mains electric clocks; (*f*) the highly accurate quartz-crystal and atomic clocks used for astronomical purposes. *See* Clock.

Horse Chestnut, one of the large forest trees, with ample branches, and full foliage, and much esteemed for parks and ornamental grounds. The flowers, which appear in May, are white tinged with red and yellow. The tree is native to the mountainous regions of northern Greece. *See also* Chestnut.

Horse Guards, the building in Whitehall which until 1872 was the headquarters of the Commander-in-Chief of the British Army. The archway is still sentinelled by mounted guards.

Horse Latitudes, the latitudes of the sub-tropical high pressure systems, between the trade winds and the prevailing westerlies, characterised by light variable winds and low humidity.

Hospitallers, Knights, were of the order of St. John of Jerusalem, at first devoted to the aid of the sick, but afterwards military monks, who became prominent figures in the Crusades of the 12th cent. They adopted the Benedictine black habit with the eight-pointed cross worn by the modern St. John's Ambulance Brigade. In 1309 they took Rhodes, but were expelled by the Ottomans in 1522. In 1530 the emperor Charles V gave them the island of Malta, which as Knights of Malta, they held until 1798, when they were dislodged by Napoleon. The Knights still survive as a sovereign order, with headquarters in Rome. See **Templars** and **Teutonic Order.**

Hottentots, name given to certain African natives by Dutch settlers in the 17th cent. They used to occupy the greater part of Cape Colony and though driven out a number still survive in S.W. Africa. Appear to be related to the Bushmen, though their culture is more advanced. In addition to herding, they practise some farming and know how to smelt iron.

Hounds are dogs that were originally bred and trained for hunting, such as the greyhound, foxhound, bloodhound, wolfhound, deerhound, beagle, harrier, etc., but now often kept also as domestic dogs. The greyhound, deerhound and wolfhound hunt by sight, the others, with the bloodhound first in order, track by scent.

House Flies are world-wide and prolific. Their eggs are hatched within 24 hours of being laid, and full maturity is attained in a month. They feed mainly on decayed animals and vegetable matter.

Hovercraft, or air cushion vehicle, is a craft which is lifted on a pad of air underneath it. This pad or cushion must be at a pressure higher than that of the atmosphere and it is made by sucking in air above the craft and ejecting it in a downward stream all round the lower edge. The stream is guided by a flexible skirt and the high pressure air pad is contained partly by the skirt and partly by the air stream itself which forms a continuous air curtain all round the vehicle. Hovercraft are being intensively developed and there are variations in the basic scheme just described and also in the means of propulsion which can be by air or water jets or propellers. Hovercraft were devised by Cockerell in the 1950s and a full-scale example appeared before the British public in June 1959. Craft of over 100 tonnes are made commercially and much bigger ones conceived. The air pad support means that hovercraft can move over land, water or marsh. Cross-Channel hovercraft were introduced in 1966.

Howler Monkey, a genus of South American monkey noted for a laryngeal conformation which enables it to emit a loud reverberant noise something between a yell and a howl, as the name suggests.

Huanuco-bark, a medicinal bark, brought from the Peruvian town of that name, and derived from the *Cinchona micrantha* tree.

Huguenots, a name applied to the French Protestant communities of the 16th and 17th cent. Henry of Navarre, by the Edict of Nantes in 1598, granted them religious freedom, but more than a quarter of a century before—24 August 1572—thousands had been put to death in the massacre of St. Bartholomew. The revocation of the Edict of Nantes by Louis XIV in 1685 drove thousands into exile in England, Holland, Germany and America.

Humanism. See Section J.

Humble-bee or **Bumble-bee,** the common name of the insects of the genus *bombus,* of the Hymenoptera order. They live in small communities comprising males, females and drones, their habitations being underground. They do not have one queen bee only like the hive bee, but several females occupy the same nest, and these alone live through the winter, breeding and forming new colonies in the spring. Their sting does not have a barb like the honey bee's.

Humidity, the state of the atmosphere with respect to the water-vapour it contains. "Absolute humidity" is defined as the density of the vapour present, while "relative humidity", more frequently employed indicates the degree of saturation, *i.e.,* the ratio of the actual vapour pressure to the saturation vapour pressure at the particular temperature, expressed as a percentage.

Humming Birds are so called because of the humming noise made by the vibration of their wings in flying. They are of radiant plumage, and are among the smallest birds. The smallest bird in the world is the Fairy or Princess Helen's humming bird of Cuba, whose body is only 5·7 cm long. There are from four to five hundred species, and they are confined wholly to North and South America, being most numerous in the tropical latitudes. They have long, slender bills and tubular tongues which reach down

into flowers to suck up the nectar on which they feed.

Hummum, the original name for what is now called the Turkish Bath in this country. One of the first of these baths to be established in London was the Hummums in Covent Garden.

Hundred, the ancient divisional name given to a portion of a county for administration or military purposes. It is supposed to imply the territory occupied by a hundred families; or the space of a hundred hides of land, or the capacity of providing 100 soldiers. Each hundred had its hundred court, with powers similar to those of a manor court, but this was abolished in 1867 by County Court Act.

Hundred Days, the interval of time between Napoleon Bonaparte's entry into Paris after his escape from Elba and his departure after his abdication, extending from 20 March 1815 to 28 June. During this period occurred the battle of Waterloo, 18 June. See **L128.**

Hundred Years' War, a term applied to the almost incessant contest between England and France, lasting from 1338 to 1453, including such famous battles as Crécy, Poitiers and Agincourt, and engaging successively Edward III, Henry V and Henry VI, among English kings.

Huns, a fierce Asiatic race which swept over eastern Europe in the 4th cent. Under Attila about the middle of the 5th cent, they obtained control of a large portion of central and eastern Europe, forcing even Rome to pay tribute. Their defeat at Châlons-sur-Marne in 451 by a mixed army of Romans, Goths and Teutonic tribes, and the death of Attila in 453, terminated their empire.

Hurdy-Gurdy, an Italian rustic musical stringed instrument of the lute order, the sounds of which are produced by the action of a rosined wheel turned by the left hand, the notes being made by the fingering of the right hand.

Hussites. See Section J.

Hurricane. See **Cyclone, Wind.**

Hydra, an aquatic animal of simple structure, whose body is in the form of a cylindrical tube, with a disc-shaped base by which it attaches itself to any shifting substance. Its mouth is surrounded by tentacles by which it catches its food. The Hydra has the power of reproducing lost parts.

Hydrates are compounds containing water of crystallisation.

Hydraulic Ram, a form of automatic pump, used to raise water to a height by the action of its own falling velocity.

Hydraulics, the science of applied hydrodynamics, or water-machine engineering, ranging from pumps to marine engines.

Hydrocarbons are compounds of carbon and hydrogen. They include the *paraffins,* which are saturated compounds (*e.g.,* methane); the ethylene, acetylene and other series which are unsaturated; compounds with ring structures, *e.g.,* benzene, naphthalene and anthracene. Petroleum is composed almost entirely of hydrocarbons.

Hydrochloric Acid, a solution of hydrogen chloride gas in water, and resulting in considerable quantities as a by-product of the soda-ash or salt-cake manufacture. Its solution forms the common hydrochloric or muriatic acid of commerce. It is present to the extent of nearly half a per cent, in the digestive juice secreted by the stomach.

Hydrocyanic Acid, cyanide of hydrogen or prussic acid; very poisonous, and of the odour of bitter almonds. It is formed by the action of acids on sodium or potassium cyanide. Used to kill wasps (and in the gas chamber in the USA). It is a very important chemical on account of the reactions of its derivatives in many synthetic fields. Discovered by Scheele in 1782.

Hydroelectric Schemes. The sun's energy has been indirectly exploited in the past by harnessing the energy of the winds and rain. The climate is due, essentially, to differential heating of the earth. The resulting convection currents in the air (the motion of which is complicated by the rotation of the earth) give rise to winds. Moisture is collected from the sea and deposited high up on mountains as rain. Some of the gravitational energy may be collected as hydropower. Simple windmills or waterwheels are so undependable that they have not been used to any extent since the beginning of the Industrial Revolution. However, the modern form of the waterwheel—the hydroelectric generation plant —is extensively used in mountainous countries and about a third of the world's electricity is produced by this means. The essential requirements for a modern hydroelectric scheme are a river with a sufficient flow of water to provide the required power, a large "head" of water so that a cheap, compact turbine can be used and a dam so that water can be stored until it is required. In some cases a hydroelectric scheme is made economic by being associated with an irrigation or drainage scheme. Such multi-purpose schemes are especially important in India and Pakistan, where most hydro projects are of this type. Other well-known examples include the Snowy Mountains scheme in Australia and the Aswan High Dam in Egypt. Although over 90 per cent of the electricity in certain individual countries, notably Norway, Sweden, Switzerland and Uganda is produced from hydroelectric schemes, only a relatively small fraction of the total potential has been exploited. This fraction varies from about a third in Western Europe to a quarter in the United States to a very small fraction in Alaska, Canada, Africa and the hinterland of Asia.

Hydrofluoric Acid is obtained by distillation of fluorspar with sulphuric acid, and is a compound of fluorine and hydrogen. Its action is highly corrosive; a valuable agent in etching on glass, and a rapid decomposer of animal matter.

Hydrogen, symbol H, the simplest element, atomic number (**F11(2)**) of 1, colourless, and the lightest of all substances. Cavendish in 1766 was the first to recognise that it was an element. It is 14·4 times as light as air, and is found in a free state in volcanic regions. It can be obtained by the action of metals on acids, and forms an explosive mixture with air, burning with oxygen to form water. Commercially it is used to produce the very hot flame of the oxyhydrogen blowpipe for cutting metals; to fill balloons and airships; to harden certain oils and render them suitable for margarine- and soap-production. The gas can be liquefied, and the presence of the isotope deuterium was detected by Urey in 1931 in the residue of the evaporated liquid. The third isotope, tritium, is very rare. *See also* **Deuterium, Tritium.**

Hydrography, the science of water measurement, as applied to seas, rivers, lakes, currents, rocks, reefs, etc., and embracing the whole art of navigation.

Hydrometer, an instrument for measuring the specific gravity of liquids, especially for ascertaining the strength of spiritous liquors and solutions. It is usually in the form of a glass bulb, to the lower end of which a smaller bulb, containing mercury, is attached which forces the instrument to sink into the liquid which it is to test. The larger bulb has a scale fixed to it, and the indication on this scale of the sinking point shows the specific gravity. There are many varieties: Twaddell's—a pear-shaped bulb containing mercury: Beaumé's, of similar construction, but applicable to liquids both heavier and lighter than water: Sykes', largely employed for determinining the strength of alcohol: and Nicholson's, used for taking the specific gravities of solids.

Hydropathy, the method of treating disease with water, either by bathing or drinking. Natural springs of special chemical and therapeutic properties, such as sulphur springs, and other mineral sources, have been used since prehistoric times for this purpose. It is probably one of the most ancient methods of cure. Recently the beneficial effects of pure water treatment have been advocated. Hydropathic establishments have been set up in many health resorts.

Hydroponics, or soilless growth, is the craft and science of growing plants in liquid nutrients instead of soil. Originally a laboratory technique, hydroponics has become since the 1930s a practical method of vegetable, fruit and flower production on both small and large scale. Basically, the growing plants have their roots in troughs of nutrient solution, either in or out of doors. Advantages include: much higher

crop yields; the close control of weeds and diseases; quicker growth; and, very important, the possibilities of growing food in places where ordinary agriculture would be impracticable, *e.g.*, deserts and stony land, city roofs, in houses and in remote situations like Antarctic stations. Hydroponics is widely practised and contributes usefully to agriculture and horticulture in many countries, including the USA, Britain, India and France. Its value in spaceships and planetary colonies has often been pointed out by technological prophets.

Hydrostatics, the science of the pressure and equilibrium of liquids that are non-elastic.

Hydrozoa are a class of water animals of the *Coelenterata* phylum to which hydra (*q.v.*) belongs. In one order of the hydrozoa, free-swimming colonies showing marked division of labour between the individual units occur; this order includes the Portuguese man-of-war.

Hyena, a nocturnal carnivore with powerful jaws. The striped hyenas inhabit N. Africa and S.W. India. The brown hyenas with long shaggy hair are natives of S. Africa. The spotted, or laughing hyena, noted for the peculiar cry from which its name is derived, is also confined to Africa.

Hygrometer, an instrument for measuring the amount of water vapour in the atmosphere. A simple form of hygrometer, known as the wet-and-dry bulb, consists of two vertical thermometers affixed to a frame. One bulb is exposed to the air, and the other is covered with muslin which dips into a water-bath to keep it moist. If the air is saturated, it takes up no moisture from the wet bulb and the two thermometers read the same. If the air is not saturated, evaporation takes place from the wet bulb, latent heat is absorbed from the air and the temperature of the wet bulb is lower than that of the dry bulb. Relative humidity and dew-point of the air can then be derived from suitable tables. Hygrometers depending upon the expansion of human hair and goldbeater's skin and the deposition of dew on a polished surface, when cooled sufficiently, are also in general use. *See* **Humidity.**

Hymenoptera, the order of insects to which bees, wasps, hornets, ants and sawflies belong. They have a well-defined waist, two pairs of membranous wings coupled together, mouth parts modified for biting or sucking; the females possess an ovipositor used for depositing eggs and is sometimes modified for stinging. There are about 70,000 species in this order and many live in highly organised communities. *See also* **Ichneumon Fly.**

Hyperbola. A curve described by certain comets that go round the sun and never return.

Hypsometer, an instrument formerly used by mountaineers to find the height above sea-level by indirectly measuring the atmospheric pressure by determining the boiling point of water at the particular height. Based on the fact that as pressure decreases with height so the boiling point is lowered. Superseded by the aneroid barometer.

I

Ibex, wild goats of several species found in the mountain regions of Europe, Asia and Africa. The male has exceedingly large curved ridged horns. The species that lives in the Alps is called the Steinbock or bouquetin.

Ibis, belongs to a family of birds related to the stork. The sacred ibis of ancient Egypt is now extinct in Egypt but is found in the lakes and swamps of the Sudan near the Upper Nile. It has white and black plumage and a long curved beak. Other species are found elsewhere, the Glossy Ibis (black plumage glossed with purple and green) occasionally visiting England.

Ibo (properly Igbo), a large tribe of S.E. Nigeria, numbering between 5 and 6 million. After the end of British rule they were active in their struggle for national independence and under their leader, Ojukwu, embarked upon the secessionist state of Biafra and the unsuccessful civil war against Federal forces. The Hausa and the Yoruba are the other main Nigerian groups.

Ice is frozen water. It is a colourless, crystalline and brittle solid. Being only 92% as dense as water, it floats on the latter; the expansion which occurs as water changes into ice causes the fracture of water-pipes, though the fracture only becomes obvious when the ice melts and leaks out through the crack. The temperature at which ice forms is 0°C, 32°F. Ice can be melted by pressure, and the ease and smoothness with which one is able to skate on ice depends on this phenomenon.

Ice Ages. Periods during which the continents were partly or largely covered by ice-sheets and glaciers. The present-day ice-sheets of Greenland and Antarctica are relics of the most recent ice age (one of the eight major ones during the past 700,000 years), which began in the Pleistocene and ended about 10,000 years ago. During this last great glaciation ice sheets covered the northern part of Europe, Asia and North America. There is strong evidence that periodic changes in the earth's orbit around the sun caused the ice ages. The earth is now in one of its warm periods though there are signs that a moderate cooling trend has begun.

Icebergs are detached masses of glacier which subside into the sea and float as wind or current may take them. About one-ninth of an iceberg is above sea-level. The North Atlantic is the chief home of icebergs, which reach the ocean from the ice-clad plateaux of Greenland. Some of these floating masses of ice are of enormous proportions, and constitute in the spring and early summer seasons a great menace to the safety of ships, as was disastrously shown in the *Titanic* catastrophe of 1912. For some years past these menaces to N. Atlantic shipping have been kept under close observation by vessels specially detailed for this work.

Ice-breaker, a special heavy bow-plated ship for forcing a way through ice and used especially at ports of the Baltic Sea and the Great Lakes region of Canada which freeze during the winter months. The Soviet atomic ice-breaker *Lenin*, the first of its kind in the world, launched in December 1957, was designed to cut a channel through ice of any thickness. Her performance allowed the sea-route to the north of Siberia to be kept open throughout the year. Russia has now several nuclear-powered icebreakers.

Icelandic Literature, the old Norse literature, centred about Iceland, which includes numerous works of poetry, mythology and history of interest and importance. Much of this literature is in the saga form. *See also* **Edda.**

Iceland Moss, a kind of lichen (*Cetraria islandica*) which grows in great quantities in the mountain regions of Iceland and other Northern countries. It possesses certain nutritive qualities and is of some value in medicine.

Iceland Spar, a colourless form of calcite (calcium carbonate), frequently found in association with metallic ores; it has the power to produce strong double refraction of light so that two images are seen of an object viewed through a piece of Iceland spar. It was formerly used in optical apparatus for producing polarised light.

Iceni, an ancient British race who in early times lived in Norfolk and other parts of Eastern England. Their most famous ruler was Queen Boadicea, who led her people against the Romans in A.D. 61.

Ice Plant, also called "dew plant" and "diamond plant". A South African mesembryanthemum commonly grown in British gardens. Introduced in 1690.

Ice Saints, St. Mamertus, St. Pancras and St. Servatius, so called because of the legendary cold on these Saints' Days, namely, 11–13 May.

Ichneumon, the Egyptian mongoose, popularly known as "Pharaoh's Rat". It is of great use in checking the multiplication of reptiles. It is frequently domesticated.

Ichneumon Fly, a numerous group of parasitic hymenopterous insects abounding in many lands, and all having the peculiarity of depositing their eggs in the bodies of other insects. It destroys swarms of caterpillars, which become the unwilling hosts of its progeny.

Ichthyology, the natural history of fishes.

Ichthyosaurus was a gigantic marine reptile of the Mesozoic age. The fossils are mostly found in the lias formation. Some were over 9 m.

Icon, an image of a sacred personage used in the home or in churches for devotional purposes by Christians of the Eastern Orthodox faith. Icons can be painted on wood, perhaps with the figures picked out against a golden background, or they can be cast in bronze, in the form of a crucifix, diptych (*q.v.*) or triptych with details in coloured enamels. Subjects are taken from the life of Christ or of the Saints. In churches several icons are sometimes placed together on a screen (the iconostasis, which divides the altar and sanctuary from the main body of the church). The earliest preserved icons date from the 12th cent. Icons were venerated in Russia until the Revolution and remain, still in their archaic stylised form of mediaeval origin, a characteristic feature of the Orthodox Church to this day.

Ides, in the ancient Roman Calendar, the 15th of March, May, July, October, and the 13th of all other months; always the eighth day after the Nones.

Idiom, an expression characteristic of a country, district, dialect or language, which usually gives strength and force to a phrase or sentence. The idioms of a language are its distinctive marks, and the best writers are the most idiomatic.

Idris, a famous giant belonging to the myths of Wales, commemorated by a chair of rock on the top of the Cader Idris mountain in Gwynedd.

Igneous Rocks are such as have been molten under conditions of great heat at some stage in their history: *e.g.*, granite, basalt. *See* **F9(1).**

Ignis Fatuus or **"Will-o'-the-wisp",** a phosphorescent light which may often be seen on summer and autumn evenings hovering over marshy ground or graveyards. Its nature is hardly understood, though it is generally believed to be the result of the spontaneous combustion of the gases from decaying organic matter. In olden times when marshy grounds were more common than now, this "dancing light" was very frequently visible and was regarded with superstition.

Iguana, large South American lizard, with a long tail, a scaly back and head, a thick fleshy tongue and a prominent dew-lap in the throat. Specimens of the different species average 1·2–1·5 m in length, and they live mostly in trees, though they are equally at home on land or in the water. The flesh of some species is good eating, as are also the eggs.

Iguanodon, a genus of extinct dinosaurs, whose fossils are found in the Jurassic and Cretaceous rocks. Iguanodons were 4·5–7·6 m long, and walked on their hind legs, the front legs being small and adapted for grasping the branches of trees on the leaves of which they fed.

Ilex, mentioned by classical authors, the holm- or holly-oak, which flourishes round the Mediterranean. To botanists Ilex is the genus to which the holly and maté plant belong.

Iliad, the great epic poem of ancient Greece attributed to Homer (*c.* 700 B.C.). It consists of ancient folk tale and saga, welded into an artistic unity, having as plot the carrying off of Helen by Paris to Troy and the subsequent siege of Troy. *See* **Section I.**

Illuminated MSS. of great value and beauty of decoration exist in most public museums and in many private collections, some of them being of great antiquity, especially those of ancient Egypt executed on papyri. Greek and Latin specimens are also numerous, and the British Museum contains fine examples of all these kinds and also an extensive collection of mediaeval English MSS.

Illuminati. *See* **Section J.**

Ilmenite, a mineral widespread in igneous rocks: chemically it is an oxide of iron and titanium. Rich deposits have recently been found in the Allard Lake area of Quebec: the Travancore sands are also a source of ilmenite.

Immortality. *See* **Section J.**

Immortelles are wreaths, crosses or other designs made from what are called everlasting flowers, which are obtained from certain plants of the Composite order, and retain their colours and compactness for a long time. Immortelles are largely used as mementoes for decorating graves, especially in France.

Impeachment, a special arraignment, usually before Parliament or other high tribunal, of a person charged with some offence against the State. The custom in England was for the impeachment to be made in the House of Commons, and the trial to be before the House of Lords. The first instance occurred in 1376 when Lord Latimer was impeached. With present parliamentary procedure, impeachment is no longer necessary, since the Cabinet is responsible for the individual actions of its ministers, who, acting as a team, must carry the Commons with them, or resign, when it falls to the Leader of the Opposition to form a new Cabinet. Other famous impeachments were those of the Lord High Chancellor Francis Bacon (1621), Earl of Strafford and Archbishop Laud (1640), Warren Hastings (1788), the last being that of Lord Melville (1805). Under the constitution of the United States public officials may be impeached by the House of Representatives and tried by the Senate. A famous case was that of President Andrew Johnson who was saved from impeachment in 1868 by one vote. Had President Nixon not resigned in 1974 he would have been impeached for the affair of the tapes and his abuse of executive privilege.

Imperialism. *See* **Section J.**

Impressionism, the most important and influential movement in 19th cent. European painting. It gained its name, at first contemptuously, in 1874 from a picture painted by Claude Monet and named by the artist *Impression: soleil levant*, which showed the play of light on water with the observer looking straight into the rising sun. Although intended to be the ultimate form of naturalism the inspiration of the school had been the scientific study of light with an attempt to render the play of light on the surface of objects. Feeling that putting a line around a form was bound to cause it to look unnatural, they used bright colours corresponding to the spectrum and unmixed on the palette, and noted that an object of any given colour casts a shadow tinged with the complementary one (*e.g.*, red-green, yellow-blue). Hence bright sunlight was represented in clear yellows and orange with violet shadows. The first Impressionist exhibition held in Paris in 1874 aroused derision with its paintings by Monet, Renoir, Sisley, Pissaro, Cézanne and Degas among others. Impressionism subsequently led to the entirely artistic and anti-naturalist movement of Post-impressionism. Cézanne, who felt that he wanted to produce "something solid and durable, like the art of the museums" was only dubiously impressionist, as were also Degas and Renoir. Of course, in the wider sense of the word (*i.e.*, the recording of an ephemeral impression of a scene), Whistler, Turner and even Rembrandt used the technique.

Impressment, the forced seizure of persons for military service resorted to by many countries before the establishment of conscription. Press gangs forcibly recruited men for British warships especially during the Napoleonic wars, but such measures were abandoned after about 1850.

Imprimatur, originally an official licence to print and an important formula in the early days of printing. The term is now used in the wider significance of authority, or endorsement.

Incas, an Indian people who inhabited ancient Peru, founded a great empire and reached a high level of civilisation; overthrown by the Spaniards in 1533.

Incense, an aromatic resinous substance which, under combustion, exhales a pungent odour, and is used, mixed with certain fragment perfumes, in the celebration of Mass in Roman Catholic churches. Olibanum or frankincense is ordinarily the leading ingredient.

Incisors, the sharp-edged cutting teeth at the front of mammalian jaws. Rodents have long, sharp incisor teeth. Elephant tusks are modified incisors.

Independence Day, commemorates the adoption of the Declaration of Independence on 4 July 1776. 4 July is celebrated as a holiday in the USA.

Index. The name given to a list of books, prepared by papal authority, which are declared to be dangerous to faith and morals, and therefore forbidden to Roman Catholics, called the *Index librorum prohibitorum*. One of the reforms of the Vatican Council was the closing in 1966 of the Curia office which judged writings for the Church's Index of forbidden books, though the Index itself still remains. The Pope ordered that nothing should be placed on the Index until the author had been given a chance of explaining his views. The first Index was issued by Pope Pius IV, in 1559.

Indian Mutiny. This turning-point in the history of modern India occurred in 1857–58. The ostensible cause was the serving out to the native troops of cartridges greased with animal fat, for contact with this was forbidden both by the Hindu and Mohammedan faiths. A rebellious feeling, however, had long been developing, and when the Sepoys at Meerut in May 1857 refused to obey the English officers, overpowered and put them to death, the mutiny spread like wildfire. The rebels took Delhi and Lucknow, and for many months terrible massacres and atrocities were committed; men, women and children were slain in thousands. Order was re-established in the autumn of 1858 when the governing power was transferred from the East India Company to the Crown.

Indicators, substances which by a marked change in colour are used to indicate the course of a chemical reaction. Litmus paper, for instance, is red with acids and blue with alkalis. In biological work some radioactive substances are used as tracer elements.

Indigo, the substance obtained from the plant *Indigofera tinctoria*, a native of S. Asia, India being the chief producing country. The colouring matter is the result of the decomposition and fermentation of a glucoside contained in the plant. This is afterwards dried and becomes the caked indigo of commerce. Natural indigo has been eclipsed by artificial indigo, a coal-tar dye which came into commercial production at the end of the last century, and which is cheaper and more uniform in quality.

Indium, a scarce lead-coloured metallic element, no. 49, symbol In, found in zinc blende in Saxony and certain other ores. Discovered in 1863 by Reich and Richter. It is an important material in the manufacture of transistors.

Indulgence. In the Roman Catholic Church the remission granted by ecclesiastical authority to a repentant sinner of the temporal punishment still due after the guilt of sin has been forgiven by God. The indiscriminate sale of Indulgences by Tetzel and other Papal agents in the 16th cent. was one of the grievances which led to the Reformation (*see* **Section J**); the Council of Trent made such traffic unlawful.

Indulgence, Declaration of, was the proclamation by which James II suspended the penal laws against Roman Catholics and Dissenters. It was issued in 1688, but the clergy as a body refused to obey, and the trial of the Seven Bishops and their acquittal by a jury followed. An invitation was thereupon sent to William of Orange to become King.

Industrialisation is simply a name for industrial development. It is customarily used in particular to designate the course of events in a hitherto underdeveloped country which is seeking to increase its wealth and productivity by the introduction of more advanced techniques and by the establishment of industries previously not carried on within it. The word usually covers not only the development of modern industrial production but also the provision of electric power-stations, irrigation works and transport and other developments designed to improve production in any field by methods involving large capital investments. The outstanding example in our time of rapid industrialisation has been the Soviet Union, which, unable to get the capital from abroad, had to carry it through by ruthless restriction of the people's consuming power so as to achieve an unprecedentedly high ratio of investment to total production. Industrialisation has in practice meant a high concentration on the expansion of the basic heavy industries and of power supply, coupled with much slower development of the industries supplying consumer goods and of agricultural production; but there is no reason why this should always be the case. It may well be that in most underdeveloped countries development can but be devoted largely to the industries making consumers' goods and to measures designed to increase agricultural production and productivity.

Industrial Revolution. The name, first given by Engels in 1844, to describe the radical changes that took place in Britain during *c.* 1730–1850 to transform a mainly agricultural country into one predominantly industrial. It began with the mechanisation of the textile industry (Hargreave's spinning jenny, 1764, Arkwright's water-frame, 1769, Crompton's mule, 1770, and Watt's steam-engine, 1785), with subsequent major developments in mining, transport and industrial organisation. It was based on Britain's rich mineral resources, particularly coal and iron ore. With the use of the steam-engine as power, industry became concentrated round the coalfields and the great new industrial towns developed—Birmingham, Manchester, Newcastle and Glasgow. Britain became supreme in constructional ironwork (Telford, George and Robert Stephenson). Canals, bridges, railways and ships were built, and great advances were made in the practical application of scientific principles. Aided by colonial exploitation Britain became the most prosperous country in the world. The new industrial capitalists began to replace the country squires as ruling class. But the great accumulation of wealth at one pole of society was matched at the other by poverty and misery, for child labour, long working hours, low wages and slums were features of the industrial revolution in its infancy. As with all great technological developments, the industrial revolution produced related changes in all fields of social life—in politics, art, religion, literature and morals, and with the rise of democracy, social reforms.

Inertia, a term used in mechanics for the property of matter by which it offers resistance to a change in its state of rest or in its state or direction of motion.

Inertial Navigation, an automatic method of dead-reckoning which at present finds its chief application in guided missiles, submarines and aircraft. Navigation by this means is carried out with reference to inertial space (*i.e.,* space which is stationary with respect to the fixed stars) and not to the surface of the earth as in normal navigation (latitude and longitude). This is done by means of high-accuracy gyroscopes combined with highly sensitive accelerometers in an apparatus known as the Ship's Inertial Navigation System. The American nuclear-powered submarine *Nautilus* pioneered the new north-west passage under the polar ice pack by this method of dead-reckoning in August 1958.

Inflorescence, a flowering shoot. Many arrangements of the flowers are possible and there are many kinds of inflorescence; *e.g.,* the spike, catkin, umbel, capitulum (in composites).

Inflation. *See* **Section G.**

Infra-red Rays *or* **Radiation.** This is the range of rays which come between the visible red rays and the ultra-short Hertzian radiation. The wavelengths involved range between 0·75 micron (0·75 × 10⁻⁶m) and 100 micron (1 millimetre). Infra-red rays penetrate haze; hence landscapes obscured by haze or cloud can be photographed using plates sensitive to infra-red. Many substances strongly absorb these rays and thereby become hot; this happens in toasting bread. Many industries use infra-red lamps for drying paints and lacquers. Very important to chemists, as a tool in the investigation of the structure of compounds, since various groups of elements absorb infra-red radiation at a characteristic frequency. Infra-red astronomy has developed in recent years.

Infula, a sacred fillet, of woollen material, worn on the forehead by priests, magistrates and rulers in Roman times, also by persons fleeing for protection to sanctuary. Later, each of the two lappets of a bishop's mitre.

Ingoldsby Legends, a series of whimsical metrical tales full of droll humour written by the Rev. R. H. Barham, and first published in *Bentley's Miscellany* in 1837. The best known is the *Jackdaw of Rheims.*

Ink, a liquid pigment ordinarily made from an infusion of nut-galls, copperas and gum arabic. Shumac is substituted for nut-galls for inferior inks. An acid is sometimes added to prevent oxidation, and for the blue-black inks a small quantity of solution of indigo serves for colouring. Copying ink contains glycerine or sugar, which keeps the ink moist. Lampblack used to be the leading ingredient in printer's ink but now new methods of manufacturing have been developed. Marking ink is composed of a solution of nitrate of silver, gum, ammonia and carbonate of soda. For red, blue and other coloured inks, colouring solutions are used, for example, Prussian blue. The earliest examples of ink writing (on wooden tablets) ever found in Britain were recovered from the well of a Roman villa (3rd cent. A.D.) during excavations in 1954 at Chew Stoke, Somerset.

Ink Sac, a glandular organ found in squids and other cephalopods which contains an inky solution. When roused the animal discharges the contents of the ink sac into the water, to make a cloud through which its enemies cannot see. The pigment, sepia, comes from the ink sac of the cuttlefish.

Inns of Court, the four bodies in London which enjoy the privilege of calling candidates to the bar after they have studied for a certain number of terms and passed certain examinations. The Inns are: the Inner Temple, the Middle Temple, Lincoln's Inn and Gray's Inn.

Inquisition, a Roman Catholic ecclesiastical court which became a formidable weapon of the Church in the 13th cent. under Pope Innocent III in dealing with charges of heresy. It was effectively set up in the various Catholic countries of the Continent, obtaining its fullest and most sweeping organisation in Spain in the days of Ferdinand and Isabella, when Torquemada was made Grand Inquisitor, and used its powers with terrible severity. *See* **Auto-da-fé.** In the 18th cent. its influence began to wane, and the jurisdiction of the Congregation of the Holy Office at Rome was limited to the suppression of heretical literature (*see* **Index**). Recently, the Congregation for the Doctrine of Faith (CDF), as it is now called, called into question the orthodoxy of two of the Roman Catholic Church's most respected theologians.

Insectivorous Plants, plants which trap insects with special mechanisms. Plant enzymes or bacteria digest the prey, providing the plants with nitrogen usually scarce in the soil in which they grow. The most common British species are the Sun-dew and the Bladderwort.

Insects. This huge class of invertebrate animals (*see* **Arthropods** (**F36**)) includes about 100,000 species. Insects are ubiquitous except in the sea, only a very few species being adapted to marine existence. Characteristic features are: the body is divided into three parts, head, thorax and abdomen: the head carries a pair of antennae, the thorax three pairs of legs and usually two pairs of wings. The most primitive insects constituting the sub-class *Apterygota* are wingless. The other sub-class, *Pterygota,* is divided into the *Exopterygota* (*Hemimetabola*), which have a simple metamorphosis, *e.g.,* cockroach, and the *Endopterygota* (*Holometabola*), with a complex metamorphosis, *e.g.,* butterfly, bee. Although many are parasitic on man, animals and plants, innumerable animals and some plants use them as food, and many flowering plants are dependent on a variety of insects for pollination leading to the development of seeds and fruits. *See* **F36(1), 41(1).**

Insignia, marks or badges of office or honour, such as stars, ribbons, crosses, medallions or other designating objects, worn by members of special Orders or holders of prominent offices.

Instinct. *See* **F40(2).**

Institut de France was formed in 1795, and after various modifications was in 1832 organised on its present basis. Its five academies are—the Académie Française, Académie des Inscriptions et Belles-Lettres, Académie des Sciences, Académie des Beaux-Arts, Académie des Sciences morales et politiques. It is restricted to 40 members.

Instruments, Musical. Musical instruments may be classified in a number of ways, but in general they fall into one of the three main classes, String, Wind and Percussion, according to how the sound in produced. **Stringed Instruments** are those which produce the sound by the vibration of a string: (a) by plucking, as in Harp, Lyre, Psaltery, Zither, Lute, Guitar, Balalaika, Ukelele, Harpsichord; (b) by friction (bowed), as in Crwth, Rebec, Viol, Violin, Marine Trumpet, Hurdy-Gurdy; (c) by striking (hammered), as in Dulcimer, Pianoforte, Clavichord; (d) by wind (blown), as in the Aeolian Harp. **Wind Instruments** are those in which the air in the instruments is set in vibration: (a) by blowing into a tube (flue-voiced), as in Recorder, Pandean Pipe, Flute, Organ; (b) by means of reeds (reed-voiced), as in Oboe, Clarinet, Saxophone, Bagpipe, Cor Anglais, Bassoon, Organ reed-stops; (c) those in which the sound is produced by the vibration of the player's lips against the mouthpiece (lip-voiced), as in Bugle, Horn, Trumpet, Tuba, Trombone, Saxhorn, Flügelhorn, Cornet. In a modern orchestra these are known as the *Brass*; instruments of the flute, oboe and clarinet families as the *Woodwinds*. Then there are the **Percussion Instruments**, which include the Drums, Cymbals, Tambourines, Castenets.

Insulator, a substance that will not conduct electric current. Many solids, liquids and gases are important insulators—rubber, cotton, silk, plastics, porcelain, glass, air, oil. If the applied voltage is too high, all insulators will "break down", *i.e.*, conduct electricity perhaps with resulting breakage, puncture or charring. Thermal insulators will not conduct heat; they are usually the same kinds of substance as electrical insulators.

Insulin is a hormone which controls the supply of sugar from the blood to muscles. The breakdown of sugar provides energy. In diabetes there is a lack of insulin, causing a build-up of blood sugar which can be released by the injection of insulin. It is secreted by the islet tissue of the pancreas, from which it was isolated in 1922 by Banting and Best. Dr. F. Sanger of Cambridge won the 1958 Nobel Prize in Chemistry for isolating and identifying its amino acid components. Prof. Dorothy Hodgkin and her team at the Dept. of Molecular Biophysics at Oxford succeeded in determining the structure of insulin, a task which would not have been possible without the electronic computer. In 1980 insulin became the first product of genetic engineering techniques to reach clinical trials.

Intelligence. Intelligence has been variously defined as the innate potential of a person to learn and understand; to make appropriate judgments; to see the relationships between things; to profit from experience; or to meet adequately new problems and conditions in life. There are many lines of evidence to show that intellectual capacity is closely related to heredity and influenced by environmental factors. The idea of intelligence testing was first devised by the French psychologist Binet at the beginning of this century. He was asked by the French government to invent a test which would weed out backward children in state schools, and thus save public money and avoid holding back the work of the class by teaching children who were incapable of learning at a given standard. Briefly, a series of problems are given to a large number of children and it is thus found out which series can be solved by the average child of a given age-group; if a child of 7 can only pass the tests suitable to the average child of 6, then his mental age is 6. The intelligence quotient or I.Q. is discovered by dividing his mental age by his chronological age and multiplying by 100. A gifted child can usually be spotted at an early age. Although I.Q. tests are the standard method of estimating intelligence, they are not universally accepted as a criterion; a teacher's general judgment may be the best assessment. High intelligence may be inherited, but fail to develop to the full because facilities for education are not available. Recent research suggests that the growth of the brain may be permanently affected by undernutrition at the time of its fastest growth (the last weeks before birth and, to a lesser extent, the first weeks after birth). At this vulnerable period even quite minor deprivation can affect the rate and ultimate extent of growth of the brain. This has significance not only for the severely under-nourished babies in the poor parts of the world, but for babies of low birth weight in our own communities in the Western world.

Interest is the payment made for the use of borrowed money over time. The rate of interest is the rate per cent per annum charged for such loans. There are many such rates, varying with the plenty or scarcity of borrowable money, with the length of time for which the loans are made, and with the degree of risk, if any, that the loans will not be duly repaid. Short-term loans are usually cheaper than long-term: the lowest rates are usually for "call money" repayable immediately on demand. These are used principally in short-term financial transactions, such as bill discounting. Bank loans, though usually made for fairly short terms, command higher rates. Long-term loans are made chiefly to public authorities, or as bonds or debentures to business concerns. The rates obtained vary with the demand and the supply of such accommodation.

Interferon, identified in 1957 as a defence protein produced in animal cells, is also produced in human immune systems. Its use as a possible anti-cancer agent as well as for other complaints has been limited by extraction problems. Modern production is likely to be by genetic engineering. In 1980 the amino acid sequence was determined for the 150 residues in human interferon.

International Date Line, a line along the 180° meridian marking the difference in time between E. and W. For the westward-bound traveller crossing the line the date would be put forward one day, for the eastward-bound, back one day. To avoid difference of date in adjacent land areas, the line deviates from the 180° meridian where this crosses land.

Introit, the psalm sung by the choir as the priest approaches the altar to celebrate the Eucharist.

Inuit. *See under* **Eskimo (L41).**

Invention of the Cross, a Roman Catholic festival held on 3 May, to celebrate the finding of the alleged True Cross at Calvary by the Empress St. Helena in 326. Also included in the Church of England calendar. *See* **Holy Rood.**

Iodine, a non-metal element, no. 53, symbol I, member of the halogen family (*q.v.*), a substance formerly exclusively obtained from the ribbonwrack seaweeds. These were burnt and the ashes (kelp) extracted with water. After concentrating the iodides, these were distilled with manganese dioxide and sulphuric acid to yield iodine vapour which was condensed in stoneware bottles. Nearly all iodine now in use is derived from the iodine salt present in Chile saltpetre (natural sodium nitrate). Iodine is used in photography, as an antiseptic solution in alcohol or potassium iodide (tincture of iodine), and in medicine. Discovered by Courtois in 1812.

Ionosphere. Although a certain degree of ionisation occurs at all levels of the atmosphere due to cosmic rays and the radioactivity of rocks, etc., the ionosphere is normally denoted as the region above about 70 km where the ultra-violet component of sunlight is able to ionise a significant fraction of the atoms and molecules present. This ionisation causes the reflection of radio waves by which the ionosphere was initially discovered and for many years, explored. The nomenclature of the ionospheric layers—"D" region up to about 95 km, "E" region 95 km to about 180 km, and "F" region above 180 km—is due to the historical observations of radio wave reflections from "layers". Satellite and rocket observations have shown that the structure is in fact more continuous. Solar flares and aurora cause enhancements of the electron density in the ionosphere, which may result in the disturbance of radio communications over large distances (radio blackouts). *See also* **Atmosphere, Aurora, Magnetosphere.**

Ions, electrically charged atoms, or groups of atoms. Atoms of the metals lose electrons to become positively charged ions, *e.g.*, the sodium ion (Na^+) has one electron less than the atom. The non-metal ions are negatively charged, *e.g.*, the chloride ion (Cl^-) has one electron more than the atom. Similarly, a group like the sulphate ion ($SO_4{}^{2-}$) has more electrons than the constituent atoms. Thus, the hydrogen atom without its electron is a hydrogen ion or *proton* and the helium atom without its two electrons is a helium ion or *alpha-particle*. When an electric force is applied to certain solutions, the ions into which molecules of the dissolved substance are broken up are attracted to the oppositely charged electrodes, their movements constituting an electric current through the solution. In the same way gases, including air, conduct electricity by virtue of free ions (*see* **F14**(1)). Combustion, radioactivity and ultra-violet and cosmic radiations produce ionisation. *See* **F23**.

Iridium, a white and very hard metallic element, no. 77, symbol Ir, discovered by Tennant in 1804. It occurs naturally as an alloy with platinum or osmium; tips for fountain-pen nibs have been made from the former native alloy. The former standard metre was composed of platinum-iridium alloy (*see* **Metre**) as are parts of scientific apparatus and surgical tools that must be non-corrodible.

Iris, the typical genus of the botanical order *Iridacae,* with tuberous rhizomes and swordshaped leaves, many of the family having beautiful flowers. About 100 species of Iris are recorded from the northern temperate zone, the most common species wild in Britain being the yellow flag. Orris root, used in perfumery, comes from another iris species.

Iron is a metallic element, no. 53, symbol Fe (Latin *ferrum*), occurring widely in nature in such ores as haematite, loadstone (magnetic iron oxide), spathic ore and iron pyrites. It is extracted by a process known as smelting, with coke and limestone in a furnace. Its many uses are familiar, the most important being in the manufacture of cast- and wrought-iron products and of steels, which are alloys mainly of iron with added carbon and various metals. Iron rust is formed by the action of oxygen and water, and is a coating of iron oxide. *See* **Smelting.**

Ironclads, ships of war cased in iron or steel plates of sufficient thickness to resist projectiles. They were first introduced (1858) in the French Navy, and in 1860 the first British ironclad, the *Warrior*, was launched.

Iron Curtain. In a speech at Fulton, USA, on 5 March 1946, Sir Winston Churchill used this phrase to describe the dividing line behind which, he said, lie all the capitals of the ancient States of Central and Eastern Europe—Warsaw, Berlin, Prague, Vienna, Budapest, Belgrade, Bucharest and Sofia. The Iron Curtain was symbolised by the Berlin Wall (dividing that city in half) and the rival military groupings of NATO and the Warsaw Pact. The dramatic changes in Eastern Europe in 1989 (*see* **Section C Part II**) have ended this old division of Europe.

Ironsides were Cromwell's special troopers, so called because of their solidity and firmness in battle.

Irrational Number, a number such as the square root of two, or pi, which cannot be expressed as the ratio of two whole numbers. *See* **Rational Number,** and *Pi.*

Irredentists, a political party organised in Italy about 1878 with the object of incorporating within Italy neighbouring regions. Also a person, group or party advocating policies for the restoration to their country of territory formerly belonging to it but later lost.

Irrigation, an artificial method of providing water for the growth of plants on lands where the natural supply of water is deficient. For many hundreds of years techniques of irrigation have been slow and primitive (*e.g.*, tanks, inundation canals and the Archimedes screw) and consequent inefficiencies include large water losses by evaporation and seepage, and the watering of only a small area. New developments in perennial irrigation, using barrages, large reservoirs and pumping stations, permit vast tracts of land to be irrigated. Yet these are not without their problems as witnessed after the construction of the Aswan High Dam on the Nile where complex problems of delta erosion and dam lake silting ensued. Irrigation also serves the pur-

pose of supplying *warmth* in winter; *e.g.*, in the English water-meadows, and in the more highly developed Italian *marcite* and winter-meadows, where the water is mostly applied in winter when there is plenty of rain. There are several other functions of irrigation; *e.g.*, washing out of excess salts and the renewing of fertility by the addition of alluvium.

Islam. *See* **Section J.**

Isobars are the lines drawn on charts linking together points of equal barometric pressure.

Isochasms, lines connecting places at which there is an equal probability of seeing an aurora, taking the average over a number of years, based on the auroral catalogue of Fritz.

Isomers are chemical compounds having the same composition but different structural arrangements, and consequently different physical and chemical properties. For example, ethyl alcohol and methyl ether are isomers, since the molecules of both are built up of two atoms of carbon, six of hydrogen and one of oxygen, *viz.*, C_2H_6O; ethyl alcohol, C_2H_5OH; and methyl ether, CH_3OCH_3.

Isotherms are lines drawn on charts through points of equal temperature.

Isotopes. When one talks of an element, say, uranium or lead, the name of the element is a generic name for a collection of uranium species and lead species. The different species are called isotopes. For any particular element, the number and arrangement of electrons around the nucleus are the same in all the isotopes, so all the isotopes have the same chemical properties. Soddy has described isotopes as "elements, the atoms of which have similar outsides but different insides". For example, in the nucleus of the uranium isotopes, U 235, U 238 and U 239, there are respectively 143, 146 and 147 neutrons, but all have 92 protons. The isotopes have different atomic weights, in this instance respectively 235, 238 and 239. But all have the same chemical properties. *See* **F12**(1).

Ivory, the dentine substance of which the tusks of the elephant, hippopotamus, walrus, etc., are composed. The tusks of the African elephant sometimes weigh as much as 45 kg, and reach a length of 2·4–2·7 m.

Ivory Gull, a small, beautifully shaped sea-bird with striking all-white plumage and black legs which breeds on the rocky shores of the Arctic, being found farther north than any other bird; it occasionally wanders south in the winter.

J

Jabiru, the Brazilian name for the giant stork of South America.

Jacamar, from *Jacameri,* the Brazilian name for a smallish bird with long, sharply pointed bill and brilliant plumage which inhabits the tropical regions of South America east of the Andes. These birds are seen sitting motionless on trees, darting off at intervals, like flycatchers, to catch insects on the wing.

Jacanas, small water birds with immensely long toes which enable them to walk on water lily leaves. They are sometimes called "lilytrotters" and are found in tropical Africa and America. They live in swamps and feed on seeds and insects. Sometimes brilliantly coloured.

Jack, a small schooner-rigged vessel, used in the Newfoundland fisheries; a pike; an oscillating lever; a device used in roasting meat.

Jackal, *Canis aureus,* a small wild dog related to the wolf and resembling a fox. The Common Jackal is found in S.E. Europe, India and Sri Lanka; other species inhabit Africa and Egypt. The jackal is a well-known scavenger. It hunts singly or in pairs, unlike the wolf, which usually hunts in packs.

Jackdaw, one of the smaller members of the Crow family. This European bird is typically black with grey collar. It is easily tamed, makes an amusing pet and delights in making off with and taking to its nest bright objects, such as silverware.

Jacobins, a French revolutionary club or party, formed in 1789, and accustomed to meet at a Jacobin convent, hence the name. It became a controlling force in the Revolution, especially in the movement which led to the Terror. Robespierre was its chief spokesman.

Jacobites, adherents of the Stuart cause after the abdication of James II. First James himself, then his son (the Old Pretender), and later his grandson (the Young Pretender) tried to fan the flame of rebellion in Scotland and Ireland, but after the defeat at Culloden in 1746 the cause was lost. Also the name of the monophysite heretics of Syria, so named after their leader Jacobus Baradaeus in the 6th cent. A.D.

Jade, an exquisite kind of hardstone, ranging in colour from a whitish green to a deep mauvish brown. It can be translucent or opaque and sometimes it is veined. Jade is the common name for two minerals—the rarer *jadeite* (found in Burma, Tibet and China), a sodium-aluminium-silicate, and *nephrite* (found in New Zealand, China, Turkestan and Siberia), a calcium-magnesium silicate. The presence of small quantities of other chemicals accounts for the wide range of shades. In China jade has for centuries been looked upon with great veneration, magical powers have been ascribed to it, and it has been fashioned into ritual objects, also into miniature sculptures of animals or even whole landscapes, charming to look at and incredibly skilfully made. The Chinese word for jade is *yü*, used as a symbol for all that is noble, beautiful and pure.

Jaguar, a South American carnivorous animal resembling the leopard, but larger and more powerful. It preys on other animals but rarely attacks man.

Jainism. *See* Section J.

Janeite, a devotee of Jane Austen and her writings.

Janissaries, an élite band of Ottoman foot soldiers who acted as the Sultan's bodyguard. They were conscripts, raised by the "tribute of children" from conquered Christian countries, mainly Serbia and Albania. First recruited under Murad I (14th cent.). They were not allowed to marry. They gained great power under the Ottoman Empire. In 1826 the Sultan Mahmud II had them massacred.

January, the first month of the year, named after Janus, the two-faced god of the Romans. It was the *Wolf monath* and *Aefter Yule* of the Saxons.

Jasmine, a graceful climber belonging to the olive family with odoriferous blossom, originally a Persian plant, but now acclimatised in many varieties in almost all parts of the world. Two species of jasmine (the common jasmine and the Spanish jasmine) yield oils used in perfumery.

Jasper, a precious stone of the chalcedony variety, opaque, and coloured red, brown, yellow and sometimes green. It was greatly esteemed by the ancients, the Bible having numerous allusions to it.

Jay, a gaily-coloured bird of the Crow family, of many species—the Blue jay of N. America, the Canada jay, sometimes called "whisky jack", the Siberian jay and the British jay, fawn-coloured with black and whitish crest and bright blue feathers in the wings. It lives in woods and like the magpie, takes the eggs and young of small nesting birds.

Jazz a rhythmical syncopated music characterised by a strong element of improvisation in the performance, probably originating among the Negro population of the Southern States of the USA. It became popular during the first world war and, in a commercialised form, has held the popular field ever since. Modern dance music and popular songs are based on the jazz idiom, which has also had a profound effect upon more serious contemporary music.

Jean, a stout kind of twilled cotton cloth much worn in olden times, and resembling fustian. Blue jeans, adopted by American city youngsters from farmworkers, are now the fashion elsewhere and worn not only as overalls by workmen but by both sexes in leisure time.

Jelly-fish. The jelly-fishes, which have gelatinous, translucent bodies fringed at the margin with delicate tentacles, constitute the coelenterate order *Scyphozoa*. The mouth, with a squarish opening, is seen on the underside, and there are four horseshoe-shaped sex organs.

Jerboa, small jumping mammals of the Rodent order. These mice-like animals have long tufted tails and very long hind legs, the front legs not being used for locomotion.

Jeremiad, any utterance or writing in which sorrow or complaint is the chief characteristic, so named as recalling the style of the "Lamentations of Jeremiah", in the Old Testament.

Jerusalem Chamber, a room in Westminster Abbey, deriving its name from the circumstance of its having originally been decorated with a view of Jerusalem. Henry IV died in this chamber, and the Committee for the Revision of the Bible met there in 1870 and later.

Jesuits, members of the Roman Catholic religious order founded by Ignatius Loyola in 1540. A long and vigorous course of study is prescribed before they are admitted into the privileges of full membership. They are required to take the vows of voluntary poverty, perfect chastity, perfect obedience and complete submission to the Pope with regard to the Mission of the Order. Pope Paul VI gave them the particular mission of initiating a dialogue with atheists.

Jet, a deep black fossil substance admitting of a high polish and much used for jewellery, ornaments and trimming. It is a form of lignite, the most important British deposit being found near Whitby, where jet manufacture has been an established industry for a long period.

Jet Engine, an aeroplane engine which derives its thrust from the high velocity of the gases it ejects. The essential units in a jet engine are a rotary compressor and a gas turbine, the latter driving the compressor. The first reliable, high-performance jet propulsion engine for aircraft was invented by Sir Frank Whittle.

Jet Stream, a meteorological term coined in 1946 to describe the relatively narrow belt of strong winds (160–320 km/h) at levels in the atmosphere from 5–11 km. These winds are important in forecasting weather, and can be a valuable aid to aircraft. From the ground, where there may be little wind, the jet stream can sometimes be seen as high cirrus cloud moving across the sky at high speed.

Jew's Harp. The name is believed to be a corruption of "jaws harp". This instrument consists of a metal frame with a central tongue of spring steel. The frame is pressed against the teeth, and the tongue of the harp is twanged with the finger, the mouth acting as a resonating chamber. By altering the shape of the mouth the resonant frequency and therefore the note can be varied.

Jockey Club, the governing body that, although possessing no legal status, frames rules and laws by which horse-racing and turf matters are regulated. The club-house is at Newmarket.

John Bull, the typical figure of an Englishman, bluff, big and burly. Arbuthnot's *History of John Bull* is supposed to have originated the character.

John Dory, a fish found in most temperate seas and common in British waters. It is of a golden-yellow colour (*jaune doré*), has a high dorsal fin with long filaments projecting from the spines, very protractile jaws and is much valued as a table fish. According to legend the dark spot on each side of its body is the thumbprint of St. Peter who took a coin from the fish's mouth (Matt. XVII 24–7).

John o' Groat's House, W. of Duncansby Head, Caithness, popularly named as the northernmost point of Scotland. According to legend the house, which has now disappeared, was built in octagonal form by a Dutchman Jan de Groot who came to live there in the 16th cent. The site is marked and an inn was erected near it in 1876.

Jongleurs were minstrels and jesters who wandered from town to town singing songs, playing musical instruments, dancing and giving entertainments in mediaeval France and Norman England. Jongleurs were low-born in contrast to the Troubadours, who were often of the nobility.

Joule, a unit of energy in the SI system of units,

defined as the work done when the point of application of a force of one newton is displaced through a distance of one metre in the direction of the force. Named after J. P. Joule (1818–89). The relationship between mechanical energy and heat energy is called the mechanical equivalent of heat and was found by Joule to be 778 ft lbf in lb °F units, or 4·18 × 10⁷ ergs in gram °C units, or 1 Nm in SI units. See **F20(1)**.

Judaism. See **Section J.**

Julian Calendar, named after Julius Caesar, who in 45 B.C., finding the Roman year 90 days in advance of the real time, was the first to adopt the calculation of time by the solar year, the average length being fixed at 365¼ days. There was still an overplus of a few minutes every year, and this was rectified by the Gregorian Calendar, introduced in Italy in 1582 and adopted in England in 1752, from which date what is called the "New Style" begins.

July, the seventh month of the year, named after Julius Caesar. It was the *Maed monath* (Meadmonth) of the Saxons.

June, the sixth month of the year, containing 30 days and deriving its name from Juno. It was the *Sear* (Dry) *monath* of the Saxons.

Jupiter is the largest of the planets, 11 times the diameter of the earth, 318 times its mass but only one fourth its density. It is the fifth farthest from the sun and is the second brightest. Our knowledge of Jupiter, its fifteen moons, its ring and its magnetosphere was enormously increased in 1979 by data from the Voyager 1 and 2 space-probes which passed the planet at distances of 349,000 km and 722,000 km on March 5 and July 9 respectively. Jupiter is a gaseous planet composed mainly of hydrogen and helium like the sun, possibly with a small molten core of silicates. The centre is presumed to be at a very high temperature (30,000°C) and enormous pressures—a hundred million earth atmospheres—which make hydrogen not only liquid but metallic. This metallic fluid leads to intense magnetic fields. Jupiter's large magnetosphere is distorted by the solar wind and contains trapped high energy particles in radiation belts which would be lethal to man. Its existence was first inferred from its radio emissions and was confirmed by Pioneer 11 in 1974. Jupiter's outer gaseous surface is very cold (−120°C) and consists of three layers of crystal clouds (ice ammonium hydrogensulphide and ammonia) interspersed with gaseous hydrogen and helium. It shows massive persistent features like the swirling high pressure Red Spot (larger when first seen in 1664 but which could hold two earths) and the neighbouring white oval formations. All these features are in relative motion, some moving east and others west which account for Jupiter's banded appearance. The persistence of the features arises because Jupiter has no terrain to break them up and because the surface temperature is low. Lightning continuously flashes over the Jovian surface and at the poles there are large auroras caused by an electric current of five million amperes which flows from the poles out to Io, one of the four moons discovered in 1610 by Galileo. The others are Europa, Ganymede and Callisto. The fourteenth moon was discovered in 1979 by Voyager 2 at the outer edge of the thin ring of particles discovered by Voyager 1, which also discovered high plumes due to volcanic activity on Io, the first seen beyond earth (although a recent suggestion is that the plumes are caused by the electric current). Io's sulphurous surface shows no meteoric craters and Europa's smooth ice surface shows only a few impacts and is probably young, unlike the older Ganymede and Callisto whose ice-crust surfaces have many. Ganymede's crust has been reworked, however, by extensive tectonic movements. Ganymede is now known to be the largest moon in the solar system, larger than the planet Mercury. A fifteenth moon was discovered in 1980 by scientists analysing photographs taken by Voyager I in 1979. See **F8**.

Jurassic Formation, a series of rocks (the evidences of which are most marked in the Jura Mountains) coming between the Cretaceous and Triassic groups and including the Oolite and the Lias. It is a formation rich in fauna, abounding in echinoids, lamellibranchs, ammonites and belemnites; large reptiles, marine and land, are common, as are the plants called cyads. In Britain the Jurassic outcrop extends from the Dorset coast to the Yorkshire moors. See **F48**.

Jury, a body of private citizens chosen and sworn to hear and pass verdict upon evidence brought forward at a trial, inquest or inquiry. The origin of the English jury is obscure but it is thought to have been introduced by the Normans. The jurors are the sole judges of the true facts upon the evidence laid before them. Under the Criminal Justice Act of 1967 their verdicts in criminal courts in England and Wales no longer have to be unanimous but may be by a majority of 10 to 2. The age limit has recently been reduced from 21 to 18 and raised from 60 to 65. In Scotland 45 jurors are summoned in criminal cases, of whom 15 are chosen by ballot, and majority verdicts are accepted: not guilty, not proven and guilty.

Jute, the name given to the fibre of a plant grown largely in Bangladesh in the Ganges delta and used for the manufacture of coarse cloths, cordage and sacks. Calcutta is the biggest jute-manufacturing centre of the world, as Dundee was in the 19th cent.

Jutes, a Low German race who in the 5th cent. invaded the south-eastern part of England, establishing themselves in Kent and making Canterbury their capital.

Juvenile Courts. This is a special kind of Magistrates' Court to deal with accused persons under the age of seventeen. The Magistrates chosen are specially qualified for the work, and where possible a woman is appointed as one of the magistrates who constitute the Court. The Court is held in private away from the ordinary court room. The object of the Juvenile Court is to introduce into the trial a plan to reform the offender by providing for the care and protection which he may need, by removal from undesirable surroundings, and by subsequent education or training. In these objectives the Court has the co-operation of social workers, including Probation Officers (q.v.). Radical changes in methods of preventing and treating juvenile delinquency are contained in the Children and Young Persons Act, 1969, the result of the findings of two White Papers, 1965 and 1968. They emphasise the necessity of helping and supporting the child as far as possible in his own family and community, with resort to formal procedures only where he is exposed to moral danger, or control is necessary in the interest of society or of the child. The minimum age for prosecution will be raised from 10 to 12 when the Government is satisfied that "local authorities and other services have the necessary capacity to cope with this change". Children who are below prosecutable age will be dealt with by social casework or by care proceedings.

K

Kangaroo, pouched (marsupial) mammals of Australia and adjacent islands. There are over 20 species, the smaller ones being known as "wallabies". Kangaroos leap in a succession of springy bounds 3–6 m long, the forefeet not touching the ground. They can reach a height of over 2 m and a weight of 90 kg. First seen by white men when Capt. Cook's expedition visited Australia in 1770. Related genera include the tree kangaroos, rat kangaroos and the Tasmanian Jerboa kangaroo.

Kaolin or **China Clay** is an essential ingredient in hard-paste porcelain (q.v.). It results from the decomposition of felspar, and is widely found in China, Japan and the USA. The richest deposits in Europe are in Cornwall, near Limoges in France, and in Czechoslovakia.

Karst, geological formations typical of limestone regions in which the drainage is by underground channels. Rain water carries part of the limestone away in solution, leaving the surface dry and barren and pitted with innumerable hollows. The name comes from the Karst (Slav *Kras*) region of N.W. Yugoslavia where the rocks are massive pure limestone; the barren plateau is characterised by fissures, caves and subterranean rivers.

Kelvin. Lord Kelvin, an important 19th-cent.

physicist, gave his name to the kelvin, symbol K, a measure of temperature on the absolute scale. The Kelvin scale is a development of the scale invented by Celsius (*q.v.*) for everyday use, long known as the "centigrade" scale; the degree interval on both scales is the same. The conversion formula for the absolute or Kelvin scale is $K = C + 273 \cdot 15$. *See* **Absolute Temperature.**

Kestrel, the most common British falcon, well known for its habit of hovering for minutes at a time with vibrating wings and then swooping down to attack mice and insects. The male has spotted chestnut-brown back, greyish head and tail, which has a broad black band near tip.

Ketones. A class of organic compounds, related to aldehydes, of general formula R_2CO (where R is an organic radical). The simpler ketones, especially acetone, are widely used as solvents for lacquers, synthetic rubber and polymers, such as cellulose acetate and perspex. More complex ketones occur in nature, and some are used in the perfumery industry, muscone (from the musk deer (*q.v.*)) is an example.

Kew Gardens, officially known as the Royal Botanic Gardens, are among the most celebrated gardens in the world. They were started in 1759 by Princess Augusta of Saxe-Gotha, widow of Frederick, Prince of Wales, and mother of George III. They remained private property until 1841, when control passed to the Commissioners of Woods and Forests. They now cover 121 hectares and are administered by the Min. of Agriculture, Fisheries and Food. Since 1841 the gardens have been open to the public, and form one of the most attractive resorts near London. They suffered severe damage in the 1987 hurricane.

Keys, House of, is the Manx representative assembly. *See* **Tynwald.**

Keystone, the stone which occupies the centre and highest point of an arch and is usually the last to be inserted.

Khaki, a clay-coloured cloth adopted for uniforms in the British Army in the time of the war with the Boers, and used in the first and second world wars. First used by Indian regiments.

Kilderkin, once a common liquid measure in England, representing 18 gallons or 82 litres.

Kilogram, unit of mass, defined as the mass of the international prototype kilogram of platinum-iridium kept at the International Bureau of Weights and Measures at Sèvres. A remeasurement of Avogadro's Number (**F24(1)**) may lead to an atomic standard of mass (the second and the metre are already defined in atomic terms), but this will depend on the precision with which atoms can be counted.

Kilowatt. Unit of power, equal to one thousand watts. *See* **Watt.**

Kinetic Art denotes works of art which actually move or give the illusion of so doing. An early exponent of kinetic art was the American sculptor Alexander Calder (1898–1976) when he launched his famous "mobiles" in the early 1950s. Since then, constructions which rotate, jump, blink with lights, etc. have been made by many artists and the genre is being further elaborated upon today. Kinetic painters give a visual illusion of movement to their pictures by the use of particular colour contrasts or by a skilful play with spirals, squares, etc. in black and white, sometimes with colours blended in. An interesting exponent of the style is the English artist Bridget Riley (b. 1931).

Kinetic Energy, the energy (*q.v.*) possessed by a particle or body in virtue of its motion. If the motion is destroyed, *e.g.*, by the impact of the body with an obstacle, the kinetic energy vanishes, being turned into some other form of energy such as heat and sound. If the body has mass m and speed v its kinetic energy (leaving out corrections due to relativity) is $\frac{1}{2}mv^2$.

King Crab, remarkable arthropods now classified separately from both Arachnids and Crustacea which they resemble, inhabiting the sea coasts of America, Japan, India and Malay Peninsula, carrying a shield-shaped shell, and having a long pointed spine projecting from the posterior. The body comprises three separate sections articulated together. These crabs—in America known commonly as the horseshoe crab because of their shape—are from 45–60 cm in length. Fossil king crabs are found as far back as the Silurian. There are about six living species.

Kingfisher, a well-known family of brilliant-plumaged birds, found in all continents, comprising some 250 species and sub-species. The British kingfisher, *Aceldo atthis*, haunts the rivers and streams, and is one of the most beautiful of native birds, having iridescent blue-green, white and rich chestnut in its plumage and bright-red feet. All kingfishers have long, dagger-shaped bills. In the Malayan region, New Guinea, the Moluccas and Australia, the varieties are very numerous. The quaint *Laughing Jackass* of Australia is among the largest of the kingfisher family. The European kingfisher is the bird of the Greek legend of the Halcyon.

King-of-Arms, the name of the chief officials of the Heralds' College. There are several in England —the principal being those of the Garter, Norroy and Ulster, Clarenceux. *See* **Heralds' College.**

Kiosk, a word of Russian or Turkish origin meaning a small open pavilion of light construction much used in Eastern countries as a place of shade and rest. Similar structures are common in the streets of Paris as news and advertisement stands, and in London as telephone boxes.

Kirimon (*Kiri no go Mon*) and **Kikumon** (*Kiki no go Mon*), the two Japanese imperial crests, the first a design of leaves, stems and flowers of the Paulownia plant, and the other representing the sixteen-petalled chrysanthemum.

Kite, name of several birds of prey, widely distributed, related to the hawks and eagles, graceful in flight, and distinguished by their long wings and deeply forked tails. The red kite, light chestnut brown, once the most familiar bird of prey in Britain, seen scavenging the streets of London, is now the rarest, and found only in Wales. The Egyptian kite and the pariah kite of India, notorious for their daring thefts, are closely related to the black kite, a smaller European species, with less forked tail and blackish-brown plumage.

Kittiwake, a beautiful white and pearl-grey gull with black legs, dark eyes and greenish-yellow bill. Its range is wide, and includes the British Isles, where it is a local resident. The flight of this only truly oceanic gull, which except in the breeding-season is generally found offshore, is graceful, swift and buoyant. A triangular black patch, noticeable on the ends of the wings when open, is characteristic of the species, as is the call kitti-wake, from which the bird derives its name. It nests in colonies on the ledges of caves and steep sliffs.

Kiwi, flightless, stoutly-built birds of New Zealand now very rare and carefully protected by the Government. They are little larger than a domestic hen, and lay astonishingly large eggs for their size. Incubation and care of chicks fall to the male bird. They have rudimentary wings concealed by the plumage, and the feathers are hair-like. They are nocturnal.

Knighthood is a degree of honour or title common in Europe since the Middle Ages, and was at first exclusively a military order. In Great Britain the four main orders of knighthood are those of the Garter, the Bath, the Thistle and St. Patrick; in addition to which there are several other orders, such as the Order of St. Michael and St. George, the Star of India, etc. There are also Knights Bachelors not associated with any special order. The title is not hereditary, and therefore ·ranks below that of a baronet, though both are entitled to the prefix "Sir".

Knot, a nautical measure of speed (1 sea mile per hour), and formerly measured by a log-line, divided by knots at equal distances $\frac{1}{120}$ of a geographical mile. The number of knots travelled by the ship in a half a minute corresponded to the numbers of sea miles it travelled per hour. A sea mile is equal to about $1\frac{1}{8}$ of a statute mile or $1 \cdot 9$ km. Also, a grey and white wading bird, usually a winter visitor to Britain found in flocks on the coast.

Knout, a whip of many thongs, often fatal in its effects, formerly used in Russia for flogging criminals.

Koala, the Australian arboreal marsupial mammal

that looks like a toy teddy-bear, with ashy-grey fur, bushy ears and rudimentary tail. It feeds on the leaves and shoots of certain eucalyptus trees, and is not more than 60 cm in length.

Kohl, a powder prepared from antimony or burnt almond shells, and in common use by the women of the East for darkening the eyelids.

Koto, a musical instrument in general use in Japan consisting of a series of 13 silken strings stretched across a curved wooden surface, and played with the fingers. Each string is 1·5 m long, and has a separate bridge so fixed as to give the vibration necessary for the note it has to produce. It is a sort of horizontal harp, and in the hands of an expert player is capable of giving forth excellent music.

Kremlin, the citadel or walled city within a Russian city which during the Middle Ages served as an administrative and religious centre and offered protection. That of Moscow, now the headquarters of the Russian government, contains the cathedral where the Tsars were crowned, an imperial palace and the "King of Bells" (*see* **Bells**). Its walls which are topped with towers were built in the 15th cent.

Krypton, one of the rare gas elements, no. 36, symbol Kr, occurring in the air to the extent of 1 part in 20 million. It was discovered in 1898 by Ramsay and Travers. It is used in gas-filled electric lamps.

Kusti, the sacred cord or girdle of the Parsees, consisting of 72 threads—the number of the chapters of the *Yasna*—and two branches, each branch containing six knots, together standing for the 12 months of the year.

Kyrie Eleison ("Lord, have mercy"), the name of a common form of prayer in the Anglican, Roman Catholic and Greek Churches; also applied to the English Church responses after the recital of the commandments.

Kyrle Society, named after Pope's "Man of Ross", John Kyrle, founded by Miss Miranda and Miss Octavia Hill in 1875, and having for its object, the decoration of workmen's clubs, hospitals, etc. and the promotion among the poor of a taste for literature, music and outdoor recreation.

L

Labarum, the standard of Constantine the Great, adopted after his conversion to Christianity, marked with his seal and represented upon the coinage.

Labourers, English Statute of, was passed 1350–51, with the object of compelling labourers to accept a certain rate of wages and not leave their employers' service, the Plague having rendered labourers so scarce that they were in great demand and had been insisting on higher pay. These enactments were bitterly opposed and led to the "Peasants' Revolt", headed by Wat Tyler.

Labradorite, a felspar rich in calcium and of a pearly lustre on cleavage, found in masses in igneous rocks, the best samples of which come from Labrador.

Labyrinth, or **Maze,** a combination of roads and passages so constructed as to render it difficult for anyone ignorant of the clue to trace the way to the central part. The Egyptian labyrinth near Lake Moeris had 3,000 rooms, half of them subterranean and the remainder above ground. The labyrinth in Crete, according to Greek myth, was built by Daedalus to house the Minotaur. There was one at Lemnos, renowned for its stalactite columns; and another at Clusium constructed by Porsenna, King of Etruria, about 520 B.C. The labyrinth in which Fair Rosamond was concealed was at Woodstock. Hampton Court maze dates from the 16th cent.

Labyrinthodonts, gigantic fossil amphibians which get their name from the curious labyrinthine structure of their teeth, probably an evolutionary link between fishes and reptiles. They occur in the Carboniferous, Permian and Triassic formations, and remains have been found in Britain and other parts of Europe. Their heads were long, and their footprints, by which they were discovered, closely resemble the prints of the human hand.

Lac, a resinous matter deposited on the branches of a number of tropical trees by the females of the lac insect, the exudation including eggs and a viscous covering. At the gathering time the twigs are broken off and dried in the sun, when the insects die, and the lac that remains is termed *stick-lac.* From this, by the removal of extraneous accretions and dissolving, *seed-lac* is produced. *Shell-lac* is seed-lac after it has been melted and otherwise prepared, and this is the best known of the lacs, being used in printing and the manufacture of varnishes and sealing-wax, and for other commercial purposes.

Lace, a delicate fabric of linen, silk or cotton threads, made by hand or machinery, and worked in various ornamental designs. The kinds of lace are many, deriving their distinctive names either from the method employed in production or from the place where any special variety was originally made. The best-known makes are pillow or bobbin-lace, woven and plaited by hand; needle-point lace, worked by the needle over a traced design; and machine lace, which practically dates from Heathcote's invention of the early part of the 19th cent. Some of the most famed laces are the following: *Alençon,* a needle-point lace; *Brussels,* a very fine kind, with needle-point sprigs and flowers; *Chantilly,* a silk variety with flowers and open-work; *Cluny,* a netlace with darned stitch; *Honiton,* a delicate kind with dainty sprigs and figures; *Mechlin,* generally made in one piece and very varied in design; and *Valenciennes,* or bobbin lace, of great durability, the pattern and ground of which are made at the same time, being one of the best and most costly of laces, now manufactured mainly in Belgium. Nottingham is famous for its lace.

Lace-Wings, insects with frail, transparent and much-veined wings whose grubs eat large numbers of insect pests such as aphids. The eggs are borne at the ends of threads attached to plants.

Ladybird, the common name of a large family of beetles—the *Coccinellidae.* The insect is usually of a red or yellow colour with small black or coloured spots. Ladybirds are of good service to the gardener because their larvae feed on aphids. There are about 2,000 species.

Lady-Day, the day of the festival of the Annunciation of the Virgin Mary, 25 March. One of the four English quarter days.

Lake Dwelling, the name given to certain prehistoric habitations which were thought to have stood on platforms over lakes, like villages in certain Pacific islands. Recent excavations at the Lake of Burgäschi in Switzerland show that the prehistoric Swiss pile dwellings probably stood on the shores of lakes, not on platforms over the water. Also found at Mere and Glastonbury, Somerset.

Lakes are bodies of water collected in depressions of the earth's surface. The most notable lakes are the Great Lake series of North America, including Superior, Michigan, Huron, Erie and Ontario, all discharging into the St. Lawrence River. Africa has an enormous area of lakes, including the Mobutu Seso and the Victoria, forming the sources of the White Nile. Smaller lakes are numerous in other countries—Switzerland, Finland, Italy, England, Ireland, Scotland, all having their lake regions, where the scenery is invariably beautiful and romantic. The Kariba Dam (Zimbabwe–Zambia border) and the Nasser (Egypt) are the largest man-made lakes in the world.

Lake School, the name given, at first in ridicule, to a distinguished trio of poets—Wordsworth, Coleridge and Southey—who made their homes in the English Lake District.

Lamellibranchs (Pelecypods), the class of aquatic, bi-valve molluscs to which the oysters, cockles, mussels, clams and scallops belong. In these animals the body, which is compressed laterally, is enclosed in two hinged shells held together by muscular action. The gills are thin plates hence the name "lamellibranchs". *See* **F36**(1), **41**(1).

Lamination, stratification on a very fine scale, as in shales.

Lammas Day is one of the oldest of the Church festivals, probably derived from the loaf-mass (*hlafmaesse*) of the Anglo-Saxons. It occurs on 1 August. In the olden times it was the day when loaves were given in place of first-fruit offerings.

Lammergeyer, the bearded vulture of alpine regions, resembling an eagle in appearance. It has a white head with black tufts at base of the bill, and its general plumage is dark brown, nearly black. It is found in the remote mountain ranges from southern Spain and parts of Africa to China, and is becoming scarce.

Lampblack, a carboniferous pigment obtained from flame-smoke, and now produced in specially constructed furnaces in which bodies rich in carbon, such as tar, resin, petroleum, etc., are burned. The smoke or soot resulting is collected from the sides of the furnace, and forms lampblack. It finds use in making printer's ink, black paint, etc. Being a very pure form of carbon, it is also utilised in the manufacture of dynamo brushes and arc-lamp carbons.

Lamprey. Eel-like fish having no scales, bones, paired fins or jaws. They attach themselves by their mouths to fish whose blood they suck. Together with the hagfishes, the lampreys are placed in a special class—the Cyclostomes. There are three British lampreys.

"Lancet", the name of a noted English medical journal, established in 1823 by Dr. Wakley.

Land Crab, a family of crabs (*Gecarinidae*) which live mainly on land, though migrating to the seas to deposit their eggs.

Land League, an association formed in 1879, with Parnell as president, for compelling a reduction in the rents of land, and a reconstruction of the land laws in Ireland, and in case of non-compliance refusing to pay rent. For a time this League exercised great political influence and was an important aid to the Home Rule agitation.

Landrail, popularly known as the Corncrake, was a regular summer visitor to Britain two generations ago, but no longer. Its harsh and piercing note was a familiar sound in English cornfields. It is decreasing almost everywhere.

Landslip, a sudden downward sliding under gravity of large masses of rock, soil, etc.; often set off by earthquake shock or saturation of a particular stratum with water. Many serious landslides have occurred from time to time. In 1618, an earthfall happened at Plurs, on Lake Como, involving the destruction of many buildings and the loss of numerous lives. In 1806 a portion of Rossberg mountain in Switzerland slipped from its position, and falling into the valley below buried many villages and hamlets and over 800 people. A chalk cliff 30–45 m high and 1·2 km long fell at Lyme Regis, in Dorset, in 1839, doing great damage. Over 200 people were killed by a landslip in Naini Tal, in India, in 1880; and at Quebec, in 1889, a rocky eminence called Cape Diamond gave way, many buildings being destroyed and lives lost. Notable landslips in recent times have occurred at Amalfi (Italy) in 1924, at Murchiston (New Zealand) in 1929, at Aberfan (Wales) in 1966 and near St. Gervais (France) in 1970.

Langue d'oc and Langue d'oïl, the two principal mediaeval French dialects, *oc* and *oïl* being their respective words for the affirmative particle (modern French *oui*). *Langue d'oc*, spoken south of the Loire, was the language of the troubadors. Provençal, one of its dialects had a literary revival in the 19th cent. under the influence of the poet Frédéric Mistral. *Langue d'oïl* was spoken in northern France, and it was the dialect of the Paris region which developed into modern French.

Lantern Fly, bugs belonging to the family *Fulgoridae* in which the head is drawn out to form a lantern-like structure. In no instance is the "lantern" luminous, though naturalists used to think it was.

Lanthanides, the fourteen metallic elements following lanthanum in the Periodic Table, *i.e.*, the elements cerium (no. 58) to lutetium (no. 71). They are also known as the rare-earth metals, though they are in fact all more terrestrially abundant than, for instance, mercury or arsenic (with the exception of the unstable

radioactive element promethium, no. 61). The lanthanide atoms are distinguished by having an incomplete inner electron sub-shell (the 4f level), this feature giving them interesting magnetic properties. For instance, gadolinium, holmium and dysprosium are ferromagnetic (*see* **F22**) at low temperatures. Chemically, the lanthanides behave similarly, being highly reactive metals usually forming trivalent salts. *See* **Periodic Table, F65.**

Lapis Lazuli, an azure-blue mineral, being a silicate of aluminium and sodium. The pigment ultramarine is made by grinding it, though artificial ultramarine has largely superseded it. The mineral (also called *lazurite*) has been used as a gemstone since ancient times.

Lapwing or **Green Plover**, familiar British bird on moors and marshlands with iridescent greenish-black plumage, white underparts and black crest. Often called "peewit" from its cry. Protected under Protection of Birds Act, 1967.

Larboard is the old nautical term indicating the left-hand side of a ship, and changed by Admiralty order to "port" in 1844. Starboard is the right-hand side.

Larch, a familiar coniferous tree in the mountain regions of northern Europe, and though not native to Britain, the Common Larch is successfully cultivated in various parts of the kingdom. It is one of the best of all turpentine-yielding trees, and the bark is valued for tanning. The larch is an unusual conifer in being deciduous.

Lark, a family of song birds (*Alaudidae*) of many species, some of which—notably the skylark—are famed for their habit of soaring into the air, singing all the while. They build their nests on the ground in the open country and, except for the black lark of Russia, have streaked brown plumage. The skylark and woodlark are the best known British species, while the crested lark and shore lark are among the occasional visitors. Africa has the greatest number of larks; America has only one species, the horned lark.

Larkspur, the common name of the genus *Delphinium*, a favourite flower introduced into British gardens from Switzerland in 1573. The common larkspur is *D. consolida*.

Larva, the undeveloped form of any animal which, before maturity undergoes metamorphosis, usually different from the adult in structure and habits.

Laser. A remarkable kind of light source that was discovered in 1960. With the laser it is possible to probe the behaviour of matter under the influence of enormous energy densities, range and survey vast distances to microscopic accuracy and send millions of telephone and television messages between any two points that can see each other with telescopes. Laser light, in contrast to natural light, is coherent and can be expressed as a regular progression of waves carrying energy along a particular path. Thus the essential difference is that laser light is an orderly sort of wave motion in contrast to ordinary light which is inherently unsteady and therefore an inefficient carrier of information in time. The name *maser*, which is the microwave parent of the laser, derives from the expression "microwave amplification by the stimulated emission of radiation". Upon application to light wavelengths the microwave part of the name lost its meaning and the term maser became generally descriptive of any device in which stimulated emission dominates.

Laser Fusion is a method by which it has been proposed that thermonuclear reactions may be controlled and exploited as a source of energy (*see* **Nuclear Fusion**). The idea is to irradiate a millimetre-sized pellet of a mixture of frozen deuterium and tritium with a short ($\sim 10^{-9}$ s) but very intense pulse of energy in the form of laser light. This has the effect of both compressing the pellet by a factor of at least a thousand and heating it to about 10^8 °C. Under these conditions, thermonuclear reactions (principally $^2D + {}^3T \rightarrow {}^4He + {}^1n$) proceed sufficiently fast that a net output of energy is obtained before the pellet explosively separates. Formidable technical problems need to be solved before laser fusion can become a practical proposition. These include the development of efficient high-powered lasers and the design of a suitable reactor that can withstand up to 100 micro-hydrogen bomb explosions per second. It is still not clear whether this method of controlling nuclear fusion is more practical than the more conventional approach involving the magnetic confinement of plasmas.

Latent Heat is the quantity of heat required to convert 1 gram of a substance from one form into another. For example, when a solid changes into a liquid or a liquid into a gas, the addition of heat to bring about the change produces no rise in temperature, the energy being absorbed in the form of latent heat. An equal amount is released when the process is reversed. The latent heat of fusion of ice is about 79·6 calories per gram, that of the vaporisation of water about 539 calories per gram.

Lateran Councils were the religious conventions held in the Lateran basilica at Rome for deciding important questions of Church doctrine. The most brilliant was that of 1215 which pronounced in favour of a Crusade. *See* Ecumenical Council.

Lateran Treaty, 1929, between Italy and the Vatican established the Vatican City as an independent sovereign state.

Laterite refers to any tropical soil or soil horizon rich in hydrated ferric and aluminium oxides which harden when exposed to the atmosphere. It is difficult to cultivate and is commonly used for bricks and road metal. Laterite buildings have been known to withstand the weathering for many centuries and a number of fine examples are found in India and S.E. Asia.

Latin America. The Spanish-speaking, Portuguese-speaking and French-speaking countries of N. America, S. America, Central America and the W. Indies. *See* Section K.

Latitude of a point on the earth's surface is its angular distance from the equator, measured on the surface of the earth in degrees, minutes and seconds. Thus the equator is 0° Lat. and the poles 90° Lat. (N. or S.). First determined by Hipparchus of Nicaea about 160 B.C. Latitude introduces zones of climate, *e.g.,* tropical rain, subtropical steppe and desert, temperate rain and polar.

Laughing Gas. *See* Nitrous oxide.

Launce *or* **Sand Eel,** a family of eel-like sea fishes found in large numbers on the coasts of North America and Europe. There are two species common to British waters. These fishes are of a bright silvery hue, and live much in the sand underneath the water. They are prized as human food and as bait.

Laurentian Shield refers to the Pre-Cambrian rocks in the region of the Upper Lakes of Canada, nearly 5 million sq km in extent. Of enormous importance to Canada on account of the mineral wealth, forests yielding valuable timber and wood-pulp, and water-power.

Lava, the molten rock which is erupted from a volcanic vent or fissure. Also the same material which has cooled and solidified.

Lawn, very fine sun-bleached linen, in olden time called "cloth of Rheims".

Lead, a soft malleable metallic element, no. 82, symbol Pb (Latin *plumbum*), occurring in numerous ores, which are easily smelted. Its most important source is the mineral galena which consists chiefly of lead sulphide; rarely is it found free. Lead is largely used in plumbing on account of its pliability, and in nuclear reactors as a shield against radiation because of its very high density. As an alloy element it combines in the formation of type metal, stereo metal, shot metal, pewter and many other compounds. Oxides of lead are used in some types of glass and in the manufacture of paints (red lead). All lead compounds are poisonous. Leading producers of lead are the United States (Missouri), Australia (Broken Hill) and the Soviet Union.

Leaf Miners, insect larvae which tunnel between the upper and lower skins of leaves. Most leaf miners are caterpillars of tiny moths; some sawfly larvae have the same habit.

Leagues, or combinations of kings, countries, communities, have been frequent since the kings of Canaan united against the Israelites. Among the most famous leagues may be mentioned the Holy or Catholic League, which

prevented the recognition of Henry IV as King of France until he became a Roman Catholic; and the League of Augsburg against Louis XIV of France in 1686.

League of Nations, was founded on 10 January 1920, with the object of promoting international peace and security. The original members were the signatories to the Peace Treaties at Versailles, and membership grew to fifty-three as new nations and ex-enemy States were admitted. Two notable absentees were the United States and Soviet Russia, the latter not being represented until 1934. Germany was a member from 1926 to 1933. The League had an Assembly which met at Geneva every year and a Council which met five or six times a year. The Permanent Court of International Justice (now under the UN) sits at The Hague. The League held its last Assembly at Geneva in April 1946. Its place was taken by the United Nations. The International Labour Organisation, set up by the League of Nations, met in April 1944 at Philadelphia and resumed its old quarters at Geneva under the UN in 1946.

Leap Year *or* **Bissextile,** was fixed by Julius Caesar, 45 B.C., the addition of one day in every four years bringing the measure of the calendar year even with the astronomical year with three minutes per year over. The Gregorian Calendar corrected this by dropping leap year at the centuries not divisible by 400. For instance, 1700, 1800 and 1900 were not leap years.

Learning. *See* **F40(2).**

Leather was made in ancient Egypt, Greece and Rome, and has through succeeding centuries played an important part in the service of man. It consists of the dressed hides or skins of animals after the process of tanning has been gone through. Untanned skins are known as pelts. Leather is classed either according to the skins from which it is made or the system of preparation employed. The best-known kinds are morocco, kid, Russian, chamois, Cordovan, grained, patent, russet, tan, calf, Hungarian.

Leech, an aquatic blood-sucking worm, mostly found in fresh-water ponds. Each end of the body is provided with a sucker, but that at the head end has jaws and teeth. The medicinal leech has three jaws. The leech attaches itself with avidity to animal bodies and sucks until glutted. Its saliva contains an anti-coagulant.

Leeward, a nautical term, meaning the sheltered side of a vessel—that is, the opposite side to that from which the wind is blowing.

Legion, a body of Roman troops, varying in numbers at different periods. A legion was divided into 10 cohorts, and every cohort into three maniples. Three legions composed the Roman army of occupation in Britain.

Legion of Honour, the French order for distinguished services, military or civil, was instituted by Napoleon I in 1802, and confirmed and modified under later rules. There are five grades—Grands Croix, Grands Officiers, Commandeurs, Officiers and Chevaliers.

Legume, the fruit typical of the pea, bean family, or *Leguminosae.*

Lemming, small light-brown rodents with dark spots, abounding in Scandinavian countries and in Siberia, about 12 cm long, with a short stump of a tail. The migrations of the lemming are famous, probably caused by overbreeding when food is plentiful. So insistent is the urge to keep moving that these animals will march on into the sea in their thousands and be drowned.

Lemur, almost the most primitive member of the primate order of mammals (to which man, apes and monkeys also belong). They are noted for having strong plant toes enabling them to use their feet as hands, and also well-developed thumbs on the hands. They have long squirrel-like tails, fox-shaped heads and large staring eyes. True lemurs are confined to the Malagasy Rep.; closely related are the "bush-babies" of S. Africa.

Lend-Lease. During the earlier phases of the second world war the bulk of British investments in the USA had to be either sold or pledged to Americans in payment for dollar supplies. After the United States entered the war this drain was stopped by the Lend-Lease arrangement, under which Great Britain met the costs of American consumption in Great Britain, while the United States paid for British supplies from America. This arrangement was abruptly terminated on the ending of hostilities; and Great Britain and other belligerent countries found themselves without means of paying in dollars for indispensable American supplies, including the foodstuffs, materials and capital goods needed for economic reconstruction. In these circumstances Great Britain negotiated with the United States and also with Canada a large loan, which was used for buying dollar supplies and played an inportant part in helping the West European economies to maintain themselves and feed their people while they were carrying through the earlier stages of post-war reconstruction. These loans involved large charges for interest and amortisation in future years, but proved far too small to meet the dollar deficit for more than a short period. In face of this situation the United States launched the Marshall Plan.

Lenses, pieces of transparent material designed to focus an image of an illuminated object. Usually of glass, but plastic lenses are common, and quartz, etc. are used for special purposes. The surfaces of the simplest lenses are parts of spheres. Lenses which are thickest, or thinnest, at the centre are called convex and concave respectively. Lenses of complex shape are often used in microscopes, etc. Electron lenses are arrangements of electric or magnetic fields which focus beams of electrons, *e.g.*, on to T.V. screens.

Lent, the forty days' period of fasting that precedes Easter.

Lepidoptera, the order of insects with scaly wings and bodies, to which the 90,000 butterflies and moths belong.

Leptons. A group of particles which include electrons, neutrinos and muons. All are much lighter than protons or any baryons *(q.v.).* See **F16.**

Lepus, the constellation of the Hare, situated under the Orion group, and one of the constellations with which the ancients were familiar.

Lettres de Cachet, sealed letters which the kings of France issued to their agents to secure the imprisonment of distrusted or disliked persons without trial. Abolished in 1789.

Levée, a State reception held by the Sovereign or his representative and attended by men only.

Lewis, a contrivance for stone-lifting, the principle of which was known to the ancient Romans; it consists of two dovetail tenons of iron or other metal, expanded by an intervening key in a dovetail-shaped mortice in the stone, and shackled by a ringed bolt to the hoisting chain.

Leyden Jar, the earliest form of electrical condenser. Its invention is usually credited to Muschenbroeck of Leyden (1745). It consisted of a jar coated inside and out with tinfoil for about two-thirds of its height and having its inner coating connected with the top by a brass knob and chain. The jar was charged by connecting it to an electrostatic machine.

Lias, a geological term referring to the lower section of the Jurassic group, and mainly comprising shales and limestones.

Liberalism. See **Section J.**

Libraries, before the invention of printing, were few, and collected together at enormous cost. At Nineveh remains of libraries, consisting of tablets of baked clay, have been discovered. There were two libraries at Alexandria containing a vast collection of rolls or volumes, founded by Ptolemy I Soter (367–382 B.C.) and established by Ptolemy II Philadelphus (309–246 B.C.). Among the great libraries of later times may be mentioned the Vatican Library at Rome, moved to its present premises in 1588; the Royal Library in Paris which later became the Bibliothèque Nationale; The Astor Library, New York; and in England, the Bodleian Library, Oxford, and the British Library (see below). Since 1850 public libraries have been established in all the chief cities and towns of the kingdom. The first lending library was opened in Edinburgh in 1726. In most villages there is a "county library centre" to which collections of books are sent by the County Library. In Great Britain there are 24,000 centres of this kind in village clubs, halls, shops, schools and even homes. In some counties

there is a library van or the bibliobus, as it has been called by a French writer. This travelling library tours on a pre-arranged time-table so that everyone knows exactly when it will arrive. The British Library in London, the National Library of Scotland, in Edinburgh, that of Wales in Aberystwyth, the Bodleian Library of Oxford and the Cambridge University Library comprise the "copyright" libraries, entitled to receive a copy of each new book and journal published in Britain. The British Library Act 1972 brought together into a single organisation (a) the former British Museum Library (the books remaining in the Museum) and the Science Reference Library in Holborn and Bayswater, the whole now being known as the British Library, Reference Division; (b) the former National Lending Library for Science and Technology and its arts and humanities counterpart, the National Central Library, together now known as the British Library, Lending Division, and located at Boston Spa, Yorkshire. It is intended by 1993 to rehouse Reference Division in a single new building in London, near Euston Station. Lending Division, remains in Yorkshire. UNESCO is currently (1990) mounting a campaign to rebuild the Alexandria Library, one of antiquity's most celebrated centres of learning.

Libretto (It. booklet), the literary text of an opera or oratorio. Usually the composer and the librettist collaborate in the writing of an opera, but several composers (*e.g.*, Wagner) wrote their own librettos. Boito, librettist to Verdi for *Otello* and *Falstaff*, himself composed two operas *Mefistofele* and *Nerone*. Most famous of Italian opera librettists was the poet and dramatist Metastasio (1698–1782). His librettos were set to music by many composers, including Gluck, Handel, Mozart, Rossini.

Licence is a permission given to do some act, which without such permission, it would be unlawful to do. Licences are required for keeping dogs, for operating a television receiving set, for driving a motor vehicle, for killing game, for setting up as a bookmaker, for selling beer, wines and spirits, tobacco, etc. and for importing certain items such as arms, ammunition, radioactive materials, animals, plants, drugs and explosives.

Lichens. In every lichen, two plants are associated, one being an alga and the other a fungus. The fungus derives its food from the alga; probably the alga gains too from the association, being protected against desiccation by the fungus (an example of symbiosis). Lichens are the first plants to colonise bare rocks.

Life-Boats were invented by three men, Lionel Lukin who converted a coble into a boat for saving life in 1785; William Wouldhave, who discovered how to make a boat right herself if she capsized; and Henry Greathead, who built a life-boat, partly from Wouldhave's model, in 1789. This boat was stationed at South Shields, which was the first permanent life-boat station to be established. It was not until 1851 that the first life-boat able to self-right was built, and a motor was first installed in a life-boat in 1904. The Arun life-boats, launched in 1971, have twin 460 h.p. diesel engines with a maximum speed of 18.5 knots. All coastal life-boats in this country are maintained by the Royal National Lifeboat Institution founded by Sir William Hillary in 1824. It is supported entirely by voluntary contributions, and has saved over 107,500 people. Its headquarters are in Poole, Dorset. In 1990, it cost over £17m. to maintain the service.

Light, a particular kind of electromagnetic disturbance capable of travelling through space, and some kinds of matter, and of affecting our eyes to cause vision. Its finite speed was first demonstrated by O. Römer, using observations of the eclipses of Jupiter's satellites in 1675. In 1860 Maxwell showed that light waves are electromagnetic. Since Einstein's theory of relativity (1905) it has been generally realised that the speed of light is a fundamental natural constant. Visible light with wavelengths between about 4 and 7×10^{-5} cm is only a small part of the electromagnetic spectrum. The speed of light in vacuum is about $2 \cdot 997925 \times 10^{8}$ m/s.

Light Year, a measure of astronomical distance,

equal to the distance light travels in a period of one year. A light year is $9·463 \times 10^{12}$ km but the unit parsec is now preferred. (1 pc = 3·2616 l.y.).

Lighthouses, to warn ships of dangerous places and indicate coasts, points, harbours, etc., have existed since the building of the Pharos, a tower of white marble 183 m high, built by Ptolemy II Philadelphus at Alexandria about 280 B.C. In early lighthouses the lights were simple fires. The most famous and one of the earliest British lighthouses is the Eddystone (q.v.). Dungeness lighthouse, opened in 1960, is very modern in design, capable of automatic operation and the first of its kind to incorporate the xenon electric arc lamp as a source of illumination. The electric fog signal consists of sixty loud-speaker units built into the tower just below the lantern, giving a honeycomb effect. The lighthouses of England and Wales, the Channel Islands and Gibraltar are under the control of Trinity House; Commissioners of Northern Lighthouses control those of Scotland; and the Commissioners of Irish Lights control the coasts of Ireland. Particulars of lights in all parts of the world are published for the guidance of navigation in the *Admiralty Lists of Lights,* compiled annually by the British Admiralty. Under the 1987 Pilotage Act, responsibility for pilotage now rests with harbour authorities.

Lightning, the flash of a discharge of electricity between two clouds, or between a cloud and the earth, when the strength of the electric fields becomes so great as to break down the resistance of the intervening air. With "forked" lightning the actual path, often branched, is visible, while with "sheet" lightning the flash is hidden by the clouds which themselves are illuminated. "Ball" lightning or fireballs is the name given to the luminous balls which have been seen floating in the air during a thunderstorm. The Boys camera has provided much information regarding the sequence of events in a lightning discharge. It is found that a flash consists of a number of separate strokes, usually four or five, and that the discharge of electricity to earth begins with a faintly luminous "leader" moving downwards and branching at intervals. As the ground is approached a much brighter luminosity travels back along the conducting channels, lighting up with several branches. The multiple strokes which follow in fractions of a second have the same "return" nature and are rarely branched. Lightning flashes to earth damage structures, cause loss of life and endanger overhead power systems, often interrupting electricity supply. Such storms generally affect radio transmissions and present hazards to aircraft. Thunderclouds may develop energy far exceeding that of our largest power generating stations.

Lightning Conductor, a metal rod, the upper part of which is of copper with a conical point, the lower portion being iron, which extends into the earth. Its effect is to gather to itself the surrounding electricity and discharge it into the earth, thus preventing its falling upon the protected building. In ships, lightning conductors are fixed to the masts and carried down through the ship's keel-sheathing. Benjamin Franklin was the first to realise the possibilities of lightning protection and, in 1752, carried out his famous experiment of drawing electricity from thunder-clouds, with the aid of a sharp-pointed conductor fixed to a kite.

Lillibulero, an old marching song arranged by Purcell. With words by Wharton, it is said to have "sung James II out of three kingdoms". Used by the B.B.C. during the second world war as a station identification signal preceding news bulletins.

Lily Family (Liliaceae), one of the largest families of flowering plants, with 200 genera and 2,500 species. It includes the true lilies (*Lilium*), tulips and hyacinths. Vegetables belonging to the family are the onion and asparagus.

Limes, trees of the genus *Tilia,* including some 30 species spread over north temperate regions. The word is a corruption of "linden". Limes native to Britain are the small-leaved *T. cordata* and the broad-leaved *T. platyphyllos.* The hybrid *T. vulgaris* was introduced into Britain from the Continent during the 17th

cent. and is frequently seen in streets and parks. Lime-wood was used by Grinling Gibbons for his fruit, flower and bird decorations.

Limestones, sedimentary rocks composed wholly or largely of calcium carbonate and formed by two main processes, (1) organic (skeletal remains of organisms), e.g., chalk (q.v.) and (2) chemical (precipitation of calcium carbonate), e.g., oolite (q.v.). Marble is limestone that will polish after cutting.

Linen, a textile fabric manufactured from flax fibre, known to the ancient Egyptians, and first manufactured in England under Henry III by Flemish weavers. The greatest linen-manufacturing region in the world is Northern Ireland (largely yarns and the lighter types of fabrics); Scotland produces coarse linens and canvas as well as household linens.

Ling, a sea-fish common on the coasts of Britain, and abounding in more northern waters. It averages about 1 m in length, and is a voracious feeder, living chiefly on small fish. Ling is also the name applied to *Calluna vulgaris,* the plant commonly called "heather".

Linseed, the seed of the flax plant, containing, apart from its fibrous substance, certain oily and nitrogenous matter of considerable commercial value. This yields linseed oil, and some of the residue is used to make cattle food.

Lion, the most impressive of the Cat family. It is chiefly found in open bush country in Africa, being comparatively rare in Asia. Its large square head, its flowing mane (in the males only) and its tufted tail distinguish it. From tip to tip it can reach a length of 3m; a weight of 225 kg.

Lion and Unicorn, the supporting figures of the royal arms of Great Britain, date from the union of Scotland with England (1603) at the accession of James I (James VI of Scotland), the lion representing England and the unicorn Scotland.

Liqueurs are essences combined with alcoholic liquid, and are of many kinds, named according to their flavouring or place of production, and include Maraschino, Chartreuse, Curaçao, Benedictine, Noyau, Kümmel, etc.

Liquid, the name given to matter in such state that it takes its shape from the containing vessel. The volume it occupies is independent of the container, however. *See* **F20(2).**

Liquid Crystals form a special class of substance and are true liquids in that they flow easily and can be poured. However, unlike ordinary liquids, liquid crystals have their molecules arranged with geometrical regularity in one or two dimensions, so that they have a certain internal structure similar to that of solid crystals. They are fairly complicated chemicals with somewhat elongated molecules. Liquid crystals are of interest to biologists as well as to chemists and physicists, and not just because they account for the iridescence of beetles. Some body fluids are in fact liquid crystals. There are also technological applications because of their unique electrical and optical properties. They are receiving increasing attention for these reasons.

Litanies were first used in church processions in the 5th cent. The first English litany was commanded to be recited in the Reformed churches by Henry VIII in 1544.

Lithium, a soft metallic element, no. 3, symbol Li, similar to sodium. It is very reactive and is stored under paraffin oil. It is the lightest metal element.

Lithography, the art of drawing on stone and printing therefrom, was discovered by Alois Senefelder about 1796, and was introduced into England a few years later. Many improvements in the art have been made, especially in chrome-lithography and photo-lithography.

Litre, a metric measure, was abolished in 1964 as a scientific unit of volume, but remains as a special name for the cubic decimetre and as an everyday unit, e.g., a litre of petrol.

Liturgy, the name given to the Church ritual, though strictly applying only to the portion used in the celebration of the Eucharist or Lord's Supper. The Anglican liturgy is laid down in the Book of Common Prayer (1662). Temporary powers granted by Parliament in

1965 to the Church to make changes in the form of worship were made permanent in 1974. The Alternative Service Book was introduced in 1980.

Liverworts (Hepatics), a class of simple green plants related to the mosses. Liverworts are most common in damp situations, such as the banks of ditches. The majority of British species are leafy, only some are thalloid.

Lizard, the name given to a diversified order of reptiles, of which there are about 1,600 species. They include the geckos, chameleons, glass snakes, skinks and blind worms.

Llama, mammals related to the camels, from which they differ in small size, absence of the humps, and more woolly coat. The domestic llama of S. America is used as a beast of burden, also providing wool, meat and milk. *See also* **Alpaca, Guanaco.**

Loadstone *or* **Lodestone,** an oxide of iron, found chiefly in Sweden and Norway. Its scientific name is magnetite. It has the power of attracting pieces of iron and served as the first magnets used in compasses. One of the class of non-metallic magnetic materials nowadays known as "ferrites" (*q.v.*).

Lobby Correspondents are political correspondents of newspapers who do not report the actual proceedings of Parliament—this is done by Parliamentary Correspondents—but interpret political news and events.

Lobsters are marine crustacean animals existing in large numbers in the northern seas of Europe and America and in fair proportion on some parts of the British coasts, especially in the neighbourhood of the Channel Islands.

Locarno, Treaty of, 1925, whereby Germany, France and Belgium undertook to maintain their present frontiers and to abstain from the use of force against each other. Hitler broke the pact by re-occupying the Rhineland, the demilitarisation of which had been recognised by Germany.

Locust, insects of the grasshopper family, but much more powerful. They are inhabitants of hot countries, and often make their appearance in untold millions, like clouds, devastating all the vegetation that comes within their course. The locust-tree (*Ceratonia siliqua*) is supposed to have furnished food to St. John the Baptist in the wilderness, and its "beans" have accordingly been styled "St. John's Bread".

Loess, a deposit of silt or marl laid down by wind action. The biggest loess deposits are in Asia, the source of the dust of which they are composed probably being the deserts of Central Asia. Large deposits in Europe are thought to have originated from the edge of ice sheets during the Ice Age.

Logarithms, a system of calculation invented by John Napier in 1614, and developed by Henry Briggs a few years later. Thus if a number is expressed as the power of another number, *i.e.*, if $a = b^n$, then n is said to be the logarithm of a to base b, written $\log_b a$. Common logs are to base 10 and Napierian to base $2{\cdot}7182818\ldots$, expressed as e.

Lombards, a German people, originating on the Elber, who settled in Italy in the 6th cent., occupying northern and central regions, and establishing a kingdom with Pavia as capital. They were conquered by Charlemagne in 774, but left their name to the region of Lombardy. Lombard Street, London, takes its name from the Lombard merchants and bankers who came to settle there in the 12th cent.

London Clay, geological stratum which occupies much of the London Basin and part of the Hampshire Basin. It represents the lower stratum of the Eocene. Outside the metropolis, brickfields utilise the clay for brickmaking. Water held down in the Chalk by this impervious stratum is tapped by a number of artesian wells in London. The tunnels of the underground run through the London Clay.

London University is recognised as one of the great universities of the world. Originated in the foundation of a non-sectarian college in Gower Street in 1828. Among the chief colleges are: University College London, King's College, (inc. former Chelsea College and Queen Elizabeth), Imperial College of Science and Technology, London School of Economics, School of Oriental and African Studies, Queen Mary and Westfield, Birkbeck, together with Royal Holloway and Bedford New College. London University was the first to throw open all degrees to women (1878). Goldsmiths' College revealed plans to become part of London University in 1988.

Long Distance Walks. The National Parks and Access to the Countryside Act 1949 provided for the establishment in England and Wales of Long Distance Footpaths and Bridleways. The following walks have been opened: Pennine Way (the first long-distance footpath, a magnificent hill walk of 270 miles from Edale in Derbyshire along the Pennines over the Cheviots and the Scottish border): Pembrokeshire Coast Path (from St. Dogmael's to Amroth, 170 miles); Offa's Dyke Path (176 miles along the marches of Wales, one of the most important remaining earthworks of its kind in northwestern Europe); South Downs Way (Beachy Head to Buriton in Hants, 80 miles); South-West Peninsula Coast path (Minehead to Poole Harbour, 520 miles); Coast to Coast Walk from Robin Hood's Bay to St. Bee's (190 miles); Ridgeway (Avebury to Ivinghoe Beacon, 90 miles); Pilgrim's Way (Winchester to Canterbury, 116 miles); Cotswold Way (Bath to Chipping Campden, 95 miles); West Highland Way (Glasgow to Fort William, 100 miles). In 1987 plans were announced for a 180-mile Thames footpath. In 1989 the 83-mile Centenary Way was opened, from York to the North Sea at Filey. *See also* **National Parks.**

Longitude of a point on the earth's surface is the angle which the meridian through the poles and that point makes with some standard meridian. The meridian through Greenwich is usually accepted as the standard meridian and the longitude is measured east or west of that line. As the earth revolves through 360° in 24 h, 15° longitude represent 1 hour's difference in apparent time.

Long Parliament (1640–60), marked the end of Charles I's 11-year attempt to govern without Parliament. It carried through what has come to be called "the English Revolution" and was the parliament of the civil war (1642–49).

Lord Lieutenant is the Queen's representative in the county, and his office is now largely ceremonial. On his recommendation the magistrates or Justices of the Peace are appointed by the Lord Chancellor. The office was created in 1549 to take over the military duties of the sheriff.

Lords, House of, the Upper House of the British Parliament composed of Lords Spiritual and Lords Temporal. The former consist of the two Archbishops and twenty-four English Bishops and the latter of hereditary Peers, Peeresses and Life Peers. The right of the Lords to veto Bills passed by the Commons is restricted by the Parliament Acts of 1911 and 1949. The Lord Chancellor presides over the House of Lords. Under the Peerage Act 1963 a peerage may be disclaimed for life. *See* **Section D.**

Louse, parasitic insect found on the skin of birds and mammals. The two sub-species that parasitise man are the body louse and the head louse. Typhus can be transmitted by lice.

Louvre, one of the old royal palaces of Paris, was built in its present form partly by Francis I and added to by later monarchs, Louis XIV completing the edifice. Napoleon I turned it into a museum and enriched it with the plunder of many foreign art galleries. The great extension to the Louvre building begun by Napoleon I was completed under Napoleon III in 1857. Much injury was done to the building during the Commune of 1871. Amongst other famous treasures it houses the Venus de Milo and Leonardo da Vinci's masterpiece, *La Gioconda.*

LSD (d-lysergic acid diethylamide). This hallucinogenic drug has achieved wide notoriety because of its use by certain people to give themselves abnormal mental experiences. Doctors have frequently warned against the dangers of its use. It is active in extremely small quantities and a dose as small as a fifty-millionth part of a gram can cause marked disturbances of the mental function in man. LSD has been used in the study of mental disease because it produces symptoms very similar to mental disorders such as schizophrenia.

Luddites, a combination of workmen formed in

1811, in a period of great distress, with the object of destroying the new textile machinery then being largely adopted, which they regarded as the cause of their troubles. Their first outbreak was at Nottingham, and was stated to have been started by a young apprentice named Ned Ludd. Afterwards, serious Luddite riots occurred in various parts of the country, especially in West Yorkshire, where many people were killed, mills were destroyed and numbers of rioters were tried and executed. Charlotte Brontë used the period in her novel, *Shirley.*

Lunatic Fringe, term used by Theodore Roosevelt to characterise adherents of reform movements who refuse to recognise the difficulty of practical administration and insist upon immediate fulfilment of an extreme programme.

Lutecium, element (no. 71) of the rare-earth metal group discovered in 1907 by Urbain. Symbol Lu.

Lutheranism. *See* **Section J.**

Lynx, cats of sturdy build, with tufted ears and spotted fur, inhabiting many parts of the world, including Northern and Central Europe. They commit serious ravages among sheep and goats.

Lyon King of Arms, the President of the Scottish Lyon Court, and head of the heraldic organisation for Scotland.

Lyre-Bird, a remarkable family of Australian birds, the males of which possess a beautiful lyre-shaped tail. The bird is not more than 38 cm long, but its tail, displayed during its remarkable courtship dance, is 58 cm in length. There are two species: the Superb and Albert's Lyrebird.

M

Macaque. A family of monkeys which includes the Barbary ape (specimens of which live on Gibraltar), the Rhesus macaque (the organ grinder's monkey and the one used for experimental work in the investigation of disease), the Bonnet monkey of southern India and Sri Lanka, the Crab-eating and the Pig-tailed monkeys of south-eastern Asia.

Macaw, a genus of large parrots with brilliant scarlet and sky-blue plumage, with interminglings of green. Native to South and Central America.

McCarthyism, the term given to the wave of anti-Communist hysteria, associated with the name of Senator McCarthy (1908–57). The campaign lasted from early 1947 to late 1954.

Mace, originally a weapon of offence, now an ensign of authority borne before officers of state and other dignitaries. In the House of Commons the mace is handed to an official of the Crown by the Sergeant-at-Arms at the close of a parliamentary session.

Mach Number. Unit of flight speed. The ratio of speed of flight to speed of sound under same conditions of pressure and density. Speed of sound at sea-level is 762 mile/h (1,226 km/h), so flight speed of 381 mile/h (613 km/h) is equivalent to a Mach Number of ½. At supersonic speeds the Mach Number is greater than 1; subsonic speeds, less than 1.

Mackerel, a sea-fish existing in large numbers in the northern Atlantic off America and Europe. They are beautiful fish with a streamlined body and among the fastest fish in the sea.

Macromolecules are very large molecules about 10,000 times or more as heavy as ordinary small molecules like hydrogen. Most are built up from a large number of simple sub-units, *i.e.*, are polymers (*q.v.*). The term macromolecule is often used in biology, *e.g.*, starch and cellulose are biological macromolecules, both built from glucose sub-units. Other important ones are proteins and nucleic acids. The properties of macromolecules depend on the sub-units of which they are composed.

Mad Cow Disease, popular name for Bovine Spongiform Encephalopathy (BSE). A fatal brain disease in cattle rather similar to scrapies in sheep, which had caused the destruction of more than 10,000 cattle in Britain by early 1990.

Madder, one of the most important of dye-stuffs, largely used in producing Turkey-red dye, but now superseded by synthetic alizarin. Natural madder is the root of the *Rubia tinctorum.*

Maelstrom, a great whirlpool. The most famous is

that off the coast of Norway, between the islands of Moskenës and Mosken, of the Lofoten group the power of which has been much exaggerated.

Mafia. A term which is connected with Italo-American organised crime. Historically, remoteness from the central government of Italy encouraged the growth in Sicily in the 19th cent. of *mafiosi*, key-men who gained power through fear and violence. Contemporary police records give details of *mafia* behaviour in defending their authority. Emigration of vast numbers of southern Italians to the United States led to a new type of urban *mafioso* who became connected with gangsterism and vice. Sometimes called the *Cosa Nostra*, the organisation has infiltrated city governments and is reputed to be in control of drug smuggling and other illegal operations. In Italy neo-fascist groups have made use of the *mafia* in acts of terrorism, especially in the north.

Magellan, Clouds of, the name given to a pair of small galaxies, satellite systems of our own galaxy, visible only from the southern hemisphere. On account of their relative nearness to the earth (186,000 light-years), they are receiving much attention from astronomers.

Magenta, a blue-red aniline dye discovered in 1859 by Sir W. H. Perkin, and named after the great battle of that year between the French and Austrians.

Magic. *See* **Section J.**

Magistrates *or* **Justices of the Peace** preside over petty sessional and juvenile courts and are appointed by the Lord Chancellor on the recommendation of the Lord Lieutenant of the County. Most J.P.s are laymen and are unpaid. In certain big towns a legally-qualified, paid, full-time magistrate is appointed, known as a stipendiary magistrate. In London stipendiaries are known as Metropolitan Stipendiary Magistrates. J.P.s are no longer appointed over the age of 60 and they must retire when they reach 70. By the Justices of the Peace Act, 1968, *ex officio* J.P.s are abolished, except for the Lord Mayor and aldermen of the City of London.

Magma, molten rock material rich in volatile constituents prior to its eruption at the surface. With the loss of volatiles it becomes lava.

Magna Carta was sealed by King John at Runnymede on 15 June 1215, in obedience to the insistent demands of the barons and has been confirmed many times by later monarchs. It was not a revolutionary document. It laid down what the barons took to be the recognised and fundamental principles for the government of the realm and bound king and barons alike to maintain them. Its main provisions were that no man should be punished without fair trial, that ancient liberties generally should be preserved, and that no demands should be made by an overlord to his vassal (other than those recognised) without the sanction of the great council of the realm.

Magnesium, a metallic element, no. 12, symbol Mg, first isolated in 1808 by Sir Humphry Davy, who prepared it by electrolysing the chloride. Its chief ores are magnesite and dolomite. Industrially it is obtained by electrolysis. Many important light alloys contain magnesium. The metal burns with a very bright light, and for this reason it is used in photographers' flash bulbs and also in firework manufacture.

Magnetic Storms. These are the effects of magnetospheric storms observed world-wide at ground level as fluctuations of as much as 5% in the earth's magnetic field. The largest effects are observed at high latitudes, in the auroral ovals, and are due to electric currents flowing in the ionosphere and between the ionosphere and the magnetosphere. There may be concurrent disruption of radio communications. *See* **Magnetosphere.**

Magnetism, originally the name given to the quality of attraction for iron possessed by lodestone (*q.v.*). Now known to be a phenomenon inseparably connected with electricity (**F21**). Strong magnetic attraction is possessed by a comparatively small class of substances; iron, nickel and cobalt are the most common elements, but there are several less well known, *e.g.*, gadolinium. Many alloys have valuable magnetic properties which make possible numberless technical devices. New magnetic substances are always being developed (see **Ferrites**). The earth acts like a huge magnet with its axis inclined at about 11° to the axis of rotation, the magnetic poles being on the Boothia Peninsula (North Canada) and South Victoria Land (Antarctica). The magnetic field at the surface consists of the regular field of a magnetised sphere with an irregular field superimposed upon it. Variation in the magnetic forces occurs from place to place and from time to time, and maps showing the distribution over the globe of points of the same declination (i.e., the angle which the magnetic meridian makes with the geographical one) are of the utmost importance in navigation. Little is known regarding the origin of the main (regular) field of the earth, but it is believed that the irregularities are due to the presence of intense electric currents in the upper atmosphere and local magnetisation of rock strata. In 1967 the discovery was claimed of isolated magnetic poles, i.e., north and south magnetic poles existing separately, just as positive and negative electrical charges exist separately. If this is confirmed it will probably rank as one of the most important experimental results of the 20th cent., because of its significance for the theory of electromagnetism and fundamental particles. Magnetic field strengths are measured in gauss (c.g.s.) or tesla (S.I.) units.

Magnetohydro-dynamics. A current-carrying wire always experiences a force if it is in a magnetic field. This is the well-known electrodynamic force, and electric motors work because of it. If the current is carried in a fluid, e.g., a liquid metal or a plasma, these forces cause bodily movements to the fluid, which are in general very difficult to calculate. The forces are then called *magnetohydro-dynamic forces*. Now magnetic fields are themselves produced by electric currents; so a current flowing in a fluid produces a magnetic field, which then reacts on the fluid itself by means of the magnetohydro-dynamic forces. In the Harwell machine Zeta, used in studying the technical problems of thermonuclear reactions, this effect acts so as to constrict the electric discharge on to the axis of the tube and thus keeps it away from the walls. This action is assisted by an extra magnetic field produced by a separate current flowing in metallic conductors outside the tube. Thus the hot plasma is contained by magneto-hydro-dynamic forces and not at all by the material tube wall. In practical devices of the future magnetic forces may have to sustain plasma pressure of 60 atmospheres—a pressure for which a thick steel wall would normally be used! See also **Plasma Physics**.

Magnetosphere. The magnetic field of the earth prevents the plasma of the solar wind from directly impinging on the earth's upper atmosphere and ionosphere. The cavity thus maintained within the solar wind is known as the magnetosphere. The tenuous plasma within this cavity is partly of solar and partly of terrestrial origin, from the solar wind and the ionosphere respectively. These plasmas are subject to large perturbations, known as magnetospheric storms, triggered by fluctuations within the solar wind. These storms generate intense auroral displays, magnetic field fluctuations at ground level, and often major disturbances of the upper atmosphere and ionosphere which may result in disruption of radio communications. The inner parts of the magnetosphere contain the Van Allen radiation belts (q.v.). On the sunward side the magnetosphere extends to between 12 and 20 earth radii. However, on the side of the earth away from the sun it extends, like a comet tail, for many millions of km. Jupiter's large magnetic field produces a large magnetosphere, one of the largest features in our planetary system being as large as the sun itself.

Magnificat, the hymn of the Virgin Mary, given in Luke 1, 46 beginning in the Vulgate with the words "Magnificat anima mea Dominum" ("My soul doth magnify the Lord").

Magnitude in astronomy is a measure of the apparent brightness of a star, which is inversely proportional to the square of its distance. A low number indicates a bright star, and a high one a faint star. The *absolute magnitude* is a measure of *real* brightness, i.e., the brightness a star would have at a standard distance away of 10 parsecs (32·6 light years). The distance can be calculated if the apparent and absolute magnitudes are known.

Magpie, a well-known bird of the crow family, of glossy black and white plumage, famed for its mischievous propensities.

Magyars, the Hungarian race who came to eastern Europe from S.W. Asia and settled in Hungary in the 10th cent. Their language belongs to the Finno-Ugrian group.

Mahdi an Arab leader of great influence, invested with powers akin to those of a Messiah in the Mohammedan mind. The title was taken by Mohammed Ahmed, who overran the Egyptian Sudan, and in 1885 went on to capture Khartoum.

Maidenhair Tree or **Ginkgo.** This tree takes its name from the shape of its leaves, which resemble those of the maidenhair fern. Widely cultivated in China and Japan. It is the only survivor of an order of gymnosperms which flourished in Mesozoic times. Botanically interesting because the male gametes are motile.

Malmaison, château at Rueil-Malmaison, a western suburb of Paris. It derives its name from having been inhabited in the 11th cent. by the Norman brigand Odon, and afterwards, according to the tradition, by evil spirits, exorcised by the monks of St. Denis. It was the residence of Napoleon and of the Empress Josephine after her divorce. She died there in 1814 as the result of a chill caught while showing the Russian Emperor round the grounds. In 1900 it was given to the nation.

Mamluks, commonly known as Mameluks, were originally—in the 13th cent.—a bodyguard of Turkish and Circassian slaves in the service of the Sultan of Egypt, and attained such influence that in 1250 they were strong enough to appoint one of their own body to the throne of Egypt. After that a succession of Mamluk Sultans reigned down to 1517. Then the Turks annexed Egypt, and the Mamluks were taken into the service of the Beys. They again came to the front after Napoleon's conquest of Egypt, and for a time resumed governmental sway; but in 1811 they were massacred by order of Mehemet Ali.

Mammoth, extinct elephants of gigantic size. In 1799 the first perfectly preserved specimen was found in Siberia in a block of ice. It was in prehistoric times an inhabitant of Britain and other parts of Europe, as well as of Asia and America.

Mammoth Cave of Kentucky, one of the largest known limestone caverns in the world, with subterranean passages at different levels, lakes and rivers (the Echo R. flows 110 m below the surface); stalactites and stalagmites abound.

Manatee, an aquatic mammal of the sea cow (Sirenia) order of mammals, averaging when full grown from 3–3·6 m in length, with shovel-shaped tail, and forelimbs and nails which almost give the appearance of arms and hands. Gentle and trusting they are under threat from man. Protected in Florida. In spite of their ungainly aspect, they are believed to have given rise to the legend of mermaids.

Manchus, originally nomads inhabiting northern Manchuria who invaded China early in the 17th cent. A Manchu dynasty occupied the imperial throne of China from 1644 to 1911.

Mandarin, the name given to a powerful Chinese official, civil or military, under the old régime, whose rank was shown by the wearing of a button on the cap. Mandarin is the major language of N. China.

Manganese, a metallic element, no. 25, symbol Mn, discovered by Scheele, 1774. It is silver-white, not very hard (it forms a hard alloy with carbon), brittle, and tarnishes when exposed to air. Its chief ore is pyrolusite (manganese dioxide). Steels containing manganese are very tough, used for making machine parts.

Maniple, eucharistic vestment worn over left arm.

Manna, a tree of the ash genus, *Fraxinus ornus*, growing in the South of Europe and in the East and exuding a sweet substance which is gathered, boiled and eaten.

Manometer, instrument used to measure gas

pressure. Usually a U-tube containing water or mercury, one end open to the atmosphere, the other to the gas whose pressure is to be measured. More sensitive for small pressures than the Bourdon gauge.

Mansion House, the official residence of the Lord Mayor of London, stands opposite to the Bank of England, and was erected in 1739–53 from the designs of George Dance.

Mantis. Large insects belonging to the same order as the locusts and grasshoppers. The manner in which the forelegs are held, as though in suppliance, has gained for these insects the common name of "praying mantis". They are distributed throughout the warmer countries of the world.

Manx, the Celtic dialect (Manx Gaelic) of the Isle of Man, now on the point of extinction.

Maoism. See Section J.

Maoris, the race living in New Zealand at the time it was first visited by Captain Cook in 1769. They are believed to have migrated from Polynesia about 1350. Up to 1871 they were frequently in arms against the European settlers but their high intelligence and stamina enabled them to adapt themselves and the New Zealand laws have encouraged equal citizenship. They number *c.* 295,000 (1990). During 1990, there were celebrations to mark the 150th anniversary of the Treaty of Waitangi between the Maoris and the Europeans.

Maple, trees native to the northern hemisphere. There are over 100 species. The sycamore is the best-known species growing in Britain. The sugar maple abounds in Canada and the eastern parts of the United States. The sugar is tapped by boring holes in the tree in February and March, and the juice that escapes is collected and evaporated. The maple-leaf is the Canadian national emblem.

Maquis, name of the dense scrub in Mediterranean France and Corsica, providing good cover for bandits and outlaws. The French resistance movement adopted the name Maquis during the German Occupation, 1940–45.

Marble is limestone in its hardest and most crystalline form. There are many varieties—33 were used in the building of the Paris Opera House—but white is the purest and rarest. White marble was used by the ancient Greeks for their temples and statues. Among the famous marbles of Italy are the Carrara and Siena marbles, which were used by Renaissance sculptors. Devonshire and Derbyshire yield some beautiful marbles and Connemara furnishes a serpentine-marble.

March, the third month of the year, and the first of the old Roman Calendar. It was named after the god Mars, and was the *Hlyd* (storm) *monath* of the Anglo-Saxons.

Mardi Gras, the last day of the Carnival in France, Shrove Tuesday.

Marionettes are puppets moved by strings. They originated in the *Fantoccini* of the 15th cent. which had such a vogue in Italy and elsewhere on the Continent. The English *Punch and Judy* is a version of Punchinello.

Marmoset, small monkeys confined to the New World. Very squirrel-like in appearance, with long bushy tails, and thick woolly fur, they are pretty little animals and the smallest of all monkeys. There are claws, not nails, on their digits, the big toe excepted.

Maronite, Christian sect living mainly in the Lebanon and Syria. Now part of the Catholic Church.

Marprelate Tracts, seditious pamphlets written with great maliciousness by a group of Elizabethan puritans about 1586, and intended to discredit the episcopacy, caused a great sensation in their time, and led to the execution of their supposed author, John Penry.

Marquess *or* **Marquis,** the title next in precedent to that of duke. The first English marquess was Rovery de Vere, Earl of Oxford, who was honoured by Richard II, in 1385.

Mars, the fourth nearest planet to the sun (*see* **F8**). The enormous amount of new information from the recent visits to Mars, primarily by the US *Mariner* and *Viking* spacecraft, in 1971 and 1976 respectively, has revolutionised our understanding of the planet. Where the brief glimpses of the planet by the early *Mariner 6*

and *7* missions showed a dead, barren world, not unlike the moon, the 1971 and 1976 missions showed that the planet's surface displayed many contrasts—the ancient crated terrains glimpsed previously, enormous volcanos, far larger than any on earth, vast wastelands, particularly near the polar regions, scoured by wind-blown dust over many aeons, and most tantalising, in many regions water had set unmistakable marks. We see the plains which have been subject to torrential deluges of rain in, probably, a number of different episodes over hundreds of millions of years. Other regions, extending over hundreds of km, show great gorges and canyons cut by catastrophic floods, when some natural dam has burst, releasing the pent-up waters of a gigantic lake or sea. This pictorial evidence, and more detailed information of the atmosphere and surface obtained from the *Viking* spacecraft tell us that there must have been episodes in the planet's history when its climate was quite different from that observed today. The atmosphere, if only for brief interludes, must have been much denser, and warmer, and rain must have been able to fall. Mars is today too cold and dry for water but there are polar ice caps, and the nature of the meteoric craters suggests that the surface is rock over ice and solid carbon dioxide. The search for life carried out by *Viking* produced much new information, but no traces of organic compounds as evidence, or precursors, of life. Mars has two small moons, Phobos and Deimos.

Marseillaise, the French national hymn, written and composed by Rouget de L'Isle, a French engineer officer, who was inspired to write it in 1792 to encourage the Strasburg conscripts. It immediately became popular, and received its name from the fact that it was sung by the Marseillaise troops while marching into Paris.

Marshalsea, a former prison in Southwark, London, closed 1849. It existed as early as Edward III's time and was used as a jail for royal servants convicted of offences. In its later days it became a debtors' prison. Dickens described it in *Little Dorrit.*

Marston Moor, near York, was the scene of the famous battle between Prince Rupert and Cromwell on 2 July 1644. Cromwell's victory was the turning-point in the Civil War.

Marsupials, members of the order of pouched mammals. Except for the opossums of America, all marsupials occur in Australasia, and include the kangaroos, wallabies and wombats.

Martello Towers, circular forts erected on the coasts of England, Ireland and the Channel Isles early in the 19th cent. as defences against the threatened Napoleonic invasion. So called from the circular fort at Mortella (Corsica), which resisted an English sea attack in 1794.

Marten, carnivorous animals of the weasel family; one species (the Pine Marten) was once common in Britain. Most famous for their fur are the Siberian Sable and the American Marten.

Martial Law is a term loosely employed to indicate the suspension of the administration of normal civil law and its replacement by military authority.

Martin, a well-known bird-visitor to Britain. It belongs to the swallow family, and the two species that spend their summers here are the house-martin, which makes its nest of mud under the eaves of houses, and the sand martin, which builds in sandy banks.

Martinmas *or* **St. Martin's Day,** falls on 11 November, and is one of the Scottish quarter days. St. Martin was a popular Saint with our ancestors and Martinmas was a busy time for the mediaeval housewife. It was the date when "Martlemas Beef" was dried in the chimney, and enough bacon and mutton cured to last until the spring, because, owing to the scarcity of winter fodder, fresh meat could seldom be obtained. This diet of dried meat without vegetables caused scurvy. St. Martin (c. 316–400) was regarded as the patron saint of drinking and jovial meetings, as well as of reformed drunkards. The late spell of fine weather sometimes occurring at Martinmas is called St. Martin's Summer.

Martyrs. People who suffer death in testimony to their faith. Stephen (Acts 6; 7) was the first Christian martyr in 39. The first English martyr was St. Alban, 286, and in Tudor times many eminent churchmen went to the stake. The Smithfield martyrs' memorial church used to be St. Peter's, St. John Street, Clerkenwell. When that church was demolished the memorial moved to the Church of St. James, Clerkenwell Green.

Marxism. *See* **Section J.**

Mason and Dixon Line, boundary line between Pennsylvania and Maryland, for long a source of dispute, drawn up by two English surveyors, Charles Mason and Jeremiah Dixon, between 1763 and 1767. It came to designate the boundary dividing the slave states from the free states of America, and is still used in distinguishing the "North" from the "South".

Masques were light dramatic compositions set to music and performed on special occasions. One of the best-known examples is Milton's "Comus", which was given at Ludlow Castle in 1634.

Mass, the service in the Roman Catholic Church defined as the Propitiary Sacrifice of Calvary, reoffered by the Priest acting *in persona Christi.* It was first celebrated in Latin in the 4th cent., and was introduced into England in the 7th cent. The use of a vernacular language was sanctioned by the Second Vatican Council (1965).

Mass Spectrograph, an instrument for separating isotopes. It works by sorting electrified particles according to their masses; the particles stream through a magnetic and possibly an electric field, and the lightest particles undergo the greatest deflection.

Massorah, a collection of criticisms on the Hebrew text of the Scriptures, and rules for its correct interpretation.

Mast, a long round piece of timber or tubular steel or iron, standing upright in a vessel, and supporting the yards, sails and rigging in general. The earliest ships had only one mast, carrying a simple sail. The number increased until there were 4 or 5, or even more. Above the lower mast of a sailing-ship comes the topmast, and above that, the topgallantmast and royalmast. The position of each mast is indicated by a prefix, as foremast, foretopmast, foretopgallantmast, foreroyalmast, mainmast, maintopmast, etc. The foremast is in the fore of the ship, the mainmast in the centre and the mizzen nearest the stern. In large vessels nowadays the mast does not extend to the keel, as it formerly did, but is usually stopped at the second deck.

Master of the Revels was an important Court official upon whom devolved the arrangement of Court festivities. The office is at least as old as the time of Edward III. By 1737 it seems to have died.

Master of the Rolls, one of the English judges, formerly a judge of Chancery, but since 1881 a judge of the Court of Appeal only. He has charge of the rolls or records of Chancery and ranks next to the Lord Chancellor and Lord Chief Justice.

Mastodon, an extinct order of quadruped closely resembling the elephant in structure, but is larger.

Materials Science is a blend of science and technology; it is the use of scientific research methods to study and improve materials for practical use. The deeper understanding so obtained enables scientists to design new substances with hitherto unknown combinations of properties that are useful in engineering, aircraft, nuclear power, surgery, etc. Materials science institutes or university departments will usually contain an assortment of chemists, physicists, metallurgists, ceramicists, engineers and others because materials science brings to bear on materials a great many specialised techniques. The scientific study of materials is bringing continual improvement in metals, ceramics, plastics, fibres and many valuable combinations of these.

Mathematics is a body of knowledge expressed in a language of symbols. *Pure* mathematics studies the propositions that can be deduced in this language by applying definite rules of reasoning to sets of axioms. In *Applied* mathematics, the mathematical language is used, often with great effect, to discuss problems of the real world, such as mechanics, statistics and science generally. In range, subtlety, complexity and depth mathematics is unsurpassed among the intellectual disciplines and its study has attracted some of the most brilliant men in history.

Matins, the first of the canonical hours or services of the day in the Roman Catholic Church and Morning Prayer in the Anglican Church. The daily service in the Roman breviary (*q.v.*) used to consist of eight offices or "hours", fixed by canon, for prayer and devotion but since the second Vatican Council the structure has been simplified. Formerly, Matins was recited or sung at midnight, Lauds at sunrise, Prime at 6 a.m., Terce at 9 a.m., Sext at midday, Nones at 3. p.m., Vespers at sunset and Compline before retiring for the night. Lauds are now commonly joined to Matins.

Matrix, a rectangular array of numbers considered as a single mathematical object. There are special rules for multiplying and adding matrices and they are often used in mathematics, physics and elsewhere to simplify calculations and as a notational device.

Mau-Mau, a secret, anti-European, terrorist movement which agitated the Kikuyu tribe of Kenya during the years 1953–57. Mau-Mau was a symptom of native insecurity and discontent; emergency powers were lifted in November 1959, and large-scale reforms were instituted. Kenya attained independence in December 1963 with Mr. Jomo Kenyatta as the Prime Minister.

Maundy Thursday, the day before Good Friday, commemorates the Last Supper. "Maundy" derives from Christ's command (mandatum) to his disciples on that day to love one another. It was the custom in the monasteries for the monks to wash the feet of the poor on this day, and for many centuries the sovereigns of England, through their almoners, have distributed money, food and clothing to "as many old men and as many old women as the Sovereign is years of age". The Royal Maundy ceremony is still observed, maundy coins being struck from standard silver.

Mausoleum, a special place of sepulture, generally for the reception of the remains of members of a royal or other family of distinction. The name is derived from the tomb of King Mausolus at Halicarnassus, erected 352 B.C., and forming one of the seven wonders of the ancient world. Another mausoleum of antiquity is that of Hadrian in Rome.

Mauve, a colouring matter produced from lichens by Dr. Stenhouse in 1848, but in 1856 obtained from aniline by William Perkin (1838–1907), who gave it the name Mauveen. This was the first synthetic organic dyestuff ever to be produced, which led to the building up of the great synthetic dyestuffs industry (which Germany dominated before the first world war).

May, the fifth month of the year, but the third of the ancient Roman calendar. Supposed to be named after Maia, the mother of Mercury, to whom sacrifices were offered on the first day of this month. In England in former days May Day was made the occasion of many festivities, including the crowning of the May Queen, dancing round the Maypole, etc.

"Mayflower", the name of the ship which in 1620 conveyed the Pilgrim Fathers, 101 in number, from England to America. *See* **Pilgrim Fathers.**

May Fly. *See* **Ephemoptera.**

Mazarin Bible, an edition of the Latin Vulgate, acknowledged as the masterpiece of the Gutenberg press (1456). It was the first book completely printed from movable types. It is called the Mazarin Bible because the first copy to capture the attention of scholars was found in the library of Cardinal Mazarin, in Paris. Sometimes called the Gutenberg or the 42-line Bible.

Mean. In statistics and mathematics generally understood to be the arithmetic mean. The geometric mean between two quantities is the square root of their product. *See* **Average.**

Mechanical Equivalent of Heat. *See* **Joule.**

Medals, as decorations for military service, were first issued in this country by Charles I, who ordered medals for gallantry to be distributed to certain soldiers in 1643. Medals were also issued to officers and men who were victorious against the Dutch fleet in 1653. After Lord Howe's victory in 1794 a naval medal was instituted. Medals were also struck for the victory of Waterloo, and since that time special medals have been issued in connection with all our wars. The Victoria Cross, a special reward for personal gallantry, was instituted in 1856. The George Cross for gallantry instituted in 1940 ranks next to the Victoria Cross. The Military Cross was instituted in 1914.

Megalith, a prehistoric monument, consisting of a large single stone or a group of such stones, in a circle as at Stonehenge or in burial chambers as at New Grange, Ireland. Megalithic monuments have been constructed by different peoples in different parts of the world since the third millennium B.C.

Meiosis, special type of cell division by which the gametes or sex cells are generated, resulting in the sperm or ovum receiving only half the number of chromosomes found in a somatic cell. *See* **Mitosis.**

Mendelian Law. *See* **F30(2).**

Mendicant Friars, certain religious orders which spread over Europe in the 13th cent., and comprised the Franciscans, Dominicans, Augustines and Carmelites. Originally they depended entirely on alms.

Mercator's Projection, a method of indicating meridians and parallels of latitudes on maps, introduced by Mercator in the 16th cent., and still universally used in navigators' charts.

Mercury, the smallest of the planets (approx. one-twentieth of the earth's mass) is the closest to the sun at a little more than one-third of the earth's average distance. It appears to resemble the earth in its interior and has about the same density but its surface resembles the moon and is heavily cratered. Mercury was visited by Mariner 10 which passed within a few hundred kilometres in March 1974 and which relayed pictures on the two following passes in September 1974 and March 1975 before control of its altitude was lost. It nevertheless continues to revisit Mercury every 176 days (two mercurian years). Mariner 10 was guided to Mercury by the gravitational field of Venus before it became a satellite of the smallest planet. The relayed pictures showed that the planet has an approximately 59-day rotation period exactly two thirds of its orbital period of 88 days. This relationship means that unlike on earth the seasonal variations are with longitude not latitude. Surface temperatures vary from 400°C to − 200°C and there is virtually no atmosphere except a thin envelope of helium gas. Mariner 10 measured a small magnetic field at the surface about 1% of the earth's but much stronger than for Venus or Mars.

Mercury *or* **Quicksilver,** element no. 80, symbol Hg (Latin *hydrargyrum*) is one of the oldest-known metals, whose chief ore is the sulphide, cinnabar, found in certain parts of Spain, China, Japan and South America. It is liquid at ordinary temperature and is used in the construction of barometers and thermometers. Alloys of mercury are called amalgams. It is also of great value in medicine. The metal is used in the mercury-vapour (or "sunlight") lamp, since the vapour gives a bright yellow-white glow in an electric discharge.

Mercy-killing, taking the life of a person suffering from a painful and incurable disease. The killer is often actuated by a good *motive*—the desire to relieve hopeless suffering; but the *intention* is to kill, and the act, in English law, is therefore a crime. (It is not necessary for the prosecution to prove any motive.)

Meridian, an imaginary circle extending through the North and South Poles and any given place. When the sun is at its midday height at any place it is "on the meridian"; hence the terms ante-meridian (a.m.) and post-meridian (p.m.). *See also* **Greenwich Mean Time.**

Merino Sheep were imported into England from Spain in 1788 and had great influence in improving native breeds, especially in regard to the quality of the wool.

Merit, Order of, founded by King Edward VII in 1902 as a special distinction for eminent men and women without conferring a knighthood upon them. The Order has twenty-four British companions in addition to foreign honorary members limited in number, as the choice of members is, by the Sovereign's pleasure. Lord Kelvin was the founder companion. Florence Nightingale (1907), Professor Dorothy Hodgkin (1965), Dame Veronica Wedgwood (1969) and Mother Theresa of Calcutta (honorary member, 1983) are the only women to have received this coveted decoration. Awarded to violinist Yehudi Menuhin, 1987.

Merovingians, the name given to the family that ruled over France from about 500 to 750. Clovis was first of the line and Childeric the last. The "long-haired kings" have become the centre of much recent speculative history.

Mesons (from Greek *meso* = middle), a family of unstable particles of mass between that of an electron and that of a proton. Some are positive, some negative, some neutral. No stable meson is known, the longest-lived particle having a lifetime of only two-millionths of a second. The first of these particles was discovered in cosmic radiation in 1937 and called the mu-meson or *muon*. In 1947 a heavier type was discovered called the pi-meson or *pion* which behaved like the meson predicted on theoretical grounds by Yukawa in 1935. The pion is connected with the theory of nuclear forces. *See also* **F15, 16.**

Mesozoic. The geological era, including the Triassic, Jurassic and Cretaceous rocks.

Metamorphic Rocks are such geological deposits as have undergone alterations of structure and mineral reorganisation. The most active agents in producing these metamorphic changes are heat, water and pressure. *See* **F9(1).**

Metamorphosis, period of development from egg to adult, during which the animals have different forms, as found, *e.g.,* in the life histories of frog and butterfly.

Meteorites are small bodies, asteroids, or fragments of asteroids, which survive their fiery passage through the earth's atmosphere and hit the ground. The present surfaces of the moon, Mars and Mercury tell us that all the planets have been subjected since their formation to bombardment by meteorites. Though some large craters are still to be found on the earth, most have disappeared due to extensive weathering over thousands of millions of years. In some meteorites iron and nickel are the chief metals (siderites), others are like rock (aerolites). The iron meteorites are more common amongst those which have been preserved, but falls of rock-like meteorites occur more frequently. At L'Aigle in France in 1803 from 2000 to 3000 meteorite stones fell; this fall is famous because it convinced scientists that meteorites really came from outside our atmosphere. The largest meteorite stone actually known to have fallen to earth is one which descended in Emmott County, Iowa, in 1870, weighing 197 kg. A meteorite weighing no less than 37 tonnes found in Greenland is now in New York. On 30 June 1908, an enormous object fell in Siberia in a sparsely-inhabited region. A hot blast destoyed all trees within a radius of about 8–16 km, the explosion waves being recorded by barographs as far distant as London, Washington and Batavia. There is still controversy about the nature of the Siberian meteorite, whether it was an asteroid or possibly the nucleus of a small comet.

Meteorology, the science of the atmosphere considered as a heat engine. Deals with weather, climate, optical phenomena, atmospheric electricity, physical processes such as radiation and precipitation, the dynamics and structure of cyclones, anticyclones, etc. Wide application to problems of aviation, agriculture, commerce and shipping. Meteorological observing stations are in operation all over the world, and on the simultaneous or synoptic reports of their instrument readings and estimates of pressure, temperature, humidity, speed and direction of wind, rain, character and amount of cloud, visibility, etc., forecasts, gale, snow and frost warnings are based. Instruments carried by earth satellites (*e.g., Tiros, Nimbus*) outside the atmosphere can make systematic observations on a world-wide basis of the atmospheric circulation, through observation of cloud cover and of the thermal radiation into space from the atmosphere. Such observations together with the use of computers are of great importance for weather analysis and forecasting. The main communications centre for the UK is at the headquarters of the Meteorological Office at Bracknell, Berkshire, where the collection, editing and re-transmission of weather messages continue according to strict schedules day and night throughout the year.

Meteors or more commonly, "shooting stars", are small objects which enter the upper atmosphere to burn up in a bright streak of light. Their origin is mainly in the dust particles ejected in large quantities from comets. Some, particularly the larger and more brilliant ones, called fireballs, are debris of asteroids. Those which reach the earth's surface are called meteorites (q.v.).

Methane. The simplest hydrocarbon, compounded of one carbon atom and four hydrogen atoms. This gas occurs over marshes and swamps, where it is liberated in the decay of vegetable matter. It is the main constituent of natural gas, and also occurs in coal-mines, where it is called "fire-damp" because of the explosive character of its mixture with air. Formerly this natural gas was removed from the coal seams and ran to waste; now in many countries (including Britain) it is being used for commercial purposes.

Methylated Spirit, a mixture of 90 parts by volume ethyl alcohol, 9¼ parts wood naphtha (methyl alcohol), ¼ part crude pyridine, together with small amounts of petroleum oil and methyl violet dye. Industrial methylated spirit consists of a mixture of 95 parts by volume ethyl alcohol and 5 parts wood naphtha. It is used as a solvent and a fuel.

Metre, the rhythmical pattern of Verse.

Metre, unit of length in the metric system; since 1983 has been redefined as "the length of the path travelled by light in vacuum during a time interval of 1/299 792 458 of a second". This definition replaces that adopted in 1960 which used the wavelength of the orange-red line of krypton-86. Before that the "international prototype metre" was the distance between marks on the platinum-iridium bar placed at Sèvres in 1889.

Metric System, the system of weights and measures based on the gram and the metre, smaller and larger units being decimals and multiples of the primary units respectively. A decimal currency was adopted in France in 1795 and the metric system of weights and measures in 1799. (In that year the quadrant of the earth was surveyed and the standard metre adopted.) Nevertheless the change was accepted slowly, and as late as 1837 the French Government had to pass a law forbidding the use of the old measures. Since then the metric system has been adopted in most of the continental countries and is used universally in scientific work. Although there have been many attempts to get the system adopted in Britain, it was not until 1965 that the Government encouraged the adoption of the metric system of weights and measures. The changeover to decimal coinage was made in 1971; the system of weights and measures in industry is now mainly metric. See **F66–69** for **SI** units.

Mezzotint, a technical method for producing graphic work and works of art. A copper plate is made rough by close cross-hatching, so that a print from it produces an even black. When parts of the cross-hatching are scraped away, these areas will come out white when printed. By skilful use of his tools, the artist or technician can produce pictures finely graded from black to white and with a velvety black as background. The principles of the method were known and practised, for instance, by Rembrandt, but mezzotint became most popular for the reproduction of famous paintings from the end of the 18th cent.

Mica. The mica of commerce is a nearly transparent mineral, which has great heat-resisting power, and can be split into thin plates. The most important micas are muscovite (potassium mica), the commoner variety, phlogopite (magnesium mica) and biotite (the magnesium and iron mica).

Michael, St., and George, St., an order of knight-

hood originally founded for the Ionian Isles and Malta in 1818, and reorganised in 1869, so as to admit Crown servants connected with the Colonies. The Earl of Derby, Earl Russell and Earl Grey were the first of the new knights.

Michaelmas Day, the festival day of St. Michael and All Angels, 29 September, one of the English quarter days.

Microbe, a term proposed by Sédillot in 1878 to denote any microscopic organism, vegetable or animal, or found on the borderland between the two great natural kingdoms. The term is commonly used, but not by scientists.

Microelectronics, a rapidly developing technology of the 1960s which reduces entire electronic circuits to minute size and embeds them in tiny chips of solid material. These are then called integrated circuits. A circuit consisting of, say, a dozen transistors and fifty resistors can be built into a small piece of semiconductor (q.v.) measuring not more than a couple of millimetres in any direction. Hundreds of these circuits can be made simultaneously in penny-size wafers of silicon about one-hundredth of an inch thick. There are great advantages in cheapness, reliability, robustness and speed of electronic performance. The small size is in itself an advantage in space vehicles and medical instruments. Applications to missile control systems, computers and communications equipment are no doubt only the first fruits of this new achievement of the current technological revolution.

Micrometer, an instrument for measuring minute distances; usually attached to the eye-pieces of a microscope or telescope, and consisting of two very fine hairs or wires stretched across the field of view, one fixed, the other movable. It was invented by William Gascoigne in the 17th cent. and improved by later inventors. Sir Joseph Whitworth made one in 1858 to measure the millionth part of an inch.

Micro-organisms, the collective term applied to several types of organism, the most important of which are fungi, viruses, bacteria and protozoa. It is a classification of convenience in biological studies. These organisms are generally simple in their environmental requirements (e.g., have simple nutritional needs) and in cellular organisation. This makes them very suitable for modern biological research. Much of the information on the nature of the genetic code (**F32(2)**) was obtained from experiments on these organisms.

Microphone, device for converting the acoustic energy of sound waves into waves of electrical energy, used in sound amplifying systems. Developed independently by Edison (1877) and Hughes (1878).

Microscope, invented about 1590 by Janssen, and improved by Galileo, Fontana and others, is an instrument which by a lens system magnifies minute objects. Microscopes are simple, compound and binocular. See also **Electron Microscope.**

Middle Ages (c. A.D. 400–1500), usually considered to be the period between the decline and fall of the Western Roman Empire and the fall of Constantinople to the Turks (see **A4–7**). The period covers (a) an earlier part ending with the 12th cent. (sometimes called the Dark Ages) when science was dead, when theology was the main preoccupation, and when the language of the learned West was Latin; and (b) a later age of Arabian influence when alchemy and astrology (at that time indistinguishable from astronomy) were central interests, technology was advancing, and Greek learning was transmitted by Arab scholars. Characteristic features of the mediaeval scene were monasticism (**Section J**), the Crusades (q.v.), Gothic art (q.v.), feudalism (**Section J**), and the supremacy of Islam in the field of learning. The period came to an end with the general decline of Christendom and the ushering in of the Renaissance (**Section J**). The term "Middle Ages" was coined by the 17th-cent. German historian Christoph Keller.

Midrash, name given to the homiletical interpretation of some of the Hebrew Scriptures in which allegory and legendary illustration were freely used. Compiled by Jewish rabbis from c. A.D. 200.

Millenary Petition was presented to James I in 1603, on behalf of nearly 1000 Puritan Ministers against certain of the rites and ceremonies of the Church of England. The Hampton Court Conference was the outcome of this petition.

Millennium, a period of a thousand years. The term is specifically used of the period of a thousand years during which, according to Rev. xx. 1–5, Christ will reign in person on earth. The Millenarians are a sect that interprets the "Millennium" as beginning with the commencement of the 6001st year from the Creation, which, according to Archbishop Ussher (1581–1650), was in 4004 B.C.

Millipede. Arthropods (F36) allied to the centipedes, from which they differ in having two pairs of legs to each body segment (except the first three) instead of one pair. Worm-like in shape but with a pair of antennae on the head, they can do much harm to garden plants, unlike centipedes which are beneficial.

Millstone-Grit, a series of grits and sandstones of deltaic origin underlying the coal measures of the Carboniferous system and attaining in England a thickness in parts of 1,525 m. It is from this rock that millstones have been made from time immemorial.

Mimicry, protective similarity of an animal to another animal or to inanimate objects. Examples of the former are the hover flies, which mimic wasps and bees; of the latter, leaf insects, stick insects and caterpillars that look like dead twigs.

Mink. Semi-aquatic mammals closely related to polecats. There is one American species and one European. The fur, which varies light to dark brown, is soft and thick, and is among the most valuable of commercial furs. They now live in the wild in the British Isles.

Minnesingers were minstrel poets of Germany who, during the 12th and 13th cent., composed and sang verses of heroism and love. They were of knightly rank, the counterpart of the French troubadours. See **E3(2).**

Minnow, a small fresh-water fish of the carp family, abounding in all the waters of Europe; it has a mottled back and silvery belly, and forms a popular bait for trout.

Minstrels were originally specially appointed instrumentalists and singers—pipers, harpers and gleemen—engaged by barons and manorial lords to amuse their tenants. Later, minstrels assumed nomadic habits, made their way into the houses of the great and were generally welcome. By Elizabeth's time, however, they were too numerous, and were classed as "rogues and vagabonds", along with actors.

Miracle Plays, mediaeval verse plays, popular in England in the 15th cent., were usually religious in character, representing some of the dramatic incidents of the Bible.

Mirage, an optical illusion caused by unequal temperatures in different layers of the atmosphere near the earth's surface. These temperature variations alter the refracting power of the air and cause light rays to be curved, making the air act as a huge distorting lens. This can happen at sea, in deserts and elsewhere and various types of mirage are known. A common kind in deserts curves light from the sky so that it appears to come from the ground, deceiving the observer into thinking that the sky is reflected in a lake of water. Inverted images of hills, trees, etc. also look as if reflected in the non-existent lake.

Mishna, the first part of the Talmud, setting forth the "Oral Law" of the Jews.

Missal, the name of the mass-book of the Roman Church compiled 492–96 by Pope Gelasius I. The missal used until recently was sanctioned by the Council of Trent, 1546–63, but the current missal was authorised by Pope Paul VI in 1969 following the Second Vatican Council. In the Anglican Communion the Book of Common Prayer superseded the Missal in 1549.

Mistle Thrush receives its name from its partiality to the mistletoe-berry. Larger than the song-thrush, with spotted breast rather than speckled.

Mistletoe, a parasitic evergreen with white berries used as a decoration at Christmas-time. The familiar mistletoe of Europe is the *Viscum album*, which grows on the boughs of lime,

willow, apple, poplar, maple, ash, hawthorn but seldom on oak-trees. It was sacred to the Druids, and in Norse mythology it was a mistletoe dart that killed the god Baldur.

Mistral, a cold, dry, northerly wind peculiar to the French coast of the Mediterranean.

Mitosis, cell division whereby each daughter cell receives the same number of chromosomes as the parent cell. When the gametes (sex cells) are formed a special type of division occurs (meiosis) in which the number of chromosomes is halved. See **F34(1).**

Mitre, the twofold pointed head-dress of bishops and certain abbots of the Western Church and occasionally of other ecclesiastics.

Moa, the name for several species of ostrich-like extinct birds related to the New Zealand kiwi. The largest species, *Diornis maximus*, stood 2·6 m high, the smallest, *Anomalopteryx parva*, was nearer the size of a turkey. This wingless bird became extinct several centuries ago because of hunting by the Maoris from whom the name comes.

Moabite Stone, a stone of the 9th cent. B.C. containing the earliest known inscription in Phoenician characters, and discovered in the highlands of Moab in 1868. It is now in the Louvre, Paris. It records the campaign between Moab and Israel (c. 850 B.C.), an account of which is given in the Old Testament (2 Kings 3:27).

Moderator, a material used to slow down neutrons in an atomic pile. Examples of moderators are pure graphite and heavy water. See **Nuclear Reactors.**

Mohole Project, a scheme to bore through the earth's crust to take samples of the mantle rocks beneath. Drilling trials, led by an American team of geophysicists, began in 1961 near the island of Guadalupe off the Mexican coast in the Pacific. The project, however, was cancelled in 1966 on account of the escalating cost. Russian geophysicists started on a similar experiment, boring through land rocks where the digging is much deeper and higher temperatures are met with. The name "Anti-Cosmos" was given to the project. The boundary between the earth's crustal and mantle rocks is known as the Mohorovičić Discontinuity, or, more simply, as the Moho. The technology of deep sea drilling came from this project.

Molasses, sugar-cane juice in its uncrystallised form after boiling. The crystallised part is the raw sugar. Used to make rum.

Mole, a small burrowing animal with long, sensitive nose, about the size of a small rat, with short legs and forefeet armed with strong claws for digging in the earth. Their subterranean dwellings are of curiously ingenious construction, and they do not often leave them except to make raids on mice, frogs, snails, etc. The earth-worm, however, is the mole's chief item of food. Not to be confused with the vole which has a blunt nose.

Mole, or gram molecular weight. See **F24(1).**

Molecular Biology, a rapidly expanding branch of science mainly concerned with cell structure and function at a molecular level, in particular with genes and enzymes and the interaction between the two. Recent work in Britain has led to the unravelling of the structure of DNA, the hereditary substance of the genes, and has played a major part in uncovering the molecular mechanism of the transfer of hereditary information and the nature of the genetic code. Crystallisation of the first enzyme (urease) took place in 1929; the gene as a definite chemical entity was discovered in 1943. See **F29(1).**

Molecule. A group of atoms held together by chemical forces. See **F14, F23,** *also* **Macromolecule.**

Molybdenum, element no. 42, symbol Mo, a fairly hard white metal with properties resembling those of chromium. Its commonest ore is the sulphide, molybdenite. The chief use of the metals is in the manufacture of alloy steels.

Monasticism. See **Section J.**

Monazite, a cerium mineral containing some thorium. Occurs as grains, often as sand ("monazite sands"), derived from granites. Deposits occur in India (Travancore), Russia, Norway, Malagasy Rep., S. Africa, Brazil, USA.

Monday, the second day of the week, called by the Anglo-Saxons *Monandaeg* (moon-day).

Mongoose, species of mammals related to the civets, feeding on vermin and reptiles. These animals, which have long tails and short legs, occur in Africa and Asia (especially India). The biggest mongoose is the Egyptian ichneumon, and this has been introduced into the W. Indies because of its ability to kill large poisonous snakes.

Monitor, a family of lizards most resembling dragons. There are about 30 species widely distributed over the tropical parts of Asia, Australia and Africa.

Monroe Doctrine, a principle of American policy declining any European intervention in political affairs of the American continent, outlined by President Monroe in 1823. At the same time interference was disclaimed with existing European colonies in the Western Hemisphere. The American Civil War hampered the application of the doctrine for some time, but afterwards the United States firmly insisted on it. The Doctrine is not international law, but a national policy of the USA.

Monsoons, regular persistent winds which blow at certain seasons in middle latitudes, mainly in South and East Asia. Their occurrence is related to the great changes of pressure which take place between summer and winter over the land mass. In India the south-west monsoon (June–October) is moisture-laden from its long passage over the sea and in the higher regions, especially, there is heavy rainfall. Sudden reversal of the wind results in the cold north-east monsoon (October–March) which is dry on account of the shelter afforded by the mountain ranges to the north. Frequently the term "monsoon" is applied to denote the associated rainfall without reference to the actual winds.

Monstrance, an ornamental transparent receptacle in which the Sacred Host is carried in procession or exposed for adoration.

Month, the 12th part of the calendar year. A lunar month is the interval of new moon to new moon or full moon to full moon; mean length, 29 days, 12 hours, 44 minutes, 2·87 seconds. A sidereal month represents the time of the moon's revolution from a given star back to the same again, 27 days, 7 hours, 43 minutes, 11·5 seconds. In English law, since 1926, a month, unless otherwise expressed, means a calendar month.

Monument of London, a 202 ft (61·6 m) column, overlooking Billingsgate, designed by Wren and erected (1671–77) to mark the starting-point of the Great Fire of London (1666). The original inscription upon it ascribed the fire to "the treachery and malice of the popish faction", which stood until 1831, when the words were erased as objectionable. The black marble staircase has 345 steps (311 to the balcony).

Moon, the earth's satellite, 3,475 km in diameter and 384,400 km distant from the earth. It rotates in the same time as it revolves round the earth (27 days 7 hours 43 minutes), so that the same face is always presented to the earth. The lunar surface is pockmarked by innumerable collisions with solid particles of all sizes. Unlike the earth, it is unprotected by any atmosphere and for aeons of time it has been exposed to every kind of cosmic influence, including the parching effect of solar radiation. All moonlight derives from the sun but on the whole it is a pretty poor reflector. The exploration of the moon by means of rockets began in 1959 when the Russian *Luna 2* crashlanded on the plains of the *Mare Imbrium*. 1969 will be remembered as the year of the U.S. *Apollo* triumphs when man first set foot on the moon. The samples of lunar rock and dust brought back to earth by the *Apollo* astronauts and the Soviet *Luna* unmanned automatic stations are being studied by lunar scientists. Samples date back further than any found on Earth as yet. The most famous, known as the Genesis Rock, is 4,100 million years old. The exploration of the moon at close range by means of spacecraft was made possible only by parallel developments in several branches of technology—rocket propulsion, long-range radio and television transmission, electronic computer control.

Moorhen, a widely distributed bird of the rail family, a common resident in the British Isles.

The adult is blackish with white under tail coverts, a white line on the flanks and a yellow-tipped bill. The frontal shield and the base of the bill are vermilion. It bobs its head, flirts its tail and dives well. The nest is usually placed close to the water's edge or on an overhanging branch. In feeding the young the parents are sometimes helped by their offspring of a previous brood of the season. In N. America the bird is known as the Florida Gallinule.

Moors, the name given to the Moslems who live in N.W. Africa and to those who once lived in Spain. In 711 Moorish Arabs invaded Spain and spread beyond the Pyrenees into France, where they were driven back by the end of the century. Spain, however, remained virtually under Moorish domination until the 11th cent. and during that period was the most civilised and prosperous part of Western Europe. In the arts and sciences the impact of Moorish culture was profound and lasting. Examples of the brilliant splendour of Moorish architecture are still to be seen in Toledo, Córdoba, Seville and Granada. During the long struggle for the Christian reconquest thousands were killed and expelled, and in 1492 Granada, their last remaining kingdom, was forced to surrender. They were virtually exterminated by the Inquisition, and the last were expelled in 1609.

Moose, the largest members of the deer family. The N. American Moose stands 1·6–2 m high, and has huge palmate antlers. There is another New World species, occurring in Alaska. The European species is known as the elk.

Morse Alphabet, a system of dots and dashes intended to be used in combination with the indicator in telegraphy; but usually read by sound, the receiving operator writing down the words in the system as transmitted. This system of signals was invented by the American inventor and artist Samuel Finley Breese Morse (1791–1872) of Charlestown, Massachusetts.

Mosaic, art of arranging small pieces of coloured glass, marble, or other materials in such a fashion as to produce a decorative pattern. Some of the best examples of Byzantine mosaics are to be seen at Ravenna, Rome, Venice and Sicily.

Mosque, a Mohammedan church, the greatest being that of Santa Sophia at Istanbul, now converted into a museum of Byzantine art.

Mosquito, small two-winged flies with long legs and slender body. Their larvae are aquatic. The females of some species are blood-suckers, and thus come to transmit the blood parasites which cause malaria and yellow fever, for example. See **DDT** *and* **Gammexane**.

Mosses. With liverworts, mosses comprise an important group of relatively simple non-vascular land plants, the bryophytes (**F42**). In the main they are small plants, the largest between 30–70 cm high, having been recorded in the Southern Hemisphere. Mosses rarely occur singly, but usually form cushions or small colonies on moist soil, bark, wood, rock or walls. The genus *sphagnum* known as "peat" or "bog moss" is of commercial value in horticulture. In Lancashire and Cheshire lowland moors in which sphagnum is common are known as "mosses". Reindeer moss is a lichen and Spanish moss a seed plant.

Moths, of the insect order, *Lepidoptera*, differing from butterflies which have clubbed antennae, in having feathery, sometimes thin, pointed antennae, rarely clubbed. Most are nocturnal, and the pupae are usually brown and enclosed in a cocoon unlike those of the butterfly, which are usually naked. See also **Lepidoptera.**

Motion, Laws of. According to Newton: (1) A body continues in its state of rest or uniform motion in a straight line except in so far as it is compelled by external forces to change that state. (2) Rate of change of momentum is proportional to the applied force, and takes place in the direction in which the force acts. (3) To every action there is an equal and opposite reaction. These laws are the basis of almost all engineering and everyday mechanics. Corrections to them have been made by relativity and the quantum theory. See **F17, 19.**

Mule, a cross between a male ass and a horse mare; a hinny is a cross between an ass mare and a horse stallion. Also the name of the spinning machine invented by Crompton in 1779 which combined the principle of Hargreaves' spinning jenny with the machine invented by Arkwright.

Mullions, the vertical bars dividing the lights in a window, forming a highly decorative feature in the Tudor period of English Gothic architecture. The cross-beam or horizontal bar of wood or stone in a mullioned window is styled a transom. *See* **Windows.**

Munich Agreement. In September 1938 Mr. Neville Chamberlain and M. Daladier, British and French Premiers, reached agreement with Hitler at Munich for the dismemberment of Czechoslovakia, primarily for the benefit of Germany. Czechoslovakia itself was not consulted, nor Russia who with Britain and France had jointly pledged themselves to uphold the independence of Czechoslovakia. Hitler had been threatening that country for some time, but every concession had been met by further demands. After three visits to Germany, during which Hitler raised his demands, the British and French statesmen gave way. Mr. Chamberlain declared on return that he had secured "Peace in our Time". The Agreement was the subject of much controversy. Hitler seized Czechoslovakia in March 1939.

Muscles. *See* **F37(1).**

Musk Deer, a small deer of the Himalayas, standing about 51 cm high. It is grey in colour, slightly brindled, and carries a small pouch in the abdominal region, containing what is commercially known as musk, an article which is of great value in the manufacture of various perfumes. The active constituent of musk, muscone, is now made synthetically. The species has become rare on account of its slaughter for its musk.

Mutton Bird, an Australian name of controversial origin for a shearwater or petrel, *e.g.*, the Short-tailed and Sooty Shearwaters and the Great-winged, Kermadec, and White-headed Petrels. The young are taken by hand from their burrows for human food.

Myrrh, a resinous substance obtained from a tree of the natural order *Amyridaceae,* growing plentifully in Ethiopia and Arabia. Its use for embalming, medical and aromatic purposes may be traced back to the most remote times.

Mysteries, Greek, secret mystic ceremonies of the ancient Greeks, religious drama accompanied by dancing, the most well known being the Eleusinian and Orphic ceremonies.

Mystery Plays were mediaeval religious dramas performed at great ecclesiastical festivals, particularly in France and Bavaria, staging the Nativity, Passion and Resurrection stories from the Gospels.

N

Nadir, one of the two poles of the horizon, the other being the zenith. The nadir is the pole vertically below the observer's feet.

Nahum, one of the books of the Minor Prophets of the Old Testament. It is a prophecy of doom on the approaching sack of Nineveh which fell in 612 B.C. to the Medes and Babylonians.

Nantes, Edict of, was a decree promulgated by Henry IV of France in 1598, giving full freedom of worship to the Protestants of the country. It was the revocation of this edict in 1685 by Louis XIV that drove hundreds of thousands of French Huguenots to this country.

Naphtha, a liquid combustible believed to have been one of the ingredients of "Greek fire". Naphtha is a light, highly inflammable oil obtained by distilling petroleum, shale oil, or coal tar. The petroleum naphtha consists of a mixture of paraffins; that from shale contains olefines as well as paraffins. Coal-tar naphtha contains xylol.

Naphthalene is an aromatic hydrocarbon; it is obtained from coal tar, and its derivatives are much used in the manufactures of colours for dyers and printers. "Moth balls" are made of naphthalene.

Narcotic, a medical dictionary definition is that a narcotic is a drug that produces stupor; complete insanity or sleep. In terms of drug addiction, a narcotic has been defined as altering and distorting the user's perception of himself and of the external world, being taken primarily for that purpose.

Nardus, a genus of coarse grasses, growing on bleak upland heaths and hill slopes. *Nardus stricta,* known as "mat-weed", is a British species.

Narghile, an oriental tobacco pipe so constructed that smoke passes through water and up a long flexible tube before reaching lips of the smoker.

Narrative Art, a type of art popular during the late 19th cent. based on the principle: "every picture tells a story"—*e.g.*, such paintings as the little Royalist boy surrounded by his anxious family and confronted across a table by the Roundheads bearing the title: "When did you last see your father?" The term, although often applied derisively, suitably describes many works of considerable artistic merit: *e.g.*, Hogarth's *Marriage à la Mode,* his series of eight engravings entitled *A Rake's Progress,* the Bayeux Tapestry, and many Babylonian and Egyptian friezes.

Naseby, Battle of, was fought on 14 June 1645, between the Royalists under the command of Prince Rupert and the King, and the Parliamentarians under Fairfax and Cromwell. Charles I was decisively defeated.

National Anthem, a musical composition with words, officially adopted for ceremonial use as an expression of patriotism and loyalty to a national cause. The national anthem of the United Kingdom, "God save the King (Queen)", probably dates from the late-17th cent, to mid-18th cent. It was sung in 1745, the year of the landing of the Young Pretender. It had no one composer and was probably a recasting of folk-tunes and plainsong. Resemblances can be traced in pieces by Purcell and John Bull.

National Assembly, the name taken by the body responsible for the opening stages of the French Revolution and subsequently by other sovereign bodies in France and elsewhere.

National Covenant, an oath and declaration subscribed to by the Scottish Presbyterians in 1638 to maintain their religion against Charles I's episcopalianising designs.

National Gallery, established in 1824 at Pall Mall, London, with the Angerstein Collection of 38 pictures, purchased for £60,000, as a nucleus. The existing building which was opened in 1838 has been enlarged several times. The National Gallery at Millbank, the Tate Gallery, was given to the nation by Sir Henry Tate in 1897.

Nationalisation is the taking over by the State of the ownership and operation of an industry or service—*e.g.*, coal-mining, railway, transport, gas and electricity. Where this is done without revolution, compensation is usually paid to the previous owners at what is regarded as a fair market price; the compensation is sometimes paid in cash, but more often in fixed-interest-bearing bonds issued either by the State or by the administration of the nationalised service, which is usually a publicly appointed Board or Corporation acting, with greater or lesser autonomy, under the direction of a Minister responsible to Parliament. In some cases the State becomes a partner with private investors in the ownership of a particular enterprise, *e.g.*, oil companies.

National Marine Reserves have been created under the 1981 Wildlife and Countryside Act. The first statutory marine reserve, the island of Lundy, off the Devon coast, was designated in 1986. The second (designated in 1990) is the island of Skomer in the Pembrokeshire Coast National Park.

National Parks. Under the National Parks Act 1949 a National Parks Commission was set up to create National Parks in England and Wales. Ten have been established: Peak District, Lake District, Snowdonia, Yorkshire Dales, Exmoor, Brecon Beacons, Dartmoor, Pembrokeshire Coast, North York Moors and Northumberland. They cover an area of some 13,618 km², or 9 per cent of the total area of England and Wales. It is not intended to change the character of these territories but to control their development so as to harmonise with the two dominant principles: (a) that the characteristic beauty of the landscape within the Park area shall be preserved and (b) that the visiting public shall have ample access and facilities for recreation and enjoyment. The establishment of a new national park has been proposed for mid-Wales. The Commission also has power to designate areas in England and Wales outside the national parks as "areas of outstanding natural beauty". Thirty-three areas had been designated by 1977: Gower, Quantock Hills, Lleyn, Surrey Hills, Dorset, Northumberland Coast, Cannock Chase, Shropshire Hills, Malvern Hills, Cornwall, N. Devon, S. Devon, E. Devon, E. Hampshire, Isle of Wight, Forest of Bowland, Chichester Harbour, Solway Coast, Chilterns, Sussex Downs, Cotswolds, Anglesey, South Hampshire Coast, Kent Downs, Norfolk Coast, Dedham Vale, Suffolk Coast and Heaths, Wye Valley, Arnside and Silverdale, Lincolnshire Wolds, Mendip Hills, North Wessex Downs, Isles of Scilly. Under the Countryside Act, 1968, the National Parks Commission has been reconstituted as the Countryside Commission. In 1988, a special statutory authority was established to manage the 120 miles of waterways constituting the Norfolk Broads. *See also* **Long Distance Walks** and **National Marine Reserves.**

National Physical Laboratory, situated at Teddington, is one of the world's largest and best-equipped laboratories. It conducts research in its three main groups: Measurement, Materials and Engineering Sciences, and maintains British primary standards and physical units. First established in 1900 and managed by the Royal Society, it is now under the control of the Dept. of Trade and Industry, but will become an agency under privatisation.

National Portrait Gallery, established in 1856, and now located in a building in St. Martin's Lane adjoining the National Gallery. Contains portraits of eminent people in British history and a valuable collection of medals and autographs.

National Rivers Authority (NRA), established in July 1989, has overall responsibility for the management of rivers, water resources and protection of the water environment. It operates through 10 regional units.

National Trust, founded in 1895. "A non-profit-making organisation incorporated by Act of Parliament for the purposes of promoting the permanent preservation of lands and buildings of historic interest or natural beauty for the benefit and access of the people." As a consequence of gifts and public-spirited individuals the Trust now owns many hectares of magnificent scenery and property. Since 1946 lands and houses may be given to the Nationl Trust in lieu of death duties. Between 1971 and 1990, membership grew sixfold to more than 1·6m.

Nativity. There are three nativity festivals of the Christian Church: Christmas, 25 December, festival of birth of Christ; the birthday of the Virgin Mary (8 September); and of St. John the Baptist (24 June).

NATO, the North Atlantic Treaty Organisation, established 4 April 1949. A defence grouping of Western European states, America and Canada. Britain is a member. The Russian equivalent is the Warsaw Pact (signed May 1955). NATO's Secretary-General is Manfred Wörner. NATO's 40th anniversary in 1989 was marked by the collapse of communism in Eastern Europe

Natterjack, a curious warty, prominent-eyed, brown toad (*Bufo calamita*), having a bright yellow line down the middle of its back. It utters a muttering sort of croak, hence its name.

Naturalism in painting has been defined as "a direct and spontaneous approach to nature"—to landscape primarily. Constable, Turner and Boudin were among the great naturalist painters of the 19th cent. Naturalistic drama attempts to record as faithfully as possible the actual experiences of life without too much concern for artistic form.

Natural Numbers, the counting numbers 1, 2, 3, 4, 5, ...

"Nautical Almanac", published under the authority of the Admiralty, is always issued four years in advance, and contains information specially prepared for the use of navigators and astronomers. It first appeared in 1767.

Nautilus, a term now applied only to the pearly-shelled nautilus, the sole surviving example of the four-gilled section of the *Cephalopoda*. Its fossil relatives are called Ammonites. The spiral shell is divided into a number of compartments, the animal living in the last and largest chamber. There are three or four species, all living in tropical seas. The Paper Nautilus is not related to the Pearly Nautilus, belonging to the same order as the octopus.

Nave is the body or main open portion of a cathedral or church, and extends from the chief entrance to the choir, or chancel, and is usually flanked by aisles.

Neanderthal, the name of the valley lying between Düsseldorf and Wuppertal, where in a limestone cave a skull of a very early species of prehistoric man was discovered in 1856. *See* **F55.**

Nekton, term used to differentiate actively swimming aquatic organisms (*e.g.*, fishes) from the "drifters" or plankton.

Nelson Column, in Trafalgar Square, London, designed by Mr. William Railton, was chosen from among a number of designs—temples, obelisks and various sculptural groups—sent in as a result of a competition held in 1839. The erection of the column was begun in 1840. Twenty-six years later the lions designed by Landseer were set up at the foot of the completed column. The statue of Nelson himself was made by E. H. Bailey and the bronze reliefs at the base executed by Carew, Woodington, Ternouth and Watson, representing the Battles of the Nile, St. Vincent, Copenhagen and Trafalgar. Height 52 m, executed in Dartmoor granite from Foggin Tor quarries, at a cost of £46,000.

Néné *or* **Hawaiian Goose.** At the Severn Wildfowl Trust at Slimbridge Sir Peter Scott saved this bird from extinction.

Neo-Classical Style, term applied to the revival of classical logic and order after the extravagances of Rococo (*q.v.*), beginning in France in the mid-18th cent. and finding expression in architecture and the decorative arts. The style retains some of the daintiness of Rococo, furniture is on a small scale, often gilt, and silks and porcelain favour pastel shades. Straight lines take the place of the wild curvatures of Rococo and classical details like festoons and urn forms are used in many contexts and materials. Its English version is closely associated with the name of the architect Robert Adam whose light and graceful adaptations of Greek and Roman forms were introduced into English country houses. In France the style is sometimes called *Style Louis XVI*, though its dates, c. 1750–c. 1790 do not exactly coincide with the reign of that monarch. Eventually the Neo-Classical style merges into Empire (*q.v.*).

Neodymium, element no. 60, symbol Nd, belonging to the rare earth metals. Discovered 1885.

Neo-Impressionism, a development of Impressionism (*q.v.*) by Seurat and Signac during the 1880s who devised the method of painting known as *pointillism* (the application of pure colours in minute touches to form a composite whole, based on a knowledge of the laws of colour and optics). One of the best-known examples of this technique is Seurat's *Sunday Afternoon on the Grand Jatte.*

Neon, inert gas present in air to the extent of about 1 part in 65,000. The crimson glow produced when an electric discharge passes through the gas is familiar in advertising signs. Element no. 10, symbol Ne.

Nepotism, the bestowal of patronage by reason of relationship rather than of merit (*e.g.* by certain early Popes).

Neptune. Apart from Pluto this is the most distant of the planets, estimated to be about $4,497 \times 10^6$ km from the sun, and taking about 165 years to revolve around it. Discovered by the German astronomer Galle on 23 September 1846, after its existence had been predicted by Leverrier and Adams. The planet was visited by Voyager 2 in 1989, its last planetary stop. This revealed Neptune has at least six moons (not just Triton and Nereid as previously thought) as well as some form of clouds.

Neptunium, element no. 93, symbol Np, one of the four new elements discovered during the progress of the atomic bomb project in the second world war, Neptunium is formed when a neutron enters nucleus of Uranium 238, and it decays radioactively to yield plutonium.

Neutrino, a neutral particle which carries energy and spin and although possessing little or no mass plays an important part in the interaction of other fundamental particles. The discovery that there are in fact two distinct neutrinos, each with its counterpart, was discovered in 1962 as a result of an experiment made with the 30,000 million-electronvolt proton accelerator at Brookhaven. *See* **F16.**

Neutron, a neutral particle present in all atomic nuclei except the hydrogen nucleus which is a single proton. In the development of nuclear science and technology the neutron has played a most important role and neutrons produce the radioisotopes now widely used in medicine, agriculture and industry. Neutrons and protons are termed nucleons. *See* **F11(2), 16.**

Neutron Bomb, a thermonuclear fusion weapon which produces increased lethal radiation while the destructive blast and fallout are significantly less than for a fission weapon of equivalent yield; it kills organic life while sparing property, except within a small radius. In 1978 President Carter reserved his decision on production; in 1981 the new Reagan administration decided to go ahead and stockpile the weapon. *See also* **F13(2).**

New Deal. The measures taken by President Roosevelt in USA in 1933 to overcome the great economic crisis which broke out at the end of 1929 and to restore the social security threatened by it. The measures were drawn up by a group of experts called a Brains Trust and they provided for recovery by a programme of public works, including large-scale construction of houses and large-scale assistance to farmers. Loans were granted and authorities formed to stimulate activities which reduced the workless from 17 millions to between 7 and 10 millions. Unemployment relief was regulated and enlarged; and social insurance (which for decades had been a subject of dispute, being held to be contrary to American principles of self-help) was introduced. Many of the changes have become a permanent part of American legislation though some laws were repealed as being unconstitutional.

Newgate Prison was situated at the western end of Newgate Street, opposite the Old Bailey at the site of one of the old London city gates. There is a record of a prison upon this spot in the 13th cent. Later a new one was built by the executors of Richard Whittington, but this was destroyed by the Great Fire in 1666. Still another new prison on this site was erected between 1778 and 1780. In the Gordon Riots of the latter year it was destroyed by fire and re-erected. It was not used as a prison after 1880 and was demolished in 1902–3.

Newspapers. The first news-books to be published at regular intervals in Britain appeared in 1662 with news of what was going on abroad translated from German and Italian news-sheets. Licence to print was obtained from the Star Chamber, which until its abolition in 1641 allowed only the printing of foreign news. With the lifting of the ban on domestic news the Press became free. In the reign of Queen Anne English newspapers employed writers of great intellectual power and versatility. Despite the newspaper tax introduced in 1712, the number of newspapers published in London in 1776 had increased to 53, though the standard of writing was below that of earlier times. The development of the Press was greatly assisted in the 19th cent. by the abolition of the "taxes on knowledge", by the introduction of the cheap postal system and by improvements in printing, distribution, collection of news and advertising. The *London Gazette,* founded in 1665 (and still appearing twice weekly as the official organ of the Government), is the oldest newspaper living. *The Times,* known throughout the world, began as the *Daily Universal Register* in 1785, and adopted its present title in 1788. The *Manchester Guardian* (renamed *Guardian* in 1959), once a provincial now a major national newspaper with a world-wide reputation, began as a weekly in 1821, and became a daily in 1855. The *Scotsman,* founded as a weekly in 1817 and estab-

lished as a daily in 1855, and the *Glasgow Herald,* which began as the *Glasgow Advertiser* in 1783, are the leading Scottish newspapers. During 1989, the last national newspapers left Fleet St., most moving east to new sites in Docklands. *See also* **D14–15.**

Newt, amphibian of lizard shape and mottled markings. There are three British species, the largest being the Great-Crested Newt (*Triturus cristatus*), which attains a length of 15 cm.

Newton, the unit of force in the SI system of units. Under its influence a body with a mass of 1 kilogram will accelerate at a rate of 1 metre per second each second.

Newton's Rings. Concentric circular rings, due to the phenomenon of interference, which are seen around the point of contact of a slightly convex lens with a flat plate of glass.

New Towns. Under the New Town Act 1946 and subsequent Acts 33 new towns have been designated in Britain; 23 are in England and Wales, five in Scotland and four in Northern Ireland. They are: Basildon, Bracknell, Crawley, Harlow, Hatfield, Hemel Hempstead, Milton Keynes, Northampton, Peterborough, Stevenage and Welwyn (to relieve housing problems in the Greater London area); Aycliffe, Corby, Cwmbran, Peterlee and Washington (to serve the special needs of their areas); Newtown (to help stem rural depopulation in mid-Wales); Runcorn and Skelmersdale (to meet the overspill needs of Liverpool and north Merseyside); Telford and Redditch (to take population from Birmingham); Warrington (expanded to take people from Liverpool and Manchester); Central Lancashire New Town (new regional city based on existing towns of Preston, Leyland and Chorley). The five Scottish new towns are Cumbernauld, East Kilbride, Glenrothes, Irvine and Livingston. In Northern Ireland Craigavon is being developed as a new city; Antrim and Ballymena are becoming centres of economic growth; Londonderry and the surrounding district have been designated as an area of special development. The population of the new towns in Great Britain is about 1·7 million. The expansion of large existing towns like Northampton, Peterborough and Warrington means that they are becoming regional centres. A major reversal in Government policy was announced in 1976 to the effect that development resources in future were to be directed towards inner-city areas to halt their decline. In 1987, increased sales of the assets of new towns were announced.

New Year's Day, 1 January. The first New Year's festival of which we have record is that constituted by Numa 713 B.C., and dedicated to Janus.

Nibelungenlied, the German epic of the early 13th cent. comprising numerous mythical poems or sagas. Wagner's *The Ring of the Nibelungs* was based on Norse legends and the Nibelungenlied.

Nicene Creed, a summary of the principles of Christian faith, first issued in 325 by the Council of Nicaea (summoned by the emperor Constantine the Great) for the purpose of thwarting the Arian heresy and asserting the godhead of Christ. Date of Easter fixed at Council of Nicaea.

Nickel, silver-coloured metallic element, no. 28, symbol Ni, fairly soft though harder than iron. Chief source of the metal is the nickel sulphide in iron-copper pyrites deposits in Ontario. Chief uses are: in electroplating, in coins, as an element in alloy steels. A novel method of making pure nickel (by treating the metal with carbon monoxide and heating the resulting liquid, nickel carbonyl) was developed in 1890 by Mond. This discovery led to many technical advances in industrial chemistry, one of which is the production of catalysts.

Night Heron, a stocky, short-legged heron of black and white plumage, red eyes and yellowish legs, crepuscular except in breeding season, and an occasional visitor to Britain.

Nightingale, a familiar singing bird which visits the southern counties of England every summer, and is sometimes found as far north as Yorkshire. It is a shy, brown bird, not often seen, but the song of the male, usually heard in the late evening or at early morn, is of remarkable sweetness and variety. After its wooing period is over its song ceases.

Nightjar, nocturnal, insectivorous bird, owl-like in appearance, with mottled brown plumage of "dead leaf" pattern, and a churring song. It is a common breeding visitor to the British Isles, April to September, and lays its eggs on bare ground.

Niobium is a metal element, no. 41, symbol Nb, related to vanadium. Technical development has been slow because of its rare occurrence, although niobium is now used in ferrous alloys to increase resistance to corrosion and produce steel which can be used at high temperatures.

Nitre *or* **Saltpetre**, is now mostly manufactured by the double decomposition of sodium nitrate and potassium chloride. Its chief use is the manufacture of gunpowder and fireworks. It has been manufactured in England since 1625.

Nitrogen, a non-combustible gaseous element, no. 7, symbol N, devoid of taste or smell, and constituting nearly four-fifths of the atmospheric air. Nitrogen compounds are essential to plants and animals, and are used in fertilisers.

Nitro-Glycerine, an explosive yellow fluid produced by mixing small quantities of glycerine with a combination of one part of nitric acid and two parts of sulphuric acid. By itself it is a dangerously explosive substance to handle. In 1867, Nobel produced dynamite, a safe explosive made by absorbing nitro-glycerine in kieselguhr.

Nitrous Oxide, a compound of nitrogen and oxygen possessing mild anaesthetic power. Termed "laughing gas" on account of its exhilarating effect. It is still used in dentistry, and for minor operations and has proved useful in a new technique for finding leaks in water mains.

Nobel Prizes. The Nobel Foundation was established at the beginning of the century to give effect to the wishes expressed by Alfred Nobel in his Will. By the terms of the Will the judges are the Swedish Academy of Science, the Caroline Medico-Surgical Institute, the Swedish Academy and five members of the Norwegian Storting. The award of a Nobel Prize is accepted as the highest form of international recognition in the field in which it is given: physics, chemistry, medicine, literature, peace and, since 1969, economics.

Nones were dates of the Roman calendar which fell on the 5th of each month, excepting March, May, July and October, when they fell on the 7th.

Norman Architecture is English Romanesque (*q.v.*), which flourished from the time of the Norman Conquest and was gradually superseded through a transition period (*c.* 1175–1200) by the introduction of the pointed arch characteristic of the Early English (first Gothic style). Typical of Norman churches are the round arches, thick walls, massive cylindrical columns, with throughout the basic pattern of the square and the circle. Some churches (*e.g.*, the Temple church in London or the chapel at Ludlow Castle) are wholly circular. Roofs in the early days were flat and towers, usually placed at the "crossing", were square but occasionally round; the spire of all these towers have perished, but it seems likely that they were squat and pyramidal.

North-East Passage, from the North Atlantic to Bering Strait has been rapidly developed by the USSR in recent years as a northern sea route to render accessible vast areas of northern Siberia. Attempts to find a North-East passage were made by Englishmen and Dutchmen in the 16th cent. but they were always defeated by the ice, for the sea is completely frozen for some 4,800 km for 9 months of the year. A Swede succeeded in sailing from Europe to Japan via the Arctic in the late 19th cent. *See also* **Arctic Exploration.**

North-West Passage, from the Atlantic to the Pacific through the Arctic Seas, has been the dream of navigators for centuries. Attempts to find it were made in the 16th and early 17th cent. by John and Sebastian Cabot, Frobisher, Gilbert, Davis, Hudson and Baffin. Two centuries later Ross, Parry, Franklin and others made the attempt; but it was not until 1903–5 that Amundsen, discoverer of the South Pole, made the complete voyage in the *Gjoa*. The Canadian icebreaker *Labrador* was the first deep-draft vessel to traverse the North-West Passage (1954) and the US tanker *Manhattan* was the first commercial vessel to do so (1969).

Notre Dame, the famous Paris cathedral, was founded in 1163, and is one of the finest specimens of Gothic architecture in Europe.

November, the 9th month of the year originally, but from *c.* 700 B.C., when Numa added January and February, it became the 11th month.

Nuclear Energy. Atomic nuclei consist of protons and neutrons joined in various proportions **(F11)**. The heaviest naturally occurring nucleus contains 238 particles (92 protons, 146 neutrons) and is uranium 238 (U^{238}); the lightest is hydrogen, which consists of 1 proton. Neutrons and protons attract one another by very strong forces which are not at all well understood; they are called *nuclear forces*. Consequently it requires energy to be supplied if a nucleus is to be pulled apart into its constituent particles. The energy is required to overcome the attractions of the nuclear forces. Conversely, when the particles rush together to form a nucleus energy is released in the form of heat or radiation. The energy released when protons and neutrons coalesce to form a nucleus is called *Binding Energy.* The binding energy of a nucleus divided by the number of particles involved is called the binding energy per particle, which we will call B. It is very difficult to overestimate the importance of B to the human race. B varies from nucleus to nucleus, and the exact form of its variation is only roughly understood at the present time. But the most significant thing is that B is greatest for elements of medium atomic weight and lowest at the heavy (uranium) and light (hydrogen) ends of the periodic table. This means that if middleweight nuclei can be formed either from heavy ones or from light ones, B increases and *energy is released in either case.*

Nuclear Fission. *See* **F13(1).**

Nuclear Fusion. If light nuclei are hurled at high speeds into intimate contact they sometimes coalesce and release binding energy (*see* **Nuclear Energy**). This has been studied in laboratories where powerful and energy-consuming machines accelerate small numbers of particles for purely experimental purposes. If useful amounts of energy are to be gained these fusion reactions will have to occur on a bigger scale in an apparatus from which the resulting heat can be extracted in a controlled way. The one "useful" fusion device so far made is the thermonuclear bomb ("H-bomb"). Thermonuclear is the important word. If a suitable gas can be raised to a very high temperature the nuclei are stripped of their electrons and all particles move with very high speeds. The gas is then called a plasma. High enough temperatures will make speeds great enough for fusion reactions to occur and nuclear energy to be released. This is a thermonuclear reaction. For example, in deuterium gas, at temperatures over a million degrees Centigrade, the deuterium nuclei (*i.e.*, heavy hydrogen nuclei consisting of 1 proton joined to 1 neutron) interact to produce helium nuclei. To obtain a net gain in energy from this process, the temperature must be raised to about 100 million degrees C and maintained long enough; otherwise the energy released is less than that required to heat the fuel and to make up for heat losses. Many attempts to study the staggering technical problems are being made, and fusion research is very active in Britain, the USA, Japan and the Soviet Union. The joint European Torus (JET) fusion research project sited at Culham near Oxford aims to develop a new source of energy for the generation of electricity for the 21st cent. Claims by American scientists in 1989 to have achieved 'room temperature' fusion were greeted with scepticism.

Nuclear Power Stations. In 1989 Britain generated some 20 per cent of her electricity for public supply in nuclear power stations. There are 15 nuclear power stations which produce electricity for the national grid controlled by the electricity authorities and four controlled by the Atomic Energy Authority or British Nuclear Fuels plc. Eight of the 15 nuclear power stations operated by the electricity authorities are at Bradwell, Essex (1962), Hunterston "A", Scotland (1964), Hinkley Point "A", Somerset (1965), Trawsfynydd, Wales (1966), Dungeness "A", Kent (1966), Sizewell, Suffolk (1966),

Oldbury, Avon (1968) and Wylfa, Anglesey (1970). They have all been developed from the classic Calder Hall type, burning natural uranium inserted in a graphite moderator and cooled by carbon dioxide gas. They are called Magnox stations because the fuel elements of natural uranium rods are encased in magnesium alloy cans. A second nuclear power programme is based on the advanced gas cooled reactor (AGR) at Windscale, and include the reactors at Dungeness "B", (1983) and those at Hinkley Point "B", Hunterston "B", Hartlepool (Cleveland) and Heysham (Lancashire). In 1987, after the Layfield Report, the Government gave approval for the Sizewell B project which will be Britain's first pressurised water reactor. Closure of the Berkeley (Gloucs) nuclear power station, built in 1962, began in 1989. In November 1989, AGRs and the half-built Sizewell B PWR were withdrawn from planned privatisation. They will be run by a new public sector nuclear electricity company.

Nuclear Reactors are pieces of apparatus designed to permit nuclear chain reactions to occur under controlled conditions. (Uncontrolled chain reactions are dangerous, *e.g.* atomic bombs.) The success of a reactor depends on the neutrons reaching the U^{235} nuclei to produce more fissions and not being wasted in irrelevant processes or simply escaping through the wall of the apparatus (neutrons are quite difficult to contain). The neutrons leaving the scene of fission are rapidly moving, and they stand more chance of causing another fission if they are slowed down. Consequently a material other than the uranium has to be present to facilitate this, and it is called a moderator. A useful moderator is pure graphite. Thus a reactor may consist of alternate blocks of uranium and graphite. If the reactor is too small so many neutrons escape that there are not enough to keep the chain reaction going. The reactor must therefore be greater than a certain *critical size*. In order to intensify or damp down the chain reaction it is arranged for pieces of neutron-absorbing material, such as cadmium, to be inserted or withdrawn as required. While the chain reaction is proceeding countless numbers of fissions are occurring, each one liberating energy which turns into heat. The temperature therefore increases, and to prevent a catastrophic rise, cooling has to be provided. The reactor therefore has cooling pipes through which a fluid coolant is pumped. The coolant carries the heat away and, in a reactor designed to produce electrical power, the heat is taken to steam-raising boilers and the high-pressure steam is led to turbines which drive the electric generators. What has been briefly described is the type of reactor first used for serious power production at Calder Hall (1956). This is a graphite-moderated, gas-cooled reactor using as fuel natural uranium (*i.e.*, fissile U^{235} greatly diluted with U^{238}). Other thermal types of nuclear reactor are the advanced gas-cooled reactor (AGR), the high temperature reactor (HTR), the steam-generating heavy-water (SGHWR) and the light-water reactor (LWR). It is also possible to make reactors work without slowing the neutrons with a moderator; these are called *fast reactors*. The design of the prototype fast reactor (PFR) at Dounreay is based on experience gained with the Dounreay experimental fast breeder reactor (closed 1977 after 17 years' safe operation) which was the first to produce electricity on a commercial scale (1962) and achieved the highest power output of any of its type in the world. These fast reactors can produce new nuclear fuel in the course of their operation and therefore offer great economies; but they are more difficult to develop than thermal reactors. The fuel is made from the mixed oxides of plutonium and uranium and the coolant is liquid sodium metal. The Government has still to make a decision whether and when to go ahead with a commercial fast breeder reactor.

Environmental considerations are likely to be increasingly topical. Most of the products of the fission process are of necessity radioactive isotopes: they could be gaseous, like krypton, xenon and tritium or solid like strontium, caesium, zirconium and ruthenium. There are also present the new radioactive elements pluto-nium, curium, actinium, etc. Further, in both the nuclear reactor and in the plant which is used to chemically treat and reprocess the nuclear fuel, radioactivity will be induced in associated structural materials, to varying degrees. In this latter case, unlike the former, the radioactive waste with which one is left can to a great extent be selected and is largely overshadowed in importance by the waste arising from the fission and breeding processes. Even if the whole of the UK electrical power was produced by nuclear means, the volumes of such wastes would be relatively small and need in principle tens of acres of storage area. Much of the activity would decay in a decade, a great deal more in a century, but that associated with the elements bred from uranium, would be present for thousands of years: Pu^{239} has a half-life of 25,000 years. Segregation of the various types of activity is feasible; their incorporation into physically and chemically stable form has received a great deal of study so that storage, readily monitored even for many generations, seems entirely possible. The radioactive properties of these wastes can only be changed by nuclear reactions. Bombardment with neutrons or other highly energetic particles can bring about such reactions so that forms of "nuclear incineration" are feasible but are not yet fully explored.

Nucleic Acids. Living matter is built up of cells each of which has a nucleus surrounded by cytoplasm. Cell nuclei are composed chiefly of substances called nucleoproteins, which consist of a protein attached to a nucleic acid (this original name is still used, although nucleic acids are found in the cytoplasm as well as the nucleus). Nucleic acids are complex organic structures made up of chains of compounds called nucleotides (**F32(2)**). Nucleotide molecules have a sugar group attached to a nitrogenous base and a phosphate group. Only two sugar groups are found in the nucleotides, ribose, giving rise to ribonucleic acids (RNAs, found mainly in the cytoplasm) and deoxyribose, which forms deoxyribonucleic acids (DNAs, found mainly in cell nuclei). Seven different nitrogenous bases have been isolated, so that a number of different nucleotides are possible. A repeating, regular pattern of nucleotides is linked by the phosphate groups, forming nucleic acids. The functions of nucleic acids are of fundamental importance. They are concerned in the process of transmission of inherited qualities in reproduction and in building up body proteins. See **F34**.

Nuremberg Trial. On 21 November 1945, an International Military Tribunal, consisting of one American, one British, one Russian and one French member, began the trial of twenty-four Nazi leaders. There were four counts: the conspiracy of Nazism; wars of aggression; war crimes; and crimes against humanity. Twelve were condemned to hanging of whom ten were hanged on 16 October 1946. Goering committed suicide; Bormann is now presumed dead; Papen, Schacht and Fritsche were acquitted. The rest received varying terms of imprisonment.

Nuthatch, name of a number of tree-creeping birds, plump, with a short tail, bluish-grey plumage and black stripe under eye. Nest in holes and wedge nuts in bark of trees, hammering them to get a kernel. There are three European species, one, *Sitta europaea*, resident in England.

Nylon, a generic term for any long-chain synthetic polymeric amide which has recurring amide groups as an integral part of the main polymer chain, and which is capable of being formed into a filament in which the structural elements are orientated in the direction of the axis. The first nylon of commercial interest was made in 1935, and the world's first nylon factory—in the United States—began production in 1940.

O

Oak, a tree of the genus *Quercus*, including some 300 species distributed over the northern hemisphere and into the tropics. Two species are native to Britain, where the oak is the commonest tree (1 in 3)—*Q. petraea*, more common in the west and north on shallower, lighter soils, and *Q. robur*, more common in the south on deeper, heavier soils. Oak timber is much prized for its strength and durability, and from the time of the Spanish Armada to Nelson's day was in great demand for naval construction. It has always been used for building, flooring, furniture and cabinet work. The oak is attacked by many insects, the round nut-like oak galls, or oak-apples, being produced by the sting of certain minute gall wasps.

"Oaks", a famous race for three-year-old fillies run at Epsom three days after the "Derby".

Obelisk, a tapering monolithic column, square at the base and pyramidal at the top, regarded by the ancient Egyptians as a sacred stone and usually found at the entrance to the sun temples. Many were transported from Egypt and set up at various times: there is one in the Place de la Concorde in Paris, and one on the Embankment in London—Cleopatra's Needle—originally erected at Heliopolis, centre of the sun-cult, by Tuthmosis III *c.* 1500 B.C.

Observatories. *See* **Astronomy** *and* **Telescope.**

Occam's Razor. *See* **Section J.**

Ocean, comprises the great body of water which covers seven-tenths of the surface of the earth, and has an average depth of 3·2 km. The principal oceans are the Pacific, Atlantic, Indian and Arctic. The greatest ocean depth is in the Pacific, in the Mindanao Deep, 37,782 ft (11,524 m). *See* **F9(2)** *and* **Oceanography.**

Ocean Currents are well-defined streams running over certain portions of the ocean and caused mainly by wind-friction, slope of the sea surface and differences in density of the water, all movements being influenced by the deflective forces due to the earth's rotation. The climatic importance of the great ocean currents is that they constitute one means whereby heat is transferred from lower to higher latitudes.

Oceanography is the scientific study of the world ocean, *i.e.*, the single connected body of water that covers 70·8 per cent of the earth's surface. Modern oceanography dates from the voyage of HMS *Challenger* (1872–6) during which wide-ranging observations of the ocean were made, for the first time going well beyond what was directly required to assist shipping. Since then oceanography has matured into a highly technical and interdisciplinary science which may be roughly divided into: biological oceanography (the study of marine organisms and marine ecology); chemical oceanography (concerned with the composition of sea-water); physical oceanography (the study of ocean currents, tides and waves and the role played by the oceans in climate and weather); and geological oceanography (concerned with the formation, composition and evolution of the ocean basins). Oceanographic knowledge is essential to allow exploitation of the enormous food, mineral and energy resources of the ocean with the minimum damage to the ocean environment. However, close international co-operation (through such bodies as the Law of Sea Conference) will also be necessary in order to avoid such hazards as overfishing and marine pollution. By 1982 about one third of the world's oil and gas came from offshore wells and recently vast deposits of metal-rich nodules have been located on the ocean floor.

Ocelot, the most common wild cat of S. America. It is about 1·2 m in length, including tail, and of a grey or tawny colour and spotted. Closely related to the Leopard cats.

Octane Number, the index of the knock-rating of petrol. It is based on the arbitrary scale in which iso-octane (which does not cause "knocking") has a value of 100, and normal heptane (which is prone to "knocking") has a value of 0. A good fuel for modern cars must have an octane number greater than 80.

Octarch, the kings of the English heptarchy, Hengist (455) being the first, and Egbert (800) the last.

October, the 10th month, but the 8th in the old Roman calendar. It was held sacred to Mars.

Octopus, a genus of marine molluscs with eight tentacles that bear suckers.

Odyssey, Homer's epic setting forth the incidents of the wanderings of Odysseus on his way back to Ithaca after the Siege of Troy.

Oersted, a unit of magnetic-field intensity in the c.g.s. system.

Offa's Dyke, largest remaining earthwork in Britain, supposed to have been built by Offa (A.D. 757–96) as a defensive boundary line between the English settlers and the dispossessed Welsh of Gwynedd, Powys and Gwent. *See also* **Long Distance Walks.**

Ohm's Law, propounded by G. S. Ohm in 1826, is expressed in the equation: electromotive force (in volts) = current (in amperes) × resistance (in ohms). The ohm is the unit of electrical resistance in the metre-kilogram-second system.

Oil. The great expansion in energy demand over recent years has been met to a large extent by petroleum oil. This contains a wide range of hydrocarbon molecules of varying complexity. The various components are separated from each other by making use of their different boiling points. Crude oil is heated in the base of a fractionating tower; the various components condense at different temperatures in trays at different levels of the tower. The fraction of a given composition can be increased by "cracking" or breaking down the heavier hydrocarbons into lighter ones. The total world reserves of petroleum oil are still uncertain since large parts of the world are still not fully prospected. The cutback and the rise in the price of Middle Eastern oil following the 1973 Arab-Israeli war has now been succeeded by a glut of oil and falling prices. In 1988, British oil production amounted to 114m tonnes.

Okapi, nocturnal ruminant mammal, smaller than the giraffe, chestnut brown in colour with zebra-striped legs, native to the African Congo.

Olbers' Comet was discovered in 1815 by Olbers the German astronomer. Olbers also discovered the asteroids Pallas and Vesta (1802–07).

Old Red Sandstone, the continental rocks formed during the Devonian. *See* **F48.**

Olefines, a series of hydrocarbons, in which the hydrogen atoms are double the number of carbon. The first member of the series is ethylene.

Oléron Laws *or* **Judgments**, were a code of maritime laws, introduced into England in the reign of Richard I in the 12th cent. Oléron is an island off the west coast of France, opposite the mouth of the Charente.

Olive. This small tree, whose fruit yields olive oil, is a native of the eastern Mediterranean countries, but has been introduced into cultivation elsewhere. The green unripe fruit is pickled in brine for table olives.

Olympiads were periods of four years which elapsed between each celebration of the Olympic games, held at Olympia in honour of Zeus. These festivals included competitions in literature, art, drama, rhetoric, music and gymnastics, and they were continued, with intervals, from 776 B.C. to A.D. 394. Athletic revivals have taken place at Athens 1896, Paris 1900, St. Louis 1904, London 1908, Stockholm 1912, Antwerp 1920, Paris 1924, Amsterdam 1928, Los Angeles 1932, Berlin 1936, London 1948, Helsinki 1952, Melbourne 1956, Rome 1960, Tokyo 1964, Mexico City 1968, Munich 1972, Montreal 1976, Moscow 1980, Los Angeles 1984 and Seoul in 1988. Barcelona has been chosen for 1992. The first Winter Olympics were held at Chamonix in 1924; the next are at Albertville in 1992.

Onomasticians are scientists who study the fascinating subject of names—names of places and names of people—to find out their origins. They tell us, for example, that Cambridge is an Anglo-Norman corruption of *Grantabrycg* = bridge over the Granta; that Harrow-on-the-Hill was an early Anglo-Saxon settlement—"heathen temple on the hill"; that we owe the ridings of Yorkshire to the Vikings (Old Norse *thrithungr* = third part); that in Scotland *-ton* and *-toun* indicate not a town but a hamlet or village. Onomasticians are also concerned with international standardisation of place names.

Onyx *or* **Sardonyx**, a variety of chalcedony built up of different-coloured layers, which are parallel and straight (not curved as in agate).

Oolite, a geological term for the Jurassic oolitic

limestones existing through a long stretch of country extending from Yorkshire to Dorset. It abounds in fossils of molluscs and reptiles. The term "oolite" derives from the fact that these rocks are made of egg-shaped particles of calcium carbonate.

Opal, a mineral consisting of hydrous silica, occurring in numerous varieties and colours. Opals have been prized as gems since at least 400 B.C. but the secret of their unique internal "fire" or opalescence has only recently been learned. It is a result of the diffraction of light by a regular array of tiny silica spheres, about 100 nm in diameter, of which gem opals are now known to be composed. Opal miners are called gougers. Chief source—the Andanooka and Coober Pedy fields of South Australia.

Opera. *See* **Section E.**

Opium was known to the ancients, and used by them as a medicine. It is obtained from the poppy (*Papaver somniferum*), the unripe "head" or seed capsule of that flower yielding a juice which when dried becomes the opium of commerce. The poppy is cultivated in India, Iran, Turkey, Macedonia and China for the sake of this juice, which yields various alkaloids, such as morphine, narcotine, codeine, etc. These days the drug is rarely used medicinally.

Opossum, marsupial mammals found in the more southerly of the United States, South America and Australasia. They are arboreal except for the water-opossum, which eats fish.

Optics, the branch of physics which investigates the nature and properties of light and the phenomena of colour. Burning lenses were known to the ancient Greeks and Ptolemy wrote a treatise on optics A.D. 150. Lenses as visual aids were known in ancient China but eyeglasses were not in use until the 13th cent. Spectacles were in more general use after the invention of printing in the 15th cent. The camera obscura was invented in the 16th cent. and the telescope and microscope at the beginning of the 17th cent.

Oracles were in ancient times supposed to be words spoken by the gods, and it was the custom on important occasions to consult them about the future. The Greeks had the Oracles of Zeus at Dodona, and Apollo at Delphi, while the Romans consulted the Oracles of Mars, Fortune and others.

Orange, a fruit growing in most sub-tropical climates and in universal demand. It is grown on an evergreen tree that attains a height of about 6 m at maturity.

Orang-utan, one of the largest of the anthropoid apes, found only in the swampy forests of Borneo and Sumatra. When full-grown it stands over 1·2 m in height and weighs about 67 kg.

Orchestra, a group of instruments and instrumentalists whose playing is under the direction of a conductor. The composition of a typical symphony orchestra is as follows: STRINGS: 1st Violin (16), 2nd Violin (16), Viola (12), Violoncello (12), Double Bass (8). WOOD-WIND: Flute (3–4), Piccolo (1), Oboe (3), Cor Anglais (1), Bass Oboe (1), Clarinet (3), Bass Clarinet (1), Bassoon (3), Contra-bassoon (1). BRASS: Horn (6), Trumpet (5), Trombone (3–4), Tuba (2). PERCUSSION: Timpani (3–6), Side Drum (1), Bass Drum (1), Cymbals (1), Harp (2).

Orders in Council are issued by the sovereign on the advice of a few selected members of the Privy Council. They must not seriously alter the law of the land. Another class of Orders in Council are issued by authority of an Act of Parliament for the carrying out of its provisions.

Ordination, the ceremony of installing ministers or clergymen in clerical offices, has existed from the earliest times. In the Anglican and Roman Catholic Churches the rites of Ordination are performed by bishops; among Nonconformists the power of ordination rests with the governing bodies of the different Churches.

Organ is a musical wind instrument of ancient origin whose tones are produced by the vibrations of air in pipes of varying length. Basically, an organ consists of a number of pipes grouped in rows or ranks according to their special tone-character. The air is fed by

bellows or, in modern organs, by a rotary fan electrically driven. Each rank is controlled by a slider, and the knob that controls the slider is called a stop. The organist pulls out the stops to give the tones he wants, the other pipes being kept out of action by the slider. When a particular note on the keyboard is depressed the player may hear, by pulling out the appropriate stop, not only the normal pitch but the note in several octaves. A stop of which the notes are of normal pitch is called an 8-foot stop, a 16-foot stop would give an octave lower, a 4-foot stop an octave higher and a 2-foot stop two octaves higher. The hand keyboard is called a manual, and the foot keyboard the pedal board. The basic tone of an organ is its diapason tone, and is normally of 8-foot length and pitch. Most large organs have four manual keyboards and one pedal board. The most important manual is the great organ which comprises the majority of basic stops. The next in importance is the swell organ, so called because the pipes are enclosed in a box fitted with movable shutters operated by a swell-pedal. The effect provides a controlled crescendo or diminuendo. The tone of a typical English swell has a reedy character. The third manual controls the choir organ—a collection of stops suitable for vocal accompaniment. The fourth manual controls the solo organ—a group of stops which, singly or in combination, may provide a solo melody which the remainder of the organ accompanies. The pedal keyboard controls most of the bass stops. In some very large organs there is a fifth manual controlling the echo organ. This is a small group of stops usually set high in the roof of the building to give the effect of distant music. Most church organs have two or three manuals. Modern cinema organs may have some normal stops but rely chiefly on a number of effects unknown to the straight organ.

Organic Chemistry. The chemistry of compounds containing carbon and usually associated with living organisms. *See* **F23.**

Oriel Window is a window projected from the front of a building, rectangular, triangular, or pentagonal. The ordinary bay window and bow window are varieties of Oriel. When an Oriel window does not reach to the ground it usually rests upon moulded sills supported by corbels.

Oriflamme, the name of the original banner of the abbey of St. Denis, and adopted by Louis VI as his standard. It remained the national emblem of France for three centuries. The flag was of red silk, the outer edge being cut in the form of flames.

Original Sin, according to Christian doctrine the corruption that is born with us, as a result of Adam's fall.

Orioles, brilliantly coloured birds, members of the passerine family *Oriolidae,* found in the tropical regions of Asia, Africa and Australia. The golden oriole, perhaps the most beautiful of them all, with brilliant yellow plumage, black wings and tail, winters in Africa, visits England and is known to have nested here.

Orion, a famous constellation of the heavens, comprising nearly a hundred stars, all visible to the naked eye. It contains three stars of the second magnitude in a line, and these are called "Orion's Belt".

Ormer, a shellfish (*Haliotis tuberculata*) which occurs in the Channel Islands and on parts of the French coast. It is considered a great delicacy.

Ornithology, the scientific study of birds.

Ornithorhynchus. *See* **Duckbill.**

Orogeny, large-scale earth movements, including faulting and folding and sometimes igneous activity, which produce a linear belt of mountains, *e.g.,* the Alpine orogeny in Europe which produced the Alps.

Orphism. *See* **Section J.**

Orphrey, the name of an ornamental strip richly embroidered on ecclesiastical vestments.

Orrery, an instrument used in the 18th and early 19th cent. which showed the motions of the planets round the sun and the satellites round their primaries. The first orrery made was named after Charles Boyle, Earl of Orrery.

Orthodox Eastern Church. *See* **Section J.**

Osborne House, near Cowes, in the Isle of Wight. Queen Victoria's favourite winter-residence, and where she died. It was given to the nation by Edward VII, and is now a convalescent home.

Osier, a species of willow growing in damp soils and yielding branches utilised in basket-making.

Osmium, a very hard, bluish-white metallic element, no. 76, symbol Os, of the platinum group and one of the heaviest of known metals. It is obtained from certain sands of South America, California, Australia and Russia. The alloy of osmium and iridium (osmiridium) provides tips for gold fountain-pen nibs.

Osmosis, the process by which absorption of liquids through semi-permeable membranes takes place. A solution exerts osmotic pressure (O.P.) or suction in proportion to concentration but also depending on kind of dissolved substance. The roots of the higher plants are covered with fine root-hairs, within the cell-walls of which the sap is normally of a higher concentration than the dissolved matter in the surrounding soil. The root-hairs, therefore, draw into themselves these weaker salt-solutions. (The explanation of water and salt exchanges is complicated by the selective ability of some cells (*e.g.*, roots) to accept or reject particular dissolved substances along with the water. The absorption of salts by a plant is selective, each plant selecting through the semi-permeable membranes of its root-hairs those substances which are most suited to itself.)

Osprey (*Pandion haliaëtus*), a large and magnificent bird of prey, dark brown above and nearly white below. The head is whitish with a dark band from eye to nape. To the British Isles it is a rare passage migrant. In 1955, thanks to the energy and vigilance of the Royal Society for the Protection of Birds, a pair nested in a Scots pine in Inverness-shire and reared three young. Since then more young ospreys have been safely fledged in this sanctuary. The food consists almost entirely of fish, which the bird seizes with its talons. The so-called osprey plumes in fact come from the egret.

Ostrich, the largest living bird, related to the rhea, emu and extinct moa, now found only on the sandy plains of Africa and parts of S.W. Asia. The male has beautiful white plumes on wings and tail. The wings are useless in flight, but the birds have a fleetness of foot exceeding that of the swiftest horse. An ostrich's egg weighs 1·3 kg.

Otary, any seal which has external ears (as opposed to the *true seals* which lack them). The eared seals make up the family *Otariidae,* which includes the Sea-lion and the Fur-seal of the N. Pacific.

Otter, an aquatic carnivorous mammal widely distributed over Europe, and at one time very common in England and Wales. The otter averages about 60 cm in length, exclusive of tail, has web-feet and is a very expert swimmer. Otters are harmless and their hunting is a cruel and senseless blood sport. They are now protected in England.

Ounce or **Snow Leopard,** a very beautiful pale spotted cat from the Himalayas about the size of a labrador retriever but with a long furry tail.

Outcrop. Where a bed of rock appears at the surface of the ground, there is an outcrop of the particular rock. The mining of outcrop coal is called open-cast mining.

Oviparous, a zoological term referring to animals which lay eggs to be hatched outside the body of the parent.

Ovipositor, the organ by means of which female insects lay their eggs.

Owls, nocturnal birds of prey, distributed over the greater part of the world. Their forward-looking eyes, embedded in rings of feathers, give them a characteristic "owl-like" appearance, and their plumage, usually a mottled blend of browns and greys, is so soft that their flight is almost noiseless. Owls live on small mammals, reptiles, birds, insects and fish, and are very valuable birds to the farmer. British owls include the barn owl (screech owl), short-eared owl, long-eared owl, tawny owl, little owl. In many English counties the barn owl is now (1990) nearly extinct.

Ox, the popular name of the mammals included

in the genus *Bos.* They are hollow-horned ruminants and hoofed quadrupeds, and include the various classes of domestic cattle as well as the different wild species. The adult male is called a bull, the female a cow and the young a calf. The best-known breeds of domesticated cattle are the Durham or Shorthorn, the Angus, the Jersey, Ayrshire, Suffolk and Hereford.

Oxalic Acid, an organic acid obtained from numerous plants, such as sorrel and rhubarb, and produced artificially for commercial purposes from sawdust, treated with caustic potash or caustic soda. It combines with metals to form oxalates; used in the manufacture of ink.

Oxford Clay, a geological formation consisting of a bed of blue clay *c.* 200 m thick, and forming the lower portion of the Upper Jurassic. It makes good bricks.

Oxford Movement. *See* **Tractarianism, Section J.**

Oxford University. The early history of the university is obscure. There was a school at Oxford as early as 1115 and it is known that Robert Pullen, a theologian from Paris, lectured there in 1133. Allusions to Oxford as the most celebrated centre of learning in England occurred in a work of Gerald of Wales in 1184–5. The earliest colleges to be founded were University College (1249), Balliol (about 1263), Merton (1264). In 1571 the university was reorganised and granted a Charter of Incorporation by an Act of Elizabeth. Other colleges and halls with their dates of foundation are: All Souls (1438), Brasenose (1509), Christ Church (1546), Corpus Christi (1517), Exeter (1314), Hertford (1874), Jesus (1571), Keble (1868), Linacre (1962), Lincoln (1427), Magdalen (1458), New College (1379), Nuffield (1937), Oriel (1326), Pembroke (1624), Queen's (1340), St. Anthony's (1950), St. Catherine's (1962), St. Cross (1965), St. Edmund Hall (1270), St. John's (1555), St. Peter's (1929), Trinity (1554), Wadham (1612), Wolfson (1965), Worcester (1714), Campion Hall (1962), St. Benet's Hall (1964), Mansfield (1886), Regent's Park (1958), Greyfriar's Hall (1953). The original women's colleges were:—Lady Margaret Hall (1878), Somerville (1879), St. Hugh's (1886), St. Hilda's (1893), St. Anne's (1952). Women were not admitted to degrees (though allowed to sit for examination) till 1920. Since 1974 almost all colleges have admitted both men and women students. In 1989, Manchester College became a permanent private hall of the University.

Oxygen is the most abundant of all terrestrial elements, no. 8, symbol O. In combination, this gaseous element forms about 46% of the earth's crust; one-fifth of the atmosphere; eight-ninths by weight of all water. Discovered independently by Scheele (*c.* 1773) and Priestley (1774). It is colourless, tasteless and odourless, and forms the chief life-supporting element of animal and vegetable life.

Oyster, a bivalve mollusc, of the genus *Ostrea,* having very numerous species and abounding in nearly all seas. The shell is rough and irregular. Oysters are exceedingly prolific, spawning in May and June. In England and Scotland deep-sea oysters are not allowed to be sold between 15 June and 4 August, and other kinds between 14 May and 4 August. In Ireland, no oysters may be taken between 1 May and 1 September, except in certain waters. The Whitstable oyster beds have existed since pre-Roman times; "clocks" are dead oysters.

Oystercatcher, a wading bird with black and white plumage and long, orange bill, inhabiting estuaries and sea-shores. Feeds on mussels, shell fish, etc., but not oysters.

Ozone, a modified form of oxygen, containing three atoms of oxygen per molecule instead of two. It is prepared by passing oxygen through a silent electric discharge. When present in air to the extent of 1 part in 4 million parts of air it kills bacteria, and has been used for this purpose in ventilating systems, *e.g.*, that of underground railways. It is present in extremely small quantities in the lower atmosphere but is comparatively plentiful at heights between 12 and 50 km. As ozone absorbs ultraviolet light of certain wavelengths spectroscopic methods, involving the analysis of sunlight, are chiefly used in ozone determination. *See also* **Atmosphere.**

P

Paca, a genus of large rodents found in Central and South America, and resembling the guinea-pig. It is of nocturnal habits, has streaked and spotted fur and lives on fruits and plants.

Pacific Ocean. The first European to recognise the Pacific as distinct from the Atlantic was the Spanish explorer, Vasco Nuñez de Balboa, who discovered its eastern shore from a peak in Panama in 1513. The first European to sail upon it was Magellan, who entered it by the strait that bears his name in 1520. Sir Francis Drake was the first Englishman to sail upon it in 1577. The world's greatest known ocean depth is in the Mindanao Trench, off the Philippines, 37,782 ft (11,524 m).

Pagan, a person who does not worship God; a heathen. The word is derived from the Latin *paganus* (a countryman or uncultivated person). In the Middle Ages the term was used largely to describe Mohammedans (Moors, Saracens, etc.).

Pagoda, the name given in China, India and other Asiatic countries to a high pyramidal tower, usually, but not necessarily, connected with a temple.

Palaeontology, the science which is devoted to the investigation of fossils: animal (palaeozoology) and plants (palaeobotany). By studying the markings and fossils of living things in the stratified rocks, palaeontologists have been able to establish with astonishing accuracy a record of the evolution of life through geological time. The geologist at the same time with the evidence of the fossils has been able to work out the order and the age of the rocks. *See also* **Section F.**

Palatinate, a term formerly applied to two German regions, historically related, the Upper and Lower Palatinates. Now provinces of Bavaria.

Pale, the name given to the part of Ireland colonised by the English and comprising portions of the counties of Louth, Dublin, Meath and Kildare. The Anglo-Norman rulers were styled "Lords of the Pale".

Palimpsests are ancient MSS. or parchments which have been partly effaced and used for fresh writings. Many valuable MSS. were thus lost, but sometimes the second writing has been washed out, enabling the original writings to be deciphered. Among such restorations are a dialogue of Cicero's, a part of a book of Livy.

Palladium, a scarce metallic element, no. 46, symbol Pd, similar to platinum, with which it is usually found. It is an expensive metal, with desirable properties as a catalyst in reactions involving hydrogen, since it has a remarkable capacity for absorbing this gas; for example, coal gas and air will inflame in the presence of palladium at room temperature. It forms a silver-white alloy with gold, and this is used in some kinds of jewellery. It is used in expensive watches to make non-magnetic springs.

Pallium, a vestmental ornamentation of white wool presented by the Pope to archbishops on their appointment, and the sign of Papal confirmation.

Palm, a large straight-trunked plant or tree common to tropical countries, and usually fruit yielding, such as dates, coconuts, etc. Many commodities useful to man are obtained from plants of the Palm family (*Palmaceae*).

Palm Sunday, the Sunday before Easter, upon which occasion it is customary to carry palms to the churches in some countries, in commemoration of Christ's entry into Jerusalem for the Feast of the Passover, when the people went forth to greet Him with palm branches.

Panama Canal. In 1903 the United States signed a treaty with Panama (which had previously seceded from Columbia) which gave the United States rights in perpetuity over a 16 km-wide strip of land extending across the isthmus for the purposes of building and running the canal. The canal connects the Atlantic and Pacific Oceans, is just over 80 kilometres long (with sea approaches) and the depth varies from 12 to 26 m. It is constructed above sea-level, with locks, and has been available for commercial shipping since 3 August 1914. Agreement was reached in 1978 for the waterway to be turned over to Panama by the end of the century. In 1989, the canal handled *c.* 12,000 ships. *See* **Section C** for the 1989 U.S. invasion of Panama.

Panda, *or* **Cat-Bear,** is related to the Raccoon. There are two kinds, the Red or True Panda, resembling a large domestic cat, which lives in the eastern Himalayas and S.W. China, and the Giant Panda, which is more like a bear in appearance and inhabits the mountains of western China. Both frequent the dense bamboo forests of those regions.

Pangolin, the scientific name of the "scaly ant-eater", a toothless mammal, found in W. Africa and S.E. Asia. It has a long extensible tongue which it uses in catching ants and termites, its chief food. When attacked the pangolin rolls itself into a ball, and its scales assume the form of sharp spikes. Pangolins have an Order of their own—the Pholidota, the scale-bearers.

Pantagruel, the leading character in one of the satires of Rabelais.

Pantheon, the famous temple in Rome, originally consecrated to the gods, built by Agrippa in 27 B.C. and rebuilt in the 2nd cent. by Hadrian. Its splendid dome and portico make it one of the most interesting architectural monuments of ancient days. Since the 7th cent. it has been used as a Christian church.

Panther, another name for the leopard, *Panthera pardus*, related to the lion, carnivorous, active climber, found in India, and other parts of Asia, also in Africa.

Papal Infallibility. *See* **Section J.**

Paper has been known in one form or another from very early times. The papyrus reeds of the Nile swamps served the ancient Egyptians for sheets upon which to inscribe their records. The Chinese and Japanese, centuries later, were using something more akin to modern paper in substance, an Asiatic paper-mulberry, yielding a smooth fibrous material, being utilised. With the spread of learning in Western Europe the necessity of a readier medium made itself felt and paper began to be manufactured from pulped rags and other substances. The first known English paper-mill was Sele mill near Stevenage, built about 1490, which produced the paper for an edition of Chaucer in 1498. Other mills were set up under Elizabeth, using linen and cotton as raw material. Other papermaking staples were later introduced, such as surat, esparto grass and wood-pulp. The chief raw material in the world paper industry is wood-pulp, the main exporters being the timber-growing countries of Canada, Sweden and Finland. Canada is the world's chief producer of newsprint.

Papyrus, the earliest known paper made in Egypt at a very remote period from a large species of reed, *Cyperus papyrus*. This plant is to be found all over tropical Africa, especially in the "sudd" region of the White Nile.

Parachute, the umbrella-shaped safety device used in emergency by the crew and passengers of aircraft. The first parachute descent from a great height was made in 1797 by André Garnerin who dropped 915 m from a balloon. Rate of descent for a parachute jump is about 5 m/s.

Paraclete (the Holy Ghost, or Comforter), the name used in the English translations of St. John's Gospel, and adopted by Abelard to designate the convent in Champagne founded by him, of which Héloïse became the abbess.

Paradise, a Persian word used by the translators of the Old Testament to designate the Garden of Eden, and since meaning any place of happiness.

Paraffin, a mixture of hydrocarbons of higher boiling point than petrol. Paraffin was first obtained by distillation of coal, the process being discovered about 1830. About 1848, Mr. James Young procured it from mineral oil, and Irish peat also yielded it. The main source of paraffin supply today is crude petroleum. Used in the manufacture of candles, for waterproofing and numerous other purposes.

Parakeets, various small parrots of vivid plumage native to Australia, Polynesia, Asia and Africa. One of the loveliest of the parakeets is the budgerigar of Australia.

Parallax, the change in direction of a body caused by a change in position of the observer. If the parallax is measured (in degrees of angle) and the distance between the two observation points is known the distance of the observed body can be calculated. The distance of heavenly bodies has been found this way. The first stellar distances were so obtained in 1838 by Henderson, Struve and Bessel. Stellar distances are so great that even when the two observations are made at opposite points of the earth's orbit round the sun, the parallax is always less than 1·0″ of arc. See **Aberration.**

Parameter, a number which is fixed for the application of a theory to one particular situation but may be different for other situations. For example, in a theory of motion near the surface of a planet the acceleration due to gravity may be regarded as a parameter constant for a particular planet but differing from planet to planet. The word is often used in a similar way in discussions of economic affairs.

Parapsychology. See **Section J.**

Parchment, made chiefly from the skins of animals, usually of goats and sheep, was employed in olden times before printing was invented and superseded papyrus as writing material. Vegetable parchment, invented by W. E. Gaine in 1853, though not equal in strength and durability to skin parchment, is about five times stronger than ordinary paper. Vellum is parchment made from the skins of young calves or lambs.

Paris University, of which the Sorbonne forms a part was founded in the 12th cent. and is one of the greatest educational institutions of Europe.

Parliament, is the name given to the supreme legislature of the United Kingdom. It consists of the Queen, the Lords spiritual and temporal and the Commons. It meets in two houses: the House of Lords (the Upper or Second Chamber) and the House of Commons. It derives from the Anglo-Saxon *Witans* (see **Witan**). The Statute of Westminster (1275) first uses "parlement" of the Great Council in England, which comes from the French word meaning discourse. See **Section D.**

Parliamentary Correspondents sit in the Press Gallery of the House of Commons and describe its proceedings for the news media either by impressions or a summary of the debate.

Parquetry, the name of a style of flooring consisting of small rectangular wooden blocks laid down according to geometrical pattern.

Parrot, the popular name of a widely distributed family of tropical birds, including the African grey parrot, the green parrot of South America —both familiar cage pets in this country—and the various parakeets, cockatoos, macaws, lories, etc. Many of these birds possess a remarkable gift of imitating sound, especially human voices.

Parsec, modern unit of astronomical distance, the distance at which the diameter of the earth's orbit subtends an angle of 1 arc second. 1 parsec (pc) = 3·0857 × 10¹³ km.

Parthenogenesis. The development of animals from unfertilised eggs. The drones of the honey bee are parthenogenetic, and the phenomenon is also common among aphids.

Parthenon, the famous Temple of Athena on the Acropolis at Athens, was built under the rule of Pericles between 447 B.C. and 432 B.C. It was made wholly of marble without mortar. The famous sculptured friezes, known as the Elgin Marbles, are now in the British Museum.

Partridge, a well-known British game-bird. Close time: 2 February to 31 August. Two species are common in Britain.

Passport is an official document issued to a person by his own government, certifying to his citizenship and permitting him to travel abroad. Passports to British subjects are granted by the Foreign and Commonwealth Office, authorise bearer to leave the country and guarantee him the state's protection. Passports (1990) cost £15—and are issued for a period of 10 years. Children over 16 require separate passports. Parents of children under 16 who require passports should make application on form (B). A simplified form of travel document (British visitor's passport) is issued for British subjects wishing to pay short visits to certain foreign countries for a fee of £7·50—valid for 12 months. For those making frequent visits abroad a 94-page passport was first issued in 1973, which costs £30 (1990). From July 1988, British citizens began

using a common wine-coloured EEC passport. Existing blue passports will remain valid until they expire. They will disappear entirely after 31 December 1999.

Patricians, the aristocracy of ancient Rome.

Paul's Cathedral, St., is the third cathedral church to be built on the site. It was preceded by a Norman building which was practically destroyed by the Great Fire in 1666. This followed a Saxon church which was burnt in 1086. The present building was designed by Sir Christopher Wren. The foundation stone was laid in 1675 and the structure was completed in 1710. It cost a little under £748,000. Its central feature is the dome, crowned by its cupola and lantern with the golden ball and cross. It escaped serious damage during the air raids of the second world war.

*p*C **Value,** introduced by Dr. C. L. Whittles in 1935 as a measure of salinity of aqueous solutions (soil extract, irrigation water, etc.); defined as the negative logarithm of specific electrical conductivity in reciprocal ohms. Alone or joined with **p**H (*q.v.*) is useful as an index of osmotic pressure (see **Osmosis**) and related hindrance to plant growth resulting from excess of fertiliser or soil salts. If manuring is balanced, growth is best about *p*C 3.3.

Peacock, a bird of large size and beautiful plumage, its characteristic feature being a tail of brilliant "eyed" feathers, which it can erect and spread out, the males possessing resplendent feathering to a much greater extent than the females. It is related to the pheasant; one species is found wild in the forests of India, and another inhabits Burma and the Malayan regions, in Africa there is the Congo Peacock.

Peanut, Groundnut *or* **Monkey Nut.** A member of the pea family native to S. America, but now cultivated in many parts of the world. After pollination, the flower stalk bends down and buries the pod containing the peas ("nuts") in the ground. The oil from these "nuts" can be used for margarine manufacture.

Pearl is produced by certain shelled molluscs, chiefly the oyster. The inner surface of the shells of the pearl oyster yield "mother-of-pearl", and distinct pearls are believed to be morbid secretions, caused by some external irritation. Many fine pearls are found in the actual body of the oyster. The Persian Gulf, Sri Lanka, the north-west coast of Western Australia, many Pacific islands and the Gulf of Mexico are among the most productive pearl-fishing grounds. In ancient times Britain was renowned for its pearl fisheries, the pearls being obtained from a species of fresh-water mussel. Western Australia has produced a 40-grain pearl, the finest the world has seen. The largest pearl ever found was the "Beresford-Hope Pearl", which weighed 1,800 grains, over six times as much as the oyster that produced it.

Peat, decayed vegetable matter found mostly in marshy positions, and common in Ireland and Scotland. Peat is coal in its first stage of development; burnt for fuel in many cottages.

Peccary, a pig-like animal native to the Americas. There are two species: the collared peccary and the white-lipped peccary, the latter being a vicious and dangerous animal.

Pelican, a genus of bird with long depressed bill pouched underneath, thus able to hold fish in reserve. It has immense wings and webbed feet. Eight species.

Pemmican, venison or other meat, sliced, dried, pounded and made into cakes, used by explorers and others when out of reach of fresh meat.

Penguin, a genus of flightless, fish-eating sea-birds of the southern hemisphere. They are stout-bodied, short-necked and of small, moderate or large size. The Emperor and King Penguins make no nest but protect and incubate the single egg by carrying it in the down feathers between the feet and the body. Other species brood in the usual way and may lay as many as three eggs. Penguins use their flippers for swimming under water. All 17 species are bluish-grey or blackish above and white below. They are very sociable and breed in colonies.

Penicillin. An antibiotic drug produced by the mould *Penicillium notatum*, and discovered by Sir Alexander Fleming in 1928. It is one of the most effective chemotherapeutic agents known.

The mould produces a number of penicillins, all of which are effective antibiotics. *See* **P9(1), 22(2).**

Peninsular War lasted from 1808 to 1814. Fought in Spain and Portugal (the Iberian peninsula) by the British, Spanish and Portuguese forces, chiefly under Wellington, against the French. The latter were defeated.

Pentagon, government office in Washington (the largest in the world), housing many thousands of military and civilian workers in the War Department of the United States (Army, Navy and Air Force).

Pentateuch, the first five books of the Old Testament—Genesis, Exodus, Leviticus, Numbers and Deuteronomy. Referred to in the Gospel of Mark as "the book of Moses".

Pepys Diary, by Samuel Pepys, was first published in 1825. It gives a picture of the social life of the period 1 January 1660 to 31 May 1669. He bequeathed the manuscript, together with his library, to Magdalene College, Cambridge.

Perch, a well-known family of fresh-water fish, with dark striped sides. The common perch of British rivers and lakes falls an easy prey to the angler because of its voracity.

Perfumes are essences or odours obtained from floral and other substances. The chief flower perfumes are those obtained from rose, jasmine, orange flower, violet and acacia. Heliotrope perfume is largely obtained from vanilla and almonds. Among the aromatic herbs which yield attractive perfumes are the rosemary, thyme, geranium, lavender, etc., while orange peel, citron peel, musk, sandalwood, patchouli and other vegetable products are largely drawn upon. In recent times chemistry has been called into play in aid of the perfumer, and many of the popular perfumes of today are chemically prepared in simulation of the scents of the flowers or other natural substances the names of which they bear. *See* **Musk Deer.**

Perigee, the closest point of the orbit of an object such as a satellite to the earth. The opposite of apogee (*q.v.*).

Perihelion. That point in a planet's orbit when it is nearest to the sun; opposite of aphelion. The earth is at perihelion ($1 \cdot 47 \times 10^8$ km) in mid-winter, about 3 January.

Peripatus, an animal which stands as a link between the annelid worms and the arthropods. Wormlike with short unjointed legs it breathes by a system of air tubes like those in insects. Certain other points of internal structure point to a relationship with annelid worms. There are some fifty species, the best known being the S. African *Peripatus capensis*.

Perjury, the offence of giving false evidence. The ancient Romans threw the perjurer from the Tarpeian Rock, and after the Empire was Christianised, those who swore falsely upon the Gospel had their tongues cut out. The usual punishment in England from the 16th to the 19th cent. was the pillory, fine and imprisonment.

Permian Formation, a group of rocks lying between the Trias and the Carboniferous strata. It has three subdivisions, Upper, Middle and Lower Permian. *See* **F48.**

Per Procurationem signature means that the subject of the correspondence has been put into the writer's care by his principal for him to use his personal judgment in the matter, and that he is authorised to sign on behalf of his principal. Normally contracted to *per pro* or *p.p.*

Peruke, the name given to the wigs worn by men in the latter half of the 18th cent. The custom of wearing wigs was gradually superseded by powdering the natural hair. Wigs are still worn by the Speaker of the House of Commons, judges and barristers.

Petrel, the name given to a member of a large, widely-distributed family of sea-birds of great diversity of size and colouring and distinguished by tube-like external nostrils. They usually skim low over the waves, and some, for this reason, are known as shearwaters. The storm petrel or Mother Carey's chicken occasionally patters along the surface, and is often called Little Peter—a reference to St. Peter walking on the water. Except when breeding, petrels are always at sea. They mostly nest in holes and crevices on islands and lay one egg, which

is invariably white. The storm petrel, Leach's petrel, Manx shearwater and the fulmar petrel are resident in the British Isles. *See also* **Mutton Bird.**

Petroleum. *See* **Oil.**

Pewter, alloy of tin and lead formerly used for making household utensils and ornaments.

pH Value. Introduced in 1909 by the Danish chemist Sørensen to indicate hydrogen-ion concentration on the basis of electrical conductivity and a view of ionisation since discarded; is now taken as a logarithmic scale of acidity or alkalinity of aqueous solutions: acidity 0–7, neutrality at $7 \cdot 0$, alkalinity 7–14. The *pH* of blood is about $7 \cdot 6$ (faintly alkaline).

Phalanger, pouched marsupial mammals. They are arboreal and superficially resemble squirrels. There are two genera of flying phalangers or flying squirrels, which have a remarkable membrane along each side of the body enabling the animals to glide through the air. The members of the phalanger family are confined to the Australasian and oriental regions.

Phalangid, a member of the arachnid family Phalangida: popularly known as "harvesters".

Phalanx, a name applied by the ancient Greeks to a body of pike-men drawn up in close array, with overlapping shields, and eight, ten or more rows deep. The Macedonians stood sixteen rows deep. As many as 500 men could be in the front row.

Pharisees and Sadducees, two ancient Jewish sects. *See* **Judaism, Section J.**

Pharmacopoeia, an official publication containing information on the recognised drugs used in medicine. Each country has its own pharmacopoeia. The British Pharmacopoeia (B.P.) is published under the direction of the General Medical Council. The Pharmaceutical Society issues the British Pharmaceutical Codex (B.P.C.); there is also an International Pharmacopoeia (2 vols.) which is issued by the World Health Organisation.

Pharos, the name of the first lighthouse, built by Ptolemy II about 280 B.C., on the Isle of Pharos, at the entrance to the harbour of Alexandria. It was said to be 180 m high but this is doubtful. One of the "seven wonders".

Pheasant, game birds related to the partridges, quails, peacocks, chickens and turkeys, males distinguished by their brilliant plumage and long tapering tail. First found by the Greeks in Georgia where the River Phasis flows through to the Black Sea. Close time: 2 February to 30 September.

Phillippics, the oration delivered by Demosthenes, 352–341 B.C., against Philip of Macedon—remarkable for their acrimonious invective. The word was also used for Cicero's speeches against Antony. In modern use, any impassioned invective.

Philosopher's Stone. *See* **Alchemy, Section J.**

Phosphorus is a non-metal element, no. 15, symbol P. Most familiar as a waxy, yellow solid which is spontaneously inflammable in air. It has chemical similarities to arsenic, like which it is very poisonous. It was discovered by Brandt in urine in 1669. It is found in most animal and vegetable tissues. It is an essential element of all plants and of the bones of animals. In combination with various metals it forms different phosphates, which are largely utilised as manures. The chief commercial use of phosphorus is in the preparation of matches.

Photoelectric Cell, a device which gives a useful electrical response to light falling on it. There are several kinds depending on the different effects which light may have on a suitably chosen solid (usually a semiconductor), viz., the emission of electrons from the surface ("photo-emissive cell"); change in electrical resistance ("photoconducting cell"); generation of electric current from a specially designed sensitive structure ("barrier layer" or "photo-voltaic cell", "solar battery"). Different cells respond differently to lights of various wavelength and must be chosen for each application. *See also* **Solar Battery.**

Photogrammetry, the science of measurement from photographs taken from an aircraft. Aerial photography has many uses and is of great value to military intelligence and for map-making.

Photon. When light behaves like a stream of discrete particles and not like waves, the particles are called photons. See **F14, 16.**

Photosynthesis. See **F32**(1), **43**(2).

Phrenology. See **Section J.**

Phylloxera, a genus of plant-lice related to the aphids, which attacks the grape vine. Many vineyards of France, in common with the rest of Europe, were replanted with immune vines grafted on immune stocks from California in 1879 after being ravaged by the insect (which came from America). Curiously enough, the remedy also came from America, the vine stocks there being immune to *phylloxera.*

Pi is the unique number denoted by the Greek letter π and obtained by dividing the length of the circumference of any circle by its diameter. Its value is approximately 3·14159.

Picts, inhabitants of Scotland in pre-Roman times, are held by some historians to be a branch of the old Celtic race, by others to have been of Scythian origin. They occupied the north-eastern portion of Scotland, and were subdued by the Scots in Argyll in the 9th cent., Kenneth MacAlpin becoming king of a united kingdom of the Picts and Scots—the kingdom of Alban.

Pike, a familiar fresh-water fish abundant in the temperate regions of both hemispheres. It forms good sport for the angler in rivers and lakes, and sometimes attains a weight of from 9–13 kg. It is extremely voracious, is covered with small scales and has a ferocious-looking head.

Pilchard, a fish of the herring family, but with smaller scales and more rounded body. It appears off the Cornish coasts in vast shoals every summer.

Pilgrimage. The undertaking of a journey to a distant place or shrine to satisfy a religious vow or secure spiritual benefit, was resorted to in early Christian times. The first recorded pilgrimage is that of the Empress Helena to Jerusalem in 326. In thhe Middle Ages pilgrimages became common, and were undertaken by monarchs and people of rank in all Christian countries. Moslems have been making pilgrimages to Mecca since the death of the Prophet, such duty being enjoined by the Koran. Among the great centres of Christian pilgrimages are Jerusalem, Rome, the tomb of Becket at Canterbury and the holy places of Lourdes and La Salette in France.

Pilgrimage of Grace (1536), the rising in Lincolnshire and Yorkshire in the reign of Henry VIII against religious innovations and the dissolution of the smaller monasteries, which overlapped with discontents caused by taxation, rising prices, enclosures and land speculation. The insurrection was followed by many executions.

Pilgrim Fathers, the 101 English Puritans who, after living some years in exile in Holland, to escape persecution in their own country, set sail for America in the *Mayflower,* 6 September 1620, landing at Plymouth, Mass., 4 December. They founded the settlement of Plymouth, and are regarded as the pioneers of American colonisation although 13 years earlier a small Virginian colony had been established.

Pillory, a wooden instrument of punishment in use in England until 1837. It consisted of a pair of movable boards with holes through which the culprit's head and hands were put, and was usually erected on a scaffold. While a person was undergoing this punishment the mob generally pelted him with stones and rubbish, sometimes to his serious injury. People convicted of forgery, perjury or libel were often condemned to the pillory, but from 1816–1837 the only offence for which it could be inflicted was perjury.

Pine, a conifer of the genus *Pinus,* which flourishes all over the northern hemisphere and includes 80–90 species, which afford valuable timber and yield turpentine and tar. The Scots Pine, *Pinus silvestris,* with its blue-green, short needles, set in pairs, and its rosy-orange branches, is native to Britain, as it is to the whole of Europe. It provides the red and yellow deal in everyday use.

Pitcairn Islanders were originally the mutineers of the *Bounty.* They took possession of the island in 1790, and it was not until 1814 that their whereabouts was ascertained, accidentally, by a passing ship. The mutineers, under their leader, Adams, had settled down to a communal existence, married Tahitian women and increased so in numbers that in the course of years they were too many for the island to support, and in 1856 they were removed by the British Government to Norfolk Island. A small number returned to Pitcairn.

Pitchblende *or* **Uraninite,** a relatively scarce mineral. It is nearly all uranium oxide, but lead, thorium, etc., are also present. Pitchblende from Joachimstal in Czechoslovakia was the material in which radium was discovered by the Curies. Other major sources are the Great Lakes region of Canada and Zaire.

Placebo, medical treatment that the therapist uses deliberately although he knows it is without any specific effect on the condition being treated. There may be various medical reasons for using placebos, *e.g.,* for the beneficial psychological effect on people who like to feel something is being done for them; for differentiating during clinical trials of a new treatment between those persons given the real thing and a control or comparison group of persons given a placebo or inactive imitation.

Plainsong, a style of musical composition sung in unison (all voices singing the same tune without harmony), familiar in the Western Church from very early times and still performed, principally in the Roman Catholic Church. Though restrained and contemplative in spirit, it is capable of expressing deep emotion. See **E3**(2).

Planetarium, a complex optical system which projects into the interior of a dome a replica of all the phenomena of the sky that can be seen by the naked eye, *e.g.,* sun, moon, planets, stars, comets, meteors, aurora, eclipses and clouds. There is a planetarium in the Marylebone Road, London. The world's largest (opened in 1987) is at Miyazaki, Japan.

Planets, the name given to such celestial bodies as revolve round the sun in elliptical orbits. The name was first used by the Greeks to indicate their difference from the fixed stars. There are nine major planets, Mercury, Venus, Earth, Mars, Jupiter, Saturn, Uranus, Neptune and Pluto. There are also a large number of minor planets or asteroids. Saturn, Uranus and Jupiter are ringed. Many important questions can be answered by means of probes sent to the neighbourhood of the planets. These include the measurement of the magnetic field, if any, of the planets, the study of their atmospheres, much of which can be done without actually penetrating to the surface. With instruments landed gently on the surface it is possible to investigate surface conditions and composition by many methods. Even without a soft-landing information on these questions can be obtained by photography and subsequent transmission of the picture back to earth by some form of television scanning. The US Mars probe *Mariner IV* transmitted pictures of the Martian surface in 1965, the Russian *Venus IV* in 1967 made a soft-landing on Venus, and the US *Pioneer 11* came within 43,000 km of Jupiter in December 1974. Two US *Voyager* spacecraft were launched in 1977 flying by Jupiter (1979), Saturn (1980, 1981) Uranus (1986) and Neptune (1989), sending back exciting new data. *See* under their names for further details.

Plankton, a word which first came into biological use in 1886 to describe the usually microscopic plants and animals floating, swimming and drifting in the surface waters of the sea. To be distinguished from *nekton* (swimming animals like fishes and squids) and *benthos* (plants and animals living on the sea bottom, like fixed algae, sponges, oysters, crabs, etc.). Of great economic importance, providing food for fish and whales.

Plantagenets, the kings who reigned in England between 1154 and 1485 and included the Houses of Lancaster and York. More correctly they are styled Angevins, from Anjou, of which Geoffrey, father of Henry II, was Count, and whose badge was a sprig of broom (*Planta genista*).

Plasma Physics is the physics of wholly ionised gases, *i.e.,* gases in which the atoms initially present have lost practically the whole of the electrons that usually surround their nuclei, so that the gas consists of a mixture of two components, positively charged ions and negatively charged electrons. The physical properties of a *plasma* are very different from those of an unionised gas. In particular, a plasma has a high electrical conductivity and can carry large currents. *See also* **Nuclear Fusion.**

Plastics, a broad term covering those substances which become plastic when subjected to increased temperatures or pressures. The Plastics Industry is based on synthetic organic examples of this group. There are two classes of plastics: the *thermoplastic,* which become plastic every time they are heated (*e.g.* cellulosic plastics) and *thermosetting,* which undergo chemical change when heated, so that once set they cannot be rendered plastic again (*e.g.,* Bakelite). Plastics are composed of long-chained molecules, *e.g.,* polyethylene.

Plate Tectonics, the contemporary and by now well-developed theory of the movements of the earth's crust. The view is that the surface of the Earth consists of about a dozen rigid plates, some larger than continents, some much smaller, all in ceaseless motion relative to one another. Their separation and approach and their friction and collision are closely related to the evolution of mountain ranges, oceans and rift valleys and to phenomena like earthquakes and volcanoes. *See* **F9.**

Platinum, a metallic element, no. 78, symbol Pt. It is a scarce white metal generally allied with iridium, osmium, ruthenium and palladium. It can only be melted in an oxyhydrogen or electric furnace, but can be rolled out into a film-like sheet, or drawn out to the finest wire; being resistant to acids it is termed a noble metal.

Platonic Solids, five regular solid figures known to the ancient world. They are: the tetrahedron (4 triangular faces), cube (6 square faces), octahedron (8 triangular faces), dodecahedron (12 five-sided faces), icosahedron (20 triangular faces). All the faces and angles of each solid are identical.

Pleiades, famous cluster of stars in the constellation of Taurus. Of the seven principal stars in the group, one is rather faint, and many myths have sprung up about this "lost Pleiad". *See also* **I23.**

Pleistocene, the geological period that succeeded the Pliocene. During the Pleistocene, also known as the *Great Ice Age,* there were four cold periods, when the ice sheets covered northern Europe and N. America, separated by warm periods when the glaciers drew back into the mountains. From recent studies based on rock magnetic measurements the transition to Pleistocene took place *c.* 1,850,000 years ago.

Pliocene, the geological period preceding the Pleistocene, and the last major division of the Tertiary strata. It began about fifteen million years ago. *See* **Section F.**

Plough Monday, the first Monday after the Epiphany, when in olden times the rustic population returned to work after the Christmas festivities.

Plover, wading birds, widely distributed over marshy places of Europe. Several species occur in Britain, including the Golden-plover, which breeds on the moors of Devon, Somerset, Wales, N.E. Yorkshire and Scotland, and the Ringed plover, Kentish plover and Dotterel.

Pluto, the last planet to be discovered was searched for following the 1914 predictions of P. Lowell and discovered by C. W. Tombaugh at the Flagstaff Observatory in Arizona in January 1930. Generally the most distant of the planets its orbit is much more elliptical than the other planetary orbits and so it sometimes approaches the sun closer than Neptune. It was thought to be different from the other outer Jovian planets which are gaseous and to consist of rock covered in frozen methane gas. Recently the size of Pluto has been revised downwards by interferometric measurement of its diameter. The latest value is between 3,000 and 3,500 km, close to the size of our moon. Pluto's own moon, Charon, was also detected by earth-based telescopes using special photometric measurements. *See* **F8.**

Plutonium, a chemical element, no. 94, symbol Pu, capable of nuclear fission in the same way as Uranium 235. Not until after it had been synthesised in atomic piles during the second world war was it shown to occur in infinitesimally small traces in nature. Its synthesis in the atomic pile depends on the capture by Uranium 238 nuclei of neutrons; immediate product of this reaction is the element neptunium, but this undergoes rapid radioactive disintegration to plutonium.

Poet Laureate is the poet attached to the royal household, an office officially established in 1668, though its origins go back to the early Middle Ages, when minstrels were employed at the courts of English kings. Chaucer, Skelton and Spenser, though not court poets, were all unofficial poets laureate. Ben Jonson has been called the first "official laureate" (1616), but the office was not officially recognised until 1668, when Dryden was formally granted the office. It is customary for the poet laureate to write verse in celebration of events of national importance. Ted Hughes (*see* **B33**) became Poet Laureate in December 1984 after the death of Sir John Betjeman.

Pogrom. Russian word meaning "destruction". First used to describe the Csarist attacks on the Jews in 1881 in Russia. In 1938 Hitler ordered a general pogrom in Germany: all synagogues were destroyed and nearly all Jewish shops and homes, Jewish hospitals and children's homes suffered. During the subsequent war Jews of central Europe were systematically exterminated in cold blood by the Nazis.

Poitiers, Battle of, was fought on 19 September 1356, during the Hundred Years' War, when Edward the Black Prince gained a complete victory over John, King of France, who was taken prisoner and brought to London.

Polecat, an animal of a dark-brown colour, about 46 cm in length, exclusive of tail; the ears and face-markings are white or light brown. It is carnivorous and belongs to the weasel family.

Pole-Star is of the second magnitude, and the last in the tail of the Little Bear constellation. Being near the North pole of the heavens—never more than about one degree from due north—it always remains visible in the Northern hemisphere; hence its use as a guide to seamen.

Police, a regular force established for the preservation of law and order and the prevention and detection of crime. The powers they have vary from country to country and with the type of government; the more civilised and democratic the state, the less police intervention. England, compared with countries abroad, was slow to develop a police force, and it was not until 1829 that Sir Robert Peel's Metropolitan Police Act established a regular force for the metropolis, later legislation establishing county and borough forces maintained by local police authorities throughout England and Wales. Up to that time police duties were discharged by individual constables and watchmen appointed by local areas in England and Wales. The police service in Great Britain today is organised in a number of forces (43 in England and Wales and 6 regional and 2 combined forces in Scotland). In Northern Ireland there is a single force (the Royal Ulster Constabulary). In England and Wales the forces are defined according to area of responsibility:

1. County forces, under a police committee consisting of local councillors and magistrates.

2. Combined forces, covering more than one county, also under a police committee consisting of local councillors and magistrates and representatives from each constituent area.

3. The Metropolitan Police Force, covering an area within a 15-mile (24-km) radius of Charing Cross, but excluding the City of London, under the control of the Home Secretary. Strength *c.* 26,000.

4. The City of London force operating in the area of the city, under the Court of Common Council.

In Scotland the police authority is the regional or island council. Police ranks are: chief constable, assistant chief constable, chief superintendent, superintendent, chief inspector, inspector, sergeant and constable. In the Metropolitan Police area the chief officer is the Commissioner of Police of the Metropolis.

Central authority rests with the Home Secretary in England and Wales and the Secretary of State for Scotland. In the present troubles in Northern Ireland responsibility for law and order is retained at Westminster.

Poll Tax, popular name for the Community Charge, which replaces the rates. It was introduced in Scotland in April 1989 and in England and Wales in April 1990 despite great public opposition. *See* **Section H, Special Topic.**

Pollution of the atmosphere is due chiefly to the incomplete combustion of fuels, especially coal, large particles of soot being deposited fairly quickly close to their place of origin and smaller particles (including smoke) remaining suspended in the air for a long time. Invisible air pollutants include sulphur dioxide from power stations and home heating, and carbon monoxide from cars. The introduction of more efficient furnaces, the washing of flue gases and the introduction of smokeless zones have assisted in the abatement of smoke and other forms of pollution. "Smog" (smoke-laden fog) which reduces visibility to zero and affects the respiratory organs, is liable to occur when the air near the earth is cooled below the dew-point temperature by radiation on a still, cloudless night when an accumulation of smoke over a large city cuts off daylight and produces gloom, and absence of wind or vertical currents prevents the lower layers of the air from getting away. Such conditions are associated with the smoke-laden atmosphere of large industrial towns during a winter anticyclone. During the great London smog of 1952 there were 2,000 deaths over and above those expected for the time of year. Since the Clean Air Act of 1956 pollution by smoke and sulphur dioxide has continued to diminish in London, winter sunshine has increased by 70 per cent, and fish now live in the Thames. Some other pollution problems which have been in the public eye are: disposal of nuclear waste (**L89**), acid rain (**L3**), contamination of coastal waters and shores by oil slicks; possibility of depletion of the ozone layer (**L92**). This layer protects us from excessive amounts of ultraviolet radiation and there has been concern that it is being depleted because of pollution with fluorocarbons (**L45**). The carbon dioxide balance is being disturbed by the burning of fossil fuels (**L22**) and it has been calculated that doubling of carbon dioxide concentration would increase earth's surface temperature by 2–3°C.

Polonium, a radioactive element, no. 84, symbol Po, discovered by Madame Curie in 1898, and named after her native land of Poland.

Polymerisation is the linking together of small molecules to make a large long-chain molecule. The general name for polymers of ethylene is Polythene, a wax-like plastic solid which because of its special qualities is used in a variety of ways today.

Polytheism. *See* **God and Man, Section J.**

Pomology, the science of fruit-growing.

Pontifex, the title assigned in ancient Rome to members of the college of pontifices. "Pontifex maximus" was the official head of Roman religion. It was as "pontifex maximus" that Julius Caesar revised the calendar in 46 B.C., and when after the rise of Christianity the Popes took over the title the revision fell to them.

Pope, The, the head of the Roman Catholic Church, recognised by that Church as the lawful successor of St. Peter. He is elected by the body of Cardinals. Since 1870, when the King of Italy deposed the holder from temporal power, no Pope had left the Vatican between appointment and death until 1929, when peace was made between the Church and State in Italy and compensation was paid to the Holy See for the loss of temporal power. Cardinal Karol Wojtyla, Archbishop of Cracow, was elected Pope John Paul II in 1978, following the sudden death of Pope John Paul I.

Porcelain. The word is thought to be derived from the Italian *porcellana,* indicating the texture of a piglet. The majority of porcelain made on the continent was of "hard-paste", or true porcelain, similar to that discovered by the Chinese as early as the T'ang Dynasty (A.D. 618–907). It was composed of *kaolin* (china-clay) and *petuntse* (china-stone) which when fired in a kiln at a temperature of *c.* 1300°C became an extremely hard and translucent material. The recipe of "hard-paste" porcelain remained a secret of the Chinese until 1709, when it was re-discovered in Europe by Johann Böttger of the Meissen factory (popularly known as Dresden). Aided by disloyal Meissen workmen, factories were later established at Vienna, Venice and in many parts of Germany. Plymouth and Bristol were the only English factories to produce this type of porcelain, from 1768 to 1781. Elsewhere, both in England and France, the material manufactured was known as "soft-paste" or artificial porcelain which was made by blending varying white-firing clays with the ingredients of glass. The French factory of Sèvres began to make some hard-paste porcelain by 1768 and by the 19th cent. such porcelain was the only type being made throughout the whole of the continent. In England Josiah Spode is credited with the introduction of "bone-china" about 1794. This hybrid-paste was quickly adopted by many other factories and remains the most popular type of English porcelain.

Porphyry, a form of crystalline rock of many varieties that in ancient Egypt was quarried and used for the decorative portions of buildings and vessels. The term is applied generally to the eruptive rocks in which large well-formed crystals of one mineral are set in a matrix of other minerals.

Porpoise, a highly intelligent marine mammal of the dolphin and whale family, and a common inhabitant of northern seas. Porpoises travel in shoals, their progression being marked by constant leapings and plungings. Their average length is from 1·2–1·5 m. There are several species, nearly all being confined to northern oceans.

Port, a special kind of red Portuguese wine, taking its name from Oporto. It was little known in England until the Methuen Treaty of 1703, when it was permitted to be imported at a low duty.

Portland Vase, one of the most renowned specimens of ancient art, long in the possession of the Portland family. In 1810 it was loaned to the British Museum. Here it was shattered in 1845 by a stone from a maniac's hand, but has been skilfully restored. It is said to have been found in the 17th cent. in an ancient tomb near Rome. It was purchased from the Barberini family in 1770 by Sir Wm. Hamilton, subsequently sold to the Duchess of Portland. The vase, which is actually a two-handled urn, stands about 25 cm high, is of transparent dark blue glass, ornamented with figures cut in relief in overlaid white opaque glass. It was purchased by the British Museum in 1945. *See also* **Glass.**

Portreeve in olden times was an official appointed to superintend a port or harbour, and before the name of mayor was used the chief magistrate of London was styled the Portreeve.

Positivism. *See* **Section J.**

Positron, the "positive electron", an atomic particle having the same mass but an electric charge equal but opposite to that of an electron. It was discovered in 1932. *See also* **F16.**

Post-Impressionism, a term introduced by Roger Fry to describe the exhibition of paintings sponsored by himself in London (1910–11) officially entitled "Manet and the Post-Impressionists". The exhibition included paintings by Manet, Cézanne, Gauguin, Van Gogh, Seurat, Signac, works by Matisse, Rouault and the *Fauves (q.v.),* and sculpture by Maillol. In a second exhibition, held in 1912, Picasso and the Cubists were also represented. The term therefore refers to the movement in modern art which reacted against the transient naturalism of the Impressionists by concerning itself primarily with colour, form and solidity. Most artists today would include Cézanne, Van Gogh and Gauguin as the main Post-Impressionists and maintain that it prepared the way for Fauvism, Cubism and Expressionism.

Potassium, a metal, no. 19, symbol K (German *Kalium*). It is similar to sodium, reacting violently with water. It was discovered by Sir Humphry Davy in 1807, and is now generally obtained by the electrolysis of fused potassium hydroxide or chloride/fluoride mixture. Its principal minerals are caranallite and kainite, and it is relatively common in rocks, accounting for about 2¼% of the earth's crust. An essential element for healthy plant growth; the ashes of plants are relatively rich in potassium.

Potsdam Agreement was signed by Truman, Stalin and Attlee in August 1945. By this Agreement a Council of Foreign Ministers was established, representing the five principal Powers: China, France, Soviet Russia, the United Kingdom and United States of America, with the task of drawing up the peace treaties for submission to the United Nations. It laid down, *inter alia*, that German militarism and Hitlerism should be destroyed; that industrial power should be so reduced that Germany would never again be in a position to wage aggressive war; that surplus equipment should be destroyed or transferred to replace wrecked plant in allied territories; that Germany should be treated as an economic whole; and that local self-government should be restored on democratic lines as rapidly as was consistent with military security. The Potsdam Agreement became a dead letter with the creation of a communist régime in the Russian zone of Germany, and marked the beginning of the "cold war".

Prado Gallery, the great public picture collection of Madrid, containing a superb collection of paintings by Velasquez, Murillo, Raphael, Titian, Dürer, Van Dyck, Rubens and Goya.

Pragmatism. *See* **Section J.**

Prefect, chief magistrates in ancient Rome. The title is now applied to the chiefs of administration of the departments of France.

Pre-Raphaelite Brotherhood was the name given to their school of thought by three British artists, Dante Gabriel Rossetti, J. E. Millais and W. Holman Hunt, who in 1848 revolted against the academic art of their time and advocated a return to the style of the Italian painters prior to Raphael—the simple naturalism of the Primitives, such as Botticelli, Fra Angelico and Filippo Lippi. Thus they avoided the use of heavy shadows and painted on a white ground in bright colours—a technique which aroused the ire of those used to the dark and murky canvases of the contemporary romantic artists. Although they held these principles in common the three members of the "P.R.B.", as it was popularly called, were really quite different in other respects. Thus Rossetti (who for some reason is always thought of as the typical Pre-Raphaelite) produced works of a highly romanticised mediaevalism which, apart from certain aspects of technique, bear not the slightest resemblance to the sentimental naturalism of Millais or the much more dramatic realism of Holman Hunt (*e.g.*, in *The Scapegoat*). The Brotherhood was later joined by a number of lesser artists, but its works are not commonly accepted with enthusiasm today when the general feeling is that they are sentimental and religiose rather than the product of deeply-felt emotions. Ruskin in his writings defended their work but the movement came to an end in 1853.

Presbyterianism. *See* **Section J.**

Press-Gang, a body of sailors employed to impress men into naval service, frequently resorted to in England, especially during the war with France in the early 19th cent. Press gangs were not used after about 1850.

Primitive Art. The word "primitive" has a number of different meanings: (1) the art of prehistoric communities (*e.g.*, the famous animal cave-drawings of the Aurignacians, *c.* 25,000 B.C., at Altamira in Spain); (2) the art of modern primitive communities (*e.g.*, Bushman rock-paintings); (3) child art; (4) peasant art which springs from a spontaneous desire to impart beauty to objects of daily use and shows a tendency towards abstraction. Peasant art has many features in common the world over, the woodcarving of the Norsemen being almost indistinguishable from that of the Maoris; (5) the modern school of primitive painting in which naïveté of presentation is either the aim of a highly sophisticated mind (*e.g.*, the self-taught French painter Le Douanier Rousseau (d. 1910), or arises naturally from a simple one (the American "grandma" Moses (d. 1961) who began to paint in her seventies).

Printing by movable types was first used in Europe in 1454 by Johann Gutenberg, a citizen of Mainz. The invention is also claimed for Laurens Koster of Haarlem. It was introduced into England by Caxton, who set up a printing press in Westminster in 1476. Gothic characters were first used, being superseded by Roman letters in 1518. In 1798 Earl Stanhope replaced the wood printing press by one of iron. In 1814 Friedrich Koenig applied the principle of steam power to the press. Mr. John Walter, of *The Times* newspaper, was the first to use the steam press. Improvements were introduced by Applegarth and Cowper in 1828 and great strides were made in 1858 when the Hoe machine was put on the market. Then came the Walter press in 1866 which printed on continuous rolls of paper from curved stereotyped plates. The Monotype machine casts single letters and the Linotype whole lines. The term letterpress is used for all printing methods using plates where the characters stand in *relief*. The other main printing methods are *intaglio* and *planographic*. The development of computer technology using electronic methods has introduced a new era in printing.

The Privy Council is the Sovereign's own council, consisting of about 300 persons who have reached eminence in some branch of public affairs (Cabinet ministers must be Privy Counsellors), on whose advice and through which the Sovereign exercises his or her statutory and a number of prerogative powers. From it have sprung many organs of the constitution and many of our government departments have grown from committees of the Privy Council. For example the Judiciary or courts of justice have grown from the Sovereign's Council sitting as a Court of Justice, and today the Judicial Committee of the Privy Council is a body of distinguished lawyers acting as a Court of Appeal from courts of the Commonwealth.

Probation Officers are attached to particular Courts, sometimes a Magistrates' or a higher court. Sometimes an offender is not sentenced to punishment, but is released "on probation", that is on the condition that he behaves well and follows directions given by the Court or by a probation officer. Such an officer is a trained man (or woman) who advises, assists and befriends people who are placed under his supervision by a court of law. The probation officer, by his assessment of the social background of the offender, can advise the court upon the wisdom of putting the offender on probation. The probation officer by his understanding can so befriend an offender as to provide a basis for his rehabilitation. He undertakes the "after care" of those released from prison or Borstal.

Productivity. Physical productivity is the output of products during a time unit, *e.g.*, so many products per man hour, or day, or year. Total productivity is the sum of all the units of product created during the given time. Labour productivity is the part of the total that is attributed to labour as a factor of production. Productivity of capital is the element attributed to capital as a factor. Productivity of land is the element attributed to the natural powers of the soil, as distinct from what is contributed by the application to it of capital or labour. The term productivity is also used to refer not to the quantity of output, but to its money value.

Propane, a colourless inflammable gas made of carbon and hydrogen; formula C_3H_8. It is easily liquefied and transported liquid in cylinders and tanks. In this form it is familiar as a "portable gas supply" for domestic and industrial uses. It is sometimes mixed with butane (*q.v.*) for this purpose. Propane occurs in natural gas and is a by-product of oil refining.

Proteins are the main chemical substances of living matter: they are a part of every living cell and are found in all animals and plants. All proteins are basically constructed of carbon hydrogen, oxygen and nitrogen, and some contain sulphur, phosphorus (nucleoproteins) and iron (haemoglobin). Proteins are built up of very long chains of amino-acids connected by amide linkages (the synthetic polymers such as "nylon" and casein plastics (from milk) are built up of the same linkages). The structure of protein molecules allows a variety of function. Enzymes, which bring about chemical reactions in living cells, are proteins having specific properties. See **F32–3**, *also* Diet, Section P.

Proton, a basic constituent of the atomic nucleus, positively charged, having a mass about 1836 times that of the electron. It is a positive hydrogen ion. See **F13(2), 16.**

Prout's hypothesis. The English chemist William Prout (1785–1850) advanced the idea that all atoms are made of hydrogen, and their weights are exact multiples of the weight of a hydrogen atom. With the modification that neutrons as well as protons occur in the nucleus, Prout's belief, though rejected for many years, has been substantially vindicated.

Provost, a Scottish official similar in rank to an English mayor. The Provosts of Edinburgh, Glasgow, Aberdeen, Perth and Dundee are styled Lords Provost. The title of provost is also given to the heads of certain colleges.

Prud'hommes (Prudent Men), **Councils of,** were French trade tribunals, of masters and workmen, formed to decide on disputes. Originally a mediaeval institution, they were revived by Napoleon in 1806, and were carried on by the Third Republic.

Psalms, Book of, for many years attributed to David, but present-day scholars are of opinion that the psalms were written by a series of authors at different times and for different purposes, and that few, if any, were written by David. The Holy Scriptures contain 150.

Psychedelism. See Section J.

Psychic Research. See Section J.

Psychoanalysis. See Section J.

Ptarmigan, birds of the grouse family, one species of which inhabits the Scottish Highlands. In the winter the bird assumes a white plumage.

Ptomaines, amino acids produced during the putrefaction of proteins of animal origin. Not a cause of food poisoning, as was once generally supposed, which is almost invariably due to certain specific bacteria.

Publicans, under the Roman Empire, were people who farmed the public taxes. It is this class of officials that is alluded to in the "publicans and sinners" phrase in the New Testament.

Public Corporations, statutory bodies which operate major industries and services in the public interest, *e.g.,* UK Atomic Energy Authority, Bank of England, B.B.C., Electricity Authorities, Gas Council, British Coal Corporation, British Steel Corporation, British Railways Board, the Post Office, British National Oil Corporation, British Nuclear Fuels, British Airports Authority. They are accountable to Parliament but their staffs are not civil servants. The present government is pursuing a policy of privatisation of many of these bodies, and several (*e.g.* British Gas plc) are now public companies.

Public Schools. The Public Schools Act of 1864 named nine "public" schools: Eton, Harrow, Rugby, Winchester, Westminster, Shrewsbury, Charterhouse, St. Paul's and Merchant Taylors. Today the term embraces many more, and can be applied to all those schools which are financed by bodies other than the State and whose headmasters belong to the Headmasters' Conference as distinct from the Headmasters' Association. There are about 200 such schools in Britain, including among others: Bedford School (founded 1552); Bradfield College, Berks. (1850); Charterhouse, Godalming (1611); Cheltenham College (1841); Christ's Hospital, Horsham (1553); City of London (1442); Clifton College, Bristol (1862); Dulwich College (1619); Eton College (1440); Felsted, Dunmow, Essex (1564); Haileybury College (1862); Harrow (1571); King Edward's, Birmingham (1552); King's School, Canterbury (600); Malvern College (1865); Manchester Grammar School (1515); Marlborough College (1843); Merchant Taylors' (1561); Mill Hill (1807); Oundle (1556); Radley College, Abingdon (1847); Repton, Derbyshire (1557); Rugby School (1567); St. Albans (948); St. Paul's (1509); Sevenoaks School (1418); Sherborne (1550); Shrewsbury School (1552); Stonyhurst College (1593); Stowe School, Bucks. (1923); Tonbridge (1553); Uppingham, Leics. (1584); Warwick (914); Wellington College (1859); Westminster (1560); Winchester College (1382). Public schools for girls include: Christ's Hos-

pital, Hertford (1552), Cheltenham Ladies' College (founded by Miss Beale in 1853), North London Collegiate School (founded by Miss Buss in 1850), Roedean (1885), Wycombe Abbey (1806). Many public schools are now co-educational. It is now proposed to rename Public Schools as Independent Schools.

Pulsars, cosmic objects discovered in 1967 by the Radio Astronomy group at Cambridge; of great scientific interest, since they are probably neutron stars, and extremely dense. Unlike quasars (*q.v.*) they are nearby objects within our own galaxy. See **F5.**

Puma, mountain-lion or cougar, a large wild cat found throughout the Americas. It looks like a lean greyish lioness.

Pyramidology. See Section J.

Pyramids of Egypt, on the west bank of the Nile, are vast stone or brick-built structures with inner chambers and subterranean entrances, built by the Pharaohs as royal tombs and dating from about 3000 B.C. The most celebrated are at Gizeh built during the 4th dynasty. The largest, originally 147 m high, is called the Great Pyramid, one of the seven wonders of the world, built by the Pharaoh Khufu, better known as Cheops, and there he was buried. 100,000 men, according to Herodotus, being employed for 20 years upon it. Chephren, successor of Cheops, erected the second pyramid, and the third was built by Mycerinus, a son of Cheops. The pyramid at Meidum built by King Snefru, founder of the 4th dynasty, is the most imposing of all.

Pythons, large snakes, non-poisonous and destroying their prey by crushing it. Some species may reach 9 m in length, and prey upon deer and other small mammals. Found in Asia, Africa and Australia. They lay eggs.

Q

Quadrant, an astronomical instrument for measuring altitudes, superseded for navigational purposes in modern times by the sextant. It consists of a graduated arc of 90° with a movable radius for measuring angles on it.

Quai d'Orsay. An embankment in Paris where the French Foreign Office is situated.

Quail, an edible bird of the partridge family, of which only one species, the Common Quail, is found in England. It is not more than 20 cm long. It is found in most of the warmer regions of the world. In England and Wales the Quail is covered by the Wild Bird Protection Acts.

Quantum Theory. The rapid development of quantum theory has been almost entirely due to the experimental and theoretical study of the interactions between electromagnetic radiation and matter. One of the first steps was taken when it was discovered that the electrons emitted from metals due to the action of ultra-violet radiation have an energy which is not related to the intensity of the incident radiation, but is dependent on its wavelength. Einstein showed in 1905 that this could only be explained on the basis that energy is transferred between radiation and matter in finite amounts, or *quanta,* which are inversely proportional to wavelength. See **F17(2).**

Quarks are hypothetical subnuclear particles recently postulated by theoretical physicists concerned with the so-called elementary particles. There may be three kinds, possibly more, all carrying electrical charges which are fractions of those carried by familiar particles like electrons and protons. This and other special properties of quarks make them suitable for explaining the existence of the large number of other particles referred to on **F16–17.** The physical existence of quarks may be demonstrated by experiment at any time and if this happens it will be an exciting triumph for speculative theoretical physics. See **F15(2).**

Quartering, in heraldry, is the disposition of various escutcheons or coats of arms in their proper "quarters" of the family shield, in such order as indicates the alliances with other families.

Quartermaster, a military officer charged with the provisioning and superintendence of soldiers in camp or barracks, and holding the equivalent rank to a lieutenant. The Quartermaster-General is an officer who presides over the provisioning department of the whole army. A Quartermaster in the Navy is a petty officer responsible to the Officer of the Watch; at sea for the correct steering of the ship and in harbour for the running of the ship's routine.

Quarto, a sheet of paper folded twice to make four leaves, or eight pages; abbreviated to "4to".

Quartz is a common and usually colourless mineral, occurring both crystallised and massive. In the first form it is in hexagonal prisms, terminating in pyramids. When pure its specific gravity is 2·66. It is one of the constituents of granite, gneiss, etc. Among the quartz varieties are *rock crystal* (colourless), *smoky quartz* (yellow or brown), *amethyst* (purple), *rose quartz* (pink) and *milky quartz* (white). Quartz veins in metamorphic rocks may yield rich deposits of gold. Mining for gold in the rock is termed quartz-mining.

Quasars, or in preferred terminology, quasi-stellar radio-sources, form a new class of astronomical objects, first identified in the period 1960 to 1962. They have enormous energy output, and are at vast distances. Many are strong sources of radio waves and fluctuate in intensity. There is still controversy over the nature of these objects. We presently consider that the intense emission comes from a relatively small region at the centre of peculiar galaxies. While a plausible explanation would be the existence of a gigantic black hole formed by the gravitational collapse of the nucleus of the galaxy, dragging in surrounding material, including entire star systems, our information is not yet conclusive. *See* **F5.**

Queen Anne's Bounty, established by Queen Anne in 1704 for the augmentation of the maintenance of the poor clergy. Since 1 April 1948 Queen Anne's Bounty and the Ecclesiastical Commissioners ceased to exist and became embodied in the Church Commissioners for England.

Queen's (or **King's**) **Speech** is the speech prepared by the Government in consultation with the Queen and delivered by Her Majesty in person or by her deputy, at the opening or closing of a Parliamentary session.

Quinine, a vegetable alkaloid obtained from the bark of several trees of the *Cinchona* genus. It is colourless and extremely bitter. The drug, sulphate of quinine, is one of the most valuable medicines, forming a powerful tonic. It is antiperiodic, antipyretic and antineuralgic. In cases of malaria it is the most efficacious remedy of natural origin known.

Quirinal, one of the seven hills of Rome.

Quisling, term which came into use during the second world war to denote traitor, collaborator or fifth-columnist. After Vidkun Quisling, who became head of the puppet government after the German invasion of Norway in 1940.

Quorum, the number of members of any body or company necessary to be present at any meeting or commission before business can be transacted. The House of Commons needs a quorum of 40, the Lords a quorum of 3.

R

Rabbi, a Jewish term applied to specially ordained officials who pronounce upon questions of legal form and ritual, and also generally accorded to any Jewish scholar of eminence.

Raccoon, plantigrade carnivorous mammals common to the American continent. There are several species. The common Raccoon (*Procyon lotor*) is about 60 cm long, with a bush ringed tail and sharp snout. Its skin is valuable.

Race. In the old text-books anthropologists were much concerned with the differences between the various races of Man; they described the Black Man (Negro), the Yellow Man (Mongol), the Red Man (American Indian), the Brown Man (Indian), and the White Man (European). Those who study Man from this point of view further subdivide each group into others. Thus White Man may be divided into

Nordic, Alpine and Mediterranean; Black Man into Hamitic, Bushman and so on. Each of these groups tends to have physical traits which its members hold in common, although, of course, there are no *pure* racial types. All existing races have been fairly thoroughly mixed. What, in view of recent experience, is really important, is that races or even nations do not have psychological traits—at least not *innate* traits. Anthropology dismisses all theories of a superior race as unscientific: there is not the slightest evidence that one race differs in any way from another in its psychological potentialities; Jews, Irish, Scots, Italians do differ (so do the inhabitants of Edinburgh and London): but their differences are due to their situation and not to anything inborn. *See* **Racism, Section J.**

Raceme, an inflorescence in which the main stem bears stalked flowers, *e.g.,* lupin, foxglove. The youngest flowers at the tip of this axis.

Radar. The basic principle of radar is very similar to that of sight. We switch on a light in the dark, and we *see* an object because the light waves are reflected from it and return to our eye, which is able to detect them. Similarly, the radar station *sees* an object because the invisible radio waves sent out from the transmitter are reflected from it and return to the receiver, which is able to detect them. Thus radar is the use of radio signals that man broadcasts.

The utilisation of radio waves for the detection of reflecting surfaces began with the classical experiment of the late Sir Edward Appleton in 1925, which he conducted in order to demonstrate the existence of the Heaviside layer in the upper atmosphere. During the course of the last war developments took place which tremendously improved the methods and instruments used. As in the case of so many of the inventions primarily developed for the purpose of waging war, many useful applications have been found for radar in times of peace, and, in particular, it has proved of great service as an aid to aerial and marine navigation, and in meteorology and astronomy. Radar astronomy investigates the solar system with the echoes of signals sent out from the Earth.

Radiation, energy emitted in the form of a beam of rays or waves, *e.g.,* acoustic (sound) radiation from a loudspeaker, radiant heat from a fire, *β*-radiation from a radioactive substance. The radiation of electromagnetic waves from a body depends on its temperature, the amount of energy radiated per second being proportional to the fourth power of the absolute temperature. The hotter the body, the shorter the wavelengths of the radiation; thus the colour of a glowing body depends on its temperature. Of paramount importance to us is radiation from the sun. Amongst other radiations, the sun sends ultra-violet, visible and infra-red (heat) waves. The principal gases of the atmosphere are transparent to practically all of the solar and sky radiation and also that which the earth re-transmits to space. Carbon dioxide and water vapour, however, strongly absorb certain types, the latter, as clouds, playing an important rôle in regulating the temperature of the globe. The cooling of the ground on a clear night is a result of the outgoing long-wave radiation exceeding that coming down from the sky; at sunrise cooling ceases as the incoming radiation becomes sufficient to compensate for the loss of heat.

Radiation, Cosmic. *See* **F3(2).**

Radio. The theory of electromagnetic waves—of which the radio wave is one—was originated by the British physicist James Clerk Maxwell (**F14**). He showed that both electrical and optical phenomena in space are essentially similar in character, and that the waves if short in wavelength are those of light, and if of longer wavelength those of radio waves. Heinrich Hertz made many useful discoveries about the waves themselves, and about their behaviour under differing conditions, and also about the apparatus for producing them. Marconi developed the use of radio waves as a practical means of communication.

Radio methods are vital for the transmission of observed data from space vehicles back to earth, a process known as "telemetering". This is done by converting the observations into electrical pulses which actuate a suitable radio transmitter so that it radiates a signal, in coded form, which can be received at a ground station and decoded. The transmission of such a signal can also be remotely controlled by means of signals from the earth. Photographic and television techniques may also be employed for obtaining the desired information and sending it back to earth, as in the case of the Russian picture of the reverse side of the moon and the American pictures of the lunar surface. The information may be stored within the spacecraft for a time, and then, upon receipt of a particular radio signal from the earth transmitted by the spacecraft at a time convenient for its reception. Soviet scientists, by a special technique, were able in the case of their *Venus IV* probe (October 1967) to parachute an instrumented canister from the spacecraft so that it could descend slowly to the surface of the planet—a feat described by Sir Bernard Lovell, who was recording the enterprise at Jodrell Bank, as "an experiment of classic elegance". Another breath-taking achievement was the transformation of the faintest of signals from a billion miles away into superb pictures of the planet Saturn and its rings (*see* **Voyagers 1 and 2**). *See also* **Radio Astronomy, Telemetry.**

Radioactivity is the spontaneous transformation of atomic nuclei, accompanied by the emission of ionising radiations. It was discovered in 1896 by Becquerel, who noticed that salts containing uranium sent off radiations which, like X-rays, can blacken a photographic plate. Two years later Marie and Pierre Curie discovered several new chemical elements which possessed the same property, but many times more intense than uranium; the most important of these was radium. Shortly afterwards it was established, mainly by Rutherford, that three types of radiations called α-, β- and γ-rays, are emitted from radioactive substances. It was also Rutherford who, jointly with Soddy, deduced that the emission of the radiations is associated with the spontaneous disintegration of atoms which result in the transformation of one radioactive substance into another. A series of such transformations ends when a stable element is produced. All of the heavy radio-active elements can be arranged in three radio-active series, called, the uranium, thorium and actinium series. Initially, radioactivity was thought to be a property confined only to a few elements occurring in nature. In 1934, how-ever, Irene and Frederick Joliot-Curie dis-covered that ordinary elements can be trans-formed into radioactive forms by subjecting them to bombardment with α-particles. Following this, it was found that beams of other fast particles produced in accelerators can also render ordinary substances radioactive. Nowadays it is known that radioactivity is a general property of matter; any chemical element can be produced in one or more radio-active forms, or isotopes. *See* **F12(1).**

Radio Astronomy. The science of radio astro-nomy makes use of radio apparatus and tech-niques for the observation of events occurring in far distant parts of the universe, and, in so doing, is able to enlarge upon the observational field of optical astronomy in a remarkable way. By means of radio telescopes it is possible to observe parts of the universe so far distant that the radio waves received have taken thousands of millions of years to travel from their source to the earth, and thus to observe happenings which may have occurred near the beginning of the history of the universe. Thus radio astronomy works with signals that are broad-cast by objects in space.

There are two main types of radio telescope. The first, known as the interferometer, uses aerials spaced at large distances to obtain very high angular resolution. Indeed, the so-called very long baseline interferometers (VLBI) use receivers with separations of many thousands of km to obtain higher resolution than any opti-cal telescope. The second, and "steerable", type, is that of the radio telescope at Jodrell Bank, Cheshire, which consists of an enormous concave metal bowl, with the radio aerials at its centre. This, though it has a lower "reso-lution", can be directed or "steered" on to any part of the sky which is above the horizon. The interferometers, particularly the VLBI, have been used to examine the fine structure of many objects, including the nuclei of large and un-usual galaxies. The jet-like structures recently found in several galaxies are of particular in-terest. As well as exploring the structure of gas clouds and clusters in our own galaxy and in more distant ones, several of the large steer-able telescopes have been used as radar anten-nae, for example to explore the surface of the cloud-covered Venus, and to locate suitable landing sites for the *Viking* spacecraft exploring Mars. Increasingly the radio telescope is used as one of an armoury of instruments available to explore the nature of objects of astronomical interest, such as pulsars or quasars.

Radiocarbon Dating is a method of dating the origin of organic materials or objects by observ-ing their radioactivity. It is of great import-ance to archaeology because it enables pre-historic dates back to about 50,000 B.C. to be established for animal and vegetable remains. It works because cosmic rays (*q.v.*) entering the atmosphere create neutrons which convert nitrogen in the air to radioactive carbon. This forms radioactive carbon dioxide and gets in-corporated into animals and vegetables through-out the world along with ordinary carbon di-oxide in a definite ratio, approximately 1 radio carbon atom to 0.8×10^{13} ordinary carbon atoms. When the tissue dies it stops inter-changing its carbon with the atmosphere, *e.g.*, by breathing, and the radioactive carbon in it gradually turns into nitrogen emitting a β-particle (*see* **F12(1)**). The radiocarbon con-tent decreases by about 1% in 88 years. By measuring the proportion of radioactive carbon left in, say, dead wood, and comparing it with living wood, the age of the dead sample can be calculated. This needs careful laboratory experiments. It is now believed that the pro-portion of radioactive carbon in the atmosphere varied from time to time in the past because changes in the earth's magnetic field affected the cosmic rays. This has to be allowed for in calculating the radiocarbon date. One use of radiocarbon dating has been to trace the spread of agriculture through the world from its origin in the Near East *c.* 7000 B.C. *See also* **Tree rings.**

Radiosonde, a weather station in miniature carried aloft by a free balloon to heights normally in the neighbourhood of 16 km. Signals representa-tive of values of atmospheric pressure, tem-perature and humidity are transmitted sim-ultaneously by radio to ground receiving apparatus. The position of the balloon at any instant can be determined by radar, enabling the speed and direction of the upper winds to be deduced.

Radium, a radioactive metallic element, no. 88, symbol Ra, discovered by Marie and Pierre Curie in 1898. Atomic weight 226. Radiotherapy (use of X-rays from radium) is used in the treatment of cancer.

Radon, a radioactive gaseous element, no. 86, symbol Rn, formed by radioactive decay of radium. Its discovery completed the series of ele-ments known as the inert (or rare) gases.

Rain. When moist air rises into lower tempera-tures and becomes saturated, condensation takes place on the numerous hygroscopic par-ticles present in the atmosphere. If the tem-perature is above freezing a cloud of small droplets is formed. These droplets may then grow larger by coalescing with each other as they pass through the cloud until their weight is great enough to make them fall to the earth as rain. In clouds which extend above freezing level, snow and rain both form from the prefer-ential growth of ice crystals at the expense of liquid water droplets. If the resultant ice particle melts as it falls to earth, it gives rain: if not it gives snow. *See also* **Acid Rain.**

Rainbow, a beautiful colour effect visible to an ob-server with back to the sun and facing a rain shower, caused by the refraction and reflection of sunlight in minute water-droplets in the air. From high in the air it would be possible to see a rainbow as a complete circle, but from the ground the most that can be seen is a semicircle when the sun is just on the horizon; the higher the sun is, the smaller the arc of the rainbow. When conditions are suitable two bows are seen, the secondary with the colours of the spectrum reversed. The colours the rainbow are seven; red, orange, yellow, green, blue, indigo and violet—the colours of the spectrum. See also **Aurora.**

Raingauge, an instrument consisting of a deep metal funnel whose stem dips into a graduated glass jar from which the depth of the rain water collected can be read. Continuous records of rainfall are provided by self-registering instruments.

Rain Making is a facility long desired by mankind, especially in the drought-ridden regions, and attempted throughout history by numerous non-scientific means. Since the second world war it has been proved that clouds can sometimes be made to rain or snow by dropping into them from an aeroplane very cold particles of solid carbon dioxide or by burning a solution containing silver iodide. This makes the moisture of the cloud form tiny ice crystals which grow big and finally fall out of the cloud. The process is quite complicated and not fully understood. The practical exploitation is somewhat chancy at present, but experiments have been made in many countries and the United States has a considerable programme of study. As well as scientific there are commercial and legal problems; premature commercial exploitation has resulted in disillusionment in some cases.

Rambouillet, a royal French château (14th cent., rebuilt 18th cent.), near Paris, and the official summer residence of the President of the French Republic. Also the name of the famous literary salon of the Marquise de Rambouillet (1588-1665).

Rampant, in heraldry, is a term applied to the figure of an animal with forelegs elevated, the dexter uppermost. When the animal is shown side-faced it is *rampant displayed,* when fullface, *rampant guardant;* when looking back *rampant reguardant;* and when in sitting position *rampant sejant.*

Rape, a cruciferous plant yielding coleseed or rapeseed, extensively grown in all parts of Europe and India. Rape oil is made from the seeds and as oilcake is a valuable animal feeding-stuff.

Rare Gases (also called **Inert Gases**). These are a group of elements which are chemically inert, comprising helium, neon, argon, krypton, xenon and radon. Cavendish in 1785 noticed that there was in air some gas which was not oxygen, nitrogen or carbon dioxide, but it was not until 1894 that the first of the rare gases was found by Rayleigh and Ramsay. This they called argon (inert). After the discovery of helium in 1895 Kayser, Rayleigh and Travers soon isolated the other gases except radon, which was later detected as a radioactive decay product of radium. Some of these inert gases are used to fill electric-light bulbs, and helium is used in balloons, since it is very light and non-imflammable.

Rat, a well-known group of rodent embracing many species. The *brown rat* appeared in Europe early in the 18th cent., coming from the East and entering by way of Russia; now it is widespread and met with in Britain and all parts of the Continent. The *black rat,* which was the common rat before the arrival of the brown species, is a smaller animal and now comparatively scarce. There are numerous other kinds, all of them gross feeders, and existing in such numbers in many places as to constitute a pest.

Rational Number, a number which can be expressed as a ratio of two whole numbers. Examples are 2, ½, 0·3, −8. See Irrational Number.

Rationalism. See **Section J.**

Rattlesnake, venomous snakes which obtain their name from the possession of a rattle in the end of their tail, consisting of horny pieces so arranged that when vibrated they make a rattling sound. They are only found in N. and S. America.

Raven, a black-plumaged bird of the crow family, with raucous voice and massive bill. Occurs in many parts of Europe, Asia and America. Ravens are easily domesticated and form interesting pets.

Dickens had one which he described in *Barnaby Rudge.*

Ray, fish with a very flat body and broad and fleshy pectoral fins, related to the sharks. There are about 140 species. In Britain they are generally called *skate.*

Razorbill, a sea-bird of the auk family, having a high, furrowed bill and black-and-white plumage. It inhabits rocky cliffs during the breeding season, and at other times is mostly out on the open sea.

Realism is a vague term. As a movement in art it can be said to have started with Gustave Courbet in the mid-19th cent. in his revolt against the classicism of Ingres and the romanticism of Delacroix. He was a man of strong radical views, and like Zola, Balzac and Flaubert in literature, turned to the actuality of everyday life, recording it with frankness and vigour. Some young English painters, notably Bratby, of the "kitchen sink" school, practise what some describe as social realism. In another sense, realism is an attitude concerned with interpreting the essential nature of the subject, revealing truths hidden by the accidentals of ordinary visual appearance. Thus form becomes more significant than content. Beginning with Cézanne and Van Gogh this trend passes on to Cubist and Abstract painting. See also **Section J** (philosophy).

Record Office, in Chancery Lane, London, the place where the Public Records of England are preserved, including Domesday Book. More modern records are held at Kew. Modern records are subject to a 30-year restriction on access. Sensitive records may be closed for 100 years.

Rectifier, an electrical device which will allow electric current to flow in one direction only and can therefore be used for turning alternating current into direct current. Since electricity is usually supplied in alternating form and frequently needed in direct form, rectifiers are of very common use in both industry and the home, for example in radio and television and for battery chargers. Rectifying properties are possessed by a number of different devices, one of which is a thermionic diode (*see* **Valve**). Very large valves filled with mercury vapour are often used for rectifying heavy currents for industrial purposes. Many other rectifiers use semiconductors in close contact with metals or with other semiconductors because such junctions have the property of passing electric current easily only in one direction.

Recusants, people who refused to attend the Anglican Church or to acknowledge the ecclesiastical supremacy of the Crown in the 16th and 17th cent.

Recycling, the process of sorting and re-using waste products. By no means a new idea, and already much used in industry and by the whole community in war-time, recycling assumes prominence when materials are scarce and prices high. There is much evidence from several countries that the public responds well to properly organised schemes for the collection, sorting and re-use of paper, plastic, glass, metals and other waste products common in industrialised countries.

Redstart, a small bird of the Thrush family of handsome plumage and striking song. Two species visit Great Britain: the Common Redstart, with bright chestnut rump and tail, white forehead and black cheeks, favours wooded country, and the Black Redstart, with black breast and throat, chestnut tail and white wing bars, prefers rocky ground or ruins, and breeds in S. England.

Redwing, a bird of the Thrush family which finds its way to this country for the winter. Resembles the song thrush, but distinguished by smaller size, buffish-white eye-stripe, chestnut flanks and underwings. It has bred in Scotland and on Fair Isle.

Redwood *or* **Sequoia.** This genus of coniferous tree comprises two species of Redwoods occurring in N.W. America. Specimens of one species, the Giant Redwood, reach a height of over 90 m and a thickness of 11 m. The age of the largest, the General Sherman tree, is put at 3,500 years.

Referendum and Initiative, two methods by which the wishes of electors may be expressed with regard to proposed legislation. It is developed to the highest extent in Switzerland. In a *Referendum* some specific matter is referred to the electors. The *Initiative* is the means by which electors can compel their representatives to consider a specific issue. Gen. de Gaulle made use of the referendum in seeking the consent of the French nation for his policies. The British Labour Government held a referendum in June 1975, asking voters whether they felt the nation should remain in or withdraw from the European Economic Community. An Act of Parliament was required to authorise the referendum (which was something new in British constitutional history), and a further Act would have been necessary if the majority had been in favour of withdrawal. The result was for continued membership.

Reformation. *See* Section J.

Reform Bills. The principal Bills have been passed for the reform of the Parliamentary franchise. The first was the great Reform Bill of 1832, introduced by Lord John Russell and enacted under the Whig administration of Lord Grey. In addition to a sweeping redistribution of seats, this Act greatly extended the franchise but still left many people without the right to vote. The second Bill, passed by Disraeli in 1867, by giving the vote to workers in towns, established household suffrage. A third Bill, passed in 1884 under a Gladstone ministry, removed the distinction between borough and county franchise, enfranchised agricultural workers, and thus gave the vote to all men over 21. Women had to wait until 1918 to get the vote at the age of 30. The Representation of the People (Equal Franchise) Act, 1928, gave them the right to be registered as Parliamentary electors at the age of 21, thus making England into a true democracy. The Representation of the People Act, 1948, abolished the representation of the universities and the separate representation of the City of London and the business-premises vote. The Representation of the People Act, 1969, reduced the minimum voting age from 21 to 18.

Refraction. The change of direction which light rays undergo when passing from one medium to another. The phenomenon is due to the fact that in different media light (and other forms of radiation) has different speeds.

Refractory, a substance capable of standing high temperatures and therefore useful for making furnaces and allied apparatus. Some insulating refractories are fire-clay, alumina, porcelain, carborundum, graphite and silica. Some refractory metals are platinum, molybdenum, tungsten, tantalum and the alloys nichrome, chromel, alumel.

Regency Style is the English version of the French Empire (*q.v.*) and approximately covers the period of the regency of Prince George, later George IV, from 1810 to 1820. It is somewhat less austere than the French style, and contains elements of the fantastic and exotic absent from Empire. The most famous monument of Regency style is the Royal Pavilion at Brighton, built for the Prince Regent by John Nash. (Regency style should not be confused with the *Régence* style in France, fashionable during the regency period between the death of Louis XIV in 1715 and the ascent to the throne of Louis XV in 1723. Here the English equivalent is Queen Anne style.)

Reindeer, a genus of deer horned in both sexes, occurring only in northerly regions. It has an average height of 1·3 m, is very fleet of foot and the Laplanders utilise it for draught purposes and for food.

Relativity. The laws of relativity have been substantially proved and have revolutionised our ideas as to the nature of space, time, matter and energy and forced us to think along new lines. In 1949 a new theory by Einstein was announced which sets forth in a series of equations the laws governing both gravitation and electromagnetism, which is said to bridge the gap that separates the universe of the stars and galaxies and the universe of the atom. At present the one is explained by relativity, and the other rests on the quantum theory. *See* **F17–19.**

Relief in sculpture is of three kinds—high relief

(*alto-relievo*), in which the figures stand out to the extent of one-half of their natural proportions, low-relief (*basso-relievo*) when the figures project but slightly; and middle-relief (*mezzo-relievo*), when the projection is intermediate.

Renaissance. *See* **Section J.**

Republican Party of the United States was born by the fusion in 1854 of the group who called themselves National Republicans, having split from the Democrats over tariffs in 1825, and the northern Democrats, both of them being opposed to slavery. It came to power when Abraham Lincoln was elected President in 1860 and won 14 of the 18 presidential elections held between 1860 and 1932. It was defeated in 1932 largely as a result of the economic depression and reached its lowest ebb in the years of Roosevelt's New Deal (*q.v.*) The Party went on being defeated every four years until Eisenhower's victory in 1952. Nixon narrowly failed to defeat Kennedy in 1960 and Goldwater was decisively beaten by Lyndon Johnson in 1964. In 1968 and again in 1972 Nixon was successful in winning the Presidency. His fall from power in the aftermath of Watergate made 1974 a bad year for the Republican Party. In 1980 and in 1984, Ronald Reagan won landslide victories. George Bush completed a trio of Republican victories in 1988. The symbol of the Party is an elephant, the invention of Thomas Nast, a cartoonist, in 1874.

Requiem. Properly a mass for the dead, the term is extended to cover musical settings by Palestrina, Mozart, Verdi and others.

Reredos, the ornamental screen at the back of the altar or communion table. It is often of a highly decorative character and is an architectural feature in many churches in Spain. Other examples are to be found in the following cathedrals in England: Southwark, St. Albans, Winchester, Durham and Liverpool.

Resins, natural resins are vegetable compounds largely employed in the industrial arts. They comprise india-rubber, amber, mastic, copal, etc. "Synthetic resins" is a term sometimes used as a synonym for "plastics".

Reuter, an international news agency, organised since 1941 as a trust and owned by the newspapers of Britain, Australia and New Zealand, founded by Baron J. de Reuter in 1849.

Rhea, a large flightless bird, the "ostrich" of S. America, distinguished from the ostrich proper by smaller size, longer beak, larger wings, no tail and 3 toes instead of 2. There are 2 species.

Rheology, science of flow. *See* **F21(1).**

Rhesus Factor. *See* Index to Section P.

Rhinoceros, a large almost hairless animal related to the horse. Two kinds in Africa and several others in Asia. They have a horn, sometimes two, over the snout composed of modified hair. Most are leaf eaters but the largest species, the white rhino of South Africa, is a grazer. They have been much hunted for their horns. The numbers of African black rhinos have fallen from 100,000 in 1962 to less than 4,000 in 1990.

Rhodium, a metallic element, no. 45, symbol Rh, discovered by Wollaston in 1804. It is found in platinum ores in small amounts, generally less than 2 per cent. With platinum it gives a very hard and durable alloy. It is also used, instead of silver, in putting the reflecting layer on a mirror.

Ribbon Fish *or* **Oarfish,** a deep-sea fish, deriving its name from its ribbon-like shape. Though fairly long, it is only a few centimetres thick. The ribbon fish is rarely met with because of its habitat, and most of what is known about it has been learnt from specimens cast ashore.

Rice, a grain-yielding grass, of which thousands of strains are known today, extensively cultivated in China, India and certain parts of America, and forming the main food of the peoples of China, Japan, India and S.E. Asia. Some 95 per cent. of the world's rice is produced and consumed in the Orient. The grain with the husk is known as "paddy". Arrack, an alcoholic liquor, is made from fermented rice seeds.

Richter Scale, a series of numbers used to record the relative magnitude of earthquakes. Devised by F. Richter of the California Institute of Technology. An earthquake is given a number on the scale by measuring the amplitude of earth movements, *i.e.*, the size of the to and fro motion in an earthquake wave, with a special instrument called a seismometer. The reading is corrected by calculation to allow for the distance of the instrument from the earthquake and the corrected results by observers at different places agree quite well. The scale is logarithmic, *i.e.*, earthquakes differing by one unit on the Richter scale are a factor 10 different in amplitude. An earthquake allotted zero on the scale would give a reading of 10^{-6} m on a standard seismometer 100 km from the centre of the earthquake. Smaller disturbances would have negative values on the scale. The largest known earthquakes had Richter values between $+8$ and $+9$, *i.e.*, they had 10^{+8} to 10^{+9} bigger amplitudes than earthquakes of magnitude zero. It is a widespread misconception that the scale has an upper limit of 10; there are no upper or lower limits to the scale.

Rime, a crystalline deposit of ice formed on objects exposed to wet fog at the same time as frost.

Rinderpest *or* **Cattle Plague,** is a highly contagious disease affecting cattle, sheep and other ruminants. In Europe the disease has been eradicated, but it was formerly very widespread and caused great loss of life among cattle. The disease is caused by a filtrable virus, and is attended by fever and congestion of the mucous membranes.

Ring Dove *or* **Wood Pigeon,** a blue-grey bird, distinguished from other pigeons by larger size (41 cm), white wing-bar, glossy green-and-purple neck and white half-collar. It is very common in Britain.

Rituale, the book of rites used in the Roman Catholic Church for the administration of certain sacraments and other church ceremonies. Like the Roman breviary, it dates in its present form from the Council of Trent.

RNA (Ribonucleic Acid). *See* **Nucleic Acids.**

Roaring Forties, name applied to the prevailing westerly winds over the oceans in the temperate latitudes of the Southern Hemisphere. Because unimpeded by large land areas the winds are more regular and stronger than the westerlies in the Northern Hemisphere.

Robin (or Redbreast). A small bird with olive-brown upper parts and orange-red forehead, throat and breast; both sexes look alike. The young are speckled, lacking the red breast. Its wide European distribution includes the British Isles, where it is the national bird. It also occurs in N. Africa and W. Asia. The nest is placed in a great variety of situations including holes in banks, trees and walls; in sheds, amongst ivy and sometimes in old tins. Nesting-boxes are readily adopted, but care should be taken to ensure that the entrance-hole is small enough to exclude starlings. Robins are pugnacious and defend their territories with vigour. Their attractive appearance, trustful disposition, engaging ways and sweet song make them extremely popular. The name robin is also applied to a number of very different birds, one of which, the American Robin, occasionally wanders to Europe.

Rock Dove, the grey pigeon *Columbia livia* of Europe and Asia, ancestor of the domestic pigeons as Darwin was the first to show.

Rockets for use in war were first studied by Sir William Congreve early in the 19th cent., and proved very destructive in siege operations. They were invented by the Chinese as long ago as the 11th cent. The Germans devised the huge V2 rocket, carrying a ton of explosive, which was used near the end of the war to bombard London. Rockets are propelled by the burning of fuel (*e.g.*, oxygen or nitric acid), the exhaust, being ejected at high velocity, thrusts the rocket forward. For the study of the properties of the atmosphere vertical sounding rockets are used. Rocket flight in outer space was first presented as practicable by the Russian rocket expert, K. E. Tsiolkovsky, in 1903. The provision of sufficient launching velocity involves the use of rocket motors with adequate thrust. To launch a satellite into an orbit circulating within a few hundred kilometres of the surface a velocity of 29,000 km/h must be imparted. This may be done by using a multi-stage launching system. When the first-stage

motor has burned out it drops off, so that, when the second-stage motor ignites, it does not have to support the weight of the first-stage, and so on. If the launching velocity is increased to 40,000 km/h the vehicle will not return to the neighbourhood of the earth but pass out of the range of the earth's gravitational pull completely. Unless the launching velocity reaches 161,000 km/h it will not escape from the sun and will become an artificial planet. *See also* **Space Research.**

Rock Magnetism. The study of naturally occurring magnetism in rocks is a subject which has gained considerable importance in recent years. There are two principal reasons for this. One is that this so-called "fossillised magnetism" may be able to tell us more about the past history of the earth's magnetic field. The other is that after many years of heated dispute between geologists rock magnetism promises to settle once and for all the controversy as to whether or not the continents have changed their relative positions in past times (continental drift theory (*q.v.*)). This branch of geophysical research, in addition to its academic interest, may well have important economic consequences. It might, for instance, become possible to locate mineral deposits once accumulated under special conditions at certain latitudes but now drifted to other places. Salt and similar deposits formed by the continuous evaporation of solutions in hot countries are one example; oil may well be another. There has been a *steady* change in rock magnetisation direction with geological time. It is now known with some accuracy that the most recent reversal took place 700,000 years ago. It has been found that the older the rock, the farther removed is its fossil magnetisation from the present field.

Rococo, an architectural style which was, in effect, the final stage of **Baroque** (*q.v.*). The name first came into use about 1830 to describe the period 1720–70 and means "shell-shaped" (French *Rocaille*), since the shell was a favourite motif in Rococo ornamentation. At about the beginning of the 18th cent. the heavy older type of Baroque began to show even less restraint than had characterised it in the past; it became still less utilitarian, and showed a kind of playful lighthearted vitality which manifested itself in a wealth of ornamental invention. Baroque was flamboyant and robust, Rococo dainty, graceful and smiling. Its ornaments are frequently asymmetrical, and in this Rococo is unique among the historical styles of Europe. In architecture Rococo is naturally found in those areas where the Baroque had flourished, *i.e.*, Munich, Prague, Vienna and Dresden. In painting, the best expressions of Rococo are to be seen in the works of the French painters Watteau (d. 1721), Boucher (d. 1770), a favourite of Mme de Pompadour, and famous as a decorator of boudoirs, and Fragonard (d. 1806). (As in the case of Baroque, it was typical of Rococo that the sculpture, painting and the decorative arts of a building all expressed the same spirit.)

Roe, popular name given to organs in fish which produce eggs and sperms. "Hard roe" is that of the female and consists of eggs; that of the male is the soft roe or milt.

Roe Deer (*Capreolus capreolus*) deer native to Europe and found in England and Scotland but not Ireland. "Roebuck" is the name of the male adult.

Roller, a tropical Old World bird of the *Coraciidae* family, related to the hoopoe, kingfisher and bee-eater, of strikingly brilliant blue, chestnut, greenish-blue plumage. There are fifteen species, one of which breeds in the far north and visits the British Isles on its migrations to and from its winter quarters in Africa.

Romanesque Architecture, prevailed throughout Europe from the mid-10th to the 13th cent., and implies an art which developed from that of the Romans. Notable in Romanesque style were the rounded arch and masonry vaulting. Romanesque led to the graceful and more complex Gothic (*q.v.*). The Italians never regarded Gothic highly and Romanesque churches, generally based on the basilican plan (oblong with double colonnades and a semi-circular apse at the end), continued to be built there until the beginning of the 15th cent. Some of the best examples can be seen at Pisa (11th cent.), Florence (San Miniato, 1013), Lucca (12th cent.) and Milan (the 12th cent. San Ambrogio, most famous of all). In Germany Romanesque architure flourished longer than in France or England; the most famous churches are in the valley of the Rhine, at Cologne (completely destroyed during the second world war), Mainz and Speyer. In France Romanesque churches are found in Burgundy, Provence and Normandy. For English Romanesque *see* **Norman Architecture.**

Roman Roads, highways constructed by the Romans. They were of great durability. The best known British roads were Ermine Street (London, Lincoln, York), Fosse Way (Lincoln through Leicester, Cirencester, Bath, Exeter), Watling Street (Channel Ports, London to Shropshire).

Romanticism, a term for a movement in the arts— whether in music, painting, sculpture or literature—which seeks to give expression to the artist's feelings about his subject rather than to be concerned with form or reality. The romantic view is that art is nature seen through a temperament; the realist view is that art is a slice of life. In painting Delacroix (1798–1863) is the romantic artist *par excellence* with his uncontrolled expression of the passions and love of the exotic. In literature the Romantic movement reached its finest form in the works of Goethe, Schiller and Heine; in the poetry of Byron, Keats, Wordsworth, Shelley and Blake; and in the writings of Victor Hugo. Since Romanticism is partly a matter of temperament in the artist just as Classicism is, it may be found at all times and places, although whether or not it becomes predominant depends on contemporary taste. Cubism, for example, with its attention to form is classical whereas Surrealism with its attention to content is romantic. *See also* **Romantic Movement, Section J.**

Roman Walls were built as frontier barriers under the Emperors Hadrian (76–138) and Antoninus Pius (86–161). Hadrian's works, linking Wallsend-on-Tyne with Bowness-on-Solway, comprised a twenty-foot stone wall, ditches, turrets, "milecastles", fortresses and a double earthen mound, or "Vallum". Impressive ruins are still visible at Chesters and Housesteads. Antoninus Pius, Hadrian's successor, made a further advance, but the turf wall which he built between Forth and Clyde was soon abandoned. Septimius Severus (146–211) restored Hadrian's wall after the assassination of Commodus and the subsequent civil wars. It was finally abandoned between 380 and 390. Archaeologists from Lancaster University have recently excavated the Roman fort of Ravenglass (Roman Glannaventa) on the Cumbrian coast and believe it to have been built as an extension to Hadrian's wall.

Rood Screen, an ornamental partition, separating the choir from the nave in a church, and supporting a crucifix or rood.

Rook, a member of the crow family, abounding in most parts of the British Isles and found in Europe, Asia and N. Africa. It has been introduced into New Zealand. Rooks usually nest in colonies in tall trees. They are highly intelligent birds, and their ways have long been the subject of much careful study.

Rosary, a circular chain of beads, used by Catholics when reciting a particular form of prayer. Each bead represents an entire prayer, and the combined prayers constitute the Rosary.

Roses, Wars of the (1455–85), between the rival houses of York and Lancaster, for the possession of the English crown, began in the reign of Henry VI and ended with the death of Richard III on Bosworth Field. The emblem or badge of the Lancastrians was the red rose and of the Yorkists the white rose. All rivalry between The Roses ended by the marriage of Henry VII, the Lancastrian, with the Princess Elizabeth, daughter of Edward IV, the Yorkist.

Rosetta Stone, discovered in 1799 by the French at Rosetta in Egypt, and deposited in the British Museum. It is a piece of black basalt about 91 cm long, and contains a decree of the Egyptian priests of Ptolemy V Epiphanes (205–181 B.C.)

in (1) hieroglyphics, (2) demotic and (3) Greek characters. It was the three different inscriptions on the same stone that enabled hieroglyphic writing to be deciphered.

Rotten Row, a corruption of *route de roi* (king's drive), the famous riding resort in Hyde Park.

Rouge et Noir, a well-known gambling card game played on a table divided into two sections and marked with two black and two red lozenges. Any number of players can take part, and the money is staked on the red or black spaces. The cards are dealt out, first to Noir, until the pips aggregate more than 30; then in like manner to the Rouge, and the packet coming nearest to 31 wins the stakes.

Roulette, a gambling game played on a table carrying a revolving wheel divided into 37 compartments. Each compartment bears a number, 0 (zero) and 1 to 36. The numbers are mixed and do not follow any particular order. Of these 37 numbers 18 are black and 18 are red, whereas zero is green. The players stake their money on any compartment, colour or combination of numbers they please. The wheel is whirled round and a ball is set rolling in the opposite direction, dropping finally into one of the compartments, thus deciding the winning number and colour.

Roundhead. In the reign of Charles I and later, a Puritan or member of the Parliamentary party who wore his hair cut short. It was originally a term of derision applied by the Royalists, who usually wore ringlets.

Round Towers, high circular towers with conical roof and massive masonry walls, built during the early Middle Ages (*c.* 10th cent.). It is believed that they served as refuges and lookouts. These buildings are numerous in Ireland, and two remain in Scotland, at Brechin, which is attached to the church, and at Abernethy.

Royal Academy of Arts was founded in London in 1768, under the patronage of George III. The early exhibitions of the Academy were held first in Pall Mall, and later in Somerset House where the exhibitions continued to be held until 1836, when the National Gallery being built, the Academy moved its quarters to that building. In 1869 the present Royal Academy at Burlington House was opened. List of presidents: Sir Joshua Reynolds (1768), Benjamin West (1792), James Wyatt (1805), B. West (1806), Sir Thomas Lawrence (1820), Sir M. A. Shee (1830), Sir C. Eastlake (1850), Sir F. Grant (1866), Lord Leighton, (1878), Sir J. E. Millais (1896), Sir E. J. Poynter (1896), Sir Aston Webb (1919), Sir F. Dicksee (1924), Sir William Llewellyn (1928), Sir E. Lutyens (1938), Sir A. J. Munnings (1944), Sir Gerald F. Kelly (1949), Sir A. E. Richardson (1954), Sir Charles Wheeler (1956), Sir Thomas Monnington (1966), Sir Hugh Casson (1976) and Roger de Grey (1984). The Academy holds an exhibition of pictures, statuary and architectural designs every summer.

Royal Hospital, Chelsea, built by Wren, was opened in 1694 as an institution for invalid soldiers.

Royal Institution, established 1799, and incorporated by Royal Charter in 1800 for "the promotion, extension and diffusion of Science and of Useful Knowledge". It was in the building of the Institution that Faraday conducted his experiments. Today it has extensive research laboratories. Famous also for its Christmas lectures designed for a juvenile audience.

Royal Society was founded in 1660 and incorporated by Royal Charter in 1662. Viscount Brouncker being named the first president. Its *Philosophical Transactions* date from 1665. Among those who served as president of the Royal Society are Sir Christopher Wren, Pepys, Sir Isaac Newton, Sir Joseph Banks, Sir Humphry Davy, Prof. T. H. Huxley, Lord Rayleigh, Sir Archibald Geikie, Sir J. J. Thomson, O.M., Prof. Sir C. Sherrington, O.M., G.B.E., Lord Rutherford, O.M., Sir William Henry Bragg, O.M., Sir Henry Dale, O.M., Sir Robert Robinson, O.M., Lord Adrian, O.M., Sir Cyril Hinshelwood, O.M., Lord Florey, O.M., Lord Blackett O.M. (1965), Sir Alan Hodgkin, O.M. (1970), Lord Todd O.M. (1975), Sir Andrew Huxley (1980).

Rubber, substance obtained from the milky juice (latex) exuded by certain tropical trees and shrubs after tapping. Demand spread so rapidly in the 19th cent. that plantations were established wherever the tree would grow. Seeds of the Para rubber tree (*Hevea brasiliensis*) native to the Amazon basin were obtained by Kew, the young plants shipped to Ceylon and it was from these cultivated trees that the vast plantations of Malaysia and Indonesia developed. Recent years have seen great advances in the production of synthetic rubber.

Rubicon, a small river falling into the Adriatic, and forming one of the Italian boundaries, the crossing of which anciently involved decisive action and constituted a declaration of war. Thus the phrase "crossing the Rubicon", denoting an act from which there is no withdrawal.

Rubidium, a metallic element, no. 37, symbol Rb, most closely resembling potassium. It is silver-white and very soft, and was discovered in 1861 by Bunsen and Kirchhoff, using the spectroscope. It is rare, occurring in small amounts in the mica called lepidolite and in potash salts of the Stassfurt deposits in Germany.

Rubrics are instructions in regard to the ceremonies of the Church, appearing in red in the Prayer Book.

Ruby is a deep red variety of Corundum (aluminium oxide); one of the most valued of precious stones. Burma yields some of the finest, and rubies of inferior colour are found in Thailand, Sri Lanka, South Africa and Brazil.

Rudd, a fresh-water fish of wide distribution, plentiful in the rivers of Britain. It is of a reddish-gold colour, with a greenish-blue beard.

Ruff, a bird related to the common sandpiper, at one time common in the Fen districts. The males have a ruff of feathers round the neck in the breeding season. The female is the Reeve.

Ruffe *or* **Pope,** a small fresh-water fish common in most parts of central Europe, and similar in appearance to the ordinary perch. It is found in British rivers.

"Rule, Britannia!" the national sea-song of England, was written by James Thomson (1700–48), the author of the "Seasons", and set to music by Dr. Arne about 1740. The poet's words were "Britannia, rule the waves!" but it is usually rendered "Britannia rules the waves."

Rum, a ardent spirit distilled from molasses, and containing from 40 to 50 per cent. of alcohol. It is chiefly manufactured in the West Indies, and derives its special flavour from a volatile oil.

Ruminants, animals that chew the cud, being provided with a compartmented stomach, enabling them to swallow food, and later to bring it back to the mouth for mastication; *e.g.,* sheep, goats, oxen, etc. While in the rumen, or storage compartment, some digestion of food, especially cellulose, takes place by bacterial action.

Runcible spoon, a kind of fork used for pickles having three broad prongs. The word was used by Edward Lear about 1870 as a nonsense word and may be derived from *Rouncival* meaning large or huge from the bones said to have been dug up at *Roncesvalles* where Roland fell. Rouncival peas are the large peas called "marrowfats".

Runes, certain characters of an alphabet found in inscriptions in the Germanic languages, found cut into buildings and implements of stone or wood in many parts of northern Europe, including Britain. The runic alphabet originally had 24 letters. Scholars agree that some of the runes derive from Greek and others from Latin.

Ruskin College, the first residential college for working people, founded at Oxford in 1899 by Mr. Walter Vrooman, an American.

Rusts, parasitic fungi, some common species of which have reddish spores which in a mass have a rusty appearance. A well-known species is the Wheat Rust (*Puccinia graminis*), which has an alternative host in the barberry.

Ruthenium, a greyish-white metallic element, no. 44, symbol Ru, discovered by Claus in 1845. It is harder and more brittle than platinum, in whose ores it occurs.

Rutile, mineral titanium dioxide. It is found in many igneous rocks, and in gneisses and schists, Its commonest colour is reddish-brown.

S

Sabaoth, a Hebrew word, meaning an army or host, and applied sometimes to the Supreme Being, *e.g.,* "the Lord of Hosts" (Rom. ix. 29).

Sabbath and Sunday. Sunday, or the Lord's Day, is the first day of the week in the Christian year. It was substituted for the Jewish Sabbath in the 1st cent. A.D. as the Christian day of worship in commemoration of the Resurrection. The Sabbath, in the Jewish system, was the last day of the week (Saturday in the Christian calendar), designated as the day of religious rest in the fourth commandment of the Decalogue. It was the Puritans at the time of the Reformation who applied the term Sabbath to the Christian Sunday and the two terms have been used indiscriminately ever since.

Sabbatical Year was instituted by the Jews in ancient times for the purpose of giving the soil a rest from cultivation. This was every seventh year. In universities a sabbatical year is a year of absence from duty for the purpose of study and travel, granted to professors at certain intervals.

Sable, a furred mammal of the weasel family mainly inhabiting Siberia. It is bright brown in colour, and has a long, bushy tail. American sable is a marten.

Saccharin, a white crystalline solid manufactured from toluene, 550 times as sweet as cane sugar. It is used as a sweetening agent; as a substitute for sugar when sugar is forbidden, as in certain diseases, or when there is a shortage. It has no value as a food.

Safety Lamp, as used in coal-mines, was invented by Sir Humphry Davy in 1816. The flame is enclosed in a cage of fine-meshed wire which allows air to enter and promote burning, but conducts away the heat generated in combustion so that no product of combustion escapes at a temperature high enough to ignite explosive gases in the mine.

Sainfoin, a widely cultivated forage plant, especially adapted for sheep. It is of strong, leafy growth and bears bright red flowers. It belongs to the same family of flowering plants as peas and beans.

St. Elmo's Fire, a glowing brush-like discharge of electricity which takes place from sharp-pointed objects on mountains or the masts of ships exposed to the intense electric fields of thunder-clouds.

Saints' Days. In the liturgy of the Roman Catholic church a saint is commemorated and his intercession sought on a special day (saint's day), usually the anniversary of his death. Pope Paul decreed that from 1 January 1970 the following saints were to be dropped from the calendar; Christopher, Catherine of Alexandria, Alexis, Pudenzia, Susan, Margaret, Viviana, Eustace, Martina, Venantius and Domitilla. Many others, including our own Saint George, and Nicholas (Santa Claus) have been demoted though they may be venerated locally. There are now only 153 saints' days in addition to those in honour of the Apostles, Saint Joseph and the Virgin Mary. The festival of All Saints is on 1 November.

Salamanders are amphibia superficially resembling lizards, from which they differ in having a moist skin and no scales.

Salic Law was probably instituted in France in the 5th cent. for the purpose of excluding females from inheriting the Crown. The Bourbons introduced the same law into Spain, but this was abolished by decree in 1830 to enable Isabella II to succeed.

Salmon, a fish notable for its habit of returning from the sea to spawn in the river where it was itself hatched. Their origin can be inferred from the chemical composition of certain blood proteins. Salmon from the two sides of the Atlantic migrate to communal feeding grounds off Greenland.

Saltpetre. *See* **Nitre.**

Salvarsan, the organic arsenical compound asphenamine, which Ehrlich discovered was able to kill inside the human body the spirochaete germ that causes syphilis. Also known as "606". It has been superseded by neosalvarsan.

Salvation Army. *See* **Section J.**

Samarium, metallic element, no. 62, symbol Sm, one of the lanthanides (**L72**).

San Andreas Fault, is the dividing line between the North American plate and the North Pacific Ocean plate where "plate" means one of the rigid sections of the earth's crust as conceived in the theory of plate tectonics (*q.v.*). The fault runs roughly north-west-south-east in California passing near San Francisco. The Pacific Ocean bed and the North American continent are sliding past each other along this fault at about 5 cm per year. As at all plate-to-plate boundaries—another is the Western Pacific coast—the San Andreas fault is the scene of great earthquake activity. Between 1934 and 1970 there were over 7,000 earthquakes severer than magnitude 4 on Richter scale (*q.v.*) in and near southern California. Because of large population centres, the activity of San Andreas region is studied with great care and some apprehension about a repeat of the San Francisco earthquake of 1906 which caused displacements of up to 6·4 m along the San Andreas Fault. *See also* **F9**.

Sandering, small wading bird of sandpiper family; breeds in tundra regions of far north, and is seen on sandy beaches of Britain as a winter visitor. Conspicuous white wing stripe and, like Curlew, Sandpiper, Knot, Dunlin and other members of sandpiper family, has marked change of plumage between winter and summer.

Sandpiper, small- to medium-sized wading birds of several species whose migratory powers are so great that they are found in most parts of the world. They include the Common Sandpiper, a bird about 18 cm long, greenish-brown head and back, white under-parts; beak long and slender. Purple, Wood and Curlew-Sand-pipers.

Sans-culottes (French = without knee breeches), a term applied by the French aristocrats to the revolutionary leaders during the French Revolution who wore long trousers instead of knee breeches.

Sanskrit is the language of ancient India, spoken by the Brahmins, and existing in early Oriental literature. It was the language of literature and government and is now confined to temples and places of learning. Its relationship to the modern Indian languages is rather like that of Latin and Greek to modern European languages.

Saponin. The term is a generic one applied to a range of organic compounds which produce frothy, soapy solutions. Saponins are extracted from the soapwort root, horse chestnut seeds, etc. Saponin is the basis of the "foam" used for fire fighting; it can be used like soap to make insecticides and fungicides adhere to the leaves of plants. Also used as detergents.

Sapphic Verse, a form of verse said to have been invented by Sappho, the lyric poetess of Lesbos, who flourished about 600 B.C.

Sapphire, a valuable deep blue variety of Corundum (aluminium oxide) found mostly in India, Sri Lanka and Northern Italy. Synthetic sapphire is often used for gramophone styli.

Saracen, the name given in classic times to the Arab tribes of Syria and adjacent territories. In the Middle Ages the current designation among the Christians for their Muslim enemies.

Sarcophagus, the name given to a stone coffin, such as was used by the ancient Egyptians, Greeks, and Romans, for receiving the remains of their famous dead. These sarcophagi were often decorated with rich carvings and sculptures.

Sassanides were a dynasty of Persian rulers descended from Artaxerxes from 226 to 625.

Satellite Communication, the system for transmitting telephone and television signals over long distances. Satellites orbiting the earth at a height of *c.* 35,700 km above the Atlantic, Pacific and Indian oceans provide a global coverage. They take exactly 24 h to complete one orbit and so appear to stay in the same place. *Telstar,* launched in the summer of 1969, took only 2·5 h and was therefore within range of the earth stations on each side of the Atlantic for very short periods. The global satellite system Intelsat (International Telecommunications Satellite Organisation) was founded in 1964 to establish a world-wide system on a commercial basis. The first generation of Intelsat satellites to be launched from Florida was *Early Bird,* which went into service in June 1965. Further series have been introduced since then. For example, in 1981 Intelsat had five satellites covering the Atlantic, Indian and Pacific oceans. The Intelsat 5 type of satellite weighs nearly 2,000 kg and can handle two television channels and 12,000 telephone calls simultaneously. Post may now be sent by satellite through Intelpost which began operating in 1980 and links New York City, Washington D.C., Toronto, Amsterdam, Bonn and London.

Satrap, the name given to the governor of a province (satrapy) in the ancient Persian monarchy.

Saturday, the seventh day of the week (the Jewish Sabbath), derived name from planet Saturn.

Saturn, the sixth planet in order from the sun, from which it is distant 1427×10^6 km and around which it makes a revolution in 29.46 years (**F8**). It is 120,200 km in diameter or 9.42 times as large as the Earth and rotates on its axis in 10h 14 min. Saturn is noted for its magnificent ring system which is composed of myriads of ice-covered particles. Among the planet's 17 moons are Mimas, Enceladus, Tethys, Dione, Titan, Rhea, Hyperion, Iapetus and Phoebe. Titan is the largest (radius 2400 km), being the second largest satellite in the solar system, about the size of planet Mercury. Galileo was the first to observe that Saturn was ringed; Christiaan Huygens the first to study the nature of the rings; and Jacques Cassini the first to suggest that they were composed of myriads of particles. Our knowledge of the planet and its moons and rings has been greatly increased by the camera observations of the spacecrafts Pioneer 11 (flyby Sept 1979), Voyager 1 (flyby autumn 1980) and Voyager 2 (flyby Aug 1981). *See* **Voyager 1 and 2, L127.**

Saturnalia, festivals held in ancient Rome in honour of the god Saturnus.

Sawfly. These insects are considered to be the most primitive members of the order (*Hymenoptera*) to which the bees and wasps belong. In appearance they resemble somewhat the latter, but there is no waist separating thorax and abdomen. The ovipositor is never used as a sting; usually it is saw-like so that the female can use it to make incisions into tissues of plants where the eggs are laid. The larvae look like caterpillars of butterflies and moths.

Saxons, a Teutonic race originally inhabiting what is now Holstein. By the 7th cent. they had, with the Angles and Jutes, conquered and colonised most of England.

Scallop, marine bivalve molluscs of the genus *Pecten,* which is widely distributed. The scalloped edge to the shell results from a pattern of radiating groves. Related to the oyster.

Scandium, a metallic element, no. 21, symbol Sc. It was discovered in 1879 by Nilson, and occurs in small quantities in certain rarer minerals such as wolframite.

Scarabaeidae, a family of beetles (Scarabs) widely distributed through Africa and Asia and the inner parts of Europe. It is to this genus that the "Sacred Beetle" of the Egyptians belongs, and numerous representations of it are found on ancient monuments.

Sceptre, the staff or rod used since ancient times to symbolise supreme authority. The sceptre used for the coronation of Queen Elizabeth II is the one made for Charles II. It is about 90 cm long and tipped with a jewelled cross.

Schism, an ecclesiastical term for division in a church. The East–West Schism was the separation of the Greek Church from the Latin, finally established in 1054. The Great Schism was the division in the Roman Catholic Church from 1378 to 1415, when there were two lines of popes, one at Rome and one at Avignon. *See* **J11.**

Schist, the geological name of certain metamorphic rocks composed for the most part of mineral with thin plate-like crystals (*e.g.,* mica) so that the layers of a schist are closely parallel. Quartz occurs in schists, and where it preponderates the term "quartz schist" is applied.

Scientific Units. The International Bureau of Weights and Measures at Sèvres near Paris, is the custodian of accurate scientific measurement in terms of internationally agreed units.

Methods of measurement are continually being improved and measurements of new kinds coming into use. In defining units certain principles have evolved which can be expressed as a statement of priorities:

(i) units should be so defined that measurements made in one laboratory should be reproducible in another with as much consistency as possible;

(ii) units of all kinds should, so far as practical, form an interrelated system based on as few fundamental units as possible;

(iii) the fundamental units adopted should have a natural basis, independent of particular man-made objects such as metal bars or weights. An invariable universal natural standard was achieved for the metre in 1958 when it was defined in terms of the wavelength of a line in the spectrum of krypton-86. This was changed in 1983. See **L82** and **S.I. Units.**

Schoolmen, the great scholastic philosophers of the Middle Ages who devoted themselves to the study and exposition of questions of religious inquiry, and attempted to reconcile the teaching of the Church with that of Aristotle. The chief Schoolmen were Archbishop Anselm, Albertus Magnus, Thomas Aquinas, Peter Lombard, Duns Scotus. See also **Section J.**

Scorpion. The scorpions constitute an order of the arthropods. Distinctive features are the pair of powerful claws at the head and a "sting" at the tail, which curves over the back in attack or defence so that it points forwards. The poison injected by the sting is potent, causing instant death in spiders, centipedes, etc., and acute discomfort to humans. The idea that a cornered scorpion can sting itself to death is a myth; scorpions are immune to their own poison.

Scorpion Fly. The scorpion fly, of which there are less than 500 species, constitute a separate order of insects, the *Mecoptera*. They have 2 pairs of membranous wings, and gain their popular name because in some species the end of the abdomen is turned up, though it does not function as a sting.

Scree *or* **Talus,** the mass of loose, angular rock fragments which accumulate towards the bottom of hill-sides and mountain-sides. These fragments have been detached by weathering processes, in particular frost action.

Scythians, nomadic conquerors and skilled horsemen (9th–3rd cent. B.C.) who inhabited much of Southern Europe and Asiatic Russia.

Sea Anemones *or* **Actinaria,** an order of marine animals of the coelenterate class *Antozia.* They form a large and varied group of about 1,100 species and occur in many beautiful colours, flower-like in form.

Sea Butterfly, marine molluscs which propel themselves by two "wings", or side expansions of the foot. They constitute the order called *Pteropoda.*

Sea Cow. See **Manatee.**

Sea Cucumbers *or* **Holothurians.** These animals constitute the class of echinoderms called *Holothuroidea.* They are elongated and wormlike, with a ring of about twenty tentacles round the mouth. There are about 500 species.

Sea Eagle, a genus of flesh-eating birds related to the true eagles, kites and other birds of prey. Examples are the Bald Eagle, emblem of the USA, White-tailed Eagle (Grey Sea Eagle), and Steller's Sea Eagle of the Pacific coast of Asia. Last known in Britain in 1911, but successfully reintroduced from Norway in 1976 to the coast of Scotland.

Sea Elephant *or* **Elephant Seal,** a curious genus of seal, the males of which possess a proboscis of *c.* 30 cm in length that suggests an elephant's trunk. They are found on the coast of California and in certain parts of the Southern Ocean; their blubber has a commercial value.

Sea Gravimeter, an instrument to determine the density of the earth's crust beneath the oceans of the world. Designed by Dr. A. Graf of Munich and Dr. J. Lamar Worzel of Columbia University, it can detect changes of one-millionth of the value of gravity at the earth's surface.

Sea Hare, a genus of molluscs (*Aplysia*), so-called

because of resemblance to a crouching hare. The shell is thin curved plate largely sunk in the animal's body. They have four tentacles, occur in Britain in the laminaria or ribbon wrack zone, and discharge a purple fluid when molested.

Sea Horse, sea-fish (*Hippocampus*), very numerous in the tropics and comprising some twenty species. Their bodies are ringed and they have prehensile tails. Their heads are horse-shaped, and they swim in a vertical position.

Seal, a marine mammal of the *Phocidae* family. They are found in the cold seas of the world, including the waters around Britain. In 1988, over 17,000 perished in the outbreak of deadly seal distemper.

Sea Lily. A class of echinoderms, the sea lilies may be roughly described as "stalked starfishes". There are about 400 living species and several thousand extinct species are known. Otherwise called Crinoids.

Sea Mouse, a genus of marine worms called *Aphrodite*, oval in shape, 20–23 cm long, iridescent, covered with fine bristles.

Seasons comprise the four natural divisions of the year, and are due to the inclinations of the earth's axis to the plane of the ecliptic (*q.v.*). See **Section Z.**

Sea Squirts *or* **Tunicates.** These animals are placed in the sub-phylum called *Urochorda*; found growing in rounded, jelly-like masses on rocks near low-water level. They get their name through the water jets they discharge.

Sea Urchin, species forming the class *Echinoidae.* The body is globular and covered with spines which may be used for both defence and locomotion. The main organs of locomotion are, however, the tube feet, as in starfishes.

Secondary Sexual Characters, characters of animals which are distinctive of sex, but have no direct connection with the reproductive process. Examples are: the mane of the lion and the antlers of some deer.

Secretary Bird, so called because of the quill-like plumes about its ears, is a bird of prey related to the eagles and vultures; common in Africa, and of considerable service as an exterminator of snakes. It is a large bird about 1·2 m in height.

Sedimentary Rocks. See **F9(1).**

Seismology, the branch of geophysics devoted to the study of earthquakes and other earth movements. The instruments used for the registration of earth tremors are termed seismographs and consist in principle of a pendulum system, the supporting framework following the ground movement and the bob remaining at rest, thus setting up a relative movement between two parts. In order to record the displacements completely, at one station, three seismographs are necessary to show the two horizontal and the vertical components of the motion. Apart from detection and study of waves from earthquakes, sensitive seismographs are now widely used in geophysical prospecting, particularly in the search for oilfields. See also **Richter Scale.**

Selenium, a non-metallic element, no. 34, symbol Se; related to sulphur it is a dark red colour, and solid, found associated with sulphur, iron, pyrites, etc., though only in small quantities. It is a semiconductor (*q.v.*) and its special electrical properties have led to its use in photoelectric cells and rectifiers. Selenium is widely used in the chemical industry as a catalyst (*q.v.*) in producing aromatic hydrocarbons from less useful hydrocarbons. Also used in making some types of glass.

Semiconductors, substances with numerous special and useful electrical properties. These include:

(i) they conduct electricity much better than do insulators, but much less well than metals (hence their name);

(ii) their power to conduct depends strongly on their temperatures—which makes them useful for temperature sensitive devices;

(iii) they are sensitive to light—hence their use in photoelectric cells and solar batteries;

(iv) when in contact with metals, or with other suitable semiconductors, they form a boundary layer which conducts electricity much better one way than the other—this is the basis of many rectifiers some of which, called crystal diodes, are an important component in radios and electronic devices;

(v) their electrical properties can be greatly influenced by putting in minute amounts of impurity, this enables semiconductor devices, especially transistors, to be made with carefully selected properties.

Semiconductors were known to Faraday, but the semiconductor age really arrived with the invention of the transistor (q.v.) in 1947. The ubiquitous transistor is only one of very many semiconductor devices which perform a variety of functions in technical apparatus of all kinds. Semiconductors used in technology are usually small crystals, frequently of germanium or silicon, and their robustness and small power consumption often make them superior to other devices, such as thermionic valves, which they often replace. Other semiconducting materials are cadmium sulphide, selenium lead telluride, indium antimonide. See also **F22(1)**.

Senate, the higher governing Assembly of a Legislature. The word, applied primarily to the Roman council, is also used to denote the upper chamber in the legislatures of France, the United States, and other countries. In certain universities the governing body is also called the Senate.

Sensitive Plant. A species of Mimosa (*Mimosa pudica*), whose leaves are extremely sensitive to touch, shaking and burning.

Sepia, the "ink" of the cuttlefish. See **Ink Sac.**

September, the ninth month of the year, and the seventh of the old Roman calendar; hence the name, from Septimus. The designation was several times changed by the Emperors, but none of the new names survived for long.

Septuagesima Sunday, the third Sunday before Lent.

Septuagint, the Greek translation of the Old Testament made by Alexandrian Jews between 250 B.C. and 100 B.C. from Hebrew texts now lost. There are many differences between the Septuagint and the Massoretic version (A.D. 900), and therefore it is of great value for textual criticism. The symbol for the Septuagint is LXX.

Serfs, the name given to the peasants formerly existing in Russia, who answered to the condition of the feudal "villeins" of England. They were attached to the soil and were transferred with it in all sales or leases. Serfdom existed in Prussia until 1807 and in Russia until 1861.

Serpentine, a mineral: chemically a hydrous silicate of magnesium. Green serpentine is used as an ornament stone. Fibrous serpentine is called asbestos.

Serval, a collie-dog-sized cat, long-limbed and spotted, from Africa. Preys on a variety of animals, from lizards to small antelope. Black servals occur mainly in mountainous regions.

Set, both in everyday speech (as in tea set, chess set) and in mathematics, a set is a collection of things. The members of the set can be specified by listing them or by describing the properties necessary for membership of the set, e.g., the set of ginger-haired boxers. Set theory is a very important branch of mathematics founded by a great mathematician, Georg Cantor (1845–1918). Its development has influenced many other branches of mathematics. Perhaps one reflection of its fundamental nature is to be found in the fact that many schoolchildren, even of tender age, are now learning set theory and confounding parents who did not hear of it at school when they were there.

Settlement, Act of, passed in 1701, assigned the Crown to the House of Hanover in case of Anne's death without children. The decision represented the determination of the squires and the Anglican Church never again to trust themselves to a Roman Catholic king.

Seven Champions of Christendom, as set forth in mediaeval literature, were St. George of England, St. Andrew of Scotland, St. Patrick of Ireland, St. David of Wales, St. James of Spain, St. Denis of France, and St. Antony of Italy.

Seven Churches of Asia, referred to in the Revelation of St. John, were those of Ephesus, founded by St. Paul in 57, Smyrna, Pergamos, Thyatira, Sardis, Philadelphia (Lydia) and Laodicea (Phrygia), all in W. Asia Minor.

Seven Wonders of the World were: 1. The Pyramids of Egypt; 2. the tomb of Mausolus, King of Caria (hence the word mausoleum); 3. the Temple of Diana at Ephesus; 4. the Walls and Hanging Gardens of Babylon; 5. the Colossus at Rhodes; 6. the Ivory and Gold Statue of Jupiter Olympus; and 7. the Pharos, or Watch Tower, built at Alexandria by Ptolemy Philadelphus, King of Egypt.

Seven Years War was waged by Frederick the Great and England against Austria, France, and Russia, from 1756 to 1763. It resulted in the retention of Silesia by Prussia, the breaking of French power in India and the strengthening of our Indian Empire.

Severn Barrage, a barrier across the River Severn estuary proposed with a view to extracting useful electrical energy from tidal power. Essentially the idea is to let the tidal water flow into a reservoir upstream from the barrage and then to flow seaward under gravity through specially designed hydroelectric generators situated on the barrage. Tidal power has been harnessed in a French project and there is little doubt that the Severn scheme is technically feasible. However, environmental, economic and social factors enter the matter and are influencing consideration of its overall desirability. See also **Tidal Power.**

Sexagesima Sunday is the 2nd Sunday before Lent.

Sextant, a reflecting instrument for measuring the angular distances of objects. It is of special importance in navigation and surveying, and contains 60 degrees described on a graduated arc. A small telescope is attached and there are also a couple of mirrors which reflect the distant objects so as to enable them to be accurately observed. The invention is attributed to John Hadley, and to Thomas Godfrey independently, about 1780. The principle had been foreseen, and its application described, at earlier dates by Newton, Halley and Hooke.

Shad, a marine fish belonging to the same genus as the herring. It is found along the Atlantic Coast of the USA, and ascends rivers to spawn.

Shagreen, shark's skin: also untanned leather of peculiar grain made from skins of wild asses, camels and horses.

Shalloon, a kind of cloth manufactured from wool and worsted, and used chiefly for women's dresses and coat linings. It gets its name from the fact that it was originally made at Châlons-sur-Marne. It was called "chalouns" by Chaucer and "shalloons" by Swift.

Shamrock, the three-leaved clover-like plant native to Ireland and its national emblem.

Shark, a large and powerful ocean fish, comprising many species, very widely distributed, but most numerous in tropical seas. They have formidable teeth and are the most carnivorous of all fishes. They usually attain a large size, the whale-shark being often of a length of 15 m. Commercially the shark yields shagreen from its skin, the fins are made into gelatine, and an oil is obtained from the liver.

Sheep, a well-known family of ruminants of great utility as wool-producers, and for food. From the earliest times sheep have been a source of wealth to England. So much were they valued in the 15th and 16th cent., that their exportation was frequently prohibited. Sheep are classified under (1) longwools; (2) shortwools; and (3) mountain breeds. Most of the longwools carry Leicester blood in their ancestry and the shortwooled Down breeds carry the blood of the Southdown. The Southdown produced the present Suffolk, one of the most popular breeds. Cheviot is an important mountain breed. Of the foreign breeds the most valued are the Merino sheep of Spain, which yield a fine long wool. Australia, USSR, China, New Zealand, India, Argentina, South Africa, Turkey, Iran, UK are the chief wool-producing countries in the world.

Shelduck, a handsome genus of surface-feeding ducks, one of which, the common shelduck, is an inhabitant of Great Britain. It is a beautiful white-and-chestnut plumaged bird with dark-green head and neck and red bill. Another species, the ruddy shelduck, appears in Britain only occasionally.

Shellac. This resin is the secretion of the lac

insect (*Coccus lacca*), which occurs in forests of Assam and Thailand. It is used for making varnish and in the manufacture of gramophone records. *See also* **Lac.**

Sherardizing. Process for coating steel or iron parts with zinc to prevent corrosion; this is done by heating the parts in a closed rotating drum containing zinc dust.

Shilling has been an English coin from Saxon times, but it was not of the value of 12 pence until after the Conquest. It is interchangeable with the 5 new pence decimal piece which came into circulation in 1968. A new, smaller 5p coin will be introduced after 1991.

Ships have existed from prehistoric times. There is mention of one that sailed from Egypt to Greece in 1485 B.C., and in 786 B.C. the Tyrians built a double-decked vessel. No double-decked ship was known in England, however, before the *Royal Harry* was built by Henry VII, and it was not until the 17th cent. that ship-building was carried on in Great Britain as a prominent industry.

Shoddy, the name given to a kind of cloth mainly composed of woollen or worsted rags, torn up and re-fabricated by powerful machinery. It was first made at Batley in Yorkshire about 1813, and became a very important industry employing many thousands of people at Batley and the neighbouring town of Dewsbury.

Shot, the name given to solid projectiles fired from guns. In the time of Henry V stone shot was used, later leaden shot, then iron shot, and finally steel shot, introduced by Sir Joseph Whitworth.

Shrike, a large and varied family of birds of hawk-like behaviour found in all continents except S. America. The Red-backed Shrike, which winters in Africa, is a breeding visitor to England and Wales. It is commonly called the "Butcher Bird" from the way it impales its prey (small birds and insects) on thorn-twigs. The other species on the British list are the Great Grey Shrike, the Lesser Grey Shrike, the Woodchat Shrike, and the Masked Shrike.

Shrove Tuesday, the day before the first day of Lent, receiving its name from the old custom of shriving, or making confession, on that day. In England the day has always been associated with the making of pancakes.

Sicilian Vespers, the term applied to the terrible massacre of French people in Sicily in 1282. The French under Charles of Anjou were then in occupation of the island and had been guilty of many cruelties. It began at Palermo on Easter Monday at the hour of vespers and resulted in the expulsion of the French king and the introduction of Spanish rule.

Silence, Tower of, or *dakhma*, a tower about 8 m high, built by the Parsees for their dead. The corpse is taken inside by professional corpse-bearers and left to be consumed by vultures. Parsees do not burn or bury their dead, and the *dakhma* is to protect the living and the elements from defilement.

Silicon, an important non-metallic element, no. 14, symbol Si, it is related to carbon. Next to oxygen, it is the most abundant constituent of the earth's crust (27% by weight). It occurs in many rocks, and its oxide occurs in many forms (*e.g.* quartz, sand, flint, agate, chalce-dony, opal, etc.). Principally used as a semi-conducting material for making transistors and similar devices. The circuitry of the computer is etched on a chip of silicon.

Silicones are synthetic organic derivatives of silicon which because of their high resistance to heat and moisture have special uses, *e.g.*, lubri-cants, heat-resistant resins and lacquers, and water-repellent finishes. Silicones are com-pounds in which the molecules consist of chains of atoms of silicon and oxygen alternately. Silicones were developed in the United States from discoveries first made by Prof. F. S. Kipping at Nottingham University. Manu-facture began in Britain in 1950, and in the form of fluids, resins, rubbers and greases they find wide use in industry. The largest plant in Europe is in Glamorgan.

Silk, the name given to a soft glossy fabric manu-factured from the fine thread produced by the silkworm. It was known to, and highly prized by the ancients, being at one time paid for, weight for weight, with gold. The manufacture of silk was carried on in Sicily in the 12th cent., later spreading to Italy, Spain and France, where Lyons has been the great centre of pro-duction from 1450 to this day. It was not manufactured in England before 1604; but when certain French refugees established them-selves at Spitalfields in 1688, the industry was developed and became of importance. In the 18th cent. the Lombes of Derby achieved great success in this industry. Japan, China, Italy, and Korea are the chief silk-producing countries.

Silkworm, the larva of a species of moth, *Bombyx mori.* It is native to China, and has been cultivated with success in India, Iran, Turkey and Italy. The silkworm of commerce feeds on mulberry leaves and produces a cocoon of silk varying in colour from white to orange. The cocoon is the silken habitation constructed by the worm for its entrance upon the pupal condi-tion, and to obtain the silk the pupa is killed by immersing in hot water.

Sill, a sheet-like mass of igneous rock which has been intruded parallel with the stratification of the country rock, cf. a dyke.

Silurian. This geological period is one of the major subdivisions of the Palaeozoic era. Its beginning is estimated at 440 million years ago, and the period lasted about 40 million years. Maximum thickness of the Silurian strata in Britain measures 4,575 m. *See* **F48.**

Silver, a white precious metallic element, no. 47, symbol Ag (Latin *argentum*) found in a free state, also in certain combinations, and in a variety of ores. The chief silver-producing regions are the Andes and Cordilleras. Peru, Bolivia and Mexico have yielded vast supplies of the metal since the 16th century, and Colorado and Nevada in the United States have also been very prolific in silver yield. In England standard silver (that used for coinage) formerly contained 92½ per cent. fine silver and 7½ per cent. alloy, but when the price rose to 89½d. per oz and the coins be-came worth more than the face value, the Coinage Act of 1920 was passed, reducing the fineness to half. To provide silver bullion for industry and for a fund towards the redemption of our silver debt to America, it was decided in 1946 to replace the United Kingdom silver coinage by one made of cupro-nickel (75 per cent. copper, 25 per cent. nickel). Maundy money, however, is of the original silver standard. Silver chloride and bromide are light-sensitive compounds and are used in photography.

Simony, the offence of trading in church offices, has been contrary to English law since the time of Edward VI. Elizabeth also promulgated laws against simony. In 1879 a Royal Com-mission reported on the law and existing practice as to the sale, exchange and resignation of benefices. The position is now controlled by the Benefices Act 1898, the Amendment Measure 1923, and the Benefices Rules 1926.

Sinn Fein (*Irish* = ourselves alone), Irish national-istic movement founded in 1905 which de-veloped into a mass republican party and tri-umphed in the establishment of the Irish Free State. An extremist group has survived which represents politically the outlawed IRA. In Northern Ireland Sinn Fein was legalized in 1974.

Sins, The Seven Deadly or Capital sins are pride, avarice, lust, anger, gluttony, envy, sloth.

Sirius, the dog-star, so called because of its situa-tion in the mouth of the Dog (Canis Major): it is the brightest star in the sky, and is also one of the nearest to us.

Sirocco, a warm, southerly, often dust-laden, wind blowing across Mediterranean lands from the Sahara, in advance of an eastward-moving depression over the Mediterranean.

Siskin, a small bird of the finch family, common in Northern regions, nesting in Britain. The common Siskin has a yellow-green colour and is a lively, swift-flying bird with a stout bill.

Sistine Chapel, the chapel of the Pope in the Vati-can, renowned for its frescoes by Michelangelo.

S.I. Units (Système International d'Unités) form an internationally recognised system of metric units for scientific and technical quantities. The basic units of length, time, mass, electric current, temperature, amount of substance, and luminous intensity are, respectively the metre, second, kilogram, ampere, kelvin (*see* **Absolute Temperature**) mole (*see* **F24**) and candela. The S.I. was recommended for general adoption by a number of international organisations such as the General Conference on Weights and Measures (1960). Many countries have made or are making the S.I. the only legally recognised set of Units. Gt. Britain's decision to "go metric" has brought general use of S.I. units in its train. These units command the widespread though not absolutely unanimous support of industrialists, technologists, and scientists. Many have urged their adoption to end the confusing multiplicity of units on the world scene. *See also* **F66–69**.

Six Articles, The Statute of the, was passed in 1539 for compelling adhesion to the chief doctrines of Roman Catholic faith: transubstantiation, communion in one kind only for the laity, vows of chastity, celibacy of the clergy, private masses and auricular confession; those who refused to subscribe to the Articles were treated as heretics. The Act was repealed in 1547.

Skink. The skinks constitute a large family of lizards with large smooth scales, under each of which is a bony plate. The largest species, found in Australia, is about 61 cm long. Some skinks have adopted a burrowing habit and degeneration of the limbs is associated with this. The Common Skink is a small species *c.* 12 cm long, living in deserts of N. Africa.

Skua, falcon-like marine birds related to the gulls found throughout the world. Known as "Robber Birds" because they steal not only the young and eggs of other birds (including penguins) but also their food, which they force them to disgorge in mid-air. The Arctic Skua breeds as far south as Scotland. The Great Skua breeds in both Antarctica and Arctica. Other species are the Pomarine, the Long-tailed, and McCormick's Skua.

Skunk, a North American mammal of the weasel family, with short legs and long bushy tail. All fifteen species are black and white, some being striped and the rest spotted. It secretes and ejects at will a foul-smelling fluid.

Sky. The blue colour of the sky on a summer's day is the result of the scattering of light waves by particles of dust and vapour in the earth's atmosphere. Blue light having almost the smallest wavelength in the visible spectrum (0·00004 cm) is scattered laterally about 10 times as much as the red (0·00007 cm).

Skyscraper. Owing to lack of ground space, increasing cost of land, and growth of modern cities, buildings are being made higher than broader; hence the name. The structures are constructed of steel framework usually clothed in concrete or reinforced concrete. The first modern skyscraper of steel skeletal construction was the Home Insurance Building in Chicago, designed (1883) by William Le Baron. The New York skyscrapers include the World Trade Center building (110 stories), Empire State building (102 stories), Chrysler (77 stories), Rockefeller Center (70 stories), and 60 Wall Tower (67 stories). The tallest building in Britain, recently built, is National Westminster Bank tower, dominating the city skyline (183 m), topping the British Telecom radio tower by 6 m. The tallest *structure* in Britain is the IBA mast at Belmont, Lincs., (387.1m).

Slate, fine-grained clayey rocks which have undergone metamorphism. They cleave easily, and it is this property of cleavage which makes them a valuable source of roofing material. Important quarries producing mainly green slate are in the Coniston–Ambleside area of the Lake District.

Slavery. In its earlier forms, as in the times of ancient Greece and Rome, in the feudal ages, when vassalage and villeinage existed, and in the serfdom of Russia and other northern nations, slavery was attended by many inhumanities and evils; but perhaps in the negro slavery system which prevailed in the British colonies for upwards of 200 years and in certain parts of the United States up to 1865, it attained its highest point of cruelty. In 1833 the Act of Emancipation was passed, emancipating all slaves in British territories, though slavery continued to be tolerated in northern Nigeria, Sierra Leone and in the Anglo-Egyptian Sudan long after that date. Even today slavery and

forced labour are still prevalent in some parts of the world.

Slide Rule, an instrument which consists of two logarithmic scales sliding alongside each other. By its use multiplication, division, extraction of roots, etc., are speedily carried out.

Sloth, a curious family of mammals, only found in Central and South America. They dwell almost entirely in the trees, proceeding from branch to branch with their bodies hanging downwards, their weight being supported by their large hook-like claws. They eat foliage.

Slow-Worm, a species of lizard found in Britain which lacks legs. Silver with longitudinal brown stripes, it lives almost entirely on slugs.

Smelting. The process of heating an ore with a reducing agent to convert ore into metal, and with a flux to convert rocky impurities into a slag that will float on top of the molten metal. Slag and metal can then be tapped separately. An example is iron smelting; the reducing agent is coke, and limestone is added as the flux; the smelting is carried out in a blast furnace.

Snake. The snakes constitute the important reptilian order *Ophidia*. Snakes have a scaly, cylindrical, limbless body, lidless eyes, forked tongue, and the upper and lower jaws joined by an elastic ligament. All snakes have teeth used for seizing prey, and the poisonous varieties are furnished with poison fangs in the upper jaw. These fangs have hollow modified teeth and the venom passes into them from a special gland situated behind the angle of the mouth. Some 2,500 species of snakes are known, divided into 13 families. There are 3 British species—the grass-snake, smooth-snake, and adder.

Snipe, a wading bird, long-legged, with long, slender, straight bill, brown plumage, and zigzag flight. The Common Snipe breeds locally throughout Britain; the Great Snipe and small Jack Snipe are occasional visitors. The close season is February 1 to August 11.

Snow. When water vapour condenses at high levels at a temperature below freezing (sublimation), a cloud of ice particles is-formed. If these frozen droplets are small, they fall slowly and gradually assume a feathery crystalline structure, reaching the earth as snowflakes if the temperature remains below freezing.

Socialism. *See* **Section J.**

Soda, carbonate of sodium, is now mainly obtained by certain processes of manufacture from common salt. It was formerly obtained from the ashes of plants. Bicarbonate of sodium is the primary product in the Solvay or Ammonia-soda method for commercial manufacture of soda; it is also formed when carbon dioxide is passed into strong soda solution. The bicarbonate is used in medicine and in the preparation of baking powder.

Sodium, a metallic element, no. 11, symbol Na (Latin *Natrium*), first obtained by Sir Humphry Davy in 1807 from caustic soda by means of the electric battery. Its chloride is *common salt*; the deposits of salt (*e.g.*, in Cheshire and at Stassfurt) have come into existence through the drying up of inland seas. Salt occurs in sea-water to the extent of about 3 per cent.; the Dead Sea contains about 22 per cent. The blood of animals is maintained at a level of about 0·6% sodium chloride. That there is sodium in the sun's atmosphere was confirmed in 1859 by Kirchhoff from his spectroscopic observations. Liquid sodium metal has properties which make it suitable as a coolant in some nuclear reactors; a technique of handling this very reactive liquid has had to be developed.

Software, the internal programmes and operating procedures of a computer as opposed to its hardware. This includes system software designed to make the computer usable as well as programmes intended for particular applications (*e.g.* commercial or scientific calculations).

Soil Erosion occurs when the soil is removed from an area at a faster rate than soil formation. This situation usually occurs as a result of man's interference with the natural balance of the environment by the removal of natural vegetation, overgrazing or by poor farming techniques. Soil thus exposed is then removed by the wind (as in the Dust Bowl in the 1930s) or by rain in the form of gully or sheet erosion (as in the Tennessee Valley, USA). Methods introduced to stop soil erosion include contour ploughing, afforestation and dry farming techniques.

Solar Battery, one of the innumerable devices made possible by the development of semi-conducting materials, notably germanium and silicon. This device creates an electric current from light falling on it. The current can be put to use or stored in storage batteries. The energy of the current is derived from the sunlight, and the solar battery is thus an *energy converting* apparatus. Solar batteries have provided power for the instruments in satellites.

Solar Wind, a continuous stream of electrically charged particles blowing outwards from the sun, supplemented from time to time by intense outbursts from particular regions of the sun's surface. These streams of protons and electrons on encountering the earth's magnetic field distort it and cause magnetic storms (*q.v.*) and aurorae (*q.v.*).

Soldering is a means of joining together two pieces of material, usually metals, by melting a third metal (the solder) into the joint. The solder solidifies in the pores of the other metals and holds them together. The materials to be joined are not themselves melted so the technique requires less heat than welding. Solders are alloys; there are many kinds depending on the materials to be joined and the strength of joint desired. *See* **Welding.**

Solstice, an astronomical term indicating the point at which the sun is most distant from the equator. *See* **Seasons, Section Z.**

Soundings at sea, to determine depth at any point, have been taken in all seas, and with considerable accuracy. A deep reading was that of the *Challenger* expedition in 1873, near St. Thomas's in the North Atlantic, when 3,875 fathoms (7,091 m) were sounded. In 1851 H.M.S. *Challenger* recorded the then maximum ocean depth in the Marianas Trench (W. Pacific) by echo-sounding as between 5,882 and 5,950 fathoms (10,764 and 10,800 m). Another deep was located in the S. Pacific in 1952–53 of 5,814 fathoms (10,640 m) in the Tonga Trench, 290 km S. of Tonga Tabu. Since then even greater depths have been recorded, in the Marianas Trench and the Mindanao Deep. *See* **Pacific Ocean.**

Southern Cross, popular name of *Crux,* a constellation of the Southern hemisphere, consisting of four bright stars in the form of a Latin cross. It has been called the pole-star of the south and is indispensable to seafarers.

South Sea Bubble, the name given to a series of financial projects which began with the formation of the South Sea Company in 1711 and ended nine years later in disaster after a mania of speculation. The idea behind the parent scheme was that the state should sell certain trading monopolies in the South seas in return for a sum of money to pay off the National Debt (which stood at £51,300,000 in 1719 when the scheme started). The idea fascinated the public, fabulous profits being dreamt of, and the price of the stock rose out of all proportion to the earnings of the Company. Many dishonest speculative ventures sprang up in imitation with the inevitable result that thousands were ruined. All classes had joined in the gamble and a Committee of Secrecy set up by the House of Commons in December 1720 to investigate the affairs of the Company proved that there had been fraud and corruption on a large scale in the affairs of the Company. Sir Robert Walpole, an opponent of the scheme from the outset, dealt with the crisis.

Space Flight. The Soviet Union was the first country to launch a man into space and bring him safely back to earth. This epoch-making event took place on 12 April 1961, when Yuri Gagarin, tragically killed in an air crash in 1968, circled the earth in a spaceship weighing about 4,826 kg. It was launched by rocket in an elliptical orbit with greatest height 300 km and least 175 km. The inclination of the orbit to the equator was 65° 4′, and the period of revolution was 89 min. 6s. Since then, the Russian *Vostok* cosmonauts Titov (17 orbits), Nikolaev (64 orbits), Popovich (48 orbits), Bykovsky (81 orbits), Tereshkova, the first woman space traveller (48 orbits), the *Voskhod* cosmonauts Komarov, Feoktistov and Yegorov

(16 orbits), Belyaev and Leonov (17 orbits), the American *Mercury* astronauts Glenn (3 orbits), Carpenter (3 orbits), Schirra (6 orbits), Cooper (22 orbits), the *Gemini* astronauts Grissom and Young (3 orbits), McDivitt and White (62 orbits), Cooper and Conrad (120 orbits), Borman and Lovell (206 orbits), Schirra and Stafford (15 orbits), Armstrong and Scott (6·6 orbits), Stafford and Cernan (44 orbits), Young and Collins (43 orbits), Conrad and Gordon (44 orbits), Lovell and Aldrin (60 orbits) were among the first to complete successful missions in space. Leonov was the first to perform the extra-vehicular (EVA) experiment (1965), *i.e.,* to leave an orbiting spaceship and float in space. Russia was the first to achieve an automatic docking (link-up) between two unmanned spacecraft in orbital flight (October 1967), and of two unmanned spacecraft (January 1969). The American *Apollo* mission was accomplished when Armstrong and Aldrin became the first men to set foot on the moon (July 1969). A joint Soviet-American project culminated in a *Soyuz–Apollo* link-up 225 km up on 17 July 1975. On 11 January 1978 two Soviet spacecraft docked with an orbiting laboratory, the first triple link-up in space. The longest endurance record is held by Valentin Lebedev and Anatoly Berezevoy (211 days in space aboard *Salyut 7* in 1982). The first free walk in space was made by two American astronauts on 7 February 1984 from the space shuttle *Challenger.* The *Challenger* disaster in January 1986 disrupted America's space programme.

Space Research. By space research we mean scientific research work which can only be carried to otherwise inaccessible observing locations by rocket propulsion. Such propulsion does not rely on the presence of an atmosphere to provide oxygen so that it is capable in principle of conveying objects to unlimited distances. The subject of space research is, therefore, one which is concerned with scientific applications in various fields of a single highly specialised and powerful technique. It is not a single discipline, but can provide data of great importance for many, such as the physics of the earth, the sun, moon and other bodies of the solar system, astronomy, geodesy and the study of gravitation. The prospect of investigating the biological conditions on different planets such as Mars and Venus is also opened, as well as that of experimental biological studies under conditions of zero gravity. Although the results of many aspects of space research are vital for those concerned with the practical realisation of manned travel in space, space research is largely a branch of pure science, independent of any applications which may stem from it. The major technical problems involved are:

    (*a*) Launching of the instrument-containing vehicle with the necessary velocity.
    (*b*) Guidance and control of the vehicle so it pursues the desired path.
    (*c*) Tracking the vehicle to determine its actual path and the position on the path at any time.
    (*d*) Transmission of the data, recorded by the instruments, back to the earth.
    (*e*) Satisfactory operation of scientific instruments in the environment within the vehicle.
    (*f*) Provision of adequate power supplies to operate the equipment within the vehicle for sufficiently long periods.

It is important to distinguish three distinct types of vehicle—the vertical sounding rocket, the artificial earth satellite, and the deep space probe. The track of a vertical sounding rocket is mainly vertical, and the whole path to the highest point and back is traversed in a few minutes only. An earth satellite circulates in an orbit round the earth in the same way as does our natural satellite, the moon. If it approaches the earth at any point within 160 km of the surface the air resistance causes the path to spiral in so rapidly that the vehicle is eventually burnt up by air friction within the dense atmosphere after an orbital life of a few months only. It follows that artificial satellite vehicles are only useful as instrument containers if the distance of closest approach (the perigee distance) is not much less than 160 km. For the study of the properties of the atmosphere at lower altitudes down to the limit (32 km) attainable by balloons, vertical sounding rockets must be used. It is a great advantage for work at higher altitudes to use satellites, as it is then possible to make systematic observations for months at a time from a great number of positions relative to the earth. During recent years both the American and Russian space programmes have developed the concept of space stations for providing facilities for continuous manned observatories and laboratories in the future. There have now been successful soft landings on Mars and Venus, and "fly by" visits to Jupiter and Saturn. Voyager 2 left Saturn in Aug. 1981 visiting the planets Uranus (1986) and Neptune (1989) and continuing beyond. See also **Voyagers 1 and 2.**

Space Shuttle. The first reusable manned space vehicle, *Columbia*, was launched on 12 April 1981 from Cape Canaveral, Florida. It orbited the earth 36 times and returned on 14 April landing in California after a flight of 34 h 22 min with its two crew members controlling its landing. The 1986 *Challenger* disaster was a severe blow.

Spanish Civil War, 1936 to 1939. The war began with a revolt by the Fascist General Franco against the Republic which had succeeded the Monarchy in 1931. Germany and Italy aided the rebels who besieged Madrid for over 2 years. An International Brigade was formed to help the Republic, but the Spanish Government was faced with the greater part of the Army, and very effective assistance from Italy and Germany. Those powers seized the opportunity to have a curtain-raiser to the world conflict which they intended to precipitate. After a total loss of a million men the Fascists overpowered the Republic.

Sparrow, name given to finch-like birds found in most parts of the world, of which the House Sparrow *Passer domesticus*, is the most familiar of British birds. Also native to Britain is the rural Tree Sparrow, distinguished from the male House Sparrow by its chestnut crown. Other European species are the Italian, Spanish and Rock Sparrows.

Specific Gravity, defined as the ratio of the mass of a particular volume of a substance to the mass of an equal volume of water at 4°C. See **Hydrometer.**

Spectroscopy. Newton's arrangement with the prism was the first spectroscope; its function was to separate out the colour components of a source of light. Two hundred years elapsed before this apparatus was developed into a precise scientific instrument, capable of measuring both the wavelength and intensity of each colour component. In this form it is called a spectrometer. All atoms and molecules have well defined characteristic spectra which can be used to recognise them. In order to produce emission spectra it is necessary to energise the material under investigation by some means, such as by heating in a flame. The resulting radiation then consists largely of sharp bright lines, characteristic of the material. Absorption spectra are produced by interposing the experimental material between a white light source and the spectrometer. Then dark lines are seen, corresponding to absorptions of energy, in exactly the same places as the bright lines are observed in the emission spectra. Spectroscopic techniques have now been developed to such an extent that accurate measurements of wavelength and intensity are possible not only in the visible region, but over almost the whole of the electromagnetic spectrum. Two of the most useful types for the chemist are infrared spectroscopy which reveals absorption characteristic of the type of chemical bonds because of their different bond vibration frequencies and nuclear magnetic resonance spectroscopy which operates in the radiofrequency region. It reveals the structure environments of atoms containing particular nuclei. Not only does spectroscopy play an important rôle in probing the structure of matter, but it can be applied in the field of astronomy. The use of radio wave spectroscopy has led to the discovery of several new types of stellar object, and this data is now producing a complete re-

appraisal of our understanding of the universe. See **F14(2).**

Sphinx, in Greek mythology, a winged creature with a woman's head and a lion's body. The sphinx of ancient Egypt represented the pharaoh in a divine form.

Spiritualism. See **Section J.**

Spirituals, negro melodies with religious inspiration and which are still spontaneously created, but have also passed into art-music.

Sponge. See **Porifera, F36(1).**

Spoonbill, a long-legged, marsh bird, closely related to the ibis and stork, remarkable for its snowwhite plumage and broad, flat, spoon-shaped bill. The European species has not bred in England since the beginning of the 17th cent., but is still a regular summer visitor from the Netherlands, where it nests in colonies in reed beds and islets.

Sputniks, the name of the Russian earth satellites first launched during the period of the International Geophysical Year. *Sputnik I*, launched 4 October 1957, became the first man-made earth satellite. *Sputnik II*, launched a month later carried a dog as passenger. *Sputnik III*, launched in May 1958, and weighing well over 2 tonnes, became the first fully-equipped laboratory to operate in space. The father of space travel with rockets was a Russian—Konstantin Eduardovich Tsiolkovsky—the centenary of whose birth practically coincided with the launching of the first earth satellite.

Stalactites are deposits of calcium carbonate formed on the roofs and sides of limestone caves, and in tunnels, under bridges, and other places where the carbonic acid of rain-water percolates through and partly dissolves the limestone, resulting in the growth of icicle-like forms that often assume groupings. The water that drops from these may deposit further calcium carbonate, which accumulates and hardens into sharp mounds or hillocks called stalagmites.

Standard Deviation. In statistics it is often desirable to compare the variability or "spread" of different sets of data. For example, two kinds of light bulb could have the same average life but one kind could be more uniform or consistent than the other. The standard deviation is one of the commonest measures of spread. It is found as follows. If x is one of the data and $\bar{x}$ is the mean of all the x's, then $x - \bar{x}$ is called the deviation. Every deviation is now squared and the average squared deviation calculated. The standard deviation is then the square root of the average squared deviation. The lifetimes of the more uniform kind of light bulb would have a smaller standard deviation than those of the more erratic one.

Star Chamber, an ancient tribunal of state in existence in 1487 and possibly earlier, charged with the duty of trying offences against the government, unfettered by the ordinary rules of law. It was in effect a Privy Council entrusted with judicial functions. Under Charles I the Star Chamber was used by the King and his party to persecute opponents; and in 1641 a Bill carried in both Houses abolished it.

Starling (*Sturnus vulgaris*), a well-known European bird now common in many parts of the world. It has handsome iridescent blackish plumage and nests in holes and crevices. Flocks of starlings are often seen wheeling in the air; thousands roost on buildings in the heart of London. Other European species are the Spotless and Rose-coloured starlings. The latter sometimes wanders to the British Isles.

States-General, national assembly in which the chief estates of the realm were represented as separate bodies. The name, though not the institution, has survived in the Netherlands, where the two houses of parliament are known as states-general. In France the states-general consisted of three orders, clergy, nobility and commons. Philip IV first summoned it in 1302 to support him in his quarrel with Pope Boniface VIII. While absolute monarchy was establishing itself it met rarely, and not at all from 1614 until 1789, when it was convoked as a last resort by Louis XVI. But when it met it declared itself the National Assembly which marked the beginning of the revolution.

Statistics is a science that deals with the collection of numerical facts and the evaluation of their significance. The word is also used to refer to the facts themselves as in "trade statistics". This important science gives precise meanings to words like "average" and to statements like "this set of data is significantly different from that". In a world in which more and more information is becoming available in numerical form (I.Q.s, examination results, tax yields, health records, road accidents, etc.) the proper—as opposed to the misleading—use of statistics cannot be over-emphasised. Many young people can now study statistics at school and college, and governments and industries employ many statisticians. See **Average**.

Statute of Westminster 1931. An Act of parliament which gave a basis of equality to the British Dominions. The Dominions as well as the United Kingdom were defined by the Balfour Memorandum of 1926 as "autonomous communities within the British Empire, equal in status, in no way subordinate one to another in any aspect of their domestic or external affairs, though united by a common allegiance to the Crown, and freely associated as members of the British Commonwealth of Nations". The Statute was the sequel. The Dominions are sovereign States governed solely by their own Parliaments and Governments.

Steam Engine, a machine whereby steam becomes the active agent of the working of machinery, and of very wide application. The leading types of steam engine are: (a) condensing, or low-pressure engines, where the steam is generated by a boiler; (b) non-condensing, in which the cylinder exhausts its steam into the open air. Engines of the latter type are used where portable engines are required.

Steam-hammer, invented (1839) by the Scottish engineer James Nasmyth. Consists basically of a vertical steam cylinder atop two legs with piston-rod passing through cylinder base and attached to a tup (hammer) of from 100 kg to 15 tonnes which rests on an anvil. The tup slides in V grooves on inside of legs. Length of stroke and therefore weight of blow can be accurately controlled from a light tap to a massive punch. It made possible the forging in one piece of multi-throw crankshafts for marine engines, etc. and the mass production of high-class axles and wheels, con rods and buffers, etc. for locomotives and rolling stock.

Stearin is the portion of fatty matters and oils which remains solid at an ordinary temperature, and is a compound of stearic acid with glycerine. It is largely used in the manufacture of candles. With caustic soda stearin forms a soap (sodium stearate), which is present in most commercial soaps which contain sodium palmitate and oleate in addition.

Steel, an alloy of iron and carbon, with varying proportions of other minerals. The famous blades of Damascus and steels of Toledo were made by the cementation and crucible method. The metal produced by the "Bessemer process" (q.v.) is of the highest value for structural purposes, rails, etc. In recent years the technique known as continuous casting has been developed which bypasses some major steps in the conventional process of steel-making.

Stereophonic Broadcasting. A person having normal hearing is able to determine the direction from which a sound reaches him by virtue of the fact that he has two ears, and, therefore, the sound will reach one of them a fraction of a second before it reaches the other. This difference in arrival time allows the brain to calculate direction. It will, therefore, be apparent that if the same person listens to, say, an orchestral concert in a large hall he will be able to determine—even with his eyes shut—the approximate position of a particular instrument with respect to the rest of the orchestra. If, however, he listens at home to a broadcast of the same concert, then, due to the fact that he hears the music after it has been picked up by a single microphone located at one point and radiated over a single-channel transmission system, he will be unable to allocate a definite position to any instrument. The aim of stereophonic broadcasting, or sound reproduction therefore, is to restore the listener's ability to locate the position in space of the various sources of sound and to follow movement. To do this it is necessary to use two microphones in the studio—to simulate the two human ears—and to transmit their outputs, through two similar, but separate, chains of equipment, to two radio receivers and their two loudspeakers, which must be placed some distance apart, in the listener's home. The fundamental work on two-channel stereophony was done by A. D. Blumlein (1903–42), an electronics engineer and inventor of E.M.I. Ltd., his original patent being dated 1931.

Stereotype, a metal cast taken from movable type which has been set up in the ordinary way. The first to introduce the process in practical form in this country was William Ged, of Edinburgh, who made stereotype plates in 1730. An impression of the type matter is first taken by means of a mould of prepared plaster of Paris or moistened sheets of specially prepared paper and when molten stereo metal is poured upon the mould and allowed to cool and harden, the stereo plate is formed, and can be printed from as a solid block for some time.

Steroids. A class of structurally related compounds, based on a system of condensed rings of carbon and hydrogen, which are widely distributed in animals and plants. Included in the steroid family are sterols, found in all animal cells, vitamin D, sex hormones, bile acids and cortisone, a drug used in the treatment of rheumatic fever.

Stickleback, a family of small spiny-finned fish widely distributed in both fresh and salt water. Male constructs roofed nest held together by sticky secretion from glands near kidneys. Several females deposit eggs therein which he jealously guards until after young are hatched.

Stirrup, a loop of metal U-shaped strap suspended from the sides of the saddle, used for mounting and to support the horseman's foot. Some authorities allege their use as far back as the early Iron Age, and it is generally believed that they were used in battle in A.D. 378, when the Gothic cavalry defeated the legionaries of the Emperor Valens at Adrianople. Stirrups relieved the tension of the rider's knees and so enabled him to be armed from top to toe.

Stoat, a slender, carnivorous mammal with short legs, related to the weasels. The stoat is distinguished from the latter by its longer tail, which has a black tip. The black tip is retained even in the winter when the animal turns white, the fur then being known as "ermine". It is found in northern latitudes, and is abundant in Arctic America.

Stoma (pl. **stomata**), microscopic pores on the surfaces of leaves through which gaseous exchanges take place and water is lost. It has been estimated that a single maize plant bears 200 million stomata, usually closed at night.

Stone-Flies, comprise the order of insects called *Plecoptera*, which includes some 700 species, of which about thirty occur in Britain. The wings are membranous, and two long, thread-like feelers protrude at the tail end. The larvae are aquatic.

Stonehenge, a remarkable collection of Bronze Age monuments on Salisbury Plain. The site which contains ditches, earthwork-banks and megaliths (large stones) has long been recognised for its architectural innovations (the trilithon or free-standing arch and the circle of dressed and lintelled stone blocks) and for its astronomical, numerical and geometrical properties. The building and rebuilding, according to modern archaeological research, lasted from about 2100 to 1600 B.C.

Stork, a family of heron-like birds with long bills, freely distributed over Europe, Asia, Africa and S. America. The White Stork is an occasional visitor to England, and, more rarely, the Black Stork; these are the only two European storks.

Stratosphere, a layer of the earth's atmosphere which lies between the tropopause (c. 12 km above the earth) and the stratopause (c. 50 km). The ozone layer lies within the stratosphere and is responsible for the relatively high temperature there. The region is less turbulent than the troposphere, and is usually clear of clouds and other "weather", making it attractive for air transport.

Stratum (pl. **strata**), a bed or layer of rock.

Strontium. This silver-white metallic element, no. 38, was discovered by Hope and Klaproth in 1793, and isolated by Sir Humphry Davy in 1808. The chief strontium minerals are celestite (sulphate) and strontianite (carbonate). Compounds of strontium give a brilliant colour to fireworks and signal flares. Radioactive isotopes of strontium (strontium-90) are formed as fission products in nuclear explosions and tend to collect in bone on account of the chemical similarity of strontium and calcium (q.v.). This hazard is a cause of great alarm. See **Fall-out.**

Sturgeon, a large fish found in northern seas and rivers with five rows of bony plates along the back and sides and pointed mouth with four barbels. Caviare is prepared from sturgeon ova.

Sublimation, when a solid substance is heated and turns into vapour without passing through the liquid stage and then condenses as a solid on a cold surface, it is said to "sublime" and the process is called "sublimation". Iodine behaves in this way, and sublimation is used as a method of purifying it.

Submarine, the first submarine, the *Nautilus*, was designed by Robert Fulton and tried out in the river Seine and in the sea off Brest in 1801. The idea was too revolutionary to find acceptance and it was not until electricity for under-water propulsion became available that the submarine underwent extensive development. Britain became interested about 1900 and the Germans developed it and made it into an instrument of warfare. The first voyage under the North Pole was made in 1958 by the American nuclear-powered submarine *Nautilus* (q.v.). The Royal Navy's nuclear submarine fleet includes 4 Polaris vessels—HMS *Resolution* (1968), *Renown* (1969), *Repulse* (1969), *Revenge* (1970), each armed with 16 missiles with thermonuclear warheads. The Government in March 1982 decided to replace the Polaris force with a new fleet of Trident II submarines at a cost of £7,500m. The Labour Party opposes this decision. Britain's nuclear strategic force is assigned to NATO.

Suez Canal, connecting the Mediterranean and the Red Sea, was built by the French engineer Ferdinand de Lesseps and opened in 1869. An Egyptian company, *Canal Maritime de Suez*, was formed in 1866 with a capital of 200 million francs. The British Government acquired 176,602 shares out of a total of 400,000 for £4 million (value 31 March 1956, £28,982,544). Under the Convention of 1888 all nations were granted freedom of navigation without discrimination in peace or war. The right was recognised by Egypt in the Anglo-Egyptian Agreement of 1954, under which Britain agreed to give up the Suez base. The Suez Canal Company was nationalised by the Egyptian Government without warning in 1956, since when it has been widened and deepened and the average time of transit reduced. The waterway which had been closed to all shipping since the Middle East war of 1967, was reopened in 1975.

Suffragette, member of the Women's Suffrage Movement who in the early part of this century agitated to obtain the parliamentary vote. The movement ended in 1918, when women of 30 were given the vote. In 1928 a Bill was passed which granted equal suffrage to men and women. The leaders of the Women's Suffrage Movement were Mrs. Pankhurst and her two daughters, Sylvia and Dame Christabel, Mrs. Fawcett, Annie Kenney and others.

Sugar, to the chemist the term is a generic one covering a group of carbohydrates, including cane sugar (sucrose), glucose, fructose, and maltose. In ordinary parlance sugar means sucrose, which is obtained from the sugar cane, sugar beet or sugar maple.

Sulphur, element no. 16, is a brittle, crystalline solid, symbol S, abounding in the vicinity of volcanoes. It is yellow in colour. It occurs in combination with other elements, as sulphates and sulphides, and allied with oxygen, hydrogen, chlorine, etc., is of great commercial utility. Used in its pure state it constitutes the inflammable element in gunpowder; it is also used for matches and for making sulphuric acid.

Sulphuric Acid, a compound of great commercial importance, used in a variety of manufactures, and composed of sulphur, oxygen and hydrogen. Extremely corrosive, and is present in acid rain (q.v.).

Sun, the centre of our solar system, is only one of millions of stars in our galaxy. The earth

orbits the sun, which has a diameter of 1·39 million km, at a distance of 149·6 million km. The sun thus has a volume a million times that of the earth. At the surface, the gravitational field is 28 times that at the earth's surface. It rotates on its axis from east to west, though not as a solid, the solar equator turning once in about 25½ days and the poles in about 34 days. Large spots are observed on the sun which form and disappear at irregular intervals. The area of the disc covered by the spots, however, reaches a maximum roughly every 11 years, when the sun's heat seems rather greater than usual and magnetic storms more frequent (sunspot cycle). Spectrum analysis shows that the sun is composed of many elements found in the earth. Its surface temperature is about 6,000°C. Observations made in 1964–65 (Year of the Quiet Sun) complemented those obtained during the International Geophysical Year 1957–58, when the sun was remarkably active. The earth is in the outer atmosphere of the sun and subject to its winds and storms. The apparently inexhaustible heat of the sun, which has maintained life on the earth for millions of years, is derived from the destruction of matter, involved in the transmutation of hydrogen nuclei into helium nuclei, in which process about four million tonnes of matter are destroyed every second. At this rate of conversion the sun will go on radiating for 30,000 million years. The Soviet space rocket *Lunik I*, fired on 2 January 1959, became the first artificial planet of the sun. *See also* **F8.**

Superconductor, a metal in a state in which its electrical resistance has entirely vanished so that electric currents can flow indefinitely without generating heat or decreasing in strength. The superconducting state of metals was first discovered in mercury by Onnes in Leiden in 1911. There are many magnetic and thermal properties associated with superconductivity and the phenomenon as a whole has proved to be of great scientific interest: it resisted explanation till about 1957. In the meantime many metals and alloys were found to show the property but only at very low temperatures—below c. −260°C. There is a growing number of practical applications, e.g., coils of superconducting wire (kept very cold by liquid helium) can be made to carry enough electric current to produce strong magnetic fields. Such fields are very constant and do not require the large supply of electrical power that ordinary electromagnets need. By 1987, scientists were on the point of developing a revolutionary material that would superconduct (i.e. lose all electrical resistance) at *room temperature*. Such a development would revolutionise computers, power transmission and medicine.

Supersonic Speed, a speed greater than the speed of sound (in air at sea-level sound waves travel at about 1223 km/h). When a body travels at a speed which is greater than the speed at which disturbances themselves can travel, a mechanism exists for the generation of waves of enhanced intensity. Thus aircraft travelling at supersonic speeds produce shock waves in the air somewhat analogous to the bow waves of fast-moving ships. These shock waves are regions of intensely disturbed air which produce the sonic boom effect so distressing to people living near supersonic routes. *Supersonic* is not to be confused with *ultrasonic* (q.v.).

Surface Tension. The surfaces of fluids behave in some respects as though they were covered by a stretched elastic membrane. This property is called "surface tension". The action of detergents may be attributed in part to a reduction in the surface tension of water, allowing it to wet the surface of dirty articles.

Surrealism. The aim of the Surrealist school of painting and sculpture is to overcome the barriers between conscious and unconscious mind, the real and unreal worlds of waking and dreaming. As such it has a long and respectable ancestry, although the term was not in use until 1922 when it was picked by André Breton from Guillaume Apollinaire who had used it in connection with certain works by Chagall. However, Bosch in the 15th cent., Fuseli and Goya in the 18th, and many other purveyors of the weird and fantastic were the forerunners of modern Surrealism. The modern movement has broadly speaking taken two different directions: the first was towards complete fantasy and absurdity which took the form of "found objects"—*e.g.* a bird-cage filled with sugar-cubes and a thermometer, a bottle-dryer, a bicycle wheel, or abstract works with strange and apparently irrelevant titles such as Paul Klee's *Twittering Machine*; the second towards highly detailed and realistic paintings of objects placed in strange juxtapositions—*e.g.*, Salvador Dali's trees with limp watches drooping over their branches or Georgio de Chirico's deserted and classical-looking streets with long arcaded perspectives and a lone statue or a bunch of bananas in the foreground. On the whole Surrealism has spent its initial force and become almost respectable; its idea of strange juxtapositions, now widely commercialised, finds a place in advertisement illustrations and in the more sophisticated forms of window-dressing.

Swans, large, graceful birds which together with the ducks and geese form the family Anatidae. There are three European species with white plumage; the Mute Swan distinguished by its orange bill with black knob (less prominent in female), a familiar sight on the rivers and ornamental lakes of Great Britain. Two wild swans are winter visitors here, the Whooper and Bewick's Swan. The "pen" (female) and "cob" (male) mate for life and the young swans are called "cygnets".

Swan-upping. The annual marking of the Thames swans which takes place during the third week of July. This ancient ceremony dates back to the 15th cent. when all the Thames swans were declared to be Royal birds owned by the Crown. Two city guilds—the Vintners' and Dyers' Companies—own about a third of the 200 swans now on the Thames. This privilege was granted to them by King Edward IV in return for money grants. Vintners' birds are marked with a nick on each side of the bill, the Dyers' with a nick on the right side only. The Queen's birds are unmarked.

Sweet Potato. This plant (*Ipomoea batatas*), which is a climbing perennial belonging to the convolvulus family, has thick roots that are rich in starch, and are eaten like potatoes. A native of the W. Indies and Central America, new varieties of sweet potato have been bred which stand cooler climates and can be grown as far north as Cape Cod. The sweet potato of New Zealand is called the Kumara.

Swift, a bird so-called from the extreme speed of its flight, resembling a swallow but related to the humming-bird. It has long, scythe-like wings, sooty-black plumage and greyish-white chin. There are several species inhabiting most parts of the world, particularly the tropics. The British breeding bird is among the latest to return from Africa and the earliest to go. Swifts are the only birds to use saliva for their nests. One oriental species builds its nest entirely from saliva.

Sword, hand weapon of metal used in open combat, characterised by a longish blade. During the Middle Ages the most famous blades were those made by the Arabs at Damascus and those made at Toledo.

Symbiosis. When two organisms live together and both derive mutual benefit from the association, the partnership is known as symbiosis. An example is the symbiosis of an alga and a fungus in lichens; another is the ordinary pea plant and the bacteria which live in the nodules on the pea's roots.

Synapse is the point of association between one nerve cell and another. The nervous impulse travelling along one nerve has to be transmitted to the next across a minute gap. This is the synaptic gap. The mode of transmission is chemical though it was at first thought to be electrical. The impulse arriving at the synapse releases a chemical transmitter which diffuses across the gap and stimulates an impulse in the adjacent nerve cell.

Syndicalism. *See* **Section J.**

Synod, an assembly of the clergy of a particular church, state, province, or diocese. The Synod of Whitby (664) settled the dispute between the Celtic and the Roman churches in the matter of

Easter in favour of the Roman system of reckoning.

Synoptic Charts. These are meteorological charts used in forecasting on which weather conditions at a network of stations, at a standard hour of observation, are recorded, using symbols of the international weather code. Surface weather maps have been drawn regularly for more than a hundred years and the modern advance is the drawing of other maps showing conditions in the upper air. The plotting is done quickly by computer.

Synoptists. The writers of the first three Gospels whose narratives in the main agree, though Matthew and Luke add material not found in Mark (written first); all three differ from John's Gospel.

T

Taiping Rebellion, 1850–64, most famous of China's many peasant uprisings. It took place in Hunan (the province where Mao Tse-Tung was born) and was savagely suppressed with the help of foreign powers.

Taj Mahal, the white marble mausoleum built at Agra by Shah Jehan in memory of his favourite wife who died 1629. Over 20,000 men were occupied for over 20 years in its erection.

Takahe or Notornis, large New Zealand bird of the rail family which for many years was believed to be extinct. Small colony found in 1948 in remote valley of mountainous part of the S. Island. The bird is strictly protected.

Take-Over Bid describes an offer made to all the shareholders of a company to purchase their shares at a named price and conditional upon acceptance by the holders of a named proportion of the total share issue. If accepted the purchaser thus gains control of the company.

Tallage, in Norman times, were taxes levied by the Crown upon lands of the royal demesnes. The levying of tallage was taken away by a statute of 1340 which required the consent of Parliament for all direct taxes.

Tammany, an organisation founded in New York (*c.* 1786) and formed from a benevolent society named after an Indian chief. It came to exert a powerful influence over political movements in that city. The leaders of the organisation used their power when their party was successful at the polls to appoint their nominee to every prominent office, and exacted bribes for concessions and privileges, and generally Tammany rule has meant wholesale corruption. Of this there was ample evidence in the disclosures of the Tween and other Tammany frauds, and in the fact that the "Boss" usually contrived to make himself wealthy.

Tantalum, a scarce bluish metallic element, no. 73, symbol Ta, discovered by Ekeburg in 1802. Chemically related to vanadium and niobium, it is usually associated with the latter in nature. For several purposes it can be used in place of platinum, and it finds application in the making of surgical instruments. Tantalum is very hard, and resistant to acids (other than hydrofluoric acid); it is used in alloys.

Taoism. *See* **Section J.**

Tapestry, a fabric largely used in former times for wall decoration and hangings. It was known to the ancient Greeks, but in its modern form came into prominence in the 15th and 16th cent., when it was manufactured in a marked degree of excellence by the weavers of Flanders, especially those of Arras. The manufacture was introduced into England early in the 17th cent., and was attended by considerable success. At the present day the term is applied to worsted cloths for furniture coverings, and there are also various kinds of tapestry carpets now made. The most famous tapestries of olden times were the Aubusson Tapestry and the Savonnerie. The Gobelin Tapestry factory, originated in Paris in the reign of Francis I, is still a national establishment. *See also* **Bayeux Tapestry.**

Tapirs. The tapirs constitute a family close to the horse family and the rhinoceros in the Ungulate order. They have four toes on the front feet and three on the hind. The snout is drawn out into a short trunk. The largest tapir is the Malayan tapir, which stands 1 m at the shoulder. Four species occur in C. and S. America.

Tar is a dark viscid product obtained from the destructive distillation of wood, coal, peat, etc. Wood tar is acid owing to the presence of acetic acid ("pyroligneous acid"). The highest proportion of coal tar goes into road making. Distillation of coal tar yields many valuable compounds, including benzene, phenol (carbolic acid), naphthalene and creosote; the final residue after distillation is pitch. Based on the chemical manipulation of compounds from coal tar is the preparation of many perfumes, food essences, drugs, antiseptics and plastics.

Tarpeian Rock at Rome received its name from the tradition that Tarpeia, the daughter of the Governor of the Citadel who betrayed the fortress of the Sabines, was crushed to death by their shields and buried beneath the rock. From this height persons guilty of treason were hurled to death.

Tate Gallery, named after its founder, Sir Henry Tate, at Millbank, S.W., was opened in 1897; Sir Henry Tate bore the cost of the building (£80,000) and also gave the nucleus of the present collection. "The Turner Wing", the gift of Sir Joseph Duveen, was added in 1910.

Tayberry, a high-yielding new fruit, dark red with a strong, sweet flavour, which is a cross between a raspberry and a blackberry.

Tay Bridge spans the Tay at Dundee, opened for rail traffic on 20 June 1887. A previous bridge, completed in 1877, was blown down on 28 December 1879, as a train was passing over it. A new bridge was opened on 18 August 1966 for road traffic, 2,244 m in length, the longest road bridge in Britain.

Tea was introduced into England about the middle of the 17th cent., when it was a great luxury, and fetched from £6 to £10 a pound. It is an Asiatic plant, native properly to China, Japan and India. Up to about 1885 most of the tea imported into this country came from China, the bulk now comes from India and Sri Lanka.

Teal, the smallest of the European ducks and next to the Mallard the commonest British species. It is a handsome bird and a very swift flier, but not as swift as the Garganey or Summer Teal.

Telecommunications. The sending of messages over a distance. The term is generally applied to the sending of messages by telegraph, telephone, radio, television or radar. The first submarine telegraph cable between England and France was laid in 1850 and, following Hertz's investigations into electric waves, Marconi's invention led to Britain being linked with Europe by wireless telegraphy in 1899. The first permanently successful telegraph cable across the Atlantic was laid in 1866. The first telephone service between London and Paris was opened in 1891. The electro-magnetic telephone was invented by Alexander Graham Bell, a Scottish-born American, in 1876. The first submarine telephone cable to span the Atlantic was laid in 1956 connecting Britain with Canada and the United States, and many submarine telephone cables have since been laid including the Commonwealth cable system completed in 1967. The spectacular advances in space research depended on the new tools of work provided by parallel developments in telecommunications, e.g., long-range radio and television transmission, electronic computer control. See also **Satellite Communication, Radar, Radio Television.**

Telemetry, measurement at remote distances by means of a radio-link from the object (missile or satellite) to the ground. The third Russian sputnik, for instance, carried apparatus for measuring, among other things, the pressure and composition of the atmosphere, and the intensity of different kinds of radiation from the sun. Its radio transmitter, powered by solar-energy batteries, sent out the information in coded form by means of uninterrupted signals at 20·005 megacycles with a duration of 150–300 milli-seconds. Radio telemetry from inside the body is increasingly used in medical and biological research; miniature radio transmitters can be swallowed or implanted in man or animal to detect physiological conditions.

Telepathy and **Clairvoyance.** See Section J.

Teleprinter, a telegraph transmitter with a type-writer keyboard, by which characters of a message are transmitted electrically in combinations of 5 units, being recorded similarly by the receiving instrument, which then translates the matter mechanically into printed characters. The telex service provides direct person-to-person transmission of written messages.

Telescope, an optical instrument for viewing objects at a distance, "the astronomer's intelligencer". Lippershey is credited with construction of the first in 1608; Galileo constructed several from 1609 and Newton was the first to construct a reflecting telescope. The ordinary telescope consists of an object-glass and an eye-lens, with two intermediates to bring the object into an erect position. A lens brings it near to us, and the magnifier enlarges it for inspection. A refracting telescope gathers the rays together near the eye-piece and is necessarily limited as to size, but the reflecting telescope collects the rays on a larger mirror, and these are thrown back to the eye-piece. The world's largest reflectors are at Mount Pastukhov, Caucasus (6 m), Mount Palomar, California (200 in), Mount Wilson, California (100 in), the McDonald Observatory at Mount Locke, Texas (82 in), and the Victoria B.C. Observatory (183 cm). The *Hale* 200 in telescope at Mount Palomar has revealed objects never before photographed; it is able to probe space and photograph remote galaxies out to a limiting distance of 2,000 million light years. The *Schmidt* telescope at Mount Palomar has been used to make a huge photographic map of the universe. The 98 in *Isaac Newton* telescope has been moved from the Royal Observatory at Herstmonceux, Sussex, to La Palma, Canary Is. The giant steerable radio telescope built by Manchester University at Jodrell Bank, Cheshire, has a 250 ft reflector. The largest single radio dish in the world is the non-steerable 300 m instrument at Arecibo in Puerto Rico. Another instrument of radio astronomy is the interferometer which consists of spaced aerials. The biggest of these is in New Mexico. In 1990, the project to put the Hubble Space Telescope into space became reality. Weighing 11 tons, it is the biggest-ever astronomical observatory and will reveal secrets of the universe from 15 billion years ago. See also **F3, Astronomy, Radio Astronomy.**

Teletext, the system of displaying printed information and simple diagrams on domestic television screens. Two public services are available in Britain—CEEFAX (Seeing Facts), broadcast by the BBC, and ORACLE (Optical Reception of Announcements by Coded Line Electronics), by the Independent Broadcasting Authority. Teletext makes use of some of the spare lines available in the ordinary 625-line television picture, the signals being translated into written display on the screen by means of a special decoding adaptor built into the set or attached to it. User access to the information, broadcast as separate "pages", is obtained by using a pocket calculator-sized keypad. Teletext services in Britain at present offer a wide range of subject material, including weather forecasts, news headlines, sport and financial statistics, in six colours plus white. It is also possible to superimpose news flashes over ordinary programmes. All the information is provided by specially created editorial units and the pages are transmitted in rapid rotation, a one-hundred page "magazine" taking up to 25 seconds in all. CEEFAX and ORACLE pages are made up of a maximum of 24 lines of 40 characters, the same standard format as that of Viewdata. Viewdata links the television set with computerised information via the telephone and is regarded as almost limitless in application as it would be possible to make use of data offered through the global communications satellite system.

Television, or the transmission of images of moving objects by radio. To understand the problems of television it is necessary to consider the action of the human eye. Basically the eye consists of a lens which projects an image of the scene before it upon the retina, a light-sensitive screen at the back of the eye. The retina is made up of several millions of tiny light sensitive elements, each quite separate and distinct from its neighbours, and each separately connected to the brain by an individual fibre in the optic nerve. Thus the eye is a very complex organ, and it is able to pick out numbers of tiny details from a scene and convey each detail separately and simultaneously to the brain. It does not send a blend of different points of light and shade in the same way that the ear sends a blend of different sounds; if it did the brain would receive a completely unintelligible blur. From this it is clear that a television system which transmitted a mixture of detail would be useless; it must transmit all the details in a scene separately, yet almost simultaneously, and re-assemble them at such a speed that the eye cannot observe the building-up process. A means of doing this was provided by Nipkow in 1884, when he invented his famous scanning disc, and later Weiller invented the mirror drum for the same purpose. Such mechanical devices as these held the field for many years and in 1923 Baird in this country and Jenkins in America were both using them for the experiments which, in 1925, led to the successful transmission of shadows and simple outlines. It was not until 1926, however, that the first practical demonstration of television, as we understand it, took place when Baird transmitted by radio moving pictures of living human faces over a short distance. The B.B.C. began televised broadcasts in 1930; the I.T.A. in 1955. The first television exchange across the Atlantic was made in July 1962 by way of the *Telstar* satellite.

Tellurium, a relatively scarce element, no. 52, symbol Te, discovered in 1782 by von Reichenstein. Chemically it behaves rather like sulphur; its salts are known as tellurides. It occurs chiefly combined with metals in ores of gold, silver, copper and lead. It is a semiconductor, and some of its compounds (also semiconductors) are coming into use in technical devices.

Templars were soldier knights organised in the 12th cent. for the purpose of protecting pilgrims in their journeyings to and from Jerusalem, and obtained their name from having had granted to them by Baldwin II a temple for their accommodation. At first they were non-military, and wore neither crests nor helmets, but a long wide mantle and a red cross on the left shoulder. They were established in England about 1180. During the crusades they rendered valuable service, showing great bravery and devotion. In the 12th cent. they founded numerous religious houses in various parts of Europe and became possessed of considerable wealth. It was this that caused their downfall. Kings and Popes alike grew jealous of their influence, and they were subjected to much persecution, and Pope Clement V abolished the Order in 1312. Edward II in 1308 seized all the property of the English Templars. The English possessions of the Order were transferred to the Hospitallers of St. John, afterwards called the Knights of Malta. *See also* **Hospitallers, Knights, Teutonic Order.**

Temple, a building dedicated to the worship of a deity or deities. Those built by the ancient Greeks at Olympia, Athens and Delphi were the most famous. The Temple of Diana at Ephesus was another. The Temple of Solomon at Jerusalem was destroyed and rebuilt several times; Herod's Temple was destroyed by the Romans in A.D. 70.

Temple Bar, an historic gateway (designed by Sir Christopher Wren in 1672) that until 1877 stood at the junction of the Strand and Fleet Street, London, dividing the City from Westminster. It was re-erected at the entrance to Theobald's Park, near Cheshunt, Herts., in 1888.

Terbium, an element, no. 65, symbol Tb, discovered in 1842 by Mosander, belonging to the group of rare-earth metals.

Teredo, the scientific name of the ship-worm, a peculiar bivalve mollusc, which lodges itself when young on the bottoms of wooden ships and bores its way inwards, causing much injury.

Termites, also known as *White Ants,* though they are not related to the true ants and are placed in an entirely different insect order (*Isoptera*). They abound in the tropics and also occur in temperate countries, though only two species are common in Europe. There is no British species. They live in colonies and their nests

take the form of mounds of earth and wood, cemented together with saliva, and up to 6 m in height. Five separate castes are recognised, three of them being capable of reproduction, and the other two are sterile.

Tern. This slender, gull-like bird has long pointed wings, a deeply-forked tail, pale grey and white plumage, black cap, and is a very graceful flier. There are several species, some of which are summer migrants to Britain. The Arctic tern winters in the Antarctic, returning to find a nesting place in the spring.

Terracotta Army, the thousands of life-sized figures in fired clay of soldiers who were to guard China's Emperor Qiu Shihuangdi after his death in the 3rd century B.C. Discovered by peasants digging a well in 1974, at Xian, it is often referred to as the Eighth Wonder of the World.

Terrapin, a kind of fresh-water tortoise. There are several species widely distributed in the Northern Hemisphere.

Tertiary Rocks, in geology the rocks formed during the Caenozoic era comprising the Eocene, Oligocene, Miocene and Pliocene periods. *See* **F48.**

Teutonic Order, of German military knights, was founded in the Holy Land at the end of the 12th cent. for succouring the wounded of the Christian army before Acre. They were dispersed in the 15th cent. but the Order continued to exist until 1809, when Napoleon I confiscated its properties. In 1840 the order was resuscitated in Austria as a semi-religious knighthood. *See also* **Hospitallers, Knights, Templars.**

Textured Vegetable Protein, often referred to as TVP, is an edible protein material given a fibrous texture in the course of its manufacture from agricultural products. Nutritionally the material resembles meat and the extent to which it also resembles meat in succulence, flavour, feel in the mouth, suitability for chewing, etc. depends on the sophistication of the manufacturing technique and on the skill of the cook. The common starting material is the soya bean which is rich in protein and oil. The latter is removed, also for use in the food industry, and the residue is further processed to concentrate the protein and to remove unwanted flavours. A paste of suitable consistency is then forced under pressure through small holes and solidified as fibres. Bound together with a suitable binder and appropriately flavoured, these fibres form a lump of protein substance analagous to meat.

Thallium, a blue-grey metallic element, no. 81, symbol Tl, discovered by Crookes in 1861. It is obtained from the flue dust resulting from the burning of pyrites for sulphuric acid manufacture.

Thanksgiving Day, a national holiday in the United States, observed on the fourth Thursday in November: instituted by the Pilgrim Fathers in 1621 to celebrate their first successful harvest.

Theodolite. The instrument used by surveyors for measuring angles in the horizontal and vertical planes; also used in meteorology for following balloons to measure windspeed etc.

Therm. The charges for gas for lighting and heating (formerly reckoned at per cubic foot) are now based on the calorific, or heat, value of the gas, and the unit used is termed a therm. The therm is 100,000 British thermal units.

Thermionic Emission is the departure of charged particles from matter under the influence of heat. The higher the temperature the greater the flow of escaping particles. The most common example is the emission of electrons from red-hot electrodes—this is the basic phenomenon made use of in thermionic valves (*see* **Valve**). If the hot electrode (the cathode) is enclosed in an evacuated or gas-filled bulb, the emitted electrons can be collected at another electrode (the anode) and will flow through an external circuit back to the emitter. Thus an electric current has been generated by heat.

Thermodynamics, a term first applied by Joule to designate that branch of physical science which treats of the relations of heat to work. What is called the first law of thermodynamics is thus stated by Clerk Maxwell: "When work is transformed into heat, or heat into work, the quantity of work is mechanically equivalent to the quantity of heat." In one of its many formulations, the second law asserts that "the heat tends to flow from a body of hotter temperature to one that is colder, and will not naturally flow in any other way". *See* **F20.**

Thermo-electric Devices. If two wires of different materials are formed into a loop and if the two joins are kept at different temperatures a current flows in the loop. This was discovered by Seebeck in 1822, and the device is called a thermocouple. The electric current could in principle be made to drive some useful machine, and the energy comes from the heat that is absorbed by the thermocouple—if one part of the thermocouple is not hotter than the others it will not work. It has long been realised that this is a device that converts heat directly into electricity without raising steam and driving dynamos as in a power-station. However, until recently nobody has used thermocouples for much besides temperature measurement, for which they are exceedingly useful. The new development is the manufacture of semiconductors (*q.v.*); for the thermo-electric effects of these new materials are much greater than those of metals. A material much studied in this connection is a compound of bismuth and tellurium, bismuth telluride. It now seems practicable to generate useful electricity from suitably designed thermocouples. For example, the USSR produces a thermo-electric device which uses the heat from the chimney of a domestic oil-lamp to produce enough electricity to work a radio. Presumably this is very useful in remote parts with no electricity supply. But the possibilities do not stop there. Indeed, an eminent Russian authority has stated that thermocouples could produce electricity direct from the warmth of sunlight on a scale and at a cost comparable with conventional fuel-burning power-stations. Even if solar energy cannot be so used, it might be possible to use the heat of nuclear reactors, but this means that the thermo-electric devices would have to stand up to very heavy radioactivity and still work. It is not surprising, however, that many firms are showing great interest in thermo-electricity.

Thermometer, an instrument by which the temperature of bodies is ascertained. The most familiar kind of thermometer consists of a glass tube with a very small bore, containing, in general, mercury or alcohol. This expands or contracts with variation in the temperature, and the length of the thread of mercury or alcohol gives the temperature reading on a scale graduated in degrees. Various forms of thermometer are used for particular purposes. *See also* **F66–69.**

Thermonuclear Reactions. *See* **Nuclear Fusion.**

Thirty-nine Articles. *See* **Articles.**

Thistle, Order of. *See* **Knighthood.**

Thorium, a scarce, dark grey, metal element, no. 90, symbol Th, discovered by Berzelius in 1828. All substances containing thorium are radioactive. Chief source of thorium is monazite sand, big deposits of which occur in Travancore (India), Brazil and the USA. Considered important as a potential source of atomic energy since the discovery that it can be transmuted into U^{233}, which is capable of fission like U^{235}.

Thrush, a large family of song-birds of the *Passeriform* order, distributed all over the world. The British species include the robin, redstart, nightingale, song-thrush (or mavis), blackbird, mistle-thrush, ring-ouzel of the mountains and large numbers of migrant fieldfares and redwings from northern Europe are winter visitors.

Thunder, the sound heard after the occurrence of a lightning flash. It is due to vibrations of the air along the path of the flash, which are set up by the sudden heating (and expansion) followed by the rapid cooling (and contraction) to which the air is subjected. It is unusual for thunder to be heard more than 16 km away, the distance being estimated roughly by allowing 1 km for every 3 seconds which elapse between seeing the flash and hearing the thunder. Continued rolling of thunder results from the zig-zag nature of the flash and the multiple strokes of which it is composed, variations in the energy developed along the path, and echo effects. Thunderstorms are caused by powerful rising currents

of air within towering cumulonimbus clouds and are most frequent during the afternoons and evenings of sunny summer days.

Thursday, the 5th day of the week, named after Thor, the Scandinavian deity. To the Romans Thursday was *dies Jovis*, or Jupiter's day.

Tiananmen Square, central square in Beijing (Peking). Scene of 1989 massacre. *See* **Section C, Part II.**

Tidal Power. The principle of exploiting the energy of the tides is similar to hydro-power since it involves the harnessing of falling water. A barrage across a bay or estuary is filled during flow tide and closed during ebb tide creating a difference in level. When the water is allowed to fall towards the lower side of the barrage it operates a turbine which drives a generator. More sophisticated schemes would incorporate pumped storage facilities. An essential requirement is a large tidal range in order to get a sufficient head of water. Although a 240MW scheme was completed in the 1960s on the River Rance in France, it is believed that the economics of tidal power are generally insufficiently favourable for the method to be widely used. *See also* **Hydroelectric Schemes** and **Severn Barrage.**

Tides, the periodical rise and fall of the waters of the ocean and its arms, are due to the gravitational effect of the moon and sun. Newton was the first to give a general explanation of the phenomenon of the tides. He supposed the ocean to cover the whole earth and to assume at each instant a figure of equilibrium, under the combined gravitational influence of earth, sun and moon, thus making and controlling the tides. At most places there are two tides a day, and the times of high- and low-water vary according to the positions of the sun and moon relative to the earth. When earth, moon and sun are in line (at full moon and new moon) the gravitational pull is greatest and we get "spring" tides. When sun and moon are at right angles (first and third quarters of the moon's phases) we get the smaller "neap" tides.

Tiers État, the lowest of the three estates of the realm as reckoned in France—nobility, clergy and commons (*tiers état*)—prior to the Revolution.

Tiger, a powerful carnivorous animal of the cat family, which occurs in India and certain other parts of Asia. Its skin is of a tawny yellow, relieved by black stripings of great beauty of formation. Some tigers attain a length of from 3 to 3·6 m.

Time. The measurement of time has become of increasing importance to man with the advance of civilisation. It was at first almost inevitably based on the succession of night and day, the waxing and the waning of the moon, and on the changing seasons of the year, and the astronomical observation of these three periodic effects has served as the basis of time measurement until recent years. The precision of the observations has continually increased, and clocks have been developed for dividing the day into smaller units. The clocks were adjusted so as to keep in step with the rotation of the earth on its axis, but during recent years an atomic standard of time has been developed, and clocks are now adjusted so as to keep in step with the natural period of an atomic vibration. *See* **Clock, Greenwich Mean Time, British Standard Time.**

Tin is a white, metal element, no. 50, symbol Sn (Latin *Stannum*), whose commonest ore is cassiterite (tin oxide), which occurs in Malaya, Indonesia, Bolivia, Zaïre, Nigeria and Cornwall. It protects iron from rusting, and the tin coating on tinplate is applied by dipping the thin steel sheet in molten tin or by electrolysis. Tin alloys of importance include solder, bronze, pewter and Britannia metal.

Tit *or* **Titmouse,** a small insectivorous bird of the woodlands and forests, bright of plumage and very active and agile, often seen hanging upside down searching for food. There are over fifty species, eight of which occur in Britain: the Great and Blue Tits, familiar in gardens and countryside, the Cole Tit, Marsh Tit, Willow Tit, Bearded Tit, Long-tailed or "Bottle" Tit and the Scottish Crested Tit.

Titanium, a scarce metallic element, no. 22, symbol Ti, difficult to extract from ores, found in association with oxygen in rutile, anatase and brookite, as well as with certain magnetic iron ores. It combines with nitrogen at a high temperature. Discovered by the Rev. William Gregor in 1791. Titanium alloys, being very resistant to stress and corrosion, and combining strength with lightness, and finding wide application not only in marine and chemical engineering but in the building of aircraft, rockets, and the nuclear-energy field. Titanium dioxide is now widely used in making paints.

Tithes, an ecclesiastical tax consisting of a tenth part of the annual produce known to the ancient Jews, and first imposed by Christian authorities in the 4th cent., although not made compulsory in England before the 9th cent. Tithes derived from land are termed "praedial", those derived from cattle being styled "mixed", while others are personal. After the passing of the Tithes' Commutation Act of 1836, tithes were gradually converted into rent charges, and to-day the old form of tithes exists only to a small degree. For details, consult Tithe Act of 1936.

TNT (Trinitrotuluene). A high explosive formed by the action of a mixture of nitric and sulphuric acids on toluene. Not highly sensitive to shock, it can be used in shells without danger, and is exploded by a time, or detonator, fuse. Apart from wartime applications, it is used in blasting in quarries and mines.

Toad, an amphibian, differing from the frog in having a dry, warty skin, a heavier, squat build and shorter limbs. It has a similar metamorphosis, is largely nocturnal, and will wander far from water after the breeding season. Two toads occur in Britain, the Common Toad and the Natterjack. The latter have a narrow light stripe running down the middle of the back.

Tobacco is made from the leaves of various narcotic plants of the *Nicotiana* family, which contain a volatile oil and an alkaloid called nicotine. Tobacco is largely grown in America, India, Japan, Turkey, Greece, Canada, Italy, Indonesia, Bulgaria, Philippines, France, Zaïre, China, Zimbabwe, Zambia, S. Africa, S. America and other countries of a warm climate. It undergoes various processes of preparation. The leaves are first dried, then cut into small pieces, moistened and compressed, and in this form it is known as cut or "shag" tobacco; when moistened with syrup or treacle and pressed into cakes, it is Cavendish; when twisted into string form, it is "twist" or "pig-tail". For cigars the midribs of the dry leaves are removed, and what is left is moistened and rolled into cylindrical shape. For snuff, the tobacco leaves are moistened and allowed to ferment, then dried, powdered and scented. *See* **Section P (Respiratory System)** for the connection between smoking and lung cancer.

Tolls. Payments for privileges of passage were first exacted in respect of ships passing up rivers, tolls being demanded on the Elbe in 1109. Tolls for land passage are said to have originated in England in 1269, toll-bars being erected at certain distances on the high-roads in the 17th cent., where toll had to be paid for all vehicles passing to and fro. After about 1825 they began to disappear, but still linger on some country roads and bridges. Tolls on London river bridges ceased in 1878-79. Today, tolls are a feature of European motorways and major bridges (*e.g.* Severn) and tunnels (*e.g.* Dartford).

Tonic Sol-Fa, a system of musical notation in which monosyllables are substituted for notes. Thus the major diatonic scale is represented by the Doh, Ray, Me, Fah, Soh, La, Te, Doh. The system was invented by a Miss Glover of Norwich in about 1840 and has proved of great assistance in the teaching of music in schools.

Tonsure, the shaven part of the head of a Roman Catholic ecclesiastic, dates from the 5th or 6th cent. In the Roman Catholic Churches only a circle, or a crown, is shaved, while in the Greek Church shaving is forbidden.

Topaz, a transparent mineral gem, being a silicate and fluoride of aluminium and generally found in granite rocks. Its colour is yellow, but it also occurs in pink and blue shades. The best kinds come from Brazil.

Topiary, the art of clipping and trimming trees, shrubs, etc., into ornamental shapes. In Britain this art goes back before Elizabethan times when gardens were formal and the shapes simple and symmetrical. By the end of Queen Anne's reign topiary had become much more elaborate, and all kinds of fanciful shapes were produced. Pliny in his *Letters* tells how box hedges were clipped into different shapes in Roman times.

Topology is a branch of mathematics which studies geometrical objects from the point of view of their general shape rather than their precise measurements. For example, from the point of view of topology a ring doughnut and a picture frame have the same shape because they both have one single hole through them. Topology is used, for example, to deduce geometrical facts about an irregularly shaped object such as the Earth from the geometry of a regular object such as a perfect sphere of the same general shape. Topology is an important tool in other parts of mathematics.

Tornado, a violent whirlwind, characterised by a black, funnel-shaped cloud hanging from heavy cumulonimbus and travelling at speeds up to 60 km/h. Tornadoes vary in diameter from less than a metre to a kilometre and occur frequently in the Mississippi region of the USA, where it has been estimated that the circling winds of the vortex may reach a velocity of 600 km/h. In West Africa the term is applied to thundery squalls.

Tortoises and Turtles, are cold-blooded reptiles, four-footed and encased in a strong shell protection, the shells of some species being of beautifully horny substance and design, once in much demand for combs, spectacle frames and ornamental work. It is the custom to designate the land species as tortoises and the aquatic kinds as turtles. The green turtle, so called because its fat has a green tinge, is in great demand for soup. Together the tortoises and turtles make up the reptilian order called *Chelonia,* the biggest representatives of which are the giant land tortoises of the Galapagos Islands, reaching a weight of 225 kg and living a century. Some of these giant tortoises are even said to have lived 200 or 300 years.

Toucan, a South and Central American family of brilliantly coloured birds, remarkable for their huge bills. Toucans live on fruit, are of arboreal habits, and nest in holes. There are about 37 species.

Touchstone, a kind of jasper called by the ancients "Lydian stone", of economic value in testing the quality of metal alloys, especially gold alloys. The testing process is very simple. The alloy is drawn across the broken surface of the Touchstone, and from the nature of the mark or streak it makes the quality of the alloy can be ascertained.

Tourmaline, a mineral occurring in different colours in prismatic crystals. It is a well-known example of a pyro-electric crystal, *i.e.*, one that has a permanent electric polarisation. A double silicate of aluminium and boron, it occurs in Cornwall, Devon, S. America and Asia.

Tournaments were equestrian contests between military knights and others armed with lances, and frequent in the Middle Ages. The Normans introduced them to England.

Tower of London was built as a fortress by William the Conqueror. It was a royal palace in the Middle Ages and later used as a garrison and prison. Many distinguished prisoners were executed there, or on the neighbouring Tower Hill, including Anne Boleyn, Catherine Howard, Lady Jane Grey, the 2nd Earl of Essex, and the Duke of Monmouth. The Chapel Royal of St. Peter ad Vincula in the Tower was built in 1105 and took its present shape in the reign of Henry VII. The Crown Jewels are kept at the Tower, and in the Armoury a fine collection of armour is preserved. The attendant staff are called Yeomen Warders of the Tower. Their style of dress is of the Tudor period.

Trade-Mark, a mark used in relation to goods for the purpose of indicating a connection in the course of trade between the goods and some person having the right, either as a proprietor or registered user, to use the mark. Trade-marks can be registered, the registration holding good for 7 years and being renewable thereafter indefinitely for periods of 14 years. Infringement of a registered trade-mark renders the infringer liable to damages.

Trade Winds form part of the circulation of air round the great permanent anticyclones of the tropics and blow inwards from north-east (Northern Hemisphere) and south-east (Southern Hemisphere) towards the equatorial region of low pressure. Atlantic trades are more regular than those of the Pacific. The belts may extend over 2,400 km of latitude and, together with the Doldrums, move north and south in sympathy with the seasonal changes in the sun's declination, the average annual range being about 5 degrees of latitude.

Trafalgar, Battle of, was fought off Cape Trafalgar on 21 October 1805, between the British under Nelson and the French and Spanish under Villeneuve and Gravina. It was a complete victory for the British, but Nelson was killed.

Trafalgar Square. The site has often been referred to as the finest in Europe. It was conceived originally as a square by John Nash (1752–1835) when the project was considered of linking Whitehall with Bloomsbury and the British Museum. It was to be named after the new monarch as King William the Fourth's Square but on the suggestion of George Ledwell Taylor (a property owner near the site) alteration to the more popular name Trafalgar Square was agreed to by the King. On the north side the National Gallery was planned by Nash and erected by William Wilkins on the place of the Royal Mews—a work of William Kent a century before. The lay-out was the idea of Charles Barry but he did not approve the erection of the Nelson column (which see). His idea was for the square to have a grand flight of steps from the north side with sculptural figures of Wellington and Nelson but the Commons decided otherwise and the column as designed by William Railton was begun in 1840. The two fountains by Barry were supplanted in 1948 by ones designed (1938) by Sir Edwin Lutyens. Executed in Portland stone they are flanked by some bronze sculptures. In the same year memorial busts of Lords Jellicoe and Beatty were placed by the north wall.

Transept. The cross aisles of a church, projecting at right angles from the nave or choir.

Transistor. An electronic device consisting of a small piece of semiconducting solid (usually germanium or silicon) to which contact is made at appropriate places by three wires. The three parts resemble in function (not construction or behaviour) the cathode, anode, and grid of a thermionic valve, and transistors can perform many of the operations that valves have hitherto been used for in radio, television, etc. They possess several advantages over valves since there is no need for evacuated glass bulbs nor for a heated emitter to give off electrons. This leads to much greater compactness and economy as well as to a much longer life. Nevertheless, there are certain limitations to their use, and they are not yet suitable as substitutes for valves in all cases. The device was invented by the Americans Bardeen, Brattain and Shockley in 1948.

Transubstantiation. *See* **Section J.**

Treasure-Trove, a legal term applying to treasure (coin, bullion, gold or silver articles) found hidden in the earth or other place, for which no owner can be discovered. The treasure legally belongs to the Crown, but it is the practice to return to the finder all articles not required for national museums and to reward him with the full market value of such as may be retained. It is the duty of the finder to report to the Coroner for the district in which the find is made who holds an inquest to find whether the discovery be treasure-trove or no. In England concealment is a criminal offence. *See also* **Wreck.**

Tree Frog, occurs most commonly in America and Australasia. The common European tree frog is a brilliant green animal, the adhesive discs at the tips of its fingers and toes enabling it to cling to trees, etc., with ease.

Tree Rings as Natural Calendar. The approximate relationship between radiocarbon dating (*q.v.*) and true calendar age for the past 7,000 years has been established from measurements on tree-rings. Because one tree-ring is formed annually and its thickness is characteristic of the climatic conditions during its growth, it is possible, by comparing distinctive groups of rings, to date a series of trees. By using the long-lived Bristle Cone pines, tree-rings dating back to 500 B.C. have been obtained. It has been found that the radiocarbon age around, say, 3000 B.C. is too young by *c.* 600 years and because of short-term fluctuations near, say, 2000 B.C., a particular radiocarbon age can correspond to more than one true calendar age. These corrections are far less than those proved necessary after the publication of the first radiocarbon dates. Tree-rings (based on the measurement of deuterium in wood) can also show the pattern of temperature fluctuations over hundreds of years and thus make it possible to trace climatic changes before written records began. The term for tree-ring dating is dendrochronology.

Tree Shrew, an arboreal insectivorous mammal of Asia belonging to the family *Tupaiidae*. Tree shrews are related to the shrews, though in appearance they resemble squirrels except for their sharply pointed snout. They occur in Borneo, Thailand, China and Malaya.

Trent, Council of, the longest and one of the most important in the history of the Roman Catholic Church, was convened to combat the doctrines of Martin Luther. It first sat in 1545, the last sitting being in 1563. At this Council the general policy, principles and dogmas of the Roman Catholic Church were settled.

Triassic *or* **Trias,** the earliest geological period in the Mesozoic era, which began some 225 million years ago. Triassic formations 7,600 m thick occur in the Alps. Modern insects were appearing, and also small reptile-like mammals. Other important Triassic animals were: dinosaurs, ichthyosaurs (marine reptiles), and pterosaurs (flying reptiles). *See* **Section F.**

Tribunes, name assigned to officers of different descriptions in ancient Rome. The original tribunes were the commanders of contingents of cavalry and infantry. The most important tribunes were the tribunes of the plebs, first elected in 494 B.C. as the outcome of the struggle between the patrician and the plebeian orders. They held the power of veto and their persons were sacred.

Trichoptera. This is the insect order comprising the Caddis-flies. These are moth-like insects having hairs on the wings. They are usually found fluttering weakly near water. The larvae are aquatic and are remarkable for the cases (caddis cases) which they build out of sticks, small stones, sand grains, and shells.

Tricolour, the flag of the French Republic since 1789, consisting of three nearly equal vertical bands of blue, white and red (ratio 90:99:111).

Trilobites, extinct marine arthropods, most abundant in the Cambrian and Ordovician systems. Their appearance may be roughly described as resembling that of a woodlouse, and like that animal the trilobites were capable of rolling their bodies up into a ball.

Trinity. The Christian doctrine that God exists in three persons, all co-equal, and indivisible, of the same substance—God the Father, God the Son (who became incarnate as Jesus), begotten of the Father, and God the Holy Ghost, proceeding from Father and Son. The system denying the Trinity is Unitarianism. *See* **Section J.**

Trinity House, on Tower Hill, London, was incorporated in 1514 as an association for piloting ships, and has ever since been entrusted with various matters connected with the regulation of British navigation. Since 1854 the lighthouses of the country have been under its supervision. The acting Elder Brethren act as Nautical Assessors in Marine cases which are tried by the High Court of Justice. Under the 1987 Pilotage Act, Trinity House lost its responsibility as the principal pilotage authority in Britain to local harbour authorities.

Trireme, an ancient vessel with three rows of oars of great effectuality in early naval warfare. Mentioned by Thucydides. It was a long, narrow vessel propelled by 170 rowers. The Romans copied it from the Greeks.

Tritium, a radioactive isotope of hydrogen which has three times the weight of the ordinary hydrogen atom. It is produced by bombarding an isotope of lithium with neutrons and has a half-life of 12¼ years, decaying with the emission of β-particles (electrons).

Triumvirate, a term used to denote á coalition of three persons in the exercise of supreme authority. The first Roman triumvirate was that of Pompey, Julius Caesar, and Crassus, 60 B.C.: the second was that of Mark Antony, Octavus and Lepidus, 43 B.C.

Tropic-Bird, a long-tailed sea bird, of which there are 3 species (the Red-billed, the White-tailed, and the Red-tailed), frequenting the tropical regions of the Atlantic, Pacific and Indian oceans. They are commonly called Bo'sun Birds.

Troposphere. The atmospheric layer which extends from the earth's surface to the stratosphere. As a general rule temperature falls as altitude increases. *See* **Atmosphere.**

Troubadours, lyric poets who flourished from the 12th to the end of the 13th cent., chiefly in Provence and the north of Italy. They were often knightly amateurs, and cultivated a lyrical poetry intricate in metre and rhyme and usually of a romantic amatory strain, written in the *langue d'oc.* They did much to cultivate the romantic sentiment in days when society was somewhat barbaric and helped considerably in the formation of those unwritten codes of honour which served to mitigate the rudeness of mediaeval days. *See also* **Jongleurs.**

Trouvère *or* **Trouveur,** mediaeval poet of northern France, whose compositions were of a more elaborate character—epics, romances, fables, and chansons de geste—than those of the troubadour of the south. The poetry was written in the *langue d'oïl.* Flourished between the 12th and 13th cent.

Truffles are subterranean edible fungi much esteemed for seasoning purposes. There are many species, and they are found in considerable quantities in France and Italy, less commonly in Britain. They are often met with under beech or oak trees, and prefer calcareous soils, but there are no positive indications on the surface to show where they are, and they are not to be cultivated. Hogs, and sometimes dogs, are used to scent them out, the former, by reason of their rooting propensities, being the most successful in the work.

Tsetse, an African dipterous fly belonging to the same family as the house-fly. It is a serious economic pest as it transmits the protozoon causing African sleeping sickness when it pierces human skin in order to suck blood.

Tsunami, a seismic sea wave originating from any one of several submarine geological phenomena such as volcanic explosions, landslides of earth movements. Tsunamis are extremely long wavelength waves which travel in the open ocean at speeds up to 640 km/h. In deep water their height is only barely perceptible, but on reaching shallow coastal water they may attain heights of up to 30 m and can cause devastation to low-lying areas. The Pacific Ocean, whose rim is a seismically active area, is particularly susceptible to tsunamis. Following the damage caused by a tsunami which struck the volcanic islands of Hawaii on 1 April 1946, an early warning system has been in operation. Tsunamis are often incorrectly referred to as tidal waves.

Tuatara or **Sphenodon,** a reptile of great antiquity, the sole surviving species of the *Rhynchocephalia,* found in New Zealand. It has a rudimentary third eye on the top of the head; this is called the pineal eye and corresponds to tissue which in mammals forms the pineal gland.

Tube Foot, the characteristic organ of locomotion of starfishes and kindred animals. They are arranged in pairs along the underside of the arms, and their sucker-like ends can grip a surface very tightly. The action of the suckers depends on hydraulic pressure.

Tudor Period extends from 1485 to 1603. The first Tudor sovereign was Henry VII, descended from Owen Tudor; then followed Henry VIII, Edward VI, Mary and Elizabeth, the last of the line.

Tuesday, the third day of the week, named from the Saxon deity Tuisto, Tiw or Tuesco. To the Romans it was the day of Mars.

Tuileries, a French royal and imperial palace dating from 1564. It was attacked by insurgents during the outbreaks of 1792, 1830 and 1848, and was burned down during the Commune of Paris in 1871.

Tumulus, a mound of earth raised over the bodies of the dead. The mound of Marathon, enclosing the bodies of the Athenians who were killed in the famous battle with the Persians, is a celebrated tumulus. Such mounds were commonly raised over the tombs of the distinguished dead in ancient times, and sometimes enclosed heavy structures of masonry. The Roman "barrows" were tumuli. Evidence of such mounds are frequent in prehistoric remains.

Tuna *or* **Tunny,** a large marine fish belonging to the mackerel family, frequenting the warm waters of the Atlantic, Pacific and Mediterranean. Tuna fisheries are an important industry.

Tundra, the vast treeless plains lying in northern N. America and northern USSR where long severe winters and permanently frozen subsoils (permafrost) have resulted in specially adapted plant communities. The summer thaw and impervious permafrost cause waterlogging of lowland areas and marsh plants occur on these sites. In summer the ground cover of lichens and mosses with some flowering plants is distinctive. Stunted willows and birches occur in certain sites.

Tungsten, a hard, brittle metallic element, no. 74, symbol W (it was formerly called wolfram), silver to grey in colour. Its chief ores are wolframite (iron and manganese tungstate) and scheelite (calcium tungstate). Tungsten is alloyed in steel for the manufacture of cutting tools; also in the non-ferrous alloy stellite. Electric lamp filaments are made from tungsten. Tungsten carbide is one of the hardest substances known and is used for tipping tools.

Turbines propelled by steam provide power for the propulsion of many ships, and on land steam turbines are a principal source of power, being used in large central electricity stations, for instance, to convert heat energy into electrical energy. Gas turbines have recently come into use in aeroplanes, and gas-turbine railway locomotives are being developed. The first gas-turbine ship had its trials in 1947, just half a century after the first steam-turbine ship.

Turbot, a large flat fish, highly valued as food. It often attains from 13 to 18 kg in weight. Its flesh is white and firm. It is confined to European waters, and is caught by line or trawl.

Turkey, a fowl of American origin, brought to Europe from America soon after the discovery of that country. It was a domesticated bird in England in the first half of the 16th cent.

Turpentine, an oily substance obtained from coniferous trees, mostly pines and firs. It is widely used especially in making paints and varnishes, and also has medicinal properties.

Turquoise, formerly called Turkey-Stone, is a blue or greenish-blue precious stone, the earliest and best specimens of which came from Persia. It is composed of a phosphate of aluminium, with small proportions of copper and iron. India, Tibet, and Silesia yield turquoises, and a variety is found in New Mexico and Nevada. It derives its name from the fact that the first specimens were imported through Turkey.

Turtle Dove, a summer visitor from Africa to southern England. It is a small, slender bird with reddish-brown upper parts, pinkish throat, black tail with white edges, and a repeated purring note.

Tweed. A rough-surfaced fabric of the twilled type, usually all-wool, though cheaper kinds may include cotton. Of a soft, open, flexible texture, it may have a check, twill or herringbone pattern. Harris, Lewis, Bannockburn and Donegal tweeds are well known. "Tweeds" is said to have been written in error by a clerk for "twill".

Twelfth Night is the eve of the feast of the Epiphany, and in olden times was made the occasion of many festivities. It was the most popular festival next to Christmas, but is now little observed.

Twilight is the light which is reflected from the upper portion of the earth's atmosphere when the sun is below the horizon (before sunrise or after sunset). The term is most usually understood to refer, however, to the evening light; the morning light we call dawn. The twilight varies in duration in different countries, according to the position of the sun. In tropical countries it is short; in the extreme north it continues through the night.

Tyburn, a former small tributary of the Thames, which gave its name to the district where now stands the Marble Arch, Hyde Park. Here public executions formerly took place.

Tycoon, the title by which the commander-in-chief of the Japanese army (virtually the ruler of Japan) was formerly described by foreigners. (In Japanese *taikun* means great lord or prince.) The term is now applied, usually in a derogatory sense, to an influential business magnate.

Tympanum is, in architectural phraseology, the triangular space at the back of a pediment, or, indeed, any space in a similar position, as over window or between the lintel and the arch of a doorway. In ecclesiastical edifices the tympanum is often adorned with sculpture.

Tynwald, the title given to the Parliament of the Isle of Man, which includes the Governor and Council (the Upper House), and the House of Keys, the representative assembly. This practically constitutes Home Rule, the Acts passed by the Tynwald simply requiring the assent of the Sovereign.

U

Uhlan, a light cavalry soldier armed with lance, pistol, and sabre and employed chiefly as skirmisher or scout. Marshal Saxe had a corps of them in the French Army; and in the Franco-German war of 1870 the Prussian Uhlans won fame.

Ultramarine, a sky-blue pigment obtained from *Lapis lazuli,* a stone found in Tibet, Iran, Siberia and some other countries. A cheaper ultramarine is now produced by grinding and heating a mixture of clay, sulphur, carbonate of soda and resin.

Ultrasonics, sound waves of frequency so high as to be inaudible to humans, *i.e.,* above 15,000 Hz (Hz is SI unit for cycle per sec.). Ultrasonic waves are commonly produced by causing a solid object to vibrate with a suitable high frequency and to impart its vibrations to the air or other fluid. The object may be a quartz or other crystal in which vibrations are excited electrically, or a nickel component which is magnetically energised. There are numerous technical applications, *e.g.* submarine echo soundings, flaw detection in castings, drilling glass and ceramics, emulsification. Ultrasonic waves are an important tool of research in physics. Bats produce very loud sounds when they are flying, but at ultrasonic frequencies (20,000 to 150,000 Hz), so that we cannot ourselves hear them.

Ultra-Violet Rays. These are invisible electromagnetic rays whose wavelengths are less than 3900 A. (Angstrom = one hundred-millionth of a centimetre.) The sun's radiation is rich in ultra-violet light, but much of it never reaches the earth, being absorbed by molecules of atmospheric gases (in particular, ozone) as well as by soot and smoke particles. One beneficial effect of ultra-violet light on human beings is that it brings about synthesis of vitamin-D from certain fatty substances (called sterols) in the skin. The wavelengths which effect this vitamin synthesis also cause sun tan and sun burn. Ultra-violet lamps (which are mercury-vapour discharge lamps) are also used for sterilising the air inside buildings, their rays being lethal to bacteria. Many substances fluoresce under ultra-violet light; for instance, zinc silicate glows green, while cadmium borate throws out red light. This phenomenon is applied practically in fluorescent lamps, the light of requisite hue being secured by judicious mixture of the fluorescent materials which coat the lamp.

Umbra, the full shadow of the earth or moon during an eclipse; the half shadow is called penumbra.

Unciae. The Romans took over the Egyptian cubit and divided it into 16 digits as well as into 12 parts called *unciae,* the *uncia* being the origin of the inch.

Underdeveloped Countries are those in which economic structure and development are held back, or, as some would have it, countries which are underdeveloped in the transitive sense of the word. The causes of the condition of underdevelopment are complex but two opposing sets of theories dominate discussion. On the one hand there are those theories that attribute underdevelopment to the internal characteristics of the underdeveloped countries themselves. This is the doctrine of original underdevelopment as it implies that such countries are responsible for their own underdevelopment. On the other hand there are the theories that ascribe underdevelopment directly to the distortions of economic structure and the exploitation involved in the relations between the developed and underdeveloped countries. The expansion of capitalism from its birthplace in Western Europe has created a world-wide production system and market (*i.e.*, a world economy from which no country is completely isolated) structured and determined by the imperatives of capital accumulation in the developed countries. This view implies that the state and process of underdevelopment in one part of the world is inevitable as long as there is development in another. Development and underdevelopment are then mutually interdependent. *See also* **Section G, Part III.**

Unicorn, a fabulous single-horned animal. In heraldry its form is horse-like, with the tail of a lion and pointed single horn growing out of the forehead. In the Middle Ages the unicorn was a symbol of virginity.

Union of Great Britain and Ireland was proposed in the Irish Parliament in January 1799 after the 1798 Rebellion and came into force on 1 January 1801. The troubled history of Ireland, associated with the question of self-government, nationalism, land and religion, culminated in the Easter revolution of 1916. A treaty giving the 26 southern counties independence in 1921, as the Irish Free State, was followed by a period of internal dissension. In 1937 a new constitution was enacted in Eire in which no reference was made to the Crown. This, however, left in force the External Relations Act of 1936 and with its repeal in 1948, Eire separated itself from the British Crown and thus severed the last constitutional link with the Commonwealth, and became an independent Republic.

Union, Treaty of, was the treaty by which Scotland became formally united to England, the two countries being incorporated as the United Kingdom of Great Britain, the same Parliament to represent both, Scotland electing sixteen peers and forty-five members of the House of Commons. Uniformity of coins, weights, and measures was provided for, Scottish trade laws and customs were assimilated to those of England, and as regards religion and the practices of the law, Scotland was to continue as before. This Act was ratified on 1 May 1707.

Universe in astronomy means not only the star system (of which the sun and planets are a small part) but all the countless star systems or nebulae which may be separated from each other by millions of light-years. See **F3–8.**

Universities are institutions of higher education whose principal objects are the increase of knowledge over a wide field through original thought and research and its extension by the teaching of students. Such societies existed in the ancient world, notably in Greece and India, but the origin of the University as we know it today lies in mediaeval Europe, the word *universitas* being a contraction of the Latin term for corporations of teachers and students organised for the promotion of higher learning. The earliest bodies to become recognised under this description were at Bologna and Paris in the first half of the 12th cent.; Oxford was founded by an early migration of scholars from Paris, and Cambridge began with a further migration from Oxford. Other Universities sprang up all over Europe, including three in Scotland—St. Andrews (1411), Glasgow (1451) and Aberdeen (1494)—which were followed by Edinburgh in 1582. These six bodies remained the only Universities in Great Britain until the foundation in 1826–29 of University and King's Colleges in London (resulting in the establishment of the University of London in 1836) and of the University of Durham in 1832. There are (1990) thirty-four Universities in England: Aston, Bath, Birmingham, Bradford, Bristol, Brunel, Buckingham, Cambridge, The City, Durham, East Anglia, Essex, Exeter, Hull, Keele, Kent, Lancaster, Leeds, Leicester, Liverpool, London, Loughborough, Manchester, Newcastle, Nottingham, Oxford, Reading, Salford, Sheffield, Southampton, Surrey, Sussex, Warwick and York. Other institutions of university standard are the University of Manchester Institute of Science and Technology; the Manchester Business School; the London Graduate School of Business Studies; Cranfield Institute of Technology; and the Royal College of Art. Formed from colleges of technology, art and design, commerce and other institutions, thirty polytechnics have been established in England and Wales as centres of higher education. Wales has one University (The University of Wales with colleges at Aberystwyth, Bangor, Cardiff and Swansea) in addition to the Welsh National School of Medicine, the Institute of Science and Technology, and St. David's, Lampeter. Scotland now has eight: Aberdeen, Dundee (1967), Edinburgh, Glasgow, Heriot-Watt (1966), St. Andrews, Stirling (1967), and Strathclyde (1964), Britain's first technological University. Northern Ireland has two: Queen's University, Belfast and the New University of Ulster at Coleraine. The Open University received its charter in 1969; it provides degrees and other courses together with radio and television programmes and began its broadcasts in January 1971. The Republic of Ireland has the University of Dublin (Trinity College, Dublin), and the National University of Ireland with colleges at Dublin, Cork and Galway. In the USA the development of higher education has left the Universities less sharply defined than in Europe and the Commonwealth, among the best known being Harvard (1636), Yale (1701), Princeton (1746), Columbia (1754), Cornell (1865), California (Berkeley), Massachusetts Institute of Technology. In 1973 the United Nations University was established with headquarters in Tokyo. In Britain, Universities receive aid from the State mainly in the form of grants from the Universities Funding Council (est. 1989) which oversees the distribution of state finance. But they are selfgoverning institutions free from State control. In 1983, the private institution at Buckingham received its charter.

Uranium, a metallic element, no. 92, symbol U, discovered by Klaproth in 1789 in pitchblende. It is a white metal which tarnishes readily in air. Great developments have followed the discovery that the nucleus of the uranium isotope U^{235} undergoes fission, and uranium minerals have become very important since it was found that atomic energy could be released controllably by taking advantage of fission. Before atomic energy work began to take the major part of the world's output of uranium minerals, the chief users of uranium compounds were the ceramics and textile industries. *See also* **Nuclear Reactors, Nuclear Fission, F13(1).**

Uranus. This planet was discovered by Herschel in 1781. Its diameter is *c.* 51,800 km and its mean distance from the sun is $2,869 \cdot 6 \times 10^6$ km. It has five small satellites and is surrounded by five very thin rings (first seen 1977). Uranus rotates on its side so that each pole faces the sun every half-revolution of the planet round the sun, *i.e.*, every 42 years. Uranus has 5 moons—Miranda, Ariel, Umbriel, Titania and Oberon. Voyager 2 visited Uranus (Jan. 1986) and Neptune (Sept. 1989). *See* **F8** and **Voyager.**

Urea, the final product in mammals of the breakdown of nitrogenous waste, *e.g.*, excess aminoacids. It is very soluble in water and is excreted in urine. In 1828 Wöhler synthesised urea from inorganic matter. This was the first laboratory synthesis of an organic substance and refuted the idea that living creatures or life force are necessary to create such substances.

Ursa Major and **Ursa Minor** ("Greater Bear" and "Lesser Bear"), two celebrated constellations, each of seven stars, in the northern celestial hemisphere, familiar since ancient times. Ursa Major has also been called "the Plough", "Charles's (Charlemagne's) Wain" or "the Wagon". The "Pointers" in this group of bright stars point to the brightest star in Ursa Minor, the Pole Star. Called the Big Dipper and the Little Dipper in the USA.

V

Valency. A term used by chemists to describe the combining ability of an element with respect to hydrogen. Thus oxygen, which forms water, H_2O, with hydrogen is said to have a valency of two, nitrogen (forms ammonia, NH_3) three, and carbon (forms methane, CH_4) four. Chlorine forms hydrogen chloride, HCl, and is said to be monovalent. This empirical approach cannot account for valency in such compounds as carbon monoxide, CO, which appears to require both elements to have the same valency. With the discovery of the electron it was realised that the concept of valency and chemical bonds is intimately concerned with the electronic structure of atoms, and theories have been advanced to explain why the same element can have different valencies in different compounds. Iron, for example, can have a valency of two ($FeCl_2$, ferrous chloride) or three ($FeCl_3$, ferric chloride). *See* **F11(1), F24(2)** and **Table of Elements (F64).**

Valentine's Day (14 February), is a festival in celebration of St. Valentine, one of the Christian martyrs of the 3rd cent. A sweetheart or Valentine is chosen on that day and letters or tokens sent secretly to the object of affection.

Valhalla, in Scandinavian mythology, is the special Paradise to which the souls of warriors slain in battle were transported.

Valkyries, the chosen handmaidens of Odin, appointed to serve at the Valhalla banquets. Their most important office, however, according to the Norse mythology, was to ride through the air at a time of battle and point out the heroes who were to fall. It is one of these Valkyries who is made the heroine of Wagner's opera *"Die Walküre".*

Valve, an electronic device consisting of two or more metal plates (electrodes) usually enclosed in an evacuated glass bulb. One of the electrodes is heated causing electrons to be emitted. If a positive voltage is applied to the other electrode, the electrons will move towards it and the valve must conduct electricity. The current will only flow in one direction as the electrons are emitted only from one direction. A valve with two electrodes is called a diode, but by putting in one or more intermediate electrodes the flow of current can be sensitively controlled and the valves are then called triodes, pentodes, etc., according to the total number of electrodes in them. Valves have found extensive applications in amplifiers, rectifiers, oscillators and many electronic devices, but have now been superseded by transistors in many applications where it is advantageous to have greater reliability, smaller power consumption and smaller size.

Vanadium, a scarce metallic element, no. 23, symbol V, whose chief ores are carnotite and patronite. Some iron ores contain it. Most of the vanadium commercially produced finds its way into vanadium steels, which are used for tools and parts of vehicles, being hard, tough and very resistant to shocks. The oxide is used as a catalyst in industry, especially in making sulphuric acid.

Van Allen Belts. One of the most remarkable discoveries made during the IGY, 1957–58, was that the earth is surrounded by a great belt of radiation. Evidence came from *Sputnik II* (which carried the dog Laika) and from the American satellites, *Explorers I* and *III*. The American scientist, J. A. van Allen, was able to explain the puzzling data collected from these satellites. Subsequent observations with deep space-probes showed that there are in fact two zones of high intensity particle radiation surrounding the earth, one concentrated at a distance of about 1,600 km, the other at about 24,000 km. A close relation exists between the shapes of the zones and the earth's magnetic field. Recent evidence suggests that Jupiter also is surrounded by a dense belt of trapped high-energy particles.

Vatican, the Papal residence at Rome, a famous palace on the hill adjacent to St. Peter's. Its museum is a rich treasure-house of literary and artistic objects. Works of Michelangelo glorify the Sistine Chapel.

Vauxhall Gardens, a famous London pleasure resort from the early part of the 18th to the middle of the 19th cent. It was here that many great singers appeared, where the earliest balloon ascents were made, and where there were fine displays of fireworks.

Venus, the brightest of all the planets, whose orbit lies between the orbits of Mercury and Earth, is second in order from the sun (*see* **F8**). It approaches the earth to within 40 million km. It moves around the sun in the same direction as Earth and the other planets but rotates in the opposite sense. It has been visited by a number of American and Russian probes, some flybys, some soft-landings, others atmospheric probes. Venus has 100 times the atmospheric pressure of the earth and temperatures of 500°C. It is covered in a very thick cloud mainly of carbon dioxide which some scientists believe acts like a green-house trapping the heat from the sun. Complex reactions occur in the atmosphere and the rain consists mainly of sulphuric and hydrochloric acid. The cloud rotates about six times faster than Venus rotates and swirls into the polar regions like giant whirlpools. The terrain has been studied by radar, much of it ground-based, but a vast amount of information has come from the Pioneer Venus orbiter which mapped 98 per cent of the surface in two (earth) years. There are two major continents, Aphrodite Terra, about half the size of Africa, and the smaller Ishtar Terra, about the size of Australia, which consists of a very high plateau (c. 3,300 m) and a mountain range dominated by Maxwell Montes (at 10,600 m higher than Everest). Aphrodite Terra has a deep trench 2,900 m below "sea level". Most of the planet (60 per cent) is relatively flat.

Venus Fly-trap, a well-known insectivorous plant (*Dionaea muscipula*) occurring in Carolina in damp mossy places. It is related to the Sundew. The leaf is the organ that catches the insects. The leaf blade is in two halves, hinged along the centre line. Each half bears three sensitive hairs called "trigger hairs". When an insect touches a trigger, the two halves of the leaf clap together, trapping the insect between them, when it is digested by a secretion (digestive enzymes) from the leaf, which afterwards absorbs the soluble products.

Vernalization. Seeds which, after being exposed to a low temperature, produce plants that flower earlier than usual are said to have been "vernalized". This technique of seed treatment devised by Lysenko is called vernalization. It is claimed to have been widely used in Russia to obtain cereal crops in places where climatic conditions are favourable for only a short season.

Versailles, Treaty of. The Peace Treaty, 1919, ending the first world war. The first half was devoted to the organisation of the League of Nations. Among the territorial changes Germany ceded Alsace-Lorraine to France, Posen and the Corridor to Poland. Germany undertook to disarm, to abolish universal military service, to keep only a small army of 100,000 and a small navy. Her colonies were to be shared out among the Allies under League Mandates. Reparations were to be paid, but were gradually reduced and entirely ceased in 1932. Hitler took unilateral action against the Treaty especially in regard to rearmament and the annexation of Austria. This policy eventually led to the Second World War.

Victoria and Albert Museum, in Kensington, London, was begun in 1852 as the Museum of Ornamental Art at Marlborough House. The present building was completed in 1909. It has the following departments: Architecture and Sculpture, Conservation, Ceramics, Paintings, Prints and Drawings, Oriental Library Metalwork, Museum Services (inc. Information and Slide Loan Service), Textiles, Furniture and Woodwork. Education (into which the old Circulation Dept., has been absorbed), and Theatre Museum. A controversial restructuring of these departments is now (1989) taking place. The V. & A. also administers the Wellington Museum (Apsley House, Piccadilly), Ham House (Richmond, Surrey), and Osterley Park House (Middx). The Bethnal Green Museum (The Museum of Childhood) is a branch of the V. & A., opened 1872.

Victoria Cross, an order of merit for conspicuous valour, awarded to members of the Army, Navy and Air Force, was established in 1856.

Videotape recording (VTR), technique for recording television programmes on to magnetic tape. The original means of storing programmes for broadcast or library purposes was by filming productions from high-quality monitors, an expensive and slow process, since the film had to be chemically developed and edited in the conventional way. The difficulty in establishing an instant play-back system along the lines of the sound tape recording system lay in the high speed and large amount of tape needed to accommodate the picture signal. The BBC experimented with a machine called VERA (Vision Electronic Recording Apparatus), but it was an American machine, the Ampex VR100, which provided the break-through. This recorded the picture across a wider tape rather than along it, and moving at a slower speed. Tapes, in colour or black and white, now run for about 90 minutes and can be used many times by erasing and re-recording, accuracy of editing is achieved to the second by re-recording chosen sequences on to a second machine.

Vienna Congress, sat at Vienna from September 1814 to June 1815, and settled the delineation of the territories of the various European nations after the defeat of Napoleon. The Treaty of Vienna which resulted gave Sri Lanka, Mauritius, Cape Colony, Heligoland, Malta and part of Guyana to England; Belgium, Holland and Luxemburg were united in the Kingdom of the Netherlands; Austria took Lombardy-Venetia; Russia took part of Poland; and Prussia, part of Saxony and the Rhenish province. Except for one or two changes the clauses of the treaty were maintained for over forty years.

Vikings. Scandinavian pirates who from the 8th to the 10th cent. were the terror of northern waters. Sometimes the Viking raids reached south to the Mediterranean and east to the White Sea. Their leader Rurik founded the first Russian kingdom of Novgorod in A.D. 862. The Icelandic Vikings under Eric the Red discovered Greenland in A.D. 982 and a warm period in world climate allowed many to settle there. Their expeditions took them to Labrador and Newfoundland. They excelled in shipbuilding, were fine sailors and craftsmen.

Vinyl Plastics are polymers made from derivatives of ethylene, examples are polyvinyl chloride (PVC), which is used in making plastic pipes and kitchen utensils, among other things; polyvinyl acetate used in the paint industry and in bonding laminated articles like plywood; and polystyrene (polyvinyl benzene) used in making electrical fittings and for lenses.

Viper, a family of poisonous snakes in which the venom-conducting fangs hinge forward when the snake bites. One species is found in Britain, the common viper or adder.

Virus. *See* Index to P, **F31**(2).

Visibility is defined by the distance at which the farthest of a series of objects, specially selected to show against the skyline or in good contrast with their background, can be distinguished. Visibility depends chiefly upon the concentration of water or dust particles suspended in the air. Instruments are available to measure the obscurity of the atmosphere more directly, including that at night. A large lapse rate of temperature and a strong wind are favourable to good visibility; a small lapse rate, calm or light wind favourable to bad visibility. Fog is when the visibility is less than 1,000 m; mist or haze when it is between 1,000 and 2,000 m. *See* **Pollution.**

Viscount, a title of rank coming between that of Earl and Baron. The title originally stood for

deputy-earl. The first English Viscount was Viscount Beaumont, created in 1440.

Vitamins, name of a group of organic substances found in relatively minute amounts in certain foodstuffs, essential for growth and the maintenance of normal bodily structure and function. The Hungarian biochemist Szent-Györgyi, who first isolated vitamin C or ascorbic acid, defined the vitamin as "a substance that makes you ill if you don't eat it!" See **F32**(1), **Index to P**.

Volcanoes are vents through which magma reaches the surface as lava flows, or as the solid products, *e.g.*, ashes and bombs, of explosive eruption. The vent may be cylindrical or it may be a long fissure. The former type usually builds up cones, *e.g.*, Vesuvius. Notable active volcanoes are Etna, Vesuvius and Stromboli, in Italy; Hekla in Iceland; and Mont Pelée in Martinique. The last-named was in violent eruption in 1902, when the chief town of St. Pierre was completely destroyed. Volcanic eruptions are sometimes linked with brilliant sunset phenomena, *e.g.*, the Indonesian island of Krakatoa (1883), whose atmospheric and tidal effects were recorded all over the world, and Agung on the island of Bali (1963), which had been dormant for 120 years. A new fissure volcano (Surtsey) developed off the coast of Iceland in 1963.

Vole, a small rodent with blunt nose, round face and short tail. Three kinds occur in Britain: the field, the bank and the water vole.

Volt, the electromotive force unit, named after Alessandro Volta (1745–1827), and defined in terms of the coulomb, the second and the joule.

Voyagers 1 and 2. These spacecraft were launched from Earth on 5 Sept. 1977 and 20 Aug. 1977 respectively as a follow-on mission to the earlier and successful Pioneer 10 and 11 spacecraft. Both were targeted initially to swing by Jupiter (*q.v.*), with Voyager 1 on the faster trajectory, to make the next phase of investigation of Jupiter and its moons, before continuing to Saturn (*q.v.*) and beyond, using the enormous gravitational field of Jupiter to assist them in their journeys. (It was this planet's gravitational field that flung Pioneer 10 (launched 1972) into space in June 1983 to make it the first man-made object to leave the solar system.) Voyager 1, in flying through the Jovian system in 1979, discovered the unique features of Io, the most volcanically active object yet found in the solar system, photographed the ice-covered moons—Europa, Ganymede and Callisto—and made many new discoveries of Jupiter, the largest and most massive planet of the solar system. Voyager 1 began surveying Saturn in Aug. 1980, and continued sending back a vast amount of new data, including some 18,000 pictures of the planet, its moons and, perhaps most spectacularly, its fascinating and complex system of rings. The measurements included infra-red and ultra-violet measurements of the structure of the planet's atmosphere, as well as data on the magnetic field and charged particle environment of the planet. When the spacecraft passed through one of the "gaps" of the ring system on 12 Nov. 1980, it made a series of fascinating revelations. The flyby of Saturn by Voyager 2 in Aug. 1981 was carefully planned to obtain the maximum of new information to complement that obtained from Voyager 1 to help understand some of the perplexing new phenomena, and revealed even more new features of this beautiful and still enigmatic planet. Even after its Saturn flyby, the work of Voyager 2 was far from complete: its swing by Saturn redirected it toward Uranus, on which it provided our first close-up data in Jan. 1986, and from there it continued to Neptune in 1989, taking maximum advantage of a unique arrangement of all four of the outer planets, Jupiter, Saturn, Uranus and Neptune, which only occurs once every 200 years. Voyager 1, which would not pass particularly close to any planet after Saturn, carries a multi-lingual goodwill message as well as musical selections to far outside our solar system. It will not reach its nearest star, Sirius, for 360,000 years. In March 1990, Voyager 1 beamed back its last colour photographs before leaving the solar system for outer space. By then it was 3,500 million miles from Earth, travelling at 37,000 mph.

Vraic, a name for seaweed in the Channel Islands, where it is extensively used as a manure.

Vulgate, a term used to designate the Latin version of the Scriptures sanctioned by the Council of Trent. The work of St. Jerome in the late 4th cent. A.D. and still the official Bible of the Roman Catholic Church.

Vulture, a famous bird of prey of two distinctive groups; that of the Old World, whose nostrils are separated by a bony partition, and the New World vulture, which has no such division. Vultures feed on carrion and are the great scavengers of tropical regions. The European species are the Egyptian vulture, Griffon vulture, Black vulture and Bearded vulture. Vultures have no feathers on the head and neck.

W

Wading Birds, *Charadriiformes*, an order of migratory, long-legged, long-billed birds, frequenting marshes and shallow waters. They include the plovers, avocets, stilts, oystercatchers, curlews, phalaropes, godwits, dunlins, sandpipers, redshanks, greenshanks, snipe, woodcocks, the pratincole of the Mediterranean and the sun bittern of tropical America. Many species breed in Britain.

Wagtails, familar long-tailed small birds, the most common British species being the Pied or Water (with sub-species White) Grey and the Yellow (sub-species Blue). Wagtails nest in holes and are active of habit.

Walloons, name given to the French-speaking population of the southern provinces of Belgium, in contrast to the Flemings or Dutch-speaking population of the northern provinces. The Walloon areas contain the mining and heavy industries of the country.

Walpurgis Night, the night before 1 May, when witches and creatures of evil are supposed to have liberty to roam. Named after St Walpurgis, an English nun, who went on a mission to Germany in the 8th cent.

Walrus, a very large marine mammal, related to the seals having in the upper jaw two large curved tusks, which average in length from 38 to 60 cm. It lives on bi-valve molluscs, and inhabits the Arctic seas. An adult walrus can exceed 4 m in length and weigh over a tonne.

Wankel Engine *or* **Rotary Engine,** is an internal combustion engine invented by Felix Wankel in the 1930s and greatly developed since by large automobile firms in several countries. The ordinary internal combustion engine has to convert reciprocating motion of the pistons into rotary motion. In the Wankel engine the explosion of the fuel and air mixture drives a moving part (the rotor) directly into rotatory motion, and the rotor itself opens and closes the fuel inlet and exhaust ports. The three spaces between the triangular rotor and its specially shaped housing act successively as intake, compression, explosion and exhaust chambers as the rotor revolves. There are no valves and far fewer moving parts than in an ordinary piston engine. The Wankel engine is claimed to have many advantages in that it is smaller and lighter for a given horse-power, relatively simple, quieter and freer from vibration, and could contribute to pollution control. There are cars now on sale with the Wankel engine and continuous research and development will no doubt test in practice the claim of some protagonists that this engine is the agent of a technological revolution in the automobile.

Wapentake, the ancient name given in the northern countries to territorial divisions corresponding to the Hundreds of southern counties.

Warblers, a family of small, lively song-birds closely related to the flycatchers and thrushes. Represented in Britain by about 36 species, including the chiffchaff, one of the earliest spring visitors, willow-wren, wood-warbler, blackcap, garden-warbler, whitethroat, sedge and grasshopper-warbler.

Warsaw Pact. *See under* **NATO, L86.**

Water is the simplest compound of hydrogen and oxygen. It is formed when an electric spark is passed through a mixture of the gases, and is a product of combustion of all hydrogen-containing compounds, *e.g.*, petrol, coal, coal gas and wood. Water is essential to living matter, and is the medium which carries food to animals and plants. Salts in hard water may be removed by distillation of the water or by a process known as ion-exchange (water softening). Pure water freezes at 0°C and boils at 100°C and is used as a standard of temperature on this scale. It has a maximum density at 4°C. Heating water above 100°C converts it into steam, which is used under pressure to convert heat energy into useful work, as in electrical power stations and steam engines. Water gas is a mixture mainly of carbon monoxide and hydrogen formed by blowing steam and oxygen through red-hot coke: it is used as a fuel. Water is one of the very few compounds which freezes from the surface down rather than from the bulk of the liquid up. This property has important consequences on the preservation of life in rivers and lakes when they are frozen.

Water Hyacinth (*Eichhornia crassipes*), a beautiful aquatic plant native to Brazil which has spread to other favourable equatorial regions of the world causing havoc on account of its abnormal rate of reproduction away from its natural environment. In recent years it has invaded the Nile and the Zaïre, forming vast floating carpets which block the channels, clog the paddles of river craft and deoxygenate the water, killing the fish. It is being held in check by spraying with the herbicide 2,4-D.

Waterloo, Battle of, was fought on 18 June 1815. The Allies (British, German and Dutch) under Wellington and Blücher defeated the French under Napoleon, ending Napoleon's career.

Waterloo Bridge, crossing the Thames, was built by Rennie, and opened in 1817. It had nine arches, each 120 ft (36 m) span, was built of granite, and had a length (including approaches) of 2,456 ft (749 m). The present bridge, completed in 1942, and formally opened 10 December 1945, is a fine example of reinforced concrete construction. (Architect, Sir Giles Gilbert-Scott.)

Watling Street, the name of the old Roman road which ran from the Channel ports by way of London to Shropshire. See also **Roman Roads.**

Watt. A unit of electrical power equivalent to 1 joule of work per second, named after James Watt (1736–1819). See **F66–69.**

Waxbill, a small Oriental and African bird of the *Estrildidae* family, with wax-like bill and beautifully variegated plumage. The Java sparrow, and the Blue-breasted waxbill are attractive, and often find their way into cages.

Wayz-Goose, the name given to a festive gathering of people employed in printing and other works, so called from the fact that in earlier times a goose was the principal dish of the feast.

Weasel. A carnivore mammal found in Britain, smallest member of the group including the Stoat, Polecat, and Pine-marten, about 20 cm long. Its fur is reddish on the upper side of the animal, white on the under side; it may all turn white in winter with the exception of the tail.

Weather is generally accepted as being the current state of the atmosphere, particularly as regards its pressure and temperature, wind, cloud and precipitation. Many other features such as fog, sunshine duration, humidity, pressure tendency, may be added to the list, all items of which are routinely observed by specially instrumented stations usually sponsored by the national meteorological services. Day-to-day changes in the weather as experienced by the individual are due to the passage of circulation systems, many of which bring clearly recognisable areas of "good" (*i.e.*, calm and sunny) weather as frequently occurs in anticyclones and "bad" (*i.e.*, cold, windy, cloudy and rainy) weather. Clearly, the weather in any place at any time is primarily determined by the frequency and intensity of synoptic-scale weather circulation systems (*c.* 3,000 km across). Local weather (over areas of *c.* 100 km) may be heavily influenced by topography, *e.g.*, valley fogs, frost hollows.

Weather Lore. Before instruments were invented to measure atmospheric conditions, man relied on his own observation of wind and sky, behaviour of birds and animals, and came to associate certain phenomena with types of weather. Many popular weather rhymes have survived the centuries, and as long as forecasting is confined to the next 24 hours there is perhaps something to be said for them, particularly those dealing with the winds. What is very unlikely is that next year's summer can be predicted from this year's winter, or that one month's weather is related to that of another. The study of past records reveals too many exceptions for such predictions to be of much use in forecasting.

Weaver Bird, the popular name for a large group of finch-like birds belonging to the family *Ploceidae*, found principally in Africa but also in Southern Asia, Australia, and Europe and remarkable for their habit of building nests formed of blades of grass dexterously interwoven and suspended from the boughs of trees.

Weaving. The interlacing of two or more threads at right angles to form a fabric is a craft that has been practised since ancient times. The main principle of the weaving loom is the same to-day as it was thousands of years ago; a warp extends lengthwise through the loom, the threads being held in separate regular order by being passed through a reed or "slay", while the weft is crossed through alternating threads of the warp by means of a shuttle which holds the weft. Thus the fabric is built up. Weaving was done by hand up to the early part of the 19th cent., when Cartwright's steam-power loom was introduced. The Jacquard loom for weaving figured designs dates from 1801.

Wedding Anniversaries are: first, Paper; second, Cotton; third, Leather; fourth, Fruit and Flower; fifth, Wooden; sixth, Sugar; seventh, Woollen; eighth, Bronze; ninth, Pottery; tenth, Tin; twelfth, Silk and Fine Linen; fifteenth, Crystal; twentieth, China; twenty-fifth, Silver; thirtieth, Pearl; thirty-fifth, Coral; fortieth, Ruby; fiftieth, Golden; fifty-fifth, Emerald; sixtieth, Diamond; sixty-fifth, Blue Sapphire; seventieth, Platinum.

Wednesday, the 4th day of the week, derived its name from Woden or Odin, the Norse god of war.

Weights and Measures. See **F66–69.**

Welding is a means of joining together two pieces of material, often metals, by heating the joint until the substances melt locally, run together, and then solidify. The heating can be by burning gas (*e.g.*, oxy-acetylene welding) or electric current (electric arc welding). Techniques exist for welding anything from hair-like wires to massive steel plates. See **Soldering.**

Werewolf, a man or woman, who according to mediaeval belief, could be turned by witchcraft or magic into a wolf, eat human flesh or drink human blood and turn into himself again. This belief was widely held in Europe, and similar superstitions prevail among most primitive peoples, *e.g.*, the "leopard man" of certain African tribes. Lycanthropy (from Gr. = wolf-man) is a form of madness in which the patient imagines himself a beast. See **Section J.**

Westminster Abbey stands on the site of an old church and Benedictine foundation of the 7th cent. It was rebuilt under Edward the Confessor, and again under Henry III, and important additions were made by Edward II, Edward III, Richard II, Richard III and Henry VII, the latter erecting the beautiful eastern chapel in the perpendicular style which bears his name. The west towers and gable were designed by Hawksmoor (1661–1736). The Abbey contains tombs of many sovereigns, of the Unknown Warrior, and many other illustrious men are commemorated by monuments.

Westminster Cathedral, seat of the Roman Catholic Archbishop of Westminster. It was designed by J. F. Bentley and built betwen 1895 and 1910. It is of red brick, in early Christian Byzantine style with a domed campanile, 283 ft (86 m) high, and a decorative interior.

Westminster Hall, adjoining the House of Parliament, was built as a Banqueting Hall by William Rufus, and many courtly festivals were held there in succeeding centuries. King John established the Law Courts there. It now forms a gigantic hallway, leading to the Houses of Parliament. Charles I, Sir Thomas More, and Warren Hastings were tried there.

Whale, a completely aquatic mammal; the fore-limbs are modified to form fin-like paddles and there is virtually no external trace of the hind-limbs. There are two major groups of whales—the *Toothed Whales*, including the Sperm-whale (Cachalot), Dolphin, Killer-whales and Porpoises; and the *Whalebone Whales*. In the latter a series of whalebone plates grow down from the roof of the mouth, and, being frayed at their edges into a hairy fringe, together constitute a filtering mechanism. The animal takes in sea water containing minute organisms on which it feeds; the mouth is then closed and the tongue raised when the water is forced out through the filter, on which is left the food. As the tongue is lowered, the whalebone plates straighten up, flicking the food on to the tongue, which transfers it to the gut. Most whale oil is obtained from the thick layer of fat under the skin (blubber), but in the Sperm-whale there is a large reserve of oil in the head. One of the major users of sperm oil is the leather industry. Ambergris used in perfumery comes from the intestine of whales. The number of whales that may be killed in a season is limited by International Convention. The three main whaling nations are Japan, Norway and the Soviet Union.

Whiskers in physics and materials science (*q.v.*) are tiny rods of crystal, thinner than human hair and perhaps 1 cm long. Their importance lies in the fact that such crystals are free from the defects described on **F21**. They are also free from surface cracks and steps. This means they are immensely strong because failures of strength in ordinary solids are due to imperfections and cracks of one kind or another. Large numbers of whiskers of strong solids like graphite, silicon, or silicon carbide embedded in a matrix of softer matter such as plastic or metal would make a very strong new material. Many laboratories are developing such substances.

White Elephant, a term in common use to designate a gift that causes the recipient more trouble or cost than it is worth; derived from an old-time custom of the Kings of Thailand who presented a white elephant to a courtier whom it was desired to ruin.

Whitehall Palace, built within sight of Westminster by Hubert de Burgh, Earl of Kent, round about 1240, was the residence of the Archbishops of York until Wolsey presented it to Henry VIII in 1530. From then until 1697, when it was burned down, it continued to be the favourite town residence of royalty, and to the Stuarts especially it was a great centre of court festivities. In those days, with its grounds, it extended from the Strand to the river. The only portion of Whitehall Palace now standing is the Banqueting Hall built by Inigo Jones, on a scaffold projected from the front of which Charles I was beheaded. A block of government buildings has been built on part of the site of the old Palace.

White House, the official residence at Washington of the President of the United States.

Whitsuntide, the festival celebrating the descent of the Holy Ghost and occurring seven weeks after Easter.

Widow Bird, certain species of African weaver birds with predominantly black plumage. In the breeding season the male birds are strikingly beautiful, with scarlet and buff markings and long tail feathers. They are social parasites and trick other birds into rearing their young.

Wigeon, a surface-feeding duck of northern Europe, known in Britain more as a winter visitor than a nesting bird. It feeds in flocks in the muddy estuaries and has a characteristic "whee-oo" call.

Willow, a water-side-loving tree of the genus *Salix*, to which the osiers belong. The best cricket-bat blades are made from a white willow, *S. alba* var. *caerulea*, a fine tree with bluish-green leaves, mostly found in Essex. Willow is also used for polo balls. Weeping willow, *S. babylonica*, is native to China and is the willow seen on Old China willow-pattern plates.

Wind, air set in motion by special atmospheric conditions, is of various degrees, from a slight rustling breeze to a hurricane. Winds are *constant,* as in trade winds or anti-trade winds; *periodic,* as in monsoons and other wind-visitations occurring according to influences of season; *cyclonic* and *anti-cyclonic,* when their motion is spiral: *whirlwinds, hurricanes,* and *tornados,* when high temperature and great density induce extreme agitation. Ordinarily, a wind is named from the point of the compass from which it blows, or it may be expressed in degrees from true north. The *sirocco,* the *mistral,* and the *simoom* are local forms of winds of great velocity. A *blizzard* is a biting blast of icy temperature. *See also* **Beaufort Scale,** Section Z.

Windmills were in use in the East in ancient times, but were not much seen in Europe before the 13th cent. Wind sawmills were invented by a Dutchman in the 17th cent., and one was erected near the Strand in London in 1633. Great improvements have been made in these mills, especially in the United States, where, by the application of the windshaft principle, much space is saved and the mills can be used for pumping, grinding and other purposes.

Windows (Old Norse *vindauga* = wind-eye), an opening in a wall of a building to admit light and air, and to afford a view of what is outside. In northern Europe windows, as the derivation of the word implies, were first used for ventilation and glass was not used in private houses before the end of the 12th cent. In early Gothic (12th cent.) windows were still small and narrow, with rounded heads. In Early English (13th cent.) they became longer and the heads pointed. In the Decorated period (14th cent.) windows were mullioned (divided by slender bars into panes) and the pointed heads often traceried. In Tudor times when the Renaissance had found its way to England, windows were larger and the bay-window (projecting from the wall) and the oriel window (*q.v.*) were much in vogue; in the late 18th cent. curved bays (called bow-windows) became fashionable. Sash windows (invented by the English) with wooden frames and divided into equal rectangular panes were used in Queen Anne and Georgian houses. Their design was influenced by a passion for symmetry; they were very efficient ventilators. The French window reaches to the floor and has double casements opening as doors. A Dormer window is a vertical window set on the sloping side of a roof. One of the main features of modern architecture is the large area devoted to windows, a development made possible by improved heating systems. Windows are now mass-produced in stock sizes and patterns.

Windsor Castle, the famous British royal residence on the banks of the Thames, as it now stands, was mainly built by Henry III, though a royal residence had existed there from the time of the Conqueror. Additions were made by Henry VIII, Elizabeth and Charles II. Windsor Park and Forest comprise over 5,200 ha.

Wine, the fermented juice of the freshly-gathered grape. There are innumerable varieties, each obtaining its distinctive character from the species of wine producing the grape, the locality of the vineyard, method of cultivation, etc. Wines are of three main kinds: *sparkling,* as in champagne, due to their having been bottled before fermentation is complete; *beverage,* when the must has been fermented out before bottling. Such wines include the famous red and white wines of Burgundy, Bordeaux and the Rhône valley and the white wines of the Rhine, Moselle and Loire valleys. Wines are *fortified* by the addition of alcohol either after fermentation is complete (*e.g.,* Sherry) or during fermentation (*e.g.,* Port). The principal wine-producing countries are: France, Italy, Algeria, Spain, Portugal, Romania, Argentina, Yugoslavia, USA, USSR, Greece, W. Germany, Hungary.

Witan *or* **Witenagemot,** the name given to the king's council of "wise men" in Anglo-Saxon times, composed of the archbishops, bishops, abbots of the greater abbeys, earldormen and influential thanes.

Witchcraft. *See* Section J.

Woad, a plant (*Isastis tinctoria*) that in olden days was largely used in England for the blue dye obtained from the leaves. It is a biennial plant belonging to the same family (*Cruciferae*) as the wallflower.

Wolves, well-known carnivorous animals still found in many parts of Europe, but not existing in Britain since the middle of the 17th cent. They usually hunt in packs.

Women's Liberation Movement. See Section J.

Woodcock, a wading bird, valued for its flesh. It is a member of the snipe family, and breeds in Britain. The parent bird is able to carry its young between its thigh and body when flying to and from the feeding spots. It is one of the birds protected by the Game Laws.

Woodpecker, a familiar tree-climbing, insectivorous bird of conspicuous plumage, of which four species are found in Britain, the green woodpecker or yaffle (because of its harsh cry), the great spotted, the lesser spotted, and the wryneck. They build in the hollows of trees. Yaffle has a long sticky tongue for licking up ground insects, especially ants. The great and lesser woodpeckers obtain insects by digging into tree trunks with strong, chisel-like bills, spearing the insects with a sharp tongue. The metallic drumming sound made by the birds in spring is thought to be caused by their beaks hammering away at some hard resounding substance.

Wood's Metal, an alloy with a very low melting point (65°C, which is under 150°F) so that a spoon made of it will melt when used to stir a cup of tea. Contains bismuth 4 parts, lead 2 parts, tin 1 part, cadmium 1 part. Its use as a heat exchanger has now been largely superseded by silicone oils, which have a wider temperature range.

Woodworm. Four beetles are mainly responsible for woodworm damage: common furniture beetle (*Anobium punctatum*), powder post beetle (*Lyctus brunneus*), death watch beetle (*Xestobium rufovillosum*), and house longhorn beetle (*Hylotrupes bajulus*). Particular attention should be paid to wood in damp, dark and out-of-the-way places, and the backs and under-neaths of furniture. The most frequent cause of woodworm damage is the common furniture beetle (*q.v.*).

Wool is a fibre, made up of very long protein molecules. It has been largely grown and used in the manufacture of cloth in England since before the Roman invasion. It is grown on the backs of sheep, and is of various kinds, according to the breed of sheep from which it is derived. Wool differs from hair in that it has a wavy, serrated fibre, its curl being a notable characteristic, whereas hair has a smooth surface comparatively free from serratures. Long wools are mostly used for the manufacture of worsted goods, and short wools for woollen cloths, though the improvements in machinery in recent years have enabled manufacturers to utilise short wools to a great extent for dress fabrics as well as for woollens. The finest wools are obtained from the fleece of the Spanish merino sheep. Australia, USSR, New Zealand, Argentina and South Africa are the greatest wool-producing countries.

Woolsack, the name given to the seat occupied by the Lord Chancellor in the House of Lords. It is a large square bag of wool, without back or arms, covered with red cloth. At the time when it was first used, in the reign of Edward III, wool was the great staple commodity of the country and, it is said, chosen for the seat of judges as a constant reminder of the main source of the national wealth. The Lord Chancellor is said to be "appointed to the woolsack".

World Population. According to United Nations sources world population in 1989 was some c. 5,100 million, an increase of 200 million in three years. More than half the total live in Asia (56·9 per cent). Different countries are at different stages in a demographic transition from the stability provided by a combination of high birth rate and high death rate to that provided by a combination of low birth rate and low death rate. Their recent population history and current trend of growth, the age-structure of their population, and consequently their population potential for the near future are all widely different. Most rapid growth is in Africa with rates of over 3 per cent in some countries. In most European countries the rate is less than 1 per cent. A baby girl born in Norway may expect to live the longest (77·6 years) and a baby boy in Sweden (72·1 years),

but a baby born in some African countries may not live to reach 40 years. It is estimated that about one in 25 of all human beings who have ever lived are alive today. It took 115 years for the world's population to rise from one to two thousand million; in a further 35 years it rose from two thousand million to three; in the last 15 years from four to five thousand million. It is estimated to reach six billion in 1999 and seven billion in 2010. Life expectancy in Britain today (1990) is 72 for men and 77 for women (compared to 48 and 51 in 1906).

Wreck, the name given to trove found under water, usually from a maritime wreck. Finds must be brought to the notice of the Official Receiver of Wrecks, an officer of H.M. Customs and Excise.

Wren, a family of small passerine birds possessing upturned tails and most abundant in South America. The British species is an interesting singing bird with a surprising loud note for its size.

X

Xenon a rare gaseous element, no.54, symbol Xe, occurring in minute quantities in the atmosphere, discovered by Sir William Ramsay and M. W. Travers in 1898. See **Rare Gases.**

X-Rays were discovered in 1895 by Professor Röntgen, of Wurzburg. X-rays are produced when heavy metal atoms (*e.g.* tungsten) are struck by electrons of sufficient energy. X-rays are now commonly used to examine the internal structure of many opaque objects. In medicine, industry and for security, examination may be conducted without physical invasion. X-rays may also be used to probe the structure of matter, for example the atomic structure of crystals. The discovery in the 1960s that cosmic objects emitted intense X-rays has led to many important new astronomical phenomena being discovered. See **F12.**

Xylem, the woody tissue of higher plants whose function is to conduct water and mineral salts upwards, and to provide mechanical support.

Y

Yacht, a light vessel now much used for pleasure trips and racing. The first yachting club was the Cork Harbour Club, started about 1720; and in 1812 the Royal Yacht Squadron was founded at Cowes. The Royal Thames Yacht Club dates from 1823. The most famous international yachting trophy is *The America's Cup* (*q.v.*).

Yak, a curious, long-haired ox, found in Tibet used as a beast of burden, and also kept for milk and meat.

Yard, a standard measure of 36 in, the word being derived from the Saxon gryd, or rod. The yard and pound are now defined by reference to the metre and the kilogram: yard = 0·9144 of a metre; pound = 0·45359237 of a kilogram. By international agreement the metre is defined by reference to the wavelength of krypton-86 light.

Yellowhammer, a common British bird of the bunting family, of lemon-yellow and brown plumage. Nests on or near the ground.

Yeomen of the Guard are a body of Foot Guards established in the reign of Henry VII for the protection of the Royal Person. Yeomen are now about 100 in number, and their duties consist in being present on ceremonial State occasions, the yearly distribution of Maundy Money, and the searching of the vaults of the Houses of Parliament on Guy Fawkes' day. "Beefeater" is the nickname of both Yeomen of the Guard and Yeomen Warders of the Tower, and they both wear the style of dress of the

Tudor period, but with one distinction, the Yeomen of the Guard wear a cross belt, the Warders do not.

Yeti, opinions differ as to whether this is a mythical inhabitant of the Himalayas, a primitive primate or bear. Evidence to date is inconclusive.

Yoga. *See* **Section J.**

York Minster, one of the oldest and finest of English cathedrals, is 160 m long, its nave is 73 m broad, and the central tower is 66 m high. The present edifice, in parts, dates back to the 12th cent., but a church stood on the site in the 7th cent. In 1829 it was set on fire by a lunatic named Jonathan Martin. In July 1984, a serious fire caused by lightning wrought severe damage to the south transept.

Ytterbium, a chemical, no.70, symbol Yb, element discovered by Urbain in 1907; one of the group of rare earth metals.

Yttrium, a chemical element, no.39, symbol Y, discovered by Mosander in 1842. It is found in a few rare minerals such as gadolinite, xenotine, fergusonite and euxenite. One of the group of rare earth metals.

Z

Zamboni Pile, a dry galvanic battery, which can provide small amounts of high-voltage current over a very long time. At Oxford a couple of Zamboni piles have kept a bell ringing for over a hundred years. These piles in the second world war were perfected and produced in quantity, being the most convenient source of current for infra-red signalling devices.

Zebra, an African quadruped of whitish-grey colour, with regular black stripings, perhaps the most beautiful member of the Equine family. Rather larger than an ass and smaller than the horse, it has a tufted tail, is of light build, wild and fleet of foot. The Zebra may be threatened with extinction—already the fate of the Quagga species—because of its slaughter by man for its beautiful skin.

Zen Buddhism. *See* **Section J.**

Zenith, the highest point in the heavens above an observer's head, the opposite pole to the nadir.

Zero, the cypher signifying nothing originally came from China. The West is indebted to the Arabs for it, who themselves obtained it from India and passed it to European mathematicians towards the end of the Middle Ages. The zero has also been found in Babylonian cuneiform. The Greeks had no such symbol, which hindered the development of their mathematics. The use of zero led to the invention of decimal fractions and to the later developments in astronomy, physics and

chemistry. For absolute zero on the temperature scale *see* **Absolute Temperature.**

Zinc, a familiar metallic element, no.30, symbol Zn, known to the ancients, and used by them in the making of brass. It occurs as the sulphide, carbonate, etc. The ores of zinc are crushed, roasted and reduced with coal. In combination with copper it constitutes the familiar alloy called brass, and zinc itself is much used for roofing and other protective purposes. Zinc ores are mined in Canada, the USA, Mexico, Poland, Australia, Russia, Italy, Spain and many other parts of the world. Zinc smelting is carried on in most industrial countries, including Great Britain.

Zionism. *See* **Section J.**

Zirconium, metallic element, no.40, symbol Zr, was discovered by Klaproth in the sand of the rivers of Sri Lanka in 1789. The crystalline metal is white, soft and ductile; in its amorphous condition it is a blue-black powder. Zirconium is used in atomic reactors as containers for fuel elements, since it does not absorb neutrons.

Zodiac, an imaginary zone or belt of the sky enclosing the circuit over which the principal planets travel. It is divided into 12 equal spaces of 30 degrees each, comprising respectively the 12 signs of the zodiac—Aries, Taurus, Gemini, Cancer, Leo, Virgo, Libra, Scorpio, Sagittarius, Capricornus, Aquarius and Pisces. The idea of the zodiac originated with the Babylonians about 2000 B.C. and passed by way of the Greeks to the Western world.

Zodiacal Light, a faint cone of light occasionally seen stretching along the zodiac from the western horizon after evening twilight or the eastern horizon before morning twilight. It is believed to be due to the scattering of the sun's light by dust particles in orbit round the sun and extending beyond the earth. Recent observations at the high altitudes station at Chacaltaya in the Andes suggest that the dust is travelling round the sun in regular planetary orbits.

Zonda, a warm moist wind in Argentina of great velocity blowing from the north or northwest, and, like the Sirocco in Southern Europe, causes much discomfort. It happens when a depression is moving across the pampas, bringing with it a mass of air from the humid tropics. It is followed by a refreshing wind from the south east.

Zoological Gardens of London were opened in 1828, and belong to the Zoological Society of London. They contain one of the largest and most varied collections of living animals in the world. The Society maintains an open-air zoo at Whipsnade, on the edge of Dunstable Downs; this was opened in 1931.

Zoology, the branch of science concerned with animal life, embracing many aspects such as anatomy, behaviour, classification, distribution and ecology. *See* **Section F, Part IV.**

Zoroastrianism. *See* **Section J.**

CALENDAR 1991

CHRONOLOGICAL CYCLES AND ERAS

Dominical Letter	F		Julian Period (year of)		6704
Epact	14		Roman Indiction		14
Golden Number (Lunar Cycle)	XVI		Solar Cycle		12

Era	Year	Begins		Era	Year	Begins	
Byzantine	7500	14	Sept	Grecian (Seleucidae)	2303	14	Sept
Roman (A.U.C.)	2744	14	Jan			(or 14 Oct)	
Nabonassar	2740	26	Apr	Indian (Saka)	1913	22	Mar
Japanese	2651	1	Jan	Diocletian	1708	11	Sept

RELIGIOUS CALENDARS

Epiphany	6	Jan	Low Sunday		7	Apr
Septuagesima Sunday	27	Jan	Rogation Sunday		5	May
Quinquagesima Sunday	10	Feb	Ascension Day—Holy Thursday		9	May
Ash Wednesday	13	Feb	Whit Sunday—Pentecost		19	May
Quadragesima Sunday	17	Feb	Trinity Sunday		26	May
Palm Sunday	24	Mar	Corpus Christi		30	May
Good Friday	29	Mar	First Sunday in Advent		1	Dec
Easter Day	31	Mar	Christmas Day		25	Dec
Passover, First day of (Pesach)	30	Mar	Day of Atonement (Yom Kippur)		18	Sept
Feast of Weeks (Shavuot)	19	May	Tabernacles, First day of (Succoth)		23	Sept
Jewish New Year (5752)	9	Sept				
(Rosh Hashanah)						
Islamic New Year (1412)	13	July	Ramadan, First day of		17	Mar

All Jewish and Islamic dates above are tabular dates, which begin at sunset on the previous evening and end at sunset on the date tabulated. In practice, Islamic fasts and festivals are determined by an actual sighting of the appropriate New Moon.

CIVIL CALENDAR—UNITED KINGDOM

Accession of Queen Elizabeth II	6	Feb	The Queen's Official Birthday	8	June
St David (Wales)	1	Mar	Birthday of Prince Philip,		
Commonwealth Day	11	Mar	Duke of Edinburgh	10	June
St Patrick (Ireland)	17	Mar	Remembrance Sunday	10	Nov
Birthday of Queen Elizabeth II	21	Apr	Birthday of the Prince of Wales	14	Nov
St George (England)	23	Apr	St Andrew (Scotland)	30	Nov
Coronation Day	2	June			

LITERARY COMPANION

This section is arranged in five parts. The first provides a concise introduction to the history of the English Novel. The second provides a survey of English poetry. The third examines the literature of the United States and Canada. The fourth section contains a glossary of literary terms whilst the final section features special topics including in this edition a survey of contemporary Caribbean literature.

TABLE OF CONTENTS

TABLE OF CONTENTS

LITERARY COMPANION

I. THE ENGLISH NOVEL

INTRODUCTION

Definition

A novel is a fictitious prose narrative, usually of more than 50,000 words in length. It often deals with characters and actions that give readers an illusion of reality, but it can also be fanciful or fantastic. Its elements conventionally include a plot or story, personages, dialogue and a setting. Some novels contain such poetic elements as symbol, metaphor and rhythmical construction. Just as the content and general approach of novels show many variations, so the techniques in their writing greatly differ: narratives told in the first or third persons, in the form of letters and from different points of view are amongst the devices of presentation that have been used.

Types

Certain types can be defined, although they cannot always be clearly distinguished from one another.

The *picaresque novel* has a *picaro* (Spanish: "rogue") at the centre of its action, but sometimes this main character is an innocent or foolish person. Many adventures, described comically, satirically or realistically, befall him and influence him. A famous example is Lesage's *Gil Blas* (1715, 1724, 1735). Fielding's *Tom Jones* (1749) and Dickens' *Pickwick Papers* (1836-7) are in this tradition, which has been widely followed in England.

The *Bildungsroman* (German: "formation novel") relates the upbringing and education of the hero, as in Goethe's *Wilhelm Meister's Apprenticeship* (1795-6) and Dickens' *David Copperfield* (1849-50).

Psychological novels, exploring character, motives and relationships, were first established in France, with Madame de La Fayette's *La Princesse de Clèves* (1678) and the Abbé Prévost's *Manon Lescaut* (1731). Richardson's *Pamela* (1740) belongs to this category of fiction, which is often considered the most significant of all the kinds, reaching great profundity in the work of Dostoevsky (1821-81), Tolstoy (1828-1910) and Henry James (1843-1916).

Social novels, with the aim of exposure and reform of abuses and injustice, were prominent in the nineteenth century. Examples are Mrs Gaskell's *Mary Barton* (1848) and Charles Kingsley's *Alton Locke* (1850). Balzac's numerous novels, collected as *La Comédie humaine* (1842-8), and many by Dickens (*e.g. Little Dorrit*, 1855-6) are social novels in a more comprehensive sense, depicting characteristics of French and English society respectively.

The *novel of manners* is a sophisticated presentation of social codes of behaviour, especially amongst the leisured classes. Meredith's *The Egoist* (1878) partly belongs to this type.

Naturalistic novels, like those in Emile Zola's series, *Les Rougon-Macquart* (1871-93), and many by George Gissing (1857-1903), emphasise the power of environment in moulding human character.

Regional novels, by Thomas Hardy (1840-1928) and Arnold Bennett (1867-1931), amongst others, place importance on the traditions and influences of particular areas of a country.

In *adventure* and *detective* novels, the story or plot is a principal feature, as in Wilkie Collins' *The Moonstone* (1868) and Robert Louis Stevenson's *Treasure Island* (1883). The thriller, a variation of this type, is marked by excitement and violence, as in the James Bond novels of Ian Fleming (1908-64).

The *historical novel* deals with the past, sometimes mixing fact and fiction, such as the novels of Sir Walter Scott (1771-1832), Flaubert's *Salammbô* (1862) and Tolstoy's *War and Peace* (1863-9).

Fantasy has become increasingly popular, especially in the form of *science fiction*; Jules Verne (1828-1905) was one of the earliest and most widely read writers of this genre. English writers who have used this kind of fiction include H. G. Wells (1866-1946) and John Wyndham (1903-69). J. R. R. Tolkien (1892-1973) created a new "legendary" world in *The Lord of the Rings* (1954-5).

Purpose

The purpose of a novel varies with its type. Anthony Trollope's statement, made in his study of Thackeray (1879), has a fundamental validity: "the object of a novel should be to instruct in morals while it amuses." At one extreme, some novels are expressly meant to teach, such as some Victorian children's novels and social novels (*e.g.* many written by Charles Kingsley). At the other, some novels are meant simply as entertainment, such as detective stories and much science fiction. Trollope's term, "morals", is difficult to define, but one can say that the aim of most novels is to reveal and stimulate thought about aspects of human behaviour both individually and in personal and social relationships. Apart from these generalisations, the specific purposes of some English novels are described separately in the following survey.

Rise and popularity of the novel

Though stories in verse and prose are as old as human life itself, the novel, as we know it today, became established in the late seventeenth and early eighteenth centuries. Its rise is related to changes in the climate of ideas during that period, with its increasing emphasis on the rational and the actual. Influenced by such thinkers as Sir Isaac Newton (1642-1727) and John Locke (1632-1704), philosophers investigated the ordinary, physical world rather than the world of metaphysical speculation. At the same time, the reading public had increased in numbers, especially amongst the middle classes. This public wanted to read about the behaviour of realistic people in credible surroundings. One result in England was the publication of novels by Defoe, Richardson, Fielding and Smollett in the first half of the eighteenth century.

THE EIGHTEENTH CENTURY

Daniel Defoe

Daniel Defoe (c.1661-1731) is regarded as the first notable English novelist. After many years as a political pamphleteer, he published *Robinson Crusoe* (1719), based on accounts of the actual adventures of the mariner, Alexander Selkirk. The book is written with convincing, detailed realism. Robinson Crusoe's practical approach to his predicament and his powerful individualism make him an admirable character who can be seen to have a universal significance. We are shown a man confronted by adversity and yet overcoming it by means of his resourcefulness and holding to his belief in a providential God. The basic idea of a person shipwrecked on an island had a wide appeal, which was reflected in many imitations, including *The Swiss Family Robinson* (1813) by Johann Rudolf Wyss. Defoe's other novels include *Captain Singleton* (1720), *Moll Flanders* (1722), *Colonel Jack* (1722) and *Roxana* (1724). He claimed that *Moll Flanders* had a moral purpose, in that from every part of it "something may be learned, and some just and religious inference is drawn." But it survives because of its lively and uninhibited representation of the personality and doings of its disreputable, resilient heroine, who (like Robinson Crusoe) tells her own story. Formally, Defoe is an unsophisticated writer, who relies mostly on his invention of incident to keep his narrative in motion. His strength lies in his powers of observation and in his rendering of particulars, conveyed in straightforward prose, so that readers feel that they are experiencing things that actually happened.

Richardson, Fielding, Smollett and Sterne

The first great period of the English novel is 1740-71, when four important novelists flourished: Samuel Richardson (1689-1761), Henry Fielding (1707-54), Laurence Sterne (1713-68) and Tobias Smollett (1721-71). George Saintsbury, in *The English Novel* (1913), aptly called them the "remarkable exponents of a new kind of Human Comedy."

Richardson was a printer who was compiling a

collection of model letters to suit various occasions when he thought of writing an epistolary novel. The outcome was *Pamela* (1740), in which the letters reveal the story of Pamela, a servant girl, who resists her master's attempts to seduce her but finally agrees to marry him. *Clarissa* (1747–8), also written in the form of letters, tells of the tragedy of its heroine, who dies after her rape by the libertine, Lovelace. Containing a million words, it is probably the longest novel in English. Richardson's third and last epistolary novel, *Sir Charles Grandison* (1754), centres upon the scrupulously gentlemanly conduct of its hero. These are not novels of external action but are explorations of human psychology, especially of the thoughts and emotions of the young women involved. Their main theme is sexual passion and the moral problems that arise from it. The novels are admired for their sensitive portrayals of emotional and mental processes, realistically presented by means of the letters written by the characters.

Henry Fielding's first novel, *Joseph Andrews* (1742), was conceived partly as a satire on *Pamela*, which he thought hypocritical and sentimental. In picaresque style, he relates the adventures of Joseph Andrews, who is supposedly Pamela's brother, and his companion, Parson Adams. His intention in this "comic epic in prose", as he called it, was to expose the ridiculous. He therefore displays and comments upon hypocritical and affected behaviour in several walks of life. Parson Adams is one of the great humorous characters of English literature and yet he epitomises a true Christian goodness. Fielding's ironic approach reached an extreme in *Jonathan Wild* (1743), in which he treats the villainous thief who is the hero as if he were a great man. *Tom Jones* (1749), his masterpiece, gives us in an ingenious plot the history of a young man of unknown birth: his boyhood in the country, his journey to London and his escapades when he gets there. The book is full of vivid characters and episodes and contains much moral comment from the author himself. *Amelia* (1751) is concerned with the misfortunes of the heroine and her husband and with her patience and virtue. An experienced playwright, Fielding uses dramatic devices and events, sometimes involving physical action. His comedy is occasionally coarse and boisterous but often drily ironical. The reader is frequently aware of his authorial presence and he intervenes directly in the narrative. Like many of his contemporaries, he acknowledges the influence of the classics of Greek and Latin literature and here and there writes in a mock-heroic style. He is the opposite of Richardson, as Dr Johnson said to Boswell: "there was as great a difference between them as between a man who knew how a watch was made (*i.e.* Richardson), and a man who could tell the hour by looking on the dial-plate (*i.e.* Fielding)."

Tobias Smollett is superficially reminiscent of Fielding in his novels: *Roderick Random* (1748), *Peregrine Pickle* (1751), *Ferdinand, Count Fathom* (1753), *Sir Lancelot Greaves* (1760–61) and *Humphry Clinker* (1771). All of them recount the wanderings and adventures of their heroes and can therefore be described as picaresque, although *Humphry Clinker* is an epistolary novel. Smollett depicts an often brutal world with a mixture of relish and repulsion and his novels have a remarkable vivacity of invention. The episodes on board ship in *Roderick Random*, for example, give an unforgettable picture of the cruelties and rigours of eighteenth-century seafaring life.

Laurence Sterne stands apart from the novelists of his time and indeed can still be regarded as unique. *Tristram Shandy* (1760–67) is an eccentric, digressive composition. Chronological order and the sequence of cause and effect do not apply to Sterne's handling of his subject-matter—the hero is not born till half way through the novel, for instance. The personages talk of this and that, the author intervenes at will, a chapter may break off suddenly or may be blank, and so on. Despite this whimsicality and the flux of ideas and impressions, characters, such as My Uncle Toby and the Widow Wadman, are fully realised and an atmosphere of gentle humanity prevails.

Although one cannot draw clear lines of influence, it is possible to see these four novelists—Richardson, Fielding, Smollett and Sterne—as representatives of kinds of approaches to fiction that were apparent in the next two centuries. Richardson displays the interest in psychological introspection characteristic of the work of many twentieth-century writers. The emphasis laid by Fielding and Smollett upon external action has its counterpart in the broad humour and simple characterisation of some nineteenth-century novels. Modern experiments in the form of the novel remind us of Sterne's rejection of the rational development of narrative.

Later Eighteenth-Century Novelists

After the middle of the century, no outstanding English novelist emerged until Scott and Jane Austen started to write fiction at its end. But a few memorable novels appeared, including Oliver Goldsmith's *The Vicar of Wakefield* (1766) and Fanny Burney's *Evelina* (1778). Horace Walpole's *The Castle of Otranto* (1765) is important as the first Gothic novel. This type contained mystery and terror, often associated with the supernatural and a medieval setting. Its famous exponents came later: Mrs Ann Radcliffe, who wrote *The Mysteries of Udolpho* (1794) and Matthew Gregory ("Monk") Lewis, who wrote *The Monk* (1796). The most celebrated is Mary Shelley's *Frankenstein* (1818).

THE EARLY NINETEENTH CENTURY

Sir Walter Scott

The Gothic novels just mentioned are typical of Romantic literature, of whom one of the principal representatives in Britain and Europe in the early years of the nineteenth century was Sir Walter Scott (1771–1832). In his own time and for long afterwards, Scott was regarded as akin to Shakespeare in his comprehensive renderings of human life and his powers of imagination. He was a prolific author, who wrote poems, dramas, short stories, biographies and histories as well as the following novels: *Waverley* (1814), *Guy Mannering* (1815), *The Antiquary* (1816), *The Black Dwarf* (1816), *Old Mortality* (1817), *Rob Roy* (1818), *The Heart of Midlothian* (1818), *The Bride of Lammermoor* (1819), *A Legend of Montrose* (1819), *Ivanhoe* (1820), *The Monastery* (1820), *The Abbot* (1820), *Kenilworth* (1821), *The Pirate* (1822), *The Fortunes of Nigel* (1822), *Peveril of the Peak* (1822), *Quentin Durward* (1823), *Saint Ronan's Well* (1824), *Redgauntlet* (1824), *The Betrothed* (1825), *The Talisman* (1825), *Woodstock* (1826), *The Fair Maid of Perth* (1828), *Anne of Geierstein* (1829), *Count Robert of Paris* (1832) and *Castle Dangerous* (1832). These are historical novels, set in many different places and periods. *Waverley* takes place in Scotland during the 1745 Jacobite Rebellion; *Ivanhoe* in the England of Richard I; and *Quentin Durward* in fifteenth-century France during the reign of Louis XI.

Scott presents a great range of characters, from the lowliest peasants to monarchs, and mingles actual and fictional personages convincingly together. He enables us to see in their adventures, attitudes and relationships the forces of history at work. Their private lives are affected by public events. He imaginatively recreates history in his novels, which also show his sympathy for—and understanding of—all kinds of people, whatever their religious or political beliefs. His narratives are vigorously inventive, with colourful and dramatic scenes, as adaptations for opera, films and television have demonstrated. Having once read them, the reader will recall such things as Waverley's journeyings in the Highlands of Scotland, the battles in *Rob Roy*, Jeanie Deans' interviews with the Duke of Argyll and Queen Caroline in *The Heart of Midlothian*, and Meg Merrilies' roadside curses upon the Laird of Ellangowan in *Guy Mannering*. His memorable characters are often Scots, such as Jeanie Deans, Meg Merrilies, Dominie Sampson (in *Guy Mannering*) and Jonathan Oldbuck (in *The Antiquary*), but also noteworthy are Caleb Balderstone (in *The Bride of Lammermoor*) and Diana Vernon (in *Rob Roy*). His portrait of King James I in *The Fortunes of Nigel* is a remarkably convincing representation of an historical personage. But some of his heroes and women characters tend to be colourless and commonplace. Scott was not greatly concerned with psychological probings or with profound moral or religious issues. He used a huge canvas on which he portrayed the actions of people of every kind and degree in specific places and historical periods. He rendered "the being of the age" (in George Lukács' phrase) and the richness and variety of human life within that age.

Jane Austen

No novelist could be more different from Scott than Jane Austen, as he himself recognised. In an admiring comment on her work, he wrote: "The big bow-bow strain I can do myself like any now going, but the exquisite touch which renders ordinary commonplace things and characters interesting from the truth of the description and sentiment, is denied to me." Jane Austen (1775–1817) wrote only six novels, which were published as follows: *Sense and Sensibility* (1811), *Pride and Prejudice* (1813), *Mansfield Park* (1814), *Emma* (1816), *Northanger Abbey* and *Persuasion* (both 1818). The dates of composition are sometimes different: for example, *Northanger Abbey*, which was published posthumously, was one of her earliest books, begun in 1798. She also wrote shorter stories and fragments, which are conveniently collected in one volume in the *Oxford Jane Austen*.

She based her novels on the people and places with which she was familiar: the upper middle-class society of southern England, particularly Hampshire, the county in which she was born and lived for most of her life. Her work, she modestly wrote, was "that little bit (two inches wide) of ivory, in which I work with so fine a brush as produces little effect after much labour." Her subject-matter is the relationships between men and women, especially those concerned with love and marriage, and she accepts the social code of her class and period. She uses no exciting or ingenious plots, no startlingly dramatic incidents. She ignores doings and people outside the small circle in which her characters move. Yet working within these conventions of subject-matter and social code, she illuminates wider areas of human conduct. In *Persuasion*, for example, she tells the story of Anne Elliot, who had rejected the suit of Captain Wentworth, the man she truly loved, because she yielded to the well-meant advice of Lady Russell, a close friend of her family. Anne and Captain Wentworth, who have met again seven years afterwards, slowly but surely re-establish their loving relationship and eventually marry. Questions raised include the rights and wrongs of persuasion, the place of love and money in marriage, the pressures of family vanity, and motives of men and women respectively when they fall in love. Moral issues like these are treated by Jane Austen with irony and wit as well as sympathy.

Her dialogue and passages of description contain much that is subtle and drily amusing, revealing her as an author who views folly and pretension with amused disfavour and who values the qualities of prudence and tolerance. Elizabeth Bennett in *Pride and Prejudice* comes close to her ideal of what a person should be like and some words that she gives to her can represent the novelist's own approach: "I hope I never ridicule what is wise and good. Follies and nonsense, whims and inconsistencies do divert me, I own, and I laugh at them whenever I can." Jane Austen's characters come alive through their dialogue and reflections and through the novelist's observations. She constructs her novels neatly and with a feeling of inevitability so that they have an effortless artistic unity. Although she wrote at the time of the Romantic Movement, she remained cool and rational; it is significant that Charlotte Brontë attacked her for lacking warmth and enthusiasm. But her clarity of style and form, her comedy and wit and, above all, her penetrating analyses of behaviour and motive have led to her justifiably being regarded today as one of the greatest of English novelists.

Minor Novelists of the 1820s and 1830s

Between the time of Scott and the time of Dickens, who shot to fame in 1836, there flourished many minor novelists. The most enduring of these is Thomas Love Peacock (1785–1866), who wrote *Headlong Hall* (1816), *Melincourt* (1817), *Nightmare Abbey* (1818), *Maid Marian* (1822), *The Misfortunes of Elphin* (1829), *Crotchet Castle* (1831) and *Gryll Grange* (1860). These were mostly comic, satirical novels of ideas, wittily satirising fashionable thinkers and intellectual tendencies of the age. Peacock's usual device is to place his characters round a dinner-table and to record their conversation. In this way, he could poke fun at the Gothic Novel, Byronic gloom and German romanticism (in *Nightmare Abbey*), modern trends in education and agriculture (in *Crotchet Castle*) and Rousseau's views on natural

man (in *Melincourt*). Some of his characters are caricatures of living people: Scythrop is Shelley (in *Nightmare Abbey*) and Mr Fax is Malthus (in *Melincourt*). His is a rational voice, puncturing what he considered to be the pretensions and affectations of the Romantic Movement. The elegance and polish of his dialogues at the dinner-table make his novels a permanent delight.

Humour of a more obvious sort is present in the once-popular novels of Theodore Hook (1788–1841), such as *Sayings and Doings* (1826–9), but these are now forgotten. They are worth mentioning if only because some critics have seen Hook as a precursor of Dickens. "Fashionable" or "silver-fork" novels, relating the intrigues, customs and speech of high society, were also widely read at this time. Amongst the authors of these were Mrs Catherine Gore (1799–1861) and Edward Bulwer-Lytton (1803–73), whose *Pelham* (1828) still has a little amusing life in it. Bulwer-Lytton achieved fame, too, with his "Newgate Novels", such as *Paul Clifford* (1830) and *Eugene Aram* (1832), which depicted criminal life in a romanticised and even glamorous manner. Scott's prestige and influence led to the production of historical novels. Bulwer-Lytton's *The Last Days of Pompeii* (1834) and some by William Harrison Ainsworth (1805–82)—for example, *The Tower of London* (1840)—are readable, but those by G. P. R. James (1799–1860) have fallen into oblivion. These minor comic, "fashionable", "Newgate" and historical novels have little intrinsic interest for most readers today, although the student of the period will find them valuable for the insights they give, sometimes unwittingly, into the tastes and prejudices of the 1830s.

Undeserving of neglect, however, are the energetic novels of Captain Frederick Marryat (1792–1848). Like several naval officers of the period, he wrote seafaring fiction, beginning with *Frank Mildmay* (1829). *Peter Simple* (1834) and *Mr Midshipman Easy* (1836) were amongst the novels that followed. *Snarleyyow* (1837) is a macabre comedy about an apparently immortal dog. Towards the end of his writing career, Marryat turned to juvenile fiction, which included *Masterman Ready* (1841–2), *The Settlers in Canada* (1844) and *The Children of the New Forest* (1847). His novels are extrovert entertainments, full of vigour and knockabout comedy, written in an unpretentious prose style. Parts of them are reminiscent of Smollett and, more interestingly, of Dickens, who was one of his closest friends.

Some distinctively Scots novels were published at this time. John Galt (1779–1839) wrote *The Annals of the Parish* (1821), which chronicles the doings of a country parish in Scotland, and *The Entail* (1823), a tragicomedy of protracted disputes about an inheritance. Outstandingly original in form and content is *The Private Memoirs and Confessions of a Justified Sinner* (1824) by James Hogg (1770–1835). This story of evil and damnation, a narration followed by a confession, is centred upon the "sinner", who is encouraged in his wickedness by a friend, who—it becomes clear—is the Devil.

This period between Scott and Dickens was therefore productive of novels of great variety. If one had to choose amongst so many writers of fiction (and they have not all been named here), one could point to Peacock, Galt, Hogg and Marryat as novelists worth remembering, with Bulwer-Lytton and Ainsworth not far behind them. All were suddenly outshone, however, in 1836 by the dazzling appearance of Dickens on the scene.

THE EARLY VICTORIAN NOVELISTS

Charles Dickens

Charles Dickens (1812–70), who first came to public notice with sketches and articles in periodicals (collected as *Sketches by Boz* in 1835–6), achieved fame with *Pickwick Papers* (1836–7). This was rapidly followed by *Oliver Twist* (1838), *Nicholas Nickleby* (1838–9), *The Old Curiosity Shop* (1840–41), *Barnaby Rudge* (1841), *A Christmas Carol* (1843) and *Martin Chuzzlewit* (1843–4). These early books were exuberant and original in invention of every kind: colourful characterisation, vivid episodes, extravagant humour, pathos and evocation of the macabre, and an unfailingly fluent, fresh prose style. Many of Dickens' fictional personages immediately became household words: Mr Squeers, Little Nell, Scrooge and Mrs Gamp, to name only four from the books just listed. Similarly, sayings and phrases entered the English language, such as Oliver Twist's asking for more and Mrs Gamp's remarks about her imaginary friend, Mrs Harris. Dickens's tragic powers, especially those displayed in *The Old Curiosity Shop*, were found deeply moving. His evident concern for children, the poor and the deprived appealed to the humanitarian instincts of many of his contemporaries. On the other hand, his comedy made a tremendous impact, as in the *Pickwick Papers*, where Mr Pickwick's adventures and Sam Weller's sayings gave great joy to thousands of readers.

Dombey and Son (1846–8) seems to mark a turning-point in Dickens' career. It is more carefully unified than its predecessors and it relies less on exaggeration of plot and feelings; its central theme of pride is all-important. Dickens' next novel, *David Copperfield* (1849–50), with its suggestions of autobiography, is written in a calmly flowing manner, although it contains characters and incidents as striking as anything he invented: Mr Micawber, Uriah Heep, the storm at Yarmouth. Its subject-matter, concerned chiefly with the private and domestic affections, is, we feel, the product of mature contemplation.

The later novels of Dickens are *Bleak House* (1852–3), *Hard Times* (1854), *Little Dorrit* (1855–7), *A Tale of Two Cities* (1859), *Great Expectations* (1860–61), *Our Mutual Friend* (1864–5) and *The Mystery of Edwin Drood* (unfinished, 1870). They are more sombre than the earlier books. They are constructed with some care and they often deal with specific themes and subjects: the intricacies and deceits of the law (*Bleak House*), the opposition of utilitarian and imaginative values (*Hard Times*), the inefficiencies, irresponsibilities and materialism of mid-Victorian society (*Little Dorrit* and *Our Mutual Friend*) and snobbery (*Great Expectations*).

As we read a Dickens novel, we enter a self-sufficient imaginative world. He has many of the characteristics of a poet. This impression of a fertile, comprehensive imagination is enhanced in his later books by his use of motifs and symbols, such as the fog in *Bleak House*, the prisons in *Little Dorrit* and the dust-heaps and the River Thames in *Our Mutual Friend*. Although he has often been said to draw caricatures rather than characters, the people he creates spring to life on the page. In any case, some of his characters have a convincing truth about them—for example, his self-tormented people, like Miss Wade in *Little Dorrit* and Bradley Headstone in *Our Mutual Friend*. He has an amazing ability to distinguish his numerous characters from one another by their idiosyncrasies of speech. His plots are over-complicated, in a melodramatic mode, but they help to increase the tensions and mysteries that are so important in his stories and also help to hold together the many elements of his complex narratives. It should be remembered that his novels were written and published as serials, which partly accounts for some of his repetitions and exaggerations.

Dickens has astonishing powers of observation, seeing people and things as no one had seen them before, especially their peculiarities and strange resemblances. Allied to these powers is his ability to animate everybody and everything, so that even the furniture in a room can seem to have an active life of its own. He conveys all of this in vital prose, which is capable of expressing a wide range of particulars and moods. His purpose in writing, apart from sheer entertainment, is to put forward a message of hope and love, which he trusts will triumph over evil and over the vices and narrow-mindedness of materialism and a mechanical, uncaring social system.

Dickens' strengths as a novelist include his striking characterisation, his versatile prose, his power to evoke laughter, tears and fears, and his fundamental, positive "message". In the force and extent of his imagination, he stands next to Shakespeare.

William Makepeace Thackeray

William Makepeace Thackeray (1811–63) wrote miscellaneous prose and verse in the 1830s. *Catherine* (1839–40) and *Barry Lyndon* (1844), his first novels, were written partly to satirise the contemporary vogue for "Newgate Novels". *Vanity Fair* (1847–8) established him as major novelist. This book, set in the period of the Regency, tells the related stories of two contrasted women, Amelia Sedley and Becky Sharp. One of its principal purposes is to expose the shams and pretensions of high society, as is indicated by its title, which Thackeray took from Bunyan's *Pilgrim's Progress*. *Pendennis* (1848–50), like *David Copperfield*, is coloured by autobiographical reminiscence. Its eponymous hero encounters temptations during his youth in the country, at Oxbridge and in the London literary world. Thackeray turned to the eighteenth century, his favourite historical period, for the background of *Henry Esmond* (1852), whose melancholy, meditative hero is tormented by his love for Beatrix Esmond and is also active in military and political affairs, including an unsuccessful attempt to put the Old Pretender on the English throne. *The Newcomes* (1853–5) is a chronicle of the loves, intrigues, successes and disappointments of the Newcome family, centred upon Clive and his father, Colonel Newcome. Thackeray's last important novel was *The Virginians* (1857–9), which continues the story of the Esmond family into later generations, set mostly in America during the War of Independence. His career as a novelist ended with *Philip* (1861–2) and the unfinished *Denis Duval* (1864).

During his lifetime and for long afterwards, Thackeray was frequently contrasted with Dickens. Unlike the latter, he avoided complicated plots and caricatures. His narratives flow smoothly from one incident or tableau to another. Thackeray's aim was to be as truthful as possible in his portrayal of people. He disliked the falsities he detected in such novelists as Bulwer-Lytton. His characters, therefore, are often ambiguously conceived, since he refused to simplify what he saw as complexity. A good man like Dobbin in *Vanity Fair* can be ridiculous on occasions; a man as honourable as Henry Esmond can love a woman as fickle and hard-hearted as Beatrix; a schemer like Becky Sharp is sometimes sympathetically described by the author. Like Fielding, whom he admired, Thackeray sought to reveal and mock hypocrisy and cant, especially in the middle and aristocratic classes, from which his fictional personages invariably came. One topic that engaged his attention was snobbery, which he deplored. Yet gentlemanliness was all-important to him, as personified in Colonel Newcome.

Thackeray has been called both cynical and sentimental. On one hand, he shows that conduct is not always what it appears to be; on the other, he depicts some people, especially when they are female, with fulsome affection. In all his work he is a moralist, relating the behaviour, thoughts and motives of his characters to those of his readers and people in general. Commentary, description, dialogue and story-telling are blended in his novels. Furthermore, the novels connect with one another, since characters recur; Pendennis, for example, tells the story of the Newcomes. This fact increases that sense of an actual, fully realised world which many critics have found to be characteristic of Thackeray's fiction.

The Brontës

Charlotte Brontë (1816–55) wrote *Jane Eyre* in 1847. Its second edition, by the way, was dedicated to Thackeray. This novel, which has never lost its power to enthrall the reader, uses a melodramatic plot, coincidence and exaggeration. But these devices, poetically and imaginatively realised by the author, intensify the reality of the passion that informs the book: Jane's sufferings, anger, independent spirit and feelings of love. These are brought close to us by the first-person narration. Her two great temptations, first towards an illicit relationship with Rochester and secondly towards the loveless religious life that St John Rivers offers her, are necessary, we feel, so that she can deserve the final, hard-won happiness that she finds. It is therefore a convincing psychological and moral novel as well as one of dramatic impetus.

Charlotte Brontë's second published novel was *Shirley* (1849), set in the north of England during the Napoleonic Wars and Luddite Riots. In it, we read of the fortunes of Caroline Helstone and Shirley Keeldar. One of its themes is the independence of women, though the book ends conventionally with the happy marriage of each of the heroines. *Villette* (1853) is a strangely-constructed novel, to the point of clumsiness, although its mysterious opening and conclusion are remarkable. But more importantly, its love story of Lucy Snowe, the English teacher in Villette (*i.e.* Brussels), and Paul Emanuel, the

Belgian schoolmaster she meets there, is one of the most sincere and moving in English fiction. *The Professor*, Charlotte Brontë's first novel (written in 1846), was published posthumously in 1857. Basically, it has the same story as *Villette*, though roles and sexes are reversed: an English schoolmaster in Brussels falls in love with a Swiss pupil. It is a novel not to be underrated, since it has a calm air of truthfulness.

Charlotte Brontë was essentially a Romantic novelist, dealing with emotional issues. As already noted, she had a low opinion of Jane Austen's coolness. Her sister, Emily Brontë (1818–48), was even more intense in her treatment of passion. *Wuthering Heights* (1847), her only novel, concerns two generations of the Linton and Earnshaw families in Yorkshire and how they are tormented by the ferocity of Heathcliff, who was brought into their lives as a boy found in the streets of Liverpool. The love between him and Catherine Earnshaw is all-consuming, destructive and yet immortal. *Wuthering Heights*, which has been called a dramatic poem, is full of the most violent emotions, paradoxically made even more intense by the perspective in which they are placed by the various narrators of the story. The construction of the novel—its points of view and its time-shifts—is notable, as are its imagery and passages of poetic description. As in *Jane Eyre*, the settings are important: the interiors of the houses, the Yorkshire moors and the changing seasons.

Anne Brontë (1820–49) echoes some of the themes explored by her sisters. *Agnes Grey* (1847) is about a governess's life and *The Tenant of Wildfell Hall* (1848) is a melodramatic tale of mystery, drunkenness and love.

Anthony Trollope

Anthony Trollope (1815–82) wrote forty-seven novels, of which the best-known are contained in two "series". The Barsetshire Novels, dealing with the lives of the clergy and others in a fictional country district, are *The Warden* (1855), *Barchester Towers* (1857), *Doctor Thorne* (1858), *Framley Parsonage* (1861), *The Small House at Allington* (1864) and *The Last Chronicle of Barset* (1867). The Palliser Novels, which are mostly political, are *Can You Forgive Her?* (1864), *Phineas Finn* (1869), *The Eustace Diamonds* (1873), *Phineas Redux* (1874), *The Prime Minister* (1876) and *The Duke's Children* (1880). Other novels worth noting are *The Three Clerks* (1858), *Orley Farm* (1862), *The Vicar of Bullhampton* (1870) and *The Way We Live Now* (1875).

As Trollope himself said in his *Autobiography* (1883), he was a realist and not a sensational novelist. His novels are firmly constructed and written plainly and explicitly, without the poetic imagination of Dickens and the Brontës or the elegant subtlety of Thackeray (whom he admired above all contemporary novelists). Nathaniel Hawthorne, the American novelist, wrote that Trollope's novels were "solid and substantial, written on the strength of beef and the inspiration of ale, and just as real as if some giant had hewn a great lump out of the earth and put it under a glass case, with all its inhabitants going about their daily business, and not suspecting that they were being made a show of." If you want to have an accurate impression of what daily life was like amongst the upper middle-classes of England in the 1850s, then a reading of *Barchester Towers*, for example, will supply you with details of customs, dress, furniture and manner of speech. Apart from this characteristic, Trollope provides the reader with interesting and entertaining plots. The accusations of theft made against the Reverend Josiah Crawley and the ensuing complications make *The Last Chronicle of Barset* a fascinating novel. *The Eustace Diamonds* is another well-constructed tale of intrigue, about Lizzie Greystock's determination to retain an heirloom, a diamond necklace.

Trollope is especially skilful in working out the conflicts between public and private lives, in clerical and political matters above all: the disputes over the wardenship of Hiram's Hospital in *The Warden* and *Barchester Towers* and the jockeyings for power and influence in the Palliser novels. No other English novelist has so comprehensively treated this perpetually relevant subject, though C. P. Snow's *The Masters* (1951) is a modern example influenced by Trollope. He draws his characters with humour and sympathy but he occasionally disconcertingly interrupts his narration with authorial comments, as Henry James noted disapprovingly. He unquestioningly accepts Victorian standards of morality and conduct and sees everything from the standpoint of an upper-middle class English gentleman. Trollope was proud of his craftsmanship and almost without exception his novels are carefully constructed. They remain reliably readable and amusing without being too demanding.

Benjamin Disraeli, Mrs Gaskell and Charles Kingsley

Three novelists who flourished in the mid-nineteenth century were Benjamin Disraeli (1804–81), Mrs Elizabeth Gaskell (1810–65) and Charles Kingsley (1819–75). Like many of their contemporaries, they were perturbed by the social conditions of England brought about by industrialisation. As a result, they wrote influential novels that highlighted the problems of capital and labour and the sufferings of the poor.

Disraeli's first novels (*e.g. Henrietta Temple*, 1837) were of the "fashionable" kind already discussed but in the 1840s he produced three that were concerned with politics and society: *Coningsby* (1844), *Sybil* (1845) and *Tancred* (1847). Disraeli, who at that time was already prominent as a politician, developed his theories of Conservatism in the first of these, using the education, career and ideas of its hero, Coningsby, as the basis of his story. The alternative title of *Sybil* is *The Two Nations*, by which Disraeli denotes the rich and the poor. He dramatises the issues by means of the love between Sybil, the daughter of a Chartist, and Charles Egremont, a member of the aristocracy. In *Tancred*, the eponymous hero, the son of a Duke, journeys to the Holy Land to seek guidance towards true belief and conduct.

Mrs Gaskell's social novels were *Mary Barton* (1848) and *North and South* (1854–5). The first, which is set in Manchester, vividly evokes the appalling conditions of the working class, which Mrs Gaskell knew at first hand. She sensationalises the problem by using a melodramatic plot, involving murder committed by the heroine's father, but there is no escaping the fact that it is a gripping novel that not surprisingly made a considerable impression upon readers in mid-Victorian England. *North and South* contrasts two regions of England, as its title implies, through the medium of its heroine, Margaret Hale, who leaves southern England to live in the industrial north. Mrs Gaskell sympathetically presents a balanced view of social problems, indicating some of the virtues as well as the shortcomings of the employers, personified in John Thornton, with whom Margaret falls in love. Mrs Gaskell's other novels include *Cranford* (1851–3), a quiet and charming account of life amongst genteel middle-class ladies in a northern village in the 1830s; *Ruth* (1853), a harrowing tale of seduction and desertion; *Sylvia's Lovers* (1863); and *Wives and Daughters* (1864–6, unfinished), about the characters and family relationships in a provincial town.

Charles Kingsley's interests as a clergyman and Christian Socialist inspired *Alton Locke* (1850), which is about working-class London and Chartism, and *Yeast* (1851), which is concerned with problems of rural England. As in all his books, Kingsley writes with enthusiasm and commitment, not hesitating to preach his social sermons when the occasion prompts. For the student of political and religious ideas of the period, these two novels are valuable sources. Kingsley also wrote historical novels: *Hypatia* (1853), *Westward Ho!* (1855) and *Hereward the Wake* (1866). *The Water Babies* (1863) is a lively, didactic story for children.

George Eliot

George Eliot (the pseudonym of Mary Ann Evans, 1819–80), wrote three long short stories, *Scenes of Clerical Life* (1857) and then the following novels: *Adam Bede* (1859), *The Mill on the Floss* (1860), *Silas Marner* (1861), *Romola* (1862–3), *Felix Holt, the Radical* (1866), *Middlemarch* (1871–2) and *Daniel Deronda* (1876). The first three novels are set in rural England, recalling the Warwickshire where she was born and brought up. *Adam Bede* is the tragic story of Hetty Sorrel, a village girl who is seduced, bears an illegitimate child and is convicted of infanticide. *The Mill on the Floss* is concerned mainly with the life, loves and emotional vicissitudes of Maggie Tulliver, who has some of the characteristics of the author herself. *Silas Marner* tells of an unhappy, miserly weaver, who regains his love of humanity after bringing up a child who has found her way to his cottage door. All, then, are about comparatively humble people and all sympathetically render the seasons, scenes, activities and speech of country life.

For her fourth novel, George Eliot turned to a completely different setting and period, as if to challenge her powers of invention: *Romola* is an historical novel, set in late fifteenth-century Florence, at the time of Machiavelli and Savonarola. It is a moving and exciting account of the conflicts of personal and public issues and of treachery and love. *Felix Holt* has the political events of 1832 as its background, although its principal interest lies in Esther's personal relationships and in the disputes over the ownership of an estate. By general agreement, *Middlemarch* is George Eliot's masterpiece. This long, complex novel has four interwoven plots revealing various themes: love and marriage, ambition, religious hypocrisy and the pressures exerted by a provincial environment. *Daniel Deronda* has two plots and themes, again interrelated: the character and unhappy marriage of Gwendolen Harleth and the revelation of Daniel's Jewish parentage.

George Eliot brought great seriousness of purpose to the novel. Like the other Victorian novelists, she made moral teaching an essential part of her fiction. Although she had lost her belief in orthodox Christianity, she held to the ideals of duty and personal responsibility. She explores these fundamental doctrines of hers through her characters and plots and through much authorial comment. In *Silas Marner*, for example, she shows how Godfrey Cass tries to ignore his past actions that have caused distress to himself and others and how instead he hopes that Chance will come to his aid. To make the point clear to her readers, she writes a long passage, almost like a sermon, on the error of not facing the consequences of one's actions and of trusting to Fortune. Nevertheless, she constantly shows sympathy and tolerance towards her characters. She can express her pity for such people as Casaubon, Rosamond Vincy and Bulstrode in *Middlemarch* whereas a novelist who saw personality in simpler terms would deplore or condemn their faults. Perhaps more than any previous novelist, she describes and analyses the sheer complexity of character, with the result that her portraits, especially of women, have great profundity—Maggie Tulliver in *The Mill on the Floss*, Mrs Transome in *Felix Holt*, Dorothea in *Middlemarch* and Gwendolen Harleth in *Daniel Deronda*. Some of her personages, especially rural folk in her earlier novels, are presented with humour—Mrs Poyser in *Adam Bede* and Maggie's aunts and uncles in *The Mill on the Floss*.

George Eliot was scrupulous in the construction of her novels, allowing few digressions or inessential characters. The villagers' "chorus" in *Silas Marner*, for example, is necessary for our understanding of their opinions of the main characters and of the kind of existence, past and present, amongst which those characters must live. By the standards of the time, she avoids exaggeration and highly coloured incidents. Because of her wise moral concern, her understanding of psychology, and her care over the structure of her novels, George Eliot is regarded nowadays as one of the greatest English novelists.

Charles Reade, Wilkie Collins, and Sensation Novels

From about 1860 onwards, "sensation novels" were enormously popular. Their ingredients could include crime, detection, and passionate and illicit love-affairs; they had, too, a highly emotional atmosphere. Two of the best-known were *Lady Audley's Secret* (1862) by Mary Elizabeth Braddon (1837–1915) and *Uncle Silas* (1864) by J. Sheridan Le Fanu (1814–73).

Dickens, Charles Reade and Wilkie Collins have sometimes been called "sensation novelists" although that is too limiting a description of them. Charles Reade (1814–84), an original and lively author, wrote two famous historical novels: *Peg Woffington* (1853), recounting an episode in the life of the eighteenth-century actress, and *The Cloister and the Hearth* (1861), a romance set in fifteenth-century Europe. His novels dealing with contemporary social abuses include *It is never too late to Mend* (1853), in which he exposes brutalities in the prisons, and *Hard Cash* (1863), in which he describes conditions in a lunatic asylum. Wilkie Collins (1824–89),

a friend and associate of Dickens, was a prolific writer. His most enduring novels, with ingenious plots, are *The Woman in White* (1860), *No Name* (1862) and *The Moonstone* (1868), which is often called the first English detective story.

THE LATE VICTORIAN PERIOD

George Meredith

George Meredith (1828–1908) was a substantial poet as well as a novelist. After writing an Oriental fantasy, *The Shaving of Shagpat* (1856), he wrote *The Ordeal of Richard Feverel* (1859), *Evan Harrington* (1860), *Emilia in England* (1864, retitled *Sandra Belloni*, 1886), *Rhoda Fleming* (1865), *Vittoria* (1867), *The Adventures of Harry Richmond* (1871), *Beauchamp's Career* (1876), *The Egoist* (1879), *The Tragic Comedians* (1880), *Diana of the Crossways* (1885), *One of our Conquerors* (1891), *Lord Ormont and his Aminta* (1894) and *The Amazing Marriage* (1895). Of these novels, *The Ordeal of Richard Feverel*, *The Egoist* and *Diana of the Crossways* are generally accounted the best.

Richard Feverel is brought up by his father, Sir Austin, according to a System, which should train him to be a perfect English gentleman, who would avoid making the kind of disastrous marriage that the baronet had suffered. The fine plans break down. Richard marries a girl of unsuitable birth and quickly becomes corrupted in London society. Not unexpectedly, there is a tragic end to everything. But the novel is remarkable for its disparate elements: its irony and satire, not only in situation but also in the wry comments of Adrian Harley; its passages of poetic description; the melodramatic turns of the plot; its humour and its pathos. *The Egoist*, in contrast, is perfectly organised, reminiscent of a comedy of manners in the theatre, especially in its denouement. Its comedy lies in the exposure of the egoism of the central character, Sir Willoughby Patterne, but the play of wit is modified by the sympathetic portrayal of Clara Middleton, to whom Sir Willoughby is engaged to be married, and the delightfully fresh portrayal of Crossjay Patterne, a twelve-year-old boy. *Diana of the Crossways* is about a witty, attractive young woman, involved in divorce proceedings and a love affair.

One difficulty in approaching Meredith's novels is his prose style, which is elaborate and allusive and becomes increasingly so in his later work. But it is genuinely witty and poetic. For beauty of detail and evocation of romantic feeling, little in Victorian imaginative prose can rival such passages as the descriptions of the first meetings between Lucy and Richard in *The Ordeal of Richard Feverel* and of Vernon Whitford sleeping under the blossoming cherry tree in *The Egoist*. Like Fielding, Meredith set great store by the ability of comedy to reveal and rectify affectation. "Comedy is the foundation of good sense," he wrote in his *Essay on Comedy* (1877). Another relevant definition comes at the beginning of *The Egoist*: "Comedy is a game played to throw reflections upon social life, and it deals with human nature in the drawing-room of civilized men and women." His theory is brilliantly put into practice in the final chapters of *The Egoist*, when devices and revelations of different kinds bring about Sir Willoughby's humiliation.

Some elements of Meredith's technique are worth remark. He uses recurring motifs and phrases, forming parts of unifying patterns of comment: the ironical quotations from Sir Austin's "Pilgrim's Scrip" and Mrs Mountstewart Jenkinson's phrase about Clara Middleton, "a dainty rogue in porcelain", for example. Allusions can have a poetic resonance, like those he makes to *The Tempest* when describing the young love of Richard and Lucy. He draws significance and beauty from what may seem conventional symbols: the broken porcelain vase in *The Egoist*, for instance. His handling of his characters' psychology is occasionally elusive, but he has meaningful insights to offer and can be seen to be anticipating the "stream of consciousness" in parts of *The Egoist*, notably in "Clara's Meditations". Amongst his main themes are the tensions between appearance and reality (as in Evan Harrington's social position contrasted with his humble birth) and the independence of women (as shown in the fortunes of Clara and Diana).

Meredith was lionised towards the end of his life, but he is unjustly neglected today. At the least, he should be read for the new possibilities he found in the novel-form and for the risks he took. Apart from his importance in the history of the English novel, there is much in his writing that the modern reader will find intrinsically rewarding.

Thomas Hardy

The career of Thomas Hardy (1840–1928) divides into two parts. In the nineteenth century, up to 1896, he published novels. He then abandoned the writing of prose fiction and for the rest of his life concentrated on poetry (see **M28**). He divided his novels into three groups. First, there are "Novels of Character and Environment", which comprise *Under the Greenwood Tree* (1872), *Far from the Madding Crowd* (1874), *The Return of the Native* (1878), *The Mayor of Casterbridge* (1886), *The Woodlanders* (1887), *Tess of the D'Urbervilles* (1891) and *Jude the Obscure* (1896). Secondly, there are the "Romances and Fantasies": *A Pair of Blue Eyes* (1873), *The Trumpet-Major* (1880), *Two on a Tower* (1882) and *The Well-Beloved* (1892). Thirdly, there are the "Novels of Ingenuity": *Desperate Remedies* (1871), *The Hand of Ethelberta* (1876) and *A Laodicean* (1881). Hardy's major works are those in the first of these categories, with the possible additions of *A Pair of Blue Eyes*, *Desperate Remedies* and *The Trumpet-Major*. As well as these novels, Hardy wrote a considerable number of short stories.

His novels are set in Wessex, by which Hardy means Dorset and the adjacent counties of southwest England. This was the region where he was born and where he lived for most of his life. The scenery, occupations, customs, traditions and speech of Wessex all play vital parts in his narratives. One subject of his is the contrast between the rural world and the world outside, seen most dramatically when an outsider comes into the community or a former inhabitant returns. Fancy Day's coming to Mellstock in *Under the Greenwood Tree*, Sergeant Troy's arrival in *Far from the Madding Crowd* and the return of Clym Yeobright and Grace Melbury from the Continent to their native English villages in *The Return of the Native* and *The Woodlanders* respectively are examples of this kind of conflict. Hardy's great respect for traditional custom is evident in his loving rendering of typical country tasks and events: cider-making, tending sheep, felling trees, cutting furze, threshing wheat, lighting bonfires on 5 November, marriage ceremonies, and so on. Following George Eliot's practice, he uses conversation of village people as sources of commentary and local history. A setting can take on a symbolic function, as Egdon Heath does in *The Return of the Native* or the woods do in *The Woodlanders*. A character can become symbolically identified with his occupation and surroundings, like Diggory Venn in *The Return of the Native*.

Hardy's view of life was fatalistic, since he believed that the human situation was, in Lord David Cecil's words, "a struggle between man on the one hand and, on the other, an omnipotent and indifferent fate." One of his most forthright statements of this belief occurs at the end of *Tess of the D'Urbervilles* when he reports the execution of the heroine: "'Justice' was done, and the President of Immortals, in Aeschylean phrase, had ended his sport with Tess." His novels therefore contain much that is pessimistic and melancholy. The last two, *Tess of the D'Urbervilles* and *Jude the Obscure*, are the most tragic of all. Jude and Sue Bridehead, the central characters of the last novel, find all their aspirations concerning love, marriage, education and religious belief confounded and defeated and their story ends with the death of Jude and the resignation of Sue to unhappiness.

As an aspect of Hardy's deterministic view of life, he believed in the importance of chance, accident and coincidence. A trivial or thoughtless action, such as Bathsheba Everdene's throwing up a hymn book to see whether it falls open or shut (in *Far from the Madding Crowd*), can have unforeseen, appalling consequences. "Life's Little Ironies" and "Satires of Circumstance", titles of collections of his short stories and verse respectively, can be appropriately applied to much that he wrote. His novels are full of strange, striking episodes, in line with his theory that the artist was justified in using exaggeration and distortion to make his points effectively. Readers of Hardy always remember such things as the slaughter of the pig in *Jude the Obscure*, the sale of Henchard's wife in *The Mayor of Casterbridge*, the death of Mrs Yeobright on the heath in *The Return*

of the *Native* and Sergeant Troy's first encounter with Bathsheba in *Far from the Madding Crowd*. Such scenes and events are there for their emotional impact and for the illumination they shed on key motives and developments in the novels.

Hardy's stories are mostly about the tragedies and disappointments of love between men and women. A favourite plot of his depends on the relationship of a woman with two or three men (e.g. Fancy Day, Eustacia Vye, Anne Garland and Tess). Women play a dominant part in his novels. He draws them with sympathy and understanding and he is especially interested in the personalities and actions of strong-willed women or women striving for independence and a life of their own (Sue Bridehead is a famous example). Amongst his men characters, those who are tortured by misgivings, remorse and disappointment are dramatically presented, as witness Henchard, Boldwood and Jude.

Henry James

The importance of Henry James (1843–1916) in the history of the English and American novel is very great indeed. His practice and the theories he expounded in his essay, "The Art of Fiction" (1884), and in the Prefaces to his novels, have been widely influential in this century. An American by birth, James lived and worked in England for most of his life, writing short stories, travel books, essays and numerous novels.

It is convenient to divide the novels into three groups, corresponding to three stages in his career. A favourite theme of his early work is the mutual influences of European and American culture. Principal works of this period are *Roderick Hudson* (1875), *The American* (1877), *The Europeans* (1878), *Daisy Miller* (1879), *Washington Square* (1881), *The Portrait of a Lady* (1881), *The Bostonians* (1886) and *The Princess Casamassima* (1886). His middle period, in which his technique becomes more complex and his subject-matter frequently concerned with English topics, includes *The Tragic Muse* (1890), *The Spoils of Poynton* (1897), *What Maisie Knew* (1897), *Turn of the Screw* (1898), *The Awkward Age* (1899) and *The Sacred Fount* (1901). James's most difficult novels, which show a return to his interest in the tensions between English and American values, are the final three: *The Wings of a Dove* (1902), *The Ambassadors* (1903) and *The Golden Bowl* (1904).

As a man who had experienced life in the United States and Europe, James was fascinated by the differences in culture between the Old and the New Worlds. On the one hand were the newness, potentiality and democracy of America (wonderfully evoked in the opening chapter of *The Europeans*) and on the other hand were the history and achievements of Europe. In his opinion, expressed in his study of Nathaniel Hawthorne, "it takes a great deal of history to produce a little literature" and "it needs a complex social machinery to set a writer in motion." His most famous treatment of the issues involved in this opposition of two ways of life is *The Portrait of a Lady*, which many critics think is his most fully accomplished work of fiction. Isabel Archer, an American girl, comes to England and Europe. She is attractive, frank and eager for adventure and experience. Having rejected two suitors and having inherited a fortune from her uncle, she makes a disastrously ill-judged marriage with an expatriate American but finally decides to endure the consequences of her error. The novel is rich in characterisation: apart from Isabel, the most intriguing personages are Ralph Touchett (her cousin, an invalid) and Madame Merle (a cosmopolitan woman, who arranges Isabel's marriage). James reveals, with understanding, tenderness and wit, the virtues and the weaknesses of Isabel. Moreover, he gives a wise and analytical picture of many aspects of human behaviour, relating them where appropriate to the society and culture of the United States, Europe and England. The theme of the young American woman who visits Europe with tragic consequences is repeated in *The Wings of a Dove*, with Milly Theale as the girl in question. *The Europeans*, one of James' earliest books, is a brief, elegant but searching presentation of the same basic subject; in that novel the scene is the United States, which the Europeans visit.

James was also interested in exploring the problems and corruptions of contemporary English society, as embodied in the contents of the house and the avarice for them displayed in *The Spoils of*

Poynton. Or there are what the critic F. R. Leavis has called the "egotistic squalors" revealed in the comings and goings of the divorced people and spouses in *What Maisie Knew.* His fascination for observing the effects of corruption of a directly personal kind, irrespective of social pressures, is memorably realised in *The Turn of the Screw.*

He believed intensely in the importance of technique and form for the novelist, who held a "sacred office", in his view. The novelist had a duty, he maintained, to tell the truth and to impart to his fiction an "air of reality". In order to accomplish that aim, the writer had to ensure that the novel was an organic whole, with each of its parts contributing to the totality. James called some nineteenth-century novels "large, loose, baggy monsters" and sought in his own work to practise a strict control over his material. His novels are accordingly tautly constructed and written in the most meticulous prose style. This style in the later novels is difficult and subtle and some critics have thus accused him of sacrificing life and warmth for the sake of brilliant intellectual structures. Meredith and Hardy in their different ways broke with some of the conventions of the Victorian novel; but James departed radically from many of its features and can be regarded as the first of the modern novelists.

Robert Louis Stevenson and the Adventure Novel

Robert Louis Stevenson (1850–94), essayist, poet, travel-writer and novelist, achieved fame with *Treasure Island* (1883) and *Dr Jekyll and Mr Hyde* (1886). His subsequent novels include *Kidnapped* (1886), *The Black Arrow* (1888), *The Master of Ballantrae* (1889), *Catriona* (1893) and *Weir of Hermiston* (unfinished, 1896). With Lloyd Osbourne, his stepson, he wrote *The Wrong Box* (1889), *The Wrecker* (1892) and *The Ebb-Tide* (1894).

Stevenson was as scrupulous a writer as Henry James, one of his friends and correspondents. His novels are precisely and elegantly shaped and are expressed in clear, economical prose. He wrote that the artist's "one main and necessary resource" was his compulsion to "omit what is tedious or irrelevant, and suppress what is tedious and necessary." Action and the revelation of character through action form the main material of his novels. *Treasure Island*, written for boys, is a masterpiece of construction, beginning quietly but ominously, building up suspense with the discovery of Long John Silver's true nature and coming to a climax on the island with the battles between the pirates and Jim Hawkins and his friends. It has incidents and devices that stick in the mind (the black spot, the pirates' chorus) and colourful personages (Long John Silver, Ben Gunn). *Kidnapped* is admirable adventure fiction with an authentic feeling for place and period: Scotland in the years just after the '45 Jacobite Rebellion. Both books gain in immediacy through their first-person narration.

The Master of Ballantrae, set in post-1745 Scotland, is a remarkable tale of evil and persecution, personified in its leading character, the Master. It has a relentless urgency and a number of unforgettable scenes, such as the duel between the Master of Ballantrae and his brother by candlelight out-of-doors on a frosty night. Although Stevenson emphasised action rather than psychology, at least two of his characters have become household words: Long John Silver and Dr Jekyll, alias Mr Hyde.

The adventure novel or "romance" became popular towards the end of the nineteenth century. With Stevenson's successful *Treasure Island* in mind, Rider Haggard (1856–1925) wrote *King Solomon's Mines* (1885), followed by *She* (1887) and many other books of the same kind. G. A. Henty (1832–1902) wrote prolifically, producing some eighty novels for boys. Other adventures and romances were Conan Doyle's Sherlock Holmes stories (beginning in 1887 with *A Study in Scarlet*) and novels of exciting action, Stanley Weyman's historical novels from 1893 onwards, Anthony Hope Hawkins' *The Prisoner of Zenda* (1894), Bram Stoker's *Dracula* (1897) and E. W. Hornung's Raffles stories from 1899 onwards. The adventure novels of John Buchan (1875–1940) include *Prester John* (1910), *The Thirty-Nine Steps* (1915), *Greenmantle* (1916) and *Mr Standfast* (1919).

Naturalism: Gissing and Moore

Naturalism, which is sometimes used as a synonym for realism, was a literary movement associated mostly with the novels of Emile Zola (1840–1902). Writers who held the doctrine maintained that novels should be as physically detailed as possible, that novelists should use scientific methods of description and analysis and that they should emphasise the importance of environment. The subject-matter of naturalistic novels tended to be about the harsh realities of the lives of the poor and to concentrate on the least ideal aspects of human nature.

George Gissing (1857–1903) was one exponent of naturalism in England, writing about the poverty and miseries of working-class existence in novels such as *The Nether World* (1889). *New Grub Street* (1891) surveys writers' lives, contrasting the success of the unprincipled Jasper Milvain with the wretched life and death of the uncompromising Edwin Reardon. George Moore (1852–1933), strongly influenced by Zola and Maupassant, wrote *Esther Waters* (1894), as well as a variety of other novels. In an objective and yet poignant manner, he relates the hardships suffered by Esther from the time she goes into domestic service as a seventeen-year-old girl.

Naturalism: Arnold Bennett

Arnold Bennett (1867–1931) also modelled his novels on those of the French naturalists. Flaubert, the Goncourt brothers, Zola and Maupassant had established aesthetic ideals for him in their objectivity and precision of language. A writer of dogged productivity, he wrote over thirty novels, beginning with *A Man from the North* (1898). The first of importance was *Anna of the Five Towns* (1902), the title of which makes clear its setting in the Potteries, the midland region of England which is the environment of most of his best fiction. His reputation was established with *The Old Wives' Tale* (1908), a long, detailed study of Sophia and Constance Baines, two sisters, from youth to age. His achievement here is his skilful handling of Time, which E. M. Forster declared was the "real hero" of the book. *Clayhanger* (1910), *Hilda Lessways* (1911) and *These Twain* (1915) are collectively known as *The Clayhanger Family.* Set in the Five Towns, the first two deal respectively with the young lives of Edwin Clayhanger and Hilda Lessways and the third with their married life together. *The Card* (1911) is a lighter story about the agreeable rogue, Denry Machin. *Riceyman Steps* (1923) is a grim novel about a miserly second-hand bookseller in Clerkenwell; it is a tale of meanness, squalor, illness and death and is one of the most powerful of all Bennett's novels.

Bennett is meticulously realistic, supplying explicit details of the environment, thoughts and actions of his characters. He is a regional novelist, who shows us panoramic and close-up pictures of the places where his personages live. *The Old Wives' Tale* opens with a description of the county of Staffordshire, which surrounds his heroines, as he points out. The focus moves to the Five Towns, to St Luke's Square, to the Baines's shop and finally to the showroom. Bennett slowly completes his picture of the two girls, the shop and the town. Similarly, Edwin at the beginning of *Clayhanger* is shown standing on a canal bridge in a precisely depicted location in the Five Towns. Such accumulation of detail, leaving little to the imagination, was adversely criticised by later novelists, notably Virginia Woolf. But it gives a photographic verisimilitude to Bennett's stories. He is not an idealist or moralist; he is content to display to us his personages and their doings. He is not without sympathy and humour, he is inventive, he can give meaning to trivial and mundane happenings and he constructs his novels solidly.

THE TWENTIETH CENTURY

Rudyard Kipling

Rudyard Kipling (1865–1936) was another author sensitive to the aesthetic shaping of his work. He was primarily a poet and writer of short stories, but two novels of his are *The Light that Failed* (1890) and *Kim* (1901). The former, with its tragic account of the blindness that overcomes Dick Heldar, may be melodramatic and sentimental, but it has a compelling emotional drive that makes it hard to put down. *Kim* evokes the India of the Raj, which Kipling knew intimately as a child and young man.

Its central character, the boy Kim, travels through India with a Tibetan lama and becomes involved in espionage organised by the British Secret Service. He is therefore torn between the demands of two ways of life: the contemplative and the active. The novel can be appreciated on several levels: as an adventure story, as an unrivalled description of the peoples, customs and scenes of India, as a glorification as well as a criticism of British imperialism, and as a presentation of conflicts of ideas and loyalties.

H. G. Wells

H. G. Wells (1866–1946) was a prolific and versatile writer whose abiding interests were science and socialist politics. He made his name with scientific romances, which include *The Time Machine* (1895), *The Island of Dr Moreau* (1896), *The Invisible Man* (1897), *The War of the Worlds* (1898) and *The First Men on the Moon* (1901). Although Jules Verne's books were known in England, these were the first thoroughgoing examples of science fiction in English. Based on the sound scientific knowledge he had acquired as a London University student, his stories were daringly imaginative but convincing and still rank among the best of their kind. Their startling subject-matter includes travelling into the future, the coming of Martians to England and journeying to the moon, all realised in credible detail. Wells also wrote social comedies, typically featuring a "little man" of the lower middle class: *Love and Mr Lewisham* (1900), *Kipps* (1905) and *The History of Mr Polly* (1910). He explored social problems in a more serious manner in a third group of novels, including *Tono-Bungay* (1909), *Ann Veronica* (1909) and *The New Machiavelli* (1911). With the exception of *Mr Britling Sees It Through* (1916), his later novels lack the vigour and imagination of his earlier novels and are little read today.

Unlike James, Stevenson, Bennett and Kipling, Wells was impatient with the novel as an art-form, since for him its entertainment value and message were of prime importance. In his science fiction, he wanted to make his readers aware of the potentialities of technological discovery. His social novels had clear lessons to impart. *The History of Mr Polly* is an enjoyable story of the misfortunes and eventual happiness of its hero, with Dickensian humour in its characterisation (*e.g.* Uncle Pentstemon), Mr Polly's pathetically comic aspirations and actions (*e.g.* his conversation with the schoolgirl sitting on a wall and his attempted suicide) and his misuse of language. At the same time, Wells is making serious points about a system of society and education that can starve Mr Polly's imagination and stunt any possibilities of a fulfilled existence for him. The main purpose of *Ann Veronica* is an argument for women's liberation. *Tono-Bungay* is concerned with the world of commerce and *The New Machiavelli* with the world of politics, with relevance to the corruptions which Wells saw in Edwardian England.

Psychological subtlety and experiments with formal techniques have little part in Wells' novels, which succeed in their intention of giving much pleasure blended with instruction. His prose style is spontaneous and lively, sweeping the reader along. His instinctive skills and many-sidedness make him a novelist of considerable achievement.

Joseph Conrad

In contrast to the novels of Bennett and Wells, those by Joseph Conrad (1857–1924) are innovatory in a number of respects. Although he was Polish by birth, he served in the British Merchant Navy for many years and wrote all his novels in English. The principal ones are *Almayer's Folly* (1895), *An Outcast of the Islands* (1896), *The Nigger of the Narcissus* (1897), *Lord Jim* (1900), *The Heart of Darkness* (1902), *Typhoon* (1902), *Nostromo* (1904), *The Secret Agent* (1907), *Under Western Eyes* (1911), *Chance* (1913), *Victory* (1915) and *The Rover* (1923). Conrad also wrote short stories and some books in collaboration with Ford Madox Ford (1873–1939), who was a considerable novelist in his own right.

Conrad's experience as a seaman is reflected in the settings he uses: Malaysia and the Indian Ocean (as in *Lord Jim*), the Congo (*The Heart of Darkness*) and South America (*Nostromo*). London, however, is the setting of *The Secret Agent*. In such places a typical Conrad hero confronts dangers and is compelled to make immediate choices. Conrad concerns himself not so much with the relationships between people as the relationships between an individual person and circumstances. Questions of moral decision, heroism and cowardice, loyalty and treachery are therefore basic to his novels. In *Lord Jim*, Jim jumps overboard from the *Patna*, which he mistakenly thinks is about to sink. Tormented by self-accusations of despicable conduct, he seeks to redeem himself. But after achieving a measure of redemption as the respected "Lord Jim", he makes another error of judgment, which brings about his death. Conrad may show us, too, how a sensitive man may be inferior at a moment of crisis to one of little imagination. A solid and stupid man like Captain MacWhirr in *Typhoon* triumphs over the terrible storm and brings his ship to safety.

To demonstrate the complexity of arriving at a true account of happenings and motives, Conrad disrupts chronology and uses various narrators. *Lord Jim* begins with Jim as a water clerk, recounts how the *Patna* hit something below the surface of the sea, and continues with the court of enquiry. At this point, Marlow (a narrator Conrad uses in several books) intervenes. Largely through him, we are given a vivid sense of the way Jim feels defeated and only then do we arrive at the crucial event: the desertion of the *Patna*. Thus chronological order is replaced by a dramatic, significant order. Perspective and shades of meaning are gained by Conrad's using the memories and prejudices of different story-tellers. In *Nostromo*, the events are narrated by the omniscient novelist and also by Captain Mitchell, Decoud (in a letter), Dr Monyghan (in his reflections) and Nostromo. Readers have to work hard at piecing together the mosaic of action and thought and are consequently made aware of the ambiguities and subtleties of human behaviour. Unity is derived from central themes: Jim's agonies of conscience in *Lord Jim*, the storm in *Typhoon* and the silver mine in *Nostromo*.

Conrad's use of English has its awkwardnesses, especially in colloquial speech, but these are outweighed by the scrupulous way in which he expresses shades of meaning and realises people and things in concrete detail. His novels have great depth and integrity, revealing (in the words of F. R. Leavis) both "keen sensibility" and "exceptional awareness".

Ford Madox Ford and Dorothy Richardson

The principal novels of Ford Madox Ford (1873–1939), who influenced Conrad and collaborated with him (*see above*), are *The Good Soldier* (1915), *Some Do Not* (1924), *No More Parades* (1925), *A Man Could Stand Up* (1926) and *The Last Post* (1928). The last four are known as the Tietjens tetralogy, after their principal character. In the interests of what he saw as truthful presentation, Ford used experimental techniques in his fiction, including time-shifts, different viewpoints and "*progression d'effet*" (i.e., carrying on the story faster as it progresses). Together with authorial "invisibility" and irony, these methods give his narratives a sense of elusiveness and open up fascinating possibilities of interpretation. His psychological depictions (of Tietjens and Dowell, the protagonist of *The Good Soldier*, for example) are subtle and complex. Ford was concerned to explore such moral issues as honour and fidelity and also the codes and assumptions of society and class.

Dorothy Richardson (1873–1957) was one of the first English novelists fully to use the technique of the "stream of consciousness", which is associated particularly with the work of Virginia Woolf and James Joyce (*see below*). Her sequence of twelve novels, published between 1915 and 1938 and collectively known as *Pilgrimage*, have the "consciousness" of her heroine, Miriam, at their centre.

John Galsworthy, Hugh Walpole and Somerset Maugham

Three novelists who achieved immense popularity and yet who never rose high in critical esteem (at least in England) were John Galsworthy (1867–1933), Sir Hugh Walpole (1884–1941) and W. Somerset Maugham (1874–1965).

Galsworthy, who was also famous as a playwright, is remembered for *The Forsyte Saga*, which consists of *The Man of Property* (1906), *In Chancery* (1920) and *To Let* (1921). The Forsyte story continues in *A Modern Comedy*, consisting of *The White Monkey*

(1924), *The Silver Spoon* (1926) and *Swan Song* (1928). The substance of these six novels is the relationships and intrigues of a wealthy upper-middle class family from the 1880s to the 1920s. The books have a comforting readability and a documentary value in their charting the outlook, habits and possessions of the family. Galsworthy was awarded the Nobel Prize for Literature in 1932.

Walpole's books have proved to be less durable. *Mr Perrin and Mr Traill* (1911), about the cruel rivalry of two schoolmasters, still has vitality. But once-favoured novels, such as *Jeremy* (1919), *The Cathedral* (1922) and the four known as *The Herries Chronicle* (1930–33) are little read today.

Somerset Maugham began in naturalistic style with *Liza of Lambeth* (1897). Equally successful as a playwright and a short-story writer, Maugham wrote *Of Human Bondage* (1915), *The Moon and Sixpence* (1919), *Cakes and Ale* (1930), *The Razor's Edge* (1944) and many other novels. His range is wide and he is always a supreme entertainer. His sardonic attitude may disturb some, but most readers find that this gives an edge to his clear, fluent narratives. Although he has been called superficial, no one can deny his sheer readability.

E. M. Forster

Besides Conrad, four novelists of the first half of the twentieth century extended the possibilities of the form: E. M. Forster, Virginia Woolf, James Joyce and D. H. Lawrence.

E. M. Forster (1879–1970) wrote *Where Angels Fear to Tread* (1905), *The Longest Journey* (1907), *A Room with a View* (1908), *Howards End* (1910) and *A Passage to India* (1924). *Maurice* was written in 1914, but because of its homosexual theme was not published till 1971. After 1924, Forster wrote no more novels.

In all his writings, fiction and nonfiction, Forster is liberal and humanist in outlook. He always set great store by loving personal relationships and was suspicious of conceptions of duty, patriotism and imperialism. In a notorious statement in his essay, "What I Believe" (1939), he said: "I hate the idea of causes, and if I had to choose between betraying my country and betraying my friend, I hope I should have the guts to betray my country." Later in the same essay, he declared that he distrusted Great Men and believed in an aristocracy of the "sensitive, the considerate and the plucky".

His novels are elegant, drily humorous and witty, but at the same time they contain elements of the poetical and the mystical. The motto, "Only connect", which appears on the title page of *Howards End*, expresses one of his tenets. To bring out its implications, he will place two sets of ideas in opposition and show the tensions and connections between them. In *Where Angels Fear to Tread*, Lilia, an English girl from the conventional middle-classes, outrages her family when she marries Gino, an Italian dentist. After her death, they make attempts to "rescue" her baby. The comedy and the message of the novel, therefore, derive from the interactions between English and Mediterranean ways of life. The opposition in *Howards End* is that between the world of "telegrams and anger" and the world of culture and the finer feelings.

Forster's most ambitious novel, *A Passage to India*, is concerned with the mutual misunderstandings between the Indians and the ruling English in the India of 1910–20. The narrow-minded English community is angered by Dr Aziz' apparent assault on Adela Quested in the Marabar Caves. The principal characters are Fielding, the well-meaning and humane schoolmaster; Dr Aziz, impulsive and warm-hearted; Mrs Moore, the elderly, visionary Englishwoman; and Adela, herself, who—like Fielding—has good intentions but is bewildered by her encounter with India. Forster carefully patterns his novel, writes amusing and lively description and dialogue and conveys a sense of the incomprehensibility and fascination of India felt by English people. As always, he seeks to inculcate the truth that love and understanding at the personal level are vital in all circumstances.

In *Aspects of the Novel* (1927), Forster deplored the need to tell a story in the novel. But his novels contain much that is amusing and thought-provoking: surprises in the plot, realistic dialogue, economical but convincing characterisation and unexpected authorial generalisations. Altogether, we get the impression of a sharp but tolerant perception of the virtues and frailties of mankind.

Virginia Woolf

E. M. Forster was associated with the Bloomsbury Group, although he was never a fully committed member of it. The relations and friends who formed the Group between 1905 and the 1930s (Lytton Strachey, Maynard Keynes, Virginia Woolf and her sister Vanessa Bell, Clive Bell, Duncan Grant, Roger Fry and others) saw themselves as rational, enlightened people who rejected the intolerance and narrow-minded morality of the Victorians. They valued love, friendship and the arts.

One of the central figures of the Bloomsbury Group was Virginia Woolf (1882–1941), whose career as a novelist began with two fairly conventional books: *The Voyage Out* (1915) and *Night and Day* (1919). She proceeded to experiment in both form and content and all her subsequent novels are works of originality, breaking with traditional approaches and methods: *Jacob's Room* (1922), *Mrs Dalloway* (1925), *To the Lighthouse* (1927), *Orlando* (1928), *The Waves* (1931), *The Years* (1937) and *Between the Acts* (1941).

Virginia Woolf was opposed to the technique of such Edwardian novelists as Bennett, Wells and Galsworthy. In her opinion, they were materialists, who were "concerned not with the spirit but with the body". Their painstaking renderings of a solid, exterior world meant, she argued, that the inner meaning of life escaped them. What she attempted to do, on the other hand, was to capture the transience and subtlety of experience and thought. In a famous statement, she said that "Life is not a series of gig lamps symmetrically arranged; life is a luminous halo, a semi-transparent envelope surrounding us from the beginning of consciousness to the end." Modern authors should therefore "record the atoms as they fall upon the mind in the order in which they fall" and "trace the pattern, however disconnected and incoherent in appearance, which each sight or incident scores upon the consciousness." To achieve these ends, she uses as a means the "stream of consciousness" technique. She takes us inside her characters' minds, revealing the flow of their thoughts and emotions, past, present and future. The trivial and the grand are fused; the exterior world impinges now and then; repetitions, allusions, memories blend together.

A typical example of this technique is the scene of the dinner-party in *To the Lighthouse*. Outwardly, Mrs Ramsay, the hostess, is serving the food and making unremarkable conversation with her guests. But we are witnesses of the interior lives of these people. The reflections of Mrs Ramsay, Lily Briscoe, Charles Tansley and William Bankes make a delicately woven texture of thoughts and emotions, adding to what we have already learned earlier in the novel.

Realising the difficulty of giving a clear shape to the intangible, Virginia Woolf uses repeated phrases and objects as focal points, such as the royal car in *Mrs Dalloway* and the lighthouse and Lily Briscoe's painting in *To the Lighthouse*. Her prose is supple and quietly rhythmical and contains memorable and beautiful imagery. Her novels have a refined artistry—too rarefied in the opinion of some, who have criticised her for narrowness of social range and for creating people who all share her own delicate sensitivity. But she is one of the most discerning and subtle of psychological novelists.

James Joyce

James Joyce (1882–1941), an exact contemporary of Virginia Woolf, was the most far-reaching innovator in the English novel of this century. His comparatively small output began with a collection of short stories, *Dubliners* (1914), economically realistic evocations of the frustrated lives of ordinary inhabitants of the Irish city. *A Portrait of the Artist as a Young Man* (1916) is an autobiographical novel. This was followed by his masterpiece, *Ulysses* (1922). His last book was *Finnegans Wake* (1939).

Joyce used the stream of consciousness technique, carrying it to greater lengths than Virginia Woolf. It can be seen in its purest form in Molly Bloom's soliloquy at the end of *Ulysses*, where her drifting mental processes as she lies half-asleep are rendered in unpunctuated prose that moves from one apparently disconnected thought to another. His most astonishing innovations were linguistic. *A Portrait of the Artist* begins with childish-sounding language mirroring the boy's immaturity. Throughout the book, his stages of development are recorded in appropriate levels of prose. *Ulysses* is written in widely varied styles of English, most obviously in the scene where Stephen and Bloom await the birth of a baby. The conception and growth of the child are reflected in Joyce's imitations of English prose from Anglo-Saxon times to the end of the nineteenth century. His most extreme linguistic experimentation is in *Finnegans Wake*, a book of such intensive verbal coinage and word-play that it can be said to be written in a new language, for which a key is necessary.

Joyce also employs allusions and symbols, which enrich his meaning once they are interpreted (which again can be a difficult process). *Ulysses* has indirect allegiances to Homer's epic poem, the *Odyssey*, but it is filled with the actuality of one day in Dublin: 16 June 1904. It contains numerous other emblems, references and echoes, making it a fascinatingly complex picture of human experience. His psychological explorations of character are associated with the life and traditions of Ireland, for although Joyce exiled himself from his native country as a young man its politics, religion and customs are inseparable from his work.

Stephen Daedalus, the hero of *A Portrait of the Artist as a Young Man*, is the fictional equivalent of Joyce. His education, temptations and artistic credo make the main subject-matter of the book. Stephen reappears as one of the central characters of *Ulysses*, in which his companion during the day's adventures is a middle-aged Jew, Leopold Bloom. Using their particular situations in early twentieth-century Ireland, Joyce creates a universal impression of the emotions and problems of humanity, by means of interior monologue, sensuous description, individualised dialogue and allusion. In *A Portrait of the Artist*, Stephen said that the highest form of literature is the dramatic. In that form, "the artist, like the God of creation, remains within or behind or beyond or above his handiwork, invisible, refined out of existence, indifferent, paring his fingernails." By fully and uncompromisingly presenting his characters' innermost thoughts and by withholding authorial moral judgement, Joyce aimed to achieve the ideal that Stephen desired.

D. H. Lawrence

D. H. Lawrence (1885–1930) differed in many remarkable aspects from James Joyce and Virginia Woolf in his approach to writing novels. He brought an urgency and spontaneity and, above all, a poetic sense to prose fiction. He was a prolific author, who produced numerous short stories, travel books, poems, plays and essays besides novels. His principal novels are *The White Peacock* (1911), *Sons and Lovers* (1913), *The Rainbow* (1915), *Women in Love* (1920), *The Lost Girl* (1921), *Aaron's Rod* (1922), *Kangaroo* (1923), *The Plumed Serpent* (1926) and *Lady Chatterley's Lover* (1928).

As a novelist, Lawrence considered himself "superior to the saint, the scientist, the philosopher, and the poet", since in his opinion the novel dealt with the complete human being instead of a particular aspect. "The novel," he declared, "is the one bright book of life." His main theme is the tensions, joys and sorrows that exist in personal relationships: those between parents and children, husbands and wives, and other people in love. *Sons and Lovers*, his most famous book, centres upon the semi-autobiographical hero, Paul Morel, whose attachment to his mother inhibits his love for Miriam. The novel is also deeply concerned with the opposition between Paul's sensual coal-mining father and his refined, sensitive mother. *The Rainbow*, to which *Women in Love* is a kind of sequel, shows three generations of the Brangwyn family: the conflict and mutual understanding inherent in passionate marriages and love-affairs and the disputes and reconciliations between parents and children are revealed as repeating themselves through a long period of time. But no summaries can convey the subtleties of Lawrence's handling of the psychological and moral issues involved.

For Lawrence, "blood" and instinct were the dominating forces of life, superior in strength to the dictates of reason, and he saw his task as a novelist to transmit these forces through the medium of words. The result is that his novels lack conventional form. What matters is the internal lives of his characters and not their external actions, except when these actions reveal significant behaviour. He therefore concentrates on episodes of intensity and he will, where necessary, ignore the reader's expectations of an even time-scale and the clear development of plot and character. "You mustn't look into my novel for the old stable *ego* of character," he wrote. "There is another *ego*, according to whose action the individual is unrecognisable, and passes through, as it were, allotropic states which it needs a deeper sense than any we've been used to exercise, to discover and are states of the same single radically unchanged element." His writing consequently has a great emotional impact and gives the feeling of complete fidelity to life as it actually is, with its contradictions and uncertainties. But Lawrence's uncompromising frankness and refusal to conform to literary and social conventions led to the censorship and banning of some of his books, notably *Lady Chatterley's Lover*, which was too sexually explicit for contemporary English standards—it was not published in Britain in unexpurgated form until 1960.

Lawrence's descriptions of the physical appearance of his characters and their surroundings are direct and sensuous; his prose rhythms and choice of words remind us that he was a poet. Places he lived in inspired many of his settings: the Midlands countryside in *The White Peacock*, Australia in *Kangaroo*, Mexico in *The Plumed Serpent*. His imagery is rich in suggestion and is typically drawn from natural and religious sources. In *The Rainbow*, for example, the rainbow itself, doorways, archways and rural scenery and occupations evoke important aspects of the characters' lives and motives and give unity to the novel.

It has been argued that Lawrence was not always in touch with reality because the intense level at which his personages live lacks credibility. Some critics have deplored his preaching, his lack of humour and his repetitiveness. Some of these criticisms are justified only if the criterion of naturalism is rigorously applied. Most people will agree that his great novels—*Sons and Lovers*, *The Rainbow* and *Women in Love*—are masterpieces of psychological insight and moral profundity.

Other Novelists of the 1920s and 1930s

Although Ronald Firbank (1886–1926) began publishing his work in 1905, his slight, artificial novels seem to represent the frivolous side of the 1920s. Amongst them are *Vainglory* (1915), *Caprice* (1917), *Valmouth* (1919), *The Flower beneath the Foot* (1923), *Prancing Nigger* (1924) and *Concerning the Eccentricities of Cardinal Pirelli* (1926). The wit and fantasy of these books can also be related to the aestheticism of the 1890s.

One of the most influential writers of the two decades was Aldous Huxley (1894–1963). An intellectual and polymath, Huxley wrote satirical, comic novels of ideas, which have affinities with those of Peacock. They include *Crome Yellow* (1921), *Antic Hay* (1923) and *Those Barren Leaves* (1925). *Point Counterpoint* (1928) consists mainly of brilliant conversation pieces, in which the participants (e.g. Rampion, who is based on D. H. Lawrence) exchange ideas on philosophy, politics, religion, the arts and society. Of Huxley's later novels, the most important are *Brave New World* (1932), which is set six hundred years hence, *Eyeless in Gaza* (1936) and *Island* (1962).

Evelyn Waugh (1903–66) made his reputation with comic, witty, mocking novels: *Decline and Fall* (1928), *Vile Bodies* (1930), *Black Mischief* (1932), *A Handful of Dust* (1934), *Scoop* (1938) and *Put Out More Flags* (1942). Waugh's books of this period are characterised by an air of satirical detachment, black comedy and farce, the fertile invention of entertaining personages and episodes and a pointed prose style. They remain freshly amusing, though some readers dislike their apparent heartlessness. *Brideshead Revisited* (1945), with its nostalgic recollections of events centred upon a great country house, is, in contrast, a romantic and even sentimental novel. *The Loved One* (1948), a satire on American funeral customs, marked a return to his earlier manner. Waugh's last considerable work, which some consider to be his masterpiece, was a trilogy: *Men at Arms* (1952), *Officers and Gentlemen* (1955) and *Unconditional Surrender* (1961), later united as *Sword of Honour* (1965). Though this book contains much comedy, it is a sympathetic portrayal of the doubts and anxieties during the Second World War of its central figure, Guy Crouchback, a Roman Catholic and army officer.

The first novels of George Orwell (pseudonym of Eric Blair, 1903–50) reflect the period: *Burmese Days* (1934), *A Clergyman's Daughter* (1935), *Keep the Aspidistra Flying* (1936) and *Coming up for Air* (1939). His most celebrated were his last two: *Animal Farm* (1945), which is a short fable satirising revolution and dictatorship, and *Nineteen Eighty-Four* (1949), which is a grim picture of a future authoritarian world.

Christopher Isherwood (1904–86) wrote *All the Conspirators* (1928), but made his reputation with the plays he wrote with W. H. Auden in the 1930s and with his two novels about Germany in the last days of the Weimar Republic: *Mr Norris Changes Trains* (1935) and *Goodbye to Berlin* (1939). The narrator of these says "I am a camera" and consequently records his experiences in a spare, objective manner, which nevertheless evokes the emotions of himself and the other characters. Isherwood's other novels, which are varied in content, include *Prater Violet* (1946) and *Down There On A Visit* (1962).

Much of the fiction of Firbank, Huxley, Waugh, Orwell and Isherwood therefore reflects the spirit of the age. But other novelists of the time were free from contemporary preoccupations. The two most famous novels of John Cowper Powys (1872–1963) are *Wolf Solent* (1929) and *A Glastonbury Romance* (1932), which are conceived on a grand scale and are full of a metaphysical awareness of the forces of Nature. His brother, T. F. Powys (1875–1953), is best known for *Mr Weston's Good Wine* (1927). The novels of Ivy Compton-Burnett (1892–1969) are set at the end of the nineteenth century in a stylised world of middle-class families in country houses. Their titles, whose similarities denote the unchanging nature of the novels, include *Pastors and Masters* (1925), *Men and Wives* (1931), *A House and its Head* (1935), *A Family and a Fortune* (1939), *Manservant and Maidservant* (1947), *Two Worlds and their Ways* (1949), *A Father and his Fate* (1957), *The Mighty and their Fall* (1961) and *A God and his Gifts* (1963). Through the medium of mannered conversation, Ivy Compton-Burnett presents stories of wrong-doing, sin and crime. Aspects of evil are coolly exposed by means of her highly artificial narration.

J. B. Priestley (1894–1984) wrote *The Good Companions* (1929), which was a huge success, and followed this with numerous realistic, entertaining novels, including *Angel Pavement* (1930).

Graham Greene

Graham Greene (b. 1904) has been writing novels for over sixty years as well as short stories, plays, autobiography, essays and criticism. He began with *The Man Within* (1929) and his subsequent novels are *Stamboul Train* (1932), *It's a Battlefield* (1934), *England Made Me* (1935), *A Gun for Sale* (1936), *Brighton Rock* (1938), *The Confidential Agent* (1939), *The Power and the Glory* (1940), *The Ministry of Fear* (1943), *The Heart of the Matter* (1948), *The Third Man* (1950), *The End of the Affair* (1951), *Loser Takes All* (1955), *The Quiet American* (1955), *Our Man in Havana* (1958), *A Burnt-Out Case* (1961), *The Comedians* (1966), *Travels with my Aunt* (1969), *The Honorary Consul* (1973), *The Human Factor* (1978), *Doctor Fischer of Geneva* (1980), *Monsignor Quixote* (1982), *The Tenth Man* (1985; written 1944) and *The Captain and the Enemy* (1988).

Greene's novels are gripping and exciting, since they contain the basic features of such popular fiction as thrillers, adventure stories and spy stories. Their settings are dangerous or exotic places, such as Mexico (*The Power and the Glory*), West Africa (*The Heart of the Matter*), the Congo (*A Burnt-Out Case*), Haiti (*The Comedians*) and Argentina (*The Honorary Consul*). His vivid descriptions of places and people and his fast-moving pace are cinematic and many of his novels have been turned into successful films. Enmeshed in challenging circumstances, his characters are compelled to make moral choices and, in doing so, to face problems of loyalty and faith. As Greene is a Roman Catholic, these problems are generally related to religious belief. Pinkie, the young Roman Catholic criminal in *Brighton Rock*, is dedicated to evil but is opposed by the warm-hearted Ida, who has firm ideas of Right and Wrong, untroubled by theological considerations. Scobie in *The Heart of the Matter*, a self-tormented Catholic, chooses to commit the sin of suicide as a result of his entanglements in unhappy relationships with women. In his novella, *Doctor Fischer of Geneva*, Greene uses memorable, macabre events and

strange—even grotesque—characterisation to stimulate thought about profound issues: greed, power, love, revenge and death.

Greene's settings, characters and themes, especially from *Brighton Rock* onwards, are fused into complete statements about the springs of human conduct. The environment, which has sometimes been called "Greeneland", can symbolise and emphasise the dangers experienced by the characters. Because of the quantity and quality of his achievement, Graham Greene is widely considered to be the outstanding English novelist of the past fifty years. This opinion received official recognition when he was appointed a Companion of Honour in 1966 and awarded the O.M. in 1986.

THE NOVEL SINCE 1940

Novelists of the 1940s

Some writers who began their literary careers in the 1930s became more prominent in the war and post-war years. Joyce Cary (1888–1957) began by writing novels set in Nigeria, where he had worked as a government official: *Aissa Saved* (1932), *An American Visitor* (1933), *The African Witch* (1936) and *Mister Johnson* (1939). He followed these with two books about childhood: *Charley is my Darling* (1940) and *A House of Children* (1941). Then there came a trilogy centred upon three characters, Gulley Jimson, Sara Monday and Wilcher: *Herself Surprised* (1941), *To Be a Pilgrim* (1942) and *The Horse's Mouth* (1944), which is generally accounted his best novel. Another trilogy, centred upon Chester Nimmo, was *Prisoner of Grace* (1952), *Except the Lord* (1953) and *Not Honour More* (1955). A further notable novel is *A Fearful Joy* (1949). Cary's most famous works, *Mister Johnson* and *The Horse's Mouth*, are exuberant, inventive and full of *joie de vivre*, largely owing to their central characters, Mister Johnson, an African clerk, and Gulley Jimson, a painter and rogue.

L. P. Hartley (1895–1972) wrote a trilogy dealing with the fortunes of a brother and sister in the early years of this century: *The Shrimp and the Anemone* (1944), *The Sixth Heaven* (1946) and *Eustace and Hilda* (1947). *The Go-Between* (1953) is a vivid, delicate evocation of a boy's being caught up in adult sexual intrigue of Edwardian country house life.

The sensitive, psychologically penetrating novels of Elizabeth Bowen (1899–1973) include *The House in Paris* (1935), *The Death of the Heart* (1938), *The Heat of the Day* (1949)—usually said to be her greatest achievement, *A World of Love* (1955) and *Eva Trout* (1969).

Henry Green (pseudonym of Henry Yorke, 1905–73) wrote *Blindness* (1926), *Living* (1929), *Party Going* (1939), *Caught* (1943), *Loving* (1945), *Back* (1946), *Concluding* (1948), *Nothing* (1950) and *Doting* (1952). He explores personal relationships in rhythmical prose, much dialogue, imagery and symbols. His novels are some of the most imaginative works of the period.

In contrast, the novels of C. P. Snow (1905–80) are heavily realistic, often dealing with people in the midst of public affairs (in, for example, government and university circles). His best-known novels form the *Strangers and Brothers* sequence: *Strangers and Brothers* (1940), *The Light and the Dark* (1947), *Time of Hope* (1949), *The Masters* (1951), *The New Men* (1954), *Homecomings* (1956), *The Conscience of the Rich* (1958), *The Affair* (1960), *Corridors of Power* (1964), *The Sleep of Reason* (1968) and *Last Things* (1970).

The quiet, perceptive novels of Elizabeth Taylor (1912–75) include *At Mrs Lippincote's* (1945), *A View of the Harbour* (1947), *A Wreath of Roses* (1949), *Angel* (1957) and *Mrs Palfrey at the Claremont* (1971).

Samuel Beckett

As a young man, Samuel Beckett (1906–89) was a friend and associate of James Joyce, whose stream-of-consciousness technique influenced his writing. He first came into prominence in England in 1955 when his English version of his play, *Waiting for Godot*, originally written in French, was performed in London. His novel, *Murphy* (1938), set in London, is written in a fairly traditional manner. *Watt*, completed about 1944, was published in 1953. Three short novels, first written in French and in the form of monologues, comprise a trilogy: *Malone Dies* (1951; English version, 1956), *Molloy* (1951; English version, 1955) and *The Unnamable* (1953; English version, 1958). Like much of Beckett's work, which includes plays, short prose pieces and poems, these three novels are characterised by moods of negation, despair and hopelessness but also by elements of grim humour. Beckett was awarded the Nobel Prize for Literature in 1969.

The 1950s: Anthony Powell, Lawrence Durrell, Angus Wilson and Barbara Pym

Anthony Powell (b. 1905) wrote some amusing novels in the 1930s, rather like those of Evelyn Waugh: *Afternoon Men* (1931), *Venusberg* (1932), *From a View to a Death* (1933), *Agents and Patients* (1936) and *What's Become of Waring?* (1939). His major work, a sequence called *A Dance to the Music of Time*, began to appear in the 1950s: *A Question of Upbringing* (1951), *A Buyer's Market* (1952), *The Acceptance World* (1955), *At Lady Molly's* (1957), *Casanova's Chinese Restaurant* (1960), *The Kindly Ones* (1962), *The Valley of Bones* (1964), *The Soldier's Art* (1966), *The Military Philosophers* (1968), *Books Do Furnish A Room* (1971), *Temporary Kings* (1973) and *Hearing Secret Harmonies* (1975). Its subject is the relationships of a large circle of friends and acquaintances spanning a period of sixty years and including about three hundred characters. It is written with gentle irony and sharp observation of psychology, manners and social class. Powell has also written *O, How the Wheel Becomes It!* (1983) and *The Fisher King* (1986).

Lawrence Durrell (b. 1912) published his best-known novels in this decade. *The Alexandria Quartet* consists of *Justine* (1957), *Balthazar* (1958), *Mountolive* (1958) and *Clea* (1960). These complex, erotic and exotic novels are notably experimental in their treatment of time. Durrell's other novels include *Tunc* (1968), *Nunquam* (1970), *Monsieur* (1974), *Livia* (1978), *Constance* (1982), *Sebastian* (1983) and *Quinx* (1985).

Angus Wilson (b. 1913) first achieved success with two collections of short stories, *The Wrong Set* (1949) and *Such Darling Dodos* (1952). His novels are *Hemlock and After* (1952), *Anglo-Saxon Attitudes* (1956), *The Middle Age of Mrs Eliot* (1958), *The Old Men at the Zoo* (1961), *Late Call* (1964), *No Laughing Matter* (1967), *As If By Magic* (1973) and *Setting the World on Fire* (1980). An admirer of Dickens, Dostoevsky, Proust and Virginia Woolf, Angus Wilson writes in a realistic, detailed manner with convincing renderings of conversation, although this air of realism does not preclude him from using fantasy and symbolism, especially in his later work. The people and milieux he deals with are predominantly middle-class. His subject-matter is personal relationships, often amongst middle-aged men and women. Class is an important element in some of his work, which is remarkably varied.

Barbara Pym (1913–80) wrote quiet fiction typically dealing with the lives of single, middle-class women in a sympathetic, observant manner, tinged with comedy. Her novels include *Some Tame Gazelle* (1950), *Excellent Women* (1952), *Jane and Prudence* (1953), *Less than Angels* (1955), *A Glass of Blessings* (1958), *No Fond Return of Love* (1961), *Quartet in Autumn* (1977), *The Sweet Dove Died* (1978), *A Few Green Leaves* (1980), *An Unsuitable Attachment* (1982; written 1961–63); *Crampton Hodnet* (1985; written 1939–40); *An Academic Question* (1986; written 1970–71) and *Civil to Strangers and Other Writings* (1987; written 1936, 1940–41).

Kingsley Amis, John Wain and Northern Working-Class Novelists

Other novelists of the 1950s took a disillusioned, ironical look at the postwar world, just as many of the new poets and playwrights of the period did. Distrusting anything grandiose and experimental, they wrote in wryly amusing and observant ways about people of no particular privileges, wealth or pretensions. William Cooper's *Scenes of Provincial Life* (1950), with its significant title, was a forerunner of the disrespectful, non-metropolitan stance which they adopted.

The most accomplished of these writers is Kingsley Amis (b. 1922), whose novels are *Lucky Jim* (1954), *That Uncertain Feeling* (1955), *I Like It Here* (1958), *Take a Girl Like You* (1960), *One Fat Englishman* (1963), *The Anti-Death League* (1966), *I Want It Now*

(1968), *The Green Man* (1969), *Girl, 20* (1971), *The Riverside Villas Murder* (1973), *Ending Up* (1974), *The Alteration* (1976), *Jake's Thing* (1978), *Russian Hide-and-Seek* (1980), *Stanley and the Women* (1984), *The Old Devils* (1986), *Difficulties with Girls* (1988) and *The Folks That Live on the Hill* (1990). As a moral novelist, Amis writes with economy, precision, wit and cynical commonsense, constantly puncturing affectations and falsity. *Lucky Jim*, with its account of the fortunes and misfortunes of a provincial university teacher, has become one of the classic comic novels of the past thirty years.

Another versatile novelist is John Wain (b. 1925), whose *Hurry on Down* (1953) achieved the same kind of status and popularity as *Lucky Jim*. His other novels include *Living in the Present* (1955), *The Contenders* (1958), *A Travelling Woman* (1959), *Strike the Father Dead* (1962), *The Young Visitors* (1965), *A Winter in the Hills* (1974), *Young Shoulders* (1982) and *Where the Rivers Meet* (1988).

Novelists writing of life amongst the working classes, especially in the north of England, also came to the fore in the 1950s. John Braine (1922–86) wrote *Room at the Top* (1957) about a go-getting young man, Joe Lampton. His subsequent novels, which vary in theme, include *The Vodi* (1959), *Life at the Top* (1962), *The Crying Game* (1964), *Stay With Me Till Morning* (1970), *The Queen of a Distant Country* (1972), *Waiting for Sheila* (1976), *One and Last Love* (1981) *The Two of Us* (1984) and *These Golden Days* (1985). Alan Sillitoe (b. 1928) made his reputation with *Saturday Night and Sunday Morning* (1958) and went on to write novels of different kinds, including *The General* (1960), *Key to the Door* (1961), *The Death of William Posters* (1965), *A Start in Life* (1970), *Travels in Nihilon* (1971), *Raw Material* (1972), *A Flame of Life* (1974), *The Widower's Son* (1976), *The Storyteller* (1979), *The Second Chance* (1981), *Her Victory* (1982), *Down from the Hill* (1984), *Life Goes On* (1985), *Out of the Whirlpool* (1988) and *The Open Door* (1989). Stan Barstow (b. 1928) wrote *A Kind of Loving* (1960); the best-known of his other novels is *A Raging Calm* (1968) and his latest is *Give Us This Day* (1989). The first novel by David Storey (b. 1933) was *This Sporting Life* (1962), about Rugby League football. His other books include *Radcliffe* (1965), *Pasmore* (1972), *Saville* (1976), *A Prodigal Child* (1982) and *Present Times* (1984). *Room at the Top, Saturday Night and Sunday Morning, A Kind of Loving* and *This Sporting Life*, stand together as the most famous novels of northern working-class life of the 1950s.

Fantasy and Experiment

Amis, Wain, Braine, Sillitoe, Barstow and Storey are mainly realistic novelists writing without linguistic experimentation or poetic devices. Their subject-matter, point of view and style are down-to-earth. Others of their contemporaries and near-contemporaries used new fictional forms or explored more imaginative areas. J. R. R. Tolkien (1892–1973) wrote *The Lord of the Rings* (1954–5), a trilogy about an imaginary world that for many readers has the power and attraction of genuine mythology. Mervyn Peake (1911–68) created a fantastic, grotesque world in *The Gormenghast Trilogy: Titus Groan* (1946), *Gormenghast* (1950) and *Titus Alone* (1959). Sir William Golding (b. 1911) achieved great success with *Lord of the Flies* (1954), his story of shipwrecked boys who revert to a primitive, savage state. His other novels are *The Inheritors* (1955), *Pincher Martin* (1956), *Free Fall* (1959), *The Spire* (1964), *The Pyramid* (1967), *Darkness Visible* (1979), *Rites of Passage* (1980), *The Paper Men* (1984), *Close Quarters* (1987) and *Fire Down Below* (1989). In complex, imaginative ways, Golding explores profound questions of morality, especially the nature of sin and evil. His novels are often difficult but original in technique and content.

Muriel Spark (b. 1918) has written *The Comforters* (1957), *Robinson* (1958), *Memento Mori* (1959), *The Bachelors* (1960), *The Ballad of Peckham Rye* (1960), *The Prime of Miss Jean Brodie* (1961), *The Girls of Slender Means* (1963), *The Mandelbaum Gate* (1965), *The Public Image* (1968), *The Driver's Seat* (1970), *Not to Disturb* (1971), *The Hothouse by the East River* (1973), *The Abbess of Crewe* (1974), *The Takeover* (1976), *Territorial Rights* (1979), *Loitering with Intent* (1981), *The Only Problem* (1984) and *A Far Cry from Kensington* (1988). Her novels are wittily written and sometimes fantastic. She presents the reader with provocative studies of moral and metaphysical issues. Her characterisation is vivid and memorable (*e.g.* Miss Brodie). There is occasionally an element of the fairy tale or myth in her novels (*e.g. The Ballad of Peckham Rye*).

Doris Lessing (b. 1919), a novelist deeply concerned with psychological, political and social tensions (especially in Africa), has also experimented with techniques of fiction. Her novels include *The Grass is Singing* (1950), the *Children of Violence* series (1952–69), *The Golden Notebook* (1962), *The Good Terrorist* (1985) and *The Fifth Child* (1988).

One of the most prolific and inventive of postwar English novelists is Iris Murdoch (b. 1919). Her novels are *Under the Net* (1954), *The Flight from the Enchanter* (1956), *The Sandcastle* (1957), *The Bell* (1958), *A Severed Head* (1961), *An Unofficial Rose* (1962), *The Unicorn* (1963), *The Italian Girl* (1964), *The Red and the Green* (1965), *The Time of the Angels* (1966), *The Nice and the Good* (1968), *Bruno's Dream* (1969), *A Fairly Honourable Defeat* (1970), *An Accidental Man* (1971), *The Black Prince* (1973), *The Sacred and Profane Love Machine* (1974), *A Word Child* (1975), *Henry and Cato* (1976), *The Sea, The Sea* (1978), *Nuns and Soldiers* (1980), *The Philosopher's Pupil* (1983), *The Good Apprentice* (1985) *The Book and the Brotherhood* (1987) and *The Message to the Planet* (1989). A professional philosopher as well as a novelist, Iris Murdoch raises philosophical issues in her fiction by implication, although she maintains that she writes primarily to entertain her readers. Her books contain numerous characters and incidents and often have complicated plots. Their surface attractions are considerable: narrative pace, lively descriptions of people and places, striking episodes and realistic, entertaining dialogue. She uses symbols (the bell and the sea in the appropriately titled novels, for example) and mysterious happenings and coincidences. She stimulates thought about such problems as intentions, appearance and reality, truth and falsity and the part played in life by contingency and chance.

The 1960s

Anthony Burgess (b. 1917) became well known in this decade with *A Clockwork Orange* (1962). He is a productive, versatile and experimental novelist, whose many other works include *Inside Mr Enderby* (1963), *The Napoleon Symphony* (1974), *Earthly Powers* (1980), *The End of the World News* (1982), *Enderby's Dark Lady* (1984), *The Kingdom of the Wicked* (1985), *The Pianoplayers* (1986) and *Any Old Iron* (1989).

Paul Scott (1920–78) is concerned in his principal novels with the English in India. These are the *Raj Quartet*—which consists of *The Jewel in the Crown* (1966), *The Day of the Scorpion* (1968), *The Tower of Silence* (1971) and *A Division of the Spoils* (1976)— and *Staying On* (1977).

John Fowles (b. 1926) is an ingenious and innovatory novelist, whose books include *The Collector* (1963), *The Magus* (1966, revised 1977), *The French Lieutenant's Woman* (1969), *Daniel Martin* (1977), *Mantissa* (1982) and *A Maggot* (1985).

A number of African and West Indian novelists writing in English established themselves at this time. Chinua Achebe (b. 1930), a Nigerian, wrote *Things Fall Apart* (1958), followed by various novels and collections of short stories. V. S. Naipaul (b.1932), a Trinidadian, became acknowledged as one of the leading novelists of the period. His novels include *The Mystic Masseur* (1957), *A House for Mr Biswas* (1961), *Mr Stone and the Knights Companion*

(1963), *The Mimic Men* (1967), *In a Free State* (1971), *Guerrillas* (1975), *A Bend in the River* (1979) and *The Enigma of Arrival* (1987). He was knighted in 1990.

Edna O'Brien (b. 1932) began her career in this decade with three novels that humorously and poignantly portrayed the lives and loves of young Irish women: *The Country Girls* (1960), *The Lonely Girl* (1962) and *Girls in their Married Bliss* (1964). Her other books include *August is a Wicked Month* (1965), *Johnny I Hardly Knew You* (1977) and *The High Road* (1988). After the publication of *Wide Sargasso Sea* (1966), interest revived in the novels of Jean Rhys (1894–1979), including *Good Morning, Midnight* (1939). *Wide Sargasso Sea* is a sympathetic, brilliantly imaginative account of the early life in the West Indies of Mr Rochester's first wife, Charlotte Brontë's fictional character in *Jane Eyre*. The prevalent tone of Jean Rhys's novels is one of sadness and anguish, as experienced and expressed by a lonely suffering woman.

Margaret Drabble (b. 1939) has written novels that subtly explore human relationships, often with women at their centre. These are *A Summer Bird-Cage* (1963), *The Garrick Year* (1965), *The Millstone* (1965), *Jerusalem the Golden* (1967), *The Waterfall* (1969), *The Needle's Eye* (1972), *The Realms of Gold* (1975), *The Ice Age* (1977), *The Middle Ground* (1980) *The Radiant Way* (1987), and *A Natural Curiosity* (1989).

The 1970s and after

Beryl Bainbridge (b. 1934) is a comically observant, ironical novelist who made her name with *The Bottle Factory Outing* (1974). Her other novels include *Harriet Said* (1972), *Sweet William* (1975), *A Quiet Life* (1976), *Injury Time* (1977), *Young Adolf* (1978), *Another Part of the Wood* (1979), *Winter Garden* (1980), *Watson's Apology* (1984), *Filthy Lucre* (1986) and *An Awfully Big Adventure* (1989).

Malcolm Bradbury (b. 1932) and David Lodge (b. 1935), both teachers and critics of literature, became well-known in the 1970s as novelists. They are associated particularly with "campus novels" dealing with the academic life. Bradbury's novels include *Eating People is Wrong* (1959), *Stepping Westward* (1965), *The History Man* (1975), *Rates of Exchange* (1983) and *Cuts* (1987). Lodge's include *The British Museum is Falling Down* (1965), *Changing Places* (1975), *How Far Can You Go?* (1980), *Small World* (1984) and *Nice Work* (1988).

For details of other present-day novelists, see Fiction in the 1980s (**M52-3**).

THE ENGLISH NOVEL IN PERSPECTIVE

This survey has been confined to the English novel, which should be seen in the perspective of the great European and American novels of the past two or three centuries. Its qualities—its particular strengths and weaknesses—can be truly judged only by considering it in relation to the work of such acknowledged masters as Cervantes; Stendhal, Balzac, Flaubert, Zola and Proust; Tolstoy and Dostoevsky; Goethe and Thomas Mann; Hawthorne, Melville and Mark Twain; Manzoni and Svevo. Comparisons are especially important when we look at modern novelists, since much of today's most significant fiction in English comes from the United States (*see* **M32-44**). It is necessary, therefore, to realise that this survey of the English novel deals with just one area of an extensive field.

II. SURVEY OF ENGLISH POETRY

INTRODUCTION

This section contains a brief outline of the development of English poetry. It ranges in time from the age of Chaucer, through Shakespeare and the Elizabethan period, onto the genius of Milton and the later Romantic flowering, before concluding with the Victorian era and the contemporary poetry of our own time. Many of the literary terms encountered here, which may be new to readers, are defined in the Glossary of Literary Terms (*see* **M44-50**). The section is intended to provide not only a starting point for all those interested in our poetic heritage, but also an easy reference guide for more general use.

CHAUCER AND HIS SUCCESSORS

Chaucer, Langland and others

The basic structure, grammar and vocabulary of English as we know it today were in existence by the middle of the fourteenth century, although pronunciation and spelling were markedly different and various dialects were spoken and written. The first great poet to make full use of the resources of this language, as used in the south-east, was Geoffrey Chaucer (1340–1400). He was at first influenced by French, Italian and Latin literature and he had extensive experience as a courtier and diplomat. These factors help to account for the range of style and content in his verse. One of his earliest works was a translation of part of the thirteenth century French allegorical poem, the *Roman de la Rose*, by Guillaume de Loris and Jean de Meung. His first independent work was the *Book of the Duchess* (*c.* 1370), written in commemoration of Blanche of Lancaster, the wife of John of Gaunt. It is a typical "dream poem" of the period, in which the Black Knight tells the sleeping poet of the virtues and beauties of the Duchess. In the *House of Fame* (unfinished; *c.* 1380), also a "dream poem", an eagle takes the poet on a flight to the house named in the title, discoursing on love, fame and other matters. The *Parliament of Fowls* (*c.* 1380), a third "dream poem", presents a St Valentine's Day debate amongst the birds on their choice of mates. In the late 1380s, Chaucer wrote *Troilus and Criseyde* in five books, recounting the tragic love story which he took from Boccaccio's *Il Filostrato* (*c.* 1335). The characterisation, especially of Pandarus, the go-between, is striking and convincing. Throughout the long poem, Chaucer conveys the drama, irony, pathos and humour of a complex situation in assured and subtle language. Love is again the subject of the *Legend of Good Women*, an unfinished "dream poem" roughly contemporary with *Troilus and Criseyde*, in which the poet tells the stories of nine women renowned for their fidelity.

Chaucer's masterpiece is the *Canterbury Tales*, which were probably begun about 1387 but were not completed. In the Prologue, Chaucer tells how a large group of pilgrims to Thomas Becket's shrine at Canterbury meet in April at the Tabard Inn in Southwark. He describes twenty-one of these in word-portraits. Each is supposed to tell two tales on the way to Canterbury and another two on the return journey. These tales are placed in a framework of dialogue amongst the pilgrims and of separate prologues. But the scheme was left unfinished and only twenty-four of the stories exist. The characters are varied in status and personality, and include a knight, his squire, many representatives of the Church, the wife of Bath, a merchant and a physician. Through Chaucer's vivid presentation, we are given a direct and realistic impression of aspects of English social life in the late fourteenth century. Their tales greatly differ in subject and style, sometimes corresponding to the personality of their supposed narrators. For example, the "Knight's Tale" is noble and chivalrous; the "Miller's Tale" and the "Reeve's Tale" are ribald and high-spirited; the "Prioress's Tale" is the pathetic story of the murder of the child, Hugh of Lincoln; the "Nun's Priest's Tale" is a version of the fable about the fox who tricks the cock.

Chaucer's metres include octosyllabics (*e.g.*, the *Book of the Duchess*), rhyme royal (*e.g.*, *Troilus and Criseyde*) and iambic pentameter (*e.g.*, the Prologue to the *Canterbury Tales*). Once modern readers have mastered his language and some aspects of pronunciation (remembering that the final "e" was usually spoken as a separate syllable), they can appreciate his directness and clarity, his precise observation and his constant play of quiet humour and irony, a typically English characteristic. His mature poetry has an effortless air and can be delightfully entertaining, especially in the portraits in the Prologue to the *Canterbury Tales:*

There was also a nun, a Prioress,
That of her smiling was full simple and coy;
Her greatest oath was but by Saint Loy;
And she was clepèd Madam Eglantine. . .

In his humanistic approach, his awareness of European tradition and his use of accentual verse, Chaucer is the ancestor of many of the English poets. On the other hand, *Piers Plowman*, probably written by William Langland (1330?–1386?) at periods between 1367 and 1386, belongs to the older English tradition of alliterative verse and religious allegory. In visions, Piers sees first a "field full of folk" all about their earthly business and then personifications of Holy Church, the Seven Deadly Sins and other attributes. The poem presents us with descriptions and discussions of religious, moral and social issues, emphasising the necessity of Christianity and a righteous life. Although the dialect in which the poem is written poses problems for the modern reader and uncertainties about versions of the text prevent it from being seen clearly as a unity, these difficulties are worth overcoming in

order to appreciate the power and beauty of many of its passages, including the opening:

In a somer seson whan soft was the sonne,
I shope [dressed] me in shroudes as I a shepe
    [shepherd] where,
In habite as an heremite unholy of workes,
Went wyde in this world wondres to hear.

John Gower (1330?–1408) wrote in French, Latin and English. His *Confessio Amantis* (*c.* 1390) contains over 33,000 octosyllabic lines in English, recounting numerous stories concerned with the Seven Deadly Sins and such matters as love, evil and the duties of princes. John Lydgate (1370?–1450?) who was influenced by Chaucer, wrote prolifically. Amongst his lengthy poems is the *Fall of Princes* (1431–38).

The Scottish Chaucerians

The above term has long been used to describe four Scottish poets, who may have been influenced by Chaucer to some extent. King James I (1394–1437) almost certainly wrote the *Kingis Quair* (*i.e.*, the "King's Book", *c.* 1424). In rhyme royal, the verses tell of the poet's seeing a lady walking in the garden below his prison window and of his subsequent dream, in which he visits the gods in heaven. Robert Henryson (1430?–1506?) translated and rehandled the *Moral Fables of Aesop* in thirteen poems and a brief prologue, all in rhyme royal. His *Testament of Cresseid*, again in rhyme royal, is something like a sequel to Chaucer's *Troilus and Criseyde*, relating the fate of the heroine, who is betrayed and afflicted with leprosy. Henryson's poems are not as sophisticated and urbane in tone as Chaucer's, but they combine a sense of morality with comic observation and comment. The output of William Dunbar (1460?–1513) is varied. Some of his poems are in the courtly tradition, their language rooted in Latin and French, for example, the "Thrissil and the Rois", celebrating the marriage of King James IV and Princess Margaret Tudor, whereas others are vigorously alliterative and colloquial, for example, "Tua Mariit Wemen and the Wedo" (*i.e.*, "Two Married Women and the Widow"), on the subject of unhappy marriage. Dunbar satirises aspects of Scottish life and society, sometimes irreverently and coarsely. In other moods, he is celebratory, reflective or moralistic. The "Lament for the Makaris" grieves for the loss of such "makers" as the "noble Chaucer", expressing a wider fear and melancholy in its Latin refrain, "Timor mortis conturbat me." Gavin Douglas (1475?–1522) combines Scottish and Latin traditions of poetry in his translation in rhyming couplets of Virgil's *Aeneid*. Amongst his original prologues to the separate books, that to Book VII, describing winter in Scotland, is remarkable for its force and precision.

The Ballads

Ballads are narrative poems (or songs, to be more accurate) telling tales mostly of war, heroism, death and love. Some of the most celebrated come from the Borders, commemorating events in the numerous hostilities that occurred in that area of Britain. Their authors and dates are unknown since they were sung or recited and not written down at first, though manuscripts exist from the thirteenth century onwards. Because of their oral origin, they are usually composed in stanzas of four short lines rhyming *abcb*, they often use the devices of question and answer and repetition, and they are expressed in unadorned language. Their dramatic power can be felt, for example, in "Sir Patrick Spens", with its economic narrative of drowning in shipwreck:

Lang, lang may our ladies wait
Wi' the tear blinding their ee,
Afore they see Sir Patrick's ships
Come sailing o'er the sea.

"Edward, Edward", with its refrains and repetitive questions and answers, culminating in Edward's curse upon his mother, is another ballad of great emotional impact. Some Romantic poets, notably Coleridge, admired the ballads and occasionally imitated their form and content.

THE TUDOR AGE

John Skelton

The poetry of John Skelton (1460?–1529) is sometimes close to doggerel, but it has energy, exuberance and strength of emotion. He usually wrote in very short rhyming lines with two or three irregular stresses in each, a distinctive style known, in fact, as Skeltonic. One must quickly read each poem as a whole, since Skelton achieves his effect by means of accumulation. "Speke Parrot" (1521) and "Why Come Ye Not to Court?" (1522–23) are satires, including attacks on Cardinal Wolsey. "Philip Sparrow" (c. 1508) laments the death of a pet bird and "The Tunning of Elinor Rumming" (c. 1508) is a comic and grotesque description of a woman alehouse keeper and her customers:

> Her loathly lere [face]
> Is nothing clear,
> But ugly of cheer,
> Droopy and drowsy,
> Scurvy and lousy,
> Her face all bowsy,
> Comely crinkled,
> Wondrously wrinkled,
> Like a roast pig's ear,
> Bristled with hair.

Though a poet at the court of King Henry VIII, Skelton writes in a popular, colloquial idiom, moving so rapidly that Robert Graves called him "helter-skelter John".

Wyatt and Surrey

Sir Thomas Wyatt (1503–42), who admired and translated the Italian poet, Petrarch (1304–74), has an historical importance in our literature since he introduced the sonnet into English. The best-known of Wyatt's sonnets is "My galley charged with forgetfulness". Most of his poems are lyrics in various metres, which have been criticised for their irregularities of rhythm but which have also been praised for their flexibility and their meaningful use of stress. There is a feeling of personal directness in some of his poems:

> They flee from me, that sometime did me seek
>   With naked foot, stalking in my chamber.
> I have seen them gentle, tame, and meek,
>   That now are wild, and do not remember
>   That sometime they put themselves in
>   danger
> To take bread from my hand; and now
>   they range
> Busily seeking with a continual change.

Many of Wyatt's poems first appeared posthumously in the collection, *Tottel's Miscellany* (1557), in which forty of the poems of Henry Howard, Earl of Surrey (1517?–47) were also printed. Surrey wrote sonnets (e.g., "The soote season, that bud and bloom forth brings") in the form later known as Shakespearean. In his translation of Books II and IV of Virgil's *Aeneid*, Surrey was the first English poet to use blank verse. His poetry is technically accomplished with a "literary" quality to it, making it less forthright than Wyatt's.

THE ELIZABETHAN AGE

Spenser

Usually regarded as the most significant poet since Chaucer, Edmund Spenser (1552?–99) established himself as an important writer with the *Shepherd's Calendar* (1579), which was dedicated to Sir Philip Sidney. In this, he used the pastoral genre, as did many poets of the period. The poem consists of "twelve Eclogues proportionable to the twelve months" from January to December and contains a variety of forms and metres, including rhyming couplets (e.g., "February" and "May"), six-lined stanzas (e.g., "October" and "December") and the elaborate verses of "Ye dainty nymphs" ("April"). As customary in Spenser, the vocabulary and syntax are deliberately archaic, in an attempt to devise a heightened, artificial diction appropriate to poetry. In the "General Argument of the Whole Book", the contemporary commentator, "E.K.", says that the eclogues are of three kinds: the "plaintive" (i.e., 1,6,11 and 12); the "recreative", about

love or the "commendation of special personages" (3,4,8): and the "moral", which "for the most part be mixed with some satirical bitterness" (2,5,7,9,10). The divisions are not, however, as clear as this scheme suggests: for example, love is the predominant theme of January. March, June and December, and a singing match is described in August. Furthermore, modern commentators have analysed subtleties of structure, noting, for instance, the circularity achieved by having Colin, one of the characters in the poem, speak both the January and December eclogues. *Amoretti*, a sequence of eighty-nine sonnets, was published with *Epithalamion* in 1595. The sonnets are conventional, idealised tributes to the lady the poet loves. The best-known of them is Sonnet 75: "One day I wrote her name upon the strand." *Epithalamion* and *Prothalamion* (1596) are celebrations of love and marriage. Spenser's other works include *Four Hymns* to Love and Beauty and *Astrophel*, a pastoral elegy on the death of Sidney (all 1596).

The *Fairie Queene* (1590, 1596), one of the longest poems in the English language, was intended to contain twelve books of twelve cantos each, but Spenser completed only six and part of a seventh. He conceived it as an allegory of twelve "moral virtues", explaining its plan in a letter to Sir Walter Raleigh; the basis of the scheme is that Gloriana, the Faerie Queene (i.e., Queen Elizabeth I), sends forth a knight on each of twelve days to redress a certain wrong. The completed books exemplify Holiness, Temperance, Chastity, Friendship, Justice and Courtesy. Book 1, for example, tells how the Red Cross Knight (Holiness) and Una (Truth) encounter such dangers as a lion (Reason), Archimago (Satan) and Duessa (the false Church of Rome). There are many layers and aspects of moral, religious and historical allegory in the poem, which also contains numerous plots and over two hundred major characters. Although the full power of Spenser's achievement cannot always be appreciated without interpretation of the allegory, his use of metre and language has led to his being called "the poet's poet". The principal technical feature of the *Faerie Queene* is the Spenserian stanza, exploited for the purpose of detailed, flowing description, narrative and comment, reaching a climax in the final Alexandrine. Other features are alliteration, assonance, repetition and subtle variation of rhythm. The result is a work of perfect technique, smoothness and musicality that evokes a dream-world of romance and chivalry, as shown at the beginning of Book 1, Canto 1:

> A gentle knight was pricking on the plain,
> Ycladd in mightie armes and silver shielde,
> Wherein old dints of deepe wounds did remaine,
> The cruell markes of many a bloudy fielde:
> Yet armes till that time did he never wield:
> His angry steede did chide his foming bitt,
> As much disdayning to the curbe to yield:
> Full jolly knight he seemd, and faire did sitt,
> As one for knightly giusts and fierce encounters
>   fitt.

Sidney, sonneteers and others

Sir Philip Sidney (1554–1586) wrote *Astrophel and Stella*, a series of sonnets and lyrics, between 1580 and 1584. These poems on the writer's love for his mistress were followed by many sonnet-sequences, including Henry Constable's *Diana* (1592), Samuel Daniel's *Delia* (1592), Thomas Lodge's *Phillis* (1593) and Michael Drayton's *Idea's Mirror* (1594). Spenser's *Amoretti* and Shakespeare's sonnets, to be described later, also belong to this genre, which (as C.S. Lewis has pointed out) is not so much narrative as a "prolonged lyrical meditation" on love and associated matters. Songs and lyrics, often on the theme of love, were also widely written and collected in anthologies like *Tottel's Miscellany* of songs and sonnets (mentioned above) and *England's Helicon* (1600); they appear, too, in the drama and prose romances of the time. Out of the many poets who wrote lyrics, Nicholas Breton (1545?–1626), Thomas Campion (1576–1620) and Richard Barnfield (1574–1627) should be remembered. Apart from sonnets and lyrics, the Elizabethan poets wrote in diverse forms and kinds: translations from the classics, satire, chronicles, narrative, and religious and reflective verse were all produced in the late sixteenth and early seventeenth centuries. Obviously, one cannot generalise about the styles of such prolific production, but it is possible to say that characteristic features are euphony of words and rhythms and fanciful comparisons and imagery.

Marlowe and Shakespeare

The most inventive and powerful verse of the age is in the drama, of which the favoured medium was blank verse. In his plays from *Tamburlaine* (1587?) onwards, Christopher Marlowe (1564–93) realised much of the potential of the form, using it above all for effects of nobility and terror. Then William Shakespeare (1564–1616) in his thirty-eight plays, most of which were written in blank verse, developed its technical possibilities to the full, as well as making incomparable use of vocabulary, imagery, syntax and sound.

Apart from his plays, Marlowe wrote *Hero and Leander* (1593?), which was completed by George Chapman (1559–1634). This poem, in rhyming couplets, tells of the love of the protagonists in sensuous terms, evoking passion and physical beauty. His lyric, "Come live with me and be my love", is one of the best-known poems of the period.

Shakespeare's non-dramatic poetry consists of *Venus and Adonis* (1593), the *Rape of Lucrece* (1594), the sonnets (probably written in the 1590s; published 1609), possibly *A Lover's Complaint* (printed with the sonnets), the *Phoenix and the Turtle* (1601) and miscellaneous poems in a collection attributed to him, the *Passionate Pilgrim* (1599). There are also the songs in a number of his plays. *Venus and Adonis*, written in six-line stanzas rhyming *ababcc*, tells of the goddess' love for Adonis, who does not requite her love and who is killed by the boar he is hunting. Probably influenced by Marlowe's *Hero and Leander*, the poem is remarkable for its eloquent, sensuous presentation of love and desire, verging on the erotic, and of the animals and countryside. Its most admired passages include Venus' address to Adonis ("Bid me discourse, I will enchant thine ear"), the description of Adonis' horse with his "hot courage and his high desire" and the simile of the snail

... whose tender horns being hit,
Shrinks backward in his shelly cave with pain,
And there, all smothered up, in shade doth sit,
Long after fearing to creep forth again.

The *Rape of Lucrece*, in rhyme royal, also treats the subject of sexual desire, Tarquin's rape of Lucrece. Less romantic and imaginative than *Venus and Adonis* and with fewer memorable passages, the poem has a strong, rhetorical force. Shakespeare's 154 sonnets, in the form thenceforth known as Shakespearean, seem to fall into two groups: the first 126 are addressed to a young man and most of the rest to a "dark lady". Much speculation continues concerning the circumstances of the publication of the sequence and the identities of the addressees and the "rival poet" who is alluded to in some of the sonnets. The sequence ranges over various aspects of love, time, eternity and poetic creation and encompasses many moods. Nearly all the sonnets have an originality and force of language far removed from the competent smoothness of so many of those in contemporary sequences. Amongst the most esteemed are Numbers 12 ("When I do count the clock that tells the time"), 18 ("Shall I compare thee to a summer's day?"), 30 ("When to the sessions of sweet silent thought"), 60 ("Like as the waves towards the pebbled shore"), 73 ("That time of year thou mayst in me behold"), 116 ("Let me not to the marriage of true minds / Admit impediments") and 129 ("Th'expense of spirit in a waste of shame / Is lust in action"). The *Phoenix and the Turtle*, in quatrains, is a somewhat cryptic tribute to the chaste marriage of two birds, symbolising "Beauty, truth, and rarity / Grace in all simplicity." Because of its sparingly expressed, rational-sounding argument, it has been classed as Metaphysical. Shakespeare's songs, over twenty in all, are in various lyrical measures, often dealing lightly and memorably with the universal themes of love and death (*e.g.*, "It was a lover and his lass" in *As You Like It* and "Fear no more the heat of the sun" in *Cymbeline*).

THE SEVENTEENTH CENTURY

The Metaphysical Poets

The characteristics of the Metaphysical Poets are the treatment of love and religion in philosophical,

intellectual and witty verse, which typically includes ingenious imagery and comparisons. Such characteristics were present to some extent in the poetry of Sir Walter Raleigh (1554?–1618) and Ben Jonson (1572?–1637) but are fully exemplified in the work of John Donne (1572–1631), George Herbert (1593–1633), Richard Crashaw (1613–49), Abraham Cowley (1618–67), Henry Vaughan (1621–95) and Andrew Marvell (1621–78). The Metaphysical Poets were attempting, in the words of Douglas Bush, "to create a medium fitted to render the realistic questionings, complexities, and diversities of private experience in a world of changing values".

John Donne's early poems, probably written in the 1590s, were satires, elegies and love-poems. Their rhythms are sometimes emphatically irregular, conveying the urgency of a speaking voice. The images and allusions are drawn from all branches of learning and experience, including philosophy, mathematics, cartography, astronomy and voyages of exploration. His elaboration of the simile of a pair of compasses, compared to a pair of lovers, in "A Valediction: Forbidding Mourning", is a typical example of a metaphysical "conceit" in its wit, aptness and development:

If they be two, they are two so
As stiff twin compasses are two,
Thy soul the fixed foot, makes no show
To move, but doth, if th'other do.

And though it in the centre sit,
Yet when the other far doth roam,
It leans, and hearkens after it,
And grows erect, as that comes home.

The opening lines of some of his poems have an exclamatory force (*e.g.*, "Busy old fool, unruly sun" and "For God's sake, hold your tongue and let me love"). In the latter part of his poetic career, Donne, who had become the Dean of St Paul's, wrote "divine poems", of which the Holy Sonnets are the most renowned. These include "At the round earth's imagined corners, blow / Your trumpets, Angels" and "Death be not proud, though some have called thee / Mighty and dreadful".

Compared to Donne's dramatic style, that of George Herbert is more measured, though intense in its feelings and sometimes unusual in its imagery and choice of words. His poems, which are exclusively religious, were collected in *The Temple* (1633), published posthumously. He gives particularity to his religious message by the use of worldly and domestic metaphors and similes: a "sweet and virtuous soul" is like "seasoned timber" [which] "never gives"; Love (*i.e.*, Heavenly Love) welcomes him as a guest: " 'You must sit down,' says Love, 'and taste my meat:/So I did sit and eat." A master of poetic technique, Herbert uses many interesting and complicated stanza forms.

Marvell's work is sophisticated and witty and yet penetrated by deeply-felt emotion. This fusion of intellectual control and feeling is shown, for example, in his "Horatian Ode upon Cromwell's Return from Ireland" (1650), which balances praise for the hero of the title with admiration for the demeanour of King Charles I at his execution: "He nothing common did or mean / Upon that memorable scene." The same combination of qualities is evident in one of the most famous of English love poems, "To his Coy Mistress" (*c.* 1670).

Henry Vaughan's primary importance is as a religious poet, as represented in his collection, *Silex Scintillans* (1650). His work blends mysticism and limpidity of expression, clearly shown in the first lines of "The World": "I saw Eternity the other night / Like a great ring of pure and endless light, / All calm, as it was bright."

The Caroline Poets

The term, Caroline Poets, is used for a number who flourished in the reign of King Charles I (1625–49). Robert Herrick (1591–1674) wrote mainly lyrical verse, gracefully dealing with love (sometimes in a mildly erotic manner), death, transience and eternity, and aspects of religion. "Fair daffodils, we weep to see / You haste away so soon" is one of the most popular of his numerous poems, which were mostly collected in *Hesperides* (1648). Thomas Carew (1594–1640), Sir John Suckling (1609–42) and Richard Lovelace (1618–57), all of whom were attached to the royal court, are known as the Cavalier Poets. Following the example of Ben Jonson, they wrote polished and urbane verse in various lyrical forms. Like Herrick's, their verse has been frequently anthologised and shares with his the qualities of memorability and elegance, *e.g.*, Lovelace's "To Althea, from Prison".

Milton

John Milton (1608–74) brought great dedication and learning to the writing of poetry. Modelling his work on the classics of Ancient Greece and Rome, he wrote at first in Latin as well as in English. The other profound influence on all his work was the Christian religion, allied to his belief in personal and social liberty. For about twenty years, in the middle of his career, he wrote no poetry but instead put his creative energies into the writing of prose in support of the Puritan, anti-Royalist cause. His first notable poem was the "Hymn on the Morning of Christ's Nativity" (1629), written in stanzas of skilfully elaborate rhythm and rhyme (*aabccbdd*) and with imagery and description that universalise the theme. "L'Allegro" and "Il Penseroso" (*c.* 1632), in rhyming tetrameter couplets, respectively depict the happy and thoughtful man. *Comus* (1634), a masque presented at Ludlow Castle, celebrates chastity and virtue in the person of the Lady, who resists the temptations of Comus. Written mostly in blank verse, varied with some heroic couplets and lyrics, this poetic drama displays Milton's richness of vocabulary, allusion and imagery. *Lycidas* (1637), an elegy in memory of Edward King, combines blank and rhymed verse. Based on classical precedents, it has nobility and eloquence transcending any particular personal expression of grief. It meditates not only on death and fame but also "foretells the ruin of our corrupted clergy". Milton's seventeen sonnets, in the Petrarchan form, are similarly characterised by elevated feeling and style. The most famous of these is "On his Blindness" (1655–65), which ponders the question of his usefulness to God's service and ends with a line asserting faith and patience: "They also serve who only stand and wait."

Paradise Lost (1667), a blank verse epic in twelve books, has as its theme the Fall of Man as a consequence of his "first disobedience" in the Garden of Eden. Milton declares his intention in the poem to "justify the ways of God to men". The work opens with a description of Satan and the rebellious angels in Hell and their debates. It continues with Satan's journey to Eden, which is presented in evocative detail, and with great debates on theological issues amongst the principal personages, including Satan, Adam, Eve and the Archangel Raphael. The conclusion of the epic is the expulsion of Adam and Eve from Paradise. The poem, which was dictated by the blind poet, is composed in a Latinised style, making frequent use of inversion and a Latin-based vocabulary. Combined with the steady rhythm, these features give the desired effect of elevation and splendour:

> Hail, holy Light, offspring of Heaven
>   first-born,
> Or of the Eternal coeternal beam
> May I express thee unblamed? since God is
>   light,
> And never but in unapproached light
> Dwelt from eternity, dwelt then in thee,
> Bright effluence of bright essence increate.
> Or hear'st thou rather pure ethereal stream,
> Whose fountain who shall tell? Before the sun,
> Before the heavens thou wert, and at the voice
> Of God, as with a mantle didst invest
> The rising world of waters dark and deep,
> Won from the void and formless infinite.

Paradise Regained (1671), in five books, tells of Christ's resistance to Satan's temptation in the wilderness and is therefore a sequel to the preceding epic. *Samson Agonistes* (1671), a tragic poetic drama modelled on Ancient Greek tragedy, presents the heroic self-sacrifice of the blinded Samson, based on the Biblical story. Its blank verse is remarkable for its varied rhythms. Like much of Milton's poetry, it includes extensive meditation and debate on religious ideas, including the justice of the "ways of God". It also contains vivid evocations of character. Milton's grave and learned style and his general air of sublimity in his treatment of tremendous subject-matter were widely admired and imitated for at least a century and a half after his death.

The Restoration Poets

Some of the poetry written after the Restoration in 1660 represents a reaction against Puritan morality and seriousness. It is ironical, cynical, worldly and occasionally coarse in tone. It deals with urban life, politics and sex in rhythms and vocabulary not far from those in colloquial English. The poet who typifies this mood and style is John Wilmot, Earl of Rochester (1647–80), who wrote love lyrics, epistles, lampoons and satires, such as "The Maimed Debauchee' (a self-portrayal) and "Upon Nothing". His work has energy and wit, and some critics have seen it as linking Metaphysical poetry to that of the Augustan age.

Dryden

John Dryden (1631–1700), the first Poet Laureate, is important as a poet, critic, dramatist and translator. His poetry is mostly "occasional", that is, prompted by external, topical events. His *Heroic Stanzas* (1659) were "consecrated to the memory" of Cromwell and yet his *Astraea Redux* (1660) was on the "happy restoration" of Charles II. *Annus Mirabilis* (1667), called "an historical poem", deals with the war with Holland and the Great Fire of London. Dryden's principal poetic works are generally considered to be his two satires: *Absalom and Achitophel* (first part, 1681; second part, mostly written by Nahum Tate, 1682) and *MacFlecknoe* (1682). The first of these depicts and comments on the intrigues of Lord Shaftesbury (Achitophel) to ensure that the Duke of Monmouth (Absalom) should succeed to the throne of King Charles II (King David). Ingeniously based on the Biblical story (in II *Samuel*), the poem consists of character portraits, speeches by the protagonists and authorial comment, presenting the case for the exclusion of Monmouth and yet at the same time evincing some sympathy for Absalom. Two of the most telling passages are those describing Achitophel ("Of these the false Achitophel was first, / A name to all succeeding ages curst") and Zimri, *i.e.*, the Duke of Buckingham ("A man so various that he seemed to be / Not one, but all mankind's epitome"). *MacFlecknoe* is a personal satire, mocking the pretensions of the poet and dramatist, Thomas Shadwell (1642?–92) and thus condemning literary dullness and stupidity. Both poems, though alluding to contemporary political and literary matters, can still be appreciated in themselves for their wit, humour and assurance of structure. Dryden's other important long poems are *Religio Laici* (1682), a defence of the Church of England, and the *Hind and the Panther* (1687), which defends Roman Catholicism (following Dryden's conversion to that faith in 1685). In addition he wrote odes (*e.g.*, in memory of Mrs Anne Killigrew, 1686; *A Song for Saint Cecilia's Day*, 1687; and *Alexander's Feast*, 1697), songs and lyrics, verse epistles, translations, and prologues and epilogues to plays.

Dryden wrote mostly in heroic couplets and aimed to achieve clarity and precision in his verse, which is therefore typical of the new, rational climate of ideas prevalent in the late seventeenth century. One feature of his satirical and topical verse is the use of argument. His poetry thus represents a fresh stage in the history of English poetry, which became correct and disciplined, according to its practitioners, who found distasteful the exuberance and freedom of Elizabethan and Metaphysical verse. They looked for their models in classical and French literature, admiring above all others the writers of the Augustan period in Rome. In fact, the term "English Augustans" is often used for Dryden, Pope, Swift, Johnson and many other writers of prose and poetry in the late seventeenth century and throughout the eighteenth century.

THE EIGHTEENTH CENTURY

Pope

Alexander Pope (1688–1744) dominated English poetry in the early eighteenth century. Following Dryden, who had shown the exactness and flexibility of expression possible in the heroic couplet, he exploited the full resources of the medium. The technical devices he uses include significant rhymes, variation of rhythm, the caesura to emphasise balance and contrast, and alliteration. His range of vocabulary and allusion is very wide and he is able to incorporate many tones of voice in his poetry: conversational, solemn, angry, confiding, high-spirited, and so on. Pope is a master of economical expression, reinforced by the tight metrical pattern of the heroic couplet.

In *An Essay on Criticism* (1711), he expressed the principles and practice of neo-classical poetry, asserting the necessity to follow the "Ancients" and to observe decorum and precision of style. The *Rape of the Lock* (final version, 1714) is a mock-heroic poem on the subject of the wrongful clipping of a lock of Belinda's hair. It is an elegant, amusing poem, with satirical and serious elements, especially in its treatment of behaviour in high society. *Verses to the Memory of an Unfortunate Lady* and *Eloisa to Abelard* (1711) are, in contrast, charged with passion and sensibility. Pope's translation of Homer's *Iliad* (1715–20) and *Odyssey* (1725–26), which established his fame, stands on its own feet as a brilliant English poem. In the following years, Pope increasingly turned to the writing of satire. The *Dunciad* (first version, 1728; second version, 1743) was a comprehensive attack on dullness and stupidity, perhaps influenced by Dryden's *MacFlecknoe*. Its climax is impressive, ending with the triumph of Chaos and Night:

Lo! thy dread Empire, Chaos, is restored;
Light dies before thy uncreating word:
Thy hand, great Anarch, lets the curtain fall;
And Universal Darkness buries all.

His four *Moral Essays* (1733–34), four Epistles to different people on the characters of men and women and the use of riches, show his concern for practical ethics as well as the satire of folly and weakness. *An Essay on Man* (1733–34) presents a philosophical view of the "nature and state of Man" with respect to the Universe, himself, society and happiness, based on the optimistic view that God's creation is purposeful and well-ordered and that "Whatever is, is right." Pope wrote a number of *Imitations of Horace*, predominantly satirical, between 1733 and 1738, and described and explained his work and his belief in the efficacy of satire in the *Epistle to Arbuthnot* (1735). This last-named poem, which is essential reading for an understanding of Pope's outlook, contains the famous word-portraits of Atticus (*i.e.*, Addison) and Sporus (*i.e.*, Lord John Hervey):

Let Sporus tremble—"What? That thing of silk,
Sporus, that mere white curd of ass's milk?
Satire or sense, alas, can Sporus feel,
Who breaks a butterfly upon a wheel?"
Yet let me flap this bug with gilded wings,
This painted child of dirt, that stinks and stings;
Whose buzz the witty and the fair annoys,
Yet wit ne'er tastes, and beauty ne'er enjoys.

Pope's weapon was satire, as he said, since he believed that by this means he could destroy pretence and foolishness. He is a poet of wit and polished technique, and at the same time one who excelled in philosophical and descriptive verse.

Swift, Goldsmith and Johnson

Jonathan Swift (1667–1745) is best-known as a writer of prose, particularly *Gulliver's Travels* (1726), but he wrote numerous poems throughout his career, from 1690 to 1737. Unlike his friend, Pope, he generally used rhyming iambic tetrameters. As he himself said, his poems "chiefly consist either of humour or satire", expressed in rapid conversational, lively verse, which is direct, original and non-literary. Like Pope and other contemporary satirists, he took human shortcomings as one of his main subjects:

Vain human kind! fantastic race!
Thy various follies, who can trace?
Self-love, ambition, envy, pride,
Their empire in our hearts divide.

("Verses on the Death of Dr Swift", 1731). He enjoys depicting some of the more squalid and repellent aspects of behaviour and physique, as in "A Beautiful Young Nymph Going to Bed" (1731). But his poetry is invariably vigorous and fresh.

Samuel Johnson (1709–84) wrote two major poems, *London* (1738) and the *Vanity of Human*

Wishes (1749), imitations respectively of Juvenal's Third and Tenth Satires. Each, in heroic couplets, is a formal, carefully considered work, sometimes Latinised in vocabulary and structure. In *London*, Thales, the imaginary speaker about to leave the capital, surveys the social and political corruption of the city "in these degenerate days", where "all are slaves to gold, / Where looks are merchandise, and smiles are sold." The *Vanity of Human Wishes* explores different manifestations of the subject announced in the title: political preferment, learning and military glory, for example, are shown to be ultimately vain. Great men like Cardinal Wolsey and King Charles XII of Sweden die in disgrace and oblivion. The latter's fate is summed up in four lines admired by T.S. Eliot:

His fall was destined to a barren strand,
A petty fortress, and a dubious hand;
He left the name, at which the world grew pale,
To point a mortal, or adorn a tale.

Johnson's other notable poems are the "Prologue Spoken by Mr Garrick at the Opening of the Theatre in Drury Lane" (1747), "A Short Song of Congratulation" (1780) and "On the Death of Dr Robert Levet" (1783). His poetry has weight and dignity, and so contrasts with that of Swift.

The *Deserted Village* (1770) is the most famous poem by Oliver Goldsmith (1730?–74), who affectionately describes life in "Sweet Auburn! the loveliest village of the plain," in the days before trade and the accumulation of wealth led to the destruction of rural "mirth and manners". The preacher and schoolmaster are praised for their dedication to the welfare of the villagers. Thanks to the discipline of the heroic couplet, the poet's affection, tempered with humour, never becomes sentimentality, as shown in the witty description of the schoolmaster:

In arguing too, the parson owned his skill
For e'en though vanquished, he could argue still.

Retaliation (unfinished 1774), in anapaestic tetrameters, is a collection of mock-epitaphs on the poet's friends, including Burke, Garrick and Reynolds. Two popular short poems are the "Elegy on the Death of a Mad Dog" and the song, "When Lovely Woman Stoops to Folly", both from his novel, the *Vicar of Wakefield* (1766).

Topographical and Reflective Poetry

Much of the poetry of Dryden, Pope and Johnson represents one of the main streams that run through the literature of the late seventeenth century and the eighteenth century. It is written in heroic couplets and has a rational approach. It is often satirical and deals with public, political and social subjects, associated with urban life. Excess, over-enthusiasm and undue flights of fancy are alien to it. Alongside this stream flowed another, though not always completely separately. Some poets, using a variety of metres and verse-forms, dealt with the countryside and the seasons, non-classical history and mythology, and the tenderer emotions of mourning, melancholy and regret. The most famous of these were James Thomson, Thomas Gray, William Collins and William Cowper. Minor poets of the same tendency were Edward Young (1683–1765), who wrote *Night Thoughts* (1742–45); Robert Blair (1699–1746), who wrote *The Grave* (1743), and James Beattie (1735–1803), who wrote *The Minstrel* (1771–74). At one time, literary historians called these poets "Pre-Romantic", since some of the features of Romanticism can be discerned in their work. Though rooted in eighteenth century conventions, it can be related to the interest aroused by the "Gothic" (Horace Walpole's novel, the *Castle of Otranto*, was published in 1765), the supposed poems of the Gaelic bard, Ossian (largely composed by James MacPherson in the 1760s), and Thomas Percy's *Reliques of Ancient English Poetry* (1765), a collection of traditional songs and ballads.

James Thomson (1700–48) wrote *The Seasons* (first published in collected form in 1730), consisting of four separate poems ("Spring", "Summer", "Autumn", and "Winter") and "A Hymn". In Miltonic blank verse, the poet describes and reflects upon the seasonal characteristics, activities and products, sometimes in the typical poetic diction of the period (*e.g.*, "copious exhalations" for "fogs", "household feathery people" for "cocks and hens", and frequent personifications) but on other occasions in particular detail, enhanced by the movement of his syntax and metre (e.g., the description of "the keener tempests" of snow in "Winter"). Amongst Thomson's other poems are the Castle of Indolence (1748), which is an allegory in Spenserian stanzas, and "Rule, Britannia!" (1740, in Alfred: a Masque, by David Mallett and Thomson in collaboration).

Thomas Gray (1716–71) was an erudite poet, whose work is full of reminiscences of classical and English literature. His ode "On the Spring" (1748) is an accomplished exercise in poetic diction. Contemporary with this are his odes "On the Death of a Favourite Cat, Drowned in a Tub of Gold Fishes" (related in a humorous, mock-heroic manner) and "On a Distant Prospect of Eton College", with its regret for lost happiness and forecasts of misfortune (its ending has become proverbial: ". . . where ignorance is bliss / 'Tis folly to be wise"). Gray's Elegy Written in a Country Churchyard (1751) can claim to be the best-known poem in the English language. It is a reflection in four-lined stanzas on the humble, unknown dead who lie buried in the churchyard and whose abilities, for good or ill, were never realised:

> Far from the madding crowd's ignoble strife
> Their sober wishes never learned to stray;
> Along the cool sequestered vale of life
> They kept the noiseless tenor of their way.

The poem ends with a depiction of the sad elegiast himself and with his epitaph. The perennial appeal of the poem lies in its memorable phraseology, its calm and sympathetic tone of voice and (to use the words of Dr Johnson) in its abundance of "images which find a mirror in every mind, and . . . sentiments to which every bosom returns an echo". In the Progress of Poesy and The Bard (1757), Gray was one of the first English poets to use the Pindaric Ode strictly, following a pattern of strophe, antistrophe and epode, in conjunction with an elaborate stanza-form and elevated language. The Progress of Poesy pays tribute to the power of "the rich stream of music" represented by poetry and traces its world-wide presence and development, ending with praise of Shakespeare ("Nature's Darling"), Milton and Dryden, and with a hope that the present-day poet can follow their example. The Bard tells of a Welsh bard's curse upon King Edward I and of his foretelling the story of his descendants, coming to a climax with an ecstatic description of Queen Elizabeth I. These two Odes may present difficulties with their allusions and complexities of construction but achieve their aim of nobly evoking the power of poetry and the vicissitudes of the monarchy.

William Collins (1721–59) was also a learned poet, writing in a Miltonic style on such "romantic" subjects as the evening, death, the poetical character and Highland "popular superstitions". His unrhymed "Ode to Evening" (1747) shows his accomplishments at their best, as in the four lines:

> Now Air is hushed, save where the weak-eyed bat,
> With short shrill shriek flits by on leathern wing,
>   Or where the beetle winds
>   His small but sullen horn.

William Cowper (1731–1800) was a prolific writer, often on quiet, domestic themes and the pleasures of the countryside and pet animals (e.g., "Epitaph on a Hare" 1783). He wrote hymns (e.g., "God moves in a mysterious way"), humorous verses (e.g., "John Gilpin" 1782) and poems that convey his own melancholy and despair (e.g., "On the Receipt of My Mother's Picture out of Norfolk" 1790 and "The Castaway" 1799). One of his longest poems, The Task (1785), in six blank verse Books, is a meditation and description, ranging over contemporary events and the rural scenes with which he was familiar—the passages on winter are especially notable. His style in his lyrical verse is unpretentious and clear, with a precision of metre and vocabulary. Perhaps more than any other eighteenth century poet, he moved away from Augustan formality, though everything he wrote is carefully controlled.

Smart, Chatterton and Crabbe

Christopher Smart (1722–71) wrote a certain amount of conventional verse but produced two remarkable, ecstatic poems, A Song to David (1763) and Jubilate Agno (1758–63, not published until 1939), characterised by elaborate symbolism, imagery and repetition.

Thomas Chatterton (1752–70) has mostly an historical importance for two reasons. First, in his so-called Rowley poems (c. 1769), which he pretended were written by a fifteenth century poet, he shows the mid-eighteenth century interest in the "Gothic". Secondly, his poverty and suicide led to his being considered in the Romantic period as the archetype of the neglected, suffering creative genius.

The works of George Crabbe (1754–1832) include The Village (1783), The Borough (1810), Tales (1812) and Tales of the Hall (1819). Mainly using rhyming couplets, Crabbe realistically portrays scenes and tales of rural life. "Peter Grimes", one section of The Borough, tells the tale of the fate of a fisherman, a "lost, lone man, so harassed and undone", tormented by the memories of the cruelty and murder he had committed. Familiar today in Benjamin Britten's operatic version (1945), the original poem has a disciplined pathos typical of the author. Though Crabbe's best work belongs to the nineteenth century and is contemporary with Romantic poetry, its language and form can be called Augustan. On the other hand, his detailed descriptions and his sympathies for the poor make it possible to relate him to the Romantic movement.

THE ROMANTIC POETS

Blake and Burns

Romanticism, with its interest in imagination, the individual personality, liberty, Nature, children and simple people, clearly manifested itself in the poetry of William Blake (1757–1827) and Robert Burns (1759–96). Blake's Poetical Sketches (1783) contain work imitative of Spenser and Milton but also fresh, lyrical verse, such as the song, "How sweet I roamed from field to field" and the "Mad Song". Songs of Innocence (1789), like most of Blake's works, was issued as an "illuminated" book, with the text and designs etched, printed and coloured by him, to form an integrated whole of words and pictures. This collection of lyrics was followed by Songs of Experience (1794), the complete book "showing the two contrary states of the human soul", to use Blake's own description. Using simple words, rhythms and stanza-forms, Blake sings in Songs of Innocence of love, tenderness and joy, as in "The Echoing Green," "The Lamb" and "Nurse's Song". This feeling is summarised in the first stanza of "The Divine Image":

> To Mercy, Pity, Peace and Love
> All pray in their distress;
> And to these virtues of delight
> Return their thankfulness.

In Songs of Experience, the emotions are those of anger, sorrow and suffering, epitomised in "The Sick Rose":

> O Rose, thou art sick!
> The invisible worm
> That flies in the night,
> In the howling storm,
>
> Has found out thy bed
> Of crimson joy,
> And his dark secret love
> Does thy life destroy.

Instead of the lamb, Blake now writes of "The Tyger". Blake's "prophetic books", including the Book of Thel (1789), Milton (1804–08) and Jerusalem (1804–20), are largely inaccessible to the general reader because of their mythology and symbolism devised by the poet, although some passages can be appreciated for intrinsic power and beauty. The prefatory lyric to Milton, "And did those feet in ancient time / Walk upon England's mountains green?" is familiar as a hymn in Parry's setting. All of Blake's work is individual and eccentric; it has an anti-rational approach to style and content. Blake conceived poetry as a religious and imaginative medium of expression.

Burns's poetry is based on Scottish literary conventions and traditions and owes something to such forebears as Allan Ramsay (1686–1758) and Robert Fergusson (1750–1774) and to popular songs and ballads. Poems, Chiefly in the Scottish Dialect appeared in 1786. Much of Burns's subsequent career consisted in his writing and adapting Scots songs. His narrative, satirical and epistolary poems are vigorous in metre and language; they are full of a delight in life and express a comic view of pretension and hypocrisy. "Tam O'Shanter", for example, in rhyming iambic tetrameters, is about the pursuit of the tipsy Tam riding home from the inn by a crowd of witches including "ae winsome wench and wawlie", to whom he had gleefully roared out, "Well done, Cutty-sark!" "Holy Willy's Prayer," in Burns's favourite six-line stanza, is a satirical portrait of a smug Calvinist. His hundreds of lyrical poems, often meant to be sung to Scottish airs, include "My luve is like a red, red rose", "Comin' thro' the rye", "A man's a man for a' that" and "Auld Lang Syne". Burns's poetry is popular in all senses of the word, dealing with the lives, loves, thoughts and desires of ordinary people, based on late eighteenth century Scottish life but also on a wide, instinctive understanding of life in general.

Wordsworth and Coleridge

William Wordsworth (1770–1850) and Samuel Taylor Coleridge (1772–1834) brought out *Lyrical Ballads* (1798), one of the key books of the English Romantic Movement. Most of the poems in the collection were by Wordsworth; the most famous of Coleridge's contributions was the "Rime of the Ancient Mariner". Wordsworth's aim, stated in his Preface, "was to choose incidents and situations from common life, and to relate or describe them, throughout, as far as was possible, in a selection of language really used by men." He writes, for example, of children and simple people, in such poems as "We are Seven" and "The Idiot Boy", using a style of extreme simplicity. "Tintern Abbey", in which he reflects on the power of Nature, is written in blank verse with a more formal vocabulary. In the ten years between 1797 and 1807, Wordsworth produced most of his best poetry. Although he modified the simple language of *Lyrical Ballads*, he invariably wrote in a plain style, with few ornaments and no extraneous musical effects. His choice of words is precise and they are exactly placed syntactically. Matthew Arnold said that "Nature herself seems . . . to take the pen out of his hand, and to write for him with her own bare, sheer, penetrating power." An example is the opening stanza of "Resolution and Independence" (1807):

> There was a roaring in the wind all night;
> The rain came heavily and fell in floods;
> But now the sun is rising calm and bright;
> The birds are singing in the distant woods;
> Over his own sweet voice the stock-dove broods;
> The jay makes answer as the magpie chatters;
> And all the air is filled with the pleasant noise of waters.

For Wordsworth, "Nature" meant partly the "rocks and stones and trees", the sky, the wind and the sea, animals and plants, particularly of the Lake District, and partly human nature, particularly as seen in unsophisticated people. The relationship between Nature and the human mind was the constant theme of his poetry.

In "Michael" (1800), the old shepherd of the title had lived for more than eighty years amongst the mountains, valleys and fields, which "had impressed / So many incidents upon his mind / Of hardship, skill or courage, joy or fear". The growth of the poet's own mind is traced in *The Prelude* (first version, 1805; revised and published posthumously, 1850), a poem in twelve books written in blank verse, intended as a preliminary to a philosophical poem, *The Recluse*, which was never completed, though *The Excursion*, its second part, was published in 1814. In the first two books especially, Wordsworth recalls scenes and moments which inspired him with a feeling that there was a vital force in the universe. Whilst skating on the frozen lakes, for instance, he sensed Presences and Visions that haunted him.

He wrote many sonnets in the Petrarchan form, ranging over many subjects. These sonnets include "Composed upon Westminster Bridge" (1802), "The world is too much with us" (1807), "Personal Talk" (1807) and "Surprised by joy" (1815). His

"Ode: Intimations of Immortality from Recollections of Early Childhood" (1807), in elaborate stanzas, celebrates the innocence and visionary powers he associated with childhood, the beginning of our earthly life, when "trailing clouds of glory" we come "From God, who is our home". The "Extempore Effusion upon the Death of James Hogg" (1835) is written in memory of Hogg, Scott, Coleridge, Lamb, Crabbe and Mrs Hemans.

Wordsworth is a philosophical, ethical poet, who sought to communicate with people in general and not with a privileged few, since for him the definition of a poet was "a man speaking to men". Two people who strongly influenced him were his sister, Dorothy Wordsworth (1771–1855), and Coleridge.

In his *Biographia Literaria* (1817), Coleridge recalled his co-operation with Wordsworth in *Lyrical Ballads*, pointing out that his own "endeavours should be directed to persons and characters supernatural, or at least romantic", but that he should treat them so truthfully that he would "procure for these shadows of imagination that willing suspension of disbelief for the moment, which constitutes poetic faith." The "Rime of the Ancient Mariner", his principal contribution to the collection, is an imitation of a traditional ballad, narrating the tale of the mariner's wanton killing of an albatross, the consequent fate that befell the ship and his companions, and his involuntary blessing of the beautiful water-snakes, which led to the lifting of the curse and his compulsion to tell everyone of the lesson he had learned: "He prayeth well, who loveth well / Both man and bird and beast." The vivid, economical depictions in the poem are much admired:

> All in a hot and copper sky,
> The bloody sun, at noon,
> Right up above the mast did stand,
> No bigger than the moon.

"Christabel" (written 1797–1800; published 1816), an unfinished "Gothic" narrative of magical powers, moonlight, castles and beautiful ladies, is written in rhyming lines of varying lengths, with four stresses in each line—the variations, Coleridge explained, are "in correspondence with some transition in the nature of the imagery or passion". "Kubla Khan" (written 1798; published 1816) is also unfinished. In his introductory remarks, Coleridge says that he dreamt the poem during a three hours' sleep, but was interrupted while writing it down by "a person on business from Porlock". Its fifty-four lines give a sensuous picture of a "pleasure-dome", its gardens, a 'deep romantic chasm", a river, caverns and ocean, and end with a vision of "an Abyssinian maid" playing "on her dulcimer". All three of these poems, therefore, represent the kind Coleridge agreed to write for *Lyrical Ballads*, though the last two were published later and independently. Amongst his other poems, three meditations on human relationships and Nature should be mentioned: "This Lime-Tree Bower My Prison" (1797), "Frost at Midnight" (1798) and "Dejection: an Ode" (1802).

Scott and Southey

Sir Walter Scott (1771–1832) achieved great fame with his verse narratives: the *Lay of the Last Minstrel* (1805), *Marmion* (1808), the *Lady of the Lake* (1810), *Rokeby* (1813), and others. They are historical stories of adventure, heroism and love, told in vigorously rhythmical, rhyming lines, usually iambic tetrameters. Though popular in Scott's time and for long afterwards, they are little read today. Scott also wrote songs and lyrics, including "Lochinvar" (in *Marmion*), "Proud Maisie is in the wood" (in the *Heart of Midlothian*, 1818) and "Look not thou on beauty's charming" (in the *Bride of Lammermoor*, 1819).

Robert Southey (1774–1843) also wrote a number of long narrative poems, such as *Thalaba* (1801) and the *Curse of Kehama* (1810), but as a poet is remembered nowadays only for a few ballads and lyrics: the "Holly Tree" (1798), the "Battle of Blenheim" (1798), "God's Judgement on a Wicked Bishop" (1799), the "Inchcape Rock" (1803) and the "Cataract of Lodore" (1823). His verse has unobtrusive qualities of precision of observation and expression and has suffered some undeserved neglect.

Byron, Shelley and Keats

George Gordon, Lord Byron (1788–1824) became the archetypal Romantic figure in Britain and Europe, not just because of his poetry but also because of his aristocratic birth, his looks, his unconventional morals, his identification with the cause of Greek independence and his early death. His narrative poems of colourful adventures, travel and love, sometimes partly autobiographical, brought him enormous popularity. These include *Childe Harold's Pilgrimage* (1812, 1816, 1818), the *Giaour* (1813), the *Bride of Abydos* (1813), the *Corsair* (1814), *Manfred* (1817), *Beppo* (1818), *Mazeppa* (1819) and *Don Juan* (1819–24). The central figure in many of them is a Byronic hero—a man at odds with the world, melancholy, heroic and defiant. The settings and events are highly coloured and exotic and the moods are those of excitement and passion, as in the description of the eve of the Battle of Waterloo in *Childe Harold's Pilgrimage*:

> There was a sound of revelry by night,
> And Belgium's Capital had gathered then
> Her Beauty and her Chivalry, and bright
> The lamps shone o'er fair women and brave
>   men;
> A thousand hearts beat happily; and when
> Music arose with its voluptuous swell,
> Soft eyes looked love to eyes which spake
>   again,
> And all went merry as a marriage bell;
> But hush! hark! a deep sound strikes like a rising
>   knell!

Satire, cynicism and disrespect are also characteristic of his verse, jauntily expressed in strong rhythms and unexpected, daring rhymes, shown fully in *Don Juan*, where he sometimes indulges in sharp, amusing authorial comments, achieving the sense of a personal, speaking voice in the medium of the *ottava rima*. The "Vision of Judgment" (1822), written in the same metre, is a satire on Southey, the Poet Laureate, and on the recently-dead King George III. Byron wrote songs and lyrics, the best-known of which is "So, we'll go no more a-roving" (1817). The *Prisoner of Chillon* (1816), in rhyming iambic tetrameters and told in the first person, is an affecting account of the prisoner's sufferings, partly alleviated by the "carol of a bird" that said "a thousand things" to him in his incarceration. Byron's prolific output of verse is fluent and encompasses a wide range of emotions, though some critics have thought it lacking in profundity.

Byron's friend, Percy Bysshe Shelley (1792–1822), was predominantly a lyrical poet, though he wrote some stinging satire and politically committed verse. *Queen Mab* (1813), in blank verse interspersed with lyrics, is an attack on tyranny, religion, selfish commercialism and war, with a prophecy of their destruction. Much of his poetry is inspired by a similar love of freedom and idealism, for example, his poetic drama, *Prometheus Unbound* (1820). His sonnet, "Ozymandias", ironically portrays the ruined statue of a "King of Kings". Shelley's lyrical poetry has a rapidity of movement and a sense of lightness and grace. Its imagery is typically of the wind, clouds, sky and water. Favourite descriptive words of his include "blue" and "azure". The title of André Maurois' biography of the poet, *Ariel* (1924), conveys this sense of an ethereal being. The "Ode to the West Wind" (1819), the "Ode to a Skylark" (1820) and "The Cloud" exemplify this characteristic. The delicacy of his verse is shown in a poem like the following:

> Music, when soft voices die,
> Vibrates in the memory;
> Odours, when sweet violets sicken,
> Live within the sense they quicken.
>
> Rose leaves, when the rose is dead,
> Are heaped for the beloved's bed;
> And so thy thoughts, when thou art gone,
> Love itself shall slumber on.

Some of Shelley's poetry is marked by a tender and occasional self-pitying melancholy, for example, "Stanzas written in Dejection Near Naples", "Rarely, rarely comest thou, / Spirit of Delight!" and "A Lament" (all published posthumously, 1824). "Adonais" (1821), in Spenserian stanzas, is an eloquent elegy on the death of John Keats. Critical opinion is divided on Shelley's achievement.

Some commentators see his poetry as vague and diffuse, whereas others see it as representing the high point of English lyricism.

The poetry of John Keats (1795–1821) is, in contrast, rich and sensuous. In a letter to Shelley, he advised him to "load every rift of [his subject] with ore". He published three volumes of verse: *Poems* (1817), *Endymion* (1818) and *Lamia, Isabella, The Eve of St Agnes, and Other Poems* (1820). The first line of *Endymion*, "A thing of beauty is a joy for ever", is the key to the main theme of his work. "Beauty" for Keats was associated with a passionate appreciation of flowers and lush vegetation, music and bird song, sweet scents and tastes, cool water in summer heat, and so on. He presents such experiences in highly descriptive, concentrated language, as in the description of the meal in the narrative poem, the "Eve of St Agnes":

> And still she slept an azure-lidded sleep,
> In blanchèd linen, smooth, and lavender'd,
> While he from forth the closet brought a heap
> Of candied apple, quince, and plum, and gourd;
> With jellies smoother than the creamy curd,
> And lucent syrops, tinct with cinnamon;
> Manna and dates, in argosy transferr'd
> From Fez; and spiced dainties, every one,
> From silken Samarcand to cedar'd Lebanon.

His famous Odes, written in complex stanza-forms, explore the implications of beauty in our lives: in the "Nightingale" and "Grecian Urn" odes, the contrasts between the transience of human mortality and the immortality of the bird's song and the work of art respectively; in "Melancholy", the relationship between sad and joyful feelings; in "Autumn", the affirmation explicit in the fruition of the season. Keats attempted a Miltonic style of poetry in "Hyperion" (in the 1820 volume) and the "Fall of Hyperion" (published posthumously), but left both poems unfinished. A spontaneous apprehension and presentation of experience was the principle he sought to put into practice, expressed in his phrase, "negative capability" (*see* the Glossary of Literary Terms **M48**). Many would consider Keats to be the quintessential Romantic poet because of the worlds of beauty and emotion he evokes in highly-charged words and imagery.

Moore and Clare

Two very different poets typify features of Romanticism. Thomas Moore (1779–1852) wrote a widely-read Oriental poem, *Lalla Rookh* (1817). Between 1807 and 1834, he wrote *Irish Melodies*, lyrics intended to be sung to Irish airs. These include such popular songs as "Believe me, if all those endearing young charms" and "Oft in the stilly night".

John Clare (1793–1864) wrote *Poems Descriptive of Rural Life and Scenery* (1820), the *Village Minstrel* (1821), the *Shepherd's Calendar* (1827) and the *Rural Muse* (1835), followed by other poems published posthumously. As the titles of his volumes suggest, his subjects were mainly rural: the seasons, flowers, birds and animals. His later poems especially also deal with the joys and pains of love and often have a melancholy tone. Clare's style is clear and simple in the best sense, with sharp and original perceptions.

THE VICTORIANS AND AFTER

Tennyson, Browning and Arnold

The Victorian poets to a large extent followed and developed the conventions of style and subject-matter established by the Romantic poets. They used all kinds of verse and metrical forms; they emphasised the imagination rather than reason; they dealt with the more elevated emotions of love, melancholy, honour, religious faith and doubt, self-sacrifice, and so on; they used language for euphonious effects. Principal influences were Spenser, Shakespeare, the Elizabethan lyrists and sonneteers, and Milton. On the other hand, they held the Metaphysical Poets, Dryden and Pope in low regard. In line with the tendency of the Victorian age, they introduced into their verse a strong element of morality and what Matthew Arnold called "high seriousness". Although these were general features of much of the poetry of the time, there were notable exceptions (Browning, for example).

Alfred Tennyson (1809–92) can be regarded as the

leading poet of the Victorian age. His poetry, which shows the typical characteristics outlined above, was popular and respected, and it was appropriate that he should be appointed Poet Laureate in 1850. His first volumes of poetry appeared in 1830, 1832 and and 1842. His subsequent major works were *The Princess* (1847), a "medley" (as he described it) of narrative and lyrics; *In Memoriam* (1850), a sequence of 132 poems, with a Prologue and Epilogue; *Maud* (1855), a monodrama; *Idylls of the King* (1859–85), fourteen poems on the Arthurian legend; and *Enoch Arden* (1864), a narrative. Tennyson's verse is mellifluous, making skilful use of all the available devices of sound, including rhythm, alliteration, assonance and onomatopoeia. This quality, combined with easy comprehensibility, gives his writing an immediate appeal:

Dry clash'd his harness in the icy caves
And barren chasms, and all to left and right
The bare black cliff clang'd round him, as he based
His feet on juts of slippery crag that rang
Sharp-smitten with the dint of armèd heels—
And on a sudden, lo! the level lake,
And the long glories of the winter moon.

(*Morte d'Arthur*, 1842). His descriptions are minutely particular, especially in such early poems as "Mariana", where we read, for example, of the "rusted nails", "a sluice with blackened waters", a poplar "all silver-green with gnarled bark" and a "blue fly" that sang "in the pane". Melancholy is a frequent mood in Tennyson's poems, partly caused by the effect on the poet of the sudden death in 1833 of his friend, Arthur Hallam.

He sometimes expresses a tension between the temptation to indulge oneself in a dream world of "art" and the need to shoulder one's worldly responsibilities. This conflict is shown in various ways in the "Lady of Shalott", the "Palace of Art", and the "Lotos Eaters" (all 1832, revised 1842). He reflects contemporary issues of concern, raised by class distinction, industrialisation, education, technological inventions, geological investigation and the idea of evolution. "Locksley Hall" (1842) expresses both optimism and pessimism about the age, but moves towards a feeling of confidence: "Forward, forward let us range . . ." The fullest exploration of questions of faith and doubt is in *In Memoriam*, where the poet's grief for Hallam is related to his feelings about science, religion, love and immortality. Eventually, but with many fluctuations, the poet's fears and misgivings yield to confidence in God's goodness. If his faith "had fallen asleep", then

A warmth within the breast would melt
The freezing reason's colder part,
And like a man in wrath the heart
Stood up and answered "I have felt."

As Poet Laureate, Tennyson produced official poems, of which the most famous are "Ode on the Death of the Duke of Wellington" (1852) and the "Charge of the Light Brigade" (1854). It is possible, then, to see Tennyson today as a writer versifying Victorian problems (and offering solutions) but also as a poet of unsurpassed technical accomplishment, above all in verbal music and description.

Robert Browning (1812–89), the other dominant poet of the Victorian period, was slow to win popular recognition, because of the difficulty and the unusual nature of his first poems, e.g., *Pauline* (1833), *Paracelsus* (1835) and—most notorious—*Sordello* (1840). He made his name with two collections, *Men and Women* (1855) and *Dramatis Personae* (1864), and set the seal on his reputation with the *Ring and the Book* (1868–69), a blank verse narrative in twelve books of murder and trial in seventeenth century Italy. Browning's poetic style is at an opposite extreme to Tennyson's in that it is rough, exclamatory and contorted. His syntax is disrupted and broken, and he uses interjections, colloquialisms and strange words. The poems are therefore sometimes obscure but at the same time they give an impression of excitement and energy. One of his favourite forms was the blank verse dramatic monologue, spoken by someone at a moment of crisis or significance. The reader of the monologue is plunged into the speaker's thoughts, which may unwittingly reveal weaknesses and faults of character. Fra Lippo Lippi, in the poem of that

title (1855), arrested by the watch in the streets of Florence, tells the story of his life, with its conflicts between the flesh and the spirit and with the way he upsets religious opinion by his painting physical actuality in a realistic manner. "Bishop Blougram's Apology" (1855) is a worldly priest's explanation of how he temporises with the spirit of the age. These monologues are psychological, moral and ethical studies, which express doubts and difficulties but which affirm the necessity to work and strive, summarised in the lines from "Andrea del Sarto" (1855):

Ah, but a man's reach should exceed his grasp,
Or what's a heaven for?

Browning's love poems, in a variety of forms and metres, are also direct and dramatic in their conveying a depth of intimate feeling. In "Two in the Campagna" (1855), he attempts to recapture the moment of ecstasy, first by means of a metaphor of a spider's thread but then concluding:

Just when I seemed about to learn!
Where is the thread now? Off again!
The old trick! Only I discern—
Infinite passion, and the pain
Of finite hearts that yearn.

In its analyses of tormented psychological states, in its unconventional poetic language and in its occasional obscurity, Browning's poetry anticipates some of the features of twentieth century poetry.

The poetry of Matthew Arnold (1822–88), one of the most influential of social and literary critics, belongs mostly to the early part of his career. The *Strayed Reveller* (1849), *Empedocles on Etna* (1852), *Poems* (1853), *Poems: Second Series* (1855) and *New Poems* (1867) are the principal volumes. His use of metre is sometimes free by Victorian standards, in such reflective poems as "A Summer Night" (1852) and "Dover Beach" (1867), but he also uses the sonnet (*e.g.*, "Shakespeare", 1849), blank verse (*e.g.*, "Sohrab and Rustum", 1853) and Keats-like stanzas (*e.g.*, the "Scholar Gipsy", 1853 and "Thyrsis", 1866). His expression is very much in the Romantic tradition, with "poetic" archaisms and highly descriptive phraseology and imagery in some of his poems. He is concerned to express the moral dilemmas of the age, in which many, including himself, had lost their religious faith. The "Scholar Gipsy", for example, begins with a sensuous evocation of a "half-reap'd field" on an August day and then describes the ghostly visits of the long-dead "scholar gipsy" to favourite haunts in the Oxford countryside. The poet urges the "gipsy" to escape all connection with the modern world:

O born in days when wits were fresh and clear,
And life ran gaily as the sparkling Thames;
Before this strange disease of modern life,
With its sick hurry, its divided aims,
Its head o'ertaxed, its palsied hearts, was rife—
Fly hence, our contact fear!
Still fly, plunge deeper in the bowering wood!
Averse, as Dido did with gesture stern
From her false friend's approach in Hades turn,
Wave us away, and keep thy solitude!

"Dover Beach" expresses a similar escapist attitude. Now that the "Sea of Faith" has retreated from our shores, the only recourse, the poet declares, is to find fulfilment in personal relationships: "Ah, love, let us be true / To one another!" Arnold's air of sadness and resignation, mirroring the mood of some of his contemporaries, makes a fascinating complement to the inspiriting, amusing mood of his critical prose.

Clough, Patmore and Meredith

Arthur Hugh Clough (1819–61) is remembered mostly for "Say not the struggle nought availeth", the "Latest Decalogue" and the song from *Dipsychus* with its chorus "How pleasant it is to have money" (all published posthumously). His wit and originality of content and metre are shown in his long, spirited poems, the *Bothie of Tober-na-Vuolich* (1848), a "Long Vacation Pastoral" in hexameters about a student's reading party, and *Amours de Voyage* (1858), an epistolary narrative in freely-used hexameters.

Coventry Patmore (1823–96) wrote, amongst other poems, the *Angel in the House* (1854–56), two sequences of twelve cantos each, framed by Prologues and Epilogues, on the theme of married love.

George Meredith (1828–1909), better known as a novelist, wrote poetry as individual in expression as his prose. Besides many poems on Nature (*e.g.*, those collected in "A Reading of Earth" 1885), he wrote *Modern Love* (1862), a deeply-felt sequence of fifty sixteen-line "sonnets" tracing the disintegration of a marriage. The most memorable of these are Numbers 1 ("By this he knew she wept with waking eyes"), 16 ("In our old shipwrecked days there was an hour"), 43 ("Mark where the pressing wind shoots javelin-like" and 50 ("Thus piteously Love closed what he begat").

The Pre-Raphaelites and Swinburne

The term, "Pre-Raphaelite," strictly applies to the movement in English painting in the mid-nineteenth century but by extension it is conveniently used to describe the poetry of Dante Gabriel Rossetti (1828–82), William Morris (1834–96) and others. Influenced by painting, medieval legends, Blake, Keats and Tennyson, they valued beauty of expression and form instead of conforming to ideas of morality and "high seriousness". Pre-Raphaelite poetry is pictorial, its language and subject-matter is often archaic, it tends to be sad and morbid, and it uses mystical symbolism drawn from religion and myth. Rossetti's "Blessed Damozel" (1849) is a perfect example, with its visualisation of the "damozel" in heaven as "one of God's choristers":

She had three lilies in her hand,
And the stars in her hair were seven.

She thinks of her earthly lover, who will join with her one day, amongst her handmaidens and Christ the Lord. All of this scene is realised in clear, concrete detail, like that in a Pre-Raphaelite painting by Rossetti himself. Rossetti's sonnets (1881), mainly on the theme of love, are rich in their presentation of physical experience (*e.g.*, "Nuptial Sleep" and "Barren Spring"). He also wrote "sonnets for pictures", the most striking of which is "*For A Venetian Pastoral*" by Giorgione.

William Morris's principal volumes of verse were the *Defence of Guinevere* (1858), the *Life and Death of Jason* (1867), the *Earthly Paradise* (1868–70) and the *Story of Sigurd the Volsung* (1877). Some of his poems, written in conventionally romantic language, with some archaisms, are descriptive (*e.g.*, the twelve on the months of the year in the *Earthly Paradise*). Others are narratives, which are ballad-like in the simple phraseology and their dramatic approach (*e.g.*, the "Haystack in the Floods"). Morris's favourite subject-matter was legendary and historical, from Norse and medieval sources.

Christina Rossetti (1830–94), the sister of Dante Gabriel Rossetti, can be mentioned here as a poet associated with the Pre-Raphaelites by relationship and friendship. *Goblin Market* (1862), a lively "fairy" poem of rhythmical virtuosity, was followed by numerous poems of a clarity and delicacy very different from the dense texture of her brother's poems and often concerned with personal and Christian themes.

Stylistically and personally, Algernon Charles Swinburne (1837–1909) has connections with the Pre-Raphaelite poets. He created a sensation with *Atalanta in Calydon* (1865), a poetic drama, and *Poems and Ballads* (1866). His powerful, hypnotic rhythms, alliteration and assonance were allied to subject-matter that was frequently sensual, morbid and pagan (*e.g.*, in "Faustine" and "Laus Veneris"). His subsequent volumes included *Songs before Sunrise* (1871), dedicated to Mazzini and expressing his enthusiasm for the cause of Italian independence, and a second series of *Poems and Ballads* (1878). In Swinburne can be seen the culmination—and some would say the decadence—of Romantic content and style. He exploited more fully than any other English poet the possibilities of word-music in the English language, making this the predominant feature of his verse as, for example, in *Atalanta in Calydon*:

For winter's rains and ruins are over,
And all the season of snows and sins;
The days dividing lover and lover,
The light that loses, the night that wins;

And time remembered is grief forgotten,
And frosts are slain and flowers begotten,
And in green underwood and cover
Blossom by blossom the spring begins.

Gerard Manley Hopkins

The poetry of Gerard Manley Hopkins (1844–89) was not published in his lifetime. His friend and fellow-poet, Robert Bridges (1844–1930) brought out an edition of his poems in 1918. His first major work was the "Wreck of the *Deutschland*" (1876), which was followed by shorter poems in various forms, typically celebrating natural beauty (*e.g.*, "Spring", "The Windhover" and "Hurrahing in Harvest") and praising and commemorating admirable human beings (*e.g.*, "Felix Randal" and "Henry Purcell"). Towards the end of his life he wrote the so-called "terrible sonnets", expressing moods of near-despair and anguish. As a Jesuit priest, he wrote all his poetry with a Christian purpose. Nature was a proof and a symbol of God's presence. "The world is charged with the grandeur of God" is the first line of one of his sonnets, and his poetry continually describes and analyses the relationship of ourselves and this earth to the Creator. In "Spring", for example, he devotes the octave of the sonnet to an evocation of the sights, sounds and vitality of the season, and then in the sestet sees the season as a sign of the beginning of life in Eden and as a representation of the "innocent mind and Mayday in girl and boy", which he prays Christ to capture.

Hopkins sought to present the essential quality and energy of all things in as particular and meaningful detail as possible, using the terms "inscape" and "instress" to express the achievement and the process (*see* Glossary of Literary Terms). In this respect, he has been compared to the Pre-Raphaelite painters and poets. Hopkins' original use of language made his work unpublishable in the Victorian age. He invented new compound words, used archaic, dialect and technical vocabulary, made grammatical experiments, used exclamations, questions, breaks and pauses, manipulated syntax for effects of emphasis and shock, elided and compressed. He made intensive use of alliteration, assonance and onomatopoeia, as for example, in "The Wreck of the *Deutschland*":

. . . How a lush-kept plush-capped sloe
    Will, mouthed to flesh-burst,
Gush!—flush the man, the being with it, sour or
    sweet,
Brim, in a flash full!

He devised a system of "sprung rhythm" (*see* Glossary), which depended on patterns of stress in order to bring metre close to the rhythms of the speaking voice. The opening of "Carrion Comfort", one of the "terrible sonnets", shows his fusion of rhythm and syntax to convey effect—in this instance, the effect of a mind suffering the tortures of doubt:

No worst, there is none. Pitched past pitch of
    grief,
More pangs will, schooled at forepangs, wilder
    wring.
Comforter, where, where is your comforting?
Mary, mother of us, where is your relief?
My cries heave, herds-long; huddle in a main, a
    chief
Woe, world-sorrow; on an age-old anvil wince
    and sing—
The lull, then leave off. Fury had shrieked "No
    ling-
ering! Let me be fell: force I must be brief."

The intensity and innovation of Hopkins' poetry were seen in the 1920s and after as characteristics which anticipated some of the developments in the verse of this century.

Poets of the 1890s

The aesthetic spirit of the 1890s, typified by Oscar Wilde, Max Beerbohm, Aubrey Beardsley and the *Yellow Book*, was apparent in a number of poets, who to various degrees wrote on such subjects as sensual love, religious rituals, visual beauty, sickness and death, using language that was studiedly euphonious and lushly descriptive. Besides Wilde (1854–1900), these poets included Francis

Thompson (1859–1907), Arthur Symons (1865–1945), Ernest Dowson (1867–1900) and Lionel Johnson (1867–1902). W. B. Yeats, whose work is described later, was associated with some of the writers and tendencies of this period.

THE TWENTIETH CENTURY

Thomas Hardy

By the beginning of the twentieth century, the reaction against the manner and matter of Victorian verse had become apparent. Some critics and poets, including Philip Larkin, have seen the poetry of Thomas Hardy (1840–1928) as essentially "modern" in that it has an individual clarity and sincerity that owes little to literary convention. Although Hardy had written poetry from the mid-nineteenth century onwards, he did not start publishing it until 1898, when his *Wessex Poems* appeared. In this and subsequent volumes Hardy published almost a thousand poems altogether. He also wrote *The Dynasts* (1904–08), an "epic-drama" mostly in blank verse, and the *Famous Tragedy of the Queen of Cornwall* (1923), a "play for mummers" in blank and rhymed verse. Hardy's poems are lyrical, sometimes echoing traditional songs and ballads. He speaks to us as he wants to speak, however, disregarding notions of correctness. As a result his expression is sometimes awkward but more often it is striking and memorable. Poignancy and irony pervade some of his verse. Hardy can relate an episode or describe a scene and bring out its moving implications, as in *Satires of Circumstance* (1914) and in such poems as the "Choirmaster's Burial" and "At the Railway Station, Upway". After the death of his first wife in 1912, he wrote a number of poems in loving memory of her, which many consider to be his best poetic work. An example is "The Voice", which begins:

> Woman much missed, how you call to me, call
> to me,
> Saying that now you are not as you were
> When you had changed from the one who was
> all to me,
> But as at first, when our day was fair.

As in his novels, Hardy expresses a sense of Fate (*e.g.*, in the "Convergence of the Twain", an ironical poem on the sinking of the *Titanic*) and pessimism. This latter feeling is sometimes moderated by hope (as in the "Darkling Thrush", in which the bird seems to know of a "blessed Hope", of which the poet is unaware) and acceptance of things as they are (as in "He Never Expected Much", a reflection on his eighty-sixth birthday). In his independence of spirit and style and his uncertainty about received truths of belief and morality, Hardy represents a twentieth century outlook.

Rudyard Kipling

Rudyard Kipling (1865–1936) has remained one of the most popular of English poets since the publication of *Departmental Ditties* (1886) and *Barrack-Room Ballads* (1892). These were followed by numerous poems, some of which appeared in his volumes of short stories. Influenced by music-hall songs, amongst other precedents, Kipling wrote verse of amazing vitality with a vigorous use of colloquialism and rhythm and with a gift for coining phrases and lines that once read stick in the mind: "Oh, East is East, and West is West, and never the twain shall meet" (the "Ballad of East and West"), the "Glory of the Garden", the "Female of the Species", and so on. His aggressiveness, certainty and championship of imperialism (though all these traits are not as clear-cut as they may seem) have made him uncongenial to some readers. But his poetry is capable of expressing powerful, complex emotions (*e.g.*, "Danny Deever") and clear "lessons" of morality in an unignorable way (*e.g.*, the "Gods of the Copybook Headings" and "If"). As in his prose, Kipling is always supremely technically accomplished.

W. B. Yeats

The poetic career of William Butler Yeats (1865–1939) lasted for over fifty years. At first, in the 1880s and 1890s, his poetry was lyrical and narrative, drawing on Celtic mythology and Irish traditions and influenced by Romantic and Pre-Raphaelite

writing. To this period belong such poems as the "Lake Isle of Innisfree" and "Down by the Salley Gardens" (both 1889). He became increasingly interested in symbolism and the occult so that a number of his poems, in for example, *The Rose* (1893) have a mystical quality. Later volumes show a change of poetic style and attitude towards plainer, barer expression. He found, as he said in "A Coat" (1914), that "there's more enterprise / In walking naked." Poems like "In Memory of Major Robert Gregory" (1919) and "Easter 1916" (1921) have the tone of the speaking voice as it describes, commemorates and meditates. Yeats' maturity of style can be experienced in "Among School Children" (1928), which begins in straightforward, precise description ("I walk through the long schoolroom questioning"), continues with memories of childhood and youth and reaches a climax with reflections on appearance and reality ("How can we know the dancer from the dance?"). Yeats continued until his death to write in a way that blends profound meditation and imaginative vision with an immediacy of language.

Ireland formed much of his subject-matter—its legends, history and contemporary affairs. These topics were sometimes mingled with personal interests and obsessions: his love for Maud Gonne, his protests at old age and his analyses of creativity. Ceremony, order and tradition were important to him. Yeats' fascination by the occult and his construction of complex, visionary systems of his own pose difficulties of interpretation in his later poems. Recurrent symbols and motifs are, however, of a universal kind, as these include the rose, the tower and its winding stairs, Troy, swans and dolphins. Much of what he believed and tried to practise is summed up in one of his last poems, "Under Ben Bulben" (1938), in which he adjures Irish poets to learn their trade and "sing whatever is well made."

The Georgian Poets

At the same time as Hardy, Yeats and T. S. Eliot were in their different ways breaking with Victorianism, some English poets were modifying its principles and practice in a more conservative manner. W. H. Davies (1871–1940), Ralph Hodgson (1871–1962), Walter de la Mare (1873–1956), Edward Thomas (1878–1917), James Stephens (1882–1950) and Rupert Brooke (1887–1915) are amongst those writers sometimes designated as Georgians: their work appeared in a series of five anthologies called *Georgian Poetry* from 1912 onwards, edited by Edward Marsh (1872–1953), an amateur of the arts. They wrote short, lyrical verse on limited, unambitious subjects drawn from the countryside or their own experience and emotions. Their aim was to emphasise beauty and to write in an undemanding, pleasant way, eschewing experiment and the heaviness of Victorian structures and didacticism. Many of their poems consequently became popular anthology pieces and school texts: Davies's "Leisure", de la Mare's "The Listeners", and Brooke's "Grantchester" are three examples. Edward Thomas rose above the limitations of the "group" and wrote poems of exact observation and scrupulous expression. Rupert Brooke is also associated with the First World War poets, who are described later (*see* **M29**).

John Masefield (1878–1967), who was Poet Laureate from 1930 until his death, should be mentioned here. His *Salt-Water Ballads* (1902) and *Reynard the Fox* (1919) were admired for their vigour. Some of his poems have been widely anthologised, including "Sea Fever" and "Cargoes".

For Imagism, which was an important poetic movement at this time, *see* **M47**.

T. S. Eliot

Thomas Stearns Eliot (1888–1965), more than any other poet, exemplified Modernism in English poetry. At the beginning of his career, he decisively parted from insularity and worn-out Victorian conventions and created verse that was alive to the complexities of the twentieth century, shown in its rhythmical patterns, its cosmopolitan air, its detachment and allusiveness. As he acknowledged, he owed a great debt to Ezra Pound (1885–1972), who not only wrote poems himself but also encouraged and shaped those of Eliot, notably the *Waste Land*. Eliot's earliest published poems include "Preludes", "Portrait of a Lady", the "Love Song of J. Alfred

Prufrock" and "Rhapsody on a Windy Night" (in *Prufrock and other Observations*, 1917). These are characterised by urban settings and imagery, suggested by London and Paris, and are written in strongly rhythmical, rhyming lines of varying lengths. "Prufrock", the outstanding poem of this group, is marked by self-deprecation and irony, with touches of wry humour. Eliot's next poems, collected in 1920, include "Gerontion", and some written in strict quatrains: "Burbank with a Baedeker: Bleistein with a Cigar", "Sweeney Erect", "A Cooking Egg" and "Sweeney Among the Nightingales".

The *Waste Land* (1922) consists of five sections: "The Burial of the Dead", "A Game of Chess", "The Fire Sermon", "Death by Water" and "What the Thunder Said." It is a highly allusive poem, incorporating references to literature, mythology and anthropology, and composed in a variety of metres and patterns. Further complexity and obscurity are caused by its fragmentary nature. The title refers to the devastation and hopelessness of the post-war world and also to spiritual barrenness on a universal scale. Eliot had in mind the myth of the Fisher King, the legend of the Holy Grail and other primitive beliefs, all alluding to loss, death and salvation. The poem in its very form indicates disintegration but moves towards hope at the end. After the futility and paralysis of the *Hollow Men* (1925), came the promise of religious comfort in *Ash-Wednesday* (1930), a sequence of six reflections that contain images and visions that reflect the poet's recent conversion to Christianity. References to the Virgin Mary, prayers to God, pictures of natural beauty and Biblical phraseology show the distance Eliot has moved from the settings and moods of his earlier verse. *Journey of the Magi* (1927) and *A Song for Simeon* (1928) had already dealt with specifically Christian subjects.

Four Quartets (published as a whole in 1943) consists of four poems, each divided into five "movements": *Burnt Norton* (1936), *East Coker* (1940), *The Dry Salvages* (1941) and *Little Gidding* (1942). The starting-point for each poem is a place that held personal or historical associations for the poet. For example, East Coker is the village in Somerset from which his ancestors emigrated to America in the seventeenth century. *Four Quartets* is a work that gravely meditates on time, eternity, religious beliefs and artistic creativity. Its language, form and metre are unspectacular, with a sense of weight and careful appropriateness, giving the poem serenity and nobility. In contrast, *Old Possum's Book of Practical Cats* (1939) is a collection of skilful, comic word-portraits. Eliot's completed poetic dramas are *Murder in the Cathedral* (1935), *The Family Reunion* (1939), *The Cocktail Party* (1950), *The Confidential Clerk* (1954) and *The Elder Statesman* (1959). After experimenting with different modes of dramatic language, he settled in his last three plays on a lightly-stressed blank verse, in an attempt to combine the movement of colloquial speech with formal metre. In all that he wrote, Eliot showed that it was possible to create a distinctively twentieth century form, style and approach, innovatory and yet based on tradition.

Poetry of the First World War

When the war broke out in 1914, Rupert Brooke seemed to speak for his generation when he wrote about it in glorious terms of patriotism, chivalry and nobility in five sonnets. "The Soldier" ("If I should die, think only this of me"), the most popular of these, expressed a dignified, self-sacrificing love of England. Siegfried Sassoon (1886–1967), however, wrote caustically of the realities of war as he witnessed it in the trenches: the suffering and death of ordinary soldiers made a bitter contrast with the cheerful platitudes uttered by officers and people at home in England (*e.g.*, "Blighters", "Base Details" and "The General"). His brevity, witty rhymes and sharply-accented metres give Sassoon's war poems a strong impact. Wilfred Owen (1893–1918), encouraged by Sassoon, wrote essentially about the "pity" of war. "Dulce et Decorum Est" ironically juxtaposes the sight and sound of men "drunk with fatigue" and subjected to a gas attack with the fine-sounding Latin motto. "Anthem for Doomed Youth", a sonnet, works out in Romantic phraseology and imagery the funeral rites of young men killed in battle (for example, the "shrill, demented choirs of wailing shells"). Owen's realism is qualified by a tenderness seldom present in Sassoon's poetry. Isaac Rosenberg (1890–1918) wrote urgent, free verse with pictorial

and dramatic qualities in tones of sympathy, anger and excitement. "Break of Day in the Trenches" has a melancholy apprehension of suffering touched with humour, symbolised by a "queer sardonic rat", whereas "Louse Hunting" depicts the "demons' pantomime" of nude soldiers hunting the vermin by candle-light. Under the pressure of war, these poets and others shed pretension and unnecessary decoration in order to reveal the truth as they saw it. They were writing "modern" poetry parallel to that being produced by Yeats and Eliot, although their subject-matter was inevitably more limited.

D. H. Lawrence

The prolific writings of D. H. Lawrence (1885–1930) included nearly a thousand poems written from 1906 onwards and appearing in such collections as *Look! We Have Come Through!* (1917), *Birds, Beasts and Flowers* (1923), and *Pansies* (1929). Lawrence's favourite medium was free verse, shaped by the demands of his subject, conveying emphasis and movement and generally giving a forthright impression of spontaneity. As he wrote to Edward Marsh, he "always tried to get an emotion out in its own course, without altering it". Animals, birds and flowers were among his most treated topics and he always sought to present their essential nature to the reader, using repetition and sensuous words and imagery and making clear his own personal responses. "Snake" is a famous example, in which the sinuosity, beauty and fearsomeness of the reptile are described along with the poet's ambivalent feelings of admiration, anxiety and shame. The sequence, "Tortoises", blends immediacy of presentation with a consideration of religious and sexual implications. Other poems have as their subjects death and the power of the imagination (*e.g.*, the "Ship of Death" and "Bavarian Gentians"). Some, especially squibs written in the later part of his career, have a satirical sting (*e.g.*, the "Oxford Voice"). Lawrence's poems are explorations of the same themes that pervade his novels and the style of his verse is close to that of his prose.

Poetry of the 1930s

The 1930s began with economic depression, saw the establishment of European dictatorships and ended with the outbreak of the second world war. A number of young poets wrote about the concerns of the age in their verse: W. H. Auden (1907–73), Cecil Day Lewis (1904–72), Louis MacNeice (1907–63) and Stephen Spender (b. 1909). Coming from similar upper middle-class backgrounds and all educated at Oxford, they also had in common, to begin with, an anti-establishment, "left-wing" attitude. Their poetic language was grounded in colloquial usage, their imagery and references were urban, technological and scientific, they used regular metrical patterns and they were sometimes elliptical and obscure. Topicality of allusion and moods of foreboding and fear and (to some extent) political propaganda were features of their verse. Eliot and Hopkins were among their influences. All four wrote poetry in subsequent years and by then had diverged in different directions, but they are so closely identified with the 1930s that it is this early work that will be mostly considered here.

Auden published *Poems* (1928), *Poems* (1930), *The Orators* (1932), *Look Stranger!* (1936), *Spain* (1937), *Another Time* (1940), and many other volumes, sometimes in collaboration. Influenced by Skelton, Hardy, Edward Thomas, Eliot, Old English poetry and traditional verse, he attacked his themes with liveliness, wit and sometimes self-conscious cleverness, shown, for example, in his striking opening lines: "To ask the hard question is simple;" " 'O where are you going?' said reader to rider;" "Lay your sleeping head, my love, / Human on my faithless arm." Typical "landscapes" were those of northern England, moors, mines and factories and typical references were those to public school life, solitary leaders and heroes, and psychoanalysis. In his later poems especially, he showed linguistic and metrical virtuosity, experimenting with metres (including syllabics) and using outlandish words. Auden's poems of the 1930s capture ominous moods engendered by the political and social developments of the time, for example "Consider" (1930) with its "handsome and diseased youngsters" and its "immeasurable neurotic dread" and "The Witnesses"

(1932) with "the hooded women, the humpbacked surgeons, / And the Scissor Man". His economy of phrasing, strong rhythms and unexpected references combine to make Auden's poems memorable evocations of their age. His later prolific output, with a few exceptions (*e.g.*, "In Praise of Limestone" 1948; "The Shield of Achilles" 1952), lacks the impact achieved by his work of the 1930s.

Day Lewis, MacNeice and Spender unite a more conventional lyrical style with topical concerns of the period. Day Lewis's "You That Love England" begins with such things as "the slow movement of clouds in benediction" and goes on to address the "victims/Of a run-down machine" who will be leaders "when zero hour is signalled". MacNeice's principal political poem is *Autumn Journal* (1939), a record of the Munich days, but "Snow" and "Sunday Morning", two short poems which are widely admired, have no reference to contemporary affairs. Typical "thirties" poems by Spender are "The Express" (1932), "Pylons" (1933) and "An Elementary School Class Room" (1939). As already indicated, it is important to remember that their poems of this decade are only a fraction of the four poets' output, which in every case is abundant and varied.

Dylan Thomas and others

Dylan Thomas (1914–53) published the following collections of poetry: *Eighteen Poems* (1934), *Twenty-Five Poems* (1936), the *Map of Love* (1939), *New Poems* (1943), *Deaths and Entrances* (1946) and *Collected Poems* (1952). Amongst the influences on his writing were such "romantic" authors as Marlowe, De Quincey, Blake, Keats and Lawrence. He was obsessed with words, especially with their sounds, as he himself said. Although the metre and form of his poems are strict and ingenious, his language and imagery are exuberant, derived from an emotional approach: "I make one image ... let it breed another, let that image contradict the first." Thomas wrote on the universal themes of Nature, life, death and childhood, using sexual, religious and natural imagery and symbolism. His first famous poem, "The Force that through the Green Fuse drives the Flower", depends for its effect on such words and ideas as "green", "red", "blood", "water", "clay", "wind", "heaven" and "stars", giving an impression of the surging forces of creation and destruction that affect all existence. Death is the theme of "And Death Shall Have No Dominion", "After the Funeral", "A Refusal to Mourn the Death, by Fire, of a Child in London" and "Do not go gentle into that Good Night". Thomas's later poems often deal with childhood and innocence—"Fern Hill", for example, a tumbling, lush description of boyhood joys, tinged with the knowledge of their inevitable end. His romantic, passionate rendering of human experience, relying on emotional and not rational responses from the reader, is the antithesis of the way in which Eliot and Auden were writing.

The early poems of Edith Sitwell (1887–1964) include the witty *Façade* (1922), but many think her greatest achievements belong to the 1940s, with musical, symbolic and mysterious poems like "Still Falls the Rain" (subtitled, "The Raids, 1940. Night and Dawn") and "Lullaby".

A number of poets in the 1940s took up a "romantic" stance, including those in the movement called "The New Apocalypse". Associated with this trend were Henry Treece (1911–66) and George Barker (b. 1913). The poets of the Second World War also inclined towards neo-romanticism: Alun Lewis (1915–44), Keith Douglas (1920–44) and Sidney Keyes (1922–43).

The 1950s

After the death of Dylan Thomas, a strong reaction occurred against his style of writing, shown in the work of those poets collectively known as "The Movement". These poets included D. J. Enright (b, 1920), Donald Davie (b, 1922), Kingsley Amis (b, 1922), Philip Larkin (1922–85), John Wain (b, 1925), Elizabeth Jennings (b. 1926), and Thom Gunn (b. 1929), who were all represented in *New Lines* (1956), an anthology edited by Robert Conquest (b. 1917), who also contributed to it. They aimed to write empirical, rational verse with an "intellectual backbone". Their subject-matter was unpretentious and precisely delineated and their

approach to it was quiet, ironical and downbeat. The language and rhythms of their poetry called no attention to themselves but were plain and unemphatic. Amongst the older poets they admired were Robert Graves (1895–1985) and William Empson (1906–84). In addition, Philip Larkin, for one, admired the work of Sir John Betjeman (1906–84), whose witty verse in traditional form and style on such topics as English suburban life and the Church of England led to great popularity and the office of Poet Laureate. His first volume of *Collected Poems* (1958) was a best seller.

Larkin emerged as the leading poet of "The Movement". After the *North Ship* (1945), which contained derivative verse (Yeats was a powerful influence), he published *The Less Deceived* (1955), the *Whitsun Weddings* (1964) and *High Windows* (1974). His *Collected Poems*, edited by Anthony Thwaite, appeared in 1988. His poetry is often melancholy and regretful, but it is written with sympathy and a dry humour. He blends colloquialism with formality, as in "Church Going", in which after observing and gently mocking "some brass and stuff / Up at the holy end" he at length concludes that "A serious house on serious earth it is." Like other "Movement" poets, Larkin has no grand theories, beliefs or philosophy, but accepts, sometimes reluctantly, things as they are.

Ted Hughes (b. 1930), the present Poet Laureate, came into prominence with the *Hawk in the Rain* (1957) and *Lupercal* (1960). Many other volumes of verse have followed, including *Wolfwatching* (1989). Unlike the "Movement" poets, Hughes writes forcefully and dramatically, with strongly-stressed rhythms and emphatic words. The energy, violence and cruelty of Nature, especially in the form of animals, birds and fish, are typical subjects of his poetry. "Hawk Roosting", celebrates the domination of this bird of prey over other creatures, and "Thrushes" celebrates the instinctive purposiveness of the birds' activities. Geoffrey Hill (b.1932), an intense, complex poet, began with *For the Unfallen* (1959). Subsequent collections include *King Log* (1968) and *Tenebrae* (1978).

The 1960s and after

Seamus Heaney (b. 1939), like Ted Hughes, is a poet who powerfully presents physical reality. In his early poems, collected in, for example, *Death of a Naturalist* (1966), *Wintering Out* (1972) and *North* (1975), this reality is conveyed in terms of Irish rural life and work, with emphases on earth, mud, rain, digging and so on. His language is dense and weighty, making effective use of clusters of consonants and monosyllables. He was elected Professor of Poetry at Oxford in 1989. Douglas Dunn (b. 1942) made his name with *Terry Street* (1969) and has published several other collections subsequently. Poets who began publishing their work in the 1970s include Tony Harrison (b. 1937), Craig Raine (b. 1944), James Fenton (b. 1949). Blake Morrison (b. 1950) and Andrew Motion (b. 1952). But a great many poets are active and it is impossible in this brief survey to choose any more for mention. Readers are therefore advised to consult the several comprehensive anthologies of modern verse that are available. Finally, they should bear in mind the fact that this short history has been confined (for reasons of space) to poetry written in the United Kingdom and that consequently only one part of the poetry of the English-speaking world has been considered here. For North American poetry, *see* **M32–44.**

LIGHT VERSE

Alongside serious English verse runs a stream of light verse, which deals with non-serious and sometimes superficial topics, usually in amusing ways. It can be satirical, nonsensical, warmly humorous, complimentary, impolite, appreciative or critical. Its primary aim is entertainment. It can take numerous forms but it is characterised by polished technique; rhythm and rhyme can be used to brilliant effect.

Some serious poets have occasionally written light verse, including Marvell, Gray, Cowper, Byron, Keats, Tennyson, Eliot and Auden. As this selection of names indicates, it can be found in most literary periods. Writers famous for light verse before 1800 include Matthew Prior (1664–1721), John Gay (1685–1732) and John Wolcot (known as "Peter Pindar," 1738–1819). But light verse flourished particularly in the nineteenth century and in the first half of the twentieth century. This development could be due to the "dissociation of sensibility" (*see* Glossary of Literary Terms, **M45**), to the widening of the reading public and to the extension of poetic form and subject-matter associated with the Romantic Movement.

One of the first prominent writers of light verse in the nineteenth century was Richard Harris Barham (1788–1845). Using the pseudonym, Thomas Ingoldsby, he composed the *Ingoldsby Legends* (first collected in 1840). These lengthy poems, often grotesque or Gothic, tell high-spirited and fantastic stories in ingenious rhymes and emphatic metres (often anapaests). The most popular is "The Jackdaw of Rheims," about the bird's theft of the Cardinal's ring. The Cardinal cursed the unknown thief

... in eating, he cursed him in drinking,
He cursed him in coughing, in sneezing, in winking,
He cursed him in sitting, in standing, in lying;
He cursed him in walking, in riding, in flying,
He cursed him in living, he cursed him dying!

Barham's contemporary, Thomas Hood (1799–1845) wrote serious verse (*e.g.*, the *Dream of Eugene Aram*, 1831; the "Song of the Shirt," 1843), but was a prolific comic poet, as shown in such collections as *Whims and Oddities* (1st series, 1826; 2nd series, 1827) and *Hood's Own; or, Laughter from Year to Year* (1839). He writes on all kinds of subjects, sometimes topics of the day, and is remarkable for his witty word-play, particularly his use of puns:

Ben Battle was a soldier bold,
   And used to war's alarms;
But a cannon-ball took both his legs,
   So he laid down his arms.

A *tour de force* is "No!", beginning with "No sun—no moon!", continuing with over forty more similar negatives and ending with "November!" "The Broken Dish" is a serio-comic reflection on the transience of life, based on the odd comparison: "life's as frail as dishes:"

Walking about their groves of trees,
Blue bridges and blue rivers,
How little thought them two Chinese,
They'd both be smash'd to shivers!

In contrast to Barham and Hood, Winthrop Mackworth Praed (1802–39) wrote sophisticated pieces (published in periodicals) about the life and manners of contemporary fashionable society—in other words, *vers de société*. He is urbane, precise, witty and amusing, as in "Goodnight to the Season" (1827), "A Letter of Advice (1828), "Arrivals at a Watering-Place" (1829) and "A Letter, from a Lady in London to a Lady at Lausanne" (probably 1831):

His stories and jests are delightful;—
   Not stories or jests, dear, for *you;*—
The jests are exceedingly spiteful,
   The stories not always *quite* true.
Perhaps to be kind and veracious
   May do pretty well at Lausanne;
But it never would answer,—good gracious!
   Chez nous, in a talented man.

Punch, established in 1841, carried much light verse in its columns, including work by William Makepeace Thackeray (1811–63), who also published verse elsewhere: the "Ballad of Bouillabaisse" (1849), "Little Billee" (1849) and the "Sorrows of Werther" (1855) have always been popular.

One aspect of light verse is nonsense, with which we associate two writers above all: Edward Lear (1812–88) and Lewis Carroll (the pseudonym of Charles Lutwidge Dodgson, 1832–98). Unlike most of the poets in this survey, both wrote for children, who were beginning to form a significant part of a writer's public. Edward Lear's principal publications were the *Book of Nonsense* (1846), *Nonsense Songs, Stories, Botany and Alphabets* (1871), *More Nonsense* (1871) and *Laughable Lyrics* (1877). The first of these books was a collection of over one hundred limericks (but with the last line echoing the first) illustrated by himself. The second contained such famous poems as the "Owl and the Pussycat" and "The Jumblies"; the third more limericks, amongst other things; the fourth included the "Dong with the Luminous Nose," the "Pelican Chorus" and the "Pobble who has no Toes." Apart from their comic invention, Lear's verses have intrinsic poetic qualities: imagina-

tion, beauty of language, memorable phraseology and rhythm:

They dined on mince, and slices of quince,
   Which they ate with a runcible spoon;
And hand in hand, on the edge of the sand,
   They danced by the light of the moon,
      The moon,
      The moon,
They danced by the light of the moon ("Owl and the Pussycat").

Many of Lewis Carroll's poems were included in *Alice's Adventures in Wonderland* (1865) and *Through the Looking-Glass, and What Alice Found There* (1871). Some were parodies. For example, "You are old, father William" and "Will you walk a little faster?", both from *Alice in Wonderland*, imitate poems by Southey and Mary Howitt respectively. But all triumphantly exist in their own right, possessing similar poetic attributes to those associated above with Lear. Besides the two just mentioned, the "Walrus and the Carpenter," "Beautiful Soup" and the "White Knight's Song" have become classics of nonsense verse. One of the most remarkable is "Jabberwocky," with its newly invented vocabulary:

'Twas brillig, and the slithy toves
   Did gyre and gimble in the wabe:
All mimsy were the borogroves,
   And the mome raths outgrabe.

The *Hunting of the Snark* (1876) is a long poem, subtitled "An Agony, in Eight Fits," telling of the quest for the "snark" undertaken by a crew comprising a Boots, a "maker of Bonnets and Hoods," a Barrister, a Broker, a Billiard-marker, a Banker and a Beaver. It is a nonsensical narrative and yet with a logic of its own. Many regard it as a masterpiece of Victorian verse. Amongst Carroll's other poems, "Hiawatha's Photographing," a parody of Longfellow, is noteworthy. There is general agreement that the work of Edward Lear and Lewis Carroll is pre-eminent in nineteenth-century light verse.

C. S. Calverley (1831–84) published *Verses and Translations* (1861), *Fly Leaves* (1872) and other collections. His verse is polished and quietly amusing, sometimes making use of parody and literary allusion. "The Schoolmaster," "On the Rhine" and "Peace" are amongst his most popular poems. The final stanza of "Companions, a Tale of a Grandfather," shows his economy of phrase and his humorous approach slightly tinged with pathos:

Was I haply the lady's suitor?
   Or her uncle? I can't make out—
Ask your governess, dears, or tutor.
   For myself, I'm in hopeless doubt
As to why we were there, who on earth we were,
   And what this is all about.

W. S. Gilbert (1836–1911), best-known for the Savoy operas he wrote with Arthur Sullivan, first became famous with the publication of his *Bab Ballads* (illustrated by himself), collected in 1869. These were lively, fairly short narratives, mostly written in jaunty ballad metre, recounting absurd events, as in the "Yarn of the 'Nancy Bell' ". The songs he wrote as parts of the libretti for the Savoy operas are inseparably associated with Sullivan's music but some of them can be appreciated by themselves for their linguistic verve and dexterity, for example, "I am the very model of a modern Major-General" (the *Pirates of Penzance)* and the Lord Chancellor's "nightmare" song from *Iolanthe.* J. K. Stephen (1859–92), whose verse was collected in *Lapsus Calami* (1898), wrote entertainingly, smiling at contemporary writers (as in "To R. K.", where he longs for a time "When the Rudyards cease from Kipling/ And the Haggards ride no more") and at Wordsworth, in his parody of the sonnet, "Two voices are there."

Throughout the period surveyed so far and well into the twentieth century, light verse continued to appear regularly in *Punch.* Two of its editors, Sir Owen Seaman (1861–1936) and E. V. Knox (1881–1971), were highly skilled, prolific versifiers. So were A. A. Milne (1882–1956) and A. P. Herbert (1890–1971), both of whom contributed to *Punch* as well as publishing light verse elsewhere.

The light verse of Hilaire Belloc (1870–1953), a writer of great versatility, includes his *Cautionary Tales* (1907), such as "Lord Lundy" and "Henry

King" ("The Chief Defect of Henry King/Was chewing little bits of String"). There is some similarity of style and approach between these and the earlier *Ruthless Rhymes* (1899) by Harry Graham (1874–1936). G.K. Chesterton (1874–1936), also a varied and productive writer, wrote a good deal of lively light verse, which is nevertheless strong in feeling and forceful in expression (e.g., "Wine and Water" and the "Song against Grocers," 1914). His friend, E.C. (i.e., Edmund Clerihew) Bentley (1875–1956), invented an abidingly popular form of comic verse, the clerihew, and published his *Biography for Beginners* in 1905. Such "biographies" as the following are amongst the most quoted and most imitated of all verses:

Sir Christopher Wren
Said, "I am going to dine with some men.
If anybody calls
Say I am designing St. Paul's."

The work, however, of the American poet, Ogden Nash (1902–71), is inimitable. In many collections, from 1931 onwards, he wrote verse in uneven, tumbling lines and ingenious rhymes, using puns and startling comparisons. He wittily observes the human condition (as in "Middle-aged life is merry, and I love to lead it") and he punctures social and literary pretension (as in "Very Like a Whale," where he mocks the use of simile and metaphor).

Few writers today concentrate exclusively on light verse, although many examples can be found in the work of William Plomer (1903–73), John Betjeman (1906–84) and Gavin Ewart (b.1916). One poet who comments amusingly on topics of the day in *Punch, Radio Times* and elsewhere is Roger Woddis (b.1917). The best light verse, as perhaps this survey has shown, forms a body of poetic work admirable for its wit and inventiveness and for its craftsmanship.

III. NORTH AMERICAN LITERATURE

AMERICA

Introduction

The assumptions underlying the writing of American literature have changed considerably since the early New England settlers, who compared their situation in the New World to that of the Children of Israel in the wilderness, wrote about their sense of exile. Today even those American writers who criticize the values of their native land do so in the secure conviction that it has an autonomous culture that can, and frequently does, totally ignore outside influences. Yet common characteristics, linking the diverse range of American writing that has appeared in the last three hundred years, are not difficult to identify.

The United States has always been quick to assimilate newcomers and the predominant social model of the 'melting-pot' has meant that successive waves of immigrants, from the English exiles of the sixteenth and seventeenth centuries to the Hispanics and Vietnamese of today, have rapidly come to see themselves as Americans. From very early on the Frontier ethic offered the promise of material and spiritual fulfilment to the individual. While its importance in the formation of the American character was not generally recognized until 1893, when the historian Frederick Jackson Turner's paper "The Significance of the Frontier in American History" articulated the thesis that the Frontier experience was a crucial factor in the shaping of the national psyche, the freedom and opportunities offered by the new land had long been a magnet drawing immigrants from the Old World. Turner argued that the encounter with the Frontier inculcated values of self-reliance in the settler and that this gave rise to an egalitarian and individualistic national character. Today the Frontier experience is a thing of the past, but the American Dream lives on in the form of a dream of capitalist success (which has been attacked by several writers, including Scott Fitzgerald, Arthur Miller and Edward Albee).

Significant changes have occurred in American writing in recent years, particularly with regard to the representation of the older American values and minorities. Since the changes in social attitudes in the 1960s and the publication of works like Dee Brown's *Bury My Heart at Wounded Knee: An Indian History of the American West* (1971), the American Indian has ceased to be portrayed as an evil outsider or romanticized noble savage (a European stereotype popularized in America by the work of James Fenimore Cooper). Similarly black American writing has now achieved widespread recognition and previously ignored classic works by women writers, like Kate O'Flaherty Chopin's *The Awakening (see* **M35**), have begun to receive the attention they merit.

Distinctions between highbrow and lowbrow art have never been strong in America and the culture has given birth to numerous popular forms, including such literary genres as the Western and the detective novel.

Early Puritan Writing

The most important early body of American

writing was that produced by the Puritan refugees who settled New England in the seventeenth century. Their work has influenced many later American writers and the American character more generally. It includes homiletic prose, autobiography (in which, as in classic religious autobiographies such as St. Augustine's *Confessions* and Bunyan's *Grace Abounding to the Chief of Sinners*, the prime subject of investigation is the writer's spiritual development) and tracts about government, important in the Puritans' attempt to develop a just theocratic society away from the persecution they had suffered in the Old World. The most significant Puritan prose writers include John Winthrop, Cotton Mather and Samuel Sewall. Puritan poetry habitually explores the predicament of God's "Elect", those who are seen to have achieved salvation in terms of their Calvinist beliefs. The most popular Puritan poet in his own day was Michael Wigglesworth. Today the work of Edward Taylor and Ann Bradstreet is more highly regarded. Both poets are typically Puritan in their use of analogical modes of expression, in which parallels are drawn between the material and spiritual; both anticipate Emily Dickinson (*see* **M35**) in their capacity for writing about religious faith in terms of simple, domestic details and events.

Eighteenth-century American Writing

Although the first major figures in American literature do not appear until the nineteenth century, there is a considerable amount of eighteenth-century writing which is of continuing interest in one way or another. In the Southern colonies of Virginia and Maryland local presses published a variety of works, with political writing centred on the colonies' relationship with England dominant after 1750. Benjamin Franklin's *Autobiography* (first complete version 1818) is a quintessentially American work, a plain tale of an ordinary man's rags-to-riches success story. Michel-Guillaume St. John de Crèvecoeur's *Letters from an American Farmer* (1782) attempts to define the distinctiveness of the American identity while giving a picture of aspects of American life at the time. Tom Paine's pamphlet *Common Sense* (1776) was enormously influential in promoting the case for American Independence. Thomas Jefferson, the prime drafter of the *Declaration of Independence* (1776), is the most important of the group of philosopher-statesmen who provided the basis for the American Republic. He also wrote *Notes on the State of Virginia* (1774) and was a fine prose stylist, who is rightly remembered by posterity as a literary as well as a political figure. Philip Freneau, whose lyrics include "The Wild Honeysuckle" and "The Indian Burying Ground", is the most noteworthy poet of the period. Charles Brockden Brown's *Wieland* (1798) is an outstanding early example of the American psychological Gothic tradition later to be pursued by Hawthorne and Poe. By the end of the century political independence from Britain was secure and, while some Americans had, like Washington Irving's mythical Rip Van Winkle, slept through its coming, a new era of cultural nationalism was assured.

Washington Irving (1783–1859)

Irving was the first American writer to achieve an international reputation. His first significant work was *A History of New York* (1809), a mock-history of the original Dutch colony, written under the pseudonym of Diedrich Knickerbocker. It was followed by *The Sketch-Book of Geoffrey Crayon* (1819–20), in which his most famous stories, "The Legend of Sleepy Hollow" and 'Rip Van Winkle', first appeared. Both these stories were derived from German originals, but Irving, who spent over twenty years of his life in Europe and was a friend of Scott, thoroughly Americanized them. The persona of Geoffrey Crayon was based on the eighteenth-century literary type of the foolish, sentimental traveller employed by writers like Goldsmith and Sterne and the delicate comedy of Irving's best sketches is reminiscent of the work of these writers. He also wrote *Bracebridge Hall* (1822), an Americanized version of the Flying Dutchman legend, *A Tour of the Prairies* (1835), *Astoria* (1836) and biographies of Oliver Goldsmith and George Washington.

James Fenimore Cooper (1789–1851)

The son of a wealthy landowner after whom the town where he spent much of his life—Cooperstown, New York—was named, Cooper was the first important American novelist to treat the subject of the Frontier. In his five "Leatherstocking" novels—*The Pioneers* (1823), *The Last of the Mohicans* (1826), *The Prairie* (1827), *The Pathfinder* (1840) and *The Deerslayer* (1841)—Cooper created the legendary character of Natty Bumppo, a civilized man who prefers the wilderness and the company of Indians to town life and a character who is in many ways a prototype for the Western hero. Widely regarded as the American Walter Scott, Cooper was a romantic novelist whose work was criticized by later chroniclers of frontier life like Mark Twain for its verbosity, wooden characterization and lack of realism. Cooper's knowledge of the Frontier *was* sketchy—he never went within a thousand miles of the Plains landscape in which Natty Bumppo, moving west to avoid the encroachments of civilization, dies in *The Prairie*—and he enjoyed his celebrity status as a major American writer when he lived for a period in Europe (1826–33), but the novels of the Leatherstocking Series succeed despite this, as expressions of a mythic vision of American individualism and the promise of the Frontier. It is in this that Cooper's enduring claim to fame lies. His numerous other novels include *Precaution* (1820), *The Spy* (1821), *The Pilot* (1824) and *Afloat and Ashore* (1844). In *The American Democrat* (1838) he outlined his republican political beliefs, while adhering to an essentially aristocratic view of society.

Edgar Allan Poe (1809–49)

One of the early masters of the short story form, Poe was also an outstanding poet and critic. After being orphaned at the age of three, he was brought up by his wealthy godfather John Allan with whom he enjoyed an uneasy relationship until around 1830. He attended school in England and had brief periods at the University of Virginia and in the U.S. army. In 1836 he married his thirteen-year-old cousin Virginia Clemm. He was distraught when she died of tuberculosis in 1847. In the latter part of his life he was often in poverty, and was given to bouts of alcoholism, after one of which he died prematurely. Poe is best known for his stories of the supernatural, which habitually focus on abnormal states of mind and demonstrate a greater concern with psychological terror than with what he saw as the "pseudo-horror" of Germanic Gothic fiction. "The Fall of the House of Usher", "The Masque of the Red Death" and "The Pit and the Pendulum" are among his finest work in this vein. They exemplify his belief in the importance of aesthetic unity, which was one of the main precepts of his critical writing, and are typical of his fiction in their use of powerful symbolism and striking special effects. Poe is also widely regarded as the father of modern detective fiction and in stories like "The Murders in the Rue Morgue" and "The Purloined Letter" the analytical powers by which his detective C. Auguste Dupin solves bizarre crimes anticipate the deductive reasoning of Sherlock Holmes. Poe's most famous collection of stories is *Tales of the*

Grotesque and Arabesque (1840), but this only contains a fraction of his best work. He wrote one novel, *The Narrative of Arthur Gordon Pym* (1838), a strange tale of polar travel which blends science with romance. Like his prose, his verse is characterized by sensual language and richly suggestive romantic imagery. His best known poems include "The Raven" and "Annabel Lee". Poe achieved little fame in his own day, but has been very influential since his death. His work was particularly admired by Baudelaire and the French Symbolists.

Ralph Waldo Emerson (1803–82) and Transcendentalism

Emerson was the leading figure in one of the most important philosophical movements in nineteenth-century America, Transcendentalism. Born into a family of clerics—both his father and grandfather were ministers—Emerson became a Unitarian pastor in Boston, but subsequently forsook the cloth. After travelling in Europe where he met Carlyle, Wordsworth and Coleridge, who were influential in the formation of his philosophy, he began to develop a faith which questioned Unitarian doctrines by emphasizing the essential divinity of man and the natural world. The Swedish mystic Swedenborg and Oriental philosophy were also important influences in the shaping of Emerson's Transcendentalist beliefs, which form the basis of his many essays. Among the most famous of these are "Nature", "The Over-Soul", "The American Scholar" and "Self-Reliance". His volumes of essays include *Nature* (1836), *Essays* (1841; second series 1844), *Representative Men* (1850) and *English Traits* (1856).

Transcendentalism was essentially idealistic (Plato was one of the heroes celebrated in *Representative Men*) and it took issue with the Calvinist determinism which had been paramount in New England thought until this time. While in one sense a highly localized phenomenon, its assertion of the capacity of individuals to control their own destiny is quintessentially American and can be related to the myth of the Frontier. Emerson lived a fairly retiring life in Concord, Massachusetts, though he frequently gave public lectures and was involved in the attempt to establish a cooperative community at Brook Farm, Massachusetts (1841–7). His essays were very widely read in the late nineteenth century and early twentieth century, both in America and abroad, but their popularity has declined since. Other leading figures in the Transcendentalist movement included Henry David Thoreau (*see* **M34**), George Ripley, Margaret Fuller and Bronson Alcott.

Nathaniel Hawthorne (1804–64)

Born in Salem, Massachusetts, Hawthorne was descended from an early New England Puritan family and had an ancestor who had presided as a judge at the Salem witch trials. Most of his fiction is concerned with the Puritan past and he explored its legacy in the present in his novel *The House of the Seven Gables* (1851) and also in the introductory "Custom House" section of his masterpiece, *The Scarlet Letter* (1850). Although he was briefly involved with the Transcendentalists' utopian Brook Farm community in 1841, Hawthorne's work represents a counter-strain in the American imagination and shares the Puritans' Calvinist view of character as being largely predetermined. Hawthorne criticized the Brook Farm community in his novel *The Blithedale Romance* (1852) and in one of his most famous stories "The Celestial Railroad" (a contemporary reworking of *The Pilgrim's Progress*), he satirized the perfectibilitarian beliefs of the Transcendentalists. Hawthorne's sophisticated use of allegory also demonstrates his debt to his Puritan literary forebears. Like the work of these predecessors, his fiction traces analogical correspondences between the material and the moral or spiritual. However in his hands allegory became a more complex mode, with individual symbols often carrying multiple meanings. His allegorical method can be seen in the operation of the central symbol of *The Scarlet Letter*, the letter of the title—an "A" (for "Adultress")—which the heroine Hester Prynne is forced by her seventeenth-century Puritan community to wear on her dress as a badge of shame.

Several possible significances are suggested for the letter and by the end its force has been completely transformed as Hester frees herself from the sense of guilt society has imposed on her.

Hawthorne's use of allegory marked an important step forward in American writing and led directly to the complex symbolism of Melville. At the same time his equation of the physical and spiritual has parallels with Emersonian thought and in this respect his Calvinist pessimism and Emerson's Transcendentalist optimism can be seen as opposite sides of the same coin. In the 1850s Hawthorne was American Consul in Liverpool and visited Italy, an experience which provided the setting for his novel *The Marble Faun* (1860). The Puritan past is also the prime focus of interest in Hawthorne's many fine short stories, which include "My Kinsman, Major Molineux", "Young Goodman Brown", "The Minister's Black Veil" and "Rappaccini's Daughter". These mainly appeared in *Twice-Told Tales* (1837; second series 1842) and *Mosses from an Old Manse* (1846). He also published the novel *Fanshawe* (1828) and the children's book *Tanglewood Tales* (1853).

Henry David Thoreau (1817–62)

After Emerson, in whose house he lived as an assistant and handyman from 1841–3, Thoreau is the most important figure in the Transcendentalist movement. He is best known for *Walden* (1854), a work in which he describes his experiences living alone in a hut he had built himself on Emerson's property at Walden Pond, near Concord. He moved in on 4 July, American Independence Day, 1845 and remained there until September 1847, keeping a journal of his daily activities. *Walden* is a seminal American book which provides an account of practical self-reliance that complements Emerson's altogether more idealistic and abstract emphasis on the capabilities of the individual. For those uninterested in Transcendentalism, it still offers a *Robinson Crusoe*-like record of a solitary existence lived close to nature and a naturalist's meditations on the ecological balance of the natural world. Thoreau's article "Civil Disobedience" (1849), in which he argues for the primacy of the individual conscience in matters of moral decision, may be seen as another expression of the self-reliance advocated by Transcendentalism. It grew out of his experience of having spent a night in prison for refusing to pay a poll tax which he felt supported slavery and influenced such later champions of nonviolent protest as Gandhi and Martin Luther King. The only other volume Thoreau published before his death was *A Week on the Concord and Merrimack Rivers* (1849). In later years his relationship with Emerson, which he once referred to as a 'long tragedy', became less close, as they both found one another increasingly contentious. He died an early death from tuberculosis. His several posthumously published works include *The Maine Woods* (1864) and *Cape Cod* (1865). Today his reputation which was dwarfed by Emerson's in his lifetime has outstripped that of his master.

Harriet Beecher Stowe (1811–96)

The daughter of a Congregationalist pastor, Harriet Beecher Stowe had an evangelical upbringing and was a staunch advocate of humanitarian causes throughout her life. She became one of the most popular novelists in nineteenth-century America after the publication of her classic novel about slavery, *Uncle Tom's Cabin*, in 1852. *Uncle Tom* was originally serialized in an abolitionist magazine with a limited circulation, but within a year of its book publication had sold 300,000 copies. Its writing was influenced by the demands of serial publication; it is essentially episodic in form and contains sentimental plot manipulations reminiscent of Dickens's serialized novels. While its prime target was the inhumanity of slavery, it reflected Stowe's belief that slave-holding was an index of a more general malaise in society. Generally regarded as an artless piece of writing, *Uncle Tom* succeeds because of its vivid characters and incidents and its passionate moral commitment. Abraham Lincoln referred to Stowe as the "little lady who made this big war [the American Civil War]". Twentieth-century assessments have been less kind to her, and her book has been attacked by black commentators such as James Baldwin for its creation of a stereotypical compliant black man in the title character. Other aspects of her liberal vision, such as her representation of the position of women in nineteenth-century America, continue to be regarded favourably. None of Stowe's other works, which include *The Mayflower* (1843), a collection of her sketches, and *Dred* (1856), a second novel about slavery, achieved anything like the success of *Uncle Tom's Cabin*.

Walt Whitman (1819–92)

Widely regarded as the most strikingly original and influential poet of nineteenth-century America, Whitman first found his distinctive poetic voice in *Leaves of Grass* (1855). In poems like 'Song of Myself' he created the distinctive "I" persona that was to be the hallmark of his verse. This was a representative democratic speaker who proclaimed his affinity and equality with all Americans: "I celebrate myself, and sing myself,/ And what I assume you shall assume,/ For every atom belonging to me as good belongs to you". Both his doctrine of universal brotherhood and his use of free-form verse as a correlative of his subject-matter were highly innovatory, though the latter owed a partial debt to the Romantic poets' belief in organic form. The language of *Leaves of Grass* was also considered highly unusual; it combines the American vernacular with technical terms, foreign words and neologisms.

Whitman's poetry was not initially popular and it was attacked for its sexual candidness, but in later life he became the centre of a literary circle. After the publication of the first edition of *Leaves of Grass*, he kept revising and adding to it and it went through ten editions before his death. During the Civil War he worked as a nurse in Washington and published two volumes of poetry about the war, *Drum Taps* (1865) and *Sequel to Drum Taps* (1865–6), which included his famous elegies for Abraham Lincoln, "When Lilacs Last in the Dooryard Bloom'd" and "O Captain! My Captain!". The 1871 edition of *Leaves of Grass* included his last important long poem "Passage to India" (from which E. M. Forster took the title of his novel), which celebrated the opening of the transcontinental railroad and the Suez Canal. Whitman was also a stirring prose writer: his most important prose works are the Preface to *Leaves of Grass* (1855) and *Democratic Vistas* (1871). He cultivated an image of vigorous robustness, but never married and there is speculation that he may have been homosexual. After 1873, when he had a stroke, he was a semi-invalid. Whitman's poetry has influenced writers as different from one another as Ezra Pound, Wallace Stevens and Allen Ginsberg.

Herman Melville (1819–92)

After working in a bank, as a schoolteacher and, briefly, as a cabin boy on a voyage to England, Melville spent the years 1841–4 at sea. His experiences on whalers and ashore in the Pacific region provided the basis for his most significant fiction. In the decade after he returned to America he published *Typee* (1846), *Omoo* (1847), *Mardi* (1849), *Redburn* (1849), *White-Jacket* (1850), *Moby Dick* (1851) and *Pierre* (1852). While *Typee* and *Omoo*, which were romanticized accounts of his time in the South Seas, met with a favourable reception, the remainder of these works in which he employed an increasingly complex allegorical mode, were poorly received by the public and Melville abandoned the attempt to support himself by writing. His subsequent fiction, which includes *Piazza Tales* (1856)—a volume in which his novellas "Benito Cereno" and "Bartleby" appeared—and *The Confidence Man* (1857), a satire on American materialism, largely deserted the sea. From 1866 to 1885 he worked as an Inspector of Customs. In the late 1850s he turned to writing poetry and between 1866 and 1891 published four volumes of verse. Melville became friendly with Hawthorne at the time he was writing his masterpiece *Moby Dick* and the novel shows a debt to the older writer in its fascination with darker aspects of human personality and its use of a symbolic method which represents an extension of Hawthorne's allegorical technique. It tells the story of Captain Ahab's obsessive hunt for the white whale Moby Dick, which has injured him in his youth. It offers a rattling good sea story and an encyclopaedic amount of detail about whaling, but far more is involved than just this. Ahab's search is as much metaphysical as literal, a Faustian quest for the infinite, and ultimately he suffers a tragic fate. The sole survivor from his crew is the narrator Ishmael, who like many of the heroes of classic nineteenth-century fiction—Natty Bumppo, Hester Prynne and Huckleberry Finn among them—is an outsider figure. At the end of his life Melville left the uncompleted manuscript of one of his finest tales *Billy Budd*, which was eventually published in 1924, by which time his genius had been recognized.

Emily Dickinson (1830–86)

Widely regarded as one of the two finest American poets of the nineteenth century (the other being Whitman), Emily Dickinson was born, lived and died in Amherst, Massachusetts. She led a reclusive existence almost totally devoid of external incident during most of her adult life, only leaving Amherst on a few occasions. Less than ten of her poems were published during her own lifetime, but since her death and the first appearance of a volume of her work in 1890 her reputation has grown steadily, particularly in recent years. Dickinson's major themes are death, renunciation, the privacy of the life of the individual soul and Nature. She writes about them in a slow-moving short verse line which perfectly expresses her minimalist vision. Initially regarded mainly as a love poet who expressed a sense of romantic disappointment in impressionist lyrics, she has increasingly come to be seen as a poet in the New England tradition, writing about her unorthodox Puritan faith in imagistic verse which defies easy paraphrase. Her highly subjective vision also appears to owe a debt to Emersonian individualism. In recent years her poetry has been the object of feminist interpretation. Ultimately, however, the cryptic complexities of her spare, economic verse (most of her poems are twenty lines or less in length) resist easy categorization.

Mark Twain (1835–1910)

Mark Twain (whose real name was Samuel Langhorne Clemens) is widely regarded as the first great writer of the American West. He actually came from Missouri, which in his own day was considered part of the South-West, and his style as a writer owes much to the traditions of humour in South-Western journalism. Twain was brought up in the pre-Civil War South in Hannibal, Missouri, a town which provided the basis for the Mississippi towns of his fiction, most notably the St. Petersburg of *Tom Sawyer* and *Huckleberry Finn*. As a young man he worked as a printer and Mississippi riverboat pilot, an experience which he chronicled in *Life on the Mississippi* (1883). When the outbreak of the Civil War stopped traffic on the river, Twain went to Carson City, Nevada, at the time of "silver fever" there, and later recorded his impressions of the West in *Roughing It* (1872). After achieving success as a public lecturer, an occupation he was to engage in for most of his life, he travelled to Europe and the Near East and in *The Innocents Abroad* (1869), his first major work, recorded the comic and irreverential responses of a naive American to the culture of the Old World. After his marriage to Olivia Langdon in 1870 he lived in Hartford, Connecticut. Twain is best known as the author of two novels about boyhood, *The Adventures of Tom Sawyer* (1876) and *The Adventures of Huckleberry Finn* (1884). While *Tom Sawyer* offers a playful satirical treatment of the Romanticism of the American South, a theme that concerned Twain in all his fiction, it remains essentially a boy's book. *Huckleberry Finn*, Twain's masterpiece, offers a far more probing social analysis, as the ingenuous first-person narrator Huck, who describes his raft journey down the Mississippi with the runaway slave Jim, unwittingly exposes the shortcomings of Southern society. The novel provides a celebration of the Frontier ethic and the freedom of the individual with the idyllic life Huck and Jim lead aboard the raft standing in marked contrast to the corruption they encounter whenever they step ashore. It has also been widely praised for its innovative and influential use of vernacular American speech. Twain made a great deal of money from his writing, but in later years ran into financial difficulties because of his involvement in speculative printing and publishing ventures. In his later works, such as *The Tragedy of Pudd'n head Wilson* (1894) and the long

short story "The Man That Corrupted Hadleyburg" (1899), his humour assumed a darker hue as his vision of man and society became increasingly pessimistic. This strain is most prominent in the posthumously published *Letters from the Earth* (1962), in which humour is outweighed by a misanthropic indictment of the human condition. Twain's other works include the comic short story which first made him famous, "The Celebrated Jumping Frog of Calaveras County" (1865), *A Tramp Abroad* (1880), *The Prince and the Pauper* (1881), *A Connecticut Yankee in King Arthur's Court* (1889) and *Following the Equator* (1897).

Kate O'Flaherty Chopin (1851–1904)

Kate Chopin (*née* O'Flaherty), the daughter of an Irish father and a Creole mother, grew up in fashionable St. Louis society. She lived an unconventional life for a Southern woman. Her masterpiece, the novel *The Awakening* (1899), caused a furore when first published, being widely attacked for its alleged immorality. Set on a Creole island, it charts the sexual awakening of a young wife and mother who questions the norms of female behaviour in her day. Distressed by the outcry occasioned by *The Awakening*, Chopin wrote no further fiction. Previously she had published the novel, *At Fault* (1890) and two collections of short stories, *Bayou Folk* (1894) and *A Night in Acadie* (1897), notable for their vivid pictures of the Creole and Cajun life she had come to know while married and living in Louisiana (1870–82). In recent years *The Awakening* has received the recognition which Chopin, ahead of her time in her quest for women's emancipation, failed to find while alive.

Henry James (1843–1916); Edith Wharton (1862–1937)

One of the greatest of American novelists, Henry James lived for much of his life in Europe and found his major subject in the "international theme", the contrast of American innocence and European experience. This dominated his fiction from his early novels *Roderick Hudson* (1876) and *The American* (1877) to his late masterpieces, *The Ambassadors* (1903) and *The Golden Bowl* (1904). It achieved its most classic expression in *The Portrait of a Lady* (1881), in which the heroine Isabel Archer, an innocent abroad in Europe, rejects the possibility of a conventional marriage to an English aristocrat for the enlarged possibilities that seem to be offered by a union with the sophisticated Europeanized American Gilbert Osmond, who subsequently proves to be a poseur and fortune-hunter. Isabel's quest for self-fulfilment makes her a quintessential American protagonist—a kind of Transcendentalist within the novel of manners context—and, if initially she appears naive, by the end of the story she has acquired considerable dignity and emerges as a genuine tragic heroine. James's work is considered more fully elsewhere (*see* **M10**).

Edith Wharton was a friend of Henry James and her fiction shares his concern with moral values and belief in the importance of literary form. Like James she lived for many years in Europe and produced her best work within the framework of the novel of manners, sometimes using the international theme. Her first important novel *The House of Mirth* (1905) was written before she left for Europe. It is a satire of the upper échelons of New York society, into which she had been born, written more in the style of Jane Austen than James. Her masterpiece *The Age of Innocence* (1920), like *The Portrait of a Lady*, deals with the situation of an independent American woman in Europe. *Ethan Frome* (1911), a less typical novel, is a tragedy set in the New England countryside. In all Wharton published about forty books. Her other works include the novels *The Custom of the Country* (1913), *The Old Maid* (1924) and *Hudson River Bracketed* (1929) and the autobiographical *A Backward Glance* (1964), which gives an interesting account of how the newly moneyed classes took over from the old conservative aristocracy as the leaders of New York society.

Theodore Dreiser (1871–1945) and the Naturalists

During the late nineteenth century, at a time when Naturalism was becoming an increasingly popular mode in France and England, America produced a crop of novelists who were intent on offering a more realistic picture of humanity and society than had hitherto appeared in the country's literature. William Dean Howells was the first great exponent of realism in American fiction and wrote influential essays on Zola and Tolstoy. In his own day he was a more widely respected novelist than his friend Mark Twain. His best known novel *The Rise of Silas Lapham* (1885) dramatizes conflicts in nineteenth-century American society through its story of a self-made millionaire who tries to find acceptance in genteel society. Howells became a mentor to Stephen Crane after the publication of the latter's *Maggie: A Girl of the Streets* (1893), a novel which aroused a great deal of controversy when it first appeared. Crane published one other important work before his early death at the age of twenty-nine. This was *The Red Badge of Courage* (1895), a classic novel of a young man's initiation during the Civil War, which extended the gritty realism of the Naturalists into a new area. Other important naturalistic works from this period include Frank Norris's *McTeague* (1899) and *The Octopus* (1901) and the less well-known Harold Frederic's *The Damnation of Theron Ware* (1896).

It was, however, in Theodore Dreiser that America found its most important practitioner of Naturalism, though his greatness has not always been acknowledged by academics who have found his style clumsy. Dreiser grew up in poverty and his novels reflect the determinist conviction that human beings are the sum total of the economic, social and biological influences that have gone into their making. His first novel *Sister Carrie* (1900), the story of a country girl who is seduced in the big city, elicited a generally hostile reception because it withheld condemnation of the allegedly loose-moralled heroine, preferring to see her as the victim of forces beyond her control. Based on a famous murder case, Dreiser's masterpiece *An American Tragedy* (1925) follows a similar naturalistic approach in its account of the fortunes of Clyde Griffiths, a young man of lowly origins whose social-climbing leads him to murder the girl who loves him in order to marry a socialite. *Jennie Gerhardt* (1911), *The Financier* (1912) and *The Titan* (1914) are among the best of Dreiser's other novels.

Willa Cather (1873–1947)

Cather grew up in Nebraska and, while she subsequently moved to New York, was the first great novelist of the Prairies. In *O Pioneers!* (1913), the finest of her Prairie novels *My Antonia* (1918) and *A Lost Lady* (1923) she wrote about the lives of immigrant women brought up on the Great Plains. *My Antonia* utilized a more complex point of view than her previous novels, that of a male narrator who has only had spasmodic contact with the eponymous heroine over a period of years and this provided a perspective which enabled Cather to explore her theme of the problem of relationships in the vast spaces of the West with greater depth. Her most autobiographical novel *The Song of the Lark* (1915) and *Lucy Gayheart* (1935) are about the need for the artist to escape from constricting influences. In her later fiction Cather turned to the historical past for subjects, writing about nineteenth-century New Mexico in *Death Comes for the Archbishop* (1927), the novel widely regarded as her master-piece, and seventeenth-century Quebec in *Shadows on the Rock* (1931).

Robert Frost (1874–1963)

Often thought of as America's best loved poet, Frost was born in California, but spent most of his life in New England. After working at a variety of occupations, he moved in 1912 to New England, where he lived for three years and published his first volumes, *A Boy's Will* (1913) and *North of Boston* (1914). In these collections he discovered his distinctive poetic terrain, rural life in New England and more specifically in the New Hampshire countryside. He was, however, far more than a regional poet and both the apparent simplicity of his verse and the bucolic persona he sometimes cultivated are deceptive. He drew on a broad and urbane range of earlier writing, including the Latin pastoral, and was essentially a metaphysical poet, though his verse has none of the obscurity of

imagery of an Emily Dickinson. Frost was a master of prosody and particularly adept in the form of the dramatic monologue. His main volumes of verse were *Mountain Interval* (1916), *New Hampshire* (1923), *The West-Running Brook* (1928), *Collected Poems* (1930), *A Further Range* (1936), *A Witness Tree* (1942), *Steeple Bush* (1947) and *In the Clearing* (1962). *A Masque of Reason* (1945) and *A Masque of Mercy* (1947) are blank verse plays. "Mending Wall", "The Death of the Hired Man", "After Apple-Picking" and "Stopping by Woods on a Snowy Evening" are among his most popular poems.

Sherwood Anderson (1876–1941); Sinclair Lewis (1885–1951)

Sherwood Anderson was over forty when his best known novel, *Winesburg, Ohio*, a probing study of small-town American life appeared in 1919. He had grown up in a small Ohio town himself and had worked as an advertising man and paint factory manager prior to becoming a writer. Like most of Anderson's fiction, *Winesburg, Ohio* depicts the individual at odds with industrial society. The novel is really a collection of interlinked short stories, in each of which one of the town's inhabitants tells a young reporter on the local newspaper of his or her innermost fears or hopes. Anderson's other novels include *Windy McPherson's Son* (1916), *Marching Men* (1917), *Poor White* (1920), *Many Marriages* (1923) and *Dark Laughter* (1925), all of which depict the problems of living in mechanized society. He also excelled as a short story writer and *Horses and Men* (1923) and *Death in the Woods* (1933) are among his collections of work in this genre. The sentimentality of *Dark Laughter* was parodied by Hemingway in his early novel *The Torrents of Spring* (1926), but in reality, like Faulkner, he owed a considerable stylistic debt to Anderson.

Sinclair Lewis was the first American novelist to win the Nobel Prize for Literature, an award which was conferred on him in 1930. His fiction is best known for its satire of bourgeois America's smug-ness and hypocrisy, though, like Anderson, he demon-strates some affection for the world he pillories. *Main Street* (1920) lays bare the narrow-mindedness of small-town life; *Babbitt* (1922) exposes the short-comings of a representative American businessman and the name of the central character has become synonymous with philistinism; *Elmer Gantry* (1927) explores the charlatanism of another American type, the self-seeking evangelist. Lewis's fiction is no longer as popular as it was earlier in the century, but the above novels and *Arrowsmith* (1925) and *Dodsworth* (1929) continue to be read.

Eugene O'Neill (1888–1953)

Widely regarded as America's finest dramatist, O'Neill was strongly influenced by the experiences of his early years spent travelling with his actor parents. His brother became an alcoholic and his mother a drug addict. His adult life was also dogged by tragedy: he was twice divorced, suffered from tuberculosis as a young man and had a paralytic stroke in his late fifties; his eldest son committed suicide and he disowned his daughter Oona after she married the actor Charlie Chaplin, a man three times her age. Tormented family relationships are at the heart of O'Neill plays as different from one another as *Long Day's Journey into Night* (1956; written 1940), a primarily naturalistic study of addiction, and *Mourning Becomes Electra* (1931), his version of the *Oresteia* trilogy. The mode of his plays varies considerably, ranging from the natural-ism of *Anna Christie* (1921) and *Desire under the Elms* (1924) to the expressionism of *The Emperor Jones* (1920) and the technically innovative *The Hairy Ape* (1922). What links all O'Neill's drama is an attempt to probe beyond the surface of everyday life in order to lay bare fundamental, usually tragic aspects of human behaviour. *The Iceman Cometh* (1946), a tragedy about the death of illusions, is widely regarded as his finest work. His other plays include *All God's Chillun Got Wings* (1924), *The Great God Brown* (1926), *Strange Interlude* (1928), *A Moon for the Misbegotten* (1947) and his only comedy *Ah, Wilderness!* (1933).

Wallace Stevens (1879–1955)

One of the great masters of twentieth-century verse, Stevens worked for most of his life as an insurance company executive. Many of his best poems, including "Sunday Morning", "Disillusionment of Ten O'Clock", "The Emperor of Ice Cream" and "The Idea of Order at Key West", are characterized by the use of striking and often bizarre images that have been compared with those of the surrealists. A brilliant technician, Stevens attempted, through his delicately-shaped philosophical verse, to provide an answer to nihilism. In long poems like "Notes towards a Supreme Fiction" and "The Comedian as the Letter C" he discussed the poet's role in transforming reality. Much of his best work appeared in his first volume *Harmonium* (1923). His middle period was less productive, but in later life he produced further major work in *The Auroras of Autumn* (1950) and *Selected Poems* (1953). His other volumes of verse include *Ideas of Order* (1935), *The Man with the Blue Guitar* (1937), *Transport to Summer* (1947) and *Opus Posthumous* (1957). *The Necessary Angel* (1951) is a collection of his essays.

Ezra Pound (1885–1972) and the Imagists

A major figure in the development of modernist verse, Pound was one of the most erudite, influential and controversial of twentieth-century poets. He lived through several literary epochs and was at the centre of movements such as Imagism and Vorticism. In 1908 he settled in Europe, where he spent most of his subsequent life—in Italy, France and England. There he became the leader of the Imagists, a group of poets who included his American contemporaries H.D. (Hilda Doolittle), a very fine poet herself, Amy Lowell and, for a while, William Carlos Williams (see below). The Imagists attempted to replace what they saw as the outmoded and stale forms of Victorian verse with a new poetic, based on a style of direct representation aimed at breaking down the distance between subject and object.

Pound's first important poem was 'Homage to Sextus Propertius' (1918), a work which typified his practice of producing highly original poetry from what might appear to be derivative material. He helped promote the work of numerous other major avant-garde writers of the day, including James Joyce and T. S. Eliot and played an important part in the shaping of Eliot's greatest poem *The Waste Land* (1922). (The American-born Eliot's work is discussed in the 'English Poetry' section.) In Paris in the 1920s Pound was associated with Gertrude Stein and the generation of expatriate writers who had migrated there. In the 1930s he lived in Italy, became increasingly attracted to the social changes being introduced by Mussolini and, during World War II, broadcast fascist propaganda. From 1946 to 1958 he was confined to a mental hospital in Washington. After his release he spent the remaining years of his life in Italy. Pound's eclectic reading enabled him to combine a wide variety of poetic traditions, including Classical, medieval Italian, Japanese, Chinese and Provençal verse. His *Hugh Selwyn Mauberley* (1920) examines the problems facing the artist in the machine age. Written over a period of almost half a century and published in sections between 1919 and 1959, Pound's masterpiece is *The Cantos* (1964). It is one of the great American poetic sequences, a work of vast scope based on Dante and utilizing a good deal of free translation. Though fragmentary and often obscure, *The Cantos* offers an epic consideration of the history of civilization and is the summation of Pound's poetic achievement.

William Carlos Williams (1883–1963)

As a young man Williams studied medicine at the University of Pennsylvania and both there and subsequently in Europe, he was associated with Pound and H.D. While his early work shares many of the concerns of the Imagists, including their belief in metaphor and their repudiation of didacticism and sentimentalism, he subsequently distanced himself from them, rejecting their dense allusiveness for a style rooted in vernacular American idioms. This style attempts to communicate directly, presenting things themselves rather than ideas about things, and making poetry out of everyday language. Williams's best known work is *Paterson* (1946–58), a five-volume philosophical poem based on the New Jersey town where he grew up and spent most of his adult life practising as a doctor.

His reputation has grown steadily and he is now regarded as one of the major American poets of the century. His other volumes of verse include *Al Que Quiere!* (1917), *Sour Grapes* (1921), *Collected Later Poems* (1950; revised 1963), *Collected Earlier Poems* (1951), *Journey to Love* (1955) and *Pictures from Brueghel* (1962). Williams also wrote a considerable body of fiction including a trilogy of novels about an immigrant family: *White Mule* (1937), *In the Money* (1940) and *The Build-Up* (1952). In *In the American Grain* (1925), a collection of essays on seminal American figures from Eric the Red and Columbus to Edgar Allan Poe and Abraham Lincoln, Williams offers a personal view of American history.

F. Scott Fitzgerald (1896–1940)

Born in St. Paul, Minnesota, Scott Fitzgerald wrote much of his best fiction about the provincial Mid West's encounter with a romantic world, variously represented by the American East, Europe and Hollywood. After failing to graduate from Princeton, Fitzgerald was surprised, on the publication of his first novel *This Side of Paradise* (1920) to find himself acclaimed as a 'Prophet of the Jazz Age', since he felt himself an outsider in the sophisticated permissive Eastern world about which he wrote. A week after this novel was published he married the Southern belle Zelda Sayre and much of his subsequent fiction was loosely based on their relationship. In his masterpiece *The Great Gatsby* (1925), the narrator Nick Carraway describes, in a richly-textured poetic prose, the eponymous hero's attempt to recapture the lost love of his youth, an endeavour which Nick relates to the idealism of early versions of the American Dream, a romantic vision seen to be anachronistic in the present. During the 1920s and 1930s the Fitzgeralds lived for long periods in Europe, particularly on the Riviera and in Paris. Zelda suffered the first of a number of breakdowns in 1930 and after 1934 spent long periods in sanatoria (she died in a sanatorium fire in 1948). After *Gatsby* Fitzgerald found it difficult to write and he chronicled his sense that he was dissipating his talent in his next novel *Tender is the Night* (1934). Set in Europe, it tells the story of an idealistic psychiatrist who falls in love with and marries one of his more exotic patients, but subsequently declines over a period of years, while his wife climbs back to health. During his last years, Fitzgerald lived in Hollywood where he worked as a scriptwriter. He died of a heart attack while in the process of writing *The Last Tycoon* (1941), a novel about a Hollywood film producer, said to be based on the 'boy wonder' Irving Thalberg. *The Pat Hobby Stories* (1962) also deal with Hollywood. Fitzgerald's other works include the novel *The Beautiful and Damned* (1922), a collection of short autobiographical pieces collected together as *The Crack-Up* (1945) and many fine short stories, among the best of which are 'The Diamond as Big as the Ritz', 'Winter Dreams' and 'The Rich Boy'.

William Faulkner (1897–1962)

The greatest novelist of the American South, Faulkner spent nearly all his life in Lafayette County, Mississippi, which provided him with the setting for most of his fiction, his mythical Yoknapatawpha County. Yoknapatawpha functions in much the same way as James Joyce's Dublin, as a microcosm in which archetypal human conflicts are acted out. So Faulkner is at one and the same time a regional writer and a novelist who explores broad mythic issues. His first major novel *The Sound and the Fury* (1929) uses a complex fictional technique, in which stream-of-consciousness monologues—one of them "a tale told by an idiot"—provide a highly unconventional modernist reworking of the form of the family saga. Like most of Faulkner's best work, it makes few concessions to the reader, who has to build up a gradual picture of events and their possible significances from the clues which are offered. As *I Lay Dying* (1930), a tragi-comic account of a Southern family's journey with the dead mother's corpse, employs an even more fragmentary stream-of-consciousness technique and, like *The Sound and the Fury*, questions notions of what constitutes mental normality. Novels like the sensational *Sanctuary* (1931), *Light in August* (1932) and *Intruder in the Dust* (1948) explore the pernicious legacy of Southern racial prejudice, while also demonstrating a vision of endurance and survival that crosses ethnic boundaries. Faulkner's 'Snopes trilogy'—*The Hamlet* (1940), *The Town* (1957) and *The Mansion* (1959)—charts the rise of the entrepreneurial horse-trading Snopes family, which threatens the traditional fabric of Southern society. His masterpiece *Absalom, Absalom!* (1936), in which events from the nineteenth-century are filtered through the consciousness of Quentin Compson, who has committed suicide in *The Sound and the Fury*, and *A Fable* (1954), set in World War I, employ Christian myth to provide allegorical commentary on their historical subjects. Faulkner's other novels include *The Wild Palms* (1939), *Requiem for a Nun* (1951), a sequel to *Sanctuary*, and *The Reivers* (1962). *The Unvanquished* (1938) and *Go Down, Moses* (1942) are among the best of his collections of short stories. Faulkner won the 1949 Nobel Prize for Literature.

Ernest Hemingway (1899–1961)

Born in Michigan, Ernest Hemingway lived much of his life outside the United States—in France, Spain and the Caribbean. He first went abroad in 1918 as a wartime Red Cross ambulance driver in Italy, where he was wounded. This experience provided the basis for his novel, *A Farewell to Arms* (1929) and helped shape the characteristic Hemingway protagonist of the Wounded Hero, a man who suffers as much from a psychic wound as a physical one and who has to accommodate himself to life through practising the Code of "grace under pressure". Jake Barnes, the hero of Hemingway's first major novel, and in many ways his finest, *The Sun Also Rises* (U.K. title *Fiesta*) (1926) is such a hero, as is Nick Adams—the main figure in the short stories of *In Our Time* (1925)—a character who undergoes a series of initiations first in the Michigan woods and then in wartime Italy. In this volume Hemingway's much imitated but seldom equalled understated style first appeared; it is a style based on what he called the "iceberg principle", the notion that eight-ninths of the subject should be kept below the surface. Apparently hard-boiled and unsentimental, Hemingway's style provides a powerful vehicle for the expression of emotion and for the articulation of his Code.

He frequently wrote about male activities such as bullfighting, big game hunting and fishing, as well as war, and his work has lost some popularity in recent years because of its alleged embodiment of "macho" values. His other novels include *To Have and Have Not* (1937), *For Whom the Bell Tolls* (1940), a novel about the Spanish Civil War, which he reported as a journalist, *Across the River and into the Trees* (1950) and the posthumous *Islands in the Stream* (1970). The novella *The Old Man and the Sea* (1952) marked a return to his best work after a period of decline and he was awarded the Nobel Prize for Literature in 1953. His other volumes of short stories include *Men Without Women* (1927) and *Winner Take Nothing* (1933). *Death in the Afternoon* (1932) is a classic study of bullfighting; *Green Hills of Africa* (1935) is about big game hunting; and *A Moveable Feast* (1964) is a memoir of Paris in the 1920s. During his later years Hemingway lived mainly in Cuba, but after the revolution there in 1959 he returned to the United States, where he committed suicide by shooting himself in 1961.

John Steinbeck (1902–68)

Steinbeck's novels move between social realism and sentimental romanticism and, although widely acknowledged as a major novelist, he has frequently been criticized as a would-be radical, whose vision lacks ideological consistency. His best fiction responds to the plight of the dispossessed of the Depression years. The exploitation of agricultural workers driven off the land and forced to move to California is the central subject of his finest novel *The Grapes of Wrath* (1939), a work which both protests about social injustice and celebrates the human capacity for endurance. Steinbeck also treated the plight of migrant workers in *In Dubious Battle* (1936) and *Of Mice and Men* (1937). In *Tortilla Flat* (1935) and *Cannery Row* (1945) he wrote about a Monterey community of social outsiders, focussing on their essential good humour and mutual support-systems. His other fiction includes the novels *The Moon is Down* (1942), *The Wayward Bus* (1947), *East of Eden* (1952) and *The*

Winter of our Discontent (1961) and a volume of short stories, *The Long Valley* (1938). Steinbeck was awarded the Nobel Prize for Literature in 1962.

Nathanael West (1903–40)

Nathanael West wrote four fine satirical novellas before his untimely death in a car crash. *The Dream Life of Balso Snell* (1931), a surrealist fantasy, was written in Paris where West lived from 1924 to 1931. In the tragi-comic *Miss Lonelyhearts* (1933), generally regarded as West's best work, the male agony columnist of the title finds himself increasingly unable to deal with his daily mailbag of letters chronicling the sufferings of his correspondents. *A Cool Million* (1934) is another scathing satire, this time of the American rags-to-riches myth. Like his contemporary Scott Fitzgerald, West frequently exposed the destructiveness underlying the American success myth and his last work *The Day of the Locust* (1939) was a Hollywood novel which outdid Fitzgerald in its satiric intensity, even if it lacked the subtlety of analysis of Fitzgerald's Hollywood fiction.

Early Black American Writing; the Harlem Renaissance

Significant black American writing first appeared in the nineteenth-century, with books by authors like Frederick Douglass, whose autobiography *Narrative of the Life of Frederick Douglass* (1845) is generally regarded as the finest of the numerous 'slave narratives' that played an important part in the abolitionist crusade, and Charles Chesnutt, best known for his novel *The Conjure Woman* (1899). In the 1920s the first important black literary movement emerged in the work of the writers of the Harlem Renaissance. Leading figures in this group were the Jamaican-born novelist and poet Claude McKay and the poets Countee Cullen and Langston Hughes. While Cullen employed a fairly traditional poetic technique, Hughes introduced black language forms and jazz and blues themes and rhythms into his verse. Other significant works by black writers in the early part of this century include Jean Toomer's volume of short stories *Cane* (1923) and James Weldon Johnson's autobiography *Along this Way* (1933). W. E. B. DuBois's enormously influential *The Souls of Black Folk* (1903), which attempted to identify the distinctive qualities of black identity and culture, was a seminal text in advancing black awareness of social discrimination.

Other Poets and Novelists, 1900–50

Other important poets from the first half of the century include Edwin Arlington Robinson, Carl Sandburg, Vachel Lindsay, Edgar Lee Masters, e. e. cummings (who always used democratic lower case letters for his initials), Marianne Moore and Hart Crane.

Other prominent novelists from the inter-war years include the authors of two important trilogies, John Dos Passos, whose massive *U.S.A.* trilogy (1930–6) reflects the penchant for social realism in the American fiction of the 1930s, and James T. Farrell, whose three Chicago novels about Studs Lonigan (1932–5) show a similar concern with the urban predicament and the radical politics of the day. Thomas Wolfe's novels, of which *Look Homeward, Angel* (1929) and its sequel *Of Time and the River* (1935) are the best known, are passionate accounts of an artist's quest for fulfilment.

Three Southern Women Novelists

The writing of Eudora Welty mainly deals with the Mississippi area from which she originated. She is particularly noted for her memorable characters and vivid use of the language of the region. *Delta Wedding* (1946), the story of a plantation family, is her best-known novel; her volumes of short stories include *A Curtain of Green* (1941) and *The Golden Apples* (1949). Welty won the Pulitzer Prize for her novel *The Optimist's Daughter* (1972).

Both Carson McCullers and Flannery O'Connor died young, after suffering from serious illnesses: McCullers had a series of crippling strokes while still in her twenties; O'Connor was the victim of a form of lupus in the latter part of her life. Much of McCullers's work deals with the disabled, the lonely and the socially marginalized. Her first novel *The*

Heart is a Lonely Hunter (1940) is centred on a deaf-mute. *The Member of the Wedding* (1946) is a delicately realized portrait of an adolescent girl's longing for emotional fulfilment. Her other works include *Reflections in a Golden Eye* (1941) and *The Ballad of the Sad Café* (1951), a collection of short stories which takes its title from a novella included in the volume.

While McCullers is in many ways a Gothic novelist, she seldom exploits the sensational potential of her material. Flannery O'Connor writes in a similar vein, but makes no attempt to understate the bizarre and violent. Plot elements in her fiction include a sodomite rape and a man who blinds himself with quicklime. A committed Catholic herself, O'Connor explores the fanatical aspects of Southern religious belief. She published two novels, *Wise Blood* (1952) and *The Violent Bear It Away* (1960), and two short story collections, *A Good Man is Hard to Find* (1955) and *Everything that Rises Must Converge* (1965).

Black Fiction since the Harlem Renaissance

Both Richard Wright and James Baldwin followed the American expatriates of the inter-war years to France. Wright's most famous novel *Native Son* (1940), the story of Bigger Thomas, who dies in the electric chair after killing a rich white girl and a poor black girl, has been hailed as a black *American Tragedy*. His other work includes *Uncle Tom's Children* (1938), a collection of four stories, his autobiography *Black Boy* (1945) and the novel *The Outsider* (1953). Baldwin's fiction moves between fierce indictments of the racism of American society and sensitive investigations of the personal dilemmas of individuals, black and white, homosexual and heterosexual. His first novel *Go Tell It on the Mountain* (1953) is about an adolescent growing up in the depressed Harlem environment of his own youth. *Giovanni's Room* (1956), a novel narrated by a bisexual American in Paris, was seen as questioning prevalent notions of human sexual response at the time of its appearance. *Another Country* (1962), Baldwin's finest novel, charts the course of a number of relationships which cross ethnic and sexual boundaries and provides vivid commentary on problems of national, racial and gender identity. His non-fiction includes three collections of essays, in which racial issues and fragmentary autobiography loom large: *Notes of a Native Son* (1955), *Nobody Knows My Name* (1961) and *The Fire Next Time* (1963), a grim warning of racial apocalypse.

Ralph Ellison's only novel *Invisible Man* (1952) is widely regarded as the finest black American novel to have appeared to date. It is a complex allegory which follows the protagonist's journey from the rural South, where he is expelled from a black college, to New York, a job in a factory making *white* paint, Harlem race riots and involvement with a corrupt black brotherhood. At well as being a brilliant novel about the black experience, *Invisible Man* is also a classic story of country innocence struggling to find its feet in the sophisticated city.

Recent years have seen the emergence of two outstanding black women novelists. Alice Walker is best known for her novel *The Color Purple* (1983), which depicts the struggles of mutually supportive women in the harsh Southern world of the inter-war years. *Meridian* (1976) tells a more contemporary story, that of a young black woman who lives through the Civil Rights Movement of the 1960s and gradually learns how to resist oppression. *You Can't Keep a Good Woman Down* (1981) is a collection of Walker's short stories. In *The Temple of My Familiar* (1989) Walker presents history from the viewpoint of the dispossessed. Toni Morrison's novels are mainly concerned with the black struggle for community. They include *Sula* (1974), which interrogates stereotypical representations of black women, *Song of Solomon* (1977), a probing examination of family life, and her finest work to date, *Beloved* (1987), a historical novel set in nineteenth-century Virginia.

The Detective Novel

While Edgar Allan Poe's C. Auguste Dupin was the first literary detective, it was Nick Carter, who first appeared in a magazine story of 1886 and subsequently figured as the hero of over 500 paperback novels published between 1895 and 1935, who popularized the figure of the detective in America. The 1920s saw the emergence of the most popular type of the American detective, the hard-

boiled private eye, in Carroll John Daly's Race Williams. It was Daly who established many of the conventions within which two of the best known American crime fiction writers, Dashiell Hammett and Raymond Chandler, wrote. Unlike the hero of the classic British detective story—as typified by Sherlock Holmes, Hercule Poirot and Lord Peter Wimsey—the hard-boiled private eye is a self-employed small businessman trying to eke out a living while retaining a modicum of self-respect in a corrupt urban environment (such as Chandler's "mean streets" of Los Angeles). Whereas in the typical British detective story, a super-sleuth solves crimes that appear to be little more than minor aberrations in a morally stable social world, represented by the enclosed environment of the fictions (such as an English country house or a Nile steamer), the private eye has to deal with a sprawling and seemingly anarchic social reality and his own code of values is the sole moral repository of the fiction. Hammett created the detectives the Continental Op, who appears in *Red Harvest* (1929) and *The Dain Curse* (1929), and Sam Spade, hero of *The Maltese Falcon* (1930).

Raymond Chandler's Philip Marlowe is the most famous hard-boiled detective. He made his début in *The Big Sleep* (1939) and subsequently appeared in *Farewell, My Lovely* (1940), *The High Window* (1942), *The Lady in the Lake* (1943), *The Little Sister* (1949), *The Long Goodbye* (1953) and *Playback* (1958). His character is a blend of tough cynicism and sentimentality; his wisecracking idiom takes the slangy, laconic style developed by Daly and Hammett to an extreme, which in the later novels verges on parody. Other noteworthy American detectives include Ellery Queen, the protagonist of more than thirty novels and numerous short stories by his namesake, Rex Stout's Nero Wolfe, the prolific Erle Stanley Gardner's Perry Mason, Ross Macdonald's Lew Archer and Mickey Spillane's Mike Hammer. Gardner specialized in clever legal twists and courtroom climaxes. Spillane has provided a variation on the type of the hard-boiled detective in creating a private eye who, in novels like *I, the Jury* (1947) and *Vengeance is Mine* (1950), steps outside the law to exact a brutal revenge for crimes which society appears to be incapable of punishing.

The Western Novel

While aspects of the myth of the American West can be traced back to Fenimore Cooper, its key features took shape in the popular dime-novels of the late nineteenth-century, show-business attractions like Buffalo Bill's (William Cody's) travelling Wild West Show and the Hollywood Westerns of the silent movie era. The dime-novels mythologized historical figures like Wild Bill Hickok, Wyatt Earp and Calamity Jane, who were usually very different from their fictional representations. Hickok's reputation, for example, was established by his shooting a man in the back.

The first great popular Western novel was Zane Grey's highly romantic bestseller *Riders of the Purple Sage* (1912). Along with Owen Wister's classic novel about Wyoming cowboys, *The Virginian* (1902), and films starring the actors "Bronco Billy" Anderson, William S. Hart and Tom Mix, it helped establish the Western as a major American art form, celebrating the individualistic values central to the Frontier ethic. Jack Schaefer's *Shane* (1949) typifies a classic Western formula, in which the hero is a loner who reluctantly takes up his guns in order to defend a threatened community. Other classic Western novelists include Max Brand and the prolific Louis L'Amour, author of the epic *How the West Was Won* (1962). In recent years the Western has declined in popularity, but it has been revivified by works such as Thomas Berger's *Little Big Man* (1964) which treat the legends of the West in an irreverential way. Tom Robbins's *Even Cowgirls Get the Blues* (1976), a novel of the contemporary West which describes the picaresque odyssey of its hitchhiking heroine, involves a playful postmodernist reworking of Western mythologies.

Saul Bellow (1915–) and the Jewish-American Novel

Widely regarded as the finest living American novelist, Bellow has written a succession of penetrating studies of the struggles of harassed, usually Jewish heroes to maintain humanist values in contemporary American society. In the novella *Seize the Day* (1956), *Herzog* (1964) and *Humboldt's Gift* (1975), which are among his finest treatments of this endeavour, he discusses the quest for human freedom and right values within the framework of a dazzling battery of intellectual ideas. His first novel *Dangling Man* (1944), which deals with the psychological conflicts of a protagonist who is waiting to be called up in World War II, shows the influence of the French existentialist novel. *The Victim* (1947) is his most obviously 'Jewish' novel in that it takes anti-semitism as a theme, but it subtly suggests that both the persecuted Jew at the centre of the story and his Gentile tormentor, who insists he has ruined his career, are victims. The picaresque novels *The Adventures of Augie March* (1953) and *Henderson the Rain King* (1959) respectively take a Jewish *schlemiehl*, or clown, and a Gentile millionaire as their protagonists. Bellow's other books include the novels *Mr. Sammler's Planet* (1970) and *The Dean's December* (1982), the novella *A Theft* (1989), the non-fiction *To Jerusalem and Back* (1976), and *Mosby's Memoirs* (1969), a volume of short stories. While his novels employ a range of styles, Bellow is essentially a realist novelist and his fiction owes a debt to Dreiser. He won the Nobel Prize for Literature in 1976. Other significant works of Jewish-American fiction include Bernard Malamud's *The Assistant* (1957) and *The Fixer* (1966), Philip Roth's outrageous comedy *Portnoy's Complaint* (1969) and E. L. Doctorow's *The Book of Daniel* (1971).

Arthur Miller (1915–)

Miller is a primarily naturalistic dramatist writing in the tradition of Ibsen, whose *An Enemy of the People* he has adapted. His first important work *All My Sons* (1947) illustrates the Ibsenite theses that individuals cannot escape the consequences of their past actions, nor isolate themselves from the society around them. His masterpiece *Death of a Salesman* (1949) is perhaps the finest example of a form popular in the American theatre, the tight-knit family tragedy. Its ordinary hero Willy Loman is destroyed by his belief in a dream of capitalist success, a latter-day version of the American Dream, which is now seen to lack the purity of vision of the Frontier ethic. In *The Crucible* (1953) Miller retells the story of the Salem witch trials as an allegory of the McCarthyite anti-Communist purges that were taking place in America in the 1950s, but the dilemma facing the play's hero John Proctor, who is forced to choose between death or dishonour, transcends these particular origins and has affinities with the choices faced by such tragic protagonists as Sophocles' Antigone and Shaw's St. Joan. Miller was brought up in a Brooklyn Jewish family and has written two plays which deal with aspects of the holocaust, *After the Fall* (1964) and *Incident at Vichy* (also 1964). His other plays include *A View from the Bridge* (1955), *The Price* (1968) and *The Archbishop's Ceiling* (1977). He is the author of the novel *Focus* (1945) and wrote the screenplay for the film *The Misfits* (1961), in which his second wife Marilyn Monroe starred.

Tennessee Williams (1911–83)

With *The Glass Menagerie* (1945) Tennessee Williams, the finest playwright of the American South, found his distinctive dramatic terrain. The play is centred on the characters Amanda and Laura Wingfield, a mother and daughter, both of whom live through illusions. Williams's subsequent fantasists include his greatest creation, Blanche Du-Bois in *A Streetcar Named Desire* (1947), one of the masterpieces of the post-war American theatre. Set in New Orleans, it tells the story of a fading Southern belle who prides herself on her refinement, though she has been dismissed from her job as a schoolteacher because of promiscuity. Williams's protagonists are invariably outsiders: they include artists, foreigners, the physically disabled, the mentally disturbed and the sexually unconventional. They become victims in a variety of ways: Blanche is raped; Catharine in *Suddenly Last Summer* (1958) is lobotomized; Val in *Orpheus Descending* (1957) is lynched. Williams's other plays include *The Rose Tattoo* (1951), *Camino Real* (1953), *Cat on a Hot Tin Roof* (1955), *Sweet Bird of Youth* (1959) and *Night of the Iguana* (1961). He wrote one novel *The Roman Spring of Mrs. Stone* (1950). A number of his plays have been turned into highly

successful films and his collaboration with the director Elia Kazan was particularly fruitful. Superficially very different from Arthur Miller, Williams shares common ground with the other major American dramatist of the post-war period in his repeated examination of the conflicts between reality and fantasy.

Other American Dramatists

Significant American plays of the inter-war years include the left-wing Clifford Odets's *Waiting for Lefty* (1935) and *Awake and Sing* (also 1935), Lillian Hellman's *The Children's Hour* (1934), which deals with the consequences of a schoolchild's charge of lesbianism against two of her teachers, and *The Little Foxes* (1939), a study of a ruthless Southern family, and Thornton Wilder's *Our Town* (1938), a play about a small New England town notable in its day for its lack of scenery. In the post-war period, the most acclaimed dramatist after Miller and Williams has been Edward Albee. His plays include the ferocious marital comedy *Who's Afraid of Virginia Woolf?* (1962) and the absurdist *The Zoo Story* (1958), *The American Dream* (1960) and *A Delicate Balance* (1966). The two most interesting dramatists to have emerged in recent years are David Mamet, author of *American Buffalo* (1975) and *Glengarry Glen Ross* (1983) and Sam Shepard, author of *True West* (1981) and *Fool for Love* (1983).

Postmodernists, Absurdists and Fabulists

Since the 1960s many of the finest writers of American fiction have deserted realist modes. The main characteristics of their writing have been an emphasis on the way notions of "reality" are linguistically constructed, a distrust of linear narrative, a use of self-referential devices which undermine the notion that fiction offers a version of real life transferred to the printed page and open-endedness. The novels and short stories of John Barth, one of the major proponents of fictional post-modernism, frequently rework what he has called the "exhausted" forms of previous centuries. His self-reflexive fiction includes *Lost in the Funhouse* (1968), *Chimera* (1972), and two novels written in eighteenth-century modes, *The Sot-Weed Factor* (1960) and *Letters* (1979). Other important fictional postmodernists include Donald Barthelme, whose best work has been done in the form of the short "fiction" pioneered by the Argentinian writer Jorge Luis Borges, and Richard Brautigan, author of *Trout Fishing in America* (1967) and *The Hawkline Monster: A Gothic Western* (1974). The most important figure writing in this vein has been the enigmatic Thomas Pynchon, a writer who has succeeded in obscuring his own personality as thoroughly as he loses the central character of his mammoth *Gravity's Rainbow* (1973). His other novels, which draw heavily on communications theory and relate the pattern-making instincts of the human mind to the paranoiac's vision, are *V* (1963), *The Crying of Lot 49* (1966), a short and entertaining book, which provides the best introduction to his difficult oeuvre and *Vineland* (1990). Similar to the postmodernists in their use of black humour are the absurdist novelists Joseph Heller and Kurt Vonnegut. Both have written satires of the futility of war—Heller in *Catch-22* (1961) and Vonnegut in *Slaughterhouse-Five* (1969)—which comment on American society more generally. Heller's other novels include *Something Happened* (1974), *Good as Gold* (1979) and *Picture This* (1988). Vonnegut's numerous novels—most notably *The Sirens of Titan* (1959)—utilize the conventions of science-fiction, a genre which, along with other forms of fantasy fiction, has become enormously popular in the United States in recent years. Leading American science-fiction writers include Philip K. Dick, author of *The Man in the High Castle* (1962) and *Do Androids Dream of Electric Sheep?* (1968), and Ursula Le Guin, author of *The Left Hand of Darkness* (1969). Marge Piercy's *Woman on the Edge of Time* (1976) contrasts a vision of a future utopia in which gender roles are unknown with the heroine's present situation as a helpless victim in a mental hospital.

Other Post-War Novelists

J. D. Salinger's immensely popular *The Catcher in the Rye* (1951) tells the story of two days in the life of its narrator/protagonist, the mixed-up adolescent Holden Caulfield, who describes his encounters with a "phoney" society in a vernacular American idiom reminiscent of *Huckleberry Finn*. Salinger's subsequent fiction is mainly concerned with the members of the precocious and hypersensitive Glass family. It includes *For Esmé—with Love and Squalor* (1953), a collection of short stories, and two volumes which each contain two novellas: *Franny and Zooey* (1961) and *Raise High the Roof Beam, Carpenters and Seymour: An Introduction* (1963).

Norman Mailer first achieved recognition for his World War II novel *The Naked and the Dead* (1948) and has gone on to publish a broad range of fiction, including *The Deer Park* (1955), a Hollywood novel, *An American Dream* (1965), which offers a searing critique of American society in the guise of a murder story, *Why Are We in Vietnam?* (1967) and *Ancient Evenings* (1983), a massive novel set in the Egypt of the Pharaohs. Mailer's more recent work has established his reputation as one of the finest American journalists of the century. His non-fiction includes *Advertisements for Myself* (1959), *The Armies of the Night* (1968), *Miami and the Siege of Chicago* (1968) and (in collaboration) *Marilyn* (1973), a biography of Marilyn Monroe. Since the publication of *The Prisoner of Sex* (1971), he has frequently been cast in the role of an adversary of the Women's Liberation Movement. He won the Pulitzer Prize for *The Executioner's Song* (1979).

Other notable post-war American fiction includes the Russian émigré Vladimir Nabokov's *Lolita* (1958) and *Pale Fire* (1962), Jack Kerouac's classic novel of the Beat generation, *On The Road* (1957), John Updike's *Rabbit, Run* (1960), *Couples* (1968) and *S.* (1988), John Hawkes's *The Lime Twig* (1960), Ken Kesey's *One Flew over the Cuckoo's Nest* (1962), William Styron's *The Confessions of Nat Turner* (1967) and *Sophie's Choice* (1979), Marilyn French's *The Women's Room* (1978), John Irving's *The World According to Garp* (1978), *The Hotel New Hampshire* (1981) and *A Prayer for Owen Meany* (1989) and Maxine Hong Kingston's *Tripmaster Monkey* (1989). Joan Didion, author of *A Book of Common Prayer* (1977) and *Democracy* (1984), first attracted recognition as a major exponent of the "New Journalism" with her volumes *Slouching towards Bethlehem* (1968) and *The White Album* (1979). The use of fictional techniques in factual narratives has become commonplace in recent American writing and can be seen in Truman Capote's *In Cold Blood* (1965) and the journalism of Tom Wolfe, author of *The Kandy-Kolored Tangerine-Flake Streamline Baby* (1965), *Radical Chic and Mau-Mauing the Flak Catchers* (1970) and *The Right Stuff* (1975).

Post-War American Poetry

The 1950s and 1960s saw the rise of the Beat Generation of poets, whose leading figure was the Whitmanesque Allen Ginsberg, best known for his *Howl* (1956). The Beat Movement was centred on San Francisco and also included Lawrence Ferlinghetti and Gregory Corso. In addition to flouting social taboos, it took issue with received notions of poetry, often advocating the importance of sound over sense. The Black Mountain Poets, so called because of their association with Black Mountain College in North Carolina, also endeavoured to formulate a new poetic in which, according to the leading figure in the group, Charles Olson, "projective" or closed verse—verse of the kind engendered by print and its conventions—was to be rejected for a poetry based on the openness of "energy-discharge". Olson's *Maximus Poems* (1953–61) show the influence of Pound and Williams. Other members of the group included Robert Creeley, Denise Levertov, Edward Dorn and Robert Duncan.

A number of "confessional" writers are among the best poets of the post-war period. Robert Lowell's poetry habitually places the individual at the centre of crises which stem from the pressures of the modern social climate. John Berryman and Sylvia Plath, who both committed suicide, evince a similar sense of personal angst. However, Berryman, particularly in *Homage to Mistress Bradstreet* (1956), relates personal dilemmas to a wider American context of isolation and lost faith. Plath, who began writing as a student of Lowell, became something of a cult figure after her marriage to the English poet Ted Hughes and early death in 1963. Her best known collection is *Ariel* (1965) and she

also wrote the novel *The Bell Jar* (1963). Among the many other important American poets of recent decades are Randall Jarrell, Robert Penn Warren, Theodore Roethke, John Ashbery, Adrienne Rich, James Merrill and Elizabeth Bishop.

CANADA

English-Canadian writing is one of the country's two main literatures, the other being French-Canadian. However, simply to see Canada in terms of these "two solitudes" (the title of a 1945 novel by Hugh MacLennan—see below) is to misrepresent the nature of its culture and society. When European colonists first settled Eastern Canada in the seventeenth century, it was, of course, already populated by numerous groups of Amerindian and Inuit peoples with long cultural traditions of their own, traditions that quickly came under threat from the new Canadians. Since the late nineteenth century Canada's demographic make-up has become increasingly multi-cultural with the advent of groups of Chinese (who particularly came into Western Canada to help with the building of the trans-continental railroad, completed in 1885), Ukrainians and Middle Europeans (mainly in the first half of this century) and, most recently, East and West Indians. Whereas in the United States the emphasis has been on assimilating the many waves of immigrants that have come into the country into the American melting-pot, in Canada there has been the attempt, particularly in recent years, to create a "mosaic" of cultural diversity.

Where literature is concerned, however, there was until recent times little emphasis on Canada's distinctiveness, let alone the variety (ethnic, regional and cultural) within its borders. Despite earlier waves of nationalist activity (most notably in the 1880s and 1920s), prior to the late 1960s many English-Canadian writers felt the need to migrate abroad in search of literary fame. Among such writers were Morley Callaghan, a contemporary of Hemingway and Fitzgerald in the Paris of the 1920s, an experience which he describes in *That Summer in Paris* (1963), and Mordecai Richler, whose *St. Urbain's Horseman* (1971) is a classic account of two young Canadians in England, "reared to believe in the cultural thinness of their blood". Other works by these writers include Callaghan's novels *Such is My Beloved* (1934) and *More Joy in Heaven* (1937) and Richler's *The Apprenticeship of Duddy Kravitz* (1959) and *Joshua Then and Now* (1980). English-Canadian writers who stayed home found that the absence of a locally-controlled publishing industry generally obliged them to submit their works to houses in London and New York and to write for an international readership. In Quebec the situation was different. There pride in the province's Francophone culture established a strong sense of the distinctiveness of local writing prior to the 'sixties. This helped to provide an inspiration for English-Canadian writers who, in the 1960s, began to group themselves together to form small publishing houses and to promote the idea of a local culture. Within a comparatively short period of time, the situation changed dramatically and today, within the country, a book's "Canadian-ness" can generally be guaranteed to boost rather than diminish its sales.

At the same time Canadian fiction and poetry have taken giant steps forwards. Unshackled by a clearly defined cultural tradition, English-Canadian writing has been free to develop in new and exciting ways and today it has emerged as one of the finest national literatures in the world, even if it remains comparatively little known internationally. Its neglect abroad may in part be attributed to the nationalist phase of the late 1960s and 1970s, which occasioned a certain inward-lookingness, a veering away from internationalism as a corrupting influence. Today Canadian writing has emerged from this cocoon and writers like Margaret Atwood, Robertson Davies and Alice Munro have acquired major international reputations. Other writers await discovery and similar acclaim.

Nineteenth-century English-Canadian Writing

Among the most important early English-Canadian prose writers are John Richardson, whose *Wacousta* (1832) is a Romantic novel in the tradition of Scott and Fenimore Cooper, and Thomas Haliburton, whose *The Clockmaker* (1836–40) is a collection of satirical sketches about a Yankee pedlar, Sam Slick, a vivid vernacular figure who is arguably the most engaging character in nineteenth-century Canadian writing. While *The Clockmaker* adopts a comic mode, its primary purpose was to criticize social attitudes in Haliburton's native Nova Scotia, mainly through the "home truths" put into the mouth of Sam Slick.

The experience of settler women is well represented in *Roughing It in the Bush* (1852) by Susanna Moodie, *The Backwoods of Canada* (1836) and *The Canadian Settler's Guide* (1854) by Moodie's sister Catharine Parr Traill and *Winter Studies and Summer Rambles in Canada* (1838) by Anna Brownell Jameson. All three writers offer commentary on the predicament of the English gentlewoman transplanted into a frontier environment, but, unlike the two sisters, Jameson, who moved in higher social circles, writes from the standpoint of a transient in Canada. In recent years these books have enjoyed a new vogue, as contemporary writers like Margaret Atwood and Margaret Laurence have turned to Moodie and Traill as Canadian women precursors.

The last decades of the nineteenth century saw the first flowering of English-Canadian poetry in the form of the work of the "Confederation Poets": Bliss Carman, Charles G. D. Roberts (Carman's cousin), Archibald Lampman and Duncan Campbell Scott. These writers did a great deal to establish a Canadian tradition in poetry. Though much of their verse is characterized by a late Romanticism, their poetry attempts to encompass Canadian themes and, sometimes, idioms. Thus Lampman writes about the northern bush and Scott the problems of the country's Indian inhabitants, while all four poets are concerned with the problem of adapting European models of nature poetry to the Canadian landscape. Along with Ernest Thompson Seton, author of *Wild Animals I Have Known* (1898) and *Lives of the Hunted* (1901), Roberts also helped to establish the animal story as a highly popular Canadian form.

Stephen Leacock (1869–1944)

Commonly regarded as a Canadian Mark Twain, Leacock is best known as a humorist. Beginning with *Literary Lapses* (1910), he became a prolific writer of humorous books, while also pursuing a highly successful career as a political economist at Montreal's McGill University. Most of his books are collections of sketches, but some of the finest of them have more overall unity: *Sunshine Sketches of a Little Town* (1912) is a gently satirical account of life in the small Canadian town of "Mariposa" (based on Orillia, Ontario, where Leacock had a summer home); *Arcadian Adventures with the Idle Rich* (1914) is a more probing satire of the moneyed American élite; *My Discovery of England* (1922) wittily inverts the method of many travel-books by using provincial standards to evaluate a metropolitan culture. Leacock's other books include *Nonsense Novels* (1911), *Moonbeams from the Larger Lunacy* (1915), *My Discovery of the West* (1937), *My Remarkable Uncle* (1942) and *Last Leaves* (1945).

Emily Carr (1871–1945)

One of Canada's finest painters, Emily Carr is also an important prose writer. Her art, which is notable for its vivid use of bright colours and dramatic brush strokes, frequently took the culture of the Indians of British Columbia as its subject and her first book *Klee Wyck* (1942) is a collection of short stories that also celebrates their culture. *The Book of Small* (1942) is based on her own childhood in Victoria, B.C. *The House of All Sorts* (1944) describes her experiences running a boarding house in Victoria. In addition to providing insights into Indian mores, Carr's writing offers excellent commentary on late Victorian and early twentieth-century Canadian provincial life.

E. J. Pratt (1882–1964)

Although he is generally considered the first major Canadian poet of this century, much of Pratt's technically assured work is concerned with Victorian ideological conflicts, such as the challenge offered by Darwinism to conventional Christian faith. Thus *The Titanic* (1935) questions the achievements of technological "progress". His best known works, *Brébeuf and his Brethren* (1940) and *Towards the Last Spike* (1952) are both poems of epic scope

with subjects drawn from Canadian history: the former deals with the massacre of a group of early missionaries by the Iroquois and is about the difficulties of establishing a European culture in Canada; the latter takes the building of the transcontinental railroad, a metaphoric as well as a physical expression of national unity, as its subject.

Earle Birney (1904–   )

One of Canada's most important poets, Birney has written in a wide variety of styles and about a vast range of subjects, Canadian and international. His early verse demonstrates a belief in the power of art as an agent for social change. During the 1930s he was a controversial figure because of his Trotskyite views. This early writing makes extensive use of myth and is strongly influenced by a knowledge of early English culture (he began his career as a scholar of medieval literature). Subsequently he adopted an absurdist view of life and has written verse in which North American idioms loom much larger. His most important works include the comic picaresque novel *Turvey* (1949) and the verse drama *The Damnation of Vancouver* (1952).

Hugh MacLennan (1907–   )

One of Canada's best known novelists, Hugh MacLennan is primarily a writer of social realist fiction dealing with the Canadian situation. For much of his life he has taught and lectured in Montreal and his novels frequently have a didactic thrust. Though sometimes regarded as a simple nationalist, he takes a complex view of the Canadian experience, seeing Canada as occupying a middle ground between the values of classical civilization and contemporary materialism. His best fiction includes his first novel *Barometer Rising* (1941), set in Halifax in World War I and outstanding when it first appeared for its precise realization of a Canadian city, *Two Solitudes* (1945), a novel set in Quebec which explores the social, cultural and linguistic separateness of Francophone and Anglophone Canada, and *The Watch That Ends the Night* (1959), another novel rooted in a very specific Canadian environment, but one which also treats the personal theme of coming to terms with a spouse's death. *Voices in Time* (1980), a science-fiction work about a post-nuclear holocaust world, reviews twentieth-century Western history and stands as a sober warning against the destruction of civilization.

Robertson Davies (1913–   )

For many years Davies's contribution to Canadian writing was as a dramatist and contributor to the Peterborough *Examiner*, for which he wrote a weekly column under the pseudonym "Samuel Marchbanks". This writing is collected in three books, of which the best is *The Table Talk of Samuel Marchbanks* (1949). *The Papers of Samuel Marchbanks* (1986) is a compendium of the three earlier volumes. His plays include the one-act *Overlaid* (1948), *A Jig for the Gypsy* (1954) and *Hunting Stuart and Other Plays* (1972). It is, however, as a novelist that Davies is now known. He has written groups of linked novels, which include "The Salterton Trilogy"—*Tempest-Tost* (1951), *Leaven of Malice* (1954) and *A Mixture of Frailties* (1958) and his best work, "The Deptford Trilogy"—*Fifth Business* (1970), *The Manticore* (1972) and *World of Wonders* (1975). Each part of this trilogy is written in a confessional first-person mode, which in some way reflects the characters' common origins in the small Ontario town that gives the trilogy its name. At the same time it is an extremely cosmopolitan work with a broad mythic framework and incorporates a good deal of specialist knowledge on such subjects as hagiography, Jungian psychology and carnival shows. *The Rebel Angels* (1981), *What's Bred in the Bone* (1985) and *The Lyre of Orpheus* (1988) are the constituent volumes of his most recent sequence, "The Cornish Trilogy".

Al Purdy (1918–   )

Although his first collection of verse appeared in 1944, Purdy did not really discover his distinctive poetic voice until the 1960s, though there are hints of it in *The Crafte So Longe to Lerne* (1959). Then, in volumes like *Poems for All the Annettes* (1962) and *The Cariboo Horses* (1965), he began to write in the idiomatic vein that has made him the finest Canadian poet of his generation. A self-taught man, Purdy writes about an eclectic range of themes, but several of his best poems, like "The Country North of Belleville" and "My Grandfather's Country" are reflections on the Canadian landscape and its past. His other volumes of verse include *North of Summer* (1968), *In Search of Owen Roblin* (1974) and *The Stone Bird* (1981). Most of his best work is collected in *Being Alive* (1978).

Margaret Laurence (1926–87)

Margaret Laurence is best known for her "Manawaka" novels, a sequence based on the small Manitoba town in which she grew up. These began with *The Stone Angel* (1964), a classic study of old age in which a ninety-year-old Scots-Presbyterian woman attempts to come to terms with both her past and present. *A Jest of God* (1966), well-known from the film adaptation *Rachel, Rachel* which loses much of the force of the novel by moving the setting from small-town Canada to the United States, is a study of the conflicts experienced by a much younger protagonist, a thirty-four-year-old spinster schoolteacher; *The Fire-Dwellers* (1969) takes this heroine's married sister as its central figure to provide another angle of vision on the problems encountered by women in provincial Canada. *The Diviners* (1974) is Laurence's longest novel and arguably her finest. A more technically complex work than any of her previous fiction, it is both an interrogation of received notions of Western Canadian history and culture and an account of the writer-protagonist's quest for identity. Laurence also published a volume of short stories about Manawaka, *A Bird in the House* (1970), and both fiction and non-fiction about Africa, where she lived for several years.

Contemporary Western Canadian Fiction

In recent years writers in several parts of Canada have asserted the distinctiveness of their regional context and its difference from that of the "centre", usually equated with Ontario. This has happened particularly in Canada's Maritime provinces, where poets like Alden Nowlan and novelists like Ernest Buckler have produced work rooted in the local environment, and in Western Canada, an area made up of two distinct regions: the Prairies and the very different landscape of British Columbia.

A tradition of writing in the Prairies, an area that remained unsettled until the late nineteenth-century, began to emerge in the 1920s with the novels and non-fictional prose of the German-born Frederick Philip Grove. This tradition developed in the 1940s with the publication of Sinclair Ross's *As for Me and My House* (1941) and W. O. Mitchell's *Who Has Seen the Wind* (1947). Meanwhile Emily Carr (see above), Ethel Wilson, whose most highly regarded novel *Swamp Angel* (1954) is typical of her sensitive studies of women in crisis, and Sheila Watson, whose classic modernist novel *The Double Hook* (1959) incorporated symbolism based on the myths of the Western Canadian Indians, pioneered a narrative tradition in British Columbia. Recently Western Canadian writing has really come of age with the work of three major novelists—Margaret Laurence, Robert Kroetsch and Rudy Wiebe—and the emergence of fine poets like Eli Mandel, Andrew Suknaski and Kroetsch, who also works in this genre. The tradition established by the novelists has been continued by younger writers like Jack Hodgins, author of the *The Invention of the World* (1977) and *The Honorary Patron* (1987) and Aritha Van Herk, author of *Judith* (1978) and *No Fixed Address* (1986).

Although Robert Kroetsch (1927–) lived in America for many years, virtually all of his fiction is rooted in his native Alberta. His novels, which have become increasingly innovatory, are particularly concerned with the problem of gender relations in the Western Plains and with representing a landscape characterized by its unstructured vastness. *The Studhorse Man* (1969) is the mock-odyssey of the eponymous Albertan hero who tramps the Prairies in search of a mare for his stallion to "cover". In *Gone Indian* (1973), another comic picaresque, an American graduate student follows in the steps of "Grey Owl", the Englishman-turned-Indian Archie Belaney. *Badlands* (1975) is about a 1916 expedition to discover dinosaur bones, but this male narrative is complemented by a female one, in which the expedition leader's daughter whose de-

velopment has been stultified by her father undertakes her own quest in the early 1970s. Kroetsch's other novels include *The Words of My Roaring* (1966), *What the Crow Said* (1978) and *Alibi* (1983). He is also the author of a gradually-accumulating poetic autobiography *Field Notes* (Vol. I, 1981; Vol. II, 1985), in which the self is seen as non-unitary and is explored through a complex examination of ancestral objects and other problematic formative influences. Kroetsch is widely regarded as one of Western Canada's most important literary theorists.

Rudy Wiebe (1934–) grew up in a Mennonite community in Northern Saskatchewan and most of his fiction is about Prairie minorities. *Peace Shall Destroy Many* (1962) tells the story of a young Mennonite torn between the demands of his community and a desire for individual expression. *The Blue Mountains of China* (1970) is a panoramic novel, in which discrete sections survey the Mennonite experience in Russia, Paraguay and Canada. *Temptations of Big Bear* (1973), another large-scale work, is centred on the figure of the late nineteenth-century Cree Indian chief who defied central Canadian authority. It employs numerous perspectives and blends fiction and documentary in a reassessment of Western Canadian history. *The Scorched-Wood People* (1977) is a similarly epic account of the struggles of the Métis (mixed French and Indian) peoples. A distinctive quality of Wiebe's fiction is its bringing together of a Christian viewpoint and experimental technique. He has also written *The Mad Trapper* (1980) and *My Lovely Enemy* (1983).

Timothy Findley (1930–)

Timothy Findley was an actor and Hollywood dialogue-writer before becoming a full-time author in the early 1960s. His novel *The Wars* (1977) catalogues the horrors of trench warfare in World War I through a narrative technique that gradually collapses the distance between narrator and reader to a point where the latter is made to feel an agent in the formulation of history. *Famous Last Words* (1981), which takes the form of the personal testament of Ezra Pound's character Hugh Selwyn Mauberley, is another powerful study of the horrors of history. Centred on World War II, it examines the part played by artistic élitism in the fascist threat to civilization. *Not Wanted on the Voyage* (1984) is a vividly inventive reworking of the story of the Great Flood. Findley has also published *The Last of the Crazy People* (1967), *The Butterfly Plague* (1969), *The Telling of Lies* (1986) and a volume of short stories, *Dinner Along the Amazon* (1984).

Alice Munro (1931–)

Munro has been described as one of the finest living short story writers and it is in this form that all her best work has been written. Her particular terrain has been small-town Ontario and the emotional lives of its women; she views this world through a style that initially appears to be made up of realistic snapshots, but proves on closer investigation to contain Gothic undercurrents. Similarly, what appear to be everyday, ordinary emotions are frequently shown to conceal hidden depths. Her books *Lives of Girls and Women* (1971) and *Who Do You Think You Are?* (U.K. title *The Beggar Maid*) (1978) are collections of short stories about the same characters, but Munro has preferred to refer to them as "story-sequences" rather than novels. She has also written *Dance of the Happy Shades* (1968), *Something I've Been Meaning to Tell You* (1974), *The Moons of Jupiter* (1982) and *The Progress of Love* (1987).

Margaret Atwood (1939–)

Canada's most highly acclaimed living writer, Atwood has produced major work as novelist, short story writer, poet and critic. The verse in her early volumes *The Circle Game* (1966), *The Animals in that Country* (1968) and *The Journals of Susanna Moodie* (1970) uses myth and archetype to explore issues of psychic identity, particularly as they relate to Canada. Her novel *Surfacing* (1972) is similar in that it charts the narrator/protagonist's inner journey to rediscover the truth about her past which she has suppressed. *Lady Oracle* (1976) is a brilliantly funny treatment of the role-playing that social stereotyping forces on women (and to a lesser extent men) and parodies and satirizes a number of fictional and other discourses. Set in the near future, *The Handmaid's Tale* (1986) offers a chilling picture of a dystopia in which women's roles have been reduced to a series of functions that prevent the expression of individuality. Her other novels are *The Edible Woman* (1969), *Life Before Man* (1979), *Bodily Harm* (1981) and *Cat's Eye* (1989). Her shorter fiction includes *Dancing Girls* (1977) and *Bluebeard's Egg* (1983). *Procedures for Underground* (1970), *Power Politics* (1971), *Two-Headed Poems* (1978) and *True Stories* (1981) are among her other volumes of verse. Atwood is also the author of a best-selling book about Canadian writing, *Survival: A Thematic Guide to Canadian Literature* (1971) and editor of *The Oxford Book of Canadian Verse in English* (1982).

Contemporary Canadian Drama

No English-Canadian dramatist has achieved the international reputation of Quebec's Michel Trem-

blay, but recent decades have seen the emergence of a thriving Anglophone theatre. George Ryga is notable for plays, like *The Ecstasy of Rita Joe* (1967), which is about an Indian woman living a marginalized existence in the city, that have championed the predicament of minorities. James Reaney, also an important poet, is best known as a dramatist for his trilogy *The Donnellys* (1975–77) about the murder of a family in nineteenth-century rural Ontario, which utilizes a dazzling array of theatrical devices, among them dance, mime and puppetry. Robertson Davies (*see above*) is also the author of an impressive body of dramatic work. Prominent Western Canadian dramatists include Ken Mitchell and Sharon Pollock, author of *Blood Relations* (1979), a complex treatment of the legend of Lizzie Borden, the late nineteenth-century spinster alleged to have murdered her father and stepmother with an axe.

IV. GLOSSARY OF LITERARY TERMS

acatalectic. Having the complete number of syllables in a line of verse. *See* **catalectic** *and* **hypercatalectic.**

accentual verse. Verse (like most English verse) which is measured by the number and pattern of stresses in a line and not by the number or quantitative value of syllables. *See* **metre** *and* **syllabic verse.**

act. Principal division of a dramatic work, sometimes subdivided into scenes.

aestheticism. A movement that flourished in the 1880s and 1890s and that considered beauty, not morality, as the most important principle in literary and artistic work. Its key phrase was "Art for art's sake." Two of its chief exponents in England were Walter Pater and Oscar Wilde.

affective fallacy. A phrase coined by M. C. Beardsley and W. K. Wimsatt (1946), who contended that it was false to criticise a poem on the basis of its psychological effects on the reader because as a result "the poem itself, as an object of specifically critical judgement, tends to disappear." *See* **Intentional fallacy** *and* **New Critics.**

alexandrine. A line of verse containing six iambic feet. *See* **metre.**

alienation. The principle, propounded by Bertolt Brecht (1898–1956), that actors and audience should remain detached from a dramatic performance and not become identified with the rôles and action.

allegory. A narrative or description in prose or verse with a hidden meaning or moral message, *e.g.*, Spenser's *Faerie Queene* and Bunyan's *Pilgrim's Progress.*

alliteration. The use of the same consonants in close proximity, often in verse, for the sake of euphony, memorability or emotional effect, *e.g.*,

"the *l*ow *l*ast edge of the *l*ong *l*one *l*and"
(Swinburne, "A Forsaken Garden").

See **assonance.**

ambiguity. Unclear or contradictory meaning. Positively, complexity of meaning and tone, as analysed in William Empson's *Seven Types of Ambiguity* (1930).

amphibrach. *See* **metre.**

anabasis. The progress of an action to a climax, especially in a drama.

anacoluthon. An inconsistency of construction in a sentence, so that the latter part does not grammatically fit with the earlier part, *e.g.*, "One of the prettiest touches was *when*, at the relation of the queen's death ... *how* attentiveness wounded his daughter" (Shakespeare, *The Winter's Tale*, V, ii).

anacreontic. Applied to light-hearted poetry praising such pleasures as wine, women and song, *e.g.*, Abraham Cowley's *Anacreontics*. (From Anacreon, Greek poet of the sixth century B.C.)

anacrusis. An additional syllable or half-foot at the beginning of a line of verse, *e.g.*,

"Cŏld / ănd cleár- / cŭt fáce / whў cŏme / yŏŭ so crú- /
ĕllў méek?"

(Tennyson, "Maud").

anagnorisis. The discovery or recognition, originally by the protagonist of a Greek tragedy, of a truth that leads to the resolution of the drama, *e.g.*, Othello's discovery of Desdemona's innocence. (Term from Aristotle's *Poetics*.)

anapaest. *See* **metre.**

anaphora. The repetition of a word or phrase at the beginning of consecutive phrases or sentences, *e.g.*,

"*For gold* his sword the hireling ruffian draws,
For gold the hireling judge distorts the laws"
(Johnson, *The Vanity of Human Wishes*).

anti-hero. A principal character who has no traditional heroic qualities but who is diffident, cowardly, foolish and not particularly estimable, *e.g.*, the eponymous hero of Kingsley Amis's *Lucky Jim.*

anti-novel. Loosely used for some twentieth century novels (by Beckett and Robbe-Grillet, for example) with minimal regard for such conventional features as plot and development of character. *See* **nouveau roman.**

antistrophe. In the Greek *chorus* (*q.v.*) and the *Pindaric Ode* (*q.v.*) the response to the *strophe* (*q.v.*), written in the same metrical form.

antithesis. The balanced juxtaposition of words or phrases for the sake of emphasis or contrast, widely used in eighteenth-century prose and verse, *e.g.*,

"But sometimes Virtue starves, while Vice is fed"
(Pope, *Essay on Man*).

apocope. The omission of the final letter, syllable or sound of a word, *e.g.*, the poetic use of "th' " for "the."

aposiopesis. Breaking off a sentence, usually for dramatic effect, *e.g.*,

"I will have such revenges on you both
That all the world shall—I will do such things—
What they are yet I know not"
(Shakespeare, *King Lear*, II, iv).

apostrophe. Address to a person or a personified quality, place or thing, *e.g.*, "Ye distant spires, ye antique towers" (Gray, "Ode on a Distant Prospect of Eton College"); "Stern Daughter of the Voice of God!" (Wordsworth, "Ode to Duty").

apron stage. A stage, like that in the Elizabethan theatre, which projects beyond the proscenium arch into the audience.

art for art's sake. *See* **aestheticism.**

assonance. The use of the same vowel-sounds in close proximity, often in verse, for the sake of euphony, memorability or emotional effect, *e.g.*, 'And deep-asleep he seemed" (Tennyson, "The Lotus-Eaters"). *See* **alliteration.**

asyndeton. The omission of a conjunction between words, phrases or clauses, *.e.g.*,

"And dreams of home,
Waving from window, spread of welcome,
Kissing of wife under single sheet"
(W. H. Auden, "The Wanderer").

See **ellipsis.**

Augustan. Referring to the reign of the Emperor Augustus (27 B.C.–14 A.D.), when Virgil, Horace and Ovid wrote, or to the neo-classical period in English literature between *c.* 1670 and 1790, when such writers as Dryden, Addison, Pope, Swift and Johnson conformed to the Augustan principles of reason, order and decorum. *See* **classical** *and* **neo-classicism.**

ballad. A narrative poem (often anonymous) telling of heroic or tragic deeds, typically written in quatrains of alternating four and three stresses and rhyming *abcb* or *abab*, *e.g.*, "Sir Patrick Spens." *See* **quatrain** and **M18**.

ballade. A poem of three eight-line stanzas (rhyming *ababbcbc*) and one four-line envoi (*bcbc*) with a refrain at the end of each of its four sections, *e.g.*, those written by Hilaire Belloc. *See* **envoi**.

bathos. An anticlimax or sudden descent from the sublime to the commonplace, intentional or unintentional, *e.g.*, the last two lines of Tennyson's "Enoch Arden":

"And when they buried him the little port
Had seldom seen a costlier funeral."

belles-lettres. Elegant, polished prose writing, especially essays, *e.g.*, those written by Max Beerbohm.

Bildungsroman. Literally, "formation novel" (German), *i.e.*, one that relates the upbringing, education and development of its hero, *e.g.*, Goethe's *Wilhelm Meister's Apprenticeship*. *See* **M4**.

black comedy. Comedy that finds amusement in what are conventionally regarded as tragic, sick or pessimistic people and situations, *e.g.*, Joe Orton's *Loot*.

blank verse. Unrhymed iambic pentameter (*see* **metre**), as used in Shakespeare's plays, Milton's *Paradise Lost* and Wordsworth's *Prelude*.

bouts-rimés. Literally, "rhymed ends" (French), *i.e.*, rhyming words supplied in advance to which lines must be fitted.

bowdlerise. To expurgate, from the Rev. Thomas Bowdler (1754–1825), who removed what he considered to be coarse expressions from the plays in his *Family Shakespeare*.

burlesque. A ludicrous, mocking imitation in prose or verse of a literary or dramatic work, *e.g.*, the Duke of Buckingham's *The Rehearsal*, a burlesque of seventeenth-century heroic plays. *See* **heroic tragedy**.

caesura. A break in a line of poetry, often towards the middle, sometimes used to emphasise the antithesis or comparison, *e.g.*,

"Willing to wound, / and yet afraid to strike"
(Pope, *Epistle to Arbuthnot*).

See **antithesis**.

canon. Authentic works of an author or standard works of literature (as studied on academic courses, for example).

canto. A division of a long poem, perhaps consisting of many **stanzas** (*q.v.*), as in Byron's *Don Juan*.

catachresis. A misuse or incorrect application of a word, *e.g.*, "chronic" to mean "severe".

catalectic. Describing a line of verse with one or more syllables missing in the final foot, *e.g.*,

"Rúin / seíze thĕe, / rúthlĕss / kíng!"
(Gray, "The Bard").

See **acatalectic**, **hypercatalectic** *and* **metre**.

catalyst. A substance that alters the rate of a chemical reaction but itself remains unchanged. T. S. Eliot used the term as an analogy in his theory of the poet's impersonality: "the more perfect the artist, the more completely separate in him will be the man who suffers and the mind which creates" ("Tradition and the Individual Talent," 1919).

catastrophe. The tragic climax of a drama or narrative.

catharsis. The purgation of pity and terror by means of the representation of those emotions in tragedy (Aristotle, *Poetics*). *See* **tragedy**.

character. A seventeenth-century genre of writing illustrating individual and social human types ("a modest man", "a shopkeeper", *etc.*), *e.g.*, John Earle's *Microcosmography*. More widely, a fictional personage, defined by E. M. Forster in *Aspects of the Novel* (1927) as either "flat" ("constructed round a single idea or quality") or "round" (with the "incalculability of life about it").

chiasmus. A "laying crosswise" of elements in a sentence, *i.e.*, the order of words in one of two parallel clauses or phrases is inverted in the other, *e.g.*,

"Love without end, and without measure grace"
(Milton, *Paradise Lost*).

chorus. A group of actors in Greek drama providing a commentary on the action; a device adapted, for example, by Shakespeare in *King Henry V* and T. S. Eliot in *Murder in the Cathedral*.

classical. Showing a regard for the values and forms of Ancient Greek and Latin literature and so having qualities of order, restraint, reason and precision. *See* **Augustan** *and* **neo-classical**.

clerihew. Comic biographical poem in the form of a *quatrain* (*q.v.*) with lines of various length, rhyming *aabb*, named after its inventor Eric Clerihew Bentley (1875–1956). *See* **M32**.

comedy. A literary or dramatic work, or aspect of it, that is amusing in various ways. More particularly, a work with a happy ending, *e.g.*, a comedy by Shakespeare. *See* **black comedy**.

comedy of ideas. A play (or novel) that is entertainingly and wittily concerned with ideas, problems and theories, *e.g.*, the novels of Thomas Love Peacock and the plays of Bernard Shaw.

comedy of manners. A play concerned with the behaviour and intrigues of elegant, sophisticated society, *e.g.*, Congreve's *The Way of the World* and Wilde's *The Importance of Being Earnest*.

conceit. An ingenious or highly fanciful example of imagery, perhaps using elaborate figures of speech and word-play, often associated with the *Metaphysical Poets* (*q.v.*), *e.g.*, Donne's comparison of two lovers' souls with a pair of compasses ("A Valediction: Forbidding Mourning").

couplet. Two successive rhyming lines. *See* **heroic couplet** *and* **rhyming couplet**.

dactyl. *See* **metre**.

decasyllable. A line of verse of ten syllables, often synonymous with the iambic pentameter. *See* **metre**.

deconstruction. A theory and method of textual analysis that emphasises the infinite number of uncertainties and ambiguities that exist in any literary work. *See* **post-structuralism**.

defamiliarisation. A conception of artistic technique held by the Russian Formalist, Victor Shklovsky, who maintained that art enables us to experience the world afresh by means of making things unfamiliar and thus increasing "the difficulty and duration of perception". *See* **formalism**.

diaeresis. The separation of a diphthong into two sounds, sometimes indicated by a mark (¨) placed over the second vowel, *e.g.*, "Noël".

dialogue. Conversation between two or more people in a literary or dramatic work. Also, a separate genre often used for the discussion of ideas, *e.g.*, Landor's *Imaginary Conversations*.

didactic. Applied to a literary work in prose or verse that aims to instruct the reader lightly or seriously, *e.g.*, Pope's poem, *An Essay on Criticism*.

diegesis. The process of authorial explanations, commentaries and narrative in a fictional work as distinct from the direct display of characters and action by such means as dialogue. Sometimes used in criticism as the opposing term to *mimesis* (*q.v.*). (From Plato's *Republic*.)

dirge. A funeral song or poem, *e.g.*, Shelley's "Autumn: A Dirge". *See* **elegy** *and* **threnody**.

dissociation of sensibility. T. S. Eliot's term (in "The Metaphysical Poets," 1921) to explain the failure of post seventeenth-century poets to amalgamate "disparate experience" to form "new wholes". There was a separation of feeling from thought in their work.

distich. Two lines of verse expressing a complete idea.

dithyramb. A passionate, rapturous poem, *e.g.*, Dryden's "Alexander's Feast".

doggerel. Rough, technically incompetent verse, often comic, vulgar or abusive, *e.g.*, some of the street ballads of the nineteenth century.

donnée. A situation or idea given or suggested to an author, who then bases a literary work on it, *e.g.*, an anecdote at the dinner-table led to Henry James's *The Spoils of Poynton*.

dramatic irony. Words or a situation on the stage understood by the audience in a different way from the way the characters understand them, *e.g.*, Duncan's speech, "This castle hath a pleasant seat . . .", spoken on the eve of his murder there (Shakespeare, *Macbeth*, I, vi).

dramatic monologue. Poem with one speaker addressing a listener or listeners and revealing, knowingly or unknowingly, important aspects of his character and situation, *e.g.*, Browning's "Fra Lippo Lippi."

eclogue. A fairly short pastoral poem often in the form of a dialogue, the ten *Eclogues* of Virgil.

elegiac stanza. Quatrain of four iambic pentameters rhyming *abab*, as used in Gray's "Elegy in a Country Churchyard".

elegy. A poem of mourning or lament, *e.g.*, Milton's "Lycidas" and Shelley's "Adonais". *See* **dirge** *and* **threnody.**

elision. The suppression of a vowel or syllable in verse for the sake of metrical correctness, *e.g.*, "ta'en" for "taken".

ellipsis. The omission of words, especially in poetry, to achieve compression, complexity or surprise, *e.g.*, in passages of T. S. Eliot's *The Waste Land. See* **asyndeton.**

emblem. A symbolic picture with a motto and explanation, associated with allegorical and figurative writing in such seventeenth century works as Francis Quarles' *Emblems*, a collection of religious poems.

end-stopped. Describing a self-contained line of verse that ends with a punctuation mark, *e.g.*,

"Black is the beauty of the brightest day!
The golden ball of Heaven's eternal fire,
That danced with glory on the silver waves,
Now wants the glory that inflamed his beams"
(Marlowe, *Tamburlaine*, 2nd Part, II, iv).

See **enjambment.**

enjambment. The running-on of one line of verse into another without a grammatical break, *e.g.*,

"Nay, but this dotage of our general's
O'er flows the measure . . ."
(Shakespeare, *Antony and Cleopatra*, I, i).

envoi. The short final stanza of a poem, especially a *ballade* (*q.v.*), addressed as parting words to a person or persons, emphasising the subject of the poem.

epic. A long narrative poem in an elevated style celebrating heroic personages and deeds, *e.g.*, Homer's *Iliad* and *Odyssey.*

epic simile. A long, elaborately developed comparison, as found in some epic poems. Sometimes termed *Homeric simile. See* **simile.**

epigram. A pointed, witty saying or verse that can be sarcastic, complimentary or amusing, *e.g.*,

"Swans sing before they die; 'twere no bad thing
Did certain persons die before they sing"
(Coleridge).

epigraph. A quotation or motto at the beginning of a work or of a section of it, *e.g.*, "Mistah Kurtz—he dead" (quotation from Conrad's *Heart of Darkness* prefixed to T. S. Eliot's *The Hollow Men*).

epilogue. The final section of work, serving such purposes as pointing a moral or summarising, *e.g.*, Rosalind's concluding speech in Shakespeare's *As You Like it.*

epiphany. James Joyce's term for a significant moment of revelation that a writer should record: "a sudden spiritual manifestation, whether in the vulgarity of speech or of gesture or in a memorable phase of the mind itself" (Joyce, *Stephen Hero*).

epistolary novel. A novel written in the form of letters, *e.g.*, Samuel Richardson's *Clarissa* and Laclos' *Les Liaisons dangereuses.*

epode. In the Greek *chorus* (*q.v.*) and the *Pindaric Ode* (*q.v.*), the third and last section, coming after the *antistrophe* (*q.v.*).

essay. A fairly short discussion in prose (or, more rarely, in verse) of any topic, light-hearted or serious in tone and formal or informal in style, as written by Bacon, Addison and Lamb.

euphemism The use of a mild, pleasant term to express something disagreeable, harsh or vulgar, *e.g.*, "And lo, he had answered to his name, and stood in the presence of The Master" (Thackeray, *The Newcomes*), meaning "He had died"; "visually challenged" meaning "blind" or "partly blind".

euphony. Agreeable sound in verse or prose achieved by such means as metre, rhyme, alliteration and assonance, enhanced by the meanings and associations of the words chosen, frequently found, for example, in the poems of Tennyson.

euphuism. Highly elaborate, prose style, as found in John Lyly's *Euphues* (1579-80).

eye-rhyme. A rhyme that is visually correct but orally incorrect, *e.g.*, "love" and "rove", though in considering older poetry changes in pronunciation must be borne in mind. Also, Spenser's practice of adjusting spelling to make a rhyme clear to both eye and ear.

fable. A short prose or verse narrative, often with animals as characters, intended to convey a moral lesson, as written, for example, by Aesop, La Fontaine and John Gay.

fabula. In Formalist criticism, a story as it would

actually have happened chronologically and objectively, as distinct from its literary treatment in a specific text, which is termed the *sjuzet. See* **formalism.**

farce. A comedy of broad, absurd and slapstick humour, often of frantic pace and technical ingenuity, *e.g.*, Ben Travers' *Rookery Nook.*

fashionable novel. A novel about life in high society written in an inflated, sentimental style, popular in the 1820s and 1830s, *e.g.*, Disraeli's *The Young Duke. See* **M6.**

foot. *See* **metre.**

foregrounding. Emphasis and prominence achieved in literary work by such means as linguistic deviation from normal usage.

formalism. A critical theory and method developed by critics in Russia *c.* 1913–30 (*e.g.*, Shklovsky and Jakobson) that concentrated on the analysis of literary works as self-sufficient structures and paid little or no attention to biographical and social influences.

fourteener. A line of verse containing fourteen syllables arranged as seven iambic feet. *See* **metre.**

free verse. Verse with no regular metrical pattern or length of line but with its form sometimes determined by its meaning, *e.g.*, D. H. Lawrence's "Snake". Also known as *vers libre.*

genre. A kind or type of literary work defined by its form and/or its purpose, *e.g.*, comedy, satire, ode.

Georgian poetry. Poetry written between *c.* 1910 and 1925, during the reign of George V, in short, lyrical forms and of easy comprehensibility, typically dealing with English rural subjects in an affectionate and nostalgic manner. The principal poets included W. H. Davies, Walter de la Mare, James Stephens, Edward Thomas and Edmund Blunden. *See* **M28.**

Gothic novels. Melodramatic novels of the late eighteenth and early nineteenth centuries dealing with terror, mystery and the supernatural, often in medieval settings, *e.g.*, M. G. Lewis's *The Monk. See* **M5.**

grand style. A plain, natural and noble style of poetry, as found in Homer (termed thus by Matthew Arnold).

great tradition. Phrase used by the critic F. R. Leavis to denote certain novelists "significant in terms of that human awareness they promote", *i.e.*, Jane Austen, George Eliot, Henry James and Joseph Conrad (*The Great Tradition*, 1948). Leavis would later have added Dickens and D. H. Lawrence to the tradition.

haiku. Japanese verse form of seventeen syllables in three lines of five, seven and five syllables, conveying a single, sharp impression of an image or mood.

half-rhyme. Rhyme in which the consonants are the same but the vowels are different, *e.g.*, "leaves"/ "lives", "simmer"/"summer" (taken from Wilfred Owen's "Miners").

hamartia. The flaw or defect in a tragic hero that leads to his downfall (Aristotle, *Poetics*).

hemistich. Half a line of verse, divided at the *caesura* (*q.v.*).

hendecasyllabic. A line of verse of eleven syllables, as used by the Latin poet, Catullus, but rarely found in English.

hendiadys. Expression of a compound notion by two elements co-ordinated by "and" instead of by one element subordinated to the other, *e.g.*, "waving to him *while hands and courtesy*" (Tennyson, "Gareth and Lynette") for "courteous white hands."

heptameter. *See* **metre.**

heroic couplet. A pair of rhyming iambic pentameters, so called because the metre was used in seventeenth century "heroic" plays and poems by Dryden and others. (*See* **heroic tragedy.**) The prevalent metrical form in the eighteenth century. *See* **metre** *and* **rhyming couplet.**

heroic tragedy. Late seventeenth-century type of drama, dealing in an elevated manner with themes of love and honour, written in *heroic couplets* (*q.v.*), *e.g.*, John Dryden's *The Conquest of Granada.*

hexameter. *See* **metre.**

historical novel. A novel set in past times, sometimes mixing fictional and factual characters and events, *e.g.*, Sir Walter Scott's *Ivanhoe. See* **M4.**

Homeric simile. *See* **epic simile** *and* **simile.**

homonym. A word having the same sound and sometimes the same spelling as another but a different meaning, *e.g.*, "fast": "rapid"; "fast": "abstinence"; "fast": "fixed".

homophone. A word having the same pronunciation as another but a different meaning and spelling, *e.g.*, "son" and "sun".

hubris. In Greek tragedy, the arrogance of a hero or heroine who ignores divine commands and who is therefore brought to ruin, e.g., the behaviour of Creon in Sophocles' *Antigone*.

hypallage. Transference of epithet from the normal substantive to an unexpected one, *e.g.*, "Who sees his true love in her *naked bed*" (Shakespeare, *Venus and Adonis*).

hyperbaton. Transposition of words out of normal order or separation of words usually associated together, *e.g.*,

"So much I hate a *breaking* cause to be
Of heavenly oaths"
(Shakespeare, *Love's Labour's Lost*, V, ii).

hyperbole. Exaggeration for the sake of emphasis or comedy, *e.g.*,

"There emerged from scores of by-streets, lanes, and nameless turnings, innumerable people, carrying their dinners to the bakers' shops"
(Dickens, *A Christmas Carol*).

hypercatalectic. Describing a line of verse with an extra syllable, *e.g.*,

"Thĕ slĭngs / aňd ař- / rŏws ŏf / oŭtráge-/ oŭs fór-/ tŭne"
(Shakespeare, *Hamlet*, III, i).

See **acatalectic, catalectic** *and* **metre.**

hysteron proton. Reversal of normal or temporal order, *e.g.*,

"Take, eat; this is my body"
(*St. Matthew*, ch. 26)

"Th'Antoniad, the Egyptian admiral,
With all their sixty, fly and turn the rudder"
(Shakespeare, *Antony and Cleopatra*, III, x).

idyll. A poem, pleasing and contented in tone, on an innocent, rural subject, of the type written by the Ancient Greek poet, Theocritus. More widely, a poem conveying a feeling of calm happiness.

imagery. Figures of speech and other devices of language used to convey sensuous and imaginative impressions to the reader.

Imagism. A poetic movement and theory, flourishing *c.* 1909–14, which emphasised direct treatment of subject-matter, concreteness, extreme economy of language and the rhythm of phrases rather than the rhythm of regular metres. The principal Imagist poets were Richard Aldington, H.D. (*i.e.*, Hilda Doolittle), F. S. Flint, Amy Lowell and Ezra Pound.

imitation. In particular, the practice, commended in the eighteenth century, of copying and adapting classical models (*e.g.*, Pope's *Imitations of Horace*). More generally, synonymous with *mimesis* (q.v.).

inscape. Gerard Manley Hopkins' term for the particular, unique, distinctive identity of a thing, an identity which the poet should capture in his work. *See* **instress.**

instress. Hopkins' term for the natural energy that determines an *inscape* (q.v.) and that maintains its existence: "the blue [of the sky] was charged with simple instress" (Hopkins' *Journal*, 1871).

intentional fallacy. A phrase coined by M. C. Beardsley and W. K. Wimsatt (1946), who argued that the "design or intention of the author is neither available nor desirable as a standard for judging the success of a work of literary art." *See* **affective fallacy** *and* **New Critics.**

interlude. In the sixteenth century a play performed in the midst of festivities. It could be farcical, romantic or religious and was sometimes indistinguishable from a *morality play* (q.v.). John Heywood's interludes are amongst the best-known.

internal rhyme. The rhyming of two or more words within one line of verse, *e.g.*,

"When you're lying *awake* with a dismal *headache*, and repose is taboo'd by anxiety"
(Gilbert, *Iolanthe*).

See **rhyme.**

inversion. The reversal of normal syntax, usually by putting the verb before the subject, as in poetic language imitating Latin word-order, *e.g.*, the opening six lines of Milton's *Paradise Lost*: "Of

Man's first disobedience ... sing heavenly Muse". *See* **Latinism.**

irony. The use of words (verbal irony) or situations (situational irony) to convey the opposite of what is really meant or what might naturally be expected. It can be comic, tragic or satirical, *e.g.*, Fielding's description of Blifil as "this worthy young man" (*Tom Jones*), the remark made by Jane Austen's Mr Bennet about Mr Collins' "talent of flattering with delicacy" (*Pride and Prejudice*) and Thomas Hardy's portrayal of Jude's death in the midst of student festivities at Christminster (*Jude the Obscure*). *See* **dramatic irony.**

Johnsonian. In the literary style and manner of Dr Samuel Johnson (1709–84), *e.g.*, using weighty, well-balanced sentences and a Latinised vocabulary and expressing a pragmatic, common-sense attitude to life and literature.

Lake Poets. The English Romantic poets, Wordsworth, Coleridge and Southey, who lived in the Lake District. *See* **M24.**

lampoon. A personal satire, often malicious and coarse in tone, *e.g.*, Henry Carey's "Namby-Pamby" (a poem on the poet, Ambrose Philips). *See* **satire.**

langue. A language considered as a whole, abstract system, which all its speakers have in common. (Term used by the linguist, Ferdinand de Saussure.) *See* **parole.**

Latinism. Word, phrase, idiom or construction that imitates a Latin one. Characteristics can include sentence-inversion (*see* **inversion**), placing adjectives after and around substantives (see the first example below) and the use of many words (often learned and abstract) derived from Latin (see the second example), *e.g.*,

"I come to pluck your *berries harsh and crude*,
And with *forc'd fingers rude*
Shatter your leaves before the mellowing year"
(Milton, "Lycidas")

"A *doctrine* so *extraordinary* and so *sublime* must *inevitably command the veneration of the people*" (Gibbon, *Decline and Fall of the Roman Empire*).

lay. A narrative or lyrical poem recounting romantic or adventurous deeds, *e.g.*, Scott's *Lay of the Last Minstrel*.

Leavisite. Pertaining to the ideas and followers of F. R. Leavis (1895–1978), whose rigorous literary criticism was informed by a serious moral concern. *See* **great tradition.**

lexis. The vocabulary of a language, which therefore consists of lexical items (which can include words and brief phrases).

limerick. A comic five-line verse-form in anapaests (*see* **metre**), rhyming *aabba*, ideally with a surprising last line.

litotes. An understatement, particularly one that uses the negative, often made for the purposes of irony or emphasis, *e.g.*, "Mrs Blifil was not over and above pleased with the behaviour of her husband" (Fielding, *Tom Jones*); "No little band of yet remembered names" (Wordsworth, *The Prelude*, I). *See* **meiosis.**

loose sentence. A sentence with the main clause first, followed by subordinate clauses, *e.g.*, "*There can be no doubt* that this remarkable man owed the vast influence which he exercised over his contemporaries at least as much to his gloomy egotism as to the real power of his poetry" (Macaulay, *Byron*). *See* **periodic sentence.**

lyric. A short poem of a song-like nature, expressing a single—often personal—mood. For numerous examples, see Palgrave's *Golden Treasury*.

macaronic. Describing comic or burlesque verse written in mixed languages or languages adapted and distorted, *e.g.*, "Charmer virumque I sing, Jack plumigeramque Arabellam" (first line of "Narrative Macaronic Verses" by Frank Sidgwick).

malapropism. A word used in the wrong sense, sometimes for comic effect, *e.g.*, "I would have her instructed in *geometry*, that she might know something of the *contagious* countries" (Mrs Malaprop in Sheridan's *The Rivals*, I, ii).

masque. A courtly entertainment, popular in the late sixteenth and early seventeenth centuries, consisting of artificial, fantastic dramatic action, dancing, songs, and elaborate costumes and settings, *e.g.*, Ben Jonson's *Masque of Oberon*.

meiosis. An understatement, often used for purposes of emphasis or comedy, *e.g.*,

"A small accident had happened, which somewhat disconcerted them; and this was no other than the thief's escape"

(Fielding, *Joseph Andrews*)

"But she is in her grave, and, oh,
The difference to me!"
(Wordsworth, "She dwelt among the untrodden ways").

See litotes.

melodrama. Extravagant drama of heightened emotions, characterised by sentimentality and sensationalism, *e.g.*, Leopold Lewis' *The Bells*, in which Henry Irving gave a famous performance.

metaphor. A figure of speech of comparison stating an identity rather than a likeness, *i.e.*, something is said to be that which it only resembles, *e.g.*, "I fall upon the thorns of life" (Shelley, "Ode to the West Wind"); "the very honey of earthly joy" (Cowley, "The Wish").

Metaphysical Poets. Seventeenth century poets, including John Donne, George Herbert, Henry Vaughan, Richard Crashaw and Andrew Marvell, whose subject-matter was usually love or religion. Their poems contain striking imagery, wit, intense passion and powers of argument and persuasion. (Term first used by Dr Johnson, who may have been influenced by a phrase of Dryden's.) *See* **M20**.

metonymy. The application of the name of an attribute to that of the thing meant, *e.g.*, "Dickens" for "the works of Dickens"; "the Bench" for "the magistrates".

metre. The measure of lines of verse, which in English is basically accentual (*q.v.*). Each group of syllables (usually two or three) is a **foot**. These feet of stressed syllables (marked with ˊ) and unstressed syllables (marked with ˘) are often classified as follows: iambus (˘ˊ); trochee (ˊ˘); spondee (ˊˊ); pyrrhic (˘˘); anapaest (˘˘ˊ); dactyl (ˊ˘˘); amphibrach (˘ˊ˘). The number of feet in a line is indicated as follows: monometer (1); dimeter (2); trimeter (3); tetrameter (4); pentameter (5); hexameter (6); heptameter (7). An *iambic pentameter*, for example, is therefore a line of five iambic feet, *e.g.*,

"Bělín- / dă smiled, / and áll / thĕ world / wăs gáy"
(Pope, *The Rape of the Lock*).

Metrical variation, however, is a common feature of English verse.

Miltonic. Pertaining to the work of John Milton (1608–74), with reference to his Latinised syntax and vocabulary, his blank verse, his sonnets and his Protestant theology and outlook. *See* **M21**.

mimesis. Plato's term for artistic imitation or representation, which he thought necessarily false. Aristotle saw it as a basic function of art, stating that the "objects of imitation are the actions of men". The term can also denote more particularly the direct representation of speech and action in a literary work. *See* diegesis.

miracle plays. Fourteenth and fifteenth century plays, sometimes known as Mystery Plays, consisting of dramatised episodes from the Bible, from the Creation to the Day of Judgement, acted by members of trade guilds, usually on Corpus Christi day. Cycles survive from York, Coventry, Wakefield and Chester.

mock heroic. The satirical or comic application of heroic or epic styles, conventions, situations and characters to trivial or vulgar subjects, *e.g.*, Pope's *The Rape of the Lock*.

monodrama. A dramatic work for one character or performer, *e.g.*, Tennyson's poem, "Maud".

monologue. A prose or verse composition spoken by one character or performer, either as a separate work or as part of a work, *e.g.*, Beckett's *Krapp's Last Tape*. *See* **dramatic monologue**, **monodrama** *and* **soliloquy**.

morality plays. Allegorical dramas of the late fifteenth and early sixteenth centuries, in which personified virtues and vices contend for a man's soul, *e.g.*, *Everyman*.

morpheme. The smallest linguistic unit which has a grammatical function and an independent meaning, *e.g.*, sang, bread, -ing, -ed.

mystery plays. *See* miracle plays.

myth. Story of unknown origin expressing and explaining universal and religious experience (*e.g.*, fertility and seasonal change) often by means of the deeds of a hero or god. *See* **Section I Classical Mythology**.

Naturalism. Originating in nineteenth century France, a literary movement that aimed at presenting the reality of life, with an emphasis on environment, objectivity and amorality. Prominent naturalistic novelists included Zola, Gissing and Bennett. *See* **realism** *and* **M11**.

negative capability. John Keats' phrase (in a letter, 1817) for the quality, found in such great poets as Shakespeare, "of being in uncertainties, mysteries, doubts, without any irritable reaching after fact and reason".

neo-classicism. The theory and application, particularly in the eighteenth century, of the classical values and rules of reason, order and decorum, as shown in the work of Dryden, Pope and Johnson, who emulated Homer, Virgil, Horace, Juvenal and other writers of Ancient Greece and Rome. *See* **Augustan** *and* **classical**.

neologism. A new word or phrase, or an old word used in a new sense, *e.g.*, "agnostic" (coined by T. H. Huxley) and "prestigious" (meaning "having prestige" instead of "juggling").

New Critics. American group of critics, including Cleanth Brooks, R. P. Blackmur, Robert Penn Warren, John Crowe Ransom and W. K. Wimsatt, who were active in the late 1930s and the 1940s and who advocated close textual analysis, free of biographical and contextual associations. *See* **affective fallacy** *and* **intentional fallacy**.

Newgate novels. Crime novels of the 1820s and 1830s that tended to romanticise criminals and highwaymen, *e.g.*, Bulwer Lytton's *Paul Clifford* and W. H. Ainsworth's *Rookwood*. *See* **M6**.

nouveau roman. Type of French novel that began in the 1950s and that rejected conventional characterisation and plot, as written by Alain Robbe-Grillet. *See* **anti-novel**.

novel. *See* **M4**–**M17** for definitions, types and history.

novella. A short novel, *e.g.*, Conrad's *Typhoon* and D. H. Lawrence's *The Fox*.

objective correlative. T. S. Eliot's term (in his essay on *Hamlet*, 1919) for "a set of objects, a situation, a chain of events which shall be the formula" of a particular emotion expressed in art.

octave. *See* **sonnet**.

ode. A lyrical poem of elaborate structure and elevated diction written to celebrate or commemorate a noble, beautiful or admirable subject or theme, *e.g.*, Keats' "Ode to a Nightingale" and Tennyson's "Ode on the Death of the Duke of Wellington." *See* **Pindaric Ode**.

onomatopoeia. The use or invention of words to imitate sounds, *e.g.*, "buzz", "hiss", "swish", or the imitative effect of such word usage as Tennyson's "murmuring of innumerable bees" ("Come down, O maid").

ottava rima. Eight iambic pentameters (*see* **metre**) rhyming *abababcc*, as in Byron's *Don Juan*.

oxymoron. Combination of two contradictory terms in one expression, *e.g.*, "fearful joy" (Gray) and "sweet unrest" (Keats).

palindrome. A word, sentence or verse that reads the same backwards or forwards, *e.g.*, "level", "A man, a plan, a canal—Panama."

parable. A short, often realistic story told to exemplify a doctrine or moral, as told by Christ in the New Testament, *e.g.*, "The Sower" and "The Good Samaritan".

paradox. An apparent contradiction or absurdity often designed to upset conventional opinion and to indicate a truth, *e.g.*, G. K. Chesterton's "If we are to be international we must be national" and "The subtle man is always immeasurably easier to understand than the natural man."

parataxis. Arrangement of clauses without conjunctions. *e.g.*, "After a painful struggle I yielded to my fate: I sighed as a lover, I obeyed as a son; my wound was insensibly healed by time, absence, and the habits of a new life" (Gibbon, *Autobiography*).

parody. A comic or satirical imitation of an original work or of the characteristic style of a writer or literary movement, *e.g.*, Max Beerbohm's "Scruts" (a parody of Arnold Bennett) and Henry Reed's "Chard Whitlow" (a parody of T. S. Eliot's *Four Quartets*).

parole. An actual, individual utterance of language, as distinct from *langue* (*q.v.*). (Term used by the linguist, Ferdinand de Saussure.)

paronomasia. A play on words. *See* **pun**.

pastoral poetry. Poetry dealing in an idealised way with rustic life, especially the lives and emotions of shepherds and shepherdesses, *e.g.*, Spenser's *Shepherd's Calendar*.

pathetic fallacy. The false belief that human emotions exist in non-human things and phenomena. Such appearances are "entirely unconnected with any real power or character in the object, and only imputed to it by us", *e.g.*, "the cruel, crawling foam" (Ruskin, *Modern Painters*, where he coined, discussed and illustrated the term, 1856).

pentameter. *See* metre.

periodic sentence. A sentence that begins with subordinate clauses and ends with the main clause, *e.g.*, "Since then the imaginary right of vengeance must be at last remitted, because it is impossible to live in perpetual hostility, and equally impossible that of two enemies, either should first think himself obliged by justice to submission, *it is surely eligible to forgive early*" (Samuel Johnson, essay in *The Rambler*). *See* loose sentence.

peripeteia. In drama, a sudden change of fortune, "the reverse of what is expected from the circumstances of the action" (Aristotle, *Poetics*), as in Sophocles' *Oedipus Tyrannus*, where the messenger, meaning to make Oedipus happy, reveals the secret of his birth, with tragic consequences.

periphrasis. Roundabout speech or circumlocution, *e.g.*, Mr Micawber's speeches in Dickens' *David Copperfield*.

persona. A character or narrator who can in some cases be thought to be the author in disguise, *e.g.*, Stephen Daedalus in Joyce's *Portrait of the Artist as a Young Man*.

personification. Representation of a thing or quality as a person, *e.g.*, "There Honour comes, a pilgrim grey" (William Collins, "Ode").

Petrarchan sonnet. *See* sonnet.

phoneme. The minimum significant sound-unit in language, either consonant-type or vowel-type, *e.g.*, "*meat*," "*boy*".

picaresque novel. A novel with a rogue as its hero, undergoing many adventures, *e.g.*, Smollett's *Peregrine Pickle*. See M4.

Pindaric Ode. An ode modelled on the Greek odes of Pindar (518–438 B.C.) consisting of a **strophe**, **antistrophe** and **epode** (qq.v.) in complex stanzas, this three-part structure often being repeated at least once, *e.g.*, Thomas Gray's "Progress of Poesy". *See* ode.

pleonasm. Using more words than are needed, either unconsciously or deliberately for emphasis, *e.g.*, 'at this moment of time" (for "now") and "most unkindest cut of all" (Shakespeare, *Julius Caesar*).

plot. The sequence or complex of connected events in a fictional narrative or drama, with (in Forster's definition in *Aspects of the Novel*, 1927) "a sense of causality" to distinguish it from *story* (q.v.).

poetic diction. Words, phrases and syntax prescribed specifically for poetic use, especially in the eighteenth century and including *periphrasis* (q.v.) (*e.g.*, "the finny tribe" for "fish"), personification and Latinised structures and expressions.

poetic prose. Prose using such devices as rhythm, elaborate imagery, figures of speech and symbols, conventionally associated with poetry, to be found, for example, in some of George Meredith's descriptive passages in his novels.

portmanteau word. One word formed by combining two or more words, *e.g.*, "smog," a combination of "smoke" and "fog". (Term coined by Lewis Carroll in *Through the Looking-Glass*.)

poststructuralism. A development of *structuralism* (q.v.), which concentrates on the power of language as a creative force within itself and the indeterminate number of possibilities of meaning and interpretation. *See* deconstruction.

practical criticism. Exercises in the close analysis of texts, as advocated and practised by the critic and teacher I. A. Richards (in *Practical Criticism*, 1929).

prolegomenon. An introduction, sometimes of a learned nature, *e.g.*, R. B. McKerrow's *Prolegomena for the Oxford Shakespeare*.

prolepsis. Anticipatory use of an epithet, *e.g.*, "the two brothers and their murder'd man" (Keats, "Isabella") and " 'I'm killed, Sire!' " (Browning, "Incident in the French Camp").

prologue. The introductory section of a work with such functions as setting the scene, whetting the appetite of audience or reader and giving preliminary explanations, *e.g.*, the opening Chorus of Shakespeare's *Romeo and Juliet*.

prosody. The study of versification, including

rhythm, rhyme and stanza forms, as in George Saintsbury's *History of English Prosody*.

pun. A play on words, *e.g.*,

"I cannot say '*whore*':
 It does ab*hor* me now I speak the word"
                    (Shakespeare, *Othello*, IV ii)

"They went and *told* the sexton, and
 The sexton *toll'd* the bell"
              (Thomas Hood, "Sally Brown").

pyrrhic. *See* metre.

quatrain. A four-lined stanza (q.v.).

realism. In the nineteenth century, the theory and practice of a belief that art (*e.g.*, the novel) should be a precise, truthful representation of life, associated in France with Balzac and the Goncourt brothers, amongst others. Sometimes synonymous with **naturalism** (q.v.).

Revenge Tragedy. Popular seventeenth century type of drama, derived from Seneca's plays (1st century A.D.), in which revenge, ghosts and terror are prominent, *e.g.*, Kyd's *The Spanish Tragedy*.

rhetorical question. A question which does not require an answer but which is put for purposes of emphasis, *e.g.*, "Were they again to advance their money on pledges which had been forfeited over and over again?" (Macaulay, "Milton").

rhyme. Identity of sound from the last stressed vowel to the end, sometimes used in conventional patterns, such as **rhyming couplets**, **sonnets** and the **Spenserian stanza** (qq.v.).

rhyme royal. A stanza of seven iambic pentameters rhyming *ababbcc*, used, for example, in Chaucer's *Troilus and Criseyde*. *See* metre.

rhyming couplet. The same as **heroic couplet** (q.v.), but rhyming couplets in iambic tetrameter (*not* known as heroic couplets) are also frequently used, *e.g.*, in Swift's poems. *See* metre.

rhythm. Regular recurrence of stress or of long or short sounds, especially in poetry, analysed by the process of **scansion**. *See* metre. More widely, patterns of event or motif in various literary compositions, including novels.

roman à clef. A novel about actual people disguised as fictional personages, *e.g.*, Aldous Huxley's *Point Counterpoint*.

roman-fleuve. A long series of inter-related novels, *e.g.*, Proust's *A la Recherche du temps perdu*.

romance. A term of many meanings, including a medieval poetic or prose story of chivalry and love (*e.g.*, Malory's *Morte Darthur*); later, a work dealing with adventures in a fanciful and unrealistic manner (*e.g.*, Shakespeare's *The Winter's Tale*); in modern times, a glamorous, sentimental story of love (*e.g.*, the "romantic novels" published by Mills and Boon).

Romanticism. In literature, the movement at the end of the eighteenth and the beginning of the nineteenth centuries identified with individual expression, sensibility, imagination, emotion, the love of Nature and "simple" people (such as peasants and children) and a wide variety of literary forms. In part the movement was a reaction against **neo-classicism** (q.v.). Leading Romantic writers in English literature were Scott, Wordsworth, Coleridge, Byron, Shelley and Keats. *See* **M23–25**.

rondeau. A form of verse, originally French, in which lines are repeated at regular intervals. A typical pattern is *aabba*; *aab* and refrain; *aabba* and refrain, all octosyllabic. Written by some minor nineteenth century English poets, *e.g.*, Austin Dobson.

run-on line. See enjambment.

saga. An ancient Icelandic or Scandinavian prose tale of heroes and great deeds, mostly oral in origin.

samizdat. Self-published, typescript, underground Russian literature expressing opinions and viewpoints unacceptable to the government.

sapphics. A classical, quantitative metre consisting of three longer lines and one shorter.

satire. Prose or verse composition ridiculing and criticising vice and folly by such means as **irony** (q.v.), sarcasm, the **mock-heroic** (q.v.), **parody** (q.v.) and invective. John Dryden said that "the true end of satire is the amendment of vices by correction" (*Absalom and Achitophel*, "To the Reader"). Famous examples include Swift's *Modest Proposal* and Pope's *Dunciad*.

scansion. The process of analysing **metre** (q.v.).

semiology. The science of studying signs, especially those used in systems of communication (including objects, gestures and clothes as well as language). *See* **semiotics**.

semiotics. The study of patterns of behaviour in communication, particularly through the use of linguistics. More broadly, synonymous with *semiology (q.v.)*.

sensation novel. Mid-nineteenth century English novels of crime, detection and passion, with an atmosphere of excitement, suffering and suspense, *e.g.*, M. E. Braddon's *Lady Audley's Secret*. *See* **M9**.

sestet. *See* **sonnet**.

sestina. Elaborate verse-form of six six-line stanzas ending with a three-line **envoi** *(q.v.)*.

Shakespearean sonnet. *See* **sonnet**.

signified and **signifier.** Saussure's terms for the concept and its oral or written verbal "sound image", indissolubly but arbitrarily connected to each other.

simile. A figure of speech in which two things or actions are likened to each other, usually by means of "as" or "like", *e.g.*,

"Your face, my Thane, is as a book where men
May read strange matters"
(Shakespeare, *Macbeth*, I, v)

"From the earth thou springest
Like a cloud of fire"
(Shelley, "To a Skylark").

sjuzet. *See* **fabula**.

soliloquy. A solo utterance often by a character in a play talking to himself or thinking aloud, as if there were no audience, *e.g.*, Hamlet's "To be or not to be . . .".

sonnet. Poem of fourteen iambic pentameters. The two main forms are the Petrarchan (after Petrarch, 1304–74), consisting of an **octave** (eight lines usually rhyming *abbaabba*) stating the theme and a **sestet** (six lines using different rhymes in various patterns) commenting on the theme or modifying it; the Shakespearean, consisting of three quatrains (usually rhyming *ababcdcdefef*) presenting the theme and a final **rhyming couplet** *(gg)* summarising or clinching the theme. *See* **metre**, **quatrain** *and* **rhyming couplet**.

Spenserian stanza. Eight iambic pentameters followed by one iambic hexameter (or **alexandrine**, *q.v.*) rhyming *ababbcbcc*, as used in Spenser's *Faerie Queene*. *See* **metre** and **M19**.

spondee. *See* **metre**.

sprung rhythm. Gerard Manley Hopkins' metrical system, dependent on measuring stresses and not on regular numbers of feet and syllables; hence, like the rhythms of common speech, written prose, music and folk poetry.

stanza. A formal arrangement of a group of lines of poetry, usually in a rhyming pattern.

stichomythia. Interchange of short, one-line speeches in dramatic verse, *e.g.*, some of the dialogue between King Richard and Queen Elizabeth in Shakespeare's *King Richard III*, IV, iv.

story. A tale, or the general, complete action of a narrative work, ranging more widely than the **plot** *(q.v.)*.

stream of consciousness. Term coined by the philosopher William James (1890) to denote the unending, formless flow of human thoughts and emotions. Some novelists, *e.g.*, James Joyce and Virginia Woolf, have conveyed this "stream" by various techniques (*e.g.*, loose syntax and light punctuation) in order to explore the consciousness of their characters.

strophe. The first section of the Greek **chorus** or the Pindaric Ode *(q.v.)*.

structuralism. As applied to literature, a complex form of textual analysis concentrating on formal linguistic and thematic patternings, as practised, for example, by Roland Barthes.

sub-plot. A plot of lesser importance but sometimes used as a parallel or foil to the main plot, *e.g.*, the Falstaff-Prince Hal sub-plot in Shakespeare's *King Henry IV, Part 1*. *See* **plot**.

syllabic verse. Poetry written in metre measured by the number of syllables in each line, *e.g.*, some of W. H. Auden's later verse.

syllepsis. A figure of speech in which one word has the same syntactical relationship to two or more other words but different meanings, *e.g.*, The nymph may "lose her heart, or necklace, at a ball" (Pope, *The Rape of the Lock*). Sometimes synonymous with **zeugma** *(q.v.)*.

symbolism. Artistic movement of the 1890s, mostly originating amongst French writers (*e.g.*, Mallarmé and Valéry), using mystical, occult and magical images and musical, evocative language. More widely, the use of objects, actions, scenes and structures to represent or suggest significant themes and ideas in a literary work, *e.g.*, the dust heaps and the Thames in Dickens' *Our Mutual Friend* and the rose, the tower, Troy and swans in Yeats' poetry.

synaesthesia. Combination of different sense impressions, as described in Baudelaire's sonnet, "Correspondances". They are often evoked in a single phrase, *e.g.*, "dark music" (Isaac Rosenberg, "Louse Hunting") and "squealing light" (Edith Sitwell, "Gold Coast Customs").

syncope. The cutting short or contraction of a word, especially in poetic usage, *e.g.*, "e'er" for "ever".

synecdoche. A figure of speech in which the part represents the whole or the whole represents the part, *e.g.*, "the multitude of Coketown, generically called 'the Hands'" (*i.e.*, the factory-workers, Dickens, *Hard Times*) and "England" for "the English cricket team".

tercet. A three-lined stanza, particularly as used in terza rima *(q.v.)*.

terza rima. Verse-form of three-lined stanzas rhyming *aba, bcb, cdc*, etc., usually iambic pentameters, as used in Shelley's "Ode to the West Wind."

tetrameter. *See* **metre**.

theme. The central idea or topic of a literary work.

threnody. A poem of lamentation. *See* **dirge** and **elegy**.

touchstones. Criteria of excellence in poetry provided by the "lines and expressions of the great masters", *e.g.*, Homer, Dante, Shakespeare and Milton (Matthew Arnold's term and definition, "The Study of Poetry," 1880).

tragedy. "An imitation of some action that is important, entire, and of proper magnitude . . . effecting through pity and terror the correction and refinement of such passions' (Aristotle, *Poetics*). A drama that ends sadly, especially with the downfall of a flawed hero. *See* **catharsis**, **hamartia** *and* **peripeteia**.

tragi-comedy. A drama that mixes elements of tragedy and comedy, *e.g.*, Shakespeare's *Measure for Measure*.

trimeter. *See* **metre**.

triolet. Verse-form of eight lines and two rhymes, in which the fourth line repeats the first and the eighth line repeats the second, popular with some late nineteenth century minor poets, including Austin Dobson.

triplet. Three rhyming lines, usually iambic pentameters, sometimes used for variation or emphasis in a poem of **rhyming** or **heroic couplets**.

trochee. *See* **metre**.

trope. A figure of speech in general.

unities. Theory partly deriving from Aristotle's *Poetics* and fully formulated by Castelvetro (1505–71) that a drama should conform to the three unities of Action (*i.e.*, there must be no digressions), Time (*i.e.*, the action in performance should correspond as nearly as possible to the duration of the action in real life) and Place (*i.e.*, its scene should not change).

ut pictura poesis. "As a picture, so a poem", *i.e.*, "a poem is like a picture," a much-discussed formulation by the Latin poet, Horace, in his *Art of Poetry*.

vers de société. Light, elegant verse dealing with people and behaviour in polite society, *e.g.*, the poems of W. M. Praed. *See* **M31**.

vers libre. The same as **free verse** *(q.v.)*.

verse. Originally a metrical line; more commonly, a stanza or versification and verse composition in general.

villanelle. Verse-form of five **tercets** *(q.v.)* and one **quatrain** *(q.v.)* with two rhymes. The first line ends the second and fourth tercet; the third line ends the first, third and fifth tercets; the first and third lines then end the final quatrain, *e.g.*, William Empson's "Missing Dates."

zeugma. A figure of speech in which a single epithet or verb is applied to two substantives but is appropriate to only one of them, *e.g.*, "See Pan with flocks, with fruits Pomona crowned" (Pope, *Windsor Forest*). Sometimes used to mean the same as **syllepsis** *(q.v.)*.

V. SPECIAL TOPICS

MAJOR LITERARY PRIZES

The following is a selection of major literary prizes awarded since 1980, unless otherwise indicated.

James Tait Black Memorial Prizes (1918)

Two prizes of £1,500 each, one for the best biography or work of that nature and the other for the best work of fiction written in English and first published in Britain in the year of the award.

1980   Robert Bernard Martin, *Tennyson: The Unquiet Heart*
       J. M. Coetzee, *Waiting for the Barbarians*
1981   Victoria Glendinning, *Edith Sitwell: A Unicorn among Lions*
       { Salman Rushdie, *Midnight's Children*
       { Paul Theroux, *The Mosquito Coast*
1982   Richard Ellmann, *James Joyce*
       Bruce Chatwin, *On the Black Hill*
1983   Alan Walker, *Franz Liszt: The Virtuoso Years*
       Jonathan Keates, *Allegro Postillions*
1984   Lyndall Gordon, *Virginia Woolf: a Writer's Life*
       { J. G. Ballard, *Empire of the Sun*
       { Angela Carter, *Nights at the Circus*
1985   { David Nokes, *A Hypocrite Reversed*
       { Robert Edric, *Winter Garden*
1986   { D. Felicitas Corrigan, *Helen Waddell*
       { Jenny Joseph, *Persephone*
       { Ruth Dudley Edwards, *Victor Gollancz: a Biography*
1987   { George Mackay Brown, *The Golden Bird: Two Orkney Stories*
1988   Brian McGuinness, *Wittgenstein: A Life: Young Ludwig (1889–1921)*
       Piers Paul Read, *A Season in the West*
1989   Ian Gibson, *Federico García Lorca: A Life*
       James Kelman, *A Disaffection*

Booker Prize for Fiction (1968)

£20,000 for the best full-length novel in English written by a citizen of Britain, the Commonwealth, the Republic of Ireland, or South Africa.

1980   Sir William Golding, *Rites of Passage*
1981   Salman Rushdie, *Midnight's Children*
1982   Thomas Keneally, *Schindler's Ark*
1983   J. M. Coetzee, *Life and Times of Michael K*
1984   Anita Brookner, *Hotel du Lac*
1985   Keri Hulme, *The Bone People*
1986   Kingsley Amis, *The Old Devils*
1987   Penelope Lively, *Moon Tiger*
1988   Peter Carey, *Oscar and Lucinda*
1989   Kazuo Ishiguro, *The Remains of the Day*

Duff Cooper Memorial Prize (1954)

Approximately £250 and a specially bound copy of Duff Cooper's autobiography, *Old Men Forget*, for a book published in English or French in the previous two years on a subject of history, biography, politics or poetry.

1980   Robert Bernard Martin, *Tennyson: the Unquiet Heart*
1981   Victoria Glendinning, *Edith Sitwell: a Unicorn among Lions*
1982   Richard Ellmann, *James Joyce*
1983   Peter Porter, *Collected Poems*
1984   Hilary Spurling, *Ivy Compton-Burnett*
1985   Ann Thwaite, *Edmund Gosse: A Literary Landscape*
1986   Alan Crawford, *C. R. Astxee: Architect, Designer and Romantic Socialist*
1987   Robert Hughes, *The Fatal Shore*
1988   Humphrey Carpenter, *A Serious Character: the Life of Ezra Pound*
1989   Ian Gibson, *Federico García Lorca: a Life*

Prix Goncourt (1903)

Fifty francs for the best prose work in French.

1980   Yves Navarre, *Le Jardin d'acclimatation*
1981   Lucien Bodard, *Anne-Marie*
1982   Dominique Fernandez, *Dans la main de l'ange*
1983   Frédérick Tristan, *Les Egarés*
1984   Marguerite Duras, *L'Amant*
1985   Yann Queffelec, *Les Noces Barbares*
1986   Michel Host, *Valet de Nuit*
1987   Tahar Ben Jelloun, *La Nuit sacrée*
1988   Erik Orsenna, *L'Exposition Coloniale*
1989   Jean Vautrin, *Un grand pas vers le bon Dieu*

Hawthornden Prize (1919)

£750 for a work of imaginative literature by a British subject under forty-one years of age.

1980   Christopher Reid, *Arcadia*
1981   Douglas Dunn, *St. Kilda's Parliament*
1982   Timothy Mo, *Sour Sweet*
1983   Jonathan Keates, *Allegro Postillions*
1984   }
1985   } No awards
1986   }
1987   Colin Thubron, *Behind the Wall*
1988   Alan Bennett, *Talking Heads*

Somerset Maugham Awards (1947)

£5,000, to be used for a period or periods of foreign travel, for promising authors, British subjects by birth, under 35 years old. Poetry, fiction, criticism, biography, history, philosophy, belles-lettres, and travel books are eligible, but not dramatic works.

1980   Max Hastings, *Bomber Command*
       Christopher Reid, *Arcadia*
       Humphrey Carpenter, *The Inklings*
1981   Julian Barnes, *Metroland*
       Clive Sinclair, *Hearts of Gold*
       A. N. Wilson, *The Healing Art*
1982   William Boyd, *A Good Man in Africa*
       Adam Mars-Jones, *Lantern Lecture*
1983   Lisa St. Aubin de Teran, *Keepers of the House*
1984   Peter Ackroyd, *The Last Testament of Oscar Wilde*
       Timothy Garton Ash, *The Polish Revolution: Solidarity*
       Sean O'Brien, *The Indoor Park*
1985   Blake Morrison, *Dark Glasses*
       Jeremy Reed, *By the Fisheries*
       Jane Rogers, *Her Living Image*
1986   Patricia Ferguson, *Family Myths and Legends*
       Adam Nicolson, *Frontiers*
       Tim Parks, *Tongues of Flame*
1987   Stephen Gregory, *The Cormorant*
       Ganni Kinsky, *Isaac Campion*
       Andrew Motion, *The Lamberts*
1988   Jimmy Burns, *The Land that lost its Heroes*
       Carol Ann Duffy, *Selling Manhattan*
       Matthew Kneale, *Whore Banquets*
1989   Robert Christiansen, *Romantic Affinities*
       Allan Hollinghurst, *The Swimming-Pool Library*
       Deirdre Madden, *The Bird of the Innocent Wood*

Nobel Prize for Literature (1901)

The income from the trust fund (approximately £1,750,000) is annually distributed amongst five prizes: Physics, Chemistry, Physiology and Medicine, Literature and Peace.

1980   Czeslaw Milosz
1981   Elias Canetti
1982   Gabriel Garcia Márquez
1983   William Golding
1984   Jaroslav Seifert
1985   Claude Simon

1986	Wole Soyinka
1987	Joseph Brodsky
1988	Naguib Mahfouz
1989	Camilo José Cela

W. H. Smith Literary Award (1959)

£10,000 for any type of book that has made an outstanding contribution to English Literature, written by a citizen of the U.K. or the Commonwealth.

1980	Thom Gunn, *Selected Poems*
1981	Isabel Colegate, *The Shooting Party*
1982	George Clare, *Last Waltz in Vienna*
1983	A. N. Wilson, *Wise Virgin*
1984	Philip Larkin, *Required Writing*
1985	David Hughes, *The Pork Butcher*
1986	Doris Lessing, *The Good Terrorist*
1987	Elizabeth Jennings, *Collected Poems*
1988	Robert Hughes *The Fatal Shore*
1989	Christopher Hill, *A Turbulent, Seditious and Factious People: John Bunyan and his Church*
1990	V. S. Pritchett, *A Careless Widow, and Other Stories.*

The Betty Trask Awards (1984)

£19,000 in all for first novels, published or unpublished, by writers under the age of 35. They are for works of a romantic or traditional—and not experimental—nature.

1984	Ronald Frame, *Winter Journey*
	Claire Nonhebel, *Cold Showers*
1985	Susan Kay, *Legacy*
1986	Tim Parks, *Tongues of Flame*
	Patricia Ferguson, *Family Myths and Legends*
1987	James Maw, *Hard Luck*
1988	Alex Martin, *The General Interruptor*
	Candia McWilliam, *A Case of Knives*
1989	Nigel Watts, *The Life Game*
	William Riviere, *Watercolour Sky*
	Paul Horton, *Harry's Last Wedding*
	Alasdair McKee, *Uncle Harry's Last Stand*

Whitbread Literary Awards (1971)

Up to 1985, the awards were given in separate categories as shown below: Novel (N), Biography (B), Poetry (P), Children's Book (CB), First Book (FB), First Novel (FN), Autobiography (A), Short Story (SS).

From 1986, a nomination goes forward from each of the following categories: Novel, First Novel, Children's Novel, Biography or Autobiography, and Poetry. Each nomination carries an award of £1,750. From these, one Book of the Year is chosen and its author receives an additional £20,250.

1980	David Lodge, *How Far Can You Go?* (N)
	Leon Garfield, *John Diamond* (CB)
	David Lodge, *How Far Can You Go?* (Book of the Year)
1981	Maurice Leitch, *Silver's City* (N)
	Nigel Hamilton, *Monty: The Making of a General* (B)
	Jane Gardam, *The Hollow Land* (CB)
	William Boyd, *A Good Man in Africa* (FN)
1982	John Wain, *Young Shoulders* (N)
	Edward Crankshaw, *Bismarck* (B)
	W. J. Corbett, *The Song of Pentecost* (CB)
	Kenneth Rose, *King George V* (B)
	Roald Dahl, *The Witches* (CB)
	John Fuller, *Flying to Nowhere* (FN)
1984	Christopher Hope, *Kruger's Alp* (N)
	Peter Ackroyd, *T. S. Eliot* (B)
	Barbara Willard, *The Queen of the Pharisees' Children* (CB)
	James Buchan, *A Parish of Rich Women* (FN)

	Diane Rowe, *Tomorrow is our Permanent Address* (SS)
1985	Douglas Dunn, *Elegies* (Book of the Year).
1986	Kazuo Ishiguro, *An Artist of the Floating World* (Book of the Year)
1987	Christopher Nolan, *Under the Eye of the Clock* (Book of the Year)
1988	Paul Sayer, *The Comforts of Madness* (Book of the Year)
1989	Richard Holmes, *Coleridge: Early Visions* (Book of the Year)

FICTION IN THE 1980s

When we consider fiction in the 1980s, we have to bear in mind the fact that over 5,000 works of fiction, including reprints, are published annually in Great Britain. Amongst these are many best-sellers, which receive little or no critical attention. Literary historians and critics discuss "serious" novels and it is to these that awards and prizes are given. Meanwhile, the authors read most widely today include Jeffrey Archer, Agatha Christie, Jackie Collins, Catherine Cookson, Frederick Forsyth, Dick Francis, Arthur Hailey, Jack Higgins, Robert Ludlam, Sidney Sheldon and Wilbur Smith. These best-sellers are of various types: thrillers, stories of adventure, espionage, sex and horror, historical romances and science fiction. Their emphasis is on action and suspense and on convincing and realistic settings and not on psychological or moral investigation, traditionally the marks of the serious novel. They are an important phenomenon, indicating popular taste and commercial factors in the world of authorship and publication. Another relevant fact is the increase in the number, value and prestige of literary awards (*see* **M51**). Whether or not the conditions attached to eligibility for such prizes influence writers' style and subject-matter, the general result has been a heightened awareness of serious fiction amongst the reading public.

Academic critics and teachers have recently paid much attention to literary theory. Discussion of the ways in which language works, narrative and structure may have influenced novelists, particularly those of the younger generation, and may also have led some readers to expect subtler and more experimental works of fiction. Hence in this decade a good deal of interest has been shown in the writing of the Argentinian author, Jorge Luis Borges (1899–1986). One of the great successes of the 1980s was Umberto Eco's *The Name of the Rose* (1983), a mystery story set in a medieval monastery, composed with careful, self-conscious technique. This was followed by *Foucault's Pendulum* (1989). Another Italian writer whose innovatory style has been widely admired is Italo Calvino, whose *If on a Winter's Night a Traveller* (1981) is recognised as an outstanding achievement in contemporary fiction. As well as these, other translated works have made an impact, in different ways widening horizons, which have tended to remain narrow in the English novel. Typical examples are Marguerite Duras' *L'Amant* (1984), Carlos Fuentes' *Christopher Unborn* (1989), Isabel Allende's *The House of the Spirits* (1985), Milan Kundera's *The Unbearable Lightness of Being* (1984), Mario Vargas Llosa's *The Real Life of Aljerando Mayta* (1986), Gabriel Garcia Marques' *Love in the Time of Cholera* (1988), Georges Perec's *Life: A User's Manual* (1987), Leonid Borodin's *Partings* (1987) and Günter Grass's *The Rat* (1987). (Please note that the publication dates are those of the English translations). Novelists writing in English but not of English descent have also added new dimensions to fiction: Salman Rushdie's *The Satanic Verses* (1988), which caused world-wide anger amongst Moslems, Kajuo Ishiguo's *An Artist in the Floating World* (1986) and Timothy Mo's *Sour Sweet* (1982) are examples. Also, there are the New Literatures in English, emanating from past and present countries of the Commonwealth. *See* **M53–6**.

Major American novelists produced important and often challenging work: John Barth's *Letters* (1980), *Sabbatical* (1982) and *The Tidewater Tales* (1988), Saul Bellow's *The Dean's December* (1982), *More Die of Heartbreak* (1987), *A Theft* (1989) and *The Bellarosa Connection* (1989), Joseph Heller's

Good as Gold (1979), *God Knows* (1984) and *Picture This* (1988), Norman Mailer's *Ancient Evenings* (1983) and *Tough Guys Don't Dance* (1984), Philip Roth's *The Anatomy Lesson* (1984), *The Prague Orgy* (1985) and *The Counterlife* (1987), William Styron's *Sophie's Choice* (1979), Gore Vidal's *Creation* (1981), *Duluth* (1983), *Lincoln* (1984), *Empire* (1987) and *Hollywood* (1989), Karl Vonnegut's *Dead-Eye Dick* (1983), *Galapagos* (1985) and *Bluebeard* (1988), and John Updike's *S* (1988). Amongst younger American writers, John Irving published *The World According to Garp* (1978), *The Hotel New Hampshire* (1981), *The Cider House Rules* (1985) and *A Prayer for Owen Meany* (1989). Heller, Mailer and Vidal all set novels in ancient historical periods: the reign of the Biblical King David (Heller), Ancient Egypt (Mailer) and the 6th and 5th centuries BC (Vidal). Vidal has also written a number of novels dealing with periods of American history, as some of the above titles will indicate. (*See also* **M39–41**)

Historical novels have long been popular, but some novelists of the present day have brought fact and fiction even closer together in books that some people have termed "faction." Truman Capote's *In Cold Blood* (1966) was one of the first of this type in that he vividly recreated the actual events and psychological motivation associated with some brutal murders. Mailer's *The Executioner's Song* (1971) is a detailed examination of the case of a murderer who insists on execution. Thomas Keneally writes virtually a historical study of Oskar Schindler, a German industrialist who helped to save Jews from death in the Second World War, in *Schindler's Ark* (1983). Julian Barnes, who established a reputation with *Metroland* (1980), was shortlisted for the Booker Prize with *Flaubert's Parrot* (1984), which is like a collection of reflective and critical essays on the 19th century French novelist. He has also written *A History of the World in 10½ Chapters* (1989). J. M. Ballard's *Empire of the Sun* (1984) draws on autobiographical memories of Shanghai under Japanese occupation in the war. Bruce Chatwin's *The Songlines* (1987) is to some extent a travel and anthropological book about the aborigines.

Some long-established English novelists continued to produce significant work: Anthony Powell, Lawrence Durrell, William Golding, Angus Wilson, Kingsley Amis, Anthony Burgess, Graham Greene, Iris Murdoch, Margaret Drabble, Beryl Bainbridge and others have remained active, as reference to The English Novel (**M4–17**) will show. D. M. Thomas became famous with the publication of *The White Hotel* (1981), which combines the themes of psychoanalysis and the Holocaust in a dazzling display of styles and with some direct and vivid description. Other novels of his, also original in form, are *Ararat* (1983), *Swallow* (1984), *Sphinx* (1986) and *Summit* (1987). Martin Amis, who achieved instant success with *The Rachel Papers* (1973), went on to write *Dead Babies* (1975), *Success* (1978), *Other People* (1981), *Money* (1984), *Einstein's Monsters* (1987) and *London Fields* (1989). The striking feature of his work is linguistic virtuosity, revealing human behaviour and social attitudes in the contemporary world in startling and witty prose.

Two writers of fiction with the power to disturb readers with their perception of the darker and more macabre aspects of life are Angela Carter and Ian McEwen. One of Angela Carter's more remarkable books is *Nights at the Circus* (1984), about a winged female circus performer in Victorian London; others are *The Bloody Chamber* (1979), *Come unto these Yellow Sands* (1985) and *Black Venus* (1985). Ian McEwen's books include *The Cement Garden* (1978), *The Comfort of Strangers* (1981) and *The Child in Time* (1987). A. N. Wilson is a prolific writer of fiction, biography and criticism. His novels include *The Sweets of Pimlico* (1977), *Unguarded Hours* (1978), *Lead Kindly Light* (1979), *The Healing Art* (1980), *Who Was Oswald Fish?* (1981), *Wise Virgin* (1982), *Scandal* (1983), *Gentlemen in England* (1985) and *Incline our Hearts* (1988). In contrast to many of the novelists surveyed so far, Wilson is traditional in approach, writing comic, entertaining novels, reminiscent of those by Evelyn Waugh. Another novelist whose work has something of a conventional form is William Boyd: *A Good Man in Africa* (1981), his highly successful first novel, has been followed by *An Ice-Cream War* (1982), *Stars and Bars* (1984) and *The New Confessions* (1987). The innovative novels of Peter

Ackroyd include *The Last Testament of Oscar Wilde* (1983), *Hawksmoor* (1985), *Chatterton* (1987) and *First Light* (1989).

Basing her story on her own experiences as a young married woman in Venezuela, Lisa St Aubin di Teran wrote *Keepers of the House* (1982). Her subsequent novels include *The Slow Train to Milan* (1983), *The Tiger* (1984), *The Bay of Silence* (1986) and *Black Idol* (1987). Fay Weldon, a versatile and combative author, writes entertainingly, putting the woman's point of view, at a time when feminist literary and cultural criticism has become influential. Thanks partly to a memorable television adaptation, *The Life and Loves of a She-Devil* (1984), a fantastic and disturbing serio-comedy, has enjoyed wide popularity. In quieter vein, Anita Brookner's *Hotel du Lac* (1984), which won the Booker Prize, sensitively conveys the feelings of a single woman involved in a disappointing love affair.

So far we have looked mainly at serious novelists, as clearly distinct from those listed earlier as bestsellers. But some are difficult to classify (as far as such classification is useful). Richard Adams' *Watership Down* (1972) made him a bestselling author on a large scale; he subsequently wrote *Shardik* (1975), *The Plague Dogs* (1977), *The Girl on a Swing* (1980), *Maia* (1984) and *Traveller* (1989). Tom Sharpe's numerous exuberant comedies of the 1970s, such as *Blott on the Landscape* (1975), have been followed by others in the 1980s, such as *Vintage Stuff* (1982). One of the most subtle thriller writers, John Le Carré, who made his name with *The Spy Who Came in from the Cold* (1963), continues to produce his scrupulously crafted books. The most recent are *The Honourable Schoolboy* (1982), *The Little Drummer Girl* (1983), *A Perfect Spy* (1986) and *The Russia House* (1989).

We have today therefore a varied and continuously interesting literary scene, in which no English novelists seem to predominate, though when we are so close to so many books it is difficult to see things in proportion. In conclusion, it should be pointed out that posthumous or revised works by previous masters of the novel have recently been published. Terence Kilmartin revised Scott Moncrieff's translation of Proust's *A la recherche du temps perdu* (1981) and translated a hitherto unknown version of one of the volumes, *Albertine Gone* (1989). D. H. Lawrence's *Mr Noon*, hitherto only partially published, came out in a full version in 1983. A corrected text of Joyce's *Ulysses* was issued in 1984. Ernest Hemingway's *The Garden of Eden* was published in 1987.

CONTEMPORARY CARIBBEAN LITERATURE

Introduction

During the 1950s the British publication of a number of highly acclaimed West Indian novels launched Caribbean writing on the international scene as one of the most exciting of the new literatures in English. Writers like George Lamming, Sam Selvon and V. S. Naipaul, who emerged during this decade, were joined in the 1960s by other major figures, including the poets Derek Walcott and Edward Kamau Brathwaite and the novelist Wilson Harris, so that a body of West Indian literature now exists which can stand comparison with the best in the world.

Most of these writers have continued to be productive in the last decade (though Lamming has published no major new work since 1972). Today, however, a new generation of West Indian writers has come to the fore, both in the Caribbean and in Britain, and it is speaking in different tones. Although the subject-matter of contemporary Caribbean literature demonstrates continuity with what went before—quests for identity and protests against social injustice remain central themes—in important respects the new writing is beginning to chart previously unexplored territory. The most distinctive changes in recent Caribbean literature include a greater stress on the writer's responsibility to the community, the emergence of women's voices (largely neglected by publishers until the 'eighties') and a movement from the "literary" to the "oral", a significant shift in societies where the written tradition was formerly the prerogative of the colonial ruling classes.

New Work by Established Novelists

V. S. Naipaul, whose novels such as *A House for Mr Biswas* (1961), *The Mimic Men* (1967), *Guerrillas* (1975) and *A Bend in the River* (1979) have made him one of the most highly regarded of living writers despite his comparatively low reputation in the Caribbean, a region about which he has written in detached and sometimes disdainful terms, has continued to produce important work in the 1980s, though most of his recent output has been non-fiction. His *The Return of Eva Perón with the Killings in Trinidad* (1980) brings together four of his essays—on Argentina, Abdul Malik (also known as Michael X)—the black power "radical", executed for murder in 1975, Zaire and Joseph Conrad. *Among the Believers: An Islamic Journey* (1981) is an examination of four non-Arab Muslim societies—Iran, Pakistan, Malaysia and Indonesia—which presents itself as a personal attempt to explain the "Islamic revival". The picture of contemporary Islam which emerges is for the most part a negative one: the beliefs examined are represented as confusing and contradictory; the "believers'" passionate conviction is seen as a force which is unable to implement greatly needed social change. The book has been criticised by Muslim intellectuals, who have argued that it is superficial, biased towards Western rationalism and guilty of identifying the Islamic revival with fanaticism.

Naipaul's next two books, *Finding the Centre* (1984) and *The Enigma of Arrival* (1987) incorporate more autobiography than anything else he has written to date. The former work contains his "Prologue to an Autobiography" and a travel-piece about a journey to the Ivory Coast. The two essays have much in common, for each—like so much of Naipaul's work—is concerned with an endeavour to locate signification: the quest for "the centre" comes to stand for both the attempt by marginalised countries and peoples to find order, and for the writer's search for kernels of narrative which can express this predicament. *The Enigma of Arrival* calls itself a "novel", but is in fact mainly autobiography—it can be seen as the autobiography promised by the title of the first piece in *Finding the Centre*. Set mainly in Wiltshire, where Naipaul had by the time of its publication lived for many years, it also deals with the making of the English landscape. This is presented as a multi-layered, constructed environment and the writer-protagonist's particular situation—he is a tenant on a decaying Victorian-Edwardian estate—becomes a central image of the Condition of England, as perceived by one of its former colonials. Naipaul's most recent book *A Turn in the South* (1989) is a non-fiction work about the American South. He was awarded a knighthood in the 1990 New Year's Honours List.

Wilson Harris

During the 1980s Wilson Harris, who began his career as a novelist with *Palace of the Peacock* (1960), continued to produce complex and probing fictions about cross-cultural identity in an exploratory mode which takes issue with the European conventions of the novel form and has made him one of the most distinctive stylists currently writing in English. Like his earlier work, his recent novels *The Angel at the Gate* (1982), *Carnival* (1985) and *The Infinite Rehearsal* (1987) engage in an endeavour to create an alternative mode of perception and to find spiritual renewal in apparently "dead" experience. Other established novelists who produced new fiction in the 'eighties include Sam Selvon, who completed his "Moses trilogy" of novels about the experiences of Caribbean migrants in Britain—the first two parts were *The Lonely Londoners* (1956) and *Moses Ascending* (1975)—with *Moses Migrating* (1983), in which his fictional protagonist goes back to his native Trinidad for Carnival, and John Hearne, whose novel *The Sure Salvation* (1981), an account of a nineteenth-century slave ship's voyage across the Atlantic, is his finest work to date.

Recent Developments in Fiction

Significant figures to have emerged in the novel in the last two decades include Earl Lovelace, whose *The Dragon Can't Dance* (1979) and *The Wine of Astonishment* (1982) are brilliant explorations of aspects of Trinidadian popular culture and the oral tradition. The former is about a group of Port of Spain residents preparing for Trinidad's annual Carnival and investigates whether the event offers genuine release or only temporary escapism. The latter, which is centred on two forms of folk expression in the colonial period, the Spiritual Baptist Church and stickfighting, is narrated by a countrywoman and is one of the finest Caribbean novels yet to be written in Creole.

Garth St. Omer is a meticulous stylist whose novellas about middle-class alienation in St. Lucia, which include *J-, Black Bam and the Masqueraders* (1972), have yet to secure the reputation they deserve. N. D. Williams's *Ikael Torass* (1976) is about a young West Indian university student's quest for cultural authenticity; it contains some vivid satire of Caribbean intellectual life. Caryl Phillips's novel *A State of Independence* (1986) describes a West Indian's return to his native island at the time of its independence celebrations and illustrates some of the difficulties surrounding this kind of homecoming and the failure of the islanders to achieve real freedom—like Naipaul's *In a Free State* (1971), the title of the work suggests the ironies of "independence".

Women Writers

Recent years have seen the publication of a number of fine novels by women writers. Foremost among these are Erna Brodber's *Jane and Louisa Will Soon Come Home* (1980) and Merle Collins's *Angel* (1987). *Jane and Louisa Will Soon Come Home* is a complex, poetic exploration of the Jamaican female psyche. It shows how colonial brainwashing inculcates negative responses to their sexuality in Black women and suggests ways in which this process can be opposed by local folk traditions, embodied within the novel on both thematic and formal levels. Brodber's second novel, *Myal* (1988), which is about the reclamation of submerged identity through the Afro-Caribbean religious cult that gives the novel its title, was the winner of the Caribbean and Canadian region of the 1989 Commonwealth Writers' Prize.

Angel is one of a group of fine 'eighties novels which examine the gradual growth to maturity of a young female protagonist against a background of social change within her society. In the 1950s and 1960s a spate of novels about boyhood in the Caribbean, of which Lamming's *In the Castle of My Skin* (1953) and Michael Anthony's *The Year in San Fernando* (1965) are the most prominent examples, emerged without there being a similar interest shown in girlhood. This has been remedied in the 1980s with the appearance, not only of *Angel*, but also of Jamaica Kincaid's account of growing up in Antigua, *Annie John* (1985), and Zee Edgell's similar study of girlhood in colonial Belize, *Beka Lamb* (1982). Both these works are also noteworthy as coming from countries which hitherto had been unrepresented in novels by local authors. *Angel* does a similar job of putting Grenada on the literary map, again through a narrative which focuses on an independent girl's growing awareness of the injustices practised in the society around her, and is also notable for its highly effective use of Creole language forms and its account of the 1983 American invasion of Grenada. Janice Shinebourne's *Timepiece* (1986) and Grace Nichols's *Whole of a Morning Sky* (1986) are both Guyanese novels set in the troubled era of the country's late colonial period, which explore how individuals' lives are affected by the political climate in which they must move.

The 1980s have also seen the emergence of a major Caribbean short story writer, Olive Senior, who has long played an important part in Jamaican cultural life as an editor and poet as well as a fiction-writer, but only achieved international prominence with the publication of her collection of stories *Summer Lightning* (1986), the overall winner of the first Commonwealth Writers' Prize in 1987. Senior's fiction deals particularly with rural Jamaica and with the experiences of children gradually learning about adult relationships and the class hierarchies of the world around them; it displays a deft use of the full range of the Jamaican linguistic continuum. Her second collection of stories, *Arrival* of the Snake Woman, appeared in 1989. Talking of Trees (1985) is a collection of her poetry and she is the editor of A-Z of Jamaican Heritage (1983).

Black British Fiction

Fiction which deals with the Black experience in Britain is now markedly different from the work of the first generation of post-war immigrants and early accounts of "exile" in the "Mother Country", such as Lamming's The Emigrants (1954) and Selvon's The Lonely Londoners, novels written by authors for whom England was an important matrix even if their relationship with this "homeland" was at best an uneasy one, have been supplanted by works that frequently express a sense of "unbelonging" (to borrow from the title of a novel by Joan Riley—see below).

Events such as the Notting Hill riots in the 1950s and Enoch Powell's "rivers of blood" speech in the late 1960s created a mood of disillusionment among many Caribbean immigrants and their descendants. In fiction this is reflected in the more pessimistic representation of the predicament of West Indians living in London in Lamming's second novel set in Britain, Water with Berries (1971), and the 'eighties have seen the emergence of writers who use the novel to document the new Black British realities in an uncompromising manner. Prominent among these are Caryl Phillips (see also above), whose The Final Passage (1985) tells the tragic story of a small islander who comes to London, and Joan Riley, whose novels, The Unbelonging (1985), Waiting in the Twilight (1987) and Romance (1988) are the most significant works by a British-based Black woman writer to date. Riley, who was born in Jamaica and spent her early years there, writes of the problems of women who have migrated from the Caribbean to Britain and their struggle to build a decent life in England in the face of discrimination and marginalisation. Other Black British novels include David Simon's Railton Blues (1983), Faustin Charles's The Black Man of Brixton (1985) and Amon Saba Saakana's Blues Dance (1985).

Drama

Recent literary production shows a shift away from major works by individual artists, who may not always be in tune with the aspirations of the community about which they write (in some cases because they were products of the late colonial educational system), towards writing which demonstrates more collective awareness. Drama has always been a community form and as such has occupied a special place in attempts to construct a relevant Caribbean tradition. In recent years it too has seen a valuable contribution from women, most notably the very popular Jamaican theatre collective Sistren, a group which has striven to give dramatic expression to the experiences of ordinary working women. Derek Walcott, who as dramatist, director and theatre critic has done more than anyone else (with the possible exception of the theatre historian and playwright Errol Hill) to found a Caribbean theatrical tradition, remains the region's most important dramatist. His 'eighties plays include The Last Carnival (1982) and A Branch of the Blue Nile (1983).

Other writers who have made important contributions to the growth of the region's theatre include Errol John, Roderick Walcott (Derek's twin brother), Mustapha Matura, Alwin Bully, Dennis Scott and Trevor Rhone. Caryl Phillips's Strange Fruit (1980) and Edgar White's The Nine Night (1983) are among the most interesting plays to have been premièred in England in the 'eighties. The decade has also seen an increasing awareness of the omnipresence of drama in everyday Caribbean life and the work of performers like the raconteurs Louise Bennett and Paul Keens-Douglas, the poets Michael Smith and Jean "Binta" Breeze (see below) and the calypsonians The Mighty Sparrow and David Rudder attest to the importance of drama in other Caribbean art forms.

New Work by Established Poets

During the last decade Derek Walcott has further enhanced his reputation as one of the finest poets currently writing in English. The verse of The Star-

Apple Kingdom (1980) and The Fortunate Traveller (1982) is centred on the figure of a modern-day Odysseus, who finds himself "a colonial upstart at the end of an empire,/a single, circling, homeless satellite", glad to be rid of colonial rule but finding himself still engaged in a love affair with the former master's language.

Even a Creole poem like "The Spoiler's Return" (in The Fortunate Traveller), in which The Mighty Spoiler, a famous Trinidadian calypsonian of the 1950s, returns from the grave to comment on the state of contemporary Port of Spain, discusses its relationship to the European literary tradition in comparing calypso to Augustan satire. The place of a poet caught between two cultures is also a major theme of Midsummer (1984), a sequence of fifty-four poems, which follows the seasonal cycle of a year, from summer to summer. The Arkansas Testament (1987), is another richly imagistic attempt, on Walcott's part, to relate his Caribbean heritage to his experience of other cultures. It shows an increasing absorption with charting the ways in which language shapes responses to the natural world, a concern which has been important in all Walcott's poetry. His Collected Poems, 1948–1984 appeared in 1986.

The region's other leading poet Edward Kamau Brathwaite has followed his 'sixties trilogy of poems about the Black diaspora in the New World, The Arrivants (1967–9) with a second trilogy: Mother Poem (1977) is about the maternal legacy of his native Barbados; Sun Poem (1982) explores the male history of the island and is based on the imagery of the seven colours of the rainbow; X/Self (1987), like The Arrivants, brings together the various landscapes of the Afro-Caribbean experience in a wide range of linguistic registers. All Brathwaite's work is concerned with disseminating knowledge about the region's neglected folk forms and oral traditions and his History of the Voice (1984) is a prose account of the development of "nation language" (a neologism he has coined to replace "dialect", which he argues has pejorative connotations) in Anglophone Caribbean poetry.

After Walcott and Brathwaite

In the wake of Walcott and Brathwaite, a number of other very fine poets came to the fore in the Caribbean. They included Mervyn Morris, Wayne Brown and Dennis Scott. More recently, both within the Caribbean and Britain, the tendency has been towards performance poetry and today a situation has been reached where the oral tradition has taken over from the literary as the main voice of West Indian verse. Leading figures in this movement, in addition to Louise Bennett (who has been a pioneer of the use of oral forms since as long ago as the late 1930s) and Brathwaite, have been Linton Kwesi Johnson and Benjamin Zephaniah in Britain and, in Jamaica, the late Michael Smith and the "dub poets", who are heavily influenced by reggae rhythms. Johnson, whose poetry became extremely popular as a result of concert performances (a medium he has now largely deserted), is best known for the poems in his first collection, Dread, Beat and Blood (1975); Michael Smith for It a Come (1986), especially the memorable 'Mi cyan believe it'. In neither case, however, does the written version of the poetry offered in the volumes mentioned do justice to their real nature. In Smith's case in particular, his highly dramatic delivery meant that performance was the real medium of his work with recordings managing to capture only part of the effect and scribal transcription even less.

Two other fine collections of verse, David Dabydeen's Slave Song (1984), winner of the 1984 Commonwealth Poetry Prize, and Fred D'Aguiar's Mama Dot (1985), are both by British-based poets of Guyanese descent. Both draw on their Guyanese early years—Dabydeen in a violent style, which articulates the rage of the slave and D'Aguiar in a more restrained and reflective voice—and demonstrate a consummate skill in blending oral and literary elements.

After years of being marginalised women's voices have begun to assert themselves in oral and other forms and Jean "Binta" Breeze, Valerie Bloom, Grace Nichols and Lorna Goodison have all achieved considerable success in recent years. Nichols's I is a long memoried woman (1983), winner of the 1983 Commonwealth Poetry Prize, examines the horrors of the Middle Passage crossing and subsequent alienation in the New World from a woman's point of view. Lorna Goodison's poetry is outstanding for its sensitive response to women's family relationships and its use of a range of Jamaican voices (often there are several in a single short poem) which reflect the diversity in the country's linguistic continuum and the versatility it allows. Her volumes of verse are *Tamarind Season* (1980), *I Am Becoming My Mother* (1986) and *Heartease* (1988). Bloom, whose writing and performances have been compared with Louise Bennett, and Breeze, whose performances demonstrate similar dramatic skills to those of Michael Smith, draw on the richness of the oral tradition.

RECENT SHAKESPEAREAN SCHOLARSHIP

The Background

Shakespeare's plays have been acted and printed in countless productions, versions and editions for the past 400 years. His poems, especially the sonnets, have been widely read and discussed (*see* **M20**). Readers, performers and audiences have responded differently to Shakespeare according to the times in which they lived. Here are just three examples. In the eighteenth century, the Age of Reason, some people thought that he constructed his plays incorrectly, since he ignored the three "unities" (*see* **M50**) and used unrealistic plots. But during the Romantic and Victorian periods, many thought of Shakespeare as a godlike figure, who created such profound and universal characters as Hamlet and King Lear. Then in the middle of the twentieth century, critics analysed the plays as dramatic poems, concentrating on the complexity of Shakespeare's language. Through all the changes in fashion, Shakespeare has almost always been regarded as the greatest English writer and as one of the world's literary giants, though Voltaire, Tolstoy and Shaw disagreed with this view. As well as analysing Shakespeare's work, scholars have sought to establish and develop the comparatively few facts about his life; tiny new pieces of documentary evidence still occasionally turn up. There is always something new to say about Shakespeare, with constantly changing interpretations of his work on the stage and in the academic's study. The past ten years have seen a number of remarkable developments, which will be surveyed here.

The Shakespearean Bibliography

First, to put these recent developments in perspective, let us look at some of the vast bibliography that Shakespeare has generated. There are the famous editions: Heminge and Condell's *First Folio* (1962), which collected thirty-six of his plays; the editions of Nicholas Rowe (1709), Alexander Pope (1725), Lewis Theobald (1733), Samuel Johnson (1765), and Edmund Malone (1790 and later); W. G. Clark and W. A. Wright's Cambridge Shakespeare (1863–66), on which the Globe edition (1864) was based; the New Cambridge and the two series of Arden editions published in this century. Landmarks in criticism include Dryden's comments in his *Essay of Dramatic Poesy* (1688), the Prefaces by Pope and Johnson to their editions, A. W. Schlegel's lectures *On Dramatic Art and Literature* (1809–11), Coleridge's observations and lectures in the early nineteenth century, Hazlitt's *Characters of Shakespeare's Plays* (1817), G. G. Gervinus's *Shakespeare* (1849–50; translated into English as *Shakespeare Commentaries*), A. C. Bradley's *Shakespearean Tragedy* (1904), L. C. Knights's "How Many Children Had Lady Macbeth?" (1933), critical studies by G. Wilson Knight from the 1930s to the 1980s, and Jan Kott's *Shakespeare Our Contemporary* (1964). Important biographical work can be represented by J. O. Halliwell-Phillipps's *Outlines of the Life of Shakespeare* (final edition, 1887), Edward Dowden's *Shakespeare: a Critical Study of his Mind and Art* (1875), Sidney Lee's *Life of Shakespeare* (1898), E. K. Chambers's *William Shakespeare: a Study of Facts and Problems* (1930), A. L. Rowse's *William Shakespeare* (1963), and Samuel Schoenbaum's *William Shakespeare: a Documentary Life* (1975).

Between 1985 and 1989, some 150 new books on Shakespeare in general were added to the British Library; in addition, the library received many reprints, editions of the plays and poems, and studies of individual works.

The New Oxford Shakespeare

The new Oxford Shakespeare was published in 1986–7, consisting of three volumes: the *Complete Works* in modern spelling, the *Complete Works: Original-Spelling Edition*, and *A Textual Companion*, all edited by Stanley Wells, Gary Taylor, John Jowett, and William Montgomery. Taking as their principle that performance was the end to which the plays were created, the editors have sought to present the "texts of Shakespeare's plays as they were acted in the London playhouses which stood at the centre of his professional life." They disagree with the widely adopted process of making an acceptable text by means of conflating any early versions that may exist. Instead, their view is that Shakespeare revised his plays with theatrical effectiveness in mind. They have included some unconventional material. They print both the 1608 Quarto and 1623 First Folio versions of *King Lear*, *The Two Noble Kinsmen*, passages from *Sir Thomas More*, and a number of short poems, including the controversial "Shall I die?" and some epitaphs. The name Sir John Oldcastle is used instead of Sir John Falstaff in *King Henry IV, Part 1*, and the original titles are restored to two of the plays: *King Henry VI, Part 2* is called *The First Part of the Contention* and *King Henry VIII* is called *All is True*.

As well as the additions to the Shakespeare canon admitted to the Oxford Shakespeare, others have been proposed, without gaining wide acceptance. Eric Sams brought out an edition of *Shakespeare's Edmund Ironside: the Lost Play* (1986), arguing that the play, which exists as an anonymous manuscript in the British Library, is an early work that was written and acted in about 1588. Peter Levi's booklet, *New Verses by Shakespeare* (1988), which is mostly a reprint of an Appendix to his *Life and Times of William Shakespeare* (1986), argues for the authenticity of some lines in a Huntington Library manuscript. In *Elegy by W.S.: a Study in Attribution* (1989), Donald W. Foster suggests that Shakespeare possibly wrote "A Funeral Elegy," a lengthy poem published in 1612 in memory of William Peter. A collection of critical essays edited by Maurice Charney, *"Bad" Shakespeare: Revaluations of the Shakespeare Canon* (1988), radically reassesses several of the plays. Regarding further biographical material, we must mention here E. A. J. Honigmann's *Shakespeare: the Lost Years* (1985), in which he powerfully argues the case that the playwright worked as a schoolmaster and actor in Lancashire for periods from 1580 onwards.

New Directions of Criticism

The criticism of Shakespeare has taken a number of new directions in recent years, or at least has developed some of the "close reading" principles and practice associated with the New Critics (*see* **M48**). Critics who use structuralism (*see* **M50**) consider Shakespearean texts as linguistic structures in themselves and not as reflections of a real world outside. Those who practise poststructuralism (*see* **M49**) and deconstruction (*see* **M45**) go further in that they consider no text as fixed and final. In the words of Terence Hawkes, the texts "are endlessly, like language itself, in free play." They therefore insist that it is impossible to make meaningful statements about the psychological realism or otherwise of Shakespeare's characters, or to establish one stable version of a play or poem. In this last respect, deconstructionist critics agree with the Oxford editors, though arguing from different premises. Out of the many books and articles that have adopted these approaches, a lively and stimulating study is Malcolm Evans's aptly titled *Signifying Nothing: Truth's True Contents in Shakespeare's Text* (1986; 2nd edition, 1989). Other critics whose work has had a considerable impact have pursued the question of the ways in which different conceptions of Shakespeare have been formed at different periods, particularly in the twentieth century. Gary Taylor's *Reinventing Shakespeare* (1990) is a comprehensive survey of this kind. A simple example of varying reconstructions of Shakespeare is the contrast between the films of *King Henry V* made by Laurence Olivier and Kenneth Branagh in 1944 and 1989 respectively. The former was romantically patriotic, as befitted the national mood in the last days of the Second World War, whereas the latter reflected the more cynical and disillusioned mood of half a century later. Left-wing critics have discussed, in such collections as Graham Holderness's *The Shakespeare Myth* (1988), the formation by bourgeois critical and popular opinion of Shakespeare as a cultural artefact—as a token sometimes of a complacent liberalism and Englishness. Terence Hawkes, in *That Shakespeherian Rag: Essays on a Critical Process* (1986), explores, among other subjects, interpretations of Shakespeare developed by Walter Raleigh and John Dover Wilson when they were subjected to the pressures and propaganda of the First World War. "New Historicism", when applied to Shakespeare, explores the mutual relationships between his plays and the social and cultural environment of his time, as in Stephen Greenblatt's *Shakespearean Negotiations: the Circulation of Social Energy in Renaissance England* (1988). Feminist critiques have included Marilyn French's *Shakespeare's Division of Experience* (1982), which discusses the playwright's presentation of women, Catherine Belsey's *The Subject of Tragedy: Identity and Difference in Renaissance Drama* (1985), and Germaine Greer's *Shakespeare* (1986). The Marxist critic, Terry Eagleton has written a compact and vigorous study, *William Shakespeare* (1986). Some of these new approaches are exemplified in *Alternative Shakespeares* (1985), a collection of essays edited by John Drakakis. A concise yet detailed survey by Terence Hawkes is available in one of the most valuable of recent background books: *The Cambridge Companion to Shakespeare Studies* (1986), edited by Stanley Wells. If we try to sum up the tendencies of these editorial and critical activities, we can say that they modify or contradict the view that Shakespeare's work is immutable in expression and content, that they think of it primarily in theatrical terms, and that they question ideas of status and the canon.

Alongside the books and articles that break new ground, those of a more traditional approach have appeared. William Empson's *Essays on Shakespeare* (1986) were posthumously published; his close textual readings and provocative interpretations have similarities, however, to some of the new criticism. A. L. Rowse, who has written prolifically on Shakespeare as well as editing and modernising his texts, brought out *Shakespeare's Self-Portrait* (1985). Basing this anthology on his assertion that "all writers write out of their own experience," he chooses passages from the plays and poems to show Shakespeare's opinions on such subjects as himself, the theatre, the Dark Lady, and places he knew. Two straightforward, useful studies are Philip Edwards's *Shakespeare: a Writer's Progress* (1986) and Richard Dutton's *Shakespeare: a Literary Life* (1989).

As if to emphasise the tendency to see the plays as first and foremost scripts for the playhouse, there have been numerous performances in London, Stratford-on-Avon, and other places in recent years. In London alone, some twenty-five different productions were staged in each of the years 1987 and 1988. These included Sir Peter Hall's *Cymbeline*, *The Winter's Tale*, and *The Tempest*, as his farewell as the artistic director of the National Theatre (1988), and Adrian Noble's trilogy, *The Plantagenets* (1988), based on *King Henry VI, Parts 1,2,* and *3*, and *King Richard III*, for the Royal Shakespeare Company.

The Discovery of the Rose Theatre

At the beginning of 1989, the remains of the Rose Theatre were discovered on the south bank of the Thames, near Southwark Bridge. Built in 1587 and pulled down in 1605, the Rose staged Marlowe's plays, Kyd's *Spanish Tragedy*, and Shakespeare's *King Henry VI, Part 1* and *Titus Andronicus*. From this important discovery, which has for the first time provided tangible detail concerning an Elizabethan playhouse, scholars have deduced that the Rose was a comparatively small, polygonal structure. A drawing made by C. Walter Hodges for the Museum of London, based on the evidence from the

excavation, shows a three-storey, twelve-sided building with a thatched roof. Later in 1989, some remains of the Globe Theatre, about 100 yards from the Rose, were also found and were scheduled as an ancient monument. A textual discovery was an anonymous Elizabethan manuscript notebook sold by Sotheby's on 18 December 1986 to the British Library for £165,000. This contains, among other material, extracts from *King Henry IV, Part 1,* possibly predating the first publication of the play in 1598 and showing some otherwise unrecorded textual variants.

THE DETECTIVE STORY

Editor's Note: The year 1990 marks the centenary of the birth of Agatha Christie, one of the greatest names in detective story writing. This article is part appreciation of her gifts.

In a detective story, an amateur or professional detective solves the mystery of the identity of a criminal, who is usually a murderer. Thrillers and spy fiction emphasise excitement, action and violence. They may overlap with the detective story, which has, however, investigation and deduction as its primary purpose; the reader is led to—and sometimes cleverly misled from—the solution, which should be both logical and unexpected. The ten "rules" drawn up in Ronald Knox's "Decalogue" of 1929 stress the qualities of fair play and logic that should exist; the eighth of the rules states that "the detective must not light on any clues which are not instantly produced for the inspection of the reader."

Edgar Allan Poe

Crime, mystery and investigation have always existed in narrative, but the detective story as we think of it today originated in five of Edgar Allan Poe's *Tales of Mystery and Imagination* (1845): "The Murders in the Rue Morgue," "The Mystery of Marie Roget," "The Purloined Letter," "The Gold-Bug," and " 'Thou Art the Man'" (*see* **M33**). In C. Auguste Dupin, who features in the first three of these, Poe created (to quote his own words) a typical "analyst ... fond of enigmas, of conundrums, of hieroglyphics, exhibiting in his solutions of each a degree of *acumen* which appears to the ordinary apprehension preternatural." Apart from the archetypal detective, Poe's stories contain such elements as the locked room, concealment by means of the obvious, and the surprising solution. Two English progenitors were Dickens and Wilkie Collins (*see* **M6–7, 9**). In *Bleak House* (1852–53), Dickens created Inspector Bucket (based on Inspector Charles Field of the Metropolitan Police), who investigates several interconnected mysteries, including the murder of Mr Tulkinghorn, the lawyer, and the disappearance of Lady Dedlock. Dickens's last novel, *The Mystery of Edwin Drood* (1870), tantalisingly left unfinished, concerns the disappearance of Edwin Drood, the nephew of John Jasper, who seems to have murdered him. Wilkie Collins, an adept at contriving complex plots, wrote *The Moonstone* (1868). This highly ingenious novel about the theft of the diamond of the title, told from various narrative viewpoints, remains one of the most accomplished stories of detection. The investigator is Sergeant Cuff, a man with "a face as sharp as a hatchet" and eyes "of a steely light grey." Emile Gaboriau (1832–74) is the father of the *roman policier* in France; his first crime story, *L'Affaire Lerouge*, appeared in 1866. His detective, M. Lecoq, is sometimes seen as the forerunner of Sherlock Holmes.

Sherlock Holmes

Holmes, the most famous of all fictional detectives, appeared in *A Study in Scarlet,* a short novel written by Arthur Conan Doyle (1859–1930) for *Beeton's Christmas Annual* in December 1887. *The Sign of Four* followed, in *Lippincott's Magazine* in February 1890. Then came the short stories in the *Strand* magazine from 1891 onwards, collected as *The Adventures of Sherlock Holmes* (1892) and *The Memoirs of Sherlock Holmes* (1894). Having "killed off" Holmes, Conan Doyle was compelled to resurrect him in further stories and novellas: *The Hound of the Baskervilles* (1902), *The Return of Sherlock Holmes* (1905), *The Valley of Fear* (1915), *His Last Bow* (1917), and *The Case-Book of Sherlock Holmes* (1927). Holmes, with his eccentricities and powers of deduction, his stolid companion, Dr. Watson, his chambers at 221B Baker Street and the memorable cases he was involved in have always generated enormous enthusiasm and devotion. Because of their ingenuity, characterisation and evocation of late-Victorian London, the stories have become classics of their kind.

Sexton Blake

A sub-Holmes is Sexton Blake, who seems to have first appeared in 1893 in "The Missing Millionaire" in Harmsworth's *Halfpenny Marvel*; the author was Hal Meredeth, who perhaps was also known as Harry Blyth. Sexton Blake and his assistant, Tinker, subsequently figured in countless stories by as many as two hundred different writers. A number of other sleuths came on the scene at the same time, since (as E. S. Turner remarked in *Boys Will Be Boys*) "the setting up of private detectives was a major literary industry of the 'nineties." Two of the most popular were Nelson Lee and Nick Carter. Doyle's brother-in-law, E. W. Hornung, created A. J. Raffles, gentleman and burglar, in *The Amateur Cracksman* (1899). Contemporary French works were those of Maurice Leblanc (1864–1941), whose detective made his début in a book of short stories named after him, *Arsène Lupin, gentleman-cambrioleur* (1907), and Gaston Leroux (1868–1927), whose *Le Mystère de la chambre jaune* was published in the same year. Notable practitioners of the *genre* a few years later were G. K. Chesterton and E. C. Bentley (*see* **M32**). The former wrote fifty stories in five volumes about the feats of detection of the unassuming priest, Father Brown, beginning with *The Innocence of Father Brown* (1911). As we would expect from the author, paradox and wit are brilliantly deployed. Bentley's *Trent's Last Case* (1913), about the murder of the millionaire, Sigsbee Manderson, has been described as "one of the great cornerstones of the detective story." The 170 books by Edgar Wallace (1875–1932) include many thrillers and detective stories; *The Mind of Mr J. G. Reeder* (1925) is often considered to be one of his best. By 1920, then, a formidable array of fictional detectives had been created: Dupin, Lecoq, Sherlock Holmes, Father Brown and Arsène Lupin. Along with them, a considerable appetite for detective fiction had been stimulated among the reading public.

The Golden Age

As a result, perhaps, the 1920s and 1930s saw what has often been called the "golden age" of the detective story. Writing in 1942, Howard Haycraft (in *Murder for Pleasure*) considered that the "Big Five" of the period were Dorothy L. Sayers, Agatha Christie, R. Austin Freeman, Freeman Wills Crofts, and H. C. Bailey. Freeman (1862–1943), who wrote his first detective novel, *The Red Thumb Mark*, in 1907, produced over thirty books, many of them featuring the physician, Dr Thorndyke, as the investigator. Among the sixty or so books written by H. C. Bailey (1878–1961) are many (usually collections of short stories) about his detective, the kindly, whimsical Reggie Fortune. Freeman Wills Crofts (1879–1957) was also prolific, writing over thirty books, the best of which are sometimes said to be *The Cask* (1920) and *Inspector French's Greatest Case* (1925). As the last title indicates, his detective was a professional, unlike so many of the eccentric amateurs popular in the fiction of the time.

Agatha Christie

Of the five writers mentioned in the previous paragraph, Agatha Christie (1890–1976) and Dorothy L. Sayers (1893–1957) are still household words. Agatha Christie wrote over eighty crime novels and volumes of short stories between 1920 and her death. Hercule Poirot, her famous Belgian detective, appeared in the very first of these, *The Mysterious Affair at Styles* (1920), and her other well-known investigator, Miss Marple, was introduced in *Murder at the Vicarage* (1930). Her fiction, written in an undemanding, conversational style, contains amazingly clever plots and surprising but rational solutions. As the years have passed, her stories have gained a period charm, evocative of comfortable, middle-class England. Among her widely admired novels are *The Murder of Roger Ackroyd* (1926), *The ABC Murders* (1936), and *Death on the Nile* (1937). The work of Dorothy L. Sayers is more self-consciously literary but is also original and striking in its puzzles and solutions. Lord Peter Wimsey, her aristocratic and accomplished hero, elegantly solves the mysteries in such novels as *The Nine Tailors* (1934) and *Gaudy Night* (1935).

Other writers of the "golden age" in England include John Rhode (1884–1965), the creator of Dr Priestley; Francis Iles (who also wrote as Anthony Berkeley, 1893–1971), whose most famous book is *Malice Aforethought* (1931); Nicholas Blake (the pseudonym of Cecil Day Lewis—*see* **M29**); John Dickson Carr (also known as Carter Dickson, 1906–77), who made a speciality of the "locked room" mystery; and Michael Innes (the pseudonym of J. I. M. Stewart, b. 1906). Marjorie Allingham (1904–66) began writing at this time, creating her detective, Albert Campion, and achieving one of her greatest successes in 1952 with *Tiger in the Smoke*. Ngaio Marsh (1899–1982) wrote more than thirty novels, including *Final Curtain* (1947).

The American Writers

In the U.S.A., one of the remarkable detective story writers of the period was S. S. Van Dine (the pseudonym of Willard Huntington Wright, 1888–1939), whose Philo Vance became a hugely popular sleuth in twelve novels, such as *The "Canary" Murder Case* (1927). For other American writers of the *genre* at this time, *see* **M39**. Georges Simenon (1903–89), who wrote hundreds of books, began writing his Inspector Maigret novels in 1929. There are eighty-four of these, as well as eighteen short stories. They differ from the English and American detective story in that they depend on characterisation (particularly that of Maigret himself), environment and atmosphere for their full effect. They have a casual, realistic and compelling air about them; it has been well said that Simenon "discovered the criminal's identity at the same time as Maigret."

Simenon and many of the novelists of the "golden age" continued writing until fairly recent times. Others who came into prominence in the post-war years were Patricia Highsmith (b. 1921) and Ed McBain (the pseudonym of Evan Hunter, b. 1926) in the U.S.A., and Edmund Crispin (the pseudonym of Bruce Montgomery, 1921–78), H. R. F. Keating (b. 1926), and Peter Dickinson (b. 1927) in England.

Contemporary Writers

Three of the most admired detective novelists of the present day in this country are P. D. James (b. 1920), whose first book, *Cover Her Face* (1962), introduced readers to Inspector Adam Dalglish; Ruth Rendell (b. 1930); and Dick Francis (b. 1920), whose books have a racing setting. Memorable sleuths, striking scenes and intricate plots are still being created as they have been for the past century and a half.

MEDICAL
MATTERS

Here we give a brief summary of up-to-date medical knowledge, including recent developments in areas such as leukaemia and bronchial asthma. It must not be allowed to replace your doctor, who should be consulted immediately if you are worried. An index ensures easy reference. The section also examines the problem of AIDS and the proposed reform of the National Health Service.

TABLE OF CONTENTS

MEDICAL MATTERS

PART I. INTRODUCTION.

In earlier editions of Pears the Medical Section took the form of a dictionary. More recently we have attempted something different: a small medical textbook for the layman. We have two reasons for this. Firstly, we feel that there are some readers who would like to have an overall picture of modern medicine and learn something of the progress in its various fields. They may like to read the section through as a continuous narrative. Secondly, there are always readers (probably the majority) who simply want to use the section as a ready-reference guide and to that end, rather than have an alphabetically arranged collection of snippets of information (which can be unsatisfying), we have grouped diseases under bodily 'systems'. We have made no attempt to produce a *dictionary* of symptoms because self-diagnosis is foolish. However, we have retained an alphabetical index (Part IV) for easy reference.

The plan in this section is to deal with diseases according to either (a) their cause (*e.g.*, the infections due to bacteria or viruses) or (b) the body system affected (*e.g.*, the nervous system, the heart and blood vessels, the lungs and so on). We cannot emphasise too strongly that this section is not intended as a substitute for seeking medical advice. It is one thing to satisfy curiosity or try and solve a puzzle about a disease, condition or collection of symptoms by "looking it up" but quite another to try and diagnose one's own disease, condition or collection of symptoms in the same way. In other words, this section is no substitute for a doctor and when you are ill, unless you know it to be a trivial, or relatively trivial, self-limiting condition, you must get medical advice. It is easy to listen to and believe unqualified opinions and to take and act on advice from unqualified persons. However, it is unwise to do so because although doctors are sometimes wrong (just as are lawyers, architects, judges and veterinary surgeons) the unqualified are much more likely to be wrong. So choose a doctor you can trust, and then believe what he tells you and carry out his advice. There is no use in complaining about the whole medical profession just because you are dissatisfied with your own G.P. If you are, you should sign on with another.

Of recent years there has been a veritable explosion in medical information for the layman through newspapers, magazines, books, radio and television (collectively referred to as "the media") and among the more intelligently perceptive of doctors' patients there is now a much greater understanding of "how the body works" and how it can go wrong. Progress in treatment of some diseases has been rapid and, with the more ready access to specialist medical journals in which reports of drug and other trials appear which journalists now have, such news gets into a patient's hands very quickly, albeit often prematurely. The G.P. simply cannot keep up with advances in all fields and is therefore occasionally confronted by a patient who asks him why he cannot have this "new drug" for his rheumatoid arthritis, for example, a new drug which may not at that stage even have reached the market place.

Modern Medicine

Much in medicine which is now taken for granted (that for the majority of diseases caused by identifiable organisms there is a specific drug treatment, for example) was undreamed of even as recently as 50 years ago. Progress in diagnosis, in preventive medicine and in treatment, both medical and surgical, has been so rapid as to be almost breathtaking. A doctor retiring from active practice in 1985 will have seen smallpox completely eradicated, poliomyelitis practically banished (at least from the U.K.), tuberculosis become curable, coronary artery disease relievable surgically and he will have witnessed the dramatic purge in the field of molecular biology and of the research by immunologists and geneticists into their efforts to control parasitic diseases like bilharzia, malaria and river blindness that affect millions of people in the Third World. One aspect of medicine and medicinal thinking still resistant to progress in understanding in spite of continued research is the effect of mind on body. Many of us still like to think that our bodies are just something we have got into, like cars, that ill-health is simply something that has "gone wrong" in one system or another and that therefore provided we find the appropriate expert (a chest physician, a gastro-enterologist or an ophthalmic surgeon, for example) to correct the fault, we will recover. Whereas that idea holds good for a broken leg, for instance, with many diseases the idea that mind can be totally separated from the "defective" part just isn't good enough. You cannot simply divorce your stomach, your bowels, your liver or your heart from your "self". They are all part of you and react, as you yourself react, to all the stresses and anxieties, fears and worries and the hundred and one other factors that are part and parcel of modern living. It is true that most of your stomach can be removed, your gall-bladder entirely so and with the aid of a dialysing machine or a transplant you can get by without your kidneys. As with your car, old or diseased parts can be repaired or totally replaced; even your heart, conventionally the very "seat" of the emotions.

Mens sana in corpore sano—a sound mind in a sound body. Your body and its many parts may be helped to normal function by modern medicines and surgery but, in general, it will only stay that way if you can rid yourself of all those emotional blemishes—anger, frustration, fear, worry and anxiety—which trouble you. Easier said than done, of course, but a good physician can help with good advice, with medicines if necessary—or simply with his ear. Emotional stress can not only inhibit healing of such things as duodenal or gastric ulcers but may even *cause* them. There are many diseases now recognised which are known to be associated with stress factors if not actually caused by them. Mainly these are diseases of the digestive tract or of the heart and blood vessels and you will find some of them discussed in the appropriate sections.

The state of the mind has more influence on bodily functions than you might think and recovery from many serious conditions can be slowed or hastened, depending on your state of mind. Every doctor has had experience of the patient who "loses the will to live", a situation which is unfortunately commoner than the reverse.

A word about preventive medicine—or helping yourself to health. A great deal of nonsense has been talked about the healthy life; at one time we were told to take eighteen chews to each bite, to do deep breathing, to take plenty of exercise, to get lots of fresh air, to eat regularly (or to indulge in peculiar diets). But more recently eminent doctors have cast doubt on most of these fancies. Moderate exercise is necessary to health, but athletes who indulge in violent exercise have not always been noted for longevity. Fresh air is pleasant and stimulating, but, where actual breathing is concerned, it is no better than the air in most rooms. Certainly, one of the problems of our time is air pollution, but at present we are considering ordinary fresh air in comparison with the air indoors, and, in this case, the experts say there is little difference so far as health is concerned.

A balanced diet containing correct amounts of the basic food substances is essential, but there is no evidence that when, or at what intervals, you eat makes the slightest difference—unless you are a sufferer from stomach ulcer, in which case it is necessary that the intervals between meals should not be too long. The whole business of having meals at fixed intervals is nothing but a social convention, and in modern life obviously a matter of convenience. (*See* **Diet, P39**).

Sleep, too, is a necessity. But different people require vastly different amounts of sleep. Some manage on as little as three hours, others seem to believe that they need ten or more. The importance of the dream process is referred to in **Introduction to Psychology, Q15(1)**.

In a number of studies of men and women who lived to a ripe old age it was found that the only factors in common between them were that they had a good balanced diet of healthy food, that they had contented minds, and that they were interested in something which gave them an aim in life. They also came of long-lived families—for living a long and healthy life depends partly upon heredity.

So the main rules of health are:
(1) Don't abuse your body—*i.e.*, exercise it, feed it sensibly and in moderation and don't poison it with cigarette smoke (yours or anyone else's), with alcohol or with other drugs
(2) Think postively about health—make it a purpose for living
(3) Turn your thoughts away from those bodily functions (digestion, circulation, breathing and so on) which can look after themselves. Introspection leads to hypochondriasis, and
(4) Choose your parents for *their* longevity!

The Development of Medicines
A great surgeon, the first of the moderns, was Ambrose Paré, who died in 1590, and one of his best known sayings was: "I apply the dressing, but God heals the wound." He was quite right; for until about sixty years ago, or even less, all the physician could do was to put the patient in as favourable a state as possible to enable his body to cure itself. That is to say, there were hardly any specific drugs—drugs that had a direct effect on the disease. There was quinine, discovered by the Spaniards in America, which was specific for malaria, and there were iron (specific for anaemia) and digitalis (specific for certain types of heart disease), but otherwise nothing until the nineteenth century, when Paul Ehrlich discovered salvarsan, which is specific for syphilis. Ehrlich died in 1914, having conceived the brilliant idea of drugs; which he described as "magic bullets"—*i.e.*, drugs which, like bullets, would be aimed at the real cause of the disease. They would, that is to say, be specific.

Since then a large number of such drugs have been discovered. For example, the antibiotics, such as penicillin, discovered in 1928 by Fleming at St. Mary's Hospital, Paddington. Later, Florey and Chain in Oxford, helped in the war years by the vast resources of the American pharmaceutical industry, were able to make penicillin available to the public in sufficient quantities by new techniques of production. Penicillin is practically non-poisonous (although it is possible to become allergic to it, sometimes with serious results). It can kill some germs in a dilution of one part of penicillin to one hundred million parts of water; it is effective against streptococci, the cause of blood-poisoning, sepsis in wounds, and many other diseases; and also against the germs of anthrax, gonorrhea, meningitis of some types, syphilis—a whole list of plagues which have troubled man for centuries. Blood-poisoning, whether from wounds or childbirth, used to be almost incurable—now the rate of cure is 80–90 per cent.; anthrax and gonorrhœa have an almost 100 per cent. rate of cure. In pneumonia the rate is about 90 per cent., and early syphilis can be cured in a week, instead of the previous two to three years.

But that was only the beginning. Other antibiotics—streptomycin, tetracycline, erythromycin, and many others—are helping to wipe out the terrible scourges of the human race, in particular, in the case of streptomycin, tuberculosis. The sulpha group of drugs—sulphadiazine, sulphadimidine, etc.—have also proved a great boon. Then there are the new drugs which have created a revolution in psychiatry—the tranquillisers which relieve anxiety, the drugs which clear up certain types of depression, and substances such as chlorpromazine which make it possible to nurse formerly violent patients in the wards of a general hospital. The antihistamine drugs help in allergies, anticoagulants are of value after heart attacks and levodopa mitigates some of the distressing features of Parkinson's Disease.

No drug, old or new, is completely safe—if we define "safe" as meaning having absolutely no potential for harm. The household aspirin, widely used in a variety of conditions for its analgesic (pain-relieving) and antipyretic (fever-reducing) qualities, can cause bleeding from the stomach and small intestine. Phenacetin, at one time a component of compound codeine tablets but now withdrawn, can—with prolonged use—damage the kidney. Chloramphenicol, a powerful antibiotic effective in typhoid fever, typhus and whooping cough, can damage the blood-forming cells of the bone marrow producing an agranulocytosis which can be fatal.

Clearly, in any one case, the doctor must weigh up the advantages and disadvantages of this or that drug before prescribing. Minor, self-limiting illnesses do not require potent, potentially toxic remedies. Chloramphenicol is rarely justified in whooping cough, but would never be withheld from a patient with typhoid fever.

Man is a unique species. A new chemical compound promising in animal experiments, for example, as an anti-inflammatory agent, apparently safe when given, say, to mice in a dose 100 times that required to produce that anti-inflammatory effect may, over a long period of time in man, not only have no effect but make his hair fall out or perhaps cause retention of urine. Nevertheless, some animal species do react like man, or vice versa, and it is possible to make reasonably accurate extrapolations from animals to man in terms of drug effect. It is also possible to estimate the toxicity of a drug for man from its toxicity in certain animal species but the ultimate test, both of the effectiveness and the toxicity of a new drug, comes only when it is given to man.

Thalidomide was unique. In every animal test used throughout the drug industry at that time—it was introduced in the late 1950s—it had a clean bill of health. It was chemically related to other drugs which had been in use for a long time. Overdosage with other sedatives such as the barbiturates was common at that time, although less so now. Overdosage with thalidomide was unlikely to prove fatal. It was marketed in Europe and in Britain as a "safe sedative". The tragic results that followed its ingestion by women in the early weeks of pregnancy are now well known. Babies were born with severe deformities of limbs, internal organs or both. That effect could not have been foretold from any animal tests then in use. Since that date new drugs have been subjected to rigorous testing in various animal species to check the effect on foetal development as a statutory requirement, along with the older tests for toxicity which had always been undertaken by reputable drug companies.

The thalidomide disaster of the early 1960s led directly to the setting up of regulatory drug agencies in most countries of the world. In Britain the introduction and clinical testing of new compounds is controlled by the Medicines and Environmental Health Division of the Department of Health and Social Security, statutory machinery set up by the Medicines Act 1968, which followed the purely voluntary scheme of control under what was known as the Dunlop Committee after Sir Derrick Dunlop, its first chairman.

The development and introduction of new drugs is now very strictly controlled. No new drug can be marketed in Britain without the Medicines Commission being satisfied about its efficacy and its safety. We would need space in this edition almost the size of the complete Medical Section to describe fully the workings of the Commission and the limitations that the requirements of the Medicines Act inevitably place on the development and introduction of new remedies. The time from the initial synthesis of a novel compound likely to be of value to its eventual appearance in the pharmacy on prescription is now eight to 10 years. The cost is measured in millions of pounds because, for each successful drug, there will have been many thousands of unsuccessful ones.

Briefly, no new drug or modification of an old one can be sold, whether or not on prescription, unless it has been granted a product licence by the Department of Health and Social Security through its Medicines and Environmental Health Division. Many stages have to be passed to acquire that licence, from the granting of certificates to allow the drug to be tested initially in a limited way in patients in a strictly controlled manner by investigators approved by the Commission, to permission for extension of those trials at a later date to include larger numbers of patients or more investigators, to perhaps a "monitored release"—that is, to enable its use in, say, hospitals only—to the final release on the granting of a full product licence. Thus, the Medicines Commission has control at all stages.

Furthermore, all the stages are dependent on production of evidence relating to the safety and efficacy of the drug, evidence which may take the drug company months, sometimes years, to produce and which, of course, must be acceptable to the Commission. Trials may be stopped at any time, for example, if evidence of side effects of an undesirable nature come to light during clinical testing, or when evidence from some other similar compound indicates a likely risk in the use of the drug in question. Of course, "acceptable" means that the strict criteria which have been laid down by the specialist committees appointed to deal with all the various aspects of drug development, such as toxicology, adverse reactions and so forth, have been met. Experts serve on these committees which meet regularly, but the day-to-day running of the Medicines Commission is in the hands of full-time medically qualified personnel as well as pharmacists, pharmacologists and toxicologists. In addition, outside consultant opinion can be sought.

As well as all these rigid controls on development and testing in the early stages, there is also a scheme of surveillance for untoward side effects. These are the action, or actions, of a drug apart from its main one. Take the well-known side effect of drowsiness which occurs with certain antihistamine drugs: the main action, the one for which the drug is prescribed, is the mitigation of the effects of allergy, such as urticaria. Drowsiness would be an unwanted effect if the patient is not incapacitated and is able to do his usual job. On the other hand, some antihistamines have an appetite-stimulating effect which could, of course, be a useful attribute in certain situations or even allow the drug to be used solely for that purpose, the anti-allergic effect then being incidental.

An adverse reaction is a type of side effect which by definition, is unwanted and potentially harmful. The intestinal bleeding associated with aspirin, or the depressive effects of some of the earlier drugs used to lower blood pressure, such as reserpine and methyldopa, are good examples. When new drugs first become licensed for marketing and are prescribed by doctors on a gradually increasing scale it is important that adverse reactions such as those are reported. Every doctor in the National Health Service, whether in general practice or in hospital, has access to a stock of special record cards on which he can record in a standard way the details of any untoward reaction occurring in his patient during the prescribing of a new or existing drug, and which he has good reason to believe is associated with the taking of that drug. These record cards are posted to the DHSS which has a special unit to deal with them. A doctor noticing, for example that one of his patients developed, say, double vision during treatment with a new antidepressant could not assume in the absence of other firm evidence that the two events were necessarily connected. However, if 100 cards are received by the DHSS reporting the same kind of event, there is good circumstantial evidence that those events are likely to be connected with drug administration. This adverse reaction reporting system, although voluntary, is working well and is an effective "early warning system" for drug toxicity

We have come a long way since thalidomide, but have had to steer between the Scylla of stifling innovation in drug research by excessive control of development and the Charybdis of the free-for-all, profit-motivated bonanzas of the pre-thalidomide era. No system can be perfect, and it is fair to say that had it been necessary, for example, for aspirin, penicillin and streptomycin to be put through the system as we have set it up now they would probably never have reached the market and thence the patient.

Mention must of course be made of the surgical advances and progress in anaesthesia. Hardly a week goes by without operations being undertaken which seemed inconceivable even as short a time as 40 years ago. Transplantation and re-plantation (the re-attachment of severed limbs) are regularly reported; haemodialysis (the 'cleansing' of blood in patients with irreversible kidney disease) is now often undertaken in the patient's own home where, with appropriate adaptation and the modern kidney machine, he or she can run the procedure—single-handed in many instances—and still keep his or her job; and the laser beam is used to deal with detached retinas or to obliterate tiny, microscopic blood vessel 'bubbles' (aneurysms) in the back of the eye while the patient is conscious and cooperative. The list grows daily.

Social Medicine.

Medicine has passed through many phases from the time when disease was regarded as a punishment from the gods or a sign of devil possession to the present era, when increasingly there is a tendency to look on society as the patient. Indeed, one commonly hears doctors and sociologists nowadays talking about "the sick society."

The early primitive stage came to an end—at least in one part of the world—when in Greece, many centuries before Christ, Hippocrates and others began to teach that all diseases were due to natural causes. But after the first ray of hope the outlook began to deteriorate when, during the Middle and Dark Ages (that is, from the fall of the Roman Empire right up to the fifteenth century), there was a return to the belief in devil possession and supernatural causes.

Eighteenth-century medicine in Europe was materialistic, regarding the body as a machine. It was founded upon a sort of pseudo-science—although, of course, there were always individual exceptions, physicians such as Sydenham in England, who, avoiding all theories, based their work on observation of the patient. This mechanistic approach persisted right through the nineteenth century, but medicine became more and more truly scientific, and the century saw the most rapid advances in the field ever known until our own times: the discovery of germs by Pasteur, of antiseptics to combat them by Lister, of vaccination by Jenner and anaesthetics by the American Wells and the Scot Simpson. The use of the microscope by Virchow, who was a German, brought great advances in the understanding of disease and Ehrlich, another German, conceived, as we have already seen, the idea of "magic bullets" which would attack the germs at the root of a disease without harming the patient. But one of the greatest of all these great men is perhaps the least known. His name was Edwin Chadwick.

From the earliest period of recorded history human communities had been constantly ravaged by great plagues which swept over their lands year after year, killing untold millions. The Black Death of 1348-9 wiped out almost half the population of Europe. But, even in the first quarter of the nineteenth century in London, tens of thousands died from typhus, typhoid, and small-pox—and not only these, for periodically cholera would be brought into the country by travellers from abroad.

In the face of these terrible visitations the individual physician was helpless. He could not treat each one of the many sick even had he known how, and Chadwick's claim to fame rests on the fact that he was the first man to think in terms of *social* control of diseases, by so dealing with their causes that they were prevented from arising at all. In order to wipe out typhoid and cholera, he argued, we must ensure clean water supplies; for these diseases are caused by germs carried in polluted water. In order to attack typhus and plague, one must get rid of the lice which carry the germs of typhus and the rat-fleas which carry the germs of plague (including, of course, the rats, which, in turn, carry the fleas).

Chadwick was born in a Lancashire farmhouse where the children were washed every day all over, and he ruthlessly drove an obsession with cleanliness into the heads of his countrymen until, later in the century, it was possible for the German philosopher Treitschke to tell his class in Berlin: "The English think soap is civilisation." Although this remark was meant cynically, there is little doubt that soap, if it is not civilisation in itself, has played a greater part in making civilisation possible than many more elaborate remedies. A population riddled with chronic infectious illness has neither the time nor the energy to apply to the arts or sciences, and soap did a great deal to reduce infection.

One of the first Public Health measures was introduced by Chadwick and others when they brought in legislation to purify the water supply of London. Previously, the citizens had used water from the Thames (they still do, but only after it has been filtered and sterilised at the waterworks!), and from filthy, refuse-laden ponds and springs. Later, Chadwick helped to found the Poor Law Commission, and produced a Report in 1842, the principal suggestions of which were: a municipal water supply for all towns; scientific drainage both in town and country; and an independent health service with large powers for dealing with those who endangered the lives of others by polluting water or causing nuisances. He also proposed a national service for interment of the dead; for in those days bodies often remained for days in the overcrowded homes of the poor without burial.

What has the twentieth century contributed to the concept of social health? Well, of course, there has been a great deal of legislation along the lines initiated by Chadwick to control disease, and a great many other measures have been introduced concerned with the idea of positive health—not merely preventing bad health, but trying to bring about the highest possible state of good health.

Orange juice, milk, and good meals for school-children brought about a transformation in child health which became apparent to the least observant. And the National Health service is in the direct line of descent from early nineteenth-century legislation.

But in future years it is probable that the main achievement of the twentieth century will prove to be its extension of the term "social health" to cover every aspect of community life, not only in such subjects as bodily health and its control of social means, but also such problems as mental illness, crime, delinquency, drug addiction, and so on. What we are now asking ourselves is: how far are these problems produced by society itself, and if this is the case, how far can we go in preventing them by social means?

Community medicine takes the view that these problems can never be dealt with solely by moral-ising and retribution, but only by dispassionately analysing causes and dealing with them. In this century we have developed a social con-science. Not always, it is true, a very well-informed social conscience, but at least this is a good beginning. There are organisations for dealing scientifically with delinquency, for dealing with problem children, for spreading knowledge about cancer in order to show people that it can be successfully treated if taken in time. We can well say with John Donne, who died in 1631, that "no man is an island ... every man's death diminisheth me; for I am involved in mankind." This is the attitude of twentieth-century com-munity medicine.

Summary. Perhaps we can sum up our pro-gress in the past century and a half more dramatically in terms of hard facts.

Before that time a surgical operation was never undertaken except under the gravest circum-stances. There were no anaesthetics and no anti-septics, and the operation was carried out by a surgeon in a filthy tail-coat, stained with the con-gealed blood of countless operations (indeed the surgeons of that time took pride in the dirty condi-tion of their coats as showing how much experience they had previously had). Germs and the part they play in producing disease were unknown, and Paul Ehrlich had not yet been born, so there were no "magic bullets" to attack syphilis, or sera for diphtheria and other diseases. The mentally ill were simply locked up with little treatment and subjected to such indignities as the strait-jacket and the padded cell; now they are given treatment which becomes more effective each year, the padded cell and strait-jacket have gone, and in very few hospitals are the ward doors locked.

In the earlier years of this century you would very likely have died if you had developed pneumonia, "childbed fever" after the birth of a child, men-ingitis, dysentery, typhoid, or tuberculosis. With such infections as blood-poisoning you would have had practically no chance at all. Today, the sulpha drugs and the antibiotics have changed all that. Syphilis and gonorrhoea were lifelong tragedies both to the patient and his family, but now they, too, can be conquered. With scientific research and its application proceeding at a brisk pace many diseases are now being brought under control.

The National Health Service has brought the possibility of good treatment equally to all, and it is up to us to see that all these facilities are used to the full by all who need them.

PART II. DISEASES ARRANGED BY CAUSE OR BODY SYSTEM AFFECTED

THE INFECTIOUS DISEASES.
INTRODUCTION.

INFECTIOUS diseases are those which are caused by an invasion of the body by organisms from outside (the word "organism" simply means other living things, and we are using this word because, as will be seen later, it is not only what are known as "germs" which can cause infection). We know, too, that what is generally typical about this group is: (a) that the disease can be passed on from one person to another, and (b) that it is usually accompanied by a raised temperature or fever. Now (a), of course, is always true, because the definition of an infectious disease is one that can be passed on to others, but (b) is not always true, because a few infections produce little or no temperature, and also because it is possible to have a raised temperature (again in only a few cases) without any infection. For example, certain types of brain injury, tumour, or haemorrhage can produce a raised—or lowered—temperature, and so can the injection of some foreign substance such as milk into the muscles. This is known as "protein shock," and was at one time used in the treatment of certain illnesses. Finally, solutions of dead germs, such as the antityphoid vaccine given to protect troops during the War, may lead when injected to very high temperatures. But, by and large, we are entitled to suppose that the patient with a raised temperature is probably suffering from an infection.

Types of Infection.

As we have seen, it is not only germs which cause infections—so from now on we shall give germs their proper name of "bacteria." Here is a list of the chief offenders which are liable to attack our bodies: bacteria, spirochaetes, viruses, fungi, amoebae, worms and other parasites. Of these, bacteria and viruses are by far the most important, but let us look at them all more closely.

Bacteria are tiny living things which can be seen only under a fairly powerful microscope. Some are grouped like bunches of grapes (staphylococci) or in strings or chains (streptococci). They are given these names because "staphylos" is the Greek word for a bunch of grapes, and "streptos" means a chain. Yet others are comma-shaped (such as the cholera vibrio), or shaped like a drumstick—a rod with a small knob at the end (the tetanus bacillus, which causes lockjaw).

It would be a mistake to think that all bacteria are harmful; for without some species we could not survive for long. Bacteriologists divide them according to their behaviour in the human body into three groups: saprophytic, parasitic or pathogenic, and symbiotic. The *saprophytic* organisms are the bacteria normally found in the skin, mouth, and intestines; they do us neither harm nor good. The *parasitic*, or as they are more usually called, pathogenic (*i.e.*, disease-producing) organisms, are the harmful ones with which we are naturally more concerned. Lastly, there are the *symbiotic* organisms, which, whilst taking something from the body, give something in return. For example, cattle would not be able to digest the cellulose of the grass they eat were it not for helpful bacteria in the lower parts of the intestines, and there are certain bacteria in the large intestine of man which produce vitamins.

Bacteria have two peculiar characteristics: each reproduces by splitting into two separate individuals as often as every twenty minutes in favourable circumstances like an open wound. If no bacterium were destroyed, one individual could produce a mass of bacteria larger than the whole world in a matter of a few weeks (since each of the offspring also divides into two, which in turn divide again—the progression goes: one gives birth to two, these two to four, the four to eight, eight to sixteen, sixteen to thirty-two, and so on—you will see, if you work it out, that in a short period the figure becomes astronomical). Fortunately, many bacteria have accidents, so for the present the world is safe! The other curious thing about bacteria is that, barring accidents, they are potentially immortal. Under ideal conditions in which no bacteria were killed, none would die; for a bacterium there is no death from old age, no corpse except when it is actively destroyed. It simply goes on dividing, dividing, and subdividing for ever.

How, then, are bacteria destroyed? Briefly, the answer is that most are destroyed by the natural defences of the body of whatever host they are preying on; others are destroyed by antiseptics and the new drugs; and many are destroyed when they are excreted from the body in the sputum or through the bowels and land in places where they are dried up and cannot survive—although some bacteria in such circumstances can form what are called "spores," rather like the seed of plants, so making it possible for them to survive in a state of suspended animation for months on end until picked up accidentally by another unfortunate host. Finally, bacteria, in addition to all these possibilities, face another danger: they may themselves develop disease. This disease is caused by even more minute organisms known as bacteriophages (viruses which affect bacteria), discovered by F. W. Twort in 1915. Attack by bacteriophage causes whole groups of bacteria (known as "colonies") to disintegrate and become harmless.

Although bacteriophage has been used in the treatment of some diseases in human beings, this method has now been largely given up, since the new drugs are infinitely more effective.

Spirochaetes. Spirochaetes, like bacteria, are minute organisms, but differ in being shaped somewhat like a corkscrew and in being able to move (which many bacteria cannot do). Their progress is produced by a sideways wriggling motion. The two main diseases caused by spirochaetes are syphilis and spirochaetal jaundice. Spirochaetal jaundice is carried by rats, and is common in those who work in mines. It is now rare in Britain, but still occurs in Japan, Egypt, and Malaysia; the infection is passed through the skin where the excreta of infected rats mingles with water on damp ground in the mine where miners kneel. Infection may also occur through eating infected food.

Viruses. Unlike bacteria, viruses are too small to be seen under an ordinary microscope. They can, however, be photographed in some cases under an electron microscope, which uses a magnetic field instead of a glass lens and a stream of electrons in place of a beam of light. Viruses cause such diseases as typhus, measles, mumps, poliomyelitis, smallpox, and chickenpox—not to mention such plant and animal diseases as tobacco mosaic disease and foot-and-mouth disease, which often have serious economic consequences. Other virus diseases are psittacosis (an infection of parrots and similar birds which can be transmitted to Man), swine fever in pigs, influenza in Man, and myxomatosis in rabbits. They also cause, it is believed, the common cold.

The main characteristics of viruses are, first, that they can only grow in living cells—unlike bacteria, which readily grow in the laboratory on plates containing a jelly made from meat, broth, gelatin, milk, and other delicacies. The scientist, therefore, must keep them in portions of living tissue kept alive outside the body. Secondly, they are so small that they pass through the pores of the finest filter. Thirdly, a first attack usually produces immunity for life. Second attacks of the common virus diseases mentioned above are very rare; but unfortunately, this rule does not apply to influenza or the common cold. Fourthly, there is reason to believe that viruses represent an extraordinary intermediate stage between the living and non-living; they can, for instance, be produced in crystalline form and yet are just as dangerous when "thawed out." Lastly, the virus diseases have proved for the most part to be little affected by the new antibiotics and other drugs, although vaccination in smallpox and the injection of sera from infected patients in other infections may give immunity for longer or shorter periods.

The two great practical problems that doctors face with viruses are: (i) many viruses are unknown because of the difficulty of growing them outside the body in suitable tissue culture. They cannot therefore be conveniently identified in specimens from the patient, as bacteria can; and (ii) they are unaffected by antibiotics like penicillin. It has been a great step forward to grow viruses artificially in tissue culture, in which they are identified indirectly by the effects they have on the cultural *cells*. But since we do not know exactly how to grow some viruses (like those of infective hepatitis) they have still not been seen.

When we recover from a viral illness like chickenpox, we probably do so by producing virus-killing substances inside our own cells. Scientists are currently searching for these substances in case they can be used, like penicillin, to cure viral disease.

Fungi. Some infections are caused by fungi—that is to say organisms belonging to the same group as moulds, mushrooms, and toadstools. Penicillin and some other antibiotics are produced from moulds, so, as in the case of bacteria, some fungi are helpful; they even help to destroy each other, as bacteria do. For example actinomyces, which can cause infection of the jaw and other tissues, is destroyed by penicillin.

Most fungal infections are trivial and limited to the skin. But, although trivial, they can be unsightly and uncomfortable. Ringworm of the scalp, dhobie itch—an infection of the groin spread by infected underclothing—and so-called "athlete's foot" are caused by a fungus.

Amoebae. Amoebae are small, single-cell organisms, the largest of which (a harmless type found in stagnant ponds in Britain and elsewhere) is just visible to the naked eye. It is about the size of the head of a pin. Amoebae move, in the species which are capable of moving, by pushing forward a part of the cell in the appropriate direction and causing the rest to flow into the advancing portion. Like bacteria, they reproduce by dividing into halves, each of which becomes a new amoeba.

The main human disease caused by amoebae is amoebic dysentery (not to be confused with bacillary dysentery).

Parasites. These may live on the skin like lice (which can carry typhus) or fleas (carriers of plague) or the parasites of scabies which burrow into the skin, or they may live part of their time in the blood or other tissues, like malaria. They often have complicated life-cycles involving other hosts (like mosquitoes) at certain stages of development.

Worms. Worms are intestinal parasites, but the only common types found in Britain are threadworms, the tiny thread-like worms which cause irritability and itching in the skin of children, less often in adults; round-worms, somewhat resembling the ordinary garden earthworm, which seldom lead to symptoms; and tapeworms, which may reach a length of 3 or even 6 m. Many parasitic worms (like parasites elsewhere) lead a double life—they spend part of their life in the human intestine and the other part in the muscles of another animal. The tapeworm, for example, whilst in the human intestine, lays eggs which pass out of the body in the excreta, and are then swallowed by pigs, especially in those parts of the world where human excreta are used as manure in the fields. In the pig, the eggs form cysts in the muscles—meat infected in this way is known as "measly pork"—and when, in turn, the meat is eaten by man, the process in the intestine begins all over again.

Less common types, from our point of view, are the Russian tape-worm (which, as befits a Russian, grows to nearly 9 m!); this type is spread by caviare or undercooked infected fish. The small, leaf-shaped liver fluke lays eggs which are passed into canals or pools in tropical countries in the urine of infected people, hatch out and enter a water snail, and finally leave the snail in the form of small parasites which pierce the skin of bathers, whence they pass to the liver and subsequently the bladder and rectum. This is a serious condition, as is also filariasis (another tropical disease), for which, unlike bilharzia—caused by the liver fluke—no cure is known. The tropical disease known as loa-loa is caused by a variety of filaria.

How the Infection is Spread.

Infection is spread in many ways, some of which have already been mentioned. In the common fevers found in Europe and elsewhere one of the most frequent ways is by *droplet infection*—that is to say, by minute drops carrying the germs which are coughed or sneezed into the air by someone already suffering from the disease. Such droplets can be projected into the air for 3m or more, and when breathed in by someone within range infection may result. Next commonest

mode of spread is perhaps by *infected food, water,* and the dirty hands of those who prepare food: cholera, dysentery, food-poisoning, and typhoid are spread in this way. Spread by *direct contact* is found in the venereal diseases (usually, but not always, spread by sexual intercourse with someone who already has the disease), and, of course, lice, fleas, and other parasites, including the scabies mite, are spread by contact with the infested individual—or sometimes with his clothes or bed linen. Spread through an *intermediary host,* whether it be lice, fleas, or mosquitoes carrying infection, or the various means adopted by worms, has already been described above, so no more need be said. Lastly, the infection may result from *bacteria already within the body;* for example, the bacillus coli which lives in the large intestine is there harmless, but if it gets into the bladder or the ureters (the tubes leading from kidney to bladder) a quite unpleasant result may follow in the form of cystitis or pyelitis.

How the Body Deals with Infection.

The body has many mechanisms of defence against intruders, but suffice it to say here that there are two main ones. First, substances known as antibodies and antitoxins are produced in the blood—the antitoxins to neutralise the poisons produced by the invaders, the antibodies to render them helpless, for example, by causing them to clump together so that they can more easily be dealt with by the second defence mechanism. This second mechanism is provided by the white cells in the blood, some of which (the phagocytes) act like amoebae and swallow up and destroy the germs. Antibodies and antitoxins can be transferred from one individual to another and are used in medicine both to prevent infection and to cure it. This is known as immunisation, and can be active or passive. Active immunisation is produced by injecting either a solution of dead bacteria, as in the case of antityphoid injections, or by injecting live, but weakened, strains of the organism, as in the case of smallpox vaccination. In both cases the body is stimulated to produce its own immune substances. Passive immunisation is used either for people who have been in recent contact with infection or who are already ill, and in this case the antitoxins produced in another person who has had the illness are injected in the form of serum—*i.e.,* the liquid part of the blood without the blood cells. All these natural defences are inefficient in the ill, the underfed, the very young, and the very old.

The mechanisms of the response of the body to infection is the broad field of study of the immunologist.

Antiseptics.

The earliest antiseptic was carbolic acid, used by Lister in his operating-theatre in the form of a fine spray directed throughout the operation on the wound, or sometimes in the form of steam from a kettle containing a solution of carbolic. But carbolic is dangerous, and since Lister's time many more useful antiseptics have been discovered. Acriflavine, thymol, and other old favourites have been discarded too. The various forms of carbolic are still used to disinfect drains, but, to tell the truth, the use of antiseptics nowadays is very limited. In surgery the *antiseptic* method has given way to the *aseptic* method—instead of fighting sepsis we see to it that no possibility of sepsis is present before operating; all instruments, the surgeons' and nurses' hands, the skin, are sterilised—the instruments by boiling, the dressings by dry heat, the hands by soap and water, and almost the only antiseptic used is to clean the patient's skin in the area to be operated on.

Antiseptics are used as first-aid treatment for cuts and wounds, but should be applied only once as a general rule—that is, when the wound is first received. The trouble with antiseptics is that as well as killing germs they also kill the surrounding tissues, which antibiotics never do.

Antiseptic sprays to purify the air of a room or to destroy germs lurking in the dust on the sick-room floor—or any other floor—are practically useless. To quote the *British Medical Journal*: "There is no good scientific evidence that any of the chemical air-disinfectants can control the spread of infection in places such as schools, offices, or cinemas. Nor is there good evidence that any substantial effect on the spread of illness can be obtained by disinfection of dust."

Neither is there any good reason to believe that mouth-washes and gargles have any effect other than making the mouth feel fresher and (temporarily) removing mouth odour—by covering it up with the scent of the antiseptic. Mouthwashes are in contact with the bacteria for far too short a time to have any damaging result, and, in the case of tonsillitis and other diseases, all the important bacteria are hidden far out of any danger from gargles.

Antibiotics.

Some antibiotics—penicillin, streptomycin, erythromycin and so on—have already been mentioned (*see* **P4**). In recent years many others have been introduced—ampicillin, gentamycin, cephalexin. Indiscriminate use of these drugs (*e.g.* for trivial complaints) has led to problems, the most important being the development of resistance by previously sensitive organisms. It is not always convenient or possible to be able to identify the particular germ responsible for an infection and determine to which drug it is sensitive, but if there is an initial clinical response, it can be assumed that the "right" drug has been used. It is important to have a full course of treatment—which usually means ten days minimum.

Other problems are hypersensitivity (allergic) reactions which can take many forms. Once hypersensitivity to one of the antibiotics has been identified (penicillin hypersensitivity is not rare) the patient must be made aware of this, and so protect himself from unwitting prescribing by another doctor. Hospital and GP records are clearly marked in such instances but it is very important that the patient himself knows.

Antibiotics are only available on prescription, at least in the U.K., but medicine cupboards are full of them, accumulated from unfinished courses. Self-prescribing is tempting but ill-advised; antibiotics must always be given under medical supervision. Side effects are common and some are dangerous. Repeated use may lead to rapid overgrowth of fungi *e.g.* thrush (Candida albicans) normally present in harmless numbers in the alimentary tract with serious, sometimes fatal results.

General Treatment of Fevers.

Fevers are ordinarily heralded in by a rise in temperature which is noticeable either by a flushed face or by alternate sensations of heat and cold. A patient with a high temperature may have shivering attacks known as "rigors." Tell the doctor.

A high temperature does not necessarily (especially in a child) mean that the trouble is serious but the lay person should always treat it as such and certainly call a doctor if the patient is a child or an elderly person. The majority of fevers are of a viral origin and usually self limiting. The patient tends to improve rapidly once the temperature is controlled.

Even the trained physician finds it difficult to tell one fever from another in the early days; for most of the common fevers begin in more or less the same way. It is only when a rash or some other more definite sign becomes evident that a certain diagnosis can be made, and these may not show themselves until the patient has been feeling "run-down" and fevered for some days. A clinical thermometer is a useful tool and inexpensive to buy. The more recent fever scans applied directly to the forehead also give an immediate and fairly accurate temperature reading. Control of temperature is important, especially in young children, where a high fever may produce a convulsion. A febrile convulsion is a frightening experience for any parent, particularly as their child may have seemed quite well a few minutes previously. High temperature, twitching, and increased irritation may herald the onset. Emergency management involves keeping the child on its side to avoid inhalation of vomit,

clearing debris around his mouth, removing his clothes and sponging him with lukewarm water. Get someone to summon medical help, but never leave an unconscious child alone. Above all, do not panic as the initial episode will usually soon pass.

Briefly, then, the way to treat a fever in the early stages before the doctor comes, and before one knows exactly what is wrong, is as follows:

(1) Put the patient to bed. The child is probably better on the living room sofa where he will feel less isolated and is more easily observed.

(2) Give plenty of clear fluids; water, water and fruit juice, weak tea or lemonade.

(3) Give small amounts of easily digested food but only if the patient requires it.

(4) Aspirin is no longer recommended for the treatment of feverish children, and should not be given to children under 12 years of age. This is because it has been linked to the development of "Reye's Syndrome", an acute encephalopathy or inflammation of the brain with delirium, convulsions and coma. Although very rare, "Reye's Syndrome" carries a high mortality.

Adults with a history of Peptic Ulcer or chronic indigestion should also avoid Aspirin because of the possible risk of a gastro-intestinal bleed.

Paracetamol is now the treatment of choice to reduce temperature and relieve headache and elixir preparations are available for children. The dose may be repeated 4/6 hourly and there are no gastro-intestinal side effects.

Medicines containing Paracetamol should be stored in a safe place as overdosage, accidental or otherwise, may cause liver damage without initial drowsiness or loss of consciousness. Symptoms may not be apparent for a number of days.

Other methods of cooling a feverish patient involve removing excess clothing, administering tepid baths or sponging with lukewarm water. Simply standing at an open door and allowing the cool outside air to waft around the feverish child, can have an immediate effect.

THE INFECTIOUS FEVERS.

The remarks made above apply to the management of *any* fever, and we are now going to discuss particular infectious diseases, beginning with the common childhood fevers, then passing on to less common ones, tropical diseases, and worm and parasitic infestations.

The common infectious fevers are caused by bacteria or viruses, and it is useful to know the meaning of the following terms: *incubation period* is the time which elapses between being infected and developing symptoms; *prodromal period* is the time which elapses between the end of the incubation period and the appearance of a rash; *quarantine period*, the maximum time during which a person who has been in contact with the infection may develop the disease—it is usually two days more than the incubation period; *isolation period* the time a patient is supposed to be isolated.

Virus Diseases.

First, we shall take the common virus diseases, measles, chickenpox, and rubella or German measles, then the other virus diseases, mumps, infective hepatitis, viral pneumonia, and some less common conditions which do not always produce a typical rash as in the case of the first three.

In nearly all of these fevers there is a long incubation period, and one infection gives immunity for life.

Measles. The incubation period is 10–11 days. The first sign is the appearance of symptoms rather like a severe cold. The eyes become red, and exposure to light is unpleasant, the nose runs, the throat becomes inflamed, and a dry, harsh cough develops. There may be headache and the temperature rises to 39°C or more. Usually the patient is a child, and especially typical is the development of so-called Koplik's spots, which are small, bluish-white, raised spots seen on the inside of the cheek at the back of the mouth. The rash begins on the fourth day of the prodromal period, i.e., 14 days after the initial infection. It shows on the forehead and behind the ears, spreading within a day downwards over the whole body; in another two days it starts to disappear, but often leaves behind a sort of brownish staining which may last for one to two weeks.

Measles can be serious, especially in very young children because of its complications, such as bronchopneumonia and infection of the ear, which can now be treated with antibiotics. These drugs have no effect on the measles virus, but only on the secondarily invading bacteria which have invaded the lungs and ear during the illness. The illness can be attenuated or lessened by injection of antibodies (gamma globulin) from an immune adult, and this is often worth while in the very young. Effective vaccination is now available.

Rubella or German Measles. Incubation period 14–19 days. A mild fever, similar to measles except that the rash is usually the first sign that anything is wrong, and the temperature is rarely above 38°C. The eyes may be pink, and there are enlarged glands at the back of the neck. The rash disappears completely in thirty-six hours. There are no complications.

German measles, in itself, is harmless, but if a woman gets the disease in the early months of pregnancy malformations in the child may appear at birth. Vaccination is advised if a girl has not contracted the disease by the time she reaches puberty. There is no special treatment except the general rules for fevers given above.

Chickenpox. Incubation period 14–15 days, but may be more variable. In children chickenpox is a mild fever which begins with the appearance of tiny blisters on the chest and back. These later spread outwards to the legs, arms and face, and cause itching. Treatment is the general one for fevers already described. Calamine lotion or dusting powder will be helpful for the irritation, and the child's nails should be cut short to prevent scratching and infection of the spots. Whereas children are usually little bothered by chickenpox, young adults may be much more drastically affected—a temperature of 40°C is not uncommon, and then there may be severe headache.

Mumps. Incubation period 17–18 days. Everyone knows the typical appearance of the patient with mumps—the swelling in the salivary glands in front of the ears which makes the face look full. This causes pain later on, and it may be difficult to open the mouth. Temperature is not usually high (about 38°C). Although uncomfortable, mumps is rarely dangerous, but orchitis—swelling of the testicles—is sometimes a complication. Fluid diet should be given if eating is painful, with mouth-washes, and rest in bed.

Infective Hepatitis. "Hepatitis" means inflammation of the liver, and infective hepatitis, which is much the commonest cause of jaundice in young adults, is a viral infection of the liver. The main symptoms are fever, followed by jaundice, which is first noticed in the whites of the eyes as yellow staining, then in the skin. The urine becomes coloured also, and this is most easily noticed if, on shaking in a bottle, the froth shows coloration. If the froth remains white, no jaundice is present. Treatment is a matter for the doctor, but great care should be taken, both by the patient and those in contact with him, to wash the hands thoroughly after urinating or defaecating, after handling utensils from the sickroom, and both before and after eating; for the disease is very infectious.

Viral Pneumonia. Pneumonia is usually caused by bacteria, and when we speak of pneumonia, that is the type we ordinarily refer to. Viral pneumonia is known by doctors as "pneumonitis," and is believed to be closely related to influenza. There is no specific treatment so far, and since diagnosis is a specialist matter little more need be said except that the symptoms in general resemble those of ordinary pneumonia. Psittacosis, another virus disease, can also lead to pneumonia, and although there is no specific treatment for virus infections of the lungs, it is always worth while trying the antibiotics or sulpha drugs in view of the possibility that the lung condition may be caused by a secondary invasion of bacteria.

Influenza. While serious epidemics of influenza take the form of a very dramatic and often fatal disease—for example, the epidemic of "Spanish 'flu" which followed the First World War killed more people than the actual fighting—the milder type more usually seen is difficult to distinguish from the common cold. In fact, many people who complain of "a dose of the 'flu" are suffering from simple colds.

However, a sudden onset, aching in the muscles of the back and legs, and redness of the eyes, would suggest influenza, and especially typical is the depression and weakness which follow influenza but not a cold. The measures suggested above for the general treatment of fever should be applied; but the depression and weakness which follow influenza may need special treatment by the doctor.

Colds. Although everyone thinks he, or she, knows what a "cold" is, the issue is not so simple; for the symptoms of fever, running nose, and a run-down, "headachy" feeling are found in many illnesses. They may be observed, as we have seen, in the early stages of measles before the arrival of the rash, or in a number of other fevers, such as whooping cough. Mild attacks of influenza (see above) may resemble the common cold, and blocking of the nose with discharge and fever may be due to sinusitis—although here there is usually pain above, between, or below the eyes. Colds can be caused by any one of thirty different viruses known as "rhinoviruses" as well as by others which cause influenza, or infect glands (adenoviruses). This is why a single cold does not confer immunity on the sufferer. It is probable that you will not catch a cold from the same virus, at least for the rest of the year, but there are all those others waiting to infect you with other colds in buses, tubes, and other crowded places. Like all infections, do not forget that the best way to avoid them is to keep generally well, and in a good nutritional state. Do not spend money on injections or other vaccines. They do not work, probably because of the multiplicity of viruses involved. It is unlikely that adding vitamins or mineral supplements to normal diet will do any good at all provided you are eating sensibly. The vogue for prophylactic or therapeutic treatment of colds with massive doses of vitamin C has recently received much attention from scientists attempting, with little success, to prove the effect by controlled clinical trial and to find a rational basis for its use.

Poliomyelitis.

Polio, or infantile paralysis as it used to be known, is caused by a virus which has a particular affinity for the nerve cells of the spinal cord and which results in paralysis of those muscles under the control of the particular group of cells infected. Rarely, the infection is widespread in the nerve tissue causing paralysis of muscles of swallowing and respiration as well as those of the trunk and limbs. The usual pattern is for a single muscle group to be affected, for example, the muscles controlling the movements of the arm at the shoulder. Such paralysis may be transient with complete recovery, partial with some residual weakness, or total, leaving a "flail limb" which is wasted and powerless.

At one time in this country epidemics of polio-myelitis were common, mainly affecting children and young adults. There is no doubt that mild forms of the disease were always occurring in very young children, forms never diagnosed as such but conferring a natural immunity in later life.

In common with other infections, poliomyelitis begins with a mild or moderate pyrexia, with a sore throat, headache, nausea and perhaps actual vomiting, some five to 10 days after contact with the virus. There may be rigidity of the neck muscles. Paralysis, if it occurs, will become apparent about the second or third day of illness. This stage may last two or three weeks, by which time the temperature will have subsided and the paralysis started to improve. There is no specific treatment and medical care is confined to sympto-matic relief. Difficulty with swallowing and breathing calls for special nursing measures. In severe cases, artificial means of maintaining respiration may have to be continued for months, or for the rest of the patient's life. Many severely paralysed polio victims of the post-war epidemics —the self-styled "responauts"—depend for their lives on artificial respirators ("iron lungs").

With the development of the oral vaccine early in the 1960s, and its introduction into the im-munisation schedule in this country, the disease has now virtually disappeared from Great Britain.

Smallpox. In previous editions we stated that "since the introduction of vaccination it (small-pox) is comparatively rare in industrialised coun-tries." In the 88th edition we reported that small-pox (*variola major*) had now been eradicated throughout the world. The less serious form of the disease, *variola minor*, is still found in some parts of Africa, but all the signs are that it, too, will soon be eradicated. The last case of *variola major* occurred in Bangladesh in 1975. With the disappearance of the disease vaccination will become unnecessary; however, the World Health Organisation is planning to store vaccine (which can be done almost indefinitely at a temperature of $-20°C$) in sufficient quantities to vaccinate many millions of people should the need ever arise again. We made no excuse therefore for leaving out of that edition of *Pears*, for the first time in its long history, the detailed description of the disease.

Glandular Fever. Sometimes called infectious mononucleosis, since one of its features is an in-crease in a certain type of white cell—the monocyte—and a change in its microscopic charac-teristics. It is caused by a virus (the Epstein-Barr), predominantly affects young children and adults and although often taken a protracted course, it is not in itself a serious infection. The main symptoms are fever, enlargement of lymph glands in the neck and a sore throat. A transient body rash may be seen occasionally, particularly during or after the treat-ment of the sore throat with penicillin or one of its synthetic cousins such as ampicillin. Diagnosis without laboratory tests on the blood (the Paul-Bunnel test) may not be easy although the com-bination of sore throat, swollen neck glands and a rash is highly suspicious. The disease is self-limiting and there is no treatment.

Typhus. This disease used to be known as "jail fever," because it was frequent in prisons; but overcrowding, poverty, and bad hygienic surroundings anywhere are suitable conditions for epidemics of typhus. Improved conditions in industrialised countries have made it unusual, since typhus is carried from one person to another by infected body lice. It is due to the organism *Rickettsia prowazekii*, which displays both bac-terial and viral characteristics.

Typhus comes on suddenly with a rise in temperature to about 39°C, but within four days it may be as high as 42°C. There may, or may not, be a rash at this time, and in the second week, when the temperature is at its highest, there is delirium, weakness, and a feeble pulse. The typical typhus rash appears about the fifth day as reddish blotches on the chest, abdomen, and wrists.

Typhus is, needless to say, very serious but responds to modern antibiotics. Preventive measures are directed towards eradicating lice.

Rabies. Finally, we shall deal very briefly with a number of less common virus diseases, beginning, as is appropriate, with *hydrophobia* or *rabies*, since it was in this infection that the great French scientist Louis Pasteur (1822–95) showed the possibility of prevention by vaccination. Unlike Jenner, with his ready-made cowpox virus, which is the virus of smallpox weakened by natural passage through cows, Pasteur had to weaken the rabies virus by passing it through rabbits. The rabbits were infected, and after death the spinal cord was dried and powdered, a solution passed through another rabbit, and so on until the virus was sufficiently weakened.

Rabies is spread by the bite of infected animals, usually dogs, cats, or wolves, who are driven mad by the disease; in Trinidad, however, it has been spread by vampire bats. Those who are bitten usually show no symptoms for six weeks or more, but sooner or later convulsions and delirium arise, which within four to five days are fatal.

There is no cure once the symptoms have developed, but antirabies serum, followed by anti-rabies inoculation as soon as possible, prevents illness in the majority of cases. Dogs should be muzzled in areas where the disease is common, but quarantining imported dogs has made the infection almost unknown here.

Psittacosis. This is another virus disease which is of interest mainly in that it is spread by birds of the parrot group, such as parrots, love-birds, macaws, and the rest. It occasionally occurs here in people who have been in contact with birds of this type, and is serious both to the bird and to its owner. Quarantine regulations greatly reduced the risk of infection in Britain. They were lifted a few years ago but concern over recent outbreaks, not only of psittacosis but a number of economically important diseases such as fowl pest, led to their reintroduction in 1976.

The symptoms of psittacosis are fever, cough, and bronchitis. The disease is especially danger-ous to old people, but it responds to the same anti-biotics as typhus.

Sandfly Fever, or phlebotomus fever, *Dengue*, or breakbone fever, and *Trench Fever* are all some-what similar conditions in that they resemble influenza and are rarely fatal. They are all due to viruses, spread in the first case by sandflies in tropical climates; in the second by mosquitoes in tropical climates; and in the third by lice in temperate climates. They are all typical "soldiers' diseases"; the first two were common in the Middle East and Far East during the last War, the third during the First World War in France.

Yellow Fever. Of all the virus diseases, seven can now be prevented, or largely prevented, by vaccination—smallpox, measles, German measles, rabies, poliomyelitis (if started early enough), influenza and yellow fever. Yellow fever is carried by a mosquito known as Stegomyia, common in South and Central America and in African ports. For its spread, it therefore needs: a hot climate, the stegomyia mosquito, and an infected person.

In 1898 the United States was at war with Spain in Central America, where yellow fever was a serious problem. Following this war the United States, by this time acutely aware of this terrible disease, asked a Dr. G. E. Waring to deal with it in Havana, where it was rife. But Waring died of yellow fever, as had many millions before him, without knowing its cause, and it was left to Walter Reed, who died in 1902, to prove the con-nection between the mosquito and yellow fever. By a vigorous war on the mosquito, the disease has been eradicated from Havana and the West In-dian islands, and Reed's discovery made possible the building of the Panama Canal.

In yellow fever there is a sudden high tempera-ture, aching of limbs and head, jaundice, and black vomit; the pulse-rate falls as the fever rises. Previous vaccination seems to be preventive if undertaken in time.

Conclusion.

All these virus diseases have this in common: that for many there is no specific cure, although some (see above) can be prevented by vaccination, or by the social control of the creatures carrying the virus. Some of the larger viruses (psittacosis) are destroyed by certain antibiotics. There is usually a long incubation period. Finally the question will sometimes arise of protecting some people from German measles or measles with gamma globulin containing another person's antibodies to the disease. This may be considered for measles in very young patients or to protect the foetus in pregnant mothers in contact with German measles.

Bacterial Diseases.

Bacterial diseases differ from virus infections in a number of respects; their incubation period tends to be shorter: having the disease once does not often confer lifelong protection; and unlike virus diseases, most bacterial diseases respond to one of the antibiotics or sulphonamides. In many cases it is possible to inoculate against the disease to prevent it occurring, as we have seen is possible with only a few of the virus diseases.

Scarlet Fever and Other Streptococcal Infections. In the days, not so long ago, before the arrival of chemotherapy (sulphonamides) and antibiotics, streptococci were very much feared and even caused a high mortality, particularly in such susceptible groups as children, and mothers and babies in maternity hospitals. They are still taken very seriously in the latter and rightly so, although one wonders how much of the mystique is simply a hangover from the days, fifty years ago, when many mothers died from "childbed fever." All signs of infection, such as fever, during the puerperium (the period following childbirth) must be promptly dealt with by a doctor, and only occasionally now is there real cause for anxiety provided treatment is prompt and rigorous.

Scarlet fever is much less common and very much less serious an illness than it used to be, partly because of the effective treatments available today, but also because of a definite but unexplained reduction in its severity. Perhaps the streptococcus has changed, and certainly the improved physical condition of people who are now much better fed and housed than they were, has helped to ward off the terrors of this disease as of so many other infections. The classical picture of signs and symptoms is now so rarely seen that it will not be further described.

The importance of streptococcal infections has shifted from the initial infection, such as a sore throat, to some serious conditions which occasionally arise as a result of some form of delayed sensitivity to the bacteria. Acute rheumatism or rheumatic fever (not to be confused with ordinary aches and pains nor with rheumatoid arthritis) occasionally arise in people who have had a sore throat a few weeks before. Since the streptococcus is not the direct cause of the damage which may consequently occur in the heart or kidney, the antibiotics are no answer except sometimes to keep off further streptococcal invasions.

Diphtheria. This used to be an extremely serious disease, but immunisation has made it almost unknown; it is important, therefore, that all children should be immunised. There are many modern and up-to-date doctors who have qualified since the war who have never seen a case because it has become so rare, and in spite of the propaganda of certain ill-informed people, this saving of children's lives is entirely the result of nationwide inoculation during the war and since. The following description is of historic interest only, and will remain so if a high level of inoculation is kept up by parents.

In a typical case of diphtheria the incubation period is about three days; the patient is a child who becomes ill and pale-looking (*i.e.*, the onset is not sudden, as in many fevers, but insidious); the temperature is only slightly raised to, perhaps, 37° or 38°C, and although there may be no complaint of sore throat, examination will reveal inflammation with—and this is typical of diphtheria —a grey membrane spread over the tonsils, the palate, and the back of the mouth generally. The diphtheria germ does not spread within the body. It stays at the place where it entered (in this case the throat) and sends its toxins throughout the body.

Even after the acute phase is over the patient must not be allowed to walk, because the diphtheria toxin is particularly poisonous to the heart. The ordinary rule is at least one or two months in bed.

Diphtheria also occurs in the larynx—in preinoculation days many children choked to death with this form of the infection; in the nose; and, although this is not generally known, wounds can be infected. The so-called "Desert sores" of the North African campaign seem to have been caused by diphtheria-like organisms.

Diphtheria may lead to paralysis of the throat, with difficulty in speaking or swallowing, and paralysis of the eyes or limbs; these are due to neuritis caused by the influence of the toxin on the nerves.

Whooping Cough. For many years whooping cough has been regarded merely as a bother to the patient and a nuisance to others, as, in fact, a trivial disease. Unfortunately, this is not so; because statistics show that it caused more deaths than polio, diphtheria, scarlet fever, and measles put together.

Whooping cough begins in a child as an ordinary cold with cough and slight fever, and this stage lasts for a week or ten days. Then the "paroxysmal stage" begins as a series of coughs following in rapid succession, during which time the patient is unable to breathe. The "whoop" is caused by the noisy indrawing of breath when the fit stops. The face may become blue and congested. Bronchitis is usually present, and bronchopneumonia may result as a complication, so inoculation of all children before the disease has a chance to strike them is most important.

Once whooping cough has begun, there is no specific treatment, although modern drugs can reduce the frequency of the fits of coughing. The antibiotic chloramphenicol has been used for this disease, but the general opinion is that it is ordinarily of little benefit. Chinese physicians once described whooping cough as the "hundred-days cough," and the cough may, indeed, continue for at least a hundred days. There is an effective vaccine.

Food Poisoning Diseases.

Strictly speaking there is no such thing as "food poisoning" if one is thinking of "poisoning" in terms of anything apart from germs. But not so long ago it used to be thought that decomposition of food in itself produced poisons known as "ptomaines" which were deadly to those who swallowed them. All food poisoning is caused by infection of food with bacteria and by no other cause—unless of course, we are thinking of the kind of poisoning which is the concern of the lawyer rather than the medical man.

Here we are considering those diseases which are commonly spread by contaminated food or drink. The classification is not scientific, but then no scientific classification has as yet been devised. First, we shall deal with typhoid, paratyphoid, and dysentery—uncommon here in Britain, although Sonné dysentery is fairly frequent. Then there is gastro-enteritis (which means irritation of the stomach and intestines), which is caused by staphylococci and the germs of the salmonella group, and lastly botulism, which is rare.

Typhoid and Paratyphoid. These diseases are spread by infected water, food, or hands— especially uncooked food, such as milk, salads, oysters, and shellfish. Flies, too, play some part in spreading the disease. Some people are "carriers" and carry and excrete the germs without being themselves affected; for example, "Typhoid Mary," a carrier in the United States in the early years of this century, spent a large part of her life in custody as a public danger, although she did not show any symptoms of typhoid. Nevertheless, this woman caused a great deal of illness in others in her chosen profession of cook.

The influence of Chadwick's propaganda for pure water supplies is shown by the fact that deaths from typhoid, still 332 per 1,000,000 in 1870, fell to 198 per 1,000,000 at the beginning of this century. In the 1920s the death-rate was only 25 per 1,000,000, and now it is even less.

Typhoid fever begins like most fevers with headache, raised temperature, and general feeling of unwellness. This stage lasts about a week, and then the rash appears in the form of rose-red spots on the front of the chest and abdomen and on the back. In the second week there is great weakness, sometimes diarrhoea, flatulence, and mental dullness, together with dry and cracked lips and tongue. The third week is the week, in hopeful cases, of gradual decrease in temperature and other symptoms, and the fourth week is the week of convalescence.

Complications are perforation of the intestine (which needs surgical treatment), delirium, and bronchitis.

Paratyphoid fever is a milder form of typhoid (there are two forms, A and B); ordinarily it can be diagnosed only by scientific tests. The main thing is to inoculate contacts with T.A.B. vaccine and to protect food supplies; treatment is with chloramphenicol.

Dysentery. Dysentery may be caused either by a bacterium or an amoeba; the first type is known as bacillary dysentery, the latter as amoebic dysentery (which is dealt with under tropical diseases). Infection is spread in much the same way as in typhoid. There is high fever, abdominal pain, and diarrhoea, at first consisting of faecal matter, then blood and mucus. In severe cases the death-rate used to be over 20 per cent.

Various bacilli cause dysentery. The common tropical types are the Shiga and Flexner groups, but in this country most epidemics are due to the milder Sonné group.

However, in all these infections sulphaguanidine, ampicillin or tetracycline bring rapid relief, but care must be taken to avoid infection of other people.

Diarrhoea and Vomiting. Leaving out typhoid and paratyphoid fevers and dysentery, there is a group of infections known as "D. and V."—diarrhoea and vomiting. In Britain D. & V. is mostly due to:

(1) Salmonella infection.
(2) Staphylococcal infections.
(3) Other bacteria, ordinarily harmless, such as bacillus coli, when present in sufficient numbers.

Salmonella Infections are the most serious of this group; they affect the small intestine and produce vomiting, severe abdominal pain, and diarrhoea. These symptoms occur about one day after eating infected food and usually clear up within about two weeks, but occasionally death results. Salmonella bacteria are most likely to be found in meat, eggs powder, vegetables, and ducks' eggs, but staphylococci are liable to grow in milk products, such as ice-cream and cream buns. Food poisoning from staphylococci is seldom severe, and recovery takes place in about a week. Nevertheless, it is extremely infectious, and causes a great deal of lost time in industry and temporary illness in institutions; for it is in such situations that it is most likely to occur.

Staphylococcal Food Poisoning has greatly increased in recent years, so it is important to know what circumstances are likely to cause it. The reason for its increase has nothing to do, as many people suppose, with the greater use of canned foods, but it has much to do with the greater use of communal feeding and canteen meals. It is

possible for bacterial toxins in infected food to bring about illness even when the canning process has killed the bacteria, but it is certainly extremely rare. Canned foods, in fact, are much safer than so-called "fresh" foods in this respect—except when they have been opened, left about, and then re-heated. The same applies to the re-heating of any kind of food.

The real enemy is the canteen worker with a boil, a discharging nose, dirty hands, or a septic finger. Occasionally food may be infected in the larder by rats or mice, but the sort of canteen or restaurant where this can happen has little to commend it. Frankly, these infections are caused by dirty or stupid people who do not realise that their sore finger or boil can become someone else's diarrhoea and vomiting. Where children are concerned, the outlook is potentially more serious, and in the early part of this century the Summer-time "procession of baby coffins" was all too familiar. Infection is much more common in artificially fed babies or in older children who eat infected ice-cream. However trivial the condition may seem, diarrhoea and vomiting with fever in a child should never be ignored. Those in charge of canteens or restaurants must ensure that staff is supervised, that anyone with a septic infection is put off duty, and that all know about washing after visiting the lavatory and absolute cleanliness.

Bacilli normally present in the intestine, such as bacillus coli, can cause infections if absorbed in large amounts, or if of a different strain from those in the patient's intestine. They are not usually serious.

Botulism. Now uncommon, this is the disease which used to be known as "ptomaine poisoning" on the theory that it was caused by poisons produced by bad food apart from germs. In the 1920s a party of picnickers at Loch Maree in the Scottish Highlands developed botulism and a number died, with the result that the disease attracted much public attention. Botulism is caused by a germ, the bacillus botulinus, which is peculiar in that, like tetanus, its poison attacks the nervous system rather than the intestines, resulting in fits, double vision, paralysis beginning in the face and spreading downwards, and difficulty in swallowing. It is found in tinned fruits or vegetables containing the toxin even when the germ has been killed, but, as we have already seen, the toxin comes from the bacilli, not from decomposition of food as such (in fact, food does not decompose in the absence of germs). Death is common in botulism, but an antitoxin is now available which, if used in time, can cure the disease.

Tuberculosis. No disease causes more public concern, and no disease is more difficult to describe, than tuberculosis; for, like the streptococcus or the staphylococcus, the tubercle germ can attack many different parts of the body and manifest itself in many ways. Furthermore, it is a widely spread disease, infecting not only humans but also cattle, birds and reptiles. But here we shall be concerned with those types common to Man—the human and bovine (*i.e.*, the type occurring in cattle which can be spread to man by infected milk).

The tubercle bacillus is particularly hardy, so that when coughed or spat out on the ground it continues to be infectious for a long time. Infection is therefore caused by: (a) drinking infected milk; (b) droplet infection through having germs coughed in the face; (c) breathing in infected dust. In other words, tuberculosis is caused by absorption through either the lungs or the intestines; the former is common in adults, the latter in children.

But there is a good deal more to the problem than this; we know, for example, that over 90 per cent. of people in industrial countries have been infected with T.B. in early life and have conquered the infection. So the question arises: what conditions predispose to T.B.—why do some people get over the early infection and others not? There are two answers to this question: one is certain—that those who are impoverished and do not get enough food are liable to T.B.; the second is not so certain—that mental stress plays some part. Yet there is reasonably good evidence that such stress as a broken love-affair can cause lowered resistance to breakdown so that when germs are encountered infection will occur.

In children, lung tuberculosis is not common, but tuberculosis of the bones and glands is, as is also infection in the abdomen, the kidney or spine, and, worst of all, tuberculous meningitis. These are often of the bovine type from infected milk. Ordinarily, T.B. in children is less serious than adult infections; but tuberculous meningitis used to be almost invariably fatal until streptomycin was discovered.

Adult tuberculosis usually occurs in the lungs or the pleura—the thin membrane surrounding the lungs. In younger people miliary tuberculosis, which is a form of T.B. blood-poisoning or septicaemia, is a very serious condition, and the infection spreads throughout the whole body in a few weeks.

Lung infection begins gradually in someone who has previously felt unwell. There may be cough, and later blood-stained sputum (although blood which is coughed up does not necessarily prove that T.B. is present). Whatever means of treatment is used, the struggle between disease and patient is likely to be fairly long, but the outlook is now good. The closure of the Swiss sanatoria is due partly to modern disbelief that air in one place is better than that in another, but mainly to improved treatment.

Prevention depends on legal action ensuring tuberculosis-free herds of cattle; on control of spread of the disease by those "open" cases who carry germs in their sputum; on the use of vaccination in childhood with B.C.G. vaccine (which you can ask your doctor about).

Many methods are used in treatment: drugs, such as streptomycin, isoniazid, and P.A.S., lung surgery, rest, and so on. At any rate, tuberculosis is being got under control, but anyone who is worried can get a free X-ray at the nearest Mass Radiography Centre. There are skin tests to show whether there is susceptibility to T.B.

Septicaemia. Commonly known as "blood-poisoning." This is one of those diseases of which textbooks prior to the Second World War used to say: "death usually occurs."

Blood-poisoning occurs generally by spread from some septic area such as a wound (or even a small prick), after childbirth, or any place where certain germs have got admission to the body. The most usual germ is the streptococcus, although the pneumococcus—which ordinarily causes pneumonia—and the staphylococcus may also cause septicaemia.

Fever comes on suddenly and rises rapidly with headaches, sweating, and shivering. The patient is obviously very ill, and later there is wasting and delirium. The white blood cells increase in number. Septicaemia sometimes occurs without any apparent local infection in those who are weak and debilitated.

Pyaemia is a type of septicaemia which leads to the formation of numerous abscesses throughout the body. Its symptoms are the same as described above, except that the causative germ is usually the staphylococcus, and abscesses are found which may need surgical treatment.

However, in both conditions the state of affairs has been revolutionised by the use of the sulpha drugs and antibiotics; cure is now the rule rather than the exception.

Septicaemia should be suspected when any small wound or cut is followed by high temperature and the symptoms described above.

The word *"Toxaemia"* is used when the germs stay in their original position and produce symptoms by spreading their toxins throughout the body. Tetanus, diphtheria, and some kinds of childbirth infection come into this category; the symptoms may vary from mild disturbance to severe illness.

Meningitis means inflammation of the meninges, the covering which, like a layer of plastic, lies over the brain and spinal cord, just as the pleura covers the lungs and the peritoneum covers internal organs in the abdomen. (Hence inflammation of the pleura is known as pleurisy, and inflammation of the peritoneum as peritonitis.)

Various germs may cause meningitis, for example, the bacillus of tuberculosis, the pneumococcus, which ordinarily causes pneumonia, and the streptococcus or staphylococcus, but ordinarily the word refers to *Cerebrospinal Meningitis* or "spotted fever" caused by the meningococcus and occurring at times as an epidemic. It is commonest in the years from infancy to the early twenties, and begins suddenly with headache, vomiting, and fever. The temperature rises quickly, and pain develops in the back and legs; on the second or third day a rash appears on the body, and particularly on the inside of the thighs. Later there is stiffness of the neck, the head may be drawn back, vomiting persists, and the headache can be so severe as to cause the patient to scream with pain.

Fortunately, this type of meningitis (and most of the others) respond to treatment with antibiotics or the sulpha drugs, so the risks are very much less than formerly.

Pneumococcal Meningitis is an unusual complication of pneumonia, and the septic types (*strepto-coccal* or *staphylococcal*) arise either following an infected fracture of the skull or from infection of the ear or mastoid.

Tuberculous Meningitis has already been mentioned; originally always fatal, it is now treatable with streptomycin.

All these diseases are very much a matter for specialist and hospital treatment, but it is worth while mentioning *benign lymphocytic meningitis*, in which, although all the symptoms of meningitis are present, recovery without specific treatment is invariable. Meningitis, which was during the First World War and after what polio is to us now, is no longer common, and when taken in time is easily treated.

Tetanus is usually known as "lockjaw" because there may be difficulty in opening the mouth, although this is simply part of a spasm of all the muscles of the body. The tetanus bacillus is found in rich soil—hence the disease is less common in desert areas—and tetanus resembles rabies in that: (*a*) it enters at a wound; (*b*) it affects the nervous system; (*c*) it results in fits and ultimately death.

However, active immunisation with T.T. (tetanus toxoid) has resulted in the disease becoming uncommon, and even when developed, treatment with antitoxin, anaesthetics, and curare may lead to cure.

The bacillus is anaerobic (*i.e.*, does not use oxygen) and is most likely to occur in such situations as when a man digging manure or working in his garden sticks a fork through his foot, or, in war-time, when he is wounded in soil contaminated with manure.

Undulant fever, also known as Malta fever or abortus fever, falls into two types: melitensis, which infects goats, and abortus, cattle and pigs. Man gets the disease by reason of close contact with or drinking the milk of infected animals. (The name abortus is given because abortion is produced in cattle and sows.)

In Undulant Fever, as one would suppose, the fever goes up and down for two to three weeks; it may then go down and rise again, persisting for many months. The disease may occur in Britain, but modern drugs are on the whole successful in dealing with it. A striking feature of the disease is the combination of a high temperature with an appearance of relative well-being.

Another disease carried by mammals is *Glanders* or *Farcy*, spread by horses. In glanders there is discharge from the nose and sometimes pneumonia. Occasionally the disease is fatal. In farcy abscesses form, usually along the lymph vessels. Both conditions are very contagious, and treatment is a matter for a specialist; infected horses should be destroyed.

Cholera. Cholera could be classified under the head of food-poisoning, because it is mainly spread by infected water (however, like typhoid, it can also be spread by flies, infected food, and carriers); it could also be classified as a tropical disease, since, although it used to be found in Europe, it is now mainly rife in India.

Also like typhoid, cholera is caused by a bacillus, and can be prevented by early inoculation and care over food supplies—boiling water and milk, washing uncooked foods in chlorinated water, and keeping flies away.

The fever begins in the usual way with a short incubation period, followed by abdominal pain, severe vomiting, and diarrhoea. Later with the loss of fluid from the body there may be cramps in the muscles, diarrhoea increases, and the motions become of the typical "rice-water" type —*i.e.*, there is no solid matter, and the appearance is that of water to which a little milk has been added. This stage is followed by collapse, with low pulse and cold hands and feet. Death, if adequate treatment is not available, results in about 70 per cent. of cases.

Anthrax. The bacillus of anthrax, like that of tuberculosis, can exist outside the body for long periods, and, like that of tetanus, then takes the form of spores or seed-like bodies. It is spread by infected cattle and horses, which get the disease from eating grass containing spores.

In human beings the form the disease takes depends on where the germ alights; sometimes it comes from infected shaving-brushes, when it causes a large sore, like a boil, on the face, known as "malignant pustule"; sometimes it develops in those who inhale the dust from infected hides or wool (hence the name "wool-sorters' disease," which is a form of bronchitis with blood-stained sputum); lastly it may arise through eating infected meat, when the result is intestinal anthrax.

In all cases the outlook is serious. Death is common, preceded by a high temperature, skin symptoms in the first instance, lung symptoms in the second, and food-poisoning symptoms in the third. Penicillin or tetracycline may be effective.

Diseases Caused by Fungi.

There are only two important groups of disease caused by fungus: the serious *actinomycosis* and the relatively harmless, if unpleasant, *ringworm*. Ringworm or tinea will be dealt with later; it affects the hair, the body, the groin (dhobie itch, already referred to), and the feet (athlete's foot). Actinomycosis is spread by a fungus in barley and grasses which may reach the human mouth, settle around bad teeth, and thence pass to the lungs, the bone of the jaw, and even to the intestines or brain. Fortunately, this unpleasant fungus, which was once difficult to eradicate, has proved susceptible to penicillin.

The Venereal Diseases.

The venereal diseases are those caused—or at least that is what the name means—by the goddess of love, Venus. Venus, of course, causes a great deal of trouble, but venereal disease is not necessarily the worst she can do. Venereal disease is spread by sexual intercourse with an infected person.

Gonorrhoea is the result of an infection by the gonococcus (*Neisseria gonorrhoea*) and ordinarily comes on after an incubation period of three to seven days. However, babies can get an infection of the eyes, known as ophthalmia, from their mother if she is infected, and gonorrhoea in young children is often the result of being in contact with infected towels or clothes. The disease in adults is evident when there is a thick, creamy discharge from the sexual organs and sometimes pain on passing water; in infants ophthalmia is prevented by the use of silver nitrate eye-drops at birth. Gonorrhoea is fairly easily cured by the use of sulpha drugs or penicillin; but unfortunately venereal disease is increasing in recent years and drug-resistant forms are becoming more common.

Syphilis is a serious venereal disease caused by a spirochete (*Treponema pallidum*). Stories about lavatory seats are simply stories, although it is occasionally possible to get syphilis by other than sexual means: for example, it has happened that a man playing football has been infected through his hand being grazed by the teeth of someone with syphilis. But this is very unusual, although kissing can spread the disease. Children, too, can be born with syphilis (the so-called congenital syphilis).

Adult syphilis begins with a sore, known as a hard chancre, at the point where the spirochete of syphilis has entered; this may be on the lips, through kissing; on the sexual organs, through intercourse; and very rarely, as explained above, elsewhere. In a short time the chancre disappears and all may seem to be well, but this primary stage is followed by a secondary stage with sore throat, a rash, headache, and enlargement of glands. This, if left alone, also clears up, but is followed by the tertiary stage, in which a chronic infection develops in some part of the body which, presumably, is most susceptible in the particular individual. Thus there may be chronic syphilis of the skin, the bones, the heart, liver, or nervous system.

In the nervous system, the commonest forms are the two diseases of *tabes dorsalis*, in which the spinal cord is infected, and G.P.I. (general paralysis of the insane), in which the brain and mind are affected. These will be discussed under Nervous Diseases.

In congenital syphilis the pregnant mother gives her child syphilis. Such infants are often stillborn or premature, they look wizened, like little old men, and amongst other symptoms are eye disease, "snuffles," a flattened nose, and when the adult teeth appear the front ones may be notched at the biting surface.

The treatment, of course, is very much a matter for a specialist, but diagnosis is usually made through the Wassermann blood test. It was for syphilis that Ehrlich produced his "magic bullet"—an arsenical drug, known as salvarsan, which could attack the organism selectively without harming the body and was the first of the modern specific drugs. Present-day treatment is with penicillin. G.P.I. was once treated with malarial therapy with some success. Penicillin alone is often adequate.

It is important to understand that venereal disease can only be transmitted during sexual intercourse (or with intimate acts associated with it—*e.g.*, "oral sex"), that promiscuity therefore increases the risk, that not all lesions in, on or around the genitals are necessarily venereal disease and that *fear* of contracting it is widespread in many communities. If in doubt consult your own doctor or attend one of the many special clinics which can be found in most cities. Their location is usually advertised in conveniences and other public places. Delay is certainly dangerous.

Chancroid produces small septic ulcers around the sex organs, with swelling of the local glands in the groin, which may suppurate. It is caused by a bacillus, and can usually be cleared up by sulpha drugs within a week. Scabies and lice often pass from one body to another during sexual intercourse, but are not usually thought of as venereal in origin, although in many cases they are.

Tropical Diseases.

Nothing is more difficult than to define the term "tropical diseases." One might define them as the diseases which occur in tropical climates— but then measles occurs there too; and if they are defined as those diseases which are found *only* in the tropics, the solution is no easier, since leprosy, cholera, smallpox, and typhus are usually listed as tropical diseases, yet were found in this country until fairly recently—and the odd case still is.

But what a story could be told about the conquest of those infections which were—and many still are—the scourge of humanity! One day when generals and dictators are forgotten we shall remember that great international army of physicians and bacteriologists who have saved millions of lives and infinitely reduced human suffering: Koch and Ehrlich of Germany, Pasteur and Roux of France, Ross and Jenner of Britain, Reed of America, Noguchi of Japan, and many others. We shall remember how the Jesuit priests brought quinine from Peru to Europe in 1638, the first drug to save people from malaria; how in tropical heat Ronald Ross (1857-1932) peered for hours through his microscope to discover the connection between malaria and the mosquito until the sweat running from his brow rusted the instrument; how Major Walter Reed's work in Havana (1851-1902) made possible the building of the Panama Canal, and think, too, of the American soldiers who died in helping him to find the cause of yellow fever. In mentioning Jenner once more, we should recall Lady Mary Montagu (1689–1762), who brought the practice of vaccination to England from Turkey—or, rather, the practice of "variolation," which meant inoculating with the pus from smallpox cases. This was, of course, a dangerous practice, but the idea was there. Noguchi, one of the great bacteriologists of the nineteenth century, was the son of a poor peasant. He often had to steal to get enough bread even to keep alive, but was later to help in our understanding of syphilis and many tropical diseases.

Yet there is still much to do. Take, for example, the case of Egypt, one of the world's poorest countries, supporting with the help of water from the Nile about 36 million people. But if the river gives food and drink it does other things; for it carries the disease of bilharzia, which kills thousands of peasants yearly. In the villages of Egypt as many as 90–100 per cent. of the population suffer from this terrible disease. The infantile mortality rate is the second highest in the world—29·5 per cent.—seven times higher than that of Holland; the average expectation of life amongst the lower classes is thirty-one years, of the upper classes fifty to sixty years. The country is ridden with bilharzia, ankylostomiasis, malaria, plague, amoebic dysentery, typhus, tuberculosis, and pellagra. Blindness, due to trachoma and other diseases, affects tens of thousands. Such a situation cannot be treated simply by pouring drugs into the country; what is necessary is social control, to enforce purification of the water supplies, the use of insecticides to kill the disease-bearing pests, and removal of the causes of extreme poverty (tuberculosis and vitamin deficiencies which are common in Egypt are diseases of malnutrition).

Relapsing Fever, common in India and Africa, may be louse- or tick-borne; the germ is a spirochaete, similar to that of syphilis, but the disease is non-venereal. Relapsing fever gets its name from the fact that the temperature remains high (39°–41°C) for about a week, returns to normal for a week, and rises again. There may be three to five relapses of this sort. Penicillin is effective; lice or ticks must be eradicated.

Epidemic Jaundice (also known as Weil's disease or—if you prefer it—ictero-haemorrhagica spirochaetosis), is also caused by a spirochaete, and spread by rats. Now it is rarely found in Europe, although it occurred in the trenches during the First World War, in men working in sewers, and in the women who worked in the fish market of Aberdeen, which at one time was rat-infested. It is rarely fatal, but leads to high fever and jaundice. Penicillin in high dosage or tetracycline may help.

Yaws is also a spirochaetal disease, common in the tropics and particularly in children. It is unpleasant, but not serious, and tends to clear up in a year or so. There are raspberry-like growths on the skin, which disappear with the drugs used in syphilis (although the condition is non-venereal). The Wassermann reaction, positive to syphilis, is also positive in yaws.

Leprosy. Whereas syphilis, relapsing fever, epidemic jaundice, and yaws are caused by spirochaetes, leprosy is caused by a bacillus resembling the bacillus of tuberculosis. Leprosy, in fact, should not be included here at all, for it is non-spirochaetal, and not necessarily a tropical infection. Apart from the difficulty of classification, many popular beliefs about the disease are untrue. It is *not* the oldest disease afflicting man; *not* a disease confined to tropical countries; it is *not* very catching; *not* hereditary, *not* incurable; in leprosy the fingers and toes do *not* drop off; it is *not* a divine punishment for wrongdoing. So there are many misunderstandings about this disease, and placing it in the wrong part of the medical section is probably the least.

Leprosy is a serious disease not because of disfiguring light-coloured skin patches and lumps, but because it destroys peripheral nerves. Leprosy may disappear spontaneously, or it may progress until the face is lion-like and the hands and feet wasted and ulcerated. The disease rarely kills, but it is the world's greatest crippler.

Leprosy was once fairly common in colder Western countries, though its extent was exaggerated. The great majority of the 15 million people who suffer from leprosy live in tropical countries, but it still exists in Iceland, Japan, Korea and some of the southern states of the United States. Prolonged and intimate contact with an "open" case is said to be the main mode of infection, but only one infected husband in twenty passes leprosy to his wife.

The sulphone drugs have revolutionised the treatment of leprosy. Given early diagnosis and adequate treatment, the great majority of sufferers could be cured. Established deformity (such as claw hand, drop foot, paralysed eyelids) can be mitigated by reconstructive surgery, although lost sensation cannot be restored.

In the past, only Christian missions were concerned with the plight of the leprosy sufferer. Now, non-sectarian voluntary agencies, Governments and the World Health Organisation have joined in the fight against the disease. Enough is known to control the disease, but not enough is being done, as only one victim in five is at present getting treatment.

Plague is another disease caused by bacteria, common in Europe at one time, but now largely restricted to Asia. Nevertheless, it caused millions of deaths in Europe during the years 1348–49 and 1665 and was the "Black Death," which, indeed, changed the course of history. Interested readers may read Hans Zinsser's *Rats, Lice, and History* about this aspect of the disease. Plague is carried by the bite of the rat flea, but, once people become infected, spread may occur from one to the other by droplet infection—*i.e.*, by coughing and sneezing. After an incubation period of two to ten days, fever develops, rather like severe influenza, and in a day or two the glands in the groin begin to swell, followed perhaps by swelling of the glands elsewhere. This is the usual type of plague, but it is also possible to get disease of the lungs from droplet infection and blood-poisoning from infection of the blood-stream. Both the latter types are almost invariably fatal, and even the glandular type (bubonic plague) has a mortality of about 80 per cent. The vaccine has given place to streptomycin and sulpha drugs which are also used on contacts.

Although we have little space to discuss the subject of plagues and epidemics in general, it is worth noting that serious epidemics have almost always followed wars, revolutions, and economic and political collapse. Thus the Black Death followed the break-up of the Roman Empire, and, in the fourteenth century, accompanied the end of mediaeval civilisation. The Napoleonic wars were followed by other epidemics, and the wars of the 1830s in Europe were followed by influenza. In the most widespread outburst of influenza after the First World War, more people were killed by the disease than in all the fighting of four years. It is a reflection on the peculiar mentality of Man that this devastating epidemic, which affected almost the whole world, occupies little space in his history books—we still, with few exceptions, regard history as the doings of kings, queens, and generals. Yet, in 1918, 20 million men, and women, and children died from influenza, and no cure has, as yet, been found! Later we shall see that many millions of people die yearly from starvation or vitamin deficiencies. But these facts—the real facts of life—we rarely hear about.

Protozoal Diseases.

Nearly all the diseases caused by protozoa are tropical diseases, although one of the best-known protozoans is the harmless amoeba found in British ponds. Protozoal diseases are caused by these organisms, large in comparison with bacteria, which are really one-celled plants. Viruses are neither animals nor plants, are much smaller than the other two groups, and have some distinctive characteristics described elsewhere.

The only important diseases caused by protozoa are sleeping sickness or trypanosomiasis, malaria, and amoebic dysentery (as contrasted with bacillary dysentery), another disease, leishmaniasis—also known by the numerous names of kala-azar, dum-dum fever, and, in milder form, Delhi boil, Oriental sore, or Baghdad sore—will also be mentioned briefly. These infections are few, but important in their influence on Man; for, as Dr. Clark-Kennedy has pointed out, malaria until recently was responsible for one-fifth of all human sickness, sleeping sickness not so long ago caused a large part of Central Africa to be uninhabitable, and in some areas of the tropics there are probably more people with, than without, amoebic dysentery.

Malaria. The word, of course, means "bad air," just as "influenza" means "influence"—in Italian *influenza di freddo*—the influence of cold. Human beings have a natural tendency to suppose that, when two events occur together, then one must be caused by the other. Yet, although malaria and "bad air" may often go together, and influenza and cold, it does not follow that bad air (whatever that may be) causes malaria nor that cold causes influenza. In fact, the anopheles mosquito carries the amoeba of malaria, and the mosquito prefers climates which some people might describe as "bad," but it is the amoeba, not the air, which causes the disease. Anyhow, the unfortunate mosquito might well use the phrase honoured by many generations of schoolmasters: "It hurts me more than it hurts you!" For the mosquito, too, is sick, and passes on its sickness to the person it bites.

There are several types of plasmodium—which is the scientific name for this amoeba—producing attacks of fever varying in severity and frequency: benign tertian, quartan, and malignant quartan. Entering the body from the mosquito bite, the parasites penetrate the blood cells, multiply there, and finally burst into the blood stream. When this happens the temperature rises, and then they return to the cells to carry out once more the same procedure. Depending on the type, the attacks of fever may be at intervals of three or four days, severe or milder. When someone with malaria is bitten by a mosquito the infection can be transmitted to the next person it meets, but malaria is not infectious from one person to another directly. Quinine, of course, is the time-honoured remedy, but many other drugs are now available: mepacrine, primaquine, chloroquine and some sulpha drugs. The drug must be taken long enough for the infection to die out, otherwise relapses can occur even after leaving a malarial country (but it is only fair to say that, just as some people continue to give themselves the title of "Major" when they have left the army, so others long in Britain continue to describe attacks of cold or 'flu as "my old malaria again," when, to say the least of it, they are exaggerating).

Important as are the drugs used in the treatment of malaria, even more so is the control of the parasite-bearing mosquito. The eggs of mosquitoes hatch in water, and there the young or larval forms can be attacked by pouring oil on the surface of pools so that they are unable to breathe, or by introducing small fish which have a partiality for them. Adult mosquitoes can be killed by insecticides or kept away by repellent creams or nets over beds. Prophylaxis with anti-malaria before entering and while living in known malarial zones is important.

Blackwater Fever is a sequel to malaria in tropical Africa and some parts of India. Rather illogically, it is described as "Blackwater," although the urine is red and the skin is yellow but the result is due to breaking down of the red blood cells by some malarial toxin. Possibly too much quinine may help in producing the illness. Treatment is to give plenty of fluids and no quinine or any other anti-malarial drugs in the early stages. The death-rate is about 25 per cent.

Trypansomiasis or sleeping sickness—not to be confused with *sleepy* sickness—is essentially an African disease (although also found in tropical America) spread by the tsetse fly. Its cause is the type of protozoan known as a trypanosome, almond-shaped with vibrating membranes at the sides which enable it to move through the bloodstream, rather like a flat fish in the water.

There are three stages of the disease: first, the stage of fever with enlarged glands and a rapid pulse; which may continue off and on for three years; secondly, the stage of trembling hands, legs, and tongue, vacant expression, and slow and stumbling speech; thirdly, and lastly, the stage of low temperature, apathy, wasting of the muscles, and possibly death.

Treatment is with pentamidine, suramin or melarsoprol—which give good results in early cases. Preventive measures in infected areas include the destruction of tsetse flies by insecticide, the cutting down of forests near rivers which are inhabited by tsetse flies, and some authorities have suggested the shooting of big game which may form a "reservoir" of the parasites, whence tsetse flies can carry them to human beings. For similar reasons infected people should not be allowed to move to noninfected areas.

Amoebic Dysentery, also known as *Amoebiasis*, is caused by the *Entamoeba histolytica*, an amoeba whose cysts are found in food and water, or spread by infected fingers or flies. There is mild fever and diarrhoea which contains blood. The disease may become chronic, and can cause abscesses, usually in the liver but sometimes in the lungs. Amoebiasis is treated with chloroquine or nitroimidazoles.

Leishmaniasis, kala-azar, or dum-dum fever, is another amoebic disease, probably spread in this instance by the bite of sandflies. It is also known as tropical splenomegaly—enlargement of the spleen in ordinary language—since infection results in enlargement of the spleen and liver, low, irregular fever, and death within a year or so. A milder form, affecting the skin, is known as Delhi boil, Oriental sore, or Baghdad sore, does not lead to kala-azar, and is fairly readily cured. The cure for both conditions is to give injections of antimony compounds which reduce the death-rate from kala-azar from 80 per cent, to about 5 per cent.

Diseases Caused by Parasitic Worms.

Many types of worms infest human beings and other animals. They are interesting for such reasons as their size (which may range from the almost invisible to 9 m or more), their life histories, and their serious or trivial consequences on their hosts. We shall mention only a few groups here, and mainly the ones likely to be met with in Europe—the tapeworms, the roundworms, and the threadworms—although some tropical types will be described briefly.

Tapeworms, as we have seen earlier, like many other types of intestinal worm, lead a double life. What usually happens is that the worm breeds in the human intestine, the eggs pass out in the faeces, and are then swallowed by animals eating contaminated material. In the animal the eggs hatch out into larvae—primitive forms which penetrate the muscle, forming cysts—and Man is infected in turn by eating its meat. Thus *Taenia solium* gets into the flesh of pigs, which, if imperfectly cooked (measly pork), causes infestation of the intestine in Man. It reaches a length of about 3 m. *Taenia saginata*, which reaches a length of about 6 m, is spread in imperfectly cooked beef, and in Baltic countries *Dibothriocephalus latus* gets into the human intestine from caviare or undercooked fish. It reaches the awesome length of 9 m.

Now all the worms we have mentioned so far are found in the human intestine, and the cysts, which are much more dangerous and unpleasant, in the animal's muscles. But in some worms the reverse happens, with the adult in the animal's intestines and the cysts in Man. Thus in Australia the dog tapeworm (*Taenia echinococcus*) produces cysts in both sheep and Man. This is known as hydatid disease, and may remain unsuspected until cysts in the lungs, liver, or elsewhere become infected or rupture. *Trichinella spiralis* is similar in action, being found in the intestines of pigs and getting into the muscles or other organs of Man. The main difference is that this worm migrates from the pig's intestines into its muscles, whence it reaches Man in under-cooked pork meat or sausages. The muscular cysts cause swellings and sometimes pain. There are changes in the blood, swelling of the face and leg in the early stages, and fever. A minor epidemic occurred in England in 1941. *Taenia echinococcus* and *Trichinella spiralis* are small—not more than 0·5 cm in length—but are more serious in their consequences than the large worms. Treatment is very difficult, and ordinarily all that can be done is to deal with individual cysts when they make themselves apparent.

The large tapeworms, *Taenia solium* and *saginata* and *Dibothriocephalus latus*, produce varying symptoms or none at all. Usually they are not discovered until some segments of the worm are excreted, but there may be mild indigestion, excessive hunger, and occasionally anaemia. However, when the worm is discovered the patient, not unnaturally, is likely to become anxious and uncomfortable at the thought of "having" a tapeworm; these symptoms are caused by the worry rather than the worm.

Treatment is, of course, a matter for a doctor, who now has a number of very effective drugs to choose from. One has to make sure that the head of the worm has been removed, otherwise it will continue to grow.

Roundworms are similar both in appearance and size to ordinary earth-worms and the eggs reach Man, not from an animal, but from the contaminated fingers of someone else who handles food. They give rise to no symptoms, and are noticed only when discharged in the faeces or occasionally vomited up. Piperazine is an effective treatment.

Threadworms, as the name suggests, are like small 0·5–1 cm long pieces of white thread. They are very common in children, and live mainly in the caecum—*i.e.*, the part of the large intestine near the appendix. The males, which are the smaller ones, remain there, but the females pass down towards the rectum at night-time and lay their eggs in the area around the anus. Infection is by contaminated hands handling food—especially uncooked food—and water. Threadworms are not serious, and cause few symptoms other than itching around the anus and between the legs, but heavily infected children may show symptoms of anaemia. The nervousness often shown by such children is usually the result of the irritation produced by the worms in the anal region. Infection is not common in adults, and in children tends to disappear at puberty.

Treatment is, in theory, simple; for the worms are easily destroyed by a number of drugs, such as piperazine. Ointment is applied to the itching area, and the child should be prevented from scratching. However, since the eggs may lie about the house for some time, reinfection often happens, especially if there are several small children in the home who may pass the disease from one to another.

The idea that intestinal worms in general are likely to cause loss of weight by absorbing food eaten by the patient is largely mistaken; for although it is true that they do live on this food, the amount taken is certainly not enough to be significant.

Tropical Worms. Bilharzia has been mentioned before in connection with its frequency in Egypt, although it is also found in other parts of Africa, Arabia, and Iraq. There are two main types: one infecting the bladder (*Schistosomum haematobium*), the other the rectum (*Schistosomum*

mansoni). *Bilharzia* is more correctly known as *schistosomiasis*.

The parasite's fantastic life-history begins when a man bathes in infected water, and the small swimming forms known as cercariae pierce and enter his skin—or they may enter the body by drinking infected water. From the skin they pass to the portal vein below the liver, remain there six weeks until they become adult and then swim against the blood-stream down to the pelvis, where the female lays eggs which have a sharp spine. The eggs penetrate into the bladder or rectum—depending on the type of fluke—and pass out in the faeces or urine. If they enter water they hatch out into small moving forms which seek out a water-snail, develop further in its body, and leave it in the form of cercariae ready to find a new human victim. The female fluke is slender and round, about 2·5 cm in length, the male, flat and leaf-shaped, is about 2 cm long, and, as we have seen, their grisly courting takes place in the portal vein, whence the impregnated female passes to the bladder (*haematobium*) or rectum (*mansoni*) to lay her eggs.

Infection results in raised temperature and, in the urinary type, blood in the urine; in the intestinal type blood is found in the faeces, and there are symptoms resembling dysentery—*e.g.*, diarrhoea. Treatment in both cases is with antimony tartrate or niridazole. Needless to say, attempts should be made at prevention by telling people to avoid infected canals (usually easier said than done), and by periodically cutting off the water supply to the canals to kill the snails.

Hookworm Disease, or ankylostomiasis, is found in many parts of the world, especially in miners who work on damp ground. The tiny worm enters the body usually through the feet, passes through the blood-stream to the lungs, eats through into one of the bronchial tubes, climbs the windpipe, and passes down the oesophagus into the stomach to end up in the duodenum. It causes anaemia, can be fairly readily cured, but is occasionally fatal.

Elephantiasis. Some types of parasitic worm are spread by insects. Thus in *Filiariasis* mosquitoes inject by their bites the infantile forms of a tiny worm which enters the lymphatic channels; there the blockade they cause leads to the swelling of the legs and the lower part of the body, known as elephantiasis.

PHYSICAL INJURIES AND FIRST AID.

This section which lists emergencies in alphabetical order is designed for rapid reference. Yet it would be wise to make sure now of knowing very thoroughly the parts dealing with Bleeding, Burns, Resuscitation, Shock and Unconsciousness, situations which are immediately life threatening.

Nothing can teach first aid as effectively as attending one of the many courses organised by the three main organisations:

St. John's Ambulance Association, 1, Grosvenor Crescent, London, S.W.1.
British Red Cross Society, 9, Grosvenor Crescent, London, S.W.1.
St. Andrew's Ambulance Association, Milton Street, Glasgow, C.4.

Their local addresses are in the telephone directory; enquiry will get details of classes held at various hours of the day.

Purpose of First Aid.

First aid is not treatment proper (which is "Second Aid"). It aims to save life, to prevent further harm or suffering and to keep the victim in the best condition until taken over by a doctor or a nurse.

Under ordinary circumstances attempts to do more can be detrimental. If you limit your help to what is outlined here you cannot go wrong.

General Principles.

There are two priorities:

1. That the patient must breathe.
   (—*see* Choking, Resuscitation, Unconsciousness)
2. That severe bleeding is controlled.
   (—*see* Bleeding)

In any accident scene try to judge quickly which person most needs immediate attention. Treat a victim where he is; do not move him unless the surroundings suggest immediate danger (*e.g.*, fire, fumes, collapsing building).

Handle the patient with gentleness and sympathy yet achieve an atmosphere of reassurance and confidence by firm instructions and methodical actions.

Clear away a crowd (always demoralising to the victim) and use likely bystanders to telephone for an ambulance when necessary. Let your message be clear and written if possible. Let it clearly state the exact locality, the number of patients and the nature of their troubles. Always guard against shock (*q.v.*).

Asthma Attacks.

Breathing becomes very difficult, harsh and wheezing, fighting against air passages narrowed in spasm. Fear aggravates and relaxation relieves spasm. Show calm confidence.

1. Allow fresh air ventilation. Loosen tight clothes.
2. Help the mechanics of breathing by telling the patient
   to sit upright with a straight back but all the rest of the body relaxed;
   to direct breathing movements from the lower part of the chest.
3. Give him medicines he has prescribed for the emergency but avoid overdose.

Bleeding.

Treat mild bleeding as for wounds (*q.v.*).
For severe bleeding aim to let the blood clot by stopping or slowing the flow.

1. Immediately firmly press the edges of the wound together between fingers and thumb or press the palm of the hand hard down on it. (Maintain this at least ten minutes.)
2. Lay the patient down: elevate a bleeding limb (unless you suspect it to be fractured).
3. Slip a thick pad (handkerchief, gauze, wool) under your hand. Replace the hand pressure with a firmly bound bandage (stocking, belt, scarf).
4. If blood still leaks out add another pad and bandage.
5. Protect against shock (*q.v.*).

Nose Bleeding.

1. Have the patient sit up.
2. Get him to pinch between finger and thumb the whole lower half of the nose and maintain this for at least ten minutes. Repeat another ten minutes if necessary.
3. Tell him not to sniff or blow his nose.

Ear Bleeding.

1. Bandage or tape a loosely covering dressing (gauze, handkerchief) over the ear.
2. Lay the patient down towards the injured side.—*Nose or ear bleeding which follows a blow to the head may signify a fractured skull which needs immediate medical attention.*

Tooth Socket Bleeding.

This may follow after a dental extraction. Get the patient to bite hard on to a big pad (gauze, bunched-up handkerchief) placed over the bleeding area. He maintains pressure at least ten minutes sitting with a hand under his chin and the elbow on a table.

Blood Vomited.

This could appear black due to the effect of stomach acids.

1. Lay the patient down, on his side, with his head low.
2. Give him nothing to eat or drink.
3. Get a doctor or ambulance.
4. Guard against shock (*q.v.*).

Blood Coughed Up (*see also* Chest Injury).
Blood from the Back Passage.
Blood in the Urine.

However slight and brief the loss, always seek a doctor's opinion.

Blisters

Leave them intact and protect them with a simple dressing. But if they are so big as to be in the way and need flattening:—

1. Boil a needle for ten minutes: leave it in the water until needed.
2. Wash the blister area with soap and water.
3. Holding the needle by one end pierce the blister at two opposite points. Press down with clean cloth to squeeze the fluid out.
4. Dress it like a wound (*q.v.*).

Burns (*see also* Chemical Burns).

1. Put out flames the quickest way: a douche of water; smothering with cloth (rug, coat, blanket).
2. Remove burnt clothes, but leave on what is adherent to the skin.
3. Cool the burnt part with cold water for at least ten minutes, longer if pain persists. Plunge a limb in a bucket or sink. Cover other parts with a thick cloth soaked in water; renew it if it dries.
4. Lay the patient down; keep a burnt limb elevated; remove possibly constricting things (rings, bracelets) from a burnt region before it swells.
5. Dress the burn as a wound (*q.v.*).
6. Guard against shock (*q.v.*)—in severe burns give to drink half a cupful of tepid water with a pinch of salt and sugar every ten or fifteen minutes.

Car Accidents.

1. Urgently stop severe bleeding (*q.v.*) or give resuscitation (*q.v.*) where this is needed; treat choking (*q.v.*). Unless they are at risk from fire or fumes leave the injured where they are. Look for victims thrown into ditches or over walls and hedges.
2. Minimise risks by forbidding smoking (petrol leak), by switching off the ignition and applying the brakes.
3. Set your own car off the road if possible; at night have its light shining on the scene.
4. Detail bystanders (wearing or carrying white objects at night) to stop approaching traffic some 200 yards on either side.
5. Send a message for help (written down) detailing the exact place, the number injured and the injuries.
6. Give other first aid to those in the cars without trying to move them: attempts to pull them out, especially from a distorted car, can do great harm. Leave to the rescue services.

Chemical Burns.

Rapidly wash away the chemical with copious free-flowing water. Remove any contaminated clothing.
The contaminated eye, closed in painful spasm, may need gently forcing open; let the water flow on it without force and bend the patient towards the affected side so that the washings flow off at once.

Chest Injury.

Where there has been a severe blow or deep wound to the chest, possibly followed by blood being coughed up:

1. Clear the mouth of any obstruction (blood, vomit, dentures).
2. If there is an open wound at once close it with the palm of your hand firmly applied. While you keep it there, improvise a thick pad

(towel, cloth, handkerchief, sock) to replace your hand. Tape or bandage it securely to make an air-tight seal.

3. Loosen tight clothing.

4. Lay the patient down *towards* the injured side. If he has difficulty in breathing have him half propped up with head and shoulders raised.

5. Cover him loosely.

6. Get ambulance urgently.

Choking.

1. With your fingers try to clear any obstruction (food, toy, dentures) from the back of the throat.

2. If this fails tell the patient to relax, to bend well forward; give a hard slap between the shoulder blades. This may loosen the obstruction so that the patient can cough it out. A small child you place head down over your arm or your bent knee. Try up to four separate slaps.

If back slapping fails try to force the matter out by pressure:

1. Patient standing: stand behind him; put both your arms round his waist. Patient lying: turn him on his back; kneel astride him.

2. Place your fist (thumb side first) on his abdomen *between his navel and the lower end of his breast bone*; cover your fist with your other hand.

3. Make firm thrust inwards and upwards. This may propel the obstruction out of his windpipe. Try up to four separate thrusts. If these fail continue alternating four slaps and four thrusts. After each of these be ready to remove immediately any matter propelled into the mouth.

After receiving thrusts the patient must be checked by a doctor lest internal damage has occured.

If an obstruction is not cleared and the patient ceases breathing and collapses begin resuscitation (*q.v.*).

Always remember that in the unconscious the tongue may fall back and be an obstruction. *See* Unconsciousness.

Cold Effects. *See* Exposure and Hypothermia.

Cramp.

Cramps may follow severe loss of body fluid and minerals—as with severe repeated diarrhoea, vomiting or sweating. Slowly give tepid drinks containing a small pinch of table salt to each cupful or with diluted meat or yeast extracts.

Sudden cramp in a single muscle can be stopped by having the patient strongly stretch the muscle. In the front of the arm; straighten the elbow and swing the arm back. In the front of the thigh bend the knee and swing the leg back. In the back of the thigh: straighten the knee and swing the leg forward. In the calf: bend the foot up at the ankle while straightening the leg.

Diabetes.

Under certain circumstances a diabetic treated with insulin may suddenly collapse through sugar deficiency. Passing through phases of weakness, vagueness, sweating, tremor, uncoordinated actions and slurred speech he may go into a coma.

If he is conscious give him two teaspoonfuls (or lumps) of glucose or sugar in water. Failing this, give anything sweet; jam, honey, chocolate. This should clear him rapidly but repeat the dose after ten minutes.

If he is unconscious send for medical help urgently. Give nothing by mouth and put the patient in the recovery position (*q.v.*).

Ear—object in.

Do not try to poke it out.

A small object (*e.g.*, insect) can sometimes be floated up and out by lying the patient down with the ear uppermost and pouring in a little water or olive oil. But do not try this if the ear drum is possibly damaged or the ear is painful.

Electric Shock.

At once disconnect the current (at the switch or by pulling a plug out). If you cannot do this do not touch the patient but knock him away from his contact with dry non-conducting material; wooden stick, light furniture, folded thick garment.

He may need resuscitation (*q.v.*). He may have sustained a fracture (*q.v.*) or a burn. He may recover, only to collapse later; keep watch and send him to hospital.

Beware of very high voltage currents, as from wires of electric pylons: keep at least 20 feet away and do not try to rescue until the electricity authority has cut the current.

Epileptic Attack.

The patient may suddenly become unconscious, fall and soon begin convulsive jerkings, and sometimes frothing at the mouth.

1. Do not try to stop the jerking, but protect him from banging against furniture. Move the furniture or push cloth in position as buffer.

2. Clear froth from the mouth.

3. Once the convulsions stop put him in the recovery position (*q.v.*)—but beware lest he sustained a fracture (*q.v.*) in falling.

A succession of closely following attacks is dangerous: get medical aid at once.

Exposure.

A hill climber or a worker inadequately dressed against cold weather becomes slow, inefficient, clumsy, drowsy. Eventually he collapses and if not properly treated may die.

1. Put him to rest.

2. If you can, get him into a warm shelter. Otherwise protect him with screens of clothes or blankets and poles.

3. If he is conscious give warm drinks (cocoa, chocolate, tea). On no account give alcohol.

4. Get wet cold clothes off him if possible and put him in warm dry covers (sleeping bag, blankets). A plastic sheet over those helps to retain heat. Include the head, leaving only the face free.

See also Hypothermia.

Gradual rewarming is given when the patient has become cold gradually. However, when exposure has been sudden, as with falling in extremely cold water, you can warm up fast by putting the patient in a bath at about 40° C. (103° F.).

Eye Injury.

Fix a loosely covering pad over the eye and get medical aid.—Do NOT use drops or ointments.—If the wound is severe and painful keep the patient on his back and cover both eyes (since movement of the good eye entails that of the injured one).

Eye—Object In.

Have the patient seated in a good light and stand behind him. If you can see the object on the white of the eye try to lift it off gently with the rolled-up and moistened twist of a handkerchief. If it does not come easily it may be embedded; leave it alone.

If it is within the coloured part of the eye leave it for a doctor to treat.

If you cannot see it look under the lids. The lower lid you pull down as he looks upwards. The upper lid you must evert as he looks down; lay a matchstick along the "hinge" of the lid; firmly grasp the edge of the lid and roll it up over the matchstick.

Fainting.

Lay the patient down with his legs higher than his head (if this is not possible, get him seated with his head bent low between his knees); loosen any tight clothes: tell him to breathe deeply and slowly. He should soon recover. A drink of water (provided he is conscious) will help.

If he has fainted fully treat as for unconsciousness (*q.v.*).

Fractures.

Always suspect a broken bone where a blow or crush near a bone is followed by pain, swelling, deformity, weakened or restricted movement. Not all these features are always present: sometimes relatively slight pain is the only one.

Your task is to prevent movement which could worsen the condition by shifting a broken edge of bone into an important organ, or by making it pierce hitherto unbroken skin (with a risk of infection). No one will blame you for undue caution—but all will hold you responsible if you allow a fractured bone to do more damage by movement which could have been avoided.

When a fracture is suspected:—

1. Warn the patient not to move and bystanders not to try to lift him.
2. At once control any severe bleeding (q.v.). Dress any wound (q.v.) temporarily.
3. Now immobilise the fractured area including the joint at either end. The best splint is the patient's own body; e.g., injured arm secured against chest, injured leg against good leg (move the good leg up to the injured one). Or a thin board or rolled-up newspaper, well buffered with cloths and towels tied round it can be slipped under a fore-arm and wrist. Between the injured part and the splinting surface fill any hollows with firm padding of wool, or bunched-up cloth, socks, handkerchiefs. Tie the whole firmly with bandages (or stocking, thin towels) making the knots over the splint (not the hurt part) and avoiding bandage directly over the level at which you suspect the fracture. Work gently; do not lift or move the injured part.
4. Help to reduce shock (q.v.).

These are the general principles. How best to apply them for individual fractures you can learn from first aid courses.

If you expect expert help (doctor, nurse, ambulance) to arrive soon, then omit step 3 above and keep the patient lying still.

The fractured spine. When a blow or fall gives a painful back or neck, the vertebral column may be fractured. Inexpert moving may possibly drive a bone fragment into the spinal cord of nerves, causing paralysis or loss of feeling. It is most important to let the patient lay still until experienced first aiders take over. Keep him warm with a loose covering of blanket or coat.

Frostbite.

Do not heat the area directly or put it in hot water. Do not rub it.

1. Remove any wet cover (e.g., glove).
2. Remove any tight object (garter, ring, bracelet).
3. Cover the area loosely with dry material and let it warm up slowly. Fingers can be tucked under clothes into the opposite armpit. Nose, chin or ear can be covered with a dry hand.

Hanging.

Support the victim by his legs. Get the cord cut and be prepared to receive his weight as he falls. Loosen the cord round the neck. Act fast. Get medical help.

See also **Choking** *and* **Resuscitation.**

Head Injuries.

Blows to the head can cause fracture of the skull and also brain damage.

Fracture of the skull is not always obvious. Skin may swell over the site. Sometimes a fracture of the base of the skull (the body platform within the head at eye and ear level which supports the brain) may show up by bruising round an eye or by blood loss from ear or nose (*see* **Bleeding**).

Brain Damage may be of two kinds:—

Concussion, a temporary "shaking up" of brain tissue causing immediate "knock-out" unconsciousness. Recovery is in anything from a few seconds to several hours.

Compression of the brain develops from bleeding within the skull, from displacement of a fractured bone or from general swelling of the damaged brain tissues within the hard unyielding skull. The patient gradually (minutes or hours) becomes comatose and perhaps unconscious. This condition is dangerous.

The patient is unconscious—*see* unconsciousness.

The patient is dazed: put him in the recovery position (q.v.) and watch him closely while awaiting help.

The patient recovers after a knock-out (concussion). He may yet develop features of compression as well. However much he wants to carry on, keep him at rest, under observation and get medical advice.

In all cases remember that head injuries are often accompanied by injuries to other parts of the body.

Heart Attack.

Sudden heart attacks may produce:—

severe gripping pain in the centre of the chest, sometimes spreading to the neck, shoulder or arm; fast weak pulse; breathlessness; pallor and blueness; sweating.

or sudden painless breathlessness with slight cough and very wet bubbly breathing.

In either case send urgently for medical help. Get the patient to rest (in bed if possible). If he is very breathless it will be easier for him to be in a sitting position, against banked-up pillows. Otherwise have him laying down.

Loosen tight clothes. Keep him warmly but loosely covered. Mop any sweat from the face.

Heat Effects.

Heat Exhaustion. Anyone working in an unusually hot atmosphere is helped to remain cool by copious sweating which extracts heat from the body as it evaporates off the skin. But this loss of fluid also carries with it essential minerals from the body. The patient may collapse with his temperature normal or just a little raised; his skin is pale, moist and sunken, his pulse fast and weak. Muscles depleted of minerals go into cramp.

Let him rest in a cool place and give him (slowly) fruit juices or water with half a teaspoonful of salt added to each pint.

Heat Stroke happens in unusually hot and moist areas in rare industrial circumstances and in some tropical zones. Evaporation of sweat cannot take place in an atmosphere already saturated with water vapour. The patient becomes burning hot with a red dry skin and a fast forceful pulse. He may suddenly collapse and go into coma.

He must rest, have his clothes removed and be fanned or sponged down with cold (but not iced) water. The condition is dangerous and needs medical help.

Hypothermia.

Small babies and the elderly are specially susceptible to cold, e.g., overnight in a poorly heated bedroom. They become lethargic, comatose and then unconscious. Extremely cold to touch, even under bedclothes, the skin is white (though in babies it may be deceptively pink). Death may follow.

Cover the patient well including the head, leaving the face free. Put him in the recovery position (q.v.). Warm him GRADUALLY by warming the whole room and by giving slowly warm (not hot) drinks. Do NOT give alcohol. Do NOT use electric blankets or hot-water bottles.

Insect Bites.

Cool with water or (better) smooth in anti-histamine cream.

If a bee sting has been left in the skin pull it out with fine tweezers: apply these well down near the skin so that they do not squeeze in any venom left at the free top of the sting.

Lightning.

As for electric shock (q.v.) except that the patient can be touched at once as he bears no electric charge. Put a dry dressing over any skin burns.

Nose Bleed. *See* Bleeding.

Nose—Object in.

Do not try to probe it. Unless GENTLE nose blowing gets it out consult a doctor.

Poisoning.

Do not try to administer antidotes. Do not give salt solutions.

If the patient is unconscious.

Treat as for unconsciousness (*q.v.*).

If he is conscious.

Give, slowly, soothing drinks to dilute the poison (water, barley water, milk and water).

Put him in the recovery position (*q.v.*) while awaiting the ambulance. He may lose consciousness.

In all cases.

Get the patient urgently to hospital.

Send with him any remaining poison or empty container and a sample of any vomit.

Keep a close watch on him all the time you are with him.

Poisoning by pesticides (weed or insect killers).

The patient must be at complete rest. If his clothes and skin are contaminated with the poison (splashes, spray droplets) remove clothes and wash the skin copiously with water (avoid contaminating yourself). If he is conscious give sweetened drinks.

Poisoning by gases.

Get the victim rapidly out of the contaminated atmosphere, but do not venture within this unless you have a lifeline and respirator, with others to safeguard you.

Recovery Position.

This safeguards the patient's comfort and breathing if he is unconscious, or comatose, or likely to lose consciousness. It consists in having him—

laying on his side;

with lower arm and leg stretched out straight behind him;

upper leg and arm bent forward at right angles at hip, knee, shoulder, elbow;

face tilted slightly downwards and head bent backwards (NO pillow).

This ensures a clear airway and lets any fluid in the mouth (saliva, blood, vomit) flow out and not choke the patient.

To get him in position:

1. Empty his pockets; remove items like bracelet or wrist watch. Put his belongings away safely. Loosen tight clothing.
2. Kneel alongside him.
3. Straighten his arms alongside his body; tuck the nearer hand below his hip.
4. Put one of your hands under his face to protect it as your other hand pulls him at the hip over towards you, on his side.
5. Adjust the limbs.
6. Cover him with a blanket or coat.

However, do not move the patient if circumstances suggest he received a heavy blow to the backbone. In that case ensure free breathing by keeping his head bent well back (never sideways). Be ready to clear immediately any vomit from his mouth.

Resuscitation.

This is the attempt to restore life to someone who has stopped breathing. NEVER try it unless this really is the case; you will do harm if the patient has collapsed but is still breathing. Do not try it if the problem is that of fighting against choking (*q.v.*).

In cases of drowning do not try to tip the patient up to drain out water; this wastes valuable time.

(It is best to have learnt the technique in organised first aid classes, practising only on a manikin.)

Artificial Respiration.

Act very quickly:—

1. Get the patient on his back.
2. Bend his head fully backwards and keep it thus all the time.

3. With fingers rapidly clear out any obstructing matter from mouth and throat.
4. Hold his mouth open (keep your fingers clear of his lips) and pinch his nose shut.
5. Take a deep breath in: open your mouth wide and seal your lips round his mouth: breathe firmly into his mouth. The air going in should make his chest rise. Do not blow more forcibly than is needed to achieve this.
6. Lift your mouth off. His chest will now sink as air comes out. Meantime you take another breath in.
7. Continue by repeating the breathing processes of steps 5 and 6.

The first four breaths you give quickly. Thereafter time yourself by the rise and the natural fall of the patient's chest.

With small children you need not pinch the nose, but let your mouth seal over both the nose and mouth of the patient. Much gentler blowing is needed, and quite small puffs are right for babies.

Keep on until medical authority takes over.

If patient vomits turn his head to one side and clear out the mouth. Then resume artificial respiration, with the first four breaths quick ones.

Successful artificial respiration should soon improve the patient's colour, and later you may find he begins to breathe for himself, even if only weakly. Watch this closely, for he may cease again.

Heart Compression.

If there is no improvement it may be necessary to add heart compression to artificial respiration. This, however, cannot be safely learnt except from first aid class teaching and demonstration. (See the Introduction to this section.)

Shock.

Failure of the heart and of the circulation of the blood may follow any serious injury (bleeding, wounds, burns, fractures). This can happen in minutes or hours according to the severity of the lesion.

In first aid terms this dangerous physical condition is called Shock. The patient is pale, cold, sweating, faint or comatose, with weak and fast pulse and breathing.

Try to prevent or to minimise the development of shock before it appears by applying the following simple but valuable measures to every badly hurt patient.

1. At once stop severe bleeding (*q.v.*).
2. Treat the patient where he is (unless you both are in an area of danger).
3. Lie him down: keep his head low and his legs raised (but avoid movement where a fracture is suspected).
4. Loosen tight clothing.
5. Keep him warm by covering below and loosely above him—but do not use hot-water bottles.
6. Gently dress any wounds—with the minimum of disturbance.
7. Guard his mental state. Be sympathetic but as optimistically reassuring as possible. Never whisper to others. Never assume that because the patient appears unconscious he cannot hear and understand what is said near him.

Do not give the badly injured patient anything to drink. This could worsen his condition and risk vomiting and choking, especially if he becomes unconscious or needs an anaesthetic. If he is very thirsty let him refresh himself by sucking a moistened handkerchief.

Snake Bite.

The adder is the only dangerous snake in Britain. Its bite can cause collapse and great pain, but only very rarely is it fatal.

1. Lay the patient down.
2. Wipe or wash the bite area. Put on a dry dressing.
3. Cover the area with a thick pad and bandage it in position so that it presses down very firmly.

4. Immobilise the bitten part as if it were a fracture (q.v.).
5. Get the patient rapidly to hospital.
6. Reassure him about his recovery. Give aspirin or paracctamol to minimise pain.

You NEVER cut or suck the bite, or apply chemicals. You NEVER use a tourniquet.

Sprains.

These are stretched and torn ligaments at a joint. Immediately after it happens you can reduce the swelling and pain which will follow by applying a cold compress—a cloth soaked in cold water and then wrung out to be just moist. Keep it in position half an hour, and renew it if it gets dry.

Otherwise support the joint firmly with layers of cotton wool interleaved between turns of crepe bandaging. Beware of making it so tight that it interferes with circulation in the limb.

A severe sprain may be difficult to distinguish from a fracture. If in doubt treat as for the latter.

Strains.

A strain is an overstretching of muscle fibres, and is very like a sprain except that it does not necessarily happen at a joint. Treat it as a sprain.

Strokes.

Some part of the brain has sudden damage of its blood supply. The results are as variable as are the functions of the brain: e.g., poor feeling or power in hand, arm or leg, altered speech, loss of bladder control, paralysis of one side, or unconsciousness.

A mild effect may be the forerunner of more serious damage. Get the patient to bed, if necessary in the recovery position (q.v.), and keep him under observation until the doctor arrives.

Unconsciousness.

In first aid finding the cause of unconsciousness is less important than protecting the patient's breathing. The unconscious patient lying on his back and with head straight or bent towards the chest is at risk of choking from his lax tongue, flopping against and obstructing his throat. Correct positioning prevents this. Act methodically:—

1. Has the patient stopped breathing? He will urgently need resuscitation (q.v.).
2. Is his airway blocked making breathing difficult? Clear any material from his mouth. Bend his head straight back at the neck (but do not twist or turn it), and keep it there (see Choking).
3. Arrest any severe bleeding (q.v.).
4. Dress any wounds (q.v.).
5. Consider the possibilities of fractures (q.v.). If you suspect they might be present do not move him (specially important if he might have injured the backbone); stay by his head to ensure its proper position and to clear out immediately any fluid (saliva, blood, vomit) which threatens to choke.

If he can be moved:—

6. Turn him into the recovery position (q.v.)

Two other important points are that you NEVER try to give anything by mouth to the unconscious or comatose, and that you realise how much you must guard your speech, since these patients may overhear and understand what is spoken near them.

Wounds.

The general treatment is simple, and should avoid the use of antiseptics or ointments.

1. At once control any severe bleeding (q.v.).

2. Sit or lay the patient down.
3. Put a clean temporary dressing on the wound.
4. Wash your hands. Prepare dressings and bandages.
5. Wash *around* the wound (but not the open wound itself) with swabs or clean material moistened with soap and water. Use a fresh swab or material area for each stroke.
6. Cover the wound with a large dry dressing. Over this place a thick soft pad. Bandage firmly.
7. Put the injured part at rest.
8. Take measures against shock (q.v.).

Dressings. Gauze from freshly opened pack. Or improvise from clean handkerchief or small towel, held by corners, allowed to fall open and then refolded so that inside surface comes to outside. A leg or arm can be slipped inside a pillowcase.

Padding. Cotton wool. Or improvise from bunched clean handkerchief, sock.

Bandages can be improvised from stockings, necktie, belt.

Object embedded in wound. Do not try to remove it. Cover it with a clean dressing and over this place a "frame" of padding to surround the side of the object and protect above it. You can now apply further padding and bandages without pressing on the object.

Tetanus (lockjaw) is a risk in wounds contaminated with soil or from animals or thorns. Get medical advice.

St. John's Ambulance Brigade.

Readers of *Pears* will be interested to know that the Brigade celebrated its centenary in 1987. From its origins over a century ago, the organisation now boasts some 62,000 volunteers who deal with over 300,000 casualties each year. These casualties can range from minor upsets such as nose bleeds to victims of heart attacks and broken limbs. The work of the St. John's Ambulance is divided into two aspects: the Brigade, which provides volunteers to give first-aid at public meetings *etc.*, and the Association, which is engaged in the task of spreading first-aid education.

THE BLOOD.

INTRODUCTION.

Doctors who have made a special study of the blood are known as haematologists. Haematology itself is a complex subject because blood itself is complex and its many functions are not easy to describe and only a brief account will be given here. A few basic facts to begin with:

Blood consists of a fluid, called plasma, in which are suspended red and white blood cells and in which are dissolved many substances from the simple ones like glucose to the complex like hormones, proteins and fats. Total blood volume amounts to about five litres; the blood donor gives about half a litre at a session and feels no ill effects. Loss of a litre or more induces surgical shock (q.v. **Physical Injuries and First Aid**). The cells in blood are either red or white. Red cells are red because they carry a protein called haemoglobin which is capable of carrying oxygen. There are about five million red cells for each cubic millilitre of blood (that is an average sized drop), a total of five thousand million circulating in the body at any one time. The life of a red cell is about six weeks; new ones are constantly replacing old ones which are "buried" by the spleen.

The haemoglobin from dead cells is recycled; new cells are generated in the marrow of bones, including the breast bone, from which samples of marrow can be taken by a technique known as sternal puncture. Such samples are studied with a microscope to establish diagnoses of various blood disorders. White cells are of five basic types, the names of which need not concern us here. Each type has a specific function—some act as bacterial scavengers, some are concerned with antibodies (q.v.) and some with the general defence system of the body which is concerned with the development and maintenance of immunity to various diseases both bactericidal and viral. There are also non-cell particles derived from large cells which the marrow produces. These are platelets, which are concerned with blood clotting. They have the capacity to "stick" to any gaps in blood vessels (such as may be caused by injury or, in the minutest of blood vessels, "wear and tear") and initiate blood clotting. All these types of cells can be studied in the test tube after taking a sample from the patient. This is known as venepuncture, a simple and virtually painless procedure, carried out by doctor or nurse or trained "phlebotomist", by inserting a needle on the end of a syringe into a dilated vein in the crook of the arm. Marrow samples can also be taken, as we have said, from the breast bone—but that is a very different procedure, requiring local anaesthetic and much more skill. For the patient it is not a comfortable procedure either.

The fluid part of the blood, plasma, is more the province of the biochemist than the haematologist. The immunologist is also interested in plasma and all three disciplines tend to overlap to some degree. Plasma can be studied in the same way as whole blood. A venepuncture is carried out, a chemical added to stop clotting and the cells can then be removed in a centrifuge. If blood is allowed to clot in the test tube, the cells are all caught up in the clot and the plasma remains liquid and can be poured off. It is then known as serum. Plasma contains substances which are either dissolved, that is, in solution, or are held "in suspension". By this is meant that the plasma forms an emulsion because protein and fat particles are not soluble and can only form suspensions in this way. The protein and fat particles are in suspension in a like manner. The substances both in solution and in suspension are much too numerous to be dealt with here.

The functions of blood are manifold, but essentially blood is a transport medium, concerned with moving gases (oxygen and carbon dioxide), moving food (protein, carbohydrate, fat, minerals and vitamins) and eliminating waste products.

Red Cell Diseases.

These are of two main groups leading to a shortage of red cells (anaemia), or an excess (polycythaemia). The former is much the more common and there are many different kinds. In all of them the shortage of red cells results in a depletion of the capacity of the blood to carry oxygen. This means that the heart must work harder to send more blood than usual to the tissues, and even so the tissues will often go short. The patient will be persistently tired and listless, and if the anaemia is severe the action of the brain and heart will be seriously impeded, even leading to fainting, cardiac pain, and breathlessness on exertion. All these symptoms, however, can be caused by many other conditions. The only way to be sure they are due to anaemia is by a proper examination of the blood, and even this will not lead to the truth if the picture has been spoilt by the patient taking iron tonics and other remedies of his own accord. Therefore do not dose yourself with tonics, in case you really have anaemia. You may make it impossible to arrive at a proper diagnosis later.

Haemorrhagic Anaemia. Anaemia, a shortage of red cells, may be due to a variety of causes, singly or in combination. One very obvious cause is loss of blood or haemorrhage. Following the sudden loss of a half-litre of blood or more, the red-cell-producing bone marrow "factory" will step up its production; but even if it is adequately supplied with all the raw materials such as iron, it may well take many weeks to build up the numbers to normal. A very severe degree of haemorrhagic anaemia is usually treated by blood transfusion. Milder degrees can be treated by taking extra iron, often over a long period of time. The supply of iron for making new red-cell pigment is nearly always the bottle-neck which limits production. Haemorrhagic anaemia can commonly occur, however, without a sudden severe haemorrhage. From what has been said about the constant replacement of red cells as they wear out, it must be obvious that even if there is only a slight failure to keep pace with the numbers lost, several months of such a failure can eventually deplete the numbers to the level of very severe anaemia. This situation is common when small amounts of blood are being continuously or repeatedly lost, and here again it is a shortage of dietary iron which is the usual cause of the failure to replace the lost red cells. Normal menstrual loss in women and girls whose diet is on the border-line of iron deficiency is a common cause of progressive tiredness and lack of energy. Where the menstrual flow is heavier than usual, or where it is frankly excessive in older women due to the various common gynaecological disorders, serious anaemia is surprisingly common. During pregnancy a great deal of iron is lost by the mother to the baby, and this, together with the inevitable blood loss at delivery, often makes for a very tired mother indeed, just at the time when there is an enormous amount of work to be done to manufacture milk and attend to all the extra household tasks of baby care. For these reasons it is almost routinely advisable to build up stocks of iron throughout the pregnancy by remembering to take the pills provided. Men as well as women can lose small amounts of blood continuously in later life from gastro-intestinal conditions such as piles, ulcers, and tropical infestations such as hookworm; and here again the anaemia may be just as severe in the long run as that which inevitably follows a sudden, massive haemorrhage. One extra word of warning. Do not assume because you are pale that you are anaemic. Pallor is a very poor guide, because it is dependent on so many other things, like the blood vessels in your skin, and its thickness and translucency. Nothing but a blood test (which is so easy for your doctor to do) can really tell you if you are anaemic. And if your anaemia is due to a blood-losing condition, then that too must be treated. So do not be tempted to treat yourself, and never delay seeing your doctor about any unexplained bleeding.

Haemolytic Anaemia occurs when for any reason, there are more blood cells than usual being destroyed in the body. This may be because the cells are abnormally fragile, or because normal cells have been attacked by something to which you are allergic, or rarely because you have become sensitive to your own red cells. Sometimes unborn babies have severe haemolytic anaemia, due to an incompatability of blood group (Rh factor) between the mother and the baby, and the same sort of thing happens if incompatible blood is given by mistake in blood transfusion. Up to a point, in mild haemolytic anaemia, the bone marrow can keep pace with the increased loss of cells, but beyond this point anaemia develops. After incompatible blood transfusions a very dangerous situation results from the effects of the destruction of red cells and the liberation of their products into the blood. One form of jaundice is often produced in haemolytic anaemia, the patient becoming yellow because of the breakdown products of red cells circulating in excess as bile pigments. These latter are normally always present to a small extent due to the normal, comparatively small, rate of destruction of effete red cells.

Aplastic Anaemia is the term given to anaemia due to a virtually total failure of the bone marrow red-cell factory. Sometimes this occurs for no obvious reason. It is sometimes due to a heavy dose of radioactivity or X-rays knocking out the cells of the "factory." It may even be due to cancer cells growing in the bone marrow cavity and not leaving sufficient room for the red marrow cells. It is fortunate that aplastic anaemia is very rare, because it can only be treated by blood transfusions every few weeks for the rest of the patient's life. Very occasionally there have been exceptions to this rule, when the patient's marrow has re-awakened for no apparent reason and suddenly begins to make red cells again. Some marrow diseases have been apparently successfully treated with bone marrow grafts but the technique is of very recent development and it is probably too early for a full assessment of the potential to be made.

Pernicious Anaemia. This is a fairly uncommon anaemia, which has a very interesting story. The processes by which red cells are manufactured are many and complex, and depend, like so many other bodily activities, on the supply of a vitamin containing cobalt, called vitamin B_{12}. This is nearly always present in more than adequate quantities in the diet, but in order for it to be absorbed from the intestine, there must also be a substance called "intrinsic factor" which is normally made by the lining of the stomach. People with pernicious anaemia have suffered a degeneration of the lining of their stomachs, probably because, for some reason, they have become "sensitive" to this part of their own tissue. This kind of civil war within the body is known as an "auto-immune" disease, and is comparable in type with some forms of haemolytic anaemia. In other words they destroy their own stomach lining, fail to produce "intrinsic factor," and as a result fail to absorb vitamin B_{12} into the body. Faced with a failure in the supply of this essential substance, the bone marrow produces too few red cells, and the few that are produced are deformed, much too large, and very fragile. In addition to its role in blood formation, vitamin B_{12} is essential to the normal functioning of the spinal cord, and in long-standing cases of untreated pernicious anaemia, there is often a resulting neurological disability.

Nowadays pernicious anaemia is treated by small occasional injections of the vitamin, whose other name is cyanocobalamin. A similar molecule, without the cobalt atom, is now used. This is called hydroxycobalamin.

Polycythaemia. Too many red cells per cubic millilitre of blood can be found without there being an increase of the total number of red cells in the body. This occurs in dehydration, when there is a loss of plasma without a comparable loss of cells, and is called haemo-concentration. Alternatively, the bone marrow can manufacture more cells than usual as a response to living for long periods at high altitudes. The beneficial result can be that the blood can carry normal amounts of oxygen, even though the supply (in the rarefied air) is reduced. Finally there is a red cell disease in which the bone marrow factory gets out of control and produces too many cells with no beneficial results. The number in the blood can be double the normal and the blood becomes so thick that the heart has difficulty pumping it round the body. This disease (*polycythaemia rubra vera*) used to be treated by repeatedly bleeding the patient to reduce the numbers of cells. It is now treated very successfully with carefully judged amounts of radioactive phosphorus or certain other "antimitotic" chemicals which reduce the rate of multiplication of bone marrow cells.

White Cell Diseases.

Diseases of the white cells are very much less common but are inevitably serious.

Agranulocytosis. In this condition the number of those white cells which are responsible for phagocytosis of bacteria falls precipitously. The result is that one of the main bodily defences against infection fails, and the patient may die from an overwhelming invasion of germs with accompanying high fever. The usual cause is abnormal sensitivity to certain drugs, often those which are in widespread use and only give trouble in the occasional case. One example among hundreds is the antibiotic chloramphenicol which specifically kills typhoid bacteria and is used for that purpose. It is believed that about one patient in 60,000 becomes sensitive to it and agranulocytosis often fatally follows. The fact that almost any drug *can* do this to some people and yet be quite safe for the majority, is one good reason not to dose yourself unnecessarily with over-the-counter medicines.

Leukaemia. Leukaemia comprises a spectrum of diseases which involve the abnormal production of white blood cells. Immature or blast cells are produced at an increased rate and tend to infiltrate various areas of the body, for example, bone marrow, lymph nodes and spleen. They are also found in the peripheral blood and cerebral spinal fluid. In spite of their large numbers these cells, because of their abnormality, are unable to deal effectively with infection and anaemia, sepsis and fever can result. The cause of this type of cancer is open to some speculation but we know there is an increased incidence in those with Down's Syndrome and other chromosomal abnormalities. Viral infections may also be implicated and there is almost certainly an association with ionising radiation. This latter fact was proved by the increased incidence of leukaemia in those who survived the atomic explosion in Japan at the end of the Second World War. Pregnant women should not be subject to X-Rays as this may cause an increased incidence of leukaemia in their children.

Cases of leukaemia are known to occur in clusters or small groups in certain areas. Sometimes this is thought to be associated with natural radiation arising from rock structures. However, it is also suspected that there is an increased incidence around atomic power stations and plants which reprocess nuclear waste. In particular, a great controversy has raged about the incidence of leukaemia around the Sellafield reprocessing plant with some authorities insisting that the rate of occurrence is no greater than normal. However, those working and living in the area have always felt this to be untrue and recent research has suggested that workers exposed to small amounts of radioactive material may suffer abnormal spermatic development so that the tendency to leukaemia may be passed on to their unborn children who may be prone to the disease later in life.

The outcome of the illness largely depends on the specific type. Chronic lymphatic leukaemia for example, which tends to affect older people, may have no clinical signs or symptoms. In fact, it can run a very indolent course, require no treatment and be compatible with a normal lifespan. On the other hand, acute myeloid leukaemia which tends to affect younger adults is a very serious disease with an acute onset and which if not treated can prove to be rapidly fatal.

In childhood, leukaemia is the most common form of malignant disease but nevertheless, it is quite rare with an incidence of approximately 25 per 1,000,000 children. Over 85% of all children develop the type known as acute lymphoblastic leukaemia. With modern treatment, a remission (that is to say, a disease free period) can be induced in over 90% of children and cure rates are very high. Presenting features of acute leukaemia are tiredness, lethargy, abnormal susceptibility to infection, excessive bruising and occasionally bone or joint pain. A blood count usually helps in the diagnosis but this needs to be confirmed by examination of the bone marrow. Treatment involves repeated courses of cytotoxic drugs, sometimes combined with radiotherapy. For those with more resistant forms of the illness, bone marrow transplantation can often provide a cure. Treatment is best performed in specialist centres where the expertise is available to deal with the complicated drug regimes. With modern treatment the outlook for all forms of leukaemia has improved. For children, in particular, the outlook has been dramatically transformed and in a great many cases a cure can be successfully achieved.

Hodgkin's disease, Lymphosarcoma and Reticulo acoma. These are diseases which are in some ways akin to *leukaemia.* Abnormal cells are found in the reticulo-edothelial system and proliferate in a disorganised manner, causing enlargement of lymph nodes (glands), spleen and sometimes the liver.

Hodgkin's disease, named after a 19th cent. Guy's physician, has been the subject of much research and therapeutic trial. At special centres in London and elsewhere, earlier diagnosis and new methods of ascertaining the extent of the disease process have led to advances in surgical and medical treatment which show much promise. If treated early the disease can be apparently halted or even eradicated.

Hæmorrhagic or Bleeding Diseases.

Whenever blood vessels are damaged by injury, there is a remarkable series of mechanisms which automatically come into operation to stem the flow of blood. There is a constriction of all the smaller vessels in the locality. Platelets stick together and release substances which help the vessels to stay constricted as well as others necessary to blood clotting, and yet others which help to bind the clot tightly together. Later, materials appear to prevent too much clotting, and eventually the clot is removed altogether as healing proceeds. There are some very complicated diseases of this blood-conserving mechanism which can lead to abnormal bleeding, sometimes beneath the skin to produce bruising or even smaller leaks; sometimes leading to a greater loss of blood, particularly following a wound. In some kinds of *purpura* (bleeding tendency) the blood vessels are the cause of the trouble, having become fragile and leaky for a number of reasons. This happens in old age (*senile purpura*), in scurvy, or vitamin C deficiency, as an occasional accompaniment to infective diseases, or as an immunological effect on the lining of blood vessels when the patient becomes sensitised to certain substances (*Schönlein-Henoch* or *anaphylactoid purpura*). The latter often follows a streptococcal sore throat, just as rheumatic fever and acute nephritis do; and as well as the purpura there may be joint pains and nephritis. Just as almost any drug or chemical will cause agranulocytosis in some people, so it can also cause anaphylactoid purpura.

Purpura may also be due to a lack of platelets, known as thrombocytopenia (a shortage of thrombocytes or platelets). This can happen if the bone marrow factory is depressed, since this is where platelets too are made. It is therefore a common accompaniment of leukaemia or aplastic anaemia. Or there can be increased destruction of platelets in some diseases of the spleen. Platelets normally last eight to ten days, but their lifespan can be shortened in heart failure, and following massive transfusions, or often for no apparent reason ("idiopathic" thrombocytopenia), when removal of the spleen can sometimes help.

Finally, defects of the *clotting mechanism* will lead to a bleeding tendency, and since the mechanism itself is very complex, so is the variety of things which can upset it. The liver provides the blood with many of the substances required for clotting, so it is not surprising that a clotting defect commonly accompanies liver disease. One necessary substance for blood clotting is called "anti-haemophilic factor" and is missing from people who have inherited the disease *haemophilia*. These people may die of haemorrhage from quite small cuts or minor surgical procedures.

THE HEART AND BLOOD-VESSELS.

INTRODUCTION.

The heart consists of about 350g of muscle which makes up the walls of its four chambers. Anatomically the human heart closely resembles the sheeps' hearts to be found in a butcher's shop. Indeed it would be an instructive exercise to dissect one of these in the order described below, since there is no other way of properly appreciating what the chambers, valves, etc., are really like. There are two quite separate pumps in the heart—one on the owner's right (or on your *left* if you are looking at the front of someone else), and one on his left. The right heart collects spent, deoxygenated, "venous" blood which returns there from the whole of the body, and gives it the comparatively small push required to drive it through the adjacent lungs. The left heart collects the revitalised, oxygenated "arterial" blood as it trickles

away from the lungs, and gives it the enormous push required to build up the arterial blood-pressure, so that it can be forced through all the tissues of the body. As may be expected, the right heart chambers have much thinner walls than the left, since their muscle has less work to do. This will help you get your bearings with the sheep's heart. The tip, or apex, is the lowest part. The thick-feeling side is the left, the thin the right; and the great vessels are at the top.

The upper chamber on the right, or right atrium, has two large openings into it through which all the spent blood arrives from the upper and lower great veins (the superior and inferior venae cavae). Cut open the thin wall of the right atrium with scissors between these two holes to lay open the interior of the chamber, noting the "auricle" or "dog's ear" that forms a small cul-de-sac. The whole chamber is sometimes, inaccurately, called the auricle. You should be able to push a finger downwards into the lower chamber—the right ventricle—through a communicating hole guarded by the three thin cusps of the *tricuspid valve*. These will not obstruct your finger, since they are designed to permit blood flow in the same direction. When the atrium is full of blood, it squeezes its contents through the tricuspid valve into the right ventricle; and when, a split second later, the ventricle is full and contracts, the three cusps come together to prevent the blood from flowing backwards into the atrium again. Instead the spent blood is driven onwards through the *pulmonary valve* (in the upper part of the right ventricle), through the pulmonary artery, to be delivered to the lungs. The pulmonary valve has three very well-defined cusps which prevent blood from coming back into the ventricle as it relaxes to receive more blood from the atrium before the next contraction or beat. It is possible to pass a blade of the scissors from the opened-out right atrium, through the tricuspid valve towards the tip of the heart, and cut along the right border of the heart through the thickness of the ventricular muscle. Then cut upwards again, passing the scissors blade through the pulmonary valve and open up the *pulmonary artery*. If you have done this successfully you will have followed the path taken by the spent blood through the right heart to the lungs. Notice the thick round bands of muscle lining the ventricle, and notice too that you have not entered the left heart, which has no connection with the right except in some congenital malformations (see later). The same dissection can now be made of the left heart. Open up the *left atrium*, noting its "dog's ear" or "auricle," pass the scissors down into the *left ventricle* through the two rather flimsy cusps of the *mitral valve*. Notice how much thicker is the muscle of the left ventricle, and cut upwards through the three well-formed cusps of the *aortic valve* into the main artery of the body—the *aorta*. The aorta as it leaves the left heart is distinguishable from the pulmonary artery as it leaves the right, partly by the extreme toughness of the aortic wall (it has to withstand so much more blood-pressure); and partly by the entrances or orifices of the two small branches given off by the aorta, just beyond the valve cusps, which go to supply the heart muscle itself with blood. These are the *coronary arteries* which are so necessary for the heart's own survival.

The amount of blood pumped in unit time, or the *cardiac output*, can be varied a great deal, according to the needs of the moment. This is accomplished by altering both the heart rate and the stroke volume, the amount expelled per beat. Every minute, the healthy adult man at rest shifts about 5 litres of blood through the heart—an amount equivalent to all the blood he possesses. When exercise is taken, or in response to anxiety or fear, this is stepped up many times, so that the muscles can receive a greatly augmented supply of the materials required for action. The controlling mechanisms which allow these changes to be made automatically are partly organised in the brain by the so-called *cardiac centre*; and partly by local mechanical and chemical stimuli to the heart muscle itself. The cardiac centre is continuously receiving information through nerves about the physical and chemical state of the circulation, and also from the mind; which is partly how certain emotions make the heart beat faster. All the information is integrated, and a cardiac output continuously arranged which is appropriate for current demands.

Cardiac Neurosis. In ordinary circumstances at rest, most healthy people are not conscious of their heart-beat. However, there are many perfectly healthy people whose hearts slip in an extra beat occasionally. Sometimes their owners are aware of this and become unnecessarily alarmed. Their fear causes palpitations (a pounding of the heart) and the tension mounts. An undue anxiety about the tricks played by a healthy heart sometimes leads people to interpret minor pains in the chest, or even indigestion, as grave symptoms of heart disease, and the consequent anxiety leads to still worse symptoms. If you are one of these worried people, take your worries to your doctor, and let him decide for you whether there is anything wrong. A hundred to one there isn't, and then you will have to find something else to worry about, or better still give up the habit altogether. Many people secretly worry about heart disease and high blood-pressure for years, when very often they are worrying unnecessarily. Even if there is cause for worry, so much can be done for these conditions (as it can for cancer) provided medical advice is taken early in the course of the disease. Remember, too, that the slight feeling of giddiness when you get up suddenly from having been lying down, is often experienced by most normal people; but if you get frightened by it you will begin to breathe more quickly and deeply; and this in itself will make you feel even more faint—and so on.

Heart Failure. When the cardiac output of blood is too little for the requirements of the body, a state of *circulatory failure* has arisen, and when this is due primarily to the heart itself being at fault, it is more properly called *heart failure*. As will be seen, heart failure is not a disease, but the common result of a large number of different diseases. The signs and symptoms produced are caused by two sorts of process: (*a*) tissues of the body have too little blood flow through them and are therefore undersupplied; (*b*) blood accumulates and stagnates in tissues, causing congestion, since the failing heart cannot move forward the amount of blood presented to it in the great veins. Often the left or right side of the heart fails disproportionately. In *left heart failure* the lungs are congested because they are the territory from which the left heart is failing to move blood. The patient has great difficulty with his breathing, and in advanced cases may not be able to breathe when he lies down, because the lungs become so congested and waterlogged. In *right heart failure* the main veins are congested and the other parts of the body become swollen with excess tissue fluid, mainly in the lower parts such as the legs and ankles. This swelling with fluid is called oedema, and in heart failure is only partly due to the mechanics of the failing heart. It is mainly due to a poorly understood retention of sodium in the body, a situation in which excess water is also retained. Whatever the type of heart failure it is always likely to be a changing condition, since the amount of failure will depend as much on the demands being made as on the state of the heart. For instance, in mild cases at rest when the required cardiac output is small, there may be no signs or symptoms. These may only appear on exertion. Heart failure will be referred to again later under the various conditions which cause it.

Treatment of heart failure is quite logical. It is aimed at correcting the imbalance between supply and demand of blood, and at the removal of the accumulated excess fluid. We can therefore (*a*) reduce the body's demand for blood; (*b*) increase the supply or cardiac output; and (*c*) promote the excretion of sodium and fluid. Demand for blood is reduced by rest, both physical and mental, and by reduction of weight, since obesity (being overweight) is an additional demand on the cardiovascular system. The cardiac output can be increased by administering a "tonic" to the heart muscle in the form of *digitalis*, which is a powerful heart stimulant derived from fox-

glove leaf. Fluid (and hence salt) accumulation can be helped by restricting the intake of salt and by giving drugs which promote its excretion by the kidneys (diuretics). Very occasionally, very large accumulations of fluid in the legs, abdomen, or thorax, are tapped and drained physically, with needles. These remarks on treatment, as elsewhere in the Medical Section, are of course very general and must not encourage anyone to treat himself for such a potentially serious condition as heart failure. Even such a simple measure as doing without salt can be practised quite unnecessarily by many people for years, simply as a result of reading a paragraph like the above. The most they accomplish is to make their food taste horribly dull. If you need to reduce salt intake you should be in your doctor's care, and so please let him decide.

Congenital Heart Disease. It has been estimated that of all the babies born who survive at least one month, there will be about one in every two hundred with some form of congenital heart disease; that is to say that the heart will have failed to develop properly in embryonic life. In some cases this is associated with a virus disease of the mother (commonly rubella, or German measles) or with certain drugs taken by the mother (e.g. thalidomide) at a time, very early in pregnancy, when organs are assuming their adult shape. Parents should see to it that their daughters get German measles before they grow up; and drugs of all kinds should be avoided where possible during early pregnancy. In most cases of congenital heart disease, however, there is no known cause, and it seems that the manner of formation of the embryonic heart is so delicate that it can be thrown out of gear very easily, perhaps even by chance. Scores of different types of defect occur, singly and in combination. Any of the valves may be anatomically defective—either failing to close properly (*incompetence*) or being too tight (*stenosis*); the great vessels (pulmonary artery and aorta) may be switched round, or *transposed*, so that they emerge from the wrong ventricle; there may be defects in the wall (*septum*) which separates the atria or the ventricles on each side (*septal defect*, or "hole in the heart"); or there may be a persistence of the vessel which in the foetus normally by-passes the lungs by joining the pulmonary artery to the aorta (*patent ductus arteriosus*). This vessel normally closes at the time of birth when the first breaths are taken, and subsequently disappears, so that the whole output of the heart is then sent round the lungs. Detecting congenital heart disease early is one of the purposes of routine post-natal check-up examinations of the baby. Exact diagnosis requires very complicated techniques, and sometimes the structural defect can be corrected by surgery, with almost miraculous results.

Rheumatic Heart Disease. Acute rheumatic fever is not to be confused with other forms of rheumatism. Many tissues of the body (particularly the heart) are attacked, as well as the joints, and the trouble is due to a sensitivity which has developed to certain bacteria (*haemolytic streptococci*) which have probably caused a sore throat about three weeks before the onset of the disease. Why acute rheumatism only rarely follows streptococcal sore throat is poorly understood, but this is no consolation to the one per cent or so of the population whose hearts bear its scars. During the acute phase of the illness which usually occurs before the age of fifteen, inflammatory damage occurs to the valves, the heart muscle, and the sac in which the heart lives, the *pericardium*. So there is a *valvulitis* or *endocarditis*, a *myocarditis* and a *pericarditis*. There may be acute heart failure at this stage if the heart is severely affected. The better-known results of rheumatic heart disease, however, are caused in the ensuing years by scarring of the healed valves. The valves are thickened and deformed. They may have lost their elasticity and stretch, so that they do not close properly (*incompetence*); or they may contract and tighten (*stenosis*). In both cases the heart chamber situated next to the affected valve has to work progressively harder, either because it gets no rest in between beats (in *incompetence*); or it has to force the blood through too narrow a hole (in *stenosis*). The end result is some variety of heart failure (**P27**). Although there are other causes of valvular heart disease which will now be mentioned, rheumatic fever is by much the commonest, and much valve trouble can be blamed on rheumatic fever even when the patient has no recollection of ever having suffered from it. The other, much rarer, causes may be syphilis, congenital valvular anomaly, healed bacterial endocarditis, atherosclerosis, and mechanical injury.

The most commonly affected valve is the mitral, usually causing *mitral stenosis*, in which the opening between the left atrium and the left ventricle will sometimes only admit one finger-tip instead of three fingers as it should. In time the left atrium becomes much enlarged as it overworks to force blood through this narrow orifice. Later still a back pressure develops in the lungs causing congestion and breathlessness; and even later the right ventricle is strained as it tries to force blood into the already congested lung. This is a classic example of the march of trouble backwards from the site of the damaged valve involving first the chamber "behind" it (the left atrium), then the territory "behind" that (the lungs), then the pulmonary arteries taking blood to the lungs, and finally the right ventricle trying to send blood to the pulmonary artery. This steady march of events is usually very slow, and can commonly take twenty years or longer from the initial attack of acute rheumatism to the severer symptoms of advanced mitral stenosis. Treatment is both medical and surgical. The heart failure is treated medically as already described. These days surgical reopening of the valve is almost commonplace, either by inserting a finger through the left auricle and breaking down the constriction, or by opening up the heart and re-shaping the valve under direct vision. The latter involves the additional problem of by-passing the heart by the use of some sort of external pump and poses additional problems, even though from other points of view it is obviously more convenient. As always with major surgical procedures much of the problem is in selecting the patients who will benefit from the operation and in whom it is feasible. Quite often there are other valves involved, mainly the aortic or tricuspid or both, and the hydrostatic or "plumbing" problems can be extremely complex. With luck, however, combined with good judgement and good surgery, the lives of incapacitated patients can be transformed by mitral, and other valvular, surgery. Recently a great deal of progress has been made in designing new "ball-in-basket" valves of man-made materials to replace damaged natural valves. The *aortic valve* is stenosed or narrowed by other degenerative processes besides rheumatism. *Tricuspid stenosis* is nearly always rheumatic in origin.

Coronary Heart Disease. This is the term used whenever the blood supply to the heart muscle (through the coronary arteries) is reduced to such an extent that the heart muscle suffers from a lack of supplies. It has a number of causes, but the only really common one is partial obstruction of the coronary arteries by a condition known as *atheroma* or *atherosclerosis*, and sometimes inaccurately called *arteriosclerosis*. This arterial disease is described later (**P29**). It takes the form of swellings or lumps on the lining of the artery which, if they become large enough to interfere seriously with the flow of blood, produce a blood starvation or *ischaemia* of the tissue being supplied. Obviously, the smaller the artery, the more easily will a lump of given size impede the flow. Equally obviously the greater the demand for blood, as in exercise, the more blood "starvation" there will be. There are two degrees of coronary artery disease: one in which the blood flow is reduced to the point where the increased demands of hard work cannot be met, and this results in *angina pectoris* due to *coronary insufficiency*; the other is when the coronary artery becomes completely blocked, preventing the flow of blood altogether, usually by a *thrombus* or clot of blood, and this is *coronary thrombosis*.

Angina Pectoris. Whenever activity is increased in any muscle, the demands for oxygen and nutriments from the blood-stream increase,

and as these are used up there is an increased production of waste products known as metabolites. To meet the demands for a greater supply and a more efficient waste-disposal, the blood flow through the exercising muscle must always be increased. If sufficient increase does not occur, not only will there be a shortage of supplies, but there will also be a pile-up of metabolites in the muscle which cannot be carried away. It is mainly because of these latter that pain is caused in ischaemic, or blood-starved muscle, and pain is one of the chief symptoms when heart muscle becomes ischaemic. One important mechanism for increasing blood flow normally to exercising muscle is by automatically dilating the vessels concerned. Diseased vessels, such as coronary arteries when they are affected by atheroma, are not so easily dilated, although certain drugs which are powerful dilators of arterioles can accomplish a great deal, albeit temporarily. The measures taken to relieve the pain and blood-starvation of angina are two-fold. The patient can reduce the demands of the heart by a few minutes' rest, and a drug (usually nitroglycerin) can be taken to dilate the coronary vessels of supply. Another obvious long-term way to reduce demands is for the overweight patient to eat less, and reduce the load of extra body weight on his circulation. It is very frustrating, to say the least, that such an incapacitating and often lethal condition should be caused by the narrowing or blockage of only 5 or 8 cm of narrow piping about 3·5 mm wide. It is now possible to treat some forms of coronary artery disease by surgical means.

Heart Attack or *Coronary Thrombosis.* It should readily be understood from the above description that heart attacks will vary in their severity according to the amount of heart muscle deprived of blood; and this in turn will depend on where in the coronary artery the obstruction occurs. Most usually it is the left ventricular muscle which is cut off from supplies and dies, either in part or in all of its thickness. Since it is the left ventricle which does most of the work of pumping blood to the body, serious heart failure (**P27**) is to be expected. If too much muscle is killed, the heart will simply stop, and the patient will suddenly die. It is much more usual, however, for enough muscle to be left for survival, albeit with a greatly reduced cardiac efficiency. A heart attack is usually accompanied by severe pain, similar to the pain of angina but more severe, and unrelieved by rest or by the patient's usual drugs. Very occasionally the event occurs apparently without pain, or with so little that it is ignored. These so-called "silent" coronary attacks can make diagnosis extremely difficult. Since the doctor depends very considerably with heart attacks on an exact, spontaneous description of symptoms for his diagnosis, no description will be given here. There are many over-anxious people who will read these words and could be misled into an unspontaneous description of their own symptoms, and this could make the task of treating them such a problem that they could even be mis-diagnosed as a result. If you have the smallest worry that your chest pain is due to your heart, take your anxiety to your doctor without delay. He will almost certainly be able to re-assure you; and if it happens to be your heart after all, you will have taken the first sensible step towards proper treatment. Dangerous as heart attacks are, they are by no means the death warrant that many lay people think, any more than cancer is. The treatment for a true heart attack is urgent and prolonged. Patients must be at complete rest and their pain relieved quickly. The area of heart muscle they have lost must be allowed to heal with a good, firm scar, and this can take three months of rest, often in hospital.

You can help to avoid a heart attack by not smoking, avoiding obesity and living a physically active life. Avoid sudden exercise, however, when you are not in training. Surgeons are able to replace diseased coronary arteries in some patients with small veins taken from other parts of the body.

Blood-pressure. The blood is normally under great pressure in the arterial system, since it is this which forces it into all the tissues of the body.

It is therefore no more meaningful to say you have "blood-pressure" than to say you have a temperature. You would be very badly off without. Blood-pressure which is too high, however, can give rise to problems, though not always. It is another of those conditions like angina and cancer, which engender much anxiety among people even when they do not suffer from them. For this reason doctors are often unwilling to disclose a patient's blood-pressure and because of this they unjustifiably earn a reputation for unreasonable secrecy. They are themselves to blame for the general public anxiety as the following true story shows. Some years ago a lady in her fifties wished to accompany her husband to a post abroad which was to last four years. All arrangements had been made—the husband resigned his previous job, sold the house, etc.—when it was discovered that she had a high blood-pressure, and she was very solemnly advised by the rather elderly doctor not to go. There was great consternation and emotional upheaval, not least because of the inconvenience involved. Eventually she was allowed to go at her own risk. The husband's job lasted eight years instead of four, during which the lady was in no way inconvenienced by her blood-pressure; except that she worried interminably about it. On returning home to retire she began to think she had angina, and elaborate hospital investigation revealed that, as might be expected, her arteries were not as young as they used to be. She was undoubtedly suffering from mild angina, but not as badly as she thought. The opportunity then arose, in her late sixties, to go abroad yet again, and this she did, living a quite strenuous life, and one which she enjoyed. She returned home again, twenty years after she had gone abroad for the first time, able to run a home and still with very little inconvenience from her blood-pressure. There is no doubt that it had been very high all that time, and it is also certain that she will die one day, although it may well not be of her blood-pressure. How much better it would have been for her not to have been told it was high in the first place and to have avoided all these years of anxiety. It is not being suggested here that high blood-pressure is a trivial condition, but that it is for doctors to worry about rather than patients! If you ever find out your own blood-pressure, never try to work out for yourself what the figures mean. It is much too complicated. Finally, it should be mentioned that high blood-pressure may occasionally be associated with, or "secondary to," certain kidney diseases (*nephritis*) including a strange condition known as *toxaemia of pregnancy*, which lasts only as long as the pregnancy, provided great care is taken. Most high blood-pressure is, however, "primary", and without any known association or cause.

Low Blood-pressure. Some people seem normally to have surprisingly low blood-pressure all the time. There is nothing whatever wrong with this; indeed it may even be beneficial. At least they are unlikely ever to suffer the effects of high blood-pressure. The sudden low blood-pressure of circulatory failure or shock (**P27**) is another matter and must be urgently treated.

Irregularities of the Heart-beat. How quickly or how slowly the heart beats is largely under the control of the cardiac centre in the brain and the level of certain hormones in the blood. The *regularity* of the beat, however, is controlled by the so-called pace-maker in the wall of the right atrium, and by the way impulses from the pace-maker travel through specialised conducting heart cells (the bundle of His and its branches) to the ventricles. When any part of this elaborate mechanism is upset, either by altering the biochemical or electrical conditions of these specialised tissues, or by killing some of them off by deprivation of blood supply in the course of a heart attack, disordered rhythm can result. Increase (*tachycardia*) or decrease (*bradycardia*) in rate is nearly always a normal response to exercise, or anxiety. Very occasional irregularity, such as the mis-timing of an occasional beat is also quite normal in some people, although many are alarmed by it. Persistent irregularity, however, is abnormal. Its true nature can usually be elucidated by making an electrical record of the heart-beat—

an electro-cardiogram. The commonest causes are varieties of coronary artery diseases or rheumatic heart disease.

Pericarditis. The heart beats inside a bag or sac. At every beat its outer surface slides against the lining of the sac, lubricated by a small amount of fluid. This is the pericardial sac, the *pericardium* being strictly the lubricated membrane which lines the sac and which also covers the outer surface of the heart. Sometimes inflammation occurs—*pericarditis*—and the sliding surfaces become roughened and even separated by a fluid effusion. Very occasionally, so much fluid accumulates that the heart's action is seriously impeded. Pericarditis may be due to infection or to rheumatic fever, and it usually overlies the area of damaged muscle after a heart attack. This illustrates something which people rarely appreciate—that inflammation is not by any means always due to infection by bacteria. The last two varieties of pericarditis are quite free from germs (sterile).

Myocarditis. A term loosely applied to disorders affecting the heart muscle. There are lots of very rare causes. The really common ones are due to acute or chronic rheumatic causes or to coronary artery disease, both of which are described above.

Endocarditis or inflammation of the lining of the heart is a term loosely applied to any disorder of the valves or heart lining. All varieties of rheumatic valvular disease (**P27**) are included. Bacterial endocarditis in its several forms usually involves valves already damaged by rheumatic disease. It is a complication which is still much to be feared, though somewhat less so now that antibiotic drugs are available.

Atheroma or *Atherosclerosis.* This is the condition referred to above in which lumps arise on the lining of arterial blood-vessels. Although it is therefore a disease of the arteries, its importance lies in the way blood flow is held up, either by the lumps themselves, or by thrombosis ultimately blocking the narrowed portion of the pipework. The effects on the body are therefore those of depriving the tissues of blood. It is an astonishing fact that in England and America, more people die of the consequences of atheroma than of any other single disease, including all forms of cancer put together. Furthermore, cancer is mainly a disease of old age, whereas many of the effects of atheroma on men occur in early middle age. If narrowing of the artery is going to do significant harm it is easy to see that it will be of more consequence in those parts of the body where small-bore vessels are supplying tissues whose functions are necessary for life. Exactly such a situation exists in the heart and in the brain. An additional factor is that the arrangement of the blood supply in these tissues is such that any particular area has only one vessel leading to it. This is unusual among the tissues generally, where several alternative, or "collateral" vessels usually supply an area, and where others can take over if one becomes obstructed. We have, therefore, a situation in which perhaps the most important tissues —the heart and the brain—run the greatest risk of deprivation, and this leads to angina and coronary thrombosis on the one hand, and cerebral thrombosis and haemorrhage ("stroke illness") on the other, accounting jointly for about one death in every five. In addition, the effects of atheromatous narrowing are often felt in the legs, where the blood supply to the muscles is inadequate for exercise, leading to intermittent pain comparable with that in the heart in similar circumstances. This is called *intermittent claudication*, or intermittent closing of the leg arteries. In its most severe forms, it leads to the need for amputation, although in most cases early treatment can avoid this. It is small wonder that there is intensive research into the causes of atheroma, as with cancer, but it is probably true to say that we still know rather more about cancer. A lot of attention has been given to the amounts of certain fats in the circulating blood, particularly cholesterol. This fat is found in larger amounts in the blood of sufferers from atheroma, and is also found in the arterial lumps themselves.

Efforts have therefore been made to reduce blood cholesterol by modifications of the diet, but it has been extremely difficult to prove that this has done any good. Many other factors are known to contribute to atheroma, and hence to heart attacks and strokes, some of which can be reduced and others not. Such factors are age, obesity, high blood-pressure, and smoking cigarettes. People who lead an active life, like bus conductors, seem to have less trouble than others who are less active, like bus drivers. Sudden severe exercise, however, is bad if you are not used to it. It is better, and life saving, to take regular, moderate exercise. Women have less atheroma than men, until the menopause when they begin to catch up, so that hormones have something to do with it. Serious starvation, such as occurred in the German-occupied territories of Holland and Scandinavia and in the concentration camps conferred one benefit—a freedom from atheroma, but obviously we cannot all starve, and the puzzle remains. Like many of the more important outstanding medical puzzles, there is no single factor responsible, and this is what makes it difficult to solve.

Aortic Disease. The aorta, the main artery of the body, running from the left ventricle down through the chest and abdomen, also suffers from atheroma, but is too wide (about 2·5 cm across) to become obstructed. However, weaknesses occur in the thickness of its wall, sometimes due to syphilis but nowadays much more usually due to atheroma, which results in a ballooning out of a part of the vessel, rather like you sometimes see in an old bicycle inner tube. In days gone by these *aneurysms,* as the dilations are called, reached an enormous size, and would wear away the breastbone and ribs, to appear as large pulsating masses on the chest. Now that advanced syphilis is less common, atheromatous aneurysm, with a predilection for the abdominal aorta, is the one most commonly seen; and these days it is treated by replacement of the diseased portion of vessel. *Dissecting aneurysms* of the aorta are another variety in which the blood, under high pressure, somehow finds its way in between the layers of the aortic wall and then suddenly rips up and down the whole length of the vessel, separating (or dissecting) one layer from another in its path. Sometimes it tracks back towards the heart and suddenly fills the pericardium with blood to stop the heart's action altogether.

Embolism. This term refers to any foreign object travelling in the circulation and becoming impacted when it reaches a vessel too small for it to pass through. It may be a thrombus (**P30**), a collection of cancer cells, a group of bacteria, a chunk of infected pus from an abscess, a collection of fat droplets or even a bubble of air. If it originates in a vein it travels to the right heart and to the lungs. If it comes from the left heart or an artery, it will impact in any part of the arterial tree. Reasonably enough an arterial embolus will commonly end up in those parts of the body with the richest blood supply, like the brain, the kidneys, the liver or the bone marrow. A thrombotic embolus will cause death of the tissue in the area previously supplied by the blocked vessel, a condition known as *infarction.* Perhaps the commonest source of thrombotic embolism is the lining of the heart chambers where a thrombus has occurred at the site of muscle damaged by a heart attack. Massive pulmonary (lung) embolism is usually the result of the thrombosis of the leg veins in people kept immobile following surgery or childbirth. That is why postoperative patients are got out of bed for a while as soon as the first day after the operation. The cells of a cancer embolus usually die; but if they survive, a new cancer deposit begins to grow where the embolus impacts, and this is one of the ways cancer may spread. An infected embolus may infect the vessel wall when it impacts, producing a weakness which may give way. Air embolism, if enough insoluble gas enters the circulation, can kill by making so much froth in the heart chambers as to impede the normal pumping action. If bubbles pass the lungs and enter the brain, all sorts of neurological disorders like scores of tiny strokes arise. The same sort of thing happens all over the body in the *"bends"* or *"caisson"* disease,

in which the blood literally boils. It is due to a too rapid return to normal pressure from regions of high pressure at great depths or from pressurised chambers. Fat embolism sometimes occurs after fractures, due to marrow fat entering damaged veins and being carried away to the lungs.

Thrombosis. This is not quite the same as clotting. It is the mass which arises when platelets adhere to the lining of blood-vessels or heart chambers. Blood clot accumulates among layers of deposited platelets and the thrombus therefore has structure, unlike pure blood clot. Thrombosis usually occurs when the lining of the vessel or chamber is damaged by atheroma or inflammation, or when the circulation becomes very stagnant. One danger is that it will become dislodged and travel as an embolus during the first week or ten days of its existence. After this time it is usually firmly incorporated into the vessel walls by cells which migrate into it from the surrounding tissue. The other danger is, of course, that the tissue previously supplied by the blocked vessel will die before a collateral circulation can be established. As previously explained, this is called infarction. All the technical terms in this section are used elsewhere and can be looked up.

Varicose Veins. When veins become swollen they also often become tortuous (wriggly), and particularly on the surface of the leg look very unsightly. They are, however, a sign of a sluggish circulation, and are often due to disease in small valves within the veins which normally prevent the blood from pooling backwards, down towards the feet. They are often a normal maternal accompaniment of pregnancy and disappear after the child is born. If allowed to persist, the sluggish circulation allows the formation of unpleasant ulcers, mainly in elderly people. Treatment is according to severity. In the early stages they are helped by supportive stockings. Later, often as an out-patient, the sufferer may have to have them removed or obliterated by a surgeon.

Raynaud's Disease. This is a strange condition in which the finger tips and in severe cases all the fingers or the whole hand respond in an exaggerated way to cold. The vessels supplying the hand are constricted and the fingers go white as the blood drains from them. Then the capillaries dilate and become distended and filled with blood. But owing to stagnation it is venous and blue, and the fingers are therefore blue. Now we have all experienced this in very cold weather, but sufferers from Raynaud's disease, nearly always women, respond even to very slight cold, like putting their hands into cold water. Even emotional stress will start the process off. In very severe cases the fingers will be so deprived of blood for so long, that sores will develop and fingers can even be lost, but this is very rare, and can be avoided by an operation to cut the nerves which supply the circular muscle of the vessels concerned. In most cases it is sufficient to avoid getting the hands cold.

Frostbite. Strictly speaking, this is literally a freezing of the tissues. Although their freezing point might be expected to be close to that of water, it usually only occurs at temperatures below −13° C. The patient may feel a pricking feeling at first, and feel an area of firmer, pale skin on the cheeks, nose, ears, fingers, or toes. If these parts are numb with cold, the onset of frostbite may not be felt, and will often only be noticed by others. In countries where extreme cold is prevalent, it is usual for complete strangers to stop each other in the street and point it out when they see it. It is important not to rub the affected part nor to apply direct heat in any form. Rapid warming can be harmful; re-warming by close application of body temperature is good treatment, *e.g.,* fingers can be firmly held in the armpit or a warm hand closely applied to an ear or a nose.

THE RESPIRATORY SYSTEM.

INTRODUCTION.

When air is drawn in during the process of breathing, it is brought into very close contact with the blood passing through the lungs. In this way the air we breathe in, which contains 20 per cent oxygen, is confronted with "spent" blood returning from the tissues which contains much less, and oxygen therefore diffuses into the blood from the air. At the same time, the waste gas, carbon dioxide, passes by diffusion in the reverse direction from the blood into the air, because there is much more carbon dioxide in the returning "spent" blood than the tiny amount in the air we breathe. The blood is therefore continually circulating through the lungs and exchanging carbon dioxide for oxygen from the air we breathe in. When we breathe out, we disperse the carbon dioxide into the atmosphere.

When the air enters the nose or mouth, it passes into the windpipe or *trachea*, through the vocal cords in the pharynx. The trachea is held open all the time by rings of cartilage and is lined by a mucus-secreting membrane covered by millions of tiny "hairs" or cilia. These continuously waft a sheet of sticky mucus upwards, which traps any dust or other small particles we may have inhaled, until a collection of this material in the pharynx stimulates us to cough and expel the phlegm, usually to be swallowed. At its lower end, the trachea or windpipe divides into two, the right and left main *bronchus*. Each main bronchial tube enters a lung, one on each side, and proceeds to divide repeatedly within the lung until the air is being carried by more and more smaller and ever smaller tubes called *bronchioles*. There are many millions of these on each side, and each one ends in a collection of very small balloon-like structures —the air sacs or *alveoli*. If you were to cut across a lung and examine the cut surface in a good light, you would see that it is a spongy tissue, with many millions of tiny holes, each one just visible to the naked eye. These are the air sacs. In their walls run the blood capillaries, each one of which is a branch of the vessels carrying "spent" blood from the right side of the heart. At this stage, the blood is only separated from the air in the sacs by the walls of the capillaries and of the air sacs themselves. Both structures are extremely thin, making for easy diffusion of the gases between blood and air.

The action of breathing is accomplished by two muscular mechanisms. One is by the muscles which move the ribs, and the other by the diaphragm, a sheet of muscle which runs across the body, separating the chest cavity from the abdominal cavity. These muscles are all actuated by nerves, just as all other muscles are. Those running to the muscles of breathing are organised by a mechanism in the brain known as the *respiratory centre*. It is this centre—one of the so-called vital centres of the brain—which receives information from many different sources, and translates it into instructions for the breathing mechanism. Thus, when you run for a bus, you will automatically breathe more deeply and more quickly because the respiratory centre has been informed about all the extra carbon dioxide in your blood which has been produced by the exercising leg muscles. Even the conscious instructions involved when you blow a trumpet, inflate a balloon, or during speaking, all pass first to the respiratory centre. It is the death of the cells of this and other vital centres of the brain that is the ultimate cause of death in everyone who dies.

Bronchitis may be acute or chronic. It is an inflammation of the lining mucous membrane of the larger air passages or bronchi, and results in much more secretion than the amount normally produced, mixed with some pus. The acute form is often caused by viruses, with "secondary" infection from bacteria. It may sometimes be caused by irritant gases, like the sulphur dioxide in smog. The chronic, or long-standing form of bronchitis is often associated with *emphysema*, in which the small air sacs of the lung architecture are destroyed or distorted, leaving larger spaces than normal, often surrounded by fibrous scar tissue. Such an arrangement makes the normal gaseous exchange difficult between air and blood. While the exact cause of chronic bronchitis is difficult to discover, because it is such a mixture of

causes, it is mainly associated with older age groups, particularly men, in damp foggy climates like ours in Britain, with polluted town air and especially with smoking. Smoking also makes any existing bronchitis much worse. Bronchitis can cause even more trouble than lung cancer, since instead of dying in a short time, the bronchitic lives for many years in chronic sickness. About 30,000 people die of bronchitis each year. It isn't smart to smoke. Patients cough, and produce varying amounts of sputum, or phlegm. They often wheeze like asthmatics. This may go on for many years before the right side of the heart begins to fail (**P27**). Gradually, during this time, the chest tends to become barrel-shaped. Treatment consists of getting the patient to stop smoking or otherwise contaminating his lungs, preventing infection, particularly during winter months, with germ-killing antibiotics, and breathing exercises. The outlook for chronic bronchitis and emphysema is nevertheless not good, although many patients continue with their disease for many years, provided they take constant care to obey instructions and stop smoking.

Bronchial Asthma is a condition in which the finer air passages become constricted due to an allergic response. In addition, an increased secretion tends to obstruct them and the patient wheezes. In many cases it can be shown that he is allergic to a particular component of dust, or, less commonly, a foodstuff. This is the same sort of thing as occurs in the upper respiratory passages in hay fever, but the effect is on a different, lower part of the respiratory system. Many other cases are due to respiratory infection of some sort, probably combined with an allergy to the bacteria causing it. A predisposition to asthma is often inherited. Once a patient has become asthmatic, his attacks will be triggered off by such additional things as emotional stress, changes in temperature (particularly sudden cold), irritating fumes or smoke, and physical exertion. These are secondary factors, and although much of the treatment is concerned with them, it is unlikely that any of them is a sole cause of the condition. Treatment is directed at the relief of the breathing difficulty and of the wheezing, as well as the control of the causative factors. Many useful drugs are available to dilate the contracted air passages and reduce the obstructing secretions. Asthma in children often gets better as the patient grows up. Asthma is another condition made much worse by smoking.

A tiny living mite about 0·3 millimetres long exists in large numbers in nearly all mattresses and floor dust. This is the cause of much asthma, and in such cases it is often very helpful to vacuum-clean mattresses and floors frequently. For recent advances in treating this disease, *see* **P62**.

Bronchiectasis. In this condition the bronchial air passages are abnormally and permanently dilated, and the normal structure of the walls destroyed. It is thought to be caused by obstructions of the tubes which lead to dilatation of the parts beyond. Secretions accumulate, and since they cannot easily drain away, they become infected. The infection helps to complete the process of destruction of structures in the bronchial wall. The patient has a chronic cough which often produces large quantities of purulent sputum, and there are often recurrent episodes of pneumonia. Diagnosis is made by a special X-ray examination—a bronchogram—in which a material, opaque to X-rays, is dropped into the air passages. This shows up the dilated and distorted tubes. In some cases, where the disease is localised to one part of the lung, it is often a good idea to cut out that portion, and this is particularly true in young people. Vigorous physiotherapy, involving drainage of the lungs by placing the patient in a suitable posture, together with antibiotic drugs for the infection, are other forms of treatment.

Cystic Fibrosis is an inborn disease which affects chiefly the lungs and the digestive system. It is sometimes called *Fibrocystic disease of the Pan-*

creas, and sometimes "Mucoviscidosis". Until it was medically recognised forty years ago, children affected usually died from pneumonia in the first year of life. This, of course, was before antibiotics were available for the treatment of infections. Today, cystic fibrosis is known to be the commonest genetically determined disorder affecting children in Britain. One child in 2,000 receives one of the abnormal genes from each parent. Such a child therefore has a double dose of the harmful gene, and will have the disease from birth. One person in 25 of the general population carries only one of these abnormal genes, and such an individual will not have the disease, but will be a carrier of the abnormal gene. If such a seemingly normal carrier marries another carrier, there is a one in four chance of each of their children being affected. The children, therefore, who actually develop cystic fibrosis have inherited the disease *equally* from both parents, who are carriers, but are themselves unaffected by the disease. Although much has been learned about cystic fibrosis in the past forty years, there remain many unsolved problems, and we still cannot define precisely the biochemical fault which causes it. The prospects for survival into reasonably healthy adult life are steadily improving, but they depend upon early diagnosis and careful management through childhood. In cystic fibrosis most of the damage is caused by the excessive viscidity, or stickiness, of the mucus which is produced in the breathing tubes as a lubricant, and also in the ducts of the pancreatic gland which provides enzymes to help digestion. Being thick and sticky, instead of thin and slimy as in the normal, this mucus tends to block the passages instead of keeping them clear. The pancreatic cells are permanently destroyed. The gland cannot secrete pancreatic enzymes, and the food, especially protein and fat, is not properly absorbed. This deficiency can be compensated fairly well by giving pancreatic extract by mouth with every meal, and by dietary care.

The major clinical problem is in the lungs. The lung passages normally have a thin coating of mucus which is propelled steadily upwards, and is completely renewed in less than one hour. It moves more suddenly on coughing. In cystic fibrosis this upward movement is slowed down and interrupted. There is difficulty in keeping the passages clear, especially when infection with bacteria or viruses greatly increases the amount of mucus. This results in intermittent blocking of the air passages, difficulty in breathing, incomplete use of the lungs, and persistent local pockets of infection. If such infectious processes are not controlled, areas of lung will be destroyed, chronic infection will persist, and multiple lung cavities will develop. These predispose to further infection, interfering with the natural development of the lung—a process not normally complete until halfway through childhood—thus adding to the respiratory problems which the child will face in later life. Unless a correct diagnosis is made and proper treatment instituted before the first serious lung infection has occurred, the resulting lung damage may well be permanent.

Pneumonia. This is an infection of the lung tissue, rather than of the air passages. The lung is the only internal organ which is directly exposed to the air, and since there are germs of all kinds in the air, it is a source of surprise that pneumonia is not a much more common event in all of us. The answer lies, as with all infections, in the fact that it is not simply (or even mainly) bacteria which cause disease, but our own lack of resistance to them. If we allow germs to thrive and multiply by being unhealthy or run down or undernourished, infective disease will occur. If we are fit, the entry of those same harmful germs into the body causes us no inconvenience, unless we are very young, or very old, or unless the invasion of germs is abnormally overwhelming. This helps to explain why pneumonia is so often quoted as a cause of death. In most cases it is merely a terminal event occurring in the elderly sick, whose normal resistance is so far reduced by their illness that they succumb to an invasion which they would normally not notice. There are two main kinds of pneumonia, and in both the air sacs

become filled with inflammatory secretions, making the normally porous lung tissue as solid as liver. In *lobar pneumonia,* a whole segment (or lobe) of the lung becomes solid. In *bronchopneumonia,* areas of lung tissue surrounding the smaller bronchioles become consolidated, leaving normal porous lung tissue in between. Bronchopneumonia is the one which occurs in the rather stagnant lungs of people who are already ill or bedridden. Both forms respond to treatment with the appropriate antibiotics, provided any underlying debility does not interfere with the patient's own resistance. In the terminal bronchopneumonia of fatal illness, it is sometimes considered kinder not to treat the additional pneumonia. *Pleurisy* is a natural complication, and before the days of antibiotic drugs *lung abscess* was very much feared. Another form of pneumonia—*viral pneumonia*—is referred to in **P9(2)**.

Pneumoconiosis. This is a term which refers to a large group of different diseases, all of which are caused by breathing in some form of dust over a very long period of time. It is therefore an occupational hazard of certain trades. We have already mentioned the mechanisms of mucus secretion in the air passages which normally trap small particles from the air, and prevent them reaching the lung. However, in some occupations there is so much dust breathed in over the months and years that these normal barriers are defeated. About a quarter of the earth's crust consists of silicon, in quartz, flint, or sand. *Silicosis* occurs in people who have worked for many years in trades like mining, stone crushing, sandblasting, or metal grinding, who are often breathing silicon dust in high concentration. When the particles arrive in the air sacs, they set up an irritant chemical reaction which produces nodules of scar tissue. Silicosis for some reason predisposes to tuberculosis. Emphysema also occurs and there is a general impairment of respiratory function. Coalminer's pneumoconiosis is similar to silicosis but not identical with it. It is more prevalent in some coalfields than others, owing to the different composition of the dust to which these unfortunate men are daily exposed. It is hoped that modern mining methods will help to reduce this dread disease. Asbestos is a complex silicate of magnesium, calcium, and iron. *Asbestosis* is caused by inhaling its fine fibres. *Berylliosis* is caused by compounds of beryllium, used in the manufacture of fluorescent lamps. *Farmer's lung* is a pneumoconiosis caused by inhaling hay and grain dust, and is similar to *bagassosis* and *byssinosis* caused by sugar cane and cotton dust respectively. The newest pneumoconiosis to be reported is *mushroom worker's lung,* caused by something in the compost in which mushrooms are commercially grown.

Pulmonary Embolism. This catastrophic, yet quite common condition has already been briefly referred to (**P30(1)**). It is a cause of tragic, sudden death in people who have had operations or have given birth to babies some days previously, or who have been bedridden for any other cause. The first event is that the blood in the veins of the legs becomes stagnant, due to the lack of exercise; and together with the tendency to clot which often follows surgery or childbirth, the whole length of a leg vein may be obstructed for twelve inches or more by an elongated clot of blood. This does little harm to the circulation of the leg, since there are plenty of other veins for returning blood to the heart. The danger is that the clot will become dislodged and be swept upwards towards the heart by the flow of returning blood. When this happens it is carried by way of the right auricle and ventricle into the pulmonary vessels which normally carry spent blood to the lungs. Here, for the first time, it enters vessels which are getting smaller as they divide, and it then impacts in the main pulmonary artery. The patient, who may have been recovering very well, suddenly collapses and not unusually dies there and then. At autopsy a long coiled-up mass of clot is found obstructing the pulmonary vessels. It often can be seen to form a cast of the leg vein and even bears the marks of the small venous valves which are present at its site of origin. With the dramatic advances being made in chest surgery, it is now sometimes possible in selected cases to operate to remove the clot. Success clearly depends on the patient's surviving long enough to be taken to the operating theatre for the major operation of *pulmonary embolectomy.* Three quarters of all cases of pulmonary embolism die within two hours, and therefore the best hope would be to prevent the occurrence altogether. This is not at present possible, but clotting in leg veins can be discouraged by early exercise following surgery and childbirth. Patients often resent having to get up the next day because it is so uncomfortable. Herein, however, lies their best hope of avoiding pulmonary embolism.

Haemoptysis. This means coughing up blood or blood-stained material. It must be distinguished from *haematemesis*, in which the blood is vomited from the stomach. It must always be taken seriously because of the underlying lung disease which may be present. No one who coughs up blood, in however small a quantity, should neglect to inform their doctor so that its source can be determined. Haemoptysis occurs in a variety of lung disease, some of which is not serious but much of which must be treated immediately if it is not to become so. This is a suitable place to repeat our general rule that you should see your doctor without delay if you have any unexplained bleeding from any part of the body, however well you feel. And this includes haemoptysis.

Fat Embolism. Liquid fat sometimes enters the bloodstream following extensive crush injuries to soft tissue and bone. It splits up into millions of small globules which are carried to the lungs, and impact in small blood vessels there, producing obstruction of the lung circulation and consequent difficulties in breathing.

Lung Cancer. This is one of the commonest, nastiest and most incurable forms of cancer which can occur. It is also probably the easiest to prevent. Each year over 32,000 people die of lung cancer in Great Britain, all but 5,000 of them men. Every year the toll goes on. There has been no reasonable doubt for several years now that it is associated with cigarette smoking, and the evidence is overwhelming. However, in spite of this certain knowledge, smoking continues to increase, and every year there are more and more people dying unpleasantly of lung cancer. It seems that nothing the health authorities can do is able to stop it. Intensive campaigns of public advertising of the dangers, and well organised instruction in schools have so far made no impression whatever on the smoking habits even of people who accept the evidence. The only group of people who are known to have stopped smoking are British doctors, very many of whom have given it up, and it is easy to show that giving it up has saved them from the disease. Their colleagues who have not done so have continued to die. Undoubtedly a large factor contributing to the failure of anti-smoking propaganda is the enormous expenditure by the tobacco manufacturers on very clever advertising, amounting to many millions of pounds each year. Moreover they spend a pitiful fraction of this amount on their own research into the harmful effects of their own product, which has so far discovered nothing which was not already known by research doctors many years ago. Another problem is that it takes a number of years to get cancer. It is not like an infectious disease which is caught a few days after exposure to the bacteria concerned. It may be fifteen or twenty years before the cancer begins, and many smokers are apparently unwilling to look so far ahead. Furthermore, not everyone who smokes dies this way; and so a smoker can gamble with his life and hope it will not be him. The present writer once had to perform a series of post-mortem examinations on people who died of lung cancer, and this helped him to stop smoking completely, having smoked more than twenty cigarettes a day for several years. Not everyone can have this incentive. The main

encouragement to smoke probably comes from other people. Schoolboys are easily impressed when their teachers and parents stop smoking. They are not likely to fear the habit when these same people smoke openly. The smoking doctor is also a powerful stimulus to people to carry on smoking.

Lung cancer grows in the wall of a main bronchial air passage. If it grows inwards it can obstruct the air way, choking that part of the lung it is supplying with air. This causes collapse and infection of the lung and may lead to *lung abscess.* The patient will then cough up blood-stained infected and purulent material. Such a case is comparatively lucky, since the disease declares itself early by producing symptoms. In others, the lump may grow outwards into the surrounding lung and produce no symptoms at all in the early stages. Indeed, it may spread to other parts of the body, like brain or bone or liver before causing any trouble to the patient. If this happens he may go to his doctor because of fits, changes of personality, or fracture, only to discover that the origin of the trouble is in the lung.

The chances of cure are negligible, although much can be done to relieve the pain and suffering of the last stages of the illness. Not more than one in twenty patients is alive two years after it is first diagnosed. Surgery, by removing the lung, and irradiation of the growth are the standard palliative treatment. It is not the practice of the Medical Section to alarm the reader unnecessarily, but if only a few are induced to stop giving themselves such a horrible disease, then writing in this way will have been justified.

Secondary Cancer of the Lung. In nearly all forms of cancer, the big problem is that it spreads to other parts of the body. If this were not so it could be eradicated by surgical removal more often than it is. One common way in which it spreads from any part of the body is by entering the bloodstream and being carried as clumps of living cancer cells to distant parts. When these come to rest in smaller blood vessels, they begin to grow and colonise the new environment. Such new colonies are called *secondary deposits* or *metastases.* It so happens that all veins (except portal veins of the liver) lead to the right heart and thence directly to the lungs, and for this reason the lungs are a very common site of *secondary* cancer, which may have begun in the bowel, or breast, or indeed anywhere else in the body. Other common sites of secondary, blood-borne cancer are the brain, liver, bone marrow, and kidney, since all of them have an abundant blood supply, and there is therefore a high chance of the travelling cells arriving there. Secondary cancer of the lung usually consists of several lumps scattered throughout the lung. Lung cancer itself is usually only one growth. One of the main reasons for the success of early diagnosis is that treatment may be possible before blood-borne and other means of spread have occurred. Unfortunately, in the case of primary cancer of the lung, even early diagnosis is of little avail, but in many other common cancers permanent cure is possible if treatment is begun early enough.

Pleurisy. The chest is lined by one layer of a thin membrane called the *pleura.* The lungs are covered and enclosed by a second, continuous layer of this same membrane. When the lungs move during respiration, the pleura covering the lungs rubs against the pleura lining the chest, lubricated by a very thin layer of pleural fluid separating the two pleura. Whenever the pleural surface becomes inflamed, this is known as *pleurisy.* It is nearly always due to inflammatory disease of the adjoining lung, and is therefore not strictly a disease in its own right. For example, pneumonia, tuberculosis, lung cancer, or a lung infarct (**P30(2)**) will produce a pleurisy if the area of diseased lung adjoins the lung surface. Sometimes the area of inflamed inner pleura will tend to stick to its outer layer or rub painfully against it, producing a sharp pain when the patient breathes. Sometimes a large effusion of fluid is produced which separates the two layers and collapses the lung by occupying space in the chest which the lung should be occupying. This latter is more usual in tuberculosis or cancer.

The lung can be collapsed by the entry of anything between the normally adjacent layers of pleura. For example, air can be introduced, either deliberately to rest the lung in tuberculosis, or by accidental penetrating wounds of the chest wall, or by accidental rupture of the emphysematous lung (*q.v.*). This condition is called *pneumothorax* or "air in the chest." Bleeding into the cavity between the pleura is called *haemothorax*.

THE DIGESTIVE TRACT AND LARGE INTESTINE.

INTRODUCTION.

The digestive tract consists of the mouth, pharynx, oesophagus (or gullet), stomach, small intestine, large intestine (or colon), rectum, and anus. The small intestine is very long, and is subdivided into the duodenum, jejunum, and ileum. It ends at the junction of the ileum with the caecum, where there is a small blind side-tube, the appendix. The caecum leads into the colon. The whole tract has two main mechanical functions and two main biochemical ones. Mechanically, food has to be chewed in the mouth and further minced up by muscular squeezing, mainly by the stomach. It has also to be propelled along by an orderly series of squeezing movements known as *peristalsis*. While it is still in the digestive tract, food has to be digested. That is to say, it has to be broken down chemically into suitable materials for absorption into the system, and secondly, it has to be absorbed across the wall of the intestine into the blood stream, itself a highly complex biochemical process. The blood stream it now enters is a special part of the circulation, the "portal" system, which travels directly to the liver without first passing to the heart. In the liver the broken-down foods are processed and issued in their new form into the general, or "systemic" circulation, by which they are finally carried to all the tissues of the body.

As the food passes along the digestive tract (or, as it is sometimes called, the alimentary canal), it is mixed with various secretions which are either made in the wall of the tract, or by organs outside the wall connected to the main pathway by small tubes. Examples of the latter are bile, manufactured by the liver and sent into the duodenum through the bile ducts; and pancreatic juice, which comes from the pancreas down the pancreatic ducts, also into the duodenum. These secretions are either digestive juices concerned with splitting up the foodstuffs so that they can be absorbed, or they have a lubricant so that the gut contents slide along easily under the influence of peristalsis. Roughly speaking, it may be said that digestive juices give place to lubricant secretions at the junction between the small and large intestine.

The constituents of the diet are dealt with in a later section. The principal classes with whose digestion we are now concerned are carbohydrates, proteins, and fats.

Carbohydrates are sugars and starches. There are many sugars, which may exist alone, in pairs, or with lots of them stuck together. Alone they are such things as glucose or fructose. Common table sugar is a substance called sucrose, formed by sticking one glucose molecule to one fructose molecule. Starch is lots of glucose molecules all stuck together. Digestion of carbohydrates consists of splitting up sugars and starch into single sugars like glucose, since only single sugars can be absorbed into the system. The splitting is done by digestive *enzymes* which are found in the juices secreted into the digestive tract. Sugar-splitters are found in the saliva of the mouth, in the pancreatic juice of the duodenum, and in the duodenum's own juice from its own wall. On the face of it, you might think it would be better to eat glucose which needs no digestion and can be absorbed in

this form, than to eat starch which has first to be split; and so a lot of money has been made out of a gullible public by the sale of glucose drinks and powder. In fact digesting starch is no problem whatever, even for the sick, who can obtain their carbohydrate energy just as easily (and much more cheaply) from potatoes as from expensive glucose. The end result of eating both is the same. The starch-splitting enzyme in saliva is mixed with the food as it is chewed, and it is therefore probably a good idea to chew it well. However, even if the food is bolted it does not seem to matter very much. People without teeth (neither their own nor dentures) seem to digest their carbohydrate quite well, presumably by means of their pancreatic juice at a later stage.

Proteins, which are found in meat, cheese, and eggs, have very large molecules consisting of lots of small ones strung together. Unlike starch, in which all the component glucose molecules are identical, the amino acids of which proteins are composed come in many different types. They all contain nitrogen, and there are about twenty-seven varieties. One protein differs from another in the proportions of the mixture and the order in which they are stuck together. Only single amino acids can be absorbed from the food, and so protein digestion again consists of splitting the material down into its building bricks. There is a strong protein splitting enzyme in the gastric (or stomach) juice called pepsin, whose job it is to split the long amino-acid chains into shorter chains. Several other protein-splitters in the duodenal and pancreatic juice contrive to break the smaller chains into individual amino acids which are then absorbed and sent to the liver for processing.

Fats mainly consist of glycerol to which are attached three fatty acid molecules for each molecule of glycerol. An enzyme in pancreatic juice splits the fatty acids off the glycerol, but would have some difficulty penetrating the globules of fat without the help of bile. One of the constituents of bile (bile salts) has detergent properties like washing-up powder and breaks the fat globules up into a very fine suspension so that the enzyme can get at the fat. Some fat particles of this size can even be absorbed as such, without preliminary splitting.

The processes by which all these enzymic secretions are produced are very finely controlled. They are very expensive to make in terms of energy and raw materials, and so it would be very wasteful to produce them all the time, even when there was no food to digest. And so the body has some very well designed automatic arrangements for sampling the foods as they are eaten and passed on, which ensure that exactly the right kind of juice is waiting in every part of the digestive tract for whatever food arrives. As soon as the food is digested the supply of enzymes is automatically switched off, so that there is very little waste of precious materials. It is, of course, beyond the scope of this account to describe the control mechanisms. Suffice it to say that they are operated partly by nerve reflexes which signal the imminent arrival of food, and partly by special hormones produced in various parts of the gut wall. The best secretion is affected even by psychological factors, so that pleasant company and surroundings, attractive appearance of the food, and an eager anticipation of it all make for good digestion and good health. These psychological factors are all capable of proper scientific investigation and proof. The poor health of those who habitually and irregularly bolt unpalatable food is probably due to such factors as these. So is the failure of appetite in the depressed, the anxious adult, or the scolded child.

Nearly all the digestion which has been described occurs in the stomach and upper part of the small intestine (the duodenum, jejunum, and upper ileum). Almost all absorption of the products of digestion occurs in the small intestine which is long and intricately folded to give it a large surface area for this purpose. The colon, or large intestine, is adapted for conserving water, by removing it from the residual waste material. This has then to be eliminated, and being rather dry its passage has to be lubricated by suitable secretions of mucus.

Constipation.

Here, perhaps we had better mention the morbid question of constipation, about which so many people are obsessed and hold such pronounced views. First of all, what is it? For some people it is entirely normal only to pass motions about once or twice a week. For others the normal frequency is once or twice a day. What is abnormal? The answer is that the only thing worth worrying about is only pronounced change of bowel habit, particularly in middle-aged and older people. By a change is meant a change from that individual person's normal routine. Such a pronounced change—either in the direction of constipation or diarrhoea—is worth consulting your doctor about if it persists for more than a week or two. Otherwise, forget your bowels and leave them to work naturally as they know best. Many believe that constipation is the root of all evil, that it causes a mysterious condition known to them (although, alas, not to doctors) as "auto-intoxication." Sedulously fostered by the manufacturers of patent medicines, their beliefs range from the notion that headaches, spotty skin, muddy skin, and tiredness are caused by constipation, to the more extreme idea that the whole system is being poisoned and that, if the bowels do not work, the individual will shortly die. Of course, all this is the merest rubbish; for, as Professor Samson Wright, whose *Applied Physiology* is one of the most famous of medical text-books, has pointed out, there is no such thing as absorption of poisonous products from the bowel. There is no such thing as "auto-intoxication." "The symptoms of constipation," he writes, "are largely due to distension and mechanical irritation of the rectum." It has been shown that an enema removes these symptoms *immediately*, which would not be the case if they were due to poisons in the blood, and exactly the same symptoms can be produced by packing the rectum with cotton-wool. Wright mentions the case of a man who went for just over a year without bowel motion, and at the end of that time, although his abdomen was distended and he felt some discomfort, he was not noticeably ill. Needless to say, telling these facts to the purgative addict will only make him annoyed, but it is as well to note that if no known diseases are due to constipation (although constipation may be a symptom of another disease), the regular use of purgatives *can* cause disease.

Constipation should be treated first by diet containing plenty of roughage—bran and oatmeal are excellent—plenty of stewed and fresh fruits, and at least 1¼ litres of fluid should be taken daily. Failing that, one of the best things to take is a proprietary product prepared from senna pods. Never to be taken regularly are liquid paraffin, castor oil, preparations of aloes, Epsom salts, and all the other dreadful stuff that people swill down.

Oesophagus.

The oesophagus, or gullet, is more than a simple tube for taking the food from the mouth to the stomach. It is normally closed except when swallowing, and the act of swallowing is very complicated. When the material to be swallowed arrives in the back of the throat there is an automatic mechanism which opens the top end of the oesophagus to receive it, and from then onwards everything happens automatically. The next portion of the tube opens and the top closes strongly, so that the food (or drink) is propelled forcibly down the next segment. Then the part below this relaxes and the material is squeezed further downwards and so on until it arrives in the stomach. This squeezing (or milking) action is akin to the action known as peristalsis which propels contents in other parts of the gut. Thus when you see someone swallowing a glass of beer very quickly in warm weather, it is not going "down the hatch" under the influence of gravity, however much it may look like it. It is perfectly possible to swallow the same, or any other liquid, standing on your head. Getting into that position is the only difficult part. Sometimes this complicated swallowing mechanism gets out of order, leading to difficulties of swallowing, or *dysphagia*.

Another disorder known as *hiatus hernia* occurs at the lower end of the oesophagus as it meets the stomach. At this point the oesophagus has to pass through the diaphragm, the sheet of muscle which separates the chest from the abdomen. The muscular fibres of the diaphragm are normally arranged in a ring around the oesophagus. These help to keep the lower end shut, so that the acid contents of the stomach do not regurgitate upwards, causing inflammation (*oesophagitis*) or heartburn. A hiatus hernia is when muscle fibres get slack, and the upper end of the stomach can even slide upwards into the chest. People with hiatus hernia get heartburn after meals, and particularly when they bend down or lie down. Except for very severe forms, which need surgical repair, the treatment is to eat less at a time, reduce the acidity with a suitable antacid and reduce weight so that the weight of the abdomen does not press upwards so much. The other disease of the oesophagus, quite unrelated to the above, is *cancer of the oesophagus*, the cause of which is still unknown in most cases. When cancer occurs in the wall of any tube, it will often encircle the tube and gradually narrow the way through. This is what happens in the oesophagus, leading to difficulty in swallowing, particularly solids. It is a condition usually, of rather elderly men, although it is sometimes associated with a special form of severe anaemia in women. Treatment is in some way to keep the passage open, either by transplanting a new tube, or more usually, by removing the constricted piece and joining up the remainder.

The Stomach and Duodenum.

By far the commonest diseases of the stomach and duodenum are *gastric ulcer* and *duodenal ulcer*. They are actually the same condition in two different sites and are often classed together as *peptic ulcer* or *acid-peptic disease*. The ulcers, which are rather like sores on the lining of the stomach or duodenum, may be "acute" or "chronic." Acute ulcers tend to be small and there are often several of them. Chronic ulcers are usually single. They may be small, or they may be several centimetres across. Chronic ulcers smoulder for months and even years, like a sore which will not heal, and a great deal of scar tissue forms in their depths. Thus they may in time erode their way right through the wall of the stomach, destroying all its layers, and begin to eat into surrounding structures like the pancreas or liver. The fact that they do not perforate more frequently is due to all the fibrous scar tissue which is formed during the slow eroding process. Healing of such a destructive ulcer is nevertheless common, and the great problem is how to help the natural healing process to win against the ulcer's tendency to erode. Better still would be to discover the cause, and prevent it happening in the first place. This extremely common affliction is confined to the human species and has been known since the earliest times. It does not vary very much with diet or with social class. Although occurring at all ages, it usually begins between the ages of twenty and forty, and is most commonly found in men between forty-five and fifty-five. Gastric ulcer is four times, and duodenal ulcer ten times more common in men than in women. It is always due to an inability of the lining to stand up to the normal digestive activity of the stomach contents. These are normally acid and contain a powerful enzyme for digesting proteins. Again it is perhaps more surprising that we all do not digest our own stomachs, rather than that some unfortunate people do digest small areas slowly. In certain abnormal conditions when the stomach stops making acid, ulcers always heal. However, in some ulcers occur without excessive secretion of acid and many heal without the acid being neutralised with antacids. All this points to the main trouble being in the response of the lining to acid rather than to the acid itself. Nevertheless, the most effective treatment at present known involves regulating gastric secretion, and particularly its acidity. It is also known that peptic ulcers are more common in people whose occupations involve administrative and professional responsibility, competitive effort and nervous tension, long periods of anxiety or frustration. Presumably the higher nervous system influences these events by the same nerves, which normally help to control secretion.

The main symptom of peptic ulcer is pain, and this usually responds well to proper doses of antacids. Many different varieties are available and a lot of money is made from selling them. When indigestion persists for longer than a few days it is always better to see your doctor so that a proper diagnosis can be made and the best remedies begun. Many other causes exist for similar pains, and you should not try to make the diagnosis yourself. It may be necessary to analyse your gastric secretions in the hospital laboratory. Almost certainly you will have a special X-ray examination, and since the stomach cannot easily be seen on a normal X-ray, they will have to show it up by making you drink a white material containing barium. This will be seen as a silhouette of the stomach and duodenal contents. Searching for an ulcer this way is a highly skilled matter and is performed by doctors specially trained in radiology.

Until recently, no drugs capable of influencing the course of peptic ulcer in any significant manner were available and the physician had to rely on general measures, such as rest, diet and the administration of antacids to relieve pain and discomfort; episodes of acute haemorrhage were not uncommon and required surgical intervention if life were threatened.

However, recent advances in our knowledge of gastric and duodenal pathology have led to the development of at least two therapeutic agents of which the newest, *cimetidine*, is highly effective. Developments in fibre-optic technology have contributed greatly to progress in peptic ulcer treatment. The gastro-enterologist can now pass a *flexible* instrument, the *gastroduodenal endoscope* (the gastroscope is a *rigid* tube), under mild sedation through the patient's gullet and into the stomach and duodenum and view the lesions directly. Once an ulcer is diagnosed, the time has come to stop treating yourself with antacids from the chemist's counter, and to take the ones your doctor decides are best. Smoking should be stopped by ulcer patients (as, indeed, by everyone else, but that is another matter) because it inhibits healing. Alcohol tends to increase acid secretion and should be avoided. It is also *extremely important* to avoid taking any form of aspirin, even in quite small amounts, since this can lead to very serious bleeding from the ulcer. The ulcer patient should be warned that hundreds of proprietary preparations contain aspirin and all of them are dangerous for him. Search for the formula in small print on the label before taking any remedy, looking particularly for acetyl salicylic acid—the correct name for aspirin. Even some widely sold "hang-over" remedies which are sold for "upset-stomach" contain large quantities of aspirin. Some of the patients with "upset stomach" are, of course, ulcer patients, and some even die of haemorrhage following the ingestion of aspirin.

The main complications of peptic ulcer are bleeding, perforation, and a narrowing of the pylorus, or lower part, known as *pyloric stenosis*. Bleeding is caused by the eroding ulcer eating away at one of the many blood vessels in the stomach or duodenal wall. It leads to the passing of "altered" blood in the stool (*melaena*), or to the vomiting of blood (*haematemesis*). When the initial bleeding occurs, the patient may feel suddenly faint, and a little later will notice the black, tarry colour of his stool. This is sometimes confused with a similiar colour when the patient is taking iron. Peptic ulcer is not the only cause of this very serious haemorrhage, which constitutes a hospital emergency whatever its cause. The treatment, like that of every large haemorrhage, is blood transfusion which must be continued until the bleeding stops, or until the patient is sufficiently fit for surgery, should that be deemed necessary. Perforation is perhaps the most serious complication of peptic ulcer, leading to the spilling of stomach contents within the abdominal cavity. Treatment is invariably surgical, either the closure of the perforation or the partial removal of the stomach.

Surgical removal of part of the stomach is often the only way to treat a peptic ulcer which has had its chance to heal in other ways. It is tempting for the patient to "have it out and done with," but the time for surgery is a matter of fine judgment. So many ulcers heal by medical means if you give them a chance, and operations are for those which persistently refuse, or which become complicated.

Stomach Cancer. The stomach is a fairly common site for primary cancer. There is no known reason for this, and it is particularly important to stress that we know of no connection whatever between the peptic ulcers which have just been discussed and cancer. Stomach cancer used to be the commonest cancer of men, but the current rise of lung cancer has pushed it into second place. There are some strange geographical differences in its distribution. For example, it is much commoner in Japan and Scandinavia than in England or the U.S.A. It is difficult to see any reason for this in dietary habits. In Wales it causes three times as many deaths as in South-East England. All this is very puzzling, as is so much of our information about cancer generally. One of the main problems with stomach cancer is that it often causes the patient no inconvenience and thus produces no symptoms of note until the disease is far advanced and it is difficult to do much. Treatment is by surgical removal of the growth, and even in the most advanced cases a great deal can often be done to make the patient more comfortable.

The Small Intestine.

The small intestine runs from the stomach to the caecum and comprises the duodenum, jejunum, and ileum in that order. On a more cheerful note it may be remarked that it is very rarely the site of cancer. Its main problems arise in connection with defects in absorption mechanisms, with obstructions, and with a strange inflammatory condition known as *regional enteritis*. Most obstructions are due not to blockages of the tube, but to failures of peristaltic propulsion, the process which is briefly described above under "oesophagus." Such a failure is called *ileus*. When peristalsis stops for any reason, the result is severe dehydration and loss of important chemicals like sodium and chloride from the body. This is because about 9 litres of fluid enter the small intestine each day in the form of digestive juices, and all of this has to be pushed onwards to be reabsorbed into the system at lower levels. If peristalsis fails, this bulk of fluid remains in the small intestine, or is vomited. In both cases it is lost to the body itself, leading to serious dehydration and illness. Treatment is by very careful replacement by transfusion of the fluid and the chemicals lost, and by removal of the trapped fluid within the intestine through a tube threaded down through the mouth.

Regional enteritis or *ileitis* is sometimes known as *Crohn's disease*. It is a very mysterious condition in which the normally supple wall of the small intestine becomes inflamed and gradually replaced by thick fibrous scar tissue, so that it looks and feels like a thick garden hose. Loops of inflamed gut stick together, and channels open between them, and if the disease progresses a mass of adherent, thickened intestine results to which everything in the neighbourhood also adheres. However, for some unknown reason some cases do not progress downhill in this way and get better spontaneously. Surgical treatment is necessary for the majority, however, particularly those with advanced disease leading to complications such as obstruction or perforation. Sometimes an early case can be resolved by cutting out the length of affected gut, although recurrences are unfortunately common.

Appendicitis. This must be one of the best-known surgical diseases of the intestinal tract.

The appendix is a narrow, blind-ended side tube attached to the caecum near the end of the small intestine. Appendicitis is when it becomes obstructed, or infected, or both. From its position it is almost predictable that it will get obstructed sooner or later by pieces of faecal matter which pass its entrance and which are normally infected. The surprising thing is that it does not happen more often. Once this has occurred, however, a closed abscess forms, and as the abscess distends the appendix, it first weakens its wall, making it gangrenous, and then bursts into the abdominal cavity causing *peritonitis* (see later). It would be useless and misleading to describe the symptoms of acute appendicitis in detail, since it is difficult even for experienced doctors to distinguish them from those of several other conditions. Suffice it to say that any severe, persisting pain in the abdomen, whether continuous or intermittent, whether associated with diarrhoea or not, should lead the sufferer to a doctor for a quick diagnosis. Germ-killing antibiotics are useless against appendicitis, and any laxative is extremely dangerous as it may cause an acutely inflamed appendix to perforate.

The Large Intestine or Colon.

The two main serious diseases of the colon are ulcerative colitis and cancer in its various forms. *Ulcerative colitis* is yet another mysterious disease in which severe ulceration of the lining of the colon gives rise most frequently to diarrhoea with the passage of blood and mucus. In fact it can be like dysentery, and it has often been considered to be due to some form of infection. Unfortunately no particular germ can routinely be found in these cases, and the situation is endlessly confused by the presence in the normal bowel of lots of different germs anyway. Nevertheless the ulcerated lining of the bowel certainly does get infected by the germs normally present, and this makes the disease worse. Therefore germ-killing antibiotics are often helpful in alleviating symptoms and can lead to an earlier settling down of the condition, although not to a cure. It has long been known that certain kinds of psychological upset are often associated, but here again the disease is so unpleasant for the sufferer that he is to be forgiven some despondency as a result of, rather than as a cause of, his troubles. It is also suspected that ulcerative colitis may be an auto-immune disease; that is it may represent rejection by the patient of his own colonic lining in a manner somewhat comparable to the tissue rejection which often follows organ transplantation. Some of the more alarming complications are perforation through the wall of the ulcerated bowel, and sometimes massive haemorrhage occurs. The mainstay of medical treatment is the drug *sulphasalazine* together with dietary measures and the occasional use of other drugs to minimise symptoms. Surgery may be required to relieve obstruction, deal with perforation, remove chronically affected parts of the bowel, etc.

Cancer of the Colon and Rectum. This is another very common form of cancer, which can often be completely cured by surgical removal of the growth provided it is caught in the early stages before it has spread. The commonest symptom is a change in bowel habit, either towards constipation or, more often, towards diarrhoea, in the second half of life. There may be rectal bleeding, or the passage of mucus, and there may be abdominal pain. We cannot too often repeat that any such change of bowel habit, or any unexplained bleeding from any site should lead the patient promptly to his doctor.

Diverticulitis. Some people have small pockets or sacs in the wall of the colon known as diverticula. A minority of these sometimes get inflamed, and this is *diverticulitis.* Occasionally perforation occurs.

Hernia or Rupture. This is a condition in which abdominal contents, usually a loop of intestine, protrude forwards through the muscular wall of the abdomen. The wall consists of a sheet of muscle fibres running in several directions. They normally become tense when we cough, or strain, or in getting up from a recumbent position. There are places in the groin on each side where there is a way through the muscle for the spermatic cord in the male. In many men a weakness can arise at this point, and if it persists, the way through may enlarge and allow loops of bowel to emerge from behind the muscle sheet to appear as a lump under the skin of the groin. On relaxation the lump can be made to disappear by pushing the contents back the way they came; and they will re-emerge when the patient strains. This is an extremely common complaint in men, and it should be treated by an operation in which the muscle wall is repaired. Some men, however, neglect to have their rupture treated until one day it proceeds to "strangulate." This is the term used when the muscle tightens around the neck of the protruding loop of bowel, cutting off its blood supply. From then onwards the loop becomes gangrenous and the intestine is obstructed by having a part of itself nipped outside the abdominal wall. The patient is in severe pain, vomits continuously, and quickly is liable to get into such a poor condition that surgical relief is difficult. It is therefore a surgical emergency, and it would have been better to have had the relatively simple repair operation earlier and at leisure. Hernia in the region of the groin is of two types: *inguinal hernia* and *femoral hernia*, the difference between them being technical and of no consequence to the patient. They nearly always occur in men. Other types of hernia less frequently occur in both sexes. *Incisional hernia* is when the muscle wall has been weakened at the site of an old abdominal operation and has failed to heal properly. *Umbilical hernia* occurs owing to the natural weakness of the abdominal wall at the navel, and is so common in babies as to be almost normal. When a baby cries and thereby puts a strain on his abdominal wall, a lump often appears in the region of the navel, and this can be very alarming for the parents. They should of course show it to their doctor who will nearly always be able to reassure them. It is self-healing without operation in the majority of cases.

Peritonitis. The cavity of the abdomen in which the intestines and other organs lie is called the peritoneal cavity, and it is lined by a thin membrane called the peritoneum. When this becomes inflamed the condition is a serious one and is called *peritonitis*. Inflammation may be bacterial, as occurs following a burst appendix and the spillage of bacteria and pus in the cavity. It may be a sterile peritonitis as often follows perforation of a peptic ulcer, when the inflammation is caused by the acid contents of the stomach. It is always very dangerous, probably because of the large surface area afforded by the peritoneum for the absorption of inflammatory toxins.

Haemorrhoids are simply varicose veins in the rectal and anal regions. They are very common, and are caused probably in about equal degrees by inherited weakness of the veins, strain such as heavy lifting, and constipation (this is one of the very few conditions in which constipation may do some damage, due to the mechanical pressure of hardened faeces in the rectum on the veins). Pregnant women are liable to develop haemorrhoids or "*piles,*" as they are commonly called, owing to the pressure of the baby's head in the pelvis. Haemorrhoids may be external or internal, the former being in the anal region below the sphincter, the latter in the rectum; the two usually go together. There may be no symptoms, but the veins are liable to bleed, to get thrombosed (*i.e.,* a clot forms within) or to become infected. When clotting or infection occurs the piles enlarge and tend to be pushed out through the anus during defaecation, when they form extremely painful external swellings. Treatment in simple cases may be by the use of suppositories—cones of a firm grease containing suitable medicaments which are inserted in the rectum—in other cases the veins may be injected, as with varicose veins of the leg, in order to close them, but when there is much bleeding, thrombosis, infection, or interference with bowel movements they should be removed surgically.

THE LIVER.

The liver is the largest organ and has such a wide variety of known functions (to say nothing of the unknown) that it is also one of the most complicated. Nearly all of its functions are biochemical, and it is often called the laboratory of the body. Medical students, when asked to enumerate the functions of the liver, usually stick at about twenty-five, nearly all of them to do with general metabolism: that is the biochemical processing of substances taking part in structure or as body fuel. For example, the liver makes proteins from the amino-acids absorbed from the gut, and breaks down amino-acids and manufactures a waste product (urea) from them. It stores carbohydrates as glycogen, and conducts many of the processes necessary to turn carbohydrates into energy. It manufactures prothrombin with the help of vitamin K, and this is essential for blood clotting. It makes bile and secretes it into the gall bladder and bile ducts (see later). The three main constituents of bile (cholesterol, bile pigment or bilirubin, and bile acids) all have to be processed, or metabolised, in the liver during the production of bile. Vitamin B_{12} and iron are also stored and dealt with there, and these are involved in preventing various forms of anaemia (q.v.); and in addition to all these things the liver is the place where harmful substances, both from within the body and from outside it, are dealt with and rendered harmless. This last function of "detoxication" is often accomplished by making the offending molecules suitable for rapid excretion by the kidneys, or by altering their chemical shape to make them harmless.

Nearly all of these very different things are done by one single type of cell: the liver cell, and it is one of the remarkable features of the design that this cell can be so versatile. There also have to be some very efficient transport systems in the liver, in addition to the usual blood supply and venous drainage possessed by all other tissues.

One of these is the "portal venous system." Whenever a substance is absorbed across the gut wall from any part of the intestine into the interior of the body it enters the special draining blood vessels of the portal system, which are arranged throughout the length of the digestive tract. All these veins eventually unite in the main portal vein which enters the liver. Everything absorbed from the gut is therefore taken first to the liver to be processed. After this the products are carried away from the liver in the ordinary veins to the heart, and are distributed to the rest of the body by the arterial system. The liver has arteries of its own by which it receives oxygen and nutriment like any other tissue. The fourth transport system collects the bile as it is formed within the liver and delivers it to the gall bladder and bile ducts, which eventually drain it into the duodenum.

Portal Hypertension means high blood pressure in the portal venous system, and is the usual accompaniment to *cirrhosis* (see later). When the terminations of the portal veins in the liver are strangled and obstructed by cirrhotic disease, this tends to blow them up, or dilate them with blood. There is a natural escape route for the portal blood where the lower end of the oesophagus or gullet joins the upper end of the stomach. At this place some of the portal veins draining the stomach are connected with the ordinary veins draining the oesophagus so that when pressure rises in the portal system, blood tends to be diverted into these connecting veins, and they in turn become dilated, or varicose. Trouble begins when these dilated connecting veins, which bulge inwards into the oesophagus, are damaged by food particles passing across them and bleed severely into the stomach. The patient vomits large quantities of blood (*haematemesis*) or passes tarry altered blood in the stool (*melaena*). The other main cause of these is the bleeding which occasionally accompanies peptic ulcer (q.v.).

A second complication of portal hypertension (and hence of cirrhosis) is *ascites*, in which large amounts of a lymph-like fluid accumulate in the abdominal cavity. The fluid contains a great deal of precious protein and salt which is lost to the body economy. Ascites also sometimes accompanies cancerous deposits in the abdomen.

Jaundice means being yellow because there is too much yellow bile pigment circulating in the blood, and there are three main possible causes for this. The term "yellow jaundice," like "gastric stomach" is therefore unnecessarily redundant: there is no other kind.

Bile pigment comes from broken-down red blood cells, which normally come to the end of their time after existing for about 120 days. The breakdown products of red cells can always be found in the blood of normal people, but there is normally insufficient colour to show. Abnormal amounts of colour build up quite logically in any of the following three circumstances:

(1) If too many red cells are being destroyed and even the normal liver cannot deal with the amount of bile pigment produced, it piles up in the blood, and *haemolytic jaundice* is the result. The expression simply means jaundice due to (abnormally large) red-cell destruction.

(2) If the liver cells are themselves sick and unable to cope even with the normal amounts of pigment from normal red-cell destruction. Here too the pigment will pile up and cause *hepatocellular jaundice*, or liver-cell jaundice.

(3) If the bile ducts carrying bile away from the liver are blocked, then bile will pile up behind the blockage and re-enter the blood stream, causing *obstructive jaundice*. In this case the rate of red-cell breakdown is normal, and the liver cells are normal: at least for a time.

It is enormously important for the treatment of jaundice for the doctor to diagnose its type correctly, since the treatment varies from surgical relief of obstruction to the medical treatment of viral infection or of excess red-cell destruction. The so-called differential diagnosis of jaundice is often exceptionally difficult, and sometimes requires some very sophisticated laboratory tests and X-rays. At other times it is extremely easy and is obvious from a cursory glance at the urine and the stool. In any case all jaundice is a highly technical matter for the doctor who must be consulted early.

There is a special jaundice of newborn babies which resembles haemolytic jaundice and can occasionally have serious consequences for the developing brain (*kernicterus*) if it is allowed to become too severe. When this is threatened, steps are taken to reduce the level of circulating bile pigment by replacement of the baby's blood or by other means.

The commonest cause of hepatocellular jaundice is infective or viral hepatitis. Obstructive jaundice is usually due either to blockage by gallstones (q.v.) or by a lump pressing on the bile ducts from an adjacent cancer. This can often be quite satisfactorily relieved by surgery.

Infective Hepatitis. There is a group of disorders affecting the liver which are caused by viruses. The incubation period is often very long, and the sickness and other debility caused is often quite severe and prolonged. One variety, known as serum sickness, is now much less common than a few years ago. It used to be transmitted by using the same needle for injections into several different people, or from transfusing contaminated blood. A greater awareness of the problem, and the use of disposable needles and syringes has cut down the incidence.

Cirrhosis. There are many different kinds of cirrhosis, the commonest of which has already been mentioned under *portal hypertension* above. In all cases, liver cells are slowly poisoned and are killed off over a long period of time. In response to this, the surviving liver cells undergo cell division, trying to make good the numbers lost, and at the same time fibrous scar tissue replaces the damaged tissue throughout the organ. The result is a hard, knobbly liver. The many "knobs" are spherical areas of regenerated new cells, and they are separated by thickened bands of scar tissue. All of this destroys the normal architecture and leads to the portal hypertension and ascites mentioned above. In some countries (*e.g.*, France and the United States) excessive alcohol is the main cause of the original liver damage which starts it all off. In others (*e.g.*, Bantu South Africa) it seems to be nutritional starvation of the liver. In England much less than half the cases are due to alcohol, and many are thought to be due to a previous episode of infective hepatitis (*q.v.*), but this is not certain. Infective hepatitis is quite common but cirrhosis is comparatively rare. So that the great majority of people do not progress from one to the other. One day soon the treatment for advanced cirrhosis will be to replace the liver by transplantation, but there are still many problems to overcome before this can become routine.

Cancer of the Liver. Cancer of the liver is quite common, but it is nearly always cancer which has spread in the blood stream from other parts of the body. The liver is a favourite site for such secondary deposits, since it has a large blood supply and will receive a generous helping of anything being carried. It is also a very "fertile soil" for the cancer seedlings to grow in. Primary cancer of the liver is uncommon, and only occurs in a few cases of pre-existing cirrhosis.

Gallstones. These are "stones" formed by some of the major constituents of bile coming out of solution and forming solid bodies. They are very common, and often cause no trouble at all. When they do, it is usually a colicky intermittent severe pain. This is due to the muscular walls of the bile passages contracting in an effort to expel an obstructing stone into the duodenum. The second common trouble arising from gallstones is obstructive jaundice, described above. It is small consolation to gallstone sufferers that the stones are often very pretty, often being composed of beautiful cholesterol crystals coloured by varying shades of bile. If they contain calcium they will be visible on an X-ray. Otherwise they are not seen. Stones often occur in conjunction with inflammation of the gall bladder, known as *cholecystitis.* The treatment for gallstones is to remove them surgically together with the gall bladder if they are causing persistent symptoms. Ways of avoiding surgery by dissolving them in substances taken by mouth are under investigation.

The Pancreas.

This is a soft, elongated gland lying behind the stomach; it is about 12·5 cm long and 5 cm wide. Within its tissues lies the duct, which, when it leaves the pancreas, passes into the duodenum near the point of entry of the bile-duct. This duct transmits the juices containing enzymes which aid in the digestion in the small intestine. The pancreas, however, has two main functions: not only does it manufacture these important digestive juices, but in certain specialised areas, known as the islets of Langerhans, it manufactures insulin, the hormone which makes it possible for the body to utilise sugar. *Diabetes mellitus* or ordinary diabetes is a chronic disorder usually caused by a deficient secretion of insulin. The unused sugar accumulates in the blood and acts as a poison, which, in extreme cases, sends the patient into coma and may—indeed, in former times, usually did—result in death. The treatment of diabetes was revolutionised by the discovery of the hormone insulin by Banting and Best in 1921. On the whole, diabetes is more severe in young people than in the elderly, but with correct treatment it is possible for all cases to lead a perfectly normal life except for dietary restrictions and insulin injections. Not to be confused with *Diabetes insipidus* (**P43**(1)).

DIET.

When considering diet, and the effect it has on our health and well-being, there is more to it than just the things we eat. We must also know about what our body does with the food, and it would be unscientific not to acknowledge the effects of our psychological make-up and our nutritional beliefs on what we eat, what we do with it, and how well (or ill) we feel as a result.

For example, a deep-rooted conviction that brown eggs or free-range poultry are better for us than white eggs or intensively reared birds is entirely unsupported by any evidence. However, if we believe such a thing sufficiently, we will not only eat the "better" ones, but we will feel happier and more secure afterwards, and this is likely to make us healthier. Food fads can occasionally be dangerous, as when extreme vegetarians become ill through lack of certain vitamins (*e.g.* B$_{12}$) which are present only in the foods they exclude. But this is so rare, even among strict vegetarians, that such danger can virtually be ignored. On the whole (and vegetarianism is probably a good example of this) food faddism often leads to a sense of health and well-being in the believer, and should not be attacked by the rest of us for that. It is an accepted fact that personal misfortune, even when it is severe, is more easily withstood by those with strong religious conviction than by others. In the same way, a firm attachment to a theory of what is good for you can produce a feeling of well-being and genuine good health, when another person on exactly the same food intake will not feel so fit. These factors—religious belief, food faddism, or the bedside manner of a kind or persuasive doctor —are commonly dismissed by free-thinking people because they are not "true" or "real." All three, however, can materially affect our health just as can a shock, a personal tragedy or being in love. The trouble starts, and the magic ceases to work, when adherents declaim their beliefs as *ex cathedra* truths and expect the rest of us to swallow them as wholly (or holy) as they do.

Thus there are genuine *facts* about food, and fallacies too; and as well as these there is a no-man's-land between in which one man's fact is another man's fallacy.

The basic constituents of any diet are protein, fats, carbohydrates, water, vitamins, minerals, salts, and indigestible roughage. All are chemicals whose structure and function are reasonably well understood. Even the mystical differences between fine table wines, so beloved of the connoisseur and gourmet, are reasonably well understood in chemical terms. Perhaps that is a pity.

Much nonsense is talked, especially by nutritionists, about minimal daily requirements. In general terms, however, requirements can be described in terms of how many calories there are in the total intake of proteins, fats, and carbohydrates per day, and how these are distributed between the three classes of food. The other substances mentioned above are only required in trace or small amounts except for water; and roughage is only required as a mechanical stimulus to bowel movement.

During the process of digestion (described on **P34-5**) all proteins are split into their constituent amino acids; all carbohydrates are split into their constituent simple sugars and most fats are converted into fatty acids and glycerol. At this stage, and not until this stage, all these simpler building bricks derived from the three classes of food are absorbed into the body proper, and taken to the liver and other tissues. Here they are "metabolised." That is to say they are either burned as fuel for the various processes of the body; or they are built up again into proteins, fats, and carbohydrates of the special kinds the body needs. They will either be used to rebuild structures suffering ordinary wear and tear or they will be stored. Many of them will be converted into a different class from the one they came from when they entered the body. For example, excess carbohydrate is converted into fat; or if there is a shortage of carbohydrate, some will be made out of the protein amino-acids which would normally have been used for tissue growth and repair. Thus it is only a generalisation to say that dietary carbohydrates are fuel and proteins are for building bodily structure. The body can convert one into the other, and spoil the calculation.

There is a great deal of confusion in people's minds about *energy*, and that is why the word *fuel* has been used above in connection with carbohydrates. The lay person uses energy as a term meaning something which allows us to leap about, running and jumping and skipping and dancing, and which keeps us from getting tired and run down. Thus, the food industry tells us, we need potatoes or breakfast cereals for these activities or for a hard day's work. This is a deliberate commercial confidence trick, and the scientist is largely to blame. He originally handed out the word energy to an eager food industry and an unsuspecting public, forgetting to explain that he meant it in the strictly scientific sense of fuel for bodily processes. It simply is not true that more potatoes, or more cornflakes will make you more active. Indeed the reverse is the case, and after a certain point they will only be converted into fat and reduce your activity. The nutritionist measures energy as calories, which are units of heat, and it is certainly true that you must eat enough of these each day if you wish to remain alive, let alone active.

All the three main classes of food provide calories, and in an ordinary well-balanced diet about 15% are provided by protein. Carbohydrates produce most of the remainder. Each gram of fat contains about twice the calories of a similar quantity of carbohydrate. We simply eat less fat than carbohydrate, because fat has a "high satiety value." It takes away the appetite for more. Proteins are mostly found in meat, fish, eggs, cheese, and milk. However, there is quite a lot of protein in many predominantly starchy foods like bread, and such grains as wheat, rice, and corn. Carbohydrates are mainly found in bread, potatoes, sugar, pastry, sweets, and so forth. That is one of the words which fortunately seems to be used by both scientists and laymen in much the same sense.

Some substances are absolutely essential to the body if life is to continue, even if they are only needed in trace amounts. These are substances which the body's own factories (like the liver) cannot make for themselves, even if they are provided with the correct ingredients.

One group of such substances are the *vitamins.* Some of these are found in predominantly fatty foods (milk, butter, cheese and so on) and are known as the fat-soluble vitamins—Vitamins A, D, E and K; the others are water-soluble—the Vitamin B group and Vitamin C. All have now been chemically identified, are manufactured and can be bought over a pharmacist's counter. The myth has grown up that if a little is good for one then a lot more will be better and there are a great many vitamin enthusiasts who consume vast quantities of such manufactured products in the belief that by doing so they will induce extra vitality and energy. Unless your diet is unbalanced in some way (a vegetarian diet may be grossly deficient in Vitamin B_{12}) you will not need extra vitamins.

Fortunately, most people buy food because they like it, not because it does them good; and provided they have normal dietary tastes they will usually get a perfectly adequate selection of the things we have spoken of as necessary for good health. The main danger in England is to have a surfeit and become overweight. In addition there are certain times of life when conscious attention should be paid to what is necessary. For example babies and nursing mothers have special dietary needs and will hear about them from their Health Visitor or from their Welfare Clinic or Doctor. Elderly people living alone are also prone to dietary deficiencies for reasons ranging from poverty to loss of appetite or inability to look after themselves properly.

Recent surveys have revealed some interesting facts about people's attitude to food and their knowledge of it. For example, half the people asked knew that meat was a source of protein, a third mentioned eggs and a fifth cheese, fish, and milk. But practically no one knew there was protein in bread. Yet in England about a fifth of our daily protein intake comes from bread, and nearly a third from cereals as a whole. Fish is well known as a source of protein, but did you know that on average we only obtain 4% of our daily protein from fish—less than we get from

potatoes (5%)? No one seems to know that potatoes are an important source of vitamin C, although fruit and vegetables are well-known sources. Calcium is recognised in milk, but most people forget its presence in cheese. Most people are very confused about iron. Why does everyone think it is mainly in green vegetables, when these are really such a poor source? For our daily requirement of iron we would each have to eat 1 kg. spring greens or peas; or 2 kg. of sprouts! In fact meat provides one of our best sources, and one-fifth of our daily needs is contained in bread.

Since most of the people who read *Pears* live in England let us return finally to our commonest nutritional disease, or our commonest form of malnutrition in these islands: obesity. Call it "being overweight" if you like, but acknowledge that it means being fat. Being fat is not only unattractive and unsightly but it is dangerous to health and carries a high mortality. Ask any life insurance company how they view your chances if you are overweight and you will find they are as worried about it as if you had high blood pressure, or smoke heavily. It is a particularly important cause of heart disease. However, it is very important to know exactly what we mean by fatness. Many girls who are not at all fat think they are, and this leads them to diet unnecessarily. On the other hand there are people who do not appreciate they are overweight. Here is a table which shows what your weight should be according to your height.

DESIRABLE WEIGHTS FOR MEN AND WOMEN ACCORDING TO HEIGHT AND FRAME, AGES 25 AND OVER

Men Height (in shoes 2·5 cm heels)	Weight in kilograms (in indoor clothing)		
	Small frame	Medium frame	Large frame
157	51–54·5	53·5–59	57–64
160	52–56	55–60·5	59–65·5
162	53·5–57	56–62	60–67
165	55–59	58–63	61–69
167	56–60·5	59–65	63–71
170	58–62	61–67	64·5–73
172	60–64	63–69	67–75·5
175	62–66	64·5–71	68·5–77
177	63·5–68	66–72·5	70·5–79
180	65·5–70	68–75	72–81
183	67–72	70–77	74–83·5
185	69–73·5	72–79·5	76–86
188	71–76	73·5–82	78·5–88
190	72·5–77·5	76–84	81–90·5
193	74·5–79·5	78–86	82·5–93

Women Height (in shoes 5 cm heels)	Weight in kilograms (in indoor clothing)		
	Small frame	Medium frame	Large frame
147	42–44·5	43·5–48·5	47–54
150	43–46	44·5–50	48–55·5
152	43·5–47	46–51	49·5–57
155	45–48·5	47–53	51–58
157	46–50	48·5–54	52–59·5
160	48–51	50–55·5	53·5–61
162	49–53	51–57	55–63
165	50·5–54	53–59	57–64·5
167	52–56	54·5–61	59–66
170	53·5–58	56–63	60·5–68
172	55·5–59·5	58–65	62–70
175	57–61	60–67	64–72
177	59–63·5	62–68·5	66–74
180	61–65·5	63·5–70·5	68–76
183	63–67	65·5–72	69·5–78·5

If you are overweight according to these tables you need to slim, and the question is how? Answer: by will-power. There is no other satisfactory method than to decide to eat less, and to eat as little carbohydrate as possible. For the time being eat as much meat, fruit, green vegetables, and as much fat as you like, but no sugar, starch, sweets, cakes, pastry, or biscuits, and no eating between meals. And cut down on beer and other alcoholic drinks. In case you are tempted to eat "slimming" foods, be aware that there is no such thing. There is nothing you can eat which will cause you to lose weight, in spite of what the advertisement says. In special cases doctors will prescribe tablets to suppress appetite, but they are too dangerous for general use without supervision, and they do not work as well as will-power. At the same time take more exercise. Walk to work. If you make a real and genuine effort for three months without success, you should ask your doctor for advice. Almost certainly you will have to admit you have not really tried. Good luck!

NUTRITIONAL DISORDERS.

Nutritional Deficiency and Malnutrition.—Until quite recently a consideration of malnutrition would have merely led to an account of how too little food, or a deficiency of certain articles in the diet, produced deficiency diseases at the time of the restriction. For example lack of vitamins of various kinds gives rise to such diseases as rickets, scurvy, beri-beri, and pellagra; and an overall shortage of food to general starvation. These may be considered the immediate or concurrent effects of a poor diet. Modern nutritionists, however, are beginning to be concerned with two more kinds of nutritional disorders; and although the study of both kinds is in its infancy, both will be introduced in this account.

The first deals with the effects of comparatively small amounts of harmful constituents in our diet, introduced either voluntarily or involuntarily, and consumed for a long period of time; and the second with the lasting effects on our adult well-being of nutritional deficiencies in early life even though they have long since been corrected.

When viewed in this light, one or other of these three kinds of nutritional disorder may at this moment be affecting almost every individual in every part of the world, "privileged" or "under-privileged." Let us first define some terms.

Undernutrition, strictly speaking, means a state of affairs in which the quality of the diet is perfectly good. There is the correct balance of the various dietary constituents and all the necessary components are present: but there is simply too little of it. Many hundreds of millions of people throughout the underprivileged world are suffering and dying from this kind of under-nutrition, and the simplicity of the problem must be appreciated: they simply need more food of the kind they are at present getting, and which can often be produced locally.

Malnutrition means an imbalance of the various constituents: a relative lack or excess of one or more of them. It usually leads to conditions which are, from the point of view of medical treatment, much more difficult to deal with. And therefore doctors often class them as "more serious."

The diseases of malnutrition range from the widespread protein deficiencies in other parts of the underprivileged world to *obesity* in our own better-off industrial countries, which is usually due to excess carbohydrate. Make no mistake about it: obesity (or being overweight) is a widespread disease of nutritional imbalance, and it kills. It is the commonest form of malnutrition in (for example) England and America today, and is a consequence of the sophistication of our diet in modern times. Between one-fifth and one-tenth of the population of the United States is more than 20% overweight, and to be 10% or 15% overweight is almost the rule nowadays in people over thirty. There are high authorities in the world of nutritional science who attribute all this overfed malnutrition to the consumption of refined sugar, or sucrose. They say it is not only the amount of refined sugar we put in our tea or on our breakfast cereals, but also the amount in sweet cakes, biscuits, drinks, chocolates and sweets, and so forth. For some people it adds up to a phenomenal quantity each day. According to this school of thought we are not so

much suffering from a surfeit of carbohydrates or starches, but from this single sugar, sucrose. It is interesting to reflect on the recent banning of the artificial sweetener, cyclamate, by many governments. This substance, having been used extensively throughout the world as an apparently harmless non-fattening substitute for sugar, was suddenly banned in America because in very large doses (equivalent to the amount taken in hundreds of cups of coffee per day for a long time) it was found to produce cancer in rats. It has never been shown to do humans any harm, whereas the effects of sugar in producing an overweight population, thereby indirectly kill tens of thousands of British people each year. This is a fascinating example of the difficulties confronting our legislators in making balanced judgments when deciding to ban a foodstuff, a drug, or an artificial fertiliser.

Much the most widespread form of malnutrition, however, is a variety protein-lack which is part of a collection of nutritional diseases known as *Protein-Calorie Deficiency*. In very large underprivileged areas of the world, the childhood population receives such an inadequate diet that children live continuously on the brink of nutritional disaster. It only requires a small extra restriction or stress to topple them over into one of the clinical conditions to be described. At this stage they cease to be merely hungry. They become nutritionally ill. Sometimes the force which produces the disaster is a community catastrophe like a famine, an earthquake, or a war. Sometimes it is a family catastrophe like the loss of a lactating mother or a parental delinquency. Parents abandon young children as often in Africa as anywhere else. Sometimes the clinical nutritional disease is unmasked by a common childhood illness like measles, or gastro-enteritis which the well-fed child would have overcome. The starved child reveals his malnutrition instead and frequently dies. When the precipitating cause of the "epidemic" of malnutrition is a war or other national calamity, our newspapers and television screens carry distressing pictures of thin skeletal, pot-bellied children, and the conscience of a few is touched. It is insufficiently realised that these scenes can be witnessed anywhere in the continents of Africa and Asia, and in large parts of Central and South America any day of the week in normal times. The war has not been the cause, but is only the precipitating factor which has revealed the chronic malnutrition in more children than would normally exhibit it openly.

Protein-Calorie Deficiency is a collection of different kinds of childhood malnutrition. Some are due predominantly to deficiency of protein and are collectively called Kwashiorkor, a West African word meaning "red-haired boy" (see below). Others are mainly due to a severe deficiency of overall foodstuffs and are called *Marasmus*. But in any real-life situation the severe *mal*nutrition of Kwashiorkor exists side-by-side with all gradations between itself and the severe *under*nutrition of Marasmus, so that many intermediate forms of "marasmic kwashiorkor" are described. In Kwashiorkor the child is typically listless, apathetic, whining, with a reddish discoloration of the hair, a peeling, scaly skin, and with much extra fluid in his tissues causing oedema. He is so listless as not even to be hungry. In marasmus the child is ravenously hungry. He is extremely thin and "starved" looking and is quite a different picture.

There is good reason to believe that even when protein-calorie deficiency is successfully treated, there will always be some lasting restriction of mental function, particularly if the malnutrition occurred as early as the first year of life. This is especially true in situations of appalling poverty in towns, where thousands of babies are not breast-fed because their mothers are at work. Many of them die. Some of them are no heavier than their birth weight at one year of age. Breast feeding in an underprivileged community is an essential insurance for childhood health and survival.

Two new avenues of nutritional inquiry were mentioned at the beginning of this section. The impact of very long continued intake of refined sugar over many years on our bodily health is an example of one of them. Scientists and others are also becoming alarmed at the effects of modern food additives when taken, even in small amounts, over a long period. These additives include colouring matter, decolorising chemicals, taste "enhancers," and so forth, which are present in everyone's diet in a "civilised community." We are as unable to avoid a constant dosage with them as if they had been added to our water supply. It is, however, difficult to strike a balanced attitude. It is one thing to suspect that these additives are harmful and quite another to prove it. Naturally if any of them are shown to produce harm in animals given reasonable quantities they are invariably withdrawn. But in practice it is extremely difficult for animal experiments to mimic the conditions of human intake, especially as the human life span involves eating the substance concerned in small quantities for several decades. Thus it is easy to postulate the harmful effects of monosodium glutamate (a very common taste enhancer) but practically impossible to prove the question either way. It is not sufficient to condemn "chemicals." All natural foods consist of chemicals, and so do we.

The other new topic in nutrition is more soundly based on animal experiment. It has been repeatedly found that if animals do not grow quickly enough at certain early periods of life, they not only become small, but they remain smaller than they should be even when they are subsequently given as much as they like to eat. This is true of all animals and birds so far studied. For example, if rats are suckled in large families it is found that they are smaller by the time they are weaned (3 weeks of age) than those suckled in small families. The interesting thing is that if they are then given as much as they want to eat for the rest of their lives, the small animals from the larger families never catch up to the others. Whereas if their growth is not restricted until later in their "childhood," full "catch-up" is possible soon after normal diet is resumed. In other words there is a critical time in early life when growth can be permanently affected. At the moment it is difficult to know whether the same is true of humans and, if so, when is our period of vulnerability. There is some suggestion that the corresponding critical period in humans is during the last part of gestation in the uterus, and the first year or so of postnatal life. This new idea may turn out to be very important for world nutrition. Since there will not be enough food for all the children all the time, it may become important to concentrate our aid to underprivileged countries on certain sections of the population only. It may be a good idea to see that pregnant mothers and small babies are specially fed. In this way we may be able to put off the periods of inevitable malnutrition until a time of life when it is recoverable. Such a plan would also go a long way to safeguarding the development of the brain which also occurs mostly at the same early time of life.

We shall now describe some of the better-known nutritional deficiencies, bearing in mind that vitamin deficiencies are virtually unknown in the better-off countries. No one in England need spend money buying vitamins, as has been emphasised in the preceding section. Vitamin deficiency can still occur, however, in elderly people living alone and not having a well-balanced diet. It also occurs for similar reasons in alcoholics, vagrants, etc., and very occasionally in small children.

Beri-beri is a group of diseases usually confined to the Far East where a diet of polished rice results in a poor intake of vitamin B_1 (thiamine). In one form there is oedema (*q.v.*); in another the peripheral nerves are affected leading to tingling and numbness. A similar condition is occasionally seen in alcoholics and diabetics. Treatment is with thiamine, and with other vitamins too, since most sufferers are going short of more than one.

Pellagra is found among maize-eating populations and is due to a deficiency of several vitamins including niacin, another member of the B group of vitamins. There is dermatitis on exposed skin, and soreness of the mouth and tongue, with gastro-enteritis.

Scurvy is due to vitamin C deficiency. In children bone growth is affected. At all ages there is bleeding into the skin (bruising), impaired wound healing, mental depression, and anaemia. Most fresh fruit and vegetables contain vitamin C and a diet containing these prevents the disease.

Vitamin A deficiency is commonly found in children in some underprivileged countries. It causes permanent blindness, with thickening opacity and dryness of the whites of the eyes leading to ulceration of the eye. Beyond a certain stage, therefore, a child's sight cannot be saved. The only real hope is prevention, with an adequate diet.

Rickets, another disease of early childhood, is caused by deficiency of vitamin D. Bones are not properly calcified, and their softness leads to deformities of the legs and many other bones. Vitamin D can either be eaten in the diet or produced under the skin under the influence of sunlight. Therefore rickets commonly occurs when both the diet and the sunlight are inadequate. It was once very common in industrial England, and is still to be seen very occasionally there and in impoverished urban communities in the United States.

THE ENDOCRINE GLANDS.

Glands are structures or organs which manufacture secretions (except for *lymph glands* which are not glands at all and should be called *lymph nodes*). The secretions are of two main kinds. The first are passed down tubes, or ducts, or are secreted directly into the hollow organs, and act locally. Good examples are the salivary glands which make saliva and pass it down ducts into the mouth for digestion of its contents and lubrication. These are *exocrine glands*. The second kind have no ducts, and secrete their product straight into the blood stream. This secretion is called a *hormone* and it is carried to all parts of the body by the blood where it acts at a distance on some remote part. These are the *endocrine glands* or *ductless glands*, and a number of them will be discussed in this section.

The first hormone, or "chemical messenger," was discovered by the British physiologist Starling in 1904, but the effects of removing some of the endocrine glands were known centuries before when removal of the male testes (castration) was practised to procure a form of manpower safe for the harem, to salvage a good male alto voice for the church choir, or to convert a rooster into a more eatable capon.

Anterior Pituitary.—Many of the endocrine glands do not act as separate autonomous organs in spite of their great differences. They are organised into a well-disciplined band by a "master-gland" called the anterior pituitary. Somebody once called it the "conductor of the endocrine orchestra" and the phrase is still repeated *ad nauseam* in students' examination papers. The pituitary, consisting of its two parts, anterior and posterior, is not much bigger than a pea and it sits right in the middle of the skull, centrally beneath the brain and joined to the brain by a short stalk. This astonishing tiny nodule of tissue produces at least eight important hormones.

One of these is *growth hormone*, which is necessary for normal growth, and also has an influence on insulin. An excess causes *gigantism* and *acromegaly*, often coinciding with diabetes, and too little results in a form of dwarfism. Three others, known as *gonadotrophic hormones* regulate the cyclical and other activities of the reproductive organs and lactating breast. Another, *thyrotrophic hormone*, regulates thyroid activity, *Adrenocorticotrophic hormone*, or *ACTH*, as its name implies, looks after the activities of another important endocrine gland, the adrenal cortex. And there are several others.

Hypopituitarism, including *Simmonds' disease* and *Sheehan's disease*, results from destruction of the anterior pituitary. It is extremely rare, and is usually associated with difficult childbirth involving very severe bleeding. There are disturbances of all the functions mentioned above, particularly thyroid and adrenal failure (q.v.) with upset sexual function. Treatment is by replacing the lost hormones.

Hyperpituitarism, including *gigantism* and *acromegaly*, results from over-activity of the anterior pituitary, and is usually due to a tumour or overgrowth of the gland. In acromegaly the growth hormone is produced in excess over a long period of time in an adult. This results in overgrowth of all the organs except the brain, and it is characteristic to find enlarged extremities—feet, hands, and jaw. In gigantism the same has occurred during childhood before the bones have stopped growing and the result is a person who may be 2 m tall or more.

Posterior Pituitary. The posterior part of the gland is really a quite separate gland. The main hormone it produces is concerned with the excretion of urine by the kidney (antidiuretic hormone). Deficiency of the hormone results in *Diabetes Insipidus*, not to be confused with *Diabetes Mellitus* or "sugar diabetes." In diabetes insipidus, the patient produces enormous quantities of dilute urine. He consequently has a prodigious thirst and consumes astonishing quantities of fluids. Treatment is by replacing the missing hormone.

Thyroid. The thyroid gland in the neck secretes an iodine containing hormone called thyroxine. Excess of it causes *hyperthyroidism*, *thyrotoxicosis*, or *Graves' disease.* Lack of it produces *cretinism* in the growing child or *myxoedema* in the adult. Thyroxine is concerned with the metabolic rate of cells throughout the body, or the rate at which they work, as well as with the proper growth of developing tissues, especially the brain. Too much thyroxine as in thyrotoxicosis leads to over-activity, warm sweatiness in an over-excitable patient whose pulse is rapid and who is eating ravenously to try to replace the wasted energy. In spite of his appetite he is very thin, and he often has bulging eyes for a reason not understood. Treatment is by drugs which neutralise the thyroxine or by cutting out some of the gland. A *cretin* is a child usually born with insufficient thyroid. He is destined to grow poorly, and to mental subnormality of a permanent and distressing kind. If the condition is diagnosed soon after birth treatment with thyroxine can avert most of the trouble. In myxoedema, thyroxine is deficient in an adult. They become slow in all their bodily processes, the hair thins and their flesh is puffy with a dry, wrinkled skin. Treatment is by thyroid replacement. *Goitre* simply means enlargement of the gland. It may be accompanied by overactivity or underactivity, or with little functional change. One variety (Derbyshire neck) occurs in areas short of iodine in the soil and drinking water.

Adrenal Cortex. The adrenal or suprarenal glands sit, as the name implies, one on top of each kidney. There are two distinct parts: the cortex or outside which secretes steroid hormones, and the *adrenal medulla*, or core, which secretes adrenalin. There are many different steroid hormones in the adrenal cortical secretion, which look after such divers matters as sodium and potassium balance, sexual function, the reaction of the body to stress, and the regulation of sugar levels. *Addison's disease* (not to be confused with Addisonian anaemia) results from adrenal cortical insufficiency, and is often due to destruction of the gland by tuberculosis. There is weariness, malaise, pigmentation of skin creases and mucous membranes. They are short of sodium and have excess potassium. Treatment is with cortisone (replacement of the missing hormone) and by extra salt by mouth for the lack of sodium. *Cushing's disease* is due to excessive adrenal cortical function, and sometimes also occurs in patients treated with cortisone for other purposes. They have a striking redistribution of fat in the face, neck, and trunk, with stretch marks similar to those acquired by most women during pregnancy. The facial obesity makes them "moon-faced," and female patients may suffer masculinisation with deepening of the voice and hirsutism.

Testis. The male testes, as well as producing sperm are also endocrine glands producing steroid hormones known as androgens. They are mainly concerned with maintaining secondary sex characteristics. At the time of puberty the controlling secretions from the anterior pituitary begin to appear and androgens are produced. There is a whole range of rare disorders, resulting in everything from precocious puberty to delayed puberty. It should be borne in mind that the normal time of puberty can vary by several years from one boy to another.

Ovary. The human ovary has two functions: to produce ova, or eggs; and to produce two hormones, oestrogen and progesterone. These functions begin at puberty, one of whose features in the female is the onset of menstruation, or menarche. Just as in boys, the timing of normal puberty is very variable, but on the average, girls achieve puberty before boys. As social conditions improve, the age of menarche is getting younger generation by generation. All the secondary sex characteristics are under the control of the ovarian hormones which are released in response to the appropriate anterior pituitary hormones. The changes which occur in the womb and elsewhere in the intervals between menstrual periods and the periods themselves are controlled by a cyclical or rhythmic secretion, first of oestrogen and then of progesterone, by the ovary. This cycle is upset by pregnancy to allow the development of the embryo. It can also be upset by taking certain combinations of the two hormones by mouth. These can prevent the formation of ova, and are a popular form of contraception. In late middle age, the ovaries lose their function, the menstrual cycles cease to occur, and reproductive life is at an end. This is called the *menopause* or "change of life," and is sometimes accompanied for a time by distressing symptoms due to a temporary imbalance between oestrogen and progesterone. Many sexual functions, however, continue well after the menopause into old age, and these can include a continuing libido or sexual desire.

Parathyroid. Four tiny parathyroid glands are buried behind the thyroid gland and are responsible for regulating the body calcium and phosphate. They are therefore particularly important for the building and maintenance of bones and teeth. Since a proper calcium level in the blood is necessary for muscle (including heart muscle) contraction, and for correct functioning of nerves, disorders of the parathyroids can give rise to muscular spasms as well as loss of bone calcium. The latter can result in fragility and fractures. Overactivity of the glands leads to too much calcium and the formation of stones especially in the kidney.

Pineal. We end this section with a mystery gland. Like the pituitary it is small—about the size of a pea—and sits well back at the base of the brain. It was endowed in ancient times with metaphysical properties all of which remain speculative. In fish and lizards and certain lower vertebrates it is a kind of third eye, and receives light. In higher mammals, like ourselves, it is so far from any source of light that it could scarcely do so. It can be removed without harm. Indeed it normally becomes calcified and inactive about the time of puberty, and its position seen on X-rays of the skull can be a good guide to whether the brain is being pushed to one side by an abnormal mass.

THE URINARY SYSTEM.

Everyone knows what kidneys look like—in fact, the term "kidney-shaped" is used to describe other objects. Within the kidneys the blood-vessels carrying waste materials subdivide and finally end up in little coils or glomeruli through which waste products are filtered into the other system, the system of tubes which, beginning as tiny cups around the glomeruli, become larger and larger until they join the ureter passing out at the foot of the kidney, the hilum, a point at which both the veins and tubes enter and leave. The kidneys, of course, lie one on each side in the loins, so that if one puts one's hands on the hips and then slides them farther back they will cover the area over the left and right kidney. The ureters pass down on each side to the bladder, which is the storage tank of the products excreted by the kidneys, and lies in the mid-line down low in the abdomen; it is somewhat pear-shaped, and at its base in men there lies the prostate gland— a gland which apparently has few functions but can be a nuisance. Its only known function is that it adds something to the semen from the testes without which the semen would be sterile. Then, from the base of the bladder a single tube, the urethra, passes to the outside. One can, in fact, visualise the urinary system as a capital Y, in which the two upper limbs are the ureters, the place where they meet is the bladder, and the single limb at the foot is the urethra. Clearly, then, there may be diseases of the kidneys, of the ureters, of the bladder, of the prostate gland, or of the urethra.

The amount of urine may be increased or diminished. It is *increased* in the following conditions: after drinking excess of fluids; after taking drugs (known as *diuretics*) which are given to increase the flow; in diabetes of both types—mellitus and insipidus; in some types of chronic kidney disease; and finally, in emotional states of excitement. It is *decreased* in the following conditions: acute nephritis; any disease in which fluid is being lost in other ways, such as diarrhoea or sweating in fevers; when the fluid intake is small; and when both ureters are blocked by stones. Passing a great deal of urine is known as *polyuria*, passing very little as *oliguria*, passing frequent small amounts is simply called *frequency*. Normally, the urine is acid, but in infections of the bladder it may become alkaline owing to decomposition by bacteria. Abnormal substances, or normal substances in abnormal quantities, may occur in the urine and give the doctor an indication of what is wrong. In fact, urine analysis is a very important part of medical diagnosis. Thus urea is a normal content of urine which is increased in fevers, wasting diseases, or diabetes; the amount of urea is to some extent a measure of the degree of tissue breakdown. Uric acid is found in small quantities in normal urine, but the amount is increased in fevers and after an attack of gout (uric acid is important in the causation of gout, but has nothing at all to do with rheumatism in general, so one may disregard the advertisements in the popular Press showing unpleasant pictures of joints with sharp crystals of uric acid which are alleged to cause the pain of rheumatic disease). Oxalates are not ordinarily found in urine, but, since they occur in such foods as rhubarb and strawberries, and some people are unable to deal with them, such individuals may develop stones or have pain on passing urine after eating oxalate-containing fruits.

Two very important substances which ought not to be in normal urine are albumen and sugar. Albumen is a protein, and its presence in the urine indicates that the filters of the kidney are leaking —they are allowing protein to pass out which ought to remain in the body. Albumen is easily tested for, and its presence may indicate kidney disease or nephritis as it is usually called by doctors. On the other hand, small amounts of albumen occur in fevers and in nervous conditions —*functional albuminuria*. Sugar, too, should not be present, but its presence does not necessarily indicate diabetes; for small amounts may occur in nervous conditions or in some people after taking large quantities of carbohydrate.

Blood in the urine may give it an appearance which varies from bright red to a dark, smoky colour. It is found in many diseases: acute nephritis, stone, tumours, poisoning by certain drugs, infections such as bilharzia or malaria, papilloma (*i.e.*, non-malignant tumour of the bladder), after injury, in high blood-pressure,

scurvy, and blood diseases. Sometimes it occurs for no known reason at all.

It will be remembered (or if it is not, you can look it up on **P27** (2)) that streptococcal infection of the throat may cause in some people disease of the valves in the heart or endocarditis. In such cases, although the germ is found in the throat, it is not found in the heart or indeed anywhere else in the body. *Acute nephritis* occurs in the same circumstances, with the sole difference that the kidneys instead of the heart are affected. The disease appears to be an allergic reaction to the toxins of the streptococcus. The patient, often a child, has a sore throat (and even this may be absent or fail to be noticed) or sometimes the infection may arise in other sites: after scarlet fever, erysipelas, burns, and disease of the ear. A few days later there is headache, vomiting, pain in the loins, slight rise in temperature, and especially typical is *dropsy* or oedema. This begins in the face, first around the eyelids, and then affects the ankles; later it may become more general and affect the rest of the body. Blood and albumen are found in the urine, and the blood-pressure is slightly raised. The outlook is usually good if the kidneys are rested by reducing the amount of protein taken in and also the amounts of salt and water. When this is done, the inflammation soon goes and no permanent harm results. In other cases, however, if treatment is inadequate or the condition severe, the symptoms may go, but the albumen found in the urine persists. This means that permanent damage has been done, and although there may be nothing else to show for many years, *chronic nephritis* develops. In this case, the blood-pressure continues to rise, and since the filters of the kidneys no longer work efficiently, urea, the principal waste-product of the body to be excreted in the urine, is retained in the blood and only small amounts escape from the system. Hence chronic nephritis sooner or later leads to heart failure or haemorrhage in the brain from the rising blood-pressure, or to the form of poisoning known as *uraemia* which results from the retention of urea in the blood. Uraemia may come on suddenly or gradually, but ends in progressive coma, drowsiness, and unconsciousness. There may be convulsions similar to those of epilepsy, high fever, and difficulty in breathing to complicate the picture.

Another type of nephritis which seems to have nothing at all to do with streptococcal infections, and the cause of which is completely unknown, is *nephrosis*. Developing in early adult life, its onset is insidious, and the patient first shows signs of oedema in his white and puffy face and the swelling of his legs. (It should be said here that if you have swelling of the ankles or elsewhere, you would be foolish to jump to conclusions; for such swelling is common in many diseases—in heart disease, in allergic conditions, in neurotic illness, and even just from hot weather.) When the urine is examined in a case of nephrosis it is found to be full of albumen and, as in chronic nephritis, the blood urea starts to rise. The end-results of nephrosis are the same as those of chronic nephritis and depend upon the damage originally done.

The modern diuretics of the thiazide group help to control the oedema and, provided enough healthy tissue remains, remove both the fluid and the waste-products.

In recent years there have been considerable advances in the development of the artificial kidney. Once only used within hospital, artificial kidneys or dialysers as they are known, can now be used in patients' own homes, thus obviating in some cases long journeys to hospital twice a week for treatment. Dialysis is a relatively temporary measure; renal transplants now offer real hope to many sufferers although there are far more suitable recipients than there are potential donors.

Pyelitis is an infection of the pelvis of the kidney, that is to say, of the part where the ureter leaves the kidney. It is usually caused by the bacillus coli, which is normally present in the body, or by the streptococcus. These germs may reach the ureter through the blood-stream or may pass upwards from the bladder. Obstruction anywhere in the urinary tract which causes the urine to stagnate is liable to cause pyelitis. Symptoms come on suddenly, with high fever, pain in the loin (the infection is usually on one side only, and is commoner in women), and pain in the abdomen. When urine is passed there is a burning sensation, and it is passed frequently and in small amounts. On examination, the urine is found to be highly acid and full of bacillus coli or whatever the causative germ may be. Pyelitis is fairly readily treated by the antibiotics or sulpha drugs. Plenty of fluids should be given and the urine made alkaline by administration of alkalis.

Cystitis means inflammation of the bladder, either acute or chronic, and its causes are much the same as in the case of pyelitis. There is pain over the lower abdomen, frequency, and sometimes slight fever. The treatment is as for pyelitis. *Urethritis* is an inflammation of the urethra, with burning pain on passing water and frequency. The most serious cause (although it can usually be easily dealt with now) is gonorrhoea. But non-specific urethritis is common, and in this case various germs or none may bring about pain and frequency; there is often a large neurotic element. Urethritis should be regarded as probably due to gonorrhoea, which has already been discussed elsewhere, when there is a thick, creamy discharge from the penis or discharge in women following sexual intercourse with an infected person.

Kidney stones or Renal calculi sometimes form, and, as in the case of gall-stones, what causes them is not certain. They may be caused by disorders of metabolism—that is, in the inability of the body to deal with calcium, proteins, uric acid, and other products; or by vitamin deficiency, obstruction in the urinary tract, and urinary infections. But when a stone or stones are formed various events may occur: thus it may remain in the kidney and cause no symptoms; or it may cause repeated attacks of pain, infection, and blood in the urine (haematuria); or it may completely block the passage of urine from the kidney to such a degree that it degenerates and becomes useless; or, lastly, it may pass into the ureter, and when this occurs very severe pain, known as *renal colic*, will occur. A stone passing down the ureter into the bladder may become stuck in the urethra, although this is uncommon, since a stone small enough to get down the ureters is likely to be capable of manoeuvring through the rest of the tract. In fact, about 80–90 per cent. of stones are passed spontaneously. Stones not passed spontaneously may have to be removed by operation, but whether this is undertaken or not depends on various factors, such as the general health of the patient, the amount of trouble caused by the stone, and the health of the other kidney —for it is dangerous to operate on one kidney unless one is sure that the other is functioning efficiently.

If a stone blocks the passage of urine on one side for any length of time *hydronephrosis* may result, in which the part where the ureter enters the kidney swells with the retained urine. Ultimately much of the kidney may be destroyed by the back-pressure. The same effect may be produced by kinking of the ureter or anything else which causes obstruction. Sometimes children are born with hydronephrosis, and when the dilation is due to kinking of the tube the condition may be intermittent, with attacks of renal colic during which only small amounts of urine are passed; this is followed with relief and the passage of large quantities.

Tumours and Cysts. The kidney may also be the site of tumours and cysts which produce pain in the loins, sometimes a lump over the kidney which can be felt, and blood in the urine. Cancer of the bladder is a serious condition in which the bladder may have to be removed, so the urinary flow has then to be directed elsewhere. Either the ureters are brought out on to the skin surface, a procedure known as *cutaneous ureterostomy*, or they are implanted in the large bowel, so that the urine flows out with the faeces. This is described as *uretero-colostomy*.

There may also be benign tumours of the bladder or *papillomas*, which are soft and bleed easily; a great deal of blood is passed, but there is usually little or no pain. In this, and similar, diseases of the bladder examination of the inside of the organ is carried out by means of a cystoscope, a

thin tube which is passed up the urethra and has a small electric light at the end which enables the surgeon to see what is going on. Instruments may also be passed through the tube, and simple papillomas can be cauterised. Similar instruments are used in the examination of the stomach (gastroscope) and the bronchial tubes (bronchoscope). When some obstruction in the outlet of the bladder or in the urethra occurs the bladder, of course, fills with urine, which cannot be passed, and very painful dilation occurs. In this case an attempt may be made to pass a catheter, a thin rubber tube, into the bladder to relieve the tension, or if this fails a *suprapubic cystotomy* is performed—an incision is made in the abdomen over the bladder and a tube inserted into it, through which the urine escapes. This is ordinarily a temporary expedient, and later when the patient's health has improved an attempt will be made to remove the cause of obstruction. The most common cause of such obstruction is *enlargement of the prostate gland* at the base of the bladder, which surrounds this area and the beginning of the ureter. About 40 per cent. of men over sixty have some degree of obstruction due to this cause, and about 20 per cent. of these require operation. The gland is about the size of a walnut, and, as we have seen, its function is to supply part of the fluid which makes up the semen, the male sex secretion. Enlargement of the prostate may be benign or malignant, and, although nobody knows just why, such benign enlargement tends to occur in most men in later life. There may be no symptoms, but characteristically there is frequency during the day and the need to get up at night to pass water. The flow of urine being impeded by constriction of the urethra, the passage is less forceful than normal, and there is a tendency for dribbling to occur. If the obstruction is severe and not relieved the back-pressure may be transmitted to the ureters and kidneys, resulting finally in kidney failure and uraemia. The prostate, except in cases of very mild enlargement, has to be removed either through the abdomen or through the perineum (the part of the body lying between the sex organs and the anus). Sometimes, in less serious cases, it is possible without an incision to cut away the obstructing part by an electrocautery inserted, as is a cystoscope, through the urethra. Prostatectomy was once a serious operation, all the more so because the patient was usually elderly and not in good condition, but new techniques and the use of antibiotics have greatly improved the outlook.

Cancer of the Prostate is a potentially serious disease, but if diagnosed early and is localised, can often be cured by radiotherapy. If the disease spreads, or has spread at the time of diagnosis, it can often be controlled by various hormone treatments or by drugs, or by other forms of radiation. Even when the disease has spread, its progress can sometimes be slow.

THE NERVOUS SYSTEM.

The nervous system consists of the Central Nervous System and the Peripheral Nervous System. The brain and spinal cord make up the former. The latter consists of the nerve fibres by which the Central Nervous System is connected to all parts of the body. Human beings have a more complicated brain than any other animal species, but it is only its complexity which makes it different from the brains of other mammals like rats and pigs and cows. We do not have the largest brains, since whales, for example, have much larger ones. Ours is not even the largest for the size of the body. Mice and dolphins and several other creatures have relatively larger brains when compared with body weight. Furthermore the cells and materials of which our brain is composed are virtually identical with those in other mammals, and its living properties are also the same.

Before describing some of the diseases of the nervous system it will be helpful to say a little about how it is made and how it works. Each human brain probably contains about ten thousand million (10,000,000,000) nerve cells and perhaps four or five times this number of supporting "glial" cells. Each nerve cell has many long thin branching projections, called dendrites, rather like the branches of a tree, leading to many thousands of "twigs" for each single nerve cell. At the end of each "twig" there is a special structure called a *synapse* by which contact is made with other nerve cells. It is through these connections that very large numbers of nerve cells give information (or send impulses) to each other so that they can be co-ordinated. As well as these dendritic branches, each nerve cell gives off one large trunk called the *axon*, down which final messages are sent as the result of all the information it receives from its dendrites. Some axons are many feet long. Some end in another synapse, by which the outgoing message is passed to yet another nerve cell. Some axons, those of the peripheral nerves, end directly on organs like muscles or glands, instructing them and making them work.

Messages are passed along dendrites and axons as electrical impulses. These are generated in the nerve cell "body." They are modified according to information received from other nerve cells and propagated down the axon. It is this superficial resemblance to a series of electrical cables which has given rise to comparisons of the brain with a telephone system or a computer, and as long as it is realised how infinitely more complicated each brain is than any known computer, the comparison is not a bad one. However, the brain generates its own electric power from the fuel brought in its own blood supply; and no spare parts or spare cables are available if the originals should get damaged, except in peripheral nerves. Furthermore the contact of one nerve cell with another through a synapse is not an electrical contact, and neither is the contact between a nerve and the muscle or other organ it is controlling. In both cases the connection is chemical. Thus when an electrical impulse arrives at the end of the nerve fibre, a chemical is released into the gap between it and the next nerve or organ, and it is this chemical which carries the stimulus forward. There is also an arrangement to neutralise the chemical transmitter when the impulse has been transmitted. So the resemblance to a telephone exchange or computer can sometimes be misleading.

Many of the nerve axons which transmit electrical impulses are clothed in fatty *myelin sheaths*, a little like the plastic insulation around an electric wire. Here again the resemblance is only partial, since the myelin sheaths are interrupted at regular intervals and these gaps in the insulation play an important role in transmitting the impulse. One of the important functions of the non-nervous *glial* cells of the brain is to manufacture and maintain the myelin sheaths.

Most of the functions of the brain are quite unknown, and even the ones we know about are very poorly understood. It is assumed to be the organ of higher mental function, of the mind and intellect; but there is surprisingly little evidence for this, and no one has any idea what physical structures or mechanisms subserve these functions. The brain is known to control all bodily functions by means of *motor* and other nerves which carry impulses from the brain outwards to all parts of the body. Sometimes these are under our voluntary control; mostly they are involuntary, reflex or automatic. Reflex actions are the result of impulses passed inwards from the body towards the brain by means of sensory nerves. Information arriving in the brain about the various sensations like heat, pain, touch, position, the need for saliva or gastric juice or even the thought or smell of food, are acted on in the various "centres" in the brain. These send out instructions down the "motor" or "secretary" nerves which instruct the muscles or glands to take appropriate action. Thus a *reflex* has a "sensory ending" which appreciates some sort of sensation. This is converted into an electrical impulse which is sent towards the brain or spinal cord along a sensory or "afferent" nerve. The impulse arrives at a "centre" in the central nervous system which co-ordinates all the relevant information and issues instructions. These travel as impulses outwards, along "efferent" nerves towards "effector" organs like muscles or glands, and an appropriate action occurs automatically. The pathway from sensory ending to effector organ is called a *reflex arc*. Many reflex activities are partly under voluntary control, although

mainly automatic. If you touch something hot you will automatically withdraw your hand. But if it is a hot china cup which has cost you a lot of money, you are capable of overriding the tendency to drop it, at least for a time. Breathing is automatic, but it can also be controlled, again at least for a time.

Clearly the brain is a very delicately organised piece of machinery, and its cells are extremely specialised for their job. Achieving this kind of specialised perfection brings many difficulties, however, and the brain cells have become highly dependent on the proper functioning of the other body systems, especially the blood circulation, the respiratory system, and the systems regulating the detailed nutrient composition of the blood. Failure of these systems, even for a very short time, can damage the nerve cells. Nearly all death, from whatever original cause, is produced this way, by an ultimate interference with nerve cell function.

We have already mentioned that the brain and spinal cord are unable to repair or replace any components which get damaged. The vulnerability of the brain is even more obvious when it is realised how easily damage and destruction can occur. For example, unless a rich supply of oxygen and glucose is continuously arriving in the blood stream, brain cells will cease to function in a few seconds and will die in a few minutes, and they can never be replaced. This is in marked contrast to other tissues of the body. The leg, for example, may carry on for over half an hour without any blood at all because the muscle and other cells can find other ways of surviving. Thus the brain can be permanently damaged if the blood contains insufficient oxygen (through asphyxia), insufficient glucose, or if the blood supply is blocked or if the blood pressure falls. All these are likely to happen to any of us at any time, and so there are elaborate mechanisms trying to prevent them occurring. Most of the subject of physiology is concerned with the mechanisms designed to protect the brain, and most of us ultimately die because they eventually fail. One of the clever features of the body design is that all the mechanisms which protect the brain from a supply failure are controlled by the brain itself. Thus the brain has itself been made to control the heart beat and the breathing and the many other systems which are needed for its own survival.

In all that follows concerning disease of the nervous system it will be seen that the effects of neurological disease on the patient are the direct result of something going wrong with one of the structures or mechanisms we have described.

Diagnostic Techniques in Neurology. The doctor has many ways of testing the nervous system, most of which test its various functions as outlined in the introduction. Thus tests of sensation, muscular movement and reflexes of all kinds as well as the special functions of taste, smell, vision, hearing, speech and intellect play a part. A great deal can be learned about the brain by *arteriography*. In this test a radio opaque substance is put into the arteries supplying the brain, and an X-ray picture taken immediately afterwards shows up all the blood vessels. *Ventriculography* is an X-ray examination after gas has been introduced into the brain cavities or ventricles which are normally filled with *cerebrospinal fluid*; *myelography* is an X-ray of the spinal cord after a radio-opaque substance has been injected into the space between the spinal cord and the bony vertebral canal which houses it.

The development of the EMI Scanner, a relatively new concept in diagnostic radiology, has now made most of those "invasive" diagnostic techniques unnecessary. The equipment needed is expensive and is presently only available at a very few centres. Sometimes *radioactive isotopes* are put into the blood stream and carried into the brain where they can be detected from outside the skull by counters. *Electroencephalography* measures the electrical waves generated by the brain by placing electrodes on the scalp. *Electromyography* does the same for muscles.

Consciousness and Unconsciousness (Coma). Everyone knows what consciousness is until he tries to define it. Full consciousness is generally taken to imply not only wakefulness but the total complement of human mental faculties. In clinical medicine, however, something less than this is usually meant. For example a demented person, or one whose memory is lost (*amnesia*), or one whose powers of speech are lost (*aphasia*) may still be "conscious." There is really a continuous gradation between full consciousness and coma, passing through drowsiness and even "stupor" in which condition a patient can be aroused from coma but sinks back into it when left alone. Many different things can cause coma ranging from swelling of the brain, compressing it in its rigid box of bone, to disorders in other body systems resulting in a failure to provide for the brain's needs. Examples of the first are bleeding within the brain or *brain tumours*, both of which occupy space and can only do so by producing compression. In the second category are asphyxia preventing oxygen from reaching the brain, lack of glucose in the blood, circulatory failure in which there is insufficient blood, or insufficient blood pressure. Fainting is a comparatively minor example.

Sleep and Insomnia. Nobody knows what causes sleep, why it is necessary, and how it helps. It is quite different from coma or even stupor, since as much oxygen and glucose is necessary asleep as awake. Insomnia is experienced by everyone at some time, and for some reason is very distressing if it persists. There are three forms: failing to get to sleep, intermittent wakefulness, and awaking early. Nearly all insomniacs sleep more than they think. They should eat light evening meals and avoid stimulants like tea and coffee after mid-day. Elderly people should realise they need less sleep. Being cold or having a full bladder can be a cause. Or simply not being tired. Sedative drugs are a last resort, but they can be useful in "breaking the habit" of wakefulness. Obviously there may be psychological factors such as anxiety and excitement. *Narcolepsy*, or a true inability to keep awake is comparatively rare. Both narcolepsy and insomnia are really extreme examples of what all normal people suffer from occasionally.

Headache is man's most common pain. Here again we must distinguish between the very common varieties of comparatively trivial significance and the rare ones due to serious causes. Some headaches are due to continuous tightness in muscles of the scalp, and are often "nervous" or psychological in origin. Others result from nose blockage and congestion, sinus problems, eye strain, toothache, etc. Migraine is a special kind and will be described below. Very occasionally indeed headache is due to serious disease like brain tumour. Most headache results from "living it up" or being "run down," or both. The headache of alcoholic hangover is probably due to dehydration. It can often be avoided by consuming a great quantity of water (a half litre or so, before going to bed), but few people are prepared to do this in the circumstances. Be careful when using aspirin, which is a useful remedy for headache, since it is very dangerous for people with stomach complaints like gastritis or gastric or duodenal ulcer. Occasionally aspirin makes the stomach bleed, and this can be so severe as to kill. A safer pain killer is paracetamol. Be particularly careful in treating "hang-over" headaches by patent fizzy remedies. They are very effective, but often contain large quantities of aspirin described in small print by its proper name as acetyl salicylic acid.

Migraine. This is a very special variety of "sick headache" and requires special treatment under medical supervision. It has many different forms, but usually there is a definite sequence of events. An attack often starts with some alteration of vision. The patient has shimmering blind spots or other visual disorders. This is followed by a well localised severe headache which may end in nausea or vomiting. The whole thing is caused by a poorly understood disorder of the blood vessels. There are special drugs, mostly derivatives of ergot, which are effective, especially if used when the first signs of an attack appear. Although there is a direct physical cause for an attack, it is also certain that some of the trouble is psychological tenseness. People with migraine are often rather anxious, striving and perfectionist people. Also it has been noticed that attacks are much less frequent when the necessary pills are being carried available for use. However, as with all other conditions which are partly "psychological" in origin they are none the less distressing for the patient. It simply means that the treatment is also partly psychological in encouraging him to come to terms with his problems.

Ménière's Disease is one of the conditions in which the organ of balance in the middle ear is affected, giving rise to *vertigo*, a form of giddiness. It usually begins in middle life in the same sort of person who sometimes has migraine. There is buzzing in the ears and some intermittent loss of hearing as well as vertigo. During an attack the patient may be unable to walk because of his loss of balance, and nausea and vomiting are common. Treatment is by special drugs, and occasionally an operation on the ear is necessary.

Epilepsy is a symptom, not a disease, which is common at all ages but especially children. It has been attributed to St. Paul, Julius Caesar, Napoleon, and (with more justice perhaps) to Dostoyevsky. Many varieties of attack occur often in the same patient, the commonest and best known being the *grand mal* or major seizure. In this the patient falls down unconscious and rigid and the jaw is clenched, so that there is danger of the tongue being bitten. This so-called tonic phase is followed, within a minute or so, by a clonic phase in which the limbs contract rhythmically. The attack ends with the patient going limp and gradually recovering consciousness, a process which may take up to an hour. Occasionally the patient has a brief warning, most often an indescribable feeling in the stomach. There are two common forms of minor seizure, one occurring mainly in children and the other more often in adults. The common minor attacks in children are often called *petit mal* or *absence*, which well describes the instantaneous and brief loss of consciousness often unaccompanied by any change in posture. Recovery is equally instantaneous. On the other hand, in the other forms of epilepsy which arise from various parts of the brain, but especially from the lobe under the temporal region, there is often a warning similar to that which may precede a major seizure. In these cases the patient shows only confusion, no definite loss of posture, but automatic activity such as fumbling with buttons, muttering, and grimacing. Following these attacks there may be a quite prolonged period of confusion in which the patient may wander away and occasionally may be violent. Criminal acts are very rarely carried out in this state.

A large number of people have had one or two fits in their lives, particularly at times of physical or psychological stress. "Fever" or "Febrile" convulsions (often called teething fits in the past) are extremely common in young children and are often thought of as something different from epilepsy since the attacks rarely continue in later years. This form of epilepsy and some cases of *petit mal* are the only forms in which hereditary factors are important in the causation, and these are the least serious forms of epilepsy. They are very rarely associated with serious physical or psychological disturbances. Most other forms of epilepsy are due to a scar or other area of brain damage. It is a proportion of these cases which develop the psychological disturbances that are occasionally very serious.

Not every patient who has had one or two fits need necessarily take regular anticonvulsant drugs; that is drugs which damp down the abnormal excessive activity of the brain that leads to the attacks. Many drugs are available of which the most important are phenobarbitone, phenytoin and clonazepam. The succinimides and troxidones are effective only against minor seizures. The choice is a matter of skilled medical judgment. Patients often find it difficult to get work because of the reluctance of employers to take on someone who may be more prone to accidents and whose fits may distress other workers. Obviously there are some jobs which epilepsy sufferers should not do because of the danger involved (from for example, moving machinery), and they should not drive a car. A few cases are so severe that work is almost impossible, but employers have a duty whenever possible to employ these people whose mental health may suffer greatly if they are made to feel outcasts and who ordinarily are as efficient, or even more so, as the next man. It is also hoped that employees will become less prejudiced about epilepsy as the general public become less ignorant about medical matters.

Congenital Malformations. The proper shape of the brain and spinal cord is achieved quite early in development by about the thirteenth week after conception. During this time very slight changes in the foetal environment can produce disastrous malformations. The drug thalidomide, for example, operated on other body systems while they were passing through this phase of construction. Some viruses can do the same thing. Most malformations are without known cause, but it is certain that something went wrong at this very early stage, and it only needs a very minor interference with the normal process to do the permanent damage. At about this time the bones of the spine are beginning to enclose, or form a roof over the developing spinal cord. Sometimes they fail to complete the process, resulting in *spina bifida.* If the coverings of the cord protrude through the defect, this is a *meningocele*, and if the cord itself protrudes it is a *meningomyelocele.* The whole protrusion may be covered with skin, but if it is not, the cord soon becomes infected. The effect on the patient is variable, according to the amount of damage to the nerve fibres in the cord, and there are varying degrees of paralysis and loss of sensation below the area involved together with loss of bowel and bladder control. Much help is often obtained from surgical repair, but many cases remain in a distressing condition always, and the only really useful attack on the problem is research to find the cause and prevent it happening. The same is true of the *malformations of the brain.* In one of these, hydrocephaly, the narrow channel is blocked which transmits the cerebrospinal fluid from the chambers within the brain where it is secreted to the outer coverings to be taken back into the blood stream. Blockage of the channel (or aqueduct) results in distension of the brain by fluid, enlargement of the head, and mental retardation. Sometimes a by-pass valve can be inserted to restore normal fluid circulation with very gratifying results.

Cerebral Palsy is a physically disabling condition of impaired muscle co-ordination caused before, during or shortly after birth by damage to or maldevelopment in the portion of the brain which controls movement. There are 3 main types: *spasticity, athetosis,* and *ataxia* depending on what area of the brain has been affected. Inherited defects do not play a large part in cerebral palsy. The general incidence of the disorder is thought to be 2.5 per 1,000 births. For further information and advice contact: the Spastics Society, 12 Park Crescent, London W1N 4EQ.

Motor Neurone Disease. This is a group of distressing diseases usually occurring in people over 40, in whom the parts of the brain and spinal cord which look after muscular movement degenerate. The group includes *Amyotrophic Lateral Sclerosis, Progressive Muscular Atrophy, Progressive Bulbar Palsy,* and *Primary Lateral Sclerosis.* The results are paralysis or weakness with wasting of the muscles of the body, including those concerned with arms, legs, breathing, speaking, etc. Nothing whatever is known of the cause. It is uncommon, but this is little comfort to the sufferer.

Parkinson's Disease, formerly known as The Shaking Palsy, derives its present name from the London physician James Parkinson (1755–1824) whose description established it as a clinical entity. It is one of the commonest illnesses to affect the human brain with more than one in 1,000 of the population as a whole (though one in 100 of those above 60 years of age) suffering from it. The average age of onset is about 55 though one in seven contract it in their thirties or forties. It has three classical features: shaking (or tremor), muscular rigidity and poverty of movement. A stooping, shuffling gait and a mask-like loss of facial expression are common. It is a progressive disease affecting patients in variable degrees of severity and different degrees of progression. A good deal can now be done to help these patients with drugs and since the condition results from a malfunctioning of brain cells which produce a chemical 'messenger' known as dopamine replacement of this substance by the drug levodopa (often accompanied by an additive in a combined preparation) is often the first line of treatment. Occasionally younger patients have benefited from surgical destruction of small areas of diseased brain. It is important to remember that many elderly people have some tremor of the head or hands called *Senile Tremor* and this is *not* Parkinson's Disease. It is merely one of the features of achieving advanced seniority as a citizen. The Parkinson's Disease Society of 36 Portland Place, London W1N 3DG sponsors, from monies raised, medical research as well as promoting patient welfare.

Chorea. This is a group of diseases in which there is involuntary muscle movement, weakness, and emotional instability. There will be clumsiness, awkward gait, twitching of limbs, face, hands, trunk, or tongue. They include *Acute Chorea* or *St. Vitus' Dance* occurring in children from 5 to 15, *Hereditary or Huntington's Chorea* occurring in a well-defined genetic pattern and beginning later, between 35 and 50. *Tics* or habit spasms are not part of these diseases but are often of psychological origin. They are usually eye blinking, head shaking.

Stroke Illness or Cerebrovascular Diseases. Strokes are due to diseases of the brain's blood vessels which either burst or get blocked. The same blood-vessel disorders cause heart attacks by blocking the coronary arteries supplying the heart. Strokes and heart attacks together kill more people than any other single cause including cancer. They account for one death in every five. Perhaps less is known of the cause of this disease than is known about cancer, and much more research is needed to find out if it is to be prevented. The cause of the commonest cancer (of the lung) is now known and it can be prevented by stopping smoking. Perhaps the prevention of strokes and heart attacks will mean an equally difficult abstinence from all those foods which make us fat. At least it is known that being overweight leads to death from these causes, just as smoking may lead to death from lung cancer.

If any artery supplying blood to any part of the brain is blocked, the territory supplied will die; and the bodily functions for which that part of the brain is responsible will cease. The process is called *infarction* of the brain, the dead area being an *infarct.* The blockage is usually due to thrombosis (*see* **P30**) of the blood within a vessel, a *thrombus* being a rather complicated clot with a structure of its own. The underlying cause is the arterial disease, atheroma (*see* **P29**) together with stagnation of the circulation. About one blockage in ten is due to a small piece of a much larger thrombus in the heart chambers being flung into the blood stream and impacting in the distant vessel in the brain. This is *cerebral embolism* (*see* **P30**). If the area of dead or infarcted brain is not too large the patient will recover from his unconsciousness, but will be left with permanent loss of function (paralysis, etc.) related to that part of the brain.

When a blood vessel supplying the brain bursts, this causes *cerebral haemorrhage* or apoplexy. The vessel may be on the surface (*subarachnoid haemorrhage*) or in the depths of the tissue (*intracerebral haemorrhage*). Strokes tend to occur in older people, because the associated arterial disease is a product of age and high blood pressure. Occasionally a subarachnoid haemorrhage occurs in a younger person with an unsuspected malformation of the arteries of the base of the brain known as a *berry aneurysm.* This is a small berry-sized blown-out balloon due to a defect in the wall of the vessel. Berry aneurysms can often be treated surgically. Intracerebral haemorrhage carries a very poor outlook, however, since much brain tissue is often destroyed by the escaping blood, especially the deep tissues responsible for the vital functions. Haemorrhage within the brain cavity can also be caused by injury (*see concussion and compression*, **P21**).

Inflammatory Diseases of the Nervous System. The membranes covering the brain are called the meninges. Inflammation of these, nearly always by blood-borne infection or infection following injury, is called *meningitis.* Cerebrospinal or spotted fever which used to be common and very much feared was only one variety caused by a germ called "meningococcus." It is now rare. Almost any other germ may cause meningitis, and when the germ is susceptible to one of the antibiotics it is usually treatable. It will usually be necessary to identify the germ by taking a sample of cerebrospinal fluid from a convenient space around the spinal cord in the lower back. When the disease is caused by the tubercle bacillus (*tuberculous meningitis*) the problem is more difficult because the patient is often not so obviously ill until the later, less treatable stages. *Cerebral abscess,* or abscess of the brain is very serious because it occupies space in the closed box of the skull and compresses the brain, as well as being a destructive process. It may arise due to an infected piece of tissue or pus being carried to the brain in the blood stream from a distant site in the lungs or heart. When the brain or cord tissue is itself inflamed it is called *encephalitis* (brain) or *myelitis* (cord) or *encephalo-myelitis* (both). These conditions are comparatively uncommon.

Herpes zoster (Shingles) is a common viral infection of the nervous system which affects sensory nerve roots where they enter the spinal cord. The initial symptoms are of pain in the area supplied by the affected nerves—commonly one side of the trunk, the buttock or the face—followed by the appearance of blisters. Treatment is symptomatic, as there is no specific remedy. Soothing lotions may be applied to the blisters and analgesics given for the pain. The disease is fairly short-lived, but neuralgia may persist for weeks after the blisters have healed.

Shingles is interesting in that it is not a *primary* viral infection, but the result of reactivation of the varicella/zoster virus (so called because it causes *either* chicken pox or shingles) which has lain dormant in nerve root cells, probably since childhood. Primary infection with the virus at whatever age causes chicken pox, not shingles; if an adult who has never had chicken pox or shingles comes into contact with a child with chicken pox or an adult with shingles, he is likely to contract the former but not the latter.

Shingles is infectious from the time the blisters appear until they have crusted over and healed. However, it is not as infectious as chicken pox.

Multiple sclerosis is the most important of the *demyelinating diseases* in which the myelin or "fatty" sheaths which insulate nerve fibres appear to disintegrate. This occurs patchily and seemingly randomly throughout the central nervous system (*i.e.* the brain and spinal cord) and results in interference with the passage of impulses through the affected nerves. Changes in sensation, balance or muscular co-ordination occur at varying intervals of time and spaced out over months or years in such a way as to appear unconnected. There is at present no reliable, objective diagnostic test for multiple sclerosis and diagnosis has to be made from the history of such episodic symptoms. The cause is unknown, but from various pieces of evidence such as the odd distribution of the disease in the world (the incidence is very much higher in Scandinavia and Scotland than on the Equator) one theory is that multiple sclerosis is the result of a recrudescence of a dormant viral infection which may be picked up during the teenage years. It is commonly held that once diagnosis of MS is made it means a sentence of years of increasingly severe disablement which will progress relentlessly and inexorably and reduce the patient to a helpless vegetable state in twenty or thirty years. That may be the case, but in fact such a gloomy picture is very uncommon. Much research has gone into the natural history of MS and it is clear that there are seven distinct patterns of the disease. These cover a wide range of symptom patterns from that characterised by a sudden onset of symptoms with relatively few relapses after the first year, to that manifested by sudden onset followed by unremitting relapses causing progressively greater degrees of physical impairment which may indeed lead to much distressing disability and relatively early death. But between these two extremes, of which the first is far the commonest form for the disease to take and the latter relatively infrequent, there lies a whole range of disease patterns and prediction is difficult.

The Multiple Sclerosis Society exists to sponsor research, to care for patients and to give advice and support to friends and relatives. For more information write to them at their offices at 286 Munster Road, Fulham, London, SW6 6BE.

Brain Tumours. The brain is no exception to the rule that any cell in any tissue of the body can suddenly begin to disobey the body's rules regarding its growth and multiplication. A totally unknown mechanism governs how many cells of a certain type there ought to be and calls a halt to cell multiplication when this number is reached. Every now and then one of them turns a blind eye and goes on dividing, and the result is a tumour, or lump, of anarchic cells which obey no rules. Tumours are commonest in cells which normally go on dividing throughout life, in order to replace those lost by wear and tear. Examples are the cells lining the air passages in the lung, or the alimentary tract in the stomach or large bowel. Fortunately for the brain there is little cell division once it has grown. Nerve cells cannot divide at all in adult life, and the supporting glial cells only do so in response to injury. Therefore primary brain tumours are much less common than those elsewhere. Also many brain tumours like many of those elsewhere, are benign or "innocent" tumours. They are not cancerous, and need only be removed for the patient to be completely cured. The brain, however, is at two major disadvantages compared with other tissues when it comes to tumours. One is that all tumours as they grow take up space, and space in the skull is already fully occupied. Thus even an innocent tumour can compress the brain within its rigid box of bone and become most dangerous until it is removed. The second disadvantage is due to the very large blood supply of the brain. Cancer in other parts of the body spreads partly by sending small pieces of itself to other tissues by way of the blood stream, and those tissues like liver, lung, kidney, and brain which have a big blood supply naturally receive more than their share of other tissues' tumour. These secondary deposits, or *metastases,* cause compression and other trouble in the brain much more frequently than the brain's own primary tumours. Indeed convulsions or other signs of brain disorder may be the first indication that there is a primary tumour in the lung or breast or elsewhere.

Diseases of Peripheral Nerves. Compared with the nerves of the central nervous system (brain and spinal cord), the peripheral nerves are comparatively rarely affected by disease. They have some similarities of structure with central nerve fibres in that their fibres are often covered with myelin sheaths and are arranged in bundles. A special feature, however, is that they are enclosed by connective tissue sheaths and it is probably these which allow a peripheral nerve to grow again, or regenerate, after it has been cut or damaged. Central nerve fibres are unable to do this. After *injury of a peripheral nerve* the part away from the centre is cut off from its parent cell body and it dies. All function, whether motor or sensory, is lost. But in the course of many months the central surviving part grows into the connective tissue sheaths which act like tubes to guide the new nerve to its destination. Provided the cut ends are close enough together and correctly aligned, and provided enough fibres reach their correct destination, good functional recovery is possible.

A disorder of a peripheral nerve is called a *neuropathy* and means nothing more than that. There are many kinds. One of the most distressing is *trigeminal neuralgia,* again fortunately rare. The trigeminal or fifth cranial nerve has a motor and sensory territory on the face. In this condition there are paroxysmal episodes of extremely severe pain which may resist all treatment except destruction of the nerve itself with consequent facial paralysis and loss of sensation. At the other more trivial extreme are the occasions when a leg "goes to sleep" or gets "pins and needles" after crossing it and pressing on a nerve for too long. *Bell's Palsy* is sudden loss of function of the seventh cranial nerve and there is again paralysis on one side of the face which usually recovers in time. Some bacterial diseases, especially leprosy, invade the nerves themselves. Chronic alcoholism may affect the nerves, as may diabetes, probably by interfering with the nutrition of the nerve cell. So may exposure to arsenic or lead or an unpleasant nerve poison which may contaminate cooking oil known as TOCP, or triorthocresylphosphate.

Muscular Dystrophies. These are a series of diseases of muscle in which there is progressive wasting and weakness of muscle, the causes of which are entirely unknown. They are divided up according to the age of onset and the muscles involved. *Duchenne's muscular dystrophy* occurs in the first decade of life. It affects most of the muscles eventually, including the heart muscle and those concerned with breathing, and so the outlook is not good. Other forms are inherited. The Muscular Dystrophy Group (Nattrass House, 35 Macaulay Rd. London SW4 0QP) gives great assistance to sufferers.

Myasthenia Gravis. This is a strange disorder of the mechanism which transmits instructions from nerve to muscle at the "neuromuscular junction," leading to extreme weakness.

MENTAL ILLNESS

Conventionally mental illness is divided into two categories, psychosis (madness), and neurosis (exaggerated symptoms of commonly experienced states). The dividing line is not a clear one though, since even the acts of a madman are understandable if you accept his view of the world. Psychoses are themselves divided into: *organic*, implying that we can identify a physical cause, and *functional*, where the brain structure appears to be intact but its performance is abnormal. This division is now seen to be very blurred since there are physical diseases and drugs which can lower the threshold for response, or alter a person's perceptions so that he appears to be mad, albeit temporarily. The more research is done, the more organic causes are found for abnormal behaviour, and the more hope is raised for successful medical intervention.

Organic Psychoses.

The organic psychoses result from actual damage to the brain. This damage can be caused by disease, as in syphilis; by tumours; by dietary deficiencies, as in inadequate vitamin B12 absorption; by poisons such as alcohol and lead; by drugs such as LSD or amphetamine; by problems of blood circulation such as heart failure or atheroma; and by genetic inheritance. The onset of illness can be either an acute confusional state or a chronic reaction known as *dementia*. The acute episode is characterised by an impairment of consciousness which may vary from difficulty in holding on to the point of a story, to actual coma. The chronic reaction, on the other hand, does not affect consciousness but intellect, memory and personality. Characteristically, memory for recent events is lost, while that for remote ones is preserved. About one in ten men and women over the age of 65 is likely to be affected. Since it is the most commonly and voluntarily ingested poison, it is worth giving a special mention to alcohol. It is hard to define what is meant by the term 'alcoholic', but anyone whose daily intake of alcohol exceeds 5 units is generally agreed to qualify. (A unit of alcohol is a half pint of beer, or a single measure of spirits, or a glass of wine). Alcohol-related disabilities can be classed as social, psychological and physical. Social problems are often noticed first, and include failure to perform an expected role as parent or spouse or at work, or breaking social rules as in driving offences. Psychological difficulties include increased depression and personality deterioration. *Delirium Tremens*, (DTs), is an acute confusional state involving intense fear and restlessness with hallucinations. Most alcoholics experience blackouts ranging from momentary lapses to memory loss involving several hours. Intellectual impairment can occur and may be permanent, even after alcohol is abandoned.

Other physical problems associated with alcoholism include a doubled death rate, liver damage, gastritis, anaemia, increased rates of cancer, and infections such as TB. Sexual incompetence is common. The children of alcoholic mothers are at increased risk of deformity and growth retardation.

Functional Psychoses.

Functional psychoses broadly fall into two categories: *Schizophrenia* and *Manic Depressive Psychosis*. Schizophrenia was a term introduced by Eugene Bleuler in 1911 to describe a group of illnesses in which there was a splitting of the psychic functioning so that the association between two ideas was bizarre, and mood seemed inappropriate to the circumstances. Nowadays schizophrenia is diagnosed on the presence of certain accepted symptoms such as a lack of insight, auditory hallucinations especially of voices discussing the patient in derogatory terms, the idea that radio and TV programmes refer to him directly, unreasonable suspicions, or a flatness of response. However, the concept has been challenged by workers such as Thomas Szasz, who regards it as a medical fiction, and Scheff, who believed that many of the symptoms arose from being labelled 'Mad'. It seems that schizophrenia occurs in all societies, but in less developed countries appears to be more acute yet to offer better prospects for recovery. About one person in a hundred will develop the condition, and there is an increased risk where close relations are affected. There are many theories of causation though an inheritance factor is clear, but there is argument about what this factor might be, and the extent to which its influence is affected by life events. Theories invoking abnormalities in the substances responsible for the transmission of signals within the brain itself are supported by the fact that some symptoms of schizophrenia can be induced experimentally. But as yet the physical theories are not wholly proven. The concept of the 'Schizophrenogenic' mother who causes illness in her child, and the theory that abnormal dominance patterns in the family are the cause have proved equally hard to verify. The 'Double Bind' hypothesis of Bateson, that an emotionally disturbed parent, who says one thing to a child but at the same time suggests a deeper, contradictory, message will eventually cause the child to withdraw into a fantasy world, is another explanation. The Personal Construct Theory of Bannister and Fransella says that we build up constructs and relationships between them in order to understand our world. In this theory if the construct of Generous-Mean is linked with those of Honest–Dishonest and Gentle–Violent, then we expect someone we know to be generous to be also honest and gentle. If these associations are weak or inconsistent, then the world is a chaotic and fearful place. Whatever the role of early experience in the causation of schizophrenia it is clear that current stress brings on an attack.

The treatment of schizophrenia was revolutionised by the introduction in the 1950s of phenothiazine drugs which not only tranquillise but also have specific anti-psychotic effects. The fact that schizophrenic patients are increasingly returned to their community, able to function, is due in large part to these pharmacological advances, and to the concept of 'milieu therapy' involving group activities, recreation and occupational therapies.

Manic Depressive Psychosis is characterised by swings of mood between depression and elation without apparent cause, and in this form is called the *bipolar* state. More frequently, the disease is *unipolar*, showing only periods of depression interspersed with periods of normality. The difficulty in defining depression as an illness is firstly to distinguish it from a symptom, and secondly to make a distinction between normal and morbid depression which is depression of greater severity and duration than would be expected in a given population from the apparent cause. This last is a very subjective rating and this makes depression a difficult subject for research. The expectancy that one will suffer a depressive illness in one's lifetime is about one to three per cent, with females more likely than males. Generally it is accepted as a phenomenon of later life, but can occur at any age. In depression the major symptom is of a persisting sad, despairing mood, especially severe on waking up. Agitation or marked slowing down may be present, and hallucinations are not uncommon.

Ideas of unworthiness, guilt and persecution are frequent, loss of appetite, loss of weight, loss of sexual drive and loss of menstruation are also common. The causation of depressive illness is another area where authorities are in dispute, and theories abound. Seligman points to learned helplessness as a cause. In his experiments animals exposed to repeated stresses beyond their control, exhibited apathy, difficulty in accepting that they could do anything to help themselves, loss of appetite, and reduced sociability. The idea that depression is the result of aggressive feelings which cannot be channelled out and so are turned in on oneself, is a simplified view of what Freud said. Some support is lent to this idea by the fact that depressive illness is less common in time of war. Certain biochemical changes have been found in the brains of depressed patients, and the anti-depressant drugs work in ways to correct these imbalances, but whether these intra-cellular changes are cause or effect, and how this comes about, is still not entirely clear. Treatment is by specific anti-depressant drugs of which there are now many, by psychotherapy of various kinds, and much more rarely now by Electro-convulsive therapy (ECT) which can be life-saving in very severe cases. Treatment with lithium is often successful in reducing the severity of mood swings.

Mania is a state of elation, hurried speech, and physical overactivity. Irritability is common if the patient is frustrated. Grandiose plans are made and money can be lavishly spent. Gradually as the illness progresses the sufferer becomes confused, angry, hallucinated, incoherent and exhausted. Treatment is usually by tranquillising drugs.

Neurosis.

Neurosis as we now understand it is a concept we owe to Freud, and to him, too, we owe the distinction between the neurotic disorders of *hysteria*, *anxiety* and *obsessionality*, and the disorders of *personality*. Those in the latter category, while having no detectable disease, are treated by psychiatrists as if they had, and this is a decision of society as a whole since the alternative is to refer such people to the legal or social services. Because the category of neurosis is so vague, it is hard to put a figure on how many people may be affected, but researchers in General Practice consultations estimate about one in ten women, and half that many men are at risk. The reason for this disparity is not clear, but may be due to factors such as the greater freedom for expression of frustration enjoyed by men in our society than women. The majority of neurotic illnesses clear up, and may do so spontaneously, although obsessional and hypochondriacal symptoms are more persistent than others. Obsessional neurotics display recurring ruminations and rituals. Obsessional ruminations are thoughts which are felt to be foreign, yet cannot be denied, they give rise to uncomfortable tension and anxiety, and often the rituals are designed to combat and control the symptoms in a magical way. Frequent hand washing to allay fears of contamination is an example. Indecisiveness is another symptom which may be crippling, as in the case of a gardener who, asked to weed out weak seedlings, could only progress a few inches down the first row because he could not decide what to do about a medium-sized plant. Compulsive checking that the gas taps are off, or the doors locked, may lead in extreme cases to an inability to leave the house. Treatment is difficult, the present approach being behaviour modification techniques such as *modelling*, where the therapist shows by example that there is no danger in a feared situation; Flooding, where the patient is, so to speak, thrown in at the deep end and shown that he can in fact swim when he thought that he could not; Thought Stopping; and Relaxation techniques.

Anxiety neurosis as a pathological state where anxiety is either unrelated to a recognisable threat, or the degree of anxiety is out of proportion to the threat. The mechanism of our response to a threat appears to depend on the level at which the threat is perceived, if at a conscious level, the response is fear, if at an unconscious level, the response is anxiety. Symptoms include weakness, dizziness, sweating and tiredness. The physical symptoms are themselves unpleasant and increase the feelings of being threatened. Treatment may be by reassurance and explanation, by psychotherapy aimed at bringing the threat into conscious appraisal, or by drugs which are now widely, and often inappropriately, prescribed. Phobic anxiety occurs when unreasonable fear is focused on a particular object or situation, and leads to avoidance, Agoraphobia, literally a fear of the Market Place, claustrophobia, fear of enclosed spaces, and animal phobias are well recognised. Social phobias, such as fear of eating in public or fear of vomiting are often harder for the sufferer to acknowledge. Phobic states are often associated with a traumatic event in the past, and avoidance through fear leads to a form of conditioning which reinforces the fear. Gradually the sufferer extends the range of feared and avoided stimuli. Behavioural therapy offers the chance to reverse this process.

Much is made of the manipulative nature of neurotics, and the idea of secondary gain, where the neurotic is perceived as getting the better of those around him by organising his, and other people's, lives to fit in with his symptoms. Certainly neurotic people can be very irritating in their demands and social failings, but their conscious experience is of personal suffering, their gains are at an unconscious level, and one cannot but be saddened by the waste their lives represent.

Suicide as a completed act is on the decline, but the rate of attempted suicide is rising. Most attempts are preceded by a warning of intention, often quite explicit. Men, especially alcoholic or physically ill men, are more likely to complete the attempt than are women for whom the attempt itself, rather than the ending of life, seems to be the important feature.

Mental Illness in Childhood.

Mental illness in childhood refers to psychoses specific to children such as autism, to emotional disorders, and to disorders of conduct. Because children are dependent on their families, much interest has centred on relationships within the family and on maternal deprivation as factors in the creation of childhood difficulties. The work of Bowlby highlighted problems consequent on the infant's need for attachment being denied, and he expressed the view that poor early experiences led to failures in later life to develop social relationships. Autism is a state where the child displays abnormalities of language, indifference to people, and ritual behaviour. Autistic children do not grow into schizophrenics, they grow up into autistic adults, and most remain severely handicapped. Phobias and obsessional behaviour are common in children and usually appear and disappear rapidly, especially with prompt intervention. Depressive illness is rare before puberty and where depressive features are seen it is usually in response to environment.

Conduct disorders include persistent lying, stealing, disobeying, truanting, fighting or setting fires. The distinction from delinquency is important since the latter implies breaking the law which is quite common in adolescence. There is a high correlation between these behaviours and difficulty in reading, though whether this is because of a shared impairment or the result of educational frustration is not clear. Treatment is by careful assessment of the family situation, and by social and educational intervention. The future is not rosy though, since about half the antisocial boys in one long-term study went on to be antisocial men in later life.

Anorexia Nervosa is usually a disorder of adolescent girls in which food avoidance, weight loss, failure of menstruation and overactivity predominate. Anorexics often display a distorted view of their own bodies, being unable to see how thin they have become. The underlying difficulty may be a need to control something in their life at a time of actual dependence on parents, or an attempt to avoid the challenge of puberty and the demands, particularly of sexuality, that adulthood makes. Treatment is by behaviour modification, supervised weight gain, and psychotherapy. Bulimia Nervosa is a variant in which meals, often very large meals, are eaten and then vomiting is induced to get rid of them.

THE SKIN

The skin in the course of development before birth is particularly closely associated with the nervous system. It is therefore not surprising that so many skin diseases are influenced by emotional states. Other causes of skin disease are infectious, glandular disorders, vitamin deficiencies, and the numerous conditions for which no cause has been discovered, but which presumably are due to metabolic disorders.

One of the commonest skin symptoms is *itching* or *pruritus*. It may accompany many different general diseases, for example diabetes and jaundice. It may also be troublesome during the menopause (the change of life in women), in old age, or in nervous conditions. Sedatives and sex hormones sometimes help the itching during the menopause, and there are ointments which may be useful.

Itching in the region of the anus and genital organs is relatively common. It may be caused by worms, by irritating vaginal discharge, or by sugar in the urine, as in diabetes. The alteration in the normal bacteria of the bowel which follows treatment with various antibiotics also often causes anal pruritus and soreness. In many cases however the itching has some psychological cause. In treatment it is important to avoid ointments and creams which contain a local anaesthetic, because these substances can cause severe allergic reactions if used for longer than a few days, and may thus make the condition much worse. Treatment with a local corticosteroid application is more effective and safer.

Parasites, such as the *scabies* mite or *lice* can cause severe and persistent itching. The scabies mite is very small, and since it burrows under the skin surface, is unlikely to be seen; it is the cause of itching most commonly between the fingers and on the front of the wrists. The itching is worst when the body becomes heated, as in bed. Treatment consists of painting the body from head to foot with benzyl benzoate application, followed the next day by a hot bath. Since scabies is contracted through close personal contact with an infested person it is often desirable for several or all members of a family to be treated at the same time, even though only one of them may be affected. Lice are specialists, one type of which affects the scalp, another the body, and a third the genital area. Head lice are destroyed by lethane, body lice by insecticides and genital (pubic) lice by shaving off hair and washing. Obviously, the clothes, especially in the case of body lice, should be disinfested, by using a hot iron particularly over the seams, which lice (for some inexplicable reason) seem to favour. Apart from the discomfort they cause, lice are dangerous as potential carriers of typhus fever.

Baldness, or *Alopecia*, is a very common condition, as is manifested by the extraordinary number of preparations advertised as curing it. When many preparations are offered for the treatment of one condition it is a fair judgment to assume that none of them is likely to be effective. There are, in fact, two types of baldness; one, which is much the commoner, is hereditary, and cannot be influenced in the slightest by any treatment, the other, *alopecia areata*, is caused by nervous stress, and would recover in most cases by itself, whether one used a solution of soot and water or the most expensive "hair food." There is no such thing as a hair food, any more than there is such a thing as a nerve food, and although it is probable that hair hygiene may delay baldness, it certainly cannot prevent it. All hair tonics and "foods" are useless, and their uselessness is only equalled by their costliness. Those who have lost their hair and find it growing again after using some alleged tonic are people who have had *alopecia areata* and whose hair would have grown back anyhow. In women the hair often thins out soon after a pregnancy, but a few months later it usually returns to normal.

Seborrhoea is a condition in which there is over-activity of the sebaceous glands. The most usual form it takes is *dandruff*. However, it takes other forms, and those who have dandruff may also have rashes on the face, shoulders, and chest. In these areas there is a patchy, greasy, and often itchy, rash which does not clear up until the primary condition in the scalp is dealt with. The scalp should be washed with one of the modern sulphur-containing shampoos at least twice a week, and the affected parts on the face and chest can be dealt with by the use of a sulphur lotion (*not* on any account by greasy ointments). Seborrhoea is not in itself difficult to treat, but since the condition depends on over-secretion of sebum, the skin lubricant, treatment may have to be persisted in during the years of early adulthood, when it is most active.

Erythema Intertrigo is, quite simply, the sort of irritation which occurs usually from excessive sweating under the armpits, between the legs, and under the breasts in women. All that need be done is to wash frequently and to dust the affected areas after washing with powder. This is the condition which, in the tropics, is known as "prickly heat" and elsewhere as a "sweat rash." In some people *hyperhidrosis* or *excessive sweating* is a problem, especially when the sweating is accompanied with body odour—the sort of thing that, according to the advertisements, "even your best friends won't tell you." There is little need for anyone in these days to suffer in this way: for the cosmetic firms have produced many highly efficient deodorants which not only control odour but also control the amount of sweating. Chlorophyll, which has been much advertised as removing odours, is effective when applied directly to surfaces which give off an unpleasant smell. It is however ineffective when taken by mouth, and does not prevent body odours. Stale sweat smells bad because it is decomposed by bacteria, and this type of body odour can be largely prevented by preparations containing harmless antiseptic and anti-perspirants.

Erysipelas is an infection of the skin caused by the haemolytic streptococcus. It begins as a red, raised area anywhere on the body where the germs have been able to enter through a small crack or cut in the skin. The red area advances and spreads over the body until the disease is got under control. Erysipelas is very infectious, and those who look after the patient should wash their hands thoroughly after contact. At one time the disease used to spread as an epidemic throughout the hospital wards, but this is very rare nowadays. Treatment is, of course, a matter for the doctor.

Chilblains are common in cold weather, especially in those with poor circulation. Ordinarily they occur in the toes and fingers, but may appear on the nose and ears. The part affected becomes swollen, dusky, and there is pain and itching, sometimes leading to ulceration. Protection of the body, especially the hands and feet, from cold is the best and the only really effective way of preventing chilblains. Warm lined gloves and footwear, and arm stockings or trousers should be worn outdoors. Adequate heating of rooms is essential: a temperature between 18° and 21°C is recommended. Most tablets, medicines, ointment, or creams for chilblains are useless. A skin affection caused by heat is rather grandiosely described as *erythema ab igne*, and used frequently to be seen on the legs of ladies addicted to roasting their legs before the fire. It takes the form of red patches on the front of the legs and can be removed only by avoiding the cause.

Dermatitis means "inflammation of the skin," and therefore the word could be, strictly speaking, applied to any skin disease. In fact the term is used almost interchangeably with the term *eczema*. There are three main types of dermatitis or eczema. The first, *primary irritant dermatitis* results from injury of the skin by some powerful chemical, such as strong alkali or turpentine. The second, *contact dermatitis* is due to sensitisation of the skin to some substance which is normally liable to cause this type of allergic sensitivity; examples are nickel (in jewellery and suspender buckles), epoxy resins, rubber additives, primulas and chrysanthemums, and even ingredients of cosmetics. Contact dermatitis may continue for a long time, even after the patient is no longer in contact with the offending material. The third type is often called *constitutional eczema*. Although the skin is apt to react adversely to various irritants and sensitisers the major part is played by the personality, and there is often a history of eczema, hay fever or asthma in the family. Treatment is more difficult, but local corticosteroids and tar, sedatives and psychological treatment can be of great help. Infantile eczema also belongs in this category, but in most patients it disappears as the child grows up.

Impetigo is an infectious skin disease caused primarily by the streptococcus, but later often infected with staphylococci. It usually occurs on the face, and takes the form of blisters filled with pus on a red base; when the blisters burst their place is taken by yellow crusts. Impetigo is very infectious and easily spread by the fingers, dirty towels, or cloths; therefore, one of the first necessities is to prevent infection of others or reinfection of oneself by avoiding scratching and using a different towel each day, which must on no account be used by anyone else. Treatment is simple with an antibacterial ointment, so the main issue is prevention of contamination.

Urticaria or *Nettlerash* is a familiar skin disease in which itching weals appear on the skin, usually for no obvious reason. It is not infectious, and can be caused by nervous stress, certain drugs, allergy to some foods, or even exposure of the skin to cold. In some people it is possible to write on the skin with a fingernail: the "writing" appears in the form of weals. This is known as *dermographism*; it occurs in many normal persons as well as in many patients with urticaria. The antihistamine drugs are the most useful in the treatment of urticaria. Urticarial swelling of the tongue or throat requires urgent medical attention.

Acne, or *"Blackheads,"* is a condition found on the face and shoulders; its appearance is so familiar that no description is necessary. Acne is one of those conditions which is the end result of many factors. There is, first, a greasy skin, the result of glandular upset (which is why the disease usually occurs in adolescence); secondly, there is infection of the skin; and thirdly, there is blockage of the sebaceous ducts, which ordinarily allow the grease from the skin to pass out on to the surface. Since the condition starts with excess secretion of grease, ointments should never be used, and probably the best applications are drying lotions containing some sulphur preparation which inhibits secretion of grease. The face should be frequently washed, and it is possible now to obtain detergent solutions which are both antiseptic and prevent grease formation. In severe cases ultraviolet ray treatment may be necessary.

Rosacea. As has already been implied elsewhere, although the wages of sin may be extremely unpleasant, the wages of extreme virtue may be no less troublesome. Thus *rosacea*, in which the nose and cheeks become red and greasy and the skin coarsened, occurs alike to chronic alcoholics and elderly ladies with no vices other than a preference for strong tea. Both cases are associated with indigestion, since; regrettable as it may seem, strong tea and alcohol are about equally liable to cause the gastritis which may be at the root of this complaint. However, in many patients the chronic flushing is caused in other ways and psychological factors are important.

Lichen Planus is one of the numerous skin diseases which seem to be due to nervous states of tension. It may occur on any part of the body, but is most common on the front of the forearms

and legs. The rash takes the form of nodules which are lilac in colour and have a dent on the top; when these disappear a stain is left behind. There is severe itching. Treatment is a matter for a doctor, as it also is in the case of *psoriasis*, a very common disease of largely unknown origin, which is extremely resistant to treatment. It tends to run in families. It takes the form of slightly raised papules, usually on the elbows and knees; typically the papules are covered with dry, silvery-looking scales. Apart from the rash, the patient is usually in perfectly good health and there is no itching. Many drugs have been used in psoriasis, notably chrysarobin, and while it is not difficult to cause the rash (which may occur anywhere on the body) to disappear in one area or even in all areas for a time it has a strong tendency to return.

Warts, or *Verrucae* are familiar enough. They are caused by a virus, and are, theoretically at least, contagious (although having removed many warts, the writer has never found them contagious). Most frequently they are found on the hands, but may occur elsewhere. Treatment is best carried out by a doctor, who will use a cautery, a caustic carbon dioxide frozen into "snow." A curious feature of the common wart is that it can sometimes be caused to disappear by suggestion, which is presumably why so many old wives charms are not necessarily without effect. Different altogether from the common wart is the *plantar wart*, which occurs on the soles of the feet and often causes a good deal of discomfort. It is best dealt with by a chiropodist or in bad cases by a skin specialist since it is highly infectious.

Ichthyosis is a disorder of skin formation with which some unfortunate people are born. The oil and sweat-producing glands do not function well and the skin is dry and scaly like the skin of a fish. It is, however, possible to help the condition, which does not affect the general health, by frequent alkaline baths to wash off the scales, and the subsequent use of lanolin to replace the lacking oil. Large doses of vitamin A seem to help in some cases, and there have been reports in the medical Press of cases being helped by hypnosis; this, however, is very much a matter for speculation.

Cancer, Rodent Ulcer, and Cysts. Cancer of the skin occurs mostly in old people, and takes the form of what is described as an *epithelioma*. It is most common on the face or hands, and usually appears as a nodule which breaks down and produces an ulcer. The glands may later be affected, but such cancers can almost invariably be cured unless a considerable time has elapsed during which they have been neglected. *Rodent ulcer* is a form of ulcer which appears on the inner corner of the eye or the side of the nose in old people. It does not spread over the body, but acts by eating into the tissues in the area where it has started. X-ray or operation is necessary, but the outlook is good. *Cysts* on the skin are due to blockage of the sebaceous glands. They may become very large, and are best removed, as they may become infected. They do not turn into cancer, and there is no such thing as "male" and "female" cysts. It does sometimes happen that *moles*, especially of the bluish-black type, may become malignant, so it is perhaps best to have them removed surgically when they exist. *All moles which change in appearance or size should be at once referred to a doctor.*

Skin Grafts.

These are a very complex subject which can be only briefly discussed here. They are used basically for a number of conditions in which large areas of skin have been removed from the body, as in burns or serious accidents. In other cases, as in plastic surgery, grafts may be used to make a new nose, eyelids, and so on. The following are the main types:

Pinch Grafts are small, circular pieces of skin cut from some other part of the body. (The former method of using grafts from another person has been given up almost completely, since such grafts—except in the case of identical twins—never "take.") The small pieces are laid on the area without skin and gradually grow together. *Split-thickness grafts* are grafts removed from another part of the body by an instrument known as a dermatome, which cuts sections about 10 by 20 cm. containing part of the deep layers of the skin.

In *Full-thickness Grafts*, on the other hand, the whole thickness of the skin is removed from elsewhere and applied to an area which has to bear friction or heavy weights, such as the hand or the foot. Lastly, and this is largely used in plastic surgery, there is the *Pedicle graft*, which, unfortunately, although it is certainly the most exciting type, is rather difficult to describe. Briefly, if one, for example, wants to make a new nose, one cuts an area of skin and underlying fat about 5 cm wide and 12·5–15 cm long in the abdomen. One end, however, remains attached so that it gets adequate blood-supply. The problem is how to get this tissue to the nose, and this is done by a complicated process of leap-frog. First, the free end of the graft is attached to the forearm, whilst its "root" remains in the original site, and when it begins to grow and get its blood-supply from the arm, the original "root" is cut. So we now have a "sausage" of tissue attached to the arm. The arm is then lifted to the face and kept firmly in position there until the new free part becomes attached. It is then detached from the arm, modelled to the correct shape, and grows where the nose used to be!

THE JOINTS.

Rheumatism is a word most doctors wish did not exist. This is partly because they do not understand it, but mainly because it is a condition which strictly does not exist: which is small comfort to the many millions of people who are more or less totally incapacitated by it. The truth is it is used for a hotch-potch of very real diseases, in all of which there is pain and stiffness of what is called the musculo-skeletal system, *i.e.*, the muscles and the joints. It may mainly involve the joints, in which case it should have been called arthritis; or it may involve other structures near the joints like tendons, muscles and fibrous tissue. Joints may either suffer from inflammation or degeneration or both, and the trouble may be acute or chronic or both; so it is easy to see what a mix-up the subject becomes, especially when we must include the joints of the spine as well as the limbs, feet and hands.

A good deal of arthritis used to be due to various germs, but these types are much less common now that the infections causing them have become rarer or better treated. They used to include gonorrhoea, tuberculosis, septic joints, syphilis, brucellosis, typhoid fever, dysentery and so on. The importance of *Rheumatic fever*, which is a reaction to an infection (streptococcal sore throat) rather than being actually caused by the streptococcus, is not because it involves the joints. This arthritis quickly clears up, but there may also be disease of the heart which may be serious and has been described on **P27**.

Rheumatoid arthritis is a completely different condition in which there is non-infective inflammation of connective tissues throughout the body. In the joints, the normally smooth, lubricated synovial membrane lining the joint cavity becomes scarred, leading to distortion, especially of smaller joints like those of the hand. Another characteristic feature is its capacity to vary in severity from time to time, with a strong tendency to unexplainable periods when it gets better or worse. This makes it extremely difficult to know whether any form of treatment is being useful, since any response may have occurred in any case. As in all diseases which behave like this, especially those in which medical men are also baffled, there

are almost as many theories and treatments as there are doctors. It has never been satisfactorily shown to be caused by infection, faulty nutrition, "glands," emotions or personality disturbance, nor is it convincingly inherited. The best current theory links it with an increased sensitivity reaction, perhaps to the body's own tissues, known as "autoimmunity." From the patient's point of view there is swelling and deformity of the joints with tenderness on pressure and pain on movement. Treatment involves a lengthy and complicated regime of rest, relief of pain with aspirin, exercises and the application of heat, with attention to general physical and mental health. At some stage adrenal corticosteroids (cortisone and its derivatives) are often tried, but although these can give great relief they have to be very carefully used to avoid very unpleasant side-effects.

Osteoarthritis is another completely different condition closely related to the normal processes of ageing. Therefore it occurs in older people and tends to be in larger, weight-bearing joints of the spine, hips and knees rather than in the hand; although the end joint of the fingers is commonly affected. Hard wear and tear, especially that caused by overweight, or injury may be the beginning of it. It is *not* due to diet, and dieting has no part in treatment except in those who need to slim. Physiotherapy, including heat, is helpful. It is not such a relentless condition as rheumatoid arthritis and patients should be reassured about this.

Fibrositis and other vague forms of "rheumatism" are very often manifestations of psychological problems. This does not make them any less real, but it directs treatment towards the mental state rather than to the joints and muscles.

EYES, EARS, NOSE AND THROAT.

Diseases of the *eyes* are very specialised and only very general information can be given here. The most common is inflammation of the conjunctiva causing redness and usually due to infection or some irritant substance or dust. If it persists and leads to hard crusts of yellow pus on waking in the morning, get it seen by a doctor for treatment probably with antibiotics. First-aiders are usually instructed how to remove small particles of grit from under the lids. It is important that these should not scratch the front of the eye—your window on the world—as this may lead to scarring and poor vision. So, above all, do not rub them in. Also, if you are fishing one out of someone else's eye, see it before removing it. Do not have a general sweep round in vague hopes of finding it. If in any doubts, obtain skilled help. Remember the eyes are part of the brain: the only visible part. Perhaps this is why people's eyes are so revealing.

Conditions such as glaucoma, cataract and disorders of vision are beyond the scope of this section.

Foreign bodies in the ears and nose are a constant minor problem with children. In these cases, whether they be peas, beads or peanuts, do *not* attempt to fish them out. They are doing no harm where they are, provided the child can be prevented from fiddling with them. Get him to a doctor who knows far better than you do about the delicate structures of the ear drum or the internal nose just behind the object, and has the proper gadget to get it out.

Sore throats are a nuisance we all have to put up with from time to time. If they last more than a few days they should be treated professionally. Persistent or recurrent sore throats are often due to over-eager treatment with antibiotics not allowing the body to learn how to fight the germs itself. Never prescribe antibiotics for yourself, especially in lozenge form, and only expect your doctor to give them when other measures have failed.

Tonsils and their inflammation may be a problem. It is comparatively rarely that they should be removed, yet every year hundreds of thousands of innocent children are subjected to this ritual cruelty to satisfy the misconceptions of their parents and the greed (or ignorance) of some surgeons. Of course there are many children who benefit so much from having tonsils out that the operation (which has real dangers) is worth doing. But please allow your doctor to decide if it is necessary, and do not pressurise him into re-commending it. (The same is true of *circumcision*, for which there are no hygienic, and practically no medical indications. If your reasons for inflicting this cruel assault on your little boy are religious or emotional, then please admit it: but do not pretend it is "necessary" or even medically helpful.)

DISEASES OF WOMEN.

The *internal sexual organs* of a woman, like the urinary system, can best be described as shaped like a capital Y. At the tips of the arms of the Y are the female sex glands, the ovaries: the two arms running downwards are the Fallopian tubes: the point where the arms meet is the womb or uterus: the single leg of the Y is the vagina. These are the *primary sexual organs* of a woman and they undergo regular cyclical changes in response to the control exercised over them by the pituitary gland, situated in the base of the skull. This control is mediated by chemical messengers (hormones) secreted into the circulation. The ovaries also secrete hormones, oestrogen, and progesterone, and a delicate hormonal balance is maintained between the pituitary gland and the ovaries. Each month an egg cell (ovum) matures and is released from the ovary, usually midway between two menstrual periods: the ovum is wafted along the Fallopian tubes by waves of contraction and if fertilised embeds in the lining of the uterus which has been conditioned to nourish it by the ovarian hormones. If it is not fertilised the ovum escapes from the uterus, altered hormone levels then cause the lining of the uterus to be shed (this is menstrua-tion), usually about 14 days after ovulation. After menstruation a new cycle begins; another ovum matures and a fresh lining grows in the uterus. These cyclical changes recur from puberty to the menopause. Menstruation does not occur during pregnancy, of which a missed period is often the first sign. However, women do miss periods even though they are not pregnant, and this usually means that some minor and temporary change has occurred in the hormone balance. If three consecutive periods are missed it is wise to consult a doctor.

The *breasts* are called *secondary sexual organs* and are also under the influence of the ovarian hor-mones. Two conditions which need treatment are *mastitis* and *cancer of the breast*, both of which are characterised by lumps within the breast tissue. Mastitis may be uncomfortable but is not dangerous and can be treated medically, whereas cancer is more serious. The distinction between mastitis and cancer can only be made by a doctor and any woman who discovers a lump in her breast must seek medical aid *at once*.

Abscesses also occur in the breast, nearly always when the mother is feeding her child. Here again, a lump appears, the breast becomes red and very tender, and the woman may be feverish. Treatment with antibiotics is sometimes successful, especially if the mother consults her doctor quickly, otherwise treatment is by a small operation.

The Ovaries. The two commonest diseases of the ovaries are cysts and disorders arising from hormonal imbalance. The symptoms of ovarian disease are usually abdominal or low back pains, and heavy and painful loss during the periods, which may become irregular. These signs should be taken as a warning to consult a doctor.

The Fallopian Tubes. Infection of the Fal-lopian tubes is called salpingitis. The membrane lining the tubes is continuous with the lining of the uterus, hence an infection is rarely confined to a circumscribed area in either the tubes or the uterus, and pelvic inflammatory disease is a better name for this condition. Pelvic inflammatory disease often follows an abortion, or childbirth where part of the afterbirth (placenta) has been retained, or can spread from an infection in a nearby organ, for example the appendix. In-fection is sometimes conveyed by the blood from another septic source in the body. The gono-coccus is another cause of infection. The disease is characterised by pain and tenderness in the lower part of the abdomen, accompanied by fever, general malaise and frequently (but not invariably) a vaginal discharge. The treatment of pelvic inflammatory disease is usually medical and is the same irrespective of the primary site of infection. Before the introduction of antibiotics the disease often became chronic and the Fallopian tubes were frequently blocked by a cicatrising scar, a cause of subsequent sterility.

The Uterus. This is a hollow muscular organ and both its musculature and its lining membrane can be the site of disease. *Fibroids* are non-malignant muscular tumours which develop in many women. The main symptom is a heavy menstrual loss and surgical removal of the uterus (hysterectomy) is often necessary. This is a major operation, but modern anaesthesia and operative techniques minimise the discomfort. Hysterectomy does not impair sexual pleasure, but no more babies can be conceived. Infection of the lining of the uterus is usually part of a generalised pelvic inflammatory disease (see Fallopian tubes).

Cancer of the Uterus and Cervical Smears. The uterus is pear-shaped and consists of a body and neck. The wide end is uppermost (the body) and the narrow neck (cervix) projects into the top of the vagina. Cancer of the cervix is commonest in middle-aged women who have married young and have had a large family; cancer of the body of the uterus usually occurs after the menopause and is more common in nulliparous women. The symptoms are variable and it is sufficient to emphasise that any woman who has unexpected bleeding, especially after intercourse, whether her periods have stopped or not, *must* see her doctor at once. The treatment depends on individual circumstances, but is usually by operation. It is now possible to detect cancer of the cervix long before symptoms develop and at a stage when the disease can be eradicated by a relatively small operation. This early detection has been made possible by the development of exfoliative cytology. Cells taken from the cervix (without discomfort to the woman) are examined under a microscope. This test is popularly known as the "cancer test" or "cervical smear." A cervical smear is often taken as part of the routine gynaecological examination by consultants, general practitioners, and family planning doctors, and is also being included in some population screening programmes. It is a big step forward in pre-ventive medicine and may ultimately solve the problem of cancer of the cervix. Every woman between the ages of 25 and 60 should seize any chance to have this test done.

Prolapse means a sagging down of the uterus into the vagina and the cervix may even appear at the outside. It is a result of frequent childbirth and laxness of the ligaments which support the uterus: weakness of the vaginal walls often occurs at the same time. The symptoms of uterine prolapse are low back pain and a heavy dragging feeling in the lower abdomen: these are often overshadowed by the distressingly embarrassing incontinence which results from lax vaginal walls. The stress of only a sneeze, a cough, or a giggle often causes the involuntary escape of urine. The cure is operative and very rewarding.

Dysmenorrhoea or pain with the periods, is very common and most women experience this symptom at some time or another. Very often a girl's first periods are troublesome, but dysmenorrhoea develops after a year or two: this suggests that a psychological element is involved. Dysmenorrhoea is a symptom which has many varying causes, and the sensible thing to do, if pain is troublesome, is to see a doctor.

Amenorrhoea means stopping of the periods in a young woman. It may signify pregnancy or glandular disease or it can be purely psychological.

Abortion means the death and expulsion of a foetus before the 28th week of pregnancy. Abortion may happen spontaneously (*i.e.* naturally) or be deliberately induced. If deliberate, it may be legal or illegal (although a woman who aborts herself commits no offence) and the Abortion Act 1967 defines those conditions in which abortion is legal. The two main symptoms of abortion are bleeding and abdominal pain. Any bleeding occurring during pregnancy ought to be reported at once. Pain starts in the back and lower abdomen and is usually spasmodic in character, and like colic it works up to a peak and then temporarily passes off. Any pregnant woman with pain and bleeding should go to bed at once and send for her doctor. When doctors are convinced that a pregnancy should be terminated then an abortion by safe surgical means may be performed in hospital.

FAMILY PLANNING

The Family Planning Service.

In Britain a service of *free* family planning advice and supplies is in operation, that is, *free* to the consumer. The service is the responsibility of the Department of Health and Social Security which delegates its running mainly to Area Health Authorities and Family Doctors. The service is available to men and women irrespective of age, marital status and nationality.

Sources of the Service.

1. *Area Health Authorities:* provide Family Planning Clinics in local Health Centres and sometimes in other buildings—*e.g.*, those taken over from the Family Planning Association. Some require an appointment but others provide a "walkin" service at certain specified times.
2. *Family Doctors:* 90% of doctors in the Health Service primary care sector (GPs) have contracted to supply family planning to women *either* (a) just for their own patients *or* (b) for any woman who wishes to consult them. This service may be either (i) methods excluding the intra-uterine device ("IUCD" or "coil") or (ii) methods including the provison of IUCDs.
3. *Hospitals:* supply the service mainly
   (a) for the patients of that hospital referred from other departments and
   (b) for patients referred to their family planning clinics by the patients' own doctors (usually for IUCDs).
4. *Private Sector:*
   1. The Family Planning Association still provides clinics in some areas, including some special vasectomy clinics.
   2. Brook Advisory Centres operate in certain places and tend to specialise in advising the young.
   3. The Marie Stopes Clinic is in London (and advertises in the press).
   4. The British Pregnancy Advisory Service provides a pregnancy advisory service in some areas.
   5. Some Family Practitioners undertake vasectomies.
   6. Some hospital consultant surgeons do private vasectomies, female sterilisations and reversals of sterilisation operations.

How to find out about the Family Planning Service in your area.

Anyone wishing to use the service can obtain the address of a clinic or a family doctor from any one of a number of sources.

1. *The Citizens Advice Bureau:* the address is in the telephone directory.
2. *The telephone directory:* Area Health Authority clinics are usually under the heading Health and subheading Clinic for each Health Authority. Private clinics will be under their own names.
3. *Area Health Authorities:* (H.Q. telephone number usually in Directory) Health Centres; Health Visitors; Nurses; Midwives; Family Doctors;* Any clinic (baby, dental etc.)
4. *Family doctors' surgeries.*
5. *School nurses, school teachers, school counsellors.*
6. *Social workers.*

N.B. If a person goes to a family doctor she may be required to sign a form to the effect that the doctor has undertaken to provide her with contraception for the following 12 months. This is not binding on her and if for any reason she is unable to return to that doctor, or does not wish to, she may still obtain help elsewhere, *e.g.*, at a clinic or from another doctor. The patient has the choice.

At most, but not all, family planning clinics an appointment system operates.

* The list of Family Doctors issued by the Family Practitioners Committees is available in Public Libraries and Post Offices. Doctors in the list who offer Family Planning Services have "C" or "C +" after their names.

METHODS OF FAMILY PLANNING

Methods Used by the Woman.

"The pill" ("combined oral contraceptive pill").

This consists of two female type hormones, oestrogen (usually pronounced as if the first "o" were another "e", that is eestrogen), and progestogen.

Preparations:

Many different combinations of these two hormones are marketed. Nowadays most formulae contain 30–50 units (micrograms) of oestrogen, whereas twelve years ago most contained 100 units. Even the amount of progestogen has been reduced to the bare minimum which is effective. Most pills have the same amount of hormone throughout the course but some recently produced pills have differing amounts of progestogen during the course, giving the lowest total amount of hormone per month.

Mode of action:

The pill works by stopping the egg cell from being shed from the ovary, and if no egg cell is shed, no fertilisation can take place. They are thus virtually 100% effective as a contraceptive, the tiny proportion of failure which occurs being almost invariably due to human error, *e.g.*, forgetting to take the pill.

The Menstrual Cycle.

Some people may like to have a more detailed description of the way in which the pill affects the normal menstrual cycle.

The menstrual cycle begins thus: A tiny part of the base of the brain (the *hypothalamus*) sends out a hormone called Releasing Factor (R.F.), which stimulates the pituitary gland to release a hormone called follicle stimulating hormone (F.S.H.). This in turn stimulates a group of folicles or egg sacs in the ovary. Each egg sac is a small fluid-filled bubble lined with special cells and containing an immature egg cell. The lining cells are stimulated to produce oestrogen and more and more of this accumulates in the blood stream. Eventually by "negative feed back" the oestrogen causes the pituitary gland to decrease the production of F.S.H. (*i.e.* high level of oestrogen → low level F.S.H.), and by "positive feedback" causes the pituitary gland to produce a sudden surge of another hormone called luteinising hormone, L.H. (*i.e.*, high level oestrogen → high level of L.H.). This L.H. causes the largest egg sac bubble to burst, releasing the egg cell, which is caught by the fringe at the free end of the uterine tube and wafted down the tube into the uterus, during which time it can be fertilised. Meanwhile the burst bubble in the ovary turns yellow and is called the "yellow body" (or *corpus luteum*). This produces both oestrogen and another hormone progesterone which are both vital for the continuation and promotion of any pregnancy. If no pregnancy occurs the yellow body collapses after 14 days, the lining of the uterus is shed in menstruation, the level of oestrogen (and progesterone) in the blood drops, and this causes the pituitary gland to step up the output of F.S.H. again.

The combined pill consists of oestrogen and progestogen, similar to those hormones produced by the "yellow body". These act on the pituitary gland as they would in a pregnancy and prevent the release of F.S.H. and L.H., so that egg cells are neither prepared nor released. Thus, taking the pill is in some ways like being constantly pregnant, which until the present century was probably the most natural and likely way for a woman in the fertile age group to be.

Method of taking the pill.

A woman starts to take the pill initially on the 1st day of a normal period, or on the 5th day of a normal period, depending on the particular pill. If she starts on the first day, she is protected from risk of pregnancy immediately. If she starts on the fifth day she is not protected until she has taken 14 pills. The pill is taken for 21 days followed by a rest interval of 7 days and this pattern is repeated indefinitely. The pills are provided in packets of 21. (There is one pill which is supplied in packs of 22 and a rest interval of only 6 days is required.) During the seven days without the pill the "pill period" comes. This is not a true period, but is simply due to stopping the pill, when such lining of the womb as has been allowed to form, is shed.

Protection from pregnancy is maintained unless:

    she is more than 4–12 hours late in taking a pill (depending on the pill dosage)
    she misses a pill
    she has diarrhoea or vomiting so that the pill is lost before it can be absorbed.

If protection is lost she should continue to take the pills in the ordinary way but use other contraceptives, *e.g.*, the sheath, as well until the end of that packet of pills.

A few pills are put up in packets with 7 inactive tablets as well as 21 active tablets, so that a pill is taken every day. These are useful for people who find the "on-off" regime difficult to remember.

Other drugs and the pill.

A few drugs hasten the breakdown of the pill in the body and so make it less effective. Such drugs include some of those used to treat epilepsy and some, but not by any means all, antibiotics, some drugs for treating rheumatism and one or two other drugs more rarely used. Conversely, the pill is suspected of making some other drugs less effective, for example some drugs for treating depression. It is always advisable for a woman to remind any doctor who is prescribing for her that she is taking the pill.

The pill is the commonest method of birth control being used in Britain. 28% of the 11 million women in the fertile age group 15–44 use it, according to the Family Planning Association estimate 1979. In the under-30 age group, recent estimates are that about 70% are using it. In spite of the fact that the pill affects in some degree, usually slight or moderate, much body chemistry and therefore many body systems, rather as pregnancy does, most people feel no different on the pill.

Pill problems and side-effects

Connected with "pill period".

Occasionally slight bleeding happens during the days when pills are being taken, particularly when a woman first starts to take the pill. If it is very slight it is called "spotting", if rather heavier, *i.e.*, necessitating the wearing of some sort of protection, it is referred to as "breakthrough bleeding". If this is in the first month or two of pill-taking it usually settles down spontaneously. If later on, a change of pill may be indicated. It can be due to erratic pill-taking, *i.e.*, being late taking a pill, or forgetting to take a pill, or it can be caused by having to take one of a very few other drugs which have the effect of hastening the breakdown of the pill in the body so that it does not have time to be effective. It is best to consult your doctor if bleeding happens, particularly if it happens when drug treatment is given. To be absolutely safe in those circumstances it is wise to use other contraceptives, *e.g.*, sheaths, as well until the end of that packet of pills.

Other side effects.

Occasionally, and usually in the early weeks of pill-taking, other side effects are experienced such as nausea, breast tenderness, headaches or weight gain. If these are troublesome and do not settle the pill may have to be changed or even, rarely, stopped. Some symptoms such as depression, general leg aches, and decreased interest in sex, are more doubtfully attributable to the pill and may have some quite other cause, but all these problems should be discussed with the doctor.

Headaches: Migraine headaches are usually one-sided, often associated with feeling sick or with actual vomiting and sometimes with disturbances of vision. Sometimes these headaches seem to improve when a woman takes the pill, but more often they seem to become more frequent. Sometimes they come only in the pill-free week. Often a change to a pill with a lower dose of oestrogen, or even to a progestogen-only pill, will eliminate such headaches.

It is advisable to stop taking the pill if

    (a) *migraine occurs for the first time* when the pill is taken or
    (b) migraine becomes "focal".

By "focal" is meant that other localised symptoms are experienced such as attacks of tingling or weakness on one side of the body, brief episodes of difficulty in speaking or visual disturbances such as transient loss of part of the field of vision. This might be a sign of a brief loss of blood supply to a part of the brain and a warning of the danger of stroke.

Headaches other than migraine: these are of course not uncommon in women who are not taking the pill. They are not uncommon in men. If they should increase when the pill is taken then changing the pill to one with a lower dose of oestrogen, or with a different progestogen (or even to one containing progestogen only) will help.

Blood pressure: In most women the blood pressure rises very slightly on the pill. In a few, it rises to above the normal level. Having a blood pressure higher than normal over a period of time renders a person more liable to diseases of the circulation. Fortunately the blood pressure is easy to monitor regularly.

Blood clotting: Blood clotting is a normal function of the body and is the body's way of sealing a cut or otherwise injured blood vessel. In women who take the pill various factors which influence blood clotting both in the blood itself and in the blood vessel wall, are altered, so that although the blood is slightly more liable to clot, the clot is more liable to be dissolved. The net result is still a slightly increased tendency to blood clotting (thrombosis).

Blood clotting or thrombosis can occur in a vein, or in an artery.

In a vein: It can extremely rarely occur in a normal vein in a person who is not taking the pill. It is only about four times more likely (or four times less unlikely) in a person taking the pill. If it occurs, it is usually in the deep veins of the leg, mainly because blood flow tends to be slowest there. It usually causes relatively little localised damage but very occasionally a piece of the blood clot can break off and be swept in the blood stream through the heart and into the lungs where it can block a blood vessel and even occasionally prove fatal.

N.B. Moderate varicose veins with no evidence of any past thrombosis are not reasons for not taking the pill.

In an artery (thrombosis) is due to the fact that "hardening of the arteries" (atherosclerosis) affects almost everyone and in the developed world has usually begun by the age of 20. Roughened patches on the artery wall allow blood clots to form on them and occasionally to block them. The pill slightly increases the risk of this happening, again by about 4–5 times. Other factors which more strongly increase the likelihood of this happening are smoking, which at less than 15 cigarettes/day increases the risk by 5 times and at more than 20 cigarettes/day increases the risk by 10 times,

increasing age, particularly the age of 35 years and older,

high blood pressure and

abnormal blood fats. A few people have these from birth, but this is a disorder which runs in families and can be detected by a blood test.

Clotting in an artery of the heart muscle is called coronary thrombosis. Clotting in an artery of the brain, and bleeding from an artery of the brain, which can result from a weak patch in a blood vessel and/or high blood pressure, are known as cerebral thrombosis or a stroke.

In October 1983 the results of one American and one British study of cancer among women using oral contraceptives were published in the medical press. The first of these appeared to suggest that long-term use of certain types of pill by younger women (under 25) may be associated with an increased risk of breast cancer; other previously published studies had shown no such connection. The British study showed that a group of women who had chosen to take a combined oral contraceptive had an increased incidence of cancer of the neck of the womb (cervical cancer) in comparison with a similar group of women who had elected to use intra-uterine contraceptive devices (*e.g.,* the coil). Both studies suggested that the progestogen content of mixed pills could be implicated. All the women in the pill group who had been found to have invasive cervical cancer were treated effectively.

The Committee on Safety of Medicines considered both these studies very carefully and concluded that women should be prescribed pills which had the lowest progestogen content but that there was no need for any woman to make an immediate change. Furthermore, the Committee endorsed the British study authors' recommendation that all long-term users of oral contraceptives should have regular cervical cytology examinations ("smears"). Of course, your family or clinic doctor will have all the Committee of Safety of Medicine's information and will know which pill to recommend.

Helpful side effects: the pill almost always prevents period pains. It also frequently reduces the unpleasant effects of "premenstrual tension" which some women experience, including feelings of depression, irritability and tenseness.

The Progestogen-only pill.

This pill, as its name implies, contains only one hormone, progestogen. It is sometimes called the mini-pill but as this name is also occasionally used for very low dose combined pills, it will be better to call it the progestogen-only pill, or P-O-P.

Until the past year or two this pill was used mainly by women who were breast feeding as it is 98 per cent effective as a contraceptive, but does not diminish the milk flow. A very small amount of the hormone does get into the milk; it is not known whether this can affect the baby but it is thought that it does not.

Recently the P-O-P is being more widely used, particularly by women over the age of 35, and also by younger women. It is probably the next most effective method of birth control to the combined pill, having a failure rate of rather less than 2 pregnancies among 100 women taking it for a year.

Mode of action: The P-O-P works mainly by making the secretion from the neck of the womb (the cervix) scanty and thick so that the sperms do not get through. The pill does not as a rule stop the egg cell from being shed, so that the periods which come are natural periods, though they may be lighter than usual because the pill does make the lining of the uterus thinner and less suitable for a fertilised egg cell to settle in. It also probably slows down the transporting of the egg cell in the uterine tubes by diminishing the waves of movement in them which normally help to get the egg cell into the uterus.

Side effects: There are two slight risks with the P-O-P. One is the slight risk of unwanted pregnancy. The other is the risk of the nuisance of irregular bleeding.

The irregular bleeding may take the form of more frequent, usually slight, bleeding or less frequent bleeding. Sometimes the periods cease altogether, or become extremely infrequent. This means that the very small amount of hormone in the pill is having a similar effect on the pituitary gland to that of the combined pill, so that it does not stimulate egg release in the ovaries. Provided it is ascertained that the pill-taker is not pregnant, the contraceptive effect is excellent in these people, and probably because the dose of hormone is so small the pituitary gland seems to recover its normal functions very rapidly when this pill is stopped. In general tests have shown that the P-O-P has far less effect on body chemistry than has the combined pill. Blood clotting and blood pressure seem to be little affected.

Method of taking the P-O-P.

The P-O-P is taken continuously and without breaks. Starting on the first day of a period it is taken every day. Because the effect on the secretion from the neck of the womb is greatest for the first six hours after taking it, it is advisable for it to be taken about six or seven o'clock in the evening, so that protection is high at bed time when intercourse is most likely. Because the effect rapidly declines after 24 hours it should be taken at the same time every day and not more than 2 hours late, otherwise the protection is broken. It takes about 2 weeks for the protection to build up initially, and the same after any break in protection due, for example, to being late taking a pill, missing a pill or pills or having a stomach upset.

The Coil or Intra Uterine Contraceptive Device (I.U.C.D.).

Coils are devices which are inserted into the uterus and remain there until a pregnancy is desired. All are made of plastic, some have very fine copper wire wound round them to increase their effectiveness. They are all highly effective, having a failure rate of about 2 pregnancies per 100 women using it for a year.

Various shapes of coils are used. The copper wire covered ones are the Copper 7, Gravgard, the Copper 1 and the Multiload. The plastic only ones are the Lippes loop and the Saf-T coil.

Each device has a thread attached to it which passes through the neck of the womb into the vagina. This can be pulled by the doctor when the coil is to be removed. A woman should never try to remove her coil herself.

The mode of action is not entirely clear, but the coil seems to prevent the fertilised egg cell from embedding in the uterus.

The method is generally considered to be more suitable for women who have had a baby than for those who have not, because in the latter the very slight risk of an infection ensuing is 7 times greater. An infection could occasionally, if untreated, proceed to involve the uterine tubes, even rarely sealing them. A woman fitted with a coil not infrequently has slightly longer and heavier and occasionally more painful periods than were usual for her.

The coil is used by about 5% of the 11 million women in the fertile age group 15–44 (F.P.A. estimate 1979).

The Cap or Diaphragm.

The cap or diaphragm is a circle of soft rubber with a firm rim which is inserted by the woman into the vagina so that it covers the neck of the womb (the cervix) and so physically prevents sperms from entering it. It is always used with a sperm-killing jelly or cream. There are a few different shapes of cap. Most are flat, but some are variations on a thimble shape and fit closely over the cervix. One of these is also made in plastic and can be used by a person who is allergic to rubber. The suitable cap size has to be estimated and the cap first fitted by a doctor (or nurse).

Method of use:

The cap can be put in anything up to 3 hours before intercourse, or longer if more sperm-killing preparation (spermicide) is inserted. The cap should be left in for 6–8 hours after intercourse, and if this happens again before 6 hours have elapsed, more spermicide is inserted and the cap is left in for a further 6 hours. It is then removed, washed with soft soap and water and stored in its box.

The cap has the advantage of being absolutely harmless to health. It does not affect the periods or the body systems or chemistry in any way.

It is slightly less effective than either pill or coil. The failure rate has been estimated variously as 2–8 per 100 women using it for a year, probably varying with the conscientiousness of the user.

It is used by about 3% of women in the fertile age group (F.P.A. estimate 1979).

Method Used by the Man.

The sheath (or condom or French letter or "Durex"). The sheath is made of very fine rubber, nowadays almost always including a lubricant and sometimes including a spermicide. Most have a teat-shaped end to receive the semen.

Method of use: The air should be squeezed out of the teat end before the sheath is put on so that there is room for the semen and the sheath will not burst. The sheath should then be unrolled on to the erect penis before the penis makes any contact with the woman, as there can be a drop of fluid which contains sperms and is quite sufficient to make her pregnant. The man should hold the sheath in place when he withdraws. Unless the sheath contains spermicide the woman should always use a spermicidal pessary or foam in addition.

Advantages: Sheaths are completely harmless and in fact can give some protection against sexually transmitted diseases ("V.D.") They are readily available—*free* (when *prescribed* by the doctor) from all Area Health Authority Family Planning Clinics and on payment from chemists' shops and from slot machines which are found mainly in public houses, hotels, garages and service stations and sometimes in clubs, restaurants and holiday camps.

The failure rate is variously estimated at between 0·4 and 6 per 100 couples using it for a year and can be very low if the method is conscientiously used. The method is second only to the pill in the number of people using it—25 per cent of couples where the woman is in the fertile age-group (F.P.A. estimate 1979).

Natural Methods of Birth Control.

These unfortunately are not very reliable. They are all based on the woman finding out when her egg cell is shed, *i.e.*, her "ovulation time", and avoiding intercourse around that time. Sperms can live in the vagina for up to 3 days and the egg cell lives for at least 48 hours after it is shed.

There are two methods of detecting ovulation time. The *Calendar method* involves the woman in recording the length of her menstrual cycle for *at least* 6 months before it can any way be relied on. The woman must make a note of the first day of bleeding of each cycle. The last day of the cycle is the day before the next onset of bleeding. The calculation of the "safe period" is made by deducting 18 from the shortest cycle and 11 from the longest. For example, with a shortest cycle of 25 days and a longest of 31 the safe period would be *before* day 7 and *after* day 20 (25 − 18 = 7; 31 − 11 = 20). If only the safe period around day 20 is used the method is considererably more reliable.

The *Temperature method* is based on the fact that immediately after ovulation there is a distinct rise in body temperature which persists until the next period starts. The method involves taking the temperature first thing every morning *before* eating, drinking or smoking and plotting it on a chart each day. The safe period begins about four days *after* ovulation (as detected by the rise in temperature) and continues until the next menstrual period begins.

Other more accurate home-methods of finding the moment of ovulation are being explored, including tests on the mucus from the cervix, which becomes thin, clear and "stringy" at ovulation times; tests on vaginal enzymes; and even urine tests, but no simple test requiring no expertise is yet available.

Coitus interruptus, withdrawal or "being careful".

This should be mentioned in this section on "natural methods" because it is probably used at some time by many couples, though less than a generation ago. It means that the man withdraws his penis before climax or ejaculation. This requires great will-power at the height of sexual excitation. Even if withdrawal is achieved, it may be too late. There are enough sperms in the drop of fluid which emerges from the penis in the early stages of sexual stimulation to cause a pregnancy. The method is therefore highly fallible, frustrating and often futile—akin to "shutting the stable door..." Although it cannot be recommended, it is a method requiring no expert help or artificial equipment, and is better than nothing. The failure rate is at least 17%.

Sterilisation.

Sterilisation of the woman. Tubal tie or tubal ligation.

This means cutting the tubes which carry the egg cells from the ovary to the uterus. Although this is not a major operation it may involve a general anaesthetic and an abdominal operation. It can now sometimes be done through a very small cut under a local anaesthetic with an instrument called a laparascope, which can shine a light into the abdomen through a quite narrow tube. At operation the uterine tubes are cut and a piece taken out before each end is sealed. In addition the cut end nearest the uterus may also be embedded in the uterine wall to make doubly sure that the two ends do not rejoin. Sometimes the tubes are not cut but gold clips are put on to close the lumens of the tubes.

The operation must be regarded as irreversible as it is extremely rarely possible to reverse it.

Sterilisation of the man. Vasectomy.

Vasectomy means cutting the tubes which carry the sperms into the semen or seminal fluid, which is the fluid produced during intercourse.

The testicles have two functions. One is to produce sperms. The other is to produce the hormone testosterone which gives a man his maleness, for example his deep voice and his beard, and his sex drive. The hormone is carried in the blood stream. The sperms are carried in special tubes called the *vas deferens* which run under the skin of the scrotum. Thus the tubes are easily accessible to the surgeon. At operation the tube on each side is cut and a small piece is removed. This is to leave a gap to prevent the cut ends from re-uniting. The cut ends are sealed and the skin cut closed. The operation takes 15–20 minutes, can be done under general or local anaesthetic, and causes minimal discomfort afterwards. The result of the operation is that the sperms formed in the testicle do not get through to the penis. They go on being formed, but are gradually broken down again and reabsorbed by the blood stream. The sperms which are already in the *vas* beyond the cut end will still go into the seminal fluid, and it may be 3 months before they have all been ejected. A sample of fluid is usually checked about 2 months after the operation, and another 2 weeks later. There is no visible change in the fluid, only under the microscope it can be seen that there are no sperms in it. Nor is there any change in a man's virility, potency or sex drive. A man should have the operation only if he is sure he will not wish for further children. Although in some cases it may be possible to reverse the operation and give him back his fertility this can never be certain. He should be prepared to accept that it is irreversible.

DRUG ABUSE AND DRUG DEPENDENCE.

This section of earlier editions of *Pears* was simply called "Addiction." This word is still much used, but is gradually being replaced by the terms in the present title, because ideas about the nature of the problem and methods of dealing with it are changing. Addiction is a word that conjures up rather 19th century ideas in the minds of readers: opium dens, inscrutable orientals, Sherlock Holmes injecting himself with cocaine—basically a phenomenon of foreign origin, rather frightening if its implications were not literary rather than factual, and not of great significance in Great Britain.

Drug Abuse.

It is now realised by doctors, research scientists, social workers, and the police—if still not by society as a whole—that the truth is quite different. The *abuse* of drugs in this country is at present of large proportions, increasing rapidly and showing no signs of diminishing. It is responsible each year for thousands of deaths by suicide and by accidental overdosage; for an enormous but virtually unmeasurable amount of private suffering; and for the loss to society, in terms of reduced working efficiency, of millions of man-hours every year. It has nothing to do with opium smoking which was never in any case more than the eccentricity of the few. Opium is virtually unused in medicine these days and the amount of smuggling, always small, is now negligible. The problems today arise chiefly from the misuse of drugs given by doctors for their effects on the central nervous system—the pain-killers, sleeping pills, "stimulants," and "tranquillisers."

Drugs and Medicines.

To the doctor, any substance is a drug that can be introduced into the body from outside, and that is capable of producing some detectable effect. Most such substances have a beneficial use. They are "medicines," and as such are given by doctors in suitable cases. Others, for example, nicotine (in cigarettes), alcohol (in beer, wine, or spirits), and carbon monoxide (in coal gas), are of doubtful benefit and of certain harm and are used by doctors, if at all, only under certain very special and usually experimental conditions.

Medicines may be classified under four main headings. First, there are those like quinine, or penicillin and other so-called antibiotics, that actually cure diseases by eradicating the organism (bacteria or other parasites) that cause disturbance of normal bodily function. Second, drugs such as insulin or the steroids overcome in the unhealthy the lack of some necessary substance a healthy body manufactures for itself: they must usually continue to be given for life. Third are the drugs which relieve the signs of disease—for example, there are many new drugs that lower the blood pressure or increase the output of urine—without being able to put right the disturbed basic situation which is the cause of the trouble. Fourth are drugs to relieve the patient's symptoms—which make him feel better, less breathless, take away his pain, help him to sleep, and so on—although we seldom know why they are able to do this. Indeed, in many cases we suspect that they are acting mainly as a token of help from doctor to patient, and so encouraging his body to fight a more successful battle on its own behalf.

There is no doubt that the genuine advances in beneficial drugs during the last forty years have been enormous; but the very successes of the penicillins, tetracyclines, antimalarials, hormones, and so on have bred in the public and in the medical profession itself an attitude of uncritical wonder. There have been relatively few drugs in the first and second categories mentioned above; and in the field of mental health, the importance of which is now so rightly emphasised, there are virtually none. Yet drugs which act upon the brain are often received as if they were curative although they may pose fresh problems rather than solve the old. Thus, although there are many drugs which act upon the mind, few do this in any fundamental sense; they relieve pain and anxiety, bring sleep and lessening of stress, and may allow the patient to recuperate himself during the relief they provide. But often this deeper change does not occur—sometimes because the doctor has not clearly seen his part in helping to bring it about—and then the symptomatic relief may come to be sought for its own sake.

Dangers of Long-term Medication with Drugs acting on the Brain.

1. *Toxic effects.* Drugs which act upon the nervous system, like any others, have characteristic toxic or unwanted effects of their own (incidentally, these may become apparent rapidly; even, on rare occasions, after only a single dose). Such effects may have little or nothing to do with the desired effects for which they are being prescribed and taken. For example, it has only come to be realised quite recently that aspirin is liable to cause bleeding, which is occasionally serious, from the lining of the stomach in a large proportion of people who take aspirin regularly; or that phenacetin, another substance very frequently present in analgesics (*i.e.*, pain relievers) that can be bought from chemists without prescription, may lead (after prolonged use) to kidney damage. Some drugs may cause rashes and other allergic reactions in susceptible subjects; and jaundice, fainting, tremors, and motor disorders are known to occur in some patients taking a variety of other drugs.

2. *"Rebound."* The body works in such a way, over a variety of its activities, that it tends to return to a "neutral" position after it has departed from this for any reason. For example, over-eating tends to be followed by a lessening of appetite, at least for a time; the runner makes up for his air-deficit during the race by breathing more deeply thereafter; and if, at rest, you breathe for a time more rapidly and deeply than you need, this period will be followed by one in which you breathe *less* often than usual until the balance is restored. These illustrations—and there are others—have nothing to do with drugs; but in a similar way, it seems that if a continued pain, or an unpleasant emotional state such as anxiety or depression is changed into its opposite, or removed altogether by the use of a drug, the prior state may return with increased force when the drug is no longer taken. The "rebound" phenomenon, naturally, encourages the patient to take another dose, and so on.

3. *Habit formation.* This alternation of mood-changed-by-drug with the disturbed mood itself leads to the habit of taking the drug. The patient comes to rely upon it and to take it anyway, even before the unpleasant state has returned. At this stage he is said to be "habituated"; he has a psychological need for the drug, and later may become disturbed at the possibility that it will not be available when he needs it. This might not matter so greatly, if it were not that continued use of drugs in this way has physical consequences as well.

4. *Tolerance and habituation.* The body also tends to restore its own balance when drugs are given, too. It "learns" surprisingly quickly how to deal with substances with which it has never before been confronted, so that it eliminates subsequent doses more and more quickly and completely. Thus the effect of each successive dose is smaller and lasts for progressively shorter periods of time. To counter this, the patient tends to increase the dose: and the vicious circle continues. At this point he has become physically dependent upon the drug: and he may suffer physically—sometimes so severely that he dies—if supplies are not continued.

As he increases the dose in this way, so his tolerance of its effects increases, to such an extent that after prolonged use he may be taking doses of a drug that are five or ten times greater than those which will kill somebody not dependent upon them in this way. It sometimes happens that a patient develops a renewed craving at some point after a course of treatment, in which the dose of drug has been reduced without removing the underlying cause of his dependence. He may then obtain and use the dose he habitually took before treatment, not knowing that his body will have lost its tolerance of such doses. That dose is now as high for him as for any other person and so may be lethal. There has been a number of deaths for this reason.

Factors in the Causation of Dependence.

The risk of becoming dependent upon a drug is governed by three main factors; the drug itself, the personality of the individual who takes it, and the circumstances in which it is taken. Most adults have taken alcohol at one time or another, unless it is against their code to do so; yet *relatively* few are dependent upon it (relatively few, but many too many; more than half a million in the United Kingdom alone). Many of us have had morphine or some other strong analgesic for medical reasons, without becoming dependent upon it (whatever so-called addicts say, it is extremely rare for anyone to become dependent on an opiate because he was introduced to it in a medical setting). On the other hand, if we start to take such a drug "for kicks"—as more and more people, particularly teen-agers and young adults are doing—it is extremely probable that we shall become dependent upon it, and sooner rather than later at that. It is also probable that each one of us would become dependent, were he obliged to take it regularly, for long enough, and in sufficient dosage. Thus, although there are personalities—psychopathic, immature, or unstable—that are more prone than others to become dependent if they are exposed to the drug, there are also drugs that are more likely than others to cause such dependence no matter to whom they are given. The extent of the dependence will vary; with some, it is never physiological but remains psychological (but not the less real or disturbing for that). Also, the rate at which dependence develops may vary; and the picture presented by the dependent subject—the extent to which his normal life is impaired, or to which he becomes dangerous to himself or others—varies as well. In a very much oversimplified way, some of these relationships will now be summarised for certain substances.

Heroin, morphine and cocaine are usually injected. Barbiturates (sleeping pills) and amphetamines ("Benzedrine") are tablets or capsules, and marihuana ("reefer," hashish) is smoked in cigarettes. Heroin and cocaine are now usually taken together. Combinations of drugs often act differently from their individual constituents and patients dependent upon them are even more difficult to treat. Barbiturate and amphetamine, also, are often mixed (as in "purple hearts"). There is considerable *psychological* dependence on heroin, morphine, cocaine, and amphetamine, but much less with marihuana. *Physiological* dependence is great with heroin and morphine, less with barbiturates, alcohol, and amphetamine in that order, and virtually nil with cocaine and marihuana. Personality plays a greater part in initiating dependence on alcohol, marihuana, and barbiturates than with the others. Heroin, cocaine, and morphine are the cause of more antisocial tendencies in dependent people than alcohol, barbiturates, and amphetamine. The chief danger of marihuana (mere possession of which is illegal) seems to be that the search for it will lead the searcher into localities where his risk of exposure to even more dangerous influences is greatly increased. It is thus sometimes argued that if it were legal to consume marihuana, the number of young people who yearly become dependent upon the other more dangerous drugs would in fact decrease. There is as yet no evidence for or against this proposition. The number of drug dependent people in U.K. is rising fast for heroin and cocaine. This number is very large for alcohol, and is increasing in the case of barbiturates and marihuana. Very few people are dependent on morphine, and the number is not growing.

Treatment.

Exhortations, imprisonment, and other moralistic or legalistic approaches are useless. Treatment of any person dependent upon a drug is a matter for a qualified psychotherapist. It is liable to be time-consuming and frustrating for patient and doctor, and it is frequently unsuccessful. At present, there are too few specialists or centres where treatment can be obtained, although it is to be hoped that this situation will change as the problem is increasingly seen by our society to be of exceptional gravity.

When there is little or no chance of cure, prevention is certainly the best treatment. Drugs should only be taken on the prescription of a doctor: and the patient should remind him from time to time, if this be necessary, that he would like to dispense with his drugs as soon as the doctor thinks it possible. It should also be remembered that there is often no need to reach for the aspirin (or any other drug that anyone can buy from the chemist without prescription) at the first sign of a headache—or to reach for it at all to help one sleep or relax, for which purpose such drugs are in any case pharmacologically useless. A wait for ten minutes is good discipline, and will frequently resolve the problem to an extent that makes a drug unnecessary.

PART III. SPECIAL TOPICS

THE PROBLEM OF AIDS.

AIDS, the Acquired Immune Deficiency Syndrome, is the result of infection by a virus known as HIV (Human Immunodeficiency Virus), which was formerly called HTLV(111).

History.

The disease seems to have spread to man in Africa and then to the rest of the world via Haiti. It was first recognised in 1981 and is now reaching epidemic proportions. By 1990, nearly 200,000 cases in over 150 countries had been reported. Contact with the virus, which is spread primarily by blood and semen, may result in:—

(1) *The disease AIDS.* The virus damages the T-lymphocytes which play an important part in the normal defence system. As a result the normal immune response is suppressed so that the AIDS victim is affected by illnesses which are usually quite rare *e.g.* Karposi sarcoma, rare lymphomas and lung infections (pneumocystis pneumonia). Lethargy, weight loss and glandular swelling may herald its onset. As yet there is no effective vaccine and the mortality rate is over 50%. However, drugs such as Zidovudine (AZT) may help some patients and delay the progression of the disease. Trials are still continuing.

(2) *A carry state.* Such people have antibodies to the AIDS virus and may transmit it to others but they themselves seem perfectly well.

Although we can document the number of people with AIDS (c.3,250 in England and Wales by May 1990) it is much more difficult to estimate the percentage of people carrying the virus in the general population (perhaps up to 10 million or more worldwide). Nor is it certain how many of those with AIDS antibodies will eventually develop the disease. Recent evidence suggests approximately 30% will do so over a 5 year period.

The virus is transmitted as follows:—

(a) By sexual intercourse with an infected person; penetrative anal intercourse seems to carry the greatest risk especially to the recipient partner. In Europe and USA, therefore, the majority of victims have been homosexual males.

(b) By contaminated blood products and equipment. Drug abusers who share hypodermic needles are another high risk category. Many haemophiliacs were the unfortunate victims of the first onslaught of the disease. This was because they received contaminated factor V111, which had been concentrated from the serum of many donors. However, proper screening and testing has now brought this problem under control.

(c) From mother to child via the placenta.

In Africa, where a large number of prostitutes are affected, heterosexual intercourse acts as a significant means of spread. In the UK heterosexual transmission of the virus is rare, but there is a great concern that the pattern may change. It is, therefore, advisable to restrict sexual activity to a familiar partner, to avoid multiple sexual encounters and to practice "safe sex". The sharing of razors and toothbrushes with strangers should be avoided. Although the virus has been isolated in tears and saliva, there is no evidence that these fluids are involved in the spread of infection to others.

Those concerned about the possibility of AIDS can undergo the HIV test. They should, however, receive skilled medical counselling before doing so, and afterwards if it is positive. The test detects antibodies to the disease and not the presence of the virus itself. HIV antibodies may not appear for at least 3 months after the last high risk activity.

Apart from the medical aspects, those who are HIV positive face other considerable problems. Mortgages and life assurance are difficult to obtain and entry may be denied to certain countries. AIDS is clearly with us to stay, and society needs to adopt a more sympathetic and tolerant attitude towards those unfortunate enough to have been affected by the virus.

ADVANCES IN BRONCHIAL ASTHMA

Bronchial asthma is a condition in which the smaller respiratory passages become narrowed by an allergic response and blocked with inflammatory exudate. This gives rise to symptoms of chest tightness, breathlessness and wheezing. In recent years the condition seems to have become more common and now it is estimated that up to 12% of children are affected and 5% of the adult population. In addition, well over 50% of asthmatics are not diagnosed. In spite of a whole range of safe and effective therapy, more than 2,000 people die of this illness every year. This is largely due to a misunderstanding and under-estimation of the illness by both parents and doctors. The conception that asthma is largely emotional in origin is now very out-dated.

Asthmatics can be divided into two groups. In more than half, symptoms begin in childhood and are part of the Atopic Syndrome, that is to say, a triad of asthma, eczema and hayfever, which has a tendency to run in families. Attacks occur in episodes and may be triggered by infection, exertion or the presence of the house dust-mite. Sometimes the attacks can be seasonal, depending on the presence of grass pollen or fungal spores. Alcohol and tobacco smoke can also act as trigger factors.

Late Onset Asthma

Not all asthmatics wheeze and one of the characteristic early features, particularly in children, is a persistent dry nocturnal cough. Asthma occurring in adult life is usually known as "Late Onset Asthma". There is no history of allergy or of similar problems in the family but it is often associated with nasal polyps. Late onset asthma is more resistant to treatment, but in both groups, the outlook is good and after a number of acute exacerbations, perhaps lasting several years, many people become symptom free or have only minor problems. Very few people become seriously incapacitated.

Treatment is directed at easing acute episodes and preventing their recurrence. Beta₂ receptor stimulants such as Salbutamol and Terbutaline are now the most widely used drugs; they are usually given in inhaler form because their onset of action is immediate, whereas tablets take much longer to be absorbed and work. These help to dilate the respiratory airways and have a wide margin of safety; two puffs can be given every 4–6 hours. The need for increasing administration is a sign that the condition is becoming unstable and prophylactic therapy should be instigated. Many people, particularly the young and elderly, have difficulty in using pressurised aerosol inhalers, in that they are unable to co-ordinate their breathing with the administration of the drug. A wide variety of alternatives are available, for example, dry powder inhalers which are actuated by inspiration – young children can usually manage these. Spacer devices which can be fitted on to ordinary inhalers are provided with a one-way valve so that the inhalant

is not dissipated but can be taken into the lungs in the patient's own time. These devices are often bulky and some of the new inhalers are breath activated. For those who suffer from more severe attacks, broncho-dilator drugs can be given by a nebuliser. Nebulisers are electrically powered and give a high concentration of drug which is administered by placing a mask over the patient's nose and mouth. Unfortunately, they are not available on the National Health Service.

For young children, a plastic coffee cup can provide an inexpensive substitute. A small hole is cut in the base of the cup and the mouthpiece of an ordinary inhaler is inserted, the open end of the cup is placed over the child's nose and mouth and the usual dose of inhaler is given. The coffee cup acts as a reservoir so that most of the spray can be usefully inhaled without waste.

Preventive Therapy

Patients who have frequent or severe attacks should be on some form of preventive therapy and again, this should be administered in an aerosol form. Intal or Disodium Cromoglycate is a very useful drug which helps to stabilise the lining of the cells in the bronchial tubes and so make them less susceptible to allergic stimuli. Small doses of inhaled steroid have a similar effect in dampening down the inflammatory response which is a major component of an asthmatic attack. For those who suffer from persistent episodes, this treatment should be taken on a regular basis. An acute attack which does not readily respond to broncho-dilator drugs can often be successfully treated by a short course of oral steroids. Patients often worry about the potential "side effects" of steroids but as these are only given in very short courses, any problems are likely to be minimal. Indeed steroids can be life-saving and it is far better to start a course in the early stages of an attack, than wait until the condition is critical. Soluble preparations are available for children and can be dissolved in milk or juice. Parents should gain experience of handling these drugs themseves, so that severe attacks can be aborted in the early stages.

A peak flow meter is a very simple device which can often give early warning as to when a patient's condition is becoming less stable, and indicate when steroids might be used. Peak flow meters measure the rate at which air is exhaled from a forced expiration. Normal values vary depending on age and sex but the device is simple to use and can easily be handled by children.

Many asthmatics have only minor symptoms but for those who have frequent problems, the importance of using regular preventive medication cannot be overstressed. Studies have shown that, in the majority of fatal cases, no form of preventive medicine was being used. Although nebulisers are often extremely effective, they can induce a false sense of security and the necessity for their frequent use should be an indication that further treatment is necessary.

Emergency Problems

Severe asthma, especially if it lasts for 24 hours, should be treated as an emergency and often requires hospitalisation. It is characterised by breathlessness, poorly relieved by broncho-dilator drugs, a fast pulse rate, irritability and exhaustion. Paradoxically, wheezing is not always present and the serious nature of the problem may be un-recognised. In such cases, oxygen and intravenous medication is essential. Such a situation is called Status Asthmaticus and requires urgent medical assessment. Appointment systems in general practice often work against asthmatics and if the patient or his relatives feel there is cause for concern, they should insist on being seen straight away.

NATIONAL HEALTH SERVICE REFORMS

In April 1990, the controversial changes outlined in the Government's White Paper "Working for Patients" became law. The plan involves the most profound change ever applied to the National Health Service since its inception and covers all areas both in Hospital and General Practice. Hospitals will be allowed a degree of self government and will be partially able to opt out of the NHS system. Those offering specialist services will be able to recruit patients from a much wider area. The new contract for general practice completely alters the whole basis on which GP's work and are paid. These changes have caused considerable dismay in the medical profession and have been widely resisted by the British Medical Association. In a referendum involving all GPs on the acceptability of the new contract, nearly 76% voted for outright rejection. The Secretary of State was, however, unwilling to make further alterations and the contract was imposed after some minor modifications.

As most people's contact with the health service is through their own General Practitioner, the following will give a brief outline of the changes which are to be expected from April. GPs have now to be more accessible to their patients and their working hours have to be spread over 5 days per week. In addition, they are now required to retire at the age of 70. They are also expected to live within a reasonable distance from their main surgery. Since November, patients have been able to change their doctor without his/her permission.

Financial incentives are to be given to those practices who look after their own patients during out of hours periods so that the reliance on deputising service is discouraged. Newly registered patients are expected to be given a full medical check and doctors will be required to offer a consultation to every patient between the ages of 16 and 74 who has not been seen within the preceding 3 years. For patients over the age of 75, doctors are required by their Terms of Service, to offer a consultation or a visit at the patient's home, to be done on a yearly basis. Financial encouragement is to be given to those doctors who undertake health promotion clinics such as Stress Management, Alcohol Control, Anti-Smoking and Well Person Clinics. In addition, GPs will be encouraged to undertake minor surgery and child surveillance. The uptake of immunisations and cervical smears are to be encouraged by offering GPs significant rewards for achieving high targets within their practice.

Each practice will have to produce a leaflet detailing the members of staff available and their qualifications. An annual report must also be produced and returned to the local Family Practitioner Committee. These reports need to include details of patients' referrals to other services in the NHS, listing the numbers sent to hospital as In-Patients and those referred to different specialities as Out-Patients. Furthermore, full details of those referred for pathological or X-ray Investigations

will need to be given. Each General Practitioner will also be given a budget for prescribing which he will not be expected to exceed. The changes give great powers to the local Family Practitioner Committee and Health Boards, who will be obliged to monitor all GPs referrals and prescriptions. Each practitioner will be expected to be answerable regarding his referral rates and prescribing habits. The Secretary of State is also keen that as many practices as possible should become "Budget Holders". "Budget Holding" involves the allocation of large sums of money to GPs who will be responsible for the major part of patient care, so that the practice will itself meet the cost of investigations and most operations. Doctors would need to negotiate with hospitals who offer the "best buy" available for particular types of treatment.

Opposition to the Proposals

The British Medical Association and other bodies which represent doctors are opposed to these proposals because they feel that they are not in the best interests of patients. They feel it is wrong to put cash limits on clinical care, and consider that the Doctor/Patient relationship will be undermined by the patient's knowledge that his GP has financial considerations to balance against his medical welfare. There is also concern that doctors will have to spend more time on financial and administrative matters which might be better spent dealing with their patient's clinical problems. Community Health Councils and other patient groups are also concerned that individuals may not be able to get the services that they require at their local hospital and that they may be obliged to travel great distances to receive the treatment they need.

While many of the changes to be implemented would seem to be beneficial to patients the undue haste with which the contract has been worked out and imposed against the will of the majority of the medical profession must give cause for concern. Furthermore, the absence of pilot studies or detailed evaluation is also a cause for disquiet. It is extremely difficult to apply financial considerations to health matters and the popular press has already seized on alarmist reports of patients being removed from their doctor's lists because they may involve their practice in excessive expense. The Secretary of State has made it clear that such action will not be tolerated, but doctors have at present the right to remove patients without giving any reason. The medical profession is angry and disgruntled and only time will tell whether the changes have resulted in significant benefits to their patients.

PART IV. INDEX AND GLOSSARY

Abortus fever. *See* **Undulant fever**, 14 (2).

Abrasion. Any injury which rubs off the surface skin.

Acidity. *See* **Peptic ulcer**, 35 (2).

Acne, 53 (1).

Acromegaly, 43 (1).

Actinomycosis, 15 (1).

Acute chorea or St. Vitus' dance, 48 (2).

Acute nephritis, 44 (2).

Addison's disease, 43 (1).

Adrenal cortex, 43 (1).

Adrenocorticotrophic hormone (ACTH), 42 (2).

Agranulocytosis, 25 (2).

Aids, 61–2

Alcoholism, 50 (1).

Allergy. Abnormal sensitivity to any substance which does not affect normal people.

Alopecia, 52 (1).

Amenorrhœa, 56 (1).

Amnesia, 47 (1).

Amoebae, 8 (1).

Amoebic dysentery. 17 (2).

Amphetamine, 61 (1).

Amyotrophic lateral sclerosis, 48 (1).

Anaemias, 24–25.

Anaesthetic. Any drug used to abolish pain during an operation.

Anencephaly, 48 (1).

Aneurism, 30 (1).

Angina pectoris, 28 (1).

Ankylosis. Partial or complete fixation of a joint as after some types of arthritis. In other cases deliberately produced by surgery.

Ankylostomiasis, 18 (2).

Anorexia nervosa, 51 (2).

Anterior pituitary, 42 (2).

Anthrax, 15 (1).

Antibiotics, 9 (1).

Antibodies, 8 (2).

Antihistamine drugs, 4 (2), 5 (1).

Antiseptics, 8 (2).

Anxiety neurosis, 51 (2).

Aortic diseases, 30 (1).

Aphasia, 47 (1).

Aplastic anaemia, 24 (2).

Appendicitis, 36 (2).

Arteriography, 46 (2).

Arthritis, 54 (1).

Artificial respiration (kiss of life), 22 (1).

Ascites, 38 (2).

Aspirin, 60 (2), 36 (1); *see also* **Headache**.

Asthma, 31 (2).

Atheroma or Atherosclerosis, 39 (2).

Athlete's foot, 8 (1), 15 (1).

Autism, 51 (2).

Backache. A symptom which may be caused by many different diseases—sometimes disease of the vertebrae themselves, sometimes strain of the ligaments, and sometimes inflammation or spasm of the surrounding muscles. "Lumbago" is usually due to inflammation of the muscles in the small of the back. Backache from purely local causes may be treated temporarily by applying heat in the form of a kaolin poultice or a rubber hot-water bottle and taking two aspirin tablets a day. On the other hand, many cases of backache are due to disease elsewhere. The most important thing is to find out the cause, and therefore a doctor should be consulted.

Bacteria, 7 (1). **Bacterial diseases**, 12–15.

Bacteriophage, 7 (2).

Baldness, 52 (1).

Barbiturates, 61 (1).

Bell's palsy, 50 (1).

Beri-beri, 42 (1).

Berry aneurysm, 48 (2).

Bilharzia, 18 (1), 16 (1).

Birth control, 56–59.

Blackwater fever, 17 (1).

Bladder. *See under* **Urinary diseases**, 44–45.

Bleeding diseases, 26 (1).

Blood, function of the, 24 (1).

Blood, diseases of the, 24–26.

Blood Groups. Human blood plasma contains factors which clump, or agglutinate, the red cells of some other people's blood. The main blood groups are called A, B, AB, and O. The plasma of group A blood contains an anti-B factor and *vice versa*, so that people of groups A and B cannot accept each other's blood. Group AB contains neither anti-A nor anti-B factor and people with this group can therefore receive transfusions from both but can give to neither. Group O contains both anti-A and anti-B, and can therefore receive blood only from group O but can donate blood to all groups. It is important that transfused cells should not be agglutinated by the factors in the recipient's plasma. Apart from the so-called ABO system, there are several other blood groupings, one of which is mentioned under **Rhesus Factor.**

Blood poisoning (septicaemia), 14 (1).

Blood-pressure, 28 (2).

Blood-vessels, diseases of the, 29 (2)–30.

Botulism, 13 (2).

Brain. *See under* **Nervous system**, 45–50.

Brain tumour, 49 (2).

Breasts, 55 (1).

Bronchial asthma, 31 (2), 62.

Bronchial carcinoma, *See* Lung cancer.

Bronchiectasis, 31 (2).

Bronchitis, 31 (1).

Bulimia nervosa, 51 (2).

Burns and Scalds, 19 (2).

Cachexia. Extreme wasting due to disease.

Caesarean operation. When the abdomen has to be opened to remove the child. (Named after Julius Caesar, who is said to have been born in this way.)

Caisson disease, 30 (1).

Cancer of the breast, 55 (1).

Cancer of the cervix, 55 (2).

Cancer of the colon, 37 (1).

Cancer of the liver, 39 (1).

Cancer of the lung, 33 (1), 33 (2).

Cancer of the oesophagus, 35 (2).

Cancer of the rectum, 37 (1).

Cancer of the stomach, 36 (2).

Cancer test (cervical smear), 55 (2).

Carbohydrates. The scientific name for sugars, starches and cellulose, 34 (1), 39–40.

Carbuncle. A large boil.

Cardiac neurosis, 27 (1).

Cataract, 54 (2).

Cerebral abscess, 49 (1).

Cerebral embolism, 48 (2).

Cerebral haemorrhage or apoplexy, 48 (2).

Cerebral palsy, 48 (1).

Cerebrovascular diseases, *see* **Stroke illness.**

Chadwick, Sir Edwin (1800–90). English social reformer, 6 (1).

Haematemesis. Vomiting of blood, 33 (1), 36 (1).
Haematuria. The passing of blood in the urine, 44 (1).
Haemoglobin. The red pigment in the blood.
Haemolytic anaemia, 24 (2).
Haemophilia, 26 (1).
Haemoptysis. The spitting-up of blood, 33 (1).
Haemorrhage anaemia, 24 (1).
Haemorrhagic diseases, 26 (1).
Haemorrhage of the brain, 48 (2).
Haemorrhoids, 37 (2).
Hair. *See* **Alopecia,** 52 (1).
Headache, 47 (1). *See also* **Migraine.**
Head injuries, 21 (1).
Health: general principles, 3 (2).
Heart: how it works, 26–7.
Heart attack, 28 (2).
Heart beat, 29 (1).
Heart failure, 27 (1).
Hepatic. Concerning the liver.
Hepatitis, infective, 10 (1), 38 (2).
Hereditary or Huntington's chorea, 48 (2).
Hernia, 37 (1).
Heroin, 61 (1).
Herpes zoster, 49 (1).
Hiatus hernia, 35 (2).
Hodgkin's disease, 25 (2).
Hookworm disease, 18 (2).
Hormones. *See* **Endocrine glands.**
Hydrocephaly, 48 (1).
Hydronephrosis, 45 (1).
Hyperpituitarism, 43 (1).
Hypochondriasis, the unfounded belief that one is suffering from a serious disease.
Hysteria, 51 (1).

Ichthyosis, 53 (2).
Immunity, 8 (2).
Impetigo, 53 (1).
Incubation period. *See* **Infectious Fevers,** 9 (2).
Infantile paralysis. *See* **Poliomyelitis,** 10 (2).
Infarction, 30 (1), 48 (2).
Infection, how spread, 8 (1).
Infectious diseases, 6–18.
Infective hepatitis, 10 (1), 38 (2).
Infectious mononucleosis, 11 (1).
Inflammatory diseases of the nervous system, 49 (1).
Influenza, 10 (2).
Injuries, 18–23.
Insomnia, 47 (1).
Insulin. *See* **Diabetes,** 39 (1). For psychiatric use *see* **Psychosis,** 50 (2).
Intermittent claudication, 29 (2).
Itching, 52 (1).

Jaundice, 38 (2), 24 (2).
Jenner, Sir Edward (1749–1823). English physician, 15 (2).
Joints, Diseases of the, 54 (1).

Kala-azar, 17 (2).
Kidney diseases, 43–45.
Kidneys, function of, 43 (2).
Kidney stones, 45 (1).
Koch, Robert (1843–1910). German bacteriologist, 15 (2).
Kwashiorkor, 41 (2).

Large intestine, diseases of the, 37 (1).
Leishmaniasis (kala-azar or dum-dum fever), 17 (2).
Leprosy, 16 (1).
Leukaemia, 25 (2).
Lice. *See* **Parasites,** 8 (1), 52 (1).

Lichen planus, 53 (1).
Lister, Joseph (1827–1912). English surgeon who founded modern antiseptic surgery, 5 (2).
Liver, function of the, 38 (1).
Liver and gall-bladder, diseases of the, 38 (1).
Lockjaw. *See* **Tetanus,** 14 (2).
Lung cancer, 33 (1).
Lymph nodes, 25 (2), 42 (2).
Lymphosarcoma, 25 (2).

Malaria, 17 (1).
Malnutrition, 41 (1).
Malta fever (undulant fever), 14 (2).
Manic depression, 50 (2).
Marasmus, 41 (2).
Measles, 9 (2).
Medicines: classification, 22 (1).
Melancholia. *See* **Manic-depressive insanity,** 50 (2).
Menière's disease, 47 (2).
Meningitis, 14 (1), 49 (1).
Menopause, 43 (2).
Mental illnesses, 50.
Metastases or secondary deposits, 49 (2).
Migraine, 47 (1).
Minot, George Richards (1885–1950). American physician and pathologist, specialised in diseases of the blood, 25 (1).
Mitral stenosis, 28 (1).
Motor nerves, 46 (1).
Motor neurone disease, 48 (1).
Multiple sclerosis or disseminated sclerosis or "creeping paralysis", 49 (1).
Mumps, 10 (1).
Muscular dystrophies, 50 (1).
Myasthenia gravis, 50 (1).
Myelin sheaths, 46 (1).
Myelitis, 49 (1).
Myelography, 46 (2).
Myxoedema, 43 (1).

Narcolepsy, 47 (1).
National Health Service, 6 (2).
Nephritis, acute and chronic, 44 (2).
Nephrosis, 44 (2).
Nerve cells, 45 (1).
Nervous system, diseases of, 45–50.
Nettlerash, 53 (1).
Neurology: diagnostic techniques, 46 (2).
Neurosis, 51 (1).
Nutritional disorders, 41–2.

Obsessional neurosis, 51 (1).
Oedema (dropsy), 27 (1), 44 (2).
Oesophagitis, 35 (2).
Olfactory. To do with the sense of smell.
Ophthalmia, 15 (1).
Orthopaedics. A branch of medicine dealing with the surgery of bones and joints.
Osteoarthritis, 54 (2).
Ovary, 43 (2), 55 (1).

Palpitation. *See* **Tachycardia,** 29 (1).
Pancreas, 39 (1).
Papilloma, 45 (1).
Parasites, 8 (1), 52 (1).
Parasitic worms: diseases, 17 (2).
Parathyroid glands, 43 (2).
Paré, Ambroise (c. 1510–90). French army surgeon, 4 (1).
Parkinson's disease, 48 (1).
Pasteur, Louis (1822–95). French chemist, 5 (2), 11 (2), 15 (2).

AN INTRODUCTION TO PSYCHOLOGY

This section is concerned with the scientific study of mental life, a territory whose rich mysteries are only just beginning to be understood. It represents a unique layperson's guide to one of the most exciting experimental sciences of today.

TABLE OF CONTENTS

AN INTRODUCTION TO PSYCHOLOGY

The purpose of this section is to provide a general introduction to the young but expanding science of psychology. The topic itself is of course enormously broad and can only be summarised at best. However, it is hoped it will serve to give some idea of the fascinating material that psychologists study and also of their occasionally remarkable, and always interesting findings. The section also aims to dispel some of the illusions that have surrounded the subject and thus to define its boundaries more clearly.

I. INTRODUCTION.

What is a Psychologist?

The popular image of a psychologist is a fairly well-defined one—a person who treats mental illness in the way that a doctor treats physical ones. Although this picture is changing as psychologists are increasingly called upon for expert comment by the media, it is perpetuated by the countless novels, films and TV programmes in which the characters are "in analysis" or undergoing "therapy". While it is true that the study of mental illness and its treatment is certainly one facet of psychology (and is an area whose inherent bizarreness makes it especially fascinating), it only constitutes a small part of psychological inquiry. The majority of psychologists are concerned with the workings of the "normal" brain, although a little reflection on the immense variety in human behaviour between historically and geographically separated cultures may indicate that clearcut ideas about "normality" are perhaps impossible.

This section, therefore, begins with a clarification of the role of psychologists, and follows with a brief introduction to their principal fields of study—the brain and behaviour. After this we take in turn the main areas of study which may lead to an understanding of the psychological side of human nature. These are: perception, attention and memory (collectively referred to as Information Processing); Learning and Motivation; Emotion; Thinking; and Individual Differences in terms of personality and intelligence.

One of the main sources of confusion in people's minds arises from puzzlement over the distinction between four commonly used words which, while differing in meaning in important respects, are almost invariably lumped together as one. These are (1) Psychiatry, (2) Psychoanalysis, (3) Psychotherapy, and (4) Psychology. The words do look and sound rather similar but it is not difficult, once the right definitions have been given, to sort the four clearly out in one's mind. Let's take psychiatry first.

(1) **Psychiatry** concerns the treatment of mental diseases or illnesses by medical means and it is a specialist branch of medicine, entered through the medical profession and taught at hospitals or universities. A psychiatrist therefore is quite invariably a doctor of medicine with ordinary medical degrees but with a postgraduate training in mental illness and its treatment. No one may call himself a psychiatrist unless so qualified, and no one may prescribe drugs or surgery in treating mentally sick individuals unless he is medically qualified. There is an important point of issue here, for in Britain, and many other countries, people not trained as psychiatrists may nevertheless diagnose and treat mental illnesses—provided that they do not use drugs or surgery to do so.

(2) **Psychoanalysis** is a particular form of examination or diagnosis of an individual's mental state based on the theories of the mind and personality advanced by Sigmund Freud and his colleagues or followers, and the reader may like to turn to the entry on the subject in **Section J**. An interesting feature of psychoanalysis is that, unlike psychiatry, it may be practised without medical or academic qualifications on the part of the analyst. A special training at a recognised institute is normally undertaken, with the would-be practitioners themselves undergoing thorough, and often lengthy, psychoanalysis. Such training is not normally available to individuals without psychological or medical qualifications.

(3) **Psychotherapy** is the practice of treating mental diseases or illnesses by more or less *any* means. Thus, strictly speaking, the psychiatrist, the psychoanalyst and the clinical psychologist (*see below*) are all psychotherapists—as are any other individuals using reputable methods who offer therapy for the mind, even without formal qualifications. In England, the Tavistock Institute is one of the primary training centres, offering a wide range of courses in various aspects of psychotherapy.

(4) **Psychology** is the study of the mind and behaviour. Its area has broadened somewhat in the last century as we have learned that one cannot consider the mind as totally isolated from the body. Psychologists also study the behaviour and brain of animals wherever such studies throw light on human behaviour. It is important to realise that psychologists are first and foremost trained as scientists rather than as medical experts and do not necessarily take much interest in abnormalities of the brain and mental processes. Those psychologists who do, however, may take a postgraduate training in clinical psychology. This is one of three professional qualifications open to British psychologists and enables the individual concerned to work in hospital or related settings in a therapeutic capacity. The other qualifications are in educational and occupational psychology, and the holders typically work in school and industrial environments providing expert assessments and advice on both individuals and institutional practices.

It is obvious that there is a good deal of overlap between all these professions and in the following section we shall be entering the territory of psychiatry and psychoanalysis to some extent, but mainly concerning ourselves with psychology—the science and study of the human mind, personality, and behaviour.

1. The Brain.

From the moment of our birth our body is controlled and dominated by a single but complex organ, a library, switchboard, signal-box, computer, and many other things all rolled into one—the brain (*see* **F40(1), P46**).

It is encased in a hard shell of bone and is equipped with sensors for detecting food or danger at a distance (eyes, ears *etc.*). At birth the brain is closer to its adult size than any other organ and has almost the full complement of brain cells. Over approximately the next 20 years the brain reaches its maximum weight: 1,375 grammes in the male (about three pounds) and slightly less in the female. Once full grown, the brain loses about one gramme in weight per year. If relative brain size determined intelligence, however, the human would be outstripped by animals such as the mouse; clearly it is the kind of brain which is important.

The brain's proper functioning determines the

"normality" of one's behaviour and the part one can play in society; its efficiency and computational power one's intelligence, and to some extent one's creativity and ability to adapt to the environment; its storage capacity and retrieval system one's potential to learn and remember. Although these abilities are found in other animals, nowhere are they as highly developed as in Man.

The brain is the main focus of interest for the psychologist, for there can be little doubt that the key to the understanding of human personality and behaviour lies locked up within it. Its complexity of course is daunting, but thanks to physiological and anatomical studies it is possible to get at least a general idea of what's going on. In the first place the brain acts as the principal co-ordinator of messages coming in from the various sense organs, and then as the dispatch point for the appropriate responses. This coordinating centre is best developed in man, and is present in most of the "higher" animals.

Simpler creatures, however, such as amoeba and certain tiny worms, get along without any important co-ordinator of nervous impulses and respond diffusely to changes in the environment—moving away from things that "annoy" or damage them and towards food or other "pleasant" things. Such animals are literally the slaves of their environment, incapable of setting up goals to achieve and with no facility for computing the sequences of any action. One important branch of the evolutionary tree shows a steady trend towards increasing brain size and, with it, freedom from this slavery.

In the second place the brain acts as the storehouse of information which the senses have gathered at some time in the individual's life. To us it may seem "obvious" that we have a memory—a device for looking at things that took place in the past—and indeed it is hard to imagine ourselves without one. However, a large number of creatures get by with only the most limited of memory systems. Clearly a good deal must depend upon how long an animal is to live. If its life-span is to be brief, then it need not set aside much room to store information from its past. If it is to live for many years, survive in a changing and generally rather dangerous environment, and learn by its mistakes and its previous achievements, then this ability to refer back to the past is obviously essential. In human beings mechanisms of learning and memory are of vital importance and we will devote a good deal of this section to discussing the way in which psychologists study these.

The third primary function of the brain is to provide the computing and decision-making processes which dictate so much of human and higher animal behaviour.

Finally, the brain is also the seat of two of the most elusive and controversial human phenomena studied by psychologists: *consciousness* and *personality*. Determining their existence and/or relevance in non-humans is even more problematic.

2. How Does the Brain Divide up its Functions?

Nowadays we rather take for granted that important things such as thinking, remembering, etc., are mediated through the brain and it comes as something of a shock to recall that early philosophers located the majority of such processes in the heart or the stomach! Even today, a good deal of controversy exists over exactly which part of the brain does what and, as we shall see when we discuss the contradictory experimental evidence later, there is even a suggestion that certain processes are dealt with by the brain *as a whole* rather than by some specific part.

In the first place the brain is composed of a vast number of cells—the building blocks of all living systems—which in this case have become highly specialised and stretched out, rather like telephone lines. These are known as nerve or neural cells or, yet again, as neurones. They act as communication units, receiving electrical signals from other parts of the body. Brain anatomists are able to trace the routes of whole chains of cells starting at, say, the finger tips and finishing up in a particular section of the brain where such tactile messages are gathered and interpreted. On the whole messages from the

eyes tend to finish up in the back of the brain, or occipital lobes; messages from the ears, nose, etc., on the side, or temporal lobes. In the front are the frontal lobes (unsurprisingly): in Man these comprise a large area of brain tissue richly interconnected with almost all other parts of the central nervous system. Parts of the frontal lobes are more involved with output than input—the so-called motor areas which dispatch the signals commanding the various parts of the body to move. The frontal lobes' other functions are as varied as their anatomical connections. A recent review described their activities under the following headings: sensory, perception and construction functions; attention; abnormal states of awareness; flexibility and planning; language; memory; thinking and personality. Such a list summarises (almost) the whole gamut of psychology. Finally, parts of the brain must be involved in the storage of information, yet the location of these regions remains as controversial today as it was a generation ago.

The Cerebral Cortex.

All these areas we have been talking about up till now are known as the cerebral *cortex* and they are located on the outer surface of the brain itself—*i.e.*, right up against the inside of the skull. The cortex is pinkish-grey in colour hence its popular name—"grey matter". You should by now have gathered that the cortex deals largely with psychological factors closely tied up with consciousness and awareness—seeing, hearing, thinking, remembering, etc. This ties in rather nicely with its alternative name, the neocortex (or new tissue), for in evolutionary terms this part of the brain is "new." In general, the closer that an animal species approximates to man, the greater the proportion of its brain is assigned to neocortex, and the more the particular animal is capable of independent, deliberate and purposeful activity.

Tucked in beneath the cerebral cortex, growing out of the spinal cord, are the so-called lower centres—the old brain. Here in a number of specialised blocks are located the control centres which deal with the most automatic (but no less important) bodily functions such as cardiac activity, respiration, temperature, etc., and which it is unnecessary or inconvenient to keep under conscious control. Damage or injury to these centres is generally very serious, whereas damage to the outer layer of the brain, even when extensive, can sometimes have surprisingly little effect on the individual's way of life.

To sum up, we note that the brain is divided into two major functional areas in evolutionary terms—the old and the new. The former largely deals with the vital automatic processes, and the latter with the receiving and interpreting of sensory input and the decision-making processes which guide our interaction with the outside world. Clearly this is an enormously simplified picture (specific aspects of this topic are dealt with in greater detail later) and the brain and central nervous system (CNS) is complicated almost beyond description, with much of its mechanics and rules of operation still poorly understood. How then can one set out to study it properly and unravel its secrets?

3. Methods of Studying the Brain.

Psychologists and physiologists favour many approaches to finding out how the brain works, and while it won't be possible to look at them all in this section it will be worthwhile spending a bit of time on some of the most important lines of attack. Some of the following methods, as we shall see, are really possible only with animals as the experimental subjects, and others are more suited for research on human beings.

(1) *Brain Anatomy.*

This is perhaps the most obvious and logical method of all, but it has one serious and insurmountable drawback. As an analogy, suppose that one wanted to find out how a motor-car engine worked and that one had no prior knowledge of its operation. Studying brain anatomy is the equivalent of getting hold of a complete engine and taking it apart to examine its components. The chances are that with a relatively simple device, such as an automobile engine, any intelligent person would begin to see the principles of its operation. However, until they had actually watched the engine at work and studied the effect of, say, depressing the accelerator or pulling out the choke, their comprehension of the device might be rather limited and distorted.

The same problem applies equally to the anatomical study of dead (non-functioning) brains. Furthermore, there is an even greater problem: one of complexity. Whereas the average motor-car engine probably contains a maximum of about 1,000 discrete and separate components, some of which are rather large and "obvious," the brain contains about *ten thousand million* neurones or nerve cells and no large obvious "moving parts" to give the anatomist useful clues. It is little wonder therefore that while students of the brain adopting post mortem dissection have, in the course of the last few centuries, acquired a pretty clear picture of the way in which the brain is laid out—an anatomical atlas so to speak—most of the principles of cerebral *operation* are still more or less unknown.

(2) Surgical Tissue Destruction.

To return to our rather inexact analogy with the motor-car engine, let us assume that our investigator finds himself with a working, running engine to play with. Let us also assume that he has already made himself pretty familiar with the anatomy of the "dead" engine and has perhaps formed some hypotheses as to what certain parts of it do. For example, he might have a suspicion that the carburettor and the sparking plugs were particularly important, or that a key to the complete device working was that the pistons should move up and down in the cylinders. One of the first things he might do would be to systematically remove what he considered to be important parts of the engine and note how its performance was affected. Using this technique of selective removal he might soon begin to confirm or reject his hunches and a gradual comprehension of the function and capabilities of the engine would build up in his mind. He might find that whereas the removal of one sparking plug did not stop the engine, it would lower its pulling power. Removal of the carburettor in toto would be calamitous, while twiddling with it might have unpredictable effects, making it run better or worse. On the other hand, filing bits off the iron cylinder block would make no difference whatsoever. Once again the psychophysiologist is faced with something immensely more complex when he studies the brain, but there is nevertheless obviously something to be gained by adopting a similar procedure with the working or living system.

The systematic removal or destruction of parts of cerebral tissue has, in fact, been one of the most rewarding approaches adopted by brain scientists, though there are naturally severe limitations to the technique. In the first place such surgery cannot be performed on human beings, except where it is a necessary feature of therapeutic brain surgery (*e.g.*, as when removing a brain tumour) and can only be justified in living animals in the interest of serious and clearly defined scientific research. In the second place, the very act of surgery itself probably introduces side-effects which serve to complicate the picture. However, this technique, when skilfully used, has led to some informative experiments.

(3) Electroencephalography.

As we have said earlier, the principal building blocks of the brain are the neurones, specialised cells devoted to the transmission of information from one part of the body to the other. This transmission is effected by a change in the electrical potential of the cell along its long stem. The main bodies of cells tend to be pressed up against one another and when a change in potential occurs in one, this tends to trigger off a similar response in a neighbouring cell at a junction point known as a *synapse*. Incidentally, the long stems of the cells (which may be a yard or more in length in certain parts of the body) are covered by an insulating fatty sheath which prevents the electrical "message" leaking out en route and which makes them strangely similar to the kind of electrical wires and cables we use in telecommunications. With 10 thousand million cells jammed up together in the head, all of them propagating electrical signals in one way or another, it should not surprise anyone to learn that sensitive recording devices can be used to get a picture of the overall electrical activity going on in the brain.

Studies of this type (electroencephalography, or EEG for short) could not begin until suitable recording machines had been developed and thus, although scientists had been pretty confident that the brain was a potent source of electrical energy since the middle of the 19th cent., it was not until the 1920s that anyone was able to get a readable picture of this. The pioneers in this technique were the physiologists Berger and Adrian, who attached little electrodes to the outside of the human scalp and by hooking these up to amplifiers and then to special recording pens were able to get a kind of plot of the electrical activity going on within. To their surprise what emerged was not just meaningless electrical "noise" but rather a series of precise and elegant rhythms, the frequency and amplitude of these depending upon the part of the brain where the electrodes were applied.

EEG has proved invaluable in medicine, as certain disruptions of the "normal" brain wave pattern can give clear indications of the presence of epilepsy or deep-lying brain tumours. EEG has been used in the study of alertness, sleep and dreaming. A sleeping person goes through a series of stages each with a characteristic EEG pattern. When the individual is deeply asleep, and not exhibiting *rapid eye movements* (REMs), the EEG is characterized by large low frequency ("delta") waves. When a sleeping individual is making REMs their EEG more closely resembles that found in the waking state, and if woken from REM sleep they frequently report that they have just been dreaming.

A brief change in the EEG may be produced by a single presentation of a word or a picture, but the effect may well be lost in the overall pattern. Repeated presentation of the stimulus, and averaging of the EEG by computer, cancels out the other waves leaving a clear *average evoked response* or *potential* (AEP) caused by the stimulus. Psychological research with AEPs has begun to indicate that they may be related to important aspects of information processing (*see* **Q7**).

(4) Microelectrode Recording.

For all practical purposes the record obtained by the EEG is a gross, overall view of the brain at work. The waves and rhythms encountered must, at the least, represent the sum of the activity of literally hundreds of thousands of neural cells, presumably firing more or less in synchrony. Going back once more to the motor-car analogy, the EEG could be likened to a garage mechanic listening with a stethoscope to the pulsing of an engine when running at high speed. Changes of speed, adjustments in carburation of timing, etc., would give characteristically different running sounds, but little if anything could be deduced about the state of activity of an individual component unless it were a very large one. Much the same limitations, only on a gigantic scale, surround the use of the EEG as a device for measuring specific aspects of brain activity.

Quite recently, however, an interesting technological development has occurred which allows a more precise and delicate analysis of cortical cell firing to be undertaken—in fact it allows even the output from a single neural cell to be monitored. This technique involves the use of what are known as microelectrodes, tiny slivers of metal, thousandths of an inch in diameter, which when in contact with an electrical source—in this instance the body of a nerve cell or neurone—transmit a pulse of electricity to an amplifier and recording apparatus. We shall discuss the remarkable findings which have come from experiments of this kind later in the section on "Perception." Microelectrode techniques, incidentally, can on occasions be used with human subjects. In such cases, naturally the opportunity arises when an individual is undergoing brain surgery for, say, the removal of a cerebral tumour. In these circumstances with the patient's permission, the surgeon may perform experiments to study single cell responses.

(5) *Neurochemical Methods*

Owing to limited space and the complexity of techniques used, this topic will be treated very briefly. In the last 20 years or so, psychologists, in collaboration with biochemists and pharmacologists, have attempted to unravel the detailed chemistry of the brain. It has become clear that there are a large number of naturally occurring chemicals, called *neurotransmitters*, which act as chemical messengers between different nerve cells, encouraging or inhibiting the electrical impulses which travel along them. One of the primary goals has been to understand the specific mental functions which may be served by a particular neurotransmitter. In this regard, studies have shown that certain drugs may affect performance on some psychological tasks but not others. However, more detailed investigations usually reveal that this kind of analysis is not so straightforward; the neurochemical systems are both dynamic and interrelated. A drug may principally affect a particular neurotransmitter in a certain way, but this often leads to subtle physical reactions which attempt to compensate for the enforced change, along with "knock-on effects" on other brain chemicals.

Bearing in mind the preceding note of caution, important research has revealed that certain mental illnesses and brain diseases may be related to deficiencies in neurotransmitter systems. Furthermore, prescribed drugs designed to remedy the neurochemical imbalances have, in some cases, given a great deal of symptomatic relief, if not a total "cure".

(6) *Brain Scanning*

In recent years it has become possible to take an X-ray of a patient's brain. This technique entered clinical practice in the UK in 1972, and is now a routine part of medical examinations in neurology and psychiatry. Brain scans are referred to as CT, or *computerised tomography*, scans because the two-dimensional images are "photographed" in several slices at different levels roughly parallel to the top of the skull (*tomos*: cut). A CT scanner sends a narrow beam of X-rays through the head. A detector measures the amount of radiation which passes through and as the X-ray beam is moved around the head a computer system converts information on transmitted radiation into images which are captured on film. The many refinements on the basic procedure, since 1972, have led to the much higher image quality obtained by contemporary scanners.

The development of CT scanning has enabled clinicians to detect whether a patient's symptoms relate to a localised brain injury, such as those produced by a stroke or a brain tumour. (The procedure is safe as the dose of radiation is very small.) Early detection of tumours is vital in enhancing the effectiveness of surgery, and conversely increasing the diagnostic power of the doctor has lead to a reduction in unnecessary brain operations. In neuropsychological research, CT scans make it possible to relate the results of psychological testing to the approximate location of the patient's brain damage while the patient is still alive, thus allowing the researcher to make some inferences about the normal function of the damaged brain tissue. Previously, only those patients unfortunate enough to die shortly after the psychological testing could provide such information.

There is currently a proliferation of new brain-scanning technologies which do not use X-rays. Rather these techniques rely on the radioactive emissions from the atoms in special gases inhaled by the patient (emission tomographies) or by the magnetic properties of the atomic particles actually making up the brain tissue (magnetic resonance imaging, MRI, which gives the clearest pictures). Although the images in emission tomography are not as clear as CT or MRI scans they give dynamic indications of the blood flow in various brain regions as the blood supply delivers the inhaled gases to the brain. Researchers are just beginning to study this information about the *working* brain whilst the patient performs different psychological tasks.

4. Methods for Studying Behaviour.

Psychologists are interested not merely in the structure of the brain in humans and animals but also, of course, in their behaviour. "Behaviour" refers to the way in which the organism interacts with its environment (with the reasons for a particular behaviour constituting the important related question of Motivation—*see* **Q14**). A study of what, when and how a creature does something can tell one a good deal about the rules that govern behaviour. How, then, have psychologists gone about this study?

(1) *Introspection*

The oldest and perhaps most obvious method of studying the brain was simply to think about it! This was the method adopted by early philosophers who believed that if one was sufficiently logical and intelligent one could work out the solution to practically anything. Unfortunately, while the brain, mind, etc., might seem to be an ideal subject for its own thought process, this method of analysis—known as introspection—just doesn't seem to work in the way that it should. The principal problem is that much of the brain's activities are exceedingly rapid and automatic, as anyone can demonstrate for themselves. For example, turn your head and look at an object on the wall. It will be "perceived" and recognised apparently instantaneously. Even if you can detect a faint lag between the act of inspection and the act of *perception*, it is quite impossible to describe the steps or stages in the process. Much the same applies to other important mental faculties. One cannot, merely by thinking about it, say how one actually *learns* something, or how one calls an item up from memory. It was realising the relative hopelessness of this quest which led philosophers interested in the brain to convert themselves in the middle part of the 19th cent., into psychologists and adopt an experimental rather than an intellectual approach to the problem. However, it should be equally clear (though many psychologists seem to have forgotten this) that there is much important psychological material which is not readily amenable to experimental analysis, or which cannot be approached in the first instance only through some measure of introspection. Studies of 'creativity' and the altered states of consciousness reported by artists, or the distortions of perceptions and personality induced by hallucinogenic drugs, are examples of psychological research which began, of necessity, from introspections. These examples illustrate the point that when studying the brain we should not ignore the mind's power to look in on itself.

(2) *Behavioural Research*

In 1913, J. B. Watson proposed that introspection was not valid as a scientific method for understanding mind, arguing instead that the experimental analysis of behaviour was essential, thus founding a school of thought which became known as Behaviourism (*see* **J7–8**). In an effort after precision, this approach led to the laboratory study of a small number of species (*e.g.* rats) used as surrogate humans in a limited range of experimental tasks. Behaviourist methods were particularly influential in the United States in the immediate post-war period. They concentrated on understanding the animals' learning of connections between the stimuli presented to them (S; *e.g.*, a light coming on in the rat's cage) and the responses which they emitted (R; *e.g.*, pressing a lever to obtain a food pellet). Behaviourists considered these S–R connections to be "stamped in" if S and R occurred together sufficiently often, and that, once learned, R would follow S in a reflex, automatic way.

The greatest difficulties with the early Behaviourists' position were in their pretension to provide a *complete* theory of brain and mind, and with their insistence that any intervening mental processes between S and R (such as the rat having a mental "map" of the cage in which the stimuli occurred) were either non-existent or else unimportant in determining learning. Gradually, as we shall see in the section on Learning (**Q14**), this view was contradicted by evidence, and the Behaviourist hard-line softened; the pretence that animals were no more than bundles of completely automatic reflexes was slowly abandoned. Nonetheless, Behaviourists conducted many ingenious experiments obtaining results that are still valid; and systematic laboratory procedures, derived from their methods, are widely used with animals today, by psychologists who would probably describe themselves as "behavioural" rather than behaviourist.

Despite the relative demise of Behaviourism from its heyday, radical proponents such as B. F. Skinner, as recently as the 1970s, were suggesting that psychologists should concentrate on simply unearthing lawful relationships between stimuli and responses.

(3) Behavioural Research in Natural Habitats

The science of *ethology* (*see* **F40(2)**) has emerged since the Second World War, partly as a reaction to the rather dry and confining methods of early Behaviourism. Its leading figures were two European zoologists: Konrad Lorenz and Niko Tinbergen. Ethology is concerned with studying animals' behaviour under natural conditions, and ethologists emphasised *instinct* (innate unlearned behaviour) as their central explanatory idea (in contrast to the Behaviourists, who focussed on learned behaviour). From the way, for example, in which a bird builds its nest, learns to sing a song specific to its species, and displays certain types of behaviour in courtship or defence of its territory, coupled with a knowledge of its brain organisation, one should be able to learn something about brain-behaviour relationships.

Ethologists studied many species in natural habitats and concluded that much animal behaviour consisted in *fixed action patterns*: instinctive behaviour which is highly similar from one occasion to another. These behaviour patterns seemed to be triggered without learning by highly specific releasing stimuli. Male sticklebacks, for example, will attack a crude model stickleback with a red underside (as a male rival) but not an accurate model without the red belly. Gradually, however, it was realised that even these kinds of instinct are subject to modification by learning. Attempts to apply similar explanations to complex human behaviour (so-called *sociobiology*) have been highly controversial. This is hardly surprising when sociobiologists wish to claim that the darker sides of our natures (*e.g.*, fighting wars or racism) are "natural" and "pre-programmed" in the genetics of our species.

(4) Experimental Psychology in Human Subjects

Human experimental psychology started in the latter part of the nineteenth century largely as the result of the pioneering work of the German physiologist and psychologist Wilhelm Wundt. Wundt's importance does not derive from the specific body of writing and experiments which he left behind, nor was he the first individual to realise that one can actually subject the raw material of human mental activity to experimental analysis. Rather, his influence lies in the fact that he was the first actually to conduct such experiments, in his own purpose-built laboratory, publishing his findings in his own journal. Wundt concentrated on perception and related themes and he conducted the first studies of *reaction time*: the delay between being given the signal to make a response and actually beginning it.

The Wundtian experimental tradition has continued to the present day. In psychology labs, human subjects are subjected to legion scientific investigations, measuring the speed, extent and characteristics of their reactions to a wide variety of material presented to them (words and other text, pictures, shapes, abstract patterns, detailed questionnaires and self-rating scales). The advent of cheap microcomputers has given further impetus to human psychological research; for many researchers the microcomputer is an invaluable tool, almost an entire laboratory in itself, used for presenting materials and recording responses in a controlled manner.

This concludes our condensed survey of some of the principal methods used by psychologists and their colleagues in attempting to get to grips with their exciting and challenging field. The reader may have been surprised by a number of things, one of which must surely be how very much wider is the territory covered by psychology than is commonly believed.

5. What do Psychologists Study?

We now come to examine the main areas making up the subject matter of psychology. There are all kinds of ways of subdividing this material, and as the topic is so immense (and enlarging rapidly all the time) one or two important aspects will have to be left aside. We shall only refer in passing to industrial psychology and ergonomics, and much of the material of social psychology (and its relationship with sociology) will have to be passed over. The way in which behaviour changes across the human lifespan—developmental psychology—will also not be covered here. The reader should notice some overlap between the headings of the following sections, confirming that the separation is largely for the purpose of explanation. Living organisms are entities, whole units which comprise more than their constituent parts: the various domains of their behaviour are similarly integrated and interdependent.

Anyone reading this introduction seriously will find that acquiring a first formal background in psychology will necessitate thinking as a physiologist, a philosopher, an anthropologist, and a good experimental scientist all rolled into one. This will turn out to be less complicated than one might imagine.

II. INFORMATION PROCESSING.

Since the 1950s and '60s the dominant approach in psychology has been to treat the human brain as an *information processing* device, an approach which may be generally referred to as *cognitive* psychology. Cognition means "knowing", and *cognitive* psychology has concentrated on all the routes which we use in knowing: perceiving; remembering; thinking; reasoning; plus our language functions. As was noted above, the Behaviourist doctrine held that in the study of behaviour the organism could be considered as a "black box" into which stimuli (S) were fed and from which responses (R) were emitted. Cognitive psychology, in marked contrast, seeks to analyse the structure and function of the black box. However, this analysis need not wait until one has a complete fine-grained physiological knowledge of the central nervous system; parallel progress may be made by generating models for a *conceptual* nervous system (a term coined first by the Canadian, Donald Hebb) at a more coarse-grained level of analysis.

With the physiological constraints for models of the brain not yet known, the cognitive psychologists of the '60s and '70s set about building box-and-arrow models which traced the flow of information through parts of the conceptual nervous system. The boxes represented key sub-units involved in information processing and the arrows the interconnections between them. However, many of the boxes were so broad in their content and function (*e.g.* "perceptual analysis") and labelled in so descriptive a way (*e.g.* "short-term memory") that these models often tended to do little but restate the problem. The black box of Behaviourist psychology had proliferated into a large number of smaller black boxes. The overall approach, and these models, reflected the recent invention of the electronic computer and the flow diagrams of computer engineers and programmers: cognitive psychology was dominated by the metaphor of "the mind as a computer".

Although cognitive psychology has become less glib in its use of box-diagrams, the basic approach persists today as the dominant philosophy in psychology. The central idea of "information" has already been noted above but may need a little more explanation. Its scientific meaning is rather broader than our everyday notions of information as facts from sources such as newspapers, history books or timetables. When psychologists talk about information they are concerned with the influence of one thing (*e.g.* a person, object *etc.*) on another. For example, when you look at the sun or a bright light, photons from the luminous object strike the retina or sensitive layer at the back of the eye. As the result of this the retina changes its state slightly and in due course passes signals back to the brain. Now the interaction between the sun and the retina, odd though it may seem at first, constitutes an exchange of information, and when the message finally reaches the brain and the sun is recognised for what it is, the information has flowed all the way from sun to brain.

If this appears to be an odd use of the word "information," then this is probably because one has tended to think that information can only be conveyed through words or numbers and "meaningful" conversations. The more one considers this limited point of view, however, the less reasonable it seems. If one looks at a painting, which contains neither numbers nor words, but a picture of, say, a ship at sea, then most people will agree that it is conveying information (the artist originating it whenever he painted the picture). In fact we can use this analogy to add that the painting itself can be looked upon as a kind of information store since the artist who set the whole process going could easily be dead and gone, and yet his message continues to be conveyed.

If one feels reasonably comfortable in talking of the sun as an emitter of information to the eye, then one has made a critical advance in understanding cognitive psychology.

1. Perception.

The first domain of information processing which we shall consider is Perception: the gathering and decoding of information. Decoding is vital; for example, when we spoke of the retina sending signals up to the brain where the sun is "recognised" we should note that what reaches the brain is not a kind of miniature sun but rather a pattern of nerve impulses which need to be interpreted. Firstly, however, we shall consider how the information is received and gathered.

The Five Senses

Simple creatures, such as amoeba, react in a generalised way to objects in their environment. The reason for this is that they have no specialised equipment to allow them to detect what is taking place, or about to take place, around them, and no computing centre capable of selecting alternative modes of behaviour. As we ascend the evolutionary scale we note increasing specialisation of the body's cells, the development of devices capable of scanning the external environment and increasingly complex co-ordinating nervous centres (brains). By the time we reach Man and other advanced animals, the individual is not merely reacting to his/her environment but consciously aware of its flux, able to predict many changes before they can effect his/her body physically, and frequently manipulating it significantly to suit his/her ends. This immense versatility is dependent upon information from the environment being fed into the nervous system for processing, and the devices which the body has developed to gather this information are known as the senses—vision, hearing, touch, taste, and smell. For this reason, if we are to get anywhere with understanding the operation of the brain we will need to know a fair bit about the sense organs that feed it.

Perhaps the most useful information from the brain's point of view would be that which concerns the detection of food, a mate, or danger (*e.g.* predators) at a distance. Thus, animals have developed remarkable sensory abilities. In Man, for example, a tone of 2,000 Hz can be heard when the movement of air particles against the eardrum is smaller than the diameter of a hydrogen molecule. If our ears were more sensitive than this then they would respond to the random movement of molecules in the air. Man's visual system is even more sensitive—a rod receptor in the retina (*see below*) can be triggered by perhaps a single quantum of light (the smallest amount of light which exists). Based on this, the amount of mechanical energy needed to lift a pea by only two cm would be enough, if converted to light energy, to give a brief sensation of light to everyone who has ever lived on the Earth. Owing to space limitations and to the fact that vision is the best understood of our senses, we shall concentrate here on the visual system and visual perception.

The Eye

Our eyes are geared to detecting radiation over a particular frequency range which we call "light". The actual spectrum detected by the eye covers electromagnetic waves (*see* **F14(1)**) whose wavelengths range from about 380 nm to about 720 nm (1 nm = 10^{-9}m). All this means is that the distance from peak to peak of the waves which constitute the light is very small indeed—far less than a thousandth of a millimetre in fact. Note, however, that not only can the eye detect the 380 nm and the 720 nm waves quite easily but it can also discriminate between them and a whole lot of other wavelengths in between as well. In fact we call the 380 nm waves "violet," the 720 nm "red," those of about 500 nm "green," etc. Remember the minute wavelengths involved and you will appreciate that whichever part of the eye handles this kind of information must be very sensitive indeed. This fabulous bit of equipment, one of the most remarkable of all biological systems, is called the retina.

The Retina

Situated in a layer at the back of the eye, the retina is a kind of screen on to which rays of light are focused by the *lens* after having passed through a window at the front, which is called the *cornea*. How does the retina detect the light rays and then transmit the relevant information to the brain? What follows is necessarily a much-simplified explanation.

The retina is a densely packed mass of neural cells, made special by the fact that they contain light-sensitive substances known as *photopigments*. These substances change their state rapidly when the photons from a light source strike them, and this change, which is really a high-speed chemical reaction, acts as the trigger which "fires" the cell. This in turn sends a pulse of electrical activity up the neurone's long stem in the direction of the brain. After it has fired, the cell then requires a brief period to recover its normal state and for the minute portion of bleached pigment to regenerate, during which time (known as the *refractory period*) it will not fire again. Multiply all this by one hundred million, which is the approximate number of cells in the retina, and you will get some idea of the frenzied activity contributing to the process of vision. To complicate matters there are at least two major types of visual receptors, the *cones* and the *rods*. Primarily, the cones tend to handle the higher levels of luminance met in daytime and also mediate colour vision, while the rods, which are far more sensitive, tend to come into play in the dusk or dark. The shift from cone to rod vision, which, like most of the body's basic functions, is entirely automatic, is something we all experience regularly in our daily life. Walk out of the sun into a dark room and for a moment one is "blinded." Walk out of a dark room into the sun and again one is "blinded." Actually all that is happening is that the visual system is having to shift from one set of receptors to another and sometimes the lag in the switchover is dramatically apparent.

The cones are concentrated in the centre of the retina, the *fovea*, and the rods are located more peripherally. You may have noticed this distribution of receptors in operation—in daytime your vision is best directly in front of you, whereas in very dim lighting objects at the edge of your visual field may be seen rather better. You may also have noticed how your peripheral vision is remarkably insensitive to colour. If not, a simple experiment will demonstrate this. Make a small mark on a piece of paper and fix your gaze on it with one eye closed. From the side, slowly bring a small coloured item closer to the central spot. If you can manage to keep your eye still, and avoid glancing sideways, you will be surprised how far in you need to bring the object in order to determine its colour with certainty. This experiment shows that the rods, used in peripheral vision, play little part in seeing in colour. Colour vision is a major function of the more centrally-located cones.

Colour Vision

As long ago as 1802, Thomas Young noted that any colour can be made from different combinations of almost any set of three wavelengths. He suggested that the eye contained three types of receptor, each sensitive to one of the psychologically "pure" (primary) colours: red, green and blue. Subsequent investigations confirmed that the cones are of three types, containing photopigments which preferentially absorb light of specific wavelengths. (In fact, the specific wavelengths correspond to yellow, green and blue light, but the receptors are called red, green and blue cones in deference to Young.) Colour-blind individuals have defects in these systems; in common forms of colour-blindness the red cones are filled with green photopigment or vice versa, and this condition is commoner in males because the gene responsible for these photopigments is *sex-linked*.

Yellow is also a psychologically pure colour, and so theorists after Young wanted to accommodate this fact. Almost a century after Young, Ewald Hering noted that the four primary colours fell into two pairs of complementary or opposing colours: red/green and blue/yellow. (Try imagining a reddish green or a bluish yellow; a difficult feat compared with imagining yellowish greens or reddish blues.) Hering further suggested that there must be two types of receptor, responding to red or green and blue or yellow respectively. Moreover, Hering introduced the notion of *opponent processes*, which have become popular in other areas of psychology. This simply means that he considered his red-green receptor to respond to red and green light in opposing fashion, *e.g.* excited by red and inhibited by green. A reddish green sensation in the brain is therefore impossible as the red-green receptor must be either firing more rapidly (red) or more slowly (green) than it does in the dark. Reddish blues are possible, for example, as the red-green receptor may be firing in a way which indicates "red" and the blue-yellow receptor may simultaneously fire at a rate indicating "blue".

In fact, single-cell recordings in the retina have confirmed Hering's general ideas also, but they apply to *ganglion* cells and not cones. Ganglion cells are connected to rods and cones via one small intervening neurone, and the long stems of the ganglion cells leave the eye for the brain in a bundle known as the *optic nerve*. The electrical signals from the various types of cone are fed to the corresponding ganglion cells. For example, in blue light the blue cones send an excitatory signal to the blue-yellow ganglion cell which therefore fires more rapidly. In green light, the green cones send an inhibitory signal to the red-green ganglion cell, which therefore fires more slowly. Cones may also send inhibitory signals to ganglion cells of the alternative type. Another kind of ganglion cell responds to the overall brightness of colours and these cells receive excitatory inputs from all types of cone.

Negative Afterimages

Further evidence for retinal processing of colour comes from negative afterimages. These are easily demonstrated by finding a brightly coloured shape, perhaps in a book. Stare at it for a few minutes. Then, look quickly away to a white surface and you should see a short-lasting, hazy image of the shape. It will appear in the complementary colour of the patch at which you were staring.

Two processes give rise to these afterimages: photopigment bleaching and neural rebound in the adapted ganglion cells. When a colour strikes the retina, the three types of cone will not all respond equally; one will be stimulated the most and its constituent photopigment will be bleached out to a greater degree. These cones will therefore respond less upon switching to a balanced source of illumination (a white surface), leaving a more vigorous net response from the other cones, and hence a sensation of the complementary colour. Prolonged stimulation of cones also leads to *adaptation*, an important process by which the receptors stabilize, becoming progressively less responsive to the adapting stimulus. This stabilisation is accompanied by an increase in sensitivity to any changes *away* from the steady state which has developed. Thus, the inhibition of the firing rate of a red/green ganglion cell under green light will

gradually be reduced. On switching to a white stimulus the excitatory response to the red wavelengths will be normal but, contrary to normal, will not be cancelled out by an inhibitory response to the green wavelengths since this has been temporarily reduced. The net 'red' response contributes to an after-effect in the complementary colour.

Having dealt with these important processes in the retina, we should turn our attention to more central (brain-based) processes in perception.

Perception by Analysis from the Bottom Up

We have stressed the way in which the raw sensory data (a pattern of nerve impulses) have to be decoded to be perceived as a representation of the world. One view of this decoding process is that there exists a hierarchy of *features*, from the simple to the complex, which our brain is equipped to detect. First, the simple features are extracted by the appropriate brain cells, and the outputs of these cells are fed to further detector cells which respond to ever more complex features until the whole percept is constructed. Perceptual analysis which moves from lower to higher levels is referred to as *bottom up* processing. This analytic model of perception cannot work, for obvious reasons which we shall consider below. However, such thinking was encouraged by the findings from single-cell recordings carried out by two Americans, Hubel and Wiesel, in the late 1950s and early 1960s. They were awarded the Nobel Prize for their work in 1981.

The Work of Hubel and Wiesel

We last mentioned the optic nerve at the point where it left the eye. After passing through a neural junction (synapse) in the thalamus, its neural messages reach the primary visual, or occipital cortex, at the rear of the brain. It was in this region that Hubel and Wiesel attempted to understand the way in which individual brain cells respond to visual stimuli. Their recordings were taken from deeply anaesthetised cats, whose heads were held in a fixed position and eyelids kept open. The results suggested that some visually-responsive cells behaved in orderly, and quite straightforward, ways.

All brain cells have a certain degree of background, or spontaneous, electrical activity; that is, a rate of electrical firing in the cell which appears random and unrelated to any stimuli "out in the world". However, the most straightforward, or *simple*, cells discovered by Hubel and Wiesel did not have much spontaneous activity, nor did they respond to overall changes in level of illumination. However, for a particular cell there was a relatively small region of space (the *receptive field*) in which certain visual stimuli could provoke sharp increases in cell "firing" over and above the background rate. For simple cells, the most effective stimuli were small bars of a fixed width. Some cells responded most strongly to vertical bars of light within their receptive field, and did not show any increases in firing rate to horizontal bars. Bars of intermediate orientation produced intermediate degrees of neural response. Other cells fired maximally to other orientations. Moreover, within the receptive field there were excitatory regions (shaped like the light bar) in which turning on the bar of light would lead to increased cell firing, flanked by inhibitory regions in which cell firing decreased when the light was turned on.

Hubel and Wiesel also found evidence for *complex* and *hypercomplex* cells; their receptive fields were larger, the cells were more spontaneously active and they responded specifically to more complex visual stimuli such as moving bars in certain orientations, and bars of a specific orientation and length. They believed that the cells were connected in a serial fashion, starting with the simple cells, which passed their information on to the complex and, via them, to the hypercomplex cells; a hierarchical series of visual feature detectors, in just the kind of arrangement which would be necessary for "bottom up" analysis of the visual world. Although there are some quibbles about exactly how one should think about the stimuli to which these cells respond (as "bars" with edges, or as patterns with light and dark regions), this work has proved remarkably reliable and has been repeated and extended many times in a range of species. Despite this striking evidence, one is forced to consider a number of difficulties with bottom-up models of perception.

Inadequacies of Strongly Bottom-Up Models of Perception

The first problems are neurobiological. There is now some evidence that the more complex cells noted by Hubel and Wiesel are directly connected to the thalamus, bypassing the simple cell stage. More seriously still, some complex cells have been shown to respond faster than simple cells to visual inputs; this does not bode well for the view which suggests that the complex cells do further "work" on the partially analysed output of the simple cells.

Other problems derive from the phenomena highlighted by the *Gestalt school* of psychology in the early part of this century. (A simple introduction to Gestalt theory is given in **Section J**.) A central element of their *holistic* philosophy is summed up in the well-known aphorism: "the whole is more than the sum of its parts". They believed that there are certain innate *laws of perceptual organisation* which reflect this idea. For instance, if dots are drawn reasonably close together on the page, in the shape of a ring, one does not simply experience a number of individual dots. Rather, we perceive a definite form: a circle. Indeed, this overall percept can be so strong that we may not perceive the individual elements at all. (Think of a TV screen with images which consist of thousands of spots of light on the tube.)

Without an unreasonable proliferation in the number of basic features for which the brain has detector cells, it is not clear how a percept of this kind would arise from a number of distinct dots analysed bottom up; the feature analysers would stop at the perception of the individual dots.

A more contemporary analysis of this kind of difficulty is to note the influence of *context* on perception. Write a B on a piece of paper with a little gap between the vertical stroke and the loops; now write a 13 with the digits perhaps a little closer together than normal. In terms of raw sensory data (an optical image and corresponding pattern of electrical activity in the retina) these drawings are more or less equivalent. Now try drawing an ambiguous figure which could serve as either a 13 or a B. Copy it exactly onto another sheet of paper. Surround one figure with numbers, *e.g.* 11 13 15, and the other with letters, *e.g.* A B C. Show the two sheets to your friends and ask them what they see: in the one instance they will see the number 13, in the other a letter B; their perceptions are given by the context and the effect it has on their expectations. Alternatively, consider the spoken words "ice cream" and "I scream". The sound patterns are identical in fluent speech, yet we can understand them, *in context*, in spoken sentences. Try it on your friends again: ask them what they hear when you say "⟨ìskrēm⟩ in the cinema"; see if their perceptions vary when you supply the contexts "when I'm hungry I eat . . ." or "Sometimes when it's a horror film . . .".

In contrast to the bottom-up processes discussed above, this kind of effect is evidence for *top-down* influences at work in perception. These influences are so named because "higher" conceptual levels of thinking, reflecting our stored mental model of the world and its regularities, are constraining the interpretation which our perceptual system puts on the raw sensory data. The use of the word "interpretation" was deliberate here, to emphasize the active, constructive nature of perception in which top-down influences play so vital a part.

Out closing comments on perception will concern the age-old debate about the extent to which we arrive in the world innately equipped, through our genetic constitution, to perceive it, and, conversely, the extent to which we have literally to learn to see. This debate has been called the *nature-nurture* controversy.

Perceptual Development and the Nature-Nurture Controversy

There are a variety of ways in which this issue has been addressed experimentally. The first, and most direct, involves the study of the perceptual abilities of newborn babies. Of course, there are restrictions on the kinds of experimental task which can be employed with very young infants, and special procedures have had to be devised. Moreover, if an ability is absent in the new-born and only develops some time after birth, it does not conclusively prove that it is largely a learned ability with little contribution from genetic programming. Many features of the human condition are inherent in our genes but only emerge after a *maturation* period following birth. It is as if the genetic message contains a number of time-switches which program the genetic event to occur at the appropriate later stage. One may think of a variety of such events, such as beginning to walk, or puberty, for example. Barring medical disorders, these events seem to occur in their own good time and are little affected by environmental influences, although the time of onset obviously varies from individual to individual.

The infant's visual apparatus is somewhat immature at birth. The optic nerve is thinner and softer than the adult's, and its insulating myelin sheath is incomplete until about four months of age. The retina, however, is fairly well developed, possessing rods and cones. Discrimination between colours is possible at four months. Reactions to bright light can be detected in the womb, and a five-day old infant will look for different amounts of time at stimuli of different brightnesses. This seems to suggest that very basic perceptual abilities are probably largely innate.

Bower's Experiments

Psychologists have studied higher perceptual abilities in infants. One important feature of adult perception, termed *size constancy*, has been investigated, notably by Tom Bower. Size constancy is taken as yet further evidence of the active, interpretive nature of perception; it refers to the observation that we perceive an object as constant in size despite the fact that the retinal image which it produces gets smaller as the object is viewed from greater distances. It is considered that we use a number of other complex clues to judge the distance of the object, and then use this information to convert the image-size on the retina into a perception of the object's size in keeping with its inferred distance.

Bower trained two-, and three-, month old infants to turn and look at a 30 cm cube from a distance of one metre. He did this by rewarding each glance at the cube with a game of "peek-a-boo" (much loved by children this age). Then he replaced the cube with one of two others. One was 30 cm in size and was viewed from three metres distance (producing a smaller image on the retina); the other cube was 90 cm and viewed from three metres (producing a retinal image of the same size as the original cube). Would the infant continue to respond to the cube of the same actual size (*i.e.* show size constancy) or respond according to the cube with the same-sized retinal image? The former turned out to be true: the infants made nearly three times as many responses to the 30 cm, than the 90 cm, cube. Very young infants have some degree of size constancy, it seems, at least over the distances involved in this experiment.

Cross-cultural Research

Size constancy and the nature-nurture question has been studied via other means, notably through *cross-cultural* research. Here, the goal is to see to what extent perceptual phenomena are universal to all human societies. If other cultures, with widely differing social and physical environments, do not exhibit the same phenomena as have been observed in Western subjects, then we may conclude that these phenomena are influenced by environmental factors.

The Bambuti pygmies live in the dense Congo rain forests, an environment without open spaces or distances larger than a forest clearing. One such pygmy, on being taken for the first time to the open plains, asked about the insects he could see. The psychologist informed him that they were buffalo grazing, whereupon the pygmy took great offence: he had seen buffalo in the forest and they were large creatures! As they drove toward the buffalo, the pygmy was amazed to see the creatures 'grow' before his eyes and became convinced that witchcraft was being used to deceive him. Clearly size constancy does not develop to the same extent in environments where the distance of objects only varies over a narrow range. Additionally, cross-cultural studies have shown that colour perception is fairly universal (we note this again in the section on Thinking), but visual illusions may be more powerful in some cultures than others.

Studies, such as the above, have been coupled with other kinds of investigation. These have involved: animals reared in restricted perceptual environments; cataract patients, blind from birth, who have had their sight surgically restored; and volunteers who have worn goggles, for many weeks, which distort their visual images. The general conclusion is that, apart perhaps from very elementary processes, our perceptual abilities are the product of an *interaction* between the environment and our genetic constitution, a conclusion which is held to be true in many other areas of psychology also, as we shall see.

In the following section, we shall see something of what psychologists have learned about attention, particularly with respect to the selective processes which allow us to focus on the relevant aspects of our perceptual environments. Such selection seems essential if we are not to be overwhelmed by the sheer volume of perceptual information impinging on our sense systems.

2. Attention.

The Scottish psychologist Neville Moray has reflected that psychologists use the term attention in a multitude of distinct ways. We shall restrict ourselves to the two most widespread, and important, uses of the term: *selective* and *divided* attention. These are opposing sides of the same coin, respectively referring to the ability to screen out irrelevant information while concentrating on a single task and, conversely, to the ability to do two things at once.

Many relatively simple models of selective processes in attention emerged after the Second World War. They were strongly influenced by the recent developments in telecommunications technology and, like all information-processing models, by the birth of computers. It was known that for a given communication system, there was a physical limit on the rate at which units of information, in electrical form, could be passed along the system. The idea was transferred to the brain: it was argued that there must be an upper rate at which it too can process the information impinging upon it. Clearly, then, there had to be a *filter* at some point which reduced the mass of incoming information to single stream of input. If the brain was successful in performing a particular task, then the selected "stream" of input must be flowing at a rate below the brain's upper limit. This kind of model can be regarded as strongly *serial* in nature, the chunks of incoming information being dealt with one after another. This again reflected the serial technologies of the period.

As an aside, it should be noted that, more recently, psychological models have switched to a greater emphasis on *parallel* processing. Under parallel schemes, processing is carried out on many independent streams of information simultaneously. The switch is partially the result of Man's relisation that the mammalian brain has a massive degree of parallelity in its neural circuitry (a single neurone receives inputs from many other neurones at once). We return to this point in our discussion of computer "intelligence" below.

The archetypal "filter" model of attention was that of Donald Broadbent. The research debate seemed to focus on locating the stage at which the filter came into operation, and on the related question of determining the features of information with which the filter made its selections. One psychologist has characterised the research as a search for the "bottle-neck" in attention. The classic experimental task, used in such research, is a *shadowing* procedure.

Shadowing Experiments

The subject is played two different passages of spoken prose, via headphones, one passage to each ear. The task is to follow one ear, *i.e.* passage, exclusively, and the subject's accuracy and speed in doing so is checked by having him/her repeat back the attended passage as quickly and accurately as possible (hence the term shadowing). Subjects can learn to shadow complex prose read at quite fast rates, but do not retain much conscious awareness of what was presented to the ignored ear.

In fact, Broadbent's model suggested that knowledge about the meaning of the unattended message should not be processed, because this kind of feature was not used by the filter in selecting information. Rather, the filter was conceived of as using the cruder, physical features of the input information in achieving its selection. This explains why shadowing a message on one ear whilst ignoring the message on the other ear is so readily possible (the messages come from different physical locations). However, subjects did show limited awareness of meaning from unattended passages—they were reliably accurate in noticing, without forewarning, the presence of their own name, for example. Perhaps the filter allowed a limited degree of meaning information through, but only sufficient that highly important entities needing less information for detection, such as one's own name, could be consciously spotted. In fact, there are now a number of experiments demonstrating a degree of processing for meaning in unattended and unimportant material.

Nonetheless, the conclusion from shadowing studies would seem to be that (a) some kind of highly efficient filtering system is at work, and that (b) when we give one task our full focussed attention it is not possible to perform another task which involves complex meaningful analysis. This conflicts with the picture in other experimental tasks.

Failures of Selective Attention: The Stroop Effect

You can demonstrate one of these failures for yourself. Get some coloured pen and two sheets of paper. On one write 30 letter strings (*e.g.* XXXXX, ZZZZ, AAAAAAA etc). Write an approximately equal number in each of the colours which you have available. On the other sheet write a series of 30 colour words (RED, BLUE, GREEN etc), but make sure that you write them in an ink of inappropriate colour (*e.g.* RED in blue ink etc.). Get some friends to read through each sheet, identifying, as quickly as possible, *the* colour of the *ink* for each word. If you time their overall time to read each sheet, you should find that they will tend to be slower, and/or make more errors, in naming the ink of inappropriate colour-words than in identifying the ink of nonsense letter-strings. The effect has been repeatedly demonstrated in more controlled conditions, and is called the *Stroop effect* after the psychologist who discovered it in the 1930s. It is a failure of selective attention: the subjects are supposed to select one feature (the colour of the ink) but cannot avoid processing the meaning of the colour word; when this does not match the ink, they are slowed down by the conflict and perhaps make errors in naming the ink (saying the name of the word, not the ink). Here they are doing two things at once, even although it is not helpful to do so.

What might explain the differences in outcome between the Stroop and shadowing tasks? One possibility might be to do with the links between the stimuli and their responses. Through reading aloud, one forms a strong habit of linking written words to their spoken form. It is hard to "turn off" the habit in the Stroop test, and the effort required to do so interferes with the efficiency of the task at hand (saying the ink colour aloud). Thus, the selectivity of attention appears low. It is interesting to note that when the Stroop task is reversed, and subjects have to name the word and ignore the conflicting colour of the ink, the effect is much weaker. We do not have so strong a habit for seeing a colour and saying its name aloud.

In the shadowing task one is required to make an "unnatural" kind of response: we do not listen to one conversation at a party, ignoring others going on around us, by repeating back every word which is spoken in the conversation to which we are listening. When we take part in a shadowing experiment, we may therefore be well able to "hitch" just one prose passage to our speech output, leaving the other effectively "decoupled" from any response. Hence, the selectivity of attention seems very high. In fact, when shadowing experiments are turned into monitoring experiments (the subjects just have to concentrate on one passage, without shadowing it) their knowledge of material in the unattended passage improves dramatically.

Following from what has just been said on the importance of the response systems which are in use, and the strength of habitual links between the stimuli and the responses, we may be able to explain some experimental studies in which subjects have, after practice, been able to perform two difficult tasks, at the same time, with little penalty to either task. For example, pianists have been able to shadow spoken prose while playing quite difficult pieces unknown to them prior to the experiment. Similarly, typists have been able to shadow spoken prose while copy-typing previously unseen material from written scripts. Clearly, the capacity to do two tasks at once, and the ability to focus single-mindedly on just one task, are attributes of human information processing which vary from context to context, as well as from individual to individual.

We have thus seen something of how the brain selects and processes incoming sensory information. The next section deals with how that information is remembered.

3. Memory.

In the discussion of Behaviourist psychology above we noted the psychologist's idea of learning: a change in behaviour brought about by an interaction of an organism with its environment. (Learning will be considered at greater length in its own section below.) This definition is rather more general than the everyday use of the word "learning" which tends to be used interchangeably with the word "memory". For psychologists, learning and memory are distinct, both historically and experimentally; for example, learning experiments have tended to be conducted with animals, whilst studies of memory have used human subjects.

A Definition of Memory

Here we shall consider memory for a particular piece of information to be an awareness of having previously encountered it. The words of the previous sentence, what you had for breakfast this morning, the capital of France, and specific episodes and facts from your early childhood are all items you have encountered previously and your awareness of these pieces of information, when prompted (by the examples given), constitutes a series of recollections. Other individuals may be made aware of one's act of remembering, i.e. of one's changes in mental state, when it is explicitly communicated to them ("I had a bowl of muesli this morning"). Of course, the information may not have been encoded entirely accurately in the first place, and in the intervening period may have suffered some erosion, confusion with other information and/or reorganisation; all these contribute to forgetting.

Our definition has a number of implications. First, it places animal memory on an uncertain footing—how can we be sure that an animal is aware of previously encountering something except by inference from a change in its behaviour? Similarly, the current vogue for research into human memory without awareness (called implicit memory) is something of a contradiction in terms. Here, the subject studies some materials (such as a list of pictures) without attempting to memorise them. After a delay, the experimenter can observe a change in the way the subject processes these pictures (e.g. s/he names the subject of the picture more rapidly) without being aware (remembering) that the particular pictures had been studied earlier. Both these examples fall under our definition of learning. In Man, we accept that awareness of the past occurs even when the only change in outward behaviour is some form of explicit communication about the past (as long as the communication concurs with the facts). In this way, memory may therefore be considered to be a specific kind of learning, with learning defined in the general terms set out above.

More typically, psychologists would also use the term learning to describe improvements in memory over repeated exposures to the same information. The reader's memory for the precise wording of the

previous sentence will be improved by re-reading it, and this change is usually referred to as learning. The first experimental studies of memory, as we shall see, investigated this latter kind of learning.

Early Studies of Memory

In 1879, a German scholar of indendent means, Hermann Ebbinghaus, initiated the first program of experimental investigations into memory. His experiments were simple and highly controlled, and he often used himself as the subject. Ebbinghaus was particularly concerned with rates of learning and rates of forgetting of information.

What materials did he use in his experiments? Ebbinghaus realised that previous experience with a particular type of material might influence the time course of learning and forgetting, and so he devised the nonsense syllable—material which he believed would be completely novel and free of meaning. His nonsense syllables each comprised a consonant followed by a vowel followed by a consonant (e.g. wux, caz, jek), and similar materials were widely used in the study of memory until the 1970s. In recent years nonsense syllables have been largely replaced with familiar words as it has become clear that subjects often tried to remember the nonsense syllables by "converting" them to similar real words.

What kind of memory task did Ebbinghaus use? He devised a savings method, in which the amount of information retained after study is inferred from the saving in amount of study time subsequently needed to relearn the information after a delay. Using 70 lists, each containing 16 nonsense syllables, Ebbinghaus showed that each repetition of a list during initial study saved him approximately the same amount of time in his relearning of the list the next day: about 12 seconds saved for each repetition during learning. Modern research has shown that this experimental rule (that the amount of learning is directly proportional to the total amount of time spent learning) only seems to apply to the rote rehearsal of relatively meaningless materials such as those adopted by Ebbinghaus.

Ebbinghaus' studies of forgetting produced very different kinds of curve from those he found for learning: the amount of forgetting he observed was greatest in the first minutes and hours after learning, with relatively little additional forgetting occurring over the ensuing hours and days.

After two years of these beautifully executed experiments, Ebbinghaus moved on to other topics and left posterity with little by way of theoretical conclusions. Perhaps his greatest contribution was to show that an apparently intractable problem could be attacked experimentally, provided the experimenter was prepared to simplify the problem drastically. In 1932, Frederick Bartlett strongly criticized the Ebbinghaus approach, arguing that the simplifications which he had used excluded almost everything that is central to human memory. Bartlett believed that memory is determined by the subject's active search for meaning rather by passive responses to experimental materials.

Meaning and Memory

Bartlett's experiments investigated the retention of meaningful materials such as short stories. Subjects heard a story and then attempted to recall it on several subsequent occasions without hearing the story again. Across time, subjects' reproductions tended to become shorter and more coherent from their point of view, although less accurate in objective terms. Bartlett felt that this was the result of an active "effort after meaning" in the remembering process; parts of the story which did not fit in with subjects' expectations or beliefs were often omitted or were rationalised to fit better. For example, a supernatural element in a Red Indian folk story "Something black came out of his mouth" (describing the life spirit leaving an Indian after a battle) was recalled by one subject, six months after reading the passage, as "he foamed at the mouth".

Bartlett's findings represent another example of top-down influences at work in information processing. The subjects may be considered to have a model of the world, of events and scenarios which occur in that world, and of the way stories report those events. This model has been variously described as a *schema* or *script*. The schema actively alters the way in which the story is interpreted and stored. Probably, supernatural elements did not fit very well with the schema used by Bartlett's English subjects, leaving gaps in their mental representation of the story. When the story was retrieved some time later, the schema may have come into effect again, offering likely suggestions for filling in the gaps in the plot. Again, supernatural happenings would not be typical candidates for Westerners.

The use of rigidly controlled (Ebbinghaus) or richly meaningful (Bartlett) materials remains a major separation in the study of memory today, although few would question the importance of active, meaning-orientated information processing, as suggested by Bartlett.

Models of Memory

Models of memory have existed from the time of the Greeks at least; Plato used the metaphors of a block of wax, for the mind, and the imprint of a seal, for the lasting memory trace left by our experiences. Later, he also used the analogy of an aviary in which specific birds (memories) have to be searched out from the mass. Ideas did not advance particularly until the end of the 19th cent.: William James (brother of the novelist Henry James), for example, described the process of remembering by analogy with the way we "rummage about a house for a lost object". James did, however, make other important introspective observations; notably, that new experiences do not disappear from consciousness immediately, but remain in our awareness for a brief period afterwards. He regarded memory over this short period, which he termed *primary* memory, as referring not to the genuine past but to the "rearward portion" of the present moment. He contrasted this with *secondary* memory which involved the recollection of experiences, cut off from present awareness, by intervening time and experience. Unfortunately, the subsequent rise of Behaviourism meant that James' introspections were ignored for many years.

The Modal Model

By the 1960s, however, a broad consensus about memory was emerging, with many of the proposed models being essentially identical. This status was acknowledged by calling these ideas the *modal* model (the mode, in statistics, is the outcome which occurs most frequently). A central element in this model was the distinction between primary and secondary memory, now more commonly referred to as *short-term* and *long-term* memory (or STM and LTM), respectively. Long-term memory is a somewhat confusing term, referring, at its shortest time scale, to time periods of 10 seconds or so. Memories over periods of years are typically now called *remote* or very long-term memories.

STM and LTM were conceived of as memory "stores" in which varying amounts of information could be held, and manipulated, for varying periods of time. In addition there were considered to be very short-lived stores which resided in the sensory systems themselves (sensory stores). Most people have direct experience of their sensory stores at work: it is a common experience occasionally not to hear what someone has said, and, in the time it takes to request a repetition, for the original message to 'echo' round the system and be understood.

The modal model proposed that information first entered sensory storage where basic processes of identification were carried out. Then information was passed to the brain's control station: STM. Here, as in the filter model of attentional control, key information-processing decisions took place: which information was to receive full attention and therefore enter into awareness; what kind of processing was to be carried out on this material; *etc. etc.* STM was considered to be of limited capacity, thus putting strict limits on our span of awareness. To see these limits, one can construct a series of random lists of digits. Make some lists contain one more digit than the previous (*e.g.* 5 9 2; 3 8 6 1; 7 9 8 4 6 *etc.*) and read them to a friend, at one digit per second, starting with the short lists. They should listen and try to repeat back the sequence exactly. At some point, around the 7 digit

level, the friend will no longer be able to do this accurately. This is called the *digit span* technique and has been widely used to assess STM.

An example shows how useful a temporary store of ongoing information can be. To understand the previous sentence, or this one, the reader must keep in mind the beginning of the sentence in order to comprehend the latter parts and the sentence as a whole. Of course, we should not want to store all the information which we encounter (some of these sentences are less relevant than others). Thus, in the modal model only some of the information in STM was transferred to LTM, the remainder passing from awareness for ever. In LTM, which had practically no limits on its capacity, the transferred information was stored as a near-permanent memory trace, which could allow the information to re-enter awareness at a later date.

Testing the Modal Model Experimentally

The modal model represents an intuitively appealing way of thinking about memory, but how has it fared in the hands of research psychologists? There is considerable evidence which lends weight to some kind of distinction between STM and LTM. For example, one may construct a list of perhaps 20 unrelated words, and read them to subjects. They are instructed to memorize the list because at the end they will be asked to recall the words in any order they like (a test termed *free* recall). If you do this yourself with some friends as subjects, you will probably observe that they show a marked tendency to remember best the words from the last few positions in the list. This reliable finding is called the *recency effect*, as the more recent items are preferentially recalled. Advocates of the modal model were quick to suggest that the effect represented recall from STM which was more efficient than the recall from LTM for the middle portions of the list. This claim grew stronger when it was shown that interposing a time delay (filled with some irrelevant mental activity), between the end of the list and beginning to recall the items, substantially reduced the recency effect.

Research with brain-damaged patients also contributed important observations. Limited damage, from a variety of causes, to subcortical structures in the brain, can lead to an *amnesic syndrome*. Sometimes it is only the memory of these patients which may be affected. More specifically still, in some cases, it seems that LTM is selectively damaged. The patients can show a normal digit span, and a normal recency effect in the face of woeful recall of items from earlier in the list. Despite this evidence supporting the STM/LTM distinction, studies of a head- injured patient, K.F., carried out in England in the 1970s, effectively ruled out the specific requirement of the modal model that information in LTM must first pass through STM. This individual, and others studied subsequently, had damage to the left parietal cortex and seemed to suffer a selective problem with STM for spoken material. His digit span was reduced to one or two items and he did not show a recency effect in recalling a list of words. However, it was claimed that his LTM was normal, even for spoken verbal material.

Revising the Modal Model

Memory psychologists have sought different routes out of this difficulty. One idea, pioneered by the English psychologist, Alan Baddeley, has been to propose that STM (renamed *working* memory) can be split up into a number of separate subsystems which handle different kinds of information. The best studied subsystem is considered to deal with sound-based linguistic information, the so-called *phonological* code (phonemes are the basic sounds which go together to make words). Evidence for the importance of phonology comes from a number of sources. Firstly, the recency effect is more marked in the free recall of word lists which are spoken, rather than silently read. Also, short-term recall of letters is more difficult if the letters sound similar, than if they do not. Try this on your friends once again with T E G C V B (similar) and S Y K H L O (dissimilar) as the sequences. Thus, the patient K.F. would be considered to have a selective problem with this phonological STM subsystem, and he would be expected to have deficient LTM for spoken, verbal material if the other, undamaged STM subsystems could not come to the rescue by recoding the incoming information in alternative, non-phonological, ways. For example, a word to be remembered can be processed in terms of its meaning rather than its sounds. (Analysis of this kind is referred to as *semantic* processing.)

Levels of Processing

The emphasis on the *coding* of information in memory, while down-playing the importance of separate stores for various kinds and amounts of information, represents another alternative to the modal model: the *levels of processing* approach. Basically, the idea was that certain ways of processing new information would lead to better memory. For example, with words, it was felt that there were three basic levels of analysis: in terms of visual, phonological or semantic features. It was also proposed that these corresponded to differences in the complexity, or *depth*, of the processing, with semantic analysis being the deepest, and thus leading to the best memory. These claims were backed up by experiments. Giving experimental subjects instructions to concentrate on the sound (phonology) of words ("Does it rhyme with dog?") often produced much inferior memory on a later surprise test, relative to that of subjects oriented towards the meaning (semantics) of the words ("Is it a living thing?").

There were problems with this simple idea. The first is a logical one. Proponents of the levels of processing approach were asked to provide a means for deciding which of two levels of processing was the deeper, before doing an experiment to test the effects on memory. They could not: the idea that semantic processing is somehow deeper and more complex than phonological processing was just an intuition.

More problematic still was a series of investigations, from Canada, by Endel Tulving and his colleagues. They showed that the kind of processing during the study of the words did not determine later memory in a simple way. Rather, it was the degree of overlap, between this processing and the processing of the clues provided in the memory test, which seemed critical. For example, imagine you were asked to judge whether the word "frog" rhymed with "dog". Sometime later you are given a surprise memory test for the word, but are given a clue (a *retrieval cue*) that it rhymed with the word "log". Your memory will be better in this case than if you had performed "deeper", semantic processing of the word originally, such as judging whether it was a living thing. As another illustration, try recalling the months of the year in alphabetical order! The retrieval cue is a positive hindrance, as the alphabetical properties of the names of the months are not strongly represented in our memory.

Tulving put these ideas together in a general principle which he called *encoding specificity*. Although people have quibbled with some of the details of his ideas, few psychologists would quarrel with the general notion that the relationship between encoding (study) and retrieval (test) is vital to successful remembering.

Storage of Information

Thus far, we have neglected an issue central to the whole topic—the storage of information. Let us consider a gramophone record. Some information, perhaps music, is encoded by the recording and pressing processes into a series of ridges in the vinyl. The record then acts as a store of the musical information until it is required later, whereupon it is decoded by a stylus, plus amplifiers and speakers, into sounds not too dissimilar from those originally encoded. Information must be stored in the brain in some loosely analogous way. It flows from the sensory receptors, is processed, interpreted and encoded by our perceptual mechanisms and then is held in store. This storage allows the information to be remembered later and may affect subsequent behaviour (learning). Current ideas about the neurobiological bases of the storage process will be discussed in the section on Learning, because the relevant research has, of necessity, largely used animal subjects with the animal learning procedures discussed in that section.

III. LEARNING AND MOTIVATION.

We saw in the previous section how psychologists now consider mental processes in terms of the flow of information between psychological subsystems. In this section we shall look at the more basic psychological questions of how and why behaviours are acquired or changed as a result of past experience: the questions of learning and motivation.

1. Learning.

By the turn of the century more and more psychologists were beginning to follow the lead of their physiological cousins in bringing animals into the research laboratory. Indeed, strains of white rats were specially bred for this purpose. However, there were a number of basic problems. With humans, one may get the subject to learn something—a list of words or whatever—simply by using verbal instructions. With animals, researchers hit upon another strategy: using *reward*. One of the first to adopt this approach was the American, Edward Thorndike.

Thorndike and the Law of Effect

Thorndike noticed that cats kept in a cage would eventually, after a lucky accident, learn to open a simple latch to escape from the cage. With practice, their behaviour would become more effective and they would come to open the latch more quickly. (This echoes the results in human subjects; Ebbinghaus, you will recall, showed that memory after a delay improved as the number of learning trials on the previous day was increased.) However, Thorndike also noticed that the hungry cats learned much faster if their escape from the cage was rewarded with food. He thus concluded that a second factor, the *effect* of the learned behaviour, was critical for learning. This idea became known as the *law of effect*. Consider any act (*e.g.* opening the cage latch), which in a given situation (*e.g.* being in the cage) produces "satisfaction" (*e.g.* the pleasurable aspects of food for a hungry cat). The law of effect states that such an act becomes associated with the situation and is more likely to recur when the situation is encountered again, *i.e.* learning will take place.

Thorndike also found a converse relationship for "discomforting" effects: acts which lead to these effects in a particular situation were *less* likely to be repeated in that situation. His terms "satisfaction" and "discomfort" have now been replaced by their modern equivalents, *reward* and *punishment*, which may be collectively referred to as *reinforcement*. However, animal experimenters still train their subjects by making the outcomes of the behaviour in question either rewarding (*e.g.* food pellets) or punishing (*e.g.* electric shock).

There are a number of puzzles in the law of effect: for example, how does the food, or the pleasurable states it induces, forge the association in the animal's brain, between situations and actions? The problem is particularly striking for situations and actions early in a sequence of behaviour, bearing in mind that the food is consumed at the end. To consider these problems properly we shall need to begin by understanding one of the most important concepts of 20th cent. science: the *conditioned reflex*.

Pavlov and the Conditioned Reflex

A Russian physiologist, Ivan Pavlov, won the Nobel Prize in 1904 for his work on salivation and digestion in dogs. His experimental set-up involved collecting the saliva from his experimental dogs via a tube connected to their salivary ducts. Pavlov, or one of his assistants, showed the dogs a bowl of food, a sight which stimulated the automatic, innate salivation reflex in the animals (in much the same way that a sharp tap below the kneecap would induce a leg-jerk reflex in you or me). It was some incidental observations which Pavlov made whilst conducting this research which have proved so important to psychology.

Pavlov noticed that the dogs, after being in these experiments for some time, would begin to salivate as soon as he, or his assistants, entered the laboratory. He realised that this was important; the animals were reacting to the experimenter as some kind of *signal* for food, and *learning* to salivate in response to that signal. In studying this phenomenon further, Pavlov used more arbitrary signals (such as electric bells and buzzers) which were sounded at various time intervals before, during and after the presentation of the food. After repeated pairing of these signals with the food, the signal alone could produce salivation, a phenomenon today referred to as *conditioning*. The salivation in response to the signal alone is referred to as a *conditioned response*. This terminology is, in fact, a mistranslation of the original Russian, which meant *conditional* response. The term "conditional response" better emphasises the fact that salivation in response to the bells or buzzers is conditional on the bell or buzzer having been previously presented along with the food. The bell or buzzer is known as the *conditioned stimulus*. By contrast, the food always (*i.e.* unconditionally) produces a salivation response (it is an unlearned, innate reflex) and thus is an *unconditioned stimulus* producing an *unconditioned response*.

Conditioned salivation only occurred if the signal preceded the food by a brief interval; signals following food produced no salivation. If the signal continued to be presented, but without being followed by food, the conditioned salivation response, initially present, soon declined. This process is known as *extinction*. In one of Pavlov's experiments, nine presentations of the noise alone without food, one every three minutes, was sufficient to extinguish the conditioned response which had previously been established. However, extinction is not usually permanent: given a break in the presentation of the conditioned stimulus, the conditioned response will usually show some spontaneous recovery when the conditioned stimulus is re-presented, and the conditioned response will be relearned to previous levels more rapidly than before.

Pavlov's theory of these processes was a strongly physiological one. He felt that the pathways of nerve cells responsible for the original automatic reflex (*e.g.* salivation of food) had been modified in some way to "tag on" a new, and previously irrelevant, stimulus (such as a bell) which could elicit the response. Pavlov believed that conditioned and unconditioned responses were essentially identical, both being automatic and reflex-like. As we shall see, his findings had a major impact on Western ideas about learning.

The Rise of Behaviourism

We have earlier outlined the Behaviourist tradition in Western psychology, which was developing before Pavlov's discoveries were published. The strongest advocates of the Behaviourist doctrine, such as J. B. Watson, felt that, in principle, it should be possible to give a complete explanation of human or animal psychology in descriptive, mechanical terms concerning the outward manifestations of behaviour. This, for example, led Watson to the extreme view that thinking was merely "sub-vocal speech", and was better described in terms of minor muscle movements in the throat, mouth and tongue, than in terms of electrical activity patterns in the higher centres of the brain.

It is easy to see why Pavlov's discovery of conditioned reflexes was so readily welcomed by the Behaviourists. Here, at the root of possibly all behaviour, lay a simple physiological principle. By understanding it, and applying it properly, one could mould the behaviour patterns of living things in any direction considered appropriate; psychological malfunctions could be corrected; education and training could be made simple. For a brief period, the "golden goal" of the new scientific psychology was to see Man as a complex mass of innate and conditioned reflex arcs: a biological machine. It is also interesting to note that Pavlov's research found favour with the newly-developed Communist ideology of the Soviet Union, offering, as it did, an explanation for human behaviour which did away with metaphysical and religious notions such as the "soul".

One might concede that an animal, in a highly artificial laboratory situation, salivating in response to a bell, could behave pretty much as a biological machine. However, how would these conditioning phenomena cope in dealing with a real behaviour "out in the wild", or even the more complex sequences of actions which laboratory animals can be trained to perform? Here, in essence, we are returning to the question marks which we raised over the law of effect.

Consider a dog which has been trained in a Pavlovian way to associate a light with food. It is now faced with a series of doors, behind one of which some food is located, and this "target" door changes from trial to trial. Next, the light is switched on, for a brief period, above the door behind which the food is concealed. The dog soon learns to run up to the appropriate door. Watson's explanation of this type of learning drew upon the fact that the dog has a powerful reflex to approach food. In similar fashion to conditioned salivation reflexes, the initial training with the light would lead to a conditioned reflex to approach the light. This reflex then carries over to the situation where the light is above the door. The light serves to set the appropriate sequence of reflex actions in motion, in similar fashion to turning a key to start a car. Even although the light had disappeared well before the dog reached the door in question, the Behaviourist argument holds that the light had set up the appropriate muscular posture to send the dog in the correct direction, and then is no longer needed as a guide.

More troublesome still is the case in which the dog is restrained after the appearance of the light, yet still seems to "show interest" in the door signalled by the light, and when released a minute or so later, still tends to go to the correct door. In this instance is it not easier to argue that the animal has some kind of internal representation of a goal, an expectancy of food behind the door? Early Behaviourist thinking was adamant that sequences of conditioned muscular movements were all one needed to explain behaviour. Thus, the dog, even after the delay, was still adopting the appropriate posture, rather as a hunting dog freezes to point to the prey.

At this time of radical Behaviourism, Watson produced what he believed to be irrefutable evidence for the dominance of the muscular activity, even on a task as complex as learning to run a maze. In this rather cruel-sounding experiment he trained rats to find their way through a detailed maze. He then proceeded to eliminate by surgery all normal sensory equipment—eyes, ears, smell, etc., leaving only the sense of touch. These grossly deprived animals nevertheless still managed to find their way through the maze, allowing him to conclude that, in line with the conditioned-reflex notion, the animals were relying predominantly on a chain of muscle reflexes. For a brief period this dramatic experiment seemed to clinch the Behaviourist case. But then came a counter-experiment, even more drastic. A psychologist called Lashley repeated Watson's experiment, but this time also removed the sense of touch by spinal surgery. The wretched creatures even now managed to stagger through the maze—though they were certainly no longer equipped with proper muscular responses. Lashley, correctly, felt this dealt with the ultra-simple Behaviourist argument and that somehow or other the animals must be retaining some kind of general directional sense, a sort of "notion" as to where the exit lay.

Shortly after these experiments were conducted, Watson was fired from his professorship at Johns Hopkins University, and he took up a successful career in advertising. His dismissal was for another pioneering line of research—on human physiological responses during sexual intercourse. The problem in the eyes of the University, and for Watson's wife no doubt, was that the subjects of these experiments were Watson himself and his research assistant.

Subsequent Developments in Learning Research

Out of respect for Pavlov's research, the conditioning which he observed is now often referred to as *classical* conditioning. A later Behaviourist, B. F. Skinner, distinguished another kind of conditioning which he referred to as *operant* conditioning (it is also known as *instrumental* conditioning). By way of contrast, he referred to classical conditioning as *respondent*. Skinner believed that one could distinguish between learned actions which involved innate reflexes (the domain of respondent conditioning) and learning through which a non-innate sequence of behavioural operations (operants) came under the control of a particular stimulus.

Skinner developed the notions of the reinforcing (rewarding and punishing) consequences of behaviours, and proposed that these served to change the future probability of the behaviours concerned. In other words, he expanded upon the earlier "law of effect". The reinforcing properties of actions could either be natural (*e.g.* consuming food or suffering pain), or acquired via association with natural reinforcers (*e.g.* if receipt of food habitually follows the pressing of a lever, then the action eventually comes to be reinforcing in its own right). The problem of complex chains of behaviours (which we noted when discussing the law of effect) could be explained by arguing that earlier actions in the sequence are reinforced by acquired reinforcers such as the opportunity to carry out later actions. The later actions are considered to be reinforced by the food itself.

It is still a matter of debate as to whether operant and classical conditioning are truly distinct, although the intricacies of the argument are beyond the scope of this section. In sum, however, Skinner believed that reinforcement was critical to learning, by automatically strengthening or weakening the preceding actions. It is this point which subsequent evidence has shown to be in need of some kind of modification.

Experiments with rats showed that they could learn something about a maze, even when they were not given food on exit from the maze. Learning took place merely through exposure to the maze itself. Reinforcement was needed, however, to demonstrate that this learning had taken place. Thus, rats previously exposed to the maze without reinforcement learned faster than naïve rats (newcomers to the maze) when both were subsequently trained in the maze with food rewards. In the reinforced test, it is as if the rat may build up an expectation that food will be available at the exit of the maze, and then the rats with previous (unreinforced) experience in the maze become *motivated* to exit the maze, drawing upon their earlier, and previously latent, learning. In other words, there can often be a discrepancy between what has been learned and the degree to which the learning is observable through changes in performance (outward behaviour). The discrepancy may reflect the degree to which the organism is motivated to perform by available, or expected, reinforcers. We shall return to these themes in our discussion of motivation (*see* **Q18**).

Social Learning Theory

The preceding reformulation of the role of reinforcers in learning has been taken up by *social learning theory*. Its proponents believe that much of our social behaviour is learned by observation of a role model (hence this learning is referred to as *modelling* or *observational learning*). The learning which has occurred need not be reinforced at the time, but will be demonstrated whenever the social situation seems likely to reinforce it. Hence, a young boy may observe one of his parents appearing to get relief from life's stresses and strains by frequent alcohol-drinking. When older, should the child be confronted with high degrees of stress, social learning theory would predict that he would be more likely to turn to alcohol than would a person without those earlier learning experiences.

Much of the modern research in this area is concerned with working out which aspects of "models" increase the chances that their behaviour will be imitated by the observer. One key factor seems to be the degree to which the observer perceives the model as similar to him- or herself. Thus, social learning theory has been used to explain the perpetuation of sex-roles, with boys tending to imitate the behaviour of their fathers rather than that of their mothers.

As will be clear, the vast majority of research on conditioning has been performed with animal subjects. Much uncertainty and debate surrounds the degree to which these simple forms of learning are involved in human behaviour. The question has

been intensified in the wake of the information processing revolution in psychology: cognitive psychology is not usually framed in terms of conditioning concepts, and many researchers believe that cognition may often involve more elaborate, and evolutionarily recent, forms of mental operations.

However, work early in the century indicated an important role for conditioning in neurotic disorders *Phobias* are a form of neurosis in which a disproportionate fear, often for something quite specific, can have a profoundly debilitating effect on the individual's lifestyle and welfare. Typical phobia-provoking stimuli are birds, spiders, dirt or unfamiliar surroundings. Conditioning explanations for such disorders became favoured after Watson and a colleague induced a specific fear in an eleven-month old boy called Albert. They did this using classical conditioning procedures. Over a seven-week period they paired a fear-provoking stimulus (striking an iron bar with a hammer just behind the infant's head) with the presence of a white rat on seven occasions. The conditioned fear response to the rat, presented alone, persisted over a one-month period and *generalised* to other living, and non-living, furry things. One would hope that Watson had intended to extinguish this acquired fear but he did not get the chance as the infant's mother removed him from the hospital!

Shortly after this, however, another colleague of Watson succeeded in extinguishing a naturally occurring phobia in a two-year old boy called Peter. Peter's fear of rabbits was reduced in stages. First, Peter ate his lunch with the rabbit caged some distance away from him. In 17 stages, spanning 40 training sessions, the rabbit was moved gradually nearer, then released, and eventually placed on Peter's lap with Peter eating his lunch and stroking the rabbit with his free hand. This case was an early instance of a method known as *systematic desensitisation*; it is still widely used today to treat a range of naturally-occurring phobias. Related techniques, derived from conditioning theory, are used with other neurotic disorders.

It is therefore clear that some aspects of human behaviour are prone to conditioning processes. But whatever one's preferred model for learning, the behavioural change must be accompanied by underlying changes in the brain. It is to these neurobiological processes which we now turn our attention.

2. The Neurobiology of Learning.

We should recall that the initial attraction of Pavlov's discoveries was that the basic unit of learning consisted of a simple physiological system. For example, a light would strike the retina and cause retinal cells to fire. In turn, these would excite cortical cells. However, in the conditioning process these cells would develop links to the cell pathways controlling the sets of muscles which carried out some reflex action. Hence, the light itself could come to elicit the muscular reflex. By this account, the conditioning experience must be represented in a particular set of connections between neurones in a particular part of the brain. We shall refer to the representation of learning in the brain as an *engram* or *memory trace*. As we have already mentioned, Karl Lashley was one of the first of many psychologists who have gone "in search of the engram".

Lashley's Search for the Engram

Lashley performed many experiments, which involved the surgical destruction of brain tissue in rats, with the hope of *locating* the region of the brain in which their learning experiences had been stored. His data caused a shock of disbelief at the time and still present an obstacle today, more than 50 years on, for theorists who wish to argue that memory traces are located in a particular area of the brain.

Lashley took a large number of rats and trained them until they were highly familiar with a complicated maze. He then proceeded to remove from each rat a small portion of cortical tissue, taking a different area but an equivalent amount from each rat. In due course he had removed from his collection of rats the equivalent of one complete brain, though no individual animal had has more than 5 per cent of its cortical tissue destroyed. He then took another set of rats, trained them in the maze, and again removed the equivalent of a brain, but this time taking 10 per cent from each rat. With a further sample he went through the procedure again, but removed a quarter of each rat's brain, and in his final group he had a limited number of animals each of which had had half its cortex removed.

If the engram consisted of a series of linked cells then one might expect that they would be found in a relatively small region of the brain. Interrupting the chain at any point should presumably destroy the learning, or at least grossly handicap it. Thus, very poor performance would be expected from, say, one or two rats in which the removed region of cortex had been involved in the conditioned reflexes used for negotiating a route round the maze. The remainder of the rats, in whom the engram had not been destroyed, would show little loss of performance. By inspection of the rats' brains at post-mortem, Lashley hoped to be able to determine which part of the brain was critical for the storage of maze-learning experiences.

To Lashley's amazement, and to everyone else's for that matter, he found that his first group of rats, each of whom had lost about 5 per cent of cortical tissue, were apparently totally unaffected by the surgery, running the maze just as well as they did before! The rats with bigger chunks of tissue removed were slightly more affected, but even those with only half a brain left were still able to run the maze fairly competently. The loss of learning seemed to be somewhat proportional to the amount of tissue removed, but *not in any way to the area removed*! In other words, the mysterious engram did not seem to be located in any single spot, and Lashley was forced to conclude that it looked as though learning and memory were a function of the whole brain rather than just part of it.

However, the intuitively powerful appeal of localised memory traces has meant that Lashley's experiments did not close the book on the issue. For a start, maze behaviour will be affected by removal of brain tissue involved in maze performance (physically getting around the maze) as well as maze learning. (We noted the distinction between learning and performance in discussing reinforcers above.) Consider, for example, the effect of removing tissue involved in the visual perception of the maze itself or the control of movement about the maze. Lashley's observed reductions in maze *performance* may have come about for a variety of reasons, thus explaining the variety of brain tissue which seemed to be involved.

The quest for the engram, and for understanding the relevant brain processes continued; the next really major contribution came in the 1940s from an American surgeon called Wilder Penfield.

Penfield's Brain Stimulation Studies

During some brain surgery, part of the surface of the cortex is exposed after a section of the skull has been removed. The brain itself is insensitive to pain, as it lacks the relevant cells, and so surgery can proceed with only a local anaesthetic to allow incisions in the scalp. Thus, the patient can remain conscious throughout. Penfield's operations required him to stimulate the surface of the cortex with an electrode. He noted that when the temporal lobes were stimulated, some of his patients recalled "experiences". For instance, one patient said: "Something brings back a memory. I can see the Seven-Up bottling company". Penfield was so impressed by these detailed and vivid recollections of apparently trivial past events that he suggested that "the record of man's experience is complete" and that it was located in the temporal cortex.

I have heard the following said many times: "hasn't it been shown that our memories record everything in our lives, even although we can't access them?". This is testimony to the influence of Penfield's studies. However, a more detailed look at his evidence shows it to be less impressive. Of 250 patients stimulated on the temporal lobe, only 40 reported "recollections". It appears that true recollections were rare in these 40 cases; in even the most-genuine sounding responses, it has been suggested that the content is really more akin to a dream than a memory.

It would be premature, on the basis of Penfield's data, to argue that the temporal cortex is the storage site for our memory traces. However, patients with brain-damage to temporal cortex sometimes show a lack of knowledge about the properties of everyday objects and concepts, as if their stored model of the world is no longer completely normal. More recently, in research on the neurobiology of memory, the "location question" has taken second place to attempts at understanding the microscopic mechanisms of memory storage.

Microscopic Mechanisms of Learning and Memory

Most experts believe that memory is stabilised, or *consolidated*, in some way, but there is great disagreement about the possible mechanisms of this process, and about the time for which it continues after the initial encoding of the experience. Estimates for this time period range from under a second to several years! Most researchers agree, however, that stable memory traces depend upon physical changes at the synapses between neurones in the brain. Such cellular changes may well require alterations in the production of protein molecules by the cells involved. (Proteins are critically involved in the structure and biochemical activities of cells—see **F31–32**.) Drugs which block the synthesis of proteins in the brain, when given at the time of encoding, severely impair the degree of learning. Furthermore, protein synthesis is enhanced in the brains of animals who have learned a task compared with those who have not.

The detailed interpretation of the technically complex research, noted above, has proved very controversial. Additionally, such research suggested a phenomenon which has been more hotly disputed still. If memories are in some way dependent upon the large molecules which control protein synthesis, then it may be possible to transfer these molecules to a different brain from the one which originally achieved the learning. Would the learning of the new "host" brain be affected by these molecules?

To test this notion, one group of animals (*e.g.* rats, or species of flatworms) are trained in a simple conditioning experiment. After learning, these animals are killed. They are then either fed to untrained animals or chemicals extracted from their brains are injected into the untrained animals. Studies have been somewhat unreliable, but there does seem to be some benefit produced by transferring these brain chemicals: the recipients learn the task more rapidly than did their predecessors. If the effect is genuine, its mechanism remains a complete mystery, but could represent a "toning-up" effect applying to learning in general. Such a non-specific view would avoid the implausible notion that the specific learning experience is somehow represented in the molecular structure of certain brain chemicals themselves.

Long-term Potentiation (LTP)

One of the most exciting developments in research on memory storage is the discovery of the phenomenon of *long-term potentiation* (LTP). There is a neural pathway which runs from the cortex to an important subcortical brain structure called the *hippocampus*, which lies beneath the temporal cortex. If this pathway is stimulated with high-frequency electrical signals for brief periods, the sensitivity of the hippocampus to later stimulation is increased. This increase in sensitivity is the phenomenon of LTP, and it may last for weeks or even months under some conditions. Thus, it is possible that natural electrical signals along this pathway, the neural signals concerning incoming sensory information, may also produce LTP on their first occurrence. When the same sensory information appears again, some time later, the incoming neural signals will produce a high rate of response in the hippocampus, because of the LTP. This high rate of response may correspond to, or produce, the feeling of familiarity which is characteristic of our memories.

One view of LTP is that it reflects a change in the hippocampal neurones at those sites where the hippocampus receives chemical messengers (the neurotransmitters mentioned in the introductory section) from the cortex. The ability of the hippocampus to "capture" the chemical messengers depends on the number of receiving sites (*receptors*) it possesses; LTP may increase the number of these sites. The real excitement about LTP is that it may be an electro-chemical storage system for the rather complex, organised memory traces which humans probably possess. In animal studies, drugs which prevent LTP from occurring seem to affect only complex tasks; learning via simple conditioning is unaffected. Of course, it is a moot point whether the memory processes involved in complex animal tasks are really any "closer" to human memory than those used in conditioning procedures, but if they are, then our understanding of the basic physiological processes at work in learning and memory may be about to take off.

We have considered what kinds of relationship may be learned and a little of how the brain may represent that learning. The final part of this section considers the 'why' of learning: *motivation*.

3. Motivation.

The layperson's view of psychology often includes an emphasis on the study of motivation. It is felt that psychologists are especially concerned with analysing the *reasons* for a particular pattern of behaviour. This is partly true, for a science of behaviour (psychology) must also be a science of the causes of behaviour (motivation). The wide variety of psychological schools of thought is well represented in accounts of motivation, although each school has its own conceptualisation of the motives underlying behaviour. *Psychoanalytic* approaches (**J43–44**) focus on unconscious, and often long-standing, motives and wishes; *humanistic* psychologists (who concentrate on the nature, and experience, of being human rather than on observable behaviour) emphasise the importance of personal growth and fulfilment; *ethologists* (see Introductory section) have suggested a plethora of instincts with a primary controlling (*i.e.* motivating) role in behaviour. Motivation from the perspective of learning theory is intimately related to the idea of reinforcement, as we have already noted, and has also often been linked with attempts to understand the neurobiological processes involved. These latter two aspects will form the primary focus in this section.

Drives and Homeostasis

Homeostasis refers to the equilibrium, or balance, which is maintained in most of the physiological systems of a healthy organism. Rather in the same way as a thermostat regulates the operation of a heating system to produce a more-or-less steady temperature in one's house, the body is designed to keep many of its physiological states within narrow limits (*e.g.* body temperature, oxygen and carbon dioxide levels, cellular levels of water, minerals and nutrients). When a warm-blooded animal is too hot or too cold, certain automatic reflexes, such as sweating or shivering, occur. These reflexes serve to restore body temperature to a constant, optimum level.

Early attempts to explain motivation essentially viewed it in terms of homeostatic mechanisms. For example, a prolonged period without food or drink was thought to produce a physiological imbalance, or *need*, for these substances. Appropriate behaviours, eating or drinking, were therefore the product of eliminating the need and the aversive states associated with it (hunger or thirst), and had the desired result of restoring the prior physiological equilibrium.

Motivation as need-reduction was soon expanded, particularly by the American Clarke Hull, with the broader concept of a *drive*. A male rat will learn to press a lever for the opportunity of sexual contact with a female, in the absence of any physiological need. Sex hormones in the blood are partly responsible for triggering sexual arousal, but are not maintained at a constant, homeostatic level. Thus, the notion of a sex-drive was created to explain this phenomenon. Other kinds of behaviour seemed to demand the existence of various other drives: curiosity; aggression; *etc. etc.* Drives were viewed as unpleasant physiological states (internal conditions) which are triggered, without the need for learning, by certain stimuli, which may themselves be either external or internal. The drives act to energise behaviour in general; certain behaviours, initially carried out by chance, serve to reduce the

unpleasant aspects of the drive state. This drive-reduction is the reinforcing property which then strengthens the link between these behaviours and the stimuli present when the behaviours are executed. Hence, the animal learns to execute mating behaviours when sexually aroused, and to eat when hungry.

To explain the more abstract motivations which typify the human condition (*e.g.* the needs for money, self-fulfilment, knowledge, power, fame), drive-theory had to be extended. It was therefore proposed that originally neutral stimuli could acquire drive-eliciting properties by classical conditioning processes. These *secondary*, learned drives were therefore seen as arising from the repeated pairing of a neutral stimulus with one or more of the *primary* drive states (hunger, thirst, sex *etc.*). The primary drives, by contrast, are induced by stimuli to which we are genetically-programmed to respond. Thus, if the absence of money is accompanied repeatedly by hunger (elicited by internal and external signals related to the absence of food), then the absence of money, of itself, will produce a secondary drive state. Furthermore, in the same way that the person will work to receive food to reduce hunger, s/he will work to get money to reduce the money-drive. Such conceptualisations are obviously very close to the notion of a secondary, or acquired, reinforcer which was discussed earlier.

In the previous examples, some of the drives are homeostatic in nature, and we previously referred to them as "needs". There is some possibility that this kind of drive could be directly measured, at least in principle. If a person's blood-sugar level has fallen, or the extent of their bodily dehydration is known, then one may have an independent measure of the strength of their hunger or thirst. Non-homeostatic drives do not have this property. Suppose you are obtaining great pleasure from watching a television programme. According to drive-reduction explanations, certain drives (such as a curiosity drive) were high and you are watching TV because this behaviour has previously led to a pleasurable reduction in these particular drives. How can one measure the curiosity drive, and its subsequent reduction, except in terms of a tendency to watch TV—the very phenomenon which the drive states were supposed to be explaining? This logical difficulty is not unique to drive-reduction theories, but permeates all psychological models of motivation.

Another serious problem comes from the fact that drives seem to be *increased*, rather than decreased, by the very behaviours which are supposed to reduce them. Imagine that you are hungry. It is true that eating will ultimately reduce this drive, but the initial effect of eating, say, the first mouthful, seems to be to increase the desire for food and the rate of consumption. Experiments with rats have confirmed this in the domain of the sex-drive. Males removed after mounting a female, but before ejaculating, will subsequently run faster along an alley to reach her.

Many researchers became concerned to delineate the regions of the brain which are responsible for motivated behaviour. Activities such as eating, drinking, mothering, mating, and aggression seem to involve *hypothalamic* and *midbrain* structures. This conclusion was reached not only through experimental destructions of brain tissue, but also via electrical stimulation of the relevant regions.

Electrical Brain Stimulation and Motivation

In 1954, James Old and Peter Milner accidentally discovered that electrical brain stimulation could reinforce behaviour. They stimulated the *septal* region of the animal's brain each time it went into the corner of its cage and noticed that it repeatedly returned to that corner of the cage. Moreover, when they arranged things so that the rat could control its own brain stimulation by pressing a lever in its cage, they found that the rats would press the switch more than 700 times per hour (compared with rates of about 25 presses per hour for food pellets). Subsequent studies have reported pressing rates considerably higher still. Indeed, a *self-stimulating* rat will prefer self-stimulation to eating or drinking, and will often press the lever to the point of physical exhaustion. This behaviour is strongly motivated but does not appear to satiate in the way that a drive-reduction model would predict; note that the other kinds of motivated behaviour which we have considered (eating, drinking, sexual activity etc.) are accompanied by satiety in healthy individuals.

Other brain stimulation studies have also shown the inadequacy of drive-reduction theories. Stimulation of the lateral part of the hypothalamus will make rats, even those recently satiated by large meals, press a lever for food pellets. The stimulation seems to make the rat hungry, and by a drive hypothesis this should be an unpleasant state. So, the brain stimulation which produces the hunger-like state should be aversive; yet, the converse is actually true. A rat will learn to press a lever which turns on this kind of stimulation, and the same is true for brain stimulation which triggers mating, drinking or aggressive behaviours.

There is, rather unsatisfactorily, we must leave motivation, having considered the most widely studied type of explanation and having discovered that it is heavily flawed. Nonetheless, the other approaches to motivation, which we noted earlier, usually lack compelling supporting evidence and suffer from similar logical and philosophical difficulties.

IV. EMOTION.

In this brief section we shall concentrate on emotions, although exactly what these are is extraordinarily hard to define. In common parlance, they are our "feelings". While acknowledging the importance of the subjective experience of emotions, psychologists have also focused upon their physiological and behavioural characteristics. Of course, these various aspects may be related: subjective ratings of emotional state often vary in tandem with physiological measures recorded at the same time during a psychological experiment. The links are not absolute, as shown, for instance, by the fact that crying (a behavioural act) may be either an expression of sadness or joy. In order to understand the following evidence relating to theories of emotion, we will first need to consider some relevant measurement techniques.

The Autonomic Nervous System and Emotion

The nervous system is divided into central and peripheral components. The central nervous system incorporates the brain and spinal cord, and is thus the major focus for psychologists. The peripheral nervous system includes the autonomic nervous system (ANS) which receives and sends nerve signals to our various internal organs (e.g. heart, stomach, some glands etc.). One only has to think of the physical sensations which accompany emotional states to know that the ANS activity is a feature of emotions.

Unobtrusive measurement of ANS responses, via psychophysiological reading, has been a key technique in emotion research, particularly for states of anxiety, stress, pain and fear. The responses which have been recorded are not particularly surprising. They include: increases in heart rate and blood pressure; decreases in blood flow to the skin (which explains why people often "go pale" when they are experiencing strong emotions); changes in breathing patterns; increases in sweat glands of the palms (hence "sweaty palms"); increases in muscular tension (hence the trembling which accompanies some emotions); and also an increase in high-frequency electrical activity in EEG recordings. Each of these responses is part of a "fight-flight" system, found across much of the animal kingdom. The reaction pattern serves to prepare the animal for the rapid physical exertions needed in the primitive behaviours of fighting or fleeing.

There has been considerable argument as to whether different emotions are characterised by differing patterns in these autonomic responses. A small degree of specificity has been observed in some studies, but the majority of findings contribute to the view that the physiological arousal associated with emotions is relatively general: physiological responses vary with the intensity of emotional experience, but not with the distinctive subjective qualities of that experience.

Having briefly considered these physiological yardsticks of emotion, we are now able to turn to some of the actual ideas which researchers have pursued. To begin, we shall consider facial expression.

Facial Expression and Emotion

The great biologist and founder of evolutionary theory, Charles Darwin (see **B18**) wrote about the expression of emotions in animals and Man in the 1870s. Darwin saw emotions as evidence for the continuity of behaviour across the evolutionary scale. (We have already commented that emotions in Man are accompanied by the same kinds of physiological responses that are found in animals preparing to fight or flee from danger.) Darwin based his arguments on observations both of animals, in zoos and the wild, and of the preliterate cultures which he encountered on his scientific voyages.

In the realm of facial expression, Darwin noted that some expressions seemed to be identical, in both their structure and function, for humans of widely differing racial and cultural origins, in individuals born blind or sighted, and in infants and adults. He also observed some similarities with the expressions of lower animals, particularly those of our closest evolutionary cousins, the apes and monkeys. Darwin concluded, on this basis, that many facial expressions were probably innate, that is, they develop without learning on the basis of genetic information.

Ekman and his Colleagues

Almost a century later, the universality of human facial expressions was pursued more experimentally by Ekman and his colleagues. They used photographs containing facial expressions judged to be prototypical of a basic set of emotions (happiness, fear, disgust, anger, sadness, and surprise). The photographs all used Caucasian subjects. Observers were asked to provide the verbal label which related to the expression shown. Subjects from literate societies (USA, Japan, Brazil) showed agreements of around 90%, and this high level of agreement has been replicated in subsequent studies. Subjects from preliterate cultures (Borneo, New Guinea) were much more variable but still agreed far more often than would be expected by chance. Agreement here ranged from 90% for happiness to 31% for disgust. These studies were subject to a number of criticisms, most importantly that the preliterate subjects may have had considerable experience of Westerners and their expressions, perhaps through the watching of movies in some cases.

Evidence from New Guinea

Later studies of New Guineans, who had had little contact with Westerners and had seen no movies, produced much higher levels of agreement using a simpler task. The subjects had to select, from a choice of three, the picture depicting the emotion relevant to the character in a story which they had just heard. Agreement on disgust, for instance, rose to over 80%. The agreements are even more impressive when one considers that much emotional communication is achieved via changes in facial expression, and the experimental materials were limited to still photographs. Clearly, there is a high degree of universality in emotions conveyed via facial expression, but, of course, this need not imply the strongly innate model proposed by Darwin.

Other theorists have also concentrated upon facial expression by suggesting variously that information from the facial muscles, fed back to the brain, may either cause emotional experiences, or may be an essential component or modifier of emotion. These facial feedback views led to experiments in which subjects were told to accentuate or suppress their natural facial reactions to emotionally salient stimuli. The effects of these manipulations on subjects' self-ratings of emotional states have been rather small and variable and are plagued by difficulties of interpretation. For example, could not the effects of exaggerating an expression be caused by the effort involved in doing this, rather than by a specific emotional mechanism?

William James and Emotion

William James was one of the first psychologists

to theorise about emotion. However, rather than suggesting that behaviours reflect emotional states (a person cries because s/he is sad), James argued the opposite case saying that "We feel sorry because we cry; angry because we strike; afraid because we tremble." His position is similar to, but more general than, the facial feedback models mentioned above. We have already noted that James relied on introspection rather than experimental evidence, but he did suggest empirical tests of his theory. Notably, he proposed that one might counteract undesired emotional tendencies by performing actions associated with opposing emotional states. This principle is embodied in some contemporary treatments of emotional disorders: therapies for phobias, derived from learning theory (see **Q16**), are sometimes accompanied by relaxation training which produces responses directly in opposition to those normally associated with fear.

Recent work has shown that autonomic responses are not beyond our conscious control, as was once thought. By electrically recording and amplifying the signals from the ANS, they may be played back to an experimental subject. Training a subject with this *biofeedback* technique has allowed ANS responses, such as heart rate, to be brought under voluntary control to some extent. Biofeedback trained subjects, who were then instructed to increase their heart rate in anticipation of mild electric shocks, reported experiencing more pain when the shocks were delivered than subjects decreasing their heart rate before the shock. This outcome is consistent with James' theory, because it looks as if distress was influenced by the rate at which the heart was beating, rather than the increased heart beat being a reflection of, or reaction to, the painful experience. The story is not quite so simple, in that the experimental effect was only obtained for those subjects who had indicated a good knowledge of physiological responses to stress in questionnaires completed prior to the experiment.

In the 1920s, James' views on emotion came under fierce attack from Cannon, who cited a number of objections. At the time they were considered conclusive, but now the picture is less clear. For example, Cannon claimed that artificial stimulation of the physiological changes typical of strong emotions did not lead to emotional experience. Injection of adrenaline produces the physiological reactions, but does it lead to the experience of emotions? Cannon believed not.

In the early studies, subjects seemed to report "as-if" emotions: "I feel as if I were going to weep without knowing why". However, there was nothing in the situation which could have been construed as eliciting the quasi-emotional state, thus perhaps allowing the separation between the physiological and subjective experience. Research in which potential emotional sources for physiological states were present may give a different picture: it is to this research which we now turn.

Emotions as Attributions

Stanley Schachter, like James, believed that physiological changes preceded subjective emotions rather than vice versa. However, unlike James, he argued that the same state of general arousal could underlie any emotion. James believed that particular physical changes led to the experience of particular emotions. In Schachter's model, the occurrence of arousal leads to a cognitive search for an explanation of the arousal. If someone has just been exercising vigorously then their aroused state would not give rise to emotional experience because the arousal can be *attributed* to nonemotional causes. However, when a potential emotional source is present, the arousal can be attributed to emotion. Thus, depending on context, the same state of arousal could, in principle, give rise to emotional states as diverse as joy and rage. Schachter's theory is known as a two-process account of emotions because both the arousal and attributional processes are necessary for emotions to be experienced. If it were true, then it would represent another instance of top-down influences (the emotional context) on the processing of information (the perception of the arousal state).

The Schachter and Singer Hypothesis

In one of the classic experiments of modern psychology, Schachter and Singer set out to test the view of emotion as attributions. Arousal was manipulated by injecting subjects with adrenaline or a placebo, and the subjects were either correctly informed of the likely effects of the drug or told to expect no side-effects at all. A confederate of the experimenters, while ostensibly waiting to take part in the same experiment, was used to provide a manipulation of the emotional context. The confederate acted in a euphoric way or exhibited anger at the "insulting" questionnaire which he and the real subject were both completing. The subject's emotional state was assessed via self-rating scales and by independent judges who evaluated the extent to which they joined in with the behaviour shown by the confederate.

Some support for Schachter and Singer's hypothesis was gleaned from the fact that subjects who expected physiological changes were less affected by the behaviour of the confederate; their emotional behaviour changed much less during the experiment than the subjects misinformed about the effects of the drug. However, their conclusion that subjects were "readily manipulable into the disparate feeling states of anger and euphoria" was stretching the point, particularly as the average self-rating for each experimental group was to the happy side of neutral! Subsequent researchers have also been heavily critical of the methods employed in the original study, but often failed to improve upon them greatly. The results from these later studies have also not been strongly supportive of the theory. Nevertheless, Schachter and Singer's conclusions have been widely cited and their attributional framework has been influential in a wide variety of areas of psychological inquiry.

Finally, we shall complete our review of emotion by noting the regions of the brain which seem to be critical. The close links with the structures involved in motivation should be borne in mind.

Emotion and the Brain

The limbic system is a set of interconnected, and largely subcortical, structures which represent an evolutionarily "old" part of the brain. The hypothalamus is a structure intimately connected to the limbic system, and we have already noted its central role in drive-related behaviours such as eating and drinking. These two regions are critical for emotion. Surgical destruction of the neocortex in cats, leaving only the hypothalamus and lower brain structures, has produced a phenomenon known as *sham rage* in which normally unprovocative stimuli can elicit a generalised emotional response. As noted in our discussion of motivation, electrical stimulation of particular brain sites can have quite specific effects upon behaviour; indeed, aggression or fear can be either enhanced or reduced in this way. However, additional modifying influences from other brain structures, such as neocortex, must be important, as a study by Karl Probram shows. Identical surgical destructions of a structure known as the *amygdala* (part of the limbic system) increased or decreased aggressive behaviour depending upon whether the animal was placed in a competitive environment or not.

When a number of multiple murderers were found to have tumours growing in their limbic systems, it was but a small step to attempt to reproduce the placating effects of surgical destruction which had been observed in animals. Control of profoundly disruptive ("psychopathic") behaviour via surgical removal of brain tissue was therefore attempted, but evaluations of its benefits were of poor scientific standards. These *psychosurgical* procedures were more prevalent in the middle of this century; nowadays effective drugs are available and there are much greater concerns about the intellectual side-effects of the operations. Nonetheless, a few medical centres still employ psychosurgical techniques for the control of extremely intractable behavioural and emotional problems; it is a point to which we shall return when discussing neuroses in the later section on personality. Before moving on to personality, and other differences between individuals, the next section will consider the process of thinking in more general terms than hitherto.

V. THINKING.

What is thought? This question has perplexed philosophers for thousands of years and will continue to do so. For reasons of brevity we shall simply consider the highly influential psychological model of thought put forward by Kenneth Craik in the 1940s. Craik argued that the major goal of thinking was to create a "model of reality" in our heads, via the use of internal symbols and concepts. A scientist generates a theory to account for a set of experimental data, perhaps using a set of specialised symbols (*e.g.* mathematical formulae) to represent the theory. In Craik's model, thinking was a similar attempt to make sense of the enormous amount of "data" about the external world which the human being encounters. In the same way as the scientist's theory, our models of the world allow us to make predictions about the future which guide our behaviour and make it more efficient. The start of the dominant information-processing approach to psychology (*see* **Section II Q7**) can perhaps be traced back to Craik's ideas. Indeed, in our earlier discussions of perception and memory it was argued that we are active interpreters of the external world, with our interpretations strongly guided by the influences from our mental model of reality—the so-called top-down influences.

While this view of thought focusses attention on its logical, abstract and explanatory aspects, it should be mentioned that less analytical modes of thought have also been considered by psychologists. *Everyday* thinking may not always be particularly logical as social considerations (harmonising with the other humans who inhabit our world) may conflict with straightforward logic. *Artistic* and *creative* thinking are, by definition, more holistic and imaginative than analytical, although not necessarily without their own rules and structures. *Lateral* thinking, popularised by the writings of De Bono, requires insight over and above straightforward deduction. To achieve it, the thinker often has to ignore the powerful influences of his or her model of the world, or at least temporarily restructure the model, to allow the problem to be seen in a new light.

1. Conceptual Thinking.

The information processing model of thought stresses the need for a mental "code" with which to represent the world. Although we know little about this code, in biological terms, we may be confident that *concepts* play an important part at the psychological level. We need concepts for reasons of economy: if we treated all events and things individually then we should soon be overwhelmed by the amount of information bombarding us. By having a concept of an apple, say, we can link our experience with a particular apple to the general concept, at least for the period over which the particular apple is relevant. Moreover, the concept represents what we know about apples; thus, if we cut open a particular apple we would expect it to contain a core which is not especially nice to eat.

Some concepts are absolute or *classical*: they have a number of key properties which apply to every instance without exception. All "bachelors" share a single common property—they are not married. However, many everyday concepts are *probabilistic*: most people's concept of "bird" will probably contain the feature "can fly" with some degree of prominence, but of course it is only *probable* that a particular bird can fly; chickens and penguins cannot.

Hypothesis-Testing as a Means of Acquiring Concepts

In order to learn about a particular concept one might construct a hypothesis about its defining features and then test the hypothesis against a number of examples, just as the scientist tests his or her theories against particular sets of experimental data. While this approach would work well for classical concepts, it would not be so efficient for probabilistic concepts as it might take a long time for one to encounter an instance of a non-flying bird and so force a revision of the original (mistaken) hypothesis that all birds can fly. Nonetheless, hypothesis-testing has received a good deal of experimental psychological study, and this kind of thinking is held in such high esteem in the West

that many intelligence tests (see the following section) include items requiring the acquisition of abstract concepts by hypothesis-testing. Given this, the reader may be surprised to learn that even supposedly intelligent individuals are often rather biased in the way that they approach the testing of a hypothesis.

In a classic series of experiments, two British psychologists, Wason and Johnson-Laird, investigated bias in the testing of hypotheses, particularly the tendency to seek confirming instances, rather than those which might lead to the rejection of the hypothesis. One experiment involved subjects studying four cards with characters on both sides placed before them thus:

  A   K   4   7

The subjects were allowed to turn over two cards only. Which two should they choose to test the hypothesis that "If a card has a vowel on one side then it has an even number on the other side."? Which cards would you choose? Most subjects chose the card with "A" on it: if it had an even number on the other side then the hypothesis was supported; if it had an odd number on it then the hypothesis was rejected (although the experiment overall suggests that this second aspect was not important in guiding the subjects to their choice). Most subjects also picked the card bearing a 4: this card can support the hypothesis (if a vowel is present on the other side), but if a consonant appears there, the hypothesis is *not* refuted (check the hypothesis closely). Subjects seem to be suffering from another bias which leads them to generate a second, complementary hypothesis "If it has an even number on one side then it must have a vowel on the other side" which the 4-card would test most effectively. Few subjects selected the 7-card because it offers no prospect of confirming the hypothesis, yet if a vowel appears on the other side of this card the hypothesis is rejected.

The analysis of conceptual thinking leads us naturally on to consider language. In language, concepts are often represented by a single word. As a child acquires language s/he has to perform a considerable conceptual feat in learning that when a parent points to a dog and says "dog" the adult is referring to the class of animals rather than to that particular animal, or to some feature such as its eye or tail. The child's errors on the way to successfully bringing together the concept, and the symbol (word) which serves to represent it, are informative; one psychologist has reported how his child used the word "bah" (bath) to refer not only to baths but to water in sinks and swimming pools, the sea, pictures of water and even a blue-coloured label.

2. Language and Thought.

The example at the end of the previous section implies the widely held view that language is built on existing mental structures, such as concepts. The eminent mathematician Noam Chomsky founded the discipline of psycholinguistics with just such a view of language. Chomsky felt that human thought processes are reflected in the *deep* structure of language, this deep structure being universal to all human languages. Chomsky also argued that as the child develops, given a minimum amount of language input from the parents, a genetically-programmed *language acquisition device* operates to extract a set of grammatical rules specific to the language taught to the child. These rules are then used to transform the deep structure of thoughts into the linguistic *surface structures*: the actual language which can be produced by the child. Hence, the thought (deep structure) that "John likes Mary" can be expressed by a number of surface forms: "John likes Mary"; "Mary is liked by John"; "Does John like Mary?" *etc. etc.*

It should be obvious that such ideas of mental structures contrast starkly with Behaviourist notions of language. In his book, *Verbal Behaviour*, the prominent Behaviourist, B. F. Skinner, attempted to account for language in terms of simple learning principles derived from the animal laboratory: the child learns to *associate* particular speech sounds ("dog") with the animals given that name; *imitates* others saying these words; and is *reinforced* by parents' smiles and verbal approbation ("That's right, clever girl"). It was Chomsky's damning review of Skinner's book which, perhaps more than any other single event, was responsible for the demise of radical Behaviourism. For example, Chomsky wanted Skinner to explain how English speakers could perceive the inherent grammatical nature of nonsense sentences such as "Colourless green ideas sleep furiously" when they had never heard this combination of speech sounds before, and thus never associated them with anything nor imitated them, and certainly had never been reinforced them for producing the sentence.

Linguistic Relativity

Some philosophers (notably Wittgenstein) and psychologists (Sapir and Whorf) have, however, advanced the alternative position that thought actually depends on, or is relative to, language. This idea, called *linguistic relativity*, is more than the Watsonian notion that thought is merely "sub-vocal speech". Rather it is suggesting that the way in which our language divides up external reality, referring to some of its aspects and not others, actually shapes our mental model of the world. It is known that Eskimos have a number of different words for "snow" whereas Westerners have only one; linguistic relativity proposes that it is the existence of the linguistic terms which allows the Eskimos to perceive and think about the differences between the types of snow. Of course, critics of these ideas have argued that "snow" is more important to the Eskimos' way of life, and so it is more relevant for them to have terms to describe its characteristics (say, for navigating about their snow-bound landscape). Westerners may indeed be able to perceive the differences between the snow-types but have not bothered to give each of them a different label. When snow becomes more relevant, say to skiers, distinguishing terms emerge (*e.g.* "powder").

Has psychological research cast any light on this chicken-and-egg problem? The question has been most thoroughly pursued via an analysis of the use of basic colour terms in differing languages. The conclusion seems to be that perceptions and thoughts about colour seem to be pretty universal, even for peoples whose languages have a very small number of colour names, thus failing to give any support to the idea of linguistic relativity.

3. Artificial Intelligence and Artificial Languages.

In the final part of this section we shall turn our attention towards artificial forms of "thought" (by computers) and our attempts to teach artificial "languages" to animals. These topics seem destined always to provoke controversy and heated debate, probably because they are perceived as striking to the very core of human nature: if a mass of electronic circuit boards and wires can "think", or a humble ape can enter the human domain of language, our very uniqueness as humans seems called into question. Clearly, such an atmosphere may impede the scientific processes supposedly at work in trying to answer the questions.

Can a Machine Think?

Perhaps putting this question in so blunt a form is unhelpful, and the cynic may argue that the answer depends upon what one considers thinking to be. One of the more insightful views on this issue came from the computer scientist Alan Turing, who took a rather pragmatic, or *operational*, stance, now referred to as the "Turing test". Basically, one should imagine two computer screens producing output in some form, perhaps responding to questions which one types in at a keyboard. Both screens produce responses to the questions, but one is controlled by another human sitting at another computer console, the other by a computer, programmed with the appropriate software. (Both the computer and the human are attempting to conceal their true identity.) Turing's simple idea was that when the investigator cannot reliably identify the computer from the human, then it can be argued that the computer is capable of thought. For an idea of what this might seem like, the reader is recommended to read David Lodge's novel "*Small World*" in which a character has various dialogues with a computer program called Eliza (a real program of this name does actually exist).

Despite the obvious philosophical complexities of this field, *artificial intelligence* (AI), as it is called, is a burgeoning discipline to which psychologists are contributing. Some workers are developing *expert systems*, computer software which carries out a specific practical task in an efficient way. If it is a task which humans also can perform, then the program may be influenced by the way in which humans are considered to be operating, but this is not necessarily a primary concern. Other workers are using the AI approach to gain insights into human information processing. For example, a particular program may carry out a task, and the output it produces can be compared to that from a human attempting the task, say, in its relative speed on various elements or its pattern of errors. If there is a strong similarity in the output, then some AI researchers argue that this increases the likelihood that the human is approaching the task using a "mental formula" akin to that programmed into the computer.

It is just beginning to be understood that traditional ways of programming computers gave them a rather different set of abilities from those of humans. For example, consider two valid, if complex, English sentences:

A: "The notes that the lecturer that the University hired dropped scattered all over the floor."

B: "The train that the girl that the man rushed past saw whistled loudly."

For humans, sentence A is quite easy to understand because we can use our knowledge of word meaning and the world (top-down influences again) in *parsing* the sentence, *i.e.* putting each verb with each noun. For sentence B this is not possible, as both trains and people can rush past or whistle loudly. We have to rely purely on the rules of grammar to structure the sentence, and we find this quite hard work. AI programmers have written accurate language parsers, but they have great difficulty in building in the kind of influences that allow us to understand A more rapidly than B.

Parallel and Distributed Processing Models

Partly as a result of the kind of difficulties described above, a new approach to AI has been attracting great interest in recent years: so-called PDP (*parallel, distributed processing*) models. These have been inspired by the architecture of the brain itself, in which each nerve cell may contact, and be directly contacted by, many hundreds of other nerve cells. Information can therefore flow along these many channels in parallel; the shift away from the emphasis on serial processing (*see above*) has been one of the major changes in contemporary psychology. We have already seen how information must be, to some extent, distributed throughout the brain: hence, the difficulties in determining where memory traces reside. In keeping with this, PDP models store information throughout a network of simulated nerve cells via the precise pattern of firing (some cells "on", some cells "off") of all the cells in the network. In this way, such models can also simulate another feature of biological systems: resistance to damage. Brain cells are dying continuously without replacement in the adult brain and yet there is typically only a mild decline in performance over many years. Similarly, PDP models demonstrate little change when the AI programmer "destroys" a number of the cells in the program.

Can we Communicate with Other Species?

Psychologists have also turned their attentions to intelligence in other non-human systems. Could we teach the pinnacle of human intellect—language—to our nearest evolutionary relatives, the apes? Attempts in the 1950s to teach a chimp to speak proved impossible because chimps lack the necessary vocal apparatus to produce human speech sounds. Undeterred, a husband and wife team in the States, the Gardners, raised a chimp called Washoe in their own home almost as a child. Bypassing the chimp's vocal restrictions, they tried to teach Washoe the American sign language for the deaf. She acquired a vocabulary of over 100 signs, and would accurately name objects, depicted in pictures, with the appropriate sign. Washoe also appeared to combine these signs in a crude approximation of a human sentence: one famous combination being "Baby in my cup" on being shown a doll placed in her drinking cup. Other observations by the Gardners showed that Washoe could combine signs to fill in gaps in her vocabulary describing a swan as a "water bird" (*i.e.* from two signs which were in her vocabulary). It thus seems that the chimp could appreciate and utilize the symbolic nature of her artificial language.

Project Nim and Beyond

In a rigorous attempt to extend this area of research, Herb Terrace undertook extensive sign-language training with a chimp whom he mischievously named Nim Chimpsky. Although initial indications were promising, and Nim rapidly acquired a large vocabulary of signs, detailed analysis of thousands of feet of videotape revealed the extent to which Nim imitated, and was subtly cued by, his trainers. Terrace concluded that true language (which for him was the acquisition of sentences) was beyond the chimp, who could deal with pretty much his every need via single words (signs). Think how many of our basic requirements can be met with single word utterances.

Although Terrace's findings were something of a body-blow to the whole area of research, more promising work has emerged since, notably from three sources. In Hawaii, researchers have succeeded in teaching dolphins simple command "sentences" via arm gestures or underwater sounds. The dolphins have been successful in interpreting the information conveyed via the order of the words in these commands, such as "put the frisbee from the bottom of the tank through the hoop floating at the surface", and performed well on combinations of words heard or seen for the first time.

David Premack has obtained good results in teaching several chimps via a system of coloured plastic tokens. Teaching the language may have affected the chimps' abilities to understand abstract concepts; for example, while all the chimps can match half an apple to half an apple, only the language-trained chimps appear able to match half an apple to half a cylinder of water.

Finally, Francine Patterson has been teaching sign-language to a gorilla named Koko for over 10 years. Unlike Nim, Koko is claimed to imitate very little and has been filmed signing to herself in the absence of her trainers. Furthermore, there is some evidence that she has deliberately lied to her trainers via her signs. Most spectacularly of all, Patterson reports that another gorilla, called Michael, has told her a story via sign-language. In it, Michael describes men chasing gorillas and hitting them on the neck with a rock. Patterson believes this may refer to the time when Michael was captured by hunters and his parents were killed. Although such reports approach testimony rather than scientific fact, they strongly suggest an intellect which we should respect.

VI. INDIVIDUAL DIFFERENCES.

Thus far, we have been interested in the psychological abilities of humans in general, or, put another way, in the psychology of a representative member of the species. In this final section, we shall consider the variations between members of our species, and shall largely confine our discussion to two domains of interest: *personality* and *intelligence*.

As should be obvious, these have been areas of inquiry in which practical applications have often been a powerful driving force. Industry provides a demand for tests which can predict suitability for, and success in, a particular job; educationalists have believed that separating children in terms of ability may allow better tailoring of teaching to the individual, thus providing better education for all. The pragmatic approach to this need for tests has led the majority of researchers down a technological, rather than a scientific, path: if the test "works" (in the sense exemplified above), then who cares if there is little by way of theory to guide the researcher's intuition in its construction? Psychological testing has therefore developed into a rather separate discipline, referred to as *psychometrics*, concerned with the technical aspects of psychological measurement and test construction.

Before considering some important psychometric principles, it should also be noted that work on

individual differences has been dogged by socio-political controversy. Predictably, researchers who attempt to differentiate individuals have also become interested in questions of group differences, say, in terms of race or sex. Work which has produced evidence for differences between such groupings, in terms of ability, for example, has been stirred into the melting pot of conflicts between egalitarian and individualistic politics. The policy implications of these kinds of research become particularly strong when some researchers additionally claim that these individual differences are largely inherited. The value of rehabilitating the criminal, or teaching the "unintelligent" child, must be strictly limited if their characteristics are largely determined by their genetic constitution.

1. Psychometric Principles and Techniques.

Imagine that you want a quick test of an individual's wealth which avoids the embarrassment of asking them directly. You hit upon the idea of counting the number of times the person mentions money, or money-related themes, in a five-minute period. How accurate would such a test be? Two basic factors will go a long way towards determining the answer: the *validity* and *reliability* of your test. *Face* validity is really a question of plausibility—clearly the proposed test has more face validity than, say, counting the number of farm animals an individual mentions! *Construct* validity is more important, and is the actual degree to which your test, under ideal conditions, accurately measures that which it is supposed to measure (the *construct* under investigation, in this case personal wealth).

In the present example, it would not be difficult to ascertain the construct validity of our test. We could take a number of individuals, who seemed likely to vary in wealth, and go through a lengthy determination of their actual wealth in each case. We could then compute the degree of relationship, via a statistic called a *correlation*, between actual wealth and our rough-and-ready estimate. The problem for abstract constructs such as personality and intelligence, or specific aspects of these notions, is that there is no absolute yardstick with which to validate our test—we cannot ring up the "intellectual bank" and ask how much intelligence a person has. This problem has forced some psychologists to take a very pragmatic stance on the nature of intelligence itself, with the famous pronouncement that "intelligence is what intelligence tests measure". However, test validation is also attempted by using a variety of imperfect yardsticks. If the test is related to them all, then it may be reasonably valid. One such imperfect yardstick for intelligence tests is current (or even future) scholastic achievement, to which most widely-used tests have been shown to be moderately related.

In fact, the above estimation of the construct validity of our "money-mentioning measure" would be contaminated by the reliability of the measure itself. Our measure has a number of factors which make it less than perfectly reliable. First, it is likely that situational factors would affect the degree to which an individual talks about money (more so in the bank or while shopping than when watching sport). Thus, any single five-minute period is not likely to be a reliable guide as to the average tendency to talk about money. Secondly, there may be some doubt as to what constitutes talking about money, or money-related themes. One judge of our subject's conversation might score it differently from another. Psychologists, then, make strenuous efforts to maximise the reliability of their tests, for example, by increasing the number of questions in the test (equivalent to sampling many five-minute periods in the above example).

Finally, we must explore a little further the statistical methods used in psychological test construction. The notion of a correlation has already been mentioned; it is simply a measure of the degree of relationship between two measures. Across a group of adult humans, height and weight tend to be fairly closely related. As one increases, so does the other; in statistical terms, they show a positive correlation.

Personality Tests

Many personality tests involve asking the subjects

a number of questions about themselves: "Do you usually take the initiative in making new friends?"; "Would you rate yourself as a lively individual?"; "Are you inclined to be moody?"; "Does your mind often wander while you are trying to concentrate?". Across a group of individuals, the first two of the above four questions tend to be answered "yes" by the same individuals, *i.e.* the answers correlate. Similarly, answers to the latter two questions also tend to correlate. Equally importantly, there is no tendency for correlation of answers between the two pairs of questions.

More sophisticated analyses of patterns of correlation can be applied over a large number of questions like these, in order to group together those questions which tend to be answered in related ways. These techniques are called *factor analysis* and the clusters of items emerging from such analyses are thus called factors. In the example above, the former pair of questions cluster with others into a factor which the British psychologist Hans Eysenck has called *extroversion*, whilst the latter pair form part of a factor called *neuroticism* (emotional instability). Hence, answers to the questions which are members of the extroversion factor are added together to give an overall extroversion score. There is nothing arbitrary about these factors themselves, since they are objectively determined by the answers which are given by a sample of individuals. However, the name given to the factor (*e.g.* extroversion) is fairly arbitrary, being guided only by intuitions about the personality trait to which all of the member questions may relate.

An important point about factor analysis is that it can be pursued at a variety of levels. For instance, factor analysis has also revealed that there are sub-groupings of items within those which cluster to form Eysenck's extroversion factor. One sub-group seems to be concerned with the individual's sociability; another seems to relate to a lack of reflectiveness about oneself and the world; *etc. etc.* What factor analysis *cannot* tell us, is the level which offers the best description of reality. For example, factor analysis offers no clues as to whether extroversion itself, or only its sub-factors, or both these levels of analysis, are related to separate brain structures.

Factor analysis has also been used in intelligence testing. Often, scores on individual tests, rather than answers to individual questions, enter into the analysis. The outcome is rather different also, in that performances on most tests are inter-related to some degree, *i.e.* a general factor (referred to as *g*) emerges from the factor analysis. (No such general factor is found in personality questionnaires.) Again, the fact that success at a test of mechanical, practical intelligence (*e.g.* constructing an electric lamp from components) tends to be related to success at solving verbal analogies (*e.g.* flurry is to blizzard as drizzle is to ???) does not imply that the brain lacks specialised subsystems which deal separately with the two types of task. Indeed, studies of brain-damaged patients, who can do one but not the other, provide rather strong evidence that such subsystems do exist. The emergence of *g* therefore may suggest that some property like efficiency may be common to all of the separate systems.

Equipped now with an understanding of the basic tools used in testing individual differences, we may proceed to consider Eysenck's theory of personality in a little more detail. Among the many theories of personality, it merits the recent description as a "colossus bestriding the field of psychology", for two reasons. As we shall see, it attempts to trace an explanatory path from the level of brain systems to behaviour patterns. Furthermore, it has generated an immense amount of (largely confirmatory) experimental data.

2. Eysenck's Model of Personality.

In common with most theories of personality, Eysenck's suggests a small number of basic personality traits. We have already mentioned two (extroversion and neuroticism); he has included a third, which nowadays is taken to reflect a propensity for anti-social behaviour or *psychopathy*. Eysenck has developed, over many years, a standard questionnaire to assess these traits, using questions similar to the examples given above.

At the biological level, Eysenck argued that human beings vary in the speed of production, and the strength, of the neural signals which they produce. He also distinguished between excitatory and inhibitory neural signals (as we have at an earlier point). He went on to suggest that individuals who have slow-developing and relatively weak excitatory neural signals, along with fast-developing and strong inhibitory signals, tend to develop extroverted patterns of behaviour. Introverts were considered to have the converse neural characteristics. Eysenck's model was thus somewhat paradoxical. At the behavioural level, the sociable, gregarious and outgoing extrovert, a "doer" rather than a thinker, is clearly the more activated and uninhibited; yet Eysenck maintained that the brains of these individuals were in an underaroused, inhibited state.

The Yerkes–Dodson Law

The paradox is resolved by suggesting that individuals are striving for a middling level of brain arousal. It is thought that this will be optimal for most psychological functions; indeed one of the oldest laws in psychology, the *Yerkes–Dodson Law*, makes just such a statement. Thus, the extrovert's overactive behaviour may be viewed as a search for stimulation which can raise his/her level of brain arousal to a more optimal state. The overaroused brain of the introvert, by contrast, shies away from arousing situations in an attempt to lower levels of brain arousal.

The amount of data consistent with Eysenck's link between brain arousal and extroversion is enormous. For example, as time progresses while performing a long and boring psychological task, there is a reliable drop-off in the accuracy of responding, which is thought to reflect a continuous fall in brain arousal to levels below the middle range optimal for the task. One would therefore predict that extroverts would show this drop-off earlier than introverts: this has been found in many studies.

Criminality and Neuroses

It was also predicted that extroverts, in a reasonably non-arousing test situation, would lack the necessary brain arousal to show strong conditioned responses. This prediction has been generally confirmed, although some authorities believe it is particularly true when punishing rather than rewarding outcomes is involved. Eysenck viewed social conscience as largely a conditioned emotional response, built up by punishing reinforcers such as parental disapproval and disciplining methods. Thus, it was predicted that criminality, interpreted as the lack of a conditioned social conscience, would be associated with extroversion. Eysenck's investigations of prisoners in the main confirmed these predictions, particularly when one took his dimension of anti-social behaviour into account. However, more recent evaluations of the evidence have concluded that the search for distinctive personality profiles in criminals has not been particularly successful; if anything, criminals tend to be highly neurotic rather than highly extroverted.

Eysenck's neuroticism dimension is less well characterised in physiological terms, but is considered to be linked to the autonomic nervous system (ANS) which controls our internal organs. These organs, as we have seen earlier, respond to changes in our emotional state. Hence, a neurotic individual with a very active ANS would be expected to form pronounced reactions to emotionally significant stimuli, such as the conditioned phobic reactions described in the section on Learning. For the reasons of their ready conditionability to most kinds of stimuli (discussed in the preceding paragraph), introverts also are predicted to be more prone to phobias. Indeed, individuals with clinical neuroses (*see* **P51**), including phobias and obsessions, do score very highly on Eysenck's neuroticism scale, and tend to be classified as introverts on the extroversion scale.

The central (brain) components of the ANS include the limbic system, a region of the brain long connected with emotionality. Surgical removal of various parts of the limbic system (or closely-related structures), which has been attempted as a treatment for severe emotional disturbances and neuroses, does seem to produce reductions in the

Q25

(originally high) neuroticism scores of the patients concerned.

Eysenck's theory of personality, and many others, share an assumption that personality traits are stable, enduring phenomena reflecting an individual's habitual predisposition to behave in certain ways. In fact the notion is conveyed by our use of the word trait, and is inherent in a belief that personality is largely inherited (which is Eysenck's position). We shall return to the debate on this latter point, but for the moment must mention the *situationists*: psychologists who believed that persons are typified by inconsistency of behaviour across situations.

3. The Person–Situation Interaction.

Many studies have illustrated inconsistency in individuals' behaviour. A classic series of experiments from the 1920s illustrated that children's characteristics (*e.g.* honesty) in one situation (*e.g.* the classroom) were not related to their characteristics in another setting (*e.g.* the home). Based on findings such as these, Mischel advocated that traits measured in personality tests predict behaviour less effectively than a knowledge of the situation in which the individual will be placed. This line of thought concords with everyday observation to a degree: an extrovert will be more subdued at a funeral than at a party. However, there is also a powerful sense that, whatever the situation, we continue to be the same unique individual.

Social learning theorists, such as Mischel, use experimental methods which set out to study change in various situations, rather than behavioural stability. (Remember that social learning theory gives a central role to learning from models, and is interested in the variations in our learning from models with different characteristics.) Later, Mischel conceded that his case had been overstated and adopted a modified view which maintained that individuals acquire a characteristic *cognitive style* from their past learning experiences. This cognitive style, like the other top-down influences which we have discussed, determines the interpretation which is put on the current situation. Some people may have a cognitive style which is essentially optimistic, always seeking to put a "good face" on the situation while others may suffer from a converse tendency and an associated proneness to depression. Modern psychological treatments for depression have included the teaching of coping strategies which are aimed at enabling the sufferer to re-orient their cognitive style in more favourable directions.

In Mischel's later formulation of his model, he highlighted the now widely-held viewpoint that behaviour is determined by the *interaction* of the person and the situation or environment. This is a simple message, akin to the interactions observed between genetic and environmental influences on behaviour (which are discussed at a number of other points), and is one which we psychologists keep encountering but are prone to forget.

4. Intelligence.

In turning our focus primarily to intelligence, we begin with a brief history of mental testing.

In 1905, a French psychologist named Alfred Binet published a series of tests of intellectual ability that are still used, in revised form, today. The tests were arranged in order of difficulty and distributions of scores were obtained from samples of normal children of differing ages. The test was the first to provide the detailed descriptions of testing procedures which are necessary for reliability between different testers. In a revision of the test, Binet hit upon the idea of the *mental age*, a device for comparing children of differing abilities and actual (*chronological*) ages. If a child performed on Binet's tests at the level of an average 10-year-old, then the child had a mental age of 10.

In 1916, the test was revised at Stanford University for the first time and has thereafter been known as the Stanford–Binet scale. In the 1916 revision, the newly devised concept of the *intelligence quotient* or IQ was incorporated. At that time, IQ was defined as the ratio of the mental age to the chronological age, expressed as a percentage. Thus, if our child with the mental age of 10 was actually only 8 years old, his/her IQ would be 125 (10/8 × 100).

In the 1960 revision of the Stanford–Binet, a new way of computing IQ was added. This method relies upon the statistical properties of the distribution of IQ scores within a large normal sample. Basically, the scores tend to cluster about a central value, and as the scores move out progressively from the average (central score), a smaller and smaller proportion of the sample achieve these scores. By adjusting the number of points awarded for each test item, it is possible to arrange things so that the average, and most frequent, score for the sample is 100. More importantly, the new method of scoring IQs depended upon knowing the degree of scatter (*variance*) about the central value in the sample of scores. From this knowledge, it can be calculated that an IQ of 115 will only be exceeded by approximately one-sixth of the normal population, an IQ of 85 will be exceeded by all but one-sixth. More importantly, for these well-developed, standardised and reliable IQ tests, such as the Stanford–Binet, the error in any individual IQ score is likely to be quite small. Typically, one can be 95% (or more) certain that the score which is actually achieved in an individual test lies within plus or minus 10 IQ points of the "true" score, *i.e.* that which the individual would achieve when unaffected by chance factors.

Despite the care which went into the construction and scoring of published IQ tests, concerns began to arise about their content. Many seemed solely designed to measure the success of an individual's education rather than an individual's intellectual potential. For example, tests of vocabulary and general knowledge appear in many widely-used tests. Does the poor vocabulary of an ill-educated person mean that they are less intelligent? This notion of intelligence as potential, rather than realised, ability is acknowledged in Cattell's distinction between *fluid* and *crystallised* intelligence. The latter represents the extent to which an individual's intellectual potential has been brought out, or crystallised, by their education. A vocabulary test depends heavily on crystallised intelligence. Fluid intelligence is closer to many people's notion of true intelligence—as a capacity to think flexibly in new areas where previous knowledge counts for little. A moment's reflection will reveal how difficult it is to design a test which cannot be assisted in some way by having had more formal education. For example, educated individuals tend to be more accustomed to being tested in general, and this may bring some benefits to performance.

Bias in IQ Tests

When researchers looked into differences between racial groups, as was mentioned earlier, the issue of bias in the IQ tests became more acute. Blacks in America did seem to score more poorly than whites. For theorists such as Jensen and Eysenck (who is a major researcher in intelligence also), these findings fitted with their view of intelligence as a largely inherited entity. On the opposing side, it was argued that the educational and cultural biases in the question matter and the very wording of IQ test items specifically disadvantaged working class blacks with low levels of education. Indeed, it was suggested that their lack of education may have deprived such individuals of the elaborate language systems needed to succeed in such tests.

The pioneering research of Bill Labov on Black American language showed that the poorest kids in violent ghettoes possessed an elaborate and rule-governed language system, although this was only demonstrable using black researchers who did not test the youths in formal settings, but prompted them to use language in natural contexts. However, the structure and code of their language was quite different from the English of white, middle-class Americans—the English taught in schools and used for IQ tests. Studies with IQ tests written in the black vernacular reversed the performance of blacks and whites on more standard tests.

Researchers in intelligence now seek to use *culture-free* or *culture-fair* tests: ones for which successful performance depends as little as possible on cultural and educational experiences. Often these tests are non-verbal in nature and have little need for written or oral instructions. Some have been validated by showing that they correlate with measures of the overall complexity of the EEG trace recorded from the brain of the subjects. Also, a test recently attracting much interest as a bias-free measure of intelligence is the so-called *inspection time*. This is the speed with which an individual can make a simple perceptual decision (*e.g.* deciding which of two short lines is the longer) for visual material presented for only a few milliseconds. Subjects who can do this accurately at shorter durations of the visual display are claimed to be more intelligent.

Although it is hard to see how culture or education could have very marked effects on IQ tests such as inspection time, cross-cultural studies show how careful we must be in classifying certain behaviours, rather than others, as intelligent.

Cross-Cultural Studies of Intelligent Thinking

Anthropologically-minded psychologists have studied the perceptions, thought and language of many "primitive" societies from the early part of this century onwards. Two recent examples will serve to show how arbitrary Western notions of intelligence can be.

The first concerns the *conservation* problem, devised by the Swiss developmental psychologist, Jean Piaget. In this task, children up to the age of seven or so fail to appreciate that the amount, or mass, of physical substances does not change as the substances are physically altered. Thus, the children state that when water is poured from a short, fat beaker to a long, tall beaker there is more water present in the taller beaker. These errors are very widespread in Western children and they disappear with age. They have been taken to reflect a stage of immature thought processes through which the child must pass in order to acquire basic adult intellectual powers.

These errors have been observed in studies of Aboriginal adults. Are we really to infer that the adult Aborigine is no more intelligent than a 7-year-old European child? It seems unlikely, given that the Aborigines are famed for their abilities at desert survival and they have not been observed pouring their limited water supplies into ever taller storage vessels to make them last longer!

The other example concerns an African tribe called the Kpelle, from Liberia. They seemed to fail at many basic Western tests of intelligence, including those requiring sorting objects into abstract categories. Abstract categories, concepts and relationships are a lynchpin of Western IQ tests. Given 20 objects from four groups (food, tools *etc.*), Kpelle subjects tended to produce two groups of ten rather than four groups of five objects. Often their justifications for this were that "a wise man would do things in the way this was done". Exasperated, the tester hit upon the idea of asking them how a fool would sort the objects. With these instructions, four groups of five were produced!

If intelligence tests are somewhat arbitrary, or at least heavily influenced by culture and context, then perhaps it is not surprising that the definition of intelligence has been so elusive. However, some researchers have believed that it, like personality, may be genetically determined and have sought evidence for their claim and for the *extent* to which this is so. The view promoted in this article has been that much of behaviour is a product of the interaction between innate (genetic, natural) and learned (environmental, nurtured) influences. Such a view might lead one to conclude that a quest to determine that intelligence is, say, "80% genetic" is less important than trying to understand the complex ways in which an individual's genetic makeup interacts with his/her environment to produce their observed patterns of behaviour and thought. Nonetheless, we shall close with a brief review of some of the methods for estimating heritability in both intelligence and personality.

5. Estimating Heritability.

Take a group of individuals, such as a series of families, for which one knows the degree of genetic variation between the individuals. One then takes a characteristic, such as IQ performance or a personality trait score, and measures it for those same individuals. By using correlations it is possible to arrive at a statistical estimate of the degree to which variations in the characteristic of interest are related to variations in genetic constitution; this is the process of estimating *heritability*.

For both intelligence and personality, heritability estimates, derived from *kinship* studies described above, have been high. Consider a pair of siblings (brothers and sisters); we know that they share 50% of the same genes. We know also that identical, or *monozygotic* (MZ), twin brothers share 100% of the same genes. The correlations in IQ, or a personality score, across a set of siblings are almost always lower than between a set of MZ twins, for whom the correlations are sometimes so high that they are indistinguishable from the correlations for single individuals tested on two separate occasions. Thus, the correlations fall as the degree of shared genetic material drops. This is reflected in other relationships: cousins, or grandparents and grandchildren, show much weaker relationships in IQ or personality scores than either siblings or twins.

The problem for the genetic model is that the environments in which the individuals exist will also become progressively more similar as blood-relationships get stronger. It is not unreasonable, even, to argue that MZ twins will tend to be brought up in more similar environments than ordinary brothers and sisters or non-identical twins, thus explaining the greater similarity in the MZ twins' IQ or personality scores. Indeed, non-identical (or *dizygotic*, DZ) twins, who are no more genetically alike than ordinary siblings often show stronger correlations in scores than ordinary siblings. This is likely to be the product of greater similarity in environmental influences.

To get around these difficulties, researchers have tried to find cases in which chance has separated environmental and genetic influences. Adoption has been seen as one such possibility. It is even possible to find MZ twins who have been each adopted to separate, genetically-unrelated families. Even when reared in these supposedly differing environments, the MZ twins continue to have very high correlations in their IQ or personality measures. Unfortunately for the scientists, adoption is not a truly random process, and it is the case that adoptive parents are selected for certain characteristics and may be matched to potential adoptees. Hence, it is likely that the adoptive environments for each member of the twin-pairs may have been quite similar.

In summary, these studies may suggest a role for both genetics and the environment in determining IQ and personality, although there are intrinsic difficulties with even the most ingenious research designs. Moreover, we have already noted that the question being addressed in this research may not be the most informative. Soon these researchers may turn their inventive minds towards the more important issue of the actual mechanisms by which the environment affects the translation of genetic information into behaviour: this is surely one of the most basic, and tricky, questions in psychology.

VII. FURTHER READING.

The following represents a short selection of introductory psychology texts, each of which has a broad coverage, is clearly written, and should be easily comprehensible to the non-specialist.

Atkinson, R. L., Atkinson, R. C., & Hilgard, E. R. (1983). *Introduction to psychology* (8th edn.). New York: Harcourt Brace Jovanovich.

Carlson, N. R. (1984). *Psychology: The science of behaviour*. Boston: Allyn & Bacon.

Gross, R. D. (1987). *Psychology: The science of mind and behaviour*. London: Hodder & Stoughton.

Lloyd, P., & Mayes, A. (Eds.). (1984). *Introduction to psychology: An integrated approach*. London: Fontana.

Miller, G. A. (1962). *Psychology: The science of mental life*. London: Penguin.

Radford, J., & Grover, E. (Eds.). (1980). *A textbook of psychology*. London: Sheldon Press.

SPORTING COMPANION

Association Football, Athletics, Badminton, Baseball, Basketball, Billiards, Bowls, Cricket, Golf, Greyhound Racing, Hockey, Horse Racing, Lawn Tennis, Motor Racing, Rifle Shooting, Rowing and Sculling, Rugby League, Rugby Union, Show Jumping, Snooker, Speedway, Squash Rackets and Table Tennis. A Special Topic in this edition looks at the growing popularity of American Football.

SPORTING COMPANION

ASSOCIATION FOOTBALL

FOOTBALL LEAGUE CHAMPIONS

1950–1	Tottenham H	1964–5	Manchester U	1978–9	Liverpool
1951–2	Manchester U	1965–6	Liverpool	1979–80	Liverpool
1952–3	Arsenal	1966–7	Manchester U	1980–1	Aston Villa
1953–4	Wolverhampton W	1967–8	Manchester C	1981–2	Liverpool
1954–5	Chelsea	1968–9	Leeds U	1982–3	Liverpool
1955–6	Manchester U	1969–70	Everton	1983–4	Liverpool
1956–7	Manchester U	1970–1	Arsenal	1984–5	Everton
1957–8	Wolverhampton W	1971–2	Derby C	1985–6	Liverpool
1958–9	Wolverhampton W	1972–3	Liverpool	1986–7	Everton
1959–60	Burnley	1973–4	Leeds U	1987–8	Liverpool
1960–1	Tottenham H	1974–5	Derby C	1988–9	Arsenal
1961–2	Ipswich T	1975–6	Liverpool	1989–90	Liverpool
1962–3	Everton	1976–7	Liverpool		
1963–4	Liverpool	1977–8	Nottingham F		

FOOTBALL ASSOCIATION CHALLENGE CUP WINNERS

1950–1	Newcastle U	1964–5	Liverpool	1978–9	Arsenal
1951–2	Newcastle U	1965–6	Everton	1979–80	West Ham U
1952–3	Blackpool	1966–7	Tottenham H	1980–1	Tottenham H
1953–4	West Bromwich A	1967–8	West Bromwich A	1981–2	Tottenham H
1954–5	Newcastle U	1968–9	Manchester C	1982–3	Manchester U
1955–6	Manchester C	1969–70	Chelsea	1983–4	Everton
1956–7	Aston Villa	1970–1	Arsenal	1984–5	Manchester U
1957–8	Bolton W	1971–2	Leeds U	1985–6	Liverpool
1958–9	Nottingham F	1972–3	Sunderland	1986–7	Coventry City
1959–60	Wolverhampton W	1973–4	Liverpool	1987–8	Wimbledon
1960–1	Tottenham H	1974–5	West Ham U	1988–9	Liverpool
1961–2	Tottenham H	1975–6	Southampton	1989–90	Manchester U
1962–3	Manchester U	1976–7	Manchester U		
1963–4	West Ham U	1977–8	Ipswich T		

LITTLEWOODS CHALLENGE CUP WINNERS

1960–1	Aston V	1970–1	Tottenham H	1980–1	Liverpool
1961–2	Norwich C	1971–2	Stoke C	1981–2	Liverpool
1962–3	Birmingham C	1972–3	Tottenham H	1982–3	Liverpool
1963–4	Leicester C	1973–4	Wolverhampton W	1983–4	Liverpool
1964–5	Chelsea	1974–5	Aston V	1984–5	Norwich C
1965–6	West Bromwich A	1975–6	Manchester C	1985–6	Oxford U
1966–7	Queen's Park R	1976–7	Aston V	1986–7	Arsenal
1967–8	Leeds U	1977–8	Nottingham F	1987–8	Luton T
1968–9	Swindon T	1978–9	Nottingham F	1988–9	Nottingham F
1969–70	Manchester C	1979–80	Wolverhampton W	1989–90	Nottingham F

SCOTTISH LEAGUE CHAMPIONS

1950–1	Hibernian	1964–5	Kilmarnock	1978–9	Celtic
1951–2	Hibernian	1965–6	Celtic	1979–80	Aberdeen
1952–3	Rangers	1966–7	Celtic	1980–1	Celtic
1953–4	Celtic	1967–8	Celtic	1981–2	Celtic
1954–5	Aberdeen	1968–9	Celtic	1982–3	Dundee U
1955–6	Rangers	1969–70	Celtic	1983–4	Aberdeen
1956–7	Rangers	1970–1	Celtic	1984–5	Aberdeen
1957–8	Hearts	1971–2	Celtic	1985–6	Celtic
1958–9	Rangers	1972–3	Celtic	1986–7	Rangers
1959–60	Hearts	1973–4	Celtic	1987–8	Celtic
1960–1	Rangers	1974–5	Rangers	1988–9	Rangers
1961–2	Dundee	1975–6	Rangers	1989–90	Rangers
1962–3	Rangers	1976–7	Celtic		
1963–4	Rangers	1977–8	Rangers		

SCOTTISH FOOTBALL ASSOCIATION CUP WINNERS

1950–1	Celtic	1964–5	Celtic	1978–9	Rangers
1951–2	Motherwell	1965–6	Rangers	1979–80	Celtic
1952–3	Rangers	1966–7	Celtic	1980–1	Rangers
1953–4	Celtic	1967–8	Dunfermline A	1981–2	Aberdeen
1954–5	Clyde	1968–9	Celtic	1982–3	Aberdeen
1955–6	Hearts	1969–70	Aberdeen	1983–4	Aberdeen
1956–7	Falkirk	1970–1	Celtic	1984–5	Celtic
1957–8	Clyde	1971–2	Celtic	1985–6	Aberdeen
1958–9	St Mirren	1972–3	Rangers	1986–7	St Mirren
1959–60	Rangers	1973–4	Celtic	1987–8	Celtic
1960–1	Dunfermline A	1974–5	Celtic	1988–9	Celtic
1961–2	Rangers	1975–6	Rangers	1989–90	Aberdeen
1962–3	Rangers	1976–7	Celtic		
1963–4	Rangers	1977–8	Rangers		

SCOTTISH LEAGUE CUP WINNERS

1950–1	Motherwell	1964–5	Rangers	1978–9	Rangers
1951–2	Dundee	1965–6	Celtic	1979–80	Dundee U
1952–3	Dundee	1966–7	Celtic	1980–1	Dundee U
1953–4	East Fife	1967–8	Celtic	1981–2	Rangers
1954–5	Hearts	1968–9	Celtic	1982–3	Celtic
1955–6	Aberdeen	1969–70	Celtic	1983–4	Rangers
1956–7	Celtic	1970–1	Rangers	1984–5	Rangers
1957–8	Celtic	1971–2	Partick T	1985–6	Aberdeen
1958–9	Hearts	1972–3	Hibernian	1986–7	Rangers
1959–60	Hearts	1973–4	Dundee	1987–8	Rangers
1960–1	Rangers	1974–5	Celtic	1988–9	Rangers
1961–2	Rangers	1975–6	Rangers	1989–90	Aberdeen
1962–3	Hearts	1976–7	Aberdeen		
1963–4	Rangers	1977–8	Rangers		

WORLD CUP WINNERS

1930	Uruguay	1958	Brazil	1974	W Germany
1934	Italy	1962	Brazil	1978	Argentina
1938	Italy	1966	England	1982	Italy
1950	Uruguay	1970	Brazil	1986	Argentina
1954	W Germany				

EUROPEAN CHAMPIONS' CUP WINNERS

1955–6	Real Madrid	1967–8	Manchester U	1979–80	Nottingham F
1956–7	Real Madrid	1968–9	A C Milan	1980–1	Liverpool
1957–8	Real Madrid	1969–70	Feyenoord	1981–2	Aston V
1958–9	Real Madrid	1970–1	Ajax	1982–3	Hamburg SV
1959–60	Real Madrid	1971–2	Ajax	1983–4	Liverpool
1960–1	Benfica	1972–3	Ajax	1984–5	Juventus
1961–2	Benfica	1973–4	Bayern Munich	1985–6	Steaua Bucharest
1962–3	A C Milan	1974–5	Bayern Munich	1986–7	FC Porto
1963–4	Inter Milan	1975–6	Bayern Munich	1987–8	PSV Eindhoven
1964–5	Inter Milan	1976–7	Liverpool	1988–9	A C Milan
1965–6	Real Madrid	1977–8	Liverpool	1989–90	A C Milan
1966–7	Glasgow C	1978–9	Nottingham F		

EUROPEAN NATIONAL CUP–WINNERS' CUP

1961	Fiorentina	1971	Chelsea	1981	Dynamo Tbilisi
1962	Atletico Madrid	1972	Glasgow R	1982	Barcelona
1963	Tottenham H	1973	A C Milan	1983	Aberdeen
1964	Sporting Lisbon	1974	Magdeburg	1984	Juventus
1965	West Ham U	1975	Dynamo Kiev	1985	Everton
1966	Borussia Dortmund	1976	Anderlecht	1986	Dynamo Kiev
1967	Bayern Munich	1977	Hamburg SV	1987	Ajax
1968	A C Milan	1978	Anderlecht	1988	Mechelen
1969	Sl Bratislava	1979	Barcelona	1989	Barcelona
1970	Manchester C	1980	Valencia	1990	Sampdoria

UEFA CUP WINNERS

1958	Barcelona	1970	Arsenal	1981	Ipswich T
1960	Barcelona	1971	Leeds U	1982	Gothenburg
1961	A S Roma	1972	Tottenham H	1983	Anderlecht
1962	Valencia	1973	Liverpool	1984	Tottenham H
1963	Valencia	1974	Feyenoord	1985	Real Madrid
1964	Real Zaragossa	1975	Borussia M	1986	Real Madrid
1965	Ferencvaros	1976	Liverpool	1987	Gothenburg
1966	Barcelona	1977	Juventus	1988	B Leverkusen
1967	Dynamo Zagreb	1978	PSV Eindhoven	1989	Napoli
1968	Leeds U	1979	Borussia M	1990	Juventus
1969	Newcastle U	1980	Eintracht F		

EUROPEAN NATIONS COMPETITION

1960	USSR	1972	W Germany	1984	France
1964	Spain	1976	Czechoslovakia	1988	Holland
1968	Italy	1980	W Germany		

ATHLETICS

1988 OLYMPIC GAMES (SEOUL, SOUTH KOREA)

Men

100 metres C Lewis US 9·92s
200 metres J Deloach US 19·75s
400 metres S Lewis US 43·87s
800 metres P Ereng Kenya 1 min 43·45s
1,500 metres P Rono Kenya 3 min 35·96s
5,000 metres J Ngugi Kenya 13 min 11·70s
10,000 metres M B Boutayeb Morocco 27 min 21·46s
Marathon G Bordin Italy 2h 10 min 32s
4 × 100 metres relay USSR 38·19s
4 × 400 metres relay USA 2 min 56·16s
110 metres hurdles R Kingdom US 12·98s
400 metres hurdles A Phillips US 47·19s
3,000 metres steeplechase J Kariuka Kenya 8 min 5·51s

20 kilometres walk J Pribilinec Czech. 1h 19 min 57s
50 kilometres walk W Iwanenko USSR 3h 38 min 29s
High jump G Awdejenko USSR 2·38 metres
Long jump C Lewis USA 8·72 metres
Triple jump C Markow Bulgaria 17·61 metres
Pole vault S Bubka USSR 5·90 metres
Shot put U Timmermann E Germany 22·47 metres
Discus throw J Schult E Germany 68·82 metres
Javelin throw T Korjus Finland 84·28 metres
Hammer throw S Litwinow USSR 84·80 metres
Decathlon C Schenk E Germany 8,488 pts

Women

100 metres F Griffith-Joyner USA 10·54s	4 × 400 metres relay USSR 3 min 15·18s
200 metres F Griffith-Joyner USA 21·34s	100 metres hurdles J Donkowa Bulgaria 12·38s
400 metres O Brysgina USSR 48·65s	400 metres hurdles D Flintoff-King Australia 53·17s
800 metres S Wodars USSR 1 min 56·10s	High jump L Ritter USA 2·03 metres
1,500 metres P Ivan Romania 3 min 53·96s	Long jump J Joyner-Kersee USA 7·40 metres
3,000 metres T Samolenko USSR 8 min 26·96s	Discus throw M Hellmann E Germany 72·30 metres
10,000 metres O Bondarenko USSR 31 min 5·21s	Javelin throw P Felke E Germany 74·68 metres
Marathon R Mota Portugal 2h 25 min 40s	Shot put N Lissowskaja USSR 22·24 metres
4 × 100 metres relay USA 41·98s	Heptathlon J Joyner-Kersee USA 7,291 pts

OLYMPIC RECORDS

Men

100 metres 9·92 C Lewis US 1988 Seoul	3,000 metres steeplechase 8 min 5·51s J Kariuki Kenya 1988 Seoul
200 metres 19·75s J Deloach US 1988 Seoul	20 kilometres walk 1h 19 min 57s J Pribilinec Czech 1988 Seoul
400 metres 43·86s L Evans US 1968 Mex C	50 kilometres walk 3h 38 min 29s W Iwanenko USSR 1988 Seoul
800 metres 1 min 43s J Cruz Brazil 1984 Los A	
1,500 metres 3 min 32·53s S Coe GB 1984 Los A	High jump 2·38m G Awdejenko USSR 1988 Seoul
5,000 metres 13 min 5·59s S Aouita Mor 1984 Los A	Long jump 8·90m R Beamon US 1968 Mex C
10,000 metres 27 min 21·46s M B Boutayeb Mor 1988 Seoul	Triple jump 17·61m C Markow Bulgaria 1988 Seoul
Marathon 2h 9 min 21s C Lopes Por 1984 Los A	Pole vault 5·90m S Bubka USSR 1988 Seoul
4 × 100 metres relay 37·83s US 1984 Los A	Shot put 22·47m U Timmermann E Ger 1988 Seoul
4 × 400 metres relay 2 min 56·16s US 1968 Mex C 2 min 56·16s US 1988 Seoul	Discus throw 68·82m J Schult E Ger 1988 Seoul
110 metres hurdles 12·98s R Kingdom US 1988 Seoul	Javelin throw 94·58m M Nemeth Hun 1976 Mont
	Hammer throw 84·80 S Litwinow USSR 1988 Seoul
400 metres hurdles 47·19s A Philips US 1988 Seoul	Decathlon 8,797 pts D Thompson GB 1984 Los A

Women

100 metres 10·54s F Griffith-Joyner US 1988 Seoul	100 metres hurdles 12·38s J Donkowa Bulg 1988 Seoul
200 metres 21·34s F Griffith-Joyner US 1988 Seoul	400 metres hurdles 53·17s D Flintoff-King Australia 1988 Seoul
400 metres 48·65s O Brysgina USSR 1988 Seoul	
800 metres 1 min 53·43s N Olizarenko USSR 1980 Mos	High jump 2·70m U Meyfarth W Ger 1984 Los A
1,500 metres 3 min 53·96s P Ivan Romania 1988 Seoul	Long jump 7·40m J Joyner-Kersee US 1988 Seoul
3,000 metres 8 min 26.53s T Samolenko USSR 1988 Seoul	Shot put 22·41m I Slupianek E Ger 1980 Mos
10.000 metres 31 min 5·21s O Bondarenko USSR 1988 Seoul	Discus throw 72·30m M Hellmann E Ger 1988 Seoul
Marathon 2h 25 min 40s R Mota Portugal 1988 Seoul	Javelin throw 74·68m P Kelke E Ger 1988 Seoul
4 × 100 metres relay 41·60s E Ger 1980 Mos	Heptathlon 7,291 pts J Joyner-Kersee 1988 Seoul
4 × 400 metres relay 3 min 15·18s USSR 1988 Seoul	

1986 EUROPEAN CHAMPIONSHIPS (STUTTGART)

Men

100 metres L Christie GB 10·15s	20 kilometres walk J Priblinec Czech 1h 21 min 15·00s
200 metres V Krylov USSR 20·52s	50 kilometres walk H Gauder E Ger 3h 40 min 55·50s
400 metres R Black GB 44·59s	
800 metres S Coe GB 1 min 44·50s	High jump I Paklin USSR 2·34m
1,500 metres S Cram GB 3 min 41·095s	Long jump R Emmiyan USSR 8·41m
5,000 metres J Buckner GB 13 min 10·19s	Triple jump C Markov Bulgaria 17·66m
10,000 metres S Mei Italy 27 min 56·79s	Pole vault S Bubka USSR 5·85m
Marathon G Bordin Italy 2h 10 min 54s	Shot put W Guenthoer Swiz 22·22m
4 × 100 metres relay USSR 38·29s	Discus throw R Ubartes USSR 67·08m
4 × 400 metres relay GB 3 min 47·30s	Javelin throw K Tafelmeier W Ger 84·76m
110 metres hurdles S Cariston France 13·20s	Hammer throw Y Sedykh USSR 86·74m
400 metres hurdles H Schmid W Ger 48·65s	Decathlon D Thompson GB 8,811 pts
3,000 metres steeplechase H Metzer E Ger 8 min 16·65s	

Women

100 metres M Goehr E Ger 10·91s	10 kilometre walk M Cruz Diaz Spain 46 min 9s
200 metres H Drechsler E Ger 21·71s	4 × 100 metres relay E Ger 41·84s
400 metres M Koch E Ger 48·22s	4 × 400 metres relay E Ger 3 min 16·87s
800 metres N Olisarenko USSR 1 min 57·15s	High jump S Kostadinova Bulgaria 2·00m
1,500 metres R Agletdinova USSR 4 min 1·19s	Long jump H Drechster E Ger 7·27m
3,000 metres O Bondarenko USSR 8 min 33·99s	Shot put H Krieger E Ger 21·10m
10,000 metres I Kristiansen Norway 30 min 23·25s	Discus throw D Sachse E Ger 71·36m
Marathon R Mota Portugal 2h 28m 38·00s	Javelin throw F Whitbread GB 76·32m
100 metres hurdles J Donkowa Bulgaria 12·38s	Heptathlon A Behmer E Ger 6,717 pts
400 metres hurdles M Stepanova USSR 53·32s	

1990 COMMONWEALTH GAMES (AUCKLAND)

Men

100 metres L Christie Eng 9·93s	3,000 metres steeplechase J. Kariuki Ken 8 min 20·64s
200 metres M Adam Eng 20·33s	
400 metres D Clark Aus 44·60s	30 kilometres walk G. Leblanc Can 2h 8 min 25s
800 metres S Tirop Ken 1 min 45·98s	High jump N Saunders Ber 2·36m
1,500 metres P Elliot Eng 3 min 33·39s	Long jump W Alli Nig 8·39m
5,000 metres A Lloyd Aus 13 min 24·86s	Triple jump M. Hadjiandreou Cyp 16·95m
10,000 metres E Martin Eng 28 min 8·57s	Pole vault S Arkell Aus 5·35m
Marathon D Wakiihuri Ken 2h 10 min 27s	Shot put S Williams Eng 18·54m
4 × 100 metres relay Eng 38·67s	Discus throw A Olukoju Nig 62·62m
4 × 400 metres relay Ken 3 min 2·48s	Javelin throw S Backley Eng 86·02m
110 metres hurdles C Jackson Wal 13·08s	Hammer throw S Carlin Aus 75·66m
400 metres hurdles K Akabusi Eng 48·89s	Decathlon M Smith Can 8,525 pts

Women

100 metres M Ottey Jam 11·02s	High jump T Murray NZ 1·88m
200 metres M Ottey Jam 22·76s	Long jump J Flemming Aus 6·78m
400 metres F Jusuf Nig 51·08s	4 × 100 metres relay Aus 43·87s
800 metres D Edwards Eng 2 min 00·25s	4 × 400 metres relay Eng 3 min 28·08s
1,500 metres A Chalmers Can 4 min 08·41s	Shot put M Augee Eng 18·48m
3,000 metres A Chalmers Can 8 min 38·38s	Discus throw L-M Vizaniari Aus 56·38m
10,000 metres E McColgan Scot 32 min 23·56s	Javelin throw T Sanderson Eng 65·72m
Marathon L Martin Aus 2 h 25 min 28s	Heptathlon J Fleming Aus 6,695 pts
100 metres hurdles K Morley Wal 12.91s	10 kilometre walk K Saxby Aus 45m 03s
400 metres hurdles S Gunnell Eng 55.38s	

BADMINTON

ALL ENGLAND CHAMPIONSHIPS

Men's singles

1950–2	W P Soon (Malaya)	1977	F Delfs (Denmark)
1953–4	E B Choong (Malaya)	1978	L S King (Indonesia)
1955	W P Soon (Malaya)	1979	L S King (Indonesia)
1956–7	E B Choong (Malaya)	1980	P Padukone (India)
1958	E Kops (Denmark)	1981	L S King (Indonesia)
1959	T J Hok (Indonesia)	1982	M Frost (Denmark)
1960–3	E Kops (Denmark)	1983	L Jin (China)
1964	K A Nielsen (Denmark)	1984	M Frost (Denmark)
1965	E Kops (Denmark)	1985	Z Jianhua (China)
1966	T A Huang (Malaya)	1986	M Frost (Denmark)
1967	E Kops (Denmark)	1987	M Frost (Denmark)
1968–74	R Hartono (Indonesia)	1988	I Frederiksen (Denmark)
1975	S Pri (Denmark)	1989	Y Yang (China)
1976	R Hartono (Indonesia)	1990	Z Jianhua (China)

Women's singles

1950	T Ahm (Denmark)	1974	H Yuki (Japan)
1951	A S Jacobsen (Denmark)	1975	H Yuki (Japan)
1952	T Ahm (Denmark)	1976	G Gilks (GB)
1953	M Ussing (Denmark)	1977	H Yuki (Japan)
1954	J Devlin (US)	1978	G Gilks (GB)
1955–6	M Varner (US)	1979	L Koppen (Denmark)
1957–8	J Devlin (US)	1980	L Koppen (Denmark)
1959	H M Ward (GB)	1981	S A Hwang (Korea)
1960	J Devlin (US)	1982	Z Ailing (China)
1961–4	G C K Hashman (née Devlin) (US)	1983	Z Ailing (China)
1965	U H Smith (GB)	1984	L Lingwei (China)
1966–7	G C K Hashman (US)	1985	H Aiping (China)
1968	E Twedberg (Sweden)	1986	Kim Yun Ja (Korea)
1969	H Yuki (Japan)	1987	K Larsen (Denmark)
1970	E Takenaka (Japan)	1988	Gu Jiaming (China)
1971	E Twedberg (Sweden)	1989	Li Lingwei (China)
1972	N Nakayama (Japan)	1990	S Susanti (Indonesia)
1973	M Beck (GB)		

BASEBALL (US)

WORLD SERIES WINNERS

1958	New York Yankees	1969	New York Mets	1980	Philadelphia Phillies
1959	Los Angeles Dodgers	1970	Baltimore Orioles	1981	Los Angeles Dodgers
1960	Pittsburgh Pirates	1971	Pittsburgh Pirates	1982	St Louis Cardinals
1961	New York Yankees	1972	Oakland Athletics	1983	Baltimore Orioles
1962	New York Yankees	1973	Oakland Athletics	1984	Detroit Tigers
1963	Los Angeles Dodgers	1974	Oakland Athletics	1985	Kansas City Royals
1964	St Louis Cardinals	1975	Cincinnati Reds	1986	New York Mets
1965	Los Angeles Dodgers	1976	Cincinnati Reds	1987	Minnesota Twins
1966	Baltimore Orioles	1977	New York Yankees	1988	Los Angeles Dodgers
1967	St Louis Cardinals	1978	New York Yankees	1989	Oakland Athletics
1968	Detroit Tigers	1979	Pittsburgh Pirates		

BASKETBALL

WORLD CHAMPIONS

Men

1950	Argentina	1967	USSR	1978	Yugoslavia
1954	USA	1970	Yugoslavia	1982	USSR
1959	Brazil	1974	USSR	1986	USA
1963	Brazil				

Women

1953	USA	1967	USSR	1983	USSR
1957	USA	1971	USSR	1986	USA
1959	USSR	1975	USSR		
1964	USSR	1979	USA		

CARLSBERG NATIONAL CHAMPIONSHIP

1973	London LSK	1981	Sunderland	1986	Kingston
1974	C Palace	1982	C Palace	1987	BCP London
1975	EAS Islington	1983	Sunderland	1988	Murray Livingstone
1976-7-8		1984	Solent	1989	Glasgow R
-9-80	C Palace	1985	Manchester		

CARLSBERG NATIONAL LEAGUE

1973	Avenue (Leyton)	1979	Doncaster	1985	Kingston
1974	C Palace	1980	C Palace	1986	Manchester U
1975	EAS Islington	1981	Birmingham	1987	Portsmouth
1976-7		1982-3	C Palace	1988	Portsmouth
-8	C Palace	1984	Solent	1989	Oldham

BILLIARDS

WORLD CHAMPIONS (professional)

1951	C McConachy (NZ)	1980	F Davis (E)	1986	R Foldvari (A)
1968	R Williams (W)	1982	R Williams (W)	1987	N Dagley (E)
1971	R Williams (W)	1983	R Williams (W)	1988	N Dagley (E)
1973	R Williams (W)	1984	M Wildman (E)	1989	M Russell (E)
1974	R Williams (W)	1985	R Edmonds (E)	1990	M Russell (E)
1976	R Williams (W)				

UNITED KINGDOM CHAMPIONS (professional)

1947	J Davis	1979	R Williams	1987	N Dagley
1948	S Smith	1980	J Karnehem	1988	I Williamson
1950	J Barrie	1981	R Williams	1989	M Russell
1951	F Davis	1983	M Wildman	1990	M Russell

BOWLS

EBA NATIONAL CHAMPIONSHIPS
Single-handed

1960	D J Bryant	1970	H Kershaw	1980	T Buller
1961	P A Line	1971	D J Bryant	1981	A Thompson
1962	C Mercer	1972	D J Bryant	1982	C Ward
1963	C S Graham	1973	D J Bryant	1983	J Bell
1964	P A Line	1974	W C Irish	1984	W Richards
1965	R E Lewis	1975	D J Bryant	1985	R Keating
1966	D J Bryant	1976	A O'Connell	1986	W Richards
1967	W C Irish	1977	C Ward	1987	B A Holt
1968	N R Groves	1978	C Burch	1988	R Bray
1969	J Davidson	1979	D J Cutler	1989	J Ottaway

CRICKET

TEST MATCHES

England v. Australia
(first played 1876)
Won: England 88   Australia 101   Drawn: 79
England v. South Africa
(first played 1888)
Won: England 46   South Africa 18   Drawn: 38
England v. West Indies
(first played 1928)
Won: England 21   West Indies 39   Drawn: 35
England v. New Zealand
(first played 1929)
Won: England 30   New Zealand 4   Drawn: 32
England v. India
(first played 1932)
Won: England 30   India 11   Drawn: 34
England v. Pakistan
(first played 1954)
Won: England 13   Pakistan 5   Drawn: 29
England v Sri Lanka
(first played 1982)
Won: England 2 Sri Lanka 0 Drawn: 1

BRITANNIC (formerly SCHWEPPES) COUNTY CHAMPIONSHIP

1950	Lancashire	1963	Yorkshire	1977	Kent
	Surrey	1964	Worcestershire		Middlesex
1951	Warwickshire	1965	Worcestershire	1978	Kent
1952	Surrey	1966	Yorkshire	1979	Essex
1953	Surrey	1967	Yorkshire	1980	Middlesex
1954	Surrey	1968	Yorkshire	1981	Nottinghamshire
1955	Surrey	1969	Glamorgan	1982	Middlesex
1956	Surrey	1970	Kent	1983	Essex
1957	Surrey	1971	Surrey	1984	Essex
1958	Surrey	1972	Warwickshire	1985	Middlesex
1959	Yorkshire	1973	Hampshire	1986	Essex
1960	Yorkshire	1974	Worcestershire	1987	Nottinghamshire
1961	Hampshire	1975	Leicestershire	1988	Worcestershire
1962	Yorkshire	1976	Middlesex	1989	Worcestershire

NATWEST (formerly GILLETTE) TROPHY

1963	Sussex	1972	Lancashire	1981	Derbyshire
1964	Sussex	1973	Gloucestershire	1982	Surrey
1965	Yorkshire	1974	Kent	1983	Somerset
1966	Warwickshire	1975	Lancashire	1984	Middlesex
1967	Kent	1976	Northamptonshire	1985	Essex
1968	Warwickshire	1977	Middlesex	1986	Sussex
1969	Yorkshire	1978	Sussex	1987	Nottinghamshire
1970	Lancashire	1979	Somerset	1988	Middlesex
1971	Lancashire	1980	Middlesex	1989	Warwickshire

REFUGE ASSURANCE LEAGUE

1969	Lancashire	1976	Kent	1983	Yorkshire
1970	Lancashire	1977	Leicestershire	1984	Essex
1971	Worcestershire	1978	Hampshire	1985	Essex
1972	Kent	1979	Somerset	1986	Hampshire
1973	Kent	1980	Warwickshire	1987	Worcestershire
1974	Leicestershire	1981	Essex	1988	Worcestershire
1975	Hampshire	1982	Sussex	1989	Lancashire

BENSON & HEDGES CUP

1972	Leicestershire	1978	Kent	1984	Lancashire
1973	Kent	1979	Essex	1985	Leicestershire
1974	Surrey	1980	Northamptonshire	1986	Middlesex
1975	Leicestershire	1981	Somerset	1987	Yorkshire
1976	Kent	1982	Somerset	1988	Hampshire
1977	Gloucestershire	1983	Middlesex	1989	Nottinghamshire

RELIANCE WORLD CUP

1975	West Indies
1979	West Indies
1983	India
1987	Australia

GOLF

OPEN CHAMPIONSHIP

1950	A D Locke (SA)	1964	A Lema (US)	1978	J Nicklaus (US)
1951	M Faulkner (GB)	1965	P W Thomson (Aus)	1979	S Ballesteros (Spain)
1952	A D Locke (SA)	1966	J Nicklaus (US)	1980	T Watson (US)
1953	B Hogan (US)	1967	R de Vicenzo (Arg)	1981	W Rogers (US)
1954	P W Thomson (Aus)	1968	G J Player (SA)	1982	T Watson (US)
1955	P W Thomson (Aus)	1969	A Jacklin (GB)	1983	T Watson (US)
1956	P W Thomson (Aus)	1970	J Nicklaus (US)	1984	S Ballesteros (Spain)
1957	A D Locke (SA)	1971	L Trevino (US)	1985	S Lyle (GB)
1958	P W Thomson (Aus)	1972	L Trevino (US)	1986	G Norman (Aus)
1959	G J Player (SA)	1973	T Weiskopf (US)	1987	N Faldo (GB)
1960	K D G Nagle (Aus)	1974	G J Player (SA)	1988	S Ballesteros (Spain)
1961	A Palmer (US)	1975	T Watson (US)	1989	M Calcavecchia (US)
1962	A Palmer (US)	1976	J Miller (US)		
1963	R J Charles (NZ)	1977	T Watson (US)		

GREYHOUND RACING

THE DERBY
(All races photo-timed since 1953 and run over 500 metres from 1975)

	Owner	Greyhound	Trainer	Time(s)
1960	Mrs B J Dash's	Duleek Dandy	W H Dash, Private	29·15
1961	Mr D Heale's	Palm's Printer	P J McEvoy, Clapton	28·84
1962	Mr P J Dunphy's	The Grand Canal	P J Dunphy, Ireland	29·09
1963	Mr S J Barrett's	Lucky Boy Boy	J Bassett, Clapton	29·00
1964	Mr S Donohue's	Hack Up Chieftain	P Stagg, Belle Vue	28·92
1965	Messrs V R & P V Leah's	Chittering Clapton	A Jackson, Clapton	28·82
1966	Miss P Wallis & Sir R Adeane's	Faithful Hope	P Keane, Clapton	28·52
1967	Mr N Finson's	Tric-Trac	R Hookway, Owlerton	29·00
1968	HRH The Duke of Edinburgh's	Camira Flash	R Singleton, White City	28·69
1969	Mr H Orr's	Sand Star	H Orr, Ireland	28·76
1970	Mr R A Young's	John Silver	B Tompkins, Private	29·01
1971	Mr H G White's	Dolores Rocket	H G White, Private	28·74
1972	Messrs B Stanley & G & B Marks'	Patricia's Hope	A Jackson, Clapton	28·55
1973	Messrs G & B Marks & J O'Connor's	Patricia's Hope	J O'Connor, Ireland	28·66
1974	Mr J DeMulder & Miss L Walker's	Jimsun	G DeMulder, Hall Green	28·76
1975	Mr D M Law's	Tartan Khan	G Lynds, Bletchley	29·57
1976	Mr R H Lancaster's	Mutts Silver	P Rees, Wimbledon	29·38
1977	Mr R Bacci's	Balliniska Band	E Moore, Belle Vue	29·16
1978	Mrs S Pearce's	Lacca Champion	P Mullins, Private	29·42
1979	Mr R H Hadley's	Sarah's Bunny	G DeMulder, Hall Green	29·53
1980	Mr A McLean's	Indian Joe	J Hayes, Ireland	29·69
1981	Mr S Barnett's	Parkdown Jet	G McKenna, Ireland	29·57
1982	Mr L James'	Laurie's Panther	T Duggan, Romford	29·60
1983	Mr J J Quinn's	I'm Slippy	Mrs B Tompkins, Coventry	29·40
1984	Mr J Duffy's	Whisper Wishes	C Coyle, Maidstone	29·43
1985	Mr D J Hawthorn	Pagan Swallow	P Rees, Wimbledon	29·04
1986	Mr A Smee	Tico	A Hitch, Slough	28·69
1987	Mr T Alali	Signal Spark	G Buggs, Walthamstow	28·83
1988	Mr F Smith	Hitch-the-Lid	J McGee	28·53
1989	Mr G McKenna	Lartigue Note	G McKenna	28·79

HOCKEY

OLYMPIC CHAMPIONS

1908	England		1952	India		1976	New Zealand
1920	Gt Britain		1956	India		1980	India
1928	India		1960	Pakistan		1984	Pakistan
1932	India		1964	India		1988	Gt Britain
1936	India		1968	Pakistan			
1948	India		1972	W Germany			

HORSE RACING

THE DERBY

	Horse	Jockey	Owner
1950	Galcador	W Johnstone	M Boussac
1951	Arctic Prince	C Spares	Mr J McGrath
1952	Tulyar	C Smirke	The Aga Khan
1953	Pinza	G Richards	Sir V Sassoon
1954	Never Say Die	L Piggott	Mr R S Clark
1955	Phil Drake	F Palmer	Mme Volterra
1956	Lavandin	W Johnstone	M Wertheimer
1957	Crepello	L Piggott	Sir V Sassoon
1958	Hard Ridden	C Smirke	Sir V Sassoon
1959	Parthia	W H Carr	Sir H de Trafford
1960	St Paddy	L Piggott	Sir V Sassoon
1961	Psidium	R Poincelet	Mrs Arpad Plesch
1962	Larkspur	N Sellwood	Mr R Guest
1963	Relko	Y Saint-Martin	M F Dupré
1964	Santa Claus	A Breasley	Mr J Ismay
1965	Sea Bird II	T P Glennon	Mr M J Ternynck
1966	Charlottown	A Breasley	Lady Z Wernher
1967	Royal Palace	G Moore	Mr H J Joel
1968	Sir Ivor	L Piggott	Mr R R Guest
1969	Blakeney	E Johnson	Mr A Budgett

THE DERBY

	Horse	Jockey	Owner
1970	Nijinsky	L Piggott	Mr C W Engelhard
1971	Mill Reef	G Lewis	Mr P Mellon
1972	Roberto	L Piggott	Mr J Galbreath
1973	Morston	E Hide	Mr A Budgett
1974	Snow Knight	B Taylor	Mrs N Philips
1975	Grundy	P Eddery	Dr C Vittadini
1976	Empery	L Piggott	Mr B Hunt
1977	The Minstrel	L Piggott	Mr R Sangster
1978	Shirley Heights	G Starkey	Lord Halifax
1979	Troy	W Carson	Sir M Sobell
1980	Henbit	W Carson	Mrs A Plesch
1981	Shergar	W R Swinburn	The Aga Khan
1982	Golden Fleece	P Eddery	Mr R Sangster
1983	Teenoso	L Piggott	Mr E Moller
1984	Secreto	C Roche	Mr L Miglitti
1985	Slip Anchor	S Cauthen	Lord Howard de Walden
1986	Shahrastani	W R Swinburn	The Aga Khan
1987	Reference Point	S Cauthen	Mr L Freedman
1988	Kahyasi	R Cochrane	The Aga Khan
1989	Nashwan	W Carson	H. Al-Maktoum
1990	Quest for Fame	P Eddery	K Abdulla

THE GRAND NATIONAL

	Horse	Jockey	Owner
1950	Freebooter	J Power	Mrs L Brotherton
1951	Nickel Coin	J A Bullock	Mr J Royle
1952	Teal	A P Thompson	Mr H Lane
1953	Early Mist	B Marshall	Mr J H Griffin
1954	Royal Tan	B Marshall	Mr J H Griffin
1955	Quare Times	P Taffe	Mrs W H E Welman
1956	ESB	D Dick	Mrs L Carver
1957	Sundew	F Winter	Mrs G Kohn
1958	Mr What	A Freeman	Mr D Coughlan
1959	Oxo	M Scudamore	Mr J E Bigg
1960	Merryman II	G Scott	Miss W H S Wallace
1961	Nicolaus Silver	H Beasley	Mr C Vaughan
1962	Kilmore	F Winter	Mr N Cohen
1963	Ayala	P Buckley	Mr P B Raymond
1964	Team Spirit	G W Robinson	Mr J Goodman
1965	Jay Trump	C Smith	Mrs M Stephenson
1966	Anglo	T Norman	Mr S Levy
1967	Foinavon	J Buckingham	Mr C P T Watkins
1968	Red Alligator	B Fletcher	Mr J Manners
1969	Highland Wedding	E Harty	Mr T H McKay, jun.
1970	Gay Trip	P Taaffe	Mr A Chambers
1971	Specify	J Cook	Mr F W Pontin
1972	Well to Do	G Thorner	Capt T Forster
1973	Red Rum	B Fletcher	Mr N Le Mare
1974	Red Rum	B Fletcher	Mr N Le Mare
1975	L'Escargot	T Carberry	Mr R Guest
1976	Rag Trade	J Burke	Mr P Raymond
1977	Red Rum	T Stack	Mr N Le Mare
1978	Lucius	B R Davis	Mrs D Whitaker
1979	Rubstic	M Barnes	Mr J Douglas
1980	Ben Nevis	C Fenwick	Mr R Stewart, jun.
1981	Aldaniti	R Champion	Mrs V Embericos
1982	Grittar	C Saunders	Mr F Gilman
1983	Corbiere	B de Haan	Mr B Burrough
1984	Hallo Dandy	N Doughty	Mr R Shaw
1985	Last Suspect	H Davies	Anne, Duchess of Westminster
1986	West Tip	R Dunwoody	Mr P Luff
1987	Maori Venture	S Knight	Mr J Joel
1988	Rhyme 'n' Reason	B Powell	Miss J Reed
1989	Little Polvier	J Frost	Mr E Harvey
1990	Mr Frisk	M Armytage	Mrs L Duffey

LAWN TENNIS

DAVIS CUP

1950–3	Australia	1973	Australia	1982	USA
1954	USA	1974	South Africa	1983	Australia
1955–7	Australia	1975	Sweden	1984	Sweden
1958	USA	1976	Italy	1985	Sweden
1959–62	Australia	1977	Australia	1986	Australia
1963	USA	1978–9	USA	1987	Sweden
1964–7	Australia	1980	Czechoslovakia	1988	W Germany
1968–72	USA	1981	USA	1989	W Germany

WIMBLEDON CHAMPIONSHIPS

Men's Singles

1950	J E Patty (US)	1964	R Emerson (Aus)	1978	B Borg (Sweden)
1951	R Savitt (US)	1965	R Emerson (Aus)	1979	B Borg (Sweden)
1952	F A Sedgman (Aus)	1966	M Santana (Spain)	1980	B Borg (Sweden)
1953	E V Seixas (US)	1967	J D Newcombe (Aus)	1981	J P McEnroe (US)
1954	J Drobny (Czech)	1968	R Laver (Aus)	1982	J Connors (US)
1955	M A Trabert (US)	1969	R Laver (Aus)	1983	J P McEnroe (US)
1956	L A Hoad (Aus)	1970	J D Newcombe (Aus)	1984	J P McEnroe (US)
1957	L A Hoad (Aus)	1971	J D Newcombe (Aus)	1985	B Becker (W Ger)
1958	A J Cooper (Aus)	1972	S R Smith (US)	1986	B Becker (W Ger)
1959	A Olmedo (Peru)	1973	J Kodes (Czech)	1987	P Cash (Aus)
1960	N A Fraser (Aus)	1974	J Connors (US)	1988	S Edberg (Sweden)
1961	R Laver (Aus)	1975	A R Ashe (US)	1989	B Becker (W Ger)
1962	R Laver (Aus)	1976	B Borg (Sweden)		
1963	C R McKinley (US)	1977	B Borg (Sweden)		

Women's Singles

1950	A L Brough (US)	1964	M E Bueno (Braz)	1978	M Navratilova (Czech)
1951	D J Hart (US)	1965	M Smith (Aus)	1979	M Navratilova (US)
1952	M Connolly (US)	1966	B-J King (US)	1980	E F Cawley (née Goolagong)
1953	M Connolly (US)	1967	B-J King (US)		(Aus)
1954	M Connolly (US)	1968	B-J King (US)	1981	C Evert-Lloyd (US)
1955	L Brough (US)	1969	A Jones (GB)	1982	M Navratilova (US)
1956	S J Fry (US)	1970	M Court (née Smith (Aus)	1983	M Navratilova (US)
1957	A Gibson (US)	1971	E F Goolagong (Aus)	1984	M Navratilova (US)
1958	A Gibson (US)	1972	B-J King (US)	1985	M Navratilova (US)
1959	M E Bueno (Braz)	1973	B-J King (US)	1986	M Navratilova (US)
1960	M E Bueno (Braz)	1974	C Evert (US)	1987	M Navratilova (US)
1961	A Mortimer (GB)	1975	B-J King (US)	1988	S Graf (W Ger)
1962	J R Susman (US)	1976	C Evert (US)	1989	S Graf (W Ger)
1963	M Smith (Aus)	1977	S V Wade (GB)		

Men's Doubles

1950	J E Bromwich & A K Quist	1970	J D Newcombe & A D Roche
1951	K McGregor & F A Sedgman	1971	R Emerson & R Laver
1952	K McGregor & F A Sedgman	1972	R A Hewitt & F D McMillan
1953	L A Hoad & K R Rosewall	1973	J S Connors & I Nastase
1954	R N Hartwig & M G Rose	1974	J D Newcombe & A D Roche
1955	R N Hartwig & L A Hoad	1975	V Gerulaitis & A Mayer
1956	L A Hoad & K R Rosewall	1976	B E Gottfried & R Ramirez
1957	G Mulloy & J E Patty	1977	R L Case & G Masters
1958	S Davidson & U Schmidt	1978	R A Hewitt & F D McMillan
1959	R Emerson & N A Fraser	1979	P Fleming & J P McEnroe
1960	R H Osuna & R D Ralston	1980	P McNamara & P McNamee
1961	R Emerson & N A Fraser	1981	P Fleming & J P McEnroe
1962	R A Hewitt & F S Stolle	1982	P McNamara & P McNamee
1963	R H Osuna & A Palafox	1983	P Fleming & J P McEnroe
1964	R A Hewitt & F S Stolle	1984	P Fleming & J P McEnroe
1965	J D Newcombe & A D Roche	1985	H P Gunthardt & B Taroczy
1966	K N Fletcher & J D Newcombe	1986	J Nystrom & W Wilander
1967	R A Hewitt & F D McMillan	1987	K Flach & R Seguso
1968	J D Newcombe & A D Roche	1988	K Flach & R Seguso
1969	J D Newcombe & A D Roche	1989	J Fitzgerald & A Jarryd

Women's Doubles

1950	A L Brough & W Dupont	1970	R Casals & B-J King
1951	S J Fry & D J Hart	1971	R Casals & B-J King
1952	S J Fry & D J Hart	1972	B-J King & B Stove
1953	S J Fry & D J Hart	1973	R Casals & B-J King
1954	A L Brough & W Dupont	1974	E Goolagong & P Michel
1955	A Mortimer & J A Shilcock	1975	A K Kiyomura & K Sawamatsu
1956	A Buxton & A Gibson	1976	C Evert & M Navratilova
1957	A Gibson & D R Hard	1977	R L Cawley & J C Russell
1958	M E Bueno & A Gibson	1978	G E Reid & W M Turnbull
1959	J Arth & D R Hard	1979	B-J King & M Navratilova
1960	M E Bueno & D R Hard	1980	K Jordan & A Smith
1961	K Hantze & B-J Moffitt	1981	M Navratilova & P H Shriver
1962	B-J Moffitt & J R Susman	1982	M Navratilova & P H Shriver
1963	M E Bueno & D R Hard	1983	M Navratilova & P H Shriver
1964	M Smith & L R Turner	1984	M Navratilova & P H Shriver
1965	M E Bueno & B-J Moffitt	1985	K Jordan & P D Smylie
1966	M E Bueno & N Richey	1986	M Navratilova & P H Shriver
1967	R Casals & B-J King	1987	C Khode-Kilsch & H Sukova
1968	R Casals & B-J King	1988	S. Graf & G. Sabatini
1969	M Court & J A Tegart	1989	J Novotna & H Sukova

WIMBLEDON CHAMPIONSHIPS

Mixed Doubles

1950	E W Sturgess & A L Brough	1970	I Nastase & R Casals
1951	F A Sedgman & D J Hart	1971	O K Davidson & B-J King
1952	F A Sedgman & D J Hart	1972	I Nastase & R Casals
1953	E V Seixas & D J Hart	1973	O K Davidson & B-J King
1954	E V Seixas & D J Hart	1974	O K Davidson & B-J King
1955	E V Seixas & D J Hart	1975	M C Riessen & B M Court
1956	E V Seixas & S J Fry	1976	A D Roche & F Durr
1957	M G Rose & D R Hard	1977	R A J Hewitt & G R Stevens
1958	R N Howe & L Coghlan	1978	F D McMillan & B F Stove
1959	R Laver & D R Hard	1979	R A J Hewitt & G R Stevens
1960	R Laver & D R Hard	1980	J R Austin & T Austin
1961	F Stolle & L R Turner	1981	F D McMillan & B F Stove
1962	N A Fraser & W Dupont	1982	K Curren & A E Smith
1963	K N Fletcher & M Smith	1983	J M Lloyd & W Turnbull
1964	F Stolle & L R Turner	1984	J M Lloyd & W Turnbull
1965	K N Fletcher & M Smith	1985	P McNamee & M Navratilova
1966	K N Fletcher & M Smith	1986	K Flach & K Jordan
1967	O K Davidson & B-J King	1987	M J Bates & J M Durie
1968	K N Fletcher & M Court	1988	S Stewart & Z Garrison
1969	F Stolle & A Jones	1989	J Pugh & J Novotna

MOTOR RACING

World Champion Drivers

1950	G Farina (It)	1964	J Surtees (GB)	1978	M Andretti (US)
1951	J M Fangio (Arg)	1965	J Clark (GB)	1979	J Scheckter (SA)
1952	A Ascari (It)	1966	J Brabham (Aus)	1980	A Jones (Aus)
1953	A Ascari (It)	1967	D Hulme (NZ)	1981	N Piquet (Braz)
1954	J M Fangio (Arg)	1968	G Hill (GB)	1982	K Rosberg (Fin)
1955	J M Fangio (Arg)	1969	J Stewart (GB)	1983	N Piquet (Braz)
1956	J M Fangio (Arg)	1970	J Rindt (Austria)	1984	N Lauda (Austria)
1957	J M Fangio (Arg)	1971	J Stewart (GB)	1985	A Prost (Fr)
1958	M Hawthorn (GB)	1972	E Fittipaldi (Braz)	1986	A Prost (Fr)
1959	J Brabham (Aus)	1973	J Stewart (GB)	1987	N Piquet (Braz)
1960	J Brabham (Aus)	1974	E Fittipaldi (Braz)	1988	A Senna (Braz)
1961	P Hill (US)	1975	N Lauda (Austria)	1989	A Prost (Fr)
1962	G Hill (GB)	1976	J Hunt (GB)		
1963	J Clark (GB)	1977	N Lauda (Austria)		

RIFLE SHOOTING

Queen's/King's Prize Winners

1950	R Greig	1964	A Harris	1978	G R Graham
1951	G Boa	1965	J Allen	1979	A St G Tucker
1952	A Kinnier-Wilson	1966	R Hampton	1980	A Marion
1953	N McCaw	1967	J Powell	1981	G M Ayling
1954	G Twine	1968	A Parke	1982	L Peden
1955	L Fenwick	1969	F Little	1983	A Marion
1956	G Twine	1970	G F Arnold	1984	D Richards
1957	J Love	1971	R M Stevens	1985	J Bloomfield
1958	R Fulton	1972	R P Rosling	1986	G Cox
1959	I Mallabar	1973	K M Pilcher	1987	C Ogle
1960	G Westling	1974	F Harris	1988	J Pugsley
1961	N Beckett	1975	C M Y Trotter	1989	J M A Thompson
1962	P Hall	1976	W H Magnay		
1963	K Pilcher	1977	D A Friend		

ROWING AND SCULLING

THE UNIVERSITY BOAT RACE

		min	s	lengths			min	s	lengths
1952	Oxford	20	23	canvas	1972	Cambridge	18	36	9½
1953	Cambridge	19	54	8	1973	Cambridge	19	21	13
1954	Oxford	20	23	4½	1974	Oxford	17	35	5½
1955	Cambridge	19	10	16	1975	Cambridge	19	27	3¾
1956	Cambridge	18	36	1¼	1976	Oxford	16	58	6½
1957	Cambridge	19	1	2	1977	Oxford	19	28	7
1958	Cambridge	18	15	3½	1978	Oxford	19	00	†
1959	Oxford	18	52	6	1979	Oxford	20	33	3½
1960	Oxford	18	59	1	1980	Oxford	19	20	canvas
1961	Cambridge	19	22	4¼	1981	Oxford	18	11	8
1962	Cambridge	19	46	5	1982	Oxford	18	21	3¼
1963	Oxford	20	47	5	1983	Oxford	19	7	4½
1964	Cambridge	19	18	6½	1984	Oxford	16	45*	3¾
1965	Oxford	18	17	4	1985	Oxford	17	11	4¾
1966	Oxford	19	12	3½	1986	Cambridge	17	58	7
1967	Oxford	18	52	3½	1987	Oxford	20	11	4
1968	Cambridge	18	22	3½	1988	Oxford	17	35	5½
1969	Cambridge	18	4	4	1989	Oxford	18	27	2½
1970	Cambridge	20	22	3	1990	Oxford	17	15	2¼
1971	Cambridge	17	58	10					

* Record time   †Cambridge sank   Won: Cambridge 69   Oxford 66: 1 dead heat

RUGBY LEAGUE

LEAGUE CHAMPIONS

1950–1	Workington T	1964–5	Halifax	1977–8	Widnes
1951–2	Wigan	1965–6	St Helens	1978–9	Hull K R
1952–3	St Helens	1966–7	Wakefield T	1979–80	Bradford N
1953–4	Warrington	1967–8	Wakefield T	1980–1	Bradford N
1954–5	Warrington	1968–9	Leeds	1981–2	Leigh
1955–6	Hull	1969–70	St Helens	1982–3	Hull
1956–7	Oldham	1970–1	St Helens	1983–4	Hull K R
1957–8	Hull	1971–2	Leeds	1984–5	Hull K R
1958–9	St Helens	1972–3	Dewsbury	1985–6	Halifax
1959–60	Wigan	1973–4	Salford	1986–7	Wigan
1960–1	Leeds	1974–5	St Helens	1987–8	Widnes
1961–2	Huddersfield	1975–6	Salford	1988–9	Widnes
1962–3	Swinton/Hunslet	1976–7	Featherstone R	1989–90	Wigan
1963–4	Swinton/Oldham				

CHALLENGE CUP WINNERS

1950	Warrington	1964	Widnes	1978	Leeds
1951	Wigan	1965	Wigan	1979	Widnes
1952	Workington T	1966	St Helens	1980	Hull K R
1953	Huddersfield	1967	Featherstone R	1981	Widnes
1954	Warrington	1968	Leeds	1982	Hull
1955	Barrow	1969	Castleford	1983	Featherstone R
1956	St Helens	1970	Castleford	1984	Widnes
1957	Leeds	1971	Leigh	1985	Wigan
1958	Wigan	1972	St Helens	1986	Castleford
1959	Wigan	1973	Featherstone R	1987	Halifax
1960	Wakefield T	1974	Warrington	1988	Wigan
1961	St Helens	1975	Widnes	1989	Wigan
1962	Wakefield T	1976	St Helens	1990	Wigan
1963	Wakefield T	1977	Leeds		

RUGBY UNION

THORN-EMI COUNTY CHAMPIONS

1950	Cheshire	1964	Warwickshire	1978	N Midlands
1951	E Midlands	1965	Warwickshire	1979	Middlesex
1952	Middlesex	1966	Middlesex	1980	Lancashire
1953	Yorkshire	1967	Durham/Surrey	1981	Northumberland
1954	Middlesex	1968	Middlesex	1982	Lancashire
1955	Lancashire	1969	Lancashire	1983	Gloucestershire
1956	Middlesex	1970	Staffordshire	1984	Gloucestershire
1957	Devon	1971	Surrey	1985	Middlesex
1958	Warwickshire	1972	Gloucestershire	1986	Warwickshire
1959	Warwickshire	1973	Lancashire	1987	Yorkshire
1960	Warwickshire	1974	Gloucestershire	1988	Lancashire
1961	Cheshire	1975	Gloucestershire	1989	Durham
1962	Warwickshire	1976	Gloucestershire	1990	Middlesex
1963	Warwickshire	1977	Lancashire		

COURAGE LEAGUE

1987–8	Leicester	1988–9	Bath	1989–90	Wasps

INTERNATIONAL CHAMPIONS

1950–1	Ireland	1964–5	Wales	1977–8	Wales
1951–2	Wales	1965–6	Wales	1978–9	Wales
1952–3	England	1966–7	France	1979–80	England
1953–4	England	1967–8	France	1980–1	France
	France	1968–9	Wales	1981–2	Ireland
	Wales	1969–70	France	1982–3	France
1954–5	France		Wales		Ireland
	Wales	1970–1	Wales	1983–4	Scotland
1955–6	Wales	1971–2	Not completed	1984–5	Ireland
1956–7	England	1972–3	England	1985–6	France
1957–8	England		France		Scotland
1958–9	France		Ireland	1986–7	France
1959–60	England		Scotland	1987–8	Wales
	France		Wales		France
1960–1	France	1973–4	Ireland	1988–9	France
1961–2	France	1974–5	Wales	1989–90	Scotland
1962–3	England	1975–6	Wales		
1963–4	Scotland	1976–7	France		
	Wales				

SHOW JUMPING

ROYAL INTERNATIONAL HORSE SHOW 1989

	Country	Rider	Horse
King George V			
Gold Cup	Gt Britain	Michael Whitaker	Next Didi
Q Elizabeth Cup	Gt Britain	Janet Hunter	Everest Lisnamarrow
Grand Prix	Gt Britain	Michael Whitaker	Next Didi

HORSE OF THE YEAR SHOW 1989

Rover Classic	Gt Britain	Nick Skelton	Burmah Serenade
Norwich Union International	Gt Britain	Steven Smith	Brook Street Picnic
NM Financial International	Holland	Jos Lansink	Optiebeurs Libero

OLYMPIA INTERNATIONAL SHOW 1989

Crosse & Blackwell Grand Prix	W Ger	F Sloothaak	Optiebeurs Walzerkoenig

SNOOKER

WORLD CHAMPIONS

1927–46	J Davis (E)	1971	J Spencer (E)	1983	S Davis (E)
1947	W Donaldson (S)	1972	A Higgins (I)	1984	S Davis (E)
1948–9	F Davis (E)	1973–6	R Reardon (W)	1985	D Taylor (I)
1950	W Donaldson (S)	1977	J Spencer (E)	1986	J Johnson (E)
1951	F Davis (E)	1978	R Reardon (W)	1987	S Davis (E)
1952	H Lindrum (Aus)	1979	T Griffiths (W)	1988	S Davis (E)
1964–8	J Pulman (E)	1980	C Thorburn (Can)	1989	S Davis (E)
1969	J Spencer (E)	1981	S Davis (E)	1990	S Hendry (S)
1970	R Reardon (W)	1982	A Higgins (I)		

UNITED KINGDOM CHAMPIONS

1977	P Fagan	1982	T Griffiths	1987	S Davis
1978	D Mountjoy	1983	A Higgins	1988	D Mountjoy
1979	J Virgo	1984	S Davis	1989	S Hendry
1980	S Davis	1985	S Davis		
1981	S Davis	1986	S Davis		

MERCANTILE CREDIT CLASSIC CHAMPIONS

1984	S Davis	1987	S Davis	1989	D Mountjoy
1985	W Thorne	1988	S Davis	1990	S James
1986	J White				

ROTHMANS GRAND PRIX CHAMPIONS

R Reardon		1985	S Davis	1988	S Davis
1983	T Knowles	1986	J White	1989	S Davis
1984	D Taylor	1987	S Hendry		

BENSON & HEDGES MASTERS

1978	A Higgins	1983	C Thorburn	1988	S Davis
1979	P Mans	1984	J White	1989	S Hendry
1980	T Griffiths	1985	C Thorburn	1990	S Hendry
1981	A Higgins	1986	C Thorburn		
1982	S Davis	1987	D Taylor		

PEARL ASSURANCE BRITISH OPEN CHAMPIONS

1985	S Francisco	1987	J White	1989	T Meo
1986	S Davis	1988	S Hendry	1990	R Chaperon

CAR CARE WORLD TEAM CUP

1979	Wales	1983	England	1988	Australia
1980	Wales	1985	Ireland	1989	England
1981	England	1986	Ireland		
1982	Canada	1987	Ireland		

SPEEDWAY

WORLD CHAMPIONS

1950	F Williams (W)	1964	B Briggs (NZ)	1978	O Olsen (Denmark)
1951	J Young (Aus)	1965	B Knutsson (Sw)	1979	I Mauger (NZ)
1952	J Young (Aus)	1966	B Briggs (NZ)	1980	M Lee (E)
1953	F Williams (W)	1967	O Fundin (Sw)	1981	B Penhall (US)
1954	R Moore (NZ)	1968	I Mauger (NZ)	1982	B Penhall (US)
1955	P Craven (E)	1969	I Mauger (NZ)	1983	E Muller (W. Ger)
1956	O Fundin (Sw)	1970	I Mauger (NZ)	1984	E Gundersen (Den)
1957	B Briggs (NZ)	1971	O Olsen (Den)	1985	E Gundersen (Den)
1958	B Briggs (NZ)	1972	I Mauger (NZ)	1986	H Nielsen (Den)
1959	R Moore (NZ)	1973	J Szczakiel (Pol)	1987	H Nielsen (Den)
1960	O Fundin (Sw)	1974	A Michanek (Sw)	1988	E Gundersen (Den)
1961	O Fundin (Sw)	1975	O Olsen (Denmark)	1989	H Nielsen (Den)
1962	P Craven (E)	1976	P Collins (E)		
1963	O Fundin (Sw)	1977	I Mauger (NZ)		

SQUASH RACKETS

HI-TEC BRITISH OPEN CHAMPIONSHIP

1950–5	Hashim Khan (Pak)	1969	G B Hunt (Aus)	1984	Jahangir Khan (Pak)
1956	Roshan Khan (Pak)	1970–3	J P Barrington (GB)	1985	Jahangir Khan (Pak)
1957	Hashim Khan (Pak)	1974	G B Hunt (Aus)	1986	Jahangir Khan (Pak)
1958–61	Azam Khan (Pak)	1975	Q Zaman (Pak)	1987	Jahangir Khan (Pak)
1962	Mohibullah Khan	1976–81	G B Hunt (Aus)	1988	Jahangir Khan (Pak)
	(Pak)	1982	Jahangir Khan (Pak)	1989	Jahangir Khan (Pak)
1963–6	A A AbouTaleb	1983	Jahangir Khan (Pak)	1990	Jahangir Khan (Pak)
	(UAR)				
1967–8	J P Barrington (GB)				

TABLE TENNIS

WORLD CHAMPIONSHIP

Men

1950	R Bergmann (Eng)	1959	Jung Kuo-Tuan (China)	1975	I Jonyer (Hungary)
1951	J Leach (Eng)	1961	Chuang Tse-Tung (China)	1977	M Kohno (Japan)
1952	H Satoh (Japan)	1963	Chuang Tse-Tung (China)	1979	S Ono (Japan)
1953	F Sido (Hungary)	1965	Chuang Tse-Tung (China)	1981	Guo Yuehua (China)
1954	I Ogimura (Japan)	1967	N Hasegawa (Japan)	1983	Guo Yuehua (China)
1955	T Tanaka (Japan)	1969	S Itoh (Japan)	1985	Jiang Jialing (China)
1956	I Ogimura (Japan)	1971	S Bengtsson (Sweden)	1987	Jiang Jialing (China)
1957	T Tanaka (Japan)	1973	Hsi En-Ting (China)	1989	Jan-ove Waldner (Sweden)

Women

1950–5	A Rozeanu (Romania)	1971	Lin Hui-Ching (China)	1983	Cao Yanhua (China)
1956	T Okawa (Japan)	1973	Hu Yu-Lang (China)	1985	Cao Yanhua (China)
1957	F Eguchi (Japan)	1974	M Alexandra (Romania)	1987	He Zhili (China)
1959	K Matsuzaki (Japan)	1975	Pak Yung Sun (Korea	1989	Qiao Hong (China)
1961	Chiu Chung-Hui (China)		DPR)		
1963	K Matsuzaki (Japan)	1977	Pak Yung Sun (Korea		
1965	N Fukazu (Japan)		DPR)		
1967	S Morisawa (Japan)	1979	Ge Xinai (China)		
1969	T Kowada (Japan)	1981	Tong Ling (China)		

SPECIAL TOPIC

FOCUS ON
AMERICAN FOOTBALL

Introduction.

The game of American Football is one of the fastest growing sports in the world. In its home base of North America the game has long captured the imagination of local sports fans but in the last decade domestic leagues have begun to form throughout the world. In Europe the game has leapt in popularity in countries such as the United Kingdom, West Germany, Holland, Finland and even soccer-crazy Italy and it is these nations that are hoping for a franchise in the new World American Football League which is planned for 1991. Japan, which has already taken baseball to its heart, now has established American Football leagues as have both Australia and New Zealand. In China, when recordings of a Super Bowl are broadcast some six weeks after the game, it is estimated that 300 million people will watch.

The Schedule

The reasons for the success of this game are numerous, but all are related to the way that the National Football League (NFL) in the U.S.A. has prospered under the guidance of its recently retired Commissioner, Pete Rozelle. One of Rozelle's predecessors, Bert Bell, once said that: "On any given Sunday, any team in this league can defeat any other." This statement was undoubtedly true and remains so today. The 28 NFL teams are split into two conferences, the National (NFC) and the American (AFC). In turn these conferences are split into three geographical divisions, East, West and Central. Each team will play its own divisional rivals twice, at home and away, the rest of the 16 game schedule will be geared to its final position in the previous season. This has the effect of making the successful teams of the previous year play a tougher schedule than those that finished beneath them.

In addition to this schedule bias, the weaker teams are given another huge advantage. At the end of each season the best of the college players, whose games are followed with as much interest as the NFL itself, are drafted into the League. The team with the worst record gets the first pick from the hundreds of graduating college stars, moving on until the team that won the Super Bowl gets the final pick. This is then repeated for twelve rounds until eventually 336 highly skilled and experienced youngsters have been drafted into the NFL.

The NFL also has a structure that ensures that every team will still have a chance to be the Super Bowl Champions until late into their 16 game schedule. The winners of each of the six divisions automatically go through to the play-offs, but both conferences hold two wild card slots for the teams with the best records after the divisional winners. Ten teams therefore go into the sudden death play-offs over the Christmas and New Year holiday period but most of the other eighteen will have been fighting to the last game to try and clinch one of the wild card berths.

Popularity of American Football.

It is perhaps to television that the game owes much of its popularity – the game could have been invented for this medium. The many natural pauses are tailor-made for commercial breaks and instant replays from every imaginable angle. The spectacle of the game itself, the appearance and apparel of its participants, the cheerleaders, marching bands and capacity crowds are the result of spectacular marketing by the NFL organisation and in a sporting world where so many governing bodies seem to have become embroiled in controversy, inefficiency and amateurism, American Football's image is strong and attractive to millions of sports fans across the globe. This was proved on 26 January 1986 when Super Bowl XX became the most watched programme in recorded television history. On that day, as the Chicago Bears beat the New England Patriots, 127 million Americans, 6 million Britons, 6 million Italians and the sports fans of another 56 countries watched the game – then six weeks later so did the Chinese. In fact, of the ten most-watched programmes in recorded history, eight of them are Super Bowls.

A Brief History.

The game of American Football evolved from the College rugby and soccer games of the 1860s and it was in 1876 that the first rules of the game were drawn up at the Massasoit Convention. Back in 1867 Rutgers and Princeton played a match that has widely been recorded as the first American Football game although the rules were more like those of soccer than those of the modern game. The man who perhaps had most to do with shaping the game as we now know it was Walter Camp who, amongst other changes, brought about the five-yard pitch marks which gave the game its "Grid-iron" nickname.

The game meanwhile was also developing in Canada and when McGill University travelled south to play Harvard, four of the fifteen men were too ill to travel, so the game was played with eleven men a side thus creating a precedent that has remained unchanged.

Up to this point the game had been played mainly by middle-class Ivy League college students, but in the heart of the Mid-West, a new breed of professional player was coming into existence. In 1892 William Heffelfinger, or Pudge as he was universally known, was paid $500 to play for Allegheny Athletic Association. He lived up to their faith in him by scoring the only touchdown as local rivals from Pittsburgh were beaten 6–0. Numerous clubs were set up in this predominantly working-class area and one of these was the Morgan Athletic Club formed in 1899. Over the years the club has changed its name and location on more than one occasion and via Chicago, St. Louis and now Phoenix, seems for the time being at least to have settled as the Phoenix Cardinals, the oldest surviving franchise in the NFL.

Growing Pains.

The professional game went through a fairly rocky period for the first quarter of this century with College Football holding the main area of interest. It was in the late 1920s that the NFL began to take a more organised approach and many of the less well administered teams went to the wall. In 1933 the League was split into Eastern and Western Divisions and the first inter-divisional Championship game saw the Western Division's Chicago Bears beat the Eastern Division's New York Giants 23–21 at Wrigley Field in Chicago. Three Years later the College draft was introduced and Jay Berwanger, a half-back from the University of Chicago, was picked by the Philadelphia Eagles. Berwanger was traded to the Chicago Bears but ironically never played a game of professional football.

All through its existence the NFL had been threatened by rival leagues but most attempts foundered at an early stage. In 1959 a league was formed that seemed to have the credentials to match the NFL's superiority. Conceived by Lamar Hunt of Dallas, it was named the American Football League, successfully recruited eight franchises, organised a College draft and negotiated its own television contracts. There followed years of bitter wrangling and seemingly endless litigation which were finally settled in a series of secret meetings in 1966. The two leagues agreed to merge and expand. A four year plan of integration was agreed and during the transitional period, it was decided to hold a "World Championship" decider between the winners of each league. The first ever Super Bowl was planned for 15 January 1967.

The First 'Super Bowl'.

Nearly 62,000 people turned up to the Los Angeles Coliseum that day to watch the Green Bay Packers of the NFL play the Kansas City Chiefs from the AFL. Green Bay kept the established league's pride intact by winning 35–10, thanks to coach Vince Lombardi and an inspired display by quarter-back Bart Starr, who was voted the first-ever Super Bowl Most Valuable Player (MVP). One year later in Super Bowl II at the Orange Bowl in Miami, Starr, Lombardi and Green Bay were back again. This time they faced the AFL's Oakland Raiders who fared no better than the Chiefs, going down 33–14, and again Starr won the MVP award. Vince Lombardi then announced his retirement from the game. Sadly, two years later at the age of 57, he died of cancer. In recognition of his achievements the Super Bowl trophy was named after him.

Super Bowl III brought together two of the finest quarter-backs who have ever played professional football-Joe Nameth of the AFL's New York Jets and Johnny Unitas of the NFL's Baltimore Colts. Unitas, then a veteran, and the Colts were the clear favourites, but is was Nameth, the young pretender to the title of MVP, who led the Jets to a shock 16–7 victory and the first proof of true equality between the leagues was seen. The AFL consolidated its reputation over the next two seasons as Kansas City returned to beat the Minnesota Vikings 23–7 in Super Bowl IV and then Baltimore, who had transferred leagues, still quarter-backed by Johnny Unitas, beat the Dallas Cowboys 16–13 with almost the last kick of the game in Super Bowl V, the first such game to be played on artificial turf. It was during this 1970 season that the leagues completed their merger and each formed itself into three regional divisions introducing the first wild card and play-off games. This format, apart from the addition of a second wild card per league in 1978, remains the same today.

The Ascendancy of the Dolphins.

The next five years of Super Bowl history were dominated by two teams and two young coaches who are still at the helm of the same teams today. Although the Miami Dolphins and coach Don Shula lost Super Bowl VI to Dallas, they returned to record two consecutive victories against the Washington Redskins and the Minnesota Vikings in Super Bowls VII and VIII. In three seasons the Dolphins had won 44 of the 51 games played and created a still unbeaten record of three consecutive Super Bowl appearances.

Super Bowls IX and X saw the emergence of the Pittsburgh Steelers under the guidance of Chuck Noll. Led by quarter-back Terry Bradshaw, who picked up both MVP awards, the Steelers not only matched the Miami double but were back again three years later to win two more in succession, giving Chuck Noll the distinction of being the only coach to lead his team to four Super Bowl victories.

The 1980s saw the game progress dramatically. In spite of yet another attempted rival league, the USFL, which failed after only two full seasons, and two damaging players' strikes in 1982 and 1988, the game increased its world-wide popularity. In the United Kingdom, an inspired decision by Channel 4 television to bring the weekly American games to our screens ensured that the current teams of the San Francisco 49ers, the New York Giants, the Miami Dolphins and the Denver Broncos, along with the modern day giants of the game such as Joe Montana, Lawrence Taylor, Dan Marino and John Elway, are household names on both sides of the Atlantic.

The 1989 Season.

The 1989 season confirmed the San Francisco 49ers as the team of the eighties, Their 55–10 defeat of the Denver Broncos in New Orleans was their fourth Super Bowl triumph of the decade and quarter-back Joe Montana, now aged 33 with 3 Super Bowl MVP awards, is widely considered the greatest player of all time. The fact that San Francisco achieved their triumph with a new coach, George Seifert who had taken over from Bill Walsh (who had retired to the television commentary booth at the end of his last season), testifies to the remarkable spirit of this franchise.

The Denver Broncos, who have been the dominant AFC team, have now lost 3 of the last 4 Super Bowls and 4 out of 4 overall. They must be wondering if, for the time being at least, they have lost the chance for the ultimate prize. The regular 16 game season had seen San Francisco and Denver dominate their particular conferences and it was entirely fitting that they were the teams that lined up for Super Bowl XXIV.

For the other teams the season held much less cause for satisfaction. The once dominant Dallas Cowboys won only one of their 16 games. Dallas, dispensing with their coach Tom Landry after 29 years, also traded their brilliant running-back Hershel Walker to the ambitious Minnesota Vikings and in return received a host of young Viking hopefuls. With the addition of No. 1 draft choice, quarter-back Troy Aikman, Dallas now look set to rebuild some of their former glories. Minnesota, however, took a calculated gamble with Walker who was brought in for an all out attempt to reach the Super Bowl, a plan that seemed to be working until they came across the 49ers in the divisional play-offs when they were comprehensively beaten.

Chuck Noll and his Pittsburgh Steelers seemed to be heading the same way as Dallas, when, after two defeats by a combined total of 92–10 in their opening games, the press speculated on the end of Noll's long career. However, he rallied the Steelers to an impressive come-back which saw them reach the play-offs and throw down a real challenge for next season. Other coaches out of work included Mike Shanahan at the Los Angeles Raiders, who replaced him with the NFL's first black coach, Art Shell, a trend that will, or should, be continued as over 50% of the game's professionals are black. Houston Oilers, the league's "bad boy" team, surprisingly dismissed Jerry Glanville who led them to the play-offs. He now replaces Marion Campbell at the Atlanta Falcons.

The teams that should provide a challenge next season in the AFC are Eastern Champions Buffalo Bills and runners-up Miami, the consistent Cleveland Browns and Pittsburgh from the Central Division and Art Shell's Los Angeles Raiders from the West. In the NFC, San Francisco again will be the team to beat but close on their heels will be teams such as the Philadelphia Eagles and the New York Giants from the Eastern Division. The Green Bay Packers, after years in comparative obscurity, and San Francisco's own divisional rivals, the New Orleans Saints and the Los Angeles Rams, have all shown that they have the ability to perform at the highest level.

For the other teams it will probably be a year of continued rebuilding but because of the parity of the system there are few, if any, teams that do not hold genuine hopes of reaching a play-off position and a place in the much coveted Super Bowl XXV. As the game develops world-wide, even cities like London, Rome and Sydney can look forward to the possibility of a genuine World Championship team in the foreseeable future.

WORLD CHAMPIONSHIP SUPER BOWL WINNERS

I	Green Bay Packers	IX	Pittsburgh Steelers	XVII	Washington Redskins
II	Green Bay Packers	X	Pittsburgh Steelers	XVIII	Los Angeles Raiders
III	New York Jets	XI	Oakland Raiders	XIX	San Francisco 49ers
IV	Kansas City Chiefs	XII	Dallas Cowboys	XX	Chicago Bears
V	Baltimore Colts	XIII	Pittsburgh Steelers	XXI	New York Giants
VI	Dallas Cowboys	XIV	Pittsburgh Steelers	XXII	Washington Redskins
VII	Miami Dolphins	XV	Oakland Raiders	XXIII	San Francisco 49ers
VIII	Miami Dolphins	XVI	San Francisco 49ers	XXIV	San Francisco 49ers

DICTIONARY
OF
COMPUTING

This section in *Pears* provides a
concise glossary of the key terms
and vocabulary used in the world
of computers in the 1990s.

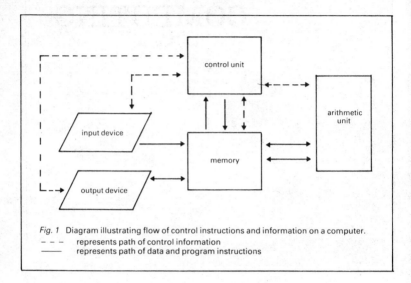

Fig. 1 Diagram illustrating flow of control instructions and information on a computer.
- - - represents path of control information
——— represents path of data and program instructions

Fig. 2

DICTIONARY OF COMPUTING

A

Access Time. Time taken to access an item of data from main memory or some device.

Accumulator. Register in the **ALU** on which all arithmetic and logical operations are performed.

Acorn. Firm which makes the BBC series of microcomputers. Now part of Olivetti.

Acoustic Coupler. Device to link a computer to the telephone network by sending sound waves to it or receiving them from it. It fits over the telephone and since there is no electrical link it is slow.

ADA. Computer language, originated at US department of defence in late 1970s. Similar to Pascal but is large and takes more time to learn.

ADC. = **Analogue to Digital Converter.**

Address. Each element in the main memory has an address so that the computer knows where to access the information it contains.

Address Bus *see* **Bus.**

AI = **Artificial Intelligence.**

ALGOL. Computer language. ALGOL60, devised in 1960 is no longer used much but was an important step in language development. ALGOL68 is a sophisticated language designed to match our own thought which can ask the computer to process instructions in **parallel.**

Algorithm. A sequence of instructions which leads to the answer to a problem, usually a mathematical one. Thus an algorithm may be used to find the square root of any specified number.

ALU. = **Arithmetic and Logical Unit.**

Amstrad. British firm which makes popular cheap word processors and microcomputers.

Analogue Computer. Type of computer which creates electrical circuitry which mimics physical systems or corresponds to sets of equations. It provides answers to certain types of problems by measuring the currents and voltages in this circuitry. *cf.* **digital computer.**

Analogue to Digital Converter. Device for measuring an electrical signal by converting it into a binary number which can be stored by a computer as data.

APL. A computer language. It is **interpretative** and **interactive**, very concise and used for mathematical applications.

Apple. American firm, one of the earliest manufacturers of microcomputers. *See* **Macintosh.**

Application Generator. Program to assist in creating other programs, thus speeding up program writing and making it easier.

Application Program. Program specific to a particular application as opposed to a **systems program** or **utility program.**

Applications Programmer. One who writes application programs.

Apricot. British firm which makes microcomputers, formerly ACT.

Architecture. Design of a computer.

Archiving. Storing data, *e.g.* on magnetic tapes, for possible retrieval later.

Arithmetic and Logical Unit. Part of a computer where all arithmetic operations such as multiplication and all logical operations such as AND operations are performed.

Array. Set of similar entities which have indices. A set of values b[1], b[2], ... b[n] is a one dimensional array. Similarly a matrix, a set of values A[i, j] where i and j are integers with a finite range of values, is a two dimensional array, because there are two indices. The entities b[i] or A[i,j] do not have to be numbers but can be anything one likes, such as other arrays or **strings.**

Array Processor. Computer capable of performing identical operations simultaneously on **arrays**, thus achieving an enormous increase in speed.

Artificial Intelligence. Apparent intelligence of computer enabling it to solve certain problems such as playing chess.

ASCII. Acronym for American Standard Code for Information Interchange. ASCII code is a code for representing all digits, both upper and lower case letters, punctuation marks and additional characters such as RETURN as numbers between 0 and 127.

Assembler. Program for converting **assembly language** instructions into machine code. *cf.* **disassemble.**

Assembly Language. Next language higher than **machine code.** Instructions are easily remembered equivalents to machine code instructions.

Asynchronous Transmission. If data communication between devices is asynchronous each character is sent on its own with a suitable start and stop element. Thus the clocks of the sending and receiving devices do not need to be synchronised over a long period of time. This saves equipment overheads but is slower than **synchronous transmission.**

Atari. US maker of microcomputers.

B

Background Job. *See* **Multitasking.**

Backing Store. Memory such as disk which is not part of the main memory of the computer and which is therefore slower.

Backup. To make a copy of material so that if original material is lost the backup remains.

Backus Naur Notation. Very compact notation for representing the **syntax** of a computer language, but difficult at first and unsuitable for learning the language.

Bandwidth. *See* **Carrier Frequency.**

Bar Chart. Way of graphically representing data as a set of bars.

Bar Code. Set of bars of varying width to be found on merchandise at a supermarket. It is read by a bar code scanner connected to a computer which returns the price.

Baseband Transmission. When data is transmitted from one device to another without modulation. *See* **Carrier Frequency.**

BASIC. Computer language, Acronym for Beginners All-purpose Symbolic Instruction Code. Originated at Dartmouth College, USA in 1960s and widely used in microcomputers. Is normally used with **interpreters** and not **compilers** but good compilers do exist.

Batch Processing. Occurs when a job for a computer is not done immediately but put in a queue along with other jobs. The batch of jobs is done when the computer is less busy, often at night. It is thus much cheaper than **on-line** or **real-time processing.**

Baud Rate. Rate at which data is transmitted in bits per second.

BBC Microcomputer. *See* **Acorn.**

BCD. Binary Coded Decimal. A representation of numbers, not in **binary** but in **denary** with each digit represented by a four bit code.

Binary. Computers usually represent numbers in binary notation, *i.e.* using 2 as a base so that the only digits allowed are 0 and 1. *e.g.* 1011 would represent the number $1 \times 2^3 + 0 \times 2^2 + 1 \times 2^1 + 1 \times 2^0 = 11$. *cf.* **denary.**

Binary Code. A complete machine code program, represented in binary.

Binary Coded Decimal. = **BCD.**

BIOS. Basic Input Output System. Part of **operating system** dealing with sending data to and from devices such as VDU or disk drives.

Bit. Unit of information which has two values, 0 or 1.

Bit Map. Representation of what is on the screen as a sequence of bits. When these bits are put together this is equivalent to a large sequence of numbers. *cf.* **raster.**

Boolean. After George Boole, Irish logician *c.* 1850. Boolean algebra is the algebra of logic, Boolean operators are logical operators and Boolean variables are ones which can just take one of two values, True or False.

Boot, Bootstrap. When a computer is started or re-started it has to load its main memory with various routines from the **backing store**, and set up various values. This process is called booting. A cold boot occurs when the machine is switched on, a warm boot when the machine is already on but reset.

Borland. US software company.

Bottom Up. Method of programming in which the detailed programming is designed first and larger units in the program are designed later, *cf.* **Top Down, Structured Programming.**

Broadcast Network. Type of network in which all nodes receive the signal transmitted by any other node. However only that node with the correct address will retain the message.

Bubble Memory. Type of serial access memory which is based on moving around magnetic bubbles in a magnetic film.

Bucket. The **backing store** can be regarded as divided into well divided regions called buckets.

Buffer Memory. Temporary store for data being transmitted from one device to another. It is to prevent the computer being delayed from other operations while the slow process of transmission takes place.

Bug. An error in a program.

Bus. Pathway along which data travels. It usually consists of many lines in parallel. Data stored in the main memory travels along the data bus. An address bus is also required to tell the memory element with that address to store the data transmitted by the data bus or alternatively to transmit its own contents.

Bus Topology. Network topology in which there is a main transmission bus and all the **nodes** and **terminals** are connected to it by T-junctions.

Byte. Sequence of 8 **bits.** A byte can represent any number between 0 and 2^8-1.

C

C. Computer language which contains both the elements of **assembly language** and a high level language, thus allowing both the execution speed and precision of assembly language as well as the structured programming of a high level language. **The Unix Operating System** is largely programmed in C.

Cables. For connecting devices. Coaxial cable is a conducting wire in the centre surrounded by insulator surrounded by another conductor and is expensive. Twisted wire is just a pair of twisted wires which is cheaper but can pick up electrical interference more easily. Ribbon cable is a set of several parallel wires laid out like a ribbon.

Cache Memory. Very high speed memory in a powerful computer into which data and instructions are loaded from main memory ready for execution.

CAD. Computer Aided Design, a computer system to aid the design of new products. It will comprise sophisticated graphics software, and a memory retrieval system.

Cambridge Ring. Network with **ring topology.**

Carrier Frequency. When information is transmitted over a long distance the electrical signal is usually modulated with a carrier frequency so that frequencies on either side of the carrier are required to transmit the signal. The difference between highest and lowest frequency is the **bandwidth.**

Cassette. A form of **serial access** backing store often used with microcomputers. Ordinary radio-cassettes and cassette drives can be used but they are much slower and more inconvenient than floppy disks.

Cathode Ray Tube. = **CRT.**

CDC. Control Data Corporation, a US computer manufacturer.

Central Processor Unit. = **CPU.**

Centronics Interface. Interface between two devices allowing **parallel transmission** of data in one direction only. Is commonly used by microcomputers to output to printers.

Character. Is a letter of either case, or a digit or punctuation mark or other symbol. Can be represented by a number between 0 and 255 as in **ASCII** and hence by a single **byte.**

Check Bit. Additional bit which is added to a series of bits to check whether they are correct. Used when data is transmitted.

Chip. = **Integrated Circuit.**

Chip Card, Intelligent Card, Smart Card. Card with magnetic strip on it containing personal details, such as bank balance, credit limit.

CISC. Complex Instruction Set Computer, reverse of **RISC.**

Clock. Each computer has a clock which synchronises operations inside it. The clock speed for personal computers is of the order of 8 MHz, but for a powerful mainframe may be 100 MHz, thus enabling it to run much faster. Also the mainframe may be able to perform more in a single clock cycle.

Clone. Computer of similar design to another computer. *See* **Compatible.**

CMOS. Complementary Metal Oxide Silicon. A type of silicon chip with both p-channel and n-channel transistors requiring very little power.

Coaxial Cable. *See* **Cable.**

COBOL. Computer language widely used in a business environment.

Collating Sequence. When **sorting** is done a collating sequence is used to define which **key** comes first. Normally "a" comes before "b" but the collating sequence might be redefined so that the order is different.

Command. This is a command which is interpreted by the **operating system** and not by a language. *cf.* **statement.**

Command Mode. Often BASIC interpreters allow the user to send BASIC instructions to be executed immediately by the computer instead of being part of a program. Such a statement is not normally preceded by a line number. Thus "PRINT 3.4*5.6" is executed immediately and not as part of a program.

Commodore. American computer manufacturer.

Compact Disk. = **Optical Disk.**

Compatible. Usually refers to a computer of similar design to some other computer and which can use the same software and peripherals.

Compiler. Program for converting programs written in a high-level language into machine code or assembly language.

Complementary Metal Oxide Silicon. = **CMOS.**

Computer Aided Design. = **CAD.**

Console. Keyboard and VDU which control a computer.

Coprocessor. Add-on for a computer which may either be placed inside it or outside connected by a cable. It often performs functions which would otherwise be performed by the host computer. A floating-point coprocessor would intercept all commands to perform floating-point operations and do them itself.

Copy Protection. Techniques to prevent unauthorized copies of software working such as putting laser burn marks on a floppy which cannot be copied.

CP/M. Control Program for Microcomputers. An early **operating system** for 8 bit microcomputers written by Digital Research.

cps. Characters per second. Measure of printer speed.

CPU. Central Processor Unit. The heart of a computer which comprises the control unit and the **ALU.** The control unit runs the computer and decodes machine code instructions making them ready for execution.

CRT. = Cathode Ray Tube. Most VDUs use CRTs as a screen. A beam of electrons is fired at a fluorescent screen. The direction of the beam is varied to strike the screen at different parts. On striking the screen that part of the screen fluoresces and appears bright.

Cursor. This is usually a flashing arrow on the screen which indicates the point on the screen where the next character that is typed appears.

D

DAC. = Digital to Analogue Converter.

Daisywheel Printer. Commonly used with microprocessors. All the permitted characters are embossed on a wheel called the daisywheel. The wheel is rotated until the correct character is opposite the ribbon and a hammer strikes the daisywheel on the opposite side pressing the daisy wheel into the ribbon and against the paper, causing the character to be printed. The daisywheel is then moved one character length horizontally, ready for the next character to be printed. At the end of a line the paper is wound on as in an ordinary typewriter. Output is usually of high quality but slow and noisy.

Data Base/Bank. This is a large store of knowledge, usually too big to be stored in the main memory and which is normally held on a magnetic disk for random access. The design of data bases is an important branch of computing, but basically there are three types, hierarchical, network and relational. The relational is currently most favoured. The Data Base Administrator (DBA) is the person in charge of the Data Base. The Data Base Management System (DBMS) is a suite of programs which allow the DBA to define the files that are kept, their names and how they are updated. The Query Language allows a user to interrogate a Data Base. The Schema is a complete description of the files kept. A Sub-Schema is a sub-set of this available to a particular user. In a large system different users will have access to different information and hence to different sub-schemas. The Dictionary is a file containing the names of all the files and the names and types of their fields, *etc.*

Data Capture. Refers to acquisition of data which may take place in many ways, some of which are manual, like typing in people's addresses, others automatic such as converting voltages into numbers using an ADC and automatically recording them on a disk.

Data Communication. The transfer of data from one device or computer to another.

Data Processing. The processing of data to obtain information in a form that can be readily assimilated or presented as a report to users. The Data Processing Manager is usually a senior person in an organisation.

DBMS. *See* **Data Base.**

Debug. Remove **bugs,** *i.e.* errors from a program.

DEC. Digital Electronic Corporation, a US computer manufacturer which specialises in medium size computers, *e.g.* the **VAX** and in networks. It is after IBM and Unisys in size.

Decision Table. Table in a special format which shows what set of actions to take in any set of contingencies.

Dedicated. Designed to do a particular job. Thus any computer with the right set of programs can act as a word processor but a dedicated word processor is a computer specially designed to do this.

Default Value. Value a computer or program assumes to be correct unless the user states the contrary. *e.g.* a program may assume the number of days in a year is 365, as default, but give the user the opportunity to change this to 366.

Demodulator. Device to convert a modulated electrical signal back to its original form. *See* **Carrier Frequency.**

Denary. The way we ourselves represent numbers using 10 as a base so that $123 = 1 \times 10^2 + 2 \times 10^1 + 3 \times 10^0$. *cf.* **binary.**

Desktop Publishing. Usually refers to the organising of text and graphics so that a computer can create an output like a newspaper, *i.e.* with text and graphics of any size and at any place.

Device Driver. A piece of software which enables a computer to send output to a particular device. *e.g.* to enable an IBM PC to write to an Epsom FX85 printer, the PC will need a device driver which will cause it to send the coded signals that the Epsom will understand, along with the text, through its output port to the printer. A laser printer would require a different device driver.

DFS. Disk Filing System. *See* **DOS.**

Diagnostics. Routines which tell the user where the errors in his work lie. Thus one compiler may have better diagnostics than another, making it easier for a programmer to correct the faults in his program.

Digital Computer. Most computers are digital. They are like digital watches in which the time can only change by discrete steps, unlike analogue watches with hands which move continuously from one position to another. In digital computers numbers change discontinuously but because numbers are represented by many significant figures digital computers are more accurate than **analogue computers**. For certain types of problems analogue computers are faster.

Digital Research. US software company which produces the **CP/M operating system, GEM** and WIMP.

Digital to Analogue Converter. DAC, device for converting a number into a voltage equal to that number.

Direct Access Memory. = **RAM.**

Direct Instruction. Instruction in **command mode.**

Disable. *See* **Enable.**

Disassemble. Opposite process to assemble, turn Machine Code instructions into **assembly language.**

Disk/Disc. *See* **Floppy, Hard Disk, Optical Disk.**

Disk Drive. Device for reading and writing information from a disk.

Disk Operating System/Disk Filing System *see* **DOS.**

Diskette = **Floppy.**

DOS. Disk Operating System, the part of the **operating system** which manages input/output to files on the floppy or hard disks. In **PCs** it may mean more than this, being the whole operating system and which is loaded into the computer from disk.

Dot Matrix Printer. A printer whose characters are a matrix of small dots, sometimes 9 by 5, but often more. It prints by striking pins through a ribbon against the paper. Such printers are capable of up to 240 **cps** and noisy. It is not restricted to a set of characters like a **daisywheel** but may make a copy of anything on the screen, such as graphs or generate new characters. It can often operate in two modes, Draft which is fast and of poor quality, and Near Letter Quality (NLQ), which is usually slower and of a quality approaching that of a daisywheel. This may be achieved by increasing the matrix grid by moving the head and paper very slightly and striking the character four times with different sets of pins.

Download. Memory to memory transfer of data from a large computer to a small one. *cf.* **upload.**

Drum. Drum coated with magnetic material for **backing store** similar in principle to a **hard disk.**

Dumb Terminal. A terminal to a computer which has little or no processing capability of its own.

Dump. Transfer of data from one medium to another, often for security or to scrutinise it.

Duplex. Mode of transmission between two devices. Full duplex means data can pass in either direction simultaneously. Half Duplex means in both directions but not simultaneously and Simplex means it can pass in one direction only.

Dynamic RAM. This form of solid state memory consists of charged capacitors. Since there is always a current leakage it has to be recharged from time to time. At this time the memory is in Burst Mode and is unavailable for other uses.

E

EAROM/EAPROM. Electrically Alterable ROM. A ROM which can be reprogrammed electrically without losing all its memory or having to be removed from its socket.

EBCDIC Code. An 8-bit character code rather like ASCII which is largely used with IBM equipment.

EFTPOS. Electronic Fund Transfer at Point Of Sale. Enables customers with a magnetic card to have money electronically transferred from their bank to the shop where they buy goods.

Eight Bit Microprocessor. A microprocessor such as the MOS Technology 6502 that the BBC and the Apple use, whose internal registers have 8 bits.

Electromagnetic Eavesdropping. Computers, especially their VDUs can generate electromagnetic radiation which can be picked up from outside and decoded. This can be prevented by screening, *i.e.* enclosing rooms in a wire mesh, radio jamming and other techniques. It is not illegal.

Electronic Mail. Many large organisations have an internal electronic mail system by which a user can send a message to be placed in the electronic mail box at some specified address. When the user of that address logs in he will be told he has mail and he can have it displayed and printed out if he wishes. Telex is a world-wide electronic mail system.

Embedded Command. Files created by word processors contain embedded commands. Such a command may state where the margins are, whether text is to be underlined or not, *etc.*

Emulation. A computer may have software which allows it to 'emulate' another computer, *i.e.* imitate it and run the same programs.

Enable. To enable a device is to make it active. Thus to enable a printer is to cause it to start printing.

'Disable' is the reverse process so that if the screen is disabled what the user types no longer appears on the screen.

Encipher/Encrypt. Encipher the data of some file so that it cannot be read by someone who does not have the password.

Environment Manager. There now exist software packages for microcomputers providing an environment in which many applications packages can be run. These perform tasks such as drawing, graph plotting, desktop publishing, word processing, data communications, spreadsheets, *etc.* and can use a **mouse** for convenience. Such environment managers are the **Macintosh** system, produced by **Apple**, **GEM** produced by **Digital Research**, Windows produced by **Microsoft**, *etc.* Each manager has its own suite of **device drivers** allowing output to a wide range of printers, graph plotters and screens, *etc.* Application packages are not interchangeable between environment managers.

EPROM. Erasable Programmable Read Only Memory. ROM chip which can be programmed. The contents of the ROM can be erased by placing in a container which exposes it to ultraviolet radiation. It can then be reprogrammed.

Ethernet. Widely used **local area network** with **bus architecture**, **broadcast system** and which is connected with **coaxial cable**.

Exception Reporting. A system by which something is only brought to the attention of the manager or operator if it lies outside certain limits, *e.g.* if the temperature of a building falls below 10°C or above 30°C a report is automatically made by the computer in control and sent to the manager. Similarly if profits on a product fall below zero the directors would be notified automatically.

Expansion Board/Card. Cards containing a large amount of electronic circuitry which can be inserted into a microcomputer to give it extra capabilities such as displaying on two screens.

Expert System. Form of **data base**, a wide body of knowledge in a computer which enables it to give expert replies to a particular field of questions. It differs from an ordinary Data Base because it interrogates the user at several stages and at the final stage comes out with a number of possible answers.

F

Facsimile Transmission/Fax. Transfer of information in the form of a printed page, *i.e.* as a photocopy. This involves transmitting far more bytes of information than just transmitting text.

Fanfold Paper. A very long strip of paper folded backwards and forwards into sheets. The paper lies in a box and the printer draws it out as it prints. The sheets are separated by tearing along the folds or by cutting.

Feedback. Negative feedback is designed to produce an effect opposite to naturally occurring oscillations and hence to cause stability. Positive feedback is the reverse and leads to instability. *See* Process Control.

Field *see* **Record.**

Field Effect Transistor FET, type of **transistor** with high gain, *i.e.* amplification.

Fifth Generation Computer. Computers still in planning stage. To be capable of at least 100 Megaflops, **parallel processing and constructed using VLSI.** Will be able to use **non-procedural languages** and **expert systems**.

File. Material stored under a single name, the name of the file in a medium such as disk or magnetic tape. The material could be a program, data or text, *etc.*

Firmware. Software which has been frozen into a chip or set of chips so that it can only be changed by replacing the chip(s).

First Generation Computer. Early computer using thermionic valves before invention of transistors.

First Generation Language. Machine code or assembly language.

Floating Point Number. Number which can have a decimal point in it, such as $1.3 * 10^9$ and does not have to be an integer.

Floppy. A light round disk coated with magnetic material inside a protective envelope designed for the storage of up to 2 MBytes of information. The **disk drive** rotates the disk inside the sta-

tionary envelope and its read/write head is positioned above a radial slot in the envelope. The head can move along the slot and thereby access all of the surface of the disk for reading and writing. Widely used on microcomputers for **non-volatile** storage of programs and data.

Flow Chart. Diagrammatic representation of a program indicating how the computer flows from one part of the program to another as it executes it instructions.

Foreground Job. In multitasking the job which has priority over all other jobs.

Format. A magnetic track is divided into concentric tracks and each track is divided by radial lines drawn from the centre into sectors. Formatting is preparing the surface of a disk for use by a particular computer. The computer itself can usually perform this. PC compatible computers can usually read each other's disks but the BBC micro and the Apple are different.

FORTRAN. The earliest high level computer language, developed in 1954 by IBM. Still in wide use for scientific purposes and now exists in several dialects.

Fourth Generation Computer. Very powerful computers already in existence using LSI and sometimes capable of **parallel processing**.

Fourth Generation Language/4GL. Language supporting **non-procedural programming**, a **data base**, control over graphics and presentation of reports, user friendly and human orientated.

Friction Feed. Situation where the paper in a printer is held by friction between two rubber wheels which drive it forward when required *cf.* **tractor-feed**.

Function Keys. Keys on microcomputers which can be programmed to represent many key strokes. Pressing such a key is equivalent to a **macro**, *i.e.* pressing a specified sequence of keys in succession.

G

Gallium Arsenide. Alternative to silicon for making transistors. Harder to work with but much faster and resistant to electromagnetic radiation. May eventually replace silicon for some applications.

Garbage Collection. Removal of unwanted files from the disk or other storage medium. Performed regularly on main frames.

Gate. Device to perform a logical operation such as AND or OR. It has several inputs and just one output whose value depends on the inputs. In a binary digital computer each input can take just one of two values which may be voltages. These can be represented by 0 and 1. The same applies to the output. Logic, O, is usually equivalent to false and 1 to true. An AND gate produces output equal to true only when all the inputs are true and output false when any input is false. Similarly an OR gate produces an output equal to true if any of the inputs are true.

GEM. Graphics Environment Manager. *See* **Environment Manager.**

Gigabyte. One thousand million **bytes**.

Gigaflop. One thousand million floating-point operations per sec.

Glitch. Unwanted electrical pulse.

Golf Ball Printer. Similar in operation to a **daisywheel** except that the characters are embossed on a small cylinder called a golf ball instead of a daisywheel. The golf ball has to be able to move up and down as well as rotate.

Graphics. The art of displaying graphs, pictures and designs on a screen, causing 3 dimensional objects to appear to rotate, zooming pictures, *etc.*

H

Hacking. Now normally means obtaining unauthorized access to files on computers and which has become illegal in many countries.

Handshake. When two devices are put into communication handshaking signals have to pass between them to ensure there is proper communication.

Hard copy. The output of data on to some large scale physical medium such as the printer.

Hard Disk. Type of **backing store**. One or more disks coated with magnetic material, mounted on a spindle and rotating continuously. There may be several read/write heads for reading from and writing to the disk. These can move radially so as to access all **tracks** on the disk. Some disks are removable from the drive. Winchester disks are a special type of non-removable hard disk which are sealed from the atmosphere and widely used on microcoputers since they have become relatively cheap.

Hardwired. A program that is hardwired into a computer is an integral part of the computer and cannot readily be changed, see **firmware**.

Hash (1) Character looking like '♯'. (2) Method of allocating storage to records in random access memory. The key is used to generate a hash address where the record is stored by a pseudo-random algorithm. The algorithm ensures there is a roughly even distribution of records over the memory space.

Head Crash. Occurs when the read/write head of a computer disk drive crashes into the disc and physical damage is done and data lost.

Hex/Hexadecimal Representation. Numbers in hex are represented to base 16. In addition to digits 0 to 9, the characters A to F are required, representing 10 to 15. Thus 1B3 is a number in hex but 1G3 is not.

High Level Language. A language in which a single instruction such as $x = (5 + y) \times 3$ may have to be broken down into several instructions in a low level language such as **assembly language**.

Host. In a network there may be several computers which do the processing required by users at the terminals. Such computers are called 'hosts'. A user may sometimes determine which host he uses.

I

IBM. International Business Machines, US computer manufacturer, easily the largest in the world.

IBM Compatible. A microcomputer that is IBM compatible can readily exchange software and peripherals with the IBM Personal Computer.

Icon. Symbol that appears on the screen to indicate the type of a particular file. Used by **environment managers.**

Impact Printer. Printer that works by striking something against the paper, *e.g.* **daisywheel, golf ball, matrix, line printer.**

Inference Engine. Part of **expert system** that draws conclusions from data supplied.

Ink Jet Printer. Printer which works by firing drops of ink at the paper. Is fast, very quiet and can print in many colours.

Integer. In programming an integer variable can only hold integers.

Integrated Circuit. Complex circuit on a chip containing many transistors. *See* **LSI, VLSI.**

Intel. US manufacturer of chips. The Intel 8086, 8088, 80286 and 80386 are all **microprocessors** used in the IBM range of PCs.

Intelligent Terminal. Terminal which has considerable processing capability of its own.

Interactive. Interactive computing is when the user is continually interacting with the computer.

Interface. Often means a device which is inserted between two other devices to enable them to interact.

International Business Machines = IBM.

Interpreter. Program that accepts one line of a program at a time and converts it into machine code instructions for immediate execution. Interpreters execute programs more slowly than compiled programs because when a statement is in a loop it has to be interpreted each time the program goes round the loop whereas a compiler only compiles the statement once. Interpreters are often used with **BASIC** on microcomputers with small memories because the interpreter is usually a much smaller program than a compiler and the compiled program is much larger than the **source program.** Also the user does not have to wait for the source program to be compiled.

Interrupt. It enables a microprocessor to handle many devices simultaneously. Such a device will send an interrupt to the microprocessor which will then suspend operations in order to execute a routine to deal with the interrupt and then return to its previous operations. A maskable interrupt is one that can be disabled by software and does not require immediate attention, whereas a non-maskable interrupt cannot be disabled and must always be serviced immediately.

J

Joystick. A device like a car gear lever which can be attached to a microcomputer and which can move a figure round the screen. Often used for games.

Justification. In word processing left-justification ensures the text on a line starts at the left-hand margin. Right-justification means the line is filled out with spaces or whatever to ensure the last word on a line ends on the right margin. Also refers, when printing out numbers in a table, to ensuring numbers in the same column have their decimal points aligned above and below each other.

K

Key *see* **Record.**

Kilobyte. One thousand **bytes.**

Knowledge Engineer. A programmer who designs an **expert system.**

L

LAN = Local Area Network.

Language. Means of expressing instructions in a way a computer with a suitable **translator** will understand.

Laptop, Lap Computer = Portable Computer.

Large Scale Integration = LSI.

Laser Disk = Optical Disk.

Laser Printer. Printer using a laser. Such printers are very fast and quiet but do not normally print in colour and usually use **sheet feed.** Their price is coming down so rapidly they are being used with microcomputers. They can print any picture and not just characters. They store a whole page in their internal memory at a time. This means the **resolution** with which they print pictures or graphs depends on the amount of memory they have.

LCD = Liquid Crystal Display.

Lexical Scan. Stage in compilation. The replacement of **reserved words** in a program written in a high level language with tokens, *i.e.* special characters which mean that word. Also the recognition of variables as such.

Light Pen. Wand with photosensitive cell at its tip. Such a pen can be used to read **bar codes** and other **optical marks.** It can also be used to draw on whatever part of the screen it is placed over.

Line Feed. Character which when sent to a printer causes it to advance one line. It does not cause a carriage return which requires a separate character.

Line Printer. Impact printer commonly used with main frames or minicomputers which prints out a line of text at a time. Normally used with tractor feed and fanfold paper, printing out the results of each job after it has been completed. The usual mechanism is to have a wheel with embossed characters on it at each character position. All the wheels are simultaneously rotated until the correct character is opposite the paper. They are linked and together pressed into the paper. Line printers do not normally print lower case characters. Variants of the line printer are the barrel printer and chain printer.

Line Spacing. In typing and word processing the spacing between lines of text.

Linker, Linkage Editor. Program which is able to combine separately compiled programs into a single object code which is ready for execution when called.

Liquid Crystal Display (LCD). Used in digital watches and pocket calculators. Liquid crystals change their reflectivity when current is passed through them but do not emit light. They use very little power so they have virtually replaced Light Emitting Diodes which require more power.

LISP. List Processing Language. A symbol manipulation language originated at MIT in 1965. LISP operates solely on groups of symbols. It is widely used in **Artificial Intelligence.**

List. To list a program or file is to print it out, either on a VDU or on paper.

Local Area Network (LAN). Network over a small area such as a building or buildings on the same site.

Logic Bomb. Code deliberately inserted into a program to cause it to behave unexpectedly when triggered by some event. The planting of logic bombs is usually malicious and criminal and can cause enormous expense.

LOGO. Interactive language designed in the late 1960s for teaching children.

LSI. Large Scale Integration. Technique of making **Integrated Circuits** with 100 to 1000 transistors per chip.

M

Machine Code. The language of the computer itself. All programs written in other languages have to be converted to machine code before execution.

Macintosh. Widely used microcomputer produced by **Apple Computers.** A large number of general purpose application packages can be purchased for it. Its desktop publishing and drawing facilities were pioneers in this field. *See* **Environment Manager.** It was originally designed for people to use the application packages rather than write their own programs although compilers are now available. It is not IBM compatible.

Macro. Sequence of key strokes or characters. Some word processors have macro facility so that if the same set of key strokes are often used a macro can be defined to be that set. Then the macro can be called instead of making all the key strokes. Macros have a similar meaning in **assembly language** but here are assumed to be a set of instructions.

Main Frame. Powerful computer with a large number of peripherals which can support a **multiuser operating system** and a **network.** Cost usually over £150,000.

Main Memory. This is usually the solid state memory of a computer and which is used for rapidly storing and retrieving data while calculations are being performed. *See* **Memory.**

Megabyte. One million **bytes.**

Megaflop. One million floating point instructions per sec. *cf.* **MIPS.**

Memory. Region of computer where it can store information and recall it when necessary. There are a large number of methods in use. *See* **Main Memory, RAM, Dynamic RAM, Volatile Memory, Non-Volatile Memory, Disc, Cache Memory, Virtual Memory.**

Microcode/Microprogram. Programs which are at a lower level than machine code and are hardwired into the **CPU.** A machine code instruction such as addition calls up the microcode routine which executes this instruction.

Microcomputer. Small computer which can sit on a desk and probably costs under £10,000. The **CPU** consists of a single chip called a microprocessor.

Microprocessor. Single chip designed to act as the **CPU** of a computer.

Microsoft. US software company which created the MSDOS **operating system** for IBM compatibles.

Minicomputer. Computer between a microcomputer and a mainframe in size costing roughly between £10,000 and £200,000. It will be capable of acting as **host** computer to a network if required.

MIPS. Unit of computer speed, million instructions per sec. This is somewhat different from a **Megaflop** since an instruction may be simpler than a floating-point operation but on the other hand in **parallel processing** may represent many operations carried out in parallel.

Modem. Short for Modulator-demodulator. *See* **Carrier Frequency.** An interface required when an electrical signal is to be transmitted to or received from a long distance. Sometime used to mean **acoustic coupler.**

Modula. Computer language. Development of Pascal, allowing structured programming and

including methods of describing **parallel processing.**

Module. Self contained part of a program. It is recommended that a large program be developed in modules, water tight compartments. This reduces the number of logical paths through the program and simplifies the debugging and testing procedures. A module should interface with the rest of the program through as few parameters as possible.

Monitor. (1) **VDU.** (2) **Operating system** or control program.

Monolithic. Describes structure of program. It means it is not divided into modules and is only recommended for small programs.

MOS. Metal Oxide Silicon. A silicon chip has these three layers. The metal is a conductor, the oxide is an insulator and the silicon is a semiconductor.

MOSFET. Metal Oxide Silicon Field Effect Transistor. A **field effect transistor** based on silicon.

Motherboard. Printed circuit board holding the main components of a computer.

Motorola. US manufacturer of chips.

Mouse. Device which is placed on a flat surface and moved about on it. When attached to a microcomputer this causes a cursor on the screen to follow its motion. It provides a very convenient method of manipulating the cursor and **environment managers** are usually designed for a mouse although the cursor can be moved using the cursor keys instead.

MSDOS. The **operating system** designed by Microsoft for 16 bit microprocessors and IBM compatibles.

Multiplexer. Device to accept input from several channels and output the same data through one channel. The multiplexer serves each channel in turn, often for a given **time-slice.** The output from the multiplexer may be processed by a computer or transmitted a long distance. It then passes through a demultiplexer which causes the data to be split up into several channels as appropriate. A multiplexer is an economy device which allows an expensive item to do the work of several.

Multitasking. This occurs when a computer has several tasks on hand simultaneously. It may **time-slice** the tasks. Alternatively some tasks have priority and go into the **foreground** while others go into the background.

Multiuser. This is more sophisticated than **multitasking.** A multiuser **operating system** allows a computer to undertake work submitted by several users simultaneously, often by **time-slicing.**

N

Network. Set of devices such as the telephone system which are linked and can transmit data to and from each other.

Nibble. 4 bits, *i.e.* half a **byte.**

Node. In **networks** a node is an interconnection between several lines.

Noise. In electronics this is a random signal. When it is significant compared with the intended signal errors in data communication arise. When listening to radio this causes an undesirable background noise.

Non-Procedural Language. Computer language in which the user specifies the desired result rather than the means by which it is achieved.

Non-Volatile Memory. Memory whose contents are retained when the computer is switched off. Disks, tapes and cassettes are non-volatile. Solid state memory is usually volatile although computers often have batteries which maintain a small amount of CMOS memory.

O

Object Code/Program. After a program (**source code**) written in a high level language has been compiled the result is an object code. It is a machine code program ready for execution.

Occam. Computer language designed for the **transputer,** exploiting its **parallel processing** capability.

OCR = Optical Character Recognition.

Octal. Representation of numbers using 8 as a base.

Offline. A device is offline when it is not being driven by the computer to which it is attached. It is then driven by its own controls. The reverse of **online**.

OMR = Optical Mark Recognition.

One's Complement. Way of storing negative numbers. All the binary digits are reversed, 1 becoming 0 and vice versa. Hence 0 has two representations. *cf.* **two's complement**.

Online. A device which is online is accepting commands from a computer. *cf.* **Offline.**

Online Processing. This refers to processing that is done while the user waits. It is often done at a terminal connected to a powerful computer which serves many terminals. *cf.* **batch processing, real time processing.**

Opcode. In a machine or assembly language instruction an opcode is the part which states which operation is to be performed, *e.g.* copy, multiply. The other part is the operand part, which may for example contain the address of the number to be operated on.

Open. A file cannot be read from or written to until it has been opened for reading or writing or both. A program using a data file should include a statement to open that file and after use a statement to close it.

Open Systems Interconnection. This is an attempt to standardise data communication over a **wide area network.** It is based on seven layers. Data passing from a user at A to a user at B goes down from layer 7 at A to layer 1 with **protocol** messages added at each layer. It is then transmitted to B and stripped of these additions as it rises from layer 1 to 7 and passed to the user.

Operand. Something that is operated on.

Operating System. Program or set of programs that allow the user to interface with the computer. It provides the user with a set of commands such as running a program, copying files, obtaining a list of stored files, *etc.* The operating system can be replaced by another or updated if required.

Operator. (1) Person who controls a computer as opposed to one who just uses it. (2) In mathematics an operator transforms an entity or entities into something else. Thus the multiplication operator acting on 5 and 3 produces 15, the operator $+1$ acting on 4 gives 5.

Optical Character Recognition, OCR. Techniques of scanning printed text, recognising the characters and storing them.

Optical Disk (Compact Disk, Laser Disk). An optical disk can store over 2 **gigabytes.** There are various technologies for writing to an optical disk. Some require that it be done by the manufacturer, others allow the user to write on it once, others many times. A laser is used to read from the disk.

Optical Fibre. An optical fibre can carry far more information than a copper wire of the same size. Because it does this in the form of light it is not subject to electrical interference and transmission losses are also much lower. Optical fibre is replacing ordinary wire for communications.

Optical Mark Recognition, OMR. Technique for recognising marks such as ink filled squares or **bar codes.**

Optimisation. The attempt to produce the best possible. A compiler with optimisation tries to produce extra efficient code which will run faster at execution time. Optimisation is also a branch of numerical analysis which deals with minimising functions.

Oracle. Relational **data base** produced by Relational Software which supports the data base language SQL.

OSI = Open Systems Interconnection.

P

PABX = Private Automatic Branch Exchange.

Package. Usually refers to a suite of programs.

Packet Switching. Method of communication over long distance by dividing messages into packets. Each packet is sent to its destination and there they are reassembled into the message. Packets may take different routes as this makes more economical use of the telephone lines.

Parallel Connection. When two devices are connected in parallel the data does not just pass down a single wire but several wires simultaneously. Thus a byte might pass through 8 wires. Parallel is good for transmission over short distances as the overhead of extra wires is less. *cf.* **Serial Connection.**

Parallel Interface. When two devices are connected in parallel each requires a parallel interface, an electronic device for emitting and receiving the signals.

Parallel Processing. Some computers are able to do many calculations simultaneously. This is known as parallel processing. This is not the same as multitasking where tasks are divided into **time-slices** which are performed sequentially although the computer may be so fast they appear to be performed simultaneously.

Parity Bit Checking. This occurs if when a character is transmitted an extra bit is transmitted and is chosen so that the sum of bits is always either even or odd. If the received character is checked and found to have the wrong parity the character has to be retransmitted. Since it is statistically unlikely that two bits will be incorrect in one character this is effective in removing errors.

Pascal. Computer language. Originated in Zurich *c.* 1970, designed for **structured programming** and allows complex data structures.

Password. Used for security. A password will probably be required to log in at a computer terminal. Further passwords may be required in order to access certain files.

PC Compatible. More or less equivalent to **IBM Compatible.** PC is short for Personal Computer.

PCB = Printed Circuit Board.

PCDOS. Operating system for IBM PC. Almost identical to **MSDOS.**

Peek. To read a memory cell of a computer by directly addressing it. *cf.* **Poke.**

Peripheral. Device which can be attached to a computer such as a printer, disk drive, *etc.*

PICK. Operating system named after its designer, Richard Pick. It includes a **relational database management system,** a **query language,** a version of **BASIC,** a stored procedure processor that allows the production of sequences of commands and various facilities concerning input and output.

Pie Graph. Graph presenting a distribution as a pie with slices in it. *e.g.* in expenditure the size of a particular slice would be proportional to the expenditure on the item that slice represents.

PIN = Personal Identification Number.

Pipelining. Pipelining is where the operands of an instruction appear to pass through a pipe. Before the result emerges other instructions have entered the pipe. The pipe contains several instructions in different stages of execution. Pipelining speeds up execution and is now even applied to microcomputers.

Pitch. In typing and word processing the pitch is the number of characters printed per inch in horizontal movement.

Pixel. In **raster graphics** a pixel is the smallest element that can be displayed. Higher **resolution** requires more pixels per square inch.

Poke. To alter a memory cell of a computer by directly addressing it. *cf.* **Peek.**

Polish. Notation for writing mathematical expressions without using brackets, attributable to a Polish logician, Lucasiewicz. It can be applied by all computers which have **stacks.** Reverse Polish is Polish written in reverse order.

Polling. When a device serves many inputs it may poll each input in turn to see whether it requires a service such as data transfer or a program to be executed.

Port. Plug in the back of a device for connection to another device.

Portable. A program is portable if it can be used on a wide variety of computers.

Portable Computer. They vary in size from pocket through brief case to suitcase. Many can plug into a larger computer for data transfer or to act as a terminal. The lighter ones usually use **LCD** for display.

Power Cleaner. Mains electricity is liable to surges when switches are pressed. A power cleaner is a device to keep mains power at a constant level.

Printed Circuit Board, PCB. Board with an electrical circuit on it, not assembled manually but automatically by a deposition technique. A PCB may have sockets in it for insertion of a chip. Computers are largely constructed out of PCBs.

Printer. Device for printing text. *See* **Daisywheel, Dot Matrix, Laser, Line Printer.**

Private Automatic Branch Exchange (PABX). Local telephone network. Modern ones can often be used as a computer network.

Procedural Language. Normal computer language, in which the programmer specifies the actions taken to achieve the required result. *cf.* **non-procedural language.**

Procedure. Set of statements written in a high level language designed to achieve a particular effect on a specified set of variables. The same procedure can be called on a different set of variables, *e.g.* a procedure might be designed to evaluate the average of a set of results. The use of procedures both shortens and adds clarity to a program.

Process Control. Technique by which a process, such as a chemical reaction, is controlled by a computer in **real time** mode acting as a **servomechanism**. **Transducers** are required to tell the computer of the state of the system. This is compared with the ideal state: The computer calculates what action to take and sends the appropriate signals to actuators such as valves, which change the state of the system under control.

Program. Sequence of instructions to a computer in an appropriate computer language. A program enables a computer to do a particular task by telling it how to do it.

Program Generator. = Application Generator.

PROLOG. Computer language, **non-procedural**, originated at Manchester University 1970–75. Applications to **artificial intelligence**, Mathematical Logic, education, **relational databases**, *etc.*

PROM. Programmable Read Only Memory. Chip which can be programmed only once by somebody who has a PROM burner.

Prompt. When a computer is ready to accept further instructions from the user it produces a symbol on the screen called a prompt and waits for an instruction.

Protocol. Convention used by two devices when they exchange data. Program used to send **handshaking** messages.

Q

Query Language. Language used to extract information from a **data base.**

R

RAM. Acronym for **Random Access Memory** although in fact nowadays it usually refers to just **main memory** and excludes disk memory.

Random Access Memory. Strictly speaking this means memory in which any section can be accessed without having to access the previous part (*cf.* **Serial Memory**). This includes disk memory. *cf.* **RAM**.

Raster. A screen using a **CRT** is continually refreshed and requires a substantial memory. The most common display technique is to regard the screen as a very large number of dots (**pixels**) which may be black, white or coloured. This is called raster technique, a raster being a horizontal line of pixels. The complete set of rasters forms a **bit map**. This can be sent to certain types of printer if required for exact reproduction of the screen. If a **CRT** is used the screen is scanned in horizontal lines. *cf.* **vector graphics.**

Read. Usually means read some data from a file into the **main memory** of a computer.

Read Only Memory. = ROM.

Real. In programming a **real** variable can hold **floating point numbers.** It is stored as a mantissa and an exponent part.

Real/Elapsed Time Clock. Clock which keeps track of date and time even when the computer is switched off.

Real Time Processing. Processing which has to be done immediately. *e.g.* in air line bookings a customer wants to know straight away if a seat is available and if a seat is booked this has to be entered in the **data base** immediately. *See* **Process control.**

Record. Many data files are divided into records, *e.g.* a company personnel file would have a record for each employee. Each record has a set of fields, *e.g.* employee number, name, salary, sex, *etc.* According to the type of file these fields may or may not have a fixed amount of memory assigned to each. Sex only requires one bit to specify and 32 bits is usually adequate to specify employee number, but some people's names are very much longer than others. It is easier to manipulate a file whose records are all of the same length but this is uneconomical in memory space. One or more of these fields may be a key, used for indexing or sorting. If the file is sorted alphabetically on that key it means the records are reordered so that the keys are in alphabetical sequence.

Register. Usually means a special memory cell inside the **CPU** for rapid access.

Relocatable. A program may be compiled in such a manner that the **object code** can be run in any part of the **main memory** of a computer in which case it is relocatable. Other types of object code may be required to be run at predetermined addresses. Relocatable codes are essential in multitasking.

Reserved Words. Any high level language such as **BASIC** has words such as GOTO or FOR which are part of its language. These are reserved words and cannot be used by a programmer as the name of a variable or subroutine.

Resident Software. Part of the **operating system** which always lies in the **main memory**, either because it is **hardwired** in or because it is loaded on **boot up** and is not deleted.

Resolution. The resolution of a VDU or printer is the fineness of detail it can display. It can be measured in **pixels** per square inch. In monochrome VDUs it may be specified as a frequency, roughly that with which the scanning beam can change from black to white.

Response Time. Time taken by a computer to respond to an instruction. *e.g.* in air line booking it may be the average time taken to find out whether a particular seat is available.

Return/Enter Key. Key on keyboard which normally causes the cursor to do a carriage return.

Reverse/Inverse Video. Display mode in which light and dark are interchanged so that a letter appears in dark on a light background.

RGB. Red, Green and Blue, the primary colours used on all colour displays.

Ring Topology. Network topology in which all devices are connected in a ring. The messages pass in one direction only and each device relays the message on to the next.

RISC. Reduced Instruction Set Computer. Its **machine code** has fewer basic instructions. This allows a smaller and therefore faster microprocessor. The Acorn Archimedes computer uses RISC technology. *cf.* **CISC.**

Robot. Automaton designed to perform some manual task.

ROM. Read Only Memory. A chip which has been preprogrammed and cannot be changed. It is equivalent to memory which can be read from but not written to.

Rounding Error. When a computer does a calculation such as multiplication the result may be rounded off to the nearest binary digit. More usually the **CPU** is designed to **truncate** the number, which is quicker but less satisfactory.

RS232C. A frequently used serial interface. Although the RS232C standard allows for 25 pin connection in practice, it is often used with only three lines, namely transmitted data, received data and signal ground.

Run. To run a program is to cause it to be executed.

S

Scroll. After all the screen has been filled up with text when another line is to be typed all the text moves up one line, the top line disappears and the new line appears on the bottom. This is called scrolling or vertical scrolling. Horizontal scrolling is the same in the horizontal direction and occurs when there is more text on a line than the screen will take.

Second Generation Computer. Computers after 1957 in which transistors replaced valves.

Sector. *See* **Track.**

Semantics. The meanings of words in the context of a computer language. The statement "LET X =

LOG(Y)" in **BASIC** is semantically incorrect if Y is negative since the logarithm of a negative number is not allowed. However it is **syntactically** correct since a compiler will understand it and convert it to machine code. The program will fail in **run** time however.

Semiconductor. Material with variable conductivity. Essential ingredient of **transistors**.

Sensor. *See* **Transducer**.

Sequential/Serial Access. This describes a memory device which only allows items to be read or written one after another as on a tape. *c.f.* **Random Access Memory**. This is suitable for some purposes such as **dumping** but for others would be unacceptably slow. To change part of a serial access file the whole file must be rewritten.

Serial Interface. Interface to allow **serial transmission**. *cf.* **Parallel Transmission**.

Serial Port. Outlet plug for serial transmission.

Serial Transmission. Occurs when data is transmitted from one device to another by sending it one bit after another. A **serial interface** is more complicated than a **parallel interface** since it has to put the data in sequence for transmission and on arrival put 8 bits into a single byte of memory. Over a long distance it is more economical as it requires fewer wires.

Servo Mechanism. A device that corrects natural instabilities. *e.g.* a bicycle rider who can stay balanced. *See* **Process Control**.

Sheet Feeder. Part of a printer which accepts sheets of paper and automatically feeds in the next when the previous one has been used.

Signal. Varying electrical voltage or current which conveys information.

Silicon. Element. Most widely used ingredient of **semiconductors**.

Simplex. *See* **Duplex**.

Simulation. A computer can simulate a physical system. This can be used to predict the behaviour of that system. Another use is for training, such as flight simulators for pilots.

Sixteen Bit Microprocessor. Microprocessor whose internal registers have 16 bits such as those used for the IBM compatible PCs.

Software. Programs for computers.

Solid State. Concerning the physics of solids. Transistors are solid state devices.

Sort. To order data in some fashion. *See* **Record**.

Source Code/Program. Program in high level language before it has been compiled. *cf.* **Object Code**.

Speech Synthesis. Programs have been written which accept text as data and cause sounds to be created which imitate a person speaking that text.

Spike. = **Glitch**.

Spool. To cause output that would otherwise go to a printer or screen to go instead to **backing memory** such as a file on a disk. This is useful on mainframes when the output is much faster than the printer can take. It is also useful for obtaining text files in microcomputers. Despooling is the reverse process by which a spooled file is printed out and then destroyed.

Spreadsheet. This is a matrix of numbers and text in which a large variety of manipulations on columns, rows or single elements are allowed. By **horizontal** or **vertical scrolling** a far larger matrix than appears on a single screen can be viewed.

Sprites. Small figures or characters which can move around the screen. They are not usually standard symbols but defined in a program.

Stack, Push Down Stack. Feature of most computers. A **word** transferred to the stack goes in at the top and pushes all other words stored in the stack down one position. In the reverse process a word pulled from the stack comes off the top and all other stored words rise one position. It is a LIFO list (Last In First Out) and is a rapid form of temporary storage.

Statement. Instruction written in a programming language. *cf.* **Command**.

Static RAM. This type of RAM requires a continuous supply of current to maintain its memory but does not have to be recharged from time to time. *cf.* **Dynamic RAM**.

Status Line. Line on the screen during word processing stating file being worked on, page, line number, position *etc.*

Stop Code. = **Embedded Command**.

Streaming Tape. Tape used for backing up contents of a hard disk.

String. Type of variable in a program. It comprises a set of characters.

Structured Programming. This is slightly more comprehensive than modular programming, which means programming in **modules**. It aims to result in programs which are easy to understand, debug and modify.

Subroutine. = **Procedure**.

Supercomputer. Very powerful **mainframe** capable of at least 10 **megaflops**.

Supervisor. = **Operating System** or most basic part of Operating System.

Synchronous Transmission. Method of **serial transmission** where each bit is transmitted on a regular time sequence over an extended period. Faster than asynchronous transmission but requires exact synchronisation of clocks at both ends.

Syntax. The syntax of a language determines which statements in it are grammatically correct. In **BASIC** a statement like LET X = *Y is syntactically incorrect and if submitted to a compiler would produce a compile time error.

System Disk. Disk with the **operating system** on it, which can be loaded into the computer.

Systems Analysis. A systems analyst is a person who acts as an interface between user and programmer. Systems analysis consists of discovering from the user exactly what is required, the resources of time, money and equipment available to achieve the required result and presenting the problem to a programmer to work on. It may involve design of a new system.

Systems Program. Systems programs are at a deeper level than **application programs**, usually written in a low level language. They may be extensions of the **operating system** or widely used **Utility Programs**.

T

Tape Streamer. = **Streaming Tape**.

Teleprinter. Printer at a computer terminal for printing output received from a distant source.

Terminal. Device attached to a **network** which can receive or transmit data. There is usually at least one **host** computer in the network which can accept commands from the terminal. *See* **Dumb/Intelligent Terminal**.

Terminal Emulator. Program or device used by one make of **terminal** to make it behave according to the standard used by another make of terminal. It enables one make of terminal to be replaced by another.

Thermal Printer. Non-impact printer which is quiet. It may require special paper which it burns to provide the script. Another technology is to apply heat to a special ribbon which causes it to transfer ink to the paper.

Third Generation Computer. Generation of computers in which integrated circuits replaced individual transistors. Originated *c.* 1965.

Time Sharing. When several jobs are being processed by a computer in time sharing mode the computer works for a period of time, called a time slice, on one job and then moves on to the next job. A job may require several time slices before completion.

Time Slice. *See* **Time sharing**.

Toggle. A key may be used as a toggle switch so that if it is pressed once the computer passes from mode A to mode B. Pressing it again causes it to return to mode A.

Token. (1) In programming, a **reserved word** or symbol in a computer language, such as "GOTO" in **BASIC**, may be stored in a file as a single character called a token, thus saving main memory or filing space. (2) *see* **Token Ring**.

Token Ring. Ring network devised by **IBM**. A control token circulates round the ring and a device can only transmit data when it possesses the token, thus preventing collisions of transmitted data.

Top Down. Method of programming in which the general outline is decided first and the work becomes increasingly detailed as it progresses. *cf.* bottom up.

Track. A floppy or hard disk is divided into concentric circles for recording called tracks. The tracks are divided into sectors, a sector containing the smallest amount of data that can be transferred.

Tractor Feed. Device attached to a printer for accepting continuous **fanfold paper** with punched holes in its sides. The tractor feed has sprockets which engage these holes and move the paper on keeping it always in the correct position. *cf.* **Friction feed**.

Transducer. Device for converting a physical quantity such as temperature or the position of an arm into an electrical voltage or current.

Transistor. Device using the variable conductivity of **semiconductors**. This conductivity is often controlled by a third terminal so that the transistor acts as an amplifier.

Translator, Language Processor. Program which translates a program written in one language into one written in another language. The conversion is usually done from a higher level language into a lower level language. **Compilers** and **assemblers** are both translators.

Transparent. Something is transparent to the user if he is not made aware of its existence. *e.g.* someone using a computer at a distant terminal will find the transmission transparent to him, *i.e.* he will not be aware of the **handshaking** or **check** bits used when sending messages.

Transputer. 32-bit microprocessor with an internal memory capable of **parallel processing**.

Truncate. To cut off the least significant bits of a binary number in order to make it fit into the **word** length of a computer. It is not equivalent to **rounding**.

Two's Complement. Usual way of storing negative numbers in a computer. The absolute value of the number is subtracted from 0, the borrow at the beginning being ignored. It is the **one's complement** + 1. There is no sign bit. The leftmost bit is 0 for positive and 1 for negative numbers.

U

Unisys. Computer manufacturer, after **IBM** in size.

Unix Operating System. Very **portable** and widely used **operating system**. Originated at Bell Laboratories in 1969.

Upload. Memory to memory transfer from a small computer to a large one. *cf.* **download**.

Upward Compatible. A program for a **PC compatible** computer would be upward compatible with the **MSDOS** 2.0 **operating system** if it could be run under all MSDOS operating systems with a number at least as great as 2.0, *i.e.* later versions of MSDOS.

User Conflict. Some data filing systems do not allow two users to simultaneously access the same file. In this case there is user conflict.

Utility Program. Program that is designed for general use, such as a **word processor**, rather than for a specific application.

V

Validation. The checking of data by a computer to see that it lies within reasonable ranges and is consistent.

VDU. = **Visual Display Unit**. The screen of a computer or **terminal**. Sometimes called a monitor.

Vector Graphics. The technology of screen display with a cathode ray tube in which the beam can move in any direction. *cf.* **raster graphics** where the path is a set of horizontal lines.

Very Large Scale Integration. = **VLSI**.

Virtual Memory. Backing store such as the hard disk can be made to appear to the user as addressable memory with addresses outside the allowed **main memory**. Such memory is called virtual memory. It is achieved by copying temporarily unwanted data in the main memory on to the hard disk and using that main memory area to hold currently required data on the hard disk.

Visual Display Unit. = **VDU**.

VLSI. = Very Large Scale Integration. The technology of making **integrated circuits** with more than 1000 transistors on them.

Voice Band. The minimum range of frequencies required to comprehend a human voice, usually 300–3000 Hz. A voice grade channel is one which can transmit this range of frequencies, modulated if necessary.

Voice Synthesis. = **Speech Synthesis**.

Volatile Memory. Memory such as solid state memory whose contents are lost when the computer is switched off.

W

Wafer. A narrow slice of pure silicon crystal which is in turn cut up into silicon chips.

Wide Area Network (WAN). Network over a wide area such as the telephone system.

Winchester Disk. *See* **Hard Disk**.

Window. The screen can be divided into windows, a window being an area used to display something. *e.g.* a word processor can simultaneously display two different files by dividing the screen into two windows.

Word. The computer memory is divided into small units called words. In a BBC B micro each word is 8 bits, in a PC compatible, 16 bits and in a large mainframe it may be over 64 bits. The IBM PC normally uses 1 word to store an **integer** and 2 words to store a **real variable** although for double precision twice as many words are used. A word can also be divided up in order to hold more than one number or character.

Word Processor. (1) Suite of programs that allows a computer to do word processing. (2) A computer with incorporated software designed to do word processing. *See* **Dedicated**.

WORM. Acronym for Write Once Read Many. **Optical disk** technology which allows the user to write data on to an optical disk. The data cannot be erased, hence the name. Because of this WORM disks can provide a valuable legal record. WORM disks can store a very large amount of information very cheaply and a read/write drive costs about £10,000 in 1988.

Write. To copy data on to some **non-volatile** memory such as a disk.

Write Protect. Floppy disks are usually made with a notch which when covered prevents them from being written to or erased from. Tapes and cassettes have similar devices to protect the data they contain.

WYSIWYG. Acronym for What You See Is What You Get. A word processor is WYSIWYG if the user can see on the screen as he types in material exactly how it will appear when printed out.

THE ENVIRONMENT

This section provides a brief introduction to the study of the environment in both the rich and poor countries of the world. It examines such topical subjects as energy problems, pollution, food resources, ecology and the quality of life. A special topic looks at recent developments in Antarctica.

TABLE OF CONTENTS

THE ENVIRONMENT

Editor's Note This section was specially written for *Pears* by Israel Berkovitch, a leading writer on environmental matters.

1. INTRODUCTION

Even at the base camp for climbing Mt Everest, at an altitude of 17,500 feet, tons of rubbish were found to have been dumped, despoiling the environment. This extreme example of a widespread human tendency (though now cleared up by a Strathclyde University expedition in November 1988) recalls to mind the warning issued earlier by Mrs Indira Gandhi, then Prime Minister of India. When inaugurating the 12th World Energy Congress in 1983, she neatly summed up the environmental challenge in these words. "We should be good guests on earth, neither too demanding nor disturbing its delicate balance. We should allow it to renew itself for those who are to follow".

In more formal terms, the Report of the World Commission on Environment and Development (known after its Chairman as the Bruntland Commission) urged sustainable development. This in essence means a process of establishing a continuous and reasonable balance between exploiting natural resources and protecting the natural environment. This section in *Pears* is devoted to examining what are current environmental trends, considered worldwide but with special attention to the European community and Britain, and what needs to be done to ensure that mankind—now extensively plundering this planet—does indeed become a better guest. In recent years concern has grown among the informed public at the risks to the environment arising from man's activities and at the associated hazard of a major recoil that would damage mankind itself. An important stage in the development of world awareness was the holding of a United Nations (UN) Conference on the Human Environment in Stockholm in 1972. It called for an official organisation with a global commitment "to safeguard and enhance the environment for present and future generations of man".

A UN Environment Programme (UNEP) was quickly set up with Headquarters in Nairobi, Kenya. Responding to a decision of the UN General Assembly it has issued annual reports on the state of the environment. The topics covered in the first ten years are indicated in the table below. These widespread concerns were also reflected in environmental programmes forming part of the activities of several other UN agencies. Among them were those dealing with food and agriculture, health, education, atomic energy, meteorology, and maritime activities. Many of the developed nations set up relevant government ministries. In the UK a number of ministries were linked in 1970 into a Department of the Environment.

These changes signified greater understanding of the fact that human activities interact on each other and on our surroundings so that events in one

FIG. 1: TOPICS TREATED IN ANNUAL STATE OF THE ENVIRONMENT REPORTS

Subject area	Topic	Year
The atmosphere	Climatic changes and their causes	1974 *, 1976, 1980
	Possible effects of ozone depletion	1976
The marine environment	Oceans	1975 *
Freshwater environment	Water resources and quality	1974,* 1976
	Ground water	1981
Land environment	Land resources	1974 *
	Raw materials	1975 *
	Firewood	1977 *
Food and agriculture	Food shortages, hunger, and losses of agricultural land	1974,* 1976, 1977
	Use of agricultural and agro-industrial residues	1978
	Resistance to pesticides	1979
Environment and health	Toxic substances and effects	1974,* 1976 *
	Heavy metals and health	1980
	Cancer	1977
	Malaria	1978
	Schistosomiasis	1979
	Biological effects of ozone depletion	1977
	Chemicals in food chain	1981
Energy	Energy conservation	1975,* 1978
	Firewood	1977
Environmental pollution	Toxic substances	1974 *
	Chemicals and the environment:	
	—possible effects of ozone depletion	1977
	—chemicals and the environment	1978
	Noise pollution	1979
Man and environment	Human stress and societal tension	1974 *
	Outer limits	1975 *
	Population	1975,* 1976 *
	Tourism and environment	1979
	Transport and the environment	1980
	Environmental effects of military activity	1980
	The child and the environment	1980
Environmental management achievements	The approach to management	1974,* 1976
	Protection and improvement of the environment	1977
	Legal and institutional arrangements	1976 *
	Environmental economics	1981

* Brief treatment.

place affect people and conditions in others and at other times. So the subject embraces such others as what we mean by quality of life, ecology, effects of population trends, food and energy supplies, reclaiming land and creating new environment, and the trends in pollution. We shall see these issues as interacting parts of a system that includes all living things, the air, water and soil, accessible parts of the earth's crust, and the exchange of radiation with the rest of the universe, the most important part being the receipt of vast amounts of energy from the sun. Whether we can meet the challenge and find ways of living in equilibrium with that environment depends on ourselves. Those of us living in the developed (or "industrialised") countries have the greater responsibility. We have greater wealth, more technology, better educated populations than the less-developed countries whose poverty limits the extent to which they can help themselves.

On the tenth anniversary of the seminal Stockholm conference, UNEP issued a comprehensive report on progress and a mercifully shorter summary *The State of the Environment 1972–1982.* Under the same title, altering only the date, UNEP has continued to issue annual reports. That for 1986 for instance, dealt with health and environment; the 1987 report reviewed cumulative changes 1981–1986; in 1988 the report covered the public and the environment. The 1989 report concentrated on two subjects; greenhouse gases and climate, and hazardous waste. These are discussed in the relevant sections below. Readers may also wish to consult **Section G, Part III** on the **Less Developed Economies** and **Section F, Part V** on Development Anthropology.

2. QUALITY OF LIFE

The concept of quality of life is difficult to define since it depends on the criteria used to judge human welfare. Yet these must certainly include "recognition of the inherent dignity and of the equal and inalienable rights of all members of the human family" set out in the Universal Declaration of Human Rights adopted in 1948 by the UN. This states that all human beings are born free and equal in dignity and rights, naming among these the right to life, liberty and security of person, freedom from slavery, from torture or degrading treatment, from arbitrary arrest, and arbitrary interference. In the economic and social spheres it covers the right to social security, to work, to rest and leisure, to a standard of living adequate for health and wellbeing, including food, clothing and medical care, and to education. Policies directed at ensuring that man lives in equilibrium with his environment must be kept consistent with these humane requirements.

For example, it would not be acceptable to argue that the need to conserve resources demanded that consumption levels should be kept low in the countries that are at present poor; nor would it be consistent with the view that all human beings are equal to suggest that population should be more severely controlled in the poorer countries than in the richer ones. These are not "abstract" questions. They have arisen forcefully at several UN conferences. And the Stockholm Conference endorsed this wider view in its 26 Principles. The environment, it declared, should be "of a quality that permits a life of dignity and well-being". And so policies that promote apartheid, discrimination and foreign domination "stand condemned and must be eliminated". Representatives of the world's nations went on to agree that "environmental deficiencies generated by conditions of under-development and natural disasters pose grave problems and can best be remedied by accelerated development through the transfer of substantial quantities of financial and technological assistance as a supplement to the domestic effort of the developing countries". And the most terrible threat to the quality of life also received due mention: "Man and his environment must be spared the effects of nuclear weapons and all other means of mass destruction. States must strive to reach prompt agreement on ... complete destruction of such weapons."

The Quality of Working Life.

Several of the industrial countries now have projects to improve the *quality of working life,* particularly for workers in operations likely to induce stress. These are seen as production or clerical jobs with forced uniform pacing especially when the pace is rapid; repetitiveness and very short time cycles leading to monotony, triviality and meaninglessness in work; large impersonal organisations and also objectives that seem distant and unreal. To combat these undesirable features, Reg Sell in the UK Department of Employment recommended in 1983 that for a job to satisfy human needs it is likely to have these characteristics:

some freedom on how it should be carried out * responsibility for work and equipment * some variety of task, pace or skills * some feedback from supervisors and "customers" * some understanding of how it fits into a total product or process * choice of whether to work as an individual or in a team * a reasonable goal giving a sense of achievement * some opportunity to learn * an understanding of their role and how it fits in with other roles * avoiding role conflict such as pressure for output and for safety * a reasonable physical environment * discussion with people affected by any changes including advances in technology.

The programme continues with a Work Research Unit aiming "to encourage industry and commerce to adopt measures that can lead to better economic performance through improving the Quality of Working Life". Developing people as a resource, they add, means that we must look at ways of both increasing their contribution to the running of business and of satisfying their needs as human beings.

There have also been big advances in attention to health and safety at work in the industrial countries, although this is less marked in the developing countries and companies of the industrial countries sometimes take advantage of this. The EC Social Action Programme (1973) includes the improvement of living and working conditions. It specifies that this must apply to disadvantaged groups including migrant workers, women workers, physically handicapped and young workers. Decisions since that date aim "to help ensure that wellbeing is spread fairly through all areas and all social groups so that conditions of competition are 'harmonised' through member states"—though progress has inevitably been hindered by heavy unemployment.

This programme is being continuously updated as part of what is called "The Social Dimension of the Internal Market". In respect of the health and safety activities, the EC Joint Research Centre has compiled several data bases on harmful chemical substances.

A major development by the EC—though alas opposed by the UK government—was the adoption in December 1989 of a Social Charter by its constituent governments by a vote of 11 to 1. (*see* **Section C Part I**).

Clean water.

A UN Conference on Human Settlements (HABITAT) in 1976 became the first international forum to set out the need for a global approach to supplying safe water and proper sanitation. In 1980 the UN General Assembly launched the International Drinking Water Supply and Sanitation Decade, intended to promote these objectives during the period 1980–1990. This was also designated the UN Decade for Women and it was noted that lack of water particularly places burdens on women; there was correspondingly, a call for women to participate fully in planning and implementing water supply projects.

The great significance of this effort is that the World Health Organisation (WHO) estimates that 80 per cent of all sickness and disease is due to inadequate water or sanitation. This includes diarrhoea, trachoma, debilitation due to parasitic worms, and malaria. The action needed is seen as a combined operation involving a clean water supply, sanitation and related programmes of health education as an integral part of the total development process. The burdens created by the threats to health and to life itself by not having clean water, and the economic and social costs, all seriously undermine the quality of life in the affected areas.

As the end of the 1980s approached, UNEP reported that the state of water supply and sanitation continued to be a matter of deep concern. Most of the people in country areas of developing countries still do not have safe water supplies, nor sanitation facilities. In 1989, UN agencies estimated that "over 1·2 billion (thousand million) lack safe drinking water and over 1·4 billion lack safe sanitation. This leads to 1 billion cases of diarrhoea per year—4·6 million children die—and more than 200 million cases of schistosomiasis." UNEP notes that the debt burden of developing countries has contributed to slowing down investment in projects for drinking water and sanitation. Charities and voluntary agencies such as Water Aid and Oxfam are active in helping people in poorer countries to provide themselves with safe water.

Though generally industrial countries have cleaner water supplies, an ironic twist is that the EC, during 1989, was considering taking legal action against the UK for extensive infringements of EC law agreed by the UK, concerning water purity. During 1989, the UK water industry was privatised, and in October 1989 the Environment Secretary relaxed pollution standards for 835 sewage works to minimise risks of prosecution of the resulting water companies.

Arms and Disarmament.

Environmental effects of a nuclear war (*Nuclear war: the aftermath* Pergamon, 1983) are the subject of an evaluation by the Swedish Academy of Sciences. In agreement with other international studies by Soviet and American scientists, this drew attention to the further consequences beyond the obvious effects of tens of millions of immediate and delayed deaths. Widespread fires, including burning forests, would result in a heavy pall of smoke. This would be so thick and extensive that it would darken the world, cause freezing temperatures, interfere with photosynthesis, and damage crops and entire ecosystems. To assess these conclusions, the International Council of Scientific Unions set up its own project on environmental consequences of nuclear war under a UK Chairman. A further scientific Working Group with a largely different membership set up by the UN to make an independent appraisal endorsed the findings of the earlier studies and concluded (see the journal *Environment* June 1988) "The direct effects of a major nuclear exchange could kill hundreds of millions; the indirect effects could kill billions".

The UN has held Special Sessions for Disarmament in 1978, 1982 and 1988, declared 1970–1980 as a Disarmament Decade, issued excellent reports on the widespread damage done by increasing armaments to all civil developments in addition to that done directly by the many wars. At the Special Sessions, the assembled governments adopted a resolution including these words: "Mankind is confronted with a choice—we must halt the arms race and proceed to disarmament or face annihilation". Yet the explosive power of arms in the world continues to increase. In a further effort, the General Assembly in 1982 unanimously declared 1986 as the International Year of Peace, calling on all nations in that year to "give evidence of their commitment to peace".

The first signs of a material breakthrough came in December 1987 when the Soviet Union and the USA signed a treaty on eliminating their intermediate range and shorter range missiles, known as the INF Treaty (though this is reliably estimated to involve only 2% of the available nuclear weapons). And at the United Nations in December 1988, Mr Mikhail Gorbachev, of the Soviet Union, called for further agreed disarmament and announced unilateral reductions in conventional Soviet arms. A successful summit meeting in December 1989 between Presidents Gorbachev and Bush, and a contemporary sweeping movement towards democratisation in Eastern Europe, have all helped to reduce international tensions. Opinion polls show that public opinion in the West is now strongly in favour of further negotiated reductions in arms. There is now a gleam of hope that this could be the beginning of the beginning of an end to the arms race.

3. ECOLOGY

The study of living beings in their environment—ecology—is reviewed systematically as a general subject in the section on biology (*see* **F44–7**). Here we aim to examine briefly some of the effects of man's own activities. On a world scale they are discussed in the UNEP ten-year survey noted earlier and in its later annual reports.

"Compared with the magnitude of the problem, the action being taken by Governments and the international community to promote conservation and sustainable use of biological diversity is inadequate in the extreme"; this is the sombre warning in UNEP's report for 1989. Rapid destruction of natural environments is reducing both the number of species and the amount of genetic variation within individual species.

Up to 7 million hectares of cultivated land are being lost each year through soil degradation. Africa is seriously affected. There have been widespread famines, malnutrition and deaths due to drought and desertification in a major crisis. On a global basis, forests are disappearing with most of the losses in humid parts of Africa, Asia and Latin America. Though trees are being planted, afforestation is lagging far behind the rate of deforestation. This results in loss of firewood for poor people and of genetic resources—of plant life and the associated animal life. Protecting wildlife and genetic resources is of major concern. A Convention on International Trade in Endangered Species that came into force in 1975 is receiving increasing (nominal) support, with 95 countries subscribing to it in 1989, though countries do not necessarily enforce it vigorously. The UK "representative" for this Convention is the Nature Conservancy Council. It publishes a World Checklist of Threatened Amphibians and Reptiles.

There is nothing new in mankind modifying the "assemblage" of plants and animals (biomes) and even causing their extinction in areas like Europe that are densely populated and highly developed. But this process seems to be accelerating. Often the fertility of the land and the stability of the soil have been put at risk, particularly in poorer areas. "About 1,000 species of birds and mammals are currently threatened with extinction; about 10 per cent of flowering plant species are also threatened with elimination or are dangerously rare" says UNEP. Its World Conservation Strategy recognises the need to ensure development while sustaining the productivity of natural renewable resources, protecting wildlife and genetic diversity. Sources of anxiety are the rate at which tropical rain forests and forests in semi-arid zones are being destroyed—in Asia, Latin America and notably in Africa. "Slash-and-burn" techniques of agriculture and shortage of fuelwood both contribute to the damage. A report (*Fuelwood: the energy crisis that won't go away* Earthscan. 1984) based on research funded by UN and the World Bank, indicates that much more tree-planting is needed. But the basic difficulty is people's poverty. Otherwise they could use coal or oil.

Deserts are advancing in many areas of tropical deciduous forests, savannahs, grasslands and steppes. In 1980 it was estimated that the desert had claimed 27 million hectares of previously irrigated land, 173 million hectares of rainfed croplands and 3,071 million hectares of rangelands. A re-appraisal in 1984 by Dr. M K Tolba, Director of the UN Action to combat desertification, made grim reading. Seven years after the nations adopted a Plan of Action the global threat has increased. 35% of the world's land is at risk, threatening 850 million people. The main cause is over-cultivation, over-grazing, bad irrigation, deforestation. Massive resources need to be invested, but local communities must be involved and neighbouring nations must co-operate. No single measure was seen as the answer. The Plan of Action is based on promoting social and economic progress in the countries affected with many detailed measures then built in to the Plan to improve land management, to conserve both land and water resources. The integrated plans may include mulching, fixing dunes, irrigating, planting arid zone plants and trees.

Areas of temperate evergreen forests and broad-leaf deciduous forests—generally in North America and Europe—remained fertile. But a new threat has emerged in temperate zones from acid precipitation since coniferous forests in particular are known to be sensitive. UNEP also found that parts of the

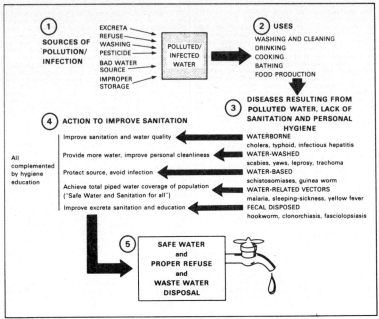

FIG. 2: PATHS TO SAFE WATER AND SANITATION

Source: "International Drinking Water Supply and Sanitation Decade 1981–90" (United Nations).

FIG. 3: AVERAGE ATMOSPHERIC CO_2 CONCENTRATION
(as measured at Mauna Loa, Hawaii)

Source: "The State of the Environment 1972–82" (United Nations Environment Programme).

Arctic tundra were threatened. This wilderness is an ecosystem that provides grazing ground for nomadic tribes, but there has been damage by the search for minerals, particularly oil and gas, and by installing equipment for hydropower.

On the positive side can be noted no fewer than fourteen international agreements arising from the Stockholm Conference, and specialist conferences on desertification and on forests. Conservation measures are being introduced in many states to save endangered species of plants and animals. Several germplasm banks, including banks for micro-organisms, have been established.

Because of the crucial role of the tree in land ecosystems, UNEP launched a project "For every child a tree" with an associated booklet *Trees as a guide to ecology*. This emphasises the importance of trees in respect of climate, protecting watersheds against flooding, helping to reduce sedimentation in rivers, providing suitable habitats for wildlife, promoting soil productivity, preventing erosion and leaching of soils, and acting as "sinks" for excess carbon dioxide in the air. Over 100 countries are now collaborating in a global network of gene banks to house the World Base Collection of crop germoplasm. There is a similar network of Micro-biological Resources Centres for microbial genetic resources, and the beginnings of a scheme for animal genetic resources. And a further positive international measure has been the international moratorium on commercial whaling imposed by the International Whaling Commission. This is tarnished only by the continued insistence of the Japanese on killing 300 whales a year, ostensibly for 'scientific' purposes 'in order to assess stocks'.

4. POPULATION

Years of studies, forecasts, warnings and exhortations by population analysts of the manifold risks to mankind in the continuing growth of our numbers have at last, slowly, begun to have effect. Growth rates for population have declined overall. In the 1950s the growth rate was 2% per year but the United Nations Population Fund (UNFPA) in 1989 estimated the rate at 1·6% per year. Yet in Africa, there has been a marked increase in rates and there have been only small changes in South-East Asia and South Asia. The pace of improvement in infant and child mortality is alas slowing down. But it is expected that the use of Oral Rehydration Therapy to treat dehydration in infants will greatly help in saving lives.

UNFPA reports that world population passed 5 thousand million (billion) in 1987 and is expected to reach 6·25 billion by the turn of the century. They reckon that growth will not stop for perhaps another century when world population will be about twice its present level. Most of these people will be born in the developing world. Developed countries have generally made the transition to low birth and death rates, high life expectancies and fairly stable population.

". . . a country's people should be a resource not a liability" points out UNFPA. "Problems arise when a population is out of balance with the resources required to sustain it, or when population is growing at such a rapid rate as to overtake the ability of governments . . . to provide proper services like health care and education, employment opportunities, and adequate housing." In many countries, large increases have been accompanied by rising living standards. But in developing countries, notably in Africa, rapid growth of population has occurred alongside decline in food, nutrition, drinking water and sanitation.

It is now widely realised that family size involves much more than successful contraception advice. For example, high death rates of children are a cause as well as an effect of high birth rates. Research has consistently shown that the education of women is of key importance. Educated women are more likely to use health services, they are less vulnerable to the risks of childbirth, they take more advantage of community services and have smaller families.

UNFPA concludes that five key factors determine family size: women's status in society, maternal and child health care, information and access to family planning services, family income and education for women. Family planning programmes need to build on these factors.

The World Bank estimates that increasing family planning spending in Africa from the current $100 million to about $640 million by the year 2000 would raise the rate of using contraceptives from 3% to 25% and would yield a financial return larger than the outlay.

UNFPA had earlier adopted decisions that such programmes must be carried out in ways that respect the principle of voluntary decisions and are in keeping with cultural and religious values. It is

also realised that if women marry young it not only has a major effect on family size but also damages the health of women and reduces their status in the family and the community. UNFPA proposes that child marriage is "recognised" as a violation of human rights.

Yet—in keeping with the points made above (Quality of Life)—the Declaration on Population and Development emphasises that all couples have the basic right to decide freely and responsibly the number of their children. But when they exercise this right they should take into account their responsibility to the community. Furthermore improving the status of women influences family life and size. These points endorse and develop those made at the first population conference. They logically lead to the final current recommendation that comprehensive population programmes are needed based on active co-operation between governments and communities.

Mortality and Health Policy.

When death rates go down, there is a delay before birth rates decline. It is as though people need time to adjust themselves. In assessing progress this must be allowed for. Improvements in death rates can be judged by expectation of life at birth. For the world as a whole, this is estimated to have risen from 47·0 years during 1950–55 to 58·9 in 1980–85. Though life expectation was lower in developing countries, it rose at a faster rate than in the developed ones where it changed from 65·2 to 73 over the same period.

High infant mortality is a harrowing, but marked, feature of the developing world. But overall this index fell from about 164 per thousand live births in 1950 to 82 in 1985 and may now be lower. Nevertheless, even the reduced rate means that millions of children annually die before their first birthday. The corresponding figures for developed countries were a fall from 56 to 17 per thousand live births. Here too no single factor is involved. Improvements in preventing child deaths are attributed to better sanitation and public health, notably in controlling epidemic diseases. Further reductions in deaths depend on better health services, living conditions and nutrition.

Urbanisation.

In search of a better life, people have moved in their millions from country to town, from poorer countries to richer, and—before the present widespread unemployment—from countries with abundant labour to those short of labour. The resulting problems have been aggravated by the further millions who have moved due to wars and political upheavals. In 1982 it was estimated that there were almost 10 million unsettled refugees. The poor people who have moved into towns have led to numbers in towns growing at 3 per cent per annum though world population as a whole was then growing at 1·7 per cent per annum. In the developing countries town populations are increasing at an estimated 4 per cent per annum. Nearly half the world population, it is reckoned, will be in towns in the year 2000.

As well as becoming a heavy burden on the resources of and organisation of the towns, this can be a severe drain on the countryside. For those who move are often the young or educated who could be most valuable to the countryside. It is therefore essential to invest in the country areas and to stimulate medium-sized cities to try and stem the flight to the large cities. In a study published in 1983, the International Institute for Applied Systems Analysis (IIASA) comments further that the peak age range for migration throughout the world is between 18 and 24. They add that the movement from country to town is ending in the industrial countries, where large cities are no longer gaining in populations but often losing people: examples include Rotterdam, New York, London, Paris, Stockholm, Amsterdam and Leipzig-Halle.

UNEP estimates that by the year 2000, the developing regions will have about 61 cities with populations over 4 million, compared to about 25 cities in the developed regions. All this strains the capacities of governments to provide basic services. Poor people live in shanty towns, with many social hazards—dirty water, no sanitation, liability to crime and drug addiction, liability to natural disasters and industrial accidents. To develop a strategy for action against these major evils, UN agencies held a conference in November 1989 concentrating on health.

Population Density in England and Wales.

Though these discussions often tend to centre on the problems of crowded countries remote from our shores—and very much on the extra problems faced by the poorer ones—Britain is very directly involved. Statistics issued by the European Community show the UK with 233 inhabitants per square kilometre well above the Community average. If we exclude heavily populated city states and island states, this puts us among the most densely populated countries.

For 1986, the population of the United Kingdom was estimated at 56·763 millions. It had increased in the decade to 1971 by 5·3%, and from then to 1981 by 0·6%. The projection by the Office of Population Censuses and Surveys available in 1989 was that the UK population would grow to 58·859 millions by the year 2000, and to 60·015 millions by the year 2025. Earlier studies have indicated that little change in the proportions of those over pensionable age is expected between 1990 and 2001 but marked increases in the proportion over 75.

5. FOOD

During the 1980s a series of TV reports on starving people notably in sub-Saharan Africa provoked a great wave of public concern in West Europe, the Soviet Union and USA. Governments and voluntary organisations poured in a stream of both food and transport in a belated attempt to minimise the human toll. Yet ironically there had been bumper wheat crops in the developed countries and the EEC had tens of millions of tonnes of corn in store. The UN Food and Agriculture Organisation (FAO) had earlier commented that prospects were "curiously mixed". FAO acknowledged that food production is indeed rising—yet there is persistent malnutrition. In 1987 UNEP estimated that the total calorie and protein content of current food production was more than twice the minimum requirement of the world population, yet famine and malnutrition remained widespread. A combination of factors was responsible, notably inequitable access to resources. On present trends, demand for food and agricultural products in developing countries would double by the year 2000.

Because of the continuing conditions of severe food shortage in many poor countries and their further deterioration, all too often, into actual famine, international bodies have taken decisions to try and minimise these risks—although the deeds have been far inferior to the grand words. Three major initiatives have been the establishment of the following:

International Emergency Food Reserve (IEFR)

Global Information and Early Warning System (GIEWS)

Food Security Assistance Scheme (FSAS).

Some success is being achieved by the GIEWS which has 98 participating governments. It receives and analyses a large amount of relevant information and alerted the world to impending severe food shortages in 1977 and 1980 in the Sahel and in sub-Saharan Africa; urgent action was taken and famines averted. Of twenty-three requests for food aid in recent years, GIEWS has issued alerts at least two months in advance for twenty-one of those situations. The warnings have been duly issued as the situations deteriorated. But the famine in 1984 developed because governments refused to take action. Following the upsurge in public concern, the EEC decided to set up its own warning system.

FSAS has also made progress. In over fifty countries it has helped improve food storage facilities, stock management, transport and port facilities, and helped set up national warning systems. But because there is still no international grain agreement, including arrangements for internationally held stocks, there is no assured buffer

stock that would stabilise prices and help developing countries. It should be added, in reply to criticisms of food aid, that officers of the World Food Programme say they take care to use it in ways that avoid inducing dependence and they aim to build up capacities to produce food. For example, food may be given to poor landless labourers in exchange for work on land development or as interim supplies during land reform schemes. On these projects as a whole, FAO reports both progress and also unmet targets for aid. Another contentious area is the need to use fertilisers and pesticides. Against them are the arguments that they are expensive for poor farmers and that it should be possible to farm without using "chemicals" liable to add to environmental pollution. But the UN appraisals are that more food is needed to relieve malnourishment of the world's poorest people. 60 per cent of this increase must come from higher yields. Present cereal yields in tonnes per hectare are West Europe 3·5, USA 4·3, Asia 2·15, South America 1·95 and Africa 1·05. Much more fertiliser is needed to increase yields in developing countries and improved seeds. Then the crop must be protected by pesticides and good storage. Developing countries have severe losses due to rotting and pests. Strategies of governments must shift to helping the world's smallholders directly by aid, education, promoting co-operatives, providing seeds, equipment, storage, etc.—and credit to buy these urgent needs. And the crisis area for many years was Africa. But FAO notes that in all aid activities environment must be preserved; conservation is emphasised as a pre-condition of food security.

Turning to fishing—we see that through a UN Convention on the Law of the Sea, the world's nations have indicated that they recognise the risks of over-fishing. Nations can now declare 200-mile exclusive economic zones and exclusive fishing zones and control the catch at a level that is sustainable. By 1986, 161 countries had signed and developing nations seem to be beginning to benefit from the new fisheries regime which offers the promise of allowing them to manage fishing resources for optimum, that is long-term, benefits.

However, despite the glimmers of hope, hunger remains widespread and FAO estimates over 400 million people to be at least malnourished today. Its studies of future trends (*Agriculture; towards 2000* FAO) indicate the urgency of helping the poorest countries to raise the level of their farming by using fertiliser, introducing conservation measures for soil, trees and gathered crops, and planting an optimum mix of crops on all cultivable land.

Early in 1984, FAO issued the result of a further study with the International Institute for Applied Systems Analysis (IIASA) on Third World land resources. Carefully analysing country by country they concluded that these could feed more people living there than the number living now. But they had to upgrade their farming practices. This could meet all food needs in 81 countries, and provide some surplus. They needed to open new areas for cultivation, expand irrigation and move up "to an intermediate level of farming technology"; this meant using improved seeds, enhancing and conserving soil, applying fertilisers and pest-controlling chemicals. Upgrading farming technology was urgent. But all these developments would need aid of several kinds from the more advanced countries to help them achieve balance between developing their agriculture and the needs of their populations.

An entirely different problem has also been the subject of review by the UN as part of its Global Environment Monitoring System (GEMS). A report "Chemical Contaminants of Food" (1988) on levels of selected pesticides, industrial chemicals and natural toxins—with reservations—was generally reassuring. After checking for such pollutants as lead, mercury, polychlorinated biphenyls, DDT, aldrin and dieldrin, and for aflatoxins, the researchers decided that current levels, particularly in the industrialized countries, were well within established health criteria.

6. ENERGY

There has been growing concern about the major environmental impacts of energy production, transport and use. For both this reason and the normal

TABLE: CLASSIFICATION OF COUNTRIES

Developing Countries			
Low income			

Oil importers

Afghanistan	Equatorial Guinea	Madagascar	Sierra Leone
Bangladesh	Ethiopia	Malawi	Somalia
Benin	Fiji	Mali	Sri Lanka
Bhutan	Ghana	Mozambique	Sudan
Burkina Faso	Guinea	Nepal	Surinam
Burma (Myanmar)	Guinea-Bissau	Niger	Tanzania
Burundi	Haiti	Pakistan	Togo
Cape Verde	India	Rwanda	Uganda
Central African	Kampuchea	Sao Tome and	Vietnam
Republic	Lao PDR	Principe	Zaïre
Chad			

Oil exporters

China

Middle income			

Oil importers

Argentina	Greece	Lebanon	Portugal
Barbados	Guatemala	Lesotho	Senegal
Bolivia	Guyana	Liberia	Singapore
Botswana	Honduras	Mauritania	Thailand
Brazil	Hong Kong	Mongolia	Turkey
Cameroon	Israel	Morocco	Uruguay
Chile	Ivory Coast	Nicaragua	Yemen Arab Rep.
Colombia	Jamaica	Panama	Yemen, PDR
Costa Rica	Jordan	Papua New Guinea	Yugoslavia
Cuba	Kenya	Paraguay	Zambia
Dominican Republic	Korea, PDR	Philippines	Zimbabwe
El Salvador	Korea, Republic of		

Oil exporters

Algeria	Gabon	Malaysia	Syrian Arab Republic
Angola	Indonesia	Mexico	Trinidad and Tobago
Congo, PR	Iran	Nigeria	Tunisia
Ecuador	Iraq	Peru	Venezuela
Egypt			

Industrial Market Economies			
Australia	France	Japan	Spain
Austria	Germany, Federal	Luxembourg	Sweden
Belgium	Republic of	Netherlands	Switzerland
Canada	Iceland	New Zealand	United Kingdom
Denmark	Ireland	Norway	United States
Finland	Italy		

High Income Oil Exporters			
Bahrain	Kuwait	Oman	Saudi Arabia
Brunei	Libya	Qatar	United Arab Emirates

Centrally Planned Economies			
Albania	German Democratic	Hungary	Romania
Bulgaria	Republic	Poland	USSR
Czechoslovakia			

Source: Based on the classification used in the *World Development Report 1983*. It does not include all countries with less than one million population and without production (or prospects of future production) of oil, gas, and coal.

desire to improve economy there have been efforts to increase the efficiency of using energy particularly in the developed countries. These efforts have achieved some success as shown by steady decreases in industrial countries in total energy needed per unit growth of GNP for many years.

Nevertheless, commercial energy consumption has increased more than threefold over the last three decades. Most of this usage (85%) is in the countries described in UN publications as the industrial market economies and the centrally-planned economies (that is the capitalist and communist industrialized countries). The BP Statistical Review of World Energy 1989 (BP 1989) reports a total primary energy demand of 8073·5 million tonnes oil equivalent (mtoe) for 1988, a rise of 3·7% on the previous year. Within this, nuclear energy consumption grew by 8%, despite 'political uncertainty'.

An important negative factor was that the steady improvement in energy economy noted above slowed worldwide in 1988. In the industrial nations forming the Organisation for Economic Co-operation and Development (OECD) for the first time for many years energy consumption grew in step with Gross Domestic Product.

During 1989 there was a major wave of concern about the contribution to the greenhouse effect, which is discussed below. Public pressure about pollution by sulphur dioxide led to the EC agreeing that by the end of this century sulphur dioxide emissions will be cut by two thirds and there will be corresponding cuts in other pollutants. But, in addition to the commercially traded fuels, large parts of the population in the developing world use firewood and they are suffering what is called the "firewood catastrophe". In several countries the time needed to collect a day's firewood is now a full day's work. Forest cover is diminishing as we noted earlier, the estimated loss being 250,000 sq km a year. The International Institute for Environment and Development has urged a combination of solutions for Africa that may be of wider application—village woodlots, increased tree growing on private land, better forest management, and rational use of crop residues. Even in the industrial countries, there is now growing attention to "energy forestry"—short rotation forestry for energy. There are programmes in Sweden, UK and in other European countries.

The World Bank estimates that the developing countries (*see* Table) account for one-fourth of the world's production and one-fifth of the world's consumption of commercial energy. (Incidentally, energy estimates have to differentiate between commercial energy and that based on collected sources such as firewood or cow-dung which do not enter into statistics.) But the shares of the developing countries in both consumption and production are rising rapidly. By 1995 the Bank expects them to account for one third of (commercial) production and one fourth of consumption. So, as a group, the developing countries are thought likely to continue to be net exporters of commercial energy to the rest of the world.

Reserves.

According to BP 1989, the ratios of proved reserves to annual production for the fossil fuels are as follows: 41·0 for oil (89 years in Saudi Arabia and some other Middle East producers, who hold a dominant position in total quantities); 58·0 for natural gas (where the USSR and the Middle East together account for two thirds of the world's resources); for coal, the figure is 218. Thus coal has by far the largest reserves and these reserves are more evenly distributed. Nevertheless, USSR, China and the USA have much larger quantities than any other area.

As noted above, worldwide consumption of nuclear energy has continued to rise despite the uncertainties arising from public concern. In 1987 it was estimated to have provided over 5% of world primary (commercially traded) energy consumption.

"Green Energy".

In using renewable forms of energy, there is naturally no comparable problem of reserves, and for many years there has been growing interest in finding economical ways of applying these sources. However, in practice, only hydro-electricity contributes on a large enough scale to commercial supplies to be listed in statistical tables. In 1988, this source contributed just under 7% worldwide, though some countries, notably Norway, depend heavily on hydro-electricity. There are many other sources of renewable energy with excellent or virtually infinite "reserves". Most are not yet economic in areas within easy reach of an electrical grid network and come into their own only in special circumstances. Yet they are, worldwide, active areas of research. They include "passive" solar (building in such a way as to collect solar heat) and active solar (heating water, heating space, photovoltaic *i.e.* converting solar energy to electrical directly). Then there are geothermal (tapping the earth's heat deep down), and a variety of approaches to biofuels. This may be simply salvaging fuel from domestic waste, from straw, wood wastes and forest thinnings. More elaborate is gaining gaseous fuels from wet wastes—landfill gas tapped from fermented tipped waste, sewage and industrial effluent gas, animal and crop wastes. Small scale hydropower is economic in isolated places, such as small inhabited islands; wave power (that is the up and down movement alone) continues to be studied, while using tidal power, which depends on the height difference between high and low tide is the subject of major scientific studies, including the question of its own environmental effects. Wind power has received more attention recently and many countries have active programmes, notably the USA, Denmark and the Netherlands; there are experimental units in the UK, but the Department of Energy classifies this area as "promising but uncertain". It should also be noted that even where such sources appear to be operating as ordinary commercial ventures—for example industrial pro-

duction of wind turbines in Denmark for use in "wind farms" in California, USA—they are in fact heavily subsidised in both countries as development projects. Naturally among environmentalists there is great interest in these renewable sources. Yet many have shrewdly noted that these apparently benign and non-polluting sources can introduce their own environmental problems. Among them is UNEP's Dr. Tolba who devoted a major section of his 1983 report to environmental aspects of energy farms. These are areas of land or water devoted exclusively to growing plants for energy. They may be specially selected fast growing trees, conventional crops or water plants. But conditions have to be right. Care must be taken to ensure that they do not in poor areas absorb resources better used for producing food, do not impoverish the soil or destroy important wildlife habitats, cause pollution or possibly affect the climate. UNEP is not arguing against "green energy". The comment on these sources concludes "Biomass is an important renewable source of energy," but many factors "will have to be carefully assessed at an early stage to make sure that 'green energy' is developed in an appropriate and environmentally sound way."

7. MAJOR THREATS TO THE BIOSPHERE

The Greenhouse Effect.

The atmosphere keeps us warm, like the glass in a greenhouse. Without the atmosphere, the Earth's surface temperature would average about minus 20°C instead of the current plus 15°C. UNEP summarises the effect in this way.

"Sunlight heats up the sea, land and vegetation. The warmed surface of the earth then radiates heat back towards space, but this outward flow of radiation is at much longer wavelengths than sunlight, in the infra-red part of the spectrum. On its way out some of this infra-red radiation is absorbed by trace gases. Nitrogen and oxygen ... play no part in the process. But relatively tiny parts of the trace gases—notably carbon dioxide and water vapour—trap the heat that keeps the planet inhabitable."

However human activities have been accentuating this heating. The concentration of carbon dioxide (CO_2) has increased largely due to burning of fossil fuels. And the effects are enhanced by other strongly heat-absorbing gases, notably methane, nitrous oxide, ozone and the chlorofluorocarbons (CFCs) used mainly as refrigerants, foaming agents and aerosol propellants.

Global warming in the range 1 to 3°C would lead to the seas rising due to ice melting and water expansion and would flood low-lying parts. These include many densely packed cities. It would cause climatic instability affecting ecosystems and agriculture.

Natural processes produce CO_2 from living organisms and decomposing vegetation. But these amounts were generally taken up by photosynthesis and by the oceans. Human activities release extra carbon dioxide by burning fuels and by destroying forests and other vegetation. "Halting destruction of rain forests would provide the best way of limiting the rise of carbon dioxide" states a study by the Royal Society (the UK academy of sciences). This is again a situation where there are many studies but relatively little action to report. In the Netherlands, studies by their Environmental Laboratory led to a National Environmental Policy Plan during 1989 which was being considered by the authorities. In the UK a House of Commons Select Committee of all parties made a range of recommendations for energy policy to mitigate the greenhouse effect. At the core of their detailed proposals were that "no one other than governments can realistically be expected to fund or coordinate this basic R & D" and "market mechanisms alone will not produce an adequate response to global warming". Expert evidence of UK government departments submitted to the UN shows that Britain could save 60% of its fuel bill over 15 years and cut the emission of greenhouse gases. What is required is encouragement of better technology for producing electricity and improved insulation of factories and homes. But Department of Energy forward estimates are based on assuming that little will be done and carbon dioxide will rise by 73% by the year 2020.

Yet ultimately the problem is global, particularly since the developing world will need greatly increased amounts of energy to raise their living standards and therefore technical and financial help in achieving this safely. So preventing the buildup of greenhouse gases, like the further problem of the ozone hole discussed below, will need urgent international measures and integrity in carrying them out.

The Ozone Hole.

In the atmosphere, there is a layer of ozone (O_3) largely concentrated in the stratosphere especially between altitudes of 20 and 30 km. Though ozone in the troposphere is a harmful constituent, the ozone in the stratosphere protects the earth including ourselves from ultraviolet radiation (UV) coming from the sun. This UV would otherwise do immense damage to life. The Natural Environment Research Council (UK) claim to have been the first to have discovered that an "ozone hole" had developed over Antarctica. After much debate about its causes, scientific opinion eventually agreed that this was due to the greatly increased use of chlorofluorocarbons (CFCs), largely as aerosol propellants, foaming agents and refrigerants. Though they were regarded as chemically inert materials, under conditions in the atmosphere with intense solar radiation, they have liberated chlorine atoms which reacted with the ozone. Changes in the amount of chlorine oxide were inversely correlated with the ozone. As the chlorine oxide amounts increased the ozone amount fell.

A wide range of effects was expected. Among them were increases in skin cancers, damage to crops and animals, and changes in world weather patterns. In September 1987 a conference of the world's major producing and consuming nations, convened by the UN, agreed to reduce the release of CFCs by 50% by the end of the century (The "Montreal Protocol"). Later information suggested that this might be too little and too late. During 1988, the EC Commission took the view that CFCs must be phased out entirely by that date. Correspondingly, ICI, Du Pont and 12 other major producers worldwide were reported at the end of 1988 to have extended collaborative programmes on alternatives to the CFCs. These cover toxicology, and environmental effects including stratospheric and tropospheric ozone effects, global warming and acid deposition. They examined hydrofluorocarbons (HFCs) and hydrochlorofluorocarbons (HCFCs) which are thought to be suitable. Both companies announced they were planning to phase out CFCs. Though final results from the combined Programme for Alternative Fluorocarbon Toxicity Testing are not due until 1993, ICI and Du Pont felt confident enough to have started building plants to manufacture the replacement compounds in 1989.

In general industrial countries (including UK) expect to eliminate most of the CFCs used for aerosols during 1989 and 1990. Reducing their use in refrigeration and as blowing agents for foamed plastics will be slower. The use of halons in fire-fighting equipment is also being restricted.

Representatives of developing countries have pointed out that they will need assistance from industrial countries in achieving improvements in their living standards while avoiding using materials liable to deplete the ozone layer.

8. RECLAIMING LAND

In manufacturing manmade islands, new land area is created and thus new environment. They may be built up solidly from the sea-bottom by filling up with sand or gravel, or built up on supports, or floating and tethered. For a crowded country with no suitable land for accommodating growth in population or activities—like Japan or the Netherlands—either recovering land from the shallows at the edge of the sea or creating new land, provides the necessary extra space. Incidentally, in judging the state of crowdedness of a country the overall population density may be misleading. For instance, the density for the Netherlands is quoted by the *1981 Demographic Yearbook* as 3·49 per hectare, but if the water-covered areas are deducted, the density becomes 4·21; similar considerations apply to Japan, which has mountainous areas, so that only 18 per cent of its land is usable as living and working space.

But apart from pure space considerations, islands can also be useful for locating industrial or other activities that many people find a nuisance—like storing oil, running airports, manufacturing products where the process creates noises or smells. In these cases, they remove these activities from intruding on other people's environments. In some cases, work is set up at sea because there lies the material that is to be worked, *e.g.* Britain's North Sea oil and gas or Japan's coal. Islands may be sternly functional, such as those in the North Sea; but they may be elegantly dressed up like the so-called THUMS islands near the Long Beach Harbour of Los Angeles in Southern California to avoid changing the visual character of a holiday district.

The oldest man-made island is a Japanese one built in 1640 to permit trading with Dutch traders who were not allowed to set foot ashore within the country. But the Dutch also have a long history of both land reclamation and building islands. Both countries continue to be highly active today in such projects. Port Island City—covering 436 hectares and a fully equipped city and port—and Rokko island, which promises to be larger, are both off Kobe. A further Japanese major project has been Aquapolis, an off-shore island as a conference and exhibition centre. Professor John Allen, a British designer active in promoting similar ventures, has proposed similar developments for the Mediterranean leisure industries where they are running short of space.

On an even bigger scale, though still at the planning stage is a "vast steel metropolis" 200 miles offshore from Tokyo. It will be home for no fewer than 2 million people, with all facilities including golf courses, swimming pools and horse riding clubs.

9. POLLUTION

Though there has always been a certain amount of concern about pollution since the start of the Industrial Revolution, this was largely an interest of relatively limited numbers of concerned people. But during the 1960s there was a great upsurge of anxiety which was reflected internationally by the calling of the Stockholm UN Conference referred to earlier.

In response to the rising public pressures, action has been taken mainly in the industrial countries, even though sometimes reluctantly and with many warnings from industry and governments about the costs. In many areas there has been a gratifying improvement. In the UK, for example, the diagrams prepared by the Warren Spring Laboratory show how the smoke emissions from coal combustion have fallen by over 85% since 1960. This is a combined effect of the Clean Air Acts, ensuring that consumers burn coal in appliances that do not make smoke, and the change to other fuels.

Urban concentration of smoke in 1985–6 was about one tenth of that in 1962–3 but the improvement seems to have halted in the later parts of the 1980s. Sulphur dioxide emissions have also fallen (by about 75% over the same period) and also appear to show the same halt in improvement recently. Lead emissions have also shown a marked reduction of pollution in response to effective campaigns reflecting public concern. These emissions fell by 60% in the 11 years to 1986 and the current interest in lead-free petrol is likely to continue this welcome trend. Lead in the atmosphere has been linked with damaging effects on the IQ of young children.

Turning to UK rivers, the proportion of water length classified as poor or grossly polluted in non-tidal rivers and canals fell from 13% in 1958 to 7% in 1980; in tidal rivers, polluted length fell 27% in 1958 to 16% in 1980. Yet here too there appears to have been a change in the years since 1980, with rivers now again becoming more polluted. One important and consistent adverse trend has been the increase in nitrate concentrations over at least 30 years, including doubling over the last twenty years. This is thought to be due to changes in agricultural practices, including increased fertiliser use. This influences the quality of drinking water. Here, pressure from the EC is leading to discussions of control on agricultural practices. Similar pressures have been applied to the UK in respect of our often seriously contaminated bathing beaches.

Considering the world as a whole—a UNEP report in 1988 was disturbingly headed "Are we poisoning our peoples?" Global air monitoring indicates that two thirds of the world's city dwellers breathe air that contains "disturbingly high levels" of sulphur dioxide and dust. Trends are for improvements in general in the most industrialised countries while quality is getting worse in many developing ones. The survey also covered nitrogen dioxide, carbon monoxide and lead. It found that in many developing countries emissions of all five pollutants are increasing. These are serious tendencies in view of the harmful effects of the pollutants, the often poor nutrition (and therefore resistance) of the poor city-dwellers, the growing tendency to industrialisation, and growth of city-dwelling in developing countries.

The assessment of water quality was equally worrying. Information was collected on more than 50 factors. They included bacteria, nitrates, faecal coliforms, dissolved oxygen and heavy metals. The study found very severe pathogen pollution, causing infant deaths in developing countries, in many streams and rivers in central and tropical South America, the Indian sub-continent and south east Asia. Though African rivers are poorly documented, they are thought to present the same features. The WHO makes the macabre observation that "inadequate water supply, insanitary excreta disposal, and vector-infested water courses are held responsible for more than half of the six million diarrhoeal infant mortalities recorded each year in the Third World."

The seas are also suffering increased pollution and by 1988 there were 820 marine and coastal protected areas in the world. There were several outbreaks of algal blooms in 1987 and 1988. Disquiet over waste incineration at sea eventually led eight North Sea countries to agree to reduce the practice by 76% by the end of 1990, and to phase it out by 1994. A further international agreement to stop ships dumping plastics at sea took effect in December 1988.

This generally mixed picture continued into the 1989 UNEP Report. The most positive features were that public attention is now strongly alerted and authorities are now making agreements and clean-up plans. It seems likely that the degree of fulfilment of these plans will depend on the consistency of public pressures.

Radioactivity.

There has been great public anxiety over risks due to radioactivity and this insidious form of pollution is monitored by public agencies in all the industrial countries, with increased attention since the Chernobyl (see **L25**) disaster (and public acknowledgement of earlier UK disasters). There was a peak of strontium-90 in milk in 1964 and this has fallen steadily due to the virtual elimination of testing of nuclear weapons in the atmosphere. Radioactivity due to liquid effluents from processing factories (such as Sellafield), experimental stations (of UKAEA), and power stations of the CEGB has been the subject of extensive protests. However, they are all officially monitored and "exposure pathways" are examined in terms of the maximum exposure of the people most likely to suffer, called the "critical group". This is a calculation that takes account of both dose rates and the length of period of occupancy of the area emitting the radiation. It is then expressed as a percentage of the dose limit recommended by the International Commission on Radiological Protection. Dumping of low-level radioactive waste in the sea reached a stalemate in 1983. Official advisers in and out of government considered that this was a safe procedure at a named mid-Atlantic site. But objections by the public, backed by a ban by the National Union of Seamen, led to a halt in this programme.

UK and EC objectives for radiological protection are officially based on the recommendations of the International Commission on Radiological Protection (ICRP). And, though eternal vigilance is of course necessary and local conditions may need attention, the overall problems of radiation exposure tend to be exaggerated. Our radiation exposure in the UK consists of some 87% from natural sources and 13% from man-made sources.

Of the latter, medical irradiation provides almost the whole of the dose. Cosmic rays bombard the earth and produce radioactive material as they pass through the atmosphere; the ground contains naturally occurring uranium, radon and thoron. The food we eat and the air we breathe are slightly radioactive, so that our bodies are also slightly radioactive.

In line with ICRP recommendations, current official objectives in the UK are these:

"a all practices giving rise to radioactive wastes must be justified, *i.e.* the need for the practice must be established in terms of its overall benefit;

b radiation exposure of individuals and the collective dose to the population arising from radioactive wastes shall be reduced to levels which are as low as reasonably achievable, economic and social factors being taken into account;

c the effective dose equivalent from all sources, excluding background radiation and medical procedures, to representative members of a critical group should not exceed 1 mSv in any one year; however, effective dose equivalents of up to 5 mSv are permissible in some years provided that the total does not exceed 70 mSv over a lifetime".

Yet there remain important sources of concern. The EC is setting up what they call "a defence system" in the event of a further nuclear accident to provide information to governments and public on foodstuff standards. A further area (radon) is discussed below. Yet a third area of concern is the disposal of waste from military, nuclear power, industrial and medical use. In the UK a Nuclear Industry Waste Executive (NIREX) has been set up to dispose of all nuclear wastes "in such a way that future generations will be fully protected". The EC is reviving monitoring provisions of the Euratom Treaty to strengthen controls on movements of nuclear waste.

But the largest problem on earth is posed by the military nuclear waste of the USA where the safety aspects have been handled very secretively. Their military plants for making plutonium are now publicly acknowledged to have produced an appalling record of contamination worse than the whole series of civilian power disasters worldwide. The costs of cleaning these up are estimated by the US government to be $1·8 billion pa for the next 20 years.

Electromagnetic Compatibility.

So much electrical and electronic equipment is now being introduced into homes, industry, commerce and transport that there is growing concern about "electromagnetic pollution". This means that this type of equipment may be disturbing or being disturbed by other such equipment. In November 1987, the EC Commission issued a proposal for a Directive to ensure that all equipment has to be constructed so that "the electromagnetic disturbance it generates does not exceed a level allowing other electronic and electrical apparatus to operate as intended; and so that it is itself adequately immune to enable it to operate as intended".

Interior Environment.

Since most people in the industrialised countries spend most of their time indoors, the interior environment is also of great importance. In recent years there has been concern about the effects of radon-222, a naturally occuring radioactive gas. This is formed by radioactive decomposition of radium. It comes out of the ground, particularly in and around areas of igneous rock such as granite. In the open air it disperses, but in buildings it may accumulate. The gas itself decays into minute solid particles. If these are breathed in, they can be deposited in the lungs. In the UK the main areas with radon concentrations at a level that may cause concern are in some parts of Devon and Cornwall. The danger was first discovered in Sweden; research on limiting exposure is in progress particularly in Sweden, Britain, and the USA. For example in Britain there is now a Householders Guide to Radon.

More generally, there is liable to be some level of concentration of volatile organic pollutants in buildings, particularly in tightly sealed air-conditioned buildings. Plastics, varnishes, paints, organic filling for cavity walls, upholstery and its dyes are all suspected of possibly emitting slowly volatile pollutants. Some people tend to become ill in air-conditioned buildings and there is considerable—but inconclusive—discussion on the relative importance of psychological and chemical factors in causing these difficulties.

Noise.

One important area that does not show much progress is noise. Over the last twenty years the level of noise in urban areas has generally risen mainly because of traffic on land and in the air. This is a difficult area because of the trouble in measuring noise levels and interpreting their effects. But action is being taken by the EC with the aim of bringing this type of nuisance under better control. In Britain there has been a Noise Abatement Act, 1960 and the Control of Pollution Act, 1974 with a section on noise. But the situation remains confused.

There have been big increases in the numbers of complaints to Environmental Health Officers (who can issue Abatement Notices) as well as further complaints to transport bodies about road traffic and aircraft noise. However from 1986 all aircraft on the UK register have had to have a noise certificate. And measures to reduce aircraft noise at source have been accompanied by providing sound insulation grants for buildings near the larger airports. Noise due to motor vehicles can be dealt with by prosecution, by the issue of written warnings by police or (since 1986) by the issue of fixed penalty notices. In respect of domestic noise the two major sources of complaint have been amplified music (generally from neighbours' flats) and barking dogs.

An EC Directive (86/188) requires workers to be protected from risks due to exposure to noise at work. The most effective way is to quieten machines at source. Methods of test are being internationally standardised. In the UK, noise data will be required on all machines producing more than 85 dB(A). By 1992 a Directive is due to extend this to machinery producing more than 70 dB(A). In addition approved designs of ear muffs will have to be available for those cases where noise cannot be reduced to safe levels.

The Disposal of Wastes.

Worldwide, landfill sites used for dumping hazardous wastes have been found unsatisfactory. Corrosive materials, poisonous organics and metals have been left in unsafe condition. UNEP has been active in urging governments to research the issue and to take action. One of the actions has been the Global Convention to control transboundary movements of hazardous wastes, (Basle Convention), adopted in March 1989. It followed the revelations of dumping of such wastes by industrial countries in African states with no facilities for properly controlling the dumps. Industrial countries have also suffered from "cowboy" dumping practices, inadequate laws, and inadequate inspection arrangements, which have even led to homes being built on poisonous dumps. Reducing waste at its source, recycling it and reusing it are strongly recommended by UNEP. Both pressure groups and commercial interests urge separating metals from waste, burning the remainder safely and utilising the heat generated.

In the UK the House of Commons Environment Committee investigating toxic waste made this withering indictment in 1989: "Never in any of our enquiries into environmental problems have we experienced such consistent and universal criticism of existing legislation and of central and local government as we have during the course of this enquiry."

The total waste arising each year in Britain alone is estimated by the Royal Commission on Environmental Pollution as 500 million tonnes. Several waste collection authorities do collect separately glass, waste paper and abandoned vehicles for reclamation. For waste that is dangerous to life because it is corrosive, flammable, or toxic there are

special regulations and a Controlled Waste Inspectorate. But surveys leading to TV programmes in 1988 showed that these arrangements are not working effectively. Dangerous waste remains accessible even to children playing.

Britain, alas, has been confirmed by a Royal Fine Art Commission report in 1989 as having more litter in public places and therefore being filthier than other countries. A large part of this is due to lack of personal discipline. But a further important aspect is the financial "squeeze" by the government on local authorities that has led to reductions in street cleaning. The UK government has threatened new litter laws if voluntary action fails to clean the streets but there has been no mention of additional finance to aid local authorities.

Dr. Tolba, Director of UNEP, has acknowledged that controls over many aspects of pollution are being introduced in the developed countries, but draws attention nevertheless to features of the environment scene that need urgent attention. They include the dangers of the enormous numbers of chemicals in commercial use (though he acknowledges the many benefits, too). Dr. Tolba reckons 70,000 are on the market, half of them in quantity. Many of these may be dangerous and the wastes generated in their manufacture may also be so. Probably the most notorious case was that at Minamata in Japan where mercury compounds discharged to sea poisoned local people; but many other cases are known.

10. RESEARCH AND ACTION

Research.

The International Council of Scientific Unions has set up a major programme to study global change as part of the international geosphere-biosphere programme. They have set out to answer these specific questions:
* How is the chemistry of the global atmosphere regulated, and what is the role of terrestrial processes producing and consuming trace gases?
* How do ocean biogeochemical processes influence and respond to climate change?
* How does vegetation interact with physical processes in the hydrological cycle?
* How will climate change affect terrestrial ecosystems?
UK environmental research organisations are actively involved.

The "Green" Movement.

"Throughout the last few years environment policy has steadily moved towards the top of the political agenda" said the retiring European Commissioner for the Environment, Mr. Stanley Clinton Davis in November 1988. The EC itself had passed some 60 items of relevant legislation in the previous four years. And the Community's basic treaties have been revised to include a separate chapter on environment for the first time. Reflecting the growing public concern a range of "Green" organisations has been set up. In West Germany there are even 42 Green MPs forming a highly influential group within the Bundestag. In the UK the Green Party startled the established political parties in the European Parliament elections (June 1989) by gaining 15% of the votes, though they failed to win a seat. Such bodies as Friends of the Earth, Greenpeace, Worldwide Fund for Nature and others continue to press through publications and demonstrations, for greater commitment to green issues by people and government. Some of the most spectacular of these have been "direct actions" by Greenpeace which has an International Board and offices in 20 countries. They have included placing themselves between whales and harpoonists, driving inflatables under barrels of toxic waste to prevent sea dumping, climbing of smoke stacks to draw attention to acid rain. More recently, in 1988 they obstructed the building of a French airstrip in Antarctica, that threatened bird colonies. With other organisations, they have exposed the many breaches of the agreement by the International Whaling Commission, noted earlier, to halt commercial whaling (these breaches are mainly through exploiting on false premises the exception allowed for "scientific research").

The combined effects of public opinion and similar green activities in many countries has led commercial companies, governments and the established political parties also to pay at least lip service to environmental issues. The EC launched a European Year of the Environment 1987–88, organising a conference on industry and environmental protection in 1988. Lead is being phased out of petrol, and in June 1989 the EC issued a Directive on catalytic convertors for car exhausts and setting strict limits on emissions of nitrogen oxides, carbon monoxide and unburnt hydrocarbons.

The UK government, during 1988–89, often expressed strong concern but in general failed to back these statements with financial support. They reduced funding for energy efficiency, allowed salaries for pollution inspectors to fall behind those of their peers in industry so that both the Chief and the Deputy Chief Inspectors of Pollution and a large proportion of their staff resigned. Staff were also cut from the Natural Environment Research Council. During 1989 the government announced a large road programme, and decreases in subsidy to rail, forcing the railways to increase fares above the rate of inflation and driving away passengers; these were measures that would aggravate the greenhouse effect.

However, at the end of 1989, the UK government issued an Environment Protection Bill which included a global approach—known as 'integrated pollution control'—to emissions to air, land and water at the same time. Other features were
* new powers for local authorities
* public access to more information
* stricter controls over waste disposal, and encouragement of recycling
* the Nature Conservancy Council was to be split into separate bodies for England, Scotland and Wales.
* stricter measures against litter louts
* new environmental controls for work with Genetically Modified Organisms.
They also planned to ban straw burning, and to tighten controls over harmful chemicals. Critics naturally welcomed positive features but pointed out the need for big increases in government as well as industry financing to give effect to the measures. Both the Chemical Industries Association and Friends of the Earth estimated that large increases in numbers of technically qualified pollution inspectors would be needed. A variety of nature interests deplored the breakup of the Nature Conservancy Council.

11. ENVIRONMENTAL ORGANISATIONS

Some organisations connected with care of the environment:

Ark, 498–500 Harrow Rd., London W9 3QA

British Society for Social Responsibility in Science, 9 Poland St., London W1V 3DG

Council for Environmental Conservation, Zoological Gardens, Regents Park, London NW1 4RY

Council for Environmental Education, University of Reading, London Rd., Reading RG1 5AO

Council for the Protection of Rural England, 4 Hobart Place, London SW1W 0HY

Countryside Commission, Crescent Place, Cheltenham, Glos GL50 3RA

Earthscan, 10 Percy St., London W1P 0DR

Environment, Department of, Marsham St., London SW1 3PY

Field Studies Council, 62 Wilson St., London EC2A 2BU

Friends of the Earth, 26–28 Underwood St., London N1 7JQ

Green Alliance, 60 Chandos Place, London WC2N 4HG

Greenpeace Ltd., 30–31 Islington Green, London N1 8XE

Health and Safety Commission, 259 Old Marylebone Rd., London NW1 5RR

Health Education Council, 78 New Oxford St., London WC1A 1AH

Industrial Air Pollution Inspectorate, Romney House, 43 Marsham St., London SW1P 3PY

Institution of Environmental Health Officers, Chadwick House, Rushforth St., London SE1 0RB

Institution of Public Health Engineers, 13 Grosvenor Place, London SW1X 7EN

Living Earth, 10 Upper Grosvenor St., London W1X 9PA

National Radiological Protection Board, Chilton, Didcot, Oxon OX11 0RQ

National Society for Clean Air, 136 North St., Brighton, BN1 1RG

Natural Environment Research Council, North Star Avenue, Swindon SN2 1EU

Nature Conservancy Council, 20 Belgrave Square, London SW1X 8PY

Oxfam, Banbury Rd., Oxford, OX2 7DZ

Royal Commission on Environmental Pollution, Church House, Gt. Smith St., London SW1P 3BL

Royal Society of Health, 13 Grosvenor Place, London SW1X 7EN

Science and Engineering Research Council, North Star Ave, Swindon, Wilts, SN2 1ET.

United Nations Information Centre, 20 Buckingham Gate, London SW1E 6LB

United Nations Educational, Scientific and Cultural Organisation, 7 Place de Fontenoy, 75700 Paris, France

United Nations Environment Programme, PO Box 30552, Nairobi, Kenya

Warren Spring Laboratory, PO Box 20, Gunnels Wood Rd., Stevenage, Herts SG1 2BX

World Health Organisation, Division of Environmental Health, Avenue Appia, 1211 Geneva 27, Switzerland

Worldwatch Institute, 1776 Massachusetts Avenue NW, Washington DC, 20036 USA

World Wide Fund For Nature, Panda House, Weyside Park, Godalming, Surrey GU17 1QU

12. CHRONOLOGY

Chronology of some of the events connected with care of the environment since 1945[1]:

1946 Simon Report on Domestic Fuel Policy which included measures for preventing domestic smoke
First Smokeless Zone legislation (Manchester Corporation Act)

1951 First smokeless zone established—in Coventry

1952 Ridley Report on use of fuel and power resources recommended measures for smoke prevention
London smog disaster, with death toll of 4,000

1954 Final Report of Beaver Committee on Air Pollution

1955 Whole City of London declared a smokeless zone

1956 Clean Air Act

1958 National Society for Clean Air (formerly Smoke Abatement) Incorporated

1960 Radioactive Substances Act

1962 Smog in London with death toll of 750

1968 Clean Air Act

1970 Department of the Environment established by combining several existing ministries
Royal Commission on Environmental Pollution established

1972 UN Conference on the Human Environabatement section on which legislation to the present day has been based

1974 Control of Pollution Act
Health and Safety at Work, etc., Act

1976 5th Report of Royal Commission on Environmental Pollution recommended an inspectorate for all forms of pollution

1979 Government decided to "axe" the Clean Air Council
1st International Agreement on transnational air pollution by governments of ECE (UN)

1980 First air quality standards in UK, by EC Directive

1981 Wildlife and Countryside Act

1982 White Paper on radioactive waste management
Special Session (10th anniversary) of UNEP
Convention on Conservation of Antarctic Marine Living Organisms came into effect protecting all marine organisms within its boundary
3rd UN Conference on Law of the Sea adopted a Convention including sections on exploitation of resources, conservation, preserving the marine environment. But US and UK (among others) refused to sign.

1983 9th Report of Royal Commission on Environmental Pollution recommending lead-free petrol was accepted by Government and will aim for this to apply throughout Europe
Royal Society agreed to investigate acidification of surface waters in Norway and Sweden with their Scientific Academies

1984 Government announced it is planning new powers for controlling pesticides.

1985 EC Directive on Environmental Impact Assessment

1986 New 'Central Unit on Environmental Issues' set up within Department of the Environment
Chemical explosion at Chernobyl Nuclear Power Station, Ukraine, USSR, spreads radioactive cloud over a large part of Europe
Unified Inspectorate of Pollution set up
Commission of the European Communities publishes proposed Fourth Environmental Action Programme

1987 European Year of the Environment until March 1988
Montreal Protocol on Substances that Deplete the Ozone Layer

1988 Commission of the European Communities issues range of proposals including rules for protecting the ozone layer, for municipal waste incineration, for tighter control of hazardous waste, for protecting habitats of wild fauna and flora, measures against air pollution by vehicles, controlling production of gases relevant to "greenhouse effect"

1989 Massive pollution of Alaska coastline after oil spillage from *Exxon Valdez*.
Basle Convention to control transboundary movements of hazardous wastes
Government published Environmental Protection Bill
EC Directive on controlling gases from car exhausts

¹This list draws heavily on *History of Pollution and its Control* kindly supplied by the National Society for Clean Air.

13. GLOSSARY OF TERMS

Acid Rain	Acid deposition from the atmosphere; one third truly in rain, two thirds deposits as gas or fine particles
Atmosphere	The 'envelope' of gases surrounding the earth
Basle Convention	UNEP's Global Convention to control transboundary movements of hazardous waste
Biosphere	Regions of earth's surface occupied by living matter
Cairo Guidelines	UNEP's Cairo Guidelines and Principles for Environmentally Sound Management of Hazardous Wastes
Cairo Programme	UNEP'S Programme for African Co-operation in environmentally sound development
Catalyst	Substance that aids a chemical change without itself being consumed
CITES	UNEP's Convention on International Trade in Endangered Species
CFC	Chlorofluorocarbon
Clean Technology	SERC programme to make manufacturing environmentally cleaner
CO₂	Chemical formula for carbon dioxide
Ecosystems	Systems of interacting organisms in their habitats
GEMS	UNEP's Global Environment Monitoring System
Geosphere	The solid surface of the earth
Greenhouse effect	Rise in atmospheric temperature due mainly to man-made greenhouse gases
Greenhouse gases	Gases that absorb some of the outward heat radiation from the earth; they include carbon dioxide, water vapour, methane, nitrous oxide, ozone and CFCs
Greenhouse Potential	Contribution to greenhouse effect compared with that of CO_2 as unity
H No (eg **H1211**)	Halon number designation system
Halon	Halogenated hydrocarbon firefighting agents (contain bromine and so have high ozone depletion potential)
Hazardous waste	In Cairo Guidelines "wastes … likely to cause danger to health or the environment"
HCFC	Hydrochlorofluorocarbon with low ozone depletion potential
HFA	Hydrofluoroalkane (includes HFCs and HCFCs)
HFC	Hydrofluorocarbon (contains no chlorine and so has zero ozone depletion potential)
Infoterra	UNEP's information network on environmental problems
IRPTC	UNEP'S International Register of Potentially Toxic Chemicals
Montreal Protocol	Agreement formulated by UNEP to phase out substances that deplete the ozone layer
Ozone	A form of oxygen with three atoms in the molecule; chemical formula O_3
Ozone Depletion Potential	The potential for depleting ozone compared with that of refrigerant R11 as unity
'Ozone layer'	Refers to ozone in the stratosphere mainly 20 to 30 km above the earth's surface; absorbs incoming short-wave UV from the sun and protects living organisms
R No (eg **R11, R12**)	Refrigerant number designation system identifying CFCs, HFCs, HCFCs
SERC	(UK) Science and Engineering Research Council
Stratosphere	Layer of atmospheric air above the troposphere
Three-way catalyst	A catalyst used in car engine exhausts that speeds conversions of carbon monoxide, nitrous oxide and unburnt hydrocarbons

Troposphere The part of the atmosphere between the earth's surface and upwards to about 12 km

UNEP United Nations Environment Programme, set up in 1972; promotes environmental action and awareness

SPECIAL TOPIC

FOCUS ON ANTARCTICA

In 1990 the signatories of the Antarctic Treaty were due to hold a Special Conference to discuss establishing a Wilderness Park to protect that continent. Proposed by Australia and France, this concept is opposed by the UK government and some other signatories of the Convention on the Regulation of Antarctic Mineral Resource Activities (CRAMRA).

Current Status.

What is the current status of the vast Antarctic region and how has this dispute arisen? In 1961 an Antarctic Treaty established Antarctica as a de-militarized zone to be used for peaceful purposes only. It therefore became the first nuclear-weapon-free zone. Covering the whole area south of the 60 degree South parallel, the Treaty included provisions for international scientific co-operation, and it simply set aside disputes over territorial claims or sovereignty. The frozen continent covers 10% of the world's surface and contains 90% of the world's ice. The world's lowest temperature, minus 89·2°C, was recorded there at the Vostock base of the USSR. Greenpeace reports that there are now 70 scientific bases on the continent, 42 of them inhabited all the year round.

The 12 original countries were in due course joined by 27 others, representing a total of about 80% of the world's population, who acceded to the Treaty. With a group of associated agreements this Treaty has kept the region free of conflict. The set of agreements are known as the Antarctic Treaty System (ATS). They include conventions on Conservation of Antarctic Seals 1972, Conservation of Antarctic Marine Living Resources (CCAMLR), 1980, and the contentious CRAMRA, 1988. All Consultative Parties of the main Antarctic Treaty meet every two years. So far they have adopted by consensus a total of 164 Recommendations, mainly concerned with conservation and environmental protection but also covering such matters as postal services, air safety, and telecommunications. There is even a Code of Conduct for Antarctic Expeditions and Station Activities to minimise any harmful environmental effects, and there are Guidelines on evaluating the environmental impact of scientific research programmes. A joint Scientific Committee on Antarctic Research (SCAR) advises the Consultative Parties.

Before the Treaty, seven Claimant States had claimed sovereignty over parts of Antarctica (some overlapping). This issue was in effect "frozen" by the terms of the Treaty. The convention CCAMLR aims to manage and conserve the Antarctic marine ecosystem. Extending beyond the area covered by the Treaty it includes the waters around South Georgia and the South Sandwich Islands. The UK has a long history of exploration and research in the area. Currently, the British Antarctic Survey researches on solar terrestrial processes, the geoenvironment, geological studies, the Southern Ocean ecosystem and the dynamics of the terrestrial and freshwater ecosystems. It was the UK Natural Environment Research Council (NERC) that discovered the ozone 'hole' in the stratosphere above Antarctica leading to further research and the urgent international action discussed earlier (**Y11**).

CRAMRA.

The CRAMRA convention was adopted by consensus among 33 countries. It is due to come into effect once 16 of the Consultative Parties have ratified it. Several countries now wish to replace it with a total ban on mineral activity. CRAMRA is intended "to provide for the effective regulation of Antarctic mineral resource activities, should these ever prove to be practicable". The UK government strongly supports CRAMRA claiming that it is "fundamentally prohibitive . . . will permit only the relatively benign activity of prospecting". The convention states that "No Antarctic mineral resource activity shall take place until it is judged . . . that the activity . . . would not cause . . ." followed by a list of possible types of environmental damage; it also requires a capacity to monitor key environmental parameters. Denying that the Antarctic environment is "fragile", the UK government adds that the physical characteristics are virtually unalterable by human activity in the Antarctic; the main threats are said to arise from human activity outside the Antarctic apart from the risks to ecosystems such as overwhaling.

Though Australia took part in the negotiations, it finally decided not to sign the convention but to work towards a Comprehensive Convention on Protecting the Environment. With extensive public support the Australian government comments that there is an underlying assumption in CRAMRA that mining could be consistent with protecting the environment, with due safeguards; the Australians question this. France is working closely with Australia and they are supported by India and four other countries.

Other objections have come from the United Nations (UN) General Assembly. At its 44th Session (June 1989) the Assembly reaffirmed earlier resolutions stating that the whole international community was entitled to information on Antarctica and to decide on the minerals question. It "expressed deep regret" about the CRAMRA convention being adopted in a way that excluded the UN. Furthermore, though the apartheid regime of South Africa was suspended from the UN, it had been allowed to participate in meetings about Antarctica and should "urgently" be excluded said the UN Assembly. These resolutions were in effect rejected by several of the Consultative Parties who abstained from voting and took the view that member states of the UN with no direct connection in Antarctica should not interfere.

Greenpeace, proposing that the Antarctic should be an area

* where wilderness values are paramount;
* where there is full protection of flora and fauna (terrestrial and marine) and the environment (including atmosphere);
* of peace, free of weapons and military activities

"believes that mineral activities are totally incompatible with these principles". It therefore supports the Comprehensive Conservation Convention, opposing all mineral activities. Its own activities have included five expeditions to Antarctica. The expedition for 1989/90, with the *M V Gondwana*, is largely devoted to the effect man has already had on the continent. Its expeditions have already shown that the agreed conventions are being flouted. Even the existing scientific settlements are contaminating the area and not using waste disposal methods meeting the Code of Conduct; they are burning waste, dumping waste, they have abandoned old bases to rot leaving debris and leaking oil drums. Tourism—including accidents to ships—is also causing environmental damage.

There seem good grounds for the general public to take more interest and ask more questions about preserving this great wilderness.

GENERAL
COMPENDIUM

A collection of useful tables and
data on a variety of unrelated subjects, including the British
monarchy, United States Presidents, phases of the moon, sunrise
and sunset, eclipses, Roman
numerals, foreign phrases, national
currencies and the Beaufort wind
scale.

TABLE OF CONTENTS

GENERAL COMPENDIUM

ENGLISH MONARCHS
(A.D. 827–1603)

Monarch	Accession	Died	Age	Reigned

I.—BEFORE THE CONQUEST.
SAXONS AND DANES

Monarch	Accession	Died	Age	Reigned
Egbert	827	839	—	12
Ethelwulf	839	858	—	19
Ethelbald	858	860	—	2
Ethelbert	858	865	—	7
Ethelred	865	871	—	6
Alfred the Great	871	899	50	28
Edward the Elder	899	924	54	25
Athelstan	924	939	45	15
Edmund	939	946	25	7
Eadred	946	955	32	9
Eadwig	955	959	18	3
Edgar	959	975	32	17
Edward the Martyr	975	978	17	3
Ethelred II ("the Unready")	978	1016	48	37
Edmund Ironside	1016	1016	27	Apr.–Nov.
Canute the Dane	1017	1035	40	18
Harold I	1035	1040	—	5
Hardicanute	1040	1042	24	2
Edward the Confessor	1042	1066	62	24
Harold II	1066	1066	44	Jan.–Oct.

II.—FROM THE CONQUEST TO THE PRESENT DAY.
NORMANS

Monarch	Accession	Died	Age	Reigned
William I	1066	1087	60	21
William II	1087	1100	43	13
Henry I	1100	1135	67	35
Stephen, Count of Blois	1135	1154	50	19

PLANTAGENETS

Monarch		Accession	Died	Age	Reigned
Henry II		1154	1189	56	35
Richard I		1189	1199	42	10
John		1199	1216	50	17
Henry III		1216	1272	65	56
Edward I		1272	1307	68	35
Edward II		1307	dep. 1327	43	20
Edward III		1327	1377	65	50
Richard II		1377	dep. 1399	34	22
Henry IV	Lancaster	1399	1413	47	13
Henry V		1413	1422	34	9
Henry VI		1422	dep. 1461	49	39
Edward IV	York	1461	1483	41	22
Edward V		1483	1483	13	Apr.–June
Richard III		1483	1485	32	2

TUDORS

Monarch	Accession	Died	Age	Reigned
Henry VII	1485	1509	53	24
Henry VIII	1509	1547	56	38
Edward VI	1547	1553	16	6
Jane	1553	1554	17	9 days
Mary I	1553	1558	43	5
Elizabeth I	1558	1603	69	44

THE BRITISH MONARCHY
(1603 to the Present day)

Monarch	Accession	Died	Age	Reigned
STUARTS				
James I (VI of Scotland)	1603	1625	59	22
Charles I.	1625	beh. 1649	48	24
COMMONWEALTH DECLARED, MAY 19, 1649				
Oliver Cromwell, Lord Protector . . .	1653–8	—	—	—
Richard Cromwell, Lord Protector. . .	1658–9	—	—	—
STUARTS (RESTORATION)				
Charles II	1660	1685	55	25
James II (VII of Scotland)	1685	dep. 1688	68	3
Interregnum Dec. 11, 1688 to Feb. 13, 1689				
William III and Mary II	1689	1702	51	13
		1694	33	6
Anne.	1702	1714	49	12
HOUSE OF HANOVER				
George I	1714	1727	67	13
George II	1727	1760	77	33
George III	1760	1820	81	59
George IV	1820	1830	67	10
William IV	1830	1837	71	7
Victoria	1837	1901	81	63
HOUSE OF SAXE-COBURG				
Edward VII	1901	1910	68	9
HOUSE OF WINDSOR				
George V	1910	1936	70	25
Edward VIII	1936	Abd. 1936	—	325 days
George VI	1936	1952	56	15
Elizabeth II	1952			

SCOTTISH MONARCHS
(1034–1603)

Monarch		Accession	Died
Duncan I	Son of Malcolm II	1034	1040
Macbeth	Slayed Duncan in 1040	1040	1057
Malcolm III (Canmore)	Son of Duncan I	1058	1093
Donald Ban	Brother of Malcolm Canmore	1093	—
Duncan II	Son of Malcom Canmore, by first marriage	1094	1094
Donald Ban	Restored	1094	1097
Edgar	Son of Malcolm Canmore, by second marriage	1097	1107
Alexander I	Son of Malcolm Canmore	1107	1124
David I	Son of Malcolm Canmore	1124	1153
Malcolm IV (the Maiden)	Son of Henry, eldest son of David I	1153	1165
William I (the Lion)	Brother of Malcolm the Maiden	1165	1214
Alexander II	Son of William the Lion	1214	1249
Alexander III	Son of Alexander II, by second marriage	1249	1286
Margaret, Maid of Norway	Daughter of Eric II of Norway, granddaughter of Alexander III	1286	1290
John Baliol	Grandson of eldest daughter of David, Earl of Huntingdon, brother of William the Lion	1292	1296
Robert I (Bruce)	Great-grandson of 2nd daughter of David, Earl of Huntingdon, brother of William the Lion	1306	1329
David II	Son of Robert I, by second marriage	1329	1371
Robert II (Stewart)	Son of Marjorie, daughter of Robert I by first marriage, and Walter the Steward	1371	1390
Robert III	(John, Earl of Carrick) son of Robert II	1390	1406
James I	Son of Robert III	1406	1437
James II	Son of James I	1437	1460
James III	Eldest son of James II	1460	1488
James IV	Eldest son of James III	1488	1513
James V	Son of James IV	1513	1542
Mary	Daughter of James V, by second marriage	1542	1587
James VI (ascended the Throne of England 1603)	Son of Mary, by second marriage	1567	1625

BRITISH PRIME MINISTERS

	Party	Served
George II, 1727–60		
Sir Robert Walpole	Whig	1721–42
Earl of Wilmington	Whig	1742–3
Henry Pelham	Whig	1743–54
Duke of Newcastle	Whig	1754–6
Duke of Devonshire	Whig	1756–7
Duke of Newcastle	Whig	1757–60
George III, 1760–1820		
Duke of Newcastle	Whig	1760–2
Earl of Bute	Tory	1762–3
George Grenville	Whig	1763–5
Marquis of Rocking-ham	Whig	1766
Earl of Chatham	Tory	1766–8
Duke of Grafton	Whig	1766–9
Lord North	Tory	1770–82
Marquis of Rocking-ham	Whig	1782
Earl of Shelburne	Whig	1782–3
Duke of Portland	Coalition	1783
William Pitt	Tory	1783–1801
Viscount Sidmouth	Tory	1801–4
William Pitt	Tory	1804–6
Lord Grenville	Whig	1806–7
Duke of Portland	Tory	1807–9
Spencer Perceval (assassinated)	Tory	1809–12
George IV, 1820–30		
Earl of Liverpool	Tory	1812–27
George Canning	Tory	1827
Viscount Goderich	Tory	1827
Duke of Wellington	Tory	1827–30
William IV, 1830–7		
Earl Grey	Whig	1830–4
Viscount Melbourne	Whig	1834
Sir Robert Peel	Tory	1834–5
Viscount Melbourne	Whig	1835–7
Victoria, 1837–1901		
Viscount Melbourne	Whig	1837–41
Sir Robert Peel	Tory	1841–6
Lord John Russell	Whig	1846–52
Earl of Derby	Tory	1852
Earl of Aberdeen	Peelite	1852–5
Viscount Palmerston	Liberal	1855–8
Earl of Derby	Tory	1858–9
Viscount Palmerston	Liberal	1859–65

	Party	Served
Earl Russell	Liberal	1865–6
Earl of Derby	Conservative	1866–8
B. Disraeli	Conservative	1868
W. E. Gladstone	Liberal	1868–74
B. Disraeli	Conservative	1874–80
W. E. Gladstone	Liberal	1880–5
Marquis of Salisbury	Conservative	1885–6
W. E. Gladstone	Liberal	1886
Marquis of Salisbury	Conservative	1886–92
W. E. Gladstone	Liberal	1892–4
Earl of Rosebury	Liberal	1894–5
Marquis of Salisbury	Conservative	1895–1901
Edward VII, 1901–10		
Marquis of Salisbury	Conservative	1901–2
A. J. Balfour	Conservative	1902–5
Sir H. Campbell-Bannerman	Liberal	1905–8
H. H. Asquith	Liberal	1908–10
George V, 1910–36		
H. H. Asquith	Liberal	1910–15
H. H. Asquith	Coalition	1915–16
D. Lloyd George	Coalition	1916–22
A. Bonar Law	Conservative	1922–3
S. Baldwin	Conservative	1923–4
J. R. MacDonald	Labour	1924
S. Baldwin	Conservative	1924–9
J. R. MacDonald	Labour	1929–31
J. R. MacDonald	National	1931–5
S. Baldwin	National	1935–6
Edward VIII, 1936		
George VI, 1936–52		
S. Baldwin	National	1936–7
N. Chamberlain	National	1937–39
N. Chamberlain	War Cabinet	1939
W. S. Churchill	War Cabinet	1940–45
W. S. Churchill	Caretaker	1945
C. R. Attlee	Labour	1945–51
Sir W. S. Churchill	Conservative	1951–2
Elizabeth II, 1952–		
Sir W. S. Churchill	Conservative	1952–5
Sir A. Eden	Conservative	1955–7
H. Macmillan	Conservative	1957–63
Sir A. Douglas-Home	Conservative	1963–4
H. Wilson	Labour	1964–70
E. Heath	Conservative	1970–4
H. Wilson	Labour	1974–6
J. Callaghan	Labour	1976–9
Mrs. M. Thatcher	Conservative	1979–

PRESIDENTS OF THE UNITED STATES

The terms are for four years; only President F. D. Roosevelt has served more than two terms.

	Party	Served
1. George Washington	Fed.	1789–97
2. John Adams	Fed.	1797–1801
3. Thomas Jefferson	Rep.	1801–9
4. James Madison	Rep.	1809–17
5. James Monroe	Rep.	1817–25
6. John Quincey Adams	Rep.	1825–9
7. Andrew Jackson	Dem.	1829–37
8. Martin Van Buren	Dem.	1837–41
9. William H. Harrison (died in office)	Whig	1841
10. John Tyler	Whig	1841–5
11. James K. Polk	Dem.	1845–9
12. Zachary Taylor (died in office)	Whig	1849–50
13. Millard Fillmore	Whig	1850–3
14. Franklin Pierce	Dem.	1853–7
15. James Buchanan	Dem.	1857–61
16. Abraham Lincoln (assassinated)	Rep.	1861–5
17. Andrew Johnson	Rep.	1865–9
18. Ulysses S. Grant	Rep.	1869–77
19. Rutherford B. Hayes	Rep.	1877–81
20. James A. Garfield (assassinated)	Rep.	1881
21. Chester A. Arthur	Rep.	1881–5

	Party	Served
22. Grover Cleveland	Dem.	1885–9
23. Benjamin Harrison	Rep.	1889–93
24. Grover Cleveland	Dem.	1893–7
25. William McKinley (assassinated)	Rep.	1897–1901
26. Theodore Roosevelt	Rep.	1901–9
27. William Howard Taft	Rep.	1909–13
28. Woodrow Wilson	Dem.	1913–21
29. Warren G. Harding (died in office)	Rep.	1921–3
30. Calvin Coolidge	Rep.	1923–9
31. Herbert C. Hoover	Rep.	1929–33
32. Franklin D. Roosevelt (died in office)	Dem.	1933–45
33. Harry S. Truman	Dem.	1945–53
34. Dwight D. Eisenhower	Rep.	1953–61
35. John F. Kennedy (assassinated)	Dem.	1961–3
36. Lyndon B. Johnson	Dem.	1963–9
37. Richard M. Nixon (resigned)	Rep.	1969–74
38. Gerald R. Ford	Rep.	1974–6
39. James Carter	Dem.	1976–81
40. Ronald Reagan	Rep.	1981–9
41. George Bush	Rep.	1989–

FOREIGN PHRASES

Fr., French.   Gr., Greek.   Ger., German.   It., Italian.   L., Latin.   Sp., Spanish

à bas (Fr.), down, down with.

ab extra (L.), from without.

ab incunabilis (L.), from the cradle.

ab initio (L.), from the beginning.

ab intra (L.), from within.

à bon chat, bon rat (Fr.), to be a good cat, a good rat; well attacked and defended; tit for tat; a Rowland for an Oliver.

à bon marche (Fr.), cheap, a good bargain.

à bras ouverts (Fr.), with open arms.

absente reo (L.), the accused being absent.

absit invidia (L.), let there be no ill-will; envy apart.

ab uno disce omnes (L.), from one specimen judge of all the rest; from a single instance infer the whole.

ab urbe conditâ (L.), from the building of the city; *i.e.,* Rome.

a capite ad calcem (L.) from head to heel.

à chaque saint sa chandelle (Fr.), to each saint his candle; honour where honour is due.

à cheval (Fr.), on horseback.

à compte (Fr.) on account; in part payment.

à corps perdu (Fr.), with might and main.

à couvert (Fr.), under cover; protected; sheltered.

ad astra (L.), to the stars.

ad calendas Græcas (L.), at the Greek calends; *i.e.,* never, as the Greeks had no calends in their mode of reckoning.

à demi (Fr.), by halves; half-way.

a Deo et rege (L.), from God and the king.

ad hoc (L.), arranged for this purpose; special.

ad hominem (L.), to the man; to an individual's interests or passions; personal.

adhuc sub judice lis est (L.), the case has not yet been decided.

a die (L.), from that day.

ad infinitum (L.), to infinity.

ad interim (L.), in the meantime.

ad libitum (L.), at pleasure.

ad modum (L.), after the manner of.

ad nauseam (L.), to disgust or satiety.

ad referendum (L.), for further consideration.

ad rem (L.), to the purpose; to the point.

ad valorem (L.), according to the value.

affaire d'amour (Fr.), a love affair.

affaire d'honneur (Fr.), an affair of honour; a duel.

affaire de cœur (Fr.), an affair of the heart.

a fortiori (L.), with stronger reason.

à gauche (Fr.), to the left.

à genoux (Fr.), on the knees.

à haute voix (Fr.), aloud.

à huis clos (Fr.), with closed doors; secretly.

à belle étoile (Fr.), under the stars; in the open air.

à la bonne heure (Fr.), well timed; all right; very well; as you please.

à l'abri (Fr.), under shelter.

à la mode (Fr.), according to the custom or fashion.

à la Tartuffe (Fr.), like Tartuffe, the hero of a celebrated comedy by Molière; hypocritically.

al fresco (It.), in the open air; out-of-doors.

al più (It.), at most.

alter ego (L.), another self.

à merveille (Fr.), to a wonder; marvellously.

amor patriæ (L.), love of country.

amour-propre (Fr.), self-love, vanity.

ancien régime (Fr.), the ancient or former order of things.

anguis in herba (L.), a snake in the grass.

anno Christi (L.), in the year of Christ.

anno Domini (L.), in the year of our Lord.

anno mundi (L.), in the year of the world.

annus mirabilis (L.), year of wonders; wonderful year.

ante bellum (L.), before the war.

ante lucem (L.), before light.

ante meridiem (L.), before noon.

à outrance (Fr.), to the utmost; to extremities; without sparing.

à pied (Fr.), on foot.

à point (Fr.), to a point, just in time, exactly right.

a posse ad esse (L.), from possibility to reality.

ariston metron (Gr.), the middle course is the best; the golden mean.

arrière-pensé (Fr.), hidden thought; mental reservation.

au courant (Fr.), fully acquainted with.

audi alteram partem (L.), hear the other side.

au fait (Fr.), well acquainted with; expert.

au fond (Fr.), at bottom.

auf Wiedersehen! (Ger.), till we meet again.

au revoir (Fr.), adieu; till we meet again.

au pis aller (Fr.), at the worst.

aut vincere aut mori (L.), either to conquer or to die; death or victory.

a verbis ad verbera (L.), from words to blows.

a vinculo matrimonii (L.), from the bond of matrimony.

à volonte (Fr.), at pleasure.

a vostra salute (It.) ⎫
à votre santé (Fr.) ⎬ to your health.
a vuestra salud (Sp.) ⎭

bas bleu (Fr.), a blue-stocking; a literary woman.

beau monde (Fr.), the world of fashion.

beaux esprits (Fr.), men of wit, gay spirits.

beaux yeux (Fr.), fine eyes; good looks.

ben trovato (It.), well or cleverly invented.

bête noire (Fr.), a black beast; a bugbear.

bon gré mal gré (Fr.), with good or ill grace; willing or unwilling.

bonhomie (Fr.), good-nature; artlessness.

bonne bouche (Fr.), a delicate or tasty morsel.

bon vivant (Fr.), a good liver; a gourmand.

brutum fulmen (L.), a harmless thunderbolt.

canaille (Fr.), rabble.

candida Pax (L.), white-robed Peace.

casus belli (L.), that which causes or justifies war.

causa sine qua non (L.), an indispensable cause or condition.

caveat emptor (L.), let the buyer beware (or look after his own interest).

cela va sans dire (Fr.), that goes without saying; needless to say.

ceteris paribus (L.), other things being equal.

chacun à son goût (Fr.), every one to his taste.

cogito, ergo sum (L.), I think, therefore I exist.

comme il faut (Fr.), as it should be.

compos mentis (L.), sound of mind; quite sane.

compte rendu (Fr.), an account rendered; a report or statement drawn up.

conditio sine qua non (L.), a necessary condition.

conseil de famille (Fr.), a family consultation.

consensus facit legem (L.), consent makes the law.

consilio et animis (L.), by wisdom and courage.

consilio et prudentia (L.), by wisdom and prudence.

constantia et virtute (L.), by constancy and virtue.

contra bonos mores (L.), against good manners.

contretemps (Fr.), an unlucky accident; a hitch.

cordon bleu (Fr.), blue ribbon; a cook of the highest class.

cordon sanitaire (Fr.), a line of guards to prevent the spreading of contagion or pestilence.

corpus delicti (L.), the body or substance of a crime or offence.

corrigenda (L.), things to be corrected.

coup de grâce (Fr.), a sudden decisive blow in politics; a stroke of policy.

coup de soleil (Fr.), sunstroke.

credat Judæus Apella (L.), let Apella, the superstitious Jew, believe it (I won't); tell that to the marines.

cucullus non facit monachum (L.), the cowl does not make the friar.

cui bono? (L.), For whose advantage is it? to what end?

culpam pœna premit comes (L.), punishment follows hard upon crime.

cum grano salis (L.), with a grain of salt; with some allowance.

cum privilegio (L.), with privilege.

currente calamo (L.), with a fluent pen.

da locum melioribus (L.), give place to your betters.

damnant quod non intelligunt (L.), they condemn what they do not comprehend.

data et accepta (L.), expenditures and receipts.

de bon augure (Fr.), of good augury or omen.

de bonne grâce (Fr.), with good grace; willingly.

de die in diem (L.), from day to day.

de facto (L.), in point of fact; actual or actually.

dei gratia (L.), by God's grace.

de jure (L.), from the law; by right.

de mal en pis (Fr.), from bad to worse.

de novo (L.), anew.

deo volente (L.), God willing; by God's will.

de profundis (L.), out of the depths.

dernier ressort (Fr.), a last resource.

deus ex machina (L.), one who puts matters right at a critical moment; providential intervention.

dies non (L.), a day on which judges do not sit.

distingué (Fr.), distinguished; of genteel or elegant appearance.

dolce far niente (It.), a sweet doing-nothing; sweet idleness.

double entente (Fr.), a double meaning; a play on words.

dramatis personæ (L.), characters of the drama or play.

dum spiro, spero (L.), while I breathe, I hope.

ecce homo! (L.), behold the man!

eheu! fugaces labuntur anni (L.), alas! the fleeting years glide by.

einmal ist keinmal (Ger.), just once doesn't count.

en avant (Fr.), forward.

en badinant (Fr.), in sport; in jest.

en déshabillé (Fr.), in undress.

en famille (Fr.), with one's family; in a domestic state.

enfant terrible (Fr.), a terrible child, or one that makes disconcerting remarks.

enfin (Fr.), in short; at last; finally.

en passant (Fr.), in passing; by the way.

en plein jour (Fr.), in broad day.

en rapport (Fr.), in harmony; in agreement; in relation.

en règle (Fr.), according to rules; in order.

entente cordiale (Fr.), cordial understanding, especially between two states.

entre nous (Fr.), between ourselves.

en vérité (Fr.), in truth; verily.

e pluribus unum (L.), one out of many; one composed of many.

esprit de corps (Fr.), the animating spirit of a collective body, as a regiment, learned profession or the like.

et sequentes, et sequentia (L.), and those that follow.

et tu, Brute! (L.), and thou also, Brutus!

ex animo (L.), heartily; sincerely.

ex capite (L.), from the head; from memory.

ex cathedra (L.), from the chair or seat of authority, with high authority.

exceptio probat regulam (L.), the exception proves the rule.

ex curia (L.), out of court.

ex dono (L.), by the gift.

exeunt omnes (L.), all go out or retire.

exit (L.), he goes out.

ex mero motu (L.), from his own impulse, from his own free will.

ex nihilo nihil fit (L.), out of nothing, nothing comes; nothing produces nothing.

ex officio (L.), in virtue of his office.

ex post facto (L.), after the deed is done; retrospective.

face à face (Fr.), face to face.

façon de parler (Fr.), manner of speaking.

faire bonne mine (Fr.), to put a good face upon the matter.

fait accompli (Fr.), a thing already done.

fama clamosa (L.), a current scandal; a prevailing report.

faute de mieux (Fr.), for want of better.

faux pas (Fr.), a false step; a slip in behaviour.

festina lente (L.), hasten slowly.

fiat justitia, ruat cœlum (L.), let justice be done though the heavens should fall.

fiat lux (L.), let there be light.

fide et amore (L.), by faith and love.

fide et fiducia (L.), by fidelity and confidence.

fide et fortitudine (L.), with faith and fortitude.

fidei defensor (L.), defender of the faith.

fide non armis (L.), by faith, not by arms.

fide, sed cui vide (L.), trust, but see whom.

fides et justitia (L.), fidelity and justice.

fides Punica (L.), Punic faith; treachery.

filius nullius (L.), a son of nobody; a bastard.

finis coronat opus (L.), the end crowns the work.

flagrante bello (L.), during hostilities.

flagrante delicto (L.), in the commission of the crime.

floreat (L.), let it flourish.

fons et origo (L.), the source and origin.

force majeure (Fr.), irresistible compulsion; war, strike, Act of God, etc.

forensis strepitus (L.), the clamour of the forum.

fortuna favet fortibus (L.), fortune favours the bold.

functus officio (L.), having performed one's office or duty; hence, out of office.

gaudeamus igitur (L.), so let us be joyful!

genius loci (L.), the genius or guardian spirit of a place.

gradu diverso, via una (L.), the same road by different steps.

grande parure } (Fr.), full dress.
grande toilette }

guerra al cuchillo (Sp.), war to the knife.

Hannibal ante portas (L.), Hannibal before the gates; the enemy close at hand.

hiatus valde deflendus (L.), a chasm or deficiency much to be regretted.

hic et nunc (L.), here and now.

hic et ubique (L.), here and everywhere.

hic jacet (L.), here lies.

hic labor, hoc opus est (L.), this is a labour, this is a toil.

hic sepultus (L.), here buried.

hoc genus omne (L.), all of this sort or class.

hoi polloi (Gr.), the many; the vulgar; the rabble.

hominis est errare (L.), to err is human.

homme de robe (Fr.), a man in civil office.

homme d'affair (Fr.), a man of business.

homme d'esprit (Fr.), a man of wit or genius.

honi soit qui mal y pense (O. Fr.), evil to him who evil thinks.

honores mutant mores (L.), honours change men's manners or characters.

hors de combat (Fr.), out of condition to fight.

hors de propos (Fr.), not to the point or purpose.

hors d'œuvre (Fr.), out of course; out of order.

ich dien (Ger.), I serve.

idée fixe (Fr.), a fixed idea.

id est (L.), that is.

il a diable au corps (Fr.), the devil is in him.

Ilias malorum (L.), an Iliad of ills; a host of evils.

il penseroso (It.), the pensive man.

il sent le fagot (Fr.), he smells of the faggot; he is suspected of heresy.

imperium in imperio (L.), a state within a state; a government within another.

in actu (L.), in act or reality.

in articulo mortis (L.), at the point of death; in the last struggle.

in capite (L.), in chief.

in curia (L.), in court.

index expurgatorius } (L.), a list of books prohibited
index prohibitorius } to Roman Catholics.

in esse (L.), in being; in actuality.

in extenso (L.), at full length.

in extremis (L.), at the point of death.

in memoriam (L.), to the memory of; in memory.

in nubibus (L.), in the clouds.

in petto (It.), in (my) breast; to one's self.

in re (L.), in the matter of.

in sano sensu (L.), in a proper sense.

in situ (L.), in its original situation.

in vino veritas (L.), there is truth in wine; truth is told under the influence of intoxicants.

ipse dixit (L.), he himself said it; a dogmatic saying or assertion.

ipsissima verba (L.), the very words.

ipso facto (L.), in the fact itself.

ipso jure (L.), by the law itself.

jacta est alea (L.), the die is cast.

je ne sais quoi (Fr.), I know not what.

joci causa (L.), for the sake of a joke.

labor omnia vincit (L.), labour conquers everything.

l'allegro (It.), the merry man.

lapsus linguæ (L.), a slip of the tongue.

lares et penates (L.), household goods.

laus Deo (L.), praise to God.

le beau monde (Fr.), the fashionable world.

lector benevole (L.), kind or gentle reader.

le jeu n'en vaut pas la chandelle (Fr.), the game is not worth the candle; the object is not worth the trouble.

le mot de l'énigme (Fr.), the key to the mystery.

le point du jour (Fr.), daybreak.

lèse-majesté (Fr.), high-treason.

lettre de cachet (Fr.), a sealed letter containing private orders; a royal warrant.

lex loci (L.), the law or custom of the place.

lex non scripta (L.), unwritten law; common law.

lex scripta (L.), written law; statute law.

locum tenens (L.), a deputy.

lucri causa (L.), for the sake of gain.

magnum opus (L.), a great work.

mala fide (L.), with bad faith; treacherously.

mal à propos (Fr.), ill-timed; out of place.

malgré nous (Fr.), in spite of us.

malheur ne vient jamais seul (Fr.), misfortunes never come singly.

malum in se (L.), evil or an evil in itself.

mardi gras (Fr.), Shrove Tuesday.

mariage de convenance (Fr.), marriage from motives of interest rather than of love.

mauvais goût (Fr.), bad taste.

mauvaise honte (Fr.), false modesty.

mea culpa (L.), my fault; by my fault.

me judice (L.), I being judge; in my opinion.

mens agitat molem (L.), mind moves matter.

mens legis (L.), the spirit of the law.

mens sana in corpore sano (L.), a sound mind in a sound body.

meo periculo (L.), at my own risk.

meo voto (L.), according to my wish.

mise en scène (Fr.), the getting up for the stage, or the putting on the stage.

modus operandi (L.), manner of working.

more suo (L.), in his own way.

motu proprio (L.), of his own accord.

multum in parvo (L.), much in little.

mutatis mutandis (L.), with suitable or necessary alteration.

nervus probandi (L.), the sinews of the argument.

nihil ad rem (L.), irrelevant.

nil desperandum (L.), there is no reason to despair.

noblesse oblige (Fr.), rank imposes obligations; much is expected from one in good position.

nolens volens (L.), willing or unwilling.

nom de guerre (Fr.), a false or assumed name.

non compos mentis (L.), not of sound mind.

non sequitur (L.), it does not follow.

nosce te ipsum (L.), know thyself.

nota bene (L.), mark well.

nudis verbis (L.), in plain words.

obiter dictum (L.), a thing said by the way.

omnia vincit amor (L.), love conquers all things.

ora pro nobis (L.), pray for us.

O tempora! O mores! (L.), O the times! O the manners (or morals)!

ouï-dire (Fr.), hearsay.

padrone (It.), a master; a landlord.

par excellence (Fr.), by way of eminence.

pari passu (L.), at an equal pace or rate of progress.

particeps criminis (L.), an accomplice in a crime.

pas de quoi (Fr. abbrev. Il n'y a pas de quoi), don't mention it.

passim (L.), everywhere; in all parts of the book, chapter, etc.

pâté de foie gras (Fr.), goose-liver paté.

pater patriæ (L.), father of his country.

patres conscripti (L.), the conscript fathers; Roman senators.

pax vobiscum (L.), peace be with you.

per ardua ad astra (L.), through rough ways to the stars; through suffering to renown.

per capita (L.), by the head or poll.

per contra (It.), contrariwise.

per diem (L.), by the day; daily.

per se (L.), by itself; considered apart.

pied-à-terre (Fr.), a resting-place; a temporary lodging.

pis aller (Fr.), the worst or last shift.

plebs (L.), the common people.

poco a poco (It.), little by little.

poste restante (Fr.), to remain in the post-office till called for.

prima facie (L.), at first view or consideration.

primus inter pares (L.), first among equals.

pro forma (L.), for the sake of form.

pro patria (L.), for our country.

pro tanto (L.), for so much; for as far as it goes.

pro tempore (L.), for the time being.

quid pro quo (L.), one thing for another; tit for tat; an equivalent.

qui m'aime, aime mon chien (Fr.), love me, love my dog.

qui tacet consentit (L.), he who is silent gives consent.

quod erat demonstrandum (L.), which was to be proved or demonstrated.

quod erat faciendum (L.), which was to be done.

quod vide (L.), which see; refer to the word just mentioned.

quo jure? (L.), by what right?

raison d'être (Fr.), the reason for a thing's existence.

re (L.), in the matter or affair of.

reculer pour mieux sauter (Fr.), to draw back in order to make a better spring.

reductio ad absurdum (L.), the reducing of a position to a logical absurdity.

requiescat in pace (L.), may he (or she) rest in peace.

respice finem (L.), look to the end.

respublica (L.), the commonwealth.

revenons à nos moutons (Fr.), let us return to our sheep; let us return to our subject.

re vera (L.) in truth.

sans peur et sans reproche (Fr.), without fear and without reproach.

sans rime ni raison (Fr.), without rhyme or reason.

sans souci (Fr.), without care.

sartor resartus (L.), the botcher repatched; the tailor patched or mended.

sauve qui peut (Fr.), let him save himself who can.

savoir-faire (Fr.), the knowing how to act; tact.

savoir-vivre (Fr.), good-breeding; refined manners.

semper idem (L.), always the same.

seriatim (L.), in a series; one by one.

sic passim (L.), so here and there throughout; so everywhere.

sicut ante (L.), as before.

sine die (L.), without a day being appointed.

sine mora (L.), without delay.

sine qua non (L.), without which, not; indispensable condition.

sotto voce (It.), in an undertone.

spirituel (Fr.), intellectual; witty.

stet (L.), let it stand; do not delete.

sub judice (L.), under consideration.

sub pœna (L.), under a penalty.

sub rosa (L.), under the rose; privately.

sub voce (L.), under such or such a word.

sui generis (L.), of its own or of a particular kind.

summum bonum (L.), the chief good.

tableau vivant (Fr.), a living picture; the representation of some scene by a group of persons.

tant mieux (Fr.), so much the better.

tant pis (Fr.), so much the worse.

tempora mutantur, nos et mutamur in illis (L.), the times are changing and we with them.

tempus fugit (L.), time flies.

tête-à-tête (Fr.), together in private.

tiers état (Fr.), the third estate; the commons.

to kalon (Gr.), the beautiful; the chief good.

to prepon (Gr.), the becoming or proper.

tour de force (Fr.), a feat of strength or skill.

tout à fait (Fr.), wholly; entirely.

tout à l'heure (Fr.), instantly.

toute de suite (Fr.), immediately.

tu quoque (L.), thou also.

ubique (L.), everywhere.

ubi supra (L.), where above mentioned.

ultra licitum (L.), beyond what is allowable.

ultra vires (L.), beyond powers or rights conferred by law.

urbi et orbi (L.), to the city (Rome), and the world.

utile dulci (L.), the useful with the pleasant.

ut infra (L.), as below.

ut supra (L.), as above stated.

vade in pace (L.), go in peace.

variæ lectiones (L.), various readings.

variorum notæ (L.), the notes of various commentators.

vede et crede (L.), see and believe.

veni, vidi, vici (L.), I came, I saw, I conquered.

verbatim et literatim (L.), word for word and letter for letter.

verbum sat sapienti (L.), a word is enough for a wise man.

ver non semper viret (L.), spring is not always green.

vexata quæstio (L.), a disputed question.

via media (L.), a middle course.

via trita, via tuta (L.), the beaten path is the safe path.

vice versa (L.), the terms of the case being reversed.

videlicet (L.), that is to say; namely.

vi et armis (L.), by force of arms; by main force; by violence.

vigilate et orate (L.), watch and pray.

vita brevis, ars longa (L.), life is short; art is long.

viva regina! (L.), long live the queen!

vivat rex! (L.), long live the king!

viva voce (L.), by the living voice; orally.

voilà (Fr.), behold; there is; there are.

voilà tout (Fr.), that's all.

volo, non valeo (L.), I am willing, but unable.

vox populi, vox Dei (L), the voice of the people is the voice of God.

MAJOR NATIONAL CURRENCIES

Country	Currency
Albania	Lek
Argentina	Austral
Australia.	Dollar
Austria	Schilling
Belgium/Lux. . . .	Franc
Belize	Dollar
Bolivia	Peso Boliviano
Brazil	Cruzeiro
Bulgaria	Lev
Burma	Kyat
Canada	Dollar
Chile	Peso
China	Renminbi
Colombia.	Peso
Costa Rica	Colón
Cuba	Peso
Czechoslovakia . . .	Koruna
Denmark.	Krone
Dominican Republic. .	Peso
Ecuador	Sucre
Egypt	Pound
El Salvador	Colón
Ethiopia	Dollar
Finland	Markka
France	Franc
Germany (E.) . . .	Mark
Germany (Fed. Rep.) .	D. Mark
Greece	Drachma
Guatemala	Quetzal
Guyana	Dollar
Haiti	Gourde
Hong Kong	Dollar
Hungary.	Forint
Iceland	Króna
India	Rupee
Indonesia	Rupiah
Iran	Rial
Iraq	Dinar
Israel	Shekel
Italy	New Lira
Jamaica	Dollar
Japan	Yen
Jordan	Dinar
Kenya	K. Shilling
Lebanon	Pound
Malaysia	Ringgit
Mexico	Peso
Morocco	Dirham
Netherlands	Guilder
New Zealand	Dollar
Nicaragua	Córdoba
Nigeria	Naira
Norway	Krone
Pakistan	Rupee
Panama	Balboa
Paraguay	Guaraní
Peru	Inti
Philippines	Peso
Poland	Zloty
Portugal	Escudo
Romania.	Leu
Saudi Arabia	Rial
South Africa	Rand
Spain	Peseta
Sri Lanka	Rupee
Sweden	Krona
Switzerland	Franc
Syria	Pound
Tanzania.	T. Shilling
Thailand	Baht
Trinidad and Tobago . .	T.T. Dollar
Tunisia	Dinar
Turkey	Lira
United Arab Emirates . .	Dirham
United Kingdom . . .	Pound
U.S.A.	Dollar
U.S.S.R.	Rouble
Uruguay	Peso
Venezuela	Bolivar
Yugoslavia	Dinar
Yemen Arab Rep. . . .	Riyal
Yemen South	Dinar
Zaïre	Zaïre
Zambia	Kwacha

ROMAN NUMERALS

I 1		LXX . . . 70	
II 2		LXXX . . . 80	
III 3		LXXXVIII . 88	
IV 4		XC 90	
V 5		XCIX. . . 99	
VI 6		C 100	
VII 7		CX 110	
VIII 8		CXI . . . 111	
IX 9		CXX . . . 120	
X 10		CC 200	
XI 11		CCXX . . . 220	
XII 12		CCC . . . 300	
XIII 13		CCCXX . . 320	
XIV 14		CD 400	
XV 15		D. 500	
XVI 16		DC 600	
XVII 17		DCC . . . 700	
XVIII 18		DCCC. . . 800	
XIX 19		CM . . . 900	
XX 20		XM 990	
XXX 30		M. 1000	
XL 40		MD 1500	
L. 50		MDCCC . . 1800	
LV 55		MCMLXXX . 1980	
LX 60		MM . . . 2000	

INTERNATIONAL TIME-TABLE (GMT)

Place	Time h	Place	Time h
Adelaide	21 30	Melbourne	22 00
Amsterdam	13 00	Montreal	07 00
Ankara	14 00	Moscow	15 00
Athens	14 00	Nairobi	15 00
Auckland		New York	07 00
(N.Z.)	24 00	Oslo	13 00
Belgrade	13 00	Ottawa	07 00
Berlin	13 00	Panama	07 00
Bombay	17 30	Paris	13 00
Brisbane	22 00	Peking	20 00
Brussels	13 00	Perth (W.A.)	20 00
Budapest	13 00	Prague	13 00
Buenos Aires	09 00	Quebec	07 00
Cairo	14 00	Rangoon	18 30
Calcutta	17 30	Rio de Janeiro	09 00
Cape Town	14 00	Rome	13 00
Chicago	06 00	San Francisco	04 00
Copenhagen	13 00	St. John's	
Gibraltar	13 00	(N.F.)	08 30
Helsinki	14 00	Singapore	19 30
Hobart	22 00	Stockholm	13 00
Hong Kong	20 00	Sydney	22 00
Istanbul	14 00	Tehran	15 30
Jerusalem	14 00	Tokyo	21 00
London	12 00	Toronto	07 00
Madeira	12 00	Vancouver	04 00
Madrid	13 00	Vienna	13 00
Malta	13 00	Winnipeg	06 00
Mauritius	16 00	Yokohama	21 00

GREEK ALPHABET

A	α	Alpha	N	ν	nu
B	β	beta	Ξ	ξ	xi
Γ	γ	gamma	O	o	omicron
Δ	δ	delta	Π	π	pi
E	ε	epsilon	P	ρ	rho
Z	ζ	zeta	Σ	σ	sigma
H	η	eta	T	τ	tau
Θ	θ	theta	Υ	υ	upsilon
I	ι	iota	Φ	ϕ	phi
K	κ	kappa	X	χ	chi
Λ	λ	lambda	Ψ	ψ	psi
M	μ	mu	Ω	ω	omega

BANK AND PUBLIC HOLIDAYS

The number of public holidays in England and Wales comprise at present six bank holidays (New Year's Day, Easter Monday, May Day, Spring and Late Summer Holidays at the end of May and August respectively, and Boxing Day), with also two common law holidays (Good Friday and Christmas Day); in Scotland seven bank holidays (New Year's Day, January 3, Good Friday, May Day, Spring and Late Summer Holidays at the beginning of May and August respectively, and Christmas Day); and in Northern Ireland seven bank holidays (New Year's Day, St. Patrick's Day, Easter Monday, May Day, Spring Late Summer Holidays at the end of May and August respectively, and Boxing Day) plus two other public holidays (Easter Tuesday and the anniversary of the Battle of the Boyne).

1991   Bank Holidays in England and Wales—Jan 1, Mar 29, Apr 1, May 6, May 27, Aug 26, Dec 25, Dec 26.
          Northern Ireland—Jan 1, Mar 18, Mar 29, Apr 1, May 6, May 27, July 12, Aug 26, Dec 25, Dec 26.
          Scotland—Jan 1, Jan 2, Mar 29, May 6, May 27, Aug 5, Dec 25, Dec 26.

Note: There are holidays in lieu of other public holidays which fall at weekends. In Scotland and Northern Ireland a general holiday is not necessarily observed on the same day as a bank holiday.

THE SEASONS

	1990			1991		
	d	h	m	d	h	m
Vernal Equinox—Spring begins	Mar 20	21	19	Mar 21	03	02
Summer Solstice—Summer begins	June 21	15	33	June 21	21	19
Autumnal Equinox—Autumn begins	Sept 23	06	55	Sept 23	12	48
Winter Solstice—Winter begins	Dec 22	03	07	Dec 22	08	54

(All times are in GMT)

THE COUNTRY CODE

GUARD AGAINST THE RISK OF FIRE. Great damage is done every year to crops, plantations, woodlands, and heaths. A match or cigarette thrown away or a pipe carelessly knocked out, picnic fires not properly put out or lighted near dry crops, can quickly start a blaze.

FASTEN ALL GATES. If animals get out of a field they stray. As a result they may do serious damage to crops, suffer injury on the roads, or eat food that is harmful.

KEEP DOGS UNDER CONTROL. Animals are easily frightened, even by small, playful dogs. Stillbirths may be the result.

KEEP TO THE PATHS ACROSS FARM LAND. Crops are damaged by treading; flattened crops are difficult to harvest. Grass is a valuable crop.

AVOID DAMAGING FENCING, HEDGES, AND WALLS. If these are damaged, gaps will be caused. Where a man goes, an animal may follow.

LEAVE NO LITTER. Litter is not just unsightly, but often a danger as well. Broken glass and tins may injure animals and harm machinery.

SAFEGUARD WATER SUPPLIES. Countrymen often depend on wells and streams for water for themselves and for their animals.

PROTECT WILD LIFE, PLANTS, AND TREES. Wild animals should not be disturbed, plants uprooted, or trees treated roughly.

GO CAREFULLY ON COUNTRY ROADS. If there is no footpath, walkers are generally safer on the right, facing on-coming traffic. Care and patience are needed by motorists when passing farm animals.

RESPECT THE LIFE OF THE COUNTRYSIDE. Many of the machines and much of the business stock of which the farmer depends for his livelihood have to be kept in the open. Take care not to damage them.

THE BEAUFORT SCALE OF WIND FORCE

Beaufort number	Wind	Effect on land	Speed	
			mile/h	Knots
0	Calm	Smoke rises vertically	Less than 1	Less than 1
1	Light air	Direction shown by smoke but not by wind vanes	1–3	1–3
2	Light breeze	Wind felt on face; leaves rustle; wind vanes move	4–7	4–6
3	Gentle breeze	Leaves and twigs in motion; wind extends light flag	8–12	7–10
4	Moderate breeze	Raises dust, loose paper and moves small branches	13–18	11–16
5	Fresh breeze	Small trees in leaf begin to sway	19–24	17–21
6	Strong breeze	Large branches in motion; whistling in telegraph wires; difficulty with umbrellas	25–31	22–27
7	Moderate gale	Whole trees in motion; difficult to walk against wind	32–38	28–33
8	Fresh gale	Twigs break off trees; progress impeded	39–46	34–40
9	Strong gale	Slight structural damage occurs; chimney pots and slates blown off	47–54	41–47
10	Whole gale	Trees uprooted and considerable structural damage	55–63	48–56
11	Storm	Widespread damage, seldom experienced in England	64–75	57–65
12	Hurricane	Winds of this force rarely encountered outside tropical revolving storms[1]	Above 75	Above 65

[1] The most notable recent exception was the tremendous storm which devastated Southern England on the night of 15/16 October 1987. Storms of great severity also battered Britain in January and February 1990.

SUNRISE AND SUNSET FOR LONDON, 1991

		Rise h m	Set h m			Rise h m	Set h m			Rise h m	Set h m
Jan	1	08 06	16 02	May	7	05 23	20 33	September	3	06 15	19 44
	8	08 05	16 10		14	05 11	20 44		10	06 27	19 28
	15	08 00	16 20		21	05 01	20 54		17	06 38	19 12
	22	07 53	16 32		28	04 53	21 03		24	06 49	18 56
	29	07 44	16 44								
				June	4	04 47	21 11	October	1	07 00	18 40
Feb	5	07 33	16 57		11	04 44	21 18		8	07 12	18 24
	12	07 21	17 09		18	04 43	21 21		15	07 24	18 09
	19	07 08	17 22		25	04 44	21 22		22	07 36	17 54
	26	06 53	17 35						29	06 48	16 40
March	5	06 38	17 47	July	2	04 48	21 21	November	5	07 00	16 28
	12	06 23	17 59		9	04 54	21 17		12	07 13	16 16
	19	06 07	18 11		16	05 02	21 11		19	07 25	16 07
	26	05 51	18 23		23	05 11	21 03		26	07 36	15 59
					30	05 20	20 53				
April	2	06 35	19 35					December	3	07 46	15 54
	9	06 19	19 46	August	6	05 31	20 41		10	07 55	15 52
	16	06 04	19 58		13	05 42	20 28		17	08 01	15 52
	23	05 49	20 10		20	05 53	20 14		24	08 05	15 55
	30	05 36	20 21		27	06 04	19 59		31	08 06	16 01

Note: These times are in GMT, except between 0100 on 31 Mar and 0100 on 27 Oct when the times are in BST (1 hour in advance of GMT).

PHASES OF THE MOON, 1991

	New Moon d h m			First Quarter d h m			Full Moon d h m			Last Quarter d h m	
Jan	15 23 50	Jan	23 14 21	Jan	30 06 10	Jan	7 18 35				
Feb	14 17 32	Feb	21 22 58	Feb	28 18 25	Feb	6 13 52				
Mar	16 08 10	Mar	26 06 03	Mar	30 07 17	Mar	8 10 32				
Apr	14 19 38	Apr	21 12 39	Apr	28 20 58	Apr	7 06 45				
May	14 04 36	May	20 19 46	May	28 11 37	May	7 00 46				
June	12 12 06	June	19 04 19	June	27 02 58	June	5 15 30				
July	11 19 06	July	18 15 11	July	26 18 24	July	5 02 50				
Aug	10 02 28	Aug	17 05 01	Aug	25 09 07	Aug	3 11 25				
Sept	8 11 01	Sept	15 22 01	Sept	23 22 40	Sept	1 18 16				
Oct	7 21 39	Oct	15 17 33	Oct	23 11 08	Oct	1 00 30				
Nov	6 11 11	Nov	14 14 02	Nov	21 22 56	Oct	30 07 10				
Dec	6 03 56	Dec	14 09 32	Dec	21 10 23	Nov	28 15 21				
								Dec	28 01 55		

Note: All times are in GMT.

ECLIPSES, 1991

1. An annular eclipse of the Sun on 15–16 January is visible as a partial eclipse from the south eastern part of the Indian Ocean, the Southern Ocean, Oceania, Australasia, the western part of Antarctica and the Pacific Ocean. The eclipse begins on 15 January at 20h 51m and ends on 16 January at 02h 55m. The annular phase begins on 15 January at 22h 00m just off the west coast of Australia, crosses the extreme south western part of Australia, Tasmania, the central part of New Zealand and ends on 16 January at 01h 46m in the South Pacific Ocean. The maximum duration of the annular phase is 7m 55s.

2. A total eclipse of the Sun on 11 July. The path of totality begins in the North Pacific Ocean, passes along the western coast of Central America, crosses the centre of Colombia and ends in the centre of Brazil. The partial phase is visible from the Pacific Ocean, the southern half of North America, Central America, the Caribbean, South America except the extreme south, and the Atlantic Ocean. The eclipse begins at 16h 29m and ends at 21h 43m, the total phase begins at 17h 23m and ends at 20h 49m. The maximum duration of totality is 6m 54s.

3. A partial eclipse of the Moon on 21 December is visible from Iceland, Greenland, Arctic regions, north west of South America, Central America, North America, the Pacific Ocean except the extreme eastern part, Australasia except the extreme west, Asia except the south western part and the extreme north of Scandinavia. The eclipse begins at 10h 01m and ends at 11h 05m. The time of maximum eclipse is 10h 33m when 0.09 of the Moon's diameter is obscured.

Source: H.M. Nautical Almanac Office. Reproduced with permission from data supplied to the Science and Engineering Council.

THE COMMONWEALTH

The Commonwealth of Nations is a free association of independent member nations and their dependencies. The political status of the member nations listed below is clarified and given legal substance in the *Statute of Westminster* drawn up in 1931, before the Commonwealth was founded, by the United Kingdom and the Dominions. The original Dominions were Australia, Canada, Irish Free State, Newfoundland, New Zealand and South Africa.

MEMBERS OF THE COMMONWEALTH, MAY 1990

Country	Capital	Status	Date of Joining	Population
1. Antigua and Barbuda	St. John's	M	1981	80,000 (est. 1985)
2. Australia	Canberra	M	1931	15,970,000 (est. 1986)
3. The Bahamas	Nassau	M	1973	231,000 (est. 1985)
4. Bangladesh	Dhaka	R	1972	98,657,000 (est. 1985)
5. Barbados	Bridgetown	M	1966	253,000 (est. 1985)
6. Belize	Belmopen	M	1981	166,000 (est. 1985)
7. Botswana	Gaborone	R	1966	1,085,000 (est. 1985)
8. Brunei	Bandar Seri Begawan	M*	1984	227,000 (est. 1986)
9. Canada	Ottawa	M	1931	25,354,000 (est. 1986)
10. Cyprus	Nicosia	R	1961	665,200 (est. 1985)
11. Dominica	Roseau	R	1978	76,000 (est. 1985)
12. The Gambia	Banjul	R	1965	643,000 (est. 1985)
13. Ghana	Accra	R	1957	13,588,000 (est. 1985)
14. Grenada	St. George's	M	1974	112,000 (est. 1985)
15. Guyana	Georgetown	R	1966	790,000 (est. 1985)
16. India	New Delhi	R	1947	751,000,000 (est. 1985)
17. Jamaica	Kingston	M	1962	2,337,000 (est. 1985)
18. Kenya	Nairobi	R	1963	20,333,000 (est. 1985)
19. Kiribati	Tarawa	R	1979	64,000 (est. 1985)
20. Lesotho	Maseru	M*	1966	1,528,000 (est. 1985)
21. Malawi	Lilongwe	R	1964	7,059,000 (est. 1985)
22. Malaysia	Kuala Lumpur	M*	1957	16,100,000 (est. 1986)
23. Maldives	Male	R	1982(S)	177,000 (est. 1985)
24. Malta	Valletta	R	1964	343,000 (est. 1986)
25. Mauritius	Port Louis	M	1968	1,020,000 (est. 1985)
26. Namibia	Windhoek	R	1990	1,300,000 (est. 1990)
27. Nauru	Nauru	R	1968(S)	8,000 (est. 1985)
28. New Zealand	Wellington	M	1931	3,254,000 (est. 1985)
29. Nigeria	Lagos	R	1960	95,198,000 (est. 1985)
30. Pakistan	Islamabad	R	1947*	102,200,000 (est. 1987)
31. Papua New Guinea	Port Moresby	M	1975	3,329,000 (est. 1985)
32. St. Kitts and Nevis	Basseterre	M	1983	47,000 (est. 1987)
33. St. Lucia	Castries	M	1979	130,000 (est. 1985)
34. St. Vincent and the Grenadines	Kingstown	M	1979(S)	104,000 (est. 1985)
35. Seychelles	Victoria	R	1976	65,000 (est. 1985)
36. Sierra Leone	Freetown	R	1961	3,670,000 (est. 1987)
37. Singapore	Singapore	R	1965	2,613,000 (est. 1987)
38. Solomon Islands	Honiara	M	1978	270,000 (est. 1985)
39. Sri Lanka	Colombo	R	1948	15,800,000 (est. 1985)
40. Swaziland	Mbabane	M*	1968	647,000 (est. 1985)
41. Tanzania	Dar es Salaam	R	1961	23,200,000 (est. 1987)
42. Tonga	Nuku'Alofa	M*	1970	97,000 (est. 1985)
43. Trinidad and Tobago	Port of Spain	R	1962	1,185,000 (est. 1985)
44. Tuvalu	Funafuti	M	1978(S)	8,000 (est. 1985)
45. Uganda	Kampala	R	1962	16,789,000 (est. 1987)
46. United Kingdom	London	M	1931	56,125,000 (est. 1985)
47. Vanuatu	Port Vila	R	1980	142,000 (est. 1985)
48. Western Samoa	Apia	M*	1970	163,000 (est. 1985)
49. Zambia	Lusaka	R	1964	6,666,000 (est. 1985)
50. Zimbabwe	Harare	R	1980	8,640,000 (est. 1987)

M   = Monarchy under Queen Elizabeth, represented by Governor-General in all countries except Britain.
M* = Country with its own monarchy. Brunei is a Sultanate.
R   = Republic.
(S) = Special Member.
*   = Pakistan left in 1972, rejoining in 1989.

Dependencies of Britain

Anguilla	Gibraltar
Bermuda	Hong Kong (until 1997)
British Antarctic Territory	Montserrat
British Indian Ocean Territory	Pitcairn Islands Group
British Virgin Isles	St. Helena and Dependencies (Ascension,
Cayman Islands	Tristan da Cunha)
Falkland Islands and Dependencies	Turks and Caicos Islands
(South Georgia, South Sandwich Islands)	

Territories of Member Countries

Australia Norfolk Island, Heard Island, McDonald Island, Cocos (Keeling) Islands, Christmas Island, Asmore and Cartier Islands, Coral Sea Islands
New Zealand Cook Islands, Niue, Tokelau Islands

The Channel Islands and the Isle of Man are dependent territories of the crown and do not form part of the United Kingdom. They have their own legislative assemblies and legal and administrative systems.

INDEX

Each section has a letter and, where appropriate, the column is given in brackets after the page number, *e.g.*, F8(1), G25(2). Some of the sections are alphabetically arranged and index themselves. Their contents are not included here except where it is anticipated some special difficulty may arise. The sections "Medical Matters" and "The World of Music" have each a separate index and glossary.

M

N